The Britich Empire

ca. 1913

A.Kitzinger

THE MIDDLE AGES
David / Simpson

THE SIXTEENTH CENTURY
Logan / Greenblatt

THE EARLY SEVENTEENTH CENTURY
Lewalski / Maus

THE RESTORATION AND THE EIGHTEENTH CENTURY
Lipking / Noggle

THE ROMANTIC PERIOD
Stillinger / Lynch

THE VICTORIAN AGE
Christ / Robson

THE TWENTIETH CENTURY AND AFTER
Stallworthy / Ramazani

The Norton Anthology
of English Literature

EIGHTH EDITION

VOLUME 2

The Norton Anthology of English Literature

EIGHTH EDITION
VOLUME 2

Stephen Greenblatt, *General Editor*
COGAN UNIVERSITY PROFESSOR OF THE HUMANITIES, HARVARD UNIVERSITY

M. H. Abrams, *Founding Editor Emeritus*
CLASS OF 1916 PROFESSOR OF ENGLISH EMERITUS, CORNELL UNIVERSITY

W • W • NORTON & COMPANY • *New York* • *London*

W. W. Norton & Company has been independent since its founding in 1923, when William Warder Norton and Mary D. Herter Norton first published lectures delivered at the People's Institute, the adult education division of New York City's Cooper Union. The Nortons soon expanded their program beyond the Institute, publishing books by celebrated academics from America and abroad. By mid-century, the two major pillars of Norton's publishing program— trade books and college texts—were firmly established. In the 1950s, the Norton family transferred control of the company to its employees, and today—with a staff of four hundred and a comparable number of trade, college, and professional titles published each year— W. W. Norton & Company stands as the largest and oldest publishing house owned wholly by its employees.

Editor: Julia Reidhead
Managing Editor, College: Marian Johnson
Developmental Editor: Kurt Wildermuth
Electronic Media Editor: Eileen Connell
Production Manager: Diane O'Connor
Associate Editor: Erin Granville
Copy Editors: Alice Falk, Katharine Ings, Candace Levy, Alan Shaw, Ann Tappert
Permissions Managers: Nancy Rodwan, Katrina Washington
Text Design: Antonina Krass
Art Research: Neil Ryder Hoos

Composition by Binghamton Valley Composition
Manufacturing by RR Donnelley

The Library of Congress has cataloged another edition as follows:

The Norton anthology of English literature / Stephen Greenblatt, general editor ; M.H. Abrams, founding editor emeritus.—8th ed.
p. cm.
Includes bibliographical references and indexes.

ISBN 0-393-92713-X (v. 1) — ISBN 0-393-92531-5 (v. 1: pbk.)
ISBN 0-393-92715-6 (v. 2) — ISBN 0-393-92532-3 (v. 2: pbk.)

1. English literature. 2. Great Britain—Literary collections. I. Greenblatt, Stephen, 1943– II. Abrams, M. H. (Meyer Howard), 1912–
PR1109.N6   2005
820.8—dc22
2005052313

W. W. Norton & Company, Inc., 500 Fifth Avenue, New York, N.Y. 10110
www.wwnorton.com

W. W. Norton & Company Ltd., Castle House, 75/76 Wells Street, London WIT 3QT

1 2 3 4 5 6 7 8 9 0

Contents

Preface to the
Eighth Edition

The outpouring of English literature overflows all boundaries, including the capacious boundaries of *The Norton Anthology of English Literature*. But these pages manage to contain many of the most remarkable works written in English during centuries of restless creative effort. We have included epic poems and short lyrics; love songs and satires; tragedies and comedies written for performance on the commercial stage, and private meditations meant to be perused in silence; prayers, popular ballads, prophecies, ecstatic visions, erotic fantasies, sermons, short stories, letters in verse and prose, critical essays, polemical tracts, several entire novels, and a great deal more. Such works generally form the core of courses that are designed to introduce students to English literature, with its history not only of gradual development, continuity, and dense internal echoes, but also of sudden change and startling innovation.

One of the joys of literature in English is its spectacular abundance. Even within the geographical confines of England, Scotland, Wales, and Ireland, where the majority of texts brought together in this collection originated, one can find more than enough distinguished and exciting works to fill the pages of this anthology many times over. The abundance is all the greater if one takes, as the editors of these volumes do, a broad understanding of the term *literature*. In the course of several centuries, the meaning of the term has shifted from the whole body of writing produced in a particular language to a subset of that writing consisting of works that claim special attention because of their unusual formal beauty or expressive power. Certain literary works, arousing enduring admiration, have achieved sufficient prominence to serve as widespread models for other writers and thus to constitute something approximating a canon. But just as in English-speaking countries there have never been academies empowered to regulate the use of language, so too there have never been firmly settled guidelines for canonizing particular texts. Any individual text's claim to attention is subject to constant debate and revision; established texts are jostled both by new arrivals and by previously neglected claimants; and the boundaries between the literary and whatever is thought to be "nonliterary" are constantly challenged and redrawn. The heart of this collection consists of poems, plays, and prose fiction, but, like the language in which they are written, these categories are themselves products of ongoing historical transformations, and we have included many texts that call into question any conception of literature as only a limited set of particular kinds of writing. English literature as a field arouses not a sense of order but what Yeats calls "the emotion of multitude."

Following the lead of most college courses, we have separated off, on pragmatic grounds, English literature from American literature, but, in keeping with the multinational, multicultural, and hugely expansive character of the language, we have incorporated, particularly for the modern period, a substantial number of texts by authors from other countries. This border-crossing is not a phenomenon of modernity only. It is fitting that among the first works here is *Beowulf*, a powerful epic written in the Germanic language known as Old English about a singularly restless Scandinavian hero. *Beowulf*'s remarkable translator in *The Norton Anthology of English Literature*, Seamus Heaney, is one of the great contemporary masters of English literature—he was awarded the Nobel Prize for Literature in 1995—but it would be potentially misleading to call him an "English poet" for he was born in Northern Ireland and is not in fact English. It would be still more misleading to call him a "British poet," as if the British Empire were the most salient fact about the language he speaks and writes in or the culture by which he was shaped. What matters is that the language in which Heaney writes is English, and this fact links him powerfully with the authors assembled in these volumes, a linguistic community that stubbornly refuses to fit comfortably within any firm geographical or ethnic or national boundaries. So too, to glance at other authors and writings in the anthology, in the sixteenth century William Tyndale, in exile in the Low Countries and inspired by German religious reformers, translated the New Testament from Greek and thereby changed the course of the English language; in the seventeenth century Aphra Behn deeply touched her readers with a story that moves from Africa, where its hero is born, to South America, where Behn herself may have witnessed some of the tragic events she describes; and early in the twentieth century Joseph Conrad, born in Ukraine of Polish parents, wrote in eloquent English a celebrated novella whose vision of European empire was trenchantly challenged at the century's end by the Nigerian-born writer in English, Chinua Achebe.

A vital literary culture is always on the move. This principle was the watchword of M. H. Abrams, the distinguished literary critic who first conceived *The Norton Anthology of English Literature*, brought together the original team of editors, and, with characteristic insight, diplomacy, and humor, oversaw seven editions and graciously offered counsel on this eighth edition. Abrams wisely understood that the dense continuities that underlie literary performance are perpetually challenged and revitalized by innovation. He understood too that new scholarly discoveries and the shifting interests of readers constantly alter the landscape of literary history. Hence from the start he foresaw that, if the anthology were to be successful, it would have to undergo a process of periodic revision and reselection, an ambitious enterprise that would draw upon the energy and ideas of new editors brought in to work with the seasoned team.

The Eighth Edition of *The Norton Anthology of English Literature* represents the most thoroughgoing instance in its long publishing history of this generational renewal. Across the whole chronological breadth of the volumes, new editors joined forces with the existing editors in a spirit of close collaboration. The revitalized team has considered afresh each of the selections and rethought all the other myriad aspects of the anthology. In doing so, we have, as in past years, profited from a remarkable flow of voluntary corrections and suggestions proposed by teachers, as well as students, who view the anthology with a loyal but critical eye. Moreover, we have again solicited and received detailed information on the works actually assigned, proposals for deletions and additions, and suggestions for improving the editorial matter, from over two hundred reviewers from around the world, almost all of them teachers who use the book in a course. The active participation of an engaged and dedicated community of readers has been crucial as the editors of the *Norton Anthology* grapple with the task of retaining (and indeed strengthening) the selection of more traditional texts even while adding many texts that reflect the transformation and expansion of the field of English studies. The great challenge (and therefore the interest) of the task is linked to the space constraints that even these hefty volumes must observe. The virtually limitless resources of the anthology's Web site make at least some of the difficult choices less vexing, but the editorial team kept clearly in view the central importance in the classroom of the printed pages. The final decisions on what to include were made by the editors, but we were immeasurably assisted by our ongoing collaboration with teachers and students.

With each edition, *The Norton Anthology of English Literature* has offered a broadened canon without sacrificing major writers and a selection of complete longer texts in which readers can immerse themselves. Perhaps the most emblematic of these longer texts are the two great epics *Beowulf* and *Paradise Lost*. To the extensive list of such complete works, the Eighth Edition has added many others, including Sir Thomas More's *Utopia*, Samuel Johnson's *Rasselas* (restored to its entirety), Eliza Haywood's *Fantomina*, Robert Louis Stevenson's *The Strange Case of Dr. Jekyll and Mr. Hyde*, Tom Stoppard's *Arcadia*, and Brian Friel's *Translations*.

Though this latest edition of *The Norton Anthology of English Literature* has retained the works that have traditionally been identified and taught as the principal glories of English literature, many of the newer selections reflect the fact that the *national* conception of literary history, the conception by which English Literature meant the literature of England or at most of Great Britain, has begun to give way to something else. Writers like William Butler Yeats (born in Dublin), Hugh MacDiarmid (born in Dumfriesshire, Scotland), Virginia Woolf (born in London), and Dylan Thomas (born in Swansea, Wales) are now being taught, and are here anthologized, alongside such writers as Nadine Gordimer (born in the Transvaal, South Africa), Alice Munro (born in Wingham, Ontario), Derek Walcott (born on Saint Lucia in the West Indies), V. S. Naipaul (born in Trinidad), and Salman Rushdie (born in Bombay, India). English literature, like so many other collective enterprises in our century, has ceased to be principally about the identity of a single nation; it is a global phenomenon.

We have in this edition continued to expand the selection of writing by women in all of the historical periods. The sustained work of scholars in recent years has recovered dozens of significant authors who had been marginalized or neglected by a male-dominated literary tradition and has deepened our understanding of those women writers who had managed, against considerable odds, to claim a place in that tradition. The First Edition of the *Norton Anthology* included 6 women writers; this Eighth Edition includes 67, of whom 16 are newly added and 15 are reselected or expanded. Poets and dramatists whose names were scarcely mentioned even in the specialized literary histories of earlier generations—Aemilia Lanyer, Lady Mary Wroth, Elizabeth Cary, Margaret Cavendish, Mary Leapor, Anna Letitia Barbauld, Charlotte Smith, Letitia Elizabeth Landon, and many others—now appear in the company of their male contemporaries. There are in addition four complete long prose works by women—Aphra Behn's *Oroonoko*, Eliza Haywood's *Fantomina*, Jane

Austen's *Love and Friendship,* and Virginia Woolf's *A Room of One's Own*—along with new selections from such celebrated fiction writers as Maria Edgeworth, Jean Rhys, Katherine Mansfield, and Doris Lessing.

The novel is, of course, a stumbling block for an anthology. The length of many great novels defies their incorporation in any volume that hopes to include a broad spectrum of literature. At the same time it is difficult to excerpt representative passages from narratives whose power often depends upon amplitude or upon the slow development of character or upon the onrushing urgency of the story. Therefore, better to represent the achievements of novelists, the publisher is making available the full list of Norton Critical Editions—more than 180 titles—including the most frequently assigned novels: Jane Austen's *Pride and Prejudice,* Mary Shelley's *Frankenstein,* Charles Dickens's *Hard Times,* Charlotte Brontë's *Jane Eyre,* and Emily Brontë's *Wuthering Heights.* A free Norton Critical Edition may be packaged with Volume 1 or 2 clothbound, paperbound, or three-volume package.

Building on an innovation introduced in the Seventh Edition, the editors have included for each of the periods several clusters that gather together short texts illuminating the cultural, historical, intellectual, and literary concerns of the age. In the Eighth Edition we have rethought, streamlined, and more closely coordinated these clusters with three aims: to make them easier to teach in the space of a class meeting or two, to make them more lively and accessible, and to heighten their relevance to the surrounding works of literature. Hence, for example, a new cluster for the Middle Ages, "Christ's Humanity," broaches one of the broadest and most explosive cultural and literary movements of the period, a movement that brought forth new kinds of readers and writers and a highly contested cultural politics of the visual. Similarly, a new cluster for the eighteenth century, "Liberty," goes to the heart of a central and momentous contradiction: on the one hand, the period's passionate celebration of liberty as the core British value, and, on the other hand, its extensive and profitable engagement in the slave trade. The implications of this contradiction, as the conjoined texts demonstrate, ripple out through English philosophy, law, and literature. Another new cluster, to take a final example, focuses on the fraught relationship between nation and language in the twentieth and twenty-first centuries. Through the vast extent of the former British Empire and, more recently, through American economic and political power, the English language has displaced or commingled with indigenous languages in many parts of the world. In consequence, imaginative writers from India to Africa, from the Caribbean to Hong Kong, have grappled with the kind of vexed questions about linguistic and national identity that have been confronted by generations of Welsh, Scottish, and Irish writers. The political, psychological, and cultural complexity of these questions is evident in the array of texts brought together in the "Nation and Language" cluster, while their rich literary potential is fully apparent in Brian Friel's powerful play *Translations.* We supplement the topical clusters for each period by several more extensive topical selections of texts, with illustrations, on the anthology Web site.

Now, as in the past, cultures define themselves by the songs they sing and the stories they love to tell. But the central importance of visual media in contemporary culture has heightened our awareness of the ways in which songs and stories have always been closely linked to the images that societies have fashioned. The Eighth Edition of *The Norton Anthology of English Literature* features sixty pages of color plates (in seven new color inserts). In addition, black-and-white engravings and illustrations by Hogarth, Blake, and Dante Gabriel Rossetti provide compelling examples of the hybrid art of the "visual narrative." In selecting visual material—from the Sutton Hoo treasure of the seventh century to Anish Kapoor's immense *Marsyas* in the twenty-first century—the editors sought to provide images that conjure up, whether directly or indirectly, the individual writers in each section; that relate specifically to individual works in the anthology; and that shape and illuminate the culture of a particular literary period. We have tried to choose visually striking images that will interest students and provoke discussion, and our captions draw attention to important details and cross-reference related texts in the anthology.

Period-by-Period Revisions

The scope of the extensive revisions we have undertaken can be conveyed more fully by a list of some of the principal texts and features that have been added to the Eighth Edition.

The Middle Ages. The period, edited by Alfred David and James Simpson, is divided into three sections: Anglo-Saxon Literature, Anglo-Norman Literature, and Middle English Literature of the Fourteenth and Fifteenth Centuries. The heart of the Anglo-Saxon section is the great epic *Beowulf,* in an acclaimed translation, specially commissioned for *The Norton Anthology of English Literature,* by Seamus Heaney. The selection of Anglo-Saxon texts has been newly augmented with the alliterative poem *Judith* and with King Alfred's preface to the *Pastoral Care.* The Anglo-Norman section—a key bridge between the Anglo-Saxon period and the time of Chaucer—includes two clusters of texts: "Legendary Histories of Britain" traces the origins of Arthurian romance in the accounts of Geoffrey of Monmouth, Wace, and Layamon. "Celtic Contexts" explores the complex multilingual situation of the period, represented by the Old Irish "Exile of the Sons of Uisliu"; newly added, the conclusion of Thomas of England's *Le Roman de Tristan,* which comes from Irish, Welsh, and Breton sources and was written down in Old French; and Marie de France's magnificent Breton lay *Lanval,* one of the period's principal texts, as well as her *Chevrefoil,* in a new verse translation by Alfred David. A tale from the *Confessio Amantis* of John Gower, a new author, complements the generous selections from Chaucer's *Canterbury Tales.* We have added new selections from the remarkable Margery Kempe and from Langland's *Piers Plowman* and an important new topical cluster, "Christ's Humanity." Our representation of medieval drama has been strengthened by the addition of the powerful *York Play of the Crucifixion.*

The Sixteenth Century. For the first time with this edition, the anthology includes the whole of Thomas More's *Utopia,* the visionary masterpiece that helped to shape the modern world. Edited by George Logan and Stephen Greenblatt, this period includes five other complete longer texts: Book 1 of Spenser's *Faerie Queene,* Marlowe's *Hero and Leander* and *Doctor Faustus,* and Shakespeare's *Twelfth Night* and *King Lear.* The selection of poems offers new works by Wyatt, five additional sonnets by Sidney, five additional sonnets by Shakespeare, and two sonnets by a poet introduced here for the first time, Richard Barnfield. In addition we provide modern prose translations of several of Petrarch's *rime* in order to show their close relationship with sonnets by Wyatt, Sidney, and Ralegh. The cluster on the period's bitter religious controversies, "Faith in Conflict," has been redesigned in order to better represent the Catholic as well as the Protestant position. A new cluster, "Women in Power," greatly expands the selections from Queen Elizabeth and sets her writings alongside those of three compelling new figures: Mary Tudor ("Bloody Mary"), Lady Jane Grey, the tragic queen for nine days, and Mary, Queen of Scots, Elizabeth's cousin and prisoner. The topic as a whole provides insight into the strange position of female rulers attempting to shape their public performances in a society that ordinarily allowed little scope for women's shaping power.

The Early Seventeenth Century. At the heart of this section, edited by Barbara Lewalski and Katharine Eisaman Maus, is John Milton's Paradise Lost, presented in its entirety. Other complete longer works include John Donne's soul-searching Satire 3, Aemilia Lanyer's country-house poem "The Description of Cookham," three major works by Ben Jonson (The Masque of Blackness, Volpone [freshly edited by Katharine Eisaman Maus], and the Cary-Morison ode), John Webster's tragedy The Duchess of Malfi, and Milton's Lycidas. Significant additions have been made to the works of Donne, Jonson, Bacon, Carew, and Hobbes. Three newly conceived topical clusters will help teachers organize the rich profusion of seventeenth-century texts. "The Gender Wars" offers the stark contrast between Joseph Swetnam's misogynistic diatribe and Rachel Speght's vigorous response. "Forms of Inquiry" represents the vital intellectual currents of the period by bringing together reselected texts by Bacon, Burton, Browne, and Hobbes. And introducing riveting reports on the trial and execution of Charles I, political writings by the conservative Filmer and the revolutionaries Milton and Winstanley, and searching memoirs by Lucy Hutchinson, Edward Hyde, Earl of Clarendon, Lady Anne Halkett, and Dorothy Waugh, "Crisis of Authority" shows how new literary forms arose out of the trauma of political conflict.

The Restoration and the Eighteenth Century. In response to widespread demand and our own sense of its literary merit, the editors, Lawrence Lipking and James Noggle, include the complete text of Samuel Johnson's philosophical fable Rasselas. We introduce as well Fantomina, a novella of sexual role-playing by an author new to the anthology, Eliza Haywood. Other complete longer texts in this section include Dryden's satires Absolom and Achitophel and MacFlecknoe, Aphra Behn's novel Oroonoko, Congreve's comedy The Way of the World, Pope's Essay on Criticism, The Rape of the Lock, and Epistle to Dr. Abuthnot, Gay's Beggar's Opera, Hogarth's graphic satire "Marriage A-la-Mode," Johnson's Vanity of Human Wishes, Gray's "Elegy Written in a Country Churchyard," and Goldsmith's "The Deserted Village." Additions have been made to the works of John Wilmot, Second Earl of Rochester, and Mary Leapor, and the selection from Joseph Addison and Sir Richard Steele has been recast. "Liberty," a new thematic cluster on freedom and slavery, brings together texts by John Locke, Mary Astell, Anthony Ashley Cooper, Third Earl of Shaftesbury, David Hume, Edmund Burke, and others.

The Romantic Period. The principal changes introduced by the editors, Jack Stillinger and Deidre Shauna Lynch, center on significantly increased attention to women writers of both poetry and prose. There are more poems by Anna Letitia Barbauld, Charlotte Smith (including the great long work Beachy Head and a substantial selection from The Emigrants), Mary Robinson, Joanna Baillie, and Felicia Hemans. Mary Wollstonecraft and Dorothy Wordsworth are now joined by two new woman authors, Maria Edgeworth and Jane Austen. Mary Shelley is represented by two works, her introduction to The Last Man and her story "The Mortal Immortal" (*Frankenstein,* formerly in the anthology, is now available in a Norton Critical Edition). There are additional poems by Robert Burns, William Wordsworth, Percy Bysshe Shelley, and John Keats and new prose pieces by Sir Walter Scott, Charles Lamb, and John Clare. A new topic, "The Gothic and the Development of a Mass Readership," focuses on the controversial history of a genre that continues to shape popular fiction and films. Writings by Horace Walpole, William Beckford, Ann Radcliff, and "Monk" Lewis, together with commentaries and reviews by contemporaries such as Anna Barbauld and Samuel Taylor Coleridge, illuminate the promise and menace that this period saw in a mode of writing that opened up a realm of nightmarish terror to literary exploration.

The Victorian Age. Among the major additions to this section, edited by Carol Christ and Catherine Robson, are Robert Louis Stevenson's *The Strange Case of Doctor Jekyll and Mr. Hyde;* two new long poems—Elizabeth Barrett Browning's poem *The Runaway Slave at Pilgrim's Point* and Dante Gabriel Rossetti's *Jenny;* a new complete text of FitzGerald's *The Rubáiyát of Omar Kayyam;* and Rudyard Kipling's *The White Man's Burden* and *If.* Kipling's novella *The Man Who Would Be King* and Oscar Wilde's comedy *The Importance of Being Earnest* continue to be featured, as does the poetry of Tennyson, Robert Browning, Elizabeth Barrett Browning, Dante Gabriel Rossetti, Christina Rossetti, and others. Along with the widely assigned "Victorian Issues" clusters (Evolution, Industrialism, and the "Woman Question"), we present the topic "Empire and National Identity." This is an innovative and highly teachable sequence of paired texts, grappling with fiercely contentious issues that repeatedly arose across the empire's vast extent.

The Twentieth Century and After. A host of new writers and topics mark this major revision by the editors, Jon Stallworthy and Jahan Ramazani. The section now features two brilliant plays, Brian Friel's *Translations* and Tom Stoppard's *Arcadia,* both of which have vital connections to literary and cultural issues that extend throughout these volumes. The many writers introduced to the anthology for the first time include the Indian poet A. K. Ramanujan, the Canadian poet Anne Carson, and the English poet Carol Ann Duffy. There are new stories by E. M. Forster and Jean Rhys, a new selection from J. M. Coetzee's *Waiting for the Barbarians,* and new poems by W. B. Yeats, W. H. Auden, Derek Walcott, and Ted Hughes. There is, as before, a remarkable array of complete longer texts, including Hardy's "On the Western Circuit," Conrad's *Heart of Darkness,* Woolf's *A Room of One's Own,* Eliot's *The Waste Land,* Mansfield's "The Garden Party" and "The Daughters of the Late Colonel," Beckett's *Endgame,* Lessing's "To Room Nineteen," Pinter's *The Dumb Waiter,* Achebe's *Things Fall Apart,* and Naipaul's *One Out of Many.* And two new, highly innovative topics will enable teachers to introduce students to major aspects of the period's cultural scene. The first, "Modernist Manifestos," brings together the radical experiments of T. E. Hulme, Ezra Pound, H. D., Wyndham Lewis, and Mina Loy. The second, "Nation and Language," gets to the heart of the questions that face colonial and postcolonial writers who must grapple with the power, at once estranging and liberating, of the English language. The voices in this cluster, Claude McKay, Hugh MacDiarmid, Louise Bennett, Brian Friel, Kamau Brathwaite, Wole Soyinka, Tony Harrison, Ngũgĩ wa Thiong'o, Salman Rushdie, and John Agard, bear eloquent witness to the global diffusion of English, the urgency of unresolved issues of nation and identity, and the rich complexity of literary history. That history is not a straightforward sequence. Seamus Heaney's works, to which two new poems have been added, provide the occasion to look back again to Heaney's translation of *Beowulf* at the beginning of the anthology. This translation is a reminder that the most recent works can double back upon the distant past, and that words set down by men and women who have crumbled into dust can speak to us with astonishing directness.

Editorial Procedures

The Eighth Edition adheres to the core principles that have always characterized *The Norton Anthology of English Literature*. Period introductions, headnotes, and annotation are designed to enhance students' reading and, without imposing an interpretation, to give students the information they need to understand each text. The aim of these editorial materials is to make the anthology self-sufficient, so that it can be read anywhere—in a coffee bar, on a bus, or under a tree. Above all, we have tried always to keep in mind the actual classroom situation. Teachability is central to every aspect of these volumes.

Our fidelity to a trusted and well-tried format may make it difficult for long-time users to take in, at first glance, how thoroughgoing and extensive the revisions to the Eighth Edition actually are. The editorial team undertook to rethink and update virtually everything in these pages, from the endpaper maps, scrutinized for accuracy by Catherine Robson and redrawn by cartographer Adrian Kitzinger, to the appendix on English money, which, thanks to James Noggle's clever chart, now provides, at a glance, answers to the perennial question, But what was money actually worth? Similarly, "Religions in England," rewritten by Katharine Maus, and "Geographic Nomenclature," revised by Jahan Ramazani, quickly and elegantly illuminate what students have often found obscure. Each volume of the anthology includes a "Poems in Process" section, revised and expanded by Deidre Lynch with the help of Alfred David and James Simpson, which reproduces from manuscripts and printed texts the genesis and evolution of a number of poems whose final form is printed in that volume. And, thanks to the thoroughgoing work of James Simpson, we now have a freshly conceived and thoroughly rewritten "Literary Terminology" appendix, recast as a quick-reference alphabetical glossary with examples from works in *The Norton Anthology of English Literature*.

Drawing upon the latest scholarship and upon classroom experience, the editors have substantially rewritten the period introductions and headnotes. We have updated as well the bibliographies and have carefully revised the timelines. And we have provided in-text references to the *Norton Literature Online* Web site. With all aspects of the anthology's apparatus our intention is to facilitate direct and informed access to the extraordinary works of literature assembled here.

The Norton Anthology of English Literature prides itself on both the scholarly accuracy and the readability of its texts. To ease students' encounter with some works, we have normalized spelling and capitalization in texts up to and including the Romantic period—for the most part they now follow the conventions of modern English; we leave unaltered, however, texts in which such modernizing would change semantic or metrical qualities. From the Victorian period onward, we have restored the original spelling and punctuation to selections retained from the previous edition.

We continue other editorial procedures that have proved useful in the past. After each work, we cite the date of first publication on the right; in some instances, this date is followed by the date of a revised edition for which the author was responsible. Dates of composition, when they differ from those of publication and when they are known, are provided on the left. We have used square brackets to indicate titles supplied by the editors for the convenience of readers. Whenever a portion of a text has been omitted, we have indicated that omission with three asterisks. If the omitted portion is important for following the plot or argument, we have provided a brief summary within the text or in a footnote. Finally, we have reconsidered annotations throughout and increased the number of marginal glosses for archaic, dialect, or unfamiliar words.

Additional Resources

With the Eighth Edition of *The Norton Anthology of English Literature,* the publisher is proud to launch an extensive new resource—Norton Literature Online (*wwnorton.com/literature*)—the gateway to all of the outstanding online literature resources available from Norton. Students who activate the password included in each new copy of the anthology will find at Norton Literature Online a deep and broad array of general resources, among them a glossary of literary terms, advice on writing about literature and using MLA documentation style, study aids and quizzes, a portrait gallery featuring 380 authors, more than 100 maps, and over 90 minutes of recorded readings and musical selections. To encourage students to explore Norton Literature Online, cross-references in the anthology draw attention to relevant materials, notably to the 27 topical clusters (augmenting the 17 in-text topics) in the much-praised Norton Topics Online site. Prepared by the anthology editors, each topic includes an introduction, a gathering of annotated texts and images, and study questions and research links. For use with the Eighth Edition, three entirely new Twentieth Century topics—"Imagining Ireland," "Modernist Experiment," and "Representing the Great War"—and a recast Romantic topic, "The Satanic and Byronic Hero," have been added, among other updates and improvements. Norton Literature Online is also the portal to the Online Archive (*wwnorton.com/nael/noa*), which offers more than 150 downloadable texts from the Middle Ages through the early Victorian period, as well as some 80 audio files. An ongoing project, the Online Archive is being expanded with all public-domain texts trimmed from *The Norton Anthology of English Literature* over six editions. A new feature of the archive, a Publication Chronology, lists over 1,000 texts and the edition of the anthology in which each was introduced, dropped, and sometimes reintroduced. As such, the table, and the archive of texts now being assembled (a massive project of a few years' duration) are a unique window on changing interests in the teaching of English literature over four decades.

Teaching with The Norton Anthology of English Literature: *A Guide for Instructors* has been reconceived for ease of use and substantially rewritten by Sondra Archimedes, University of California, Santa Cruz, Elizabeth Fowler, University of Virginia, Laura Runge, University of South Florida, and Philip Schwyzer, University of Exeter. The Guide offers extensive help with teaching a course, from planning, to developing a syllabus and course objectives, to preparing exams. For authors and works, the Guide entries provide a "hook" to start class discussion; a "Quick Read" section to help instructors review essential information about a text or author; teaching suggestions that call out interesting textual or contextual features; teaching clusters of suggested groups or pairs of texts; and discussion questions. Built into the *Guide for Instructors* is a freestanding Media Guide, by Philip Schwyzer, which offers specific suggestions for integrating the anthology's rich multimedia resources with the text and for incorporating them into traditional or distance-learning courses. Finally, the Norton Resource Library (*wwnorton.com/nrl*), also by Philip Schwyzer, offers instructors brief period introductions and "class sessions" to facilitate close reading, art galleries and literary links, enhanced period timelines, essay assignments, sample syllabi, and instructions for customizing the material. These materials are compatible with WebCT and other course management systems.

The editors are deeply grateful to the hundreds of teachers worldwide who have helped us to improve *The Norton Anthology of English Literature*. A list of the advisors who prepared in-depth reviews and of the instructors who replied to a detailed questionnaire follows on a separate page, under Acknowledgments. The editors would like to express appreciation for their assistance to Elizabeth Anker (University of Virginia), Sandie Byrne (Oxford University), Timothy Campbell (Indiana University), Sarita Cargas (Oxford University), Jason Coats (University of Virginia), Joseph W. Childers (University of California, Riverside), Daniel Cook (University of California, Davis), Linda David, Christopher Fanning (Queens University), William Flesch (Brandeis University), Robert Folkenflik (University of California, Irvine), Robert D. Fulk (Indiana University), Omaar Hena (University of Virginia), Tom Keirstead (Indiana University), Shayna Kessel (University of Southern California), Joanna Lipking (Northwestern University), Ian Little (Liverpool University), Tricia Lootens (University of Georgia), Erin Minear (Harvard University), Elaine Musgrave (University of California, Davis), J. Morgan Myers (University of Virginia), Kate Nash (University of Virginia), Ruth Perry (M.I.T.), Emily Peterson (Harvard University), Kate Pilson (Harvard University), Jane Potter (Oxford Brookes University), Leah Price (Harvard University), Angelique Richardson (Exeter University), Philip Schwyzer (Exeter University), and Ramie Targoff (Brandeis University). We especially thank John W. Sider (Westmont College) for his meticulous review of standing annotations and myriad suggestions for improvements. We also thank the many people at Norton who contributed to the Eighth Edition: Julia Reidhead, who served not only as the inhouse supervisor but also as an unfailingly wise and effective collaborator in every aspect of planning and accomplishing this Eighth Edition; Marian Johnson, managing editor for college books, who kept the project moving forward with a remarkable blend of focused energy, intelligence, and common sense; Kurt Wildermuth, developmental and project editor; Alice Falk, Katharine Ings, Candace Levy, Alan Shaw, and Ann Tappert, manuscript editors; Eileen Connell, electronic media editor; Diane O'Connor, production manager; Nancy Rodwan and Katrina Washington, permissions managers; Toni Krass, designer; Neil Ryder Hoos, art researcher; Erin Granville, associate editor; and Catherine Spencer, editorial assistant. All these friends provided the editors with indispensable help in meeting the challenge of representing the unparalleled range and variety of English literature.

We dedicate this Eighth Edition of *The Norton Anthology of English Literature* to our friend, mentor, and inspiring guide M. H. Abrams. His shaping power over these volumes and the profession it serves will long endure.

Acknowledgments

Among our many critics, advisors, and friends, the following were of especial help toward the preparation of the Eighth Edition, either by offering advice or by providing critiques of particular periods of the anthology: Daniel Albright (University of Rochester), David L. Anderson (Butler County Community College), Judith H. Anderson (Indiana University), David Barnard (University of Regina), Ian Baucom (Duke University), Dr. Richard Beadle (St John's College, Cambridge University), Elleke Boehmer (Nottingham Trent University), Scott Boltwood (Emory and Henry College), Joseph Bristow (University of California, Los Angeles), James Chandler (University of Chicago), William Cohen (University of Maryland, College Park), Helen Cooper (Oxford University), Valentine Cunningham (Oxford University), Timothy Drake (Queen's University), Ian Duncan (University of California), Elizabeth Hanson (Queen's University), Brean Hammond (University of Nottingham), Claudia Johnson (Princeton University), Emrys Jones (Oxford University), Suzanne Keen, Shanya Kessel (University of Southern California), Bruce King, Rebecca Krug (University of Minnesota), David Kuijt (University of Maryland), John Leonard (University of Western Ontario), Peter Lindenbaum (Indiana University), Jesse Matz (Kenyon College), Brian May (Northern Illinois University), Father Germain Marc'hadour (Angers, France), Vincent Gillespie (Oxford University), Leah S. Marcus (Vanderbilt University), Paula McDowell (Rutgers University), Clarence H. Miller (St. Louis University), Tyrus Miller (University of California, Santa Cruz), Michael Moses (Duke University), Barbara Newman (Northwestern University), Michael North (University of California, Los Angeles), Stephen Orgel, (Stanford University), Ruth Perry (Massachusetts Institute of Technology), Adela Pinch (University of Michigan), David Porter (University of Michigan), Laura Quinney (Brandeis University), Alan Richardson (Boston College), Phillip Rogers (Queen's University), Mary Beth Rose (University of Illinois at Chicago), Elizabeth Scala (University of Texas), Nigel Smith (Princeton University), Janet Sorensen (Indiana University), Michele Stanco (Università degli Studi di Napoli "Frederico"), Marta Straznicky (Queen's University), Helen Thompson (Northwestern University), Blakey Vermeule (Northwestern University), Richard Wendorf (Boston Athenæum), Johnny Wink (Ouachita Baptist University), David Wyatt (University of Maryland), Steven Zwicker (Washington University, St. Louis).

The editors would like to express appreciation and thanks to the hundreds of teachers who provided reviews: Laila Abdalla (Central Washington University), Avis Adams (Green River Community College), Kimberly VanEsveld Adams (Elizabethtown College), Thomas Amarose (Seattle Pacific University), Mark Addison Amos (Southern Illinois University, Carbondale), M. G. Aune (North Dakota State College), E. Baldwin (University of Victoria), Jackson Barry (University of Maryland, College Park), Elisa E. Beshero-Bondar (The

Pennsylvania State University), Thomas Bestul (University of Illinois at Chicago), J. Christopher Bittenbender (Eastern University), Dr. K Blumerich (Grand Valley State University), Karl Boehler (University of Wisconsin, Osh Kosh), Bruce Brandt (South Dakota State University), Caroline Breashears (St. Lawrence University), Dr. Chris Brooks (Wichita State University), M. Brown (SUNY, Morrisville), Jennifer Bryan (Oberlin College), Kristin Bryant (Portland Community College), Stephen Buhler (University of Nebraska-Lincoln), Michel Camp (Jackson State Community College), Joseph Candido (University of Arkansas, Fayetteville), Tim Carens (College of Charleston), Cynthia Caywood (University of San Diego), Merlin Cheney (Weber State University), William Christmas (San Francisco State University), Caroline Cherry (Eastern University), Joyce Coleman (University of North Dakota), Brian Connery (Oakland University), Kevin L. Cope (Louisiana State University, Baton Rouge), J. Cortelloni (Lincoln College), Richard Cox (Abilene Christian University), Joanne Craig (Bishop's University), S. B. Darrell (Southern Indiana University), J. A. Dane (University of South California), M. V. Davidson (University of Wisconsin, La Crosse), William Dawson (University of Missouri), Danette DiMarco (Slippery Rock University), Michael Doerrer (University of Maryland, College Park), Alfred J. Drake (California State University, Fullerton), George Drake (Central Washington University), Ende Duffy (University of California, Santa Barbara), Judy Elsley (Weber State University), Dan Embree (Mississippi State University), Audrey Fisch (New Jersey City University), Annette Federico (James Madison University), Robert Forman (St. John's University), Thomas Frosch (City University of New York, Queens), Dr. Donald Fucci (Ramapo College), Mark Fulk (Buffalo State College), Kevin Gardner (Baylor University), Robert Geary (James Madison University), Marc Geisler (Western Washington University), Jason Gieger (California State University, Sacramento), Cynthia Gilliatt (James Madison University), Julia Giordano (Nassau Community College), Stephen Glosecki (University of Alabama at Birmingham), William Gracie (Miami University of Ohio), Kenneth Graham (University of Waterloo), Loren C. Gruber (Missouri Valley College), Leigh Harbin (Angelo State University), H. George Hawn (Towson University), Douglas Hayes (Winona State University), Aeron Haynie (University of Wisconsin, Green Bay), Regina Hewitt (University of South Florida), Matthew Hill (University of Maryland, College Park), Jim Hoogenakker (Washburn University), Robert Hoskins (James Madison University), Kathy Houff (University of Georgia), Claudia House (Nashville State Tech Community College), Darren Howard (University of California, Los Angeles), Rebecca Kajs (Anne Arundel Community College), Bridget Keegan (Creighton University), Erin Kelly (University of Maryland), Julie Kim (Northeastern Illinois University), Jackie Kogan (California State University, Northridge), Neal Kramer (Brigham Young University), Deborah Knuth (Colgate University), E. Carole Knuth (Buffalo State College), Wai-Leung Kwok (San Francisco State University), Elizabeth Lambert (Gettysburg College), Mary Lenard (University of Wisconsin, Parkside), George Evans Light (Mississippi State University), Henry Limouze (Wright State University), Sherry Little (San Diego State), Debbie Lopez (University of Texas, San Antonio), Susan Lorsch (Hofstra University), Thomas Lyons (University of Colorado, Boulder), Susan Maher (University of Nebraska, Omaha), Phoebe Mainster (Wayne State University), W. J. Martin (Niagara University), Nicholas Mason (Brigham Young University), Ian McAdam (University of Lethbridge), Ruth McAdams (Tarrant County College), John McCombe (University of Dayton), Kristen McDermott (Central Michigan University), Joseph McGowan (University of San Diego), Christian Michener (St. Mary's University, Minnesota), D. Keith Mikolavich (Diablo Valley College), Nicholas Moschovakis (George Washington University), Gwendolyn Morgan (Montana State University), Daniel Mosser (Virginia Polytechnic Institute), K. D. Neill (University of Victoria, British Columbia), Douglas Nordfor (James Madison University), Michael North (University of California, Los Angeles), Bernie O'Donnell (University of Florida). Michael Olmert (University of Maryland, College Park), C. R. Orchard (Indiana University of Pennsylvania), Jennifer Panek (University of Ottawa), Cynthia Patton (Emporia State University), James Persoon (Grand Valley State University), Sara Pfaffenroth (County College of Morris), John Pfordreshen (Georgetown University), Jennifer Phegley (University of Missouri, Kansas City), Trey Philpotts (Arkansas Technical University), Brenda Powell (University of St. Thomas, St. Paul), Tison Pugh (University of Central Florida), Katherine Quinsey (University of Windsor), Eric Reimer (University of Montana), Kathryn Rummel (California Polytechnic State University), Harbindar Sanghara (University of Victoria, Canada), William Scheuede (University of South Florida), Michael Schoenfeldt (University of Michigan), R. M. Schuler (University of Victoria, British Columbia), D. Schwartz (Cal Poly, Saint Louis Obispo), Michael Schwartz (California State University, Chico), Richard Sha (American University), George Shuffelton (Carleton College), Brandie Sigfried (Brigham Young University), Elizabeth Signorotti (Binghamton University), Dawn Simmons (Ohio State University), Erik Simpson (Grinnell College), Sarah Singer (Delaware County Community College), Dr. Mary-Antoinette Smith (Seattle University), Jonathan Smith (University of Michigan, Dearborn), Nigel Smith (Princeton University), Malinda Snow (Georgia State University), Jean Sorenson (Grayson County College), C. Spinks (Trinity College), Donald Stone (City University of New York, Queens), Kevin Swafford (Bradley University), Andrew Taylor (University of Ottawa), Rebecca Totaro (Florida Gulf Coast University), Bente Videbaek (State University New York, Stony Brook), Joseph Viscome (University of North Carolina, Chapel Hill), Jennie Wakefield (Clemson University), David Ward (University of Pittsburgh), Tracy Ware (Queen's University), Alexander Weiss (Radford University), Lachlan Whalen (Marshall University), Christopher Wheatley (Catholic University of America), C. Williams (Mississippi State University), Jodi Wyett (Xavier University, Cincinnati), Jiyeon Yoo (University of California, Los Angeles), Richard Zeikowitz (University of South Alabama).

The Norton Anthology of English Literature

EIGHTH EDITION
VOLUME 2

The Romantic Period
1785–1830

1789–1815: Revolutionary and Napoleonic period in France.—1789:
The Revolution begins with the assembly of the States-
General in May and the storming of the Bastille on July 14.—
1793: King Louis XVI executed; England joins the alliance
against France.—1793–94: The Reign of Terror under
Robespierre. 1804: Napoleon crowned emperor.—1815:
Napoleon defeated at Waterloo
1807: British slave trade outlawed (slavery abolished throughout
the empire, including the West Indies, twenty-six years
later)
1811–20: The Regency—George, Prince of Wales, acts as regent for
George III, who has been declared incurably insane
1819: Peterloo Massacre
1820: Accession of George IV

The Romantic period, though by far the shortest, is at least as complex and
diverse as any other period in British literary history. For much of the twentieth
century, scholars singled out five poets—Wordsworth, Coleridge, Byron, Percy
Shelley, and Keats, adding Blake belatedly to make a sixth—and constructed
notions of a unified Romanticism on the basis of their works. But there were
problems all along: even the two closest collaborators of the 1790s, Wordsworth and Coleridge, would fit no single definition; Byron despised both Coleridge's philosophical speculations and Wordsworth's poetry; Shelley and Keats
were at opposite poles from each other stylistically and philosophically; Blake
was not at all like any of the other five.

Nowadays, although the six poets remain, by most measures of canonicity,
the principal canonical figures, we recognize a greater range of accomplishments. In 1798, the year of Wordsworth and Coleridge's first *Lyrical Ballads,*
neither of the authors had much of a reputation; Wordsworth was not even
included among the 1,112 entries in David Rivers's *Literary Memoirs of Living
Authors of Great Britain* of that year, and *Lyrical Ballads* was published anonymously because, as Coleridge told the publisher, "Wordsworth's name is
nothing—to a large number of people mine *stinks*." Some of the best-regarded
poets of the time were women—Anna Barbauld, Charlotte Smith, Mary Robinson—and Wordsworth and Coleridge (junior colleagues of Robinson when
she was poetry editor of the *Morning Post* in the late 1790s) looked up to them
and learned their craft from them. The rest of the then-established figures
were the later eighteenth-century poets who are printed at the end of volume
1 of this anthology—Gray, Collins, Crabbe, and Cowper in particular. Only
Byron, among the now-canonical poets, was instantly famous; and Felicia

Hemans and Letitia Landon ran him a close race as best-sellers. The Romantic period had a great many more participants than the six principal male poets and was shaped by a multitude of political, social, and economic changes.

REVOLUTION AND REACTION

Following a widespread practice of historians of English literature, we use "Romantic period" to refer to the span between the year 1785, the midpoint of the decade in which Samuel Johnson died and Blake, Burns, and Smith published their first poems, and 1830, by which time the major writers of the preceding century were either dead or no longer productive. This was a turbulent period, during which England experienced the ordeal of change from a primarily agricultural society, where wealth and power had been concentrated in the landholding aristocracy, to a modern industrial nation. And this change occurred in a context of revolution—first the American and then the more radical French—and of war, of economic cycles of inflation and depression, and of the constant threat to the social structure from imported revolutionary ideologies to which the ruling classes responded by the repression of traditional liberties.

The early period of the French Revolution, marked by the Declaration of the Rights of Man and the storming of the Bastille, evoked enthusiastic support from English liberals and radicals alike. Three important books epitomize the radical social thinking stimulated by the Revolution. Mary Wollstonecraft's *A Vindication of the Rights of Men* (1790) justified the French Revolution against Edmund Burke's attack in his *Reflections on the Revolution in France* (1790). Tom Paine's *Rights of Man* (1791–92) also advocated for England a democratic republic that was to be achieved, if lesser pressures failed, by popular revolution. More important as an influence on Wordsworth and Percy Shelley was William Godwin's *Enquiry Concerning Political Justice* (1793), which foretold an inevitable but peaceful evolution of society to a final stage in which property would be equally distributed and government would wither away. But English sympathizers dropped off as the Revolution followed its increasingly grim course: the accession to power by Jacobin extremists, intent on purifying their new republic by purging it of its enemies; the "September Massacres" of the imprisoned nobility in 1792, followed by the execution of the king and queen; the new French Republic's invasion of the Rhineland and the Netherlands, which brought England into the war against France; the guillotining of thousands in the Reign of Terror under Robespierre; and, after the execution in their turn of the men who had directed the Terror, the emergence of Napoleon, first as dictator then as emperor of France. As Wordsworth wrote in *The Prelude*,

> become Oppressors in their turn,
> Frenchmen had changed a war of self-defence
> For one of Conquest, losing sight of all
> Which they had struggled for. . . . (11.206–09)

Napoleon, the brilliant tactician whose rise through the ranks of the army had seemed to epitomize the egalitarian principles of the Revolution, had become an arch-aggressor, a despot, and would-be founder of a new imperial dynasty. By 1800 liberals found they had no side they could wholeheartedly espouse. Napoleon's defeat at Waterloo in 1815 proved to be the triumph, not of progress and reform, but of reactionary despotisms throughout continental Europe.

In England this was a period of harsh, repressive measures. Public meetings were prohibited, the right of habeas corpus (the legal principle protecting individuals from arbitrary imprisonment) was suspended for the first time in over a hundred years, and advocates of even moderate political change were charged with treason. Efforts during these war years to repeal the laws that barred Protestants who did not conform to the Anglican Church from the universities and government came to nothing: in the new climate of counter-revolutionary alarm, it was easy to portray even a slight abridgement of the privileges of the established Church as a measure that, validating the Jacobins' campaigns to de-Christianize France, would aid the enemy cause. Another early casualty of this counterrevolution was the movement to abolish the slave trade, a cause supported initially by a wide cross-section of English society. In the 1780s and 1790s numerous writers, both white (Barbauld, Robinson, Coleridge, and Wordsworth) and black (Ottobah Cugoano and Olaudah Equiano), attacked the greed of the owners of the West Indian sugar plantations and detailed the horrors of the traffic in African flesh that provided them with their labor power. But the bloodshed that accompanied political change in France strengthened the hand of apologists for slavery, by making any manner of reform seem the prelude to violent insurrection. Parliament rejected a bill abolishing the trade in 1791, and sixteen years—marked by slave rebellions and by the planters' brutal reprisals—elapsed before it passed a new version of the bill.

The frustration of the abolitionist cause is an emblematic chapter in the larger story of how a reactionary government sacrificed hopes of reform while it mobilized the nation's resources for war. Yet this was the very time when economic and social changes were creating a desperate need for corresponding changes in political arrangements. For one thing, new classes inside England—manufacturing rather than agricultural—were beginning to demand a voice in government proportionate to their wealth. The "Industrial Revolution"—the shift in manufacturing that resulted from the invention of power-driven machinery to replace hand labor—had begun in the mid-eighteenth century with improvements in machines for processing textiles, and was given immense impetus when James Watt perfected the steam engine in 1765. In the succeeding decades steam replaced wind and water as the primary source of power for all sorts of manufacturing processes, beginning that dynamic of ever-accelerating economic expansion and technological development that we still identify as the hallmark of the modern age. A new laboring population massed in sprawling mill towns such as Manchester, whose population increased by a factor of five in fifty years. In agricultural communities the destruction of home industry was accompanied by the acceleration of the process of enclosing open fields and wastelands (usually, in fact, "commons" that had provided the means of subsistence for entire communities) and incorporating them into larger, privately owned holdings. Enclosure was by and large necessary for the more efficient methods of agriculture required to feed the nation's growing population (although some of the land that the wealthy acquired through parliamentary acts of enclosure they in fact incorporated into their private estates). But enclosure was socially destructive, breaking up villages, creating a landless class who either migrated to the industrial towns or remained as farm laborers, subsisting on starvation wages and the little they could obtain from parish charity. The landscape of England began to take on its modern appearance—the hitherto open rural areas subdivided into a checkerboard of fields enclosed by hedges and stone walls, with the factories of the cities casting a pall of smoke over vast areas of cheaply built houses and slum tenements. Meanwhile, the population was increasingly polarized into what Disraeli later called the "Two Nations"—the two classes of capital and labor, the rich and the poor.

No attempt was made to regulate this shift from the old economic world to the new, since even liberal reformers were committed to the philosophy of laissez-faire. This theory of "let alone," set out in Adam Smith's *The Wealth of Nations* in 1776, holds that the general welfare can be ensured only by the free operation of economic laws; the government should maintain a policy of strict noninterference and leave people to pursue, unfettered, their private interests. On the one hand, laissez-faire thinking might have helped pave the way for the long-postponed emancipation of the slave population of the West Indies; by 1833, when Parliament finally ended slavery, the anomaly that their unfree labor represented for the new economic and social orthodoxies evidently had become intolerable. But for the great majority of the laboring class at home, the results of laissez-faire and the "freedom" of contract it secured were inadequate wages and long hours of work under harsh discipline and in sordid conditions. Investigators' reports on the coal mines, where male and female children of ten or even five years of age were harnessed to heavy coal-sledges that they dragged by crawling on their hands and knees, read like scenes from Dante's *Inferno*. With the end of the war in 1815, the nation's workforce was enlarged by demobilized troops at the very moment when demand for manufactured goods, until now augmented by the needs of the military, fell dramatically. The result was an unemployment crisis that persisted through the 1820s. Since the workers had no vote and were prevented by law from unionizing, their only recourses were petitions, protest meetings, and riots, to which the ruling class responded with even more repressive measures. The introduction of new machinery into the mills resulted in further loss of jobs, provoking sporadic attempts by the displaced workers to destroy the machines. After one such outbreak of "Luddite" machine-breaking, the House of Lords—despite Byron's eloquent protest—passed a bill (1812) making death the penalty for destroying the frames used for weaving in the stocking industry. In 1819 hundreds of thousands of workers organized meetings to demand parliamentary reform. In August of that year, a huge but orderly assembly at St. Peter's Fields, Manchester, was charged by saber-wielding troops, who killed nine and severely injured hundreds more; this was the notorious "Peterloo Massacre," so named with sardonic reference to the Battle of Waterloo, and condemned by Shelley in his poem for the working class "England in 1819."

Suffering was largely confined to the poor, however, while the landed classes and industrialists prospered. So did many merchants, who profited from the new markets opened up as the British Empire expanded aggressively, compensating with victories against the French for the traumatic loss of America in 1783. England's merchants profited, too, thanks to the marketing successes that, over time, converted once-exotic imports from these colonies into everyday fare for the English. In the eighteenth century tea and sugar had been transformed in this way, and in the nineteenth century other commodities followed suit: the Indian muslin, for instance, that was the fabric of choice for gentlemen's cravats and fashionable ladies' gowns, and the laudanum (Indian opium dissolved in alcohol) that so many ailing writers of the period appear to have found irresistible. The West End of London and new seaside resorts like Brighton became in the early nineteenth century consumers' paradises, sites where West Indian planters and nabobs (a Hindi word that entered English as a name for those who owed their fortunes to Indian gain) could be glimpsed displaying their purchasing power in a manner that made them moralists' favorite examples of nouveau riche vulgarity. The word *shopping* came into English usage in this era. Luxury villas sprang up in London, and the prince regent, who in 1820 became George IV, built himself palaces and pleasure domes, retreats from his not very onerous public responsibilities.

But even, or especially, in private life at home, the prosperous could not escape being touched by the great events of this period. French revolutionary principles were feared by English conservatives almost as much for their challenge to the "proper" ordering of the relations between men and women as for their challenge to traditional political arrangements. Yet the account of what it meant to be English that developed in reaction to this challenge—an account emphasizing the special virtues of the English sense of home and family—was in its way equally revolutionary. The war that the English waged almost without intermission between 1793 and 1815 was one that in an unprecedented manner had a "home front": the menaced sanctuary of the domestic fireside became the symbol of what the nation's military might was safeguarding. What popularity the monarchy held on to during this turbulent period was thus a function not of the two King Georges' traditional exercise of a monarch's sovereign powers but instead of the publicity, tailored to suit this nationalist rhetoric, that emphasized each one's domestic bliss within a "royal family." Conceptions of proper femininity altered as well under the influence of this new idealization and nationalization of the home, this project (as Burke put it) of "binding up the constitution of our country with our dearest domestic ties."

And that alteration both put new pressures on women and granted them new opportunities. As in earlier English history, women in the Romantic period were provided only limited schooling, were subjected to a rigid code of sexual behavior, and (especially after marriage) were bereft of legal rights. In this period women began, as well, to be deluged by books, sermons, and magazine articles that insisted vehemently on the physical and mental differences between the sexes and instructed women that, because of these differences, they should accept that their roles in life involved child rearing, housekeeping, and nothing more. (Of course, in tendering this advice promoters of female domesticity conveniently ignored the definitions of duty that industrialists imposed on the poor women who worked in their mills.) Yet a paradoxical byproduct of the connections that the new nationalist rhetoric forged between the well-being of the state and domestic life was that the identity of the patriot became one a woman might attempt, with some legitimacy, to claim. Within the framework created by the new accounts of English national identity, a woman's private virtues now had a public relevance. They had to be seen as crucial to the nation's welfare. Those virtues might well be manifested in the work of raising patriotic sons, but, as the thousands of women in this period who made their ostensibly natural feminine feelings of pity their alibi for participation in abolitionism demonstrated, they could be turned to nontraditional uses as well.

The new idea that, as the historian Linda Colley has put it, a woman's place was not simply in the home but also in the nation could also justify or at least extenuate the affront to proper feminine modesty represented by publication— by a woman's entry into the public sphere of authorship. "Bluestockings"— educated women—remained targets of masculine scorn. This became, none- theless, the first era in literary history in which women writers began to com- pete with men in their numbers, sales, and literary reputations: just in the category of poetry, some nine hundred women are listed in J. R. de J. Jackson's comprehensive bibliography, *Romantic Poetry by Women*. These female authors had to tread carefully, to be sure, to avoid suggesting that (as one male critic fulminated) they wished the nation's "affectionate wives, kind mothers, and lovely daughters" to be metamorphosed into "studious philosophers" and "busy politicians." And figures like Wollstonecraft, who in the *Vindication of the Rights of Woman* grafted a radical proposal about gender equality onto a more orthodox argument about the education women needed to be proper mothers, remained exceptional. Later women writers tended cautiously to either ignore her example or define themselves against it.

Only in the Victorian period would Wollstonecraft's cause of women's rights rally enough support for substantial legal reform to begin, and that process would not be completed until the twentieth century. In the early nineteenth century the pressures for political reform focused on the rights of men, as distinct from women. Middle-class and working-class men, entering into stra- tegic and short-lived alliances, made the restructuring of the British electoral system their common cause. Finally, at a time of acute economic distress, and after unprecedented disorders that threatened to break out into revolution, the first Reform Bill was passed in 1832. It did away with the rotten boroughs (depopulated areas whose seats in the House of Commons were at the disposal of a few noblemen), redistributed parliamentary representation to include the industrial cities, and extended the franchise. Although about half the middle class, almost all the working class, and all women remained without a vote, the principle of the peaceful adjustment of conflicting interests by parliamen- tary majority had been firmly established. Reform was to go on, by stages, until Britain acquired universal adult suffrage in 1928.

"THE SPIRIT OF THE AGE"

Writers working in the period 1785–1830 did not think of themselves as "Romantic"; the word was not applied until half a century later, by English historians. Contemporary reviewers treated them as independent individuals, or else grouped them (often maliciously, but with some basis in fact) into a number of separate schools: the "Lake School" of Wordsworth, Coleridge, and Robert Southey; the "Cockney School," a derogatory term for the Londoners Leigh Hunt, William Hazlitt, and associated writers, including Keats; and the "Satanic School" of Percy Shelley, Byron, and their followers.

Many writers, however, felt that there was something distinctive about their time—not a shared doctrine or literary quality, but a pervasive intellectual and imaginative climate, which some of them called "the spirit of the age." They had the sense that (as Keats wrote) "Great spirits now on earth are sojourning," and that there was evidence of the experimental boldness that marks a literary renaissance. In his "Defence of Poetry" Shelley claimed that the literature of the age "has arisen as it were from a new birth," and that "an electric life burns" within the words of its best writers, "less their spirit than the spirit of the age." He explained this spirit as an accompaniment of revolution, and others agreed. Francis Jeffrey, the foremost conservative reviewer of the day, connected "the revolution in our literature" with "the agitations of the French Revolution, and the discussions as well as the hopes and terrors to which it gave occasion." Hazlitt, who devoted a series of essays entitled *The Spirit of the Age* to assessing his contemporaries, maintained that the new poetry of the school of Wordsworth "had its origin in the French Revolution."

The imagination of many Romantic-period writers was preoccupied with revolution, and from that fact and idea they derived the framework that enabled them to think of themselves as inhabiting a distinctive period in history. The deep familiarity that many late-eighteenth-century Englishmen and -women had with the prophetic writings of the Bible contributed from the start to their readiness to attribute a tremendous significance to the political transformations set in motion in 1789. Religious belief predisposed many to view these convulsions as something more than local historical events and to cast them instead as harbingers of a new age in the history of *all* human beings. Seeing the hand of God in the events in France and understanding those events as the fulfillment of prophecies of the coming millennium came easily to figures such as Barbauld, Coleridge, Wollstonecraft, and, above all, Blake: all were affiliated with the traditions of radical Protestant Dissent, in which accounts of the imminence of the Apocalypse and the coming of the Kingdom of God had long been central. A quarter-century later, their millenarian interpretation of the Revolution would be recapitulated by radical writers such as Percy Shelley and Hazlitt, who, though they tended to place their faith in notions of progress and the diffusion of knowledge and tended to identify a rational citizenry and not God as the moving force of history, were just as convinced as their predecessors were that the Revolution had marked humanity's chance to start history over again (a chance that had been lost but was perhaps recoverable).

Another method that writers of this period took when they sought to salvage the millennial hopes that had, for many, been dashed by the bloodshed of the Terror involved granting a crucial role to the creative imagination. Some writers rethought apocalyptic transformation so that it no longer depended on the political action of collective humanity but depended instead (in a shift from the external to the internal) on the individual consciousness. The new heaven and earth promised in the prophecies could, in this account, be gained by the individual who had achieved a new, spiritualized, and visionary way of seeing. An apocalypse of the imagination could liberate the individual from time, from what Blake called the "mind-forg'd manacles" of imprisoning orthodoxies and from what Percy Shelley called "the curse which binds us to be subjected to the accident of surrounding impressions."

Wordsworth, whose formulations of this notion of a revolution in imagination would prove immensely influential, wrote in *The Prelude* the classic description of the spirit of the early 1790s. "Europe at that time was thrilled with joy, / France standing on top of the golden hours, / And human nature seeming born again" (6.340–42). "Not favored spots alone, but the whole earth, / The beauty wore of promise" (6.117–18). Something of this sense of possibility and anticipation of spiritual regeneration (captured in that phrase "born again") survived the disenchantment with politics that Wordsworth experienced later in the decade. His sense of the emancipatory opportunities brought in by the new historical moment carried over to the year 1797, when, working in tandem, he and Coleridge revolutionized the theory and practice of poetry. The product of their exuberant daily discussions was the *Lyrical Ballads* of 1798.

POETIC THEORY AND POETIC PRACTICE

Wordsworth undertook to justify those poems by means of a critical manifesto, or statement of poetic principles, which appeared first as a short Advertisement in the original *Lyrical Ballads* and then as an extended Preface to the second edition in 1800, which he enlarged still further in the third edition of 1802. In it he set himself in opposition to the literary ancien régime, those writers of the eighteenth century who, in his view, had imposed on poetry artificial conventions that distorted its free and natural expression. Many of Wordsworth's later critical writings were attempts to clarify, buttress, or qualify points made in this first declaration. Coleridge said that the Preface was "half a child of my own brain"; and although he developed doubts about some of Wordsworth's unguarded statements, he did not question the rightness of Wordsworth's attempt to overthrow the reigning tradition. Of course, many writers in eighteenth-century England had anticipated Wordsworth's attempt, as well as the definitions of the "authentic" language of poetry it assumed. Far from unprecedented, efforts to displace the authority of a poet such as Pope can be dated back to only a few years after Pope's death in 1744; by 1800 readers were accustomed to hear, for instance, that Pope's propensities for satire had derailed true poetry by elevating wit over feeling. Moreover, the last half of the eighteenth century, a time when philosophers and moralists highlighted in new ways the role that emotional sensitivity ("sensibility") plays in mental and social life, had seen the emergence of many of the critical concepts, as well as a number of the poetic subjects and forms, that later would be exploited by Wordsworth and his contemporaries.

Wordsworth's Preface nevertheless deserves its reputation as a turning point in literary history, for Wordsworth gathered up isolated ideas, organized them into a coherent theory, and made them the rationale for his own achievements. We can safely use concepts in the Preface as points of departure for a survey of some of the distinctive elements in the poetry of the Romantic period—especially if we bear in mind that during this era of revolution definitions of good poetry, like definitions of the good society, were sure to create as much contention as consensus.

The Concept of the Poet and the Poem

Seeking a stable foundation on which social institutions might be constructed, eighteenth-century British philosophers had devoted much energy to demonstrating that human nature must be everywhere the same, because it everywhere derived from individuals' shared sensory experience of an external world that could be objectively represented. As the century went on, however, philosophers began emphasizing—and poets began developing a new language for—individual variations in perception and the capacity the receptive consciousness has to filter and to re-create reality. This was the shift Wordsworth registered when in the Preface he located the source of a poem not in outer nature but in the psychology of the individual poet, and specified that the essential materials of a poem were not the external people and events it represented but the inner feelings of the author, or external objects only after these have been transformed by the author's feelings. Wordsworth in 1802 described all good poetry as, at the moment of composition, "the spontaneous overflow of powerful feelings." Other Romantic theories concurred by referring to the mind, emotions, and imagination of the poet for the origin, content, and defining attributes of a poem. Using a metaphor that parallels Wordsworth's "overflow," and that Wordsworth would revive in a late poem, Mary Robinson and Coleridge identified some of their key poems of the 1790s as "effusions"—ardent outpourings of feeling. Coleridge subsequently drew on German precedents and introduced into English criticism an account of the organic form of literary works; in this account the work is conceptualized as a self-originating and self-organizing process, parallel to the growth of a plant, that begins with a seedlike idea in the poet's imagination, grows by assimilating both the poet's feelings and the materials of sensory experience, and evolves into an organic whole in which the parts are integrally related to each other and to the whole.

In keeping with the view that poetry expresses the poet's feelings, the lyric poem written in the first person, which for much of literary history was regarded as a minor kind, became a major Romantic form and was often described as the most essentially poetic of all the genres. And in most Romantic lyrics the "I" is no longer a conventionally typical lyric speaker, such as the Petrarchan lover or Cavalier gallant of Elizabethan and seventeenth-century love poems, but one who shares recognizable traits with the poet. The experiences and states of mind expressed by the lyric speaker often accord closely with the known facts of the poet's life and the personal confessions in the poet's letters and journals. This reinvention of the lyric complicated established understandings of the gender of authorship. It may not be an accident, some critics suggest, that Wordsworth in the Preface defines poetry as "the real language of men" and the Poet as a "man speaking to men": Wordsworth, who began to publish when women such as Robinson and Charlotte Smith occupied the vanguard of the new personal poetry, might have decided that to establish the distinctiveness of his project he needed to counterbalance his emphasis on his feelings with an emphasis on those feelings' "manly" dignity. This is not to say that women writers' relationship to the new ideas about poetry was straightforward either. In one of her prefaces Smith says that she anticipates being criticized for "bringing forward 'with querulous egotism,' the mention of myself." For many female poets the other challenge those ideas about poetry posed might have consisted in their potential to reinforce the old, prejudicial idea that their sex—traditionally seen as creatures of feeling rather than intellect—wrote about their own experiences because they were capable of nothing else. For male poets the risks of poetic self-revelation were different—and in some measure they were actively seized by those who, like Coleridge and Shelley, intimated darkly that the introspective tendency and emotional sensitivity that made someone a poet could also lead him to melancholy and madness.

It was not only the lyric that registered these new accounts of the poet. Byron confounded his contemporaries' expectations about which poetic genre was best suited to self-revelation by inviting his audience to equate the heroes of *Childe Harold, Manfred,* and *Don Juan* with their author, and to see these fictional protagonists' experiences as disclosing the deep truths of his secret self. Wordsworth's *Prelude* represents an extreme instance of this tendency to self-reference. Though the poem is of epic length and seriousness, its subject is not, as is customary in an epic, history on a world-changing scale but the growth of the poet's mind.

The Prelude exemplifies two other important tendencies. Like Blake, Coleridge in early poems, and later on Shelley, Wordsworth presents himself as, in his words, "a chosen son" or "Bard." That is, he assumes the persona of a poet-prophet, a composite figure modeled on Milton, the biblical prophets, and figures of a national music, the harp-playing patriots, Celtic or Anglo-Saxon, whom eighteenth-century poets and antiquarians had located in a legendary Dark Ages Britain. Adopting this bardic guise, Wordsworth puts himself forward as a spokesman for civilization at a time of crisis—a time, as Wordsworth said in *The Prelude,* of the "melancholy waste of hopes o'erthrown." (Spokesman is appropriate here: almost always, the bardic poet-prophet was a distinctively male persona.) *The Prelude* is also an instance of a central literary form of English, as of European, Romanticism—a long work about the crisis and renewal of the self, recounted as the story of an interior journey taken in quest of one's true identity and destined spiritual home and vocation. Blake's *Milton,* Keats's *Endymion* and *Fall of Hyperion,* and, in Victorian poetry, Elizabeth Barrett Browning's *Aurora Leigh* also exemplify this form. Late in the period there are equivalent developments in prose: spiritual autobiographies (Coleridge's *Biographia Literaria,* Thomas De Quincey's *Confessions of an English Opium Eater*) undergo a revival, at the same time that Lamb and Hazlitt rediscover the essay as a medium of self-revelation.

Spontaneity and the Impulses of Feeling

Wordsworth defined good poetry not merely as the overflow but as the "*spontaneous* overflow" of feelings. In traditional poetics, poetry had been regarded as supremely an art—an art that in modern times is practiced by poets who have assimilated classical precedents, are aware of the "rules" governing the kind of poem they are writing, and (except for the happy touches that, as Pope said, are "beyond the reach of art") deliberately employ tested means to achieve premeditated effects on an audience. But to Wordsworth, although the composition of a poem originates from "emotion recollected in tranquillity" and may be preceded and followed by reflection, the immediate act of composition must be spontaneous—arising from impulse and free from rules. Keats listed as an "axiom" a similar proposition—that "if poetry comes not as naturally as the leaves to a tree it had better not come at all."

Other Romantics voiced similar declarations of artistic independence from inherited precepts, sometimes in a manner involving, paradoxically, a turn from the here-and-now toward a remote, preliterate, and primitive past. If the ancient bard was a charismatic figure for many Romantics, this was in part because imagining the songs he might have sung made it easier to think about an alternative to the mundane language of modernity—about a natural, oral poetry, blissfully unconscious of modern decorums. (Though they chafed against this expectation, writers from the rural working class—Burns and later John Clare—could be expected, by virtue of their perceived distance from the restraint and refinement of civilized discourse, to play a comparable role inside modern culture, that of peasant poet or natural genius.) When, after Waterloo, writers like Byron, Hunt, and the Shelleys traveled to Italy, taking these bardic ideals with them, they became enthralled with the arts of the improvisatore and improvisatrice, men and women whose electrifying oral performances of poetry involved no texts but those of immediate inspiration. One of the writers who praised and emulated that rhapsodic spontaneity, Percy Shelley, thought it "an error to assert that the finest passages of poetry are produced by labor and study." He suggested instead that these were the products of an unconscious creativity: "A great statue or picture grows under the power of the artist as a child in the mother's womb."

The emphasis in this period on the spontaneous activity of the imagination is linked to a belief (which links the Romantics' literary productions to the poetry and fiction of sensibility written earlier in the eighteenth century) in the essential role of passion, whether in the province of art, philosophy, or morality. The intuitive feelings of "the heart" had to supplement the judgments of the purely logical faculty, "the head." "Deep thinking," Coleridge wrote, "is attainable only by a man of deep feeling"; hence, "a metaphysical solution that does not tell you something in the heart is grievously to be suspected as apocryphal."

Romantic "Nature Poetry"

Wordsworth identified *Lyrical Ballads* as his effort to counteract the degradation in taste that had resulted from "the increasing accumulation of men in cities": the revolution in style he proposed in the Preface was meant in part to undo the harmful effects of urbanization. Because he and many fellow writers kept their distance from city life, and because natural scenes so often provide the occasions for their writing, Romantic poetry for present-day readers has become almost synonymous with "nature poetry." In the Essay that supplements his Preface, Wordsworth portrays himself as remedying the failings of predecessors who, he argues, were unable truthfully to depict natural phenomena such as a moonlit sky: from Dryden to Pope, he asserts, there are almost no images of external nature "from which it can be inferred that the eye of the Poet had been steadily fixed upon his object." Neither Romantic theory nor practice, however, justifies the opinion that Romantic poets valued description for its own sake, though many poems of the period are almost unmatched in their ability to capture the sensuous nuances of the natural scene, and the writers participated enthusiastically in the touring of picturesque scenery that was a new leisure activity of their age. But in the Essay Supplementary to the Preface, Wordsworth's complaint against eighteenth-century poetic imagery continues: take an image from an early-eighteenth-century poem, and it will show no signs either, he says, that the Poet's "feelings had urged him to work upon it in the spirit of genuine imagination." For Wordsworth the ability to observe objects accurately is a necessary but not sufficient condition for poetry, "as its exercise supposes all the higher qualities of the mind to be passive, and in a state of subjection to external objects." And while many of the great Romantic lyrics—Wordsworth's "Tintern Abbey," Coleridge's "Frost at Midnight," Keats's "Nightingale," Smith's *Beachy Head*— remark on an aspect or a change of aspect in the natural scene, this serves only as stimulus to the most characteristic human activity, that of thinking. The longer Romantic "nature poems" are in fact usually meditative, using the presented scene to suggest a personal crisis; the organizing principle of the poem involves that crisis's development and resolution.

In addition, Romantic poems habitually endow the landscape with human life, passion, and expressiveness. Many poets respond to the outer universe as a vital entity that participates in the feelings of the observer (an idea of sympathetic exchange between nature and humanity that Mary Shelley, however, would probe fiercely in her novel *The Last Man*). James Thomson and other descriptive poets of the eighteenth century had depicted the created universe as giving direct access to the deity. In "Tintern Abbey" and other poems, Wordsworth not only exhibits toward the landscape attitudes and sentiments that human beings had earlier felt for God; he also loves it in the way human beings love a father, a mother, or a beloved. Still, there was a competing sense, evident especially in the poetry of Blake and Percy Shelley, that natural objects were meaningful primarily for the correspondences linking them to an inner or spiritual world. In their poems a rose, a sunflower, a cloud, or a mountain is presented not as something to be observed and imaged but as an object imbued with a significance beyond itself. "I always seek in what I see," Shelley said, "the likeness of something beyond the present and tangible object." And by Blake, mere nature, as perceived by the physical eye, was spurned "as the dust upon my feet, no part of me." Annotating a copy of Wordsworth's 1815 *Poems*, Blake deplored what *he* perceived as Wordsworth's commitment to unspiritualized observation: "Natural objects always did, and now do, weaken, deaden, and obliterate imagination in men."

The Glorification of the Ordinary

Also discussing Wordsworth, Hazlitt declared his school of poetry the literary equivalent of the French Revolution, which translated political change into poetical experiment. "Kings and queens were dethroned from their rank and station in legitimate tragedy or epic poetry, as they were decapitated elsewhere. . . . The paradox [these poets] set out with was that all things are by nature, equally fit subjects for poetry; or that if there is any preference to give, those that are the meanest [i.e., most humble] and most unpromising are the best." Hazlitt had in mind Wordsworth's statement that the aim of *Lyrical Ballads* was "to choose incidents and situations from common life" and to use a "language really spoken by men": for Wordsworth's polemical purposes, it is in "humble and rustic life" that this language is found. Later eighteenth-century writers had already experimented with the simple treatment of simple subjects. Burns—like the young Wordsworth, a sympathizer with the Revolution—had with great success represented "the rural scenes and rural pleasures of [his] natal Soil," and in a language aiming to be true to the rhythms of his regional Scots dialect. Women poets especially—Barbauld, Robinson, Baillie—assimilated to their poems the subject matter of everyday life. But Wordsworth underwrote his poetic practice with a theory that inverted the traditional hierarchy of poetic genres, subjects, and styles: it elevated humble life and the plain style, which in earlier theory were appropriate only for the pastoral, the genre at the bottom of the traditional hierarchy, into the principal subject and medium for poetry in general. And in his practice, as Hazlitt also noted, Wordsworth went further and turned for the subjects of serious poems not only to humble country folk but to the disgraced, outcast, and delinquent—"convicts, female vagrants, gypsies . . . idiot boys and mad mothers." Hence the scorn of Lord Byron, who facetiously summoned ghosts from the eighteenth century to help him demonstrate that Wordsworth's innovations had been taking literature in the wrong direction:

> "Peddlers," and "Boats," and "Wagons"! Oh! ye shades
> Of Pope and Dryden, are we come to this?

Yet Wordsworth's project was not simply to represent the world as it is but, as he announced in his Preface, to throw over "situations from common life . . . a certain coloring of imagination, whereby ordinary things should be presented to the mind in an unusual aspect." No one can read his poems without noticing the reverence with which he invests words that for earlier writers had been derogatory—words such as "common," "ordinary," "everyday," "humble." Wordsworth's aim was to shatter the lethargy of custom so as to refresh our sense of wonder in the everyday, the trivial, and the lowly. In the eighteenth century Samuel Johnson had said that "wonder is a pause of reason"—"the effect of novelty upon ignorance." But for many Romantics, to arouse in the sophisticated mind that sense of wonder presumed to be felt by the ignorant and the innocent—to renew the universe, Percy Shelley wrote, "after it has been blunted by reiteration"—was a major function of poetry. Commenting on the special imaginative quality of Wordsworth's early verse, Coleridge remarked: "To combine the child's sense of wonder and novelty with the appearances, which every day for perhaps forty years had rendered familiar . . . this is the character and privilege of genius." Contributing to this poetry of the child's-eye view, Baillie and Barbauld wrote poems centered on an observer's effort to imagine the unknowable perspective of beings for whom thought and sensation are new or not begun—in Baillie's case, a "waking infant," in Barbauld's, a "little invisible being who is expected soon to become visible" but is still in its mother's womb.

The Supernatural, the Romance, and Psychological Extremes

In most of his poems, Coleridge, like Wordsworth, dealt with everyday things, and in "Frost at Midnight" he showed how well he too could achieve the effect of wonder in the familiar. But Coleridge tells us in *Biographia Literaria* that, according to the division of labor that organized their collaboration on *Lyrical Ballads*, his assignment was to achieve wonder by a frank violation of natural laws and of the ordinary course of events: in his poems "the incidents and agents were to be, in part at least, supernatural." And in *The Rime of the Ancient Mariner, Christabel,* and "Kubla Khan," Coleridge opened up to modern poetry a realm of mystery and magic. Stories of bewitchings, hauntings, and possession—shaped by antiquated treatises on demonology, folklore, and Gothic novels—supplied him with the means of impressing upon readers a sense of occult powers and unknown modes of being.

Materials like these were often grouped together under the rubric "romance," a term that would some time after the fact give the "Romantic" period its name. On the one hand romances were writings that turned, in their quest for settings conducive to supernatural happenings, to "strange fits of passion" and strange adventures, to distant pasts, faraway places, or both— Keats's "perilous seas, in faery lands forlorn" or the China of "Kubla Khan." On the other hand romance also named a homegrown, native tradition of literature, made unfamiliar and alien by the passage of time. For many authors, starting with Horace Walpole, whose *Castle of Otranto* (1764) began the tradition of Gothic fiction, writing under the banner of romance meant reclaiming their national birthright: a literature of untrammeled imagination— associated, above all, with Spenser and the Shakespeare of fairy magic and witchcraft—that had been forced underground by the Enlightenment's emphasis on reason and refinement. Byron negotiated between romance's two sets of associations in *Childe Harold,* having his hero travel in far-off Albania and become entranced by the inhabitants' savage songs, but also giving the poem the subtitle "A Romaunt" (an archaic spelling of romance) and writing it in Spenserian stanzas. This was the same stanzaic form, neglected for much of the eighteenth century, that Keats drew on for *The Eve of St. Agnes,* the poem in which he proved himself a master of that Romantic mode that establishes a medieval setting for events that violate our sense of realism and the natural order. The Romantic period's "medieval revival" was also promoted by women: Robinson, for instance (author of "Old English," "Monkish," and "Gothic" Tales), as well as Letitia Landon, Felicia Hemans, Joanna Baillie, and others, women who often matched the arch-medievalist Sir Walter Scott in the historical learning they brought to their compositions.

The "addition of strangeness to beauty" that Walter Pater near the end of the nineteenth century would identify as a key Romantic tendency is seen not only in this concern with the exotic and archaic landscapes of romance, but also in the Romantic interest in the mysteries of mental life and determination to investigate psychological extremes. Wordsworth explored visionary states of consciousness that are common among children but violate the categories of adult judgment. Coleridge and De Quincey shared an interest in dreams and nightmares and in the altered consciousness they experienced under their addiction to opium. In his odes as in the quasi-medieval "ballad" "La Belle Dame sans Merci" Keats recorded strange mixtures of pleasure and pain with extraordinary sensitivity, pondering the destructive aspects of sexuality and the erotic quality of the longing for death. And Byron made repeated use of the fascination of the forbidden and the appeal of the terrifying yet seductive Satanic hero.

There were, of course, writers who resisted these poetic engagements with fantasized landscapes and strange passions. Significant dissent came from women, who, given accounts of their sex as especially susceptible to the delusions of romantic love, had particular reason to continue the Enlightenment program and promote the rational regulation of emotion. Barbauld wrote a poem gently advising the young Coleridge not to prolong his stay in the "fairy bower" of romance but to engage actively with the world as it is. Often satirical when she assesses characters who imagine themselves the pitiable victims of their own powerful feelings, Jane Austen had her heroine in *Persuasion,* while conversing with a melancholy, Byron-reading young man, caution him against overindulgence in Byron's "impassioned descriptions of hopeless agony" and "prescribe" to him a "larger allowance of prose in his daily study." And yet this heroine, having "been forced into prudence in her youth," has "learned romance as she grew older." The reversal of the sequence that usually orders the story line of female socialization suggests a receptivity to romance's allure that links even Austen to the spirit of the age.

Individualism and Alienation

Another feature of Byron's poetry that attracted notice and, in some quarters, censure was its insistence on his or his hero's self-sufficiency. Hazlitt, for instance, borrowed lines from Shakespeare's *Coriolanus* to object to Byron's habit of spurning human connection "[a]s if a man were author of himself, / And owned no other kin." The audacious individualism that Hazlitt questions here (a questioning that he carries on in part by enacting his own reliance on others and supplementing his words with Shakespeare's) was, however, central to the celebrations of creativity occupying many Romantic-period writers:

indeed, in the Preface to *Lyrical Ballads*, Wordsworth (as if anticipating and preemptively defying Hazlitt) had already characterized his poetic experimentation as an exercise in artistic self-sufficiency. The Preface has been read as a document in which Wordsworth, proving himself a self-made man, arranges for his disinheritance—arranges to cut himself off, he says, "from a large portion of the phrases and figures of speech which from father to son have long been regarded as the common inheritance of Poets." The German philosophers who generated many of the characteristic ideas of European Romanticism had likewise developed an account of how individuals might author and create themselves. In the work of Kant and others, the human mind was described as creating the universe it perceived and so creating its own experience. Mind is "not passive," Kant's admirer Coleridge wrote, but "made in God's image, and that too in the sublimest sense—the Image of the *Creator*." And Wordsworth declared in *The Prelude* that the individual mind "Doth, like an Agent of the one great Mind, / Create, creator and receiver both." The Romantic period, the epoch of free enterprise, imperial expansion, and boundless revolutionary hope, was also an epoch of individualism in which philosophers and poets alike put an extraordinarily high estimate on human potentialities and powers.

In representing this expanded scope for individual initiative, much poetry of the period redefined heroism and made a ceaseless striving for the unattainable its crucial element. Viewed by moralists of previous ages as sin or lamentable error, longings that can never be satisfied—in Percy Shelley's phrase, "the desire of the moth for a star"—came to be revalued as the glory of human nature. "Less than everything," Blake announced, "cannot satisfy man." Discussions of the nature of art developed similarly. The German philosopher Friedrich Schlegel's proposal that poetry "should forever be becoming and never be perfected" supplied a way to understand the unfinished, "fragment" poems of the period (Coleridge's "Kubla Khan" most famously) not as failures but instead as confirmations that the most poetic poetry was defined as much by what was absent as by what was present: the poem, in this understanding, was a fragmentary trace of an original conception that was too grand ever to be fully realized. This defiant attitude toward limits also made many writers impatient with the conceptions of literary genre they inherited from the past. The result was that, creating new genres from old, they produced an astonishing variety of hybrid forms constructed on fresh principles of organization and style: "elegiac sonnets," "lyrical ballads," the poetic autobiography of *The Prelude*, Percy Shelley's "lyric drama" of cosmic reach, *Prometheus Unbound*, and (in the field of prose) the "historical novels" of Scott and the complex interweaving of letters, reported oral confessions, and interpolated tales that is Mary Shelley's *Frankenstein*. Blake went furthest: the composite art of word and image and "illuminated printing" he created for his poems daringly reinvented the concept of the book.

In this context many writers' choice to portray poetry as a product of solitude and poets as loners might be understood as a means of reinforcing the individuality of their vision. (The sociability of the extroverted narrator of *Don Juan*, who is forever buttonholing "the gentle reader," is exceptional—Byron's way of harkening back to the satire of the eighteenth century.) And the pervasiveness of nature poetry in the period can be attributed to a determination to idealize the natural scene as a site where the individual could find freedom from social laws, an idealization that was easier to sustain when nature was, as often in the era, represented not as cultivated fields but as uninhabitable wild wastes, unploughed uplands, caves, and chasms. Rural *community*, threatened by the enclosures that were breaking up village life, was a tenuous presence in poetry as well.

Wordsworth's imagination is typically released, for instance, by the sudden apparition of a single figure, stark and solitary against a natural background; the words "solitary," "by one self," "alone" sound through his poems. In the poetry of Coleridge, Shelley, and Byron (before *Don Juan* launched Byron's own satire on Byronism), the desolate landscapes are often the haunts of disillusioned visionaries and accursed outlaws, figures whose thwarted ambitions and torments connect them, variously, to Cain, the Wandering Jew, Satan, and even Napoleon. A variant of this figure is Prometheus, the hero of classical mythology, who is Satan-like in setting himself in opposition to God, but who, unlike Satan, is the champion rather than the enemy of the human race. Mary Shelley subjected this hero, central to her husband's mythmaking, to ironic rewriting in *Frankenstein:* Victor Frankenstein, a "Modern Prometheus," is far from championing humankind. For other women writers of the period, and for Shelley in novels following *Frankenstein,* the equivalent to these half-charismatic, half-condemnable figures of alienation is the woman of "genius." In a world in which—as Wollstonecraft complained in the *Rights of Woman*— "all women are to be levelled by meekness and docility, into one character of . . . gentle compliance," the woman who in "unfeminine" fashion claimed a distinctive individuality did not gain authority but risked ostracism. As for the woman of genius, in writings by Robinson, Hemans, and Landon particularly, her story was often told as a modern variation on ancient legends of the Greek Sappho, the ill-fated female poet who had triumphed in poetry but died of love. Pressured by the emergent Victorianism of the 1820s and playing it safe, Hemans and Landon especially were careful to associate genius with self-inflicted sorrow and happiness with a woman's embrace of her domestic calling.

WRITING IN THE MARKETPLACE AND THE COURTS

Even Romantics who wished to associate literature with isolated poets holding mute converse with their souls had to acknowledge that in real life the writer did not dwell in solitude but confronted, and was accountable to, a crowd. For many commentators the most revolutionary aspect of the age was the spread of literacy and the dramatic expansion of the potential audience for literature. This revolution, like the Revolution in France, occasioned a conservative reaction: the worry, frequently expressed as books ceased to be written exclusively for an elite, that this bigger audience (by 1830, about half England's population of fourteen million) would be less qualified to judge or understand what it read. Beginning in 1780, more members of the working classes had learned to read as a result of lessons provided in Sunday schools (informal sites for the education of the poor that long antedated state-supported schools). At the same time reading matter became more plentiful and cheaper, thanks to innovations in retailing—the cut-rate sales of remaindered books and the spread of circulating libraries where volumes could be "rented"—and thanks to technological developments. By the end of the period, printing presses were driven by steam engines, and the manufacture of paper had been mechanized; publishers had mastered publicity, the art (as it was called) of "the puff." Surveying the consequences of these changes, Coleridge muttered darkly about that "misgrowth," "a Reading Public," making it sound like something freakish. Books had become a big business, one enrolling increasing numbers of individuals who found it possible to do without the assistance of wealthy patrons and who, accordingly, looked to this public for their hopes of survival. A few writers became celebrities, invested with a glamor that formerly had been reserved for royalty and that we nowadays save for movie stars. This was the case for the best-selling Byron, particularly, whose enthusiastic public could by the 1830s purchase dinner services imprinted with illustrations from his life and works.

How such popular acclaim was to be understood and how the new reading public that bestowed it (and took it away) could possibly be reformed or monitored when, as Coleridge's term "misgrowth" suggests, its limits and composition seemed unknowable: these were pressing questions for the age. Opponents of the French Revolution and political reform at home pondered a frightening possibility: if "events . . . [had] made us a world of readers" (as Coleridge put it, thinking of how newspapers had proliferated in response to the political upheavals), it might also be true that readers could *make* events in turn, that the new members of the audience for print would demand a part in the drama of national politics. Conservatives were well aware of arguments conjecturing that the Revolution had been the result of the invention of the printing press three centuries before. They certainly could not forget that Paine's *Rights of Man*—not the reading matter for the poor the Sunday-school movement had envisioned—had sold an astonishing two hundred thousand copies in a year. Distributed by clubs of workers who pooled money for this purpose, read aloud in alehouses or as listeners worked in the fields, those copies reached a total audience that was much more numerous still.

However, the British state had lacked legal provisions for the prepublication censorship of books since 1695, which was when the last Licensing Act had lapsed. Throughout the Romantic period therefore the Crown tried out other methods for policing reading and criminalizing certain practices of authoring and publishing. Paine was in absentia found guilty of sedition, for instance, and in 1817 the radical publisher William Hone narrowly escaped conviction for blasphemy. Another government strategy was to use taxes to inflate the prices of printed matter and so keep political information out of the hands of the poor without exactly violating the freedom of the press. In the meantime worries about how the nation would fare now that "the people" read were matched by worries about how to regulate the reading done by women. In 1807 the bowdlerized edition was born, as the Reverend Thomas Bowdler and his sister Henrietta produced *The Family Shakespeare,* concocting a Bard who, his indelicacies expurgated, could be sanctioned family fare.

Commentators who condemned the publishing industry as a scene of criminality also cited the frequency with which, during this chaotic time, best-selling books ended up republished in unauthorized, "pirated" editions. Novels were the pirates' favorite targets. But the radical underground of London's printing industry also appropriated one of the most politically daring works of Percy Shelley, *Queen Mab,* and by keeping it in print, and accessible in cheap editions, thwarted attempts to posthumously sanitize the poet's reputation. And in 1817 Robert Southey, the Poet Laureate, was embarrassed to find his insurrectionary drama of 1794, *Wat Tyler,* republished without his permission. There was no chance, Southey learned, that the thieves who had filched his intellectual property and put this souvenir of his youthful radicalism back into circulation would be punished: the judiciary ruled that copyright law was for the law-abiding and did not apply to "sedition."

OTHER LITERARY FORMS

Prose

Although we now know the Romantic period as an age of poetry, centered on works of imagination, nonfiction prose forms—essays, reviews, political pamphlets—flourished during the epoch, as writers seized the opportunity to speak to and for the era's new audiences. In eighteenth-century England, prose, particularly in the urbane, accessible style that writers such as Addison and Hume cultivated in their essays, had been valued as the medium of sociable exchange that could integrate different points of view and unify the public space known as the "republic of letters." That ideal of civil discussion came under pressure in the Romantic period, however, since by then many intellectuals were uncertain whether a republic of letters could survive the arrival of those new readers, "the people," and whether in this age of class awareness such a thing as a unified public culture was even possible. Those uncertainties are never far from the surface in the masterpieces of Romantic prose—a category that ranges from the pamphleteering that drew Burke, Wollstonecraft, and Paine into the Revolution controversy of the 1790s, to the periodical essays, with suggestive titles like *The Watchman* and *The Friend,* in which Coleridge turned controversialist, to the magazine writing of Hazlitt, Lamb, and De Quincey in the 1820s.

The issue of how the writer should relate to audience—as watchman or friend?—was especially tricky, because this period, when so many more people defined themselves as readers, saw the emergence of a new species of specialist reader. This was the critic, who, perhaps problematically, was empowered to tell all the others what to read. Following the establishment in 1802 of the *Edinburgh Review* and in 1809 of the *Quarterly Review,* a new professionalized breed of book reviewer claimed a degree of cultural authority to which eighteenth-century critics had never aspired. Whereas later-eighteenth-century periodicals such as the *Monthly Review* and *Critical Review* had aimed to notice almost everything in print, the *Edinburgh* and *Quarterly* limited themselves to about fifteen books per issue. The selectivity enabled them to make decisive statements about what would count as culture and what would fall beyond the pale. They also conceptualized criticism as a space of discipline, in which the reputations of the writers under review were as likely to be marred as they were to be made. The stern Latin motto of the *Edinburgh* (founded by lawyers) translates as "the judge is condemned when the guilty go free." The continuing tension in the relations between criticism and literature and doubt about whether critical prose can be literature—whether it can have artistic value as well as social utility—are legacies from the Romantic era. Hazlitt wondered self-consciously in an essay on criticism whether his was not in fact a critical rather than a poetical age and whether "no great works of genius appear, because so much is said and written about them."

Hazlitt participated importantly in another development. In 1820 the founding editor of the *London Magazine* gathered a group of writers, Hazlitt, Lamb, and De Quincey, who in the *London's* pages collectively developed the Romantic form known as the familiar essay: intimate-feeling commentaries, often presented as if prompted by incidents in the authors' private lives, on an eclectic range of topics, from pork to prize-fighting. In some of his essays, Hazlitt modeled an account of the individual's response to works of art as most important not for how, for instance, it prepares that person for public citizenship, but for what it helps him discover about his personality. For their essays Lamb and De Quincey developed a style that harkened back to writers who flourished before the republic of letters and who had more idiosyncratic eccentricities than eighteenth-century decorum would have allowed. Though these essayists were very differently circumstanced from the Romantic poets who were their friends—paid by the page and writing to a deadline, for a start—their works thus parallel the poets' in also turning toward the personal and subjective. One consequence of the essayists' cultivation of intimacy and preference for the impressionistic over the systematic is that, when we track the history of prose to the 1820s, we see it end up in a place very different from the one it occupies at the start of the Romantic period. Participants in the Revolution controversy of the 1790s had claimed to speak for all England. By the close of the period the achievement of the familiar essay was to have brought the medium of prose within the category of "the literary"—but by distancing it from public life.

Drama

Whether the plays composed during the Romantic period can qualify as literature has been, by contrast, more of a puzzle. England throughout this period had a vibrant theatrical culture. Theater criticism, practiced with flair by Hazlitt and Lamb, emerged as a new prose genre; actors like Sarah Siddons and Edmund Kean numbered the poets among their admirers and found their way into Romantic poetry; Mary Robinson was known as an actor before she was known as an author. But there were many restrictions limiting what could be staged in England and many calls for reform. As places where crowds gathered, theaters were always closely watched by suspicious government officials. The English had habitually extolled their theater as a site of social mixing—a mirror to the political order in that it supplied all the classes in the nation (those who, depending on how their tickets were priced, frequented the box, the pit, or the gallery) with another sort of representative assembly. But during this era *disorder* seemed the rule: riots broke out at Covent Garden in 1792 and 1809. The link between drama and disorder was one reason that new dramas had to meet the approval of a censor before they could be performed, a rule in place since 1737. Another restriction was that only the theaters royal (in London, Drury Lane and Covent Garden) had the legal right to produce "legitimate" (spoken word) drama, leaving the other stages limited to entertainments—pantomimes and melodramas mainly—in which dialogue was by regulation always combined with music. An evening's entertainment focused on legitimate drama would not have been so different. The stages and auditoriums of the two theaters royal were huge spaces, which encouraged their managers to favor grandiose spectacles or, more precisely, multimedia experiences, involving musicians, dancers, and artists who designed scenery, besides players and playwrights.

This theatrical culture's demotion of *words* might explain why the poets of the era, however stagestruck, found drama uncongenial. Nonetheless, almost all tried their hands at the form, tempted by the knowledge that the plays of certain of their (now less esteemed) contemporaries—Hannah Cowley and Charles Maturin, for example—had met with immense acclaim. Some of the poets' plays were composed to be read rather than performed: "closet dramas," such as Byron's *Manfred,* Shelley's *Prometheus Unbound,* and most of Baillie's *Plays on the Passions,* permitted experimentation with topic and form. Others were written expressly for the stage, but their authors were hampered by their inexperience and tendency, exacerbated by the censorship that encouraged them to seek safe subject matter in the past, to imitate the style of Elizabethan and Jacobean drama. There were exceptions to this discouraging record. Coleridge's tragedy *Remorse,* for instance, was a minor hit and ran for twenty nights in 1813. The most capable dramatist among the poets was, surprisingly, Percy Shelley. His powerful tragedy *The Cenci* (1820), the story of a monstrous father who rapes his daughter and is murdered by her in turn, was deemed unstageable on political rather than artistic or technical grounds. It had no chance of getting by the Examiner of Plays; indeed, by thematizing the unspeakable topic of incest, Shelley predicted his own censoring.

The Novel

Novels at the start of the Romantic period were immensely popular but—as far as critics and some of the form's half-ashamed practitioners were concerned—not quite respectable. Loose in structure, they seemed to require fewer skills than other literary genres. This genre lacked the classic pedigree claimed by poetry and drama. It attracted (or so detractors declared) an undue proportion of readers who were women, and who, by consuming its escapist stories of romantic love, risked developing false ideas of life. It likewise attracted (so some of these same critics complained) too many *writers* who were women. (By the 1780s women were publishing as many novels as men.) Because of its popularity, the form also focused commentators' anxieties about the expansion of the book market and commercialization of literature: hence late-eighteenth-century reviewers of new novels often sarcastically described them as mass-produced commodities, not authored exactly, but instead stamped out automatically in "novel-mills." Matters changed decisively, however, starting around 1814. Reviews of Scott's *Waverley* series of historical novels and then a review that Scott wrote of Jane Austen's *Emma* declared a renaissance—"a new style of novel." By this time, too, the genre had its historians, who delineated the novel's origins and rise and in this manner established its particularity against the more reputable literary forms. It was having a canon created for it too; figures like Barbauld and Scott compiled and introduced collections of the best novels. So equipped, the novel began to endanger poetry's long-held monopoly on literary prestige.

There had in fact been earlier signs of these new ambitions for the genre, although reviewers did not then know what to make of them. The last decade of the eighteenth century saw bold experiments with novels' form and subject matter—in particular, new ways of linking fiction with philosophy and history. Rather than, as one reviewer put it, contentedly remaining in a "region of their own," some novels showed signs of having designs on the real world. The writers now known as the Jacobin novelists used the form to test political theories and represent the political upheavals of the age. Thus in *Caleb Williams, or, Things as They Are,* the philosopher William Godwin (husband of Mary Wollstonecraft and father of Mary Shelley) set out, he said, to "write a tale, that shall constitute an epoch in the mind of the reader, that no one, after he had read it, shall ever be exactly the same": the result was a chilling novel of surveillance and entrapment in which a servant recounts the persecutions he suffers at the hands of the master whose secret past he has detected. (The disturbing cat-and-mouse game between the two gets rewritten two decades later as the conclusion to *Frankenstein,* a novel that, among many other things, represents Shelley's tribute to the philosophical fictions of her parents.) Loyalists attacked the Jacobins with their own weapons and, in making novels their ammunition, contributed in turn to enhancing the genre's cultural presence.

Another innovation in novel-writing took shape, strangely enough, as a recovery of what was old. Writers whom we now describe as the Gothic novelists revisited the romance, the genre identified as the primitive forerunner of the modern novel, looking to a medieval (i.e., "Gothic") Europe that they pictured as a place of gloomy castles, devious Catholic monks, and stealthy ghosts. These authors—first Walpole, followed by Clara Reeve, Sophia Lee, Matthew Lewis, and the hugely popular Ann Radcliffe—developed for the novel a repertory of settings and story lines meant to purvey to readers the pleasurable terror of regression to a premodern, prerational state. This Gothic turn was another instance of the period's "romance revival," another variation on the effort to renew the literature of the present by reworking the past. Gothic fiction was thus promoted in terms running parallel to those in accounts of the powers of poetry: when novels break with humdrum reality, Anna Barbauld explained, "our imagination, darting forth, explores with rapture the new world which is laid open to its view, and rejoices in the expansion of its powers."

Possibly this "new world" was meant to supply Romantic-period readers with an escape route from the present and from what Godwin called "things as they are." Certainly, the pasts that Gothic novelists conjure up are conceived of in fanciful, freewheeling ways; it is comical just how often a Radcliffe heroine who is supposed to inhabit sixteenth-century France can act like a proper English girl on the marriage market in the 1790s. But even that example of anachronism might suggest that some Gothic novelists were inviting readers to assess their stories as engaging the questions of the day. Gothic horrors gave many writers a language in which to examine the nature of power—the elements of sadism and masochism in the relations between men and women, for instance. And frequently the Gothic novelists probe the very ideas of historical accuracy and legitimacy that critics use against them, and meditate on who is authorized to tell the story of the past and who is not.

The ascendancy of the novel in the early nineteenth century is in many ways a function of fiction writers' new self-consciousness about their relation to works of history. By 1814 the novelist and historian encroached on each other's territory more than ever. This was not exactly because nineteenth-century novelists were renewing their commitment to probability and realism (although, defining themselves against the critically reviled Gothic novelists, many were), but rather because the nature of things historical was also being reinvented. In light of the Revolution, history's traditional emphasis on public affairs and great men had begun to give way to an emphasis on beliefs, customs, everyday habits—the approach we now identify with social history. Novelists pursued similar interests: in works like *Castle Rackrent,* Maria Edgeworth, for instance, provides an almost anthropological account of the way of life of a bygone Ireland. The only novelist before Scott whom the influential *Edinburgh Review* took seriously, Edgeworth builds into her "national tales" details about local practices that demonstrate how people's ways of seeing are rooted in the particularities of their native places. Scott learned from her, incorporating her regionalism into his new style of historical novels, in which, with deeply moving results, he also portrayed the past as a place of adventure, pageantry, and grandeur.

Scott and Edgeworth establish the master theme of the early-nineteenth-century novel: the question of how the individual consciousness intermeshes with larger social structures, of how far character is the product of history and how far it is not. Jane Austen's brilliance as a satirist of the English leisure class often prompts literary historians to compare her works to witty Restoration and eighteenth-century comedies. But she too helped bring this theme to the forefront of novel-writing, devising new ways of articulating the relationship between the psychological history of the individual and the history of society, and, with unsurpassed psychological insight, creating unforgettable heroines who live in time and change. As with other Romantics, Austen's topic is revolution—revolutions of the mind. The momentous event in her fictions, which resemble Wordsworth's poetry in finding out the extraordinary in the everyday, is the change of mind that creates the possibility of love. Contrasting his own "big bow-wow strain" with Austen's nuance, Scott wrote that Austen "had a talent for describing the involvements and feelings and characters of ordinary life, which is to me the most wonderful I ever met with." Nineteenth-century reviewers of his triumphant *Waverley* series were certain that Scott's example foretold the future of novel-writing. He, however, recognized the extent to which Austen had also changed the genre in which she worked, by developing a new novelistic language for the workings of the mind in flux.

Additional information about the Romantic Period, including primary texts and images, is available at Norton Literature Online (www.wwnorton.com/literature). Online topics are

- *Tintern Abbey*, Tourism, and Romantic Landscape
- The Satanic and Byronic Hero
- The French Revolution
- Romantic Orientalism

THE ROMANTIC PERIOD

TEXTS	CONTEXTS
1773 Anna Letitia Aikin (later Barbauld), *Poems*	
1774 J. W. von Goethe, *The Sorrows of Young Werther*	
	1775 American War of Independence (1775–83)
1776 Adam Smith, *The Wealth of Nations*	
1778 Frances Burney, *Evelina*	
1779 Samuel Johnson, *Lives of the English Poets* (1779–81)	
	1780 Gordon Riots in London
1781 Immanuel Kant, *Critique of Pure Reason*. Jean-Jacques Rousseau, *Confessions*. J. C. Friedrich Schiller, *The Robbers*	
	1783 William Pitt becomes prime minister (serving until 1801 and again in 1804–06)
1784 Charlotte Smith, *Elegiac Sonnets*	1784 Death of Samuel Johnson
1785 William Cowper, *The Task*	
1786 William Beckford, *Vathek*. Robert Burns, *Poems, Chiefly in the Scottish Dialect*	
	1787 W. A. Mozart, *Don Giovanni*. Society for the Abolition of the Slave Trade founded
1789 Jeremy Bentham, *Principles of Morals and Legislation*. William Blake, *Songs of Innocence*	1789 Fall of the Bastille (beginning of the French Revolution)
1790 Joanna Baillie, *Poems*. Blake, *The Marriage of Heaven and Hell*. Edmund Burke, *Reflections on the Revolution in France*	1790 J. M. W. Turner first exhibits at the Royal Academy
1791 William Gilpin, *Observations on the River Wye*. Thomas Paine, *Rights of Man*. Ann Radcliffe, *The Romance of the Forest*	1791 Revolution in Santo Domingo (modern Haiti)
1792 Mary Wollstonecraft, *A Vindication of the Rights of Woman*	1792 September Massacres in Paris. First gas lights in Britain
1793 William Godwin, *Political Justice*	1793 Execution of Louis XVI and Marie Antoinette. France declares war against Britain (and then Britain against France). The Reign of Terror
1794 Blake, *Songs of Experience*. Godwin, *Caleb Williams*. Radcliffe, *The Mysteries of Udolpho*	1794 The fall of Robespierre. Trials for high treason of members of the London Corresponding Society
	1795 Pitt's Gagging Acts suppress freedom of speech and assembly in Britain

TEXTS	CONTEXTS
1796 Matthew Gregory Lewis, *The Monk*	
	1797 Death of complications resulting from childbirth of Mary Wollstonecraft
1798 Joanna Baillie, *Plays on the Passions*, volume 1. Bentham, *Political Economy*. Thomas Malthus, *An Essay on the Principle of Population*. William Wordsworth and Samuel Taylor Coleridge, *Lyrical Ballads*	**1798** Rebellion in Ireland
1800 Maria Edgeworth, *Castle Rackrent*. Mary Robinson, *Lyrical Tales*	
	1801 Parliamentary Union of Ireland and Great Britain
	1802 Treaty of Amiens. *Edinburgh Review* founded. John Constable first exhibits at the Royal Academy
	1804 Napoleon crowned emperor. Founding of the republic of Haiti
1805 Walter Scott, *The Lay of the Last Minstrel*	**1805** The French fleet defeated by the British at Trafalgar
1807 Wordsworth, *Poems in Two Volumes*	**1807** Abolition of the slave trade in Britain
1808 Goethe, *Faust*, part 1	**1808** Ludwig van Beethoven, *Symphonies* 5 and 6
	1809 *Quarterly Review* founded
	1811 The Prince of Wales becomes regent for George III, who is declared incurably insane
1812 Lord Byron, *Childe Harold's Pilgrimage*, cantos 1 and 2. Felicia Hemans, *The Domestic Affections*	**1812** War between Britain and the United States (1812–15)
1813 Jane Austen, *Pride and Prejudice*	
1814 Walter Scott, *Waverley*. Wordsworth, *The Excursion*	
	1815 Napoleon defeated at Waterloo. Corn Laws passed, protecting economic interests of the landed aristocracy
1816 Byron, *Childe Harold,* cantos 3 and 4. Coleridge, *Christabel*, "Kubla Khan." Percy Shelley, *Alastor*	
1817 Byron, *Manfred*. Coleridge, *Biographia Literaria* and *Sibylline Leaves*. John Keats, *Poems*	**1817** *Blackwood's Edinburgh Magazine* founded. Death of Princess Charlotte. Death of Jane Austen
1818 Austen, *Northanger Abbey*. Keats, *Endymion*. Thomas Love Peacock, *Nightmare Abbey*. Mary Shelley, *Frankenstein*	

TEXTS	CONTEXTS
1819 Byron, *Don Juan*, cantos 1 and 2	1819 "Peterloo Massacre" in Manchester
1820 John Clare, *Poems Descriptive of Rural Life*. Keats, *Lamia, Isabella, The Eve of St. Agnes, and Other Poems*. Percy Shelley, *Prometheus Unbound*	1820 Death of George III; accession of George IV. *London Magazine* founded
1821 Thomas De Quincey, *Confessions of an English Opium-Eater*. Percy Shelley, *Adonais*	1821 Deaths of Keats in Rome and Napoleon at St. Helena
	1822 Franz Schubert, *Unfinished Symphony*. Death of Percy Shelley in the Bay of Spezia, near Lerici, Italy
1824 Letitia Landon, *The Improvisatrice*	1824 Death of Byron in Missolonghi
1827 Clare, *The Shepherd's Calendar*	
1828 Hemans, *Records of Woman*	1828 Parliamentary repeal of the Test and Corporation Acts excluding Dissenters from state offices
	1829 Catholic Emancipation
1830 Charles Lyell, *Principles of Geology* (1830–33). Alfred Tennyson, *Poems, Chiefly Lyrical*	1830 Death of George IV; accession of William IV. Revolution in France
	1832 First Reform Bill

ANNA LETITIA BARBAULD
1743–1825

Anna Barbauld, born Anna Letitia Aikin, received an unusual education from her father, a minister and a teacher, after 1758, at the Warrington Academy in Lancashire, the great educational center for the Nonconformist community, whose religion barred them from admission to the universities of Oxford and Cambridge. Over the course of the eighteenth century, Dissenting academies such as Warrington had developed a modern curriculum in the natural sciences, as well as in modern languages and English literature. This progressive educational program deviated significantly from the classics-based curriculum, scarcely altered since the sixteenth century, that was supplied by the old universities. Barbauld benefited from the curriculum the Dissenters had designed with their sons in mind and mastered French and Italian, and then Latin and Greek, while still a girl.

She made her literary debut with *Poems,* which went through five editions between 1773 and 1777 and immediately established her as a leading poet. In 1774 she married Rochemont Barbauld, a Dissenting minister, and with him comanaged a school at Palgrave, in Suffolk. Thereafter, becoming increasingly famous and respected in literary circles as (according to the custom of the day) "Mrs. Barbauld," she divided her time between the teaching of younger pupils at Palgrave and a series of writings focused on education, politics, and literature. She published *Devotional Pieces* (1775), three volumes of *Lessons for Children* (1778–79), and *Hymns in Prose for Children* (1781), all of which were reprinted many times. William Hazlitt records a common experience in recalling that he read her works "before those of any other author, male or female, when I was learning to spell words of one syllable in her storybooks for children."

She wrote political pamphlets in the 1790s, opposing Britain's declaration of war against France, defending democratic government and popular education, and campaigning for the repeal of the Test Acts that had long excluded Nonconformist Protestants (those who would not subscribe, as a "test" of their loyalty, to the thirty-nine Articles of the Established Church) from the public life of the nation. Her 1791 "Epistle to William Wilberforce" attacked Britain's involvement in the slave trade. She accompanied her poetry and political writing with editing, producing an edition of William Collins's poems (1797), six volumes of the correspondence of the mid-eighteenth-century novelist Samuel Richardson (1804), fifty volumes of *The British Novelists* (beginning in 1810), and a popular anthology of poetry and prose for young women called *The Female Speaker* (1811). *The British Novelists* was the first attempt to establish a national canon in fiction paralleling the multivolume collections of British poets (such as the one associated with Samuel Johnson's prefaces) that had been appearing since the 1770s. Her introductory essay, "On the Origin and Progress of Novel-Writing," is a pioneering statement concerning the educational value of novels.

Barbauld's last major work in poetry was *Eighteen Hundred and Eleven* (1812), a bitter diagnosis of contemporary British life and politics, which lamented the war with France (then in its seventeenth year), the poverty of leadership, the fallen economy, colonialism, and the failure of genius (at the conclusion, the Spirit of Genius emigrates to South America). Critics, even the more liberal ones, were antagonized by a woman writer's use of the scourge of Juvenalian satire, and their response was anguished and unanimously negative; and Barbauld seems not to have attempted another long work after this (she was, by this time, in her late sixties). After Barbauld's death, her niece Lucy Aikin brought out her aunt's *Works* (two volumes), including several previously unpublished pieces.

The Mouse's Petition[1]

*Found in the trap where he had been confined all night by Dr. Priestley,
for the sake of making experiments with different kinds of air*

"Parcere subjectis, et debellare superbos."
—Virgil

Oh hear a pensive prisoner's prayer,
For liberty that sighs;
And never let thine heart be shut
Against the wretch's cries.

5   For here forlorn and sad I sit,
Within the wiry gate;
And tremble at th' approaching morn,
Which brings impending fate.

If e'er thy breast with freedom glow'd,
10   And spurn'd a tyrant's chain,
Let not thy strong oppressive force
A free-born mouse detain.

Oh do not stain with guiltless blood
Thy hospitable hearth;
15   Nor triumph that thy wiles betray'd
A prize so little worth.

The scatter'd gleanings of a feast
My frugal meals supply;
But if thine unrelenting heart
20   That slender boon deny,

The cheerful light, the vital air,
Are blessings widely given;
Let nature's commoners enjoy
The common gifts of heaven.

25   The well-taught philosophic mind
To all compassion gives;
Casts round the world an equal eye,
And feels for all that lives.

If mind, as ancient sages taught,[2]
30   A never dying flame,

1. Addressed to the clergyman, political theorist, and scientist Joseph Priestley (1733–1804), who at this time was the most distinguished teacher at the Nonconformist Protestant Warrington Academy, where Barbauld's father was also a member of the faculty. The imagined speaker (the petitioning mouse) is destined to participate in just the sort of experiment that led Priestley, a few years later, to the discovery of "phlogiston"—what we now call oxygen. Tradition has it that when Barbauld showed him the lines, Priestley set the mouse free. According to Barbauld's modern editors, the poem was many times reprinted and was a favorite to assign students for memorizing. The Latin epigraph is from *The Aeneid* 6.853, "To spare the humbled, and to tame in war the proud."
2. Lines 29–36 play on the idea of transmigration of souls, a doctrine that Priestley believed until the early 1770s.

Still shifts through matter's varying forms,
In every form the same,

Beware, lest in the worm you crush
A brother's soul you find;
35 And tremble lest thy luckless hand
Dislodge a kindred mind.

Or, if this transient gleam of day
Be *all* of life we share,
Let pity plead within thy breast
40 That little *all* to spare.

So may thy hospitable board
With health and peace be crown'd;
And every charm of heartfelt ease
Beneath thy roof be found.

45 So, when destruction lurks unseen,
Which men, like mice, may share,
May some kind angel clear thy path,
And break the hidden snare.

ca. 1771   1773

An Inventory of the Furniture in Dr. Priestley's Study

A map of every country known,[1]
With not a foot of land his own.
A list of folks that kicked a dust
On this poor globe, from Ptol. the First;[2]
5 He hopes,—indeed it is but fair,—
Some day to get a corner there.
A group of all the British kings,
Fair emblem! on a packthread swings.
The Fathers, ranged in goodly row,[3]
10 A decent, venerable show,
Writ a great while ago, they tell us,
And many an inch o'ertop their fellows.
A Juvenal to hunt for mottos;
And Ovid's tales of nymphs and grottos.[4]
15 The meek-robed lawyers, all in white;
Pure as the lamb,—at least, to sight.
A shelf of bottles, jar and phial,°   *vial*
By which the rogues he can defy all,—
All filled with lightning keen and genuine,
20 And many a little imp he'll pen you in;

1. The maps, historical charts, books, and scientific apparatus are all part of the "furniture" (furnishings) of Joseph Priestley's study (see the first note to the preceding poem).
2. Ptolemy I (ca. 367–283 B.C.E.), founder of the Ptolemaic dynasty in Egypt.
3. The works of the Catholic Church Fathers.
4. Ovid's *Metamorphoses* and the works of the Roman satirist Juvenal.

Which, like Le Sage's sprite, let out,
Among the neighbours makes a rout;[5]
Brings down the lightning on their houses,
And kills their geese, and frights their spouses.
25 A rare thermometer, by which
He settles, to the nicest pitch,
The just degrees of heat, to raise
Sermons, or politics, or plays.
Papers and books, a strange mixed olio,
30 From shilling touch° to pompous folio;   *cheap pamphlet*
Answer, remark, reply, rejoinder,
Fresh from the mint, all stamped and coined here;
Like new-made glass, set by to cool,
Before it bears the workman's tool.
35 A blotted proof-sheet, wet from Bowling.[6]
—"How can a man his anger hold in?"—
Forgotten rimes, and college themes,
Worm-eaten plans, and embryo schemes;—
A mass of heterogeneous matter,
40 A chaos dark, nor land nor water;—
New books, like new-born infants, stand,
Waiting the printer's clothing hand;—
Others, a motley ragged brood,
Their limbs unfashioned all, and rude,
45 Like Cadmus' half-formed men appear;[7]
One rears a helm, one lifts a spear,
And feet were lopped and fingers torn
Before their fellow limbs were born;
A leg began to kick and sprawl
50 Before the head was seen at all,
Which quiet as a mushroom lay
Till crumbling hillocks gave it way;
And all, like controversial writing,
Were born with teeth, and sprung up fighting.
55   "But what is this," I hear you cry,
"Which saucily provokes my eye?"—
A thing unknown, without a name,
Born of the air and doomed to flame.

ca. 1771   1825

A Summer Evening's Meditation[1]

'Tis past! The sultry tyrant of the south
Has spent his short-lived rage; more grateful° hours   *pleasing*
Move silent on; the skies no more repel

5. In René LeSage's *Le Diable Boiteux* (1707), a laboratory-created spirit lifts the roofs from the neighbors' houses, exposing their private lives and creating havoc.
6. Presumably a local printer.
7. Armed men created when Cadmus sowed the earth with the teeth of a dragon he had killed

(Ovid's *Metamorphoses* 3.95–114).
1. This poem looks backward to poems such as William Collins's "Ode to Evening" (1747), Anne Finch's "A Nocturnal Reverie" (1713), and even to Milton's description in book 2 of *Paradise Lost* of Satan's daring navigation of the realm of Chaos. At the same time Barbauld's excursion-and-return

The dazzled sight, but with mild maiden beams
5   Of tempered lustre court the cherished eye
To wander o'er their sphere; where, hung aloft,
Dian's bright crescent, like a silver bow
New strung in heaven, lifts high its beamy horns
Impatient for the night, and seems to push
10 Her brother° down the sky. Fair Venus shines   *Apollo*
Even in the eye of day; with sweetest beam
Propitious shines, and shakes a trembling flood
Of softened radiance from her dewy locks.
The shadows spread apace; while meekened² Eve,
15 Her cheek yet warm with blushes, slow retires
Through the Hesperian gardens of the west,
And shuts the gates of day. 'Tis now the hour
When Contemplation from her sunless haunts,
The cool damp grotto, or the lonely depth
20 Of unpierced woods, where wrapt in solid shade
She mused away the gaudy hours of noon,
And fed on thoughts unripened by the sun,
Moves forward; and with radiant finger points
To yon blue concave swelled by breath divine,
25 Where, one by one, the living eyes of heaven
Awake, quick kindling o'er the face of ether
One boundless blaze; ten thousand trembling fires,
And dancing lustres, where the unsteady eye,
Restless and dazzled, wanders unconfined
30 O'er all this field of glories; spacious field,
And worthy of the Master: he, whose hand
With hieroglyphics elder than the Nile
Inscribed the mystic tablet, hung on high
To public gaze, and said, "Adore, O man!
35 The finger of thy God." From what pure wells
Of milky light, what soft o'erflowing urn,
Are all these lamps so fill'd? these friendly lamps,
For ever streaming o'er the azure deep
To point our path, and light us to our home.
40 How soft they slide along their lucid spheres!
And silent as the foot of Time, fulfill
Their destined courses: Nature's self is hushed,
And, but° a scattered leaf, which rustles through   *except for*
The thick-wove foliage, not a sound is heard
45 To break the midnight air; though the raised ear,
Intensely listening, drinks in every breath.
How deep the silence, yet how loud the praise!
But are they silent all? or is there not
A tongue in every star, that talks with man,
50 And woos him to be wise? nor woos in vain:
This dead of midnight is the noon of thought,
And Wisdom mounts her zenith with the stars.

structure anticipates the high flights (and returns) of later lyrics by Coleridge, Percy Shelley, and Keats. But her account of the journey, with its references to Diana's crescent (line 7) and Venus's sweetest beams (10 and 11) is *differently* gendered: this soul that launches "into the trackless deeps" (82) is clearly female.
2. Softened, made meek.

At this still hour the self-collected soul
Turns inward, and beholds a stranger there
55 Of high descent, and more than mortal rank;
An embryo God; a spark of fire divine,
Which must burn on for ages, when the sun,—
Fair transitory creature of a day!—
Has closed his golden eye, and wrapt in shades
60 Forgets his wonted journey through the east.

Ye citadels of light, and seats of Gods!
Perhaps my future home, from whence the soul,
Revolving° periods past, may oft look back   *Meditating on*
With recollected tenderness on all
65 The various busy scenes she left below,
Its deep-laid projects and its strange events,
As on some fond and doting tale that soothed
Her infant hours—O be it lawful now
To tread the hallowed circle of your courts,
70 And with mute wonder and delighted awe
Approach your burning confines. Seized in thought,
On Fancy's wild and roving wing I sail,
From the green borders of the peopled Earth,
And the pale Moon, her duteous fair attendant;
75 From solitary Mars; from the vast orb
Of Jupiter, whose huge gigantic bulk
Dances in ether like the lightest leaf;
To the dim verge, the suburbs of the system,
Where cheerless Saturn 'midst his watery moons[3]
80 Girt with a lucid zone,° in gloomy pomp,   *belt*
Sits like an exiled monarch: fearless thence
I launch into the trackless deeps of space,
Where, burning round, ten thousand suns appear,
Of elder beam, which ask no leave to shine
85 Of our terrestrial star, nor borrow light
From the proud regent of our scanty day;
Sons of the morning, first-born of creation,
And only less than Him who marks their track,
And guides their fiery wheels. Here must I stop,
90 Or is there aught beyond? What hand unseen
Impels me onward through the glowing orbs
Of habitable nature, far remote,
To the dread confines of eternal night,
To solitudes of vast unpeopled space,
95 The deserts of creation, wide and wild;
Where embryo systems and unkindled suns
Sleep in the womb of chaos? fancy droops,
And thought astonished stops her bold career.
But O thou mighty mind! whose powerful word
100 Said, thus let all things be, and thus they were,[4]
Where shall I seek thy presence? how unblamed

---

3. Saturn marked the outmost bounds of the solar
system until the discovery of Uranus in 1781.

4. An echo of Genesis 1.3.

      Invoke thy dread perfection?
      Have the broad eyelids of the morn beheld thee?
      Or does the beamy shoulder of Orion
105 Support thy throne? O look with pity down
      On erring, guilty man! not in thy names
      Of terror clad; not with those thunders armed
      That conscious Sinai felt, when fear appalled
      The scattered tribes;⁵—thou hast a gentler voice,
110 That whispers comfort to the swelling heart,
      Abashed, yet longing to behold her Maker.

      But now my soul, unused to stretch her powers
      In flight so daring, drops her weary wing,
      And seeks again the known accustomed spot,
115 Drest up with sun, and shade, and lawns, and streams,
      A mansion fair, and spacious for its guest,
      And full replete with wonders. Let me here,
      Content and grateful, wait the appointed time,
      And ripen for the skies: the hour will come
120 When all these splendours bursting on my sight
      Shall stand unveiled, and to my ravished sense
      Unlock the glories of the world unknown.

1773

Epistle to William Wilberforce, Esq. on the Rejection of the Bill for Abolishing the Slave Trade[1]

      Cease, Wilberforce, to urge thy generous aim!
      Thy Country knows the sin, and stands the shame!
      The Preacher, Poet, Senator in vain
      Has rattled in her sight the Negro's chain;
5   With his deep groans assail'd her startled ear,
      And rent the veil that hid his constant tear;
      Forc'd her averted eyes his stripes to scan,
      Beneath the bloody scourge laid bare the man,
      Claim'd Pity's tear, urg'd Conscience' strong control,
10 And flash'd conviction on her shrinking soul.
      The Muse too, soon awak'd, with ready tongue
      At Mercy's shrine applausive° paeans rung;   *approving*
      And Freedom's eager sons, in vain foretold
      A new Astrean reign,° an age of gold: *reign of justice*
15 She knows and she persists—Still Afric bleeds,
      Uncheck'd, the human traffic still proceeds;
      She stamps her infamy to future time,

---

5. When God came down to deliver the Ten Commandments "there were thunders and lightnings . . . so that all the people . . . trembled" (Exodus 19.16).

1. On April 18, 1791, the politician and humanitarian Wilberforce (1759–1833) presented a motion in the House of Commons to abolish the slave trade. The motion was rejected a day later by a vote of 163 to 88. Sixteen years passed before the trade was outlawed in the British West Indies (1807), and another twenty-six before it was abolished in the rest of the British Empire (1833).

And on her harden'd forehead seals the crime.
    In vain, to thy white standard gathering round,
20 Wit, Worth, and Parts and Eloquence are found:
In vain, to push to birth thy great design,
Contending chiefs, and hostile virtues join;
All, from conflicting ranks, of power possest
To rouse, to melt, or to inform the breast.
25 Where seasoned tools of Avarice prevail,
A Nation's eloquence, combined, must fail:
Each flimsy sophistry by turns they try;
The plausive° argument, the daring lie,   *specious*
The artful gloss, that moral sense confounds,
30 Th' acknowledged thirst of gain that honour wounds:
Bane of ingenuous minds, th' unfeeling sneer,
Which, sudden, turns to stone the falling tear:
They search assiduous, with inverted skill,
For forms of wrong, and precedents of ill;
35 With impious mockery wrest the sacred page,
And glean up crimes from each remoter age:
Wrung Nature's tortures, shuddering, while you tell,
From scoffing fiends bursts forth the laugh of hell;
In Britain's senate, Misery's pangs give birth
40 To jests unseemly, and to horrid mirth—
Forbear!—thy virtues but provoke our doom,
And swell th' account of vengeance yet to come;
For, not unmark'd in Heaven's impartial plan,
Shall man, proud worm, contemn his fellow-man?
45 And injur'd Afric, by herself redrest,
Darts her own serpents at her Tyrant's breast.
Each vice, to minds deprav'd by bondage known,
With sure contagion fastens on his own;
In sickly languors melts his nerveless frame,
50 And blows to rage impetuous Passion's flame:
Fermenting swift, the fiery venom gains
The milky innocence of infant veins;
There swells the stubborn will, damps learning's fire,
The whirlwind wakes of uncontrol'd desire,
55 Sears the young heart to images of woe,
And blasts the buds of Virtue as they blow.°   *bloom*
    Lo! where reclin'd, pale Beauty courts the breeze,
Diffus'd on sofas of voluptuous ease;
With anxious awe, her menial train around,
60 Catch her faint whispers of half-utter'd sound;
See her, in monstrous fellowship, unite
At once the Scythian, and the Sybarite;[2]
Blending repugnant vices, misallied,
Which *frugal* nature purpos'd to divide;
65 See her, with indolence to fierceness join'd,
Of body delicate, infirm of mind,
With languid tones imperious mandates urge;
With arm recumbent wield the household scourge;

2. I.e., the contraries of pastoral wildness and effeminate voluptuousness.

And with unruffled mien, and placid sounds,
70 Contriving torture, and inflicting wounds.
    Nor, in their palmy walks and spicy groves,
The form benign of rural Pleasure roves;
No milk-maid's song, or hum of village talk,
Sooths the lone Poet in his evening walk:
75 No willing arm the flail unwearied plies,
Where the mix'd sounds of cheerful labour rise;
No blooming maids and frolic swains are seen
To pay gay homage to their harvest queen:
No heart-expanding scenes their eyes must prove
80 Of thriving industry, and faithful love:
But shrieks and yells disturb the balmy air,
Dumb sullen looks of woe announce despair,
And angry eyes through dusky features glare.
Far from the sounding lash the Muses fly,
85 And sensual riot drowns each finer joy.
    Nor less from the gay East, on essenc'd wings,
Breathing unnam'd perfumes, Contagion springs;
The soft luxurious plague alike pervades
The marble palaces, and rural shades;
90 Hence, throng'd Augusta° builds her rosy bowers,   *London*
And decks in summer wreaths her smoky towers;
And hence, in summer bow'rs, Art's costly hand
Pours courtly splendours o'er the dazzled land:
The manners melt—One undistinguish'd blaze
95 O'erwhelms the sober pomp of elder days;
Corruption follows with gigantic stride,
And scarce vouchsafes his shameless front to hide:
The spreading leprosy taints ev'ry part,
Infects each limb, and sickens at the heart.
100 Simplicity! most dear of rural maids,
Weeping resigns her violated shades:
Stern Independance from his glebe° retires,   *cultivated land*
And anxious Freedom eyes her drooping fires;
By foreign wealth are British morals chang'd,
105 And Afric's sons, and India's, smile aveng'd.
    For you, whose temper'd ardour long has borne
Untir'd the labour, and unmov'd the scorn;
In Virtue's fasti° be inscrib'd your fame,   *records*
And utter'd yours with Howard's honour'd name,[3]
110 Friends of the friendless—Hail, ye generous band!
Whose efforts yet arrest Heav'n's lifted hand,
Around whose steady brows, in union bright,
The civic wreath, and Christian's palm unite:
Your merit stands, no greater and no less,
115 Without, or with the varnish of success;
But seek no more to break a Nation's fall,
For ye have sav'd yourselves—and that is all.
Succeeding times your struggles, and their fate,
With mingled shame and triumph shall relate,

3. John Howard (1726–1790), philanthropist and prison and public health reformer.

120 While faithful History, in her various page,
Marking the features of this motley age,
To shed a glory, and to fix a stain,
Tells how you strove, and that you strove in vain.

1791   1791

The Rights of Woman[1]

Yes, injured Woman! rise, assert thy right!
Woman! too long degraded, scorned, opprest;
O born to rule in partial° Law's despite,   biased
Resume thy native empire o'er the breast!

5   Go forth arrayed in panoply° divine;   suit of armor
That angel pureness which admits no stain;
Go, bid proud Man his boasted rule resign,
And kiss the golden sceptre of thy reign.

Go, gird thyself with grace; collect thy store
10 Of bright artillery glancing from afar;
Soft melting tones thy thundering cannon's roar,
Blushes and fears thy magazine° of war.   storehouse of arms

Thy rights are empire: urge no meaner claim,—
Felt, not defined, and if debated, lost;
15 Like sacred mysteries, which withheld from fame,
Shunning discussion, are revered the most.

Try all that wit and art suggest to bend
Of thy imperial foe the stubborn knee;
Make treacherous Man thy subject, not thy friend;
20 Thou mayst command, but never canst be free.

Awe the licentious, and restrain the rude;
Soften the sullen, clear the cloudy brow:
Be, more than princes' gifts, thy favours sued;—
She hazards all, who will the least allow.

25 But hope not, courted idol of mankind,
On this proud eminence secure to stay;
Subduing and subdued, thou soon shalt find
Thy coldness soften, and thy pride give way.

Then, then, abandon each ambitious thought,
30 Conquest or rule thy heart shall feebly move,

---

1. A response—seemingly favorable until the last two stanzas—to Mary Wollstonecraft's *A Vindication of the Rights of Woman* (1792). In chapter 4 of *Vindication*, Wollstonecraft had singled out Barbauld's poem "To a Lady with Some Painted Flowers" as evidence that even women of sense were capable of adopting the masculine-centered gender code that identified the feminine with the ornamental and the frivolous.

> In Nature's school, by her soft maxims taught,
> That separate rights are lost in mutual love.

ca. 1792–95   1825

To a Little Invisible Being
Who Is Expected Soon to Become Visible

Germ of new life, whose powers expanding slow
For many a moon their full perfection wait,—
Haste, precious pledge of happy love, to go
Auspicious borne through life's mysterious gate.

5   What powers lie folded in thy curious frame,—
Senses from objects locked, and mind from thought!
How little canst thou guess thy lofty claim
To grasp at all the worlds the Almighty wrought!

And see, the genial season's warmth to share,
10 Fresh younglings° shoot, and opening roses glow!   young plants
Swarms of new life exulting fill the air,—
Haste, infant bud of being, haste to blow!°   bloom

For thee the nurse prepares her lulling songs,
The eager matrons count the lingering day;
15 But far the most thy anxious parent longs
On thy soft cheek a mother's kiss to lay.

She only asks to lay her burden down,
That her glad arms that burden may resume;
And nature's sharpest pangs her wishes crown,
20 That free thee living from thy living tomb.

She longs to fold to her maternal breast
Part of herself, yet to herself unknown;
To see and to salute the stranger guest,
Fed with her life through many a tedious moon.

25 Come, reap thy rich inheritance of love!
Bask in the fondness of a Mother's eye!
Nor wit nor eloquence her heart shall move
Like the first accents of thy feeble cry.

Haste, little captive, burst thy prison doors!
30 Launch on the living world, and spring to light!
Nature for thee displays her various stores,
Opens her thousand inlets of delight.

If charmed verse or muttered prayers had power,
With favouring spells to speed thee on thy way,

35 Anxious I'd bid my beads° each passing hour,   *offer a prayer*
    Till thy wished smile thy mother's pangs o'erpay.° *more than compensate*

ca. 1795?   1825

Washing-Day

      . . . and their voice,
    Turning again towards childish treble, pipes
    And whistles in its sound.[1]

    The Muses are turned gossips; they have lost
    The buskined° step, and clear high-sounding phrase,   *tragic, elevated*
    Language of gods. Come then, domestic Muse,
    In slipshod measure loosely prattling on
5   Of farm or orchard, pleasant curds and cream,
    Or drowning flies, or shoe lost in the mire
    By little whimpering boy, with rueful face;
    Come, Muse; and sing the dreaded Washing-Day.
    Ye who beneath the yoke of wedlock bend,
10 With bowed soul, full well ye ken° the day   *know*
    Which week, smooth sliding after week, brings on
    Too soon;—for to that day nor peace belongs
    Nor comfort;—ere the first gray streak of dawn,
    The red-armed washers come and chase repose.
15 Nor pleasant smile, nor quaint device of mirth,
    E'er visited that day: the very cat,
    From the wet kitchen scared, and reeking hearth,
    Visits the parlour,—an unwonted° guest.   *unaccustomed*
    The silent breakfast-meal is soon dispatched;
20 Uninterrupted, save by anxious looks
    Cast at the lowering sky, if sky should lower.
    From that last evil, O preserve us, heavens!
    For should the skies pour down, adieu to all
    Remains of quiet: then expect to hear
25 Of sad disasters,—dirt and gravel stains
    Hard to efface, and loaded lines at once
    Snapped short,—and linen-horse° by dog thrown down,   *drying rack*
    And all the petty miseries of life.
    Saints have been calm while stretched upon the rack,
30 And Guatimozin[2] smiled on burning coals;
    But never yet did housewife notable
    Greet with a smile a rainy washing-day.
    —But grant the welkin° fair, require not thou   *sky*
    Who call'st thyself perchance the master there,
35 Or study swept or nicely dusted coat,
    Or usual 'tendance;—ask not, indiscreet,
    Thy stockings mended, though the yawning rents
    Gape wide as Erebus;° nor hope to find   *the underworld*

1. Loosely quoted from Shakespeare's *As You Like*   who was tortured and executed by the Spanish
It 2.7.160–62.   conquistadors.
2. The last Aztec emperor (Cuanhtémoc, d. 1525),

Some snug recess impervious: shouldst thou try
40   The 'customed garden walks, thine eye shall rue
The budding fragrance of thy tender shrubs,
Myrtle or rose, all crushed beneath the weight
Of coarse checked apron,—with impatient hand
Twitched off when showers impend: or crossing lines
45   Shall mar thy musings, as the wet cold sheet
Flaps in thy face abrupt. Woe to the friend
Whose evil stars have urged him forth to claim
On such a day the hospitable rites!
Looks, blank at best, and stinted courtesy,
50   Shall he receive. Vainly he feeds his hopes
With dinner of roast chicken, savoury pie,
Or tart or pudding:—pudding he nor tart
That day shall eat; nor, though the husband try,
Mending what can't be helped, to kindle mirth
55   From cheer deficient, shall his consort's brow
Clear up propitious:—the unlucky guest
In silence dines, and early slinks away.
I well remember, when a child, the awe
This day struck into me; for then the maids,
60   I scarce knew why, looked cross, and drove me from them;
Nor soft caress could I obtain, nor hope
Usual indulgencies; jelly or creams,
Relic of costly suppers, and set by
For me, their petted one; or buttered toast,
65   When butter was forbid; or thrilling tale
Of ghost or witch, or murder—so I went
And sheltered me beside the parlour fire:
There my dear grandmother, eldest of forms,
Tended the little ones, and watched from harm,
70   Anxiously fond, though oft her spectacles
With elfin cunning hid, and oft the pins
Drawn from her ravelled stocking, might have soured
One less indulgent.—
At intervals my mother's voice was heard,
75   Urging dispatch: briskly the work went on,
All hands employed to wash, to rinse, to wring,
To fold, and starch, and clap,° and iron, and plait.   *flatten*
Then would I sit me down, and ponder much
Why washings were. Sometimes through hollow bowl
80   Of pipe amused we blew, and sent aloft
The floating bubbles; little dreaming then
To see, Mongolfier,[3] thy silken ball
Ride buoyant through the clouds—so near approach
The sports of children and the toils of men.
85   Earth, air, and sky, and ocean, hath its bubbles,[4]
And verse is one of them—this most of all.

1797

3. Brothers Joseph-Michel and Jacques-Étienne Mongolfier successfully launched the first hot-air balloon, at Annonay, France, in 1783.

4. Cf. Shakespeare's *Macbeth* 1.3.77: "The earth hath bubbles, as the water has."

CHARLOTTE SMITH
1749–1806

The melancholy of Charlotte Smith's poems was no mere literary posture. After her father married for the second time, she herself was married off, at the age of fifteen, and bore a dozen children (three of whom died in infancy or childhood), before permanently separating from her husband, Benjamin Smith, because of his abusive temper, infidelities, and financial irresponsibility. She began writing to make money when her husband was imprisoned for debt in 1783. Her first book, *Elegiac Sonnets, and Other Essays by Charlotte Smith of Bignor Park, in Sussex,* came out in 1785 and went through nine expanding editions in the following sixteen years.

Beginning with the 1788 publication of *Emmeline,* Smith also enjoyed considerable success as a novelist, rapidly producing nine more novels within the decade, including *Desmond* (1792), *The Old Manor House* (1793), *The Banished Man* (1794), and *The Young Philosopher* (1798). The liberal political views espoused in these fictions made the books key contributions to the Revolution Controversy in Britain. This was also the case with her eight-hundred-line blank verse poem *The Emigrants* (1793), which both evokes the suffering endured by political refugees from France and links their plight to that of the poet herself, who as a woman has discovered the emptiness of her native land's "boast / Of equal law." Such views earned Smith a place of dishonor, alongside Mary Wollstonecraft and Anna Letitia Barbauld, in Richard Polwhele's conservative satire *The Unsex'd Females* (1797), which scolds her for having suffered "her mind to be infected with the Gallic mania." We are more likely now to follow Stuart Curran, Smith's modern editor, and hail *The Emigrants* as "the finest piece of extended blank verse in English between Cowper's *The Task* (1785) and Wordsworth's unpublished initial version of *The Prelude* (1799)."

The sonnet as a form, after its great flourishing in the Renaissance in the hands of Sidney, Spenser, Shakespeare, Donne, and Milton, dropped out of fashion in the eighteenth century. It was, Samuel Johnson declared in his *Dictionary* (1755), "not very suitable to the English language." Its revival toward the end of that century—by Coleridge in the 1790s; Wordsworth (who wrote some five hundred sonnets beginning in 1802); and in the next generation, Shelley and Keats—was largely the result of Smith's influential refashioning of the sonnet as a medium of mournful feeling. Coleridge noted in the introduction to his privately printed "sheet of sonnets" in 1796 that "Charlotte Smith and [William Lisle] Bowles are they who first made the Sonnet popular among the present English"; but Bowles's *Fourteen Sonnets* of 1789, imitating those that Smith first published five years earlier (which by 1789 had reached a fifth edition), rode on a wave of popularity of the form that she had already established.

Coleridge in his 1796 introductory essay on the sonnet, using Smith as a principal example, remarked that "those Sonnets appear to me the most exquisite, in which moral Sentiments, Affections, or Feelings, are deduced from, and associated with, the scenery of Nature." Subsequently, of course, the connecting of feelings and nature became a central theme and strategy in Romantic poetry, especially in the genre that has come to be known as "the greater Romantic lyric." But Smith's engagement with nature differs from Coleridge's and Wordsworth's in its quasi-scientific insistence on the faithful rendering of detail: it is not surprising to learn that she addressed a sonnet to the "goddess of botany." That close-up view of nature is rendered exquisitely in her last long poem, the posthumously published *Beachy Head* (1807).

FROM ELEGIAC SONNETS

Written at the Close of Spring

The garlands fade that Spring so lately wove,
    Each simple flower, which she had nursed in dew,
Anemonies,[1] that spangled every grove,
    The primrose wan, and hare-bell mildly blue.
5 No more shall violets linger in the dell,
    Or purple orchis variegate the plain,
Till Spring again shall call forth every bell,
    And dress with humid hands her wreaths again.—
Ah! poor humanity! so frail, so fair,
10   Are the fond visions of thy early day,
Till tyrant passion, and corrosive care,
    Bid all thy fairy colors fade away!
Another May new buds and flowers shall bring;
Ah! why has happiness—no second Spring?

1784

To Sleep

Come, balmy Sleep! tired nature's soft resort!
    On these sad temples all thy poppies shed;
And bid gay dreams, from Morpheus'° airy court,   *Greek god of sleep*
    Float in light vision round my aching head!
5 Secure of all thy blessings, partial° Power!   *friendly*
    On his hard bed the peasant throws him down;
And the poor sea boy, in the rudest hour,
    Enjoys thee more than he who wears a crown.[1]
Clasp'd in her faithful shepherd's guardian arms,
10   Well may the village girl sweet slumbers prove
And they, O gentle Sleep! still taste thy charms,
    Who wake to labor, liberty, and love.
But still thy opiate aid dost thou deny
To calm the anxious breast; to close the streaming eye.

1784

To Night

I love thee, mournful, sober-suited Night!
    When the faint moon, yet lingering in her wane,
And veil'd in clouds, with pale uncertain light
    Hangs o'er the waters of the restless main.

1. Anemonies. *Anemony Nemeroso.* The wood Anemony [Smith's note].
1. "Wilt thou upon the high and giddy mast / seal up the ship boy's eyes, and rock his brains / In cradle of the rude impetuous surge?" Shakespeare's *Henry IV* [Smith's note; "imperious surge" in the original].

5   In deep depression sunk, the enfeebled mind
     Will to the deaf cold elements complain,
     And tell the embosom'd grief, however vain,
   To sullen surges and the viewless wind.
   Though no repose on thy dark breast I find,
10   I still enjoy thee—cheerless as thou art;
     For in thy quiet gloom the exhausted heart
   Is calm, though wretched; hopeless, yet resign'd.
   While to the winds and waves its sorrows given,
   May reach—though lost on earth—the ear of Heaven!

1788

Written in the Church-Yard at Middleton in Sussex[1]

Press'd by the Moon, mute arbitress of tides,
   While the loud equinox its power combines,
   The sea no more its swelling surge confines,
But o'er the shrinking land sublimely rides.
5   The wild blast, rising from the Western cave,
   Drives the huge billows from their heaving bed;
   Tears from their grassy tombs the village dead,
And breaks the silent sabbath of the grave!
With shells and sea-weed mingled, on the shore
10   Lo! their bones whiten in the frequent wave;
   But vain to them the winds and waters rave;
They hear the warring elements no more:
While I am doom'd—by life's long storm opprest,
To gaze with envy on their gloomy rest.

1789

On Being Cautioned against Walking on an Headland Overlooking the Sea, Because It Was Frequented by a Lunatic

Is there a solitary wretch who hies
   To the tall cliff, with starting pace or slow,
And, measuring, views with wild and hollow eyes
   Its distance from the waves that chide below;
5   Who, as the sea-born gale with frequent sighs
   Chills his cold bed upon the mountain turf,
With hoarse, half-utter'd lamentation, lies

1. Middleton is a village on the margin of the sea, in Sussex, containing only two or three houses. There were formerly several acres of ground between its small church and the sea, which now, by its continual encroachments, approaches within a few feet of this half ruined and humble edifice. The wall, which once surrounded the churchyard, is entirely swept away, many of the graves broken up, and the remains of bodies interred washed into the sea: whence human bones are found among the sand and shingles on the shore [Smith's note].

Murmuring responses to the dashing surf?
In moody sadness, on the giddy brink,
10   I see him more with envy than with fear;
He has no *nice felicities* that shrink[1]
From giant horrors; wildly wandering here,
He seems (uncursed with reason) not to know
The depth or the duration of his woe.

1797

The Sea View[1]

The upland shepherd, as reclined he lies
On the soft turf that clothes the mountain brow,
Marks the bright sea-line mingling with the skies;
Or from his course celestial, sinking slow,
5   The summer-sun in purple radiance low,
Blaze on the western waters; the wide scene
Magnificent, and tranquil, seems to spread
Even o'er the rustic's breast a joy serene,
When, like dark plague-spots by the Demons shed,
10   Charged deep with death, upon the waves, far seen,
Move the war-freighted ships; and fierce and red,
Flash their destructive fire.—The mangled dead
And dying victims then pollute the flood.
Ah! thus man spoils Heaven's glorious works with blood!

1797

The Emigrants[1]

From *Book 1*

SCENE, *on the Cliffs to the Eastward of the Town of
Brighthelmstone in Sussex.*

TIME, *a Morning in November, 1792.*

Slow in the Wintry Morn, the struggling light
Throws a faint gleam upon the troubled waves;

1. " 'Tis delicate felicity that shrinks / when rocking winds are loud." Walpole [Smith's note; the passage from Walpole has not been identified].
1. Suggested by the recollection of having seen, some years since, on a beautiful evening of Summer, an engagement between two armed ships, from the high down called the Beacon Hill, near Brighthelmstone [Smith's note, referring to a location near Brighton].
1. As the Revolution unfolded in France, growing numbers of aristocrats, aghast at their loss of power and increasingly in fear for their lives, abandoned their estates and riches and sought refuge in England. Following the new Republic's abolition of state religion and confiscation of Church lands, these nobles were joined in their exile by Catholic clerics. Book 1 of *The Emigrants* traces how these people cope, and fail to cope, with the disintegra-

tion of the system that had sanctioned their social privilege. It is set, as Smith indicates, in November 1792, just after the downfall of the French monarchy and the declaration of a Republic. Its "scene" is atop the cliffs at Brighthelmstone (Brighton), across the Channel from France. Book 2, set five months later, at a time following the execution of Louis XVI and the outbreak of war between Britain and France, narrates how the emigrants, forming a counterrevolutionary army, invade France to wage war on their own countrymen. Here Smith emphasizes the situation of the women this foolhardy army leaves behind, abandoned to an unwanted independence in a strange land.
Smith dedicated *The Emigrants* to William Cowper, whose easy, informal blank verse in *The Task* (1785) was an immediate influence on her own.

Their foaming tops, as they approach the shore
And the broad surf that never ceasing breaks
5   On the innumerous pebbles, catch the beams
Of the pale Sun, that with reluctance gives
To this cold northern Isle, its shorten'd day.
Alas! how few the morning wakes to joy!
How many murmur at oblivious night
10   For leaving them so soon; for bearing thus
Their fancied bliss (the only bliss they taste!),
On her black wings away!—Changing° the dreams   *exchanging*
That sooth'd their sorrows, for calamities
(And every day brings its own sad proportion)
15   For doubts, diseases, abject dread of Death,
And faithless friends, and fame and fortune lost;
Fancied or real wants; and wounded pride,
That views the day star,° but to curse his beams.   *the sun*
      Yet He, whose Spirit into being call'd
20   This wond'rous World of Waters; He who bids
The wild wind lift them till they dash the clouds,
And speaks to them in thunder; or whose breath,
Low murmuring o'er the gently heaving tides,
When the fair Moon, in summer night serene,
25   Irradiates with long trembling lines of light
Their undulating surface; that great Power,
Who, governing the Planets, also knows
If but a Sea-Mew falls, whose nest is hid
In these incumbent° cliffs; He surely means   *overhanging*
30   To us, his reasoning Creatures, whom He bids
Acknowledge and revere his awful° hand,   *awe-inspiring*
Nothing but good: Yet Man, misguided Man,
Mars the fair work that he was bid enjoy,
And makes himself the evil he deplores.
35   How often, when my weary soul recoils
From proud oppression, and from legal crimes
(For such are in this Land, where the vain boast
Of equal Law is mockery, while the cost
Of seeking for redress is sure to plunge
40   Th' already injur'd to more certain ruin
And the wretch starves, before his Counsel pleads)
How often do I half abjure Society,
And sigh for some lone Cottage, deep embower'd
In the green woods, that these steep chalky Hills
45   Guard from the strong South West; where round their base
The Beach² wide flourishes, and the light Ash
With slender leaf half hides the thymy° turf!—   *abounding in thyme*
There do I wish to hide me; well content
If on the short grass, strewn with fairy flowers,
50   I might repose thus shelter'd; or when Eve
In Orient crimson° lingers in the west,   *the setting sun*
Gain the high mound, and mark these waves remote
(Lucid tho' distant), blushing with the rays
Of the far-flaming Orb, that sinks beneath them;

2. Possibly a variant spelling of *beech* (the tree).

55 For I have thought, that I should then behold
The beauteous works of God, unspoil'd by Man
And less affected then, by human woes
I witness'd not; might better learn to bear
Those that injustice, and duplicity
60 And faithlessness and folly, fix on me:
For never yet could I derive relief,
When my swol'n heart was bursting with its sorrows,
From the sad thought, that others like myself
Live but to swell affliction's countless tribes!
65 —Tranquil seclusion I have vainly sought;
Peace, who delights in solitary shade,
No more will spread for me her downy wings,
But, like the fabled Danaïds—or the wretch,
Who ceaseless, up the steep acclivity,
70 Was doom'd to heave the still rebounding rock,[3]
Onward I labour; as the baffled wave,
Which yon rough beach repulses, that returns
With the next breath of wind, to fail again.—
Ah! Mourner—cease these wailings: cease and learn,
75 That not the Cot sequester'd, where the briar
And wood-bine wild, embrace the mossy thatch,
(Scarce seen amid the forest gloom obscure!)
Or more substantial farm, well fenced and warm,
Where the full barn, and cattle fodder'd round
80 Speak rustic plenty; nor the statelier dome
By dark firs shaded, or the aspiring pine,
Close by the village Church (with care conceal'd
By verdant foliage, lest the poor man's grave
Should mar the smiling prospect of his Lord),
85 Where offices° well rang'd, or dove-cote stock'd,   *outbuildings*
Declare manorial residence; not these
Or any of the buildings, new and trim
With windows circling towards the restless Sea,
Which ranged in rows, now terminate my walk,
90 Can shut out for an hour the spectre Care,
That from the dawn of reason, follows still
Unhappy Mortals,'till the friendly grave
(Our sole secure asylum) "ends the chace."[4]
Behold, in witness of this mournful truth,
95 A group approach me, whose dejected looks,
Sad Heralds of distress! proclaim them Men
Banish'd for ever[5] and for conscience sake
From their distracted Country, whence the name
Of Freedom misapplied, and much abus'd
100 By lawless Anarchy, has driven them far
To wander; with the prejudice they learn'd

3. In Greek mythology Sisyphus was condemned forever to push a rock uphill, only to have it roll back down just before it reached the top. The Danaides were condemned to pour water into leaky vessels.
4. I have a confused notion, that this expression, with nearly the same application, is to be found in [Edward] Young: but I cannot refer to it [Smith's note; the quotation has never been identified].
5. Catholic clergymen, banished from France by the revolutionists.

From Bigotry (the Tut'ress of the blind),
Thro' the wide World unshelter'd; their sole hope,
That German spoilers, thro' that pleasant land
105 May carry wide the desolating scourge
Of War and Vengeance;[6] yet unhappy Men,
Whate'er your errors, I lament your fate:
And, as disconsolate and sad ye hang
Upon the barrier of the rock, and seem
110 To murmur your despondence, waiting long
Some fortunate reverse that never comes;
Methinks in each expressive face, I see
Discriminated° anguish; there droops one,   *distinct, marked*
Who in a moping cloister long consum'd
115 This life inactive, to obtain a better,
And thought that meagre abstinence, to wake
From his hard pallet with the midnight bell,
To live on eleemosynary bread,°   *alms*
And to renounce God's works, would please that God.
120 And now the poor pale wretch receives, amaz'd,
The pity, strangers give to his distress,
Because these strangers are, by his dark creed,
Condemn'd as Heretics—and with sick heart
Regrets° his pious prison, and his beads.[7]—   *recalls with regret*
125 Another, of more haughty port, declines
The aid he needs not; while in mute despair
His high indignant thoughts go back to France,
Dwelling on all he lost—the Gothic dome,
That vied with splendid palaces;[8] the beds
130 Of silk and down, the silver chalices,
Vestments with gold enwrought for blazing altars;
Where, amid clouds of incense, he held forth
To kneeling crowds the imaginary bones
Of Saints suppos'd, in pearl and gold enchas'd,°   *decoratively set*
135 And still with more than living Monarchs' pomp
Surrounded; was believ'd by mumbling bigots
To hold the keys of Heaven, and to admit
Whom he thought good to share it.—Now alas!
He, to whose daring soul and high ambition
140 The World seem'd circumscrib'd; who, wont to dream
Of Fleuri, Richelieu, Alberoni,[9] men
Who trod on Empire, and whose politics
Were not beyond the grasp of his vast mind,
Is, in a Land once hostile, still prophan'd

6. An Austro-Prussian army invaded France in August 1792 but was driven back.
7. Lest the same attempts at misrepresentation should now be made, as have been made on former occasions, it is necessary to repeat, that nothing is farther from my thoughts, than to reflect invidiously on the Emigrant clergy, whose steadiness of principle excites veneration, as much as their sufferings compassion. Adversity has now taught them the charity and humility they perhaps wanted, when they made it a part of their faith, that salvation could be obtained in no other religion than their own [Smith's note].
8. Let it not be considered as an insult to men in fallen fortune, if these luxuries (undoubtedly inconsistent with their profession) be here enumerated.—France is not the only country, where the splendour and indulgences of the higher, and the poverty and depression of the inferior Clergy, have alike proved injurious to the cause of Religion [Smith's note].
9. Three cardinals who held important political offices.

145 By disbelief, and rites un-orthodox,
The object of compassion.—At his side,
Lighter of heart than these, but heavier far
Than he was wont, another victim comes,
An Abbé—who with less contracted brow
150 Still smiles and flatters, and still talks of Hope;
Which, sanguine as he is, he does not feel,
And so he cheats the sad and weighty pressure
Of evils present;—Still, as Men misled
By early prejudice (so hard to break),
155 I mourn your sorrows; for I too have known
Involuntary exile; and while yet
England had charms for me, have felt how sad
It is to look across the dim cold sea,
That melancholy rolls its refluent° tides   *ebbing*
160 Between us and the dear regretted land
We call our own—as now ye pensive wait
On this bleak morning, gazing on the waves
That seem to leave your shore; from whence the wind
Is loaded to your ears, with the deep groans
165 Of martyr'd Saints and suffering Royalty,
While to your eyes the avenging power of Heaven
Appears in aweful anger to prepare
The storm of vengeance, fraught with plagues and death.
Even he of milder heart, who was indeed
170 The simple shepherd in a rustic scene,
And,'mid the vine-clad hills of Languedoc,
Taught to the bare-foot peasant, whose hard hands
Produc'd¹ the nectar he could seldom taste,
Submission to the Lord for whom he toil'd;
175 He, or his brethren, who to Neustria's sons°   *the men of Normandy*
Enforc'd religious patience, when, at times,
On their indignant hearts Power's iron hand
Too strongly struck; eliciting some sparks
Of the bold spirit of their native North;
180 Even these Parochial Priests, these humbled men,
Whose lowly undistinguish'd cottages
Witness'd a life of purest piety,
While the meek tenants were, perhaps, unknown
Each to the haughty Lord of his domain,
185 Who mark'd them not; the Noble scorning still
The poor and pious Priest, as with slow pace
He glided thro' the dim arch'd avenue
Which to the Castle led; hoping to cheer
The last sad hour of some laborious life
190 That hasten'd to its close—even such a Man
Becomes an exile; staying not to try
By temperate zeal to check his madd'ning flock,

1. See the finely descriptive Verses written at Montauban in France in 1750, by Dr. Joseph Warton. Printed in Dodsley's *Miscellanies*, Vol. IV, page 203 [Smith's note; the lines begin, "Tarn, how delightful wind thy willow'd waves, / But ah! they fructify a land of slaves! / In vain thy barefoot, sunburnt peasants hide / With luscious grapes yon hill's romantic side; / No cups nectareous shall their toils repay . . ."]. Languedoc is in southern France, just above the Pyrenees.

Who, at the novel sound of Liberty
(Ah! most intoxicating sound to slaves!),
195 Start into licence.—Lo! dejected now,
The wandering Pastor mourns, with bleeding heart,
His erring people, weeps and prays for them,
And trembles for the account that he must give
To Heaven for souls entrusted to his care.—
200 Where the cliff, hollow'd by the wintry storm,
Affords a seat with matted sea-weed strewn,
A softer form reclines; around her run,
On the rough shingles,° or the chalky bourn,   pebbles
Her gay unconscious children, soon amus'd;
205 Who pick the fretted stone, or glossy shell,
Or crimson plant marine: or they contrive
The fairy vessel, with its ribband sail
And gilded paper pennant: in the pool,
Left by the salt wave on the yielding sands,
210 They launch the mimic navy.—Happy age!
Unmindful of the miseries of Man!—
Alas! too long a victim to distress,
Their Mother, lost in melancholy thought,
Lull'd for a moment by the murmurs low
215 Of sullen billows, wearied by the task
Of having here, with swol'n and aching eyes
Fix'd on the grey horizon, since the dawn
Solicitously watch'd the weekly sail
From her dear native land, now yields awhile
220 To kind forgetfulness, while Fancy brings,
In waking dreams, that native land again!
Versailles² appears—its painted galleries,
And rooms of regal splendour; rich with gold,
Where, by long mirrors multiply'd, the crowd
225 Paid willing homage—and, united there,
Beauty gave charms to empire.—Ah! too soon
From the gay visionary pageant rous'd,
See the sad mourner start!—and, drooping, look
With tearful eyes and heaving bosom round
230 On drear reality—where dark'ning waves,
Urg'd by the rising wind, unheeded foam
Near her cold rugged seat. * * *

1793

Beachy Head¹

On thy stupendous summit, rock sublime!
That o'er the channel rear'd, half way at sea

2. Louis XIV's opulent palace, south of Paris.
1. This is the longest of several works left in manuscript when Smith died in October 1806 and published in the posthumous volume *Beachy Head and
Other Poems* the following year. It is not known to
what degree Smith considered the poem finished.
Beachy Head is the southernmost point of Sussex,
near Eastbourne and directly across the Channel
from the French town of Dieppe.

The mariner at early morning hails,[2]
I would recline; while Fancy should go forth,
5   And represent the strange and awful hour
Of vast concussion;[3] when the Omnipotent
Stretch'd forth his arm, and rent the solid hills,
Bidding the impetuous main flood rush between
The rifted shores, and from the continent
10 Eternally divided this green isle.
Imperial lord of the high southern coast!
From thy projecting head-land I would mark
Far in the east the shades of night disperse,
Melting and thinned, as from the dark blue wave
15 Emerging, brilliant rays of arrowy light°   *dawn*
Dart from the horizon; when the glorious sun
Just lifts above it his resplendent orb.
Advances now, with feathery silver touched,
The rippling tide of flood; glisten the sands,
20 While, inmates of the chalky clefts that scar
Thy sides precipitous, with shrill harsh cry,
Their white wings glancing in the level beam,
The terns, and gulls, and tarrocks, seek their food,[4]
And thy rough hollows echo to the voice
25 Of the gray choughs,[5] and ever restless daws,
With clamour, not unlike the chiding hounds,
While the lone shepherd, and his baying dog,
Drive to thy turfy crest his bleating flock.

The high meridian° of the day is past,   *noon*
30 And Ocean now, reflecting the calm Heaven,
Is of cerulean hue; and murmurs low
The tide of ebb, upon the level sands.
The sloop, her angular canvas shifting still,
Catches the light and variable airs
35 That but a little crisp the summer sea,
Dimpling its tranquil surface.

Afar off,
And just emerging from the arch immense
Where seem to part the elements, a fleet
Of fishing vessels stretch their lesser sails;
40 While more remote, and like a dubious spot
Just hanging in the horizon, laden deep,
The ship of commerce richly freighted, makes
Her slower progress, on her distant voyage,
Bound to the orient climates, where the sun

---

2. In crossing the Channel from the coast of France, Beachy-Head is the first land made [Smith's note].
3. Alluding to an idea that this Island was once joined to the continent of Europe, and torn from it by some convulsion in Nature. I confess I never could trace the resemblance between the two countries. Yet the cliffs about Dieppe, resemble the chalk cliffs on the Southern coast. But Normandy has no likeness whatever to the part of England opposite to it [Smith's note].
4. Terns. *Sterna hirundo*, or Sea Swallow. Gulls. *Larus canus*. Tarrocks. *Larus tridactylus* [Smith's note].
5. Gray choughs. *Corvus Graculus*, Cornish Choughs, or, as these birds are called by the Sussex people, Saddle-backed Crows, build in great numbers on this coast [Smith's note].

45   Matures the spice within its odorous shell,
      And, rivalling the gray worm's filmy toil,
      Bursts from its pod the vegetable down;[6]
      Which in long turban'd wreaths, from torrid heat
      Defends the brows of Asia's countless castes.
50   There the Earth hides within her glowing breast
      The beamy adamant,[7] and the round pearl
      Enchased° in rugged covering; which the slave,   *enclosed*
      With perilous and breathless toil, tears off
      From the rough sea-rock, deep beneath the waves.
55   These are the toys of Nature; and her sport
      Of little estimate in Reason's eye:
      And they who reason, with abhorrence see
      Man, for such gaudes and baubles, violate
      The sacred freedom of his fellow man—
60   Erroneous estimate! As Heaven's pure air,
      Fresh as it blows on this aërial height,
      Or sound of seas upon the stony strand,
      Or inland, the gay harmony of birds,
      And winds that wander in the leafy woods;
65   Are to the unadulterate taste more worth
      Than the elaborate harmony, brought out
      From fretted stop, or modulated airs
      Of vocal science.—So the brightest gems,
      Glancing resplendent on the regal crown,
70   Or trembling in the high born beauty's ear,
      Are poor and paltry, to the lovely light
      Of the fair star,° that as the day declines   *Venus*
      Attendent on her queen, the crescent moon,
      Bathes her bright tresses in the eastern wave.
75   For now the sun is verging to the sea,
      And as he westward sinks, the floating clouds
      Suspended, move upon the evening gale,
      And gathering round his orb, as if to shade
      The insufferable brightness, they resign
80   Their gauzy whiteness; and more warm'd, assume
      All hues of purple. There, transparent gold
      Mingles with ruby tints, and sapphire gleams,
      And colours, such as Nature through her works
      Shews only in the ethereal canopy.
85   Thither aspiring Fancy fondly soars,
      Wandering sublime thro' visionary vales,
      Where bright pavilions rise, and trophies, fann'd
      By airs celestial; and adorn'd with wreaths
      Of flowers that bloom amid elysian bowers.
90   Now bright, and brighter still the colours glow,
      Till half the lustrous orb within the flood
      Seems to retire: the flood reflecting still
      Its splendor, and in mimic glory drest;

6. Cotton. *Gossypium herbaceum* [Smith's note]. The worm's "filmy toil" in line 46 produces silk.
7. Diamonds, the hardest and most valuable of precious stones. For the extraordinary exertions of the Indians in diving for the pearl oysters, see the account of the Pearl fisheries in Percival's *View of Ceylon* [Smith's note].

Till the last ray shot upward, fires the clouds
95   With blazing crimson; then in paler light,
Long lines of tenderer radiance, lingering yield
To partial darkness; and on the opposing side
The early moon distinctly rising, throws
Her pearly brilliance on the trembling tide.

100   The fishermen, who at set seasons pass
Many a league off at sea their toiling night,
Now hail their comrades, from their daily task
Returning; and make ready for their own,
With the night tide commencing:—The night tide
105   Bears a dark vessel on, whose hull and sails
Mark her a coaster⁸ from the north. Her keel
Now ploughs the sand; and sidelong now she leans,
While with loud clamours her athletic crew
Unload her; and resounds the busy hum
110   Along the wave-worn rocks. Yet more remote
Where the rough cliff hangs beetling° o'er its base,   *projecting*
All breathes repose; the water's rippling sound
Scarce heard; but now and then the sea-snipe's⁹ cry
Just tells that something living is abroad;
115   And sometimes crossing on the moonbright line,
Glimmers the skiff, faintly discern'd awhile,
Then lost in shadow.

            Contemplation here,
High on her throne of rock, aloof may sit,
And bid recording Memory unfold
120   Her scroll voluminous—bid her retrace
The period, when from Neustria's hostile shore°   *Normandy*
The Norman launch'd his galleys, and the bay
O'er which that mass of ruin¹ frowns even now
In vain and sullen menace, then received
125   The new invaders; a proud martial race,
Of Scandinavia² the undaunted sons,

8. Ship that sails along the coast.
9. In crossing the channel this bird is heard at night, uttering a short cry, and flitting along near the surface of the waves. The sailors call it the Sea Snipe; but I can find no species of sea bird of which this is the vulgar name. A bird so called inhabits the Lake of Geneva [Smith's note].
1. Pevensey Castle [Smith's note].
2. The Scandinavians (modern Norway, Sweden, Denmark, Lapland, &c.) and other inhabitants of the north, began towards the end of the 8th century, to leave their inhospitable climate in search of the produce of more fortunate countries.
The North-men made inroads on the coasts of France; and carrying back immense booty, excited their compatriots to engage in the same piratical voyages: and they were afterwards joined by numbers of necessitous and daring adventurers from the coasts of Provence and Sicily.
In 844, these wandering innovators had a great number of vessels at sea; and again visiting the coasts of France, Spain, and England, the follow-

ing year they penetrated even to Paris: and the unfortunate Charles the Bald, king of France, purchased at a high price, the retreat of the banditti he had no other means of repelling.
These successful expeditions continued for some time; till Rollo, otherwise Raoul, assembled a number of followers, and after a descent on England, crossed the channel, and made himself master of Rouen, which he fortified. Charles the Simple, unable to contend with Rollo, offered to resign to him some of the northern provinces, and to give him his daughter in marriage. Neustria, since called Normandy, was granted to him, and afterwards Brittany. He added the more solid virtues of the legislator to the fierce valour of the conqueror—converted to Christianity, he established justice, and repressed the excesses of his Danish subjects, till then accustomed to live only by plunder. His name became the signal for pursuing those who violated the laws; as well as the cry of Haro, still so usual in Normandy. The Danes and Francs produced a race of men celebrated for their

Whom Dogon, Fier-a-bras, and Humfroi led
To conquest: while Trinacria to their power
Yielded her wheaten garland; and when thou,
130   Parthenope! within thy fertile bay
Receiv'd the victors—

           In the mailed ranks
Of Normans landing on the British coast
Rode Taillefer; and with astounding voice
Thunder'd the war song daring Roland sang
135   First in the fierce contention: vainly brave,
One not inglorious struggle England made—
But failing, saw the Saxon heptarchy[3]
Finish for ever.——Then the holy pile,[4]
Yet seen upon the field of conquest, rose,
140   Where to appease heaven's wrath for so much blood,
The conqueror bade unceasing prayers ascend,
And requiems for the slayers and the slain.
But let not modern Gallia° form from hence   *France*
Presumptuous hopes, that ever thou again,
145   Queen of the isles! shalt crouch to foreign arms.
The enervate sons of Italy may yield;
And the Iberian, all his trophies torn
And wrapp'd in Superstition's monkish weed,
May shelter his abasement, and put on
150   Degrading fetters. Never, never thou!
Imperial mistress of the obedient sea;
But thou, in thy integrity secure,
Shalt now undaunted meet a world in arms.

England! 'twas where this promontory rears
155   Its rugged brow above the channel wave,
Parting the hostile nations, that thy fame,
Thy naval fame was tarnish'd, at what time
Thou, leagued with the Batavian, gavest to France[5]

---

valour; and it was a small party of these that in 983, having been on a pilgrimage to Jerusalem, arrived on their return at Salerno, and found the town surrounded by Mahometans, whom the Salernians were bribing to leave their coast. The Normans represented to them the baseness and cowardice of such submission; and notwithstanding the inequality of their numbers, they boldly attacked the Saracen camp, and drove the infidels to their ships. The prince of Salerno, astonished at their successful audacity, would have loaded them with the marks of his gratitude; but refusing every reward, they returned to their own country, from whence, however, other bodies of Normans passed into Sicily (anciently called Trinacria); and many of them entered into the service of the emperor of the East, others of the Pope, and the duke of Naples was happy to engage a small party of them in defence of his newly founded dutchy. Soon afterwards three brothers of Coutance, the sons of Tancred de Hauteville, Guillaume Fier-a-bras, Drogon, and Humfroi, joining the Normans established at Aversa, became masters of the fertile island of Sicily; and Robert Guiscard joining them,

the Normans became sovereigns both of Sicily and Naples (Parthenope). How William, the natural son of Robert, duke of Normandy, possessed himself of England, is too well known to be repeated here. William sailing from St. Valori, landed in the bay of Pevensey; and at the place now called Battle, met the English forces under Harold: an esquire (ecuyer) called Taillefer, mounted on an armed horse, led on the Normans, singing in a thundering tone the war song of Rollo. He threw himself among the English, and was killed on the first onset. In a marsh not far from Hastings, the skeletons of an armed man and horse were found a few years since, which are believed to have belonged to the Normans, as a party of their horse, deceived in the nature of the ground, perished in the morass [Smith's note].
3. The seven kingdoms of Saxon England.
4. Battle Abbey was raised by the Conqueror, and endowed with an ample revenue, that masses might be said night and day for the souls of those who perished in battle [Smith's note].
5. In 1690, King William being then in Ireland, Tourville, the French admiral, arrived on the coast

One day of triumph—triumph the more loud,
160 Because even then so rare. Oh! well redeem'd,
Since, by a series of illustrious men,
Such as no other country ever rear'd,
To vindicate her cause. It is a list
Which, as Fame echoes it, blanches the cheek
165 Of bold Ambition; while the despot feels
The extorted sceptre tremble in his grasp.

From even the proudest roll° by glory fill'd,   *historical record*
How gladly the reflecting mind returns
To simple scenes of peace and industry,
170 Where, bosom'd in some valley of the hills
Stands the lone farm; its gate with tawny ricks°   *hay stacks*
Surrounded, and with granaries and sheds,
Roof'd with green mosses, and by elms and ash
Partially shaded; and not far remov'd
175 The hut of sea-flints built; the humble home
Of one, who sometimes watches on the heights,[6]
When hid in the cold mist of passing clouds,
The flock, with dripping fleeces, are dispers'd
O'er the wide down; then from some ridged point
180 That overlooks the sea, his eager eye
Watches the bark that for his signal waits
To land its merchandize:—Quitting for this
Clandestine traffic his more honest toil,
The crook abandoning, he braves himself
185 The heaviest snow-storm of December's night,
When with conflicting winds the ocean raves,
And on the tossing boat, unfearing mounts
To meet the partners of the perilous trade,
And share their hazard. Well it were for him,
190 If no such commerce of destruction known,
He were content with what the earth affords
To human labour; even where she seems
Reluctant most. More happy is the hind,°   *peasant*
Who, with his own hands rears on some black moor,
195 Or turbary,° his independent hut   *peat bog*
Cover'd with heather, whence the slow white smoke
Of smouldering peat arises——A few sheep,
His best possession, with his children share

---

of England. His fleet consisted of seventy-eight large ships, and twenty-two fire-ships. Lord Torrington, the English admiral, lay at St. Helens, with only forty English and a few Dutch ships; and conscious of the disadvantage under which he should give battle, he ran up between the enemy's fleet and the coast, to protect it. The queen's council, dictated to by Russel, persuaded her to order Torrington to venture a battle. The orders Torrington appears to have obeyed reluctantly: his fleet now consisted of twenty-two Dutch and thirty-four English ships. Evertson, the Dutch admiral, was eager to obtain glory; Torrington, more cautious, reflected on the importance of the stake. The consequence was, that the Dutch rashly sailing on were surrounded, and Torrington, solicitous to recover this false step, placed himself with diffi-culty between the Dutch and French;—but three Dutch ships were burnt, two of their admirals killed, and almost all their ships disabled. The English and Dutch declining a second engagement, retired towards the mouth of the Thames. The French, from ignorance of the coast, and misunderstanding among each other, failed to take all the advantage they might have done of this victory [Smith's note].

6. The shepherds and labourers of this tract of country, a hardy and athletic race of men, are almost universally engaged in the contraband trade, carried on for the coarsest and most destructive spirits, with the opposite coast. When no other vessel will venture to sea, these men hazard their lives to elude the watchfulness of the Revenue officers, and to secure their cargoes [Smith's note].

The rugged shed when wintry tempests blow;
200 But, when with Spring's return the green blades rise
Amid the russet heath, the household live
Joint tenants of the waste° throughout the day,   *uncultivated land*
And often, from her nest, among the swamps,
Where the gemm'd sun-dew grows, or fring'd buck-bean,[7]
205 They scare the plover,[8] that with plaintive cries
Flutters, as° sorely wounded, down the wind.   *pretending to be*
Rude, and but just remov'd from savage life
Is the rough dweller among scenes like these,
(Scenes all unlike the poet's fabling dreams
210 Describing Arcady[9])—But he is free;
The dread that follows on illegal acts
He never feels; and his industrious mate
Shares in his labour. Where the brook is traced
By crowding osiers,° and the black coot[1] hides   *willows*
215 Among the plashy reeds, her diving brood,
The matron wades; gathering the long green rush[2]
That well prepar'd hereafter lends its light
To her poor cottage, dark and cheerless else
Thro' the drear hours of Winter. Otherwhile
220 She leads her infant group where charlock° grows   *wild mustard*
"Unprofitably gay,"[3] or to the fields,
Where congregate the linnet and the finch,
That on the thistles, so profusely spread,
Feast in the desert; the poor family
225 Early resort, extirpating with care
These, and the gaudier mischief of the ground;
Then flames the high rais'd heap; seen afar off
Like hostile war-fires flashing to the sky.[4]
Another task is theirs: On fields that shew
230 As° angry Heaven had rain'd sterility,   *as if*
Stony and cold, and hostile to the plough,
Where clamouring loud, the evening curlew[5] runs
And drops her spotted eggs among the flints;
The mother and the children pile the stones
235 In rugged pyramids;—and all this toil
They patiently encounter; well content
On their flock bed[6] to slumber undisturb'd
Beneath the smoky roof they call their own.
Oh! little knows the sturdy hind, who stands
240 Gazing, with looks where envy and contempt
Are often strangely mingled, on the car°   *carriage*
Where prosperous Fortune sits; what secret care
Or sick satiety is often hid,
Beneath the splendid outside: *He* knows not

7. Sun-dew. *Drosera rotundifolia.* Buck-bean. *Menyanthes trifoliatum* [Smith's note].
8. Plover. *Tringa vanellus* [Smith's note].
9. Arcadia, an imagined land of peace and simplicity.
1. Coot. *Fulica aterrima* [Smith's note].
2. A reedy plant burned for light.
3. "With blossom'd furze, unprofitably gay." Goldsmith [Smith's note, citing *The Deserted Village*, line 194].
4. The Beacons formerly lighted up on the hills to give notice of the approach of an enemy. These signals would still be used in case of alarm, if the Telegraph [the signaling apparatus] now substituted could not be distinguished on account of fog or darkness [Smith's note].
5. Curlew. *Charadrius oedienemus* [Smith's note].
6. A bed stuffed with tufts of wool.

245   How frequently the child of Luxury
Enjoying nothing, flies from place to place
In chase of pleasure that eludes his grasp;
And that content is e'en less found by him,
Than by the labourer, whose pick-axe smooths
250   The road before his chariot; and who doffs
What *was* an hat; and as the train pass on,
Thinks how one day's expenditure, like this,
Would cheer him for long months, when to his toil
The frozen earth closes her marble breast.
255   Ah! who *is* happy? Happiness! a word
That like false fire,° from marsh effluvia born,   *will-o'-the-wisp*
Misleads the wanderer, destin'd to contend
In the world's wilderness, with want or woe—
Yet *they* are happy, who have never ask'd
260   What good or evil means. The boy
That on the river's margin gaily plays,
Has heard that Death is there.—He knows not Death,
And therefore fears it not; and venturing in
He gains a bullrush, or a minnow—then,
265   At certain peril, for a worthless prize,
A crow's, or raven's nest, he climbs the boll°   *bole, trunk*
Of some tall pine; and of his prowess proud,
Is for a moment happy. Are *your* cares,
Ye who despise him, never worse applied?
270   The village girl is happy, who sets forth
To distant fair, gay in her Sunday suit,
With cherry colour'd knots, and flourish'd shawl,
And bonnet newly purchas'd. So is he
Her little brother, who his mimic drum
275   Beats, till he drowns her rural lovers' oaths
Of constant faith, and still increasing love;
Ah! yet a while, and half those oaths believ'd,
Her happiness is vanish'd; and the boy
While yet a stripling, finds the sound he lov'd
280   Has led him on, till he has given up
His freedom, and his happiness together.
I once was happy, when while yet a child,
I learn'd to love these upland solitudes,
And, when elastic as the mountain air,
285   To my light spirit, care was yet unknown
And evil unforseen:—Early it came,
And childhood scarcely passed, I was condemned,
A guiltless exile, silently to sigh,
While Memory, with faithful pencil, drew
290   The contrast; and regretting, I compar'd
With the polluted smoky atmosphere
And dark and stifling streets, the southern hills
That to the setting Sun, their graceful heads
Rearing, o'erlook the frith,° where Vecta[7] breaks   *firth, inlet*

---

7. Vecta. The Isle of Wight, which breaks the force of the waves when they are driven by southwest winds against this long and open coast. It is somewhere described as "Vecta shouldering the Western Waves" [Smith's note].

295 With her white rocks, the strong impetuous tide,
     When western winds the vast Atlantic urge
     To thunder on the coast.—Haunts of my youth!
     Scenes of fond day dreams, I behold ye yet!
     Where 'twas so pleasant by thy northern slopes
300 To climb the winding sheep-path, aided oft
     By scatter'd thorns: whose spiny branches bore
     Small woolly tufts, spoils of the vagrant lamb
     There seeking shelter from the noon-day sun;
     And pleasant, seated on the short soft turf,
305 To look beneath upon the hollow way
     While heavily upward mov'd the labouring wain,°   wagon
     And stalking slowly by, the sturdy hind
     To ease his panting team, stopp'd with a stone
     The grating wheel.

                         Advancing higher still
310 The prospect widens, and the village church
     But little, o'er the lowly roofs around
     Rears its gray belfry, and its simple vane;
     Those lowly roofs of thatch are half conceal'd
     By the rude arms of trees, lovely in spring,[8]
315 When on each bough, the rosy-tinctur'd bloom
     Sits thick, and promises autumnal plenty.
     For even those orchards round the Norman Farms,
     Which, as their owners mark the promis'd fruit,
     Console them for the vineyards of the south,
     Surpass not these.

320   Where woods of ash, and beech,
     And partial copses, fringe the green hill foot,
     The upland shepherd rears his modest home,
     There wanders by, a little nameless stream
     That from the hill wells forth, bright now and clear,
325 Or after rain with chalky mixture gray,
     But still refreshing in its shallow course,
     The cottage garden; most for use design'd,
     Yet not of beauty destitute. The vine
     Mantles the little casement; yet the briar
330 Drops fragrant dew among the July flowers;
     And pansies rayed, and freak'd and mottled pinks
     Grow among balm, and rosemary and rue;
     There honeysuckles flaunt, and roses blow
     Almost uncultured:° Some with dark green leaves   uncultivated
335 Contrast their flowers of pure unsullied white;
     Others, like velvet robes of regal state
     Of richest crimson, while in thorny moss
     Enshrined and cradled, the most lovely, wear
     The hues of youthful beauty's glowing cheek.—

8. Every cottage in this country has its orchard; and I imagine that not even those of Herefordshire, or Worcestershire, exhibit a more beautiful prospect, when the trees are in bloom, and the "Pri- mavera candida e vermiglia," is every where so enchanting [Smith's note, quoting Petrarch's sonnet 310, "pure and ruddy spring"].

340 With fond regret I recollect e'en now
     In Spring and Summer, what delight I felt
     Among these cottage gardens, and how much
     Such artless nosegays, knotted with a rush
     By village housewife or her ruddy maid,
345 Were welcome to me; soon and simply pleas'd.

     An early worshipper at Nature's shrine,
     I loved her rudest scenes—warrens,° and heaths,   *land for breeding*
     And yellow commons, and birch-shaded hollows,
     And hedge rows, bordering unfrequented lanes
350 Bowered with wild roses, and the clasping woodbine
     Where purple tassels of the tangling vetch[9]
     With bittersweet, and bryony inweave,[1]
     And the dew fills the silver bindweed's[2] cups.—
     I loved to trace the brooks whose humid banks
355 Nourish the harebell, and the freckled pagil;[3]
     And stroll among o'ershadowing woods of beech,
     Lending in Summer, from the heats of noon
     A whispering shade; while haply there reclines
     Some pensive lover of uncultur'd flowers,°   *wildflowers*
360 Who, from the tumps° with bright green mosses clad,   *hillocks, mounds*
     Plucks the wood sorrel,[4] with its light thin leaves,
     Heart-shaped, and triply folded; and its root
     Creeping like beaded coral; or who there
     Gathers, the copse's pride, anémones,[5]
365 With rays like golden studs on ivory laid
     Most delicate: but touch'd with purple clouds,
     Fit crown for April's fair but changeful brow.

     Ah! hills so early loved! in fancy still
     I breathe your pure keen air; and still behold
370 Those widely spreading views, mocking alike
     The Poet and the Painter's utmost art.
     And still, observing objects more minute,
     Wondering remark the strange and foreign forms
     Of sea-shells; with the pale calcareous° soil   *chalky*
375 Mingled, and seeming of resembling substance.[6]
     Tho' surely the blue Ocean (from the heights
     Where the downs westward trend, but dimly seen)
     Here never roll'd its surge. Does Nature then

---

9. Vetch. *Vicia sylvatica* [Smith's note].
1. Bittersweet. *Solanum dulcamara*. Bryony. *Bryonia alba* [Smith's note].
2. Bindweed. *Convolvulus sepium* [Smith's note].
3. Harebell. *Hyacinthus non scriptus*. Pagil. *Primula veris* [Smith's note].
4. Sorrel. *Oxalis acetosella* [Smith's note].
5. Anémones. *Anemóne nemorosa*. It appears to be settled on late and excellent authorities, that this word should not be accented on the second syllable, but on the penultima. I have however ventured the more known accentuation, as more generally used, and suiting better the nature of my verse [Smith's note].
6. Among the crumbling chalk I have often found shells, some quite in a fossil state and hardly distinguishable from chalk. Others appeared more recent; cockles, muscles, and periwinkles, I well remember, were among the number; and some whose names I do not know. A great number were like those of small land snails. It is now many years since I made these observations. The appearance of sea-shells so far from the sea excited my surprise, though I then knew nothing of natural history. I have never read any of the late theories of the earth, nor was I ever satisfied with the attempts to explain many of the phenomena which call forth conjecture in those books I happened to have had access to on this subject [Smith's note].

Mimic, in wanton mood, fantastic shapes
380   Of bivalves, and inwreathed volutes,[7] that cling
To the dark sea-rock of the wat'ry world?
Or did this range of chalky mountains, once[8]
Form a vast basin, where the Ocean waves
Swell'd fathomless? What time these fossil shells,
385   Buoy'd on their native element, were thrown
Among the imbedding calx:° when the huge hill   *lime*
Its giant bulk heaved, and in strange ferment
Grew up a guardian barrier, 'twixt the sea
And the green level of the sylvan weald.[9]

390   Ah! very vain is Science' proudest boast,
And but a little light its flame yet lends
To its most ardent votaries; since from whence
These fossil forms are seen, is but conjecture,
Food for vague theories, or vain dispute,
395   While to his daily task the peasant goes,
Unheeding such inquiry; with no care
But that the kindly change of sun and shower,
Fit for his toil the earth he cultivates.
As little recks the herdsman of the hill,
400   Who on some turfy knoll, idly reclined,
Watches his wether° flock, that deep beneath   *male sheep*
Rest the remains of men, of whom is left[1]
No traces in the records of mankind,
Save what these half obliterated mounds
405   And half fill'd trenches doubtfully impart
To some lone antiquary; who on times remote,
Since which two thousand years have roll'd away,
Loves to contemplate. He perhaps may trace,
Or fancy he can trace, the oblong square
410   Where the mail'd legions, under Claudius,[2] rear'd
The rampire,° or excavated fosse° delved;   *rampart / ditch*
What time the huge unwieldy Elephant[3]

7. Spiral-shelled mollusks such as periwinkles. "Bivalves": hinge-shelled mollusks such as clams and oysters.
8. The theory here slightly hinted at, is taken from an idea started by Mr. White [Smith's note, referring to Gilbert White, author of *The Natural History and Antiquities of Selborne*, 1789].
9. The Sussex Weald, a wooded tract of land between the North and South Downs.
1. These Downs are not only marked with traces of encampments, which from their forms are called Roman or Danish; but there are numerous tumuli [burial mounds] among them. Some of which having been opened a few years ago, were supposed by a learned antiquary to contain the remains of the original natives of the country [Smith's note].
2. That the legions of Claudius [10 B.C.E.–54 C.E.] were in this part of Britain appears certain. Since this emperor received the submission of Cantii, Atrebates, Irenobates, and Regni, in which latter denomination were included the people of Sussex [Smith's note].
3. In the year 1740, some workmen digging in the park at Burton in Sussex, discovered, nine feet below the surface, the teeth and bones of an elephant; two of the former were seven feet eight inches in length. There were besides these, tusks, one of which broke in removing it, a grinder not at all decayed, and a part of the jaw-bone, with bones of the knee and thigh, and several others. Some of them remained very lately at Burton House, the seat of John Biddulph, Esq. Others were in possession of the Rev. Dr. Langrish, minister of Petworth at that period, who was present when some of these bones were taken up, and gave it as his opinion, that they had remained there since the universal deluge [the Flood]. The Romans under the Emperor Claudius probably brought elephants into Britain. Milton, in the Second Book of his History [of Britain], in speaking of the expedition, says that "He like a great eastern king, with armed elephants, marched through Gallia." This is given on the authority of Dion Cassius, in his Life of the Emperor Claudius. It has therefore been conjectured, that the bones found at Burton might have been those of one of these elephants, who perished there soon after its

Auxiliary reluctant, hither led,
From Afric's forest glooms and tawny sands,
415   First felt the Northern blast, and his vast frame
Sunk useless; whence in after ages found,
The wondering hinds, on those enormous bones
Gaz'd; and in giants[4] dwelling on the hills
Believed and marvell'd.—

Hither, Ambition come!
420   Come and behold the nothingness of all
For which you carry thro' the oppressed Earth,
War, and its train of horrors—see where tread
The innumerous° hoofs of flocks above the works   *countless*
By which the warrior sought to register
425   His glory, and immortalize his name.—
The pirate Dane,[5] who from his circular camp
Bore in destructive robbery, fire and sword
Down thro' the vale, sleeps unremember'd here;
And here, beneath the green sward, rests alike
430   The savage native,[6] who his acorn meal
Shar'd with the herds, that ranged the pathless woods;
And the centurion, who on these wide hills
Encamping, planted the Imperial Eagle.°   *the Roman standard*
All, with the lapse of Time, have passed away,
435   Even as the clouds, with dark and dragon shapes,
Or like vast promontories crown'd with towers,
Cast their broad shadows on the downs: then sail
Far to the northward, and their transient gloom
Is soon forgotten.

But from thoughts like these,
440   By human crimes suggested, let us turn
To where a more attractive study courts
The wanderer of the hills; while shepherd girls
Will from among the fescue[7] bring him flowers,
Of wonderous mockery; some resembling bees
445   In velvet vest, intent on their sweet toil,[8]
While others mimic flies,[9] that lightly sport

---

landing; or dying on the high downs, one of which, called Duncton Hill, rises immediately above Burton Park, the bones might have been washed down by the torrents of rain, and buried deep in the soil. They were not found together, but scattered at some distance from each other. The two tusks were twenty feet apart. I had often heard of the elephant's bones at Burton, but never saw them; and I have no books to refer to. I think I saw, in what is now called the National Museum at Paris, the very large bones of an elephant, which were found in North America: though it is certain that this enormous animal is never seen in its natural state, but in the countries under the torrid zone of the old world. I have, since making this note, been told that the bones of the rhinoceros and hippopotamus have been found in America [Smith's note].

4. The peasants believe that the large bones sometimes found belonged to giants, who formerly lived on the hills. The devil also has a great deal to do with the remarkable forms of hill and vale: the Devil's Punch Bowl, the Devil's Leaps, and the Devil's Dyke, are names given to deep hollows, or high and abrupt ridges, in this and the neighbouring county [Smith's note].

5. The incursions of the Danes were for many ages the scourge of this island [Smith's note].

6. The Aborigines of this country lived in woods, unsheltered but by trees and caves; and were probably as truly savage as any of those who are now termed so [Smith's note].

7. The grass called Sheep's Fescue (*Festuca ovina*), clothes these Downs with the softest turf [Smith's note].

8. *Ophrys apifera*, Bee Ophrys, or Orchis found plentifully on the hills, as well as the next [Smith's note].

9. *Ophrys muscifera*. Fly Orchis. Linnæus, misled by the variations to which some of this tribe are really subject, has perhaps too rashly esteemed all those which resemble insects, as forming only one

In the green shade, or float along the pool,
But here seen perch'd upon the slender stalk,
And gathering honey dew. While in the breeze
450 That wafts the thistle's plumed seed along,
Blue bells wave tremulous. The mountain thyme[1]
Purples the hassock° of the heaving mole,   *tuft of grass*
And the short turf is gay with tormentil,[2]
And bird's foot trefoil, and the lesser tribes
455 Of hawkweed;[3] spangling it with fringed stars.—
Near where a richer tract of cultur'd land
Slopes to the south; and burnished by the sun,
Bend in the gale of August, floods of corn;
The guardian of the flock, with watchful care,[4]
460 Repels by voice and dog the encroaching sheep—
While his boy visits every wired trap[5]
That scars the turf; and from the pit-falls takes
The timid migrants,[6] who from distant wilds,
Warrens, and stone quarries, are destined thus
465 To lose their short existence. But unsought
By Luxury yet, the Shepherd still protects
The social bird,[7] who from his native haunts
Of willowy current, or the rushy pool,
Follows the fleecy crowd, and flirts and skims,
In fellowship among them.

470   Where the knoll
More elevated takes the changeful winds,
The windmill rears its vanes; and thitherward
With his white load,° the master travelling,   *load of grain*
Scares the rooks rising slow on whispering wings,
475 While o'er his head, before the summer sun
Lights up the blue expanse, heard more than seen,
The lark sings matins; and above the clouds
Floating, embathes his spotted breast in dew.

species, which he terms Ophrys insecti fera. See *English Botany* [Smith's note].
1. Blue bells. *Campanula rotundifolia.* Mountain thyme. *Thymus serpyllum.* "It is a common notion, that the flesh of sheep which feeds upon aromatic plants, particularly wild thyme, is superior in flavour to other mutton. The truth is, that sheep do not crop these aromatic plants, unless now and then by accident, or when they are first turned on hungry to downs, heaths, or commons; but the soil and situations favourable to aromatic plants, produce a short sweet pasturage, best adapted to feeding sheep, whom nature designed for mountains, and not for turnip grounds and rich meadows. The attachment of bees to this, and other aromatic plants, is well known." Martyn's Miller [Smith's note, citing Thomas Martyn's revision of Philip Miller's *The Gardener's and Botanist's Dictionary,* 1797–1807].
2. Tormentil. *Tormentilla reptans* [Smith's note].
3. Bird's foot trefoil. *Trifolium ornithopoides.* Hawkweed. *Hieracium,* many sorts [Smith's note].
4. The downs, especially to the south, where they

are less abrupt, are in many places under the plough; and the attention of the shepherds is there particularly required to keep the flocks from trespassing [Smith's note].
5. Square holes cut in the turf, into which a wire noose is fixed, to catch Wheatears. Mr. White [*Natural History of Selborne*] says, that these birds (*Motacilla oenanthe*) are never taken beyond the river Adur, and Beding Hill; but this is certainly a mistake [Smith's note].
6. These birds are extremely fearful, and on the slightest appearance of a cloud, run for shelter to the first rut, or heap of stone, that they see [Smith's note].
7. The Yellow Wagtail. *Motacilla flava.* It frequents the banks of rivulets in winter, making its nest in meadows and corn-fields. But after the breeding season is over, it haunts downs and sheepwalks, and is seen constantly among the flocks, probably for the sake of the insects it picks up. In France the shepherds call it *La Bergeronette,* and say it often gives them, by its cry, notice of approaching danger [Smith's note].

Beneath the shadow of a gnarled thorn,
480 Bent by the sea blast[8] from a seat of turf
With fairy nosegays strewn, how wide the view![9]
Till in the distant north it melts away,
And mingles indiscriminate with clouds:
But if the eye could reach so far, the mart
485 Of England's capital, its domes and spires
Might be perceived.—Yet hence the distant range
Of Kentish hills,[1] appear in purple haze;
And nearer, undulate the wooded heights,
And airy summits,[2] that above the mole
490 Rise in green beauty; and the beacon'd ridge
Of Black-down[3] shagg'd with heath, and swelling rude
Like a dark island from the vale; its brow
Catching the last rays of the evening sun
That gleam between the nearer park's old oaks,
495 Then lighten up the river, and make prominent
The portal, and the ruin'd battlements[4]
Of that dismantled fortress; rais'd what time
The Conqueror's successors fiercely fought,
Tearing with civil feuds the desolate land.
500 But now a tiller of the soil dwells there,
And of the turret's loop'd and rafter'd halls
Has made an humbler homestead—Where he sees,
Instead of armed foemen, herds that graze
Along his yellow meadows; or his flocks
505 At evening from the upland driv'n to fold.—

In such a castellated mansion once
A stranger chose his home; and where hard by
In rude disorder fallen, and hid with brushwood
Lay fragments gray of towers and buttresses,
510 Among the ruins, often he would muse.—
His rustic meal soon ended, he was wont
To wander forth, listening the evening sounds
Of rushing milldam,[5] or the distant team,
Or night-jar, chasing fern-flies:[6] the tir'd hind

8. The strong winds from the south-west occasion almost all the trees, which on these hills are exposed to it, to grow the other way [Smith's note].
9. So extensive are some of the views from these hills, that only the want of power in the human eye to travel so far, prevents London itself being discerned. Description falls so infinitely short of the reality, that only here and there, distinct features can be given [Smith's note].
1. A scar of chalk in a hill beyond Sevenoaks in Kent, is very distinctly seen of a clear day [Smith's note].
2. The hills about Dorking in Surry; over almost the whole extent of which county the prospect extends [Smith's note]. "Mole" refers to the cliffs descending to the sea.
3. This is an high ridge, extending between Sussex and Surry. It is covered with heath, and has almost always a dark appearance. On it is a telegraph [Smith's note].
4. In this country there are several of the for-

tresses or castles built by Stephen of Blois [King of England, 1135–54], in his contention for the kingdom, with the daughter of Henry the First, the empress Matilda. Some of these are now converted into farm houses [Smith's note].
5. I.e., the water in the dammed millstream.
6. Dr. Aikin remarks, I believe, in his essay "On the Application of Natural History to the Purposes of Poetry," how many of our best poets have noticed the same circumstance, the hum of the Dor Beetle (Scaraboeus stercorarius) among the sounds heard by the evening wanderer. I remember only one instance in which the more remarkable, though by no means uncommon noise, of the Fern Owl, or Goatsucker, is mentioned. It is called the Night Hawk, the Jar Bird, the Churn Owl, and the Fern Owl, from its feeding on the Scaraboeus solstitialis, or Fern Chafer, which it catches while on the wing with its claws, the middle toe of which is long and curiously serrated, on purpose to hold them. It was this bird that was intended to be

515   Pass'd him at nightfall, wondering he should sit
       On the hill top so late: they from the coast
       Who sought by-paths with their clandestine load,
       Saw with suspicious doubt, the lonely man
       Cross on their way: but village maidens thought
520   His senses injur'd; and with pity say
       That he, poor youth! must have been cross'd in love—
       For often, stretch'd upon the mountain turf
       With folded arms, and eyes intently fix'd
       Where ancient elms and firs obscured a grange,°   *farm*
525   Some little space within the vale below,
       They heard him, as complaining of his fate,
       And to the murmuring wind, of cold neglect
       And baffled hope he told.—The peasant girls
       These plaintive sounds remember, and even now
530   Among them may be heard the stranger's songs.

       Were I a Shepherd on the hill
          And ever as the mists withdrew
       Could see the willows of the rill
       Shading the footway to the mill
535   Where once I walk'd with you—

       And as away Night's shadows sail,
          And sounds of birds and brooks arise,
       Believe, that from the woody vale
       I hear your voice upon the gale
540   In soothing melodies;

       And viewing from the Alpine height,
          The prospect dress'd in hues of air,
       Could say, while transient colours bright
       Touch'd the fair scene with dewy light,
545   'Tis, that *her* eyes are there!

       I think, I could endure my lot
          And linger on a few short years,
       And then, by all but you forgot,
       Sleep, where the turf that clothes the spot
550   May claim some pitying tears.

       For 'tis not easy to forget
          One, who thro' life has lov'd you still,
       And you, however late, might yet

---

described in the Forty-second sonnet. I was mistaken in supposing it as visible in November; it is a migrant, and leaves this country in August. I had often seen and heard it, but I did not then know its name or history. It is called Goatsucker (*Caprimulgus*), from a strange prejudice taken against it by the Italians, who assert that it sucks their goats; and the peasants of England still believe that a disease in the backs of their cattle, occasioned by a fly, which deposits its egg under the skin, and raises a boil, sometimes fatal to calves, is the work of this bird, which they call a Puckeridge. Nothing can convince them that their beasts are not injured by this bird, which they therefore hold in abhorrence [Smith's note, referring at the beginning to John Aikin's *An Essay on the Application of Natural History to Poetry*, 1777, and in the middle to sonnet 42 in her own *Elegiac Sonnets*].

With sighs to Memory giv'n, regret°   *recall with regret*
555   The Shepherd of the Hill.

Yet otherwhile it seem'd as if young Hope
Her flattering pencil gave to Fancy's hand,
And in his wanderings, rear'd to sooth his soul
Ideal bowers of pleasure.—Then, of Solitude
560   And of his hermit life, still more enamour'd,
His home was in the forest; and wild fruits
And bread sustain'd him. There in early spring
The Barkmen[7] found him, e'er the sun arose;
There at their daily toil, the Wedgecutters[8]
565   Beheld him thro' the distant thicket move.
The shaggy dog following the truffle hunter,[9]
Bark'd at the loiterer; and perchance at night
Belated villagers from fair or wake,
While the fresh night-wind let the moonbeams in
570   Between the swaying boughs, just saw him pass,
And then in silence, gliding like a ghost
He vanish'd! Lost among the deepening gloom.—
But near one ancient tree, whose wreathed roots
Form'd a rude couch, love-songs and scatter'd rhymes,
575   Unfinish'd sentences, or half erased,
And rhapsodies like this, were sometimes found.—

Let us to woodland wilds repair
     While yet the glittering night-dews seem
To wait the freshly-breathing air,
580   Precursive of the morning beam,
That rising with advancing day,
Scatters the silver drops away.

An elm, uprooted by the storm,
     The trunk with mosses gray and green,
585   Shall make for us a rustic form,
     Where lighter grows the forest scene;
And far among the bowery shades,
Are ferny lawns and grassy glades.

Retiring May to lovely June
590   Her latest garland now resigns;
The banks with cuckoo-flowers[1] are strewn,
     The woodwalks blue with columbines,[2]

---

7. As soon as the sap begins to rise, the trees intended for felling are cut and barked. At which time the men who are employed in that business pass whole days in the woods [Smith's note].
8. The wedges used in ship-building are made of beech wood, and great numbers are cut every year in the woods near the Downs [Smith's note].
9. Truffles are found under the beech woods, by means of small dogs trained to hunt them by the scent [Smith's note].
1. Cuckoo-flowers. *Lychnis dioica.* Shakespeare describes the Cuckoo buds as being yellow [*Love's Labor's Lost* 5.2.871]. He probably meant the numerous Ranunculi, or March marigolds (*Caltha palustris*) which so gild the meadows in Spring; but poets have never been botanists. The Cuckoo flower is the *Lychnis floscuculi* [Smith's note].
2. Columbines. *Aquilegia vulgaris* [Smith's note].

And with its reeds, the wandering stream
Reflects the flag-flower's[3] golden gleam.

595   There, feathering down the turf to meet,
      Their shadowy arms the beeches spread,
While high above our sylvan seat,
      Lifts the light ash its airy head;
And later leaved, the oaks between
600   Extend their boughs of vernal green.

The slender birch its paper rind
      Seems offering to divided love,
And shuddering even without a wind
      Aspens, their paler foliage move,
605   As if some spirit of the air
Breath'd a low sigh in passing there.

The Squirrel in his frolic mood,
      Will fearless bound among the boughs;
Yaffils[4] laugh loudly thro' the wood,
610   And murmuring ring-doves tell their vows;
While we, as sweetest woodscents rise,
Listen to woodland melodies.

And I'll contrive a sylvan room
      Against the time of summer heat,
615   Where leaves, inwoven in Nature's loom,
      Shall canopy our green retreat;
And gales that "close the eye of day"[5]
Shall linger, e'er they die away.

And when a sere and sallow hue
620   From early frost the bower receives,
I'll dress the sand rock cave for you,
      And strew the floor with heath and leaves,
That you, against the autumnal air
May find securer shelter there.

625   The Nightingale will then have ceas'd
      To sing her moonlight serenade;
But the gay bird with blushing breast,[6]
      And Woodlarks[7] still will haunt the shade,
And by the borders of the spring
630   Reed-wrens[8] will yet be carolling.

---

3. Flag-flower. *Iris pseudacorus* [Smith's note].
4. Yaffils. Woodpeckers (*Picus*); three or four species in Britain [Smith's note].
5. "And liquid notes that close the eye of day." Milton [Sonnet 1, "O Nightingale"]. The idea here meant to be conveyed is of the evening wind, so welcome after a hot day of Summer, and which appears to sooth and lull all nature into tranquillity [Smith's note].

6. The Robin (*Motacilla rubecula*), which is always heard after other songsters have ceased to sing [Smith's note].
7. The Woodlark (*Alauda nemorosa*), sings very late [Smith's note].
8. Reed-wrens (*Motacilla arundinacea*), sing all the summer and autumn, and are often heard during the night [Smith's note].

The forest hermit's lonely cave
  None but such soothing sounds shall reach,
Or hardly heard, the distant wave
  Slow breaking on the stony beach;
635 Or winds, that now sigh soft and low,
  Now make wild music as they blow.

And then, before the chilling North
  The tawny foliage falling light,
Seems, as it flits along the earth,
640   The footfall of the busy Sprite,
Who wrapt in pale autumnal gloom,
  Calls up the mist-born Mushroom.

Oh! could I hear your soft voice there,
  And see you in the forest green
645 All beauteous as you are, more fair
  You'd look, amid the sylvan scene,
And in a wood-girl's simple guise,
  Be still more lovely in mine eyes.

Ye phantoms of unreal delight,
650   Visions of fond delirium born!
Rise not on my deluded sight,
  Then leave me drooping and forlorn
To know, such bliss can never be,
  Unless Amanda loved like me.

655 The visionary, nursing dreams like these,
Is not indeed unhappy. Summer woods
Wave over him, and whisper as they wave,
Some future blessings he may yet enjoy.
And as above him sail the silver clouds,
660 He follows them in thought to distant climes,
Where, far from the cold policy of this,
Dividing him from her he fondly loves,
He, in some island of the southern sea,[9]
May haply build his cane-constructed bower
665 Beneath the bread-fruit, or aspiring palm,
With long green foliage rippling in the gale.
Oh! let him cherish his ideal bliss—
For what is life, when Hope has ceas'd to strew
Her fragile flowers along its thorny way?
670 And sad and gloomy are his days, who lives
Of Hope abandon'd!

             Just beneath the rock
Where Beachy overpeers the channel wave,

9. An allusion to the visionary delights of the newly discovered islands [Polynesia], where it was at first believed men lived in a state of simplicity and happiness; but where, as later enquiries have ascertained, that exemption from toil, which the fertility of their country gives them, produces the grossest vices; and a degree of corruption that late navigators think will end in the extirpation of the whole people in a few years [Smith's note].

Within a cavern mined by wintry tides
Dwelt one,[1] who long disgusted with the world
675 And all its ways, appear'd to suffer life
Rather than live; the soul-reviving gale,
Fanning the bean-field, or the thymy° heath,   *abounding in thyme*
Had not for many summers breathed on him;
And nothing mark'd to him the season's change,
680 Save that more gently rose the placid sea,
And that the birds which winter on the coast
Gave place to other migrants; save that the fog,
Hovering no more above the beetling cliffs
Betray'd not then the little careless sheep[2]
685 On the brink grazing, while their headlong fall
Near the lone Hermit's flint-surrounded home,
Claim'd unavailing pity; for his heart
Was feelingly alive to all that breath'd;
And outraged as he was, in sanguine youth,
690 By human crimes, he still acutely felt
For human misery.

              Wandering on the beach,
He learn'd to augur from the clouds of heaven,
And from the changing colours of the sea,
And sullen murmurs of the hollow cliffs,
695 Or the dark porpoises,[3] that near the shore
Gambol'd and sported on the level brine
When tempests were approaching: then at night
He listen'd to the wind; and as it drove
The billows with o'erwhelming vehemence
700 He, starting from his rugged couch, went forth
And hazarding a life, too valueless,
He waded thro' the waves, with plank or pole
Towards where the mariner in conflict dread
Was buffeting for life the roaring surge;
705 And now just seen, now lost in foaming gulphs,
The dismal gleaming of the clouded moon
Shew'd the dire peril. Often he had snatch'd
From the wild billows, some unhappy man
Who liv'd to bless the hermit of the rocks.
710 But if his generous cares were all in vain,
And with slow swell the tide of morning bore
Some blue swol'n cor'se° to land; the pale recluse   *corpse*
Dug in the chalk a sepulchre—above
Where the dank sea-wrack° mark'd the utmost tide,   *refuse from the sea*

1. In a cavern almost immediately under the cliff called Beachy Head, there lived, as the people of the country believed, a man of the name of Darby, who for many years had no other abode than this cave, and subsisted almost entirely on shell-fish. He had often administered assistance to shipwrecked mariners; but venturing into the sea on this charitable mission during a violent equinoctial storm, he himself perished. As it is above thirty years since I heard this tradition of Parson Darby (for so I think he was called): it may now perhaps be forgotten [Smith's note].
2. Sometimes in thick weather the sheep feeding on the summit of the cliff, miss their footing, and are killed by the fall [Smith's note].
3. Dark porpoises. *Delphinus phocœna* [Smith's note].

715 And with his prayers perform'd the obsequies
For the poor helpless stranger.

                    One dark night
The equinoctial wind blew south by west,
Fierce on the shore;—the bellowing cliffs were shook
Even to their stony base, and fragments fell
720 Flashing and thundering on the angry flood.
At day-break, anxious for the lonely man,
His cave the mountain shepherds visited,
Tho' sand and banks of weeds had choak'd their way.—
He was not in it; but his drowned cor'se
725 By the waves wafted, near his former home
Receiv'd the rites of burial. Those who read
Chisel'd within the rock, these mournful lines,
Memorials of his sufferings, did not grieve,
That dying in the cause of charity
730 His spirit, from its earthly bondage freed,
Had to some better region fled for ever.

1806   1807

MARY ROBINSON
1757?–1800

Mary Robinson, whom the *Dictionary of National Biography*, at the beginning of a long entry, describes as "actress, author, and mistress of George, Prince of Wales," lived a more sensational life than any other poet of the period, Byron and Shelley included. Her father was a Bristol whaler, her mother a woman of "genteel background" who, after her husband deserted the family, ran a school for girls. At fifteen Mary was married to Thomas Robinson, an articled law clerk who seemed a good match but quickly proved a gambler and libertine; he was arrested for debt, and Mary and her infant daughter spent a year with him in debtors' prison, where, to pass the time, she began writing poetry. Her first pieces appeared in a two-volume *Poems* published under the patronage of the duchess of Devonshire in 1775.

In December 1776, accepting a long-standing invitation of David Garrick, the actor-manager of the Drury Lane theater, Robinson made her stage debut as Juliet, and for the next four years she was constantly before the public—in thirty or more principal roles, nine of them in plays by Shakespeare. A beauty and leader of fashion, she attracted many suitors and was painted by many of the leading portraitists of the day, including George Romney, Thomas Gainsborough, and Sir Joshua Reynolds, president of the Royal Academy. At a command performance of *The Winter's Tale* in December 1779, playing the role of Perdita, Robinson captivated the teenaged prince of Wales and, after negotiating financial compensation in the form of a £20,000 bond (because she would have to give up her acting career), became his mistress. As a royal mistress, she was even more exposed to the public eye than she had been on the stage; years after the prince abandoned her, ribald speculation about the erotic adventures of "Perdita" continued to engross gossip columnists and satiric cartoonists. Robinson's attempt, following the prince's desertion, to sue for the promised £20,000 failed, but through the efforts of the Whig parliamentarian Charles James Fox, another famous man who may have been her lover, she received an annuity from the prince of £500 per year. At twenty-five she formed an attachment with Banastre Tarleton, an army officer who had just returned from the war in America and was embarking on a career in Parliament. That attachment lasted ten years, until Tarleton married an heiress. Robinson was by this time in poor health and, as a consequence of either a miscarriage (in some accounts) or rheumatic fever (in others), was paralyzed from the waist down. Even in this condition she made a striking public figure, as four liveried servants, covering their arms with long white sleeves, bore her from the opera house to her waiting carriage. A savvy self-publicist, she appears to have been well aware of the part she played in the spectacle that was fashionable London, accepting and even embracing (in the words of her modern editor, Judith Pascoe) her role as "the most attractive object in a large urban display."

Literature became Robinson's principal activity and source of income when she was in her early thirties. In 1788 and 1789, writing under the pen name "Laura Maria" and sending her verse to the papers the *World* and the *Oracle*, she entered into a passionate poetical correspondence with "Della Crusca" (pseudonym of the poet Robert Merry, who had already participated in a similar public flirtation in the periodical press, in the series of love poems he exchanged with "Anna Matilda," the poet Hannah Cowley). When, in her *Poems* of 1791, Robinson reprinted some of these "effusions" of feeling, she attracted six hundred subscribers. In 1796 she contributed to the English revival of the sonnet with her Petrarchan series *Sappho and Phaon*. In the 1790s she also authored seven novels, beginning in 1792 with *Vacenza, or The Dangers of Credulity*. She succeeded Robert Southey in the influential office of poetry editor of the *Morning Post* in 1799. Other writings by Robinson include her political tracts *Impartial Reflections on the Present Situation of the Queen of France* (1793) and *Thoughts on the Condition of Women, and on the Injustice of Mental Subordination* (1799) and her posthumous *Memoirs* (1801), an autobiography whose description of a woman's poetic vocation makes it (like Robinson's critical discussion of the Greek poet of passion Sappho) exceptional in an era now better known for its models of masculine artistry.

Robinson is one of the accomplished writers of blank verse in the 1790s (as in "London's Summer Morning") as well as one of the most irrepressibly musical in many different forms of rhyme. Outspokenly liberal in its politics, good-humored, satirical, and sentimental by turns, her late verse in particular exemplifies what Stuart Curran calls "the new realism that will impel English poetry into the nineteenth century." *Lyrical Tales* (1800), the final volume of Robinson's poetry to be published in her lifetime, appeared the month before the second edition of Wordsworth and Coleridge's *Lyrical Ballads*—from the same publisher and printer and in exactly the same format and typography (Wordsworth, in reaction, tried to change his own title to *Poems by W. Wordsworth*). Robinson's "The Poor Singing Dame" is modeled on the most popular of Wordsworth's 1798 ballads, "Goody Blake and Harry Gill." Wordsworth in turn based one of his pieces ("The Seven Sisters; or, The Solitude of Binnorie") on the elaborate metrical scheme of Robinson's "The Haunted Beach," a poem that prompted Coleridge to exclaim to Southey, when he first saw it in the *Morning Post*, "the Metre—ay! that Woman has an Ear." Coleridge admired her "undoubted Genius," and Robinson returned the compliment in one of her last poems, "To the Poet Coleridge," a shrewd reading of "Kubla Khan" sixteen years before it first got into print.

January, 1795[1]

Pavement slipp'ry, people sneezing,
Lords in ermine, beggars freezing;
Titled gluttons dainties carving,
Genius in a garret starving.

5 Lofty mansions, warm and spacious;
Courtiers cringing and voracious;
Misers scarce the wretched heeding;
Gallant soldiers fighting, bleeding.

Wives who laugh at passive spouses;
10 Theatres, and meeting-houses;
Balls, where simp'ring misses languish;
Hospitals, and groans of anguish.

Arts and sciences bewailing;
Commerce drooping, credit failing;
15 Placemen° mocking subjects loyal;   *political appointees*
Separations, weddings royal.

Authors who can't earn a dinner;
Many a subtle rogue a winner;
Fugitives for shelter seeking;
20 Misers hoarding, tradesmen breaking.°   *going bankrupt*

Taste and talents quite deserted;
All the laws of truth perverted;
Arrogance o'er merit soaring;
Merit silently deploring.

25 Ladies gambling night and morning;
Fools the works of genius scorning;
Ancient dames for girls mistaken,
Youthful damsels quite forsaken.

Some in luxury delighting;
30 More in talking than in fighting;
Lovers old, and beaux decrepid;
Lordlings empty and insipid.

Poets, painters, and musicians;
Lawyers, doctors, politicians:
35 Pamphlets, newspapers, and odes,
Seeking fame by diff'rent roads.

Gallant souls with empty purses;
Gen'rals only fit for nurses;
School-boys, smit with martial spirit,
40 Taking place of vet'ran merit.

1. First published in the *Morning Post* as the work of "Portia."

Honest men who can't get places,
Knaves who shew unblushing faces;
Ruin hasten'd, peace retarded;
Candor spurn'd, and art rewarded.

1795   1806

London's Summer Morning

Who has not wak'd to list the busy sounds
Of summer's morning, in the sultry smoke
Of noisy London? On the pavement hot
The sooty chimney-boy, with dingy face
5   And tatter'd covering, shrilly bawls his trade,
Rousing the sleepy housemaid. At the door
The milk-pail rattles, and the tinkling bell
Proclaims the dustman's° office; while the street   *trash collector's*
Is lost in clouds impervious. Now begins
10 The din of hackney-coaches, waggons, carts;
While tinmen's shops, and noisy trunk-makers,
Knife-grinders, coopers, squeaking cork-cutters,
Fruit-barrows, and the hunger-giving cries
Of vegetable venders, fill the air.
15 Now ev'ry shop displays its varied trade,
And the fresh-sprinkled pavement cools the feet
Of early walkers. At the private door
The ruddy housemaid twirls the busy mop,[1]
Annoying the smart 'prentice, or neat girl,
20 Tripping with band-box[2] lightly. Now the sun
Darts burning splendor on the glitt'ring pane,
Save where the canvas awning throws a shade
On the gay merchandise. Now, spruce and trim,
In shops (where beauty smiles with industry)
25 Sits the smart damsel; while the passenger°   *passerby*
Peeps through the window, watching ev'ry charm.
Now pastry dainties catch the eye minute
Of humming insects, while the limy snare[3]
Waits to enthral them. Now the lamp-lighter
30 Mounts the tall ladder, nimbly venturous,
To trim the half-fill'd lamp; while at his feet
The pot-boy[4] yells discordant! All along
The sultry pavement, the old-clothes-man cries
In tone monotonous, and side-long views
35 The area for his traffic: now the bag
Is slily open'd, and the half-worn suit
(Sometimes the pilfer'd treasure of the base
Domestic spoiler), for one half its worth,
Sinks in the green abyss. The porter now
40 Bears his huge load along the burning way;

1. An echo of Jonathan Swift's urban pastoral "A
Description of the Morning" (1709), in which Moll
whirls "her mop with dex'trous airs" (line 7).

2. Box for hats, gloves, etc.
3. Sticky substance used to catch insects.
4. Servant from a nearby pub.

And the poor poet wakes from busy dreams,
To paint the summer morning.

1795–1800   1800

The Camp[1]

Tents, *marquees,* and baggage waggons;
Suttling houses,[2] beer in flaggons;
Drums and trumpets, singing, firing;
Girls seducing, *beaux* admiring;
5   Country lasses gay and smiling,
City lads their hearts beguiling;
Dusty roads, and horses frisky;
Many an *Eton boy* in whisky;[3]
Tax'd carts full of farmer's daughters;
10   Brutes condemn'd, and man—who slaughters!
Public-houses, booths, and castles;
Belles of fashion, serving vassals;
Lordly Gen'rals fiercely staring,
Weary soldiers, sighing, swearing!
15   *Petit maitres*° always dressing—   *fops*
In the glass themselves caressing;
Perfum'd, painted, patch'd and blooming
Ladies—manly airs assuming!
Dowagers of fifty, simp'ring
20   Misses, for a lover whimp'ring—
Husbands drill'd to household tameness;
Dames heart sick of wedded sameness.
Princes setting girls a-madding—
Wives for ever fond of gadding—
25   Princesses with lovely faces,
Beauteous children of the Graces!
Britain's pride and Virtue's treasure,
Fair and gracious, beyond measure!
Aid de Camps, and youthful pages—
30   Prudes, and vestals° of all ages!—   *virgins*
Old coquets, and matrons surly,
Sounds of distant *hurly burly!*
Mingled voices uncouth singing;
Carts, full laden, forage bringing;
35   Sociables,[4] and horses weary;
Houses warm, and dresses airy;
Loads of fatten'd poultry; pleasure
Serv'd (TO NOBLES) without measure.
Doxies[5] who the waggons follow;
40   Beer, for thirsty hinds° to swallow;   *farm boys*

---

1. Robinson's description of the social world of a
military camp was published in the *Morning Post,*
on Aug. 1, 1800, as the work of "Oberon," king of
the fairies.
2. Establishments selling provisions to soldiers.
3. Besides being a drink, a whisky was a fashionable two-wheeled carriage. Eton, the famous public school, is in Windsor, where a military camp
had been established.
4. Carriages with facing seats.
5. Mistresses, perhaps prostitutes.

Washerwomen, fruit-girls cheerful,
ANTIENT LADIES—*chaste* and *fearful*!
Tradesmen, leaving shops, and seeming
More of *war* than profit dreaming;
45 Martial sounds, and braying asses;
Noise, that ev'ry noise surpasses!
All confusion, din, and riot—
NOTHING CLEAN—and NOTHING QUIET.

1800

The Poor Singing Dame

Beneath an old wall, that went round an old castle,
  For many a year, with brown ivy o'erspread,
A neat little hovel, its lowly roof raising,
  Defied the wild winds that howl'd over its shed:
5 The turrets, that frown'd on the poor simple dwelling,
  Were rock'd to and fro, when the tempest would roar,
And the river, that down the rich valley was swelling,
  Flow'd swiftly beside the green step of its door.

The summer sun gilded the rushy roof slanting,
10 The bright dews bespangled its ivy-bound hedge,
And above, on the ramparts, the sweet birds were chanting,
  And wild buds thick dappled the clear river's edge.
When the castle's rich chambers were haunted and dreary,
  The poor little hovel was still and secure;
15 And no robber e'er enter'd, nor goblin nor fairy,
  For the splendors of pride had no charms to allure.

The Lord of the castle, a proud surly ruler,
  Oft heard the low dwelling with sweet music ring,
For the old Dame that liv'd in the little hut cheerly,
20 Would sit at her wheel, and would merrily sing:
When with revels the castle's great hall was resounding,
  The old Dame was sleeping, not dreaming of fear;
And when over the mountains the huntsmen were bounding
  She would open her lattice, their clamors to hear.

25 To the merry-ton'd horn she would dance on the threshold,
  And louder, and louder, repeat her old song:
And when winter its mantle of frost was displaying,
  She caroll'd, undaunted, the bare woods among:
She would gather dry fern, ever happy and singing,
30 With her cake of brown bread, and her jug of brown beer,
And would smile when she heard the great castle-bell ringing,
  Inviting the proud—to their prodigal cheer.

Thus she liv'd, ever patient and ever contented,
  Till envy the Lord of the castle possess'd,
35 For he hated that poverty should be so cheerful,

While care could the fav'rites of fortune molest;
He sent his bold yeomen with threats to prevent her,
And still would she carol her sweet roundelay;
At last, an old steward relentless he sent her—
40   Who bore her, all trembling, to prison away!

Three weeks did she languish, then died broken-hearted,
Poor Dame! how the death-bell did mournfully sound!
And along the green path six young bachelors bore her,
And laid her for ever beneath the cold ground!
45   And the primroses pale 'mid the long grass were growing,
The bright dews of twilight bespangled her grave,
And morn heard the breezes of summer soft blowing
To bid the fresh flow'rets in sympathy wave.

The Lord of the castle, from that fatal moment
50   When poor singing Mary was laid in her grave,
Each night was surrounded by screech-owls appalling,
Which o'er the black turrets their pinions would wave!
On the ramparts that frown'd on the river, swift flowing,
They hover'd, still hooting a terrible song,
55   When his windows would rattle, the winter blast blowing,
They would shriek like a ghost, the dark alleys among!

Wherever he wander'd they follow'd him crying,
At dawnlight, at eve, still they haunted his way!
When the moon shone across the wide common they hooted,
60   Nor quitted his path till the blazing of day.
His bones began wasting, his flesh was decaying,
And he hung his proud head, and he perish'd with shame;
And the tomb of rich marble, no soft tear displaying,
O'ershadows the grave of the Poor Singing Dame!

1799–1800   1800

The Haunted Beach

Upon a lonely desart Beach,
   Where the white foam was scatter'd,
A little shed uprear'd its head,
   Though lofty barks° were shatter'd.   *ships*
5   The sea-weeds gath'ring near the door
   A somber path display'd;
And, all around, the deaf'ning roar
Re-echo'd on the chalky shore,
   By the green billows made.

10   Above a jutting cliff was seen
   Where Sea Birds hover'd, craving;
And all around the craggs were bound
   With weeds—for ever waving.

And here and there, a cavern wide
15   Its shad'wy jaws display'd;
And near the sands, at ebb of tide,
A shiver'd mast was seen to ride
    Where the green billows stray'd.

And often, while the moaning wind
20   Stole o'er the Summer Ocean,
The moonlight scene was all serene,
    The waters scarce in motion;
Then, while the smoothly slanting sand
    The tall cliff wrapp'd in shade,
25   The Fisherman beheld a band
Of Spectres gliding hand in hand—
    Where the green billows play'd.

And pale their faces were as snow,
    And sullenly they wander'd;
30   And to the skies with hollow eyes
    They look'd as though they ponder'd.
And sometimes, from their hammock shroud,
    They dismal howlings made,
And while the blast blew strong and loud
35   The clear moon mark'd the ghastly crowd,
    Where the green billows play'd!

And then above the haunted hut
    The Curlews screaming hover'd;
And the low door, with furious roar,
40   The frothy breakers cover'd.
For in the Fisherman's lone shed
    A murder'd man was laid,
With ten wide gashes in his head,
And deep was made his sandy bed
45   Where the green billows play'd.

A shipwreck'd Mariner was he,
    Doom'd from his home to sever;
Who swore to be through wind and sea
    Firm and undaunted ever!
50   And when the wave resistless roll'd,
    About his arm he made
A packet rich of Spanish gold,
And, like a British sailor bold,
    Plung'd where the billows play'd!

55   The Spectre band, his messmates brave,
    Sunk in the yawning ocean,
While to the mast he lash'd him fast,
    And brav'd the storm's commotion.
The winter moon upon the sand
60   A silv'ry carpet made,
And mark'd the Sailor reach the land,

And mark'd his murd'rer wash his hand
Where the green billows play'd.

And since that hour the Fisherman
65   Has toil'd and toil'd in vain;
For all the night the moony light
Gleams on the specter'd main!
And when the skies are veil'd in gloom,
The Murd'rer's liquid way
70   Bounds o'er the deeply yawning tomb,
And flashing fires the sands illume,
Where the green billows play!

Full thirty years his task has been
Day after day more weary;
75   For Heav'n design'd his guilty mind
Should dwell on prospects dreary.
Bound by a strong and mystic chain,
He has not pow'r to stray;
But destin'd mis'ry to sustain,
80   He wastes, in Solitude and Pain,
A loathsome life away.

1800

To the Poet Coleridge[1]

Rapt in the visionary theme!
    Spirit divine! with thee I'll wander,
Where the blue, wavy, lucid stream,
    'Mid forest glooms, shall slow meander!
5 With thee I'll trace the circling bounds
    Of thy new Paradise extended;
And listen to the varying sounds
    Of winds, and foamy torrents blended.

Now by the source which lab'ring heaves
10   The mystic fountain, bubbling, panting,
While gossamer° its net-work weaves,   *filmy cobweb*
    Adown the blue lawn slanting!
I'll mark thy *sunny dome*, and view
    Thy *caves of ice*, thy fields of dew!
15 Thy ever-blooming mead, whose flow'r
    Waves to the cold breath of the moonlight hour!
Or when the day-star, peering bright
    On the grey wing of parting night;
While more than vegetating pow'r
20   Throbs grateful to the burning hour,

1. This poem is a tribute to, and running commentary on, Coleridge's "Kubla Khan," which Robinson read in manuscript (Coleridge had drafted it in 1797 but did not publish it until 1816).

As summer's whisper'd sighs unfold
Her million, million buds of gold;
Then will I climb the breezy bounds,
    Of thy new Paradise extended,
25 And listen to the distant sounds
    Of winds, and foamy torrents blended!

Spirit divine! with thee I'll trace
Imagination's boundless space!
With thee, beneath thy *sunny dome,*
30   I'll listen to the minstrel's lay,
    Hymning the gradual close of day;
In *caves of ice* enchanted roam,
Where on the glitt'ring entrance plays
The moon's-beam with its silv'ry rays;
35   Or, when the glassy stream,
       That through the deep dell flows,
Flashes the noon's hot beam;
    The noon's hot beam, that midway shows
Thy flaming temple, studded o'er
40 With all Peruvia's° lustrous store!   *Peru's*
There will I trace the circling bounds
    Of thy new Paradise extended!
And listen to the awful sounds,
    Of winds, and foamy torrents blended!

45 And now I'll pause to catch the moan
    Of distant breezes, cavern-pent;
Now, ere the twilight tints are flown,
Purpling the landscape, far and wide,
On the dark promontory's side
50   I'll gather wild flow'rs, dew besprent,°   *sprinkled*
And weave a crown for thee,
Genius of Heav'n-taught poesy!
While, op'ning to my wond'ring eyes,
Thou bidst a new creation rise,
55 I'll raptur'd trace the circling bounds
    Of thy rich Paradise extended,
And listen to the varying sounds
    Of winds, and foaming torrents blended.

And now, with lofty tones inviting,
60 Thy nymph, her dulcimer swift smiting,
Shall wake me in ecstatic measures!
Far, far remov'd from mortal pleasures!
    In cadence rich, in cadence strong,
Proving the wondrous witcheries of song!
65   I hear her voice! thy *sunny dome,*
    Thy *caves of ice,* aloud repeat,
    Vibrations, madd'ning sweet,
Calling the visionary wand'rer home.
She sings of thee, O favor'd child
70   Of *minstrelsy,* sublimely wild!

Of thee, whose soul can feel the tone
Which gives to airy dreams *a magic* all thy own!

Oct. 1800   1801

WILLIAM BLAKE
1757–1827

What William Blake called his "Spiritual Life" was as varied, free, and dramatic as his "Corporeal Life" was simple, limited, and unadventurous. His father was a London tradesman. His only formal education was in art: at the age of ten he entered a drawing school, and later he studied for a time at the school of the Royal Academy of Arts. At fourteen he entered an apprenticeship for seven years to a well-known engraver, James Basire, and began reading widely in his free time and trying his hand at poetry. At twenty-four he married Catherine Boucher, daughter of a market gardener. She was then illiterate, but Blake taught her to read and to help him in his engraving and printing. In the early and somewhat sentimentalized biographies, Catherine is represented as an ideal wife for an unorthodox and impecunious genius. Blake, however, must have been a trying domestic partner, and his vehement attacks on the torment caused by a possessive, jealous female will, which reached their height in 1793 and remained prominent in his writings for another decade, probably reflect a troubled period at home. The couple was childless.

The Blakes for a time enjoyed a moderate prosperity while Blake gave drawing lessons, illustrated books, and engraved designs made by other artists. When the demand for his work slackened, Blake in 1800 moved to a cottage at Felpham, on the Sussex seacoast, to take advantage of the patronage of the wealthy amateur of the arts and biographer William Hayley (also a supporter of Charlotte Smith), who with the best of narrow intentions tried to transform Blake into a conventional artist and breadwinner. But the caged eagle soon rebelled. Hayley, Blake wrote, "is the Enemy of my Spiritual Life while he pretends to be the Friend of my Corporeal."

At Felpham in 1803 occurred an event that left a permanent mark on Blake's mind and art—an altercation with one John Schofield, a private in the Royal Dragoons. Blake ordered the soldier out of his garden and, when Schofield replied with threats and curses against Blake and his wife, pushed him the fifty yards to the inn where he was quartered. Schofield brought charges that Blake had uttered seditious statements about king and country. Since England was at war with France, sedition was a hanging offense. Blake was acquitted—an event, according to a newspaper account, "which so gratified the auditory that the court was . . . thrown into an uproar by their noisy exultations." Nevertheless Schofield, his fellow soldier Cock, and other participants in the trial haunted Blake's imagination and were enlarged to demonic characters who play a sinister role in *Jerusalem*. The event exacerbated Blake's sense that ominous forces were at work in the contemporary world and led him to complicate the symbolic and allusive style by which he veiled the radical religious, moral, and political opinions that he expressed in his poems.

The dominant literary and artistic fashion of Blake's youth involved the notion that the future of British culture would involve the recovery, through archaeology as well as literary history, of an all but lost past. As an apprentice engraver who learned to draw by sketching the medieval monuments of London churches, Blake began his artistic career in the thick of that antiquarianism. It also informs his early lyric poetry. *Poetical Sketches*, published when he was twenty-six, suggests Blake's affinities with a group of later-eighteenth-century writers that includes Thomas Warton, poet and student of Middle English romance and Elizabethan verse; Thomas Gray, translator from Old Icelandic and Welsh and author, in 1757, of "The Bard," a poem about the English conquest of Wales; Thomas Percy, the editor of the ballad collection *Reliques of Ancient English Poetry* (1765); and James Macpherson, who came before the public in the 1760s claiming to be the translator of the epic verse of a third-century Gaelic bard named Ossian. Like these figures, Blake located the sources of poetic inspiration in an archaic native tradition that, according to the prevailing view of national history, had ended up eclipsed after the seventeenth century, when French court culture, manners, and morals began their cultural ascendancy. Even in their orientation to a visionary culture, the bards of Blake's later Prophetic Books retain an association with this imagined version of a primitive past.

Poetical Sketches was the only book of Blake's to be set in type according to customary methods. In 1788 he began to experiment with relief etching, a method that he called "illuminated printing" (a term associating his works with the illuminated manuscripts of the Middle Ages) and used to produce most of his books of poems. Working directly on a copper plate with pens, brushes, and an acid-resistant medium, he wrote the text in reverse (so that it would print in the normal order) and also drew the illustration; he then etched the plate in acid to eat away the untreated copper and leave the design standing in relief. The pages printed from such plates were colored by hand in water colors, often by Catherine Blake, and stitched together to make up a volume. This process was laborious and time-consuming, and Blake printed very few copies of his books; for example, of *Songs of Innocence and of Experience* only twenty-eight copies (some of them incomplete) are known to exist; of *The Book of Thel*, sixteen; of *The Marriage of Heaven and Hell*, nine; and of *Jerusalem*, five.

To read a Blake poem without the pictures is to miss something important: Blake places words and images in a relationship that is sometimes mutually enlightening and sometimes turbulent, and that relationship is an aspect of the poem's argument. In this mode of relief etching, he published *Songs of Innocence* (1789), then added supplementary poems and printed *Songs of Innocence and of Experience* (1794). The two groups of poems represent the world as it is envisioned by what he calls "two contrary states of the human soul."

Gradually Blake's thinking about human history and his experience of life and suffering articulated themselves in the "Giant Forms" and their actions, which came to constitute a complete mythology. As Blake's mythical character Los said, speaking for all imaginative artists, "I must Create a System or be enslaved by another Man's." This coherent but constantly altering and enlarging system composed the subject matter first of Blake's "minor prophecies," completed by 1795, and then of the major prophetic books on which he continued working until about 1820: *The Four Zoas, Milton,* and *Jerusalem*.

In his sixties Blake gave up poetry to devote himself to pictorial art. In the course of his life, he produced hundreds of paintings and engravings, many of them illustrations for the work of other poets, including a representation of Chaucer's Canterbury pilgrims, a superb set of designs for the Book of Job, and a series of illustrations of Dante, on which he was still hard at work when he died. At the time of his death, Blake was little known as an artist and almost entirely unknown as a poet. In the mid-nineteenth century he acquired a group of admirers among the Pre-Raphaelites, who regarded him as a precursor. Since the mid-1920s Blake has finally come into his own, both in poetry and in painting, as one of the most dedicated, intellectually challenging, and astonishingly original artists. His marked influence ranges from William Butler Yeats, who edited Blake's writings and modeled his own system of mythology on Blake's, to Allen Ginsberg and other Beat writers, Philip Pullman's *His Dark Materials* trilogy, and the graphic novels of the present day.

The explication of Blake's cryptic prophetic books has been the preoccupation of many scholars. Blake wrote them in the persona, or "voice," of "the Bard! / Who Present, Past, & Future sees"—that is, as a British poet who follows Spenser, and especially Milton, in a lineage going back to the prophets of the Bible. "The Nature of my Work," he said, "is Visionary or Imaginative." What Blake meant by the key terms *vision* and *imagination*, however, is often misinterpreted by taking literally what he, speaking the traditional language of his great predecessors, intended in a figurative sense. "That which can be made Explicit to the Idiot," he declared, "is not worth my care." Blake was a born ironist who enjoyed mystifying his well-meaning but literal-minded friends and who took a defiant pleasure in shocking the dull and complacent "angels" of his day by being deliberately outrageous in representing his work and opinions.

Blake declared that "all he knew was in the Bible" and that "The Old & New Testaments are the Great Code of Art." This is an exaggeration of the truth that all his prophetic writings deal, in various formulations, with some aspects of the overall biblical plot of the creation and the Fall, the history of the generations of humanity in the fallen world, redemption, and the promise of a recovery of Eden and of a New Jerusalem. These events, however, Blake interprets in what he calls "the spiritual sense." For such a procedure he had considerable precedent, not in the neoplatonic and occult thinkers with whom some modern commentators align him, but in the "spiritual" interpreters of the Bible among the radical Protestant sects in seventeenth- and eighteenth-century England. In *The French Revolution, America: A Prophecy, Europe: A Prophecy,* and the trenchant prophetic satire *The Marriage of Heaven and Hell*—all of which Blake wrote in the early 1790s while he was an ardent supporter of the French Revolution—he, like Wordsworth, Coleridge, Southey, and a number of radical English theologians, represented the contemporary Revolution as the purifying violence that, according to biblical prophecy, portended the imminent redemption of humanity and the world. (For discussion of these apocalyptic expectations, see "The French Revolution" at Norton Literature Online.) In Blake's later poems Orc, the fiery spirit of violent revolution, gives way as a central personage to Los, the type of the visionary imagination in the fallen world.

BLAKE'S MYTHMAKING

Blake's first attempt to articulate his full myth of humanity's present, past, and future was *The Four Zoas,* begun in 1796 or 1797. A passage from the opening statement of its theme exemplifies the long verse line (what Blake called "the march of long resounding strong heroic verse") in which he wrote his Prophetic Books and will serve also to outline the Books' vision:

> Four Mighty Ones are in every Man; a Perfect Unity
> Cannot Exist, but from the Universal Brotherhood of Eden,
> The Universal Man. To Whom be Glory Evermore, Amen. . . .
> Los was the fourth immortal starry one, & in the Earth
> Of a bright Universe Empery attended day & night
> Days & nights of revolving joy, Urthona was his name
> In Eden; in the Auricular Nerves of Human life
> Which is the Earth of Eden, he his Emanations propagated. . . .
> Daughter of Beulah, Sing
> His fall into Division & his Resurrection to Unity.

Blake's mythical premise, or starting point, is not a transcendent God but the "Universal Man" who is God and who incorporates the cosmos as well. (Blake elsewhere describes this founding image as "the Human Form Divine" and names him "Albion.") The Fall, in this myth, is not the fall of humanity away from God but a falling apart of primal people, a "fall into Division." In this event the original sin is what Blake calls "Selfhood," the attempt of an isolated part to be self-sufficient. The breakup of the all-inclusive Universal Man in Eden into exiled parts, it is evident, serves to identify the Fall with the creation—the creation not only of man and of nature as we ordinarily know them but also of a separate sky god who is alien from humanity. Universal Man divides first into the "Four Mighty Ones" who are the Zoas, or chief powers and component aspects of humanity, and these in turn divide sexually into male Spectres and female Emanations. (Thus in the quoted passage the Zoa known in the unfallen state of Eden as Urthona, the imaginative power, separates into the form of Los in the fallen world.) In addition to Eden there are three successively lower "states" of being in the fallen world, which Blake calls Beulah (a pastoral condition of easy and relaxed innocence, without clash of "contraries"), Generation (the realm of common human experience, suffering, and conflicting contraries), and Ulro (Blake's hell, the lowest state, or limit, of bleak rationality, tyranny, static negation, and isolated Selfhood). The fallen world moves through the cycles of its history, successively approaching and falling away from redemption, until, by the agency of the Redeemer (who is equated with the human imagination and is most potently operative in the prophetic poet), it will culminate in an apocalypse. In terms of his controlling image of the Universal Man, Blake describes this apocalypse as a return to the original, undivided condition, "his Resurrection to Unity."

What is confusing to many readers is that Blake alternates this representation of the Fall (as a fragmentation of the one Primal Man into separate parts) with a different kind of representation, in terms of two sharply opposed ways of seeing the universe. In this latter mode the Fall is a catastrophic change from imaginative insight (which sees the cosmos as unified and humanized) to sight by the physical eye (which sees the cosmos as a multitude of isolated individuals in an inhuman and alien nature). In terms of this distinction, the apocalypse toward which Blake as imaginative artist strives unceasingly will enable men and women once again to envision all beings as participant in the individual life that he calls "the Universal Brotherhood of Eden"— that is, a humanized world in which all individuals, in familial union, can feel at home.

The text for Blake's writings is that of *The Complete Poetry and Prose of William Blake,* edited by David V. Erdman and Harold Bloom (rev. ed., Berkeley, 1982). Blake's erratic spelling and punctuation have been altered when the original form might mislead the reader. The editors are grateful for the expert advice of Joseph Viscomi and Robert Essick in editing the selections from Blake.

All Religions Are One[1]

The Voice of one crying in the Wilderness[2]

The Argument. As the true method of knowledge is experiment the true faculty of knowing must be the faculty which experiences. This faculty I treat of.

PRINCIPLE 1st. That the Poetic Genius is the true Man, and that the body or outward form of Man is derived from the Poetic Genius. Likewise that the forms of all things are derived from their Genius, which by the Ancients was call'd an Angel & Spirit & Demon.

PRINCIPLE 2d. As all men are alike in outward form, So (and with the same infinite variety) all are alike in the Poetic Genius.

PRINCIPLE 3d. No man can think write or speak from his heart, but he must

1. This and the following two selections are early illuminated works, probably etched in 1788. They are directed both against 18th-century Deism, or "natural religion" (which bases its religious tenets not on scriptural revelation, but on evidences of God in the natural or "organic" world), and against Christian orthodoxy, whose creed is based on a particular Scripture. In this selection Blake ironically accepts the Deistic view that all particular religions are variants of the one true religion but rejects the Deists' "Argument" that this religion is grounded on reasoning from sense experience. He attributes the one religion instead to the innate possession by all people of "Poetic Genius"—that is, of a capacity for imaginative vision.

2. Applied in the Gospels (e.g., Matthew 3.3) to John the Baptist, regarded as fulfilling the prophecy in Isaiah 39.3. Blake applies the phrase to himself, as a later prophetic voice in an alien time.

intend truth. Thus all sects of Philosophy are from the Poetic Genius, adapted to the weaknesses of every individual.

PRINCIPLE 4. As none by travelling over known lands can find out the unknown, So from already acquired knowledge Man could not acquire more. Therefore an universal Poetic Genius exists.

PRINCIPLE 5. The Religions of all Nations are derived from each Nation's different reception of the Poetic Genius, which is every where call'd the Spirit of Prophecy.

PRINCIPLE 6. The Jewish & Christian Testaments are An original derivation from the Poetic Genius. This is necessary from the confined nature of bodily sensation.

PRINCIPLE 7th. As all men are alike (tho' infinitely various), So all Religions & as all similars have one source.

The true Man is the source, he being the Poetic Genius.

1788

There Is No Natural Religion[1]

[a]

The Argument. Man has no notion of moral fitness but from Education. Naturally he is only a natural organ subject to Sense.

I. Man cannot naturally Percieve but through his natural or bodily organs.

II. Man by his reasoning power can only compare & judge of what he has already perciev'd.

III. From a perception of only 3 senses or 3 elements none could deduce a fourth or fifth.

IV. None could have other than natural or organic thoughts if he had none but organic perceptions.

V. Man's desires are limited by his perceptions; none can desire what he has not perciev'd.

VI. The desires & perceptions of man, untaught by any thing but organs of sense, must be limited to objects of sense.

Conclusion. If it were not for the Poetic or Prophetic character the Philosophic & Experimental would soon be at the ratio of all things, & stand still unable to do other than repeat the same dull round over again.

1788

There Is No Natural Religion[1]

[b]

I. Man's perceptions are not bounded by organs of perception; he percieves more than sense (tho' ever so acute) can discover.

1. In this selection Blake presents his version of English empiricism, which derives all mental content (including the evidences from which, in "natural religion," reason is held to prove the existence of God) from perceptions by the physical senses.
1. In this third document Blake presents his asser-

tions (in opposition to those in the preceding tract) that knowledge is not limited to the physical senses, but is as unbounded as the infinite desires of humankind and its godlike capacity for infinite vision.

II. Reason, or the ratio² of all we have already known, is not the same that it shall be when we know more.
[III lacking]
IV. The bounded is loathed by its possessor. The same dull round even of a universe would soon become a mill with complicated wheels.
V. If the many become the same as the few when possess'd, More! More! is the cry of a mistaken soul. Less than All cannot satisfy Man.
VI. If any could desire what he is incapable of possessing, despair must be his eternal lot.
VII. The desire of Man being Infinite, the possession is Infinite & himself Infinite.
Application. He who sees the Infinite in all things sees God. He who sees the Ratio only sees himself only.
Therefore God becomes as we are, that we may be as he is.

1788

FROM SONGS OF INNOCENCE AND OF EXPERIENCE¹

SHEWING THE TWO CONTRARY STATES OF THE HUMAN SOUL

FROM SONGS OF INNOCENCE

Introduction

Piping down the valleys wild
Piping songs of pleasant glee
On a cloud I saw a child,
And he laughing said to me,

5   "Pipe a song about a Lamb";
So I piped with merry chear;
"Piper pipe that song again"—
So I piped, he wept to hear.

---

2. In Latin *ratio* signifies both "reason" and "calculation." Blake applies the term derogatorily to the 18th-century concept of reason as a calculating faculty whose operations are limited to sense perceptions.
1. *Songs of Innocence* was etched in 1789, and in 1794 was combined with additional poems under the title *Songs of Innocence and of Experience*; this collection was reprinted at various later times with varying arrangements of the poems. In his songs of innocence Blake assumes the stance that he is writing "happy songs / Every child may joy to hear," but they do not all depict an innocent and happy world; many of them incorporate injustice, evil, and suffering. These aspects of the fallen world, however, are represented as they appear to a "state" of the human soul that Blake calls "innocence" and that he expresses in a simple pastoral language, in the tradition both of Isaac Watts's widely read *Divine Songs for Children* (1715) and of the picture-books for child readers pioneered by mid-eighteenth-century booksellers such as John Newbery. The vision of the same world, as it appears to the "contrary" state of the soul that Blake calls "experience," is an ugly and terrifying one of poverty, disease, prostitution, war, and social, institutional, and sexual repression, epitomized in the ghastly representation of modern London. Though each stands as an independent poem, a number of the songs of innocence have a matched counterpart, or "contrary," in the songs of experience. Thus "Infant Joy" is paired with "Infant Sorrow," and the meek "Lamb" reveals its other aspect of divinity in the flaming, wrathful "Tyger."

Title page for *Songs of Innocence*
(1789)

"Drop thy pipe thy happy pipe
10 Sing thy songs of happy chear";
So I sung the same again
While he wept with joy to hear.

"Piper sit thee down and write
In a book that all may read"—
15 So he vanish'd from my sight.
And I pluck'd a hollow reed,

And I made a rural pen,
And I stain'd the water clear,
And I wrote my happy songs
20 Every child may joy to hear.

1789

The Ecchoing Green

The Sun does arise,
And make happy the skies.
The merry bells ring

To welcome the Spring.
5   The sky-lark and thrush,
The birds of the bush,
Sing louder around,
To the bells' chearful sound.
While our sports shall be seen
10   On the Ecchoing Green.

Old John with white hair
Does laugh away care,
Sitting under the oak,
Among the old folk.
15   They laugh at our play,
And soon they all say:
"Such, such were the joys.
When we all, girls & boys,
In our youth-time were seen,
20   On the Ecchoing Green."

Till the little ones weary
No more can be merry
The sun does descend,
And our sports have an end:
25   Round the laps of their mothers,
Many sisters and brothers,
Like birds in their nest,
Are ready for rest;
And sport no more seen,
30   On the darkening Green.

1789

The Lamb[1]

Little Lamb, who made thee?
Dost thou know who made thee?
Gave thee life & bid thee feed,
By the stream & o'er the mead;
5   Gave thee clothing of delight,
Softest clothing wooly bright;
Gave thee such a tender voice,
Making all the vales rejoice!
Little Lamb who made thee?
10   Dost thou know who made thee?

Little Lamb I'll tell thee,
Little Lamb I'll tell thee!
He is callèd by thy name,

---

1. The opening of this poem mimes the form of the catechistic questions and answers customarily used for children's religious instruction.

For he calls himself a Lamb;
15 He is meek & he is mild,
He became a little child;
I a child & thou a lamb,
We are callèd by his name.
Little Lamb God bless thee.
20   Little Lamb God bless thee.

1789

The Little Black Boy

My mother bore me in the southern wild,
And I am black, but O! my soul is white;
White as an angel is the English child,
But I am black as if bereav'd of light.

5 My mother taught me underneath a tree,
And sitting down before the heat of day,
She took me on her lap and kissèd me,
And pointing to the east, began to say:

"Look on the rising sun: there God does live
10 And gives his light, and gives his heat away;
And flowers and trees and beasts and men receive
Comfort in morning, joy in the noon day.

"And we are put on earth a little space,
That we may learn to bear the beams of love,
15 And these black bodies and this sun-burnt face
Is but a cloud, and like a shady grove.

"For when our souls have learn'd the heat to bear,
The cloud will vanish; we shall hear his voice,
Saying: 'Come out from the grove, my love & care,
20 And round my golden tent like lambs rejoice.' "

Thus did my mother say, and kissèd me;
And thus I say to little English boy:
When I from black and he from white cloud free,
And round the tent of God like lambs we joy,

25 I'll shade him from the heat till he can bear
To lean in joy upon our father's knee.
And then I'll stand and stroke his silver hair,
And be like him, and he will then love me.

1789

The Chimney Sweeper

When my mother died I was very young,
And my father sold me while yet my tongue
Could scarcely cry " 'weep! 'weep! 'weep! 'weep!"[1]
So your chimneys I sweep & in soot I sleep.

5   There's little Tom Dacre, who cried when his head
That curl'd like a lamb's back, was shav'd, so I said,
"Hush, Tom! never mind it, for when your head's bare,
You know that the soot cannot spoil your white hair."

And so he was quiet, & that very night,
10   As Tom was a-sleeping he had such a sight!
That thousands of sweepers, Dick, Joe, Ned, & Jack,
Were all of them lock'd up in coffins of black;

And by came an Angel who had a bright key,
And he open'd the coffins & set them all free;
15   Then down a green plain, leaping, laughing they run,
And wash in a river and shine in the Sun.

Then naked & white, all their bags left behind,
They rise upon clouds, and sport in the wind.
And the Angel told Tom, if he'd be a good boy,
20   He'd have God for his father & never want joy.

And so Tom awoke; and we rose in the dark
And got with our bags & our brushes to work.
Tho' the morning was cold, Tom was happy & warm;
So if all do their duty, they need not fear harm.

1789

The Divine Image

To Mercy, Pity, Peace, and Love,
All pray in their distress,
And to these virtues of delight
Return their thankfulness.

5   For Mercy, Pity, Peace, and Love,
Is God, our father dear:
And Mercy, Pity, Peace, and Love,
Is Man, his child and care.

For Mercy has a human heart,
10   Pity, a human face,
And Love, the human form divine,
And Peace, the human dress.

1. The child's lisping attempt at the chimney sweeper's street cry, "Sweep! Sweep!"

Then every man of every clime,
That prays in his distress,
15 Prays to the human form divine,
Love, Mercy, Pity, Peace.

And all must love the human form,
In heathen, Turk, or Jew.
Where Mercy, Love, & Pity dwell,
20 There God is dwelling too.

1789

Holy Thursday[1]

'Twas on a Holy Thursday, their innocent faces clean,
The children walking two & two, in red & blue & green;
Grey headed beadles[2] walkd before with wands as white as snow,
Till into the high dome of Paul's they like Thames' waters flow.

5 O what a multitude they seemd, these flowers of London town!
Seated in companies they sit with radiance all their own.
The hum of multitudes was there, but multitudes of lambs,
Thousands of little boys & girls raising their innocent hands.

Now like a mighty wind they raise to heaven the voice of song,
10 Or like harmonious thunderings the seats of heaven among.
Beneath them sit the agèd men, wise guardians of the poor;
Then cherish pity, lest you drive an angel from your door.[3]

ca. 1784   1789

Nurse's Song

When the voices of children are heard on the green
And laughing is heard on the hill,
My heart is at rest within my breast
And everything else is still.

5 "Then come home my children, the sun is gone down
And the dews of night arise;
Come, come, leave off play, and let us away
Till the morning appears in the skies."

"No, no, let us play, for it is yet day
10 And we cannot go to sleep;

1. In the Anglican Church the Thursday celebrating the ascension of Jesus (thirty-nine days after Easter). It was the custom on this day to march the poor (frequently orphaned) children from the charity schools of London to a service at St. Paul's Cathedral.

2. Lower church officers, one of whose duties is to keep order.

3. Cf. Hebrews 13.2: "Be not forgetful to entertain strangers: for thereby some have entertained angels unawares."

Besides, in the sky, the little birds fly
And the hills are all coverd with sheep."

"Well, well, go & play till the light fades away
And then go home to bed."
15 The little ones leaped & shouted & laugh'd
And all the hills ecchoèd.

ca. 1784   1789

Infant Joy

"I have no name,
I am but two days old."
What shall I call thee?
"I happy am,
5 Joy is my name."
Sweet joy befall thee!

Pretty joy!
Sweet joy but two days old,
Sweet joy I call thee;
10 Thou dost smile,
I sing the while—
Sweet joy befall thee.

1789

FROM SONGS OF EXPERIENCE

Introduction

Hear the voice of the Bard!
Who Present, Past, & Future sees;
Whose ears have heard
The Holy Word
5 That walk'd among the ancient trees;[1]

Calling the lapsèd Soul[2]
And weeping in the evening dew,
That might controll[3]
The starry pole,
10 And fallen, fallen light renew!

---

1. Genesis 3.8: "And [Adam and Eve] heard the voice of the Lord God walking in the garden in the cool of the day." The Bard, or poet-prophet, whose imagination is not bound by time, has heard the voice of the Lord in Eden.
2. The syntax leaves it ambiguous whether it is "the Bard" or "the Holy Word" who calls to the fallen ("lapsèd") soul and to the fallen earth to stop the natural cycle of light and darkness.
3. The likely syntax is that "Soul" is the subject of "might controll."

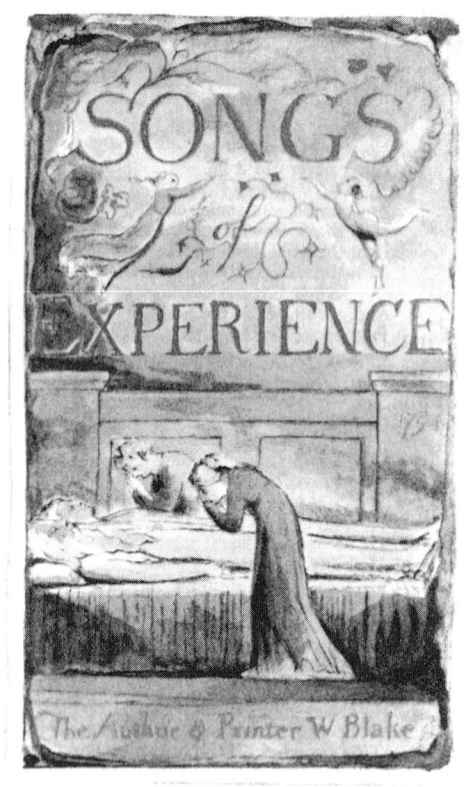

Separate title page for *Songs of
Experience* (1794)

"O Earth, O Earth, return!
Arise from out the dewy grass;
Night is worn,
And the morn
15   Rises from the slumberous mass.

"Turn away no more;
Why wilt thou turn away?
The starry floor
The watry shore[4]
20   Is giv'n thee till the break of day."

1794

Earth's Answer[1]

Earth rais'd up her head,
From the darkness dread & drear.

---

4. In Blake's recurrent symbolism the starry sky
("floor") signifies rigid rational order, and the sea
signifies chaos.

1. The Earth explains why she, the natural world,
cannot by her unaided endeavors renew the fallen
light.

Her light fled:
Stony dread!
5   And her locks cover'd with grey despair.

"Prison'd on watry shore
Starry Jealousy does keep my den,
Cold and hoar
Weeping o'er
10   I hear the Father of the ancient men.[2]

"Selfish father of men,
Cruel, jealous, selfish fear!
Can delight
Chain'd in night
15   The virgins of youth and morning bear?

"Does spring hide its joy
When buds and blossoms grow?
Does the sower
Sow by night,
20   Or the plowman in darkness plow?

"Break this heavy chain
That does freeze my bones around;
Selfish! vain!
Eternal bane!
25   That free Love with bondage bound."

1794

The Clod & the Pebble

"Love seeketh not Itself to please,
Nor for itself hath any care;
But for another gives its ease,
And builds a Heaven in Hell's despair."

5   So sang a little Clod of Clay,
Trodden with the cattle's feet;
But a Pebble of the brook,
Warbled out these metres meet:

"Love seeketh only Self to please,
10   To bind another to its delight;
Joys in another's loss of ease,
And builds a Hell in Heaven's despite."

1794

2. This is the character that Blake later named "Urizen" in his prophetic works. He is the tyrant who binds the mind to the natural world and also imposes a moral bondage on sexual desire and other modes of human energy.

Holy Thursday

Is this a holy thing to see,
In a rich and fruitful land,
Babes reduced to misery,
Fed with cold and usurous hand?

5   Is that trembling cry a song?
Can it be a song of joy?
And so many children poor?
It is a land of poverty!

And their sun does never shine,
10   And their fields are bleak & bare,
And their ways are fill'd with thorns;
It is eternal winter there.

For where-e'er the sun does shine,
And where-e'er the rain does fall,
15   Babe can never hunger there,
Nor poverty the mind appall.

1794

The Chimney Sweeper

A little black thing among the snow
Crying " 'weep, 'weep," in notes of woe!
"Where are thy father & mother? say?"
"They are both gone up to the church to pray.

5   "Because I was happy upon the heath,
And smil'd among the winter's snow;
They clothed me in the clothes of death,
And taught me to sing the notes of woe.

"And because I am happy, & dance & sing,
10   They think they have done me no injury,
And are gone to praise God & his Priest & King,
Who make up a heaven of our misery."

1790–92   1794

Nurse's Song

When the voices of children are heard on the green
And whisperings are in the dale,
The days of my youth rise fresh in my mind,
My face turns green and pale.

⁵ Then come home my children, the sun is gone down
And the dews of night arise;
Your spring & your day are wasted in play,
And your winter and night in disguise.

1794

The Sick Rose

O Rose, thou art sick.
The invisible worm
That flies in the night
In the howling storm

⁵ Has found out thy bed
Of crimson joy,
And his dark secret love
Does thy life destroy.

1794

The Fly

Little Fly
Thy summer's play
My thoughtless hand
Has brush'd away

⁵ Am not I
A fly like thee?
Or art not thou
A man like me?

For I dance
¹⁰ And drink & sing,
Till some blind hand
Shall brush my wing.

If thought is life
And strength & breath,
¹⁵ And the want
Of thought is death;

Then am I
A happy fly,
If I live,
²⁰ Or if I die.

1794

"The Tyger"

The Tyger[1]

Tyger! Tyger! burning bright
In the forests of the night,
What immortal hand or eye
Could frame thy fearful symmetry?

5   In what distant deeps or skies
Burnt the fire of thine eyes?
On what wings dare he aspire?
What the hand dare seize the fire?

And what shoulder, & what art,
10   Could twist the sinews of thy heart?
And when thy heart began to beat,
What dread hand? & what dread feet?

---

1. For the author's revisions while composing "The Tyger," see "Poems in Process," in the appendices to this volume.

What the hammer? what the chain?
In what furnace was thy brain?
15 What the anvil? what dread grasp
Dare its deadly terrors clasp?

When the stars threw down their spears[2]
And water'd heaven with their tears,
Did he smile his work to see?
20 Did he who made the Lamb make thee?

Tyger! Tyger! burning bright
In the forests of the night,
What immortal hand or eye
Dare frame thy fearful symmetry?

1790–92   1794

My Pretty Rose Tree

A flower was offerd to me;
Such a flower as May never bore,
But I said, "I've a Pretty Rose-tree,"
And I passed the sweet flower o'er.

5 Then I went to my Pretty Rose-tree,
To tend her by day and by night.
But my Rose turnd away with jealousy,
And her thorns were my only delight.

1794

Ah Sun-flower

Ah Sun-flower! weary of time,
Who countest the steps of the Sun,
Seeking after that sweet golden clime
Where the traveller's journey is done;

5 Where the Youth pined away with desire,
And the pale Virgin shrouded in snow,
Arise from their graves and aspire,
Where my Sun-flower wishes to go.

1794

2. "Threw down" is ambiguous and may signify that the stars either "surrendered" or "hurled down" their spears.

The Garden of Love

I went to the Garden of Love,
And saw what I never had seen:
A Chapel was built in the midst,
Where I used to play on the green.

5 And the gates of this Chapel were shut,
And "Thou shalt not" writ over the door;
So I turn'd to the Garden of Love,
That so many sweet flowers bore,

And I saw it was filled with graves,
10 And tomb-stones where flowers should be;
And Priests in black gowns were walking their rounds,
And binding with briars my joys & desires.

1794

London

I wander thro' each charter'd[1] street,
Near where the charter'd Thames does flow,
And mark in every face I meet
Marks of weakness, marks of woe.

5 In every cry of every Man,
In every Infant's cry of fear,
In every voice, in every ban,[2]
The mind-forg'd manacles I hear:

How the Chimney-sweeper's cry
10 Every blackning Church appalls,
And the hapless Soldier's sigh
Runs in blood down Palace walls.

But most thro' midnight streets I hear
How the youthful Harlot's curse
15 Blasts the new-born Infant's tear,[3]
And blights with plagues the Marriage hearse.[4]

1794

1. "Given liberty," but also, ironically, "preempted as private property, and rented out."
2. The various meanings of *ban* are relevant (political and legal prohibition, curse, public condemnation) as well as "banns" (marriage proclamation).
3. Most critics read this line as implying prenatal blindness, resulting from a parent's venereal disease (the "plagues" of line 16) by earlier infection from the harlot.
4. In the older sense: "converts the marriage bed into a bier." Or possibly, because the current sense of the word had also come into use in Blake's day, "converts the marriage coach into a funeral hearse."

The Human Abstract[1]

Pity would be no more,
If we did not make somebody Poor;
And Mercy no more could be,
If all were as happy as we;

5   And mutual fear brings peace,
Till the selfish loves increase;
Then Cruelty knits a snare,
And spreads his baits with care.

He sits down with holy fears,
10 And waters the ground with tears;
Then Humility takes its root
Underneath his foot.

Soon spreads the dismal shade
Of Mystery over his head;
15 And the Catterpiller and Fly
Feed on the Mystery.

And it bears the fruit of Deceit,
Ruddy and sweet to eat;
And the Raven his nest has made
20 In its thickest shade.

The Gods of the earth and sea,
Sought thro' Nature to find this Tree,
But their search was all in vain:
There grows one in the Human Brain.

1790–92   1794

Infant Sorrow

My mother groand! my father wept.
Into the dangerous world I leapt,
Helpless, naked, piping loud;
Like a fiend hid in a cloud.

5   Struggling in my father's hands,
Striving against my swadling bands;
Bound and weary I thought best
To sulk upon my mother's breast.

1794

---

1. The matched contrary to "The Divine Image" in *Songs of Innocence.* The virtues of the earlier poem, "Mercy, Pity, Peace, and Love," are now represented as possible marks for exploitation, cruelty, conflict, and hypocritical humility.

A Poison Tree

I was angry with my friend:
I told my wrath, my wrath did end.
I was angry with my foe:
I told it not, my wrath did grow.

5   And I waterd it in fears,
Night & morning with my tears;
And I sunnèd it with smiles,
And with soft deceitful wiles.

And it grew both day and night,
10 Till it bore an apple bright.
And my foe beheld it shine,
And he knew that it was mine,

And into my garden stole,
When the night had veild the pole;
15 In the morning glad I see
My foe outstretchd beneath the tree.

1794

To Tirzah[1]

Whate'er is Born of Mortal Birth
Must be consumèd with the Earth
To rise from Generation free;
Then what have I to do with thee?[2]

5   The Sexes sprung from Shame & Pride,
Blow'd° in the morn, in evening died;   *blossomed*
But Mercy changd Death into Sleep;
The Sexes rose to work & weep.

Thou, Mother of my Mortal part,
10 With cruelty didst mould my Heart,
And with false self-deceiving tears
Didst bind my Nostrils, Eyes, & Ears.

Didst close my Tongue in senseless clay
And me to Mortal Life betray.
15 The Death of Jesus set me free;
Then what have I to do with thee?

ca. 1805

1. Tirzah was the capital of the northern kingdom
of Israel and is conceived by Blake in opposition to
Jerusalem, capital of the southern kingdom of
Judah, whose tribes had been redeemed from captivity. In this poem, which was added to late versions of *Songs of Experience*, Tirzah is represented
as the mother—in the realm of material nature and
"Generation"—of the mortal body, with its restrictive senses.
2. Echoing the words of Christ to his mother at
the marriage in Cana, John 2.4: "Woman, what
have I to do with thee? mine hour is not yet come."

A Divine Image[1]

Cruelty has a Human Heart
And Jealousy a Human Face,
Terror, the Human Form Divine,
And Secrecy, the Human Dress.

5   The Human Dress is forgèd Iron,
The Human Form, a fiery Forge,
The Human Face, a Furnace seal'd,
The Human Heart, its hungry Gorge.°   *maw, stomach*

1790–91

The Book of Thel   Although Blake dated the etched poem 1789, its composition probably extended to 1791, so that he was working on it at the time he was writing the *Songs of Innocence* and some of the *Songs of Experience. The Book of Thel* treats the same two "states"; now, however, Blake employs the narrative instead of the lyrical mode and embodies aspects of the developing myth that was fully enacted in his later prophetic books. And like the major prophecies, this poem is written in the fourteener, a long line of seven stresses.

    The name *Thel* possibly derives from the Greek word for "wish" or "will" and may be intended to suggest the failure of desire, because of timidity, to fulfill itself. Thel is represented as a virgin dwelling in the Vales of Har, which seems equivalent to the sheltered state of pastoral peace and innocence in Blake's *Songs of Innocence*. Here, however, Thel feels useless and unfulfilled, and appeals for comfort, unavailingly, to various beings who are contented with their roles in Har. Finally, the Clay invites Thel to try the experiment of assuming embodied life. Part 4 (plate 6) expresses the brutal shock of the revelation to Thel of the experience of sexual desire—a revelation from which she flees in terror back to her sheltered, if unsatisfying, existence in Har.

    Some commentators propose that Thel is an unborn soul who rejects the ordeal of an embodied life in the material world. Others propose that Thel is a human virgin who shrinks from experiencing a life of adult sexuality. It is possible, however, to read Blake's little myth as comprehending both these areas of significance. The reader does not need to know Blake's mythology inside and out to recognize the broad symbolic reach of this poem in ordinary human experience—the elemental failure of nerve to meet the challenge of life as it is, the timid incapacity to risk the conflict, physicality, pain, and loss without which there is no possibility either of growth or of creativity.

---

1. Blake omitted this poem from all but one copy of *Songs of Experience*, probably because "The Human Abstract" served as a more comprehensive and subtle contrary to "The Divine Image" in *Songs of Innocence*.

The Book of Thel

PLATE i[1]

Thel's Motto

Does the Eagle know what is in the pit?
Or wilt thou go ask the Mole?
Can Wisdom be put in a silver rod?
Or Love in a golden bowl?[2]

PLATE 1

1

The daughters of Mne[3] Seraphim led round their sunny flocks,
All but the youngest; she in paleness sought the secret air,
To fade away like morning beauty from her mortal day;
Down by the river of Adona her soft voice is heard,
5 And thus her gentle lamentation falls like morning dew:

"O life of this our spring! why fades the lotus of the water?
Why fade these children of the spring? born but to smile & fall.
Ah! Thel is like a watry bow, and like a parting cloud,
Like a reflection in a glass, like shadows in the water,
10 Like dreams of infants, like a smile upon an infant's face,
Like the dove's voice, like transient day, like music in the air.
Ah! gentle may I lay me down, and gentle rest my head,
And gentle sleep the sleep of death, and gentle hear the voice
Of him that walketh in the garden in the evening time."[4]

15 The Lilly of the valley breathing in the humble grass
Answer'd the lovely maid and said: "I am a watry weed,
And I am very small, and love to dwell in lowly vales;
So weak, the gilded butterfly scarce perches on my head;
Yet I am visited from heaven, and he that smiles on all
20 Walks in the valley and each morn over me spreads his hand,
Saying: 'Rejoice, thou humble grass, thou new-born lilly flower,
Thou gentle maid of silent valleys and of modest brooks;
For thou shalt be clothed in light, and fed with morning manna,
Till summer's heat melts thee beside the fountains and the springs
25 To flourish in eternal vales.' Then why should Thel complain?

1. The plate numbers identify the page, each with its own pictorial design, as originally printed by Blake. These numbers are reproduced here because they are frequently used in references to Blake's writings.
2. Ecclesiastes 12.5–6 describes a time when "fears shall be in the way . . . and desire shall fail: because man goeth to his long home, and the mourners go about the streets: Or ever the silver cord be loosed, or the golden bowl be broken." Per-

haps Blake changed the silver cord to a rod to make it, with the golden bowl, a sexual symbol.
3. There has been much speculation about this curious term. It may be an abbreviation for the name "Mnetha," the goddess of the Vales of Har in Blake's earlier poem *Tiriel*.
4. Genesis 3.8: "And they heard the voice of the Lord God walking in the garden in the cool of the day."

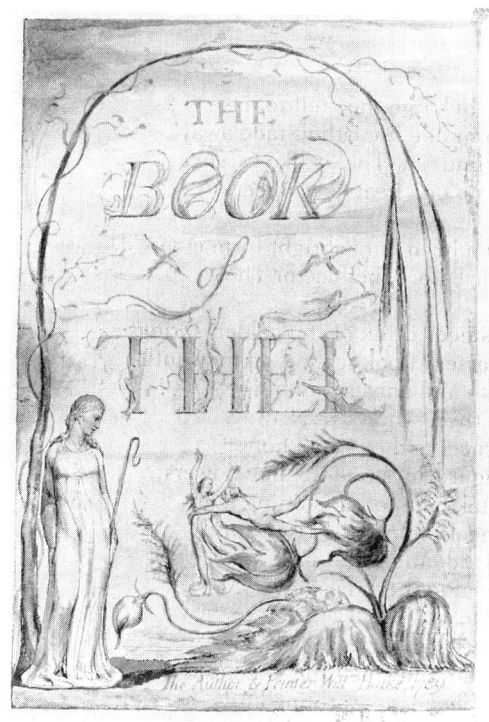

Title page of *The Book of Thel*
(1789), plate ii. Copy N, ca. 1815

PLATE 2

Why should the mistress of the vales of Har utter a sigh?"

She ceasd & smild in tears, then sat down in her silver shrine.

Thel answerd: "O thou little virgin of the peaceful valley,
Giving to those that cannot crave, the voiceless, the o'ertired;
5   Thy breath doth nourish the innocent lamb, he smells thy milky garments,
He crops thy flowers, while thou sittest smiling in his face,
Wiping his mild and meekin° mouth from all contagious taints.   *humble*
Thy wine doth purify the golden honey; thy perfume,
Which thou dost scatter on every little blade of grass that springs,
10 Revives the milkèd cow, & tames the fire-breathing steed.
But Thel is like a faint cloud kindled at the rising sun:
I vanish from my pearly throne, and who shall find my place?"

"Queen of the vales," the Lilly answered, "ask the tender cloud,
And it shall tell thee why it glitters in the morning sky,
15 And why it scatters its bright beauty thro' the humid air.
Descend, O little cloud, & hover before the eyes of Thel."
The Cloud descended, and the Lilly bowd her modest head,
And went to mind her numerous charge among the verdant grass.

PLATE 3

2

"O little Cloud," the virgin said, "I charge thee tell to me,
Why thou complainest not when in one hour thou fade away:
Then we shall seek thee but not find; ah, Thel is like to Thee.
I pass away, yet I complain, and no one hears my voice."

5   The Cloud then shew'd his golden head & his bright form emerg'd,
Hovering and glittering on the air before the face of Thel.

"O virgin, know'st thou not our steeds drink of the golden springs
Where Luvah[5] doth renew his horses? Look'st thou on my youth,
And fearest thou because I vanish and am seen no more,
10   Nothing remains? O maid, I tell thee, when I pass away,
It is to tenfold life, to love, to peace, and raptures holy:
Unseen descending, weigh my light wings upon balmy flowers,
And court the fair eyed dew, to take me to her shining tent;
The weeping virgin trembling kneels before the risen sun,
15   Till we arise link'd in a golden band, and never part,
But walk united, bearing food to all our tender flowers."

"Dost thou O little Cloud? I fear that I am not like thee;
For I walk through the vales of Har and smell the sweetest flowers,
But I feed not the little flowers; I hear the warbling birds,
20   But I feed not the warbling birds; they fly and seek their food;
But Thel delights in these no more, because I fade away,
And all shall say, 'Without a use this shining woman liv'd,
Or did she only live to be at death the food of worms?'"

The Cloud reclind upon his airy throne and answer'd thus:

25   "Then if thou art the food of worms, O virgin of the skies,
How great thy use, how great thy blessing! Every thing that lives
Lives not alone, nor for itself; fear not, and I will call
The weak worm from its lowly bed, and thou shalt hear its voice.
Come forth, worm of the silent valley, to thy pensive queen."

30   The helpless worm arose, and sat upon the Lilly's leaf,
And the bright Cloud said on, to find his partner in the vale.

PLATE 4

3

Then Thel astonish'd view'd the Worm upon its dewy bed.

"Art thou a Worm? Image of weakness, art thou but a Worm?
I see thee like an infant wrapped in the Lilly's leaf;
Ah, weep not, little voice, thou can'st not speak, but thou can'st weep.

5. The earliest mention in Blake's work of one of his "Giant Forms," the Zoas. Luvah is the mythical embodiment of the passional and sexual aspect of humankind. He is represented here, like the Greek Phoebus Apollo, as the driver of the chariot of the sun; he repairs to the Vales of Har simply to rest and water his horses. The cloud in this passage describes the cycle of water, from cloud to rain and (by the vaporizing action of the sun on water) back to the cloud.

5 Is this a Worm? I see thee lay helpless & naked, weeping,
And none to answer, none to cherish thee with mother's smiles."

The Clod of Clay heard the Worm's voice, & raisd her pitying head;
She bow'd over the weeping infant, and her life exhal'd
In milky fondness; then on Thel she fix'd her humble eyes.

10 "O beauty of the vales of Har! we live not for ourselves;
Thou seest me the meanest thing, and so I am indeed;
My bosom of itself is cold, and of itself is dark,

PLATE 5

But he that loves the lowly, pours his oil upon my head,
And kisses me, and binds his nuptial bands around my breast,
And says: 'Thou mother of my children, I have lovèd thee,
And I have given thee a crown that none can take away.'
5 But how this is, sweet maid, I know not, and I cannot know;
I ponder, and I cannot ponder; yet I live and love."

The daughter of beauty wip'd her pitying tears with her white veil,
And said: "Alas! I knew not this, and therefore did I weep.
That God would love a Worm, I knew, and punish the evil foot
10 That, wilful, bruis'd its helpless form; but that he cherish'd it
With milk and oil I never knew; and therefore did I weep,
And I complaind in the mild air, because I fade away,
And lay me down in thy cold bed, and leave my shining lot."

"Queen of the vales," the matron Clay answered, "I heard thy sighs,
15 And all thy moans flew o'er my roof, but I have call'd them down.
Wilt thou, O Queen, enter my house? 'tis given thee to enter
And to return; fear nothing, enter with thy virgin feet."

PLATE 6

4

The eternal gates' terrific porter lifted the northern bar:[6]
Thel enter'd in & saw the secrets of the land unknown.
She saw the couches of the dead, & where the fibrous roots
Of every heart on earth infixes deep its restless twists:
5 A land of sorrows & of tears where never smile was seen.

She wanderd in the land of clouds thro' valleys dark, listning
Dolours & lamentations; waiting oft beside a dewy grave,
She stood in silence, listning to the voices of the ground,
Till to her own grave plot she came, & there she sat down,
10 And heard this voice of sorrow breathed from the hollow pit:

"Why cannot the Ear be closed to its own destruction?
Or the glistning Eye to the poison of a smile?

---

6. Homer, in *Odyssey* 13, described the Cave of the Naiades, of which the northern gate is for mortals and the southern gate for gods. The neoplatonist Porphyry had allegorized it as an account of the descent of the soul into matter and then its return.

Why are Eyelids stord with arrows ready drawn,
Where a thousand fighting men in ambush lie?
15 Or an Eye of gifts & graces, show'ring fruits & coinèd gold?
Why a Tongue impress'd with honey from every wind?
Why an Ear, a whirlpool fierce to draw creations in?
Why a Nostril wide inhaling terror, trembling, & affright?
Why a tender curb upon the youthful burning boy?
20 Why a little curtain of flesh on the bed of our desire?"

The Virgin started from her seat, & with a shriek
Fled back unhinderd till she came into the vales of Har.

1789–91

Visions of the Daughters of Albion

This work, dated 1793 on the title page, is one of Blake's early illuminated books, and like his later and longer works is written in what Blake called "the long resounding strong heroic verse" of seven-foot lines. Unlike the timid heroine of *The Book of Thel,* the virgin Oothoon dares to break through into adult sexuality (symbolized by her plucking a marigold and placing it between her breasts) and sets out joyously to join her lover Theotormon, whose realm is the Atlantic Ocean. She is stopped and raped by Bromion, who appears as a thunderstorm (1.16–17). The jealous Theotormon, condemning the victim as well as the rapist, binds the two "back to back" in a cave and sits weeping on the threshold. The rest of the work consists of monologues by the three characters, who remain fixed in these postures. Throughout this stage tableau the Daughters of Albion serve as the chorus who, in a recurrent refrain, echo the "woes" and "sighs" of Oothoon, but not her call to rebellion.

This simple drama is densely significant, for as Blake's compressed allusions indicate, the characters, events, and monologues have diverse areas of application. Blake's abrupt opening word, which he etched in very large letters, is *Enslav'd,* and the work as a whole embodies his view that contemporary men, and even more women, in a spiritual parallel to shackled black slaves, are in bondage to oppressive concepts and codes in all aspects of perception, thought, social institutions, and actions. As indicated by the refrain of the Daughters of Albion (that is, contemporary Englishwomen), Oothoon in one aspect represents the sexual disabilities and slavelike status of all women in a male-dominated society. But as "the soft soul of America" (1.3) she is also the revolutionary nation that had recently won political emancipation, yet continued to tolerate an agricultural system that involved black slavery and to acquiesce in the crass economic exploitation of her "soft American plains." At the same time Oothoon is represented in the situation of a black female slave who has been branded, whipped, raped, and impregnated by her master.

Correlatively, the speeches of the boastful Bromion show him to be not only a sexual exploiter of women and a cruel and acquisitive slave owner but also a general proponent of the use of force to achieve mastery in wars, in an oppressive legal system, and in a religious morality based on the fear of hell (4.19–24). Theotormon is represented as even more contemptible. Broken and paralyzed by the prohibitions of a puritanical religion, he denies any possibility of achieving "joys" in this life, despairs of the power of intellect and imagination to improve the human condition and, rationalizing his own incapacity, bewails Oothoon's daring to think and act other than he does.

Oothoon's long and passionate oration that concludes the poem (plates 5–8) celebrates a free sexual life for both women and men. Blake, however, uses this open and unpossessive sexuality to typify the realization of all human potentialities and to represent an outgoing altruism, as opposed to an enclosed self-centeredness, "the self-love that envies all." To such a suspicious egotism, as her allusions indicate, Oothoon attributes the tyranny of uniform moral laws imposed on variable individuals, a rigidly institutional religion, the acquisitiveness that drives the system of commerce, and the property rights in another person that are established by the marriage contract.

Blake's poem reflects some prominent happenings of the years of its composition, 1791–93. This was not only the time when the revolutionary spirit had moved from America to France and effected reverberations in England, but also the time of rebellions by black slaves in the Western Hemisphere and of widespread debate in England about the abolition of the slave trade. Blake, while composing the *Visions*, had illustrated the sadistic punishments inflicted on rebellious slaves in his engravings for J. G. Stedman's *A Narrative, of a Five Years' Expedition, against the Revolted Negroes of Surinam* (see David Erdman, *Blake: Prophet against Empire*, chap. 10). Blake's championing of women's liberation parallels some of the views expressed in the *Vindication of the Rights of Woman* published in 1792 by Mary Wollstonecraft, whom Blake knew and admired, and for whom he had illustrated a book the year before.

Visions of the Daughters of Albion

The Eye sees more than the Heart knows.

PLATE iii

The Argument

I loved Theotormon
And I was not ashamed
I trembled in my virgin fears
And I hid in Leutha's[1] vale!

5   I plucked Leutha's flower,
And I rose up from the vale;
But the terrible thunders tore
My virgin mantle in twain.

PLATE 1

Visions

ENSLAV'D, the Daughters of Albion weep: a trembling lamentation
Upon their mountains; in their valleys, sighs toward America.

For the soft soul of America, Oothoon[2] wandered in woe,
Along the vales of Leutha seeking flowers to comfort her;
5 And thus she spoke to the bright Marygold of Leutha's vale:

---

1. In some poems by Blake, Leutha is represented as a female figure who is beautiful and seductive but treacherous.
2. The name is adapted by Blake from a character in James Macpherson's pretended translations, in the 1760s, from the ancient British bard Ossian. After her husband goes off to war, Macpherson's Oithona is abducted, raped, and imprisoned by a rejected suitor.

Frontispiece, *Visions of the Daughters of Albion* (1793), plate i. Copy P, ca. 1815

"Art thou a flower! art thou a nymph! I see thee now a flower,
Now a nymph! I dare not pluck thee from thy dewy bed!"

The Golden nymph replied: "Pluck thou my flower Oothoon the mild.
Another flower shall spring, because the soul of sweet delight
10 Can never pass away." She ceas'd & closd her golden shrine.

Then Oothoon pluck'd the flower saying, "I pluck thee from thy bed,
Sweet flower, and put thee here to glow between my breasts,
And thus I turn my face to where my whole soul seeks."

Over the waves she went in wing'd exulting swift delight;
15 And over Theotormon's reign took her impetuous course.

Bromion rent her with his thunders. On his stormy bed
Lay the faint maid, and soon her woes appalld his thunders hoarse.

Bromion spoke: "Behold this harlot here on Bromion's bed,
And let the jealous dolphins sport around the lovely maid;
20 Thy soft American plains are mine, and mine thy north & south:
Stampt with my signet[3] are the swarthy children of the sun:
They are obedient, they resist not, they obey the scourge:
Their daughters worship terrors and obey the violent.

PLATE 2

Now thou maist marry Bromion's harlot, and protect the child
Of Bromion's rage, that Oothoon shall put forth in nine moons' time."[4]

---

3. A small seal or stamp. The allusion is to the branding of black slaves by their owners.

4. Pregnancy enhanced the market value of a female slave in America.

Then storms rent Theotormon's limbs; he rolld his waves around,
And folded his black jealous waters round the adulterate pair;
5 Bound back to back in Bromion's caves terror & meekness dwell.

At entrance Theotormon sits wearing the threshold hard
With secret tears; beneath him sound like waves on a desart shore
The voice of slaves beneath the sun, and children bought with money,
That shiver in religious caves beneath the burning fires
10 Of lust, that belch incessant from the summits of the earth.

Oothoon weeps not: she cannot weep! her tears are locked up;
But she can howl incessant, writhing her soft snowy limbs,
And calling Theotormon's Eagles to prey upon her flesh.[5]

"I call with holy voice! kings of the sounding air,
15 Rend away this defiled bosom that I may reflect
The image of Theotormon on my pure transparent breast."

The Eagles at her call descend & rend their bleeding prey;
Theotormon severely smiles; her soul reflects the smile,
As the clear spring mudded with feet of beasts grows pure & smiles.

20 The Daughters of Albion hear her woes, & eccho back her sighs.

"Why does my Theotormon sit weeping upon the threshold,
And Oothoon hovers by his side, perswading him in vain?
I cry, 'Arise O Theotormon, for the village dog
Barks at the breaking day, the nightingale has done lamenting,
25 The lark does rustle in the ripe corn, and the Eagle returns
From nightly prey, and lifts his golden beak to the pure east,
Shaking the dust from his immortal pinions to awake
The sun that sleeps too long. Arise my Theotormon, I am pure;
Because the night is gone that clos'd me in its deadly black.'
30 They told me that the night & day were all that I could see;
They told me that I had five senses to inclose me up,
And they inclos'd my infinite brain into a narrow circle,
And sunk my heart into the Abyss, a red round globe hot burning,
Till all from life I was obliterated and erased.
35 Instead of morn arises a bright shadow, like an eye
In the eastern cloud,[6] instead of night a sickly charnel house,
That Theotormon hears me not! to him the night and morn
Are both alike: a night of sighs, a morning of fresh tears;

PLATE 3

And none but Bromion can hear my lamentations.

"With what sense is it that the chicken shuns the ravenous hawk?
With what sense does the tame pigeon measure out the expanse?
With what sense does the bee form cells? have not the mouse & frog

5. The implied parallel is to Zeus's punishment of Prometheus for befriending the human race, by setting an eagle to devour his liver.
6. The contrast is between the physical sun perceived by the constricted ("inclos'd," line 32) sensible eye and "the breaking day" (line 24) of a new era perceived by Oothoon's liberated vision.

5 Eyes and ears and sense of touch? yet are their habitations
And their pursuits as different as their forms and as their joys.
Ask the wild ass why he refuses burdens, and the meek camel
Why he loves man; is it because of eye, ear, mouth, or skin,
Or breathing nostrils? No, for these the wolf and tyger have.
10 Ask the blind worm the secrets of the grave, and why her spires
Love to curl round the bones of death; and ask the rav'nous snake
Where she gets poison, & the wing'd eagle why he loves the sun,
And then tell me the thoughts of man, that have been hid of old.[7]

"Silent I hover all the night, and all day could be silent,
15 If Theotormon once would turn his loved eyes upon me.
How can I be defild when I reflect thy image pure?
Sweetest the fruit that the worm feeds on, & the soul prey'd on by woe,
The new wash'd lamb ting'd with the village smoke, & the bright swan
By the red earth of our immortal river:[8] I bathe my wings,
20 And I am white and pure to hover round Theotormon's breast."

Then Theotormon broke his silence, and he answered:

"Tell me what is the night or day to one o'erflowd with woe?
Tell me what is a thought? & of what substance is it made?
Tell me what is a joy? & in what gardens do joys grow?
25 And in what rivers swim the sorrows? and upon what mountains

PLATE 4

Wave shadows of discontent? and in what houses dwell the wretched
Drunken with woe, forgotten, and shut up from cold despair?

"Tell me where dwell the thoughts, forgotten till thou call them forth?
Tell me where dwell the joys of old! & where the ancient loves?
5 And when will they renew again & the night of oblivion past?
That I might traverse times & spaces far remote and bring
Comforts into a present sorrow and a night of pain.
Where goest thou, O thought? to what remote land is thy flight?
If thou returnest to the present moment of affliction
10 Wilt thou bring comforts on thy wings and dews and honey and balm,
Or poison from the desart wilds, from the eyes of the envier?"

Then Bromion said, and shook the cavern with his lamentation:

"Thou knowest that the ancient trees seen by thine eyes have fruit;
But knowest thou that trees and fruits flourish upon the earth
15 To gratify senses unknown? trees beasts and birds unknown:
Unknown, not unpercievd, spread in the infinite microscope,
In places yet unvisited by the voyager, and in worlds
Over another kind of seas, and in atmospheres unknown?

7. Oothoon implies that "thoughts" (powers of conceiving a liberated life in a better world) are as innate to human beings as instinctual patterns of behavior are to other species of living things.
8. "Red earth" is the etymological meaning of the Hebrew name "Adam" (cf. *The Marriage of Heaven and Hell* 2.13, p. 111). The "immortal river," accordingly, may refer to the "river" that "went out of Eden" (Genesis 2.10).

Ah! are there other wars, beside the wars of sword and fire?
20 And are there other sorrows, beside the sorrows of poverty?
And are there other joys, beside the joys of riches and ease?
And is there not one law for both the lion and the ox?[9]
And is there not eternal fire, and eternal chains?
To bind the phantoms of existence from eternal life?"

25 Then Oothoon waited silent all the day and all the night,

PLATE 5

But when the morn arose, her lamentation renewd.
The Daughters of Albion hear her woes, & eccho back her sighs.

"O Urizen![1] Creator of men! mistaken Demon of heaven:
Thy joys are tears! thy labour vain, to form men to thine image.
5 How can one joy absorb another? are not different joys
Holy, eternal, infinite! and each joy is a Love.

"Does not the great mouth laugh at a gift? & the narrow eyelids mock
At the labour that is above payment? and wilt thou take the ape
For thy councellor? or the dog for a schoolmaster to thy children?
10 Does he who contemns poverty, and he who turns with abhorrence
From usury, feel the same passion, or are they moved alike?
How can the giver of gifts experience the delights of the merchant?
How the industrious citizen the pains of the husbandman?
How different far the fat fed hireling with hollow drum,
15 Who buys whole corn fields into wastes,[2] and sings upon the heath:
How different their eye and ear! how different the world to them!
With what sense does the parson claim the labour of the farmer?
What are his nets & gins° & traps? & how does he surround him   snares
With cold floods of abstraction, and with forests of solitude,
20 To build him castles and high spires, where kings & priests may dwell?
Till she who burns with youth, and knows no fixed lot, is bound
In spells of law to one she loaths; and must she drag the chain
Of life, in weary lust? must chilling murderous thoughts obscure
The clear heaven of her eternal spring? to bear the wintry rage
25 Of a harsh terror, driv'n to madness, bound to hold a rod
Over her shrinking shoulders all the day, & all the night
To turn the wheel of false desire, and longings that wake her womb
To the abhorred birth of cherubs in the human form
That live a pestilence & die a meteor & are no more;
30 Till the child dwell with one he hates, and do the deed he loaths,
And the impure scourge force his seed into its unripe birth
E'er yet his eyelids can behold the arrows of the day?[3]

9. The last line of *The Marriage of Heaven and Hell* proclaims: "One Law for the Lion & Ox is Oppression."
1. This is the first occurrence of the name "Urizen" in Blake (the name can be pronounced either as "your reason" or as an echo of "horizon"). Oothoon's liberated vision recognizes the error in the way God is conceived in conventional religion.
2. Probably a compressed allusion both to the wealthy landowner who converts fertile fields into a game preserve and to the recruiting officer ("with hollow drum") who strips the land of its agricultural laborers.
3. The reference is to the begetting of children, both in actual slavery and in the metaphoric slavery of a loveless marriage, from generation to generation.

"Does the whale worship at thy footsteps as the hungry dog?
Or does he scent the mountain prey, because his nostrils wide
35 Draw in the ocean? does his eye discern the flying cloud
As the raven's eye? or does he measure the expanse like the vulture?
Does the still spider view the cliffs where eagles hide their young?
Or does the fly rejoice because the harvest is brought in?
Does not the eagle scorn the earth & despise the treasures beneath?
40 But the mole knoweth what is there, & the worm shall tell it thee.
Does not the worm erect a pillar in the mouldering church yard,

PLATE 6

And a palace of eternity in the jaws of the hungry grave?
Over his porch these words are written: 'Take thy bliss O Man!
And sweet shall be thy taste & sweet thy infant joys renew!'

"Infancy, fearless, lustful, happy! nestling for delight
5 In laps of pleasure; Innocence! honest, open, seeking
The vigorous joys of morning light, open to virgin bliss,
Who taught thee modesty, subtil modesty? Child of night & sleep,
When thou awakest wilt thou dissemble all thy secret joys,
Or wert thou not awake when all this mystery was disclos'd?
10 Then com'st thou forth a modest virgin, knowing to dissemble,
With nets found under thy night pillow to catch virgin joy,
And brand it with the name of whore, & sell it in the night,
In silence, ev'n without a whisper, and in seeming sleep.[4]
Religious dreams and holy vespers light thy smoky fires;
15 Once were thy fires lighted by the eyes of honest morn.
And does my Theotormon seek this hypocrite modesty,
This knowing, artful, secret, fearful, cautious, trembling hypocrite?
Then is Oothoon a whore indeed! and all the virgin joys
Of life are harlots, and Theotormon is a sick man's dream,
20 And Oothoon is the crafty slave of selfish holiness.

"But Oothoon is not so; a virgin fill'd with virgin fancies
Open to joy and to delight where ever beauty appears.
If in the morning sun I find it, there my eyes are fix'd

PLATE 7

In happy copulation; if in evening mild, wearied with work,
Sit on a bank and draw the pleasures of this free born joy.

"The moment of desire! the moment of desire! The virgin
That pines for man shall awaken her womb to enormous joys
5 In the secret shadows of her chamber; the youth shut up from
The lustful joy shall forget to generate & create an amorous image
In the shadows of his curtains and in the folds of his silent pillow.[5]

4. Oothoon contrasts the natural, innocent sensuality of an infant to the sort of modesty characterizing the adult virgin, a false modesty that, Mary Wollstonecraft had observed in her *Vindication of* the *Rights of Woman*, is "merely a respect for the opinion of the world."
5. Blake is describing masturbation.

Are not these the places of religion? the rewards of continence?
The self enjoyings of self denial? Why dost seek religion?
10 Is it because acts are not lovely, that thou seekest solitude,
Where the horrible darkness is impressed with reflections of desire?

"Father of Jealousy,⁶ be thou accursed from the earth!
Why hast thou taught my Theotormon this accursed thing?
Till beauty fades from off my shoulders, darken'd and cast out,
15 A solitary shadow wailing on the margin of non-entity.

"I cry, Love! Love! Love! happy happy Love! free as the mountain wind!
Can that be Love, that drinks another as a sponge drinks water?
That clouds with jealousy his nights, with weepings all the day,
To spin a web of age around him, grey and hoary! dark!
20 Till his eyes sicken at the fruit that hangs before his sight.
Such is self-love that envies all! a creeping skeleton
With lamplike eyes watching around the frozen marriage bed.

"But silken nets and traps of adamant⁷ will Oothoon spread,
And catch for thee girls of mild silver, or of furious gold;
25 I'll lie beside thee on a bank & view their wanton play
In lovely copulation bliss on bliss with Theotormon:
Red as the rosy morning, lustful as the first born beam,
Oothoon shall view his dear delight, nor e'er with jealous cloud
Come in the heaven of generous love; nor selfish blightings bring.

30 "Does the sun walk in glorious raiment on the secret floor

PLATE 8

Where the cold miser spreads his gold? or does the bright cloud drop
On his stone threshold? does his eye behold the beam that brings
Expansion to the eye of pity? or will he bind himself
Beside the ox to thy hard furrow? does not that mild beam blot
5 The bat, the owl, the glowing tyger, and the king of night?
The sea fowl takes the wintry blast for a cov'ring to her limbs,
And the wild snake the pestilence to adorn him with gems & gold.
And trees & birds & beasts & men behold their eternal joy.
Arise you little glancing wings, and sing your infant joy!
10 Arise and drink your bliss, for every thing that lives is holy!"⁸

Thus every morning wails Oothoon, but Theotormon sits
Upon the margind ocean conversing with shadows dire.

The Daughters of Albion hear her woes, & eccho back her sighs.

1791–93   1793

<hr/>

6. I.e., Urizen (5.3), the God who prohibits the
satisfaction of human desires.
7. A legendary stone believed to be unbreakable.
(The name is derived from the Greek word for

diamond.)
8. This last phrase is also the concluding line of
"A Song of Liberty," appended to *The Marriage of
Heaven and Hell.*

The Marriage of Heaven and Hell
This, the most immediately accessible of Blake's longer works, is a vigorous, deliberately outrageous, and at times comic onslaught against timidly conventional and self-righteous members of society as well as against stock opinions of orthodox Christian piety and morality. The seeming simplicity of Blake's satiric attitude, however, is deceptive.

Initially, Blake accepts the terminology of standard Christian morality ("what the religious call Good & Evil") but reverses its values. In this conventional use Evil, which is manifested by the class of beings called Devils and which consigns wrongdoers to the orthodox Hell, is everything associated with the body and its desires and consists essentially of energy, abundance, actions, and freedom. Conventional Good, which is manifested by Angels and guarantees its adherents a place in the orthodox Heaven, is associated with the Soul (regarded as entirely separate from the body) and consists of the contrary qualities of reason, restraint, passivity, and prohibition. Blandly adopting these conventional oppositions, Blake elects to assume the diabolic persona—what he calls "the voice of the Devil"—and to utter "Proverbs of Hell."

But this stance is only a first stage in Blake's complex irony, designed to startle the reader into recognizing the inadequacy of conventional moral categories. As he also says in the opening summary, "Without Contraries is no progression," and "Reason and Energy" are both "necessary to Human existence." It turns out that Blake subordinates his reversal of conventional values under a more inclusive point of view, according to which the real Good, as distinguished from the merely ironic Good, is not abandonment of all restraints but a "marriage," or union of the contraries, of desire and restraint, energy and reason, the promptings of Hell and the denials of Heaven—or as Blake calls these contraries in plate 16, "the Prolific" and "the Devouring." These two classes, he adds, "should be enemies," and "whoever tries to reconcile them seeks to destroy existence." Implicit in Blake's satire is the view that the good and abundant life consists in the sustained tension, without victory or suppression, of co-present oppositions.

When Blake composed this unique work in the early 1790s, his city of London was teeming with religious mystics, astrologers, and sometimes bawdy freethinkers who were determined to challenge the Established Church's monopoly on spirituality and who were reviving the link, created in the seventeenth century, between enthusiasm in religion and political revolution. The work is also a response to the writings of the visionary Swedish theologian Emanuel Swedenborg, whom Blake had at first admired but then had come to recognize as a conventional Angel in the disguise of a radical Devil. In plate 3 the writings of Swedenborg are described as the winding clothes Blake discards as he is resurrected from the tomb of his past self, as a poet-prophet who heralds the apocalyptic promise of his age. Blake shared the expectations of a number of radical English writers, including the young poets Wordsworth, Coleridge, and Southey, that the French Revolution was the violent stage that, as the biblical prophets foresaw, immediately preceded the millennium. The double role of *The Marriage* as both satire and revolutionary prophecy is made explicit in *A Song of Liberty*, which Blake etched in 1792 and added as a coda.

The Marriage of Heaven and Hell

PLATE 2

The Argument

Rintrah[1] roars & shakes his fires in the burdend air;
Hungry clouds swag on the deep.
Once meek, and in a perilous path,
The just man kept his course along
5   The vale of death.
Roses are planted where thorns grow,
And on the barren heath
Sing the honey bees.

Then the perilous path was planted,
10   And a river, and a spring,
On every cliff and tomb;
And on the bleached bones
Red clay[2] brought forth;

Till the villain left the paths of ease,
15   To walk in perilous paths, and drive
The just man into barren climes.

Now the sneaking serpent walks
In mild humility,
And the just man rages in the wilds
20   Where lions roam.

Rintrah roars & shakes his fires in the burdend air;
Hungry clouds swag on the deep.

PLATE 3

As a new heaven is begun, and it is now thirty-three years since its advent, the Eternal Hell revives. And lo! Swedenborg[3] is the Angel sitting at the tomb; his writings are the linen clothes folded up. Now is the dominion of Edom, & the return of Adam into Paradise; see Isaiah xxxiv & XXXV Chap.[4]

1. Rintrah plays the role of the angry Old Testament prophet Elijah as well as of John the Baptist, the voice "crying in the wilderness" (Matthew 3), preparing the way for Christ the Messiah. It has been plausibly suggested that stanzas 2–5 summarize the course of biblical history to the present time. "Once" (line 3) refers to Old Testament history after the Fall; "Then" (line 9) is the time of the birth of Christ. "Till" (line 14) identifies the era when Christianity was perverted into an institutional religion. "Now" (line 17) is the time of the wrathful portent of the French Revolution. In this final era the hypocritical serpent represents the priest of the "angels" in the poem, while "the just man" is embodied in Blake, a raging poet and prophet in the guise of a devil. "Swag" (line 2): sag, hang down.
2. In Hebrew the literal meaning of "Adam," or created man. The probable reference is to the birth of the Redeemer, the new Adam.
3. Emanuel Swedenborg (1688–1772), Swedish scientist and religious philosopher, had predicted, on the basis of his visions, that the Last Judgment and the coming of the Kingdom of Heaven would occur in 1757. This was precisely the year of Blake's birth. Now, in 1790, Blake is thirty-three, the age at which Christ had been resurrected from the tomb; correspondingly, Blake rises from the tomb of his past life in his new role as imaginative artist who will redeem his age. But, Blake ironically comments, the works he will engrave in his resurrection will constitute the Eternal Hell, the contrary brought into simultaneous being by Swedenborg's limited New Heaven.
4. Isaiah 34 prophesies "the day of the Lord's vengeance," a time of violent destruction and blood-

Without Contraries is no progression. Attraction and Repulsion, Reason and Energy, Love and Hate, are necessary to Human existence.

From these contraries spring what the religious call Good & Evil. Good is the passive that obeys Reason. Evil is the active springing from Energy.

Good is Heaven. Evil is Hell.

PLATE 4

The Voice of the Devil

All Bibles or sacred codes have been the causes of the following Errors:

1. That Man has two real existing principles; Viz: a Body & a Soul.

2. That Energy, calld Evil, is alone from the Body, & that Reason, calld Good, is alone from the Soul.

3. That God will torment Man in Eternity for following his Energies.

But the following Contraries to these are True:

1. Man has no Body distinct from his Soul; for that calld Body is a portion of Soul discernd by the five Senses, the chief inlets of Soul in this age.

2. Energy is the only life, and is from the Body; and Reason is the bound or outward circumference of Energy.

3. Energy is Eternal Delight.

PLATE 5

Those who restrain desire, do so because theirs is weak enough to be restrained; and the restrainer or reason usurps its place & governs the unwilling.

And being restraind, it by degrees becomes passive, till it is only the shadow of desire.

The history of this is written in *Paradise Lost*,[5] & the Governor or Reason is call'd Messiah.

And the original Archangel, or possessor of the command of the heavenly host, is calld the Devil or Satan, and his children are call'd Sin & Death.[6]

But in the Book of Job, Milton's Messiah is call'd Satan.[7]

For this history has been adopted by both parties.

It indeed appear'd to Reason as if Desire was cast out; but the Devil's account is, that the Messi[PLATE 6]ah fell, & formed a heaven of what he stole from the Abyss.

This is shewn in the Gospel, where he prays to the Father to send the comforter or Desire that Reason may have Ideas to build on;[8] the Jehovah of

shed; Isaiah 35 prophesies the redemption to follow, in which "the desert shall . . . blossom as the rose," "in the wilderness shall waters break out, and streams in the desert," and "no lion shall be there," but "an highway shall be there . . . and it shall be called The way of holiness" (cf. "The Argument," lines 3–11, 20). Blake combines with these chapters Isaiah 63, in which "Edom" is the place from which comes the man whose garments are red with the blood he has spilled; for as he says, "the day of vengeance is in mine heart, and the year of my redeemed is come." Blake interprets this last phrase as predicting the time when Adam would regain his lost Paradise. Also relevant is Genesis 36.1, where the Edomites are identified as the descendants of the disinherited Esau, cheated out of his father's blessing by Jacob.

5. What follows, to the end of this section, is Blake's "diabolical" reading of Milton's *Paradise Lost*. For other Romantic comments on the magnificence of Milton's Satan see "The Satanic and Byronic Hero" at Norton Literature Online.
6. Satan's giving birth to Sin and then incestuously begetting Death upon her is described in *Paradise Lost* 2.745ff.; the war in heaven, referred to three lines below, in which the Messiah defeated Satan and drove him out of heaven, is described in 6.824ff.
7. In the Book of Job, Satan plays the role of Job's moral accuser and physical tormentor.
8. Possibly John 14.16–17, where Christ says he "will pray the Father, and he shall give you another Comforter . . . Even the Spirit of truth."

the Bible being no other than he who dwells in flaming fire. Know that after Christ's death, he became Jehovah.

But in Milton, the Father is Destiny, the Son, a Ratio[9] of the five senses, & the Holy-ghost, Vacuum!

Note. The reason Milton wrote in fetters when he wrote of Angels & God, and at liberty when of Devils & Hell, is because he was a true Poet and of the Devil's party without knowing it.

A Memorable Fancy[1]

As I was walking among the fires of hell, delighted with the enjoyments of Genius, which to Angels look like torment and insanity, I collected some of their Proverbs; thinking that as the sayings used in a nation mark its character, so the Proverbs of Hell shew the nature of Infernal wisdom better than any description of buildings or garments.

When I came home, on the abyss of the five senses, where a flat sided steep frowns over the present world, I saw a mighty Devil folded in black clouds, hovering on the sides of the rock; with cor[PLATE 7]roding fires he wrote the following sentence[2] now perceived by the minds of men, & read by them on earth:

> How do you know but ev'ry Bird that cuts the airy way,
> Is an immense world of delight, clos'd by your senses five?

Proverbs of Hell[3]

In seed time learn, in harvest teach, in winter enjoy.
Drive your cart and your plow over the bones of the dead.
The road of excess leads to the palace of wisdom.
Prudence is a rich ugly old maid courted by Incapacity.
5 He who desires but acts not, breeds pestilence.
The cut worm forgives the plow.
Dip him in the river who loves water.
A fool sees not the same tree that a wise man sees.
He whose face gives no light, shall never become a star.
10 Eternity is in love with the productions of time.
The busy bee has no time for sorrow.
The hours of folly are measur'd by the clock; but of wisdom, no clock can
    measure.
All wholsom food is caught without a net or a trap.
Bring out number, weight, & measure in a year of dearth.
15 No bird soars too high, if he soars with his own wings.
A dead body revenges not injuries.
The most sublime act is to set another before you.
If the fool would persist in his folly he would become wise.

---

9. The Latin *ratio* means both "reason" and "sum." Blake applies the term to the 18th-century view, following the empiricist philosophy of John Locke, that the content of the mind, on which the faculty of reason operates, is limited to the sum of the experience acquired by the five senses.
1. A parody of what Swedenborg called "memorable relations" of his literal-minded visions of the eternal world.

2. The "mighty Devil" is Blake, as he sees himself reflected in the shiny plate on which he is etching this very passage with "corroding fires," i.e., the acid used in the etching process. See also the third from last sentence in plate 14.
3. A "diabolic" version of the Book of Proverbs in the Old Testament, which also incorporates sly allusions to 18th-century books of piety such as Isaac Watts's *Divine Songs*.

Folly is the cloke of knavery.
20 Shame is Pride's cloke.

PLATE 8

Prisons are built with stones of Law, Brothels with bricks of Religion.
The pride of the peacock is the glory of God.
The lust of the goat is the bounty of God.
The wrath of the lion is the wisdom of God.
5   The nakedness of woman is the work of God.
Excess of sorrow laughs. Excess of joy weeps.
The roaring of lions, the howling of wolves, the raging of the stormy sea,
    and the destructive sword, are portions of eternity too great for the eye
    of man.
The fox condemns the trap, not himself.
Joys impregnate. Sorrows bring forth.
10 Let man wear the fell of the lion, woman the fleece of the sheep.
The bird a nest, the spider a web, man friendship.
The selfish smiling fool & the sullen frowning fool shall be both thought
    wise, that they may be a rod.
What is now proved was once only imagin'd.
The rat, the mouse, the fox, the rabbit watch the roots; the lion, the tyger,
    the horse, the elephant, watch the fruits.
15 The cistern contains; the fountain overflows.
One thought fills immensity.
Always be ready to speak your mind, and a base man will avoid you.
Every thing possible to be believ'd is an image of truth.
The eagle never lost so much time as when he submitted to learn of the
    crow.

PLATE 9

The fox provides for himself, but God provides for the lion.
Think in the morning, Act in the noon, Eat in the evening, Sleep in the
    night.
He who has sufferd you to impose on him knows you.
As the plow follows words, so God rewards prayers.
5   The tygers of wrath are wiser than the horses of instruction.
Expect poison from the standing water.
You never know what is enough unless you know what is more than
    enough.
Listen to the fool's reproach! it is a kingly title!
The eyes of fire, the nostrils of air, the mouth of water, the beard of earth.
10 The weak in courage is strong in cunning.
The apple tree never asks the beech how he shall grow, nor the lion the
    horse, how he shall take his prey.
The thankful reciever bears a plentiful harvest.
If others had not been foolish, we should be so.
The soul of sweet delight can never be defil'd.
15 When thou seest an Eagle, thou seest a portion of Genius; lift up thy head!
As the catterpiller chooses the fairest leaves to lay her eggs on, so the priest
    lays his curse on the fairest joys.

To create a little flower is the labour of ages.
Damn braces; Bless relaxes.
The best wine is the oldest, the best water the newest.
20 Prayers plow not! Praises reap not!
Joys laugh not! Sorrows weep not!

PLATE 10

The head Sublime, the heart Pathos, the genitals Beauty, the hands & feet
    Proportion.
As the air to a bird or the sea to a fish, so is contempt to the contemptible.
The crow wish'd every thing was black, the owl that every thing was white.
Exuberance is Beauty.
5 If the lion was advised by the fox, he would be cunning.
Improvement makes strait roads, but the crooked roads without
    Improvement are roads of Genius.
Sooner murder an infant in its cradle than nurse unacted desires.
Where man is not, nature is barren.
Truth can never be told so as to be understood, and not be believ'd.
10   Enough! or Too much.

PLATE 11

The ancient Poets animated all sensible objects with Gods or Geniuses,
calling them by the names and adorning them with the properties of woods,
rivers, mountains, lakes, cities, nations, and whatever their enlarged & numerous senses could perceive.

And particularly they studied the genius of each city & country, placing it
under its mental deity.

Till a system was formed, which some took advantage of & enslav'd the
vulgar by attempting to realize or abstract the mental deities from their objects;
thus began Priesthood,

Choosing forms of worship from poetic tales.

And at length they pronounced that the Gods had ordered such things.

Thus men forgot that All deities reside in the human breast.

PLATE 12

A Memorable Fancy[4]

The Prophets Isaiah and Ezekiel dined with me, and I asked them how they
dared so roundly to assert that God spake to them; and whether they did not
think at the time that they would be misunderstood, & so be the cause of
imposition.

Isaiah answer'd: "I saw no God, nor heard any, in a finite organical perception; but my senses discover'd the infinite in every thing, and as I was then
perswaded, & remain confirm'd, that the voice of honest indignation is the
voice of God, I cared not for consequences, but wrote."

Then I asked: "Does a firm perswasion that a thing is so, make it so?"

He replied: "All poets believe that it does, & in ages of imagination this firm

---

4. Blake parodies Swedenbo.g's accounts, in his *Memorable Relations,* of his conversations with the inhabitants during his spiritual trips to heaven.

perswasion removed mountains; but many are not capable of a firm perswasion of any thing."

Then Ezekiel said: "The philosophy of the East taught the first principles of human perception. Some nations held one principle for the origin & some another; we of Israel taught that the Poetic Genius (as you now call it) was the first principle and all the others merely derivative, which was the cause of our despising the Priests & Philosophers of other countries, and prophecying that all Gods [PL 13] would at last be proved to originate in ours & to be the tributaries of the Poetic Genius; it was this that our great poet, King David, desired so fervently & invokes so pathetically, saying by this he conquers enemies & governs kingdoms; and we so loved our God, that we cursed in his name all the deities of surrounding nations, and asserted that they had rebelled; from these opinions the vulgar came to think that all nations would at last be subject to the Jews."

"This," said he, "like all firm perswasions, is come to pass, for all nations believe the Jews' code and worship the Jews' god, and what greater subjection can be?"

I heard this with some wonder, & must confess my own conviction. After dinner I ask'd Isaiah to favour the world with his lost works; he said none of equal value was lost. Ezekiel said the same of his.

I also asked Isaiah what made him go naked and barefoot three years? He answered, "the same that made our friend Diogenes,[5] the Grecian."

I then asked Ezekiel why he eat dung, & lay so long on his right & left side?[6] He answered, "the desire of raising other men into a perception of the infinite; this the North American tribes practise, & is he honest who resists his genius or conscience only for the sake of present ease or gratification?"

PLATE 14

The ancient tradition that the world will be consumed in fire at the end of six thousand years is true, as I have heard from Hell.

For the cherub with his flaming sword is hereby commanded to leave his guard at the tree of life;[7] and when he does, the whole creation will be consumed, and appear infinite and holy, whereas it now appears finite & corrupt.

This will come to pass by an improvement of sensual enjoyment.

But first the notion that man has a body distinct from his soul is to be expunged; this I shall do, by printing in the infernal method, by corrosives, which in Hell are salutary and medicinal, melting apparent surfaces away, and displaying the infinite which was hid.[8]

If the doors of perception were cleansed every thing would appear to man as it is, infinite.

For man has closed himself up, till he sees all things thro' narrow chinks of his cavern.

5. Greek Cynic (4th century), whose extreme repudiation of civilized customs gave rise to anecdotes that he had renounced clothing. In Isaiah 20.2–3 the prophet, at the Lord's command, walked "naked and barefoot" for three years.
6. The Lord gave these instructions to the prophet Ezekiel (4.4–6).
7. In Genesis 3.24, when the Lord drove Adam and Eve from the Garden of Eden, he had placed Cherubim and a flaming sword at the eastern end "to keep the way of the tree of life."
8. See n. 2, p. 113.

PLATE 15

A Memorable Fancy

I was in a Printing house[9] in Hell & saw the method in which knowledge is transmitted from generation to generation.

In the first chamber was a Dragon-Man, clearing away the rubbish from a cave's mouth; within, a number of Dragons were hollowing the cave.

In the second chamber was a Viper folding round the rock & the cave, and others adorning it with gold, silver, and precious stones.

In the third chamber was an Eagle with wings and feathers of air; he caused the inside of the cave to be infinite; around were numbers of Eagle-like men, who built palaces in the immense cliffs.

In the fourth chamber were Lions of flaming fire, raging around & melting the metals into living fluids.

In the fifth chamber were Unnam'd forms, which cast the metals into the expanse.

There they were receiv'd by Men who occupied the sixth chamber, and took the forms of books & were arranged in libraries.[1]

PLATE 16

The Giants[2] who formed this world into its sensual existence, and now seem to live in it in chains, are in truth the causes of its life & the sources of all activity; but the chains are the cunning of weak and tame minds which have power to resist energy; according to the proverb, the weak in courage is strong in cunning.

Thus one portion of being is the Prolific, the other, the Devouring; to the Devourer it seems as if the producer was in his chains, but it is not so; he only takes portions of existence and fancies that the whole.

But the Prolific would cease to be Prolific unless the Devourer as a sea received the excess of his delights.

Some will say, "Is not God alone the Prolific?" I answer, "God only Acts & Is, in existing beings or Men."

These two classes of men are always upon earth, & they should be enemies; whoever tries [PLATE 17] to reconcile them seeks to destroy existence.

Religion is an endeavour to reconcile the two.

Note. Jesus Christ did not wish to unite but to separate them, as in the Parable of sheep and goats! & he says, "I came not to send Peace but a Sword."[3]

Messiah or Satan or Tempter was formerly thought to be one of the Ante-diluvians[4] who are our Energies.

A Memorable Fancy

An Angel came to me and said: "O pitiable foolish young man! O horrible! O dreadful state! consider the hot burning dungeon thou art preparing for thyself to all eternity, to which thou art going in such career."

9. A covert pun runs through this section: workers, ink-blackened, who did the dirty work in the printing houses of the period were humorously known as "printer's devils."
1. In this "Memorable Fancy" Blake allegorizes his procedure in designing, etching, printing, and binding his works of imaginative genius.

2. In this section human creative energies, called "the Prolific," in their relation to their indispensable contrary, "the Devourer."
3. Matthew 10.34. The parable of the sheep and the goats is in Matthew 25.32–33.
4. Those who lived before Noah's Flood.

I said: "Perhaps you will be willing to shew me my eternal lot, & we will contemplate together upon it and see whether your lot or mine is most desirable."

So he took me thro' a stable & thro' a church & down into the church vault at the end of which was a mill; thro' the mill we went, and came to a cave; down the winding cavern we groped our tedious way till a void boundless as a nether sky appeared beneath us, & we held by the roots of trees and hung over this immensity, but I said: "If you please, we will commit ourselves to this void, and see whether Providence is here also, if you will not I will." But he answered: "Do not presume, O young man, but as we here remain, behold thy lot which will soon appear when the darkness passes away."[5]

So I remaind with him sitting in the twisted [PLATE 18] root of an oak; he was suspended in a fungus which hung with the head downward into the deep.

By degrees we beheld the infinite Abyss, fiery as the smoke of a burning city; beneath us at an immense distance was the sun, black but shining; round it were fiery tracks on which revolv'd vast spiders, crawling after their prey, which flew, or rather swum in the infinite deep, in the most terrific shapes of animals sprung from corruption; & the air was full of them, & seemed composed of them; these are Devils, and are called Powers of the air. I now asked my companion which was my eternal lot? He said, "Between the black & white spiders."

But now, from between the black & white spiders a cloud and fire burst and rolled thro the deep, blackning all beneath, so that the nether deep grew black as a sea & rolled with a terrible noise. Beneath us was nothing now to be seen but a black tempest, till looking east between the clouds & the waves, we saw a cataract of blood mixed with fire, and not many stones' throw from us appeared and sunk again the scaly fold of a monstrous serpent. At last to the east, distant about three degrees, appeared a fiery crest above the waves. Slowly it reared like a ridge of golden rocks till we discovered two globes of crimson fire, from which the sea fled away in clouds of smoke. And now we saw it was the head of Leviathan;[6] his forehead was divided into streaks of green & purple like those on a tyger's forehead; soon we saw his mouth & red gills hang just above the raging foam, tinging the black deep with beams of blood, advancing toward [PLATE 19] us with all the fury of a spiritual existence.

My friend the Angel climb'd up from his station into the mill. I remain'd alone, & then this appearance was no more, but I found myself sitting on a pleasant bank beside a river by moon light, hearing a harper who sung to the harp, & his theme was: "The man who never alters his opinion is like standing water, & breeds reptiles of the mind."

But I arose, and sought for the mill, & there I found my Angel, who surprised asked me how I escaped?

I answered: "All that we saw was owing to your metaphysics: for when you ran away, I found myself on a bank by moonlight hearing a harper. But now we have seen my eternal lot, shall I shew you yours? He laughd at my proposal;

5. The "stable" is that where Jesus was born, which, allegorically, leads to the "church" founded in his name and to the "vault" where this institution effectually buried him. The "mill" in Blake is a symbol of mechanical and analytic philosophy; through this the pilgrims pass into the twisting cave of rationalistic theology and descend to an underworld that is an empty abyss. The point of this Blakean equivalent of a carnival funhouse is that only after you have thoroughly confused yourself by this tortuous approach, and only if you then (as in the next two paragraphs) stare at this topsy-turvy emptiness long enough, will the void gradually assume the semblance of the comic horrors of the fantasized Hell of religious orthodoxy.
6. The biblical sea monster.

but I by force suddenly caught him in my arms, & flew westerly thro' the night, til we were elevated above the earth's shadow; then I flung myself with him directly into the body of the sun. Here I clothed myself in white, & taking in my hand Swedenborg's volumes, sunk from the glorious clime, and passed all the planets till we came to Saturn. Here I staid to rest & then leap'd into the void between Saturn & the fixed stars.[7]

"Here," said I, "is your lot, in this space, if space it may be calld." Soon we saw the stable and the church, & I took him to the altar and open'd the Bible, and lo! it was a deep pit, into which I descended, driving the Angel before me. Soon we saw seven houses of brick;[8] one we enterd; in it were a [PLATE 20] number of monkeys, baboons, & all of that species, chaind by the middle, grinning and snatching at one another, but withheld by the shortness of their chains. However, I saw that they sometimes grew numerous, and then the weak were caught by the strong, and with a grinning aspect, first coupled with & then devourd, by plucking off first one limb and then another till the body was left a helpless trunk. This, after grinning & kissing it with seeming fondness, they devourd too; and here & there I saw one savourily picking the flesh off of his own tail. As the stench terribly annoyd us both, we went into the mill, & I in my hand brought the skeleton of a body, which in the mill was Aristotle's Analytics.[9]

So the Angel said: "Thy phantasy has imposed upon me, & thou oughtest to be ashamed."

I answerd: "We impose on one another, & it is but lost time to converse with you whose works are only Analytics."

Opposition is true Friendship.

PLATE 21

I have always found that Angels have the vanity to speak of themselves as the only wise; this they do with a confident insolence sprouting from systematic reasoning.

Thus Swedenborg boasts that what he writes is new; tho' it is only the Contents or Index of already publish'd books.

A man carried a monkey about for a shew, & because he was a little wiser than the monkey, grew vain, and conceiv'd himself as much wiser than seven men. It is so with Swedenborg; he shews the folly of churches & exposes hypocrites, till he imagines that all are religious, & himself the single [PLATE 22] one on earth that ever broke a net.

Now hear a plain fact: Swedenborg has not written one new truth. Now hear another: he has written all the old falshoods.

And now hear the reason: He conversed with Angels who are all religious, & conversed not with Devils, who all hate religion, for he was incapable thro' his conceited notions.

Thus Swedenborg's writings are a recapitulation of all superficial opinions, and an analysis of the more sublime, but no further.

7. In the Ptolemaic world picture, Saturn was in the outermost planetary sphere; beyond it was the sphere of the fixed stars.
8. The "seven churches which are in Asia," to which John addresses the Book of Revelation 1.4.

Blake now forces on the angel his own diabolic view of angelic biblical exegesis, theological speculation and disputation, and Hell.
9. Aristotle's treatises on logic.

Have now another plain fact: Any man of mechanical talents may from the writings of Paracelsus or Jacob Behmen[1] produce ten thousand volumes of equal value with Swedenborg's, and from those of Dante or Shakespear, an infinite number.

But when he has done this, let him not say that he knows better than his master, for he only holds a candle in sunshine.

A Memorable Fancy

Once I saw a Devil in a flame of fire, who arose before an Angel that sat on a cloud, and the Devil utterd these words:

"The worship of God is, Honouring his gifts in other men, each according to his genius, and loving the [PLATE 23] greatest men best. Those who envy or calumniate great men hate God, for there is no other God."

The Angel hearing this became almost blue; but mastering himself, he grew yellow, & at last white, pink, & smiling, and then replied:

"Thou Idolater, is not God One? & is not he visible in Jesus Christ? and has not Jesus Christ given his sanction to the law of ten commandments, and are not all other men fools, sinners, & nothings?"

The Devil answer'd; "Bray a fool in a mortar with wheat, yet shall not his folly be beaten out of him.[2] If Jesus Christ is the greatest man, you ought to love him in the greatest degree. Now hear how he has given his sanction to the law of ten commandments: did he not mock at the sabbath, and so mock the sabbath's God?[3] murder those who were murderd because of him? turn away the law from the woman taken in adultery?[4] steal the labor of others to support him? bear false witness when he omitted making a defence before Pilate?[5] covet when he pray'd for his disciples, and when he bid them shake off the dust of their feet against such as refused to lodge them?[6] I tell you, no virtue can exist without breaking these ten commandments. Jesus was all virtue, and acted from im[PLATE 24]pulse, not from rules."

When he had so spoken, I beheld the Angel, who stretched out his arms embracing the flame of fire, & he was consumed and arose as Elijah.[7]

Note. This Angel, who is now become a Devil, is my particular friend; we often read the Bible together in its infernal or diabolical sense, which the world shall have if they behave well.

I have also The Bible of Hell,[8] which the world shall have whether they will or no.

One Law for the Lion & Ox is Oppression.

1790–93   1790–93

PLATE 25

1. Jakob Boehme (1575–1624), a German shoemaker who developed a theosophical system that has had persisting influence on both theological and metaphysical speculation. Paracelsus (1493–1541), a Swiss physician and a pioneer in empirical medicine, was also a prominent theorist of the occult.
2. Proverbs 27.22: "Though thou shouldst bray a fool in a mortar among wheat with a pestle, yet will not his foolishness depart from him." "Bray": pound into small pieces.
3. Mark 2.27: "The sabbath was made for man."
4. Cf. John 8.2–11.
5. Cf. Matthew 27.13–14.
6. Matthew 10.14: "Whosoever shall not receive you . . . when ye depart . . . shake off the dust of your feet."
7. In 2 Kings 2.11 the prophet Elijah "went up by a whirlwind into heaven," borne by "a chariot of fire."
8. I.e., the poems and designs that Blake is working on.

A Song of Liberty[1]

1. The Eternal Female groand! it was heard over all the Earth.

2. Albion's coast is sick, silent; the American meadows faint!

3. Shadows of Prophecy shiver along by the lakes and the rivers and mutter across the ocean. France, rend down thy dungeon![2]

4. Golden Spain, burst the barriers of old Rome!

5. Cast thy keys, O Rome,[3] into the deep down falling, even to eternity down falling,

6. And weep.[4]

7. In her trembling hands she took the new born terror, howling.

8. On those infinite mountains of light now barr'd out by the Atlantic sea,[5] the new born fire stood before the starry king![6]

9. Flag'd with grey brow'd snows and thunderous visages, the jealous wings wav'd over the deep.

10. The speary hand burned aloft, unbuckled was the shield, forth went the hand of jealousy among the flaming hair, and [PLATE 26] Hurl'd the new born wonder thro' the starry night.

11. The fire, the fire, is falling!

12. Look up! look up! O citizen of London, enlarge thy countenance! O Jew, leave counting gold! return to thy oil and wine. O African! black African! (Go, wingèd thought, widen his forehead.)

13. The fiery limbs, the flaming hair, shot like the sinking sun into the western sea.

14. Wak'd from his eternal sleep, the hoary element[7] roaring fled away:

15. Down rushd, beating his wings in vain, the jealous king; his grey brow'd councellors, thunderous warriors, curl'd veterans, among helms, and shields, and chariots, horses, elephants; banners, castles, slings and rocks,

16. Falling, rushing, ruining! buried in the ruins, on Urthona's dens;

17. All night beneath the ruins; then, their sullen flames faded, emerge round the gloomy king,

18. With thunder and fire, leading his starry hosts thro' the waste wilderness [PLATE 27] he promulgates his ten commands, glancing his beamy eyelids over the deep in dark dismay,

19. Where the son of fire in his eastern cloud, while the morning plumes her golden breast,

1. Blake etched this poem in 1792 and sometimes bound it as an appendix to The Marriage of Heaven and Hell. It recounts the birth, manifested in the contemporary events in France, of the flaming Spirit of Revolution (whom Blake later called Orc), and describes his conflict with the tyrannical sky god (whom Blake later called Urizen). The poem ends with the portent of the Spirit of Revolution shattering the ten commandments, or prohibitions against political, religious, and moral liberty, and bringing in a free and joyous new world. "Albion's" (line 2): England's.
2. The political prison, the Bastille, was destroyed by the French revolutionaries in 1789.

3. The keys of Rome, a symbol of Papal power.
4. Echoing, among others, John 11.35 ("Jesus wept") and Revelation 18.11 (which states that at the fall of Babylon, "the merchants of the earth shall weep and mourn for her").
5. The legendary continent of Atlantis, sunk beneath the sea, which Blake uses to represent the condition before the Fall.
6. Blake often uses the stars, in their fixed courses, as a symbol of the law-governed Newtonian universe.
7. The sea, which to Blake represents a devouring chaos, such as had swallowed Atlantis.

20. Spurning the clouds written with curses, stamps the stony law[8] to dust, loosing the eternal horses from the dens of night, crying:

"Empire is no more! and now the lion & wolf shall cease."[9]

Chorus

Let the Priests of the Raven of dawn, no longer in deadly black, with hoarse note curse the sons of joy. Nor his accepted brethren, whom, tyrant, he calls free, lay the bound or build the roof. Nor pale religious letchery call that virginity, that wishes but acts not!
For every thing that lives is Holy.

1792   1792

8. I.e., the Ten Commandments (verse 18), which the "finger of God" had written on "tables [tablets] of stone" (Exodus 31.18).
9. Cf. Isaiah's prophecy, 65.17–25, of "new heav-
ens and a new earth," when "The wolf and the lamb shall feed together, and the lion shall eat straw like the bullock."

FROM BLAKE'S NOTEBOOK[1]

Mock on, Mock on, Voltaire, Rousseau

Mock on, Mock on, Voltaire, Rousseau;[2]
Mock on, Mock on, 'tis all in vain.
You throw the sand against the wind,
And the wind blows it back again;

5   And every sand becomes a Gem
Reflected in the beams divine;
Blown back, they blind the mocking Eye,
But still in Israel's paths they shine.

The Atoms of Democritus
10 And Newton's Particles of light[3]
Are sands upon the Red sea shore,
Where Israel's tents do shine so bright.

Never pain to tell thy love

Never pain to tell thy love
Love that never told can be,

1. A commonplace book in which Blake drew sketches and jotted down verses and memoranda between the late 1780s and 1810. It is known as the Rossetti manuscript because it later came into the possession of the poet and painter Dante Gabriel Rossetti. These poems were first published in imperfect form in 1863, then transcribed from the manuscript by Geoffrey Keynes in 1935.
2. Blake regards both Voltaire and Rousseau, French writers often hailed as the authors of the Revolution, as representing rationalism and Deism.
3. Newton in his *Opticks* hypothesized that light consisted of minute material particles. Democritus (460–362 B.C.E.) proposed that atoms were the ultimate components of the universe.

For the gentle wind does move
Silently, invisibly.

5   I told my love, I told my love,
I told her all my heart,
Trembling, cold, in ghastly fears—
Ah, she doth depart.

Soon as she was gone from me
10   A traveller came by
Silently, invisibly—
O, was no deny.

I askèd a thief

I askèd a thief to steal me a peach,
He turned up his eyes;
I ask'd a lithe lady to lie her down,
Holy & meek she cries.

5   As soon as I went
An angel came.
He wink'd at the thief
And smild at the dame—

And without one word said
10   Had a peach from the tree
And still as a maid
Enjoy'd the lady.

1796

And did those feet[1]

And did those feet in ancient time
Walk upon England's mountains green?
And was the holy Lamb of God
On England's pleasant pastures seen?

5   And did the Countenance Divine
Shine forth upon our clouded hills?
And was Jerusalem builded here,
Among those dark Satanic Mills?[2]

1. These quatrains occur in the preface to Blake's prophetic poem *Milton*. There is an ancient belief that Jesus came to England with Joseph of Arimathea, the merchant who is identified in the Gospels as making the arrangements for Christ's burial following the crucifixion. Blake adapts the legend to his own conception of a spiritual Israel, in which the significance of biblical events is as relevant to England as to Palestine. By a particularly Blakean irony, this poem of mental war in the service of apocalyptic desire is widely used as a hymn, national anthem, or school song by just those establishment figures whom Blake would call "angels."
2. There may be an allusion here to industrial England, but the mill is also Blake's symbol for a mechanistic and utilitarian worldview, according to which, as he said elsewhere, "the same dull round, even of a universe" becomes "a mill with complicated wheels."

Bring me my Bow of burning gold,
10 Bring me my Arrows of desire,
Bring me my Spear; O clouds unfold!
Bring me my Chariot of fire!

I will not cease from Mental Fight,
Nor shall my Sword sleep in my hand,
15 Till we have built Jerusalem
In England's green & pleasant Land.

ca. 1804–10   ca. 1804–10

From A Vision of the Last Judgment[1]

For the Year 1810
Additions to Blake's Catalogue of Pictures &c

The Last Judgment [will be] when all those are Cast away who trouble Religion with Questions concerning Good & Evil or Eating of the Tree of those Knowledges or Reasonings which hinder the Vision of God turning all into a Consuming fire. When Imaginative Art & Science & all Intellectual Gifts, all the Gifts of the Holy Ghost, are lookd upon as of no use & only Contention remains to Man, then the Last Judgment begins, & its Vision is seen by the Imaginative Eye of Every one according to the situation he holds.

[PAGE 68] The Last Judgment is not Fable or Allegory but Vision. Fable or Allegory are a totally distinct & inferior kind of Poetry. Vision, or Imagination, is a Representation of what Eternally Exists, Really & Unchangeably. Fable or Allegory is Formd by the daughters of Memory. Imagination is Surrounded by the daughters of Inspiration, who in the aggregate are calld Jerusalem. [PAGE 69] Fable is Allegory, but what Critics call The Fable is Vision itself. [PAGE 68] The Hebrew Bible & the Gospel of Jesus are not Allegory, but Eternal Vision, or Imagination of All that Exists. Note here that Fable or Allegory is Seldom without some Vision. *Pilgrim's Progress* is full of it, the Greek Poets the same; but Allegory & Vision ought to be known as Two Distinct Things, & so calld for the Sake of Eternal Life. Plato has made Socrates say that Poets & Prophets do not know or Understand what they write or Utter; this is a most Pernicious Falshood. If they do not, pray is an inferior Kind to be calld Knowing? Plato confutes himself.[2]

The Last Judgment is one of these Stupendous Visions. I have represented it as I saw it. To different People it appears differently, as [PAGE 69] every thing else does; for tho on Earth things seem Permanent, they are less permanent than a Shadow, as we all know too well.

1. In this essay Blake describes and comments on his painting of the Last Judgment, now lost, which is said to have measured seven by five feet and to have included a thousand figures. The text has been transcribed and rearranged, as the sequence of the pages indicates, from the scattered fragments in Blake's Notebook. The opening and closing parts are reprinted here as Blake's fullest, although cryptic, statements of what he means by "vision." These sections deal with the relations of imaginative vision to allegory, Greek fable, and the biblical story; to uncurbed human passion and intellectual power; to conventional and coercive virtue; to what is seen by the "corporeal" eye; to the arts; and to the Last Judgment and the apocalyptic redemption of humanity and of the created world—an apocalypse that is to be achieved through the triumph over the bodily eye by human imagination, as manifested in the creative artist.
2. In Plato's dialogue *Ion*, in which Socrates traps Ion into admitting that, because poets compose by inspiration, they do so without knowing what they are doing.

The Nature of Visionary Fancy, or Imagination, is very little Known, & the Eternal nature & permanence of its ever Existent Images is considered as less permanent than the things of Vegetative & Generative Nature; yet the Oak dies as well as the Lettuce, but Its Eternal Image & Individuality never dies, but renews by its seed. Just so the Imaginative Image returns by the seed of Contemplative Thought. The Writings of the Prophets illustrate these conceptions of the Visionary Fancy by their various sublime & Divine Images as seen in the Worlds of Vision. * * *

Let it here be Noted that the Greek Fables originated in Spiritual Mystery [PAGE 72] & Real Visions, Which are lost & clouded in Fable & Allegory, while the Hebrew Bible & the Greek Gospel are Genuine, Preservd by the Saviour's Mercy. The Nature of my Work is Visionary or Imaginative; it is an Endeavour to Restore what the Ancients calld the Golden Age.

[PAGE 69] This world of Imagination is the World of Eternity; it is the Divine bosom into which we shall all go after the death of the Vegetated body. This World of Imagination is Infinite & Eternal, whereas the world of Generation, or Vegetation, is Finite & Temporal. There Exist in that Eternal World the Permanent Realities of Every Thing which we see reflected in this Vegetable Glass of Nature.

All Things are comprehended in their Eternal Forms in the Divine [PAGE 70] body of the Saviour, the True Vine of Eternity, The Human Imagination, who appeard to Me as Coming to Judgment among his Saints & throwing off the Temporal that the Eternal might be Establishd. Around him were seen the Images of Existences according to a certain order suited to my Imaginative Eye. * * *

[PAGE 87] Men are admitted into Heaven not because they have curbed & governd their Passions, or have No Passions, but because they have Cultivated their Understandings. The Treasures of Heaven are not Negations of Passion, but Realities of Intellect from which All the Passions Emanate Uncurbed in their Eternal Glory. The Fool shall not enter into Heaven, let him be ever so Holy. Holiness is not The price of Enterance into Heaven. Those who are cast out Are All Those who, having no Passions of their own because No Intellect, Have spent their lives in Curbing & Governing other People's by the Various arts of Poverty & Cruelty of all kinds. Wo Wo Wo to you Hypocrites! Even Murder the Courts of Justice, more merciful than the Church, are compelld to allow, is not done in Passion but in Cool Blooded Design & Intention. The Modern Church Crucifies Christ with the Head Downwards.

[PAGE 92] Many persons such as Paine & Voltaire,[3] with some of the Ancient Greeks, say: "We will not converse concerning Good & Evil; we will live in Paradise & Liberty." You may do so in Spirit, but not in the Mortal Body as you pretend, till after the last Judgment; for in Paradise they have no Corporeal & Mortal Body—that originated with the Fall & was calld Death & cannot be removed but by a Last Judgment; while we are in the world of Mortality we Must Suffer. The Whole Creation Groans to be deliverd; there will always be as many Hypocrites born as Honest Men & they will always have superior Power in Mortal Things. You cannot have Liberty in this World without what you call Moral Virtue, & you cannot have Moral Virtue without the Slavery of that half of the Human Race who hate what you call Moral Virtue.

---

3. Blake represents Thomas Paine, author of *The Rights of Man* (1791), and Voltaire, the great author of the French Enlightenment, as proponents of the possibility of restoring an earthly paradise by political revolution. Such had been Blake's own view in the early 1790s (see, e.g., *The Marriage of Heaven and Hell*, p. 110).

* * *

Thinking as I do that the Creator of this World is a very Cruel Being, & being a Worshipper of Christ, I cannot help saying: "The Son, O how unlike the Father!" First God Almighty comes with a Thump on the Head. Then Jesus Christ comes with a balm to heal it.

The Last Judgment is an Overwhelming of Bad Art & Science. Mental Things are alone Real; what is Calld Corporeal Nobody Knows of its dwelling Place; it is in Fallacy & its Existence an Imposture. Where is the Existence Out of Mind or Thought? Where is it but in the Mind of a Fool? Some People flatter themselves that there will be No Last Judgment, & [PAGE 95] that Bad Art will be adopted & mixed with Good Art, That Error or Experiment will make a Part of Truth, & they Boast that it is its Foundation. These People flatter themselves; I will not Flatter them. Error is Created; Truth is Eternal. Error or Creation will be Burned Up, & then & not till then Truth or Eternity will appear. It is Burnt up the Moment Men cease to behold it. I assert for My self that I do not behold the Outward Creation & that to me it is hindrance & not Action; it is as the Dirt upon my feet, No part of Me. "What," it will be Questioned, "When the Sun rises, do you not see a round Disk of fire somewhat like a Guinea?"[4] O no no, I see an Innumerable company of the Heavenly host crying "Holy Holy Holy is the Lord God Almighty." I question not my Corporeal or Vegetative Eye any more than I would Question a Window concerning a Sight: I look thro it & not with it.

1810   1810

Two Letters on Sight and Vision[1]

To Dr. John Trusler (Aug. 23, 1799)

Revd Sir

I really am sorry that you are falln out with the Spiritual World, Especially if I should have to answer for it. I feel very sorry that your Ideas & Mine on Moral Painting differ so much as to have made you angry with my method of Study. If I am wrong, I am wrong in good company. I had hoped your plan comprehended All Species of this Art, & Especially that you would not regret that Species which gives Existence to Every other, namely Visions of Eternity. You say that I want somebody to Elucidate my Ideas. But you ought to know that What is Grand is necessarily obscure to Weak men. That which can be made Explicit to the Idiot is not worth my care. The wisest of the Ancients considerd what is not too Explicit as the fittest for Instruction, because it rouzes the faculties to act. I name Moses, Solomon, Esop, Homer, Plato.

But as you have favored me with your remarks on my Design, permit me in return to defend it against a mistaken one, which is, That I have supposed Malevolence without a Cause.[2]—Is not Merit in one a Cause of Envy in

---

4. A gold coin worth twenty-one shillings.
1. Blake wrote these pronouncements about the difference between "corporeal" sight and imaginative vision at times when a friend, a patron, or the need for money was putting pressure on him to turn from his visionary art to more fashionable modes of representation. The first letter is a pas-

sionate response to John Trusler (1735–1820), clergyman and author, who had objected to some of Blake's visionary art.
2. Blake had made a watercolor drawing (which has survived) illustrating Malevolence. He described this design in an earlier letter: "A Father, taking leave of his Wife & Child, Is watch'd by two Fiends

another, & Serenity & Happiness & Beauty a Cause of Malevolence? But Want of Money & the Distress of A Thief can never be alleged as the Cause of his Thievery, for many honest people endure greater hardships with Fortitude. We must therefore seek the Cause elsewhere than in want of Money, for that is the Miser's passion, not the Thief's.

I have therefore proved your Reasonings Ill proportioned, which you can never prove my figures to be. They are those of Michael Angelo, Rafael, & the Antique, & of the best living Models. I perceive that your Eye is perverted by Caricature Prints,[3] which ought not to abound so much as they do. Fun I love, but too much Fun is of all things the most loathsom. Mirth is better than Fun, & Happiness is better than Mirth—I feel that a Man may be happy in This World. And I know that This World Is a World of Imagination & Vision. I see Every thing I paint In This World, but Every body does not see alike. To the Eyes of a Miser a Guinea is more beautiful than the Sun, & a bag worn with the use of Money has more beautiful proportions than a Vine filled with Grapes. The tree which moves some to tears of joy is in the Eyes of others only a Green thing that stands in the way. Some See Nature all Ridicule & Deformity, & by these I shall not regulate my proportions; & Some Scarce see Nature at all. But to the Eyes of the Man of Imagination Nature is Imagination itself. As a man is, So he Sees. As the Eye is formed, such are its Powers. You certainly Mistake when you say that the Visions of Fancy are not to be found in This World. To Me This World is all One continued Vision of Fancy or Imagination, & I feel Flatterd when I am told So. What is it sets Homer, Virgil, & Milton in so high a rank of Art? Why is the Bible more Entertaining & Instructive than any other book? Is it not because they are addressed to the Imagination, which is Spiritual Sensation, & but mediately to the Understanding or Reason? Such is True Painting, and such was alone valued by the Greeks & the best modern Artists. Consider what Lord Bacon says, "Sense sends over to Imagination before Reason have judged, & Reason sends over to Imagination before the Decree can be acted." See Advancem^t of Learning, Part 2, P. 47 of first Edition.

But I am happy to find a Great Majority of Fellow Mortals who can Elucidate My Visions, & Particularly they have been Elucidated by Children, who have taken a greater delight in contemplating my Pictures than I even hoped. Neither Youth nor Childhood is Folly or Incapacity. Some Children are Fools, & so are some Old Men. But There is a vast Majority on the side of Imagination or Spiritual Sensation.

To Engrave after another Painter is infinitely more laborious than to Engrave one's own Inventions. And of the Size you require my price has been Thirty Guineas, & I cannot afford to do it for less. I had Twelve for the Head I sent you as a Specimen; but after my own designs, I could do at least Six times the quantity of labour in the same time, which will account for the difference of price, as also that Chalk Engraving is at least six times as laborious as Aqua tinta. I have no objection to Engraving after another Artist. Engraving is the profession I was apprenticed to, & should never have attempted to live by any thing else, If orders had not come in for my Designs & Paintings, which I have the pleasure to tell you are Increasing Every Day.

---

incarnate, with intention that when his back is turned they will murder the mother & her infant."

3. Pictures of people with ludicrously exaggerated features.

Thus If I am a Painter, it is not to be attributed to Seeking after. But I am contented whether I live by Painting or Engraving.

I am Revd Sir Your very obedient servant,

William Blake

To George Cumberland[4] (Apr. 12, 1827)

Dear Cumberland

I have been very near the Gates of Death & have returned very weak & an Old Man feeble & tottering, but not in Spirit & Life not in The Real Man The Imagination which Liveth for Ever. In that I am stronger & stronger as this Foolish Body decays. I thank you for the Pains you have taken with Poor Job.[5] I know too well that a great majority of Englishmen are fond of The Indefinite, which they Measure by Newton's Doctrine of the Fluxions of an Atom,[6] a Thing that does not Exist. These are Politicians & think that Republican Art[7] is Inimical to their Atom. For a Line or Lineament is not formed by Chance; a Line is a Line in its Minutest Subdivision[s]; Strait or Crooked, It is Itself, & Not Intermeasurable with or by any Thing Else. Such is Job, but since the French Revolution Englishmen are all Intermeasurable One by Another; Certainly a happy state of Agreement, to which I for One do not Agree. God keep me from the Divinity of Yes & No too, The Yea Nay Creeping Jesus, from supposing Up & Down to be the same Thing, as all Experimentalists must suppose.

You are desirous, I know, to dispose of some of my Works & to make [them] Pleasing. I am obliged to you & to all who do so. But having none remaining of all that I had Printed, I cannot Print more Except at a great loss, for at the time I printed those things I had a whole House to range in; now I am shut up in a Corner, therefore am forced to ask a Price for them that I scarce expect to get from a Stranger. I am now Printing a Set of the Songs of Innocence & Experience for a Friend at Ten Guineas, which I cannot do under Six Months consistent with my other Work, so that I have little hope of doing any more of such things. The Last Work I produced is a Poem Entitled "Jerusalem the Emanation of the Giant Albion," but find that to Print it will Cost my Time the amount of Twenty Guineas. One I have Finishd; it contains 100 Plates but it is not likely that I shall get a Customer for it.[8]

As you wish me to send you a list with the Prices of these things they are as follows:

	£	s	d
America	6.	6.	0
Europe	6.	6.	0
Visions &^c	5.	5.	0
Thel	3.	3.	0
Songs of Inn. & Exp.	10.	10.	0
Urizen	6.	6.	0

4. A businessman who was an old and loyal friend of Blake and a buyer of his illuminated books. Blake wrote this letter only four months before he died on Aug. 4, 1827.
5. Cumberland was trying to interest his friends in buying a set of Blake's engravings, *Illustrations of the Book of Job*.
6. Isaac Newton's *Method of Fluxions* (1704)

announced his discovery of the infinitesimal calculus. To Blake, Newton was the archrepresentative of materialist philosophy.
7. I.e., a free art, not subject to authoritarian control, and suited to the free citizens of a republic (rather than the subjects of a monarch).
8. This single colored copy of Blake's *Jerusalem* survives in the Mellon Collection.

The Little Card⁹ I will do as soon as Possible, but when you Consider that I have been reduced to a Skeleton, from which I am slowly recovering, you will I hope have Patience with me.

Flaxman¹ is Gone & we must All soon follow, every one to his Own Eternal House, Leaving the Delusive Goddess Nature & her Laws to get into Freedom from all Law of the Members into The Mind, in which every one is King & Priest in his own House. God Send it so on Earth as it is in Heaven.

I am, Dear Sir, Yours Affectionately

WILLIAM BLAKE

9. A small illustrated name card that Blake executed for Cumberland; it was his last engraving.
1. John Flaxman, a well-known sculptor of the time and illustrator of Homer and Dante, had died the preceding December.

ROBERT BURNS
1759–1796

When Robert Burns published his first volume of *Poems* in 1786, he was immediately hailed by the Edinburgh establishment as an instance of the natural genius, a "Heaven-taught ploughman" whose poems owed nothing to literary study, but instead represented the spontaneous overflow of his native feelings. Burns took care to call attention to those qualities in his verse—the undisciplined energy and rustic simplicity—that suited the temper of an age worried that modern refinement and propriety had undermined the vigor of poetry. But even though he cast himself (in the half-modest, half-defiant words of his Preface to *Poems*) as someone "unacquainted with the necessary requisites for commencing Poet by rule," Burns was in fact a widely read (although largely self-educated) man and a careful craftsman who turned to two earlier traditions for his poetic models. One of these was an oral tradition of folklore and folk song. The other was the highly developed literary tradition of poetry written in the Scots dialect of English.

His father—William Burnes, as he spelled his name—was a God-fearing and hard-working farmer of Ayrshire, a county in southwestern Scotland, who, unable to make a go of it in a period of hard times and high rents, died in 1784 broken in body and spirit. Robert, with his brother Gilbert, was forced to do the heavy work of a man while still a boy and began to show signs of the heart trouble of which he was to die when only thirty-seven. Although his father had the Scottish esteem for education and saw to it that his sons attended school whenever they could, Burns's education in literature, theology, politics, and philosophy came mainly from his own reading. At the age of fifteen, he fell in love and was inspired by that event to write his first song. "Thus," he said, "with me began Love and Poesy." After he reached maturity, he practiced at both. He began a series of love affairs, fathering in 1785 the first of a number of illegitimate children. He also extended greatly the range and quantity of his attempts at poetry. So rapid was his development that by the time he published the Kilmarnock edition, at the age of twenty-seven, he had written all but a few of his greatest long poems.

The Kilmarnock volume (so named from the town in which it was published) is one of the most remarkable first volumes by any British poet, and it had a great and immediate success. Burns was acclaimed "Caledonia's Bard" and championed by intellectuals and gentlefolk when he visited the city of Edinburgh soon after his book came out. The peasant-poet demonstrated that he could more than hold his own as an urbane conversationalist and debater. But he was also wise enough to realize that once the novelty wore off, his eminence in this society would not endure. He had a fierce pride that was quick to resent any hint of contempt or condescension toward himself as a man of low degree. His sympathies were democratic, and even in 1793 and 1794, when partisans of parliamentary reform were being prosecuted for sedition in Edinburgh and Glasgow, he remained (like William Blake in London) an outspoken admirer of the republican revolutions in America and France. In religion, too, he was a radical. Against the strict Calvinism of the Presbyterian kirk (church) in which he had been raised, Burns was known to profess "the Religion of Sentiment and Reason." A letter of December 1789, in which he seizes the chance to play a free-thinking Son "of Satan," merrily proclaims his intention to take up a theme that will, he says, be "pregnant with all the stores of Learning, from Moses & Confucius to [Benjamin] Franklin & [Joseph] Priestl[e]y—in short . . . I intend to write Baudy." Burns's satires on the kirk and taste for bawdy vulgarity could offend. Furthermore, his promiscuity gained him considerable notoriety, less because womanizing was out of the common order for the time than because he flaunted it. Many of the friendships that he made in high society fell apart, and Burns's later visits to Edinburgh were less successful than the first.

In 1788 Burns was given a commission as excise officer, or tax inspector, and he settled down with Jean Armour, a former lover, now his wife, at Ellisland, near Dumfries, combining his official duties with farming. This was the fourth farm on which Burns had worked; and when it, like the others, failed, he moved his family to the lively country town of Dumfries. Here he was fairly happy, despite recurrent illness and a chronic shortage of money. He performed his official duties efficiently and was respected by his fellow townspeople and esteemed by his superiors; he was a devoted family man and father; and he accumulated a circle of intimates to whom he could repair for conversation and conviviality. In 1787 James Johnson, an engraver, had enlisted Burns's aid in collecting Scottish folk songs for an anthology called *The Scots Musical Museum*. Burns soon became the real editor for several volumes of this work, devoting all of his free time to collecting, editing, restoring, and imitating traditional songs, and to writing verses of his own to traditional dance tunes. Almost all of his creative work during the last twelve years of his life went into the writing of songs for the *Musical Museum* and for George Thomson's *Select Collection of Original Scottish Airs*. This was for Burns a devoted labor of love and patriotism, done anonymously, for which he refused to accept any pay, although badly in need of money; and he continued the work when he was literally on his deathbed.

Because of its use of Scots dialect, the language spoken by most eighteenth-century Scottish people (lower and upper class alike), and because, in addition, of its lyricism and engagement with folk culture, Burns's verse is often said to anticipate William Wordsworth's idea of a poetry founded on "a selection of language really used by men." This account is based primarily on his songs. By far the major portion of the poems that he published under his own name are concerned with men and manners and are written in the literary forms that had been favored by earlier eighteenth-century poets. They include brilliant satire in a variety of modes, a number of fine verse epistles to friends and fellow poets, and one masterpiece of mock-heroic (or at any rate seriocomic) narrative, "Tam o' Shanter." It can be argued that, next to Pope, Burns is the greatest eighteenth-century master of these literary types. (Byron would later claim those forms for his own generation.) Yet Burns's writings in satire, epistle, and mock-heroic are remote from Pope's in their heartiness and verve, no less than in their dialect and intricate stanza forms. The reason for the difference is that Burns turned for his models not to Horace and the English neoclassic tradition but to the native tradition that had been established in the golden age of Scottish poetry by Robert Henryson, William Dunbar, Gavin Douglas, and other Scottish Chaucerians of the fifteenth and sixteenth centuries. He knew this literature through his eighteenth-century Scottish predecessors, especially Allan Ramsay and Robert Fergusson, who had collected some of the old poems and written new ones based on the old models. Burns improved greatly on these predecessors, but he derived from them much that is characteristic in his literary forms, subjects, diction, and stanzas.

Burns's songs, which number more than three hundred, have, however, in themselves been enough to sustain his poetic reputation. They made him, for a start, a central figure for his contemporaries' discussions of how music, valued by them for awakening sympathies that reason could not rouse, might serve as the foundation of a national identity. (William Wordsworth would explore this new notion of "national music"—of ethnically marked melody—in his 1805 poem "The Solitary Reaper.") But beyond being the bard of Scots nationalism, Burns is a songwriter for all English-speaking people. Evidence of that standing is supplied each New Year's Eve, when, moved once again to acknowledge their common bondage to time, men and women join hands and sing "Auld Lang Syne," to an old tune that Burns refitted with his new words.

The texts printed here are based on *The Poems and Songs of Robert Burns*, ed. James Kinsley, 3 vols. (Oxford, 1968).

Green grow the rashes[1]

Chorus

Green grow the rashes,° O;   rushes
Green grow the rashes, O;
The sweetest hours that e'er I spend,
Are spent among the lasses, O.

I

5   There's nought but care on ev'ry han',
    In ev'ry hour that passes, O:
    What signifies the life o' man,
    An' 'twere na for the lasses, O.
        Chorus

2

    The warly° race may riches chase,   worldly
10   An' riches still may fly them, O;
    An' tho' at last they catch them fast,
    Their hearts can ne'er enjoy them, O.
        Chorus

3

    But gie me a canny° hour at e'en,   quiet
    My arms about my Dearie, O;
15 An' warly cares, an' warly men,
    May a' gae tapsalteerie,° O!   topsy-turvy
        Chorus

4

    For you sae douse,° ye sneer at this,   sober
    Ye're nought but senseless asses, O:
    The wisest Man[2] the warl' saw,
20   He dearly lov'd the lasses, O.
        Chorus

1. Burns's revision of a song long current in a number of versions, most of them bawdy. A recording of this song may be found at Norton Literature Online.
2. King Solomon.

5
Auld Nature swears, the lovely Dears
Her noblest work She classes, O:
Her prentice° han' she try'd on man,   *apprentice*
An' then She made the lasses, O.
Chorus

1784   1787

Holy Willie's Prayer[1]

And send the Godly in a pet to pray—
POPE

Argument

Holy Willie was a rather oldish batchelor Elder in the parish of Mauchline,
and much and justly famed for that polemical chattering which ends in tippling
Orthodoxy, and for that Spiritualized Bawdry which refines to Liquorish Devotion.—In a Sessional process with a gentleman in Mauchline, a Mr. Gavin
Hamilton, Holy Willie, and his priest, Father Auld, after full hearing in the
Presbytry of Ayr, came off but second best; owing partly to the oratorical
powers of Mr. Robt. Aiken, Mr. Hamilton's Counsel; but chiefly to Mr. Hamilton's being one of the most irreproachable and truly respectable characters
in the country.—On losing his Process, the Muse overheard him at his devotions as follows—

O thou that in the heavens does dwell!
Wha, as it pleases best thysel,
Sends ane to heaven and ten to h-ll,
          A' for thy glory!
5   And no for ony gude or ill
          They've done before thee.[2]

I bless and praise thy matchless might,
When thousands thou has left in night,
That I am here before thy sight,
10   For gifts and grace,
A burning and a shining light
          To a' this place.

1. This satire, in the form of a dramatic
monologue, was inspired by William Fisher, a self-
righteous elder in the same Ayrshire parish that in
1785 had forced Burns and Betty Paton to do public penance in church for "fornication," and is
directed against a basic Calvinist tenet of the old
Scottish kirk. Holy Willie assumes that he is one
of a small minority, God's "elect"—in other words
that he has been predestined for grace, no matter
what deeds he does in this world. The sessional
processes were court proceedings carried on under
the auspices of the Kirk. The epigraph is from *The
Rape of the Lock.*
2. Here as elsewhere Burns use the virtuosic

stanza form known as the "standard Habbie"
(named for "The Life and Death of Habbie Simpson" a ballad in this form by Robert Sempill, a
17th-century poet, who, also hailing from the west
of Scotland, was a countryman of Burns's). In each
sestet three lines of iambic tetrameter that rhyme
aaa are followed by a dimeter rhyming *b*, another
line of tetrameter rhyming *a*, and a final dimeter
rhyming *b*. Associated at its origins with the troubadour poetry of Europe, the form came to Scotland during the Renaissance and had been revived
in the 18th century by Ramsay and Fergusson as
a distinctively national Scots measure.

What was I, or my generation,
That I should get such exaltation?
15 I, wha deserv'd most just damnation,
   For broken laws
Sax° thousand years ere my creation,   *six*
   Thro' Adam's cause!

When from my mother's womb I fell,
20 Thou might hae plunged me deep in hell,
To gnash my gooms, and weep, and wail,[3]
   In burning lakes,
Where damned devils roar and yell
   Chain'd to their stakes.

25 Yet I am here, a chosen sample,
To shew thy grace is great and ample:
I'm here, a pillar o' thy temple
   Strong as a rock,
A guide, a ruler and example
30   To a' thy flock.

O Lord thou kens what zeal I bear,
When drinkers drink, and swearers swear,
And singin' there, and dancin' here,
   Wi' great an' sma';
35 For I am keepet by thy fear,
   Free frae them a'.

But yet—O Lord—confess I must—
At times I'm fash'd° wi' fleshly lust;   *troubled*
And sometimes too, in warldly trust
40   Vile Self gets in;
But thou remembers we are dust,
   Defil'd wi' sin.

O Lord—yestreen°—thou kens°—wi' Meg—   *yesterday / knowest*
Thy pardon I sincerely beg!
45 O may't ne'er be a living plague,
   To my dishonor!
And I'll ne'er lift a lawless leg
   Again upon her.

Besides, I farther maun° avow,   *must*
50 Wi' Leezie's lass, three times—I trow°—   *believe*
But Lord, that Friday I was fou°   *drunk*
   When I cam near her;
Or else, thou kens, thy servant true
   Wad never steer° her.   *molest*

---

3. An echo of Matthew 8.12, "the children of the kingdom shall be cast out into outer darkness: there shall be weeping and gnashing of teeth."

55   Maybe thou lets this fleshly thorn
     Buffet thy servant e'en and morn,[4]
     Lest he o'er proud and high should turn,
         That he's sae gifted;
     If sae, thy hand maun e'en be borne
60   Untill thou lift it.

     Lord bless thy Chosen in this place,
     For here thou has a chosen race:
     But God, confound their stubborn face,
         And blast their name,
65   Wha bring thy rulers to disgrace
         And open shame.

     Lord mind Gaun Hamilton's[5] deserts!
     He drinks, and swears, and plays at cartes,°   *cards*
     Yet has sae mony taking arts
70   Wi' Great and Sma',
     Frae God's ain priest the people's hearts
         He steals awa.

     And when we chasten'd him therefore,
     Thou kens how he bred sic a splore,°   *disturbance*
75   And set the warld in a roar
         O' laughin at us:
     Curse thou his basket and his store,
         Kail° and potatoes.   *broth*

     Lord hear my earnest cry and prayer
80   Against that Presbytry of Ayr!
     Thy strong right hand, Lord, make it bare
         Upon their heads!
     Lord visit them, and dinna spare,
         For their misdeeds!

85   O Lord my God, that glib-tongu'd Aiken!
     My very heart and flesh are quaking
     To think how I sat, sweating, shaking,
         And piss'd wi' dread,
     While Auld wi' hingin° lip gaed sneaking   *hanging*
90   And hid his head!

     Lord, in thy day o'vengeance try him!
     Lord visit him that did employ him!
     And pass not in thy mercy by them,
         Nor hear their prayer;
95   But for thy people's sake destroy them,
         And dinna spare!

---

4. An echo of 2 Corinthians 12.7, "there was given to me a thorn in the flesh, the messenger of Satan to buffet me, lest I should be exalted above measure."

5. Burns's friend Gavin Hamilton, whom Holy Willie had brought up on moral charges before the Kirk Session of the Presbytery of Ayr. As Burns explains in the Argument, Hamilton was successfully defended by his counsel, Robert Aiken (referred to in line 85).

But Lord, remember me and mine
Wi' mercies temporal and divine!
That I for grace and gear° may shine,   *wealth*
100   Excell'd by nane!
And a' the glory shall be thine!
Amen! Amen!

1789   1789

To a Mouse

*On Turning Her up in Her Nest with the Plough,
November, 1785*[1]

Wee, sleeket,° cowran, tim'rous beastie,   *sleek*
O, what a panic's in thy breastie!
Thou need na start awa sae hasty,
          Wi' bickering brattle![2]
5   I wad be laith° to rin an' chase thee   *loath*
          Wi' murd'ring pattle!°   *plowstaff*

I'm truly sorry Man's dominion
Has broken Nature's social union,
An' justifies that ill opinion,
10   Which makes thee startle,
At me, thy poor, earth-born companion,
          An' fellow mortal!

I doubt na, whyles,° but thou may thieve;   *sometimes*
What then? poor beastie, thou maun° live!   *must*
15   A daimen-icker in a thrave[3]
          'S a sma' request:
I'll get a blessin wi' the lave,°   *remainder*
          An' never miss 't!

Thy wee-bit housie, too, in ruin!
20   It's silly wa's° the win's are strewin!   *frail walls*
An' naething, now, to big° a new ane,   *build*
          O' foggage° green!   *coarse grass*
An' bleak December's winds ensuin,
          Baith snell° an' keen!   *bitter*

25   Thou saw the fields laid bare an' waste,
An' weary Winter comin fast,
An' cozie here, beneath the blast,
          Thou thought to dwell,
Till crash! the cruel coulter° past   *cutter blade*
30   Out thro' thy cell.

---

1. Burns's brother claimed that this poem was
composed while the poet was actually holding the
plow.

2. With headlong scamper.
3. An occasional ear in twenty-four sheaves.

That wee-bit heap o' leaves an' stibble°   *stubble*
Has cost thee monie a weary nibble!
Now thou 's turn'd out, for a' thy trouble,
    But° house or hald,[4]   *without*
35 To thole° the Winter's sleety dribble,   *endure*
    An' cranreuch° cauld!   *hoarfrost*

But Mousie, thou art no thy-lane,°   *not alone*
In proving foresight may be vain:
The best laid schemes o' Mice an' Men
40   Gang aft agley,[5]
An' lea'e us nought but grief an' pain,
    For promis'd joy!

Still, thou art blest, compar'd wi' me!
The present only toucheth thee:
45 But Och! I backward cast my e'e,
    On prospects drear!
An' forward tho' I canna see,
    I guess an' fear!

1785   1786

To a Louse

On Seeing One on a Lady's Bonnet at Church

Ha! whare ye gaun, ye crowlan° ferlie!°   *crawling / wonder*
Your impudence protects you sairly:°   *sorely*
I canna say but ye strunt° rarely,   *strut*
    Owre gawze and lace;
5 Tho' faith, I fear ye dine but sparely,
    On sic a place.

Ye ugly, creepan, blastet wonner,°   *wonder*
Detested, shunn'd, by saunt an' sinner,
How daur ye set your fit° upon her,   *foot*
10   Sae fine a Lady!
Gae somewhere else and seek your dinner,
    On some poor body.

Swith,° in some beggar's haffet° squattle;°   *swift / locks / sprawl*
There ye may creep, and sprawl, and sprattle,°   *struggle*
15 Wi' ither kindred, jumping cattle,
    In shoals and nations;
Whare horn nor bane[1] ne'er daur unsettle,
    Your thick plantations.

Now haud you there, ye're out o' sight,
20 Below the fatt'rels,° snug and tight,   *ribbon ends*

4. Hold, holding (i.e., land).
5. Go oft awry.

1. I.e., fine-tooth comb made of horn or bone ("bane").

Na faith ye yet!² ye'll no be right,
  Till ye've got on it,
The vera tapmost, towrin height
  O' Miss's bonnet.

25 My sooth! right bauld ye set your nose out,
As plump an' gray as onie grozet:°   *gooseberry*
O for some rank, mercurial rozet,°   *rosin*
  Or fell,° red smeddum,°   *sharp / powder*
I'd gie you sic a hearty dose o't,
30   Wad dress your droddum!°   *buttocks*

I wad na been surpriz'd to spy
You on an auld wife's flainen toy,°   *flannel cap*
Or aiblins° some bit duddie° boy,   *perhaps / ragged*
  On 's wylecoat;°   *undershirt*
35 But Miss's fine Lunardi,³ fye!
  How daur ye do 't?

O Jenny dinna toss your head,
An' set your beauties a' abread!°   *abroad*
Ye little ken what cursed speed
40   The blastie's° makin!   *creature's*
Thae° winks and finger-ends, I dread,   *those*
  Are notice takin!

O wad some Pow'r the giftie gie us
To see oursels as others see us!
45 It wad frae monie a blunder free us
  An' foolish notion:
What airs in dress an' gait wad lea'e us,
  And ev'n Devotion!⁴

1785   1786

Auld Lang Syne¹

Should auld acquaintance be forgot
  And never brought to mind?
Should auld acquaintance be forgot,
  And auld lang syne!

Chorus

5 For auld lang syne, my jo,
  For auld lang syne,
We'll tak a cup o' kindness yet
  For auld lang syne.

2. Confound you!
3. A balloon-shaped bonnet, named after Vincenzo Lunardi, who made a number of balloon flights in the mid-1780s.
4. I.e., even pretended piety.
1. Long ago.

And surely ye'll be° your pint stowp!°   *pay for / pint cup*
10   And surely I'll be mine!
And we'll tak a cup o' kindness yet,
    For auld lang syne.
        Chorus

We twa hae run about the braes°   *slopes*
   And pou'd° the gowans° fine;   *pulled / daisies*
15   But we've wander'd many a weary fitt,
   Sin° auld lang syne.   *since*
        Chorus

We twa hae paidl'd in the burn°   *stream*
   Frae morning sun till dine;°   *dinner, noon*
But seas between us braid° hae roar'd,   *broad*
20   Sin auld lang syne.
        Chorus

And there's a hand, my trusty fiere!°   *friend*
   And gie's a hand o' thine!
And we'll tak a right gude-willie-waught,°   *cordial drink*
   For auld lang syne.
        Chorus

1788   1796

Afton Water[1]

Flow gently, sweet Afton, among thy green braes,°   *slopes*
Flow gently, I'll sing thee a song in thy praise;
My Mary's asleep by thy murmuring stream,
Flow gently, sweet Afton, disturb not her dream.

5   Thou stock dove whose echo resounds thro' the glen,
Ye wild whistling blackbirds in yon thorny den,
Thou green crested lapwing thy screaming forbear,
I charge you disturb not my slumbering Fair.

How lofty, sweet Afton, thy neighbouring hills,
10   Far mark'd with the courses of clear winding rills;
There daily I wander as noon rises high,
My flocks and my Mary's sweet Cot° in my eye.   *cottage*

How pleasant thy banks and green vallies below,
Where wild in the woodlands the primroses blow;
15   There oft as mild ev'ning weeps over the lea,
The sweet scented birk° shades my Mary and me.   *birch*

Thy chrystal stream, Afton, how lovely it glides,
And winds by the cot where my Mary resides;

1. The Afton is a small river in Ayrshire.

How wanton thy waters her snowy feet lave,
20　As gathering sweet flowerets she stems thy clear wave.

Flow gently, sweet Afton, among thy green braes,
Flow gently, sweet River, the theme of my lays;
My Mary's asleep by thy murmuring stream,
Flow gently, sweet Afton, disturb not her dream.

1789   1792

Tam o' Shanter: A Tale[1]

Of Brownyis and of Bogillis full is this buke.
GAWIN DOUGLAS.

When chapman billies[2] leave the street,
And drouthy° neebors neebors meet,　　　　　　　　　*thirsty*
As market-days are wearing late,
An' folk begin to tak the gate;°　　　　　　　　　　　*road*
5　While we sit bousing at the nappy,°　　　　　　　　*strong ale*
And getting fou° and unco° happy,　　　　　　*drunk / very*
We think na on the lang Scots miles,
The mosses, waters, slaps,° and styles,　　　*gaps (in walls)*
That lie between us and our hame,
10　Whare sits our sulky sullen dame,
Gathering her brows like gathering storm,
Nursing her wrath to keep it warm.

This truth fand° honest Tam o' Shanter,　　　　　　　*found*
As he frae Ayr ae night did canter,
15　(Auld Ayr, wham ne'er a town surpasses,
For honest men and bonny lasses).

O Tam! hadst thou but been sae wise,
As ta'en thy ain wife Kate's advice!
She tauld thee weel thou was a skellum,°　　*good-for-nothing*
20　A blethering,° blustering, drunken blellum;°　*chattering / babbler*
That frae November till October,
Ae market-day thou was nae sober;
That ilka° melder,[3] wi' the miller,　　　　　　　　　　*every*

Thou sat as lang as thou had siller;° *silver, money*
25 That every naig° was ca'd° a shoe on, *nag / driven*
The smith and thee gat roaring fou on;
That at the Lord's house, even on Sunday,
Thou drank wi' Kirkton Jean till Monday.
She prophesied that late or soon,
30 Thou would be found deep drown'd in Doon;
Or catch'd wi' warlocks in the mirk,° *night*
By Alloway's auld haunted kirk.

Ah, gentle dames! it gars° me greet° *makes / weep*
To think how mony counsels sweet,
35 How mony lengthen'd sage advices,
The husband frae the wife despises!

But to our tale: Ae market-night,
Tam had got planted unco right;
Fast by an ingle,° bleezing° finely, *fireplace / blazing*
40 Wi' reaming swats,° that drank divinely; *foaming new ale*
And at his elbow, Souter° Johnny, *shoemaker*
His ancient, trusty, drouthy crony;
Tam lo'ed him like a vera brither;
They had been fou for weeks thegither.
45 The night drave on wi' sangs and clatter;
And ay the ale was growing better:
The landlady and Tam grew gracious,
Wi' favours secret, sweet, and precious:
The Souter tauld his queerest stories;
50 The landlord's laugh was ready chorus:
The storm without might rair° and rustle, *roar*
Tam did na mind the storm a whistle.

Care, mad to see a man sae happy,
E'en drown'd himsel amang the nappy:
55 As bees flee hame wi' lades o' treasure,
The minutes wing'd their way wi' pleasure:
Kings may be blest, but Tam was glorious,
O'er a' the ills o' life victorious!

But pleasures are like poppies spread,
60 You seize the flower, its bloom is shed;
Or like the snow falls in the river,
A moment white—then melts for ever;
Or like the borealis race,
That flit ere you can point their place;
65 Or like the rainbow's lovely form
Evanishing amid the storm.—
Nae man can tether time or tide;
The hour approaches Tam maun° ride; *must*
That hour, o' night's black arch the key-stane,
70 That dreary hour, he mounts his beast in;
And sic a night he taks the road in,
As ne'er poor sinner was abroad in.

The wind blew as 'twad blawn its last;
The rattling showers rose on the blast;
75 The speedy gleams the darkness swallow'd;
Loud, deep, and lang, the thunder bellow'd:
That night, a child might understand,
The Deil had business on his hand.

Weel mounted on his gray mare, Meg,
80 A better never lifted leg,[4]
Tam skelpit° on thro' dub° and mire,   *slapped / puddle*
Despising wind, and rain, and fire;
Whiles holding fast his gude blue bonnet;
Whiles crooning o'er some auld Scots sonnet;
85 Whiles glowring° round wi' prudent cares,   *staring*
Lest bogles° catch him unawares.   *hobgoblins*
Kirk-Alloway was drawing nigh,
Whare ghaists° and houlets° nightly cry.—   *ghosts / owls*

By this time he was cross the ford,
90 Whare in the snaw, the chapman smoor'd;[5]
And past the birks° and meikle stane,°   *birches / big stone*
Whare drunken Charlie brak's neck-bane;
And thro' the whins, and by the cairn,[6]
Whare hunters fand the murder'd bairn;
95 And near the thorn, aboon the well,
Where Mungo's mither hang'd hersel.—
Before him Doon pours all his floods;
The doubling storm roars thro' the woods;
The lightnings flash from pole to pole;
100 Near and more near the thunders roll:
When, glimmering thro' the groaning trees,
Kirk-Alloway seemed in a bleeze;°   *blaze*
Thro' ilka bore° the beams were glancing;   *hole*
And loud resounded mirth and dancing.—

105 Inspiring bold John Barleycorn!
What dangers thou canst make us scorn!
Wi' tippeny,[7] we fear nae evil;
Wi' usquabae,° we'll face the devil!—   *whisky*
The swats sae ream'd in Tammie's noddle,
110 Fair play, he car'd na deils a boddle.[8]
But Maggie stood right sair astonish'd,
Till, by the heel and hand admonish'd,
She ventured forward on the light;
And, vow! Tam saw an unco° sight!   *strange*
115 Warlocks and witches in a dance;
Nae cotillion brent° new frae France,   *brand*

4. Compare this "lifted leg" to Willie's use of the term about himself in line 47 of "Holy Willie's Prayer." Tam's horse, Meg (also called Maggie), occasions the poem's bawdiest wordplay.
5. The peddler smothered.
6. Stones heaped up as a memorial. "Whins": furze (an evergreen shrub).
7. Twopenny (usually of weak beer).
8. I.e., he didn't care a farthing about devils (a "boddle" is a very small copper coin).

But hornpipes, jigs, strathspeys,[9] and reels,
Put life and mettle in their heels.
A winnock-bunker° in the east,   *window seat*
120   There sat auld Nick, in shape o' beast;
A touzie tyke,° black, grim, and large,   *shaggy dog*
To gie them music was his charge:
He screw'd the pipes and gart° them skirl,°   *made / screech*
Till roof and rafters a' did dirl.°—   *rattle*
125   Coffins stood round, like open presses,
That shaw'd the dead in their last dresses;
And by some devilish cantraip° slight   *charm, trick*
Each in its cauld hand held a light.—
By which heroic Tam was able
130   To note upon the haly° table,   *holy*
A murderer's banes in gibbet airns;°   *irons*
Twa span-lang,[1] wee, unchristened bairns;
A thief, new-cutted frae a rape,°   *rope*
Wi' his last gasp his gab° did gape;   *mouth*
135   Five tomahawks, wi' blude red-rusted;
Five scymitars, wi' murder crusted;
A garter, which a babe had strangled;
A knife, a father's throat had mangled,
Whom his ain son o' life bereft,
140   The grey hairs yet stack° to the heft;   *stuck*
Wi' mair o' horrible and awefu',
Which even to name wad be unlawfu'.

As Tammie glowr'd, amaz'd, and curious,
The mirth and fun grew fast and furious:
145   The piper loud and louder blew;
The dancers quick and quicker flew;
They reel'd, they set, they cross'd, they cleekit,°   *joined hands*
Till ilka carlin° swat and reekit,   *old woman*
And coost her duddies to the wark,[2]
150   And linket° at it in her sark![3]   *tripped lightly*

Now, Tam, O Tam! had thae been queans,°   *girls*
A' plump and strapping in their teens,
Their sarks, instead o' creeshie flannen,°   *greasy flannel*
Been snaw-white seventeen hunder linnen![4]
155   Thir° breeks o' mine, my only pair,   *these*
That ance were plush, o' gude blue hair,
I wad hae gi'en them off my hurdies,°   *buttocks*
For ae blink o' the bonie burdies!°   *bonny (pretty) girls*

But wither'd beldams,° auld and droll,   *hags*
160   Rigwoodie° hags wad spean° a foal,   *bony / wean*
Lowping° and flinging on a crummock,°   *leaping / staff*
I wonder didna turn thy stomach.

9. Slow Highland dance.
1. Two spans long (a span is the distance from outstretched thumb to little finger).
2. Cast off her clothes for the work.

3. Shirt (underclothes).
4. Very fine linen, woven on a loom with seventeen hundred strips.

But Tam kend what was what fu' brawlie,°   *finely*
There was ae winsome wench and wawlie°   *strapping*
165 That night enlisted in the core,°   *corps*
(Lang after kend on Carrick shore;
For mony a beast to dead she shot,
And perish'd mony a bony boat,
And shook baith meikle corn and bear,°   *barley*
170 And kept the country-side in fear:)
Her cutty° sark, o' Paisley harn,°   *short / yarn*
That while a lassie she had worn,
In longitude tho' sorely scanty,
It was her best, and she was vauntie.°—   *proud*
175 Ah! little kend thy reverend grannie,
That sark she coft° for her wee Nannie,   *bought*
Wi' twa pund Scots ('twas a' her riches),
Wad ever grac'd a dance of witches!

But here my Muse her wing maun cour;°   *lower*
180 Sic flights are far beyond her pow'r;
To sing how Nannie lap and flang,
(A souple jade° she was, and strang),   *disreputable woman*
And how Tam stood, like ane bewitch'd,
And thought his very een° enrich'd;   *eyes*
185 Even Satan glowr'd, and fidg'd fu' fain,[5]
And hotch'd° and blew wi' might and main: *jerked*
Till first ae caper, syne° anither,   *then*
Tam tint° his reason a' thegither,   *lost*
And roars out, 'Weel done, Cutty-sark!'
190 And in an instant all was dark:
And scarcely had he Maggie rallied,
When out the hellish legion sallied.

As bees bizz out wi' angry fyke,°   *fuss*
When plundering herds° assail their byke;°   *herdsmen / hive*
195 As open° pussie's mortal foes,   *begin to bark*
When, pop! she starts before their nose;
As eager runs the market-crowd,
When 'Catch the thief!' resounds aloud;
So Maggie runs the witches follow,
200 Wi' mony an eldritch° skreech and hollow.   *unearthly*

Ah, Tam! Ah, Tam! thou'll get thy fairin'!°   *deserts*
In hell they'll roast thee like a herrin!
In vain thy Kate awaits thy comin!
Kate soon will be a woefu' woman!
205 Now, do thy speedy utmost, Meg,
And win the key-stane of the brig;[6]
There at them thou thy tail may toss,
A running stream they dare na cross.

5. Fidgeted with pleasure.
6. It is a well known fact that witches, or any evil spirits, have no power to follow a poor wight any farther than the middle of the next running stream.—It may be proper likewise to mention to the benighted traveler, that when he falls in with *bogles*, whatever danger may be in his going forward, there is much more hazard in turning back [Burns's note]. "Brig": bridge.

But ere the key-stane she could make,
210 The fient a tail she had to shake!
For Nannie, far before the rest,
Hard upon noble Maggie prest,
And flew at Tam wi' furious ettle;°   *intent*
But little wist she Maggie's mettle—
215 Ae spring brought off her master hale,°   *whole*
But left behind her ain gray tail:
The carlin claught° her by the rump,   *clutched*
And left poor Maggie scarce a stump.[7]

Now, wha this tale o' truth shall read,
220 Ilk man and mother's son, take heed:
Whene'er to drink you are inclin'd,
Or cutty-sarks run in your mind,
Think, ye may buy the joys o'er dear,
Remember Tam o' Shanter's mare.

1790   1791

Such a parcel of rogues in a nation

Fareweel to a' our Scotish fame,
    Fareweel our ancient glory;
Fareweel even to the Scotish name,
    Sae fam'd in martial story!
5 Now Sark rins° o'er the Solway sands,   *runs*
    And Tweed rins to the ocean,
To mark whare England's province stands,
    Such a parcel of rogues in a nation!

What force or guile could not subdue,
10   Thro' many warlike ages,
Is wrought now by a coward few,
    For hireling traitors' wages.
The English steel we could disdain,
    Secure in valor's station;
15 But English gold has been our bane,
    Such a parcel of rogues in a nation!

O would, or I had seen the day
    That treason thus could sell us,
My auld grey head had lien in clay,
20   Wi' BRUCE and loyal WALLACE![1]
But pith and power,° till my last hour,   *with all my strength*
    I'll mak this declaration;
We're bought and sold for English gold,
    Such a parcel of rogues in a nation!

1792

7. I.e., she had no tail left at all.
1. For Bruce and Wallace, see the notes to the next poem.

Robert Bruce's March to Bannockburn[1]

[SCOTS, WHA HAE]

Scots, wha hae wi' Wallace[2] bled,
Scots, wham Bruce has aften led,
Welcome to your gory bed,—
   Or to victorie.—

5 Now's the day, and now's the hour;
See the front o' battle lour;
See approach proud Edward's power,
   Chains and Slaverie.—

Wha will be a traitor-knave?
10 Wha can fill a coward's grave?
Wha sae base as be a Slave?
   —Let him turn and flie:—

Wha for Scotland's king and law,
Freedom's sword will strongly draw,
15 Free-man stand, or Free-man fa',
   Let him follow me.—

By Oppression's woes and pains!
By your Sons in servile chains!
We will drain our dearest veins,
20   But they *shall* be free!

Lay the proud Usurpers low!
Tyrants fall in every foe!
Liberty's in every blow!
   Let us Do—or Die!!!

1793   1794, 1815

A Red, Red Rose[1]

O my Luve's like a red, red rose,
   That's newly sprung in June;
O my Luve's like the melodie
   That's sweetly played in tune.

5 As fair art thou, my bonie lass,
   So deep in luve am I;

1. Burns's words are set to the old tune to which, it was said, Robert Bruce's Scottish army had marched when it went to battle against the English invaders in 1314. This marching song is at once a historical reconstruction and an anthem for the Revolutionary 1790s. Burns's turn to songwriting in these last few years of his life might, the critic Marilyn Butler has suggested, have had to do with the fact that songs like these, transmitted aurally, were more likely than compositions in other modes to slip past the scrutiny of a censorious government.
2. Sir William Wallace (ca. 1272–1305), the great Scottish warrior in the wars against the English.
1. Like many of Burns's lyrics, this one incorporates elements from several current folk songs.

And I will love thee still, my Dear,
Till a' the seas gang dry.

Till a' the seas gang dry, my Dear,
10   And the rocks melt wi' the sun:
O I will love thee still, my Dear,
While the sands o' life shall run.

And fare thee weel, my only Luve!
And fare thee weel, a while!
15   And I will come again, my Luve,
Tho' it were ten thousand mile!

1794   1796

Song: For a' that and a' that[1]

Is there, for honest Poverty
    That hangs his head, and a' that;
The coward-slave, we pass him by,
    We dare be poor for a' that!
5   For a' that, and a' that,
    Our toils obscure, and a' that,
The rank is but the guinea's stamp,°   *inscription on a coin*
The Man's the gowd° for a' that.   *gold*

What though on hamely fare we dine,
10   Wear hodden grey,[2] and a' that.
Gie fools their silks, and knaves their wine,
    A Man's a Man for a' that.
For a' that, and a' that,
    Their tinsel show, and a' that;
15   The honest man, though e'er sae poor,
    Is king o' men for a' that.

Ye see yon birkie° ca'd a lord,   *fellow*
    Wha struts, and stares, and a' that,
Though hundreds worship at his word,
20   He's but a coof° for a' that.   *dolt*
For a' that, and a' that,
    His ribband, star and a' that,
The man of independant mind,
    He looks and laughs at a' that.

25   A prince can mak a belted knight,
    A marquis, duke, and a' that;
But an honest man's aboon° his might,   *above*
    Guid faith he mauna fa' that![3]

1. This song was set to a dance tune, known as   2. A coarse cloth of undyed wool.
Lady Macintosh's Reel, that Burns had drawn on   3. Must not claim that.
for previous songs.

For a' that, and a' that,
30   Their dignities, and a' that,
The pith o' Sense, and pride o' Worth,
Are higher rank than a' that.

Then let us pray that come it may,
As come it will for a' that,
35 That Sense and Worth, o'er a' the earth
Shall bear the gree,° and a' that.   *win the prize*
For a' that, and a' that,
It's coming yet for a' that,
That Man to Man the warld o'er,
40   Shall brothers be for a' that.

1795   1795

The Revolution Controversy and the "Spirit of the Age"

In a letter to Byron in 1816, Percy Shelley called the French Revolution "the master theme of the epoch in which we live"; and in various letters and essays, he declared that, as the result of the repercussions of the Revolution, the literature of England "has arisen as it were from a new birth," and that "the electric life that burns" within the great poets of the time expresses "less their spirit than the spirit of the age." (See, for example, the concluding paragraph of Shelley's "Defence of Poetry," page 849.) With these judgments many of Shelley's contemporaries concurred. Writers during Shelley's lifetime were obsessed with the possibility of a drastic and inclusive change in the human condition; and the works of the period cannot be understood historically without awareness of the extent to which their distinctive themes, plot forms, imagery, and modes of imagining and feeling were shaped first by the boundless promise, then by the tragedy, of the great events in neighboring France. And for a number of young poets in the early years (1789–93), the enthusiasm for the Revolution had the impetus and intensity of a religious awakening, because they interpreted the events in France in accordance with the apocalyptic prophecies in the Hebrew and Christian Scriptures; that is, they viewed these events as fulfilling the promise, guaranteed by an infallible text, that a short period of retributive and cleansing violence would usher in an era of universal peace and felicity equivalent to a restored Paradise. (See "The French Revolution: Apocalyptic Expectations" at Norton Literature Online.) Even after what they considered the failure of the revolutionary promise—signaled by the execution of the king and queen, the massacres during the Reign of Terror under Robespierre, and later the wars of imperial conquest under Napoleon—these poets did not surrender their hope for a radical transformation of the political and social world. Instead, they transferred the basis of that hope from violent political revolution to an inner revolution in the moral and imaginative nature of the human race.

The Revolution began with the storming of the Bastille and freeing of a handful of political prisoners by an angry mob of Parisians on July 14, 1789. A month later, the new French National Assembly passed the Declaration of the Rights of Man. Six weeks after that (in early October), citizens marched to the royal palace at Versailles, southwest of the city, and arrested King Louis XVI and his queen, Marie Antoinette, confining them to the Tuileries palace in Paris. These happenings were quickly reported in the London newspapers. The British liberals applauded; the radicals were ecstatic; many ordinary people were confused by the events, which seemed to promise improvement of the common lot but at the cost of toppling long-standing traditions of royalty and aristocracy.

One reaction on the English side of the Channel was the so-called war of pamphlets, initiated by Richard Price's sermon *A Discourse on the Love of Our Country,* which he delivered on November 4, 1789, a month after the imprisonment of the French king and queen. The controversy accelerated in the wake of Edmund Burke's response to Price a year later, *Reflections on the Revolution in France,* which itself drew more than fifty further responses, among which the two most famous are Mary Wollstonecraft's *A Vindication of the Rights of Men* and Thomas Paine's *Rights of Man.* The works of Burke and Wollstonecraft and part 1 of Paine's *Rights* appeared in a very short span, from November 1790 to March 1791.

All four writers in this section are concerned with the same questions: justification of hereditary rule, ownership of property, interpretation of the English constitution, and the "rights of men"—and women—in things such as (in Price's words) "liberty of conscience in religious matters," the "right to resist power when abused," the "right to chuse our own governors; to cashier them for misconduct; and to frame a government for ourselves." But the extracts have been chosen mainly to illustrate the *tones* of the debate: celebratory in Price, congratulating himself and his audience on having lived to see "Thirty Millions of people, indignant and resolute, spurning at slavery, and demanding liberty with an irresistible voice"; blatantly sensationalist in Burke, depicting the rude treatment of the king and especially the queen, in her nightgown ("almost naked"), "forced to abandon the sanctuary of the most splendid palace in the world, which they left swimming in blood, polluted by massacre, and strewed with scattered limbs and mutilated carcases"; forthrightly contemptuous in Wollstonecraft, who describes Burke's work as "many ingenious arguments in a very specious garb"; basically pointed and plain in Paine: "I am contending for the rights of the *living*, and against their being willed away, and controuled and contracted for, by the . . . assumed authority of the dead."

RICHARD PRICE

Richard Price (1723–1791) was a Unitarian minister in London and a writer on moral philosophy, population, and the national debt, among other topics. The full title of his sermon, which prompted Burke's *Reflections* and in turn the scores of responses to Burke, is *A Discourse on the Love of Our Country, Delivered on Nov. 4, 1789, at the Meeting-House in the Old Jewry, to the Society for Commemorating the Revolution in Great Britain.* The London Revolution Society had been founded a year earlier to mark the hundredth anniversary of the "bloodless" Glorious Revolution of 1688, which ended the short reign of King James II and produced the Declaration of Right, establishing a limited monarchy and guaranteeing the civil rights of privileged classes. The first two-thirds of the extracts given here commemorate that Revolution; in the final third, beginning "What an eventful period is this!" Price greets with religious fervor "two other Revolutions, both glorious," the American and the French. The *Discourse* went through six editions in its first year of publication.

From A Discourse on the Love of Our Country

We are met to thank God for that event in this country to which the name of THE REVOLUTION has been given; and which, for more than a century, it has been usual for the friends of freedom, and more especially Protestant Dissenters, under the title of the REVOLUTION SOCIETY, to celebrate with expressions of joy and exultation. * * * By a bloodless victory, the fetters which despotism had been long preparing for us were broken; the rights of the people were asserted, a tyrant expelled, and a Sovereign of our own choice appointed in his room. Security was given to our property, and our consciences were emancipated. The bounds of free enquiry were enlarged; the volume in which are the words of eternal life, was laid more open to our examination; and that *aera* of light and liberty was introduced among us, by which we have been made an example to other kingdoms, and became the instructors of the world.

Had it not been for this deliverance, the probability is, that, instead of being thus distinguished, we should now have been a base people, groaning under the infamy and misery of popery and slavery. Let us, therefore, offer thanksgivings to God, the author of all our blessings. * * *

It is well known that King James was not far from gaining his purpose; and that probably he would have succeeded, had he been less in a hurry. But he was a fool as well as a bigot. He wanted courage as well as prudence; and, therefore, fled, and left us to settle quietly for ourselves that constitution of government which is now our boast. We have particular reason, as Protestant Dissenters, to rejoice on this occasion. It was at this time we were rescued from persecution, and obtained the liberty of worshipping God in the manner we think most acceptable to him. It was then our meeting houses were opened, our worship was taken under the protection of the law, and the principles of toleration gained a triumph. We have, therefore, on this occasion, peculiar reasons for thanksgiving.—But let us remember that we ought not to satisfy ourselves with thanksgivings. Our gratitude, if genuine, will be accompanied with endeavours to give stability to the deliverance our country has obtained, and to extend and improve the happiness with which the Revolution has blest us.—Let us, in particular, take care not to forget the principles of the Revolution. This Society has, very properly, in its Reports, held out these principles, as an instruction to the public. I will only take notice of the three following:

First: The right to liberty of conscience in religious matters.

Secondly: The right to resist power when abused. And,

Thirdly: The right to chuse our own governors; to cashier them for misconduct; and to frame a government for ourselves.

* * *

I would farther direct you to remember, that though the Revolution was a great work, it was by no means a perfect work; and that all was not then gained which was necessary to put the kingdom in the secure and complete possession of the blessings of liberty.—In particular, you should recollect, that the toleration then obtained was imperfect. It included only those who could declare their faith in the doctrinal articles of the church of England. It has, indeed, been since extended, but not sufficiently; for there still exist penal laws on account of religious opinions, which (were they carried into execution) would shut up many of our places of worship, and silence and imprison some of our ablest and best men.—The TEST LAWS are also still in force; and deprive of eligibility to civil and military offices, all who cannot conform to the established worship. It is with great pleasure I find that the body of Protestant Dissenters, though defeated in two late attempts to deliver their country from this disgrace to it, have determined to persevere. Should they at last succeed, they will have the satisfaction, not only of removing from themselves a proscription they do not deserve, but of contributing to lessen the number of public iniquities. For I cannot call by a gentler name, laws which convert an ordinance appointed by our Saviour to commemorate his death, into an instrument of oppressive policy, and a qualification of rakes and atheists for civil posts.—I have said, *should* they succeed—but perhaps I ought not to suggest a doubt about their success. And, indeed, when I consider that in Scotland the established church is defended by no such test—that in Ireland it has been abolished—that in a great neighbouring country it has been declared to be an indefeasible right of all citizens to be equally eligible to public offices—that

in the same kingdom a professed Dissenter from the established church holds
the first office in the state—that in the Emperor's dominions *Jews* have been
lately admitted to the enjoyment of equal privileges with other citizens—and
that in this very country, a Dissenter, though excluded from the power of
executing the laws, yet is allowed to be employed in *making* them.—When, I
say, I consider such facts as these, I am disposed to think it impossible that
the enemies of the repeal of the Test Laws should not soon become ashamed,
and give up their opposition.

But the most important instance of the imperfect state in which the Revolution left our constitution, is the *inequality of our representation*. I think,
indeed, this defect in our constitution so gross and so palpable, as to make it
excellent chiefly in form and theory. You should remember that a representation in the legislature of a kingdom is the *basis* of constitutional liberty in it,
and of all legitimate government; and that without it a government is nothing
but an usurpation. When the representation is fair and equal, and at the same
time vested with such powers as our House of Commons possesses, a kingdom
may be said to govern itself, and consequently to possess true liberty. When
the representation is partial, a kingdom possesses liberty only partially; and if
extremely partial, it only gives a *semblance* of liberty; but if not only extremely
partial, but corruptly chosen, and under corrupt influence after being chosen,
it becomes a *nuisance,* and produces the worst of all forms of government—a
government by corruption, a government carried on and supported by spreading venality and profligacy through a kingdom. May heaven preserve this kingdom from a calamity so dreadful! It is the point of depravity to which abuses
under such a government as ours naturally tend, and the last stage of national
unhappiness. We are, at present, I hope, at a great distance from it. But it
cannot be pretended that there are no advances towards it, or that there is no
reason for apprehension and alarm.

           ✢   ✢   ✢

What an eventful period is this! I am thankful that I have lived to it; and I
could almost say, *Lord, now lettest thou thy servant depart in peace, for mine
eyes have seen thy salvation* [Luke 2.29–30]. I have lived to see a diffusion of
knowledge, which has undermined superstition and error—I have lived to see
the rights of men better understood than ever; and nations panting for liberty,
which seemed to have lost the idea of it.—I have lived to see THIRTY MILLIONS
of people, indignant and resolute, spurning at slavery, and demanding liberty
with an irresistible voice; their king led in triumph, and an arbitrary monarch
surrendering himself to his subjects.—After sharing in the benefits of one
Revolution, I have been spared to be a witness to two other Revolutions, both
glorious.——And now, methinks, I see the ardour for liberty catching and
spreading; a general amendment beginning in human affairs; the dominion of
kings changed for the dominion of laws, and the dominion of priests giving
way to the dominion of reason and conscience.

Be encouraged, all ye friends of freedom, and writers in its defence! The
times are auspicious. Your labours have not been in vain. Behold kingdoms,
admonished by you, starting from sleep, breaking their fetters, and claiming
justice from their oppressors! Behold, the light you have struck out, after setting *America* free, reflected to *France,* and there kindled into a blaze that lays
despotism in ashes, and warms and illuminates *Europe!*

Tremble all ye oppressors of the world! Take warning all ye supporters of slavish governments, and slavish hierarchies! Call no more (absurdly and wickedly) REFORMATION, innovation. You cannot now hold the world in darkness. Struggle no longer against increasing light and liberality. Restore to mankind their rights; and consent to the correction of abuses, before they and you are destroyed together.

1789

EDMUND BURKE

The great statesman and political theorist Edmund Burke (1729–1797) read Price's *Discourse* in January 1790 and immediately began drafting his *Reflections on the Revolution in France* as a reply in the form of a letter (as the lengthy subtitle describes it) "Intended to Have Been Sent to a Gentleman in Paris" (a Frenchman who had written to Burke soliciting the British parliamentarian's opinion of events in his country). The work was published at the beginning of November and was an instant bestseller: thirteen thousand copies were purchased in the first five weeks, and by the following September it had gone through eleven editions. Clearly, part of its appeal to contemporary readers lay in the highly wrought accounts of the mob's violent treatment of the French king and queen (who at the time Burke was writing were imprisoned in Paris and would be executed three years later, in January and October 1793). *Reflections* has become the classic, most eloquent statement of British conservatism favoring monarchy, aristocracy, property, hereditary succession, and the wisdom of the ages. Earlier in his career Burke had championed many liberal causes and sided with the Americans in their war for independence; opponents and allies alike were surprised at the strength of his conviction that the French Revolution was a disaster and the revolutionists "a swinish multitude."

From Reflections on the Revolution in France

* * * All circumstances taken together, the French revolution is the most astonishing that has hitherto happened in the world. The most wonderful things are brought about in many instances by means the most absurd and ridiculous; in the most ridiculous modes; and apparently, by the most contemptible instruments. Every thing seems out of nature in this strange chaos of levity and ferocity, and of all sorts of crimes jumbled together with all sorts of follies. In viewing this monstrous tragi-comic scene, the most opposite passions necessarily succeed, and sometimes mix with each other in the mind; alternate contempt and indignation; alternate laughter and tears; alternate scorn and horror.

* * *

You will observe, that from Magna Charta to the Declaration of Right,[1] it has been the uniform policy of our constitution to claim and assert our lib-

---

1. The Magna Carta, the "great charter" of English personal and political liberty, dates from 1215. The Declaration of Right, another corner- stone of the English constitution, was a product of the Glorious Revolution of 1688.

erties, as an *entailed inheritance*[2] derived to us from our forefathers, and to be transmitted to our posterity; as an estate specially belonging to the people of this kingdom without any reference whatever to any other more general or prior right. By this means our constitution preserves an unity in so great a diversity of its parts. We have an inheritable crown; an inheritable peerage; and an house of commons and a people inheriting privileges, franchises, and liberties, from a long line of ancestors.

This policy appears to me to be the result of profound reflection; or rather the happy effect of following nature, which is wisdom without reflection, and above it. A spirit of innovation is generally the result of a selfish temper and confined views. People will not look forward to posterity, who never look backward to their ancestors. Besides, the people of England well know, that the idea of inheritance furnishes a sure principle of conservation, and a sure principle of transmission; without at all excluding a principle of improvement. It leaves acquisition free; but it secures what it acquires. Whatever advantages are obtained by a state proceeding on these maxims, are locked fast as in a sort of family settlement; grasped as in a kind of mortmain[3] for ever. By a constitutional policy, working after the pattern of nature, we receive, we hold, we transmit our government and our privileges, in the same manner in which we enjoy and transmit our property and our lives. The institutions of policy, the goods of fortune, the gifts of Providence, are handed down, to us and from us, in the same course and order. Our political system is placed in a just correspondence and symmetry with the order of the world, and with the mode of existence decreed to a permanent body composed of transitory parts; wherein, by the disposition of a stupendous wisdom, moulding together the great mysterious incorporation of the human race, the whole, at one time, is never old, or middle-aged, or young, but in a condition of unchangeable constancy, moves on through the varied tenour of perpetual decay, fall, renovation, and progression. Thus, by preserving the method of nature in the conduct of the state, in what we improve we are never wholly new; in what we retain we are never wholly obsolete. By adhering in this manner and on those principles to our forefathers, we are guided not by the superstition of antiquarians, but by the spirit of philosophic analogy. In this choice of inheritance we have given to our frame of polity the image of a relation in blood; binding up the constitution of our country with our dearest domestic ties; adopting our fundamental laws into the bosom of our family affections; keeping inseparable, and cherishing with the warmth of all their combined and mutually reflected charities, our state, our hearths, our sepulchres, and our altars.

Through the same plan of a conformity to nature in our artificial institutions, and by calling in the aid of her unerring and powerful instincts, to fortify the fallible and feeble contrivances of our reason, we have derived several other, and those no small benefits, from considering our liberties in the light of an inheritance. Always acting as if in the presence of canonized forefathers, the spirit of freedom, leading in itself to misrule and excess, is tempered with an awful gravity. This idea of a liberal descent inspires us with a sense of habitual native dignity, which prevents that upstart insolence almost inevitably adher-

2. An entail is a legal device that prescribes the line of succession along which a piece of family property must pass and that thereby prevents future generations of heirs from making their own decisions about that property.
3. A legal term (literally, "dead hand") for the perpetual holding of lands by an ecclesiastical or other corporation.

ing to and disgracing those who are the first acquirers of any distinction. By this means our liberty becomes a noble freedom. It carries an imposing and majestic aspect. It has a pedigree and illustrating ancestors. It has its bearings and its ensigns armorial. It has its gallery of portraits; its monumental inscriptions; its records, evidences, and titles. We procure reverence to our civil institutions on the principle upon which nature teaches us to revere individual men; on account of their age; and on account of those from whom they are descended. All your sophisters[4] cannot produce any thing better adapted to preserve a rational and manly freedom than the course that we have pursued, who have chosen our nature rather than our speculations, our breasts rather than our inventions, for the great conservatories and magazines of our rights and privileges.

             *   *   *

Far am I from denying in theory; full as far is my heart from withholding in practice (if I were of power to give or to withhold) the *real* rights of men. In denying their false claims of right, I do not mean to injure those which are real, and are such as their pretended rights would totally destroy. If civil society be made for the advantage of man, all the advantages for which it is made become his right. It is an institution of beneficence; and law itself is only beneficence acting by a rule. Men have a right to live by that rule; they have a right to justice; as between their fellows, whether their fellows are in politic function or in ordinary occupation. They have a right to the fruits of their industry; and to the means of making their industry fruitful. They have a right to the acquisitions of their parents; to the nourishment and improvement of their offspring; to instruction in life, and to consolation in death. Whatever each man can separately do, without trespassing upon others, he has a right to do for himself; and he has a right to a fair portion of all which society, with all its combinations of skill and force, can do in his favor. In this partnership all men have equal rights; but not to equal things. He that has but five shillings in the partnership, has as good a right to it, as he that has five hundred pound has to his larger proportion. But he has not a right to an equal dividend in the product of the joint stock; and as to the share of power, authority, and direction which each individual ought to have in the management of the state, that I must deny to be amongst the direct original rights of man in civil society; for I have in my contemplation the civil social man, and no other. It is a thing to be settled by convention.

             *   *   *

* * * History, who keeps a durable record of all our acts, and exercises her awful censure over the proceedings of all sorts of sovereigns, will not forget, either those events, or the aera of this liberal refinement in the intercourse of mankind. History will record, that on the morning of the 6th of October 1789, the king and queen of France, after a day of confusion, alarm, dismay, and slaughter, lay down, under the pledged security of public faith, to indulge nature in a few hours of respite, and troubled melancholy repose. From this sleep the queen was first startled by the voice of the centinel at her door, who cried out to her, to save herself by flight—that this was the last proof of fidelity

---

4. Persons reasoning with clever and fallacious arguments (from the name given to a sect of paid teachers of rhetoric and philosophy in ancient Athens).

he could give—that they were upon him, and he was dead. Instantly he was cut down. A band of cruel ruffians and assassins, reeking with his blood, rushed into the chamber of the queen, and pierced with an hundred strokes of bayonets and poniards the bed, from whence this persecuted woman had but just time to fly almost naked, and through ways unknown to the murderers had escaped to seek refuge at the feet of a king and husband, not secure of his own life for a moment.

This king, to say no more of him, and this queen, and their infant children (who once would have been the pride and hope of a great and generous people) were then forced to abandon the sanctuary of the most splendid palace in the world, which they left swimming in blood, polluted by massacre, and strewed with scattered limbs and mutilated carcases. Thence they were conducted into the capital of their kingdom. Two had been selected from the unprovoked, unresisted, promiscuous slaughter, which was made of the gentlemen of birth and family who composed the king's body guard. These two gentlemen, with all the parade of an execution of justice, were cruelly and publickly dragged to the block, and beheaded in the great court of the palace. Their heads were stuck upon spears, and led the procession; whilst the royal captives who followed in the train were slowly moved along, amidst the horrid yells, and shrilling screams, and frantic dances, and infamous contumelies, and all the unutterable abominations of the furies of hell, in the abused shape of the vilest of women. After they had been made to taste, drop by drop, more than the bitterness of death, in the slow torture of a journey of twelve miles, protracted to six hours, they were, under a guard, composed of those very soldiers who had thus conducted them through this famous triumph, lodged in one of the old palaces of Paris, now converted into a Bastile[5] for kings.

* * *

I hear that the august person, who was the principal object of our preacher's triumph,[6] though he supported himself, felt much on that shameful occasion. As a man, it became him to feel for his wife and his children, and the faithful guards of his person, that were massacred in cold blood about him; as a prince, it became him to feel for the strange and frightful transformation of his civilized subjects, and to be more grieved for them, than solicitous for himself. It derogates little from his fortitude, while it adds infinitely to the honor of his humanity. I am very sorry to say it, very sorry indeed, that such personages are in a situation in which it is not unbecoming in us to praise the virtues of the great.

I hear, and I rejoice to hear, that the great lady, the other object of the triumph, has borne that day (one is interested that beings made for suffering should suffer well) and that she bears all the succeeding days, that she bears the imprisonment of her husband, and her own captivity, and the exile of her friends, and the insulting adulation of addresses, and the whole weight of her accumulated wrongs, with a serene patience, in a manner suited to her rank and race, and becoming the offspring of a sovereign distinguished for her piety and her courage;[7] that like her she has lofty sentiments; that she feels with the

5. The Bastille was France's political prison.
6. A reference to Price's exclamation, in the final selection printed above from A Discourse on the Love of Our Country, that he has lived to see the French "king led in triumph . . . an arbitrary monarch surrendering himself to his subjects." "August person": King Louis XVI.
7. Marie Antoinette was the daughter of Maria Theresa, empress of Austria.

dignity of a Roman matron; that in the last extremity she will save herself from the last disgrace,[8] and that if she must fall, she will fall by no ignoble hand.

It is now sixteen or seventeen years since I saw the queen of France, then the dauphiness,[9] at Versailles; and surely never lighted on this orb, which she hardly seemed to touch, a more delightful vision. I saw her just above the horizon, decorating and cheering the elevated sphere she just began to move in,—glittering like the morning-star, full of life, and splendor, and joy. Oh! what a revolution! and what an heart must I have, to contemplate without emotion that elevation and that fall! Little did I dream when she added titles of veneration to those of enthusiastic, distant, respectful love, that she should ever be obliged to carry the sharp antidote against disgrace concealed in that bosom; little did I dream that I should have lived to see such disasters fallen upon her in a nation of gallant men, in a nation of men of honor and of cavaliers. I thought ten thousand swords must have leaped from their scabbards to avenge even a look that threatened her with insult.—But the age of chivalry is gone.—That of sophisters, oeconomists, and calculators, has succeeded; and the glory of Europe is extinguished for ever. Never, never more, shall we behold that generous loyalty to rank and sex, that proud submission, that dignified obedience, that subordination of the heart, which kept alive, even in servitude itself, the spirit of an exalted freedom. The unbought grace of life, the cheap defence of nations, the nurse of manly sentiment and heroic enterprize is gone! It is gone, that sensibility of principle, that chastity of honor, which felt a stain like a wound, which inspired courage whilst it mitigated ferocity, which ennobled whatever it touched, and under which vice itself lost half its evil, by losing all its grossness.

This mixed system of opinion and sentiment had its origin in the antient chivalry; and the principle, though varied in its appearance by the varying state of human affairs, subsisted and influenced through a long succession of generations, even to the time we live in. If it should ever be totally extinguished, the loss I fear will be great. It is this which has given its character to modern Europe. It is this which has distinguished it under all its forms of government, and distinguished it to its advantage, from the states of Asia, and possibly from those states which flourished in the most brilliant periods of the antique world. It was this, which, without confounding ranks, had produced a noble equality, and handed it down through all the gradations of social life. It was this opinion which mitigated kings into companions, and raised private men to be fellows with kings. Without force, or opposition, it subdued the fierceness of pride and power; it obliged sovereigns to submit to the soft collar of social esteem, compelled stern authority to submit to elegance, and gave a domination vanquisher of laws, to be subdued by manners.

But now all is to be changed. All the pleasing illusions, which made power gentle, and obedience liberal, which harmonized the different shades of life, and which, by a bland assimilation, incorporated into politics the sentiments which beautify and soften private society, are to be dissolved by this new conquering empire of light and reason. All the decent drapery of life is to be rudely torn off. All the superadded ideas, furnished from the wardrobe of a moral imagination, which the heart owns, and the understanding ratifies, as

8. Like the women of classical Rome when they endured defeat, Marie Antoinette, Burke suggests, will kill herself to preserve her chastity rather than suffer the disgrace of rape.
9. I.e., wife of the dauphin, who was heir to the throne of France.

necessary to cover the defects of our naked shivering nature, and to raise it to dignity in our own estimation, are to be exploded as a ridiculous, absurd, and antiquated fashion.

On this scheme of things, a king is but a man; a queen is but a woman; a woman is but an animal; and an animal not of the highest order. All homage paid to the sex[1] in general as such, and without distinct views, is to be regarded as romance and folly. Regicide, and parricide, and sacrilege, are but fictions of superstition, corrupting jurisprudence by destroying its simplicity. The murder of a king, or a queen, or a bishop, or a father, are only common homicide; and if the people are by any chance, or in any way gainers by it, a sort of homicide much the most pardonable, and into which we ought not to make too severe a scrutiny.

On the scheme of this barbarous philosophy, which is the offspring of cold hearts and muddy understandings, and which is as void of solid wisdom, as it is destitute of all taste and elegance, laws are to be supported only by their own terrors, and by the concern, which each individual may find in them, from his own private speculations, or can spare to them from his own private interests. In the groves of *their* academy, at the end of every visto, you see nothing but the gallows. Nothing is left which engages the affections on the part of the commonwealth. On the principles of this mechanic philosophy, our institutions can never be embodied, if I may use the expression, in persons; so as to create in us love, veneration, admiration, or attachment. But that sort of reason which banishes the affections is incapable of filling their place. These public affections, combined with manners, are required sometimes as supplements, sometimes as correctives, always as aids to law. The precept given by a wise man, as well as a great critic, for the construction of poems, is equally true as to states. *Non satis est pulchra esse poemata, dulcia sunto.*[2] There ought to be a system of manners in every nation which a well-formed mind would be disposed to relish. To make us love our country, our country ought to be lovely.

But power, of some kind or other, will survive the shock in which manners and opinions perish; and it will find other and worse means for its support. The usurpation which, in order to subvert antient institutions, has destroyed antient principles, will hold power by arts similar to those by which it has acquired it. When the old feudal and chivalrous spirit of *Fealty*,[3] which, by freeing kings from fear, freed both kings and subjects from the precautions of tyranny, shall be extinct in the minds of men, plots and assassinations will be anticipated by preventive murder and preventive confiscation, and that long roll of grim and bloody maxims, which form the political code of all power, not standing on its own honor, and the honor of those who are to obey it. Kings will be tyrants from policy when subjects are rebels from principle.

When antient opinions and rules of life are taken away, the loss cannot possibly be estimated. From that moment we have no compass to govern us; nor can we know distinctly to what port we steer. Europe undoubtedly, taken in a mass, was in a flourishing condition the day on which your Revolution was compleated. How much of that prosperous state was owing to the spirit of our old manners and opinions is not easy to say; but as such causes cannot be indifferent in their operation, we must presume, that, on the whole, their operation was beneficial.

1. Homage paid to women.
2. It is not enough for poems to have beauty; they must be sweet, tender, affecting (Latin; Horace's

Ars Poetica 99).
3. Fidelity of a vassal or feudal tenant to his lord.

We are but too apt to consider things in the state in which we find them, without sufficiently adverting to the causes by which they have been produced, and possibly may be upheld. Nothing is more certain, than that our manners, our civilization, and all the good things which are connected with manners, and with civilization, have, in this European world of ours, depended for ages upon two principles; and were indeed the result of both combined; I mean the spirit of a gentleman, and the spirit of religion. The nobility and the clergy, the one by profession, the other by patronage, kept learning in existence, even in the midst of arms and confusions, and whilst governments were rather in their causes than formed. Learning paid back what it received to nobility and to priesthood; and paid it with usury,[4] by enlarging their ideas, and by furnishing their minds. Happy if they had all continued to know their indissoluble union, and their proper place! Happy if learning, not debauched by ambition, had been satisfied to continue the instructor, and not aspired to be the master! Along with its natural protectors and guardians, learning will be cast into the mire, and trodden down under the hoofs of a swinish multitude.

If, as I suspect, modern letters owe more than they are always willing to own to antient manners, so do other interests which we value full as much as they are worth. Even commerce, and trade, and manufacture, the gods of our oeconomical politicians, are themselves perhaps but creatures; are themselves but effects, which, as first causes, we choose to worship. They certainly grew under the same shade in which learning flourished. They too may decay with their natural protecting principles. With you, for the present at least, they all threaten to disappear together. Where trade and manufactures are wanting to a people, and the spirit of nobility and religion remains, sentiment supplies, and not always ill supplies their place; but if commerce and the arts should be lost in an experiment to try how well a state may stand without these old fundamental principles, what sort of a thing must be a nation of gross, stupid, ferocious, and at the same time, poor and sordid barbarians, destitute of religion, honor, or manly pride, possessing nothing at present, and hoping for nothing hereafter?

I wish you may not be going fast, and by the shortest cut, to that horrible and disgustful situation. Already there appears a poverty of conception, a coarseness and vulgarity in all the proceedings of the assembly and of all their instructors. Their liberty is not liberal. Their science is presumptuous ignorance. Their humanity is savage and brutal.

* * *

1790

---

4. Interest.

MARY WOLLSTONECRAFT

The first of the many published replies to Burke's *Reflections* was by Mary Wollstonecraft (1759–1797), who appears elsewhere in this anthology as author of *A Vindication of the Rights of Woman* (1792), the landmark work in the history of feminism, and *Letters Written during a Short Residence in Sweden, Norway, and Denmark* (1796). Toward the end of 1790, when Burke's *Reflections* came out, she was working in London as a writer and translator for the radical publisher Joseph Johnson. Reading Burke, she was outraged at the weakness of his arguments and the exaggerated rhetoric with which he depicted the revolutionists as violators of royalty and womanhood. Always a rapid writer, she composed her reply, *A Vindication of the Rights of Men*, in a matter of days, and Johnson's printer set it in type as fast as the sheets of manuscript were turned in. It was published anonymously in November, less than a month after Burke's *Reflections* first appeared, and a second edition (this time with her name on the title page) was called for almost immediately.

From A Vindication of the Rights of Men

Advertisement

Mr. Burke's Reflections on the French Revolution first engaged my attention as the transient topic of the day; and reading it more for amusement than information, my indignation was roused by the sophistical arguments, that every moment crossed me, in the questionable shape of natural feelings and common sense.

Many pages of the following letter were the effusions of the moment; but, swelling imperceptibly to a considerable size, the idea was suggested of publishing a short vindication of the *Rights of Men*.

Not having leisure or patience to follow this desultory writer through all the devious tracks in which his fancy has started fresh game, I have confined my strictures, in a great measure, to the grand principles at which he has levelled many ingenious arguments in a very specious garb.

A Letter to the Right Honorable Edmund Burke

Sir,

It is not necessary, with courtly insincerity, to apologize to you for thus intruding on your precious time, nor to profess that I think it an honor to discuss an important subject with a man whose literary abilities have raised him to notice in the state. I have not yet learned to twist my periods, nor, in the equivocal idiom of politeness, to disguise my sentiments, and imply what I should be afraid to utter: if, therefore, in the course of this epistle, I chance to express contempt, and even indignation, with some emphasis, I beseech you to believe that it is not a flight of fancy; for truth, in morals, has ever appeared to me the essence of the sublime; and, in taste, simplicity the only criterion of the beautiful. But I war not with an individual when I contend for the *rights of men* and the liberty of reason. You see I do not condescend to cull my words to avoid the invidious phrase, nor shall I be prevented from giving a manly definition of it, by the flimsy ridicule which a lively fancy has interwoven with the present acceptation of the term. Reverencing the rights of humanity, I shall dare to assert them; not intimidated by the horse laugh that you have raised, or waiting till time has wiped away the compassionate tears which you have elaborately labored to excite.

From the many just sentiments interspersed through the letter before me, and from the whole tendency of it, I should believe you to be a good, though a vain man, if some circumstances in your conduct did not render the inflexibility of your integrity doubtful; and for this vanity a knowledge of human nature enables me to discover such extenuating circumstances, in the very texture of your mind, that I am ready to call it amiable, and separate the public from the private character.

* * *

Quitting now the flowers of rhetoric, let us, Sir, reason together; and, believe me, I should not have meddled with these troubled waters, in order to point out your inconsistencies, if your wit had not burnished up some rusty, baneful opinions, and swelled the shallow current of ridicule till it resembled the flow of reason, and presumed to be the test of truth.

I shall not attempt to follow you through "horse-way and foot-path;"[1] but, attacking the foundation of your opinions, I shall leave the superstructure to find a center of gravity on which it may lean till some strong blast puffs it into the air; or your teeming fancy, which the ripening judgment of sixty years has not tamed, produces another Chinese erection,[2] to stare, at every turn, the plain country people in the face, who bluntly call such an airy edifice—a folly.

The birthright of man, to give you, Sir, a short definition of this disputed right, is such a degree of liberty, civil and religious, as is compatible with the liberty of every other individual with whom he is united in a social compact, and the continued existence of that compact.

Liberty, in this simple, unsophisticated sense, I acknowledge, is a fair idea that has never yet received a form in the various governments that have been established on our beauteous globe; the demon of property has ever been at hand to encroach on the sacred rights of men, and to fence round with awful pomp laws that war with justice. But that it results from the eternal foundation of right—from immutable truth—who will presume to deny, that pretends to rationality—if reason has led them to build their morality[3] and religion on an everlasting foundation—the attributes of God?

I glow with indignation when I attempt, methodically, to unravel your slavish paradoxes, in which I can find no fixed first principle to refute; I shall not, therefore, condescend to shew where you affirm in one page what you deny in another; and how frequently you draw conclusions without any previous premises:—it would be something like cowardice to fight with a man who had never exercised the weapons with which his opponent chose to combat, and irksome to refute sentence after sentence in which the latent spirit of tyranny appeared.

I perceive, from the whole tenor of your Reflections, that you have a mortal antipathy to reason; but, if there is any thing like argument, or first principles, in your wild declamation, behold the result:—that we are to reverence the rust of antiquity, and term the unnatural customs, which ignorance and mistaken self-interest have consolidated, the sage fruit of experience: nay, that, if we do discover some errors, our *feelings* should lead us to excuse, with blind love, or unprincipled filial affection, the venerable vestiges of ancient days. These are gothic[4] notions of beauty—the ivy is beautiful, but, when it insidiously destroys the trunk from which it receives support, who would not grub it up?

Further, that we ought cautiously to remain for ever in frozen inactivity, because a thaw, whilst it nourishes the soil, spreads a temporary inundation; and the fear of risking any personal present convenience should prevent a

---

1. Shakespeare's *King Lear* 4.1.57.
2. Chinese pagodas were popular ornaments in late-18th-century British landscaping.
3. As religion is included in my idea of morality, I should not have mentioned the term without specifying all the simple ideas which that comprehen-

sive word generalizes; but as the charge of atheism has been very freely banded about in the letter I am considering, I wish to guard against misrepresentation [Wollstonecraft's note].
4. Barbarous.

struggle for the most estimable advantages. This is sound reasoning, I grant, in the mouth of the rich and short-sighted.

Yes, Sir, the strong gained riches, the few have sacrificed the many to their vices; and, to be able to pamper their appetites, and supinely exist without exercising mind or body, they have ceased to be men.—Lost to the relish of true pleasure, such beings would, indeed, deserve compassion, if injustice was not softened by the tyrant's plea—necessity; if prescription was not raised as an immortal boundary against innovation. Their minds, in fact, instead of being cultivated, have been so warped by education, that it may require some ages to bring them back to nature, and enable them to see their true interest, with that degree of conviction which is necessary to influence their conduct.

The civilization which has taken place in Europe has been very partial, and, like every custom that an arbitrary point of honour has established, refines the manners at the expence of morals, by making sentiments and opinions current in conversation that have no root in the heart, or weight in the cooler resolves of the mind.—And what has stopped its progress?—hereditary property—hereditary honors. The man has been changed into an artificial monster by the station in which he was born, and the consequent homage that benumbed his faculties like the torpedo's[5] touch;—or a being, with a capacity of reasoning, would not have failed to discover, as his faculties unfolded, that true happiness arose from the friendship and intimacy which can only be enjoyed by equals; and that charity is not a condescending distribution of alms, but an intercourse of good offices and mutual benefits, founded on respect for justice and humanity.

✻ ✻ ✻

It is necessary emphatically to repeat, that there are rights which men inherit at their birth, as rational creatures, who were raised above the brute creation by their improvable faculties; and that, in receiving these, not from their forefathers but, from God, prescription can never undermine natural rights.

A father may dissipate his property without his child having any right to complain;—but should he attempt to sell him for a slave, or fetter him with laws contrary to reason; nature, in enabling him to discern good from evil, teaches him to break the ignoble chain, and not to believe that bread becomes flesh, and wine blood, because his parents swallowed the Eucharist with this blind persuasion.

There is no end to this implicit submission to authority—some where it must stop, or we return to barbarism; and the capacity of improvement, which gives us a natural sceptre on earth, is a cheat, an ignis-fatuus,[6] that leads us from inviting meadows into bogs and dung-hills. And if it be allowed that many of the precautions, with which any alteration was made, in our government, were prudent, it rather proves its weakness than substantiates an opinion of the soundness of the stamina, or the excellence of the constitution.

But on what principle Mr. Burke could defend American independence, I cannot conceive; for the whole tenor of his plausible arguments settles slavery on an everlasting foundation. Allowing his servile reverence for antiquity, and prudent attention to self-interest, to have the force which he insists on, the slave trade ought never to be abolished; and, because our ignorant forefathers,

---

5. Stingray, a fish with a whiplike tail that gives an electric shock to those it touches.
6. The phosphorescent light (also known as will o' the wisp) that is said to appear in marshy landscapes and lead travelers off the path of safety.

not understanding the native dignity of man, sanctioned a traffic that outrages every suggestion of reason and religion, we are to submit to the inhuman custom, and term an atrocious insult to humanity the love of our country, and a proper submission to the laws by which our property is secured.—Security of property! Behold, in a few words, the definition of English liberty. And to this selfish principle every nobler one is sacrificed.—The Briton takes place of the man, and the image of God is lost in the citizen! But it is not that enthusiastic flame which in Greece and Rome consumed every sordid passion: no, self is the focus; and the disparting rays rise not above our foggy atmosphere. But softly—it is only the property of the rich that is secure; the man who lives by the sweat of his brow has no asylum from oppression; the strong man may enter—when was the castle of the poor sacred? and the base informer steal him from the family that depend on his industry for subsistence.

❖   ❖   ❖

But, among all your plausible arguments, and witty illustrations, your contempt for the poor always appears conspicuous, and rouses my indignation. The following paragraph in particular struck me, as breathing the most tyrannic spirit, and displaying the most factitious feelings. "Good order is the foundation of all good things. To be enabled to acquire, the people, without being servile, must be tractable and obedient. The magistrate must have his reverence, the laws their authority. The body of the people must not find the principles of natural subordination by art rooted out of their minds. They *must* respect that property of which they *cannot* partake. *They must labor to obtain what by labor can be obtained; and when they find, as they commonly do, the success disproportioned to the endeavor, they must be taught their consolation in the final proportions of eternal justice.* Of this consolation, whoever deprives them, deadens their industry, and strikes at the root of all acquisition as of all conservation. He that does this, is the cruel oppressor, the merciless enemy, of the poor and wretched; at the same time that, by his wicked speculations, he exposes the fruits of successful industry, and the accumulations of fortune, (ah! there's the rub)[7] to the plunder of the negligent, the disappointed, and the unprosperous."

This is contemptible hard-hearted sophistry, in the specious form of humility, and submission to the will of Heaven.—It is, Sir, *possible* to render the poor happier in this world, without depriving them of the consolation which you gratuitously grant them in the next. They have a right to more comfort than they at present enjoy; and more comfort might be afforded them, without encroaching on the pleasures of the rich: not now waiting to enquire whether the rich have any right to exclusive pleasures. What do I say?—encroaching! No; if an intercourse were established between them, it would impart the only true pleasure that can be snatched in this land of shadows, this hard school of moral discipline.

I know, indeed, that there is often something disgusting in the distresses of poverty, at which the imagination revolts, and starts back to exercise itself in the more attractive Arcadia of fiction. The rich man builds a house, art and taste give it the highest finish. His gardens are planted, and the trees grow to recreate the fancy of the planter, though the temperature of the climate may rather force him to avoid the dangerous damps they exhale, than seek the umbrageous retreat. Every thing on the estate is cherished but man;—yet, to

---

7. Cf. Shakespeare's *Hamlet* 3.1.67. The "rub" is the flaw in the reasoning.

contribute to the happiness of man, is the most sublime of all enjoyments. But if, instead of sweeping pleasure-grounds, obelisks, temples, and elegant cottages,[8] as *objects* for the eye, the heart was allowed to beat true to nature, decent farms would be scattered over the estate, and plenty smile around. Instead of the poor being subject to the griping hand of an avaricious steward, they would be watched over with fatherly solicitude, by the man whose duty and pleasure it was to guard their happiness, and shield from rapacity the beings who, by the sweat of their brow, exalted him above his fellows.

I could almost imagine I see a man thus gathering blessings as he mounted the hill of life; or consolation, in those days when the spirits lag, and the tired heart finds no pleasure in them. It is not by squandering alms that the poor can be relieved, or improved—it is the fostering sun of kindness, the wisdom that finds them employments calculated to give them habits of virtue, that meliorates their condition. Love is only the fruit of love; condescension and authority may produce the obedience you applaud; but he has lost his heart of flesh who can see a fellow-creature humbled before him, and trembling at the frown of a being, whose heart is supplied by the same vital current, and whose pride ought to be checked by a consciousness of having the same infirmities.

* * *

1790

8. A reference to the vogue for picturesque landscaping on aristocratic estates.

THOMAS PAINE

Although he was born and lived his first thirty-seven years in England, Thomas Paine (1737–1809) enters the debate as a visitor from America, where by writing *Common Sense* (1776) and the sixteen *Crisis* pamphlets, beginning "These are the times that try men's souls" (1776–83), he had served as the most effective propagandist for American independence. His *Rights of Man: Being an Answer to Mr. Burke's Attack on the French Revolution*, published in March 1791 with a dedication "To George Washington, President of the United States of America," has the full weight of the American revolutionary experience behind it and is the strongest statement against hereditary monarchy of any of the works replying to Burke in this "war of pamphlets." Paine published a second part of *Rights of Man* the following year and, when charged with treason by the British, fled to France, where he was made a citizen and a member of the Convention. With the fall of the more moderate Girondists, he was imprisoned by the Jacobins for a year in 1793–94, during which he wrote his last famous work, *The Age of Reason* (1794).

From Rights of Man

Among the incivilities by which nations or individuals provoke and irritate each other, Mr. Burke's pamphlet on the French Revolution is an extraordinary instance. Neither the people of France, nor the National Assembly, were troubling themselves about the affairs of England, or the English Parliament; and why Mr. Burke should commence an unprovoked attack upon them, both in parliament and in public, is a conduct that cannot be pardoned on the score of manners, nor justified on that of policy.

There is scarcely an epithet of abuse to be found in the English language with which Mr. Burke has not loaded the French nation and the National Assembly. Every thing which rancor, prejudice, ignorance or knowledge could suggest, are poured forth in the copious fury of near four hundred pages. In the strain and on the plan Mr. Burke was writing, he might have written on to as many thousands. When the tongue or the pen is let loose in a frenzy of passion, it is the man, and not the subject, that becomes exhausted.

Hitherto Mr. Burke has been mistaken and disappointed in the opinions he had formed of the affairs of France; but such is the ingenuity of his hope, or the malignancy of his despair, that it furnishes him with new pretences to go on. There was a time when it was impossible to make Mr. Burke believe there would be any revolution in France. His opinion then was, that the French had neither spirit to undertake it, nor fortitude to support it; and now that there is one, he seeks an escape by condemning it.

✻ ✻ ✻

There never did, there never will, and there never can exist a parliament, or any description of men, or any generation of men, in any country, possessed of the right or the power of binding and controuling posterity to the *"end of time,"* or of commanding for ever how the world shall be governed, or who shall govern it; and therefore, all such clauses, acts or declarations, by which the makers of them attempt to do what they have neither the right nor the power to do, nor the power to execute, are in themselves null and void.—Every age and generation must be as free to act for itself, *in all cases*, as the ages and generations which preceded it. The vanity and presumption of governing beyond the grave, is the most ridiculous and insolent of all tyrannies. Man has no property in man; neither has any generation a property in the generations which are to follow. The parliament or the people of 1688, or of any other period, had no more right to dispose of the people of the present day, or to bind or to controul them *in any shape whatever*, than the parliament or the people of the present day have to dispose of, bind or controul those who are to live a hundred or a thousand years hence. Every generation is, and must be, competent to all the purposes which its occasions require. It is the living, and not the dead, that are to be accommodated. When man ceases to be, his power and his wants cease with him; and having no longer any participation in the concerns of this world, he has no longer any authority in directing who shall be its governors, or how its government shall be organized, or how administered.

I am not contending for nor against any form of government, nor for nor against any party here or elsewhere. That which a whole nation chooses to do, it has a right to do. Mr. Burke says, No. Where then *does* the right exist? I am contending for the rights of the *living*, and against their being willed away, and controuled and contracted for, by the manuscript assumed authority of the dead; and Mr. Burke is contending for the authority of the dead over the rights and freedom of the living. ✻ ✻ ✻

✻ ✻ ✻

"We have seen," says Mr. Burke, "the French rebel against a mild and lawful Monarch, with more fury, outrage, and insult, than any people has been known to rise against the most illegal usurper, or the most sanguinary tyrant."—This is one among a thousand other instances, in which Mr. Burke shews that he is ignorant of the springs and principles of the French revolution.

It was not against Louis the XVIth, but against the despotic principles of the government, that the nation revolted. These principles had not their origin in him, but in the original establishment, many centuries back; and they were become too deeply rooted to be removed, and the augean stable[1] of parasites and plunderers too abominably filthy to be cleansed, by any thing short of a complete and universal revolution. When it becomes necessary to do a thing, the whole heart and soul should go into the measure, or not attempt it. That crisis was then arrived, and there remained no choice but to act with determined vigor, or not to act at all. The King was known to be the friend of the nation, and this circumstance was favorable to the enterprise. Perhaps no man bred up in the style of an absolute King, ever possessed a heart so little disposed to the exercise of that species of power as the present King of France. But the principles of the government itself still remained the same. The Monarch and the monarchy were distinct and separate things; and it was against the established despotism of the latter, and not against the person or principles of the former, that the revolt commenced, and the revolution has been carried.

Mr. Burke does not attend to the distinction between *men* and *principles*; and therefore, he does not see that a revolt may take place against the despotism of the latter, while there lies no charge of despotism against the former.

The natural moderation of Louis the XVIth contributed nothing to alter the hereditary despotism of the monarchy. All the tyrannies of former reigns, acted under that hereditary despotism, were still liable to be revived in the hands of a successor. It was not the respite of a reign that would satisfy France, enlightened as she was then become. A casual discontinuance of the *practice* of despotism, is not a discontinuance of its *principles*; the former depends on the virtue of the individual who is in immediate possession of power; the latter, on the virtue and fortitude of the nation. In the case of Charles I and James II of England, the revolt was against the personal despotism of the men;[2] whereas in France, it was against the hereditary despotism of the established government. But men who can consign over the rights of posterity for ever on the authority of a moldy parchment, like Mr. Burke, are not qualified to judge of this revolution. It takes in a field too vast for their views to explore, and proceeds with a mightiness of reason they cannot keep pace with.

But there are many points of view in which this revolution may be considered. When despotism has established itself for ages in a country, as in France, it is not in the person of the King only that it resides. It has the appearance of being so in show, and in nominal authority; but it is not so in practice, and in fact. It has its standard every where. Every office and department has its despotism founded upon custom and usage. Every place has its Bastille,[3] and every Bastille its despot. The original hereditary despotism resident in the person of the King, divides and subdivides itself into a thousand shapes and

1. King Augeas's stable, housing three thousand oxen and neglected for decades, was a classical symbol of filth and corruption. Hercules cleaned it by changing the course of a river.
2. Charles I was overthrown by the Civil War and executed in 1649. His son, James II, was dethroned in the Glorious Revolution of 1688.
3. France's political prison (where the French Revolution began on July 14, 1789).

forms, till at last the whole of it is acted by deputation. This was the case in France; and against this species of despotism, proceeding on through an endless labyrinth of office till the source of it is scarcely perceptible, there is no mode of redress. It strengthens itself by assuming the appearance of duty, and tyrannises under the pretence of obeying.

When a man reflects on the condition which France was in from the nature of her government, he will see other causes for revolt than those which immediately connect themselves with the person or character of Louis XVI. There were, if I may so express it, a thousand despotisms to be reformed in France, which had grown up under the hereditary despotism of the monarchy, and became so rooted as to be in a great measure independent of it. Between the monarchy, the parliament, and the church, there was a *rivalship* of despotism; besides the feudal despotism operating locally, and the ministerial despotism operating every where. But Mr. Burke, by considering the King as the only possible object of a revolt, speaks as if France was a village, in which every thing that passed must be known to its commanding officer, and no oppression could be acted but what he could immediately control. Mr. Burke might have been in the Bastille his whole life, as well under Louis XVI as Louis XIV and neither the one nor the other have known that such a man as Mr. Burke existed. The despotic principles of the government were the same in both reigns, though the dispositions of the men were as remote as tyranny and benevolence.

What Mr. Burke considers as a reproach to the French Revolution (that of bringing it forward under a reign more mild than the preceding ones), is one of its highest honors. The revolutions that have taken place in other European countries, have been excited by personal hatred. The rage was against the man, and he became the victim. But, in the instance of France, we see a revolution generated in the rational contemplation of the rights of man, and distinguishing from the beginning between persons and principles.

But Mr. Burke appears to have no idea of principles, when he is contemplating governments. "Ten years ago," says he, "I could have felicitated France on her having a government, without enquiring what the nature of that government was, or how it was administered." Is this the language of a rational man? Is it the language of a heart feeling as it ought to feel for the rights and happiness of the human race? On this ground, Mr. Burke must compliment every government in the world, while the victims who suffer under them, whether sold into slavery, or tortured out of existence, are wholly forgotten. It is power, and not principles, that Mr. Burke venerates; and under this abominable depravity, he is disqualified to judge between them.—Thus much for his opinion as to the occasions of the French Revolution. * * *

* * *

As to the tragic paintings by which Mr. Burke has outraged his own imagination, and seeks to work upon that of his readers, they are very well calculated for theatrical representation, where facts are manufactured for the sake of show, and accommodated to produce, through the weakness of sympathy, a weeping effect. But Mr. Burke should recollect that he is writing History, and not *Plays*; and that his readers will expect truth, and not the spouting rant of high-toned exclamation.

When we see a man dramatically lamenting in a publication intended to be believed, that, "*The age of chivalry is gone! that The glory of Europe is extin-*

guished for ever! that *The unbought grace of life* (if any one knows what it is), *the cheap defence of nations, the nurse of manly sentiment and heroic enterprize, is gone!"* and all this because the Quixote age of chivalric nonsense is gone, What opinion can we form of his judgment, or what regard can we pay to his facts? In the rhapsody of his imagination, he has discovered a world of windmills, and his sorrows are, that there are no Quixotes to attack them. But if the age of aristocracy, like that of chivalry, should fall, and they had originally some connection, Mr. Burke, the trumpeter of the Order, may continue his parody to the end, and finish with exclaiming, *"Othello's occupation's gone!"*[4]

Notwithstanding Mr. Burke's horrid paintings, when the French Revolution is compared with that of other countries, the astonishment will be, that it is marked with so few sacrifices; but this astonishment will cease when we reflect that *principles*, and not *persons*, were the meditated objects of destruction. The mind of the nation was acted upon by a higher stimulus than what the consideration of persons could inspire, and sought a higher conquest than could be produced by the downfall of an enemy. * * *

1791

4. Shakespeare's *Othello* 3.3.362 (Othello's feeling, when he thinks Desdemona has been unfaithful, that his life is over). "Quixote" as an adjective, referring to the hero of Cervantes's romance, who famously mistakes windmills for his foes the giants, means "insanely idealistic."

MARY WOLLSTONECRAFT
1759–1797

Mary Wollstonecraft's father inherited a substantial fortune and set himself up as a gentleman farmer. He was, however, both extravagant and incompetent, and as one farm after another failed, he became moody and violent and sought solace in heavy bouts of drinking and in tyrannizing his submissive wife. Mary was the second of five children and the oldest daughter. She later told her husband, William Godwin, that she used to throw herself in front of her mother to protect her from her husband's blows, and that she sometimes slept outside the door of her parents' bedroom to intervene if her father should break out in a drunken rage. The solace of Mary's early life was her fervent attachment to Fanny Blood, an accomplished girl two years her senior; their friendship, which began when Mary was sixteen, endured and deepened until Fanny's death.

At the age of nineteen, Mary Wollstonecraft left home to take a position as companion to a well-to-do widow living in Bath, where for the first time she had the opportunity to observe—and scorn—the social life of the upper classes at the most fashionable of English resort cities. Having left her job in 1780 to nurse her dying mother through a long and harrowing illness, Wollstonecraft next went to live with the Bloods, where her work helped sustain the struggling family. Her sister Eliza meanwhile had married and, in 1784, after the birth of a daughter, suffered a nervous breakdown. Convinced that her sister's collapse was the result of her husband's cruelty and abuse, Wollstonecraft persuaded her to abandon husband and child and flee to London. Because a divorce at that time was not commonly available, and a fugitive wife could be forced to return to her husband, the two women hid in secret quarters while awaiting the grant of a legal separation. The infant, automatically given into the father's custody, died before she was a year old.

The penniless women, together with Fanny Blood and Wollstonecraft's other sister, Everina, established a girls' school at Newington Green, near London. The project flourished at first, and at Newington, Wollstonecraft was befriended by the Reverend Richard Price, the radical author who was soon to play a leading role in the British debates about the Revolution in France, and whose kindly guidance helped shape her social and political opinions. Blood, although already ill with tuberculosis, went to Lisbon to marry her longtime suitor, Hugh Skeys, and quickly became pregnant. Wollstonecraft rushed to Lisbon to attend her friend's childbirth, only to have Fanny die in her arms; the infant died soon afterward. The loss threw Wollstonecraft (already subject to bouts of depression) into black despair, which was heightened when she found that the school at Newington was in bad financial straits and had to be closed. Tormented by creditors, she rallied her energies to write her first book, *Thoughts on the Education of Daughters* (1786), a conventional and pious series of essays, and took up a position as governess for several daughters in the Anglo-Irish family of Viscount Kingsborough, a man of great wealth whose seat was in County Cork, Ireland.

The Kingsboroughs were well intentioned and did their best to introduce Wollstonecraft into the busy trivialities of their social life. But the ambiguity of her position as governess, halfway between a servant and a member of the family, was galling. An antagonism developed between Wollstonecraft and Lady Kingsborough, in part because the children feared their mother and adored their governess. Wollstonecraft was dismissed. She returned to London, where Joseph Johnson in 1788 published *Mary, a Fiction*, a novel, as Wollstonecraft described it, about "the mind of a woman who has thinking powers." Johnson also published her book for children, *Original Stories from Real Life*, a considerable success that was translated into German and quickly achieved a second English edition illustrated with engravings by William Blake. Wollstonecraft was befriended and subsidized by Johnson, the major publisher in England of radical and reformist books, and she took a prominent place among the writers (including notables such as Barbauld and Coleridge) whom he regularly entertained at his rooms in St. Paul's Churchyard. She published translations from French and German (she had taught herself both languages) and began reviewing books for Johnson's newly founded journal, the *Analytical Review*. Though still in straitened circumstances, she helped support her two sisters and her improvident and importunate father, and was also generous with funds—and with advice—to one of her brothers and to the indigent family of Fanny Blood.

In 1790 Edmund Burke's *Reflections on the Revolution in France*—an eloquent and powerful attack on the French Revolution and its English sympathizers—quickly evoked Wollstonecraft's response, *A Vindication of the Rights of Men*. This was a formidable piece of argumentation; its most potent passages represent the disabilities and sufferings of the English lower classes and impugn the motives and sentiments of Burke. This work, the first book-length reply to Burke, scored an immediate success, although it was soon submerged in the flood of other replies, most notably Tom Paine's classic *Rights of Man* (1791–92). In 1792 Wollstonecraft focused her defense of the underprivileged on her own sex and wrote, in six weeks of intense effort, *A Vindication of the Rights of Woman*.

Earlier writers in both France and England had proposed that, given equivalent educations, women would equal men in achievement. Wollstonecraft was particularly indebted to the historian Catharine Macaulay, whose *Letters on Education* (1790) she had reviewed enthusiastically. At the same time Wollstonecraft was contributing to a long-running discussion of human rights that in Britain dated back to John Locke's publication of the *Second Treatise of Civil Government* (1690). Prefaced with a letter addressed to the French politician Bishop Talleyrand, the *Vindication* was in part her rejoinder to the inconsistent actions of France's National Assembly, which in 1791 had formally denied to all Frenchwomen the rights of citizens, even as, ironically enough, it set about celebrating the "universal rights of man."

Her book was also unprecedented in its firsthand observations of the disabilities and indignities suffered by women and in the articulateness and passion with which it exposed and decried this injustice. Wollstonecraft's views were conspicuously radical at a time when women had no political rights; were limited to a few lowly vocations as servants, nurses, governesses, and petty shopkeepers; and were legally nonpersons who lost their property to their husbands at marriage and were incapable of instituting an action in the courts of law. An impressive feature of her book, for all its vehemence, is the clear-sightedness and balance of her analysis of the social conditions of the time, as they affect men as well as women. She perceives that women constitute an oppressed class that cuts across the standard hierarchy of social classes; she shows that women, because they are denied their rights as human beings, have been forced to seek their ends by means of coquetry and cunning, the weapons of the weak; and, having demonstrated that it is contrary to reason to expect virtue from those who are not free, she also recognizes that men, no less than women, inherit their roles, and that the wielding of irresponsible power corrupts the oppressor no less than it distorts the oppressed. Hence her surprising and telling comparisons between women on the one hand and men of the nobility and military on the other as classes whose values and behavior have been distorted because their social roles prevent them from becoming fully human. In writing this pioneering work, Wollstonecraft found the cause that she was to pursue the rest of her life.

In December 1792 Wollstonecraft went to Paris to observe the Revolution at firsthand. During the years that she lived in France, 1793–94, the early period of moderation was succeeded by extremism and violence. In Paris she joined a group of English, American, and European expatriates sympathetic to the Revolution and fell in love with Gilbert Imlay, a personable American who had briefly been an officer in the American Revolutionary Army and was the author of a widely read book on the Kentucky backwoods, where he had been an explorer. He played the role in Paris of an American frontiersman and child of nature, but was in fact an adventurer who had left America to avoid prosecution for debt and for freewheeling speculations in Kentucky land. He was also unscrupulous in his relations with women. The two became lovers, and Wollstonecraft bore a daughter, Fanny Imlay, in May 1794. Imlay, who was often absent on mysterious business deals, left mother and daughter for a visit to London that he kept protracting. After the publication of her book *An Historical and Moral View of the Origin and Progress of the French Revolution* (1794), Wollstonecraft followed Imlay to London, where, convinced that he no longer loved her, she tried to commit suicide. The attempt, however, was discovered and prevented by Imlay. To get her out of the way, he persuaded her to take a trip as his business envoy to the Scandinavian countries. Although this was then a region of poor or impassible roads and primitive accommodations, the intrepid Wollstonecraft traveled there for four months, sometimes in the wilds, accompanied by the year-old Fanny and a French nursemaid.

Back in London, Wollstonecraft discovered that Imlay was living with a new mistress, an actress. Finally convinced he was lost to her, she hurled herself from a bridge into the Thames but was rescued by a passerby. Imlay departed with his actress to Paris. Wollstonecraft, resourceful as always, used the letters she had written to Imlay to compose a book, *Letters Written during a Short Residence in Sweden, Norway, and Denmark* (1796), full of sharp observations of politics, the lives of Scandinavian women, and the austere northern landscape.

In the same year Wollstonecraft renewed an earlier acquaintance with the philosopher William Godwin. His *Inquiry Concerning Political Justice* (1793), the most drastic proposal for restructuring the political and social order yet published in England, together with his novel of terror, *Caleb Williams* (1794), which embodies his social views, had made him the most famed radical writer of his time. The austerely rationalistic philosopher, then forty years of age, had an unexpected capacity for deep feeling, and what began as a flirtation soon ripened into affection and (as their letters show) passionate physical love. She wrote Godwin, with what was for the time remarkable outspokenness on the part of a woman: "Now by these presents [i.e., this document] let me assure you that you are not only in my heart, but my veins, this morning. I turn from you half abashed—yet you haunt me, and some look, word or touch thrills through my whole frame. . . . When the heart and reason accord there is no flying from voluptuous sensations, do what a woman can." Wollstonecraft was soon pregnant once more, and Godwin (who had in his *Inquiry* attacked the institution of marriage as a base form of property rights in human beings) braved the ridicule of his radical friends and conservative enemies by marrying her.

They set up a household together, but Godwin also kept separate quarters in which to do his writing, and they further salvaged their principles by agreeing to live separate social lives. Wollstonecraft was able to enjoy this arrangement for only six months. She began writing *The Wrongs of Woman*, a novel about marriage and motherhood that uses its Gothic setting inside a dilapidated madhouse to explore how women are confined both by unjust marriage laws and by their own romantic illusions. On August 30, 1797, she gave birth to a daughter, Mary Wollstonecraft Godwin, later the author of *Frankenstein* and wife of Percy Shelley. The delivery was not difficult, but resulted in massive blood poisoning. After ten days of agony, she lapsed into a coma and died. Her last whispered words were about her husband: "He is the kindest, best man in the world." Godwin wrote to a friend, announcing her death: "I firmly believe that there does not exist her equal in the world. I know from experience we were formed to make each other happy."

To distract himself in his grief, Godwin published in 1798 *Memoirs of the Author of "A Vindication of the Rights of Woman,"* in which he told, with the total candor on which he prided himself, of her affairs with Imlay and himself, her attempts at suicide, and her free thinking in matters of religion and sexual relationships. In four companion volumes of her *Posthumous Works,* he indiscreetly included her love letters to Imlay along with the unfinished *Wrongs of Woman.* The reaction to these revelations was immediate and ugly. The conservative satirist the Reverend Richard Polwhele, for instance, remarked gloatingly on how it appeared to him providential that as a proponent of sexual equality Wollstonecraft should have died in childbirth—"a death that strongly marked the distinction of the sexes, by pointing out the destiny of women, and the diseases to which they are liable." The unintended consequence of Godwin's candor was that Wollstonecraft came to be saddled with a scandalous reputation so enduring that through the Victorian era advocates of the equality of women circumspectly avoided explicit reference to her *Vindication.* Even John Stuart Mill, in his *Subjection of Women* (1869), neglected to mention the work. It was only in the twentieth century, and especially in the later decades, that Wollstonecraft's *Vindication* gained recognition as a classic in the literature not only of women's rights but of social analysis as well.

From A Vindication of the Rights of Woman[1]

Introduction

After considering the historic page, and viewing the living world with anxious solicitude, the most melancholy emotions of sorrowful indignation have depressed my spirits, and I have sighed when obliged to confess, that either nature has made a great difference between man and man, or that the civilization which has hitherto taken place in the world has been very partial. I have turned over various books written on the subject of education, and patiently observed the conduct of parents and the management of schools;

---

1. The text is from the second revised edition of 1792, as edited by Carol H. Poston for the Norton Critical Edition of *A Vindication* (1975). The edi-   tors gratefully acknowledge Poston's permission to use the information in her annotations.

but what has been the result?—a profound conviction that the neglected education of my fellow-creatures is the grand source of the misery I deplore; and that women, in particular, are rendered weak and wretched by a variety of concurring causes, originating from one hasty conclusion. The conduct and manners of women, in fact, evidently prove that their minds are not in a healthy state; for, like the flowers which are planted in too rich a soil, strength and usefulness are sacrificed to beauty; and the flaunting leaves, after having pleased a fastidious eye, fade, disregarded on the stalk, long before the season when they ought to have arrived at maturity.—One cause of this barren blooming I attribute to a false system of education, gathered from the books written on this subject by men who, considering females rather as women than human creatures, have been more anxious to make them alluring mistresses than affectionate wives and rational mothers; and the understanding of the sex has been so bubbled[2] by this specious homage, that the civilized women of the present century, with a few exceptions, are only anxious to inspire love, when they ought to cherish a nobler ambition, and by their abilities and virtues exact respect.

In a treatise, therefore, on female rights and manners, the works which have been particularly written for their improvement must not be overlooked; especially when it is asserted, in direct terms, that the minds of women are enfeebled by false refinement; that the books of instruction, written by men of genius, have had the same tendency as more frivolous productions; and that, in the true style of Mahometanism, they are treated as a kind of subordinate beings, and not as a part of the human species,[3] when improvable reason is allowed to be the dignified distinction which raises men above the brute creation, and puts a natural sceptre in a feeble hand.

Yet, because I am a woman, I would not lead my readers to suppose that I mean violently to agitate the contested question respecting the equality or inferiority of the sex; but as the subject lies in my way, and I cannot pass it over without subjecting the main tendency of my reasoning to misconstruction, I shall stop a moment to deliver, in a few words, my opinion.—In the government of the physical world it is observable that the female in point of strength is, in general, inferior to the male. This is the law of nature; and it does not appear to be suspended or abrogated in favor of woman. A degree of physical superiority cannot, therefore, be denied—and it is a noble prerogative! But not content with this natural pre-eminence, men endeavor to sink us still lower, merely to render us alluring objects for a moment; and women, intoxicated by the adoration which men, under the influence of their senses, pay them, do not seek to obtain a durable interest in their hearts, or to become the friends of the fellow creatures who find amusement in their society.

I am aware of an obvious inference:—from every quarter have I heard exclamations against masculine women; but where are they to be found? If by this appellation men mean to inveigh against their ardor in hunting, shooting, and gaming, I shall most cordially join in the cry; but if it be against the imitation of manly virtues, or, more properly speaking, the attainment of those talents and virtues, the exercise of which ennobles the human character, and which raise females in the scale of animal being, when they are comprehensively termed mankind;—all those who view them with a philosophic eye must, I

2. In an archaic sense: deluded, cheated.
3. It was a common but mistaken opinion among Europeans that the Koran, the sacred text of Islam, teaches that women have no souls.

should think, wish with me, that they may every day grow more and more masculine.

This discussion naturally divides the subject. I shall first consider women in the grand light of human creatures, who, in common with men, are placed on this earth to unfold their faculties; and afterwards I shall more particularly point out their peculiar designation.

I wish also to steer clear of an error which many respectable writers have fallen into; for the instruction which has hitherto been addressed to women, has rather been applicable to *ladies*, if the little indirect advice, that is scattered through Sandford and Merton,[4] be excepted; but, addressing my sex in a firmer tone, I pay particular attention to those in the middle class, because they appear to be in the most natural state.[5] Perhaps the seeds of false refinement, immorality, and vanity, have ever been shed by the great. Weak, artificial beings, raised above the common wants and affections of their race, in a premature unnatural manner, undermine the very foundation of virtue, and spread corruption through the whole mass of society! As a class of mankind they have the strongest claim to pity; the education of the rich tends to render them vain and helpless, and the unfolding mind is not strengthened by the practice of those duties which dignify the human character.—They only live to amuse themselves, and by the same law which in nature invariably produces certain effects, they soon only afford barren amusement.

But as I purpose taking a separate view of the different ranks of society, and of the moral character of women, in each, this hint is, for the present, sufficient, and I have only alluded to the subject, because it appears to me to be the very essence of an introduction to give a cursory account of the contents of the work it introduces.

My own sex, I hope, will excuse me, if I treat them like rational creatures, instead of flattering their *fascinating* graces, and viewing them as if they were in a state of perpetual childhood, unable to stand alone. I earnestly wish to point out in what true dignity and human happiness consists—I wish to persuade women to endeavor to acquire strength, both of mind and body, and to convince them that the soft phrases, susceptibility of heart, delicacy of sentiment, and refinement of taste, are almost synonymous with epithets of weakness, and that those beings who are only the objects of pity and that kind of love, which has been termed its sister, will soon become objects of contempt.

Dismissing then those pretty feminine phrases, which the men condescendingly use to soften our slavish dependence, and despising that weak elegancy of mind, exquisite sensibility, and sweet docility of manners, supposed to be the sexual characteristics of the weaker vessel, I wish to shew that elegance is inferior to virtue, that the first object of laudable ambition is to obtain a character as a human being, regardless of the distinction of sex; and that secondary views should be brought to this simple touchstone.

This is a rough sketch of my plan; and should I express my conviction with the energetic emotions that I feel whenever I think of the subject, the dictates of experience and reflection will be felt by some of my readers. Animated by this important object, I shall disdain to cull[6] my phrases or polish my style;—I

4. *The History of Sandford and Merton*, by Thomas Day, was a very popular story for children, published in three volumes (1786–89). In it a tutor, the Reverend Mr. Barlow, frequently cites the superiority in moral principles of Harry Sandford, the son of a poor farmer, over Tommy Merton, the spoiled son of a rich family.
5. The middle class is viewed as more "natural" than the upper classes because it is uncorrupted by the artificialities of leisure-class life.
6. Be selective in.

aim at being useful, and sincerity will render me unaffected; for, wishing rather to persuade by the force of my arguments, than dazzle by the elegance of my language, I shall not waste my time in rounding periods,[7] or in fabricating the turgid bombast of artificial feelings, which, coming from the head, never reach the heart. I shall be employed about things, not words!—and, anxious to render my sex more respectable members of society, I shall try to avoid that flowery diction which has slided from essays into novels, and from novels into familiar letters and conversation.

These pretty superlatives, dropping glibly from the tongue, vitiate the taste, and create a kind of sickly delicacy that turns away from simple unadorned truth; and a deluge of false sentiments and over-stretched feelings, stifling the natural emotions of the heart, render the domestic pleasures insipid, that ought to sweeten the exercise of those severe duties, which educate a rational and immortal being for a nobler field of action.

The education of women has, of late, been more attended to than formerly; yet they are still reckoned a frivolous sex, and ridiculed or pitied by the writers who endeavour by satire or instruction to improve them. It is acknowledged that they spend many of the first years of their lives in acquiring a smattering of accomplishments;[8] meanwhile strength of body and mind are sacrificed to libertine notions of beauty, to the desire of establishing themselves,—the only way women can rise in the world,—by marriage. And this desire making mere animals of them, when they marry they act as such children may be expected to act:—they dress; they paint, and nickname God's creatures.[9]—Surely these weak beings are only fit for a seraglio![1]—Can they be expected to govern a family with judgment, or take care of the poor babes whom they bring into the world?

If then it can be fairly deduced from the present conduct of the sex, from the prevalent fondness for pleasure which takes place of ambition and those nobler passions that open and enlarge the soul; that the instruction which women have hitherto received has only tended, with the constitution of civil society, to render them insignificant objects of desire—mere propagators of fools!—if it can be proved that in aiming to accomplish them, without cultivating their understandings, they are taken out of their sphere of duties, and made ridiculous and useless when the short-lived bloom of beauty is over,[2] I presume that *rational* men will excuse me for endeavoring to persuade them to become more masculine and respectable.

Indeed the word masculine is only a bugbear: there is little reason to fear that women will acquire too much courage or fortitude; for their apparent inferiority with respect to bodily strength, must render them, in some degree, dependent on men in the various relations of life; but why should it be increased by prejudices that give a sex to virtue, and confound simple truths with sensual reveries?

---

7. I.e., in rounding out elaborate sentences. "Period": a formal sentence composed of balanced clauses.
8. The lessons in music, dancing, sketching, and needlework that were central elements in the education provided for genteel young ladies and that were supposed to enhance their value on the marriage market.
9. Hamlet, charging Ophelia with the faults characteristic of women, says: "You jig, you amble, and you lisp, and / nickname God's creatures, and make your wantonness your ignorance" (Shakespeare,

Hamlet 3.1.143–45).
1. Harem, the women's quarters in a Muslim household.
2. A lively writer, I cannot recollect his name, asks what business women turned of forty have to do in the world? [Wollstonecraft's note]. Poston, in her edition of the *Vindication*, suggests that Wollstonecraft is recalling a passage in Frances Burney's novel *Evelina* (1778), where the licentious Lord Merton exclaims: "I don't know what the devil a woman lives for after thirty; she is only in other folks' way."

Women are, in fact, so much degraded by mistaken notions of female excellence, that I do not mean to add a paradox when I assert, that this artificial weakness produces a propensity to tyrannize, and gives birth to cunning, the natural opponent of strength, which leads them to play off those contemptible infantine airs that undermine esteem even whilst they excite desire. Let men become more chaste and modest, and if women do not grow wiser in the same ratio it will be clear that they have weaker understandings. It seems scarcely necessary to say, that I now speak of the sex in general. Many individuals have more sense than their male relatives; and, as nothing preponderates where there is a constant struggle for an equilibrium, without[3] it has naturally more gravity, some women govern their husbands without degrading themselves, because intellect will always govern.

Chap. 2. The Prevailing Opinion of a Sexual Character Discussed

To account for, and excuse the tyranny of man, many ingenious arguments have been brought forward to prove, that the two sexes, in the acquirement of virtue, ought to aim at attaining a very different character: or, to speak explicitly, women are not allowed to have sufficient strength of mind to acquire what really deserves the name of virtue. Yet it should seem, allowing them to have souls, that there is but one way appointed by Providence to lead *mankind* to either virtue or happiness.

If then women are not a swarm of ephemeron[4] triflers, why should they be kept in ignorance under the specious name of innocence? Men complain, and with reason, of the follies and caprices of our sex, when they do not keenly satirize our headstrong passions and groveling vices.—Behold, I should answer, the natural effect of ignorance! The mind will ever be unstable that has only prejudices to rest on, and the current will run with destructive fury when there are no barriers to break its force. Women are told from their infancy, and taught by the example of their mothers, that a little knowledge of human weakness, justly termed cunning, softness of temper, *outward* obedience, and a scrupulous attention to a puerile kind of propriety, will obtain for them the protection of man; and should they be beautiful, every thing else is needless, for, at least, twenty years of their lives.

Thus Milton describes our first frail mother; though when he tells us that women are formed for softness and sweet attractive grace,[5] I cannot comprehend his meaning, unless, in the true Mahometan strain, he meant to deprive us of souls, and insinuate that we were beings only designed by sweet attractive grace, and docile blind obedience, to gratify the senses of man when he can no longer soar on the wing of contemplation.

How grossly do they insult us who thus advise us only to render ourselves gentle, domestic brutes! For instance, the winning softness so warmly, and frequently, recommended, that governs by obeying. What childish expressions, and how insignificant is the being—can it be an immortal one? who will condescend to govern by such sinister methods! "Certainly," says Lord Bacon, "man is of kin to the beasts by his body; and if he be not of kin to God by his spirit, he is a base and ignoble creature!"[6] Men, indeed, appear to me to act in a very unphilosophical manner when they try to secure the good conduct

3. Unless.
4. A flying insect that lives only one day.
5. Milton asserts the authority of man over woman, on the grounds that "for contemplation he

and valor formed, / For softness she and sweet attractive grace; / He for God only, she for God in him" (*Paradise Lost* 4.298ff.).
6. Francis Bacon's "Of Atheism" (1597).

of women by attempting to keep them always in a state of childhood. Rousseau[7] was more consistent when he wished to stop the progress of reason in both sexes, for if men eat of the tree of knowledge, women will come in for a taste; but, from the imperfect cultivation which their understandings now receive, they only attain a knowledge of evil.

Children, I grant, should be innocent; but when the epithet is applied to men, or women, it is but a civil term for weakness. For if it be allowed that women were destined by Providence to acquire human virtues, and by the exercise of their understandings, that stability of character which is the firmest ground to rest our future hopes upon, they must be permitted to turn to the fountain of light, and not forced to shape their course by the twinkling of a mere satellite. Milton, I grant, was of a very different opinion; for he only bends to the indefeasible right of beauty, though it would be difficult to render two passages which I now mean to contrast, consistent. But into similar inconsistencies are great men often led by their senses.

> To whom thus Eve with *perfect beauty* adorn'd.
> My Author and Disposer, what thou bidst
> *Unargued* I obey; So God ordains;
> God is *thy law, thou mine*: to know no more
> Is Woman's *happiest* knowledge and her *praise*.[8]

These are exactly the arguments that I have used to children; but I have added, your reason is now gaining strength, and, till it arrives at some degree of maturity, you must look up to me for advice—then you ought to *think*, and only rely on God.

Yet in the following lines Milton seems to coincide with me; when he makes Adam thus expostulate with his Maker.

> Hast thou not made me here thy substitute,
> And these inferior far beneath me set?
> Among *unequals* what society
> Can sort, what harmony or true delight?
> Which must be mutual, in proportion due
> Giv'n and receiv'd; but in *disparity*
> The one intense, the other still remiss
> Cannot well suit with either, but soon prove
> Tedious alike: of *fellowship* I speak
> Such as I seek, fit to participate
> All rational delight[9]—

In treating, therefore, of the manners of women, let us, disregarding sensual arguments, trace what we should endeavor to make them in order to co-operate, if the expression be not too bold, with the supreme Being.

By individual education, I mean, for the sense of the word is not precisely defined, such an attention to a child as will slowly sharpen the senses, form the temper,[1] regulate the passions as they begin to ferment, and set the understanding to work before the body arrives at maturity; so that the man may only

7. Throughout his writings Jean-Jacques Rousseau (1712–1778) argued against the notion that civilization and rationality brought moral perfection, proposing that virtuous societies were instead the primitive ones that remained closest to nature. Rousseau's opinions about women, also alluded to in this chapter, are outlined in *Émile* (1762), a blend of educational treatise and novel. In book 5 Rousseau describes the education of the perfect woman, Sophie, brought up to provide Émile with a perfect wife.
8. *Paradise Lost* 4.634–38 (Wollstonecraft's italics).
9. *Paradise Lost* 8.381–91 (Wollstonecraft's italics).
1. Temperament, character.

have to proceed, not to begin, the important task of learning to think and reason.

To prevent any misconstruction, I must add, that I do not believe that a private education[2] can work the wonders which some sanguine writers have attributed to it. Men and women must be educated, in a great degree, by the opinions and manners of the society they live in. In every age there has been a stream of popular opinion that has carried all before it, and given a family character, as it were, to the century. It may then fairly be inferred, that, till society be differently constituted, much cannot be expected from education. It is, however, sufficient for my present purpose to assert, that, whatever effect circumstances have on the abilities, every being may become virtuous by the exercise of its own reason; for if but one being was created with vicious inclinations, that is positively bad, what can save us from atheism? or if we worship a God, is not that God a devil?

Consequently, the most perfect education, in my opinion, is such an exercise of the understanding as is best calculated to strengthen the body and form the heart. Or, in other words, to enable the individual to attain such habits of virtue as will render it independent. In fact, it is a farce to call any being virtuous whose virtues do not result from the exercise of its own reason. This was Rousseau's opinion respecting men: I extend it to women, and confidently assert that they have been drawn out of their sphere by false refinement, and not by an endeavour to acquire masculine qualities. Still the regal homage which they receive is so intoxicating, that till the manners of the times are changed, and formed on more reasonable principles, it may be impossible to convince them that the illegitimate power, which they obtain, by degrading themselves, is a curse, and that they must return to nature and equality, if they wish to secure the placid satisfaction that unsophisticated affections impart. But for this epoch we must wait—wait, perhaps, till kings and nobles, enlightened by reason, and, preferring the real dignity of man to childish state,[3] throw off their gaudy hereditary trappings: and if then women do not resign the arbitrary power of beauty—they will prove that they have *less* mind than man.

I may be accused of arrogance; still I must declare what I firmly believe, that all the writers who have written on the subject of female education and manners from Rousseau to Dr. Gregory,[4] have contributed to render women more artificial, weak characters, than they would otherwise have been; and, consequently, more useless members of society. I might have expressed this conviction in a lower key; but I am afraid it would have been the whine of affectation, and not the faithful expression of my feelings, of the clear result, which experience and reflection have led me to draw. When I come to that division of the subject, I shall advert to the passages that I more particularly disapprove of, in the works of the authors I have just alluded to; but it is first necessary to observe, that my objection extends to the whole purport of those books, which tend, in my opinion, to degrade one half of the human species, and render women pleasing at the expense of every solid virtue.

Though, to reason on Rousseau's ground, if man did attain a degree of perfection of mind when his body arrived at maturity, it might be proper, in

2. Education at home.
3. Pomp, costly display.
4. John Gregory, Scottish author of a widely read

book on the education of women, *A Father's Legacy to His Daughters* (1774).

order to make a man and his wife *one*, that she should rely entirely on his understanding; and the graceful ivy, clasping the oak that supported it, would form a whole in which strength and beauty would be equally conspicuous. But, alas! husbands, as well as their helpmates, are often only overgrown children; nay, thanks to early debauchery, scarcely men in their outward form— and if the blind lead the blind, one need not come from heaven to tell us the consequence.

Many are the causes that, in the present corrupt state of society, contribute to enslave women by cramping their understandings and sharpening their senses. One, perhaps, that silently does more mischief than all the rest, is their disregard of order.

To do every thing in an orderly manner, is a most important precept, which women, who, generally speaking, receive only a disorderly kind of education, seldom attend to with that degree of exactness that men, who from their infancy are broken into method, observe. This negligent kind of guess-work, for what other epithet can be used to point out the random exertions of a sort of instinctive common sense, never brought to the test of reason? prevents their generalizing matters of fact—so they do to-day, what they did yesterday, merely because they did it yesterday.

This contempt of the understanding in early life has more baneful consequences than is commonly supposed; for the little knowledge which women of strong minds attain, is, from various circumstances, of a more desultory kind than the knowledge of men, and it is acquired more by sheer observations on real life, than from comparing what has been individually observed with the results of experience generalized by speculation. Led by their dependent situation and domestic employments more into society, what they learn is rather by snatches; and as learning is with them, in general, only a secondary thing, they do not pursue any one branch with that persevering ardour necessary to give vigor to the faculties, and clearness to the judgment. In the present state of society, a little learning is required to support the character of a gentleman; and boys are obliged to submit to a few years of discipline. But in the education of women, the cultivation of the understanding is always subordinate to the acquirement of some corporeal accomplishment; even while enervated by confinement and false notions of modesty, the body is prevented from attaining that grace and beauty which relaxed half-formed limbs never exhibit. Besides, in youth their faculties are not brought forward by emulation; and having no serious scientific study, if they have natural sagacity it is turned too soon on life and manners. They dwell on effects, and modifications, without tracing them back to causes; and complicated rules to adjust behaviour are a weak substitute for simple principles.

As a proof that education gives this appearance of weakness to females, we may instance the example of military men, who are, like them, sent into the world before their minds have been stored with knowledge or fortified by principles. The consequences are similar; soldiers acquire a little superficial knowledge, snatched from the muddy current of conversation, and, from continually mixing with society, they gain, what is termed a knowledge of the world; and this acquaintance with manners and customs has frequently been confounded with a knowledge of the human heart. But can the crude fruit of casual observation, never brought to the test of judgment, formed by comparing speculation and experience, deserve such a distinction? Soldiers, as well as women, practice the minor virtues with punctilious politeness. Where is then the sexual difference, when the education has been the same? All the difference that I can discern, arises from the superior advantage of liberty, which enables the former to see more of life.

It is wandering from my present subject, perhaps, to make a political remark; but, as it was produced naturally by the train of my reflections, I shall not pass it silently over.

Standing armies can never consist of resolute, robust men; they may be well disciplined machines, but they will seldom contain men under the influence of strong passions, or with very vigorous faculties. And as for any depth of understanding, I will venture to affirm, that it is as rarely to be found in the army as amongst women; and the cause, I maintain, is the same. It may be further observed, that officers are also particularly attentive to their persons, fond of dancing, crowded rooms, adventures, and ridicule.[5] Like the *fair* sex, the business of their lives is gallantry.—They were taught to please, and they only live to please. Yet they do not lose their rank in the distinction of sexes, for they are still reckoned superior to women, though in what their superiority consists, beyond what I have just mentioned, it is difficult to discover.

The great misfortune is this, that they both acquire manners before morals, and a knowledge of life before they have, from reflection, any acquaintance with the grand ideal outline of human nature. The consequence is natural; satisfied with common nature, they become a prey to prejudices, and taking all their opinions on credit, they blindly submit to authority. So that, if they have any sense, it is a kind of instinctive glance, that catches proportions, and decides with respect to manners; but fails when arguments are to be pursued below the surface, or opinions analyzed.

May not the same remark be applied to women? Nay, the argument may be carried still further, for they are both thrown out of a useful station by the unnatural distinctions established in civilized life. Riches and hereditary honours have made cyphers of women to give consequence to the numerical figure;[6] and idleness has produced a mixture of gallantry and despotism into society, which leads the very men who are the slaves of their mistresses to tyrannize over their sisters, wives, and daughters. This is only keeping them in rank and file, it is true. Strengthen the female mind by enlarging it, and there will be an end to blind obedience; but, as blind obedience is ever sought for by power, tyrants and sensualists are in the right when they endeavour to keep women in the dark, because the former only want slaves, and the latter a play-thing. The sensualist, indeed, has been the most dangerous of tyrants, and women have been duped by their lovers, as princes by their ministers, whilst dreaming that they reigned over them.

I now principally allude to Rousseau, for his character of Sophia is, undoubtedly, a captivating one, though it appears to me grossly unnatural; however it is not the superstructure, but the foundation of her character, the principles on which her education was built, that I mean to attack; nay, warmly as I admire the genius of that able writer, whose opinions I shall often have occasion to cite, indignation always takes place of admiration, and the rigid frown of insulted virtue effaces the smile of complacency, which his eloquent

5. Why should women be censured with petulant acrimony, because they seem to have a passion for a scarlet coat? Has not education placed them more on a level with soldiers than any other class of men? [Wollstonecraft's note].

6. Much as a zero added to a number multiplies its value by a factor of ten, in a hierarchical society women magnify the status of the men with whom they are allied.

periods are wont to raise, when I read his voluptuous reveries. Is this the man, who, in his ardor for virtue, would banish all the soft arts of peace, and almost carry us back to Spartan discipline? Is this the man who delights to paint the useful struggles of passion, the triumphs of good dispositions, and the heroic flights which carry the glowing soul out of itself?—How are these mighty sentiments lowered when he describes the pretty foot and enticing airs of his little favorite! But, for the present, I waive the subject, and, instead of severely reprehending the transient effusions of overweening sensibility, I shall only observe, that whoever has cast a benevolent eye on society, must often have been gratified by the sight of a humble mutual love, not dignified by sentiment, or strengthened by a union in intellectual pursuits. The domestic trifles of the day have afforded matters for cheerful converse, and innocent caresses have softened toils which did not require great exercise of mind or stretch of thought: yet, has not the sight of this moderate felicity excited more tenderness than respect? An emotion similar to what we feel when children are playing, or animals sporting,[7] whilst the contemplation of the noble struggles of suffering merit has raised admiration, and carried our thoughts to that world where sensation will give place to reason.

Women are, therefore, to be considered either as moral beings, or so weak that they must be entirely subjected to the superior faculties of men.

Let us examine this question. Rousseau declares that a woman should never, for a moment, feel herself independent, that she should be governed by fear to exercise her natural cunning, and made a coquetish slave in order to render her a more alluring object of desire, a *sweeter* companion to man, whenever he chooses to relax himself. He carries the arguments, which he pretends to draw from the indications of nature, still further, and insinuates that truth and fortitude, the corner stones of all human virtue, should be cultivated with certain restrictions, because, with respect to the female character, obedience is the grand lesson which ought to be impressed with unrelenting rigor.[8]

What nonsense! when will a great man arise with sufficient strength of mind to puff away the fumes which pride and sensuality have thus spread over the subject! If women are by nature inferior to men, their virtues must be the same in quality, if not in degree, or virtue is a relative idea; consequently, their conduct should be founded on the same principles, and have the same aim.

Connected with man as daughters, wives, and mothers, their moral character may be estimated by their manner of fulfilling those simple duties; but the end, the grand end of their exertions should be to unfold their own faculties and acquire the dignity of conscious virtue. They may try to render their road pleasant; but ought never to forget, in common with man, that life yields not the felicity which can satisfy an immortal soul. I do not mean to insinuate, that either sex should be so lost in abstract reflections or distant views, as to forget the affections and duties that lie before them, and are, in truth, the means appointed to produce the fruit of life; on the contrary, I would warmly

7. Similar feelings has Milton's pleasing picture of paradisiacal happiness ever raised in my mind; yet, instead of envying the lovely pair, I have, with conscious dignity, or Satanic pride, turned to hell for sublimer objects. In the same style, when viewing some noble monument of human art, I have traced the emanation of the Deity in the order I admired, till, descending from that giddy height, I have caught myself contemplating the grandest of all human sights;—for fancy quickly placed, in some solitary recess, an outcast of fortune, rising superior to passion and discontent [Wollstonecraft's note].

8. Rousseau had written in *Émile*: "What is most wanted in a woman is gentleness; formed to obey a creature so imperfect as man, a creature often vicious and always faulty, she should early learn to submit to injustice and to suffer the wrongs inflicted on her by her husband without complaint."

recommend them, even while I assert, that they afford most satisfaction when they are considered in their true, sober light.

Probably the prevailing opinion, that woman was created for man, may have taken its rise from Moses's poetical story;[9] yet, as very few, it is presumed, who have bestowed any serious thought on the subject, ever supposed that Eve was, literally speaking, one of Adam's ribs, the deduction must be allowed to fall to the ground; or, only be so far admitted as it proves that man, from the remotest antiquity, found it convenient to exert his strength to subjugate his companion, and his invention to shew that she ought to have her neck bent under the yoke, because the whole creation was only created for his convenience or pleasure.

Let it not be concluded that I wish to invert the order of things; I have already granted, that, from the constitution of their bodies, men seem to be designed by Providence to attain a greater degree of virtue.[1] I speak collectively of the whole sex; but I see not the shadow of a reason to conclude that their virtues should differ in respect to their nature. In fact, how can they, if virtue has only one eternal standard? I must therefore, if I reason consequentially, as strenuously maintain that they have the same simple direction, as that there is a God.

It follows then that cunning should not be opposed to wisdom, little cares to great exertions, or insipid softness, varnished over with the name of gentleness, to that fortitude which grand views alone can inspire.

I shall be told that woman would then lose many of her peculiar graces, and the opinion of a well known poet might be quoted to refute my unqualified assertion. For Pope has said, in the name of the whole male sex,

> Yet ne'er so sure our passion to create,
> As when she touch'd the brink of all we hate.[2]

In what light this sally places men and women, I shall leave to the judicious to determine; meanwhile I shall content myself with observing, that I cannot discover why, unless they are mortal, females should always be degraded by being made subservient to love or lust.

To speak disrespectfully of love is, I know, high treason against sentiment and fine feelings; but I wish to speak the simple language of truth, and rather to address the head than the heart. To endeavor to reason love out of the world, would be to out-Quixote Cervantes,[3] and equally offend against common sense; but an endeavor to restrain this tumultuous passion, and prove that it should not be allowed to dethrone superior powers, or to usurp the sceptre which the understanding should ever coolly wield, appears less wild.

Youth is the season for love in both sexes; but in those days of thoughtless enjoyment provision should be made for the more important years of life, when reflection takes place of sensation. But Rousseau, and most of the male writers who have followed his steps, have warmly inculcated that the whole tendency of female education ought to be directed to one point:—to render them pleasing.

Let me reason with the supporters of this opinion who have any knowledge of human nature, do they imagine that marriage can eradicate the habitude

9. The story of the creation of Eve from the rib of Adam (Genesis 2.21–22). Traditionally, the first five books of the Old Testament were attributed to the authorship of Moses.
1. In the third paragraph of her Introduction (p. 171 above), Wollstonecraft had said that men are, in general, physically stronger than women.
2. Alexander Pope's *Moral Essays* 2, "Of the Characters of Women," lines 51–52.
3. I.e., to outdo the hero of Cervantes's *Don Quixote* (1605) in trying to accomplish the impossible.

of life? The woman who has only been taught to please will soon find that her charms are oblique sunbeams, and that they cannot have much effect on her husband's heart when they are seen every day, when the summer is passed and gone. Will she then have sufficient native energy to look into herself for comfort, and cultivate her dormant faculties? or, is it not more rational to expect that she will try to please other men; and, in the emotions raised by the expectation of new conquests, endeavor to forget the mortification her love or pride has received? When the husband ceases to be a lover—and the time will inevitably come, her desire of pleasing will then grow languid, or become a spring of bitterness; and love, perhaps, the most evanescent of all passions, gives place to jealousy or vanity.

I now speak of women who are restrained by principle or prejudice; such women, though they would shrink from an intrigue with real abhorrence, yet, nevertheless, wish to be convinced by the homage of gallantry that they are cruelly neglected by their husbands; or, days and weeks are spent in dreaming of the happiness enjoyed by congenial souls till their health is undermined and their spirits broken by discontent. How then can the great art of pleasing be such a necessary study? it is only useful to a mistress; the chaste wife, and serious mother, should only consider her power to please as the polish of her virtues, and the affection of her husband as one of the comforts that render her task less difficult and her life happier.—But, whether she be loved or neglected, her first wish should be to make herself respectable,[4] and not to rely for all her happiness on a being subject to like infirmities with herself.

The worthy Dr. Gregory fell into a similar error. I respect his heart; but entirely disapprove of his celebrated Legacy to his Daughters.

He advises them to cultivate a fondness for dress, because a fondness for dress, he asserts, is natural to them. I am unable to comprehend what either he or Rousseau mean, when they frequently use this indefinite term.[5] If they told us that in a pre-existent state the soul was fond of dress, and brought this inclination with it into a new body, I should listen to them with a half smile, as I often do when I hear a rant about innate elegance.—But if he only meant to say that the exercise of the faculties will produce this fondness—I deny it.— It is not natural; but arises, like false ambition in men, from a love of power.

Dr. Gregory goes much further; he actually recommends dissimulation, and advises an innocent girl to give the lie to her feelings, and not dance with spirit, when gaiety of heart would make her feel eloquent without making her gestures immodest. In the name of truth and common sense, why should not one woman acknowledge that she can take more exercise than another? or, in other words, that she has a sound constitution; and why, to damp innocent vivacity, is she darkly to be told that men will draw conclusions which she little thinks of?[6]—Let the libertine draw what inference he pleases; but, I hope, that no sensible mother will restrain the natural frankness of youth by instilling such indecent cautions. Out of the abundance of the heart the mouth speaketh;[7] and a wiser than Solomon hath said, that the heart should be made clean,[8] and not trivial ceremonies observed, which is not very difficult to fulfill with scrupulous exactness when vice reigns in the heart.

4. I.e., morally worthy of respect.
5. I.e., "natural."
6. In A Father's Legacy to His Daughters, Gregory had advised a girl, when she dances, not "to forget the delicacy of [her] sex," lest she be "thought to discover a spirit she little dreams of"—i.e., lest she

betray her capacity for physical pleasure.
7. Matthew 12.34.
8. Psalm 51 (attributed to David, the "wiser than Solomon"), 10: "Create in me a clean heart, O God; and renew a right spirit within me."

Women ought to endeavor to purify their heart; but can they do so when their uncultivated understandings make them entirely dependent on their senses for employment and amusement, when no noble pursuit sets them above the little vanities of the day, or enables them to curb the wild emotions that agitate a reed over which every passing breeze has power? To gain the affections of a virtuous man is affectation necessary? Nature has given woman a weaker frame than man; but, to ensure her husband's affections, must a wife, who by the exercise of her mind and body whilst she was discharging the duties of a daughter, wife, and mother, has allowed her constitution to retain its natural strength, and her nerves a healthy tone, is she, I say, to condescend to use art and feign a sickly delicacy in order to secure her husband's affection? Weakness may excite tenderness, and gratify the arrogant pride of man; but the lordly caresses of a protector will not gratify a noble mind that pants for, and deserves to be respected. Fondness is a poor substitute for friendship!

In a seraglio, I grant, that all these arts are necessary; the epicure must have his palate tickled, or he will sink into apathy; but have women so little ambition as to be satisfied with such a condition? Can they supinely dream life away in the lap of pleasure, or the languor of weariness, rather than assert their claim to pursue reasonable pleasures and render themselves conspicuous by prac-tising the virtues which dignify mankind? Surely she has not an immortal soul who can loiter life away merely employed to adorn her person, that she may amuse the languid hours, and soften the cares of a fellow-creature who is willing to be enlivened by her smiles and tricks, when the serious business of life is over.

Besides, the woman who strengthens her body and exercises her mind will, by managing her family and practising various virtues, become the friend, and not the humble dependent of her husband; and if she, by possessing such substantial qualities, merit his regard, she will not find it necessary to conceal her affection, nor to pretend to an unnatural coldness of constitution to excite her husband's passions. In fact, if we revert to history, we shall find that the women who have distinguished themselves have neither been the most beau-tiful nor the most gentle of their sex.

Nature, or, to speak with strict propriety, God, has made all things right; but man has sought him out many inventions to mar the work. I now allude to that part of Dr. Gregory's treatise, where he advises a wife never to let her husband know the extent of her sensibility or affection. Voluptuous precau-tion, and as ineffectual as absurd.—Love, from its very nature, must be tran-sitory. To seek for a secret that would render it constant, would be as wild a search as for the philosopher's stone, or the grand panacea:[9] and the discovery would be equally useless, or rather pernicious to mankind. The most holy band of society is friendship. It has been well said, by a shrewd satirist, "that rare as true love is, true friendship is still rarer."[1]

This is an obvious truth, and the cause not lying deep, will not elude a slight glance of inquiry.

Love, the common passion, in which chance and sensation take place of choice and reason, is, in some degree, felt by the mass of mankind; for it is not necessary to speak, at present, of the emotions that rise above or sink

9. A medicine reputed to cure all diseases. "The philosopher's stone," in alchemy, had the power of transmuting base metals into gold.

1. Maxim 473 of La Rochefoucauld (1613–1680), the great French writer of epigrams.

below love. This passion, naturally increased by suspense and difficulties, draws the mind out of its accustomed state, and exalts the affections; but the security of marriage, allowing the fever of love to subside, a healthy temperature is thought insipid, only by those who have not sufficient intellect to substitute the calm tenderness of friendship, the confidence of respect, instead of blind admiration, and the sensual emotions of fondness.

This is, must be, the course of nature.—Friendship or indifference inevitably succeeds love.—And this constitution seems perfectly to harmonize with the system of government which prevails in the moral world. Passions are spurs to action, and open the mind; but they sink into mere appetites, become a personal and momentary gratification, when the object is gained, and the satisfied mind rests in enjoyment. The man who had some virtue whilst he was struggling for a crown, often becomes a voluptuous tyrant when it graces his brow; and, when the lover is not lost in the husband, the dotard, a prey to childish caprices, and fond jealousies, neglects the serious duties of life, and the caresses which should excite confidence in his children are lavished on the overgrown child, his wife.

In order to fulfil the duties of life, and to be able to pursue with vigour the various employments which form the moral character, a master and mistress of a family ought not to continue to love each other with passion. I mean to say, that they ought not to indulge those emotions which disturb the order of society, and engross the thoughts that should be otherwise employed. The mind that has never been engrossed by one object wants vigor—if it can long be so, it is weak.

A mistaken education, a narrow, uncultivated mind, and many sexual prejudices, tend to make women more constant than men; but, for the present, I shall not touch on this branch of the subject. I will go still further, and advance, without dreaming of a paradox, that an unhappy marriage is often very advantageous to a family, and that the neglected wife is, in general, the best mother.[2] And this would almost always be the consequence if the female mind were more enlarged: for, it seems to be the common dispensation of Providence, that what we gain in present enjoyment should be deducted from the treasure of life, experience; and that when we are gathering the flowers of the day and revelling in pleasure, the solid fruit of toil and wisdom should not be caught at the same time. The way lies before us, we must turn to the right or left; and he who will pass life away in bounding from one pleasure to another, must not complain if he acquire neither wisdom nor respectability of character.

Supposing, for a moment, that the soul is not immortal, and that man was only created for the present scene,—I think we should have reason to complain that love, infantine fondness, ever grew insipid and palled upon the sense. Let us eat, drink, and love for to-morrow we die, would be, in fact, the language of reason, the morality of life; and who but a fool would part with a reality for a fleeting shadow? But, if awed by observing the improbable[3] powers of the mind, we disdain to confine our wishes or thoughts to such a comparatively mean field of action; that only appears grand and important, as it is connected with a boundless prospect and sublime hopes, what necessity is there for false-

2. Wollstonecraft's point is that a woman who is not preoccupied with her husband (and his attentions to her) has more time and attention for her children.

3. Poston points out that this may be a misprint in the second edition for "improvable," which occurs in the first edition.

hood in conduct, and why must the sacred majesty of truth be violated to detain a deceitful good that saps the very foundation of virtue? Why must the female mind be tainted by coquetish arts to gratify the sensualist, and prevent love from subsiding into friendship, or compassionate tenderness, when there are not qualities on which friendship can be built? Let the honest heart shew itself, and *reason* teach passion to submit to necessity; or, let the dignified pursuit of virtue and knowledge raise the mind above those emotions which rather imbitter than sweeten the cup of life, when they are not restrained within due bounds.

I do not mean to allude to the romantic passion, which is the concomitant of genius.—Who can clip its wing? But that grand passion not proportioned to the puny enjoyments of life, is only true to the sentiment, and feeds on itself. The passions which have been celebrated for their durability have always been unfortunate. They have acquired strength by absence and constitutional melancholy.—The fancy has hovered around a form of beauty dimly seen— but familiarity might have turned admiration into disgust; or, at least, into indifference, and allowed the imagination leisure to start fresh game. With perfect propriety, according to his view of things, does Rousseau make the mistress of his soul, Eloisa, love St. Preux, when life was fading before her;[4] but this is no proof of the immortality of the passion.

Of the same complexion is Dr. Gregory's advice respecting delicacy of sentiment,[5] which he advises a woman not to acquire, if she have determined to marry. This determination, however, perfectly consistent with his former advice, he calls *indelicate*, and earnestly persuades his daughters to conceal it, though it may govern their conduct;—as if it were indelicate to have the common appetites of human nature.

Noble morality! and consistent with the cautious prudence of a little soul that cannot extend its views beyond the present minute division of existence. If all the faculties of woman's mind are only to be cultivated as they respect her dependence on man; if, when a husband be obtained, she have arrived at her goal, and meanly proud rests satisfied with such a paltry crown, let her grovel contentedly, scarcely raised by her employments above the animal kingdom; but, if, struggling for the prize of her high calling,[6] she look beyond the present scene, let her cultivate her understanding without stopping to consider what character the husband may have whom she is destined to marry. Let her only determine, without being too anxious about present happiness, to acquire the qualities that ennoble a rational being, and a rough inelegant husband may shock her taste without destroying her peace of mind. She will not model her soul to suit the frailties of her companion, but to bear with them: his character may be a trial, but not an impediment to virtue.

If Dr. Gregory confined his remark to romantic expectations of constant love and congenial feelings, he should have recollected that experience will banish what advice can never make us cease to wish for, when the imagination is kept alive at the expence of reason.

I own it frequently happens that women who have fostered a romantic

4. In Rousseau's *Julie, ou la Nouvelle Héloise* (1761), Julie, after a life of fidelity to her husband, reveals on her deathbed that she has never lost her passion for St. Preux, her lover when she was young. Wollstonecraft accepts the common opinion that Julie represents Madame d'Houdetot, with whom Rousseau was in love when he wrote the novel.

5. I.e., too elevated and refined a notion of what to expect in a man.

6. An echo of Philippians 3.14, where St. Paul writes, "I press toward the mark for the prize of the high calling of God in Christ Jesus."

unnatural delicacy of feeling, waste their[7] lives in *imagining* how happy they should have been with a husband who could love them with a fervid increasing affection every day, and all day. But they might as well pine married as single—and would not be a jot more unhappy with a bad husband than longing for a good one. That a proper education; or, to speak with more precision, a well stored mind, would enable a woman to support a single life with dignity, I grant; but that she should avoid cultivating her taste, lest her husband should occasionally shock it, is quitting a substance for a shadow. To say the truth, I do not know of what use is an improved taste, if the individual be not rendered more independent of the casualties of life; if new sources of enjoyment, only dependent on the solitary operations of the mind, are not opened. People of taste, married or single, without distinction, will ever be disgusted by various things that touch not less observing minds. On this conclusion the argument must not be allowed to hinge; but in the whole sum of enjoyment is taste to be denominated a blessing?

The question is, whether it procures most pain or pleasure? The answer will decide the propriety of Dr. Gregory's advice, and shew how absurd and tyrannic it is thus to lay down a system of slavery; or to attempt to educate moral beings by any other rules than those deduced from pure reason, which apply to the whole species.

Gentleness of manners, forbearance, and long-suffering, are such amiable Godlike qualities, that in sublime poetic strains the Deity has been invested with them; and, perhaps, no representation of his goodness so strongly fastens on the human affections as those that represent him abundant in mercy and willing to pardon. Gentleness, considered in this point of view, bears on its front all the characteristics of grandeur, combined with the winning graces of condescension; but what a different aspect it assumes when it is the submissive demeanour of dependence, the support of weakness that loves, because it wants protection; and is forbearing, because it must silently endure injuries; smiling under the lash at which it dare not snarl. Abject as this picture appears, it is the portrait of an accomplished woman, according to the received opinion of female excellence, separated by specious reasoners from human excellence. Or, they[8] kindly restore the rib, and make one moral being of a man and woman; not forgetting to give her all the "submissive charms."[9] How women are to exist in that state where there is to be neither marrying nor giving in marriage,[1] we are not told. For though moralists have agreed that the tenor of life seems to prove that *man* is prepared by various circumstances for a future state, they constantly concur in advising *woman* only to provide for the present. Gentleness, docility, and a spaniel-like affection are, on this ground, consistently recommended as the cardinal virtues of the sex; and, disregarding the arbitrary economy of nature, one writer has declared that it is masculine for a woman to be melancholy. She was created to be the toy of man, his rattle,

---

7. For example, the herd of Novelists [Wollstonecraft's note]. The author's reference is to women who have formed their expectations of love as it is misrepresented in the sentimental novels of their time.
8. *Vide* [see] Rousseau and Swedenborg [Wollstonecraft's note]. Rousseau's view was that a wife constituted an integral moral being only in concert with her husband. Emanuel Swedenborg (1688–1772), the Swedish theosophist, held that in the married state in heaven male and female are embodied in a single angelic form.
9. Milton says of Adam and Eve in *Paradise Lost* 4.497–99 that "he in delight / Both of her beauty and submissive charms / Smiled with superior love."
1. "For in the resurrection they neither marry, nor are given in marriage, but are as the angels of God in heaven" (Matthew 22.30).

and it must jingle in his ears whenever, dismissing reason, he chooses to be amused.

To recommend gentleness, indeed, on a broad basis is strictly philosophical. A frail being should labor to be gentle. But when forbearance confounds right and wrong, it ceases to be a virtue; and, however convenient it may be found in a companion—that companion will ever be considered as an inferior, and only inspire a vapid tenderness, which easily degenerates into contempt. Still, if advice could really make a being gentle, whose natural disposition admitted not of such a fine polish, something towards the advancement of order would be attained; but if, as might quickly be demonstrated, only affectation be produced by this indiscriminate counsel, which throws a stumbling-block in the way of gradual improvement, and true melioration of temper, the sex is not much benefited by sacrificing solid virtues to the attainment of superficial graces, though for a few years they may procure the individuals regal sway.

As a philosopher, I read with indignation the plausible epithets which men use to soften their insults; and, as a moralist, I ask what is meant by such heterogeneous associations, as fair defects, amiable weaknesses, &c.?[2] If there be but one criterion of morals, but one archetype of man, women appear to be suspended by destiny, according to the vulgar tale of Mahomet's coffin;[3] they have neither the unerring instinct of brutes, nor are allowed to fix the eye of reason on a perfect model. They were made to be loved, and must not aim at respect, lest they should be hunted out of society as masculine.

But to view the subject in another point of view. Do passive indolent women make the best wives? Confining our discussion to the present moment of existence, let us see how such weak creatures perform their part. Do the women who, by the attainment of a few superficial accomplishments, have strengthened the prevailing prejudice, merely contribute to the happiness of their husbands? Do they display their charms merely to amuse them? And have women, who have early imbibed notions of passive obedience, sufficient character to manage a family or educate children? So far from it, that, after surveying the history of woman, I cannot help, agreeing with the severest satirist, considering the sex as the weakest as well as the most oppressed half of the species. What does history disclose but marks of inferiority, and how few women have emancipated themselves from the galling yoke of sovereign man?—So few, that the exceptions remind me of an ingenious conjecture respecting Newton: that he was probably a being of a superior order, accidentally caged in a human body.[4] Following the same train of thinking, I have been led to imagine that the few extraordinary women who have rushed in eccentrical directions out of the orbit prescribed to their sex, were *male* spirits, confined by mistake in female frames. But if it be not philosophical to think of sex when the soul is mentioned, the inferiority must depend on the organs; or the heavenly fire, which is to ferment the clay, is not given in equal portions.

But avoiding, as I have hitherto done, any direct comparison of the two sexes collectively, or frankly acknowledging the inferiority of woman, according to the present appearance of things, I shall only insist that men have increased that inferiority till women are almost sunk below the standard of

---

2. In *Paradise Lost* 10.891–92 the fallen Adam refers to Eve as "this fair defect / Of Nature"; and in *Moral Essays* 2.43 Pope describes women as "Fine by defect, and delicately weak."
3. A legend has it that Muhammad's coffin hovers

suspended in his tomb.
4. A possible reminiscence of Pope's *An Essay on Man* 2.31–34: "Superior beings [i.e., angels] . . . / Admired such wisdom in an earthly shape, / And showed a Newton as we show an ape."

rational creatures. Let their faculties have room to unfold, and their virtues to gain strength, and then determine where the whole sex must stand in the intellectual scale. Yet let it be remembered, that for a small number of distinguished women I do not ask a place.

It is difficult for us purblind mortals to say to what height human discoveries and improvements may arrive when the gloom of despotism subsides, which makes us stumble at every step; but, when morality shall be settled on a more solid basis, then, without being gifted with a prophetic spirit, I will venture to predict that woman will be either the friend or slave of man. We shall not, as at present, doubt whether she is a moral agent, or the link which unites man with brutes.[5] But, should it then appear, that like the brutes they were principally created for the use of man, he will let them patiently bite the bridle, and not mock them with empty praise; or, should their rationality be proved, he will not impede their improvement merely to gratify his sensual appetites. He will not, with all the graces of rhetoric, advise them to submit implicitly their understanding to the guidance of man. He will not, when he treats of the education of women, assert that they ought never to have the free use of reason, nor would he recommend cunning and dissimulation to beings who are acquiring, in like manner as himself, the virtues of humanity.

Surely there can be but one rule of right, if morality has an eternal foundation, and whoever sacrifices virtue, strictly so called, to present convenience, or whose *duty* it is to act in such a manner, lives only for the passing day, and cannot be an accountable creature.

The poet then should have dropped his sneer when he says,

> If weak women go astray,
> The stars are more in fault than they.[6]

For that they are bound by the adamantine chain of destiny is most certain, if it be proved that they are never to exercise their own reason, never to be independent, never to rise above opinion, or to feel the dignity of a rational will that only bows to God, and often forgets that the universe contains any being but itself and the model of perfection to which its ardent gaze is turned, to adore attributes that, softened into virtues, may be imitated in kind, though the degree overwhelms the enraptured mind.

If, I say, for I would not impress by declamation when Reason offers her sober light, if they be really capable of acting like rational creatures, let them not be treated like slaves; or, like the brutes who are dependent on the reason of man, when they associate with him; but cultivate their minds, give them the salutary, sublime curb of principle, and let them attain conscious dignity by feeling themselves only dependent on God. Teach them, in common with man, to submit to necessity, instead of giving, to render them more pleasing, a sex to morals.

Further, should experience prove that they cannot attain the same degree

---

5. Rousseau doubted that a woman, of herself, was a moral agent. There had been a long dispute about the question of woman being part of humankind. In the *Summa Theologica* (Question XVII, Art. 1) St. Thomas Aquinas concedes, with Aristotle, that the "production of woman comes from a defect in the active power, or from some material indisposition, or even from some external influence, such as that of a south wind, which is moist" (English Dominican translation of St. Thomas, edited by Anton C. Pegis, *The Basic Writings of Saint Thomas Aquinas* [New York, 1945], I, 880) [Poston's note].
6. Matthew Prior, "Hans Carvel," lines 11–12, alluding to Shakespeare's *Julius Caesar* 1.2.141–42: "The fault, dear Brutus, is not in our stars, / But in ourselves."

of strength of mind, perseverance, and fortitude, let their virtues be the same in kind, though they may vainly struggle for the same degree; and the superiority of man will be equally clear, if not clearer; and truth, as it is a simple principle, which admits of no modification, would be common to both. Nay, the order of society as it is at present regulated would not be inverted, for woman would then only have the rank that reason assigned her, and arts could not be practised to bring the balance even, much less to turn it.

These may be termed Utopian dreams.—Thanks to that Being who impressed them on my soul, and gave me sufficient strength of mind to dare to exert my own reason, till, becoming dependent only on him for the support of my virtue, I view, with indignation, the mistaken notions that enslave my sex.

I love man as my fellow; but his scepter, real or usurped, extends not to me, unless the reason of an individual demands my homage; and even then the submission is to reason, and not to man. In fact, the conduct of an accountable being must be regulated by the operations of its own reason; or on what foundation rests the throne of God?

It appears to me necessary to dwell on these obvious truths, because females have been insulated, as it were; and, while they have been stripped of the virtues that should clothe humanity, they have been decked with artificial graces that enable them to exercise a short-lived tyranny. Love, in their bosoms, taking place of every nobler passion, their sole ambition is to be fair, to raise emotion instead of inspiring respect; and this ignoble desire, like the servility in absolute monarchies, destroys all strength of character. Liberty is the mother of virtue, and if women be, by their very constitution, slaves, and not allowed to breathe the sharp invigorating air of freedom, they must ever languish like exotics,[7] and be reckoned beautiful flaws in nature.

As to the argument respecting the subjection in which the sex has ever been held, it retorts on man. The many have always been enthralled by the few; and monsters, who scarcely have shewn any discernment of human excellence, have tyrannized over thousands of their fellow-creatures. Why have men of superiour endowments submitted to such degradation? For, is it not universally acknowledged that kings, viewed collectively, have ever been inferior, in abilities and virtue, to the same number of men taken from the common mass of mankind—yet, have they not, and are they not still treated with a degree of reverence that is an insult to reason? China is not the only country where a living man has been made a God.[8] *Men* have submitted to superior strength to enjoy with impunity the pleasure of the moment—*women* have only done the same, and therefore till it is proved that the courtier, who servilely resigns the birthright of a man, is not a moral agent, it cannot be demonstrated that woman is essentially inferior to man because she has always been subjugated.

Brutal force has hitherto governed the world, and that the science of politics is in its infancy, is evident from philosophers scrupling to give the knowledge most useful to man that determinate distinction.

I shall not pursue this argument any further than to establish an obvious inference, that as sound politics diffuse liberty, mankind, including woman, will become more wise and virtuous.

---

7. Hot-house plants, which do not thrive in the English climate. There is also an echo here of the language of the Mansfield Judgment of 1772, the legal decision that effectually prohibited slavery within England by declaring "the air of England . . . too pure for slaves to breathe in."
8. The emperors of China were regarded as deities.

From *Chap. 4. Observations on the State of Degradation to Which Woman Is Reduced by Various Causes*

❧   ❧   ❧

In the middle rank of life, to continue the comparison,[9] men, in their youth, are prepared for professions, and marriage is not considered as the grand feature in their lives; whilst women, on the contrary, have no other scheme to sharpen their faculties. It is not business, extensive plans, or any of the excursive flights of ambition, that engross their attention; no, their thoughts are not employed in rearing such noble structures. To rise in the world, and have the liberty of running from pleasure to pleasure, they must marry advantageously, and to this object their time is sacrificed, and their persons often legally prostituted. A man when he enters any profession has his eye steadily fixed on some future advantage (and the mind gains great strength by having all its efforts directed to one point), and, full of his business, pleasure is considered as mere relaxation; whilst women seek for pleasure as the main purpose of existence. In fact, from the education, which they receive from society, the love of pleasure may be said to govern them all; but does this prove that there is a sex in souls? It would be just as rational to declare that the courtiers in France, when a destructive system of despotism had formed their character, were not men, because liberty, virtue, and humanity, were sacrificed to pleasure and vanity.—Fatal passions, which have ever domineered over the *whole* race!

The same love of pleasure, fostered by the whole tendency of their education, gives a trifling turn to the conduct of women in most circumstances: for instance, they are ever anxious about secondary things; and on the watch for adventures, instead of being occupied by duties.

A man, when he undertakes a journey, has, in general, the end in view; a woman thinks more of the incidental occurrences, the strange things that may possibly occur on the road; the impression that she may make on her fellow-travellers; and, above all, she is anxiously intent on the care of the finery that she carries with her, which is more than ever a part of herself, when going to figure on a new scene; when, to use an apt French turn of expression, she is going to produce a sensation.—Can dignity of mind exist with such trivial cares?

In short, women, in general, as well as the rich of both sexes, have acquired all the follies and vices of civilization, and missed the useful fruit. It is not necessary for me always to premise, that I speak of the condition of the whole sex, leaving exceptions out of the question. Their senses are inflamed, and their understandings neglected, consequently they become the prey of their senses, delicately termed sensibility, and are blown about by every momentary gust of feeling. Civilized women are, therefore, so weakened by false refinement, that, respecting morals, their condition is much below what it would be were they left in a state nearer to nature. Ever restless and anxious, their over exercised sensibility not only renders them uncomfortable themselves, but troublesome, to use a soft phrase, to others. All their thoughts turn on things calculated to excite emotion; and feeling, when they should reason, their conduct is unstable, and their opinions are wavering—not the wavering produced

9. I.e., her comparison between the social expectations that shape men and those that shape women and lead them to "degradation."

by deliberation or progressive views, but by contradictory emotions. By fits and starts they are warm in many pursuits; yet this warmth, never concentrated into perseverance, soon exhausts itself; exhaled by its own heat, or meeting with some other fleeting passion, to which reason has never given any specific gravity, neutrality ensues. Miserable, indeed, must be that being whose cultivation of mind has only tended to inflame its passions! A distinction should be made between inflaming and strengthening them. The passions thus pampered, whilst the judgment is left unformed, what can be expected to ensue?— Undoubtedly, a mixture of madness and folly!

This observation should not be confined to the *fair* sex; however, at present, I only mean to apply it to them.

Novels, music, poetry, and gallantry, all tend to make women the creatures of sensation, and their character is thus formed in the mold of folly during the time they are acquiring accomplishments, the only improvement they are excited, by their station in society, to acquire. This overstretched sensibility naturally relaxes the other powers of the mind, and prevents intellect from attaining that sovereignty which it ought to attain to render a rational creature useful to others, and content with its own station: for the exercise of the understanding, as life advances, is the only method pointed out by nature to calm the passions.

Satiety has a very different effect, and I have often been forcibly struck by an emphatical description of damnation:—when the spirit is represented as continually hovering with abortive eagerness round the defiled body, unable to enjoy any thing without the organs of sense. Yet, to their senses, are women made slaves, because it is by their sensibility that they obtain present power.

And will moralists pretend to assert, that this is the condition in which one half of the human race should be encouraged to remain with listless inactivity and stupid acquiescence? Kind instructors! what were we created for? To remain, it may be said, innocent; they mean in a state of childhood.—We might as well never have been born, unless it were necessary that we should be created to enable man to acquire the noble privilege of reason, the power of discerning good from evil, whilst we lie down in the dust from whence we were taken, never to rise again.—

It would be an endless task to trace the variety of meannesses, cares, and sorrows, into which women are plunged by the prevailing opinion, that they were created rather to feel than reason, and that all the power they obtain, must be obtained by their charms and weakness:

> Fine by defect, and amiably weak![1]

And, made by this amiable weakness entirely dependent, excepting what they gain by illicit sway, on man, not only for protection, but advice, is it surprising that, neglecting the duties that reason alone points out, and shrinking from trials calculated to strengthen their minds, they only exert themselves to give their defects a graceful covering, which may serve to heighten their charms in the eye of the voluptuary, though it sink them below the scale of moral excellence?

Fragile in every sense of the word, they are obliged to look up to man for every comfort. In the most trifling dangers they cling to their support, with parasitical tenacity, piteously demanding succour; and their *natural* protector extends his arm, or lifts up his voice, to guard the lovely trembler—from what?

---

1. Pope's actual words were "Fine by defect, and delicately weak" (*Moral Essays* 2.43).

Perhaps the frown of an old cow, or the jump of a mouse; a rat, would be a serious danger. In the name of reason, and even common sense, what can save such beings from contempt; even though they be soft and fair?

These fears, when not affected, may produce some pretty attitudes; but they shew a degree of imbecility which degrades a rational creature in a way women are not aware of—for love and esteem are very distinct things.

I am fully persuaded that we should hear of none of these infantine airs, if girls were allowed to take sufficient exercise, and not confined in close rooms till their muscles are relaxed, and their powers of digestion destroyed. To carry the remark still further, if fear in girls, instead of being cherished, perhaps, created, were treated in the same manner as cowardice in boys, we should quickly see women with more dignified aspects. It is true, they could not then with equal propriety be termed the sweet flowers that smile in the walk of man; but they would be more respectable members of society, and discharge the important duties of life by the light of their own reason. "Educate women like men," says Rousseau, "and the more they resemble our sex the less power will they have over us."[2] This is the very point I aim at. I do not wish them to have power over men; but over themselves.

In the same strain have I heard men argue against instructing the poor; for many are the forms that aristocracy assumes. "Teach them to read, and write," say they, "and you take them out of the station assigned them by nature." An eloquent Frenchman has answered them, I will borrow his sentiments. But they know not, when they make man a brute, that they may expect every instant to see him transformed into a ferocious beast.[3] Without knowledge there can be no morality!

Ignorance is a frail base for virtue! Yet, that it is the condition for which woman was organized, has been insisted upon by the writers who have most vehemently argued in favor of the superiority of man; a superiority not in degree, but essence; though, to soften the argument, they have labored to prove, with chivalrous generosity, that the sexes ought not to be compared; man was made to reason, woman to feel: and that together, flesh and spirit, they make the most perfect whole, by blending happily reason and sensibility into one character.

And what is sensibility? "Quickness of sensation; quickness of perception; delicacy." Thus is it defined by Dr. Johnson;[4] and the definition gives me no other idea than of the most exquisitely polished instinct. I discern not a trace of the image of God in either sensation or matter. Refined seventy times seven,[5] they are still material; intellect dwells not there; nor will fire ever make lead gold!

I come round to my old argument; if woman be allowed to have an immortal soul, she must have, as the employment of life, an understanding to improve. And when, to render the present state more complete, though every thing proves it to be but a fraction of a mighty sum, she is incited by present gratification to forget her grand destination, nature is counteracted, or she was born only to procreate and rot. Or, granting brutes, of every description, a

2. In *Émile* Rousseau means this as a warning to women that if they are brought up to be like men, they will lose their sexual power over men.
3. Poston suggests that Wollstonecraft has in mind the comment by Mirabeau, the Revolutionary statesman, to the Abbé Sieyès, who had been rudely treated in the French Constituent Assembly in 1790: "My dear abbé, you have loosed the bull:

do you expect he is not to make use of his horns?"
4. In his *Dictionary of the English Language* (1755).
5. Jesus replies, when asked whether a brother's repeated sin should be forgiven "till seven times": "I say not unto thee, Until seven times: but, Until seventy times seven" (Matthew 18.22).

192 / Mary Wollstonecraft

soul, though not a reasonable one, the exercise of instinct and sensibility may be the step, which they are to take, in this life, towards the attainment of reason in the next; so that through all eternity they will lag behind man, who, why we cannot tell, had the power given him of attaining reason in his first mode of existence.

When I treat of the peculiar duties of women, as I should treat of the peculiar duties of a citizen or father, it will be found that I do not mean to insinuate that they should be taken out of their families, speaking of the majority. "He that hath wife and children," says Lord Bacon, "hath given hostages to fortune; for they are impediments to great enterprises, either of virtue or mischief. Certainly the best works, and of greatest merit for the public, have proceeded from the unmarried or childless men."[6] I say the same of women. But, the welfare of society is not built on extraordinary exertions; and were it more reasonably organized, there would be still less need of great abilities, or heroic virtues.

In the regulation of a family, in the education of children, understanding, in an unsophisticated sense, is particularly required: strength both of body and mind; yet the men who, by their writings, have most earnestly labored to domesticate women, have endeavored, by arguments dictated by a gross appetite, which satiety had rendered fastidious, to weaken their bodies and cramp their minds. But, if even by these sinister methods they really *persuaded* women, by working on their feelings, to stay at home, and fulfil the duties of a mother and mistress of a family, I should cautiously oppose opinions that led women to right conduct, by prevailing on them to make the discharge of such important duties the main business of life, though reason were insulted. Yet, and I appeal to experience, if by neglecting the understanding they be as much, nay, more detached from these domestic employments, than they could be by the most serious intellectual pursuit, though it may be observed, that the mass of mankind will never vigorously pursue an intellectual object,[7] I may be allowed to infer that reason is absolutely necessary to enable a woman to perform any duty properly, and I must again repeat, that sensibility is not reason.

The comparison with the rich still occurs to me; for, when men neglect the duties of humanity, women will follow their example; a common stream hurries them both along with thoughtless celerity. Riches and honors prevent a man from enlarging his understanding, and enervate all his powers by reversing the order of nature, which has ever made true pleasure the reward of labor. Pleasure—enervating pleasure is, likewise, within women's reach without earning it. But, till hereditary possessions are spread abroad, how can we expect men to be proud of virtue? And, till they are, women will govern them by the most direct means, neglecting their dull domestic duties to catch the pleasure that sits lightly on the wing of time.

"The power of the woman," says some author, "is her sensibility";[8] and men, not aware of the consequence, do all they can to make this power swallow up every other. Those who constantly employ their sensibility will have most: for

6. From Francis Bacon's essay "Of Marriage and the Single Life."
7. The mass of mankind are rather the slaves of their appetites than of their passions [Wollstonecraft's note].
8. The sentiment is a commonplace, but Wollstonecraft may be referring to Edmund Burke's

phrase: "The beauty of women is considerably owing to their weakness, or delicacy . . ." (Edmund Burke, *A Philosophical Enquiry into the Origin of Our Ideas of the Sublime and Beautiful* [London, 1759 (repr. The Scolar Press, 1970)], p. 219) [Poston's note].

example; poets, painters, and composers.[9] Yet, when the sensibility is thus increased at the expence of reason, and even the imagination, why do philosophical men complain of their fickleness? The sexual attention of man particularly acts on female sensibility, and this sympathy has been exercised from their youth up. A husband cannot long pay those attentions with the passion necessary to excite lively emotions, and the heart, accustomed to lively emotions, turns to a new lover, or pines in secret, the prey of virtue or prudence. I mean when the heart has really been rendered susceptible, and the taste formed; for I am apt to conclude, from what I have seen in fashionable life, that vanity is oftener fostered than sensibility by the mode of education, and the intercourse between the sexes, which I have reprobated; and that coquetry more frequently proceeds from vanity than from that inconstancy, which overstrained sensibility naturally produces.

Another argument that has had great weight with me, must, I think, have some force with every considerate benevolent heart. Girls who have been thus weakly educated, are often cruelly left by their parents without any provision; and, of course, are dependent on, not only the reason, but the bounty of their brothers. These brothers are, to view the fairest side of the question, good sort of men, and give as a favor, what children of the same parents had an equal right to. In this equivocal humiliating situation, a docile female may remain some time, with a tolerable degree of comfort. But, when the brother marries, a probable circumstance, from being considered as the mistress of the family, she is viewed with averted looks as an intruder, an unnecessary burden on the benevolence of the master of the house, and his new partner.

Who can recount the misery, which many unfortunate beings, whose minds and bodies are equally weak, suffer in such situations—unable to work, and ashamed to beg? The wife, a cold-hearted, narrow-minded, woman, and this is not an unfair supposition; for the present mode of education does not tend to enlarge the heart any more than the understanding, is jealous of the little kindness which her husband shews to his relations; and her sensibility not rising to humanity, she is displeased at seeing the property of *her* children lavished on an helpless sister.

These are matters of fact, which have come under my eye again and again. The consequence is obvious, the wife has recourse to cunning to undermine the habitual affection, which she is afraid openly to oppose; and neither tears nor caresses are spared till the spy is worked out of her home, and thrown on the world, unprepared for its difficulties; or sent, as a great effort of generosity, or from some regard to propriety, with a small stipend, and an uncultivated mind, into joyless solitude.

These two women may be much upon a par, with respect to reason and humanity; and changing situations, might have acted just the same selfish part; but had they been differently educated, the case would also have been very different. The wife would not have had that sensibility, of which self is the centre, and reason might have taught her not to expect, and not even to be flattered by, the affection of her husband, if it led him to violate prior duties. She would wish not to love him merely because he loved her, but on account

---

9. Men of these descriptions pour it into their compositions, to amalgamate the gross materials; and, molding them with passion, give to the inert body a soul; but, in woman's imagination, love alone concentrates these ethereal beams [Wollstonecraft's note].

of his virtues; and the sister might have been able to struggle for herself instead of eating the bitter bread of dependence.

I am, indeed, persuaded that the heart, as well as the understanding, is opened by cultivation; and by, which may not appear so clear, strengthening the organs; I am not now talking of momentary flashes of sensibility, but of affections. And, perhaps, in the education of both sexes, the most difficult task is so to adjust instruction as not to narrow the understanding, whilst the heart is warmed by the generous juices of spring, just raised by the electric fermentation of the season; nor to dry up the feelings by employing the mind in investigations remote from life.

With respect to women, when they receive a careful education, they are either made fine ladies, brimful of sensibility, and teeming with capricious fancies; or mere notable women.[1] The latter are often friendly, honest creatures, and have a shrewd kind of good sense joined with worldly prudence, that often render them more useful members of society than the fine sentimental lady, though they possess neither greatness of mind nor taste. The intellectual world is shut against them; take them out of their family or neighborhood, and they stand still; the mind finding no employment, for literature affords a fund of amusement which they have never sought to relish, but frequently to despise. The sentiments and taste of more cultivated minds appear ridiculous, even in those whom chance and family connections have led them to love; but in mere acquaintance they think it all affectation.

A man of sense can only love such a woman on account of her sex, and respect her, because she is a trusty servant. He lets her, to preserve his own peace, scold the servants, and go to church in clothes made of the very best materials. A man of her own size of understanding would, probably, not agree so well with her; for he might wish to encroach on her prerogative, and manage some domestic concerns himself. Yet women, whose minds are not enlarged by cultivation, or the natural selfishness of sensibility expanded by reflection, are very unfit to manage a family; for, by an undue stretch of power, they are always tyrannizing to support a superiority that only rests on the arbitrary distinction of fortune. The evil is sometimes more serious, and domestics are deprived of innocent indulgences, and made to work beyond their strength, in order to enable the notable woman to keep a better table, and outshine her neighbours in finery and parade. If she attend to her children, it is, in general, to dress them in a costly manner—and, whether this attention arise from vanity or fondness, it is equally pernicious.

Besides, how many women of this description pass their days; or, at least, their evenings, discontentedly. Their husbands acknowledge that they are good managers, and chaste wives; but leave home to seek for more agreeable, may I be allowed to use a significant French word, *piquant*[2] society; and the patient drudge, who fulfils her task, like a blind horse in a mill, is defrauded of her just reward; for the wages due to her are the caresses of her husband; and women who have so few resources in themselves, do not very patiently bear this privation of a natural right.

A fine lady, on the contrary, has been taught to look down with contempt on the vulgar employments of life; though she has only been incited to acquire accomplishments that rise a degree above sense; for even corporeal accomplishments cannot be acquired with any degree of precision unless the

1. I.e., energetic in running a household.   2. Stimulating.

understanding has been strengthened by exercise. Without a foundation of principles taste is superficial, grace must arise from something deeper than imitation. The imagination, however, is heated, and the feelings rendered fastidious, if not sophisticated; or, a counterpoise of judgment is not acquired, when the heart still remains artless, though it becomes too tender.

These women are often amiable; and their hearts are really more sensible to general benevolence, more alive to the sentiments that civilize life, than the square-elbowed family drudge; but, wanting a due proportion of reflection and self-government, they only inspire love; and are the mistresses of their husbands, whilst they have any hold on their affections; and the platonic friends of his male acquaintance. These are the fair defects in nature; the women who appear to be created not to enjoy the fellowship of man, but to save him from sinking into absolute brutality, by rubbing off the rough angles of his character; and by playful dalliance to give some dignity to the appetite that draws him to them.—Gracious Creator of the whole human race! hast thou created such a being as woman, who can trace thy wisdom in thy works, and feel that thou alone art by thy nature exalted above her,—for no better purpose?—Can she believe that she was only made to submit to man, her equal, a being, who, like her, was sent into the world to acquire virtue?—Can she consent to be occupied merely to please him; merely to adorn the earth, when her soul is capable of rising to thee?—And can she rest supinely dependent on man for reason, when she ought to mount with him the arduous steeps of knowledge?—

Yet, if love be the supreme good, let women be only educated to inspire it, and let every charm be polished to intoxicate the senses; but, if they be moral beings, let them have a chance to become intelligent; and let love to man be only a part of that glowing flame of universal love, which, after encircling humanity, mounts in grateful incense to God.

* * *

1792

Letters Written in Sweden, Norway, and Denmark

Writing to a friend in March 1797, the poet Robert Southey declared himself haunted by a book of travels that the firm of Joseph Johnson had published at the start of the preceding year: Mary Wollstonecraft, Southey enthused, "has made me in love with a cold climate, and frost and snow, with a northern moonlight." Wollstonecraft had set out on her arduous and sometimes dangerous five-month journey through the Scandinavian countries in June 1795, taking with her Fanny, her year-old infant, and Marguerite, a French maid who had earlier accompanied her from Paris to London. Fanny's father, Gilbert Imlay—author, inaugurator of sometimes shady commercial deals, and inveterate philanderer—had devised this scheme of sending Wollstonecraft as his business agent to the northern countries, thus leaving himself free to pursue an affair with another woman. Upon returning to London in September 1795, Wollstonecraft prepared for publication the letters that she had written to Imlay during the trip. Contemporary readers were left to speculate about the identity of the *you* to whom the letters were addressed and to ponder the suggestion that the letters' unhappy author had once been romantically involved with this unnamed correspondent. For many this tantalizingly sketchy love story gave the *Letters* their fascination. Writing in his *Memoirs* of Wollstonecraft, William Godwin declared, "If ever there was a book calculated to make a man in love with its author, this appears to me the book."

By the late eighteenth century, travel writing had begun to develop into a philosophical genre—a forum for comparative inquiries into the effects various sorts of political institutions and legal systems had on people's everyday lives and a forum in which commentators assessed the costs, as well as the benefits, of social and economic progress. Wollstonecraft had reviewed travelogues for Johnson's *Analytical Review*, and she contributed to this development in her turn with these discussions of Europe's northern fringe, a remote, unmodernized region that until then had rarely figured on travelers' itineraries. In the letters she thus remarks insightfully on the relations between rich and poor in the communities she visits, on the people's responses to the political tumults of the era, and, especially, on the situation of women and the petty despotisms of family life. Yet she also responds ardently to the sublime natural scenery of Scandinavia, and moves easily from those aesthetic contemplations to meditations on death and the possibility of an afterlife—reveries she intersperses with her sharply realistic observations of the world around her.

Carol Poston, who has edited both Wollstonecraft's *Vindications of the Rights of Woman* and her *Letters* from Scandinavia, justly describes the latter as "her most delightful work" and remarks that, in the unsystematic freedom that it permits, "it is possible that the epistolary journal is the perfect literary mode for Wollstonecraft's strengths as a writer and thinker."

From Letters Written during a Short Residence in Sweden, Norway, and Denmark

Advertisement

The writing travels, or memoirs, has ever been a pleasant employment; for vanity or sensibility always renders it interesting. In writing these desultory letters, I found I could not avoid being continually the first person—"the little hero of each tale." I tried to correct this fault, if it be one, for they were designed for publication; but in proportion as I arranged my thoughts, my letter, I found, became stiff and affected: I, therefore, determined to let my remarks and reflections flow unrestrained, as I perceived that I could not give a just description of what I saw, but by relating the effect different objects had produced on my mind and feelings, whilst the impression was still fresh.

A person has a right, I have sometimes thought, when amused by a witty or interesting egotist, to talk of himself when he can win on our attention by acquiring our affection. Whether I deserve to rank amongst this privileged number, my readers alone can judge—and I give them leave to shut the book, if they do not wish to become better acquainted with me.

My plan was simply to endeavor to give a just view of the present state of the countries I have passed through, as far as I could obtain information during so short a residence; avoiding those details which, without being very useful to travelers who follow the same route, appear very insipid to those who only accompany you in their chair.

Letter 1

Eleven days of weariness on board a vessel not intended for the accommodation of passengers have so exhausted my spirits, to say nothing of the other causes, with which you are already sufficiently acquainted, that it is with some difficulty I adhere to my determination of giving you my observations, as I travel through new scenes, whilst warmed with the impression they have made on me.

The captain, as I mentioned to you, promised to put me on shore at Arendall, or Gothenburg, in his way to Elsineur;[1] but contrary winds obliged us to pass both places during the night. In the morning, however, after we had lost sight of the entrance of the latter bay, the vessel was becalmed; and the captain, to oblige me, hanging out a signal for a pilot, bore down towards the shore.

My attention was particularly directed to the lighthouse; and you can scarcely imagine with what anxiety I watched two long hours for a boat to emancipate me—still no one appeared. Every cloud that flitted on the horizon was hailed as a liberator, till approaching nearer, like most of the prospects sketched by hope, it dissolved under the eye into disappointment.

Weary of expectation, I then began to converse with the captain on the subject; and, from the tenor of the information my questions drew forth, I soon concluded, that, if I waited for a boat, I had little chance of getting on shore at this place. Despotism, as is usually the case, I found had here cramped the industry of man. The pilots being paid by the king, and scantily, they will not run into any danger, or even quit their hovels, if they can possibly avoid it, only to fulfil what is termed their duty. How different is it on the English coast, where, in the most stormy weather, boats immediately hail you, brought out by the expectation of extraordinary profit.

Disliking to sail for Elsineur, and still more to lie at anchor, or cruise about the coast for several days, I exerted all my rhetoric to prevail on the captain to let me have the ship's boat; and though I added the most forcible of arguments, I for a long time addressed him in vain.

It is a kind of rule at sea, not to send out a boat. The captain was a good-natured man; but men with common minds seldom break through general rules. Prudence is ever the resort of weakness; and they rarely go as far as they may in any undertaking, who are determined not to go beyond it on any account. If, however, I had some trouble with the captain, I did not lose much time with the sailors; for they, all alacrity, hoisted out the boat, the moment I obtained permission, and promised to row me to the lighthouse.

I did not once allow myself to doubt of obtaining a conveyance from thence round the rocks—and then away for Gothenburg—confinement is so unpleasant.

The day was fine; and I enjoyed the water till, approaching the little island, poor Marguerite, whose timidity always acts as a feeler before her adventuring spirit, began to wonder at our not seeing any inhabitants. I did not listen to her. But when, on landing, the same silence prevailed, I caught the alarm, which was not lessened by the sight of two old men, whom we forced out of their wretched hut. Scarcely human in their appearance, we with difficulty obtained an intelligible reply to our questions—the result of which was, that they had no boat, and were not allowed to quit their post, on any pretense. But, they informed us, that there was at the other side, eight or ten miles over, a pilot's dwelling; two guineas[2] tempted the sailors to risk the captain's displeasure, and once more embark to row me over.

1. Helsingør, Denmark. "Arendall": in Norway [Wollstonecraft's note]. "Gothenburg": Göteborg, Sweden.

2. A British gold coin worth one pound and a shilling.

The weather was pleasant, and the appearance of the shore so grand, that I should have enjoyed the two hours it took to reach it, but for the fatigue which was too visible in the countenances of the sailors who, instead of uttering a complaint, were, with the thoughtless hilarity peculiar to them, joking about the possibility of the captain's taking advantage of a slight westerly breeze, which was springing up, to sail without them. Yet, in spite of their good humor, I could not help growing uneasy when the shore, receding, as it were, as we advanced, seemed to promise no end to their toil. This anxiety increased when, turning into the most picturesque bay I ever saw, my eyes sought in vain for the vestige of a human habitation. Before I could determine what step to take in such a dilemma, for I could not bear to think of returning to the ship, the sight of a barge relieved me, and we hastened towards it for information. We were immediately directed to pass some jutting rocks when we should see a pilot's hut.

There was a solemn silence in this scene, which made itself be felt. The sunbeams that played on the ocean, scarcely ruffled by the lightest breeze, contrasted with the huge, dark rocks, that looked like the rude materials of creation forming the barrier of unwrought space, forcibly struck me; but I should not have been sorry if the cottage had not appeared equally tranquil. Approaching a retreat where strangers, especially women, so seldom appeared, I wondered that curiosity did not bring the beings who inhabited it to the windows or door. I did not immediately recollect that men who remain so near the brute creation, as only to exert themselves to find the food necessary to sustain life, have little or no imagination to call forth the curiosity necessary to fructify the faint glimmerings of mind which entitles them to rank as lords of the creation.—Had they either, they could not contentedly remain rooted in the clods they so indolently cultivate.

Whilst the sailors went to seek for the sluggish inhabitants, these conclusions occurred to me; and, recollecting the extreme fondness which the Parisians ever testify for novelty, their very curiosity appeared to me a proof of the progress they had made in refinement. Yes; in the art of living—in the art of escaping from the cares which embarrass the first steps towards the attainment of the pleasures of social life.

The pilots informed the sailors that they were under the direction of a lieutenant retired from the service, who spoke English; adding, that they could do nothing without his orders; and even the offer of money could hardly conquer their laziness, and prevail on them to accompany us to his dwelling. They would not go with me alone which I wanted them to have done, because I wished to dismiss the sailors as soon as possible. Once more we rowed off, they following tardily, till, turning round another bold protuberance of the rocks, we saw a boat making towards us, and soon learnt that it was the lieutenant himself, coming with some earnestness to see who we were.

To save the sailors any further toil, I had my baggage instantly removed into his boat; for, as he could speak English, a previous parley was not necessary; though Marguerite's respect for me could hardly keep her from expressing the fear, strongly marked on her countenance, which my putting ourselves into the power of a strange man excited. He pointed out his cottage; and, drawing near to it, I was not sorry to see a female figure, though I had not, like Marguerite, been thinking of robberies, murders, or the other evil[3] which instantly, as the sailors would have said, runs foul of a woman's imagination.

---

3. Rape.

On entering, I was still better pleased to find a clean house, with some degree of rural elegance. The beds were of muslin, coarse it is true, but dazzlingly white; and the floor was strewed over with little sprigs of juniper (the custom, as I afterwards found, of the country), which formed a contrast with the curtains and produced an agreeable sensation of freshness, to soften the ardor of noon. Still nothing was so pleasing as the alacrity of hospitality—all that the house afforded was quickly spread on the whitest linen.—Remember I had just left the vessel, where, without being fastidious, I had continually been disgusted. Fish, milk, butter, and cheese, and I am sorry to add, brandy, the bane of this country, were spread on the board. After we had dined, hospitality made them, with some degree of mystery, bring us some excellent coffee. I did not then know that it was prohibited.[4]

The good man of the house apologized for coming in continually, but declared that he was so glad to speak English, he could not stay out. He need not have apologized; I was equally glad of his company. With the wife I could only exchange smiles; and she was employed observing the make of our clothes. My hands, I found, had first led her to discover that I was the lady. I had, of course, my quantum of reverences; for the politeness of the north seems to partake of the coldness of the climate, and the rigidity of its iron sinewed rocks. Amongst the peasantry, there is, however, so much of the simplicity of the golden age in this land of flint—so much overflowing of heart, and fellow-feeling, that only benevolence, and the honest sympathy of nature, diffused smiles over my countenance when they kept me standing, regardless of my fatigue, whilst they dropt courtesy after courtesy.

The situation of this house was beautiful, though chosen for convenience. The master being the officer who commanded all the pilots on the coast, and the person appointed to guard wrecks, it was necessary for him to fix on a spot that would overlook the whole bay. As he had seen some service, he wore, not without a pride I thought becoming, a badge to prove that he had merited well of his country. It was happy, I thought, that he had been paid in honor; for the stipend he received was little more than twelve pounds a year.—I do not trouble myself or you with the calculation of Swedish ducats. Thus, my friend, you perceive the necessity of *perquisites*.[5] This same narrow policy runs through every thing. I shall have occasion further to animadvert on it.

Though my host amused me with an account of himself, which gave me an idea of the manners of the people I was about to visit, I was eager to climb the rocks to view the country, and see whether the honest tars had regained their ship. With the help of the lieutenant's telescope I saw the vessel underway with a fair though gentle gale. The sea was calm, playful even as the most shallow stream, and on the vast bason[6] I did not see a dark speck to indicate the boat. My conductors were consequently arrived.

Straying further my eye was attracted by the sight of some heart's-ease[7] that peeped through the rocks. I caught at it as a good omen, and going to preserve it in a letter that had not conveyed balm to my heart, a cruel remembrance suffused my eyes; but it passed away like an April shower. If you are deep read in Shakspeare, you will recollect that this was the little western flower tinged

---

4. The law then prohibited the import or consumption of coffee.
5. Payments in addition to salary. The suggestion is of income derived from bribes or smuggling.
6. I.e., basin.

7. A small wildflower, variously colored. Wollstonecraft goes on to make the first of many veiled allusions to her faithless lover Gilbert Imlay, to whom these letters are addressed.

by love's dart, which "maidens call love in idleness."[8] The gaiety of my babe was unmixed; regardless of omens or sentiments, she found a few wild strawberries more grateful[9] than flowers or fancies.

The lieutenant informed me that this was a commodious bay. Of that I could not judge, though I felt its picturesque beauty. Rocks were piled on rocks, forming a suitable bulwark to the ocean. Come no further, they emphatically said, turning their dark sides to the waves to augment the idle roar. The view was sterile: still little patches of earth, of the most exquisite verdure, enameled with the sweetest wild flowers, seemed to promise the goats and a few straggling cows luxurious herbage. How silent and peaceful was the scene. I gazed around with rapture, and felt more of that spontaneous pleasure which gives credibility to our expectation of happiness, than I had for a long, long time before. I forgot the horrors I had witnessed in France,[1] which had cast a gloom over all nature, and suffering the enthusiasm of my character, too often, gracious God! damped by the tears of disappointed affection, to be lighted up afresh, care took wing while simple fellow feeling expanded my heart.

To prolong this enjoyment, I readily assented to the proposal of our host to pay a visit to a family, the master of which spoke English, who was the drollest dog in the country, he added, repeating some of his stories, with a hearty laugh.

I walked on, still delighted with the rude beauties of the scene; for the sublime often gave place imperceptibly to the beautiful, dilating the emotions which were painfully concentrated.

When we entered this abode, the largest I had yet seen, I was introduced to a numerous family; but the father, from whom I was led to expect so much entertainment, was absent. The lieutenant consequently was obliged to be the interpreter of our reciprocal compliments. The phrases were awkwardly transmitted, it is true; but looks and gestures were sufficient to make them intelligible and interesting. The girls were all vivacity, and respect for me could scarcely keep them from romping with my host, who, asking for a pinch of snuff, was presented with a box, out of which an artificial mouse, fastened to the bottom, sprung. Though this trick had doubtless been played time out of mind, yet the laughter it excited was not less genuine.

They were overflowing with civility; but to prevent their almost killing my babe with kindness, I was obliged to shorten my visit; and two or three of the girls accompanied us, bringing with them a part of whatever the house afforded to contribute towards rendering my supper more plentiful; and plentiful in fact it was, though I with difficulty did honor to some of the dishes, not relishing the quantity of sugar and spices put into every thing. At supper my host told me bluntly that I was a woman of observation, for I asked him *men's questions.*

The arrangements for my journey were quickly made; I could only have a car with post-horses, as I did not choose to wait till a carriage could be sent for to Gothenburg. The expense of my journey, about one or two and twenty English miles, I found would not amount to more than eleven or twelve shillings, paying, he assured me, generously. I gave him a guinea and a half. But it was with the greatest difficulty that I could make him take so much, indeed any thing for my lodging and fare. He declared that it was next to robbing me,

8. Popular name for the pansy, whose juice Oberon put on the sleeping Titania's eyes to make her dote on the next person she saw (Shakespeare's *A Midsummer Night's Dream* 2.1.165–72).

9. Pleasing.
1. Wollstonecraft had lived in France at the time of the Reign of Terror under Robespierre (1793–94).

explaining how much I ought to pay on the road. However, as I was positive, he took the guinea for himself; but, as a condition, insisted on accompanying me, to prevent my meeting with any trouble or imposition on the way.

I then retired to my apartment with regret. The night was so fine, that I would gladly have rambled about much longer; yet recollecting that I must rise very early, I reluctantly went to bed: but my senses had been so awake, and my imagination still continued so busy, that I sought for rest in vain. Rising before six, I scented the sweet morning air; I had long before heard the birds twittering to hail the dawning day, though it could scarcely have been allowed to have departed.

Nothing, in fact, can equal the beauty of the northern summer's evening and night; if night it may be called that only wants the glare of day, the full light, which frequently seems so impertinent; for I could write at midnight very well without a candle. I contemplated all nature at rest; the rocks, even grown darker in their appearance, looked as if they partook of the general repose, and reclined more heavily on their foundation.—What, I exclaimed, is this active principle which keeps me still awake?—Why fly my thoughts abroad when every thing around me appears at home? My child was sleeping with equal calmness—innocent and sweet as the closing flowers.—Some recollections, attached to the idea of home, mingled with reflections respecting the state of society I had been contemplating that evening, made a tear drop on the rosy cheek I had just kissed; and emotions that trembled on the brink of ectasy and agony gave a poignancy to my sensations, which made me feel more alive than usual.

What are these imperious sympathies? How frequently has melancholy and even misanthropy taken possession of me, when the world has disgusted me, and friends have proved unkind. I have then considered myself as a particle broken off from the grand mass of mankind;—I was alone, till some involuntary sympathetic emotion, like the attraction of adhesion,[2] made me feel that I was still a part of a mighty whole, from which I could not sever myself—not, perhaps, for the reflection has been carried very far, by snapping the thread of an existence which loses its charms in proportion as the cruel experience of life stops or poisons the current of the heart. Futurity, what hast thou not to give to those who know that there is such a thing as happiness! I speak not of philosophical contentment, though pain has afforded them the strongest conviction of it.

After our coffee and milk, for the mistress of the house had been roused long before us by her hospitality, my baggage was taken forward in a boat by my host, because the car could not safely have been brought to the house.

The road at first was very rocky and troublesome; but our driver was careful, and the horses accustomed to the frequent and sudden acclivities and descents; so that not apprehending any danger, I played with my girl, whom I would not leave to Marguerite's care, on account of her timidity.

Stopping at a little inn to bait[3] the horses, I saw the first countenance in Sweden that displeased me, though the man was better dressed than any one who had as yet fallen in my way. An altercation took place between him and my host, the purport of which I could not guess, excepting that I was the occasion of it, be it what it would. The sequel was his leaving the house angrily;

2. The physical attraction between two different   3. Feed.
substances.

202 / MARY WOLLSTONECRAFT

and I was immediately informed that he was the custom-house officer. The professional had indeed effaced the national character, for living as he did with these frank hospitable people, still only the exciseman appeared,—the counterpart of some I had met with in England and France. I was unprovided with a passport, not having entered any great town. At Gothenburg I knew I could immediately obtain one, and only the trouble made me object to the searching my trunks. He blustered for money; but the lieutenant was determined to guard me, according to promise, from imposition.

To avoid being interrogated at the town-gate, and obliged to go in the rain to give an account of myself, merely a form, before we could get the refreshment we stood in need of, he requested us to descend, I might have said step, from our car, and walk into town.

I expected to have found a tolerable inn, but was ushered into a most comfortless one; and, because it was about five o'clock, three or four hours after their dining hour, I could not prevail on them to give me any thing warm to eat.

The appearance of the accommodations obliged me to deliver one of my recommendatory letters, and the gentleman, to whom it was addressed, sent to look out for a lodging for me whilst I partook of his supper. As nothing passed at this supper to characterize the country, I shall here close my letter.

Your's truly.

Letter 4

The severity of the long Swedish winter tends to render the people sluggish; for, though this season has its peculiar pleasures, too much time is employed to guard against its inclemency. Still, as warm cloathing is absolutely necessary, the women spin, and the men weave, and by these exertions get a fence to keep out the cold. I have rarely passed a knot of cottages without seeing cloth laid out to bleach; and when I entered, always found the women spinning or knitting.

A mistaken tenderness, however, for their children, makes them, even in summer, load them with flannels; and, having a sort of natural antipathy to cold water, the squalid appearance of the poor babes, not to speak of the noxious smell which flannel and rugs retain, seems a reply to a question I had often asked—Why I did not see more children in the villages I passed through? Indeed the children appear to be nipt in the bud, having neither the graces nor charms of their age. And this, I am persuaded, is much more owing to the ignorance of the mothers than to the rudeness of the climate. Rendered feeble by the continual perspiration they are kept in, whilst every pore is absorbing unwholesome moisture, they give them, even at the breast, brandy, salt fish, and every other crude substance, which air and exercise enables the parent to digest.

The women of fortune here, as well as every where else, have nurses to suckle their children; and the total want of chastity in the lower class of women frequently renders them very unfit for the trust.[4]

You have sometimes remarked to me the difference of the manners of the country girls in England and in America; attributing the reserve of the former to the climate—to the absence of genial suns. But it must be their stars,[5] not

4. Because of the possibility that veneral disease might be transmitted via their breast milk.
5. See the quotation from Prior and the explana-

tory note in chapter 2 of *Vindication* (p. 187 above).

the zephyrs gently stealing on their senses, which here lead frail women astray.—Who can look at these rocks, and allow the voluptuousness[6] of nature to be an excuse for gratifying the desires it inspires? We must, therefore, find some other cause beside voluptuousness, I believe, to account for the conduct of the Swedish and American country girls; for I am led to conclude, from all the observations I have made, that there is always a mixture of sentiment and imagination in voluptuousness, to which neither of them have much pretension.

The country girls of Ireland and Wales equally feel the first impulse of nature, which, restrained in England by fear or delicacy, proves that society is there in a more advanced state. Besides, as the mind is cultivated, and taste gains ground, the passions become stronger, and rest on something more stable than the casual sympathies of the moment. Health and idleness will always account for promiscuous amors; and in some degree I term every person idle, the exercise of whose mind does not bear some proportion to that of the body.

The Swedish ladies exercise neither sufficiently; of course, grow very fat at an early age; and when they have not this downy[7] appearance, a comfortable idea, you will say, in a cold climate, they are not remarkable for fine forms. They have, however, mostly fine complexions; but indolence makes the lily soon displace the rose. The quantity of coffee, spices, and other things of that kind, with want of care, almost universally spoil their teeth, which contrast but ill with their ruby lips.

The manners of Stockholm are refined, I hear, by the introduction of gallantry; but in the country, romping and coarse freedoms, with coarser allusions, keep the spirits awake. In the article of cleanliness, the women, of all descriptions, seem very deficient; and their dress shews that vanity is more inherent in women than taste.

The men appear to have paid still less court to the graces. They are a robust, healthy race, distinguished for their common sense and turn for humor, rather than for wit or sentiment. I include not, as you may suppose, in this general character, some of the nobility and officers, who having traveled, are polite and well informed.

I must own to you, that the lower class of people here amuse and interest me much more than the middling, with their apish good breeding and prejudices. The sympathy and frankness of heart conspicuous in the peasantry produces even a simple gracefulness of deportment, which has frequently struck me as very picturesque; I have often also been touched by their extreme desire to oblige me, when I could not explain my wants, and by their earnest manner of expressing that desire. There is such a charm in tenderness!—It is so delightful to love our fellow-creatures, and meet the honest affections as they break forth. Still, my good friend, I begin to think that I should not like to live continually in the country, with people whose minds have such a narrow range. My heart would frequently be interested; but my mind would languish for more companionable society.

The beauties of nature appear to me now even more alluring than in my youth, because my intercourse with the world has formed, without vitiating my taste. But, with respect to the inhabitants of the country, my fancy has probably, when disgusted with artificial manners, solaced itself by joining the advantages of cultivation with the interesting sincerity of innocence, forgetting the lassitude that ignorance will naturally produce. I like to see animals sport-

6. Erotic sensuality.　　　　　　7. Softly plump.

ing, and sympathize in their pains and pleasures. Still I love sometimes to view the human face divine,[8] and trace the soul, as well as the heart, in its varying lineaments.

A journey to the country, which I must shortly make, will enable me to extend my remarks.—Adieu!

Letter 8

Tonsberg[9] was formerly the residence of one of the little sovereigns of Norway; and on an adjacent mountain the vestiges of a fort remain, which was battered down by the Swedes; the entrance of the bay lying close to it.

Here I have frequently strayed, sovereign of the waste, I seldom met any human creature; and sometimes, reclining on the mossy down, under the shelter of a rock, the prattling of the sea amongst the pebbles has lulled me to sleep—no fear of any rude satyr's approaching to interrupt my repose. Balmy were the slumbers, and soft the gales, that refreshed me, when I awoke to follow, with an eye vaguely curious, the white sails, as they turned the cliffs, or seemed to take shelter under the pines which covered the little islands that so gracefully rose to render the terrific ocean beautiful. The fishermen were calmly casting their nets; whilst the seagulls hovered over the unruffled deep. Every thing seemed to harmonize into tranquillity—even the mournful call of the bittern was in cadence with the tinkling bells on the necks of the cows, that, pacing slowly one after the other, along an inviting path in the vale below, were repairing to the cottages to be milked. With what ineffable pleasure have I not gazed—and gazed again, losing my breath through my eyes—my very soul diffused itself in the scene—and, seeming to become all senses, glided in the scarcely-agitated waves, melted in the freshening breeze, or, taking its flight with fairy wing, to the misty mountains which bounded the prospect, fancy tript over new lawns, more beautiful even than the lovely slopes on the winding shore before me.—I pause, again breathless, to trace, with renewed delight, sentiments which entranced me, when, turning my humid eyes from the expanse below to the vault above, my sight pierced the fleecy clouds that softened the azure brightness; and, imperceptibly recalling the reveries of childhood, I bowed before the awful throne of my Creator, whilst I rested on its footstool.

You have sometimes wondered, my dear friend, at the extreme affection of my nature—But such is the temperature of my soul—It is not the vivacity of youth, the hey-day of existence. For years have I endeavored to calm an impetuous tide—laboring to make my feelings take an orderly course.—It was striving against the stream.—I must love and admire with warmth, or I sink into sadness. Tokens of love which I have received have rapt me in elysium—purifying the heart they enchanted.—My bosom still glows.—Do not saucily ask, repeating Sterne's question, "Maria, is it still so warm?"[1] Sufficiently, O my God! has it been chilled by sorrow and unkindness—still nature will prevail—and if I blush at recollecting past enjoyment, it is the rosy hue of pleasure

8. An echo of Milton's *Paradise Lost* 3.44 and possibly of William Blake's "The Divine Image" (p. 85 above).
9. Tönsberg, Norway.
1. In Laurence Sterne's novel *A Sentimental Journey* (1768), Parson Yorick, a man of acute sensi-

bility, drenches his handkerchief with tears at hearing of the beautiful Maria's romantic misadventures. When Maria offers to wash the handkerchief in the stream, then dry it in her bosom, Yorick asks flirtatiously, "And is your heart still so warm, Maria?"

heightened by modesty; for the blush of modesty and shame are as distinct as the emotions by which they are produced.

I need scarcely inform you, after telling you of my walks, that my constitution has been renovated here; and that I have recovered my activity, even whilst attaining a little *embonpoint*.[2] My imprudence last winter, and some untoward accidents just at the time I was weaning my child, had reduced me to a state of weakness which I never before experienced.[3] A slow fever preyed on me every night, during my residence in Sweden, and after I arrived at Tonsberg. By chance I found a fine rivulet filtered through the rocks, and confined in a bason for the cattle. It tasted to me like a chaly-beat;[4] at any rate it was pure; and the good effect of the various waters which invalids are sent to drink, depends, I believe, more on the air, exercise and change of scene, than on their medicinal qualities. I therefore determined to turn my morning walks towards it, and seek for health from the nymph of the fountain; partaking of the beverage offered to the tenants of the shade.

Chance likewise led me to discover a new pleasure, equally beneficial to my health. I wished to avail myself of my vicinity to the sea, and bathe; but it was not possible near the town; there was no convenience. The young woman whom I mentioned to you, proposed rowing me across the water, amongst the rocks; but as she was pregnant, I insisted on taking one of the oars, and learning to row. It was not difficult; and I do not know a pleasanter exercise. I soon became expert, and my train of thinking kept time, as it were, with the oars, or I suffered the boat to be carried along by the current, indulging a pleasing forgetfulness, or fallacious hopes.—How fallacious! yet, without hope, what is to sustain life, but the fear of annihilation—the only thing of which I have ever felt a dread—I cannot bear to think of being no more—of losing myself—though existence is often but a painful consciousness of misery; nay, it appears to me impossible that I should cease to exist, or that this active, restless spirit, equally alive to joy and sorrow, should only be organized dust—ready to fly abroad the moment the spring snaps, or the spark goes out, which kept it together. Surely something resides in this heart that is not perishable—and life is more than a dream.

Sometimes, to take up my oar, once more, when the sea was calm, I was amused by disturbing the innumerable young star fish which floated just below the surface: I had never observed them before; for they have not a hard shell, like those which I have seen on the seashore. They look like thickened water, with a white edge; and four purple circles, of different forms, were in the middle, over an incredible number of fibers, or white lines. Touching them, the cloudy substance would turn or close, first on one side, then on the other, very gracefully; but when I took one of them up in the ladle with which I heaved the water out of the boat, it appeared only a colorless jelly.

I did not see any of the seals, numbers of which followed our boat when we landed in Sweden; for though I like to sport in the water, I should have had no desire to join in their gambols.

Enough, you will say, of inanimate nature, and of brutes, to use the lordly phrase of man; let me hear something of the inhabitants.

The gentleman with whom I had business, is the mayor of Tonsberg; he

2. Plumpness (French).
3. Wollstonecraft tells of these events in letters to Gilbert Imlay, January 1795.
4. Mineral water containing salts of iron, taken as a tonic.

speaks English intelligibly; and, having a sound understanding, I was sorry
that his numerous occupations prevented my gaining as much information
from him as I could have drawn forth, had we frequently conversed. The
people of the town, as far as I had an opportunity of knowing their sentiments,
are extremely well satisfied with his manner of discharging his office. He has
a degree of information and good sense which excites respect, whilst a cheerfulness, almost amounting to gaiety, enables him to reconcile differences, and
keep his neighbors in good humor.—"I lost my horse," said a woman to me;
"but ever since, when I want to send to the mill, or go out, the mayor lends
me one.—He scolds if I do not come for it."

A criminal was branded, during my stay here, for the third offense; but the
relief he received made him declare that the judge was one of the best men
in the world.

I sent this wretch a trifle, at different times, to take with him into slavery.
As it was more than he expected, he wished very much to see me; and this
wish brought to my remembrance an anecdote I heard when I was in Lisbon.[5]

A wretch who had been imprisoned several years, during which period lamps
had been put up, was at last condemned to a cruel death; yet, in his way to
execution, he only wished for one night's respite, to see the city lighted.

Having dined in company at the mayor's, I was invited with his family to
spend the day at one of the richest merchant's houses.—Though I could not
speak Danish, I knew that I could see a great deal: yes; I am persuaded that I
have formed a very just opinion of the character of the Norwegians, without
being able to hold converse with them.

I had expected to meet some company; yet was a little disconcerted at being
ushered into an apartment full of well-dressed people; and, glancing my eyes
round, they rested on several very pretty faces. Rosy cheeks, sparkling eyes,
and light brown or golden locks; for I never saw so much hair with a yellow
cast; and, with their fine complexions, it looked very becoming.

These women seem a mixture of indolence and vivacity; they scarcely ever
walk out, and were astonished that I should, for pleasure; yet they are immod-
erately fond of dancing. Unaffected in their manners, if they have no pretensions to elegance, simplicity often produces a gracefulness of deportment,
when they are animated by a particular desire to please—which was the case
at present. The solitariness of my situation, which they thought terrible, interested them very much in my favor. They gathered round me—sung to me—
and one of the prettiest, to whom I gave my hand, with some degree of cordiality, to meet the glance of her eyes, kissed me very affectionately.

At dinner, which was conducted with great hospitality, though we remained
at table too long, they sung several songs, and, amongst the rest, translations
of some patriotic French ones.[6] As the evening advanced, they became playful,
and we kept up a sort of conversation of gestures. As their minds were totally
uncultivated, I did not lose much, perhaps gained, by not being able to understand them; for fancy probably filled up, more to their advantage, the void in
the picture. Be that as it may, they excited my sympathy; and I was very much
flattered when I was told, the next day, that they said it was a pleasure to look
at me, I appeared so good-natured.

The men were generally captains of ships. Several spoke English very tol-

5. Wollstonecraft had gone to Lisbon in 1785, to
nurse her dying friend Fanny Blood.

6. To indicate sympathy with the French Revolution.

erably; but they were merely matter of fact men, confined to a very narrow circle of observation. I found it difficult to obtain from them any information respecting their own country, when the fumes of tobacco did not keep me at a distance.

I was invited to partake of some other feasts, and always had to complain of the quantity of provision, and the length of time taken to consume it; for it would not have been proper to have said devour, all went on so fair and softly. The servants wait as slowly as their mistresses carve.

The young women here, as well as in Sweden, have commonly bad teeth, which I attribute to the same causes. They are fond of finery, but do not pay the necessary attention to their persons, to render beauty less transient than a flower; and that interesting expression which sentiment and accomplishments give, seldom supplies its place.

The servants have likewise an inferior sort of food here; but their masters are not allowed to strike them with impunity. I might have added mistresses; for it was a complaint of this kind, brought before the mayor, which led me to a knowledge of the fact.

The wages are low, which is particularly unjust, because the price of clothes is much higher than provisions. A young woman, who is wet nurse to the mistress of the inn where I lodge, receives only twelve dollars[7] a year, and pays ten for the nursing of her own child; the father had run away to get clear of the expense. There was something in this most painful state of widowhood which excited my compassion, and led me to reflections on the instability of the most flattering plans of happiness, that were painful in the extreme, till I was ready to ask whether this world was not created to exhibit every possible combination of wretchedness. I asked these questions of a heart writhing with anguish, whilst I listened to a melancholy ditty sung by this poor girl. It was too early for thee to be abandoned, thought I, and I hastened out of the house, to take my solitary evening's walk—And here I am again, to talk of any thing, but the pangs arising from the discovery of estranged affection, and the lonely sadness of a deserted heart.

The father and mother, if the father can be ascertained, are obliged to maintain an illegitimate child at their joint expense; but, should the father disappear, go up the country or to sea, the mother must maintain it herself. However, accidents of this kind do not prevent their marrying; and then it is not unusual to take the child or children home; and they are brought up very amicably with the marriage progeny.

I took some pains to learn what books were written originally in their language; but for any certain information respecting the state of Danish literature, I must wait till I arrive at Copenhagen.

The sound of the language is soft, a great proportion of the words ending in vowels; and there is a simplicity in the turn of some of the phrases which have been translated to me, that pleased and interested me. In the country, the farmers use the *thou* and *thee*; and they do not acquire the polite plurals of the towns by meeting at market. The not having markets established in the large towns appears to me a great inconvenience. When the farmers have any thing to sell, they bring it to the neighboring town, and take it from house to house. I am surprised that the inhabitants do not feel how very incommodious this usage is to both parties, and redress it. They indeed perceive it; for when

7. The local currency was the rixdollar, worth about one-fifth of a British pound sterling.

I have introduced the subject, they acknowledged that they were often in want of necessaries, there being no butchers, and they were often obliged to buy what they did not want; yet it was the *custom*; and the changing of customs of a long standing requires more energy than they yet possess. I received a similar reply, when I attempted to persuade the women that they injured their children by keeping them too warm. The only way of parrying off my reasoning was, that they must do as other people did. In short, reason on any subject of change, and they stop you by saying that "the town would talk." A person of sense, with a large fortune, to insure respect, might be very useful here, by inducing them to treat their children, and manage their sick properly, and eat food dressed in a simpler manner: the example, for instance, of a count's lady.

Reflecting on these prejudices made me revert to the wisdom of those legislators who established institutions for the good of the body, under the pretext of serving heaven for the salvation of the soul. These might with strict propriety be termed pious frauds; and I admire the Peruvian pair[8] for asserting that they came from the sun, when their conduct proved that they meant to enlighten a benighted country, whose obedience, or even attention, could only be secured by awe.

Thus much for conquering the *inertia* of reason; but, when it is once in motion, fables, once held sacred, may be ridiculed; and sacred they were, when useful to mankind.—Prometheus alone stole fire to animate the first man; his posterity need not supernatural aid to preserve the species, though love is generally termed a flame; and it may not be necessary much longer to suppose men inspired by heaven to inculcate the duties which demand special grace, when reason convinces them that they are the happiest who are the most nobly employed.

In a few days I am to set out for the western part of Norway, and then shall return by land to Gothenburg. I cannot think of leaving this place without regret. I speak of the place before the inhabitants, though there is a tenderness in their artless kindness which attaches me to them; but it is an attachment that inspires a regret very different from that I felt at leaving Hull, in my way to Sweden. The domestic happiness, and good-humored gaiety, of the amiable family where I and my Frances were so hospitably received, would have been sufficient to insure the tenderest remembrance, without the recollection of the social evenings to stimulate it, when good-breeding gave dignity to sympathy, and wit, zest to reason.

Adieu!—I am just informed that my horse has been waiting this quarter of an hour. I now venture to ride out alone. The steeple serves as a land-mark. I once or twice lost my way, walking alone, without being able to inquire after a path. I was therefore obliged to make to the steeple, or wind-mill, over hedge and ditch.

Your's truly.

Letter 19

Business having obliged me to go a few miles out of town this morning, I was surprised at meeting a crowd of people of every description; and inquiring

8. Probably a reference to the Inca of Peru and his daughter Orazia in John Dryden and Robert Howard's drama *The Indian Queen* (1663). When the Aztec emperor Montezuma, as a reward for his military service, requests Orazia in marriage, the Inca, addressing him as "Thou glorious sun," says that Montezuma deserves to die for wanting to mix "such base blood" with his divine blood.

the cause, of a servant who spoke French, I was informed that a man had been executed two hours before, and the body afterwards burnt. I could not help looking with horror around—the fields lost their verdure—and I turned with disgust from the well-dressed women, who were returning with their children from this sight. What a spectacle for humanity! The seeing such a flock of idle gazers, plunged me into a train of reflections, on the pernicious effects produced by false notions of justice. And I am persuaded that till capital punishments be entirely abolished, executions ought to have every appearance of horror given to them; instead of being, as they are now, a scene of amusement for the gaping crowd, where sympathy is quickly effaced by curiosity.

I have always been of opinion that the allowing actors to die, in the presence of the audience, has an immoral tendency; but trifling when compared with the ferocity acquired by viewing the reality as a show; for it seems to me, that in all countries the common people go to executions to see how the poor wretch plays his part, rather than to commiserate his fate, much less to think of the breach of morality which has brought him to such a deplorable end. Consequently executions, far from being useful examples to the survivors, have, I am persuaded, a quite contrary effect, by hardening the heart they ought to terrify. Besides, the fear of an ignominious death, I believe, never deterred any one from the commission of a crime; because, in committing it, the mind is roused to activity about present circumstances. It is a game at hazard,[9] at which all expect the turn of the die in their own favor; never reflecting on the chance of ruin, till it comes. In fact, from what I saw, in the fortresses of Norway, I am more and more convinced that the same energy of character, which renders a man a daring villain, would have rendered him useful to society, had that society been well organized. When a strong mind is not disciplined by cultivation, it is a sense of injustice that renders it unjust.

Executions, however, occur very rarely at Copenhagen; for timidity, rather than clemency, palsies all the operations of the present government. The malefactor, who died this morning, would not, probably, have been punished with death at any other period; but an incendiary excites universal execration; and as the greater part of the inhabitants are still distressed by the late conflagration,[1] an example was thought absolutely necessary; though, from what I can gather, the fire was accidental.

Not, but that I have very seriously been informed, that combustible materials were placed at proper distances, by the emissaries of Mr. Pitt;[2] and, to corroborate the fact, many people insist, that the flames burst out at once in different parts of the city; not allowing the wind to have any hand in it. So much for the plot. But the fabricators of plots in all countries build their conjectures on the "baseless fabric of a vision";[3] and, it seems even a sort of poetical justice, that whilst this minister is crushing at home, plots of his own conjuring up,[4] that on the continent, and in the north, he should, with as little foundation, be accused of wishing to set the world on fire.

I forgot to mention, to you, that I was informed, by a man of veracity, that two persons came to the stake to drink a glass of the criminal's blood, as an

9. A game played with dice, similar to craps.
1. Earlier in that year (1795) a great fire in Copenhagen had destroyed nearly a thousand houses and public buildings. "Incendiary": arsonist.
2. William Pitt, then prime minister of England.
3. Prospero in Shakespeare's *The Tempest*

4.1.151–54: "And like the baseless fabric of this vision, . . . shall dissolve."
4. Pitt was prosecuting what he claimed to be Jacobin plots against Great Britain, at a time of war with revolutionary France.

infallible remedy for the apoplexy. And when I animadverted in the company, where it was mentioned, on such a horrible violation of nature, a Danish lady reproved me very severely, asking how I knew that it was not a cure for the disease? adding, that every attempt was justifiable in search of health. I did not, you may imagine, enter into an argument with a person the slave of such a gross prejudice. And I allude to it not only as a trait of the ignorance of the people, but to censure the government, for not preventing scenes that throw an odium on the human race.

Empiricism[5] is not peculiar to Denmark; and I know no way of rooting it out, though it be a remnant of exploded witchcraft, till the acquiring a general knowledge of the component parts of the human frame, become a part of public education.

Since the fire, the inhabitants have been very assiduously employed in searching for property secreted during the confusion; and it is astonishing how many people, formerly termed reputable, had availed themselves of the common calamity to purloin what the flames spared. Others, expert at making a distinction without a difference, concealed what they found, not troubling themselves to enquire for the owners, though they scrupled to search for plunder any where, but amongst the ruins.

To be honester than the laws require, is by most people thought a work of supererogation;[6] and to slip through the grate of the law, has ever exercised the abilities of adventurers, who wish to get rich the shortest way. Knavery, without personal danger, is an art, brought to great perfection by the statesman and swindler; and meaner knaves are not tardy in following their footsteps.

It moves my gall to discover some of the commercial frauds practiced during the present war. In short, under whatever point of view I consider society, it appears, to me, that an adoration of property is the root of all evil. Here it does not render the people enterprising, as in America, but thrifty and cautious. I never, therefore, was in a capital where there was so little appearance of active industry; and as for gaiety, I looked in vain for the sprightly gait of the Norwegians, who in every respect appear to me to have got the start of them. This difference I attribute to their having more liberty: a liberty which they think their right by inheritance, whilst the Danes, when they boast of their negative happiness, always mention it as the boon of the prince royal, under the superintending wisdom of count Bernstorff. Vassallage[7] is nevertheless ceasing throughout the kingdom, and with it will pass away that sordid avarice which every modification of slavery is calculated to produce.

If the chief use of property be power, in the shape of the respect it procures, is it not among the inconsistencies of human nature most incomprehensible, that men should find a pleasure in hoarding up property which they steal from their necessities, even when they are convinced that it would be dangerous to display such an enviable superiority? Is not this the situation of serfs in every country; yet a rapacity to accumulate money seems to become stronger in proportion as it is allowed to be useless.

Wealth does not appear to be sought for, amongst the Danes, to obtain the elegant luxuries of life; for a want of taste is very conspicuous at Copenhagen; so much so, that I am not surprised to hear that poor Matilda[8] offended the

5. In the old sense: medical practices without a scientific basis.
6. More than is required.
7. Social system that holds the peasantry in legal bondage to their masters as serfs. Andreas Peter

Bernstorff was an able administrator in the Danish foreign service.
8. Caroline Matilda, sister of the Hanoverian George III of Great Britain, was the young wife of Christian VII of Denmark. By the plotting of

rigid Lutherans, by aiming to refine their pleasures. The elegance which she wished to introduce, was termed lasciviousness: yet I do not find that the absence of gallantry renders the wives more chaste, or the husbands more constant. Love here seems to corrupt the morals, without polishing the manners, by banishing confidence and truth, the charm as well as cement of domestic life. A gentleman, who has resided in this city some time, assures me that he could not find language to give me an idea of the gross debaucheries into which the lower order of people fall; and the promiscuous amors of the men of the middling class with their female servants, debases both beyond measure, weakening every species of family affection.

I have every where been struck by one characteristic difference in the conduct of the two sexes; women, in general, are seduced by their superiors, and men jilted by their inferiors; rank and manners awe the one, and cunning and wantonness subjugate the other; ambition creeping into the woman's passion, and tyranny giving force to the man's; for most men treat their mistresses as kings do their favorites: *ergo* is not man then the tyrant of the creation?

Still harping on the same subject, you will exclaim—How can I avoid it, when most of the struggles of an eventful life have been occasioned by the oppressed state of my sex:[9] we reason deeply, when we forcibly feel.

But to return to the straight road of observation. The sensuality so prevalent appears to me to arise rather from indolence of mind, and dull senses, than from an exuberance of life, which often fructifies the whole character when the vivacity of youthful spirits begins to subside into strength of mind.

I have before mentioned that the men are domestic tyrants, considering them as fathers, brothers, or husband; but there is a kind of interregnum between the reign of the father and husband, which is the only period of freedom and pleasure that the women enjoy. Young people, who are attached to each other, with the consent of their friends, exchange rings, and are permitted to enjoy a degree of liberty together, which I have never noticed in any other country. The days of courtship are therefore prolonged, till it be perfectly convenient to marry: the intimacy often becomes very tender: and if the lover obtain the privilege of a husband, it can only be termed half by stealth, because the family is wilfully blind. It happens very rarely that these honorary engagements are dissolved or disregarded, a stigma being attached to a breach of faith, which is thought more disgraceful, if not so criminal, as the violation of the marriage vow.

Do not forget that, in my general observations, I do not pretend to sketch a national character; but merely to note the present state of morals and manners, as I trace the progress of the world's improvement. Because, during my residence in different countries, my principal object has been to take such a dispassionate view of men as will lead me to form a just idea of the nature of man. And, to deal ingenuously with you, I believe I should have been less severe in the remarks I have made on the vanity and depravity of the French,[1] had I travelled towards the north before I visited France.

The interesting picture frequently drawn of the virtues of a rising people has, I fear, been fallacious, excepting the accounts of the enthusiasm which

Crown Prince Frederick, who had become regent in 1784 when his father was judged mentally unfit to rule, she had been ordered imprisoned, but was rescued by an English ship and taken to Hanover, Germany, where she died in 1775 at the age of twenty-four.

9. Wollstonecraft had published A *Vindication of the Rights of Woman* three years earlier, in 1792.
1. See *Historical and Moral View of the French Revolution* [Wollstonecraft's note; she had published the book in 1794].

various public struggles have produced. We talk of the depravity of the French, and lay a stress on the old age of the nation; yet where has more virtuous enthusiasm been displayed than during the two last years, by the common people of France and in their armies? I am obliged sometimes to recollect the numberless instances which I have either witnessed, or heard well authenticated, to balance the account of horrors, alas! but too true. I am, therefore, inclined to believe that the gross vices which I have always seen allied with simplicity of manners, are the concomitants of ignorance.

What, for example, has piety, under the heathen or christian system, been, but a blind faith in things contrary to the principles of reason? And could poor reason make considerable advances, when it was reckoned the highest degree of virtue to do violence to its dictates? Lutherans preaching reformation, have built a reputation for sanctity on the same foundation as the catholics; yet I do not perceive that a regular attendance on public worship, and their other observances, make them a whit more true in their affections, or honest in their private transactions. It seems, indeed, quite as easy to prevaricate[2] with religious injunctions as human laws, when the exercise of their reason does not lead people to acquire principles for themselves to be the criterion of all those they receive from others.

If travelling, as the completion of a liberal education, were to be adopted on rational grounds, the northern states ought to be visited before the more polished parts of Europe, to serve as the elements even of the knowledge of manners, only to be acquired by tracing the various shades in different countries. But, when visiting distant climes, a momentary social sympathy should not be allowed to influence the conclusions of the understanding; for hospitality too frequently leads travellers, especially those who travel in search of pleasure, to make a false estimate of the virtues of a nation; which, I am now convinced, bear an exact proportion to their scientific improvements.

Adieu.

1795   1796

2. Evade or distort.

JOANNA BAILLIE
1762–1851

Joanna Baillie, who was born in Lanarkshire, Scotland, but lived in London and Hampstead from her early twenties until her death at the age of eighty-eight, is known primarily as a dramatist. Her first volume of *A Series of Plays: in Which It Is Attempted to Delineate the Stronger Passions of the Mind: Each Passion Being the Subject of a Tragedy and a Comedy*—now generally referred to as *Plays on the Passions*—appeared anonymously in 1798. It was an instant literary sensation, attracting as much speculation about its authorship as there was sixteen years later concerning Walter Scott's anonymous publication of *Waverley*. Two other volumes in the series followed in 1802 and 1812, winning acclaim for her as Britain's most distinguished woman playwright of the time—in some evaluations, the most distinguished regardless of gender. Scott compared her to Shakespeare. In a letter of 1817, Byron, just then completing his own play *Manfred*, recalled that the French author Voltaire had proposed that "the composition of a tragedy require[d] *testicles*": "If this be true," Byron continued, "Lord knows what Joanna Baillie does—I suppose she borrows them." Baillie published, all told, twenty-eight plays and exerted considerable sway over the early-nineteenth-century drama.

Her preface to the original *Series of Plays,* a seventy-page "introductory discourse" advocating naturalness of language and subject matter, influenced both the Advertisement to Wordsworth and Coleridge's *Lyrical Ballads,* which appeared six months later, and Wordsworth's longer and more famous Preface two years later. "Those works," she wrote, "which most strongly characterize human nature in the middling and lower classes of society, where it is to be discovered by stronger and more unequivocal marks, will ever be the most popular"; the writer should forsake "the enchanted regions of simile, metaphor, allegory, and description" in favor of "the plain order of things in this every-day world." Baillie's prolonged focus on both the writer's and the reader's "sympathetick curiosity" in the essay probably also influenced William Hazlitt's concept of the sympathetic imagination and, through Hazlitt, Keats's notion of the self-effacing empathic "poetical Character."

In an 1812 preface Baillie acknowledged the gap between her theory as a dramatist and her practice, admitting that her effort to "unveil" the workings of the mind was ill suited to the practical realities of the stage. In the major London theatres of her day, which were immense spaces designed principally to house spectacular scenery and light effects, only a third of the audience, she estimated, could hear the actors' lines or see their faces. (Charles Lamb had, to similar effect, argued in 1811 that readers who loved Shakespearean tragedy in the privacy of the study would have their illusions shattered when they saw it in one of these theaters.) Indeed, even when Baillie's plays were staged by stars such as Sarah Siddons and Edmund Kean, theatergoers failed to respond as enthusiastically as reading audiences had. Today, in fact, the modern reader is more likely to agree not with Scott and Byron but with Hazlitt, who declared Baillie's plan to illustrate each passion separately a heresy in dramatic art: "the passions are . . . not so in nature, or in Shakspeare." But Baillie's interest in discovering an authentic language of feeling originated in her poetry, with a volume of 1790 titled *Poems: Wherein It Is Attempted to Describe Certain Views of Nature and of Rustic Manners,* and she remains of great interest as a poet. The modern reader, admiring the homely but graceful blank verse of her "A Winter's Day," can make connections with *The Prelude* (as in the descriptions of bird snaring, ice-skating, and the old discharged soldier), *The Excursion* (the character of the Wanderer), and "Michael" (Michael's thrift, Isabel's industrious spinning wheel)—works that Wordsworth wrote more than ten years after Baillie's poem. Baillie's 1823 "Address to a Steamvessel" likewise anticipates by a decade Wordsworth's "Steamboats, Viaducts, and Railways," and it parallels, in its determination to make poetry accountable to new technology and in its mixed feelings about a modern tourist industry's marketing of picturesque nature, Wordsworth's ambivalent project in his 1810 guidebook to the Lake District. Baillie also excelled as a songwriter both in standard English (as in "Up! quit thy bower") and, like her contemporary Robert Burns, in the Scottish dialect (as in "Woo'd and married").

A Winter's Day

The cock, warm roosting 'mid his feather'd mates,
Now lifts his beak and snuffs the morning air,
Stretches his neck and claps his heavy wings,
Gives three hoarse crows and, glad his task is done,
5   Low chuckling turns himself upon the roost,
Then nestles down again into his place.

The laboring hind,[1] who on his bed of straw
Beneath his home-made coverings, coarse but warm,
Lock'd in the kindly arms of her who spun them,
10   Dreams of the gain that next year's crop should bring;
Or at some fair, disposing of his wool,
Or by some lucky and unlook'd-for bargain,
Fills his skin purse with store of tempting gold;
Now wakes from sleep at the unwelcome call,
15   And finds himself but just the same poor man
As when he went to rest.
He hears the blast against his window beat,
And wishes to himself he were a laird,°   *landowner, lord*
That he might lie a-bed. It may not be:
20   He rubs his eyes and stretches out his arms;
Heigh oh! heigh oh! he drawls with gaping mouth,
Then most unwillingly creeps from his lair,
And without looking-glass puts on his clothes.

    With rueful face he blows the smother'd fire,
25   And lights his candle at the reddening coal;
First sees that all be right among his cattle,
Then hies° him to the barn with heavy tread,   *hastens*
Printing his footsteps on the new-fall'n snow.
From out the heap'd-up mow° he draws his sheaves,   *stored grain or hay*
30   Dislodging the poor red-breast from his shelter
Where all the live-long night he slept secure;
But now, affrighted, with uncertain flight,
Flutters round walls and roof to find some hole
Through which he may escape.
35   Then whirling o'er his head, the heavy flail
Descends with force upon the jumping sheaves,
While every rugged wall and neighboring cot°   *cottage*
The noise re-echoes of his sturdy strokes.

    The family cares call next upon the wife
40   To quit her mean but comfortable bed.
And first she stirs the fire and fans the flame,
Then from her heap of sticks for winter stored
An armful brings; loud crackling as they burn,
Thick fly the red sparks upward to the roof,
45   While slowly mounts the smoke in wreathy clouds.
On goes the seething pot with morning cheer,
For which some little wistful folk await,
Who, peeping from the bed-clothes, spy well pleased
The cheery light that blazes on the wall,
50   And bawl for leave to rise.
Their busy mother knows not where to turn,

---

1. Hind does not perfectly express the condition of the person here intended, who is somewhat above a common laborer,—the tenant of a very small farm, which he cultivates with his own hands; a few cows, perhaps a horse, and some six or seven sheep being all the wealth he possessed. A class of men very common in the west of Scotland, ere political economy was thought of [Baillie's note]. "Political economy" refers to the new discipline of economics pioneered by Adam Smith at the University of Glasgow, where Baillie's father and uncle also lectured.

Her morning's work comes now so thick upon her.
One she must help to tie his little coat,
Unpin another's cap, or seek his shoe
55 Or hosen° lost, confusion soon o'er-master'd!   *breeches*
When all is o'er, out to the door they run
With new-comb'd sleeky hair and glistening faces,
Each with some little project in his head.
His new-soled shoes one on the ice must try;
60 To view his well-set trap another hies,
In hopes to find some poor unwary bird
(No worthless prize) entangled in his snare;
While one, less active, with round rosy cheeks,
Spreads out his purple fingers to the fire,
65 And peeps most wistfully into the pot.

         But let us leave the warm and cheerful house
To view the bleak and dreary scene without,
And mark the dawning of a Winter day.
The morning vapor rests upon the heights,
70 Lurid and red, while growing gradual shades
Of pale and sickly light spread o'er the sky.
Then slowly from behind the southern hills
Enlarged and ruddy comes the rising sun,
Shooting athwart the hoary waste his beams
75 That gild the brow of every ridgy bank,
And deepen every valley with a shade.
The crusted window of each scatter'd cot,
The icicles that fringe the thatched roof,
The new-swept slide upon the frozen pool,
80 All keenly glance, new kindled with his rays;
And e'en the rugged face of scowling Winter
Looks somewhat gay. But only for a time
He shows his glory to the brightening earth,
Then hides his face behind a sullen cloud.

85   The birds now quit their holes and lurking sheds,
Most mute and melancholy, where through night,
All nestling close to keep each other warm,
In downy sleep they had forgot their hardships;
But not to chant and carol in the air,
90 Or lightly swing upon some waving bough,
And merrily return each other's notes;
No, silently they hop from bush to bush,
Can find no seeds to stop their craving want,
Then bend their flight to the low smoking cot,
95 Chirp on the roof, or at the window peck,
To tell their wants to those who lodge within.
The poor lank hare flies homeward to his den,
But little burthen'd with his nightly meal
Of wither'd coleworts² from the farmer's garden,
100 A wretched scanty portion, snatch'd in fear;

2. Kale or another cabbagelike vegetable.

216 / Joanna Baillie

And fearful creatures, forced abroad by hunger,
Are now to every enemy a prey.

The husbandman lays by his heavy flail,
And to the house returns, where for him wait
105 His smoking breakfast and impatient children,
Who, spoon in hand, and ready to begin,
Toward the door cast many an eager look
To see their dad come in.
Then round they sit, a cheerful company;
110 All quickly set to work, and with heap'd spoons
From ear to ear besmear their rosy cheeks.
The faithful dog stands by his master's side
Wagging his tail and looking in his face;
While humble puss pays court to all around,
115 And purrs and rubs them with her furry sides;
Nor goes this little flattery unrewarded.
But the laborious sit not long at table;
The grateful father lifts his eyes to heaven
To bless his God, whose ever bounteous hand
120 Him and his little ones doth daily feed,
Then rises satisfied to work again.

The varied rousing sounds of industry
Are heard through all the village.
The humming wheel, the thrifty housewife's tongue,
125 Who scolds to keep her maidens to their work,
The wool-card's grating, most unmusical!
Issue from every house.
But hark! the sportsman³ from the neighboring hedge
His thunder sends! loud bark the village curs;
130 Up from her cards or wheel the maiden starts
And hastens to the door; the housewife chides,
Yet runs herself to look, in spite of thrift,
And all the little town is in a stir.

Strutting before, the cock leads forth his train,
135 And, chuckling near the barn-door 'mid the straw,
Reminds the farmer of his morning's service.
His grateful master throws a liberal handful;
They flock about it, while the hungry sparrows,
Perch'd on the roof, look down with envious eye,
140 Then, aiming well, amidst the feeders light,
And seize upon the feast with greedy bill,
Till angry partlets° peck them off the field.   hens
But at a distance, on the leafless tree,
All woe-begone, the lonely blackbird sits;
145 The cold north wind ruffles his glossy feathers;
Full oft he looks, but dares not make approach,
Then turns his yellow beak to peck his side

---

3. Since in the late 18th century only gentlemen who met certain property qualifications had the right to shoot game, this sportsman likely belongs to a higher social class than the villagers he disturbs.

And claps his wings close to his sharpen'd breast.
The wandering fowler from behind the hedge,
150 Fastens his eye upon him, points his gun,
And firing wantonly, as at a mark,
Of life bereaves him in the cheerful spot
That oft hath echo'd to his summer's song.

The mid-day hour is near; the pent-up kine cows
155 Are driven from their stalls to take the air.
How stupidly they stare! and feel how strange!
They open wide their smoking mouths to low,
But scarcely can their feeble sound be heard,
Then turn and lick themselves and, step by step,
160 Move, dull and heavy, to their stalls again.

In scatter'd groups the little idle boys,
With purple fingers molding in the snow
Their icy ammunition, pant for war;
And drawing up in opposite array,
165 Send forth a mighty shower of well-aim'd balls.
Each tiny hero tries his growing strength,
And burns to beat the foe-men off the field.
Or on the well-worn ice in eager throngs,
After short race, shoot rapidly along,
170 Trip up each other's heels, and on the surface
With studded shoes draw many a chalky line.
Untired and glowing with the healthful sport
They cease not till the sun hath run his course,
And threatening clouds, slow rising from the north,
175 Spread leaden darkness o'er the face of heaven;
Then by degrees they scatter to their homes,
Some with a broken head or bloody nose,
To claim their mother's pity, who, most skillful!
Cures all their troubles with a bit of bread.

180 The night comes on apace—
Chill blows the blast and drives the snow in wreaths;
Now every creature looks around for shelter,
And whether man or beast, all move alike
Towards their homes, and happy they who have
185 A house to screen them from the piercing cold!
Lo, o'er the frost a reverend form advances!
His hair white as the snow on which he treads,
His forehead mark'd with many a care-worn furrow,
Whose feeble body bending o'er a staff,
190 Shows still that once it was the seat of strength,
Though now it shakes like some old ruin'd tower.
Clothed indeed, but not disgraced with rags,
He still maintains that decent dignity
Which well becomes those who have served their country.
195 With tottering steps he gains the cottage door;
The wife within, who hears his hollow cough,
And pattering of his stick upon the threshold,

Sends out her little boy to see who's there.
The child looks up to mark the stranger's face,
200 And, seeing it enlighten'd with a smile,
Holds out his tiny hand to lead him in.
Round from her work the mother turns her head,
And views them, not ill pleased.
The stranger whines not with a piteous tale,
205 But only asks a little to relieve
A poor old soldier's wants.
The gentle <u>matron</u> brings the ready chair
And bids him sit to rest his weary limbs,
And warm himself before her blazing fire.
210 The children, full of curiosity,
Flock round, and with their fingers in their mouths
Stand staring at him, while the stranger, pleased,
Takes up the youngest urchin on his knee.
Proud of its seat, it wags its little feet,
215 And prates and laughs and plays with his white locks.
But soon a change comes o'er the soldier's face;
His thoughtful mind is turn'd on other days,
When his own boys were wont to play around him,
Who now lie distant from their native land
220 In honorable but untimely graves:
He feels how helpless and forlorn he is,
And big round tears course down his wither'd cheeks.
His toilsome daily labor at an end,
In comes the wearied <u>master of the house</u>,
225 And marks with satisfaction his old guest,
In the chief seat, with all the children round him.
His honest heart is fill'd with manly kindness,
He bids him stay and share their homely meal,
And take with them his quarters for the night.
230 The aged wanderer thankfully accepts,
And by the simple hospitable board,
Forgets the by-past hardships of the day.

When all are satisfied, about the fire
They draw their seats and form a cheerful ring.
235 The thrifty housewife turns her spinning-wheel;
The husband, useful even in his hour
Of ease and rest, a stocking knits, belike,
Or plaits stored rushes, which with after skill
Into a basket form'd may do good service,
240 With eggs or butter fill'd at fair or market.

Some idle neighbors now come dropping in,
Draw round their chairs and widen out the circle;
And every one in his own native way
Does what he can to cheer the social group.
245 Each tells some little story of himself,
That constant subject upon which mankind,
Whether in court or country, love to dwell.
How at a fair he saved a simple clown°   *country fellow*

From being trick'd in buying of a cow;
250 Or laid a bet on his own horse's head
Against his neighbor's bought at twice his cost,
Which fail'd not to repay his better skill;
Or on a harvest day bound in an hour
More sheaves of corn than any of his fellows,
255 Though e'er so stark,° could do in twice the time;   strong, powerful
Or won the bridal race with savory broose[4]
And first kiss of the bonny bride, though all
The fleetest youngsters of the parish strove
In rivalry against him.
260 But chiefly the good man, by his own fire,
Hath privilege of being listen'd to,
Nor dares a little prattling tongue presume,
Though but in play, to break upon his story.
The children sit and listen with the rest;
265 And should the youngest raise its lisping voice,
The careful mother, ever on the watch,
And ever pleased with what her husband says,
Gives it a gentle tap upon the fingers,
Or stops its ill-timed prattle with a kiss.
270 The soldier next, but not unask'd, begins
His tale of war and blood. They gaze upon him,
And almost weep to see the man so poor,
So bent and feeble, helpless and forlorn,
Who has undaunted stood the battle's brunt
275 While roaring cannons shook the quaking earth,
And bullets hiss'd round his defenseless head.
Thus passes quickly on the evening hour,
Till sober folks must needs retire to rest;
Then all break up, and, by their several paths,
280 Hie homeward, with the evening pastime cheer'd
Far more, belike, than those who issue forth
From city theatre's gay scenic show,
Or crowded ball-room's splendid moving maze.
But where the song and story, joke and gibe,
285 So lately circled, what a solemn change
In little time takes place!
The sound of psalms, by mingled voices raised
Of young and old, upon the night air borne,
Haply to some benighted traveler,
290 Or the late parted neighbors on their way,
A pleasing notice gives, that those whose sires
In former days on the bare mountain's side,
In deserts, heaths, and caverns, praise and prayer,
At peril of their lives, in their own form
295 Of covenanted worship offered up,
In peace and safety in their own quiet home

[Handwritten margin note: Direct comparison to a higher class life]

---

4. A race, from the bride's former home to the bridegroom's house, run by the young men attending a country wedding.

Are—(as in quaint and modest phrase is termed)
Engaged now in *evening exercise*.[5]

But long accustom'd to observe the weather,
300 The farmer cannot lay him down in peace
Till he has look'd to mark what bodes the night.
He lifts the latch, and moves the heavy door,
Sees wreaths of snow heap'd up on every side,
And black and dismal all above his head.
305 Anon the northern blast begins to rise;
He hears its hollow growling from afar,
Which, gathering strength, rolls on with doubled might,
And raves and bellows o'er his head. The trees
Like pithless saplings bend. He shuts his door,
310 And, thankful for the roof that covers him,
Hies him to bed.

*they are noble too,
in a comparitive, correlated
way to noble people*

1790

A Mother to Her Waking Infant

Now in thy dazzled half-oped eye,
Thy curled nose and lip awry,
Up-hoisted arms and noddling head,
And little chin with crystal spread,
5 Poor helpless thing! what do I see,
That I should sing of thee?

From thy poor tongue no accents come,
Which can but rub thy toothless gum:
Small understanding boasts thy face,
10 Thy shapeless limbs nor step nor grace:
A few short words thy feats may tell,
And yet I love thee well.

When wakes the sudden bitter shriek,
And redder swells thy little cheek;
15 When rattled keys thy woes beguile,
And through thine eyelids gleams the smile,
Still for thy weakly self is spent
Thy little silly[1] plaint.

But when thy friends are in distress,
20 Thou'lt laugh and chuckle ne'ertheless,

5. In the first edition of the *Winter Day*, nothing regarding family worship was mentioned: a great omission, for which I justly take shame to myself. "The Evening exercise," as it was called, prevailed in every house over the simple country parts of the West of Scotland, and I have often heard the sound of it passing through the twilight air, in returning from a late walk [Baillie's note]. Lines 281–98 are a later addition to the poem. They allude to the persecutions that, during the "Killing Times" of the mid-17th century, were endured by the Covenanters—Presbyterians who adhered to a Covenant contracted between their congregation and Christ and who therefore refused to acknowledge the Crown's authority over their forms of worship.
1. Deserving of pity (Scots dialect).

Nor with kind sympathy be smitten,
Though all are sad but thee and kitten;
Yet puny varlet° that thou art,   *rascal*
Thou twitchest at the heart.

25 Thy smooth round cheek so soft and warm;
Thy pinky hand and dimpled arm;
Thy silken locks that scantly peep,
With gold tipp'd ends, where circles deep,
Around thy neck in harmless grace,
30 So soft and sleekly hold their place,
Might harder hearts with kindness fill,
And gain our right goodwill.

Each passing clown° bestows his blessing,   *peasant*
Thy mouth is worn with old wives' kissing;
35 E'en lighter looks the gloomy eye
Of surly sense when thou art by;
And yet, I think, whoe'er they be,
They love thee not like me.

Perhaps when time shall add a few
40 Short months to thee, thou'lt love me too;
And after that, through life's long way,
Become my sure and cheering stay;
Wilt care for me and be my hold,
When I am weak and old.

45 Thou'lt listen to my lengthen'd tale,
And pity me when I am frail[2]—
But see, the sweepy spinning fly
Upon the window takes thine eye.
Go to thy little senseless play;
50 Thou dost not heed my lay.°   *song*

1790

Up! quit thy bower[1]

Up! quit thy bower, late wears the hour;
Long have the rooks caw'd round thy tower;
On flower and tree, loud hums the bee;
The wilding kid[2] sports merrily:
5 A day so bright, so fresh, so clear,
Shineth when good fortune's near.

Up! lady fair, and braid thy hair,
And rouse thee in the breezy air;

---

2. *Feeble.* In this sense the word is often applied
in Scotland [Baillie's note].
1. This song opens act 1 of Baillie's *The Beacon:*

A Serious Musical Drama in Two Acts (1812).
2. Wild young goat.

The lulling stream, that sooth'd thy dream,
10 Is dancing in the sunny beam:
And hours so sweet, so bright, so gay,
Will waft good fortune on its way.

Up! time will tell; the friar's bell
Its service sound hath chimed well;
15 The aged crone keeps house alone,
And reapers to the fields are gone:
The active day, so boon and bright,
May bring good fortune ere the night.

1812

Song: Woo'd and married and a'[1]

The bride she is winsome and bonny,
Her hair it is snooded[2] sae sleek,
And faithfu' and kind is her Johnny,
Yet fast fa' the tears on her cheek.
5 New pearlins° are cause of her sorrow,   *lace trimmings*
New pearlins and plenishing° too,   *furnishings*
The bride that has a' to borrow,
Has e'en right mickle ado,
Woo'd and married and a'!
10 Woo'd and married and a'!
Is na' she very weel aff
To be woo'd and married at a'?

Her mither then hastily spak,
"The lassie is glaikit° wi' pride;   *foolish*
15 In my pouch I had never a plack°   *farthing*
On the day when I was a bride.
E'en tak' to your wheel, and be clever,
And draw out your thread in the sun;
The gear° that is gifted,° it never   *goods, wealth / given*
20 Will last like the gear that is won.°   *earned*
Woo'd and married and a'!
Wi' havins° and toucher° sae sma',   *possessions / dowry*
I think ye are very weel aff,
To be woo'd and married at a'!"

25 "Toot, toot!" quo' her gray-headed faither,
"She's less o' a bride than a bairn;°   *child*
She's ta'en like a cout° frae the heather,   *colt*
Wi' sense and discretion to learn.
Half husband, I trow, and half daddy,
30 As humor inconstantly leans,
The chiel° maun° be patient and steady,   *man / must*

1. For a reading of "Woo'd and married and a' "
consult Norton Literature Online: Baillie's writing
in Scots needs to be heard as well as read to be
properly appreciated.
2. Bound up with a ribbon.

That yokes wi' a mate in her teens.
   A kerchief sae douce° and sae neat,   *sedate, respectable*
O'er her locks that the winds used to blaw!
35   I'm baith like to laugh and to greet,°   *weep*
   When I think o' her married at a'!"

Then out spak' the wily bridegroom;
   Weel waled° were his wordies, I ween—   *chosen*
"I'm rich, though my coffer be toom,°   *empty*
40   Wi' the blinks o' your bonny blue een.°   *eyes*
I'm prouder o' thee by my side,
   Though thy ruffles or ribbons be few,
Than if Kate o' the Croft were my bride,
   Wi' purfles³ and pearlins enow.
45   Dear and dearest of ony!
      Ye're woo'd and buikit⁴ and a'!"
   And do ye think scorn o' your Johnny,
      And grieve to be married at a'?"

She turn'd, and she blush'd, and she smiled,
50   And she looket sae bashfully down;
The pride o' her heart was beguiled,
   And she played wi' the sleeves o' her gown;
She twirled the tag o' her lace,
   And she nippet her boddice sae blue,
55   Syne° blinket sae sweet in his face,   *then*
   And aff like a maukin° she flew.   *hare*
      Woo'd and married and a'!
      Wi' Johnny to roose° her and a'!   *praise*
   She thinks hersel very weel aff,
60   To be woo'd and married at a'!

                                             1822

Address to a Steamvessel¹

Freighted with passengers of every sort,
A motley throng, thou leav'st the busy port:
Thy long and ample deck,—where scatter'd lie
Baskets and cloaks and shawls of crimson dye;
5 Where dogs and children through the crowd are straying,
And on his bench apart the fiddler playing,

---

3. Embroidered trimmings.
4. Booked, i.e., entered as betrothed in the official registry of the session clerk.
1. Steamships and sightseers were new features in Scotland's landscape in Baillie's lifetime; here she reckons with their presence. As she notes, new steamship routes enabled greater numbers of tourists, some from the industrial working classes, to visit the area's beauty spots, often the sites celebrated in the period's poetry of natural description. The mixed feelings she expresses about this change are similar to those informing the writings of Wordsworth. His sonnet "Steamboats, Viaducts, and Railways" (p. 320) acknowledges the sublime aspects of the new transportation technologies, but he later campaigned against the construction of the Kendal and Windermere Railway, and worried that the influx of visitors it would bring to the Lake District (visitors in some measure drawn there by his poetry) would "deface" the region's beauties. See "*Tintern Abbey*, Tourism, and Romantic Landscape" at Norton Literature Online.

While matron dames to tressel'd seats repair,—
Seems, on the glassy waves, a floating fair.

    Its dark form on the sky's pale azure cast,
10 Towers from this clustering group thy pillar'd mast;
The dense smoke, issuing from its narrow vent,
Is to the air in curly volumes sent,
Which coiling and uncoiling on the wind,
Trail, like a writhing serpent, far behind.
15 Beneath, as each merged wheel its motion plies,
On either side the white-churn'd waters rise,
And newly parted from the noisy fray,
Track with light ridgy foam thy recent way,
Then far diverged, in many a lustrous line
20 On the still-moving distant surface shine.

    Thou holdst thy course in independent pride;
No leave ask'st thou of either wind or tide.
To whate'er point the breeze inconstant veer,
Still doth thy careless helmsman onward steer;
25 As if the stroke of some magician's wand
Had lent thee power the ocean to command.
What is this power which thus within thee lurks
And all unseen, like a mask'd giant works?
E'en that which gentle dames at morning tea,
30 From silver urn ascending, daily see
With tressy wreathings borne upon the air
Like loosen'd ringlets of a lady's hair;
Or rising from th' enamell'd cup beneath,
With the soft fragrance of an infant's breath;
35 That which within the peasant's humble cot
Comes from the uncover'd mouth of savoury pot,
As his kind mate prepares his noonday fare,
Which cur and cat and rosy urchins share;
That which, all silver'd by the moon's pale beam
40 Precedes the mighty Geyser's up-cast stream,
What time, with bellowing din, exploded forth,
It decks the midnight of the frozen north,
While travellers from their skin-spread couches rise
To gaze upon the sight with wondering eyes.

45   Thou hast to those "in populous city pent"[2]
Glimpses of wild and beauteous nature lent,
A bright remembrance ne'er to be destroy'd,
That proves to them a treasure long enjoy'd,
And for this scope to beings erst confined,
50 I fain would hail thee with a grateful mind.
They who had nought of verdant freshness seen,
But suburb orchards choked with coleworts° green,   *cabbage plants*
Now, seated at their ease, may glide along,

2. Milton's *Paradise Lost* 9.445, from the extended simile describing Satan's entrance into Eden.

Loch Lomond's fair and fairy Isles[3] among;
55   Where bushy promontories fondly peep
At their own beauty in the nether deep,
O'er drooping birch and rowan[4] red that lave°   wash
Their fragrant branches in the glassy wave:
They who on higher objects scarce have counted
60   Than church-spire with its gilded vane surmounted,
May view within their near, distinctive ken
The rocky summits of the lofty Ben;[5]
Or see his purple shoulders darkly lower
Through the dim drapery of a summer shower.
65   Where, spread in broad and fair expanse, the Clyde[6]
Mingles his waters with the briny tide,
Along the lesser Cumbray's rocky shore,[7]
With moss and crusted lichens flecker'd o'er,
He who but warfare held with thievish cat,
70   Or from his cupboard chaced a hungry rat,
The city cobbler,—scares the wild sea-mew
In its mid-flight with loud and shrill halloo;
Or valiantly with fearful threatening shakes
His lank and greasy head at Kittywakes.[8]
75   The eyes that have no fairer outline seen,
Than chimney'd walls with slated roofs between,
Which hard and harshly edge the smoky sky,
May Arran's softly-vision'd peaks[9] descry,
Coping with graceful state her steepy sides
80   O'er which the cloud's broad shadow swiftly glides,
And interlacing slopes that gently merge
Into the pearly mist of ocean's verge.
Eyes which admired that work of sordid skill,
The storied structure of a cotton mill,
85   May wondering now behold the unnumber'd host
Of marshall'd pillars on fair Ireland's coast,
Phalanx on phalanx ranged with sidelong bend,
Or broken ranks that to the main descend,
Like Pharaoh's army on the Red Sea shore,
90   Which deep and deeper sank, to rise no more.[1]

Yet ne'ertheless, whate'er we owe to thee,
Rover at will on river, lake, and sea,
As profit's bait or pleasure's lure engage,
Offspring of Watt,[2] that philosophic sage,
95   Who in the heraldry of science ranks
With those to whom men owe high meed of thanks
For genius usefully employ'd, whose fame
Shall still be link'd with Davy's[3] splendid name;

3. Loch Lomond, lake north of Glasgow and a favorite tourist destination.
4. Mountain ash trees.
5. The mountain Ben Lomond.
6. River running through Scotland's industrial center, the city of Glasgow.
7. Island in the Firth of Clyde.
8. The common or vulgar name of a water-bird

frequenting that coast [Baillie's note].
9. Island off the west coast of Scotland.
1. See Exodus 14.28.
2. James Watt (1736–1819), Scottish engineer who developed the steam engine.
3. Humphrey Davy (1778–1829), English chemist.

Dearer to fancy, to the eye more fair
100 Are the light skiffs,° that to the breezy air   *sailboats*
Unfurl their swelling sails of snowy hue
Upon the moving lap of ocean blue:
As the proud swan on summer lake displays,
With plumage brightening in the morning rays,
105 Her fair pavilion of erected wings,
They change, and veer, and turn like living things.

With ample store of shrouding,° sails, and mast,   *rigging*
To brave with manly skill the winter blast
Of every clime,—in vessels rigg'd like these
110 Did great Columbus cross the western seas,
And to the stinted thoughts of man reveal'd
What yet the course of ages had conceal'd:
In such as these, on high adventure bent,
Round the vast world Magellan's comrades went.[4]
115 To such as these are hardy seamen found
As with the ties of kindred feeling bound,
Boasting, while cans of cheering grog they sip,
The varied fortunes of "our gallant ship";
The offspring these of bold sagacious man,
120 Ere yet the reign of letter'd lore began.

In very truth, compared to these, thou art
A daily labourer, a mechanic swart,°   *swarthy*
In working weeds array'd of homely gray,
Opposed to gentle nymph or lady gay,
125 To whose free robes the graceful right is given
To play and dally with the winds of heaven.
Beholding thee, the great of other days
And modern men with all their alter'd ways,
Across my mind with hasty transit gleam,
130 Like fleeting shadows of a feverish dream:
Fitful I gaze, with adverse humours teased,
Half sad, half proud, half angry, and half pleased.

1823   1823

4. Ferdinand Magellan (1489–1521), Portuguese navigator whose fleet undertook the first circumnavigation of the globe. Magellan did not survive the voyage.

MARIA EDGEWORTH
1768–1849

Maria Edgeworth's publishing career earned her more than £11,000—an enormous sum. It also made the novel, regularly reviled by critics in the late eighteenth century, a respectable form. After 1804, the editor Francis Jeffrey attended respectfully in the pages of his *Edinburgh Review* to each of Edgeworth's publications, remarking on how in her hands fiction had become an edifying medium for serious ideas.

Edgeworth was born in Oxfordshire on New Year's Day, 1768, the second child of Richard Lovell Edgeworth and Anna Maria Elers, who died when her daughter was five. (Richard Lovell Edgeworth married three more times, each new wife younger than her predecessor, and eventually fathered twenty-two children.) Maria Edgeworth spent most of her childhood in fashionable boarding schools in England, until her father, in a spirit of patriotism and optimism about social progress, decided to dedicate himself to the family estate in Ireland that had been his birthplace. In 1782 he sent for Maria to join him, his third wife, and Maria's half-brothers and half-sisters at Edgeworthstown, source of the Protestant Edgeworths' wealth since the early seventeenth century, when the property had been confiscated from a Catholic family. For the rest of her life, that manor house in rural County Longford would remain home for Edgeworth, who in 1802 rejected a marriage proposal from a Swedish diplomat.

Brimming over with children, with books, and (it was reported) with "ingenious mechanical devices" (some of them Richard Lovell Edgeworth's inventions), this home doubled as a laboratory for her father's experiments in education, up-to-the-minute agricultural techniques, and enlightened landlord-tenant relations. From the age of fourteen, Edgeworth assumed a central role in those experiments. She took up the business of estate management. She taught the younger children. At her father's prompting, she began a course of reading in political and economic theory, starting with Adam Smith's *The Wealth of Nations*.

Eventually Maria Edgeworth also began to write. *Letters for Literary Ladies* (1795), a novelistic defense of women's education, was followed by *The Parent's Assistant* (1796) and *Practical Education* (1798), treatises on pedagogy she coauthored with her father, and by the first of her influential collections of stories for children (*Early Lessons*, 1801). In 1800 she published *Castle Rackrent*, her masterpiece. *Rackrent* inaugurated Edgeworth's series of narratives memorializing the vanishing ways of life of rural Ireland, a project continued by *Ennui* (1809), *The Absentee* (1812), and *Ormond* (1819). Edgeworth's study of the Enlightenment social sciences is easy to trace in these regional fictions, and these concerns were a factor that helped secure their reputation among the reviewers. Not only had Edgeworth managed to associate the novel with a more intellectually prestigious discourse; by packaging her representations of Ireland's picturesque folk culture in this way, she was also able to tap the authority of a system of economic and political analysis that, in its claims to be scientifically impartial, seemed to many to offer a counterweight to the ugly prejudices that were the legacies of that nation's history of colonial conquest.

The year Richard Lovell Edgeworth settled in Ireland, 1782, seemed an auspicious moment for a reformer like him. The Parliament in Dublin had just won legislative independence, and it appeared as though penal laws targeting Catholics would soon be relaxed. But this confidence that a new era of civil harmony was dawning was quickly shattered. In 1798 armed insurrection, involving both Catholic peasants and middle-class Protestants from the North, engulfed Ireland. The rising was soon repressed, with extreme brutality. Introduced in 1800 as a security measure by a British state horrified at the news that French expeditionary forces had planned to aid the rebels, an Act of Union abolished the Dublin Parliament and incorporated Ireland into the United Kingdom. However, as Byron observed in an address to the House of Lords, to call the ensuing political situation a Union was to abuse the term: "If it must be called an Union, it is the union of the shark with his prey." The native Catholic population would long remain without civil rights. Indeed, when Edgeworth died in 1849 at the age of eighty-three, Ireland was once again a scene of violent insurrection as well as of horrendous famine.

An anecdote in Edgeworth's 1820 memoir of her father conveys a sense of the ambiguous position that the Protestant Anglo-Irish—neither English exactly, nor Irish, neither outsiders nor natives—occupied in this tense political context. Edgeworth recounts how, after their family escaped from the Catholic rebels who in 1798 occupied the countryside around Edgeworthstown, Richard Lovell Edgeworth was nearly lynched by a mob from the Protestant county town where the Edgeworths had taken refuge, who were certain (such were the suspicions aroused by his nonsectarian politics) that he was a rebel sympathizer and a French spy.

The 1802 tale that we have selected as an example of Maria Edgeworth's fiction, "The Irish Incognito"—part trickster tale from the folk tradition, part philosophical meditation on the precariousness of personal identity—also captures something of this experience of living between cultures. Starting with the first disorienting sentence, which introduces a hero who sports the ultra-English name of John Bull but who is also a native son of Cork, this treatment of cultural difference is distinguished by some slippery ironies. (A town on Ireland's south coast, Cork, of course, is home to the legendary Blarney Stone, which grants Irish people their gift of the gab.) The tale might well have promoted tolerance for British diversity among its original readers: unlike many of his namesakes of the era, this "John Bull" is eminently likeable. But (as with the more biting satires that Jonathan Swift had penned in Dublin eighty years before) it would also have perplexed these readers' preconceived notions about *who* exactly was *who* within that hybrid political entity called "the United Kingdom of Great Britain and Ireland."

The Irish Incognito[1]

Sir John Bull was a native of Ireland, *bred* and *born* in the city of Cork. His real name was Phelim O'Mooney, and he was by profession a *stocah*, or walking gentleman; that is, a person who is too proud to earn his bread, and too poor to have bread without earning it. He had always been told that none of his ancestors had ever been in trade or business of any kind, and he resolved, when a boy, never to *demean* himself and family, as his elder brother had done, by becoming a rich merchant. When he grew up to be a young man, he kept this spirited resolution as long as he had a relation or friend in the world who would let him hang upon them; but when he was shaken off by all, what could he do but go into business? He chose the most genteel, however; he became a wine merchant. I'm *only* a wine merchant, said he to himself, and that is next door to being nothing at all. His brother furnished his cellars; and Mr. Phelim O'Mooney, upon the strength of the wine that he had in his cellars, and of the money he expected to make of it, immediately married a wife, set up a gig, and gave excellent dinners to men who were ten times richer than he even ever *expected* to be. In return for these excellent dinners, his new friends bought all their wine from Mr. O'Mooney, and never paid for it; he lived upon credit himself, and gave all his friends credit, till he became a bankrupt. Then nobody came to dine with him, and every body found out that he had been very imprudent; and he was obliged to sell his gig, but not before it had broken his wife's neck; so that when accounts came to be finally settled, he was not much worse than when he began the world, the loss falling upon

1. Although written solely by Maria Edgeworth, "The Irish Incognito" forms the culminating chapter of a book that was published under both her name and her father's (her *Memoir* of her father states that he contributed passages to a few of the other chapters). This book was the *Essay on Irish Bulls*, which went through three, revised editions between 1802 and 1808, before being included, in its 1808 version, in Maria Edgeworth's eighteen-

volume collected *Tales and Novels* of 1832. That edition provides the basis for the text we give here. A "bull" is a verbal blunder, an expression containing a contradiction that goes unperceived by the speaker. To collect "Irish bulls" as the *Essay* does is, on the face of it, to contribute to a longstanding English tradition of jokes about the dim-witted Irish, but the Edgeworths' relationship to that tradition turned out to be quite complicated.

his creditors, and he being, as he observed, free to begin life again, with the advantage of being once more a bachelor. He was such a good-natured, free-hearted fellow, that every body liked him, even his creditors. His wife's relations made up the sum of five hundred pounds for him, and his brother offered to take him into his firm as partner; but O'Mooney preferred, he said, going to try, or rather to make, his fortune in England, as he did not doubt but he should by marriage, being, as he did not scruple to acknowledge, a personable, clever-looking man, and a great favourite with the sex.[2]

"My last wife I married for love, my next I expect will do the same by me, and of course the money must come on her side this time," said our hero, half jesting, half in earnest. His elder and wiser brother, the merchant, whom he still held in more than sufficient contempt, ventured to hint some slight objections to this scheme of Phelim's seeking fortune in England. He observed that so many had gone upon this plan already, that there was rather a prejudice in England against Irish adventurers.

This could not affect *him* any ways, Phelim replied, because he did not mean to appear in England as an Irishman at all.

"How then?"

"As an Englishman, since that is most agreeable."

"How can that be?"

"Who should hinder it?"

His brother, hesitatingly, said "Yourself."

"Myself !—What part of myself? Is it my tongue?—You'll acknowledge, brother, that I do not speak with the brogue."

It was true that Phelim did not speak with any Irish brogue: his mother was an English woman, and he had lived much with English officers in Cork, and he had studied and imitated their manner of speaking so successfully, that no one, merely by his accent, could have guessed that he was an Irishman.

"Hey! brother, I say!" continued Phelim, in a triumphant English tone; "I never was taken for an Irishman in my life. Colonel Broadman told me the other day, I spoke English better than the English themselves; that he should take me for an Englishman, in any part of the known world, the moment I opened my lips. You must allow that not the smallest particle of brogue is discernible on my tongue."

His brother allowed that not the smallest particle of brogue was to be discerned upon Phelim's tongue, but feared that some Irish idiom might be perceived in his conversation. And then the name of O'Mooney!

"Oh, as to that, I need not trouble an act of parliament, or even a king's letter, just to change my name for a season; at the worst, I can travel and appear incognito."

"Always?"

"No: only just till I'm upon good terms with the lady—Mrs. Phelim O'Mooney, that is to be, God willing. Never fear, nor shake your head, brother; *you* men of business are out of this line, and not proper judges: I beg your pardon for saying so, but as you are my own brother, and nobody by, you'll excuse me."

His brother did excuse him, but continued silent for some minutes; he was pondering upon the means of persuading Phelim to give up this scheme.

"I would lay you any wager, my dear Phelim," said he, "that you could not continue four days in England incognito."

2. Women.

"Done!" cried Phelim. "Done for a hundred pounds; done for a thousand pounds, and welcome."

"But if you lose, how will you pay?"

"Faith! that's the last thing I thought of, being sure of winning."

"Then you will not object to any mode of payment I shall propose."

"None: only remembering always, that I was bankrupt last week, and shall be little better till I'm married; but then I'll pay you honestly if I lose."

"No, if you lose I must be paid before that time, my good sir," said his brother, laughing. "My bet is this:—I will lay you one hundred guineas that you do not remain four days in England incognito; be upon honour with me, and promise, that if you lose, you will, instead of laying down a hundred guineas, come back immediately, and settle quietly again to business."

The word _business_ was always odious to our hero's proud ears; but he thought himself so secure of winning his wager, that he willingly bound himself in a penalty which he believed would never become due; and his generous brother, at parting, made the bet still more favourable, by allowing that Phelim should not be deemed the loser unless he was, in the course of the first four days after he touched English ground, detected eight times in being an Irishman.

"Eight times !" cried Phelim. "Good bye to a hundred guineas, brother, you may say."

"You may say," echoed his brother, and so they parted.

Mr. Phelim O'Mooney the next morning sailed from Cork harbour with a prosperous gale, and with a confidence in his own success which supplied the place of auspicious omens. He embarked at Cork, to go by long sea to London, and was driven into Deal, where Julius Cesar once landed before him, and with the same resolution to see and conquer.[3] It was early in the morning; having been very sea-sick, he was impatient, as soon as he got into the inn, for his breakfast: he was shown into a room where three ladies were waiting to go by the stage; his air of easy confidence was the best possible introduction.

"Would any of the company choose eggs?" said the waiter.

"I never touch an egg for my share," said O'Mooney, carelessly; he knew that it was supposed to be an Irish custom to eat eggs at breakfast; and when the malicious waiter afterwards set a plate full of eggs in salt upon the table, our hero magnanimously abstained from them; he even laughed heartily at a story told by one of the ladies of an Hibernian at Buxton, who declared that "no English hen ever laid a fresh egg."

O'Mooney got through breakfast much to his own satisfaction, and to that of the ladies, whom he had taken a proper occasion to call the _three graces_,[4] and whom he had informed that he was an _old_ baronet of an English family, and that his name was Sir John Bull. The youngest of the graces civilly observed, "that whatever else he might he, she should never have taken him for an _old_ baronet." The lady who made this speech was pretty, but O'Mooney had penetration enough to discover, in the course of the conversation, that she and her companions were far from being divinities; his three graces were a greengrocer's wife, a tallow chandler's widow, and a milliner. When he found that these ladies were likely to be his companions if he were to travel

---

3. The Roman expeditionary force that invaded Britain in 55 B.C.E. landed in the southeast in the vicinity of the modern-day port of Deal. A later victory in Asia Minor occasioned Caesar's boast about how he "came, saw, and conquered."

4. A flowery compliment: in classical mythology the three graces are sister goddesses who bestow beauty and charm.

in the coach, he changed his plan, and ordered a post-chaise and four.

O'Mooney was not in danger of making any vulgar Irish blunders in paying his bill at an inn. No landlord or waiter could have suspected him, especially as he always left them to settle the matter first, and then looked over the bill and money with a careless gentility, saying, "Very right," or, "Very well, sir"; wisely calculating, that it was better to lose a few shillings on the road, than to lose a hundred pounds by the risk of Hibernian miscalculation.

Whilst the chaise was getting ready he went to the custom-house to look after his baggage. He found a red-hot countryman of his own there, roaring about four and fourpence, and fighting the battle of his trunks, in which he was ready to make affidavit there was not, nor never had been, any thing contraband; and when the custom-house officer replied by pulling out of one of them a piece of Irish poplin, the Hibernian fell immediately upon the Union, which he swore was Disunion, as the custom-house officers managed it. Sir John Bull appeared to much advantage all this time, maintaining a dignified silence; from his quiet appearance and deportment, the custom-house officers took it for granted that he was an Englishman. He was in no hurry; he begged *that* gentleman's business might be settled first; he would wait the officer's leisure, and as he spoke he played so dexterously with half-a-guinea between his fingers, as to make it visible only where he wished. The custom-house officer was his humble servant immediately; but the Hibernian would have been his enemy, if he had not conciliated him by observing, "that even Englishmen must allow there was something very like a bull in professing to make a complete identification of the two kingdoms, whilst, at the same time, certain regulations continued in full force to divide the countries by art, even more than the British channel does by nature."

Sir John talked so plausibly, and, above all, so candidly and coolly on Irish and English politics, that the custom-house officer conversed with him for a quarter of an hour without guessing of what country he was, till in an unlucky moment Phelim's heart got the better of his head. Joining in the praises bestowed by all parties on the conduct of a distinguished patriot of his country, he, in the height of his enthusiasm, inadvertently called him *the Speaker*.

"The *Speaker!*" said the officer.

"Yes, the Speaker—*our* Speaker" cried Phelim, with exultation.[5] He was not aware how he had betrayed himself, till the officer smiled and said—

"Sir, I really never should have found out that you were an Irishman but from the manner in which you named your countryman, who is as highly thought of by all parties in this country as in yours: your enthusiasm does honour to your heart."

"And to my head, I'm sure," said our hero, laughing with the best grace imaginable. "Well, I am glad you have found me out in this manner, though I lose the eighth part of a bet of a hundred guineas by it."

He explained the wager, and begged the custom-house officer to keep his secret, which he promised to do faithfully, and assured him, "that he should be happy to do any thing in his power to serve him." Whilst he was uttering these last words, there came in a snug, but soft-looking Englishman, who opining from the words "happy to do any thing in my power to serve you," that O'Mooney was a friend of the custom-house officer's, and encouraged by

---

5. John Foster, Baron Oriel, the last man to serve as speaker in the Irish House of Commons, before its abolition by the Act of Union in 1801.

something affable and good-natured in our hero's countenance, crept up to him, and whispered a request—"Could you tell a body, sir, how to get out of the custom-house a very valuable box of Sèvre china that has been *laying* in the custom-house three weeks, and which I was commissioned to get out if I could, and bring up to town for a lady."

As a lady was in the case, O'Mooney's gallantry instantly made his good-nature effective. The box of Sèvre china was produced, and opened only as a matter of form, and only as a matter of curiosity its contents were examined—a beautiful set of Sèvre china and a pendule, said to have belonged to M. Egalité![6] "These things must be intended," said Phelim, "for some lady of superior taste or fortune."

As Phelim was a proficient in the Socratic art of putting judicious interrogatories, he was soon happily master of the principal points it concerned him to know: he learnt that the lady was rich—a spinster—of full age—at her own disposal—living with a single female companion at Blackheath[7]—furnishing a house there in a superior style—had two carriages—her Christian name Mary—her surname Sharperson.

O'Mooney, by the blessing of God, it shall soon be, thought Phelim. He politely offered the Englishman a place in his chaise for himself and Sèvre china, as it was for a lady, and would run great hazard in the stage, which besides was full. Mr. Queasy, for that was our soft Englishman's name, was astonished by our hero's condescension and affability, especially as he heard him called Sir John: he bowed sundry times as low as the fear of losing his wig would permit, and accepted the polite offer with many thanks for himself and the lady concerned.

Sir John Bull's chaise and four was soon ready and Queasy seated in the corner of it, and the Sèvre china safely stowed between his knees. Captain Murray, a Scotch officer, was standing at the inn door, with his eyes intently fixed on the letters that were worked in nails on the top of Sir John's trunk; the letters were P. O'M. Our hero, whose eyes were at least as quick as the Scotchman's, was alarmed lest this should lead to a second detection. He called instantly, with his usual presence of mind, to the ostler, and desired him to uncord *that* trunk, as it was not to go with him; raising his voice loud enough for all *the yard* to hear, he added—"It is not mine at all; it belongs to my friend, Mr. O'Mooney: let it be sent after me, at leisure, by the waggon, as directed, to the care of Sir John Bull."

Our hero was now giving his invention a prodigious quantity of superfluous trouble; and upon this occasion, as upon most others, he was more in danger from excess than deficiency of ingenuity: he was like the man in the fairy tale, who was obliged to tie his legs lest he should outrun the object of which he was in pursuit. The Scotch officer, though his eyes were fixed on the letters P. O'M., had none of the suspicions which Phelim was counteracting; he was only considering how he could ask for the third place in Sir John's chaise during the next stage, as he was in great haste to get to town upon particular business, and there were no other horses at the inn. When he heard that the heavy baggage was to go by the waggon, he took courage, and made his request.

6. Cousin to King Louis XVI and himself in line for the throne of France, Philippe, Duke of Orleans (1747–1793) assumed the surname Egalité ("Equality") as testimony of his support for the Revolution. The name change did not save him from the guillotine. The Duke's Sèvre—expensive porcelain manufactured near Paris—and pendule, a pendulum clock, appear to have come on the market following his execution.
7. District of London.

It was instantly granted by the good-natured Hibernian, who showed as much hospitality about his chaise as if it had been his house. Away they drove as fast as they could. Fresh dangers awaited him at the next inn. He left his hat upon the table in the hall whilst he went into the parlour, and when he returned, he heard some person inquiring what Irish gentleman was there. Our hero was terribly alarmed, for he saw that his hat was in the inquirer's hand, and he recollected that the name of Phelim O'Mooney was written in it. This the inquisitive gentleman did not see, for it was written in no very legible characters on the leather withinside of the front; but "F. Guest, hatter, Dame-street, Dublin," was a printed advertisement that could not be mistaken, and *that* was pasted within the crown. O'Mooney's presence of mind did not forsake him upon this emergency.

"My good sir," said he, turning to Queasy, who, without hearing one word of what was passing, was coming out of the parlour, with his own hat and gloves in his hand; "My good sir," continued he, loading him with parcels, "will you have the goodness to see these put into my carriage? I'll take care of your hat and gloves," added O'Mooney in a low voice. Queasy surrendered his hat and gloves instantly, unknowing wherefore; then squeezed forward with his load through the crowd, crying—"Waiter! hostler! pray, somebody put these into Sir John Bull's chaise."

Sir John Bull, equipped with Queasy's hat, marched deliberately through the defile, bowing with the air of at least an English county member[8] to this side and to that, as way was made for him to his carriage. No one suspected that the hat did not belong to him; no one, indeed, thought of the hat, for all eyes were fixed upon the man. Seated in the carriage, he threw money to the waiter, hostler, and boots, and drew up the glass, bidding the postilions drive on. By this cool self-possession our hero effected his retreat with successful generalship, leaving his new Dublin beaver behind him, without regret, as bona waviata.[9] Queasy, before whose eyes things passed continually without his seeing them, thanked Sir John for the care he had taken of his hat, drew on his gloves, and calculated aloud how long they should be going to the next stage. At the first town they passed through, O'Mooney bought a new hat, and Queasy deplored the unaccountable mistake by which Sir John's hat had been forgotten. No further *mistakes* happened upon the journey. The travellers rattled on, and neither 'stinted nor stayed'[1] till they arrived at Blackheath, at Miss Sharperson's. Sir John sat Queasy down without having given him the least hint of his designs upon the lady; but as he helped him out with the Sèvre china, he looked through the large opening double doors of the hall, and slightly said—"Upon my word, this seems to be a handsome house: it would be worth looking at, if the family were not at home."

"I am morally sure, Sir John," said the soft Queasy, "that Miss Sharperson would be happy to let you see the house to-night, and this minute, if she knew you were at the door, and who you were, and all your civility about me and the china.—Do, pray, walk in."

"Not for the world: a gentleman could not do such a thing without an invitation from the lady of the house herself."

8. One of the members of Parliament who represented the counties of England.
9. *Bona waviata* is a Latin term applied in law to stolen goods that have been thrown away by their thief, who would rather lose them than be caught red-handed. It is applied here to the hero's "beaver," a type of hat made from beaver's fur.
1. I.e., by not stinting on money or food for the horses, they avoided any delay (stay).

"Oh, if that's all, I'll step up myself to the young lady; I'm certain she'll be proud—"

"Mr. Queasy, by no means; I would not have the lady disturbed for the world at this unseasonable hour.—It is too late—quite too late."

"Not at all, begging pardon, Sir John," said Queasy, taking out his watch: "only just tea-time by me.—Not at all unseasonable for any body; besides, the message is of my own head:—all, you know, if not well taken—"

Up the great staircase he made bold to go on his mission, as he thought, in defiance of Sir John's better judgment. He returned in a few minutes with a face of self-complacent exultation, *and* Miss Sharperson's compliments, and begs Sir John Bull will walk up and rest himself with a dish of tea, and has her thanks to him for the china.

Now Queasy, who had the highest possible opinion of Sir John Bull and of Miss Sharperson, whom he thought the two people of the greatest consequence and affability, had formed the notion that they were made for each other, and that it must be a match if they could but meet. The meeting he had now happily contrived and effected; and he had done his part for his friend Sir John, with Miss Sharperson, by as many exaggerations as he could utter in five minutes, concerning his perdigious politeness and courage, his fine person and carriage, his ancient family, and vast connections and importance wherever he appeared on the road, at inns, and over all England. He had previously, during the journey, done his part for his friend Miss Sharperson with Sir John, by stating that "she had a large fortune left her by her mother, and was to have twice as much from her grandmother; that she had thousands upon thousands in the funds, and an estate of two thousand a year, called Rascàlly, in Scotland, besides plate and jewels without end."

Thus prepared, how could this lady and gentleman meet without falling desperately in love with each other!

Though a servant in handsome livery appeared ready to show Sir John up the great staircase, Mr. Queasy acted as a gentleman usher, or rather as showman. He nodded to Sir John as they passed across a long gallery and through an ante-chamber, threw open the doors of various apartments as he went along, crying—"Peep in! peep in! peep in here! peep in there!—Is not this spacious? Is not this elegant? Is not that grand? Did I say too much?" continued he, rubbing his hands with delight. "Did you ever see so magnificent and such highly-polished steel grates out of Lon'on?"

Sir John, conscious that the servant's eyes were upon him, smiled at this question, "looked superior down;" and though with reluctant complaisance he leaned his body to this side or to that, as Queasy pulled or swayed, yet he appeared totally regardless of the man's vulgar reflections. He had seen every thing as he passed, and was surprised at all he saw; but he evinced not the slightest symptom of astonishment. He was now ushered into a spacious, well lighted apartment: he entered with the easy, unembarrassed air of a man who was perfectly accustomed to such a home. His quick coup-d'oeil took in the whole at a single glance. Two magnificent candelabras stood on Egyptian tables[2] at the farther end of the room, and the lights were reflected on all sides from mirrors of no common size. Nothing seemed worthy to attract our hero's attention but the lady of the house, whom he approached with an air of dis-

---

2. Following the victory of the British Fleet against the French at the Battle of the Nile (1798), furnishings in an Egyptian style were the height of fashion.

tinguished respect. She was reclining on a Turkish sofa, her companion seated beside her, tuning a harp. Miss Sharperson half rose to receive Sir John: he paid his compliments with an easy, yet respectful air. He was thanked for his civilities to *the person* who had been commissioned to bring the box of Sèvre china from Deal.

"Vastly sorry it should have been so troublesome," Miss Sharperson said, in a voice fashionably unintelligible, and with a most becoming yet intimidating nonchalance of manner. Intimidating it might have been to any man but our hero; he, who had the happy talent of catching, wherever he went, the reigning manner of the place, replied to the lady in equal strains; and she, in her turn, seemed to look upon him more as her equal. Tea and coffee were served. *Nothings* were talked of quite easily by Sir John. He practised the art "not to admire," so as to give a justly high opinion of his taste, consequence, and knowledge of the world. Miss Sharperson, though her nonchalance was much diminished, continued to maintain a certain dignified reserve; whilst her companion, Miss Felicia Flat, condescended to ask Sir John, who had doubtless seen every fine house in England and on the continent, his opinion with respect to the furniture and finishing of the room, the placing of the Egyptian tables and the candelabras.

No mortal could have guessed by Sir John Bull's air, when he heard this question, that he had never seen a candelabra before in his life. He was so much, and yet seemingly so little upon his guard, he dealt so dexterously in generals, and evaded particulars so delicately, that he went through this dangerous conversation triumphantly. Careful not to protract his visit beyond the bounds of propriety, he soon rose to take leave, and he mingled "intrusion, regret, late hour, happiness, and honour," so charmingly in his parting compliment, as to leave the most favourable impression on the minds of both the ladies, and to procure for himself an invitation to see the house next morning.

The first day was now ended, and our hero had been detected but once. He went to rest this night well satisfied with himself, but much more occupied with the hopes of marrying the heiress of Rascàlly than of winning a paltry bet.

The next day he waited upon the ladies in high spirits. Neither of them was *visible*, but Mr. Queasy had orders to show him the house, which he did with much exultation, dwelling particularly in his praises on the beautiful high polish of the steel grates. Queasy boasted that it was he who had recommended the ironmonger who furnished the house in that line; and that his bill, as he was proud to state, amounted to *many, many* hundreds. Sir John, who did not attend to one word Queasy said, went to examine the map of the Rascàlly estate, which was unrolled, and he had leisure to count the number of lords' and ladies' visiting tickets[3] which lay upon the chimney-piece. He saw names of the people of first quality and respectability: it was plain that Miss Sharperson must be a lady of high family as well as large fortune, else she would not be visited by persons of such distinction. Our hero's passion for her increased every moment. Her companion, Miss Flat, now appeared, and entered very freely into conversation with Sir John; and as he perceived that she was commissioned to sit in judgment upon him, he evaded all her leading questions with the skill of an Irish witness, but without giving any Hibernian answers. She was fairly at a fault. Miss Sharperson at length appeared, ele-

3. The cards left by the people paying social calls on Miss Sharperson.

gantly dressed; her person was genteel, and her face rather pretty. Sir John, at this instant, thought her beautiful, or seemed to think so. The ladies interchanged looks, and afterwards Sir John found a softness in his fair one's manner, a languishing tenderness in her eyes, in the tone of her voice, and at the same time a modest perplexity and reserve about her, which altogether persuaded him that he was quite right, and his brother quite wrong *en fait d'amour*.[4] Miss Flat appeared now to have the most self-possession of the three, and Miss Sharperson looked at her, from time to time, as if she asked leave to be in love. Sir John's visit lasted a full half hour before he was sensible of having been five minutes engaged in this delightful conversation.

Miss Sharperson's coach now came to the door: he handed her into it, and she gave him a parting look, which satisfied him all was yet safe in her heart. Miss Flat, as he handed her into the carriage, said, "Perhaps they should meet Sir John at Tunbridge,[5] where they were going in a few days." She added some words as she seated herself, which he scarcely noticed at the time, but they recurred afterwards disagreeably to his memory. The words were, "I'm so glad we've a roomy coach, for of all things it annoys me to be *squeedged* in a carriage."

This word *squeedged*, as he had not been used to it in Ireland, sounded to him extremely vulgar, and gave him suspicions of the most painful nature. He had the precaution, before he left Blackheath, to go into several shops, and to inquire something more concerning his fair ladies. All he heard was much to their advantage; that is, much to the advantage of Miss Sharperson's fortune. All agreed that she was a rich Scotch heiress. A rich Scotch heiress, Sir John wisely considered, might have an humble companion who spoke bad English. He concluded that *squeedged* was Scotch, blamed himself for his suspicions, and was more in love with his mistress and with himself than ever. As he returned to town, he framed the outline of a triumphant letter to his brother on his approaching marriage. The bet was a matter, at present, totally beneath his consideration. However, we must do him the justice to say, that like a man of honour he resolved that, as soon as he had won the lady's heart, he would *candidly* tell her his circumstances, and then leave her the choice either to marry him or break her heart, as she pleased. Just as he had formed this generous resolution, at a sudden turn of the road he overtook Miss Sharperson's coach: he bowed and looked in as he passed, when, to his astonishment, he saw, *squeedged* up in the corner by Miss Felicia, Mr. Queasy. He thought that this was a blunder in etiquette that would never have been made in Ireland. Perhaps his mistress was of the same opinion, for she hastily pulled down the blind as Sir John passed. A cold qualm came over the lover's heart. He lost no time in idle doubts and suspicions, but galloped on to town as fast as he could, and went immediately to call upon the Scotch officer with whom he had travelled, and whom he knew to be keen and prudent. He recollected the map of the Rascàlly estate, which he saw in Miss Sharperson's breakfast-room, and he remembered that the lands were said to lie in that part of Scotland from which Captain Murray came; from him he resolved to inquire into the state of the premises, before he should offer himself as tenant for life. Captain Murray assured him that there was no such place as Rascàlly in that part of Scotland; that he had never heard of any such person as Miss Sharperson,

---

4. In matters concerning love (French).
5. Tunbridge Wells, a fashionable spa town in southeast England.

though he was acquainted with every family and every estate in the neighbourhood where she fabled hers to be. O'Mooney drew, from memory, the map of the Rascàlly estate. Captain Murray examined the boundaries, and assured him that his cousin the general's lands joined his own at the very spot which he described, and that unless two straight lines could enclose a space, the Rascàlly estate could not be found.

Sir John, naturally of a warm temper, proceeded, however, with prudence. The Scotch officer admired his sagacity in detecting this adventurer. Sir John waited at his hotel for Queasy, who had promised to call to let him know when the ladies would go to Tunbridge. Queasy came. Nothing could equal his astonishment and dismay when he was told the news.

"No such place as the Rascàlly estate! Then I'm an undone man! an undone man!" cried poor Queasy, bursting into tears: "but I'm certain it's impossible; and you'll find, Sir John, you've been misinformed. I would stake my life upon it, Miss Sharperson's a rich heiress, and has a rich grandmother. Why, she's five hundred pounds in my debt, and I know of her being thousands and thousands in the books of as good men as myself, to whom I've recommended her, which I wouldn't have done for my life if I had not known her to be solid. You'll find she'll prove a rich heiress, Sir John."

Sir John hoped so, but the proofs were not yet satisfactory. Queasy determined to inquire about her payments to certain creditors at Blackheath, and promised to give a decisive answer in the morning. O'Mooney saw that this man was too great a fool to be a knave; his perturbation was evidently the perturbation of a dupe, not of an accomplice: Queasy was made to "be an anvil, not a hammer."[6] In the midst of his own disappointment, our good-natured Hibernian really pitied this poor currier.[7]

The next morning Sir John went early to Blackheath. All was confusion at Miss Sharperson's house; the steps covered with grates and furniture of all sorts; porters carrying out looking-glasses, Egyptian tables, and candelabras; the noise of workmen was heard in every apartment; and louder than all the rest, O'Mooney heard the curses that were denounced against his rich heiress—curses such as are bestowed on a swindler in the moment of detection by the tradesmen whom she has ruined.

Our hero, who was of a most happy temper, congratulated himself upon having, by his own wit and prudence, escaped making the practical bull of marrying a female swindler.

Now that Phelim's immediate hopes of marrying a rich heiress were over, his bet with his brother appeared to him of more consequence, and he rejoiced in the reflection that this was the third day he had spent in England, and that he had but once been detected.—The ides of March[8] were come, but not passed!

"My lads," said he to the workmen, who were busy in carrying out the furniture from Miss Sharperson's house, "all hands are at work, I see, in saving what they can from the wreck of *the Sharperson*. She was as well-fitted out a vessel, and in as gallant trim, as any ship upon the face of the earth."

"Ship upon the face of the *yearth*!" repeated an English porter with a sneer;

---

6. I.e., Queasy has not acted but been acted upon.
7. Someone who curries favor.
8. March 15. In Shakespeare's *Julius Caesar* 1.2, a soothsayer prophesies that Caesar will meet with danger on this date.

"ship upon the face of the water, you should say, master; but I take it you be's an Irishman."

O'Mooney had reason to be particularly vexed at being detected by this man, who spoke a miserable jargon, and who seemed not to have a very extensive range of ideas. He was one of those half-witted geniuses who catch at the shadow of an Irish bull. In fact, Phelim had merely made a lapsus linguae and had used an expression justifiable by the authority of the elegant and witty lord Chesterfield,[9] who said—no, who *wrote*—that the English navy is the finest navy *upon the face of the earth!* But it was in vain for our hero to argue the point; he was detected—no matter how or by whom. But this was only his second detection, and three of his four days of probation were past.

He dined this day at Captain Murray's. In the room in which they dined there was a picture of the captain, painted by Romney. Sir John, who happened to be seated opposite to it, observed that it was a very fine picture; the more he looked at it, the more he liked it. His admiration was at last unluckily expressed: he said, "That's an incomparable, an inimitable picture; it is abso-lutely *more like than the original.*"[1]

A keen Scotch lady in company smiled, and repeated, "*More like than the original!* Sir John, if I had not been told by my relative here that you were an Englishman, I should have set you *doon*, from that speech, for an Irishman."

This unexpected detection brought the colour, for a moment, into Sir John's face; but immediately recovering his presence of mind, he said, "That was, I acknowledge, an excellent Irish bull; but in the course of my travels I have heard as good English bulls as Irish."

To this Captain Murray politely acceded, and he produced some laughable instances in support of the assertion, which gave the conversation a new turn.

O'Mooney felt extremely obliged to the captain for this, especially as he saw, by his countenance, that he also had suspicions of the truth. The first moment he found himself alone with Murray, our hero said to him, "Murray, you are too good a fellow to impose upon, even in jest. Your keen countrywoman guessed the truth—I am an Irishman, but not a swindler. You shall hear why I conceal my country and name; only keep my secret till to-morrow night, or I shall lose a hundred guineas by my frankness."

O'Mooney then explained to him the nature of his bet. "This is only my third detection, and half of it voluntary, I might say, if I chose to higgle, which I scorn to do."

Captain Murray was so much pleased by this openness, that as he shook hands with O'Mooney, he said, "Give me leave to tell you, Sir, that even if you should lose your bet by this frank behaviour, you will have gained a better thing—a friend."

In the evening our hero went with his friend and a party of gentlemen to Maidenhead, near which place a battle was to be fought next day, between two famous pugilists, Bourke and Belcher.[2] At the appointed time the com-batants appeared upon the stage; the whole boxing corps and the gentlemen *amateurs* crowded to behold the spectacle. Phelim O'Mooney's heart beat for

---

9. The hero's *lapsus linguae* (Latin for slip of the tongue) has a precedent in the writings of Philip Dormer Stanhope, the fourth earl of Chesterfield (1694–1773), whose posthumously published let-ters to his illegitimate son secured him a reputation as a wit and a schemer.

1. This bull was really made [Edgeworth's note]. George Romney (1734–1802) painted society por-traits and rural scenes.
2. The reference is to actual historical figures of the early 19th century—the bare-knuckle boxers Jem Belcher and Joe Bourke.

the Irish champion Bourke; but he kept a guard upon his tongue, and had even the forbearance not to bet upon his countryman's head. How many rounds were fought, and how many minutes the fight lasted, how many blows were *put in* on each side, or which was the *game man* of the two, we forbear to decide or relate, as all this has been settled in the newspapers of the day; where also it was remarked, that Bourke, who lost the battle, "was put into a post-chaise, and left *standing* half an hour, while another fight took place. This was very scandalous on the part of his friends," says the humane newspaper historian, "as the poor man might possibly be dying."

Our hero O'Mooney's heart again got the better of his head. Forgetful of his bet, forgetful of every thing but humanity, he made his way up to the chaise, where Bourke was left. "How are you, my gay fellow?" said he. "Can you *see at all with the eye that's knocked out?*"

The brutal populace, who overheard this question, set up a roar of laughter: "A bull! a bull! an Irish bull! Did you hear the question this Irish gentleman asked his countryman?"

O'Mooney was detected a fourth time, and this time he was not ashamed. There was one man in the crowd who did not join in the laugh: a poor Irishman, of the name of Terence McDermod. He had in former times gone out a grousing, near Cork, with our hero; and the moment he heard his voice, he sprang forward, and with uncouth but honest demonstrations of joy, exclaimed, "Ah, my dear master! my dear young master! Phelim O'Mooney, Esq.[3] And I have found your honour alive again? By the blessing of God above, I'll never part you now till I die; and I'll go to the world's end to sarve *yees*."

O'Mooney wished him at the world's end this instant, yet could not prevail upon himself to check this affectionate follower of the O'Mooneys. He, however, put half a crown into his hand, and hinted that if he wished really to serve him, it must be at some other time. The poor fellow threw down the money, saying, he would never leave him. "Bid me do any thing, barring that. No, you shall never part me. Do what you plase with me, still I'll be close to your heart, like your own shadow: knock me down if you will, and wilcome, ten times a day, and I'll be up again like a ninepin: only let me sarve your honour; I'll ask no wages nor take none."

There was no withstanding all this; and whether our hero's good-nature deceived him we shall not determine, but he thought it most prudent, as he could not get rid of Terence, to take him into his service, to let him into his secret, to make him swear that he would never utter the name of Phelim O'Mooney during the remainder of this day. Terence heard the secret of the bet with joy, entered into the jest with all the readiness of an Irishman, and with equal joy and readiness swore by the hind leg of the holy lamb that he would never mention, even to his own dog, the name of Phelim O'Mooney, Esq., good or bad, till past twelve o'clock; and further, that he would, till the clock should strike that hour, call his master Sir John Bull, and nothing else, to all men, women, and children, upon the floor of God's creation.

Satisfied with the fulness of this oath, O'Mooney resolved to return to town with his man Terence McDermod. He, however, contrived, before he got there, to make a practical bull, by which he was detected a fifth time. He got into the coach which was driving *from* London instead of that which was driving *to* London, and he would have been carried rapidly to Oxford, had not his man

3. "Esquire"—designation given to men regarded as gentlemen.

Terence, after they had proceeded a mile and a half on the wrong road, put his head down from the top of the coach, crying, as he looked in at the window, "Master, Sir John Bull, are you there? Do you know we're in the wrong box, going to Oxford?"

"Your master's an Irishman, dare to say, as well as yourself," said the coachman, as he let Sir John out. He walked back to Maidenhead, and took a chaise to town.

It was six o'clock when he got to London, and he went into a coffee-house to dine. He sat down beside a gentleman who was reading the newspaper. "Any news to-day, sir?"

The gentleman told him the news of the day, and then began to read aloud some paragraphs in a strong Hibernian accent. Our hero was sorry that he had met with another countryman; but he resolved to set a guard upon his lips, and he knew that his own accent could not betray him. The stranger read on till he came to a trial about a legacy which an old woman had left to her cats. O'Mooney exclaimed, "I hate cats almost as much as old women; and if I had been the English minister, I would have laid the *dog-tax* upon cats."[4]

"If you had been the *Irish* minister, you mean," said the stranger, smiling; "for I perceive now you are a countryman of my own."

"How can you think so, sir?" said O'Mooney: "You have no reason to suppose so from my accent, I believe."

"None in life—quite the contrary; for you speak remarkably pure English—not the least note or half note of the brogue; but there's another sort of freemason sign by which we Hibernians know one another and are known all over the globe. Whether to call it a confusion of expressions or of ideas, I can't tell. Now an Englishman, if he had been saying what you did, sir, just now, would have taken time to separate the dog and the tax, and he would have put the tax upon cats, and let the dogs go about their business." Our hero, with his usual good-humour, acknowledged himself to be fairly detected.

"Well, sir," said the stranger, "if I had not found you out before by the blunder, I should be sure now you were my countryman by your good-humour. An Irishman can take what's said to him, provided no affront's meant, with more good-humour than any man on earth."

"Ay, that he can," cried O' Mooney: "he lends himself, like the whale, to be tickled even by the fellow with the harpoon, till he finds what he is about, and then he pays away, and pitches the fellow, boat and all, to the devil. Ah, countryman! you would give me credit indeed for my good humour if you knew what danger you have put me in by detecting me for an Irishman. I have been found out six times, and if I blunder twice more before twelve o'clock this night, I shall lose a hundred guineas by it: but I will make sure of my bet; for I will go home straight this minute, lock myself up in my room, and not say a word to any mortal till the watchman cries 'past twelve o'clock,'—then the fast and long Lent of my tongue will be fairly over; and if you'll meet me, my dear friend, at the King's Arms, we will have a good supper and keep Easter for ever."

Phelim, pursuant to his resolution, returned to his hotel, and shut himself up in his room, where he remained in perfect silence and consequent safety till about nine o'clock. Suddenly he heard a great huzzaing in the street; he looked out of the window, and saw that all the houses in the street were illuminated. His landlady came bustling into his apartment, followed by wait-

4. One of several new taxes introduced by Prime Minister Pitt to finance Britain's war against France.

ers with candles. His spirits instantly rose, though he did not clearly know the cause of the rejoicings. "I give you joy, ma'am. What are you all illuminating[5] for?" said he to his landlady.

"Thank you, sir, with all my heart. I am not sure. It is either for a great victory or the peace. Bob—waiter—step out and inquire for the gentleman."

The gentleman preferred stepping out to inquire for himself. The illuminations were in honour of the peace.[6] He totally forgot his bet, his silence, and his prudence, in his sympathy with the general joy. He walked rapidly from street to street, admiring the various elegant devices. A crowd was standing before the windows of a house that was illuminated with extraordinary splendour. He inquired whose it was, and was informed that it belonged to a contractor, who had made an immense fortune by the war.

"Then I'm sure these illuminations of his for the peace are none of the most sincere," said O'Mooney. The mob were of his opinion; and Phelim, who was now, alas ! worked up to the proper pitch for blundering, added, by way of pleasing his audience still more—"If this contractor had *illuminated* in character, it should have been with *dark lanterns*."[7]

"Should it? by Jasus! that would be an Irish illumination," cried some one. "Arrah, honey! you're an Irishman, whoever you are, and have spoke your mind in character."

Sir John Bull was vexed that the piece of wit which he had aimed at the contractor had recoiled upon himself. "It is always, as my countryman observed, by having too much wit that I blunder. The deuce take me if I sport a single bon mot more this night. This is only my seventh detection, I have an eighth blunder still *to the good*; and if I can but keep my wit to myself till I am out of purgatory, then I shall be in heaven, and may sing Io triumphe[8] in spite of my brother."

Fortunately, Phelim had not made it any part of his bet that he should not speak to himself an Irish idiom, or that he should not think a bull. Resolved to be as obstinately silent as a monk of La Trappe,[9] he once more shut himself up in his cell, and fell fast asleep—dreamed that fat bulls of Basan[1] encompassed him round about—that he ran down a steep hill to escape them—that his foot slipped—he rolled to the bottom—felt the bull's horns in his side— heard the bull bellowing in his ears—wakened—and found Terence Mc-Dermod bellowing at his room door.

"Sir John Bull! Sir John Bull ! murder! murder! my dear master, Sir John Bull! murder, robbery, and reward! let me in! for the love of the Holy Virgin! they are all after you!"

"Who? are you drunk, Terence?" said Sir John, opening the door.

"No, but they are mad—all mad."

"Who?"

"The constable. They are all mad entirely, and the lord mayor, all along with your honour's making me swear I would not tell your name. Sure they are all coming armed in a body to put you in jail for a forgery, unless I run back and tell them the truth—will I?"

"First tell me the truth, blunderer!"

5. Decorating with lights as a sign of celebration.
6. Probably the truce signed between Britain and France in October 1801, temporarily suspending hostilities after eight years of war.
7. Lanterns equipped with slides that allow their light to be hidden.

8. Greek cry of triumph.
9. Alluding to the vows of silence taken by the monks of the French Abbey of La Trappe.
1. A recollection of Psalms 22.12, where the Psalmist describes his anguish at being forsaken: "strong bulls of Bashan have beset me round."

"I'll make my affidavit I never blundered, plase your honour, but just went to the merchant's, as you ordered, with the draught, signed with the name I swore not to utter till past twelve. I presents the draught, and waits to be paid. 'Are you Mr. O'Mooney's servant?' says one of the clerks after a while. No, sir, not at all, sir,' said I; 'I'm Sir John Bull's, at your sarvice.' He puzzles and puzzles, and asks me did I bring the draught, and was that your writing at the bottom of it? I still said it was my master's writing, *Sir John Bull's*, and no other. They whispered from one up to t'other, and then said it was a forgery, as I overheard, and I must go before the mayor. With that, while the master, who was called down to be examined as to his opinion, was putting on his glasses to spell it out, I gives them, one and all, the slip, and whips out of the street door and home to give your honour notice, and have been breaking my heart at the door this half hour to make you hear—and now you have it all."

"I am in a worse dilemma now than when between the horns of the bull," thought Sir John: "I must now either tell my real name, avow myself an Irishman, and so lose my bet, or else go to gaol."

He preferred going to gaol. He resolved to pretend to be dumb, and he charged Terence not to betray him. The officers of justice came to take him up: Sir John resigned himself to them, making signs that he could not speak. He was carried before a magistrate. The merchant had never seen Mr. Phelim O'Mooney, but could swear to his handwriting and signature, having many of his letters and draughts. The draught in question was produced. Sir John Bull would neither acknowledge nor deny the signature, but in dumb show made signs of innocence. No art or persuasion could make him speak; he kept his fingers on his lips. One of the bailiffs offered to open Sir John's mouth. Sir John clenched his hand, in token that if they used violence he knew his remedy. To the magistrate he was all bows and respect: but the law, in spite of civility, must take its course.

Terence MᶜDermod beat his breast, and called upon all the saints in the Irish calender when he saw the committal actually made out, and his dear master given over to the constables. Nothing but his own oath and his master's commanding eye, which was fixed upon him at this instant, could have made him forbear to utter, what he had never in his life been before so strongly tempted to tell—the truth.

Determined to win his wager, our hero suffered himself to be carried to a lock-up house, and persisted in keeping silence till the clock struck twelve! Then the charm was broken, and he spoke. He began talking to himself, and singing as loud as he possibly could. The next morning Terence, who was no longer bound by his oath to conceal Phelim's name, hastened to his master's correspondent in town, told the whole story, and O'Mooney was liberated. Having won his bet by his wit and steadiness, he had now the prudence to give up these adventuring schemes, to which he had so nearly become a dupe; he returned immediately to Ireland to his brother, and determined to settle quietly to business. His good brother paid him the hundred guineas most joyfully, declaring that he had never spent a hundred guineas better in his life than in recovering a brother. Phelim had now conquered his foolish dislike to trade: his brother took him into partnership, and Phelim O'Mooney never relapsed into Sir John Bull.

1802

WILLIAM WORDSWORTH
1770–1850

William Wordsworth was born in Cockermouth in West Cumberland, just on the northern fringe of the English Lake District. When his mother died, the eight-year-old boy was sent to school at Hawkshead, near Esthwaite Lake, in the heart of that sparsely populated region that he and Coleridge were to transform into one of the poetic centers of England. William and his three brothers boarded in the cottage of Ann Tyson, who gave the boys simple comfort, ample affection, and freedom to roam the countryside at will. A vigorous, unruly, and sometimes moody boy, William spent his free days and occasionally "half the night" in the sports and rambles described in the first two books of *The Prelude*, "drinking in" (to use one of his favorite metaphors) the natural sights and sounds, and getting to know the cottagers, shepherds, and solitary wanderers who moved through his imagination into his later poetry. He also found time to read voraciously in the books owned by his young headmaster, William Taylor, who encouraged him in his inclination to poetry.

John Wordsworth, the poet's father, died suddenly when William was thirteen, leaving to his five children mainly the substantial sum owed him by Lord Lonsdale, whom he had served as attorney and as steward of the huge Lonsdale estate. This harsh nobleman had yet to pay the debt when he died in 1802. Wordsworth was nevertheless able in 1787 to enter St. John's College, Cambridge University, where four years later he took his degree without distinction.

During the summer vacation of his third year at Cambridge (1790), Wordsworth and his closest college friend, the Welshman Robert Jones, journeyed on foot through France and the Alps (described in *The Prelude* 6) at the time when the French were joyously celebrating the first anniversary of the fall of the Bastille. Upon completing his course at Cambridge, Wordsworth spent four months in London, set off on another walking tour with Robert Jones through Wales (the time of the memorable ascent of Mount Snowdon in *The Prelude* 14), and then went back alone to France to master the language and qualify as a traveling tutor.

During his year in France (November 1791 to December 1792), Wordsworth became a fervent supporter of the French Revolution—which seemed to him and many others to promise a "glorious renovation" of society—and he fell in love with Annette Vallon, the daughter of a French surgeon at Blois. The two planned to marry, despite their differences in religion and political inclinations (Annette belonged to an old Catholic family whose sympathies were Royalist). But almost immediately after their daughter, Caroline, was born, lack of money forced Wordsworth to return to England. The outbreak of war made it impossible for him to rejoin Annette and Caroline. Wordsworth's guilt over this abandonment, his divided loyalties between England and France, and his gradual disillusion with the course of the Revolution brought him—according to his account in *The Prelude* 10 and 11—to the verge of an emotional breakdown, when "sick, wearied out with contrarieties," he "yielded up moral questions in despair." His suffering, his near-collapse, and the successful effort, after his break with his past, to reestablish "a saving intercourse with my true self," are the experiences that underlie many of his greatest poems.

At this critical point, a friend died and left Wordsworth a sum of money just sufficient to enable him to live by his poetry. In 1795 he settled in a rent-free house at Racedown, Dorsetshire, with his beloved sister, Dorothy, who now began her long career as confidante, inspirer, and secretary. At that same time Wordsworth met Samuel Taylor Coleridge. Two years later he moved to Alfoxden House, Somersetshire, to be near Coleridge, who lived four miles away at Nether Stowey. Here he entered at the age of twenty-seven on the delayed springtime of his poetic career.

Even while he had been an undergraduate at Cambridge, Coleridge claimed that

244 / WILLIAM WORDSWORTH

he had detected signs of genius in Wordsworth's rather conventional poem about his tour in the Alps, *Descriptive Sketches*, published in 1793. Now he hailed Wordsworth unreservedly as "the best poet of the age." The two men met almost daily, talked for hours about poetry, and wrote prolifically. So close was their association that we find the same phrases occurring in poems by Wordsworth and Coleridge, as well as in the remarkable journals that Dorothy kept at the time; the two poets collaborated in some writings and freely traded thoughts and passages for others; and Coleridge even undertook to complete a few poems that Wordsworth had left unfinished. This close partnership, along with the hospitality the two households offered to another young radical writer, John Thelwall, aroused the paranoia of people in the neighborhood. Already fearful of a military invasion by France, they became convinced that Words-worth and Coleridge were political plotters, not poets. The government sent spies to investigate, and the Wordsworths lost their lease.

Although brought to this abrupt end, that short period of collaboration resulted in one of the most important books of the era, *Lyrical Ballads, with a Few Other Poems*, published anonymously in 1798. This short volume opened with Coleridge's *Ancient Mariner* and included three other poems by Coleridge, some lyrics in which Words-worth celebrated the experience of nature, and a number of verse anecdotes drawn from the lives of the rural poor. (The verse forms and the subject matter of this last set of poems—which includes "Simon Lee," "We Are Seven," and "The Thorn"— make evident the debt, announced in the very title of *Lyrical Ballads*, that Words-worth's and Coleridge's book owed to the folk ballads that were being transcribed and anthologized in the later eighteenth century by collectors such as Thomas Percy and Robert Burns.) The book closed with Wordsworth's great descriptive and meditative poem in blank verse, "Tintern Abbey." This poem inaugurated what modern critics call Wordsworth's "myth of nature": his presentation of the "growth" of his mind to maturity, a process unfolding through the interaction between the inner world of the mind and the shaping force of external Nature.

William Hazlitt said that when he heard Coleridge read some of the newly written poems of *Lyrical Ballads* aloud, "the sense of a new style and a new spirit in poetry came over me," with something of the effect "that arises from the turning up of the fresh soil, or of the first welcome breath of spring." The reviewers were less enthusiastic, warning that, because of their simple language and subject matter, poems such as "Simon Lee" risked "vulgarity" or silliness. Nevertheless *Lyrical Ballads* sold out in two years, and Wordsworth published under his own name a new edition, dated 1800, to which he added a second volume of poems. In his famous Preface to this edition, planned in close consultation with Coleridge, Wordsworth outlined a critical program that provided a retroactive rationale for the "experiments" the poems represented.

Late in 1799 William and Dorothy moved back permanently to their native lakes, settling at Grasmere in the little house later named Dove Cottage. Coleridge, following them, rented at Keswick, thirteen miles away. In 1802 Wordsworth finally came into his father's inheritance and, after an amicable settlement with Annette Vallon, married Mary Hutchinson, whom he had known since childhood. His life after that time had many sorrows: the drowning in 1805 of his favorite brother, John, a sea captain; the death in 1812 of two of his and Mary's five children; a growing rift with Coleridge, culminating in a bitter quarrel (1810) from which they were not completely reconciled for almost two decades; and, from the 1830s on, Dorothy's physical and mental illness. Over these years Wordsworth became, nonetheless, increasingly prosperous and famous. He also displayed a political and religious conservatism that disappointed readers who, like Hazlitt, had interpreted his early work as the expression of a "levelling Muse" that promoted democratic change. In 1813 a government sinecure, the position of stamp distributor (that is, revenue collector) for Westmorland, was bestowed on him—concrete evidence of his recognition as a national poet and of the alteration in the government's perception of his politics. Gradually, Words-worth's residences, as he moved into more and more comfortable quarters, became standard stops for sightseers touring the Lakes. By 1843 he was poet laureate of Great

Britain. He died in 1850 at the age of eighty. Only then did his executors publish his masterpiece, *The Prelude*, the autobiographical poem that he had written in two parts in 1799, expanded to its full length in 1805, and then continued to revise almost to the last decade of his long life.

Most of Wordsworth's greatest poetry had been written by 1807, when he published *Poems, in Two Volumes;* and after *The Excursion* (1814) and the first collected edition of his poems (1815), although he continued to write prolifically, his powers appeared to decline. The causes of that decline have been much debated. One seems to be inherent in the very nature of his writing. Wordsworth is above all the poet of the remembrance of things past or, as he put it, of "emotion recollected in tranquillity." Some object or event in the present triggers a sudden renewal of feelings he had experienced in youth; the result is a poem exhibiting the discrepancy between what Wordsworth called "two consciousnesses": himself as he is now and himself as he once was. But the memory of one's early emotional experience is not an inexhaustible resource for poetry, as Wordsworth recognized. He said in *The Prelude* 12, while describing the recurrence of "spots of time" from his memories of childhood:

> The days gone by
> Return upon me almost from the dawn
> Of life: the hiding places of Man's power
> Open; I would approach them, but they close.
> I see by glimpses now; when age comes on,
> May scarcely see at all.

The past that Wordsworth recollected was one of moments of intense experience, and of emotional turmoil that is ordered, in the calmer present, into a hard-won equilibrium. As time went on, however, he gained what, in the "Ode to Duty" (composed in 1804), he longed for, "a repose which ever is the same"—but at the expense of the agony and excitation that, under the calm surface, empower his best and most characteristic poems.

Occasionally in his middle and later life a jolting experience would revive the intensity of Wordsworth's remembered emotion, and also his earlier poetic strength. The moving sonnet "Surprised by Joy," for example, was written in his forties at the abrupt realization that time was beginning to diminish his grief at the death some years earlier of his little daughter Catherine. And when Wordsworth was sixty-five years old, the sudden report of the death of James Hogg called up the memory of other poets whom Wordsworth had loved and outlived; the result was his "Extempore Effusion," in which he returns to the simple quatrains of the early *Lyrical Ballads* and recovers the elegiac voice that had mourned Lucy, thirty-five years before.

FROM LYRICAL BALLADS

Simon Lee[1]

The Old Huntsman

WITH AN INCIDENT IN WHICH HE WAS CONCERNED

In the sweet shire of Cardigan,[2]
Not far from pleasant Ivor-hall,

---

1. This old man had been huntsman to the Squires of Alfoxden. . . . I have, after an interval of 45 years, the image of the old man as fresh before my eyes as if I had seen him yesterday. The expression when the hounds were out, "I dearly love their voices," was word for word from his own lips [Wordsworth's note, 1843]. Wordsworth and Dorothy had lived at Alfoxden House, Somersetshire, in 1797–98.

An old man dwells, a little man,—
'Tis said he once was tall.
5   Full five-and-thirty years he lived
A running huntsman[3] merry;
And still the centre of his cheek
Is red as a ripe cherry.

No man like him the horn could sound,
10   And hill and valley rang with glee
When Echo bandied, round and round,
The halloo of Simon Lee.
In those proud days, he little cared
For husbandry or tillage;
15   To blither tasks did Simon rouse
The sleepers of the village.

He all the country could outrun,
Could leave both man and horse behind;
And often, ere the chase was done,
20   He reeled, and was stone-blind.°   totally blind
And still there's something in the world
At which his heart rejoices;
For when the chiming hounds are out,
He dearly loves their voices!

25   But, oh the heavy change![4]—bereft
Of health, strength, friends, and kindred, see!
Old Simon to the world is left
In liveried[5] poverty.
His Master's dead,—and no one now
30   Dwells in the Hall of Ivor;
Men, dogs, and horses, all are dead;
He is the sole survivor.

And he is lean and he is sick;
His body, dwindled and awry,
35   Rests upon ankles swoln and thick;
His legs are thin and dry.
One prop he has, and only one,
His wife, an aged woman,
Lives with him, near the waterfall,
40   Upon the village Common.

Beside their moss-grown hut of clay,
Not twenty paces from the door,
A scrap of land they have, but they
Are poorest of the poor.
45   This scrap of land he from the heath
Enclosed when he was stronger;

---

3. Manager of the hunt and the person in charge
of the hounds.
4. Milton's "Lycidas," line 37: "But O the heavy
change, now thou art gone."
5. Livery was the uniform worn by the male servants of a household.

But what to them avails the land
Which he can till no longer?

    Oft, working by her Husband's side,
50 Ruth does what Simon cannot do;
For she, with scanty cause for pride,
Is stouter° of the two.   *stronger, sturdier*
And, though you with your utmost skill
From labour could not wean them,
55 'Tis very, very little—all
That they can do between them.

    Few months of life has he in store
As he to you will tell,
For still, the more he works, the more
60 Do his weak ankles swell.
My gentle Reader, I perceive
How patiently you've waited,
And now I fear that you expect
Some tale will be related.

65 O Reader! had you in your mind
Such stores as silent thought can bring,
O gentle Reader! you would find
A tale in every thing.
What more I have to say is short,
70 And you must kindly take it:
It is no tale; but, should you think,
Perhaps a tale you'll make it.

    One summer-day I chanced to see
This old Man doing all he could
75 To unearth the root of an old tree,
A stump of rotten wood.
The mattock tottered in his hand;
So vain was his endeavour,
That at the root of the old tree
80 He might have worked for ever.

    "You're overtasked, good Simon Lee,
Give me your tool," to him I said;
And at the word right gladly he
Received my proffered aid.
85 I struck, and with a single blow
The tangled root I severed,
At which the poor old Man so long
And vainly had endeavoured.

    The tears into his eyes were brought,
90 And thanks and praises seemed to run
So fast out of his heart, I thought
They never would have done.
—I've heard of hearts unkind, kind deeds

With coldness still returning;
95 Alas! the gratitude of men
Hath oftener left me mourning.

1798   1798

We Are Seven[1]

———A simple Child,
That lightly draws its breath,
And feels its life in every limb,
What should it know of death?

5 I met a little cottage Girl:
She was eight years old, she said;
Her hair was thick with many a curl
That clustered round her head.

She had a rustic, woodland air,
10 And she was wildly clad:
Her eyes were fair, and very fair;
—Her beauty made me glad.

"Sisters and brothers, little Maid,
How many may you be?"
15 "How many? Seven in all," she said,
And wondering looked at me.

"And where are they? I pray you tell."
She answered, "Seven are we;
And two of us at Conway[2] dwell,
20 And two are gone to sea.

"Two of us in the church-yard lie,
My sister and my brother;
And, in the church-yard cottage, I
Dwell near them with my mother."

25 "You say that two at Conway dwell,
And two are gone to sea,
Yet ye are seven! I pray you tell,
Sweet Maid, how this may be."

Then did the little Maid reply,
30 "Seven boys and girls are we;
Two of us in the church-yard lie,
Beneath the church-yard tree."

1. Written at Alfoxden in the spring of 1798. . . .
The little girl who is the heroine I met within the
area of Goodrich Castle [in the Wye Valley north
of Tintern Abbey] in the year 1793 [Wordsworth's
note, 1843]. Wordsworth also tells us that, "while

walking to and fro," he composed the last stanza
first, beginning with the last line, and that Coleridge contributed the first stanza.
2. A seaport town in north Wales.

"You run about, my little Maid,
Your limbs they are alive;
35 If two are in the church-yard laid,
Then ye are only five."

"Their graves are green, they may be seen,"
The little Maid replied,
"Twelve steps or more from my mother's door,
40 And they are side by side.

"My stockings there I often knit,
My kerchief there I hem;
And there upon the ground I sit,
And sing a song to them.

45 "And often after sun-set, Sir,
When it is light and fair,
I take my little porringer,[3]
And eat my supper there.

"The first that died was sister Jane;
50 In bed she moaning lay,
Till God released her of her pain;
And then she went away.

"So in the church-yard she was laid;
And, when the grass was dry,
55 Together round her grave we played,
My brother John and I.

"And when the ground was white with snow,
And I could run and slide,
My brother John was forced to go,
60 And he lies by her side."

"How many are you, then," said I,
"If they two are in heaven?"
Quick was the little Maid's reply,
"O Master! we are seven."

65 "But they are dead; those two are dead!
Their spirits are in heaven!"
'Twas throwing words away; for still
The little Maid would have her will,
And said, "Nay, we are seven!"

1798   1798

---

3. Bowl for porridge.

Lines Written in Early Spring

I heard a thousand blended notes,
While in a grove I sate reclined,
In that sweet mood when pleasant thoughts
Bring sad thoughts to the mind.

5   To her fair works did Nature link
The human soul that through me ran;
And much it grieved my heart to think
What man has made of man.

Through primrose tufts, in that green bower,
10   The periwinkle¹ trailed its wreaths,
And 'tis my faith that every flower
Enjoys the air it breathes.

The birds around me hopped and played,
Their thoughts I cannot measure:—
15   But the least motion which they made,
It seemed a thrill of pleasure.

The budding twigs spread out their fan,
To catch the breezy air;
And I must think, do all I can,
20   That there was pleasure there.

If this belief from heaven be sent,
If such be Nature's holy plan,²
Have I not reason to lament
What man has made of man?

1798   1798

Expostulation and Reply¹

"Why, William, on that old grey stone,
Thus for the length of half a day,
Why, William, sit you thus alone,
And dream your time away?

5   "Where are your books?—that light bequeathed
To Beings else forlorn and blind!

---

1. A trailing evergreen plant with small blue flowers (U.S. myrtle).
2. The version of these two lines in the *Lyrical Ballads* of 1798 reads: "If I these thoughts may not prevent, / If such be of my creed the plan."
1. This and the following companion poem have often been attacked—and defended—as Wordsworth's own statement about the comparative merits of nature and of books. But they are a dialogue between two friends who rally one another by the usual device of overstating parts of a whole truth. In the 1798 Advertisement to *Lyrical Ballads*, Wordsworth said that the pieces originated in a conversation "with a friend who was somewhat unreasonably attached to modern books of moral philosophy." In 1843 he noted that the idea of learning when the mind is in a state of "wise passiveness" made this poem a favorite of the Quakers, who rejected religious ritual for informal and spontaneous worship.

Up! up! and drink the spirit breathed
From dead men to their kind.

"You look round on your Mother Earth,
10   As if she for no purpose bore you;
As if you were her first-born birth,
And none had lived before you!"

One morning thus, by Esthwaite lake,
When life was sweet, I knew not why,
15   To me my good friend Matthew spake,
And thus I made reply.

"The eye—it cannot choose but see;
We cannot bid the ear be still;
Our bodies feel, where'er they be,
20   Against or with our will.

"Nor less I deem that there are Powers
Which of themselves our minds impress;
That we can feed this mind of ours
In a wise passiveness.

25   "Think you, 'mid all this mighty sum
Of things for ever speaking,
That nothing of itself will come,
But we must still be seeking?

"—Then ask not wherefore, here, alone,
30   Conversing² as I may,
I sit upon this old grey stone,
And dream my time away."

Spring 1798   1798

The Tables Turned

An Evening Scene on the Same Subject

Up! up! my Friend, and quit your books;
Or surely you'll grow double:°   *double over*
Up! up! my Friend, and clear your looks;
Why all this toil and trouble?

5   The sun, above the mountain's head,
A freshening lustre mellow
Through all the long green fields has spread,
His first sweet evening yellow.

Books! 'tis a dull and endless strife:
10   Come, hear the woodland linnet,°   *small finch*

2. In the old sense of "communing" (with the "things for ever speaking").

How sweet his music! on my life,
There's more of wisdom in it.

And hark! how blithe the throstle° sings!   *song thrush*
He, too, is no mean preacher:
15   Come forth into the light of things,
Let Nature be your Teacher.

She has a world of ready wealth,
Our minds and hearts to bless—
Spontaneous wisdom breathed by health,
20   Truth breathed by cheerfulness.

One impulse from a vernal wood
May teach you more of man,
Of moral evil and of good,
Than all the sages can.

25   Sweet is the lore which Nature brings;
Our meddling intellect
Mis-shapes the beauteous forms of things:—
We murder to dissect.

Enough of Science and of Art;
30   Close up those barren leaves;°   *pages*
Come forth, and bring with you a heart
That watches and receives.

1798   1798

The Thorn[1]

I

"There is a Thorn[2]—it looks so old,
In truth, you'd find it hard to say

1. Arose out of my observing, on the ridge of Quantock Hill [in Somersetshire], on a stormy day, a thorn which I had often past, in calm and bright weather, without noticing it. I said to myself, "Cannot I by some invention do as much to make this Thorn permanently an impressive object as the storm has made it to my eyes at this moment?" I began the poem accordingly, and composed it with great rapidity [Wordsworth's note, 1843]. In the prefatory Advertisement to the 1798 *Lyrical Ballads* Wordsworth wrote, "The poem of the Thorn . . . is not supposed to be spoken in the author's own person: the character of the loquacious narrator will sufficiently shew itself in the course of the story." In the editions of 1800–05 he elaborated in a separate note that reads, in part: "The character which I have here introduced speaking is sufficiently common. The Reader will perhaps have a general notion of it, if he has ever known a man, a Captain of a small trading vessel, for example, who, being past the middle age of life, had retired upon an annuity or small independent income to some village or country town of which he was not a native. . . . Such men, having little to do, become credulous and talkative from indolence; and from the same cause . . . they are prone to superstition. On which account it appeared to me proper to select a character like this to exhibit some of the general laws by which superstition acts upon the mind. Superstitious men are almost always men of slow faculties and deep feelings: their minds are not loose but adhesive; they have a reasonable share of imagination, by which word I mean the faculty which produces impressive effects out of simple elements. . . . It was my wish in this poem to show the manner in which such men cleave to the same ideas; and to follow the turns of passion . . . by which their conversation is swayed. . . . There is a numerous class of readers who imagine that the same words cannot be repeated without tautology: this is a great error. . . . Words, a Poet's words more particularly, ought to be weighed in the balance of feeling and not measured by the space they occupy upon paper."
2. Hawthorn, a thorny shrub or small tree.

How it could ever have been young,
It looks so old and grey.
5   Not higher than a two years' child
It stands erect, this aged Thorn;
No leaves it has, no prickly points;
It is a mass of knotted joints,
A wretched thing forlorn.
10   It stands erect, and like a stone
With lichens is it overgrown.

2

"Like rock or stone, it is o'ergrown,
With lichens to the very top,
And hung with heavy tufts of moss,
15   A melancholy crop:
Up from the earth these mosses creep,
And this poor Thorn they clasp it round
So close, you'd say that they are bent
With plain and manifest intent
20   To drag it to the ground;
And all have joined in one endeavour
To bury this poor Thorn for ever.

3

"High on a mountain's highest ridge,
Where oft the stormy winter gale
25   Cuts like a scythe, while through the clouds
It sweeps from vale to vale;
Not five yards from the mountain path,
This Thorn you on your left espy;
And to the left, three yards beyond,
30   You see a little muddy pond
Of water—never dry
Though but of compass small, and bare
To thirsty suns and parching air.

4

"And, close beside this aged Thorn,
35   There is a fresh and lovely sight,
A beauteous heap, a hill of moss,
Just half a foot in height.
All lovely colours there you see,
All colours that were ever seen;
40   And mossy network too is there,
As if by hand of lady fair
The work had woven been;
And cups, the darlings of the eye,
So deep is their vermilion dye.

5

45   "Ah me! what lovely tints are there
Of olive green and scarlet bright,
In spikes, in branches, and in stars,
Green, red, and pearly white!
This heap of earth o'ergrown with moss,

50 Which close beside the Thorn you see,
So fresh in all its beauteous dyes,
Is like an infant's grave in size,
As like as like can be:
But never, never any where,
55 An infant's grave was half so fair.

6

"Now would you see this aged Thorn,
This pond, and beauteous hill of moss,
You must take care and choose your time
The mountain when to cross.
60 For oft there sits between the heap
So like an infant's grave in size,
And that same pond of which I spoke,
A Woman in a scarlet cloak,
And to herself she cries,
65 'Oh misery! oh misery!
Oh woe is me! oh misery!'

7

"At all times of the day and night
This wretched Woman thither goes;
And she is known to every star,
70 And every wind that blows;
And there, beside the Thorn, she sits
When the blue daylight's in the skies,
And when the whirlwind's on the hill,
Or frosty air is keen and still,
75 And to herself she cries,
'Oh misery! oh misery!
Oh woe is me! oh misery!' "

8

"Now wherefore, thus, by day and night,
In rain, in tempest, and in snow,
80 Thus to the dreary mountain-top
Does this poor Woman go?
And why sits she beside the Thorn
When the blue daylight's in the sky
Or when the whirlwind's on the hill,
85 Or frosty air is keen and still,
And wherefore does she cry?—
O wherefore? wherefore? tell me why
Does she repeat that doleful cry?"

9

"I cannot tell; I wish I could;
90 For the true reason no one knows:
But would you gladly view the spot,
The spot to which she goes;
The hillock like an infant's grave,
The pond—and Thorn, so old and grey;
95 Pass by her door—'tis seldom shut—

And, if you see her in her hut—
Then to the spot away!
I never heard of such as dare
Approach the spot when she is there."

10

100 "But wherefore to the mountain-top
Can this unhappy Woman go,
Whatever star is in the skies,
Whatever wind may blow?"
"Full twenty years are past and gone
105 Since she (her name is Martha Ray)³
Gave with a maiden's true good-will
Her company to Stephen Hill;
And she was blithe and gay,
While friends and kindred all approved
110 Of him whom tenderly she loved.

11

"And they had fixed the wedding day,
The morning that must wed them both;
But Stephen to another Maid
Had sworn another oath;
115 And, with this other Maid, to church
Unthinking Stephen went—
Poor Martha! on that woeful day
A pang of pitiless dismay
Into her soul was sent;
120 A fire was kindled in her breast,
Which might not burn itself to rest.

12

"They say, full six months after this,
While yet the summer leaves were green,
She to the mountain-top would go,
125 And there was often seen.
What could she seek?—or wish to hide?
Her state to any eye was plain;
She was with child,° and she was mad;   *pregnant*
Yet often was she sober sad
130 From her exceeding pain.
O guilty Father—would that death
Had saved him from that breach of faith!

13

"Sad case for such a brain to hold
Communion with a stirring child!
135 Sad case, as you may think, for one
Who had a brain so wild!

---

3. Wordsworth gives the woman the name of the victim at the center of one of the 18th century's most famous murder trials. Martha Ray, mistress to a nobleman, was murdered in 1779 by a rejected suitor, a clergyman who claimed he had been driven to the deed by "love's madness." One of the illegitimate children whom this Martha Ray bore to the earl of Sandwich was Wordsworth's and Coleridge's friend Basil Montagu.

Last Christmas-eve we talked of this,
And grey-haired Wilfred of the glen
Held that the unborn infant wrought
140 About its mother's heart, and brought
Her senses back again:
And, when at last her time drew near,
Her looks were calm, her senses clear.

14

"More know I not, I wish I did,
145 And it should all be told to you;
For what became of this poor child
No mortal ever knew;
Nay—if a child to her was born
No earthly tongue could ever tell;
150 And if 'twas born alive or dead,
Far less could this with proof be said;
But some remember well,
That Martha Ray about this time
Would up the mountain often climb.

15

155 "And all that winter, when at night
The wind blew from the mountain-peak,
'Twas worth your while, though in the dark,
The churchyard path to seek:
For many a time and oft were heard
160 Cries coming from the mountain head:
Some plainly living voices were;
And others, I've heard many swear,
Were voices of the dead:
I cannot think, whate'er they say,
165 They had to do with Martha Ray.

16

"But that she goes to this old Thorn,
The Thorn which I described to you,
And there sits in a scarlet cloak,
I will be sworn is true.
170 For one day with my telescope,
To view the ocean wide and bright,
When to this country first I came,
Ere I had heard of Martha's name,
I climbed the mountain's height:—
175 A storm came on, and I could see
No object higher than my knee.

17

" 'Twas mist and rain, and storm and rain:
No screen, no fence could I discover;
And then the wind! in sooth, it was
180 A wind full ten times over.
I looked around, I thought I saw
A jutting crag,—and off I ran,

Head-foremost, through the driving rain,
The shelter of the crag to gain;
185 And, as I am a man,
Instead of jutting crag, I found
A Woman seated on the ground.

18
"I did not speak—I saw her face;
Her face!—it was enough for me;
190 I turned about and heard her cry,
'Oh misery! oh misery!'
And there she sits, until the moon
Through half the clear blue sky will go;
And, when the little breezes make
195 The waters of the pond to shake,
As all the country know,
She shudders, and you hear her cry,
'Oh misery! oh misery!' "

19
"But what's the Thorn? and what the pond?
200 And what the hill of moss to her?
And what the creeping breeze that comes
The little pond to stir?"
"I cannot tell; but some will say
She hanged her baby on the tree;
205 Some say she drowned it in the pond,
Which is a little step beyond:
But all and each agree,
The little Babe was buried there,
Beneath that hill of moss so fair.

20
210 "I've heard, the moss is spotted red
With drops of that poor infant's blood;
But kill a new-born infant thus,
I do not think she could!
Some say, if to the pond you go,
215 And fix on it a steady view,
The shadow of a babe you trace,
A baby and a baby's face,
And that it looks at you;
Whene'er you look on it, 'tis plain
220 The baby looks at you again.

21
"And some had sworn an oath that she
Should be to public justice brought;
And for the little infant's bones
With spades they would have sought.
225 But instantly the hill of moss
Before their eyes began to stir!
And, for full fifty yards around,
The grass—it shook upon the ground!

Yet all do still aver
230 The little Babe lies buried there,
Beneath that hill of moss so fair.

22

"I cannot tell how this may be,
But plain it is the Thorn is bound
With heavy tufts of moss that strive
235 To drag it to the ground;
And this I know, full many a time,
When she was on the mountain high,
By day, and in the silent night,
When all the stars shone clear and bright,
240 That I have heard her cry,
'Oh misery! oh misery!
Oh woe is me! oh misery!' "

Mar.–Apr. 1798   1798

Lines[1]

Composed a Few Miles above Tintern Abbey, on Revisiting the Banks of the Wye during a Tour, July 13, 1798

Five years have past; five summers, with the length
Of five long winters! and again I hear
These waters, rolling from their mountain-springs
With a soft inland murmur.[2]—Once again
5 Do I behold these steep and lofty cliffs,
That on a wild secluded scene impress
Thoughts of more deep seclusion; and connect
The landscape with the quiet of the sky.
The day is come when I again repose
10 Here, under this dark sycamore, and view
These plots of cottage-ground, these orchard-tufts,
Which at this season, with their unripe fruits,
Are clad in one green hue, and lose themselves
'Mid groves and copses. Once again I see
15 These hedge-rows, hardly hedge-rows, little lines
Of sportive wood run wild: these pastoral farms,
Green to the very door; and wreaths of smoke
Sent up, in silence, from among the trees!

1. No poem of mine was composed under circumstances more pleasant for me to remember than this. I began it upon leaving Tintern, after crossing the Wye, and concluded it just as I was entering Bristol in the evening, after a ramble of 4 or 5 days, with my sister. Not a line of it was altered, and not any part of it written down till I reached Bristol [Wordsworth's note, 1843]. The poem was printed as the last item in *Lyrical Ballads*.
   Wordsworth had first visited the Wye valley and the ruins of Tintern Abbey, in Monmouthshire, while on a solitary walking tour in August 1793, when he was twenty-three years old. (See "Tintern

Abbey, Tourism, and Romantic Landscape" at Norton Literature Online.) The puzzling difference between the present landscape and the remembered "picture of the mind" (line 61) gives rise to an intricately organized meditation, in which the poet reviews his past, evaluates the present, and (through his sister as intermediary) anticipates the future; he ends by rounding back quietly on the scene that had been his point of departure.
2. The river is not affected by the tides a few miles above Tintern [Wordsworth's note, 1798 ff.]. Until 1845 the text had "sweet" for "soft," meaning fresh, not salty.

With some uncertain notice, as might seem
20 Of vagrant dwellers in the houseless woods,
Or of some Hermit's cave, where by his fire
The Hermit sits alone.

             These beauteous forms,
Through a long absence, have not been to me
As is a landscape to a blind man's eye:
25 But oft, in lonely rooms, and 'mid the din
Of towns and cities, I have owed to them
In hours of weariness, sensations sweet,
Felt in the blood, and felt along the heart;
And passing even into my purer mind,
30 With tranquil restoration:—feelings too
Of unremembered pleasure: such, perhaps,
As have no slight or trivial influence
On that best portion of a good man's life,
His little, nameless, unremembered, acts
35 Of kindness and of love. Nor less, I trust,
To them I may have owed another gift,
Of aspect more sublime; that blessed mood,
In which the burthen° of the mystery,   *burden*
In which the heavy and the weary weight
40 Of all this unintelligible world,
Is lightened:—that serene and blessed mood,
In which the affections gently lead us on,—
Until, the breath of this corporeal frame
And even the motion of our human blood
45 Almost suspended, we are laid asleep
In body, and become a living soul:
While with an eye made quiet by the power
Of harmony, and the deep power of joy,
We see into the life of things.

                     If this
50 Be but a vain belief, yet, oh! how oft—
In darkness and amid the many shapes
Of joyless daylight; when the fretful stir
Unprofitable, and the fever of the world,
Have hung upon the beatings of my heart—
55 How oft, in spirit, have I turned to thee,
O sylvan Wye! thou wanderer thro' the woods,
How often has my spirit turned to thee!

    And now, with gleams of half-extinguished thought,
With many recognitions dim and faint,
60 And somewhat of a sad perplexity,
The picture of the mind revives again:
While here I stand, not only with the sense
Of present pleasure, but with pleasing thoughts
That in this moment there is life and food
65 For future years. And so I dare to hope,
Though changed, no doubt, from what I was when first

I came among these hills; when like a roe°   *deer*
I bounded o'er the mountains, by the sides
Of the deep rivers, and the lonely streams,
70   Wherever nature led: more like a man
Flying from something that he dreads, than one
Who sought the thing he loved. For nature then
(The coarser pleasures of my boyish days,
And their glad animal movements all gone by)
75   To me was all in all.—I cannot paint
What then I was. The sounding cataract
Haunted me like a passion: the tall rock,
The mountain, and the deep and gloomy wood,
Their colours and their forms, were then to me
80   An appetite; a feeling and a love,
That had no need of a remoter charm,
By thought supplied, nor any interest
Unborrowed from the eye.—That time is past,
And all its aching joys are now no more,
85   And all its dizzy raptures.[3] Not for this
Faint° I, nor mourn nor murmur; other gifts   *lose heart*
Have followed; for such loss, I would believe,
Abundant recompense. For I have learned
To look on nature, not as in the hour
90   Of thoughtless youth; but hearing oftentimes
The still, sad music of humanity,
Nor harsh nor grating, though of ample power
To chasten and subdue. And I have felt
A presence that disturbs me with the joy
95   Of elevated thoughts; a sense sublime
Of something far more deeply interfused,
Whose dwelling is the light of setting suns,
And the round ocean and the living air,
And the blue sky, and in the mind of man:
100 A motion and a spirit, that impels
All thinking things, all objects of all thought,
And rolls through all things. Therefore am I still
A lover of the meadows and the woods,
And mountains; and of all that we behold
105 From this green earth; of all the mighty world
Of eye, and ear,—both what they half create,[4]
And what perceive; well pleased to recognise
In nature and the language of the sense,
The anchor of my purest thoughts, the nurse,
110 The guide, the guardian of my heart, and soul
Of all my moral being.

3. Lines 66ff. contain Wordsworth's famed description of the three stages of his growing up, defined in terms of his evolving relations to the natural scene: the young boy's purely physical responsiveness (lines 73–74); the postadolescent's aching, dizzy, and equivocal passions—a love that is more like dread (lines 67–72, 75–85: this was his state of mind on the occasion of his first visit); his present state (lines 85ff.), in which for the first time he adds thought to sense.
4. This line has a close resemblance to an admirable line of Young, the exact expression of which I cannot recollect [Wordsworth's note, 1798 ff.]. Edward Young in *Night Thoughts* (1744) says that the human senses "half create the wondrous world they see."

Nor perchance,
If I were not thus taught, should I the more
Suffer my genial spirits[5] to decay:
For thou art with me here upon the banks
115   Of this fair river; thou my dearest Friend,[6]
My dear, dear Friend; and in thy voice I catch
The language of my former heart, and read
My former pleasures in the shooting lights
Of thy wild eyes. Oh! yet a little while
120   May I behold in thee what I was once,
My dear, dear Sister! and this prayer I make,
Knowing that Nature never did betray
The heart that loved her; 'tis her privilege,
Through all the years of this our life, to lead
125   From joy to joy: for she can so inform
The mind that is within us, so impress
With quietness and beauty, and so feed
With lofty thoughts, that neither evil tongues,[7]
Rash judgments, nor the sneers of selfish men,
130   Nor greetings where no kindness is, nor all
The dreary intercourse of daily life,
Shall e'er prevail against us, or disturb
Our cheerful faith, that all which we behold
Is full of blessings. Therefore let the moon
135   Shine on thee in thy solitary walk;
And let the misty mountain-winds be free
To blow against thee: and, in after years,
When these wild ecstasies shall be matured
Into a sober pleasure; when thy mind
140   Shall be a mansion for all lovely forms,
Thy memory be as a dwelling-place
For all sweet sounds and harmonies; oh! then,
If solitude, or fear, or pain, or grief,
Should be thy portion,° with what healing thoughts   *inheritance, dowry*
145   Of tender joy wilt thou remember me,
And these my exhortations! Nor, perchance—
If I should be where I no more can hear
Thy voice, nor catch from thy wild eyes these gleams
Of past existence[8]—wilt thou then forget
150   That on the banks of this delightful stream
We stood together; and that I, so long
A worshipper of Nature, hither came
Unwearied in that service; rather say
With warmer love—oh! with far deeper zeal
155   Of holier love. Nor wilt thou then forget,
That after many wanderings, many years
Of absence, these steep woods and lofty cliffs,

5. Creative powers. ("Genial" is here the adjectival form of the noun *genius*.)
6. His sister, Dorothy.
7. In the opening of *Paradise Lost* 7, Milton describes himself as fallen on "evil days" and "evil tongues" and with "dangers compassed round" (lines 26–27).
8. I.e., reminders of his own "past existence" five years earlier (see lines 116–19).

And this green pastoral landscape, were to me
More dear, both for themselves and for thy sake!

July 1798   1798

Preface to *Lyrical Ballads* (1802)   To the first edition of *Lyrical Ballads*, published jointly with Coleridge in 1798, Wordsworth prefixed an "Advertisement" asserting that the majority of the poems were "to be considered as experiments" to determine "how far the language of conversation in the middle and lower classes of society is adapted to the purposes of poetic pleasure." In the second, two-volume edition of 1800, Wordsworth, aided by frequent conversations with Coleridge, expanded the Advertisement into a preface that justified the poems not as experiments, but as exemplifying the principles of all good poetry. The Preface was enlarged for the third edition of *Lyrical Ballads*, published two years later. This last version of 1802 is reprinted here.

Although some of its ideas had antecedents in the later eighteenth century, the Preface as a whole deserves its reputation as a revolutionary manifesto about the nature of poetry. Like many radical statements, however, it claims to go back to the implicit principles that governed the great poetry of the past but have been perverted in recent practice. Most discussions of the Preface, following the lead of Coleridge in chapters 14 and 17 of his *Biographia Literaria*, have focused on Wordsworth's assertions about the valid language of poetry, on which he bases his attack on the "poetic diction" of eighteenth-century poets. As Coleridge pointed out, Wordsworth's argument about this issue is far from clear. However, Wordsworth's questioning of the underlying premises of neoclassical poetry went even further. His Preface implicitly denies the traditional assumption that the poetic genres constitute a hierarchy, from epic and tragedy at the top down through comedy, satire, pastoral, to the short lyric at the lowest reaches of the poetic scale; he also rejects the traditional principle of "decorum," which required the poet to arrange matters so that the poem's subject (especially the social class of its protagonists) and its level of diction conformed to the status of the literary kind on the poetic scale.

When Wordsworth asserted in the Preface that he deliberately chose to represent "incidents and situations from common life," he translated his democratic sympathies into critical terms, justifying his use of peasants, children, outcasts, criminals, and madwomen as serious subjects of poetic and even tragic concern. He also undertook to write in "a selection of language really used by men," on the grounds that there can be no "essential difference between the language of prose and metrical composition." In making this claim Wordsworth attacked the neoclassical principle that required the language, in many kinds of poems, to be elevated over everyday speech by a special, more refined and dignified diction and by artful figures of speech. Wordsworth's views about the valid language of poetry are based on the new premise that "all good poetry is the spontaneous overflow of powerful feelings"—spontaneous, that is, at the moment of composition, even though the process is influenced by prior thought and acquired poetic skill.

Wordsworth's assertions about the materials and diction of poetry have been greatly influential in expanding the range of serious literature to include the common people and ordinary things and events, as well as in justifying a poetry of sincerity rather than of artifice, expressed in the ordinary language of its time. But in the long view other aspects of his Preface have been no less significant in establishing its importance, not only as a turning point in English criticism but also as a central document in modern culture, Wordsworth feared that a new urban, industrial society's mass media and mass culture (glimpsed in the Preface when he refers derisively to contemporary Gothic novels and German melodramas) were threatening to blunt the human mind's "discriminatory powers" and to "reduce it to a state of almost savage torpor." He attributed to imaginative literature the primary role in keeping the human beings who live in such societies emotionally alive and morally sensitive. Literature, that is, could keep humans essentially human.

From Preface to *Lyrical Ballads, with Pastoral and Other Poems* (1802)

[THE SUBJECT AND LANGUAGE OF POETRY]

The first volume of these poems has already been submitted to general perusal. It was published, as an experiment, which, I hoped, might be of some use to ascertain, how far, by fitting to metrical arrangement a selection of the real language of men in a state of vivid sensation, that sort of pleasure and that quantity of pleasure may be imparted, which a poet may rationally endeavour to impart.

I had formed no very inaccurate estimate of the probable effect of those poems: I flattered myself that they who should be pleased with them would read them with more than common pleasure: and, on the other hand, I was well aware, that by those who should dislike them they would be read with more than common dislike. The result has differed from my expectation in this only, that I have pleased a greater number than I ventured to hope I should please.

For the sake of variety, and from a consciousness of my own weakness, I was induced to request the assistance of a friend, who furnished me with the poems of the *Ancient Mariner*, the *Foster-Mother's Tale*, the *Nightingale*, and the poem entitled *Love*. I should not, however, have requested this assistance, had I not believed that the poems of my friend[1] would in a great measure have the same tendency as my own, and that, though there would be found a difference, there would be found no discordance in the colours of our style; as our opinions on the subject of poetry do almost entirely coincide.

Several of my friends are anxious for the success of these poems from a belief, that, if the views with which they were composed were indeed realized, a class of poetry would be produced, well adapted to interest mankind permanently, and not unimportant in the multiplicity, and in the quality of its moral relations: and on this account they have advised me to prefix a systematic defence of the theory upon which the poems were written. But I was unwilling to undertake the task, because I knew that on this occasion the reader would look coldly upon my arguments, since I might be suspected of having been principally influenced by the selfish and foolish hope of *reasoning* him into an approbation of these particular poems: and I was still more unwilling to undertake the task, because, adequately to display my opinions, and fully to enforce my arguments, would require a space wholly disproportionate to the nature of a preface. For to treat the subject with the clearness and coherence of which I believe it susceptible, it would be necessary to give a full account of the present state of the public taste in this country, and to determine how far this taste is healthy or depraved; which, again, could not be determined, without pointing out, in what manner language and the human mind act and re-act on each other, and without retracing the revolutions, not of literature alone,

---

1. The "friend" of course is Coleridge.

but likewise of society itself. I have therefore altogether declined to enter regularly upon this defence; yet I am sensible, that there would be some impropriety in abruptly obtruding upon the public, without a few words of introduction, poems so materially different from those upon which general approbation is at present bestowed.

It is supposed, that by the act of writing in verse an author makes a formal engagement that he will gratify certain known habits of association; that he not only thus apprizes the reader that certain classes of ideas and expressions will be found in his book, but that others will be carefully excluded. This exponent or symbol held forth by metrical language must in different eras of literature have excited very different expectations: for example, in the age of Catullus, Terence, and Lucretius and that of Statius or Claudian,[2] and in our own country, in the age of Shakespeare and Beaumont and Fletcher, and that of Donne and Cowley, or Dryden, or Pope. I will not take upon me to determine the exact import of the promise which by the act of writing in verse an author, in the present day, makes to his reader; but I am certain, it will appear to many persons that I have not fulfilled the terms of an engagement thus voluntarily contracted. They who have been accustomed to the gaudiness and inane phraseology of many modern writers, if they persist in reading this book to its conclusion, will, no doubt, frequently have to struggle with feelings of strangeness and awkwardness: they will look round for poetry, and will be induced to inquire by what species of courtesy these attempts can be permitted to assume that title. I hope therefore the reader will not censure me, if I attempt to state what I have proposed to myself to perform; and also (as far as the limits of a preface will permit) to explain some of the chief reasons which have determined me in the choice of my purpose: that at least he may be spared any unpleasant feeling of disappointment, and that I myself may be protected from the most dishonorable accusation which can be brought against an author, namely, that of an indolence which prevents him from endeavouring to ascertain what is his duty, or, when this duty is ascertained, prevents him from performing it.

The principal object, then, which I proposed to myself in these poems was to choose incidents and situations from common life, and to relate or describe them, throughout, as far as was possible, in a selection of language really used by men; and, at the same time, to throw over them a certain colouring of imagination, whereby ordinary things should be presented to the mind in an unusual way; and, further, and above all, to make these incidents and situations interesting by tracing in them, truly though not ostentatiously, the primary laws of our nature: chiefly, as far as regards the manner in which we associate ideas in a state of excitement. Low and rustic life was generally chosen, because in that condition, the essential passions of the heart find a better soil in which they can attain their maturity, are less under restraint, and speak a plainer and more emphatic language; because in that condition of life our elementary feelings co-exist in a state of greater simplicity, and, consequently, may be more accurately contemplated, and more forcibly communicated; because the manners of rural life germinate from those elementary feelings; and, from the necessary character of rural occupations, are more easily comprehended; and are more durable; and lastly, because in that con-

2. Wordsworth's implied contrast is between the naturalness and simplicity of the first three Roman poets (who wrote in the last two centuries B.C.E.) and the elaborate artifice of the last two Roman poets (Statius wrote in the 1st and Claudian in the 4th century C.E.).

dition the passions of men are incorporated with the beautiful and permanent forms of nature. The language, too, of these men is adopted (purified indeed from what appear to be its real defects, from all lasting and rational causes of dislike or disgust) because such men hourly communicate with the best objects from which the best part of language is originally derived; and because, from their rank in society and the sameness and narrow circle of their intercourse, being less under the influence of social vanity they convey their feelings and notions in simple and unelaborated expressions. Accordingly, such a language, arising out of repeated experience and regular feelings, is a more permanent, and a far more philosophical language, than that which is frequently substituted for it by poets, who think that they are conferring honour upon themselves and their art, in proportion as they separate themselves from the sympathies of men, and indulge in arbitrary and capricious habits of expression, in order to furnish food for fickle tastes, and fickle appetites, of their own creation.[3]

I cannot, however, be insensible of the present outcry against the triviality and meanness both of thought and language, which some of my contemporaries have occasionally introduced into their metrical compositions; and I acknowledge, that this defect, where it exists, is more dishonorable to the writer's own character than false refinement or arbitrary innovation, though I should contend at the same time that it is far less pernicious in the sum of its consequences. From such verses the poems in these volumes will be found distinguished at least by one mark of difference, that each of them has a worthy *purpose.* Not that I mean to say, that I always began to write with a distinct purpose formally conceived; but I believe that my habits of meditation have so formed my feelings, as that my descriptions of such objects as strongly excite those feelings, will be found to carry along with them a *purpose.* If in this opinion I am mistaken, I can have little right to the name of a poet. For all good poetry is the spontaneous overflow of powerful feelings: but though this be true, poems to which any value can be attached, were never produced on any variety of subjects but by a man who, being possessed of more than usual organic sensibility, had also thought long and deeply. For our continued influxes of feeling are modified and directed by our thoughts, which are indeed the representatives of all our past feelings; and, as by contemplating the relation of these general representatives to each other we discover what is really important to men, so, by the repetition and continuance of this act, our feelings will be connected with important subjects, till at length, if we be originally possessed of much sensibility, such habits of mind will be produced, that, by obeying blindly and mechanically the impulses of those habits, we shall describe objects, and utter sentiments, of such a nature and in such connection with each other, that the understanding of the being to whom we address ourselves, if he be in a healthful state of association, must necessarily be in some degree enlightened, and his affections ameliorated.

I have said that each of these poems has a purpose. I have also informed my reader what this purpose will be found principally to be: namely, to illustrate the manner in which our feelings and ideas are associated in a state of excitement. But, speaking in language somewhat more appropriate, it is to follow the fluxes and refluxes of the mind when agitated by the great and

---

3. It is worth while here to observe that the affecting parts of Chaucer are almost always expressed in language pure and universally intelligible even to this day [Wordsworth's note].

simple affections of our nature. This object I have endeavored in these short essays to attain by various means; by tracing the maternal passion through many of its more subtile[4] windings, as in the poems of the *Idiot Boy* and the *Mad Mother*; by accompanying the last struggles of a human being, at the approach of death, cleaving in solitude to life and society, as in the poem of the *Forsaken Indian*; by shewing, as in the stanzas entitled *We Are Seven*, the perplexity and obscurity which in childhood attend our notion of death, or rather our utter inability to admit that notion; or by displaying the strength of fraternal, or to speak more philosophically, of moral attachment when early associated with the great and beautiful objects of nature, as in *The Brothers*; or, as in the Incident of *Simon Lee*, by placing my reader in the way of receiving from ordinary moral sensations another and more salutary impression than we are accustomed to receive from them. It has also been part of my general purpose to attempt to sketch characters under the influence of less impassioned feelings, as in the *Two April Mornings, The Fountain, The Old Man Travelling, The Two Thieves*, &c., characters of which the elements are simple, belonging rather to nature than to manners,[5] such as exist now, and will probably always exist, and which from their constitution may be distinctly and profitably contemplated. I will not abuse the indulgence of my reader by dwelling longer upon this subject; but it is proper that I should mention one other circumstance which distinguishes these poems from the popular poetry of the day; it is this, that the feeling therein developed gives importance to the action and situation, and not the action and situation to the feeling. My meaning will be rendered perfectly intelligible by referring my reader to the poems entitled *Poor Susan* and the *Childless Father*, particularly to the last stanza of the latter poem.

I will not suffer a sense of false modesty to prevent me from asserting, that I point my reader's attention to this mark of distinction, far less for the sake of these particular poems than from the general importance of the subject. The subject is indeed important! For the human mind is capable of being excited without the application of gross[6] and violent stimulants; and he must have a very faint perception of its beauty and dignity who does not know this, and who does not further know, that one being is elevated above another, in proportion as he possesses this capability. It has therefore appeared to me, that to endeavour to produce or enlarge this capability is one of the best services in which, at any period, a writer can be engaged; but this service, excellent at all times, is especially so at the present day. For a multitude of causes, unknown to former times, are now acting with a combined force to blunt the discriminating powers of the mind, and, unfitting it for all voluntary exertion, to reduce it to a state of almost savage torpor. The most effective of these causes are the great national events which are daily taking place, and the increasing accumulation of men in cities, where the uniformity of their occupations produces a craving for extraordinary incident, which the rapid communication of intelligence hourly gratifies.[7] To this tendency of life and manners the literature and theatrical exhibitions of the country have conformed themselves. The invaluable works of our elder writers, I had almost said the works of Shakespeare and Milton, are driven into neglect by frantic novels, sickly and stupid German tragedies,[8] and deluges of idle and extrava-

4. Subtle.
5. Social custom.
6. Coarse.
7. This was the period of the wars against France, of industrial urbanization, and of the rapid proliferation in England of daily newspapers.

8. Wordsworth had in mind the "Gothic" terror novels by writers such as Ann Radcliffe and Matthew Gregory Lewis and the sentimental melodrama, then immensely popular in England, of August von Kotzebue and his German contemporaries.

gant stories in verse.—When I think upon this degrading thirst after outrageous stimulation, I am almost ashamed to have spoken of the feeble effort with which I have endeavoured to counteract it; and, reflecting upon the magnitude of the general evil, I should be oppressed with no dishonorable melancholy, had I not a deep impression of certain inherent and indestructible qualities of the human mind, and likewise of certain powers in the great and permanent objects that act upon it which are equally inherent and indestructible; and did I not further add to this impression a belief, that the time is approaching when the evil will be systematically opposed, by men of greater powers, and with far more distinguished success.

Having dwelt thus long on the subjects and aim of these poems, I shall request the reader's permission to apprize him of a few circumstances relating to their *style*, in order, among other reasons, that I may not be censured for not having performed what I never attempted. The reader will find that personifications of abstract ideas[9] rarely occur in these volumes; and, I hope, are utterly rejected as an ordinary device to elevate the style, and raise it above prose. I have proposed to myself to imitate, and, as far as is possible, to adopt the very language of men; and assuredly such personifications do not make any natural or regular part of that language. They are, indeed, a figure of speech occasionally prompted by passion, and I have made use of them as such; but I have endeavoured utterly to reject them as a mechanical device of style, or as a family language which writers in metre seem to lay claim to by prescription. I have wished to keep my reader in the company of flesh and blood, persuaded that by so doing I shall interest him. I am, however, well aware that others who pursue a different track may interest him likewise; I do not interfere with their claim, I only wish to prefer a different claim of my own. There will also be found in these volumes little of what is usually called poetic diction;[1] I have taken as much pains to avoid it as others ordinarily take to produce it; this I have done for the reason already alleged, to bring my language near to the language of men, and further, because the pleasure which I have proposed to myself to impart is of a kind very different from that which is supposed by many persons to be the proper object of poetry. I do not know how, without being culpably particular, I can give my reader a more exact notion of the style in which I wished these poems to be written than by informing him that I have at all times endeavoured to look steadily at my subject, consequently, I hope that there is in these poems little falsehood of description, and that my ideas are expressed in language fitted to their respective importance. Something I must have gained by this practice, as it is friendly to one property of all good poetry, namely, good sense; but it has necessarily cut me off from a large portion of phrases and figures of speech which from father to son have long been regarded as the common inheritance of poets. I have also thought it expedient to restrict myself still further, having abstained from the use of many expressions, in themselves proper and beautiful, but which have been foolishly repeated by bad poets, till such feelings of disgust are connected with them as it is scarcely possible by any art of association to overpower.

If in a poem there should be found a series of lines, or even a single line,

---

9. This practice was common in 18th-century poetry. Samuel Johnson, for instance, in *The Vanity of Human Wishes* (1749), has "Observation . . . survey[ing] mankind" and "Vengeance listen[ing] to the fool's request" (lines 1–2, 14).

1. In the sense of words, phrases, and figures of speech not commonly used in conversation or prose that are regarded as especially appropriate to poetry.

in which the language, though naturally arranged and according to the strict laws of metre, does not differ from that of prose, there is a numerous class of critics, who, when they stumble upon these prosaisms as they call them, imagine that they have made a notable discovery, and exult over the poet as over a man ignorant of his own profession. Now these men would establish a canon of criticism which the reader will conclude he must utterly reject, if he wishes to be pleased with these volumes. And it would be a most easy task to prove to him, that not only the language of a large portion of everygood poem, even of the most elevated character, must necessarily, except with reference to the metre, in no respect differ from that of good prose, but likewise that some of the most interesting parts of the best poems will be found to be strictly the language of prose, when prose is well written. The truth of this assertion might be demonstrated by innumerable passages from almost all the poetical writings, even of Milton himself. I have not space for much quotation; but, to illustrate the subject in a general manner, I will here adduce a short composition of Gray, who was at the head of those who by their reasonings have attempted to widen the space of separation betwixt prose and metrical composition, and was more than any other man curiously elaborate in the structure of his own poetic diction.[2]

> In vain to me the smiling mornings shine,
> And reddening Phoebus lifts his golden fire:
> The birds in vain their amorous descant join,
> Or cheerful fields resume their green attire:
> These ears, alas! for other notes repine;
> *A different object do these eyes require;*
> *My lonely anguish melts no heart but mine;*
> *And in my breast the imperfect joys expire;*
> Yet Morning smiles the busy race to cheer,
> And new-born pleasure brings to happier men;
> The fields to all their wonted tribute bear;
> To warm their little loves the birds complain.
> *I fruitless mourn to him that cannot hear*
> *And weep the more because I weep in vain.*

It will easily be perceived that the only part of this sonnet which is of any value is the lines printed in italics: it is equally obvious, that, except in the rhyme, and in the use of the single word "fruitless" for fruitlessly, which is so far a defect, the language of these lines does in no respect differ from that of prose.

By the foregoing quotation I have shewn that the language of prose may yet be well adapted to poetry; and I have previously asserted that a large portion of the language of every good poem can in no respect differ from that of good prose. I will go further. I do not doubt that it may be safely affirmed, that there neither is, nor can be, any essential difference between the language of prose and metrical composition. We are fond of tracing the resemblance between poetry and painting, and, accordingly, we call them sisters: but where shall we find bonds of connection sufficiently strict to typify the affinity betwixt metrical and prose composition? They both speak by and to the same organs; the

2. Thomas Gray (author in 1751 of the "Elegy Written in a Country Churchyard") had written, in a letter to Richard West, that "the language of the age is never the language of poetry." The poem that follows is Gray's "Sonnet on the Death of Richard West."

bodies in which both of them are clothed may be said to be of the same substance, their affections are kindred and almost identical, not necessarily differing even in degree; poetry[3] sheds no tears "such as Angels weep,"[4] but natural and human tears; she can boast of no celestial ichor[5] that distinguishes her vital juices from those of prose; the same human blood circulates through the veins of them both.

* * *

["WHAT IS A POET?"]

Taking up the subject, then, upon general grounds, I ask what is meant by the word "poet"? What is a poet? To whom does he address himself? And what language is to be expected from him? He is a man speaking to men: a man, it is true, endued with more lively sensibility, more enthusiasm and tenderness, who has a greater knowledge of human nature, and a more comprehensive soul, than are supposed to be common among mankind; a man pleased with his own passions and volitions, and who rejoices more than other men in the spirit of life that is in him; delighting to contemplate similar volitions and passions as manifested in the goings-on of the universe, and habitually impelled to create them where he does not find them. To these qualities he has added a disposition to be affected more than other men by absent things as if they were present; an ability of conjuring up in himself passions, which are indeed far from being the same as those produced by real events, yet (especially in those parts of the general sympathy which are pleasing and delightful) do more nearly resemble the passions produced by real events, than any thing which, from the motions of their own minds merely, other men are accustomed to feel in themselves; whence, and from practice, he has acquired a greater readiness and power in expressing what he thinks and feels, and especially those thoughts and feelings which, by his own choice, or from the structure of his own mind, arise in him without immediate external excitement.

But, whatever portion of this faculty we may suppose even the greatest poet to possess, there cannot be a doubt but that the language which it will suggest to him, must, in liveliness and truth, fall far short of that which is uttered by men in real life, under the actual pressure of those passions, certain shadows of which the poet thus produces, or feels to be produced, in himself. However exalted a notion we would wish to cherish of the character of a poet, it is obvious, that, while he describes and imitates passions, his situation is alto-gether slavish and mechanical, compared with the freedom and power of real and substantial action and suffering. So that it will be the wish of the poet to bring his feelings near to those of the persons whose feelings he describes, nay, for short spaces of time perhaps, to let himself slip into an entire delusion, and even confound and identify his own feelings with theirs; modifying only the language which is thus suggested to him, by a consideration that he describes for a particular purpose, that of giving pleasure. Here, then, he will

3. I here use the word "poetry" (though against my own judgment) as opposed to the word "prose," and synonymous with metrical composition. But much confusion has been introduced into criticism by this contradistinction of poetry and prose, instead of the more philosophical one of poetry and matter of fact, or science. The only strict antithesis to prose is metre; nor is this, in truth, a *strict* antithesis; because lines and passages of metre so naturally occur in writing prose, that it would be scarcely possible to avoid them, even were it desirable [Wordsworth's note].
4. Milton's *Paradise Lost* 1.620.
5. In Greek mythology the fluid in the veins of the gods.

apply the principle on which I have so much insisted, namely, that of selection; on this he will depend for removing what would otherwise be painful or disgusting in the passion; he will feel that there is no necessity to trick out[6] or to elevate nature: and, the more industriously he applies this principle, the deeper will be his faith that no words, which his fancy or imagination can suggest, will be to be compared with those which are the emanations of reality and truth.

But it may be said by those who do not object to the general spirit of these remarks, that, as it is impossible for the poet to produce upon all occasions language as exquisitely fitted for the passion as that which the real passion itself suggests, it is proper that he should consider himself as in the situation of a translator, who deems himself justified when he substitutes excellences of another kind for those which are unattainable by him; and endeavours occasionally to surpass his original, in order to make some amends for the general inferiority to which he feels that he must submit. But this would be to encourage idleness and unmanly despair. Further, it is the language of men who speak of what they do not understand; who talk of poetry as a matter of amusement and idle pleasure; who will converse with us as gravely about a *taste* for poetry, as they express it, as if it were a thing as indifferent as a taste for rope-dancing, or Frontiniac[7] or sherry. Aristotle, I have been told, hath said, that poetry is the most philosophic of all writing;[8] it is so: its object is truth, not individual and local, but general, and operative; not standing upon external testimony, but carried alive into the heart by passion; truth which is its own testimony, which gives strength and divinity to the tribunal to which it appeals, and receives them from the same tribunal. Poetry is the image of man and nature. The obstacles which stand in the way of the fidelity of the biographer and historian, and of their consequent utility, are incalculably greater than those which are to be encountered by the poet who has an adequate notion of the dignity of his art. The poet writes under one restriction only, namely, that of the necessity of giving immediate pleasure to a human being possessed of that information which may be expected from him, not as a lawyer, a physician, a mariner, an astronomer or a natural philosopher, but as a man. Except this one restriction, there is no object standing between the poet and the image of things; between this, and the biographer and historian there are a thousand.

Nor let this necessity of producing immediate pleasure be considered as a degradation of the poet's art. It is far otherwise. It is an acknowledgment of the beauty of the universe, an acknowledgment the more sincere because it is not formal, but indirect; it is a task light and easy to him who looks at the world in the spirit of love: further, it is a homage paid to the native and naked dignity of man, to the grand elementary principle of pleasure, by which he knows, and feels, and lives, and moves.[9] We have no sympathy but what is propagated by pleasure: I would not be misunderstood; but wherever we sympathize with pain it will be found that the sympathy is produced and carried on by subtle combinations with pleasure. We have no knowledge, that is, no general principles drawn from the contemplation of particular facts, but what

---

6. Dress up.
7. A sweet wine made from muscat grapes.
8. Aristotle in fact said that "poetry is more philosophic than history, since its statements are of the nature of universals, whereas those of history are

singulars" (*Poetics* 1451b).
9. A bold echo of the words of St. Paul, that in God "we live, and move, and have our being" (Acts 17.28).

has been built up by pleasure, and exists in us by pleasure alone. The man of science, the chemist and mathematician, whatever difficulties and disgusts they may have had to struggle with, know and feel this. However painful may be the objects with which the anatomist's knowledge is connected, he feels that his knowledge is pleasure; and where he has no pleasure he has no knowledge. What then does the poet? He considers man and the objects that surround him as acting and re-acting upon each other, so as to produce an infinite complexity of pain and pleasure; he considers man in his own nature and in his ordinary life as contemplating this with a certain quantity of immediate knowledge, with certain convictions, intuitions, and deductions which by habit become of the nature of intuitions; he considers him as looking upon this complex scene of ideas and sensations, and finding every where objects that immediately excite in him sympathies which, from the necessities of his nature, are accompanied by an overbalance of enjoyment.

To this knowledge which all men carry about with them, and to these sympathies in which without any other discipline than that of our daily life we are fitted to take delight, the poet principally directs his attention. He considers man and nature as essentially adapted to each other, and the mind of man as naturally the mirror of the fairest and most interesting qualities of nature. And thus the poet, prompted by this feeling of pleasure which accompanies him through the whole course of his studies, converses with general nature with affections akin to those, which, through labour and length of time, the man of science has raised up in himself, by conversing with those particular parts of nature which are the objects of his studies. The knowledge both of the poet and the man of science is pleasure; but the knowledge of the one cleaves to us as a necessary part of our existence, our natural and unalienable inheritance; the other is a personal and individual acquisition, slow to come to us, and by no habitual and direct sympathy connecting us with our fellow-beings. The man of science seeks truth as a remote and unknown benefactor; he cherishes and loves it in his solitude: the poet, singing a song in which all human beings join with him, rejoices in the presence of truth as our visible friend and hourly companion. Poetry is the breath and finer spirit of all knowledge; it is the impassioned expression which is in the countenance of all science. Emphatically may it be said of the poet, as Shakespeare hath said of man, "that he looks before and after."[1] He is the rock of defence of human nature; an upholder and preserver, carrying everywhere with him relationship and love. In spite of difference of soil and climate, of language and manners, of laws and customs, in spite of things silently gone out of mind and things violently destroyed, the poet binds together by passion and knowledge the vast empire of human society, as it is spread over the whole earth, and over all time. The objects of the poet's thoughts are every where; though the eyes and senses of man are, it is true, his favorite guides, yet he will follow wheresoever he can find an atmosphere of sensation in which to move his wings. Poetry is the first and last of all knowledge—it is as immortal as the heart of man. If the labours of men of science should ever create any material revolution, direct or indirect, in our condition, and in the impressions which we habitually receive, the poet will sleep then no more than at present, but he will be ready to follow the steps of the man of science, not only in those general indirect effects, but he will be at his side, carrying sensation into the midst of the

1. Cf. Shakespeare's *Hamlet* 4.4.9.27.

272 / WILLIAM WORDSWORTH

objects of the science itself. The remotest discoveries of the chemist, the botanist, or mineralogist, will be as proper objects of the poet's art as any upon
which it can be employed, if the time should ever come when these things
shall be familiar to us, and the relations under which they are contemplated
by the followers of these respective sciences shall be manifestly and palpably
material to us as enjoying and suffering beings.[2] If the time should ever come
when what is now called science, thus familiarized to men, shall be ready to
put on, as it were, a form of flesh and blood, the poet will lend his divine spirit
to aid the transfiguration, and will welcome the being thus produced, as a dear
and genuine inmate of the household of man.—It is not, then, to be supposed
that any one, who holds that sublime notion of poetry which I have attempted
to convey, will break in upon the sanctity and truth of his pictures by transitory
and accidental ornaments, and endeavour to excite admiration of himself by
arts, the necessity of which must manifestly depend upon the assumed meanness of his subject.

What I have thus far said applies to poetry in general; but especially to those
parts of composition where the poet speaks through the mouth of his characters; and upon this point it appears to have such weight that I will conclude,
there are few persons, of good sense, who would not allow that the dramatic
parts of composition are defective, in proportion as they deviate from the real
language of nature, and are coloured by a diction of the poet's own, either
peculiar to him as an individual poet, or belonging simply to poets in general,
to a body of men who, from the circumstance of their compositions being in
metre, it is expected will employ a particular language.

It is not, then, in the dramatic parts of composition that we look for this
distinction of language; but still it may be proper and necessary where the
poet speaks to us in his own person and character. To this I answer by referring
my reader to the description which I have before given of a poet. Among the
qualities which I have enumerated as principally conducing to form a poet, is
implied nothing differing in kind from other men, but only in degree. The sum
of what I have there said is, that the poet is chiefly distinguished from other
men by a greater promptness to think and feel without immediate external
excitement, and a greater power in expressing such thoughts and feelings as
are produced in him in that manner. But these passions and thoughts and
feelings are the general passions and thoughts and feelings of men. And with
what are they connected? Undoubtedly with our moral sentiments and animal
sensations, and with the causes which excite these; with the operations of the
elements and the appearances of the visible universe; with storm and sunshine, with the revolutions[3] of the seasons, with cold and heat, with loss of
friends and kindred, with injuries and resentments, gratitude and hope, with
fear and sorrow. These, and the like, are the sensations and objects which the
poet describes, as they are the sensations of other men, and the objects which
interest them. The poet thinks and feels in the spirit of the passions of men.
How, then, can his language differ in any material degree from that of all other
men who feel vividly and see clearly? It might be *proved* that it is impossible.
But supposing that this were not the case, the poet might then be allowed to
use a peculiar language, when expressing his feelings for his own gratification,
or that of men like himself. But poets do not write for poets alone, but for

2. Wordsworth is at least right in anticipating the
poetry of the machine. His sonnet "Steamboats,
Viaducts, and Railways" is an early instance, as is
Joanna Baillie's "Address to a Steamvessel."
3. Recurrence.

men. Unless therefore we are advocates for that admiration which depends upon ignorance, and that pleasure which arises from hearing what we do not understand, the poet must descend from this supposed height, and, in order to excite rational sympathy, he must express himself as other men express themselves. * * *

["EMOTION RECOLLECTED IN TRANQUILLITY"]

I have said that poetry is the spontaneous overflow of powerful feelings: it takes its origin from emotion recollected in tranquillity: the emotion is contemplated till by a species of reaction the tranquillity gradually disappears, and an emotion, kindred to that which was before the subject of contemplation, is gradually produced, and does itself actually exist in the mind. In this mood successful composition generally begins, and in a mood similar to this it is carried on; but the emotion, of whatever kind and in whatever degree, from various causes is qualified by various pleasures, so that in describing any passions whatsoever, which are voluntarily described, the mind will upon the whole be in a state of enjoyment. Now, if nature be thus cautious in preserving in a state of enjoyment a being thus employed, the poet ought to profit by the lesson thus held forth to him, and ought especially to take care, that whatever passions he communicates to his reader, those passions, if his reader's mind be sound and vigorous, should always be accompanied with an overbalance of pleasure. Now the music of harmonious metrical language, the sense of difficulty overcome, and the blind association of pleasure which has been previously received from works of rhyme or metre of the same or similar construction, an indistinct perception perpetually renewed of language closely resembling that of real life, and yet, in the circumstance of metre, differing from it so widely, all these imperceptibly make up a complex feeling of delight, which is of the most important use in tempering the painful feeling which will always be found intermingled with powerful descriptions of the deeper passions. This effect is always produced in pathetic and impassioned poetry; while, in lighter compositions, the ease and gracefulness with which the poet manages his numbers are themselves confessedly a principal source of the gratification of the reader. I might perhaps include all which it is *necessary* to say upon this subject by affirming, what few persons will deny, that, of two descriptions, either of passions, manners, or characters, each of them equally well executed, the one in prose and the other in verse, the verse will be read a hundred times where the prose is read once. * * *

I know that nothing would have so effectually contributed to further the end which I have in view, as to have shewn of what kind the pleasure is, and how the pleasure is produced, which is confessedly produced by metrical composition essentially different from that which I have here endeavoured to recommend: for the reader will say that he has been pleased by such composition; and what can I do more for him? The power of any art is limited; and he will suspect, that, if I propose to furnish him with new friends, it is only upon condition of his abandoning his old friends. Besides, as I have said, the reader is himself conscious of the pleasure which he has received from such composition, composition to which he has peculiarly attached the endearing name of poetry; and all men feel an habitual gratitude, and something of an honorable bigotry for the objects which have long continued to please them: we not only wish to be pleased, but to be pleased in that particular way in which we have been accustomed to be pleased. There is a host of arguments in these feelings; and I should be the less able to combat them successfully, as I am willing to allow, that, in order entirely to enjoy the poetry which I am recommending, it would be necessary to give up much of what is ordinarily enjoyed. But, would my limits have permitted me to point out how this pleasure is produced, I might have removed many obstacles, and assisted my reader in perceiving that the powers of language are not so limited as he may suppose; and that it is possible that poetry may give other enjoyments, of a purer, more lasting, and more exquisite nature. This part of my subject I have not altogether neglected; but it has been less my present aim to prove, that the interest excited by some other kinds of poetry is less vivid, and less worthy of the nobler powers of the mind, than to offer reasons for presuming, that, if the object which I have proposed to myself were adequately attained, a species of poetry would be produced, which is genuine poetry; in its nature well adapted to interest mankind permanently, and likewise important in the multiplicity and quality of its moral relations.

From what has been said, and from a perusal of the poems, the reader will be able clearly to perceive the object which I have proposed to myself: he will determine how far I have attained this object; and, what is a much more important question, whether it be worth attaining; and upon the decision of these two questions will rest my claim to the approbation of the public.

1800, 1802

Strange fits of passion have I known[1]

Strange fits of passion have I known:
And I will dare to tell,
But in the Lover's ear alone,
What once to me befel.

5   When she I loved looked every day
Fresh as a rose in June,
I to her cottage bent my way,
Beneath an evening moon.

Upon the moon I fixed my eye,
10   All over the wide lea;
With quickening pace my horse drew nigh
Those paths so dear to me.

And now we reached the orchard-plot;
And, as we climbed the hill,
15   The sinking moon to Lucy's cot
Came near, and nearer still.

1. This and the four following pieces are often grouped by editors as the "Lucy poems," even though "A slumber did my spirit seal" does not identify the "she" who is the subject of that poem. All but the last were written in 1799, while Words- worth and his sister were in Germany and home- sick. There has been diligent speculation about the identity of Lucy, but it remains speculation. The one certainty is that she is not the girl of Words- worth's "Lucy Gray."

In one of those sweet dreams I slept,
Kind Nature's gentlest boon!
And all the while my eyes I kept
20   On the descending moon.

My horse moved on; hoof after hoof
He raised, and never stopped:
When down behind the cottage roof,
At once, the bright moon dropped.

25   What fond and wayward thoughts will slide
Into a Lover's head!
"O mercy!" to myself I cried,
"If Lucy should be dead!"[2]

1799   1800

She dwelt among the untrodden ways[1]

She dwelt among the untrodden ways
    Beside the springs of Dove,[2]
A Maid whom there were none to praise
    And very few to love:

5   A violet by a mossy stone
    Half hidden from the eye!
—Fair as a star, when only one
    Is shining in the sky.

She lived unknown, and few could know
10   When Lucy ceased to be;
But she is in her grave, and, oh,
    The difference to me!

1799   1800

Three years she grew

Three years she grew in sun and shower,
Then Nature said, "A lovelier flower
On earth was never sown;
This Child I to myself will take;
5   She shall be mine, and I will make
A Lady of my own.[1]

2. An additional stanza in an earlier manuscript version demonstrates how a poem can be improved by omission of a passage that is, in itself, excellent poetry: "I told her this: her laughter light / Is ringing in my ears; / And when I think upon that night / My eyes are dim with tears."
1. For the author's revisions while composing this poem, see "Poems in Process," in the appendices

to this volume.
2. There are several rivers by this name in England, including one in the Lake District.
1. I.e., Lucy was three years old when Nature made this promise; line 37 makes clear that Lucy had reached the maturity foretold in the sixth stanza when she died.

"Myself will to my darling be
Both law and impulse: and with me
The Girl, in rock and plain,
10 In earth and heaven, in glade and bower,
Shall feel an overseeing power
To kindle or restrain.

"She shall be sportive as the fawn
That wild with glee across the lawn
15 Or up the mountain springs;
And hers shall be the breathing balm,
And hers the silence and the calm
Of mute insensate things.

"The floating clouds their state shall lend
20 To her; for her the willow bend;
Nor shall she fail to see
Even in the motions of the Storm
Grace that shall mould the Maiden's form
By silent sympathy.

25 "The stars of midnight shall be dear
To her; and she shall lean her ear
In many a secret place
Where rivulets dance their wayward round,
And beauty born of murmuring sound
30 Shall pass into her face.

"And vital feelings of delight
Shall rear her form to stately height,
Her virgin bosom swell;
Such thoughts to Lucy I will give
35 While she and I together live
Here in this happy dell."

Thus Nature spake—the work was done—
How soon my Lucy's race was run!
She died, and left to me
40 This heath, this calm, and quiet scene;
The memory of what has been,
And never more will be.

1799   1800

A slumber did my spirit seal

A slumber did my spirit seal;
I had no human fears:
She seemed a thing that could not feel
The touch of earthly years.

5 No motion has she now, no force;
She neither hears nor sees;

Rolled round in earth's diurnal° course,   *daily*
With rocks, and stones, and trees.

1799   1800

I travelled among unknown men

I travelled among unknown men,
   In lands beyond the sea;
Nor, England! did I know till then
   What love I bore to thee.

5   'Tis past, that melancholy dream!
   Nor will I quit thy shore
A second time; for still I seem
   To love thee more and more.

Among thy mountains did I feel
10   The joy of my desire;
And she I cherished turned her wheel
   Beside an English fire.

Thy mornings showed, thy nights concealed
   The bowers where Lucy played;
15   And thine too is the last green field
   That Lucy's eyes surveyed.

ca. 1801   1807

Lucy Gray[1]

Or, Solitude

Oft I had heard of Lucy Gray:
   And, when I crossed the wild,
I chanced to see at break of day
   The solitary child.

5   No mate, no comrade Lucy knew;
   She dwelt on a wide moor,
—The sweetest thing that ever grew
   Beside a human door!

You yet may spy the fawn at play,
10   The hare upon the green;

1. Written in 1799 while Wordsworth was in Germany, and founded on a true account of a young girl who drowned when she lost her way in a snowstorm. "The body however was found in the canal. The way in which the incident was treated and the spiritualizing of the character might furnish hints for contrasting the imaginative influences which I have endeavored to throw over common life with Crabbe's matter-of-fact style of treating subjects of the same kind" [Wordsworth's note, 1843]. George Crabbe (1765–1832) won fame in the late 18th century for his long poem *The Village*. Cf. Wordsworth's discussion, in the Preface to *Lyrical Ballads*, of how he had aimed in those poems to throw over ordinary things "a certain colouring of imagination" (p. 264).

But the sweet face of Lucy Gray
Will never more be seen.

"To-night will be a stormy night—
You to the town must go;
15   And take a lantern, Child, to light
Your mother through the snow."

"That, Father! will I gladly do:
'Tis scarcely afternoon—
The minster°-clock has just struck two,   church
20   And yonder is the moon!"

At this the Father raised his hook,
And snapped a faggot-band²
He plied his work;—and Lucy took
The lantern in her hand.

25   Not blither is the mountain roe:°   deer
With many a wanton stroke
Her feet disperse the powdery snow,
That rises up like smoke.

The storm came on before its time:
30   She wandered up and down;
And many a hill did Lucy climb:
But never reached the town.

The wretched parents all that night
Went shouting far and wide;
35   But there was neither sound nor sight
To serve them for a guide.

At day-break on a hill they stood
That overlooked the moor;
And thence they saw the bridge of wood,
40   A furlong³ from their door.

They wept—and, turning homeward, cried,
"In heaven we all shall meet;"
—When in the snow the mother spied
The print of Lucy's feet.

45   Then downwards from the steep hill's edge
They tracked the footmarks small;
And through the broken hawthorn hedge,
And by the long stone-wall;

And then an open field they crossed:
50   The marks were still the same;

2. Cord binding a bundle of sticks to be used for   3. One eighth of a mile.
fuel.

They tracked them on, nor ever lost;
And to the bridge they came.

They followed from the snowy bank
Those footmarks, one by one,
55   Into the middle of the plank;
And further there were none!

—Yet some maintain that to this day
She is a living child;
That you may see sweet Lucy Gray
60   Upon the lonesome wild.

O'er rough and smooth she trips along,
And never looks behind;
And sings a solitary song
That whistles in the wind.

1799   1800

Nutting[1]

———————— It seems a day
(I speak of one from many singled out)
One of those heavenly days that cannot die;
When, in the eagerness of boyish hope,
5   I left our cottage-threshold, sallying forth
With a huge wallet° o'er my shoulder slung,   *bag, knapsack*
A nutting-crook in hand; and turned my steps
Tow'rd some far-distant wood, a Figure quaint,
Tricked out in proud disguise of cast-off weeds°   *clothes*
10   Which for that service had been husbanded,
By exhortation of my frugal Dame[2]—
Motley accoutrement, of power to smile
At thorns, and brakes, and brambles,—and, in truth,
More ragged than need was! O'er pathless rocks,
15   Through beds of matted fern, and tangled thickets,
Forcing my way, I came to one dear nook
Unvisited, where not a broken bough
Drooped with its withered leaves, ungracious sign
Of devastation; but the hazels rose
20   Tall and erect, with tempting clusters hung,
A virgin scene!—A little while I stood,
Breathing with such suppression of the heart
As joy delights in; and, with wise restraint
Voluptuous, fearless of a rival, eyed
25   The banquet;—or beneath the trees I sate

1. Wordsworth said in 1843 that these lines, written in Germany in 1798, were "intended as part of
a poem on my own life [*The Prelude*], but struck
out as not being wanted there." He published them
in the second edition of *Lyrical Ballads*, 1800.
2. Ann Tyson, with whom Wordsworth lodged
while at Hawkshead grammar school.

Among the flowers, and with the flowers I played;
A temper known to those, who, after long
And weary expectation, have been blest
With sudden happiness beyond all hope.
30   Perhaps it was a bower beneath whose leaves
The violets of five seasons re-appear
And fade, unseen by any human eye;
Where fairy water-breaks³ do murmur on
For ever; and I saw the sparkling foam,
35   And—with my cheek on one of those green stones
That, fleeced with moss, under the shady trees,
Lay round me, scattered like a flock of sheep—
I heard the murmur and the murmuring sound,
In that sweet mood when pleasure loves to pay
40   Tribute to ease; and, of its joy secure,
The heart luxuriates with indifferent things,
Wasting its kindliness on stocks⁴ and stones,
And on the vacant air. Then up I rose,
And dragged to earth both branch and bough, with crash
45   And merciless ravage: and the shady nook
Of hazels, and the green and mossy bower,
Deformed and sullied, patiently gave up
Their quiet being: and, unless I now
Confound my present feelings with the past,
50   Ere from the mutilated bower I turned
Exulting, rich beyond the wealth of kings,
I felt a sense of pain when I beheld
The silent trees, and saw the intruding sky.—
Then, dearest Maiden,⁵ move along these shades
55   In gentleness of heart; with gentle hand
Touch—for there is a spirit in the woods.

1798   1800

The Ruined Cottage¹

First Part

'Twas summer and the sun was mounted high.
Along the south the uplands feebly glared

3. Places where the flow of a stream is broken by
rocks.
4. Tree stumps. ("Stocks and stones" is a conventional expression for "inanimate things.")
5. In a manuscript passage originally intended to
lead up to "Nutting," the maiden is called Lucy.
1. Wordsworth wrote *The Ruined Cottage* in
1797–98, then revised it several times before he
finally published an expanded version of the story
as book 1 of *The Excursion*, in 1814. *The Ruined
Cottage* was not published as an independent poem
until 1949, when it appeared in the fifth volume
of *The Poetical Works of William Wordsworth*,
edited by Ernest de Selincourt and Helen Darbishire, who printed a version known as "MS. B."

The text reprinted here is from "MS. D," dated
1799, as transcribed by James Butler in the Cornell
Wordsworth volume, *"The Ruined Cottage" and
"The Pedlar"* (1979).
    Concerning the principal narrator, introduced in
line 33, Wordsworth said in 1843, "had I been born
in a class which would have deprived me of what
is called a liberal education, it is not unlikely that
being strong in body; I should have taken to a way
of life such as that in which my Pedlar passed the
greater part of his days. . . . [T]he character I have
represented in his person is chiefly an idea of what
I fancied my own character might have become in
his circumstances."

Through a pale steam, and all the northern downs
In clearer air ascending shewed far off
5   Their surfaces with shadows dappled o'er
Of deep embattled clouds: far as the sight
Could reach those many shadows lay in spots
Determined and unmoved, with steady beams
Of clear and pleasant sunshine interposed;
10 Pleasant to him who on the soft cool moss
Extends his careless limbs beside the root
Of some huge oak whose aged branches make
A twilight of their own, a dewy shade
Where the wren warbles while the dreaming man,
15 Half-conscious of that soothing melody,
With side-long eye looks out upon the scene,
By those impending branches made more soft,
More soft and distant. Other lot was mine.
Across a bare wide Common I had toiled
20 With languid feet which by the slipp'ry ground
Were baffled still, and when I stretched myself
On the brown earth my limbs from very heat
Could find no rest nor my weak arm disperse
The insect host which gathered round my face
25 And joined their murmurs to the tedious noise
Of seeds of bursting gorse that crackled round.
I rose and turned towards a group of trees
Which midway in that level stood alone,
And thither come at length, beneath a shade
30 Of clustering elms that sprang from the same root
I found a ruined house, four naked walls
That stared upon each other. I looked round
And near the door I saw an aged Man,
Alone, and stretched upon the cottage bench;
35 An iron-pointed staff lay at his side.
With instantaneous joy I recognized
That pride of nature and of lowly life,
The venerable Armytage, a friend
As dear to me as is the setting sun.
40   Two days before
We had been fellow-travellers. I knew
That he was in this neighbourhood and now
Delighted found him here in the cool shade.
He lay, his pack of rustic merchandize
45 Pillowing his head—I guess he had no thought
Of his way-wandering life. His eyes were shut;
The shadows of the breezy elms above
Dappled his face. With thirsty heat oppress'd
At length I hailed him, glad to see his hat
50 Bedewed with water-drops, as if the brim
Had newly scoop'd a running stream. He rose
And pointing to a sun-flower bade me climb
The [   ]² wall where that same gaudy flower

2. The brackets here and in later lines mark blank spaces left unfilled in the manuscript.

Looked out upon the road. It was a plot
55 Of garden-ground, now wild, its matted weeds
Marked with the steps of those whom as they pass'd,
The goose-berry trees that shot in long lank slips,
Or currants hanging from their leafless stems
In scanty strings, had tempted to o'erleap
60 The broken wall. Within that cheerless spot,
Where two tall hedgerows of thick willow boughs
Joined in a damp cold nook, I found a well
Half-choked [with willow flowers and weeds.][3]
I slaked my thirst and to the shady bench
65 Returned, and while I stood unbonneted
To catch the motion of the cooler air
The old Man said, "I see around me here
Things which you cannot see: we die, my Friend,
Nor we alone, but that which each man loved
70 And prized in his peculiar nook of earth
Dies with him or is changed, and very soon
Even of the good is no memorial left.
The Poets in their elegies and songs
Lamenting the departed call the groves,
75 They call upon the hills and streams to mourn,
And senseless[4] rocks, nor idly; for they speak
In these their invocations with a voice
Obedient to the strong creative power
Of human passion. Sympathies there are
80 More tranquil, yet perhaps of kindred birth,
That steal upon the meditative mind
And grow with thought. Beside yon spring I stood
And eyed its waters till we seemed to feel
One sadness, they and I. For them a bond
85 Of brotherhood is broken: time has been
When every day the touch of human hand
Disturbed their stillness, and they ministered
To human comfort. When I stooped to drink,
A spider's web hung to the water's edge,
90 And on the wet and slimy foot-stone lay
The useless fragment of a wooden bowl;
It moved my very heart. The day has been
When I could never pass this road but she
Who lived within these walls, when I appeared,
95 A daughter's welcome gave me, and I loved her
As my own child. O Sir! the good die first,
And they whose hearts are dry as summer dust
Burn to the socket. Many a passenger°   *passerby, traveler*
Has blessed poor Margaret for her gentle looks
100 When she upheld the cool refreshment drawn
From that forsaken spring, and no one came
But he was welcome, no one went away
But that it seemed she loved him. She is dead,

3. Wordsworth penciled the bracketed phrase into   4. Incapable of sensation or perception.
a gap left in the manuscript.

The worm is on her cheek, and this poor hut,
105 Stripp'd of its outward garb of household flowers,
Of rose and sweet-briar, offers to the wind
A cold bare wall whose earthy top is tricked
With weeds and the rank spear-grass. She is dead,
And nettles rot and adders sun themselves
110 Where we have sate together while she nurs'd
Her infant at her breast. The unshod Colt,
The wandring heifer and the Potter's ass,
Find shelter now within the chimney-wall
Where I have seen her evening hearth-stone blaze
115 And through the window spread upon the road
Its chearful light.—You will forgive me, Sir,
But often on this cottage do I muse
As on a picture, till my wiser mind
Sinks, yielding to the foolishness of grief.
120   She had a husband, an industrious man,
Sober and steady; I have heard her say
That he was up and busy at his loom
In summer ere the mower's scythe had swept
The dewy grass, and in the early spring
125 Ere the last star had vanished. They who pass'd
At evening, from behind the garden-fence
Might hear his busy spade, which he would ply
After his daily work till the day-light
Was gone and every leaf and flower were lost
130 In the dark hedges. So they pass'd their days
In peace and comfort, and two pretty babes
Were their best hope next to the God in Heaven.
—You may remember, now some ten years gone,
Two blighting seasons when the fields were left
135 With half a harvest.⁵ It pleased heaven to add
A worse affliction in the plague of war:
A happy land was stricken to the heart;
'Twas a sad time of sorrow and distress:
A wanderer among the cottages,
140 I with my pack of winter raiment saw
The hardships of that season: many rich
Sunk down as in a dream among the poor,
And of the poor did many cease to be,
And their place knew them not. Meanwhile, abridg'd°   deprived
145 Of daily comforts, gladly reconciled
To numerous self-denials, Margaret
Went struggling on through those calamitous years
With chearful hope: but ere the second autumn
A fever seized her husband. In disease
150 He lingered long, and when his strength returned
He found the little he had stored to meet
The hour of accident or crippling age

---

5. As James Butler points out in his introduction, Wordsworth is purposely distancing his story in time. The "two blighting seasons" in fact occurred in 1794–95, only a few years before Wordsworth wrote *The Ruined Cottage*, when a bad harvest was followed by one of the worst winters on record. Much of the seed grain was destroyed in the ground, and the price of wheat nearly doubled.

Was all consumed. As I have said, 'twas now
A time of trouble; shoals of artisans
155 Were from their daily labour turned away
To hang for bread on parish charity,[6]
They and their wives and children—happier far
Could they have lived as do the little birds
That peck along the hedges or the kite
160 That makes her dwelling in the mountain rocks.
Ill fared it now with Robert, he who dwelt
In this poor cottage; at his door he stood
And whistled many a snatch of merry tunes
That had no mirth in them, or with his knife
165 Carved uncouth figures on the heads of sticks,
Then idly sought about through every nook
Of house or garden any casual task
Of use or ornament, and with a strange,
Amusing but uneasy novelty
170 He blended where he might the various tasks
Of summer, autumn, winter, and of spring.
But this endured not; his good-humour soon
Became a weight in which no pleasure was,
And poverty brought on a petted° mood   *ill-tempered*
175 And a sore temper: day by day he drooped,
And he would leave his home, and to the town
Without an errand would he turn his steps
Or wander here and there among the fields.
One while he would speak lightly of his babes
180 And with a cruel tongue: at other times
He played with them wild freaks of merriment:
And 'twas a piteous thing to see the looks
Of the poor innocent children. 'Every smile,'
Said Margaret to me here beneath these trees,
185 'Made my heart bleed,' " At this the old Man paus'd
And looking up to those enormous elms
He said, " 'Tis now the hour of deepest noon,
At this still season of repose and peace,
This hour when all things which are not at rest
190 Are chearful, while this multitude of flies
Fills all the air with happy melody,
Why should a tear be in an old man's eye?
Why should we thus with an untoward mind
And in the weakness of humanity
195 From natural wisdom turn our hearts away,
To natural comfort shut our eyes and ears,
And feeding on disquiet thus disturb
The calm of Nature with our restless thoughts?"

END OF THE FIRST PART

6. The so-called able-bodied poor were entitled to receive from the parish in which they were settled the food, the clothing, and sometimes the cash that would help them over a crisis.

Second Part

He spake with somewhat of a solemn tone:
200 But when he ended there was in his face
Such easy chearfulness, a look so mild
That for a little time it stole away
All recollection, and that simple tale
Passed from my mind like a forgotten sound.
205 A while on trivial things we held discourse,
To me soon tasteless. In my own despite
I thought of that poor woman as of one
Whom I had known and loved. He had rehearsed
Her homely tale with such familiar power,
210 With such a[n active]⁷ countenance, an eye
So busy, that the things of which he spake
Seemed present, and, attention now relaxed,
There was a heartfelt chillness in my veins.
I rose, and turning from that breezy shade
215 Went out into the open air and stood
To drink the comfort of the warmer sun.
Long time I had not stayed ere, looking round
Upon that tranquil ruin, I returned
And begged of the old man that for my sake
220 He would resume his story. He replied,
"It were a wantonness° and would demand   reckless ill-doing
Severe reproof, if we were men whose hearts
Could hold vain dalliance with the misery
Even of the dead, contented thence to draw
225 A momentary pleasure never marked
By reason, barren of all future good.
But we have known that there is often found
In mournful thoughts, and always might be found,
A power to virtue friendly; were't not so,
230 I am a dreamer among men, indeed
An idle dreamer. 'Tis a common tale,
By moving accidents⁸ uncharactered,
A tale of silent suffering, hardly clothed
In bodily form, and to the grosser sense
235 But ill adapted, scarcely palpable
To him who does not think. But at your bidding
I will proceed.
            While thus it fared with them
To whom this cottage till that hapless year
Had been a blessed home, it was my chance
240 To travel in a country far remote,
And glad I was when, halting by yon gate
That leads from the green lane, again I saw
These lofty elm-trees. Long I did not rest:

7. Wordsworth penciled the bracketed phrase into a gap left in the manuscript.
8. Othello speaks "of most disastrous chances, / Of moving accidents by flood and field, / Of hairbreadth 'scapes" (Shakespeare, *Othello* 1.3.133–35).

With many pleasant thoughts I cheer'd my way
245 O'er the flat common. At the door arrived,
I knocked, and when I entered with the hope
Of usual greeting, Margaret looked at me
A little while, then turned her head away
Speechless, and sitting down upon a chair
250 Wept bitterly. I wist not what to do
Or how to speak to her. Poor wretch! at last
She rose from off her seat—and then, oh Sir!
I cannot tell how she pronounced my name:
With fervent love, and with a face of grief
255 Unutterably helpless, and a look
That seem'd to cling upon me, she enquir'd
If I had seen her husband. As she spake
A strange surprize and fear came to my heart,
Nor had I power to answer ere she told
260 That he had disappeared—just two months gone.
He left his house; two wretched days had passed,
And on the third by the first break of light,
Within her casement full in view she saw
A purse of gold.[9] 'I trembled at the sight,'
265 Said Margaret, 'for I knew it was his hand
That placed it there, and on that very day
By one, a stranger, from my husband sent,
The tidings came that he had joined a troop
Of soldiers going to a distant land.
270 He left me thus—Poor Man! he had not heart
To take a farewell of me, and he feared
That I should follow with my babes, and sink
Beneath the misery of a soldier's life.'
This tale did Margaret tell with many tears:
275 And when she ended I had little power
To give her comfort, and was glad to take
Such words of hope from her own mouth as serv'd
To cheer us both: but long we had not talked
Ere we built up a pile of better thoughts,
280 And with a brighter eye she looked around
As if she had been shedding tears of joy.
We parted. It was then the early spring;
I left her busy with her garden tools;
And well remember, o'er that fence she looked,
285 And while I paced along the foot-way path
Called out, and sent a blessing after me
With tender chearfulness and with a voice
That seemed the very sound of happy thoughts.
    I roved o'er many a hill and many a dale
290 With this my weary load, in heat and cold,
Through many a wood, and many an open ground,
In sunshine or in shade, in wet or fair,

9. The "bounty" that her husband had been paid for enlisting in the militia. The shortage of volunteers and England's sharply rising military needs had in some counties forced the bounty up from about £1 in 1757 to more than £16 in 1796 (J. R. Western, *English Militia in the Eighteenth Century*, 1965).

Now blithe, now drooping, as it might befal,
My best companions now the driving winds
295 And now the 'trotting brooks'[1] and whispering trees
And now the music of my own sad steps,
With many a short-lived thought that pass'd between
And disappeared. I came this way again
Towards the wane of summer, when the wheat
300 Was yellow, and the soft and bladed grass
Sprang up afresh and o'er the hay-field spread
Its tender green. When I had reached the door
I found that she was absent. In the shade
Where now we sit I waited her return.
305 Her cottage in its outward look appeared
As chearful as before; in any shew
Of neatness little changed, but that I thought
The honeysuckle crowded round the door
And from the wall hung down in heavier wreathes,
310 And knots of worthless stone-crop[2] started out
Along the window's edge, and grew like weeds
Against the lower panes. I turned aside
And stroll'd into her garden.—It was chang'd:
The unprofitable bindweed spread his bells
315 From side to side and with unwieldy wreaths
Had dragg'd the rose from its sustaining wall
And bent it down to earth; the border-tufts—
Daisy and thrift and lowly camomile
And thyme—had straggled out into the paths
320 Which they were used° to deck. Ere this an hour   *accustomed*
Was wasted. Back I turned my restless steps,
And as I walked before the door it chanced
A stranger passed, and guessing whom I sought
He said that she was used to ramble far.
325 The sun was sinking in the west, and now
I sate with sad impatience. From within
Her solitary infant cried aloud.
The spot though fair seemed very desolate,
The longer I remained more desolate.
330 And, looking round, I saw the corner-stones,
Till then unmark'd, on either side the door
With dull red stains discoloured and stuck o'er
With tufts and hairs of wool, as if the sheep
That feed upon the commons[3] thither came
335 Familiarly and found a couching-place
Even at her threshold.—The house-clock struck eight;
I turned and saw her distant a few steps.
Her face was pale and thin, her figure too
Was chang'd. As she unlocked the door she said,
340 'It grieves me you have waited here so long,
But in good truth I've wandered much of late

---

1. From Robert Burns ("To William Simpson,"
line 87).
2. A plant with yellow flowers that grows on walls
and rocks.
3. Land belonging to the local community as a
whole.

And sometimes, to my shame I speak, have need
Of my best prayers to bring me back again.'
While on the board she spread our evening meal
345 She told me she had lost her elder child,
That he for months had been a serving-boy
Apprenticed by the parish. 'I perceive
You look at me, and you have cause. Today
I have been travelling far, and many days
350 About the fields I wander, knowing this
Only, that what I seek I cannot find.
And so I waste my time: for I am changed;
And to myself,' said she, 'have done much wrong,
And to this helpless infant. I have slept
355 Weeping, and weeping I have waked; my tears
Have flow'd as if my body were not such
As others are, and I could never die.
But I am now in mind and in my heart
More easy, and I hope,' said she, 'that heaven
360 Will give me patience to endure the things
Which I behold at home.' It would have grieved
Your very heart to see her. Sir, I feel
The story linger in my heart. I fear
'Tis long and tedious, but my spirit clings
365 To that poor woman: so familiarly
Do I perceive her manner, and her look
And presence, and so deeply do I feel
Her goodness, that not seldom in my walks
A momentary trance comes over me;
370 And to myself I seem to muse on one
By sorrow laid asleep or borne away,
A human being destined to awake
To human life, or something very near
To human life, when he shall come again
375 For whom she suffered. Sir, it would have griev'd
Your very soul to see her: evermore
Her eye-lids droop'd, her eyes were downward cast;
And when she at her table gave me food
She did not look at me. Her voice was low,
380 Her body was subdued. In every act
Pertaining to her house-affairs appeared
The careless stillness which a thinking mind
Gives to an idle matter—still she sighed,
But yet no motion of the breast was seen,
385 No heaving of the heart. While by the fire
We sate together, sighs came on my ear;
I knew not how, and hardly whence they came.
I took my staff, and when I kissed her babe
The tears stood in her eyes. I left her then
390 With the best hope and comfort I could give;
She thanked me for my will, but for my hope
It seemed she did not thank me.
                                        I returned
And took my rounds along this road again

Ere on its sunny bank the primrose flower
395 Had chronicled the earliest day of spring.
I found her sad and drooping; she had learn'd
No tidings of her husband: if he lived
She knew not that he lived; if he were dead
She knew not he was dead. She seemed the same
400 In person [or]⁴ appearance, but her house
Bespoke a sleepy hand of negligence;
The floor was neither dry nor neat, the hearth
Was comfortless [   ],
The windows too were dim, and her few books,
405 Which, one upon the other, heretofore
Had been piled up against the corner-panes
In seemly order, now with straggling leaves
Lay scattered here and there, open or shut
As they had chanced to fall. Her infant babe
410 Had from its mother caught the trick of grief
And sighed among its playthings. Once again
I turned towards the garden-gate and saw
More plainly still that poverty and grief
Were now come nearer to her: the earth was hard,
415 With weeds defaced and knots of withered grass;
No ridges there appeared of clear black mould,
No winter greenness; of her herbs and flowers
It seemed the better part were gnawed away
Or trampled on the earth; a chain of straw
420 Which had been twisted round the tender stem
Of a young apple-tree lay at its root;
The bark was nibbled round by truant sheep.
Margaret stood near, her infant in her arms,
And seeing that my eye was on the tree
425 She said, 'I fear it will be dead and gone
Ere Robert come again.' Towards the house
Together we returned, and she inquired
If I had any hope. But for her Babe
And for her little friendless Boy, she said,
430 She had no wish to live, that she must die
Of sorrow. Yet I saw the idle loom
Still in its place. His Sunday garments hung
Upon the self-same nail, his very staff
Stood undisturbed behind the door. And when
435 I passed this way beaten by Autumn winds
She told me that her little babe was dead
And she was left alone. That very time,
I yet remember, through the miry lane
She walked with me a mile, when the bare trees
440 Trickled with foggy damps, and in such sort
That any heart had ached to hear her begg'd
That wheresoe'er I went I still would ask
For him whom she had lost. We parted then,
Our final parting, for from that time forth

4. The word *or* was erased here; later manuscripts read "and."

445 Did many seasons pass ere I returned
Into this tract again.
                    Five tedious years
She lingered in unquiet widowhood,
A wife and widow. Needs must it have been
A sore heart-wasting. I have heard, my friend,
450 That in that broken arbour she would sit
The idle length of half a sabbath day—
There, where you see the toadstool's lazy head—
And when a dog passed by she still would quit
The shade and look abroad. On this old Bench
455 For hours she sate, and evermore her eye
Was busy in the distance, shaping things
Which made her heart beat quick. Seest thou that path?
(The green-sward now has broken its grey line)
There to and fro she paced through many a day
460 Of the warm summer, from a belt of flax
That girt her waist spinning the long-drawn thread
With backward steps.—Yet ever as there passed
A man whose garments shewed the Soldier's red,
Or crippled Mendicant in Sailor's garb,
465 The little child who sate to turn the wheel
Ceased from his toil, and she with faltering voice,
Expecting still to learn her husband's fate,
Made many a fond inquiry; and when they
Whose presence gave no comfort were gone by,
470 Her heart was still more sad. And by yon gate
Which bars the traveller's road she often stood
And when a stranger horseman came, the latch
Would lift, and in his face look wistfully,
Most happy if from aught discovered there
475 Of tender feeling she might dare repeat
The same sad question. Meanwhile her poor hut
Sunk to decay, for he was gone whose hand
At the first nippings of October frost
Closed up each chink and with fresh bands of straw
480 Chequered the green-grown thatch. And so she lived
Through the long winter, reckless and alone,
Till this reft house by frost, and thaw, and rain
Was sapped; and when she slept the nightly damps
Did chill her breast, and in the stormy day
485 Her tattered clothes were ruffled by the wind
Even at the side of her own fire. Yet still
She loved this wretched spot, nor would for worlds
Have parted hence; and still that length of road
And this rude bench one torturing hope endeared,
490 Fast rooted at her heart, and here, my friend,
In sickness she remained, and here she died,
Last human tenant of these ruined walls."
        The old Man ceased: he saw that I was mov'd;
From that low Bench, rising instinctively,
495 I turned aside in weakness, nor had power
To thank him for the tale which he had told.

I stood, and leaning o'er the garden-gate
Reviewed that Woman's suff'rings, and it seemed
To comfort me while with a brother's love
500 I blessed her in the impotence of grief.
At length [towards] the [Cottage I returned]⁵
Fondly, and traced with milder interest
That secret spirit of humanity
Which, 'mid the calm oblivious tendencies
505 Of nature, 'mid her plants, her weeds, and flowers,
And silent overgrowings, still survived.
The old man, seeing this, resumed and said,
"My Friend, enough to sorrow have you given,
The purposes of wisdom ask no more;
510 Be wise and chearful, and no longer read
The forms of things with an unworthy eye.
She sleeps in the calm earth, and peace is here.
I well remember that those very plumes,
Those weeds, and the high spear-grass on that wall,
515 By mist and silent rain-drops silver'd o'er,
As once I passed did to my heart convey
So still an image of tranquillity,
So calm and still, and looked so beautiful
Amid the uneasy thoughts which filled my mind,
520 That what we feel of sorrow and despair
From ruin and from change, and all the grief
The passing shews of being leave behind,
Appeared an idle dream that could not live
Where meditation was. I turned away
525 And walked along my road in happiness."
      He ceased. By this the sun declining shot
A slant and mellow radiance which began
To fall upon us where beneath the trees
We sate on that low bench, and now we felt,
530 Admonished thus, the sweet hour coming on.
A linnet warbled from those lofty elms,
A thrush sang loud, and other melodies,
At distance heard, peopled the milder air.
The old man rose and hoisted up his load.
535 Together casting then a farewell look
Upon those silent walls, we left the shade
And ere the stars were visible attained
A rustic inn, our evening resting-place.

THE END

1797–ca.1799   1949

---

5. The words inside the brackets were added in MS. E.

Michael[1]

A Pastoral Poem

If from the public way you turn your steps
Up the tumultuous brook of Green-head Ghyll,[2]
You will suppose that with an upright path
Your feet must struggle; in such bold ascent
5   The pastoral mountains front you, face to face.
But, courage! for around that boisterous brook
The mountains have all opened out themselves,
And made a hidden valley of their own.
No habitation can be seen; but they
10   Who journey thither find themselves alone
With a few sheep, with rocks and stones, and kites°   *hawks*
That overhead are sailing in the sky.
It is in truth an utter solitude;
Nor should I have made mention of this Dell
15   But for one object which you might pass by,
Might see and notice not. Beside the brook
Appears a straggling heap of unhewn stones!
And to that simple object appertains
A story—unenriched with strange events,
20   Yet not unfit, I deem, for the fireside,
Or for the summer shade. It was the first
Of those domestic tales that spake to me
Of Shepherds, dwellers in the valleys, men
Whom I already loved;—not verily
25   For their own sakes, but for the fields and hills
Where was their occupation and abode.
And hence this Tale, while I was yet a Boy
Careless of books, yet having felt the power
Of Nature, by the gentle agency
30   Of natural objects, led me on to feel
For passions that were not my own, and think
(At random and imperfectly indeed)
On man, the heart of man, and human life.
Therefore, although it be a history
35   Homely and rude, I will relate the same
For the delight of a few natural hearts;

1. This poem is founded on the actual misfortunes
of a family at Grasmere. For the account of the
sheepfold, see Dorothy Wordsworth's *Grasmere
Journals,* October 11, 1800 (p. 393). Wordsworth
wrote to Thomas Poole, on April 9, 1801, that he
had attempted to picture a man "agitated by two
of the most powerful affections of the human
heart; the parental affection, and the love of property, *landed* property, including the feelings of
inheritance, home, and personal and family independence." In another letter, sent, along with a
copy of the 1800 *Lyrical Ballads,* January 14, 1801,
to Charles James Fox, the leader of the opposition
in Parliament, Wordsworth commented in a similar vein on how a "little tract of land" could serve,
for the class of men whom he had represented in
"Michael," as "a kind of permanent rallying point
for their domestic feelings"; he also remarked,
with regret, that this class, "small independent *proprietors* of land," was "rapidly disappearing." The
subtitle shows Wordsworth's shift of the term "pastoral" from aristocratic make-believe to the tragic
suffering of people in what he called "humble and
rustic life."
2. A ravine forming the bed of a stream. Green-
head Ghyll is not far from Wordsworth's cottage at
Grasmere. The other places named in the poem are
also in that vicinity.

And, with yet fonder feeling, for the sake
Of youthful Poets, who among these hills
Will be my second self when I am gone.

40   Upon the forest-side in Grasmere Vale
There dwelt a Shepherd, Michael was his name;
An old man, stout of heart, and strong of limb.
His bodily frame had been from youth to age
Of an unusual strength: his mind was keen,
45 Intense, and frugal, apt for all affairs,
And in his shepherd's calling he was prompt
And watchful more than ordinary men.
Hence had he learned the meaning of all winds,
Of blasts of every tone; and, oftentimes,
50 When others heeded not, he heard the South°   *south wind*
Make subterraneous music, like the noise
Of bagpipers on distant Highland hills.
The Shepherd, at such warning, of his flock
Bethought him, and he to himself would say,
55 "The winds are now devising work for me!"
And, truly, at all times, the storm, that drives
The traveller to a shelter, summoned him
Up to the mountains: he had been alone
Amid the heart of many thousand mists,
60 That came to him, and left him, on the heights.
So lived he till his eightieth year was past.
And grossly that man errs, who should suppose
That the green valleys, and the streams and rocks,
Were things indifferent to the Shepherd's thoughts.
65 Fields, where with cheerful spirits he had breathed
The common air; hills, which with vigorous step
He had so often climbed; which had impressed
So many incidents upon his mind
Of hardship, skill or courage, joy or fear;
70 Which, like a book, preserved the memory
Of the dumb animals, whom he had saved,
Had fed or sheltered, linking to such acts
The certainty of honourable gain;
Those fields, those hills—what could they less? had laid
75 Strong hold on his affections, were to him
A pleasurable feeling of blind love,
The pleasure which there is in life itself.

    His days had not been passed in singleness.
His Helpmate was a comely matron, old—
80 Though younger than himself full twenty years.
She was a woman of a stirring life,
Whose heart was in her house: two wheels she had
Of antique form; this large, for spinning wool;
That small, for flax; and if one wheel had rest,
85 It was because the other was at work.
The Pair had but one inmate in their house,
An only Child, who had been born to them

When Michael, telling° o'er his years, began   *counting*
To deem that he was old,—in shepherd's phrase,
90   With one foot in the grave. This only Son,
With two brave sheep-dogs tried° in many a storm,   *tested*
The one of an inestimable worth,
Made all their household. I may truly say,
That they were as a proverb in the vale
95   For endless industry. When day was gone,
And from their occupations out of doors
The Son and Father were come home, even then,
Their labour did not cease; unless when all
Turned to the cleanly supper-board, and there,
100 Each with a mess of pottage and skimmed milk,
Sat round the basket piled with oaten cakes,
And their plain home-made cheese. Yet when the meal
Was ended, Luke (for so the Son was named)
And his old Father both betook themselves
105 To such convenient work as might employ
Their hands by the fire-side; perhaps to card
Wool for the Housewife's spindle, or repair
Some injury done to sickle, flail, or scythe,
Or other implement of house or field.

110   Down from the ceiling, by the chimney's edge,
That in our ancient uncouth country style
With huge and black projection overbrowed
Large space beneath, as duly as the light
Of day grew dim the Housewife hung a lamp;
115 An aged utensil, which had performed
Service beyond all others of its kind.
Early at evening did it burn—and late,
Surviving comrade of uncounted hours,
Which, going by from year to year, had found,
120 And left the couple neither gay perhaps
Nor cheerful, yet with objects and with hopes,
Living a life of eager industry.
And now, when Luke had reached his eighteenth year,
There by the light of his old lamp they sate,
125 Father and Son, while far into the night
The Housewife plied her own peculiar work,
Making the cottage through the silent hours
Murmur as with the sound of summer flies.
This light was famous in its neighbourhood,
130 And was a public symbol of the life
That thrifty Pair had lived. For, as it chanced,
Their cottage on a plot of rising ground
Stood single, with large prospect, north and south,
High into Easedale, up to Dunmail-Raise,
135 And westward to the village near the lake;
And from this constant light, so regular
And so far seen, the House itself, by all
Who dwelt within the limits of the vale,
Both old and young, was named THE EVENING STAR.

140   Thus living on through such a length of years,
The Shepherd, if he loved himself, must needs
Have loved his Helpmate; but to Michael's heart
This son of his old age was yet more dear—
Less from instinctive tenderness, the same
145 Fond spirit that blindly works in the blood of all—
Than that a child, more than all other gifts
That earth can offer to declining man,
Brings hope with it, and forward-looking thoughts,
And stirrings of inquietude, when they
150 By tendency of nature needs must fail.
Exceeding was the love he bare to him,
His heart and his heart's joy! For oftentimes
Old Michael, while he was a babe in arms,
Had done him female service, not alone
155 For pastime and delight, as is the use
Of fathers, but with patient mind enforced
To acts of tenderness; and he had rocked
His cradle, as with a woman's gentle hand.

    And, in a later time, ere yet the Boy
160 Had put on boy's attire, did Michael love,
Albeit of a stern unbending mind,
To have the Young-one in his sight, when he
Wrought in the field, or on his shepherd's stool
Sate with a fettered sheep before him stretched
165 Under the large old oak, that near his door
Stood single, and, from matchless depth of shade,
Chosen for the Shearer's covert from the sun,
Thence in our rustic dialect was called
The Clipping Tree, a name which yet it bears.
170 There, while they two were sitting in the shade,
With others round them, earnest all and blithe,
Would Michael exercise his heart with looks
Of fond correction and reproof bestowed
Upon the Child, if he disturbed the sheep
175 By catching at their legs, or with his shouts
Scared them, while they lay still beneath the shears.

    And when by Heaven's good grace the boy grew up
A healthy Lad, and carried in his cheek
Two steady roses that were five years old;
180 Then Michael from a winter coppice[3] cut
With his own hand a sapling, which he hooped
With iron, making it throughout in all
Due requisites a perfect shepherd's staff,
And gave it to the Boy; wherewith equipt
185 He as a watchman oftentimes was placed
At gate or gap, to stem or turn the flock;
And, to his office prematurely called,
There stood the urchin, as you will divine,

3. Grove of small trees.

Something between a hindrance and a help;
190 And for this cause not always, I believe,
    Receiving from his Father hire° of praise;   *wages*
Though nought was left undone which staff, or voice,
Or looks, or threatening gestures, could perform.

But soon as Luke, full ten years old, could stand
195 Against the mountain blasts; and to the heights,
Not fearing toil, nor length of weary ways,
He with his Father daily went, and they
Were as companions, why should I relate
That objects which the Shepherd loved before
200 Were dearer now? that from the Boy there came
Feelings and emanations—things which were
Light to the sun and music to the wind;
And that the old Man's heart seemed born again?

Thus in his Father's sight the Boy grew up:
205 And now, when he had reached his eighteenth year,
He was his comfort and his daily hope.

While in this sort the simple household lived
From day to day, to Michael's ear there came
Distressful tidings. Long before the time
210 Of which I speak, the Shepherd had been bound
In surety for his brother's son, a man
Of an industrious life, and ample means;
But unforeseen misfortunes suddenly
Had prest upon him; and old Michael now
215 Was summoned to discharge the forfeiture,
A grievous penalty, but little less
Than half his substance.[4] This unlooked-for claim,
At the first hearing, for a moment took
More hope out of his life than he supposed
220 That any old man ever could have lost.
As soon as he had armed himself with strength
To look his trouble in the face, it seemed
The Shepherd's sole resource to sell at once
A portion of his patrimonial fields.
225 Such was his first resolve; he thought again,
And his heart failed him. "Isabel," said he,
Two evenings after he had heard the news,
"I have been toiling more than seventy years,
And in the open sunshine of God's love
230 Have we all lived; yet if these fields of ours
Should pass into a stranger's hand, I think
That I could not lie quiet in my grave.
Our lot is a hard lot; the sun himself
Has scarcely been more diligent than I;
235 And I have lived to be a fool at last

4. Michael has guaranteed a loan for his nephew and now has lost the collateral, which amounts to half
his financial worth.

To my own family. An evil man
That was, and made an evil choice, if he
Were false to us; and if he were not false,
There are ten thousand to whom loss like this
240 Had been no sorrow. I forgive him;—but
'Twere better to be dumb than to talk thus.

    "When I began, my purpose was to speak
Of remedies and of a cheerful hope.
Our Luke shall leave us, Isabel; the land
245 Shall not go from us, and it shall be free;°   *unmortgaged*
He shall possess it, free as is the wind
That passes over it. We have, thou know'st,
Another kinsman—he will be our friend
In this distress. He is a prosperous man,
250 Thriving in trade—and Luke to him shall go,
And with his kinsman's help and his own thrift
He quickly will repair this loss, and then
He may return to us. If here he stay,
What can be done? Where every one is poor,
What can be gained?"
255   At this the old Man paused,
And Isabel sat silent, for her mind
Was busy, looking back into past times.
There's Richard Bateman,[5] thought she to herself,
He was a parish-boy[6]—at the church-door
260 They made a gathering for him, shillings, pence
And halfpennies, wherewith the neighbours bought
A basket, which they filled with pedlar's wares;
And, with this basket on his arm, the lad
Went up to London, found a master there,
265 Who, out of many, chose the trusty boy
To go and overlook his merchandise
Beyond the seas; where he grew wondrous rich,
And left estates and monies to the poor,
And, at his birth-place, built a chapel floored
270 With marble, which he sent from foreign lands.
These thoughts, and many others of like sort,
Passed quickly through the mind of Isabel,
And her face brightened. The old Man was glad,
And thus resumed:—"Well, Isabel! this scheme
275 These two days, has been meat and drink to me.
Far more than we have lost is left us yet.
—We have enough—I wish indeed that I
Were younger;—but this hope is a good hope.
Make ready Luke's best garments, of the best
280 Buy for him more, and let us send him forth
To-morrow, or the next day, or to-night:
—If he *could* go, the Boy should go to-night."

5. The story alluded to here is well known in the country. The chapel is called Ings Chapel and is on the road leading from Kendal to Ambleside [Wordsworth's note, 1802–05].

6. A poor boy supported financially by the poor rates (taxes) paid out by the wealthier members of his parish.

Here Michael ceased, and to the fields went forth
With a light heart. The Housewife for five days
285   Was restless morn and night, and all day long
Wrought on with her best fingers to prepare
Things needful for the journey of her son.
But Isabel was glad when Sunday came
To stop her in her work: for, when she lay
290   By Michael's side, she through the last two nights
Heard him, how he was troubled in his sleep:
And when they rose at morning she could see
That all his hopes were gone. That day at noon
She said to Luke, while they two by themselves
295   Were sitting at the door, "Thou must not go:
We have no other Child but thee to lose,
None to remember—do not go away,
For if thou leave thy Father he will die."
The Youth made answer with a jocund voice;
300   And Isabel, when she had told her fears,
Recovered heart. That evening her best fare
Did she bring forth, and all together sat
Like happy people round a Christmas fire.

With daylight Isabel resumed her work;
305   And all the ensuing week the house appeared
As cheerful as a grove in Spring: at length
The expected letter from their kinsman came,
With kind assurances that he would do
His utmost for the welfare of the Boy;
310   To which, requests were added, that forthwith
He might be sent to him. Ten times or more
The letter was read over; Isabel
Went forth to show it to the neighbours round;
Nor was there at that time on English land
315   A prouder heart than Luke's. When Isabel
Had to her house returned, the old Man said,
"He shall depart to-morrow." To this word
The Housewife answered, talking much of things
Which, if at such short notice he should go,
320   Would surely be forgotten. But at length
She gave consent, and Michael was at ease.

Near the tumultuous brook of Green-head Ghyll,
In that deep valley, Michael had designed
To build a Sheep-fold;[7] and, before he heard
325   The tidings of his melancholy loss,
For this same purpose he had gathered up
A heap of stones, which by the streamlet's edge
Lay thrown together, ready for the work.
With Luke that evening thitherward he walked:
330   And soon as they had reached the place he stopped,
And thus the old Man spake to him:—"My Son,

7. A sheepfold [pen for sheep] in these mountains is an unroofed building of stone walls, with different divisions [Wordsworth's note, 1802–05].

To-morrow thou wilt leave me: with full heart
I look upon thee, for thou art the same
That wert a promise to me ere thy birth,
335   And all thy life hast been my daily joy.
I will relate to thee some little part
Of our two histories; 'twill do thee good
When thou art from me, even if I should touch
On things thou canst not know of.——After thou
340   First cam'st into the world—as oft befals
To new-born infants—thou didst sleep away
Two days, and blessings from thy Father's tongue
Then fell upon thee. Day by day passed on,
And still I loved thee with increasing love.
345   Never to living ear came sweeter sounds
Than when I heard thee by our own fire-side
First uttering, without words, a natural tune;
While thou, a feeding babe, didst in thy joy
Sing at thy Mother's breast. Month followed month,
350   And in the open fields my life was passed
And on the mountains; else I think that thou
Hadst been brought up upon thy Father's knees.
But we were playmates, Luke: among these hills,
As well thou knowest, in us the old and young
355   Have played together, nor with me didst thou
Lack any pleasure which a boy can know."
Luke had a manly heart; but at these words
He sobbed aloud. The old Man grasped his hand,
And said, "Nay, do not take it so—I see
360   That these are things of which I need not speak.
—Even to the utmost I have been to thee
A kind and a good Father: and herein
I but repay a gift which I myself
Received at others' hands; for, though now old
365   Beyond the common life of man, I still
Remember them who loved me in my youth.
Both of them sleep together: here they lived,
As all their Forefathers had done; and when
At length their time was come, they were not loth
370   To give their bodies to the family mould.°   grave plot
I wished that thou should'st live the life they lived:
But, 'tis a long time to look back, my Son,
And see so little gain from threescore years.
These fields were burthened° when they came to me;   mortgaged
375   Till I was forty years of age, not more
Than half of my inheritance was mine.
I toiled and toiled; God blessed me in my work,
And till these three weeks past the land was free.
—It looks as if it never could endure
380   Another Master. Heaven forgive me, Luke,
If I judge ill for thee, but it seems good
That thou should'st go."
                              At this the old Man paused;
Then, pointing to the stones near which they stood,
Thus, after a short silence, he resumed:

385 "This was a work for us; and now, my Son,
It is a work for me. But, lay one stone—
Here, lay it for me, Luke, with thine own hands.
Nay, Boy, be of good hope;—we both may live
To see a better day. At eighty-four
390 I still am strong and hale;—do thou thy part;
I will do mine.—I will begin again
With many tasks that were resigned to thee:
Up to the heights, and in among the storms,
Will I without thee go again, and do
395 All works which I was wont to do alone,
Before I knew thy face.—Heaven bless thee, Boy!
Thy heart these two weeks has been beating fast
With many hopes; it should be so—yes—yes—
I knew that thou could'st never have a wish
400 To leave me, Luke: thou hast been bound to me
Only by links of love: when thou art gone,
What will be left to us!—But, I forget
My purposes. Lay now the corner-stone,
As I requested; and hereafter, Luke,
405 When thou art gone away, should evil men
Be thy companions, think of me, my Son,
And of this moment; hither turn thy thoughts,
And God will strengthen thee: amid all fear
And all temptation, Luke, I pray that thou
410 May'st bear in mind the life thy Fathers lived,
Who, being innocent, did for that cause
Bestir them in good deeds. Now, fare thee well—
When thou return'st, thou in this place wilt see
A work which is not here: a covenant
415 'Twill be between us; but, whatever fate
Befal thee, I shall love thee to the last,
And bear thy memory with me to the grave."

The Shepherd ended here; and Luke stooped down,
And, as his Father had requested, laid
420 The first stone of the Sheep-fold. At the sight
The old Man's grief broke from him; to his heart
He pressed his Son, he kissèd him and wept;
And to the house together they returned.
—Hushed was that House in peace, or seeming peace,
425 Ere the night fell:—with morrow's dawn the Boy
Began his journey, and when he had reached
The public way, he put on a bold face;
And all the neighbours, as he passed their doors,
Came forth with wishes and with farewell prayers,
430 That followed him till he was out of sight.

A good report did from their Kinsman come,
Of Luke and his well-doing: and the Boy
Wrote loving letters, full of wondrous news,
Which, as the Housewife phrased it, were throughout
435 "The prettiest letters that were ever seen."

Both parents read them with rejoicing hearts.
So, many months passed on: and once again
The Shepherd went about his daily work
With confident and cheerful thoughts; and now
440 Sometimes when he could find a leisure hour
He to that valley took his way, and there
Wrought at the Sheep-fold. Meantime Luke began
To slacken in his duty; and, at length,
He in the dissolute city gave himself
445 To evil courses: ignominy and shame
Fell on him, so that he was driven at last
To seek a hiding-place beyond the seas.

There is a comfort in the strength of love;
'Twill make a thing endurable, which else
450 Would overset the brain, or break the heart:
I have conversed with more than one who well
Remember the old Man, and what he was
Years after he had heard this heavy news.
His bodily frame had been from youth to age
455 Of an unusual strength. Among the rocks
He went, and still looked up to sun and cloud,
And listened to the wind; and, as before
Performed all kinds of labour for his sheep,
And for the land, his small inheritance.
460 And to that hollow dell from time to time
Did he repair, to build the Fold of which
His flock had need. 'Tis not forgotten yet
The pity which was then in every heart
For the old Man—and 'tis believed by all
465 That many and many a day he thither went,
And never lifted up a single stone.

There, by the Sheep-fold, sometimes was he seen
Sitting alone, or with his faithful Dog,
Then old, beside him, lying at his feet.
470 The length of full seven years, from time to time,
He at the building of this Sheep-fold wrought,
And left the work unfinished when he died.
Three years, or little more, did Isabel
Survive her Husband: at her death the estate
475 Was sold, and went into a stranger's hand.
The Cottage which was named the EVENING STAR
Is gone—the ploughshare has been through the ground
On which it stood;[8] great changes have been wrought
In all the neighbourhood:—yet the oak is left
480 That grew beside their door; and the remains
Of the unfinished Sheep-fold may be seen
Beside the boisterous brook of Green-head Ghyll.

Oct. 11–Dec. 9, 1800   1800

---

8. The land on which Michael's sheep had grazed has been turned over to cultivation.

Resolution and Independence[1]

1

There was a roaring in the wind all night;
The rain came heavily and fell in floods;
But now the sun is rising calm and bright;
The birds are singing in the distant woods;
5 Over his own sweet voice the Stock-dove broods;
The Jay makes answer as the Magpie chatters;
And all the air is filled with pleasant noise of waters.

2

All things that love the sun are out of doors;
The sky rejoices in the morning's birth;
10 The grass is bright with rain-drops;—on the moors
The hare is running races in her mirth;
And with her feet she from the plashy earth
Raises a mist; that, glittering in the sun,
Runs with her all the way, wherever she doth run.

3

15 I was a Traveller then upon the moor;
I saw the hare that raced about with joy;
I heard the woods and distant waters roar;
Or heard them not, as happy as a boy:
The pleasant season did my heart employ:
20 My old remembrances went from me wholly;
And all the ways of men, so vain and melancholy.

4

But, as it sometimes chanceth, from the might
Of joy in minds that can no further go,
As high as we have mounted in delight
25 In our dejection do we sink as low;
To me that morning did it happen so;
And fears and fancies thick upon me came;
Dim sadness—and blind thoughts, I knew not, nor could name.

5

I heard the sky-lark warbling in the sky;
30 And I bethought me of the playful hare:
Even such a happy Child of earth am I;
Even as these blissful creatures do I fare;
Far from the world I walk, and from all care;
But there may come another day to me—
35 Solitude, pain of heart, distress, and poverty.

1. For the meeting with the old leech gatherer, see
Dorothy Wordsworth's *Grasmere Journals*, October
3, 1800 (p. 393). Wordsworth himself tells us, in
a note of 1843, that "I was in the state of feeling
described in the beginning of the poem, while
crossing over Barton Fell from Mr. Clarkson's, at
the foot of Ullswater, towards Askam. The image
of the hare I then observed on the ridge of the
Fell." He wrote the poem eighteen months after
this event (see *Grasmere Journals*, May 4 and 7,
1802; pp. 398 and 400).

6

My whole life I have lived in pleasant thought,
As if life's business were a summer mood;
As if all needful things would come unsought
To genial° faith, still rich in genial good;   *creative*
40 But how can He expect that others should
Build for him, sow for him, and at his call
Love him, who for himself will take no heed at all?

7

I thought of Chatterton,[2] the marvellous Boy,
The sleepless Soul that perished in his pride;
45 Of Him[3] who walked in glory and in joy
Following his plough, along the mountain-side:
By our own spirits are we deified:
We Poets in our youth begin in gladness;
But thereof come in the end despondency and madness.

8

50 Now, whether it were by peculiar grace,
A leading from above, a something given,
Yet it befel, that, in this lonely place,
When I with these untoward thoughts had striven,
Beside a pool bare to the eye of heaven
55 I saw a Man before me unawares:
The oldest man he seemed that ever wore grey hairs.

9

As a huge stone is sometimes seen to lie
Couched on the bald top of an eminence;
Wonder to all who do the same espy,
60 By what means it could thither come, and whence;
So that it seems a thing endued with sense:
Like a sea-beast crawled forth, that on a shelf
Of rock or sand reposeth, there to sun itself;

10

Such seemed this Man,[4] not all alive nor dead,
65 Nor all asleep—in his extreme old age:
His body was bent double, feet and head
Coming together in life's pilgrimage;

---

2. After his early death through drug overdose, a death believed by many to have been a suicide, the poet Thomas Chatterton (1752–1770) became a prime symbol of neglected boy genius for the Romantics. He came to public attention in his hometown of Bristol in the West of England as the discoverer of the long-lost manuscripts of a local 15th-century monk named "Thomas Rowley." Rowley's works—in fact Chatterton's own inventions—included many poems. His pseudo-Chaucerian "An Excelente Balade of Charitie" used the rhyme royal stanza form that Wordsworth employs here. Reports of the frustrations that Chatterton experienced in his attempts to interest the London literary establishment in such "discoveries" provided the seed for that Romantic myth-making in which Wordsworth, Coleridge, and Keats participated.

3. Robert Burns, here considered, as Chatterton is, a natural poet who died young and poor, without adequate recognition, and who seemed to have hastened his death through dissipation.

4. In Wordsworth's analysis of this passage he says that the stone is endowed with something of life, the sea beast is stripped of some of its life to assimilate it to the stone, and the old man divested of enough life and motion to make "the two objects unite and coalesce in just comparison." He used the passage to demonstrate his theory of how the "conferring, the abstracting, and the modifying powers of the Imagination . . . are all brought into conjunction" (Preface to the *Poems* of 1815). Cf. Coleridge's brief definitions of the imagination in *Biographia Literaria*, chap. 13 (p. 477).

As if some dire constraint of pain, or rage
Of sickness felt by him in times long past,
70 A more than human weight upon his frame had cast.

11

Himself he propped, limbs, body, and pale face,
Upon a long grey staff of shaven wood:
And, still as I drew near with gentle pace,
Upon the margin of that moorish flood
75 Motionless as a cloud the old Man stood,
That heareth not the loud winds when they call;
And moveth all together, if it move at all.

12

At length, himself unsettling, he the pond
Stirred with his staff, and fixedly did look
80 Upon the muddy water, which he conned,°   studied
As if he had been reading in a book:
And now a stranger's privilege I took;
And, drawing to his side, to him did say,
"This morning gives us promise of a glorious day."

13

85 A gentle answer did the old Man make,
In courteous speech which forth he slowly drew:
And him with further words I thus bespake,
"What occupation do you there pursue?
This is a lonesome place for one like you."
90 Ere he replied, a flash of mild surprise
Broke from the sable orbs of his yet-vivid eyes.

14

His words came feebly, from a feeble chest,
But each in solemn order followed each,
With something of a lofty utterance drest—
95 Choice word and measured phrase, above the reach
Of ordinary men; a stately speech;
Such as grave Livers⁵ do in Scotland use,
Religious men, who give to God and man their dues.

15

He told, that to these waters he had come
100 To gather leeches,⁶ being old and poor:
Employment hazardous and wearisome!
And he had many hardships to endure:
From pond to pond he roamed, from moor to moor;
Housing, with God's good help, by choice or chance;
105 And in this way he gained an honest maintenance.

16

The old Man still stood talking by my side;
But now his voice to me was like a stream

5. Those who live gravely (as opposed to "loose livers," those who live for a life of pleasure).
6. Used by medical attendants to draw their patients' blood for curative purposes. A leech gath-

erer, bare legged in shallow water, stirred the water to attract them and, when they fastened themselves to his legs, picked them off.

Scarce heard; nor word from word could I divide;
And the whole body of the Man did seem
110 Like one whom I had met with in a dream;
Or like a man from some far region sent,
To give me human strength, by apt admonishment.

17

My former thoughts returned: the fear that kills;
And hope that is unwilling to be fed;
115 Cold, pain, and labour, and all fleshly ills;
And mighty Poets in their misery dead.
—Perplexed, and longing to be comforted,
My question eagerly did I renew,
"How is it that you live, and what is it you do?"

18

120 He with a smile did then his words repeat;
And said, that, gathering leeches, far and wide
He travelled; stirring thus about his feet
The waters of the pools where they abide.
"Once I could meet with them on every side;
125 But they have dwindled long by slow decay;
Yet still I persevere, and find them where I may."

19

While he was talking thus, the lonely place,
The old Man's shape, and speech—all troubled me:
In my mind's eye I seemed to see him pace
130 About the weary moors continually,
Wandering about alone and silently.
While I these thoughts within myself pursued,
He, having made a pause, the same discourse renewed.

20

And soon with this he other matter blended,
135 Cheerfully uttered, with demeanour kind,
But stately in the main; and when he ended,
I could have laughed myself to scorn to find
In that decrepit Man so firm a mind.
"God," said I, "be my help and stay[7] secure;
140 I'll think of the Leech-gatherer on the lonely moor!"

May 3–July 4, 1802   1807

I wandered lonely as a cloud[1]

I wandered lonely as a cloud
That floats on high o'er vales and hills,
When all at once I saw a crowd,

7. Support (a noun).
1. For the original experience, two years earlier, see Dorothy Wordsworth's *Grasmere Journals*, April 15, 1802 (p. 396).

A host, of golden daffodils;
5 Beside the lake, beneath the trees,
Fluttering and dancing in the breeze.

Continuous as the stars that shine
And twinkle on the milky way,
They stretched in never-ending line
10 Along the margin of a bay:
Ten thousand saw I at a glance,
Tossing their heads in sprightly dance.

The waves beside them danced; but they
Out-did the sparkling waves in glee:
15 A poet could not but be gay,
In such a jocund company:
I gazed—and gazed—but little thought
What wealth the show to me had brought:

For oft, when on my couch I lie
20 In vacant or in pensive mood,
They flash upon that inward eye
Which is the bliss of solitude;
And then my heart with pleasure fills,
And dances with the daffodils.

1804   1807

✗ My heart leaps up

My heart leaps up when I behold
A rainbow in the sky:
So was it when my life began;
So is it now I am a man;
5 So be it when I shall grow old,
Or let me die!
The Child is father of the Man;
And I could wish my days to be
Bound each to each by natural piety.[1]

Mar. 26, 1802   1807

✗ Ode: Intimations of Immortality   In 1843 Wordsworth said about this
Ode to Isabella Fenwick:

This was composed during my residence at Town End, Grasmere; two years at
least passed between the writing of the four first stanzas and the remaining part.
To the attentive and competent reader the whole sufficiently explains itself; but

1. Perhaps as distinguished from piety based on the Bible, in which the rainbow is the token of God's
promise to Noah and his descendants never again to send a flood to destroy the earth.

there may be no harm in adverting here to particular feelings or *experiences* of my own mind on which the structure of the poem partly rests. Nothing was more difficult for me in childhood than to admit the notion of death as a state applicable to my own being. I have said elsewhere [in the opening stanza of "We Are Seven"]:

> —A simple child,
> That lightly draws its breath,
> And feels its life in every limb,
> What should it know of death!—

But it was not so much from [feelings] of animal vivacity that *my* difficulty came as from a sense of the indomitableness of the spirit within me. I used to brood over the stories of Enoch and Elijah [Genesis 5.22–24; 2 Kings 2.11], and almost to persuade myself that, whatever might become of others, I should be translated, in something of the same way, to heaven. With a feeling congenial to this, I was often unable to think of external things as having external existence, and I communed with all that I saw as something not apart from, but inherent in, my own immaterial nature. Many times while going to school have I grasped at a wall or tree to recall myself from this abyss of idealism to the reality. At that time I was afraid of such processes. In later periods of life I have deplored, as we have all reason to do, a subjugation of an opposite character, and have rejoiced over the remembrances, as is expressed in the lines—

> Obstinate questionings
> Of sense and outward things,
> Fallings from us, vanishings; etc.

To that dreamlike vividness and splendor which invest objects of sight in childhood, everyone, I believe, if he would look back, could bear testimony, and I need not dwell upon it here: but having in the Poem regarded it as presumptive evidence of a prior state of existence, I think it right to protest against a conclusion, which has given pain to some good and pious persons, that I meant to inculcate such a belief. It is far too shadowy a notion to be recommended to faith, as more than an element in our instincts of immortality. * * * [W]hen I was impelled to write this Poem on the 'Immortality of the Soul,' I took hold of the notion of pre-existence as having sufficient foundation in humanity for authorizing me to make for my purpose the best use of it I could as a Poet.

When he dictated this long note to Isabella Fenwick, at the age of seventy-two or seventy-three, Wordsworth was troubled by objections that his apparent claim for the preexistence of the soul violated the Christian belief that the soul, although it survives after death, does not exist before the birth of an individual. His claim in the note is that he refers to the preexistence of the soul not in order to set out a religious doctrine but only so as to deal "as a Poet" with a common human experience: that the passing of youth involves the loss of a freshness and radiance investing everything one sees. Coleridge's "Dejection: An Ode," which he wrote (in its earliest version) after he had heard the first four stanzas of Wordsworth's poem, employs a similar figurative technique for a comparable, though more devastating, experience of loss.

The original published text of this poem (in 1807) had as its title only "Ode," and then as epigraph *"Paulo maiora canamus"* (Latin for "Let us sing of somewhat higher things") from Virgil's *Eclogue 4.*

✹ Ode

Intimations of Immortality from Recollections of Early Childhood

The Child is Father of the Man;
And I could wish my days to be
Bound each to each by natural piety.[1]

1

There was a time when meadow, grove, and stream,
The earth, and every common sight,
    To me did seem
    Apparelled in celestial light,
5   The glory and the freshness of a dream.
It is not now as it hath been of yore;—
    Turn wheresoe'er I may,
    By night or day,
The things which I have seen I now can see no more.

2

10   The Rainbow comes and goes,
      And lovely is the Rose,
      The Moon doth with delight
Look round her when the heavens are bare,
    Waters on a starry night
15   Are beautiful and fair;
    The sunshine is a glorious birth;
But yet I know, where'er I go,
That there hath past away a glory from the earth.

3

   Now, while the birds thus sing a joyous song,
20   And while the young lambs bound
     As to the tabor's[2] sound,
To me alone there came a thought of grief:
A timely utterance[3] gave that thought relief,
   And I again am strong:
25 The cataracts blow their trumpets from the steep;
No more shall grief of mine the season wrong;
I hear the Echoes through the mountains throng,
The Winds come to me from the fields of sleep,[4]
    And all the earth is gay;
30   Land and sea
    Give themselves up to jollity,
    And with the heart of May
   Doth every Beast keep holiday;—
     Thou Child of Joy,
35 Shout round me, let me hear thy shouts, thou happy
    Shepherd-boy!

---

1. The concluding lines of Wordsworth's "My heart leaps up" (p. 306).
2. A small drum often used to beat time for dancing.
3. Perhaps "My heart leaps up," perhaps "Resolution and Independence," perhaps not a poem at all.
4. Of the many suggested interpretations, the simplest is "from the fields where they were sleeping." Wordsworth often associated a rising wind with the revival of spirit and of poetic inspiration (see, e.g., the opening passage of *The Prelude,* p. 324).

4

Ye blessed Creatures, I have heard the call
    Ye to each other make; I see
The heavens laugh with you in your jubilee;
    My heart is at your festival,
40   My head hath its coronal,[5]
The fulness of your bliss, I feel—I feel it all.
    Oh evil day! if I were sullen
    While Earth herself is adorning,
      This sweet May-morning,
45   And the Children are culling
        On every side,
    In a thousand valleys far and wide,
    Fresh flowers; while the sun shines warm,
And the Babe leaps up on his Mother's arm:—
50   I hear, I hear, with joy I hear!
    —But there's a Tree, of many, one,
A single Field which I have looked upon,
Both of them speak of something that is gone:
      The Pansy at my feet
55   Doth the same tale repeat:
Whither is fled the visionary gleam?
Where is it now, the glory and the dream?

5

Our birth is but a sleep and a forgetting:
The Soul that rises with us, our life's Star,[6]
60   Hath had elsewhere its setting,
        And cometh from afar:
    Not in entire forgetfulness,
    And not in utter nakedness,
But trailing clouds of glory do we come
65   From God, who is our home:
Heaven lies about us in our infancy!
Shades of the prison-house begin to close
      Upon the growing Boy,
But He beholds the light, and whence it flows,
70   He sees it in his joy;
The Youth, who daily farther from the east
    Must travel, still is Nature's Priest,
    And by the vision splendid
    Is on his way attended;
75 At length the Man perceives it die away,
And fade into the light of common day.

6

Earth fills her lap with pleasures of her own;
Yearnings she hath in her own natural kind,
And, even with something of a Mother's mind,
80   And no unworthy aim,
    The homely[7] Nurse doth all she can

---

5. Circlet of wildflowers, with which the shepherd boys trimmed their hats in May.

6. The sun, as metaphor for the soul.
7. In the old sense: simple and friendly.

To make her Foster-child, her Inmate Man,
        Forget the glories he hath known,
And that imperial palace whence he came.

7

85 Behold the Child among his new-born blisses,
A six years' Darling of a pigmy size!
See, where 'mid work of his own hand he lies,
Fretted[8] by sallies of his mother's kisses,
With light upon him from his father's eyes!
90 See, at his feet, some little plan or chart,
Some fragment from his dream of human life,
Shaped by himself with newly-learnèd art;
        ⎧ A wedding or a festival, ⎫
        ⎩ A mourning or a funeral; ⎭
95   And this hath now his heart,
        And unto this he frames his song:
        Then will he fit his tongue
To dialogues of business, love, or strife;
        But it will not be long
100   Ere this be thrown aside,
        And with new joy and pride
The little Actor cons° another part;   studies
Filling from time to time his "humorous stage"[9]
With all the Persons, down to palsied Age,
105 That Life brings with her in her equipage;
        As if his whole vocation
        Were endless imitation.

8

Thou, whose exterior semblance doth belie
        Thy Soul's immensity;
110 Thou best Philosopher, who yet dost keep
Thy heritage, thou Eye among the blind,
That, deaf and silent, read'st the eternal deep,
Haunted for ever by the eternal mind,—
        Mighty Prophet! Seer blest!
115   On whom those truths do rest,
Which we are toiling all our lives to find,
In darkness lost, the darkness of the grave;
Thou, over whom thy Immortality
Broods like the Day, a Master o'er a Slave,
120 A Presence which is not to be put by;
Thou little Child, yet glorious in the might
Of heaven-born freedom on thy being's height,
Why with such earnest pains dost thou provoke
The years to bring the inevitable yoke,
125 Thus blindly with thy blessedness at strife?
Full soon thy Soul shall have her earthly freight,
And custom lie upon thee with a weight,
Heavy as frost, and deep almost as life!

8. Irritated; or possibly in the old sense: checkered over.
9. From a sonnet by the Elizabethan poet Samuel Daniel. In Daniel's era *humorous* meant "capri-cious" and also referred to the various characters and temperaments ("humors") represented in drama.

9

O joy! that in our embers

130   Is something that doth live,

That nature yet remembers

What was so fugitive!°   *fleeting*

The thought of our past years in me doth breed

Perpetual benediction: not indeed

135   For that which is most worthy to be blest;

Delight and liberty, the simple creed

Of Childhood, whether busy or at rest,

With new-fledged hope still fluttering in his breast:—

Not for these I raise

140   The song of thanks and praise;

But for those obstinate questionings

Of sense and outward things,

Fallings from us, vanishings;

Blank misgivings of a Creature

145   Moving about in worlds not realised,[1]

High instincts before which our mortal Nature

Did tremble like a guilty Thing surprised:

But for those first affections,

Those shadowy recollections,

150   Which, be they what they may,

Are yet the fountain light of all our day,

Are yet a master light of all our seeing;

Uphold us, cherish, and have power to make

Our noisy years seem moments in the being

155   Of the eternal Silence: truths that wake,

To perish never;

Which neither listlessness, nor mad endeavour,

Nor Man nor Boy,

Nor all that is at enmity with joy,

160   Can utterly abolish or destroy!

Hence in a season of calm weather

Though inland far we be,

Our Souls have sight of that immortal sea

Which brought us hither,

165   Can in a moment travel thither,

And see the Children sport upon the shore,

And hear the mighty waters rolling evermore.

10

Then sing, ye Birds, sing, sing a joyous song!

And let the young Lambs bound

170   As to the tabor's sound!

We in thought will join your throng,

Ye that pipe and ye that play,

Ye that through your hearts to-day

Feel the gladness of the May!

175   What though the radiance which was once so bright

Be now for ever taken from my sight,

Though nothing can bring back the hour

1. Not seeming real (see Wordsworth's comment about "this abyss of idealism" in the headnote on p. 306).

Of splendour in the grass, of glory in the flower;
We will grieve not, rather find
180 Strength in what remains behind;
In the primal sympathy
Which having been must ever be;
In the soothing thoughts that spring
Out of human suffering;
185 In the faith that looks through death,
In years that bring the philosophic mind.

11

And O, ye Fountains, Meadows, Hills, and Groves,
Forebode° not any severing of our loves!   *predict, portend*
Yet in my heart of hearts I feel your might;
190 I only have relinquished one delight
To live beneath your more habitual sway.
I love the Brooks which down their channels fret,
Even more than when I tripped lightly as they;
The innocent brightness of a new-born Day
195   Is lovely yet;
The Clouds that gather round the setting sun
Do take a sober colouring from an eye
That hath kept watch o'er man's mortality;
Another race hath been, and other palms are won.[2]
200 Thanks to the human heart by which we live,
Thanks to its tenderness, its joys, and fears,
To me the meanest flower that blows can give
Thoughts that do often lie too deep for tears.

1802–04   1807

Ode to Duty[1]

*Jam non consilio bonus, sed more eo perductus, ut non tantum recte
facere possim, sed nisi recte facere non possim.*[2]

Stern Daughter of the Voice of God![3]
O Duty! if that name thou love

2. In Greece foot races were often run for the prize of a branch or wreath of palm. Wordsworth's line echoes Paul, 1 Corinthians 9.24, who uses such races as a metaphor for life: "Know ye not that they which run in a race run all, but one receiveth the prize?"

1. This Ode . . . is on the model of Gray's "Ode to Adversity" which is copied from Horace's "Ode to Fortune." Many and many a time have I been twitted by my wife and sister for having forgotten this dedication of myself to the stern lawgiver [Wordsworth's note, 1843].
In this poem, a striking departure from his earlier forms and ideas. Wordsworth abandons the descriptive-meditative pattern of his "Tintern Abbey" and "Ode: Intimations of Immortality." Where in the Preface to *Lyrical Ballads* of 1802 he had both disparaged the 18th-century poet

Thomas Gray and rejected the personifications that were customary in 18th-century poetry, Wordsworth here reverts to a standard 18th-century form, an ode addressed to a personified abstraction.
2. Now I am not good by conscious intent, but have been so trained by habit that I not only can act rightly but am unable to act other than rightly (Latin). Added in 1837, this epigraph is an adaptation from *Moral Epistles* 120.10 by Seneca (4 B.C.E.–65 C.E.), Stoic philosopher and writer of tragedies.
3. Cf. Milton's *Paradise Lost* 9.652–54. Eve for a moment resists the serpent's recommendation of the forbidden fruit by stating, "God so commanded, and left that Command / Sole Daughter of his voice; the rest, we live / Law to ourselves, our Reason is our Law."

Who art a light to guide, a rod
To check the erring, and reprove;
5   Thou, who art victory and law
When empty terrors overawe;
From vain temptations dost set free;
And calm'st the weary strife of frail humanity!

There are who ask not if thine eye
10   Be on them; who, in love and truth,
Where no misgiving is, rely
Upon the genial sense[4] of youth:
Glad Hearts! without reproach or blot;
Who do thy work, and know it not:
15   Oh! if through confidence misplaced
They fail, thy saving arms, dread Power! around them cast.

Serene will be our days and bright,
And happy will our nature be,
When love is an unerring light,
20   And joy its own security.
And they a blissful course may hold
Even now, who, not unwisely bold,
Live in the spirit of this creed;
Yet seek thy firm support, according to their need.

25   I, loving freedom, and untried;
No sport of every random gust,
Yet being to myself a guide,
Too blindly have reposed my trust:
And oft, when in my heart was heard
30   Thy timely mandate, I deferred
The task, in smoother walks to stray;
But thee I now would serve more strictly, if I may.

Through no disturbance of my soul,
Or strong compunction[5] in me wrought,
35   I supplicate for thy control;
But in the quietness of thought:
Me this unchartered freedom tires;
I feel the weight of chance-desires:
My hopes no more must change their name,
40   I long for a repose that ever is the same.

Stern Lawgiver! yet thou dost wear
The Godhead's most benignant grace;
Nor know we any thing so fair
As is the smile upon thy face:
45   Flowers laugh before thee on their beds
And fragrance in thy footing treads;

---

4. Innate vitality.
5. In the older sense: sting of conscience, or remorse.

Thou dost preserve the stars from wrong;
And the most ancient heavens, through Thee, are fresh and strong.

To humbler functions, awful Power!
50 I call thee: I myself commend
Unto thy guidance from this hour;
Oh, let my weakness have an end!
Give unto me, made lowly wise,[6]
The spirit of self-sacrifice;
55 The confidence of reason give;
And in the light of truth thy Bondman[7] let me live!

1804   1807

The Solitary Reaper[1]

Behold her, single in the field,
Yon solitary Highland Lass!
Reaping and singing by herself;
Stop here, or gently pass!
5   Alone she cuts and binds the grain,
And sings a melancholy strain;
O listen! for the Vale profound
Is overflowing with the sound.

No Nightingale did ever chaunt
10   More welcome notes to weary bands
Of travellers in some shady haunt,
Among Arabian sands:
A voice so thrilling ne'er was heard
In spring-time from the Cuckoo-bird,
15   Breaking the silence of the seas
Among the farthest Hebrides.[2]

Will no one tell me what she sings?[3]
Perhaps the plaintive numbers° flow   *verses*
For old, unhappy, far-off things,
20   And battles long ago:
Or is it some more humble lay,
Familiar matter of to-day?
Some natural sorrow, loss, or pain,
That has been, and may be again?

---

6. Another echo from Milton. The angel Raphael had advised Adam (*Paradise Lost* 8.173–74), "Be lowly wise: / Think only what concerns thee and thy being."
7. Man in bondage, serf or slave.
1. One of the rare poems not based on Wordsworth's own experience. In a note published with the poem in 1807, Wordsworth says that it was suggested by a passage in Thomas Wilkinson's *Tours to the British Mountains* (1824), which he had seen in manuscript: "Passed a female who was reaping alone: she sung in Erse [the Gaelic lan-

guage of Scotland] as she bended over her sickle; the sweetest human voice I ever heard: her strains were tenderly melancholy, and felt delicious, long after they were heard no more." In 1803 William and Mary Wordsworth, Dorothy Wordsworth, and Coleridge toured Scotland, making a pilgrimage to Robert Burns's grave and visiting places mentioned in Walter Scott's historical notes to his *Minstrelsy of the Scottish Border*.
2. Islands off the west coast of Scotland.
3. The poet does not understand Erse, the language in which she sings.

25 Whate'er the theme, the Maiden sang
As if her song could have no ending;
I saw her singing at her work,
And o'er the sickle bending;—
I listened, motionless and still;
30 And, as I mounted up the hill,
The music in my heart I bore,
Long after it was heard no more.

Nov. 5, 1805   1807

Elegiac Stanzas

*Suggested by a Picture of Peele Castle, in a Storm,
Painted by Sir George Beaumont*[1]

I was thy neighbour once, thou rugged Pile!°   building
Four summer weeks I dwelt in sight of thee:
I saw thee every day; and all the while
Thy Form was sleeping on a glassy sea.

5   So pure the sky, so quiet was the air!
So like, so very like, was day to day!
Whene'er I looked, thy Image still was there;
It trembled, but it never passed away.

How perfect was the calm! it seemed no sleep;
10   No mood, which season takes away, or brings:
I could have fancied that the mighty Deep
Was even the gentlest of all gentle Things.

Ah! THEN, if mine had been the Painter's hand,
To express what then I saw; and add the gleam,
15   The light that never was, on sea or land,
The consecration, and the Poet's dream;

I would have planted thee, thou hoary Pile
Amid a world how different from this!
Beside a sea that could not cease to smile;
20   On tranquil land, beneath a sky of bliss.

Thou shouldst have seemed a treasure-house divine
Of peaceful years; a chronicle of heaven;
—Of all the sunbeams that did ever shine
The very sweetest had to thee been given.

25   A Picture had it been of lasting ease,
Elysian[2] quiet, without toil or strife;

1. A wealthy landscape painter who was Wordsworth's patron and close friend. Peele Castle is on
an island opposite Rampside, Lancashire, where
Wordsworth had spent a month in 1794, twelve
years before he saw Beaumont's painting.
2. Referring to Elysium, in classical mythology the
peaceful place where those favored by the gods
dwelled after death.

No motion but the moving tide, a breeze,
Or merely silent Nature's breathing life.

Such, in the fond illusion of my heart,
30   Such Picture would I at that time have made:
And seen the soul of truth in every part,
A stedfast peace that might not be betrayed.

So once it would have been,—'tis so no more;
I have submitted to a new control:
35   A power is gone, which nothing can restore;
A deep distress hath humanised my Soul.[3]

Not for a moment could I now behold
A smiling sea, and be what I have been:
The feeling of my loss will ne'er be old;
40   This, which I know, I speak with mind serene.

Then, Beaumont, Friend! who would have been the Friend,
If he had lived, of Him whom I deplore,°   *mourn*
This work of thine I blame not, but commend;
This sea in anger, and that dismal shore.

45   O 'tis a passionate Work!—yet wise and well,
Well chosen is the spirit that is here;
That Hulk° which labours in the deadly swell,   *ship*
This rueful sky, this pageantry of fear!

And this huge Castle, standing here sublime,
50   I love to see the look with which it braves,
Cased in the unfeeling armour of old time,
The lightning, the fierce wind, and trampling waves.

Farewell, farewell the heart that lives alone,
Housed in a dream, at distance from the Kind!°   *humankind*
55   Such happiness, wherever it be known,
Is to be pitied; for 'tis surely blind.

But welcome fortitude, and patient cheer,
And frequent sights of what is to be borne!
Such sights, or worse, as are before me here.—
60   Not without hope we suffer and we mourn.

Summer 1806   1807

3. Captain John Wordsworth, William's brother, had been drowned in a shipwreck on February 5, 1805. He is referred to in lines 41–42.

SONNETS

Composed upon Westminster Bridge, September 3, 1802[1]

Earth has not any thing to show more fair:
Dull would he be of soul who could pass by
A sight so touching in its majesty:
This City now doth, like a garment, wear
5   The beauty of the morning; silent, bare,
Ships, towers, domes, theatres, and temples lie
Open unto the fields, and to the sky;
All bright and glittering in the smokeless air.
Never did sun more beautifully steep
10 In his first splendour, valley, rock, or hill;
Ne'er saw I, never felt, a calm so deep!
The river glideth at his own sweet will:
Dear God! the very houses seem asleep;
And all that mighty heart is lying still!

1802   1807

It is a beauteous evening

It is a beauteous evening, calm and free,
The holy time is quiet as a Nun
Breathless with adoration; the broad sun
Is sinking down in its tranquillity;
5   The gentleness of heaven broods o'er the Sea:
Listen! the mighty Being is awake,
And doth with his eternal motion make
A sound like thunder—everlastingly.
Dear Child! dear Girl! that walkest with me here,[2]
10 If thou appear untouched by solemn thought,
Thy nature is not therefore less divine:
Thou liest in Abraham's bosom[3] all the year;
And worshipp'st at the Temple's inner shrine,
God being with thee when we know it not.

Aug. 1802   1807

1. The date of this experience was not September 3, but July 31, 1802. Its occasion was a trip to France, made possible by a brief truce in the war (see Dorothy Wordsworth's *Grasmere Journals*, July 1802, p. 400). Wordsworth's conflicted feelings about this return to France, where he had once supported the Revolution and loved Annette Vallon, inform a number of personal and political sonnets that he wrote in 1802, among them the four that follow.

2. The girl walking with Wordsworth is Caroline, his daughter by Annette Vallon. For the event described see Dorothy Wordsworth's *Grasmere Journals*, July 1802 (p. 400).

3. Where the souls destined for heaven rest after death. Luke 16.22: "And it came to pass, that the beggar died, and was carried by the angels into Abraham's bosom."

To Toussaint l'Ouverture[4]

Toussaint, the most unhappy Man of Men!
Whether the rural Milk-maid by her Cow
Sing in thy hearing, or thou liest now
Alone in some deep dungeon's earless den,
5 O miserable Chieftain! where and when
Wilt thou find patience? Yet die not; do thou
Wear rather in thy bonds a cheerful brow:
Though fallen Thyself, never to rise again,
Live, and take comfort. Thou hast left behind
10 Powers that will work for thee; air, earth, and skies;
There's not a breathing of the common wind
That will forget thee; thou hast great allies;
Thy friends are exultations, agonies,
And love, and Man's unconquerable mind.

1802   1803

September 1st, 1802[5]

We had a fellow-Passenger who came
From Calais with us, gaudy in array,
A Negro Woman like a Lady gay,
Yet silent as a woman fearing blame;
5 Dejected, meek, yea pitiably tame,
She sat, from notice turning not away,
But on our proffered kindness still did lay
A weight of languid speech, or at the same
Was silent, motionless in eyes and face.
10 She was a Negro Woman driv'n from France,
Rejected like all others of that race,
Not one of whom may now find footing there;
This the poor Out-cast did to us declare,
Nor murmured at the unfeeling Ordinance.

1802   1803

4. First published in the *Morning Post*, Feb. 2, 1803. François Dominique Toussaint, later called L'Ouverture (ca. 1743–1803), was a self-educated slave who became leader of the slave rebellion in Haiti and governor of Santo Domingo. For opposing Napoleon's edict reestablishing slavery (abolished in France and its colonial possessions in the early stages of the Revolution), Toussaint was arrested and taken to Paris in June 1802. He died in prison in April 1803.
5. First published, with the title "The Banished Negroes," in the *Morning Post*, Feb. 11, 1803. In 1827 Wordsworth added an explanatory headnote beneath the title: "Among the capricious acts of tyranny that disgraced those times, was the chasing of all Negroes from France by decree of the government: we had a Fellow-passenger who was one of the expelled."

London, 1802[6]

Milton! thou should'st be living at this hour:
England hath need of thee: she is a fen
Of stagnant waters: altar, sword, and pen,
Fireside, the heroic wealth of hall and bower,
5 Have forfeited their ancient English dower°   endowment, gift
Of inward happiness. We are selfish men;
Oh! raise us up, return to us again;
And give us manners, virtue, freedom, power.
Thy soul was like a Star, and dwelt apart:
10 Thou hadst a voice whose sound was like the sea:
Pure as the naked heavens, majestic, free,
So didst thou travel on life's common way,
In cheerful godliness; and yet thy heart
The lowliest duties on herself did lay.

Sept. 1802   1807

The world is too much with us

The world is too much with us; late and soon,
Getting and spending, we lay waste our powers:
Little we see in Nature that is ours;
We have given our hearts away, a sordid boon![7]
5 This Sea that bares her bosom to the moon;
The winds that will be howling at all hours,
And are up-gathered now like sleeping flowers;
For this, for every thing, we are out of tune;
It moves us not.—Great God! I'd rather be
10 A Pagan suckled in a creed outworn;
So might I, standing on this pleasant lea,
Have glimpses that would make me less forlorn;
Have sight of Proteus rising from the sea;
Or hear old Triton[8] blow his wreathèd horn.

1802–04   1807

6. One of a series "written immediately after my
return from France to London, when I could not
but be struck, as here described, with the vanity
and parade of our own country . . . as contrasted
with the quiet, and I may say the desolation, that
the revolution had produced in France. This must
be borne in mind, or else the reader may think that
in this and the succeeding sonnets I have exaggerated the mischief engendered and fostered among
us by undisturbed wealth" [Wordsworth's note,
1843].
7. Gift. It is the act of giving the heart away that
is sordid.
8. A sea deity, usually represented as blowing on
a conch shell. Proteus was an old man of the sea
who (in the Odyssey) could assume a variety of
shapes. The description of Proteus echoes Paradise
Lost 3.603–04, and that of Triton echoes Edmund
Spenser's Colin Clouts Come Home Againe, lines
244–45.

Surprised by joy[9]

Surprised by joy—impatient as the Wind
I turned to share the transport—Oh! with whom
But Thee, deep buried in the silent tomb,
That spot which no vicissitude can find?
5   Love, faithful love, recalled thee to my mind—
But how could I forget thee? Through what power,
Even for the least division of an hour,
Have I been so beguiled as to be blind
To my most grievous loss!—That thought's return
10   Was the worst pang that sorrow ever bore,
Save one, one only, when I stood forlorn,
Knowing my heart's best treasure was no more;
That neither present time, nor years unborn
Could to my sight that heavenly face restore.

1813–14   1815

Mutability[1]

From low to high doth dissolution climb,
And sink from high to low, along a scale
Of awful° notes, whose concord shall not fail;   awe-inspiring
A musical but melancholy chime,
5   Which they can hear who meddle not with crime,
Nor avarice, nor over-anxious care.
Truth fails not; but her outward forms that bear
The longest date do melt like frosty rime,
That in the morning whitened hill and plain
10   And is no more; drop like the tower sublime
Of yesterday, which royally did wear
His crown of weeds, but could not even sustain
Some casual shout that broke the silent air,
Or the unimaginable touch of Time.

1821   1822

Steamboats, Viaducts, and Railways[2]

Motions and Means, on land and sea at war
With old poetic feeling, not for this,

9. This was in fact suggested by my daughter
Catherine, long after her death [Wordsworth's
note]. Catherine Wordsworth died June 4, 1812,
at the age of four.
1. This late sonnet was included in an otherwise
rather uninspired sequence, Ecclesiastical Sonnets,
dealing with the history and ceremonies of the

Church of England.
2. In late middle age Wordsworth demonstrates,
as he had predicted in the Preface to Lyrical Ballads, that the poet will assimilate to his subject
matter the "material revolution" produced by science.

Shall ye, by Poets even, be judged amiss!
Nor shall your presence, howsoe'er it mar
5   The loveliness of Nature, prove a bar
To the Mind's gaining that prophetic sense
Of future change, that point of vision, whence
May be discovered what in soul ye are.
In spite of all that beauty may disown
10 In your harsh features, Nature doth embrace
Her lawful offspring in Man's art; and Time,
Pleased with your triumphs o'er his brother Space,
Accepts from your bold hands the proffered crown
Of hope, and smiles on you with cheer sublime.

1833   1835

Extempore Effusion upon the Death of James Hogg[1]

When first, descending from the moorlands,
I saw the Stream of Yarrow[2] glide
Along a bare and open valley,
The Ettrick Shepherd[3] was my guide.

5   When last along its banks I wandered,
Through groves that had begun to shed
Their golden leaves upon the pathways,
My steps the Border-minstrel[4] led.

The mighty Minstrel breathes no longer,
10 'Mid mouldering ruins low he lies;
And death upon the braes[5] of Yarrow,
Has closed the Shepherd-poet's eyes:

Nor has the rolling year twice measured,
From sign to sign, its stedfast course,
15 Since every mortal power of Coleridge
Was frozen at its marvellous source;

The rapt One, of the godlike forehead,
The heaven-eyed creature sleeps in earth:
And Lamb,[6] the frolic and the gentle,
20 Has vanished from his lonely hearth.

Like clouds that rake the mountain-summits,
Or waves that own no curbing hand,

1. Wordsworth's niece relates how he was deeply moved by finding unexpectedly in a newspaper an account of the death of the poet James Hogg. "Half an hour afterwards he came into the room where the ladies were sitting and asked Miss Hutchinson [his sister-in-law] to write down some lines which he had just composed." All the writers named here, several of Wordsworth's closest friends among them, had died between 1832 and 1835.

2. A river in the southeast of Scotland.
3. I.e., Hogg, who was born in Ettrick Forest (an area in southeast Scotland near the border with England) and worked as a shepherd. He was discovered as a writer by Sir Walter Scott and became well known as a poet, essayist, editor, and novelist.
4. Sir Walter Scott.
5. The sloping banks of a stream.
6. The essayist Charles Lamb.

How fast has brother followed brother,
From sunshine to the sunless land!

25 Yet I, whose lids from infant slumber
Were earlier raised, remain to hear
A timid voice, that asks in whispers,
"Who next will drop and disappear?"

Our haughty life is crowned with darkness,
30 Like London with its own black wreath,
On which with thee, O Crabbe![7] forth-looking,
I gazed from Hampstead's breezy heath.

As if but yesterday departed,
Thou too art gone before; but why,
35 O'er ripe fruit, seasonably gathered,
Should frail survivors heave a sigh?

Mourn rather for that holy Spirit,
Sweet as the spring, as ocean deep;
For Her[8] who, ere her summer faded,
40 Has sunk into a breathless sleep.

No more of old romantic sorrows,
For slaughtered Youth or love-lorn Maid!
With sharper grief is Yarrow smitten,
And Ettrick mourns with her their Poet dead.

Nov. 21, 1835   1835

The Prelude   *The Prelude*, now regarded as Wordsworth's crowning achievement, was unknown to the public at the time of his death in April 1850. When, three
months later, it was published from manuscript by Wordsworth's literary executors,
its title was given to it by the poet's wife, Mary. Wordsworth had referred to it variously
as "the poem to Coleridge," "the poem on the growth of my own mind," and "the
poem on my own poetical education."
　For some seventy-five years this posthumous publication of 1850 was the only
known text. Then in 1926 Ernest de Selincourt, working from manuscripts, printed
an earlier version of the poem that Wordsworth had completed in 1805. Since that
time other scholars have established the existence of a still earlier and much shorter
version of *The Prelude*, in two parts, that Wordsworth had composed in 1798–99.
The following seems to have been the process of composition that produced the three
principal versions of the poem:
　1. The *Two-Part Prelude* of 1799. Wordsworth originally planned, early in 1798,
to include an account of his own development as a poet in his projected but never-
completed philosophical poem *The Recluse*. While living in Germany during the
autumn and winter of 1798–99, he composed a number of passages about his early
experiences with nature. What had been intended to be part of *The Recluse*, however,

7. George Crabbe, the poet of rural and village
life, with whom Wordsworth contrasts himself in
his comment on "Lucy Gray" (see p. 277).

8. The poet Felicia Hemans, who died at forty-
two.

quickly evolved into an independent autobiographical poem, and by late 1799, when Wordsworth settled with his sister, Dorothy, at Grasmere, he had written a two-part, 978-line poem which describes his life from infancy, through his years at Hawkshead School, to the age of seventeen. This poem corresponds, by and large, to the contents of books 1 and 2 of the later versions of The Prelude.

2. The 1805 Prelude. Late in 1801 Wordsworth began to expand the poem on his poetic life, and in 1804 he set to work intensively on the project. His initial plan was to write it in five books, but he soon decided to enlarge it to incorporate an account of his experiences in France and of his mental crisis after the failure of his hopes in the French Revolution, and to end the poem with his settlement at Grasmere and his taking up the great task of The Recluse. He completed the poem, in thirteen books, in May 1805. This is the version that Wordsworth read to Coleridge after the latter's return from Malta (see Coleridge's "To William Wordsworth," p. 471).

3. The 1850 Prelude. For the next thirty-five years, Wordsworth tinkered with the text. He polished the style and softened some of the challenges to religious orthodoxy that he had set out in his earlier statements about the godlike powers of the human mind in its communion with nature; he did not, however, in any essential way alter its subject matter or overall design. The Prelude that was published in July 1850 is in fourteen books, it incorporated Wordsworth's latest revisions, which had been made in 1839, as well as some alterations introduced by his literary executors. The selections printed here—from W. J. B. Owen's Cornell Wordsworth volume, The Fourteen-Book Prelude (1985)—are from the manuscript of this final version. Our reasons for choosing this version are set forth in Jack Stillinger's "Textual Primitivism and the Editing of Wordsworth," Studies in Romanticism 28 (1989): 3–28.

When Wordsworth enlarged the two-part Prelude of 1799, he not only made it a poem of epic length but also heightened the style and introduced various thematic parallels with earlier epics, especially Paradise Lost. The expanded poem, however, is a personal history that turns on a mental crisis and recovery, and for such a narrative design the chief prototype is not the classical or Christian epic but the spiritual auto-biography of crisis. St. Augustine's Confessions established this central Christian form late in the fourth century. Jean-Jacques Rousseau's Confessions, published between 1780 and 1789, and quickly translated into English from French, renewed this auto-biographical form for writers of Wordsworth's generation.

As in many versions of spiritual autobiography, Wordsworth's persistent metaphor is that of life as a circular journey whose end (as T. S. Eliot put it in Four Quartets, his adaptation of the traditional form) is "to arrive where we started / And know the place for the first time" (Little Gidding, lines 241–42). Wordsworth's Prelude opens with a literal journey whose chosen goal (1.72, 106–07) is "a known Vale whither my feet should turn"—that is, the Vale of Grasmere. The Prelude narrates a number of later journeys, most notably the crossing of the Alps in book 6 and, at the beginning of the final book, the climactic ascent of Mount Snowdon. In the course of the poem, such literal journeys become the metaphoric vehicle for a spiritual journey—the quest, within the poet's memory, and in the very process of composing his poem, for his lost early self and his proper spiritual home. At its end the poem, rounding back on its beginning, leaves the poet at home in the Vale of Grasmere, ready finally to begin his great project The Recluse (14.302–11, 374–85). It is in this sense that the poem is a "prelude"—preparation for the "honorable toil" (1.626) for which, having discovered his vocation, the mature writer is ready at last.

Although the episodes of The Prelude are recognizable events from Wordsworth's life, they are interpreted in retrospect, reordered in sequence, and retold as dramas involving the interaction between the mind and nature and between the creative imagination and the force of history. And although the narrator is recognizably William Wordsworth, addressing the entire poem as a communication to his friend Coleridge, he adopts the prophetic persona, modeled on the poet-prophets of the Bible, which John Milton had adopted in narrating Paradise Lost (13.300–11). In this way

Wordsworth, like his great English predecessor, assumes the authority to speak as a national poet whose function is to reconstitute the grounds of hope in a dark time of postrevolutionary reaction and despair. As Wordsworth describes it (2.433–42), he speaks out

> in these times of fear,
> This melancholy waste of hopes overthrown,
> . . . 'mid indifference and apathy
> And wicked exultation, when good men,
> On every side, fall off, we know not how,
> To selfishness, disguised in gentle names
> Of peace and quiet and domestic love
>   . . . this time
> Of dereliction and dismay. . . .

FROM THE PRELUDE
OR
GROWTH OF A POET'S MIND

AN AUTOBIOGRAPHICAL POEM

Book First
Introduction, Childhood, and School-time

O there is blessing in this gentle breeze,
A visitant that, while he fans my cheek,
Doth seem half-conscious of the joy he brings
From the green fields, and from yon azure sky.
5 Whate'er his mission, the soft breeze can come
To none more grateful than to me; escaped
From the vast City,° where I long have pined   *London*
A discontented Sojourner—Now free,
Free as a bird to settle where I will.
10 What dwelling shall receive me? in what vale
Shall be my harbour? underneath what grove
Shall I take up my home? and what clear stream
Shall with its murmur lull me into rest?
The earth is all before me:[1] with a heart
15 Joyous, nor scared at its own liberty,
I look about; and should the chosen guide
Be nothing better than a wandering cloud,
I cannot miss my way. I breathe again;
Trances of thought and mountings of the heart
20 Come fast upon me: it is shaken off,
That burthen of my own unnatural self,
The heavy weight of many a weary day
Not mine, and such as were not made for me.
Long months of peace (if such bold word accord

1. One of many echoes from *Paradise Lost*, where the line is applied to Adam and Eve as, at the conclusion of the poem, they begin their new life after being expelled from Eden: "The world was all before them" (12.646).

25 With any promises of human life),
    Long months of ease and undisturbed delight
    Are mine in prospect;° whither shall I turn,   *anticipation*
    By road or pathway, or through trackless field,
    Up hill or down, or shall some floating thing
30 Upon the River point me out my course?
    Dear Liberty! Yet what would it avail,
    But for a gift that consecrates the joy?
    For I, methought, while the sweet breath of heaven
    Was blowing on my body, felt, within,
35 A correspondent breeze, that gently moved
    With quickening virtue,² but is now become
    A tempest, a redundant° energy,   *abundant*
    Vexing its own creation. Thanks to both,
    And their congenial° powers that, while they join   *kindred*
40 In breaking up a long continued frost,
    Bring with them vernal° promises, the hope   *springtime*
    Of active days urged on by flying hours;
    Days of sweet leisure taxed with patient thought
    Abstruse, nor wanting punctual service high,
45 Matins and vespers, of harmonious verse!³
        Thus far, O Friend!⁴ did I, not used to make
    A present joy the matter of a Song,⁵
    Pour forth, that day, my soul in measured strains,
    That would not be forgotten, and are here
50 Recorded:—to the open fields I told
    A prophecy:—poetic numbers° came   *verse*
    Spontaneously, to clothe in priestly robe
    A renovated° Spirit singled out,   *renewed*
    Such hope was mine, for holy services:
55 My own voice cheered me, and, far more, the mind's
    Internal echo of the imperfect sound;
    To both I listened, drawing from them both
    A chearful confidence in things to come.
        Content, and not unwilling now to give
60 A respite to this passion,⁶ I paced on
    With brisk and eager steps; and came at length
    To a green shady place where down I sate
    Beneath a tree, slackening my thoughts by choice,
    And settling into gentler happiness.
65 'Twas Autumn, and a clear and placid day,

2. Revivifying power. ("To quicken" is to give or restore life.)
3. I.e., verses equivalent to morning prayers (matins) and evening prayers (vespers). The opening passage (lines 1–45), which Wordsworth calls in book 7, line 4, a "glad preamble," replaces the traditional epic device, such as Milton had adopted in *Paradise Lost*, of an opening prayer to the Muse for inspiration. To be "inspired," in the literal sense, is to be breathed or blown into by a divinity (in Latin *spirare* means both "to breathe" and "to blow"). Wordsworth begins his poem with a "blessing" from an outer "breeze," which (lines 34–45) is called the "breath of heaven" and evokes in him, in response, an inner, "correspondent" breeze, a burst of inspiration. The power of this revivifying breeze and breath, at once material and spiritual, is represented in other Romantic poems, such as Coleridge's "The Eolian Harp" and Percy Shelley's "Ode to the West Wind" as well as in the opening letter of Mary Shelley's *Frankenstein*.
4. Samuel Taylor Coleridge, to whom Wordsworth addresses the whole of the *Prelude*. For Coleridge's response, after the poem was read to him, see "To William Wordsworth" (p. 471).
5. In the Preface to *Lyrical Ballads*, Wordsworth says that his poetry usually originates in "emotion recollected in tranquillity"; hence not, as in the preceding preamble, during the experience that it records.
6. I.e., "and willing to prolong the passion."

With warmth, as much as needed, from a sun
Two hours declined towards the west, a day
With silver clouds, and sunshine on the grass,
And, in the sheltered and the sheltering grove,
70 A perfect stillness. Many were the thoughts
Encouraged and dismissed, till choice was made
Of a known Vale[7] whither my feet should turn,
Nor rest till they had reached the very door
Of the one Cottage which methought I saw.
75 No picture of mere memory ever looked
So fair; and while upon the fancied scene
I gazed with growing love, a higher power
Than Fancy gave assurance of some work
Of glory, there forthwith to be begun,
80 Perhaps too there performed.[8] Thus long I mused,
Nor e'er lost sight of what I mused upon,
Save where, amid the stately grove of Oaks,
Now here—now there—an acorn, from its cup
Dislodged, through sere leaves rustled, or at once
85 To the bare earth dropped with a startling sound.
   From that soft couch I rose not, till the sun
Had almost touched the horizon; casting then
A backward glance upon the curling cloud
Of city smoke, by distance ruralized,
90 Keen as a Truant or a Fugitive,
But as a Pilgrim resolute, I took,
Even with the chance equipment of that hour,
The road that pointed tow'rd the chosen Vale.
   It was a splendid evening: and my Soul
95 Once more made trial of her strength, nor lacked
Eolian visitations;[9] but the harp
Was soon defrauded, and the banded host
Of harmony dispersed in straggling sounds;
And lastly utter silence! "Be it so;
100 Why think of any thing but present good?"
So, like a Home-bound Labourer, I pursued
My way, beneath the mellowing sun, that shed
Mild influence;[1] nor left in me one wish
Again to bend the sabbath of that time[2]
105 To a servile yoke. What need of many words?
A pleasant loitering journey, through three days
Continued, brought me to my hermitage.
I spare to tell of what ensued, the life
In common things,—the endless store of things
110 Rare, or at least so seeming, every day
Found all about me in one neighbourhood;
The self-congratulation,° and from morn   *self-rejoicing*

7. Grasmere, where Wordsworth settled with his sister, Dorothy, in December 1799.
8. I.e., *The Recluse,* which Wordsworth planned to be his major poetic work.
9. Influences to which his soul responded as an Eolian harp, placed in an open window, responds with music to gusts of a breeze. For a description of this instrument, see Coleridge's *The Eolian Harp,* n. 1, p. 426.
1. An astrological term for the effect of stars on human life.
2. That time of rest.

To night unbroken cheerfulness serene.
But speedily an earnest longing rose
115 To brace myself to some determined aim,
Reading or thinking; either to lay up
New stores, or rescue from decay the old
By timely interference: and therewith
Came hopes still higher, that with outward life
120 I might endue° some airy phantasies   *invest*
That had been floating loose about for years;
And to such Beings temperately deal forth
The many feelings that oppressed my heart.
That hope hath been discouraged; welcome light
125 Dawns from the East, but dawns—to disappear
And mock me with a sky that ripens not
Into a steady morning: if my mind,
Remembering the bold promise of the past,
Would gladly grapple with some noble theme,
130 Vain is her wish: where'er she turns, she finds
Impediments from day to day renewed.
    And now it would content me to yield up
Those lofty hopes awhile for present gifts
Of humbler industry. But, O dear Friend!
135 The Poet, gentle Creature as he is,
Hath, like the Lover, his unruly times,
His fits when he is neither sick nor well,
Though no distress be near him but his own
Unmanageable thoughts: his mind, best pleas'd
140 While she, as duteous as the Mother Dove,
Sits brooding,[3] lives not always to that end,
But, like the innocent Bird, hath goadings on
That drive her, as in trouble, through the groves:
With me is now such passion, to be blamed
145 No otherwise than as it lasts too long.
    When as becomes a Man who would prepare
For such an arduous Work, I through myself
Make rigorous inquisition, the report
Is often chearing; for I neither seem
150 To lack that first great gift, the vital Soul,
Nor general Truths, which are themselves a sort
Of Elements and Agents, Under-powers,
Subordinate helpers of the living Mind:
Nor am I naked of external things,
155 Forms, images, nor numerous other aids
Of less regard, though won perhaps with toil,
And needful to build up a Poet's praise.
Time, place, and manners do I seek, and these
Are found in plenteous store, but no where such
160 As may be singled out with steady choice:
No little band of yet remembered names
Whom I in perfect confidence might hope

---

3. An echo of Milton's reference in *Paradise Lost* to the original act of creation in his invocation to the
Holy Spirit: Thou "Dovelike satst brooding on the vast Abyss / And mad'st it pregnant" (1.21–22).

To summon back from lonesome banishment,
And make them dwellers in the hearts of men
165 Now living, or to live in future years.
Sometimes the ambitious Power of choice, mistaking
Proud spring-tide swellings for a regular sea,
Will settle on some British theme, some old
Romantic Tale by Milton left unsung:[4]
170 More often turning to some gentle place
Within the groves of Chivalry, I pipe
To Shepherd Swains, or seated, harp in hand,
Amid reposing knights by a River side
Or fountain, listen to the grave reports
175 Of dire enchantments faced, and overcome
By the strong mind, and Tales of warlike feats
Where spear encountered spear, and sword with sword
Fought, as if conscious of the blazonry
That the shield bore, so glorious was the strife;
180 Whence inspiration for a song that winds
Through ever changing scenes of votive quest,[5]
Wrongs to redress, harmonious tribute paid
To patient courage and unblemished truth,
To firm devotion, zeal unquenchable,
185 And Christian meekness hallowing faithful loves.[6]
Sometimes, more sternly moved, I would relate
How vanquished Mithridates northward passed,
And, hidden in the cloud of years, became
Odin, the Father of a Race by whom
190 Perished the Roman Empire;[7] how the friends
And followers of Sertorius, out of Spain
Flying, found shelter in the Fortunate Isles;
And left their usages, their arts, and laws
To disappear by a slow gradual death;
195 To dwindle and to perish, one by one,
Starved in those narrow bounds: but not the soul
Of Liberty, which fifteen hundred years
Survived, and, when the European came
With skill and power that might not be withstood,
200 Did, like a pestilence, maintain its hold,
And wasted down by glorious death that Race
Of natural Heroes;[8]—or I would record
How, in tyrannic times, some high-souled Man,
Unnamed among the chronicles of Kings,

4. In *Paradise Lost* 9.24–41 Milton relates that, in seeking a subject for his epic poem, he rejected "fabled Knights" and medieval romance.
5. A quest undertaken to fulfill a vow.
6. An echo of the prefatory statement to Spenser's *Faerie Queene*, line 9: "Fierce warres and faithfull loves shall moralize my song."
7. Mithridates VI, king of Pontus, was defeated by the Roman Pompey in 66 B.C.E. In his *Decline and Fall of the Roman Empire* (published between 1776 and 1788), the historian Edward Gibbon had discussed Mithridates as a historical prototype for the legendary Norse god Odin. Mithridates' determination to found a family line that would take revenge on the conquering Romans links him to other figures whom Wordsworth here considers as potential subjects for his poem, all of them battlers against tyranny.
8. Sertorius, a Roman general allied with Mithridates, fought off the armies of Pompey and others until he was assassinated in 72 B.C.E. There is a legend that after his death his followers, to escape Roman tyranny, fled from Spain to the Canary Islands (known in ancient times as "the Fortunate Isles," line 192), where their descendants flourished until subjugated and decimated by invading Spaniards late in the 15th century.

205   Suffered in silence for truth's sake: or tell
How that one Frenchman, through continued force
Of meditation on the inhuman deeds
Of those who conquered first the Indian isles,
Went, single in his ministry, across
210   The Ocean;—not to comfort the Oppressed,
But, like a thirsty wind, to roam about,
Withering the Oppressor:[9]—how Gustavus sought
Help at his need in Dalecarlia's mines:[1]
How Wallace[2] fought for Scotland, left the name
215   Of Wallace to be found, like a wild flower,
All over his dear Country, left the deeds
Of Wallace, like a family of Ghosts,
To people the steep rocks and river banks,
Her natural sanctuaries, with a local soul
220   Of independence and stern liberty.
Sometimes it suits me better to invent
A Tale from my own heart, more near akin
To my own passions, and habitual thoughts,
Some variegated Story, in the main
225   Lofty, but the unsubstantial Structure melts
Before the very sun that brightens it,
Mist into air dissolving! Then, a wish,
My last and favourite aspiration, mounts,
With yearning, tow'rds some philosophic Song
230   Of Truth[3] that cherishes our daily life;
With meditations passionate, from deep
Recesses in man's heart, immortal verse
Thoughtfully fitted to the Orphean lyre;[4]
But from this awful burthen I full soon
235   Take refuge, and beguile myself with trust
That mellower years will bring a riper mind
And clearer insight. Thus my days are passed
In contradiction; with no skill to part
Vague longing, haply bred by want of power,
240   From paramount impulse—not to be withstood;
A timorous capacity from prudence;
From circumspection, infinite delay.[5]
Humility and modest awe themselves
Betray me, serving often for a cloke
245   To a more subtile selfishness; that now
Locks every function up in blank° reserve,°   *absolute / inaction*
Now dupes me, trusting to an anxious eye
That with intrusive restlessness beats off

---

9. Dominique de Gourges, a French gentleman who went in 1568 to Florida to avenge the massacre of the French by the Spaniards there [footnote in *The Prelude* of 1850].
1. Gustavus I of Sweden (1496–1530) worked to advance Sweden's liberation from Danish rule while toiling in disguise as a miner in his country's Dalecarlia mines.
2. William Wallace, Scottish patriot, fought against the English until captured and executed in 1305. See Robert Burns's "Robert Bruce's March

to Bannockburn," p. 145.
3. I.e., *The Recluse.*
4. The lyre of Orpheus. In Greek myth Orpheus was able to enchant not only human listeners but also the natural world by his singing and playing.
5. The syntax is complex and inverted; in outline the sense of lines 238–42 seems to be: "With no ability ('skill') to distinguish between vague desire (perhaps, 'haply,' resulting from lack of power) and ruling impulse; between endless procrastination and carefulness ('circumspection')."

Simplicity, and self-presented truth.
250   Ah! better far than this, to stray about
Voluptuously,° through fields and rural walks,   *luxuriously*
And ask no record of the hours, resigned
To vacant musing, unreproved neglect
Of all things, and deliberate holiday:
255   Far better never to have heard the name
Of zeal and just ambition, than to live
Baffled and plagued by a mind that every hour
Turns recreant° to her task, takes heart again,   *unfaithful*
Then feels immediately some hollow thought
260   Hang like an interdict° upon her hopes.   *prohibition*
This is my lot; for either still I find
Some imperfection in the chosen theme;
Or see of absolute accomplishment
Much wanting, so much wanting, in myself
265   That I recoil and droop, and seek repose
In listlessness from vain perplexity;
Unprofitably travelling toward the grave,
Like a false Steward who hath much received,
And renders nothing back.⁶
                          Was it for this⁷
270   That one, the fairest of all rivers, loved
To blend his murmurs with my Nurse's song;
And, from his alder shades and rocky falls,
And from his fords and shallows, sent a voice
That flowed along my dreams? For this didst Thou,
275   O Derwent! winding among grassy holms⁸
Where I was looking on, a Babe in arms,
Make ceaseless music, that composed my thoughts
To more than infant softness, giving me,
Amid the fretful dwellings of mankind,
280   A foretaste, a dim earnest, of the calm
That Nature breathes among the hills and groves?
    When he had left the mountains, and received
On his smooth breast the shadow of those Towers
That yet survive, a shattered Monument
285   Of feudal sway, the bright blue River passed
Along the margin of our Terrace Walk;⁹
A tempting Playmate whom we dearly loved.
O many a time have I, a five years' Child,
In a small mill-race¹ severed from his stream,
290   Made one long bathing of a summer's day;
Basked in the sun, and plunged, and basked again,
Alternate all a summer's day, or scoured²
The sandy fields, leaping through flow'ry groves
Of yellow ragwort; or when rock and hill,

---

6. The reference is to Christ's parable of the steward who fails to use his talents (literally, the coins
his master has entrusted to him and, figuratively,
his God-given abilities) in Matthew 25.14–30.
7. The two-part *Prelude* that Wordsworth wrote in
1798–99 begins at this point.
8. Flat ground next to a river.

9. The Derwent River flows by Cockermouth
Castle and then past the garden terrace behind
Wordsworth's father's house in Cockermouth,
Cumberland.
1. The current that drives a mill wheel.
2. Run swiftly over.

295   The woods and distant Skiddaw's³ lofty height,
Were bronzed with deepest radiance, stood alone
Beneath the sky, as if I had been born
On Indian plains, and from my Mother's hut
Had run abroad in wantonness,° to sport,   *frolic*
300   A naked Savage, in the thunder shower.
      Fair seed-time had my soul, and I grew up
Fostered alike by beauty and by fear;
Much favoured in my birth-place, and no less
In that beloved Vale⁴ to which erelong
305   We were transplanted—there were we let loose
For sports of wider range. Ere I had told
Ten birth-days, when among the mountain slopes
Frost, and the breath of frosty wind, had snapped
The last autumnal Crocus, 'twas my joy,
310   With store of Springes° o'er my Shoulder slung,   *bird snares*
To range the open heights where woodcocks ran
Along the smooth green turf. Through half the night,
Scudding away from snare to snare, I plied
That anxious visitation;—moon and stars
315   Were shining o'er my head; I was alone,
And seemed to be a trouble to the peace
That dwelt among them. Sometimes it befel,
In these night-wanderings, that a strong desire
O'erpowered my better reason, and the Bird
320   Which was the Captive of another's toil⁵
Became my prey; and when the deed was done
I heard, among the solitary hills,
Low breathings coming after me, and sounds
Of undistinguishable motion, steps
325   Almost as silent as the turf they trod.
      Nor less, when Spring had warmed the cultured° Vale,   *cultivated*
Roved we as plunderers where the Mother-bird
Had in high places built her lodge; though mean°   *of little value*
Our object, and inglorious, yet the end°   *outcome*
330   Was not ignoble. Oh! when I have hung
Above the Raven's nest, by knots of grass
And half-inch fissures in the slippery rock
But ill-sustained; and almost (so it seemed)
Suspended by the blast that blew amain,
335   Shouldering the naked crag; Oh, at that time,
While on the perilous ridge I hung alone,
With what strange utterance did the loud dry wind
Blow through my ears! the sky seemed not a sky
Of earth, and with what motion moved the clouds!
340   Dust as we are, the immortal Spirit grows
Like harmony in music; there is a dark
Inscrutable workmanship that reconciles
Discordant elements, makes them cling together
In one society. How strange that all

3. A mountain nine miles east of Cockermouth.   head, where Wordsworth attended school.
4. The valley of Esthwaite, the location of Hawks-   5. Snare or labor.

345 The terrors, pains, and early miseries,
Regrets, vexations, lassitudes, interfused
Within my mind, should e'er have borne a part,
And that a needful part, in making up
The calm existence that is mine when I
350 Am worthy of myself! Praise to the end!
Thanks to the means which Nature deigned to employ!
Whether her fearless visitings or those
That came with soft alarm like hurtless lightning
Opening the peaceful clouds, or she would use
355 Severer interventions, ministry
More palpable, as best might suit her aim.
    One summer evening (led by her) I found
A little Boat tied to a Willow-tree
Within a rocky cave, its usual home.
360 Straight I unloosed her chain, and, stepping in,
Pushed from the shore. It was an act of stealth
And troubled pleasure, nor without the voice
Of mountain-echoes did my Boat move on,
Leaving behind her still, on either side,
365 Small circles glittering idly in the moon,
Until they melted all into one track
Of sparkling light. But now, like one who rows
(Proud of his skill) to reach a chosen point
With an unswerving line, I fixed my view
370 Upon the summit of a craggy ridge,
The horizon's utmost boundary; for above
Was nothing but the stars and the grey sky.
She was an elfin Pinnace;° lustily   *small boat*
I dipped my oars into the silent lake;
375 And, as I rose upon the stroke, my boat
Went heaving through the Water like a swan:
When, from behind that craggy Steep, till then
The horizon's bound, a huge peak, black and huge,
As if with voluntary power instinct,°   *endowed*
380 Upreared its head.[6]—I struck, and struck again,
And, growing still in stature, the grim Shape
Towered up between me and the stars, and still,
For so it seemed, with purpose of its own
And measured motion, like a living Thing
385 Strode after me. With trembling oars I turned,
And through the silent water stole my way
Back to the Covert° of the Willow-tree;   *shelter*
There, in her mooring-place, I left my Bark,—
And through the meadows homeward went, in grave
390 And serious mood; but after I had seen
That spectacle, for many days, my brain
Worked with a dim and undetermined sense
Of unknown modes of being; o'er my thoughts

6. To direct his boat in a straight line, the rower (sitting facing the stern of the boat) has fixed his eye on a point on the ridge above the nearby shore, which blocks out the landscape behind. As he moves farther out, the black peak rises into his altering angle of vision and seems to stride closer with each stroke of the oars.

There hung a darkness, call it solitude
395 Or blank desertion. No familiar Shapes
Remained, no pleasant images of trees,
Of sea or Sky, no colours of green fields,
But huge and mighty Forms, that do not live
Like living men, moved slowly through the mind
400 By day, and were a trouble to my dreams.
    Wisdom and Spirit of the Universe!
Thou Soul that art the eternity of thought,
That giv'st to forms and images a breath
And everlasting Motion! not in vain,
405 By day or star-light, thus from my first dawn
Of Childhood didst thou intertwine for me
The passions that build up our human Soul,
Not with the mean° and vulgar° works of man,   *inferior / commonplace*
But with high objects, with enduring things,
410 With life and nature, purifying thus
The elements of feeling and of thought,
And sanctifying, by such discipline,
Both pain and fear; until we recognize
A grandeur in the beatings of the heart.
415   Nor was this fellowship vouchsafed to me
With stinted kindness. In November days
When vapours, rolling down the valley, made
A lonely scene more lonesome; among woods
At noon, and 'mid the calm of summer nights,
420 When, by the margin of the trembling Lake,
Beneath the gloomy hills homeward I went
In solitude, such intercourse was mine:
Mine was it, in the fields both day and night,
And by the waters, all the summer long.
425 —And in the frosty season, when the sun
Was set, and visible for many a mile,
The cottage windows blazed through twilight gloom,
I heeded not their summons,—happy time
It was indeed for all of us; for me
430 It was a time of rapture!—Clear and loud
The village Clock toll'd six—I wheeled about,
Proud and exulting like an untired horse
That cares not for his home.—All shod with steel,°   *i.e., on skates*
We hissed along the polished ice, in games
435 Confederate, imitative of the chase
And woodland pleasures,—the resounding horn,
The Pack loud-chiming and the hunted hare.
So through the darkness and the cold we flew,
And not a voice was idle: with the din
440 Smitten, the precipices rang aloud;
The leafless trees and every icy crag
Tinkled like iron; while far distant hills
Into the tumult sent an alien sound
Of melancholy, not unnoticed while the stars,
445 Eastward, were sparkling clear, and in the west
The orange sky of evening died away.

Not seldom from the uproar I retired
Into a silent bay,—or sportively
Glanced sideway,[7] leaving the tumultous throng
450 To cut across the reflex° of a star   *reflection*
That fled, and, flying still before me, gleamed
Upon the glassy plain: and oftentimes,
When we had given our bodies to the wind,
And all the shadowy banks on either side
455 Came sweeping through the darkness, spinning still
The rapid line of motion, then at once
Have I, reclining back upon my heels,
Stopped short; yet still the solitary cliffs
Wheeled by me—even as if the earth had rolled
460 With visible motion her diurnal° round!   *daily*
Behind me did they stretch in solemn train,°   *succession*
Feebler and feebler, and I stood and watched
Till all was tranquil as a dreamless sleep.
    Ye presences of Nature, in the sky,
465 And on the earth! Ye visions of the hills!
And Souls[8] of lonely places! can I think
A vulgar hope was yours when ye employed
Such ministry, when ye, through many a year,
Haunting me thus among my boyish sports,
470 On caves and trees, upon the woods and hills,
Impressed upon all forms the characters°   *signs*
Of danger or desire; and thus did make
The surface of the universal earth
With triumph and delight, with hope and fear,
Work° like a sea?   *seethe*
475   Not uselessly employed,
Might I pursue this theme through every change
Of exercise and play, to which the year
Did summon us in his delightful round.
    —We were a noisy crew; the sun in heaven
480 Beheld not vales more beautiful than ours,
Nor saw a Band in happiness and joy
Richer, or worthier of the ground they trod.
I could record with no reluctant voice
The woods of Autumn, and their hazel bowers
485 With milk-white clusters hung; the rod and line,
True symbol of hope's foolishness, whose strong
And unreproved enchantment led us on,
By rocks and pools shut out from every star
All the green summer, to forlorn cascades
490 Among the windings hid of mountain brooks.
    —Unfading recollections! at this hour
The heart is almost mine with which I felt,
From some hill-top on sunny afternoons,
The paper-Kite, high among fleecy clouds,

---

7. Moved off obliquely.
8. Wordsworth refers both to a single "Spirit" or "Soul" of the universe as a whole (e.g., lines 401–
02) and to plural "Presences" and "Souls" animating the various parts of the universe.

495   Pull at her rein, like an impatient Courser;°   *swift horse*
      Or, from the meadows sent on gusty days,
      Beheld her breast the wind, then suddenly
      Dashed headlong, and rejected by the storm.
        Ye lowly Cottages in which we dwelt,
500   A ministration of your own was yours!
      Can I forget you, being as ye were
      So beautiful among the pleasant fields
      In which ye stood? or can I here forget
      The plain and seemly countenance with which
505   Ye dealt out your plain Comforts? Yet had ye
      Delights and exultations of your own.
      Eager and never weary, we pursued
      Our home-amusements by the warm peat-fire
      At evening, when with pencil, and smooth slate
510   In square divisions parcelled out, and all
      With crosses and with cyphers scribbled o'er,
      We schemed and puzzled, head opposed to head,
      In strife too humble to be named in verse;[9]
      Or round the naked table, snow-white deal,°   *pine or fir*
515   Cherry, or maple, sate in close array,
      And to the Combat, Lu or Whist, led on
      A thick-ribbed Army, not as in the world
      Neglected and ungratefully thrown by
      Even for the very service they had wrought,
520   But husbanded through many a long campaign.
      Uncouth assemblage was it, where no few
      Had changed their functions; some, plebeian cards
      Which Fate, beyond the promise of their birth,
      Had dignified, and called to represent
525   The Persons of departed Potentates.[1]
      Oh, with what echoes on the board they fell!
      Ironic diamonds; Clubs, Hearts, Diamonds, Spades,
      A congregation piteously akin!
      Cheap matter offered they to boyish wit,
530   Those sooty Knaves, precipitated down
      With scoffs and taunts like Vulcan[2] out of heaven;
      The paramount Ace, a moon in her eclipse,
      Queens gleaming through their Splendor's last decay,
      And Monarchs surly at the wrongs sustained
535   By royal visages.[3] Meanwhile abroad
      Incessant rain was falling, or the frost
      Raged bitterly, with keen and silent tooth;
      And, interrupting oft that eager game,

9. I.e., ticktacktoe. With his phrasing in this passage, Wordsworth pokes fun at 18th-century poetic diction, which avoided everyday terms by using elaborate paraphrases.
1. The cards have changed their functions in ways that remind us that the first version of *The Prelude* was begun soon after the downfall of the French monarchy during the Revolution. The "Potentate" cards—the kings, queens, and jacks—have over time been lost from the pack and so selected "ple-beian," or commoner, cards have come to be used in their place.
2. Roman god of fire and forge. His mother, Juno, when he was born lame, threw him down from Olympus, the home of the gods.
3. Wordsworth implicitly parallels the boys' card games to the mock-epic description of the aristocratic game of ombre in Pope's *The Rape of the Lock* 3.37–98.

From under Esthwaite's splitting fields of ice
540 The pent-up air, struggling to free itself,
Gave out to meadow-grounds and hills, a loud
Protracted yelling, like the noise of wolves
Howling in Troops along the Bothnic Main.[4]
Nor, sedulous° as I have been to trace   *diligent*
545 How Nature by extrinsic passion first
Peopled the mind with forms sublime or fair
And made me love them, may I here omit
How other pleasures have been mine, and joys
Of subtler origin; how I have felt,
550 Not seldom even in that tempestuous time,
Those hallowed and pure motions of the sense
Which seem, in their simplicity, to own
An intellectual[5] charm;—that calm delight
Which, if I err not, surely must belong
555 To those first-born° affinities that fit   *innate*
Our new existence to existing things,
And, in our dawn of being, constitute
The bond of union between life and joy.
Yes, I remember when the changeful earth
560 And twice five summers on my mind had stamped
The faces of the moving year, even then
I held unconscious intercourse with beauty
Old as creation, drinking in a pure
Organic pleasure from the silver wreaths
565 Of curling mist, or from the level plain
Of waters, colored by impending° clouds.   *overhanging*
The sands of Westmorland, the creeks and bays
Of Cumbria's° rocky limits, they can tell   *Cumberland's*
How, when the Sea threw off his evening shade,
570 And to the Shepherd's hut on distant hills
Sent welcome notice of the rising moon,
How I have stood, to fancies such as these
A Stranger, linking with the Spectacle
No conscious memory of a kindred sight,
575 And bringing with me no peculiar sense
Of quietness or peace, yet have I stood,
Even while mine eye hath moved o'er many a league[6]
Of shining water, gathering, as it seemed,
Through every hair-breadth in that field of light,
580 New pleasure, like a bee among the flowers.
Thus oft amid those fits of vulgar[7] joy
Which, through all seasons, on a Child's pursuits
Are prompt Attendants; 'mid that giddy bliss
Which like a tempest works along the blood
585 And is forgotten: even then I felt
Gleams like the flashing of a shield,—the earth
And common face of Nature spake to me
Rememberable things; sometimes, 'tis true,
By chance collisions and quaint accidents

---

4. A northern gulf of the Baltic Sea.
5. Spiritual, as opposed to sense perceptions.

6. A distance equal to approximately three miles.
7. Ordinary, commonplace.

590 (Like those ill-sorted unions, work supposed
Of evil-minded fairies), yet not vain
Nor profitless, if haply they impressed
Collateral° objects and appearances,   *secondary*
Albeit lifeless then, and doomed to sleep
595 Until maturer seasons called them forth
To impregnate and to elevate the mind.
—And, if the vulgar joy by its own weight
Wearied itself out of the memory,
The scenes which were a witness of that joy
600 Remained, in their substantial lineaments
Depicted on the brain, and to the eye
Were visible, a daily sight: and thus
By the impressive discipline of fear,
By pleasure and repeated happiness,
605 So frequently repeated, and by force
Of obscure feelings representative
Of things forgotten; these same scenes so bright,
So beautiful, so majestic in themselves,
Though yet the day was distant, did become
610 Habitually dear; and all their forms
And changeful colours by invisible links
Were fastened to the affections.°   *feelings*
                                  I began
My Story early, not misled, I trust,
By an infirmity of love for days
615 Disowned by memory,[8] fancying flowers where none,
Not even the sweetest, do or can survive
For him at least whose dawning day they cheered;
Nor will it seem to Thee, O Friend! so prompt
In sympathy, that I have lengthened out,
620 With fond and feeble tongue, a tedious tale.
Meanwhile, my hope has been, that I might fetch
Invigorating thoughts from former years;
Might fix the wavering balance of my mind,
And haply meet reproaches too, whose power
625 May spur me on, in manhood now mature,
To honorable toil. Yet should these hopes
Prove vain, and thus should neither I be taught
To understand myself, nor thou to know
With better knowledge how the heart was framed
630 Of him thou lovest, need I dread from thee
Harsh judgments, if the Song be loth to quit
Those recollected hours that have the charm
Of visionary things, those lovely forms
And sweet sensations that throw back our life,
635 And almost make remotest infancy
A visible scene, on which the sun is shining?
        One end at least hath been attained—my mind
Hath been revived; and, if this genial[9] mood
Desert me not, forthwith shall be brought down

8. I.e., he hopes that he has not mistakenly attrib-   he can no longer remember.
uted his later thoughts and feelings to a time of life   9. Productive, creative.

640   Through later years the story of my life:
The road lies plain before me,—'tis a theme
Single, and of determined bounds; and hence
I chuse it rather, at this time, than work
Of ampler or more varied argument,
645   Where I might be discomfited and lost;
And certain hopes are with me that to thee
This labour will be welcome, honoured Friend!

Book Second
School-time continued

Thus far, O Friend! have we, though leaving much
Unvisited, endeavoured to retrace
The simple ways in which my childhood walked,
Those chiefly, that first led me to the love
5   Of rivers, woods, and fields. The passion yet
Was in its birth, sustained, as might befal,
By nourishment that came unsought; for still,
From week to week, from month to month, we lived
A round of tumult. Duly° were our games   *appropriately*
10   Prolonged in summer till the day-light failed;
No chair remained before the doors, the bench
And threshold steps were empty; fast asleep
The Labourer, and the old Man who had sate,
A later Lingerer, yet the revelry
15   Continued, and the loud uproar; at last,
When all the ground was dark, and twinkling stars
Edged the black clouds, home and to bed we went,
Feverish, with weary joints and beating minds.
Ah! is there One who ever has been young
20   Nor needs a warning voice to tame the pride
Of intellect, and virtue's self-esteem?
One is there,[1] though the wisest and the best
Of all mankind, who covets not at times
Union that cannot be; who would not give,
25   If so he might, to duty and to truth
The eagerness of infantine desire?
A tranquillizing spirit presses now
On my corporeal frame, so wide appears
The vacancy between me and those days,
30   Which yet have such self-presence° in my mind,   *actuality*
That, musing on them, often do I seem
Two consciousnesses, conscious of myself
And of some other Being. A rude mass
Of native rock, left midway in the Square
35   Of our small market Village, was the goal
Or centre of these sports; and, when, returned
After long absence, thither I repaired,

---

1. I.e., "Is there anyone . . . ?"

Gone was the old grey stone, and in its place
A smart Assembly-room usurped the ground
40 That had been ours.[2] There let the fiddle scream,
And be ye happy! Yet, my Friends,[3] I know
That more than one of you will think with me
Of those soft starry nights, and that old Dame
From whom the Stone was named, who there had sate
45 And watched her table with its huckster's wares°   peddler's goods
Assiduous, through the length of sixty years.
—We ran a boisterous course, the year span round
With giddy motion. But the time approached
That brought with it a regular desire
50 For calmer pleasures, when the winning forms
Of Nature were collaterally attached[4]
To every scheme of holiday delight,
And every boyish sport, less grateful° else   pleasing
And languidly pursued.
                            When summer came,
55 Our pastime was, on bright half-holidays,
To sweep along the plain of Windermere
With rival oars; and the selected bourne°   destination
Was now an Island musical with birds
That sang and ceased not; now a sister isle,
60 Beneath the oaks' umbrageous° covert, sown   shaded
With lilies of the valley like a field;
And now a third small island,[5] where survived,
In solitude, the ruins of a shrine
Once to our Lady dedicate, and served
65 Daily with chaunted rites. In such a race,
So ended, disappointment could be none,
Uneasiness, or pain, or jealousy;
We rested in the Shade, all pleased alike,
Conquered and Conqueror. Thus the pride of strength,
70 And the vain-glory of superior skill,
Were tempered, thus was gradually produced
A quiet independence of the heart:
And, to my Friend who knows me, I may add,
Fearless of blame, that hence, for future days,
75 Ensued a diffidence and modesty;
And I was taught to feel, perhaps too much,
The self-sufficing power of solitude.
     Our daily meals were frugal, Sabine fare![6]
More than we wished we knew the blessing then
80 Of vigorous hunger—hence corporeal strength
Unsapped by delicate viands;° for, exclude   food
A little weekly stipend,[7] and we lived
Through three divisions of the quartered year

2. The Hawkshead Town Hall, built in 1790.
3. Coleridge and John Wordsworth (William's brother), who had visited Hawkshead together with William in November 1799.
4. Associated as an accompaniment.
5. The island of Lady Holm, former site of a chapel dedicated to the Virgin Mary.

6. Like the meals of the Roman poet Horace on his Sabine farm.
7. In his last year at school, Wordsworth had an allowance of sixpence a week; his younger brother Christopher, threepence. After the Midsummer and Christmas holidays (line 85), the boys received a larger sum, ranging up to a guinea.

In pennyless poverty. But now, to school
85   From the half-yearly holidays returned,
     We came with weightier purses, that sufficed
     To furnish treats more costly than the Dame
     Of the old grey stone, from her scanty board, supplied.
     Hence rustic dinners on the cool green ground,
90   Or in the woods, or by a river side,
     Or shady fountains,° while among the leaves   *springs, streams*
     Soft airs were stirring, and the mid-day sun
     Unfelt shone brightly round us in our joy.
          Nor is my aim neglected if I tell
95   How sometimes, in the length of those half years,
     We from our funds drew largely—proud to curb,
     And eager to spur on, the gallopping Steed:
     And with the cautious Inn-keeper, whose Stud
     Supplied our want, we haply might employ
100 Sly subterfuges, if the Adventure's bound
     Were distant, some famed Temple⁸ where of yore°   *long ago*
     The Druids worshipped, or the antique Walls
     Of that large Abbey which within the Vale
     Of Nightshade, to St Mary's honour built,
105 Stands yet, a mouldering Pile,° with fractured arch, *building in ruin*
     Belfry, and Images, and living Trees;
     A holy Scene!⁹—Along the smooth green Turf
     Our Horses grazed:—to more than inland peace
     Left by the west wind sweeping overhead
110 From a tumultuous ocean, trees and towers
     In that sequestered Valley may be seen
     Both silent and both motionless alike;
     Such the deep shelter that is there, and such
     The safeguard for repose and quietness.
115   Our Steeds remounted, and the summons given,
     With whip and spur we through the Chauntry¹ flew
     In uncouth race, and left the cross-legged Knight
     And the Stone-abbot, and that single Wren
     Which one day sang so sweetly in the Nave
120 Of the old Church, that, though from recent Showers
     The earth was comfortless, and, touched by faint
     Internal breezes, sobbings of the place
     And respirations, from the roofless walls
     The shuddering ivy dripped large drops, yet still
125 So sweetly 'mid the gloom the invisible Bird
     Sang to herself, that there I could have made
     My dwelling-place, and lived for ever there
     To hear such music. Through the Walls we flew,
     And down the Valley, and, a circuit made
130 In wantonness° of heart, through rough and smooth   *playfulness*
     We scampered homewards. Oh, ye rocks and streams,
     And that still Spirit shed from evening air!

8. The stone circle at Swinside, on the lower Dud-
don River, mistakenly believed at the time to have
been a Druid temple.
9. Furness Abbey, some twenty miles south of
Hawkshead.
1. A chapel endowed for masses to be sung for the
donor.

Even in this joyous time I sometimes felt
Your presence, when with slackened step we breathed[2]
135 Along the sides of the steep hills, or when,
Lighted by gleams of moonlight from the sea,
We beat with thundering hoofs the level sand.
     Midway on long Winander's Eastern shore,
Within the crescent of a pleasant Bay,
140 A Tavern[3] stood, no homely-featured House,
Primeval like its neighbouring Cottages;
But 'twas a splendid place, the door beset
With Chaises, Grooms, and Liveries,—and within
Decanters, Glasses, and the blood-red Wine.
145 In ancient times, or ere the Hall was built
On the large Island,[4] had this Dwelling been
More worthy of a Poet's love, a Hut
Proud of its one bright fire and sycamore shade.
But, though the rhymes were gone that once inscribed
150 The threshold, and large golden characters°   *letters*
Spread o'er the spangled sign-board had dislodged
The old Lion, and usurped his place in slight
And mockery of the rustic Painter's hand,
Yet to this hour the spot to me is dear
155 With all its foolish pomp. The garden lay
Upon a slope surmounted by the plain
Of a small Bowling-green: beneath us stood
A grove, with gleams of water through the trees
And over the tree-tops; nor did we want
160 Refreshment, strawberries, and mellow cream.
There, while through half an afternoon we played
On the smooth platform, whether skill prevailed
Or happy blunder triumphed, bursts of glee
Made all the mountains ring. But ere night-fall,
165 When in our pinnace° we returned, at leisure   *small boat*
Over the shadowy Lake, and to the beach
Of some small Island steered our course with one,
The Minstrel of our Troop, and left him there,
And rowed off gently, while he blew his flute
170 Alone upon the rock,—Oh then the calm
And dead still water lay upon my mind
Even with a weight of pleasure, and the sky,
Never before so beautiful, sank down
Into my heart, and held me like a dream!
175   Thus were my sympathies enlarged, and thus
Daily the common range of visible things
Grew dear to me: already I began
To love the sun; a boy I loved the sun,
Not as I since have loved him, as a pledge
180 And surety of our earthly life, a light
Which we behold, and feel we are alive;
Nor for his bounty to so many worlds,

2. Slowed to let the horses catch their breath.   4. The Hall on Belle Isle in Lake Windermere had
3. The White Lion at Bowness.   been built in the early 1780s.

But for this cause, that I had seen him lay
His beauty on the morning hills, had seen
185 The western mountain touch his setting orb,
In many a thoughtless hour, when, from excess
Of happiness, my blood appear'd to flow
For its own pleasure, and I breathed with joy;
And from like feelings, humble though intense,
190 To patriotic and domestic love
Analogous, the moon to me was dear;
For I would dream away my purposes,
Standing to gaze upon her while she hung
Midway between the hills, as if she knew
195 No other region; but belonged to thee,
Yea, appertained by a peculiar right
To thee, and thy grey huts,⁵ thou one dear Vale!
   Those incidental charms which first attached
My heart to rural objects, day by day
200 Grew weaker, and I hasten on to tell
How Nature, intervenient⁶ till this time
And secondary, now at length was sought
For her own sake. But who shall⁷ parcel out
His intellect, by geometric rules,
205 Split like a province into round and square?
Who knows the individual hour in which
His habits were first sown, even as a seed?
Who that shall point, as with a wand, and say,
"This portion of the river of my mind
210 Came from yon fountain"? Thou, my friend! art one
More deeply read in thy own thoughts; to thee
Science⁸ appears but what in truth she is,
Not as our glory and our absolute boast,
But as a succedaneum,⁹ and a prop
215 To our infirmity. No officious° slave   intrusive
Art thou of that false secondary power¹
By which we multiply distinctions, then
Deem that our puny boundaries are things
That we perceive, and not that we have made.
220 To thee, unblinded by these formal arts,
The unity of all hath been revealed;
And thou wilt doubt with me, less aptly skilled
Than many are to range the faculties
In scale and order, class the cabinet²
225 Of their sensations, and in voluble phrase³
Run through the history and birth of each
As of a single independent thing.
Hard task, vain hope, to analyse the mind,
If each most obvious and particular thought,

5. Cottages built of gray stones.
6. I.e., entering incidentally into his other concerns.
7. Is able to.
8. In the old sense: learning.
9. In medicine a drug substituted for a different drug. Wordsworth, however, uses the term to signify a remedy, or palliative.
1. The analytic faculty of the mind, as contrasted with the power to apprehend "the unity of all" (line 221).
2. To classify, as if arranged in a display case.
3. In fluent words.

230 Not in a mystical and idle sense,
But in the words of reason deeply weighed,
Hath no beginning.
           Blest the infant Babe,
(For with my best conjecture I would trace
Our Being's earthly progress) blest the Babe,
235 Nursed in his Mother's arms, who sinks to sleep
Rocked on his Mother's breast; who, when his soul
Claims manifest kindred with a human soul,
Drinks in the feelings of his Mother's eye![4]
For him, in one dear Presence, there exists
240 A virtue which irradiates and exalts
Objects through widest intercourse of sense.
No outcast he, bewildered and depressed;
Along his infant veins are interfused
The gravitation and the filial bond
245 Of nature that connect him with the world.
Is there a flower to which he points with hand
Too weak to gather it, already love
Drawn from love's purest earthly fount for him
Hath beautified that flower; already shades
250 Of pity cast from inward tenderness
Do fall around him upon aught that bears
Unsightly marks of violence or harm.
Emphatically such a Being lives,
Frail Creature as he is, helpless as frail,
255 An inmate of° this active universe.   *a dweller in*
For feeling has to him imparted power
That through the growing faculties of sense
Doth, like an Agent of the one great Mind,
Create, creator and receiver both,
260 Working but in alliance with the works
Which it beholds.[5]—Such, verily, is the first
Poetic spirit of our human life,
By uniform control of after years
In most abated or suppressed, in some,
265 Through every change of growth and of decay,
Preeminent till death.
           From early days,
Beginning not long after that first time
In which, a Babe, by intercourse of touch,
I held mute dialogues with my Mother's heart,[6]
270 I have endeavoured to display the means
Whereby this infant sensibility,
Great birth-right of our being, was in me
Augmented and sustained. Yet is a path
More difficult before me, and I fear

4. Like the modern psychologist, Wordsworth recognized the importance of earliest infancy in the development of the individual mind, although he had then to invent the terms with which to analyze the process.
5. The infant, in the sense of security and love shed by his mother's presence on outer things, perceives what would otherwise be an alien world as a place to which he has a relationship like that of a son to a mother (lines 239–45). On such grounds Wordsworth asserts that the mind partially creates, by altering, the world it seems simply to perceive.
6. I.e., both infant and mother feel the pulse of the other's heart.

275　That, in its broken windings, we shall need
　　　The chamois'[7] sinews, and the eagle's wing:
　　　For now a trouble came into my mind
　　　From unknown causes. I was left alone,
　　　Seeking the visible world, nor knowing why.
280　The props of my affections were removed,[8]
　　　And yet the building stood, as if sustained
　　　By its own spirit! All that I beheld
　　　Was dear, and hence to finer influxes°　　　　　　　　　*influences*
　　　The mind lay open, to a more exact
285　And close communion. Many are our joys
　　　In youth, but Oh! what happiness to live
　　　When every hour brings palpable access
　　　Of knowledge, when all knowledge is delight,
　　　And sorrow is not there! The seasons came,
290　And every season, wheresoe'er I moved,
　　　Unfolded° transitory qualities　　　　　　　　　　*revealed*
　　　Which, but for this most watchful power of love,
　　　Had been neglected, left a register
　　　Of permanent relations, else unknown.[9]
295　Hence life, and change, and beauty; solitude
　　　More active even than "best society,"[1]
　　　Society made sweet as solitude
　　　By inward concords, silent, inobtrusive;
　　　And gentle agitations of the mind
300　From manifold distinctions, difference
　　　Perceived in things where, to the unwatchful eye,
　　　No difference is, and hence, from the same source,
　　　Sublimer joy: for I would walk alone
　　　Under the quiet stars, and at that time
305　Have felt whate'er there is of power in sound
　　　To breathe an elevated mood, by form
　　　Or Image unprofaned: and I would stand,
　　　If the night blackened with a coming storm,
　　　Beneath some rock, listening to notes that are
310　The ghostly° language of the ancient earth,　　　*disembodied*
　　　Or make their dim abode in distant winds.
　　　Thence did I drink the visionary power;
　　　And deem not profitless those fleeting moods
　　　Of shadowy exultation: not for this,
315　That they are kindred to our purer mind
　　　And intellectual life;[2] but that the soul,
　　　Remembering how she felt, but what she felt
　　　Remembering not, retains an obscure sense
　　　Of possible sublimity, whereto
320　With growing faculties she doth aspire,
　　　With faculties still growing, feeling still

7. An agile species of antelope inhabiting mountainous regions of Europe.
8. Wordsworth's mother had died the month before his eighth birthday.
9. I.e., had it not been for the watchful power of love (line 292), the "transitory qualities" (291) would have been neglected, and the "permanent relations" now recorded in his memory would have been unknown.
1. A partial quotation of a line spoken by Adam to Eve in *Paradise Lost* 9.249: "For solitude sometimes is best society."
2. I.e., not because they are related to the nonsensuous ("intellectual") aspect of our life.

That, whatsoever point they gain, they yet
Have something to pursue.
         And not alone
'Mid gloom and tumult, but no less 'mid fair
325 And tranquil scenes, that universal power
And fitness in the latent qualities
And essences of things, by which the mind
Is moved with feelings of delight, to me
Came strengthened with a superadded soul,
330 A virtue not its own.—My morning walks
Were early;—oft before the hours of School
I travelled round our little Lake, five miles
Of pleasant wandering; happy time! more dear
For this, that One was by my side, a Friend[3]
335 Then passionately loved; with heart how full
Would he peruse these lines! for many years
Have since flowed in between us, and, our minds
Both silent to each other, at this time
We live as if those hours had never been.
340 Nor seldom did I lift our Cottage latch
Far earlier, and ere one smoke-wreath had risen
From human dwelling, or the thrush, high perched,
Piped to the woods his shrill *reveillé*,[4] sate
Alone upon some jutting eminence
345 At the first gleam of dawn-light, when the Vale,
Yet slumbering, lay in utter solitude.
How shall I seek the origin, where find
Faith in the marvellous things which then I felt?
Oft in those moments such a holy calm
350 Would overspread my soul, that bodily eyes[5]
Were utterly forgotten, and what I saw
Appeared like something in myself, a dream,
A prospect° in the mind.   *scene*
              'Twere long to tell
What spring and autumn, what the winter snows,
355 And what the summer shade, what day and night,
Evening and morning, sleep and waking thought,
From sources inexhaustible, poured forth
To feed the spirit of religious love,
In which I walked with Nature. But let this
360 Be not forgotten, that I still retained
My first creative sensibility,
That by the regular action of the world
My soul was unsubdued. A plastic° power   *shaping*
Abode with me, a forming hand, at times
365 Rebellious, acting in a devious mood,
A local Spirit of his own, at war
With general tendency, but, for the most,
Subservient strictly to external things
With which it communed. An auxiliar light

3. Identified as John Fleming in a note to the 1850   5. As opposed to the mind's eye, inner vision.
4. The signal given to awaken soldiers.

370 Came from my mind which on the setting sun
Bestowed new splendor; the melodious birds,
The fluttering breezes, fountains that ran on
Murmuring so sweetly in themselves, obeyed
A like dominion; and the midnight storm
375 Grew darker in the presence of my eye;
Hence my obeisance, my devotion hence,
And hence my transport.°   *exaltation*
            Nor should this, perchance,
Pass unrecorded, that I still° had loved   *always*
The exercise and produce of a toil
380 Than analytic industry to me
More pleasing, and whose character I deem
Is more poetic, as resembling more
Creative agency. The Song would speak
Of that interminable building reared
385 By observation of affinities
In objects where no brotherhood exists
To passive minds. My seventeenth year was come;
And, whether from this habit rooted now
So deeply in my mind, or from excess
390 Of the great social principle of life
Coercing all things into sympathy,
To unorganic Natures were transferred
My own enjoyments; or the Power of truth,
Coming in revelation, did converse
395 With things that really are;[6] I, at this time,
Saw blessings spread around me like a sea.
Thus while the days flew by and years passed on,
From Nature overflowing on my soul
I had received so much, that every thought
400 Was steeped in feeling; I was only then
Contented when with bliss ineffable
I felt the sentiment of Being spread
O'er all that moves, and all that seemeth still;
O'er all that, lost beyond the reach of thought
405 And human knowledge, to the human eye
Invisible, yet liveth to the heart;
O'er all that leaps, and runs, and shouts, and sings,
Or beats the gladsome air; o'er all that glides
Beneath the wave, yea, in the wave itself,
410 And mighty depth of waters. Wonder not
If high the transport, great the joy I felt,
Communing in this sort through earth and Heaven
With every form of Creature, as it looked
Towards the Uncreated° with a countenance   *God*
415 Of adoration, with an eye of love.[7]
One song they sang, and it was audible,

6. Wordsworth is careful to indicate that there are alternative explanations for his sense that life pervades the inorganic as well as the organic world: it may be the result either of a way of perceiving that has been habitual since infancy or of a projection of his own inner life, or else it may be the perception of an objective truth.
7. Wordsworth did not add lines 412–14, which frame his experience of the "one life" in Christian terms, until the last revision of *The Prelude*, in 1839.

Most audible, then, when the fleshly ear,
O'ercome by humblest prelude of that strain,
Forgot her functions and slept undisturbed.
420　　If this be error, and another faith
Find easier access to the pious mind,[8]
Yet were I grossly destitute of all
Those human sentiments that make this earth
So dear, if I should fail with grateful voice
425　To speak of you, Ye Mountains, and Ye Lakes,
And sounding Cataracts, Ye Mists and Winds
That dwell among the Hills where I was born.
If in my Youth I have been pure in heart,
If, mingling with the world, I am content
430　With my own modest pleasures, and have lived,
With God and Nature communing, removed
From little enmities and low desires,
The gift is yours: if in these times of fear,
This melancholy waste° of hopes o'erthrown,　　　　　*wasteland*
435　If, 'mid indifference and apathy
And wicked exultation, when good men,
On every side, fall off, we know not how,
To selfishness, disguised in gentle names
Of peace and quiet and domestic love,
440　Yet mingled, not unwillingly, with sneers
On visionary minds; if, in this time
Of dereliction and dismay,[9] I yet
Despair not of our Nature, but retain
A more than Roman confidence, a faith
445　That fails not, in all sorrow my support,
The blessing of my life, the gift is yours,
Ye Winds and sounding Cataracts, 'tis yours,
Ye Mountains! thine, O Nature! Thou hast fed
My lofty speculations; and in thee,
450　For this uneasy heart of ours, I find
A never-failing principle of joy
And purest passion.
　　　　　　Thou, my Friend! wert reared
In the great City, 'mid far other scenes;[1]
But we, by different roads, at length have gained
455　The self-same bourne.° And for this cause to Thee　　　*destination*
I speak, unapprehensive of contempt,
The insinuated scoff of coward tongues,
And all that silent language which so oft,
In conversation between Man and Man,
460　Blots from the human countenance all trace
Of beauty and of love. For Thou hast sought
The truth in solitude, and, since the days
That gave thee liberty, full long desired,

8. Compare "Tintern Abbey" lines 43–50, ending with "If this / Be but a vain belief . . ." (p. 259).
9. The era, some ten years after the start of the French Revolution, was one of violent reaction. Many earlier sympathizers were abandoning their radical beliefs, and the British government was clamping down on all forms of political expression that resembled, even faintly, French ideas.
1. A reminiscence of Coleridge's "Frost at Midnight," lines 51–52: "For I was reared / In the great city, pent 'mid cloisters dim."

To serve in Nature's Temple, thou hast been
465 The most assiduous of her Ministers,[2]
In many things my Brother, chiefly here
In this our deep devotion.
              Fare Thee well!
Health, and the quiet of a healthful mind,
Attend Thee! seeking oft the haunts of Men,
470 And yet more often living with thyself
And for thyself, so haply shall thy days
Be many, and a blessing to mankind.

From Book Third
Residence at Cambridge

[ARRIVAL AT ST. JOHN'S COLLEGE. "THE GLORY OF MY YOUTH"]

It was a dreary Morning when the Wheels
Rolled over a wide plain o'erhung with clouds,
And nothing cheered our way till first we saw
The long-roof'd Chapel of King's College lift
5 Turrets, and pinnacles in answering files
Extended high above a dusky grove.
    Advancing, we espied upon the road
A Student, clothed in Gown and tasselled Cap,
Striding along, as if o'ertasked by Time
10 Or covetous of exercise and air.
He passed—nor was I Master of my eyes
Till he was left an arrow's flight behind.
As near and nearer to the Spot we drew,
It seemed to suck us in with an eddy's force;
15 Onward we drove beneath the Castle, caught,
While crossing Magdalene Bridge, a glimpse of Cam,[1]
And at the *Hoop* alighted, famous Inn!
    My Spirit was up, my thoughts were full of hope;
Some friends I had, acquaintances who there
20 Seemed friends, poor simple School-boys! now hung round
With honor and importance: in a world
Of welcome faces up and down I roved;
Questions, directions, warnings, and advice
Flowed in upon me, from all sides; fresh day
25 Of pride and pleasure! to myself I seemed
A man of business and expence, and went
From shop to shop, about my own affairs,
To Tutor or to Tailor, as befel,
From street to street, with loose and careless mind.
30   I was the Dreamer, they the dream: I roamed
Delighted through the motley spectacle;

2. Wordsworth may be recalling the conclusion of
Coleridge's "France: An Ode" (1798), where, disillusioned about the promise of liberty by the
French Revolution, he writes that, while standing
on a "sea-cliff's verge," "O Liberty! my spirit felt
thee there." Wordsworth added lines 461–64 some
years after Coleridge's death in 1834.
1. The river that flows through Cambridge.

Gowns grave or gaudy, Doctors, Students, Streets,
Courts, Cloisters, flocks of Churches, gateways, towers.
Migration strange for a Stripling° of the Hills,   *youngster*
35 A Northern Villager! As if the change
Had waited on some Fairy's wand, at once
Behold me rich in monies; and attired
In splendid garb, with hose° of silk, and hair   *stockings*
Powdered like rimy² trees, when frost is keen.
40 My lordly dressing-gown, I pass it by,
With other signs of manhood that supplied°   *compensated for*
The lack of beard.—The weeks went roundly on
With invitations, suppers, wine and fruit,
Smooth housekeeping within, and all without
45 Liberal,° and suiting Gentleman's array!   *generous*
The Evangelist St. John my Patron was;³
Three gothic Courts are his, and in the first
Was my abiding-place, a nook obscure!
Right underneath, the College Kitchens made
50 A humming sound, less tuneable than bees,
But hardly less industrious; with shrill notes
Of sharp command and scolding intermixed.
Near me hung Trinity's loquacious Clock,
Who never let the quarters, night or day,
55 Slip by him unproclaimed, and told the hours
Twice over, with a male and female voice.
Her pealing Organ was my neighbour too;
And from my pillow, looking forth by light
Of moon or favoring stars, I could behold
60 The Antechapel, where the Statue stood
Of Newton, with his prism,⁴ and silent face:
The marble index of a Mind for ever
Voyaging through strange seas of Thought, alone.
Of College labors, of the Lecturer's room
65 All studded round, as thick as chairs could stand,
With loyal Students faithful to their books,
Half-and-half Idlers, hardy Recusants,⁵
And honest Dunces—of important days,
Examinations when the man was weighed
70 As in a balance! of excessive hopes,
Tremblings withal, and commendable fears;
Small jealousies, and triumphs good or bad,
Let others, that know more, speak as they know.
Such glory was but little sought by me
75 And little won. Yet, from the first crude days
Of settling time in this untried abode,
I was disturbed at times by prudent thoughts,

2. Covered with rime, frosted over. Fashion required the late-18th-century gentleman to wear powder in his hair.
3. Wordsworth was a student at St. John's College, Cambridge University, in 1787–91. Book 3 deals with his first year there, when he was seventeen.
4. In the west end of Trinity Chapel, adjoining St. John's College, stands Roubiliac's statue of Newton holding the prism with which he had conducted the experiments described in his *Optics* (1704).
5. Those who do not conform to college discipline, particularly regulations about religious observance.

Wishing to hope, without a hope; some fears
About my future worldly maintenance;[6]
80   And, more than all, a strangeness in the mind,
A feeling that I was not for that hour,
Nor for that place. But wherefore be cast down?
For (not to speak of Reason and her pure
Reflective acts to fix the moral law
85   Deep in the conscience; nor of Christian Hope
Bowing her head before her Sister Faith
As one far mightier),[7] hither I had come,
Bear witness, Truth, endowed with holy powers
And faculties, whether to work or feel.
90   Oft when the dazzling shew no longer new
Had ceased to dazzle, ofttimes did I quit
My Comrades, leave the Crowd, buildings and groves,
And as I paced alone the level fields
Far from those lovely sights and sounds sublime
95   With which I had been conversant, the mind
Drooped not, but there into herself returning
With prompt rebound, seemed fresh as heretofore.
At least I more distinctly recognized
Her native° instincts; let me dare to speak   innate
100   A higher language, say that now I felt
What independent solaces were mine
To mitigate the injurious sway of place
Or circumstance, how far soever changed
In youth, or *to* be changed in manhood's prime;
105   Or, for the few who shall be called to look
On the long shadows, in our evening years,
Ordained Precursors to the night of death.
As if awakened, summoned, roused, constrained,
I looked for universal things, perused
110   The common countenance of earth and sky;
Earth no where unembellished by some trace
Of that first paradise whence man was driven;
And sky whose beauty and bounty are expressed
By the proud name she bears, the name of heaven.
115   I called on both to teach me what they might;
Or, turning the mind in upon herself,
Pored, watched, expected, listened, spread my thoughts
And spread them with a wider creeping; felt
Incumbencies more awful,[8] visitings
120   Of the Upholder, of the tranquil Soul
That tolerates the indignities of Time;
And, from his centre of eternity
All finite motions overruling, lives
In glory immutable. But peace!—enough
125   Here to record I had ascended now

6. Wordsworth was troubled by his family's expectation that his success at his studies would lead to his appointment as a fellow of St. John's College at the end of his degree.
7. This pious qualification, lines 83–87, was

added by Wordsworth in late revisions of *The Prelude*. In the version of 1805, he wrote: "I was a chosen son. / For hither I had come with holy powers / And faculties, whether to work or feel."
8. I.e., the weight of more awe-inspiring moods.

To such community with highest truth.
—A track pursuing, not untrod before,
From strict analogies by thought supplied,
Or consciousnesses not to be subdued,
130 To every natural form, rock, fruit or flower,
Even the loose stones that cover the high-way,
I gave a moral life; I saw them feel,
Or linked them to some feeling: the great mass
Lay bedded in a quickening° soul, and all   *life-giving*
135 That I beheld respired with inward meaning.
Add, that whate'er of Terror or of Love
Or Beauty, Nature's daily face put on
From transitory passion, unto this
I was as sensitive as waters are
140 To the sky's influence: in a kindred mood
Of passion, was obedient as a lute
That waits upon the touches of the wind.[9]
Unknown, unthought of, yet I was most rich;
I had a world about me; 'twas my own,
145 I made it; for it only lived to me,
And to the God who sees into the heart.
Such sympathies, though rarely, were betrayed
By outward gestures and by visible looks:
Some called it madness—so, indeed, it was,
150 If child-like fruitfulness in passing joy,
If steady moods of thoughtfulness, matured
To inspiration, sort with such a name;
If prophecy be madness; if things viewed
By Poets in old time, and higher up
155 By the first men, earth's first inhabitants,
May in these tutored days no more be seen
With undisordered sight. But, leaving this,
It was no madness: for the bodily eye
Amid my strongest workings evermore
160 Was searching out the lines of difference
As they lie hid in all external forms,
Near or remote, minute or vast, an eye
Which from a tree, a stone, a withered leaf,
To the broad ocean, and the azure heavens
165 Spangled with kindred multitudes of Stars,
Could find no surface where its power might sleep;
Which spake perpetual logic to my Soul,
And by an unrelenting agency
Did bind my feelings, even as in a chain.
170   And here, O friend! have I retraced my life
Up to an eminence,° and told a tale   *high ground, hill*
Of matters which not falsely may be called
The glory of my Youth. Of genius, power,
Creation, and Divinity itself,
175 I have been speaking, for my theme has been
What passed within me. Not of outward things

9. I.e., as an Eolian harp.

Done visibly for other minds; words, signs,
Symbols, or actions, but of my own heart
Have I been speaking, and my youthful mind.
180 O Heavens! how awful is the might of Souls
And what they do within themselves, while yet
The yoke of earth is new to them, the world
Nothing but a wild field where they were sown.
This is, in truth, heroic argument,
185 This genuine prowess, which I wished to touch
With hand however weak,¹ but in the main
It lies far hidden from the reach of words.
Points have we, all of us, within our Souls,
Where all stand single: this I feel, and make
190 Breathings for incommunicable powers.²
But is not each a memory to himself?
And, therefore, now that we must quit this theme,
I am not heartless;° for there's not a man   *disheartened*
That lives who hath not known his god-like hours,
195 And feels not what an empire we inherit,
As natural Beings, in the strength of Nature.
     No more:—for now into a populous plain
We must descend.—A Traveller I am
Whose tale is only of himself; even so,
200 So be it, if the pure of heart be prompt
To follow, and if Thou, O honored Friend!
Who in these thoughts art ever at my side,
Support, as heretofore, my fainting steps.³

From Book Fourth
Summer Vacation¹

[THE WALKS WITH HIS TERRIER. THE CIRCUIT OF THE LAKE]

     Among the favorites whom it pleased me well
To see again, was one, by ancient right
95 Our Inmate, a rough terrier of the hills,
By birth and call of nature pre-ordained
To hunt the badger, and unearth the fox,
Among the impervious crags; but having been
From youth our own adopted, he had passed
100 Into a gentler service. And when first
The boyish spirit flagged, and day by day
Along my veins I kindled with the stir,
The fermentation and the vernal° heat   *springtime*
Of poesy, affecting² private shades

1. An echo of *Paradise Lost* 9.28–29, where Milton declares his subject to be as suitable for "heroic
argument" as was the warfare that traditionally had
been represented in epics.
2. This obscure assertion may mean that he tries,
inadequately, to express the inexpressible.
3. The terms of this request to Coleridge suggest

the relation to Dante of Virgil, his guide in the
Inferno.
1. Wordsworth returned to Hawkshead for his
first summer vacation in 1788.
2. "Affecting" in the sense of "preferring," but also
suggesting a degree of affectation.

105 Like a sick lover, then this Dog was used
     To watch me, an attendant and a friend
     Obsequious to my steps, early and late,
     Though often of such dilatory walk
     Tired, and uneasy at the halts I made.
110 A hundred times when, roving high and low,
     I have been harrassed with the toil of verse,
     Much pains and little progress, and at once
     Some lovely Image in the Song rose up
     Full-formed, like Venus rising from the Sea;[3]
115 Then have I darted forwards and let loose
     My hand upon his back, with stormy joy;
     Caressing him again, and yet again.
     And when at evening on the public Way
     I sauntered, like a river murmuring
120 And talking to itself, when all things else
     Are still, the Creature trotted on before—
     Such was his custom; but whene'er he met
     A passenger° approaching, he would turn   *foot traveler*
     To give me timely notice; and, straitway,
125 Grateful for that admonishment, I hushed
     My voice, composed my gait, and with the air
     And mien° of one whose thoughts are free, advanced   *look*
     To give and take a greeting, that might save
     My name from piteous rumours, such as wait
130 On men suspected to be crazed in brain.
       Those walks, well worthy to be prized and loved,
     Regretted! that word too was on my tongue,
     But they were richly laden with all good,
     And cannot be remembered but with thanks
135 And gratitude, and perfect joy of heart;
     Those walks, in all their freshness, now came back,
     Like a returning Spring. When first I made
     Once more the circuit of our little Lake,
     If ever happiness hath lodged with man,
140 That day consummate° happiness was mine,   *perfect*
     Wide-spreading, steady, calm, contemplative.
     The sun was set, or setting, when I left
     Our cottage door, and evening soon brought on
     A sober hour,—not winning or serene,
145 For cold and raw the air was, and untuned:
     But as a face we love is sweetest then
     When sorrow damps it; or, whatever look
     It chance to wear, is sweetest if the heart
     Have fulness in herself, even so with me
150 It fared that evening. Gently did my Soul
     Put off her veil, and, self-transmuted, stood
     Naked, as in the presence of her God.[4]
     While on I walked, a comfort seemed to touch

---

3. Venus, goddess of love, was born from the foam of the sea.
4. In Exodus 34.30–34, when Moses descended from Mount Sinai, he wore a veil to hide from the Israelites the shining of his face, but removed the veil when, in privacy, he talked to God.

A heart that had not been disconsolate;
155 Strength came where weakness was not known to be,
At least not felt; and restoration came,
Like an intruder, knocking at the door
Of unacknowledged weariness. I took
The balance, and with firm hand weighed myself.
160 —Of that external scene which round me lay
Little, in this abstraction, did I see,
Remembered less; but I had inward hopes
And swellings of the Spirit: was rapt and soothed,
Conversed with promises; had glimmering views
165 How life pervades the undecaying mind,
How the immortal Soul with God-like power
Informs, creates, and thaws the deepest sleep[5]
That time can lay upon her; how on earth,
Man, if he do but live within the light
170 Of high endeavours, daily spreads abroad
His being armed with strength that cannot fail.
Nor was there want of milder thoughts, of love,
Of innocence, and holiday repose;
And more than pastoral quiet 'mid the stir
175 Of boldest projects; and a peaceful end
At last, or glorious, by endurance won.
Thus musing, in a wood I sate me down,
Alone, continuing there to muse; the slopes
And heights, meanwhile, were slowly overspread
180 With darkness; and before a rippling breeze
The long lake lengthened out its hoary° line: *gray-white*
And in the sheltered coppice[6] where I sate,
Around me from among the hazel leaves,
Now here, now there, moved by the straggling wind,
185 Came ever and anon a breath-like sound,
Quick as the pantings of the faithful Dog,
The off and on Companion of my walk;
And such, at times, believing them to be,
I turned my head, to look if he were there;
190 Then into solemn thought I passed once more.

[THE WALK HOME FROM THE DANCE. THE DISCHARGED SOLDIER]

* * * 'Mid a throng
310 Of Maids and Youths, old Men and Matrons staid,
A medley of all tempers,[7] I had passed
The night in dancing, gaiety, and mirth;
With din of instruments, and shuffling feet,
And glancing forms, and tapers° glittering,   *candles*
315 And unaimed prattle flying up and down—
Spirits upon the stretch, and here and there
Slight shocks of young love-liking interspersed,
Whose transient pleasure mounted to the head,

5. "Informs" and "creates" are probably to be read as intransitive verbs, whereas "thaws" has "sleep" for its direct object.
6. A clump of small trees and underbrush.
7. Temperaments, types of character.

And tingled through the veins. Ere we retired
320   The cock had crowed; and now the eastern sky
Was kindling, not unseen from humble copse
And open field through which the pathway wound
That homeward led my steps. Magnificent
The Morning rose, in memorable pomp,
325   Glorious as e'er I had beheld; in front
The Sea lay laughing at a distance;—near,
The solid mountains shone bright as the clouds,
Grain-tinctured, drenched in empyrean light;[8]
And, in the meadows and the lower grounds,
330   Was all the sweetness of a common dawn;
Dews, vapours, and the melody of birds;
And Labourers going forth to till the fields.
    Ah! need I say, dear Friend, that to the brim
My heart was full: I made no vows, but vows
335   Were then made for me; bond unknown to me
Was given, that I should be, else sinning greatly,
A dedicated Spirit. On I walked
In thankful blessedness which yet survives.

                ✳   ✳   ✳

370   Once, when those summer Months
Were flown, and Autumn brought its annual shew
Of oars with oars contending, sails with sails,
Upon Winander's[9] spacious breast, it chanced
That—after I had left a flower-decked room
375   (Whose in-door pastime, lighted-up, survived
To a late hour) and spirits overwrought[1]
Were making night do penance for a day
Spent in a round of strenuous idleness—
My homeward course led up a long ascent
380   Where the road's watery surface, to the top
Of that sharp rising, glittered to the moon
And bore the semblance of another stream
Stealing with silent lapse[2] to join the brook
That murmured in the Vale. All else was still;
385   No living thing appeared in earth or air,
And, save the flowing Water's peaceful voice,
Sound was there none: but lo! an uncouth° shape   *strange*
Shewn by a sudden turning of the road,
So near, that, slipping back into the shade
390   Of a thick hawthorn, I could mark him well,
Myself unseen. He was of stature tall,
A span[3] above man's *common* measure tall.

8. Celestial light, referring to the universe's outermost sphere, thought to be composed of fire. "Grain-tinctured": as if dyed in the grain, dyed fast, by the dawn light.
9. Lake Windermere's.
1. Worked up to a high pitch. Wordsworth is describing a party at which the "pastime" had been dancing. The description of the meeting with the discharged soldier that follows was written in 1798

as an independent poem, which Wordsworth later incorporated in *The Prelude.*
2. Flowing. Wordsworth is remembering a description that his sister, Dorothy, had entered into her journal in January 1798, a few days before he composed this passage: "The road to the village of Holford glittered like another stream."
3. About nine inches (the distance between extended thumb and little finger).

Stiff, lank, and upright;—a more meagre° man   *emaciated*
Was never seen before by night or day.
395   Long were his arms, pallid his hands;—his mouth
Looked ghastly° in the moonlight. From behind,   *ghostly*
A mile-stone propped him; I could also ken°   *see*
That he was clothed in military garb,
Though faded, yet entire. Companionless,
400   No dog attending, by no staff sustained
He stood; and in his very dress appeared
A desolation, a simplicity
To which the trappings of a gaudy world
Make a strange background. From his lips erelong
405   Issued low muttered sounds, as if of pain
Or some uneasy thought; yet still his form
Kept the same awful steadiness;—at his feet
His shadow lay and moved not. From self-blame
Not wholly free, I watched him thus; at length
410   Subduing my heart's specious cowardice,[4]
I left the shady nook where I had stood,
And hailed him. Slowly, from his resting-place
He rose; and, with a lean and wasted arm
In measured gesture lifted to his head,
415   Returned my salutation: then resumed
His station as before; and when I asked
His history, the Veteran, in reply,
Was neither slow nor eager; but, unmoved,
And with a quiet uncomplaining voice,
420   A stately air of mild indifference,
He told, in few plain words, a Soldier's tale—
That in the Tropic Islands he had served,
Whence he had landed, scarcely three weeks past,
That on his landing he had been dismissed,[5]
425   And now was travelling towards his native home.
This heard, I said in pity, "Come with me."
He stooped, and straightway from the ground took up
An oaken staff, by me yet unobserved—
A staff which must have dropped from his slack hand
430   And lay till now neglected in the grass.
    Though weak his step and cautious, he appeared
To travel without pain, and I beheld,
With an astonishment but ill suppressed,
His ghastly figure moving at my side;
435   Nor could I, while we journeyed thus, forbear
To turn from present hardships to the past,
And speak of war, battle, and pestilence,
Sprinkling this talk with questions, better spared,
On what he might himself have seen or felt.
440   He all the while was in demeanour calm,

4. I.e., he had been deceiving himself in thinking that the motive for his delay was not cowardice.
5. The Tropic Islands are the West Indies. During the 1790s tens of thousands of soldiers were stationed there to protect Britain's colonial holdings from the French and to quell slave rebellions. Many contracted tropical diseases and died, or else were rendered unfit for further service and discharged.

Concise in answer; solemn and sublime
He might have seemed, but that in all he said
There was a strange half-absence, as of one
Knowing too well the importance of his theme,
445 But feeling it no longer. Our discourse
Soon ended, and together on we passed,
In silence, through a wood, gloomy and still.
Up-turning then along an open field,
We reached a Cottage. At the door I knocked,
450 And earnestly to charitable care
Commended him, as a poor friendless Man
Belated, and by sickness overcome.
Assured that now the Traveller would repose
In comfort, I entreated, that henceforth
455 He would not linger in the public ways,
But ask for timely furtherance° and help,   assistance
Such as his state required.—At this reproof,
With the same ghastly mildness in his look,
He said, "My trust is in the God of Heaven,
460 And in the eye of him who passes me."
The Cottage door was speedily unbarred,
And now the Soldier touched his hat once more
With his lean hand; and, in a faltering voice
Whose tone bespake reviving interests
465 Till then unfelt, he thanked me; I returned
The farewell blessing of the patient Man,
And so we parted. Back I cast a look,
And lingered near the door a little space;
Then sought with quiet heart my distant home.

From Book Fifth
Books

[THE DREAM OF THE ARAB]

45   * * * Oh! why hath not the Mind
Some element to stamp her image on
In nature somewhat nearer to her own?
Why gifted with such powers to send abroad
Her spirit, must it lodge in shrines so frail?[1]
50   One day, when from my lips a like complaint
Had fallen in presence of a studious friend,
He with a smile made answer that in truth
'Twas going far to seek disquietude,
But, on the front of his reproof, confessed
55   That he himself had oftentimes given way
To kindred hauntings. Whereupon I told
That once in the stillness of a summer's noon,
While I was seated in a rocky cave

---

1. Wordsworth is describing his recurrent fear that some holocaust might wipe out all books, the frail and perishable repositories of all human wisdom and poetry.

By the sea-side, perusing, so it chanced,
60 The famous history of the errant Knight
Recovered by Cervantes,[2] these same thoughts
Beset me, and to height unusual rose,
While listlessly I sate, and, having closed
The Book, had turned my eyes tow'rd the wide Sea.
65 On Poetry, and geometric truth,
And their high privilege of lasting life,
From all internal injury exempt,
I mused; upon these chiefly: and, at length,
My senses yielding to the sultry air,
70 Sleep seized me, and I passed into a dream.
I saw before me stretched a boundless plain,
Of sandy wilderness, all blank and void;
And as I looked around, distress and fear
Came creeping over me, when at my side,
75 Close at my side, an uncouth° Shape appeared   *strange*
Upon a Dromedary,° mounted high.   *camel*
He seemed an Arab of the Bedouin Tribes:[3]
A Lance he bore, and underneath one arm
A Stone; and, in the opposite hand, a Shell
80 Of a surpassing brightness. At the sight
Much I rejoiced, not doubting but a Guide
Was present, one who with unerring skill
Would through the desert lead me; and while yet
I looked, and looked, self-questioned what this freight
85 Which the New-comer carried through the Waste
Could mean, the Arab told me that the Stone
(To give it in the language of the Dream)
Was Euclid's Elements;[4] "and this," said he,
"This other," pointing to the Shell, "this book
90 Is something of more worth": and, at the word,
Stretched forth the Shell, so beautiful in shape,
In color so resplendent, with command
That I should hold it to my ear. I did so,—
And heard, that instant, in an unknown tongue,
95 Which yet I understood, articulate sounds,
A loud prophetic blast of harmony—
An Ode, in passion uttered, which foretold
Destruction to the Children of the Earth,
By Deluge now at hand. No sooner ceased
100 The Song than the Arab with calm look declared
That all would come to pass, of which the voice
Had given forewarning, and that he himself
Was going then to bury those two Books:
The One that held acquaintance with the stars,
105 And wedded Soul to Soul in purest bond

2. I.e., *Don Quixote*, the 17th-century novel about a man unable to distinguish between books' romantic fictions and his own reality. In the 1805 *Prelude* the dream vision that follows is that of the friend mentioned in line 51. It is, in fact, closely modeled on a dream actually dreamt by the 17th-century French philosopher Descartes and recorded by a biographer.
3. Mathematics had flourished among the Arabs—hence the Arab rider.
4. Celebrated book on plane geometry and the theory of numbers by the Greek mathematician Euclid; it continued to be used as a textbook into the 19th century.

Of Reason, undisturbed by space or time:
Th'other, that was a God, yea many Gods,
Had voices more than all the winds, with power
To exhilarate the Spirit, and to soothe,
110   Through every clime, the heart of human kind.
While this was uttering, strange as it may seem,
I wondered not, although I plainly saw
The One to be a Stone, the Other a Shell,
Nor doubted once but that they both were Books;
115   Having a perfect faith in all that passed.
Far stronger now grew the desire I felt
To cleave unto this Man; but when I prayed
To share his enterprize, he hurried on,
Reckless° of me: I followed, not unseen,   heedless
120   For oftentimes he cast a backward look,
Grasping his twofold treasure. Lance in rest,
He rode, I keeping pace with him; and now
He to my fancy had become the Knight
Whose tale Cervantes tells; yet not the Knight,
125   But was an Arab of the desert, too,
Of these was neither, and was both at once.
His countenance, meanwhile, grew more disturbed,
And looking backwards when he looked, mine eyes
Saw, over half the wilderness diffused,
130   A bed of glittering light: I asked the cause.
"It is," said he, "the waters of the Deep
Gathering upon us"; quickening then the pace
Of the unwieldy Creature he bestrode,
He left me; I called after him aloud,—
135   He heeded not; but with his twofold charge
Still in his grasp, before me, full in view,
Went hurrying o'er the illimitable Waste
With the fleet waters of a drowning World
In chase of him; whereat I waked in terror;
140   And saw the Sea before me, and the Book,
In which I had been reading, at my side.

[THE BOY OF WINANDER]

There was a Boy;[5]—ye knew him well, Ye Cliffs
And Islands of Winander!—many a time
At evening, when the earliest stars began
To move along the edges of the hills,
370   Rising or setting, would he stand alone,
Beneath the trees, or by the glimmering lake;
And there, with fingers interwoven, both hands
Pressed closely palm to palm and to his mouth
Uplifted, he, as through an instrument,
375   Blew mimic hootings to the silent owls
That they might answer him.—And they would shout

---

5. In an early manuscript version of this passage, Wordsworth uses the first-person pronoun. The experience he describes was thus apparently his own.

Across the watery Vale, and shout again,
Responsive to his call,—with quivering peals,
And long halloos, and screams, and echoes loud
380 Redoubled and redoubled; concourse wild
Of jocund din! and when a lengthened pause
Of silence came, and baffled his best skill,
Then, sometimes, in that silence, while he hung
Listening, a gentle shock of mild surprize
385 Has carried far into his heart[6] the voice
Of mountain torrents; or the visible scene
Would enter unawares into his mind
With all its solemn imagery, its rocks,
Its woods, and that uncertain heaven, received
390 Into the bosom of the steady lake.
    This Boy was taken from his Mates, and died
In childhood, ere he was full twelve years old.
Fair is the Spot, most beautiful the Vale
Where he was born: the grassy Church-yard hangs
395 Upon a slope above the Village School;
And through that Church-yard when my way has led
On summer evenings, I believe that there
A long half-hour together I have stood
Mute—looking at the grave in which he lies!
400   Even now appears before the mind's clear eye
That self-same Village Church; I see her sit
(The thronèd Lady whom erewhile we hailed)
On her green hill, forgetful of this Boy
Who slumbers at her feet, forgetful, too,
405 Of all her silent neighbourhood of graves,
And listening only to the gladsome sounds
That, from the rural School ascending, play
Beneath her, and about her. May she long
Behold a race of Young Ones like to those
410 With whom I herded! (easily, indeed,
We might have fed upon a fatter soil
Of Arts and Letters, but be that forgiven)
A race of *real* children; not too wise,
Too learnèd, or too good: but wanton,° fresh,   *playful*
415 And bandied up and down by love and hate;
Not unresentful where self-justified;
Fierce, moody, patient, venturous, modest, shy;
Mad at their sports like withered leaves in winds:
Though doing wrong and suffering, and full oft
420 Bending beneath our life's mysterious weight
Of pain, and doubt, and fear; yet yielding not
In happiness to the happiest upon earth.
Simplicity in habit, truth in speech,
Be these the daily strengtheners of their minds!

6. Thomas De Quincey responded to this line in *Recollections of the Lakes and the Lake Poets:* "This very expression, 'far,' by which space and its infinities are attributed to the human heart, and to its capacities of re-echoing the sublimities of nature, has always struck me as with a flash of sublime revelation."

425   May books and nature be their early joy!
And knowledge, rightly honored with that name,
Knowledge not purchased by the loss of power!

["THE MYSTERY OF WORDS"]

Here must we pause; this only let me add,
From heart-experience, and in humblest sense
Of modesty, that he, who, in his youth,
A daily Wanderer among woods and fields,
590   With living Nature hath been intimate,
Not only in that raw unpractised time
Is stirred to extasy, as others are,
By glittering verse; but, further, doth receive,
In measure only dealt out to himself,
595   Knowledge and increase of enduring joy
From the great Nature that exists in works
Of mighty Poets. Visionary Power
Attends the motions of the viewless° winds   *invisible*
Embodied in the mystery of words:
600   There darkness makes abode, and all the host
Of shadowy things work endless changes there,
As in a mansion like their proper home.
Even forms and substances are circumfused
By that transparent veil with light divine;
605   And, through the turnings intricate of verse,
Present themselves as objects recognized,
In flashes, and with glory not their own.

From Book Sixth
Cambridge, and the Alps

["HUMAN NATURE SEEMING BORN AGAIN"]

When the third summer freed us from restraint,[1]
A youthful Friend, he too a Mountaineer,
325   Not slow to share my wishes, took his staff,
And, sallying forth, we journeyed, side by side,
Bound to the distant Alps. A hardy slight
Did this unprecedented course imply
Of College studies and their set rewards;[2]
330   Nor had, in truth, the scheme been formed by me
Without uneasy forethought of the pain,
The censures, and ill-omening of those

---

1. After reviewing briefly his second and third
years at Cambridge, Wordsworth here describes
his trip through France and Switzerland with a college friend, Robert Jones, during the succeeding
summer vacation, in 1790. France was then in the
"golden hours" of the early period of the Revolution; the fall of the Bastille had occurred on July

14 of the preceding year.
2. Universities in Britain allow longer vacations
than those in North America, on the assumption
that they will be used for study. In the upcoming
term Wordsworth faces his final examinations. His
ranking in those will determine his career prospects.

To whom my worldly interests were dear.
But Nature then was Sovereign in my mind,
335 And mighty Forms, seizing a youthful fancy,
Had given a charter[3] to irregular hopes.
In any age of uneventful calm
Among the Nations, surely would my heart
Have been possessed by similar desire;
340 But Europe at that time was thrilled with joy,
France standing on the top of golden hours,
And human nature seeming born again.

[CROSSING SIMPLON PASS]

* * * That very day,
525 From a bare ridge we also first beheld
Unveiled the summit of Mont Blanc, and grieved
To have a soulless image on the eye
Which had usurped upon a living thought
That never more could be.[4] The wondrous Vale
530 Of Chamouny[5] stretched far below, and soon
With its dumb° cataracts, and streams of ice,   silent
A motionless array of mighty waves,
Five rivers broad and vast, made rich amends,
And reconciled us to realities.
535 There small birds warble from the leafy trees,
The eagle soars high in the element;
There doth the Reaper bind the yellow sheaf,
The Maiden spread the hay-cock in the sun,
While Winter like a well-tamed lion walks,
540 Descending from the Mountain to make sport
Among the Cottages by beds of flowers.
    Whate'er in this wide circuit we beheld,
Or heard, was fitted to our unripe state
Of intellect and heart. With such a book
545 Before our eyes we could not chuse but read
Lessons of genuine brotherhood, the plain
And universal reason of mankind,
The truths of Young and Old. Nor, side by side
Pacing, two social Pilgrims, or alone
550 Each with his humour,[6] could we fail to abound
In dreams and fictions pensively composed,
Dejection taken up for pleasure's sake,
And gilded sympathies; the willow wreath,[7]
And sober posies[8] of funereal flowers
555 Gathered, among those solitudes sublime,
From formal gardens of the Lady Sorrow,
Did sweeten many a meditative hour.
    Yet still in me with those soft luxuries

3. Privileged freedom.
4. The "image" is the actual sight of Mont Blanc, as against what the poet has imagined the famous Swiss mountain to be.
5. Chamonix, a valley in eastern France, north of

Mont Blanc.
6. Temperament, or state of mind.
7. Clichéd symbol of sorrow. "Gilded": laid on like gilt; i.e., superficial.
8. Small bunches of flowers.

Mixed something of stern mood, an under thirst
560 Of vigor seldom utterly allayed.
And from that source how different a sadness
Would issue, let one incident make known.
When from the Vallais we had turned, and clomb°   *climbed*
Along the Simplon's steep and rugged road,⁹
565 Following a band of Muleteers, we reached
A halting-place where all together took
Their noon-tide meal. Hastily rose our Guide,
Leaving *us* at the Board;° awhile we lingered,   *i.e., eating the meal*
Then paced the beaten downward way that led
570 Right to a rough stream's edge and there broke off.
The only track now visible was one
That from the torrent's further brink held forth
Conspicuous invitation to ascend
A lofty mountain. After brief delay
575 Crossing the unbridged stream, that road we took
And clomb with eagerness, till anxious fears
Intruded, for we failed to overtake
Our Comrades gone before. By fortunate chance,
While every moment added doubt to doubt,
580 A Peasant met us, from whose mouth we learned
That to the Spot which had perplexed us first
We must descend, and there should find the road,
Which in the stony channel of the Stream
Lay a few steps, and then along its banks,
585 And that our future course, all plain to sight,
Was downwards, with the current of that Stream.
Loth to believe what we so grieved to hear,
For still we had hopes that pointed to the clouds,
We questioned him again, and yet again;
590 But every word that from the Peasant's lips
Came in reply, translated by our feelings,
Ended in this, *that we had crossed the Alps.*¹
    Imagination—here the Power so called
Through sad incompetence of human speech—
595 That awful° Power rose from the Mind's abyss   *awe-inspiring*
Like an unfathered vapour² that enwraps
At once some lonely Traveller. I was lost,
Halted without an effort to break through;
But to my conscious soul I now can say,
600 "I recognize thy glory"; in such strength
Of usurpation, when the light of sense
Goes out, but with a flash that has revealed
The invisible world, doth Greatness make abode,
There harbours, whether we be young or old;
605 Our destiny, our being's heart and home,
Is with infinitude, and only there;

9. The Simplon Pass through the Alps.
1. As Dorothy Wordsworth baldly put it later on,
"The ambition of youth was disappointed at these
tidings." The visionary experience that follows
(lines 593–617) occurred not in the Alps but at the

time of writing the passage, as the 1805 text explicitly says: "Imagination! lifting up itself / Before the
eye and progress of my Song."
2. Sudden vapor from no apparent source.

With hope it is, hope that can never die,
Effort, and expectation, and desire,
And something evermore about to be.
610 Under such banners militant the Soul
Seeks for no trophies, struggles for no spoils,
That may attest her prowess, blest in thoughts
That are their own perfection and reward,
Strong in herself, and in beatitude³
615 That hides her like the mighty flood of Nile
Poured from his fount of Abyssinian clouds
To fertilize the whole Egyptian plain.
   The melancholy slackening that ensued
Upon those tidings by the Peasant given
620 Was soon dislodged; downwards we hurried fast
And, with the half-shaped road, which we had missed,
Entered a narrow chasm. The brook and road
Were fellow-Travellers in this gloomy Strait,
And with them did we journey several hours
625 At a slow pace. The immeasurable height
Of woods decaying, never to be decayed,
The stationary blasts of waterfalls,
And in the narrow rent at every turn
Winds thwarting winds, bewildered and forlorn,
630 The torrents shooting from the clear blue sky,
The rocks that muttered close upon our ears,
Black drizzling crags that spake by the way-side
As if a voice were in them, the sick sight
And giddy prospect of the raving stream,
635 The unfettered clouds, and region of the Heavens,
Tumult and peace, the darkness and the light—
Were all like workings of one mind, the features
Of the same face, blossoms upon one tree,
Characters of the great Apocalypse,
640 The types and symbols of Eternity,⁴
Of first and last, and midst, and without end.⁵

From Book Seventh
Residence in London¹

[THE BLIND BEGGAR. BARTHOLOMEW FAIR]

As the black storm upon the mountain top
620 Sets off the sunbeam in the Valley, so
That huge fermenting Mass of human-kind

3. The ultimate blessedness or happiness.
4. The objects in this natural scene are like the written words ("characters") of the Apocalypse—i.e., of the Book of Revelation, the last book of the New Testament. "Types": signs foreshadowing the future.
5. Cf. Revelation 1.8: "I am Alpha and Omega, the beginning and the ending, saith the Lord." The

phrase is repeated in Revelation 21.6, after the fulfillment of the last things. In *Paradise Lost* 5.153–65 Milton says that the things created declare their Creator, and calls on all to extol "him first, him last, him midst, and without end."
1. Wordsworth spent three and a half months in London in 1791.

Serves as a solemn background or relief
To single forms and objects, whence they draw,
For feeling and contemplative regard,
625 More than inherent liveliness and power.
How oft amid those overflowing streets
Have I gone forward with the Crowd, and said
Unto myself, "The face of every one
That passes by me is a mystery!"
630 Thus have I looked, nor ceased to look, oppressed
By thoughts of what and whither, when and how,
Until the Shapes before my eyes became
A second-sight procession, such as glides
Over still mountains, or appears in dreams.
635 And once, far-travelled in such mood, beyond
The reach of common indication, lost
Amid the moving pageant, I was smitten
Abruptly with the view (a sight not rare)
Of a blind Beggar who, with upright face,
640 Stood propped against a Wall; upon his chest
Wearing a written paper to explain
His Story, whence he came, and who he was.
Caught by the spectacle, my mind turned round
As with the might of waters; an apt type
645 This Label seemed, of the utmost we can know
Both of ourselves and of the universe;
And on the Shape of that unmoving Man,
His steadfast face, and sightless eyes, I gazed
As if admonished from another world.
650   Though reared upon the base of outward things,
Structures like these the excited Spirit mainly
Builds for herself. Scenes different there are,
Full-formed, that take, with small internal help,
Possession of the faculties—the peace
655 That comes with night; the deep solemnity
Of Nature's intermediate hours of rest,
When the great tide of human life stands still,
The business of the day to come—unborn,
Of that gone by—locked up as in the grave;[2]
660 The blended calmness of the heavens and earth,
Moonlight, and stars, and empty streets, and sounds
Unfrequent as in deserts: at late hours
Of winter evenings when unwholesome rains
Are falling hard, with people yet astir,
665 The feeble salutation from the voice
Of some unhappy woman,[3] now and then
Heard as we pass; when no one looks about,
Nothing is listened to. But these, I fear,
Are falsely catalogued;[4] things that are, are not,
670 As the mind answers to them, or the heart

2. The sonnet "Composed upon Westminster Bridge" describes a similar response to London when its "mighty heart is lying still."
3. Perhaps a prostitute.
4. Mistakenly classified, because what things *are* depends on the attitude with which they are perceived.

Is prompt or slow to feel. What say you, then,
To times when half the City shall break out
Full of one passion, vengeance, rage, or fear?
To executions,[5] to a Street on fire,
675   Mobs, riots, or rejoicings? From these sights
Take one, that annual Festival, the Fair
Holden where Martyrs suffered in past time,
And named of St. Bartholomew;[6] there see
A work completed to our hands, that lays,
680   If any spectacle on earth can do,
The whole creative powers of Man asleep!
For once the Muse's help will we implore,
And she shall lodge us, wafted on her wings,
Above the press and danger of the Crowd,
685   Upon some Shewman's platform. What a shock
For eyes and ears! what anarchy and din
Barbarian and infernal—a phantasma[7]
Monstrous in color, motion, shape, sight, sound!
Below, the open space, through every nook
690   Of the wide area, twinkles, is alive
With heads; the midway region and above
Is thronged with staring pictures, and huge scrolls,
Dumb proclamations of the Prodigies!
With chattering monkeys dangling from their poles,
695   And children whirling in their roundabouts;°   *merry-go-rounds*
With those that stretch the neck, and strain the eyes;
And crack the voice in rivalship, the crowd
Inviting; with buffoons against buffoons
Grimacing, writhing, screaming, him who grinds
700   The hurdy-gurdy,[8] at the fiddle weaves,
Rattles the salt-box,[9] thumps the Kettle-drum;
And him who at the trumpet puffs his cheeks;
The silver-collared Negro with his timbrel;°   *tambourine*
Equestrians, tumblers, women, girls, and boys,
705   Blue-breeched, pink-vested, with high-towering plumes.
—All moveables of wonder from all parts
And here, Albinos, painted-Indians, Dwarfs,
The Horse of Knowledge, and the learned Pig,[1]
The Stone-eater, the Man that swallows fire—
710   Giants, Ventriloquists, the Invisible-girl,
The Bust that speaks, and moves its goggling eyes,
The Wax-work, Clock-work, all the marvellous craft
Of modern Merlins,[2] Wild-beasts, Puppet-shews,
All out-o'th'-way, far-fetched, perverted things,[3]

5. Executions were public events in England until 1868.
6. This huge fair was long held in Smithfield, the place where, on St. Bartholomew's Day, August 24, Protestants had been executed in Queen Mary's reign (1553–58).
7. Fantasy of a disordered mind. Perhaps suggestive too of "phantasmagoria," the name given, starting in 1802, to the exhibition of optical illusions that showmen mounted by means of a kind of slide projector.

8. A stringed instrument, sounded by a turning wheel covered by rosin.
9. A wooden box, rattled and beaten with a stick.
1. Animals trained to tap out answers to arithmetic questions, etc.
2. Magicians. Merlin was the magician in Arthurian romance.
3. Cf. Milton's description of Hell as containing "Perverse, all monstrous, all prodigious things" (*Paradise Lost* 2.625).

715 All freaks of Nature, all Promethean[4] thoughts
     Of man; his dullness, madness, and their feats,
     All jumbled up together, to compose
     A Parliament of Monsters. Tents and Booths,
     Meanwhile, as if the whole were one vast mill,
720 Are vomiting, receiving, on all sides,
     Men, Women, three-years' Children, Babes in arms.
         Oh blank confusion! true epitome
     Of what the mighty City is herself
     To thousands upon thousands of her Sons,
725 Living amid the same perpetual whirl
     Of trivial objects, melted and reduced
     To one identity, by differences
     That have no law, no meaning, and no end;
     Oppression under which even highest minds
730 Must labour, whence the strongest are not free!
     But though the picture weary out the eye,
     By nature an unmanageable sight,
     It is not wholly so to him who looks
     In steadiness, who hath among least things
735 An undersense of greatest; sees the parts
     As parts, but with a feeling of the whole.

                    *   *   *

     This did I feel in London's vast Domain;
     The Spirit of Nature was upon me there;
     The Soul of Beauty and enduring life
     Vouchsafed° her inspirations; and diffused,   *granted*
770 Through meagre lines and colours, and the press
     Of self-destroying transitory things,
     Composure, and ennobling harmony.

From Book Eighth
Retrospect, Love of Nature leading
to Love of Man[1]

[THE SHEPHERD IN THE MIST]

        * * * A rambling School-boy, thus
     I felt his° presence in his own domain   *the shepherd's*
     As of a Lord and Master; or a Power
     Or Genius,° under Nature, under God   *presiding spirit*
260 Presiding; and severest solitude
     Had more commanding looks when he was there.
     When up the lonely brooks on rainy days
     Angling I went, or trod the trackless hills
     By mists bewildered, suddenly mine eyes

---

4. Of daring creativity. In Greek mythology Prometheus made man out of clay and taught him the arts.
1. In this book Wordsworth reviews the first twenty-one years of his life to trace the transfer of his earlier feelings for nature to the shepherds and other working people who inhabited the landscape he loved.

265   Have glanced upon him distant a few steps,
In size a Giant, stalking through thick fog,[2]
His sheep like Greenland bears;° or, as he stepped   *polar bears*
Beyond the boundary line of some hill-shadow,
His form hath flashed upon me, glorified
270   By the deep radiance of the setting sun:[3]
Or him have I descried in distant sky,
A solitary object and sublime,
Above all height! like an aerial cross
Stationed alone upon a spiry rock
275   Of the Chartreuse,[4] for worship. Thus was Man
Ennobled outwardly before my sight,
And thus my heart was early introduced
To an unconscious love and reverence
Of human nature; hence the human Form
280   To me became an index of delight,
Of grace, and honor, power, and worthiness.
Meanwhile this Creature, spiritual almost
As those of Books, but more exalted far;
Far more of an imaginative Form
285   Than the gay Corin of the groves, who lives
For his own fancies, or to dance by the hour
In coronal, with Phillis[5] in the midst—
Was, for the purposes of Kind,[6] a Man
With the most common; husband, father; learned,
290   Could teach, admonish, suffered with the rest
From vice and folly, wretchedness and fear;
Of this I little saw, cared less for it;
But something must have felt. * * *

From Book Ninth
Residence in France[1]

[PARIS AND ORLÉANS. BECOMES A "PATRIOT"]

—France lured me forth, the realm that I had crossed
35   So lately, journeying toward the snow-clad Alps.
But now relinquishing the scrip° and staff[2]   *knapsack*
And all enjoyment which the summer sun
Sheds round the steps of those who meet the day
With motion constant as his own, I went

2. Wordsworth borrows this image from James Thomson's *Autumn* (1730), lines 727–29.
3. A "glory" is a mountain phenomenon in which the enlarged figure of a person is seen projected by the sun on the mist, with a radiance about its head. Cf. Coleridge's "Dejection: An Ode," line 54 (p. 467).
4. In his tour of the Alps, Wordsworth had been deeply impressed by the Chartreuse, a Carthusian monastery in France, with its soaring cross visible against the sky.
5. Corin and Phillis, shepherd and shepherdess

dancing in their coronals, or wreaths of flowers, were stock characters in earlier pastoral literature.
6. I.e., in carrying out the tasks of humankind.
1. Wordsworth's second visit to France, while he was twenty-one and twenty-two years of age (1791–92), came during a crucial period of the French Revolution. This book deals with his stay at Paris, Orléans, and Blois, when he developed his passionate partisanship for the French people and the revolutionary cause.
2. Emblems of the pilgrim traveling on foot.

40   Prepared to sojourn in a pleasant Town[3]
     Washed by the current of the stately Loire.
     Through Paris lay my readiest course, and there
     Sojourning a few days, I visited
     In haste each spot, of old or recent fame,
45   The latter chiefly; from the field of Mars[4]
     Down to the suburbs of St. Anthony;[5]
     And from Mont Martyr[6] southward to the Dome
     Of Genevieve.[7] In both her clamorous Halls,
     The National Synod and the Jacobins,[8]
50   I saw the Revolutionary Power
     Toss like a Ship at anchor, rocked by storms;
     The Arcades I traversed, in the Palace huge
     Of Orleans,[9] coasted round and round the line
     Of Tavern, Brothel, Gaming-house, and Shop,
55   Great rendezvous of worst and best, the walk
     Of all who had a purpose, or had not;
     I stared, and listened with a Stranger's ears
     To Hawkers and Haranguers, hubbub wild!
     And hissing Factionists, with ardent eyes,
60   In knots, or pairs, or single. Not a look
     Hope takes, or Doubt or Fear are forced to wear,
     But seemed there present, and I scanned them all,
     Watched every gesture uncontrollable
     Of anger, and vexation, and despite,
65   All side by side, and struggling face to face
     With Gaiety and dissolute Idleness.
     —Where silent zephyrs° sported with the dust   *breezes*
     Of the Bastille,[1] I sate in the open sun,
     And from the rubbish gathered up a stone
70   And pocketed the Relic in the guise
     Of an Enthusiast; yet, in honest truth,
     I looked for Something that I could not find,
     Affecting more emotion than I felt;
     For 'tis most certain that these various sights,
75   However potent their first shock, with me
     Appeared to recompence the Traveller's pains
     Less than the painted Magdalene of Le Brun,[2]
     A Beauty exquisitely wrought, with hair
     Dishevelled, gleaming eyes, and rueful cheek
80   Pale, and bedropp'd with everflowing tears.
     But hence to my more permanent Abode[3]

---

3. Orléans, on the Loire River, where Wordsworth stayed from December 1791 until he moved to Blois early the next year.
4. The Champ de Mars, where during the Festival of the Federation in 1790 Louis XVI swore fidelity to the new constitution.
5. Faubourg St. Antoine, near the Bastille, a militant working-class district and center of revolutionary violence.
6. Montmartre, a hill on which revolutionary meetings were held.
7. Became the Panthéon, a burial place for heroes of the Revolution such as Voltaire and Rousseau.

8. The club of radical democratic revolutionists, named for the ancient convent of St. Jacques, their meeting place. "National Synod": the newly formed National Assembly.
9. The arcades in the courtyard of the Palais d'Orléans, a fashionable gathering place.
1. The political prison, which had been demolished after being stormed and sacked on July 14, 1789.
2. The painting of the weeping Mary Magdalen by Charles Le Brun (1619–1690) was a tourist attraction.
3. In Orléans.

I hasten; there by novelties in speech,
Domestic manners, customs, gestures, looks,
And all the attire of ordinary life,
85   Attention was engrossed; and, thus amused,
I stood 'mid those concussions unconcerned,
Tranquil almost, and careless as a flower
Glassed in a green-house, or a Parlour shrub
That spreads its leaves in unmolested peace
90   While every bush and tree, the country through,
Is shaking to the roots; indifference this
Which may seem strange; but I was unprepared
With needful knowledge, had abruptly passed
Into a theatre whose stage was filled,
95   And busy with an action far advanced.
Like Others I had skimmed, and sometimes read
With care, the master pamphlets of the day;[4]
Nor wanted° such half-insight as grew wild   *lacked*
Upon that meagre soil, helped out by talk
100   And public news; but having never seen
A Chronicle that might suffice to shew
Whence the main Organs[5] of the public Power
Had sprung, their transmigrations when and how
Accomplished, giving thus unto events
105   A form and body; all things were to me
Loose and disjointed, and the affections left
Without a vital interest. At that time,
Moreover, the first storm was overblown,
And the strong hand of outward violence
110   Locked up in quiet.[6] For myself, I fear
Now, in connection with so great a Theme,
To speak (as I must be compelled to do)
Of one so unimportant; night by night
Did I frequent the formal haunts of men
115   Whom, in the City, privilege of birth
Sequestered from the rest: societies
Polished in Arts, and in punctilio° versed;   *social niceties*
Whence, and from deeper causes, all discourse
Of good and evil of the time was shunned
120   With scrupulous care: but these restrictions soon
Proved tedious, and I gradually withdrew
Into a noisier world, and thus erelong
Became a Patriot;[7] and my heart was all
Given to the People, and my love was theirs.

---

4. Wordsworth probably refers to the numerous English pamphlets (including Paine's *Rights of Man*, part 1, and Wollstonecraft's *A Vindication of the Rights of Men*) published in response to Edmund Burke's attack on the revolution, *Reflections on the Revolution in France* (1790).
5. Institutions, instruments.

6. The peace that followed the storming of the Bastille in 1789 was dramatically broken when, between September 2 and 6, 1792, three thousand prisoners suspected of Royalist sympathies were summarily executed by a Paris mob.
7. I.e., became committed to the people's side in the Revolution.

From Book Tenth
France continued[1]

[THE REVOLUTION: PARIS AND ENGLAND]

Cheared with this hope,[2] to Paris I returned;
And ranged, with ardor heretofore unfelt,
50 The spacious City, and in progress passed
The Prison[3] where the unhappy Monarch lay,
Associate with his Children and his Wife,
In Bondage; and the Palace[4] lately stormed,
With roar of Cannon, by a furious Host.
55 I crossed the Square (an empty Area then!)
Of the Carousel, where so late had lain
The Dead, upon the Dying heaped; and gazed
On this and other Spots, as doth a Man
Upon a Volume whose contents he knows
60 Are memorable, but from him locked up,
Being written in a tongue he cannot read;
So that he questions the mute leaves° with pain,   *pages*
And half-upbraids their silence. But, that night,
I felt most deeply in what world I was,
65 What ground I trod on, and what air I breathed.
High was my Room and lonely, near the roof
Of a large Mansion or Hotel,° a Lodge   *town house*
That would have pleased me in more quiet times,
Nor was it wholly without pleasure, then.
70 With unextinguished taper I kept watch,
Reading at intervals; the fear gone by
Pressed on me almost like a fear to come.
I thought of those September massacres,
Divided from me by one little month,
75 Saw them and touched;[5] the rest was conjured up
From tragic fictions, or true history,
Remembrances and dim admonishments.
The Horse is taught his manage,[6] and no Star
Of wildest course but treads back his own steps;
80 For the spent hurricane the air provides
As fierce a Successor; the tide retreats
But to return out of its hiding place
In the great Deep; all things have second birth;
The earthquake is not satisfied at once;
85 And in this way I wrought upon myself

1. Book 10 deals with the period between October 1792 and August 1794.
2. I.e., hope that, with the Declaration of the Republic and the French army's recent defeat of an Austrian and Prussian invasion, there would be no more need for violence.
3. I.e., the "Temple" (it had once housed the religious Order of Templars), where starting in September 1792 the deposed king was held prisoner awaiting trial for his crimes against the people.

4. The Tuileries. On August 10, 1792, the palace was marched upon by a crowd intent on seizing Louis XVI, whose Swiss guards opened fire on the insurgents. The bodies of the thousands who died in the conflict were cremated in the great square of the "Carousel" (line 56), in front of the palace.
5. I.e., his imagination of the September massacres was so vivid as to be palpable.
6. The French *manège*, the prescribed action and paces of a trained horse.

Until I seemed to hear a voice that cried
To the whole City, "Sleep no more."[7] The Trance
Fled with the Voice to which it had given birth,
But vainly comments of a calmer mind
90   Promised soft peace and sweet forgetfulness.
The place, all hushed and silent as it was,
Appeared unfit for the repose of Night,
Defenceless as a wood where Tygers roam.

          * * * In this frame of mind,
Dragged by a chain of harsh necessity,
So seemed it,—now I thankfully acknowledge,
Forced by the gracious providence of Heaven—
225   To England I returned,[8] else (though assured
That I both was, and must be, of small weight,
No better than a Landsman on the deck
Of a ship struggling with a hideous storm)
Doubtless I should have then made common cause
230   With some who perished, haply° perished too,[9]   *perhaps*
A poor mistaken and bewildered offering,
Should to the breast of Nature have gone back
With all my resolutions, all my hopes,
A Poet only to myself, to Men
235   Useless, and even, belovèd Friend, a Soul
To thee unknown![1]

               *   *   *

What then were my emotions, when in Arms
Britain put forth her free-born strength in league,
265   O pity and shame! with those confederate Powers?[2]
Not in my single self alone I found,
But in the minds of all ingenuous Youth,
Change and subversion from that hour. No shock
Given to my moral nature had I known
270   Down to that very moment; neither lapse
Nor turn of sentiment that might be named
A revolution, save at this one time;
All else was progress on the self-same path
On which, with a diversity of pace,
275   I had been travelling: this a stride at once
Into another region.—As a light
And pliant hare-bell° swinging in the breeze   *bluebell*
On some gray rock, its birth-place, so had I
Wantoned, fast rooted on the ancient tower
280   Of my beloved Country, wishing not
A happier fortune than to wither there.

---

7. Macbeth's hallucination after his murder of the king. "Methought I heard a voice cry, 'Sleep no more, / Macbeth does murder sleep' " (Shakespeare, *Macbeth* 2.2.33–34). Louis XVI was guillotined on January 21, 1793.
8. Forced by the "harsh necessity" of a lack of money, Wordsworth returned to England late in 1792.

9. Wordsworth sympathized with the moderate party of the Girondins, almost all of whom were guillotined or committed suicide following Robespierre's rise to power in the National Convention.
1. Wordsworth did not meet Coleridge, the "beloved Friend," until 1795.
2. England joined Austria and Prussia in the war against France in February 1793.

Now was I from that pleasant station torn
And tossed about in whirlwind. I rejoiced,
Yea, afterwards, truth most painful to record!
285 Exulted, in the triumph of my Soul,
When Englishmen by thousands were o'erthrown,
Left without glory on the field, or driven,
Brave hearts, to shameful flight.[3] It was a grief,—
Grief call it not, 'twas any thing but that,—
290 A conflict of sensations without name,
Of which *he* only who may love the sight
Of a Village Steeple as I do can judge,
When, in the Congregation bending all
To their great Father, prayers were offered up,
295 Or praises, for our Country's victories,
And, 'mid the simple Worshippers, perchance
I only, like an uninvited Guest,
Whom no one owned, sate silent, shall I add,
Fed on the day of vengeance yet to come?

❉   ❉   ❉

[THE REIGN OF TERROR. NIGHTMARES]

—Domestic carnage now filled the whole year
With Feast-days;[4] old Men from the Chimney-nook,
The Maiden from the bosom of her Love,
The Mother from the Cradle of her Babe,
360 The Warrior from the Field, all perished, all,
Friends, enemies, of all parties, ages, ranks,
Head after head, and never heads enough
For those that bade them fall. They found their joy,
They made it, proudly eager as a Child
365 (If like desires of innocent little ones
May with such heinous appetites be compared),
Pleased in some open field to exercise
A toy that mimics with revolving wings
The motion of a windmill, though the air
370 Do of itself blow fresh and make the Vanes
Spin in his eyesight, *that* contents him not,
But, with the play-thing at arm's length, he sets
His front against the blast, and runs amain
That it may whirl the faster.

❉   ❉   ❉

Most melancholy at that time, O Friend!
Were my day-thoughts, my nights were miserable;
Through months, through years, long after the last beat
400 Of those atrocities, the hour of sleep
To me came rarely charged with natural gifts,

---

3. The French defeated the English in the battle of Hondschoote, September 6, 1793.
4. I.e., festivals celebrated by human slaughter ("carnage"). Wordsworth alludes ironically to the patriotic festivals created to replace Catholic feast days within the new Republic's calendar. Lines 356–63 describe the Reign of Terror organized by Robespierre's Committee of Public Safety. In 1794 a total of 1,376 people were guillotined in Paris in forty-nine days.

Such ghastly Visions had I of despair
And tyranny, and implements of death,
And innocent victims sinking under fear,
405 And momentary hope, and worn-out prayer,
Each in his separate cell, or penned in crowds
For sacrifice, and struggling with forced mirth
And levity in dungeons where the dust
Was laid with tears. Then suddenly the scene
410 Changed, and the unbroken dream entangled me
In long orations which I strove to plead
Before unjust tribunals—with a voice
Labouring, a brain confounded, and a sense
Death-like of treacherous desertion, felt
415 In the last place of refuge, my own soul.

From Book Eleventh
France, concluded[1]

[RETROSPECT: "BLISS WAS IT IN THAT DAWN." RECOURSE TO
"REASON'S NAKED SELF"]

O pleasant exercise of hope and joy![2]
For mighty were the Auxiliars° which then stood   *allies*
Upon our side, we who were strong in Love!
Bliss was it in that dawn to be alive,
But to be young was very Heaven! O times,
110 In which the meagre, stale, forbidding ways
Of custom, law, and statute, took at once
The attraction of a Country in Romance!
When Reason seemed the most to assert her rights,
When most intent on making of herself
115 A prime Enchantress—to assist the work
Which then was going forward in her name!
Not favored spots alone, but the whole earth
The beauty wore of promise—that which sets
(As at some moments might not be unfelt
120 Among the bowers of Paradise itself)
The budding rose above the rose full blown.
What Temper° at the prospect did not wake   *temperament*
To happiness unthought of? The inert
Were roused, and lively natures rapt away![3]
125 They who had fed their Childhood upon dreams,
The play-fellows of Fancy, who had made
All powers of swiftness, subtilty, and strength
Their ministers,—who in lordly wise had stirred
Among the grandest objects of the Sense,

1. Book 11 deals with the year from August 1794 through September 1795: Wordsworth's growing disillusionment with the French Revolution, his recourse to abstract theories of politics, his despair and nervous breakdown, and the beginning of his recovery when he moved from London to Race- down.
2. Wordsworth in this passage turns back to the summer of 1792, when his enthusiasm for the Revolution was at its height.
3. Enraptured; carried away by enthusiasm.

cut

130 And dealt with whatsoever they found there
As if they had within some lurking right
To wield it;—they, too, who of gentle mood
Had watched all gentle motions, and to these
Had fitted their own thoughts, schemers more mild,
135 And in the region of their peaceful selves;—
Now was it that *both* found, the Meek and Lofty
Did both find helpers to their hearts' desire,
And stuff at hand, plastic° as they could wish,—   *malleable*
Were called upon to exercise their skill,
140 Not in Utopia,—subterranean Fields,—
Or some secreted Island, Heaven knows where!
But in the very world, which is the world
Of all of us,—the place where in the end
We find our happiness, or not at all!
145   Why should I not confess that Earth was then
To me what an Inheritance new-fallen
Seems, when the first time visited, to one
Who thither comes to find in it his home?
He walks about and looks upon the spot
150 With cordial transport, moulds it and remoulds,
And is half-pleased with things that are amiss,
'Twill be such joy to see them disappear.
       An active partisan, I thus convoked°   *called up*
From every object pleasant circumstance
155 To suit my ends; I moved among mankind
With genial feelings still° predominant;   *always*
When erring, erring on the better part,
And in the kinder spirit; placable,°   *forgiving*
Indulgent, as not uninformed that men
160 See as they have been taught, and that Antiquity[4]
Gives rights to error; and aware no less
That throwing off oppression must be work
As well of licence as of liberty;
And above all, for this was more than all,
165 Not caring if the wind did now and then
Blow keen upon an eminence° that gave   *elevated ground*
Prospect so large into futurity;
In brief, a Child of Nature, as at first,
Diffusing only those affections wider
170 That from the cradle had grown up with me,
And losing, in no other way than light
Is lost in light, the weak in the more strong.
       In the main outline, such, it might be said,
Was my condition, till with open war
175 Britain opposed the Liberties of France;[5]
This threw me first out of the pale° of love,   *bounds*
Soured, and corrupted, upwards to the source,
My sentiments; was not,[6] as hitherto,
A swallowing up of lesser things in great;

4. Tradition, long use.
5. On February 11, 1793, England declared war
against France.
6. I.e., there was not (in my sentiments).

180   But change of them into their contraries;
And thus a way was opened for mistakes
And false conclusions, in degree as gross,
In kind more dangerous. What had been a pride
Was now a shame; my likings and my loves
185   Ran in new channels, leaving old ones dry,
And hence a blow that in maturer age
Would but have touched the judgement, struck more deep
Into sensations near the heart; meantime,
As from the first, wild theories were afloat
190   To whose pretensions sedulously urged[7]
I had but lent a careless ear, assured
That time was ready to set all things right,
And that the multitude so long oppressed
Would be oppressed no more.
                           But when events
195   Brought less encouragement, and unto these
The immediate proof of principles no more
Could be entrusted, while the events themselves,
Worn out in greatness, stripped of novelty,
Less occupied the mind; and sentiments
200   Could through my understanding's natural growth
No longer keep their ground, by faith maintained
Of inward consciousness, and hope that laid
Her hand upon her object; evidence
Safer, of universal application, such
205   As could not be impeached, was sought elsewhere.
    But now, become Oppressors in their turn,
Frenchmen had changed a war of self-defence
For one of Conquest, losing sight of all
Which they had struggled for:[8] and mounted up,
210   Openly in the eye of Earth and Heaven,
The scale of Liberty.[9] I read her doom
With anger vexed, with disappointment sore,
But not dismayed, nor taking to the shame
Of a false Prophet. While resentment rose,
215   Striving to hide, what nought could heal, the wounds
Of mortified presumption, I adhered
More firmly to old tenets, and, to prove[1]
Their temper, strained them more; and thus, in heat
Of contest, did opinions every day
220   Grow into consequence, till round my mind
They clung, as if they were its life, nay more,
The very being of the immortal Soul.
    This was the time when, all things tending fast
To depravation, speculative schemes
225   That promised to abstract the hopes of Man
Out of his feelings, to be fixed thenceforth

---

7. Diligently argued for.
8. In late 1794 and early 1795, French troops had successes in Spain, Italy, Holland, and Germany— even though, in the constitution written in 1790, they had renounced all foreign conquest.

9. I.e., the desire for power now outweighed the love of liberty.
1. Test. The figure is that of testing a tempered steel sword.

For ever in a purer element,
Found ready welcome.² Tempting region *that*
For Zeal to enter and refresh herself,
230   Where passions had the privilege to work,
And never hear the sound of their own names:
But, speaking more in charity, the dream
Flattered the young, pleased with extremes, nor least
With that which makes our Reason's naked self³
235   The object of its fervour. * * *

[CRISIS, BREAKDOWN, AND RECOVERY]

I summoned my best skill, and toiled, intent
280   To anatomize° the frame of social life,   *dissect*
Yea, the whole body of society
Searched to its heart. Share with me, Friend! the wish
That some dramatic tale indued with shapes
Livelier, and flinging out less guarded words
285   Than suit the Work we fashion, might set forth
What then I learned, or think I learned, of truth,
And the errors into which I fell, betrayed
By present objects, and by reasonings false
From their beginnings, inasmuch as drawn
290   Out of a heart that had been turned aside
From Nature's way by outward accidents,
And which was thus confounded more and more,
Misguided and misguiding. So I fared,
Dragging all precepts, judgments, maxims, creeds,
295   Like culprits to the bar;° calling the mind,   *courtroom*
Suspiciously, to establish in plain day
Her titles⁴ and her honors, now believing,
Now disbelieving, endlessly perplexed
With impulse, motive, right and wrong, the ground
300   Of obligation, what the rule and whence
The sanction, till, demanding formal *proof*
And seeking it in every thing, I lost
All feeling of conviction, and, in fine,°   *the end*
Sick, wearied out with contrarieties,
305   Yielded up moral questions in despair.
This was the crisis of that strong disease,
This the soul's last and lowest ebb; I drooped,
Deeming our blessed Reason of least use
Where wanted most. * * *

2. I.e., schemes that undertook to separate ("abstract") people's hopes for future happiness from reliance on the emotional part of human nature, and instead to ground those hopes on their rational natures ("a purer element"). The allusion is primarily to William Godwin's *Inquiry Concerning Political Justice* (1793), which proposed that humans' moral and political progress would be unstoppable if reason were allowed to function freely.
3. Cf. Edmund Burke's denunciation in *Reflec-*

tions on the Revolution in France (p. 152 above) of the new political theories founded on reason: "All the decent drapery of life is to be rudely torn off. All the superadded ideas, furnished from the wardrobe of a moral imagination, which the heart owns, and the understanding ratifies, as necessary to cover the defects of our naked shivering nature . . . are to be exploded as a ridiculous, absurd, and antiquated fashion."
4. Deeds to prove legal entitlements.

* * * Then it was,
Thanks to the bounteous Giver of all good!
335 That the beloved Woman[5] in whose sight
Those days were passed, now speaking in a voice
Of sudden admonition—like a brook
That does but *cross* a lonely road, and now
Seen, heard, and felt, and caught at every turn,
340 Companion never lost through many a league—
Maintained for me a saving intercourse°   communion
With my true self: for, though bedimmed and changed
Both as a clouded and a waning moon,
She whispered still that brightness would return,
345 She in the midst of all preserved me still
A Poet, made me seek beneath that name,
And that alone, my office° upon earth.   duty
And lastly, as hereafter will be shewn,
If willing audience fail not, Nature's self,
350 By all varieties of human love
Assisted, led me back through opening day
To those sweet counsels between head and heart
Whence grew that genuine knowledge fraught with peace
Which, through the later sinkings of this cause,
355 Hath still upheld me, and upholds me now
In the catastrophe (for so they dream,
And nothing less), when, finally to close
And rivet down the gains of France, a Pope
Is summoned in, to crown an Emperor:[6]
360 This last opprobrium,° when we see a people   disgrace
That once looked up in faith, as if to Heaven
For manna, take a lesson from the Dog
Returning to his vomit.[7] * * *

Book Twelfth
Imagination and Taste, how impaired and restored

[SPOTS OF TIME]

* * * I shook the habit off[1]
205 Entirely and for ever, and again
In Nature's presence stood, as now I stand,
A sensitive Being, a *creative* Soul.
There are in our existence spots of time,[2]

5. After a long separation Dorothy Wordsworth came to live with her brother at Racedown in 1795 and remained a permanent member of his household.
6. The ultimate blow to liberal hopes for France occurred when on December 2, 1804, Napoleon summoned Pope Pius VII to officiate at the ceremony elevating him to emperor. At the last moment Napoleon took the crown and donned it himself.
7. Allusion to Proverbs 26.11: "As a dog returneth to his vomit, a fool returneth to his folly."

1. The acquired habit of logical analysis, which had marred his earlier feelings for the natural world.
2. Wordsworth's account in the lines that follow of two memories from childhood was originally drafted for book 1 of the two-part *Prelude* of 1799. By transferring these early memories to the end of his completed autobiography, rather than presenting them in its opening books, he enacts his own theory about how remembrance of things past nourishes the mind. He shows that it does so, as he says, "down to this *very* time" (line 327): the

That with distinct pre-eminence retain
210   A renovating virtue,° whence, depressed   *power of renewal*
By false opinion and contentious thought,
Or aught of heavier or more deadly weight,
In trivial occupations, and the round
Of ordinary intercourse, our minds
215   Are nourished and invisibly repaired;
A virtue by which pleasure is inhanced,
That penetrates, enables us to mount,
When high, more high, and lifts us up when fallen.
This efficacious Spirit chiefly lurks
220   Among those passages of life that give
Profoundest knowledge how and to what point
The mind is lord and master—outward sense[3]
The obedient Servant of her will. Such moments
Are scattered every where, taking their date
225   From our first Childhood. I remember well
That once, while yet my inexperienced hand
Could scarcely hold a bridle, with proud hopes
I mounted, and we journied towards the hills:
An ancient Servant of my Father's house
230   Was with me, my encourager and Guide.
We had not travelled long ere some mischance
Disjoined me from my Comrade, and, through fear
Dismounting, down the rough and stony Moor
I led my horse, and, stumbling on, at length
235   Came to a bottom,° where in former times   *valley*
A Murderer had been hung in iron chains.
The Gibbet mast[4] had mouldered down, the bones
And iron case were gone, but on the turf
Hard by, soon after that fell deed was wrought,
240   Some unknown hand had carved the Murderer's name.
The monumental Letters were inscribed
In times long past, but still from year to year,
By superstition of the neighbourhood,
The grass is cleared away, and to that hour
245   The characters° were fresh and visible.   *letters*
A casual glance had shewn them, and I fled,
Faultering and faint and ignorant of the road:
Then, reascending the bare common,° saw   *field*
A naked Pool that lay beneath the hills,
250   The Beacon[5] on its summit, and, more near,
A Girl who bore a Pitcher on her head,
And seemed with difficult steps to force her way
Against the blowing wind. It was in truth
An ordinary sight; but I should need
255   Colors and words that are unknown to man
To paint the visionary dreariness
Which, while I looked all round for my lost Guide,

---

poetic imagination he brings to the composition of
this book has been revived by recollections.
3. Perception of the external world.

4. The post with a projecting arm used for hanging
criminals.
5. A signal beacon on a hill above Penrith.

Invested Moorland waste and naked Pool,
The Beacon crowning the lone eminence,
260 The Female and her garments vexed and tossed
By the strong wind.—When, in the blessed hours
Of early love, the loved One[6] at my side,
I roamed, in daily presence of this scene,
Upon the naked Pool and dreary Crags,
265 And on the melancholy Beacon, fell
A spirit of pleasure, and Youth's golden gleam;
And think ye not with radiance more sublime
For these remembrances, and for the power
They had left behind? So feeling comes in aid
270 Of feeling, and diversity of strength
Attends us, if but once we have been strong.
Oh! mystery of Man, from what a depth
Proceed thy honors! I am lost, but see
In simple child-hood something of the base
275 On which thy greatness stands; but this I feel,
That from thyself it comes, that thou must give,
Else never canst receive. The days gone by
Return upon me almost from the dawn
Of life: the hiding-places of Man's power
280 Open; I would approach them, but they close.
I see by glimpses now; when age comes on
May scarcely see at all, and I would give,
While yet we may, as far as words can give,
Substance and life to what I feel, enshrining,
285 Such is my hope, the spirit of the past
For future restoration.—Yet another
Of these memorials.
                              One Christmas-time,[7]
On the glad Eve of its dear holidays,
Feverish, and tired, and restless, I went forth
290 Into the fields, impatient for the sight
Of those led Palfreys[8] that should bear us home,
My Brothers and myself. There rose a Crag
That, from the meeting point of two highways
Ascending, overlooked them both, far stretched;
295 Thither, uncertain on which road to fix
My expectation, thither I repaired,
Scout-like, and gained the summit; 'twas a day
Tempestuous, dark, and wild, and on the grass
I sate, half-sheltered by a naked wall;
300 Upon my right hand couched a single sheep,
Upon my left a blasted hawthorn stood:
With those Companions at my side, I sate,
Straining my eyes intensely, as the mist
Gave intermitting prospect of the copse
305 And plain beneath. Ere we to School returned

---

6. Mary Hutchinson.
7. In 1783. Wordsworth, aged thirteen, was at

Hawkshead School with two of his brothers.
8. Small saddle horses.

That dreary time, ere we had been ten days
Sojourners in my Father's House, he died,[9]
And I and my three Brothers, Orphans then,
Followed his Body to the Grave. The Event,
310   With all the sorrow that it brought, appeared
A chastisement; and when I called to mind
That day so lately passed, when from the Crag
I looked in such anxiety of hope,
With trite reflections of morality,
315   Yet in the deepest passion, I bowed low
To God, who thus corrected my desires;
And afterwards, the wind and sleety rain
And all the business[1] of the Elements,
The single Sheep, and the one blasted tree,
320   And the bleak music of that old stone wall,
The noise of wood and water, and the mist
That on the line of each of those two Roads
Advanced in such indisputable shapes;[2]
All these were kindred spectacles and sounds
325   To which I oft repaired, and thence would drink
As at a fountain; and on winter nights,
Down to this *very* time, when storm and rain
Beat on my roof, or haply° at noon-day,   *perhaps*
While in a grove I walk whose lofty trees,
330   Laden with summer's thickest foliage, rock
In a strong wind, some working of the spirit,
Some inward agitations, thence are brought,[3]
Whate'er their office, whether to beguile
Thoughts over-busy in the course they took,
335   Or animate an hour of vacant ease.

From Book Thirteenth
Subject concluded

[POETRY OF "UNASSUMING THINGS"]

From Nature doth emotion come, and moods
Of calmness equally are Nature's gift:
This is her glory; these two attributes
Are sister horns that constitute her strength.[1]
5   Hence Genius, born to thrive by interchange
Of peace and excitation, finds in her
His best and purest friend, from her receives
That energy by which he seeks the truth,
From her that happy stillness of the mind

9. John Wordsworth died on December 30, 1783.
William's mother had died five years earlier.
1. Busy-ness; motions.
2. I.e., shapes one did not dare question. Cf. Hamlet's declaration to the ghost of his father: "Thou
com'st in such questionable shape / That I will

speak to thee" (Shakespeare, *Hamlet* 1.4.24–25).
3. Another instance of Wordsworth's inner
response to an outer breeze (cf. 1.33–38, p. 325).
1. In the Old Testament the horn of an animal
signifies power.

10 Which fits him to receive it, when unsought.
Such benefit the humblest intellects
Partake of, each in their degree: 'tis mine
To speak of what myself have known and felt.
Smooth task! for words find easy way, inspired
15 By gratitude and confidence in truth.
Long time in search of knowledge did I range
The field of human life, in heart and mind
Benighted, but the dawn beginning now
To reappear,[2] 'twas proved that not in vain
20 I had been taught to reverence a Power
That is the visible quality and shape
And image of right reason,[3] that matures
Her processes by steadfast laws, gives birth
To no impatient or fallacious hopes,
25 No heat of passion or excessive zeal,
No vain conceits,—provokes to no quick turns
Of self-applauding intellect,—but trains
To meekness, and exalts by humble faith;[4]
Holds up before the mind, intoxicate
30 With present objects, and the busy dance
Of things that pass away, a temperate shew
Of objects that endure; and by this course
Disposes her, when over-fondly set
On throwing off incumbrances,° to seek   *burdens*
35 In Man, and in the frame of social life,
Whate'er there is desireable and good
Of kindred permanence, unchanged in form
And function, or through strict vicissitude
Of life and death revolving.[5] Above all
40 Were re-established now those watchful thoughts
Which (seeing little worthy or sublime
In what the Historian's pen so much delights
To blazon,° Power and Energy detached   *celebrate*
From moral purpose) early tutored me
45 To look with feelings of fraternal love
Upon the unassuming things that hold
A silent station in this beauteous world.

[DISCOVERY OF HIS POETIC SUBJECT. SALISBURY PLAIN.
SIGHT OF "A NEW WORLD"]

220 Here, calling up to mind what then I saw,
A youthful Traveller, and see daily now
In the familiar circuit of my home,
Here might I pause and bend in reverence

2. I.e., he is beginning to recover from the spiritual crisis recorded in 11.293–309.
3. Wordsworth follows Milton's use of the term "right reason" to denote a human faculty that is inherently attuned to truth.
4. In the text of 1805: "but lifts / The being into magnanimity."
5. Cf. the 1802 Preface to *Lyrical Ballads* and

Wordsworth's discussion of how the plain language of rural life that he draws on for his poetry expresses "the essential passions of the heart" and how, "arising out of repeated experience and regular feelings, [it] is a more permanent, and a far more philosophical language, than that which is frequently substituted for it by poets" (p. 262 above).

To Nature, and the power of human minds,
225 To Men as they are Men within themselves.
How oft high service is performed within,
When all the external Man is rude in shew!
Not like a Temple rich with pomp and gold,
But a mere mountain Chapel that protects
230 Its simple Worshippers from sun and shower.
Of these, said I, shall be my song, of these,
If future years mature me for the task,
Will I record the praises, making Verse
Deal boldly with substantial things; in truth
235 And sanctity of passion speak of these,
That justice may be done, obeisance paid
Where it is due: thus haply° shall I teach,   *perhaps*
Inspire, through unadulterated° ears   *uncorrupted*
Pour rapture, tenderness, and hope, my theme
240 No other than the very heart of Man
As found among the best of those who live
Not unexalted by religious faith,
Nor uninformed by Books, good books, though few,
In Nature's presence: thence may I select
245 Sorrow, that is not sorrow, but delight,
And miserable love that is not pain
To hear of, for the glory that redounds
Therefrom to human kind and what we are.

                    *   *   *

* * * Dearest Friend,
If thou partake the animating faith
300 That Poets, even as Prophets, each with each
Connected in a mighty scheme of truth,
Have each his own peculiar faculty,
Heaven's gift, a sense that fits him to perceive
Objects unseen before, thou wilt not blame
305 The humblest of this band[6] who dares to hope
That unto him hath also been vouchsafed°   *given*
An insight, that in some sort he possesses
A Privilege, whereby a Work of his,
Proceeding from a source of untaught things,
310 Creative and enduring, may become
A Power like one of Nature's. To a hope
Not less ambitious once among the Wilds
Of Sarum's Plain[7] my youthful Spirit was raised;
There, as I ranged at will the pastoral downs[8]
315 Trackless and smooth, or paced the bare white roads
Lengthening in solitude their dreary line,
Time with his retinue of ages fled
Backwards, nor checked his flight until I saw
Our dim Ancestral Past in Vision clear;[9]

---

6. Wordsworth himself.
7. Salisbury Plain, which Wordsworth crossed
alone on foot in the summer of 1793. The journey
occasioned the poem *Adventures on Salisbury*

Plain.
8. Open hills used to pasture sheep.
9. Wordsworth shared the common, but mistaken,
belief of his time that Stonehenge, the giant meg-

320   Saw multitudes of men, and here and there
A single Briton clothed in Wolf-skin vest,
With shield and stone-axe, stride across the wold;[1]
The voice of Spears was heard, the rattling spear
Shaken by arms of mighty bone, in strength,
325   Long mouldered, of barbaric majesty.
I called on Darkness—but before the word
Was uttered, midnight darkness seemed to take
All objects from my sight; and lo! again
The Desert visible by dismal flames;
330   It is the Sacrificial Altar, fed
With living Men—how deep the groans! the voice
Of those that crowd the giant wicker thrills
The monumental hillocks,[2] and the pomp
Is for both worlds, the living and the dead.
335   At other moments (for through that wide waste
Three summer days I roamed) where'er the Plain
Was figured o'er with circles, lines, or mounds,
That yet survive, a work, as some divine,[3]
Shaped by the Druids, so to represent
340   Their knowledge of the heavens, and image forth
The constellations; gently was I charmed
Into a waking dream, a reverie
That with believing eyes, where'er I turned,
Beheld long-bearded Teachers with white wands
345   Uplifted, pointing to the starry sky
Alternately, and Plain below, while breath
Of music swayed their motions, and the Waste
Rejoiced with them and me in those sweet Sounds.[4]

                    *   *   *

365   Moreover, each man's mind is to herself
Witness and judge; and I remember well
That in Life's every-day appearances
I seemed about this time[5] to gain clear sight
Of a new world, a world, too, that was fit
370   To be transmitted and to other eyes
Made visible, as ruled by those fixed laws
Whence spiritual dignity originates,
Which do both give it being and maintain
A balance, an ennobling interchange
375   Of action from without, and from within;
The excellence, pure function, and best power
Both of the object seen, and eye that sees.

---

alithic structure on Salisbury Plain, had been a
temple of the Celtic priests, the Druids, and that
the Druids had there performed the rite of human
sacrifice; hence the imaginings and vision that he
goes on to relate.
1. High open country.
2. The many Bronze Age burial mounds on Salisbury Plain. "Giant wicker": Aylett Sammes, in Britannia Antiqua Illustrata (1676), had described, as
a rite of the ancient Britons, that they wove a huge

wicker structure in the shape of a man, filled it
with living humans, and set it afire.
3. Conjecture (a verb).
4. Many 18th-century antiquarians believed the
Druids to be the forerunners of the bards, the poets
whose songs kept alive the nation's traditions in the
era prior to the advent of writing.
5. 1797, the year of the start of his friendship with
Coleridge.

From Book Fourteenth
Conclusion

[THE VISION ON MOUNT SNOWDON.]

In one of those Excursions (may they ne'er
Fade from remembrance!), through the Northern tracts
Of Cambria ranging with a youthful Friend,
I left Bethgellert's huts at couching-time,
5   And westward took my way, to see the sun
Rise from the top of Snowdon.[1] To the door
Of a rude Cottage at the Mountain's base
We came, and rouzed the Shepherd who attends
The adventurous Stranger's steps, a trusty Guide;
10   Then, cheered by short refreshment, sallied forth.
—It was a close, warm, breezeless summer night,
Wan, dull, and glaring,[2] with a dripping fog
Low-hung and thick, that covered all the sky.
But, undiscouraged, we began to climb
15   The mountain-side. The mist soon girt us round,
And, after ordinary Travellers' talk
With our Conductor, pensively we sank
Each into commerce with his private thoughts:
Thus did we breast the ascent, and by myself
20   Was nothing either seen or heard that checked
Those musings or diverted, save that once
The Shepherd's Lurcher,° who, among the crags,   hunting dog
Had to his joy unearthed a Hedgehog, teased
His coiled-up Prey with barkings turbulent.
25   This small adventure, for even such it seemed
In that wild place, and at the dead of night,
Being over and forgotten, on we wound
In silence as before. With forehead bent
Earthward, as if in opposition set
30   Against an enemy, I panted up
With eager pace, and no less eager thoughts.
Thus might we wear a midnight hour away,
Ascending at loose distance each from each,
And I, as chanced, the foremost of the Band:
35   When at my feet the ground appeared to brighten,
And with a step or two seemed brighter still;
Nor was time given to ask, or learn, the cause;
For instantly a light upon the turf
Fell like a flash; and lo! as I looked up,
40   The Moon hung naked in a firmament

1. Wordsworth climbed Mount Snowdon—the highest peak in Wales ("Cambria"), and some ten miles from the sea—with Robert Jones, the friend with whom he had also tramped through the Alps (book 6). The climb started from the village of Bethgelert at "couching-time" (line 4), the time of night when the sheep lie down to sleep. This event had taken place in 1791 (or possibly 1793); Words-worth presents it out of its chronological order to introduce at this point a great natural "type" or "emblem" (lines 66, 70) for the mind, and especially for the activity of the imagination, whose "restoration" he has described in the two preceding books.
2. In north of England dialect, *glairie*, applied to the weather, means dull, rainy.

Of azure without cloud, and at my feet
Rested a silent sea of hoary mist.
A hundred hills their dusky backs upheaved
All over this still Ocean;³ and beyond,
45 Far, far beyond, the solid vapours stretched,
In Headlands, tongues, and promontory shapes,
Into the main Atlantic, that appeared
To dwindle, and give up his majesty,
Usurped upon far as the sight could reach.
50 Not so the ethereal Vault; encroachment none
Was there, nor loss;⁴ only the inferior stars
Had disappeared, or shed a fainter light
In the clear presence of the full-orbed Moon;
Who, from her sovereign elevation, gazed
55 Upon the billowy ocean, as it lay
All meek and silent, save that through a rift
Not distant from the shore whereon we stood,
A fixed, abysmal, gloomy breathing-place,
Mounted the roar of waters—torrents—streams
60 Innumerable, roaring with one voice!
Heard over earth and sea, and in that hour,
For so it seemed, felt by the starry heavens.
    When into air had partially dissolved
That Vision, given to Spirits of the night,
65 And three chance human Wanderers, in calm thought
Reflected, it appeared to me the type
Of a majestic Intellect, its acts
And its possessions, what it has and craves,
What in itself it is, and would become.
70 There I beheld the emblem of a Mind
That feeds upon infinity, that broods
Over the dark abyss, intent to hear
Its voices issuing forth to silent light
In one continuous stream; a mind sustained
75 By recognitions of transcendent power
In sense, conducting to ideal form;
In soul, of more than mortal privilege.⁵
One function, above all, of such a mind
Had Nature shadowed there, by putting forth,
80 'Mid circumstances awful° and sublime,   *awe-inspiring*
That mutual domination which she loves
To exert upon the face of outward things,
So moulded, joined, abstracted; so endowed
With interchangeable supremacy,
85 That Men least sensitive see, hear, perceive,
And cannot chuse but feel. The power which all
Acknowledge when thus moved, which Nature thus
To bodily sense exhibits, is the express

---

3. In Milton's description of God's creation of the land from the waters, "the mountains huge appear / Emergent, and their broad bare backs upheave / Into the clouds" (*Paradise Lost* 7.285–87).
4. The mist projected in various shapes over the Irish Sea, but did not "encroach" on the heavens
overhead.
5. The sense of lines 74–77 seems to be that the mind of someone who is gifted beyond the ordinary lot of mortals recognizes its power to transcend the senses by converting sensory objects into ideal forms.

Resemblance of that glorious faculty
90 That higher minds bear with them as their own.[6]
This is the very spirit in which they deal
With the whole compass of the universe:
They, from their native selves, can send abroad
Kindred mutations; for themselves create
95 A like existence; and whene'er it dawns
Created for them, catch it;—or are caught
By its inevitable mastery,
Like angels stopped upon the wing by sound
Of harmony from heaven's remotest spheres.
100 Them the enduring and the transient both
Serve to exalt; they build up greatest things
From least suggestions; ever on the watch,
Willing to work and to be wrought upon,
They need not extraordinary calls
105 To rouse them, in a world of life they live;
By sensible° impressions not enthralled,   *sensory*
But, by their quickening impulse, made more prompt
To hold fit converse with the spiritual world,
And with the generations of mankind
110 Spread over time, past, present, and to come,
Age after age, till Time shall be no more.
Such minds are truly from the Deity,
For they are powers; and hence the highest bliss
That flesh can know is theirs,—the consciousness
115 Of whom they are, habitually infused
Through every image, and through every thought,
And all affections° by communion raised   *emotions*
From earth to heaven, from human to divine.
Hence endless occupation for the Soul,
120 Whether discursive or intuitive;[7]
Hence chearfulness for acts of daily life,
Emotions which best foresight need not fear,
Most worthy then of trust when most intense:
Hence, amid ills that vex, and wrongs that crush
125 Our hearts, if here the words of holy Writ
May with fit reverence be applied, that peace
Which passeth understanding,[8]—that repose
In moral judgements which from this pure source
Must come, or will by Man be sought in vain.

�※ �※ �※

[CONCLUSION: "THE MIND OF MAN"]

And now, O Friend![9] this History is brought
To its appointed close: the discipline

---

6. The "glorious faculty" is the imagination, which transfigures and re-creates what is given to it by the senses, much as, in Wordsworth's account of this night on Snowdon, the moonlit mist transfigures the familiar landscape.
7. An echo of Archangel Raphael's account to Adam of the soul's powers of reason (*Paradise Lost* 5.488–89). Discursive reason, mainly a human

quality according to Raphael, undertakes to reach truths through a logical sequence of premises, observations, and conclusions; "intuitive" reason, mainly angelic, comprehends truths immediately.
8. Philippians 4.7: "The peace of God, which passeth all understanding." This passage of Christian piety was added by Wordsworth in a late revision.
9. Coleridge.

And consummation° of a Poet's mind   *completion*
305 In every thing that stood most prominent
Have faithfully been pictured; we have reached
The time (our guiding object from the first)
When we may, not presumptuously, I hope,
Suppose my powers so far confirmed, and such
310 My knowledge, as to make me capable
Of building up a Work that shall endure.

                 * * * Having now
Told what best merits mention, further pains
Our present purpose seems not to require,
And I have other tasks. Recall to mind
375 The mood in which this labour was begun.
O Friend! the termination of my course
Is nearer now, much nearer; yet even then,
In that distraction, and intense desire,
I said unto the life which I had lived,
380 Where art thou? Hear I not a voice from thee
Which 'tis reproach to hear?[1] Anon I rose
As if on wings, and saw beneath me stretched
Vast prospect of the world which I had been
And was; and hence this Song, which like a Lark
385 I have protracted, in the unwearied heavens
Singing, and often with more plaintive voice
To earth attempered° and her deep-drawn sighs,   *adapted*
Yet centering all in love, and in the end
All gratulant,° if rightly understood.[2]   *joyful*

                 ✼   ✼   ✼

Oh! yet a few short years of useful life,
And all will be complete, thy[3] race be run,
Thy monument of glory will be raised;
435 Then, though, too weak to tread the ways of truth,
This Age fall back to old idolatry,
Though Men return to servitude as fast
As the tide ebbs, to ignominy and shame
By Nations sink together,[4] we shall still
440 Find solace—knowing what we have learnt to know,
Rich in true happiness if allowed to be
Faithful alike in forwarding a day
Of firmer trust, joint laborers in the Work
(Should Providence such grace to us vouchsafe°)   *grant*
445 Of their deliverance, surely yet to come.
Prophets of Nature, we to them will speak
A lasting inspiration, sanctified
By reason, blest by faith: what we have loved

---

1. As he approaches the end, Wordsworth recalls the beginning of *The Prelude*. The reproachful voice is that which asked the question, "Was it for this?" in 1.269ff.
2. The poet finds that suffering and frustration are justified when seen as part of the overall design of the life he has just reviewed. The passage echoes the conclusion of Pope's *An Essay on Man* 1.291–92: "All discord, harmony not understood;/All partial evil, universal good."
3. Coleridge's.
4. I.e., though men—whole nations of them together—sink to ignominy (disgrace) and shame.

Others will love, and we will teach them how,
450   Instruct them how the mind of Man becomes
A thousand times more beautiful than the earth
On which he dwells, above this Frame of things
(Which 'mid all revolutions in the hopes
And fears of Men doth still remain unchanged)
455   In beauty exalted, as it is itself
Of quality and fabric more divine.

1798–1839   1850

DOROTHY WORDSWORTH
1771–1855

Dorothy Wordsworth has an enduring place in English literature even though she wrote almost no word for publication. Not until long after her death did scholars gradually retrieve and print her letters, a few poems, and a series of journals that she kept sporadically between 1798 and 1828 because, she wrote, "I shall give William Pleasure by it." It has always been known, from tributes to her by her brother and Coleridge, that she exerted an important influence on the lives and writings of both these men. It is now apparent that she also possessed a power surpassing that of the two poets for precise observation of people and the natural world, together with a genius for terse, luminous, and delicately nuanced description in prose.

Dorothy was born on Christmas Day 1771, twenty-one months after William; she was the only girl of five Wordsworth children. From her seventh year, when her mother died, she lived with various relatives—some of them tolerant and affectionate, others rigid and tyrannical—and saw William and her other brothers only occasionally, during the boys' summer vacations from school. In 1795, when she was twenty-four, an inheritance that William received enabled her to carry out a long-held plan to join her brother in a house at Racedown, and the two spent the rest of their long lives together, first in Dorsetshire and Somersetshire, in the southwest of England, then in their beloved Lake District. She uncomplainingly subordinated her own talents to looking after her brother and his household. She also became William's secretary, tirelessly copying and recopying the manuscripts of his poems to ready them for publication. Despite the scolding of a great-aunt, who deemed "rambling about . . . on foot" unladylike, she accompanied her brother, too, in vigorous cross-country walks in which they sometimes covered as much as thirty-three miles in a day.

All her adult life she was overworked; after a severe illness in 1835, she suffered a physical and mental collapse. She spent the rest of her existence as an invalid. Hardest for her family to endure was the drastic change in her temperament: from a high-spirited and compassionate woman she became (save for brief intervals of lucidity) querulous, demanding, and at times violent. In this half-life she lingered for twenty years, attended devotedly by William until his death five years before her own in 1855.

Our principal selections are from the journal Dorothy kept in 1798 at Alfoxden, Somersetshire, where the Wordsworths had moved from Racedown to be near Coleridge at Nether Stowey, as well as from her journals while at Grasmere (1800–03), with Coleridge residing some thirteen miles away at Greta Hall, Keswick. Her records cover the period when both men emerged as major poets, and in their achievements Dorothy played an indispensable role. In book 11 of *The Prelude*, William says that in the time of his spiritual crisis, Dorothy "maintained for me a saving intercourse /

With my true self" and "preserved me still / A Poet"; in a letter of 1797, Coleridge stressed the delicacy and tact in the responses of William's "exquisite sister" to the world of sense: "Her manners are simple, ardent, impressive. . . . Her information various—her eye watchful in minutest observation of nature—and her taste a perfect electrometer—it bends, protrudes, and draws in, at subtlest beauties & most recondite faults."

The verbal sketches of natural scenes given in the journal passages that we reprint are often echoed in Wordsworth's and Coleridge's poems. Of at least equal importance for Wordsworth was her chronicling of the busy wayfaring life of rural England. These were exceedingly hard times for country people, when the suffering caused by the displacement of small farms and of household crafts by large-scale farms and industries was aggravated by the economic distress caused by protracted Continental wars (see Wordsworth's comment in *The Ruined Cottage*, lines 133ff., p. 283). Peddlers, maimed war veterans, leech gatherers, adult and infant beggars, ousted farm families, fugitives, and women abandoned by husbands or lovers streamed along the rural roads and into William's brooding poetic imagination—often by way of Dorothy's prose records.

The journals also show the intensity of Dorothy's love for her brother. Inevitably in our era, the mutual devotion of the orphaned brother and sister has evoked psychoanalytic speculation. It is important to note that Mary Hutchinson, a gentle and openhearted young woman, had been Dorothy's closest friend since childhood, and that Dorothy encouraged William's courtship and marriage, even though she realized that it entailed her own displacement as a focus of her brother's life. All the evidence indicates that their lives in a single household never strained the affectionate relationship between the two women; indeed Dorothy, until she became an invalid, added to her former functions as William's chief support, housekeeper, and scribe a loving ministration to her brother's children.

Because the manuscript of the Alfoxden journal has disappeared, the text printed here is from the transcript published by William Knight in 1897. The selections from the Grasmere journals reproduce Pamela Woof's exact transcription of the manuscripts in the Wordsworth Library at Dove Cottage (Oxford University Press, 1991). Dorothy Wordsworth's poems, written mainly for children in her brother's household and surviving as manuscripts in one or another family commonplace book, were not collected until 1987, when Susan M. Levin edited thirty of them in an appendix ("The Collected Poems of Dorothy Wordsworth") to her *Dorothy Wordsworth and Romanticism*. The two poems included here are reprinted from this source.

From The Alfoxden Journal

Jan. 31, 1798. Set forward to Stowey[1] at half-past five. A violent storm in the wood; sheltered under the hollies. When we left home the moon immensely large, the sky scattered over with clouds. These soon closed in, contracting the dimensions of the moon without concealing her.[2] The sound of the pattering shower, and the gusts of wind, very grand. Left the wood when nothing remained of the storm but the driving wind, and a few scattering drops of rain. Presently all clear, Venus first showing herself between the struggling clouds; afterwards Jupiter appeared. The hawthorn hedges, black and pointed, glittering with millions of diamond drops; the hollies shining with broader patches of light. The road to the village of Holford glittered like another

---

1. I.e., to Coleridge's cottage at Nether Stowey, three miles from Alfoxden.

2. Cf. Coleridge's *Christabel*, lines 16–19 (p. 450).

stream. On our return, the wind high—a violent storm of hail and rain at the Castle of Comfort.[3] All the Heavens seemed in one perpetual motion when the rain ceased; the moon appearing, now half veiled, and now retired behind heavy clouds, the stars still moving, the roads very dirty.

* * *

Feb. 3. A mild morning, the windows open at breakfast, the redbreasts singing in the garden. Walked with Coleridge over the hills. The sea at first obscured by vapour; that vapour afterwards slid in one mighty mass along the sea-shore; the islands and one point of land clear beyond it. The distant country (which was purple in the clear dull air), overhung by straggling clouds that sailed over it, appeared like the darker clouds, which are often seen at a great distance apparently motionless, while the nearer ones pass quickly over them, driven by the lower winds. I never saw such a union of earth, sky, and sea. The clouds beneath our feet spread themselves to the water, and the clouds of the sky almost joined them. Gathered sticks in the wood; a perfect stillness. The redbreasts sang upon the leafless boughs. Of a great number of sheep in the field, only one standing. Returned to dinner at five o'clock. The moonlight still and warm as a summer's night at nine o'clock.

Feb. 4. Walked a great part of the way to Stowey with Coleridge. The morning warm and sunny. The young lasses seen on the hill-tops, in the villages and roads, in their summer holiday clothes—pink petticoats and blue. Mothers with their children in arms, and the little ones that could just walk, tottering by their side. Midges or small flies spinning in the sunshine; the songs of the lark and redbreast; daisies upon the turf; the hazels in blossom; honeysuckles budding. I saw one solitary strawberry flower under a hedge. The furze gay with blossom. The moss rubbed from the pailings by the sheep, that leave locks of wool, and the red marks with which they are spotted, upon the wood.[4]

* * *

Feb. 8. Went up the Park, and over the tops of the hills, till we came to a new and very delicious pathway, which conducted us to the Coombe.[5] Sat a considerable time upon the heath. Its surface restless and glittering with the motion of the scattered piles of withered grass, and the waving of the spiders' threads.[6] On our return the mist still hanging over the sea, but the opposite coast clear, and the rocky cliffs distinguishable. In the deep Coombe, as we stood upon the sunless hill, we saw miles of grass, light and glittering, and the insects passing.

Feb. 9. William gathered sticks.

Feb. 10. Walked to Woodlands, and to the waterfall. The adder's-tongue and the ferns green in the low damp dell. These plants now in perpetual motion from the current of the air; in summer only moved by the drippings of the rocks.[7] A cloudy day.

* * *

3. A tavern halfway between Holford and Nether Stowey.
4. Cf. Wordsworth's *The Ruined Cottage,* lines 330–36 (p. 287).
5. Hodder's Coombe in the Quantock Hills, near Alfoxden. A combe is a deep valley on the flank of a hill.
6. Cf. Coleridge's *The Rime of the Ancient Mariner,* line 184 (p. 435).
7. Cf. the description of the dell in Coleridge's "This Lime-Tree Bower My Prison," lines 13–20 (p. 428).

Mar. 7. William and I drank tea at Coleridge's. A cloudy sky. Observed nothing particularly interesting—the distant prospect obscured. One only leaf upon the top of a tree—the sole remaining leaf—danced round and round like a rag blown by the wind.[8]

Mar. 8. Walked in the Park in the morning. I sate under the fir trees. Coleridge came after dinner, so we did not walk again. A foggy morning, but a clear sunny day.

Mar. 9. A clear sunny morning, went to meet Mr and Mrs Coleridge. The day very warm.

Mar. 10. Coleridge, Wm, and I walked in the evening to the top of the hill. We all passed the morning in sauntering about the park and gardens, the children playing about, the old man at the top of the hill gathering furze; interesting groups of human creatures, the young frisking and dancing in the sun, the elder quietly drinking in the life and soul of the sun and air.

Mar. 11. A cold day. The children went down towards the sea. William and I walked to the top of the hills above Holford. Met the blacksmith. Pleasant to see the labourer on Sunday jump with the friskiness of a cow upon a sunny day.

✻   ✻   ✻

1798   1897

From The Grasmere Journals

1800

May 14 1800 [Wednesday]. Wm & John set off into Yorkshire[1] after dinner at ½ past 2 o'clock—cold pork in their pockets. I left them at the turning of the Low-wood bay under the trees. My heart was so full that I could hardly speak to W when I gave him a farewell kiss. I sate a long time upon a stone at the margin of the lake, & after a flood of tears my heart was easier. The lake looked to me I knew not why dull and melancholy, and the weltering on the shores seemed a heavy sound. I walked as long as I could amongst the stones of the shore. The wood rich in flowers. A beautiful yellow, palish yellow flower, that looked thick round & double, & smelt very sweet—I supposed it was a ranunculus—Crowfoot, the grassy-leaved Rabbit-toothed white flower, strawberries, geranium—scentless violet, anemones two kinds, orchises, primroses. The heckberry very beautiful, the crab coming out as a low shrub. Met a blind man, driving a very large beautiful Bull & a cow—he walked with two sticks. Came home by Clappersgate. The valley very green, many sweet views up to Rydale head when I could juggle away the fine houses, but they disturbed me even more than when I have been happier—one beautiful view of the Bridge, without Sir Michael's.[2] Sate down very often, tho' it was cold. I resolved to write a journal of the time till W & J return, & I set about keeping my resolve because I will not quarrel with myself, & because I shall give Wm Pleasure by it when he comes home again. At Rydale a woman of the village,

8. Cf. *Christabel,* lines 49ff. (p. 451).
1. William and his younger brother John, on the way to visit Mary Hutchinson, whom William was

to marry two and a half years later.
2. Sir Michael le Fleming's estate, Rydal Hall. "Without": outside or beyond.

stout & well-dressed, begged a halfpenny—she had never she said done it before—but these hard times!—Arrived at home with a bad head-ache, set some slips of privett. The evening cold, had a fire—my face now flame-coloured. It is nine o'clock. I shall soon go to bed. A young woman begged at the door—she had come from Manchester on Sunday morn with two shillings & a slip of paper which she supposed a Bank note—it was a cheat. She had buried her husband & three children within a year & a half—all in one grave—burying very dear—paupers all put in one place—20 shillings paid for as much ground as will bury a man—a stone to be put over it or the right will be lost—11/6³ each time the ground is opened. Oh! that I had a letter from William!

✳   ✳   ✳

Friday 3rd October. Very rainy all the morning—little Sally learning to mark. Wm walked to Ambleside after dinner. I went with him part of the way—he talked much about the object of his Essay for the 2nd volume of LB.⁴ I returned expecting the Simpsons—they did not come. I should have met Wm but my teeth ached & it was showery & late—he returned after 10. Amos Cottle's⁵ death in the Morning Post. Wrote to S. Lowthian.⁶

N.B. When Wm & I returned from accompanying Jones we met an old man almost double,⁷ he had on a coat thrown over his shoulders above his waistcoat & coat. Under this he carried a bundle & had an apron on & a night cap. His face was interesting. He had dark eyes & a long nose—John who afterwards met him at Wythburn took him for a Jew. He was of Scotch parents but had been born in the army. He had had a wife "& a good woman & it pleased God to bless us with ten children"—all these were dead but one of whom he had not heard for many years, a sailor—his trade was to gather leeches, but now leeches are scarce & he had not strength for it—he lived by begging & was making his way to Carlisle where he should buy a few godly books to sell. He said leeches were very scarce partly owing to this dry season, but many years they have been scarce—he supposed it owing to their being much sought after, that they did not breed fast, & were of slow growth. Leeches were formerly 2/6 [per] 100; they are now 30/. He had been hurt in driving a cart his leg broke his body driven over his skull fractured—he felt no pain till he recovered from his first insensibility. It was then late in the evening—when the light was just going away.

✳   ✳   ✳

Saturday [Oct.] 11th. A fine October morning—sat in the house working all the morning. Wm composing—Sally Ashburner learning to mark. After Dinner we walked up Greenhead Gill in search of a sheepfold.⁸ We went by Mr Oliff's & through his woods. It was a delightful day & the views looked excessively chearful & beautiful chiefly that from Mr Oliff's field where our house is to be built. The colours of the mountains soft & rich, with orange fern—The Cattle pasturing upon the hill-tops Kites sailing as in the sky above our heads—

---

3. Eleven shillings, six pence.
4. The Preface to the second edition of *Lyrical Ballads,* 1800.
5. The brother of Joseph Cottle, Bristol publisher of the first edition of *Lyrical Ballads.*
6. Sally Lowthian, who had been a servant in the house of the Wordsworths' father.
7. William's "Resolution and Independence,"

composed one and a half years later, incorporated various details of Dorothy's description of the leech gatherer. See May 4 and 7, 1802 (pp. 398 and 400), for William working on the poem he originally called "The Leech Gatherer."
8. The sheepfold (pen for sheep) in William's "Michael"; lines 1–17 of the poem describe the walk up Greenhead Ghyll.

Sheep bleating & in lines & chains & patterns scattered over the mountains. They come down & feed on the little green islands in the beds of the torrents & so may be swept away. The Sheepfold is falling away it is built nearly in the form of a heart unequally divided. Look down the brook & see the drops rise upwards & sparkle in the air, at the little falls, the higher sparkles the tallest. We walked along the turf of the mountain till we came to a Cattle track— made by the cattle which come upon the hills. We drank tea at Mr Simpson's returned at about nine—a fine mild night.

Sunday 12th October. Beautiful day. Sate in the house writing in the morning while Wm went into the Wood to compose. Wrote to John in the morning— copied poems for the LB, in the evening wrote to Mrs Rawson. Mary Jameson & Sally Ashburner dined. We pulled apples after dinner, a large basket full. We walked before tea by Bainriggs to observe the many coloured foliage the oaks dark green with yellow leaves—The birches generally still green, some near the water yellowish. The Sycamore crimson & crimson-tufted—the mountain ash a deep orange—the common ash Lemon colour but many ashes still fresh in their summer green. Those that were discoloured chiefly near the water. William composing in the Evening. Went to bed at 12 o'clock.

✻   ✻   ✻

1801

Tuesday [Nov.] 24th. A rainy morning. We all were well except that my head ached a little & I took my Breakfast in bed. I read a little of Chaucer, prepared the goose for dinner, & then we all walked out—I was obliged to return for my fur tippet & Spenser[9] it was so cold. We had intended going to Easedale but we shaped our course to Mr Gell's cottage. It was very windy & we heard the wind everywhere about us as we went along the Lane but the walls sheltered us—John Green's house looked pretty under Silver How—as we were going along we were stopped at once, at the distance perhaps of 50 yards from our favorite Birch tree it was yielding to the gusty wind with all its tender twigs, the sun shone upon it & it glanced in the wind like a flying sunshiny shower—it was a tree in shape with stem & branches but it was like a Spirit of water—The sun went in & it resumed its purplish appearance the twigs still yielding to the wind but not so visibly to us. The other Birch trees that were near it looked bright & chearful—but it was a Creature by its own self among them. We could not get into Mr Gell's grounds—the old tree fallen from its undue exaltation above the Gate. A shower came on when we were at Benson's. We went through the wood—it became fair, there was a rainbow which spanned the lake from the Island house to the foot of Bainriggs. The village looked populous & beautiful. Catkins are coming out palm trees budding— the alder with its plumb coloured buds. We came home over the stepping stones the Lake was foamy with white waves. I saw a solitary butter flower in the wood. *I* found it not easy to get over the stepping stones—reached home at dinner time. Sent Peggy Ashburner some goose. She sent me some honey— with a thousand thanks—"alas the gratitude of men has & c"[1] I went in to set

9. A close-fitting jacket worn by women and children. A tippet is a stole or scarf.
1. A quotation from William's "Simon Lee":

"Alas! the gratitude of men / Has oft'ner left me mourning."

her right about this & sate a while with her. She talked about Thomas's having sold his land—"Ay" says she I said many a time "He's not come fra London to buy our Land however" then she told me with what pains & industry they had made up their taxes interest &c &c—how they all got up at 5 o'clock in the morning to spin & Thomas carded, & that they had paid off a hundred pound of the interest. She said she used to take such pleasure in the cattle & sheep— "O how pleased I used to be when they fetched them down, & when I had been a bit poorly I would gang out upon a hill & look over t' fields & see them & it used to do me so much good you cannot think"—Molly said to me when I came in "poor Body! she's very ill but one does not know how long she may last. Many a fair face may gang before her." We sate by the fire without work for some time then Mary read a poem of Daniell upon Learning.[2] After tea Wm read Spenser now & then a little aloud to us. We were making his waistcoat. We had a note from Mrs C., with bad news from poor C very ill. William walked to John's grove—I went to meet him—moonlight but it rained. I met him before I had got as far as John Baty's he had been surprized & terrified by a sudden rushing of winds which seemed to bring earth sky & lake together, as if the whole were going to enclose him in—he was glad he was in a high Road.

In speaking of our walk on Sunday Evening the 22nd November I forgot to notice one most impressive sight—it was the moon & the moonlight seen through hurrying driving clouds immediately behind the Stone man upon the top of the hill on the Forest side. Every tooth & every edge of Rock was visible, & the Man stood like a Giant watching from the Roof of a lofty castle. The hill seemed perpendicular from the darkness below it. It was a sight that I could call to mind at any time it was so distinct.

*   *   *

1802

Thursday [*Mar. 4*]. Before we had quite finished Breakfast Calvert's man brought the horses for Wm.[3] We had a deal to do to shave—pens to make— poems to put in order for writing, to settle the dress pack up &c &. The man came before the pens were made & he was obliged to leave me with only two— Since he has left me (at ½ past 11) it is now 2 I have been putting the Drawers into order, laid by his clothes which we had thrown here & there & everywhere, filed two months' newspapers & got my dinner 2 boiled eggs & 2 apple tarts. I have set Molly on to clear the garden a little, & I myself have helped. I transplanted some snowdrops—The Bees are busy—Wm has a nice bright day. It was hard frost in the night—The Robins are singing sweetly—Now for my walk. I *will* be busy, I *will* look well & be well when he comes back to me. O the Darling! Here is one of his bitten apples! I can hardly find in my heart to throw it into the fire. I must wash myself, then off—I walked round the two Lakes crossed the stepping stones at Rydale Foot. Sate down where we always sit. I was full of thoughts about my darling. Blessings on him. I came home at the foot of our own hill under Loughrigg. They are making sad ravages in the woods—Benson's Wood is going & the wood above the River. The wind has blown down a small fir tree on the Rock that terminates John's path—I

---

2. Samuel Daniel's long poem *Musophilus: Containing a General Defense of Learning* (1599).

3. For a journey to Keswick, to visit Coleridge.

suppose the wind of Wednesday night. I read German after my return till tea time. After tea I worked & read the LB, enchanted with the Idiot Boy. Wrote to Wm then went to Bed. It snowed when I went to Bed.

* * *

Monday [Mar. 22]. A rainy day—William very poorly. Mr Luff came in after dinner & brought us 2 letters from Sara H. & one from poor Annette. I read Sara's letters while he was here. I finished my letters to M. & S. & wrote to my Br Richard. We talked a good deal about C. & other interesting things. We resolved to see Annette, & that Wm should go to Mary.[4] We wrote to Coleridge not to expect us till Thursday or Friday.

Tuesday [Mar. 23]. A mild morning William worked at the Cuckow poem.[5] I sewed beside him. After dinner he slept I read German, & at the closing in of day went to sit in the Orchard—he came to me, & walked backwards & forwards. We talked about C—Wm repeated the poem to me—I left him there & in 20 minutes he came in, rather tired with attempting to write—he is now reading Ben Jonson I am going to read German it is about 10 o'clock, a quiet night. The fire flutters & the watch ticks I hear nothing else save the Breathing of my Beloved & he now & then pushes his book forward & turns over a leaf. Fletcher is not come home. No letter from C.

* * *

Thursday [Apr.] 15th. It was a threatening misty morning—but mild. We set off after dinner from Eusemere—Mrs Clarkson went a short way with us but turned back. The wind was furious & we thought we must have returned. We first rested in the large Boat-house, then under a furze Bush opposite Mr Clarksons, saw the plough going in the field. The wind seized our breath the Lake was rough. There was a Boat by itself floating in the middle of the Bay below Water Millock—We rested again in the Water Millock Lane. The hawthorns are black & green, the birches here & there greenish but there is yet more of purple to be seen on the Twigs. We got over into a field to avoid some cows—people working, a few primroses by the roadside, wood-sorrel flower, the anemone, scentless violets, strawberries, & that starry yellow flower which Mrs C calls pile wort. When we were in the woods beyond Gowbarrow park we saw a few daffodils close to the water side.[6] We fancied that the lake had floated the seeds ashore & that the little colony had so sprung up—But as we went along there were more & yet more & at last under the boughs of the trees, we saw that there was a long belt of them along the shore, about the breadth of a country turnpike road. I never saw daffodils so beautiful they grew among the mossy stones about & about them, some rested their heads upon these stones as on a pillow for weariness & the rest tossed & reeled & danced & seemed as if they verily laughed with the wind that blew upon them over the lake, they looked so gay ever glancing ever changing. This wind blew directly over the lake to them. There was here & there a little knot & a few stragglers a few yards higher up but they were so few as not to disturb the

---

4. It had been arranged several months earlier that William was to marry Mary Hutchinson ("Sara H" is Mary's sister, with whom Coleridge had fallen in love). Now the Wordsworths resolve to go to France to settle affairs with Annette Vallon, mother of William's daughter, Caroline. William did not conceal the facts of his early love affair from his family, or from Mary Hutchinson.
5. "To the Cuckoo."
6. William did not compose his poem on the daffodils, "I wandered lonely as a cloud," until two years later. Comparison with the poem will show how extensive was his use of Dorothy's prose description (see p. 305).

simplicity & unity & life of that one busy highway—We rested again & again. The Bays were stormy & we heard the waves at different distances & in the middle of the water like the sea—Rain came on, we were wet when we reached Luffs but we called in. Luckily all was chearless & gloomy so we faced the storm—we *must* have been wet if we had waited—put on dry clothes at Dobson's. I was very kindly treated by a young woman, the Landlady looked sour but it is her way. She gave us a goodish supper. Excellent ham & potatoes. We paid 7/ when we came away. William was sitting by a bright fire when I came downstairs. He soon made his way to the Library piled up in a corner of the window. He brought out a volume of Enfield's Speaker,[7] another miscellany, & an odd volume of Congreve's plays. We had a glass of warm rum & water—We enjoyed ourselves & wished for Mary. It rained & blew when we went to bed. NB Deer in Gowbarrow park like skeletons.

Friday 16th April (Good Friday). When I undrew my curtains in the morning, I was much affected by the beauty of the prospect & the change. The sun shone, the wind has passed away, the hills looked chearful, the river was very bright as it flowed into the lake. The Church rises up behind a little knot of Rocks, the steeple not so high as an ordinary 3 story house. Bees, in a row in the garden under the wall. After Wm had shaved we set forward. The valley is at first broken by little rocky woody knolls that make retiring places, fairy valleys in the vale, the river winds along under these hills travelling not in a bustle but not slowly to the lake. We saw a fisherman in the flat meadow on the other side of the water. He came towards us & threw his line over the two arched Bridge. It is a Bridge of a heavy construction, almost bending inwards in the middle, but it is grey & there is a look of ancientry in the architecture of it that pleased me. As we go on the vale opens out more into one vale with somewhat of a cradle Bed. Cottages with groups of trees on the side of the hills. We passed a pair of twin Children 2 years old—& Sate on the next bridge which we crossed a single arch. We rested again upon the Turf & looked at the same Bridge. We observed arches in the water occasioned by the large stones sending it down in two streams—a Sheep came plunging through the river, stumbled up the Bank & passed close to us, it had been frightened by an insignificant little Dog on the other side, its fleece dropped a glittering shower under its belly—Primroses by the roadside, pile wort that shone like stars of gold in the Sun, violets, strawberries, retired & half buried among the grass. When we came to the foot of Brothers water I left William sitting on the Bridge & went along the path on the right side of the Lake through the wood—I was delighted with what I saw. The water under the boughs of the bare old trees, the simplicity of the mountains & the exquisite beauty of the path. There was one grey cottage. I repeated the Glowworm[8] as I walked along—I hung over the gate, & thought I could have stayed for ever. When I returned I found William writing a poem descriptive of the sights & sounds we saw & heard. There was the gentle flowing of the stream, the glittering lively lake, green fields without a living creature to be seen on them, behind us, a flat pasture with 42 cattle feeding to our left the road leading to the hamlet, no smoke there, the sun shone on the bare roofs. The people were at work ploughing, harrowing & sowing—Lasses spreading dung, a dog's barking now & then, cocks crowing, birds twittering, the snow in patches at the top

7. William Enfield's *The Speaker* (1774), a volume of selections suitable for elocution.
8. William's poem beginning "Among all lovely things my Love had been," composed four days earlier; "my Love" in this line is Dorothy.

of the highest hills, yellow palms, purple & green twigs on the Birches, ashes with their glittering spikes quite bare. The hawthorn a bright green with black stems under the oak. The moss of the oak glossy. We then went on, passed two sisters at work, *they first passed us,* one with two pitch forks in her hand. The other had a spade. We had some talk with them. They laughed aloud after we were gone perhaps half in wantonness, half boldness. William finished his poem before we got to the foot of Kirkstone.[9] * * *

* * *

Thursday [Apr.] 29. A beautiful morning. The sun shone & all was pleasant. We sent off our parcel to Coleridge by the waggon. Mr Simpson heard the Cuckow today. Before we went out after I had written down the Tinker (which William finished this morning)[1] Luff called. He was very lame, limped into the kitchen—he came on a little Pony. We then went to John's Grove, sate a while at first. Afterwards William lay, & I lay in the trench under the fence—he with his eyes shut & listening to the waterfalls & the Birds. There was no one waterfall above another[2]—it was a sound of waters in the air—the voice of the air. William heard me breathing & rustling now & then but we both lay still, & unseen by one another—he thought that it would be as sweet thus to lie so in the grave, to hear the *peaceful* sounds of the earth & just to know that our dear friends were near. The Lake was still. There was a Boat out. Silver How reflected with delicate purple & yellowish hues as I have seen Spar—Lambs on the island & running races together by the half dozen in the round field near us. The copses green*ish*, hawthorn green.—Came home to dinner then went to Mr Simpson. We rested a long time under a wall. Sheep & lambs were in the field—cottages smoking. As I lay down on the grass, I observed the glittering silver line on the ridges of the Backs of the sheep, owing to their situation respecting the Sun—which made them look beautiful but with some-thing of strangeness, like animals of another kind—as if belonging to a more splendid world. Met old Mr S at the door—Mrs S poorly—I got mullens & pansies—I was sick & ill & obliged to come home soon. We went to bed immediately—I slept up stairs. The air coldish where it was felt somewhat frosty.

* * *

Tuesday May 4th. William had slept pretty well & though he went to bed nervous & jaded in the extreme he rose refreshed. I wrote the Leech Gatherer[3] for him which he had begun the night before & of which he wrote several stanzas in bed this Monday morning. It was very hot, we called at Mr Simpson's door as we passed but did not go in. We rested several times by the way, read & repeated the Leech Gatherer. We were almost melted before we were at the top of the hill. We saw Coleridge on the Wytheburn side of the water. He crossed the Beck to us. Mr Simpson was fishing there. William & I ate a Luncheon, then went on towards the waterfall. It is a glorious wild solitude under that lofty purple crag. It stood upright by itself. Its own self & its shadow below, one mass—all else was sunshine. We went on further. A Bird at the top of the crags was flying round & round & looked in thinness & transparency,

9. The short lyric "Written in March."
1. William never published his comic poem "The Tinker." It was first printed in 1897.
2. I.e., no waterfall could be heard individually.

3. The poem that was published as "Resolution and Independence." For its origin see the entry for October 3, 1800 (p. 393).

shape & motion like a moth. We climbed the hill but looked in vain for a shade except at the foot of the great waterfall, & there we did not like to stay on account of the loose stones above our heads. We came down & rested upon a moss covered Rock, rising out of the bed of the River. There we lay ate our dinner & stayed there till about 4 o'clock or later—Wm & C repeated & read verses. I drank a little Brandy & water & was in Heaven. The Stags horn is very beautiful & fresh springing upon the fells. Mountain ashes, green. We drank tea at a farm house. The woman had not a pleasant countenance, but was civil enough. She had a pretty Boy a year old whom she suckled. We parted from Coleridge at Sara's Crag after having looked at the Letters which C carved in the morning. I kissed them all. Wm deepened the T with C's pen-knife.[4] We sate afterwards on the wall, seeing the sun go down & the reflections in the still water. C looked well & parted from us chearfully, hopping up upon the side stones. On the Rays we met a woman with 2 little girls one in her arms the other about 4 years old walking by her side, a pretty little thing, but half starved. She had on a pair of slippers that had belonged to some gentleman's child, down at the heels—it was not easy to keep them on—but, poor thing! young as she was, she walked carefully with them. Alas too young for such cares & such travels—The Mother when we accosted her told us that her husband had left her & gone off with another woman & how she "pursued" them. Then her fury kindled & her eyes rolled about. She changed again to tears. She was a Cockermouth woman—30 years of age a child at Cockermouth when I was—I was moved & gave her a shilling, I believe 6[d] more than I ought to have given. We had the crescent moon with the "auld moon in her arms."[5]—We rested often:—always upon the Bridges. Reached home at about 10 o'clock. The Lloyds had been here in our absence. We went soon to bed. I repeated verses to William while he was in bed—he was soothed & I left him. "This is the Spot"[6] over & over again.

❖   ❖   ❖

6th May Thursday 1802. A sweet morning we have put the finishing stroke to our Bower & here we are sitting in the orchard. It is one o'clock. We are sitting upon a seat under the wall which I found my Brother building up when I came to him with his apple—he had intended that it should have been done before I came. It is a nice cool shady spot. The small Birds are singing—Lambs bleating, Cuckow calling—The Thrush sings by Fits. Thomas Ashburner's axe is going quietly (without passion) in the orchard—Hens are cackling, Flies humming, the women talking together at their doors—Plumb & pear trees are in Blossom—apple trees greenish—the opposite woods green, the crows are cawing. We have heard Ravens. The ash trees are in blossom, Birds flying all about us. The stitchwort is coming out, there is one budding Lychnis, the primroses are passing their prime. Celandine violets & wood sorrel for ever more little—geraniums & pansies on the wall. We walked in the evening to Tail End to enquire about hurdles for the orchard shed & about Mr Luff's flower—The flower dead—no hurdles. I went to look at the falling wood—Wm also when he had been at Benson's went with me. They have left a good

4. The rock, which has since been blasted away to make room for a new road, contained the carved letters W. W., M. H., D. W., S.T.C., J. W., S. H. (M. H. and S. H. are Mary and Sara Hutchinson; J. W. is John Wordsworth.)

5. From the "Ballad of Sir Patrick Spens." Coleridge quoted the stanza, of which this phrase is part, as epigraph to "Dejection: An Ode" (p. 466).

6. William never completed this poem.

many small oak trees but we dare not hope that they are all to remain. The Ladies are come to Mr Gell's cottage. We saw them as we went & their light when we returned. When we came in we found a Magazine & Review & a letter from Coleridge with verses to Hartley & Sara H. We read the Review,[7] &c. The moon was a perfect Boat a silver Boat when we were out in the evening. The Birch Tree is all over green in *small* leaf more light & elegant than when it is full out. It bent to the breezes as if for the love of its own delightful motions. Sloe thorns & Hawthorns in the hedges.

Friday 7th May. William had slept uncommonly well so, feeling himself strong, he fell to work at the Leech gatherer—He wrote hard at it till dinner time, then he gave over tired to death—he had finished the poem.[8] ✳ ✳ ✳

✳   ✳   ✳

[*July.*] On Thursday morning, 29th, we arrived in London.[9] Wm left me at the Inn—I went to bed &c &c &c—After various troubles and disasters we left London on Saturday morning at ½ past 5 or 6, the 31st of July (I have forgot which). We mounted the Dover Coach at Charing Cross. It was a beautiful morning. The City, St. Paul's, with the River & a multitude of little Boats, made a most beautiful sight as we crossed Westminster Bridge. The houses were not overhung by their cloud of smoke & they were spread out endlessly, yet the sun shone so brightly with such a pure light that there was even something like the purity of one of nature's own grand spectacles.[1] We rode on chearfully now with the Paris Diligence before us, now behind—we walked up the steep hills, beautiful prospects everywhere, till we even reached Dover. ✳ ✳ ✳ We arrived at Calais at 4 o'clock on Sunday morning the 31st of July.[2] We stayed in the vessel till ½ past 7, then Wm went for Letters, at about ½ past 8 or 9. We found out Annette & C chez Madame Avril dans la Rue de la Tête d'or. We lodged opposite two Ladies in tolerably decent-sized rooms but badly furnished, & with large store of bad smells & dirt in the yard, & all about. The weather was very hot. We walked by the sea-shore almost every evening with Annette & Caroline or Wm & I alone. I had a bad cold & could not bathe at first but William did. It was a pretty sight to see as we walked upon the Sands when the tide was low perhaps a hundred people bathing about ¼ of a mile distant from us, and we had delightful walks after the heat of the day was passed away—seeing far off in the west the Coast of England like a cloud crested with Dover Castle, which was but like the summit of the cloud—the Evening star & the glory of the sky. The Reflections in the water were more beautiful than the sky itself, purple waves brighter than precious stones for ever melting away upon the sands. ✳ ✳ ✳

✳   ✳   ✳

[*Sept. 24 and following.*] Mary first met us in the avenue. She looked so fat and well that we were made very happy by the sight of her—then came Sara, & last of all Joanna.[3] Tom was forking corn standing upon the corn cart. We

7. The *Monthly Review* for March 1802.
8. Later entries show, however, that William kept working on the manuscript until July 4.
9. On the way to France to visit Annette Vallon and Caroline (see the entry for March 22, 1802; p. 396).
1. Cf. William's sonnet "Composed upon Westminster Bridge" (p. 317).
2. The actual date was August 1. One of the walks by the sea that Dorothy goes on to describe was

the occasion for William's sonnet "It is a beauteous evening."
3. The Wordsworths have come to Gallow Hill, Yorkshire, for the marriage of William and Mary. The people mentioned are Mary's sisters and brothers (Sara, Joanna, Tom, Jack, and George Hutchinson). Out of consideration for Dorothy's overwrought feelings, only Joanna, Jack, and Tom attended the ceremony at Brampton Church.

dressed ourselves immediately & got tea—the garden looked gay with asters & sweet peas—I looked at everything with tranquillity & happiness but I was ill both on Saturday & Sunday & continued to be poorly most of the time of our stay. Jack & George came on Friday Evening 1st October. On Saturday 2nd we rode to Hackness, William Jack George & Sara single, I behind Tom. On Sunday 3rd Mary & Sara were busy packing. On Monday 4th October 1802, my Brother William was married to Mary Hutchinson. I slept a good deal of the night & rose fresh & well in the morning—at a little after 8 o'clock I saw them go down the avenue towards the Church. William had parted from me up stairs. I gave him the wedding ring—with how deep a blessing! I took it from my forefinger where I had worn it the whole of the night before—he slipped it again onto my finger and blessed me fervently. When they were absent my dear little Sara prepared the breakfast. I kept myself as quiet as I could, but when I saw the two men running up the walk, coming to tell us it was over, I could stand it no longer & threw myself on the bed where I lay in stillness, neither hearing or seeing any thing, till Sara came upstairs to me & said "They are coming." This forced me from the bed where I lay & I moved I knew not how straight forward, faster than my strength could carry me till I met my beloved William & fell upon his bosom. He & John Hutchinson led me to the house & there I stayed to welcome my dear Mary. As soon as we had breakfasted we departed.[4] It rained when we set off. Poor Mary was much agitated when she parted from her Brothers & Sisters & her home. Nothing particular occurred till we reached Kirby. We had sunshine & showers, pleasant talk, love & chearfulness. * * * It rained very hard when we reached Windermere. We sate in the rain at Wilcock's to change horses, & arrived at Grasmere at about 6 o'clock on Wednesday Evening, the 6th of October 1802. Molly was overjoyed to see us,—for my part I cannot describe what I felt, & our dear Mary's feelings would I dare say not be easy to speak of. We went by candle light into the garden & were astonished at the growth of the Brooms, Portugal Laurels, &c &c &—The next day, Thursday, we unpacked the Boxes. On Friday 8th we baked Bread, & Mary & I walked, first upon the Hill side, & then in John's Grove, then in view of Rydale, the first walk that I had taken with my Sister.

* * *

24th December 1802, Christmas Eve. William is now sitting by me at ½ past 10 o'clock. I have been beside him ever since tea running the heel of a stocking, repeating some of his sonnets to him, listening to his own repeating, reading some of Milton's & the Allegro & Penseroso. It is a quiet keen frost. Mary is in the parlour below attending to the baking of cakes & Jenny Fletcher's pies. Sara is in bed in the tooth ache, & so we are—beloved William is turning over the leaves of Charlotte Smith's sonnets, but he keeps his hand to his poor chest pushing aside his breastplate.[5] Mary is well & I am well, & Molly is as blithe as last year at this time. Coleridge came this morning with Wedgwood.[6] We all turned out of Wm's bedroom one by one to meet him— he looked well. We had to tell him of the Birth of his little Girl, born yesterday morning at 6 o'clock.[7] W went with them to Wytheburn in the Chaise, & M & I met Wm on the Rays. It was not an unpleasant morning to the feelings—far

---

4. Dorothy accompanied William and Mary on the three-day journey back to their cottage at Grasmere.

5. Probably an undergarment covering the chest.

6. Tom Wedgwood, whose father had founded the famous pottery works, was a friend and generous patron of Coleridge.

7. Coleridge's daughter, Sara (1802–1852).

from it—the sun shone now & then, & there was no wind, but all things looked chearless & distinct, no meltings of sky into mountains—the mountains like stone-work wrought up with huge hammers.—Last Sunday was as mild a day as I ever remember—We all set off together to walk. I went to Rydale & Wm returned with me. M & S[8] went round the Lakes. There were flowers of various kinds the topmost bell of a fox-glove, geraniums, daisies—a buttercup in the water (but this I saw two or three days before) small yellow flowers (I do not know their name) in the turf a large bunch of strawberry blossoms. Wm sate a while with me, then went to meet M. & S.—Last Saturday I dined at Mr Simpson's also a beautiful mild day. Monday was a frosty day, & it has been frost ever since. On Saturday I dined with Mrs Simpson. It is today Christmas-day Saturday 25th December 1802. I am 31 years of age.—It is a dull frosty day.

*Where'd they get the money
to live like that?*

* * *

1800–02   1897

Grasmere—A Fragment

Peaceful our valley, fair and green,
And beautiful her cottages,
Each in its nook, its sheltered hold,
Or underneath its tuft of trees.

5   Many and beautiful they are;
But there is *one* that I love best,
A lowly shed, in truth, it is,
A brother of the rest.

Yet when I sit on rock or hill,
10 Down looking on the valley fair,
That Cottage with its clustering trees
Summons my heart; it settles there.

Others there are whose small domain
Of fertile fields and hedgerows green
15 Might more seduce a wanderer's mind
To wish that *there* his home had been.

Such wish be his! I blame him not,
My fancies they perchance are wild
—I love that house because it is
20 The very Mountains' child.

Fields hath it of its own, green fields,
But they are rocky steep and bare;
Their fence is of the mountain stone,
And moss and lichen flourish there.

8. Mary and her sister Sara Hutchinson.

25 And when the storm comes from the North
It lingers near that pastoral spot,
And, piping through the mossy walls,
It seems delighted with its lot.

And let it take its own delight;
30 And let it range the pastures bare;
Until it reach that group of trees,
—It may not enter there!

A green unfading grove it is,
Skirted with many a lesser tree,
35 Hazel and holly, beech and oak,
A bright and flourishing company.

Precious the shelter of those trees;
They screen the cottage that I love;
The sunshine pierces to the roof,
40 And the tall pine-trees tower above.

When first I saw that dear abode,
It was a lovely winter's day:
After a night of perilous storm
The west wind ruled with gentle sway;

45 A day so mild, it might have been
The first day of the gladsome spring;
The robins warbled, and I heard
One solitary throstle sing.

A Stranger, Grasmere, in thy Vale,
50 All faces then to me unknown,
I left my sole companion-friend
To wander out alone.

Lured by a little winding path,
I quitted soon the public road,
55 A smooth and tempting path it was,
By sheep and shepherds trod.

Eastward, toward the lofty hills,
This pathway led me on
Until I reached a stately Rock,
60 With velvet moss o'ergrown.

With russet oak and tufts of fern
Its top was richly garlanded;
Its sides adorned with eglantine
Bedropp'd with hips of glossy red.

65 There, too, in many a sheltered chink
The foxglove's broad leaves flourished fair,
And silver birch whose purple twigs
Bend to the softest breathing air.

Beneath that Rock my course I stayed,
70 And, looking to its summit high,
"Thou wear'st," said I, "a splendid garb,
Here winter keeps his revelry.

"Full long a dweller on the Plains,
I griev'd when summer days were gone;
75 No more I'll grieve; for Winter here
Hath pleasure gardens of his own.

"What need of flowers? The splendid moss
Is gayer than an April mead;
More rich its hues of various green,
80 Orange, and gold, & glittering red."

—Beside that gay and lovely Rock
There came with merry voice
A foaming streamlet glancing by;
It seemed to say "Rejoice!"

85 My youthful wishes all fulfill'd,
Wishes matured by thoughtful choice,
I stood an Inmate of this vale
How *could* I but rejoice?

ca. 1802–05   1892

Thoughts on My Sick-Bed[1]

And has the remnant of my life
Been pilfered of this sunny Spring?
And have its own prelusive sounds
Touched in my heart no echoing string?

5 Ah! say not so—the hidden life
Couchant° within this feeble frame   *lying*
Hath been enriched by kindred gifts,
That, undesired, unsought-for, came

With joyful heart in youthful days
10 When fresh each season in its Round
I welcomed the earliest Celandine
Glittering upon the mossy ground;

1. In a letter of May 25, 1832, William Wordsworth's daughter Dora mentions this as "an affecting poem which she [her aunt Dorothy] has written
on the pleasure she received from the first spring
flowers that were carried up to her when confined
to her sick room." The lines refer to half a dozen
or more poems by William, including "I wandered
lonely as a cloud" (in line 18) and "Tintern Abbey"
(lines 45–52).

With busy eyes I pierced the lane
In quest of known and *un*known things,
15 —The primrose a lamp on its fortress rock,
The silent butterfly spreading its wings,

The violet betrayed by its noiseless breath,
The daffodil dancing in the breeze,
The carolling thrush, on his naked perch,
20 Towering above the budding trees.

Our cottage-hearth no longer our home,
Companions of Nature were we,
The Stirring, the Still, the Loquacious, the Mute—
To all we gave our sympathy.

25 Yet never in those careless days
When spring-time in rock, field, or bower
Was but a fountain of earthly hope
A promise of fruits & the *splendid* flower.

No! then I never felt a bliss
30 That might with *that* compare
Which, piercing to my couch of rest,
Came on the vernal air.

When loving Friends an offering brought,
The first flowers of the year,
35 Culled from the precincts of our home,
From nooks to Memory dear.

With some sad thoughts the work was done,
Unprompted and unbidden,
But joy it brought to my *hidden* life,
40 To consciousness no longer hidden.

I felt a Power unfelt before,
Controlling weakness, languor, pain;
It bore me to the Terrace walk
I trod the Hills again;—

45 No prisoner in this lonely room,
I *saw* the green Banks of the Wye,
Recalling thy prophetic words,
Bard, Brother, Friend from infancy!

No need of motion, or of strength,
50 Or even the breathing air:
—I thought of Nature's loveliest scenes;
And with Memory I was there.

May 1832   1978

SIR WALTER SCOTT
1771–1832

Walter Scott was born in Edinburgh, but as a small boy, to improve his health, he lived for some years with his grandparents on their farm in the Scottish Border country (the part of southern Scotland lying immediately north of the border with England). This region was rich in ballad and folklore, much of it associated with the Border warfare between northern English and southern Scottish raiders. As a child Scott listened eagerly to stories about the past, especially to accounts of their experiences by survivors of the Jacobite rebellion of 1745, the last in a series of ill-fated attempts to restore to the throne of Britain the Stuart dynasty, who had been living in exile since 1688. The defeat of the ragtag army of Scottish Highland soldiers who had rallied around Charles Edward Stuart brought to an end not just the Jacobite cause but also the quasi-feudal power that the Highland chiefs had exercised over their clans. The Highlands' native traditions were suppressed by a government in London that was determined, to the point of brutality, to integrate all its Scottish subjects more fully into the United Kingdom. Ideally situated to witness these social and cultural transformations, Scott early acquired what he exploited throughout his work—a sense of history as associated with a specific place and a sense of the past that is kept alive, tenuously, in the oral traditions of the present.

Scott's father was a lawyer and he himself was trained in the law, becoming in 1799 sheriff (local judge) of Selkirkshire, a Border county, and in 1806 clerk of session—i.e., secretary to the highest civil court in Scotland—in Edinburgh. Scott viewed the law, in its development over the centuries, as embodying the changing social customs of the country and an important element in social history, and he often used it (as in *The Heart of Midlothian* and *Redgauntlet*) to give a special dimension to his fiction.

From early childhood Scott was an avid reader of ballads and poetic romances, which with his phenomenal memory he effortlessly memorized. He began his literary career as a poet, first as a translator of German ballad imitations and then as a writer of such imitations. In 1799 he set out on the collecting expedition that resulted in the *Minstrelsy of the Scottish Border* (1802–03), his compilation of Border ballads. Motivating the collection was Scott's belief that the authentic features of the Scottish character were "daily melting . . . into those of her . . . ally" (i.e., England), but he had fewer compunctions than modern folklorists about "improving" the ballads he and assistants transcribed from the recitations of elderly peasant women and shepherds. Scott turned next to composing long narrative poems set in medieval times, the best-known of which are *The Lay of the Last Minstrel* (1805), *Marmion* (1808), and *The Lady of the Lake* (1810). Although these "metrical romances" were sensational best sellers (in 1830 Scott estimated that *The Lay* had sold thirty thousand copies) and helped establish nineteenth-century culture's vogue for medieval chivalry, Scott eventually gave up poetry for prose fiction. "Byron beat me," he explained, referring to the fact that his metrical romances ended up eclipsed by his rival's even more exotic "Eastern tales."

Scott continued to write lyric poems, which he inserted in his novels. Some of the lyrics, including "Proud Maisie," are based on the folk ballad and capture remarkably the terse suggestiveness of the oral form. *Waverley* (1814), which deals with the Jacobite defeat in 1845, introduced a motif that would remain central to Scott's fiction: the protagonist mediates between a heroic but violent old world that can no longer survive and an emerging new world that will be both safer than the old one—ensuring the security of property and the rule of law—and duller, allowing few opportunities for adventure. The novels negotiate between preserving the last traces of the traditional cultures whose disappearance they chronicle—for instance, the Scots superstitions and distinctive speech forms that feature in the ghost story that Wandering Willie recounts in *Redgauntlet* and the song, "Proud Maisie," that Madge

Wildfire sings in *The Heart of Midlothian*—and representing, through the long views of the novels' impersonal narrators, the iron laws of historical development, as those were expounded in the emerging Scottish Enlightenment disciplines of political economy, sociology, and anthropology. This approach to representing change, one that acquiesces in the necessity of social progress but also nostalgically acknowledges the allure of the backward past, was timely. It appealed powerfully to a generation that, following the British victory at Waterloo, was both eager to think that a new period in its history had begun and yet reluctant to turn its back on the past, not least because devotion to its shared historical heritage might help reunify a fragmented nation. Scott did not invent the historical novel, and indeed was readier than most twentieth-century critics to acknowledge that he had been influenced by the women novelists who dominated the literary scene prior to his debut, but his example established the significance the form would henceforth claim.

Scott published all his novels anonymously, an index of how a gentleman-poet, even at the start of the nineteenth century, might find fiction a disreputable occupation. However, his authorship of "the Waverley Series" was an open secret, and Scott became the most internationally famous novelist as well as the most prolific writer of the day. In 1811 he started building his palatial country house at Abbotsford, a place that, characteristically, he both equipped with up-to-date indoor plumbing and gas lighting and stocked with antiquarian relics. There he enacted his vision of himself as a country gentleman of the old school. Though in 1820 he acquired the title of baronet and thus added a "Sir" to his name, this glamorous persona of the Scottish laird depended on his hardheaded, unromantic readiness to conceive of literature as a business. To support his expenditures at Abbotsford, Scott wrote (as Thomas Carlyle put it disapprovingly in 1838) "with the ardour of a steam-engine" and participated in a number of commercial ventures in printing and publishing. In the crash of 1826, as a result of the failure of the publishing firm of Constable, Scott was financially ruined. He insisted on working off his huge debts by his pen and exhausted himself in the effort to do so. Not until after his death were his creditors finally paid off in full with the proceeds of the continuing sale of his novels.

The Lay of the Last Minstrel[1]

Introduction

The way was long, the wind was cold,
The Minstrel was infirm and old;
His withered cheek, and tresses gray,
Seemed to have known a better day;
5   The harp, his sole remaining joy,
Was carried by an orphan boy.
The last of all the Bards was he,
Who sung of Border chivalry;

1. Scott's first metrical romance interweaves two stories and boasts more than a hundred pages of historical notes. One story is set in the 16th century and combines the Border legend of the goblin Gilpin Horner with a story of the magic spells cast by the dowager lady of Branksome, who hopes to use a long-hidden book of black arts to avenge the death of her husband at the hands of a neighboring clan. In the second story, which unfolds across the introductions and endings of the poem's six cantos, the 17th-century minstrel who tells or sings the story of this witch's plot (a lay is a song) emerges as hero. In his prose preface Scott described this minstrel, who has "survived the Revolution" of 1688, as a figure of historical transition. He has caught "somewhat of the refinement of modern poetry without losing the simplicity of his original model"—a hint that the relationship between this figure and his 17th-century listeners mirrors Scott's relationship with his 19th-century audience. But in addition to allying his authorship with his minstrel's improvised vocal performance, Scott associates himself with the power of the written word: the "wondrous book" that the Lady of Branksome seeks is buried inside the grave of a wizard suggestively named "Michael Scott."

For, well-a-day! their date was fled,
10 His tuneful brethren all were dead;
And he, neglected and oppressed,
Wished to be with them, and at rest.
No more, on prancing palfrey° borne,   *saddle horse*
He carolled, light as lark at morn;
15 No longer, courted and caressed,
High placed in hall, a welcome guest,
He poured, to lord and lady gay,
The unpremeditated lay;
Old times were changed, old manners gone,
20 A stranger² filled the Stuarts' throne;
The bigots of the iron time
Had called his harmless art a crime.
A wandering harper, scorned and poor,
He begged his bread from door to door;
25 And tuned, to please a peasant's ear,
The harp, a King had loved to hear.

He passed where Newark's stately tower
Looks out from Yarrow's birchen bower:³
The Minstrel gazed with wishful eye—
30 No humbler resting place was nigh.
With hesitating step, at last,
The embattled portal-arch he passed,
Whose ponderous grate, and massy bar,
Had oft rolled back the tide of war,
35 But never closed the iron door
Against the desolate and poor.
The Duchess marked his weary pace,
His timid mien, and reverend face,
And bade her page the menials° tell,   *servants*
40 That they should tend the old man well:
For she had known adversity,
Though born in such a high degree;
In pride of power, in beauty's bloom,
Had wept o'er Monmouth's bloody tomb!⁴

45 When kindness had his wants supplied,
And the old man was gratified,
Began to rise his minstrel pride.
And he began to talk, anon,
Of good Earl Francis, dead and gone,
50 And of Earl Walter, rest him God!⁵
A braver ne'er to battle rode;
And how full many a tale he knew,

2. William III, who in 1688 ascended to the British throne after Parliament coerced the last Stuart monarch, the Catholic James II, into fleeing to France.
3. Newark Castle, located in the Border district, at a bend of the river Yarrow.
4. The Duchess, identified in Scott's footnote as Anne, Duchess of Buccleuch, was, in addition to being a descendant of the Lady of Branksome whose black magic will figure in the minstrel's story, the widow of the duke of Monmouth. A bastard son of Charles II, Monmouth was executed in 1685 after his unsuccessful insurrection against his uncle James II.
5. In footnotes Scott identifies Earl Francis and Earl Walter as the father and grandfather of the Duchess.

Of the old warriors of Buccleuch;
And, would the noble Duchess deign
55 To listen to an old man's strain,
Though stiff his hand, his voice though weak,
He thought even yet, the sooth° to speak,   *truth*
That, if she loved the harp to hear,
He could make music to her ear.

60 The humble boon was soon obtained;
The aged Minstrel audience gained.
But, when he reached the room of state,
Where she, with all her ladies, sate,
Perchance he wished his boon denied;
65 For, when to tune his harp he tried,
His trembling hand had lost the ease,
Which marks security to please;
And scenes, long past, of joy and pain,
Came wildering o'er his aged brain—
70 He tried to tune his harp in vain.
The pitying Duchess praised its chime,
And gave him heart, and gave him time,
Till every string's according glee
Was blended into harmony.
75 And then, he said, he would full fain
He could recall an ancient strain,
He never thought to sing again.
It was not framed for village churls,
But for high dames and mighty earls;
80 He had played it to King Charles the Good
When he kept court at Holyrood;[6]
And much he wished, yet feared, to try
The long-forgotten melody.
Amid the strings his fingers strayed,
85 And an uncertain warbling made—
And oft he shook his hoary° head.   *gray with age*
But when he caught the measure wild,
The old man raised his face, and smiled;
And lightened up his faded eye,
90 With all a poet's extacy!
In varying cadence, soft or strong,
He swept the sounding chords along;
The present scene, the future lot,
His toils, his wants, were all forgot;
95 Cold diffidence, and age's frost,
In the full tide of song were lost.
Each blank, in faithless memory void,
The poet's glowing thought supplied;
And, while his harp responsive rung,
100 'Twas thus the LATEST MINSTREL sung.

1805

6. Having ascended to the throne of England in 1626, Charles I traveled to the palace of Holyrood in Edinburgh in 1633 to receive the crown of Scotland.

Proud Maisie[1]

Proud Maisie is in the wood
    Walking so early;
Sweet Robin sits on the bush,
    Singing so rarely.

5   "Tell me, thou bonny bird,
    When shall I marry me?"—
"When six braw° gentlemen   *fine*
    Kirkward shall carry ye."

"Who makes the bridal bed,
10   Birdie, say truly?"—
"The gray-headed sexton
    That delves the grave duly.

"The glowworm o'er grave and stone
    Shall light thee steady,
15   The owl from the steeple sing,
    'Welcome, proud lady.' "

1818

Wandering Willie's Tale

"Wandering Willie's Tale" forms part of *Red-gauntlet* (1824), Scott's most formally inventive novel and the last of his major fictions set in the Border Country. It is told by the blind fiddler Willie Steenson to a young gentleman of a romantic temperament, Darsie Latimer, who on a whim has joined him in his cross-country wandering and who subsequently writes down Willie's tale and sends it off in a letter to a friend in Edinburgh. (*Redgauntlet* begins, though after its first third does not continue, as a novel in letters, the eighteenth-century form that Scott revived for this book he called his "Tale of the Eighteenth Century.") Like most of Scott's fiction, then, "Wandering Willie's Tale" juxtaposes oral storytelling against written records, while also moving among several time frames: 1765, when Willie recounts to Darsie the tale he heard from his grandfather, the piper Steenie Steenson; the year—sometime in the early 1690s—when the events Steenie experienced occurred; and also the four decades prior to 1690, in which the central figure in the story, Sir Robert Redgauntlet, committed the wicked deeds for which, in the course of the tale, he will pay at last. The story likewise mixes fiction and history: Steenie's journey to the underworld, where he pursues the fictional Redgauntlet and thereby recovers a lost piece of his own past, gives Scott a device for making his reader acquainted with some central figures of seventeenth-century Scottish history.

We follow the text of the "Magnum Opus" edition of his works, which Scott prepared in 1832 and in which he officially acknowledged authorship of his novels; we omit, however, the long historical notes he added to that edition.

Scott's simulation of Willie's Scots dialect becomes easier to understand when one hears rather than reads it, so reading the tale aloud is advised. For tips on pronunciation of Scots, consult the recordings of "Tam O' Shanter," by Robert Burns, and "Woo'd and married and a'," by Joanna Baillie, both at Norton Literature Online.

---

1. The "fragment" of a song heard by the characters in *The Heart of Midlothian* who attend the insane gypsy Madge Wildfire on her deathbed (chap. 40).

FROM REDGAUNTLET

Wandering Willie's Tale

Ye maun[1] have heard of Sir Robert Redgauntlet of that Ilk, who lived in these parts before the dear years.[2] The country will lang mind him; and our fathers used to draw breath thick if ever they heard him named. He was out wi' the Hielandmen in Montrose's time; and again he was in the hills wi' Glencairn in the saxteen hundred and fifty-twa; and sae when King Charles the Second came in, wha was in sic[3] favour as the Laird of Redgauntlet?[4] He was knighted at Lonon court, wi' the King's ain sword; and being a redhot prelatist, he came down here, rampauging like a lion, with commissions of lieutenancy (and of lunacy, for what I ken[5]), to put down a' the Whigs and Covenanters in the country. Wild wark they made of it, for the Whigs were as dour as the Cavaliers were fierce, and it was which should first tire the other. Redgauntlet was aye[6] for the strong hand; and his name is kend as wide in the country as Claverhouse's or Tam Dalyell's.[7] Glen, nor dargle,[8] nor mountain, nor cave, could hide the puir hill-folk when Redgauntlet was out with bugle and bloodhound after them, as if they had been sae mony deer. And troth when they fand them, they didna mak muckle[9] mair ceremony than a Hielandman wi' a roebuck— It was just, "Will ye tak the test?"—if not, "Make ready—present—fire!"—and there lay the recusant.[1]

Far and wide was Sir Robert hated and feared. Men thought he had a direct compact with Satan—that he was proof against steel—and that bullets happed aff his buff-coat like hailstanes from a hearth—that he had a mear that would turn a hare on the side of Carrifra-gawns[2]—and muckle to the same purpose, of whilk mair anon. The best blessing they wared[3] on him was, "Deil scowp wi' Redgauntlet!"[4] He wasna a bad maister to his ain folk though, and was weel aneugh liked by his tenants; and as for the lackies and troopers that raid out wi' him to the persecutions, as the Whigs caa'd those killing times, they wad hae drunken themsells blind to his health at ony time.

---

1. Must.
2. Years of famine at the end of the 1690s. "Of that ilk": from the estate that bears the same name as the family. Willie's story concerns Redgauntlet of Redgauntlet.
3. Such.
4. This opening establishes Redgauntlet's past as a "prelatist"—supporter of what was, for most of the 17th century, Scotland's established, Episcopal Church—and a royalist. For four decades he was the foe of the Covenanters—Presbyterians, often members of Scotland's middle and lower classes, who rejected episcopacy, the spiritual authority of the bishops, and supported "Covenants" to preserve the purity of their worship. The conflict between the royalists and Covenanters began during the Civil War of the 1640s, when, on behalf of Charles I, the earl of Montrose and his Highland army battled the Presbyterian insurgents—known as the Whigs—who had sided in the war with Cromwell. In 1652, during the Interregnum that followed Charles's execution, the earl of Glencairn continued this battle: Redgauntlet, we are to understand, joined him. When Charles II was restored to the throne in 1660, the royalists and prelatists regained the upper hand. Their conflict with the Covenanters culminated, during the "killing years" of 1681–85, with massacres of the "hill

folk," called this because Presbyterian ministers who after the Restoration had been ejected from their churches had taken to conducting religious services outdoors.
5. Know.
6. Always.
7. Royalist aristocrats who led the persecutions of Covenanters in 1681–85. Folk legends held that both had diabolical powers, which Scott transfers to Redgauntlet in the following paragraph.
8. A word for river valley, perhaps of Scott's coining.
9. Much.
1. To take the Test is, according to the terms of the Test Act of 1681, to swear an oath recognizing the monarch's supremacy as head of the Church, something a Presbyterian, who recognized Christ alone as head, could not do. Redgauntlet and followers used this legal device to hunt down "recusants," i.e., those who did not conform to the Episcopal church.
2. Redgauntlet's supernaturally fleet-footed mare could turn a hare—i.e., get in front of it and change its course—while being ridden on Carrifra-gawns, a steep slope.
3. Bestowed.
4. "Devil take Redgauntlet!"

Now you are to ken that my gudesire[5] lived on Redgauntlet's grund—they ca' the place Primrose-Knowe. We had lived on the grund, and under the Redgauntlets, since the riding days,[6] and lang before. It was a pleasant bit; and I think the air is callerer[7] and fresher there than ony where else in the country. It's a' deserted now; and I sat on the broken door-cheek three days since, and was glad I couldna see the plight the place was in; but that's a' wide o' the mark.[8] There dwelt my gudesire, Steenie Steenson, a rambling, rattling chiel[9] he had been in his young days, and could play weel on the pipes; he was famous at "Hoopers and Girders"—a' Cumberland couldna touch him at "Jockie Lattin"—and he had the finest finger for the back-lill[1] between Berwick and Carlisle. The like o' Steenie wasna the sort that they made Whigs o'. And so he became a Tory, as they ca' it, which we now ca' Jacobites,[2] just out of a kind of needcessity, that he might belang to some side or other. He had nae ill-will to the Whig bodies, and liked little to see the blude rin, though, being obliged to follow Sir Robert in hunting and hosting, watching and warding,[3] he saw muckle mischief, and maybe did some, that he couldna avoid.

Now Steenie was a kind of favourite with his master, and kend a' the folks about the castle, and was often sent for to play the pipes when they were at their merriment. Auld Dougal MacCallum, the butler, that had followed Sir Robert through gude and ill, thick and thin, pool and stream, was specially fond of the pipes, and aye gae[4] my gudesire his gude word wi' the Laird; for Dougal could turn his master round his finger.

Weel, round came the Revolution,[5] and it had like to have broken the hearts baith of Dougal and his master. But the change was not a'thegether sae great as they feared, and other folk thought for. The Whigs made an unco crawing[6] what they wad do with their auld enemies, and in special wi' Sir Robert Redgauntlet. But there were ower many great folks dipped in the same doings, to mak a spick and span new warld. So parliament passed it a' ower easy; and Sir Robert, bating[7] that he was held to hunting foxes instead of Covenanters, remained just the man he was. He revel was as loud, and his hall as weel lighted, as ever it had been, though maybe he lacked the fines of the nonconformists, that used to come to stock his larder and cellar; for it is certain he began to be keener about the rents than his tenants used to find him before, and they behoved to be[8] prompt to the rent-day, or else the Laird wasna pleased. And he was sic an awsome body, that naebody cared to anger him; for the oaths he swore, and the rage that he used to get into, and the looks that he put on, made men sometimes think him a devil incarnate.

Weel, my gudesire was nae manager—no that he was a very great misguider—but he hadna the saving gift, and he got twa terms' rent in arrear. He got the first brash at Whitsunday put ower wi' fair word and piping; but when Martinmas came, there was a summons from the grund-officer to come wi'

---

5. Grandfather.
6. Period of Border warfare in the 16th century.
7. Cooler.
8. Beside the point.
9. Lad.
1. Thumbhole in the melody pipe of a bagpipe. The border between Scotland and England extends between Carlisle—chief city of the Northern English county of Cumberland (now known as Cumbria) on the west coast and Berwick on the east.
2. The Tory party in Scotland included most supporters of the Episcopal Church and, after 1688,

the Jacobites—supporters of the exiled James Stuart and his heirs.
3. Guarding.
4. Gave.
5. The Revolution of 1688, which expelled the Stuart dynasty from the British throne, and in Scotland reestablished Presbyterianism, ending the persecutions of the Covenanters. Jacobites continued to resist the Revolutionary Settlement until their last uprising in 1745.
6. Extraordinary crowing; i.e., much noise.
7. Except.
8. Were obliged to be.

the rent on a day preceese, or else Steenie behoved to flit.[9] Sair wark[1] he had
to get the siller; but he was weel-freended, and at last he got the haill[2] scraped
thegither—a thousand merks—the maist of it was from a neighbour they caa'd
Laurie Lapraik—a sly tod.[3] Laurie had walth o' gear[4]—could hunt wi' the
hound and rin wi' the hare—and be Whig or Tory, saunt or sinner, as the wind
stood. He was a professor in this Revolution warld, but he liked an orra sough
of this warld;[5] and a tune on the pipes weel aneugh at a bytime, and abune
a',[6] he thought he had gude security for the siller he lent my gudesire ower
the stocking at Primrose-Knowe.[7]

Away trots my gudesire to Redgauntlet Castle, wi' a heavy purse and a light
heart, glad to be out of the Laird's danger. Weel, the first thing he learned at
the Castle was, that Sir Robert had fretted himself into a fit of the gout,
because he did not appear before twelve o'clock. It wasna a'thegether for sake
of the money, Dougal thought; but because he didna like to part wi' my gudesire aff the grund. Dougal was glad to see Steenie, and brought him into the
great oak parlour, and there sat the Laird his leesome lane, excepting that he
had beside him a great, ill-favoured jackanape,[8] that was a special pet of his;
a cankered beast it was, and mony an ill-natured trick it played—ill to please
it was, and easily angered—ran about the haill castle, chattering and yowling,
and pinching and biting folk, especially before ill weather, or disturbances in
the state. Sir Robert caa'd it Major Weir, after the warlock that was burnt;[9]
and few folk liked either the name or the conditions of the creature—they
thought there was something in it by ordinar—and my gudesire was not just
easy in his mind when the door shut on him, and he saw himself in the room
wi' naebody but the Laird, Dougal MacCallum, and the Major, a thing that
hadna chanced to him before.

Sir Robert sat, or, I should say, lay, in a great armed chair, wi' his grand
velvet gown, and his feet on a cradle; for he had baith gout and gravel, and
his face looked as gash and ghastly as Satan's. Major Weir sat opposite to him,
in a red laced coat, and the Laird's wig[1] on his head; and aye as Sir Robert
girned[2] wi' pain, the jackanape girned too, like a sheep's-head between a pair
of tangs—an ill-faured,[3] fearsome couple they were. The Laird's buff-coat was
hung on a pin behind him, and his broadsword and his pistols within reach;
for he keepit up the auld fashion of having the weapons ready, and a horse
saddled day and night, just as he used to do when he was able to loup on
horseback, and away after ony of the hill-folk he could get speerings[4] of. Some
said it was for fear of the Whigs taking vengeance, but I judge it was just his
auld custom—he wasna gien to fear ony thing. The rental-book, wi' its black
cover and brass clasps, was lying beside him; and a book of sculduddry sangs[5]
was put betwixt the leaves, to keep it open at the place where it bore evidence

9. To move house. Rents were due on "quarter
days": Candlemas (February 2), Whitsunday (May
15), Lammas (August 1), and Martinmas (November 11).
1. Difficult work.
2. Whole.
3. Fox.
4. Lots of property.
5. I.e., in this post-Revolutionary world puritanical Laurie adheres to ("professes") his religion but
still likes an occasional ("orra") worldly song
("sough").
6. Above all.
7. I.e., the security for the loan of the rent money

is "the stocking"—cattle, farm implements, etc.—
of Steenie's farm.
8. Monkey.
9. Major Weir, a historical figure who fought in
the Covenanter cause in youth and in old age confessed to crimes that included wizardry, for which
he was executed in 1670.
1. Gentlemen in the late 17th and the 18th centuries were in the custom of wearing wigs in public.
2. Grimaced.
3. Ugly.
4. News.
5. Obscene songs.

against the Goodman of Primrose-Knowe, as behind the hand with his mails and duties.[6] Sir Robert gave my gudesire a look, as if he would have withered his heart in his bosom. Ye maun ken he had a way of bending his brows, that men saw the visible mark of a horse-shoe in his forehead, deep-dinted, as if it had been stamped there.

"Are ye come light-handed, ye son of a toom whistle?" said Sir Robert. "Zounds! if you are"—

My gudesire, with as gude a countenance as he could put on, made a leg,[7] and placed the bag of money on the table wi' a dash, like a man that does something clever. The Laird drew it to him hastily—"Is it all here, Steenie, man?"

"Your honour will find it right," said my gudesire.

"Here, Dougal," said the Laird, "gie Steenie a tass[8] of brandy down stairs, till I count the siller and write the receipt."

But they werena weel out of the room, when Sir Robert gied a yelloch that garr'd[9] the Castle rock! Back ran Dougal—in flew the livery-men—yell on yell gied the Laird, ilk ane mair awfu' than the ither. My gudesire knew not whether to stand or flee, but he ventured back into the parlour, where a' was gaun hirdy-girdie—naebody to say "come in," or "gae out." Terribly the Laird roared for cauld water to his feet, and wine to cool his throat; and hell, hell, hell, and its flames, was aye the word in his mouth. They brought him water, and when they plunged his swoln feet into the tub, he cried out it was burning; and folk say that it *did* bubble and sparkle like a seething cauldron. He flung the cup at Dougal's head, and said he had given him blood instead of burgundy; and, sure aneugh, the lass washed clotted blood aff the carpet the neist day. The jackanape they caa'd Major Weir, it jibbered and cried as if it was mocking its master; my gudesire's head was like to turn—he forgot baith siller and receipt, and down stairs he banged; but as he ran, the shrieks came faint and fainter; there was a deep-drawn shivering groan, and word gaed through the Castle, that the Laird was dead.

Weel, away came my gudesire, wi' his finger in his mouth, and his best hope was, that Dougal had seen the money-bag, and heard the Laird speak of writing the receipt. The young Laird, now Sir John, came from Edinburgh, to see things put to rights. Sir John and his father never gree'd weel. Sir John had been bred an advocate, and afterwards sat in the last Scots Parliament and voted for the Union, having gotten, it was thought, a rug of the compensations[1]—if his father could have come out of his grave, he would have brained him for it on his awn hearthstane. Some thought it was easier counting with the auld rough Knight than the fair-spoken young ane—but mair of that anon.

Dougal MacCallum, poor body, neither grat[2] nor graned, but gaed about the house looking like a corpse, but directing, as was his duty, a' the order of the grand funeral. Now, Dougal looked aye waur and waur[3] when night was coming, and was aye the last to gang to his bed, whilk was in a little round just opposite the chamber of dais,[4] whilk his master occupied while he was

---

6. Rents.
7. I.e., he bowed.
8. Cup.
9. Made.
1. Sir John is eventually to hold a seat in the Scots Parliament that will make history in 1707 by passing the Act of Union that joins the kingdoms of

England and Scotland and by this means voting itself out of existence. Like many of his peers, Sir John will take a cut ("rug") of the "compensations" offered the parliamentarians as a bribe.
2. Wept.
3. Always looked worse and worse.
4. Best bedroom.

living, and where he now lay in state, as they caa'd it, weel-a-day! The night before the funeral, Dougal could keep his awn counsel[5] nae langer; he came doun with his proud spirit, and fairly asked auld Hutcheon to sit in his room with him for an hour. When they were in the round, Dougal took ae tass of brandy to himsell, and gave another to Hutcheon, and wished him all health and lang life, and said that, for himsell, he wasna lang for this world; for that, every night since Sir Robert's death, his silver call had sounded from the state chamber, just as it used to do at nights in his lifetime, to call Dougal to help to turn him in his bed. Dougal said, that being alone with the dead on that floor of the tower (for naebody cared to wake Sir Robert Redgauntlet like another corpse), he had never daured to answer the call, but that now his conscience checked him for neglecting his duty; for, "though death breaks service," said MacCallum, "it shall never break my service to Sir Robert; and I will answer his next whistle, so be you will stand by me, Hutcheon."

Hutcheon had nae will to the wark, but he had stood by Dougal in battle and broil, and he wad not fail him at this pinch; so down the carles[6] sat ower a stoup[7] of brandy, and Hutcheon, who was something of a clerk, would have read a chapter of the Bible; but Dougal would hear naething but a blaud[8] of Davie Lindsay, whilk was the waur preparation.

When midnight came, and the house was quiet as the grave, sure aneugh the silver whistle sounded as sharp and shrill as if Sir Robert was blowing it, and up gat the twa auld serving-men, and tottered into the room where the dead man lay. Hutcheon saw aneugh at the first glance; for there were torches in the room, which showed him the foul fiend in his ain shape, sitting on the Laird's coffin! Over he cowped[9] as if he had been dead. He could not tell how lang he lay in a trance at the door, but when he gathered himself, he cried on his neighbour, and getting nae answer, raised the house, when Dougal was found lying dead within twa steps of the bed where his master's coffin was placed. As for the whistle, it was gaen anes and aye;[1] but mony a time was it heard at the top of the house on the bartizan,[2] and amang the auld chimneys and turrets, where the howlets have their nests. Sir John hushed the matter up, and the funeral passed over without mair bogle-wark.[3]

But when a' was ower, and the Laird was beginning to settle his affairs, every tenant was called up for his arrears, and my gudesire for the full sum that stood against him in the rental-book. Weel, away he trots to the Castle, to tell his story, and there he is introduced to Sir John, sitting in his father's chair, in deep mourning, with weepers and hanging cravat,[4] and a small walking rapier by his side, instead of the auld broadsword that had a hundred-weight of steel about it, what with blade, chape, and basket-hilt. I have heard their communing so often tauld ower, that I almost think I was there mysell, though I couldna be born at the time. . . .

"I wuss ye joy, sir, of the head seat, and the white loaf, and the braid laird-ship.[5] Your father was a kind man to friends and followers; muckle grace to

5. Keep quiet.
6. Fellows.
7. Cup.
8. A selection: Lindsay was a 16th-century satirical poet.
9. Tilted.
1. Once and always—i.e., forever.
2. Parapet atop a castle.
3. Ghostly occurrences.

4. Mourning dress included hat bands of white linen ("weepers") and a "hanging cravat" instead of the usual shirt frills.
5. A ceremonious speech wishing Sir John well in his new position as head of a great family: white bread ("white loaf") is mentioned as a delicacy only the rich could afford; a "braid lairdship" is a large estate.

you, Sir John, to fill his shoon—his boots, I suld say, for he seldom wore shoon, unless it were muils⁶ when he had the gout."

"Ay, Steenie," quoth the Laird, sighing deeply, and putting his napkin to his een, "his was a sudden call, and he will be missed in the country; no time to set his house in order—weel prepared Godward, no doubt, which is the root of the matter—but left us behind a tangled hesp to wind,⁷ Steenie.—Hem! hem! We maun go to business, Steenie; much to do, and little time to do it in."

Here he opened the fatal volume. I have heard of a thing they call Doomsday-book⁸—I am clear it has been a rental of back-ganging⁹ tenants.

"Stephen," said Sir John, still in the same soft, sleekit tone of a voice— "Stephen Stevenson, or Steenson, ye are down here for a year's rent behind the hand—due at last term."

Stephen. "Please your honour, Sir John, I paid it to your father."

Sir John. "Ye took a receipt then, doubtless, Stephen; and can produce it?"

Stephen. "Indeed I hadna time, an it like your honour; for nae sooner had I set doun the siller, and just as his honour Sir Robert, that's gaen, drew it till him to count it, and write out the receipt, he was ta'en wi' the pains that removed him."

"That was unlucky," said Sir John, after a pause. "But ye maybe paid it in the presence of somebody. I want but a *talis qualis* evidence,¹ Stephen. I would go ower strictly to work with no poor man."

Stephen. "Troth, Sir John, there was naebody in the room but Dougal MacCallum, the butler. But, as your honour kens, he has e'en followed his auld master."

"Very unlucky again, Stephen," said Sir John, without altering his voice a single note. "The man to whom ye paid the money is dead—and the man who witnessed your payment is dead too—and the siller, which should have been to the fore, is neither seen nor heard tell of in the repositories. How am I to believe a' this?"

Stephen. "I dinna ken, your honour; but there is a bit memorandum note of the very coins; for, God help me! I had to borrow out of twenty purses; and I am sure that ilka² men there set down will take his grit oath for what purpose I borrowed the money."

Sir John. "I have little doubt that ye *borrowed* the money, Steenie. It is the *payment* to my father that I want to have some proof of."

Stephen. "The siller maun be about the house, Sir John. And since your honour never got it, and his honour that was canna have ta'en it wi' him, maybe some of the family may have seen it."

Sir John. "We will examine the servants, Stephen; that is but reasonable."

But lackey and lass, and page and groom, all denied stoutly that they had ever seen such a bag of money as my gudesire described. What was waur, he had unluckily not mentioned to any living soul of them his purpose of paying his rent. Ae quean³ had noticed something under his arm, but she took it for the pipes.

Sir John Redgauntlet ordered the servants out of the room, and then said

---

6. Slippers.
7. A "hesp" is a length of yarn: the deceased has left behind him a confused state of affairs that requires disentangling (winding).
8. The property survey of England ordered by William the Conqueror in 1086.

9. Behind in paying.
1. Law Latin for "of some kind"; used for evidence that is acceptable only under special circumstances.
2. Every.
3. Young woman.

to my gudesire, "Now, Steenie, ye see you have fair play; and, as I have little doubt ye ken better where to find the siller than ony other body, I beg, in fair terms, and for your own sake, that you will end this fasherie;[4] for, Stephen, ye maun pay or flit."

"The Lord forgie your opinion," said Stephen, driven almost to his wit's end—"I am an honest man."

"So am I, Stephen," said his honour; "and so are all the folks in the house, I hope. But if there be a knave amongst us, it must be he that tells the story he cannot prove." He paused, and then added, mair sternly, "If I understand your trick, sir, you want to take advantage of some malicious reports concerning things in this family, and particularly respecting my father's sudden death, thereby to cheat me out of the money, and perhaps take away my character, by insinuating that I have received the rent I am demanding.—Where do you suppose this money to be?—I insist upon knowing."

My gudesire saw every thing look sae muckle against him that he grew nearly desperate—however, he shifted from one foot to another, looked to every corner of the room, and made no answer.

"Speak out, sirrah," said the Laird, assuming a look of his father's, a very particular ane, which he had when he was angry—it seemed as if the wrinkles of his frown made that selfsame fearful shape of a horse's shoe in the middle of his brow;—"Speak out, sir! I *will* know your thoughts;—do you suppose that I have this money?"

"Far be it frae me to say so," said Stephen.

"Do you charge any of my people with having taken it?"

"I wad be laith to charge them that may be innocent," said my gudesire; "and if there be any one that is guilty, I have nae proof."

"Somewhere the money must be, if there is a word of truth in your story," said Sir John; "I ask where you think it is—and demand a correct answer?"

"In hell, if you *will* have my thoughts of it," said my gudesire, driven to extremity,—"in hell! with your father, his jackanape, and his silver whistle."

Down the stairs he ran (for the parlour was nae place for him after such a word), and he heard the Laird swearing blood and wounds behind him, as fast as ever did Sir Robert, and roaring for the bailie and the baron-officer.

Away rode my gudesire to his chief creditor (him they caa'd Laurie Lapraik), to try if he could make ony thing out of him; but when he tauld his story, he got but the warst word in his wame[5]—thief, beggar, and dyvour,[6] were the saftest terms; and to the boot of these hard terms, Laurie brought up the auld story of his dipping his hand in the blood of God's saunts, just as if a tenant could have helped riding with the Laird, and that a laird like Sir Robert Redgauntlet. My gudesire was, by this time, far beyond the bounds of patience, and while he and Laurie were at deil speed the liars, he was wanchancie[7] aneugh to abuse Lapraik's doctrine as weel as the man, and said things that garr'd folk's flesh grue[8] that heard them;—he wasna just himsell, and he had lived wi' a wild set in his day.

At last they parted, and my gudesire was to ride hame through the wood of Pitmurkie, that is a' fou of black firs, as they say.—I ken the wood, but the firs may be black or white for what I can tell.—At the entry of the wood there is a wild common, and on the edge of the common, a little lonely change-

4. Annoyance.
5. Mind.
6. Good-for-nothing.

7. Unlucky.
8. Made people's flesh creep.

418 / S<small>IR</small> W<small>ALTER</small> S<small>COTT</small>

house, that was keepit then by an ostler-wife, they suld hae caa'd her Tibbie
Faw,[9] and there puir Steenie cried for a mutchkin of brandy, for he had had
no refreshment the haill day. Tibbie was earnest wi' him to take a bite of meat,
but he couldna think o't, nor would he take his foot out of the stirrup, and
took off the brandy wholely at twa draughts, and named a toast at each:—the
first was, the memory of Sir Robert Redgauntlet, and might he never lie quiet
in his grave till he had righted his poor bond-tenant; and the second was, a
health to Man's Enemy, if he would but get him back the pock of siller, or tell
him what came o't, for he saw the haill world was like to regard him as a thief
and a cheat, and he took that waur than even the ruin of his house and hauld.[1]

On he rode, little caring where. It was a dark night turned, and the trees
made it yet darker, and he let the beast take its ain road through the wood;
when, all of a sudden, from tired and wearied that it was before, the nag began
to spring, and flee, and stend, that my gudesire could hardly keep the saddle—
Upon the whilk, a horseman, suddenly riding up beside him, said, "That's a
mettle beast of yours, freend; will you sell him?"—So saying, he touched the
horse's neck with his riding-wand, and it fell into its auld heigh-ho of a stumbling trot. "But his spunk's soon out of him, I think," continued the stranger,
"and that is like mony a man's courage, that thinks he wad do great things till
he came to the proof."

My gudesire scarce listened to this, but spurred his horse, with "Gude e'en
to you, freend."

But it's like the stranger was ane that doesna lightly yield his point; for, ride
as Steenie liked, he was aye beside him at the selfsame pace. At last my gudesire, Steenie Steenson, grew half angry; and, to say the truth, half feared.

"What is it that ye want with me, freend?" he said. "If ye be a robber, I have
nae money; if ye be a leal[2] man, wanting company, I have nae heart to mirth
or speaking; and if ye want to ken the road, I scarce ken it mysell."

"If you will tell me your grief," said the stranger, "I am one that, though I
have been sair miscaa'd[3] in the world, am the only hand for helping my
freends."

So my gudesire, to ease his ain heart, mair than from any hope of help, told
him the story from beginning to end.

"It's a hard pinch," said the strange; "but I think I can help you."

"If you could lend me the money, sir, and take a lang day[4]—I ken nae other
help on earth," said my gudesire.

"But there may be some under the earth," said the stranger. "Come, I'll be
frank wi' you; I could lend you the money on bond, but you would maybe
scruple my terms. Now, I can tell you, that your auld Laird is disturbed in his
grave by your curses, and the wailing of your family, and if ye daur venture to
go to see him, he will give you the receipt."

My gudesire's hair stood on end at this proposal, but he thought his companion might be some humorsome chield that was trying to frighten him, and
might end with lending him the money. Besides he was bauld wi' brandy, and
desperate wi' distress; and he said, he had courage to go to the gate of hell,
and a step farther, for that receipt.—The stranger laughed.

Weel, they rode on through the thickest of the wood, when, all of a sudden,
the horse stopped at the door of a great house; and, but that he knew the place

9. I.e., "I am told she was called Tibbie Faw."   2. Honest.
"Ostler-wife": female keeper of a hostelry (inn).   3. Much maligned.
1. Home.   4. Extend credit for a long time.

was ten miles off, my father would have thought he was at Redgauntlet Castle. They rode into the outer court-yard, through the muckle faulding yetts,[5] and aneath the auld portcullis; and the whole front of the house was lighted, and there were pipes and fiddles, and as much dancing and deray[6] within as used to be in Sir Robert's House at Pace and Yule,[7] and such high seasons. They lap off, and my gudesire, as seemed to him, fastened his horse to the very ring he had tied him to that morning, when he gaed to wait on the young Sir John.

"God!" said my gudesire, "if Sir Robert's death be but a dream!"

He knocked at the ha' door just as he was wont, and his auld acquaintance, Dougal MacCallum,—just after his wont, too,—came to open the door, and said, "Piper Steenie, are ye there, lad? Sir Robert has been crying for you."

My gudesire was like a man in a dream—he looked for the stranger, but he was gane for the time. At last he just tried to say, "Ha! Dougal Driveower,[8] are ye living? I thought ye had been dead."

"Never fash[9] yoursell wi' me," said Dougal, "but look to yoursell; and see ye take naething frae onybody here, neither meat, drink, or siller, except just the receipt that is your ain."

So saying, he led the way out through halls and trances that were weel kend to my gudesire, and into the auld oak parlour; and there was as much singing of profane sangs, and birling[1] of red wine, and speaking blasphemy and sculduddry, as had ever been in Redgauntlet Castle when it was at the blithest.

But, Lord take us in keeping! what a set of ghastly revellers they were that sat round that table!—My gudesire kend mony that had long before gane to their place, for often had he piped to the most part in the hall of Redgauntlet. There was the fierce Middleton, and the dissolute Rothes, and the crafty Lauderdale; and Dalyell, with his bald head and a beard to his girdle; and Earlshall, with Cameron's blude on his hand; and wild Bonshaw, that tied blessed Mr Cargill's limbs till the blude sprung; and Dumbarton Douglas, the twice-turned traitor baith to country and king. There was the Bluidy Advocate MacKenyie, who, for his worldly wit and wisdom, had been to the rest as a god.[2] And there was Claverhouse, as beautiful as when he lived, with his long, dark, curled locks, streaming down over his laced buff-coat, and his left hand always on his right spule-blade, to hide the wound that the silver bullet had made.[3] He sat apart from them all, and looked at them with a melancholy, haughty countenance; while the rest hallooed, and sung, and laughed, that the room rang. But their smiles were fearfully contorted from time to time; and their laughter passed into such wild sounds, as made my gudesire's very nails grow blue, and chilled the marrow in his banes.

They that waited at the table were just the wicked serving-men and troopers, that had done their work and cruel bidding on earth. There was the Lang Lad of Nethertown, that helped to take Argyle; and the Bishop's summoner, that they called the Deil's Rattle-bag; and the wicked guardsmen, in their laced coats; and the savage Highland Amorites,[4] that shed blood like water; and

5. Great folding gates.
6. Disorderly revelry.
7. Easter and Christmas.
8. Nickname for an idler.
9. Trouble.
1. Pouring.
2. Willie's list identifies a number of the royalist aristocrats who, while alive, took the lead in persecuting the Covenanters.
3. John Graham of Claverhouse, another histori-

cal figure notorious for his ruthlessness during the killing years, and the leader of the Highland army that fought for the cause of the exiled King James Stuart in 1689: he died in battle that year, and legend reported that it took a silver bullet to kill him.
4. The "Highland host" sent into southwest Scotland in 1678 to enforce a law that legalized the evictions of people who attended Presbyterian conventicles rather than parish churches. Covenanter

many a proud serving-man, haughty of heart and bloody of hand, cringing to the rich, and making them wickeder than they would be; grinding the poor to powder, when the rich had broken them into fragments. And mony, mony mair were coming and ganging, a' as busy in their vocation as if they had been alive.

Sir Robert Redgauntlet, in the midst of a' this fearful riot, cried, wi' a voice like thunder, on Steenie Piper, to come to the board-head where he was sitting; his legs stretched out before him, and swathed up with flannel, with his holster pistols aside him, while the great broadsword rested against his chair, just as my gudesire had seen him the last time upon earth—the very cushion for the jackanape was close to him, but the creature itsell was not there—it wasna its hour, it's likely; for he heard them say as he came forward, "Is not the Major come yet?" And another answered, "The jackanape will be here betimes the morn." And when my gudesire came forward, Sir Robert, or his ghaist, or the deevil in his likeness, said, "Weel, piper, hae ye settled wi' my son for the year's rent?"

With much ado my father gat breath to say, that Sir John would not settle without his honour's receipt.

"Ye shall hae that for a tune of the pipes, Steenie," said the appearance of Sir Robert—"Play us up, 'Weel hoddled, Luckie.' "

Now this was a tune my gudesire learned frae a warlock, that heard it when they were worshipping Satan at their meetings; and my gudesire had some-times played it at the ranting[5] suppers in Redgauntlet Castle, but never very willingly; and now he grew cauld at the very name of it, and said, for excuse, he hadna his pipes wi' him.

"MacCallum, ye limb of Beelzebub," said the fearfu' Sir Robert, "bring Steenie the pipes that I am keeping for him."

MacCallum brought a pair of pipes might have served the piper of Donald of the Isles.[6] But he gave my gudesire a nudge as he offered them; and looking secretly and closely, Steenie saw that the chanter[7] was of steel, and heated to a white heat; so he had fair warning not to trust his fingers with it. So he excused himself again, and said, he was faint and frightened, and had not wind aneugh to fill the bag.

"Then ye maun eat and drink, Steenie," said the figure; "for we do little else here; and it's ill speaking between a fou man and a fasting."[8]

Now these were the very words that the bloody Earl of Douglas said to keep the King's messenger in hand, while he cut the head off MacLellan of Bombie, at the Threave Castle;[9] and that put Steenie mair and mair on his guard. So he spoke up like a man, and said he came neither to eat, or drink, or make minstrelsy; but simply for his ain—to ken what was come o' the money he had paid, and to get a discharge for it; and he was so stout-hearted by this time, that he charged Sir Robert for conscience-sake—(he had no power to say the holy name)—and as he hoped for peace and rest, to spread no snares for him, but just to give him his ain.

The appearance gnashed its teeth and laughed, but it took from a large

---

hymns compared this army to the Amorites, who in the Old Testament are the enemies of the Isra-elites.
5. Merry.
6. A powerful chief of the Western Isles of Scot-land.
7. Melody pipe of a bagpipe.

8. Proverb: a full man should not prevent a hungry man from eating.
9. In 1452 the earl of Douglas beheaded his pris-oner MacLellan while the king's messenger bear-ing orders for his release was detained at the table refreshing himself after his journey.

pocketbook the receipt, and handed it to Steenie. "There is your receipt, ye pitiful cur; and for the money, my dog-whelp of a son may go look for it in the Cat's Cradle."

My gudesire uttered mony thanks, and was about to retire, when Sir Robert roared aloud, "Stop though, thou sack-doudling son of a whore! I am not done with thee. HERE we do nothing for nothing; and you must return on this very day twelvemonth, to pay your master the homage that you owe me for my protection."

My father's tongue was loosed of a suddenty, and he said aloud, "I refer mysell to God's pleasure, and not to yours."

He had no sooner uttered the word than all was dark around him; and he sunk on the earth with such a sudden shock, that he lost both breath and sense.

How lang Steenie lay there, he could not tell; but when he came to himsell, he was lying in the auld kirkyard of Redgauntlet parochine,[1] just at the door of the family aisle, and the scutcheon[2] of the auld knight, Sir Robert, hanging over his head. There was a deep morning fog on the grass and gravestane around him, and his horse was feeding quietly beside the minister's twa cows. Steenie would have thought the whole was a dream, but he had the receipt in his hand, fairly written and signed by the auld Laird; only the last letters of his name were a little disorderly, written like one seized with sudden pain.

Sorely troubled in his mind, he left that dreary place, rode through the mist to Redgauntlet Castle, and with much ado he got speech of the Laird.

"Well, you dyvour bankrupt," was the first word, "have you brought me my rent?"

"No," answered my gudesire, "I have not; but I have brought your honour Sir Robert's receipt for it."

"How, sirrah?—Sir Robert's receipt!—You told me he had not given you one."

"Will your honour please to see if that bit line is right?"

Sir John looked at every line, and at every letter, with much attention; and at last, at the date, which my gudesire had not observed,—"From my appointed place," he read, "this twenty-fifth of November.—What!—That is yesterday!—Villain, thou must have gone to hell for this!"

"I got it from your honour's father—whether he be in heaven or hell, I know not," said Steenie.

"I will delate[3] you for a warlock to the Privy Council!" said Sir John. "I will send you to your master, the devil, with the help of a tar-barrel and a torch!"

"I intend to delate mysell to the Presbytery,"[4] said Steenie, "and tell them all I have seen last night, whilk are things fitter for them to judge of than a borrel[5] man like me."

Sir John paused, composed himsell, and desired to hear the full history; and my gudesire told it from point to point, as I have told it you—word for word, neither more nor less.

Sir John was silent again for a long time, and at last he said, very composedly, "Steenie, this story of yours concerns the honour of many a noble family besides mine; and if it be a leasing-making,[6] to keep yourself out of my danger,

1. Churchyard of Redgauntlet parish.
2. Coat of arms.
3. Report.
4. Ecclesiastical court made up of ministers and

elders from the local parishes.
5. Simple.
6. Slander.

the least you can expect is to have a redhot iron driven through your tongue, and that will be as bad as scauding your fingers with a redhot chanter. But yet it may be true, Steenie; and if the money cast up, I shall not know what to think of it.—But where shall we find the Cat's Cradle? There are cats enough about the old house, but I think they kitten without the ceremony of bed or cradle."

"We were best ask Hutcheon," said my gudesire; "he kens a' the odd corners about as weel as—another serving-man that is now gane, and that I wad not like to name."

Aweel, Hutcheon, when he was asked, told them, that a ruinous turret, lang disused, next to the clock-house, only accessible by a ladder, for the opening was on the outside, and far above the battlements, was called of old the Cat's Cradle.

"There will I go immediately," said Sir John; and he took (with what purpose, Heaven kens) one of his father's pistols from the hall-table, where they had lain since the night he died, and hastened to the battlements.

It was a dangerous place to climb, for the ladder was auld and frail, and wanted ane or twa rounds. However, up got Sir John, and entered at the turret door, where his body stopped the only little light that was in the bit turret. Something flees at him wi' a vengeance, maist dang him back ower—bang gaed the knight's pistol, and Hutcheon, that held the ladder, and my gudesire that stood beside him, hears a loud skelloch.[7] A minute after, Sir John flings the body of the jackanape down to them, and cries that the siller is fund, and that they should come up and help him. And there was the bag of siller sure aneugh, and mony orra things besides, that had been missing for mony a day. And Sir John, when he had riped[8] the turret weel, led my gudesire into the dining-parlour, and took him by the hand, and spoke kindly to him, and said he was sorry he should have doubted his word, and that he would hereafter be a good master to him, to make amends.

"And now, Steenie," said Sir John, "although this vision of yours tends, on the whole, to my father's credit, as an honest man, that he should, even after his death, desire to see justice done to a poor man like you, yet you are sensible that ill-dispositioned men might make bad constructions on it, concerning his soul's health. So, I think, we had better lay the haill dirdum[9] on that ill-deedie creature, Major Weir, and say naething about your dream in the wood of Pitmurkie. You had taken ower muckle brandy to be very certain about ony thing; and, Steenie, this receipt," (his hand shook while he held it out,)—"it's but a queer kind of document, and we will do best, I think, to put it quietly in the fire."

"Od, but for as queer as it is, it's a' the voucher I have for my rent," said my gudesire, who was afraid, it may be, of losing the benefit of Sir Robert's discharge.

"I will bear the contents to your credit in the rental-book, and give you a discharge under my own hand," said Sir John, "and that on the spot. And, Steenie, if you can hold your tongue about this matter, you shall sit, from this term downward, at an easier rent."

"Mony thanks to your honour," said Steenie, who saw easily in what corner the wind was; "doubtless I will be conformable to all your honour's commands;

7. Screech.
8. Searched.

9. Blame.

only I would willingly speak wi' some powerful minister on the subject, for I do not like the sort of soumons of appointment whilk your honour's father"—"Do not call that phantom my father!" said Sir John, interrupting him.

"Weel, then, the thing that was so like him,"—said my gudesire; "he spoke of my coming back to him this time twelvemonth, and it's a weight on my conscience."

"Aweel, then," said Sir John, "if you be much distressed in mind, you may speak to our minister of the parish; he is a douce[1] man, regards the honour of our family, and the mair that he may look for some patronage from me."

Wi' that my gudesire readily agreed that the receipt should be burnt, and the Laird threw it into the chimney with his ain hand. Burn it would not for them, though; but away it flew up the lum,[2] wi' a lang train of sparks at its tail, and a hissing noise like a squib.[3]

My gudesire gaed down to the manse,[4] and the minister, when he had heard the story, said, it was his real opinion, that though my gudesire had gaen very far in tampering with such dangerous matters, yet, as he had refused the devil's arles[5] (for such was the offer of meat and drink,) and had refused to do homage by piping at his bidding, he hoped, that if he held a circumspect walk hereafter, Satan could take little advantage by what was come and gane. And, indeed, my gudesire, of his ain accord, lang forswore baith the pipes and the brandy—it was not even till the year was out, and the fatal day passed, that he would so much as take the fiddle, or drink usquebaugh or tippeny.[6]

Sir John made up his story about the jackanape as he liked himsell; and some believe till this day there was no more in the matter than the filching nature of the brute. Indeed, ye'll no hinder some to threap,[7] that it was nane o' the Auld Enemy that Dougal and my gudesire saw in the Laird's room, but only that wanchancy creature, the Major, capering on the coffin; and that as to the blawing on the Laird's whistle that was heard after he was dead, the filthy brute could do that as weel as the Laird himsell, if no better. But Heaven kens the truth, whilk first came out by the minister's wife, after Sir John and her ain gudeman[8] were baith in the moulds.[9] And then, my gudesire, wha was failed in his limbs, but not in his judgment or memory—at least nothing to speak of—was obliged to tell the real narrative to his freends, for the credit of his good name. He might else have been charged for a warlock.

The shades of evening were growing thicker around us as my conductor finished his long narrative with this moral—"Ye see, birkie,[1] it is nae chancy thing to tak a stranger traveller for a guide, when ye are in an uncouth[2] land."

1824

---

1. Respectable.
2. Chimney flue.
3. Firecracker.
4. Minister's house.
5. Money given to bind the bargain when a servant is hired.
6. Whiskey and weak beer that was sold for two pence. Compare Burns's "Tam O'Shanter," lines

107–8: Steenie's adventure in some respects repeats Tam's.
7. Contend.
8. Husband.
9. Their graves.
1. Clever young man.
2. Strange.

SAMUEL TAYLOR COLERIDGE
1772–1834

In *The Prelude* Wordsworth, recording his gratitude to the mountains, lakes, and winds "that dwell among the hills where I was born," commiserates with Coleridge because "thou, my Friend! wert reared / In the great City, 'mid far other scenes." Samuel Taylor Coleridge had in fact been born in the small town of Ottery St. Mary, in rural Devonshire, but on the death of his father he had been sent to school at Christ's Hospital in London. He was a dreamy, enthusiastic, and extraordinarily precocious schoolboy. Charles Lamb, his schoolmate and lifelong friend, in his essay on Christ's Hospital has given us a vivid sketch of Coleridge's loneliness, his learning, and his eloquence. When in 1791 Coleridge entered Jesus College, Cambridge, he was an accomplished scholar; but he found little intellectual stimulation at the university, fell into idleness, dissoluteness, and debt, then in despair fled to London and enlisted in the Light Dragoons under the alias of Silas Tomkyn Comberbache—one of the most inept cavalrymen in the long history of the British army. Although rescued by his brothers and sent back to Cambridge, he left in 1794 without a degree.

In June 1794 Coleridge met Robert Southey, then a student at Oxford who, like himself, had poetic aspirations, was a radical in religion and politics, and sympathized with the republican experiment in France. Together the two young men planned to establish an ideal democratic community in America for which Coleridge coined the name "Pantisocracy;" signifying an equal rule by all. A plausible American real-estate agent persuaded them that the ideal location would be on the banks of the Susquehanna in Pennsylvania. Twelve men undertook to go; and because perpetuation of the scheme required offspring, hence wives, Coleridge dutifully became engaged to Sara Fricker, conveniently at hand as the sister of Southey's fiancée. The Pantisocracy scheme collapsed, but at Southey's insistence Coleridge went through with the marriage, "resolved," as he said, "but wretched." Later Coleridge's radicalism waned, and he became a conservative in politics—a highly philosophical one—and a staunch Anglican in religion.

In 1795 Coleridge met Wordsworth and at once judged him to be "the best poet of the age." When in 1797 Wordsworth brought his sister, Dorothy, to settle at Alfoxden, only three miles from the Coleridges at Nether Stowey, the period of intimate communication and poetic collaboration began that was the golden time of Coleridge's life. An annual allowance of £150, granted to Coleridge by Thomas and Josiah Wedgwood, sons of the founder of the famous pottery firm, came just in time to deflect him from assuming a post as a Unitarian minister. After their joint publication of *Lyrical Ballads* in 1798, Coleridge and the Wordsworths spent a winter in Germany, where Coleridge attended the University of Göttingen and began the lifelong study of German philosophers and critics—Kant, Schiller, Schelling, and Fichte—that helped alter profoundly his thinking about philosophy, religion, and aesthetics.

Back in England, Coleridge in 1800 followed the Wordsworths to the Lake District, settling at Greta Hall, Keswick. He had become gradually disaffected from his wife, and now he fell helplessly and hopelessly in love with Sara Hutchinson, whose sister, Mary, Wordsworth married in 1802. In accord with the medical prescription of that time, Coleridge had been taking laudanum (opium dissolved in alcohol) to ease the painful physical ailments from which he had suffered from an early age. In 1800–01 heavy dosages during attacks of rheumatism made opium a necessity to him, and Coleridge soon recognized that the drug was a greater evil than the diseases it did not cure. "Dejection: An Ode," published in 1802, was Coleridge's despairing farewell to health, happiness, and poetic creativity. A two-year sojourn on the Mediterranean island of Malta, intended to restore his health, instead completed his decline. When he returned to England in the late summer of 1806, he was a broken man, a drug addict, estranged from his wife, suffering from agonies of remorse, and subject to terrifying nightmares of guilt and despair from which his own shrieks awakened him. By 1810, when he and Wordsworth quarreled bitterly, it must have seemed that he could not fall any lower.

Under these conditions Coleridge's literary efforts, however sporadic and fragmentary, were little short of heroic. In 1808 he debuted as a speaker at one of the new lecturing institutions that sprang up in British cities in the early nineteenth century. His lectures on poetry, like his later series on Shakespeare, became part of the social calendar for fashionable Londoners—women, excluded still from universities, particularly. He wrote for newspapers and single-handedly undertook to write, publish, and distribute a periodical, *The Friend,* which lasted for some ten months beginning in June 1809. A tragedy, *Remorse,* had in 1813 a successful run of twenty performances at the Drury Lane theater. In 1816 he took up residence at Highgate, a northern suburb of London, under the supervision of the excellent and endlessly forbearing physician James Gillman, who managed to control, although not to eliminate, Coleridge's consumption of opium. The next three years were Coleridge's most sustained period of literary activity. While continuing to lecture and to write for the newspapers on a variety of subjects, he published *Biographia Literaria, Zapolya* (a drama), a book consisting of the essays in *The Friend* (revised and greatly enlarged), two collections of poems, and several important treatises on philosophical and religious subjects. In these treatises and those that followed over the next fifteen years, he emerged as the heir to the conservatism of Edmund Burke, an opponent to secularism and a defender of the Anglican Church, and an unapologetic intellectual elitist with an ambitious account of the role elites might play in modern states, outlined in his discussions of national culture and of the "clerisy" who would take responsibility for preserving it.

The remaining years of his life, which he spent with Dr. and Mrs. Gillman, were quieter and happier than any he had known since the turn of the century. He came to a peaceful understanding with his wife and was reconciled with Wordsworth, with whom he toured the Rhineland in 1828. His rooms at Highgate became a center for friends, for the London literati, and for a steady stream of pilgrims from England and America. They came to hear one of the wonders of the age, the Sage of Highgate's conversation—or monologue—for even in his decline, Coleridge's talk never lost the almost hypnotic power that Hazlitt has immortalized in "My First Acquaintance with Poets." Mary Shelley appears to have been haunted by the memory of the evening when, a small child, she hid behind a sofa to listen to Coleridge, one of her father's visitors, recite *The Rime of the Ancient Mariner,* and a stanza from that poem of dark mystery found its way into *Frankenstein,* just as her recollections of that visitor's voice contributed to her depictions of the irresistible hold her novel's storytellers have over their auditors. When he died, Coleridge left his friends with the sense that an incomparable intellect had vanished from the world.

Coleridge's friends, however, abetted by his own merciless self-judgments, set current the opinion, still common, that he was great in promise but not in performance. Even in his buoyant youth he described his own character as "indolence capable of energies"; and it is true that while his mind was incessantly active and fertile, he lacked application and staying power. He also manifested early in life a profound sense of guilt and a need for public expiation. After drug addiction sapped his strength and will, he often adapted (or simply adopted) passages from other writers, with little or no acknowledgment, and sometimes in a context that seems designed to reveal that he relies on sources that he does not credit. Whatever the tangled motives for his procedure, Coleridge has repeatedly been charged with gross plagiarism, from his day to ours. After *The Ancient Mariner,* most of the poems he completed were written, like the first version of "Dejection: An Ode," in a spasm of intense effort. Writings that required sustained planning and application were either left unfinished or, like *Biographia Literaria,* made up of brilliant sections padded out with filler, sometimes lifted from other writers, in a desperate effort to meet a deadline. Many of his speculations Coleridge merely confided to his notebooks and the ears of his friends, incorporated in letters, and poured out in the margins of his own and other people's books. Even so, it is only when measured against his own potentialities that Coleridge's achievements appear limited. In an 1838 essay the philosopher John Stuart Mill hailed the recently deceased Coleridge as one of "the two great seminal minds of England": according to Mill, Coleridge's conservatism had, along with the very different utilitarian philosophy of Jeremy Bentham (the other seminal mind identified in Mill's essay), revolutionized the political thought of the day. Coleridge was also one of the important and influential literary theorists of the nineteenth century. One of his major legacies is the notion that culture, the nation's artistic and spiritual heritage, represents a force with the power to combat the fragmentation of a modern, market-driven society and to restore a common, collective life. This was an idea that he worked out largely in opposition to Bentham's utilitarianism, the newly prestigious discipline of political economy, and the impoverished, soulless account of human nature that these systems of thought offered. And in *Biographia Literaria* and elsewhere, Coleridge raised the stakes for literary criticism, making it into a kind of writing that could address the most difficult and abstract questions—questions about, for instance, the relations between literary language and ordinary language, or between poetry and philosophy, or between perception and imagination. Above all, Coleridge's writings in verse—whether we consider the poetry of Gothic demonism in *Christabel* or the meditative conversation poems like "Frost at Midnight" or "This Lime-Tree Bower My Prison"—are the achievements of a remarkably innovative poet.

The Eolian Harp[1]

Composed at Clevedon, Somersetshire

My pensive Sara! thy soft cheek reclined
Thus on mine arm, most soothing sweet it is
To sit beside our cot, our cot o'ergrown
With white-flowered jasmin, and the broad-leaved myrtle,
5 (Meet emblems they of Innocence and Love!)
And watch the clouds, that late were rich with light,
Slow saddening round, and mark the star of eve
Serenely brilliant (such should wisdom be)
Shine opposite! How exquisite the scents
10 Snatched from yon bean-field! and the world so hushed!
The stilly murmur of the distant sea
Tells us of silence.

And that simplest lute,
Placed length-ways in the clasping casement, hark!

---

1. Named for Aeolus, god of the winds, the harp has strings stretched over a rectangular sounding box. When placed in an opened window, the harp (also called "Eolian lute," "Eolian lyre," "wind harp") responds to the altering wind by sequences of musical chords. This instrument, which seems to voice nature's own music, was a favorite household furnishing in the period and was repeatedly alluded to in Romantic poetry. It served also as one of the recurrent Romantic images for the mind—either the mind in poetic inspiration, as in the last stanza of Shelley's "Ode to the West Wind" (p. 772), or else the mind in perception, responding to an intellectual breeze by trembling into consciousness, as in this poem, lines 44–48.
   Coleridge wrote this poem to Sara Fricker, whom he married on October 4, 1795, and took to a cottage (the "cot" of lines 3 and 64) at Clevedon, overlooking the Bristol Channel. He later several times expanded and altered the original version; the famous lines 26–29, for example, were not added until 1817. Originally it was titled "Effusion XXXV" and was one of thirty-six such effusions that Coleridge included in a 1796 volume of verse; revised and retitled, it became what he called a "conversation poem"—the designation used since his day for a sustained blank-verse lyric of description and meditation, in the mode of conversation addressed to a silent auditor. This was the form that Coleridge perfected in "Frost at Midnight" and that Wordsworth adopted in "Tintern Abbey."

How by the desultory breeze caressed,
15 Like some coy maid half yielding to her lover,
   It pours such sweet upbraiding,° as must needs   *scolding*
   Tempt to repeat the wrong! And now, its strings
   Boldlier swept, the long sequacious° notes   *regularly following*
   Over delicious surges sink and rise,
20 Such a soft floating witchery of sound
   As twilight Elfins make, when they at eve
   Voyage on gentle gales from Fairy-Land,
   Where Melodies round honey-dropping flowers,
   Footless and wild, like birds of Paradise,[2]
25 Nor pause, nor perch, hovering on untamed wing!
   O the one life within us and abroad,
   Which meets all motion and becomes its soul,
   A light in sound, a sound-like power in light,
   Rhythm in all thought, and joyance[3] every where—
30 Methinks, it should have been impossible
   Not to love all things in a world so filled;
   Where the breeze warbles, and the mute still air
   Is Music slumbering on her instrument.

   And thus, my love! as on the midway slope
35 Of yonder hill I stretch my limbs at noon,
   Whilst through my half-closed eye-lids I behold
   The sunbeams dance, like diamonds, on the main,°   *ocean*
   And tranquil muse upon tranquillity;
   Full many a thought uncalled and undetained,
40 And many idle flitting phantasies,
   Traverse my indolent and passive brain,
   As wild and various as the random gales
   That swell and flutter on this subject lute!

   And what if all of animated nature
45 Be but organic harps diversely framed,
   That tremble into thought, as o'er them sweeps
   Plastic and vast, one intellectual breeze,
   At once the Soul of each, and God of All?

   But thy more serious eye a mild reproof
50 Darts, O beloved woman! nor such thoughts
   Dim and unhallowed dost thou not reject,
   And biddest me walk humbly with my God.
   Meek daughter in the family of Christ!
   Well hast thou said and holily dispraised
55 These shapings of the unregenerate[4] mind;
   Bubbles that glitter as they rise and break
   On vain Philosophy's aye-babbling° spring.   *ever babbling*
   For never guiltless may I speak of him,
   The Incomprehensible! save when with awe

2. Brilliantly colored birds found in New Guinea and adjacent islands. The native practice of removing the legs when preparing the skin led Europeans to believe that the birds were footless and spent their lives hovering in the air and feeding on nectar.
3. An archaic term for enjoyment, coined in the 16th century by Spenser and reintroduced by Coleridge.
4. Spiritually unredeemed; not born again.

60 I praise him, and with Faith that inly feels;
    Who with his saving mercies healed me,
    A sinful and most miserable man,
    Wildered and dark, and gave me to possess
    Peace, and this cot, and thee, heart-honored Maid!

1795   1796

This Lime-Tree Bower My Prison

In the June of 1797, some long-expected Friends paid a visit to the
author's cottage; and on the morning of their arrival, he met with
an accident, which disabled him from walking during the whole
time of their stay. One evening, when they had left him for a few
hours, he composed the following lines in the garden-bower.[1]

    Well, they are gone, and here must I remain,
    This lime-tree bower my prison! I have lost
    Beauties and feelings, such as would have been
    Most sweet to my remembrance even when age
5   Had dimmed mine eyes to blindness! They, meanwhile,
    Friends, whom I never more may meet again,
    On springy[2] heath, along the hill-top edge,
    Wander in gladness, and wind down, perchance,
    To that still roaring dell, of which I told;
10 The roaring dell, o'erwooded, narrow, deep,
    And only speckled by the mid-day sun;
    Where its slim trunk the ash from rock to rock
    Flings arching like a bridge;—that branchless ash,
    Unsunned and damp, whose few poor yellow leaves
15 Ne'er tremble in the gale, yet tremble still,
    Fanned by the water-fall! and there my friends
    Behold the dark green file of long lank weeds,
    That all at once (a most fantastic sight!)
    Still nod and drip beneath the dripping edge
    Of the blue clay-stone.[3]

20   Now, my friends emerge
    Beneath the wide wide Heaven—and view again
    The many-steepled tract magnificent
    Of hilly fields and meadows, and the sea,
    With some fair bark,° perhaps, whose sails light up   boat
25 The slip of smooth clear blue betwixt two Isles
    Of purple shadow! Yes! they wander on

1. The time was in fact July 1797; the visiting
friends were William and Dorothy Wordsworth
and Charles Lamb; the accident was the fault of
Mrs. Coleridge—"dear Sara," Coleridge wrote,
"accidentally emptied a skillet of boiling milk on
my foot"; and the bower consisted of lime (i.e., lin-
den) trees in the garden of Thomas Poole, next
door to Coleridge's cottage at Nether Stowey.
Coleridge related these facts in a letter to Robert

Southey, July 17, 1797, in which he transcribed
the first version of this poem. In the earliest printed
text, the title is followed by "Addressed to Charles
Lamb, of the India-House, London."
2. Elastic, I mean [Coleridge's note].
3. Cf. Dorothy Wordsworth's description of the
"low damp dell" in her Alfoxden Journal, February
10, 1798 (p. 391).

In gladness all; but thou, methinks, most glad,
My gentle-hearted Charles! for thou hast pined
And hungered after Nature, many a year,
30　In the great City pent,[4] winning thy way
With sad yet patient soul, through evil and pain
And strange calamity![5] Ah! slowly sink
Behind the western ridge, thou glorious sun!
Shine in the slant beams of the sinking orb,
35　Ye purple heath-flowers! richlier burn, ye clouds!
Live in the yellow light, ye distant groves!
And kindle, thou blue ocean! So my Friend
Struck with deep joy may stand, as I have stood,
Silent with swimming sense; yea, gazing round
40　On the wide landscape, gaze till all doth seem
Less gross than bodily; and of such hues
As veil the Almighty Spirit, when yet he makes
Spirits perceive his presence.

　　　　　　　　　　　　A delight
Comes sudden on my heart, and I am glad
45　As I myself were there! Nor in this bower,
This little lime-tree bower, have I not marked
Much that has soothed me. Pale beneath the blaze
Hung the transparent foliage; and I watched
Some broad and sunny leaf, and loved to see
50　The shadow of the leaf and stem above
Dappling its sunshine! And that walnut-tree
Was richly tinged, and a deep radiance lay
Full on the ancient ivy, which usurps
Those fronting elms, and now, with blackest mass
55　Makes their dark branches gleam a lighter hue
Through the late twilight: and though now the bat
Wheels silent by, and not a swallow twitters,
Yet still the solitary humble bee
Sings in the bean-flower! Henceforth I shall know
60　That Nature ne'er deserts the wise and pure;
No plot so narrow, be but Nature there,
No waste so vacant, but may well employ
Each faculty of sense, and keep the heart
Awake to Love and Beauty! and sometimes
65　'Tis well to be bereft of promised good,
That we may lift the Soul, and contemplate
With lively joy the joys we cannot share.
My gentle-hearted Charles! when the last rook
Beat its straight path along the dusky air
70　Homewards, I blessed it! deeming its black wing
(Now a dim speck, now vanishing in light)
Had crossed the mighty orb's dilated glory,
While thou stood'st gazing; or when all was still,

4. Despite Coleridge's claim, Charles Lamb eminently preferred London over what he called "dead
Nature." For Lamb's love of city life, see his letter
to Wordsworth at Norton Literature Online.

5. Some ten months earlier Charles Lamb's sister,
Mary, had stabbed their mother to death in a fit of
insanity.

Flew creeking o'er thy head, and had a charm
75 For thee, my gentle-hearted Charles, to whom
No sound is dissonant which tells of Life.

1797   1800

The Rime of the Ancient Mariner[1]

IN SEVEN PARTS

*Facile credo, plures esse Naturas invisibiles quam visibiles in rerum
universitate. Sed horum [sic] omnium familiam quis nobis enarrabit,
et gradus et cognationes et discrimina et singulorum munera? Quid
agunt? quae loca habitant? Harum rerum notitiam semper ambivit
ingenium humanum, nunquam attigit. Juvat, interea, non diffiteor,
quandoque in animo, tanquam in tabulâ, majoris et melioris mundi
imaginem contemplari: ne mens assuefacta hodiernae vitae minutiis
se contrahat nimis, et tota subsidat in pusillas cogitationes. Sed
veritati interea invigilandum est, modusque servandus, ut certa ab
incertis, diem a nocte, distinguamus.*

T. BURNET, *Archaeol. Phil.* p. 68.[2]

Part 1

An ancient Mariner
meeteth three gal-
lants bidden to a
wedding-feast, and
detaineth one.

It is an ancient Mariner
And he stoppeth one of three.
"By thy long grey beard and glittering eye,
Now wherefore stopp'st thou me?

The Bridegroom's doors are opened wide,   5
And I am next of kin;
The guests are met, the feast is set:
May'st hear the merry din."

He holds him with his skinny hand,
"There was a ship," quoth he.   10
"Hold off! unhand me, grey-beard loon!"
Eftsoons[3] his hand dropt he.

1. Coleridge describes the origin of this poem in the opening section of chap. 14 of *Biographia Literaria*. In a comment made to the Reverend Alexander Dyce in 1835 and in a note on "We Are Seven" dictated in 1843, Wordsworth added some details. The poem, based on a dream of Coleridge's friend Cruikshank, was originally planned as a collaboration between Coleridge and Wordsworth, to pay the expense of a walking tour they took with Dorothy Wordsworth in November 1797. Before he dropped out of the enterprise, Wordsworth suggested the shooting of the albatross and the navigation of the ship by the dead men; he also contributed lines 13–16 and 226–27.
When printed in *Lyrical Ballads* (1798), this poem was titled "The Rime of the Ancyent Marinere" and contained many archaic words and spellings, which, Wordsworth believed, hurt the sales of their volume. In later editions Coleridge revised the poem, in part by pruning those archaisms. He also added the Latin epigraph and the marginal

glosses written in the old-fashioned style of 17th-century learning.
2. "I readily believe that there are more invisible than visible Natures in the universe. But who will explain for us the family of all these beings, and the ranks and relations and distinguishing features and functions of each? What do they do? What places do they inhabit? The human mind has always sought the knowledge of these things, but never attained it. Meanwhile I do not deny that it is helpful sometimes to contemplate in the mind, as on a tablet, the image of a greater and better world, lest the intellect, habituated to the petty things of daily life, narrow itself and sink wholly into trivial thoughts. But at the same time we must be watchful for the truth and keep a sense of proportion, so that we may distinguish the certain from the uncertain, day from night." Adapted by Coleridge from Thomas Burnet, *Archaeologiae Philosophicae* (1692).
3. At once.

The wedding guest is spellbound by the eye of the old sea-faring man, and constrained to hear his tale.

He holds him with his glittering eye—
The wedding-guest stood still,
And listens like a three years' child:
The Mariner hath his will.[4]   15

The wedding-guest sat on a stone:
He cannot choose but hear;
And thus spake on that ancient man,
The bright-eyed Mariner.   20

"The ship was cheered, the harbor cleared,
Merrily did we drop
Below the kirk,[5] below the hill,
Below the light house top.

The Mariner tells how the ship sailed southward with a good wind and fair weather, till it reached the line.

The sun came up upon the left,   25
Out of the sea came he!
And he shone bright, and on the right
Went down into the sea.

Higher and higher every day,
Till over the mast at noon[6]—"   30
The wedding-guest here beat his breast,
For he heard the loud bassoon.

The Wedding Guest heareth the bridal music; but the mariner continueth his tale.

The bride hath paced into the hall,
Red as a rose is she;
Nodding their heads before her goes   35
The merry minstrelsy.

The wedding-guest he beat his breast,
Yet he cannot choose but hear;
And thus spake on that ancient man,
The bright-eyed Mariner.   40

The ship driven by a storm toward the south pole.

"And now the storm-blast came, and he
Was tyrannous and strong:
He struck with his o'ertaking wings,
And chased us south along.

With sloping masts and dipping prow,   45
As who pursued with yell and blow
Still treads the shadow of his foe,
And forward bends his head,
The ship drove fast, loud roared the blast,
And southward aye[7] we fled.   50

And now there came both mist and snow,
And it grew wondrous cold:

---

4. I.e., the Mariner has gained control of the will of the wedding guest by hypnosis—or, as it was called in Coleridge's time, by "mesmerism."

5. Church.
6. The ship had reached the equator.
7. Always.

And ice, mast-high, came floating by,
As green as emerald.

The land of ice, and of fearful sounds where no living thing was to be seen.
And through the drifts the snowy clifts   55
Did send a dismal sheen:
Nor shapes of men nor beasts we ken[8]—
The ice was all between.

The ice was here, the ice was there,
The ice was all around: 60
It cracked and growled, and roared and howled,
Like noises in a swound![9]

Till a great sea-bird, called the Albatross, came through the snow-fog, and was received with great joy and hospitality.
At length did cross an Albatross,
Thorough the fog it came;
As if it had been a Christian soul,   65
We hailed it in God's name.

It ate the food it ne'er had eat,
And round and round it flew.
The ice did split with a thunder-fit;
The helmsman steered us through!   70

And lo! the Albatross proveth a bird of good omen, and followeth the ship as it returned northward through fog and floating ice.
And a good south wind sprung up behind;
The Albatross did follow,
And every day, for food or play,
Came to the mariners' hollo!

In mist or cloud, on mast or shroud,[1]   75
It perched for vespers nine;
Whiles all the night, through fog-smoke white,
Glimmered the white moon-shine."

The ancient Mariner inhospitably killeth the pious bird of good omen.
"God save thee, ancient Mariner!
From the fiends, that plague thee thus!—   80
Why look'st thou so?"—With my cross-bow
I shot the Albatross.

Part 2

The Sun now rose upon the right:[2]
Out of the sea came he,
Still hid in mist, and on the left   85
Went down into the sea.

And the good south wind still blew behind,
But no sweet bird did follow,
Nor any day for food or play
Came to the mariners' hollo!   90

8. Knew.
9. Swoon.
1. Rope supporting the mast.

2. Having rounded Cape Horn, the ship heads north into the Pacific.

*His shipmates cry out
against the ancient
Mariner, for killing
the bird of good luck.*

And I had done a hellish thing,
And it would work 'em woe:
For all averred, I had killed the bird
That made the breeze to blow.
Ah wretch! said they, the bird to slay,   95
That made the breeze to blow!

*But when the fog
cleared off, they jus-
tify the same, and
thus make themselves
accomplices in the
crime.*

Nor dim nor red, like God's own head,
The glorious Sun uprist:
Then all averred, I had killed the bird
That brought the fog and mist.   100
'Twas right, said they, such birds to slay,
That bring the fog and mist.

*The fair breeze con-
tinues; the ship
enters the Pacific
Ocean, and sails
northward, even till
it reaches the Line.³*

The fair breeze blew, the white foam flew,
The furrow followed free;
We were the first that ever burst   105
Into that silent sea.

*The ship hath been
suddenly becalmed.*

Down dropt the breeze, the sails dropt down,
'Twas sad as sad could be;
And we did speak only to break
The silence of the sea!   110

All in a hot and copper sky,
The bloody Sun, at noon,
Right up above the mast did stand,
No bigger than the Moon.

Day after day, day after day,   115
We stuck, nor breath nor motion;
As idle as a painted ship
Upon a painted ocean.

*And the Albatross
begins to be avenged.*

Water, water, every where,
And all the boards did shrink;   120
Water, water, every where,
Nor any drop to drink.

The very deep did rot: O Christ!
That ever this should be!
Yea, slimy things did crawl with legs   125
Upon the slimy sea.

About, about, in reel and rout
The death-fires⁴ danced at night;
The water, like a witch's oils,
Burnt green, and blue and white.   130

---

3. I.e., the equator. Unless it is simply an error (Coleridge misreading his own poem), this gloss anticipates the ship's later arrival at the equator, on its trip north from the region of the South Pole, as described in lines 381–84.
4. Usually glossed as St. Elmo's fire—an atmo-
spheric electricity on a ship's mast or rigging—believed by superstitious sailors to portend disaster. Possibly the reference is instead to phosphorescence resulting from the decomposition of organic matter in the sea (see line 123).

A spirit had followed them; one of the invisible inhabitants of this planet, neither departed souls nor angels; concerning whom the learned Jew, Josephus, and the Platonic Constantinopolitan, Michael Psellus, may be consulted. They are very numerous, and there is no climate or element without one or more.

And some in dreams assured were
Of the spirit that plagued us so;
Nine fathom deep he had followed us
From the land of mist and snow.

And every tongue, through utter drought,   135
Was withered at the root;
We could not speak, no more than if
We had been choked with soot.

The shipmates, in their sore distress, would fain throw the whole guilt on the ancient Mariner: in sign whereof they hang the dead sea bird round his neck.

Ah! well-a-day! what evil looks
Had I from old and young!   140
Instead of the cross, the Albatross
About my neck was hung.

Part 3

There passed a weary time. Each throat
Was parched, and glazed each eye.
A weary time! a weary time!   145
How glazed each weary eye,

The ancient Mariner beholdeth a sign in the element afar off.

When looking westward, I beheld
A something in the sky.

At first it seemed a little speck,
And then it seemed a mist;   150
It moved and moved, and took at last
A certain shape, I wist.[5]

A speck, a mist, a shape, I wist!
And still it neared and neared:
As if it dodged a water-sprite,[6]   155
It plunged and tacked and veered.

At its nearer approach, it seemeth him to be a ship; and at a dear ransom he freeth his speech from the bonds of thirst.

With throats unslaked, with black lips baked,
We could nor laugh nor wail;
Through utter drought all dumb we stood!
I bit my arm, I sucked the blood,   160
And cried, A sail! a sail!

A flash of joy;

With throats unslaked, with black lips baked,
Agape they heard me call:
Gramercy![7] they for joy did grin,
And all at once their breath drew in,   165
As they were drinking all.

5. Knew.
6. A supernatural being that supervises the natural elements (but Coleridge may in fact have been using the term to mean water-*spout*).
7. Great thanks; from the French *grand-merci*.

And horror follows. For can it be a ship that comes onward without wind or tide?

See! see! (I cried) she tacks no more!
Hither to work us weal;[8]
Without a breeze, without a tide,
She steadies with upright keel!   170

The western wave was all a-flame.
The day was well nigh done!
Almost upon the western wave
Rested the broad bright Sun;
When that strange shape drove suddenly   175
Betwixt us and the Sun.

It seemeth him but the skeleton of a ship.

And straight the Sun was flecked with bars,
(Heaven's Mother send us grace!)
As if through a dungeon-grate he peered
With broad and burning face.   180

Alas! (thought I, and my heart beat loud)
How fast she nears and nears!
Are those her sails that glance in the Sun,
Like restless gossameres?[9]

And its ribs are seen as bars on the face of the setting Sun. The specter-woman and her death-mate, and no other on board the skeleton-ship.

Are those her ribs through which the Sun   185
Did peer, as through a grate?
And is that Woman all her crew?
Is that a Death? and are there two?
Is Death that woman's mate?

Like vessel, like crew!

Her lips were red, her looks were free,   190
Her locks were yellow as gold:
Her skin was as white as leprosy,
The Night-mare Life-in-Death was she,
Who thicks man's blood with cold.

Death and Life-in-death have diced for the ship's crew, and she (the latter) winneth the ancient Mariner.

The naked hulk[1] alongside came,   195
And the twain were casting dice;
"The game is done! I've won! I've won!"
Quoth she, and whistles thrice.

No twilight within the courts of the sun.

The Sun's rim dips; the stars rush out:
At one stride comes the dark;   200
With far-heard whisper, o'er the sea,
Off shot the spectre-bark.[2]

At the rising of the Moon,

We listened and looked sideways up!
Fear at my heart, as at a cup,
My life-blood seemed to sip!   205
The stars were dim, and thick the night,
The steersman's face by his lamp gleamed white;

8. Benefit.   1. Large ship.
9. Filmy cobwebs floating in the air.   2. Ghost ship.

From the sails the dew did drip—
Till clomb above the eastern bar
The horned Moon, with one bright star   210
Within the nether tip.³

One after another,   One after one, by the star-dogged Moon,
Too quick for groan or sigh,
Each turned his face with a ghastly pang,
And cursed me with his eye.   215

His shipmates drop   Four times fifty living men,
down dead.   (And I heard nor sigh nor groan)
With heavy thump, a lifeless lump,
They dropped down one by one.

But Life-in-Death   The souls did from their bodies fly,—   220
begins her work on   They fled to bliss or woe!
the ancient Mariner.   And every soul, it passed me by,
Like the whizz of my cross-bow!

Part 4

The wedding guest   "I fear thee, ancient Mariner!
feareth that a spirit is
talking to him.   I fear thy skinny hand!   225
And thou art long, and lank, and brown,
As is the ribbed sea-sand.

I fear thee and thy glittering eye,
And thy skinny hand, so brown."—
But the ancient Mar-   Fear not, fear not, thou wedding-guest!   230
iner assureth him of   This body dropt not down.
his bodily life, and
proceedeth to relate
his horrible penance.
Alone, alone, all, all alone,
Alone on a wide wide sea!
And never a saint took pity on
My soul in agony.   235

He despiseth the   The many men, so beautiful!
creatures of the
calm,   And they all dead did lie:
And a thousand thousand slimy things
Lived on; and so did I.

And envieth that   I looked upon the rotting sea,   240
they should live, and   And drew my eyes away;
so many lie dead.   I looked upon the rotting deck,
And there the dead men lay.

I looked to heaven, and tried to pray;
But or ever a prayer had gusht,   245
A wicked whisper came, and made
My heart as dry as dust.

3. An omen of impending evil.

I closed my lids, and kept them close,
And the balls like pulses beat;
For the sky and the sea, and the sea and the sky   250
Lay like a load on my weary eye,
And the dead were at my feet.

But the curse liveth
for him in the eye of
the dead men.

The cold sweat melted from their limbs,
Nor rot nor reek did they:
The look with which they looked on me   255
Had never passed away.

An orphan's curse would drag to hell
A spirit from on high;
But oh! more horrible than that
Is the curse in a dead man's eye!   260
Seven days, seven nights, I saw that curse,
And yet I could not die.

In his loneliness and
fixedness he yearneth
towards the journey-
ing Moon, and the
stars that still
sojourn, yet still
move onward; and

The moving Moon went up the sky,
And no where did abide:
Softly she was going up,
And a star or two beside—   265

everywhere the blue sky belongs to them, and is their appointed rest, and their native country and their
own natural homes, which they enter unannounced, as lords that are certainly expected and yet there
is a silent joy at their arrival.

Her beams bemocked the sultry main,
Like April hoar-frost spread;
But where the ship's huge shadow lay,
The charmed water burnt alway   270
A still and awful red.

By the light of the
Moon he beholdeth
God's creatures of
the great calm.

Beyond the shadow of the ship,
I watched the water-snakes:
They moved in tracks of shining white,
And when they reared, the elfish light   275
Fell off in hoary flakes.

Within the shadow of the ship
I watched their rich attire:
Blue, glossy green, and velvet black,
They coiled and swam; and every track   280
Was a flash of golden fire.

Their beauty and
their happiness.

O happy living things! no tongue
Their beauty might declare:
A spring of love gushed from my heart,

He blesseth them in
his heart.

And I blessed them unaware: 285
Sure my kind saint took pity on me,
And I blessed them unaware.

The spell begins to
break.

The selfsame moment I could pray;
And from my neck so free

The Albatross fell off, and sank   290
Like lead into the sea.

Part 5

Oh sleep! it is a gentle thing,
Beloved from pole to pole!
To Mary Queen the praise be given!
She sent the gentle sleep from Heaven,   295
That slid into my soul.

By grace of the holy
Mother, the ancient   The silly[4] buckets on the deck,
Mariner is refreshed   That had so long remained,
with rain.   I dreamt that they were filled with dew;
And when I awoke, it rained.   300

My lips were wet, my throat was cold,
My garments all were dank;
Sure I had drunken in my dreams,
And still my body drank.

I moved, and could not feel my limbs: 305
I was so light—almost
I thought that I had died in sleep,
And was a blessed ghost.

He heareth sounds
and seeth strange   And soon I heard a roaring wind:
sights and commo-   It did not come anear;   310
tions in the sky and   But with its sound it shook the sails,
the element.   That were so thin and sere.

The upper air burst into life!
And a hundred fire-flags sheen,[5]
To and fro they were hurried about!   315
And to and fro, and in and out,
The wan stars danced between.

And the coming wind did roar more loud,
And the sails did sigh like sedge;[6]
And the rain poured down from one black cloud; 320
The Moon was at its edge.

The thick black cloud was cleft, and still
The Moon was at its side:
Like waters shot from some high crag,
The lightning fell with never a jag,   325
A river steep and wide.

---

4. Simple, homely.
5. Shone. These fire-flags are probably St. Elmo's fire (see n. 4, p. 433), but Coleridge may be

describing the Aurora Australis, or Southern Lights, and possibly also lightning.
6. A rushlike plant growing in wet soil.

The bodies of the ship's crew are inspired, and the ship moves on;

The loud wind never reached the ship,
Yet now the ship moved on!
Beneath the lightning and the moon
The dead men gave a groan.   330

They groaned, they stirred, they all uprose,
Nor spake, nor moved their eyes;
It had been strange, even in a dream,
To have seen those dead men rise.

The helmsman steered, the ship moved on;   335
Yet never a breeze up blew;
The mariners all 'gan work the ropes,
Where they were wont to do;
They raised their limbs like lifeless tools—
We were a ghastly crew.   340

The body of my brother's son
Stood by me, knee to knee:
The body and I pulled at one rope,
But he said nought to me.

But not by the souls of the men, nor by dæmons⁷ of earth or middle air, but by a blessed troop of angelic spirits, sent down by the invocation of the guardian saint.

"I fear thee, ancient Mariner!"   345
Be calm, thou Wedding-Guest!
'Twas not those souls that fled in pain,
Which to their corses⁸ came again,
But a troop of spirits blest:

For when it dawned—they dropped their arms,   350
And clustered round the mast;
Sweet sounds rose slowly through their mouths,
And from their bodies passed.

Around, around, flew each sweet sound,
Then darted to the Sun;   355
Slowly the sounds came back again,
Now mixed, now one by one.

Sometimes a-dropping from the sky
I heard the sky-lark sing;
Sometimes all little birds that are,   360
How they seemed to fill the sea and air
With their sweet jargoning!⁹

And now 'twas like all instruments,
Now like a lonely flute;
And now it is an angel's song,   365
That makes the heavens be mute.

---

7. Supernatural beings halfway between mortals and gods (the type of spirit that Coleridge describes in the gloss beside lines 131–34).

8. Corpses.

9. Warbling (Middle English).

It ceased; yet still the sails made on
A pleasant noise till noon,
A noise like of a hidden brook
In the leafy month of June,   370
That to the sleeping woods all night
Singeth a quiet tune.

Till noon we quietly sailed on,
Yet never a breeze did breathe:
Slowly and smoothly went the ship,   375
Moved onward from beneath.

The lonesome spirit
from the south-pole   Under the keel nine fathom deep,
carries on the ship as   From the land of mist and snow,
far as the line, in   The spirit slid: and it was he
obedience to the
angelic troop, but   That made the ship to go.   380
still requireth   The sails at noon left off their tune,
vengeance.   And the ship stood still also.

The Sun, right up above the mast,
Had fixed her to the ocean:
But in a minute she 'gan stir,   385
With a short uneasy motion—
Backwards and forwards half her length
With a short uneasy motion.

Then like a pawing horse let go,
She made a sudden bound: 390
It flung the blood into my head,
And I fell down in a swound.

The Polar Spirit's fel-
low dæmons, the   How long in that same fit I lay,
invisible inhabitants   I have not[1] to declare;
of the element, take
part in his wrong;   But ere my living life returned,   395
and two of them   I heard and in my soul discerned
relate, one to the   Two voices in the air.
other, that penance
long and heavy for
the ancient Mariner   "Is it he?" quoth one, "Is this the man?
hath been accorded   By him who died on cross,
to the Polar Spirit,
who returneth   With his cruel bow he laid full low   400
southward.   The harmless Albatross.

The spirit who bideth by himself
In the land of mist and snow,
He loved the bird that loved the man
Who shot him with his bow."   405

The other was a softer voice,
As soft as honey-dew:
Quoth he, "The man hath penance done,
And penance more will do."

---

1. I.e., have not the knowledge.

Part 6

FIRST VOICE

"But tell me, tell me! speak again,   410
Thy soft response renewing—
What makes that ship drive on so fast?
What is the ocean doing?"

SECOND VOICE

"Still as a slave before his lord,
The ocean hath no blast;   415
His great bright eye most silently
Up to the Moon is cast—

If he may know which way to go;
For she guides him smooth or grim.
See, brother, see! how graciously   420
She looketh down on him."

FIRST VOICE

The Mariner hath been cast into a trance; for the angelic power causeth the vessel to drive northward faster than human life could endure.

"But why drives on that ship so fast,
Without or wave or wind?"

SECOND VOICE

"The air is cut away before,
And closes from behind.   425

Fly, brother, fly! more high, more high!
Or we shall be belated:
For slow and slow that ship will go,
When the Mariner's trance is abated."

The supernatural motion is retarded; the Mariner awakes, and his penance begins anew.

I woke, and we were sailing on   430
As in a gentle weather:
'Twas night, calm night, the moon was high;
The dead men stood together.

All stood together on the deck,
For a charnel-dungeon fitter: 435
All fixed on me their stony eyes,
That in the Moon did glitter.

The pang, the curse, with which they died,
Had never passed away:
I could not draw my eyes from theirs,   440
Nor turn them up to pray.

The curse is finally expiated.

And now this spell was snapt: once more
I viewed the ocean green,
And looked far forth, yet little saw
Of what had else been seen—   445

Like one, that on a lonesome road
Doth walk in fear and dread,
And having once turned round walks on,
And turns no more his head;
Because he knows, a frightful fiend   450
Doth close behind him tread.

But soon there breathed a wind on me,
Nor sound nor motion made:
Its path was not upon the sea,
In ripple or in shade.   455

It raised my hair, it fanned my cheek
Like a meadow-gale of spring—
It mingled strangely with my fears,
Yet it felt like a welcoming.

Swiftly, swiftly flew the ship,   460
Yet she sailed softly too:
Sweetly, sweetly blew the breeze—
On me alone it blew.

*And the ancient
Mariner beholdeth
his native country.* Oh! dream of joy! is this indeed
The light-house top I see?   465
Is this the hill? is this the kirk?
Is this mine own countree?

We drifted o'er the harbour-bar,
And I with sobs did pray—
O let me be awake, my God!   470
Or let me sleep alway.

The harbour-bay was clear as glass,
So smoothly it was strewn!
And on the bay the moonlight lay,
And the shadow of the moon.   475

The rock shone bright, the kirk no less,
That stands above the rock:
The moonlight steeped in silentness
The steady weathercock.

And the bay was white with silent light,   480
Till rising from the same,
*The angelic spirits
leave the dead
bodies,* Full many shapes, that shadows were,
In crimson colours came.

*And appear in their
own forms of light.* A little distance from the prow
Those crimson shadows were: 485
I turned my eyes upon the deck—
Oh, Christ! what saw I there!

Each corse lay flat, lifeless and flat,
And, by the holy rood!

A man all light, a seraph-man,[2]　　　　　　　490
On every corse there stood.

This seraph-band, each waved his hand:
It was a heavenly sight!
They stood as signals to the land,
Each one a lovely light;　　　　　　　　495

This seraph-band, each waved his hand,
No voice did they impart—
No voice; but oh! the silence sank
Like music on my heart.

But soon I heard the dash of oars,　　　　500
I heard the Pilot's cheer;
My head was turned perforce away,
And I saw a boat appear.

The Pilot and the Pilot's boy,
I heard them coming fast:　　　　　　　505
Dear Lord in Heaven! it was a joy
The dead men could not blast.

I saw a third—I heard his voice:
It is the Hermit good!
He singeth loud his godly hymns　　　　510
That he makes in the wood.
He'll shrieve[3] my soul, he'll wash away
The Albatross's blood.

Part 7

The Hermit of the wood,

This Hermit good lives in that wood
Which slopes down to the sea.　　　　　515
How loudly his sweet voice he rears!
He loves to talk with marineres
That come from a far countree.

He kneels at morn, and noon, and eve—
He hath a cushion plump:　　　　　　520
It is the moss that wholly hides
The rotted old oak-stump.

The skiff-boat neared: I heard them talk,
"Why, this is strange, I trow!
Where are those lights so many and fair,　525
That signal made but now?"

Approacheth the ship with wonder.

"Strange, by my faith!" the Hermit said—
"And they answered not our cheer!
The planks looked warped! and see those sails,

2. A shining celestial being, highest in the ranks　3. Absolve.
of the angels. "Rood": cross.

How thin they are and sere! 530
I never saw aught like to them,
Unless perchance it were

Brown skeletons of leaves that lag
My forest-brook along;
When the ivy-tod⁴ is heavy with snow, 535
And the owlet whoops to the wolf below,
That eats the she-wolf's young."

"Dear Lord! it hath a fiendish look"—
(The Pilot made reply)
"I am a-feared"—"Push on, push on!" 540
Said the Hermit cheerily.

The boat came closer to the ship,
But I nor spake nor stirred;
The boat came close beneath the ship,
And straight a sound was heard. 545

The ship suddenly sinketh. Under the water it rumbled on,
Still louder and more dread:
It reached the ship, it split the bay;
The ship went down like lead.

The ancient Mariner is saved in the Pilot's boat. Stunned by that loud and dreadful sound, 550
Which sky and ocean smote,
Like one that hath been seven days drowned
My body lay afloat;
But swift as dreams, myself I found
Within the Pilot's boat. 555

Upon the whirl, where sank the ship,
The boat spun round and round;
And all was still, save that the hill
Was telling of the sound.

I moved my lips—the Pilot shrieked 560
And fell down in a fit;
The holy Hermit raised his eyes,
And prayed where he did sit.

I took the oars: the Pilot's boy,
Who now doth crazy go, 565
Laughed loud and long, and all the while
His eyes went to and fro.
"Ha! ha!" quoth he, "full plain I see,
The Devil knows how to row."

And now, all in my own countree, 570
I stood on the firm land!

4. Clump of ivy.

The Hermit stepped forth from the boat,
And scarcely he could stand.

The ancient Mariner earnestly entreateth the Hermit to shrieve him; and the penance of life falls on him.
"O shrieve me, shrieve me, holy man!"
The Hermit crossed his brow.[5]   575
"Say quick," quoth he, "I bid thee say—
What manner of man art thou?"

Forthwith this frame of mine was wrenched
With a woful agony,
Which forced me to begin my tale;   580
And then it left me free.

And ever and anon throughout his future life an agony constraineth him to travel from land to land.
Since then, at an uncertain hour,
That agony returns:
And till my ghastly tale is told,
This heart within me burns.   585

I pass, like night, from land to land;
I have strange power of speech;
That moment that his face I see,
I know the man that must hear me:
To him my tale I teach.   590

What loud uproar bursts from that door!
The wedding-guests are there:
But in the garden-bower the bride
And bride-maids singing are:
And hark the little vesper bell,   595
Which biddeth me to prayer!

O Wedding-Guest! this soul hath been
Alone on a wide wide sea:
So lonely 'twas, that God himself
Scarce seemed there to be.   600

O sweeter than the marriage-feast,
'Tis sweeter far to me,
To walk together to the kirk
With a goodly company!—

To walk together to the kirk,   605
And all together pray,
While each to his great Father bends,
Old men, and babes, and loving friends,
And youths and maidens gay!

And to teach, by his own example, love and reverence to all things that God made and loveth.
Farewell, farewell! but this I tell   610
To thee, thou Wedding-Guest!
He prayeth well, who loveth well
Both man and bird and beast.

---

5. Made the sign of the cross on his forehead. "Shrieve me": hear my confession and grant me absolution.

He prayeth best, who loveth best
All things both great and small;   615
For the dear God who loveth us,
He made and loveth all.[6]

The Mariner, whose eye is bright,
Whose beard with age is hoar,
Is gone: and now the Wedding-Guest   620
Turned from the bridegroom's door.

He went like one that hath been stunned,
And is of sense forlorn:[7]
A sadder and a wiser man,
He rose the morrow morn.   625

1797   1798

Kubla Khan

Or, A Vision in a Dream. A Fragment

In[1] the summer of the year 1797, the Author, then in ill health, had retired to a lonely farm house between Porlock and Linton, on the Exmoor confines of Somerset and Devonshire. In consequence of a slight indisposition, an anodyne had been prescribed, from the effect of which he fell asleep in his chair at the moment that he was reading the following sentence, or words of the same substance, in *Purchas's Pilgrimage:* "Here the Khan Kubla commanded a palace to be built, and a stately garden thereunto: and thus ten miles of fertile ground were inclosed with a wall."[2] The author continued for about three hours in a profound sleep, at least of the external senses,[3] during which time he has the most vivid confidence, that he could not have composed less than from two to three hundred lines; if that indeed can be called composition in which all the images rose up before him as things, with a parallel production of the correspondent expressions, without any sensation or consciousness of effort. On awaking he appeared to himself to have a distinct recollection of

6. Coleridge said in 1830, answering the objection of the poet Anna Barbauld that the poem "lacked a moral": "I told her that in my own judgment the poem had too much; and that the only, or chief fault, if I might say so, was the obtrusion of the moral sentiment so openly on the reader as a principle or cause of action in a work of pure imagination. It ought to have had no more moral than the *Arabian Nights'* tale of the merchant's sitting down to eat dates by the side of a well and throwing the shells aside, and lo! a genie starts up and says he *must* kill the aforesaid merchant *because* one of the date shells had, it seems, put out the eye of the genie's son."
7. Bereft.
1. In the texts of 1816–29, this note began with an additional short paragraph: "The following fragment is here published at the request of a poet of great and deserved celebrity, and, as far as the Author's own opinions are concerned, rather as a psychological *curiosity*, than on the ground of any supposed *poetic* merits." The "poet of . . . celeb-

rity" was Lord Byron.
2. "In Xamdu did Cublai Can build a stately Palace, encompassing sixteene miles of plaine ground with a wall, wherein are fertile Meddowes, pleasant Springs, delightfull Streames, and all sorts of beasts of chase and game, and in the middest thereof a sumptuous house of pleasure, which may be removed from place to place." From Samuel Purchas's book of travelers' tales, *Purchas his Pilgrimage* (1613). The historical Kublai Khan founded the Mongol dynasty in China in the 13th century.
3. In a note on a manuscript copy of "Kubla Khan," Coleridge gave a more precise account of the nature of this "sleep": "This fragment with a good deal more, not recoverable, composed, in a sort of reverie brought on by two grains of opium, taken to check a dysentery, at a farmhouse between Porlock and Linton, a quarter of a mile from Culbone Church, in the fall of the year, 1797."

the whole, and taking his pen, ink, and paper, instantly and eagerly wrote down the lines that are here preserved. At this moment he was unfortunately called out by a person on business from Porlock, and detained by him above an hour, and on his return to his room, found, to his no small surprise and mortification, that though he still retained some vague and dim recollection of the general purport of the vision, yet, with the exception of some eight or ten scattered lines and images, all the rest had passed away like the images on the surface of a stream into which a stone had been cast, but, alas! without the after restoration of the latter:

> Then all the charm
> Is broken—all that phantom-world so fair
> Vanishes, and a thousand circlets spread,
> And each mis-shape[s] the other. Stay awhile,
> Poor youth! who scarcely dar'st lift up thine eyes—
> The stream will soon renew its smoothness, soon
> The visions will return! And lo! he stays,
> And soon the fragments dim of lovely forms
> Come trembling back, unite, and now once more
> The pool becomes a mirror.
> [From Coleridge's *The Picture; or, the Lover's Resolution,*
> lines 91–100]

Yet from the still surviving recollections in his mind, the Author has frequently purposed to finish for himself what had been originally, as it were, given to him. Αὔριον ἄδιον ἄσω:[4] but the to-morrow is yet to come.

As a contrast to this vision, I have annexed a fragment of a very different character, describing with equal fidelity the dream of pain and disease.[5]— 1816.

> In Xanadu did Kubla Khan   *I am*
> A stately pleasure-dome decree:
> Where Alph,[6] the sacred river, ran
> Through caverns measureless to man
> 5   Down to a sunless sea.
> So twice five miles of fertile ground
> With walls and towers were girdled round:
> And there were gardens bright with sinuous rills
> Where blossomed many an incense-bearing tree;
> 10 And here were forests ancient as the hills,
> Enfolding sunny spots of greenery.
>
> But oh! that deep romantic chasm which slanted
> Down the green hill athwart a cedarn cover!
> A savage place! as holy and enchanted
> 15 As e'er beneath a waning moon was haunted
> By woman wailing for her demon-lover!

4. I shall sing a sweeter song tomorrow (Greek; recalled from Theocritus's *Idyls* 1.145).
A number of Coleridge's assertions in this preface have been debated by critics: whether the poem was written in 1797 or later, whether it was actually composed in a "dream" or opium reverie, even whether it is a fragment or in fact complete. All critics agree, however, that this visionary poem

of demonic inspiration is much more than a mere "psychological curiosity."
5. Coleridge refers to "The Pains of Sleep."
6. Derived probably from the Greek river Alpheus, which flows into the Ionian Sea. Its waters were fabled to rise again in Sicily as the fountain of Arethusa.

And from this chasm, with ceaseless turmoil seething,
As if this earth in fast thick pants were breathing,
A mighty fountain momently was forced:
20   Amid whose swift half-intermitted burst
Huge fragments vaulted like rebounding hail,
Or chaffy grain beneath the thresher's flail:
And 'mid these dancing rocks at once and ever
It flung up momently the sacred river.
25   Five miles meandering with a mazy motion
Through wood and dale the sacred river ran,
Then reached the caverns measureless to man,
And sank in tumult to a lifeless ocean:
And 'mid this tumult Kubla heard from far
30   Ancestral voices prophesying war!

The shadow of the dome of pleasure
Floated midway on the waves;
Where was heard the mingled measure
From the fountain and the caves.
35   It was a miracle of rare device,
A sunny pleasure-dome with caves of ice!

A damsel with a dulcimer   *music, poetry*
In a vision once I saw: *inspires*
It was an Abyssinian maid,
40   And on her dulcimer she played,
Singing of Mount Abora.[7]
Could I revive within me
Create wonders
with imagination.
Her symphony and song,
To such a deep delight 'twould win me,
45   That with music loud and long,
I would build that dome in air,
That sunny dome! those caves of ice!
And all who heard should see them there,
And all should cry, Beware! Beware!
Protect the poet
in his inspiration
50   His flashing eyes, his floating hair!
Weave a circle round him thrice,[8]
And close your eyes with holy dread,
For he on honey-dew hath fed,
And drunk the milk of Paradise.[9]

ca. 1797–98   1816

7. Apparently a reminiscence of Milton's *Paradise Lost* 4.280–82: "where Abassin Kings their issue guard / Mount Amara (though this by some supposed / True Paradise) under the Ethiop line."
8. A magic ritual, to protect the inspired poet from intrusion.

9. Lines 50ff. echo in part the description, in Plato's *Ion* 533–34, of inspired poets, who are "like Bacchic maidens who draw milk and honey from the rivers when they are under the influence of Dionysus but not when they are in their right mind."

Christabel[1]

Preface

The first part of the following poem was written in the year 1797, at Stowey, in the county of Somerset. The second part, after my return from Germany, in the year 1800, at Keswick, Cumberland. It is probable, that if the poem had been finished at either of the former periods, or if even the first and second part had been published in the year 1800, the impression of its originality would have been much greater than I dare at present expect. But for this, I have only my own indolence to blame. The dates are mentioned for the exclusive purpose of precluding charges of plagiarism or servile imitation from myself. For there is amongst us a set of critics, who seem to hold, that every possible thought and image is traditional; who have no notion that there are such things as fountains in the world, small as well as great; and who would therefore charitably derive every rill they behold flowing, from a perforation made in some other man's tank. I am confident, however, that as far as the present poem is concerned, the celebrated poets[2] whose writings I might be suspected of having imitated, either in particular passages, or in the tone and the spirit of the whole, would be among the first to vindicate me from the charge, and who, on any striking coincidence, would permit me to address them in this doggerel version of two monkish Latin hexameters.

Tis mine and it is likewise yours;
But an if this will not do;
Let it be mine, good friend! for I
Am the poorer of the two.

I have only to add, that the metre of the Christabel is not, properly speaking, irregular, though it may seem so from its being founded on a new principle: namely, that of counting in each line the accents, not the syllables.[3] Though the latter may vary from seven to twelve, yet in each line the accents will be found to be only four. Nevertheless this occasional variation in number of syllables is not introduced wantonly, or for the mere ends of convenience, but in correspondence with some transition, in the nature of the imagery or passion.

Part 1

'Tis the middle of night by the castle clock,
And the owls have awakened the crowing cock;

---

1. Coleridge had planned to publish *Christabel* in the 2nd edition of *Lyrical Ballads* (1800) but had not been able to complete the poem. When *Christabel* was finally published in 1816 in its present fragmentary state, he still hoped to finish it, for the Preface contained this sentence (deleted in the edition of 1834): "But as, in my very first conception of the tale, I had the whole present to my mind, with the wholeness, no less than with the liveliness of a vision; I trust that I shall be able to embody in verse the three parts yet to come, in the course of the present year."
2. Sir Walter Scott and Lord Byron, who had read and admired *Christabel* while it circulated in man-

uscript. Coleridge has in mind Scott's *Lay of the Last Minstrel* (1805) and Byron's *Siege of Corinth* (1816), which showed the influence of *Christabel*, especially in their meter.
3. Much of the older English versification, following the example of Anglo-Saxon poetry, had been based on stress, or "accent," and some of it shows as much freedom in varying the number of syllables as does *Christabel*. The poem, however, is a radical departure from the theory and practice of versification in the 18th century, which had been based on a recurrent number of syllables in each line.

Tu—whit!——Tu—whoo!
And hark, again! the crowing cock,
5   How drowsily it crew.

Sir Leoline, the Baron rich,
Hath a toothless mastiff bitch;
From her kennel beneath the rock
She maketh answer to the clock,
10   Four for the quarters, and twelve for the hour;
Ever and aye,° by shine and shower,   *always*
Sixteen short howls, not over loud;
Some say, she sees my lady's shroud.

Is the night chilly and dark?
15   The night is chilly, but not dark.
The thin gray cloud is spread on high,
It covers but not hides the sky.
The moon is behind, and at the full;
And yet she looks both small and dull.
20   The night is chill, the cloud is gray:
'Tis a month before the month of May,
And the Spring comes slowly up this way.

The lovely lady, Christabel,
Whom her father loves so well,
25   What makes her in the wood so late,
A furlong from the castle gate?
She had dreams all yesternight
Of her own betrothed knight;
And she in the midnight wood will pray
30   For the weal° of her lover that's far away.   *well-being*

She stole along, she nothing spoke,
The sighs she heaved were soft and low,
And naught was green upon the oak,
But moss and rarest mistletoe:⁴
35   She kneels beneath the huge oak tree,
And in silence prayeth she.

The lady sprang up suddenly,
The lovely lady, Christabel!
It moaned as near, as near can be,
40   But what it is, she cannot tell.—
On the other side it seems to be,
Of the huge, broad-breasted, old oak tree.

The night is chill; the forest bare;
Is it the wind that moaneth bleak?
45   There is not wind enough in the air
To move away the ringlet curl

4. In Celtic Britain the mistletoe (a parasitic plant) had been held in veneration when it was found growing—as it rarely does—on an oak tree. (Its usual host is the apple tree.)

From the lovely lady's cheek—
There is not wind enough to twirl
The one red leaf, the last of its clan,
50 That dances as often as dance it can,
Hanging so light, and hanging so high,
On the topmost twig that looks up at the sky.

Hush, beating heart of Christabel!
Jesu, Maria, shield her well!
55 She folded her arms beneath her cloak,
And stole to the other side of the oak.
　　　What sees she there?

There she sees a damsel bright,
Drest in a silken robe of white,
60 That shadowy in the moonlight shone:
The neck that made that white robe wan,
Her stately neck, and arms were bare;
Her blue-veined feet unsandal'd were,
And wildly glittered here and there
65 The gems entangled in her hair.
I guess, 'twas frightful there to see
A lady so richly clad as she—
Beautiful exceedingly!

"Mary mother, save me now!"
70 (Said Christabel,) "And who art thou?"

The lady strange made answer meet,°　　　　　　　　　*appropriate*
And her voice was faint and sweet:—
"Have pity on my sore distress,
I scarce can speak for weariness:
75 Stretch forth thy hand, and have no fear!"
Said Christabel, "How camest thou here?"
And the lady, whose voice was faint and sweet,
Did thus pursue her answer meet:—

"My sire is of a noble line,
80 And my name is Geraldine:
Five warriors seized me yestermorn,
Me, even me, a maid forlorn:
They choked my cries with force and fright,
And tied me on a palfrey white.
85 The palfrey was as fleet as wind,
And they rode furiously behind.
They spurred amain,° their steeds were white:　　　　　*at top speed*
And once we crossed the shade of night.
As sure as Heaven shall rescue me,
90 I have no thought what men they be;
Nor do I know how long it is
(For I have lain entranced I wis⁵)

5. I believe (Coleridge's misinterpretation of the Middle English adverb *ywis*, meaning "certainly").

Since one, the tallest of the five,
Took me from the palfrey's back,
95   A weary woman, scarce alive.
Some muttered words his comrades spoke:
He placed me underneath this oak;
He swore they would return with haste;
Whither they went I cannot tell—
100 I thought I heard, some minutes past,
Sounds as of a castle bell.
Stretch forth thy hand" (thus ended she),
"And help a wretched maid to flee."

Then Christabel stretched forth her hand
105 And comforted fair Geraldine:
"O well, bright dame! may you command
The service of Sir Leoline;
And gladly our stout chivalry
Will he send forth and friends withal
110 To guide and guard you safe and free
Home to your noble father's hall."

She rose: and forth with steps they passed
That strove to be, and were not, fast.
Her gracious stars the lady blest,
115 And thus spake on sweet Christabel:
"All our household are at rest,
The hall as silent as the cell;°   *a monastery*
Sir Leoline is weak in health,
And may not well awakened be,
120 But we will move as if in stealth,
And I beseech your courtesy,
This night, to share your couch with me."

They crossed the moat, and Christabel
Took the key that fitted well;
125 A little door she opened straight,
All in the middle of the gate;
The gate that was ironed within and without,
Where an army in battle array had marched out.
The lady sank, belike through pain,
130 And Christabel with might and main
Lifted her up, a weary weight,
Over the threshold of the gate:⁶
Then the lady rose again,
And moved, as she were not in pain.

135 So free from danger, free from fear,
They crossed the court: right glad they were.
And Christabel devoutly cried
To the Lady by her side;

6. According to legend, a witch cannot cross the threshold by her own power because it has been blessed against evil spirits.

"Praise we the Virgin all divine
140 Who hath rescued thee from thy distress!"
"Alas, alas!" said Geraldine,
"I cannot speak for weariness."
So free from danger, free from fear,
They crossed the court: right glad they were.

145 Outside her kennel the mastiff old
Lay fast asleep, in moonshine cold.
The mastiff old did not awake,
Yet she an angry moan did make!
And what can ail the mastiff bitch?
150 Never till now she uttered yell
Beneath the eye of Christabel.
Perhaps it is the owlet's scritch:
For what can ail the mastiff bitch?

They passed the hall, that echoes still,
155 Pass as lightly as you will!
The brands were flat, the brands were dying,
Amid their own white ashes lying;
But when the lady passed, there came
A tongue of light, a fit of flame;
160 And Christabel saw the lady's eye,
And nothing else saw she thereby,
Save the boss of the shield of Sir Leoline tall,
Which hung in a murky old niche in the wall.
"O softly tread," said Christabel,
165 "My father seldom sleepeth well."

Sweet Christabel her feet doth bare,
And, jealous of the listening air,
They steal their way from stair to stair,
Now in glimmer, and now in gloom,
170 And now they pass the Baron's room,
As still as death with stifled breath!
And now have reached her chamber door;
And now doth Geraldine press down
The rushes[7] of the chamber floor.

175 The moon shines dim in the open air,
And not a moonbeam enters here.
But they without its light can see
The chamber carved so curiously,
Carved with figures strange and sweet,
180 All made out of the carver's brain,
For a lady's chamber meet:
The lamp with twofold silver chain
Is fastened to an angel's feet.
The silver lamp burns dead and dim;
185 But Christabel the lamp will trim.

7. Often used as a floor covering in the Middle Ages.

She trimmed the lamp, and made it bright,
And left it swinging to and fro,
While Geraldine, in wretched plight,
Sank down upon the floor below.

190 "O weary lady, Geraldine,
I pray you, drink this cordial wine!
It is a wine of virtuous powers;
My mother made it of wild flowers."

"And will your mother pity me,
195 Who am a maiden most forlorn?"
Christabel answered—"Woe is me!
She died the hour that I was born.
I have heard the grey-haired friar tell,
How on her death-bed she did say,
200 That she should hear the castle-bell
Strike twelve upon my wedding day.
O mother dear! that thou wert here!"
"I would," said Geraldine, "she were!"

But soon with altered voice, said she—
205 "Off, wandering mother!⁸ Peak and pine!
I have power to bid thee flee."
Alas! what ails poor Geraldine?
Why stares she with unsettled eye?
Can she the bodiless dead espy?
210 And why with hollow voice cries she,
"Off, woman, off! this hour is mine—
Though thou her guardian spirit be,
Off, woman, off! 'tis given to me."

Then Christabel knelt by the lady's side,
215 And raised to heaven her eyes so blue—
"Alas!" said she, "this ghastly ride—
Dear lady! it hath wildered you!"
The lady wiped her moist cold brow,
And faintly said, " 'tis over now!"

220 Again the wild-flower wine she drank:
Her fair large eyes 'gan glitter bright,
And from the floor whereon she sank,
The lofty lady stood upright;
She was most beautiful to see,
225 Like a lady of a far countrée.

And thus the lofty lady spake—
"All they who live in the upper sky,
Do love you, holy Christabel!
And you love them, and for their sake
230 And for the good which me befell,

8. A term that could designate a fit of hysteria. "Peak and pine": Shakespeare's *Macbeth* 1.3.22.

Even I in my degree will try,
Fair maiden, to requite you well.
But now unrobe yourself; for I
Must pray, ere yet in bed I lie."

235 Quoth Christabel, "So let it be!"
And as the lady bade, did she.
Her gentle limbs did she undress,
And lay down in her loveliness.

But through her brain of weal and woe
240 So many thoughts moved to and fro,
That vain it were her lids to close;
So half-way from the bed she rose,
And on her elbow did recline
To look at the lady Geraldine.

245 Beneath the lamp the lady bowed,
And slowly rolled her eyes around;
Then drawing in her breath aloud,
Like one that shuddered, she unbound
The cincture° from beneath her breast: belt
250 Her silken robe, and inner vest,
Dropt to her feet, and full in view,
Behold! her bosom and half her side——
A sight to dream of, not to tell!
O shield her! shield sweet Christabel![9]

255 Yet Geraldine nor speaks nor stirs;
Ah! what a stricken look was hers!
Deep from within she seems half-way
To lift some weight with sick assay,°   attempt
And eyes the maid and seeks delay;
260 Then suddenly as one defied
Collects herself in scorn and pride,
And lay down by the maiden's side!—
And in her arms the maid she took,
      Ah well-a-day!
265 And with low voice and doleful look
These words did say:
"In the touch of this bosom there worketh a spell,
Which is lord of thy utterance, Christabel!
Thou knowest to-night, and wilt know to-morrow
270 This mark of my shame, this seal of my sorrow;
      But vainly thou warrest,
         For this is alone in
      Thy power to declare,
         That in the dim forest
275   Thou heard'st a low moaning,
And found'st a bright lady, surpassingly fair:

---

9. In several manuscripts and the first printing, this line reads "And she is to sleep by [or with] Christ-abel."

And didst bring her home with thee in love and in charity,
To shield her and shelter her from the damp air."

The Conclusion to Part 1

It was a lovely sight to see
280   The lady Christabel, when she
Was praying at the old oak tree.
    Amid the jagged shadows
    Of mossy leafless boughs,
    Kneeling in the moonlight,
285   To make her gentle vows;
Her slender palms together prest,
Heaving sometimes on her breast;
Her face resigned to bliss or bale°—   *evil, sorrow*
Her face, oh call it fair not pale,
290   And both blue eyes more bright than clear,
Each about to have a tear.

With open eyes (ah woe is me!)
Asleep, and dreaming fearfully,
Fearfully dreaming, yet I wis,
295   Dreaming that alone, which is—
O sorrow and shame! Can this be she,
The lady, who knelt at the old oak tree?
And lo! the worker of these harms,
That holds the maiden in her arms,
300   Seems to slumber still and mild,
As a mother with her child.

A star hath set, a star hath risen,
O Geraldine! since arms of thine
Have been the lovely lady's prison.
305   O Geraldine! one hour was thine—
Thou'st had thy will! By tairn[1] and rill,
The night-birds all that hour were still.
But now they are jubilant anew,
From cliff and tower, tu—whoo! tu—whoo!
310   Tu—whoo! tu—whoo! from wood and fell![2]

And see! the lady Christabel
Gathers herself from out her trance;
Her limbs relax, her countenance
Grows sad and soft; the smooth thin lids
315   Close o'er her eyes; and tears she sheds—
Large tears that leave the lashes bright!
And oft the while she seems to smile
As infants at a sudden light!
Yea, she doth smile, and she doth weep,
320   Like a youthful hermitess,
Beauteous in a wilderness,

---

1. Tarn, a mountain pool.   2. Elevated moor, or hill.

Who, praying always, prays in sleep.
And, if she move unquietly,
Perchance, 'tis but the blood so free,
325 Comes back and tingles in her feet.
No doubt, she hath a vision sweet.
What if her guardian spirit 'twere?
What if she knew her mother near?
But this she knows, in joys and woes,
330 That saints will aid if men will call:
For the blue sky bends over all!

Part 2

"Each matin bell," the Baron saith,
"Knells us back to a world of death."
These words Sir Leoline first said,
335 When he rose and found his lady dead:
These words Sir Leoline will say,
Many a morn to his dying day!

And hence the custom and law began,
That still at dawn the sacristan,[3]
340 Who duly pulls the heavy bell,
Five and forty beads must tell[4]
Between each stroke—a warning knell,
Which not a soul can choose but hear
From Bratha Head to Wyndermere.[5]

345 Saith Bracy the bard, "So let it knell!
And let the drowsy sacristan
Still count as slowly as he can!
There is no lack of such, I ween,°   believe
As well fill up the space between.
350 In Langdale Pike° and Witch's Lair,   Peak
And Dungeon-ghyll[6] so foully rent,
With ropes of rock and bells of air
Three sinful sextons' ghosts are pent,
Who all give back, one after t'other,
355 The death-note to their living brother;
And oft too, by the knell offended,
Just as their one! two! three! is ended,
The devil mocks the doleful tale
With a merry peal from Borodale."

360 The air is still! through mist and cloud
That merry peal comes ringing loud;
And Geraldine shakes off her dread,
And rises lightly from the bed;
Puts on her silken vestments white,

3. Church officer who digs the graves and rings
the bells.
4. Pray while "telling" (keeping count on) the
beads of a rosary.

5. These and the following names are of localities
in the English Lake District.
6. Ravine forming the bed of a stream.

365 And tricks her hair in lovely plight,°   *plait*
And nothing doubting of her spell
Awakens the lady Christabel.
"Sleep you, sweet lady Christabel?
I trust that you have rested well."

370 And Christabel awoke and spied
The same who lay down by her side—
O rather say, the same whom she
Raised up beneath the old oak tree!
Nay, fairer yet! and yet more fair!
375 For she belike hath drunken deep
Of all the blessedness of sleep!
And while she spake, her looks, her air
Such gentle thankfulness declare,
That (so it seemed) her girded vests
380 Grew tight beneath her heaving breasts.
"Sure I have sinned!" said Christabel,
"Now heaven be praised if all be well!"
And in low faltering tones, yet sweet,
Did she the lofty lady greet
385 With such perplexity of mind
As dreams too lively leave behind.

So quickly she rose, and quickly arrayed
Her maiden limbs, and having prayed
That He, who on the cross did groan,
390 Might wash away her sins unknown,
She forthwith led fair Geraldine
To meet her sire, Sir Leoline.

The lovely maid and the lady tall
Are pacing both into the hall,
395 And pacing on through page and groom,
Enter the Baron's presence room.

The Baron rose, and while he prest
His gentle daughter to his breast,
With cheerful wonder in his eyes
400 The lady Geraldine espies,
And gave such welcome to the same,
As might beseem so bright a dame!

But when he heard the lady's tale,
And when she told her father's name,
405 Why waxed Sir Leoline so pale,
Murmuring o'er the name again,
Lord Roland de Vaux of Tryermaine?

Alas! they had been friends in youth;
But whispering tongues can poison truth;
410 And constancy lives in realms above;
And life is thorny; and youth is vain;

And to be wroth with one we love,
Doth work like madness in the brain.
And thus it chanced, as I divine,
415   With Roland and Sir Leoline.
Each spake words of high disdain
And insult to his heart's best brother:
They parted—ne'er to meet again!
But never either found another
420   To free the hollow heart from paining—
They stood aloof, the scars remaining,
Like cliffs which had been rent asunder;
A dreary sea now flows between;—
But neither heat, nor frost, nor thunder,
425   Shall wholly do away, I ween,
The marks of that which once hath been.

Sir Leoline, a moment's space,
Stood gazing on the damsel's face:
And the youthful Lord of Tryermaine
430   Came back upon his heart again.

O then the Baron forgot his age,
His noble heart swelled high with rage;
He swore by the wounds in Jesu's side,
He would proclaim it far and wide
435   With trump and solemn heraldry,
That they who thus had wronged the dame,
Were base as spotted infamy!
"And if they dare deny the same,
My herald shall appoint a week,
440   And let the recreant traitors seek
My tourney court[7]—that there and then
I may dislodge their reptile souls
From the bodies and forms of men!"
He spake: his eye in lightning rolls!
445   For the lady was ruthlessly seized; and he kenned
In the beautiful lady the child of his friend!

And now the tears were on his face,
And fondly in his arms he took
Fair Geraldine, who met the embrace,
450   Prolonging it with joyous look.
Which when she viewed, a vision fell
Upon the soul of Christabel,
The vision of fear, the touch and pain!
She shrunk and shuddered, and saw again—
455   (Ah, woe is me! Was it for thee,
Thou gentle maid! such sights to see?)
Again she saw that bosom old,
Again she felt that bosom cold,
And drew in her breath with a hissing sound:

7. Arena for tournaments.

460 Whereat the Knight turned wildly round,
And nothing saw, but his own sweet maid
With eyes upraised, as one that prayed.

The touch, the sight, had passed away,
And in its stead that vision blest,
465 Which comforted her after-rest,
While in the lady's arms she lay,
Had put a rapture in her breast,
And on her lips and o'er her eyes
Spread smiles like light!
                                    With new surprise,
470 "What ails then my beloved child?"
The Baron said—His daughter mild
Made answer, "All will yet be well!"
I ween, she had no power to tell
Aught else: so mighty was the spell.

475 Yet he, who saw this Geraldine,
Had deemed her sure a thing divine.
Such sorrow with such grace she blended,
As if she feared, she had offended
Sweet Christabel, that gentle maid!
480 And with such lowly tones she prayed,
She might be sent without delay
Home to her father's mansion.
                                    "Nay!
Nay, by my soul!" said Leoline.
"Ho! Bracy, the bard, the charge be thine!
485 Go thou, with music sweet and loud,
And take two steeds with trappings proud,
And take the youth whom thou lov'st best
To bear thy harp, and learn thy song,
And clothe you both in solemn vest,
490 And over the mountains haste along,
Lest wandering folk, that are abroad,
Detain you on the valley road.
And when he has crossed the Irthing flood,
My merry bard! he hastes, he hastes
495 Up Knorren Moor, through Halegarth Wood,
And reaches soon that castle good
Which stands and threatens Scotland's wastes.

"Bard Bracy! bard Bracy! your horses are fleet,
Ye must ride up the hall, your music so sweet,
500 More loud than your horses' echoing feet!
And loud and loud to Lord Roland call,
Thy daughter is safe in Langdale hall!
Thy beautiful daughter is safe and free—
Sir Leoline greets thee thus through me.
505 He bids thee come without delay
With all thy numerous array;
And take thy lovely daughter home:

And he will meet thee on the way
With all his numerous array
510 White with their panting palfreys' foam:
And by mine honour! I will say,
That I repent me of the day
When I spake words of fierce disdain
To Roland de Vaux of Tryermaine!—
515 —For since that evil hour hath flown,
Many a summer's sun hath shone;
Yet ne'er found I a friend again
Like Roland de Vaux of Tryermaine."

The lady fell, and clasped his knees,
520 Her face upraised, her eyes o'erflowing;
And Bracy replied, with faltering voice,
His gracious hail on all bestowing!—
"Thy words, thou sire of Christabel,
Are sweeter than my harp can tell;
525 Yet might I gain a boon of thee,
This day my journey should not be,
So strange a dream hath come to me;
That I had vowed with music loud
To clear yon wood from thing unblest,
530 Warned by a vision in my rest!
For in my sleep I saw that dove,
That gentle bird, whom thou dost love,
And call'st by thy own daughter's name—
Sir Leoline! I saw the same
535 Fluttering, and uttering fearful moan,
Among the green herbs in the forest alone.
Which when I saw and when I heard,
I wonder'd what might ail the bird;
For nothing near it could I see,
540 Save the grass and green herbs underneath the old tree.

"And in my dream methought I went
To search out what might there be found;
And what the sweet bird's trouble meant,
That thus lay fluttering on the ground.
545 I went and peered, and could descry
No cause for her distressful cry;
But yet for her dear lady's sake
I stooped, methought, the dove to take,
When lo! I saw a bright green snake
550 Coiled around its wings and neck,
Green as the herbs on which it couched,
Close by the dove's its head it crouched;
And with the dove it heaves and stirs,
Swelling its neck as she swelled hers!
555 I woke; it was the midnight hour,
The clock was echoing in the tower;
But though my slumber was gone by,
This dream it would not pass away—

It seems to live upon my eye!
560 And thence I vowed this self-same day,
With music strong and saintly song
To wander through the forest bare,
Lest aught unholy loiter there."

Thus Bracy said: the Baron, the while,
565 Half-listening heard him with a smile;
Then turned to Lady Geraldine,
His eyes made up of wonder and love;
And said in courtly accents fine,
"Sweet maid, Lord Roland's beauteous dove,
570 With arms more strong than harp or song,
Thy sire and I will crush the snake!"
He kissed her forehead as he spake,
And Geraldine, in maiden wise,°   manner
Casting down her large bright eyes,
575 With blushing cheek and courtesy fine
She turned her from Sir Leoline;
Softly gathering up her train,
That o'er her right arm fell again;
And folded her arms across her chest,
580 And couched her head upon her breast,
And looked askance at Christabel——
Jesu Maria, shield her well!

A snake's small eye blinks dull and shy,
And the lady's eyes they shrunk in her head,
585 Each shrunk up to a serpent's eye,
And with somewhat of malice, and more of dread,
At Christabel she looked askance!—
One moment—and the sight was fled!
But Christabel in dizzy trance
590 Stumbling on the unsteady ground
Shuddered aloud, with a hissing sound;
And Geraldine again turned round,
And like a thing, that sought relief,
Full of wonder and full of grief,
595 She rolled her large bright eyes divine
Wildly on Sir Leoline.

The maid, alas! her thoughts are gone,
She nothing sees—no sight but one!
The maid, devoid of guile and sin,
600 I know not how, in fearful wise
So deeply had she drunken in
That look, those shrunken serpent eyes,
That all her features were resigned
To this sole image in her mind;
605 And passively did imitate
That look of dull and treacherous hate!
And thus she stood, in dizzy trance,
Still picturing that look askance
With forced unconscious sympathy

610　Full before her father's view——
　　　As far as such a look could be,
　　　In eyes so innocent and blue!
　　　And when the trance was o'er, the maid
　　　Paused awhile, and inly prayed:
615　Then falling at the Baron's feet,
　　　"By my mother's soul do I entreat
　　　That thou this woman send away!"
　　　She said: and more she could not say:
　　　For what she knew she could not tell,
620　O'er-mastered by the mighty spell.

　　　Why is thy cheek so wan and wild,
　　　Sir Leoline? Thy only child
　　　Lies at thy feet, thy joy, thy pride,
　　　So fair, so innocent, so mild;
625　The same, for whom thy lady died!
　　　O by the pangs of her dear mother
　　　Think thou no evil of thy child!
　　　For her, and thee, and for no other,
　　　She prayed the moment ere she died:
630　Prayed that the babe for whom she died,
　　　Might prove her dear lord's joy and pride!
　　　　That prayer her deadly pangs beguiled,
　　　　　Sir Leoline!
　　　And wouldst thou wrong thy only child,
635　　　Her child and thine?

　　　Within the Baron's heart and brain
　　　If thoughts, like these, had any share,
　　　They only swelled his rage and pain,
　　　And did but work confusion there.
640　His heart was cleft with pain and rage,
　　　His cheeks they quivered, his eyes were wild,
　　　Dishonoured thus in his old age;
　　　Dishonoured by his only child,
　　　And all his hospitality
645　To the wrong'd daughter of his friend
　　　By more than woman's jealousy
　　　Brought thus to a disgraceful end—
　　　He rolled his eye with stern regard
　　　Upon the gentle minstrel bard,
650　And said in tones abrupt, austere—
　　　"Why, Bracy! dost thou loiter here?
　　　I bade thee hence!" The bard obeyed;
　　　And turning from his own sweet maid,
　　　The aged knight, Sir Leoline,
655　Led forth the lady Geraldine!

The Conclusion to Part 2

　　　A little child, a limber elf,
　　　Singing, dancing to itself,
　　　A fairy thing with red round cheeks,

That always finds, and never seeks,
660 Makes such a vision to the sight
As fills a father's eyes with light;
And pleasures flow in so thick and fast
Upon his heart, that he at last
Must needs express his love's excess
665 With words of unmeant bitterness.
Perhaps 'tis pretty to force together
Thoughts so all unlike each other;
To mutter and mock a broken charm,
To dally with wrong that does no harm.
670 Perhaps 'tis tender too and pretty
At each wild word to feel within
A sweet recoil of love and pity.
And what, if in a world of sin
(O sorrow and shame should this be true!)
675 Such giddiness of heart and brain
Comes seldom save from rage and pain,
So talks as it's most used to do.

1798–1800   1816

Frost at Midnight[1]

The frost performs its secret ministry,
Unhelped by any wind. The owlet's cry
Came loud—and hark, again! loud as before.
The inmates of my cottage, all at rest,
5 Have left me to that solitude, which suits
Abstruser musings: save that at my side
My cradled infant slumbers peacefully.
'Tis calm indeed! so calm, that it disturbs
And vexes meditation with its strange
10 And extreme silentness. Sea, hill, and wood,
This populous village! Sea, and hill, and wood,
With all the numberless goings on of life,
Inaudible as dreams! the thin blue flame
Lies on my low burnt fire, and quivers not;
15 Only that film,[2] which fluttered on the grate,
Still flutters there, the sole unquiet thing.
Methinks, its motion in this hush of nature
Gives it dim sympathies with me who live,
Making it a companionable form,
20 Whose puny flaps and freaks the idling Spirit
By its own moods interprets, every where

1. The scene is Coleridge's cottage at Nether Stowey; the infant in line 7 is his son Hartley, then aged seventeen months.
2. In all parts of the kingdom these films are called *strangers* and supposed to portend the arrival of some absent friend [Coleridge's note]. The "film" is a piece of soot fluttering on the bar of the grate. Cf. Cowper's *The Task* 4.292–95, in which the poet describes how, dreaming before the parlor fire, he watches "The sooty films that play upon the bars, / Pendulous and foreboding, in the view / Of superstition prophesying still, / Though still deceived, some stranger's near approach." Several editions of Cowper's poems were advertised on the verso of the last page of Coleridge's text in the 1798 volume in which "Frost at Midnight" was first published.

Echo or mirror seeking of itself,
And makes a toy of Thought.

But O! how oft,
How oft, at school, with most believing mind,
25 Presageful, have I gazed upon the bars,
To watch that fluttering stranger! and as oft
With unclosed lids, already had I dreamt
Of my sweet birth-place,[3] and the old church-tower,
Whose bells, the poor man's only music, rang
30 From morn to evening, all the hot Fair-day,
So sweetly, that they stirred and haunted me
With a wild pleasure, falling on mine ear
Most like articulate sounds of things to come!
So gazed I, till the soothing things I dreamt
35 Lulled me to sleep, and sleep prolonged my dreams!
And so I brooded all the following morn,
Awed by the stern preceptor's[4] face, mine eye
Fixed with mock study on my swimming book:
Save if the door half opened, and I snatched
40 A hasty glance, and still my heart leaped up,
For still I hoped to see the stranger's face,
Townsman, or aunt, or sister more beloved,
My play-mate when we both were clothed alike![5]

Dear Babe, that sleepest cradled by my side,
45 Whose gentle breathings, heard in this deep calm,
Fill up the interspersed vacancies
And momentary pauses of the thought!
My babe so beautiful! it thrills my heart
With tender gladness, thus to look at thee,
50 And think that thou shalt learn far other lore
And in far other scenes! For I was reared
In the great city, pent 'mid cloisters dim,
And saw nought lovely but the sky and stars.
But thou, my babe! shalt wander like a breeze
55 By lakes and sandy shores, beneath the crags
Of ancient mountain, and beneath the clouds,
Which image in their bulk both lakes and shores
And mountain crags: so shalt thou see and hear
The lovely shapes and sounds intelligible
60 Of that eternal language, which thy God
Utters, who from eternity doth teach
Himself in all, and all things in himself.
Great universal Teacher! he shall mould
Thy spirit, and by giving make it ask.

65 Therefore all seasons shall be sweet to thee,
Whether the summer clothe the general earth
With greenness, or the redbreast sit and sing

3. Coleridge was born at Ottery St. Mary, Devonshire, but went to school in London, beginning at the age of nine.
4. The Reverend James Boyer at Coleridge's school, Christ's Hospital.
5. I.e., when both Coleridge and his sister Ann still wore infant clothes, before he was deemed old enough to be breeched.

Betwixt the tufts of snow on the bare branch
Of mossy apple-tree, while the nigh thatch
70 Smokes in the sun-thaw; whether the eave-drops fall
Heard only in the trances of the blast,
Or if the secret ministry of frost
Shall hang them up in silent icicles,
Quietly shining to the quiet Moon.

Feb. 1798   1798

✗ Dejection: An Ode[1]

*Late, late yestreen I saw the new Moon,
With the old Moon in her arms;
And I fear, I fear, my Master dear!
We shall have a deadly storm.*
        Ballad of Sir Patrick Spence

1

Well! If the Bard was weather-wise, who made
The grand old ballad of Sir Patrick Spence,
This night, so tranquil now, will not go hence
Unroused by winds, that ply a busier trade
5 Than those which mould yon cloud in lazy flakes,
Or the dull sobbing draft, that moans and rakes
    Upon the strings of this Eolian lute,[2]
    Which better far were mute.
For lo! the New-moon winter-bright!
10 And overspread with phantom light,
(With swimming phantom light o'erspread
But rimmed and circled by a silver thread)
I see the old Moon in her lap, foretelling
The coming on of rain and squally blast.
15 And oh! that even now the gust were swelling,
And the slant night-shower driving loud and fast!
Those sounds which oft have raised me, whilst they awed,
    And sent my soul abroad,
Might now perhaps their wonted° impulse give,   customary
20 Might startle this dull pain, and make it move and live!

2

A grief without a pang, void, dark, and drear,
A stifled, drowsy, unimpassioned grief,

---

1. This poem originated in a verse letter of 340 lines, called "A Letter to ———," that Coleridge wrote on the night of April 4, 1802, after hearing the opening stanzas of "Ode: Intimations of Immortality," which Wordsworth had just composed. The "Letter" was addressed to Sara Hutchinson (whom Coleridge sometimes called "Asra"), the sister of Wordsworth's fiancée, Mary. It picked up the theme of a loss in the quality of perceptual experience that Wordsworth had presented at the beginning of his "Ode." In his original poem Coleridge lamented at length his unhappy marriage and the hopelessness of his love for Sara Hutchinson. In the next six months Coleridge deleted more than half the original lines, revised and reordered the remaining passages, and so transformed a long verse confession into the compact and dignified "Dejection: An Ode." He published the "Ode," in substantially its present form, on October 4, 1802, Wordsworth's wedding day—and also the seventh anniversary of Coleridge's own disastrous marriage to Sara Fricker.

2. A stringed instrument played upon by the wind (see "The Eolian Harp," n. 1, p. 426).

Which finds no natural outlet, no relief,
   In word, or sigh, or tear—
25 O Lady![3] in this wan and heartless mood,
To other thoughts by yonder throstle woo'd,
   All this long eve, so balmy and serene,
Have I been gazing on the western sky,
   And its peculiar tint of yellow green:
30 And still I gaze—and with how blank an eye!
And those thin clouds above, in flakes and bars,
That give away their motion to the stars;
Those stars, that glide behind them or between,
Now sparkling, now bedimmed, but always seen:
35 Yon crescent Moon as fixed as if it grew
In its own cloudless, starless lake of blue;
I see them all so excellently fair,
I see, not feel, how beautiful they are!

3

   My genial° spirits fail;   *creative*
40   And what can these avail
To lift the smothering weight from off my breast?
    It were a vain endeavour,
    Though I should gaze for ever
On that green light that lingers in the west:
45 I may not hope from outward forms to win
The passion and the life, whose fountains are within.

4

O Lady! we receive but what we give,
And in our life alone does nature live:
Ours is her wedding-garment, ours her shroud![4]
50   And would we aught° behold, of higher worth,   *anything*
Than that inanimate cold world allowed
To the poor loveless ever-anxious crowd,
    Ah! from the soul itself must issue forth,
A light, a glory,[5] a fair luminous cloud
55   Enveloping the Earth—
And from the soul itself must there be sent
    A sweet and potent voice, of its own birth,
Of all sweet sounds the life and element!

5

  O pure of heart! thou need'st not ask of me
60 What this strong music in the soul may be!
  What, and wherein it doth exist,
  This light, this glory, this fair luminous mist,
  This beautiful and beauty-making power.
    Joy, virtuous Lady! Joy that ne'er was given,

---

3. In the original version "Sara"—i.e., Sara Hutchinson. After intervening versions, in which the poem was addressed first to "William" (Wordsworth) and then to "Edmund," Coleridge introduced the noncommittal "Lady" in 1817.
4. I.e., nature's wedding garment and shroud are ours to give to her.

5. A "glory" is a halo. Coleridge often uses the term to identify in particular the phenomenon that occurs in the mountains when a walker sees his or her own figure projected by the sun in the mist, enlarged and with light encircling its head. Cf. Wordsworth's *Prelude* 8.268–70 (p. 368).

65 Save to the pure, and in their purest hour,
Life, and Life's effluence, cloud at once and shower,
Joy, Lady! is the spirit and the power,
Which wedding Nature to us gives in dower,
A new Earth and new Heaven,[6]
70 Undreamt of by the sensual and the proud—
Joy is the sweet voice, Joy the luminous cloud—
We in ourselves rejoice!
And thence flows all that charms or ear or sight,
All melodies the echoes of that voice,
75 All colours a suffusion from that light.

6

There was a time when, though my path was rough,
This joy within me dallied with distress,
And all misfortunes were but as the stuff
Whence Fancy made me dreams of happiness:
80 For hope grew round me, like the twining vine,
And fruits, and foliage, not my own, seemed mine.
But now afflictions bow me down to earth:
Nor care I that they rob me of my mirth,
But oh! each visitation°   *i.e., of affliction*
85 Suspends what nature gave me at my birth,
My shaping spirit of Imagination.
For not to think of what I needs must feel,
But to be still and patient, all I can;
And haply by abstruse research to steal
90 From my own nature all the natural man—
This was my sole resource, my only plan:
Till that which suits a part infects the whole,
And now is almost grown the habit of my soul.

7

Hence, viper thoughts, that coil around my mind,
95 Reality's dark dream!
I turn from you, and listen to the wind,
Which long has raved unnoticed. What a scream
Of agony by torture lengthened out
That lute sent forth! Thou Wind, that ravest without,
100 Bare crag, or mountain-tairn,[7] or blasted tree,
Or pine-grove whither woodman never clomb,°   *climbed*
Or lonely house, long held the witches' home,
Methinks were fitter instruments for thee,
Mad Lutanist! who in this month of showers,
105 Of dark brown gardens, and of peeping flowers,
Mak'st Devils' yule,[8] with worse than wintry song,
The blossoms, buds, and timorous leaves among.
Thou Actor, perfect in all tragic sounds!
Thou mighty Poet, e'en to frenzy bold!

6. The sense becomes clearer if line 68 is punctuated in the way that Coleridge punctuated it
when quoting the passage in one of his essays:
"Which, wedding Nature to us, gives in dower."
I.e., Joy marries us to Nature and gives us, for our

dowry, "a new Earth and a new Heaven," a phrase
echoing Revelation 21.1.
7. Tarn, or mountain pool.
8. Christmas as, in a perverted form, it is celebrated by devils.

110   What tell'st thou now about?
    'Tis of the rushing of a host in rout,
    With groans of trampled men, with smarting wounds—
    At once they groan with pain, and shudder with the cold!
    But hush! there is a pause of deepest silence!
115   And all that noise, as of a rushing crowd,
    With groans, and tremulous shudderings—all is over—
    It tells another tale, with sounds less deep and loud!
    A tale of less affright,
    And tempered with delight,
120   As Otway's[9] self had framed the tender lay,
    'Tis of a little child
    Upon a lonesome wild,
    Not far from home, but she hath lost her way:
    And now moans low in bitter grief and fear,
125   And now screams loud, and hopes to make her mother hear.

8

    'Tis midnight, but small thoughts have I of sleep:
    Full seldom may my friend such vigils keep!
    Visit her, gentle Sleep! with wings of healing,
    And may this storm be but a mountain-birth,[1]
130   May all the stars hang bright above her dwelling,
    Silent as though they watched the sleeping Earth!
    With light heart may she rise,
    Gay fancy, cheerful eyes,
    Joy lift her spirit, joy attune her voice;
135   To her may all things live, from pole to pole,
    Their life the eddying of her living soul!
    O simple spirit, guided from above,
    Dear Lady! friend devoutest of my choice,
    Thus mayest thou ever, evermore rejoice.

Apr. 4, 1802   1802

The Pains of Sleep[1]

Ere on my bed my limbs I lay,
It hath not been my use to pray
With moving lips or bended knees;
But silently, by slow degrees,

---

9. Thomas Otway (1652–1685), a dramatist noted for the pathos of his tragic passages. The poet originally named was "William," and the allusion was probably to Wordsworth's "Lucy Gray."
1. Probably, "May this be a typical mountain storm, short though violent," although Coleridge might have intended an allusion to Horace's phrase "the mountain labored and brought forth a mouse."
1. Coleridge included a draft of this poem in a letter to Robert Southey, September 11, 1803, in which he wrote that "my spirits are dreadful, owing entirely to the Horrors of every night—I truly dread to sleep. It is no shadow with me, but substantial Misery foot-thick, that makes me sit by my bedside of a morning, & cry—. I have abandoned all opiates except Ether be one; & that only in fits. . . . " The last sentence indicates what Coleridge did not know—that his guilty nightmares were probably withdrawal symptoms from opium. The dreams he describes are very similar to those that De Quincey represents as "The Pains of Opium" in his Confessions of an English Opium-Eater.

5 My spirit I to Love compose,
   In humble trust mine eye-lids close,
   With reverential resignation,
   No wish conceived, no thought exprest,
   Only a sense of supplication;
10 A sense o'er all my soul imprest
   That I am weak, yet not unblest,
   Since in me, round me, every where
   Eternal strength and wisdom are.

   But yester-night I prayed aloud
15 In anguish and in agony,
   Up-starting from the fiendish crowd
   Of shapes and thoughts that tortured me:
   A lurid light, a trampling throng,
   Sense of intolerable wrong,
20 And whom I scorned, those only strong!
   Thirst of revenge, the powerless will
   Still baffled, and yet burning still!
   Desire with loathing strangely mixed
   On wild or hateful objects fixed.
25 Fantastic passions! maddening brawl!
   And shame and terror over all!
   Deeds to be hid which were not hid,
   Which all confused I could not know,
   Whether I suffered, or I did:
30 For all seemed guilt, remorse or woe,
   My own or others still the same
   Life-stifling fear, soul-stifling shame.

   So two nights passed: the night's dismay
   Saddened and stunned the coming day.
35 Sleep, the wide blessing, seemed to me
   Distemper's worst calamity.
   The third night, when my own loud scream
   Had waked me from the fiendish dream,
   O'ercome with sufferings strange and wild,
40 I wept as I had been a child;
   And having thus by tears subdued
   My anguish to a milder mood,
   Such punishments, I said, were due
   To natures deepliest stained with sin,—
45 For aye entempesting anew
   The unfathomable hell within,
   The horror of their deeds to view,
   To know and loathe, yet wish and do!
   Such griefs with such men well agree,
50 But wherefore, wherefore fall on me?
   To be beloved is all I need,
   And whom I love, I love indeed.

1803   1816

To William Wordsworth

Composed on the Night after His Recitation of a Poem on the Growth of an Individual Mind[1]

Friend of the wise! and teacher of the good!
Into my heart have I received that lay°   song
More than historic, that prophetic lay
Wherein (high theme by thee first sung aright)
5   Of the foundations and the building up
Of a Human Spirit thou hast dared to tell
What may be told, to the understanding mind
Revealable; and what within the mind
By vital breathings secret as the soul
10   Of vernal° growth, oft quickens in the heart   springtime
Thoughts all too deep for words!2—

                                        Theme hard as high!
Of smiles spontaneous, and mysterious fears
(The first-born they of Reason and twin birth),
Of tides obedient to external force,
15   And currents self-determined, as might seem,
Or by some inner power; of moments awful,°   awe-inspiring
Now in thy inner life, and now abroad,
When power streamed from thee, and thy soul received
The light reflected, as a light bestowed—
20   Of fancies fair, and milder hours of youth,
Hyblean3 murmurs of poetic thought
Industrious in its joy, in vales and glens
Native or outland, lakes and famous hills!
Or on the lonely high-road, when the stars
25   Were rising; or by secret mountain-streams,
The guides and the companions of thy way!

      Of more than Fancy, of the Social Sense
Distending wide, and man beloved as man,
Where France in all her towns lay vibrating
30   Like some becalmed bark beneath the burst
Of Heaven's immediate thunder, when no cloud
Is visible, or shadow on the main.
For thou wert there, thine own brows garlanded,
Amid the tremor of a realm aglow,
35   Amid a mighty nation jubilant,
When from the general heart of human kind
Hope sprang forth like a full-born Deity!
——Of that dear Hope afflicted and struck down,
So summoned homeward, thenceforth calm and sure

1. This was the poem (later called *The Prelude*), addressed to Coleridge, that Wordsworth had completed in 1805. After Coleridge returned from Malta, very low in health and spirits, Wordsworth read the poem aloud to him during the evenings of almost two weeks. Coleridge wrote most of the present response immediately after the reading was completed, on January 7, 1807.

2. Wordsworth had described the effect on his mind of the animating breeze ("vital breathings") in *The Prelude* 1.1–44. "Thoughts . . . words" echoes the last line of Wordsworth's "Intimations" ode. Coleridge goes on to summarize the major themes and events of *The Prelude*.

3. Sweet. Hybla, in ancient Sicily, was famous for its honey.

40   From the dread watch-tower of man's absolute self,
With light unwaning on her eyes, to look
Far on—herself a glory to behold,
The Angel of the vision! Then (last strain)
Of Duty, chosen laws controlling choice,
45   Action and joy!—An Orphic song[4] indeed,
A song divine of high and passionate thoughts
To their own music chanted!

                O great Bard!
Ere yet that last strain dying awed the air,
With steadfast eye I viewed thee in the choir
50   Of ever-enduring men. The truly great
Have all one age, and from one visible space
Shed influence! They, both in power and act,
Are permanent, and Time is not with them,
Save as it worketh for them, they in it.
55   Nor less a sacred roll, than those of old,
And to be placed, as they, with gradual fame
Among the archives of mankind, thy work
Makes audible a linked lay of Truth,
Of Truth profound a sweet continuous lay,
60   Not learnt, but native, her own natural notes!
Ah! as I listened with a heart forlorn,
The pulses of my being beat anew:
And even as life returns upon the drowned,
Life's joy rekindling roused a throng of pains—
65   Keen pangs of Love, awakening as a babe
Turbulent, with an outcry in the heart;
And fears self-willed, that shunned the eye of hope;
And hope that scarce would know itself from fear;
Sense of past youth, and manhood come in vain,
70   And genius given, and knowledge won in vain;
And all which I had culled in wood-walks wild,
And all which patient toil had reared, and all,
Commune with thee had opened out—but flowers
Strewed on my corse, and borne upon my bier,
75   In the same coffin, for the self-same grave!

    That way no more! and ill beseems it me,
Who came a welcomer in herald's guise,
Singing of glory, and futurity,
To wander back on such unhealthful road,
80   Plucking the poisons of self-harm! And ill
Such intertwine beseems triumphal wreaths
Strewed before thy advancing!

                Nor do thou,
Sage Bard! impair the memory of that hour

---

4. As enchanting and oracular as the song of the legendary Orpheus. There may also be an allusion to the Orphic mysteries, involving spiritual death and rebirth (see lines 61–66). "The Angel of the vision" (line 43) probably alludes to "the great vision of the guarded mount" in Milton's "Lycidas," line 161.

Of thy communion with my nobler mind[5]
85 By pity or grief, already felt too long!
Nor let my words import more blame than needs.
The tumult rose and ceased: for peace is nigh
Where wisdom's voice has found a listening heart.
Amid the howl of more than wintry storms,
90 The halcyon[6] hears the voice of vernal hours
Already on the wing.

Eve following eve,[7]
Dear tranquil time, when the sweet sense of Home
Is sweetest! moments for their own sake hailed
And more desired, more precious for thy song,
95 In silence listening, like a devout child,
My soul lay passive, by thy various strain
Driven as in surges now beneath the stars,
With momentary stars of my own birth,
Fair constellated foam, still darting off
100 Into the darkness; now a tranquil sea,
Outspread and bright, yet swelling to the moon.

And when—O Friend! my comforter and guide!
Strong in thyself, and powerful to give strength!—
Thy long sustained Song finally closed,
105 And thy deep voice had ceased—yet thou thyself
Wert still before my eyes, and round us both
That happy vision of beloved faces—
Scarce conscious, and yet conscious of its close
I sate, my being blended in one thought
110 (Thought was it? or aspiration? or resolve?)
Absorbed, yet hanging still upon the sound—
And when I rose, I found myself in prayer.

1807   1817

Epitaph[1]

Stop, Christian Passer-by!—Stop, child of God,
And read with gentle breast. Beneath this sod
A poet lies, or that which once seem'd he.—
O, lift one thought in prayer for S. T. C.;
5 That he who many a year with toil of breath
Found death in life, may here find life in death!
Mercy for praise—to be forgiven for[2] fame
He ask'd, and hoped, through Christ. Do thou the same!

1833   1834

5. I.e., during the early association between the two poets (1797–98).
6. A fabled bird, able to calm the sea where it nested in winter.
7. The evenings during which Wordsworth read his poem aloud.
1. Written by Coleridge the year before he died.

One version that he sent in a letter had as a title: "Epitaph on a Poet little known, yet better known by the Initials of his name than by the Name Itself."
2. "For" in the sense of "instead of" [Coleridge's note].

Biographia Literaria   In March 1815 Coleridge was preparing a collected edition of his poems and planned to include "a general preface . . . on the principles of philosophic and genial criticism." As was typical for Coleridge, the materials developed as he worked on them until, on July 29, he declared that the preface had expanded to become a book in its own right, an "Autobiographia Literaria." In a characteristic Romantic reinvention of autobiography, the work merged personal experience with philosophical speculation, as well as with what Coleridge identified as "digression and anecdotes." It was to consist of two main parts, "my literary life and opinions, as far as poetry and *poetical* criticism [are] concerned" and a critique of Wordsworth's theory of poetic diction. This work was ready by September 17, 1815, but the *Biographia Literaria,* in two volumes, was not published until July 1817. The delay was caused by a series of miscalculations by his printer, which forced Coleridge to add 150 pages of miscellaneous materials to pad out the length of the second volume.

Coleridge had been planning a detailed critique of Wordsworth's theory of poetic diction ever since 1802, when he had detected "a radical difference in our theoretical opinions respecting poetry." In the selection from chapter 17, Coleridge agrees with Wordsworth's general aim of reforming the artifices of current poetic diction, but he sharply denies Wordsworth's claim that there is no essential difference between the language of poetry and the language spoken by people in real life. The other selections printed here are devoted mainly to the central principle of Coleridge's own critical theory, the distinction between the mechanical "fancy" and the organic imagination, which is tersely summarized in the conclusion to chapter 13. The definition of poetry at the end of chapter 14, develops at greater length the nature of the "synthetic and magical power . . . of imagination," which, for Coleridge, has the capacity to dissolve the divisions (between, for instance, the perceiving human subject and his or her objects of perception) that characterize human beings' fallen state.

From Biographia Literaria

From Chapter 4

[MR. WORDSWORTH'S EARLIER POEMS]

* * * During the last year of my residence at Cambridge, I became acquainted with Mr. Wordsworth's first publication, entitled *Descriptive Sketches;*[1] and seldom, if ever, was the emergence of an original poetic genius above the literary horizon more evidently announced. In the form, style, and manner of the whole poem, and in the structure of the particular lines and periods, there is a harshness and acerbity connected and combined with words and images all a-glow which might recall those products of the vegetable world, where gorgeous blossoms rise out of the hard and thorny rind and shell within which the rich fruit was elaborating. The language was not only peculiar and strong, but at times knotty and contorted, as by its own impatient strength; while the novelty and struggling crowd of images, acting in conjunction with the difficulties of the style, demanded always a greater closeness of attention than poetry (at all events than descriptive poetry) has a right to claim. It not seldom therefore justified the complaint of obscurity. In the following extract

---

1. Published 1793, the year before Coleridge left Cambridge; a long descriptive-meditative poem in closed couplets, recounting Wordsworth's walking tour in the Alps in 1790. Wordsworth describes the same tour in *The Prelude,* book 6.

I have sometimes fancied that I saw an emblem of the poem itself and of the author's genius as it was then displayed:

> 'Tis storm; and hid in mist from hour to hour,
> All day the floods a deepening murmur pour;
> The sky is veiled, and every cheerful sight:
> Dark is the region as with coming night;
> And yet what frequent bursts of overpowering light!
> Triumphant on the bosom of the storm,
> Glances the fire-clad eagle's wheeling form;
> Eastward, in long perspective glittering, shine
> The wood-crowned cliffs that o'er the lake recline;
> Wide o'er the Alps a hundred streams unfold,
> At once to pillars turned that flame with gold;
> Behind his sail the peasant strives to shun
> The West, that burns like one dilated sun,
> Where in a mighty crucible expire
> The mountains, glowing hot, like coals of fire.[2]

The poetic Psyche, in its process to full development, undergoes as many changes as its Greek namesake, the butterfly.[3] And it is remarkable how soon genius clears and purifies itself from the faults and errors of its earliest products; faults which, in its earliest compositions, are the more obtrusive and confluent because, as heterogeneous elements which had only a temporary use, they constitute the very-*ferment* by which themselves are carried off. Or we may compare them to some diseases, which must work on the humors and be thrown out on the surface in order to secure the patient from their future recurrence. I was in my twenty-fourth year when I had the happiness of knowing Mr. Wordsworth personally;[4] and, while memory lasts, I shall hardly forget the sudden effect produced on my mind by his recitation of a manuscript poem which still remains unpublished, but of which the stanza and tone of style were the same as those of *The Female Vagrant* as originally printed in the first volume of the *Lyrical Ballads*.[5] There was here no mark of strained thought or forced diction, no crowd or turbulence of imagery, and, as the poet hath himself well described in his lines on revisiting the Wye,[6] manly reflection and human associations had given both variety and an additional interest to natural objects which in the passion and appetite of the first love they had seemed to him neither to need or permit. The occasional obscurities, which had risen from an imperfect control over the resources of his native language, had almost wholly disappeared, together with that worse defect of arbitrary and illogical phrases, at once hackneyed and fantastic, which hold so distinguished a place in the *technique* of ordinary poetry and will, more or less, alloy the earlier poems of the truest genius, unless the attention has been specifically directed to their worthlessness and incongruity. I did not perceive anything particular in the mere style of the poem alluded to during its recitation, except indeed such difference as was not separable from the thought and manner; and the Spenserian stanza which always, more or less, recalls to the reader's mind

2. *Descriptive Sketches* (1815 version), lines 332ff.
3. In Greek, Psyche is the common name for the soul and the butterfly [Coleridge's note].
4. The meeting occurred in September 1795.
5. *Salisbury Plain* (1793–94), which was left in

manuscript until Wordsworth published a revised version in 1842 under the title "Guilt and Sorrow." An excerpt from *Salisbury Plain* was printed as "The Female Vagrant," in *Lyrical Ballads* (1798).
6. Wordsworth's "Tintern Abbey," lines 76ff.

Spenser's own style, would doubtless have authorized in my then opinion a more frequent descent to the phrases of ordinary life than could, without an ill effect, have been hazarded in the heroic couplet. It was not however the freedom from false taste, whether as to common defects or to those more properly his own, which made so unusual an impression on my feelings immediately, and subsequently on my judgment. It was the union of deep feeling with profound thought; the fine balance of truth in observing with the imaginative faculty in modifying the objects observed; and above all the original gift of spreading the tone, the *atmosphere,* and with it the depth and height of the ideal world, around forms, incidents, and situations of which, for the common view, custom had bedimmed all the luster, had dried up the sparkle and the dewdrops. "To find no contradiction in the union of old and new, to contemplate the Ancient of Days and all his works with feelings as fresh as if all had then sprang forth at the first creative fiat,[7] characterizes the mind that feels the riddle of the world and may help to unravel it. To carry on the feelings of childhood into the powers of manhood; to combine the child's sense of wonder and novelty with the appearances which every day for perhaps forty years had rendered familiar;

> With sun and moon and stars throughout the year,
> And man and woman;[8]

this is the character and privilege of genius, and one of the marks which distinguish genius from talents. And therefore it is the prime merit of genius, and its most unequivocal mode of manifestation, so to represent familiar objects as to awaken in the minds of others a kindred feeling concerning them, and that freshness of sensation which is the constant accompaniment of mental no less than of bodily convalescence. Who has not a thousand times seen snow fall on water? Who has not watched it with a new feeling from the time that he has read Burns' comparison of sensual pleasure

> To snow that falls upon a river
> A moment white—then gone forever![9]

In poems, equally as in philosophic disquisitions, genius produces the strongest impressions of novelty while it rescues the most admitted truths from the impotence caused by the very circumstance of their universal admission. Truths of all others the most awful and mysterious, yet being at the same time of universal interest, are too often considered as *so* true, that they lose all the life and efficiency of truth and lie bedridden in the dormitory of the soul side by side with the most despised and exploded errors." *The Friend,* p. 76, no. 5.[1]

[ON FANCY AND IMAGINATION—THE INVESTIGATION OF THE DISTINCTION IMPORTANT TO THE FINE ARTS]

This excellence, which in all Mr. Wordsworth's writings is more or less predominant and which constitutes the character of his mind, I no sooner felt than I sought to understand. Repeated meditations led me first to suspect (and a more intimate analysis of the human faculties, their appropriate marks, functions, and effects, matured my conjecture into full conviction) that fancy and

---

7. The first divine command: "Let there be light."
8. Altered from Milton's sonnet "To Mr. Cyriack Skinner upon His Blindness."

9. Altered from Burns's "Tam o' Shanter," lines 61–62.
1. A periodical published by Coleridge (1809–10).

imagination were two distinct and widely different faculties, instead of being, according to the general belief, either two names with one meaning, or at furthest the lower and higher degree of one and the same power. It is not, I own, easy to conceive a more apposite translation of the Greek *phantasia* than the Latin *imaginatio*; but it is equally true that in all societies there exists an instinct of growth, a certain collective unconscious good sense working progressively to desynonymize those words originally of the same meaning which the conflux of dialects had supplied to the more homogeneous languages, as the Greek and German: and which the same cause, joined with accidents of translation from original works of different countries, occasion in mixed languages like our own. The first and most important point to be proved is, that two conceptions perfectly distinct are confused under one and the same word, and (this done) to appropriate that word exclusively to one meaning, and the synonym (should there be one) to the other. But if (as will be often the case in the arts and sciences) no synonym exists, we must either invent or borrow a word. In the present instance the appropriation had already begun and been legitimated in the derivative adjective: Milton had a highly *imaginative*, Cowley a very *fanciful*, mind. If therefore I should succeed in establishing the actual existence of two faculties generally different, the nomenclature would be at once determined. To the faculty by which I had characterized Milton we should confine the term *imagination*; while the other would be contradistinguished as *fancy*. Now were it once fully ascertained that this division is no less grounded in nature than that of delirium from mania, or Otway's

> Lutes, lobsters, seas of milk, and ships of amber,[2]

from Shakespeare's

> What! have his daughters brought him to this pass?[3]

or from the preceding apostrophe to the elements, the theory of the fine arts and of poetry in particular could not, I thought, but derive some additional and important light. It would in its immediate effects furnish a torch of guidance to the philosophical critic, and ultimately to the poet himself. In energetic minds truth soon changes by domestication into power; and from directing in the discrimination and appraisal of the product becomes influencive in the production. To admire on principle is the only way to imitate without loss of originality. * * *

From *Chapter 13*

[ON THE IMAGINATION, OR ESEMPLASTIC[4] POWER]

* * * The IMAGINATION, then, I consider either as primary, or secondary. The primary IMAGINATION I hold to be the living power and prime agent of all human perception, and as a repetition in the finite mind of the eternal act of creation in the infinite I AM. The secondary I consider as an echo of the former, coexisting with the conscious will, yet still as identical with the primary in the *kind* of its agency, and differing only in *degree*, and in the *mode* of its operation. It dissolves, diffuses, dissipates, in order to recreate; or where this process is

---

2. Thomas Otway, in *Venice Preserved* (1682), wrote "laurels" in place of "lobsters" (5.2.151).
3. *King Lear* 3.4.59.

4. Coleridge coined this word and used it to mean "molding into unity."

rendered impossible, yet still, at all events, it struggles to idealize and to unify. It is essentially *vital,* even as all objects (*as* objects) are essentially fixed and dead.

FANCY, on the contrary, has no other counters to play with but fixities and definites. The fancy is indeed no other than a mode of memory emancipated from the order of time and space; and blended with, and modified by that empirical phenomenon of the will which we express by the word CHOICE. But equally with the ordinary memory it must receive all its materials ready made from the law of association.[5] * * *

Chapter 14

OCCASION OF THE *LYRICAL BALLADS,* AND THE OBJECTS ORIGINALLY
PROPOSED—PREFACE TO THE SECOND EDITION—THE ENSUING
CONTROVERSY, ITS CAUSES AND ACRIMONY—PHILOSOPHIC DEFINITIONS
OF A POEM AND POETRY WITH SCHOLIA.[6]

During the first year that Mr. Wordsworth and I were neighbours,[7] our conversations turned frequently on the two cardinal points of poetry, the power of exciting the sympathy of the reader by a faithful adherence to the truth of nature, and the power of giving the interest of novelty by the modifying colors of imagination.[8] The sudden charm which accidents of light and shade, which moonlight or sunset diffused over a known and familiar landscape, appeared to represent the practicability of combining both. These are the poetry of nature. The thought suggested itself (to which of us I do not recollect) that a series of poems might be composed of two sorts. In the one, the incidents and agents were to be, in part at least, supernatural; and the excellence aimed at was to consist in the interesting of the affections by the dramatic truth of such emotions as would naturally accompany such situations, supposing them real. And real in *this* sense they have been to every human being who, from whatever source of delusion, has at any time believed himself under supernatural agency. For the second class, subjects were to be chosen from ordinary life; the characters and incidents were to be such as will be found in every village and its vicinity where there is a meditative and feeling mind to seek after them, or to notice them when they present themselves.

In this idea originated the plan of the *Lyrical Ballads;* in which it was agreed that my endeavours should be directed to persons and characters supernatural, or at least romantic; yet so as to transfer from our inward nature a human interest and a semblance of truth sufficient to procure for these shadows of imagination that willing suspension of disbelief for the moment, which constitutes poetic faith. Mr. Wordsworth, on the other hand, was to propose to himself as his object to give the charm of novelty to things of every day, and to excite a feeling analogous to the supernatural, by awakening the mind's attention from the lethargy of custom and directing it to the loveliness and

5. Coleridge conceives God's creation to be a continuing process, which has an analogy in the creative perception ("primary imagination") of all human minds. The creative process is repeated, or "echoed," on still a third level, by the "secondary imagination" of the poet, which dissolves the products of primary perception to shape them into a new and unified creation—the imaginative passage or poem. The "fancy," on the other hand, can only manipulate "fixities and definites" that, linked by association, come to it ready-made from perception.
6. Additional remarks, after a philosophic demonstration.
7. At Nether Stowey and Alfoxden, Somerset, in 1797.
8. Cf. Wordsworth's account in his Preface to *Lyrical Ballads* (p. 262).

the wonders of the world before us; an inexhaustible treasure, but for which, in consequence of the film of familiarity and selfish solicitude, we have eyes yet see not, ears that hear not, and hearts that neither feel nor understand.[9]

With this view I wrote *The Ancient Mariner,* and was preparing, among other poems, *The Dark Ladie,* and the *Christabel,* in which I should have more nearly realized my ideal than I had done in my first attempt. But Mr. Wordsworth's industry had proved so much more successful and the number of his poems so much greater, that my compositions, instead of forming a balance, appeared rather an interpolation of heterogeneous matter.[1] Mr. Wordsworth added two or three poems written in his own character, in the impassioned, lofty, and sustained diction which is characteristic of his genius. In this form the *Lyrical Ballads* were published; and were presented by him, as an *experiment,*[2] whether subjects which from their nature rejected the usual ornaments and extra-colloquial style of poems in general might not be so managed in the language of ordinary life as to produce the pleasurable interest which it is the peculiar business of poetry to impart. To the second edition[3] he added a preface of considerable length; in which, notwithstanding some passages of apparently a contrary import, he was understood to contend for the extension of this style to poetry of all kinds, and to reject as vicious and indefensible all phrases and forms of style that were not included in what he (unfortunately, I think, adopting an equivocal expression) called the language of *real* life. From this preface, prefixed to poems in which it was impossible to deny the presence of original genius, however mistaken its direction might be deemed, arose the whole long-continued controversy.[4] For from the conjunction of perceived power with supposed heresy I explain the inveteracy[5] and in some instances, I grieve to say, the acrimonious passions with which the controversy has been conducted by the assailants.

Had Mr. Wordsworth's poems been the silly, the childish things which they were for a long time described as being; had they been really distinguished from the compositions of other poets merely by meanness[6] of language and inanity of thought; had they indeed contained nothing more than what is found in the parodies and pretended imitations of them; they must have sunk at once, a dead weight, into the slough of oblivion, and have dragged the preface along with them. But year after year increased the number of Mr. Wordsworth's admirers. They were found too not in the lower classes of the reading public, but chiefly among young men of strong sensibility and meditative minds; and their admiration (inflamed perhaps in some degree by opposition) was distinguished by its intensity, I might almost say, by its *religious* fervor. These facts, and the intellectual energy of the author, which was more or less consciously felt where it was outwardly and even boisterously denied, meeting with sentiments of aversion to his opinions and of alarm at their consequences, produced an eddy of criticism which would of itself have borne up the poems by the violence with which it whirled them round and round. With many parts of this preface, in the sense attributed to them and which the words undoubtedly seem to authorize, I never concurred; but, on the contrary objected to them as erroneous in principle, and as contradictory (in appearance at least)

9. Cf. Isaiah 6.9–10.
1. The first edition of *Lyrical Ballads,* published anonymously in 1798, contained nineteen poems by Wordsworth, four by Coleridge.
2. *Experiments* was the word used by Wordsworth in his *Advertisement* to the first edition.

3. Published in 1800.
4. The controversy over Wordsworth's theory and poetical practice in the literary journals of the day.
5. Deep-rooted prejudice.
6. Vulgarity.

both to other parts of the same preface and to the author's own practice in the greater number of the poems themselves. Mr. Wordsworth in his recent collection[7] has, I find, degraded this prefatory disquisition to the end of his second volume, to be read or not at the reader's choice. But he has not, as far as I can discover, announced any change in his poetic creed. At all events, considering it as the source of a controversy in which I have been honored more than I deserve by the frequent conjunction of my name with his, I think it expedient to declare once for all in what points I coincide with his opinions, and in what points I altogether differ. But in order to render myself intelligible I must previously, in as few words as possible, explain my ideas, first, of a POEM; and secondly, of POETRY itself, in *kind* and in *essence*.

The office of philosophical *disquisition* consists in just *distinction*; while it is the privilege of the philosopher to preserve himself constantly aware that distinction is not division. In order to obtain adequate notions of any truth, we must intellectually separate its distinguishable parts; and this is the technical of philosophy. But having so done, we must then restore them in our conceptions to the unity in which they actually coexist; and this is the *result* of philosophy. A poem contains the same elements as a prose composition; the difference therefore must consist in a different combination of them, in consequence of a different object proposed. According to the difference of the object will be the difference of the combination. It is possible that the object may be merely to facilitate the recollection of any given facts or observations by artificial arrangement; and the composition will be a poem, merely because it is distinguished from prose by meter, or by rhyme, or by both conjointly. In this, the lowest sense, a man might attribute the name of a poem to the well-known enumeration of the days in the several months:

> Thirty days hath September,
> April, June, and November, etc.

and others of the same class and purpose. And as a particular pleasure is found in anticipating the recurrence of sounds and quantities, all compositions that have this charm superadded, whatever be their contents, *may* be entitled poems.

So much for the superficial *form*. A difference of object and contents supplies an additional ground of distinction. The immediate purpose may be the communication of truths; either of truth absolute and demonstrable, as in works of science; or of facts experienced and recorded, as in history. Pleasure, and that of the highest and most permanent kind, may *result* from the attainment of the end; but it is not itself the immediate end. In other works the communication of pleasure may be the immediate purpose; and though truth, either moral or intellectual, ought to be the *ultimate* end, yet this will distinguish the character of the author, not the class to which the work belongs. Blessed indeed is that state of society in which the immediate purpose would be baffled by the perversion of the proper ultimate end; in which no charm of diction or imagery could exempt the Bathyllus even of an Anacreon, or the Alexis of Virgil,[8] from disgust and aversion!

But the communication of pleasure may be the immediate object of a work not metrically composed; and that object may have been in a high degree

---

7. *Poems*, 2 vols., 1815.
8. The reference is to poems of homosexual love. Bathyllus was a beautiful boy praised by Anacreon,

a Greek lyric poet (ca. 560–475 B.C.E.); Alexis was a young man loved by the shepherd Corydon in Virgil's *Eclogue* 2.

attained, as in novels and romances. Would then the mere superaddition of meter, with or without rhyme, entitle *these* to the name of poems? The answer is that nothing can permanently please which does not contain in itself the reason why it is so, and not otherwise. If meter be superadded, all other parts must be made consonant with it. They must be such as to justify the perpetual and distinct attention to each part which an exact correspondent recurrence of accent and sound are calculated to excite. The final definition then, so deduced, may be thus worded. A poem is that species of composition which is opposed to works of science by proposing for its *immediate* object pleasure, not truth; and from all other species (having *this* object in common with it) it is discriminated by proposing to itself such delight from the *whole* as is compatible with a distinct gratification from each component *part*.

Controversy is not seldom excited in consequence of the disputants attaching each a different meaning to the same word; and in few instances has this been more striking than in disputes concerning the present subject. If a man chooses to call every composition a poem which is rhyme, or measure, or both, I must leave his opinion uncontroverted. The distinction is at least competent to characterize the writer's intention. If it were subjoined that the whole is likewise entertaining or affecting as a tale or as a series of interesting reflections, I of course admit this as another fit ingredient of a poem and an additional merit. But if the definition sought for be that of a *legitimate* poem, I answer it must be one the parts of which mutually support and explain each other; all in their proportion harmonizing with, and supporting the purpose and known influences of metrical arrangement. The philosophic critics of all ages coincide with the ultimate judgment of all countries in equally denying the praises of a just poem on the one hand to a series of striking lines or distichs,[9] each of which absorbing the whole attention of the reader to itself disjoins it from its context and makes it a separate whole, instead of a harmonizing part; and on the other hand, to an unsustained composition, from which the reader collects rapidly the general result unattracted by the component parts. The reader should be carried forward, not merely or chiefly by the mechanical impulse of curiosity, or by a restless desire to arrive at the final solution; but by the pleasurable activity of mind excited by the attractions of the journey itself. Like the motion of a serpent, which the Egyptians made the emblem of intellectual power; or like the path of sound through the air; at every step he pauses and half recedes, and from the retrogressive movement collects the force which again carries him onward. "*Praecipitandus est* liber *spiritus,*"[1] says Petronius Arbiter most happily. The epithet *liber* here balances the preceding verb; and it is not easy to conceive more meaning condensed in fewer words.

But if this should be admitted as a satisfactory character of a poem, we have still to seek for a definition of poetry. The writings of Plato, and Bishop Taylor, and the *Theoria Sacra* of Burnet,[2] furnish undeniable proofs that poetry of the highest kind may exist without meter, and even without the contradistinguishing objects of a poem. The first chapter of Isaiah (indeed a very large proportion of the whole book) is poetry in the most emphatic sense; yet it would be

9. Pairs of lines.
1. "The *free* spirit [of the poet] must be hurled onward." From the *Satyricon*, by the Roman satirist Petronius Arbiter (1st century c.e.).
2. Thomas Burnet (1635?–1715), author of *The Sacred Theory of the Earth.* Bishop Jeremy Taylor

(1613–1667), author of *Holy Living* and *Holy Dying.* Coleridge greatly admired the elaborate and sonorous prose of both these writers. He took from a work by Burnet the Latin motto for *The Rime of the Ancient Mariner.*

not less irrational than strange to assert that pleasure, and not truth, was the immediate object of the prophet. In short, whatever *specific* import we attach to the word poetry, there will be found involved in it, as a necessary consequence, that a poem of any length neither can be, nor ought to be, all poetry. Yet if a harmonious whole is to be produced, the remaining parts must be preserved in *keeping*[3] with the poetry; and this can be no otherwise effected than by such a studied selection and artificial arrangement as will partake of *one*, though not a *peculiar*, property of poetry. And this again can be no other than the property of exciting a more continuous and equal attention than the language of prose aims at, whether colloquial or written.

My own conclusions on the nature of poetry, in the strictest use of the word, have been in part anticipated in the preceding disquisition on the fancy and imagination. What is poetry? is so nearly the same question with, what is a poet? that the answer to the one is involved in the solution of the other. For it is a distinction resulting from the poetic genius itself, which sustains and modifies the images, thoughts, and emotions of the poet's own mind.

The poet, described in *ideal* perfection, brings the whole soul of man into activity, with the subordination of its faculties to each other, according to their relative worth and dignity. He diffuses a tone and spirit of unity that blends and (as it were) *fuses*, each into each, by that synthetic and magical power to which we have exclusively appropriated the name of imagination. This power, first put in action by the will and understanding and retained under their irremissive,[4] though gentle and unnoticed, control (*laxis effertur habenis*)[5] reveals itself in the balance or reconciliation of opposite or discordant qualities:[6] of sameness, with difference; of the general, with the concrete; the idea, with the image; the individual, with the representative; the sense of novelty and freshness, with old and familiar objects; a more than usual state of emotion, with more than usual order; judgment ever awake and steady self-possession, with enthusiasm and feeling profound or vehement; and while it blends and harmonizes the natural and the artificial, still subordinates art to nature; the manner to the matter; and our admiration of the poet to our sympathy with the poetry. "Doubtless," as Sir John Davies observes of the soul (and his words may with slight alteration be applied, and even more appropriately, to the poetic IMAGINATION):

> Doubtless this could not be, but that she turns
> Bodies to spirit by sublimation strange,
> As fire converts to fire the things it burns,
> As we our food into our nature change.
>
> From their gross matter she abstracts their forms,
> And draws a kind of quintessence from things;
> Which to her proper nature she transforms,
> To bear them light on her celestial wings.
>
> Thus does she, when from individual states
> She doth abstract the universal kinds;

3. A term from the theory of painting for the maintenance of the harmony of a composition.
4. Continuous.
5. Driven with loosened reins (Latin).
6. Here Coleridge introduces the concept, which became central to the American New Critics of the mid-20th century, that the best poetry incorporates and reconciles opposite or discordant elements.

Which then reclothed in divers names and fates
Steal access through our senses to our minds.[7]

Finally, GOOD SENSE is the BODY of poetic genius, FANCY its DRAPERY,[8] MOTION its LIFE, and IMAGINATION the SOUL that is everywhere, and in each; and forms all into one graceful and intelligent whole.

From Chapter 17

[EXAMINATION OF THE TENETS PECULIAR TO MR. WORDSWORTH]

As far then as Mr. Wordsworth in his preface contended, and most ably contended, for a reformation in our poetic diction, as far as he has evinced the truth of passion, and the *dramatic* propriety of those figures and metaphors in the original poets which, stripped of their justifying reasons and converted into mere artifices of connection or ornament, constitute the characteristic falsity in the poetic style of the moderns; and as far as he has, with equal acuteness and clearness, pointed out the process by which this change was effected and the resemblances between that state into which the reader's mind is thrown by the pleasurable confusion of thought from an unaccustomed train of words and images and that state which is induced by the natural language of impassioned feeling, he undertook a useful task and deserves all praise, both for the attempt and for the execution. The provocations to this remonstrance in behalf of truth and nature were still of perpetual recurrence before and after the publication of this preface. * * *

My own differences from certain supposed parts of Mr. Wordsworth's theory ground themselves on the assumption that his words had been rightly interpreted, as purporting that the proper diction for poetry in general consists altogether in a language taken, with due exceptions, from the mouths of men in real life, a language which actually constitutes the natural conversation of men under the influence of natural feelings.[9] My objection is, first, that in *any* sense this rule is applicable only to *certain* classes of poetry; secondly, that even to these classes it is not applicable, except in such a sense as hath never by anyone (as far as I know or have read) been denied or doubted; and, lastly, that as far as, and in that degree in which it is *practicable,* yet as a *rule* it is useless, if not injurious, and therefore either need not or ought not to be practiced. * * *

[RUSTIC LIFE (ABOVE ALL, *LOW* AND RUSTIC LIFE) ESPECIALLY UNFAVORABLE TO THE FORMATION OF A HUMAN DICTION—THE BEST PARTS OF LANGUAGE THE PRODUCTS OF PHILOSOPHERS, NOT CLOWNS[1] OR SHEPHERDS]

As little can I agree with the assertion that from the objects with which the rustic hourly communicates the best part of language is formed. For first, if to communicate with an object implies such an acquaintance with it, as renders it capable of being discriminately reflected on; the distinct knowledge of an uneducated rustic would furnish a very scanty vocabulary. The few things, and modes of action, requisite for his bodily conveniences, would alone be

7. Adapted from John Davies's *Nosce Teipsum* ("Know Thyself"), a philosophical poem (1599).
8. Clothing.
9. Wordsworth's Preface to *Lyrical Ballads* (1800): "A selection of the real language of men in

a state of vivid sensation. . . . Low and rustic life was generally chosen. . . . The language, too, of these men is adopted."
1. Rustic people.

individualized; while all the rest of nature would be expressed by a small number of confused general terms. Secondly, I deny that the words and combinations of words derived from the objects, with which the rustic is familiar, whether with distinct or confused knowledge, can be justly said to form the *best* part of language. It is more than probable that many classes of the brute creation possess discriminating sounds, by which they can convey to each other notices of such objects as concern their food, shelter, or safety. Yet we hesitate to call the aggregate of such sounds a language, otherwise than metaphorically. The best part of human language, properly so called, is derived from reflection on the acts of the mind itself. It is formed by a voluntary appropriation of fixed symbols to internal acts, to processes and results of imagination, the greater part of which have no place in the consciousness of uneducated man; though in civilized society, by imitation and passive remembrance of what they hear from their religious instructors and other superiors, the most uneducated share in the harvest which they neither sowed or reaped. * * *

[THE LANGUAGE OF MILTON AS MUCH THE LANGUAGE OF *REAL* LIFE, YEA, INCOMPARABLY MORE SO THAN THAT OF THE COTTAGER]

Here let me be permitted to remind the reader that the positions which I controvert are contained in the sentences—"a selection of the REAL language of men"; "the language of these men (i.e., men in low and rustic life) I propose to myself to imitate, and as far as possible to adopt the very language of men." "Between the language of prose and that of metrical composition there neither is, nor can be any essential difference." It is against these exclusively that my opposition is directed.

I object, in the very first instance, to an equivocation in the use of the word "real." Every man's language varies according to the extent of his knowledge, the activity of his faculties, and the depth or quickness of his feelings. Every man's language has, first, its *individualities;* secondly, the common properties of the *class* to which he belongs; and thirdly, words and phrases of *universal* use. The language of Hooker, Bacon, Bishop Taylor, and Burke[2] differs from the common language of the learned class only by the superior number and novelty of the thoughts and relations which they had to convey. The language of Algernon Sidney[3] differs not at all from that which every well-educated gentleman would wish to write, and (with due allowances for the undeliberateness and less connected train of thinking natural and proper to conversation) such as he would wish to talk. Neither one nor the other differ half as much from the general language of cultivated society as the language of Mr. Wordsworth's homeliest composition differs from that of a common peasant. For "real" therefore we must substitute *ordinary*, or *lingua communis*.[4] And this, we have proved, is no more to be found in the phraseology of low and rustic life than in that of any other class. Omit the peculiarities of each, and the result of course must be common to all. And assuredly the omissions and changes to be made in the language of rustics before it could be transferred to any species of poem, except the drama or other professed imitation,

2. Richard Hooker (1554–1600), author of *The Laws of Ecclesiastical Polity;* Francis Bacon (1561–1626), essayist and philosopher, and Jeremy Taylor were all, together with the late-18th-century politician and opponent of the French Revolution Edmund Burke (1729–1797), lauded for their prose styles.

3. Republican soldier and statesman (1622–1683), author of *Discourses Concerning Government,* executed for his part in the Rye House Plot to assassinate Charles II.

4. The common language (Latin).

are at least as numerous and weighty as would be required in adapting to the same purpose the ordinary language of tradesmen and manufacturers. Not to mention that the language so highly extolled by Mr. Wordsworth varies in every county, nay, in every village, according to the accidental character of the clergyman, the existence or nonexistence of schools; or even, perhaps, as the exciseman, publican, or barber happen to be, or not to be, zealous politicians and readers of the weekly newspaper *pro bono publico*.[5] Anterior to cultivation the *lingua communis* of every country, as Dante has well observed, exists every where in parts and no where as a whole.[6]

Neither is the case rendered at all more tenable by the addition of the words "in a state of excitement."[7] For the nature of a man's words, when he is strongly affected by joy, grief, or anger, must necessarily depend on the number and quality of the general truths, conceptions, and images, and of the words expressing them, with which his mind had been previously stored. For the property of passion is not to *create*, but to set in increased activity. At least, whatever new connections of thoughts or images, or (which is equally, if not more than equally, the appropriate effect of strong excitement) whatever generalizations of truth or experience the heat of passion may produce, yet the terms of their conveyance must have pre-existed in his former conversations, and are only collected and crowded together by the unusual stimulation. It is indeed very possible to adopt in a poem the unmeaning repetitions, habitual phrases, and other blank counters which an unfurnished or confused understanding interposes at short intervals in order to keep hold of his subject which is still slipping from him, and to give him time for recollection; or in mere aid of vacancy, as in the scanty companies of a country stage the same player pops backwards and forwards, in order to prevent the appearance of empty spaces, in the procession of *Macbeth* or *Henry VIIIth*. But what assistance to the poet or ornament to the poem these can supply, I am at a loss to conjecture. Nothing assuredly can differ either in origin or in mode more widely from the apparent tautologies of intense and turbulent feeling in which the passion is greater and of longer endurance than to be exhausted or satisfied by a single representation of the image or incident exciting it. Such repetitions I admit to be a beauty of the highest kind; as illustrated by Mr. Wordsworth himself from the song of Deborah. "At her feet he bowed, he fell, he lay down; at her feet he bowed, he fell; where he bowed, there he fell down dead."[8]

1815   1817

From *Lectures on Shakespeare*[1]

[FANCY AND IMAGINATION IN SHAKESPEARE'S POETRY]

In the preceding lecture we have examined with what armor clothed and with what titles authorized Shakespeare came forward as a poet to demand the throne of fame as the dramatic poet of England; we have now to observe

5. For the public welfare (Latin).
6. In *De Vulgari Eloquentia* ("On the Speech of the people") Dante discusses—and affirms—the fitness for poetry of the unlocalized Italian vernacular.
7. Wordsworth: "the manner in which we associate ideas in a state of excitement."
8. Judges 5.27. Cited by Wordsworth in a note to *The Thorn* as an example of the natural repetitious-

ness of "impassioned feelings."
1. Although Coleridge's series of public lectures on Shakespeare and other poets contained much of his best criticism, he published none of this material, leaving only fragmentary remains of his lectures in notebooks, scraps of manuscript, and notes written in the margins of books. The following selections, which develop some of the principal ideas presented in *Biographia Literaria*, reproduce

and retrace the excellencies which compelled even his contemporaries to seat him on that throne, although there were giants in those days contending for the same honor. Hereafter we shall endeavor to make out the title of the English drama, as created by and existing in Shakespeare, and its right to the supremacy of dramatic excellence in general. I have endeavored to prove that he had shown himself a *poet*, previously to his appearance as a dramatic poet—and that had no *Lear*, no *Othello*, no *Henry the Fourth*, no *Twelfth Night* appeared, we must have admitted that Shakespeare possessed the chief if not all the requisites of a poet—namely, deep feeling and exquisite sense of beauty, both as exhibited to the eye in combinations of form, and to the ear in sweet and appropriate melody (with the exception of Spenser he is [the sweetest of English poets]); that these feelings were under the command of *his own will*—that in his very first productions he projected his mind out of his own particular being, and felt and made others feel, on subjects [in] no way connected with himself, except by force of contemplation, and that sublime faculty, by which a great mind becomes that which it meditates on. To this we are to add the affectionate love of nature and natural objects, without which no man could have observed so steadily, or painted so truly and passionately the very minutest beauties of the external world. Next, we have shown that he possessed fancy, considered as the faculty of bringing together images dissimilar in the main by some one point or more of likeness distinguished.[2]

> Full gently now she takes him by the hand,
> A lily prisoned in a jail of snow,
> Or ivory in an alabaster band—
> So white a friend engirts so white a foe.

Still mounting, we find undoubted proof in his mind of imagination, or the power by which one image or feeling is made to modify many others and by a sort of *fusion to force many into one*—that which after showed itself in such might and energy in *Lear*, where the deep anguish of a father spreads the feeling of ingratitude and cruelty over the very elements of heaven. Various are the workings of this greatest faculty of the human mind—both passionate and tranquil. In its tranquil and purely pleasurable operation, it acts chiefly by producing out of many things, as they would have appeared in the description of an ordinary mind, described slowly and in unimpassioned succession, a oneness, even as nature, the greatest of poets, acts upon us when we open our eyes upon an extended prospect. Thus the flight of Adonis from the enamored goddess in the dusk of evening—

> Look how a bright star shooteth from the sky—
> So glides he in the night from Venus' eye.[3]

How many images and feelings are here brought together without effort and without discord—the beauty of Adonis—the rapidity of his flight—the yearning yet hopelessness of the enamored gazer—and a shadowy ideal character thrown over the whole.—Or it acts by impressing the stamp of humanity, of human feeling, over inanimate objects * * *

---

the text of T. M. Raysor's edition—based on Coleridge's manuscripts and on contemporary reports—of *Coleridge's Shakespearean Criticism* (1930); four minor corrections in wording have been taken from R. A. Foakes's edition of Coleridge's *Lectures 1808–1819: On Literature* (1987).

2. Coleridge here applies the distinction between fancy and imagination presented in *Biographia Literaria*, chap. 13, to a passage from the narrative poem *Venus and Adonis* (lines 361–64).
3. *Venus and Adonis*, lines 815–16.

Lo, here the gentle lark, weary of rest,
From his moist cabinet mounts up on high
And wakes the morning, from whose silver breast
The sun ariseth in his majesty;
    Who doth the world so gloriously behold
    That cedar tops and hills seem burnished gold.

And lastly, which belongs only to a great poet, the power of so carrying on the eye of the reader as to make him almost lose the consciousness of words—to make him *see* everything—and this without exciting any painful or laborious attention, without any *anatomy* of description (a fault not uncommon in descriptive poetry) but with the sweetness and easy movement of nature.

Lastly, he previously to his dramas, gave proof of a most profound, energetic, and philosophical mind, without which he might have been a very delightful poet, but not the great dramatic poet. * * * But chance and his powerful instinct combined to lead him to his proper province—in the conquest of which we are to consider both the difficulties that opposed him, and the advantages.

1808

[MECHANIC VS. ORGANIC FORM][4]

The subject of the present lecture is no less than a question submitted to your understandings, emancipated from national prejudice: Are the plays of Shakespeare works of rude uncultivated genius, in which the splendor of the parts compensates, if aught can compensate, for the barbarous shapelessness and irregularity of the whole? To which not only the French critics, but even his own English admirers, say [yes]. Or is the form equally admirable with the matter, the judgment of the great poet not less deserving of our wonder than his genius? Or to repeat the question in other words, is Shakespeare a great dramatic poet on account only of those beauties and excellencies which he possesses in common with the ancients, but with diminished claims to our love and honor to the full extent of his difference from them? Or are these very differences additional proofs of poetic wisdom, at once results and symbols of living power as contrasted with lifeless mechanism, of free and rival originality as contradistinguished from servile imitation, or more accurately, [from] a blind copying of effects instead of a true imitation of the essential principles? Imagine not I am about to oppose genius to rules. No! the comparative value of these rules is the very cause to be tried. The spirit of poetry, like all other living powers, must of necessity circumscribe itself by rules, were it only to unite power with beauty. It must embody in order to reveal itself; but a living body is of necessity an organized one—and what is organization but the connection of parts to a whole, so that each part is at once end and means! This is no discovery of criticism; it is a necessity of the human mind—

---

4. Coleridge is opposing the view that because Shakespeare violates the critical "rules" based on classical drama—the unities, for instance—his dramatic successes are marred by his irregularities and reflect the work of an uncultivated genius that operates without artistry or judgment. His argument is based on a distinction between the "mechanical form" central to earlier critical assess-ments and "organic form." Mechanical form results from imposing a system of preexisting rules on the literary material. Shakespeare's organic form, on the other hand, evolves like a plant by an inner principle and according to the unique laws of its own growth, until it achieves an organic unity.

and all nations have felt and obeyed it, in the invention of meter and measured sounds as the vehicle and involucrum[5] of poetry, itself a fellow growth from the same life, even as the bark is to the tree.

No work of true genius dare want its appropriate form; neither indeed is there any danger of this. As it must not, so neither can it, be lawless! For it is even this that constitutes its genius—the power of acting creatively under laws of its own origination. How then comes it that not only single Zoili,[6] but whole nations have combined in unhesitating condemnation of our great dramatist, as a sort of African nature, fertile in beautiful monsters, as a wild heath where islands of fertility look greener from the surrounding waste, where the loveliest plants now shine out among unsightly weeds and now are choked by their parasitic growth, so intertwined that we cannot disentangle the weed without snapping the flower. In this statement I have had no reference to the vulgar abuse of Voltaire,[7] save as far as his charges are coincident with the decisions of his commentators and (so they tell you) his almost idolatrous admirers. The true ground of the mistake, as has been well remarked by a continental critic,[8] lies in the confounding mechanical regularity with organic form. The form is mechanic when on any given material we impress a predetermined form, not necessarily arising out of the properties of the material, as when to a mass of wet clay we give whatever shape we wish it to retain when hardened. The organic form, on the other hand, is innate; it shapes as it develops itself from within, and the fullness of its development is one and the same with the perfection of its outward form. Such is the life, such the form. Nature, the prime genial[9] artist, inexhaustible in diverse powers, is equally inexhaustible in forms. Each exterior is the physiognomy of the being within, its true image reflected and thrown out from the concave mirror. And even such is the appropriate excellence of her chosen poet, of our own Shakespeare, himself a nature humanized, a genial understanding directing self-consciously a power and an implicit wisdom deeper than consciousness.

1812   1930

From The Statesman's Manual

[ON SYMBOL AND ALLEGORY][1]

The histories and political economy[2] of the present and preceding century partake in the general contagion of its mechanic philosophy, and are the *prod-*

---

5. Outer covering of part of a plant.
6. Plural of "Zoilus," who in classical times was the standard example of a bad critic.
7. The French writer Voltaire (1694–1778) vexed British nationalists with his description of Shakespeare as a barbarous, irregular, and sometimes indecent natural genius.
8. August Wilhelm Schlegel (1767–1845), German critic and literary historian, whose *Lectures on Dramatic Art and Literature* (1808–09) proposed the distinction between mechanical and organic form that Coleridge develops in this lecture.
9. Creative.
1. Coleridge published *The Statesman's Manual,*

or *The Bible the Best Guide to Political Skill and Foresight* in 1816; it was intended to show that the Scriptures, properly interpreted, provide the universal principles that should guide lawmakers in meeting the political and economic emergencies of that troubled era. His discussion there of symbol, in contradistinction both to allegory and to metaphor, has been often cited and elaborated in treatments of symbolism in poetry. Coleridge's analysis, however, is directed not to poetry but to his view that the persons and events in biblical history signify timeless and universal, as well as particular and local, truths.
2. The increasingly prestigious intellectual discipline of economics.

uct of an unenlivened generalizing Understanding. In the Scriptures they are the living *educts*[3] of the Imagination; of that reconciling and mediatory power, which incorporating the Reason in Images of the Sense, and organizing (as it were) the flux of the Senses by the permanence and self-circling energies of the Reason, gives birth to a system of symbols, harmonious in themselves, and consubstantial with the truths, of which they are the *conductors*. These are the Wheels which Ezekiel beheld, when the hand of the Lord was upon him, and he saw visions of God as he sat among the captives by the river of Chebar. *Whithersoever the Spirit was to go, the wheels went, and thither was their spirit to go: for the spirit of the living creature was in the wheels also.*[4] The truths and the symbols that represent them move in conjunction and form the living chariot that bears up (for *us*) the throne of the Divine Humanity. Hence, by a derivative, indeed, but not a divided, influence, and though in a secondary yet in more than a metaphorical sense, the Sacred Book is worthily intitled *the* WORD OF GOD. Hence too, its contents present to us the stream of time continuous as Life and a symbol of Eternity, inasmuch as the Past and the Future are virtually contained in the Present. According therefore to our relative position on its banks the Sacred History becomes prophetic, the Sacred Prophecies historical, while the power and substance of both inhere in its Laws, its Promises, and its Comminations.[5] In the Scriptures therefore both Facts and Persons must of necessity have a twofold significance, a past and a future, a temporary and a perpetual, a particular and a universal application. They must be at once Portraits and Ideals.

Eheu! paupertina philosophia in paupertinam religionem ducit:[6]—A hunger-bitten and idea-less philosophy naturally produces a starveling and comfortless religion. It is among the miseries of the present age that it recognizes no medium between *Literal* and *Metaphorical*. Faith is either to be buried in the dead letter,[7] or its name and honors usurped by a counterfeit product of the mechanical understanding, which in the blindness of self-complacency confounds SYMBOLS with ALLEGORIES. Now an Allegory is but a translation of abstract notions into a picture-language which is itself nothing but an abstraction from objects of the senses; the principal being more worthless even than its phantom proxy, both alike unsubstantial, and the former shapeless to boot. On the other hand a Symbol (ὁ ἔστιν ἀεὶ ταυτηγόρικον)[8] is characterized by a translucence of the Special[9] in the Individual or of the General in the Especial or of the Universal in the General. Above all by the translucence of the Eternal through and in the Temporal. It always partakes of the Reality which it renders intelligible; and while it enunciates the whole, abides itself as a living part in that Unity, of which it is the representative. The other are but empty echoes which the fancy arbitrarily associates with apparitions of matter, less beautiful but not less shadowy than the sloping orchard or hillside pasture-field seen in the transparent lake below. Alas! for the flocks that are to be led

3. Those things that are educed—i.e., brought forth, evolved.
4. Slightly altered from the prophet Ezekiel's vision of the Chariot of God, when he had been "among the captives by the river of Chebar" (Ezekiel 1.1–20). Ezekiel was among the Jews who had been taken into captivity in Babylonia by King Nebuchadnezzar in 597 B.C.E. He was put in a community of Jewish captives at Tel-Abib on the banks of the Chebar canal.

5. Divine threats of punishment for sins.
6. Alas! a poverty-stricken philosophy leads to a poverty-stricken religion (Latin).
7. I.e., the Scriptures read entirely literally.
8. Which is always tautegorical (Greek). Coleridge coined this word and elsewhere defined "tautegorical" as "expressing the *same* subject but with a difference."
9. That which pertains to the species.

forth to such pastures! *"It shall even be as when the hungry dreameth, and behold! he eateth; but he waketh and his soul is empty: or as when the thirsty dreameth, and behold he drinketh; but he awaketh and is faint!"*[1] * * *

* * * The fact therefore, that the mind of man in its own primary and constitutional forms represents the laws of nature, is a mystery which of itself should suffice to make us religious:[2] for it is a problem of which God is the only solution, God, the one before all, and of all, and through all!—True natural philosophy is comprised in the study of the science and language of *symbols*. The power delegated to nature is all in every part: and by a symbol I mean, not a metaphor or allegory or any other figure of speech or form of fancy, but an actual and essential part of that, the whole of which it represents. Thus our Lord speaks symbolically when he says that "the eye is the light of the body."[3] The genuine naturalist is a dramatic poet in his own line: and such as our myriad-minded Shakespeare is, compared with the Racines and Metastasios,[4] such and by a similar process of self-transformation would the man be, compared with the Doctors of the mechanic school,[5] who should construct his physiology on the heaven-descended, Know Thyself.[6]

[THE SATANIC HERO][7]

* * * In its state of immanence (or indwelling) in reason and religion, the WILL appears indifferently, as wisdom or as love: two names of the same power, the former more intelligential,[8] the latter more spiritual, the former more frequent in the Old, the latter in the New Testament. But in its utmost abstraction and consequent state of reprobation,[9] the Will becomes satanic pride and rebellious self-idolatry in the relations of the spirit to itself, and remorseless despotism relatively to others; the more hopeless as the more obdurate by its subjugation of sensual impulses, by its superiority to toil and pain and pleasure; in short, by the fearful resolve to find in itself alone the one absolute motive of action, under which all other motives from within and from without must be either subordinated or crushed.

This is the character which Milton has so philosophically as well as sublimely embodied in the Satan of his Paradise Lost. Alas! too often has it been embodied in *real* life! Too often has it given a dark and savage grandeur to the historic page! And wherever it has appeared, under whatever circumstances of time and country, the same ingredients have gone to its composition; and it has been identified by the same attributes. Hope in which there is no Cheerfulness; Steadfastness within and immovable Resolve, with outward Restlessness and whirling Activity; Violence with Guile; Temerity with Cunning; and, as the result of all, Interminableness of Object with perfect Indifference of

1. Slightly altered from Isaiah 29.8.
2. This paragraph is from appendix C of *The Statesman's Manual*.
3. Matthew 6.22: "The light of the body is the eye."
4. Pietro Metastasio (1698–1782), a minor Italian poet and author of opera librettos. Jean Racine (1639–1699), the great French author of verse tragedies. Set on dissociating himself from his youthful support for the Revolution, Coleridge enjoyed finding fault with French philosophy and culture. "Naturalist": one who studies natural science.
5. I.e., learned men who hold a mechanistic philosophy of nature.

6. The Roman Juvenal, in *Satires* 11.27 of Horace (Quintas Horatius Flaccus), had said that "From Heaven it descends, 'Know Thyself.' " The original saying, "Know Thyself," was attributed by classical authors to the Delphic oracle.
7. From *The Statesman's Manual*, appendix C. Coleridge analyzes the character of Milton's Satan and goes on to recognize, and to warn his age against, the appeal of that type of Romantic hero (exemplified above all by the protagonists in Byron's romances and in his drama, *Manfred*), which was in large part modeled on the Satan of *Paradise Lost*.
8. Intellectual.
9. In its theological sense: rejection by God.

Means; these are the qualities that have constituted the COMMANDING GENIUS! these are the Marks that have characterized the Masters of Mischief, the Liberticides, and mighty Hunters of Mankind, from NIMROD[1] to NAPOLEON. And from inattention to the possibility of such a character as well as from ignorance of its elements, even men of honest intentions too frequently become fascinated. Nay, whole nations have been so far duped by this want of insight and reflection as to regard with palliative admiration, instead of wonder and abhorrence, the Molocks[2] of human nature, who are indebted, for the far larger portion of their meteoric success, to their total want of principle, and who surpass the generality of their fellow creatures in one act of courage only, that of daring to say with their whole heart, "Evil, be thou my good!"[3]—All *system* so far is power; and a *systematic* criminal, self-consistent and entire in wickedness, who entrenches villainy within villainy, and barricades crime by crime, has removed a world of obstacles by the mere decision, that he will have no obstacles, but those of force and brute matter.

1816

1. In Genesis 10.9 Nimrod is described as "a mighty hunter before the Lord." The passage was traditionally interpreted to signify that Nimrod hunted down men, hence that he was the prototype of all tyrants and bloody conquerors.
2. Molochs, monsters of evil. In the Old Testa-
ment Moloch is an idol to whom firstborn children are sacrificed. Milton adopted the name for the warlike fallen angel in Satan's company (see *Paradise Lost* 2.43–107).
3. Spoken by Satan, *Paradise Lost* 4.110.

CHARLES LAMB
1775–1834

Charles Lamb was a near contemporary of Wordsworth and Coleridge. He numbered these two poets among his close friends, published his own early poems in combination with those of Coleridge in 1796 and 1797, and supported the *Lyrical Ballads* and some of the other new poetry of his time. Yet Lamb lacks almost all the traits and convictions we think of as characteristically "Romantic." He happily lived all his life in the city and its environs. He could not abide Shelley or his poetry, and he distrusted Coleridge's supernaturalism and Wordsworth's oracular sublimities and religion of nature, preferring those elements in their poems that were human and realistic. In an age when many of the important writers were fervent radicals and some became equally fervent reactionaries, Lamb remained uncommitted in both politics and religion, and although on intimate terms with such dedicated reformers as William Hazlitt, William Godwin, Thomas Holcroft, and Leigh Hunt, he chose them as friends, as he said, not for their opinions but "for some individuality of character which they manifested." In his own writings he shared Wordsworth's concern with memories' power to transform the present moment and, like him, interjected a sense of the ideal into his representations of the actual and everyday. "The streets of London," Hazlitt wrote, assessing the essays Lamb published under the pseudonym Elia in the *London Magazine*, "are his fairy-land, teeming with wonder, with life and interest to his retrospective glance, as it did to the eager eye of childhood."

Lamb was born in London at the Inner Temple, center of the English legal profession. His father, who began his working life as a footman, was assistant to a lawyer there. His paternal as well as maternal grandparents were servants. At the age of seven he entered Christ's Hospital, the "Bluecoat School" of his essay "Christ's Hospital Five-and-Thirty Years Ago." Childhood ended early. He left the school before he was fifteen and soon thereafter became a clerk in the accounting department of the East India Company, a huge commercial house, where he remained for thirty-three years. His adult life was quiet and unadventurous, but under its calm surface lay great tragedy. When he was twenty-two his beloved sister, Mary, ten years his senior, exhausted by her labors as a dressmaker and the work of caring for her invalid parents, began to show signs of a breakdown. One day she turned in a manic rage on the little girl who was her apprentice. When Mrs. Lamb tried to intercede, her daughter stabbed her in the heart. The jury's verdict was lunacy, but the intercession of her father's former employer spared Mary permanent confinement in an asylum. Instead, she was remanded to the custody of Charles, who devoted the rest of his life to her and their common household. Mary's attacks of insanity recurred, and when the terribly familiar symptoms began to show themselves, Charles and Mary would walk arm in arm and weeping to the asylum, carrying a straitjacket with them.

Most of the time, however, Mary was her normally serene and gracious self, and shared her brother's love of company and genius for friendship. The evening gatherings at the Lambs' attracted a varied company that included many of the leading writers and artists of England. Charles drew furiously on a pipe of strong tobacco and drank copiously; as the alcohol eased his habitual stammer, his puns and practical jokes grew ever more outrageous. He had, in fact, a complex temperament, in which the playfulness overlay a somber melancholy and the eccentricity sometimes manifested a touch of malice.

To supplement his salary at the East India House, Lamb had early turned to writing in a variety of literary forms: sonnets; blank verse; a sentimental novel; a tragedy; and a farce, Mr. H——, which was hissed by the audience, including its honest author, when it was produced at Drury Lane (the uneasiness with the theater that informs his essay "On the Tragedies of Shakespeare" probably reflects this experience). He also collaborated with his sister, Mary, on a series of children's books, including the excellent Tales from Shakespeare, and wrote some brilliant critical commentaries in his anthology, important for the Elizabethan revival of that period, titled Specimens of English Dramatic Poets Who Lived about the Time of Shakespeare. Not until 1820, however, at the age of forty-five, did Lamb discover the form that would make his name, when he began to write essays for John Scott's new London Magazine.

Lamb's achievement in those contributions to the London was to accommodate the intimacies of the familiar essay, a genre dating back to Montaigne in the sixteenth century, to a modern world of magazine writing that aimed to reach a general public. The Essays of Elia make the magazine—an impersonal medium that contributed conspicuously to the information overload of the age—appear to be a forum in which a reader might really know an author. A sense of the paradoxes of that project—a sense that the illusions of personality in the personal essay might be easily debunked—is never far away in Lamb's writings, lending a fascinating edge to their charm and complicating the autobiographical impulse that seems to link them to the works of his contemporaries. Under the pseudonym Elia, which, Lamb said, was the name of an Italian clerk he had known briefly while employed in the South Sea House, Lamb projects in his essays the character of a man who is whimsical but strong-willed, self-deprecating yet self-absorbed, with strong likes and dislikes, a specialist in nostalgia and in that humor which balances delicately on the verge of pathos. But Elia is also, as Lamb noted, an anagram for "a lie": the essays' seemingly unguarded self-revelation is intertwined with the cunning of a deliberate and dedicated artist in prose. And to write about himself Lamb developed a prose style that was colored throughout by archaic words and expressions that continually alluded to literary precursors, including the works of other eccentrics such as Robert Burton and Laurence Sterne—as if he were suggesting that he was most distinctively himself when most immersed in his beloved old books.

From On the Tragedies of Shakespeare, Considered with Reference to Their Fitness for Stage Representation[1]

* * * [S]uch is the instantaneous nature of the impressions which we take in at the eye and ear at a play-house, compared with the slow apprehension oftentimes of the understanding in reading, that we are apt not only to sink the play-writer in the consideration which we pay to the actor, but even to identify in our minds, in a perverse manner, the actor with the character which he represents. It is difficult for a frequent play-goer to disembarrass the idea of Hamlet from the person and voice of Mr. K. We speak of Lady Macbeth, while we are in reality thinking of Mrs. S.[2] * * *

Never let me be so ungrateful as to forget the very high degree of satisfaction which I received some years back from seeing for the first time a tragedy of Shakespeare performed, in which these two great performers sustained the principal parts. It seemed to embody and realize conceptions which had hitherto assumed no distinct shape. But dearly do we pay all our life after for this juvenile pleasure, this sense of distinctness. When the novelty is past, we find to our cost that instead of realizing an idea, we have only materialized and brought down a fine vision to the standard of flesh and blood. We have let go a dream, in quest of an unattainable substance.

How cruelly this operates upon the mind, to have its free conceptions thus cramped and pressed down to the measure of a strait-lacing actuality, may be judged from that delightful sensation of freshness, with which we turn to those plays of Shakespeare which have escaped being performed. * * *

It may seem a paradox, but I cannot help being of opinion that the plays of Shakespeare are less calculated for performance on a stage than those of almost any other dramatist whatever. Their distinguished excellence is a reason that they should be so. There is so much in them, which comes not under the province of acting, with which eye, and tone, and gesture, have nothing to do.

The glory of the scenic art is to personate passion, and the turns of passion; and the more coarse and palpable the passion is, the more hold upon the eyes and ears of the spectators the performer obviously possesses. For this reason, scolding scenes, scenes where two persons talk themselves into a fit of fury, and then in a surprising manner talk themselves out of it again, have always been the most popular upon our stage. And the reason is plain, because the spectators are here most palpably appealed to, they are the proper judges in this war of words, they are the legitimate ring that should be formed round such "intellectual prize-fighters." Talking is the direct object of the imitation here. But in all the best dramas, and in Shakespeare above all, how obvious it is, that the form of *speaking*, whether it be in soliloquy or dialogue, is only a medium, and often a highly artificial one, for putting the reader or spectator into possession of that knowledge of the inner structure and workings of a mind in a character, which he could otherwise never have arrived at *in that form of composition* by any gift short of intuition. We do here as we do with novels written in the *epistolary form*. How many improprieties, perfect solecisms in letter-writing, do we put up with in *Clarissa*[3] and other

1. Published under Lamb's name in the magazine *The Reflector* in 1811.
2. Acclaimed actors John Philip Kemble (1757–

1823) and his sister Sarah Siddons (1755–1831).
3. Samuel Richardson's novel in letters, published 1747–48, admired across Europe for its illumina-

books, for the sake of the delight which that form upon the whole gives us.

But the practice of stage representation reduces every thing to a controversy of elocution. Every character, from the boisterous blasphemings of Bajazet[4] to the shrinking timidity of womanhood, must play the orator. * * *

The character of Hamlet is perhaps that by which, since the days of Betterton,[5] a succession of popular performers have had the greatest ambition to distinguish themselves. The length of the part may be one of their reasons. But for the character itself, we find it in a play, and therefore we judge it a fit subject of dramatic representation. The play itself abounds in maxims and reflections beyond any other, and therefore we consider it as a proper vehicle for conveying moral instruction. But Hamlet himself—what does he suffer meanwhile by being dragged forth as a public schoolmaster, to give lectures to the crowd! Why, nine parts in ten of what Hamlet does, are transactions between himself and his moral sense, they are the effusions of his solitary musings, which he retires to holes and corners and the most sequestered parts of the palace to pour forth; or rather, they are the silent meditations with which his bosom is bursting, reduced to *words* for the sake of the reader, who must else remain ignorant of what is passing there. These profound sorrows, these light-and-noise-abhorring ruminations, which the tongue scarce dares utter to deaf walls and chambers, how can they be represented by a gesticulating actor, who comes and mouths them out before an audience, making four hundred people his confidants at once? I say not that it is the fault of the actor so to do; he must pronounce them *ore rotundo*,[6] he must accompany them with his eye; he must insinuate them into his auditory by some trick of eye, tone, or gesture, or he fails. *He must be thinking all the while of his appearance, because he knows that all the while the spectators are judging of it.* And this is the way to represent the shy, negligent, retiring Hamlet.

It is true that there is no other mode of conveying a vast quantity of thought and feeling to a great portion of the audience, who otherwise would never earn it for themselves by reading, and the intellectual acquisition gained this way may, for aught I know, be inestimable; but I am not arguing that Hamlet should not be acted, but how much Hamlet is made another thing by being acted. * * *

The truth is, the Characters of Shakespeare are so much the objects of meditation rather than of interest or curiosity as to their actions, that while we are reading any of his great criminal characters,—Macbeth, Richard, even Iago,—we think not so much of the crimes which they commit, as of the ambition, the aspiring spirit, the intellectual activity, which prompts them to overleap those moral fences. * * * But when we see these things represented, the acts which they do are comparatively everything, their impulses nothing. The state of sublime emotion into which we are elevated by those images of night and horror which Macbeth is made to utter, that solemn prelude with which he entertains the time till the bell shall strike which is to call him to murder Duncan,[7]—when we no longer read it in a book, when we have given up that vantage-ground of abstraction which reading possesses over seeing, and come to see a man in his bodily shape before our eyes actually preparing

---

tion of the mysteries of the human heart.
4. Ottoman sultan; more than one dramatic character is based on this historical figure, but Lamb likely refers to a performance of Nicholas Rowe's *Tamerlane* (first staged 1701).

5. Thomas Betterton (1635?–1710), acclaimed tragedian.
6. Latin: "with well turned speech" or, literally, "with rounded mouth."
7. *Macbeth* 2.1.

to commit a murder, if the acting be true and impressive, as I have witnessed it in Mr. K.'s performance of that part, the painful anxiety about the act, the natural longing to prevent it while it yet seems unperpetrated, the too close pressing semblance of reality, give a pain and an uneasiness which totally destroy all the delight which the words in the book convey, where the deed doing never presses upon us with the painful sense of presence: it rather seems to belong to history,—to something past and inevitable, if it has any thing to do with time at all. The sublime images, the poetry alone, is that which is present to our minds in the reading.

So to see Lear acted,—to see an old man tottering about the stage with a walking-stick, turned out of doors by his daughters in a rainy night, has nothing in it but what is painful and disgusting. We want to take him into shelter and relieve him. That is all the feeling which the acting of Lear ever produced in me. But the Lear of Shakespeare cannot be acted. The contemptible machinery by which they mimic the storm which he goes out in, is not more inadequate to represent the horrors of the real elements, than any actor can be to represent Lear: they might more easily propose to personate the Satan of Milton upon a stage, or one of Michael Angelo's terrible figures. The greatness of Lear is not in corporal dimension, but in intellectual; the explosions of his passion are terrible as a volcano; they are storms turning up and disclosing to the bottom that sea, his mind, with all its vast riches. It is his mind which is laid bare. This case of flesh and blood seems too insignificant to be thought on; even as he himself neglects it. On the stage we see nothing but corporal infirmities and weakness, the impotence of rage; while we read it, we see not Lear, but we are Lear,—we are in his mind, we are sustained by a grandeur which baffles the malice of daughters and storms; in the aberrations of his reason, we discover a mighty irregular power of reasoning, immethodized from the ordinary purposes of life, but exerting its powers, as the wind bloweth where it listeth,[8] at will upon the corruptions and abuses of mankind. * * *

Lear is essentially impossible to be represented on a stage. But how many dramatic personages are there in Shakespeare, which, though more tractable and feasible (if I may so speak) than Lear, yet from some circumstance, some adjunct to their character, are improper to be shewn to our bodily eye. Othello for instance. Nothing can be more soothing, more flattering to the nobler parts of our natures, than to read of a young Venetian lady of highest extraction, through the force of love and from a sense of merit in him whom she loved, laying aside every consideration of kindred, and country, and colour, and wedding with a *coal-black Moor*—(for such he is represented, in the imperfect state of knowledge respecting foreign countries in those days, compared with our own, or in compliance with popular notions, though the Moors are now well enough known to be by many shades less unworthy of a white woman's fancy)—it is the perfect triumph of virtue over accidents,[9] of the imagination over the senses. She sees Othello's colour in his mind.[1] But upon the stage, when the imagination is no longer the ruling faculty, but we are left to our poor unassisted senses, I appeal to every one that has seen Othello played, whether he did not, on the contrary, sink Othello's mind in his colour; whether he did not find something extremely revolting in the courtship and wedded caresses of Othello and Desdemona; and whether the actual sight of the thing

<hr />

8. Echo of Christ's discussion of the mysteries of spiritual rebirth in John 3.8.
9. "Accidents" in the sense used for properties or qualities that are extraneous to—i.e., not of the essence of—an object.
1. *Othello* 1.3.247.

did not over-weigh all that beautiful compromise which we make in reading. And the reason it should do so is obvious, because there is just so much reality presented to our senses as to give a perception of disagreement, with not enough of belief in the internal motives,—all that which is unseen,—to overpower and reconcile the first and obvious prejudices. What we see upon a stage is body and bodily action; what we are conscious of in reading is almost exclusively the mind, and its movements: and this I think may sufficiently account for the very different sort of delight with which the same play so often affects us in the reading and the seeing.

1811   1811

Christ's Hospital Five-and-Thirty Years Ago[1]

In Mr. Lamb's *Works,* published a year or two since, I find a magnificent eulogy on my old school, such as it was, or now appears to him to have been, between the years 1782 and 1789. It happens very oddly that my own standing at Christ's was nearly corresponding with his; and, with all gratitude to him for his enthusiasm for the cloisters, I think he has contrived to bring together whatever can be said in praise of them, dropping all the other side of the argument most ingeniously.

I remember L. at school, and can well recollect that he had some peculiar advantages, which I and others of his schoolfellows had not. His friends lived in town, and were near at hand; and he had the privilege of going to see them almost as often as he wished, through some invidious distinction, which was denied to us. The present worthy subtreasurer to the Inner Temple[2] can explain how that happened. He had his tea and hot rolls in a morning, while we were battening upon our quarter of a penny loaf—our *crug*—moistened with attenuated small beer, in wooden piggins, smacking of the pitched leathern jack[3] it was poured from. Our Monday's milk porritch, blue and tasteless, and the pease soup of Saturday, coarse and choking, were enriched for him with a slice of "extraordinary bread and butter," from the hot loaf of the Temple. The Wednesday's mess of millet, somewhat less repugnant—(we had three banyan to four meat days[4] in the week)—was endeared to his palate with a lump of double-refined,[5] and a smack of ginger (to make it go down the more glibly) or the fragrant cinnamon. In lieu of our *half-pickled* Sundays, or *quite fresh* boiled beef on Thursdays (strong as *caro equina*[6]), with detestable marigolds floating in the pail to poison the broth—our scanty mutton scrags on

1. Christ's Hospital, London (founded in 1552 by Edward VI), was run as a free boarding school for the sons of middle-class parents in straitened financial circumstances. Its students were known as "Bluecoat Boys," from their uniform of a long blue gown and yellow stockings. Lamb had in 1813 published a magazine article, "Recollections of Christ's Hospital," that the present essay undertakes to supplement by presenting the less formal side of school life. The "I" or narrator of the essay is Elia—a device that allows Lamb to combine his own experiences (L.'s) with those of Coleridge, his older contemporary at the school.
2. Randal Norris, who had befriended young

Charles Lamb. The Inner Temple is one of the four Inns of Court, the center of the English legal profession.
3. A leather vessel coated on the outside with pitch. "Crug": bread (slang). "Small beer": beer low in alcoholic content. "Piggins": small wooden pails.
4. "Banyan . . . days": nautical term for days when no meat is served; it derives from *banian,* a member of a Hindu caste to whom meat is forbidden. "Millet": a cereal.
5. Sugar.
6. Horsemeat (Latin).

Friday—and rather more savory, but grudging, portions of the same flesh, rotten-roasted[7] or rare, on the Tuesdays (the only dish which excited our appetites, and disappointed our stomachs, in almost equal proportion)—he had his hot plate of roast veal, or the more tempting griskin[8] (exotics unknown to our palates), cooked in the paternal kitchen (a great thing), and brought him daily by his maid or aunt! I remember the good old relative (in whom love forbade pride) squatting down upon some odd stone in a by-nook of the cloisters, disclosing the viands (of higher regale than those cates which the ravens ministered to the Tishbite);[9] and the contending passions of L. at the unfolding. There was love for the bringer; shame for the thing brought, and the manner of its bringing; sympathy for those who were too many to share in it; and, at top of all, hunger (eldest, strongest of the passions!) predominant, breaking down the stony fences of shame, and awkwardness, and a troubling over-consciousness.

I was a poor friendless boy. My parents, and those who should care for me, were far away. Those few acquaintances of theirs, which they could reckon upon being kind to me in the great city, after a little forced notice, which they had the grace to take of me on my first arrival in town, soon grew tired of my holiday visits. They seemed to them to recur too often, though I thought them few enough; and, one after another, they all failed me, and I felt myself alone among six hundred playmates.

O the cruelty of separating a poor lad from his early homestead! The yearnings which I used to have towards it in those unfledged years! How, in my dreams, would my native town (far in the west) come back, with its church, and trees, and faces! How I would wake weeping, and in the anguish of my heart exclaim upon sweet Calne in Wiltshire![1]

To this late hour of my life, I trace impressions left by the recollections of those friendless holidays. The long warm days of summer never return but they bring with them a gloom from the haunting memory of those *whole-day leaves*, when, by some strange arrangement, we were turned out for the livelong day, upon our own hands, whether we had friends to go to or none. I remember those bathing excursions to the New River which L. recalls with such relish, better, I think, than he can—for he was a home-seeking lad, and did not much care for such water pastimes: How merrily we would sally forth into the fields; and strip under the first warmth of the sun; and wanton like young dace[2] in the streams; getting us appetites for noon, which those of us that were penniless (our scanty morning crust long since exhausted) had not the means of allaying—while the cattle, and the birds, and the fishes were at feed about us and we had nothing to satisfy our cravings—the very beauty of the day, and the exercise of the pastime, and the sense of liberty, setting a keener edge upon them! How faint and languid, finally, we would return, towards nightfall, to our desired morsel, half-rejoicing, half-reluctant that the hours of our uneasy liberty had expired!

It was worse in the days of winter, to go prowling about the streets objectless—shivering at cold windows of print shops, to extract a little amusement; or haply, as a last resort in the hopes of a little novelty, to pay a fifty-times

7. Overdone. "Scrags": necks.
8. The lean part of a loin of pork.
9. The prophet Elijah, who was fed by the ravens in 1 Kings 17. "Cates": delicacies.

1. Coleridge had come to school from Ottery St. Mary, Devonshire, in the southwest of England.
2. A small quick-darting fish.

repeated visit (where our individual faces should be as well known to the warden as those of his own charges) to the Lions in the Tower—to whose levee, by courtesy immemorial, we had a prescriptive title to admission.[3]

L.'s governor (so we called the patron who presented us to the foundation)[4] lived in a manner under his paternal roof. Any complaint which he had to make was sure of being attended to. This was understood at Christ's, and was an effectual screen to him against the severity of masters, or worse tyranny of the monitors. The oppressions of these young brutes are heart-sickening to call to recollection. I have been called out of my bed, and *waked for the purpose,* in the coldest winter nights—and this not once, but night after night— in my shirt, to receive the discipline of a leathern thong and eleven other sufferers, because it pleased my callow overseer, when there has been any talking heard after we were gone to bed, to make the six last beds in the dormitory, where the youngest children of us slept, answerable for an offense they neither dared to commit nor had the power to hinder. The same execrable tyranny drove the younger part of us from the fires, when our feet were perishing with snow; and, under the cruelest penalties, forbade the indulgence of a drink of water when we lay in sleepless summer nights fevered with the season and the day's sports.

There was one H——, who, I learned, in after days was seen expiating some maturer offense in the hulks.[5] (Do I flatter myself in fancying that this might be the planter of that name, who suffered—at Nevis, I think, or St. Kitts[6]— some few years since? My friend Tobin was the benevolent instrument of bringing him to the gallows.) This petty Nero actually branded a boy who had offended him with a red-hot iron; and nearly starved forty of us with exacting contributions, to the one-half of our bread, to pamper a young ass, which, incredible as it may seem, with the connivance of the nurse's daughter (a young flame of his) he had contrived to smuggle in, and keep upon the leads[7] of the *ward,* as they called our dormitories. This game went on for better than a week, till the foolish beast, not able to fare well but he must cry roast meat— happier than Caligula's minion,[8] could he have kept his own counsel—but foolisher, alas! than any of his species in the fables—waxing fat, and kicking, in the fullness of bread, one unlucky minute would needs proclaim his good fortune to the world below; and, laying out his simple throat, blew such a ram's-horn blast, as (toppling down the walls of his own Jericho)[9] set concealment any longer at defiance. The client was dismissed, with certain attentions, to Smithfield; but I never understood that the patron underwent any censure on the occasion. This was in the stewardship of L.'s admired Perry.[1]

Under the same *facile* administration, can L. have forgotten the cool impunity with which the nurses used to carry away openly, in open platters, for their own tables, one out of two of every hot joint, which the careful matron had been seeing scrupulously weighed out for our dinners? These things were

3. The Bluecoat Boys had the right of free admission to the royal menagerie, then housed in the Tower of London. "Levee": a formal morning reception.
4. I.e., who vouched for a candidate for entrance to Christ's Hospital. Lamb's patron was Samuel Salt, a lawyer and member of Parliament for whom Lamb's father served as clerk.
5. Prison ship. (In Lamb's time the plural "hulks" had come to be used for the singular.)

6. Islands in the West Indies.
7. A flat roof.
8. The favorite horse of the Roman emperor Caligula, who was fed gilded oats and appointed to the post of chief consul.
9. Joshua toppled the walls of Jericho by trumpet blasts (Joshua 6.16–20).
1. John Perry, steward of the school, described in Lamb's earlier essay. "Smithfield": a market for horses and cattle.

daily practiced in that magnificent apartment which L. (grown connoisseur since, we presume) praises so highly for the grand paintings "by Verrio,[2] and others," with which it is "hung round and adorned." But the sight of sleek, well-fed bluecoat boys in pictures was, at that time, I believe, little consolatory to him, or us, the living ones, who saw the better part of our provisions carried away before our faces by harpies; and ourselves reduced (with the Trojan in the hall of Dido)

> To feed our mind with idle portraiture.[3]

L. has recorded the repugnance of the school to *gags*, or the fat of fresh beef boiled; and sets it down to some superstition. But these unctuous morsels are never grateful[4] to young palates (children are universally fat-haters), and in strong, coarse, boiled meats, *unsalted*, are detestable. A *gag-eater* in our time was equivalent to a *ghoul*, and held in equal detestation.———suffered under the imputation.

> . . . 'Twas said
> He ate strange flesh.[5]

He was observed, after dinner, carefully to gather up the remnants left at his table (not many nor very choice fragments, you may credit me)—and, in an especial manner, these disreputable morsels, which he would convey away and secretly stow in the settle that stood at his bedside. None saw when he ate them. It was rumored that he privately devoured them in the night. He was watched, but no traces of such midnight practices were discoverable. Some reported that on leave-days he had been seen to carry out of the bounds a large blue check handkerchief, full of something. This then must be the accursed thing. Conjecture next was at work to imagine how he could dispose of it. Some said he sold it to the beggars. This belief generally prevailed. He went about moping. None spake to him. No one would play with him. He was excommunicated; put out of the pale of the school. He was too powerful a boy to be beaten, but he underwent every mode of that negative punishment which is more grievous than many stripes. Still he persevered. At length he was observed by two of his schoolfellows, who were determined to get at the secret, and had traced him one leave-day for the purpose, to enter a large worn-out building, such as there exist specimens of in Chancery Lane, which are let out to various scales of pauperism, with open door and a common staircase. After him they silently slunk in, and followed by stealth up four flights, and saw him tap at a poor wicket, which was opened by an aged woman, meanly clad. Suspicion was now ripened into certainty. The informers had secured their victim. They had him in their toils. Accusation was formally preferred, and retribution most signal was looked for. Mr. Hathaway, the then steward (for this happened a little after my time), with that patient sagacity which tempered all his conduct, determined to investigate the matter before he proceeded to sentence. The result was that the supposed mendicants, the receivers or purchasers of the mysterious scraps, turned out to be the parents of———
—, an honest couple come to decay—whom this seasonable supply had, in all

2. Antonio Verrio, Italian painter of the 17th century. While living in England, he painted a large picture of the mathematics students of Christ's Hospital being received by James II.
3. Virgil's *Aeneid* 1.464; Aeneas is inspecting the paintings in Dido's temple to Juno.
4. Pleasing.
5. Loosely quoted from Shakespeare's *Antony and Cleopatra* 1.4.67.

probability, saved from mendicancy; and that this young stork, at the expense of his own good name, had all this while been only feeding the old birds!— The governors on this occasion, much to their honor, voted a present relief to the family of————, and presented him with a silver medal. The lesson which the steward read upon RASH JUDGMENT, on the occasion of publicly delivering the medal to————, I believe would not be lost upon his auditory.—I had left school then, but I well remember————. He was a tall, shambling youth, with a cast in his eye, not at all calculated to conciliate hostile prejudices. I have since seen him carrying a baker's basket. I think I heard he did not do quite so well by himself as he had done by the old folks.

I was a hypochondriac[6] lad; and the sight of a boy in fetters, upon the day of my first putting on the blue clothes, was not exactly fitted to assuage the natural terrors of initiation. I was of tender years, barely turned of seven; and had only read of such things in books, or seen them but in dreams. I was told he had *run away*. This was the punishment for the first offense.—As a novice I was soon after taken to see the dungeons. These were little, square, Bedlam[7] cells, where a boy could just lie at his length upon straw and a blanket—a mattress, I think, was afterwards substituted—with a peep of light, let in askance, from a prison orifice at top, barely enough to read by. Here the poor boy was locked in by himself all day, without sight of any but the porter who brought him his bread and water—who *might not speak to him*—or of the beadle, who came twice a week to call him out to receive his periodical chastisement, which was almost welcome, because it separated him for a brief interval from solitude—and here he was shut up by himself *of nights* out of the reach of any sound, to suffer whatever horrors the weak nerves, and superstition incident to his time of life, might subject him to. This was the penalty for the second offense. Wouldst thou like, reader, to see what became of him in the next degree?

The culprit, who had been a third time an offender, and whose expulsion was at this time deemed irreversible, was brought forth, as at some solemn auto da fé, arrayed in uncouth and most appalling attire—all trace of his late "watchet weeds"[8] carefully effaced, he was exposed in a jacket resembling those which London lamplighters formerly delighted in, with a cap of the same. The effect of this divestiture was such as the ingenious devisers of it could have anticipated. With his pale and frighted features, it was as if some of those disfigurements in Dante[9] had seized upon him. In this disguisement he was brought into the hall (*L.'s favorite state room*), where awaited him the whole number of his schoolfellows, whose joint lessons and sports he was thenceforth to share no more; the awful presence of the steward, to be seen for the last time; of the executioner beadle, clad in his state robe for the occasion; and of two faces more, of direr import, because never but in these extremities visible. These were governors; two of whom by choice, or charter, were always accustomed to officiate at these *Ultima Supplicia;*[1] not to mitigate (so at least we understood it), but to enforce the uttermost stripe. Old Bamber Gascoigne, and Peter Aubert, I remember, were colleagues on one occasion,

6. Melancholy.
7. St. Mary of Bethlehem, an insane asylum in London.
8. Blue clothes. "Auto da fé": act of faith (literal trans.); the ceremony before the execution of

heretics under the Spanish Inquisition.
9. I.e., of the sinners in Dante's *Inferno;* see canto 20.
1. Extreme punishments (Latin).

when the beadle turning rather pale, a glass of brandy was ordered to prepare him for the mysteries. The scourging was, after the old Roman fashion, long and stately. The lictor[2] accompanied the criminal quite round the hall. We were generally too faint, with attending to the previous disgusting circumstances, to make accurate report with our eyes of the degree of corporal suffering inflicted. Report, of course, gave out the back knotty and livid. After scourging, he was made over, in his *San Benito*,[3] to his friends, if he had any (but commonly such poor runagates were friendless), or to his parish officer, who, to enhance the effect of the scene, had his station allotted to him on the outside of the hall gate.

These solemn pageantries were not played off so often as to spoil the general mirth of the community. We had plenty of exercise and recreation *after* school hours; and, for myself, I must confess that I was never happier than *in* them. The Upper and the Lower Grammar Schools were held in the same room; and an imaginary line only divided their bounds. Their character was as different as that of the inhabitants on the two sides of the Pyrenees. The Rev. James Boyer was the Upper master; but the Rev. Matthew Field presided over that portion of the apartment of which I had the good fortune to be a member. We lived a life as careless as birds. We talked and did just what we pleased, and nobody molested us. We carried an accidence, or a grammar, for form; but, for any trouble it gave us, we might take two years in getting through the verbs deponent,[4] and another two in forgetting all that we had learned about them. There was now and then the formality of saying a lesson, but if you had not learned it, a brush across the shoulders (just enough to disturb a fly) was the sole remonstrance. Field never used the rod; and in truth he wielded the cane with no great good will—holding it "like a dancer." It looked in his hands rather like an emblem than an instrument of authority; and an emblem, too, he was ashamed of. He was a good, easy man, that did not care to ruffle his own peace, nor perhaps set any great consideration upon the value of juvenile time. He came among us, now and then, but often stayed away whole days from us; and when he came it made no difference to us—he had his private room to retire to, the short time he stayed, to be out of the sound of our noise. Our mirth and uproar went on. We had classics of our own, without being beholden to "insolent Greece or haughty Rome,"[5] that passed current among us—*Peter Wilkins*—the *Adventures of the Hon. Captain Robert Boyle*—the *Fortunate Bluecoat Boy*[6]—and the like. Or we cultivated a turn for mechanic and scientific operations; making little sun-dials of paper; or weaving those ingenious parentheses called *cat cradles*; or making dry peas to dance upon the end of a tin pipe; or studying the art military over that laudable game "French and English,"[7] and a hundred other such devices to pass away the time—mixing the useful with the agreeable—as would have made the souls of Rousseau and John Locke[8] chuckle to have seen us.

Matthew Field belonged to that class of modest divines who affect to mix

2. A Roman officer who cleared the way for the chief magistrates.
3. The yellow robe worn by the condemned heretic at an auto da fé.
4. Verbs with an active meaning but passive form. "Accidence": a table of the declension of nouns and conjugation of verbs in Greek and Latin.
5. Ben Jonson's "To the Memory of . . . William Shakespeare," line 39.

6. All three were popular adventure stories or romances of the day.
7. A game in which contestants, with eyes closed, draw lines on a sheet of paper covered with dots. The winner is the contestant whose line touches the most dots.
8. Two philosophers who recommended systems of education that combined theory with practical experience.

in equal proportion the *gentleman*, the *scholar*, and the *Christian*; but, I know not how, the first ingredient is generally found to be the predominating dose in the composition. He was engaged in gay parties, or with his courtly bow at some episcopal levee, when he should have been attending upon us. He had for many years the classical charge of a hundred children, during the four or five first years of their education, and his very highest form seldom proceeded further than two or three of the introductory fables of Phaedrus.[9] How things were suffered to go on thus, I cannot guess. Boyer, who was the proper person to have remedied these abuses, always affected, perhaps felt, a delicacy in interfering in a province not strictly his own. I have not been without my suspicions, that he was not altogether displeased at the contrast we presented to his end of the school. We were a sort of Helots to his young Spartans.[1] He would sometimes, with ironic deference, send to borrow a rod of the Under Master, and then, with sardonic grin, observe to one of his upper boys, "how neat and fresh the twigs looked." While his pale students were battering their brains over Xenophon and Plato, with a silence as deep as that enjoined by the Samite, we were enjoying ourselves at our ease in our little Goshen.[2] We saw a little into the secrets of his discipline, and the prospect did but the more reconcile us to our lot. His thunders rolled innocuous for us: his storms came near, but never touched us; contrary to Gideon's miracle, while all around were drenched, our fleece was dry.[3] His boys turned out the better scholars; we, I suspect, have the advantage in temper. His pupils cannot speak of him without something of terror allaying their gratitude; the remembrance of Field comes back with all the soothing images of indolence, and summer slumbers, and work like play, and innocent idleness, and Elysian exemptions, and life itself a "playing holiday."

Though sufficiently removed from the jurisdiction of Boyer, we were near enough (as I have said) to understand a little of his system. We occasionally heard sounds of the *Ululantes*, and caught glances of Tartarus.[4] B. was a rabid pedant. His English style was cramped to barbarism. His Easter anthems (for his duty obliged him to those periodical flights) were grating as scrannel pipes.[5]—He would laugh, aye, and heartily, but then it must be at Flaccus's quibble about *Rex*[6]—or at the *tristis severitas in vultu*, or *inspicere in patinas*, of Terence[7]—thin jests, which at their first broaching could hardly have had *vis*[8] enough to move a Roman muscle.—He had two wigs, both pedantic, but of different omen. The one serene, smiling, fresh powdered, betokening a mild day. The other, an old, discolored, unkempt, angry caxon,[9] denoting frequent and bloody execution. Woe to the school, when he made his morning appearance in his *passy*, or *passionate wig*. No comet expounded surer.[1]—J. B. had a

9. A Roman of the 1st century C.E., author of a verse translation of Aesop's fables.
1. The Spartans exhibited drunken Helots (slaves) as a warning example to their children.
2. Where the Israelites dwelled, protected from the swarms of flies with which the Lord plagued the Egyptians in Exodus 8.22. "Samite": Pythagoras of Samos, Greek mathematician and philosopher (6th century B.C.E.), who forbade his pupils to speak until they had studied with him five years.
3. Judges 6.37–38. As a sign to Gideon, the Lord soaked his sheepskin while leaving the earth around it dry.
4. In the *Aeneid* 6.557–58 Aeneas hears the groans and the sound of the lash from Tartarus, the infernal place of punishment for the wicked.

"*Ululantes*": howling sufferers.
5. Harsh pipes, an echo of Milton's "Lycidas," line 124.
6. In Horace's *Satires* 1.7 there is a pun on *Rex* as both a surname and the word for *king*.
7. In Terence's *Andrea* 5.2 one character says of a notorious liar that he has "a sober severity in his countenance." In his *Adelphi* 3.3, after a father has advised his son to look into the lives of men as a mirror, the slave advises the kitchen scullions "to look into the stew pans" as a mirror.
8. Force (Latin); a term in rhetorical theory.
9. A type of wig.
1. Comets were superstitiously regarded as omens of disaster.

heavy hand. I have known him double his knotty fist at a poor trembling child (the maternal milk hardly dry upon its lips) with a "Sirrah, do you presume to set your wits at me?"—Nothing was more common than to see him make a headlong entry into the schoolroom, from his inner recess, or library, and, with turbulent eye, singling out a lad, roar out, "Od's my life, sirrah" (his favorite adjuration), "I have a great mind to whip you"—then, with as sudden a retracting impulse, fling back into his lair—and, after a cooling lapse of some minutes (during which all but the culprit had totally forgotten the context) drive headlong out again, piecing out his imperfect sense, as if it had been some Devil's Litany, with the expletory yell—*"and I* WILL, *too."*—In his gentler moods, when the *rabidus furor* was assuaged, he had resort to an ingenious method, peculiar, for what I have heard, to himself, of whipping the boy, and reading the Debates,[2] at the same time; a paragraph, and a lash between; which in those times, when parliamentary oratory was most at a height and flourishing in these realms, was not calculated to impress the patient with a veneration for the diffuser graces of rhetoric.

Once, and but once, the uplifted rod was known to fall ineffectual from his hand—when droll squinting W—— having been caught putting the inside of the master's desk to a use for which the architect had clearly not designed it, to justify himself, with great simplicity averred, that *he did not know that the thing had been forewarned.* This exquisite irrecognition of any law antecedent to the *oral* or *declaratory* struck so irresistibly upon the fancy of all who heard it (the pedagogue himself not excepted)—that remission was unavoidable.

L. has given credit to B.'s great merits as an instructor. Coleridge, in his literary life,[3] has pronounced a more intelligible and ample encomium on them. The author of the *Country Spectator*[4] doubts not to compare him with the ablest teachers of antiquity. Perhaps we cannot dismiss him better than with the pious ejaculation of C.—when he heard that his old master was on his deathbed: "Poor J. B.!—may all his faults be forgiven; and may he be wafted to bliss by little cherub boys all head and wings, with no *bottoms* to reproach his sublunary infirmities."

Under him were many good and sound scholars bred.—First Grecian[5] of my time was Lancelot Pepys Stevens, kindest of boys and men, since Co-grammar-master (and inseparable companion) with Dr. T——e. What an edifying spectacle did this brace of friends present to those who remembered the antisocialities of their predecessors!—You never met the one by chance in the street without a wonder, which was quickly dissipated by the almost immediate sub-appearance of the other. Generally arm-in-arm, these kindly coadjutors lightened for each other the toilsome duties of their profession, and when, in advanced age, one found it convenient to retire, the other was not long in discovering that it suited him to lay down the fasces[6] also. Oh, it is pleasant, as it is rare, to find the same arm linked in yours at forty, which at thirteen helped it to turn over the *Cicero De Amicitia,*[7] or some tale of Antique Friendship, which the young heart even then was burning to anticipate!—Co-

2. The record of debates in Parliament. *"Rabidus furor"*: mad rage (Latin).
3. I.e., *Biographia Literaria.*
4. Thomas Middleton, who was at school with Lamb and Coleridge, edited the magazine *Country Spectator* (1792–93) and later became bishop of Calcutta.
5. The Grecians were the small group of superior scholars selected to be sent to a university (usually

Cambridge) on a Christ's Hospital scholarship.
6. The bundle of rods, serving as the handle of an ax, carried before the Roman magistrates as a symbol of office. This is a facetious reference to the birch-rod schoolmaster habitually carried at a time when flogging was almost part of the curriculum.
7. Cicero's essay *On Friendship.*

Grecian with S. was Th——, who has since executed with ability various diplomatic functions at the Northern courts. Th—— was a tall, dark, saturnine youth, sparing of speech, with raven locks.—Thomas Fanshaw Middleton followed him (now Bishop of Calcutta), a scholar and a gentleman in his teens. He has the reputation of an excellent critic; and is author (besides the *Country Spectator*) of a *Treatise on the Greek Article*, against Sharpe. M. is said to bear his miter high in India, where the *regni novitas*[8] (I dare say) sufficiently justifies the bearing. A humility quite as primitive as that of Jewel or Hooker[9] might not be exactly fitted to impress the minds of those Anglo-Asiatic diocesans with a reverence for home institutions, and the church which those fathers watered. The manners of M. at school, though firm, were mild and unassuming.—Next to M. (if not senior to him) was Richards, author of the *Aboriginal Britons*, the most spirited of the Oxford Prize Poems; a pale, studious Grecian.—Then followed poor S——, ill-fated M——! of these the Muse is silent.[1]

> Finding some of Edward's race
> Unhappy, pass their annals by.[2]

Come back into memory, like as thou wert in the dayspring of thy fancies, with hope like a fiery column before thee—the dark pillar not yet turned—Samuel Taylor Coleridge—Logician, Metaphysician, Bard!—How have I seen the casual passer through the cloisters stand still, entranced with admiration (while he weighed the disproportion between the *speech* and the *garb* of the young Mirandola[3]), to hear thee unfold, in thy deep and sweet intonations, the mysteries of amblichus, or Plotinus[4] (for even in those years thou waxedst not pale at such philosophic draughts), or reciting Homer in his Greek, or Pindar—while the walls of the old Grey Friars[5] re-echoed to the accents of the *inspired charity-boy!*—Many were the "wit combats" (to dally awhile with the words of old Fuller) between him and C. V. Le G——, "which two I behold like a Spanish great galleon, and an English man-of-war; Master Coleridge, like the former, was built far higher in learning, solid, but slow in his performances. C. V. L., with the English man-of-war, lesser in bulk, but lighter in sailing, could turn with all tides, tack about, and take advantage of all winds, by the quickness of his wit and invention."[6]

Nor shalt thou, their compeer, be quickly forgotten, Allen, with the cordial smile, and still more cordial laugh, with which thou wert wont to make the old cloisters shake, in thy cognition of some poignant jest of theirs; or the anticipation of some more material, and, peradventure, practical one, of thine own. Extinct are those smiles, with that beautiful countenance, with which (for thou wert the *Nireus formosus*[7] of the school), in the days of thy maturer waggery, thou didst disarm the wrath of infuriated town-damsel, who, incensed by provoking pinch, turning tigress-like round, suddenly converted by thy angel look, exchanged the half-formed terrible "*bl——,*" for a gentler greeting—"*bless thy handsome face!*"

---

8. Newness of the reign (Latin).
9. Famous divines in the 16th century during the early period of the Anglican Church.
1. Lamb identified these students as Scott, who died insane, and Maunde, who was expelled from the school.
2. Altered from Matthew Prior's "Carmen Seculare" (1700). "Edward's race": applied to the students of Christ's Hospital, founded by Edward VI.
3. Pico della Mirandola, the brilliant and charming humanist and philosopher of the Italian Renaissance.

4. Neoplatonist philosophers.
5. Christ's Hospital was located in buildings that had once belonged to the Grey Friars (i.e., Franciscans).
6. Lamb adapts to Coleridge and Charles Valentine Le Grice the famous description of the wit combats between Shakespeare (the "man-of-war") and Ben Jonson (the "great galleon") in Thomas Fuller's *Worthies of England* (1662).
7. The handsome Nireus; a Greek warrior in Homer's *Iliad* 2.

Next follow two, who ought to be now alive, and the friends of Elia—the junior Le G——and F——; who impelled, the former by a roving temper, the latter by too quick a sense of neglect—ill capable of enduring the slights poor Sizars⁸ are sometimes subject to in our seats of learning—exchanged their Alma Mater for the camp; perishing, one by climate, and one on the plains of Salamanca: Le G——, sanguine, volatile, sweet-natured; F——, dogged, faithful, anticipative of insult, warmhearted, with something of the old Roman height about him.

Fine, frank-hearted Fr——, the present master of Hertford, with Marmaduke T——,⁹ mildest of missionaries—and both my good friends still—close the catalogue of Grecians in my time.

1820   1823

Detached Thoughts on Books and Reading¹

> To mind the inside of a book is to entertain one's self with the forced product of another man's brain. Now I think a man of quality and breeding may be much amused with the natural sprouts of his own.
> —Lord Foppington in *The Relapse*²

An ingenious acquaintance of my own was so much struck with this bright sally of his Lordship, that he has left off reading altogether, to the great improvement of his originality. At the hazard of losing some credit on this head, I must confess that I dedicate no inconsiderable portion of my time to other people's thoughts. I dream away my life in others' speculations. I love to lose myself in other men's minds. When I am not walking, I am reading; I cannot sit and think. Books think for me.

I have no repugnances. Shaftesbury is not too genteel for me, nor Jonathan Wild too low.³ I can read any thing which I call a *book*. There are things in that shape which I cannot allow for such.

In this catalogue of *books which are no books—biblia a-biblia*—I reckon Court Calendars, Directories, Pocket Books, Draught Boards bound and lettered at the back, Scientific Treatises, Almanacks, Statutes at Large; the works of Hume, Gibbon, Robertson, Beattie, Soame Jenyns, and, generally, all those volumes which "no gentleman's library should be without":⁴ the Histories of Flavius Josephus (that learned Jew), and Paley's *Moral Philosophy*.⁵ With these exceptions, I can read almost any thing. I bless my stars for a taste so catholic, so unexcluding.

---

8. An undergraduate at Cambridge University who receives an allowance from the college and who in former times was expected in return to perform certain menial duties. "Le G——": Samuel Le Grice, who became an army officer and died in the West Indies. "F——": Joseph Favell.
9. Marmaduke Thompson. "Fr——": Frederick William Franklin.
1. Published in the *London Magazine*, July 1822, and revised for *Last Essays of Elia* (1833), Lamb's essay, although often tongue in cheek, shrewdly challenges the hierarchies of the era's reviewers and others used to rank different kinds of writing and sort out good, tasteful readers from bad. Elia's fondness for novels from circulating libraries is as unusual as his willingness to present himself as a receptive reader first and an original author sec-

ond. For a contrast to his bookishness, see Wordsworth's "Expostulation and Reply" and "The Tables Turned" (pp. 250–52).
2. The would-be man of fashion in Sir John Vanbrugh's comedy of 1696, *The Relapse*.
3. Two extremes in 18th-century prose: the third earl of Shaftesbury (1671–1713), philosopher and essayist, and the gang leader who inspired Henry Fielding's 1743 crime novel *Jonathan Wild the Great*.
4. Elia's list begins with the types of books sold by stationers and ends with those authored by venerated and prolific moralists, philosophers, and historians of the 18th century.
5. Josephus (37–100 C.E.), historian of the Jewish people; William Paley (1743–1805), theologian and philosopher.

I confess that it moves my spleen to see these *things in books' clothing* perched upon shelves, like false saints, usurpers of true shrines, intruders into the sanctuary, thrusting out the legitimate occupants. To reach down a well-bound semblance of a volume, and hope it is some kind-hearted play-book, then, opening what "seem its leaves," to come bolt upon a withering Population Essay.[6] To expect a Steele, or a Farquhar, and find—Adam Smith.[7] To view a well-arranged assortment of blockheaded Encyclopaedias (Anglicanas or Metropolitanas) set out in an array of Russia, or Morocco,[8] when a tithe of that good leather would comfortably re-clothe my shivering folios; would renovate Paracelsus himself, and enable old Raymund Lully to look like himself again in the world.[9] I never see these impostors, but I long to strip them, to warm my ragged veterans in their spoils.

To be strong-backed and neat-bound is the desideratum of a volume. Magnificence comes after. This, when it can be afforded, is not to be lavished upon all kinds of books indiscriminately. I would not dress a set of Magazines, for instance, in full suit. The dishabille,[1] or half-binding (with Russia backs ever) is *our* costume. A Shakespeare, or a Milton (unless the first editions), it were mere foppery to trick out in gay apparel. The possession of them confers no distinction. The exterior of them (the things themselves being so common), strange to say, raises no sweet emotions, no tickling sense of property in the owner. Thomson's *Seasons*,[2] again, looks best (I maintain it) a little torn, and dog's-eared. How beautiful to a genuine lover of reading are the sullied leaves, and worn out appearance, nay, the very odour (beyond Russia), if we would not forget kind feelings in fastidiousness, of an old "Circulating Library" *Tom Jones*, or *Vicar of Wakefield!*[3] How they speak of the thousand thumbs, that have turned over their pages with delight!—of the lone sempstress, whom they may have cheered (milliner, or harder-working mantuamaker)[4] after her long day's needle-toil, running far into midnight, when she has snatched an hour, ill spared from sleep, to steep her cares, as in some Lethean cup,[5] in spelling out their enchanting contents! Who would have them a whit less soiled? What better condition could we desire to see them in?

In some respects the better a book is, the less it demands from binding. Fielding, Smollet, Sterne,[6] and all that class of perpetually self-reproductive volumes—Great Nature's Stereotypes[7]—we see them individually perish with less regret, because we know the copies of them to be "eterne."[8] But where a book is at once both good and rare—where the individual is almost the species, and when *that* perishes,

---

6. Thomas Malthus's *Essay on the Principle of Population*, first published 1798, had by 1822 been through several editions and prompted several responses, including ones by Lamb's friends Godwin and Hazlitt.
7. The early-18th-century dramatists Richard Steele and George Farquhar, contrasted with the author of *The Wealth of Nations* (1776).
8. Russia and Morocco are two varieties of leather used in book-binding.
9. Paracelsus (1493–1541) and Ramon Lull (1235–1317), authors with connections to alchemy and the search for the philosopher's stone, which could transmute base metals into gold, and for the elixir of life.
1. Negligent or casual dress.
2. James Thomson's widely read poem of natural description, published in 1730.

3. Novels by Henry Fielding and Oliver Goldsmith, published in 1748 and 1766.
4. Milliners were seamstresses specializing in bonnet-making; mantua-makers were dressmakers. Mary Lamb, a great reader of novels borrowed from circulating libraries, was a mantua-maker.
5. The waters of the river Lethe, which flowed through Hades, caused forgetfulness.
6. The novelists Tobias Smollett (1721–1771) and Laurence Sterne (1713–1768).
7. Refers to the molds that at the start of the 19th century had begun to be employed in the printing process, considerably enhancing the speed and efficiency of book production.
8. Lady Macbeth, suggesting the killing of Banquo and Fleance: "in them nature's copy's not eterne" (Shakespeare, *Macbeth* 3.2.39).

We know not where is that Promethean torch
That can its light relumine—[9]

such a book, for instance, as the *Life of the Duke of Newcastle,* by his Duch-ess[1]—no casket is rich enough, no casing sufficiently durable, to honour and keep safe such a jewel.

Not only rare volumes of this description, which seem hopeless ever to be reprinted; but old editions of writers, such as Sir Philip Sydney, Bishop Tay-lor,[2] Milton in his prose-works, Fuller[3]—of whom we *have* reprints, yet the books themselves, though they go about, and are talked of here and there, we know, have not endenizened themselves (nor possibly ever will) in the national heart, so as to become stock books—it is good to possess these in durable and costly covers. I do not care for a First Folio of Shakespeare. I rather prefer the common editions of Rowe and Tonson, without notes, and with *plates,* which, being so execrably bad, serve as maps, or modest remembrancers, to the text; and without pretending to any supposable emulation with it, are so much better than the Shakespeare gallery *engravings,* which *did.*[4] I have a community of feeling with my countrymen about his Plays, and I like those editions of him best, which have been oftenest tumbled about and handled.—On the contrary, I cannot read Beaumont and Fletcher but in Folio. The Octavo edi-tions are painful to look at.[5] I have no sympathy with them. If they were as much read as the current editions of the other poet, I should prefer them in that shape to the older one. I do not know a more heartless sight than the reprint of the *Anatomy of Melancholy.*[6] What need was there of unearthing the bones of that fantastic old great man, to expose them in a winding-sheet of the newest fashion to modern censure? what hapless stationer could dream of Burton ever becoming popular?—The wretched Malone could not do worse, when he bribed the sexton of Stratford church to let him white-wash the painted effigy of old Shakespeare,[7] which stood there, in rude but lively fashion depicted, to the very colour of the cheek, the eye, the eye-brow, hair, the very dress he used to wear—the only authentic testimony we had, however imper-fect, of these curious parts and parcels of him. They covered him over with a coat of white paint. By——, if I had been a justice of peace for Warwickshire, I would have clapt both commentator and sexton fast in the stocks, for a pair of meddling sacrilegious varlets.

I think I see them at their work—these sapient trouble-tombs.

Shall I be thought fantastical, if I confess, that the names of some of our poets sound sweeter, and have a finer relish to the ear—to mine, at least—

9. Cf. Othello's words as he contemplates Des-demona's murder (Shakespeare, *Othello* 5.2.12–13).
1. The 1667 biography of her husband by the poet and playwright Margaret Cavendish.
2. Jeremy Taylor (1613–1667), author of *Holy Living* and *Holy Dying.*
3. Anglican clergyman and antiquarian Thomas Fuller (1608–1661).
4. Illustrations by leading English artists were pro-vided for the deluxe edition of Shakespeare issued by the print seller John Boydell in 1802. Elia favors the editions that were prepared by Nicholas Rowe and his publisher Jacob Tonson starting in 1709.
5. Francis Beaumont (1585?–1616) and John Fletcher (1579–1625), Elizabeth dramatists and collaborators: Lamb's folio edition of their works is also mentioned in "Old China." Folio editions are

distinguished from octavo by size: folio is the larg-est format for books, produced when a full-sized printer's sheet is folded once, whereas an octavo book is sized for pages folded so that each is one-eighth the size of a full sheet. By Lamb's day, book formats were to an extent correlated with their contents: the more cultural authority granted the type of literature or the author, the larger the for-mat.
6. Robert Burton's vast treatise from 1621; there was an 1800 reprint. Burton's unmethodical, mot-ley prose, which seemingly broaches a thousand topics to take on one, gave Lamb a model for his style in the Elia essays.
7. Shakespeare editor Edmund Malone (1741–1812). The repainting of Shakespeare's bust occurred in 1793.

than that of Milton or of Shakespeare? It may be, that the latter are more staled and rung upon in common discourse. The sweetest names, and which carry a perfume in the mention, are, Kit Marlowe, Drayton, Drummond of Hawthornden, and Cowley.[8]

Much depends upon *when* and *where* you read a book. In the five or six impatient minutes, before the dinner is quite ready, who would think of taking up the *Fairy Queen* for a stopgap, or a volume of Bishop Andrewes' sermons?[9]

Milton almost requires a solemn service of music to be played before you enter upon him. But he brings his music, to which, who listens, had need bring docile thoughts, and purged ears.

Winter evenings—the world shut out—with less of ceremony the gentle Shakespeare enters. At such a season, the *Tempest*, or his own *Winter's Tale*—

These two poets you cannot avoid reading aloud—to yourself, or (as it chances) to some single person listening. More than one—and it degenerates into an audience.

Books of quick interest, that hurry on for incidents, are for the eye to glide over only. It will not do to read them out. I could never listen to even the better kind of modern novels without extreme irksomeness.

A newspaper, read out, is intolerable. In some of the Bank offices it is the custom (to save so much individual time) for one of the clerks—who is the best scholar—to commence upon the Times, or the Chronicle, and recite its entire contents aloud *pro bono publico*.[1] With every advantage of lungs and elocution, the effect is singularly vapid. In barbers' shops and public-houses a fellow will get up, and spell out a paragraph, which he communicates as some discovery. Another follows with *his* selection. So the entire journal transpires at length by piece-meal. Seldom-readers are slow readers, and, without this expedient no one in the company would probably ever travel through the contents of a whole paper.

Newspapers always excite curiosity. No one ever lays one down without a feeling of disappointment.

What an eternal time that gentleman in black, at Nando's,[2] keeps the paper! I am sick of hearing the waiter bawling out incessantly, "the Chronicle is in hand, Sir."

Coming in to an inn at night—having ordered your supper—what can be more delightful than to find lying in the window-seat, left there time out of mind by the carelessness of some former guest—two or three numbers of the old Town and Country Magazine, with its amusing *tête-à-tête* pictures—"The Royal Lover and Lady G——"; "The Melting Platonic and the old Beau,"— and such like antiquated scandal? Would you exchange it—at that time, and in that place—for a better book?

Poor Tobin, who latterly fell blind, did not regret it so much for the weightier kinds of reading—the *Paradise Lost*, or *Comus*, he could have *read* to him— but he missed the pleasure of skimming over with his own eye a magazine, or a light pamphlet.

I should not care to be caught in the serious avenues of some cathedral alone, and reading *Candide*.[3]

I do not remember a more whimsical surprise than having been once

8. Poet and dramatist Christopher Marlowe (1564–1593); poets Michael Drayton (1563–1631), William Drummond of Hawthornden (1585–1649), and Abraham Cowley (1610–1667).
9. Launcelot Andrewes (1551–1626).

1. For the common good (Latin).
2. Coffeehouse in London's Fleet Street.
3. Voltaire, the author of the satirical *Candide, or Optimism* (1759), was notorious for his freethinking in religious matters.

detected—by a familiar damsel—reclined at my ease upon the grass, on Primrose Hill (her Cythera),[4] reading—*Pamela*.[5] There was nothing in the book to
make a man seriously ashamed at the exposure; but as she seated herself down
by me, and seemed determined to read in company, I could have wished it
had been—any other book. We read on very sociably for a few pages; and, not
finding the author much to her taste, she got up, and—went away. Gentle
casuist, I leave it to thee to conjecture, whether the blush (for there was one
between us) was the property of the nymph or the swain in this dilemma. From
me you shall never get the secret.

I am not much a friend to out-of-doors reading. I cannot settle my spirits
to it. I knew a Unitarian minister, who was generally to be seen upon Snow-
hill (as yet Skinner's-street *was not*), between the hours of ten and eleven in
the morning, studying a volume of Lardner.[6] I own this to have been a strain
of abstraction beyond my reach. I used to admire how he sidled along, keeping
clear of secular contacts. An illiterate encounter with a porter's knot,[7] or a
bread basket, would have quickly put to flight all the theology I am master of,
and have left me worse than indifferent to the five points.[8]

There is a class of street-readers, whom I can never contemplate without
affection—the poor gentry, who, not having wherewithal to buy or hire a book,
filch a little learning at the open stalls—the owner, with his hard eye, casting
envious looks at them all the while, and thinking when they will have done.
Venturing tenderly, page after page, expecting every moment when he shall
interpose his interdict, and yet unable to deny themselves the gratification,
they "snatch a fearful joy."[9] Martin B———,[1] in this way, by daily fragments,
got through two volumes of *Clarissa*,[2] when the stallkeeper damped his laudable ambition, by asking him (it was in his younger days) whether he meant
to purchase the work. M. declares, that under no circumstances of his life did
he ever peruse a book with half the satisfaction which he took in those uneasy
snatches. A quaint poetess of our day[3] has moralised upon this subject in two
very touching but homely stanzas.

> I saw a boy with eager eye
> Open a book upon a stall,
> And read, as he'd devour it all;
> Which when the stall-man did espy,
> Soon to the boy I heard him call,
> "You, Sir, you never buy a book,
> Therefore in one you shall not look."
> The boy pass'd slowly on, and with a sigh
> He wish'd he never had been taught to read,
> Then of the old churl's books he should have had no need.
>
> Of sufferings the poor have many,
> Which never can the rich annoy:

---

4. Greek island sacred to the goddess of love. "Primrose Hill": a green space in north London.
5. Samuel Richardson's 1740 novel in letters chronicling the failed seduction of a very virtuous maidservant.
6. Theologian Nathaniel Lardner (1684–1768).
7. The padded yoke a London market porter wore to help him carry his burden.
8. The five points of Calvinist belief: Original Sin, Predestination, Irresistible Grace, Particular Redemption, and the Final Perseverance of the

Saints.
9. Cf. the description of schoolboys' play in Thomas Gray's 1742 "Ode on a Distant Prospect of
Eton College" (line 40).
1. The Lambs' friend Martin Burney, nephew of
the novelist Frances Burney.
2. A million-word novel, Samuel Richardson's
Clarissa (1747–48) took up seven volumes.
3. Mary Lamb. The poem had appeared earlier in
the Lambs' *Poetry for Children* (1809).

I soon perceiv'd another boy,
Who look'd as if he'd not had any
Food, for that day at least—enjoy
The sight of cold meat in a tavern larder.
This boy's case, then thought I, is surely harder,
Thus hungry, longing, thus without a penny,
Beholding choice of dainty-dressed meat:
No wonder if he wish he ne'er had learn'd to eat.

1822   1833

Old China

I have an almost feminine partiality for old china. When I go to see any great house, I inquire for the china closet, and next for the picture gallery. I cannot defend the order of preference, but by saying that we have all some taste or other, of too ancient a date to admit of our remembering distinctly that it was an acquired one. I can call to mind the first play, and the first exhibition, that I was taken to; but I am not conscious of a time when china jars and saucers were introduced into my imagination.

I had no repugnance then—why should I now have?—to those little, lawless, azure-tinctured grotesques, that under the notion of men and women float about, uncircumscribed by any element, in that world before perspective—a china teacup.

I like to see my old friends—whom distance cannot diminish—figuring up in the air (so they appear to our optics), yet on terra firma still—for so we must in courtesy interpret that speck of deeper blue, which the decorous artist, to prevent absurdity, had made to spring up beneath their sandals.

I love the men with women's faces, and the women, if possible, with still more womanish expressions.

Here is a young and courtly mandarin, handing tea to a lady from a salver—two miles off. See how distance seems to set off respect! And here the same lady, or another—for likeness is identity on teacups—is stepping into a little fairy boat, moored on the hither side of this calm garden river, with a dainty mincing foot, which in a right angle of incidence (as angles go in our world) must infallibly land her in the midst of a flowery mead—a furlong off on the other side of the same strange stream!

Farther on—if far or near can be predicated of their world—see horses, trees, pagodas, dancing the hays.[1]

Here—a cow and rabbit couchant,[2] and coextensive—so objects show, seen through the lucid atmosphere of fine Cathay.[3]

I was pointing out to my cousin last evening, over our Hyson[4] (which we are old-fashioned enough to drink unmixed still of an afternoon), some of these *speciosa miracula*[5] upon a set of extraordinary old blue china (a recent purchase) which we were now for the first time using; and could not help remarking how favorable circumstances had been to us of late years that we could afford to please the eye sometimes with trifles of this sort—when a passing

1. An English country dance.
2. Lying down with the head raised (term from heraldry).
3. The old European name for China.
4. A Chinese green tea.
5. Shining wonders (Latin).

sentiment seemed to overshade the brows of my companion. I am quick at detecting these summer clouds in Bridget.[6]

"I wish the good old times would come again," she said, "when we were not quite so rich. I do not mean that I want to be poor; but there was a middle state"—so she was pleased to ramble on—"in which I am sure we were a great deal happier. A purchase is but a purchase, now that you have money enough and to spare. Formerly it used to be a triumph. When we coveted a cheap luxury (and, O! how much ado I had to get you to consent in those times!)— we were used to have a debate two or three days before, and to weigh the *for* and *against*, and think what we might spare it out of, and what saving we could hit upon, that should be an equivalent. A thing was worth buying then, when we felt the money that we paid for it.

"Do you remember the brown suit, which you made to hang upon you, till all your friends cried shame upon you, it grew so threadbare—and all because of that folio Beaumont and Fletcher,[7] which you dragged home late at night from Barker's in Covent Garden? Do you remember how we eyed it for weeks before we could make up our minds to the purchase, and had not come to a determination till it was near ten o'clock of the Saturday night, when you set off from Islington,[8] fearing you should be too late—and when the old book-seller with some grumbling opened his shop, and by the twinkling taper (for he was setting bedwards) lighted out the relic from his dusty treasures—and when you lugged it home, wishing it were twice as cumbersome—and when you presented it to me—and when we were exploring the perfectness of it (*collating*, you called it)—and while I was repairing some of these loose leaves with paste, which your impatience would not suffer to be left till daybreak— was there no pleasure in being a poor man? or can those neat black clothes which you wear now, and are so careful to keep brushed, since we have become rich and finical, give you half the honest vanity with which you flaunted it about in that overworn suit—your old corbeau[9]—for four or five weeks longer than you should have done, to pacify your conscience for the mighty sum of fifteen—or sixteen shillings was it?—a great affair we thought it then—which you had lavished on the old folio. Now you can afford to buy any book that pleases you, but I do not see that you ever bring me home any nice old purchases now.

"When you came home with twenty apologies for laying out a less number of shillings upon that print after Leonardo,[1] which we christened the 'Lady Blanch'; when you looked at the purchase, and thought of the money—and thought of the money, and looked again at the picture—was there no pleasure in being a poor man? Now, you have nothing to do but to walk into Colnaghi's,[2] and buy a wilderness of Leonardos. Yet do you?

"Then, do you remember our pleasant walks to Enfield, and Potter's Bar, and Waltham,[3] when we had a holiday—holidays, and all other fun, are gone now we are rich—and the little hand-basket in which I used to deposit our

6. In Lamb's essays, his name for his sister, Mary.
7. The Elizabethan dramatic collaborators, whose plays were first collected in a large folio volume in 1647.
8. In the north of London, where the Lambs had been living.
9. A dark green cloth, almost black (hence its name, the French for raven).
1. Leonardo da Vinci (1452–1519), the great Italian painter. The painting is the one known as *Modesty and Vanity*.

2. Colnaghi was a London print seller. In the issue of the *London Magazine* in which "Old China" first appeared, the artist Thomas Griffiths Wainewright (using the signature "C. van Vinkboom") works some advice for Colnaghi into his essay: namely, to immediately "import a few impressions . . . of those beautiful plates from Da Vinci," including "Miss Lamb's favourite, 'Lady Blanche,' " as he foresees that this issue "will occasion a considerable call for them."
3. All three are suburbs to the north of London.

day's fare of savory cold lamb and salad—and how you would pry about at noontide for some decent house, where we might go in and produce our store—only paying for the ale that you must call for—and speculate upon the looks of the landlady, and whether she was likely to allow us a tablecloth—and wish for such another honest hostess as Izaak Walton has described many a one on the pleasant banks of the Lea, when he went-fishing—and sometimes they would prove obliging enough, and sometimes they would look grudgingly upon us—but we had cheerful looks still for one another, and would eat our plain food savorily, scarcely grudging Piscator[4] his Trout Hall? Now—when we go out a day's pleasuring, which is seldom, moreover, we *ride* part of the way—and go into a fine inn, and order the best of dinners, never debating the expense—which, after all, never has half the relish of those chance country snaps,[5] when we were at the mercy of uncertain usage and a precarious welcome.

"You are too proud to see a play anywhere now but in the pit. Do you remember where it was we used to sit, when we saw the *Battle of Hexham*, and the *Surrender of Calais*,[6] and Bannister and Mrs. Bland in the *Children in the Wood*[7]—when we squeezed out our shillings apiece to sit three or four times in a season in the one-shilling gallery—where you felt all the time that you ought not to have brought me—and more strongly I felt obligation to you for having brought me—and the pleasure was the better for a little shame—and when the curtain drew up, what cared we for our place in the house, or what mattered it where we were sitting, when our thoughts were with Rosalind in Arden, or with Viola at the Court of Ilyria.[8] You used to say that the gallery was the best place of all for enjoying a play socially—that the relish of such exhibitions must be in proportion to the infrequency of going—that the company we met there, not being in general readers of plays, were obliged to attend the more, and did attend, to what was going on, on the stage—because a word lost would have been a chasm, which it was impossible for them to fill up. With such reflections we consoled our pride then—and I appeal to you whether, as a woman, I met generally with less attention and accommodation than I have done since in more expensive situations in the house? The getting in indeed, and the crowding up those inconvenient staircases, was bad enough—but there was still a law of civility to woman recognized to quite as great an extent as we ever found in the other passages—and how a little difficulty overcome heightened the snug seat and the play, afterwards! Now we can only pay our money and walk in. You cannot see, you say, in the galleries now. I am sure we saw, and heard too, well enough then—but sight, and all, I think, is gone with our poverty.

"There was pleasure in eating strawberries, before they became quite common—in the first dish of peas, while they were yet dear—to have them for a nice supper, a treat. What treat can we have now? If we were to treat ourselves now—that is, to have dainties a little above our means, it would be selfish and wicked. It is the very little more that we allow ourselves beyond what the actual poor can get at that makes what I call a treat—when two people living together, as we have done, now and then indulge themselves in a cheap luxury, which both like; while each apologizes, and is willing to take

---

4. The fisherman in Izaak Walton's *Complete Angler* (1653).
5. Snacks.
6. Comedies by George Colman (1762–1836).

7. By Thomas Morton (1764–1838).
8. Rosalind in Shakespeare's *As You Like It* and Viola in his *Twelfth Night*.

both halves of the blame to his single share. I see no harm in people making much of themselves, in that sense of the word. It may give them a hint how to make much of others. But now—what I mean by the word—we never do make much of ourselves. None but the poor can do it. I do not mean the veriest poor of all, but persons as we were, just above poverty.

"I know what you were going to say, that it is mighty pleasant at the end of the year to make all meet—and much ado we used to have every Thirty-first Night of December to account for our exceedings—many a long face did you make over your puzzled accounts, and in contriving to make it out how we had spent so much—or that we had not spent so much—or that it was impossible we should spend so much next year—and still we found our slender capital decreasing—but then, betwixt ways, and projects, and compromises of one sort or another, and talk of curtailing this charge, and doing without that for the future—and the hope that youth brings, and laughing spirits (in which you were never poor till now), we pocketed up our loss, and in conclusion, with 'lusty brimmers' (as you used to quote it out of *hearty cheerful Mr. Cotton*,[9] as you called him), we used to welcome in 'the coming guest.' Now we have no reckoning at all at the end of the old year—no flattering promises about the new year doing better for us."

Bridget is so sparing of her speech on most occasions that when she gets into a rhetorical vein, I am careful how I interrupt it. I could not help, however, smiling at the phantom of wealth which her dear imagination had conjured up out of a clear income of poor—— hundred pounds a year. "It is true we were happier when we were poorer, but we were also younger, my cousin. I am afraid we must put up with the excess, for if we were to shake the superflux into the sea, we should not much mend ourselves. That we had much to struggle with, as we grew up together, we have reason to be most thankful. It strengthened and knit our compact closer. We could never have been what we have been to each other, if we had always had the sufficiency which you now complain of. The resisting power—those natural dilations of the youthful spirit, which circumstances cannot straiten—with us are long since passed away. Competence to age is supplementary youth, a sorry supplement indeed, but I fear the best that is to be had. We must ride where we formerly walked: live better and lie softer—and shall be wise to do so—than we had means to do in those good old days you speak of. Yet could those days return—could you and I once more walk our thirty miles a day—could Bannister and Mrs. Bland again be young, and you and I be young to see them—could the good old one-shilling gallery days return—they are dreams, my cousin, now—but could you and I at this moment, instead of this quiet argument, by our well-carpeted fireside, sitting on this luxurious sofa—be once more struggling up those inconvenient staircases, pushed about, and squeezed, and elbowed by the poorest rabble of poor gallery scramblers—could I once more hear those anxious shrieks of yours—and the delicious *Thank God, we are safe,* which always followed when the topmost stair, conquered, let in the first light of the whole cheerful theater down beneath us—I know not the fathom line that ever touched a descent so deep as I would be willing to bury more wealth in than Croesus had, or the great Jew R——[1] is supposed to have, to purchase

9. Charles Cotton (1630–1687), a favorite poet of Lamb's. The quotations are from his poem "The New Year." "Lusty brimmers": glasses filled to the brim.

1. Nathan Meyer Rothschild (1777–1836) founded the English branch of the great European banking house.

it. And now do just look at that merry little Chinese waiter holding an umbrella, big enough for a bed-tester,[2] over the head of that pretty insipid half Madonnaish chit of a lady in that very blue summerhouse."

1823   1823

2. Bed canopy.

JANE AUSTEN
1775–1817

Although nowadays her portrait adorns coffee mugs and T-shirts, and journalists, making much of the movie adaptations of her novels, like to imagine her as the center of attention at Hollywood parties, Jane Austen spent her short, secluded life away from the spotlight. Other members of her large family—she was one of eight children born to an Anglican clergyman and his wife—appear to have lived more in the world and closer to this turbulent period's great events than she did. Two brothers fought as naval officers in the Napoleonic War; another became the banker to the flashy London set of the prince regent; her cousin Eliza, born in India, wed a captain in the French army who perished by the guillotine. Austen, however, spent most of her life in Hampshire, the same rural area of southern England in which she was born. Her formal education was limited to a short time at boarding school. Otherwise she and her beloved sister Cassandra had to scramble, like most girls of their class, into what education they could while at home and amidst their father's books. As neither Austen daughter married, home was where these two remained the whole of their adult lives.

Jane Austen turned down a proposal of marriage in 1802, possibly intuiting how difficult it would be to combine authorship with life as a wife, mother, and gentry hostess. She had started writing at the age of twelve, for her family's amusement and her own, and in 1797 began sending work to publishers in London. At that stage they were for the most part unreceptive. In 1803 one paid £10 for the copyright of the novel we know as *Northanger Abbey,* but then declined to publish it, so that Austen had at last, after tangled negotiations, to buy it back. Finally she published *Sense and Sensibility* (1811) at her own expense, then *Pride and Prejudice* (1813) and *Mansfield Park* (1814). Next—by this time under the prestigious auspices of John Murray, who was also Byron's publisher—came *Emma* (1816) and, posthumously, after Austen's death at forty-one, *Persuasion* and a revised version of *Northanger Abbey* (both 1818). The Austen name was never publicly associated with any of these books, whose discreet title pages merely identified "a lady" as the author (though, as was also the case with Scott's Waverley novels, success made Austen's authorship an open secret). The modesty of that signature, however, is belied by the assurance of Austen's narrative voice, the confidence with which (to adapt the famous first sentence of *Pride and Prejudice*) it subjects "truths universally acknowledged" to witty critical scrutiny.

The six novels are all, in Austen's words, "pictures of domestic life in country villages." The world they depict might seem provincial and insular. For the most part the working classes are absent or present only as silent servants; the soldiers and sailors who were protecting England from Napoleon are presented mainly as welcome additions to a ball. Yet the novels also document with striking detail how, within those country villages, the boundaries that had formerly defined the category of "the gentleman" were becoming permeable under the influence of the changes wrought by revolution and war, and how competition for social status was becoming that much fiercer. Through their heroines, readers can see, as well, how harshly the hard facts of economic life bore down on gentlewomen during this period when a lady's security depended on her making a good marriage. The conundrum at the center of the fiction is whether such a marriage can be compatible with the independence of mind and moral integrity that Austen, like her heroines, cherishes.

Austen also wrote so as to explore what the novel form could be and do. Along with the reviewers of the time, she criticized the form, but unlike them, she did so to perfect it. With striking flexibility the new narrative voice that she introduced into novel writing shifts back and forth between a romantic point of view and an irony that reminds us of romance's limits—that reminds us that romance features its own sort of provincialism. At the same time Austen also distanced the novel form from the didactic agenda cultivated by her many contemporaries who were convinced that the only respectable fiction was the antiromance that weaned its readers of their romantic expectations. Her delight in mocking their preachy fictions is not only evident in the parodies that she wrote in the 1790s (including *Love and Friendship*, a forerunner of George Eliot's "Silly Novels by Lady Novelists") but is a feature of her mature novels, which as a rule conclude in ways that deviate quite flagrantly from the patterns of rewards and punishment a moralist might prefer. "I leave it to be settled by whomsoever it may concern," the narrator of *Northanger Abbey* declares in a parting shot, and in characteristic epigrammatic style, "whether the tendency of this work be altogether to recommend parental tyranny, or reward filial disobedience." "[P]ictures of perfection," Austen wrote in a letter, "make me sick and wicked."

Austen's example is so central to what the novel as a form has become that it can be difficult from our present-day vantage point to recognize the iconoclasm in her depictions of the undervalued business of everyday life. It can be hard to see how much her originality—her creation of characters who are both ordinary and unforgettable, her accounts of how they change—challenged her contemporaries' expectations about novels' plots, setting, and characterization. Her dissent from those expectations is palpable, however, in a "Plan of a Novel, According to Hints from Various Quarters," the satire Austen wrote after *Emma*, and which assembles the various "hints" she had received from well-wishers about what she should write next. The immediate occasion for the "Plan" was the series of letters Austen received from the Reverend James Stanier Clarke, librarian to the prince regent, who having conveyed to her the prince's wish that *Emma* should be dedicated to him, continued the correspondence so as to suggest topics that Austen should engage for the next novel—in particular, a historical romance about the royal house of Saxe Cobourg. Austen in reply affirmed the comic spirit of all her works: "I could not sit seriously down to write a serious Romance under any other motive than to save my Life, and if it were indispensable for me to keep it up and never relax into laughing at myself or other people, I am sure I should be hung before I had finished the first Chapter."

Love and Friendship

This work, an anarchic parody written when the author was fourteen, puts front and center Austen's gifts for ironic assassination and her sharp-eyed sense of the preachiness not simply of her period's moralists but more particularly of her period's rebels against orthodox morality. In this miniaturized novel in letters, Austen constructs a world whose inhabitants are absurdly faithful to codes of conduct they extract from their readings of novels in letters. The protagonists of *Love and Friendship* are energetic students of the clichés of fashionable sentimentalism. They adore Nature, like many poets favoring the romantic Scottish Highlands and picturesque Wales; they know that free spirits, true radicals, should elevate the dictates of the heart over the head. The young Austen calls attention to the messages about gender roles embedded in novel writers' celebrations of the strong feelings that make heroines swoon. She shares Wollstonecraft's impatience with how, as the latter put it in *A Vindication of the Rights of Woman* (see p. 170), the culture makes women slaves to their emotions—"blown about by every momentary gust of feeling." This work is usually classified among Austen's juvenilia, but it has the worldliness and bravado we expect from a much older author.

Our text modernizes the irregular spelling and, to a lesser extent, the punctuation of the manuscript, which Austen titled "Love and Freindship."

Love and Friendship

A Novel in a Series of Letters

"Deceived in Friendship & Betrayed in Love"

LETTER THE FIRST *From Isabel to Laura*

How often, in answer to my repeated entreaties that you would give my daughter a regular detail of the misfortunes and adventures of your life, have you said "No, my friend, never will I comply with your request till I may be no longer in danger of again experiencing such dreadful ones." Surely that time is now at hand. You are this day fifty-five. If a woman may ever be said to be in safety from the determined perseverance of disagreeable lovers and the cruel persecutions of obstinate fathers, surely it must be at such a time of life.

Isabel

LETTER THE SECOND *Laura to Isabel*

Although I cannot agree with you in supposing that I shall never again be exposed to misfortunes as unmerited as those I have already experienced, yet to avoid the imputation of obstinacy or ill nature, I will gratify the curiosity of your daughter; and may the fortitude with which I have suffered the many afflictions of my past life prove to her a useful lesson for the support of those which may befall her in her own.

Laura

LETTER THE THIRD *Laura to Marianne*

As the daughter of my most intimate friend I think you entitled to that knowledge of my unhappy story, which your mother has so often solicited me to give you. My father was a native of Ireland and an inhabitant of Wales; my mother was the natural daughter of a Scotch peer by an Italian opera-girl[1]— I was born in Spain and received my education at a convent in France.

When I had reached my eighteenth year I was recalled by my parents to my paternal roof in Wales. Our mansion was situated in one of the most romantic parts of the vale of Usk.[2] Though my charms are now considerably softened and somewhat impaired by the misfortunes I have undergone, I was once beautiful. But lovely as I was, the graces of my person were the least of my perfections. Of every accomplishment[3] accustomary to my sex, I was mistress. When in the convent, my progress had always exceeded my instructions, my

---

1. Illegitimate daughter of a Scottish nobleman and a woman who danced in the ballet corps of an opera company.
2. River valley in south Wales that had been celebrated by William Gilpin in his handbook for tourists in quest of picturesque scenes, *Observations on the River Wye* (1782). See "*Tintern Abbey,*

Tourism, and Romantic Landscape" at Norton Literature Online.
3. Central to the curriculum of female education, "accomplishments" were the skills in music, dance, and drawing that were supposed to make young ladies better companions for their future husbands.

acquirements had been wonderful for my age, and I had shortly surpassed my masters.

In my mind, every virtue that could adorn it was centered; it was the rendezvous of every good quality and of every noble sentiment.

A sensibility[4] too tremblingly alive to every affliction of my friends, my acquaintance, and particularly to every affliction of my own, was my only fault, if a fault it could be called. Alas! how altered now! Though indeed my own misfortunes do not make less impression on me than they ever did, yet now I never feel for those of an other. My accomplishments too, begin to fade—I can neither sing so well nor dance so gracefully as I once did—and I have entirely forgot the *Minuet Dela Cour.*[5]

Adieu.
Laura

LETTER THE FOURTH *Laura to Marianne*

Our neighbourhood was small, for it consisted only of your mother. She may probably have already told you that, being left by her parents in indigent circumstances, she had retired into Wales on economical motives. There it was our friendship first commenced. Isabel was then one and twenty—Though pleasing both in her person and manners (between ourselves) she never possessed the hundredth part of my beauty or accomplishments. Isabel had seen the world. She had passed two years at one of the first boarding schools in London, had spent a fortnight in Bath,[6] and had supped one night in Southampton.[7]

"Beware, my Laura, (she would often say) beware of the insipid vanities and idle dissipations of the metropolis of England; beware of the unmeaning luxuries of Bath and of the stinking fish of Southampton."

"Alas! (exclaimed I) how am I to avoid those evils I shall never be exposed to? What probability is there of my ever tasting the dissipations of London, the luxuries of Bath, or the stinking fish of Southampton? I who am doomed to waste my days of youth and beauty in an humble cottage in the vale of Usk."

Ah! little did I then think I was ordained so soon to quit that humble cottage for the deceitful pleasures of the world.

Adieu.
Laura

LETTER THE FIFTH *Laura to Marianne*

One evening in December as my father, my mother, and myself were arranged in social converse round our fireside, we were on a sudden greatly astonished by hearing a violent knocking on the outward door of our rustic cot.[8]

My father started—"What noise is that?" (said he.) "It sounds like a loud

---

4. Sensibility, as a term designating the individual's capacity for sensitive emotional reaction, was celebrated in much late-18th-century literature at the same time that it was studied in medicine, investigations of the human nervous system especially. Sensibility was often linked to sympathy—the ability to enter into the feelings of another person—and hence to pity and benevolence, and was in this context assessed as a source of social har-

mony.
5. Literally, the court minuet—the stately formal dance that in the 18th century would begin a ball and be followed by livelier country dances.
6. Fashionable spa town in the west of England.
7. Port town in the south of England, in Austen's home county of Hampshire.
8. Cottage.

rapping at the door"—(replied my mother.) "It does indeed." (cried I.) "I am of your opinion; (said my father) it certainly does appear to proceed from some uncommon violence exerted against our unoffending door." "Yes, (exclaimed I) I cannot help thinking it must be somebody who knocks for admittance."

"That is another point (replied he;) We must not pretend to determine on what motive the person may knock—though that someone *does* rap at the door, I am partly convinced."

Here, a second tremendous rap interrupted my father in his speech and somewhat alarmed my mother and me.

"Had we not better go and see who it is? (said she) The servants are out." "I think we had." (replied I.) "Certainly, (added my father) by all means." "Shall we go now?" (said my mother.) "The sooner the better." (answered he). "Oh! let no time be lost." (cried I.)

A third more violent rap than ever again assaulted our ears. "I am certain there is somebody knocking at the door." (said my mother.) "I think there must," (replied my father) "I fancy the servants are returned; (said I) I think I hear Mary going to the door." "I'm glad of it (cried my father) for I long to know who it is."

I was right in my conjecture; for Mary instantly entering the room informed us that a young gentleman and his servant were at the door, who had lost their way, were very cold, and begged leave to warm themselves by our fire.

"Won't you admit them?" (said I) "You have no objection, my dear?" (said my Father.) "None in the world." (replied my mother.)

Mary, without waiting for any further commands, immediately left the room and quickly returned, introducing the most beauteous and amiable youth I had ever beheld. The servant, she kept to herself.

My natural sensibility had already been greatly affected by the sufferings of the unfortunate stranger, and no sooner did I first behold him, than I felt that on him the happiness or misery of my future life must depend.

Adieu.

Laura

LETTER THE SIXTH *Laura to Marianne*

The noble youth informed us that his name was Lindsay—for particular reasons, however, I shall conceal it under that of Talbot. He told us that he was the son of an English baronet,[9] that his mother had been many years no more, and that he had a sister of the middle size. "My father (he continued) is a mean and mercenary wretch—it is only to such particular friends as this dear party that I would thus betray his failings. Your virtues, my amiable Polydore (addressing himself to my father), yours, dear Claudia, and yours, my charming Laura, call on me to repose in you my confidence." We bowed. "My Father, seduced by the false glare of fortune and the deluding pomp of title, insisted on my giving my hand to Lady Dorothea. No, never, exclaimed I. Lady Dorothea is lovely and engaging; I prefer no woman to her; but, know sir, that I scorn to marry her in compliance with your wishes. No! Never shall it be said that I obliged my father."

We all admired the noble manliness of his reply. He continued.

"Sir Edward was surprised; he had perhaps little expected to meet with so

---

9. A baronet, a member of the lower aristocracy, is entitled to be called "Sir" and can pass on his title to his son.

spirited an opposition to his will. 'Where, Edward, in the name of wonder (said he) did you pick up this unmeaning gibberish? You have been studying novels, I suspect.' I scorned to answer: it would have been beneath my dignity. I mounted my horse and, followed by my faithful William, set forwards for my aunt's."

"My father's house is situated in Bedfordshire, my aunt's in Middlesex, and, though I flatter myself with being a tolerable proficient in geography, I know not how it happened, but I found myself entering this beautiful vale, which I find is in South Wales, when I had expected to have reached my aunt's."[1]

"After having wandered some time on the banks of the Usk without knowing which way to go, I began to lament my cruel destiny in the bitterest and most pathetic manner. It was now perfectly dark, not a single star was there to direct my steps, and I know not what might have befallen me, had I not at length discerned through the solemn gloom that surrounded me a distant light, which, as I approached it, I discovered to be the cheerful blaze of your fire. Impelled by the combination of misfortunes under which I laboured, namely fear, cold, and hunger, I hesitated not to ask admittance, which at length I have gained; and now, my adorable Laura (continued he, taking my hand), when may I hope to receive that reward of all the painful sufferings I have undergone during the course of my attachment to you, to which I have ever aspired? Oh! when will you reward me with yourself?"

"This instant, dear and amiable Edward." (replied I.) We were immediately united by my father, who though he had never taken orders had been bred to the church.[2]

Adieu.
Laura

LETTER THE SEVENTH *Laura to Marianne*

We remained but a few days after our marriage in the vale of Usk. After taking an affecting farewell of my father, my mother, and my Isabel, I accompanied Edward to his aunt's in Middlesex. Philippa received us both with every expression of affectionate love. My arrival was indeed a most agreeable surprise to her, as she had not only been totally ignorant of my marriage with her nephew, but had never even had the slightest idea of there being such a person in the world.

Augusta, the sister of Edward, was on a visit to her when we arrived. I found her exactly what her brother had described her to be—of the middle size. She received me with equal surprise, though not with equal cordiality, as Philippa. There was a disagreeable coldness and forbidding reserve in her reception of me which was equally distressing and unexpected. None of that interesting sensibility or amiable sympathy in her manners and address to me which should have distinguished our introduction to each other. Her language was neither warm, nor affectionate, her expressions of regard were neither animated nor cordial; her arms were not opened to receive me to her heart, though my own were extended to press her to mine.

A short conversation between Augusta and her brother, which I accidentally

---

1. Bedfordshire is in the eastern midlands of England; Middlesex is just northwest of London; and south Wales is many miles to the southwest of both.
2. Laura's father has never been ordained. This marriage is not legal.

overheard, increased my dislike to her, and convinced me that her heart was no more formed for the soft ties of love than for the endearing intercourse of friendship.

"But do you think that my father will ever be reconciled to this imprudent connection?" (said Augusta.)

"Augusta (replied the noble youth) I thought you had a better opinion of me, than to imagine I would so abjectly degrade myself as to consider my father's concurrence in any of my affairs, either of consequence or concern to me. Tell me, Augusta, tell me with sincerity; did you ever know me consult his inclinations or follow his advice in the least trifling particular since the age of fifteen?"

"Edward (replied she) you are surely too diffident in your own praise. Since you were fifteen only!—My dear brother, since you were five years old, I entirely acquit you of ever having willingly contributed to the satisfaction of your father. But still I am not without apprehensions of your being shortly obliged to degrade yourself in your own eyes by seeking a support for your wife in the generosity of Sir Edward."

"Never, never, Augusta, will I so demean myself. (said Edward). Support! What support will Laura want which she can receive from him?"

"Only those very insignificant ones of victuals and drink." (answered she.)

"Victuals and drink! (replied my husband in a most nobly contemptuous manner) and dost thou then imagine that there is no other support for an exalted mind (such as is my Laura's) than the mean and indelicate employment of eating and drinking?"

"None that I know of so efficacious." (returned Augusta).

"And did you then never feel the pleasing pangs of love, Augusta? (replied my Edward). Does it appear impossible to your vile and corrupted palate to exist on love? Can you not conceive the luxury of living in every distress that poverty can inflict, with the object of your tenderest affection?"

"You are too ridiculous (said Augusta) to argue with; perhaps, however, you may in time be convinced that. . . ."

Here I was prevented from hearing the remainder of her speech, by the appearance of a very handsome young woman, who was ushered into the room at the door of which I had been listening. On hearing her announced by the name of "Lady Dorothea," I instantly quitted my post and followed her into the parlour, for I well remembered that she was the lady proposed as a wife for my Edward by the cruel and unrelenting baronet.

Although Lady Dorothea's visit was nominally to Philippa and Augusta, yet I have some reason to imagine that (acquainted with the marriage and arrival of Edward) to see me was a principal motive to it.

I soon perceived that, though lovely and elegant in her person and though easy and polite in her address, she was of that inferior order of beings with regard to delicate feeling, tender sentiments, and refined sensibility, of which Augusta was one.

She stayed but half an hour and neither, in the course of her visit, confided to me any of her secret thoughts, nor requested me to confide in her any of mine. You will easily imagine therefore, my dear Marianne, that I could not feel any ardent affection or very sincere attachment for Lady Dorothea.

Adieu.
Laura

LETTER THE EIGHTH *Laura to Marianne, in continuation*

Lady Dorothea had not left us long before another visitor, as unexpected a one as her Ladyship, was announced. It was Sir Edward, who, informed by Augusta of her brother's marriage, came doubtless to reproach him for having dared to unite himself to me without his knowledge. But Edward, foreseeing his design, approached him with heroic fortitude as soon as he entered the room, and addressed him in the following manner.

"Sir Edward, I know the motive of your journey here—You come with the base design of reproaching me for having entered into an indissoluble engagement with my Laura without your consent—But, Sir, I glory in the act—. It is my greatest boast that I have incurred the displeasure of my father!"

So saying, he took my hand and, whilst Sir Edward, Philippa, and Augusta were doubtless reflecting with admiration on his undaunted bravery, led me from the parlour to his father's carriage, which yet remained at the door and in which we were instantly conveyed from the pursuit of Sir Edward.

The postilions[3] had at first received orders only to take the London road; as soon as we had sufficiently reflected, however, we ordered them to drive to M——., the seat of Edward's most particular friend, which was but a few miles distant.

At M——. we arrived in a few hours; and on sending in our names were immediately admitted to Sophia, the wife of Edward's friend. After having been deprived during the course of three weeks of a real friend (for such I term your mother), imagine my transports at beholding one, most truly worthy of the name. Sophia was rather above the middle size; most elegantly formed. A soft languor spread over her lovely features, but increased their beauty.—It was the characteristic of her mind—. She was all sensibility and feeling. We flew into each other's arms and, after having exchanged vows of mutual friendship for the rest of our lives, instantly unfolded to each other the most inward secrets of our hearts—. We were interrupted in this delightful employment by the entrance of Augustus (Edward's friend), who was just returned from a solitary ramble.

Never did I see such an affecting scene as was the meeting of Edward and Augustus.

"My life! my soul!" (exclaimed the former) "My adorable angel!" (replied the latter) as they flew into each other's arms. It was too pathetic for the feelings of Sophia and myself—We fainted alternately on a sofa.[4]

Adieu.
Laura

LETTER THE NINTH *From the same to the same*

Towards the close of the day we received the following letter from Philippa.

Sir Edward is greatly incensed by your abrupt departure; he has taken back Augusta with him to Bedfordshire. Much as I wish to enjoy again your charming society, I cannot determine to snatch you from that of such dear and

---

3. The servants mounted on and guiding the horses that draw a coach.
4. A stage direction in Richard Brinsley Sheridan's comedy *The Critic* (1779) directs the actors playing the mother and son to "faint alternately in each other's arms."

deserving friends—When your visit to them is terminated, I trust you will return to the arms of your

Philippa

We returned a suitable answer to this affectionate note and, after thanking her for her kind invitation, assured her that we would certainly avail ourselves of it, whenever we might have no other place to go to. Though certainly nothing could, to any reasonable being, have appeared more satisfactory than so grateful a reply to her invitation, yet I know not how it was, but she was certainly capricious enough to be displeased with our behaviour and in a few weeks after, either to revenge our conduct, or relieve her own solitude, married a young and illiterate fortune-hunter. This imprudent step (though we were sensible[5] that it would probably deprive us of that fortune which Philippa had ever taught us to expect) could not on our own accounts excite from our exalted minds a single sigh; yet fearful lest it might prove a source of endless misery to the deluded bride, our trembling sensibility was greatly affected when we were first informed of the event. The affectionate entreaties of Augustus and Sophia that we would for ever consider their house as our home, easily prevailed on us to determine never more to leave them—. In the society of my Edward and this amiable pair, I passed the happiest moments of my life: Our time was most delightfully spent, in mutual protestations of friendship, and in vows of unalterable love, in which we were secure from being interrupted by intruding and disagreeable visitors, as Augustus and Sophia had, on their first entrance in the neighbourhood, taken due care to inform the surrounding families that, as their happiness centered wholly in themselves, they wished for no other society. But alas! my dear Marianne, such happiness as I then enjoyed was too perfect to be lasting. A most severe and unexpected blow at once destroyed every sensation of pleasure. Convinced as you must be from what I have already told you concerning Augustus and Sophia, that there never were a happier couple, I need not, I imagine, inform you that their union had been contrary to the inclinations of their cruel and mercenary parents, who had vainly endeavoured with obstinate perseverance to force them into a marriage with those whom they had ever abhorred, but, with an heroic fortitude worthy to be related and admired, they had both constantly refused to submit to such despotic power.

After having so nobly disentangled themselves from the shackles of parental authority by a clandestine marriage, they were determined never to forfeit the good opinion they had gained in the world in so doing, by accepting any proposals of reconciliation that might be offered them by their fathers—to this farther trial of their noble independence, however, they never were exposed.

They had been married but a few months when our visit to them commenced, during which time they had been amply supported by a considerable sum of money which Augustus had gracefully purloined from his unworthy father's escritoire,[6] a few days before his union with Sophia.

By our arrival their expenses were considerably increased, though their means for supplying them were then nearly exhausted. But they, exalted creatures! scorned to reflect a moment on their pecuniary distresses and would have blushed at the idea of paying their debts.—Alas! what was their reward for such disinterested behaviour? The beautiful Augustus was arrested and we were all undone. Such perfidious treachery in the merciless perpetrators of

5. Conscious, aware.   6. Writing desk.

the deed will shock your gentle nature, dearest Marianne, as much as it then affected the delicate sensibility of Edward, Sophia, your Laura, and of Augustus himself. To complete such unparalleled barbarity, we were informed that an execution in the house would shortly take place.[7] Ah! what could we do but what we did! We sighed and fainted on the sofa.

Adieu.
Laura

LETTER THE TENTH *Laura in continuation*

When we were somewhat recovered from the overpowering effusions of our grief, Edward desired that we would consider what was the most prudent step to be taken in our unhappy situation, while he repaired to his imprisoned friend to lament over his misfortunes. We promised that we would, and he set forwards on his journey to town. During his absence we faithfully complied with his desire and, after the most mature deliberation, at length agreed that the best thing we could do was to leave the house of which we every moment expected the officers of justice to take possession. We waited therefore with the greatest impatience for the return of Edward, in order to impart to him the result of our deliberations—. But no Edward appeared—. In vain did we count the tedious moments of his absence—in vain did we weep—in vain even did we sigh—no Edward returned—. This was too cruel, too unexpected a blow to our gentle sensibility—we could not support it—we could only faint—. At length, collecting all the resolution I was mistress of, I arose and, after packing up some necessary apparel for Sophia and myself, I dragged her to a carriage I had ordered, and instantly we set out for London. As the habitation of Augustus was within twelve miles of town, it was not long ere we arrived there, and no sooner had we entered Holborn[8] than, letting down one of the front glasses,[9] I enquired of every decent-looking person that we passed "If they had seen my Edward?"

But as we drove too rapidly to allow them to answer my repeated enquiries, I gained little, or indeed, no information concerning him. "Where am I to drive?" said the postilion. "To Newgate,[1] gentle youth (replied I), to see Augustus." "Oh! no, no, (exclaimed Sophia) I cannot go to Newgate; I shall not be able to support the sight of my Augustus in so cruel a confinement—my feelings are sufficiently shocked by the *recital* of his distress, but to behold it will overpower my sensibility." As I perfectly agreed with her in the justice of her sentiments, the postilion was instantly directed to return into the country. You may perhaps have been somewhat surprised, my dearest Marianne, that in the distress I then endured, destitute of any support, and unprovided with any habitation, I should never once have remembered my father and mother or my paternal cottage in the vale of Usk. To account for this seeming forgetfulness I must inform you of a trifling circumstance concerning them which I have as yet never mentioned—. The death of my parents a few weeks after my departure is the circumstance I allude to. By their decease I became the lawful inheritress of their house and fortune. But alas! the house had never been their own, and their fortune had only been an annuity[2] on their own lives.

---

7. I.e., the goods in the house, as property of a debtor who has forfeited them, will be seized by a sheriff's officer.
8. District in London.
9. Window of the coach.

1. A prison. That Augustus is thought to be there indicates he has been arrested as a thief rather than as a debtor.
2. Annual payment of a set sum.

Such is the depravity of the world! To your mother I should have returned with pleasure, should have been happy to have introduced to her my charming Sophia, and should have with cheerfulness have passed the remainder of my life in their dear society in the vale of Usk, had not one obstacle to the execution of so agreeable a scheme intervened; which was the marriage and removal of your mother to a distant part of Ireland.

Adieu.
Laura

LETTER THE ELEVENTH *Laura in continuation*

"I have a relation in Scotland (said Sophia to me as we left London) who, I am certain, would not hesitate in receiving me." "Shall I order the boy to drive there?" said I—but instantly recollecting myself, exclaimed "Alas, I fear it will be too long a journey for the horses." Unwilling however to act only from my own inadequate knowledge of the strength and abilities of horses, I consulted the postilion, who was entirely of my opinion concerning the affair. We therefore determined to change horses at the next town and to travel post[3] the remainder of the journey—. When we arrived at the last inn we were to stop at, which was but a few miles from the house of Sophia's relation, unwilling to intrude our society on him unexpected and unthought of, we wrote a very elegant and well-penned note to him containing an account of our destitute and melancholy situation, and of our intention to spend some months with him in Scotland. As soon as we had dispatched this letter, we immediately prepared to follow it in person and were stepping into the carriage for that purpose, when our attention was attracted by the entrance of a coroneted coach and four[4] into the inn-yard. A gentleman considerably advanced in years descended from it—. At his first appearance my sensibility was wonderfully affected and ere I had gazed at him a second time, an instinctive sympathy whispered to my heart, that he was my grandfather.

Convinced that I could not be mistaken in my conjecture, I instantly sprang from the carriage I had just entered, and following the venerable stranger into the room he had been shewn to, I threw myself on my knees before him and besought him to acknowledge me as his grandchild.—He started, and, after having attentively examined my features, raised me from the ground and throwing his grandfatherly arms around my neck, exclaimed, "Acknowledge thee! Yes, dear resemblance of my Laurina and my Laurina's daughter, sweet image of my Claudia and my Claudia's mother, I do acknowledge thee as the daughter of the one and the granddaughter of the other." While he was thus tenderly embracing me, Sophia, astonished at my precipitate departure, entered the room in search of me—. No sooner had she caught the eye of the venerable peer, than he exclaimed with every mark of astonishment—"Another granddaughter ! Yes, yes, I see you are the daughter of my Laurina's eldest girl; your resemblance to the beauteous Matilda sufficiently proclaims it." "Oh!" replied Sophia, "when I first beheld you the instinct of nature whispered me that we were in some degree related—But whether grandfathers, or grandmothers, I could not pretend to determine." He folded her in his arms, and whilst they were tenderly embracing, the door of the apartment opened and a most beautiful young man appeared. On perceiving him Lord St. Clair started

---

3. By speedy and expensive post coach.
4. The coach, drawn by four horses, is adorned
with the image of a crown, indicating its occupant's noble rank.

and, retreating back a few paces, with uplifted hands, said, "Another grand-child! What an unexpected happiness is this! to discover in the space of three minutes, as many of my descendants! This, I am certain, is Philander, the son of my Laurina's third girl, the amiable Bertha; there wants now but the presence of Gustavus to complete the union of my Laurina's grandchildren."

"And here he is; (said a graceful youth who that instant entered the room) here is the Gustavus you desire to see. I am the son of Agatha, your Laurina's fourth and youngest daughter." "I see you are indeed; replied Lord St. Clair—But tell me (continued he, looking fearfully towards the door) tell me, have I any other grandchildren in the house." "None, my Lord." "Then I will provide for you all without further delay—Here are four banknotes of 50£ each—Take them and remember I have done the duty of a grandfather—." He instantly left the room and immediately afterwards the house.

Adieu.

Laura

LETTER THE TWELFTH *Laura in continuation*

You may imagine how greatly we were surprised by the sudden departure of Lord St. Clair. "Ignoble grandsire!" exclaimed Sophia. "Unworthy grand-father!" said I, and instantly fainted in each other's arms. How long we remained in this situation I know not; but when we recovered we found ourselves alone, without either Gustavus, Philander, or the banknotes. As we were deploring our unhappy fate, the door of the apartment opened and "Macdonald" was announced. He was Sophia's cousin. The haste with which he came to our relief so soon after the receipt of our note spoke so greatly in his favour that I hesitated not to pronounce him, at first sight, a tender and sympathetic friend. Alas! he little deserved the name—for though he told us that he was much concerned at our misfortunes, yet by his own account it appeared that the perusal of them had neither drawn from him a single sigh, nor induced him to bestow one curse on our vindictive stars—. He told Sophia that his daughter depended on her returning with him to Macdonald Hall, and that as his cousin's friend he should be happy to see me there also. To Macdonald Hall, therefore, we went, and were received with great kindness by Janetta, the daughter of Macdonald, and the mistress of the mansion. Janetta was then only fifteen; naturally well disposed, endowed with a susceptible heart, and a sympathetic disposition, she might, had these amiable qualities been properly encouraged, have been an ornament to human nature; but, unfortunately, her father possessed not a soul sufficiently exalted to admire so promising a disposition, and had endeavoured by every means in his power to prevent its increasing with her years. He had actually so far extinguished the natural noble sensibility of her heart, as to prevail on her to accept an offer from a young man of his recommendation. They were to be married in a few months, and Graham was in the house when we arrived. *We* soon saw through his character—. He was just such a man as one might have expected to be the choice of Macdonald. They said he was sensible, well-informed, and agreeable; we did not pretend to judge of such trifles, but, as we were convinced he had no soul, that he had never read the *Sorrows of Werter*,[5] and that his hair bore not

---

5. *Sorrows of Young Werther* (1774), Goethe's novel in letters telling the story of the title character's hopeless love, was a hit in England when translated from its original German. It is often seen as a founding text of the European Romantic movement.

the slightest resemblance to auburn, we were certain that Janetta could feel no affection for him, or at least that she ought to feel none. The very circumstance of his being her father's choice, too, was so much in his disfavour, that had he been deserving her in every other respect, yet *that* of itself ought to have been a sufficient reason in the eyes of Janetta for rejecting him. These considerations we were determined to represent to her in their proper light and doubted not of meeting with the desired success from one naturally so well disposed, whose errors in the affair had only arisen from a want of proper confidence in her own opinion, and a suitable contempt of her father's. We found her, indeed, all that our warmest wishes could have hoped for; we had no difficulty to convince her that it was impossible she could love Graham, or that it was her duty to disobey her father; the only thing at which she rather seemed to hesitate was our assertion that she must be attached to some other person. For some time, she persevered in declaring that she knew no other young man for whom she had the smallest affection; but upon explaining the impossibility of such a thing she said that she believed she *did like* Captain M'Kenzie better than anyone she knew besides. This confession satisfied us and, after having enumerated the good qualities of M'Kenzie and assured her that she was violently in love with him, we desired to know whether he had ever in anywise declared his affection to her.

"So far from having ever declared it, I have no reason to imagine that he has ever felt any for me." said Janetta. "That he certainly adores you (replied Sophia) there can be no doubt—. The attachment must be reciprocal—. Did he never gaze on you with admiration—tenderly press your hand—drop an involuntary tear—and leave the room abruptly?" "Never (replied she) that I remember—he has always left the room indeed when his visit has been ended, but has never gone away particularly abruptly or without making a bow." "Indeed, my love (said I) you must be mistaken—: for it is absolutely impossible that he should ever have left you but with confusion, despair, and precipitation—. Consider but for a moment, Janetta, and you must be convinced how absurd it is to suppose that he could ever make a bow, or behave like any other person." Having settled this point to our satisfaction, the next we took into consideration was to determine in what manner we should inform M'Kenzie of the favourable opinion Janetta entertained of him—. We at length agreed to acquaint him with it by an anonymous letter which Sophia drew up in the following manner.

> Oh! happy lover of the beautiful Janetta; oh! enviable possessor of *her* heart whose hand is destined to another, why do you thus delay a confession of your attachment to the amiable object of it ? Oh! consider that a few weeks will at once put an end to every flattering hope that you may now entertain, by uniting the unfortunate victim of her father's cruelty to the execrable and detested Graham.
>
> Alas! why do you thus so cruelly connive at the projected misery of her and of yourself by delaying to communicate that scheme which had doubtless long possessed your imagination? A secret union will at once secure the felicity of both.

The amiable M'Kenzie, whose modesty, as he afterwards assured us, had been the only reason of his having so long concealed the violence of his affection for Janetta, on receiving this billet flew on the wings of love to Macdonald Hall and so powerfully pleaded his attachment to her who inspired it that, after a few more private interviews, Sophia and I experienced the satisfaction of seeing them depart for Gretna Green,[6] which they chose for the celebration of their nuptials, in preference to any other place, although it was at a considerable distance from Macdonald Hall.

Adieu.

Laura

LETTER THE THIRTEENTH *Laura in Continuation*

They had been gone nearly a couple of hours, before either Macdonald or Graham had entertained any suspicion of the affair—. And they might not even then have suspected it, but for the following little accident. Sophia, happening one day to open a private drawer in Macdonald's library with one of her own keys, discovered that it was the place where he kept his papers of consequence and amongst them some banknotes of considerable amount. This discovery she imparted to me; and having agreed together that it would be a proper treatment of so vile a wretch as Macdonald to deprive him of money, perhaps dishonestly gained, it was determined that the next time we should either of us happen to go that way, we would take one or more of the banknotes from the drawer. This well-meant plan we had often successfully put in execution; but alas! on the very day of Janetta's escape, as Sophia was majestically removing the fifth banknote from the drawer to her own purse, she was suddenly most impertinently interrupted in her employment by the entrance of Macdonald himself, in a most abrupt and precipitate manner. Sophia (who, though naturally all winning sweetness, could when occasions demanded it call forth the dignity of her sex) instantly put on a most forbidding look, and, darting an angry frown on the undaunted culprit, demanded in a haughty tone of voice "Wherefore her retirement was thus insolently broken in on?" The unblushing Macdonald, without even endeavouring to exculpate himself from the crime he was charged with, meanly endeavoured to reproach Sophia with ignobly defrauding him of his money. The dignity of Sophia was wounded; "Wretch (exclaimed she, hastily replacing the banknote in the drawer) how darest thou to accuse me of an act, of which the bare idea makes me blush?" The base wretch was still unconvinced and continued to upbraid the justly offended Sophia in such opprobrious language, that at length he so greatly provoked the gentle sweetness of her nature, as to induce her to revenge herself on him by informing him of Janetta's elopement, and of the active part we had both taken in the affair. At this period of their quarrel I entered the library and was, as you may imagine, equally offended as Sophia at the ill-grounded accusations of the malevolent and contemptible Macdonald. "Base miscreant (cried I) how canst thou thus undauntedly endeavour to sully the spotless reputation of such bright excellence? Why dost thou not suspect *my* innocence as soon?" "Be satisfied Madam (replied he) I *do* suspect it, and therefore must desire that you will both leave this house in less than half an hour."

"We shall go willingly; (answered Sophia) our hearts have long detested thee, and nothing but our friendship for thy daughter could have induced us to remain so long beneath thy roof."

"Your friendship for my daughter has indeed been most powerfully exerted

6. A town in southern Scotland, in which marriages of minors could be quickly performed without questions being asked. It was for this reason the destination of many eloping couples during the period.

by throwing her into the arms of an unprincipled fortune-hunter." (replied he.)

"Yes, (exclaimed I) amidst every misfortune, it will afford us some consolation to reflect that by this one act of friendship to Janetta, we have amply discharged every obligation that we have received from her father."

"It must indeed be a most grateful reflection, to your exalted minds." (said he.)

As soon as we had packed up our wardrobe and valuables, we left Macdonald Hall, and after having walked about a mile and a half we sat down by the side of a clear limpid stream to refresh our exhausted limbs. The place was suited to meditation—. A grove of full-grown elms sheltered us from the east—. A bed of full-grown nettles from the west—. Before us ran the murmuring brook and behind us ran the turnpike road. We were in a mood for contemplation and in a disposition to enjoy so beautiful a spot. A mutual silence, which had for some time reigned between us, was at length broke by my exclaiming— "What a lovely scene! Alas, why are not Edward and Augustus here to enjoy its beauties with us?"

"Ah! my beloved Laura (cried Sophia) for pity's sake, forbear recalling to my remembrance the unhappy situation of my imprisoned husband. Alas, what would I not give to learn the fate of my Augustus! to know if he is still in Newgate, or if he is yet hung. But never shall I be able so far to conquer my tender sensibility as to enquire after him. Oh! do not, I beseech you, ever let me again hear you repeat his beloved name—. It affects me too deeply—. I cannot bear to hear him mentioned; it wounds my feelings."

"Excuse me, my Sophia, for having thus unwillingly offended you—" replied I—and then changing the conversation, desired her to admire the noble grandeur of the elms which sheltered us from the eastern zephyr.[7] "Alas! my Laura (returned she) avoid so melancholy a subject, I entreat you.—Do not again wound my sensibility by observations on those elms. They remind me of Augustus—. He was like them, tall, majestic—he possessed that noble grandeur which you admire in them."

I was silent, fearful lest I might any more unwillingly distress her by fixing on any other subject of conversation which might again remind her of Augustus.

"Why do you not speak, my Laura?" (said she, after a short pause) "I cannot support this silence—you must not leave me to my own reflections; they ever recur to Augustus."

"What a beautiful sky! (said I) How charmingly is the azure varied by those delicate streaks of white!"

"Oh! my Laura (replied she, hastily withdrawing her eyes from a momentary glance at the sky) do not thus distress me by calling my attention to an object which so cruelly reminds me of my Augustus's blue satin waistcoat striped with white! In pity to your unhappy friend, avoid a subject so distressing." What could I do? The feelings of Sophia were at that time so exquisite, and the tenderness she felt for Augustus so poignant, that I had not the power to start any other topic, justly fearing that it might in some unforeseen manner again awaken all her sensibility by directing her thoughts to her husband.— Yet to be silent would be cruel; she had entreated me to talk.

---

7. A breeze; usually one from the west.

From this dilemma I was most fortunately relieved by an accident truly apropos;[8] it was the lucky overturning of a gentleman's phaeton,[9] on the road which ran murmuring behind us. It was a most fortunate accident as it diverted the attention of Sophia from the melancholy reflections which she had been before indulging. We instantly quitted our seats and ran to the rescue of those who but a few moments before had been in so elevated a situation as a fashionably high phaeton, but who were now laid low and sprawling in the dust—. "What an ample subject for reflection on the uncertain enjoyments of this world, would not that phaeton and the life of Cardinal Wolsey afford a thinking mind!"[1] said I to Sophia as we were hastening to the field of action.

She had not time to answer me, for every thought was now engaged by the horrid spectacle before us. Two gentlemen, most elegantly attired but weltering in their blood, was what first struck our eyes—we approached—they were Edward and Augustus—Yes, dearest Marianne, they were our husbands. Sophia shrieked and fainted on the ground—I screamed and instantly ran mad—. We remained thus mutually deprived of our senses some minutes, and on regaining them were deprived of them again.—For an hour and a quarter did we continue in this unfortunate situation—Sophia fainting every moment and I running mad as often. At length a groan from the hapless Edward (who alone retained any share of life) restored us to ourselves—. Had we indeed before imagined that either of them lived, we should have been more sparing of our grief—but as we had supposed when we first beheld them that they were no more, we knew that nothing could remain to be done but what we were about—. No sooner therefore did we hear my Edward's groan than, postponing our lamentations for the present, we hastily ran to the dear youth and kneeling on each side of him implored him not to die—. "Laura (said he, fixing his now languid eyes on me) I fear I have been overturned."

I was overjoyed to find him yet sensible—.

"Oh! tell me, Edward (said I) tell me, I beseech you, before you die, what has befallen you since that unhappy day in which Augustus was arrested and we were separated—"

"I will" (said he) and instantly fetching a deep sigh, expired—. Sophia immediately sunk again into a swoon—. *My* grief was more audible. My voice faltered, my eyes assumed a vacant stare, my face became as pale as death, and my senses were considerably impaired—.

"Talk not to me of phaetons (said I, raving in a frantic, incoherent manner)—give me a violin—. I'll play to him and soothe him in his melancholy hours—Beware, ye gentle nymphs, of Cupid's thunderbolts, avoid the piercing shafts of Jupiter—Look at that grove of firs—I see a leg of mutton—They told me Edward was not dead; but they deceived me—they took him for a cucumber—" Thus I continued, wildly exclaiming on my Edward's death—. For two hours did I rave thus madly and should not then have left off, as I was not in the least fatigued, had not Sophia, who was just recovered from her swoon, entreated me to consider that night was now approaching and that the damps began to fall. "And whither shall we go (said I) to shelter us from either?" "To that white cottage." (replied she, pointing to a neat building which

8. Opportune.
9. Type of open carriage, named for the over-adventurous charioteer of Greek mythology.
1. The reference is to Cardinal Wolsey's fall from

royal grace during the reign of Henry VIII. Laura, like any well-trained schoolgirl of the 18th century, knows how to moralize on topics from English history.

rose up amidst the grove of elms and which I had not before observed—) I agreed, and we instantly walked to it—we knocked at the door—it was opened by an old woman; on being requested to afford us a night's lodging, she informed us that her house was but small, that she had only two bedrooms, but that however, we should be welcome to one of them. We were satisfied and followed the good woman into the house, where we were greatly cheered by the sight of a comfortable fire—. She was a widow and had only one daughter, who was then just seventeen—One of the best of ages; but alas! she was very plain and her name was Bridget. . . . . . Nothing therefore could be expected from her—she could not be supposed to possess either exalted ideas, delicate feelings, or refined sensibilities—She was nothing more than a mere good-tempered, civil, and obliging young woman; as such we could scarcely dislike her—she was only an object of contempt—.

Adieu.
Laura

LETTER THE FOURTEENTH *Laura in continuation*

Arm yourself, my amiable young friend, with all the philosophy you are mistress of; summon up all the fortitude you possess, for alas! in the perusal of the following pages your sensibility will be most severely tried. Ah! what were the misfortunes I had before experienced and which I have already related to you, to the one I am now going to inform you of. The death of my father, my mother, and my husband, though almost more than my gentle nature could support, were trifles in comparison to the misfortune I am now proceeding to relate. The morning after our arrival at the cottage, Sophia complained of a violent pain in her delicate limbs, accompanied with a disagreeable headache. She attributed it to a cold caught by her continued faintings in the open air as the dew was falling the evening before. This, I feared, was but too probably the case; since how could it be otherwise accounted for that I should have escaped the same indisposition, but by supposing that the bodily exertions I had undergone in my repeated fits of frenzy had so effectually circulated and warmed my blood as to make me proof against the chilling damps of night, whereas Sophia, lying totally inactive on the ground, must have been exposed to all their severity. I was most seriously alarmed by her illness, which, trifling as it may appear to you, a certain instinctive sensibility whispered me would in the end be fatal to her.

Alas! my fears were but too fully justified; she grew gradually worse, and I daily became more alarmed for her.—At length she was obliged to confine herself solely to the bed allotted us by our worthy landlady—. Her disorder turned to a galloping consumption[2] and in a few days carried her off. Amidst all my lamentations for her (and violent you may suppose they were) I yet received some consolation in the reflection of my having paid every attention to her that could be offered in her illness. I had wept over her every day—had bathed her sweet face with my tears and had pressed her fair hands continually in mine—. "My beloved Laura (said she to me, a few hours before she died) take warning from my unhappy end and avoid the imprudent conduct which has occasioned it . . . beware of fainting-fits . . . Though at the time they may be refreshing and agreeable, yet, believe me, they will in the end, if too

---

2. A rapidly developing case of tuberculosis.

often repeated and at improper seasons, prove destructive to your constitution. . . . . My fate will teach you this . . . I die a martyr to my grief for the loss
of Augustus. . . . One fatal swoon has cost me my life. . . . Beware of swoons,
dear Laura . . . A frenzy fit is not one quarter so pernicious; it is an exercise
to the body and, if not too violent, is, I dare say, conducive to health in its
consequences—Run mad as often as you choose; but do not faint—".

These were the last words she ever addressed to me . . . It was her dying
advice to her afflicted Laura, who has ever most faithfully adhered to it.

After having attended my lamented friend to her early grave, I immediately
(though late at night) left the detested village in which she died, and near
which had expired my husband and Augustus. I had not walked many yards
from it before I was overtaken by a stagecoach, in which I instantly took a
place, determined to proceed in it to Edinburgh, where I hoped to find some
kind pitying friend who would receive and comfort me in my afflictions.

It was so dark when I entered the coach that I could not distinguish the
number of my fellow travellers; I could only perceive that they were many.
Regardless, however, of any thing concerning them, I gave myself up to my
own sad reflections. A general silence prevailed—a silence, which was by nothing interrupted but by the loud and repeated snores of one of the party.

"What an illiterate villain must that man be! (thought I to myself) What a
total want of delicate refinement must he have who can thus shock our senses
by such a brutal noise! He must, I am certain, be capable of every bad action!
There is no crime too black for such a character!" Thus reasoned I within
myself, and doubtless such were the reflections of my fellow travellers.

At length, returning day enabled me to behold the unprincipled scoundrel
who had so violently disturbed my feelings. It was Sir Edward, the father of
my deceased husband. By his side sat Augusta, and on the same seat with me
were your mother and Lady Dorothea. Imagine my surprise at finding myself
thus seated amongst my old acquaintance. Great as was my astonishment, it
was yet increased, when, on look[ing] out of [the] windows, I beheld the husband of Philippa, with Philippa by his side, on the coach-box,[3] and when, on
looking behind, I beheld Philander and Gustavus in the basket.[4] "Oh! heavens,
(exclaimed I) is it possible that I should so unexpectedly be surrounded by my
nearest relations and connections?" These words roused the rest of the party,
and every eye was directed to the corner in which I sat; "Oh! my Isabel (continued I, throwing myself across Lady Dorothea into her arms) receive once
more to your bosom the unfortunate Laura. Alas! when we last parted in the
vale of Usk, I was happy in being united to the best of Edwards; I had then a
father and a mother, and had never known misfortunes—But now deprived
of every friend but you—".

"What! (interrupted Augusta) is my brother dead then? Tell us, I entreat
you, what is become of him?" "Yes, cold and insensible[5] nymph, (replied I)
that luckless swain, your brother, is no more, and you may now glory in being
the heiress of Sir Edward's fortune."

Although I had always despised her from the day I had overheard her conversation with my Edward, yet in civility I complied with hers and Sir Edward's
entreaties that I would inform them of the whole melancholy affair. They were

3. Seat for the driver.
4. The overhanging back compartment on the outside of a stagecoach, where the passengers paying

the cheapest fares were seated.
5. Incapable of feeling, callous.

greatly shocked—Even the obdurate heart of Sir Edward and the insensible one of Augusta were touched with sorrow by the unhappy tale. At the request of your mother I related to them every other misfortune which had befallen me since we parted. Of the imprisonment of Augustus and the absence of Edward—of our arrival in Scotland—of our unexpected meeting with our grandfather and our cousins—of our visit to Macdonald Hall—of the singular service we there performed towards Janetta—of her father's ingratitude for it. . . . . of his inhuman behaviour, unaccountable suspicions, and barbarous treatment of us, in obliging us to leave the house. . . . . of our lamentations on the loss of Edward and Augustus and finally of the melancholy death of my beloved companion.

Pity and surprise were strongly depictured in your mother's countenance, during the whole of my narration, but I am sorry to say, that to the eternal reproach of her sensibility, the latter infinitely predominated. Nay, faultless as my conduct had certainly been during the whole course of my late misfortunes and adventures, she pretended to find fault with my behaviour in many of the situations in which I had been placed. As I was sensible myself, that I had always behaved in a manner which reflected honour on my feelings and refinement, I paid little attention to what she said, and desired her to satisfy my curiosity by informing me how she came there, instead of wounding my spotless reputation with unjustifiable reproaches. As soon as she had complied with my wishes in this particular and had given me an accurate detail of everything that had befallen her since our separation (the particulars of which, if you are not already acquainted with, your mother will give you), I applied to Augusta for the same information respecting herself, Sir Edward, and Lady Dorothea.

She told me that, having a considerable taste for the beauties of nature, her curiosity to behold the delightful scenes it exhibited in that part of the world had been so much raised by Gilpin's tour to the Highlands,[6] that she had prevailed on her father to undertake a tour of Scotland and had persuaded Lady Dorothea to accompany them. That they had arrived at Edinburgh a few days before and from thence had made daily excursions into the country around in the stage coach they were then in, from one of which excursions they were at that time returning. My next enquiries were concerning Philippa and her husband, the latter of whom, I learned, having spent all her fortune, had recourse for subsistence to the talent in which he had always most excelled, namely, driving, and that having sold everything which belonged to them, except their coach, had converted it into a stage, and in order to be removed from any of his former acquaintance, had driven it to Edinburgh from whence he went to Sterling[7] every other day; that Philippa, still retaining her affection for her ungrateful husband, had followed him to Scotland and generally accompanied him in his little excursions to Sterling. "It has only been to throw a little money into their pockets (continued Augusta) that my father has always travelled in their coach to view the beauties of the country since our arrival in Scotland—for it would certainly have been much more agreeable to us to visit the Highlands in a post-chaise[8] than merely to travel from Edin-

6. Gilpin's *Observations, Relative Chiefly to Picturesque Beauty . . . On Several Parts of Great Britain; Particularly the High-Lands of Scotland* (1789).
7. Stirling, a town forty miles northeast of Edin-

burgh.
8. Augusta wishes that they had hired on their own a smaller, more comfortable carriage, rather than traveling in a public stagecoach that follows a predetermined route.

burgh to Sterling and from Sterling to Edinburgh every other day in a crowded and uncomfortable stage." I perfectly agreed with her in her sentiments on the affair, and secretly blamed Sir Edward for thus sacrificing his daughter's pleasure for the sake of a ridiculous old woman, whose folly in marrying so young a man ought to be punished. His behaviour, however, was entirely of a piece with his general character; for what could be expected from a man who possessed not the smallest atom of sensibility, who scarcely knew the meaning of sympathy, and who actually snored—.

Adieu.
Laura

LETTER THE FIFTEENTH *Laura in continuation*

When we arrived at the town where we were to breakfast, I was determined to speak with Philander and Gustavus, and to that purpose as soon as I left the carriage, I went to the basket and tenderly enquired after their health, expressing my fears of the uneasiness of their situation. At first they seemed rather confused at my appearance, dreading no doubt that I might call them to account for the money which our grandfather had left me and which they had unjustly deprived me of, but finding that I mentioned nothing of the matter, they desired me to step into the basket, as we might there converse with greater ease. Accordingly I entered, and whilst the rest of the party were devouring green tea and buttered toast, we feasted ourselves in a more refined and sentimental manner by a confidential conversation. I informed them of everything which had befallen me during the course of my life, and at my request they related to me every incident of theirs.

"We are the sons, as you already know, of the two youngest daughters which Lord St. Clair had by Laurina, an Italian opera girl. Our mothers could neither of them exactly ascertain who were our fathers; though it is generally believed that Philander is the son of one Philip Jones, a bricklayer, and that my father was Gregory Staves, a stay-maker[9] of Edinburgh. This is, however, of little consequence, for as our mothers were certainly never married to either of them, it reflects no dishonour on our blood, which is of a most ancient and unpolluted kind. Bertha (the mother of Philander) and Agatha (my own mother) always lived together. They were neither of them very rich; their united fortunes had originally amounted to nine thousand pounds, but as they had always lived upon the principal of it, when we were fifteen it was diminished to nine hundred. This nine hundred, they always kept in a drawer in one of the tables which stood in our common sitting parlour, for the convenience of having it always at hand. Whether it was from this circumstance, of its being easily taken, or from a wish of being independent, or from an excess of sensibility (for which we were always remarkable), I cannot now determine, but certain it is that when we had reached our fifteenth year, we took the nine hundred pounds and ran away. Having obtained this prize we were determined to manage it with economy and not to spend it either with folly or extravagance. To this purpose we therefore divided it into nine parcels, one of which we devoted to victuals, the second to drink, the third to housekeeping, the fourth to carriages, the fifth to horses, the sixth to servants, the seventh to amusements, the eighth to clothes, and the ninth to silver buckles. Having thus

9. Maker of corsets.

arranged our expenses for two months (for we expected to make the nine hundred pounds last as long), we hastened to London and had the good luck to spend it in seven weeks and a day, which was six days sooner than we had intended. As soon as we had thus happily disencumbered ourselves from the weight of so much money, we began to think of returning to our mothers, but accidentally hearing that they were both starved to death, we gave over the design and determined to engage ourselves to some strolling company of players, as we had always a turn for the stage. Accordingly, we offered our services to one and were accepted; our company was indeed rather small, as it consisted only of the manager, his wife, and ourselves, but there were fewer to pay and the only inconvenience attending it was the scarcity of plays, which for want of people to fill the characters we could perform—. We did not mind trifles, however—. One of our most admired performances was *Macbeth,* in which we were truly great. The manager always played *Banquo* himself, his wife my *Lady Macbeth.* I did the *three witches,* and Philander acted *all the rest.* To say the truth, this tragedy was not only the best, but the only play we ever performed; and after having acted it all over England and Wales, we came to Scotland to exhibit it over the remainder of Great Britain. We happened to be quartered in that very town, where you came and met your grandfather—. We were in the inn-yard when his carriage entered and, perceiving by the arms[1] to whom it belonged, and, knowing that Lord St. Clair was our grandfather, we agreed to endeavour to get something from him by discovering the relationship—. You know how well it succeeded—. Having obtained the two hundred pounds, we instantly left the town, leaving our manager and his wife to act *Macbeth* by themselves, and took the road to Sterling, where we spent our little fortune with great *éclat.*[2] We are now returning to Edinburgh to get some preferment[3] in the acting way; and such, my dear cousin, is our history."

I thanked the amiable youth for his entertaining narration, and after expressing my wishes for their welfare and happiness, left them in their little habitation and returned to my other friends who impatiently expected me.

My adventures are now drawing to a close, my dearest Marianne; at least for the present.

When we arrived at Edinburgh, Sir Edward told me that, as the widow of his son, he desired I would accept from his hands of four hundred a year. I graciously promised that I would, but could not help observing that the unsympathetic baronet offered it more on account of my being the widow of Edward than in being the refined and amiable Laura.

I took up my residence in a romantic village in the Highlands of Scotland, where I have ever since continued, and where I can, uninterrupted by unmeaning visits, indulge, in a melancholy solitude, my unceasing lamentations for the death of my father, my mother, my husband, and my friend.

Augusta has been for several years united to Graham, the man of all others most suited to her; she became acquainted with him during her stay in Scotland.

Sir Edward, in hopes of gaining an heir to his title and estate, at the same time married Lady Dorothea—. His wishes have been answered.

Philander and Gustavus, after having raised their reputation by their per-

---

1. The coat of arms painted on the side of a nobleman's or noblewoman's carriage.
2. French: literally, brilliant display; conspicuous

success.
3. Advancement.

formances in the theatrical line at Edinburgh, removed to Covent Garden, where they still exhibit under the assumed names of *Lewis and Quick*.[4] Philippa has long paid the debt of nature;[5] her husband, however, still continues to drive the stage-coach from Edinburgh to Sterling:—

Adieu, my dearest Marianne.

Laura

1790   1922

Plan of a Novel, According to Hints from Various Quarters[1]

Scene to be in the country, heroine the daughter of a clergyman, one who after having lived much in the world had retired from it, and settled in a curacy,[2] with a very small fortune of his own.—He, the most excellent man that can be imagined, perfect in character, temper, and manners—without the smallest drawback or peculiarity to prevent his being the most delightful companion to his daughter from one year's end to the other.—Heroine a faultless character herself—, perfectly good, with much tenderness and sentiment, and not the least wit—very highly accomplished, understanding modern languages and (generally speaking) everything that the most accomplished young women learn, but particularly excelling in music—her favourite pursuit—and playing equally well on the piano forte and harp—and singing in the first stile. Her person, quite beautiful—dark eyes and plump cheeks.—Book to open with the description of father and daughter—who are to converse in long speeches, elegant language—and a tone of high, serious sentiment.—The father to be induced, at his daughter's earnest request, to relate to her the past events of his life. This narrative will reach through the greatest part of the first volume— as besides all the circumstances of his attachment to her mother and their marriage, it will comprehend his going to sea as chaplain to a distinguished naval character about the court, his going afterwards to court himself, which introduced him to a great variety of characters and involved him in many interesting situations, concluding with his opinion of the benefits to result from tythes being done away, and his having buried his own mother (heroine's lamented grandmother) in consequence of the high priest of the parish in which she died, refusing to pay her remains the respect due to them. The father to be of a very literary turn, an enthusiast in literature, nobody's enemy but his own[3]—at the same time most zealous in the discharge of his pastoral

---

4. William Thomas Lewis and John Quick were well-known actors of the late 18th century. Covent Garden: one of the two London theaters licensed by royal patent.
5. I.e., she has died.
1. "Plan of a Novel, According to Hints from Various Quarters," Austen's teasing account of the novel she *would* write if she took to heart the advice people gave her about what her fiction ought to be, is another manuscript preserved in her family. It was first published in her nephew James Austen-Leigh's *Memoir of Jane Austen* (1870). In the original manuscript, Austen supplied marginal glosses, mainly omitted here, indicating the source of each "hint" the "Plan" incorporates. Her would-be advisors included, in

addition to the Reverend James Stanier Clarke (the librarian to the prince regent), neighbors; family members, most prominently her niece Fanny Knight, a parson, J. G. Sherer, who had been displeased, Austen reported, with her "pictures of clergymen"; and William Gifford, the editor of the *Quarterly Review* as well as the advisor who had read *Emma* for the publisher John Murray.
2. I.e., settled in the position of curate, the assistant (often badly paid) to the incumbent priest of the parish.
3. For this summary of the clergyman's tale that will fill up her novel's projected first volume, Austen lifts a number of phrases directly from Clarke's letters. Clarke wished to see Austen address the benefits of the abolition of tithes (the taxes sup-

duties, the model of an[4] exemplary parish priest.—The heroine's friendship to be sought after by a young woman in the same neighbourhood, of talents and shrewdness, with light eyes and a fair skin, but having a considerable degree of wit, heroine shall shrink from the acquaintance.—From this outset, the story will proceed, and contain a striking variety of adventures. Heroine and her father never above a[5] fortnight together in one place, *he* being driven from his curacy by the vile arts of some totally unprincipled and heartless young man, desperately in love with the heroine, and pursuing her with unrelenting passion—no sooner settled in one country of Europe than they are necessitated to quit it and retire to another—always making new acquaintance, and always obliged to leave them.—This will of course exhibit a wide variety of characters—but there will be no mixture; the scene will be for ever shifting from one set of people to another—but all the good will be unexceptionable in every respect—and there will be no foibles or weaknesses but with the wicked, who will be completely depraved and infamous, hardly a resemblance of humanity left in them.—Early in her career, in the progress of her first removals, heroine must meet with the hero—all perfection of course—and only prevented from paying his addresses to her,[6] by some excess of refinement.—Wherever she goes, somebody falls in love with her, and she receives repeated offers of marriage—which she always refers wholly to her father, exceedingly angry that *he* should not be first applied to.—Often carried away by the anti-hero, but rescued either by her father or the hero—often reduced to support herself and her father by her talents and work for her bread;—continually cheated and defrauded of her hire,[7] worn down to a skeleton, and now and then starved to death—. At last, hunted out of civilized society, denied the poor shelter of the humblest cottage, they are compelled to retreat into Kamschatka[8] where the poor father, quite worn down, finding his end approaching, throws himself on the ground, and after four or five hours of tender advice and paternal admonition to his miserable child, expires in a fine burst of literary enthusiasm, intermingled with invectives again[st] holders of tythes.—Heroine inconsolable for some time—but afterwards crawls back towards her former country—having at least twenty narrow escapes of falling into the hands of anti-hero—and at last in the very nick of time, turning a corner to avoid him, runs into the arms of the hero himself, who having just shaken off the scruples which fetter'd him before, was at the very moment setting off in pursuit of her.—The tenderest and completest eclaircissement[9] takes place, and they are happily united.—Throughout the whole work, heroine to be in the most elegant society and living in high style. The name of the work *not* to be *Emma*—but of the same sort as S & S and P & P.

1816   1870

---

porting the Anglican Church and clergy) and thought his own story of having buried his mother would make good material for her novel.
4. Mr. Sherer [Austen's note].
5. Many critics [Austen's note].
6. I.e., seeking her hand in marriage.
7. Wages.
8. Kamchatka: peninsula on the eastern edge of Asia, extending into the Bering Sea, acquired by

Russia in the 18th century. The novels of Austen's contemporaries tended to be cosmopolitan in setting and often did send heroines wandering across Europe. Austen, however, may be thinking particularly of Sophie de Cottin's *Elizabeth; or Exiles of Siberia* (1806; English translation, 1809).
9. French: the clarification of mysteries and misunderstandings that brings a narrative to closure.

WILLIAM HAZLITT
1778–1830

"I started in life," William Hazlitt wrote, "with the French Revolution, and I have lived, alas! to see the end of it. . . . Since then, I confess, I have no longer felt myself young, for with that my hopes fell." He was born into a radical circle, for the elder William Hazlitt, his father, was a Unitarian minister who declared from the pulpit his advocacy both of American independence and of the French Revolution. When young William was five years old, his father took the family to America in search of liberty and founded the first Unitarian church in Boston, but four years later he returned to settle at Wem, in Shropshire. Despite the persistent attacks of reviewers and the backsliding of his once-radical friends, Hazlitt never wavered in his loyalty to liberty, equality, and the principles behind the overthrow of the monarchy in France. His first literary production, at the age of thirteen, was a letter to a newspaper in indignant protest against the mob that sacked Joseph Priestley's house, when the scientist and preacher had celebrated publicly the second anniversary of the fall of the Bastille. His last book, published in the year he died, was a four-volume life of Napoleon, in which he expressed a vehement, but qualified, admiration of Napoleon as a man of heroic will and power in the service of the emancipation of mankind.

Hazlitt was a long time finding his vocation. When he attended the Hackney College, London, between the ages of fifteen and eighteen, he plunged into philosophical studies. In 1799 he took up the study of painting and did not relinquish the ambition to become a portraitist until 1812. His first books dealt with philosophy, economics, and politics; and his first job as a journalist was as parliamentary reporter for the *Morning Chronicle*. It was not until 1813, when he was thirty-six, that he began contributing dramatic criticism and miscellaneous essays to various periodicals and so discovered what he had been born to do. Years of wide reading and hard thinking had made him thoroughly ready: within the next decade he demonstrated himself to be a highly popular lecturer on Shakespeare, Elizabethan drama, and English poetry from Chaucer to his own day; a superb connoisseur of the theater and of painting; a master of the familiar essay; and with Coleridge, one of the two most important literary critics of his time. Coleridge elaborates his theory of poetry as part of a general philosophy of human imagination and human society. Hazlitt, on the other hand, disapproves of what he calls the "modern or metaphysical school of criticism." His distinctive critical gift is to communicate what he calls his "impressions," that is, the immediacy of his firsthand responses to a passage or work of literature.

Unlike his contemporaries Coleridge, Lamb, and De Quincey, whose writings look back to the elaborate prose stylists of the earlier seventeenth century, Hazlitt developed a fast-moving, hard-hitting prose in a style that he called "plain, point-blank speaking." He wrote, indeed, nearly as fast as he talked, almost without correction and (despite the density of literary quotations) without reference to books or notes. This rapidity was possible only because his essays are relatively planless. Hazlitt characteristically lays down a topic, then piles up relevant observations and instances; the essay accumulates instead of developing; often, it does not round to a conclusion, but simply stops. Hazlitt's prose is unfailingly energetic, but his most satisfying essays, considered as works of literary art, are those that, like "My First Acquaintance with Poets," have a narrative subject matter to give him a principle of organization.

In demeanor Hazlitt was awkward and self-conscious; Coleridge described him in 1803 as "brow-hanging, shoe-contemplative, strange." He had grown up as a member of a highly unpopular minority, in both religion and politics; he found his friends deserting to the side of reaction; and his natural combativeness was exacerbated by the persistent abuse directed against him by writers in the conservative press and periodicals. In the course of his life, he managed to quarrel, in private and in print, with almost everyone whom he had once admired and liked, including Coleridge,

Wordsworth, Leigh Hunt, and even his most intimate and enduring friend, Charles Lamb. But what appealed to his admirers, as to modern readers of his essays, is his courage and uncompromising honesty, and above all his zest for life in its diversity— including even, as he announced in the title of an essay, "The Pleasure of Hating." He relished, and was able to convey completely, the particular qualities of things—a passage of poetry, a painting, a natural prospect, or a well-directed blow in a prize fight. Despite the recurrent frustrations of his fifty-two years of existence, he was able to say, with his last breath, "Well, I've had a happy life."

On Gusto[1]

Gusto in art is power or passion defining any object. It is not so difficult to explain this term in what relates to expression (of which it may be said to be the highest degree) as in what relates to things without expression, to the natural appearances of objects, as mere color or form. In one sense, however, there is hardly any object entirely devoid of expression, without some character of power belonging to it, some precise association with pleasure or pain: and it is in giving this truth of character from the truth of feeling, whether in the highest or the lowest degree, but always in the highest degree of which the subject is capable, that gusto consists.

There is a gusto in the coloring of Titian.[2] Not only do his heads seem to think—his bodies seem to feel. This is what the Italians mean by the *morbidezza*[3] of his flesh color. It seems sensitive and alive all over; not merely to have the look and texture of flesh, but the feeling in itself. For example, the limbs of his female figures have a luxurious softness and delicacy, which appears conscious of the pleasure of the beholder. As the objects themselves in nature would produce an impression on the sense, distinct from every other object, and having something divine in it, which the heart owns and the imagination consecrates, the objects in the picture preserve the same impression, absolute, unimpaired, stamped with all the truth of passion, the pride of the eye, and the charm of beauty. Rubens makes his flesh color like flowers; Albano's[4] is like ivory; Titian's is like flesh, and like nothing else. It is as different from that of other painters, as the skin is from a piece of white or red drapery thrown over it. The blood circulates here and there, the blue veins just appear, the rest is distinguished throughout only by that sort of tingling sensation to the eye, which the body feels within itself. This is gusto. Vandyke's[5] flesh color, though it has great truth and purity, wants gusto. It has

1. Hazlitt's essay, first published in 1816 in the radical journal *The Examiner*, introduces one of his distinctive critical terms. In the 17th century English writers had imported the Italian word *gusto*, meaning taste, to denote a spectator's artistic sensibility. *Gusto* also carried the sense (which remains primary today) of especially keen, zestful appreciation. Hazlitt expanded the meaning of the term so that it described not only the responsiveness of the spectator to the work of art but also the essential features of the natural or human objects that the work depicted. Keats, greatly impressed by "On Gusto," illuminated the essay's discussion of the wide range of sensuous and emotional responses evoked by art when (in a letter of December 21, 1817) he remarked regretfully about a painting by Benjamin West that "there is nothing to be intense upon; no women one feels mad to kiss; no face swelling into reality."
2. Tiziano Vecelli (ca. 1490–1576), greatest of the 16th-century Venetian painters.
3. Softness, delicacy.
4. Francesco Albani (1578–1660), Italian painter. Peter Paul Rubens (1577–1640), Flemish painter, was the most important artist of his time in northern Europe.
5. Sir Anthony Vandyke (1599–1641), Flemish portrait painter, who did some of his best-known work at the English court of Charles I.

not the internal character, the living principle in it. It is a smooth surface, not a warm, moving mass. It is painted without passion, with indifference. The hand only has been concerned. The impression slides off from the eye, and does not, like the tones of Titian's pencil,[6] leave a sting behind it in the mind of the spectator. The eye does not acquire a taste or appetite for what it sees. In a word, gusto in painting is where the impression made on one sense excites by affinity those of another.

Michael Angelo's forms are full of gusto. They everywhere obtrude the sense of power upon the eye. His limbs convey an idea of muscular strength, of moral grandeur, and even of intellectual dignity: they are firm, commanding, broad, and massy, capable of executing with ease the determined purposes of the will. His faces have no other expression than his figures, conscious power and capacity. They appear only to think what they shall do, and to know that they can do it. This is what is meant by saying that his style is hard and masculine. It is the reverse of Correggio's,[7] which is effeminate. That is, the gusto of Michael Angelo consists in expressing energy of will without proportionable sensibility, Correggio's in expressing exquisite sensibility without energy of will. In Correggio's faces as well as figures we see neither bones nor muscles, but then what a soul is there, full of sweetness and of grace—pure, playful, soft, angelical! There is sentiment enough in a hand painted by Correggio to set up a school of history painters. Whenever we look at the hands of Correggio's women or of Raphael's,[8] we always wish to touch them.

Again, Titian's landscapes have a prodigious gusto, both in the coloring and forms. We shall never forget one that we saw many years ago in the Orleans Gallery of Acteon hunting.[9] It had a brown, mellow, autumnal look. The sky was of the color of stone. The winds seemed to sing through the rustling branches of the trees, and already you might hear the twanging of bows resound through the tangled mazes of the wood. Mr. West,[1] we understand, has this landscape. He will know if this description of it is just. The landscape background of the St. Peter Martyr[2] is another well known instance of the power of this great painter to give a romantic interest and an appropriate character to the objects of his pencil, where every circumstance adds to the effect of the scene—the bold trunks of the tall forest trees, the trailing ground plants, with that tall convent spire rising in the distance, amidst the blue sapphire mountains and the golden sky.

Rubens has a great deal of gusto in his Fauns and Satyrs, and in all that expresses motion, but in nothing else. Rembrandt has it in everything; everything in his pictures has a tangible character. If he puts a diamond in the ear of a burgomaster's wife, it is of the first water; and his furs and stuffs are proof against a Russian winter. Raphael's gusto was only in expression; he had no idea of the character of anything but the human form. The dryness and poverty of his style in other respects is a phenomenon in the art. His trees are like

---

6. In the archaic sense: a painter's brush.
7. Antonio Correggio (1494–1534), Italian artist.
8. Rafaello Sanzio (1488–1520), one of the supreme painters of the high Italian Renaissance.
9. Titian's *Diana and Actaeon*, shown in a celebrated public exhibition (1798–99) of old Italian masters, most of them from the collection of the duc d'Orléans. Following the duke's execution, English investors brought his collection to London from Revolutionary France to be auctioned off. In

"On the Pleasures of Painting" Hazlitt writes that for visitors to the Orléans Gallery it was as if "Old Time had unlocked his treasures": "From that time I lived in a world of pictures."
1. Benjamin West (1738–1820) was an American-born painter of historical scenes who achieved a high reputation in England.
2. A celebrated altarpiece by Titian depicting the martyrdom of Peter, a 13th-century Dominican.

sprigs of grass stuck in a book of botanical specimens. Was it that Raphael never had time to go beyond the walls of Rome? That he was always in the streets, at church, or in the bath? He was not one of the Society of Arcadians.[3] Claude's[4] landscapes, perfect as they are, want gusto. This is not easy to explain. They are perfect abstractions of the visible images of things; they speak the visible language of nature truly. They resemble a mirror or a microscope. To the eye only they are more perfect than any other landscapes that ever were or will be painted; they give more of nature, as cognizable by one sense alone; but they lay an equal stress on all visible impressions. They do not interpret one sense by another; they do not distinguish the character of different objects as we are taught, and can only be taught, to distinguish them by their effect on the different senses. That is, his eye wanted imagination: it did not strongly sympathize with his other faculties. He saw the atmosphere, but he did not feel it. He painted the trunk of a tree or a rock in the foreground as smooth—with as complete an abstraction of the gross, tangible impression, as any other part of the picture. His trees are perfectly beautiful, but quite immovable; they have a look of enchantment. In short, his landscapes are unequaled imitations of nature, released from its subjection to the elements, as if all objects were become a delightful fairy vision, and the eye had rarefied and refined away the other senses.

The gusto in the Greek statues is of a very singular kind. The sense of perfect form nearly occupies the whole mind, and hardly suffers it to dwell on any other feeling. It seems enough for them *to be*, without acting or suffering. Their forms are ideal, spiritual. Their beauty is power. By their beauty they are raised above the frailties of pain or passion; by their beauty they are deified.

The infinite quantity of dramatic invention in Shakespeare takes from his gusto. The power he delights to show is not intense, but discursive. He never insists on anything as much as he might, except a quibble.[5] Milton has great gusto. He repeats his blows twice; grapples with and exhausts his subject. His imagination has a double relish of its objects, an inveterate attachment to the things he describes, and to the words describing them.

> ——Or where Chineses drive
> With sails and wind their *cany* waggons *light*.

> Wild above rule or art, *enormous* bliss.[6]

There is a gusto in Pope's compliments, in Dryden's satires, and Prior's tales; and among prose writers Boccaccio and Rabelais had the most of it.[7] We will only mention one other work which appears to us to be full of gusto, and that

---

3. I.e., someone who delights in the beauties of the countryside. Hazlitt adds a footnote: "Raphael not only could not paint a landscape; he could not paint people in a landscape. He could not have painted the heads or the figures, or even the dresses, of the St. Peter Martyr. His figures have always an *in-door* look, that is, a set, determined, voluntary, dramatic character, arising from their own passions, or a watchfulness of those of others, and want [lack] that wild uncertainty of expression, which is connected with the accidents of nature and the changes of the elements. He has nothing *romantic* about him."
4. Claude Lorraine (1600–1682), French painter

renowned for his landscapes and seascapes.
5. I.e., pun. In "The Preface to Shakespeare" (1765), Samuel Johnson had written that the fascinations of quibble were for Shakespeare "irresistible": "A quibble was to him the fatal Cleopatra for which he lost the world and was content to lose it."
6. *Paradise Lost* 3.438–39 and 5.297.
7. The 14th-century Italian writer Boccaccio and the 16th-century French writer Rabelais are singled out here perhaps for their bawdy comedy. "Prior's tales": a group of somewhat racy narrative poems by the early-18th-century poet Matthew Prior.

is the *Beggar's Opera.*[8] If it is not, we are altogether mistaken in our notions on this delicate subject.

1816   1817

My First Acquaintance with Poets[1]

My father was a Dissenting Minister, at Wem, in Shropshire; and in the year 1798 (the figures that compose that date are to me like the "dreaded name of Demogorgon"[2]) Mr. Coleridge came to Shrewsbury, to succeed Mr. Rowe in the spiritual charge of a Unitarian congregation there. He did not come till late on the Saturday afternoon before he was to preach; and Mr. Rowe, who himself went down to the coach, in a state of anxiety and expectation, to look for the arrival of his successor, could find no one at all answering the description but a round-faced man, in a short black coat (like a shooting jacket) which hardly seemed to have been made for him, but who seemed to be talking at a great rate to his fellow passengers. Mr. Rowe had scarce returned to give an account of his disappointment, when the round-faced man in black entered, and dissipated all doubts on the subject, by beginning to talk. He did not cease while he stayed; nor has he since, that I know of. He held the good town of Shrewsbury in delightful suspense for three weeks that he remained there, "fluttering the *proud Salopians,* like an eagle in a dovecote";[3] and the Welsh mountains that skirt the horizon with their tempestuous confusion, agree to have heard no such mystic sounds since the days of

High-born Hoel's harp or soft Llewellyn's lay![4]

As we passed along between Wem and Shrewsbury, and I eyed their blue tops seen through the wintry branches, or the red rustling leaves of the sturdy oak trees by the roadside, a sound was in my ears as of a Siren's song; I was stunned, startled with it, as from deep sleep; but I had no notion then that I should ever be able to express my admiration to others in motley imagery or quaint allusion, till the light of his genius shone into my soul, like the sun's rays glittering in the puddles of the road. I was at that time dumb, inarticulate, helpless, like a worm by the wayside, crushed, bleeding, lifeless; but now, bursting from the deadly bands that bound them,

With Styx nine times round them,[5]

my ideas float on winged words, and as they expand their plumes, catch the golden light of other years. My soul has indeed remained in its original bondage, dark, obscure, with longings infinite and unsatisfied; my heart, shut up

8. The popular comic opera by John Gay, produced in 1728.
1. This essay was written in 1823, a quarter century after the events it describes. By then Coleridge and Wordsworth had long given up their early radicalism, and both men had quarreled with Hazlitt—hence the essay's elegiac note in dealing with the genius of the two poets.
2. *Paradise Lost* 2.964–65. To mythographers of the Renaissance, Demogorgon was a mysterious and terrifying demon, sometimes described as ancestor of all the gods. He plays a central role in

Shelley's *Prometheus Unbound.*
3. Shakespeare's Roman general Coriolanus reminds his enemies that in, in his days of military glory, "like an eagle in a dove-cote, I / Fluttered your Volscians" (*Coriolanus* 5.6.115–16). "Salopians": inhabitants of Shropshire.
4. Thomas Gray's "The Bard," line 28—names of famous bards silenced by King Edward's conquest of Wales.
5. Adapted from Pope's "Ode on St. Cecilia's Day," lines 90–91.

in the prison house of this rude clay, has never found, nor will it ever find, a heart to speak to; but that my understanding also did not remain dumb and brutish, or at length found a language to express itself, I owe to Coleridge. But this is not to my purpose.

My father lived ten miles from Shrewsbury, and was in the habit of exchanging visits with Mr. Rowe, and with Mr. Jenkins of Whitechurch (nine miles farther on) according to the custom of Dissenting Ministers in each other's neighborhood. A line of communication is thus established, by which the flame of civil and religious liberty is kept alive, and nourishes its smoldering fire unquenchable, like the fires in the *Agamemnon* of Aeschylus, placed at different stations, that waited for ten long years to announce with their blazing pyramids the destruction of Troy. Coleridge had agreed to come over to see my father, according to the courtesy of the country, as Mr. Rowe's probable successor; but in the meantime, I had gone to hear him preach the Sunday after his arrival. A poet and a philosopher getting up into a Unitarian pulpit to preach the Gospel was a romance in these degenerate days, a sort of revival of the primitive spirit of Christianity, which was not to be resisted.

It was in January of 1798, that I rose one morning before daylight, to walk ten miles in the mud, and went to hear this celebrated person preach. Never, the longest day I have to live, shall I have such another walk as this cold, raw, comfortless one, in the winter of the year 1798. *Il y a des impressions que ni le temps ni les circonstances peuvent effacer. Dusse-je vivre des siècles entiers, le doux temps de ma jeunesse ne peut renaître pour moi, ni s'effacer jamais dans ma mémoire.*[6] When I got there, the organ was playing the 100th psalm, and when it was done, Mr. Coleridge rose and gave out his text, "And he went up into the mountain to pray, *himself, alone.*"[7] As he gave out this text, his voice "rose like a steam of rich distilled perfume,"[8] and when he came to the two last words, which he pronounced loud, deep, and distinct, it seemed to me, who was then young, as if the sounds had echoed from the bottom of the human heart, and as if that prayer might have floated in solemn silence through the universe. The idea of St. John came into my mind, "of one crying in the wilderness, who had his loins girt about, and whose food was locusts and wild honey."[9] The preacher then launched into his subject, like an eagle dallying with the wind. The sermon was upon peace and war; upon church and state—not their alliance but their separation—on the spirit of the world and the spirit of Christianity, not as the same, but as opposed to one another. He talked of those who had "inscribed the cross of Christ on banners dripping with human gore." He made a poetical and pastoral excursion—and to show the fatal effects of war, drew a striking contrast between the simple shepherd boy, driving his team afield, or sitting under the hawthorn, piping to his flock, "as though he should never be old,"[1] and the same poor country lad, crimped,[2] kidnapped, brought into town, made drunk, at an alehouse, turned into a wretched drummer boy, with his hair sticking on end with powder and pomatum, a long cue[3] at his back, and tricked out in the loathsome finery of the profession of blood.

6. There are some impressions that neither time nor circumstances can efface. Even if I lived whole centuries, the sweet time of my youth could not be reborn for me, nor ever erased from my memory (French). Based on Rousseau's novel in letters *La Nouvelle Héloïse* (1761), part 6, letter 7.
7. The text for Coleridge's sermon was perhaps Matthew 14.23 or John 6.15—both of which describe how Christ withdraws into the mountains to prevent the people from making him king.
8. Milton's *Comus*, line 556.
9. See Matthew 3.3–4 and Mark 1.3–6.
1. Sir Philip Sidney's *Arcadia* 1.2.
2. Tricked into enlisting in military service.
3. Pigtail. "Pomatum": perfumed hair oil.

Such were the notes our once-loved poet sung.[4]

And for myself, I could not have been more delighted if I had heard the music of the spheres. Poetry and Philosophy had met together. Truth and Genius had embraced, under the eye and with the sanction of Religion. This was even beyond my hopes. I returned home well satisfied. The sun that was still laboring pale and wan through the sky, obscured by thick mists, seemed an emblem of the *good cause*;[5] and the cold dank drops of dew, that hung half melted on the beard of the thistle, had something genial and refreshing in them; for there was a spirit of hope and youth in all nature, that turned everything into good. The face of nature had not then the brand of *Jus Divinum*[6] on it:

Like to that sanguine flower inscribed with woe.[7]

On the Tuesday following, the half-inspired speaker came. I was called down into the room where he was, and went half-hoping, half-afraid. He received me very graciously, and I listened for a long time without uttering a word. I did not suffer in his opinion by my silence. "For those two hours," he afterwards was pleased to say, "he was conversing with W. H.'s forehead!" His appearance was different from what I had anticipated from seeing him before. At a distance, and in the dim light of the chapel, there was to me a strange wildness in his aspect, a dusky obscurity, and I thought him pitted with the smallpox. His complexion was at that time clear, and even bright—

As are the children of yon azure sheen.[8]

His forehead was broad and high, light as if built of ivory, with large projecting eyebrows, and his eyes rolling beneath them, like a sea with darkened luster. "A certain tender bloom his face o'erspread,"[9] a purple tinge as we see it in the pale thoughtful complexions of the Spanish portrait painters, Murillo and Velasquez. His mouth was gross, voluptuous, open, eloquent; his chin good-humored and round; but his nose, the rudder of the face, the index of the will, was small, feeble, nothing—like what he has done. It might seem that the genius of his face as from a height surveyed and projected him (with sufficient capacity and huge aspiration) into the world unknown of thought and imagination, with nothing to support or guide his veering purpose, as if Columbus had launched his adventurous course for the New World in a scallop,[1] without oars or compass. So at least I comment on it after the event. Coleridge in his person was rather above the common size, inclining to the corpulent, or like Lord Hamlet, "somewhat fat and pursy."[2] His hair (now, alas! gray) was then black and glossy as the raven's, and fell in smooth masses over his forehead. This long pendulous hair is peculiar to enthusiasts, to those whose minds tend heavenward; and is traditionally inseparable (though of a different color) from the pictures of Christ. It ought to belong, as a character, to all who preach *Christ crucified*, and Coleridge was at that time one of those!

It was curious to observe the contrast between him and my father, who was a veteran in the cause, and then declining into the vale of years. He had been a poor Irish lad, carefully brought up by his parents, and sent to the University

---

4. The first line of Pope's "Epistle to Robert, Earl of Oxford."
5. The cause of liberty, i.e., the French Revolution.
6. The divine right (of kings).
7. I.e., the hyacinth, believed to be marked with the Greek letters "AI AI," a cry of grief. Hazlitt

quotes Milton's "Lycidas," line 106.
8. Adapted from James Thomson's *The Castle of Indolence* 2.33.
9. See Thomson's *The Castle of Indolence* 1.57.
1. Probably for *shallop*, a small boat.
2. Cf. Shakespeare's *Hamlet* 3.4.144, 5.2.230.

of Glasgow (where he studied under Adam Smith[3]) to prepare him for his future destination. It was his mother's proudest wish to see her son a Dissenting Minister. So if we look back to past generations (as far as eye can reach) we see the same hopes, fears, wishes, followed by the same disappointments, throbbing in the human heart; and so we may see them (if we look forward) rising up forever, and disappearing, like vaporish bubbles, in the human breast! After being tossed about from congregation to congregation in the heats of the Unitarian controversy, and squabbles about the American war,[4] he had been relegated to an obscure village, where he was to spend the last thirty years of his life, far from the only converse that he loved, the talk about disputed texts of Scripture and the cause of civil and religious liberty. Here he passed his days, repining but resigned, in the study of the Bible, and the perusal of the Commentators—huge folios, not easily got through, one of which would outlast a winter! Why did he pore on these from morn to night (with the exception of a walk in the fields or a turn in the garden to gather broccoli plants or kidney beans of his own rearing, with no small degree of pride and pleasure)? Here were "no figures nor no fantasies"[5]—neither poetry nor philosophy—nothing to dazzle, nothing to excite modern curiosity; but to his lackluster eyes there appeared, within the pages of the ponderous, unwieldy, neglected tomes, the sacred name of JEHOVAH in Hebrew capitals: pressed down by the weight of the style, worn to the last fading thinness of the understanding, there were glimpses, glimmering notions of the patriarchal wanderings, with palm trees hovering in the horizon, and processions of camels at the distance of three thousand years; there was Moses with the Burning Bush, the number of the Twelve Tribes, types, shadows,[6] glosses on the law and the prophets; there were discussions (dull enough) on the age of Methuselah, a mighty speculation! there were outlines, rude guesses at the shape of Noah's Ark and of the riches of Solomon's Temple; questions as to the date of the creation, predictions of the end of all things; the great lapses of time, the strange mutations of the globe were unfolded with the voluminous leaf,[7] as it turned over; and though the soul might slumber with an hieroglyphic veil of inscrutable mysteries drawn over it, yet it was in a slumber ill-exchanged for all the sharpened realities of sense, wit, fancy, or reason. My father's life was comparatively a dream; but it was a dream of infinity and eternity, of death, the resurrection, and a judgment to come!

No two individuals were ever more unlike than were the host and his guest. A poet was to my father a sort of nondescript: yet whatever added grace to the Unitarian cause was to him welcome. He could hardly have been more surprised or pleased if our visitor had worn wings. Indeed, his thoughts had wings; and as the silken sounds rustled round our little wainscoted parlor, my father threw back his spectacles over his forehead, his white hairs mixing with its sanguine hue; and a smile of delight beamed across his rugged cordial face, to think that Truth had found a new ally in Fancy! Besides, Coleridge seemed

---

3. Scottish professor of moral philosophy, author of the *Theory of Moral Sentiments* (1759) and the great economic treatise *The Wealth of Nations* (1776).
4. The American Revolution, with which a number of radical Unitarian preachers were in sympathy.
5. In Shakespeare's *Julius Caesar* Brutus's description of the carefree state of his sleeping servant,

who knows nothing of his master's plotting (2.1.230).
6. Old Testament foreshadowings of later events, or symbols of moral and theological truths. "Types": characters and events in the Old Testament believed to prefigure analogous matters in the New Testament.
7. Page.

to take considerable notice of me, and that of itself was enough. He talked very familiarly, but agreeably, and glanced over a variety of subjects. At dinner time he grew more animated, and dilated in a very edifying manner on Mary Wollstonecraft and Mackintosh.[8] The last, he said, he considered (on my father's speaking of his *Vindiciae Gallicae* as a capital performance) as a clever scholastic[9] man—a master of the topics—or as the ready warehouseman of letters, who knew exactly where to lay his hand on what he wanted, though the goods were not his own. He thought him no match for Burke, either in style or matter. Burke was a metaphysician, Mackintosh a mere logician. Burke was an orator (almost a poet) who reasoned in figures, because he had an eye for nature: Mackintosh, on the other hand, was a rhetorician, who had only an eye to commonplaces. On this I ventured to say that I had always entertained a great opinion of Burke, and that (as far as I could find) the speaking of him with contempt might be made the test of a vulgar democratical mind. This was the first observation I ever made to Coleridge, and he said it was a very just and striking one. I remember the leg of Welsh mutton and the turnips on the table that day had the finest flavor imaginable. Coleridge added that Mackintosh and Tom Wedgwood[1] (of whom, however, he spoke highly) had expressed a very indifferent opinion of his friend Mr. Wordsworth, on which he remarked to them—"He strides on so far before you that he dwindles in the distance!" Godwin[2] had once boasted to him of having carried on an argument with Mackintosh for three hours with dubious success; Coleridge told him—"If there had been a man of genius in the room, he would have settled the question in five minutes." He asked me if I had ever seen Mary Wollstonecraft, and I said I had once for a few moments, and that she seemed to me to turn off Godwin's objections to something she advanced with quite a playful, easy air. He replied, that "this was only one instance of the ascendancy which people of imagination exercised over those of mere intellect." He did not rate Godwin very high[3] (this was caprice or prejudice, real or affected) but he had a great idea of Mrs. Wollstonecraft's powers of conversation, none at all of her talent for book-making. We talked a little about Holcroft.[4] He had been asked if he was not much struck *with* him, and he said, he thought himself in more danger of being struck *by* him. I complained that he would not let me get on at all, for he required a definition of even the commonest word, exclaiming, "What do you mean by a *sensation*, sir? What do you mean by an *idea*?" This, Coleridge said, was barricadoing the road to truth: it was setting up a turnpike gate at every step we took. I forget a great number of things, many more than I remember; but the day passed off pleasantly, and the next morning Mr. Coleridge was to return to Shrewsbury. When I came down to breakfast, I found that he had just received a letter from his friend, T. Wedgwood, making him an offer of £150 a year if he chose to waive his present pursuit, and devote

8. Mary Wollstonecraft's *A Vindication of the Rights of Men* (1790) and the Scottish philosopher James Mackintosh's *Vindiciae Gallicae* ("Defense of France," 1791) were both written in opposition to Edmund Burke's *Reflections on the French Revolution* (1790). See pp. 148–67 above.
9. The Scholastics, medieval philosophers and theologians, organized their thought systematically, often under various "topics"—standard headings, or "commonplaces."
1. Son of Josiah Wedgwood (1730–1795), who founded the great pottery firm (which still exists).
2. William Godwin (1756–1836), radical philos-

opher and novelist, author of the influential *Inquiry Concerning Political Justice* (1793).
3. He complained in particular of the presumption of attempting to establish the future immortality of man "without" (as he said) "knowing what Death was or what Life was"—and the tone in which he pronounced these two words seemed to convey a complete image of both [Hazlitt's note].
4. Thomas Holcroft (1749–1809), another radical contemporary, author of plays and novels. Hazlitt completed his friend Holcroft's memoirs and published them in 1816.

himself entirely to the study of poetry and philosophy. Coleridge seemed to make up his mind to close with this proposal in the act of tying on one of his shoes. It threw an additional damp on his departure. It took the wayward enthusiast quite from us to cast him into Deva's winding vales,[5] or by the shores of old romance. Instead of living at ten miles' distance, of being the pastor of a Dissenting congregation at Shrewsbury, he was henceforth to inhabit the Hill of Parnassus, to be a Shepherd on the Delectable Mountains.[6] Alas! I knew not the way thither, and felt very little gratitude for Mr. Wedgwood's bounty. I was presently relieved from this dilemma; for Mr. Coleridge, asking for a pen and ink, and going to a table to write something on a bit of card, advanced towards me with undulating step, and giving me the precious document, said that that was his address, *Mr. Coleridge, Nether Stowey, Somersetshire;* and that he should be glad to see me there in a few weeks' time, and, if I chose, would come half-way to meet me. I was not less surprised than the shepherd boy (this simile is to be found in *Cassandra*[7]) when he sees a thunderbolt fall close at his feet. I stammered out my acknowledgments and acceptance of this offer (I thought Mr. Wedgwood's annunity a trifle to it) as well as I could; and this mighty business being settled, the poet-preacher took leave, and I accompanied him six miles on the road. It was a fine morning in the middle of winter, and he talked the whole way. The scholar in Chaucer is described as going

———sounding on his way.[8]

So Coleridge went on his. In digressing, in dilating, in passing from subject to subject, he appeared to me to float in air, to slide on ice. He told me in confidence (going along) that he should have preached two sermons before he accepted the situation at Shrewsbury, one on Infant Baptism, the other on the Lord's Supper, showing that he could not administer either, which would have effectually disqualified him for the object in view. I observed that he continually crossed me on the way by shifting from one side of the footpath to the other. This struck me as an odd movement; but I did not at that time connect it with any instability of purpose or involuntary change of principle, as I have done since. He seemed unable to keep on in a straight line. He spoke slightingly of Hume[9] (whose *Essay on Miracles* he said was stolen from an objection started in one of South's sermons—*Credat Judaeus Appella!*[1]). I was not very much pleased at this account of Hume, for I had just been reading, with infinite relish, that completest of all metaphysical *choke-pears,*[2] his *Treatise on Human Nature,* to which the *Essays,* in point of scholastic subtlety and close reasoning, are mere elegant trifling, light summer reading. Coleridge even denied the excellence of Hume's general style, which I think betrayed a want of taste or candor. He however made me amends by the manner in which

---

5. In "Lycidas," line 55, Milton associates the "wizard stream" of Deva (the river Dee in Wales) with the ancient bards. Hazlitt's point is that Coleridge will henceforth inhabit the terrain of the poetic imagination.
6. In classical mythology Mount Parnassus was sacred to the muses. In John Bunyan's allegory *Pilgrim's Progress* (1678–79), the pilgrim Christian, on his journey to the Celestial City, passes through the Delectable Mountains, where he is entertained by the shepherds.
7. A romance by the 17th-century French writer La Calprenède.

8. *The Canterbury Tales,* "General Prologue," line 309: "Souning in moral vertu was his speeche" (in Chaucer the meaning of "souning in" is either "resounding in" or "consonant with").
9. David Hume, 18th-century Scottish philosopher.
1. From Horace's *Satires* 1.5.100: "Let Appella the Jew believe it" (Latin); implying that he himself does not. Robert South (1634–1716), Anglican divine.
2. A very sour variety of pear; hence anything hard to take in.

he spoke of Berkeley.[3] He dwelt particularly on his *Essay on Vision* as a masterpiece of analytical reasoning. So it undoubtedly is. He was exceedingly
angry with Dr. Johnson for striking the stone with his foot, in allusion to this
author's theory of matter and spirit, and saying, "Thus I confute him, sir."[4]
Coleridge drew a parallel (I don't know how he brought about the connection)
between Bishop Berkeley and Tom Paine.[5] He said the one was an instance
of a subtle, the other of an acute mind, than which no two things could be
more distinct. The one was a shop-boy's quality, the other the characteristic
of a philosopher. He considered Bishop Butler[6] as a true philosopher, a profound and conscientious thinker, a genuine reader of nature and of his own
mind. He did not speak of his *Analogy*, but of his *Sermons at the Rolls' Chapel*,
of which I had never heard. Coleridge somehow always contrived to prefer the
unknown to the *known*. In this instance he was right. The *Analogy* is a tissue
of sophistry, of wire-drawn,[7] theological special-pleading; the *Sermons* (with
the Preface to them) are in a fine vein of deep, matured reflection, a candid
appeal to our observation of human nature, without pedantry and without bias.
I told Coleridge I had written a few remarks, and was sometimes foolish
enough to believe that I had made a discovery on the same subject (the *Natural
Disinterestedness of the Human Mind*)[8]—and I tried to explain my view of it to
Coleridge, who listened with great willingness, but I did not succeed in making
myself understood. I sat down to the task shortly afterwards for the twentieth
time, got new pens and paper, determined to make clear work of it, wrote a
few meager sentences in the skeleton-style of a mathematical demonstration,
stopped halfway down the second page; and, after trying in vain to pump up
any words, images, notions, apprehensions, facts, or observations, from that
gulf of abstraction in which I had plunged myself for four or five years preceding, gave up the attempt as labor in vain, and shed tears of helpless despondency on the blank unfinished paper. I can write fast enough now. Am I better
than I was then? Oh no! One truth discovered, one pang of regret at not being
able to express it, is better than all the fluency and flippancy in the world.
Would that I could go back to what I then was! Why can we not revive past
times as we can revisit old places? If I had the quaint Muse of Sir Philip Sidney
to assist me, I would write a *Sonnet to the Road between Wem and Shrewsbury*,
and immortalize every step of it by some fond enigmatical conceit. I would
swear that the very milestones had ears, and that Harmer Hill stooped with
all its pines, to listen to a poet, as he passed! I remember but one other topic
of discourse in this walk. He mentioned Paley,[9] praised the naturalness and
clearness of his style, but condemned his sentiments, thought him a mere
time-serving casuist, and said that "the fact of his work on Moral and Political
Philosophy being made a textbook in our universities was a disgrace to the
national character." We parted at the six-mile stone; and I returned homeward

3. Bishop George Berkeley, 18th-century Irish
idealist philosopher and author of an *Essay toward
a New Theory of Vision* (1709).
4. The anecdote is in James Boswell's *The Life of
Samuel Johnson.*
5. Supporter of the American and French Revolutions and author of *Common Sense* and *The
Rights of Man.* See pp. 163–67.
6. Joseph Butler, 18th-century theologian and
moral philosopher, author of the *Analogy of Religion* (1736).
7. Drawn out to great length.

8. Published as *An Essay on the Principles of
Human Action* (1805).
9. William Paley, author of *Evidences of Christianity* (1794) and *Principles of Moral and Political
Philosophy* (1785), which became a textbook for
generations of Cambridge students. With its
account of how individuals' calculations of their
best interests provide an adequate foundation for
Christian morality, Paley's utilitarian theology
would have displeased Coleridge. A "casuist" uses
reason in a slippery, deceptive manner.

pensive but much pleased. I had met with unexpected notice from a person whom I believed to have been prejudiced against me. "Kind and affable to me had been his condescension, and should be honored ever with suitable regard."[1] He was the first poet I had known, and he certainly answered to that inspired name. I had heard a great deal of his powers of conversation, and was not disappointed. In fact, I never met with anything at all like them, either before or since. I could easily credit the accounts which were circulated of his holding forth to a large party of ladies and gentlemen, an evening or two before, on the Berkeleian Theory, when he made the whole material universe look like a transparency of fine words; and another story (which I believe he has somewhere told himself)[2] of his being asked to a party at Birmingham, of his smoking tobacco and going to sleep after dinner on a sofa, where the company found him, to their no small surprise, which was increased to wonder when he started up of a sudden, and rubbing his eyes, looked about him, and launched into a three hours' description of the third heaven, of which he had had a dream, very different from Mr. Southey's *Vision of Judgment,* and also from that other *Vision of Judgment,* which Mr. Murray, the secretary of the Bridge Street Junto,[3] has taken into his especial keeping!

On my way back, I had a sound in my ears, it was the voice of Fancy: I had a light before me, it was the face of Poetry. The one still lingers there, the other has not quitted my side! Coleridge in truth met me half-way on the ground of philosophy, or I should not been won over to his imaginative creed. I had an uneasy, pleasurable sensation all the time, till I was to visit him. During those months the chill breath of winter gave me a welcoming; the vernal air was balm and inspiration to me. The golden sunsets, the silver star of evening, lighted me on my way to new hopes and prospects. *I was to visit Coleridge in the spring.* This circumstance was never absent from my thoughts, and mingled with all my feelings. I wrote to him at the time proposed, and received an answer postponing my intended visit for a week or two, but very cordially urging me to complete my promise then. This delay did not damp, but rather increased my ardor. In the meantime, I went to Llangollen Vale,[4] by way of initiating myself in the mysteries of natural scenery; and I must say I was enchanted with it. I had been reading Coleridge's description of England in his fine *Ode on the Departing Year,* and I applied it, *con amore,*[5] to the objects before me. That valley was to me (in a manner) the cradle of a new existence: in the river that winds through it, my spirit was baptized in the waters of Helicon![6]

I returned home, and soon after set out on my journey with unworn heart and untired feet. My way lay through Worcester and Gloucester, and by Upton, where I thought of Tom Jones and the adventure of the muff.[7] I remember getting completely wet through one day, and stopping at an inn (I think it was at Tewkesbury) where I sat up all night to read *Paul and Virginia.*[8] Sweet

1. Paraphrasing Adam's praise for the teaching offered to him by the archangel Raphael (*Paradise Lost* 8.648–50).
2. See Coleridge's *Biographia Literaria,* chap. 10.
3. Byron's *Vision of Judgment* is a brilliant parody of Southey's poem. Charles Murray was solicitor to an association, located at New Bridge Street in London, that prosecuted John Hunt for publishing Byron's poem in 1822 in the first number of the journal *The Liberal.* Hazlitt's "My First Acquaintance with Poets" would appear in the pages of *The Liberal* the following year. Hazlitt derisively refers

to Murray's Constitutional Association, founded to oppose "the progress of disloyal and seditious principles," as a "junto," i.e., a group formed for political intrigue.
4. In north Wales (about thirty-five miles from Wem)—a standard destination for lovers of picturesque landscapes.
5. "With love," fervently (Italian).
6. A mountain sacred to Apollo and the Muses.
7. Henry Fielding's *Tom Jones* 10.5ff.
8. A sentimental novel (1788) by the French writer Bernardin de Saint-Pierre.

were the showers in early youth that drenched my body, and sweet the drops of pity that fell upon the books I read! I recollect a remark of Coleridge's upon this very book that nothing could show the gross indelicacy of French manners and the entire corruption of their imagination more strongly than the behavior of the heroine in the last fatal scene, who turns away from a person on board the sinking vessel, that offers to save her life, because he has thrown off his clothes to assist him in swimming. Was this a time to think of such a circumstance? I once hinted to Wordsworth, as we were sailing in his boat on Grasmere lake, that I thought he had borrowed the idea of his *Poems on the Naming of Places* from the local inscriptions of the same kind in *Paul and Virginia*. He did not own the obligation, and stated some distinction without a difference in defense to his claim to originality. Any the slightest variation would be sufficient for this purpose in his mind; for whatever he added or omitted would inevitably be worth all that any one else had done, and contain the marrow of the sentiment. I was still two days before the time fixed for my arrival, for I had taken care to set out early enough. I stopped these two days at Bridgewater, and when I was tired of sauntering on the banks of its muddy river, returned to the inn and read *Camilla*.[9] So have I loitered my life away, reading books, looking at pictures, going to plays, hearing, thinking, writing on what pleased me best. I have wanted only one thing to make me happy; but wanting that, have wanted everything!

I arrived, and was well received. The country about Nether Stowey is beautiful, green and hilly, and near the seashore. I saw it but the other day, after an interval of twenty years, from a hill near Taunton. How was the map of my life spread out before me, as the map of the country lay at my feet! In the afternoon, Coleridge took me over to Alfoxden, a romantic old family mansion of the St. Aubins, where Wordsworth lived. It was then in the possession of a friend of the poet's, who gave him the free use of it.[1] Somehow, that period (the time just after the French Revolution) was not a time when *nothing was given for nothing*. The mind opened and a softness might be perceived coming over the heart of individuals, beneath "the scales that fence" our self-interest. Wordsworth himself was from home, but his sister kept house, and set before us a frugal repast; and we had free access to her brother's poems, the *Lyrical Ballads*, which were still in manuscript, or in the form of *Sybilline Leaves*.[2] I dipped into a few of these with great satisfaction, and with the faith of a novice. I slept that night in an old room with blue hangings, and covered with the round-faced family portraits of the age of George I and II and from the wooded declivity of the adjoining park that overlooked my window, at the dawn of day, could

——hear the loud stag speak.[3]

In the outset of life (and particularly at this time I felt it so) our imagination has a body to it. We are in a state between sleeping and waking, and have indistinct but glorious glimpses of strange shapes, and there is always something to come better than what we see. As in our dreams the fullness of the blood gives warmth and reality to the coinage of the brain, so in youth our ideas are clothed, and fed, and pampered with our good spirits; we breathe thick with thoughtless happiness, the weight of future years presses on the

9. A 1796 novel by Frances Burney.
1. A mistake; Wordsworth paid rent.
2. I.e., prophetic writings in a scattered state. The phrase is used by Coleridge as the title for his published poems in 1817.
3. A pleasure of country life mentioned in Ben Jonson's 1616 poem "To Sir Robert Wroth" (line 22).

strong pulses of the heart, and we repose with undisturbed faith in truth and good. As we advance, we exhaust our fund of enjoyment and of hope. We are no longer wrapped in *lamb's wool*, lulled in Elysium. As we taste the pleasures of life, their spirit evaporates, the sense palls; and nothing is left but the phantoms, the lifeless shadows of what *has been!*

That morning, as soon as breakfast was over, we strolled out into the park, and seating ourselves on the trunk of an old ash tree that stretched along the ground, Coleridge read aloud with a sonorous and musical voice, the ballad of *Betty Foy.*[4] I was not critically or skeptically inclined. I saw touches of truth and nature, and took the rest for granted. But in the *Thorn*, the *Mad Mother*, and the *Complaint of a Poor Indian Woman*, I felt that deeper power and pathos which have been since acknowledged,

In spite of pride, in erring reason's spite,[5]

as the characteristics of this author; and the sense of a new style and a new spirit in poetry came over me. It had to me something of the effect that arises from the turning up of the fresh soil, or of the first welcome breath of spring,

While yet the trembling year is unconfirmed.[6]

Coleridge and myself walked back to Stowey that evening, and his voice sounded high

Of Providence, foreknowledge, will, and fate,
Fixed fate, free will, foreknowledge absolute,[7]

as we passed through echoing grove, by fairy stream or waterfall, gleaming in the summer moonlight! He lamented that Wordsworth was not prone enough to believe in the traditional superstitions of the place, and that there was a something corporeal, a *matter-of-fact-ness*, a clinging to the palpable, or often to the petty, in his poetry, in consequence. His genius was not a spirit that descended to him through the air; it sprung out of the ground like a flower, or unfolded itself from a green spray, on which the goldfinch sang. He said, however (if I remember right), that this objection must be confined to his descriptive pieces, that his philosophic poetry had a grand and comprehensive spirit in it, so that his soul seemed to inhabit the universe like a palace, and to discover truth by intuition, rather than by deduction. The next day Wordsworth arrived from Bristol at Coleridge's cottage. I think I see him now. He answered in some degree to his friend's description of him, but was more gaunt and Don Quixote-like. He was quaintly dressed (according to the *costume* of that unconstrained period) in a brown fustian[8] jacket and striped pantaloons. There was something of a roll, a lounge in his gait, not unlike his own Peter Bell.[9] There was a severe, worn pressure of thought about his temples, a fire in his eye (as if he saw something in objects more than the outward appearance), an intense high narrow forehead, a Roman nose, cheeks furrowed by strong purpose and feeling, and a convulsive inclination to laughter about the mouth, a good deal at variance with the solemn, stately expression of the rest of his face. Chantry's bust wants the marking traits; but he was teased into making it regular and heavy; Haydon's[1] head of him, introduced into the

4. Wordsworth's *Idiot Boy*. Like the other poems mentioned, it was included in *Lyrical Ballads*.
5. Pope's *Essay on Man* 1.293.
6. James Thomson's *The Seasons: Spring*, line 18.
7. The topics debated by the fallen angels in *Paradise Lost* 2.559–60.
8. A coarse and heavy cotton cloth.
9. The rough protagonist in Wordsworth's poem *Peter Bell* (1819).
1. Sir Francis Chantry's bust of Wordsworth was sculpted in 1820. In his large-scale history painting *Christ's Entry into Jerusalem* (1817), Benjamin

Entrance of Christ into Jerusalem, is the most like his drooping weight of thought and expression. He sat down and talked very naturally and freely, with a mixture of clear gushing accents in his voice, a deep guttural intonation, and a strong tincture of the northern *burr,* like the crust on wine. He instantly began to make havoc of the half of a Cheshire cheese on the table, and said triumphantly that "his marriage with experience had not been so unproductive as Mr. Southey's in teaching him a knowledge of the good things of this life." He had been to see the *Castle Spectre* by Monk Lewis,[2] while at Bristol, and described it very well. He said "it fitted the taste of the audience like a glove." This *ad captandum*[3] merit was, however, by no means a recommendation of it, according to the severe principles of the new school, which reject rather than court popular effect. Wordsworth, looking out of the low, latticed window, said, "How beautifully the sun sets on that yellow bank!" I thought within myself, "With what eyes these poets see nature!" and ever after, when I saw the sunset stream upon the objects facing it, conceived I had made a discovery, or thanked Mr. Wordsworth for having made one for me! We went over to Alfoxden again the day following, and Wordsworth read us the story of *Peter Bell* in the open air; and the comment made upon it by his face and voice was very different from that of some later critics! Whatever might be thought of the poem, "his face was as a book where men might read strange matters,"[4] and he announced the fate of his hero in prophetic tones. There is a *chaunt* in the recitation both of Coleridge and Wordsworth, which acts as a spell upon the hearer, and disarms the judgment. Perhaps they have deceived themselves by making habitual use of this ambiguous accompaniment. Coleridge's manner is more full, animated, and varied; Wordsworth's more equable, sustained, and internal. The one might be termed more *dramatic,* the other more *lyrical.* Coleridge has told me that he himself liked to compose in walking over uneven ground, or breaking through the straggling branches of a copse wood; whereas Wordsworth always wrote (if he could) walking up and down a straight gravel walk, or in some spot where the continuity of his verse met with no collateral interruption. Returning that same evening, I got into a metaphysical argument with Wordsworth, while Coleridge was explaining the different notes of the nightingale to his sister, in which we neither of us succeeded in making ourselves perfectly clear and intelligible. Thus I passed three weeks at Nether Stowey and in the neighborhood, generally devoting the afternoons to a delightful chat in an arbor made of bark by the poet's friend Tom Poole, sitting under two fine elm trees, and listening to the bees humming round us while we quaffed our flip.[5] It was agreed, among other things, that we should make a jaunt down the Bristol Channel, as far as Linton. We set off together on foot, Coleridge, John Chester, and I. This Chester was a native of Nether Stowey, one of those who were attracted to Coleridge's discourse as flies are to honey, or bees in swarming-time to the sound of a brass pan. He "followed in the chase like a dog who hunts, not like one that made up the cry."[6] He had on a brown cloth coat, boots, and corduroy breeches, was low in stature, bowlegged, had a drag in his walk like a drover, which he assisted by a hazel

Robert Haydon included likenesses of his friends Hazlitt, Keats, and Wordsworth among figures in the crowd surrounding Christ.
2. *The Castle Spectre* (staged in 1797) was a play of Gothic horrors by Matthew Gregory Lewis, nicknamed Monk Lewis in tribute to his most famous Gothic work, the novel *The Monk* (1795).

3. "For the sake of captivating" an audience.
4. Lady Macbeth's description of her husband as the two plot King Duncan's murder (Shakespeare, *Macbeth* 1.5.60–61).
5. Spiced and sweetened ale.
6. See Shakespeare, *Othello* 2.3.337–38.

switch, and kept on a sort of trot by the side of Coleridge, like a running footman by a state coach, that he might not lose a syllable or sound that fell from Coleridge's lips. He told me his private opinion, that Coleridge was a wonderful man. He scarcely opened his lips, much less offered an opinion the whole way: yet of the three, had I to choose during that journey, I would be John Chester. He afterwards followed Coleridge into Germany, where the Kantean philosophers were puzzled how to bring him under any of their categories. When he sat down at table with his idol, John's felicity was complete; Sir Walter Scott's, or Mr. Blackwood's, when they sat down at the same table with the King,[7] was not more so. We passed Dunster on our right, a small town between the brow of a hill and the sea. I remember eying it wistfully as it lay below us: contrasted with the woody scene around, it looked as clear, as pure, as *embrowned* and ideal as any landscape I have seen since, of Gaspar Poussin's or Domenichino's. We had a long day's march—(our feet kept time to the echoes of Coleridge's tongue)—through Minehead and by the Blue Anchor, and on to Linton, which we did not reach till near midnight, and where we had some difficulty in making a lodgment. We however knocked the people of the house up at last, and we were repaid for our apprehensions and fatigue by some excellent rashers of fried bacon and eggs. The view in coming along had been splendid. We walked for miles and miles on dark brown heaths overlooking the channel, with the Welsh hills beyond, and at times descended into little sheltered valleys close by the seaside, with a smuggler's face scowling by us, and then had to ascend conical hills with a path winding up through a coppice to a barren top, like a monk's shaven crown, from one of which I pointed out to Coleridge's notice the bare masts of a vessel on the very edge of the horizon and within the red-orbed disk of the setting sun, like his own specter-ship in the *Ancient Mariner*. At Linton the character of the seacoast becomes more marked and rugged. There is a place called the Valley of Rocks (I suspect this was only the poetical name for it) bedded among precipices overhanging the sea, with rocky caverns beneath, into which the waves dash, and where the seagull forever wheels its screaming flight. On the tops of these are huge stones thrown transverse, as if an earthquake had tossed them there, and behind these is a fretwork of perpendicular rocks, something like the Giant's Causeway.[8] A thunderstorm came on while we were at the inn, and Coleridge was running out bareheaded to enjoy the commotion of the elements in the Valley of Rocks, but as if in spite, the clouds only muttered a few angry sounds, and let fall a few refreshing drops. Coleridge told me that he and Wordsworth were to have made this place the scene of a prose tale, which was to have been in the manner of, but far superior to, the *Death of Abel*,[9] but they had relinquished the design. In the morning of the second day, we breakfasted luxuriously in an old-fashioned parlor, on tea, toast, eggs, and honey, in the very sight of the beehives from which it had been taken, and a garden full of thyme and wild flowers that had produced it. On this occasion Coleridge spoke of Virgil's *Georgics*, but not well. I do not think he had much feeling for the classical or elegant. It was in this room that we found a little worn-out copy of the *Seasons*,[1] lying in a window seat, on which Coleridge exclaimed, "*That*

7. At a banquet given to George IV at Edinburgh in 1822. The publisher William Blackwood was, like his fellow Tory Sir Walter Scott (who had organized the king's visit), an ardent supporter of the unpopular monarchy.

8. A mass of rocks on the northern Irish coast.
9. The "prose tale" exists as a fragment, *The Wanderings of Cain*. The *Death of Abel* (1758) is by the once celebrated Swiss poet Salomon Gessner.
1. By James Thomson, published in 1726–30.

is true fame!" He said Thomson was a great poet, rather than a good one; his style was as meretricious as his thoughts were natural. He spoke of Cowper as the best modern poet. He said the *Lyrical Ballads* were an experiment about to be tried by him and Wordsworth, to see how far the public taste would endure poetry written in a more natural and simple style than had hitherto been attempted; totally discarding the artifices of poetical diction, and making use only of such words as had probably been common in the most ordinary language since the days of Henry II. Some comparison was introduced between Shakespeare and Milton. He said "he hardly knew which to prefer. Shakespeare appeared to him a mere stripling in the art; he was as tall and as strong, with infinitely more activity than Milton, but he never appeared to have come to man's estate; or if he had, he would not have been a man, but a monster." He spoke with contempt of Gray, and with intolerance of Pope. He did not like the versification of the latter. He observed that "the ears of these couplet-writers might be charged with having short memories, that could not retain the harmony of whole passages." He thought little of Junius[2] as a writer; he had a dislike of Dr. Johnson; and a much higher opinion of Burke as an orator and politician, than of Fox or Pitt.[3] He however thought him very inferior in richness of style and imagery to some of our elder prose writers, particularly Jeremy Taylor.[4] He liked Richardson, but not Fielding; nor could I get him to enter into the merits of *Caleb Williams*.[5] In short, he was profound and discriminating with respect to those authors whom he liked, and where he gave his judgment fair play; capricious, perverse, and prejudiced in his antipathies and distastes. We loitered on the "ribbed sea-sands,"[6] in such talk as this, a whole morning, and I recollect met with a curious seaweed, of which John Chester told us the country name! A fisherman gave Coleridge an account of a boy that had been drowned the day before, and that they had tried to save him at the risk of their own lives. He said "he did not know how it was that they ventured, but, sir, we have a *nature* towards one another." This expression, Coleridge remarked to me, was a fine illustration of that theory of disinterestedness which I (in common with Butler) had adopted. I broached to him an argument of mine to prove that *likeness* was not mere association of ideas. I said that the mark in the sand put one in mind of a man's foot, not because it was part of a former impression of a man's foot (for it was quite new) but because it was like the shape of a man's foot. He assented to the justness of this distinction (which I have explained at length elsewhere, for the benefit of the curious) and John Chester listened; not from any interest in the subject, but because he was astonished that I should be able to suggest anything to Coleridge that he did not already know. We returned on the third morning, and Coleridge remarked the silent cottage-smoke curling up the valleys where, a few evenings before, we had seen the lights gleaming through the dark.

In a day or two after we arrived at Stowey, we set out, I on my return home, and he for Germany. It was a Sunday morning, and he was to preach that day for Dr. Toulmin of Taunton. I asked him if he had prepared anything for the occasion? He said he had not even thought of the text, but should as soon as we

2. The pseudonym of the author (whose identity is still uncertain) of a series of attacks on George III and various politicians, 1769–72.
3. The liberal parliamentarian Charles James Fox (1749–1806); the Conservative prime minister William Pitt (1759–1806).
4. The 17th-century divine, author of *Holy Living*

(1650) and *Holy Dying* (1651).
5. A 1794 novel by William Godwin. Samuel Richardson and Henry Fielding, the great 18th-century novelists.
6. Echoing *The Rime of the Ancient Mariner,* line 227.

parted. I did not go to hear him—this was a fault—but we met in the evening at Bridgewater. The next day we had a long day's walk to Bristol, and sat down, I recollect, by a well-side on the road, to cool ourselves and satisfy our thirst, when Coleridge repeated to me some descriptive lines from his tragedy of *Remorse;* which I must say became his mouth and that occasion better than they, some years after, did Mr. Elliston's[7] and the Drury Lane boards,

> Oh memory! shield me from the world's poor strife,
> And give those scenes thine everlasting life.

I saw no more of him for a year or two, during which period he had been wandering in the Hartz Forest in Germany; and his return was cometary, meteorous, unlike his setting out. It was not till some time after that I knew his friends Lamb and Southey. The last always appears to me (as I first saw him) with a commonplace-book under his arm, and the first with a bon mot[8] in his mouth. It was at Godwin's that I met him with Holcroft and Coleridge, where they were disputing fiercely which was the best—*Man as he was, or man as he is to be.* "Give me," says Lamb, "man as he is *not* to be." This saying was the beginning of a friendship between us, which I believe still continues.— Enough of this for the present.

> But there is matter for another rhyme,
> And I to this may add a second tale.[9]

1823

7. Robert William Elliston, a well-known actor. Coleridge's *Remorse* was produced at Drury Lane in 1813.
8. A witticism. "Commonplace-book": a manu-script notebook of personal reflections and favorite quotations culled from one's reading.
9. Wordsworth, *Hart-Leap Well*, lines 95–96.

THOMAS DE QUINCEY
1785–1859

Born in Manchester, the son of a wealthy merchant involved in the West Indian cotton trade, De Quincey was the fourth of eight children. Before his tenth birthday he experienced the deaths of a series of family members, his father included; the loss that more than any other haunted him his entire life was that of his favorite sister and "nursery playmate," Elizabeth, two years his senior, who died suddenly in 1792. Sent from home to school at seven, De Quincey was a precocious scholar, especially in Latin and Greek, and a gentle and bookish introvert; he found it difficult to adapt himself to discipline and routine and was thrown into panic by any emergency that called for decisive action. He ran away from Manchester Grammar School and, after a summer spent tramping through Wales, broke off completely from his family and guardians and went to London in the hope that he could obtain from moneylenders an advance on his prospective inheritance. There at the age of seventeen he spent a terrible winter of loneliness and poverty, befriended only by some kindly prostitutes. These early experiences with the sinister aspect of city life later became persistent elements in his dreams of terror.

After a reconciliation with his guardians, he entered Worcester College, Oxford, on an inadequate allowance. He spent the years 1803–08 in sporadic attendance, isolated as usual, then left abruptly in the middle of his examination for the A.B. with honors because he could not face the ordeal of an oral examination.

De Quincey had been an early admirer of Wordsworth and Coleridge. No sooner did he come of age and into his inheritance than, with his usual combination of generosity and recklessness, he made Coleridge an anonymous gift of £300. He became an intimate friend of the Wordsworths at Grasmere, and when they left Dove Cottage for Allan Bank, took up his own residence at Dove Cottage to be near them. For a time he lived the life of a rural scholar, but then fell in love with Margaret Simpson, the daughter of a minor local landholder and farmer and, after she had borne him a son, married her in February 1817. This affair led to an estrangement from the Wordsworths and left him in severe financial difficulties. Worse still, De Quincey at this time became completely enslaved to opium. Following the ordinary medical practice of the time, he had been taking the drug for a variety of painful ailments; but now, driven by poverty and despair as well as pain, he indulged in huge quantities of laudanum (opium dissolved in alcohol) and was never thereafter able to free himself from addiction to what he called "the pleasures and pains of opium." It was during periods of maximum use, and especially in the recurrent agonies of cutting down his opium dosage, that he experienced the grotesque and terrifying reveries and nightmares that he wove into his literary fantasies.

Desperate for income, De Quincey at last turned to writing at the age of thirty-six. *Confessions of an English Opium-Eater,* which he contributed to the *London Magazine,* scored an immediate success and was at once reprinted as a book, but it earned him little money. In 1828 he moved with his three children to Edinburgh, to write for *Blackwood's Magazine.* For almost the rest of his life, he led a harried existence, beset by many physical ills, struggling with his indecisiveness and depression and the horrors of the opium habit, dodging his creditors and the constant threat of imprisonment for debt. All the while he ground out articles on any salable subject in a ceaseless struggle to keep his children, who ultimately numbered eight, from starving to death. Only after his mother died and left him a small income was he able, in his sixties, to live in comparative ease and freedom under the care of his devoted and practical-minded daughters. His last decade he spent mainly in gathering, revising, and expanding his essays for his "Collective Edition"; the final volume appeared in 1860, the year after his death.

De Quincey's life was chaotic, and in tone his best-known writings run the gamut from quirky wit to nightmarish sensationalism. Nonetheless, he was a conventional and conservative person—a rigid moralist, a Tory, and a faithful champion of the Church of England. Everybody who knew him testified to his gentleness, his courteous and musical speech, and his exquisite manners. Less obvious, under the surface timidity and irresolution, were the toughness and courage that sustained him through a long life of seemingly hopeless struggle.

A voracious reader (when he absconded from school, he was slowed down by a weighty trunk of books he was determined to take with him). De Quincey was a writer of encyclopedic intellectual interests and great versatility. A new twenty-one volume edition of his collected works encompasses the many essays he wrote on the philosophy and literature of Germany, as well as a book that explained the highly technical theories of value outlined by the economist David Ricardo. The collected works also include commentaries on politics and theology, numerous pieces of literary criticism (such as his "specimen of psychological criticism" "On the Knocking at the Gate in *Macbeth*") and vivid biographical sketches of the many writers he knew personally, most notably Wordsworth, Coleridge, Southey, and Lamb. His most distinctive and impressive achievements, however, are the writings that start with fact and move into macabre fantasy ("On Murder Considered as One of the Fine Arts") and especially those that begin as quiet autobiography and develop into an elaborate construction made up from the materials of his reveries and dreams (*Confessions of an English Opium-Eater, Autobiographic Sketches, Suspiria de Profundis* ["Sighs from the depths"], and "The English Mail Coach"). In these achievements De Quincey opened up to English literature the nightside of human consciousness, with its grotesque strangeness, its angst, and its pervasive sense of guilt and alienation. "In dreams," he wrote, long before Sigmund Freud, "perhaps under some secret conflict of the midnight sleeper, lighted up to the consciousness at the time, but darkened to the memory as soon as all is finished, each several child of our mysterious race completes for himself the treason of the aboriginal fall." And for these dream writings he developed a mode of organization that is based on thematic statement, variation, and development in the art of music, in which he had a deep and abiding interest. Although by temperament a conservative, De Quincey was in his writings a radical innovator, whose experiments look ahead to the materials and methods of later masters in prose and verse such as James Joyce, Franz Kafka, Virginia Woolf, and T. S. Eliot.

From Confessions of an English Opium-Eater[1]

From *Preliminary Confessions*[2]

[THE PROSTITUTE ANN]

* * * Another person there was at that time, whom I have since sought to trace with far deeper earnestness, and with far deeper sorrow at my failure. This person was a young woman, and one of that unhappy class who subsist upon the wages of prostitution. I feel no shame, nor have any reason to feel it, in avowing, that I was then on familiar and friendly terms with many women in that unfortunate condition. The reader needs neither smile at this avowal, nor frown. For, not to remind my classical readers of the old Latin proverb— "*Sine Cerere*," &c.,[3] it may well be supposed that in the existing state of my purse, my connection with such women could not have been an impure one. But the truth is, that at no time of my life have I been a person to hold myself polluted by the touch or approach of any creature that wore a human shape: on the contrary, from my very earliest youth it has been my pride to converse familiarly, *more Socratico*,[4] with all human beings, man, woman, and child,

1. The *Confessions* were published anonymously in two issues of the *London Magazine*, September and October 1821, and were reprinted as a book in the following year. In 1856 De Quincey revised the book for the collected edition of his writings, expanding it to more than twice its original length. The author was over seventy years old at the time and privately expressed the judgment that the expanded edition lacks the immediacy and artistic economy of the original. The selections here are from the version of the *Confessions* printed in 1822.

   The work is divided into three parts. The first part, "Preliminary Confessions," deals with De Quincey's early experiences—at school, in Wales, and in London—before taking opium. Part Two, "The Pleasures of Opium" (omitted here), describes the early effects on his perceptions and reveries of his moderate and occasional indulgence in the drug. Part Three, "The Pains of Opium," is an elaborate and artful representation of his fantastic nightmares; these, in modern medical opinion, are in part withdrawal symptoms, during periods when he tried to cut down his use of opium.

   In De Quincey's own lifetime, and ever since, the charge has been brought that the reports of these dreams were largely fabricated by the author.

But De Quincey always insisted that they were substantially accurate; and both the fact and the content of such anguished nightmares are corroborated by the testimony of another laudanum addict, Samuel Taylor Coleridge, in his poem "The Pains of Sleep" (1803).

2. The seventeen-year-old De Quincey had run away from school and, although originally planning to head north from Manchester so as to introduce himself to Wordsworth (whose poetry he worshipped), had ended up taking refuge in London, his whereabouts unknown to his mother and his guardians. He had slept outdoors for two months but has now been permitted, by a disreputable and seedy lawyer, to sleep in an unoccupied, unfurnished, and rat-infested house. There he and a ten-year-old girl, nameless and of uncertain parentage, huddle together for warmth, eking out a famished existence on whatever scraps he can scavenge from his landlord's frugal breakfast. He goes on to describe his friendship with a young prostitute, Ann.

3. *Sine Cerere et Baccho friget Venus*—"without Ceres and Bacchus [food and wine], love grows cold."

4. "In the manner of Socrates"; i.e., by a dialogue of questions and answers.

that chance might fling in my way: a practice which is friendly to the knowledge of human nature, to good feelings, and to that frankness of address which becomes a man who would be thought a philosopher. For a philosopher should not see with the eyes of the poor limitary[5] creature, calling himself a man of the world, and filled with narrow and self-regarding prejudices of birth and education, but should look upon himself as a Catholic[6] creature, and as standing in an equal relation to high and low—to educated and uneducated, to the guilty and the innocent. Being myself at that time of necessity a peripatetic, or a walker of the street, I naturally fell in more frequently with those female peripatetics who are technically called street-walkers. Many of these women had occasionally taken my part against watchmen who wished to drive me off the steps of houses where I was sitting. But one amongst them, the one on whose account I have at all introduced this subject—yet no! let me not class thee, oh noble-minded Ann——, with that order of women; let me find, if it be possible, some gentler name to designate the condition of her to whose bounty and compassion, ministering to my necessities when all the world had forsaken me, I owe it that I am at this time alive.—For many weeks I had walked at nights with this poor friendless girl up and down Oxford Street, or had rested with her on steps and under the shelter of porticos. She could not be so old as myself: she told me, indeed, that she had not completed her sixteenth year. By such questions as my interest about her prompted, I had gradually drawn forth her simple history. Hers was a case of ordinary occurrence (as I have since had reason to think), and one in which, if London beneficence had better adapted its arrangements to meet it, the power of the law might oftener be interposed to protect, and to avenge. But the stream of London charity flows in a channel which, though deep and mighty, is yet noiseless and underground; not obvious or readily accessible to poor houseless wanderers; and it cannot be denied that the outside air and framework of London society is harsh, cruel, and repulsive. In any case, however, I saw that part of her injuries might easily have been redressed; and I urged her often and earnestly to lay her complaint before a magistrate: friendless as she was, I assured her that she would meet with immediate attention; and that English justice, which was no respecter of persons, would speedily and amply avenge her on the brutal ruffian who had plundered her little property. She promised me often that she would; but she delayed taking the steps I pointed out from time to time: for she was timid and dejected to a degree which showed how deeply sorrow had taken hold of her young heart: and perhaps she thought justly that the most upright judge, and the most righteous tribunals, could do nothing to repair her heaviest wrongs. Something, however, would perhaps have been done: for it had been settled between us at length, but unhappily on the very last time but one that I was ever to see her, that in a day or two we should go together before a magistrate, and that I should speak on her behalf. This little service it was destined, however, that I should never realize. Meantime, that which she rendered to me, and which was greater than I could ever have repaid her, was this:—One night, when we were pacing slowly along Oxford Street, and after a day when I had felt more than usually ill and faint, I requested her to turn off with me into Soho Square: thither we went; and we sat down on the steps of a house, which, to this hour, I never pass without a pang of grief, and an inner act of homage to the spirit of that unhappy girl,

5. Limited.
6. In the sense of "inclusive in tastes and understanding."

in memory of the noble action which she there performed. Suddenly, as we sat, I grew much worse: I had been leaning my head against her bosom; and all at once I sank from her arms and fell backwards on the steps. From the sensations I then had, I felt an inner conviction of the liveliest kind that without some powerful and reviving stimulus, I should either have died on the spot—or should at least have sunk to a point of exhaustion from which all re-ascent under my friendless circumstances would soon have become hopeless. Then it was, at this crisis of my fate, that my poor orphan companion—who had herself met with little but injuries in this world—stretched out a saving hand to me. Uttering a cry of terror, but without a moment's delay, she ran off into Oxford Street, and in less time than could be imagined, returned to me with a glass of port wine and spices, that acted upon my empty stomach (which at that time would have rejected all solid food) with an instantaneous power of restoration: and for this glass the generous girl without a murmur paid out of her own humble purse at a time—be it remembered!—when she had scarcely wherewithal to purchase the bare necessaries of life, and when she could have no reason to expect that I should ever be able to reimburse her.——Oh! youthful benefactress! how often in succeeding years, standing in solitary places, and thinking of thee with grief of heart and perfect love, how often have I wished that, as in ancient times the curse of a father was believed to have a supernatural power, and to pursue its object with a fatal necessity of self-fulfillment—even so the benediction of a heart oppressed with gratitude, might have a like prerogative; might have power given to it from above to chase—to haunt—to waylay[7]—to overtake—to pursue thee into the central darkness of a London brothel, or (if it were possible) into the darkness of the grave—there to awaken thee with an authentic message of peace and forgiveness, and of final reconciliation!

I do not often weep: for not only do my thoughts on subjects connected with the chief interests of man daily, nay hourly, descend a thousand fathoms "too deep for tears";[8] not only does the sternness of my habits of thought present an antagonism to the feelings which prompt tears—wanting of necessity to those who, being protected usually by their levity from any tendency to meditative sorrow, would by that same levity be made incapable of resisting it on any casual access of such feelings:—but also, I believe that all minds which have contemplated such objects as deeply as I have done, must, for their own protection from utter despondency, have early encouraged and cherished some tranquilizing belief as to the future balances and the hieroglyphic meanings of human sufferings. On these accounts, I am cheerful to this hour; and, as I have said, I do not often weep. Yet some feelings, though not deeper or more passionate, are more tender than others; and often, when I walk at this time in Oxford Street by dreamy lamplight, and hear those airs played on a barrel-organ[9] which years ago solaced me and my dear companion (as I must always call her), I shed tears, and muse with myself at the mysterious dispensation which so suddenly and so critically separated us for ever.[1] * * *

7. From Wordsworth's "She was a phantom of delight," line 10: "To haunt, to startle, and waylay." De Quincey was an early and enthusiastic admirer of Wordsworth's poetry.
8. From the last line of Wordsworth's "Ode: Intimations of Immortality."
9. Instrument played by an organ-grinder.
1. De Quincey goes on to narrate that, having been given some money by a family friend who recognized him in the street, he had traveled to Eton to ask a young nobleman whom he knew to stand security for a loan that De Quincey was soliciting from a moneylender. When he returned to London three days later, Ann had disappeared. "If she lived," he writes, "doubtless we must have been sometimes in search of each other, at the very same moment, through the mighty labyrinths of London; perhaps, even within a few feet of each other—a barrier no wider in a London street, often amounting in the end to a separation for eternity!"

From *Introduction to the Pains of Opium*[2]

[THE MALAY]

* * * I remember, about this time, a little incident, which I mention, because, trifling as it was, the reader will soon meet it again in my dreams, which it influenced more fearfully than could be imagined. One day a Malay[3] knocked at my door. What business a Malay could have to transact amongst English mountains, I cannot conjecture: but possibly he was on his road to a seaport about forty miles distant.

The servant who opened the door to him was a young girl born and bred amongst the mountains, who had never seen an Asiatic dress of any sort: his turban, therefore, confounded her not a little: and, as it turned out that his attainments in English were exactly of the same extent as hers in the Malay, there seemed to be an impassable gulf fixed between all communication of ideas, if either party had happened to possess any. In this dilemma, the girl, recollecting the reputed learning of her master (and, doubtless, giving me credit for a knowledge of all the languages of the earth, besides, perhaps, a few of the lunar ones), came and gave me to understand that there was a sort of demon below, whom she clearly imagined that my art could exorcise from the house. I did not immediately go down: but, when I did, the group which presented itself, arranged as it was by accident, though not very elaborate, took hold of my fancy and my eye in a way that none of the statuesque attitudes exhibited in the ballets at the Opera House, though so ostentatiously complex, had ever done. In a cottage kitchen, but paneled on the wall with dark wood that from age and rubbing resembled oak, and looking more like a rustic hall of entrance than a kitchen, stood the Malay—his turban and loose trousers of dingy white relieved upon the dark paneling: he had placed himself nearer to the girl than she seemed to relish; though her native spirit of mountain intrepidity contended with the feeling of simple awe which her countenance expressed as she gazed upon the tiger-cat before her. And a more striking picture there could not be imagined, than the beautiful English face of the girl, and its exquisite fairness, together with her erect and independent attitude, contrasted with the sallow and bilious skin of the Malay, enameled or veneered with mahogany, by marine air, his small, fierce, restless eyes, thin lips, slavish gestures and adorations. Half-hidden by the ferocious-looking Malay, was a little child from a neighboring cottage who had crept in after him, and was now in the act of reverting its head, and gazing upwards at the turban and the fiery eyes beneath it, whilst with one hand he caught at the dress of the young woman for protection. My knowledge of the Oriental tongues is not remarkably extensive, being indeed confined to two words—the Arabic word for barley, and the Turkish for opium (madjoon), which I have learnt from Anastasius.[4] And, as I had neither a Malay dictionary, nor even Adelung's *Mithridates*,[5] which might have helped me to a few words, I addressed him in some lines from the Iliad; considering that, of such languages

2. It is 1816. De Quincy is living at Dove Cottage, Grasmere, and for three years has been addicted to laudanum, i.e., opium dissolved in alcohol. At this time he has succeeded in reducing his daily dosage from eight thousand to one thousand drops, with a consequent improvement in health and energy.
3. Native of the Malay peninsula in Southeast Asia.

4. *Anastasius, or Memoirs of a Greek,* was a novel published anonymously by Thomas Hope in 1819. It included a description of the physical effects of opium that De Quincey considered to be a "grievous misrepresentation."
5. *Mithridates, or The Universal Table of Languages,* by the German philologist J. C. Adelung (1732–1806).

as I possessed, Greek, in point of longitude, came geographically nearest to an Oriental one. He worshiped[6] me in a most devout manner, and replied in what I suppose was Malay. In this way I saved my reputation with my neighbors: for the Malay had no means of betraying the secret. He lay down upon the floor for about an hour, and then pursued his journey. On his departure, I presented him with a piece of opium. To him, as an Orientalist, I concluded that opium must be familiar: and the expression of his face convinced me that it was. Nevertheless, I was struck with some little consternation when I saw him suddenly raise his hand to his mouth, and (in the schoolboy phrase) bolt the whole, divided into three pieces, at one mouthful. The quantity was enough to kill three dragoons and their horses: and I felt some alarm for the poor creature: but what could be done? I had given him the opium in compassion for his solitary life, on recollecting that if he had traveled on foot from London, it must be nearly three weeks since he could have exchanged a thought with any human being. I could not think of violating the laws of hospitality, by having him seized and drenched with an emetic, and thus frightening him into a notion that we were going to sacrifice him to some English idol. No: there was clearly no help for it:—he took his leave: and for some days I felt anxious: but as I never heard of any Malay being found dead, I became convinced that he was used[7] to opium: and that I must have done him the service I designed, by giving him one night of respite from the pains of wandering.

This incident I have digressed to mention, because this Malay (partly from the picturesque exhibition he assisted to frame, partly from the anxiety I connected with his image for some days) fastened afterwards upon my dreams, and brought other Malays with him worse than himself, that ran "amuck"[8] at me, and led me into a world of troubles. * * *

From *The Pains of Opium*

[OPIUM REVERIES AND DREAMS]

I have thus described and illustrated my intellectual torpor, in terms that apply, more or less, to every part of the four years during which I was under the Circean[9] spells of opium. But for misery and suffering, I might, indeed, be said to have existed in a dormant state. I seldom could prevail on myself to write a letter; an answer of a few words, to any that I received, was the utmost that I could accomplish; and often *that* not until the letter had lain weeks, or even months, on my writing table. Without the aid of M.[1] all records of bills paid, or *to be* paid, must have perished: and my whole domestic economy, whatever became of Political Economy,[2] must have gone into irretrievable confusion.— I shall not afterwards allude to this part of the case: it is one, however, which the opium-eater will find, in the end, as oppressive and tormenting as any other, from the sense of incapacity and feebleness, from the direct embarrass-

6. Bowed down to.
7. This, however, is not a necessary conclusion: the varieties of effect produced by opium on different constitutions are infinite [De Quincey's note].
8. See the common accounts in any Eastern traveller or voyager of the frantic excesses committed by Malays who have taken opium, or are reduced to desperation by ill luck at gambling [De Quincey's note]. As a term denoting frenzy, "amuck," also spelled "amok," entered English by way of

travel literature and was used initially as a generic designation for inhabitants of the Malay peninsula.
9. Like those of Circe, the enchantress in the *Odyssey* who turned Odysseus's men into swine.
1. Margaret Simpson, whom De Quincey had married in 1817.
2. Inspired by David Ricardo's *Principles of Political Economy* (1817), De Quincey had begun to write, but never completed, a work he called *Prolegomena to All Future Systems of Political Economy*.

ments incident to the neglect or procrastination of each day's appropriate duties, and from the remorse which must often exasperate the stings of these evils to a reflective and conscientious mind. The opium-eater loses none of his moral sensibilities, or aspirations: he wishes and longs, as earnestly as ever, to realize what he believes possible, and feels to be exacted by duty; but his intellectual apprehension of what is possible infinitely outruns his power, not of execution only, but even of power to attempt. He lies under the weight of incubus and nightmare: he lies in sight of all that he would fain perform, just as a man forcibly confined to his bed by the mortal languor of a relaxing disease, who is compelled to witness injury or outrage offered to some object of his tenderest love:—he curses the spells which chain him down from motion:—he would lay down his life if he might get up and walk; but he is powerless as an infant, and cannot even attempt to rise.

I now pass to what is the main subject of these latter confessions, to the history and journal of what took place in my dreams; for these were the immediate and proximate cause of my acutest suffering.

The first notice I had of any important change going on in this part of my physical economy, was from the re-awakening of a state of eye generally incident to childhood, or exalted states of irritability. I know not whether my reader is aware that many children, perhaps most, have a power of painting, as it were, upon the darkness, all sorts of phantoms; in some, that power is simply a mechanic affection of the eye; others have a voluntary, or a semi-voluntary power to dismiss or to summon them; or, as a child once said to me when I questioned him on this matter, "I can tell them to go, and they go; but sometimes they come, when I don't tell them to come." Whereupon I told him that he had almost as unlimited a command over apparitions, as a Roman centurion[3] over his soldiers.—In the middle of 1817, I think it was, that this faculty became positively distressing to me: at night, when I lay awake in bed, vast processions passed along in mournful pomp; friezes of never-ending stories, that to my feelings were as sad and solemn as if they were stories drawn from times before Oedipus or Priam—before Tyre—before Memphis.[4] And, at the same time, a corresponding change took place in my dreams; a theater seemed suddenly opened and lighted up within my brain, which presented nightly spectacles of more than earthly splendor. And the four following facts may be mentioned, as noticeable at this time:

1. That, as the creative state of the eye increased, a sympathy seemed to arise between the waking and the dreaming states of the brain in one point— that whatsoever I happened to call up and to trace by a voluntary act upon the darkness was very apt to transfer itself to my dreams; so that I feared to exercise this faculty; for, as Midas turned all things to gold, that yet baffled his hopes and defrauded his human desires,[5] so whatsoever things capable of being visually represented I did but think of in the darkness, immediately shaped themselves into phantoms of the eye; and, by a process apparently no less inevitable, when thus once traced in faint and visionary colors, like writings in sympathetic ink,[6] they were drawn out by the fierce chemistry of my dreams, into insufferable splendor that fretted my heart.

3. A Roman officer commanding a troop of a hundred soldiers (a "century").
4. De Quincey is calling the roll of great civilizations in the past. Oedipus was the king of Thebes; Priam, the king of Troy. Tyre was the chief city of Phoenicia; Memphis, the capital of ancient Egypt.

5. When granted his rash wish that all he touched should turn to gold, King Midas was horrified to discover that his food, drink, and beloved daughter all became gold at his touch.
6. Invisible ink.

2. For this, and all other changes in my dreams, were accompanied by deep-seated anxiety and gloomy melancholy, such as are wholly incommunicable by words. I seemed every night to descend, not metaphorically, but literally to descend, into chasms and sunless abysses, depths below depths, from which it seemed hopeless that I could ever reascend. Nor did I, by waking, feel that I *had* re-ascended. This I do not dwell upon; because the state of gloom which attended these gorgeous spectacles, amounting at least to utter darkness, as of some suicidal despondency, cannot be approached by words.

3. The sense of space, and in the end, the sense of time, were both powerfully affected. Buildings, landscapes, &c. were exhibited in proportions so vast as the bodily eye is not fitted to receive. Space swelled, and was amplified to an extent of unutterable infinity. This, however, did not disturb me so much as the vast expansion of time; I sometimes seemed to have lived for 70 or 100 years in one night; nay, sometimes had feelings representative of a millennium passed in that time, or, however, of a duration far beyond the limits of any human experience.

4. The minutest incidents of childhood, or forgotten scenes of later years, were often revived: I could not be said to recollect them; for if I had been told of them when waking, I should not have been able to acknowledge them as parts of my past experience. But placed as they were before me, in dreams like intuitions, and clothed in all their evanescent circumstances and accompanying feelings, I *recognized* them instantaneously. I was once told by a near relative[7] of mine, that having in her childhood fallen into a river, and being on the very verge of death but for the critical assistance which reached her, she saw in a moment her whole life, in its minutest incidents, arrayed before her simultaneously as in a mirror; and she had a faculty developed as suddenly for comprehending the whole and every part. This, from some opium experiences of mine, I can believe; I have, indeed, seen the same thing asserted twice in modern books, and accompanied by a remark which I am convinced is true; viz. that the dread book of account, which the Scriptures speak of,[8] is, in fact, the mind itself of each individual. Of this, at least, I feel assured, that there is no such thing as *forgetting* possible to the mind; a thousand accidents may, and will, interpose a veil between our present consciousness and the secret inscriptions on the mind; accidents of the same sort will also rend away this veil; but alike, whether veiled or unveiled, the inscription remains forever; just as the stars seem to withdraw before the common light of day, whereas, in fact, we all know that it is the light which is drawn over them as a veil— and that they are waiting to be revealed, when the obscuring daylight shall have withdrawn.

Having noticed these four facts as memorably distinguishing my dreams from those of health, I shall now cite a case illustrative of the first fact; and shall then cite any others that I remember, either in their chronological order, or any other that may give them more effect as pictures to the reader.

I had been in youth, and even since, for occasional amusement, a great reader of Livy,[9] whom, I confess, that I prefer, both for style and matter, to any of the Roman historians; and I had often felt as most solemn and appalling sounds, and most emphatically representative of the majesty of the Roman people, the two words so often occurring in Livy—*Consul Romanus*;[1] especially

7. According to family report De Quincey's mother.
8. The book listing everyone's name at the Last Judgment (Revelation 20.12).

9. Titus Livius (59 B.C.E.–17 C.E.), author of a history of Rome in 142 books.
1. Roman consul (Latin); one of two officials, elected annually, who wielded the chief military

when the consul is introduced in his military character. I mean to say, that the words king—sultan—regent, &c. or any other titles of those who embody in their own persons the collective majesty of a great people, had less power over my reverential feelings. I had also, though no great reader of history, made myself minutely and critically familiar with one period of English history, viz. the period of the Parliamentary War, having been attracted by the moral grandeur of some who figured in that day, and by the many interesting memoirs which survive those unquiet times. Both these parts of my lighter reading, having furnished me often with matter of reflection, now furnished me with matter for my dreams. Often I used to see, after painting upon the blank darkness a sort of rehearsal whilst waking, a crowd of ladies, and perhaps a festival, and dances. And I heard it said, or I said to myself, "These are English ladies from the unhappy times of Charles I. These are the wives and the daughters of those who met in peace, and sat at the same tables, and were allied by marriage or by blood; and yet, after a certain day in August, 1642,[2] never smiled upon each other again, nor met but in the field of battle; and at Marston Moor, at Newbury, or at Naseby,[3] cut asunder all ties of love by the cruel saber, and washed away in blood the memory of ancient friendship."—The ladies danced, and looked as lovely as the court of George IV.[4] Yet I knew, even in my dream, that they had been in the grave for nearly two centuries.— This pageant would suddenly dissolve: and at a clapping of hands, would be heard the heart-quaking sound of *Consul Romanus*; and immediately came "sweeping by," in gorgeous paludaments, Paulus or Marius,[5] girt round by a company of centurions, with the crimson tunic hoisted on a spear,[6] and followed by the *alalagmos*[7] of the Roman legions.

Many years ago, when I was looking over Piranesi's Antiquities of Rome, Mr. Coleridge, who was standing by, described to me a set of plates by that artist, called his *Dreams*,[8] and which record the scenery of his own visions during the delirium of a fever. Some of them (I describe only from memory of Mr. Coleridge's account) represented vast Gothic halls: on the floor of which stood all sorts of engines and machinery, wheels, cables, pulleys, levers, catapults, &c. &c. expressive of enormous power put forth, and resistance overcome. Creeping along the sides of the walls, you perceived a staircase; and upon it, groping his way upwards, was Piranesi himself: follow the stairs a little further, and you perceive it come to a sudden abrupt termination, without any balustrade, and allowing no step onwards to him who had reached the extremity, except into the depths below. Whatever is to become of poor Piranesi, you suppose, at least, that his labors must in some way terminate here. But raise your eyes, and behold a second flight of stairs still higher: on which again Piranesi is perceived, but this time standing on the very brink of the abyss. Again elevate your eye, and a still more aerial flight of stairs is beheld: and again is poor Piranesi busy on his aspiring labors: and so on, until the unfin-

and judicial authority in Republican Rome.
2. The raising of the king's banner on Castle Hill, Nottingham, on August 22, 1642, signaled the beginning of the English Civil War.
3. Scenes of the defeat of King Charles's forces in the Civil War.
4. The reigning monarch at the time De Quincey was writing.
5. Lucius Paulus (d. 160 B.C.E.) and Caius Marius (d. 86 B.C.E.) were Roman generals who won famous victories. "Paludaments": the cloaks worn by Roman generals.
6. The signal which announced a day of battle [De

Quincey's note in the revised edition].
7. A word expressing collectively the gathering of the Roman war-cries [De Quincey's note in the revised edition]. The word is Greek.
8. Giovanni Piranesi (1720–1778), a Venetian especially famed for his many etchings of ancient and modern Rome. He did not publish prints called *Dreams*; De Quincey doubtless refers to his series called *Carceri d'Invenzione*, "Imaginary prisons." The description that De Quincey recalls from Coleridge's conversation is remarkably apt for these terrifying architectural fantasies.

ished stairs and Piranesi both are lost in the upper gloom of the hall.—With the same power of endless growth and self-reproduction did my architecture proceed in dreams. In the early stage of my malady, the splendors of my dreams were indeed chiefly architectural: and I beheld such pomp of cities and palaces as was never yet beheld by the waking eye, unless in the clouds. From a great modern poet[9] I cite part of a passage which describes, as an appearance actually beheld in the clouds, what in many of its circumstances I saw frequently in sleep:

> The appearance, instantaneously disclosed,
> Was of a mighty city—boldly say
> A wilderness of building, sinking far
> And self-withdrawn into a wondrous depth,
> Far sinking into splendor—without end!
> Fabric[1] it seem'd of diamond, and of gold,
> With alabaster domes, and silver spires,
> And blazing terrace upon terrace, high
> Uplifted; here, serene pavilions bright
> In avenues disposed; there towers begirt
> With battlements that on their restless fronts
> Bore stars—illumination of all gems!
> By earthly nature had the effect been wrought
> Upon the dark materials of the storm
> Now pacified: on them, and on the coves,
> And mountain-steeps and summits, whereunto
> The vapors had receded,—taking there
> Their station under a cerulean sky, &c. &c.

The sublime circumstance—"battlements that on their *restless* fronts bore stars"—might have been copied from my architectural dreams, for it often occurred.—We hear it reported of Dryden, and of Fuseli[2] in modern times, that they thought proper to eat raw meat for the sake of obtaining splendid dreams: how much better for such a purpose to have eaten opium, which yet I do not remember that any poet is recorded to have done, except the dramatist Shadwell:[3] and in ancient days, Homer is, I think, rightly reputed to have known the virtues of opium.[4]

To my architecture succeeded dreams of lakes—and silvery expanses of water:—these haunted me so much, that I feared (though possibly it will appear ludicrous to a medical man) that some dropsical state or tendency of the brain[5] might thus be making itself (to use a metaphysical word) *objective;* and the sentient organ *project* itself as its own object.—For two months I suffered greatly in my head—a part of my bodily structure which had hitherto been so clear from all touch or taint of weakness (physically, I mean), that I used to say of it, as the last Lord Orford[6] said of his stomach, that it seemed

9. The quotation is from Wordsworth's *The Excursion,* book 2, lines 834ff. It describes a cloud structure after a storm.
1. I.e., building.
2. John Henry Fuseli (1741–1825) was born in Switzerland and painted in England. He was noted for his paintings of nightmarish fantasies.
3. Thomas Shadwell was a Restoration dramatist and poet. He is now best-known as the target of Dryden's satire (in *Mac Flecknoe* and elsewhere) than as a writer in his own right.

4. In the *Odyssey,* book 4, Homer praises nepenthe (which is probably opium) as a "drug to heal all pain and anger, and bring forgetfulness of every sorrow."
5. De Quincey's sister Elizabeth died at age nine of hydrocephalus, water on the brain. "Dropsical": afflicted with dropsy—an accumulation of fluid in the bodily tissues and cavities.
6. Horace Walpole, 18th-century wit and letter writer, author of the Gothic novel *The Castle of Otranto* (1764).

likely to survive the rest of my person.—Till now I had never felt a headache even, or any the slightest pain, except rheumatic pains caused by my own folly. However, I got over this attack, though it must have been verging on something very dangerous.

The waters now changed their character—from translucent lakes, shining like mirrors, they now became seas and oceans. And now came a tremendous change, which, unfolding itself slowly like a scroll, through many months, promised an abiding torment; and, in fact, it never left me until the winding up of my case. Hitherto the human face had mixed often in my dreams, but not despotically, nor with any special power of tormenting. But now that which I have called the tyranny of the human face began to unfold itself. Perhaps some part of my London life might be answerable for this. Be that as it may, now it was that upon the rocking waters of the ocean the human face began to appear: the sea appeared paved with innumerable faces, upturned to the heavens: faces, imploring, wrathful, despairing, surged upwards by thousands, by myriads, by generations, by centuries:—my agitation was infinite,—my mind tossed—and surged with the ocean.

May 1818

The Malay has been a fearful enemy for months. I have been every night, through his means, transported into Asiatic scenes. I know not whether others share in my feelings on this point; but I have often thought that if I were compelled to forego England, and to live in China, and among Chinese manners and modes of life and scenery, I should go mad. The causes of my horror lie deep; and some of them must be common to others. Southern Asia, in general, is the seat of awful images and associations. As the cradle of the human race, it would alone have a dim and reverential feeling connected with it. But there are other reasons. No man can pretend that the wild, barbarous, and capricious superstitions of Africa, or of savage tribes elsewhere, affect him in the way that he is affected by the ancient, monumental, cruel, and elaborate religions of Indostan, &c. The mere antiquity of Asiatic things, of their institutions, histories, modes of faith, &c. is so impressive, that to me the vast age of the race and name overpowers the sense of youth in the individual. A young Chinese seems to me an antediluvian man[7] renewed. Even Englishmen, though not bred in any knowledge of such institutions, cannot but shudder at the mystic sublimity of castes[8] that have flowed apart, and refused to mix, through such immemorial tracts of time; nor can any man fail to be awed by the names of the Ganges, or the Euphrates. It contributes much to these feelings, that southern Asia is, and has been for thousands of years, the part of the earth most swarming with human life; the great *officina gentium*.[9] Man is a weed in those regions. The vast empires also, into which the enormous population of Asia has always been cast, give a further sublimity to the feelings associated with all Oriental names or images. In China, over and above what it has in common with the rest of southern Asia, I am terrified by the modes of life, by the manners, and the barrier of utter abhorrence, and want of sympathy, placed between us by feelings deeper than I can analyze. I could sooner live with lunatics, or brute animals. All this, and much more than I can say,

---

7. A person who lived in in the time before the great flood described in Genesis.
8. The reference is to the Hindu caste system of

India, with its sharp divisions between four hereditary social classes.
9. Manufactory of populations (Latin).

or have time to say, the reader must enter into before he can comprehend the unimaginable horror which these dreams of Oriental imagery, and mythological tortures, impressed upon me. Under the connecting feeling of tropical heat and vertical sunlights, I brought together all creatures, birds, beasts, reptiles, all trees and plants, usages and appearances, that are found in all tropical regions, and assembled them together in China or Indostan. From kindred feelings, I soon brought Egypt and all her gods under the same law. I was stared at, hooted at, grinned at, chattered at, by monkeys, by paroquets, by cockatoos. I ran into pagodas: and was fixed, for centuries, at the summit, or in secret rooms; I was the idol; I was the priest; I was worshiped; I was sacrificed. I fled from the wrath of Brama through all the forests of Asia: Vishnu hated me: Seeva[1] laid wait for me. I came suddenly upon Isis and Osiris: I had done a deed, they said, which the ibis and the crocodile[2] trembled at. I was buried, for a thousand years, in stone coffins, with mummies and sphinxes, in narrow chambers at the heart of eternal pyramids. I was kissed, with cancerous kisses, by crocodiles; and laid, confounded with all unutterable slimy things, amongst reeds and Nilotic mud.

I thus give the reader some slight abstraction of my Oriental dreams,[3] which always filled me with such amazement at the monstrous scenery, that horror seemed absorbed, for a while, in sheer astonishment. Sooner or later, came a reflux of feeling that swallowed up the astonishment, and left me, not so much in terror, as in hatred and abomination of what I saw. Over every form, and threat, and punishment, and dim sightless incarceration, brooded a sense of eternity and infinity that drove me into an oppression as of madness. Into these dreams only, it was, with one or two slight exceptions, that any circumstances of physical horror entered. All before had been moral and spiritual terrors. But here the main agents were ugly birds, or snakes, or crocodiles; especially the last. The cursed crocodile became to me the object of more horror than almost all the rest. I was compelled to live with him; and (as was always the case almost in my dreams) for centuries. I escaped sometimes, and found myself in Chinese houses, with cane tables, &c. All the feet of the tables, sofas, &c. soon became instinct with life: the abominable head of the crocodile, and his leering eyes, looked out at me, multiplied into a thousand repetitions: and I stood loathing and fascinated. And so often did this hideous reptile haunt my dreams, that many times the very same dream was broken up in the very same way: I heard gentle voices speaking to me (I hear every thing when I am sleeping); and instantly I awoke: it was broad noon; and my children were standing, hand in hand, at my bedside; come to show me their colored shoes, or new frocks, or to let me see them dressed for going out. I protest that so awful was the transition from the damned crocodile, and the other unutterable monsters and abortions of my dreams, to the sight of innocent *human* natures and of infancy, that, in the mighty and sudden revulsion of mind, I wept, and could not forbear it, as I kissed their faces.

---

1. Among the Hindu deities Brahma is the creative aspect of divine reality, Vishnu is its maintainer, and Shiva its destroyer.
2. The ibis (a long-legged wading bird) and the crocodile were considered sacred in ancient Egypt. Isis was the ancient Egyptian goddess of fertility.

She was the sister and wife of Osiris, whose annual death and rebirth represented the seasonal cycle of nature.
3. For a discussion of the cultural context of De Quincey's "Oriental dreams," see "Romantic Orientalism" at Norton Literature Online.

June 1819

I have had occasion to remark, at various periods of my life, that the deaths of those whom we love, and indeed the contemplation of death generally, is (*ceteris paribus*)[4] more affecting in summer than in any other season of the year. And the reasons are these three, I think: first, that the visible heavens in summer appear far higher, more distant, and (if such a solecism may be excused) more infinite; the clouds, by which chiefly the eye expounds the distance of the blue pavilion stretched over our heads, are in summer more voluminous, massed, and accumulated in far grander and more towering piles: secondly, the light and the appearances of the declining and the setting sun are much more fitted to be types and characters of the Infinite: and, thirdly (which is the main reason), the exuberant and riotous prodigality of life naturally forces the mind more powerfully upon the antagonist thought of death, and the wintry sterility of the grave. For it may be observed, generally, that wherever two thoughts stand related to each other by a law of antagonism, and exist, as it were, by mutual repulsion, they are apt to suggest each other. On these accounts it is that I find it impossible to banish the thought of death when I am walking alone in the endless days of summer; and any particular death, if not more affecting, at least haunts my mind more obstinately and besiegingly in that season. Perhaps this cause, and a slight incident which I omit, might have been the immediate occasions of the following dream; to which, however, a predisposition must always have existed in my mind; but having been once roused, it never left me, and split into a thousand fantastic varieties, which often suddenly reunited, and composed again the original dream.

I thought that it was a Sunday morning in May, that it was Easter Sunday, and as yet very early in the morning. I was standing, as it seemed to me, at the door of my own cottage. Right before me lay the very scene which could really be commanded from that situation, but exalted, as was usual, and solemnized by the power of dreams. There were the same mountains, and the same lovely valley at their feet; but the mountains were raised to more than Alpine height, and there was interspace far larger between them of meadows and forest lawns; the hedges were rich with white roses; and no living creature was to be seen, excepting that in the green churchyard there were cattle tranquilly reposing upon the verdant graves, and particularly round about the grave of a child whom I had tenderly loved,[5] just as I had really beheld them, a little before sunrise in the same summer, when that child died. I gazed upon the well-known scene, and I said aloud (as I thought) to myself, "It yet wants much of sunrise; and it is Easter Sunday; and that is the day on which they celebrate the first-fruits of resurrection. I will walk abroad; old griefs shall be forgotten today; for the air is cool and still, and the hills are high, and stretch away to heaven; and the forest-glades are as quiet as the churchyard; and, with the dew, I can wash the fever from my forehead, and then I shall be unhappy no longer." And I turned, as if to open my garden gate; and immediately I saw upon the left a scene far different; but which yet the power of dreams had reconciled into harmony with the other. The scene was an Oriental one; and there also it was Easter Sunday, and very early in the morning.

---

4. Other things being the same (Latin).
5. The child is Wordsworth's daughter Catherine,
who died at the age of four. She is the subject of
Wordsworth's sonnet "Surprised by joy."

And at a vast distance were visible, as a stain upon the horizon, the domes and cupolas of a great city—an image or faint abstraction, caught perhaps in childhood from some picture of Jerusalem. And not a bow-shot from me, upon a stone, and shaded by Judean palms, there sat a woman; and I looked; and it was—Ann! She fixed her eyes upon me earnestly; and I said to her at length: "So then I have found you at last." I waited: but she answered me not a word. Her face was the same as when I saw it last, and yet again how different! Seventeen years ago, when the lamplight fell upon her face, as for the last time I kissed her lips (lips, Ann, that to me were not polluted), her eyes were streaming with tears: the tears were now wiped away; she seemed more beautiful than she was at that time, but in all other points the same, and not older. Her looks were tranquil, but with unusual solemnity of expression; and I now gazed upon her with some awe, but suddenly her countenance grew dim, and, turning to the mountains, I perceived vapors rolling between us; in a moment, all had vanished; thick darkness came on; and, in the twinkling of an eye, I was far away from mountains, and by lamplight in Oxford Street, walking again with Ann—just as we walked seventeen years before, when we were both children.

As a final specimen, I cite one of a different character, from 1820.

The dream commenced with a music which now I often heard in dreams—a music of preparation and of awakening suspense; a music like the opening of the Coronation Anthem,[6] and which, like *that*, gave the feeling of a vast march—of infinite cavalcades filing off—and the tread of innumerable armies. The morning was come of a mighty day—a day of crisis and of final hope for human nature, then suffering some mysterious eclipse, and laboring in some dread extremity. Somewhere, I knew not where—somehow, I knew not how— by some beings, I knew not whom—a battle, a strife, an agony, was conducting—was evolving like a great drama, or piece of music; with which my sympathy was the more insupportable from my confusion as to its place, its cause, its nature, and its possible issue. I, as is usual in dreams (where, of necessity, we make ourselves central to every movement), had the power, and yet had not the power, to decide it. I had the power, if I could raise myself, to will it; and yet again had not the power, for the weight of twenty Atlantics was upon me, or the oppression of inexpiable guilt. "Deeper than ever plummet sounded,"[7] I lay inactive. Then, like a chorus, the passion deepened. Some greater interest was at stake; some mightier cause than ever yet the sword had pleaded, or trumpet had proclaimed. Then came sudden alarms: hurryings to and fro: trepidations of innumerable fugitives, I knew not whether from the good cause or the bad: darkness and lights: tempest and human faces: and at last, with the sense that all was lost, female forms, and the features that were worth all the world to me, and but a moment allowed—and clasped hands, and heart-breaking partings, and then—everlasting farewells! and with a sigh, such as the caves of hell sighed when the incestuous mother uttered the abhorred name of death,[8] the sound was reverberated—

6. Composed by George Frideric Handel for the coronation of George II in 1727.
7. In Shakespeare's *The Tempest* guilt-ridden King Alonso, believing that his son has drowned, says he will "seek him deeper then e'er plummet sounded / And with him there lie mudded" (3.3.101–02).

8. The reference is to *Paradise Lost*, book 2, lines 777ff. The "incestuous mother" is Sin, who is doubly incestuous: she is the daughter of Satan, who begot Death upon her, and she was in turn raped by her son and gave birth to a pack of "yelling Monsters."

everlasting farewells! and again, and yet again reverberated—everlasting
farewells!
And I awoke in struggles, and cried aloud—"I will sleep no more!"⁹

1821   1821

On the Knocking at the Gate in *Macbeth*[1]

From my boyish days I had always felt a great perplexity on one point in
Macbeth. It was this: The knocking at the gate which succeeds to the murder
of Duncan produced to my feelings an effect for which I never could account.
The effect was that it reflected back upon the murderer a peculiar awfulness
and a depth of solemnity; yet, however obstinately I endeavored with my
understanding to comprehend this, for many years I never could see *why* it
should produce such an effect.

Here I pause for one moment, to exhort the reader never to pay any attention
to his understanding when it stands in opposition to any other faculty of his
mind. The mere understanding, however useful and indispensable, is the
meanest[2] faculty in the human mind, and the most to be distrusted; and yet the
great majority of people trust to nothing else—which may do for ordinary life,
but not for philosophical purposes. Of this out of ten thousand instances that
I might produce I will cite one. Ask of any person whatsoever who is not previously prepared for the demand by a knowledge of the perspective to draw in
the rudest way the commonest appearance which depends upon the laws of
that science—as, for instance, to represent the effect of two walls standing at
right angles to each other, or the appearance of the houses on each side of a
street as seen by a person looking down the street from one extremity. Now, in
all cases, unless the person has happened to observe in pictures how it is that
artists produce these effects, he will be utterly unable to make the smallest
approximation to it. Yet why? For he has actually seen the effect every day of
his life. The reason is that he allows his understanding to overrule his eyes. His
understanding, which includes no intuitive knowledge of the laws of vision,
can furnish him with no reason why a line which is known and can be proved
to be a horizontal line should not *appear* a horizontal line: a line that made any
angle with the perpendicular less than a right angle would seem to him to indicate that his houses were all tumbling down together. Accordingly, he makes
the line of his houses a horizontal line, and fails, of course, to produce the
effect demanded. Here, then, is one instance out of many in which not only the
understanding is allowed to overrule the eyes, but where the understanding is
positively allowed to obliterate the eyes, as it were; for not only does the man
believe the evidence of his understanding in opposition to that of his eyes, but
(what is monstrous) the idiot is not aware that his eyes ever gave such evidence. He does not know that he has seen (and therefore *quoad* his consciousness[3] has *not* seen) that which he *has* seen every day of his life.

9. Macbeth says: "Methought I heard a voice cry
'Sleep no more, / Macbeth does murder sleep'"
(Shakespeare, *Macbeth* 2.2.33–34).
1. One of the best-known pieces of 19th-century
Shakespeare criticism, this essay, originally published pseudonymously in the *London Magazine* as
a "note from the pocket-book of a late opium-
eater," deals with the scene in *Macbeth* (2.2–3) in
which, just after they have murdered Duncan,
Macbeth and his wife are startled by a loud knocking at the gate. De Quincey exhibits the procedure
in Romantic criticism of making, as he says, the
"understanding" wait upon the "feelings."
2. Lowest.
3. I.e., so far as his consciousness is concerned.

But to return from this digression. My understanding could furnish no rea-son why the knocking at the gate in *Macbeth* should produce any effect, direct or reflected. In fact, my understanding said positively that it could not produce any effect. But I knew better; I felt that it did; and I waited and clung to the problem until further knowledge should enable me to solve it. At length, in 1812, Mr. Williams[4] made his debut on the stage of Ratcliffe Highway, and executed those unparalleled murders which have procured for him such a brilliant and undying reputation. On which murders, by the way, I must observe that in one respect they have had an ill effect, by making the con-noisseur in murder very fastidious in his taste, and dissatisfied by anything that has been since done in that line. All other murders look pale by the deep crimson of his; and, as an amateur[5] once said to me in a querulous tone, "There has been absolutely nothing *doing* since his time, or nothing that's worth speaking of." But this is wrong; for it is unreasonable to expect all men to be great artists, and born with the genius of Mr. Williams. Now, it will be remem-bered that in the first of these murders (that of the Marrs) the same incident (of a knocking at the door[6] soon after the work of extermination was complete) did actually occur which the genius of Shakespeare has invented; and all good judges, and the most eminent dilettanti,[7] acknowledged the felicity of Shake-speare's suggestion as soon as it was actually realized. Here, then, was a fresh proof that I was right in relying on my own feeling, in opposition to my under-standing; and I again set myself to study the problem. At length I solved it to my own satisfaction; and my solution is this: Murder, in ordinary cases, where the sympathy is wholly directed to the case of the murdered person, is an incident of coarse and vulgar horror; and for this reason—that it flings the interest exclusively upon the natural but ignoble instinct by which we cleave to life: an instinct which, as being indispensable to the primal law of self-preservation, is the same in kind (though different in degree) amongst all living creatures. This instinct, therefore, because it annihilates all distinctions, and degrades the greatest of men to the level of "the poor beetle that we tread on,"[8] exhibits human nature in its most abject and humiliating attitude. Such an attitude would little suit the purposes of the poet. What then must he do? He must throw the interest on the murderer. Our sympathy must be with *him* (of course I mean a sympathy of comprehension, a sympathy by which we enter into his feelings, and are made to understand them—not a sympathy of pity or approbation).[9] In the murdered person, all strife of thought, all flux and reflux of passion and of purpose, are crushed by one overwhelming panic; the fear of instant death smites him "with its petrific[1] mace." But in the mur-derer, such a murderer as a poet will condescend to, there must be raging some great storm of passion—jealousy, ambition, vengeance, hatred—which will create a hell within him; and into this hell we are to look.

4. John Williams, a sailor, had thrown London into a panic (the date was actually December 1811) by murdering the Marr family and, twelve days later, the Williamson family. De Quincey described these murders at length in the postscript to his two essays "On Murder Considered as One of the Fine Arts."
5. I.e., a fancier or follower of an art or sport.
6. By a maidservant of the Marrs, returning from the purchase of oysters for supper.
7. Lovers of the fine arts.
8. From the scene in *Measure for Measure* (3.1.77)

in which Isabella visits her brother Claudio in his prison cell the day before his execution.
9. In a note De Quincey decries "the unscholar-like use of the word sympathy, at present so gen-eral, by which, instead of taking it in its proper sense, as the act of reproducing in our minds the feelings of another, whether for hatred, indigna-tion, love, pity, or approbation, it is made a mere synonym of the word *pity*."
1. Petrifying, turning to stone (from Milton's *Par-adise Lost* 10.294).

In *Macbeth*, for the sake of gratifying his own enormous and teeming faculty of creation, Shakespeare has introduced two murderers: and, as usual in his hands, they are remarkably discriminated;[2] but—though in Macbeth the strife of mind is greater than in his wife, the tiger spirit not so awake, and his feelings caught chiefly by contagion from her—yet, as both were finally involved in the guilt of murder, the murderous mind of necessity is finally to be presumed in both. This was to be expressed; and, on its own account, as well as to make it a more proportionable antagonist to the unoffending nature of their victim, "the gracious Duncan," and adequately to expound "the deep damnation of his taking off,"[3] this was to be expressed with peculiar energy. We were to be made to feel that the human nature—i.e., the divine nature of love and mercy, spread through the hearts of all creatures, and seldom utterly withdrawn from man—was gone, vanished, extinct, and that the fiendish nature had taken its place. And, as this effect is marvelously accomplished in the *dialogues* and *soliloquies* themselves, so it is finally consummated by the expedient under consideration; and it is to this that I now solicit the reader's attention. If the reader has ever witnessed a wife, daughter, or sister in a fainting fit, he may chance to have observed that the most affecting moment in such a spectacle is *that* in which a sigh and a stirring announce the recommencement of suspended life. Or, if the reader has ever been present in a vast metropolis on the day when some great national idol was carried in funeral pomp to his grave, and, chancing to walk near the course through which it passed, has felt powerfully, in the silence and desertion of the streets, and in the stagnation of ordinary business, the deep interest which at that moment was possessing the heart of man—if all at once he should hear the deathlike stillness broken up by the sound of wheels rattling away from the scene, and making known that the transitory vision was dissolved, he will be aware that at no moment was his sense of the complete suspension and pause in ordinary human concerns so full and affecting as at that moment when the suspension ceases, and the goings-on of human life are suddenly resumed. All action in any direction is best expounded, measured, and made apprehensible, by reaction. Now, apply this to the case in *Macbeth*. Here, as I have said, the retiring of the human heart and the entrance of the fiendish heart was to be expressed and made sensible. Another world has stepped in; and the murderers are taken out of the region of human things, human purposes, human desires. They are transfigured: Lady Macbeth is "unsexed";[4] Macbeth has forgot that he was born of woman; both are conformed to the image of devils; and the world of devils is suddenly revealed. But how shall this be conveyed and made palpable? In order that a new world may step in, this world must for a time disappear. The murderers and the murder must be insulated—cut off by an immeasurable gulf from the ordinary tide and succession of human affairs—locked up and sequestered in some deep recess; we must be made sensible that the world of ordinary life is suddenly arrested, laid asleep, tranced, racked into a dread armistice; time must be annihilated, relation to things without abolished; and all must pass self-withdrawn into a deep syncope[5] and suspension of earthly passion. Hence it is that, when the deed is done, when the work of darkness is perfect, then the world of darkness passes away like a pageantry in the

2. I.e., differentiated from each other.
3. *Macbeth* 3.1.67 and 1.7.20.
4. Steeling herself to the murder, Lady Macbeth

calls on the spirits of hell to "unsex me here" (1.5.39).
5. Fainting spell.

clouds: the knocking at the gate is heard, and it makes known audibly that the reaction has commenced; the human has made its reflux upon the fiendish; the pulses of life are beginning to beat again; and the re-establishment of the goings-on of the world in which we live first makes us profoundly sensible of the awful parenthesis that had suspended them.

O mighty poet! Thy works are not as those of other men, simply and merely great works of art, but are also like the phenomena of nature, like the sun and the sea, the stars and the flowers, like frost and snow, rain and dew, hailstorm and thunder, which are to be studied with entire submission of our own faculties, and in the perfect faith that in them there can be no too much or too little, nothing useless or inert, but that, the farther we press in our discoveries, the more we shall see proofs of design and self-supporting arrangement where the careless eye had seen nothing but accident!

1823

From Alexander Pope

[THE LITERATURE OF KNOWLEDGE AND THE LITERATURE OF POWER][1]

What is it that we mean by *literature*? Popularly, and amongst the thoughtless, it is held to include everything that is printed in a book. Little logic is required to disturb *that* definition. The most thoughtless person is easily made aware that in the idea of *literature* one essential element is some relation to a general and common interest of man—so that what applies only to a local, or professional, or merely personal interest, even though presenting itself in the shape of a book, will not belong to Literature. So far the definition is easily narrowed; and it is as easily expanded. For not only is much that takes a station in books not literature; but inversely, much that really *is* literature never reaches a station in books. The weekly sermons of Christendom, that vast pulpit literature which acts so extensively upon the popular mind—to warn, to uphold, to renew, to comfort, to alarm—does not attain the sanctuary of libraries in the ten-thousandth part of its extent. The Drama again—as, for instance, the finest of Shakespeare's plays in England, and all leading Athenian plays in the noontide of the Attic stage—operated as a literature on the public mind, and were (according to the strictest letter of that term) *published* through the audiences that witnessed[2] their representation some time before they were published as things to be read; and they were published in this scenical mode of publication with much more effect than they could have had as books during ages of costly copying or of costly printing.

1. This section of a review of an 1847 edition of Pope's works (written in 1848, revised in 1858) has achieved independent status as a contribution to literary theory. In an earlier treatment of this topic in "Letters to a Young Man" (1823), De Quincey wrote that "the true antithesis to knowledge," in defining the effects of literature, "is not *pleasure*, but *power*"; then added in a footnote that he owed this distinction "to many years' conversation with Mr. Wordsworth." In his "Essay Supplementary" to the Preface to his *Poems* (1815), Wordsworth had written that "every great poet . . . has to call

forth and communicate *power*," and that for an original writer "to create taste is to call forth and bestow power, of which knowledge is the effect."
2. Charles I, for example, when Prince of Wales, and many others in his father's court, gained their known familiarity with Shakespeare not through the original quartos, so slenderly diffused, nor through the first folio of 1623, but through the court representations of his chief dramas at Whitehall [De Quincey's note]. Whitehall was a royal palace in London. It was destroyed by fire in 1698.

Books, therefore, do not suggest an idea coextensive and interchangeable with the idea of Literature; since much literature, scenic, forensic, or didactic[3] (as from lecturers and public orators), may never come into books, and much that *does* come into books may connect itself with no literary interest.[4] But a far more important correction, applicable to the common vague idea of literature, is to be sought not so much in a better definition of literature as in a sharper distinction of the two functions which it fulfills. In that great social organ which, collectively, we call literature, there may be distinguished two separate offices that may blend and often *do* so, but capable, severally, of a severe insulation, and naturally fitted for reciprocal repulsion. There is, first, the literature of *knowledge*; and, secondly, the literature of *power*. The function of the first is—to *teach*; the function of the second is—to *move*: the first is a rudder; the second, an oar or a sail. The first speaks to the *mere* discursive understanding;[5] the second speaks ultimately, it may happen, to the higher understanding or reason, but always *through* affections of pleasure and sympathy. Remotely, it may travel towards an object seated in what Lord Bacon calls *dry* light;[6] but, proximately, it does and must operate—else it ceases to be a literature of *power*—on and through that *humid* light which clothes itself in the mists and glittering *iris* of human passions, desires, and genial[7] emotions. Men have so little reflected on the higher functions of literature as to find it a paradox if one should describe it as a mean[8] or subordinate purpose of books to give information. But this is a paradox only in the sense which makes it honorable to be paradoxical. Whenever we talk in ordinary language of seeking information or gaining knowledge, we understand the words as connected with something of absolute novelty. But it is the grandeur of all truth which *can* occupy a very high place in human interests that it is never absolutely novel to the meanest of minds: it exists eternally by way of germ or latent principle in the lowest as in the highest, needing to be developed, but never to be planted. To be capable of transplantation is the immediate criterion of a truth that ranges on a lower scale. Besides which, there is a rarer thing than truth—namely, *power,* or deep sympathy with truth. What is the effect, for instance, upon society, of children? By the pity, by the tenderness, and by the peculiar modes of admiration, which connect themselves with the helplessness, with the innocence, and with the simplicity of children, not only are the primal affections strengthened and continually renewed, but the qualities which are dearest in the sight of heaven—the frailty, for instance, which appeals to forbearance, the innocence which symbolizes the heavenly, and the simplicity which is most alien from the worldly—are kept up in perpetual

3. Expository, designed to instruct. "Scenic": dramatic. "Forensic": argumentative, designed to persuade, especially in legal proceedings.
4. What are called *The Blue Books*—by which title are understood the folio reports issued every session of Parliament by committees of the two Houses, and stitched into blue covers—though often sneered at by the ignorant as so much wastepaper, will be acknowledged gratefully by those who have used them diligently as the main wellheads of all accurate information as to the Great Britain of this day. As an immense depository of faithful (*and not superannuated*) statistics, they are indispensable to the honest student. But no man would therefore class the *Blue Books* as literature [De Quincey's note].

5. I.e., a way of understanding that proceeds by argumentation and by passing from premises to conclusions. The term is usually contrasted with intuitive understanding.
6. In his essay "Of Friendship," Francis Bacon quotes Heraclitus, the early Greek philosopher, as saying "Dry light is ever the best," then goes on to distinguish between dry light and the light of an understanding, which is "ever infused and drenched" in an individual's own "affections and customs."
7. Pertaining to genius; creative. "Iris": rainbow colors. De Quincey is here referring to the way colors are the effect of the refraction of light.
8. Low, vulgar.

remembrance, and their ideals are continually refreshed. A purpose of the
same nature is answered by the higher literature, viz. the literature of power.
What do you learn from *Paradise Lost*? Nothing at all. What do you learn from
a cookery book? Something new, something that you did not know before, in
every paragraph. But would you therefore put the wretched cookery book on
a higher level of estimation than the divine poem? What you owe to Milton is
not any knowledge, of which a million separate items are still but a million of
advancing steps on the same earthly level; what you owe is *power*—that is,
exercise and expansion to your own latent capacity of sympathy with the infinite, where every pulse and each separate influx is a step upwards, a step
ascending as upon a Jacob's ladder from earth to mysterious altitudes above
the earth.[9] *All* the steps of knowledge, from first to last, carry you further on
the same plane, but could never raise you one foot above your ancient level
of earth: whereas the very *first* step in power is a flight—is an ascending movement into another element where earth is forgotten.

Were it not that human sensibilities are ventilated[1] and continually called
out into exercise by the great phenomena of infancy, or of real life as it moves
through chance and change, or of literature as it recombines these elements
in the mimicries of poetry, romance, etc., it is certain that, like any animal
power or muscular energy falling into disuse, all such sensibilities would gradually droop and dwindle. It is in relation to these great *moral* capacities of
man that the literature of power, as contradistinguished from that of knowledge, lives and has its field of action. It is concerned with what is highest in
man; for the Scriptures themselves never condescended to deal by suggestion
or cooperation with the mere discursive understanding: when speaking of man
in his intellectual capacity, the Scriptures speak not of the understanding, but
of *"the understanding heart"*[2]—making the heart, i.e. the great *intuitive* (or
nondiscursive) organ, to be the interchangeable formula for man in his highest
state of capacity for the infinite. Tragedy, romance, fairy tale, or epopée,[3] all
alike restore to man's mind the ideals of justice, of hope, of truth, of mercy,
of retribution, which else (left to the support of daily life in its realities) would
languish for want of sufficient illustration. What is meant, for instance, by
poetic justice?[4]—It does not mean a justice that differs by its object from the
ordinary justice of human jurisprudence; for then it must be confessedly a very
bad kind of justice; but it means a justice that differs from common forensic
justice by the degree in which it *attains* its object, a justice that is more omnipotent over its own ends, as dealing—not with the refractory elements of earthly
life, but with the elements of its own creation, and with materials flexible to
its own purest preconceptions. It is certain that, were it not for the Literature
of Power, these ideals would often remain amongst us as mere arid notional
forms; whereas, by the creative forces of man put forth in literature, they gain
a vernal life of restoration, and germinate into vital activities. The commonest
novel, by moving in alliance with human fears and hopes, with human instincts
of wrong and right, sustains and quickens those affections. Calling them into

9. The ladder that the patriarch Jacob saw in a
dream, reaching from the earth to heaven, on
which the angels were ascending and descending
(Genesis 28.11–12).
1. Provided with an outlet.
2. In 1 Kings 3.9 King Solomon asks the Lord for

"an understanding heart to judge thy people."
3. Epic poem (French).
4. A term in old literary criticism for the distribution of earthly rewards and punishments, at the
end of a work of literature, in proportion to the
virtues and vices of the various characters.

action, it rescues them from torpor. And hence the preeminency over all authors that merely *teach* of the meanest that *moves*, or that teaches, if at all, indirectly *by* moving. The very highest work that has ever existed in the Literature of Knowledge is but a *provisional* work: a book upon trial and sufferance, and *quamdiu bene se gesserit*.[5] Let its teaching be even partially revised, let it be but expanded—nay, even let its teaching be but placed in a better order—and instantly it is superseded. Whereas the feeblest works in the Literature of Power, surviving at all, survive as finished and unalterable amongst men. For instance, the *Principia* of Sir Isaac Newton was a book *militant*[6] on earth from the first. In all stages of its progress it would have to fight for its existence: 1st, as regards absolute truth; 2dly, when that combat was over, as regards its form or mode of presenting the truth. And as soon as a La Place,[7] or anybody else, builds higher upon the foundations laid by this book, effectually he throws it out of the sunshine into decay and darkness; by weapons won from this book he superannuates and destroys this book, so that soon the name of Newton remains as a mere *nominis umbra*,[8] but his book, as a living power, has transmigrated into other forms. Now, on the contrary, the *Iliad*, the *Prometheus* of Aeschylus, the *Othello* or *King Lear*, the *Hamlet* or *Macbeth*, and the *Paradise Lost*, are not militant, but triumphant forever as long as the languages exist in which they speak or can be taught to speak. They never *can* transmigrate into new incarnations. To reproduce *these* in new forms, or variations, even if in some things they should be improved, would be to plagiarize. A good steam engine is properly superseded by a better. But one lovely pastoral valley is not superseded by another, nor a statue of Praxiteles by a statue of Michael Angelo.[9] These things are separated not by imparity, but by disparity. They are not thought of as unequal under the same standard, but as different in *kind*, and, if otherwise equal, as equal under a different standard. Human works of immortal beauty and works of nature in one respect stand on the same footing: they never absolutely repeat each other, never approach so near as not to differ; and they differ not as better and worse, or simply by more and less: they differ by undecipherable and incommunicable differences, that cannot be caught by mimicries, that cannot be reflected in the mirror of copies, that cannot become ponderable in the scales of vulgar comparison.

Applying these principles to Pope as a representative of fine literature in general, we would wish to remark the claim which he has, or which any equal writer has, to the attention and jealous winnowing of those critics in particular who watch over public morals. Clergymen, and all organs of public criticism put in motion by clergymen, are more especially concerned in the just appreciation of such writers, if the two canons are remembered which we have endeavored to illustrate, viz. that all works in this class, as opposed to those in the literature of knowledge, 1st, work by far deeper agencies, and, 2dly, are more permanent; in the strictest sense they are κτήματα ἐς ἀεί[1] and what evil they do, or what good they do, is commensurate with the national language,

---

5. As long as it shall conduct itself well (Latin).
6. Combative. *"Principia"*: Isaac Newton's great *Philosophiae Naturalis Principia Mathematica* (Mathematical Principles of Natural Philosophy), published in 1687, set forth the laws of motion and the principle of universal gravitation.
7. Pierre-Simon, marquis de Laplace, mathematician and astronomer, author of *A Treatise on*

Celestial Mechanics (1799–1825), was known as "the Newton of France."
8. Shadow of a name (Latin).
9. Michelangelo Buonarroti (1475–1564), Renaissance sculptor, painter, architect, and poet. Praxiteles (4th century B.C.E.), Greek sculptor.
1. Everlasting possessions (Greek).

sometimes long after the nation has departed. At this hour, five hundred years since their creation, the tales of Chaucer,[2] never equaled on this earth for their tenderness, and for life of picturesqueness, are read familiarly by many in the charming language of their natal day, and by others in the modernizations of Dryden, of Pope, and Wordsworth.[3] At this hour, one thousand eight hundred years since their creation, the Pagan tales of Ovid,[4] never equaled on this earth for the gaiety of their movement and the capricious graces of their narrative, are read by all Christendom. This man's people and their monuments are dust; but *he* is alive: he has survived them, as he told us that he had it in his commission to do, by a thousand years; "and *shall* a thousand more."

All the literature of knowledge builds only ground-nests, that are swept away by floods, or confounded by the plow; but the literature of power builds nests in aerial altitudes of temples sacred from violation, or of forests inaccessible to fraud. *This* is a great prerogative of the *power* literature; and it is a greater which lies in the mode of its influence. The *knowledge* literature, like the fashion of this world, passeth away. An Encyclopedia is its abstract; and, in this respect, it may be taken for its speaking symbol—that before one generation has passed an Encyclopedia is superannuated; for it speaks through the dead memory and unimpassioned understanding, which have not the repose of higher faculties, but are continually enlarging and varying their phylacteries.[5] But all literature properly so called—literature κατ' ἐξχην[6]—for the very same reason that it is so much more durable than the literature of knowledge, is (and by the very same proportion it is) more intense and electrically searching in its impressions. The directions in which the tragedy of this planet has trained our human feelings to play, and the combinations into which the poetry of this planet has thrown our human passions of love and hatred, of admiration and contempt, exercise a power for bad or good over human life that cannot be contemplated, when stretching through many generations, without a sentiment allied to awe.[7] And of this let everyone be assured—that he owes to the impassioned books which he has read many a thousand more of emotions than he can consciously trace back to them. Dim by their origination, these emotions yet arise in him, and mould him through life, like forgotten incidents of his childhood.

1848, 1858

---

2. The *Canterbury Tales* were not made public until 1380 or thereabouts; but the composition must have cost thirty or more years; not to mention that the work had probably been finished for some years before it was divulged [De Quincey's note].
3. Following the example of various earlier poets who wrote modernized versions of Chaucer, Wordsworth had translated "The Prioress's Tale" and a section of *Troilus and Criseyde*.
4. Latin poet (43 B.C.E.–18 C.E.), author of *Metamorphoses* and other books of verse narratives.
5. I.e., preestablished texts. "Phylacteries" are leather boxes, inscribed with quotations from the Hebrew Scriptures, worn by Orthodox Jews during morning prayer.
6. In the highest degree (Greek).

7. The reason why the broad distinctions between the two literatures of power and knowledge so little fix the attention lies in the fact that a vast proportion of books—history, biography, travels, miscellaneous essays, etc.—lying in a middle zone, confound these distinctions by interblending them. All that we call "amusement" or "entertainment" is a diluted form of the power belonging to passion, and also a mixed form; and, where threads of direct *instruction* intermingle in the texture with these threads of *power*, this absorption of the duality into one representative *nuance* neutralizes the separate perception of either. Fused into a *tertium quid* [a third thing], or neutral state, they disappear to the popular eye as the repelling forces which, in fact, they are [De Quincey's note].

The Gothic and the Development of a Mass Readership

Strictly speaking, the Gothic is not "Gothic" at all, but a phenomenon that originates in the late eighteenth century, long after enlightened Europeans put the era of Gothic cathedrals, chivalry, and superstition behind them—a phenomenon that begins, in fact, as an embrace of a kind of counterfeit medievalism or as a "medieval revival." As a word they applied to a dark and distant past, Gothic gave Romantic-period writers and readers a way to describe accounts of terrifying experiences in ancient castles and ruined abbeys—experiences connected with subterranean dungeons, secret passageways, flickering lamps, screams, moans, ghosts, and graveyards. In the long run Gothic became a label for the macabre, mysterious, supernatural, and terrifying, especially the *pleasurably* terrifying, in literature generally; the link that Romantic-period writers had forged between the Gothic and antiquated spaces was eventually loosened. Even so, one has only to look, in post-Romantic literature, at the fiction of the Brontës or Poe, or, in our own not-so-modern culture, at movies or video games, to realize that the pleasures of regression the late-eighteenth-century Gothic revival provided die hard. Readers continue to seek out opportunities to feel haunted by pasts that will not let themselves be exorcised.

The Gothic revival appeared in later-eighteenth-century English garden design and architecture before it got into literature. In 1747 Horace Walpole (1717–1797), younger son of the British prime minister, purchased Strawberry Hill, an estate on the river Thames near London, and three years later set about remodeling it in what he called a "Gothick" style. Adding towers, turrets, battlements, arched doors, windows, and ornaments of every description, he created the kind of spurious medieval architecture that survives today mainly in churches and university buildings. Eventually tourists came from all over to see Strawberry Hill and went home to Gothicize their own houses.

When the Gothic made its appearance in literature, Walpole was again a trailblazer. In 1764 he published *The Castle of Otranto*, a self-styled "Gothic story" featuring a haunted castle, an early, pre-Byronic version of the Byronic hero (suitably named Manfred), mysterious deaths, a moaning ancestral portrait, damsels in distress, violent passions, and strange obsessions. Walpole's gamble—that the future of the novel would involve the reclamation of the primitive emotions of fear and wonder provided by the romances of a pre-Enlightened age—convinced many writers who came after him. By the 1790s novels trading on horror, mystery, and faraway settings flooded the book market; meanwhile in theaters new special effects were devised to incarnate ghostly apparitions on stage. It is noteworthy that the best-selling author of the terror school (Ann Radcliffe), the author of its most enduring novel (Mary Shelley), and the author of its most effective send-up (Jane Austen) were all women. Indeed, many of Radcliffe's numerous imitators (and, on occasion, downright plagiarizers) published under the auspices of the Minerva Press, a business whose very name (that of the goddess of wisdom) acknowledged the centrality of female authors and readers to this new lucrative trend in the book market. William Lane, the marketing genius who owned the Press, also set up a cross-country network of circulating libraries that stocked his ladies' volumes and made them available for hire at modest prices.

This section offers extracts from some of the most celebrated works in the Gothic mode: Walpole's *Otranto* as the initiating prototype; William Beckford's *Vathek*

(1786), which is "oriental" rather than medieval but similarly blends cruelty, terror, and eroticism; two extremely popular works by Radcliffe, the "Queen of Terror," *The Romance of the Forest* (1791) and *The Mysteries of Udolpho* (1794); Matthew Lewis's concoction of devilry, sadism, and mob violence, *The Monk* (1796). We also include an essay of 1773 in which John and Anna Letitia Aikin provide justification after the fact for Walpole's rebellion against the critical orthodoxies. According to most early critics of novels, the only *moral* fiction was probable fiction; the Aikins, however, make the business of the novelist lie as much with the pleasures of the imagination as with moral edification and the representation of real life.

Their essay suggests why Gothic reading was appealing to so many Romantic poets—visionaries who in their own way dissented from critical rules that would, drearily, limit literature to the already known and recognizable. Signs of the poets' acquaintance with the terror school of novel writing show up in numerous well-known Romantic poems—from *The Rime of the Ancient Mariner* to *Manfred*. For instance, in Keats's *The Eve of St. Agnes*, a poem that in many respects represents an idealized tale of young love, Porphyro's invasion of Madeline's bedroom has some perturbing connections with the predatory overtones of our extract from *The Monk*. And Keats's enigmatic fragment "This living hand" can be read as a brilliantly abbreviated version of the kind of tale of terror that aimed to make its reader's blood run cold.

Yet it simplifies matters to characterize the Gothic only as an influence on Romanticism. As the concluding pieces in this section suggest, the poets had a love-hate relationship with Gothic writers and, even more so, with Gothic readers. Many contemporary commentators objected to the new school of novels on moral and technical grounds: they complained, for instance, about how plot-driven they were and how cheaply they solved their mysteries. But questions about social class and literary taste were also important. In an era of revolution, in which newly literate workers were reading about "the rights of man" and crowds were starting to shape history, the very *popularity* of Gothic novels, the terror writers' capacity to move and manipulate whole crowds with their suspense and trickery, itself represented a source of anxiety. As the twentieth-century critic E. J. Clery explains, the "unprecedented capacity of the market to absorb at great speed large amounts of a particular type of literary product, the 'terrorist' novel, shook old certainties."

Many of the Romantic poets comment, accordingly, on what is scary and pernicious *about* the Gothic as well as what is scary and pernicious *in* the Gothic. And throughout their writings, the tales of terror are invoked in ways that enable the writer to construct a divide between "high" and "low" culture and to play off the passive absorption associated with the reading of the crowds against the tasteful, active reading that is (according to the writer) practiced by the elite few. In the Preface to *Lyrical Ballads*, for instance, Wordsworth identifies as a cause of English culture's modern decline the "frenetic novels" that have blunted their consumers' powers of discrimination and reduced them "to a state of almost savage torpor" (a negative version of the regression that William Hazlitt, for instance, celebrates as he describes how Radcliffe "makes her readers twice children" while she "forces us to believe all that is strange and next to impossible"). Wordsworth follows a hint that he may have found three years earlier in Coleridge's review of *The Monk* (extracted near the end of this section) and suggests that such readers inevitably need higher and higher doses of the "violent stimulants" that novelists—drug pushers of sorts—have supplied them. In this way the Preface pioneers an account of a mass readership addicted to what will kill it. In similar fashion "Terrorist Novel Writing," the short anti-Gothic satire we include near the end of this section, makes it seem, as does our extract containing Coleridge's very funny tirade against the patrons of circulating libraries, that Gothic novels were objects of utterly mindless consumption (absorbed, imbibed, but not *read*), and that terror was a commodity produced on an assembly line. The extracts with which we close this section register, in other words, a recoil from the Gothic. But Gothic themes frequently come back to haunt the critics of the mode. When they depict popular, commercialized culture's threat to individual autonomy and describe consumers as if they were zombies sunk in trances, the critics appear to rehearse nightmarish scenarios straight out of the tales of terror.

HORACE WALPOLE

Walpole's landmark work *The Castle of Otranto* initially purported to be a translation from (as the title page of the first edition put it) "the original Italian of Onuphrio Muralto, Canon of the Church of St. Nicholas at Otranto." The events related in it were supposed to have occurred in the twelfth or thirteenth century. In the second edition, however, Walpole renounced the hoax and confessed his authorship. Rather than presenting the narrative as a remarkable historical discovery, a manuscript from the lost barbaric past, he cast his "Gothic Story" as a novelty: an experiment in blending, he explained, "the ancient and modern" romance, and in combining the realism that was the hallmark of the up-to-date eighteenth-century novel with the imagination that had flourished in medieval romance and that this realism had suffocated.

When the story opens, the villainous Manfred, prince of Otranto, to get an heir to his estate, has arranged a marriage between his only son, Conrad, and the beautiful Isabella. But on his wedding day Conrad is mysteriously killed, victim of a giant helmet that falls from the sky and crushes him. Lest he should be left without male descendants, Manfred determines to divorce his present wife, Hippolita, who is past childbearing, and marry Isabella himself. In the extract given here, Isabella learns of his intention and decides to flee the castle by night. The account of her flight suggests how the Gothic novelists, lavishing attention on architectural details, make experiences of terror inseparable from the walls, ceilings, floors, and doors enclosing them.

From The Castle of Otranto

From *Chapter 1*

As it was now evening, the servant who conducted Isabella bore a torch before her. When they came to Manfred, who was walking impatiently about the gallery, he started and said hastily, "Take away that light, and begone." Then shutting the door impetuously, he flung himself upon a bench against the wall, and bade Isabella sit by him. She obeyed trembling. "I sent for you, lady," said he,—and then stopped under great appearance of confusion. "My lord!"— "Yes, I sent for you on a matter of great moment," resumed he,—"Dry your tears, young lady—you have lost your bridegroom.—Yes, cruel fate! and I have lost the hopes of my race!—but Conrad was not worthy of your beauty."— "How! my lord," said Isabella; "sure you do not suspect me of not feeling the concern I ought. My duty and affection would have always—" "Think no more of him," interrupted Manfred; "he was a sickly puny child, and heaven has perhaps taken him away that I might not trust the honours of my house on so frail a foundation. The line of Manfred calls for numerous supports. My foolish fondness for that boy blinded the eyes of my prudence—but it is better as it is. I hope in a few years to have reason to rejoice at the death of Conrad."

Words cannot paint the astonishment of Isabella. At first she apprehended that grief had disordered Manfred's understanding. Her next thought suggested that this strange discourse was designed to ensnare her: she feared that Manfred had perceived her indifference for his son: and in consequence of that idea she replied, "Good my lord, do not doubt my tenderness: my heart would have accompanied my hand. Conrad would have engrossed all my care; and wherever fate shall dispose of me, I shall always cherish his memory, and regard your highness and the virtuous Hippolita as my parents." "Curse on Hippolita!" cried Manfred: "forget her from this moment as I do. In short, lady, you have missed a husband undeserving of your charms: they shall now be better disposed of. Instead of a sickly boy, you shall have a husband in the prime of his age, who will know how to value your beauties, and who may expect a numerous offspring." "Alas! my lord," said Isabella, "my mind is too sadly engrossed by the recent catastrophe in your family to think of another marriage. If ever my father returns, and it shall be his pleasure, I shall obey, as I did when I consented to give my hand to your son: but until his return, permit me to remain under your hospitable roof, and employ the melancholy hours in assuaging yours, Hippolita's, and the fair Matilda's affliction."

"I desired you once before," said Manfred angrily, "not to name that woman: from this hour she must be a stranger to you, as she must be to me;—in short, Isabella, since I cannot give you my son, I offer you myself."—"Heavens!" cried Isabella, waking from her delusion, "what do I hear! You! My lord! You! My father-in-law! the father of Conrad! the husband of the virtuous and tender Hippolita!"—"I tell you," said Manfred imperiously, "Hippolita is no longer my wife; I divorce her from this hour. Too long has she cursed me by her unfruitfulness: my fate depends on having sons,—and this night I trust will give a new date to my hopes." At those words he seized the cold hand of Isabella, who was half-dead with fright and horror. She shrieked and started from him. Manfred rose to pursue her, when the moon, which was now up and gleamed in at the opposite casement, presented to his sight the plumes of the fatal helmet, which rose to the height of the windows, waving backwards and forwards in a tempestuous manner, and accompanied with a hollow and rustling sound. Isabella, who gathered courage from her situation, and who dreaded nothing so much as Manfred's pursuit of his declaration, cried, "Look! my lord; see, heaven itself declares against your impious intentions!"— "Heaven nor hell shall impede my designs," said Manfred, advancing again to seize the princess. At that instant the portrait of his grandfather, which hung over the bench where they had been sitting, uttered a deep sigh, and heaved its breast. Isabella, whose back was turned to the picture, saw not the motion, nor knew whence the sound came, but started, and said, "Hark, my lord! What sound was that?" and at the same time made towards the door. Manfred, distracted between the flight of Isabella, who had now reached the stairs, and yet unable to keep his eyes from the picture, which began to move, had however advanced some steps after her, still looking backwards on the portrait, when he saw it quit its panel, and descend on the floor with a grave and melancholy air. "Do I dream?" cried Manfred returning, "or are the devils themselves in league against me? Speak, infernal spectre! or, if thou art my grandsire, why dost thou too conspire against thy wretched descendant, who too dearly pays for—" Ere he could finish the sentence the vision sighed again, and made a sign to Manfred to follow him. "Lead on!" cried Manfred; "I will follow thee to the gulph of perdition." The spectre marched sedately, but dejected, to the end of the gallery, and turned into a chamber on the right hand. Manfred accompanied him at a little distance, full of anxiety and horror, but resolved. As he would have entered the chamber, the door was clapped to with violence by an invisible hand. The prince, collecting courage from this delay, would have forcibly burst open the door with his foot, but found that it resisted his utmost efforts. "Since hell will not satisfy my curiosity," said Manfred, "I will use the human means in my power for preserving my race; Isabella shall not escape me."

That lady, whose resolution had given way to terror the moment she had quitted Manfred, continued her flight to the bottom of the principal staircase. There she stopped, not knowing whither to direct her steps, nor how to escape from the impetuosity of the prince. The gates of the castle she knew were locked, and guards placed in the court. Should she, as her heart prompted her, go and prepare Hippolita for the cruel destiny that awaited her, she did not doubt but Manfred would seek her there, and that his violence would incite him to double the injury he meditated, without leaving room for them to avoid the impetuosity of his passions. Delay might give him time to reflect on the horrid measures he had conceived, or produce some circumstance in her favour, if she could for that night at least avoid his odious purpose.—Yet where conceal herself? how avoid the pursuit he would infallibly make throughout the castle? As these thoughts passed rapidly through her mind, she recollected a subterraneous passage which led from the vaults of the castle to the church of St. Nicholas. Could she reach the altar before she was overtaken, she knew even Manfred's violence would not dare to profane the sacredness of the place; and she determined, if no other means of deliverance offered, to shut herself up for ever among the holy virgins, whose convent was contiguous to the cathedral. In this resolution, she seized a lamp that burned at the foot of the staircase, and hurried towards the secret passage. The lower part of the castle was hollowed into several intricate cloisters; and it was not easy for one under so much anxiety to find the door that opened into the cavern. An awful silence reigned throughout those subterraneous regions, except now and then some blasts of wind that shook the doors she had passed, and which, grating on the rusty hinges, were re-echoed through that long labyrinth of darkness. Every murmur struck her with new terror;—yet more she dreaded to hear the wrathful voice of Manfred urging his domestics[1] to pursue her. She trod as softly as impatience would give her leave,—yet frequently stopped and listened to hear if she was followed. In one of those moments she thought she heard a sigh. She shuddered, and recoiled a few paces. In a moment she thought she heard the step of some person. Her blood curdled; she concluded it was Manfred. Every suggestion that horror could inspire rushed into her mind. She condemned her rash flight, which had thus exposed her to his rage in a place where her cries were not likely to draw anybody to her assistance.—Yet the sound seemed not to come from behind,— if Manfred knew where she was, he must have followed her: she was still in one of the cloisters, and the steps she had heard were too distinct to proceed from the way she had come. Cheered with this reflection, and hoping to find a friend in whoever was not the prince, she was going to advance, when a door that stood ajar, at some distance to the left, was opened gently: but ere her lamp, which she held up, could discover who opened it, the person retreated precipitately on seeing the light.

Isabella, whom every incident was sufficient to dismay, hesitated whether

---

1. Servants.

she should proceed. Her dread of Manfred soon outweighed every other terror. The very circumstance of the person avoiding her gave her a sort of courage. It could only be, she thought, some domestic belonging to the castle. Her gentleness had never raised her an enemy, and conscious innocence bade her hope that, unless sent by the prince's order to seek her, his servants would rather assist than prevent her flight. Fortifying herself with these reflections, and believing, by what she could observe, that she was near the mouth of the subterraneous cavern, she approached the door that had been opened; but a sudden gust of wind that met her at the door extinguished her lamp, and left her in total darkness.

1764

ANNA LETITIA AIKIN (later BARBAULD) and JOHN AIKIN

In the following essay John Aikin (1747–1822) and his sister Anna Letitia (who appears earlier in this anthology as a poet and under her married name, Barbauld) engage a question philosophers and psychologists continue to debate: why do people who listen to ghost stories around the campfire, or read Gothic novels, or watch monster movies find such frightening experience pleasing? The Aikins, members of a prominent family of religious dissenters and educators, begin by observing that it is easy to explain why we might feel satisfaction when we feel pity—that emotion is necessary for the well-being of the human community, which would fall apart were it not somehow in our own interest to feel for others. But it is by contrast more difficult to understand how morality is advanced when we delight in objects of terror. As they map out an alternative way of accounting for that amoral delight, the Aikins write an early Romantic description of the glory of the imagination; the reader's encounter with what is unknown and amazing elevates and expands the mind. The fragmentary story of a medieval knight errant that the Aikins appended to their essay was meant to give their readers a chance to test this thesis, but thanks to its handling of suspense "Sir Bertrand" soon came to be celebrated in its own right.

Published in 1773 in the Aikins' *Miscellaneous Pieces in Prose*, "On the Pleasure Derived from Objects of Terror" built on Walpole's innovation in *Otranto*. It gave the next generation of Gothic authors a critical justification for their engagement with the supernatural and for their swerve away from the didacticism that had valued fiction writers only when they seemed to be educating readers for real life. Family tradition ascribed the essay to Anna and "Sir Bertrand" to John.

On the Pleasure Derived from Objects of Terror; with Sir Bertrand, a Fragment

That the exercise of our benevolent feelings, as called forth by the view of human afflictions, should be a source of pleasure, cannot appear wonderful to one who considers that relation between the moral and natural system of man, which has connected a degree of satisfaction with every action or emotion productive of the general welfare. The painful sensation immediately arising from a scene of misery, is so much softened and alleviated by the reflex sense of self-approbation on attending virtuous sympathy, that we find, on the whole, a very exquisite and refined pleasure remaining, which makes us desirous of again being witnesses to such scenes, instead of flying from them with disgust and horror. It is obvious how greatly such a provision must conduce to the ends of mutual support and assistance. But the apparent delight with which we dwell upon objects of pure terror, where our moral feelings are not in the least concerned, and no passion seems to be excited but the depressing one of fear, is a paradox of the heart, much more difficult of solution.

The reality of this source of pleasure seems evident from daily observation. The greediness with which the tales of ghosts and goblins, of murders, earthquakes, fires, shipwrecks, and all the most terrible disasters attending human life, are devoured by every ear, must have been generally remarked. Tragedy, the most favourite work of fiction, has taken a full share of those scenes; "it has supt full with horrors"[1]—and has, perhaps, been more indebted to them for public admiration than to its tender and pathetic parts. The ghost of Hamlet, Macbeth descending into the witches' cave, and the tent scene in Richard, command as forcibly the attention of our souls as the parting of Jaffeir and Belvidera, the fall of Wolsey, or the death of Shore.[2] The inspiration of *terror* was by the antient critics assigned as the peculiar province of tragedy; and the Greek and Roman tragedians have introduced some extraordinary personages for this purpose: not only the shades of the dead, but the furies, and other fabulous inhabitants of the infernal regions. Collins, in his most poetical ode to Fear, has finely enforced this idea.

> Tho' gently Pity claim her mingled part,
> Yet all the thunders of the scene are thine.[3]

The old Gothic romance and the Eastern tale, with their genii, giants, enchantments, and transformations, however a refined critic may censure them as absurd and extravagant, will ever retain a most powerful influence on the mind, and interest the reader independently of all peculiarity of taste. Thus the great Milton, who had a strong bias to these wildnesses of the imagination, has with striking effect made the stories "of forests and enchantments drear," a favourite subject with his *Penseroso*; and had undoubtedly their awakening images strong upon his mind when he breaks out,

> Call up him that left half-told
> The story of Cambuscan bold; &c.[4]

How are we then to account for the pleasure derived from such objects? I have often been led to imagine that there is a deception in these cases; and that the avidity with which we attend is not a proof of our receiving real pleasure. The pain of suspense, and the irresistible desire of satisfying curiosity, when once raised, will account for our eagerness to go quite through an adventure, though we suffer actual pain during the whole course of it. We

---

1. Shakespeare's *Macbeth* 5.5.13.
2. The mentions of Hamlet, Macbeth, and Richard III are followed by references to the doomed husband and wife in Thomas Otway's tragedy *Venice Preserv'd* (1681); the royal advisor whose fall from grace centers the action of Shakespeare's *Henry VIII*; and Jane Shore, title character of Nicholas Rowe's tragedy of 1714.

3. Lines 44–45 in William Collins's "Ode to Fear" (1746), slightly misquoted. The speaker of this poem anticipates the Aikins in marveling over the allure of fear and its potency as a source of art.
4. Quoting lines 119 and 109–10 of Milton's poem on the delights of studious melancholy. The story of Cambuscan was left half-told in Chaucer's unfinished *Squire's Tale*.

rather chuse to suffer the smart pang of a violent emotion than the uneasy craving of an unsatisfied desire. That this principle, in many instances, may involuntarily carry us through what we dislike, I am convinced from experience. This is the impulse which renders the poorest and most insipid narrative interesting when once we get fairly into it; and I have frequently felt it with regard to our modern novels, which, if lying on my table, and taken up in an idle hour, have led me through the most tedious and disgusting pages, while, like Pistol eating his leek, I have swallowed and execrated to the end.[5] And it will not only force us through dullness, but through actual torture—through the relation of a Damien's execution, or an inquisitor's act of faith.[6] When children, therefore, listen with pale and mute attention to the frightful stories of apparitions, we are not, perhaps, to imagine that they are in a state of enjoyment, any more than the poor bird which is dropping into the mouth of the rattlesnake—they are chained by the ears, and fascinated by curiosity. This solution, however, does not satisfy me with respect to the well-wrought scenes of artificial terror which are formed by a sublime and vigorous imagination. Here, though we know before-hand what to expect, we enter into them with eagerness, in quest of a pleasure already experienced. This is the pleasure constantly attached to the excitement of surprise from new and wonderful objects. A strange and unexpected event awakens the mind, and keeps it on the stretch; and where the agency of invisible beings is introduced, of "forms unseen, and mightier far than we," our imagination, darting forth, explores with rapture the new world which is laid open to its view, and rejoices in the expansion of its powers. Passion and fancy cooperating elevate the soul to its highest pitch; and the pain of terror is lost in amazement.

Hence the more wild, fanciful, and extraordinary are the circumstance, of a scene of horror, the more pleasure we receive from it; and where they are too near common nature, though violently borne by curiosity through the adventure, we cannot repeat it or reflect on it, without an overbalance of pain. In the *Arabian Nights* are many most striking examples of the terrible joined with the marvellous: the story of Aladdin, and the travels of Sinbad are particularly excellent. The *Castle of Otranto* is a very spirited modern attempt upon the same plan of mixed terror, adapted to the model of Gothic romance. The best conceived, and most strongly worked-up scene of mere natural horror that I recollect, is in Smollett's *Ferdinand Count Fathom*;[7] where the hero, entertained in a lone house in a forest, finds a corpse just slaughtered in the room where he is sent to sleep, and the door of which is locked upon him. It may be amusing for the reader to compare his feelings upon these, and from thence form his opinion of the justness of my theory. The following fragment, in which both these manners are attempted to be in some degree united, is offered to entertain a solitary winter's evening.

---

5. Alluding to a comic scene of force-feeding in Shakespeare's *Henry V* (5.1.36–60).
6. The brutality of the public torture and execution in 1757 of Robert-François Damiens, the would-be assassin of Louis XV of France, was commented on across Europe. An act of faith, or *auto da fe*, was the form of execution that the Spanish Inquisition inflicted on heretics: the condemned were burned alive.
7. Tobias Smollett's 1753 novel of villainy and picaresque adventure.

Sir Bertrand, a Fragment

After this adventure, Sir Bertrand turned his steed towards the woulds,[8] hoping to cross these dreary moors before the curfew. But ere he had proceeded half his journey, he was bewildered by the different tracks, and not being able, as far as the eye could reach, to espy any object but the brown heath surrounding him, he was at length quite uncertain which way he should direct his course. Night overtook him in this situation. It was one of those nights when the moon gives a faint glimmering of light through the thick black clouds of a lowering sky. Now and then she suddenly emerged in full splendor from her veil; and then instantly retired behind it, having just served to give the forlorn Sir Bertrand a wide extended prospect over the desolate waste. Hope and native courage a while urged him to push forwards, but at length the increasing darkness and fatigue of body and mind overcame him; he dreaded moving from the ground he stood on, for fear of unknown pits and bogs, and alighting from his horse in despair, he threw himself on the ground. He had not long continued in that posture when the sullen toll of a distant bell struck his ears—he started up, and turning towards the sound discerned a dim twinkling light.

Instantly he seized his horse's bridle, and with cautious steps advanced towards it. After a painful march he was stopt by a moated ditch surrounding the place from whence the light proceeded; and by a momentary glimpse of moon-light he had a full view of a large antique mansion, with turrets at the corners, and an ample porch in the centre. The injuries of time were strongly marked on every thing about it. The roof in various places was fallen in, the battlements were half demolished, and the windows broken and dismantled. A drawbridge, with a ruinous gateway at each end, led to the court before the building—He entered, and instantly the light, which proceeded from a window in one of the turrets, glided along and vanished; at the same moment the moon sunk beneath a black cloud, and the night was darker than ever. All was silent—Sir Bertrand fastened his steed under a shed, and approaching the house traversed its whole front with light and slow footsteps—All was still as death—He looked in at the lower windows, but could not distinguish a single object through the impenetrable gloom. After a short parley with himself, he entered the porch, and seizing a massy iron knocker at the gate, lifted it up, and hesitating, at length struck a loud stroke. The noise resounded through the whole mansion with hollow echoes. All was still again—He repeated the strokes more boldly and louder—another interval of silence ensued—A third time he knocked, and a third time all was still. He then fell back to some distance that he might discern whether any light could be seen in the whole front—It again appeared in the same place and quickly glided away as before— at the same instant a deep sullen toll sounded from the turret. Sir Bertrand's heart made a fearful stop—He was a while motionless; then terror impelled him to make some hasty steps towards his steed—but shame stopt his flight; and urged by honour, and a resistless desire of finishing the adventure, he returned to the porch; and working up his soul to a full steadiness of resolution, he drew forth his sword with one hand, and with the other lifted up the latch of the gate. The heavy door, creaking upon its hinges, reluctantly yielded to his hand—he applied his shoulder to it and forced it open—he quitted it

8. I.e., woulds: open, elevated ground.

and stept forward—the door instantly shut with a thundering clap. Sir Bertrand's blood was chilled—he turned back to find the door, and it was long ere his trembling hands could seize it—but his utmost strength could not open it again. After several ineffectual attempts, he looked behind him, and beheld, across a hall, upon a large staircase, a pale bluish flame which cast a dismal gleam of light around. He again summoned forth his courage and advanced towards it—It retired. He came to the foot of the stairs, and after a moment's deliberation ascended. He went slowly up, the flame retiring before him, till he came to a wide gallery—The flame proceeded along it, and he followed in silent horror, treading lightly, for the echoes of his footsteps startled him. It led him to the foot of another staircase, and then vanished—At the same instant another toll sounded from the turret—Sir Bertrand felt it strike upon his heart. He was now in total darkness, and with his arms extended, began to ascend the second staircase. A dead cold hand met his left hand and firmly grasped it, drawing him forcibly forwards—he endeavoured to disengage himself, but could not—he made a furious blow with his sword, and instantly a loud shriek pierced his ears, and the dead hand was left powerless in his—He dropt it, and rushed forwards with a desperate valour. The stairs were narrow and winding, and interrupted by frequent breaches, and loose fragments of stone. The staircase grew narrower and narrower and at length terminated in a low iron grate. Sir Bertrand pushed it open—it led to an intricate winding passage, just large enough to admit a person upon his hands and knees. A faint glimmering of light served to show the nature of the place. Sir Bertrand entered—A deep hollow groan resounded from a distance through the vault— He went forwards, and proceeding beyond the first turning, he discerned the same blue flame which had before conducted him. He followed it. The vault, at length, suddenly opened into a lofty gallery, in the midst of which a figure appeared, compleatly armed, thrusting forwards the bloody stump of an arm, with a terrible frown and menacing gesture, and brandishing a sword in his hand. Sir Bertrand undauntedly sprung forwards; and aiming a fierce blow at the figure, it instantly vanished, letting fall a massy iron key. The flame now rested upon a pair of ample folding doors at the end of the gallery. Sir Bertrand went up to it, and applied the key to a brazen lock—with difficulty he turned the bolt—instantly the doors flew open, and discovered a large apartment, at the end of which was a coffin rested upon a bier, with a taper burning on each side of it. Along the room on both sides were gigantic statues of black marble, attired in the Moorish habit, and holding enormous sabres in their right hands. Each of them reared his arm, and advanced one leg forwards, as the knight entered; at the same moment the lid of the coffin flew open, and the bell tolled. The flame still glided forwards, and Sir Bertrand resolutely followed, till he arrived within six paces of the coffin. Suddenly, a lady in a shroud and black veil rose up in it, and stretched out her arms towards him—at the same time the statues clashed their sabres and advanced. Sir Bertrand flew to the lady and clasped her in his arms—she threw up her veil and kissed his lips; and instantly the whole building shook as with an earthquake, and fell asunder with a horrible crash. Sir Bertrand was thrown into a sudden trance, and on recovering, found himself seated on a velvet sofa, in the most magnificent room he had ever seen, lighted with innumerable tapers, in lustres of pure crystal. A sumptuous banquet was set in the middle. The doors opening to soft music, a lady of incomparable beauty, attired with amazing splendour entered, surrounded by a troop of gay nymphs far more fair than the Graces—She

advanced to the knight, and falling on her knees thanked him as her deliverer.
The nymphs placed a garland of laurel on his head, and the lady led him by
the hand to the banquet, and sat beside him. The nymphs placed themselves
at the table, and a numerous train of servants entering, served up the feast;
delicious music playing all the time. Sir Bertrand could not speak for astonishment—he could only return their honours by courteous looks and gestures.
After the banquet was finished, all retired but the lady, who leading back the
knight to the sofa, addressed him in these words:—[9]

1773

9. The fragment ends here.

WILLIAM BECKFORD

Beckford's *Vathek* is regularly mentioned in discussions of Gothic romance, though
its setting is Arabian rather than European, and its exquisitely detailed architecture
is futuristic rather than imitation medieval. It also has more incongruity of tone—
suppressed comedy along with melodramatic high-seriousness—than the other works
included in this section; it is Gothic, that is, in the way *The Rocky Horror Picture
Show* is Gothic. *Vathek* was written in French—"at a single sitting of three days and
two nights," according to the *Dictionary of National Biography*—and then published
in English translation as *An Arabian Tale, from an Unpublished Manuscript* (1786).
Byron was an enthusiastic admirer, drawing on the book extensively for his Eastern
tale *The Giaour* (1813).

Besides *Vathek*, Beckford (1760–1844) was known in his time for building one of
the most extraordinary and eccentric structures in the history of architecture: Fonthill
Abbey, Beckford's Gothic palace, which he furnished with rare books; medieval,
Islamic, and East Asian art; and other curiosities. Beckford endowed the Caliph
Vathek with his own zeal for collecting, making him another connoisseur of the
strange, as well as a tyrant who puts people, even little children, to death at the
slightest whim. Sated with even these unorthodox pleasures, Vathek sets out in
the course of Beckford's tale to find the city of Istakhar and "the treasures of the pre-
adamite Sultans." In the extract we have selected from the final pages, he and his
favorite companion, Nouronihar, daughter of the emir Fakreddin, arrive at the mountains surrounding Istakhar and, with the guidance of the Giaour (an evil magician),
enter the underground realm of Eblis, prince of darkness. They achieve their quest
but are doomed to suffer the agony of eternally burning hearts and, what seems even
worse, the cessation of communion with anything outside their separate selves.

For discussion of the exotic geography of Beckford's fantasy, see "Romantic Orientalism" at Norton Literature Online.

From Vathek

A deathlike stillness reigned over the mountain, and through the air. The moon
dilated, on a vast platform, the shades of the lofty columns, which reached
from the terrace almost to the clouds. The gloomy watch-towers, whose numbers could not be counted, were veiled by no roof; and their capitals, of an

architecture unknown in the records of the earth, served as an asylum for the birds of darkness, which, alarmed at the approach of such visitants, fled away croaking.

The Chief of the Eunuchs, trembling with fear, besought Vathek that a fire might be kindled. "No!" replied he, "there is no time left to think of such trifles: abide where thou art, and expect my commands." Having thus spoken, he presented his hand to Nouronihar; and, ascending the steps of a vast staircase, reached the terrace, which was flagged with squares of marble, and resembled a smooth expanse of water, upon whose surface not a leaf ever dared to vegetate. On the right rose the watch-towers, ranged before the ruins of an immense palace, whose walls were embossed with various figures. In front stood forth the colossal forms of four creatures, composed of the leopard and the griffin; and, though but of stone, inspired emotions of terror. Near these were distinguished, by the splendour of the moon, which streamed full on the place, characters like those on the sabres of the Giaour, that possessed the same virtue of changing every moment. These, after vacillating for some time, at last fixed in Arabic letters, and prescribed to the Caliph the following words:

"Vathek! thou hast violated the conditions of my parchment, and deservest to be sent back; but, in favour to thy companion, and as the meed for what thou hast done to obtain it, Eblis permitteth that the portal of his palace shall be opened, and the subterranean fire will receive thee into the number of its adorers."

He scarcely had read these words before the mountain, against which the terrace was reared, trembled; and the watch-towers were ready to topple headlong upon them. The rock yawned, and disclosed within it a stair-case of polished marble that seemed to approach the abyss. Upon each stair were planted two large torches, like those Nouronihar had seen in her vision, the camphorated vapour ascending from which gathered into a cloud under the hollow of the vault.

This appearance, instead of terrifying, gave new courage to the daughter of Fakreddin. Scarcely deigning to bid adieu to the moon and the firmament, she abandoned without hesitation the pure atmosphere, to plunge into these infernal exhalations. The gait of those impious personages was haughty and determined. As they descended, by the effulgence of the torches, they gazed on each other with mutual admiration; and both appeared so resplendent that they already esteemed themselves spiritual Intelligences.[1] The only circumstance that perplexed them was their not arriving at the bottom of the stairs. On hastening their descent with an ardent impetuosity, they felt their steps accelerated to such a degree that they seemed not walking, but falling from a precipice. Their progress, however, was at length impeded by a vast portal of ebony, which the Caliph, without difficulty, recognized. Here the Giaour awaited them, with the key in his hand. "Ye are welcome!" said he to them, with a ghastly smile, "in spite of Mahomet, and all his dependents. I will now admit you into that palace where you have so highly merited a place." Whilst he was uttering these words, he touched the enameled lock with his key; and the doors at once expanded, with a noise still louder than the thunder of mountains, and as suddenly recoiled the moment they had entered.

The Caliph and Nouronihar beheld each other with amazement, at finding themselves in a place which, though roofed with a vaulted ceiling, was so

1. Angels.

spacious and lofty that at first they took it for an immeasurable plain. But their eyes at length growing familiar to the grandeur of the objects at hand, they extended their view to those at a distance, and discovered rows of columns and arcades, which gradually diminished, till they terminated in a point, radiant as the sun, when he darts his last beams athwart the ocean. The pavement, strewed over with gold dust and saffron, exhaled so subtle an odour as almost overpowered them. They, however, went on, and observed an infinity of censers, in which ambergris[2] and the wood of aloes were continually burning. Between the several columns were placed tables, each spread with a profusion of viands, and wines of every species, sparkling in vases of crystal. A throng of Genii, and other fantastic spirits, of each sex danced lasciviously in troops, at the sound of music which issued from beneath.

In the midst of this immense hall, a vast multitude was incessantly passing, who severally kept their right hands on their hearts, without once regarding anything around them. They had, all, the livid paleness of death. Their eyes, deep sunk in their sockets, resembled those phosphoric meteors that glimmer by night in places of interment. Some stalked slowly on, absorbed in profound reverie; some, shrieking with agony, ran furiously about, like tigers wounded with poisoned arrows; whilst others, grinding their teeth in rage, foamed along, more frantic than the wildest maniac. They all avoided each other; and, though surrounded by a multitude that no one could number, each wandered at random, unheedful of the rest, as if alone on a desert which no foot had trodden.

Vathek and Nouronihar, frozen with terror at a sight so baleful, demanded of the Giaour what these appearances might mean, and why these ambulating spectres never withdrew their hands from their hearts. "Perplex not yourselves," replied he bluntly, "with so much at once; you will soon be acquainted with all: let us haste, and present you to Eblis." They continued their way through the multitude; but, notwithstanding their confidence at first, they were not sufficiently composed to examine, with attention, the various perspectives of halls and of galleries that opened on the right hand and left, which were all illuminated by torches and braziers, whose flames rose in pyramids to the centre of the vault. At length they came to a place where long curtains, brocaded with crimson and gold, fell from all parts in striking confusion. Here the choirs and dances were heard no longer. The light which glimmered came from afar.

After some time, Vathek and Nouronihar perceived a gleam brightening through the drapery, and entered a vast tabernacle, carpeted with the skins of leopards. An infinity of Elders with streaming beards, and Afrits[3] in complete armour, had prostrated themselves before the ascent of a lofty eminence, on the top of which, upon a globe of fire, sat the formidable Eblis. His person was that of a young man, whose noble and regular features seemed to have been tarnished by malignant vapours. In his large eyes appeared both pride and despair: his flowing hair retained some resemblance to that of an angel of light. In his hand, which thunder had blasted, he swayed the iron sceptre that causes the monster Ouranabad, the Afrits, and all the Powers of the abyss to tremble. At his presence, the heart of the Caliph sunk within him; and, for the first time, he fell prostrate on his face. Nouronihar, however, though greatly dismayed, could not help admiring the person of Eblis: for she expected

2. The musky secretion of the sperm whale, valued for its perfume.

3. Demons of Islamic legend.

to have seen some stupendous Giant. Eblis, with a voice more mild than might be imagined, but such as transfused through the soul the deepest melancholy, said: "Creatures of clay, I receive you into mine empire: ye are numbered amongst my adorers: enjoy whatever this palace affords: the treasures of the pre-adamite Sultans, their bickering sabres, and those talismans that compel the Dives[4] to open the subterranean expanses of the mountain of Kaf, which communicate with these. There, insatiable as your curiosity may be, shall you find sufficient to gratify it. You shall possess the exclusive privilege of entering the fortress of Aherman,[5] and the halls of Argenk, where are portrayed all creatures endowed with intelligence, and the various animals that inhabited that earth prior to the creation of that contemptible being, whom ye denominate the Father of Mankind."[6]

Vathek and Nouronihar, feeling themselves revived and encouraged by this harangue, eagerly said to the Giaour: "Bring us instantly to the place which contains these precious talismans."—"Come!" answered this wicked Dive, with his malignant grin, "come! and possess all that my Sovereign hath promised, and more." He then conducted them into a long aisle adjoining the tabernacle, preceding them with hasty steps, and followed by his disciples with the utmost alacrity. They reached, at length, a hall of great extent, and covered with a lofty dome, around which appeared fifty portals of bronze, secured with as many fastenings of iron. A funereal gloom prevailed over the whole scene. Here, upon two beds of incorruptible cedar, lay recumbent the fleshless forms of the Pre-adamite Kings, who had been monarchs of the whole earth. They still possessed enough of life to be conscious of their deplorable condition. Their eyes retained a melancholy motion: they regarded each other with looks of the deepest dejection, each holding his right hand, motionless, on his heart. At their feet were inscribed the events of their several reigns, their power, their pride, and their crimes: Soliman Raad, Soliman Daki, and Soliman Di Gian Ben Gian, who, after having chained up the Dives in the dark caverns of Kaf, became so presumptuous as to doubt of the Supreme Power. All these maintained great state, though not to be compared with the eminence of Soliman Ben Daoud.

This King, so renowned for his wisdom, was on the loftiest elevation, and placed immediately under the dome. He appeared to possess more animation than the rest. Though from time to time he laboured with profound sighs, and, like his companions, kept his right hand on his heart, yet his countenance was more composed; and he seemed to be listening to the sullen roar of a vast cataract, visible in part through the grated portals. This was the only sound that intruded on the silence of these doleful mansions. A range of brazen vases surrounded this elevation. "Remove the covers from these cabalistic depositaries," said the Giaour to Vathek, "and avail thyself of the talismans, which will break asunder all these gates of bronze, and not only render thee master of the treasures contained within them, but also of the Spirits by which they are guarded."

The Caliph, whom this ominous preliminary had entirely disconcerted, approached the vases with faltering footsteps, and was ready to sink with terror when he heard the groans of Soliman. As he proceeded, a voice from the livid lips of the Prophet articulated these words: "In my life-time, I filled a magnif-

---

4. Persian term for giants.
5. In the Zoroastrian theology of ancient Persia,

the name for the principle of evil.
6. I.e., Adam.

icent throne, having on my right hand twelve thousand seats of gold, where the Patriarchs and the Prophets heard my doctrines: on my left the Sages and Doctors, upon as many thrones of silver, were present at all my decisions. Whilst I thus administered justice to innumerable multitudes, the birds of the air, librating[7] over me, served as a canopy from the rays of the sun. My people flourished; and my palace rose to the clouds. I erected a temple to the Most High, which was the wonder of the universe: but I basely suffered myself to be seduced by the love of women, and a curiosity that could not be restrained by sublunary things. I listened to the counsels of Aherman and the daughter of Pharaoh, and adored fire and the hosts of heaven. I forsook the holy city, and commanded the Genii to rear the stupendous palace of Istakhar, and the terrace of the watch-towers, each of which was consecrated to a star. There, for a while, I enjoyed myself, in the zenith of glory and pleasure. Not only men, but supernatural Existences were subject also to my will. I began to think, as these unhappy monarchs around had already thought, that the vengeance of Heaven was asleep; when at once the thunder burst my structures asunder, and precipitated me hither: where, however, I do not remain, like the other inhabitants, totally destitute of hope; for an angel of light hath revealed that, in consideration of the piety of my early youth, my woes shall come to an end when this cataract shall for ever cease to flow. Till then, I am in torments, ineffable torments! an unrelenting fire preys on my heart."

Having uttered this exclamation, Soliman raised his hands towards heaven, in token of supplication; and the Caliph discerned through his bosom, which was transparent as crystal, his heart enveloped in flames. At a sight so full of horror Nouronihar fell back, like one petrified, into the arms of Vathek, who cried out with a convulsive sob: "O Giaour! whither hast thou brought us? Allow us to depart, and I will relinquish all thou hast promised. O Mahomet! remains there no more mercy?"—"None! none!" replied the malicious Dive. "Know, miserable Prince! thou art now in the abode of vengeance and despair. Thy heart also will be kindled, like those of the other votaries of Eblis. A few days are allotted thee, previous to this fatal period: employ them as thou wilt: recline on these heaps of gold: command the Infernal Potentates: range, at thy pleasure, through these immense subterranean domains: no barrier shall be shut against thee. As for me, I have fulfilled my mission: I now leave thee to thyself." At these words, he vanished.

The Caliph and Nouronihar remained in the most abject affliction. Their tears unable to flow, scarcely could they support themselves. At length, taking each other despondingly by the hand, they went faltering from this fatal hall, indifferent which way they turned their steps. Every portal opened at their approach. The Dives fell prostrate before them. Every reservoir of riches was disclosed to their view: but they no longer felt the incentives of curiosity, pride, or avarice. With like apathy they heard the chorus of Genii, and saw the stately banquets prepared to regale them. They went wandering on, from chamber to chamber, hall to hall, and gallery to gallery, all without bounds or limit, all distinguishable by the same lowering gloom, all adorned with the same awful grandeur, all traversed by persons in search of repose and consolation, but who sought them in vain; for every one carried within him a heart tormented in flames. Shunned by these various sufferers, who seemed, by their looks, to be upbraiding the partners of their guilt, they withdrew from them, to wait in

7. Hovering.

direful suspense the moment which should render them to each other the like objects of terror.

1786

ANN RADCLIFFE

The "Great Enchantress," Radcliffe (1764–1823) published five novels between 1789 and 1797 and a sixth posthumously in 1826, most of them tremendously popular and influential on other writers for long afterward. She shunned fame and lived in seclusion; so little was known of her that, seeking to explain the long interval between *The Italian* in 1797 and *Gaston de Blondeville* in 1826, contemporaries gossiped that Radcliffe had at last gone mad from too much imagining and had spent her final decades confined in an asylum. The rumor was without basis, but the fate it assigned to Radcliffe is the fate most feared by her heroines, who cling valiantly to reason, but who are plunged into worlds of nightmarish mystery where nothing is as it seems and where reason, at least initially, does not get them very far. A Radcliffean heroine, like Radcliffe's reader, is kept on the rack of suspense by a succession of inexplicable sights and sounds that tempt her to believe that supernatural events really do happen. The ancient castle in which she is confined, the site of these mysteries, is often located in some wilderness that the forces of law have abandoned and that has become the haunt of mercenary soldiers and picaresque bandits. For all its strangeness, however, this place frequently turns out to be a version of the heroine's long-lost home, just as her tyrannical persecutors turn out to be closely allied with the fathers, uncles, and priests who are supposed to be a young lady's protectors.

Our first extract is taken from Radcliffe's third novel, *The Romance of the Forest* (1791). In this episode, later remembered by Jane Austen as she recounted the story of the first eventful night that Catherine Morland spends as a guest at Northanger Abbey, the orphaned Adeline sets out, detectivelike, to solve a mystery. The second extract is from Radcliffe's masterpiece, *The Mysteries of Udolpho* (1794), one of her signature pieces of dreamy landscape description, representing Emily St. Aubert's reactions as she and her villainous guardian Montoni approach his castle high in the Italian Appenines.

From The Romance of the Forest

From *Chapter 8*

Adeline retired early to her room, which adjoined on one side to Madame La Motte's, and on the other to the closet formerly mentioned. It was spacious and lofty, and what little furniture it contained was falling to decay; but, perhaps, the present tone of her spirits might contribute more than these circumstances to give that air of melancholy which seemed to reign in it. She was unwilling to go to bed, lest the dreams that had lately pursued her should return; and determined to sit up till she found herself oppressed by sleep, when it was probable her rest would be profound. She placed the light on a small table, and, taking a book, continued to read for above an hour, till her mind refused any longer to abstract itself from its own cares, and she sat for some time leaning pensively on her arm.

The wind was high, and as it whistled through the desolate apartment, and shook the feeble doors, she often started, and sometimes even thought she heard sighs between the pauses of the gust; but she checked these illusions, which the hour of the night and her own melancholy imagination conspired to raise. As she sat musing, her eyes fixed on the opposite wall, she perceived the arras, with which the room was hung, wave backwards and forwards; she continued to observe it for some minutes, and then rose to examine it farther. It was moved by the wind; and she blushed at the momentary fear it had excited: but she observed that the tapestry was more strongly agitated in one particular place than elsewhere, and a noise that seemed something more than that of the wind issued thence. The old bedstead, which La Motte had found in this apartment, had been removed to accommodate Adeline, and it was behind the place where this had stood that the wind seemed to rush with particular force: curiosity prompted her to examine still farther; she felt about the tapestry, and perceiving the wall behind shake under her hand, she lifted the arras, and discovered a small door, whose loosened hinges admitted the wind, and occasioned the noise she had heard.

The door was held only by a bolt, having undrawn which, and brought the light, she descended by a few steps into another chamber: she instantly remembered her dreams. The chamber was not much like that in which she had seen the dying Chevalier, and afterwards the bier; but it gave her a confused remembrance of one through which she had passed. Holding up the light to examine it more fully, she was convinced by its structure that it was part of the ancient foundation. A shattered casement, placed high from the floor, seemed to be the only opening to admit light. She observed a door on the opposite side of the apartment; and after some moments of hesitation, gained courage, and determined to pursue the inquiry. "A mystery seems to hang over these chambers," said she, "which it is, perhaps, my lot to develope;[1] I will, at least, see to what that door leads."

She stepped forward, and having unclosed it, proceeded with faltering steps along a suite of apartments resembling the first in style and condition, and terminating in one exactly like that where her dream had represented the dying person; the remembrance struck so forcibly upon her imagination that she was in danger of fainting; and looking round the room, almost expected to see the phantom of her dream.

Unable to quit the place, she sat down on some old lumber[2] to recover herself, while her spirits were nearly overcome by a superstitious dread, such as she had never felt before. She wondered to what part of the abbey these chambers belonged, and that they had so long escaped detection. The casements were all too high to afford any information from without. When she was sufficiently composed to consider the direction of the rooms, and the situation of the abbey, there appeared not a doubt that they formed an interior part of the original building.

As these reflections passed over her mind, a sudden gleam of moonlight fell upon some object without the casement. Being now sufficiently composed to wish to pursue the inquiry, and believing this object might afford her some means of learning the situation of these rooms, she combated her remaining terrors, and, in order to distinguish it more clearly, removed the light to an outer chamber; but before she could return, a heavy cloud was driven over the

---

1. Unfold, reveal.   2. Disused furniture and the like.

face of the moon, and all without was perfectly dark: she stood for some moments waiting a returning gleam, but the obscurity continued. As she went softly back for the light, her foot stumbled over something on the floor, and while she stooped to examine it, the moon again shone, so that she could distinguish, through the casement, the eastern towers of the abbey. This discovery confirmed her former conjectures concerning the interior situation of these apartments. The obscurity of the place prevented her discovering what it was that had impeded her steps, but having brought the light forward, she perceived on the floor an old dagger: with a trembling hand she took it up, and upon a closer view perceived that it was spotted and stained with rust.

Shocked and surprised, she looked round the room for some object that might confirm or destroy the dreadful suspicion which now rushed upon her mind; but she saw only a great chair, with broken arms, that stood in one corner of the room, and a table in a condition equally shattered, except that in another part lay a confused heap of things, which appeared to be old lumber. She went up to it, and perceived a broken bedstead, with some decayed remnants of furniture, covered with dust and cobwebs, and which seemed, indeed, as if they had not been moved for many years. Desirous, however, of examining farther, she attempted to raise what appeared to have been part of the bedstead, but it slipped from her hand, and, rolling to the floor, brought with it some of the remaining lumber. Adeline started aside and saved herself, and when the noise it made had ceased, she heard a small rustling sound, and as she was about to leave the chamber, saw something falling gently among the lumber.

It was a small roll of paper, tied with a string, and covered with dust. Adeline took it up, and on opening it perceived an handwriting. She attempted to read it, but the part of the manuscript she looked at was so much obliterated that she found this difficult, though what few words were legible impressed her with curiosity and terror, and induced her to return immediately to her chamber.

1791

From The Mysteries of Udolpho

From Volume 2, Chapter 5

Towards the close of day, the road wound into a deep valley. Mountains, whose shaggy steeps appeared to be inaccessible, almost surrounded it. To the east, a vista opened, that exhibited the Apennines in their darkest horrors; and the long perspective of retiring summits, rising over each other, their ridges clothed with pines, exhibited a stronger image of grandeur, than any that Emily had yet seen. The sun had just sunk below the top of the mountains she was descending, whose long shadow stretched athwart the valley, but his sloping rays, shooting through an opening of the cliffs, touched with a yellow gleam the summits of the forest, that hung upon the opposite steeps, and streamed in full splendour upon the towers and battlements of a castle, that spread its extensive ramparts along the brow of a precipice above. The splendour of these illumined objects was heightened by the contrasted shade, which involved the valley below.

"There," said Montoni, speaking for the first time in several hours, "is Udolpho."

Emily gazed with melancholy awe upon the castle, which she understood to be Montoni's; for, though it was now lighted up by the setting sun, the gothic greatness of its features, and its mouldering walls of dark grey stone, rendered it a gloomy and sublime object. As she gazed, the light died away on its walls, leaving a melancholy purple tint, which spread deeper and deeper, as the thin vapour crept up the mountain, while the battlements above were still tipped with splendour. From those too, the rays soon faded, and the whole edifice was invested with the solemn duskiness of evening. Silent, lonely and sublime, it seemed to stand the sovereign of the scene, and to frown defiance on all who dared to invade its solitary reign. As the twilight deepened, its features became more awful in obscurity, and Emily continued to gaze, till its clustering towers were alone seen, rising over the tops of the woods, beneath whose thick shade the carriages soon after began to ascend.

The extent and darkness of these tall woods awakened terrific images in her mind, and she almost expected to see banditti start up from under the trees. At length, the carriages emerged upon a heathy rock, and, soon after, reached the castle gates, where the deep tone of the portal bell, which was struck upon to give notice of their arrival, increased the fearful emotions that had assailed Emily. While they waited till the servant within should come to open the gates, she anxiously surveyed the edifice: but the gloom that overspread it allowed her to distinguish little more than a part of its outline, with the massy walls of the ramparts, and to know that it was vast, ancient and dreary. From the parts she saw, she judged of the heavy strength and extent of the whole. The gateway before her, leading into the courts, was of gigantic size, and was defended by two round towers, crowned by overhanging turrets, embattled, where instead of banners, now waved long grass and wild plants, that had taken root among the mouldering stones, and which seemed to sigh, as the breeze rolled past, over the desolation around them. The towers were united by a curtain, pierced and embattled also, below which appeared the pointed arch of an huge portcullis, surmounting the gates: from these, the walls of the ramparts extended to other towers, overlooking the precipice, whose shattered outline, appearing on a gleam that lingered in the west, told of the ravages of war.—Beyond these all was lost in the obscurity of evening.

While Emily gazed with awe upon the scene, footsteps were heard within the gates, and the undrawing of the bolts; after which an ancient servant of the castle appeared, forcing back the huge folds of the portal, to admit his lord. As the carriage-wheels rolled heavily under the portcullis, Emily's heart sunk, and she seemed as if she was going into her prison; the gloomy court into which she passed served to confirm the idea, and her imagination, ever awake to circumstance, suggested even more terrors than her reason could justify.

1794

MATTHEW GREGORY LEWIS

Lewis's *The Monk*, published in 1796 when the author was twenty, is the most gory of the Gothic novels and one of the most vividly written (a combination guaranteed to produce a best seller). Lewis (1775–1818) appears to have been alarmed by the scandal that erupted when his authorship was revealed, but not so rattled as to alter his literary course. He went on to compose Gothic dramas for the stage and, finding new uses for the language skills honed during the education that was meant to have prepared him for a diplomatic career, played a major part in introducing German tales of terror to England.

In *The Monk* Ambrosio, abbot of a monastery in Madrid, goes from a pinnacle of self-satisfied saintliness to become one of the most depraved villains in all fiction, both an incestuous rapist and matricidal murderer. After being seduced by Matilda, a female demon who has entered his monastery disguised as a male novice named Rosario, Ambrosio, with the help of a talisman that Matilda provides, plots the rape of one of his penitents, Antonia. Within *The Monk* mob violence competes with Ambrosio's bloodlust as a source for horror, suggesting how Gothic stories, even when set in distant pasts and places, may have allowed the readers and writers of the 1790s to work through timely anxieties about the power of crowds and the threat of revolution.

In the first extract given here, Ambrosio exults in private after having delivered a spellbinding sermon to a packed church in Madrid. The second extract recounts his assault on Antonia and the discovery by her mother, Elvira, of the young woman's peril.

From The Monk

From *Chapter 2*

The monks having attended their abbot to the door of his cell, he dismissed them with an air of conscious superiority, in which humility's semblance combated with the reality of pride.

He was no sooner alone, than he gave free loose to the indulgence of his vanity. When he remembered the enthusiasm which his discourse had excited, his heart swelled with rapture, and his imagination presented him with splendid visions of aggrandizement. He looked round him with exultation; and pride told him loudly that he was superior to the rest of his fellow-creatures.

"Who," thought he, "who but myself has passed the ordeal of youth, yet sees no single stain upon his conscience? Who else has subdued the violence of strong passions and an impetuous temperament, and submitted even from the dawn of life to voluntary retirement? I seek for such a man in vain. I see no one but myself possessed of such resolution. Religion cannot boast Ambrosio's equal! How powerful an effect did my discourse produce upon its auditors! How they crowded round me! How they loaded me with benedictions, and pronounced me the sole uncorrupted pillar of the church! What then now is left for me to do? Nothing, but to watch as carefully over the conduct of my brethren, as I have hitherto watched over my own. Yet hold! May I not be tempted from those paths which till now I have pursued without one moment's wandering? Am I not a man whose nature is frail and prone to error? I must now abandon the solitude of my retreat; the fairest and noblest dames of Madrid continually present themselves at the abbey, and will use no other confessor. I must accustom my eyes to objects of temptation, and expose myself to the seduction of luxury and desire. Should I meet in that world which I am constrained to enter, some lovely female—lovely as you—Madona—!"

As he said this, he fixed his eyes upon a picture of the Virgin, which was suspended opposite to him: this for two years had been the object of his increasing wonder and adoration. He paused, and gazed upon it with delight.

"What beauty in that countenance!" he continued after a silence of some minutes; "how graceful is the turn of that head! what sweetness, yet what majesty in her divine eyes! how softly her cheek reclines upon her hand! Can the rose vie with the blush of that cheek? can the lily rival the whiteness of that hand? Oh! if such a creature existed, and existed but for me! were I permitted to twine round my fingers those golden ringlets, and press with my lips the treasures of that snowy bosom! gracious God, should I then resist the temptation? Should I not barter for a single embrace the reward of my sufferings for thirty years? Should I not abandon———Fool that I am! Whither do I suffer my admiration of this picture to hurry me? Away, impure ideas! Let me remember that woman is for ever lost to me. Never was mortal formed so perfect as this picture. But even did such exist, the trial might be too mighty for a common virtue; but Ambrosio's is proof against temptation. Temptation, did I say? To me it would be none. What charms me, when ideal and considered as a superior being, would disgust me, become woman and tainted with all the failings of mortality. It is not the woman's beauty that fills me with such enthusiasm: it is the painter's skill that I admire; it is the Divinity that I adore. Are not the passions dead in my bosom? have I not freed myself from the frailty of mankind? Fear not, Ambrosio! Take confidence in the strength of your virtue. Enter boldly into the world, to whose failings you are superior; reflect that you are now exempted from humanity's defects, and defy all the arts of the spirits of darkness. They shall know you for what you are!"

Here his reverie was interrupted by three soft knocks at the door of his cell. With difficulty did the abbot awake from his delirium. The knocking was repeated.

"Who is there?" said Ambrosio at length.

"It is only Rosario," replied a gentle voice.

From *Chapter 8*

It was almost two o'clock before the lustful monk ventured to bend his steps towards Antonia's dwelling. It has been already mentioned that the abbey was at no great distance from the strada di San Iago. He reached the house unobserved. Here he stopped, and hesitated for a moment. He reflected on the enormity of the crime, the consequences of a discovery, and the probability, after what had passed, of Elvira's suspecting him to be her daughter's ravisher. On the other hand it was suggested that she could do no more than suspect; that no proofs of his guilt could be produced; that it would seem impossible for the rape to have been committed without Antonia's knowing when, where, or by whom; and finally, he believed that his fame was too firmly established to be shaken by the unsupported accusations of two unknown women. This latter argument was perfectly false. He knew not how uncertain is the air of popular applause, and that a moment suffices to make him to-day the detestation of the world, who yesterday was its idol. The result of the monk's deliberations was that he should proceed in his enterprise. He ascended the steps leading to the house. No sooner did he touch the door with the silver myrtle than it flew open, and presented him with a free passage. He entered, and the door closed after him of its own accord.

Guided by the moon-beams, he proceeded up the stair-case with slow and cautious steps. He looked round him every moment with apprehension and anxiety. He saw a spy in every shadow, and heard a voice in every murmur of the night-breeze. Consciousness of the guilty business on which he was employed appalled his heart, and rendered it more timid than a woman's. Yet still he proceeded. He reached the door of Antonia's chamber. He stopped, and listened. All was hushed within. The total silence persuaded him that his intended victim was retired to rest, and he ventured to lift up the latch. The door was fastened, and resisted his efforts. But no sooner was it touched by the talisman than the bolt flew back. The ravisher stepped on, and found himself in the chamber where slept the innocent girl, unconscious how dangerous a visitor was drawing near her couch. The door closed after him, and the bolt shot again into its fastening.

Ambrosio advanced with precaution. He took care that not a board should creak under his foot, and held in his breath as he approached the bed. His first attention was to perform the magic ceremony, as Matilda had charged him: he breathed thrice upon the silver myrtle, pronounced over it Antonia's name, and laid it upon her pillow. The effects which it had already produced permitted not his doubting its success in prolonging the slumbers of his devoted mistress. No sooner was the enchantment performed than he considered her to be absolutely in his power, and his eyes flashed with lust and impatience. He now ventured to cast a glance upon the sleeping beauty. A single lamp, burning before the statue of St. Rosolia, shed a faint light through the room, and permitted him to examine all the charms of the lovely object before him. The heat of the weather had obliged her to throw off part of the bed-clothes. Those which still covered her Ambrosio's insolent hand hastened to remove. She lay with her cheek reclining upon one ivory arm: the other rested on the side of the bed with graceful indolence. A few tresses of her hair had escaped from beneath the muslin which confined the rest, and fell carelessly over her bosom, as it heaved with slow and regular suspiration. The warm air had spread her cheek with a higher colour than usual. A smile inexpressibly sweet played round her ripe and coral lips, from which every now and then escaped a gentle sigh, or an half-pronounced sentence. An air of enchanting innocence and candour pervaded her whole form; and there was a sort of modesty in her very nakedness, which added fresh stings to the desires of the lustful monk.

He remained for some moments devouring those charms with his eyes which soon were to be subjected to his ill-regulated passions. Her mouth half-opened seem to solicit a kiss: he bent over her: he joined his lips to hers, and drew in the fragrance of her breath with rapture. This momentary pleasure increased his longing for still greater. His desires were raised to that frantic height by which brutes are agitated. He resolved not to delay for one instant longer the accomplishment of his wishes, and hastily proceeded to tear off those garments which impeded the gratification of his lust.

"Gracious God!" exclaimed a voice behind him: "Am I not deceived? Is not this an illusion?"

Terror, confusion, and disappointment accompanied these words, as they struck Ambrosio's hearing. He started, and turned towards it. Elvira stood at the door of the chamber, and regarded the monk with looks of surprise and detestation.

A frightful dream had represented to her Antonia on the verge of a precipice. She saw her trembling on the brink: every moment seemed to threaten her fall, and she heard her exclaim with shrieks, "Save me, mother! save me!—Yet a moment, and it will be too late." Elvira woke in terror. The vision had made too strong an impression upon her mind to permit her resting till assured of her daughter's safety. She hastily started from her bed, threw on a loose nightgown, and, passing through the closet in which slept the waiting-woman, reached Antonia's chamber just in time to rescue her from the grasp of the ravisher.

His shame and her amazement seemed to have petrified into statues both Elvira and the monk. They remained gazing upon each other in silence. The lady was the first to recover herself.

"It is no dream," she cried: "it is really Ambrosio who stands before me. It is the man whom Madrid esteems a saint that I find at this late hour near the couch of my unhappy child. Monster of hypocrisy! I already suspected your designs, but forbore your accusation in pity to human frailty. Silence would now be criminal. The whole city shall be informed of your incontinence. I will unmask you, villain, and convince the church what a viper she cherishes in her bosom."

Pale and confused, the baffled culprit stood trembling before her. He would fain have extenuated his offence, but could find no apology for his conduct. He could produce nothing but broken sentences, and excuses which contradicted each other. Elvira was too justly incensed to grant the pardon which he requested. She protested that she would raise the neighbourhood, and make him an example to all future hypocrites. Then hastening to the bed, she called to Antonia to wake; and finding that her voice had no effect, she took her arm, and raised her forcibly from the pillow. The charm operated too powerfully. Antonia remained insensible; and, on being released by her mother, sank back upon the pillow.

"This slumber cannot be natural," cried the amazed Elvira, whose indignation increased with every moment: "some mystery is concealed in it. But tremble, hypocrite! All your villainy shall soon be unravelled. Help! help!" she exclaimed aloud: "Within there! Flora! Flora!"

"Hear me for one moment, lady!" cried the monk, restored to himself by the urgency of the danger: "by all that is sacred and holy, I swear that your daughter's honour is still unviolated. Forgive my transgression! Spare me the shame of a discovery, and permit me to regain the abbey undisturbed. Grant me this request in mercy! I promise not only that Antonia shall be secure from me in future, but that the rest of my life shall prove—"

Elvira interrupted him abruptly.

"Antonia secure from you? *I* will secure her. You shall betray no longer the confidence of parents. Your iniquity shall be unveiled to the public eye. All Madrid shall shudder at your perfidy, your hypocrisy, and incontinence. What ho! there! Flora! Flora! I say."

While she spoke thus, the remembrance of Agnes struck upon his mind. Thus had she sued to him for mercy, and thus had he refused her prayer! It was now his turn to suffer, and he could not but acknowledge that his punishment was just. In the mean while Elvira continued to call Flora to her assistance; but her voice was so choaked with passion, that the servant, who was buried in profound slumber, was insensible to all her cries: Elvira dared not go towards the closet in which Flora slept, lest the monk should take that opportunity to escape. Such indeed was his intention: he trusted that, could he reach the abbey unobserved by any other than Elvira, her single testimony would not suffice to ruin a reputation so well established as his was in Madrid. With this idea he gathered up such garments as he had already thrown off, and hastened towards the door. Elvira was aware of his design: she followed him, and, ere he could draw back the bolt, seized him by the arm, and detained him.

"Attempt not to fly!" said she: "you quit not this room without witnesses of your guilt."

Ambrosio struggled in vain to disengage himself. Elvira quitted not her hold, but redoubled her cries for succour. The friar's danger grew more urgent. He expected every moment to hear people assembling at her voice; and, worked up to madness by the approach of ruin, he adopted a resolution equally desperate and savage. Turning round suddenly, with one hand he grasped Elvira's throat so as to prevent her continuing her clamour, and with the other, dashing her violently upon the ground, he dragged her towards the bed. Confused by this unexpected attack, she scarcely had power to strive at forcing herself from his grasp: while the monk, snatching the pillow from beneath her daughter's head, covering with it Elvira's face, and pressing his knee upon her stomach with all his strength, endeavoured to put an end to her existence. He succeeded but too well. Her natural strength increased by the excess of anguish, long did the sufferer struggle to disengage herself, but in vain. The monk continued to kneel upon her breast, witnessed without mercy the convulsive trembling of her limbs beneath him, and sustained with inhuman firmness the spectacle of her agonies, when soul and body were on the point of separating. Those agonies at length were over. She ceased to struggle for life. The monk took off the pillow, and gazed upon her. Her face was covered with a frightful blackness: her limbs moved no more: the blood was chilled in her veins: her heart had forgotten to beat; and her hands were stiff and frozen. Ambrosio beheld before him that once noble and majestic form, now become a corse, cold, senseless, and disgusting.

This horrible act was no sooner perpetrated, than the friar beheld the enormity of his crime. A cold dew flowed over his limbs: his eyes closed: he staggered to a chair, and sank into it almost as lifeless as the unfortunate who lay extended at his feet. From this state he was roused by the necessity of flight, and the danger of being found in Antonia's apartment. He had no desire to profit by the execution of his crime. Antonia now appeared to him an object of disgust. A deadly cold had usurped the place of that warmth which glowed in his bosom. No ideas offered themselves to his mind but those of death and guilt, of present shame and future punishment. Agitated by remorse and fear, he prepared for flight: yet his terrors did not so completely master his recollection as to prevent his taking the precautions necessary for his safety. He replaced the pillow upon the bed, gathered up his garments, and, with the fatal talisman in his hand, bent his unsteady steps towards the door. Bewildered by fear, he fancied that his flight was opposed by legions of phantoms. Wherever he turned, the disfigured corse seemed to lie in his passage, and it was long before he succeeded in reaching the door.

1795   1796

ANONYMOUS

The following discussion of the "fashion" for tales of terror appeared in *The Spirit of the Public Journals for 1797*. Its wonderfully scathing humor aside, it is typical of the many Romantic-period commentaries that argued that the popularity of this new style of novel was a frightening symptom of literature's commercialization and of culture's degradation. The "recipe" with which the anonymous author concludes the squib, and which makes the point that best-selling fiction is likely to be, in a precise sense, "formula fiction," is a frequent feature of satires on novelists (Coleridge, who in our next extract refers to novels as "manufactures," i.e., as things produced mechanically rather than as works that authors compose, elsewhere wrote his own recipes for Radcliffe romances and for Walter Scott poems). Also notable is the author's tacit suggestion that the political climate has helped make "terror the order of the day": that phrase appeared in the directive that was issued in September 1793 by Robespierre's Committee of Public Safety and that inaugurated the bloodiest chapter of the Revolution in France.

Terrorist Novel Writing

I never complain of fashion, when it is confined to externals—to the form of a cap, or the cut of a lapelle; to the colour of a wig, or the tune of a ballad; but when I perceive that there is such a thing as fashion even in composing books, it is, perhaps, full time that some attempt should be made to recall writers to the old boundaries of common sense.

I allude, Sir, principally to the great quantity of novels with which our circulating libraries are filled, and our parlour tables covered, in which it has been the fashion to make *terror* the *order of the day*, by confining the heroes and heroines in old gloomy castles, full of spectres, apparitions, ghosts, and dead men's bones. This is now so common, that a Novelist blushes to bring about a marriage by ordinary means, but conducts the happy pair through long and dangerous galleries, where the light burns blue, the thunder rattles, and the great window at the end presents the hideous visage of a *murdered* man, *uttering* piercing groans, and developing shocking mysteries. If a curtain is withdrawn, there is a bleeding body behind it; if a chest is opened, it contains a skeleton; if a noise is heard, somebody is receiving a deadly blow; and if a candle goes out, its place is sure to be supplied by a flash of lightning. Cold hands grasp us in the dark, statues are seen to move, and suits of armour walk off their pegs, while the wind whistles louder than one of Handel's choruses, and the still air is more melancholy than the dead march in Saul.

Such are the dresses and decorations of a modern novel, which, as Bayes[1] says, is calculated to "elevate and surprise"; but in doing so, carries the young reader's imagination into such a confusion of terrors, as must be hurtful. It is to great purpose, indeed, that we have forbidden our servants from telling the children stories of ghosts and hobgoblins, if we cannot put a novel into their hands which is not filled with monsters of the imagination, more frightful than are to be found in Glanvil,[2] the famous *bug-a-boo* of our fore fathers.

A novel, if at all useful, ought to be a representation of human life and manners, with a view to direct the conduct in the important duties of life, and to correct its follies. But what instruction is to be reaped from the distorted ideas of lunatics, I am at a loss to conceive. Are we come to such a pass, that the only commandment necessary to be repeated is, "Thou shalt do no murder?" Are the duties of life so changed, that all the instructions necessary for a young person is to learn to walk at night upon the battlements of an old castle, to creep hands and feet along a narrow passage, and meet the devil at

1. The ludicrously self-satisfied dramatist in *The Rehearsal*, a comedy by George Villiers, duke of Buckingham (1672).

2. Joseph Glanvill, author of *Saducismus Triumphatus* (1681), which defended the belief in witchcraft.

the end of it? Is the corporeal frame of the female sex so masculine and hardy, that it must be softened down by the touch of dead bodies, clay-cold hands, and damp sweats? Can a young lady be taught nothing more necessary in life, than to sleep in a dungeon with venomous reptiles, walk through a ward with assassins, and carry bloody daggers in their pockets, instead of pin-cushions and needle-books?

Every absurdity has an end, and as I observe that almost all novels are of the terrific cast, I hope the insipid repetition of the same bugbears[3] will at length work a cure. In the mean time, should any of your female readers be desirous of catching the season of terrors, she may compose two or three very pretty volumes from the following recipe:

> *Take*—An old castle, half of it ruinous.
> A long gallery, with a great many doors, some secret ones.
> Three murdered bodies, quite fresh.
> As many skeletons, in chests and presses.
> An old woman hanging by the neck; with her throat cut.
> Assassins and desperadoes, *quant. suff.*[4]
> Noises, whispers, and groans, threescore at least.

Mix them together, in the form of three volumes, to be taken at any of the watering places,[5] before going to bed.

1798

3. Annoyances, objects of needless fear.
4. I.e., *quantum sufficit* (standard Latin phrase used in medical prescriptions): "as much as suffices."
5. Seaside resorts. The suggestion is that readers choose novels of terror as vacation reading.

SAMUEL TAYLOR COLERIDGE

Many elements in Coleridge's poetry—the account of the skeleton ship in *The Rime of the Ancient Mariner*, for instance, or the atmosphere, setting, and fragmentary plot of witchery and seduction in *Christabel*—suggest how absorbing he found the novels of the "terrorist school." His letters from the 1790s sometimes reveal him sitting up all night, trembling, he says, "like an aspen leaf" as he turns their pages. But elsewhere Coleridge's writings indicate how complex and ambivalent the Romantic poets' reaction to Gothic writing could be. As a first example we provide his scathing review, published in the *Critical Review* in February 1797, of *The Monk*. It should be noted that Coleridge's reaction to Matthew Lewis's novel is, for all its alarm, much more measured than those of most of his fellow critics.

From Review of *The Monk* by Matthew Lewis

The horrible and the preternatural have usually seized on the popular taste, at the rise and decline of literature. Most powerful stimulants, they can never be required except by the torpor of an unawakened, or the languor of an exhausted, appetite. The same phenomenon, therefore, which we hail as a favourable omen in the belles lettres[1] of Germany, impresses a degree of gloom in the compositions of our countrymen. We trust, however, that satiety will banish what good sense should have prevented; and that, wearied with fiends, incomprehensible characters, with shrieks, murders, and subterraneous dungeons, the public will learn, by the multitude of the manufacturers, with how little expense of thought or imagination this species of composition is manufactured. But, cheaply as we estimate romances in general, we acknowledge, in the work before us, the offspring of no common genius. The tale is similar to that of Santon Barsista in the Guardian.[2] Ambrosio, a monk, surnamed the Man of Holiness, proud of his own undeviating rectitude, and severe to the faults of others, is successfully assailed by the tempter of mankind, and seduced to the perpetration of rape and murder, and finally precipitated into a contract in which he consigns his soul to everlasting perdition.

The larger part of the three volumes is occupied by the underplot, which, however, is skilfully and closely connected with the main story, and is subservient to its development. The tale of the bleeding nun is truly terrific; and we could not easily recollect a bolder or more happy conception than that of the burning cross on the forehead of the wandering Jew (a mysterious character, which, though copied as to its more prominent features from Schiller's incomprehensible Armenian,[3] does, nevertheless, display great vigour of fancy). But the character of Matilda, the chief agent in the seduction of Antonio[4] appears to us to be the author's master-piece. It is, indeed, exquisitely imagined, and as exquisitely supported. The whole work is distinguished by the variety and impressiveness of its incidents; and the author everywhere discovers an imagination rich, powerful, and fervid. Such are the excellencies;—the errors and defects are more numerous, and (we are sorry to add) of greater importance.

All events are levelled into one common mass, and become almost equally probable, where the order of nature may be changed whenever the author's purposes demand it. No address is requisite to the accomplishment of any design; and no pleasure therefore can be received from the perception of *difficulty surmounted*. The writer may make us wonder, but he cannot surprise us. For the same reasons a romance is incapable of exemplifying a moral truth. No proud man, for instance, will be made less proud by being told that Lucifer once seduced a presumptuous monk. *Incredulus odit.*[5] Or even if, believing the story, he should deem his virtue less secure, he would yet acquire no lessons of prudence, no feelings of humility. Human prudence can oppose no sufficient shield to the power and cunning of supernatural beings; and the privilege of being proud might be fairly conceded to him who could rise superior to all earthly temptations, and whom the strength of the spiritual world alone would be adequate to overwhelm. So falling, he would fall with glory, and might reasonably welcome his defeat with the haughty emotions of a conqueror. As far, therefore, as the story is concerned, the praise which a romance can claim, is simply that of having given pleasure during its perusal; and so many are the calamities of life, that he who has done this, has not written uselessly. The children of sickness and of solitude shall thank him. To this praise, however, our author has not entitled himself. The sufferings which he describes are so frightful and intolerable, that we break with abruptness

1. Literature.
2. An Eastern tale published in 1713 and acknowledged by Lewis as one of his sources.
3. The mysterious villain of Friedrich Schiller's

The Ghost-seer (English translation 1795).
4. Coleridge's mistake for Ambrosio.
5. "To disbelieve is to dislike": Horace, *Art of Poetry* 1.188.

from the delusion, and indignantly suspect the man of a species of brutality, who could find a pleasure in wantonly imagining them; and the abominations which he portrays with no hurrying pencil, are such as the observation of character by no means demanded, such as "no observation of character can justify, because no good man would willingly suffer them to pass, however transiently, through his own mind." The merit of a novelist is in proportion (not simply to the effect, but) to the *pleasurable* effect which he produces. Situations of torment, and images of naked horror, are easily conceived; and a writer in whose works they abound, deserves our gratitude almost equally with him who should drag us by way of sport through a military hospital, or force us to sit at the dissecting-table of a natural philosopher. To trace the nice[6] boundaries, beyond which terror and sympathy are deserted by the pleasurable emotions,—to reach those limits, yet never to pass them,—*hic labor, hic opus est.*[7] Figures that shock the imagination, and narratives that mangle the feelings, rarely discover *genius*, and always betray a low and vulgar *taste*. Nor has our author indicated less ignorance of the human heart in the management of the principal character. The wisdom and goodness of providence have ordered that the tendency of vicious actions to deprave the heart of the perpetrator, should diminish in proportion to the greatness of his temptations. Now, in addition to constitutional warmth and irresistible opportunity, the monk is impelled to incontinence by friendship, by compassion, by gratitude, by all that is amiable, and all that is estimable; yet in a few weeks after his first frailty, the man who had been described as possessing much general humanity, a keen and vigorous understanding, with habits of the most exalted piety, degenerates into an uglier fiend than the gloomy imagination of Dante would have ventured to picture. Again, the monk is described as feeling and acting under the influence of an appetite which could not co-exist with his other emotions. The romance-writer possesses an unlimited power over situations; but he must scrupulously make his characters act in congruity with them. Let him work *physical* wonders only, and we will be content to *dream* with him for a while; but the first *moral* miracle which he attempts, he disgusts and awakens us. Thus our judgment remains unoffended, when, announced by thunders and earthquakes, the spirit appears to Ambrosio involved in blue fires that increase the cold of the cavern; and we acquiesce in the power of the silver myrtle which made gates and doors fly open at its touch, and charmed every eye into sleep. But when a mortal, fresh from the impression of that terrible appearance, and in the act of evincing for the first time the witching force of this myrtle, is represented as being at the same moment agitated by so fleeting an appetite as that of lust, our own feelings convince us that this is not improbable, but impossible; not preternatural, but contrary to nature. The extent of the powers that may exist, we can never ascertain; and therefore we feel no great difficulty in yielding a temporary belief to any, the strangest, situation of *things*. But that situation once conceived, how beings like ourselves would feel and act in it, our own feelings sufficiently instruct us; and we instantly reject the clumsy fiction that does not harmonise with them. These are the two *principal* mistakes in *judgment*, which the author has fallen into; but we cannot wholly pass over the frequent incongruity of his style with his subjects. It is gaudy where it should have been severely simple; and too often the mind is offended by phrases the most trite and colloquial,

6. Subtle.   7. "This is the effort, this is the work."

where it demands and had expected a sternness and solemnity of diction.

A more grievous fault remains, a fault for which no literary excellence can atone, a fault which all other excellence does but aggravate, as adding subtlety to a poison by the elegance of its preparation. Mildness of censure would here be criminally misplaced, and silence would make us accomplices. Not without reluctance then, but in full conviction that we are performing a duty, we declare it to be our opinion, that the Monk is a romance, which if a parent saw in the hands of a son or daughter, he might reasonably turn pale. The temptations of Ambrosio are described with a libidinous minuteness, which, we sincerely hope, will receive its best and only adequate censure from the offended conscience of the author himself. The shameless harlotry of Matilda, and the trembling innocence of Antonia, are seized with equal avidity, as vehicles of the most voluptuous images; and though the tale is indeed a tale of horror, yet the most painful impression which the work left on our minds was that of great acquirements and splendid genius employed to furnish a *mormo*[8] for children, a poison for youth, and a provocative for the debauchee. Tales of enchantments and witchcraft can never be *useful*: our author has contrived to make them *pernicious*, by blending, with an irreverent negligence, all that is most awfully true in religion with all that is most ridiculously absurd in superstition. He takes frequent occasion, indeed, to manifest his sovereign contempt for the latter, both in his own person, and (most incongruously) in that of his principal characters; and that his respect for the *former* is not excessive, we are forced to conclude from the treatment which its inspired writings receive from him. Ambrosio discovers Antonia reading—

> He examined the book which she had been reading, and had now placed upon the table. It was the Bible.
>
> "How!" said the friar to himself, "Antonia reads the Bible, and is still so ignorant?"
>
> But, upon a further inspection, he found that Elvira had made exactly the same remark. That prudent mother, while she admired the beauties of the sacred writings, was convinced that, unrestricted, no reading more improper could be permitted a young woman. Many of the narratives can only tend to excite ideas the worst calculated for a female breast: every thing is called plainly and roundly by its name; and the *annals of a brothel would scarcely furnish a greater choice of indecent expressions.* Yet this is the book which young women are recommended to study, which is put into the hands of children, able to comprehend little more than those passages of which they had better remain ignorant, and which but too *frequently inculcates the first rudiments of vice,* and gives the first alarm to the still sleeping passions. Of this was Elvira so fully convinced, that she would have preferred putting into her daughter's hands "Amadis de Gaul," or "The Valiant Champion, Tirante the White"; and *would sooner have authorised her studying the lewd exploits of Don Galaor, or the lascivious jokes of the Damsel Plazer di mi vida.* Vol.II, p. 247.

The impiety of this falsehood can be equalled only by its impudence. This is indeed as if a Corinthian harlot, clad from head to foot in the transparent thinness of the Cöan vest, should affect to view with prudish horror the naked knee of a Spartan matron! If it be possible that the author of these blasphemies

---

8. Bogeyman, object of needless dread.

is a Christian, should he not have reflected that the only passage in the scriptures,[9] which could give a *shadow* of plausibility to the *weakest* of these expressions, is represented as being spoken by the Almighty himself? But if he be an
infidel, he has acted consistently enough with that character, in his endeavours
first to influence the fleshly appetites, and then to pour contempt on the only
book which would be adequate to the task of recalming them. We believe it
not absolutely impossible that a mind may be so deeply depraved by the habit
of reading lewd and voluptuous tales, as to use even the Bible in conjuring up
the spirit of uncleanness. The most innocent expressions might become the
first link in the chain of association, when a man's soul had been so poisoned;
and we believe it not absolutely impossible that he might extract pollution
from the word of purity, and, in a literal sense, *turn the grace of God into
wantonness*.

We have been induced to pay particular attention to this work, from the
unusual success which it has experienced. It certainly possesses much real
merit, in addition to its meretricious attractions. Nor must it be forgotten that
the author is a man of rank and fortune. Yes! the author of the Monk signs
himself a LEGISLATOR![1] We stare and tremble.

1797

From Biographia Literaria

From *Chapter 3*[1]

For as to the devotees of the circulating libraries, I dare not compliment their
pass-time, or rather *kill-time*, with the name of *reading*. Call it rather a sort of
beggarly daydreaming, during which the mind of the dreamer furnishes for
itself nothing but laziness and a little mawkish sensibility; while the whole
materiel and imagery of the doze is supplied *ab extra*[2] by a sort of mental
camera obscura[3] manufactured at the printing office, which *pro tempore*[4] fixes,
reflects and transmits the moving phantasms of one man's delirium, so as to
people the barrenness of an hundred other brains afflicted with the same
trance or suspension of all common sense and all definite purpose. We should
therefore transfer this species of *amusement* (if indeed those can be said to
retire *a musis*,[5] who were never in their company, or relaxation be attributable
to those, whose bows are never bent) from the genus, *reading*, to that comprehensive class characterized by the power of reconciling the two contrary
yet co-existing propensities of human nature, namely indulgence of sloth, and
hatred of vacancy. In addition to novels and tales of chivalry in prose or rhyme

9. Ezekiel, chap. xxiii [Coleridge's note].
1. Lewis, a member of Parliament, signed himself
"M. G. Lewis, Esq., M.P." on the title page of the
second edition of *The Monk*. Worried that the public outcry over the episode Coleridge here lambastes would lead to his being charged with
obscene libel, Lewis cut the episode from the
fourth edition.
1. This paragraph makes up the first footnote to
the third chapter of Coleridge's *Biographia Literaria*, the hybrid book in which he blended autobiography with philosophical speculations and
favorite anecdotes. In the body of his text, Coleridge refers to the frequency with which his name

has been before the reading public; the footnote
(the text given here) then goes on to identify the
sort of people who for him do not count as bona
fide members of that public.
2. From the outside (Latin).
3. A device (forerunner of the modern camera)
creating a special optical effect: light passes
through a pinhole into a darkened room and creates an inverted image of the world beyond the
walls.
4. For the time being (Latin).
5. A pun linking "amusement" and *a musis*, "away
from the Muses."

(by which last I mean neither rhythm nor metre) this genus comprises as its species, gaming; swinging or swaying on a chair or gate; spitting over a bridge; smoking; snuff-taking; tête-à-tête quarrels after dinner between husband and wife; conning word by word all the advertisements of the *Daily Advertiser* in a public house on a rainy day, etc. etc. etc.

1815   1817

GEORGE GORDON, LORD BYRON
1788–1824

In his *History of English Literature,* written in the late 1850s, the French critic Hippolyte Taine gave only a few condescending pages to Wordsworth, Coleridge, Percy Shelley, and Keats and then devoted a long chapter to Lord Byron, "the greatest and most English of these artists; he is so great and so English that from him alone we shall learn more truths of his country and of his age than from all the rest together." This comment reflects the fact that Byron had achieved an immense European reputation during his own lifetime, while admirers of his English contemporaries were much more limited in number. Through much of the nineteenth century he continued to be rated as one of the greatest of English poets and the very prototype of literary Romanticism. His influence was manifested everywhere, among the major poets and novelists (Balzac and Stendhal in France, Pushkin and Dostoyevsky in Russia, and Melville in America), painters (especially Delacroix), and composers (including Beethoven and Berlioz).

Yet even as poets, painters, and composers across Europe and the Americas struck Byronic attitudes, Byron's place within the canon of English Romantic poetry was becoming insecure. The same Victorian critics who first described the Romantic period *as* a literary period warned readers against the immorality of Byron's poetry, finding in his voluptuous imagination and aristocratic disdain for the commonplace an affront to their own middle-class values: "Close thy Byron; open thy Goethe," Thomas Carlyle urged in *Sartor Resartus* (1834), meaning to redirect the nation toward healthier reading matter. After getting a glimpse of the scandalous stuff recorded in Byron's journals, Felicia Hemans ceased to wear the brooch in which she had preserved a lock of the poet's hair: she could venerate him no longer. Indeed, Byron would have had qualms about being considered a representative figure of a period that also included Wordsworth (memorialized in Byron's *Don Juan* as "Wordy") or Keats (a shabby Cockney brat, Byron claimed) or scribbling women such as Hemans. These reservations were reciprocated. Of Byron's best-known male contemporaries, only Shelley thought highly of either the man or his work (although there are signs that, among the naysayers, the negative reactions were tinged with some resentment at Byron's success in developing a style that spoke to a popular audience). Byron in fact insisted that, measured against the poetic practice of Alexander Pope, he and his contemporaries were "all in the wrong, one as much as another. . . . We are upon a wrong revolutionary poetical system, or systems, not worth a damn in itself." Pope's Horatian satires, along with Laurence Sterne's novel *Tristram Shandy,* exerted a significant influence on the style that Byron developed for his epic survey of modern folly, *Don Juan.*

Still, even as he had recourse to old-fashioned eighteenth-century models, Byron cultivated a skepticism about established systems of belief that, in its restlessness and defiance, expressed the intellectual and social ferment of his era. And through much of his best poetry, he shared his contemporaries' fascination with the internal dramas of the individual mind (although Byron explored personality in an improvisatory and mercurial manner that could not have been more different from Wordsworth's auto-biographical accounts of his psychological development). Readers marveled over the intensity of the feelings his verse communicated—"its force, fire, and thought," said the novelist Lady Sydney Morgan—and the vividness of the sense of self they found in it. Byron's chief claim to be considered an arch-Romantic is that he provided the age with what Taine called its "ruling personage; that is, the model that contempo-raries invest with their admiration and sympathy." This personage is the "Byronic hero." He is first sketched in the opening canto of *Childe Harold,* then recurs in various guises in the verse romances and dramas that followed. In his developed form, as we find it in *Manfred,* he is an alien, mysterious, and gloomy spirit, superior in his passions and powers to the common run of humanity, whom he regards with disdain. He harbors the torturing memory of an enormous, nameless guilt that drives him toward an inevitable doom. And he exerts an attraction on other characters that is the more compelling because it involves their terror at his obliviousness to ordinary human concerns and values. This figure, infusing the archrebel in a nonpolitical form with a strong erotic interest, was imitated in life as well as in art and helped shape the intellectual and the cultural history of the later nineteenth century. The literary descendants of the Byronic hero include Heathcliff in *Wuthering Heights,* Captain Ahab in *Moby-Dick,* and the hero of Pushkin's great poem *Eugene Onegin.* Byron also lived on in the guise of the Undead, thanks to the success of a novella by his former friend and traveling companion John Polidori, whose "The Vampyre" (1819) mischievously made Byron its model for the title character. Earlier Byron had in his writings helped introduce the English to the Eastern Mediterranean's legends of bloodsucking evil spirits; it was left to Polidori, however, to portray the vampire as a habitué of England's most fashionable social circles. The fact that, for all their men-ace, vampires—from Bela Lugosi's Count Dracula to Anne Rice's L'Estat—remain models of well-dressed, aristocratic elegance represents yet another tribute to the staying power of Byron's image.

Byron's contemporaries insisted on identifying the author with his fictional char-acters, reading his writing as veiled autobiography even when it dealt with supernat-ural themes. (They also read other people's writing this way: to Polidori's chagrin, authorship of "The Vampyre" was attributed to Byron.) Byron's letters and the testi-mony of his friends show, however, that, except for recurrent moods of deep depres-sion, his own temperament was in many respects opposite to that of his heroes. While he was passionate and willful, he was also a witty conversationalist capable of taking an ironic attitude toward his own activities as well as those of others. But although Byronism was largely a fiction, produced by a collaboration between Byron's imagi-nation and that of his public, the fiction was historically more important than the actual person.

Byron was descended from two aristocratic families, both of them colorful, violent, and dissolute. His grandfather was an admiral nicknamed "Foulweather Jack"; his great-uncle was the fifth Baron Byron, known to his rural neighbors as the "Wicked Lord," who was tried by his peers for killing his kinsman William Chaworth in a drunken duel; his father, Captain John Byron, was a rake and fortune hunter who rapidly spent his way through the fortunes of two wealthy wives. Byron's mother was a Scotswoman, Catherine Gordon of Gight, the last descendant of a line of lawless Scottish lairds. After her husband died (Byron was then three), she brought up her son in near poverty in Aberdeen, where he was indoctrinated with the Calvinistic morality of Scottish Presbyterianism. Catherine Byron was an ill-educated and extremely irascible woman who nevertheless had an abiding love for her son; they fought violently when together, but corresponded affectionately enough when apart, until her death in 1811.

When Byron was ten the death of his great-uncle, preceded by that of more immediate heirs to the title, made him the sixth Lord Byron. In a fashion suitable to his new status, he was sent to Harrow School, then to Trinity College, Cambridge. He had a deformed foot, made worse by inept surgical treatment, about which he felt acute embarrassment. His lameness made him avid for athletic prowess; he played cricket and made himself an expert boxer, fencer, and horseman and a powerful swimmer. Both at Cambridge and at his ancestral estate of Newstead, he engaged with more than ordinary zeal in the expensive pursuits and fashionable dissipations of a young Regency lord. As a result, despite a sizable and increasing income, he got into financial difficulties from which he did not entirely extricate himself until late in his life. In the course of his schooling, he formed many close and devoted friendships, the most important with John Cam Hobhouse, a sturdy political liberal and commonsense moralist who exerted a steadying influence throughout Byron's turbulent life.

Despite his distractions at the university, Byron found time to try his hand at lyric verse, some of which was published in 1807 in a slim and conventional volume titled *Hours of Idleness*. This was treated so harshly by the *Edinburgh Review* that Byron was provoked to write in reply his first important poem, *English Bards and Scotch Reviewers*, a vigorous satire in which he incorporated brilliant ridicule (whose tactlessness he later came to regret) of important contemporaries, including Scott, Wordsworth, and Coleridge.

After attaining his M.A. degree and his legal independence from his guardians, Byron set out with Hobhouse in 1809 on a tour through Portugal and Spain to Malta, and then to little-known Albania, Greece, and Asia Minor. There, in the classic locale for Greek love, he encountered a culture that accepted sexual relations between older aristocratic men and beautiful boys, and he accumulated materials that, sometimes rather slyly, he incorporated into many of his important poems, including his last work, *Don Juan*. The first literary product was *Childe Harold*; he wrote the opening two cantos while on the tour that the poem describes; published them in 1812 soon after his return to England; and, in his own oft-quoted phrase, "awoke one morning and found myself famous." He became the celebrity of fashionable London, and increased his literary success with a series of highly readable Eastern tales; in these the Byronic hero, represented against various exotic backdrops as a "Giaour" (an "infidel" within Muslim society), or a "Corsair" (a pirate), or in other forms, flaunts his misanthropy and undergoes violent and romantic adventures that current gossip attributed to the author. In his chronic shortage of money, Byron could well have used the huge income from these publications, but instead maintained his status as an aristocratic amateur by giving the royalties away. Occupying his inherited seat in the House of Lords, he also became briefly active on the liberal side of the Whig party and spoke courageously in defense of the Nottingham weavers who had resorted to smashing the newly invented textile machines that had thrown them out of work. He also supported other liberal measures, including that of Catholic Emancipation.

Byron was extraordinarily handsome—"so beautiful a countenance," Coleridge wrote, "I scarcely ever saw . . . his eyes the open portals of the sun—things of light, and for light." Because of a constitutional tendency to obesity, however, he was able to maintain his looks only by resorting again and again to a starvation diet of biscuits, soda water, and strong purgatives. Often as a result of female initiative rather than his own, Byron entered into a sequence of liaisons with ladies of fashion. One of these, the flamboyant and eccentric young Lady Caroline Lamb, caused him so much distress by her pursuit that Byron turned for relief to marriage with Annabella Milbanke, who was in every way Lady Caroline's opposite, for she was unworldly and intellectual (with a special passion for mathematics) and naively believed that she could reform her husband. This ill-starred marriage produced a daughter (Augusta Ada) and many scenes in which Byron, goaded by financial difficulties, behaved so frantically that his wife suspected his sanity; after only one year the union ended in a legal separation. The final blow came when Lady Byron discovered her husband's incestuous relations with his half-sister, Augusta Leigh. The two had been raised apart, so that they were almost strangers when they met as adults. Byron's affection for his sister, however guilty, was genuine and endured all through his life. This affair, enhanced by rumors about Byron's earlier liaisons with men, proved a delicious morsel even to the jaded palate of a public that was used to eating up stories of aristocratic vice. Byron was ostracized by all but a few friends and was finally forced to leave England forever on April 25, 1816.

Byron now resumed the travels incorporated in the third and fourth cantos of *Childe Harold*. At Geneva he lived for several months in close and intellectually fruitful relation to Percy and Mary Shelley, who were accompanied by Mary's stepsister, Claire Clairmont—a misguided seventeen-year-old who had forced herself on Byron while he was still in England and who in January 1817 bore him a daughter, Allegra. In the fall of 1817, Byron established himself in Venice, where he began a year and a half of debauchery that, he estimated, involved liaisons with more than two hundred women. This period, however, was also one of great literary creativity. Often working through the night, he finished his tragedy *Manfred;* wrote the fourth canto of *Childe Harold;* and then, feeling more and more trapped by the poetic modes that had won him his popularity, tested out an entirely new mode in *Beppo: A Venetian Story,* a comic verse tale about a deceived husband in which he previewed the playful narrative manner and the ottava rima stanzas of *Don Juan.* In December 1818 he began the composition of *Don Juan.*

Exhausted and bored by promiscuity, Byron in 1819 settled into a placid and relatively faithful relationship with Teresa Guiccioli, the young wife of the elderly Count Alessandro Guiccioli; according to the Italian upper-class mores of the times, having contracted a marriage of convenience, she could now with some propriety take Byron as her lover. Through the countess's nationalistic family, the Gambas, Byron became involved with a group of political conspirators seeking to end the Austrian Empire's control over northern Italy. When the Gambas were forced by the authorities to move to Pisa, Byron followed them there and, for the second time, joined the Shelleys. There grew up about them the "Pisan Circle," which in addition to the Gambas included their friends Thomas Medwin and Edward and Jane Williams, as well as the Greek nationalist leader Prince Mavrocordatos, the picturesque Irish Count Taaffe, and the adventurer Edward Trelawny, a great teller of tall tales who seems to have stepped out of one of Byron's romances. Leigh Hunt, the journalist and essayist, joined them, drawing Byron and Percy Shelley into his plan to make Italy the base for a radical political journal, *The Liberal.* This circle was gradually broken up, however, first by the Shelleys' anger over Byron's treatment of his daughter Allegra (Byron had sent the child to be brought up as a Catholic in an Italian convent, where she died of a fever in 1822); then by the expulsion of the Gambas, whom Byron followed to Genoa; and finally by the drowning of Percy Shelley and Edward Williams in July 1822.

Byron meanwhile had been steadily at work on a series of closet tragedies (including *Cain, Sardanapalus,* and *Marino Faliero*) and on his devastating satire on the life and death of George III, *The Vision of Judgment.* But increasingly he devoted himself to the continuation of *Don Juan.* He had always been diffident in his self-judgments and easily swayed by literary advice. But now, confident that he had at last found his métier, he kept on, in spite of persistent objections against the supposed immorality of the poem by the English public, by his publisher John Murray, by his friends and well-wishers, and by his extremely decorous lover, the Countess Guiccioli—by almost everyone, in fact, except the idealist Shelley, who thought *Juan* incomparably better than anything he himself could write and insisted "that every word of it is pregnant with immortality."

Byron finally broke off literature for action when he organized an expedition to assist in the Greek war for independence from the Ottoman Empire. He knew too well the conditions in Greece, and had too skeptical an estimate of human nature, to entertain hope of success; but, in part because his own writings had helped kindle European enthusiasm for the Greek cause, he now felt honor-bound to try what could be done. In the dismal, marshy town of Missolonghi, he lived a Spartan existence, training troops whom he had subsidized and exhibiting practical grasp and a power of leadership amid a chaos of factionalism, intrigue, and military ineptitude. Worn out, he succumbed to a series of feverish attacks and died just after he had reached his thirty-sixth birthday. To this day Byron is revered by the Greek people as a national hero.

Students of Byron still feel, as his friends had felt, the magnetism of his volatile temperament. As Mary Shelley wrote six years after his death, when she read Thomas Moore's edition of his *Letters and Journals*: "The Lord Byron I find there is our Lord Byron—the fascinating—faulty—childish—philosophical being—daring the world—docile to a private circle—impetuous and indolent—gloomy and yet more gay than any other." Of his contradictions Byron was well aware; he told his friend Lady Blessington: "I am so changeable, being everything by turns and nothing long— I am such a strange *mélange* of good and evil, that it would be difficult to describe me." Yet he remained faithful to his code: a determination to tell the truth as he saw it about the world and about himself (his refusal to suppress or conceal any of his moods is in part what made him seem so contradictory) and a dedication to the freedom of nations and individuals. As he went on to say to Lady Blessington: "There are but two sentiments to which I am constant—a strong love of liberty, and a detestation of cant."

The poetry texts printed here are taken from Jerome J. McGann's edition, *Lord Byron: The Complete Poetical Works* (Oxford, 1980–93).

Written after Swimming from Sestos to Abydos[1]

May 9, 1810

1

If in the month of dark December
Leander, who was nightly wont
(What maid will not the tale remember?)
To cross thy stream, broad Hellespont!

2

5   If when the wintry tempest roared
He sped to Hero, nothing loth,
And thus of old thy current pour'd,
Fair Venus! how I pity both!

3

For *me*, degenerate modern wretch,
10   Though in the genial month of May,

---

1. The Hellespont (now called the Dardanelles) is the narrow strait between Europe and Asia. In the ancient story, retold in Christopher Marlowe's *Hero and Leander*, young Leander of Abydos, on the Asian side, swam nightly to visit Hero, a priestess of the goddess Venus at Sestos, until he was drowned when he made the attempt in a storm. Byron and a young Lieutenant Ekenhead swam the Hellespont in the reverse direction on May 3,

1810. Byron alternated between complacency and humor in his many references to the event. In a note to the poem, he mentions that the distance was "upwards of four English miles, though the actual breadth is barely one. The rapidity of the current is such that no boat can row directly across. . . . The water was extremely cold, from the melting of the mountain snows."

My dripping limbs I faintly stretch,
    And think I've done a feat to-day.

4

But since he cross'd the rapid tide,
    According to the doubtful story,
15 To woo,—and—Lord knows what beside,
    And swam for Love, as I for Glory;

5

'Twere hard to say who fared the best:
    Sad mortals! thus the Gods still plague you!
He lost his labour, I my jest:
20 For he was drown'd, and I've the ague.

1810   1812

She walks in beauty[1]

1

She walks in beauty, like the night
    Of cloudless climes and starry skies;
And all that's best of dark and bright
    Meet in her aspect and her eyes:
5 Thus mellow'd to that tender light
    Which heaven to gaudy day denies.

2

One shade the more, one ray the less,
    Had half impair'd the nameless grace
Which waves in every raven tress,
10   Or softly lightens o'er her face;
Where thoughts serenely sweet express
    How pure, how dear their dwelling place.

3

And on that cheek, and o'er that brow,
    So soft, so calm, yet eloquent,
15 The smiles that win, the tints that glow,
    But tell of days in goodness spent,
A mind at peace with all below,
    A heart whose love is innocent!

June 1814   1815

---

1. From *Hebrew Melodies* (1815), a collection of
lyrics on Old Testament themes that Byron composed to accompany the musician Isaac Nathan's
settings of traditional synagogue chants. Byron
wrote these lines about his beautiful cousin by
marriage, Anne Wilmot, who at the ball where they
first met wore a black mourning gown brightened
with spangles. In their context as the opening
poem of *Hebrew Melodies*, the lines praise any one
of a number of Old Testament heroines. To hear
the poem sung to Nathan's music, consult Norton
Literature Online.

They say that Hope is happiness

Felix qui potuit rerum cognoscere causas.[1]
VIRGIL

1

They say that Hope is happiness—
But genuine Love must prize the past;
And Mem'ry wakes the thoughts that bless:
They rose the first—they set the last.

2

5   And all that mem'ry loves the most
Was once our only hope to be:
And all that hope adored and lost
Hath melted into memory.

3

Alas! it is delusion all—
10   The future cheats us from afar:
Nor can we be what we recall,
Nor dare we think on what we are.

1814   1829

When we two parted

1

When we two parted
In silence and tears,
Half broken-hearted
To sever for years,
5   Pale grew thy cheek and cold,
Colder thy kiss;
Truly that hour foretold
Sorrow to this.

2

The dew of the morning
10   Sunk chill on my brow—
It felt like the warning
Of what I feel now.
Thy vows are all broken,
And light is thy fame;
15   I hear thy name spoken,
And share in its shame.

3

They name thee before me,
A knell to mine ear;

1. Happy is he who has been able to learn the causes of things (Latin; *Georgics* 2.490).

A shudder comes o'er me—
20   Why wert thou so dear?
They know not I knew thee,
Who knew thee too well:—
Long, long shall I rue thee,
Too deeply to tell.

4

25   In secret we met—
In silence I grieve,
That thy heart could forget,
Thy spirit deceive.
If I should meet thee
30   After long years,
How should I greet thee!—
With silence and tears.

1815   1815

Stanzas for Music

There be none of Beauty's daughters
With a magic like thee;
And like music on the waters
Is thy sweet voice to me:
5   When, as if its sound were causing
The charmed ocean's pausing,
The waves lie still and gleaming,
And the lulled winds seem dreaming.

And the midnight moon is weaving
10   Her bright chain o'er the deep;
Whose breast is gently heaving,
As an infant's asleep.
So the spirit bows before thee,
To listen and adore thee;
15   With a full but soft emotion,
Like the swell of Summer's ocean.

1816   1816

Darkness[1]

I had a dream, which was not all a dream.
The bright sun was extinguish'd, and the stars
Did wander darkling° in the eternal space,   *in the dark*
Rayless, and pathless, and the icy earth

---

1. A powerful blank-verse description of the end of life on Earth. New geological sciences and an accompanying interest in what the fossil record indicated about the extinction of species made such speculations hardly less common in Byron's time than in ours. Mary Shelley would later take up the theme in her novel *The Last Man* (1826).

5 Swung blind and blackening in the moonless air;
 Morn came, and went—and came, and brought no day,
 And men forgot their passions in the dread
 Of this their desolation; and all hearts
 Were chill'd into a selfish prayer for light:
10 And they did live by watchfires—and the thrones,
 The palaces of crowned kings—the huts,
 The habitations of all things which dwell,
 Were burnt for beacons; cities were consumed,
 And men were gathered round their blazing homes
15 To look once more into each other's face;
 Happy were those who dwelt within the eye
 Of the volcanos, and their mountain-torch:
 A fearful hope was all the world contain'd;
 Forests were set on fire—but hour by hour
20 They fell and faded—and the crackling trunks
 Extinguish'd with a crash—and all was black.
 The brows of men by the despairing light
 Wore an unearthly aspect, as by fits
 The flashes fell upon them; some lay down
25 And hid their eyes and wept; and some did rest
 Their chins upon their clenched hands, and smiled;
 And others hurried to and fro, and fed
 Their funeral piles with fuel, and looked up
 With mad disquietude on the dull sky,
30 The pall of a past world; and then again
 With curses cast them down upon the dust,
 And gnash'd their teeth and howl'd: the wild birds shriek'd,
 And, terrified, did flutter on the ground,
 And flap their useless wings; the wildest brutes
35 Came tame and tremulous; and vipers crawl'd
 And twined themselves among the multitude,
 Hissing, but stingless—they were slain for food:
 And War, which for a moment was no more,
 Did glut himself again;—a meal was bought
40 With blood, and each sate sullenly apart
 Gorging himself in gloom: no love was left;
 All earth was but one thought—and that was death,
 Immediate and inglorious; and the pang
 Of famine fed upon all entrails—men
45 Died, and their bones were tombless as their flesh;
 The meagre by the meagre were devoured,
 Even dogs assail'd their masters, all save one,
 And he was faithful to a corse, and kept
 The birds and beasts and famish'd men at bay,
50 Till hunger clung° them, or the dropping dead   *withered*
 Lured their lank jaws; himself sought out no food,
 But with a piteous and perpetual moan,
 And a quick desolate cry, licking the hand
 Which answered not with a caress—he died.
55 The crowd was famish'd by degrees; but two
 Of an enormous city did survive,
 And they were enemies; they met beside
 The dying embers of an altar-place,

Where had been heap'd a mass of holy things
60   For an unholy usage; they raked up,
And shivering scraped with their cold skeleton hands
The feeble ashes, and their feeble breath
Blew for a little life, and made a flame
Which was a mockery; then they lifted up
65   Their eyes as it grew lighter, and beheld
Each other's aspects—saw, and shriek'd, and died—
Even of their mutual hideousness they died,
Unknowing who he was upon whose brow
Famine had written Fiend. The world was void,
70   The populous and the powerful—was a lump,
Seasonless, herbless,° treeless, manless, lifeless—   *without vegetation*
A lump of death—a chaos of hard clay.
The rivers, lakes, and ocean all stood still,
And nothing stirred within their silent depths;
75   Ships sailorless lay rotting on the sea,
And their masts fell down piecemeal; as they dropp'd
They slept on the abyss without a surge—
The waves were dead; the tides were in their grave,
The moon their mistress had expired before;
80   The winds were withered in the stagnant air,
And the clouds perish'd; Darkness had no need
Of aid from them—She was the universe.

1816   1816

So, we'll go no more a roving[1]

1

So, we'll go no more a roving
    So late into the night,
Though the heart be still as loving,
    And the moon be still as bright.

2

5   For the sword outwears its sheath,
    And the soul wears out the breast,
And the heart must pause to breathe,
    And love itself have rest.

3

Though the night was made for loving,
10   And the day returns too soon,
Yet we'll go no more a roving
    By the light of the moon.

1817   1830

1. Composed in the Lenten aftermath of a period of late-night carousing during the Carnival season in Venice, and included in a letter to Thomas Moore, February 28, 1817. Byron wrote, "I find 'the sword wearing out the scabbard,' though I have but just turned the corner of twenty-nine." The poem is based on the refrain of a bawdy Scottish song, "The Jolly Beggar": "And we'll gang nae mair a roving / Sae late into the nicht."

Childe Harold's Pilgrimage

Childe Harold is a travelogue narrated by a melancholy, passionate, well-read, and very eloquent tourist. Byron wrote most of the first two cantos while on the tour through Spain, Portugal, Albania, and Greece that these cantos describe. When he published them, in 1812, they made him at one stroke the best-known and most talked about poet in England. Byron took up *Childe Harold* again in 1816, during the European tour he made after the breakup of his marriage. Canto 3, published in 1816, moves through Belgium, up the Rhine, then to Switzerland and the Alps. Canto 4, published in 1818, describes Italy's great cities, in particular their ruins and museums and the stories these tell of the bygone glories of the Roman Empire.

Byron chose for his poem the Spenserian stanza, and like James Thomson (in *The Castle of Indolence*) and other eighteenth-century predecessors, he attempted in the first canto to imitate, in a seriocomic fashion, the archaic language of his Elizabethan model. (*Childe* is the ancient term for a young noble awaiting knighthood.) But he soon dropped the archaisms, and in the last two cantos he confidently adapts Spenser's mellifluous stanza to his own autobiographical and polemical purposes. The virtuoso range of moods and subjects in *Childe Harold* was a quality on which contemporaries commented admiringly. Equally fascinating is the tension between the body of the poem and the long notes (for the most part omitted here) that Byron appended to its sometimes dashing and sometimes sorrowing chronicle of his pilgrimage in the countries of chivalry and romance—notes that feature cosmopolitan reflections on the contrasts among cultures as well as sardonic, hard-hitting critiques of the evolving political order of Europe.

In the preface to his first two cantos, Byron had insisted that the narrator, Childe Harold, was "a fictitious character," merely "the child of imagination." In the manuscript version of these cantos, however, he had called his hero "Childe Burun," the early form of his own family name. The world insisted on identifying the character as well as the travels of the protagonist with those of the author, and in the fourth canto Byron, abandoning the third-person *dramatis persona,* spoke out frankly in the first person. In the preface to that canto, he declares that there will be "less of the pilgrim" here than in any of the preceding cantos, "and that little slightly, if at all, separated from the author speaking in his own person. The fact is, that I had become weary of drawing a line which every one seemed determined not to perceive."

FROM CHILDE HAROLD'S PILGRIMAGE

A ROMAUNT[1]

From Canto 1

["SIN'S LONG LABYRINTH"]

I

Oh, thou! in Hellas° deem'd of heav'nly birth,   *Greece*
Muse! form'd or fabled at the minstrel's will!
Since sham'd full oft by later lyres on earth,
Mine dares not call thee from thy sacred hill:
5 Yet there I've wander'd by thy vaunted rill;

---

1. A romance or narrative of adventure.

Yes! sigh'd o'er Delphi's long-deserted shrine,
Where, save that feeble fountain, all is still;
Nor mote° my shell awake the weary Nine[2]   *may*
To grace so plain a tale—this lowly lay° of mine.   *song*

2

10   Whilome[3] in Albion's° isle there dwelt a youth,   *England's*
Who ne in virtue's ways did take delight;
But spent his days in riot most uncouth,
And vex'd with mirth the drowsy ear of Night.
Ah, me! in sooth he was a shameless wight,°   *creature*
15   Sore given to revel and ungodly glee;
Few earthly things found favour in his sight
Save concubines and carnal companie,
And flaunting wassailers[4] of high and low degree.

3

Childe Harold was he hight:°—but whence his name   *called*
20   And lineage long, it suits me not to say;
Suffice it, that perchance they were of fame,
And had been glorious in another day:
But one sad losel[5] soils a name for aye,
However mighty in the olden time;
25   Nor all that heralds rake from coffin'd clay,
Nor florid prose, nor honied lies of rhyme
Can blazon evil deeds, or consecrate a crime.

4

Childe Harold bask'd him in the noon-tide sun,
Disporting there like any other fly;
30   Nor deem'd before his little day was done
One blast might chill him into misery.
But long ere scarce a third of his pass'd by,
Worse than adversity the Childe befell;
He felt the fulness of satiety:
35   Then loath'd he in his native land to dwell,
Which seem'd to him more lone than Eremite's[6] sad cell.

5

For he through Sin's long labyrinth had run,
Nor made atonement when he did amiss,
Had sigh'd to many though he lov'd but one,
40   And that lov'd one, alas! could ne'er be his.
Ah, happy she! to 'scape from him whose kiss
Had been pollution unto aught so chaste;
Who soon had left her charms for vulgar bliss,
And spoil'd her goodly lands to gild his waste,
45   Nor calm domestic peace had ever deign'd to taste.

2. The Muses, whose "vaunted rill" (line 5) was the Castalian spring. "Shell": lyre. Hermes is fabled to have invented the lyre by stretching strings over the hollow of a tortoise shell.
3. Once upon a time; one of the many archaisms that Byron borrowed from Spenser.
4. Noisy, insolent drinkers (Byron is thought to refer to his own youthful carousing with friends at Newstead Abbey).
5. Rascal. Byron's great-uncle, the fifth Lord Byron, had killed a kinsman in a drunken duel.
6. A religious hermit.

6

And now Childe Harold was sore sick at heart,
And from his fellow bacchanals would flee;
'Tis said, at times the sullen tear would start,
But Pride congeal'd the drop within his ee:°   *eye*
50   Apart he stalk'd in joyless reverie,
And from his native land resolv'd to go,
And visit scorching climes beyond the sea;
With pleasure drugg'd he almost long'd for woe,
And e'en for change of scene would seek the shades below.

From Canto 3

["ONCE MORE UPON THE WATERS"]

1

Is thy face like thy mother's, my fair child!
Ada![1] sole daughter of my house and heart?
When last I saw thy young blue eyes they smiled,
And then we parted,—not as now we part,
5   But with a hope.—
                    Awaking with a start,
The waters heave around me; and on high
The winds lift up their voices: I depart,
Whither I know not; but the hour's gone by,
When Albion's lessening shores could grieve or glad mine eye.

2

10   Once more upon the waters! yet once more!
And the waves bound beneath me as a steed
That knows his rider. Welcome, to their roar!
Swift be their guidance, wheresoe'er it lead!
Though the strain'd mast should quiver as a reed,
15   And the rent canvas fluttering strew the gale,
Still must I on; for I am as a weed,
Flung from the rock, on Ocean's foam, to sail
Where'er the surge may sweep, the tempest's breath prevail.

3

In my youth's summer[2] I did sing of One,
20   The wandering outlaw of his own dark mind;
Again I seize the theme then but begun,
And bear it with me, as the rushing wind
Bears the cloud onwards: in that Tale I find
The furrows of long thought, and dried-up tears,
25   Which, ebbing, leave a sterile track behind,
O'er which all heavily the journeying years
Plod the last sands of life,—where not a flower appears.

---

1. Byron's daughter Augusta Ada, born in December 1815, a month before her parents separated. Byron's "hope" (line 5) had been for a reconciliation, but he was never to see Ada again.
2. Byron wrote canto 1 at age twenty-one; he is now twenty-eight.

4

Since my young days of passion—joy, or pain,
Perchance my heart and harp have lost a string,
30   And both may jar:[3] it may be, that in vain
I would essay as I have sung to sing.
Yet, though a dreary strain, to this I cling;
So that it wean me from the weary dream
Of selfish grief or gladness—so it fling
35   Forgetfulness around me—it shall seem
To me, though to none else, a not ungrateful theme.

5

He, who grown aged in this world of woe,
In deeds, not years, piercing the depths of life,
So that no wonder waits him; nor below
40   Can love, or sorrow, fame, ambition, strife,
Cut to his heart again with the keen knife
Of silent, sharp endurance: he can tell
Why thought seeks refuge in lone caves, yet rife
With airy images, and shapes which dwell
45   Still unimpair'd, though old, in the soul's haunted cell.

6

'Tis to create, and in creating live
A being more intense, that we endow
With form our fancy, gaining as we give
The life we image, even as I do now.
50   What am I? Nothing; but not so art thou,
Soul of my thought![4] with whom I traverse earth,
Invisible but gazing, as I glow
Mix'd with thy spirit, blended with thy birth,
And feeling still with thee in my crush'd feelings' dearth.

7

55   Yet must I think less wildly:—I *have* thought
Too long and darkly, till my brain became,
In its own eddy boiling and o'erwrought,
A whirling gulf of phantasy and flame:
And thus, untaught in youth my heart to tame,
60   My springs of life were poison'd. 'Tis too late!
Yet am I chang'd; though still enough the same
In strength to bear what time can not abate,
And feed on bitter fruits without accusing Fate.

8

Something too much of this:—but now 'tis past,
65   And the spell closes with its silent seal.[5]
Long absent HAROLD re-appears at last;
He of the breast which fain no more would feel,
Wrung with the wounds which kill not, but ne'er heal;
Yet Time, who changes all, had alter'd him

---

3. Sound discordant.
4. I.e., Childe Harold, his literary creation.

5. I.e., he sets the seal of silence on his personal
tale ("spell").

70 In soul and aspect as in age: years steal
Fire from the mind as vigour from the limb;
And life's enchanted cup but sparkles near the brim.

9

His had been quaff'd too quickly, and he found
The dregs were wormwood; but he fill'd again,
75 And from a purer fount, on holier ground,
And deem'd its spring perpetual; but in vain!
Still round him clung invisibly a chain
Which gall'd for ever, fettering though unseen,
And heavy though it clank'd not; worn with pain,
80 Which pined although it spoke not, and grew keen,
Entering with every step, he took, through many a scene.

10

Secure in guarded coldness, he had mix'd
Again in fancied safety with his kind,
And deem'd his spirit now so firmly fix'd
85 And sheath'd with an invulnerable mind,
That, if no joy, no sorrow lurk'd behind;
And he, as one, might midst the many stand
Unheeded, searching through the crowd to find
Fit speculation! such as in strange land
90 He found in wonder-works of God and Nature's hand.

11

But who can view the ripened rose, nor seek
To wear it? who can curiously behold
The smoothness and the sheen of beauty's cheek,
Nor feel the heart can never all grow old?
95 Who can contemplate Fame through clouds unfold
The star which rises o'er her steep, nor climb?
Harold, once more within the vortex, roll'd
On with the giddy circle, chasing Time,
Yet with a nobler aim than in his youth's fond° prime.   *foolish*

12

100 But soon he knew himself the most unfit
Of men to herd with Man; with whom he held
Little in common; untaught to submit
His thoughts to others, though his soul was quell'd
In youth by his own thoughts; still uncompell'd,
105 He would not yield dominion of his mind
To spirits against whom his own rebell'd;
Proud though in desolation; which could find
A life within itself, to breathe without mankind.

13

Where rose the mountains, there to him were friends;
110 Where roll'd the ocean, thereon was his home;
Where a blue sky, and glowing clime, extends,
He had the passion and the power to roam;
The desert, forest, cavern, breaker's foam,

Were unto him companionship; they spake
115   A mutual language, clearer than the tome°   *book*
Of his land's tongue, which he would oft forsake
For Nature's pages glass'd° by sunbeams on the lake.   *made glassy*

14

Like the Chaldean,[6] he could watch the stars,
Till he had peopled them with beings bright
120   As their own beams; and earth, and earth-born jars,
And human frailties, were forgotten quite:
Could he have kept his spirit to that flight
He had been happy; but this clay will sink
Its spark immortal, envying it the light
125   To which it mounts, as if to break the link
That keeps us from yon heaven which woos us to its brink.

15

But in Man's dwellings he became a thing
Restless and worn, and stern and wearisome,
Droop'd as a wild-born falcon with clipt wing,
130   To whom the boundless air alone were home:
Then came his fit again, which to o'ercome,
As eagerly the barr'd-up bird will beat
His breast and beak against his wiry dome
Till the blood tinge his plumage, so the heat
135   Of his impeded soul would through his bosom eat.

16

Self-exiled Harold wanders forth again,
With nought of hope left, but with less of gloom;
The very knowledge that he lived in vain,
That all was over on this side the tomb,
140   Had made Despair a smilingness assume,
Which, though 'twere wild,—as on the plundered wreck
When mariners would madly meet their doom
With draughts intemperate on the sinking deck,—
Did yet inspire a cheer, which he forbore to check.

[WATERLOO]

17

145   Stop!—for thy tread is on an Empire's dust!
An Earthquake's spoil is sepulchered below!
Is the spot mark'd with no colossal bust?
Nor column trophied for triumphal show?[7]
None; but the moral's truth tells simpler so,
150   As the ground was before, thus let it be;—
How that red rain hath made the harvest grow!
And is this all the world has gained by thee,
Thou first and last of fields! king-making Victory?

6. A people of ancient Babylonia, expert in astronomy.
7. Referring to the triumphal arches erected in
ancient Rome to honor conquering generals, a custom Napoleon had revived.

18

And Harold stands upon this place of skulls,
155 The grave of France, the deadly Waterloo![8]
How in an hour the power which gave annuls
Its gifts, transferring fame as fleeting too!
In "pride of place" here last the eagle flew,[9]
Then tore with bloody talon the rent plain,
160 Pierced by the shaft of banded nations[1] through;
Ambition's life and labours all were vain;
He wears the shattered links of the world's broken chain.[2]

19

Fit retribution! Gaul[3] may champ the bit
And foam in fetters;—but is Earth more free?
165 Did nations combat to make *One* submit;
Or league to teach all kings true sovereignty?
What! shall reviving Thraldom again be
The patched-up idol of enlightened days?
Shall we, who struck the Lion down, shall we
170 Pay the Wolf homage? proffering lowly gaze
And servile knees to thrones? No; *prove*[4] before ye praise!

20

If not, o'er one fallen despot boast no more!
In vain fair cheeks were furrowed with hot tears
For Europe's flowers long rooted up before
175 The trampler of her vineyards; in vain years
Of death, depopulation, bondage, fears,
Have all been borne, and broken by the accord
Of roused-up millions: all that most endears
Glory, is when the myrtle wreathes a sword
180 Such as Harmodius drew on Athens' tyrant lord.[5]

21

There was a sound of revelry by night,[6]
And Belgium's capital had gathered then
Her Beauty and her Chivalry, and bright
The lamps shone o'er fair women and brave men;
185 A thousand hearts beat happily; and when
Music arose with its voluptuous swell,
Soft eyes look'd love to eyes which spake again,
And all went merry as a marriage-bell;
But hush! hark! a deep sound strikes like a rising knell!

8. Napoleon's defeat at Waterloo, near Brussels, had occurred only the year before, on June 18, 1815. The battlefield, where almost fifty thousand English, Prussian, and French soldiers were killed in a single day, quickly became a gruesome tourist attraction.
9. "Pride of place," is a term of falconry, and means the highest pitch of flight [Byron's note, which continues by referring to the use of the term in Shakespeare's *Macbeth* 2.4]. The eagle was the symbol of Napoleon.
1. The Grand Alliance formed in opposition to Napoleon.

2. Napoleon was then a prisoner at St. Helena.
3. France. Byron, like other liberals, saw the defeat of the Napoleonic tyranny as a victory for tyrannical kings and the forces of reaction throughout Europe.
4. Await the test (proof) of experience.
5. In 514 B.C.E. Harmodius and Aristogeiton, hiding their daggers in myrtle (symbol of love), killed Hipparchus, tyrant of Athens.
6. A famous ball, given by the duchess of Richmond on the eve of the battle of Quatre Bras, which opened the conflict at Waterloo.

22

190 Did ye not hear it?—No; 'twas but the wind,
Or the car rattling o'er the stony street;
On with the dance! let joy be unconfined;
No sleep till morn, when Youth and Pleasure meet
To chase the glowing Hours with flying feet—
195 But, hark!—that heavy sound breaks in once more,
As if the clouds its echo would repeat;
And nearer, clearer, deadlier than before!
Arm! Arm! and out—it is—the cannon's opening roar!

23

Within a windowed niche of that high hall
200 Sate Brunswick's fated chieftain;[7] he did hear
That sound the first amidst the festival,
And caught its tone with Death's prophetic ear;
And when they smiled because he deem'd it near,
His heart more truly knew that peal too well
205 Which stretch'd his father on a bloody bier,
And roused the vengeance blood alone could quell:
He rush'd into the field, and, foremost fighting, fell.

24

Ah! then and there was hurrying to and fro,
And gathering tears, and tremblings of distress,
210 And cheeks all pale, which but an hour ago
Blush'd at the praise of their own loveliness;
And there were sudden partings, such as press
The life from out young hearts, and choking sighs
Which ne'er might be repeated; who could guess
215 If ever more should meet those mutual eyes,
Since upon nights so sweet such awful morn could rise?

25

And there was mounting in hot haste: the steed,
The mustering squadron, and the clattering car,
Went pouring forward in impetuous speed,
220 And swiftly forming in the ranks of war;
And the deep thunder peal on peal afar;
And near, the beat of the alarming drum
Roused up the soldier ere the morning star;
While throng'd the citizens with terror dumb,
225 Or whispering, with white lips—"The foe! They come! they come!"

26

And wild and high the "Cameron's gathering" rose!
The war-note of Lochiel,[8] which Albyn's° hills   *Scotland's*
Have heard, and heard, too, have her Saxon foes:—
How in the noon of night that pibroch[9] thrills,

---

7. The duke of Brunswick, nephew of George III
of England, was killed in the battle of Quatre Bras.
His father, commanding the Prussian army against
Napoleon, had been killed at Auerstedt in 1806
(line 205).

8. "Cameron's gathering" is the clan song of the
Camerons, whose chief was called "Lochiel," after
his estate.
9. Bagpipe music, usually warlike in character.

230 Savage and shrill! But with the breath which fills
Their mountain-pipe, so fill the mountaineers
With the fierce native daring which instils
The stirring memory of a thousand years,
And Evan's, Donald's[1] fame rings in each clansman's ears!

27

235 And Ardennes[2] waves above them her green leaves,
Dewy with nature's tear-drops, as they pass,
Grieving, if aught inanimate e'er grieves,
Over the unreturning brave,—alas!
Ere evening to be trodden like the grass
240 Which now beneath them, but above shall grow
In its next verdure, when this fiery mass
Of living valour, rolling on the foe
And burning with high hope, shall moulder cold and low.

28

Last noon beheld them full of lusty life,
245 Last eve in Beauty's circle proudly gay,
The midnight brought the signal-sound of strife,
The morn the marshalling in arms,—the day
Battle's magnificently-stern array!
The thunder-clouds close o'er it, which when rent
250 The earth is covered thick with other clay,
Which her own clay shall cover, heaped and pent,
Rider and horse,—friend, foe,—in one red burial blent!

＊　＊　＊

[NAPOLEON]

36

There sunk the greatest, nor the worst of men,[3]
Whose spirit antithetically mixt
One moment of the mightiest, and again
On little objects with like firmness fixt,
320 Extreme in all things! hadst thou been betwixt,
Thy throne had still been thine, or never been;
For daring made thy rise as fall: thou seek'st
Even now to re-assume the imperial mien,°   character
And shake again the world, the Thunderer of the scene!

37

325 Conqueror and captive of the earth art thou!
She trembles at thee still, and thy wild name
Was ne'er more bruited in men's minds than now
That thou art nothing, save the jest of Fame,

1. Sir Evan and Donald Cameron, famous warriors in the Stuart cause in the Jacobite risings of 1689 and 1745.
2. The wood of Soignes is supposed to be a remnant of the "forest of Ardennes" famous in Boiardo's Orlando, and immortal in Shakespeare's As You Like It. It is also celebrated in Tacitus as being the spot of successful defence by the Germans against the Roman encroachments—I have ventured to adopt the name connected with nobler associations than those of mere slaughter [Byron's note]. Orlando Innamorato is a 15th-century Italian epic of love and adventure.
3. Napoleon, here portrayed with many characteristics of the Byronic hero.

Who wooed thee once, thy vassal, and became
330   The flatterer of thy fierceness, till thou wert
A god unto thyself; nor less the same
To the astounded kingdoms all inert,
Who deem'd thee for a time whate'er thou didst assert.

38

Oh, more or less than man—in high or low,
335   Battling with nations, flying from the field;
Now making monarchs' necks thy footstool, now
More than thy meanest° soldier taught to yield;   *lowest*
An empire thou couldst crush, command, rebuild,
But govern not thy pettiest passion, nor,
340   However deeply in men's spirits skill'd,
Look through thine own, nor curb the lust of war,
Nor learn that tempted Fate will leave the loftiest star.

39

Yet well thy soul hath brook'd the turning tide
With that untaught innate philosophy,
345   Which, be it wisdom, coldness, or deep pride,
Is gall and wormwood to an enemy.
When the whole host of hatred stood hard by,
To watch and mock thee shrinking, thou hast smiled
With a sedate and all-enduring eye;—
350   When Fortune fled her spoil'd and favourite child,
He stood unbowed beneath the ills upon him piled.

40

Sager than in thy fortunes; for in them
Ambition steel'd thee on too far to show
That just habitual scorn which could contemn
355   Men and their thoughts; 'twas wise to feel, not so
To wear it ever on thy lip and brow,
And spurn the instruments thou wert to use
Till they were turn'd unto thine overthrow:
'Tis but a worthless world to win or lose;
360   So hath it proved to thee, and all such lot who choose.[4]

41

If, like a tower upon a headlong rock,
Thou hadst been made to stand or fall alone,
Such scorn of man had help'd to brave the shock;
But men's thoughts were the steps which paved thy throne,
365   *Their* admiration thy best weapon shone;
The part of Philip's son[5] was thine, not then
(Unless aside thy purple had been thrown)
Like stern Diogenes[6] to mock at men;
For sceptred cynics earth were far too wide a den.

4. An inversion: "all who choose such lot" (i.e., who choose to play such a game of chance).
5. Alexander the Great, son of Philip of Macedon.
6. The Greek philosopher of Cynicism, contem- porary of Alexander. It is related that Alexander was so struck by his independence of mind that he said, "If I were not Alexander, I should wish to be Diogenes."

42

370   But quiet to quick bosoms is a hell,
And *there* hath been thy bane; there is a fire
And motion of the soul which will not dwell
In its own narrow being, but aspire
Beyond the fitting medium of desire;
375   And, but once kindled, quenchless evermore,
Preys upon high adventure, nor can tire
Of aught but rest; a fever at the core,
Fatal to him who bears, to all who ever bore.

43

This makes the madmen who have made men mad
380   By their contagion; Conquerors and Kings,
Founders of sects and systems, to whom add
Sophists,[7] Bards, Statesmen, all unquiet things
Which stir too strongly the soul's secret springs,
And are themselves the fools to those they fool;
385   Envied, yet how unenviable! what stings
Are theirs! One breast laid open were a school
Which would unteach mankind the lust to shine or rule:

44

Their breath is agitation, and their life
A storm whereon they ride, to sink at last,
390   And yet so nurs'd and bigotted to strife,
That should their days, surviving perils past,
Melt to calm twilight, they feel overcast
With sorrow and supineness, and so die;
Even as a flame unfed, which runs to waste
395   With its own flickering, or a sword laid by
Which eats into itself, and rusts ingloriously.

45

He who ascends to mountain-tops, shall find
The loftiest peaks most wrapt in clouds and snow;
He who surpasses or subdues mankind,
400   Must look down on the hate of those below.
Though high *above* the sun of glory glow,
And far *beneath* the earth and ocean spread,
Round him are icy rocks, and loudly blow
Contending tempests on his naked head,
405 And thus reward the toils which to those summits led.[8]

✼   ✼   ✼

52

460   Thus Harold inly said, and pass'd along,
Yet not insensibly to all which here

---

7. Learned men. But the term often carries a derogatory sense—thinkers with a penchant for tricky reasoning.

8. In the stanzas here omitted, Harold is sent sailing up the Rhine, meditating on the "thousand battles" that "have assailed thy banks."

Awoke the jocund birds to early song
In glens which might have made even exile dear:
Though on his brow were graven lines austere,
465   And tranquil sternness which had ta'en the place
Of feelings fierier far but less severe,
Joy was not always absent from his face,
But o'er it in such scenes would steal with transient trace.

53

Nor was all love shut from him, though his days
470   Of passion had consumed themselves to dust.
It is in vain that we would coldly gaze
On such as smile upon us; the heart must
Leap kindly back to kindness, though disgust
Hath wean'd it from all worldlings: thus he felt,
475   For there was soft remembrance, and sweet trust
In one fond breast,[9] to which his own would melt,
And in its tenderer hour on that his bosom dwelt.

54

And he had learn'd to love,—I know not why,
For this in such as him seems strange of mood,—
480   The helpless looks of blooming infancy,
Even in its earliest nurture; what subdued,
To change like this, a mind so far imbued
With scorn of man, it little boots to know;
But thus it was; and though in solitude
485   Small power the nipp'd affections have to grow,
In him this glowed when all beside had ceased to glow.

55

And there was one soft breast, as hath been said,
Which unto his was bound by stronger ties
Than the church links withal; and, though unwed,
490   *That* love was pure, and, far above disguise,
Had stood the test of mortal enmities
Still undivided, and cemented more
By peril, dreaded most in female eyes;
But this was firm, and from a foreign shore
495   Well to that heart might his these absent greetings pour!

✻   ✻   ✻

[SWITZERLAND][1]

68

Lake Leman° woos me with its crystal face,   *Geneva*
645   The mirror where the stars and mountains view

---

9. Commentators agree that the reference is to Byron's half-sister, Augusta Leigh.
1. Byron with his traveling companion and physician, John Polidori, spent the gloomy summer of 1816 near Geneva, in a villa rented for its proximity to the household that Percy Shelley, Mary Wollstonecraft Godwin (who would marry Shelley at the end of the year), and her half-sister Claire Clairmont had set up there. The famous ghost-story-telling contest in which these five participated, and which saw the genesis of both *Frankenstein* and Polidori's "The Vampyre," took place that June. The Shelley household's involvement in *Childe Harold* is extensive. The fair copy of this canto was in fact written out by Claire, and Percy would eventually deliver it to Byron's publisher in London.

The stillness of their aspect in each trace
Its clear depth yields of their far height and hue:
There is too much of man here, to look through
With a fit mind the might which I behold;
650   But soon in me shall Loneliness renew
Thoughts hid, but not less cherish'd than of old,
Ere mingling with the herd had penn'd me in their fold.

69

To fly from, need not be to hate, mankind;
All are not fit with them to stir and toil,
655   Nor is it discontent to keep the mind
Deep in its fountain, lest it overboil
In the hot throng, where we become the spoil
Of our infection, till too late and long
We may deplore and struggle with the coil,°   tumult
660   In wretched interchange of wrong for wrong
'Midst a contentious world, striving where none are strong.

70

There, in a moment, we may plunge our years
In fatal penitence, and in the blight
Of our own soul, turn all our blood to tears,
665   And colour things to come with hues of Night;
The race of life becomes a hopeless flight
To those that walk in darkness: on the sea,
The boldest steer but where their ports invite,
But there are wanderers o'er Eternity
670   Whose bark drives on and on, and anchored ne'er shall be.

71

Is it not better, then, to be alone,
And love Earth only for its earthly sake?
By the blue rushing of the arrowy Rhone,[2]
Or the pure bosom of its nursing lake,
675   Which feeds it as a mother who doth make
A fair but froward infant her own care,
Kissing its cries away as these awake;—
Is it not better thus our lives to wear,
Than join the crushing crowd, doom'd to inflict or bear?

72

680   I live not in myself, but I become
Portion of that around me; and to me,
High mountains are a feeling, but the hum
Of human cities torture: I can see
Nothing to loathe in nature, save to be
685   A link reluctant in a fleshly chain,
Class'd among creatures, when the soul can flee,
And with the sky, the peak, the heaving plain
Of ocean, or the stars, mingle, and not in vain.[3]

2. River rising in Switzerland and flowing through
France into the Mediterranean.
3. During the tour around Lake Geneva that they
took in late June 1816, Percy Shelley introduced

Byron to the poetry of Wordsworth and Wordsworth's concepts of nature. Those ideas are
reflected in canto 3, but the voice is Byron's own.
For his comment on being "half mad" while writing

73

And thus I am absorb'd, and this is life:
690   I look upon the peopled desart past,
As on a place of agony and strife,
Where, for some sin, to Sorrow I was cast,
To act and suffer, but remount at last
With a fresh pinion; which I feel to spring,
695   Though young, yet waxing vigorous, as the blast
Which it would cope with, on delighted wing,
Spurning the clay-cold bonds which round our being cling.

74

And when, at length, the mind shall be all free
From what it hates in this degraded form,
700   Reft of its carnal life, save what shall be
Existent happier in the fly and worm,—
When elements to elements conform,
And dust is as it should be, shall I not
Feel all I see, less dazzling, but more warm?
705   The bodiless thought? the Spirit of each spot?
Of which, even now, I share at times the immortal lot?

75

Are not the mountains, waves, and skies, a part
Of me and of my soul, as I of them?
Is not the love of these deep in my heart
710   With a pure passion? should I not contemn
All objects, if compared with these? and stem
A tide of suffering, rather than forego
Such feelings for the hard and worldly phlegm
Of those whose eyes are only turn'd below,
715   Gazing upon the ground, with thoughts which dare not glow?

76

But this is not my theme; and I return
To that which is immediate, and require
Those who find contemplation in the urn,[4]
To look on One,[5] whose dust was once all fire,
720   A native of the land where I respire
The clear air for a while—a passing guest,
Where he became a being,—whose desire
Was to be glorious; 'twas a foolish quest,
The which to gain and keep, he sacrificed all rest.

77

725   Here the self-torturing sophist, wild Rousseau,
The apostle of affliction, he who threw
Enchantment over passion, and from woe
Wrung overwhelming eloquence, first drew
The breath which made him wretched; yet he knew
730   How to make madness beautiful, and cast

canto 3, see his letter to Thomas Moore, January
28, 1817 (p. 736).
4. I.e., those who find matter for meditation in an
urn containing the ashes of the dead.

5. Jean-Jacques Rousseau, who had been born in
Geneva in 1712. Byron's characterization is based
on Rousseau's novel *La Nouvelle Héloise* and autobiographical *Confessions.*

O'er erring deeds and thoughts, a heavenly hue
Of words, like sunbeams, dazzling as they past
The eyes, which o'er them shed tears feelingly and fast.

78

His love was passion's essence—as a tree
735 On fire by lightning; with ethereal flame
Kindled he was, and blasted; for to be
Thus, and enamoured, were in him the same.
But his was not the love of living dame,
Nor of the dead who rise upon our dreams,
740 But of ideal beauty, which became
In him existence, and o'erflowing teems
Along his burning page, distempered though it seems.

* * *

85

Clear, placid Leman! thy contrasted lake,
With the wild world I dwelt in, is a thing
Which warns me, with its stillness, to forsake
800 Earth's troubled waters for a purer spring.
This quiet sail is as a noiseless wing
To waft me from distraction; once I loved
Torn ocean's roar, but thy soft murmuring
Sounds sweet as if a sister's voice reproved,
805 That I with stern delights should e'er have been so moved.

86

It is the hush of night, and all between
Thy margin and the mountains, dusk, yet clear,
Mellowed and mingling, yet distinctly seen,
Save darken'd Jura,[6] whose capt heights appear
810 Precipitously steep; and drawing near,
There breathes a living fragrance from the shore,
Of flowers yet fresh with childhood; on the ear
Drops the light drip of the suspended oar,
Or chirps the grasshopper one good-night carol more;

87

815 He is an evening reveller, who makes
His life an infancy, and sings his fill;
At intervals, some bird from out the brakes,°   thickets
Starts into voice a moment, then is still.
There seems a floating whisper on the hill,
820 But that is fancy, for the starlight dews
All silently their tears of love instil,
Weeping themselves away, till they infuse
Deep into Nature's breast the spirit of her hues.

88

Ye stars! which are the poetry of heaven!
825 If in your bright leaves we would read the fate

6. The mountain range between Switzerland and France, visible from Lake Geneva.

Of men and empires,—'tis to be forgiven,
That in our aspirations to be great,
Our destinies o'erleap their mortal state,
And claim a kindred with you; for ye are
A beauty and a mystery, and create
In us such love and reverence from afar,
That fortune, fame, power, life, have named themselves a star.

830

89

All heaven and earth are still—though not in sleep,
But breathless, as we grow when feeling most;
And silent, as we stand in thoughts too deep:—
All heaven and earth are still: From the high host
Of stars, to the lull'd lake and mountain-coast,
All is concentered in a life intense,
Where not a beam, nor air, nor leaf is lost,
But hath a part of being, and a sense
Of that which is of all Creator and defence.

835

840

90

Then stirs the feeling infinite, so felt
In solitude, where we are *least* alone;
A truth, which through our being then doth melt
And purifies from self: it is a tone,
The soul and source of music, which makes known
Eternal harmony, and sheds a charm,
Like to the fabled Cytherea's zone,[7]
Binding all things with beauty;—'twould disarm
The spectre Death, had he substantial power to harm.

845

850

91

Not vainly did the early Persian make
His altar the high places and the peak
Of earth-o'ergazing mountains, and thus take[8]
A fit and unwall'd temple, there to seek
The Spirit, in whose honour shrines are weak,
Uprear'd of human hands. Come, and compare
Columns and idol-dwellings, Goth or Greek,
With Nature's realms of worship, earth and air,
Nor fix on fond abodes to circumscribe thy prayer!

855

92

The sky is changed!—and such a change! Oh night,
And storm, and darkness, ye are wondrous strong,
Yet lovely in your strength, as is the light
Of a dark eye in woman! Far along,
From peak to peak, the rattling crags among
Leaps the live thunder! Not from one lone cloud,
But every mountain now hath found a tongue,
And Jura answers, through her misty shroud,
Back to the joyous Alps, who call to her aloud!

860

865

7. The sash of Venus, which conferred the power to attract love.
8. It is to be recollected, that the most beautiful and impressive doctrines of the Founder of Christianity were delivered, not in the *Temple*, but on the *Mount* [Byron's note].

93

And this is in the night:—Most glorious night!
870 Thou wert not sent for slumber! let me be
A sharer in thy fierce and far delight,—
A portion of the tempest and of thee!
How the lit lake shines, a phosphoric sea,
And the big rain comes dancing to the earth!
875 And now again 'tis black,—and now, the glee
Of the loud hills shakes with its mountain-mirth,
As if they did rejoice o'er a young earthquake's birth.

94

Now, where the swift Rhone cleaves his way between
Heights which appear as lovers who have parted
880 In hate, whose mining depths so intervene,
That they can meet no more, though broken-hearted;
Though in their souls, which thus each other thwarted,
Love was the very root of the fond rage
Which blighted their life's bloom, and then departed:—
885 Itself expired, but leaving them an age
Of years all winters,—war within themselves to wage.

95

Now, where the quick Rhone thus hath cleft his way,
The mightiest of the storms hath ta'en his stand:
For here, not one, but many, make their play,
890 And fling their thunder-bolts from hand to hand,
Flashing and cast around: of all the band,
The brightest through these parted hills hath fork'd
His lightnings,—as if he did understand,
That in such gaps as desolation work'd,
895 There the hot shaft should blast whatever therein lurk'd.

96

Sky, mountains, river, winds, lake, lightnings! ye!
With night, and clouds, and thunder, and a soul
To make these felt and feeling, well may be
Things that have made me watchful; the far roll
900 Of your departing voices, is the knoll[9]
Of what in me is sleepless,—if I rest.
But where of ye, oh tempests! is the goal?
Are ye like those within the human breast?
Or do ye find, at length, like eagles, some high nest?

97

905 Could I embody and unbosom now
That which is most within me,—could I wreak
My thoughts upon expression, and thus throw
Soul, heart, mind, passions, feelings, strong or weak,
All that I would have sought, and all I seek,
910 Bear, know, feel, and yet breathe—into *one* word,
And that one word were Lightning, I would speak;

9. Knell (old form).

But as it is, I live and die unheard,
With a most voiceless thought, sheathing it as a sword.

98

The morn is up again, the dewy morn,
915   With breath all incense, and with cheek all bloom,
Laughing the clouds away with playful scorn,
And living as if earth contain'd no tomb,—
And glowing into day: we may resume
The march of our existence: and thus I,
920   Still on thy shores, fair Leman! may find room
And food for meditation, nor pass by
Much, that may give us pause, if pondered fittingly.

               *   *   *

113

I have not loved the world, nor the world me;
1050   I have not flattered its rank breath, nor bow'd
To its idolatries a patient knee,—
Nor coin'd my cheek to smiles,—nor cried aloud
In worship of an echo; in the crowd
They could not deem me one of such; I stood
1055   Among them, but not of them; in a shroud
Of thoughts which were not their thoughts, and still could,
Had I not filed[1] my mind, which thus itself subdued.

114

I have not loved the world, nor the world me,—
But let us part fair foes; I do believe,
1060   Though I have found them not, that there may be
Words which are things,—hopes which will not deceive,
And virtues which are merciful, nor weave
Snares for the failing: I would also deem
O'er others' griefs that some sincerely grieve;
1065   That two, or one, are almost what they seem,—
That goodness is no name, and happiness no dream.

115

My daughter! with thy name this song begun—
My daughter! with thy name thus much shall end—
I see thee not,—I hear thee not,—but none
1070   Can be so wrapt in thee; thou art the friend
To whom the shadows of far years extend:
Albeit my brow thou never should'st behold,
My voice shall with thy future visions blend,
And reach into thy heart,—when mine is cold,—
1075   A token and a tone, even from thy father's mould.

116

To aid thy mind's development,—to watch
Thy dawn of little joys,—to sit and see

---

1. Defiled. In a note Byron refers to *Macbeth* 3.1.66 ("For Banquo's issue have I filed my mind").

Almost thy very growth,—to view thee catch
Knowledge of objects,—wonders yet to thee!
1080   To hold thee lightly on a gentle knee,
And print on thy soft cheek a parent's kiss,—
This, it should seem, was not reserv'd for me;
Yet this was in my nature:—as it is,
I know not what is there, yet something like to this.

117

1085   Yet, though dull Hate as duty should be taught,
I know that thou wilt love me; though my name
Should be shut from thee, as a spell still fraught
With desolation,—and a broken claim:
Though the grave closed between us,—'twere the same,
1090   I know that thou wilt love me; though to drain
My blood from out thy being, were an aim,
And an attainment,—all would be in vain,—
Still thou would'st love me, still that more than life retain.

118

The child of love,—though born in bitterness,
1095   And nurtured in convulsion,—of thy sire
These were the elements,—and thine no less.
As yet such are around thee,—but thy fire
Shall be more tempered, and thy hope far higher.
Sweet be thy cradled slumbers! O'er the sea,
1100   And from the mountains where I now respire,
Fain would I waft such blessing upon thee,
As, with a sigh, I deem thou might'st have been to me!

1812, 1816

Manfred   *Manfred* is Byron's first dramatic work. As its subtitle, "A Dramatic
Poem," indicates, it was not intended to be produced on the stage; Byron also referred
to it as a "metaphysical" drama—that is, a drama of ideas. He began writing it in the
autumn of 1816 while living in the Swiss Alps, whose grandeur stimulated his imagination; he finished the drama the following year in Italy.

    Manfred's literary forebears include the villains of Gothic fiction (another Manfred
can be found in Horace Walpole's *Castle of Otranto*; see p. 579) and of the Gothic
dramas Byron had encountered during his time on the board of managers of London's
Drury Lane Theatre. Manfred also shares traits with the Greek Titan Prometheus,
rebel against Zeus, ruler of the gods; Milton's Satan; Ahasuerus, the legendary Wandering Jew who, having ridiculed Christ as he bore the Cross to Calvary, is doomed
to live until Christ's Second Coming; and Faust, who yielded his soul to the devil in
exchange for superhuman powers. Byron denied that he had ever heard of Marlowe's
Doctor Faustus, and because he knew no German he had not read Goethe's *Faust,* of
which part 1 had been published in 1808. But during an August 1816 visit to Byron
and the Shelley household, Matthew Lewis (author of the Gothic novel *The Monk*;
see pp. 595 and 602) had read parts of *Faust* to him aloud, translating as he went,
and Byron worked memories of this oral translation into his own drama in a way that
evoked Goethe's admiration.

    Like Byron's earlier heroes, Childe Harold and the protagonists of some of his

Eastern tales, Manfred is hounded by remorse—in this instance, for a transgression that (it is hinted but never quite specified) is incest with his sister Astarte; it is also hinted that Astarte has taken her own life. While this element in the drama is often regarded as Byron's veiled confession of his incestuous relations with his half-sister, Augusta, and while Byron, ever the attention-seeker, in some ways courted this interpretation, the theme of incest was a common one in Gothic and Romantic writings. It features in *The Monk* and Walpole's closet drama *The Mysterious Mother* (1768), and, at about the time Byron was composing his drama, it was also being explored by Mary and Percy Shelley.

The character of Manfred is its author's most impressive representation of the Byronic Hero. Byron's invention is to have Manfred, unlike Faust, disdainfully reject the offer of a pact with the powers of darkness. He thereby sets himself up as the totally autonomous man, independent of any external authority or power, whose own mind, as he says in the concluding scene (3.4.127–40), generates the values by which he lives "in sufferance or in joy," and by reference to which he judges, requites, and finally destroys himself. In his work *Ecce Homo*, the German philosopher Friedrich Nietzsche, recognizing Byron's anticipation of his own *Übermensch* (the "superman" who posits for himself a moral code beyond all traditional standards of good and evil), asserted that the character of Manfred was greater than that of Goethe's Faust.

For more information on the context of *Manfred*, see "The Satanic and Byronic Hero" at Norton Literature Online.

Manfred

A DRAMATIC POEM

"There are more things in heaven and earth, Horatio,
Than are dreamt of in your philosophy."[1]

DRAMATIS PERSONAE

MANFRED	WITCH OF THE ALPS
CHAMOIS HUNTER	ARIMANES
ABBOT OF ST. MAURICE	NEMESIS
MANUEL	THE DESTINIES
HERMAN	SPIRITS, ETC.

The scene of the Drama is amongst the Higher Alps—partly in the Castle of Manfred, and partly in the Mountains.

Act 1

SCENE 1. MANFRED *alone.—Scene, a Gothic gallery.*[2]*—Time, Midnight.*

MANFRED The lamp must be replenish'd, but even then
It will not burn so long as I must watch:
My slumbers—if I slumber—are not sleep,
But a continuance of enduring thought,
5   Which then I can resist not: in my heart
There is a vigil, and these eyes but close
To look within; and yet I live, and bear
The aspect and the form of breathing men.

---

1. Hamlet's comment after having seen his father's ghost (Shakespeare, *Hamlet* 1.5.168–69).

2. A large chamber built in the medieval Gothic style with high, pointed arches.

But grief should be the instructor of the wise;
10   Sorrow is knowledge: they who know the most
Must mourn the deepest o'er the fatal truth,
The Tree of Knowledge is not that of Life.
Philosophy and science, and the springs
Of wonder, and the wisdom of the world,
15   I have essayed, and in my mind there is
A power to make these subject to itself—
But they avail not: I have done men good,
And I have met with good even among men—
But this avail'd not: I have had my foes,
20   And none have baffled, many fallen before me—
But this avail'd not:—Good, or evil, life,
Powers, passions, all I see in other beings,
Have been to me as rain unto the sands,
Since that all-nameless hour. I have no dread,
25   And feel the curse to have no natural fear,
Nor fluttering throb, that beats with hopes or wishes,
Or lurking love of something on the earth.—
Now to my task.—
                    Mysterious Agency!
Ye spirits of the unbounded Universe!
30   Whom I have sought in darkness and in light—
Ye, who do compass earth about, and dwell
In subtler essence—ye, to whom the tops
Of mountains inaccessible are haunts,
And earth's and ocean's caves familiar things—
35   I call upon ye by the written charm
Which gives me power upon you—Rise! appear!   [A pause.]
They come not yet.—Now by the voice of him
Who is the first among you[3]—by this sign,
Which makes you tremble—by the claims of him
40   Who is undying,[4]—Rise! appear!—Appear!   [A pause.]
If it be so.—Spirits of earth and air,
Ye shall not thus elude me: by a power,
Deeper than all yet urged, a tyrant-spell,
Which had its birth-place in a star condemn'd,
45   The burning wreck of a demolish'd world,
A wandering hell in the eternal space;
By the strong curse which is upon my soul,
The thought which is within me and around me,
I do compel ye to my will.—Appear!

[A star is seen at the darker end of the gallery; it is stationary; and a
voice is heard singing.]

FIRST SPIRIT[5]
50   Mortal! to thy bidding bow'd,
From my mansion in the cloud,

3. Arimanes, who appears in 2.4.
4. Probably God, to whom traditional magic con-
jurations often allude.

5. The Spirits, successively, are those of the Air,
Mountain, Ocean, Earth, Winds, Night, and Manfred's guiding Star.

Which the breath of twilight builds,
And the summer's sun-set gilds
With the azure and vermilion,
55   Which is mix'd for my pavilion;
Though thy quest may be forbidden,
On a star-beam I have ridd'n;
To thine adjuration° bow'd,   summons
Mortal—be thy wish avow'd!

            Voice of the SECOND SPIRIT
60   Mont Blanc⁶ is the monarch of mountains,
They crowned him long ago
On a throne of rocks, in a robe of clouds,
With a diadem of snow.
Around his waist are forests braced,
65   The Avalanche in his hand;
But ere it fall, that thundering ball
Must pause for my command.
The Glacier's cold and restless mass
Moves onward day by day;
70   But I am he who bids it pass,
Or with its ice delay.
I am the spirit of the place,
Could make the mountain bow
And quiver to his cavern'd base—
75   And what with me wouldst *Thou?*

            Voice of the THIRD SPIRIT
In the blue depth of the waters,
Where the wave hath no strife,
Where the wind is a stranger,
And the sea-snake hath life,
80   Where the Mermaid is decking
Her green hair with shells;
Like the storm on the surface
Came the sound of thy spells;
O'er my calm Hall of Coral
85   The deep echo roll'd—
To the Spirit of Ocean
Thy wishes unfold!

            FOURTH SPIRIT
Where the slumbering earthquake
Lies pillow'd on fire,
90   And the lakes of bitumen°   mineral pitch
Rise boilingly higher;
Where the roots of the Andes
Strike deep in the earth,

6. The highest mountain in the Alps. Percy Shelley paid tribute to it in a poem published in the same year
as *Manfred.*

As their summits to heaven
Shoot soaringly forth;
I have quitted my birth-place,
Thy bidding to bide—
Thy spell hath subdued me,
Thy will be my guide!

FIFTH SPIRIT

I am the Rider of the wind,
The Stirrer of the storm;
The hurricane I left behind
Is yet with lightning warm;
To speed to thee, o'er shore and sea
I swept upon the blast:
The fleet I met sailed well, and yet
'Twill sink ere night be past.

SIXTH SPIRIT

My dwelling is the shadow of the night,
Why doth thy magic torture me with light?

SEVENTH SPIRIT

The star which rules thy destiny,
Was ruled, ere earth began, by me:
It was a world as fresh and fair
As e'er revolved round sun in air;
Its course was free and regular,
Space bosom'd not a lovelier star.
The hour arrived—and it became
A wandering mass of shapeless flame,
A pathless comet, and a curse,
The menace of the universe;
Still rolling on with innate force,
Without a sphere, without a course,
A bright deformity on high,
The monster of the upper sky!
And thou! beneath its influence born—
Thou worm! whom I obey and scorn—
Forced by a power (which is not thine,
And lent thee but to make thee mine)
For this brief moment to descend,
Where these weak spirits round thee bend
And parley with a thing like thee—
What wouldst thou, Child of Clay! with me?

The SEVEN SPIRITS
Earth, ocean, air, night, mountains, winds, thy star,
Are at thy beck and bidding, Child of Clay!
Before thee at thy quest their spirits are—
What wouldst thou with us, son of mortals—say?

MANFRED Forgetfulness—
FIRST SPIRIT Of what—of whom—and why?

MANFRED   Of that which is within me; read it there—
Ye know it, and I cannot utter it.
SPIRIT   We can but give thee that which we possess:
140   Ask of us subjects, sovereignty, the power
O'er earth, the whole, or portion, or a sign
Which shall control the elements, whereof
We are the dominators, each and all,
These shall be thine.
MANFRED   Oblivion, self-oblivion—
145   Can ye not wring from out the hidden realms
Ye offer so profusely what I ask?
SPIRIT   It is not in our essence, in our skill;
But—thou mayst die.
MANFRED   Will death bestow it on me?
SPIRIT   We are immortal, and do not forget;
150   We are eternal; and to us the past
Is, as the future, present. Art thou answered?
MANFRED   Ye mock me—but the power which brought ye here
Hath made you mine. Slaves, scoff not at my will!
The mind, the spirit, the Promethean spark,[7]
155   The lightning of my being, is as bright,
Pervading, and far-darting as your own,
And shall not yield to yours, though coop'd in clay!
Answer, or I will teach you what I am.
SPIRIT   We answer as we answered; our reply
Is even in thine own words.
160   MANFRED   Why say ye so?
SPIRIT   If, as thou say'st, thine essence be as ours,
We have replied in telling thee, the thing
Mortals call death hath nought to do with us.
MANFRED   I then have call'd ye from your realms in vain;
Ye cannot, or ye will not, aid me.
165   SPIRIT   Say;
What we possess we offer; it is thine:
Bethink ere thou dismiss us, ask again—
Kingdom, and sway, and strength, and length of days—
MANFRED   Accursed! what have I to do with days?
170   They are too long already.—Hence—begone!
SPIRIT   Yet pause: being here, our will would do thee service;
Bethink thee, is there then no other gift
Which we can make not worthless in thine eyes?
MANFRED   No, none: yet stay—one moment, ere we part—
175   I would behold ye face to face. I hear
Your voices, sweet and melancholy sounds,
As music on the waters; and I see
The steady aspect of a clear large star;
But nothing more. Approach me as ye are,
180   Or one, or all, in your accustom'd forms.
SPIRIT   We have no forms beyond the elements

---

7. In Greek myth Prometheus molded man from clay, and stole fire from heaven to give it to humans.

Of which we are the mind and principle:
But choose a form—in that we will appear.
MANFRED   I have no choice; there is no form on earth
185   Hideous or beautiful to me. Let him,
Who is most powerful of ye, take such aspect
As unto him may seem most fitting.—Come!
SEVENTH SPIRIT [*appearing in the shape of a beautiful female figure*].[8]
Behold!
MANFRED   Oh God! if it be thus, and *thou*
Art not a madness and a mockery,
190   I yet might be most happy.—I will clasp thee,
And we again will be—   [*The figure vanishes.*]
My heart is crushed!   [MANFRED *falls senseless.*]

[*A voice is heard in the Incantation*[9] *which follows.*]

When the moon is on the wave,
        And the glow-worm in the grass,
And the meteor on the grave,
195   And the wisp on the morass;
When the falling stars are shooting,
And the answer'd owls are hooting,
And the silent leaves are still
In the shadow of the hill,
200   Shall my soul be upon thine,
With a power and with a sign.

Though thy slumber may be deep,
Yet thy spirit shall not sleep,
There are shades which will not vanish,
205   There are thoughts thou canst not banish;
By a power to thee unknown,
Thou canst never be alone;
Thou art wrapt as with a shroud,
Thou art gathered in a cloud;
10   And for ever shalt thou dwell
In the spirit of this spell.

Though thou seest me not pass by,
Thou shalt feel me with thine eye
As a thing that, though unseen,
15   Must be near thee, and hath been;
And when in that secret dread
Thou hast turn'd around thy head,
Thou shalt marvel I am not
As thy shadow on the spot,
20   And the power which thou dost feel
Shall be what thou must conceal.

8. This shape may be an image of Astarte, whose phantom appears in 2.3.97.
9. Byron had published this "incantation"—a magical spell—as a separate poem six months before *Manfred*, with a note explaining that the poem was "a Chorus in an unfinished Witch drama began some years ago."

And a magic voice and verse
Hath baptized thee with a curse;
And a spirit of the air
225   Hath begirt thee with a snare;
In the wind there is a voice
Shall forbid thee to rejoice;
And to thee shall Night deny
All the quiet of her sky;
230   And the day shall have a sun,
Which shall make thee wish it done.

From thy false tears I did distil
An essence which hath strength to kill;
From thy own heart I then did wring
235   The black blood in its blackest spring;
From thy own smile I snatch'd the snake,
For there it coil'd as in a brake;°   *thicket*
From thy own lip I drew the charm
Which gave all these their chiefest harm;
240   In proving every poison known,
I found the strongest was thine own.

By thy cold breast and serpent smile,
By thy unfathom'd gulfs of guile,
By that most seeming virtuous eye,
245   By thy shut soul's hypocrisy;
By the perfection of thine art
Which pass'd for human thine own heart;
By thy delight in others' pain,
And by thy brotherhood of Cain,[1]
250   I call upon thee! and compel
Thyself to be thy proper Hell![2]

And on thy head I pour the vial
Which doth devote thee to this trial;
Nor to slumber, nor to die,
255   Shall be in thy destiny;
Though thy death shall still seem near
To thy wish, but as a fear;
Lo! the spell now works around thee,
And the clankless chain hath bound thee;
260   O'er thy heart and brain together
Hath the word been pass'd—now wither!

SCENE 2. *The Mountain of the Jungfrau.*[3]—Time, Morning.—
MANFRED *alone upon the Cliffs.*

MANFRED   The spirits I have raised abandon me—
The spells which I have studied baffle me—

1. I.e., by your kinship with Cain, who murdered
his brother, Abel.
2. Cf. Satan's words in Milton's *Paradise Lost*

4.75: "Which way I fly is Hell; my self am Hell."
3. A high Alpine mountain in south-central Switzerland.

The remedy I reck'd of° tortured me;   *considered*
I lean no more on super-human aid,
5   It hath no power upon the past, and for
The future, till the past be gulf'd in darkness,
It is not of my search.—My mother Earth!
And thou fresh breaking Day, and you, ye Mountains,
Why are ye beautiful? I cannot love ye.
10   And thou, the bright eye of the universe,
That openest over all, and unto all
Art a delight—thou shin'st not on my heart.
And you, ye crags, upon whose extreme edge
I stand, and on the torrent's brink beneath
15   Behold the tall pines dwindled as to shrubs
In dizziness of distance; when a leap,
A stir, a motion, even a breath, would bring
My breast upon its rocky bosom's bed
To rest for ever—wherefore do I pause?
20   I feel the impulse—yet I do not plunge;
I see the peril—yet do not recede;
And my brain reels—and yet my foot is firm:
There is a power upon me which withholds
And makes it my fatality to live;
25   If it be life to wear within myself
This barrenness of spirit, and to be
My own soul's sepulchre, for I have ceased
To justify my deeds unto myself—
The last infirmity of evil.[4] Ay,
30   Thou winged and cloud-cleaving minister,   [*An eagle passes.*]
Whose happy flight is highest into heaven,
Well may'st thou swoop so near me—I should be
Thy prey, and gorge thine eaglets; thou art gone
Where the eye cannot follow thee; but thine
35   Yet pierces downward, onward, or above,
With a pervading vision.—Beautiful!
How beautiful is all this visible world!
How glorious in its action and itself;
But we, who name ourselves its sovereigns, we,
40   Half dust, half deity, alike unfit
To sink or soar, with our mix'd essence make
A conflict of its elements, and breathe
The breath of degradation and of pride,
Contending with low wants and lofty will
45   Till our mortality predominates,
And men are—what they name not to themselves,
And trust not to each other. Hark! the note,
                    [*The Shepherd's pipe in the distance is heard.*]
The natural music of the mountain reed—

---

4. An echo of Milton's "Lycidas," where fame is identified as "That last infirmity of a noble mind" (line 71).

For here the patriarchal days[5] are not
A pastoral fable—pipes in the liberal° air,   *free-moving*
Mix'd with the sweet bells of the sauntering herd;
My soul would drink those echoes.—Oh, that I were
The viewless° spirit of a lovely sound,   *invisible*
A living voice, a breathing harmony,
A bodiless enjoyment—born and dying
With the blest tone which made me!
        Enter from below a CHAMOIS[6] HUNTER.
CHAMOIS HUNTER   Even so
This way the chamois leapt: her nimble feet
Have baffled me; my gains to-day will scarce
Repay my break-neck travail.—What is here?
Who seems not of my trade, and yet hath reach'd
A height which none even of our mountaineers,
Save our best hunters, may attain: his garb
Is goodly, his mien° manly, and his air   *appearance*
Proud as a free-born peasant's, at this distance.—
I will approach him nearer.
MANFRED [*not perceiving the other*]   To be thus—
Gray-hair'd with anguish, like these blasted pines,
Wrecks of a single winter, barkless, branchless,
A blighted trunk upon a cursed root,
Which but supplies a feeling to decay—
And to be thus, eternally but thus,
Having been otherwise! Now furrow'd o'er
With wrinkles, plough'd by moments, not by years;
And hours—all tortured into ages—hours
Which I outlive!—Ye toppling crags of ice!
Ye avalanches, whom a breath draws down
In mountainous o'erwhelming, come and crush me—
I hear ye momently above, beneath,
Crash with a frequent conflict; but ye pass,
And only fall on things which still would live;
On the young flourishing forest, or the hut
And hamlet of the harmless villager.
CHAMOIS HUNTER   The mists begin to rise from up the valley;
I'll warn him to descend, or he may chance
To lose at once his way and life together.
MANFRED   The mists boil up around the glaciers; clouds
Rise curling fast beneath me, white and sulphury,
Like foam from the roused ocean of deep Hell,
Whose every wave breaks on a living shore,
Heaped with the damn'd like pebbles.—I am giddy.
CHAMOIS HUNTER   I must approach him cautiously; if near,
A sudden step will startle him, and he
Seems tottering already.
MANFRED   Mountains have fallen,

5. The days of the Old Testament partriarchs, who
were shepherds.

6. A goatlike antelope found in the European
mountains.

Leaving a gap in the clouds, and with the shock
Rocking their Alpine brethren; filling up
5   The ripe green valleys with destruction's splinters;
Damming the rivers with a sudden dash,
Which crush'd the waters into mist, and made
Their fountains find another channel—thus,
Thus, in its old age, did Mount Rosenberg[7]—
Why stood I not beneath it?

10 CHAMOIS HUNTER   Friend! have a care,
Your next step may be fatal!—for the love
Of him who made you, stand not on that brink!

MANFRED [*not hearing him*]   Such would have been for me a fitting tomb;
My bones had then been quiet in their depth;
15   They had not then been strewn upon the rocks
For the wind's pastime—as thus—thus they shall be—
In this one plunge.—Farewell, ye opening heavens!
Look not upon me thus reproachfully—
Ye were not meant for me—Earth! take these atoms!

[*As* MANFRED *is in act to spring from the cliff, the* CHAMOIS HUNTER
seizes and retains him with a sudden grasp.][8]

10 CHAMOIS HUNTER   Hold, madman!—though aweary of thy life,
Stain not our pure vales with thy guilty blood.—
Away with me—I will not quit my hold.

MANFRED   I am most sick at heart—nay, grasp me not—
I am all feebleness—the mountains whirl
15   Spinning around me—I grow blind—What art thou?

CHAMOIS HUNTER   I'll answer that anon.—Away with me—
The clouds grow thicker—there—now lean on me—
Place your foot here—here, take this staff, and cling
A moment to that shrub—now give me your hand,
20   And hold fast by my girdle—softly—well—
The Chalet will be gained within an hour—
Come on, we'll quickly find a surer footing,
And something like a pathway, which the torrent
Hath wash'd since winter.—Come, 'tis bravely done—
25   You should have been a hunter.—Follow me.

[*As they descend the rocks with difficulty, the scene closes.*]

Act 2

SCENE 1. *A Cottage amongst the Bernese Alps.*[9] MANFRED *and the* CHAMOIS
HUNTER.

CHAMOIS HUNTER   No, no—yet pause—thou must not yet go forth:
Thy mind and body are alike unfit
To trust each other, for some hours, at least;
When thou art better, I will be thy guide—

---

7. In 1806, ten years before the composition of *Manfred*, a huge landslide on Mount Rossberg ("Rosenberg") had destroyed four villages and killed 457 people.

8. See the color insert for John Martin's visual representation of this moment in his watercolor *Manfred on the Jungfrau*.

9. A mountain range in south-central Switzerland.

But whither?

5 MANFRED   It imports not; I do know
My route full well, and need no further guidance.
CHAMOIS HUNTER   Thy garb and gait bespeak thee of high lineage—
One of the many chiefs, whose castled crags
Look o'er the lower valleys—which of these
10 May call thee Lord? I only know their portals;
My way of life leads me but rarely down
To bask by the huge hearths of those old halls,
Carousing with the vassals; but the paths,
Which step from out our mountains to their doors,
15 I know from childhood—which of these is thine?
MANFRED   No matter.
CHAMOIS HUNTER   Well, sir, pardon me the question,
And be of better cheer. Come, taste my wine;
'Tis of an ancient vintage; many a day
'T has thawed my veins among our glaciers, now
20 Let it do thus for thine—Come, pledge me fairly.
MANFRED   Away, away! there's blood upon the brim!
Will it then never—never sink in the earth?
CHAMOIS HUNTER   What dost thou mean? thy senses wander from thee.
MANFRED   I say 'tis blood—my blood! the pure warm stream
25 Which ran in the veins of my fathers, and in ours
When we were in our youth, and had one heart,
And loved each other as we should not love,
And this was shed: but still it rises up,
Colouring the clouds, that shut me out from heaven,
30 Where thou art not—and I shall never be.
CHAMOIS HUNTER   Man of strange words, and some half-maddening sin,
Which makes thee people° vacancy, whate'er   populate
Thy dread and sufferance be, there's comfort yet—
The aid of holy men, and heavenly patience—
35 MANFRED   Patience and patience! Hence—that word was made
For brutes of burthen, not for birds of prey;
Preach it to mortals of a dust like thine,—
I am not of thine order.
                              Thanks to heaven!
CHAMOIS HUNTER   I would not be of thine for the free fame
40 Of William Tell;¹ but whatsoe'er thine ill,
It must be borne, and these wild starts are useless.
MANFRED   Do I not bear it?—Look on me—I live.
CHAMOIS HUNTER   This is convulsion, and no healthful life.
MANFRED   I tell thee, man! I have lived many years,
45 Many long years, but they are nothing now
To those which I must number: ages—ages—
Space and eternity—and consciousness,
With the fierce thirst of death—and still unslaked!
CHAMOIS HUNTER   Why, on thy brow the seal of middle age
50 Hath scarce been set; I am thine elder far.

1. The hero who, according to legend, liberated Switzerland from Austrian oppression in the 14th century.

MANFRED   Think'st thou existence doth depend on time?
It doth; but actions are our epochs: mine
Have made my days and nights imperishable,
Endless, and all alike, as sands on the shore,
55   Innumerable atoms, and one desart,
Barren and cold, on which the wild waves break,
But nothing rests, save carcases and wrecks,
Rocks, and the salt-surf weeds of bitterness.
CHAMOIS HUNTER   Alas! he's mad—but yet I must not leave him.
60 MANFRED   I would I were—for then the things I see
Would be but a distempered° dream.   *disturbed*
CHAMOIS HUNTER   What is it
That thou dost see, or think thou look'st upon?
MANFRED   Myself, and thee—a peasant of the Alps—
Thy humble virtues, hospitable home,
65   And spirit patient, pious, proud and free;
Thy self-respect, grafted on innocent thoughts;
Thy days of health, and nights of sleep; thy toils,
By danger dignified, yet guiltless; hopes
Of cheerful old age and a quiet grave,
70   With cross and garland over its green turf,
And thy grandchildren's love for epitaph;
This do I see—and then I look within—
It matters not—my soul was scorch'd already!
CHAMOIS HUNTER   And would'st thou then exchange thy lot for mine?
75 MANFRED   No, friend! I would not wrong thee, nor exchange
My lot with living being: I can bear—
However wretchedly, 'tis still to bear—
In life what others could not brook to dream,
But perish in their slumber.
CHAMOIS HUNTER   And with this—
80   This cautious feeling for another's pain,
Canst thou be black with evil?—say not so.
Can one of gentle thoughts have wreak'd revenge
Upon his enemies?
MANFRED   Oh! no, no, no!
My injuries came down on those who loved me—
85   On those whom I best loved: I never quell'd°   *killed*
An enemy, save in my just defence—
My wrongs were all on those I should have cherished—
But my embrace was fatal.
CHAMOIS HUNTER   Heaven give thee rest!
And penitence restore thee to thyself;
My prayers shall be for thee.
90 MANFRED   I need them not,
But can endure thy pity. I depart—
'Tis time—farewell!—Here's gold, and thanks for thee—
No words—it is thy due.—Follow me not—
I know my path—the mountain peril's past:—
95   And once again, I charge thee, follow not!   [*Exit* MANFRED.]

SCENE 2. *A lower Valley in the Alps.—A Cataract.*

Enter MANFRED.

It is not noon—the sunbow's rays still arch[2]
The torrent with the many hues of heaven,
And roll the sheeted silver's waving column
O'er the crag's headlong perpendicular,
5   And fling its lines of foaming light along,
And to and fro, like the pale courser's tail,
The Giant steed, to be bestrode by Death,
As told in the Apocalypse.[3] No eyes
But mine now drink this sight of loveliness;
10   I should be sole in this sweet solitude,
And with the Spirit of the place divide
The homage of these waters.—I will call her.
    [MANFRED *takes some of the water into the palm of his hand, and flings
    it in the air, muttering the adjuration. After a pause, the* WITCH OF THE
    ALPS *rises beneath the arch of the sunbow of the torrent.*]
Beautiful Spirit! with thy hair of light,
And dazzling eyes of glory, in whose form
15   The charms of Earth's least-mortal daughters grow
To an unearthly stature, in an essence
Of purer elements; while the hues of youth,—
Carnation'd like a sleeping infant's cheek,
Rock'd by the beating of her mother's heart,
20   Or the rose tints, which summer's twilight leaves
Upon the lofty glacier's virgin snow,
The blush of earth embracing with her heaven,—
Tinge thy celestial aspect, and make tame
The beauties of the sunbow which bends o'er thee.
25   Beautiful Spirit! in thy calm clear brow,
Wherein is glass'd° serenity of soul,   *reflected*
Which of itself shows immortality,
I read that thou wilt pardon to a Son
Of Earth, whom the abstruser powers permit
30   At times to commune with them—if that he
Avail him of his spells—to call thee thus,
And gaze on thee a moment.
WITCH   Son of Earth!
I know thee, and the powers which give thee power;
I know thee for a man of many thoughts,
35   And deeds of good and ill, extreme in both,
Fatal and fated in thy sufferings.
I have expected this—what wouldst thou with me?
MANFRED   To look upon thy beauty—nothing further.
The face of the earth hath madden'd me, and I
40   Take refuge in her mysteries, and pierce

---

2. This iris is formed by the rays of the sun over
the lower part of the Alpine torrents: it is exactly
like a rainbow come to pay a visit, and so close that
you may walk into it: this effect lasts until noon

[Byron's note].
3. Revelation 6.8: "And I looked, and behold a
pale horse: and his name that sat on him was
Death, and Hell followed with him."

To the abodes of those who govern her—
But they can nothing aid me. I have sought
From them what they could not bestow, and now
I search no further.
WITCH   What could be the quest
45 Which is not in the power of the most powerful,
The rulers of the invisible?
MANFRED   A boon;
But why should I repeat it? 'twere in vain.
WITCH   I know not that; let thy lips utter it.
MANFRED   Well, though it torture me,'tis but the same;
50 My pang shall find a voice. From my youth upwards
My spirit walk'd not with the souls of men,
Nor look'd upon the earth with human eyes;
The thirst of their ambition was not mine,
The aim of their existence was not mine;
55 My joys, my griefs, my passions, and my powers,
Made me a stranger; though I wore the form,
I had no sympathy with breathing flesh,
Nor midst the creatures of clay that girded me
Was there but one who—but of her anon.
60 I said, with men, and with the thoughts of men,
I held but slight communion; but instead,
My joy was in the Wilderness, to breathe
The difficult air of the iced mountain's top,
Where the birds dare not build, nor insect's wing
65 Flit o'er the herbless granite; or to plunge
Into the torrent, and to roll along
On the swift whirl of the new breaking wave
Of river-stream, or ocean, in their flow.
In these my early strength exulted; or
70 To follow through the night the moving moon,
The stars and their development; or catch
The dazzling lightnings till my eyes grew dim;
Or to look, list'ning, on the scattered leaves,
While Autumn winds were at their evening song.
75 These were my pastimes, and to be alone;
For if the beings, of whom I was one,—
Hating to be so,—cross'd me in my path,
I felt myself degraded back to them,
And was all clay again. And then I dived,
80 In my lone wanderings, to the caves of death,
Searching its cause in its effect; and drew
From wither'd bones, and skulls, and heap'd up dust,
Conclusions most forbidden.[4] Then I pass'd
The nights of years in sciences untaught,
85 Save in the old-time; and with time and toil,

4. Cf. passages from Victor Frankenstein's account of his scientific investigations. "To examine the causes of life, we must first have recourse to death"; "Who shall conceive the horrors of my secret toil, as I dabbled among the unhallowed damps of the grave . . . ?" (chap. 4).

And terrible ordeal, and such penance
As in itself hath power upon the air,
And spirits that do compass air and earth,
Space, and the peopled infinite, I made
90   Mine eyes familiar with Eternity,
Such as, before me, did the Magi,⁵ and
He who from out their fountain dwellings raised
Eros and Anteros, at Gadara,⁶
As I do thee;—and with my knowledge grew
95   The thirst of knowledge, and the power and joy
Of this most bright intelligence, until—
WITCH   Proceed.
MANFRED   Oh! I but thus prolonged my words,
Boasting these idle attributes, because
As I approach the core of my heart's grief—
100   But to my task. I have not named to thee
Father or mother, mistress, friend, or being,
With whom I wore the chain of human ties;
If I had such, they seem'd not such to me—
Yet there was one—
WITCH   Spare not thyself—proceed.
105   MANFRED   She was like me in lineaments—her eyes,
Her hair, her features, all, to the very tone
Even of her voice, they said were like to mine;
But soften'd all, and temper'd into beauty;
She had the same lone thoughts and wanderings,
110   The quest of hidden knowledge, and a mind
To comprehend the universe: nor these
Alone, but with them gentler powers than mine,
Pity, and smiles, and tears—which I had not;
And tenderness—but that I had for her;
115   Humility—and that I never had.
Her faults were mine—her virtues were her own—
I loved her, and destroy'd her!
WITCH   With thy hand?
MANFRED   Not with my hand, but heart—which broke her heart—
It gazed on mine, and withered. I have shed
120   Blood, but not hers—and yet her blood was shed—
I saw—and could not staunch it.
WITCH   And for this—
A being of the race thou dost despise,
The order which thine own would rise above,
Mingling with us and ours, thou dost forego
125   The gifts of our great knowledge, and shrink'st back
To recreant° mortality—Away!   cowardly
MANFRED   Daughter of Air! I tell thee, since that hour—
But words are breath—look on me in my sleep,

---

5. Masters of occult knowledge (plural of *magus*).
6. Byron's note to lines 92–93 identifies this figure as Iamblicus, the 4th-century Neoplatonic philos-
opher, who called up Eros, god of love, and Anteros, god of unrequited love, from the hot springs named after them at Gadara, in Syria.

Or watch my watchings—Come and sit by me!
My solitude is solitude no more,
But peopled with the Furies;—I have gnash'd
My teeth in darkness till returning morn,
Then cursed myself till sunset;—I have pray'd
For madness as a blessing—'tis denied me.
I have affronted death—but in the war
Of elements the waters shrunk from me,
And fatal things pass'd harmless—the cold hand
Of an all-pitiless demon held me back,
Back by a single hair, which would not break.
In phantasy, imagination, all
The affluence of my soul—which one day was
A Croesus in creation[7]—I plunged deep,
But, like an ebbing wave, it dash'd me back
Into the gulf of my unfathom'd thought.
I plunged amidst mankind—Forgetfulness
I sought in all, save where 'tis to be found,
And that I have to learn—my sciences,[8]
My long pursued and super-human art,
Is mortal here—I dwell in my despair—
And live—and live for ever.

WITCH   It may be
That I can aid thee.

MANFRED   To do this thy power
Must wake the dead, or lay me low with them.
Do so—in any shape—in any hour—
With any torture—so it be the last.

WITCH   That is not in my province; but if thou
Wilt swear obedience to my will, and do
My bidding, it may help thee to thy wishes.

MANFRED   I will not swear—Obey! and whom? the spirits
Whose presence I command, and be the slave
Of those who served me—Never!

WITCH   Is this all?
Hast thou no gentler answer—Yet bethink thee,
And pause ere thou rejectest.

MANFRED   I have said it.

WITCH   Enough!—I may retire then—say!

MANFRED   Retire!

                    [The WITCH disappears.]

MANFRED [alone]   We are the fools of time and terror: Days
Steal on us and steal from us; yet we live,
Loathing our life, and dreading still to die.
In all the days of this detested yoke—
This heaving burthen, this accursed breath—
This vital weight upon the struggling heart,

---

7. I.e., my imagination had at one time been, in its creative powers, as rich as King Croesus (the legendary monarch famed for his wealth). Manfred's self-description in this passage, as longing for a death that is denied him, is modeled on the legend, often treated in Romantic literature, of the Wandering Jew.

8. Occult bodies of knowledge.

170 Which sinks with sorrow, or beats quick with pain,
Or joy that ends in agony or faintness—
In all the days of past and future, for
In life there is no present, we can number
How few—how less than few—wherein the soul
175 Forbears to pant for death, and yet draws back
As from a stream in winter, though the chill
Be but a moment's. I have one resource
Still in my science—I can call the dead,
And ask them what it is we dread to be:
180 The sternest answer can but be the Grave,
And that is nothing—if they answer not—
The buried Prophet answered to the Hag
Of Endor;[9] and the Spartan Monarch drew
From the Byzantine maid's unsleeping spirit
185 An answer and his destiny—he slew
That which he loved, unknowing what he slew,
And died unpardon'd—though he call'd in aid
The Phyxian Jove, and in Phigalia roused
The Arcadian Evocators to compel
190 The indignant shadow to depose her wrath,[1]
Or fix her term of vengeance—she replied
In words of dubious import, but fulfill'd.
If I had never lived, that which I love
Had still been living; had I never loved,
195 That which I love would still be beautiful—
Happy and giving happiness. What is she?
What is she now?—a sufferer for my sins—
A thing I dare not think upon—or nothing.
Within few hours I shall not call in vain—
200 Yet in this hour I dread the thing I dare:
Until this hour I never shrunk to gaze
On spirit, good or evil—now I tremble,
And feel a strange cold thaw upon my heart,
But I can act even what I most abhor,
205 And champion human fears.—The night approaches.   [*Exit.*]

SCENE 3. *The Summit of the Jungfrau Mountain.*

Enter FIRST DESTINY.[2]
The moon is rising broad, and round, and bright;
And here on snows, where never human foot

9. The Woman of Endor, at the behest of King Saul, summoned up the spirit of the dead prophet Samuel, who foretold that in an impending battle the Philistines would conquer the Israelites and kill Saul and his sons (1 Samuel 28.7–19).
1. Plutarch relates that King Pausanias ("the Spartan Monarch") had accidentally killed Cleonice ("the Byzantine maid"), whom he desired as his mistress. Her ghost haunted him until he called up her spirit to beg her forgiveness. She told him, enigmatically, that he would quickly be freed from his troubles; soon after that, he was killed. Another

Pausanias, author of the *Description of Greece*, adds the details that King Pausanias, in the vain attempt to purge his guilt, had called for aid from Jupiter Phyxius and consulted the Evocators at Phigalia, in Arcadia, who had the power to call up the souls of the dead.
2. The three Destinies are modeled on both the witches of Shakespeare's *Macbeth* and the three Fates of classical mythology, who, in turn, spin, measure, and then cut the thread of an individual's life.

Of common mortal trod, we nightly tread,
And leave no traces; o'er the savage sea,
5 The glassy ocean of the mountain ice,
We skim its rugged breakers, which put on
The aspect of a tumbling tempest's foam,
Frozen in a moment—a dead whirlpool's image;
And this most steep fantastic pinnacle,
10 The fretwork of some earthquake—where the clouds
Pause to repose themselves in passing by—
Is sacred to our revels, or our vigils;
Here do I wait my sisters, on our way
To the Hall of Arimanes,³ for to-night
15 Is our great festival—'tis strange they come not.

A Voice without, singing
The Captive Usurper,⁴
Hurl'd down from the throne,
Lay buried in torpor,
Forgotten and lone;
20 I broke through his slumbers,
I shivered his chain,
I leagued him with numbers—
He's Tyrant again!
With the blood of a million he'll answer my care,
25 With a nation's destruction—his flight and despair.

Second Voice, without
The ship sail'd on, the ship sail'd fast,
But I left not a sail, and I left not a mast;
There is not a plank of the hull or the deck,
And there is not a wretch to lament o'er his wreck;
30 Save one, whom I held, as he swam, by the hair,
And he was a subject well worthy my care;
A traitor on land, and a pirate at sea—
But I saved him to wreak further havoc for me!

FIRST DESTINY, *answering*
The city lies sleeping;
35 The morn, to deplore it,
May dawn on it weeping:
Sullenly, slowly,
The black plague flew o'er it—
Thousands lie lowly;
40 Tens of thousands shall perish—
The living shall fly from
The sick they should cherish;
But nothing can vanquish
The touch that they die from.
45 Sorrow and anguish,

3. The name is derived from Ahriman, who in the dualistic Zoroastrian religion was the principle of darkness and evil.
4. Napoleon. The song of the first Voice alludes to Napoleon's escape from his captivity on the island of Elba in March 1815. After his defeat at the Battle of Waterloo he was imprisoned on another island, St. Helena, in October 1815.

And evil and dread,
　Envelope a nation—
The blest are the dead,
　Who see not the sight
50　　　Of their own desolation.—
This work of a night—
This wreck of a realm—this deed of my doing—
For ages I've done, and shall still be renewing!

Enter the SECOND *and* THIRD DESTINIES.

THE THREE
Our hands contain the hearts of men,
55　　　Our footsteps are their graves;
We only give to take again
The spirits of our slaves!

FIRST DESTINY　Welcome!—Where's Nemesis?[5]
SECOND DESTINY　　　　　　　　At some great work;
But what I know not, for my hands were full.
THIRD DESTINY　Behold she cometh.
　　　　　　　Enter NEMESIS.
60　FIRST DESTINY　　　　　　Say, where hast thou been?—
My sisters and thyself are slow to-night.
NEMESIS　I was detain'd repairing shattered thrones,
Marrying fools, restoring dynasties,[6]
Avenging men upon their enemies,
65　And making them repent their own revenge;
Goading the wise to madness; from the dull
Shaping out oracles to rule the world
Afresh, for they were waxing out of date,
And mortals dared to ponder for themselves,
70　To weigh kings in the balance, and to speak
Of freedom, the forbidden fruit.—Away!
We have outstaid the hour—mount we our clouds!　　　[*Exeunt.*]

SCENE 4. *The Hall of* ARIMANES.—ARIMANES *on his Throne, a Globe of Fire,
surrounded by the* SPIRITS.

Hymn of the SPIRITS
Hail to our Master!—Prince of Earth and Air!—
Who walks the clouds and waters—in his hand
The sceptre of the elements, which tear
Themselves to chaos at his high command!
5　He breatheth—and a tempest shakes the sea;
He speaketh—and the clouds reply in thunder;
He gazeth—from his glance the sunbeams flee;
He moveth—earthquakes rend the world asunder.
Beneath his footsteps the volcanos rise;

5. The Greek and Roman goddess of vengeance, particularly of the sin of hubris, overweening presumption against the gods.

6. Alluding to Byron's marriage and to the restoration of monarchies across Europe that followed the battle of Waterloo.

His shadow is the Pestilence; his path
The comets herald through the crackling skies;
And planets turn to ashes at his wrath.
To him War offers daily sacrifice;
To him Death pays his tribute; Life is his,
5   With all its infinite of agonies—
And his the spirit of whatever is!

Enter the DESTINIES *and* NEMESIS

FIRST DESTINY   Glory to Arimanes! on the earth
His power increaseth—both my sisters did
His bidding, nor did I neglect my duty!
20   SECOND DESTINY   Glory to Arimanes! we who bow
The necks of men, bow down before his throne!
THIRD DESTINY   Glory to Arimanes!—we await
His nod!
NEMESIS   Sovereign of Sovereigns! we are thine,
And all that liveth, more or less, is ours,
25   And most things wholly so; still to increase
Our power increasing thine, demands our care,
And we are vigilant—Thy late commands
Have been fulfilled to the utmost.

Enter MANFRED.

A SPIRIT   What is here?
A mortal!—Thou most rash and fatal wretch,
Bow down and worship!
30   SECOND SPIRIT   I do know the man—
A Magian° of great power, and fearful skill!   magus
THIRD SPIRIT   Bow down and worship, slave!—What, know'st thou not
Thine and our Sovereign?—Tremble, and obey!
ALL THE SPIRITS   Prostrate thyself, and thy condemned clay,
Child of the Earth! or dread the worst.
35   MANFRED   I know it;
And yet ye see I kneel not.
FOURTH SPIRIT   'Twill be taught thee.
MANFRED   'Tis taught already;—many a night on the earth,
On the bare ground, have I bow'd down my face,
And strew'd my head with ashes; I have known
40   The fulness of humiliation, for
I sunk before my vain despair, and knelt
To my own desolation.
FIFTH SPIRIT   Dost thou dare
Refuse to Arimanes on his throne
What the whole earth accords, beholding not
45   The terror of his Glory—Crouch! I say.
MANFRED   Bid *him* bow down to that which is above him,
The overruling Infinite—the Maker
Who made him not for worship—let him kneel,
And we will kneel together.
THE SPIRITS   Crush the worm!
Tear him in pieces!—
50   FIRST DESTINY   Hence! Avaunt!—he's mine.

Prince of the Powers invisible! This man
Is of no common order, as his port
And presence here denote; his sufferings
Have been of an immortal nature, like
Our own; his knowledge and his powers and will,
As far as is compatible with clay,
Which clogs the ethereal essence, have been such
As clay hath seldom borne; his aspirations
Have been beyond the dwellers of the earth,
And they have only taught him what we know—
That knowledge is not happiness, and science
But an exchange of ignorance for that
Which is another kind of ignorance.
This is not all—the passions, attributes
Of earth and heaven, from which no power, nor being,
Nor breath from the worm upwards is exempt,
Have pierced his heart; and in their consequence
Made him a thing, which I, who pity not,
Yet pardon those who pity. He is mine,
And thine, it may be—be it so, or not,
No other Spirit in this region hath
A soul like his—or power upon his soul.
NEMESIS   What doth he here then?
FIRST DESTINY   Let *him* answer that.
MANFRED   Ye know what I have known; and without power
I could not be amongst ye: but there are
Powers deeper still beyond—I come in quest
Of such, to answer unto what I seek.
NEMESIS   What wouldst *thou*?
MANFRED   Thou canst not reply to me.
Call up the dead—my question is for them.
NEMESIS   Great Arimanes, doth thy will avouch°   confirm
The wishes of this mortal?
ARIMANES   Yea.
NEMESIS   Whom would'st thou
Uncharnel?
MANFRED   One without a tomb—call up
Astarte.[7]

NEMESIS
Shadow! or Spirit!
Whatever thou art,
Which still doth inherit
The whole or a part
Of the form of thy birth,
Of the mould of thy clay,
Which returned to the earth,
Re-appear to the day!

---

7. Byron applies to Manfred's beloved the name of Astarte (also known as Ashtoreth), goddess of love and fertility, the Eastern equivalent of the Greek goddess Aphrodite.

                    Bear what thou borest,
                    The heart and the form,
                    And the aspect thou worest
95   Redeem from the worm.
                    Appear!—Appear!—Appear!
                    Who sent thee there requires thee here!

[*The Phantom of* ASTARTE *rises and stands in the midst.*]

MANFRED   Can this be death? there's bloom upon her cheek;
    But now I see it is no living hue,
00 But a strange hectic°—like the unnatural red   *feverish flush*
    Which Autumn plants upon the perish'd leaf.
    It is the same! Oh, God! that I should dread
    To look upon the same—Astarte!—No,
    I cannot speak to her—but bid her speak—
05 Forgive me or condemn me.

                            NEMESIS
                    By the power which hath broken
                    The grave which enthrall'd thee,
                    Speak to him who hath spoken,
                    Or those who have call'd thee!

10 MANFRED   She is silent,
    And in that silence I am more than answered.
    NEMESIS   My power extends no further. Prince of air!
    It rests with thee alone—command her voice.
    ARIMANES   Spirit—obey this sceptre!
    NEMESIS   Silent still!
15 She is not of our order, but belongs
    To the other powers. Mortal! thy quest is vain,
    And we are baffled also.
    MANFRED   Hear me, hear me—
    Astarte! my beloved! speak to me:
    I have so much endured—so much endure—
20 Look on me! the grave hath not changed thee more
    Than I am changed for thee. Thou lovedst me
    Too much, as I loved thee: we were not made
    To torture thus each other, though it were
    The deadliest sin to love as we have loved.
25 Say that thou loath'st me not—that I do bear
    This punishment for both—that thou wilt be
    One of the blessed—and that I shall die,
    For hitherto all hateful things conspire
    To bind me in existence—in a life
30 Which makes me shrink from immortality—
    A future like the past. I cannot rest.
    I know not what I ask, nor what I seek:
    I feel but what thou art—and what I am;
    And I would hear yet once before I perish
35 The voice which was my music—Speak to me!

For I have call'd on thee in the still night,
Startled the slumbering birds from the hush'd boughs,
And woke the mountain wolves, and made the caves
Acquainted with thy vainly echoed name,
140   Which answered me—many things answered me—
Spirits and men—but thou wert silent all.
Yet speak to me! I have outwatch'd the stars,
And gazed o'er heaven in vain in search of thee.
Speak to me! I have wandered o'er the earth,
145   And never found thy likeness—Speak to me!
Look on the fiends around—they feel for me:
I fear them not, and feel for thee alone—
Speak to me! though it be in wrath;—but say—
I reck not what—but let me hear thee once—
This once—once more!

PHANTOM OF ASTARTE   Manfred!
150   MANFRED   Say on, say on—
I live but in the sound—it is thy voice!
PHANTOM   Manfred! To-morrow ends thine earthly ills.
Farewell!
MANFRED
                  Yet one word more—am I forgiven?
PHANTOM   Farewell!
MANFRED   Say, shall we meet again?
PHANTOM   Farewell!
155   MANFRED   One word for mercy! Say, thou lovest me.
PHANTOM   Manfred!   [*The Spirit of* ASTARTE *disappears.*]
NEMESIS   She's gone, and will not be recall'd;
Her words will be fulfill'd. Return to the earth.
A SPIRIT   He is convulsed—This is to be a mortal
And seek the things beyond mortality.
160   ANOTHER SPIRIT   Yet, see, he mastereth himself, and makes
His torture tributary to his will.
Had he been one of us, he would have made
An awful spirit.
NEMESIS   Hast thou further question
Of our great sovereign, or his worshippers?
MANFRED   None.
NEMESIS   Then for a time farewell.
165   MANFRED   We meet then—
Where? On the earth?
NEMESIS   That will be seen hereafter.
MANFRED   Even as thou wilt: and for the grace accorded
I now depart a debtor. Fare ye well!   [*Exit* MANFRED.]
         [*Scene closes.*]

                        Act 3

SCENE 1. *A Hall in the Castle of* MANFRED. MANFRED *and* HERMAN.

MANFRED   What is the hour?
HERMAN   It wants but one till sunset,

And promises a lovely twilight.
MANFRED   Say,
    Are all things so disposed of in the tower
    As I directed?
HERMAN   All, my lord, are ready;
    Here is the key and casket.
5   MANFRED   It is well:
    Thou mayst retire.   [*Exit* HERMAN.]
MANFRED [*alone*]   There is a calm upon me—
    Inexplicable stillness! which till now
    Did not belong to what I knew of life.
    If that I did not know philosophy
10   To be of all our vanities the motliest,[8]
    The merest word that ever fool'd the ear
    From out the schoolman's jargon, I should deem
    The golden secret, the sought "Kalon,"[9] found,
    And seated in my soul. It will not last,
15   But it is well to have known it, though but once:
    It hath enlarged my thoughts with a new sense,
    And I within my tablets would note down
    That there is such a feeling. Who is there?
                  Re-enter HERMAN.
HERMAN   My lord, the abbot of St. Maurice[1] craves
    To greet your presence.
             Enter the ABBOT OF ST. MAURICE.
20   ABBOT   Peace be with Count Manfred!
MANFRED   Thanks, holy father! welcome to these walls;
    Thy presence honours them, and blesseth those
    Who dwell within them.
ABBOT   Would it were so, Count!—
    But I would fain confer with thee alone.
25   MANFRED   Herman, retire. What would my reverend guest?   [*Exit* HERMAN.]
ABBOT   Thus, without prelude:—Age and zeal, my office,[2]
    And good intent, must plead my privilege;
    Our near, though not acquainted neighbourhood,
    May also be my herald. Rumours strange,
30   And of unholy nature, are abroad,
    And busy with thy name; a noble name
    For centuries; may he who bears it now
    Transmit it unimpair'd!
MANFRED   Proceed,—I listen.
ABBOT   'Tis said thou holdest converse with the things
35   Which are forbidden to the search of man;
    That with the dwellers of the dark abodes,
    The many evil and unheavenly spirits
    Which walk the valley of the shade of death,
    Thou communest. I know that with mankind,

---

8. "The most diverse" or, possibly, "the most foolish" (*motley* was the multicolored suit worn by a
court jester).

9. Greek for both "the Beautiful" and "the Good."
1. In the Rhone Valley in Switzerland.
2. Position in the church.

40   Thy fellows in creation, thou dost rarely
       Exchange thy thoughts, and that thy solitude
       Is as an anchorite's,[3] were it but holy.
       MANFRED   And what are they who do avouch these things?
       ABBOT   My pious brethren—the scared peasantry—
45   Even thy own vassals—who do look on thee
       With most unquiet eyes. Thy life's in peril.
       MANFRED   Take it.
       ABBOT   I come to save, and not destroy—
       I would not pry into thy secret soul;
       But if these things be sooth, there still is time
50   For penitence and pity: reconcile thee
       With the true church, and through the church to heaven.
       MANFRED   I hear thee. This is my reply; whate'er
       I may have been, or am, doth rest between
       Heaven and myself.—I shall not choose a mortal
55   To be my mediator. Have I sinn'd
       Against your ordinances? prove and punish!
       ABBOT   My son! I did not speak of punishment,
       But penitence and pardon;—with thyself
       The choice of such remains—and for the last,
60   Our institutions and our strong belief
       Have given me power to smooth the path from sin
       To higher hope and better thoughts; the first
       I leave to heaven—"Vengeance is mine alone!"
       So saith the Lord,[4] and with all humbleness
65   His servant echoes back the awful word.
       MANFRED   Old man! there is no power in holy men,
       Nor charm in prayer—nor purifying form
       Of penitence—nor outward look—nor fast—
       Nor agony—nor, greater than all these,
70   The innate tortures of that deep despair,
       Which is remorse without the fear of hell,
       But all in all sufficient to itself
       Would make a hell of heaven—can exorcise
       From out the unbounded spirit, the quick sense
75   Of its own sins, wrongs, sufferance, and revenge
       Upon itself; there is no future pang
       Can deal that justice on the self-condemn'd
       He deals on his own soul.
       ABBOT   All this is well;
       For this will pass away, and be succeeded
80   By an auspicious hope, which shall look up
       With calm assurance to that blessed place,
       Which all who seek may win, whatever be
       Their earthly errors, so they be atoned:
       And the commencement of atonement is
85   The sense of its necessity.—Say on—

3. A person who, for religious reasons, lives in seclusion.

4. Romans 12.19: "Vengeance is mine; I will repay, saith the Lord."

And all our church can teach thee shall be taught;
And all we can absolve thee, shall be pardon'd.
MANFRED   When Rome's sixth Emperor[5] was near his last,
The victim of a self-inflicted wound,
90   To shun the torments of a public death
From senates once his slaves, a certain soldier,
With show of loyal pity, would have staunch'd
The gushing throat with his officious robe;
The dying Roman thrust him back and said—
95   Some empire still in his expiring glance,
"It is too late—is this fidelity?"
ABBOT   And what of this?
MANFRED   I answer with the Roman—
"It is too late!"
ABBOT   It never can be so,
To reconcile thyself with thy own soul,
00   And thy own soul with heaven. Hast thou no hope?
'Tis strange—even those who do despair above,
Yet shape themselves some phantasy on earth,
To which frail twig they cling, like drowning men.
MANFRED   Ay—father! I have had those earthly visions
05   And noble aspirations in my youth,
To make my own the mind of other men,
The enlightener of nations; and to rise
I knew not whither—it might be to fall;
But fall, even as the mountain-cataract,
10   Which having leapt from its more dazzling height,
Even in the foaming strength of its abyss,
(Which casts up misty columns that become
Clouds raining from the re-ascended skies)
Lies low but mighty still.—But this is past,
My thoughts mistook themselves.
15   ABBOT   And wherefore so?
MANFRED   I could not tame my nature down; for he
Must serve who fain would sway—and soothe—and sue—
And watch all time—and pry into all place—
And be a living lie—who would become
20   A mighty thing amongst the mean, and such
The mass are; I disdained to mingle with
A herd, though to be leader—and of wolves.
The lion is alone, and so am I.
ABBOT   And why not live and act with other men?
25   MANFRED   Because my nature was averse from life;
And yet not cruel; for I would not make,
But find a desolation:—like the wind,
The red-hot breath of the most lone Simoom,[6]
Which dwells but in the desert, and sweeps o'er

5. Byron transfers to Otho, the sixth emperor, a
story that the historian Suetonius tells about the
death of an earlier emperor, Nero.

6. A hot, sand-laden wind in the Sahara and Arabian deserts.

130   The barren sands which bear no shrubs to blast,
And revels o'er their wild and arid waves,
And seeketh not, so that it is not sought,
But being met is deadly; such hath been
The course of my existence; but there came
Things in my path which are no more.
135 ABBOT   Alas!
I 'gin to fear that thou art past all aid
From me and from my calling; yet so young,
I still would—
    MANFRED   Look on me! there is an order
Of mortals on the earth, who do become
140   Old in their youth, and die ere middle age,
Without the violence of warlike death;
Some perishing of pleasure—some of study—
Some worn with toil—some of mere weariness—
Some of disease—and some insanity—
145   And some of withered, or of broken hearts;
For this last is a malady which slays
More than are numbered in the lists of Fate,
Taking all shapes, and bearing many names.
Look upon me! for even of all these things
150   Have I partaken; and of all these things,
One were enough; then wonder not that I
Am what I am, but that I ever was,
Or, having been, that I am still on earth.
    ABBOT   Yet, hear me still—
    MANFRED   Old man! I do respect
155   Thine order, and revere thine years; I deem
Thy purpose pious, but it is in vain:
Think me not churlish; I would spare thyself,
Far more than me, in shunning at this time
All further colloquy—and so—farewell.   [*Exit* MANFRED.]
160 ABBOT   This should have been a noble creature: he
Hath all the energy which would have made
A goodly frame of glorious elements,
Had they been wisely mingled; as it is,
It is an awful chaos—light and darkness—
165   And mind and dust—and passions and pure thoughts,
Mix'd, and contending without end or order,
All dormant or destructive: he will perish,
And yet he must not; I will try once more,
For such are worth redemption; and my duty
170   Is to dare all things for a righteous end.
I'll follow him—but cautiously, though surely.   [*Exit* ABBOT.]

SCENE 2. *Another Chamber.* MANFRED *and* HERMAN.

HERMAN   My Lord, you bade me wait on you at sunset:
He sinks beyond the mountain.
    MANFRED   Doth he so?

I will look on him.
  [MANFRED *advances to the Window of the Hall.*]
   Glorious Orb! the idol
Of early nature, and the vigorous race
5 Of undiseased mankind, the giant sons
Of the embrace of angels, with a sex
More beautiful than they, which did draw down
The erring spirits[7] who can ne'er return.—
Most glorious orb! that wert a worship, ere
10 The mystery of thy making was reveal'd!
Thou earliest minister of the Almighty,
Which gladden'd, on their mountain tops, the hearts
Of the Chaldean° shepherds, till they pour'd   *Babylonian*
Themselves in orisons!° Thou material God!   *prayers*
15 And representative of the Unknown—
Who chose thee for his shadow! Thou chief star!
Centre of many stars! which mak'st our earth
Endurable, and temperest the hues
And hearts of all who walk within thy rays!
20 Sire of the seasons! Monarch of the climes,
And those who dwell in them! for near or far,
Our inborn spirits have a tint of thee,
Even as our outward aspects;—thou dost rise,
And shine, and set in glory. Fare thee well!
25 I ne'er shall see thee more. As my first glance
Of love and wonder was for thee, then take
My latest look: thou wilt not beam on one
To whom the gifts of life and warmth have been
Of a more fatal nature. He is gone:
30 I follow.   [*Exit* MANFRED.]

SCENE 3. *The Mountains.—The Castle of* MANFRED *at some distance.—A Terrace before a Tower.—Time, Twilight.* HERMAN, MANUEL, *and other Dependants of* MANFRED.

HERMAN 'Tis strange enough; night after night, for years,
He hath pursued long vigils in this tower,
Without a witness. I have been within it,—
So have we all been oft-times; but from it,
5 Or its contents, it were impossible
To draw conclusions absolute, of aught
His studies tend to. To be sure, there is
One chamber where none enter; I would give
The fee° of what I have to come these three years,   *ownership*
To pore upon its mysteries.
10 MANUEL   'Twere dangerous;
Content thyself with what thou knowest already.

---

7. Genesis 6.4: "There were giants in the earth in those days; and also after that, when the sons of God came in unto the daughters of men, and they bare children to them, the same became mighty men which were of old, men of renown." Byron interprets "the sons of God" as denoting disobedient angels.

HERMAN   Ah! Manuel! thou art elderly and wise,
And could'st say much; thou hast dwelt within the castle—
How many years is't?
MANUEL   Ere Count Manfred's birth,
15   I served his father, whom he nought resembles.
HERMAN   There be more sons in like predicament.
But wherein do they differ?
MANUEL   I speak not
Of features or of form, but mind and habits:
Count Sigismund was proud,—but gay and free,—
20   A warrior and a reveller; he dwelt not
With books and solitude, nor made the night
A gloomy vigil, but a festal time,
Merrier than day; he did not walk the rocks
And forests like a wolf, nor turn aside
From men and their delights.
25   HERMAN   Beshrew[8] the hour,
But those were jocund times! I would that such
Would visit the old walls again; they look
As if they had forgotten them.
MANUEL   These walls
Must change their chieftain first. Oh! I have seen
Some strange things in them, Herman.
30   HERMAN   Come, be friendly;
Relate me some to while away our watch:
I've heard thee darkly speak of an event
Which happened hereabouts, by this same tower.
MANUEL   That was a night indeed; I do remember
35   'Twas twilight, as it may be now, and such
Another evening—yon red cloud, which rests
On Eigher's[9] pinnacle, so rested then,—
So like that it might be the same; the wind
Was faint and gusty, and the mountain snows
40   Began to glitter with the climbing moon;
Count Manfred was, as now, within his tower,—
How occupied, we knew not, but with him
The sole companion of his wanderings
And watchings—her, whom of all earthly things
45   That lived, the only thing he seem'd to love,—
As he, indeed, by blood was bound to do,
The Lady Astarte, his—
                         Hush! who comes here?
                         Enter the ABBOT.
ABBOT   Where is your master?
HERMAN   Yonder in the tower.
ABBOT   I must speak with him.
MANUEL   'Tis impossible;
50   He is most private, and must not be thus
Intruded on.

8. Curse (used jocularly).   9. A peak a few miles north of the Jungfrau.

ABBOT   Upon myself I take
The forfeit of my fault, if fault there be—
But I must see him.
HERMAN   Thou hast seen him once
This eve already.
ABBOT   Sirrah! I command thee,
Knock, and apprize the Count of my approach.
HERMAN   We dare not.
ABBOT   Then it seems I must be herald
Of my own purpose.
MANUEL   Reverend father, stop—
I pray you pause.
ABBOT   Why so?
MANUEL   But step this way,
And I will tell you further.   [*Exeunt.*]

SCENE 4. *Interior of the Tower.*

MANUEL *alone*

The stars are forth, the moon above the tops
Of the snow-shining mountains.—Beautiful!
I linger yet with Nature, for the night
Hath been to me a more familiar face
Than that of man; and in her starry shade
Of dim and solitary loveliness,
I learn'd the language of another world.
I do remember me, that in my youth,
When I was wandering,—upon such a night
I stood within the Coloseum's wall,
'Midst the chief relics of almighty Rome;
The trees which grew along the broken arches
Waved dark in the blue midnight, and the stars
Shone through the rents of ruin; from afar
The watchdog bayed beyond the Tiber;[1] and
More near from out the Caesars' palace[2] came
The owl's long cry, and, interruptedly,
Of distant sentinels the fitful song
Begun and died upon the gentle wind.
Some cypresses beyond the time-worn breach
Appeared to skirt the horizon, yet they stood
Within a bowshot—where the Caesars dwelt,
And dwell the tuneless birds of night; amidst
A grove which springs through levell'd battlements,
And twines its roots with the imperial hearths,
Ivy usurps the laurel's place of growth;—
But the gladiators' bloody Circus[3] stands,

1. The river that flows through Rome.
2. The palace of the Roman emperors. It stands on the Palatine hill, immediately southwest of the Coloseum.
3. The circular arena within the Coliseum where professional gladiators fought to the death as public entertainment.

A noble wreck in ruinous perfection!
While Caesar's chambers, and the Augustan halls,
30 Grovel on earth in indistinct decay.—
And thou didst shine, thou rolling moon, upon
All this, and cast a wide and tender light,
Which soften'd down the hoar austerity
Of rugged desolation, and fill'd up,
35 As 'twere anew, the gaps of centuries;
Leaving that beautiful which still was so,
And making that which was not, till the place
Became religion, and the heart ran o'er
With silent worship of the great of old!—
40 The dead, but sceptred sovereigns, who still rule
Our spirits from their urns.—

        'Twas such a night!
'Tis strange that I recall it at this time;
But I have found our thoughts take wildest flight
Even at the moment when they should array
Themselves in pensive order.

           Enter the ABBOT.
45 ABBOT   My good Lord!
I crave a second grace for this approach;
But yet let not my humble zeal offend
By its abruptness—all it hath of ill
Recoils on me; its good in the effect
50 May light upon your head—could I say *heart*—
Could I touch *that,* with words or prayers, I should
Recall a noble spirit which hath wandered,
But is not yet all lost.
MANFRED   Thou know'st me not;
My days are numbered, and my deeds recorded:
55 Retire, or 'twill be dangerous—Away!
ABBOT Thou dost not mean to menace me?
MANFRED   Not I;
I simply tell thee peril is at hand,
And would preserve thee.
ABBOT   What dost mean?
MANFRED   Look there!
What dost thou see?
ABBOT   Nothing.
MANFRED   Look there, I say,
60 And steadfastly;—now tell me what thou seest?
ABBOT That which should shake me,—but I fear it not—
I see a dusk and awful figure rise
Like an infernal god from out the earth;
His face wrapt in a mantle, and his form
65 Robed as with angry clouds; he stands between
Thyself and me—but I do fear him not.
MANFRED Thou hast no cause—he shall not harm thee—but
His sight may shock thine old limbs into palsy.
I say to thee—Retire!

ABBOT   And, I reply—

70 Never—till I have battled with this fiend—
What doth he here?

MANFRED   Why—ay—what doth he here?
I did not send for him,—he is unbidden.

ABBOT   Alas! lost mortal! what with guests like these
Hast thou to do? I tremble for thy sake;

75 Why doth he gaze on thee, and thou on him?
Ah! he unveils his aspect; on his brow
The thunder-scars are graven; from his eye
Glares forth the immortality of hell—
Avaunt!—

MANFRED   Pronounce—what is thy mission?

SPIRIT   Come!

80 ABBOT   What art thou, unknown being? answer!—speak!

SPIRIT   The genius[4] of this mortal.—Come! 'tis time.

MANFRED   I am prepared for all things, but deny
The power which summons me. Who sent thee here?

SPIRIT   Thou'lt know anon—Come! come!

MANFRED   I have commanded

85 Things of an essence greater far than thine,
And striven with thy masters. Get thee hence!

SPIRIT   Mortal! thine hour is come—Away! I say.

MANFRED   I knew, and know my hour is come, but not
To render up my soul to such as thee:

90 Away! I'll die as I have lived—alone.

SPIRIT   Then I must summon up my brethren.—Rise! [*Other Spirits rise up.*]

ABBOT   Avaunt! ye evil ones!—Avaunt! I say,—
Ye have no power where piety hath power,
And I do charge ye in the name—

SPIRIT   Old man!

95 We know ourselves, our mission, and thine order;
Waste not thy holy words on idle uses,
It were in vain; this man is forfeited.
Once more I summon him—Away! away!

MANFRED   I do defy ye,—though I feel my soul

100 Is ebbing from me, yet I do defy ye;
Nor will I hence, while I have earthly breath
To breathe my scorn upon ye—earthly strength
To wrestle, though with spirits; what ye take
Shall be ta'en limb by limb.

SPIRIT   Reluctant mortal!

105 Is this the Magian who would so pervade
The world invisible, and make himself
Almost our equal?—Can it be that thou
Art thus in love with life? the very life
Which made thee wretched!

MANFRED   Thou false fiend, thou liest!

110 My life is in its last hour,—*that* I know,

---

4. The spirit or deity presiding over a human being from birth.

Nor would redeem a moment of that hour;
I do not combat against death, but thee
And thy surrounding angels; my past power
Was purchased by no compact with thy crew,
115 But by superior science—penance—daring—
And length of watching—strength of mind—and skill
In knowledge of our fathers—when the earth
Saw men and spirits walking side by side,
And gave ye no supremacy: I stand
120 Upon my strength—I do defy—deny—
Spurn back, and scorn ye!—
SPIRIT   But thy many crimes
Have made thee—
MANFRED   What are they to such as thee?
Must crimes be punish'd but by other crimes,
And greater criminals?—Back to thy hell!
125 Thou hast no power upon me, *that* I feel;
Thou never shalt possess me, *that* I know:
What I have done is done; I bear within
A torture which could nothing gain from thine:
The mind which is immortal makes itself
130 Requital for its good or evil thoughts—
Is its own origin of ill and end—
And its own place and time[5]—its innate sense,
When stripp'd of this mortality, derives
No colour from the fleeting things without,
135 But is absorb'd in sufferance or in joy,
Born from the knowledge of its own desert.
Thou didst not tempt me, and thou couldst not tempt me;
I have not been thy dupe, nor am thy prey—
But was my own destroyer, and will be
140 My own hereafter.—Back, ye baffled fiends!
The hand of death is on me—but not yours!

[*The Demons disappear.*]

ABBOT   Alas! how pale thou art—thy lips are white—
And thy breast heaves—and in thy gasping throat
The accents rattle—Give thy prayers to Heaven—
145 Pray—albeit but in thought,—but die not thus.
MANFRED   'Tis over—my dull eyes can fix thee not;
But all things swim around me, and the earth
Heaves as it were beneath me. Fare thee well—
Give me thy hand.
ABBOT   Cold—cold—even to the heart—
150 But yet one prayer—alas! how fares it with thee?—
MANFRED   Old man! 'tis not so difficult to die.[6]

5. The last of several echoes by Manfred of Satan's claim that "The mind is its own place, and in itself / Can make a Heaven of Hell, and a Hell of Heaven" (*Paradise Lost* 1.254–55). See also 1.1.251 and 3.1.73, above.

6. When this line was dropped in the printing of the first edition, Byron wrote angrily to his publisher: "You have destroyed the whole effect and moral of the poem by omitting the last line of Manfred's speaking."

[MANFRED *expires.*]
ABBOT   He's gone—his soul hath ta'en its earthless flight—
Whither? I dread to think—but he is gone.

1816–17   1817

Don Juan   Byron began his masterpiece (pronounced in the English fashion,
Don Joó-un) in July 1818, published it in installments beginning with cantos 1 and
2 in 1819, and continued working on it almost until his death. Initially he improvised
the poem from episode to episode. "I *have* no plan," he said, "I *had* no plan; but I had
or have materials." The work was composed with remarkable speed (the 888 lines of
canto 13, for example, were dashed off within a week), and it aims at the effect of
improvisation rather than of artful compression; it asks to be read rapidly, at a conversational pace.
     The poem breaks off with the sixteenth canto, but even in its unfinished state *Don
Juan* is the longest satirical poem, and indeed one of the longest poems of any kind, in
English. Its hero, the Spanish libertine, had in the original legend been superhuman
in his sexual energy and wickedness. Throughout Byron's version the unspoken but
persistent joke is that this archetypal lady-killer of European legend is in fact more
acted upon than active. Unfailingly amiable and well intentioned, he is guilty largely of
youth, charm, and a courteous and compliant spirit. The women do all the rest.
     The chief models for the poem were the Italian seriocomic versions of medieval
chivalric romances; the genre had been introduced by Pulci in the fifteenth century
and was adopted by Ariosto in his *Orlando Furioso* (1532). From these writers Byron
caught the mixed moods and violent oscillations between the sublime and the ridiculous as well as the colloquial management of the complex ottava rima—an eight-
line stanza in which the initial interlaced rhymes (*ababab*) build up to the comic turn
in the final couplet (*cc*). Byron was influenced in the English use of this Italian form
by a mildly amusing poem published in 1817, under the pseudonym of "Whistlecraft,"
by his friend John Hookham Frere. Other recognizable antecedents of *Don Juan* are
Jonathan Swift's *Gulliver's Travels* and Samuel Johnson's *Rasselas*, both of which had
employed the naive traveler as a satiric device, and Laurence Sterne's novel *Tristram
Shandy*, with its comic exploitation of a narrative medium blatantly subject to the
whimsy of the author. But even the most original literary works play variations on
inherited conventions. Shelley at once recognized his friend's poem as "something
wholly new and relative to the age."
     Byron's literary advisers thought the poem unacceptably immoral, and John Murray
took the precaution of printing the first two installments (cantos 1–2, then 3–5)
without identifying Byron as the author or himself as the publisher. The eleven completed cantos that followed were, because of Murray's continuing jitters, brought out
in 1823–24 by the radical publisher John Hunt. In those cantos Byron's purpose
deepened. He set out to create a comic yet devastatingly critical history of the Europe
of his own age, sending the impressionable Juan from West to East and back again,
from his native Spain to a Russian court (by way of a primitive Greek island and the
1790 siege of the Turkish town of Ismail) and then into the English gentry's country
manors. These journeys, which facilitated Byron's satire on almost all existing forms
of political organization, would, according to the scheme that he projected for the
poem as a whole, ultimately have taken Juan to a death by guillotining in Revolutionary France.
     Yet the controlling element of *Don Juan* is not the narrative but the narrator. His
running commentary on Juan's misadventures, his reminiscences, and his opinion-
ated remarks on the epoch of political reaction in which he is actually telling Juan's

story together add another level to the poem's engagement with history. The narrator's reflections also at the same time lend unity to *Don Juan*'s effervescent variety. Tellingly, the poem opens with the first-person pronoun and immediately lets us into the storyteller's predicament: "I want a hero. . . ." The voice then goes on, for almost two thousand stanzas, with effortless volubility and shifts of mood. The poet who in his brilliant successful youth created the gloomy Byronic hero, in his later and sadder life created a character (not the hero, but the narrator of *Don Juan*) who is one of the great comic inventions in English literature.

FROM DON JUAN

Fragment[1]

I would to Heaven that I were so much Clay—
    As I am blood—bone—marrow, passion—feeling—
    Because at least the past were past away—
    And for the future—(but I write this reeling
5   Having got drunk exceedingly to day
    So that I seem to stand upon the ceiling)
    I say—the future is a serious matter—
    And so—for Godsake—Hock[2] and Soda water.

From Canto 1

[JUAN AND DONNA JULIA]

I

I want a hero: an uncommon want,
    When every year and month sends forth a new one,
    Till, after cloying the gazettes with cant,
    The age discovers he is not the true one;
5   Of such as these I should not care to vaunt,
    I'll therefore take our ancient friend Don Juan,
    We all have seen him in the pantomime[1]
    Sent to the devil, somewhat ere his time.

✻   ✻   ✻

5

Brave men were living before Agamemnon[2]
    And since, exceeding valorous and sage,
35 A good deal like him too, though quite the same none;
    But then they shone not on the poet's page,

---

1. This stanza was written on the back of a page of the manuscript of canto 1. For the author's revisions while composing two stanzas of *Don Juan*, see "Poems in Process," in the appendices to this volume.
2. A white Rhine wine, from the German *Hoch-*

heimer.
1. The Juan legend was a popular subject in English pantomime.
2. In Homer's *Iliad* the king commanding the Greeks in the siege of Troy. This line is translated from a Latin ode by Horace.

And so have been forgotten—I condemn none,
    But can't find any in the present age
Fit for my poem (that is, for my new one);
40   So, as I said, I'll take my friend Don Juan.

6

Most epic poets plunge in *"medias res,"*[3]
    (Horace makes this the heroic turnpike road)[4]
And then your hero tells, whene'er you please,
    What went before—by way of episode,
45 While seated after dinner at his ease,
    Beside his mistress in some soft abode,
Palace, or garden, paradise, or cavern,
Which serves the happy couple for a tavern.

7

That is the usual method, but not mine—
50 My way is to begin with the beginning;
The regularity of my design
    Forbids all wandering as the worst of sinning,
And therefore I shall open with a line
    (Although it cost me half an hour in spinning)
55 Narrating somewhat of Don Juan's father,
And also of his mother, if you'd rather.

8

In Seville was he born, a pleasant city,
    Famous for oranges and women—he
Who has not seen it will be much to pity,
60 So says the proverb—and I quite agree;
Of all the Spanish towns is none more pretty,
    Cadiz perhaps—but that you soon may see:—
Don Juan's parents lived beside the river,
A noble stream, and call'd the Guadalquivir.

9

65 His father's name was Jóse[5]—*Don,* of course,
    A true Hidalgo,° free from every stain   *noble man*
Of Moor or Hebrew blood, he traced his source
    Through the most Gothic gentlemen of Spain;
A better cavalier ne'er mounted horse,
70 Or, being mounted, e'er got down again,
Than Jóse, who begot our hero, who
Begot—but that's to come——Well, to renew:

10

His mother was a learned lady, famed
    For every branch of every science known—
75 In every christian language ever named,
    With virtues equall'd by her wit alone,
She made the cleverest people quite ashamed,

---

3. Into the middle of things (Latin; Horace's *Art of Poetry* 148).
4. I.e., the smoothest road for heroic poetry.

5. Normally "José"; Byron transferred the accent to keep his meter.

And even the good with inward envy groan,
Finding themselves so very much exceeded
80   In their own way by all the things that she did.

11

Her memory was a mine: she knew by heart
All Calderon and greater part of Lopé,[6]
So that if any actor miss'd his part
She could have served him for the prompter's copy;
85   For her Feinagle's[7] were an useless art,
And he himself obliged to shut up shop—he
Could never make a memory so fine as
That which adorn'd the brain of Donna Inez.

12

Her favourite science was the mathematical,
90   Her noblest virtue was her magnanimity,
Her wit (she sometimes tried at wit) was Attic[8] all,
Her serious sayings darken'd to sublimity;
In short, in all things she was fairly what I call
A prodigy—her morning dress was dimity,°   cotton
95   Her evening silk, or, in the summer, muslin,
And other stuffs, with which I won't stay puzzling.

13

She knew the Latin—that is, "the Lord's prayer,"
And Greek—the alphabet—I'm nearly sure;
She read some French romances here and there,
100   Although her mode of speaking was not pure;
For native Spanish she had no great care,
At least her conversation was obscure;
Her thoughts were theorems, her words a problem,
As if she deem'd that mystery would ennoble 'em.

*   *   *

22

'Tis pity learned virgins ever wed
170   With persons of no sort of education,
Or gentlemen, who, though well-born and bred,
Grow tired of scientific conversation:
I don't choose to say much upon this head,
I'm a plain man, and in a single station,
175   But—Oh! ye lords of ladies intellectual,
Inform us truly, have they not hen-peck'd you all?

23

Don Jóse and his lady quarrell'd—why,
Not any of the many could divine,
Though several thousand people chose to try,

6. Calderón de la Barca and Lope de Vega, the
great Spanish dramatists of the early 17th century.
7. Gregor von Feinagle, a German expert on the
art of memory, who had lectured in England in

1811.
8. Athenian. Attic salt is a term for the famed wit
of the Athenians.

180   'Twas surely no concern of theirs nor mine;
     I loathe that low vice curiosity,
       But if there's any thing in which I shine
     'Tis in arranging all my friends' affairs.
     Not having, of my own, domestic cares.

24

185   And so I interfered, and with the best
     Intentions, but their treatment was not kind;
     I think the foolish people were possess'd,
       For neither of them could I ever find,
     Although their porter afterwards confess'd—
190   But that's no matter, and the worst's behind,
     For little Juan o'er me threw, down stairs,
     A pail of housemaid's water unawares.

25

     A little curly-headed, good-for-nothing,
       And mischief-making monkey from his birth;
195   His parents ne'er agreed except in doting
       Upon the most unquiet imp on earth;
     Instead of quarrelling, had they been but both in
       Their senses, they'd have sent young master forth
     To school, or had him soundly whipp'd at home,
200   To teach him manners for the time to come.

26

     Don Jóse and the Donna Inez led
       For some time an unhappy sort of life,
     Wishing each other, not divorced, but dead;
       They lived respectably as man and wife,
205   Their conduct was exceedingly well-bred,
       And gave no outward signs of inward strife,
     Until at length the smother'd fire broke out,
     And put the business past all kind of doubt.

27

     For Inez call'd some druggists and physicians,
210   And tried to prove her loving lord was *mad*,⁹
     But as he had some lucid intermissions,
       She next decided he was only *bad;*
     Yet when they ask'd her for her depositions,
       No sort of explanation could be had,
215   Save that her duty both to man and God
     Required this conduct—which seem'd very odd.

28

     She kept a journal, where his faults were noted,
       And open'd certain trunks of books and letters,
     All which might, if occasion served, be quoted;

9. Lady Byron had thought her husband might be insane and sought medical advice on the matter. This and other passages obviously allude to his wife, although Byron insisted that Donna Inez was not intended to be a caricature of Lady Byron. In her determination to preserve her son's innocence, Donna Inez also shares traits with Byron's mother.

220   And then she had all Seville for abettors,
        Besides her good old grandmother (who doted);
        The hearers of her case became repeaters,
        Then advocates, inquisitors, and judges,
        Some for amusement, others for old grudges.

29

225   And then this best and meekest woman bore
        With such serenity her husband's woes,
        Just as the Spartan ladies did of yore,
        Who saw their spouses kill'd, and nobly chose
        Never to say a word about them more—
230   Calmly she heard each calumny that rose,
        And saw *his* agonies with such sublimity,
        That all the world exclaim'd "What magnanimity!"

✻   ✻   ✻

32

        Their friends had tried at reconciliation,
250   Then their relations, who made matters worse;
        ('Twere hard to say upon a like occasion
        To whom it may be best to have recourse—
        I can't say much for friend or yet relation):
        The lawyers did their utmost for divorce,
255   But scarce a fee was paid on either side
        Before, unluckily, Don Jóse died.

33

        He died: and most unluckily, because,
        According to all hints I could collect
        From counsel learned in those kinds of laws,
260   (Although their talk's obscure and circumspect)
        His death contrived to spoil a charming cause;°   *law case*
        A thousand pities also with respect
        To public feeling, which on this occasion
        Was manifested in a great sensation.

✻   ✻   ✻

37

        Dying intestate,° Juan was sole heir   *without a will*
290   To a chancery suit, and messuages,[1] and lands,
        Which, with a long minority and care,
        Promised to turn out well in proper hands:
        Inez became sole guardian, which was fair,
        And answer'd but to nature's just demands;
295   An only son left with an only mother
        Is brought up much more wisely than another.

---

1. Houses and the adjoining lands. "Chancery suit": a case in what was then the highest English court, notorious for its delays.

38

Sagest of women, even of widows, she
    Resolved that Juan should be quite a paragon,
And worthy of the noblest pedigree:
300   (His sire was of Castile, his dam from Arragon).
Then for accomplishments of chivalry,
    In case our lord the king should go to war again,
He learn'd the arts of riding, fencing, gunnery,
    And how to scale a fortress—or a nunnery.

39

305 But that which Donna Inez most desired,
    And saw into herself each day before all
The learned tutors whom for him she hired,
    Was, that his breeding should be strictly moral;
Much into all his studies she inquired,
310   And so they were submitted first to her, all,
Arts, sciences, no branch was made a mystery
To Juan's eyes, excepting natural history.[2]

40

The languages, especially the dead,
    The sciences, and most of all the abstruse,
315 The arts, at least all such as could be said
    To be the most remote from common use,
In all these he was much and deeply read;
    But not a page of anything that's loose,
Or hints continuation of the species,
320 Was ever suffer'd, lest he should grow vicious.

41

His classic studies made a little puzzle,
    Because of filthy loves of gods and goddesses,
Who in the earlier ages made a bustle,
    But never put on pantaloons or boddices;
325 His reverend tutors had at times a tussle,
    And for their Aeneids, Iliads, and Odysseys,
Were forced to make an odd sort of apology,
For Donna Inez dreaded the mythology.

42

Ovid's a rake, as half his verses show him,
330   Anacreon's morals are a still worse sample,
Catullus scarcely has a decent poem,
    I don't think Sappho's Ode a good example,
Although Longinus[3] tells us there is no hymn
    Where the sublime soars forth on wings more ample;
335 But Virgil's songs are pure, except that horrid one
Beginning with *"Formosum Pastor Corydon."*[4]

2. Includes biology, physiology, and particularly botany, popular in the era in part because study of plants' stamens and pistils offered a form of surreptitious sex education.
3. In *On the Sublime* 10, the Greek rhetorician Longinus praises a passage of erotic longing from one of Sappho's odes.
4. Virgil's *Eclogue* 2 begins: "The shepherd, Corydon, burned with love for the handsome Alexis."

43

Lucretius' irreligion[5] is too strong
For early stomachs, to prove wholesome food;
I can't help thinking Juvenal[6] was wrong,
340   Although no doubt his real intent was good,
For speaking out so plainly in his song,
So much indeed as to be downright rude;
And then what proper person can be partial
To all those nauseous epigrams of Martial?

44

345   Juan was taught from out the best edition,
Expurgated by learned men, who place,
Judiciously, from out the schoolboy's vision,
The grosser parts; but fearful to deface
Too much their modest bard by this omission,
350   And pitying sore his mutilated case,
They only add them all in an appendix,[7]
Which saves, in fact, the trouble of an index.

                    ✻   ✻   ✻

52

For my part I say nothing—nothing—but
410   *This* I will say—my reasons are my own—
That if I had an only son to put
To school (as God be praised that I have none)
'Tis not with Donna Inez I would shut
Him up to learn his catechism alone,
415   No—No—I'd send him out betimes to college,
For there it was I pick'd up my own knowledge.

53

For there one learns—'tis not for me to boast,
Though I acquired—but I pass over *that,*
As well as all the Greek I since have lost:
420   I say that there's the place—but *"Verbum sat,"*[8]
I think I pick'd up too, as well as most,
Knowledge of matters—but no matter *what*—
I never married—but, I think, I know
That sons should not be educated so.

54

425   Young Juan now was sixteen years of age,
Tall, handsome, slender, but well knit; he seem'd
Active, though not so sprightly, as a page;
And every body but his mother deem'd
Him almost man; but she flew in a rage,

---

5. In *De Rerum Natura* (*On the Nature of Things*), Lucretius argues that the universe can be explained in entirely materialist terms without reference to any god.
6. The Latin satires of Juvenal attacked the corruption of Roman society in the 1st century C.E.
and displayed its vices.
7. Fact! There is, or was, such an edition, with all the obnoxious epigrams of Martial placed by themselves at the end [Byron's note]. Martial, another Latin poet, was a contemporary of Juvenal.
8. A word [to the wise] is sufficient (Latin).

430   And bit her lips (for else she might have scream'd),
If any said so, for to be precocious
Was in her eyes a thing the most atrocious.

55

Amongst her numerous acquaintance, all
    Selected for discretion and devotion,
435 There was the Donna Julia, whom to call
    Pretty were but to give a feeble notion
Of many charms in her as natural
    As sweetness to the flower, or salt to ocean,
Her zone to Venus,⁹ or his bow to Cupid,
440   (But this last simile is trite and stupid).

56

The darkness of her Oriental eye
    Accorded with her Moorish origin;
(Her blood was not all Spanish, by the by;
    In Spain, you know, this is a sort of sin).
445 When proud Grenada fell, and, forced to fly,
    Boabdil wept,¹ of Donna Julia's kin
Some went to Africa, some staid in Spain,
Her great great grandmamma chose to remain.

57

She married (I forget the pedigree)
450   With an Hidalgo, who transmitted down
His blood less noble than such blood should be;
    At such alliances his sires would frown,
In that point so precise in each degree
    That they bred *in and in,* as might be shown,
455 Marrying their cousins—nay, their aunts and nieces,
Which always spoils the breed, if it increases.

58

This heathenish cross restored the breed again,
    Ruin'd its blood, but much improved its flesh;
For, from a root the ugliest in Old Spain
460   Sprung up a branch as beautiful as fresh;
The sons no more were short, the daughters plain:
    But there's a rumour which I fain would hush,
'Tis said that Donna Julia's grandmamma
Produced her Don more heirs at love than law.

59

465 However this might be, the race° went on   *family line*
    Improving still through every generation,
Until it center'd in an only son,
    Who left an only daughter; my narration
May have suggested that this single one
470   Could be but Julia (whom on this occasion

9. The belt ("zone") of Venus made its wearer sexually irresistible.
1. The Moorish king of Granada (the last Islamic enclave in Spain) wept when his capital fell and he and his people were forced to emigrate to Africa (1492).

I shall have much to speak about), and she
Was married, charming, chaste,[2] and twenty-three.

60

Her eye (I'm very fond of handsome eyes)
Was large and dark, suppressing half its fire
475   Until she spoke, then through its soft disguise
Flash'd an expression more of pride than ire,
And love than either; and there would arise
A something in them which was not desire,
But would have been, perhaps, but for the soul
480   Which struggled through and chasten'd down the whole.

61

Her glossy hair was cluster'd o'er a brow
Bright with intelligence, and fair and smooth;
Her eyebrow's shape was like the aerial bow,
Her cheek all purple with the beam of youth,
485   Mounting, at times, to a transparent glow,
As if her veins ran lightning; she, in sooth,
Possess'd an air and grace by no means common:
Her stature tall—I hate a dumpy woman.

62

Wedded she was some years, and to a man
490   Of fifty, and such husbands are in plenty;
And yet, I think, instead of such a ONE
'Twere better to have TWO of five and twenty,
Especially in countries near the sun:
And now I think on't, "mi vien in mente,"[3]
495   Ladies even of the most uneasy virtue
Prefer a spouse whose age is short of thirty.

63

'Tis a sad thing, I cannot choose but say,
And all the fault of that indecent sun,
Who cannot leave alone our helpless clay,
500   But will keep baking, broiling, burning on,
That howsoever people fast and pray
The flesh is frail, and so the soul undone:
What men call gallantry, and gods adultery,
Is much more common where the climate's sultry.

64

505   Happy the nations of the moral north!
Where all is virtue, and the winter season
Sends sin, without a rag on, shivering forth;
('Twas snow that brought St. Francis back to reason);
Where juries cast up what a wife is worth
510   By laying whate'er sum, in mulct,[4] they please on
The lover, who must pay a handsome price,
Because it is a marketable vice.

2. I.e., faithful to her husband.
3. It comes to my mind (Italian).

4. By way of a fine or legal penalty.

65

Alfonso was the name of Julia's lord,
    A man well looking for his years, and who
515 Was neither much beloved, nor yet abhorr'd;
    They lived together as most people do,
    Suffering each other's foibles by accord,
        And not exactly either *one* or *two;*
    Yet he was jealous, though he did not show it,
520 For jealousy dislikes the world to know it.

* * *

69

545 Juan she saw, and, as a pretty child,
        Caress'd him often, such a thing might be
    Quite innocently done, and harmless styled,
        When she had twenty years, and thirteen he;
    But I am not so sure I should have smiled
550   When he was sixteen, Julia twenty-three,
    These few short years make wondrous alterations,
    Particularly amongst sun-burnt nations.

70

Whate'er the cause might be, they had become
    Changed; for the dame grew distant, the youth shy,
555 Their looks cast down, their greetings almost dumb,
    And much embarrassment in either eye;
    There surely will be little doubt with some
        That Donna Julia knew the reason why,
    But as for Juan, he had no more notion
560 Than he who never saw the sea of ocean.

71

Yet Julia's very coldness still was kind,
    And tremulously gentle her small hand
Withdrew itself from his, but left behind
    A little pressure, thrilling, and so bland
565 And slight, so very slight, that to the mind
    'Twas but a doubt; but ne'er magician's wand
Wrought change with all Armida's[5] fairy art
Like what this light touch left on Juan's heart.

72

And if she met him, though she smiled no more,
570   She look'd a sadness sweeter than her smile,
As if her heart had deeper thoughts in store
    She must not own, but cherish'd more the while,
    For that compression in its burning core;
        Even innocence itself has many a wile,
575 And will not dare to trust itself with truth,
    And love is taught hypocrisy from youth.

* * *

5. The sorceress in Torquato Tasso's *Jerusalem Delivered* (1581) who seduces Rinaldo into forgetting his vows as a crusader.

75

Poor Julia's heart was in an awkward state;
She felt it going, and resolved to make
595   The noblest efforts for herself and mate,
For honour's, pride's, religion's, virtue's sake;
Her resolutions were most truly great,
And almost might have made a Tarquin[6] quake;
She pray'd the Virgin Mary for her grace,
600   As being the best judge of a lady's case.

76

She vow'd she never would see Juan more,
And next day paid a visit to his mother,
And look'd extremely at the opening door,
Which, by the Virgin's grace, let in another;
605   Grateful she was, and yet a little sore—
Again it opens, it can be no other,
'Tis surely Juan now—No! I'm afraid
That night the Virgin was no further pray'd.

77

She now determined that a virtuous woman
610   Should rather face and overcome temptation,
That flight was base and dastardly, and no man
Should ever give her heart the least sensation;
That is to say, a thought beyond the common
Preference, that we must feel upon occasion,
615   For people who are pleasanter than others,
But then they only seem so many brothers.

78

And even if by chance—and who can tell?
The devil's so very sly—she should discover
That all within was not so very well,
620   And, if still free, that such or such a lover
Might please perhaps, a virtuous wife can quell
Such thoughts, and be the better when they're over;
And if the man should ask,'tis but denial:
I recommend young ladies to make trial.

79

625   And then there are such things as love divine,
Bright and immaculate, unmix'd and pure,
Such as the angels think so very fine,
And matrons, who would be no less secure,
Platonic, perfect, "just such love as mine":
630   Thus Julia said—and thought so, to be sure,
And so I'd have her think, were I the man
On whom her reveries celestial ran.

*   *   *

6. A member of a legendary family of Roman kings noted for tyranny and cruelty; perhaps a reference specifically to Lucius Tarquinus, the villain of Shakespeare's *The Rape of Lucrece.*

86

So much for Julia. Now we'll turn to Juan,
    Poor little fellow! he had no idea
Of his own case, and never hit the true one;
    In feelings quick as Ovid's Miss Medea,[7]
685 He puzzled over what he found a new one,
    But not as yet imagined it could be a
Thing quite in course, and not at all alarming,
Which, with a little patience, might grow charming.

                   *   *   *

90

Young Juan wander'd by the glassy brooks
    Thinking unutterable things; he threw
715 Himself at length within the leafy nooks
    Where the wild branch of the cork forest grew;
There poets find materials for their books,
    And every now and then we read them through,
So that their plan and prosody are eligible,
720 Unless, like Wordsworth, they prove unintelligible.

91

He, Juan (and not Wordsworth), so pursued
    His self-communion with his own high soul,
Until his mighty heart, in its great mood,
    Had mitigated part, though not the whole
725 Of its disease; he did the best he could
    With things not very subject to control,
And turn'd, without perceiving his condition,
Like Coleridge, into a metaphysician.

92

He thought about himself, and the whole earth,
730   Of man the wonderful, and of the stars,
And how the deuce they ever could have birth;
    And then he thought of earthquakes, and of wars,
How many miles the moon might have in girth,
    Of air-balloons, and of the many bars
735 To perfect knowledge of the boundless skies;
And then he thought of Donna Julia's eyes.

93

In thoughts like these true wisdom may discern
    Longings sublime, and aspirations high,
Which some are born with, but the most part learn
740   To plague themselves withal, they know not why:
'Twas strange that one so young should thus concern
    His brain about the action of the sky;
If *you* think 'twas philosophy that this did,
I can't help thinking puberty assisted.

7. In *Metamorphoses* 7 Ovid tells the story of Medea's mad infatuation for Jason.

94

745 He pored upon the leaves, and on the flowers,
    And heard a voice in all the winds; and then
    He thought of wood nymphs and immortal bowers,
    And how the goddesses came down to men:
    He miss'd the pathway, he forgot the hours,
750 And when he look'd upon his watch again,
    He found how much old Time had been a winner—
    He also found that he had lost his dinner.

              ❋   ❋   ❋

103

'Twas on a summer's day—the sixth of June:—
I like to be particular in dates,
Not only of the age, and year, but moon;
820 They are a sort of post-house, where the Fates
Change horses, making history change its tune,
    Then spur away o'er empires and o'er states,
Leaving at last not much besides chronology,
Excepting the post-obits[8] of theology.

104

825 'Twas on the sixth of June, about the hour
    Of half-past six—perhaps still nearer seven,
    When Julia sate within as pretty a bower
    As e'er held houri in that heathenish heaven
    Described by Mahomet, and Anacreon Moore,[9]
830 To whom the lyre and laurels have been given,
    With all the trophies of triumphant song—
    He won them well, and may he wear them long!

105

She sate, but not alone; I know not well
How this same interview had taken place,
835 And even if I knew, I should not tell—
People should hold their tongues in any case;
No matter how or why the thing befell,
    But there were she and Juan, face to face—
When two such faces are so,'twould be wise,
840 But very difficult, to shut their eyes.

106

How beautiful she look'd! her conscious[1] heart
Glow'd in her cheek, and yet she felt no wrong.
Oh Love! how perfect is thy mystic art,
    Strengthening the weak, and trampling on the strong,

---

8. I.e., postobit bonds (*post obitum*, "after death" [Latin]): loans to an heir that fall due after the death of the person whose estate he or she is to inherit. Byron's meaning is probably that only theology purports to tell us what rewards are due in heaven.
9. Byron's friend the poet Thomas Moore, who in

1800 had translated the *Odes* of the ancient Greek Anacreon and whose popular Orientalist poem *Lalla Rookh* (1817) had portrayed the "heathenish heaven" of Islam as populated by "houris," beautiful maidens who in the afterlife will give heroes their reward.
1. Secretly aware (of her feelings).

845   How self-deceitful is the sagest part
      Of mortals whom thy lure hath led along—
   The precipice she stood on was immense,
      So was her creed° in her own innocence.   *belief*

107
   She thought of her own strength, and Juan's youth,
850   And of the folly of all prudish fears,
   Victorious virtue, and domestic truth,
      And then of Don Alfonso's fifty years:
   I wish these last had not occurr'd, in sooth,
      Because that number rarely much endears,
855   And through all climes, the snowy and the sunny,
   Sounds ill in love, whate'er it may in money.

*   *   *

113
   The sun set, and up rose the yellow moon:
      The devil's in the moon for mischief; they
   Who call'd her CHASTE, methinks, began too soon
900   Their nomenclature; there is not a day,
   The longest, not the twenty-first of June,
      Sees half the business in a wicked way
   On which three single hours of moonshine smile—
   And then she looks so modest all the while.

114
905   There is a dangerous silence in that hour,
      A stillness, which leaves room for the full soul
   To open all itself, without the power
      Of calling wholly back its self-control;
   The silver light which, hallowing tree and tower,
910   Sheds beauty and deep softness o'er the whole,
   Breathes also to the heart, and o'er it throws
   A loving languor, which is not repose.

115
   And Julia sate with Juan, half embraced
      And half retiring from the glowing arm,
915   Which trembled like the bosom where 'twas placed;
      Yet still she must have thought there was no harm,
   Or else 'twere easy to withdraw her waist;
      But then the situation had its charm,
   And then—God knows what next—I can't go on;
920   I'm almost sorry that I e'er begun.

116
   Oh Plato! Plato! you have paved the way,
      With your confounded fantasies, to more
   Immoral conduct by the fancied sway
      Your system feigns o'er the controlless core
925   Of human hearts, than all the long array
      Of poets and romancers:—You're a bore,

A charlatan, a coxcomb—and have been,
At best, no better than a go-between.

117

And Julia's voice was lost, except in sighs,
930   Until too late for useful conversation;
The tears were gushing from her gentle eyes,
    I wish, indeed, they had not had occasion,
But who, alas! can love, and then be wise?
    Not that remorse did not oppose temptation,
935   A little still she strove, and much repented,
And whispering "I will ne'er consent"—consented.

✻ ✻ ✻

126

'Tis sweet to win, no matter how, one's laurels
    By blood or ink; 'tis sweet to put an end
To strife; 'tis sometimes sweet to have our quarrels,
    Particularly with a tiresome friend;
1005   Sweet is old wine in bottles, ale in barrels;
    Dear is the helpless creature we defend
Against the world; and dear the schoolboy spot
We ne'er forget, though there we are forgot.

127

But sweeter still than this, than these, than all,
1010   Is first and passionate love—it stands alone,
Like Adam's recollection of his fall;
    The tree of knowledge has been pluck'd—all's known—
And life yields nothing further to recall
    Worthy of this ambrosial sin, so shown,
1015   No doubt in fable, as the unforgiven
Fire which Prometheus[2] filch'd for us from heaven.

✻ ✻ ✻

133

Man's a phenomenon, one knows not what,
    And wonderful beyond all wondrous measure;
'Tis pity though, in this sublime world, that
1060   Pleasure's a sin, and sometimes sin's a pleasure;
Few mortals know what end they would be at,
    But whether glory, power, or love, or treasure,
The path is through perplexing ways, and when
The goal is gain'd, we die, you know—and then—

134

1065   What then?—I do not know, no more do you—
    And so good night.—Return we to our story:
'Twas in November, when fine days are few,
    And the far mountains wax a little hoary,
And clap a white cape on their mantles blue;

---

2. The Titan Prometheus incurred the wrath of Zeus by stealing fire from heaven for humans.

1070   And the sea dashes round the promontory,
     And the loud breaker boils against the rock,
     And sober suns must set at five o'clock.

135

     'Twas, as the watchmen say, a cloudy night;
       No moon, no stars, the wind was low or loud
1075   By gusts, and many a sparkling hearth was bright
       With the piled wood, round which the family crowd;
     There's something cheerful in that sort of light,
       Even as a summer sky's without a cloud:
     I'm fond of fire, and crickets, and all that,
1080   A lobster-salad, and champagne, and chat.

136

     'Twas midnight—Donna Julia was in bed,
       Sleeping, most probably—when at her door
     Arose a clatter might awake the dead,
       If they had never been awoke before,
1085   And that they have been so we all have read,
       And are to be so, at the least, once more—
     The door was fasten'd, but with voice and fist
     First knocks were heard, then "Madam—Madam—hist!

137

     "For God's sake, Madam—Madam—here's my master,
1090   With more than half the city at his back—
     Was ever heard of such a curst disaster!
       'Tis not my fault—I kept good watch—Alack!
     Do, pray undo the bolt a little faster—
       They're on the stair just now, and in a crack°   *moment*
1095   Will all be here; perhaps he yet may fly—
     Surely the window's not so *very* high!"

138

     By this time Don Alfonso was arrived,
       With torches, friends, and servants in great number;
     The major part of them had long been wived,
1100   And therefore paused not to disturb the slumber
     Of any wicked woman, who contrived
       By stealth her husband's temples to encumber:[3]
     Examples of this kind are so contagious,
     Were one not punish'd, all would be outrageous.

139

1105   I can't tell how, or why, or what suspicion
       Could enter into Don Alfonso's head;
     But for a cavalier of his condition°   *rank*
       It surely was exceedingly ill-bred
     Without a word of previous admonition,
1110   To hold a levee[4] round his lady's bed,
     And summon lackeys, arm'd with fire and sword,
     To prove himself the thing he most abhorr'd.

---

3. I.e., with horns that, growing on the forehead, were the traditional emblem of the cuckolded husband.
4. Morning reception.

140

Poor Donna Julia! starting as from sleep,
  (Mind—that I do not say—she had not slept)
1115 Began at once to scream, and yawn, and weep;
  Her maid Antonia, who was an adept,
Contrived to fling the bed-clothes in a heap,
  As if she had just now from out them crept:
I can't tell why she should take all this trouble
1120 To prove her mistress had been sleeping double.

141

But Julia mistress, and Antonia maid,
  Appear'd like two poor harmless women, who
Of goblins, but still more of men afraid,
  Had thought one man might be deterr'd by two,
1125 And therefore side by side were gently laid,
  Until the hours of absence should run through,
And truant husband should return, and say,
"My dear, I was the first who came away."

142

Now Julia found at length a voice, and cried,
1130   "In heaven's name, Don Alfonso, what d'ye mean?
Has madness seized you? would that I had died
  Ere such a monster's victim I had been!
What may this midnight violence betide,
  A sudden fit of drunkenness or spleen?
1135 Dare you suspect me, whom the thought would kill?
Search, then, the room!"—Alfonso said, "I will."

143

He search'd, *they* search'd, and rummaged every where,
  Closet and clothes'-press, chest and window-seat,
And found much linen, lace, and seven pair
1140   Of stockings, slippers, brushes, combs, complete,
With other articles of ladies fair,
  To keep them beautiful, or leave them neat:
Arras[5] they prick'd and curtains with their swords,
And wounded several shutters, and some boards.

144

1145 Under the bed they search'd, and there they found—[6]
  No matter what—it was not that they sought;
They open'd windows, gazing if the ground
  Had signs or footmarks, but the earth said nought;
And then they stared each others' faces round:
1150   'Tis odd, not one of all these seekers thought,
And seems to me almost a sort of blunder,
Of looking *in* the bed as well as under.

145

During this inquisition Julia's tongue
  Was not asleep—"Yes, search and search," she cried,

---

5. A tapestry hanging on a wall.   6. Perhaps a chamber pot.

1155 "Insult on insult heap, and wrong on wrong!
      It was for this that I became a bride!
    For this in silence I have suffer'd long
      A husband like Alfonso at my side;
    But now I'll bear no more, nor here remain,
1160 If there be law, or lawyers, in all Spain.

146

    "Yes, Don Alfonso! husband now no more,
      If ever you indeed deserved the name,
    Is't worthy of your years?—you have threescore,
      Fifty, or sixty—it is all the same—
1165 Is't wise or fitting causeless to explore
      For facts against a virtuous woman's fame?
    Ungrateful, perjured, barbarous Don Alfonso,
    How dare you think your lady would go on so?"

                    *   *   *

159

1265 The Senhor Don Alfonso stood confused;
      Antonia bustled round the ransack'd room,
    And, turning up her nose, with looks abused
      Her master, and his myrmidons,[7] of whom
    Not one, except the attorney, was amused;
1270   He, like Achates,[8] faithful to the tomb,
    So there were quarrels, cared not for the cause,
    Knowing they must be settled by the laws.

160

    With prying snub-nose, and small eyes, he stood,
      Following Antonia's motions here and there,
1275 With much suspicion in his attitude;
      For reputations he had little care;
    So that a suit or action were made good,
      Small pity had he for the young and fair,
    And ne'er believed in negatives, till these
1280 Were proved by competent false witnesses.

161

    But Don Alfonso stood with downcast looks,
      And, truth to say, he made a foolish figure;
    When, after searching in five hundred nooks,
      And treating a young wife with so much rigour,
1285 He gain'd no point, except some self-rebukes,
      Added to those his lady with such vigour
    Had pour'd upon him for the last half-hour,
    Quick, thick, and heavy—as a thunder-shower.

162

    At first he tried to hammer an excuse,
1290   To which the sole reply was tears, and sobs,

7. Servants, so named for the followers Achilles led to the Trojan War.
8. The *fidus Achates* ("faithful Achates") of Virgil's *Aeneid*, whose loyalty to Aeneas has become proverbial.

And indications of hysterics, whose
  Prologue is always certain throes, and throbs,
Gasps, and whatever else the owners choose:—
  Alfonso saw his wife, and thought of Job's;[9]
1295 He saw too, in perspective, her relations,
  And then he tried to muster all his patience.

163

He stood in act to speak, or rather stammer,
  But sage Antonia cut him short before
The anvil of his speech received the hammer,
1300   With "Pray sir, leave the room, and say no more,
Or madam dies."—Alfonso mutter'd "D—n her,"
  But nothing else, the time of words was o'er;
He cast a rueful look or two, and did,
He knew not wherefore, that which he was bid.

164

1305 With him retired his *"posse comitatus,"*[1]
  The attorney last, who linger'd near the door,
Reluctantly, still tarrying there as late as
  Antonia let him—not a little sore
At this most strange and unexplain'd *"hiatus"*
1310 In Don Alfonso's facts, which just now wore
An awkward look; as he resolved the case
The door was fasten'd in his legal face.

165

No sooner was it bolted, than—Oh shame!
  Oh sin! Oh sorrow! and Oh womankind!
1315 How can you do such things and keep your fame,
  Unless this world, and t'other too, be blind?
Nothing so dear as an unfilch'd good name!
  But to proceed—for there is more behind:
With much heart-felt reluctance be it said,
1320 Young Juan slipp'd, half-smother'd, from the bed.

166

He had been hid—I don't pretend to say
  How, nor can I indeed describe the where—
Young, slender, and pack'd easily, he lay,
  No doubt, in little compass, round or square;
1325 But pity him I neither must nor may
  His suffocation by that pretty pair;
'Twere better, sure, to die so, than be shut
With maudlin Clarence in his Malmsey butt.[2]

* * *

9. Job's wife advised her afflicted husband to "curse God, and die." He replied, "Thou speakest as one of the foolish women speaketh" (Job 2.9–10).
1. The complete form of the modern word *posse* (*posse comitatus* means literally "power of the

county" [Latin], i.e., the body of citizens summoned by a sheriff to preserve order in the county).
2. Clarence, brother of Edward IV and of the future Richard III, was reputed to have been assassinated by being drowned in a cask ("butt") of malmsey, a sweet and aromatic wine.

169

1345 What's to be done? Alfonso will be back
    The moment he has sent his fools away.
    Antonia's skill was put upon the rack,
        But no device could be brought into play—
    And how to parry the renew'd attack?
1350   Besides, it wanted but few hours of day:
    Antonia puzzled; Julia did not speak,
    But press'd her bloodless lip to Juan's cheek.

170

He turn'd his lip to hers, and with his hand
    Call'd back the tangles of her wandering hair;
1355 Even then their love they could not all command,
    And half forgot their danger and despair:
    Antonia's patience now was at a stand—
        "Come, come,'tis no time now for fooling there,"
    She whisper'd, in great wrath—"I must deposit
1360 This pretty gentleman within the closet."

*   *   *

173

Now, Don Alfonso entering, but alone,
    Closed the oration of the trusty maid:
    She loiter'd, and he told her to be gone,
1380   An order somewhat sullenly obey'd;
    However, present remedy was none,
        And no great good seem'd answer'd if she staid:
    Regarding both with slow and sidelong view,
    She snuff'd the candle, curtsied, and withdrew.

174

1385 Alfonso paused a minute—then begun
    Some strange excuses for his late proceeding;
    He would not justify what he had done,
        To say the best, it was extreme ill-breeding;
    But there were ample reasons for it, none
1390   Of which he specified in this his pleading:
    His speech was a fine sample, on the whole,
    Of rhetoric, which the learn'd call *"rigmarole."*

*   *   *

180

Alfonso closed his speech, and begg'd her pardon,
    Which Julia half withheld, and then half granted,
1435 And laid conditions, he thought, very hard on,
        Denying several little things he wanted:
    He stood like Adam lingering near his garden,
        With useless penitence perplex'd and haunted,
    Beseeching she no further would refuse,
1440 When lo! he stumbled o'er a pair of shoes.

181

A pair of shoes!—what then? not much, if they
    Are such as fit with lady's feet, but these
(No one can tell how much I grieve to say)
    Were masculine; to see them, and to seize,
1445 Was but a moment's act.—Ah! Well-a-day!
    My teeth begin to chatter, my veins freeze—
Alfonso first examined well their fashion,
And then flew out into another passion.

182

He left the room for his relinquish'd sword,
1450   And Julia instant to the closet flew,
"Fly, Juan, fly! for heaven's sake—not a word—
    The door is open—you may yet slip through
The passage you so often have explored—
    Here is the garden-key—Fly—fly—Adieu!
1455 Haste—haste!—I hear Alfonso's hurrying feet—
Day has not broke—there's no one in the street."

183

None can say that this was not good advice,
    The only mischief was, it came too late;
Of all experience 'tis the usual price,
1460   A sort of income-tax laid on by fate:
Juan had reach'd the room-door in a trice,
    And might have done so by the garden-gate,
But met Alfonso in his dressing-gown,
Who threaten'd death—so Juan knock'd him down.

184

1465 Dire was the scuffle, and out went the light,
    Antonia cried out "Rape!" and Julia "Fire!"
But not a servant stirr'd to aid the fight.
    Alfonso, pommell'd to his heart's desire,
Swore lustily he'd be revenged this night;
1470   And Juan, too, blasphemed an octave higher,
His blood was up; though young, he was a Tartar,[3]
And not at all disposed to prove a martyr.

185

Alfonso's sword had dropp'd ere he could draw it,
    And they continued battling hand to hand,
1475 For Juan very luckily ne'er saw it;
    His temper not being under great command,
If at that moment he had chanced to claw it,
    Alfonso's days had not been in the land
Much longer.—Think of husbands', lovers' lives!
1480 And how ye may be doubly widows—wives!

186

Alfonso grappled to detain the foe,
    And Juan throttled him to get away,

3. A formidable opponent.

And blood ('twas from the nose) began to flow;
　At last, as they more faintly wrestling lay,
1485 Juan contrived to give an awkward blow,
　And then his only garment quite gave way;
He fled, like Joseph,⁴ leaving it; but there,
I doubt, all likeness ends between the pair.

187
Lights came at length, and men, and maids, who found
1490 　An awkward spectacle their eyes before;
Antonia in hysterics, Julia swoon'd,
　Alfonso leaning, breathless, by the door;
Some half-torn drapery scatter'd on the ground,
　Some blood, and several footsteps, but no more:
1495 Juan the gate gain'd, turn'd the key about,
And liking not the inside, lock'd the out.

188
Here ends this canto.—Need I sing, or say,
　How Juan, naked, favour'd by the night,
Who favours what she should not, found his way,
1500 　And reach'd his home in an unseemly plight?
The pleasant scandal which arose next day,
　The nine days' wonder which was brought to light,
And how Alfonso sued for a divorce,
Were in the English newspapers, of course.

189
1505 If you would like to see the whole proceedings,
　The depositions, and the cause at full,
The names of all the witnesses, the pleadings
　Of counsel to nonsuit,⁵ or to annul,
There's more than one edition, and the readings
1510 　Are various, but they none of them are dull,
The best is that in shorthand ta'en by Gurney,⁶
Who to Madrid on purpose made a journey.

190
But Donna Inez, to divert the train
　Of one of the most circulating scandals
1515 That had for centuries been known in Spain,
　Since Roderic's Goths, or older Genseric's Vandals,⁷
First vow'd (and never had she vow'd in vain)
　To Virgin Mary several pounds of candles;
And then, by the advice of some old ladies,
1520 She sent her son to be embark'd at Cadiz.

191
She had resolved that he should travel through
All European climes, by land or sea,

4. In Genesis 39.7ff. the chaste Joseph flees from the advances of Potiphar's wife, leaving "his garment in her hand."
5. Judgment against the plaintiff for failure to establish his case.
6. William B. Gurney (1777–1855), official short-hand writer for the houses of Parliament and a famous court reporter.
7. The Germanic tribes that overran Spain and other parts of southern Europe in the 5th through 8th centuries, notorious for rape and violence.

To mend his former morals, or get new,
    Especially in France and Italy,
1525 (At least this is the thing most people do).
    Julia was sent into a nunnery,
And there, perhaps, her feelings may be better
Shown in the following copy of her letter:

192

"They tell me 'tis decided; you depart:
1530   'Tis wise—'tis well, but not the less a pain;
I have no further claim on your young heart,
    Mine was the victim, and would be again;
To love too much has been the only art
    I used;—I write in haste, and if a stain
1535 Be on this sheet,'tis not what it appears,
My eyeballs burn and throb, but have no tears.

193

"I loved, I love you, for that love have lost
    State, station, heaven, mankind's, my own esteem,
And yet can not regret what it hath cost,
1540   So dear is still the memory of that dream;
Yet, if I name my guilt,'tis not to boast,
    None can deem harshlier of me than I deem:
I trace this scrawl because I cannot rest—
I've nothing to reproach, nor to request.

194

1545 "Man's love is of his life a thing apart,
    'Tis woman's whole existence; man may range
The court, camp, church, the vessel, and the mart,
    Sword, gown, gain, glory, offer in exchange
Pride, fame, ambition, to fill up his heart,
1550   And few there are whom these can not estrange;
Man has all these resources, we but one,
To love again, and be again undone.

195

"My breast has been all weakness, is so yet;
    I struggle, but cannot collect my mind;
1555 My blood still rushes where my spirit's set,
    As roll the waves before the settled wind;
My brain is feminine, nor can forget—
    To all, except your image, madly blind;
As turns the needle[8] trembling to the pole
1560 It ne'er can reach, so turns to you, my soul.

196

"You will proceed in beauty, and in pride,
    Beloved and loving many; all is o'er
For me on earth, except some years to hide
    My shame and sorrow deep in my heart's core;

8. Of a compass.

1565 These I could bear, but cannot cast aside
     The passion which still rends it as before,
     And so farewell—forgive me, love me—No,
     That word is idle now—but let it go.

                    197
     "I have no more to say, but linger still,
1570   And dare not set my seal upon this sheet,
     And yet I may as well the task fulfil,
        My misery can scarce be more complete:
     I had not lived till now, could sorrow kill;
        Death flies the wretch who fain the blow would meet,
1575 And I must even survive this last adieu,
     And bear with life, to love and pray for you!"

                    198
     This note was written upon gilt-edged paper
        With a neat crow-quill, rather hard, but new;
     Her small white fingers scarce could reach the taper,[9]
1580   But trembled as magnetic needles do,
     And yet she did not let one tear escape her;
        The seal a sunflower; *"Elle vous suit partout,"*[1]
     The motto, cut upon a white cornelian;
     The wax was superfine, its hue vermilion.

                    199
1585 This was Don Juan's earliest scrape; but whether
     I shall proceed with his adventures is
     Dependent on the public altogether;
        We'll see, however, what they say to this,
     Their favour in an author's cap's a feather,
1590   And no great mischief's done by their caprice;
     And if their approbation we experience,
     Perhaps they'll have some more about a year hence.

                    200
     My poem's epic, and is meant to be
        Divided in twelve books; each book containing,
1595 With love, and war, a heavy gale at sea,
        A list of ships, and captains, and kings reigning,
     New characters; the episodes are three:
        A panorama view of hell's in training,
     After the style of Virgil and of Homer,
1600 So that my name of Epic's no misnomer.

                    201
     All these things will be specified in time,
        With strict regard to Aristotle's rules,
     The *vade mecum*[2] of the true sublime,

---

9. The candle (to melt wax to seal the letter).
1. She follows you everywhere (French). This motto was inscribed on one of Byron's seals and on a jewel he gave to John Edleston, the boy with whom he had a romantic friendship while at Cambridge. Their friendship was memorialized in

Byron's 1807 poem "The Cornelian."
2. Go with me (Latin, literal trans.); handbook. Byron is deriding the neoclassical view that Aristotle's *Poetics* proposes "rules" for writing epic and tragedy.

Which makes so many poets, and some fools;
1605 Prose poets like blank-verse, I'm fond of rhyme,
Good workmen never quarrel with their tools;
I've got new mythological machinery,[3]
And very handsome supernatural scenery.

202

There's only one slight difference between
1610 Me and my epic brethren gone before,
And here the advantage is my own, I ween;
(Not that I have not several merits more,
But this will more peculiarly be seen)
They so embellish, that 'tis quite a bore
1615 Their labyrinth of fables to thread through,
Whereas this story's actually true.

203

If any person doubt it, I appeal
To history, tradition, and to facts,
To newspapers, whose truth all know and feel,
1620 To plays in five, and operas in three acts;
All these confirm my statement a good deal,
But that which more completely faith exacts
Is, that myself, and several now in Seville,
Saw Juan's last elopement with the devil.[4]

204

1625 If ever I should condescend to prose,
I'll write poetical commandments, which
Shall supersede beyond all doubt all those
That went before; in these I shall enrich
My text with many things that no one knows,
1630 And carry precept to the highest pitch:
I'll call the work "Longinus o'er a Bottle,
Or, Every Poet his *own* Aristotle."

205

Thou shalt believe in Milton, Dryden, Pope;[5]
Thou shalt not set up Wordsworth, Coleridge, Southey;
1635 Because the first is crazed beyond all hope,
The second drunk, the third so quaint and mouthey:
With Crabbe it may be difficult to cope,
And Campbell's Hippocrene[6] is somewhat drouthy:
Thou shalt not steal from Samuel Rogers, nor—
1640 Commit—flirtation with the muse of Moore.

3. The assemblage of supernatural personages and incidents introduced into a literary work.
4. The usual plays on the Juan legend ended with Juan in hell; an early-20th-century version is Bernard Shaw's *Man and Superman.*
5. This is one of many passages, in prose and verse, in which Byron vigorously defends Dryden and Pope against his Romantic contemporaries.

6. Fountain on Mount Helicon whose waters supposedly gave inspiration. George Crabbe, whom Byron admired, was the author of *The Village* and other realistic poems of rural life. Thomas Campbell, Samuel Rogers, and Thomas Moore were lesser poets of the Romantic period; the last two were close friends of Byron and members of London's liberal Whig circles.

206

Thou shalt not covet Mr. Sotheby's Muse,
    His Pegasus,[7] nor any thing that's his;
Thou shalt not bear false witness like "the Blues,"[8]
    (There's one, at least, is very fond of this);
1645 Thou shalt not write, in short, but what I choose:
    This is true criticism, and you may kiss—
Exactly as you please, or not, the rod,
But if you don't, I'll lay it on, by G—d![9]

207

If any person should presume to assert
1650   This story is not moral, first I pray
That they will not cry out before they're hurt,
    Then that they'll read it o'er again, and say,
(But, doubtless, nobody will be so pert)
    That this is not a moral tale, though gay;
1655 Besides, in canto twelfth, I mean to show
The very place where wicked people go.

※   ※   ※

213

But now at thirty years my hair is gray—
    (I wonder what it will be like at forty?
I thought of a peruke° the other day)   wig
1700   My heart is not much greener; and, in short, I
Have squander'd my whole summer while 'twas May,
    And feel no more the spirit to retort; I
Have spent my life, both interest and principal,
And deem not, what I deem'd, my soul invincible.

214

1705 No more—no more—Oh! never more on me
    The freshness of the heart can fall like dew,
Which out of all the lovely things we see
    Extracts emotions beautiful and new,
Hived in our bosoms like the bag o' the bee:
1710   Think'st thou the honey with those objects grew?
Alas! 'twas not in them, but in thy power
To double even the sweetness of a flower.

215

No more—no more—Oh! never more, my heart,
    Canst thou be my sole world, my universe!
1715 Once all in all, but now a thing apart,

7. The winged horse symbolizing poetic inspiration. The wealthy William Sotheby, minor poet and
translator, is satirized, as Botherby, in Byron's
Beppo.
8. I.e., bluestockings, a contemporary term for
female intellectuals, among whom Byron numbered his wife (line 1644).
9. Byron's parody of the Ten Commandments

seemed blasphemous to some commentators. Radical publishers like William Hone, who in 1817
had been put on trial for the ostensible blasphemy
of political satires that used the form of the Anglican Church's creed and catechism bitterly noted a
double standard: books brought out by the ultra-
respectable John Murray were not subject to the
same reprisals as Hone's books.

Thou canst not be my blessing or my curse:
The illusion's gone for ever, and thou art
Insensible, I trust, but none the worse,
And in thy stead I've got a deal of judgment,
1720   Though heaven knows how it ever found a lodgement.

216

My days of love are over, me no more
    The charms of maid, wife, and still less of widow,
Can make the fool of which they made before,
    In short, I must not lead the life I did do;
1725   The credulous hope of mutual minds is o'er,
    The copious use of claret is forbid too,
So for a good old gentlemanly vice,
I think I must take up with avarice.

217

Ambition was my idol, which was broken
1730   Before the shrines of Sorrow and of Pleasure;
And the two last have left me many a token
    O'er which reflection may be made at leisure:
Now, like Friar Bacon's brazen head, I've spoken,
    "Time is, Time was, Time's past,"[1] a chymic treasure[2]
1735   Is glittering youth, which I have spent betimes—
My heart in passion, and my head on rhymes.

218

What is the end of fame? 'tis but to fill
    A certain portion of uncertain paper:
Some liken it to climbing up a hill,
1740   Whose summit, like all hills', is lost in vapour;
For this men write, speak, preach, and heroes kill,
    And bards burn what they call their "midnight taper,"
To have, when the original is dust,
A name, a wretched picture, and worse bust.[3]

219

1745   What are the hopes of man? old Egypt's King
    Cheops erected the first pyramid
And largest, thinking it was just the thing
    To keep his memory whole, and mummy hid;
But somebody or other rummaging,
1750   Burglariously broke his coffin's lid:
Let not a monument give you or me hopes,
Since not a pinch of dust remains of Cheops.

220

But I, being fond of true philosophy,
    Say very often to myself, "Alas!

---

1. Spoken by a bronze bust in Robert Greene's *Friar Bacon and Friar Bungay* (1594). This comedy was based on legends about the magical power of Roger Bacon, the 13th-century Franciscan monk who was said to have built with diabolical assistance a brazen head capable of speech.

2. "Chymic": alchemic; i.e., the "treasure" is counterfeit gold.
3. Byron was unhappy with the portrait bust of him recently made by the Danish sculptor Thorwaldsen.

1755 All things that have been born were born to die,
　　　 And flesh (which Death mows down to hay) is grass;[4]
　　　 You've pass'd your youth not so unpleasantly,
　　　 And if you had it o'er again—'twould pass—
　　　 So thank your stars that matters are no worse,
1760 And read your Bible, sir, and mind your purse."

221

　　　 But for the present, gentle reader! and
　　　 Still gentler purchaser! the bard—that's I—
　　　 Must, with permission, shake you by the hand,
　　　 And so your humble servant, and good bye!
1765 We meet again, if we should understand
　　　 Each other; and if not, I shall not try
　　　 Your patience further than by this short sample—
　　　 'Twere well if others follow'd my example.

222

　　　 "Go, little book, from this my solitude!
1770 I cast thee on the waters, go thy ways!
　　　 And if, as I believe, thy vein be good,
　　　 The world will find thee after many days."
　　　 When Southey's read, and Wordsworth understood,
　　　 I can't help putting in my claim to praise—
1775 The four first rhymes are Southey's every line:[5]
　　　 For God's sake, reader! take them not for mine.

From Canto 2

[THE SHIPWRECK]

8

　　　 But to our tale: the Donna Inez sent
　　　 Her son to Cadiz only to embark;
　　　 To stay there had not answer'd her intent,
60　　 But why?—we leave the reader in the dark—
　　　 'Twas for a voyage that the young man was meant,
　　　 As if a Spanish ship were Noah's ark,
　　　 To wean him from the wickedness of earth,
　　　 And send him like a dove of promise forth.

9

65　 Don Juan bade his valet pack his things
　　　 According to direction, then received
　　　 A lecture and some money: for four springs
　　　 He was to travel; and though Inez grieved,
　　　 (As every kind of parting has its stings)
70　 She hoped he would improve—perhaps believed:
　　　 A letter, too, she gave (he never read it)
　　　 Of good advice—and two or three of credit.[1]

4. An echo of Isaiah 40.6 and 1 Peter 1.24: "All flesh is grass."
5. The lines are part of the last stanza of Southey's "Epilogue to the Lay of the Laureate."
1. Letters of credit allowed travelers to obtain cash from an international network of bankers.

10

In the mean time, to pass her hours away,
  Brave Inez now set up a Sunday school
75 For naughty children, who would rather play
  (Like truant rogues) the devil, or the fool;
Infants of three years old were taught that day,
  Dunces were whipt, or set upon a stool:
The great success of Juan's education,
80 Spurr'd her to teach another generation.

11

Juan embark'd—the ship got under way,
  The wind was fair, the water passing rough;
A devil of a sea rolls in that bay,
  As I, who've cross'd it oft, know well enough;
85 And, standing upon deck, the dashing spray
  Flies in one's face, and makes it weather-tough:
And there he stood to take, and take again,
  His first—perhaps his last—farewell of Spain.

12

I can't but say it is an awkward sight
90 To see one's native land receding through
The growing waters; it unmans one quite,
  Especially when life is rather new:
I recollect Great Britain's coast looks white,
  But almost every other country's blue,
95 When gazing on them, mystified by distance,
  We enter on our nautical existence.

       *   *   *

17

And Juan wept, and much he sigh'd and thought,
130 While his salt tears dropp'd into the salt sea,
"Sweets to the sweet"; (I like so much to quote;
  You must excuse this extract, 'tis where she,
The Queen of Denmark, for Ophelia brought
  Flowers to the grave);[2] and sobbing often, he
135 Reflected on his present situation,
  And seriously resolved on reformation.

18

"Farewell, my Spain! a long farewell!" he cried,
  "Perhaps I may revisit thee no more,
But die, as many an exiled heart hath died,
140 Of its own thirst to see again thy shore:
Farewell, where Guadalquivir's waters glide!
  Farewell, my mother! and, since all is o'er,
Farewell, too dearest Julia!,"—(here he drew
  Her letter out again, and read it through).

2. Shakespeare's *Hamlet* 5.1.227.

19

145 "And oh! if e'er I should forget, I swear—
    But that's impossible, and cannot be—
    Sooner shall this blue ocean melt to air,
        Sooner shall earth resolve itself to sea,
    Than I resign thine image, Oh! my fair!
150   Or think of any thing excepting thee;
    A mind diseased no remedy can physic—"
    (Here the ship gave a lurch, and he grew sea-sick.)

20

    "Sooner shall heaven kiss earth"—(here he fell sicker)
        "Oh, Julia! what is every other woe?—
155 (For God's sake let me have a glass of liquor,
        Pedro, Battista, help me down below.)
    Julia, my love!—(you rascal, Pedro, quicker)—
        Oh Julia!—(this curst vessel pitches so)—
    Beloved Julia, hear me still beseeching!"
160 (Here he grew inarticulate with retching.)

21

    He felt that chilling heaviness of heart,
        Or rather stomach, which, alas! attends,
    Beyond the best apothecary's art,
        The loss of love, the treachery of friends,
165 Or death of those we doat on, when a part
        Of us dies with them as each fond hope ends:
    No doubt he would have been much more pathetic,
    But the sea acted as a strong emetic.[3]

              *   *   *

49

385 'Twas twilight, and the sunless day went down
        Over the waste of waters; like a veil,
    Which, if withdrawn, would but disclose the frown
        Of one whose hate is masked but to assail;
    Thus to their hopeless eyes the night was shown
390   And grimly darkled o'er their faces pale,
    And the dim desolate deep; twelve days had Fear
    Been their familiar, and now Death was here.

50

    Some trial had been making at a raft,
        With little hope in such a rolling sea,
395 A sort of thing at which one would have laugh'd,
        If any laughter at such times could be,
    Unless with people who too much have quaff'd,
        And have a kind of wild and horrid glee,
    Half epileptical, and half hysterical:—
400 Their preservation would have been a miracle.

---

3. In stanzas 22–48 (here omitted) the ship, bound for Leghorn in Italy, runs into a violent storm and is battered into a helpless, sinking wreck.

51

At half-past eight o'clock, booms, hencoops, spars,
  And all things, for a chance, had been cast loose,
That still could keep afloat the struggling tars,
  For yet they strove, although of no great use:
405 There was no light in heaven but a few stars,
  The boats put off o'ercrowded with their crews;
She gave a heel, and then a lurch to port,
And, going down head foremost—sunk, in short.

52

Then rose from sea to sky the wild farewell,
410 Then shriek'd the timid, and stood still the brave,
Then some leap'd overboard with dreadful yell,
  As eager to anticipate their grave;
And the sea yawn'd around her like a hell,
  And down she suck'd with her the whirling wave,
415 Like one who grapples with his enemy,
And strives to strangle him before he die.

53

And first one universal shriek there rush'd,
  Louder than the loud ocean, like a crash
Of echoing thunder; and then all was hush'd,
420   Save the wild wind and the remorseless dash
Of billows; but at intervals there gush'd,
  Accompanied with a convulsive splash,
A solitary shriek, the bubbling cry
Of some strong swimmer in his agony.

*   *   *

56

Juan got into the long-boat, and there
  Contrived to help Pedrillo[4] to a place;
It seem'd as if they had exchanged their care,
  For Juan wore the magisterial face
445 Which courage gives, while poor Pedrillo's pair
  Of eyes were crying for their owner's case:
Battista, though (a name call'd shortly Tita),
Was lost by getting at some aqua-vita.°   brandy

57

Pedro, his valet, too, he tried to save,
450   But the same cause, conducive to his loss,
Left him so drunk, he jump'd into the wave
  As o'er the cutter's edge he tried to cross,
And so he found a wine-and-watery grave;
  They could not rescue him although so close,
455 Because the sea ran higher every minute,
And for the boat—the crew kept crowding in it.

*   *   *

4. Juan's tutor.

66

'Tis thus with people in an open boat,
    They live upon the love of life, and bear
More than can be believed, or even thought,
    And stand like rocks the tempest's wear and tear;
525 And hardship still has been the sailor's lot,
    Since Noah's ark went cruising here and there;
She had a curious crew as well as cargo,
Like the first old Greek privateer, the Argo.[5]

67

But man is a carnivorous production,
530   And must have meals, at least one meal a day;
He cannot live, like woodcocks, upon suction,[6]
    But, like the shark and tiger, must have prey:
Although his anatomical construction
    Bears vegetables in a grumbling way,
535 Your labouring people think beyond all question,
Beef, veal, and mutton, better for digestion.

68

And thus it was with this our hapless crew,
    For on the third day there came on a calm,
And though at first their strength it might renew,
540   And lying on their weariness like balm,
Lull'd them like turtles sleeping on the blue
    Of ocean, when they woke they felt a qualm,
And fell all ravenously on their provision,
Instead of hoarding it with due precision.

❊   ❊   ❊

72

The seventh day,[7] and no wind—the burning sun
570   Blister'd and scorch'd, and, stagnant on the sea,
They lay like carcases; and hope was none,
    Save in the breeze that came not; savagely
They glared upon each other—all was done,
    Water, and wine, and food,—and you might see
575 The longings of the cannibal arise
(Although they spoke not) in their wolfish eyes.

73

At length one whisper'd his companion, who
    Whisper'd another, and thus it went round,
And then into a hoarser murmur grew,
580   An ominous, and wild, and desperate sound,
And when his comrade's thought each sufferer knew,

5. In the Greek myth the *Argo* is the ship on which Jason set out in quest of the Golden Fleece. Byron ironically calls it a "privateer" (a private ship licensed by a government in wartime to attack and pillage enemy vessels).
6. Woodcocks probe the turf with their long flexible bills, seeming to suck air as they feed.

7. On the fourth day the crew had killed and eaten Juan's pet spaniel. Byron based the episode of cannibalism that follows on various historical accounts of disasters at sea, including his grandfather Admiral Byron's 1768 narrative of his misadventure off the coast of Patagonia.

'Twas but his own, suppress'd till now, he found:
And out they spoke of lots for flesh and blood,
And who should die to be his fellow's food.

74

585 But ere they came to this, they that day shared
    Some leathern caps, and what remain'd of shoes;
And then they look'd around them, and despair'd,
    And none to be the sacrifice would choose;
At length the lots were torn up, and prepared,
590   But of materials that must shock the Muse—
Having no paper, for the want of better,
They took by force from Juan Julia's letter.

75

The lots were made, and mark'd, and mix'd, and handed,
    In silent horror, and their distribution
595 Lull'd even the savage hunger which demanded,
    Like the Promethean vulture,[8] this pollution;
None in particular had sought or plann'd it,
    'Twas nature gnaw'd them to this resolution,
By which none were permitted to be neuter—
600 And the lot fell on Juan's luckless tutor.

76

He but requested to be bled to death:
    The surgeon had his instruments, and bled
Pedrillo, and so gently ebb'd his breath,
    You hardly could perceive when he was dead.
605 He died as born, a Catholic in faith,
    Like most in the belief in which they're bred,
And first a little crucifix he kiss'd,
And then held out his jugular and wrist.

77

The surgeon, as there was no other fee,
610   Had his first choice of morsels for his pains;
But being thirstiest at the moment, he
    Preferr'd a draught from the fast-flowing veins:
Part was divided, part thrown in the sea,
    And such things as the entrails and the brains
615 Regaled two sharks, who follow'd o'er the billow—
The sailors ate the rest of poor Pedrillo.

78

The sailors ate him, all save three or four,
    Who were not quite so fond of animal food;
To these was added Juan, who, before
620   Refusing his own spaniel, hardly could
Feel now his appetite increased much more;
    'Twas not to be expected that he should,
Even in extremity of their disaster,
Dine with them on his pastor and his master.

---

8. Because Prometheus had stolen fire from heaven to give to humans, Zeus punished him by chaining
him to a mountain peak, where an eagle fed on his ever-renewing liver.

79

625 'Twas better that he did not; for, in fact,
    The consequence was awful in the extreme;
For they, who were most ravenous in the act,
    Went raging mad—Lord! how they did blaspheme!
And foam and roll, with strange convulsions rack'd,
630   Drinking salt-water like a mountain-stream,
Tearing, and grinning, howling, screeching, swearing,
And, with hyaena laughter, died despairing.

※　※　※

103

As they drew nigh the land, which now was seen
    Unequal in its aspect here and there,
They felt the freshness of its growing green,
820   That waved in forest-tops, and smooth'd the air,
And fell upon their glazed eyes like a screen
    From glistening waves, and skies so hot and bare—
Lovely seem'd any object that should sweep
Away the vast, salt, dread, eternal deep.

104

825 The shore look'd wild, without a trace of man,
    And girt by formidable waves; but they
Were mad for land, and thus their course they ran,
    Though right ahead the roaring breakers lay:
A reef between them also now began
830   To show its boiling surf and bounding spray,
But finding no place for their landing better,
They ran the boat for shore, and overset her.

105

But in his native stream, the Guadalquivir,
    Juan to lave° his youthful limbs was wont;   bathe
835 And having learnt to swim in that sweet river,
    Had often turn'd the art to some account:
A better swimmer you could scarce see ever,
    He could, perhaps, have pass'd the Hellespont,
As once (a feat on which ourselves we prided)
840   Leander, Mr. Ekenhead, and I did.[9]

106

So here, though faint, emaciated, and stark,
    He buoy'd his boyish limbs, and strove to ply
With the quick wave, and gain, ere it was dark,
    The beach which lay before him, high and dry:
845 The greatest danger here was from a shark,
    That carried off his neighbour by the thigh;
As for the other two, they could not swim,
So nobody arrived on shore but him.

9. Like Leander in the myth, Byron and Lieutenant Ekenhead had swum the Hellespont, on May 3, 1810.
See "Written after Swimming from Sestos to Abydos" (p. 611).

107

Nor yet had he arrived but for the oar,
850   Which, providentially for him, was wash'd
Just as his feeble arms could strike no more,
     And the hard wave o'erwhelm'd him as 'twas dash'd
Within his grasp; he clung to it, and sore
     The waters beat while he thereto was lash'd;
855 At last, with swimming, wading, scrambling, he
     Roll'd on the beach, half senseless, from the sea:

108

There, breathless, with his digging nails he clung
     Fast to the sand, lest the returning wave,
From whose reluctant roar his life he wrung,
860   Should suck him back to her insatiate grave:
And there he lay, full length, where he was flung,
     Before the entrance of a cliff-worn cave,
With just enough of life to feel its pain,
And deem that it was saved, perhaps, in vain.

109

865 With slow and staggering effort he arose,
     But sunk again upon his bleeding knee
And quivering hand; and then he look'd for those
     Who long had been his mates upon the sea,
But none of them appear'd to share his woes,
870   Save one, a corpse from out the famish'd three,
Who died two days before, and now had found
An unknown barren beach for burial ground.

110

And as he gazed, his dizzy brain spun fast,
     And down he sunk; and as he sunk, the sand
875 Swam round and round, and all his senses pass'd:
     He fell upon his side, and his stretch'd hand
Droop'd dripping on the oar, (their jury-mast)[1]
     And, like a wither'd lily, on the land
His slender frame and pallid aspect lay,
880 As fair a thing as e'er was form'd of clay.

[JUAN AND HAIDEE]

111

How long in his damp trance young Juan lay
     He knew not, for the earth was gone for him,
And Time had nothing more of night nor day
     For his congealing blood, and senses dim;
885 And how this heavy faintness pass'd away
     He knew not, till each painful pulse and limb,
And tingling vein seem'd throbbing back to life,
For Death, though vanquish'd, still retired with strife.

---

1. A mast put up in the place of one that has been carried away or broken.

112

His eyes he open'd, shut, again unclosed,
890   For all was doubt and dizziness; methought
He still was in the boat, and had but dozed,
    And felt again with his despair o'erwrought,
And wish'd it death in which he had reposed,
    And then once more his feelings back were brought,
895 And slowly by his swimming eyes was seen
A lovely female face of seventeen.

113

'Twas bending close o'er his, and the small mouth
    Seem'd almost prying into his for breath;
And chafing him, the soft warm hand of youth
900   Recall'd his answering spirits back from death;
And, bathing his chill temples, tried to soothe
    Each pulse to animation, till beneath
Its gentle touch and trembling care, a sigh
To these kind efforts made a low reply.

114

905 Then was the cordial pour'd, and mantle flung
    Around his scarce-clad limbs; and the fair arm
Raised higher the faint head which o'er it hung;
    And her transparent cheek, all pure and warm,
Pillow'd his death-like forehead; then she wrung
910   His dewy curls, long drench'd by every storm;
And watch'd with eagerness each throb that drew
A sigh from his heaved bosom—and hers, too.

115

And lifting him with care into the cave,
    The gentle girl, and her attendant,—one
915 Young, yet her elder, and of brow less grave,
    And more robust of figure,—then begun
To kindle fire, and as the new flames gave
    Light to the rocks that roof'd them, which the sun
Had never seen, the maid, or whatsoe'er
920 She was, appear'd distinct, and tall, and fair.

116

Her brow was overhung with coins of gold,
    That sparkled o'er the auburn of her hair,
Her clustering hair, whose longer locks were roll'd
    In braids behind, and though her stature were
925 Even of the highest for a female mould,
    They nearly reach'd her heel; and in her air
There was a something which bespoke command,
As one who was a lady in the land.

117

Her hair, I said, was auburn; but her eyes
930   Were black as death, their lashes the same hue,
Of downcast length, in whose silk shadow lies

Deepest attraction, for when to the view
Forth from its raven fringe the full glance flies,
Ne'er with such force the swiftest arrow flew;
935   'Tis as the snake late coil'd, who pours his length,
And hurls at once his venom and his strength.

*   *   *

123

And these two tended him, and cheer'd him both
    With food and raiment, and those soft attentions,
Which are (as I must own) of female growth,
980   And have ten thousand delicate inventions:
They made a most superior mess of broth,
    A thing which poesy but seldom mentions,
But the best dish that e'er was cook'd since Homer's
Achilles order'd dinner for new comers.[2]

124

985 I'll tell you who they were, this female pair,
    Lest they should seem princesses in disguise;
Besides, I hate all mystery, and that air
    Of clap-trap, which your recent poets prize;
And so, in short, the girls they really were
990   They shall appear before your curious eyes,
Mistress and maid; the first was only daughter
Of an old man, who lived upon the water.

125

A fisherman he had been in his youth,
    And still a sort of fisherman was he;
995 But other speculations were, in sooth,
    Added to his connection with the sea,
Perhaps not so respectable, in truth:
    A little smuggling, and some piracy,
Left him, at last, the sole of many masters
1000 Of an ill-gotten million of piastres.[3]

126

A fisher, therefore, was he—though of men,
    Like Peter the Apostle,[4]—and he fish'd
For wandering merchant vessels, now and then,
    And sometimes caught as many as he wish'd;
1005 The cargoes he confiscated, and gain
    He sought in the slave-market too, and dish'd
Full many a morsel for that Turkish trade,
By which, no doubt, a good deal may be made.

---

2. A reference to the lavish feast with which Achilles entertained Ajax, Phoenix, and Ulysses (*Iliad* 9.193ff.).
3. Near-Eastern coins.

4. Christ's words to Peter and Andrew, both fishermen: "Follow me, and I will make you fishers of men" (Matthew 4.19).

127

He was a Greek, and on his isle had built
1010   (One of the wild and smaller Cyclades)[5]
A very handsome house from out his guilt,
    And there he lived exceedingly at ease;
Heaven knows what cash he got, or blood he spilt,
    A sad[6] old fellow was he, if you please,
1015 But this I know, it was a spacious building,
Full of barbaric carving, paint, and gilding.

128

He had an only daughter, call'd Haidée,
    The greatest heiress of the Eastern Isles;
Besides, so very beautiful was she,
1020   Her dowry was as nothing to her smiles:
Still in her teens, and like a lovely tree
    She grew to womanhood, and between whiles
Rejected several suitors, just to learn
How to accept a better in his turn.

129

1025 And walking out upon the beach, below
    The cliff, towards sunset, on that day she found,
Insensible,°—not dead, but nearly so,—   *unconscious*
    Don Juan, almost famish'd, and half drown'd;
But being naked, she was shock'd, you know,
1030   Yet deem'd herself in common pity bound,
As far as in her lay, "to take him in,
A stranger"[7] dying, with so white a skin.

130

But taking him into her father's house
    Was not exactly the best way to save,
1035 But like conveying to the cat the mouse,
    Or people in a trance into their grave;
Because the good old man had so much "νους,"[8]
    Unlike the honest Arab thieves so brave,
He would have hospitably cured the stranger,
1040 And sold him instantly when out of danger.

131

And therefore, with her maid, she thought it best
    (A virgin always on her maid relies)
To place him in the cave for present rest:
    And when, at last, he open'd his black eyes,
1045 Their charity increased about their guest;
    And their compassion grew to such a size,
It open'd half the turnpike-gates to heaven—
(St. Paul says 'tis the toll which must be given).[9]

*   *   *

5. A group of islands in the Aegean Sea.
6. In the playful sense: wicked.
7. Cf. Matthew 25.35: "I was a stranger, and ye took me in."
8. *Nous*, intelligence (Greek); in England pronounced so as to rhyme with *mouse*.
9. 1 Corinthians 13.13: "And now abideth faith, hope, charity, these three; but the greatest of these is charity."

141

And Haidee met the morning face to face;
   Her own was freshest, though a feverish flush
Had dyed it with the headlong blood, whose race
   From heart to cheek is curb'd into a blush,
1125   Like to a torrent which a mountain's base,
   That overpowers some Alpine river's rush,
Checks to a lake, whose waves in circles spread;
Or the Red Sea—but the sea is not red.

142

And down the cliff the island virgin came,
1130   And near the cave her quick light footsteps drew,
While the sun smiled on her with his first flame,
   And young Aurora° kiss'd her lips with dew,   *dawn*
Taking her for a sister; just the same
   Mistake you would have made on seeing the two,
1135   Although the mortal, quite as fresh and fair,
Had all the advantage too of not being air.

143

And when into the cavern Haidee stepp'd
   All timidly, yet rapidly, she saw
That like an infant Juan sweetly slept;
1140   And then she stopp'd, and stood as if in awe,
(For sleep is awful)° and on tiptoe crept   *awe-inspiring*
   And wrapt him closer, lest the air, too raw,
Should reach his blood, then o'er him still as death
Bent, with hush'd lips, that drank his scarce-drawn breath.

         *   *   *

148

And she bent o'er him, and he lay beneath,
   Hush'd as the babe upon its mother's breast,
Droop'd as the willow when no winds can breathe,
1180   Lull'd like the depth of ocean when at rest,
Fair as the crowning rose of the whole wreath,
   Soft as the callow° cygnet° in its nest;   *young / swan*
In short, he was a very pretty fellow,
Although his woes had turn'd him rather yellow.

149

1185   He woke and gazed, and would have slept again,
   But the fair face which met his eyes forbade
Those eyes to close, though weariness and pain
   Had further sleep a further pleasure made;
For woman's face was never form'd in vain
1190   For Juan, so that even when he pray'd
He turn'd from grisly saints, and martyrs hairy,
To the sweet portraits of the Virgin Mary.

150

And thus upon his elbow he arose,
   And look'd upon the lady, in whose cheek

1195 The pale contended with the purple rose,
    As with an effort she began to speak;
    Her eyes were eloquent, her words would pose,
      Although she told him, in good modern Greek,
      With an Ionian accent, low and sweet,
1200 That he was faint, and must not talk, but eat.

                   *   *   *

168

And every day by day-break—rather early
    For Juan, who was somewhat fond of rest—
    She came into the cave, but it was merely
1340   To see her bird reposing in his nest;
    And she would softly stir his locks so curly,
      Without disturbing her yet slumbering guest,
    Breathing all gently o'er his cheek and mouth,
    As o'er a bed of roses the sweet south.[1]

169

1345 And every morn his colour freshlier came,
    And every day help'd on his convalescence;
    'Twas well, because health in the human frame
      Is pleasant, besides being true love's essence,
    For health and idleness to passion's flame
1350   Are oil and gunpowder; and some good lessons
    Are also learnt from Ceres[2] and from Bacchus,
    Without whom Venus will not long attack us.

170

While Venus fills the heart (without heart really
    Love, though good always, is not quite so good)
1355 Ceres presents a plate of vermicelli,—
    For love must be sustain'd like flesh and blood,—
    While Bacchus pours out wine, or hands a jelly:
      Eggs, oysters too, are amatory food;
    But who is their purveyor from above
1360 Heaven knows,—it may be Neptune, Pan, or Jove.

171

When Juan woke he found some good things ready,
    A bath, a breakfast, and the finest eyes
    That ever made a youthful heart less steady,
      Besides her maid's, as pretty for their size;
1365 But I have spoken of all this already—
    And repetition's tiresome and unwise,—
    Well—Juan, after bathing in the sea,
    Came always back to coffee and Haidee.

172

Both were so young, and one so innocent,
1370   That bathing pass'd for nothing; Juan seem'd

1. The south wind.
2. Ceres, goddess of the grain; Bacchus, god of wine and revelry.

To her, as 'twere, the kind of being sent,
  Of whom these two years she had nightly dream'd,
  A something to be loved, a creature meant
    To be her happiness, and whom she deem'd
1375 To render happy; all who joy would win
Must share it,—Happiness was born a twin.

173
It was such pleasure to behold him, such
  Enlargement of existence to partake
  Nature with him, to thrill beneath his touch,
1380   To watch him slumbering, and to see him wake:
To live with him for ever were too much;
  But then the thought of parting made her quake:
He was her own, her ocean-treasure, cast
Like a rich wreck—her first love, and her last.

174
1385 And thus a moon° roll'd on, and fair Haidee   *month*
  Paid daily visits to her boy, and took
  Such plentiful precautions, that still he
    Remain'd unknown within his craggy nook;
At last her father's prows put out to sea,
1390   For certain merchantmen upon the look,
Not as of yore to carry off an Io,[3]
  But three Ragusan vessels, bound for Scio.[4]

175
Then came her freedom, for she had no mother,
  So that, her father being at sea, she was
1395 Free as a married woman, or such other
  Female, as where she likes may freely pass,
Without even the encumbrance of a brother,
  The freest she that ever gazed on glass:°   *in a mirror*
I speak of christian lands in this comparison,
1400 Where wives, at least, are seldom kept in garrison.

176
Now she prolong'd her visits and her talk
  (For they must talk), and he had learnt to say
So much as to propose to take a walk,—
  For little had he wander'd since the day
1405 On which, like a young flower snapp'd from the stalk,
  Drooping and dewy on the beach he lay,—
And thus they walk'd out in the afternoon,
And saw the sun set opposite the moon.

177
It was a wild and breaker-beaten coast,
1410   With cliffs above, and a broad sandy shore,
Guarded by shoals and rocks as by an host,

3. A mistress of Zeus who was persecuted by his jealous wife, Hera, and kidnapped by Phoenician merchants.

4. The Italian name for Chios, an island near Turkey. "Ragusan": Ragusa (or Dubrovnik) is an Adriatic port located in what is now Croatia.

With here and there a creek, whose aspect wore
A better welcome to the tempest-tost;
And rarely ceas'd the haughty billow's roar,
1415 Save on the dead long summer days, which make
The outstretch'd ocean glitter like a lake.

178

And the small ripple spilt upon the beach
Scarcely o'erpass'd the cream of your champagne,
When o'er the brim the sparkling bumpers reach,
1420 That spring-dew of the spirit! the heart's rain!
Few things surpass old wine; and they may preach
Who please,—the more because they preach in vain,—
Let us have wine and woman, mirth and laughter,
Sermons and soda water the day after.

179

1425 Man, being reasonable, must get drunk;
The best of life is but intoxication:
Glory, the grape, love, gold, in these are sunk
The hopes of all men, and of every nation;
Without their sap, how branchless were the trunk
1430 Of life's strange tree, so fruitful on occasion:
But to return,—Get very drunk; and when
You wake with head-ache, you shall see what then.

180

Ring for your valet—bid him quickly bring
Some hock and soda-water, then you'll know
1435 A pleasure worthy Xerxes⁵ the great king;
For not the blest sherbet, sublimed with snow,
Nor the first sparkle of the desert-spring,
Nor Burgundy in all its sunset glow,
After long travel, ennui, love, or slaughter,
1440 Vie with that draught of hock and soda-water.

181

The coast—I think it was the coast that I
Was just describing—Yes, it *was* the coast—
Lay at this period quiet as the sky,
The sands untumbled, the blue waves untost,
1445 And all was stillness, save the sea-bird's cry,
And dolphin's leap, and little billow crost
By some low rock or shelve, that made it fret
Against the boundary it scarcely wet.

182

And forth they wandered, her sire being gone,
1450 As I have said, upon an expedition;
And mother, brother, guardian, she had none,
Save Zoe, who, although with due precision
She waited on her lady with the sun,

---

5. The 5th-century Persian king was said to have offered a reward to anyone who could discover a new kind of pleasure.

Thought daily service was her only mission,
1455 Bringing warm water, wreathing her long tresses,
And asking now and then for cast-off dresses.

183
It was the cooling hour, just when the rounded
Red sun sinks down behind the azure hill,
Which then seems as if the whole earth it bounded,
1460   Circling all nature, hush'd, and dim, and still,
With the far mountain-crescent half surrounded
   On one side, and the deep sea calm and chill
Upon the other, and the rosy sky,
With one star sparkling through it like an eye.

184
1465 And thus they wander'd forth, and hand in hand,
   Over the shining pebbles and the shells,
Glided along the smooth and harden'd sand,
   And in the worn and wild receptacles
Work'd by the storms, yet work'd as it were plann'd,
1470   In hollow halls, with sparry roofs and cells,
They turn'd to rest; and, each clasp'd by an arm,
Yielded to the deep twilight's purple charm.

185
They look'd up to the sky, whose floating glow
   Spread like a rosy ocean, vast and bright;
1475 They gazed upon the glittering sea below,
   Whence the broad moon rose circling into sight;
They heard the wave's splash, and the wind so low,
   And saw each other's dark eyes darting light
Into each other—and, beholding this,
1480 Their lips drew near, and clung into a kiss;

186
A long, long kiss, a kiss of youth and love,
   And beauty, all concentrating like rays
Into one focus, kindled from above;
   Such kisses as belong to early days,
1485 Where heart, and soul, and sense, in concert move,
   And the blood's lava, and the pulse a blaze,
Each kiss a heart-quake,—for a kiss's strength,
I think, it must be reckon'd by its length.

187
By length I mean duration; theirs endured
1490   Heaven knows how long—no doubt they never reckon'd;
And if they had, they could not have secured
   The sum of their sensations to a second:
They had not spoken; but they felt allured,
   As if their souls and lips each other beckon'd,
1495 Which, being join'd, like swarming bees they clung—
Their hearts the flowers from whence the honey sprung.

188

They were alone, but not alone as they
 Who shut in chambers think it loneliness;
The silent ocean, and the starlight bay,
1500 The twilight glow, which momently grew less,
The voiceless sands, and dropping caves, that lay
 Around them, made them to each other press,
As if there were no life beneath the sky
Save theirs, and that their life could never die.

189

1505 They fear'd no eyes nor ears on that lone beach,
 They felt no terrors from the night, they were
All in all to each other: though their speech
 Was broken words, they *thought* a language there,—
And all the burning tongues the passions teach
1510 Found in one sigh the best interpreter
Of nature's oracle—first love,—that all
Which Eve has left her daughters since her fall.

190

Haidee[6] spoke not of scruples, ask'd no vows,
 Nor offer'd any; she had never heard
1515 Of plight and promises to be a spouse,
 Or perils by a loving maid incurr'd;
She was all which pure ignorance allows,
 And flew to her young mate like a young bird;
And, never having dreamt of falsehood, she
1520 Had not one word to say of constancy.

191

She loved, and was beloved—she adored,
 And she was worshipp'd; after nature's fashion,
Their intense souls, into each other pour'd,
 If souls could die, had perish'd in that passion,—
1525 But by degrees their senses were restored,
 Again to be o'ercome, again to dash on;
And, beating 'gainst *his* bosom, Haidee's heart
Felt as if never more to beat apart.

192

Alas! they were so young, so beautiful,
1530 So lonely, loving, helpless, and the hour
Was that in which the heart is always full,
 And, having o'er itself no further power,
Prompts deeds eternity can not annul,
 But pays off moments in an endless shower
1535 Of hell-fire—all prepared for people giving
Pleasure or pain to one another living.

---

6. Byron said, with reference to Haidee: "I was, and am, penetrated with the conviction that women only know evil from men, whereas men have no criterion to judge of purity or goodness but woman."

193

Alas! for Juan and Haidee! they were
    So loving and so lovely—till then never,
Excepting our first parents, such a pair
1540   Had run the risk of being damn'd for ever;
And Haidee, being devout as well as fair,
    Had, doubtless, heard about the Stygian river,[7]
And hell and purgatory—but forgot
Just in the very crisis she should not.

194

1545 They look upon each other, and their eyes
    Gleam in the moonlight; and her white arm clasps
Round Juan's head, and his around hers lies
    Half buried in the tresses which it grasps;
She sits upon his knee, and drinks his sighs,
1550   He hers, until they end in broken gasps;
And thus they form a group that's quite antique,
Half naked, loving, natural, and Greek.

195

And when those deep and burning moments pass'd,
    And Juan sunk to sleep within her arms,
1555 She slept not, but all tenderly, though fast,
    Sustain'd his head upon her bosom's charms;
And now and then her eye to heaven is cast,
    And then on the pale cheek her breast now warms,
Pillow'd on her o'erflowing heart, which pants
1560 With all it granted, and with all it grants.

196

An infant when it gazes on a light,
    A child the moment when it drains the breast,
A devotee when soars the Host[8] in sight,
    An Arab with a stranger for a guest,
1565 A sailor when the prize has struck[9] in fight,
    A miser filling his most hoarded chest,
Feel rapture; but not such true joy are reaping
As they who watch o'er what they love while sleeping.

197

For there it lies so tranquil, so beloved,
1570   All that it hath of life with us is living;
So gentle, stirless, helpless, and unmoved,
    And all unconscious of the joy 'tis giving;
All it hath felt, inflicted, pass'd, and proved,
    Hush'd into depths beyond the watcher's diving;
1575 There lies the thing we love with all its errors
And all its charms, like death without its terrors.

7. The Styx, which flows through Hades.
8. The bread or wafer that a priest consecrates to celebrate Mass.
9. When a captured vessel (a "prize") lowers its flag in token of surrender.

198

The lady watch'd her lover—and that hour
    Of Love's, and Night's, and Ocean's solitude,
    O'erflow'd her soul with their united power;
1580   Amidst the barren sand and rocks so rude
She and her wave-worn love had made their bower,
    Where nought upon their passion could intrude,
And all the stars that crowded the blue space
Saw nothing happier than her glowing face.

199

1585 Alas! the love of women! it is known
    To be a lovely and a fearful thing;
For all of theirs upon that die is thrown,
    And if 'tis lost, life hath no more to bring
To them but mockeries of the past alone,
1590   And their revenge is as the tiger's spring,
Deadly, and quick, and crushing; yet, as real
Torture is theirs, what they inflict they feel.

200

They are right; for man, to man so oft unjust,
    Is always so to women; one sole bond
1595 Awaits them, treachery is all their trust;
    Taught to conceal, their bursting hearts despond
Over their idol, till some wealthier lust
    Buys them in marriage—and what rests beyond?
A thankless husband, next a faithless lover,
1600 Then dressing, nursing, praying, and all's over.

201

Some take a lover, some take drams° or prayers,   drink
    Some mind their household, others dissipation,
Some run away, and but exchange their cares,
    Losing the advantage of a virtuous station;
1605 Few changes e'er can better their affairs,
    Theirs being an unnatural situation,
From the dull palace to the dirty hovel:
Some play the devil, and then write a novel.[1]

202

Haidee was Nature's bride, and knew not this;
1610   Haidee was Passion's child, born where the sun
Showers triple light, and scorches even the kiss
    Of his gazelle-eyed daughters; she was one
Made but to love, to feel that she was his
    Who was her chosen: what was said or done
1615 Elsewhere was nothing—She had nought to fear,
Hope, care, nor love beyond, her heart beat *here*.

---

1. The impetuous Lady Caroline Lamb, having thrown herself at Byron and been after a time rejected, incorporated incidents from the affair in her novel *Glenarvon* (1816).

203

And oh! that quickening of the heart, that beat!
  How much it costs us! yet each rising throb
  Is in its cause as its effect so sweet,
1620   That Wisdom, ever on the watch to rob
Joy of its alchymy, and to repeat
  Fine truths, even Conscience, too, has a tough job
To make us understand each good old maxim,
So good—I wonder Castlereagh[2] don't tax 'em.

204

1625 And now 'twas done—on the lone shore were plighted
  Their hearts; the stars, their nuptial torches, shed
Beauty upon the beautiful they lighted:
  Ocean their witness, and the cave their bed,
By their own feelings hallow'd and united,
1630   Their priest was Solitude, and they were wed:
And they were happy, for to their young eyes
Each was an angel, and earth paradise.[3]

*   *   *

208

But Juan! had he quite forgotten Julia?
  And should he have forgotten her so soon?
  I can't but say it seems to me most truly a
1660   Perplexing question; but, no doubt, the moon
Does these things for us, and whenever newly a
  Strong palpitation rises,'tis her boon,
Else how the devil is it that fresh features
Have such a charm for us poor human creatures?

209

1665 I hate inconstancy—I loathe, detest,
  Abhor, condemn, abjure the mortal made
Of such quicksilver clay that in his breast
  No permanent foundation can be laid;
Love, constant love, has been my constant guest,
1670   And yet last night, being at a masquerade,
I saw the prettiest creature, fresh from Milan,
Which gave me some sensations like a villain.

210

But soon Philosophy came to my aid,
  And whisper'd "think of every sacred tie!"
1675 "I will, my dear Philosophy!" I said,
"But then her teeth, and then, Oh heaven! her eye!

---

2. Robert Stewart, Viscount Castlereagh, detested by Byron for the ruthlessness he had shown in 1798 as the government's chief secretary for Ireland and for the foreign policy he later pursued as foreign secretary (1812–22). His belligerence with political opponents contributed to his unpopularity. Byron refers to a famously testy speech in which Castlereagh complained of "an ignorant impatience of taxation."
3. This episode rewrites *Aeneid* 4 in which, influenced by the malicious goddess Juno's love spells, the hero Aeneas and Dido, queen of Carthage, consummate their union in the cave in which they have taken refuge from a storm.

I'll just inquire if she be wife or maid,
    Or neither—out of curiosity."
"Stop!" cried Philosophy, with air so Grecian,
1680 (Though she was masqued then as a fair Venetian).

211

"Stop!" so I stopp'd.—But to return: that which
    Men call inconstancy is nothing more
Than admiration due where nature's rich
    Profusion with young beauty covers o'er
1685 Some favour'd object; and as in the niche
    A lovely statue we almost adore,
This sort of adoration of the real
Is but a heightening of the "beau ideal."[4]

212

'Tis the perception of the beautiful,
1690   A fine extension of the faculties,
Platonic, universal, wonderful,
    Drawn from the stars, and filter'd through the skies,
Without which life would be extremely dull;
    In short, it is the use of our own eyes,
1695 With one or two small senses added, just
To hint that flesh is form'd of fiery dust.

213

Yet 'tis a painful feeling, and unwilling,
    For surely if we always could perceive
In the same object graces quite as killing
1700   As when she rose upon us like an Eve,
'Twould save us many a heart-ache, many a shilling,
    (For we must get them anyhow, or grieve),
Whereas, if one sole lady pleased for ever,
How pleasant for the heart, as well as liver!

                    *   *   *

216

In the mean time, without proceeding more
    In this anatomy, I've finish'd now
Two hundred and odd stanzas as before,
    That being about the number I'll allow
1725 Each canto of the twelve, or twenty-four;
    And, laying down my pen, I make my bow,
Leaving Don Juan and Haidee to plead
For them and theirs with all who deign to read.

4. Ideal beauty (French), a common phrase in discussions of aesthetics.

From Canto 3

[JUAN AND HAIDEE]

1

Hail, Muse! *et cetera.*—We left Juan sleeping,
   Pillow'd upon a fair and happy breast,
And watch'd by eyes that never yet knew weeping,
   And loved by a young heart, too deeply blest
5 To feel the poison through her spirit creeping,
   Or know who rested there, a foe to rest
Had soil'd the current of her sinless years,
And turn'd her pure heart's purest blood to tears.

2

Oh, Love! what is it in this world of ours
10   Which makes it fatal to be loved? Ah why
With cypress branches[1] hast thou wreathed thy bowers,
   And made thy best interpreter a sigh?
As those who dote on odours pluck the flowers,
   And place them on their breast—but place to die!
15 Thus the frail beings we would fondly cherish
Are laid within our bosoms but to perish.

3

In her first passion woman loves her lover,
   In all the others all she loves is love,[2]
Which grows a habit she can ne'er get over,
20   And fits her loosely—like an easy glove,
As you may find, whene'er you like to prove° her: *test*
   One man alone at first her heart can move;
She then prefers him in the plural number,
Not finding that the additions much encumber.

4

25 I know not if the fault be men's or theirs;
   But one thing's pretty sure; a woman planted[3]—
(Unless at once she plunge for life in prayers)—
   After a decent time must be gallanted;
Although, no doubt, her first of love affairs
30   Is that to which her heart is wholly granted;
Yet there are some, they say, who have had *none*,
But those who have ne'er end with only *one*.[4]

5

'Tis melancholy, and a fearful sign
   Of human frailty, folly, also crime,
35 That love and marriage rarely can combine,
   Although they both are born in the same clime;
Marriage from love, like vinegar from wine—

1. Signifying sorrow.
2. An epigram that Byron translates from the 17th-century French wit François de la Rochefoucauld.
3. Abandoned (from the French *planter là*, to leave in the lurch).
4. Another epigram from la Rochefoucauld.

A sad, sour, sober beverage—by time
Is sharpen'd from its high celestial flavour
40   Down to a very homely household savour.

6

There's something of antipathy, as 'twere,
    Between their present and their future state;
A kind of flattery that's hardly fair
    Is used until the truth arrives too late—
45   Yet what can people do, except despair?
    The same things change their names at such a rate;
For instance—passion in a lover's glorious,
But in a husband is pronounced uxorious.

7

Men grow ashamed of being so very fond;
50   They sometimes also get a little tired
(But that, of course, is rare), and then despond:
    The same things cannot always be admired,
Yet 'tis "so nominated in the bond,"[5]
    That both are tied till one shall have expired.
55   Sad thought! to lose the spouse that was adorning
Our days, and put one's servants into mourning.

8

There's doubtless something in domestic doings,
    Which forms, in fact, true love's antithesis;
Romances paint at full length people's wooings,
60   But only give a bust of marriages;
For no one cares for matrimonial cooings,
    There's nothing wrong in a connubial kiss:
Think you, if Laura had been Petrarch's wife,
He would have written sonnets all his life?[6]

9

65   All tragedies are finish'd by a death,
    All comedies are ended by a marriage;
The future states of both are left to faith,
    For authors fear description might disparage
The worlds to come of both, or fall beneath,
70   And then both worlds would punish their miscarriage;
So leaving each their priest and prayer-book ready,
They say no more of Death or of the Lady.[7]

10

The only two that in my recollection
    Have sung of heaven and hell, or marriage, are
75   Dante and Milton, and of both the affection
    Was hapless in their nuptials, for some bar
Of fault or temper ruin'd the connexion
    (Such things, in fact, it don't ask much to mar);

5. Spoken by Shylock in Shakespeare's *The Merchant of Venice* 4.1.254: "Is it so nominated in the bond?"
6. The 14th-century Italian poet Petrarch made Laura the subject of his sonnets but loved her only from afar.
7. Alluding to a popular ballad, "Death and the Lady."

But Dante's Beatrice and Milton's Eve
80   Were not drawn from their spouses, you conceive.

11

Some persons say that Dante meant theology
    By Beatrice, and not a mistress—I,
Although my opinion may require apology,
    Deem this a commentator's phantasy,
85   Unless indeed it was from his own knowledge he
    Decided thus, and show'd good reason why;
I think that Dante's more abstruse ecstatics
Meant to personify the mathematics.

12

Haidee and Juan were not married, but
90   The fault was theirs, not mine: it is not fair,
Chaste reader, then, in any way to put
    The blame on me, unless you wish they were;
Then if you'd have them wedded, please to shut
    The book which treats of this erroneous pair,
95   Before the consequences grow too awful;
'Tis dangerous to read of loves unlawful.

13

Yet they were happy,—happy in the illicit
    Indulgence of their innocent desires;
But more imprudent grown with every visit,
100   Haidee forgot the island was her sire's;
When we have what we like,'tis hard to miss it,
    At least in the beginning, ere one tires;
Thus she came often, not a moment losing,
Whilst her piratical papa was cruising.

14

105   Let not his mode of raising cash seem strange,
    Although he fleeced the flags of every nation,
For into a prime minister but change
    His title, and 'tis nothing but taxation;
But he, more modest, took an humbler range
110   Of life, and in an honester vocation
Pursued o'er the high seas his watery journey,
And merely practised as a sea-attorney.

15

The good old gentleman had been detain'd
    By winds and waves, and some important captures;
115   And, in the hope of more, at sea remain'd,
    Although a squall or two had damp'd his raptures,
By swamping one of the prizes; he had chain'd
    His prisoners, dividing them like chapters
In number'd lots; they all had cuffs and collars,
120   And averaged each from ten to a hundred dollars.

*   *   *

19

145 Then having settled his marine affairs,
    Despatching single cruisers here and there,
His vessel having need of some repairs,
    He shaped his course to where his daughter fair
Continued still her hospitable cares;
150   But that part of the coast being shoal and bare,
And rough with reefs which ran out many a mile,
His port lay on the other side o' the isle.

20

And there he went ashore without delay,
    Having no custom-house nor quarantine
155 To ask him awkward questions on the way
    About the time and place where he had been:
He left his ship to be hove down next day,
    With orders to the people to careen;[8]
So that all hands were busy beyond measure,
160 In getting out goods, ballast, guns, and treasure.

* * *

27

He saw his white walls shining in the sun,
210   His garden trees all shadowy and green;
He heard his rivulet's light bubbling run,
    The distant dog-bark; and perceived between
The umbrage of the wood so cool and dun
    The moving figures, and the sparkling sheen
215 Of arms (in the East all arm)—and various dyes
Of colour'd garbs, as bright as butterflies.

28

And as the spot where they appear he nears,
    Surprised at these unwonted signs of idling,
He hears—alas! no music of the spheres,
220   But an unhallow'd, earthly sound of fiddling!
A melody which made him doubt his ears,
    The cause being past his guessing or unriddling;
A pipe, too, and a drum, and shortly after,
A most unoriental roar of laughter.

* * *

38

He did not know (Alas! how men will lie)
    That a report (especially the Greeks)
Avouch'd his death (such people never die),
300   And put his house in mourning several weeks,
But now their eyes and also lips were dry;
    The bloom too had return'd to Haidee's cheeks.

---

8. To tip a vessel on its side to clean and repair its hull. "To be hove down": to weigh anchor.

Her tears too being return'd into their fount,
She now kept house upon her own account.

39

305 Hence all this rice, meat, dancing, wine, and fiddling,
    Which turn'd the isle into a place of pleasure;
The servants all were getting drunk or idling,
    A life which made them happy beyond measure.
Her father's hospitality seem'd middling,
310   Compared with what Haidee did with his treasure;
'Twas wonderful how things went on improving,
While she had not one hour to spare from loving.

40

Perhaps you think in stumbling on this feast
    He flew into a passion, and in fact
315 There was no mighty reason to be pleased;
    Perhaps you prophesy some sudden act,
The whip, the rack, or dungeon at the least,
    To teach his people to be more exact,
And that, proceeding at a very high rate,
320 He showed the royal *penchants* of a pirate.

41

You're wrong.—He was the mildest manner'd man
    That ever scuttled ship or cut a throat;
With such true breeding of a gentleman,
    You never could divine his real thought;
325 No courtier could, and scarcely woman can
    Gird more deceit within a petticoat;
Pity he loved adventurous life's variety,
He was so great a loss to good society.

*   *   *

48

Not that he was not sometimes rash or so,
    But never in his real and serious mood;
Then calm, concentrated, and still, and slow,
380   He lay coil'd like the boa in the wood;
With him it never was a word and blow,
    His angry word once o'er, he shed no blood,
But in his silence there was much to rue,
And his *one* blow left little work for *two*.

49

385 He ask'd no further questions, and proceeded
    On to the house, but by a private way,
So that the few who met him hardly heeded,
    So little they expected him that day;
If love paternal in his bosom pleaded
390   For Haidee's sake, is more than I can say,
But certainly to one deem'd dead returning,
This revel seem'd a curious mode of mourning.

50

If all the dead could now return to life,
  (Which God forbid!) or some, or a great many,
395 For instance, if a husband or his wife
  (Nuptial examples are as good as any),
No doubt whate'er might be their former strife,
  The present weather would be much more rainy—
Tears shed into the grave of the connexion
400 Would share most probably its resurrection.

51

He enter'd in the house no more his home,
  A thing to human feelings the most trying,
And harder for the heart to overcome,
  Perhaps, than even the mental pangs of dying;
405 To find our hearthstone turn'd into a tomb,
  And round its once warm precincts palely lying
The ashes of our hopes, is a deep grief,
Beyond a single gentleman's belief.

52

He enter'd in the house—his home no more,
410 For without hearts there is no home;—and felt
The solitude of passing his own door
  Without a welcome; *there* he long had dwelt,
There his few peaceful days Time had swept o'er,
  There his worn bosom and keen eye would melt
415 Over the innocence of that sweet child,
His only shrine of feelings undefiled.

53

He was a man of a strange temperament,
  Of mild demeanour though of savage mood,
Moderate in all his habits, and content
420 With temperance in pleasure, as in food,
Quick to perceive, and strong to bear, and meant
  For something better, if not wholly good;
His country's wrongs[9] and his despair to save her
Had stung him from a slave to an enslaver.

* * *

96

But let me to my story: I must own,
  If I have any fault, it is digression;
Leaving my people to proceed alone,
860 While I soliloquize beyond expression;
But these are my addresses from the throne,[1]
  Which put off business to the ensuing session:
Forgetting each omission is a loss to
The world, not quite so great as Ariosto.[2]

9. Referring to the Greek nation's subjugation by the Ottoman Empire.
1. The speeches with which the British monarch opens sessions of Parliament.

2. Byron warmly admired this poet, author of *Orlando Furioso* (1532), the greatest of the Italian chivalric romances.

97

865 I know that what our neighbours call *"longueurs,"*[3]
(We've not so good a *word*, but have the *thing*
In that complete perfection which ensures
An epic from Bob Southey[4] every spring—)
Form not the true temptation which allures
870 The reader; but 'twould not be hard to bring
Some fine examples of the *épopée*,[5]
To prove its grand ingredient is *ennui*.

98

We learn from Horace, Homer sometimes sleeps;[6]
We feel without him: Wordsworth sometimes wakes,
875 To show with what complacency he creeps,
With his dear *"Waggoners,"*[7] around his lakes;
He wishes for "a boat" to sail the deeps—
Of ocean?—No, of air; and then he makes
Another outcry for "a little boat,"
880 And drivels seas to set it well afloat.[8]

99

If he must fain sweep o'er the etherial plain,
And Pegasus[9] runs restive in his "waggon,"
Could he not beg the loan of Charles's Wain?[1]
Or pray Medea for a single dragon?[2]
885 Or if too classic for his vulgar brain,
He fear'd his neck to venture such a nag on,
And he must needs mount nearer to the moon,
Could not the blockhead ask for a balloon?

100

"Pedlars,"[3] and "boats," and "waggons!" Oh! Ye shades
890 Of Pope and Dryden, are we come to this?
That trash of such sort not alone evades
Contempt, but from the bathos' vast abyss
Floats scumlike uppermost, and these Jack Cades[4]
Of sense and song above your graves may hiss—
895 The "little boatman" and his "Peter Bell"
Can sneer at him who drew "Achitophel!"[5]

3. Boringly wordy passages of verse or prose (French).
4. Robert Southey (1774–1843), poet laureate and author of a number of epic-length narrative poems.
5. Epic poem (French).
6. Horace's *Art of Poetry* 359: "Sometimes great Homer nods."
7. A reference to Wordsworth's long narrative poem *The Waggoner* (1819).
8. In the prologue to his poem *Peter Bell* (1819), Wordsworth wishes for "a little boat, / In shape a very crescent-moon: / Fast through the clouds my boat can sail."
9. The winged horse of Greek myth.
1. The constellation known in the United States as the Big Dipper. "Wain" is an archaic term for wagon.
2. When the Argonaut Jason abandoned Medea to take a new wife, she murdered their sons to punish him, then escaped in a chariot drawn by winged dragons.
3. Wordsworth's Peddler is the narrator of the story in his early manuscript *The Ruined Cottage* (p. 280), which was later incorporated into book 1 of *The Excursion* (1814).
4. A rebel commoner who led an uprising against Henry VI in 1450.
5. I.e., John Dryden, author of the satiric *Absalom and Achitophel* (1681), whom Byron greatly admired. Wordsworth had criticized Dryden's poetry in the Essay, Supplementary to the Preface to his *Poems* (1815).

101

T' our tale.—The feast was over, the slaves gone,
 The dwarfs and dancing girls had all retired;
 The Arab lore and poet's song were done,
900 And every sound of revelry expired;
 The lady and her lover, left alone,
  The rosy flood of twilight's sky admired;—
 Ave Maria!⁶ o'er the earth and sea,
 That heavenliest hour of Heaven is worthiest thee!

102

905 Ave Maria! blessed be the hour!
  The time, the clime, the spot, where I so oft
 Have felt that moment in its fullest power
  Sink o'er the earth so beautiful and soft,
 While swung the deep bell in the distant tower,
910 Or the faint dying day-hymn stole aloft,
 And not a breath crept through the rosy air,
 And yet the forest leaves seem'd stirr'd with prayer.

103

Ave Maria! 'tis the hour of prayer!
 Ave Maria! 'tis the hour of love!
915 Ave Maria! may our spirits dare
  Look up to thine and to thy Son's above!
 Ave Maria! oh that face so fair!
  Those downcast eyes beneath the Almighty dove—
 What though 'tis but a pictured image strike—⁷
920 That painting is no idol, 'tis too like.

104

Some kinder casuists° are pleased to say,   *moralists*
 In nameless print—that I have no devotion;
But set those persons down with me to pray,
 And you shall see who has the properest notion
925 Of getting into Heaven the shortest way;
  My altars are the mountains and the ocean,
 Earth, air, stars,—all that springs from the great Whole,
 Who hath produced, and will receive the soul.

     ✻ ✻ ✻

From Canto 4

[JUAN AND HAIDEE]

3

As boy, I thought myself a clever fellow,
 And wish'd that others held the same opinion;

---

6. Hail, Mary (Latin); the opening words of a Roman Catholic prayer. *Ave Maria* is sometimes used to refer to evening (or morning), because the prayer is part of the service at these times.
7. I.e., "those downcast eyes" seize the attention.

They took it up when my days grew more mellow,
20   And other minds acknowledged my dominion:
Now my sere fancy "falls into the yellow
   Leaf,"[1] and imagination droops her pinion,°   *wing*
And the sad truth which hovers o'er my desk
Turns what was once romantic to burlesque.

4

25 And if I laugh at any mortal thing,
   'Tis that I may not weep; and if I weep,
'Tis that our nature cannot always bring
   Itself to apathy, for we must steep
Our hearts first in the depths of Lethe's[2] spring
30   Ere what we least wish to behold will sleep:
Thetis baptized her mortal son in Styx;[3]
A mortal mother would on Lethe fix.

5

Some have accused me of a strange design
   Against the creed and morals of the land,
35 And trace it in this poem every line:
   I don't pretend that I quite understand
My own meaning when I would be *very* fine,
   But the fact is that I have nothing plann'd,
Unless it were to be a moment merry,
40 A novel word in my vocabulary.

6

To the kind reader of our sober clime
   This way of writing will appear exotic;
Pulci[4] was sire of the half-serious rhyme,
   Who sang when chivalry was more Quixotic,
45 And revell'd in the fancies of the time,
   True knights, chaste dames, huge giants, kings despotic;
But all these, save the last, being obsolete,
I chose a modern subject as more meet.

7

How I have treated it, I do not know;
50   Perhaps no better than they have treated me
Who have imputed such designs as show
   Not what they saw, but what they wish'd to see;
But if it gives them pleasure, be it so,
   This is a liberal age, and thoughts are free:
55 Meantime Apollo plucks me by the ear,
And tells me to resume my story here.

*   *   *

---

1. Cf. Shakespeare's *Macbeth* 5.3.22–24: "My way of life / Is fall'n into the sere, the yellow leaf."
2. A river in Hades that brings forgetfulness of life.
3. The river in Hades into which the nymph Thetis dipped Achilles to make him invulnerable.
4. Author of the *Morgante Maggiore*, prototype of the Italian seriocomic romance from which Byron derived the stanza and manner of *Don Juan* (see headnote, p. 669).

26

Juan and Haidee gazed upon each other
   With swimming looks of speechless tenderness,
Which mix'd all feelings, friend, child, lover, brother,
   All that the best can mingle and express
205 When two pure hearts are pour'd in one another,
   And love too much, and yet can not love less;
But almost sanctify the sweet excess
By the immortal wish and power to bless.

27

Mix'd in each other's arms, and heart in heart,
210   Why did they not then die?—they had lived too long
Should an hour come to bid them breathe apart;
   Years could but bring them cruel things or wrong,
The world was not for them, nor the world's art[5]
   For beings passionate as Sappho's song;
215 Love was born *with* them, *in* them, so intense,
It was their very spirit—not a sense.

28

They should have lived together deep in woods,
   Unseen as sings the nightingale; they were
Unfit to mix in these thick solitudes
220   Call'd social, haunts of Hate, and Vice, and Care:
How lonely every freeborn creature broods!
   The sweetest song-birds nestle in a pair;
The eagle soars alone; the gull and crow
Flock o'er their carrion, just like men below.

29

225 Now pillow'd cheek to cheek, in loving sleep,
   Haidee and Juan their siesta took,
A gentle slumber, but it was not deep,
   For ever and anon a something shook
Juan, and shuddering o'er his frame would creep;
230   And Haidee's sweet lips murmur'd like a brook
A wordless music, and her face so fair
Stirr'd with her dream as rose-leaves with the air;

30

Or as the stirring of a deep clear stream
   Within an Alpine hollow, when the wind
235 Walks o'er it, was she shaken by the dream,
   The mystical usurper of the mind—
O'erpowering us to be whate'er may seem
   Good to the soul which we no more can bind;
Strange state of being! (for 'tis still to be)
240 Senseless to feel, and with seal'd eyes to see.

31

She dream'd of being alone on the sea-shore,
   Chain'd to a rock; she knew not how, but stir

---

5. An echo of Romeo's words to the impoverished apothecary: "The world is not thy friend, nor the world's law" (Shakespeare, *Romeo and Juliet* 5.1.72).

She could not from the spot, and the loud roar
Grew, and each wave rose roughly, threatening her;
245 And o'er her upper lip they seem'd to pour,
Until she sobb'd for breath, and soon they were
Foaming o'er her lone head, so fierce and high—
Each broke to drown her, yet she could not die.

32
Anon—she was released, and then she stray'd
250 O'er the sharp shingles° with her bleeding feet,   *loose pebbles*
And stumbled almost every step she made;
And something roll'd before her in a sheet,
Which she must still pursue howe'er afraid;
'Twas white and indistinct, nor stopp'd to meet
255 Her glance nor grasp, for still she gazed and grasp'd,
And ran, but it escaped her as she clasp'd.

33
The dream changed; in a cave she stood, its walls
Were hung with marble icicles; the work
Of ages on its water-fretted halls,
260 Where waves might wash, and seals might breed and lurk;
Her hair was dripping, and the very balls
Of her black eyes seemed turn'd to tears, and murk
The sharp rocks look'd below each drop they caught,
Which froze to marble as it fell, she thought.

34
265 And wet, and cold, and lifeless at her feet,
Pale as the foam that froth'd on his dead brow,
Which she essay'd in vain to clear, (how sweet
Were once her cares, how idle seem'd they now!)
Lay Juan, nor could aught renew the beat
270 Of his quench'd heart; and the sea dirges low
Rang in her sad ears like a mermaid's song,
And that brief dream appear'd a life too long.

35
And gazing on the dead, she thought his face
Faded, or alter'd into something new—
275 Like to her father's features, till each trace
More like and like to Lambro's aspect grew—
With all his keen worn look and Grecian grace;
And starting, she awoke, and what to view?
Oh! Powers of Heaven! what dark eye meets she there?
280 'Tis—'tis her father's—fix'd upon the pair!

36
Then shrieking, she arose, and shrieking fell,
With joy and sorrow, hope and fear, to see
Him whom she deem'd a habitant where dwell
The ocean-buried, risen from death, to be
285 Perchance the death of one she loved too well:
Dear as her father had been to Haidee,

It was a moment of that awful kind—
I have seen such—but must not call to mind.

37

Up Juan sprung to Haidee's bitter shriek,
290   And caught her falling, and from off the wall
Snatch'd down his sabre, in hot haste to wreak
    Vengeance on him who was the cause of all:
Then Lambro, who till now forbore to speak,
    Smiled scornfully, and said, "Within my call,
295 A thousand scimitars await the word;
Put up, young man, put up your silly sword."

38

And Haidee clung around him; "Juan,'tis—
'Tis Lambro—'tis my father! Kneel with me—
He will forgive us—yes—it must be—yes.
300   Oh! dearest father, in this agony
Of pleasure and of pain—even while I kiss
    Thy garment's hem with transport, can it be
That doubt should mingle with my filial joy?
Deal with me as thou wilt, but spare this boy."

39

305 High and inscrutable the old man stood,
    Calm in his voice, and calm within his eye—
Not always signs with him of calmest mood:
    He look'd upon her, but gave no reply;
Then turn'd to Juan, in whose cheek the blood
310   Oft came and went, as there resolved to die;
In arms, at least, he stood, in act to spring
On the first foe whom Lambro's call might bring.

40

"Young man, your sword"; so Lambro once more said:
Juan replied, "Not while this arm is free."
315 The old man's cheek grew pale, but not with dread,
    And drawing from his belt a pistol, he
Replied, "Your blood be then on your own head."
    Then look'd close at the flint, as if to see
'Twas fresh—for he had lately used the lock[6]—
320 And next proceeded quietly to cock.

41

It has a strange quick jar upon the ear,
    That cocking of a pistol, when you know
A moment more will bring the sight to bear
    Upon your person, twelve yards off, or so;
325 A gentlemanly distance,[7] not too near,
    If you have got a former friend for foe;
But after being fired at once or twice,
The ear becomes more Irish, and less nice.[8]

6. The part of the gun that explodes the charge.
7. I.e., dueling distance.

8. Finicky. Byron alludes to the propensity of hot-headed young Irishmen to fight duels.

42

Lambro presented, and one instant more
330   Had stopp'd this Canto, and Don Juan's breath,
When Haidee threw herself her boy before;
    Stern as her sire: "On me," she cried, "let death
Descend—the fault is mine; this fatal shore
He found—but sought not. I have pledged my faith;
335   I love him—I will die with him: I knew
Your nature's firmness—know your daughter's too."

43

A minute past, and she had been all tears,
    And tenderness, and infancy: but now
She stood as one who champion'd human fears—
340   Pale, statue-like, and stern, she woo'd the blow;
And tall beyond her sex, and their compeers,[9]
    She drew up to her height, as if to show
A fairer mark; and with a fix'd eye scann'd
Her father's face—but never stopp'd his hand.

44

345   He gazed on her, and she on him; 'twas strange
    How like they look'd! the expression was the same;
Serenely savage, with a little change
    In the large dark eye's mutual-darted flame;
For she too was as one who could avenge,
350   If cause should be—a lioness, though tame:
Her father's blood before her father's face
Boil'd up, and prov'd her truly of his race.

45

I said they were alike, their features and
    Their stature differing but in sex and years;
355   Even to the delicacy of their hand
    There was resemblance, such as true blood wears;
And now to see them, thus divided, stand
    In fix'd ferocity, when joyous tears,
And sweet sensations, should have welcomed both,
360   Show what the passions are in their full growth.

46

The father paused a moment, then withdrew
    His weapon, and replaced it; but stood still,
And looking on her, as to look her through,
    "Not I," he said, "have sought this stranger's ill;
365   Not I have made this desolation: few
    Would bear such outrage, and forbear to kill;
But I must do my duty—how thou hast
Done thine, the present vouches for the past.

47

"Let him disarm; or, by my father's head,
370   His own shall roll before you like a ball!"

9. I.e., she was the match in height of Lambro and Juan.

He raised his whistle, as the word he said,
  And blew; another answer'd to the call,
And rushing in disorderly, though led,
  And arm'd from boot to turban, one and all,
375 Some twenty of his train came, rank on rank;
  He gave the word, "Arrest or slay the Frank."[1]

48

Then, with a sudden movement, he withdrew
  His daughter; while compress'd within his clasp,
'Twixt her and Juan interposed the crew;
380   In vain she struggled in her father's grasp—
His arms were like a serpent's coil: then flew
  Upon their prey, as darts an angry asp,
The file of pirates; save the foremost, who
Had fallen, with his right shoulder half cut through.

49

385 The second had his cheek laid open; but
  The third, a wary, cool old sworder, took
The blows upon his cutlass, and then put
  His own well in; so well, ere you could look,
His man was floor'd, and helpless at his foot,
390   With the blood running like a little brook
From two smart sabre gashes, deep and red—
One on the arm, the other on the head.

50

And then they bound him where he fell, and bore
  Juan from the apartment: with a sign
395 Old Lambro bade them take him to the shore,
  Where lay some ships which were to sail at nine.
They laid him in a boat, and plied the oar
  Until they reach'd some galliots,[2] placed in line;
On board of one of these, and under hatches,
400 They stow'd him, with strict orders to the watches.

51

The world is full of strange vicissitudes,
  And here was one exceedingly unpleasant:
A gentleman so rich in the world's goods,
  Handsome and young, enjoying all the present,
405 Just at the very time when he least broods
  On such a thing is suddenly to sea sent,
Wounded and chain'd, so that he cannot move,
And all because a lady fell in love.

*   *   *

56

Afric is all the sun's, and as her earth
  Her human clay is kindled; full of power

---

1. Term used in the Near East to designate a Western European.

2. Small, fast galleys, propelled by both oars and sails.

For good or evil, burning from its birth,
  The Moorish blood partakes the planet's hour,
445 And like the soil beneath it will bring forth:
  Beauty and love were Haidee's mother's dower;°   *dowry*
  But her large dark eye show'd deep Passion's force,
  Though sleeping like a lion near a source.

57
Her daughter, temper'd with a milder ray,
450   Like summer clouds all silvery, smooth, and fair,
Till slowly charged with thunder they display
  Terror to earth, and tempest to the air,
  Had held till now her soft and milky way;
  But overwrought with passion and despair,
455 The fire burst forth from her Numidian° veins,   *North African*
  Even as the Simoom³ sweeps the blasted plains.

58
The last sight which she saw was Juan's gore,
  And he himself o'ermaster'd and cut down;
His blood was running on the very floor
460   Where late he trod, her beautiful, her own;
Thus much she view'd an instant and no more,—
  Her struggles ceased with one convulsive groan;
On her sire's arm, which until now scarce held
  Her writhing, fell she like a cedar fell'd.

59
465 A vein had burst, and her sweet lips' pure dyes
  Were dabbled with the deep blood which ran o'er;⁴
And her head droop'd as when the lily lies
  O'ercharged with rain: her summon'd handmaids bore
Their lady to her couch with gushing eyes;
470   Of herbs and cordials they produced their store,
But she defied all means they could employ,
  Like one life could not hold, nor death destroy.

60
Days lay she in that state unchanged, though chill
  With nothing livid,⁵ still her lips were red;
475 She had no pulse, but death seem'd absent still;
  No hideous sign proclaim'd her surely dead;
Corruption came not in each mind to kill
  All hope; to look upon her sweet face bred
New thoughts of life, for it seem'd full of soul,
480 She had so much, earth could not claim the whole.

✢   ✢   ✢

---

3. A violent, hot, dust-laden desert wind.
4. This is no very uncommon effect of the violence
of conflicting and different passions [Byron's

note].
5. I.e., though she was ashen pale.

69

545 Twelve days and nights she wither'd thus; at last,
　　Without a groan, or sigh, or glance, to show
　　A parting pang, the spirit from her past:°　　　　　　　*passed*
　　And they who watch'd her nearest could not know
　　The very instant, till the change that cast
550　　Her sweet face into shadow, dull and slow,
　　Glazed o'er her eyes—the beautiful, the black—
　　Oh! to possess such lustre—and then lack!

70

She died, but not alone; she held within
　　A second principle of life, which might
555 Have dawn'd a fair and sinless child of sin;
　　But closed its little being without light,
　　And went down to the grave unborn, wherein
　　Blossom and bough lie wither'd with one blight;
　　In vain the dews of Heaven descend above
560 The bleeding flower and blasted fruit of love.

71

Thus lived—thus died she; never more on her
　　Shall sorrow light, or shame. She was not made
Through years or moons the inner weight to bear,
　　Which colder hearts endure till they are laid
565 By age in earth; her days and pleasures were
　　Brief, but delightful—such as had not staid
Long with her destiny; but she sleeps well
By the sea shore, whereon she loved to dwell.

72

That isle is now all desolate and bare,
570　　Its dwellings down, its tenants past away;
None but her own and father's grave is there,
　　And nothing outward tells of human clay;
Ye could not know where lies a thing so fair,
　　No stone is there to show, no tongue to say
575 What was; no dirge, except the hollow sea's,
Mourns o'er the beauty of the Cyclades.

73

But many a Greek maid in a loving song
　　Sighs o'er her name; and many an islander
With her sire's story makes the night less long;
580　　Valour was his, and beauty dwelt with her;
If she loved rashly, her life paid for wrong—
　　A heavy price must all pay who thus err,
In some shape; let none think to fly the danger,
For soon or late Love is his own avenger.

74

585 But let me change this theme, which grows too sad,
And lay this sheet of sorrows on the shelf;
I don't much like describing people mad,
For fear of seeming rather touch'd myself—
Besides I've no more on this head to add;
590 And as my Muse is a capricious elf,
We'll put about, and try another tack
With Juan, left half-kill'd some stanzas back.[6]

1818–23   1819–24

Stanzas Written on the Road between Florence and Pisa

Oh, talk not to me of a name great in story—
The days of our youth are the days of our glory;
And the myrtle and ivy[1] of sweet two-and-twenty
Are worth all your laurels,[2] though ever so plenty.

5 What are garlands and crowns to the brow that is wrinkled?
'Tis but as a dead-flower with May-dew besprinkled:
Then away with all such from the head that is hoary![3]
What care I for the wreaths that can *only* give glory?

Oh FAME!—if I e'er took delight in thy praises,
10 'Twas less for the sake of thy high-sounding phrases,
Than to see the bright eyes of the dear one discover
She thought that I was not unworthy to love her.

There chiefly I sought thee, *there* only I found thee;
Her glance was the best of the rays that surround thee;
15 When it sparkled o'er aught that was bright in my story,
I knew it was love, and I felt it was glory.

Nov. 1821   1830

6. Juan's adventures continue. He is sold as a slave in Constantinople to an enamored sultana; she disguises him as a girl and adds him to her husband's harem for convenience of access. Juan escapes, joins the Russian army that is besieging Ismail, and so well distinguishes himself in the capture of the town that he is sent with dispatches to St. Petersburg. There he becomes "man-mistress" to the insatiable empress Catherine the Great. As the result of her assiduous attentions, he falls into a physical decline and, for a salutary change of scene and climate, is sent on a diplomatic mission to England. In canto 16, the last that Byron finished, he is in the middle of an amorous adventure while a guest at the medieval country mansion of an English nobleman, Lord Henry Amundeville, and his very beautiful wife.
1. Sacred to Bacchus, god of wine and revelry. "Myrtle": sacred to Venus, goddess of love.
2. A laurel crown was awarded by the Greeks as a mark of high honor.
3. White or gray with age.

January 22nd. Missolonghi

On this day I complete my thirty sixth year

'Tis time this heart should be unmoved,
   Since others it hath ceased to move:
Yet though I cannot be beloved,
           Still let me love!

5 My days are in the yellow leaf;
   The flowers and fruits of Love are gone;
The worm—the canker, and the grief
           Are mine alone!

The fire that on my bosom preys
10 Is lone as some Volcanic Isle;
No torch is kindled at its blaze
           A funeral pile!

The hope, the fear, the jealous care,
   The exalted portion of the pain
15 And power of Love I cannot share,
           But wear the chain.

But 'tis not *thus*—and 'tis not *here*
   Such thoughts should shake my Soul, nor *now*
Where Glory decks the hero's bier
20   Or binds his brow.

The Sword, the Banner, and the Field,
   Glory and Greece around us see!
The Spartan borne upon his shield
           Was not more free!

25 Awake (not Greece—she *is* awake!)
   Awake, my Spirit! think through *whom*
Thy life-blood tracks its parent lake
           And then strike home!

Tread those reviving passions down
30 Unworthy Manhood—unto thee
Indifferent should the smile or frown
           Of Beauty be.

If thou regret'st thy Youth, *why live?*
   The land of honourable Death
35 Is here:—up to the Field, and give
           Away thy Breath!

Seek out—less often sought than found—
   A Soldier's Grave, for thee the best;
Then look around, and choose thy Ground,
40   And take thy Rest!

Jan. 1824   1824

Letters[1]

To Thomas Moore[1]

Venice, January 28th, 1817

Your letter of the 8th is before me. The remedy for your plethora is simple—abstinence. I was obliged to have recourse to the like some years ago, I mean in point of *diet*, and, with the exception of some convivial weeks and days, (it might be months, now and then), have kept to Pythagoras[2] ever since. For all this, let me hear that you are better. You must not *indulge* in "filthy beer," nor in porter, nor eat *suppers*—the last are the devil to those who swallow dinner.

✲ ✲

✲ [3]

I am truly sorry to hear of your father's misfortune[4]—cruel at any time, but doubly cruel in advanced life. However, you will, at least, have the satisfaction of doing your part by him, and, depend upon it, it will not be in vain. Fortune, to be sure, is a female, but not such a b * * as the rest (always excepting your wife and my sister from such sweeping terms); for she generally has some justice in the long run. I have no spite against her, though between her and Nemesis I have had some sore gauntlets to run—but then I have done my best to deserve no better. But to *you*, she is a good deal in arrear, and she will come round—mind if she don't: you have the vigour of life, of independence, of talent, spirit, and character all with you. What you can do for yourself, you have done and will do; and surely there are some others in the world who would not be sorry to be of use, if you would allow them to be useful, or at least attempt it.

I think of being in England in the spring. If there is a row, by the sceptre of King Ludd,[5] but I'll be one; and if there is none, and only a continuance of "this meek, piping time of peace,"[6] I will take a cottage a hundred yards to the south of your abode, and become your neighbour; and we will compose such canticles, and hold such dialogues, as shall be the terror of the *Times* (including the newspaper of that name), and the wonder, and honour, and praise, of the Morning Chronicle and posterity.

I rejoice to hear of your forthcoming in February[7]—though I tremble for the "magnificence," which you attribute to the new Childe Harold.[8] I am glad you like it; it is a fine indistinct piece of poetical desolation, and my favourite. I was half mad during the time of its composition, between metaphysics, mountains, lakes, love unextinguishable, thoughts unutterable, and the night-

---

1. Three thousand of Byron's letters have survived—a remarkable number for so short a life. In general they are our best single biographical source for the poet, providing running commentary on his day-to-day concerns and activities and giving us the clearest possible picture of his complex personality, a picture relatively (but not entirely) free of the posturings that pervade both the romantic poems and the satires. The texts of our small sample here are from Leslie A. Marchand's twelve-volume edition, *Byron's Letters and Journals* (1973–82).
1. Irish poet and a good friend of Byron since they met in 1811. Moore's *Life* of Byron in 1830 is the sole source for many of Byron's letters, including this one.
2. I.e., have eaten no flesh (the disciples of the Greek philosopher-mathematician Pythagoras were strict vegetarians).
3. These asterisks (as well as those in the next paragraph and near the end of the letter) are Moore's, representing omissions in his printed text.
4. Moore's father had been dismissed from his post as barrack master at Dublin.
5. A mythical king of Britain.
6. Shakespeare's *Richard III* 1.1.24.
7. Moore's Oriental romance *Lalla Rookh.*
8. Canto 3 of *Childe Harold's Pilgrimage* (1816).

mare of my own delinquencies. I should, many a good day, have blown my brains out, but for the recollection that it would have given pleasure to my mother-in-law; and, even *then*, if I could have been certain to haunt her—but I won't dwell upon these trifling family matters.

Venice is in the *estro* of her carnival, and I have been up these last two nights at the ridotto⁹ and the opera, and all that kind of thing. Now for an adventure. A few days ago a gondolier brought me a billet without a subscription, intimating a wish on the part of the writer to meet me either in gondola or at the island of San Lazaro, or at a third rendezvous, indicated in the note. "I know the country's disposition well"—in Venice "they do let Heaven see those tricks they dare not show," &c. &c.;¹ so, for all response, I said that neither of the three places suited me; but that I would either be at home at ten at night *alone*, or at the ridotto at midnight, where the writer might meet me masked. At ten o'clock I was at home and alone (Marianna was gone with her husband to a conversazione²), when the door of my apartment opened, and in walked a well-looking and (for an Italian) *bionda*³ girl of about nineteen, who informed me that she was married to the brother of my *amorosa*, and wished to have some conversation with me. I made a decent reply, and we had some talk in Italian and Romaic (her mother being a Greek of Corfu), when lo! in a very few minutes, in marches, to my very great astonishment, Marianna S[egati], *in propria persona*, and after making polite courtesy to her sister-in-law and to me, without a single word seizes her said sister-in-law by the hair, and bestows upon her some sixteen slaps, which would have made your ear ache only to hear their echo. I need not describe the screaming which ensued. The luckless visitor took flight. I seized Marianna, who, after several vain efforts to get away in pursuit of the enemy, fairly went into fits in my arms; and, in spite of reasoning, eau de Cologne, vinegar, half a pint of water, and God knows what other waters beside, continued so till past midnight.

After damning my servants for letting people in without apprizing me, I found that Marianna in the morning had seen her sister-in-law's gondolier on the stairs, and, suspecting that his apparition boded her no good, had either returned of her own accord, or been followed by her maids or some other spy of her people to the conversazione, from whence she returned to perpetrate this piece of pugilism. I had seen fits before, and also some small scenery of the same genus in and out of our island: but this was not all. After about an hour, in comes—who? why, Signor S[egati], her lord and husband, and finds me with his wife fainting upon the sofa, and all the apparatus of confusion, dishevelled hair, hats, handkerchiefs, salts, smelling-bottles—and the lady as pale as ashes without sense or motion. His first question was, "What is all this?" The lady could not reply—so I did. I told him the explanation was the easiest thing in the world; but in the mean time it would be as well to recover his wife—at least, her senses. This came about in due time of suspiration and respiration.

You need not be alarmed—jealousy is not the order of the day in Venice, and daggers are out of fashion; while duels, on love matters, are unknown—at least, with the husbands. But, for all this, it was an awkward affair; and though he must have known that I made love to Marianna, yet I believe he

9. An Italian social gathering. "Estro": fire, fervor.   2. An evening party. Marianna Segati, wife of a
1. Shakespeare's *Othello* 3.3.206–07. The passage   Venetian draper, was Byron's current *amorosa*.
continues: "dare not show their husbands."   3. Blonde (Italian).

was not, till that evening, aware of the extent to which it had gone. It is very well known that almost all the married women have a lover; but it is usual to keep up the forms, as in other nations. I did not, therefore, know what the devil to say. I could not out with the truth, out of regard to her, and I did not choose to lie for my sake;—besides, the thing told itself. I thought the best way would be to let her explain it as she chose (a woman being never at a loss—the devil always sticks by them)—only determining to protect and carry her off, in case of any ferocity on the part of the Signor. I saw that he was quite calm. She went to bed, and next day—how they settled it, I know not, but settle it they did. Well—then I had to explain to Marianna about this never to be sufficiently confounded sister-in-law; which I did by swearing innocence, eternal constancy, &c. &c. * * * But the sister-in-law, very much discomposed with being treated in such wise, has (not having her own shame before her eyes) told the affair to half Venice, and the servants (who were summoned by the fight and the fainting) to the other half. But, here, nobody minds such trifles, except to be amused by them. I don't know whether you will be so, but I have scrawled a long letter out of these follies.

Believe me ever. &c.

To Douglas Kinnaird[1]

[DON JUAN: "IS IT NOT LIFE?"]

Venice. Octr. 26th. [1819]

My dear Douglas—My late expenditure has arisen from living at a distance from Venice and being obliged to keep up two establishments, from frequent journeys—and buying some furniture and books as well as a horse or two—and not from any renewal of the EPICUREAN system[2] as you suspect. I have been faithful to my honest liaison with Countess Guiccioli[3]—and I can assure you that *She* has never cost me directly or indirectly a sixpence—indeed the circumstances of herself and family render this no merit.—I never offered her but one present—a broach of brilliants—and she sent it back to me with her *own hair* in it (I shall *not* say of *what part* but *that* is an Italian custom) and a note to say that she was not in the habit of receiving presents of that value—but hoped that I would not consider her sending it back as an affront—nor the value diminished by the enclosure.—I have not had a whore this half-year—confining myself to the strictest adultery.——Why should you prevent Hanson from making a *peer*[4] if he likes it—I think the *"Garretting"* would be by far the best parliamentary privilege—I know of.——Damn your delicacy.—It is a low commercial quality—and very unworthy a man who prefixes "honourable" to his nomenclature. If you say that I must sign the bonds—I suppose that I must—but it is very iniquitous to make me pay my debts—you have no idea of the pain it gives one.—Pray do three things—get my property out of

---

1. Kinnaird, a friend from Cambridge days, was Byron's banker and literary agent in London.
2. I.e., money spent on pleasures of the senses.
3. Byron mentions having fallen in love with Teresa Guiccioli ("a Romagnuola Countess from Ravenna—who is nineteen years old & has a Count of fifty") in a letter of April 6, 1819. Their

relationship lasted until Byron set sail for Greece in the summer of 1823.
4. I.e., being made a peer (of the realm). John Hanson, Byron's solicitor and agent before Kinnaird took over his principal business affairs, never realized this ambition.

the *funds*—get Rochdale[5] sold—get me some information from Perry about *South America*[6]—and 4thly. ask Lady Noel not to live so very long.——As to Subscribing to Manchester—if I do that—I will write a letter to Burdett[7]—for publication—to accompany the Subscription—which shall be more radical than anything yet rooted—but I feel lazy.—I have thought of this for some time—but alas! the air of this cursed Italy enervates—and disfranchises the thoughts of a man after nearly four years of respiration—to say nothing of emission.—As to "Don Juan"—confess—confess—you dog—and be candid—that it is the sublime of *that there* sort of writing—it may be bawdy—but is it not good English?—it may be profligate—but is it not *life*, is it not *the thing*?—Could any man have written it—who has not lived in the world?—and tooled in a post-chaise? in a hackney coach? in a Gondola? against a wall? in a court carriage? in a vis a vis?[8]—on a table?—and under it?—I have written about a hundred stanzas of a third Canto—but it is damned modest—the outcry has frightened me.—I had such projects for the Don—but the *Cant* is so much stronger than *Cunt*—now a days,—that the benefit of experience in a man who had well weighed the worth of both monosyllables—must be lost to despairing posterity.—After all what stuff this outcry is—Lalla Rookh and Little—are more dangerous than my burlesque poem can be—Moore has been here—we got tipsy together—and were very amicable—he is gone on to Rome—I put my life (in M.S.) into his hands[9]—(*not* for publication) you—or any body else may see it—at his return.—It only comes up to 1816.——He is a noble fellow—and looks quite fresh and poetical—nine years (the age of a poem's education) my Senior—he looks younger—this comes of marriage and being settled in the Country. I want to go to South America—I have written to Hobhouse all about it.—I wrote to my wife—three months ago—under care to Murray—has she got the letter—or is the letter got into Blackwood's magazine?——You ask after my Christmas pye—Remit it any how—*Circulars*[1] is the best—you are right about *income*—I must have it all—how the devil do I know that I may live a year or a month?—I wish I knew that I might regulate my spending in more ways than one.—As it is one always thinks that there is but a span.—A man may as well break or be damned for a large sum as a small one—I should be loth to pay the devil or any other creditor more than sixpence in the pound.—

[scrawl for signature]

P.S.—I recollect nothing of "Davies's landlord"—but what ever Davies *says*—I will *swear* to—and *that's* more than *he* would.—So pray pay—has he a landlady too?—perhaps I may owe her something.——With regard to the bonds I will sign them but—it goes against the grain.——As to the rest—you *can't* err—so long as you *don't* pay.——Paying is executor's or executioner's work.——You may write somewhat oftener—Mr. Galignani's messenger[2] gives the outline of your public affairs—but I see no results—you have no man yet—(always excepting Burdett—& you & H[obhouse] and the Gentlemanly leaven of your two-penny loaf of rebellion) don't forget however my charge of

5. An estate that Byron had inherited in Lancashire.
6. Byron was considering the possibility of emigrating to South America, specifically to Venezuela.
7. Sir Francis Burdett, member of Parliament for Westminster, a reformer and leader of opposition to the Tories.
8. A light carriage for two persons sitting face to face.
9. Byron's famous memoirs, which were later sold to John Murray and burned in the publisher's office.
1. Letters of credit that could be exchanged for cash.
2. *Galignani's Messenger*, an English newspaper published in Paris.

horse—and commission for the Midland Counties and by the holies!—You shall have your account in decimals.—Love to Hobby—but why leave the Whigs?——

To Percy Bysshe Shelley

[KEATS AND SHELLEY]

Ravenna, April 26th, 1821

The child continues doing well, and the accounts are regular and favourable. It is gratifying to me that you and Mrs. Shelley do not disapprove of the step which I have taken, which is merely temporary.[1]

I am very sorry to hear what you say of Keats[2]—is it *actually* true? I did not think criticism had been so killing. Though I differ from you essentially in your estimate of his performances, I so much abhor all unnecessary pain, that I would rather he had been seated on the highest peak of Parnassus than have perished in such a manner. Poor fellow! though with such inordinate self-love he would probably have not been very happy. I read the review of "Endymion" in the Quarterly. It was severe,—but surely not so severe as many reviews in that and other journals upon others.

I recollect the effect on me of the Edinburgh on my first poem;[3] it was rage, and resistance, and redress—but not despondency nor despair. I grant that those are not amiable feelings; but, in this world of bustle and broil, and especially in the career of writing, a man should calculate upon his powers of *resistance* before he goes into the arena.

"Expect not life from pain nor danger free,
Nor deem the doom of man reversed for thee."[4]

You know my opinion of *that second-hand* school of poetry. You also know my high opinion of your own poetry,—because it is of *no* school. I read Cenci—but, besides that I think the *subject* essentially *un*dramatic, I am not an admirer of our old dramatists *as models.* I deny that the English have hitherto had a drama at all. Your Cenci, however, was a work of power, and poetry. As to *my* drama,[5] pray revenge yourself upon it, by being as free as I have been with yours.

I have not yet got your Prometheus, which I long to see. I have heard nothing of mine, and do not know that it is yet published. I have published a pamphlet on the Pope controversy, which you will not like. Had I known that Keats was dead—or that he was alive and so sensitive—I should have omitted some remarks upon his poetry, to which I was provoked by his *attack* upon *Pope*,[6] and my disapprobation of *his own* style of writing.

1. Byron had recently placed his four-year-old daughter, Allegra, in a convent school near Ravenna, against the wishes of her mother, Mary Shelley's stepsister Claire Clairmont.
2. In a letter to Byron, April 17, 1821: "Young Keats, whose 'Hyperion' showed so great a promise, died lately at Rome from the consequences of breaking a blood-vessel, in paroxysms of despair at the contemptuous attack on his book in the *Quarterly Review*" (see Shelley's *Adonais*, p. 822).
3. The review of Byron's *Hours of Idleness* in the *Edinburgh Review* prompted him to write his first

major satire, *English Bards and Scotch Reviewers* (1809).
4. Johnson, *The Vanity of Human Wishes*, lines 155–56 (Byron is quoting from memory).
5. *Marino Faliero*, published in London on April 21, 1821. Shelley's *The Cenci* and *Prometheus Unbound* (next paragraph) were written in 1819 and published in 1820.
6. Keats attacked Augustan poetry (but not necessarily Pope) in "Sleep and Poetry," lines 181–206. Byron's pamphlet, *Letter to ********[John Murray], on the Rev. W. L. Bowles' Strictures on*

You want me to undertake a great Poem—I have not the inclination nor the power. As I grow older, the indifference—*not* to life, for we love it by instinct—but to the stimuli of life, increases. Besides, this late failure of the Italians[7] has latterly disappointed me for many reasons,—some public, some personal. My respects to Mrs. S.

Yours ever,

B

P.S.—Could not you and I contrive to meet this summer? Could not you take a run *alone*?

---

the *Life and Writings of Pope*, had just appeared in London. His best-known comment on Keats, written a year and a half later, is canto 11, stanza 60 in *Don Juan*, beginning "John Keats, who was killed off by one critique" and ending " 'Tis strange the mind, that very fiery particle, / Should let itself be snuffed out by an Article."
7. A planned uprising by the Carbonari, a secret revolutionary society into which Byron had been initiated by the father and brother of his mistress Teresa Guiccioli, failed in Feb. 1821.

PERCY BYSSHE SHELLEY
1792–1822

Percy Bysshe Shelley, radical in every aspect of his life and thought, emerged from a solidly conservative background. His ancestors had been Sussex aristocrats since early in the seventeenth century; his grandfather, Sir Bysshe Shelley, made himself the richest man in Horsham, Sussex; his father, Timothy Shelley, was a hardheaded and conventional member of Parliament. Percy Shelley was in line for a baronetcy and, as befitted his station, was sent to be educated at Eton and Oxford. As a youth he was slight of build, eccentric in manner, and unskilled in sports or fighting and, as a consequence, was mercilessly bullied by older and stronger boys. He later said that he saw the petty tyranny of schoolmasters and schoolmates as representative of man's general inhumanity to man, and dedicated his life to a war against injustice and oppression. As he described the experience in the Dedication to *Laon and Cythna*:

> So without shame, I spake:—"I will be wise,
> And just, and free, and mild, if in me lies
> Such power, for I grow weary to behold
> The selfish and the strong still tyrannise
> Without reproach or check." I then controuled
> My tears, my heart grew calm, and I was meek and bold.

At Oxford in the autumn of 1810, Shelley's closest friend was Thomas Jefferson Hogg, a self-centered, self-confident young man who shared Shelley's love of philosophy and scorn of orthodoxy. The two collaborated on a pamphlet, *The Necessity of Atheism*, which claimed that God's existence cannot be proved on empirical grounds, and, provocatively, they mailed it to the bishops and heads of the colleges at Oxford. Shelley refused to repudiate the document and, to his shock and grief, was peremptorily expelled, terminating a university career that had lasted only six months. This event opened a breach between Shelley and his father that widened over the years.

Shelley went to London, where he took up the cause of Harriet Westbrook, the pretty and warmhearted daughter of a well-to-do tavern keeper, whose father, Shelley wrote to Hogg, "has persecuted her in a most horrible way by endeavoring to compel her to go to school." Harriet threw herself on Shelley's protection, and "gratitude and admiration," he wrote, "all demand that I shall love her *forever*." He eloped with Harriet to Edinburgh and married her, against his conviction that marriage was a tyrannical and degrading social institution. He was then eighteen years of age; his bride, sixteen. The couple moved restlessly from place to place, living on a small allowance granted reluctantly by their families. In February 1812, accompanied by Harriet's sister Eliza, they traveled to Dublin to distribute Shelley's *Address to the Irish People* and otherwise take part in the movement for Catholic emancipation and for the amelioration of that oppressed and poverty-stricken people.

Back in London, Shelley became a disciple of the radical social philosopher William Godwin, author of the *Inquiry Concerning Political Justice*. In 1813 he printed privately his first important work, *Queen Mab*, a long poem set in the fantastic frame of the journey of a disembodied soul through space, to whom the fairy Mab reveals in visions the woeful past, the dreadful present, and a utopian future. Announcing that "there is no God!" Mab decries institutional religion and codified morality as the roots of social evil, prophesying that all institutions will wither away and humanity will return to its natural condition of goodness and felicity.

In the following spring Shelley, who had drifted apart from Harriet, fell in love with the beautiful Mary Wollstonecraft Godwin, daughter of Mary Wollstonecraft and William Godwin. Convinced that cohabitation without love is immoral, he abandoned Harriet, fled to France with Mary (taking along her stepsister, Claire Clairmont), and—in accordance with his belief in nonexclusive love—invited Harriet to come live with them in the relationship of a sister. Shelley's elopement with Mary outraged her father, despite the facts that his own views of marriage had been no less radical than Shelley's and that Shelley, himself in financial difficulties, had earlier taken over Godwin's very substantial debts. When he returned to London, Shelley found that the general public, his family, and most of his friends regarded him as not only an atheist and a revolutionary but also a gross immoralist. When two years later Harriet, pregnant by an unknown lover, drowned herself in a fit of despair, the courts denied Shelley the custody of their two children. (His first child with Mary Godwin, a girl born prematurely, had died earlier, only twelve days after her birth in February 1815.) Percy and Mary married in December 1816, and in spring 1818 they moved to Italy. Thereafter he envisioned himself as an alien and outcast, rejected by the human race to whose welfare he had dedicated his powers and his life.

In Italy he resumed his restless way of life, evading the people to whom he owed money by moving from town to town and house to house. His health was usually bad. Although the death of his grandfather in 1815 had provided a substantial income, he dissipated so much of it by his warmhearted but imprudent support of William Godwin, Leigh Hunt, and other needy acquaintances that he was constantly short of funds. Within nine months, in 1818–19, both Clara and William, the children Mary had borne in 1815 and 1817, died. Grief over these deaths destroyed the earlier harmony of the Shelleys' marriage; the birth in November 1819 of another son, Percy Florence (their only child to survive to adulthood), was not enough to mend the rift.

In these circumstances, close to despair and knowing that he almost entirely lacked an audience, Shelley wrote his greatest works. In 1819 he completed *Prometheus Unbound* and a tragedy, *The Cenci*. He wrote also numerous lyric poems; a visionary call for a proletarian revolution, "The Mask of Anarchy"; a witty satire on Wordsworth, *Peter Bell the Third*; and a penetrating political essay, "A Philosophical View of Reform." His works of the next two years include "A Defence of Poetry"; *Epipsychidion*, a rhapsodic vision of love as a spiritual union beyond earthly limits; *Adonais*, his elegy on the death of Keats; and *Hellas*, a lyrical drama evoked by the Greek war for liberation from the Turks. These writings, unlike the early *Queen Mab*, are the products of a mind chastened by tragic experience, deepened by philosophical speculation, and stored with the harvest of his reading—which Shelley carried on, as his friend

Hogg said, "in season and out of season, at table, in bed, and especially during a walk," until he became one of the most erudite of poets. His delight in scientific discoveries and speculations continued, but his earlier zest for Gothic terrors and the social theories of the radical eighteenth-century optimists gave way to an absorption in Greek tragedy, Milton's *Paradise Lost,* and the Bible. Although he did not give up his hopes for a millennial future (he wore a ring with the motto *Il buon tempo verrà*— "the good time will come"), he now attributed the evils of society to humanity's own moral failures and grounded the possibility of radical social reform on a reform of the moral and imaginative faculties through the redeeming power of love. Though often represented as a simpleminded doctrinaire, Shelley in fact possessed a complex and energetically inquisitive intelligence that never halted at a fixed mental position; his writings reflect stages in a ceaseless exploration.

The poems of Shelley's maturity also show the influence of his study of Plato and the Neoplatonists. Shelley found congenial the Platonic division of the cosmos into two worlds—the ordinary world of change, mortality, evil, and suffering and an ideal world of perfect and eternal Forms, of which the world of sense experience is only a distant and illusory reflection. The earlier interpretations of Shelley as a downright Platonic idealist, however, have been drastically modified by modern investigations of his reading and writings. He was a close student of British empiricist philosophy, which limits knowledge to valid reasoning on what is given in sense experience, and within this tradition he felt a special affinity to the radical skepticism of David Hume. A number of Shelley's works, such as "Mont Blanc," express his view of the narrow limits of what human beings can know with certainty and exemplify his refusal to let his hopes harden into a philosophical or religious creed. To what has been called the "skeptical idealism" of the mature Shelley, hope in a redemption from present social ills is not an intellectual certainty but a moral obligation. Despair is self-fulfilling; we must continue to hope because, by keeping open the possibility of a better future, hope releases the imaginative and creative powers that are the only means of achieving that end.

When in 1820 the Shelleys settled finally at Pisa, he came closer to finding contentment than at any other time in his adult life. A group of friends, Shelley's "Pisan Circle," gathered around them, including for a while Lord Byron and the swashbuckling young Cornishman Edward Trelawny. Chief in Shelley's affections were Edward Williams, a retired lieutenant of a cavalry regiment serving in India, and his charming common-law wife, Jane, with whom Shelley became infatuated and to whom he addressed some of his best lyrics and verse letters. The end came suddenly, and in a way prefigured uncannily in the last stanza of *Adonais,* in which he had described his spirit as a ship driven by a violent storm out into the dark unknown. On July 8, 1822, Shelley and Edward Williams were sailing their open boat, the *Don Juan,* on the Gulf of Spezia. A violent squall swamped the boat. When several days later the bodies were washed ashore, they were cremated, and Shelley's ashes were buried in the Protestant Cemetery at Rome, near the graves of John Keats and William Shelley, the poet's young son.

Both Shelley's character and his poetry have been the subject of violently contradictory, and often partisan, estimates. His actions according to his deep convictions often led to disastrous consequences for himself and those near to him; and even recent scholars, while repudiating the vicious attacks by Shelley's contemporaries, attribute some of those actions to a self-assured egotism that masked itself as idealism. Yet Byron, who knew Shelley intimately and did not pay moral compliments lightly, wrote to his publisher John Murray, in response to attacks on Shelley at the time of his death: "You are all brutally mistaken about Shelley, who was, without exception, the *best* and least selfish man I ever knew." Shelley's politics, vilified during his lifetime, made him a literary hero to later political radicals: the Chartists in the middle of the nineteenth century, Marx and Engels at the end, and for much of the twentieth century, many of the guiding lights of the British Labour Party. As a poet Shelley was greatly admired by Robert Browning, Swinburne, and other Victorians; but in the mid-twentieth century he was repeatedly charged with intellectual and emotional immaturity, shoddy workmanship, and incoherent imagery by influential writers such as F. R. Leavis and his followers in Britain and the New Critics in America. More recently, however, many sympathetic studies have revealed the coherent intellectual understructure of his poems and have confirmed Wordsworth's early recognition that "Shelley is one of the best *artists* of us all: I mean in workmanship of style." Shelley, it has become clear, greatly expanded the metrical and stanzaic resources of English versification. His poems exhibit a broad range of voices, from the high but ordered passion of "Ode to the West Wind," through the heroic dignity of the utterances of Prometheus, to the approximation of what is inexpressible in the description of Asia's transfiguration and in the visionary conclusion of *Adonais*. Most surprising, for a poet who almost entirely lacked an audience, is the urbanity, the assured command of the tone and language of a cultivated man of the world, exemplified in passages that Shelley wrote all through his mature career and especially in the lyrics and verse letters that he composed during the last year of his life.

The texts printed here are those prepared by Donald H. Reiman and Neil Fraistat for *Shelley's Poetry and Prose*, a Norton Critical Edition, 2nd ed. (2001); Reiman has also edited for this anthology a few poems not included in that edition.

Mutability

We are as clouds that veil the midnight moon;
    How restlessly they speed, and gleam, and quiver,
Streaking the darkness radiantly!—yet soon
    Night closes round, and they are lost for ever:

5 Or like forgotten lyres,° whose dissonant strings   *wind harps*
    Give various response to each varying blast,
To whose frail frame no second motion brings
    One mood or modulation like the last.

We rest.—A dream has power to poison sleep;
10   We rise.—One wandering thought pollutes the day;
We feel, conceive or reason, laugh or weep;
    Embrace fond woe, or cast our cares away:

It is the same!—For, be it joy or sorrow,
    The path of its departure still is free:
15 Man's yesterday may ne'er be like his morrow;
    Nought may endure but Mutability.

ca. 1814–15   1816

To Wordsworth[1]

Poet of Nature, thou hast wept to know
That things depart which never may return:

---

1. Shelley's grieved comment on the poet of nature and of social radicalism after his views had become conservative.

Childhood and youth, friendship and love's first glow,
Have fled like sweet dreams, leaving thee to mourn.
5 These common woes I feel. One loss is mine
Which thou too feel'st, yet I alone deplore.
Thou wert as a lone star, whose light did shine
On some frail bark° in winter's midnight roar: *small ship*
Thou hast like to a rock-built refuge stood
10 Above the blind and battling multitude:
In honoured poverty thy voice did weave
Songs consecrate to truth and liberty,²—
Deserting these, thou leavest me to grieve,
Thus having been, that thou shouldst cease to be.

ca. 1814–15   1816

Alastor; or, The Spirit of Solitude

Shelley wrote *Alastor* in the fall and early winter of 1815 and published it in March 1816. According to his friend Thomas Love Peacock, the poet was "at a loss for a title, and I proposed that which he adopted: Alastor, or the Spirit of Solitude. The Greek word *Alastor* is an evil genius. . . . I mention the true meaning of the word because many have supposed *Alastor* to be the name of the hero" (*Memoirs of Shelley*). Peacock's definition of an *alastor* as "an *evil genius*" has compounded the problems in interpreting this work: the term *evil* does not seem to fit the attitude expressed within the poem toward the protagonist's solitary quest, the poem seems to clash with statements in Shelley's preface, and the first and second paragraphs of the preface seem inconsistent with each other. These problems, however, may be largely resolved if we recognize that, in this early achievement (he was only twenty-three when he wrote *Alastor*), Shelley established his characteristic procedure of working with multiple perspectives. Both preface and poem explore alternative and conflicting possibilities in what Shelley calls "doubtful knowledge"— matters that are humanly essential but in which no certainty is humanly possible.

By the term *allegorical* in the opening sentence of his preface, Shelley seems to mean that his poem, like medieval and Renaissance allegories such as Dante's *Divine Comedy* and Spenser's *Faerie Queene,* represents an aspiration in the spiritual realm by the allegorical vehicle of a journey and quest in the material world. As Shelley's first paragraph outlines, the poem's protagonist, for whom objects in the natural world "cease to suffice," commits himself to the search for a female Other who will fulfill his intellectual, imaginative, and sensuous needs. The second paragraph of the preface, by contrast, passes judgment on the visionary protagonist in terms of the values of "actual men"—that is, the requirements of human and social life in this world. From this point of view, the visionary has been "avenged" (punished) for turning away from community in pursuit of his individual psychic needs. The diversity of attitudes expressed within the poem becomes easier to understand if, on the basis of the many echoes of Wordsworth in the opening invocation, we identify the narrator of the story as a Wordsworthian poet for whom the natural world is sufficient to satisfy both the demands of his imagination and his need for community. This narrative poet, it can be assumed, undertakes to tell compassionately, but from his own perspective, the history of a nameless visionary who has surrendered everything in the quest for a goal beyond possibility.

In this early poem Shelley establishes a form, a conceptual frame, and the imagery

2. Perhaps an allusion to "Sonnets Dedicated to Liberty," the title that Wordsworth gave to the section of sonnets such as "London, 1802" when he republished them in his *Poems* of 1807.

for the Romantic quest that he reiterated in his later poems and that also served as a paradigm for many other poems, from Byron's *Manfred* and Keats's *Endymion* to the quest poems of Shelley's later admirer William Butler Yeats.

Alastor; or, The Spirit of Solitude

Preface

The poem entitled "ALASTOR," may be considered as allegorical of one of the most interesting situations of the human mind. It represents a youth of uncorrupted feelings and adventurous genius led forth by an imagination inflamed and purified through familiarity with all that is excellent and majestic, to the contemplation of the universe. He drinks deep of the fountains of knowledge, and is still insatiate. The magnificence and beauty of the external world sinks profoundly into the frame of his conceptions, and affords to their modifications a variety not to be exhausted. So long as it is possible for his desires to point towards objects thus infinite and unmeasured, he is joyous, and tranquil, and self-possessed. But the period arrives when these objects cease to suffice. His mind is at length suddenly awakened and thirsts for intercourse with an intelligence similar to itself. He images to himself the Being whom he loves. Conversant with speculations of the sublimest and most perfect natures, the vision in which he embodies his own imaginations unites all of wonderful, or wise, or beautiful, which the poet, the philosopher, or the lover could depicture. The intellectual faculties, the imagination, the functions of sense, have their respective requisitions on the sympathy of corresponding powers in other human beings. The Poet is represented as uniting these requisitions, and attaching them to a single image.[1] He seeks in vain for a prototype of his conception. Blasted by his disappointment, he descends to an untimely grave.

The picture is not barren of instruction to actual men. The Poet's self-centred seclusion was avenged by the furies of an irresistible passion pursuing him to speedy ruin. But that Power which strikes the luminaries of the world with sudden darkness and extinction, by awakening them to too exquisite a perception of its influences, dooms to a slow and poisonous decay those meaner spirits that dare to abjure its dominion. Their destiny is more abject and inglorious as their delinquency is more contemptible and pernicious. They who, deluded by no generous error, instigated by no sacred thirst of doubtful knowledge, duped by no illustrious superstition, loving nothing on this earth, and cherishing no hopes beyond, yet keep aloof from sympathies with their kind, rejoicing neither in human joy nor mourning with human grief; these, and such as they, have their apportioned curse. They languish, because none feel with them their common nature. They are morally dead. They are neither friends, nor lovers, nor fathers, nor citizens of the world, nor benefactors of their country. Among those who attempt to exist without human sympathy, the pure and tender-hearted perish through the intensity and passion of their

---

1. Shelley's view that the object of love is an idealized projection of all that is best within the self is clarified by a passage in his "Essay on Love," which may have been written at about the time of *Alastor:* "We dimly see within our intellectual nature . . . the ideal prototype of every thing excellent or lovely that we are capable of conceiving as belonging to the nature of men. . . . [This is] a soul within our soul. . . . The discovery of its anti-type . . . in such proportion as the type within demands; this is the invisible and unattainable point to which Love tends; and . . . without the possession of which there is no rest nor respite to the heart over which it rules."

search after its communities, when the vacancy of their spirit suddenly makes itself felt. All else, selfish, blind, and torpid, are those unforeseeing multitudes who constitute, together with their own, the lasting misery and loneliness of the world. Those who love not their fellow-beings live unfruitful lives, and prepare for their old age a miserable grave.

> "The good die first,
> And those whose hearts are dry as summer dust,
> Burn to the socket!"[2]

December 14, 1815

Alastor; or, The Spirit of Solitude

*Nondum amabam, et amare amabam, qæurebam quid amarem,
amans amare.—Confess. St. August.*[3]

Earth, ocean, air, beloved brotherhood!
If our great Mother[4] has imbued my soul
With aught of natural piety[5] to feel
Your love, and recompense the boon° with mine;[6]   *gift*
5   If dewy morn, and odorous noon, and even,°   *evening*
With sunset and its gorgeous ministers,[7]
And solemn midnight's tingling silentness;
If autumn's hollow sighs in the sere wood,
And winter robing with pure snow and crowns
10   Of starry ice the grey grass and bare boughs;
If spring's voluptuous pantings when she breathes
Her first sweet kisses, have been dear to me;
If no bright bird, insect, or gentle beast
I consciously have injured, but still loved
15   And cherished these my kindred; then forgive
This boast, beloved brethren, and withdraw
No portion of your wonted° favour now!   *customary*

Mother of this unfathomable world!
Favour my solemn song, for I have loved
20   Thee ever, and thee only; I have watched
Thy shadow, and the darkness of thy steps,
And my heart ever gazes on the depth
Of thy deep mysteries. I have made my bed
In charnels and on coffins, where black death
25   Keeps record of the trophies won from thee,
Hoping to still these obstinate questionings[8]
Of thee and thine, by forcing some lone ghost,

---

2. Wordsworth's *The Excursion* 1.519–21; the passage occurs also in *The Ruined Cottage* 96–98, which Wordsworth reworked into the first book of *The Excursion* (1814).
3. St. Augustine's *Confessions* 3.1: "Not yet did I love, though I loved to love, seeking what I might love, loving to love." Augustine thus describes his state of mind when he was addicted to illicit sexual love; the true object of his desire, which compels the tortuous spiritual journey of his life, he later discovered to be the infinite and transcendent God.

4. Nature, invoked as the common mother of both the elements and the poet.
5. Wordsworth, "My heart leaps up," lines 8–9: "And I could wish my days to be / Bound each to each by natural piety." Wordsworth also used these lines as the epigraph to his "Ode: Intimations of Immortality."
6. I.e., with my love.
7. The sunset colors.
8. Wordsworth, "Ode: Intimations of Immortality," lines 141–42: "those obstinate questionings / Of sense and outward things."

Thy messenger, to render up the tale
Of what we are. In lone and silent hours,
30   When night makes a weird sound of its own stillness,
Like an inspired and desperate alchymist
Staking his very life on some dark hope,
Have I mixed awful talk and asking looks
With my most innocent love, until strange tears
35   Uniting with those breathless kisses, made
Such magic as compels the charmed night
To render up thy charge: . . . and, though ne'er yet
Thou hast unveil'd thy inmost sanctuary,
Enough from incommunicable dream,
40   And twilight phantasms, and deep noonday thought,
Has shone within me, that serenely now
And moveless,° as a long-forgotten lyre   motionless
Suspended in the solitary dome
Of some mysterious and deserted fane,[9]
45   I wait thy breath, Great Parent, that my strain
May modulate with murmurs of the air,
And motions of the forests and the sea,
And voice of living beings, and woven hymns
Of night and day, and the deep heart of man.[1]

50   There was a Poet whose untimely tomb
No human hands with pious reverence reared,
But the charmed eddies of autumnal winds
Built o'er his mouldering bones a pyramid
Of mouldering leaves in the waste wilderness:—
55   A lovely youth,—no mourning maiden decked
With weeping flowers, or votive cypress wreath,[2]
The lone couch of his everlasting sleep:—
Gentle, and brave, and generous,—no lorn° bard   abandoned
Breathed o'er his dark fate one melodious sigh:
60   He lived, he died, he sung, in solitude.
Strangers have wept to hear his passionate notes,
And virgins, as unknown he past, have pined
And wasted for fond love of his wild eyes.
The fire of those soft orbs has ceased to burn,
65   And Silence, too enamoured of that voice,
Locks its mute music in her rugged cell.

By solemn vision, and bright silver dream,
His infancy was nurtured. Every sight
And sound from the vast earth and ambient air,
70   Sent to his heart its choicest impulses.
The fountains of divine philosophy
Fled not his thirsting lips, and all of great
Or good, or lovely, which the sacred past

---

9. Temple. The narrator calls on the Mother, his natural muse, to make him her wind harp. Cf. the opening passage of Wordsworth's *Prelude*, Coleridge's "Dejection: An Ode," and the conclusions of Shelley's "Ode to the West Wind" and *Adonais*.
1. Cf. Wordsworth, "Tintern Abbey," lines 94ff.:

"A presence . . . / Whose dwelling is . . . the round ocean and the living air, / And the blue sky, and in the mind of man: / A motion and a spirit."
2. The cypress represented mourning. "Votive": offered to fulfill a vow to the gods.

In truth or fable consecrates, he felt
75 And knew. When early youth had past, he left
His cold fireside and alienated home
To seek strange truths in undiscovered lands.
Many a wide waste and tangled wilderness
Has lured his fearless steps; and he has bought
80 With his sweet voice and eyes, from savage men,
His rest and food. Nature's most secret steps
He like her shadow has pursued, where'er
The red volcano overcanopies
Its fields of snow and pinnacles of ice
85 With burning smoke, or where bitumen lakes³
On black bare pointed islets ever beat
With sluggish surge, or where the secret caves
Rugged and dark, winding among the springs
Of fire and poison, inaccessible
90 To avarice or pride, their starry domes
Of diamond and of gold expand above
Numberless and immeasurable halls,
Frequent° with crystal column, and clear shrines   *crowded*
Of pearl, and thrones radiant with chrysolite.⁴
95 Nor had that scene of ampler majesty
Than gems or gold, the varying roof of heaven
And the green earth lost in his heart its claims
To love and wonder; he would linger long
In lonesome vales, making the wild his home,
100 Until the doves and squirrels would partake
From his innocuous hand his bloodless food,⁵
Lured by the gentle meaning of his looks,
And the wild antelope, that starts whene'er
The dry leaf rustles in the brake,° suspend   *thicket*
105 Her timid steps to gaze upon a form
More graceful than her own.

                His wandering step
Obedient to high thoughts, has visited
The awful° ruins of the days of old: *awe-inspiring*
Athens, and Tyre, and Balbec,⁶ and the waste
110 Where stood Jerusalem, the fallen towers
Of Babylon, the eternal pyramids,
Memphis and Thebes,⁷ and whatsoe'er of strange
Sculptured on alabaster obelisk,
Or jasper tomb, or mutilated sphinx,
115 Dark Æthiopia in her desert hills
Conceals. Among the ruined temples there,
Stupendous columns, and wild images
Of more than man, where marble dæmons watch
The Zodiac's⁸ brazen mystery, and dead men

---

3. Lakes of pitch, flowing from a volcano.
4. An olive-green semiprecious stone.
5. Shelley was himself a vegetarian.
6. An ancient city in what is now Lebanon. Tyre was once an important commercial city on the Phoenician coast.
7. The ancient capital of Upper Egypt. Memphis

is the ruined capital of Lower Egypt.
8. In the temple of Isis at Denderah, Egypt, the Zodiac is represented on the ceiling. Journeying among the great civilizations of the past has taken the Poet backward in time to older and older cultures—from the Greeks to the Phoenicians, the Jews, the Babylonians, and the Egyptians. Finally

120   Hang their mute thoughts on the mute walls around,[9]
      He lingered, poring on memorials
      Of the world's youth, through the long burning day
      Gazed on those speechless shapes, nor, when the moon
      Filled the mysterious halls with floating shades
125   Suspended he that task, but ever gazed
      And gazed, till meaning on his vacant mind
      Flashed like strong inspiration, and he saw
      The thrilling secrets of the birth of time.

      Meanwhile an Arab maiden brought his food,
130   Her daily portion, from her father's tent,
      And spread her matting for his couch, and stole
      From duties and repose to tend his steps:—
      Enamoured, yet not daring for deep awe
      To speak her love:—and watched his nightly sleep,
135   Sleepless herself, to gaze upon his lips
      Parted in slumber, whence the regular breath
      Of innocent dreams arose: then, when red morn
      Made paler the pale moon, to her cold home
      Wildered,° and wan, and panting, she returned.   bewildered

140   The Poet wandering on, through Arabie
      And Persia, and the wild Carmanian waste,[1]
      And o'er the aërial mountains which pour down
      Indus and Oxus[2] from their icy caves,
      In joy and exultation held his way;
145   Till in the vale of Cashmire, far within
      Its loneliest dell, where odorous plants entwine
      Beneath the hollow rocks a natural bower,
      Beside a sparkling rivulet he stretched
      His languid limbs. A vision on his sleep
150   There came, a dream of hopes that never yet
      Had flushed his cheek. He dreamed a veiled maid
      Sate near him, talking in low solemn tones.
      Her voice was like the voice of his own soul
      Heard in the calm of thought; its music long,
155   Like woven sounds of streams and breezes, held
      His inmost sense suspended in its web
      Of many-coloured woof° and shifting hues.   weave
      Knowledge and truth and virtue were her theme,
      And lofty hopes of divine liberty,
160   Thoughts the most dear to him, and poesy,
      Herself a poet. Soon the solemn mood
      Of her pure mind kindled through all her frame
      A permeating fire: wild numbers° then   verse
      She raised, with voice stifled in tremulous sobs
165   Subdued by its own pathos: her fair hands
      Were bare alone, sweeping from some strange harp

---

he reaches Ethiopia (line 115), which had been
described as the "cradle of the sciences." "Daemons": in Greek mythology, not evil spirits but
minor deities or attendant spirits.

9. I.e., by quotations inscribed in the stone.
1. A desert in southern Persia.
2. Rivers in Asia.

Strange symphony, and in their branching veins
The eloquent blood told an ineffable tale.
The beating of her heart was heard to fill
170 The pauses of her music, and her breath
Tumultuously accorded with those fits
Of intermitted song. Sudden she rose,
As if her heart impatiently endured
Its bursting burthen: at the sound he turned,
175 And saw by the warm light of their own life
Her glowing limbs beneath the sinuous veil
Of woven wind, her outspread arms now bare,
Her dark locks floating in the breath of night,
Her beamy bending eyes, her parted lips
180 Outstretched, and pale, and quivering eagerly.
His strong heart sunk and sickened with excess
Of love. He reared his shuddering limbs and quelled
His gasping breath, and spread his arms to meet
Her panting bosom: . . . she drew back a while,
185 Then, yielding to the irresistible joy,
With frantic gesture and short breathless cry
Folded his frame in her dissolving arms.
Now blackness veiled his dizzy eyes, and night
Involved° and swallowed up the vision; sleep,   *wrapped up*
190 Like a dark flood suspended in its course,
Rolled back its impulse on his vacant brain.

        Roused by the shock he started from his trance—
The cold white light of morning, the blue moon
Low in the west, the clear and garish hills,
195 The distinct valley and the vacant woods,
Spread round him where he stood. Whither have fled
The hues of heaven that canopied his bower
Of yesternight? The sounds that soothed his sleep,
The mystery and the majesty of Earth,
200 The joy, the exultation? His wan eyes
Gaze on the empty scene as vacantly
As ocean's moon looks on the moon in heaven.
The spirit of sweet human love has sent
A vision to the sleep of him who spurned
205 Her choicest gifts. He eagerly pursues
Beyond the realms of dream that fleeting shade;°   *phantom*
He overleaps the bounds. Alas! alas!
Were limbs, and breath, and being intertwined
Thus treacherously? Lost, lost, for ever lost,
210 In the wide pathless desart of dim sleep,
That beautiful shape! Does the dark gate of death
Conduct to thy mysterious paradise,
O Sleep?³ Does the bright arch of rainbow clouds,
And pendent° mountains seen in the calm lake,   *jutting, overhanging*
215 Lead only to a black and watery depth,
While death's blue vault, with loathliest vapours hung,

---

3. I.e., is death the only access to this maiden of his dream?

Where every shade which the foul grave exhales
Hides its dead eye from the detested day,
Conduct, O Sleep, to thy delightful realms?
220 This doubt with sudden tide flowed on his heart,
The insatiate hope which it awakened, stung
His brain even like despair.
                  While day-light held
The sky, the Poet kept mute conference
With his still soul. At night the passion came,
225 Like the fierce fiend of a distempered dream,
And shook him from his rest, and led him forth
Into the darkness.—As an eagle grasped
In folds of the green serpent, feels her breast
Burn with the poison, and precipitates°   *hastens*
230 Through night and day, tempest, and calm, and cloud,
Frantic with dizzying anguish, her blind flight
O'er the wide aëry wilderness:[4] thus driven
By the bright shadow of that lovely dream,
Beneath the cold glare of the desolate night,
235 Through tangled swamps and deep precipitous dells,
Startling with careless step the moon-light snake,
He fled. Red morning dawned upon his flight,
Shedding the mockery of its vital hues
Upon his cheek of death. He wandered on
240 Till vast Aornos seen from Petra's[5] steep
Hung o'er the low horizon like a cloud;
Through Balk,[6] and where the desolated tombs
Of Parthian kings[7] scatter to every wind
Their wasting dust, wildly he wandered on,
245 Day after day, a weary waste of hours,
Bearing within his life the brooding care
That ever fed on its decaying flame.
And now his limbs were lean; his scattered hair
Sered by the autumn of strange suffering
250 Sung dirges in the wind; his listless hand
Hung like dead bone within its withered skin;
Life, and the lustre that consumed it, shone
As in a furnace burning secretly
From his dark eyes alone. The cottagers,
255 Who ministered with human charity
His human wants, beheld with wondering awe
Their fleeting visitant. The mountaineer,
Encountering on some dizzy precipice
That spectral form, deemed that the Spirit of wind
260 With lightning eyes, and eager breath, and feet
Disturbing not the drifted snow, had paused
In its career: the infant would conceal
His troubled visage in his mother's robe

4. The eagle and serpent locked in mortal combat is a recurrent image in Shelley's poems (see *Prometheus Unbound* 3.1.72–73, p. 811).
5. The rock (literal trans.); "Petra's steep" is a mountain stronghold in the northern part of ancient Arabia. Aornos is a high mountain.
6. Bactria, in ancient Persia, is now part of Afghanistan.
7. The Parthians inhabited northern Persia.

In terror at the glare of those wild eyes,
265 To remember their strange light in many a dream
Of after-times; but youthful maidens, taught
By nature, would interpret half the woe
That wasted him, would call him with false° names   *mistaken*
Brother, and friend, would press his pallid hand
270 At parting, and watch, dim through tears, the path
Of his departure from their father's door.

At length upon the lone Chorasmian shore[8]
He paused, a wide and melancholy waste
Of putrid marshes. A strong impulse urged
275 His steps to the sea-shore. A swan was there,
Beside a sluggish stream among the reeds.
It rose as he approached, and with strong wings
Scaling the upward sky, bent its bright course
High over the immeasurable main.
280 His eyes pursued its flight.—"Thou hast a home,
Beautiful bird; thou voyagest to thine home,
Where thy sweet mate will twine her downy neck
With thine, and welcome thy return with eyes
Bright in the lustre of their own fond joy.
285 And what am I that I should linger here,
With voice far sweeter than thy dying notes,
Spirit more vast than thine, frame more attuned
To beauty, wasting these surpassing powers
In the deaf air, to the blind earth, and heaven
290 That echoes not my thoughts?" A gloomy smile
Of desperate hope convulsed his curling lips
For sleep, he knew, kept most relentlessly
Its precious charge,[9] and silent death exposed,
Faithless perhaps as sleep, a shadowy lure,
295 With doubtful smile mocking its own strange charms.

Startled by his own thoughts he looked around.
There was no fair fiend[1] near him, not a sight
Or sound of awe but in his own deep mind.
A little shallop[2] floating near the shore
300 Caught the impatient wandering of his gaze.
It had been long abandoned, for its sides
Gaped wide with many a rift, and its frail joints
Swayed with the undulations of the tide.
A restless impulse urged him to embark
305 And meet lone Death on the drear ocean's waste;
For well he knew that mighty Shadow loves
The slimy caverns of the populous deep.

The day was fair and sunny; sea and sky
Drank its inspiring radiance, and the wind

8. The shore of Lake Aral, about 175 miles east of the Caspian Sea.
9. I.e., the maiden in the sleeper's dream.
1. Apparently he suspects there may have been an external agent luring him to the death described in the preceding lines.
2. A small open boat.

310 Swept strongly from the shore, blackening the waves.
Following his eager soul, the wanderer
Leaped in the boat, he spread his cloak aloft
On the bare mast, and took his lonely seat,
And felt the boat speed o'er the tranquil sea
315 Like a torn cloud before the hurricane.[3]

As one that in a silver vision floats
Obedient to the sweep of odorous winds
Upon resplendent clouds, so rapidly
Along the dark and ruffled waters fled
320 The straining boat.—A whirlwind swept it on,
With fierce gusts and precipitating force,
Through the white ridges of the chafed sea.
The waves arose. Higher and higher still
Their fierce necks writhed beneath the tempest's scourge
325 Like serpents struggling in a vulture's grasp.
Calm and rejoicing in the fearful war
Of wave ruining° on wave, and blast on blast   crashing
Descending, and black flood on whirlpool driven
With dark obliterating course, he sate:
330 As if their genii were the ministers
Appointed to conduct him to the light
Of those beloved eyes, the Poet sate
Holding the steady helm. Evening came on,
The beams of sunset hung their rainbow hues
335 High 'mid the shifting domes of sheeted spray
That canopied his path o'er the waste deep;
Twilight, ascending slowly from the east,
Entwin'd in duskier wreaths her braided locks
O'er the fair front and radiant eyes of day;
340 Night followed, clad with stars. On every side
More horribly the multitudinous streams
Of ocean's mountainous waste to mutual war
Rushed in dark tumult thundering, as to mock
The calm and spangled sky. The little boat
345 Still fled before the storm; still fled, like foam
Down the steep cataract of a wintry river;
Now pausing on the edge of the riven° wave;   torn asunder
Now leaving far behind the bursting mass
That fell, convulsing ocean. Safely fled—
350 As if that frail and wasted human form,
Had been an elemental god.[4]
                              At midnight
The moon arose: and lo! the etherial cliffs[5]
Of Caucasus, whose icy summits shone
Among the stars like sunlight, and around

3. If the Poet's boat is being carried upstream on
the Oxus River from the Aral Sea to the river's
headwaters in the Hindu Kush Mountains (the
"Indian Caucasus" that is the setting for Prometheus Unbound), then the journey is taking him to
a region that the naturalist Buffon (whom Shelley
often read) had identified as the cradle of the
human race. But it is also possible that the starting
point for this journey is the Caspian Sea, in which
case the journey would end near the traditional site
of the Garden of Eden.
4. A god of one of the natural elements (see
line 1).
5. I.e., cliffs high in the air.

355 Whose cavern'd base the whirlpools and the waves
Bursting and eddying irresistibly
Rage and resound for ever.—Who shall save?—
The boat fled on,—the boiling torrent drove,—
The crags closed round with black and jagged arms,
360 The shattered mountain overhung the sea,
And faster still, beyond all human speed,
Suspended on the sweep of the smooth wave,
The little boat was driven. A cavern there
Yawned, and amid its slant and winding depths
365 Ingulphed the rushing sea. The boat fled on
With unrelaxing speed.—"Vision and Love!"
The Poet cried aloud, "I have beheld
The path of thy departure. Sleep and death
Shall not divide us long!"

                                    The boat pursued
370 The winding of the cavern. Day-light shone
At length upon that gloomy river's flow;
Now, where the fiercest war among the waves
Is calm, on the unfathomable stream
The boat moved slowly. Where the mountain, riven,
375 Exposed those black depths to the azure sky,
Ere yet the flood's enormous volume fell
Even to the base of Caucasus, with sound
That shook the everlasting rocks, the mass
Filled with one whirlpool all that ample chasm;
380 Stair above stair the eddying waters rose,
Circling immeasurably fast, and laved°   *washed*
With alternating dash the knarled roots
Of mighty trees, that stretched their giant arms
In darkness over it. I' the midst was left,
385 Reflecting, yet distorting every cloud,
A pool of treacherous and tremendous calm.
Seized by the sway of the ascending stream,
With dizzy swiftness, round, and round, and round,
Ridge after ridge the straining boat arose,
390 Till on the verge of the extremest curve,
Where, through an opening of the rocky bank,
The waters overflow, and a smooth spot
Of glassy quiet mid those battling tides
Is left, the boat paused shuddering.—Shall it sink
395 Down the abyss? Shall the reverting stress
Of that resistless gulph embosom it?
Now shall it fall?—A wandering stream of wind,
Breathed from the west, has caught the expanded sail,
And, lo! with gentle motion, between banks
400 Of mossy slope, and on a placid stream,
Beneath a woven grove it sails, and, hark!
The ghastly torrent mingles its far roar,
With the breeze murmuring in the musical woods.
Where the embowering trees recede, and leave
405 A little space of green expanse, the cove

Is closed by meeting banks, whose yellow flowers
For ever gaze on their own drooping eyes,
Reflected in the crystal calm. The wave
Of the boat's motion marred their pensive task,
410   Which nought but vagrant bird, or wanton wind,
Or falling spear-grass, or their own decay
Had e'er disturbed before. The Poet longed
To deck with their bright hues his withered hair,
But on his heart its solitude returned,
415   And he forbore.⁶ Not the strong impulse hid
In those flushed cheeks, bent eyes, and shadowy frame,
Had yet performed its ministry: it hung
Upon his life, as lightning in a cloud
Gleams, hovering ere it vanish, ere the floods
Of night close over it.
420   The noonday sun
Now shone upon the forest, one vast mass
Of mingling shade, whose brown magnificence
A narrow vale embosoms. There, huge caves,
Scooped in the dark base of their aëry rocks
425   Mocking⁷ its moans, respond and roar for ever.
The meeting boughs and implicated° leaves   *intertwined*
Wove twilight o'er the Poet's path, as led
By love, or dream, or god, or mightier Death,
He sought in Nature's dearest haunt, some bank,
430   Her cradle, and his sepulchre. More dark
And dark the shades accumulate. The oak,
Expanding its immense and knotty arms,
Embraces the light beech. The pyramids
Of the tall cedar overarching, frame
435   Most solemn domes within, and far below.
Like clouds suspended in an emerald sky,
The ash and the acacia floating hang
Tremulous and pale. Like restless serpents, clothed
In rainbow and in fire, the parasites,
440   Starred with ten thousand blossoms, flow around
The grey trunks, and, as gamesome infants' eyes,
With gentle meanings, and most innocent wiles,
Fold their beams round the hearts of those that love,
These twine their tendrils with the wedded boughs
445   Uniting their close union; the woven leaves
Make net-work of the dark blue light of day,
And the night's noontide clearness, mutable
As shapes in the weird clouds. Soft mossy lawns
Beneath these canopies extend their swells,
450   Fragrant with perfumed herbs, and eyed with blooms
Minute yet beautiful. One darkest glen
Sends from its woods of musk-rose, twined with jasmine,

---

6. The "yellow flowers" overhanging their own reflection (lines 406–08), probably narcissus, may signify the narcissistic temptation of the Poet to be satisfied with a projection of his own self. But his need for an unearthly Other revives, and "the strong impulse" (line 415) drives him on.
7. As often in Shelley, "mocking" has a double sense: mimicking as well as ridiculing the sounds of the forest (line 421).

A soul-dissolving odour, to invite
To some more lovely mystery. Through the dell,
455　Silence and Twilight here, twin-sisters, keep
Their noonday watch, and sail among the shades,
Like vaporous shapes half seen; beyond, a well,
Dark, gleaming, and of most translucent wave,
Images all the woven boughs above,
460　And each depending leaf, and every speck
Of azure sky, darting between their chasms;
Nor aught else in the liquid mirror laves
Its portraiture, but some inconstant star
Between one foliaged lattice twinkling fair,
465　Or, painted bird, sleeping beneath the moon,
Or gorgeous insect floating motionless,
Unconscious of the day, ere yet his wings
Have spread their glories to the gaze of noon.

Hither the Poet came. His eyes beheld
470　Their own wan light through the reflected lines
Of his thin hair, distinct in the dark depth
Of that still fountain; as the human heart,
Gazing in dreams over the gloomy grave,
Sees its own treacherous likeness there. He heard
475　The motion of the leaves, the grass that sprung
Startled and glanced and trembled even to feel
An unaccustomed presence, and the sound
Of the sweet brook that from the secret springs
Of that dark fountain rose. A Spirit seemed
480　To stand beside him—clothed in no bright robes
Of shadowy silver or enshrining light,
Borrowed from aught the visible world affords
Of grace, or majesty, or mystery;—
But, undulating woods, and silent well,
485　And leaping rivulet, and evening gloom
Now deepening the dark shades, for speech assuming
Held commune with him, as if he and it
Were all that was,—only . . . when his regard
Was raised by intense pensiveness, . . . two eyes,
490　Two starry eyes, hung in the gloom of thought,
And seemed with their serene and azure smiles
To beckon him.

Obedient to the light
That shone within his soul, he went, pursuing
The windings of the dell.—The rivulet
495　Wanton and wild, through many a green ravine
Beneath the forest flowed. Sometimes it fell
Among the moss with hollow harmony
Dark and profound. Now on the polished stones
It danced; like childhood laughing as it went:
500　Then, through the plain in tranquil wanderings crept,
Reflecting every herb and drooping bud
That overhung its quietness.—"O stream!

Whose source is inaccessibly profound,
Whither do thy mysterious waters tend?
505 Thou imagest my life. Thy darksome stillness,
Thy dazzling waves, thy loud and hollow gulphs,
Thy searchless° fountain, and invisible course   *undiscoverable*
Have each their type in me: and the wide sky,
And measureless ocean may declare as soon
510 What oozy cavern or what wandering cloud
Contains thy waters, as the universe
Tell where these living thoughts reside, when stretched
Upon thy flowers my bloodless limbs shall waste
I' the passing wind!"

                 Beside the grassy shore
515 Of the small stream he went; he did impress
On the green moss his tremulous step, that caught
Strong shuddering from his burning limbs. As one
Roused by some joyous madness from the couch
Of fever, he did move; yet, not like him,
520 Forgetful of the grave, where, when the flame
Of his frail exultation shall be spent,
He must descend. With rapid steps he went
Beneath the shade of trees, beside the flow
Of the wild babbling rivulet; and now
525 The forest's solemn canopies were changed
For the uniform and lightsome° evening sky.   *luminous*
Grey rocks did peep from the spare moss, and stemmed
The struggling brook: tall spires of windlestrae[8]
Threw their thin shadows down the rugged slope,
530 And nought but knarled roots[9] of antient pines
Branchless and blasted, clenched with grasping roots
The unwilling soil. A gradual change was here,
Yet ghastly. For, as fast years flow away,
The smooth brow gathers, and the hair grows thin
535 And white, and where irradiate° dewy eyes   *illumined*
Had shone, gleam stony orbs:—so from his steps
Bright flowers departed, and the beautiful shade
Of the green groves, with all their odorous winds
And musical motions. Calm, he still pursued
540 The stream, that with a larger volume now
Rolled through the labyrinthine dell; and there
Fretted a path through its descending curves
With its wintry speed. On every side now rose
Rocks, which, in unimaginable forms,
545 Lifted their black and barren pinnacles
In the light of evening, and its precipice[1]
Obscuring the ravine, disclosed above,
Mid toppling stones, black gulphs and yawning caves,
Whose windings gave ten thousand various tongues

8. Windlestraw (Scottish dial.); tall, dried stalks of grass.
9. Probably an error for "stumps" or "trunks."
1. Headlong fall (of the stream, line 540).

550 To the loud stream. Lo! where the pass expands
Its stony jaws, the abrupt mountain breaks,
And seems, with its accumulated crags,
To overhang the world: for wide expand
Beneath the wan stars and descending moon
555 Islanded seas, blue mountains, mighty streams,
Dim tracts and vast, robed in the lustrous gloom
Of leaden-coloured even, and fiery hills
Mingling their flames with twilight, on the verge
Of the remote horizon. The near° scene,   *nearby*
560 In naked and severe simplicity,
Made contrast with the universe. A pine,[2]
Rock-rooted, stretched athwart the vacancy
Its swinging boughs, to each inconstant blast
Yielding one only response, at each pause
565 In most familiar cadence, with the howl
The thunder and the hiss of homeless streams
Mingling its solemn song, whilst the broad river,
Foaming and hurrying o'er its rugged path,
Fell into that immeasurable void
570 Scattering its waters to the passing winds.

Yet the grey precipice and solemn pine
And torrent, were not all;—one silent nook
Was there. Even on the edge of that vast mountain,
Upheld by knotty roots and fallen rocks,
575 It overlooked in its serenity
The dark earth, and the bending vault of stars.
It was a tranquil spot, that seemed to smile
Even in the lap of horror. Ivy clasped
The fissured stones with its entwining arms,
580 And did embower with leaves for ever green,
And berries dark, the smooth and even space
Of its inviolated floor, and here
The children of the autumnal whirlwind bore,
In wanton sport, those bright leaves, whose decay,
585 Red, yellow, or etherially pale,
Rivals the pride of summer. 'Tis the haunt
Of every gentle wind, whose breath can teach
The wilds to love tranquillity. One step,
One human step alone, has ever broken
590 The stillness of its solitude:—one voice
Alone inspired its echoes,—even that voice
Which hither came, floating among the winds,
And led the loveliest among human forms
To make their wild haunts the depository
595 Of all the grace and beauty that endued
Its motions, render up its majesty,
Scatter its music on the unfeeling storm,
And to the damp leaves and blue cavern mould,

2. Pine trees in Shelley often signify persistence and steadfastness amid change and vicissitudes.

Nurses of rainbow flowers and branching moss,
600 Commit the colours of that varying cheek,
That snowy breast, those dark and drooping eyes.

The dim and horned[3] moon hung low, and poured
A sea of lustre on the horizon's verge
That overflowed its mountains. Yellow mist
605 Filled the unbounded atmosphere, and drank
Wan moonlight even to fulness: not a star
Shone, not a sound was heard; the very winds,
Danger's grim playmates, on that precipice
Slept, clasped in his embrace.—O, storm of death!
610 Whose sightless[4] speed divides this sullen night:
And thou, colossal Skeleton,° that, still   Death
Guiding its irresistible career
In thy devastating omnipotence,
Art king of this frail world, from the red field
615 Of slaughter, from the reeking hospital,
The patriot's sacred couch, the snowy bed
Of innocence, the scaffold and the throne,
A mighty voice invokes thee. Ruin calls
His brother Death. A rare and regal prey
620 He hath prepared, prowling around the world;
Glutted with which thou mayst repose, and men
Go to their graves like flowers or creeping worms,
Nor ever more offer at thy dark shrine
The unheeded tribute of a broken heart.

625   When on the threshold of the green recess
The wanderer's footsteps fell, he knew that death
Was on him. Yet a little, ere it fled,
Did he resign his high and holy soul
To images of the majestic past,
630 That paused within his passive being now,
Like winds that bear sweet music, when they breathe
Through some dim latticed chamber. He did place
His pale lean hand upon the rugged trunk
Of the old pine. Upon an ivied stone
635 Reclined his languid head, his limbs did rest,
Diffused and motionless, on the smooth brink
Of that obscurest° chasm;—and thus he lay,   darkest
Surrendering to their final impulses
The hovering powers of life. Hope and despair,
640 The torturers, slept; no mortal pain or fear
Marred his repose, the influxes of sense,
And his own being unalloyed by pain,
Yet feebler and more feeble, calmly fed
The stream of thought, till he lay breathing there
645 At peace, and faintly smiling:—his last sight
Was the great moon, which o'er the western line

---

3. The moon is crescent shaped with the points
rising, as in Coleridge's "Dejection: An Ode": "the
new Moon / With the old Moon in her arms."
4. Invisible, or perhaps "unseeing."

Of the wide world her mighty horn suspended,
With whose dun° beams inwoven darkness seemed   *darkened*
To mingle. Now upon the jagged hills
650   It rests, and still as the divided frame
Of the vast meteor⁵ sunk, the Poet's blood,
That ever beat in mystic sympathy
With nature's ebb and flow, grew feebler still:
And when two lessening points of light alone
655   Gleamed through the darkness, the alternate gasp
Of his faint respiration scarce did stir
The stagnate night:⁶—till the minutest ray
Was quenched, the pulse yet lingered in his heart.
It paused—it fluttered. But when heaven remained
660   Utterly black, the murky shades involved
An image, silent, cold, and motionless,
As their own voiceless earth and vacant air.
Even as a vapour° fed with golden beams   *cloud*
That ministered on⁷ sunlight, ere the west
665   Eclipses it, was now that wonderous frame—
No sense, no motion, no divinity—
A fragile lute, on whose harmonious strings
The breath of heaven did wander—a bright stream
Once fed with many-voiced waves—a dream
670   Of youth, which night and time have quenched for ever,
Still, dark, and dry, and unremembered now.

O, for Medea's wondrous alchemy,
Which wheresoe'er it fell made the earth gleam
With bright flowers, and the wintry boughs exhale
675   From vernal blooms fresh fragrance!⁸ O, that God,
Profuse of poisons, would concede the chalice
Which but one living man⁹ has drained, who now,
Vessel of deathless wrath, a slave that feels
No proud exemption in the blighting curse
680   He bears, over the world wanders for ever,
Lone as incarnate death! O, that the dream
Of dark magician in his visioned cave,¹
Raking the cinders of a crucible
For life and power, even when his feeble hand
685   Shakes in its last decay, were the true law
Of this so lovely world! But thou art fled
Like some frail exhalation;° which the dawn   *mist*
Robes in its golden beams,—ah! thou hast fled!
The brave, the gentle, and the beautiful,

5. I.e., the moon. "Meteor" was once used for any phenomenon in the skies, as our modern term "meteorology" suggests.
6. The ebbing of the Poet's life parallels the descent of the "horned moon," to the moment when only the two "points of light"—its horns—show above the hills.
7. Attended, acted as a servant to.
8. Medea brewed a magic potion to rejuvenate the dying Aeson; where some of the potion spilled on the ground, flowers sprang up (Ovid, *Metamorpho-*

ses 7.275ff.).
9. The Wandering Jew. According to a medieval legend, he had taunted Christ on the way to the crucifixion and was condemned to wander the world, deathless, until Christ's second coming.
1. Cave in which he has visions. "Dark magician": an alchemist attempting to produce the elixir of enduring life. Alchemy intrigued both Shelleys. See Mary Shelley's "The Mortal Immortal" (p. 960).

690 The child of grace and genius. Heartless things
Are done and said i' the world, and many worms
And beasts and men live on, and mighty Earth
From sea and mountain, city and wilderness,
In vesper² low or joyous orison,°   prayer
695 Lifts still its solemn voice:—but thou art fled—
Thou canst no longer know or love the shapes
Of this phantasmal scene, who have to thee
Been purest ministers, who are, alas!
Now thou art not. Upon those pallid lips
700 So sweet even in their silence, on those eyes
That image sleep in death, upon that form
Yet safe from the worm's outrage, let no tear
Be shed—not even in thought. Nor, when those hues
Are gone, and those divinest lineaments,
705 Worn by the senseless° wind, shall live alone   unfeeling
In the frail pauses of this simple strain,
Let not high verse, mourning the memory
Of that which is no more, or painting's woe
Or sculpture, speak in feeble imagery
710 Their own cold powers. Art and eloquence,
And all the shews o' the world are frail and vain
To weep a loss that turns their lights to shade.
It is a woe too "deep for tears,"³ when all
Is reft at once, when some surpassing Spirit,
715 Whose light adorned the world around it, leaves
Those who remain behind, not sobs or groans,
The passionate tumult of a clinging hope;
But pale despair and cold tranquillity,
Nature's vast frame, the web of human things,
720 Birth and the grave, that are not as they were.

1815   1816

Mont Blanc¹

Lines Written in the Vale of Chamouni

I

The everlasting universe of things
Flows through the mind, and rolls its rapid waves,
Now dark—now glittering—now reflecting gloom—
Now lending splendour, where from secret springs

---

2. Evening prayer.
3. From the last line of Wordsworth's "Ode: Intimations of Immortality": "Thoughts that do often lie too deep for tears."
1. "Mont Blanc," in which Shelley both echoes and argues with the poetry of natural description written by Wordsworth and Coleridge, was first published as the conclusion to the *History of a Six Weeks' Tour*. This was a book that Percy and Mary Shelley wrote together detailing the excursion that they and Claire Clairmont took in July 1816 to the valley of Chamonix, in what is now southeastern

France. That valley lies at the foot of Mont Blanc, the highest mountain in the Alps and in all Europe.
In the *History* Percy Shelley commented on his poem: "It was composed under the immediate impression of the deep and powerful feelings excited by the objects it attempts to describe; and, as an indisciplined overflowing of the soul rests its claim to approbation on an attempt to imitate the untamable wildness and inaccessible solemnity from which those feelings sprang." He was inspired to write the poem while standing on a bridge spanning the river Arve, which flows through the valley

5   The source of human thought its tribute brings
Of waters,—with a sound but half its own.
Such as a feeble brook will oft assume
In the wild woods, among the mountains lone,
Where waterfalls around it leap forever,
10 Where woods and winds contend, and a vast river
Over its rocks ceaselessly bursts and raves.

2

Thus thou, Ravine of Arve—dark, deep Ravine—
Thou many-coloured, many-voiced vale,
Over whose pines, and crags, and caverns sail
15 Fast cloud shadows and sunbeams: awful° scene,   *awe-inspiring*
Where Power in likeness of the Arve comes down
From the ice gulphs that gird his secret throne,
Bursting through these dark mountains like the flame
Of lightning through the tempest;—thou dost lie,
20 Thy giant brood of pines around thee clinging,
Children of elder° time, in whose devotion   *earlier, ancient*
The chainless winds still come and ever came
To drink their odours, and their mighty swinging
To hear—an old and solemn harmony;
25 Thine earthly rainbows stretched across the sweep
Of the etherial waterfall, whose veil
Robes some unsculptured[2] image; the strange sleep
Which when the voices of the desart fail
Wraps all in its own deep eternity;—
30 Thy caverns echoing to the Arve's commotion,
A loud, lone sound no other sound can tame;
Thou art pervaded with that ceaseless motion,
Thou art the path of that unresting sound—
Dizzy Ravine! and when I gaze on thee
35 I seem as in a trance sublime and strange
To muse on my own separate phantasy,
My own, my human mind, which passively
Now renders and receives fast influencings,
Holding an unremitting interchange
40 With the clear universe of things around;[3]
One legion of wild thoughts, whose wandering wings
Now float above thy darkness, and now rest
Where that or thou art no unbidden guest,

---

of Chamonix and is fed from above by the meltoff of the glacier, the Mer de Glace.

    In a letter to Thomas Love Peacock drafted in the same week as "Mont Blanc," Shelley had recalled that the count de Buffon, a French pioneer of the science we now know as geology, had proposed a "sublime but gloomy theory—that this globe which we inhabit will at some future period be changed to a mass of frost." This sense, which Shelley takes from Buffon, of a Nature that is utterly alien and indifferent to human beings (and whose history takes shape on a timescale of incomprehensible immensity) is counterposed throughout "Mont Blanc" with Shelley's interest, fueled by his reading of 18th-century skeptics such as David Hume, in questions about the human mind, its

powers, and the limits of knowledge. "All things exist as they are perceived: at least in relation to the percipient," Shelley would later write in "A Defence of Poetry" (p. 837). In "Mont Blanc" the priority that this statement gives to the mind over the external world is challenged by the sheer destructive power of the mountain.

2. I.e., not formed by humans.

3. This passage is remarkably parallel to a passage Shelley could not have read in *The Prelude*, first published in 1850, in which Wordsworth discovers, in the landscape viewed from Mount Snowdon, the "type" or "emblem" of the human mind in its interchange with nature (see *The Prelude* 14.63ff., p. 386).

In the still cave of the witch Poesy,[4]
45 Seeking among the shadows that pass by
Ghosts of all things that are, some shade of thee,
Some phantom, some faint image; till the breast
From which they fled recalls them, thou art there![5]

3

Some say that gleams of a remoter world
50 Visit the soul in sleep,—that death is slumber,
And that its shapes the busy thoughts outnumber
Of those who wake and live.—I look on high;
Has some unknown omnipotence unfurled
The veil of life and death? or do I lie
55 In dream, and does the mightier world of sleep
Spread far around and inaccessibly
Its circles? For the very spirit fails,
Driven like a homeless cloud from steep to steep
That vanishes among the viewless° gales!   *invisible*
60 Far, far above, piercing the infinite sky,
Mont Blanc appears,—still, snowy, and serene—
Its subject mountains their unearthly forms
Pile around it, ice and rock; broad vales between
Of frozen floods, unfathomable deeps,
65 Blue as the overhanging heaven, that spread
And wind among the accumulated steeps;
A desart peopled by the storms alone,
Save° when the eagle brings some hunter's bone,   *except*
And the wolf tracts° her there—how hideously   *tracks*
70 Its shapes are heaped around! rude, bare, and high,
Ghastly, and scarred, and riven.°—Is this the scene   *split*
Where the old Earthquake-dæmon[6] taught her young
Ruin? Were these their toys? or did a sea
Of fire, envelope once this silent snow?
75 None can reply—all seems eternal now.
The wilderness has a mysterious tongue
Which teaches awful doubt, or faith so mild,
So solemn, so serene, that man may be
But for such faith[7] with nature reconciled;
80 Thou hast a voice, great Mountain, to repeal
Large codes of fraud and woe; not understood
By all, but which[8] the wise, and great, and good
Interpret, or make felt, or deeply feel.

4. I.e., in the part of the mind that creates poetry.
5. I.e., the thoughts (line 41) seek, in the poet's creative faculty, some shade, phantom, or image of the Ravine of the Arve; and when the breast, which has forgotten these images, recalls them again—there, suddenly, the Arve exists.
6. A supernatural being, halfway between mortals and the gods. Here it represents the force that makes earthquakes. Shelley views this landscape as the product of violent geological upheavals in the past.
7. I.e., "simply by holding such faith." In Shelley's

balance of possibilities, the landscape is equally capable either of instilling such a Wordsworthian faith (in the possibility of reconciling humans and nature, lines 78–79) or of producing the "awful" (i.e., "awesome") doubt (that nature is totally alien to human needs and values). For Wordsworth's faith in the correspondence of Nature and human thoughts and his conviction that "Nature never did betray / The heart that loved her," see "Tintern Abbey," lines 122–23.
8. The reference is to "voice," line 80.

4

The fields, the lakes, the forests, and the streams,
85   Ocean, and all the living things that dwell
Within the dædal⁹ earth; lightning, and rain,
Earthquake, and fiery flood, and hurricane,
The torpor of the year when feeble dreams
Visit the hidden buds, or dreamless sleep
90   Holds every future leaf and flower;—the bound
With which from that detested trance they leap;
The works and ways of man, their death and birth,
And that of him and all that his may be;
All things that move and breathe with toil and sound
95   Are born and die; revolve, subside and swell.
Power dwells apart in its tranquillity
Remote, serene, and inaccessible:
And *this*, the naked countenance of earth,
On which I gaze, even these primæval mountains
100   Teach the adverting° mind. The glaciers creep   *observant*
Like snakes that watch their prey, from their far fountains,
Slow rolling on; there, many a precipice,
Frost and the Sun in scorn of mortal power
Have piled: dome, pyramid, and pinnacle,
105   A city of death, distinct with many a tower
And wall impregnable of beaming ice.
Yet not a city, but a flood of ruin
Is there, that from the boundaries of the sky
Rolls its perpetual stream; vast pines are strewing
110   Its destined path, or in the mangled soil
Branchless and shattered stand: the rocks, drawn down
From yon remotest waste, have overthrown
The limits of the dead and living world,
Never to be reclaimed. The dwelling-place
115   Of insects, beasts, and birds, becomes its spoil;
Their food and their retreat for ever gone,
So much of life and joy is lost. The race
Of man, flies far in dread; his work and dwelling
Vanish, like smoke before the tempest's stream,
120   And their place is not known. Below, vast caves
Shine in the rushing torrents' restless gleam,
Which from those secret chasms in tumult welling¹
Meet in the vale, and one majestic River,²
The breath and blood of distant lands, for ever
125   Rolls its loud waters to the ocean waves,
Breathes its swift vapours to the circling air.

5

Mont Blanc yet gleams on high:—the power is there,
The still and solemn power of many sights,

9. Intricately formed; derived from Daedalus, builder of the labyrinth in Crete.
1. This description (as well as that in lines 9–11) seems to be an echo of Coleridge's description of the chasm and sacred river in the recently pub-

lished "Kubla Khan," lines 12–24.
2. The Arve, which flows into Lake Geneva. Nearby the river Rhone flows out of Lake Geneva to begin its course through France and into the Mediterranean.

And many sounds, and much of life and death.
130 In the calm darkness of the moonless nights,
In the lone glare of day, the snows descend
Upon that Mountain; none beholds them there,
Nor when the flakes burn in the sinking sun,
Or the star-beams dart through them:—Winds contend
135 Silently there, and heap the snow with breath
Rapid and strong, but silently! Its home
The voiceless lightning in these solitudes
Keeps innocently, and like vapour broods
Over the snow. The secret strength of things
140 Which governs thought, and to the infinite dome
Of heaven is as a law, inhabits thee!
And what were thou,° and earth, and stars, and sea,   *Mont Blanc*
If to the human mind's imaginings
Silence and solitude were vacancy?

1816   1817

Hymn to Intellectual Beauty[1]

1

The awful shadow of some unseen Power
Floats though unseen amongst us,—visiting
This various world with as inconstant wing
As summer winds that creep from flower to flower.—
5 Like moonbeams that behind some piny mountain shower,[2]
It visits with inconstant glance
Each human heart and countenance;
Like hues and harmonies of evening,—
Like clouds in starlight widely spread,—
10 Like memory of music fled,—
Like aught that for its grace may be
Dear, and yet dearer for its mystery.

2

Spirit of BEAUTY, that dost consecrate
With thine own hues all thou dost shine upon
15 Of human thought or form,—where art thou gone?
Why dost thou pass away and leave our state,
This dim vast vale of tears, vacant and desolate?
Ask why the sunlight not forever
Weaves rainbows o'er yon mountain river,
20 Why aught° should fail and fade that once is shewn,   *anything*
Why fear and dream and death and birth
Cast on the daylight of this earth
Such gloom,—why man has such a scope
For love and hate, despondency and hope?

1. "Intellectual" means nonmaterial, that which is beyond access to the human senses. In this poem intellectual beauty is something postulated to account for occasional states of awareness that lend splendor, grace, and truth both to the natural world and to people's moral consciousness.
2. Used as a verb.

3

25 No voice from some sublimer world hath ever
   To sage or poet these responses given—
   Therefore the name of God and ghosts and Heaven,
   Remain the records of their vain endeavour,[3]
   Frail spells—whose uttered charm might not avail to sever,
30   From all we hear and all we see,
       Doubt, chance, and mutability.
   Thy light alone—like mist o'er mountains driven,
       Or music by the night wind sent
       Through strings of some still instrument,°   wind harp
35   Or moonlight on a midnight stream,
   Gives grace and truth to life's unquiet dream.

4

   Love, Hope, and Self-esteem, like clouds depart
   And come, for some uncertain moments lent.
   Man were immortal, and omnipotent,
40 Didst thou, unknown and awful as thou art,
   Keep with thy glorious train firm state within his heart.[4]
       Thou messenger of sympathies,
       That wax and wane in lovers' eyes—
   Thou—that to human thought art nourishment,
45   Like darkness to a dying flame![5]
       Depart not as thy shadow came,
       Depart not—lest the grave should be,
   Like life and fear, a dark reality.

5

   While yet a boy I sought for ghosts, and sped
50 Through many a listening chamber, cave and ruin,
   And starlight wood, with fearful steps pursuing
   Hopes of high talk with the departed dead.
   I called on poisonous names with which our youth is fed;[6]
       I was not heard—I saw them not—
55   When musing deeply on the lot
   Of life, at that sweet time when winds are wooing
       All vital things that wake to bring
       News of buds and blossoming,—
   Sudden, thy shadow fell on me;
60 I shrieked, and clasped my hands in extacy!

6

   I vowed that I would dedicate my powers
   To thee and thine—have I not kept the vow?
   With beating heart and streaming eyes, even now
   I call the phantoms of a thousand hours
65 Each from his voiceless grave: they have in visioned bowers

---

3. The names (line 27) represent nothing better than the feeble guesses that philosophers and poets have made in attempting to answer the questions posed in stanza 2, but these guesses also delude us as though they were magic spells.
4. I.e., "man would be immortal . . . if thou didst keep."

5. Darkness may be said to nourish the dying flame by providing the contrast that offsets its light.
6. Lines 49–52 refer to Shelley's youthful experiments with magic. The "poisonous names" may be the religious terms ("God and ghosts and Heaven") of line 27.

Of studious zeal or love's delight
Outwatched with me the envious night[7]—
They know that never joy illumed my brow
Unlinked with hope that thou wouldst free
70   This world from its dark slavery,
That thou—O awful LOVELINESS,
Wouldst give whate'er these words cannot express.

7

The day becomes more solemn and serene
When noon is past—there is a harmony
75   In autumn, and a lustre in its sky,
Which through the summer is not heard or seen,
As if it could not be, as if it had not been!
Thus let thy power, which like the truth
Of nature on my passive youth
80   Descended, to my onward life supply
Its calm—to one who worships thee,
And every form containing thee,
Whom, SPIRIT fair, thy spells did bind
To fear[8] himself, and love all human kind.

1816   1817

Ozymandias[1]

I met a traveller from an antique land,
Who said—"Two vast and trunkless° legs of stone   *without a torso*
Stand in the desert. . . . Near them, on the sand,
Half sunk a shattered visage lies, whose frown,
5   And wrinkled lip, and sneer of cold command,
Tell that its sculptor well those passions read
Which yet survive,° stamped on these lifeless things,   *outlive*
The hand that mocked them, and the heart that fed;[2]
And on the pedestal, these words appear:
10   My name is Ozymandias, King of Kings,
Look on my Works, ye Mighty, and despair!
Nothing beside remains. Round the decay
Of that colossal Wreck, boundless and bare
The lone and level sands stretch far away."

1817   1818

---

7. I.e., stayed up until the night, envious of their delight, had reluctantly departed.
8. Probably in the old sense: "to stand in awe of."
1. According to Diodorus Siculus, Greek historian of the 1st century B.C.E., the largest statue in Egypt had the inscription "I am Ozymandias, king of kings; if anyone wishes to know what I am and

where I lie, let him surpass me in some of my exploits." Ozymandias was the Greek name for Ramses II of Egypt, 13th century B.C.E.
2. "The hand" is the sculptor's, who had "mocked" (both imitated and satirized) the sculptured passions; "the heart" is the king's, which has "fed" his passions.

Stanzas Written in Dejection—
December 1818, near Naples[1]

The Sun is warm, the sky is clear,
The waves are dancing fast and bright,
Blue isles and snowy mountains wear
The purple noon's transparent might,
5   The breath of the moist earth is light
Around its unexpanded buds;
Like many a voice of one delight
The winds, the birds, the Ocean-floods;
The City's voice itself is soft, like Solitude's.

10   I see the Deep's untrampled floor
With green and purple seaweeds strown;
I see the waves upon the shore
Like light dissolved in star-showers, thrown;
I sit upon the sands alone;
15   The lightning of the noontide Ocean
Is flashing round me, and a tone
Arises from its measured motion,
How sweet! did any heart now share in my emotion.

Alas, I have nor hope nor health
20   Nor peace within nor calm around,
Nor that content surpassing wealth
The sage[2] in meditation found,
And walked with inward glory crowned;
Nor fame nor power nor love nor leisure—
25   Others I see whom these surround,
Smiling they live and call life pleasure:
To me that cup has been dealt in another measure.

Yet now despair itself is mild,
Even as the winds and waters are;
30   I could lie down like a tired child
And weep away the life of care
Which I have borne and yet must bear
Till Death like Sleep might steal on me,
And I might feel in the warm air
35   My cheek grow cold, and hear the Sea
Breathe o'er my dying brain its last monotony.

Some might lament that I were cold,
As I, when this sweet day is gone,[3]
Which my lost heart, too soon grown old,
40   Insults with this untimely moan—

---

1. Shelley's first wife, Harriet, had drowned herself; Clara, his baby daughter with Mary Shelley, had just died; and he was plagued by ill health, pain, financial worries, and the sense that he had failed as a poet.

2. Probably the Roman emperor Marcus Aurelius (2nd century C.E.), Stoic philosopher who wrote twelve books of *Meditations*.

3. I.e., as I will lament this sweet day when it has gone.

They might lament,—for I am one
Whom men love not, and yet regret;
Unlike this day, which, when the Sun
Shall on its stainless glory set,
45   Will linger though enjoyed, like joy in Memory yet.

1818   1824

A Song: "Men of England"[1]

Men of England, wherefore plough
For the lords who lay ye low?
Wherefore weave with toil and care
The rich robes your tyrants wear?

5   Wherefore feed and clothe and save
From the cradle to the grave
Those ungrateful drones who would
Drain your sweat—nay, drink your blood?

Wherefore, Bees of England, forge
10   Many a weapon, chain, and scourge,
That these stingless drones may spoil
The forced produce of your toil?

Have ye leisure, comfort, calm,
Shelter, food, love's gentle balm?
15   Or what is it ye buy so dear
With your pain and with your fear?

The seed ye sow, another reaps;
The wealth ye find, another keeps;
The robes ye weave, another wears;
20   The arms ye forge, another bears.

Sow seed—but let no tyrant reap:
Find wealth—let no impostor heap:
Weave robes—let not the idle wear:
Forge arms—in your defence to bear.

25   Shrink to your cellars, holes, and cells—
In halls ye deck another dwells.
Why shake the chains ye wrought? Ye see
The steel ye tempered glance on ye.

With plough and spade and hoe and loom
30   Trace your grave and build your tomb

---

1. This and the two following poems were written at a time of turbulent unrest, after the return of troops from the Napoleonic Wars had precipitated a great economic depression. The "Song," express-ing Shelley's hope for a proletarian revolution, was originally planned as one of a series for workers. It has become, as the poet wished, a hymn of the British labor movement.

And weave your winding-sheet—till fair
England be your Sepulchre.

1819   1839

England in 1819

An old, mad, blind, despised, and dying King;[1]
Princes, the dregs of their dull race, who flow
Through public scorn,—mud from a muddy spring;
Rulers who neither see nor feel nor know,
5   But leechlike to their fainting country cling
Till they drop, blind in blood, without a blow.
A people starved and stabbed in th' untilled field;[2]
An army, whom liberticide[3] and prey
Makes as a two-edged sword to all who wield;
10 Golden and sanguine laws[4] which tempt and slay;
Religion Christless, Godless—a book sealed;
A senate, Time's worst statute, unrepealed—
Are graves from which a glorious Phantom[5] may
Burst, to illumine our tempestuous day.

1819   1839

To Sidmouth and Castlereagh[1]

As from their ancestral oak
    Two empty ravens wind their clarion,
Yell by yell, and croak by croak,
When they scent the noonday smoke
5   Of fresh human carrion:—

As two gibbering night-birds flit
    From their bowers of deadly yew
Through the night to frighten it—
When the moon is in a fit,
10   And the stars are none, or few:—

As a shark and dogfish wait
    Under an Atlantic isle

1. George III, who had been declared insane in 1811. He died in 1820.
2. Alluding to the Peterloo Massacre on August 16, 1819. In St. Peter's field, near Manchester, a troop of cavalry had charged into a crowd attending a peaceful rally in support of parliamentary reform. "Peterloo" is an ironic combination of "St. Peter's" and "Waterloo."
3. The killing of liberty.
4. Laws bought with gold and leading to bloodshed.
5. I.e., a revolution.

1. Shelley's powerful satire is directed against Viscount Castlereagh, foreign secretary during 1812–22, who took a leading part in the European settlement after the Battle of Waterloo, and Viscount Sidmouth (1757–1844), the home secretary, whose cruelly coercive measures (supported by Castlereagh) against unrest in the laboring classes were in large part responsible for the Peterloo Massacre.
    When this poem was reprinted by Mary Shelley in 1839, it was given the title "Similes for Two Political Characters of 1819."

For the Negro-ship, whose freight
Is the theme of their debate,
15   Wrinkling their red gills the while—

Are ye—two vultures sick for battle,
Two scorpions under one wet stone,
Two bloodless wolves whose dry throats rattle,
Two crows perched on the murrained² cattle,
20   Two vipers tangled into one.

1819   1832

To William Shelley¹

1

My lost William, thou in whom
    Some bright spirit lived, and did
That decaying robe consume
    Which its lustre faintly hid,—
5 Here its ashes find a tomb,
    But beneath this pyramid²
Thou art not—if a thing divine
Like thee can die, thy funeral shrine
Is thy mother's grief and mine.

2

10 Where art thou, my gentle child?
    Let me think thy spirit feeds,
With its life intense and mild,
    The love of living leaves and weeds
Among these tombs and ruins wild;—
15   Let me think that through low seeds
Of sweet flowers and sunny grass
Into their hues and scents may pass
A portion——

1819   1824

Ode to the West Wind¹

O wild West Wind, thou breath of Autumn's being,
Thou, from whose unseen presence the leaves dead
Are driven, like ghosts from an enchanter fleeing,

2. A *murrain* is a malignant disease of domestic animals.
1. The Shelleys' son William, who died of malaria in June 1819, age three and a half years, was buried in the Protestant Cemetery in Rome. These unfinished lines were discovered among the poet's papers by his widow, Mary Shelley (the grieving mother of line 9), who published them in her husband's *Posthumous Poems* (1824).

2. The Shelleys, who left Rome shortly after William's death, ordered the construction of a small stone pyramid to mark his grave. This is not, except perhaps obliquely, a reference to the famous tomb, a 150-foot pyramid, of the 1st-century B.C.E. Roman magistrate Caius Cestius just outside the cemetery.
1. This poem was conceived and chiefly written in a wood that skirts the Arno, near Florence, and on

Yellow, and black, and pale, and hectic² red,
5   Pestilence-stricken multitudes: O Thou,
Who chariotest to their dark wintry bed

The winged seeds, where they lie cold and low,
Each like a corpse within its grave, until
Thine azure sister of the Spring³ shall blow

10   Her clarion⁴ o'er the dreaming earth, and fill
(Driving sweet buds like flocks to feed in air)
With living hues and odours plain and hill:

Wild Spirit, which art moving everywhere;
Destroyer and Preserver;⁵ hear, O hear!

2

15   Thou on whose stream, 'mid the steep sky's commotion,
Loose clouds like Earth's decaying leaves are shed,
Shook from the tangled boughs of Heaven and Ocean,

Angels⁶ of rain and lightning: there are spread
On the blue surface of thine aery surge,
20   Like the bright hair uplifted from the head

Of some fierce Mænad,⁷ even from the dim verge
Of the horizon to the zenith's height,
The locks of the approaching storm. Thou Dirge

Of the dying year, to which this closing night
25   Will be the dome of a vast sepulchre,
Vaulted with all thy congregated might

Of vapours,° from whose solid atmosphere   clouds
Black rain and fire and hail will burst: O hear!

3

Thou who didst waken from his summer dreams
30   The blue Mediterranean, where he lay,
Lulled by the coil of his chrystalline streams,⁸

---

a day when that tempestuous wind, whose temperature is at once mild and animating, was collecting the vapours which pour down the autumnal
rains [Shelley's note]. As in other major Romantic
poems—for example, the opening of Wordsworth's
Prelude, Coleridge's "Dejection: An Ode," and the
conclusion to Shelley's *Adonais*—the rising wind,
linked with the cycle of the seasons, is presented
as the correspondent in the external world to an
inner change, a burst of creative power that is paralleled to the inspiration of prophets. In many languages the words for *wind*, *breath*, *soul*, and
inspiration are identical or related. Thus Shelley's
west wind is a "spirit" (the Latin *spiritus*: wind,
breath, soul, and the root word for *inspiration*), the
"breath of Autumn's being," which on earth, sky,
and sea destroys in autumn to revive in the spring.
In some philosophical histories of the period, the
spirit of liberty was said to have deserted Europe
for the Americas. In blowing from the west, the
wind may carry liberty back again.

Shelley's sonnet-length stanza, developed from
the interlaced three-line units of the Italian *terza
rima* (*aba bcb cdc*, etc.), consists of a set of four
such tercets, closed by a couplet rhyming with the
middle line of the preceding tercet: *aba bcb cdc ded
ee*.
2. Referring to the kind of fever that occurs in
tuberculosis.
3. The west wind that will blow in the spring.
4. A high, shrill trumpet.
5. Refers to the Hindu gods Siva the Destroyer
and Vishnu the Preserver.
6. In the old sense of messengers.
7. A female worshipper who danced frenziedly in
the worship of Dionysus (Bacchus), the Greek god
of wine and vegetation. As vegetation god he was
fabled to die in the fall and to be resurrected in the
spring.
8. The currents that flow in the Mediterranean
Sea, sometimes with a visible difference in color.

Beside a pumice isle in Baiæ's bay,[9]
And saw in sleep old palaces and towers
Quivering within the wave's intenser day,

35   All overgrown with azure moss and flowers
So sweet, the sense faints picturing them! Thou
For whose path the Atlantic's level powers

Cleave themselves into chasms, while far below
The sea-blooms and the oozy woods which wear
40   The sapless foliage of the ocean, know

Thy voice, and suddenly grow grey with fear,
And tremble and despoil themselves:[1] O hear!

4

If I were a dead leaf thou mightest bear;
If I were a swift cloud to fly with thee;
45   A wave to pant beneath thy power, and share

The impulse of thy strength, only less free
Than thou, O Uncontrollable! If even
I were as in my boyhood, and could be

The comrade of thy wanderings over Heaven,
50   As then, when to outstrip thy skiey speed
Scarce seemed a vision; I would ne'er have striven

As thus with thee in prayer in my sore need.
Oh! lift me as a wave, a leaf, a cloud!
I fall upon the thorns of life! I bleed!

55   A heavy weight of hours has chained and bowed
One too like thee: tameless, and swift, and proud.

5

Make me thy lyre,[2] even as the forest is:
What if my leaves are falling like its own!
The tumult of thy mighty harmonies

60   Will take from both a deep, autumnal tone,
Sweet though in sadness. Be thou, Spirit fierce,
My spirit! Be thou me, impetuous one!

Drive my dead thoughts over the universe
Like withered leaves to quicken a new birth![3]
65   And, by the incantation of this verse,

9. West of Naples, the locale of imposing villas built in the glory days of imperial Rome. Their ruins are reflected in the waters of the bay, a sight Mary Shelley also describes in the Introduction to *The Last Man* (see p. 957).
1. The vegetation at the bottom of the sea . . . sympathizes with that of the land in the change of seasons, and is consequently influenced by the winds which announce it [Shelley's note].
2. The Eolian lyre, which responds to the wind with rising and falling musical chords.
3. This line may play on the secondary sense of "leaves" as pages in a book.

Scatter, as from an unextinguished hearth
Ashes and sparks, my words among mankind!
Be through my lips to unawakened Earth

The trumpet of a prophecy! O Wind,
70   If Winter comes, can Spring be far behind?

1819   1820

Prometheus Unbound   Shelley composed this work in Italy between the
autumn of 1818 and the close of 1819 and published it the following summer. Upon
its completion he wrote in a letter, "It is a drama, with characters and mechanism of
a kind yet unattempted; and I think the execution is better than any of my former
attempts." It is based on the *Prometheus Bound* of Aeschylus, which dramatizes the
sufferings of Prometheus, unrepentant champion of humanity, who, because he had
stolen fire from heaven, was condemned by Zeus to be chained to Mount Caucasus
and to be tortured by a vulture feeding on his liver; in a lost sequel Aeschylus reconciled Prometheus with his oppressor. Shelley continued Aeschylus's story but transformed it into a symbolic drama about the origin of evil and the possibility of
overcoming it. In such early writings as *Queen Mab*, Shelley had expressed his belief
that injustice and suffering could be eliminated by an external revolution that would
wipe out or radically reform the causes of evil, attributed to existing social, political,
and religious institutions. Implicit in *Prometheus Unbound*, on the other hand, is the
view that both evil and the possibility of reform are the moral responsibility of men
and women. Social chaos and wars are a gigantic projection of human moral disorder
and inner division and conflict; tyrants are the outer representatives of the tyranny
of our baser over our better elements; hatred for others is a product of self-contempt;
and external political reform is impossible unless we have first reformed our own
nature at its roots, by substituting selfless love for divisive hatred. Shelley thus incorporates into his secular myth—of universal regeneration by a triumph of humanity's
moral imagination—the ethical teaching of Christ on the Mount, together with the
classical morality represented in the *Prometheus* of Aeschylus.

FROM PROMETHEUS UNBOUND

A Lyrical Drama in Four Acts

Audisne hæc Amphiarae, sub terram abdite?[1]

Preface

The Greek tragic writers, in selecting as their subject any portion of their
national history or mythology, employed in their treatment of it a certain arbi-

---

1. Cicero, *Tusculan Disputations* 2.60: "Do you
hear this, O Amphiaraus, concealed under the
earth?" In Greek myth Amphiaraus was a seer.
Fleeing from an unsuccessful assault on Thebes,
he was saved from his pursuers by Zeus, who by a
thunderbolt opened a cleft in the earth that swallowed him up.
    In his *Disputations* Cicero is arguing for the
Stoic doctrine of the need to master pain and suffering. He quotes this line (a Latin translation from
Aeschylus's lost drama *Epigoni*) in the course of an
anecdote about Dionysius of Heraclea, who, tormented by kidney stones, abjures the doctrine of
his Stoic teacher Zeno that pain is not an evil. By
way of reproof his fellow-Stoic Cleanthes strikes
his foot on the ground and utters this line. Cicero
interprets it as an appeal to Zeno the Stoic master
(under the name of Amphiaraus).

trary discretion. They by no means conceived themselves bound to adhere to the common interpretation or to imitate in story as in title their rivals and predecessors. Such a system would have amounted to a resignation of those claims to preference over their competitors which incited the composition. The Agamemnonian story was exhibited on the Athenian theatre with as many variations as dramas.

I have presumed to employ a similar licence.—The *Prometheus Unbound* of Æschylus, supposed the reconciliation of Jupiter with his victim as the price of the disclosure of the danger threatened to his empire by the consummation of his marriage with Thetis. Thetis, according to this view of the subject, was given in marriage to Peleus, and Prometheus by the permission of Jupiter delivered from his captivity by Hercules.[2]—Had I framed my story on this model I should have done no more than have attempted to restore the lost drama of Æschylus; an ambition, which, if my preference to this mode of treating the subject had incited me to cherish, the recollection of the high comparison such an attempt would challenge, might well abate. But in truth I was averse from a catastrophe so feeble as that of reconciling the Champion with the Oppressor of mankind. The moral interest of the fable which is so powerfully sustained by the sufferings and endurance of Prometheus, would be annihilated if we could conceive of him as unsaying his high language, and quailing before his successful and perfidious adversary. The only imaginary being resembling in any degree Prometheus, is Satan; and Prometheus is, in my judgement, a more poetical character than Satan because, in addition to courage and majesty and firm and patient opposition to omnipotent force, he is susceptible of being described as exempt from the taints of ambition, envy, revenge, and a desire for personal aggrandisement, which in the Hero of *Paradise Lost,* interfere with the interest. The character of Satan engenders in the mind a pernicious casuistry[3] which leads us to weigh his faults with his wrongs and to excuse the former because the latter exceed all measure. In the minds of those who consider that magnificent fiction with a religious feeling, it engenders something worse. But Prometheus is, as it were, the type of the highest perfection of moral and intellectual nature, impelled by the purest and the truest motives to the best and noblest ends.

This Poem was chiefly written upon the mountainous ruins of the Baths of Caracalla, among the flowery glades, and thickets of odoriferous blossoming trees which are extended in ever winding labyrinths upon its immense platforms and dizzy arches suspended in the air. The bright blue sky of Rome, and the effect of the vigorous awakening of spring in that divinest climate, and the new life with which it drenches the spirits even to intoxication, were the inspiration of this drama.

The imagery which I have employed will be found in many instances to have been drawn from the operations of the human mind, or from those external actions by which they are expressed. This is unusual in modern Poetry; although Dante and Shakespeare are full of instances of the same kind: Dante indeed more than any other poet and with greater success. But the Greek poets, as writers to whom no resource of awakening the sympathy of their contemporaries was unknown, were in the habitual use of this power, and it is the study of their works (since a higher merit would probably be denied

2. Shelley's description of the subject of Aeschylus's lost drama, *Prometheus Unbound*, is a speculation based on surviving fragments.
3. Slippery reasoning.

me) to which I am willing that my readers should impute this singularity. One word is due in candour to the degree in which the study of contemporary writings may have tinged my composition, for such has been a topic of censure with regard to poems far more popular, and indeed more deservedly popular than mine. It is impossible that any one who inhabits the same age with such writers as those who stand in the foremost ranks of our own, can conscientiously assure himself, that his language and tone of thought may not have been modified by the study of the productions of those extraordinary intellects. It is true, that, not the spirit of their genius, but the forms in which it has manifested itself, are due, less to the peculiarities of their own minds, than to the peculiarity of the moral and intellectual condition of the minds among which they have been produced. Thus a number of writers possess the form, whilst they want the spirit of those whom, it is alleged, they imitate; because the former is the endowment of the age in which they live, and the latter must be the uncommunicated lightning of their own mind.

The peculiar style of intense and comprehensive imagery which distinguishes the modern literature of England, has not been, as a general power, the product of the imitation of any particular writer. The mass of capabilities remains at every period materially the same; the circumstances which awaken it to action perpetually change. If England were divided into forty republics, each equal in population and extent to Athens, there is no reason to suppose but that, under institutions not more perfect than those of Athens, each would produce philosophers and poets equal to those who (if we except Shakespeare) have never been surpassed. We owe the great writers of the golden age of our literature to that fervid awakening of the public mind which shook to dust the oldest and most oppressive form of the Christian Religion. We owe Milton to the progress and developement of the same spirit; the sacred Milton was, let it ever be remembered, a Republican,[4] and a bold enquirer into morals and religion. The great writers of our own age are, we have reason to suppose, the companions and forerunners of some unimagined change in our social condition or the opinions which cement it. The cloud of mind is discharging its collected lightning, and the equilibrium between institutions and opinions is now restoring, or is about to be restored.[5]

As to imitation; Poetry is a mimetic art. It creates, but it creates by combination and representation. Poetical abstractions are beautiful and new, not because the portions of which they are composed had no previous existence in the mind of man or in nature, but because the whole produced by their combination has some intelligible and beautiful analogy with those sources of emotion and thought, and with the contemporary condition of them: one great poet is a masterpiece of nature, which another not only ought to study but must study. He might as wisely and as easily determine that his mind should no longer be the mirror of all that is lovely in the visible universe, as exclude from his contemplation the beautiful which exists in the writings of a great contemporary. The pretence of doing it would be a presumption in any but the greatest; the effect, even in him, would be strained, unnatural and ineffectual. A Poet, is the combined product of such internal powers as modify the nature of others, and of such external influences as excite and sustain

---

4. I.e., Milton hoped that the overthrow of the monarchy during the Civil War would lead to England's rebirth as a republic.

5. See Shelley's similar tribute to his great contemporaries in the concluding paragraph of his "Defence of Poetry" (p. 849).

these powers; he is not one, but both. Every man's mind is in this respect modified by all the objects of nature and art, by every word and every suggestion which he ever admitted to act upon his consciousness; it is the mirror upon which all forms are reflected, and in which they compose one form. Poets, not otherwise than philosophers, painters, sculptors and musicians, are in one sense the creators and in another the creations of their age. From this subjection the loftiest do not escape. There is a similarity between Homer and Hesiod, between Æschylus and Euripides, between Virgil and Horace, between Dante and Petrarch, between Shakespeare and Fletcher, between Dryden and Pope; each has a generic resemblance under which their specific distinctions are arranged. If this similarity be the result of imitation, I am willing to confess that I have imitated.

Let this opportunity be conceded to me of acknowledging that I have, what a Scotch philosopher characteristically terms, "a passion for reforming the world:"[6] what passion incited him to write and publish his book, he omits to explain. For my part I had rather be damned with Plato and Lord Bacon, than go to Heaven with Paley and Malthus.[7] But it is a mistake to suppose that I dedicate my poetical compositions solely to the direct enforcement of reform, or that I consider them in any degree as containing a reasoned system on the theory of human life. Didactic poetry is my abhorrence; nothing can be equally well expressed in prose that is not tedious and supererogatory in verse. My purpose has hitherto been simply to familiarise the highly refined imagination of the more select classes of poetical readers with beautiful idealisms of moral excellence; aware that until the mind can love, and admire, and trust, and hope, and endure, reasoned principles of moral conduct are seeds cast upon the highway of life which the unconscious passenger tramples into dust, although they would bear the harvest of his happiness. Should I live to accomplish what I purpose, that is, produce a systematical history of what appear to me to be the genuine elements of human society,[8] let not the advocates of injustice and superstition flatter themselves that I should take Æschylus rather than Plato as my model.

The having spoken of myself with unaffected freedom will need little apology with the candid; and let the uncandid consider that they injure me less than their own hearts and minds by misrepresentation. Whatever talents a person may possess to amuse and instruct others, be they ever so inconsiderable, he is yet bound to exert them: if his attempt be ineffectual, let the punishment of an unaccomplished purpose have been sufficient; let none trouble themselves to heap the dust of oblivion upon his efforts; the pile they raise will betray his grave which might otherwise have been unknown.

---

6. This is the title of chap. 16 in *The Principles of Moral Science* (1805), by the Scottish writer Robert Forsyth.
7. Thomas Malthus's *An Essay on the Principle of Population* (1798) argued that the rate of increase in population will soon exceed the rate of increase in the food supply necessary to sustain it. William Paley wrote *Evidences of Christianity* (1794),

which undertakes to prove that the design apparent in natural phenomena, and especially in the human body, entails the existence of God as the great Designer. Shelley ironically expresses his contempt for the doctrines of both these thinkers, which he conceives as arguments for accepting uncomplainingly the present state of the world.
8. Shelley did not live to write this history.

Prometheus Unbound

Act 1

SCENE: *A Ravine of Icy Rocks in the Indian Caucasus.* PROMETHEUS *is discovered bound to the Precipice.* PANTHEA *and* IONE[1] *are seated at his feet. Time, Night. During the Scene, Morning slowly breaks.*

PROMETHEUS   Monarch of Gods and Dæmons, and all Spirits
But One,[2] who throng those bright and rolling Worlds
Which Thou and I alone of living things
Behold with sleepless eyes! regard this Earth
5 Made multitudinous with thy slaves, whom thou
Requitest for knee-worship, prayer and praise,
And toil, and hecatombs[3] of broken hearts,
With fear and self contempt and barren hope;
Whilst me, who am thy foe, eyeless° in hate,   *blinded*
10 Hast thou made reign and triumph, to thy scorn,
O'er mine own misery and thy vain revenge.—
Three thousand years of sleep-unsheltered hours
And moments—aye° divided by keen pangs   *always*
Till they seemed years, torture and solitude,
15 Scorn and despair,—these are mine empire:—
More glorious far than that which thou surveyest
From thine unenvied throne, O Mighty God!
Almighty, had I deigned[4] to share the shame
Of thine ill tyranny, and hung not here
20 Nailed to this wall of eagle-baffling mountain,
Black, wintry, dead, unmeasured; without herb,°   *vegetation*
Insect, or beast, or shape or sound of life.
Ah me, alas, pain, pain ever, forever!

No change, no pause, no hope!—Yet I endure.
25 I ask the Earth, have not the mountains felt?
I ask yon Heaven—the all-beholding Sun,
Has it not seen? The Sea, in storm or calm,
Heaven's ever-changing Shadow, spread below—
Have its deaf waves not heard my agony?
30 Ah me, alas, pain, pain ever, forever!

The crawling glaciers pierce me with the spears
Of their moon-freezing chrystals; the bright chains
Eat with their burning cold into my bones.
Heaven's winged hound, polluting from thy lips
35 His beak in poison not his own, tears up
My heart;[5] and shapeless sights come wandering by,

---

1. Ione, Panthea, and Asia (introduced in the following scene) are sisters and Oceanids—i.e., daughters of Oceanus.
2. Demogorgon (see 2.4). "Daemons": supernatural beings, intermediary between gods and mortals. Prometheus is addressing Jupiter.
3. Large sacrificial offerings.
4. I.e., you would have been all-powerful, if I had deigned.
5. The vulture, tearing daily at Prometheus's heart, was kissed by Jupiter by way of reward.

The ghastly people of the realm of dream,
Mocking me: and the Earthquake-fiends are charged
To wrench the rivets from my quivering wounds
40 When the rocks split and close again behind;
While from their loud abysses howling throng
The genii of the storm, urging the rage
Of whirlwind, and afflict me with keen hail.
And yet to me welcome is Day and Night,
45 Whether one breaks the hoar frost of the morn,
Or starry, dim, and slow, the other climbs
The leaden-coloured East; for then they lead
Their wingless, crawling Hours,[6] one among whom
—As some dark Priest hales° the reluctant victim—   drags
50 Shall drag thee, cruel King, to kiss the blood
From these pale feet,[7] which then might trample thee
If they disdained not such a prostrate slave.
Disdain? Ah no! I pity thee.[8]—What Ruin
Will hunt thee undefended through wide Heaven!
55 How will thy soul, cloven to its depth with terror,
Gape like a Hell within! I speak in grief,
Not exultation, for I hate no more,
As then, ere misery made me wise.—The Curse
Once breathed on thee I would recall.[9] Ye Mountains,
60 Whose many-voiced Echoes, through the mist
Of cataracts, flung the thunder of that spell!
Ye icy Springs, stagnant with wrinkling frost,
Which vibrated to hear me, and then crept
Shuddering through India! Thou serenest Air,
65 Through which the Sun walks burning without beams!
And ye swift Whirlwinds, who on poised wings
Hung mute and moveless o'er yon hushed abyss,
As thunder louder than your own made rock
The orbed world! If then my words had power
70 —Though I am changed so that aught evil wish
Is dead within, although no memory be
Of what is hate—let them not lose it now![1]
What was that curse? for ye all heard me speak.

FIRST VOICE: *from the Mountains*
Thrice three hundred thousand years
75   O'er the Earthquake's couch we stood;
Oft as men convulsed with fears
We trembled in our multitude.

SECOND VOICE: *from the Springs*
Thunderbolts had parched out water,
We had been stained with bitter blood,

6. The Hours were represented in Greek myth and
art by human figures with wings.
7. One of a number of implied parallels between
the agony of Prometheus and the passion of Christ.
8. At this early point occurs the crisis of the
action: the beginning of Prometheus's change of

heart from hate to compassion, consummated in
lines 303–05.
9. I.e., remember. But the word's alternative
sense, "revoke," will later become crucial.
1. Let my words not lose their power now.

80 And had run mute 'mid shrieks of slaughter
    Through a city and a solitude!

THIRD VOICE: *from the Air*
I had clothed since Earth uprose
    Its wastes in colours not their own,
And oft had my serene repose
85   Been cloven by many a rending groan.

FOURTH VOICE: *from the Whirlwinds*
We had soared beneath these mountains
    Unresting ages;—nor had thunder
Nor yon Volcano's flaming fountains
    Nor any power above or under
90   Ever made us mute with wonder!

FIRST VOICE
But never bowed our snowy crest
As at the voice of thine unrest.

SECOND VOICE
Never such a sound before
To the Indian waves we bore.—
95 A pilot asleep on the howling sea
Leaped up from the deck in agony
And heard, and cried, "Ah, woe is me!"
And died as mad as the wild waves be.

THIRD VOICE
By such dread words from Earth to Heaven
100 My still realm was never riven;
When its wound was closed, there stood
Darkness o'er the Day, like blood.

FOURTH VOICE
And we shrank back—for dreams of ruin
To frozen caves our flight pursuing
105 Made us keep silence—thus—and thus—
Though silence is as hell to us.

THE EARTH
The tongueless Caverns of the craggy hills
Cried "Misery!" then; the hollow Heaven replied,
"Misery!" And the Ocean's purple waves,
110 Climbing the land, howled to the lashing winds.
And the pale nations heard it,—"Misery!"

PROMETHEUS
I hear a sound of voices—not the voice
Which I gave forth.—Mother,° thy sons and thou   *Earth*
Scorn him, without whose all-enduring will
115 Beneath the fierce omnipotence of Jove

Both they and thou had vanished like thin mist
Unrolled on the morning wind!—Know ye not me,
The Titan, he who made his agony
The barrier to your else all-conquering foe?
120 O rock-embosomed lawns and snow-fed streams
Now seen athwart frore vapours² deep below,
Through whose o'er-shadowing woods I wandered once
With Asia, drinking life from her loved eyes;
Why scorns the spirit which informs ye, now
125 To commune with me? me alone, who checked—
As one who checks a fiend-drawn charioteer—
The falshood and the force of Him who reigns
Supreme, and with the groans of pining slaves
Fills your dim glens and liquid wildernesses?
Why answer ye not, still? brethren!

THE EARTH
130 They dare not.

PROMETHEUS
Who dares? for I would hear that curse again. . . .
Ha, what an awful whisper rises up!
'Tis scarce like sound, it tingles through the frame
As lightning tingles, hovering ere it strike.—
135 Speak, Spirit! from thine inorganic voice
I only know that thou art moving near
And love. How cursed I him?

THE EARTH
How canst thou hear
Who knowest not the language of the dead?

PROMETHEUS
Thou art a living spirit—speak as they.

THE EARTH
140 I dare not speak like life, lest Heaven's fell° King   *cruel*
Should hear, and link me to some wheel of pain
More torturing than the one whereon I roll.—
Subtle thou art and good, and though the Gods
Hear not this voice—yet thou art more than God
145 Being wise and kind—earnestly hearken now.—

PROMETHEUS
Obscurely through my brain like shadows dim
Sweep awful° thoughts, rapid and thick.—I feel   *awe-inspiring*
Faint, like one mingled in entwining love,
Yet 'tis not pleasure.

2. Through frosty vapors.

THE EARTH

No, thou canst not hear:
50   Thou art immortal, and this tongue is known
Only to those who die . . .

PROMETHEUS

And what art thou,
O melancholy Voice?

THE EARTH

I am the Earth,
Thy mother, she within whose stony veins
To the last fibre of the loftiest tree
55   Whose thin leaves trembled in the frozen air
Joy ran, as blood within a living frame,
When thou didst from her bosom, like a cloud
Of glory, arise, a spirit of keen joy!
And at thy voice her pining sons uplifted
60   Their prostrate brows from the polluting dust
And our almighty Tyrant with fierce dread
Grew pale—until his thunder chained thee here.—
Then—see those million worlds which burn and roll
Around us: their inhabitants beheld
65   My sphered light wane in wide Heaven; the sea
Was lifted by strange tempest, and new fire
From earthquake-rifted mountains of bright snow
Shook its portentous hair beneath Heaven's frown;
Lightning and Inundation vexed the plains;
70   Blue thistles bloomed in cities; foodless toads
Within voluptuous chambers panting crawled;
When Plague had fallen on man and beast and worm,
And Famine,—and black blight on herb and tree,
And in the corn and vines and meadow-grass
75   Teemed ineradicable poisonous weeds
Draining their growth, for my wan breast was dry
With grief,—and the thin air, my breath, was stained
With the contagion of a mother's hate
Breathed on her child's destroyer—aye, I heard
0   Thy curse, the which if thou rememberest not
Yet my innumerable seas and streams,
Mountains and caves and winds, and yon wide Air
And the inarticulate people of the dead
Preserve, a treasured spell. We meditate
5   In secret joy and hope those dreadful words
But dare not speak them.

PROMETHEUS

Venerable Mother!
All else who live and suffer take from thee
Some comfort; flowers and fruits and happy sounds

And love, though fleeting; these may not be mine.
190   But mine own words, I pray, deny me not.

THE EARTH

They shall be told.—Ere Babylon was dust,
The Magus Zoroaster,³ my dead child,
Met his own image walking in the garden.
That apparition, sole of men, he saw.
195   For know there are two worlds of life and death:
One that which thou beholdest, but the other
Is underneath the grave, where do inhabit
The shadows of all forms that think and live
Till death unite them, and they part no more;
200   Dreams and the light imaginings of men
And all that faith creates, or love desires,
Terrible, strange, sublime and beauteous shapes.
There thou art, and dost hang, a writhing shade
'Mid whirlwind-peopled mountains; all the Gods
205   Are there, and all the Powers of nameless worlds,
Vast, sceptred Phantoms; heroes, men, and beasts;
And Demogorgon,⁴ a tremendous Gloom;
And he, the Supreme Tyrant,⁵ on his throne
Of burning Gold. Son, one of these shall utter
210   The curse which all remember. Call at will
Thine own ghost, or the ghost of Jupiter,
Hades or Typhon,⁶ or what mightier Gods
From all-prolific Evil, since thy ruin
Have sprung, and trampled on my prostrate sons.—
215   Ask and they must reply—so the revenge
Of the Supreme may sweep through vacant shades
As rainy wind through the abandoned gate
Of a fallen palace.

PROMETHEUS

Mother, let not aught
Of that which may be evil, pass again
220   My lips, or those of aught resembling me.—
Phantasm of Jupiter, arise, appear!

IONE

My wings are folded o'er mine ears,
My wings are crossed over mine eyes,

3. Zoroaster founded in ancient Persia a dualistic religion that worshiped fire and light in opposition to the evil principle of darkness. Priests of the religion were called Magi (singular: Magus).
4. In a note to the name in a poem published in 1817, Thomas Love Peacock alludes to Milton's mention of Demogorgon (*Paradise Lost*, 2.965) and explains: "He was the Genius of the Earth, and the Sovereign Power of the Terrestrial Dæmons. He dwelt originally with Eternity and Chaos, till, becoming weary of inaction, he organised the cha-

otic elements, and surrounded the earth with the heavens. In addition to Pan and the Fates, his children were Uranus, Titæa, Pytho, Eris, and Erebus." Thus, in Peacock's account, Demogorgon is the father of the Sky, the Earth, and the Underworld, as well as the Fates.
5. The shade or simulacrum of Jupiter.
6. Hades (Pluto), king of the underworld; Typhon, a hundred-headed giant, imprisoned beneath volcanic Mount Aetna.

Yet through their silver shade appears
25 And through their lulling plumes arise
A Shape, a throng of sounds:
May it be, no ill to thee[7]
O thou of many wounds!
Near whom for our sweet sister's sake
30 Ever thus we watch and wake.

PANTHEA

The sound is of whirlwind underground,
Earthquake and fire, and mountains cloven,—
The Shape is awful like the sound,
Clothed in dark purple, star-inwoven.
35 A sceptre of pale gold
To stay steps proud, o'er the slow cloud
His veined hand doth hold.
Cruel he looks but calm and strong
Like one who does, not suffers wrong.

PHANTASM OF JUPITER

40 Why have the secret powers of this strange world
Driven me, a frail and empty phantom, hither
On direst storms? What unaccustomed sounds
Are hovering on my lips, unlike the voice
With which our pallid race hold ghastly talk
45 In darkness? And, proud Sufferer, who art thou?

PROMETHEUS

Tremendous Image! as thou art must be
He whom thou shadowest forth. I am his foe
The Titan. Speak the words which I would hear,
Although no thought inform thine empty voice.

THE EARTH

50 Listen! and though your echoes must be mute,
Grey mountains and old woods and haunted springs,
Prophetic caves and isle-surrounding streams
Rejoice to hear what yet ye cannot speak.

PHANTASM

A spirit seizes me, and speaks within:
55 It tears me as fire tears a thunder-cloud!

PANTHEA

See how he lifts his mighty looks, the Heaven
Darkens above.

IONE

He speaks! O shelter me—

7. Shelley uses the comma in the middle of lines like these to emphasize the internal rhymes.

PROMETHEUS

I see the curse on gestures proud and cold,
And looks of firm defiance, and calm hate,
260   And such despair as mocks itself with smiles,
Written as on a scroll . . . yet speak—O speak!

PHANTASM

Fiend, I defy thee! with a calm, fixed mind,
All that thou canst inflict I bid thee do;
Foul Tyrant both of Gods and Humankind,
265   One only being shalt thou not subdue.
Rain then thy plagues upon me here,
Ghastly disease and frenzying fear;
And let alternate frost and fire
Eat into me, and be thine ire
270   Lightning and cutting hail and legioned forms
Of furies, driving by upon the wounding storms.

Aye, do thy worst. Thou art Omnipotent.
O'er all things but thyself I gave thee power,
And my own will. Be thy swift mischiefs sent
275   To blast mankind, from yon etherial tower.
Let thy malignant spirit move
Its darkness over those I love:
On me and mine I imprecate°   *call down*
The utmost torture of thy hate
280   And thus devote to sleepless agony
This undeclining head while thou must reign on high.

But thou who art the God and Lord—O thou
Who fillest with thy soul this world of woe,
To whom all things of Earth and Heaven do bow
285   In fear and worship—all-prevailing foe!
I curse thee! let a sufferer's curse
Clasp thee, his torturer, like remorse,
Till thine Infinity shall be
A robe of envenomed agony;⁸
290   And thine Omnipotence a crown of pain
To cling like burning gold round thy dissolving brain.

Heap on thy soul by virtue of this Curse
Ill deeds, then be thou damned, beholding good,
Both infinite as is the Universe,
295   And thou, and thy self-torturing solitude.
An awful Image of calm power
Though now thou sittest, let the hour
Come, when thou must appear to be

8. Like the poisoned shirt of the centaur Nessus, which consumed Hercules' flesh when he put it on. The next two lines allude to the mock crowning of Christ with a crown of thorns.

That which thou art internally.
And after many a false and fruitless crime
Scorn track thy lagging fall through boundless space and time.
[*The Phantasm vanishes.*]
PROMETHEUS   Were these my words, O Parent?
THE EARTH   They were thine.
PROMETHEUS   It doth repent me: words are quick and vain;
Grief for awhile is blind, and so was mine.
I wish no living thing to suffer pain.

THE EARTH

Misery, O misery to me,
That Jove at length should vanquish thee.
Wail, howl aloud, Land and Sea,
The Earth's rent heart shall answer ye.
Howl, Spirits of the living and the dead,
Your refuge, your defence lies fallen and vanquished.

FIRST ECHO

Lies fallen and vanquished?

SECOND ECHO

Fallen and vanquished!

IONE

Fear not—'tis but some passing spasm,
The Titan is unvanquished still.
But see, where through the azure chasm
Of yon forked and snowy hill,
Trampling the slant winds on high
With golden-sandalled feet, that glow
Under plumes of purple dye
Like rose-ensanguined[9] ivory,
A Shape comes now,
Stretching on high from his right hand
A serpent-cinctured[1] wand.

PANTHEA

'Tis Jove's world-wandering Herald, Mercury.

IONE

And who are those with hydra tresses[2]
And iron wings that climb the wind,
Whom the frowning God represses
Like vapours steaming up behind,
Clanging loud, an endless crowd—

---

9. Stained blood color.
1. Mercury carries a caduceus, a staff encircled by two snakes with their heads facing each other, a symbol of peace befitting the role of Hermes/Mer-
cury as the messenger of the Gods.
2. Locks of hair resembling the many-headed snake, the hydra.

PANTHEA

These are Jove's tempest-walking hounds,³
Whom he gluts with groans and blood,
When charioted on sulphurous cloud
He bursts Heaven's bounds.

IONE

335   Are they now led, from the thin dead
On new pangs to be fed?

PANTHEA

The Titan looks as ever, firm, not proud.

FIRST FURY

Ha! I scent life!

SECOND FURY

Let me but look into his eyes!

THIRD FURY

The hope of torturing him smells like a heap
340   Of corpses to a death-bird after battle!

FIRST FURY

Darest thou delay, O Herald! take cheer, Hounds
Of Hell—what if the Son of Maia° soon   *Mercury*
Should make us food and sport? Who can please long
The Omnipotent?

MERCURY

Back to your towers of iron
345   And gnash, beside the streams of fire, and wail
Your foodless teeth! . . . Geryon, arise! and Gorgon,
Chimæra,⁴ and thou Sphinx, subtlest of fiends,
Who ministered to Thebes Heaven's poisoned wine,
Unnatural love and more unnatural hate:⁵
These shall perform your task.

FIRST FURY

350   O mercy! mercy!
We die with our desire—drive us not back!

3. I.e., the Furies, avengers of crimes committed against the gods.
4. Geryon, a monster with three heads and three bodies; the Gorgons, three mythical personages, with snakes for hair, who turned beholders into stone; the Chimera, a fabled fire-breathing monster of Greek mythology with three heads (lion, goat, and dragon), the body of a lion and a goat,

and a dragon's tail.
5. The Sphinx, a monster with the body of a lion, wings, and the face and breasts of a woman, besieged Thebes by devouring those who could not answer her riddle. Oedipus solved the riddle (causing the Sphinx to kill herself), only to marry his mother ("unnatural love"), leading to the tragic events depicted in the Greek Theban plays.

MERCURY

Crouch then in silence.—
            Awful° Sufferer!   *awe-inspiring*
To thee unwilling, most unwillingly
I come, by the great Father's will driven down
To execute a doom of new revenge.
Alas! I pity thee, and hate myself
That I can do no more.—Aye from thy sight
Returning, for a season, Heaven seems Hell,
So thy worn form pursues me night and day,
Smiling reproach. Wise art thou, firm and good,
But vainly wouldst stand forth alone in strife
Against the Omnipotent, as yon clear lamps
That measure and divide the weary years
From which there is no refuge, long have taught
And long must teach.—Even now thy Torturer arms
With the strange might of unimagined pains
The powers who scheme slow agonies in Hell,
And my commission is, to lead them here,
Or what more subtle,° foul or savage fiends   *artful*
People° the abyss, and leave them to their task.   *populate*
Be it not so! . . . There is a secret known
To thee and to none else of living things
Which may transfer the sceptre of wide Heaven,
The fear of which perplexes the Supreme . . .
Clothe it in words, and bid it clasp his throne
In intercession; bend thy soul in prayer
And like a suppliant in some gorgeous fane°   *temple*
Let the will kneel within thy haughty heart;
For benefits and meek submission tame
The fiercest and the mightiest.

PROMETHEUS
            Evil minds
Change good to their own nature. I gave all
He has; and in return he chains me here
Years, ages, night and day: whether the Sun
Split my parched skin, or in the moony night
The chrystal-winged snow cling round my hair—
Whilst my beloved race is trampled down
By his thought-executing ministers.
Such is the tyrant's recompense—'tis just:
He who is evil can receive no good;
And for a world bestowed, or a friend lost,
He can feel hate, fear, shame—not gratitude:
He but requites me for his own misdeed.
Kindness to such is keen reproach, which breaks
With bitter stings the light sleep of Revenge.
Submission, thou dost know, I cannot try:
For what submission but that fatal word,
The death-seal of mankind's captivity—

Like the Sicilian's hair-suspended sword[6]
Which trembles o'er his crown—would he accept,
400   Or could I yield?—which yet I will not yield.
Let others flatter Crime where it sits throned
In brief Omnipotence; secure are they:
For Justice when triumphant will weep down
Pity not punishment on her own wrongs,
405   Too much avenged by those who err. I wait,
Enduring thus the retributive hour[7]
Which since we spake is even nearer now.—
But hark, the hell-hounds clamour. Fear delay!
Behold! Heaven lowers° under thy Father's frown.   *cowers*

MERCURY

410   O that we might be spared—I to inflict
And thou to suffer! Once more answer me:
Thou knowest not the period[8] of Jove's power?

PROMETHEUS

I know but this, that it must come.

MERCURY

Alas!
Thou canst not count thy years to come of pain?

PROMETHEUS

415   They last while Jove must reign, nor more nor less
Do I desire or fear.

MERCURY

Yet pause, and plunge
Into Eternity, where recorded time,
Even all that we imagine, age on age,
Seems but a point, and the reluctant mind
420   Flags wearily in its unending flight
Till it sink, dizzy, blind, lost, shelterless;
Perchance it has not numbered the slow years
Which thou must spend in torture, unreprieved.

PROMETHEUS

Perchance no thought can count them—yet they pass.

MERCURY

425   If thou might'st dwell among the Gods the while
Lapped in voluptuous joy?—

---

6. I.e., the sword of Damocles, suspended by a   7. Time of retribution.
thread above the throne of Damocles, ruler of Syr-   8. The end or conclusion.
acuse in Sicily.

PROMETHEUS
I would not quit
This bleak ravine, these unrepentant pains.

MERCURY
Alas! I wonder at, yet pity thee.

PROMETHEUS
Pity the self-despising slaves of Heaven,
430 Not me, within whose mind sits peace serene
As light in the sun, throned. . . . How vain is talk!
Call up the fiends.

IONE
O sister, look! White fire
Has cloven to the roots yon huge snow-loaded Cedar;
How fearfully God's thunder howls behind!

MERCURY
435 I must obey his words and thine—alas!
Most heavily remorse hangs at my heart!

PANTHEA
See where the child of Heaven with winged feet
Runs down the slanted sunlight of the dawn.

IONE
Dear sister, close thy plumes over thine eyes
440 Lest thou behold and die—they come, they come
Blackening the birth of day with countless wings,
And hollow underneath, like death.

FIRST FURY
Prometheus!

SECOND FURY
Immortal Titan!

THIRD FURY
Champion of Heaven's slaves!

PROMETHEUS
He whom some dreadful voice invokes is here,
445 Prometheus, the chained Titan.—Horrible forms,
What and who are ye? Never yet there came
Phantasms° so foul through monster-teeming Hell   *apparitions*
From the all-miscreative brain of Jove;
Whilst I behold such execrable shapes,
450 Methinks I grow like what I contemplate
And laugh and stare in loathsome sympathy.

FIRST FURY

We are the ministers of pain and fear
And disappointment and mistrust and hate
And clinging° crime; and as lean dogs pursue   *clasping*
455   Through wood and lake some struck and sobbing fawn,
We track all things that weep and bleed and live
When the great King betrays them to our will.

PROMETHEUS

O many fearful natures in one name!
I know ye, and these lakes and echoes know
460   The darkness and the clangour of your wings.
But why more hideous than your loathed selves
Gather ye up in legions from the deep?

SECOND FURY

We knew not that—Sisters, rejoice, rejoice!

PROMETHEUS

Can aught exult in its deformity?

SECOND FURY

465   The beauty of delight makes lovers glad
Gazing on one another—so are we.
As from the rose which the pale priestess kneels
To gather for her festal° crown of flowers   *festive*
The aerial crimson falls, flushing her cheek—
470   So from our victim's destined agony
The shade which is our form invests us round,
Else we are shapeless as our Mother Night.

PROMETHEUS

I laugh° your power and his who sent you here   *mock*
To lowest scorn.—Pour forth the cup of pain.

FIRST FURY

475   Thou thinkest we will rend thee bone from bone?
And nerve from nerve, working like fire within?

PROMETHEUS

Pain is my element as hate is thine;
Ye rend me now: I care not.

SECOND FURY

                              Dost imagine
We will but laugh into thy lidless eyes?

PROMETHEUS

480   I weigh° not what ye do, but what ye suffer   *consider*
Being evil. Cruel was the Power which called
You, or aught else so wretched, into light.

THIRD FURY

Thou think'st we will live through thee, one by one,
Like animal life, and though we can obscure not
The soul which burns within, that we will dwell
Beside it, like a vain loud multitude
Vexing the self-content of wisest men—
That we will be dread thought beneath thy brain
And foul desire round thine astonished heart
And blood within thy labyrinthine veins
Crawling like agony.

PROMETHEUS

Why, ye are thus now;
Yet am I king over myself, and rule
The torturing and conflicting throngs within
As Jove rules you when Hell grows mutinous.

CHORUS OF FURIES

From the ends of the Earth, from the ends of the Earth,
Where the night has its grave and the morning its birth,
    Come, Come, Come!
O yet who shake hills with the scream of your mirth
When cities sink howling in ruin, and ye
Who with wingless footsteps trample the Sea,
And close upon Shipwreck and Famine's track
Sit chattering with joy on the foodless wrack;
    Come, Come, Come!
    Leave the bed, low, cold and red,
    Strewed beneath a nation dead;
    Leave the hatred—as in ashes
        Fire is left for future burning,—
    It will burst in bloodier flashes
        When ye stir it, soon returning;
    Leave the self-contempt implanted
    In young spirits sense-enchanted,
        Misery's yet unkindled fuel;
    Leave Hell's secrets half-unchanted
        To the maniac dreamer: cruel
    More than ye can be with hate,
        Is he with fear.
        Come, Come, Come!
We are steaming up from Hell's wide gate
And we burthen the blasts of the atmosphere,
But vainly we toil till ye come here.

IONE

Sister, I hear the thunder of new wings.

PANTHEA

These solid mountains quiver with the sound
Even as the tremulous air:—their shadows make
The space within my plumes more black than night.

FIRST FURY

525   Your call was as a winged car
Driven on whirlwinds fast and far;
It rapt° us from red gulphs of war—   *carried*

SECOND FURY

From wide cities, famine-wasted—

THIRD FURY

Groans half heard, and blood untasted—

FOURTH FURY

530   Kingly conclaves, stern and cold,
Where blood with gold is bought and sold—

FIFTH FURY

From the furnace, white and hot,
In which—

A FURY

Speak not—whisper not!
I know all that ye would tell,
535   But to speak might break the spell
Which must bend the Invincible,
    The stern of thought;
He yet defies the deepest power of Hell.

A FURY

Tear the veil!—

ANOTHER FURY

It is torn!

CHORUS

The pale stars of the morn
540   Shine on a misery dire to be borne.
Dost thou faint, mighty Titan? We laugh thee to scorn.
Dost thou boast the clear knowledge thou waken'dst for man?
Then was kindled within him a thirst which outran
Those perishing waters: a thirst of fierce fever,
545   Hope, love, doubt, desire—which consume him forever.
One° came forth, of gentle worth,   *Christ*
Smiling on the sanguine earth;
His words outlived him, like swift poison
    Withering up truth, peace and pity.
550   Look! where round the wide horizon
    Many a million-peopled city
Vomits smoke in the bright air.—
Hark that outcry of despair!
'Tis his mild and gentle ghost
555   Wailing for the faith he kindled.

Look again,—the flames almost
  To a glow-worm's lamp have dwindled:
The survivors round the embers
  Gather in dread.
      Joy, Joy, Joy!
Past ages crowd on thee, but each one remembers,
And the future is dark, and the present is spread
Like a pillow of thorns for thy slumberless head.

SEMICHORUS I

Drops of bloody agony flow
From his white and quivering brow.
Grant a little respite now—
See! a disenchanted Nation⁹
Springs like day from desolation;
To truth its state, is dedicate,
And Freedom leads it forth, her mate;
A legioned band of linked brothers
Whom Love calls children—

SEMICHORUS II

    'Tis another's—
See how kindred murder kin!
'Tis the vintage-time for Death and Sin:
Blood, like new wine, bubbles within
    Till Despair smothers
The struggling World—which slaves and tyrants win.
        [*All the* Furies *vanish, except one.*]

IONE

Hark, sister! what a low yet dreadful groan
Quite unsuppressed is tearing up the heart
Of the good Titan—as storms tear the deep
And beasts hear the Sea moan in inland caves.
Darest thou observe how the fiends torture him?

PANTHEA

Alas, I looked forth twice, but will no more.

IONE

What didst thou see?

PANTHEA

    A woeful sight—a youth°   Christ
With patient looks nailed to a crucifix.

IONE

What next?

9. Usually identified as France, breaking the spell of monarchy at the time of the Revolution.

PANTHEA
The Heaven around, the Earth below
Was peopled with thick shapes of human death,
All horrible, and wrought by human hands,
And some appeared the work of human hearts,
590   For men were slowly killed by frowns and smiles:
And other sights too foul to speak and live
Were wandering by. Let us not tempt worse fear
By looking forth—those groans are grief enough.

FURY   Behold, an emblem—those who do endure
595   Deep wrongs for man, and scorn and chains, but heap
Thousand-fold torment on themselves and him.
PROMETHEUS   Remit the anguish of that lighted stare—
Close those wan lips—let that thorn-wounded brow
Stream not with blood—it mingles with thy tears
600   Fix, fix those tortured orbs in peace and death
So thy sick throes shake not that crucifix,
So those pale fingers play not with thy gore.—
O horrible! Thy name I will not speak,
It hath become a curse.[1] I see, I see
605   The wise, the mild, the lofty and the just,
Whom thy slaves hate for being like to thee,
Some hunted by foul lies from their heart's home,
An early-chosen, late-lamented home,
As hooded ounces[2] cling to the driven hind,°   *doe*
610   Some linked to corpses in unwholesome cells:
Some—hear I not the multitude laugh loud?—
Impaled in lingering fire: and mighty realms
Float by my feet like sea-uprooted isles
Whose sons are kneaded down in common blood
615   By the red light of their own burning homes.
FURY   Blood thou canst see, and fire; and canst hear groans;
Worse things, unheard, unseen, remain behind.
PROMETHEUS   Worse?
FURY   In each human heart terror survives
The ravin it has gorged:[3] the loftiest fear
620   All that they would disdain to think were true:
Hypocrisy and custom make their minds
The fanes° of many a worship, now outworn.   *temples*
They dare not devise good for man's estate
And yet they know not that they do not dare.
625   The good want power, but to weep barren tears.[4]
The powerful goodness want: worse need for them.
The wise want love, and those who love want wisdom;
And all best things are thus confused to ill.

---

1. I.e., the name "Christ" has become, literally, a curse word, and metaphorically, a curse to humankind, in that His religion of love is used to justify religious wars and bloody oppression.
2. Cheetahs, or leopards, used in hunting (hoods were sometimes placed over their eyes to make them easier to control).
3. The prey that it has greedily devoured.
4. I.e., the good lack ("want") power except to weep "barren tears."

Many are strong and rich,—and would be just,—
But live among their suffering fellow men
As if none felt: they know not what they do.[5]
PROMETHEUS   Thy words are like a cloud of winged snakes
And yet, I pity those they torture not.
FURY   Thou pitiest them? I speak no more!   [*Vanishes.*]
PROMETHEUS   Ah woe!
Ah woe! Alas! pain, pain ever, forever!
I close my tearless eyes, but see more clear
Thy works within my woe-illumed mind,
Thou subtle Tyrant![6] . . . Peace is in the grave—
The grave hides all things beautiful and good—
I am a God and cannot find it there,
Nor would I seek it: for, though dread revenge,
This is defeat, fierce King, not victory.
The sights with which thou torturest gird my soul
With new endurance, till the hour arrives
When they shall be no types of things which are.
PANTHEA   Alas! what sawest thou?
PROMETHEUS   There are two woes:
To speak and to behold; thou spare me one.[7]
Names are there, Nature's sacred watchwords—they
Were borne aloft in bright emblazonry.[8]
The nations thronged around, and cried aloud
As with one voice, "Truth, liberty and love!"
Suddenly fierce confusion fell from Heaven
Among them—there was strife, deceit and fear;
Tyrants rushed in, and did divide the spoil.
This was the shadow of the truth I saw.
THE EARTH   I felt thy torture, Son, with such mixed joy
As pain and Virtue give.—To cheer thy state
I bid ascend those subtle and fair spirits
Whose homes are the dim caves of human thought
And who inhabit, as birds wing the wind,
Its world-surrounding ether;[9] they behold
Beyond that twilight realm, as in a glass,°   *mirror*
The future—may they speak comfort to thee!

PANTHEA

Look, Sister, where a troop of spirits gather
Like flocks of clouds in spring's delightful weather,
Thronging in the blue air!

IONE

And see! more come
Like fountain-vapours when the winds are dumb,

5. The Fury ironically echoes Christ's plea for forgiveness of his crucifiers: "Father, forgive them: for they know not what they do" (Luke 23.34).
6. Jupiter (also addressed as "fierce King," line 642).

7. I.e., spare me the woe of speaking (about what I have beheld).
8. As in a brilliant display of banners.
9. A medium, weightless and infinitely elastic, once supposed to permeate the universe.

That climb up the ravine in scattered lines.
And hark! is it the music of the pines?
670   Is it the lake? is it the waterfall?

PANTHEA

'Tis something sadder, sweeter far than all.

CHORUS OF SPIRITS[1]

From unremembered ages we
Gentle guides and guardians be
Of Heaven-oppressed mortality—
675   And we breathe, and sicken not,
The atmosphere of human thought:
Be it dim and dank and grey
Like a storm-extinguished day
Travelled o'er by dying gleams;
680   Be it bright as all between
Cloudless skies and windless streams,
    Silent, liquid and serene—
As the birds within the wind,
As the fish within the wave,
685   As the thoughts of man's own mind
    Float through all above the grave,
We make there, our liquid lair,
Voyaging cloudlike and unpent°   unconfined
Through the boundless element—
690   Thence we bear the prophecy
Which begins and ends in thee!

IONE

More yet come, one by one: the air around them
Looks radiant as the air around a star.

FIRST SPIRIT

On a battle-trumpet's blast
695   I fled hither, fast, fast, fast,
Mid the darkness upward cast—
From the dust of creeds outworn,
From the tyrant's banner torn,
Gathering round me, onward borne,
700   There was mingled many a cry—
Freedom! Hope! Death! Victory!
Till they faded through the sky
And one sound—above, around,
One sound beneath, around, above,
705   Was moving; 'twas the soul of love;
'Twas the hope, the prophecy,
Which begins and ends in thee.

1. Identified by Earth at lines 658–63.

SECOND SPIRIT

A rainbow's arch stood on the sea,
Which rocked beneath, immoveably;
And the triumphant Storm did flee,
Like a conqueror swift and proud
Between, with many a captive cloud
A shapeless, dark and rapid crowd,
Each by lightning riven in half.—
I heard the thunder hoarsely laugh.—
Mighty fleets were strewn like chaff
And spread beneath, a hell of death
O'er the white waters. I alit
On a great ship lightning-split
And speeded hither on the sigh
Of one who gave an enemy
His plank—then plunged aside to die.

THIRD SPIRIT

I sate beside a sage's bed
And the lamp was burning red
Near the book where he had fed,
When a Dream with plumes of flame
To his pillow hovering came,
And I knew it was the same
Which had kindled long ago
Pity, eloquence and woe;
And the world awhile below
Wore the shade its lustre made.
It has borne me here as fleet
As Desire's lightning feet:
I must ride it back ere morrow,
Or the sage will wake in sorrow.

FOURTH SPIRIT

On a Poet's lips I slept
Dreaming like a love-adept
In the sound his breathing kept;
Nor seeks nor finds he mortal blisses
But feeds on the aerial kisses
Of shapes that haunt thought's wildernesses.
He will watch from dawn to gloom
The lake-reflected sun illume
The yellow bees i' the ivy-bloom
Nor heed nor see, what things they be;
But from these create he can
Forms more real than living man,
Nurslings° of immortality!—   *children*
One of these awakened me
And I sped to succour thee.

IONE

Behold'st thou not two shapes from the East and West
Come, as two doves to one beloved nest,
Twin nurslings of the all-sustaining air,
755 On swift still wings glide down the atmosphere?
And hark! their sweet, sad voices! 'tis despair
Mingled with love, and then dissolved in sound.—

PANTHEA

Canst thou speak, sister? all my words are drowned.

IONE

Their beauty gives me voice. See how they float
760 On their sustaining wings of skiey grain,
Orange and azure, deepening into gold:
Their soft smiles light the air like a star's fire.

CHORUS OF SPIRITS

Hast thou beheld the form of Love?

FIFTH SPIRIT

As over wide dominions
I sped, like some swift cloud that wings the wide air's wildernesses.
765 That planet-crested Shape swept by on lightning-braided
 pinions,°   *wings*
Scattering the liquid joy of life from his ambrosial° tresses: *heavenly*
His footsteps paved the world with light—but as I past 'twas fading
And hollow Ruin yawned behind. Great Sages bound in madness
And headless patriots and pale youths who perished unupbraiding,[2]
770 Gleamed in the Night I wandered o'er—till thou, O King of sadness,
Turned by thy smile the worst I saw to recollected gladness.

SIXTH SPIRIT

Ah, sister! Desolation is a delicate thing:
It walks not on the Earth, it floats not on the air,
But treads with silent footstep, and fans with silent wing
775 The tender hopes which in their hearts the best and gentlest bear,
Who, soothed to false repose by the fanning plumes above
And the music-stirring motion of its soft and busy feet,
Dreams visions of aerial joy, and call the monster, Love,
And wake, and find the shadow Pain—as he whom now we greet.

CHORUS

780 Though Ruin now Love's shadow be,
 Following him destroyingly
  On Death's white and winged steed,
 Which the fleetest cannot flee—
  Trampling down both flower and weed,
785 Man and beast and foul and fair,

2. Without uttering reproaches.

Like a tempest through the air;
Thou shalt quell this Horseman grim,
Woundless though in heart or limb.—

PROMETHEUS

Spirits! how know ye this shall be?

CHORUS

90 In the atmosphere we breathe—
As buds grow red when snow-storms flee
From spring gathering up beneath,
Whose mild winds shake, the elder brake°   thicket
And the wandering herdsmen know
95 That the white-thorn soon will blow—
Wisdom, Justice, Love and Peace,
When they struggle to increase,
Are to us as soft winds be
To shepherd-boys—the prophecy
100 Which begins and ends in thee.

IONE

Where are the Spirits fled?

PANTHEA

Only a sense
Remains of them, like the Omnipotence
Of music when the inspired voice and lute
Languish, ere yet the responses are mute
105 Which through the deep and labyrinthine soul,
Like echoes through long caverns, wind and roll.

PROMETHEUS

How fair these air-born shapes! and yet I feel
Most vain all hope but love, and thou art far,
Asia! who when my being overflowed
110 Wert like a golden chalice to bright wine
Which else had sunk into the thirsty dust.
All things are still—alas! how heavily
This quiet morning weighs upon my heart;
Though I should dream, I could even sleep with grief
115 If slumber were denied not . . . I would fain
Be what it is my destiny to be,
The saviour and the strength of suffering man,
Or sink into the original gulph of things. . . .
There is no agony and no solace left;
120 Earth can console, Heaven can torment no more.

PANTHEA

Hast thou forgotten one who watches thee
The cold dark night, and never sleeps but when
The shadow of thy spirit falls on her?

PROMETHEUS
I said all hope was vain but love—thou lovest . . .

PANTHEA
825　Deeply in truth—but the Eastern star looks white,
And Asia waits in that far Indian vale,
The scene of her sad exile—rugged once
And desolate and frozen like this ravine;
But now invested with fair flowers and herbs
830　And haunted by sweet airs and sounds, which flow
Among the woods and waters, from the ether°　　　　　　　*purer air*
Of her transforming presence—which would fade
If it were mingled not with thine.—Farewell!

From *Act 2*

SCENE 4—*The Cave of* DEMOGORGON. ASIA *and* PANTHEA.[3]

PANTHEA　What veiled form sits on that ebon throne?
ASIA　The veil has fallen! . . .
PANTHEA　　　　　　　　　　　　I see a mighty Darkness
Filling the seat of power; and rays of gloom
Dart round, as light from the meridian Sun,
5　Ungazed upon and shapeless—neither limb
Nor form—nor outline;[4] yet we feel it is
A living Spirit.
DEMOGORGON　Ask what thou wouldst know.
ASIA　What canst thou tell?
DEMOGORGON　　　　　　　　All things thou dar'st demand.
ASIA　Who made the living world?
DEMOGORGON　　　　　　　　　　　　God.
ASIA　　　　　　　　　　　　　　　　Who made all
10　That it contains—thought, passion, reason, will,
Imagination?
DEMOGORGON　God, Almighty God.
ASIA　Who made that sense[5] which, when the winds of Spring
In rarest visitation, or the voice
Of one beloved heard in youth alone,
15　Fills the faint eyes with falling tears, which dim
The radiant looks of unbewailing flowers,
And leaves this peopled earth a solitude
When it returns no more?

---

3. Act 2 has opened with Asia—the feminine principle and embodiment of love, who was separated from Prometheus at the moment of his fall into divisive hate—in a lovely Indian valley at the first hour of the dawn of the spring season of redemption. Asia and her sister Panthea have been led, by a sweet and irresistible compulsion, first to the portal and then down into the depths of the cave of Demogorgon—the central enigma of Shelley's poem.
As the father of all that exists, Demogorgon may represent the ultimate reason for the way things

are. As such, Shelley appears to argue, Demogorgon must be a mystery inaccessible to knowledge and must be ignorant of the principle controlling him. In this scene Demogorgon can give only riddling answers to Asia's questions about the "why" of creation, good, and evil.
4. Echoing Milton's description of Death, *Paradise Lost* 2.666–73.
5. Presumably the sense by which one is aware of the "unseen Power" that Shelley calls "Intellectual Beauty" (see "Hymn to Intellectual Beauty," stanza 2, p. 766).

DEMOGORGON   Merciful God.

ASIA   And who made terror, madness, crime, remorse,
Which from the links of the great chain of things
To every thought within the mind of man
Sway and drag heavily—and each one reels
Under the load towards the pit of death;
Abandoned hope, and love that turns to hate;
And self-contempt, bitterer to drink than blood;
Pain whose unheeded and familiar speech
Is howling and keen shrieks, day after day;
And Hell, or the sharp fear of Hell?[6]

DEMOGORGON   He reigns.

ASIA   Utter his name—a world pining in pain
Asks but his name; curses shall drag him down.

DEMOGORGON   He reigns.

ASIA   I feel, I know it—who?

DEMOGORGON   He reigns.

ASIA   Who reigns? There was the Heaven and Earth at first
And Light and Love;—then Saturn,[7] from whose throne
Time fell, an envious shadow; such the state
Of the earth's primal spirits beneath his sway
As the calm joy of flowers and living leaves
Before the wind or sun has withered them
And semivital worms; but he refused
The birthright of their being, knowledge, power,
The skill which wields the elements, the thought
Which pierces this dim Universe like light,
Self-empire and the majesty of love,
For thirst of which they fainted. Then Prometheus
Gave wisdom, which is strength, to Jupiter
And with this law alone: "Let man be free,"
Clothed him with the dominion of wide Heaven.
To know nor faith nor love nor law, to be
Omnipotent but friendless, is to reign;
And Jove now reigned; for on the race of man
First famine, and then toil, and then disease,
Strife, wounds, and ghastly death unseen before,
Fell; and the unseasonable seasons drove,
With alternating shafts of frost and fire,
Their shelterless, pale tribes to mountain caves;
And in their desart° hearts fierce wants he sent   *empty*
And mad disquietudes, and shadows idle
Of unreal good, which levied mutual war,
So ruining the lair wherein they raged.
Prometheus saw, and waked the legioned hopes
Which sleep within folded Elysian flowers,
Nepenthe, Moly, Amaranth,[8] fadeless blooms;

6. The nouns "hope," "love," etc. (lines 24–28) are all objects of the verb "made" (line 19).
7. In Greek myth Saturn's reign was the golden age. In Shelley's version Saturn refused to grant mortals knowledge and science, so that it was an age of ignorant innocence in which the deepest human needs remained unfulfilled.
8. These are medicinal drugs and flowers in Greek myth. Asia is describing (lines 59–97) the various sciences and arts given to humans by Prometheus, the culture bringer.

That they might hide with thin and rainbow wings
The shape of Death; and Love he sent to bind
The disunited tendrils of that vine
65   Which bears the wine of life, the human heart;
And he tamed fire which, like some beast of prey,
Most terrible, but lovely, played beneath
The frown of man, and tortured to his will
Iron and gold, the slaves and signs of power,
70   And gems and poisons, and all subtlest forms,
Hidden beneath the mountains and the waves.
He gave man speech, and speech created thought,
Which is the measure of the Universe;
And Science struck the thrones of Earth and Heaven
75   Which shook, but fell not; and the harmonious mind
Poured itself forth in all-prophetic song,
And music lifted up the listening spirit
Until it walked, exempt from mortal care,
Godlike, o'er the clear billows of sweet sound;
80   And human hands first mimicked and then mocked[9]
With moulded limbs more lovely than its own
The human form, till marble grew divine,
And mothers, gazing, drank the love men see
Reflected in their race, behold, and perish.[1]—
85   He told the hidden power of herbs and springs,
And Disease drank and slept—Death grew like sleep.—
He taught the implicated° orbits woven   *intertwined*
Of the wide-wandering stars, and how the Sun
Changes his lair, and by what secret spell
90   The pale moon is transformed, when her broad eye
Gazes not on the interlunar[2] sea;
He taught to rule, as life directs the limbs,
The tempest-winged chariots of the Ocean,
And the Celt knew the Indian.[3] Cities then
95   Were built, and through their snow-like columns flowed
The warm winds, and the azure æther shone,
And the blue sea and shadowy hills were seen . . .
Such the alleviations of his state
Prometheus gave to man—for which he hangs
100   Withering in destined pain—but who rains down
Evil, the immedicable plague, which while
Man looks on his creation like a God
And sees that it is glorious, drives him on,
The wreck of his own will, the scorn of Earth,
105   The outcast, the abandoned, the alone?—
Not Jove: while yet his frown shook Heaven, aye when
His adversary from adamantine° chains   *unbreakable*

9. I.e., sculptors first merely reproduced but later improved on and heightened the beauty of the human form, so that the original was inferior to, and hence "mocked" by, the copy.
1. Expectant mothers looked at the beautiful statues so that their children might, by prenatal influence, be born with the beauty that makes beholders die of love.
2. The phase between old and new moons, when the moon is invisible.
3. The reference is to the ships in which the Celtic (here, non-Greco-Roman) races of Europe were able to sail to India.

Cursed him, he trembled like a slave. Declare
Who is his master? Is he too a slave?
10 DEMOGORGON   All spirits are enslaved which serve things evil:
Thou knowest if Jupiter be such or no.
ASIA   Whom calledst thou God?
DEMOGORGON   I spoke but as ye speak—
For Jove is the supreme of living things.
ASIA   Who is the master of the slave?
DEMOGORGON   —If the Abysm
15 Could vomit forth its secrets:—but a voice
Is wanting, the deep truth is imageless;
For what would it avail to bid thee gaze
On the revolving world? what to bid speak
Fate, Time, Occasion, Chance and Change? To these
20 All things are subject but eternal Love.
ASIA   So much I asked before, and my heart gave
The response thou hast given; and of such truths
Each to itself must be the oracle.—
One more demand . . . and do thou answer me
25 As my own soul would answer, did it know
That which I ask.—Prometheus shall arise
Henceforth the Sun of this rejoicing world:
When shall the destined hour arrive?
DEMOGORGON   Behold!⁴
ASIA   The rocks are cloven, and through the purple night
30 I see Cars drawn by rainbow-winged steeds
Which trample the dim winds—in each there stands
A wild-eyed charioteer, urging their flight.
Some look behind, as fiends pursued them there
And yet I see no shapes but the keen stars:
35 Others with burning eyes lean forth, and drink
With eager lips the wind of their own speed,
As if the thing they loved fled on before,
And now—even now they clasped it; their bright locks
Stream like a comet's flashing hair: they all
Sweep onward.—
40 DEMOGORGON   These are the immortal Hours
Of whom thou didst demand.—One waits for thee.
ASIA   A Spirit with a dreadful countenance
Checks its dark chariot by the craggy gulph.
Unlike thy brethren, ghastly charioteer,
45 What art thou? whither wouldst thou bear me? Speak!
SPIRIT   I am the shadow of a destiny
More dread than is my aspect—ere yon planet
Has set, the Darkness which ascends with me
Shall wrap in lasting night Heaven's kingless throne.
ASIA   What meanest thou?
50 PANTHEA   That terrible shadow⁵ floats
Up from its throne, as may the lurid° smoke   red-glaring

---

4. Demogorgon's answer is a gesture: he points to   5. Demogorgon (the "Darkness" of line 148), who
the approaching chariots ("Cars").   is ascending (lines 150–55) to dethrone Jupiter.

Of earthquake-ruined cities o'er the sea.—
Lo! it ascends the Car . . . the coursers fly
Terrified; watch its path among the stars
Blackening the night!
155 ASIA   Thus I am answered—strange!
PANTHEA   See, near the verge° another chariot stays;   *horizon*
An ivory shell inlaid with crimson fire
Which comes and goes within its sculptured rim
Of delicate strange tracery—the young Spirit
160 That guides it, has the dovelike eyes of hope.
How its soft smiles attract the soul!—as light
Lures winged insects⁶ through the lampless air.

SPIRIT
My coursers are fed with the lightning,
They drink of the whirlwind's stream
165 And when the red morning is brightning
They bathe in the fresh sunbeam;
They have strength for their swiftness, I deem:
Then ascend with me, daughter of Ocean.

I desire—and their speed makes night kindle;
170 I fear—they outstrip the Typhoon;
Ere the cloud piled on Atlas⁷ can dwindle
We encircle the earth and the moon:
We shall rest from long labours at noon:
Then ascend with me, daughter of Ocean.

SCENE 5—*The Car pauses within a Cloud on the Top of a snowy Mountain.* ASIA, PANTHEA, *and the* SPIRIT OF THE HOUR.

SPIRIT
On the brink of the night and the morning
My coursers are wont to respire,⁸
But the Earth has just whispered a warning
That their flight must be swifter than fire:
5 They shall drink the hot speed of desire!

ASIA   Thou breathest on their nostrils—but my breath
Would give them swifter speed.
SPIRIT   Alas, it could not.
PANTHEA   O Spirit! pause and tell whence is the light
Which fills the cloud? the sun is yet unrisen.
10 SPIRIT   The sun will rise not until noon.⁹—Apollo
Is held in Heaven by wonder—and the light
Which fills this vapour, as the aerial hue
Of fountain-gazing roses fills the water,

6. The ancient image of the soul, or *psyche*, was a
moth. The chariot described here will carry Asia to
a reunion with Prometheus.
7. A mountain in North Africa that the Greeks

regarded as so high that it supported the heavens.
8. Catch their breath.
9. The time of the reunion of Prometheus and
Asia.

Flows from thy mighty sister.
PANTHEA   Yes, I feel . . .
5   ASIA   What is it with thee, sister? Thou art pale.
PANTHEA   How thou art changed! I dare not look on thee;
I feel, but see thee not. I scarce endure
The radiance of thy beauty.[1] Some good change
Is working in the elements which suffer
10 Thy presence thus unveiled.—The Nereids tell
That on the day when the clear hyaline°   *glassy sea*
Was cloven at thy uprise, and thou didst stand
Within a veined shell,[2] which floated on
Over the calm floor of the chrystal sea,
15 Among the Ægean isles, and by the shores
Which bear thy name, love, like the atmosphere
Of the sun's fire filling the living world,
Burst from thee, and illumined Earth and Heaven
And the deep ocean and the sunless caves,
20 And all that dwells within them; till grief cast
Eclipse upon the soul from which it came:
Such art thou now, nor is it I alone,
Thy sister, thy companion, thine own chosen one,
But the whole world which seeks thy sympathy.
25 Hearest thou not sounds i' the air which speak the love
Of all articulate beings? Feelest thou not
The inanimate winds enamoured of thee?—List!   *[Music.]*
ASIA   Thy words are sweeter than aught else but his
Whose echoes they are—yet all love is sweet,
30 Given or returned; common as light is love
And its familiar voice wearies not ever.
Like the wide Heaven, the all-sustaining air,
It makes the reptile equal to the God . . .
They who inspire it most are fortunate
35 As I am now; but those who feel it most
Are happier still, after long sufferings
As I shall soon become.
PANTHEA   List! Spirits speak.

VOICE (*in the air, singing*)[3]
     Life of Life! thy lips enkindle
        With their love the breath between them
40   And thy smiles before they dwindle
        Make the cold air fire; then screen them
     In those looks where whoso gazes
     Faints, entangled in their mazes.

1. In an earlier scene Panthea had envisioned in a dream the radiant and eternal inner form of Prometheus emerging through his "wound-worn limbs." The corresponding transfiguration of Asia, prepared for by her descent to the underworld to question Demogorgon, now takes place.
2. The story told by the Nereids (sea nymphs) serves to associate Asia with Aphrodite, goddess of love, emerging (as in Botticelli's painting) from the Mediterranean on a seashell.
3. The voice attempts to describe, in a dizzying whirl of optical paradoxes, what it feels like to look on the naked essence of love and beauty.

Child of Light! thy limbs are burning
55   Through the vest which seems to hide them
As the radiant lines of morning
      Through the clouds ere they divide them,
And this atmosphere divinest
Shrouds thee wheresoe'er thou shinest.

60   Fair are others;—none beholds thee
      But thy voice sounds low and tender
Like the fairest, for it folds thee
      From the sight, that liquid splendour,
And all feel, yet see thee never
65   As I feel now, lost forever!

Lamp of Earth! where'er thou movest
      Its dim shapes are clad with brightness
And the souls of whom thou lovest
      Walk upon the winds with lightness
70   Till they fail, as I am failing,
Dizzy, lost . . . yet unbewailing!

ASIA

My soul is an enchanted Boat
Which, like a sleeping swan, doth float
Upon the silver waves of thy sweet singing,
75   And thine doth like an Angel sit
Beside the helm conducting it
Whilst all the winds with melody are ringing.
      It seems to float ever—forever—
      Upon that many winding River
80   Between mountains, woods, abysses,
      A Paradise of wildernesses,
Till like one in slumber bound
Borne to the Ocean, I float down, around,
Into a Sea profound, of ever-spreading sound.

85   Meanwhile thy spirit lifts its pinions°   *wings*
      In Music's most serene dominions,
Catching the winds that fan that happy Heaven.
      And we sail on, away, afar,
      Without a course—without a star—
90   But by the instinct of sweet Music driven
      Till, through Elysian garden islets
      By thee, most beautiful of pilots,
      Where never mortal pinnace° glided,   *small boat*
      The boat of my desire is guided—
95   Realms where the air we breathe is Love
Which in the winds and on the waves doth move,
Harmonizing this Earth with what we feel above.

We have past Age's icy caves,
And Manhood's dark and tossing waves

100   And Youth's smooth ocean, smiling to betray;
       Beyond the glassy gulphs we flee
       Of shadow-peopled Infancy,
       Through Death and Birth to a diviner day,[4]
       A Paradise of vaulted bowers
105   Lit by downward-gazing flowers
       And watery paths that wind between
       Wildernesses calm and green,
       Peopled by shapes too bright to see,
       And rest, having beheld—somewhat like thee,
110   Which walk upon the sea, and chaunt melodiously!

From *Act 3*

SCENE 1—*Heaven.* JUPITER *on his Throne;* THETIS *and the other Deities assembled.*

JUPITER   Ye congregated Powers of Heaven who share
       The glory and the strength of him ye serve,
       Rejoice! henceforth I am omnipotent.
       All else had been subdued to me—alone
5   The soul of man, like unextinguished fire,
       Yet burns towards Heaven with fierce reproach and doubt
       And lamentation and reluctant prayer,
       Hurling up insurrection, which might make
       Our antique empire insecure, though built
10   On eldest faith, and Hell's coeval,[5] fear.
       And though my curses through the pendulous° air   *overhanging*
       Like snow on herbless peaks, fall flake by flake
       And cling to it[6]—though under my wrath's night
       It climb the crags of life, step after step,
15   Which wound it, as ice wounds unsandalled feet,
       It yet remains supreme o'er misery,
       Aspiring . . . unrepressed; yet soon to fall:
       Even now have I begotten a strange wonder,
       That fatal Child,[7] the terror of the Earth,
20   Who waits but till the destined Hour arrive,
       Bearing from Demogorgon's vacant throne
       The dreadful might of ever living limbs
       Which clothed that awful spirit unbeheld—
       To redescend, and trample out the spark[8] . . .

25   Pour forth Heaven's wine, Idæan Ganymede,
       And let it fill the dædal[9] cups like fire
       And from the flower-inwoven soil divine

4. Asia is describing what it feels like to be transfigured—in the image of moving backward in the stream of time, through youth and infancy and birth, in order to die to this life and be born again to a "diviner" existence.
5. Of the same age.
6. "It" (as also in lines 14 and 16) is "the soul of man" (line 5).
7. The son of Jupiter and Thetis. Jupiter believes that he has begotten a child who will assume the bodily form of the conquered Demogorgon and then return to announce his victory and the defeat of the resistance of Prometheus.
8. Of Prometheus's defiance.
9. Skillfully wrought (from the name of the Greek craftsman Daedalus). Ganymede (line 25) had been seized on Mount Ida by an eagle and carried to heaven to be Jupiter's cupbearer.

Ye all triumphant harmonies arise
As dew from Earth under the twilight stars;
30   Drink! be the nectar circling through your veins
The soul of joy, ye everliving Gods,
Till exultation burst in one wide voice
Like music from Elysian winds.—
                              And thou
Ascend beside me, veiled in the light
35   Of the desire which makes thee one with me,
Thetis, bright Image of Eternity!—
When thou didst cry, "Insufferable might![1]
God! spare me! I sustain not the quick flames,
The penetrating presence; all my being,
40   Like him whom the Numidian seps[2] did thaw
Into a dew with poison, is dissolved,
Sinking through its foundations"—even then
Two mighty spirits, mingling, made a third
Mightier than either—which unbodied now
45   Between us, floats, felt although unbeheld,
Waiting the incarnation, which ascends—
Hear ye the thunder of the fiery wheels
Griding[3] the winds?—from Demogorgon's throne.—
Victory! victory! Feel'st thou not, O World,
50   The Earthquake of his chariot thundering up
Olympus?
        [*The Car of the* HOUR *arrives.* DEMOGORGON *descends and moves towards*
        the Throne of JUPITER.]
                Awful Shape, what art thou? Speak!
DEMOGORGON   Eternity—demand no direr name.
Descend, and follow me down the abyss;
I am thy child,[4] as thou wert Saturn's child,
55   Mightier than thee; and we must dwell together
Henceforth in darkness.—Lift thy lightnings not.
The tyranny of Heaven none may retain,
Or reassume, or hold succeeding thee . . .
Yet if thou wilt—as 'tis the destiny
60   Of trodden worms to writhe till they are dead—
Put forth thy might.
JUPITER   Detested prodigy!
Even thus beneath the deep Titanian prisons[5]
I trample thee! . . . thou lingerest?
                            Mercy! mercy!
No pity—no release, no respite! . . . Oh,
65   That thou wouldst make mine enemy my judge.
Even where he hangs, seared by my long revenge
On Caucasus—he would not doom me thus.—

1. This description of Jupiter's rape of Thetis is a
grotesque parody of the reunion of Prometheus
and Asia.
2. A serpent of Numidia (North Africa) whose bite
was thought to cause putrefaction.
3. Cutting with a rasping sound.

4. Ironically, and in a figurative sense: Demogorgon's function follows from Jupiter's actions.
5. After they overthrew the Titans, Jupiter and the
Olympian gods imprisoned them in Tartarus, deep
beneath the earth.

Gentle and just and dreadless, is he not
The monarch of the world? what then art thou? . . .
No refuge! no appeal— . . .
70   Sink with me then—
We two will sink in the wide waves of ruin
Even as a vulture and a snake outspent
Drop, twisted in inextricable fight,[6]
Into a shoreless sea.—Let Hell unlock
75 Its mounded Oceans of tempestuous fire,
And whelm on them° into the bottomless void   *wash them*
The desolated world and thee and me,
The conqueror and the conquered, and the wreck
Of that for which they combated.
                         Ai! Ai![7]
80 The elements obey me not . . . I sink . . .
Dizzily down—ever, forever, down—
And, like a cloud, mine enemy above
Darkens my fall with victory!—Ai! Ai!

From SCENE 4—*A Forest. In the Background a Cave.* PROMETHEUS, ASIA, PAN-
THEA, IONE, *and the* SPIRIT OF THE EARTH.[8]

                     *   *   *

[*The* SPIRIT OF THE HOUR *enters.*]
PROMETHEUS   We feel what thou hast heard and seen—yet speak.
SPIRIT OF THE HOUR   Soon as the sound had ceased whose thunder filled
    The abysses of the sky, and the wide earth,
90 There was a change . . . the impalpable thin air
    And the all-circling sunlight were transformed
    As if the sense of love dissolved in them
    Had folded itself round the sphered world.
    My vision then grew clear and I could see
95 Into the mysteries of the Universe.[9]
    Dizzy as with delight I floated down,
    Winnowing the lightsome air with languid plumes,
    My coursers sought their birthplace in the sun
    Where they henceforth will live exempt from toil,
100 Pasturing flowers of vegetable fire—
    And where my moonlike car will stand within
    A temple, gazed upon by Phidian forms,[1]
    Of thee, and Asia and the Earth, and me
    And you fair nymphs, looking the love we feel,
105 In memory of the tidings it has borne,

6. The eagle (or vulture) and the snake locked in equal combat—a favorite Shelleyan image (cf. *Alastor*, lines 227–32, p. 752).
7. Traditional Greek cry of sorrow.
8. After Jupiter's annihilation (described in scene 2), Hercules unbinds Prometheus, who is reunited with Asia and retires to a cave "where we will sit and talk of time and change / . . . ourselves unchanged." In the speech that concludes the act (reprinted here) the Spirit of the Hour describes

what happened in the human world when he sounded the apocalyptic trumpet.
9. I.e., the earth's atmosphere clarifies, no longer refracting the sunlight, and so allows the Spirit of the Hour to see what is happening on earth.
1. The crescent-shaped ("moonlike") chariot, its apocalyptic mission accomplished, will be frozen to stone and will be surrounded by the sculptured forms of other agents in the drama. Phidias (5th century B.C.E.) was the noblest of Greek sculptors.

Beneath a dome fretted with graven flowers,
Poised on twelve columns of resplendent stone
And open to the bright and liquid sky.
Yoked to it by an amphisbænic snake[2]
120   The likeness of those winged steeds will mock[3]
The flight from which they find repose.—Alas,
Whither has wandered now my partial[4] tongue
When all remains untold which ye would hear!—
As I have said, I floated to the Earth:
125   It was, as it is still, the pain of bliss
To move, to breathe, to be; I wandering went
Among the haunts and dwellings of mankind
And first was disappointed not to see
Such mighty change as I had felt within
130   Expressed in outward things; but soon I looked,
And behold! thrones were kingless, and men walked
One with the other even as spirits do,
None fawned, none trampled; hate, disdain or fear,
Self-love or self-contempt on human brows
135   No more inscribed, as o'er the gate of hell,
"All hope abandon, ye who enter here";[5]
None frowned, none trembled, none with eager fear
Gazed on another's eye of cold command
Until the subject of a tyrant's will
140   Became, worse fate, the abject of his own[6]
Which spurred him, like an outspent° horse, to death.   exhausted
None wrought his lips in truth-entangling lines
Which smiled the lie his tongue disdained to speak;
None with firm sneer trod out in his own heart
145   The sparks of love and hope, till there remained
Those bitter ashes, a soul self-consumed,
And the wretch crept, a vampire among men,
Infecting all with his own hideous ill.
None talked that common, false, cold, hollow talk
150   Which makes the heart deny the *yes* it breathes
Yet question that unmeant hypocrisy
With such a self-mistrust as has no name.
And women too, frank, beautiful and kind
As the free Heaven which rains fresh light and dew
155   On the wide earth, past: gentle, radiant forms,
From custom's evil taint exempt and pure;
Speaking the wisdom once they could not think,
Looking emotions once they feared to feel
And changed to all which once they dared not be,
160   Yet being now, made Earth like Heaven—nor pride
Nor jealousy nor envy nor ill shame,

2. A mythical snake with a head at each end; it serves here as a symbolic warning that a reversal of the process is always possible.
3. "Imitate" and also, in their immobility, "mock at" the flight they represent.

4. Biased or, possibly, telling only part of the story.
5. The inscription over the gate of hell in Dante's *Inferno* 3.9.
6. I.e., he was so abjectly enslaved that his own will accorded with the tyrant's will.

The bitterest of those drops of treasured gall,
Spoilt the sweet taste of the nepenthe,[7] love.

Thrones, altars, judgement-seats and prisons; wherein
65 And beside which, by wretched men were borne
Sceptres, tiaras, swords and chains, and tomes
Of reasoned wrong glozed on[8] by ignorance,
Were like those monstrous and barbaric shapes,
The ghosts of a no more remembered fame,
70 Which from their unworn obelisks[9] look forth
In triumph o'er the palaces and tombs
Of those who were their conquerors, mouldering round.
Those imaged to the pride of Kings and Priests
A dark yet mighty faith, a power as wide
75 As is the world it wasted, and are now
But an astonishment; even so the tools
And emblems of its last captivity
Amid the dwellings of the peopled Earth,
Stand, not o'erthrown, but unregarded now.
80 And those foul shapes, abhorred by God and man—
Which under many a name and many a form
Strange, savage, ghastly, dark and execrable
Were Jupiter,[1] the tyrant of the world;
And which the nations panic-stricken served
85 With blood, and hearts broken by long hope, and love
Dragged to his altars soiled and garlandless
And slain amid men's unreclaiming tears,
Flattering the thing they feared, which fear was hate—
Frown, mouldering fast, o'er their abandoned shrines.
90 The painted veil, by those who were, called life,[2]
Which mimicked, as with colours idly spread,
All men believed and hoped, is torn aside—
The loathsome mask has fallen, the man remains
Sceptreless, free, uncircumscribed—but man:
95 Equal, unclassed, tribeless, and nationless,
Exempt from awe, worship, degree,—the King
Over himself; just, gentle, wise—but man:
Passionless? no—yet free from guilt or pain
Which were, for his will made, or suffered them,
00 Nor yet exempt, though ruling them like slaves,
From chance and death and mutability,
The clogs of that which else might oversoar
The loftiest star of unascended Heaven
Pinnacled dim in the intense inane.[3]

7. A drug (probably opium) that brings forgetfulness of pain and sorrow.
8. Annotated, explained.
9. The Egyptian obelisks (tapering shafts of stone), brought to Rome by its conquering armies, included hieroglyphs that—because they were still undeciphered in Shelley's time—seemed "monstrous and barbaric shapes" (line 168).
1. The "foul shapes" (line 180) were statues of the gods who, whatever their names, were all really manifestations of Jupiter.
2. I.e., which was thought to be life by humans as they were before their regeneration.
3. I.e., a dim point in the extreme of empty space. The sense of lines 198–204 is if regenerate man were to be released from all earthly and biological impediments ("clogs"), he would become what even the stars are not—a pure ideal.

From *Act 4*[4]

SCENE—*A Part of the Forest near the Cave of* PROMETHEUS.

* * *

DEMOGORGON

This is the Day which down the void Abysm
555   At the Earth-born's spell[5] yawns for Heaven's Despotism,
  And Conquest is dragged Captive through the Deep;[6]
  Love from its awful° throne of patient power   *awesome*
  In the wise heart, from the last giddy hour
  Of dread endurance, from the slippery, steep,
560   And narrow verge of crag-like Agony, springs
  And folds over the world its healing wings.

Gentleness, Virtue, Wisdom and Endurance,—
These are the seals of that most firm assurance
  Which bars the pit over Destruction's strength;
565   And if, with infirm hand, Eternity,
Mother of many acts and hours, should free
The serpent that would clasp her with his length[7]—
These are the spells by which to reassume
An empire o'er the disentangled Doom.[8]

570   To suffer woes which Hope thinks infinite;
  To forgive wrongs darker than Death or Night;
    To defy Power which seems Omnipotent;
  To love, and bear; to hope, till Hope creates
  From its own wreck the thing it contemplates;
575   Neither to change nor falter nor repent:
  This, like thy glory, Titan! is to be
  Good, great and joyous, beautiful and free;
  This is alone Life, Joy, Empire and Victory.

1818–19   1820

4. The original drama, completed in the spring of 1819, consisted of three acts. Later that year Shelley added a jubilant fourth act. In Revelation 21 the apocalyptic replacement of the old world by "a new heaven and new earth" had been symbolized by the marriage of the Lamb with the New Jerusalem. Shelley's fourth act, somewhat like the conclusion of Blake's *Jerusalem,* expands this figure into a cosmic epithalamion, representing a union of divided elements that enacts everywhere the reunion of Prometheus and Asia taking place offstage.
  Shelley's model is the Renaissance masque, which combines song and dance with spectacular displays. Panthea and Ione serve as commentators on the action, which is divided into three episodes. In the first episode the purified "Spirits of the human mind" unite in a ritual dance with the Hours of the glad new day. In the second episode (lines 194–318), there appear emblematic representations of the moon and the earth, each bearing

an infant whose hour has come round at last. Shelley based this description in part on Ezekiel 1, the vision of the chariot of divine glory, which had traditionally been interpreted as a portent of apocalypse. The third episode (lines 319–502) is the bacchanalian dance of the love-intoxicated Moon around her brother and paramour, the rejuvenescent Earth.
5. Prometheus's spell—the magically effective words of pity, rather than vengefulness, that he spoke in act 1.
6. Ephesians 4.8: "When [Christ] ascended up on high, he led captivity captive."
7. A final reminder that the serpent incessantly struggles to break loose and start the cycle of humanity's fall all over again.
8. Shelley's four cardinal virtues (line 562), which seal the serpent in the pit, also constitute the magic formulas ("spells") by which to remaster him, should he again break loose.

The Cloud

I bring fresh showers for the thirsting flowers,
   From the seas and streams;
I bear light shade for the leaves when laid
   In their noon-day dreams.
5 From my wings are shaken the dews that waken
   The sweet buds every one,
When rocked to rest on their mother's° breast,   *earth's*
   As she dances about the Sun.
I wield the flail[1] of the lashing hail,
10   And whiten the green plains under,
And then again I dissolve it in rain,
   And laugh as I pass in thunder.

I sift the snow on the mountains below,
   And their great pines groan aghast;
15 And all the night 'tis my pillow white,
   While I sleep in the arms of the blast.
Sublime on the towers of my skiey bowers,
   Lightning my pilot sits;
In a cavern under is fettered the thunder,
20   It struggles and howls at fits;°   *fitfully*
Over Earth and Ocean, with gentle motion,
   This pilot is guiding me,
Lured by the love of the genii that move
   In the depths of the purple sea;[2]
25 Over the rills, and the crags, and the hills,
   Over the lakes and the plains,
Wherever he dream, under mountain or stream,
   The Spirit he loves remains;
And I all the while bask in Heaven's blue smile,[3]
30   Whilst he is dissolving in rains.

The sanguine Sunrise, with his meteor eyes,
   And his burning plumes outspread,[4]
Leaps on the back of my sailing rack,[5]
   When the morning star shines dead;
35 As on the jag of a mountain crag,
   Which an earthquake rocks and swings,
An eagle alit one moment may sit
   In the light of its golden wings.
And when Sunset may breathe, from the lit Sea beneath,
40   Its ardours of rest and of love,
And the crimson pall° of eve may fall   *rich coverlet*
   From the depth of Heaven above,

1. Either a weapon fashioned as a ball and chain or a tool for threshing grain.
2. I.e., atmospheric electricity, guiding the cloud (line 18), discharges as lightning when "lured" by the attraction of an opposite charge.
3. The upper part of the cloud remains exposed to the sun.
4. The sun's corona. "Meteor eyes": as bright as a burning meteor.
5. High, broken clouds, driven by the wind.

With wings folded I rest, on mine aëry nest,
    As still as a brooding dove.[6]
45 That orbed maiden with white fire laden
    Whom mortals call the Moon,
Glides glimmering o'er my fleece-like floor,
    By the midnight breezes strewn;
And wherever the beat of her unseen feet,
50   Which only the angels hear,
May have broken the woof,° of my tent's thin roof,   *texture*
    The stars peep behind her, and peer;
And I laugh to see them whirl and flee,
    Like a swarm of golden bees,
55 When I widen the rent in my wind-built tent,
    Till the calm rivers, lakes, and seas,
Like strips of the sky fallen through me on high,
    Are each paved with the moon and these.[7]

I bind the Sun's throne with a burning zone°   *belt, sash*
60   And the Moon's with a girdle of pearl;
The volcanos are dim and the stars reel and swim
    When the whirlwinds my banner unfurl.
From cape to cape, with a bridge-like shape,
    Over a torrent sea,
65 Sunbeam-proof, I hang like a roof—
    The mountains its columns be!
The triumphal arch, through which I march
    With hurricane, fire, and snow,
When the Powers of the Air, are chained to my chair,°   *chariot*
70   Is the million-coloured Bow;
The sphere-fire° above its soft colours wove   *sunlight*
    While the moist Earth was laughing below.

I am the daughter of Earth and Water,
    And the nursling of the Sky;
75 I pass through the pores, of the ocean and shores;
    I change, but I cannot die—
For after the rain, when with never a stain
    The pavilion of Heaven is bare,
And the winds and sunbeams, with their convex gleams,
80   Build up the blue dome of Air[8]—
I silently laugh at my own cenotaph,[9]
    And out of the caverns of rain,
Like a child from the womb, like a ghost from the tomb,
    I arise, and unbuild it again.—

1820   1820

6. An echo of Milton's description of his Muse, identified with the Holy Spirit, who "with mighty wings outspread / Dove-like sat'st brooding on the vast abyss" (*Paradise Lost* 1.20–21).
7. The stars reflected in the water.
8. The blue color of the sky. The phenomenon, as Shelley indicates, results from the way "sunbeams" are filtered by the earth's atmosphere.
9. The memorial monument of the dead cloud is the cloudless blue dome of the sky. (The point is that a cenotaph is a monument that does not contain a corpse.)

To a Sky-Lark[1]

Hail to thee, blithe Spirit!
  Bird thou never wert—
  That from Heaven, or near it,
    Pourest thy full heart
5 In profuse strains of unpremeditated art.

Higher still and higher
  From the earth thou springest
  Like a cloud of fire;
    The blue deep thou wingest,
10 And singing still dost soar, and soaring ever singest.

In the golden lightning
  Of the sunken Sun—
  O'er which clouds are brightning,
    Thou dost float and run;
15 Like an unbodied joy whose race is just begun.

The pale purple even°   *evening*
  Melts around thy flight,
  Like a star of Heaven
    In the broad day-light
20 Thou art unseen,—but yet I hear thy shrill delight,

Keen as are the arrows
  Of that silver sphere,[2]
  Whose intense lamp narrows
    In the white dawn clear
25 Until we hardly see—we feel that it is there.

All the earth and air
  With thy voice is loud,
  As when Night is bare
    From one lonely cloud
30 The moon rains out her beams—and Heaven is overflowed.

What thou art we know not;
  What is most like thee?
  From rainbow clouds there flow not
    Drops so bright to see
35 As from thy presence showers a rain of melody.

Like a Poet hidden
  In the light of thought,
  Singing hymns unbidden,
    Till the world is wrought
40 To sympathy with hopes and fears it heeded not:

---

1. The European skylark is a small bird that sings only in flight, often when it is too high to be visible.

2. The morning star, Venus.

Like a high-born maiden
  In a palace-tower,
Soothing her love-laden
  Soul in secret hour,
45 With music sweet as love—which overflows her bower:

Like a glow-worm golden
  In a dell of dew,
Scattering unbeholden
  Its aerial hue
50 Among the flowers and grass which screen it from the view:

Like a rose embowered
  In its own green leaves—
By warm winds deflowered—
  Till the scent it gives
55 Makes faint with too much sweet those heavy-winged thieves:[3]

Sound of vernal° showers   *springtime*
  On the twinkling grass,
Rain-awakened flowers,
  All that ever was
60 Joyous, and clear and fresh, thy music doth surpass.

Teach us, Sprite° or Bird,   *spirit*
  What sweet thoughts are thine;
I have never heard
  Praise of love or wine
65 That panted forth a flood of rapture so divine:

Chorus Hymeneal[4]
  Or triumphal chaunt
Matched with thine would be all
  But an empty vaunt,
70 A thing wherein we feel there is some hidden want.

What objects are the fountains
  Of thy happy strain?
What fields or waves or mountains?
  What shapes of sky or plain?
75 What love of thine own kind? what ignorance of pain?

With thy clear keen joyance
  Languor cannot be—
Shadow of annoyance
  Never came near thee;
80 Thou lovest—but ne'er knew love's sad satiety.

Waking or asleep,
  Thou of death must deem
Things more true and deep

---

3. The "warm winds," line 53.   4. Marital (from Hymen, Greek god of marriage).

Than we mortals dream,
85 Or how could thy notes flow in such a chrystal stream?

We look before and after,
   And pine for what is not—
Our sincerest laughter
   With some pain is fraught—
90 Our sweetest songs are those that tell of saddest thought.

Yet if we could scorn
   Hate and pride and fear;
If we were things born
   Not to shed a tear,
95 I know not how thy joy we ever should come near.

Better than all measures
   Of delightful sound—
Better than all treasures
   That in books are found—
100 Thy skill to poet were, thou Scorner of the ground!

Teach me half the gladness
   That thy brain must know,
Such harmonious madness
   From my lips would flow
105 The world should listen then—as I am listening now.

1820   1820

To Night

      Swiftly walk o'er the western wave,
            Spirit of Night!
      Out of the misty eastern cave
      Where, all the long and lone daylight
   5 Thou wovest dreams of joy and fear,
      Which make thee terrible and dear,
            Swift be thy flight!

      Wrap thy form in a mantle grey,
            Star-inwrought!
   10 Blind with thine hair the eyes of day,
      Kiss her until she be wearied out—
      Then wander o'er City and sea and land,
      Touching all with thine opiate wand—
            Come, long-sought!

   15 When I arose and saw the dawn
            I sighed for thee;
      When Light rode high, and the dew was gone,
      And noon lay heavy on flower and tree,

And the weary Day[1] turned to his rest,
20   Lingering like an unloved guest,
        I sighed for thee.

Thy brother Death came, and cried,
        Wouldst thou me?
Thy sweet child Sleep, the filmy-eyed,
25   Murmured like a noontide bee,
        Shall I nestle near thy side?
Wouldst thou me? and I replied,
        No, not thee!

Death will come when thou art dead,
30   Soon, too soon—
Sleep will come when thou art fled;
Of neither would I ask the boon
I ask of thee, beloved Night—
Swift be thine approaching flight,
35   Come soon, soon!

1820   1824

To ——— [Music, when soft voices die][1]

Music, when soft voices die,
Vibrates in the memory.—
Odours, when sweet violets sicken,
Live within the sense they quicken.°—   *enliven*

5   Rose leaves, when the rose is dead,
Are heaped for the beloved's bed[2]—
And so thy thoughts,[3] when thou art gone,
Love itself shall slumber on.

1821   1824

O World, O Life, O Time[1]

O World, O Life, O Time,
On whose last steps I climb,
Trembling at that where I had stood before,
When will return the glory of your prime?
5   No more, O never more!

1. Here the "Day" is the male sun, not the female "day" with whom the Spirit of Night dallies in the preceding stanza.
1. This poem was first published under the title "Memory" in Mary Shelley's edition of her husband's *Posthumous Poems* in 1824, with the two stanzas in the reverse order from what we give here. Our text is based on a version found in a notebook of Percy Shelley's now housed in the Bodleian Library at Oxford.
2. The bed of the dead rose.
3. I.e., my thoughts of thee.
1. For the author's revisions while composing this poem, see "Poems in Process," in the appendices to this volume.

Out of the day and night
A joy has taken flight—
Fresh spring and summer [   ] and winter hoar
Move my faint heart with grief, but with delight
10   No more, O never more!

1824

Chorus from *Hellas*[1]

The world's great age[2]

The world's great age begins anew,
    The golden years[3] return,
The earth doth like a snake renew
    Her winter weeds[4] outworn;
5 Heaven smiles, and faiths and empires gleam
Like wrecks of a dissolving dream.

A brighter Hellas rears its mountains
    From waves serener far,
A new Peneus[5] rolls his fountains
10   Against the morning-star,
Where fairer Tempes bloom, there sleep
Young Cyclads[6] on a sunnier deep.

A loftier Argo[7] cleaves the main,
    Fraught with a later prize;
15 Another Orpheus[8] sings again,
    And loves, and weeps, and dies;
A new Ulysses leaves once more
Calypso[9] for his native shore.

O, write no more the tale of Troy,
20   If earth Death's scroll must be!
Nor mix with Laian[1] rage the joy

1. *Hellas*, a closet drama written in the autumn of 1821, was inspired by the Greek war for independence against the Turks. ("Hellas" is another name for Greece.) In his preface Shelley declared that he viewed this revolution as foretelling the final overthrow of all tyramy. The choruses throughout are sung by enslaved Greek women. We give the chorus that concludes the drama.
2. Prophecies of wars, and rumours of wars, etc., may safely be made by poet or prophet in any age, but to anticipate however darkly a period of regeneration and happiness is a more hazardous exercise of the faculty which bards possess or fain. It will remind the reader . . . of Isaiah and Virgil, whose ardent spirits . . . saw the possible and perhaps approaching state of society in which the "lion shall lie down with the lamb," and "*omnis feret omnia tellus.*" Let these great names be my authority and excuse [Shelley's note]. The quotations are from Isaiah's millennial prophecy (e.g., chaps. 25, 45), and Virgil's prediction, in *Eclogue* 4, of a

return of the golden age, when "all the earth will produce all things."
3. In Greek myth the first period of history, when Saturn reigned.
4. Clothes (especially mourning garments) as well as dead vegetation.
5. The river in northeast Greece that flows through the beautiful vale of Tempe (line 11).
6. The Cyclades, islands in the Aegean Sea.
7. On which Jason sailed in his quest for the Golden Fleece.
8. The legendary player on the lyre who was torn to pieces by the frenzied Thracian women while he was mourning the death of his wife, Eurydice.
9. The nymph deserted by Ulysses on his voyage back from the Trojan War to his native Ithaca.
1. King Laius of Thebes was killed in a quarrel by his son Oedipus, who did not recognize his father. Shortly thereafter Oedipus delivered Thebes from the ravages of the Sphinx by answering its riddle (lines 23–24).

Which dawns upon the free;
Although a subtler Sphinx renew
Riddles of death Thebes never knew.

25   Another Athens shall arise,
        And to remoter time
Bequeath, like sunset to the skies,
        The splendour of its prime,
And leave, if nought so bright may live,
30   All earth can take or Heaven can give.

Saturn and Love their long repose
Shall burst, more bright and good
Than all who fell, than One who rose,
Than many unsubdued;[2]
35   Not gold, not blood their altar dowers°   *gifts*
But votive tears and symbol flowers.

O cease! must hate and death return?
Cease! must men kill and die?
Cease! drain not to its dregs the urn
40   Of bitter prophecy.
The world is weary of the past,
O might it die or rest at last!

1821   1822

Adonais   John Keats died in Rome on February 23, 1821, and was buried there
in the Protestant Cemetery. Shelley had met Keats, had invited him to be his guest
at Pisa, and had gradually come to realize that he was "among the writers of the
highest genius who have adorned our age" (Preface to *Adonais*). The name "Adonais"
is derived from Adonis, the handsome youth who had been loved by the goddess Venus
and slain by a wild boar. He was restored to life on the condition that he spend only
part of every year with Venus in heaven and the other part with Proserpine in the
underworld. This cycle of rebirth and death, symbolic of the alternate return of summer and winter, suggests why Adonis was central to ancient fertility myths. Shelley
in his poem gives the role of the boar to the anonymous author of a vituperative
review of Keats's *Endymion* in the *Quarterly Review*, April 1818 (now known to be
John Wilson Croker), whom Shelley mistakenly believed to be responsible for Keats's
illness and death.

    Shelley in a letter described *Adonais*, which he wrote in April–June 1821 and had
printed in Pisa in July, as a "highly wrought piece of art." Its artistry consists in part
in the care with which it follows the conventions of the pastoral elegy, established
more than two thousand years earlier by the Greek Sicilian poets Theocritus, Bion,
and Moschus—Shelley had translated into English Bion's *Lament for Adonis* and
Moschus's *Lament for Bion*. We recognize the centuries-old poetic ritual in many
verbal echoes and in devices such as the mournful and accusing invocation to a muse
(stanzas 2–4), the sympathetic participation of nature in the grieving (stanzas 14–
17), the procession of appropriate mourners (stanzas 30–35), the denunciation of

2. Saturn and Love were among the deities of a
real or imaginary state of innocence and happiness.
"All" those "who fell" [are] the Gods of Greece,
Asia, and Egypt; the "One who rose" [is] Jesus

Christ . . . and the "many unsubdued" [are] the
monstrous objects of the idolatry of China, India,
the Antarctic islands, and the native tribes of
America [Shelley's note].

unworthy practitioners of the pastoral or literary art (stanzas 17, 27–29, 36–37), and above all, in the turn from despair at the finality of human death (lines 1, 64, 190: "*He* will awake no more, oh, never more!") to consolation in the sudden and contradictory discovery that the grave is a gate to a higher existence (line 343: "Peace, peace! he is not dead, he doth not sleep").

Published first in Pisa, Italy, in 1821, *Adonais* was not issued in England until 1829, in an edition sponsored by the so-called Cambridge Apostles (the minor poet R. M. Milnes and the more famous poets Alfred Tennyson and A. H. Hallam). The appearance of this edition marked the beginning of Keats's posthumous emergence from obscurity.

Adonais

An Elegy on the Death of John Keats, Author of Endymion, Hyperion, etc.

[Thou wert the morning star among the living,
Ere thy fair light had fled—
Now, having died, thou art as Hesperus, giving
New splendour to the dead.][1]

1

I weep for Adonais—he is dead!
O, weep for Adonais! though our tears
Thaw not the frost which binds so dear a head!
And thou, sad Hour,[2] selected from all years
5   To mourn our loss, rouse thy obscure compeers,°   *companions*
And teach them thine own sorrow, say: with me
Died Adonais; till the Future dares
Forget the Past, his fate and fame shall be
An echo and a light unto eternity!

2

10   Where wert thou mighty Mother,[3] when he lay,
When thy Son lay, pierced by the shaft which flies
In darkness?[4] where was lorn° Urania   *forlorn*
When Adonais died? With veiled eyes,
'Mid listening Echoes, in her Paradise
15   She sate, while one,[5] with soft enamoured breath,
Rekindled all the fading melodies,
With which, like flowers that mock the corse° beneath,   *corpse*
He had adorned and hid the coming bulk of death.

3

O, weep for Adonais—he is dead!
20   Wake, melancholy Mother, wake and weep!
Yet wherefore? Quench within their burning bed
Thy fiery tears, and let thy loud heart keep

1. Shelley prefixed to *Adonais* a Greek epigram attributed to Plato; this is Shelley's translation of the Greek. The planet Venus appears both as the morning star, Lucifer, and as the evening star, Hesperus or Vesper. Shelley makes of this phenomenon a key symbol for Adonais's triumph over death, in stanzas 44–46.
2. Shelley follows the classical mode of personifying the hours, which mark the passage of time and turn of the seasons.
3. Urania. She had originally been the Muse of astronomy, but the name was also an epithet for Venus. Shelley converts Venus Urania, who in Greek myth had been the lover of Adonis, into the mother of Adonais.
4. Alludes to the anonymity of the review of *Endymion.*
5. I.e., the echo of Keats's voice in his poems.

Like his, a mute and uncomplaining sleep;
For he is gone, where all things wise and fair
25   Descend;—oh, dream not that the amorous Deep°   *abyss*
Will yet restore him to the vital air;
Death feeds on his mute voice, and laughs at our despair.

4

Most musical of mourners, weep again!
Lament anew, Urania!—He[6] died,
30   Who was the Sire of an immortal strain,
Blind, old, and lonely, when his country's pride,
The priest, the slave, and the liberticide,
Trampled and mocked with many a loathed rite
Of lust and blood; he went, unterrified,
35   Into the gulph of death; but his clear Sprite°   *spirit*
Yet reigns o'er earth; the third among the sons of light.[7]

5

Most musical of mourners, weep anew!
Not all to that bright station dared to climb;
And happier they their happiness who knew,
40   Whose tapers° yet burn through that night of time   *candles*
In which suns perished; others more sublime,
Struck by the envious wrath of man or God,
Have sunk, extinct in their refulgent° prime;   *radiant*
And some yet live, treading the thorny road,
45   Which leads, through toil and hate, to Fame's serene abode.

6

But now, thy youngest, dearest one, has perished—
The nursling of thy widowhood, who grew,
Like a pale flower by some sad maiden cherished,
And fed with true love tears, instead of dew;[8]
50   Most musical of mourners, weep anew!
Thy extreme[9] hope, the loveliest and the last,
The bloom, whose petals nipt before they blew°   *bloomed*
Died on the promise of the fruit, is waste;
The broken lily lies—the storm is overpast.

7

55   To that high Capital,° where kingly Death   *Rome*
Keeps his pale court in beauty and decay,
He came; and bought, with price of purest breath,
A grave among the eternal.—Come away!
Haste, while the vault of blue Italian day
60   Is yet his fitting charnel-roof! while still
He lies, as if in dewy sleep he lay;

6. Milton, regarded as precursor of the great poetic tradition in which Keats wrote. He had adopted Urania as the muse of *Paradise Lost*. Lines 31–35 describe Milton's life during the restoration of the Stuart monarchy.
7. In "A Defence of Poetry," Shelley says that Milton was the third great epic poet, along with Homer and Dante. The stanza following describes the lot of other poets, up to Shelley's own time.
8. An allusion to an incident in Keats's *Isabella*.
9. Last, as well as highest.

Awake him not! surely he takes his fill
Of deep and liquid rest, forgetful of all ill.

8

He will awake no more, oh, never more!—
65   Within the twilight chamber spreads apace,
The shadow of white Death, and at the door
Invisible Corruption waits to trace
His extreme way to her dim dwelling-place;
The eternal Hunger sits, but pity and awe
70   Soothe her pale rage, nor dares she to deface
So fair a prey, till darkness, and the law
Of change, shall 'oer his sleep the mortal curtain draw.

9

O, weep for Adonais!—The quick° Dreams,   *living*
The passion-winged Ministers of thought,
75   Who were his flocks,[1] whom near the living streams
Of his young spirit he fed, and whom he taught
The love which was its music, wander not,—
Wander no more, from kindling brain to brain,
But droop there, whence they sprung; and mourn their lot
80   Round the cold heart, where, after their sweet pain,
They ne'er will gather strength, or find a home again.

10

And one[2] with trembling hands clasps his cold head,
And fans him with her moonlight wings, and cries;
"Our love, our hope, our sorrow, is not dead;
85   See, on the silken fringe of his faint eyes,
Like dew upon a sleeping flower, there lies
A tear some Dream has loosened from his brain."
Lost Angel of a ruined Paradise!
She knew not 'twas her own; as with no stain
90   She faded, like a cloud which had outwept its rain.

11

One from a lucid° urn of starry dew   *luminous*
Washed his light limbs as if embalming them;
Another clipt her profuse locks, and threw
The wreath upon him, like an anadem,°   *rich garland*
95   Which frozen tears instead of pearls begem;
Another in her wilful grief would break
Her bow and winged reeds, as if to stem
A greater loss with one which was more weak;
And dull the barbed fire against his frozen cheek.

12

100   Another Splendour on his mouth alit,
That mouth, whence it was wont° to draw the breath   *accustomed*
Which gave it strength to pierce the guarded wit,[3]

1. The products of Keats's imagination, figuratively represented (according to the conventions of the pastoral elegy) as his sheep.
2. One of the Dreams (line 73).
3. The cautious intellect (of the listener).

And pass into the panting heart beneath
With lightning and with music: the damp death
105 Quenched its caress upon his icy lips;
And, as a dying meteor stains a wreath
Of moonlight vapour, which the cold night clips,
It flushed through his pale limbs, and past to its eclipse.

13

And others came . . . Desires and Adorations,
110 Winged Persuasions and veiled Destinies,
Splendours, and Glooms, and glimmering Incarnations
Of hopes and fears, and twilight Phantasies;
And Sorrow, with her family of Sighs,
And Pleasure, blind with tears, led by the gleam
115 Of her own dying smile instead of eyes,
Came in slow pomp;—the moving pomp might seem
Like pageantry of mist on an autumnal stream.

14

All he had loved, and moulded into thought,
From shape, and hue, and odour, and sweet sound,
120 Lamented Adonais. Morning sought
Her eastern watchtower, and her hair unbound,
Wet with the tears which should adorn the ground,
Dimmed the aerial eyes that kindle day;
Afar the melancholy thunder moaned,
125 Pale Ocean in unquiet slumber lay,
And the wild winds flew round, sobbing in their dismay.

15

Lost Echo sits amid the voiceless mountains,
And feeds her grief with his remembered lay,°   *song*
And will no more reply to winds or fountains,
130 Or amorous birds perched on the young green spray,
Or herdsman's horn, or bell at closing day;
Since she can mimic not his lips, more dear
Than those for whose disdain she pined away
Into a shadow of all sounds:[4]—a drear
135 Murmur, between their songs, is all the woodmen hear.

16

Grief made the young Spring wild, and she threw down
Her kindling buds, as if she Autumn were,
Or they dead leaves; since her delight is flown
For whom should she have waked the sullen year?
140 To Phoebus was not Hyacinth so dear[5]
Nor to himself Narcissus, as to both
Thou Adonais: wan they stand and sere[6]
Amid the faint companions of their youth,
With dew all turned to tears; odour, to sighing ruth.°   *pity*

---

4. Because of her unrequited love for Narcissus, who was enamored of his own reflection (line 141), the nymph Echo pined away until she was only a reflected sound.
5. Young Hyacinthus was loved by Phoebus Apollo, who accidentally killed him in a game of quoits. Apollo made the hyacinth flower spring from his blood.
6. Dried, withered.

17

145 Thy spirit's sister, the lorn nightingale[7]
Mourns not her mate with such melodious pain;
Not so the eagle, who like thee could scale
Heaven, and could nourish in the sun's domain
Her mighty youth with morning,[8] doth complain,°   *lament*
150 Soaring and screaming round her empty nest,
As Albion° wails for thee: the curse of Cain   *England*
Light on his head[9] who pierced thy innocent breast,
And scared the angel soul that was its earthly guest!

18

Ah woe is me! Winter is come and gone,
155 But grief returns with the revolving year;
The airs and streams renew their joyous tone;
The ants, the bees, the swallows reappear;
Fresh leaves and flowers deck the dead Seasons' bier;
The amorous birds now pair in every brake,°   *thicket*
160 And build their mossy homes in field and brere;°   *briar*
And the green lizard, and the golden snake,
Like unimprisoned flames, out of their trance awake.

19

Through wood and stream and field and hill and Ocean
A quickening life from the Earth's heart has burst
165 As it has ever done, with change and motion,
From the great morning of the world when first
God dawned on Chaos; in its stream immersed
The lamps of Heaven flash with a softer light;
All baser things pant with life's sacred thirst;
170 Diffuse themselves; and spend in love's delight,
The beauty and the joy of their renewed might.

20

The leprous corpse touched by this spirit tender
Exhales itself in flowers of gentle breath;
Like incarnations of the stars, when splendour
175 Is changed to fragrance, they illumine death
And mock the merry worm that wakes beneath;
Nought we know, dies. Shall that alone which knows
Be as a sword consumed before the sheath[1]
By sightless° lightning?—th' intense atom glows   *invisible*
180 A moment, then is quenched in a most cold repose.

21

Alas! that all we loved of him should be,
But for our grief, as if it had not been,
And grief itself be mortal! Woe is me!
Whence are we, and why are we? of what scene
185 The actors or spectators? Great and mean°   *low*
Meet massed in death, who lends what life must borrow.

7. To whom Keats had written "Ode to a Nightingale."
8. In the legend the aged eagle, to renew his youth, flies toward the sun until his old plumage is burned off and the film cleared from his eyes.
9. The reviewer of *Endymion*.
1. The "sword" is the mind that knows; the "sheath" is its vehicle, the material body.

As long as skies are blue, and fields are green,
Evening must usher night, night urge the morrow,
Month follow month with woe, and year wake year to sorrow.

22

190 *He* will awake no more, oh, never more!
"Wake thou," cried Misery, "childless Mother, rise
Out of thy sleep, and slake,° in thy heart's core,   *assuage*
A wound more fierce than his with tears and sighs."
And all the Dreams that watched Urania's eyes,
195 And all the Echoes whom their sister's song[2]
Had held in holy silence, cried: "Arise!"
Swift as a Thought by the snake Memory stung,
From her ambrosial rest the fading Splendour° sprung.   *Urania*

23

She rose like an autumnal Night, that springs
200 Out of the East, and follows wild and drear
The golden Day, which, on eternal wings,
Even as a ghost abandoning a bier,
Had left the Earth a corpse. Sorrow and fear
So struck, so roused, so rapt Urania;
205 So saddened round her like an atmosphere
Of stormy mist; so swept her on her way
Even to the mournful place where Adonais lay.

24

Out of her secret Paradise she sped,
Through camps and cities rough with stone, and steel,
210 And human hearts, which to her aery tread
Yielding not, wounded the invisible
Palms of her tender feet where'er they fell:
And barbed tongues, and thoughts more sharp than they
Rent° the soft Form they never could repel,   *tore*
215 Whose sacred blood, like the young tears of May,
Paved with eternal flowers that undeserving way.

25

In the death chamber for a moment Death
Shamed by the presence of that living Might
Blushed to annihilation, and the breath
220 Revisited those lips, and life's pale light
Flashed through those limbs, so late her dear delight.
"Leave me not wild and drear and comfortless,
As silent lightning leaves the starless night!
Leave me not!" cried Urania: her distress
225 Roused Death: Death rose and smiled, and met her vain caress.

26

"Stay yet awhile! speak to me once again;
Kiss me, so long but as a kiss may live;
And in my heartless[3] breast and burning brain

---

2. I.e., the Echo in line 127.   3. Because her heart had been given to Adonais.

That word, that kiss shall all thoughts else survive
230   With food of saddest memory kept alive,
Now thou art dead, as if it were a part
Of thee, my Adonais! I would give
All that I am to be as thou now art!
But I am chained to Time, and cannot thence depart!

27

235   "Oh gentle child, beautiful as thou wert,
Why didst thou leave the trodden paths of men
Too soon, and with weak hands though mighty heart
Dare° the unpastured dragon in his den?[4]   *challenge*
Defenceless as thou wert, oh where was then
240   Wisdom the mirrored shield, or scorn the spear?[5]
Or hadst thou waited the full cycle, when
Thy spirit should have filled its crescent sphere,[6]
The monsters of life's waste had fled from thee like deer.

28

"The herded wolves, bold only to pursue;
245   The obscene ravens, clamorous o'er the dead;
The vultures to the conqueror's banner true
Who feed where Desolation first has fed,
And whose wings rain contagion;—how they fled,
When like Apollo, from his golden bow,
250   The Pythian of the age[7] one arrow sped
And smiled!—The spoilers tempt no second blow,
They fawn on the proud feet that spurn them lying low.

29

"The sun comes forth, and many reptiles spawn;
He sets, and each ephemeral insect[8] then
255   Is gathered into death without a dawn,
And the immortal stars awake again;
So is it in the world of living men:
A godlike mind soars forth, in its delight
Making earth bare and veiling heaven,[9] and when
260   It sinks, the swarms that dimmed or shared its light
Leave to its kindred lamps[1] the spirit's awful night."

30

Thus ceased she: and the mountain shepherds came,
Their garlands sere, their magic mantles° rent;   *cloaks*
The Pilgrim of Eternity,[2] whose fame
265   Over his living head like Heaven is bent,
An early but enduring monument,

---

4. I.e., the hostile reviewers.
5. The allusion is to Perseus, who had cut off Medusa's head while avoiding the direct sight of her (which would have turned him to stone) by looking only at her reflection in his shield.
6. I.e., when thy spirit, like the full moon, should have reached its maturity.
7. Byron, who had directed against critics of the age his satiric poem *English Bards and Scotch Reviewers* (1809). The allusion is to Apollo, called

"the Pythian" because he had slain the dragon Python.
8. Insect that lives and dies in a single day.
9. As the sun reveals the earth but veils the other stars.
1. The other stars (i.e., creative minds), of lesser brilliance than the sun.
2. Byron, who had referred to his Childe Harold as one of the "wanderers o'er Eternity" (3.669).

Came, veiling all the lightnings of his song
In sorrow; from her wilds Ierne sent
The sweetest lyrist³ of her saddest wrong,
270 And love taught grief to fall like music from his tongue.

31

Midst others of less note, came one frail Form,⁴
A phantom among men; companionless
As the last cloud of an expiring storm
Whose thunder is its knell;° he, as I guess,   *funeral bell*
275 Had gazed on Nature's naked loveliness,
Actæon-like, and now he fled astray
With feeble steps o'er the world's wilderness,
And his own thoughts, along that rugged way,
Pursued, like raging hounds, their father and their prey.⁵

32

280 A pardlike° Spirit beautiful and swift—   *leopardlike*
A Love in desolation masked;—a Power
Girt round with weakness;—it can scarce uplift
The weight of the superincumbent hour;⁶
It is a dying lamp, a falling shower,
285 A breaking billow;—even whilst we speak
Is it not broken? On the withering flower
The killing sun smiles brightly: on a cheek
The life can burn in blood, even while the heart may break.

33

His head was bound with pansies overblown,
290 And faded violets, white, and pied, and blue;
And a light spear topped with a cypress cone,
Round whose rude shaft dark ivy tresses grew⁷
Yet dripping with the forest's noonday dew,
Vibrated, as the ever-beating heart
295 Shook the weak hand that grasped it; of that crew
He came the last, neglected and apart;
A herd-abandoned deer struck by the hunter's dart.

34

All stood aloof, and at his partial moan
Smiled through their tears; well knew that gentle band
300 Who in another's fate now wept his own;
As in the accents of an unknown land,
He sung new sorrow; sad Urania scanned
The Stranger's mien, and murmured: "who art thou?"
He answered not, but with a sudden hand

3. Thomas Moore (1779–1852), from Ireland ("Ierne"), who had written poems about the oppression of his native land.
4. Shelley, represented in one of his aspects— such as the Poet in *Alastor,* rather than the author of *Prometheus Unbound.*
5. Actaeon, while hunting, came upon the naked Diana bathing and, as a punishment, was turned into a stag and torn to pieces by his own hounds.
6. The heavy, overhanging hour of Keats's death.
7. Like the thyrsus, the leaf-entwined and cone-topped staff carried by Dionysus, to whom leopards (see line 280) are sacred. The pansies, which are "overblown," i.e., past their bloom, are emblems of sorrowful thought. The cypress is an emblem of mourning.

305 Made bare his branded and ensanguined° brow,   *bloodied*
     Which was like Cain's or Christ's[8]—Oh! that it should be so!

35

     What softer voice is hushed over the dead?
     Athwart what brow is that dark mantle thrown?
     What form leans sadly o'er the white death-bed,
310 In mockery of monumental stone,[9]
     The heavy heart heaving without a moan?
     If it be He,[1] who, gentlest of the wise,
     Taught, soothed, loved, honoured the departed one;
     Let me not vex, with inharmonious sighs
315 The silence of that heart's accepted sacrifice.

36

     Our Adonais has drunk poison—oh!
     What deaf and viperous murderer could crown
     Life's early cup with such a draught of woe?
     The nameless worm[2] would now itself disown:
320 It felt, yet could escape the magic tone
     Whose prelude held all envy, hate, and wrong,
     But what was howling in one breast alone,
     Silent with expectation of the song,[3]
     Whose master's hand is cold, whose silver lyre unstrung.

37

325 Live thou, whose infamy is not thy fame!
     Live! fear no heavier chastisement from me,
     Thou noteless blot on a remembered name!
     But be thyself, and know thyself to be!
     And ever at thy season be thou free
330 To spill the venom when thy fangs o'erflow:
     Remorse and Self-contempt shall cling to thee;
     Hot Shame shall burn upon thy secret brow,
     And like a beaten hound tremble thou shalt—as now.

38

     Nor let us weep that our delight is fled
335 Far from these carrion kites[4] that scream below;
     He wakes or sleeps with the enduring dead;
     Thou canst not soar where he is sitting now.—
     Dust to the dust! but the pure spirit shall flow
     Back to the burning fountain whence it came,
340 A portion of the Eternal,[5] which must glow
     Through time and change, unquenchably the same,
     Whilst thy cold embers choke the sordid hearth of shame.

8. His bloody ("ensanguined") brow bore a mark like that with which God had branded Cain for murdering Abel—or like that left by Christ's crown of thorns.
9. In imitation of a memorial statue.
1. Leigh Hunt, close friend of both Keats and Shelley.
2. Snake—the anonymous reviewer.

3. The promise of later greatness in Keats's early poems "held . . . silent" the expression of "all envy, hate, and wrong" except the reviewer's.
4. A species of hawk that feeds on dead flesh.
5. Shelley adopts for this poem the Neoplatonic view that all life and all forms emanate from the Absolute, the eternal One. The Absolute is imaged as both a radiant light source and an overflowing

39

Peace, peace! he is not dead, he doth not sleep—
He hath awakened from the dream of life—
'Tis we, who lost in stormy visions, keep
With phantoms an unprofitable strife,
And in mad trance, strike with our spirit's knife
Invulnerable nothings.—*We* decay
Like corpses in a charnel; fear and grief
Convulse us and consume us day by day,
And cold hopes swarm like worms within our living clay.

40

He has outsoared the shadow of our night;[6]
Envy and calumny° and hate and pain,   slander
And that unrest which men miscall delight,
Can touch him not and torture not again;
From the contagion of the world's slow stain
He is secure, and now can never mourn
A heart grown cold, a head grown grey in vain;
Nor, when the spirit's self has ceased to burn,
With sparkless ashes load an unlamented urn.

41

He lives, he wakes—'tis Death is dead, not he;
Mourn not for Adonais.—Thou young Dawn
Turn all thy dew to splendour, for from thee
The spirit thou lamentest is not gone;
Ye caverns and ye forests, cease to moan!
Cease ye faint flowers and fountains, and thou Air
Which like a mourning veil thy scarf hadst thrown
O'er the abandoned Earth, now leave it bare
Even to the joyous stars which smile on its despair![7]

42

He is made one with Nature: there is heard
His voice in all her music, from the moan
Of thunder, to the song of night's sweet bird;[8]
He is a presence to be felt and known
In darkness and in light, from herb and stone,
Spreading itself where'er that Power may move
Which has withdrawn his being to its own;
Which wields the world with never wearied love,
Sustains it from beneath, and kindles it above.

43

He is a portion of the loveliness
Which once he made more lovely: he doth bear
His part, while the one Spirit's plastic[9] stress
Sweeps through the dull dense world, compelling there,

fountain, which circulates continuously through the dross of matter (stanza 43) and back to its source.
6. He has soared beyond the shadow cast by the earth as it intercepts the sun's light.
7. Shelley's science is, as usual, accurate: it is the

envelope of air around the earth that, by diffusing and reflecting sunlight, veils the stars so that they are invisible during the day.
8. The nightingale, in allusion to Keats's "Ode to a Nightingale."
9. Formative, shaping.

All new successions to the forms they wear;
Torturing th' unwilling dross that checks its flight
385   To its own likeness, as each mass may bear;¹
And bursting in its beauty and its might
From trees and beasts and men into the Heaven's light.

44

The splendours of the firmament of time
May be eclipsed, but are extinguished not;
390   Like stars to their appointed height they climb
And death is a low mist which cannot blot
The brightness it may veil.² When lofty thought
Lifts a young heart above its mortal lair,
And love and life contend in it, for what°   *whatever*
395   Shall be its earthly doom,° the dead live there³   *destiny*
And move like winds of light on dark and stormy air.

45

The inheritors of unfulfilled renown⁴
Rose from their thrones, built beyond mortal thought,
Far in the Unapparent. Chatterton
400   Rose pale, his solemn agony had not
Yet faded from him; Sidney, as he fought
And as he fell and as he lived and loved
Sublimely mild, a Spirit without spot,
Arose; and Lucan, by his death approved:°   *justified*
405   Oblivion as they rose shrank like a thing reproved.

46

And many more, whose names on Earth are dark
But whose transmitted effluence cannot die
So long as fire outlives the parent spark,
Rose, robed in dazzling immortality.
410   "Thou art become as one of us," they cry,
"It was for thee yon kingless sphere has long
Swung blind in unascended majesty,
Silent alone amid an Heaven of song.
Assume thy winged throne, thou Vesper of our throng!"⁵

47

415   Who mourns for Adonais? oh come forth
Fond° wretch! and know thyself and him aright.   *foolish*
Clasp with thy panting soul the pendulous⁶ Earth;
As from a centre, dart thy spirit's light
Beyond all worlds, until its spacious might°   *power*
420   Satiate the void circumference: then shrink

---

1. I.e., to the degree that a particular substance will permit.
2. The radiance of stars (i.e., of poets) persists, even when they are temporarily "eclipsed" by another heavenly body, or obscured by the veil of the earth's atmosphere.
3. I.e., in the thought of the "young heart."
4. Poets who (like Keats) died young, before achieving their full measure of fame: the seventeen-year-old Thomas Chatterton (1752–1770) was believed to have committed suicide out

of despair over his poverty and lack of recognition, Sir Philip Sidney (1554–1586) died in battle at thirty-two, and the Roman poet Lucan (39–65 C.E.) killed himself at twenty-six to escape a sentence of death for having plotted against the tyrant Nero.
5. Adonais assumes his place in the sphere of Vesper, the evening star, hitherto unoccupied ("kingless"), hence also "silent" amid the music of the other spheres.
6. Suspended, floating in space.

Even to a point within our day and night;[7]
And keep thy heart light lest it make thee sink
When hope has kindled hope, and lured thee to the brink.

48

Or go to Rome, which is the sepulchre
425   O, not of him, but of our joy: 'tis nought
That ages, empires, and religions there
Lie buried in the ravage they have wrought;
For such as he can lend,—they[8] borrow not
Glory from those who made the world their prey;
430   And he is gathered to the kings of thought
Who waged contention with their time's decay,
And of the past are all that cannot pass away.

49

Go thou to Rome,—at once the Paradise,
The grave, the city, and the wilderness;
435   And where its wrecks° like shattered mountains rise,   *ruins*
And flowering weeds, and fragrant copses[9] dress
The bones of Desolation's nakedness
Pass, till the Spirit of the spot shall lead
Thy footsteps to a slope of green access[1]
440   Where, like an infant's smile, over the dead,
A light of laughing flowers along the grass is spread.

50

And grey walls moulder round,[2] on which dull Time
Feeds, like slow fire upon a hoary brand;[3]
And one keen pyramid with wedge sublime,[4]
445   Pavilioning the dust of him who planned
This refuge for his memory, doth stand
Like flame transformed to marble; and beneath,
A field is spread, on which a newer band
Have pitched in Heaven's smile their camp of death[5]
450   Welcoming him we lose with scarce extinguished breath.

51

Here pause: these graves are all too young as yet
To have outgrown the sorrow which consigned
Its charge to each; and if the seal is set,
Here, on one fountain of a mourning mind,[6]
455   Break it not thou! too surely shalt thou find
Thine own well full, if thou returnest home,
Of tears and gall. From the world's bitter wind

---

7. The poet bids the mourner to stretch his imagination so as to reach the poet's own cosmic viewpoint and then allow it to contract ("shrink") back to its ordinary vantage point on Earth—where, unlike Adonais in his heavenly place, we have an alternation of day and night.
8. Poets such as Keats.
9. Undergrowth. In Shelley's time the ruins of ancient Rome were overgrown with weeds and shrubs, almost as if the ground were returning to its natural state.
1. The Protestant Cemetery, Keats's burial place.

The next line is a glancing allusion to Shelley's three-year-old son, William, also buried there.
2. The wall of ancient Rome formed one boundary of the cemetery.
3. A burning log, white with ash.
4. The tomb of Caius Cestius, a Roman tribune, just outside the cemetery.
5. A common name for a cemetery in Italy is *camposanto*, "holy camp or ground." Shelley is punning seriously on the Italian word.
6. Shelley's mourning for his son.

Seek shelter in the shadow of the tomb.
What Adonais is, why fear we to become?

52

460 The One remains, the many change and pass;
Heaven's light forever shines, Earth's shadows fly;
Life, like a dome of many-coloured glass,
Stains the white radiance of Eternity,
Until Death tramples it to fragments.[7]—Die,
465 If thou wouldst be with that which thou dost seek!
Follow where all is fled!—Rome's azure sky,
Flowers, ruins, statues, music, words, are weak
The glory they transfuse with fitting truth to speak.

53

Why linger, why turn back, why shrink, my Heart?
470 Thy hopes are gone before; from all things here
They have departed; thou shouldst now depart!
A light is past° from the revolving year,   *passed*
And man, and woman; and what still is dear
Attracts to crush, repels to make thee wither.
475 The soft sky smiles,—the low wind whispers near:
'Tis Adonais calls! oh, hasten thither,
No more let Life divide what Death can join together.

54

That Light whose smile kindles the Universe,
That Beauty in which all things work and move,
480 That Benediction which the eclipsing Curse
Of birth can quench not, that sustaining Love
Which through the web of being blindly wove
By man and beast and earth and air and sea,
Burns bright or dim, as each are mirrors of[8]
485 The fire for which all thirst;[9] now beams on me,
Consuming the last clouds of cold mortality.

55

The breath whose might I have invoked in song[1]
Descends on me; my spirit's bark is driven,
Far from the shore, far from the trembling throng
490 Whose sails were never to the tempest given;
The massy earth and sphered skies are riven![2]
I am borne darkly, fearfully, afar;
Whilst burning through the inmost veil of Heaven,
The soul of Adonais, like a star,
495 Beacons from the abode where the Eternal are.

1821   1821

---

7. Earthly life colors ("stains") the pure white light of the One, which is the source of all light (see lines 339–40, n. 5). The azure sky, flowers, etc., of lines 466–68 exemplify earthly colors that, however beautiful, fall far short of the "glory" of the pure Light that they transmit but also refract ("transfuse").
8. I.e., according to the degree that each reflects.
9. The "thirst" of the human spirit is to return to the fountain and fire (the "burning fountain," line 339) that are its source.
1. Two years earlier Shelley had "invoked" (prayed to, and also asked for) "the breath of Autumn's being" in his "Ode to the West Wind" (p. 772).
2. In her 1839 edition of her husband's works, Mary Shelley asked: "who but will regard as a prophecy the last stanza of the 'Adonais'?"

When the lamp is shattered

When the lamp is shattered
The light in the dust lies dead—
When the cloud is scattered
The rainbow's glory is shed—
5   When the lute is broken
Sweet tones are remembered not—
When the lips have spoken
Loved accents are soon forgot.

As music and splendour
10   Survive not the lamp and the lute,
The heart's echoes render
No song when the spirit is mute—
No song—but sad dirges
Like the wind through a ruined cell
15   Or the mournful surges
That ring the dead seaman's knell.

When hearts have once mingled
Love first leaves the well-built nest—
The weak one is singled
20   To endure what it once possest.
O Love! who bewailest
The frailty of all things here,
Why choose you the frailest
For your cradle, your home and your bier?

25   Its passions will rock thee
As the storms rock the ravens on high—
Bright Reason will mock thee
Like the Sun from a wintry sky—
From thy nest every rafter
30   Will rot, and thine eagle home
Leave thee naked to laughter
When leaves fall and cold winds come.

1822   1824

To Jane[1] (The keen stars were twinkling)

The keen stars were twinkling
And the fair moon was rising among them,
    Dear Jane.
The guitar was tinkling
5   But the notes were not sweet 'till you sung them
    Again.—

1. Jane Williams, the common-law wife of Shelley's close friend Edward Williams.

As the moon's soft splendour
O'er the faint cold starlight of Heaven
    Is thrown—
10   So your voice most tender
To the strings without soul had then given
    Its own.

The stars will awaken,
Though the moon sleep a full hour later,
15   Tonight;
No leaf will be shaken
While the dews of your melody scatter
    Delight.
Though the sound overpowers
20 Sing again, with your dear voice revealing
    A tone
Of some world far from ours,
Where music and moonlight and feeling
    Are one.

1822   1832

A Defence of Poetry

In 1820 Shelley's good friend Thomas Love Peacock published an ironic essay, "The Four Ages of Poetry," implicitly directed against the towering claims for poetry and the poetic imagination made by his Romantic contemporaries. In this essay, which is available at Norton Literature Online, Peacock adopted the premise of Wordsworth and some other Romantic critics—that poetry in its origin was a primitive use of language and mind—but from this premise he proceeded to draw the conclusion that poetry had become a useless anachronism in his own Age of Bronze, a time defined by new sciences (including economics and political theory) and technologies that had the potential to improve the world. Peacock was a poet as well as an excellent prose satirist, and Shelley saw the joke; but he also recognized that the view that Peacock, as a satirist, had assumed was very close to that actually held in his day by Utilitarian philosophers and the material-minded public, which either attacked or contemptuously ignored the imaginative faculty and its achievements. He therefore undertook, as he good-humoredly wrote to Peacock, "to break a lance with you . . . in honor of my mistress Urania" (giving the cause for which he battled the name that Milton had used for the muse inspiring *Paradise Lost*), even though he was only "the knight of the shield of shadow and the lance of gossamere." The result was "A Defence of Poetry," planned to consist of three parts. The last two parts were never written, and even the existing section, written in 1821, remained unpublished until 1840, eighteen years after Shelley's death.

Shelley's emphasis in this essay is not on the particularity of individual poems but on the universal and permanent qualities and values that, he believes, all great poems, as products of imagination, have in common. Shelley in addition extends the term *poet* to include all creative minds that break out of the conditions of their historical time and place in order to envision such values. This category includes not only writers in prose as well as verse but also artists, legislators, prophets, and the founders of new social and religious institutions.

The "Defence" is an eloquent and enduring claim for the indispensability of the visionary and creative imagination in all the great human concerns. Few later social critics have equaled the cogency of Shelley's attack on our acquisitive society and its narrowly material concepts of utility and progress. Such a bias has opened the way to enormous advances in the physical sciences and our material well-being, but without a proportionate development of our "poetic faculty," the moral imagination. The result, Shelley says, is that "man, having enslaved the elements, remains himself a slave."

From A Defence of Poetry

or Remarks Suggested by an Essay Entitled "The Four Ages of Poetry"

According to one mode of regarding those two classes of mental action, which are called reason and imagination, the former may be considered as mind contemplating the relations borne by one thought to another, however produced; and the latter, as mind acting upon those thoughts so as to colour them with its own light, and composing from them, as from elements, other thoughts, each containing within itself the principle of its own integrity. The one[1] is the *to poiein*,[2] or the principle of synthesis, and has for its objects those forms which are common to universal nature and existence itself; the other is the *to logizein*,[3] or principle of analysis, and its action regards the relations of things, simply as relations; considering thoughts, not in their integral unity, but as the algebraical representations which conduct to certain general results. Reason is the enumeration of quantities already known; imagination is the perception of the value of those quantities, both separately and as a whole. Reason respects the differences, and imagination the similitudes of things. Reason is to Imagination as the instrument to the agent, as the body to the spirit, as the shadow to the substance.

Poetry, in a general sense, may be defined to be "the expression of the Imagination": and poetry is connate with the origin of man. Man is an instrument over which a series of external and internal impressions are driven, like the alternations of an ever-changing wind over an Æolian lyre,[4] which move it by their motion to ever-changing melody. But there is a principle within the human being, and perhaps within all sentient beings, which acts otherwise than in the lyre, and produces not melody, alone, but harmony, by an internal adjustment of the sounds or motions thus excited to the impressions which excite them. It is as if the lyre could accommodate its chords to the motions of that which strikes them, in a determined proportion of sound; even as the musician can accommodate his voice to the sound of the lyre. A child at play by itself will express its delight by its voice and motions; and every inflexion of tone and every gesture will bear exact relation to a corresponding antitype in the pleasurable impressions which awakened it; it will be the reflected image of that impression; and as the lyre trembles and sounds after the wind has died away, so the child seeks, by prolonging in its voice and motions the duration of the effect, to prolong also a consciousness of the cause. In relation to

1. The imagination. "The other" (later in the sentence) is the reason.
2. Making. The Greek word from which the English term *poet* derives means "maker," and "maker" was often used as equivalent to "poet" by Renaissance critics such as Sir Philip Sidney in his

Defence of Poesy, which Shelley had carefully studied.
3. Calculating, reasoning.
4. A wind harp (see Coleridge, "The Eolian Harp," p. 426).

the objects which delight a child, these expressions are, what poetry is to higher objects. The savage (for the savage is to ages what the child is to years) expresses the emotions produced in him by surrounding objects in a similar manner; and language and gesture, together with plastic[5] or pictorial imitation, become the image of the combined effect of those objects, and of his apprehension of them. Man in society, with all his passions and his pleasures, next becomes the object of the passions and pleasures of man; an additional class of emotions produces an augmented treasure of expressions; and language, gesture, and the imitative arts, become at once the representation and the medium, the pencil and the picture, the chisel and the statue, the chord and the harmony. The social sympathies, or those laws from which as from its elements society results, begin to develope themselves from the moment that two human beings coexist; the future is contained within the present as the plant within the seed; and equality, diversity, unity, contrast, mutual dependence, become the principles alone capable of affording the motives according to which the will of a social being is determined to action, inasmuch as he is social; and constitute pleasure in sensation, virtue in sentiment, beauty in art, truth in reasoning, and love in the intercourse of kind. Hence men, even in the infancy of society, observe a certain order in their words and actions, distinct from that of the objects and the impressions represented by them, all expression being subject to the laws of that from which it proceeds. But let us dismiss those more general considerations which might involve an enquiry into the principles of society itself, and restrict our view to the manner in which the imagination is expressed upon its forms.

In the youth of the world, men dance and sing and imitate natural objects, observing[6] in these actions, as in all others, a certain rhythm or order. And, although all men observe a similar, they observe not the same order, in the motions of the dance, in the melody of the song, in the combinations of language, in the series of their imitations of natural objects. For there is a certain order or rhythm belonging to each of these classes of mimetic representation, from which the hearer and the spectator receive an intenser and purer pleasure than from any other: the sense of an approximation to this order has been called taste, by modern writers. Every man in the infancy of art, observes an order which approximates more or less closely to that from which this highest delight results: but the diversity is not sufficiently marked, as that its gradations should be sensible,[7] except in those instances where the predominance of this faculty of approximation to the beautiful (for so we may be permitted to name the relation between this highest pleasure and its cause) is very great. Those in whom it exists in excess are poets, in the most universal sense of the word; and the pleasure resulting from the manner in which they express the influence of society or nature upon their own minds, communicates itself to others, and gathers a sort of reduplication from that community. Their language is vitally metaphorical; that is, it marks the before unapprehended relations of things, and perpetuates their apprehension, until the words which represent them, become through time signs for portions or classes of thoughts[8] instead of pictures of integral thoughts; and then if no new poets should arise to create afresh the associations which have been thus disorganized, language

5. Sculptural.
6. Following, obeying.

7. Discernible.
8. I.e., abstract concepts.

will be dead to all the nobler purposes of human intercourse. These similitudes or relations are finely said by Lord Bacon to be "the same footsteps of nature impressed upon the various subjects of the world"[9]—and he considers the faculty which perceives them as the storehouse of axioms common to all knowledge. In the infancy of society every author is necessarily a poet, because language itself is poetry; and to be a poet is to apprehend the true and the beautiful, in a word the good which exists in the relation, subsisting, first between existence and perception, and secondly between perception and expression. Every original language near to its source is in itself the chaos of a cyclic poem:[1] the copiousness of lexicography and the distinctions of grammar are the works of a later age, and are merely the catalogue and the form of the creations of Poetry.

But Poets, or those who imagine and express this indestructible order, are not only the authors of language and of music, of the dance and architecture and statuary and painting: they are the institutors of laws, and the founders of civil society and the inventors of the arts of life and the teachers, who draw into a certain propinquity with the beautiful and the true that partial apprehension of the agencies of the invisible world which is called religion.[2] Hence all original religions are allegorical, or susceptible of allegory, and like Janus[3] have a double face of false and true. Poets, according to the circumstances of the age and nation in which they appeared, were called in the earlier epochs of the world legislators or prophets:[4] a poet essentially comprises and unites both these characters. For he not only beholds intensely the present as it is, and discovers those laws according to which present things ought to be ordered, but he beholds the future in the present, and his thoughts are the germs of the flower and the fruit of latest time. Not that I assert poets to be prophets in the gross sense of the word, or that they can foretell the form as surely as they foreknow the spirit of events: such is the pretence of superstition which would make poetry an attribute of prophecy, rather than prophecy an attribute of poetry. A Poet participates in the eternal, the infinite, and the one; as far as relates to his conceptions, time and place and number are not. The grammatical forms which express the moods of time, and the difference of persons and the distinction of place are convertible with respect to the highest poetry without injuring it as poetry, and the choruses of Æschylus, and the book of Job, and Dante's Paradise would afford, more than any other writings, examples of this fact, if the limits of this essay did not forbid citation. The creations of sculpture, painting, and music, are illustrations still more decisive.

Language, colour, form, and religious and civil habits of action are all the instruments and materials of poetry; they may be called poetry by that figure of speech which considers the effect as a synonime of the cause. But poetry in a more restricted sense[5] expresses those arrangements of language, and especially metrical language, which are created by that imperial faculty, whose throne is curtained within the invisible nature of man. And this springs from

9. Francis Bacon's *The Advancement of Learning* 3.1.
1. A group of poems (e.g., "the Arthurian cycle") that deal with the same subject.
2. Here Shelley enlarges the scope of the term *poetry* to denote all the creative achievements, or imaginative breakthroughs, of humankind, including noninstitutional religious insights.
3. Roman god of beginnings and endings, often

represented by two heads facing opposite directions.
4. Sir Philip Sidney had pointed out, in his *Defence of Poesy*, that *vates*, the Roman term for "poet," signifies "a diviner, fore-seer, or Prophet."
5. I.e., restricted to specifically verbal poetry, as against the inclusive sense in which Shelley has been applying the term.

the nature itself of language, which is a more direct representation of the actions and passions of our internal being, and is susceptible of more various and delicate combinations, than colour, form, or motion, and is more plastic and obedient to the controul of that faculty of which it is the creation. For language is arbitrarily produced by the Imagination and has relation to thoughts alone; but all other materials, instruments and conditions of art, have relations among each other, which limit and interpose between conception and expression. The former[6] is as a mirror which reflects, the latter as a cloud which enfeebles, the light of which both are mediums of communication. Hence the fame of sculptors, painters and musicians, although the intrinsic powers of the great masters of these arts, may yield in no degree to that of those who have employed language as the hieroglyphic of their thoughts, has never equalled that of poets in the restricted sense of the term; as two performers of equal skill will produce unequal effects from a guitar and a harp. The fame of legislators and founders of religions, so long as their institutions last, alone seems to exceed that of poets in the restricted sense; but it can scarcely be a question whether, if we deduct the celebrity which their flattery of the gross opinions of the vulgar usually conciliates, together with that which belonged to them in their higher character of poets, any excess will remain.

We have thus circumscribed the meaning of the word Poetry within the limits of that art which is the most familiar and the most perfect expression of the faculty itself. It is necessary however to make the circle still narrower, and to determine the distinction between measured and unmeasured language;[7] for the popular division into prose and verse is inadmissible in accurate philosophy.

Sounds as well as thoughts have relation both between each other and towards that which they represent, and a perception of the order of those relations has always been found connected with a perception of the order of the relations of thoughts. Hence the language of poets has ever affected a certain uniform and harmonious recurrence of sound, without which it were not poetry, and which is scarcely less indispensable to the communication of its influence, than the words themselves, without reference to that peculiar order. Hence the vanity of translation; it were as wise to cast a violet into a crucible that you might discover the formal principle of its colour and odour, as seek to transfuse from one language into another the creations of a poet. The plant must spring again from its seed or it will bear no flower—and this is the burthen of the curse of Babel.[8]

An observation of the regular mode of the recurrence of this harmony in the language of poetical minds, together with its relation to music, produced metre, or a certain system of traditional forms of harmony of language. Yet it is by no means essential that a poet should accommodate his language to this traditional form, so that the harmony which is its spirit, be observed. The practise is indeed convenient and popular, and to be preferred, especially in such composition as includes much form and action: but every great poet must inevitably innovate upon the example of his predecessors in the exact structure

6. I.e., language, as opposed to the media of sculpture, painting, and music.
7. I.e., in meter versus in prose.
8. When the descendants of Noah, who spoke a single language, undertook to build the Tower of Babel, which would reach heaven, God cut short the attempt by multiplying languages so that the builders could no longer communicate (see Genesis 11.1–9).

of his peculiar versification. The distinction between poets and prose writers is a vulgar error. The distinction between philosophers and poets has been anticipated.[9] Plato was essentially a poet—the truth and splendour of his imagery and the melody of his language is the most intense that it is possible to conceive. He rejected the measure of the epic, dramatic, and lyrical forms, because he sought to kindle a harmony in thoughts divested of shape and action, and he forbore to invent any regular plan of rhythm which would include, under determinate forms, the varied pauses of his style. Cicero[1] sought to imitate the cadence of his periods but with little success. Lord Bacon was a poet.[2] His language has a sweet and majestic rhythm, which satisfies the sense, no less than the almost superhuman wisdom of his philosophy satisfies the intellect; it is a strain which distends, and then bursts the circumference of the hearer's mind, and pours itself forth together with it into the universal element with which it has perpetual sympathy. All the authors of revolutions in opinion are not only necessarily poets as they are inventors, nor even as their words unveil the permanent analogy of things by images which participate in the life of truth; but as their periods are harmonious and rhythmical and contain in themselves the elements of verse; being the echo of the eternal music. Nor are those supreme poets, who have employed traditional forms of rhythm on account of the form and action of their subjects, less capable of perceiving and teaching the truth of things, than those who have omitted that form. Shakespeare, Dante and Milton (to confine ourselves to modern writers) are philosophers of the very loftiest power.

A poem is the very image of life expressed in its eternal truth. There is this difference between a story and a poem, that a story is a catalogue of detached facts, which have no other bond of connexion than time, place, circumstance, cause and effect; the other is the creation of actions according to the unchangeable forms of human nature, as existing in the mind of the creator, which is itself the image of all other minds. The one is partial, and applies only to a definite period of time, and a certain combination of events which can never again recur; the other is universal, and contains within itself the germ of a relation to whatever motives or actions have place in the possible varieties of human nature. Time, which destroys the beauty and the use of the story of particular facts, stript of the poetry which should invest them, augments that of Poetry, and for ever develops new and wonderful applications of the eternal truth which it contains. Hence epitomes[3] have been called the moths of just history;[4] they eat out the poetry of it. The story of particular facts is as a mirror which obscures and distorts that which should be beautiful: Poetry is a mirror which makes beautiful that which is distorted.

The parts of a composition may be poetical, without the composition as a whole being a poem. A single sentence may be considered as a whole though it be found in a series of unassimilated portions; a single word even may be a spark of inextinguishable thought. And thus all the great historians, Herodotus, Plutarch, Livy,[5] were poets; and although the plan of these writers, especially that of Livy, restrained them from developing this faculty in its highest

---

9. I.e., in what Shelley has already said.
1. Marcus Tullius Cicero, the great Roman orator of the 1st century B.C.E.
2. See the *Filium Labyrinthi* and the *Essay on Death* particularly [Shelley's note].
3. Abstracts, summaries.
4. By Bacon in *The Advancement of Learning*

2.2.4.
5. Titus Livius (59 B.C.E.–17 C.E.) wrote an immense history of Rome. Herodotus (ca. 480–ca. 425 B.C.E.) wrote the first systematic history of Greece. Plutarch (ca. 46–ca. 120 C.E.) wrote *Parallel Lives* (of eminent Greeks and Romans).

degree, they make copious and ample amends for their subjection, by filling all the interstices of their subjects with living images.

Having determined what is poetry, and who are poets, let us proceed to estimate its effects upon society.

Poetry is ever accompanied with pleasure: all spirits on which it falls, open themselves to receive the wisdom which is mingled with its delight. In the infancy of the world, neither poets themselves nor their auditors are fully aware of the excellence of poetry: for it acts in a divine and unapprehended manner, beyond and above consciousness; and it is reserved for future generations to contemplate and measure the mighty cause and effect in all the strength and splendour of their union. Even in modern times, no living poet ever arrived at the fulness of his fame; the jury which sits in judgement upon a poet, belonging as he does to all time, must be composed of his peers: it must be impanelled by Time from the selectest of the wise of many generations. A Poet is a nightingale, who sits in darkness and sings to cheer its own solitude with sweet sounds; his auditors are as men entranced by the melody of an unseen musician, who feel that they are moved and softened, yet know not whence or why. The poems of Homer and his contemporaries were the delight of infant Greece; they were the elements of that social system which is the column upon which all succeeding civilization has reposed. Homer embodied the ideal perfection of his age in human character; nor can we doubt that those who read his verses were awakened to an ambition of becoming like to Achilles, Hector and Ulysses: the truth and beauty of friendship, patriotism and persevering devotion to an object, were unveiled to the depths in these immortal creations: the sentiments of the auditors must have been refined and enlarged by a sympathy with such great and lovely impersonations, until from admiring they imitated, and from imitation they identified themselves with the objects of their admiration. Nor let it be objected, that these characters are remote from moral perfection, and that they can by no means be considered as edifying patterns for general imitation. Every epoch under names more or less specious has deified its peculiar errors; Revenge is the naked Idol of the worship of a semi-barbarous age; and Self-deceit is the veiled Image of unknown evil before which luxury and satiety lie prostrate. But a poet considers the vices of his contemporaries as the temporary dress in which his creations must be arrayed, and which cover without concealing the eternal proportions of their beauty. An epic or dramatic personage is understood to wear them around his soul, as he may the antient armour or the modern uniform around his body; whilst it is easy to conceive a dress more graceful than either. The beauty of the internal nature cannot be so far concealed by its accidental vesture, but that the spirit of its form shall communicate itself to the very disguise, and indicate the shape it hides from the manner in which it is worn. A majestic form and graceful motions will express themselves through the most barbarous and tasteless costume. Few poets of the highest class have chosen to exhibit the beauty of their conceptions in its naked truth and splendour; and it is doubtful whether the alloy of costume, habit, etc., be not necessary to temper this planetary music[6] for mortal ears.

The whole objection, however, of the immorality of poetry[7] rests upon a misconception of the manner in which poetry acts to produce the moral

6. The music made by the revolving crystalline spheres of the planets, inaudible to human ears.
7. In the preceding paragraph Shelley has been

implicitly dealing with the charge, voiced by Plato in his *Republic,* that poetry is immoral because it represents evil characters acting evilly.

improvement of man. Ethical science[8] arranges the elements which poetry has created, and propounds schemes and proposes examples of civil and domestic life: nor is it for want of admirable doctrines that men hate, and despise, and censure, and deceive, and subjugate one another. But Poetry acts in another and diviner manner. It awakens and enlarges the mind itself by rendering it the receptacle of a thousand unapprehended combinations of thought. Poetry lifts the veil from the hidden beauty of the world, and makes familiar objects be as if they were not familiar; it reproduces[9] all that it represents, and the impersonations clothed in its Elysian light stand thenceforward in the minds of those who have once contemplated them, as memorials of that gentle and exalted content[1] which extends itself over all thoughts and actions with which it coexists. The great secret of morals is Love; or a going out of our own nature, and an identification of ourselves with the beautiful which exists in thought, action, or person, not our own. A man, to be greatly good, must imagine intensely and comprehensively; he must put himself in the place of another and of many others; the pains and pleasures of his species must become his own. The great instrument of moral good is the imagination;[2] and poetry administers to the effect by acting upon the cause. Poetry enlarges the circumference of the imagination by replenishing it with thoughts of ever new delight, which have the power of attracting and assimilating to their own nature all other thoughts, and which form new intervals and interstices whose void for ever craves fresh food. Poetry strengthens that faculty which is the organ of the moral nature of man, in the same manner as exercise strengthens a limb. A Poet therefore would do ill to embody his own conceptions of right and wrong, which are usually those of his place and time, in his poetical creations, which participate in neither. By this assumption of the inferior office of interpreting the effect, in which perhaps after all he might acquit himself but imperfectly, he would resign the glory in a participation in the cause.[3] There was little danger that Homer, or any of the eternal Poets, should have so far misunderstood themselves as to have abdicated this throne of their widest dominion. Those in whom the poetical faculty, though great, is less intense, as Euripides, Lucan, Tasso,[4] Spenser, have frequently affected[5] a moral aim, and the effect of their poetry is diminished in exact proportion to the degree in which they compel us to advert to this purpose.[6]

☆   ☆   ☆

It is difficult to define pleasure in its highest sense; the definition involving a number of apparent paradoxes. For, from an inexplicable defect of harmony in the constitution of human nature, the pain of the inferior is frequently connected with the pleasures of the superior portions of our being. Sorrow,

8. Moral philosophy.
9. Produces anew, re-creates.
1. Contentment.
2. Central to Shelley's theory is the concept (developed by 18th-century philosophers) of the sympathetic imagination—the faculty by which an individual is enabled to identify with the thoughts and feelings of others. Shelley insists that the faculty in poetry that enables us to share the joys and sufferings of invented characters is also the basis of all morality, for it compels us to feel for others as we feel for ourselves.
3. The "effect," or the explicit moral standards into which imaginative insights are translated at a particular time or place, is contrasted to the

"cause" of all morality, the imagination itself.
4. Tasso Torquato (1544–1595), Italian poet, author of *Jerusalem Delivered*, an epic poem about a crusade. Euripides (ca. 484–406 B.C.E.), Greek writer of tragedies. Lucan (39–65 C.E.), Roman poet, author of the *Pharsalia*.
5. Assumed, adopted.
6. In the following, omitted passage, Shelley reviews the history of drama and poetry in relation to civilization and morality and proceeds to refute the charge that poets are less useful than "reasoners and merchants." He begins by defining *utility* in terms of pleasure and then distinguishes between the lower (physical and material) and the higher (imaginative) pleasures.

terror, anguish, despair itself are often the chosen expressions of an approximation to the highest good. Our sympathy in tragic fiction depends on this principle; tragedy delights by affording a shadow of the pleasure which exists in pain. This is the source also of the melancholy which is inseparable from the sweetest melody. The pleasure that is in sorrow is sweeter than the pleasure of pleasure itself. And hence the saying, "It is better to go to the house of mourning, than to the house of mirth."[7] Not that this highest species of pleasure is necessarily linked with pain. The delight of love and friendship, the ecstasy of the admiration of nature, the joy of the perception and still more of the creation of poetry is often wholly unalloyed.

The production and assurance of pleasure in this highest sense is true utility. Those who produce and preserve this pleasure are Poets or poetical philosophers.

The exertions of Locke, Hume, Gibbon, Voltaire, Rousseau,[8] and their disciples, in favour of oppressed and deluded humanity, are entitled to the gratitude of mankind. Yet it is easy to calculate the degree of moral and intellectual improvement which the world would have exhibited, had they never lived. A little more nonsense would have been talked for a century or two; and perhaps a few more men, women, and children, burnt as heretics. We might not at this moment have been congratulating each other on the abolition of the Inquisition in Spain.[9] But it exceeds all imagination to conceive what would have been the moral condition of the world if neither Dante, Petrarch, Boccaccio, Chaucer, Shakespeare, Calderon, Lord Bacon, nor Milton, had ever existed; if Raphael and Michael Angelo had never been born; if the Hebrew poetry had never been translated; if a revival of the study of Greek literature had never taken place; if no monuments of antient sculpture had been handed down to us; and if the poetry of the religion of the antient world had been extinguished together with its belief. The human mind could never, except by the intervention of these excitements, have been awakened to the invention of the grosser sciences, and that application of analytical reasoning to the aberrations of society, which it is now attempted to exalt over the direct expression of the inventive and creative faculty itself.

We have more moral, political and historical wisdom, than we know how to reduce into practice; we have more scientific and economical knowledge than can be accommodated to the just distribution of the produce which it multiplies. The poetry in these systems of thought, is concealed by the accumulation of facts and calculating processes. There is no want of knowledge respecting what is wisest and best in morals, government, and political economy, or at least, what is wiser and better than what men now practise and endure. But we let "I *dare not* wait upon I *would*, like the poor cat i' the adage."[1] We want[2] the creative faculty to imagine that which we know; we want the generous impulse to act that which we imagine; we want the poetry of life: our calculations have outrun conception; we have eaten more than we can digest. The cultivation of those sciences which have enlarged the limits of the empire of man over the external world, has, for want of the poetical faculty, proportion-

---

7. Ecclesiastes 7.2.
8. I follow the classification adopted by the author of Four Ages of Poetry. But Rousseau was essentially a poet. The others, even Voltaire, were mere reasoners [Shelley's note].
9. The Inquisition had been suspended following the Spanish Revolution of 1820, the year before

Shelley wrote this essay; it was not abolished permanently until 1834.
1. The words with which Lady Macbeth encourages her husband's ambition (Shakespeare, *Macbeth* 1.7.44–45).
2. Lack.

ally circumscribed those of the internal world; and man, having enslaved the elements, remains himself a slave. To what but a cultivation of the mechanical arts in a degree disproportioned to the presence of the creative faculty, which is the basis of all knowledge, is to be attributed the abuse of all invention for abridging and combining labour, to the exasperation of the inequality of mankind? From what other cause has it arisen that these inventions which should have lightened, have added a weight to the curse imposed on Adam?[3] Poetry, and the principle of Self, of which money is the visible incarnation, are the God and Mammon of the world.[4]

The functions of the poetical faculty are two-fold; by one it creates new materials of knowledge, and power and pleasure; by the other it engenders in the mind a desire to reproduce and arrange them according to a certain rhythm and order which may be called the beautiful and the good. The cultivation of poetry is never more to be desired than at periods when, from an excess of the selfish and calculating principle, the accumulation of the materials of external life exceed the quantity of the power of assimilating them to the internal laws of human nature. The body has then become too unwieldy for that which animates it.

Poetry is indeed something divine. It is at once the centre and circumference of knowledge; it is that which comprehends all science, and that to which all science must be referred. It is at the same time the root and blossom of all other systems of thought; it is that from which all spring, and that which adorns all; and that which, if blighted, denies the fruit and the seed, and withholds from the barren world the nourishment and the succession of the scions of the tree of life. It is the perfect and consummate surface and bloom of things; it is as the odour and the colour of the rose to the texture of the elements which compose it, as the form and the splendour of unfaded beauty to the secrets of anatomy and corruption. What were Virtue, Love, Patriotism, Friendship etc.—what were the scenery of this beautiful Universe which we inhabit—what were our consolations on this side of the grave—and what were our aspirations beyond it—if Poetry did not ascend to bring light and fire from those eternal regions where the owl-winged faculty of calculation dare not ever soar? Poetry is not like reasoning, a power to be exerted according to the determination of the will. A man cannot say, "I will compose poetry." The greatest poet even cannot say it: for the mind in creation is as a fading coal which some invisible influence, like an inconstant wind, awakens to transitory brightness: this power arises from within, like the colour of a flower which fades and changes as it is developed, and the conscious portions of our natures are unprophetic either of its approach or its departure. Could this influence be durable in its original purity and force, it is impossible to predict the greatness of the results; but when composition begins, inspiration is already on the decline, and the most glorious poetry that has ever been communicated to the world is probably a feeble shadow of the original conception of the poet. I appeal to the greatest Poets of the present day, whether it be not an error to assert that the finest passages of poetry are produced by labour and study. The toil and the delay recommended by critics can be justly interpreted to mean no more than a careful observation of the inspired moments, and an artificial connexion of the spaces between their suggestions by the intertexture of con-

3. God says to Adam: "cursed is the ground for thy sake. . . . Thorns also and thistles shall it bring forth. . . . In the sweat of thy face shalt thou eat bread, till thou return unto the ground" (Genesis 3.17–19).
4. Matthew 6.24: "Ye cannot serve God and Mammon."

ventional expressions; a necessity only imposed by the limitedness of the poetical faculty itself. For Milton conceived the Paradise Lost as a whole before
he executed it in portions. We have his own authority also for the Muse having
"dictated" to him the "unpremeditated song,"[5] and let this be an answer to
those who would allege the fifty-six various readings of the first line of the
Orlando Furioso.[6] Compositions so produced are to poetry what mosaic is to
painting. This instinct and intuition of the poetical faculty is still more observable in the plastic and pictorial arts: a great statue or picture grows under the
power of the artist as a child in the mother's womb; and the very mind which
directs the hands in formation is incapable of accounting to itself for the
origin, the gradations, or the media of the process.

Poetry is the record of the best and happiest[7] moments of the happiest and
best minds. We are aware of evanescent visitations of thought and feeling
sometimes associated with place or person, sometimes regarding our own
mind alone, and always arising unforeseen and departing unbidden, but elevating and delightful beyond all expression: so that even in the desire and the
regret they leave, there cannot but be pleasure, participating as it does in the
nature of its object. It is as it were the interpenetration of a diviner nature
through our own; but its footsteps are like those of a wind over a sea, where
the coming calm erases, and whose traces remain only as on the wrinkled sand
which paves it. These and corresponding conditions of being are experienced
principally by those of the most delicate sensibility[8] and the most enlarged
imagination; and the state of mind produced by them is at war with every base
desire. The enthusiasm of virtue, love, patriotism, and friendship is essentially
linked with these emotions; and whilst they last, self appears as what it is, an
atom to a Universe. Poets are not only subject to these experiences as spirits
of the most refined organization, but they can colour all that they combine
with the evanescent hues of this etherial world; a word, or a trait in the representation of a scene or a passion, will touch the enchanted chord, and reanimate, in those who have ever experienced these emotions, the sleeping, the
cold, the buried image of the past. Poetry thus makes immortal all that is best
and most beautiful in the world; it arrests the vanishing apparitions which
haunt the interlunations[9] of life, and veiling them or in language or in form
sends them forth among mankind, bearing sweet news of kindred joy to those
with whom their sisters abide—abide, because there is no portal of expression
from the caverns of the spirit which they inhabit into the universe of things.
Poetry redeems from decay the visitations of the divinity in man.

Poetry turns all things to loveliness; it exalts the beauty of that which is
most beautiful, and it adds beauty to that which is most deformed; it marries
exultation and horror, grief and pleasure, eternity and change; it subdues to
union under its light yoke all irreconcilable things. It transmutes all that it
touches, and every form moving within the radiance of its presence is changed
by wondrous sympathy to an incarnation of the spirit which it breathes; its
secret alchemy turns to potable gold[1] the poisonous waters which flow from
death through life; it strips the veil of familiarity from the world, and lays bare
the naked and sleeping beauty which is the spirit of its forms.

All things exist as they are perceived: at least in relation to the percipient.

---

5. *Paradise Lost* 9.21–24.
6. The epic poem by the 16th-century Italian poet
Ariosto, noted for his care in composition.
7. In the double sense of "most joyous" and "most
apt or felicitous in invention."
8. Sensitivity, capacity for sympathetic feeling.

9. The dark intervals between the old and new
moons.
1. Alchemists aimed to produce a drinkable
("potable") form of gold that would be an elixir of
life, curing all diseases.

"The mind is its own place, and of itself can make a heaven of hell, a hell of heaven."[2] But poetry defeats the curse which binds us to be subjected to the accident of surrounding impressions. And whether it spreads its own figured curtain or withdraws life's dark veil from before the scene of things, it equally creates for us a being within our being. It makes us the inhabitants of a world to which the familiar world is a chaos. It reproduces the common universe of which we are portions and percipients, and it purges from our inward sight the film of familiarity which obscures from us the wonder of our being. It compels us to feel that which we perceive, and to imagine that which we know. It creates anew the universe after it has been annihilated in our minds by the recurrence of impressions blunted by reiteration.[3] It justifies that bold and true word of Tasso: *Non merita nome di creatore, se non Iddio ed il Poeta.*[4]

A Poet, as he is the author to others of the highest wisdom, pleasure, virtue and glory, so he ought personally to be the happiest, the best, the wisest, and the most illustrious of men. As to his glory, let Time be challenged to declare whether the fame of any other institutor of human life be comparable to that of a poet. That he is the wisest, the happiest, and the best, inasmuch as he is a poet, is equally incontrovertible: the greatest poets have been men of the most spotless virtue, of the most consummate prudence, and, if we could look into the interior of their lives, the most fortunate of men: and the exceptions, as they regard those who possessed the poetic faculty in a high yet inferior degree, will be found on consideration to confirm rather than destroy the rule. Let us for a moment stoop to the arbitration of popular breath, and usurping and uniting in our own persons the incompatible characters of accuser, witness, judge and executioner, let us decide without trial, testimony, or form that certain motives of those who are "there sitting where we dare not soar"[5] are reprehensible. Let us assume that Homer was a drunkard, that Virgil was a flatterer, that Horace was a coward, that Tasso was a madman, that Lord Bacon was a peculator, that Raphael was a libertine, that Spenser was a poet laureate.[6] It is inconsistent with this division of our subject to cite living poets, but Posterity has done ample justice to the great names now referred to. Their errors have been weighed and found to have been dust in the balance; if their sins "were as scarlet, they are now white as snow";[7] they have been washed in the blood of the mediator and the redeemer Time. Observe in what a ludicrous chaos the imputations of real or fictitious crime have been confused in the contemporary calumnies against poetry and poets;[8] consider how little is, as it appears—or appears, as it is; look to your own motives, and judge not, lest ye be judged.[9]

Poetry, as has been said, in this respect differs from logic, that it is not

---

2. Satan's speech, *Paradise Lost* 1.254–55.
3. Shelley's version of a widespread Romantic doctrine that the poetic imagination transforms the familiar into the miraculous and re-creates the old world into a new world. See, e.g., Coleridge's *Biographia Literaria*, chap. 4: "To carry on the feelings of childhood into the powers of manhood; to combine the child's sense of wonder and novelty with the appearances which every day for perhaps forty years has rendered familiar; . . . this is the character and privilege of genius" (p. 474).
4. "No one merits the name of Creator except God and the Poet." Quoted by Pierantonio Serassi in his *Life of Torquato Tasso* (1785).
5. Satan's scornful words to the angels who dis-

cover him after he has surreptitiously entered Eden: "Ye knew me once no mate / For you, sitting where ye durst not soar" (*Paradise Lost* 4.828–29).
6. Charges that had in fact been made against these men. The use of "poet laureate" as a derogatory term was a dig at Robert Southey, who held that honor at the time Shelley was writing. "Peculator": an embezzler of public money. Raphael is the 16th-century Italian painter.
7. Isaiah 1.18.
8. Shelley alludes especially to the charges of immorality by contemporary reviewers against Lord Byron and himself.
9. Christ's warning in Matthew 7.1.

subject to the controul of the active powers of the mind, and that its birth and recurrence has no necessary connexion with consciousness or will. It is presumptuous to determine that these[1] are the necessary conditions of all mental causation, when mental effects are experienced insusceptible of being referred to them. The frequent recurrence of the poetical power, it is obvious to suppose, may produce in the mind an habit of order and harmony correlative with its own nature and with its effects upon other minds. But in the intervals of inspiration, and they may be frequent without being durable, a poet becomes a man, and is abandoned to the sudden reflux of the influences under which others habitually live. But as he is more delicately organized than other men, and sensible[2] to pain and pleasure, both his own and that of others, in a degree unknown to them, he will avoid the one and pursue the other with an ardour proportioned to this difference. And he renders himself obnoxious to calumny,[3] when he neglects to observe the circumstances under which these objects of universal pursuit and flight have disguised themselves in one another's garments.

But there is nothing necessarily evil in this error, and thus cruelty, envy, revenge, avarice, and the passions purely evil, have never formed any portion of the popular imputations on the lives of poets.

I have thought it most favourable to the cause of truth to set down these remarks according to the order in which they were suggested to my mind, by a consideration of the subject itself, instead of following that of the treatise that excited me to make them public.[4] Thus although devoid of the formality of a polemical reply; if the view they contain be just, they will be found to involve a refutation of the doctrines of the Four Ages of Poetry, so far at least as regards the first division of the subject. I can readily conjecture what should have moved the gall of the learned and intelligent author of that paper; I confess myself, like him, unwilling to be stunned by the Theseids of the hoarse Codri of the day. Bavius and Maevius[5] undoubtedly are, as they ever were, insufferable persons. But it belongs to a philosophical critic to distinguish rather than confound.

The first part of these remarks has related to Poetry in its elements and principles; and it has been shewn, as well as the narrow limits assigned them would permit, that what is called poetry, in a restricted sense, has a common source with all other forms of order and of beauty according to which the materials of human life are susceptible of being arranged, and which is poetry in an universal sense.

The second part[6] will have for its object an application of these principles to the present state of the cultivation of Poetry, and a defence of the attempt to idealize the modern forms of manners and opinions, and compel them into a subordination to the imaginative and creative faculty. For the literature of

---

1. I.e., consciousness or will. Shelley again proposes that some mental processes are unconscious—outside our control or awareness.
2. I.e., sensitive to, conscious of. Cf. Wordsworth's Preface to *Lyrical Ballads* (p. 269): "What is a poet? . . . He is a man speaking to men: a man, it is true, endued with more lively sensibility, more enthusiasm, and tenderness, who has a greater knowledge of human nature, and a more comprehensive soul, than are supposed to be common among mankind."
3. Exposed to slander.

4. Peacock's "Four Ages of Poetry."
5. Would-be poets satirized by Virgil and Horace. "Theseids": epic poems about Theseus. Codrus (plural "Codri") was the Roman author of a long, dull *Theseid* attacked by Juvenal and others. In 1794 and 1795 the conservative critic William Gifford had borrowed from Virgil and Horace and published the *Baviad* and the *Maeviad*, hardhitting and highly influential satires on popular poetry and drama.
6. Shelley, however, completed only the first part.

England, an energetic developement of which has ever preceded or accompanied a great and free developement of the national will, has arisen as it were from a new birth. In spite of the low-thoughted envy which would undervalue contemporary merit, our own will be a memorable age in intellectual achievements, and we live among such philosophers and poets as surpass beyond comparison any who have appeared since the last national struggle for civil and religious liberty.[7] The most unfailing herald, companion, and follower of the awakening of a great people to work a beneficial change in opinion or institution, is Poetry. At such periods there is an accumulation of the power of communicating and receiving intense and impassioned conceptions respecting man and nature. The persons in whom this power resides, may often, as far as regards many portions of their nature, have little apparent correspondence with that spirit of good of which they are the ministers. But even whilst they deny and abjure, they are yet compelled to serve, the Power which is seated upon the throne of their own soul. It is impossible to read the compositions of the most celebrated writers of the present day without being startled with the electric life which burns within their words. They measure the circumference and sound the depths of human nature with a comprehensive and all-penetrating spirit, and they are themselves perhaps the most sincerely astonished at its manifestations, for it is less their spirit than the spirit of the age. Poets are the hierophants[8] of an unapprehended inspiration, the mirrors of the gigantic shadows which futurity casts upon the present, the words which express what they understand not; the trumpets which sing to battle, and feel not what they inspire: the influence which is moved not, but moves.[9] Poets are the unacknowledged legislators of the World.

1821   1840

---

7. In the age of Milton and the English Civil Wars. 9. Aristotle had said that God is the "Unmoved
8. Priests who are expositors of sacred mysteries.   Mover" of the universe.

JOHN CLARE
1793–1864

Since the mid-eighteenth century, when critics had begun to worry that the authentic vigor of poetry was being undermined in their age of modern learning and refinement, they had looked for untaught primitive geniuses among the nation's peasantry. In the early-nineteenth-century literary scene, John Clare was the nearest thing to a "natural poet" there was. An earlier and greater peasant poet, Robert Burns, had managed to acquire a solid liberal education. Clare, however, was born at Helpston, a Northamptonshire village, the son of a field laborer and a mother who was entirely illiterate, and he obtained only enough schooling to enable him to read and write. Although he was a sickly and fearful child, he had to work hard in the field, where he found himself composing verse "for downright pleasure in giving vent to my feelings." The fragments of an autobiography that he wrote later in life describe movingly, and with humor, the stratagems that as a young man he devised in order to find the time and the materials for writing. A blank notebook could cost him a week's wages. In 1820 publication of his *Poems Descriptive of Rural Life and Scenery* attracted critical attention, and on a trip to London, he was made much of by leading writers of the day.

But his celebrity soon dimmed, and his three later books of verse were financial failures. Under these and other disappointments his mind gave way in 1837, and he spent almost all the rest of his life in an asylum. The place was for him a refuge as well as a confinement, for he was treated kindly, allowed to wander about the countryside, and encouraged to go on writing his verses. Some of his best achievements are the poems composed during his madness.

Clare did not, of course, write independently of literary influences, for he had studied the poetry of James Thomson, William Cowper, Burns, Milton, Wordsworth, and Coleridge. But he stayed true to his own experience of everyday country sights and customs. His nightingale poem, written in a long-established literary tradition, has many more particulars of nature than any of those by his predecessors, and his homely mouse, in the third poem printed below, is a bit of pure rustic impressionism in a way that even Burns's moralized mouse is not (see "To a Mouse," p. 135). Some of Clare's introspective asylum poems achieve so haunting a poignancy and are spoken in so quietly distinctive a voice that they have made the great mass of manuscripts he left at his death an exciting place of discovery for recent scholars.

Those same manuscripts are a site of contention among current textual theorists. Words are everywhere misspelled in them, standard syntax is regularly ignored, and there is almost no punctuation in the lines. In his own day Clare was respelled, punctuated, and otherwise made presentable by his publisher, John Taylor (who did the same for John Keats, another of his poets who took a casual view of such matters). Modern scholars, eager to recover exactly what Clare wrote—in effect, to free him from the impositions and constraints of well-intentioned nineteenth-century editors— are restoring the idiosyncrasies but, in the process, are constructing a poet who is so full of what we would normally call mistakes as to be, for all practical purposes, inaccessible to the general reader. (For example, the manuscripts have "were" for "where," "your" for "you're," "anker" for "hanker," "hugh" for "huge.") The texts printed below, which are presented as "reading" versions of Clare's own words, are the product of a principled modernization by the editors of this anthology. They are based, where the materials are available, on authoritative manuscript versions recovered and now made standard by Eric Robinson and his associates in a succession of editions published by Oxford University Press.

The Nightingale's Nest

Up this green woodland ride° let's softly rove,   *riding path*
And list° the nightingale—she dwelleth here.   *listen to*
Hush! let the wood gate softly clap, for fear
The noise may drive her from her home of love;
5 For here I've heard her many a merry year—
At morn and eve, nay, all the livelong day,
As though she lived on song. This very spot,
Just where that old man's beard[1] all wildly trails
Rude arbours o'er the road and stops the way—
10 And where that child its blue-bell flowers hath got,
Laughing and creeping through the mossy rails°—   *fence rails*
There have I hunted like a very boy,
Creeping on hands and knees through matted thorns
To find her nest and see her feed her young.
15 And vainly did I many hours employ:

---

1. *Clematis vitalba*, a vine.

All seemed as hidden as a thought unborn.
And where these crimping° fern leaves ramp° among   *curling / shoot up*
The hazel's under-boughs, I've nestled down
And watched her while she sung; and her renown
20 Hath made me marvel that so famed a bird[2]
Should have no better dress than russet brown.
Her wings would tremble in her ecstasy,
And feathers stand on end, as 'twere with joy,
And mouth wide open to release her heart
25 Of its out-sobbing songs. The happiest part
Of summer's fame she shared, for so to me
Did happy fancies shapen her employ;[3]
But if I touched a bush or scarcely stirred,
All in a moment stopt. I watched in vain:
30 The timid bird had left the hazel bush,
And at a distance hid to sing again.
Lost in a wilderness of listening leaves,
Rich ecstasy would pour its luscious strain,
Till envy spurred the emulating thrush
35 To start less wild and scarce inferior songs;
For cares with him for half the year remain,
To damp the ardour of his speckled breast,
While nightingales to summer's life belongs,
And naked trees and winter's nipping wrongs
40 Are strangers to her music and her rest.
Her joys are evergreen, her world is wide—
Hark! there she is as usual—let's be hush—
For in this black-thorn clump, if rightly guessed,
Her curious house is hidden. Part aside
45 These hazel branches in a gentle way,
And stoop right cautious 'neath the rustling boughs,
For we will have another search to-day,
And hunt this fern-strewn thorn clump round and round;
And where this seeded wood grass idly bows,
50 We'll wade right through, it is a likely nook:
In such like spots, and often on the ground,
They'll build where rude boys never think to look—
Aye, as I live! her secret nest is here,
Upon this whitethorn stulp!° I've searched about   *stump*
55 For hours in vain. There! put that bramble by—
Nay, trample on its branches and get near.
How subtle is the bird! she started out
And raised a plaintive note of danger nigh,
Ere we were past the brambles; and now, near
60 Her nest, she sudden stops—as choking fear
That might betray her home. So even now
We'll leave it as we found it: safety's guard
Of pathless solitude shall keep it still.
See, there she's sitting on the old oak bough,

2. The nightingale had been celebrated by, among others, Chaucer, Spenser, Shakespeare, Milton, and, closer to Clare's time, William Cowper, Charlotte Smith, Mary Robinson, Coleridge, Wordsworth, and Keats. In lines 22, 24–25, and 33, Clare echoes lines 57–58 of Keats's "Ode to a Nightingale."
3. Give shape to her (the nightingale's) regular activities.

65 Mute in her fears; our presence doth retard
   Her joys, and doubt turns all her rapture chill.

      Sing on, sweet bird! may no worse hap° befall   *fate*
   Thy visions, than the fear that now deceives.
   We will not plunder music of its dower,°   *dowry, gift*
70 Nor turn this spot of happiness to thrall;°   *misery*
   For melody seems hid in every flower,
   That blossoms near thy home. These harebells all
   Seems bowing with the beautiful in song;
   And gaping cuckoo° with its spotted leaves   *a spring flower*
75 Seems blushing of the singing it has heard.
   How curious is the nest; no other bird
   Uses such loose materials, or weaves
   Their dwellings in such spots: dead oaken leaves
   Are placed without, and velvet moss within,
80 And little scraps of grass, and, scant and spare,
   Of what seems scarce materials, down and hair;
   For from man's haunts she seemeth nought to win.
   Yet nature is the builder and contrives
   Homes for her children's comfort even here;
85 Where solitude's disciples spend their lives
   Unseen save when a wanderer passes near
   That loves such pleasant places. Deep adown,
   The nest is made an hermit's mossy cell.
   Snug lie her curious eggs, in number five,
90 Of deadened green, or rather olive brown;
   And the old prickly thorn-bush guards them well.
   And here we'll leave them, still unknown to wrong,
   As the old woodland's legacy of song.

1825–30   1835

Pastoral Poesy

   True poesy is not in words,
   But images that thoughts express,
   By which the simplest hearts are stirred
   To elevated happiness.

5 Mere books would be but useless things
   Where none had taste or mind to read,
   Like unknown lands where beauty springs
   And none are there to heed.

   But poesy is a language meet,°   *suitable, proper*
10 And fields are every one's employ;°   *concern*
   The wild flower 'neath the shepherd's feet
   Looks up and gives him joy;

   A language that is ever green,
   That feelings unto all impart,

15   As hawthorn blossoms, soon as seen,
      Give May to every heart.

      The pictures that our summer minds
      In summer's dwellings meet;
      The fancies that the shepherd finds
20   To make his leisure sweet;

      The dust mills that the cowboy delves
      In banks for dust to run,[1]
      Creates a summer in ourselves—
      He does as we have done.

25   An image to the mind is brought,
      Where happiness enjoys
      An easy thoughtlessness of thought
      And meets excess of joys.

      The world is in that little spot
30   With him—and all beside
      Is nothing, all a life forgot,
      In feelings satisfied.

      And such is poesy; its power
      May varied lights employ,
35   Yet to all minds it gives the dower
      Of self-creating joy.

      And whether it be hill or moor,
      I feel where'er I go
      A silence that discourses more
40   That any tongue can do.

      Unruffled quietness hath made
      A peace in every place,
      And woods are resting in their shade
      Of social loneliness.

45   The storm, from which the shepherd turns
      To pull his beaver° down,   *beaver hat*
      While he upon the heath sojourns,
      Which autumn pleaches° brown,   *bleaches*

      Is music, aye, and more indeed
50   To those of musing mind
      Who through the yellow woods proceed
      And listen to the wind.

      The poet in his fitful glee
      And fancy's many moods
55   Meets it as some strange melody,
      And poem of the woods.

---

1. The boy tending the cows has (as an amusement) dug miniature millstreams in the dirt.

It sings and whistles in his mind,
And then it talks aloud,
While by some leaning tree reclined
60 He shuns a coming cloud,

That sails its bulk against the sun,
A mountain in the light—
He heeds not for the storm begun
But dallies with delight.

65 And now a harp that flings around
The music of the wind,
The poet often hears the sound
When beauty fills the mind.

The morn with saffron° strips and gray,   *orange-yellow*
70 Or blushing to the view,
Like summer fields when run away
In weeds of crimson hue,

Will simple shepherds' hearts imbue
With nature's poesy,
75 Who inly fancy while they view
How grand must heaven be.

With every musing mind she steals
Attendance² on their way;
The simplest thing her heart reveals
80 Is seldom thrown away.

The old man, full of leisure hours,
Sits cutting at his door
Rude fancy sticks to tie his flowers
—They're sticks and nothing more

85 With many passing by his door—
But pleasure has its bent;°   *inclination*
With him 'tis happiness and more,
Heart satisfied content.

Those box-edged borders that impart
90 Their fragrance near his door
Hath been the comfort of his heart
For sixty years and more.

That mossy thatch above his head
In winter's drifting showers
95 To him and his old partner made
A music many hours.

---

2. She (nature) demands attention (to her beauties).

It patted to their hearts a joy[3]
That humble comfort made—
A little fire to keep them dry
100   And shelter over head.

And such no matter what they call
Each all are nothing less
Than poesy's power that gives to all
A cheerful blessedness.

105   So would I my own mind employ,
And my own heart impress,
That poesy's self's a dwelling joy
Of humble quietness.

So would I for the biding° joy   *abiding, lasting*
110   That to such thoughts belong,
That I life's errand may employ
As harmless as a song.

1824–32   1935

[Mouse's Nest]

I found a ball of grass among the hay
And progged° it as I passed and went away;   *prodded*
And when I looked I fancied something stirred,
And turned again and hoped to catch the bird—
5   When out an old mouse bolted in the wheat
With all her young ones hanging at her teats;
She looked so odd and so grotesque to me,
I ran and wondered what the thing could be,
And pushed the knapweed[1] bunches where I stood,
10   When the mouse hurried from the crawling brood.
The young ones squeaked, and when I went away
She found her nest again among the hay.
The water o'er the pebbles scarce could run
And broad old cesspools[2] glittered in the sun.

1835–37   1935

A Vision

I

I lost the love of heaven above;
I spurn'd the lust of earth below;
I felt the sweets of fancied love,—
And hell itself my only foe.

---

3. The patter of the rain on the thatch (lines 93–
94) enhanced the comfort of the fire and shelter
indoors.

1. A plant with knobs of purple flowers.
2. Low spots where water has collected.

2

5 I lost earth's joys but felt the glow
   Of heaven's flame abound in me:
   Till loveliness and I did grow
   The bard of immortality.

3

   I loved, but woman fell away;
10 I hid me from her faded fame:
   I snatch'd the sun's eternal ray,—
   And wrote till earth was but a name.

4

   In every language upon earth,
   On every shore, o'er every sea,
15 I gave my name immortal birth,
   And kept my spirit with the free.

Aug. 2, 1844   1924

I Am

1

   I am—yet what I am, none cares or knows;
      My friends forsake me like a memory lost:—
   I am the self-consumer of my woes;—
      They rise and vanish in oblivion's host,
5 Like shadows in love's frenzied stifled throes:—
   And yet I am, and live—like vapours tossed

2

   Into the nothingness of scorn and noise,—
      Into the living sea of waking dreams,
   Where there is neither sense of life or joys,
10   But the vast shipwreck of my life's esteems;
   Even the dearest that I love the best
   Are strange—nay, rather, stranger than the rest.

3

   I long for scenes where man hath never trod,
      A place where woman never smiled or wept,
15 There to abide with my Creator, God,
      And sleep as I in childhood sweetly slept,
   Untroubling and untroubled where I lie,
   The grass below—above, the vaulted sky.

1842–46   1848

An Invite to Eternity

1

Wilt thou go with me, sweet maid,
Say maiden, wilt thou go with me
Through the valley depths of shade,
Of night and dark obscurity,
5 Where the path hath lost its way,
Where the sun forgets the day,
Where there's nor life nor light to see,
Sweet maiden, wilt thou go with me?

2

Where stones will turn to flooding streams,
10 Where plains will rise like ocean waves,
Where life will fade like visioned dreams
And mountains darken into caves,
Say maiden, wilt thou go with me
Through this sad non-identity,
15 Where parents live and are forgot
And sisters live and know us not?

3

Say maiden, wilt thou go with me
In this strange death of life to be,
To live in death and be the same
20 Without this life, or home, or name,
At once to be and not to be,
That was and is not—yet to see
Things pass like shadows—and the sky
Above, below, around us lie?

4

25 The land of shadows wilt thou trace
And look—nor know each other's face,
The present mixed with reasons gone
And past and present all as one?
Say maiden, can thy life be led
30 To join the living with the dead?
Then trace thy footsteps on with me—
We're wed to one eternity.

1847   1848

Clock a Clay[1]

1

In the cowslip's peeps I lie,[2]
Hidden from the buzzing fly,
While green grass beneath me lies,
Pearled wi' dew like fishes' eyes;
5   Here I lie, a Clock a Clay,
Waiting for the time o' day.

2

While grassy forests quake surprise,
And the wild wind sobs and sighs,
My gold home rocks as like to fall
10   On its pillars green and tall;
When the pattering rain drives by
Clock a Clay keeps warm and dry.

3

Day by day and night by night,
All the week I hide from sight;
15   In the cowslip's peeps I lie,
In rain and dew still warm and dry;
Day and night and night and day,
Red black-spotted Clock a Clay.

4

My home it shakes in wind and showers,
20   Pale green pillar topped wi' flowers,
Bending at the wild wind's breath,
Till I touch the grass beneath;
Here still I live, lone Clock a Clay,
Watching for the time of day.

ca. 1848   1873

The Peasant Poet

He loved the brook's soft sound,
The swallow swimming by;
He loved the daisy-covered ground,
The cloud-bedappled sky.
5   To him the dismal storm appeared
The very voice of God,
And where the evening rack° was reared   *mass of clouds*
Stood Moses with his rod.

1. The ladybird, or ladybug. The sixth and last lines allude to the children's game of telling the hour by the number of taps it takes to make the ladybird fly away home.
2. Cf. the opening lines of Ariel's song in act 5 of Shakespeare's *The Tempest:* "Where the bee sucks, there suck I: / In a cowslip's bell I lie." "Peeps": i.e., pips—single blossoms of flowers growing in a cluster. "Cowslip": a yellow primrose.

And everything his eyes surveyed,
10   The insects i' the brake,
Were creatures God Almighty made—
He loved them for His sake:
A silent man in life's affairs,
A thinker from a boy,
15   A peasant in his daily cares—
The poet in his joy.

1842–64   1920

Song

I hid my love when young while I
Couldn't bear the buzzing of a fly;
I hid my love to my despite
Till I could not bear to look at light.
5   I dare not gaze upon her face
But left her memory in each place;
Where'er I saw a wild flower lie
I kissed and bade my love goodbye.

I met her in the greenest dells,
10   Where dewdrops pearl the wood bluebells;
The lost breeze kissed her bright blue eye,
The bee kissed and went singing by.
A sunbeam found a passage there,
A gold chain round her neck so fair;
15   As secret as the wild bee's song
She lay there all the summer long.

I hid my love in field and town
Till e'en the breeze would knock me down.
The bees seemed singing ballads o'er
20   The fly's buzz turned a lion's roar;
And even silence found a tongue
To haunt me all the summer long:
The riddle nature could not prove
Was nothing else but secret love.

1842–64   1920

Song

I peeled bits o' straws and I got switches too
From the grey peeling willow as idlers do,
And I switched at the flies as I sat all alone
Till my flesh, blood, and marrow wasted to dry bone.
5   My illness was love, though I knew not the smart,
But the beauty o' love was the blood o' my heart.

Crowded places, I shunned them as noises too rude
And flew to the silence of sweet solitude,
Where the flower in green darkness buds, blossoms, and fades,
10   Unseen of a' shepherds and flower-loving maids.
The hermit bees find them but once and away;
There I'll bury alive and in silence decay.

I looked on the eyes o' fair woman too long,
Till silence and shame stole the use o' my tongue;
15   When I tried to speak to her I'd nothing to say,
So I turned myself round, and she wandered away.
When she got too far off—why, I'd something to tell,
So I sent sighs behind her and talked to mysel'.

Willow switches I broke, and I peeled bits o' straws,
20   Ever lonely in crowds, in nature's own laws—
My ballroom the pasture, my music the bees,
My drink was the fountain, my church the tall trees.
Who ever would love or be tied to a wife
When it makes a man mad a' the days o' his life?

1842–64   1920

Autobiographical Fragments[1]

[BOOKS]

My acquantance of books is not so good as later oppertunitys might have made
it for I cannot and never coud plod thro every a book in a regular mecanical
way   as I meet with [it] I dip in to it here and there and if it does not suit
I lay it down and seldom take it up again but in the same manner I read
Thompsons Seasons and Miltons Paradise Lost thro when I was a boy and
they are the only books of Poetry that I have reguraly read thro yet   as to
history I never met with the chance of getting at [it] yet and in novels my taste
is very limited   Tom Jones Robinson Crusoe and the Vicar of Wakefield are
all that I am acquainted with   they are old acquantan[ces] and I care not
to make new ones   tho I have often been offered the perusal of the Waverly
Novels I declind it and [though] the readily remaining in ignorance of them
is no trouble yet my taste may be doubted for I hear much in their praise and
believe them good—I read the vicar of Wakefield over every Winter and am
delighted tho I always feel disappointed at the end[ing] of it happily with the
partings   my mind cannot feel that it ends happily with [the] reader   I
usd to be uncommonly fond of looking over catalogues of books and am so
still   they [are] some of the earliest readings that oppertunitys allowd me
to come at   if ever I bought a penny worth of slate pencils or Wafers or a
few sheets of Paper at Drakards they were sure to be lapt[2] in a catalogue and

1. These fragments are parts of an incomplete
manuscript autobiography that Clare undertook in
the 1820s for his publisher, John Taylor. They
were published by Eric Robinson in *John Clare's
Autobiographical Writings* (1983), and a second
time, with slightly more accurate texts, by Robinson and David Powell in *John Clare by Himself*
(1996). We take our selections from the more
recent collection.
2. Wrapped, folded up. Drakard was a bookseller
at Stamford, half a dozen miles west of Clare's
native village of Helpston.

I considered them as the most va[l]uable parts of my purchase and greedily lookd over their contents and now in cutting open a new book or Magazine[3] I always naturaly turn to the end first to read the book list and take the rest as a secondary pleasure

Anticipation is the sweetest of earthly pleasures   it is smiling hope standing on tiptoes to look for pleasure—the cutting open a new book the watching the opening of a new planted flower at spring etc

          *   *   *

The first books I got hold of beside the bible and prayer book was an old book of Essays with no title and then a large one on Farming Robin hoods Garland and the Scotch Rogue—The old book of Farming and Essays belongd to an old Mr Gee who had been a farmer and who lived in a part of our house which once was his own—he had had a good bringing up and was a desent scholar and he was always pleasd to lend me them even before I coud read them without so much spelling and guesses at words so as to be able to make much of them or understand them

          *   *   *

I became acquainted with Robinson Crusoe very early in life having borrowd it of a boy at Glinton school[4] of the name of Stimson who only dare lend it me for a few days for fear of his uncles knowing of it to whom it belongd yet I had it a sufficient time to fill my fancys with new Crusoes and adventures

From these friendships I gatherd more acquaintance with books which like chances oppertunitys were but sparing

CHAPTER 5. MY FIRST ATTEMPTS AT POETRY ETC. ETC.

I now followd gardening for a while in the Farmers Gardens about the village and workd in the fields when I had no other employment to go too   poetry was a troublsome but pleasant companion anoying and cheering me at my toils

I coud not stop my thoughts and often faild to keep them till night so when I fancyd I had hit upon a good image or natural description I usd to steal into a corner of the garden and clap it down[5] but the appearance of my employers often put my fancys to flight and made me loose the thought and the muse together for I always felt anx[i]ous to consceal my scribbling and woud as leave have confessd to be a robber as a rhymer   when I workd in the fields I had more oppertunitys to set down my thoughts and for this reason I liked to work in the fields and bye and bye forsook gardening all together till I resumd at Casterton[6]   I usd to drop down behind a hedge bush or dyke and write down my things upon the crown of my hat and when I was more in a hip[7] for thinking then usual I usd to stop later at nights to make up my lost time in the day   thus I went on writing my thoughts down and correcting them at leisure spending my sundays in the woods or heaths to be alone for that purpose and I got a bad name among the weekly church goers forsaking the "church going bell" and seeking the religion of the fields tho I did it for no dislike to church for I felt uncomfortable very often but my heart burnt over the pleasures of solitude and the restless revels of rhyme that was eternaly

3. In the early 19th century, books and magazines would be bought with their pages still uncut.
4. Glinton was two miles east of Helpston.
5. Fix it in writing.
6. A village a few miles northwest of Helpston.
7. More annoyed.

sapping my memorys like the summer sun over the tinkling brook till it one day shoud leave them dry and unconsous of the thrilling joys brin[g]ing anxiety and restless cares which it had created and the praises and censures which I shall leave behind me   I knew nothing of the poets experience then or I shoud have remaind a labourer on and not livd to envy the ignorance of my old companions and fellow clowns[8]   I wish I had never known any other tho I was not known as a poet my odd habits did not escape notice they fancied I kept aloof from company for some sort of study   others believd me crazd and some put more criminal interpretations to my rambles and said I was night walking assosiate with the gipseys robbing the woods of the hares and pheasants because I was often in their company and I must confess I found them far more honest then their callumniators whom I knew to be of that description   Scandal and Fame are cheaply purchasd in a Village   the first is a nimble tongud gossip and the latter a credoulous and ready believer who woud not hesitate but believd any thing   I had got the fame of being a good scholar and in fact I had vanity enough to fancy I was far from a bad one my self while I coud puzzle[9] the village schoolmasters over my quart for I had no tongue to brag with till I was inspird with ale with solving algebrai[c] questions   for I had once struggld hard to get fame in that crab-bed wilderness but my brains was not made for it and would not reach it tho it was a mystery scarcly half unveild to my capacity yet I made enough of it to astonish their ignorance for a village schoolmaster is one of the most pretending and most ignorant of men—and their fame is often of the sort which that droll genius Peter Pindar[1] describes—Whats christend merit often wants a auth[or]

MEMORYS OF LOVE CHAPTER 6

As I grew up a man I mixd more in company and frequented dancings for the sake of meeting with the lasses for I was a lover very early in life my first attachment being a school boy affection but Mary—who cost me more ballads then sighs was belovd with a romantic or platonic sort of feeling   if I coud but gaze on her face or fancy a smile on her co[u]ntenance it was sufficient   I went away satisfied   we playd with each other but named nothing of love   yet I fancyd her eyes told me her affections   we walkd togethere as school companions in leisure hours but our talk was of play and our actions the wanton innocence of children   yet young as my heart was it woud turn chill when I touchd her hand and trembled and I fancyd her feelings were the same for as I gazd earnestly in her face a tear woud hang in her smiling eye and she woud turn to whipe it away   her heart was as tender as a birds but when she grew up to woman hood she felt her station above mine   at least I felt that she thought so for her parents were farmers and Farmers had great pretentions to somthing then so my passion coold with my reason and con-tented itself with another tho I felt a hopful tenderness one that I might one day renew the acqua[in]tance and disclose the smotherd passion   she was a beautiful girl and as the dream never awoke into reality her beauty was always fresh in my memory   she is still unmarried

8. Yokels.
9. Perplex, confound.
1. The pen name of John Wolcot, author of *The*

Lousiad (1785–95) and other poems satirizing George III.

MY FIRST FEELINGS AND ATTEMPTS AT PO[ETRY]
CHAPTER 4

I cannot say what led me to dabble in Rhy[me or] at what age I began to write
it but my first r[ude attempts took the form of] imitations of my fathers Songs
for he knew and sung a great many and I made a many things before I venturd
to comit them to writing for I felt ashamd to expose them on paper and after
I venturd to write them down my second thoughts blushd over them and [I]
burnt them for a long while but as my feelings grew into song I felt a desire
to preserve some and usd to correct them over and over till the last copy had
lost all kindred to the first even in the title   I went on some years in this
way wearing it in my memory as a secret to all   tho my parents usd to know
that my leisure was occupyd in writing yet they had no knowledge of what I
coud be doing for they never dreamd of me writing poetry   at length I
venturd to divulge the secret a little by reading imatations of some popular
song floating among the vulgar at the markets and fairs till they were common
to all but these imatations they only laughd at and told me I need never hope
to make songs like them   this mortified me often and almost made me
desist for I knew that the excelling such doggerel woud be but a poor fame if
I coud do nothing better but I hit upon an harmless deception by repeating
my poems over a book as tho I was reading it   this had the desird effect
    they often praisd them and said if I coud write as good I shoud do   I
hugd my self over this deception and often repeated it and those which they
praisd as superior to others I tryd to preserve in a hole in the wall but my
mother found out the hurd[2] and unconscously took them for kettle holders
and fire lighters when ever she wanted paper not knowing that they were any
thing farther then attempts at learning to write for they were writing upon
shop paper of all colors and between the lines of old copy books and any paper
I could get at for I was often wanting tho I saved almost every penny I had
given me on sundays or holidays to buy it instead of sweet meats and fruit and
I usd to feel a little mortified after I discoverd it but I dare not reveal the secret
by owning to it and wishing her to desist for I feard if I did she woud have
shown them to some one to judge of ther value which woud have put me to
shame so I kept the secret dissapointment to myself and wrote on suffering
her to destroy them as she pleasd but when I wrote any thing which I imagind
better then others I preservd it in my pocket till the paper was chafd thro and
destroyd by a diff[er]ent and full as vain presevation

2. Hoard.

FELICIA DOROTHEA HEMANS
1793–1835

Born in Liverpool and brought up in Wales, Felicia Hemans published her first two
volumes—*Poems* and *England and Spain, or Valour and Patriotism*—when she was
fifteen. She followed these four years later with *The Domestic Affections and Other
Poems* (1812) and from 1816 on into the 1830s produced new books of poetry almost
annually: short sentimental lyrics, tales and "historic scenes," translations, songs for

music, sketches of women, hymns for children. She also published literary criticism in magazines and wrote three plays. Her work was widely read, anthologized, memorized, and set to music throughout the nineteenth century and was especially popular and influential in the United States, where the first of many collected editions of her poems appeared in 1825. When she died she was eulogized by many poets, including William Wordsworth, Letitia Landon, and Elizabeth Barrett—a sign of the high regard in which she was held by her contemporaries.

A tablet erected by her brothers in the cathedral of St. Asaph, in north Wales, reads in part, "In memory of Felicia Hemans, whose character is best pourtrayed in her writings." But there are several characters in her poems, and some of them seem not entirely compatible with some of the others. She is frequently thought of as the poet (in the nineteenth century as "the poetess") of domestic affections, at the center of a cult of domesticity in which the home is conceptualized as a haven apart from the stresses of the public world, to which only men are suited. Her poems have been viewed as celebrations of a feminine ethic founded on women's—especially mothers'—capacities for forbearance, piety, and long suffering. Among her most popular pieces in this vein, "Evening Prayer, at a Girls' School" depicts the happy ignorance of schoolgirls whose enjoyment of life will end when they reach womanhood, and "Indian Woman's Death-Song" is the lament of a Native American woman whose husband has abandoned her, sung as she plunges in her canoe over a cataract to suicide with an infant in her arms.

Many of Hemans's longer narratives, by contrast, recount the exploits of women warriors who, to avenge personal, family, or national injustice or insult, destroy enemies in a manner not conventionally associated with female behavior. In *The Widow of Crescentius,* Stephania stalks and poisons the German emperor Otho, the murderer of her husband; in "The Wife of Asdrubal," a mother publicly kills her own children and herself to show contempt for her husband, a betrayer of the Carthaginians whom he governed; the heroine of "The Bride of the Greek Isle," boarding the ship of the pirates who have killed her husband, annihilates them (and herself) in a conflagration rivaling the monumental explosion described in "Casabianca." Among the numerous themes of her work, patriotism and military action recur frequently; there may be a biographical basis for these motifs, given that her two oldest brothers distinguished themselves in the Peninsular War and her military husband (who deserted her and their five sons in 1818) had also served in Spain. But some of her most famous patriotic and military poems are now being viewed as critiques of the virtues and ideologies they had been thought by earlier readers to inculcate. "The Homes of England," for example, has been read as both asserting and undermining the idea that all homes are equal, ancestral estates and cottages alike; and in "Casabianca," the boy's automatic steadfastness has been interpreted as empty obedience rather than admirable loyalty.

Hemans was the highest paid writer in *Blackwood's Magazine* during her day. Her books sold more copies than those of any other contemporary poet except Byron and Walter Scott. She was a shrewd calculator of the literary marketplace and a genius in her negotiations with publishers (which she carried on entirely through the mails). Her self-abasing women of the domestic affections and her scimitar-wielding superwomen of the revenge narratives exist side by side throughout her works. These and other seeming dissonances clearly enhanced the strong appeal of her poems to a wide range of readers, men as well as women.

England's Dead

Son of the ocean isle!
Where sleep your mighty dead?

Show me what high and stately pile
Is rear'd o'er Glory's bed.

5   Go, stranger! track the deep,
Free, free the white sail spread!
Wave may not foam, nor wild wind sweep,
Where rest not England's dead.

On Egypt's burning plains,
10   By the pyramid o'ersway'd,
With fearful power the noonday reigns,
And the palm trees yield no shade.[1]

But let the angry sun
From heaven look fiercely red,
15 Unfelt by those whose task is done!—
There slumber England's dead.

The hurricane hath might
Along the Indian shore,
And far by Ganges' banks at night,
20   Is heard the tiger's roar.

But let the sound roll on!
It hath no tone of dread,
For those that from their toils are gone;—
There slumber England's dead.

25 Loud rush the torrent floods
The western wilds among,
And free, in green Columbia's woods,
The hunter's bow is strung.

But let the floods rush on!
30   Let the arrow's flight be sped!
Why should *they* reck whose task is done?—
There slumber England's dead!

The mountain storms rise high
In the snowy Pyrenees,
35 And toss the pine boughs through the sky,
Like rose leaves on the breeze.

But let the storm rage on!
Let the fresh wreaths be shed!
For the Roncesvalles' field[2] is won,—
40   *There* slumber England's dead.

1. English forces defeated the French at Alexandria in the spring of 1801. The rest of the references—to 18th- and early-19th-century battles in India (lines 17–24), America (lines 25–32), Spain (lines 33–40), and on the sea (lines 41–48)—are more general.
2. Roncesvalles, the mountain pass in the Pyrenees between France and Spain, was a scene of action during the Peninsular War (1808–14).

On the frozen deep's repose
'Tis a dark and dreadful hour,
When round the ship the ice-fields close,
And the northern night clouds lower.

45   But let the ice drift on!
Let the cold-blue desert spread!
Their course with mast and flag is done,—
Even there sleep England's dead.

The warlike of the isles,
50   The men of field and wave!
Are not the rocks their funeral piles,
The seas and shores their grave?

Go, stranger! track the deep,
Free, free the white sail spread!
55   Wave may not foam, nor wild wind sweep,
Where rest not England's dead.

1822

The Landing of the Pilgrim Fathers in New England

> Look now abroad—another race has fill'd
> Those populous borders—wide the wood recedes,
> And towns shoot up, and fertile realms are till'd;
> The land is full of harvests and green meads.
> —BRYANT[1]

The breaking waves dash'd high
On a stern and rock-bound coast,
And the woods against a stormy sky
Their giant branches toss'd;

5   And the heavy night hung dark,
The hills and waters o'er,
When a band of exiles moor'd their bark
On the wild New England shore.

Not as the conqueror comes,
10   They, the true-hearted, came;
Not with the roll of the stirring drums,
And the trumpet that sings of fame;

Not as the flying come,
In silence and in fear;—
15   They shook the depths of the desert° gloom   desolate
With their hymns of lofty cheer.

---

1. The American poet William Cullen Bryant, *The Ages* (1821), lines 280–83.

Amidst the storm they sang,
  And the stars heard and the sea;
And the sounding aisles of the dim woods rang
20   To the anthem of the free!

The ocean eagle soar'd
  From his nest by the white wave's foam;
And the rocking pines of the forest roar'd—
  This was their welcome home!

25 There were men with hoary° hair   *white*
  Amidst that pilgrim band;—
Why had *they* come to wither there,
  Away from their childhood's land?

There was woman's fearless eye,
30   Lit by her deep love's truth;
There was manhood's brow serenely high,
  And the fiery heart of youth.

What sought they thus afar?
  Bright jewels of the mine?
35 The wealth of seas, the spoils of war?—
  They sought a faith's pure shrine!

Aye, call it holy ground,
  The soil where first they trod.
They have left unstain'd what there they found—
40   Freedom to worship God.

1826

Casabianca[1]

The boy stood on the burning deck
  Whence all but he had fled;
The flame that lit the battle's wreck
  Shone round him o'er the dead.

5 Yet beautiful and bright he stood,
  As born to rule the storm;
A creature of heroic blood,
  A proud, though childlike form.

1. Young Casabianca, a boy about thirteen years old, son to the Admiral of the *Orient*, remained at his post (in the Battle of the Nile) after the ship had taken fire, and all the guns had been abandoned; and perished in the explosion of the vessel, when the flames had reached the powder [Hemans's note]. The Battle of the Nile, in which Nelson captured and destroyed the French fleet in Aboukir Bay, took place on August 1, 1798. Admiral Casabianca and his son (who was in fact only ten) were among those killed by the British forces.

The flames roll'd on—he would not go
10   Without his Father's word;
That Father, faint in death below,
   His voice no longer heard.

He call'd aloud:—"Say, Father, say
   If yet my task is done?"
15 He knew not that the chieftain lay
   Unconscious of his son.

"Speak, Father!" once again he cried,
   "If I may yet be gone!
And"—but the booming shots replied,
20   And fast the flames roll'd on.

Upon his brow he felt their breath,
   And in his waving hair,
And look'd from that lone post of death
   In still, yet brave despair.

25 And shouted but once more aloud,
   "My Father! must I stay?"
While o'er him fast, through sail and shroud,
   The wreathing fires made way.

They wrapt the ship in splendour wild,
30   They caught the flag on high,
And stream'd above the gallant child,
   Like banners in the sky.

There came a burst of thunder sound—
   The boy—oh! where was he?
35 Ask of the winds that far around
   With fragments strew'd the sea!—

With mast, and helm, and pennon fair,
   That well had borne their part,
But the noblest thing which perish'd there
40   Was that young faithful heart!

1826

The Homes of England

> Where's the coward that would not dare
> To fight for such a land?
> —*Marmion*[1]

The stately Homes of England,
 How beautiful they stand!
Amidst their tall ancestral trees,
 O'er all the pleasant land.
5 The deer across their greensward bound
 Through shade and sunny gleam,
And the swan glides past them with the sound
 Of some rejoicing stream.

The merry Homes of England!
10 Around their hearths by night,
What gladsome looks of household love
 Meet in the ruddy light!
There woman's voice flows forth in song,
 Or childhood's tale is told,
15 Or lips move tunefully along
 Some glorious page of old.

The blessed Homes of England!
 How softly on their bowers
Is laid the holy quietness
20 That breathes from Sabbath-hours!
Solemn, yet sweet, the church-bell's chime
 Floats through their woods at morn;
All other sounds, in that still time,
 Of breeze and leaf are born.

25 The Cottage Homes of England!
 By thousands on her plains,
They are smiling o'er the silvery brooks,
 And round the hamlet-fanes.°   village churches
Through glowing orchards forth they peep,
30 Each from its nook of leaves,
And fearless there the lowly sleep,
 As the bird beneath their eaves.

The free, fair Homes of England!
 Long, long, in hut and hall,
35 May hearts of native proof be rear'd
 To guard each hallow'd wall!
And green for ever be the groves,
 And bright the flowery sod,
Where first the child's glad spirit loves
40 Its country and its God!

1827

1. From Sir Walter Scott's long poem *Marmion* (1808), 4.633–34, a tale of betrayal and bloody conflict between the English and the Scots. When she first published the poem, in *Blackwood's*, April

1827, Hemans used as epigraph a passage from the work of another Scottish author, Joanna Baillie's *Ethwald: A Tragedy*, part 2 (1802), 1.2.76–82.

Corinne at the Capitol[1]

*Les femmes doivent penser qu'il est dans cette carrière bien peu de
sorte qui puissent valoir la plus obscure vie d'une femme aimée et
d'une mère heureuse.*

MADAME DE STAEL[2]

Daughter of th' Italian heaven!
Thou, to whom its fires are given,
Joyously thy car° hath roll'd   chariot
Where the conqueror's pass'd of old;
5   And the festal sun that shone,
O'er three[3] hundred triumphs gone,
Makes thy day of glory bright,
With a shower of golden light.

Now thou tread'st th'ascending road,
10 Freedom's foot so proudly trode;
While, from tombs of heroes borne,
From the dust of empire shorn,
Flowers upon thy graceful head,
Chaplets° of all hues, are shed,   wreaths
15 In a soft and rosy rain,
Touch'd with many a gemlike stain.

Thou hast gain'd the summit now!
Music hails thee from below;—
Music, whose rich notes might stir
20 Ashes of the sepulchre;
Shaking with victorious notes
All the bright air as it floats.
Well may woman's heart beat high
Unto that proud harmony!

25 Now afar it rolls—it dies—
And thy voice is heard to rise
With a low and lovely tone
In its thrilling power alone;
And thy lyre's deep silvery string,

1. Hemans's poem comments on one of the most famous and controversial novels of early-19th-century Europe, *Corinne, or Italy* (1807), by the Swiss-French writer Germaine de Staël, and particularly on its second book, in which Staël's heroine, an *improvisatrice* (a poet who speaks from rhapsodic inspiration rather than texts) is crowned at the Capitol in Rome in recognition of her genius, as Petrarch had been crowned in the 14th century. Corinne's triumph is short-lived and, at the novel's close, abandoned by her English lover, she dies of a broken heart. In book 2 of *Aurora Leigh* (1857), Elizabeth Barrett Browning would again restage the scene of Corinne's coronation, marking how Staël's simultaneously inspirational and cautionary story of the unhappy female genius had come to shape women writers' understanding of poetic fame.
2. "Women must recognize that very little in this career equals in value the most obscure life of a beloved wife and happy mother." From Staël's *De l'Influence des Passions sur le Bonheur des Individus et des Nations* (*On the Influence of the Passions on the Happiness of Individuals and Nations*; 1796).
3. The trebly hundred triumphs—BYRON [Hemans's note]. From a stinging account in *Childe Harold* (4.731) of the celebrations that greeted imperial Rome's victorious heroes.

30   Touch'd as by a breeze's wing,
      Murmurs tremblingly at first,
      Ere the tide of rapture burst.

      All the spirit of thy sky
      Now hath lit thy large dark eye,
35   And thy cheek a flush hath caught
      From the joy of kindled thought;
      And the burning words of song
      From thy lip flow fast and strong,
      With a rushing stream's delight
40   In the freedom of its might.

      Radiant daughter of the sun!
      Now thy living wreath is won.
      Crown'd of Rome!—Oh! art thou not
      Happy in that glorious lot?—
45   Happier, happier far than thou,
      With the laurel[4] on thy brow,
      She that makes the humblest hearth
      Lovely but to one on earth!

1827   1827

A Spirit's Return

"This is to be a mortal,
And seek the things beyond mortality!"
                                    —MANFRED[1]

     Thy voice prevails—dear friend, my gentle friend!
     This long-shut heart for thee shall be unsealed,
     And though thy soft eye mournfully will bend
     Over the troubled stream, yet once revealed
5   Shall its freed waters flow; then rocks must close
     For evermore, above their dark repose.

     Come while the gorgeous mysteries of the sky
     Fused in the crimson sea of sunset lie;
     Come to the woods, where all strange wandering sound
10   Is mingled into harmony profound;
     Where the leaves thrill with spirit, while the wind
     Fills with a viewless° being, unconfined,   invisible
     The trembling reeds and fountains—our own dell,

4. Wreaths of laurel were bestowed on honored poets in classical antiquity.
1. A spirit's verdict on Manfred's quest, spoken just after Manfred is convulsed by the disappearance of the Phantom of his beloved Astarte (*Manfred* 2.4.158–59; see p. 658). Hemans's poem can be read as commentary on Byron's play, Percy Shelley's *Alastor,* and Keats's *Endymion* (see the note to lines 216–17 below), all of which depict a protagonist's problems in communicating with an otherworldly lover.

With its green dimness and Aeolian° breath,   *wind-blown*
15 Shall suit th' unveiling of dark records well—
Hear me in tenderness and silent faith!

Thou knew'st me not in life's fresh vernal morn—
I would thou hadst!—for then my heart on thine
Had poured a worthier love; now, all o'erworn
20 By its deep thirst for something too divine,
It hath but fitful music to bestow,
Echoes of harp-strings broken long ago.

Yet even in youth companionless I stood,
As a lone forest-bird 'midst ocean's foam;
25 For me the silver cords of brotherhood
Were early loosed; the voices from my home
Passed one by one, and melody and mirth
Left me a dreamer by a silent hearth.

But, with the fulness of a heart that burned
30 For the deep sympathies of mind, I turned
From that unanswering spot, and fondly sought
In all wild scenes with thrilling murmurs fraught,
In every still small voice and sound of power,
And flute-note of the wind through cave and bower,
35 A perilous delight!—for then first woke
My life's lone passion, the mysterious quest
Of secret knowledge; and each tone that broke
From the wood-arches or the fountain's breast,
Making my quick soul vibrate as a lyre,
40 But ministered to that strange inborn fire.
'Midst the bright silence of the mountain dells,
In noon-tide hours or golden summer-eves,
My thoughts have burst forth as a gale that swells
Into a rushing blast, and from the leaves
45 Shakes out response. O thou rich world unseen!
Thou curtained realm of spirits!—thus my cry
Hath troubled air and silence—dost thou lie
Spread all around, yet by some filmy screen
Shut from us ever? The resounding woods,
50 Do their depths teem with marvels?—and the floods,
And the pure fountains, leading secret veins
Of quenchless melody through rock and hill,
Have they bright dwellers?—are their lone domains
Peopled with beauty, which may never still
55 *Our* weary thirst of soul?—Cold, weak and cold,
Is earth's vain language, piercing not one fold
Of our deep being! Oh, for gifts more high!
For a seer's glance to rend mortality!
For a charmed rod, to call from each dark shrine
60 The oracles divine!

I woke from those high fantasies, to know
My kindred with the earth—I woke to love:

O gentle friend! to love in doubt and woe,
Shutting the heart the worshipped name above,
65 Is to love deeply—and *my* spirit's dower
Was a sad gift, a melancholy power
Of so adoring—with a buried care,
And with the o'erflowing of a voiceless prayer,
And with a deepening dream, that day by day,
70 In the still shadow of its lonely sway,
Folded me closer, till the world held nought
Save the *one* being to my centred thought.

There was no music but his voice to hear,
No joy but such as with *his* step drew near;
75 Light was but where he looked—life where he moved;
Silently, fervently, thus, thus I loved.
Oh! but such love is fearful!—and I knew
Its gathering doom:—the soul's prophetic sight
Even then unfolded in my breast, and threw
80 O'er all things round a full, strong, vivid light,
Too sorrowfully clear!—an undertone
Was given to Nature's harp, for me alone
Whispering of grief.—Of grief?—be strong, awake,
Hath not thy love been victory, O, my soul?
85 Hath not its conflict won a voice to shake
Death's fastnesses?—a magic to control
Worlds far removed?—from o'er the grave to thee
Love hath made answer; and *thy* tale should be
Sung like a lay of triumph!—Now return,
90 And take thy treasure from its bosomed urn,²
And lift it once to light!

                    In fear, in pain,
I said I loved—but yet a heavenly strain
Of sweetness floated down the tearful stream,
A joy flashed through the trouble of my dream!
95 I knew myself beloved!—we breathed no vow,
No mingling visions might our fate allow,
As unto happy hearts; but still and deep,
Like a rich jewel gleaming in a grave,
Like golden sand in some dark river's wave,
100 So did my soul that costly knowledge keep
So jealously!°—a thing o'er which to shed,   watchfully
When stars alone beheld the drooping head,
Lone tears! yet ofttimes burdened with the excess
Of our strange nature's quivering happiness.

105 But, oh! sweet friend! we dream not of love's might
Till death has robed with soft and solemn light
The image we enshrine!—Before *that* hour,
We have but glimpses of the o'ermastering power
Within us laid!—*then* doth the spirit-flame
110 With sword-like lightning rend its mortal frame;

2. Suggests an urn in which funerary ashes are kept.

The wings of that which pants to follow fast
Shake their clay-bars, as with a prisoned blast—
The sea is in our souls!

He died—*he* died
On whom my lone devotedness was cast!
115   I might not keep one vigil by his side,
I, whose wrung heart watched with him to the last!
I might not once his fainting head sustain,
Nor bathe his parched lips in the hour of pain,
Nor say to him, "Farewell!"—He passed away—
120   Oh! had *my* love been there, its conquering sway
Had won him back from death! but thus removed,
Borne o'er the abyss no sounding-line hath proved,
Joined with the unknown, the viewless—he became
Unto my thoughts another, yet the same—
125   Changed—hallowed—glorified!—and his low grave
Seemed a bright mournful altar—mine, all mine:—
Brother and friend soon left me *that* sole shrine,
The birthright of the faithful!—*their* world's wave
Soon swept them from its brink.—Oh! deem thou not
130   That on the sad and consecrated spot
My soul grew weak!—I tell thee that a power
There kindled heart and lip—a fiery shower
My words were made—a might was given to prayer,
And a strong grasp to passionate despair,
135   And a dead triumph!—Know'st thou what I sought?
For what high boon my struggling spirit wrought?—
Communion with the dead!—I sent a cry,
Through the veiled empires of eternity,
A voice to cleave them! By the mournful truth,
140   By the lost promise of my blighted youth,
By the strong chain a mighty love can bind
On the beloved, the spell of mind o'er mind;
By words, which in themselves are magic high,
Armed and inspired, and winged with agony;
145   By tears, which comfort not, but burn, and seem
To bear the heart's blood in their passion stream;
I summoned, I adjured!°—with quickened sense,   *entreated*
With the keen vigil of a life intense,
I watched, an answer from the winds to wring,
150   I listened, if perchance the stream might bring
Token from worlds afar: I taught *one* sound
Unto a thousand echoes—one profound
Imploring accent to the tomb, the sky—
One prayer to night—"Awake, appear, reply!"
155   Hast thou been told that from the viewless bourne,°   *invisible region*
The dark way never hath allowed return?
That all, which tears can move, with life is fled—
That earthly love is powerless on the dead?
Believe it not!—there is a large lone star
160   Now burning o'er yon western hill afar,
And under its clear light there lies a spot
Which well might utter forth—Believe it not!

I sat beneath that planet—I had wept
My woe to stillness, every night-wind slept;
165 A hush was on the hills; the very streams
Went by like clouds, or noiseless founts in dreams,
And the dark tree o'ershadowing me that hour,
Stood motionless, even as the gray church-tower
Whereon I gazed unconsciously:—there came
170 A low sound, like the tremor of a flame,
Or like the light quick shiver of a wing,
Flitting through twilight woods, across the air;
And I looked up!—Oh! for strong words to bring
Conviction o'er thy thought!—Before me there,
175 He, the departed, stood!—Ay, face to face,
So near, and yet how far!—his form, his mien,
Gave to remembrance back each burning trace
Within:—Yet something awfully serene,
Pure, sculpture-like, on the pale brow, that wore
180 Of the once-beating heart no token more;
And stillness on the lip—and o'er the hair
A gleam, that trembled through the breathless air;
And an unfathomed calm, that seemed to lie
In the grave sweetness of the illumined eye;
185 Told of the gulfs between our beings set,
And, as that unsheathed spirit-glance I met,
Made my soul faint:—with *fear?* Oh! *not* with fear!
With the sick feeling that in *his* far sphere
My love could be as nothing! But he spoke—
190 How shall I tell thee of the startling thrill
In that low voice, whose breezy tones could fill
My bosom's infinite? O, friend! I woke
Then first to heavenly life!—Soft, solemn, clear
Breathed the mysterious accents on mine ear,
195 Yet strangely seemed as if the while they rose
From depths of distance, o'er the wide repose
Of slumbering waters wafted, or the dells
Of mountains, hollow with sweet-echo cells;
But, as they murmured on, the mortal chill
200 Passed from me, like a mist before the morn,
And, to that glorious intercourse upborne
By slow degrees, a calm, divinely still,
Possessed my frame: I sought that lighted eye—
From its intense and searching purity
205 I drank in *soul!*—I questioned of the dead—
Of the hushed, starry shores their footsteps tread,
And I was answered:—if remembrance there,
With dreamy whispers fill the immortal air;
If thought, here piled from many a jewel-heap,
210 Be treasure in that pensive land to keep;
If love, o'ersweeping change, and blight, and blast
Find *there* the music of his home at last;
I asked, and I was answered:—Full and high
Was that communion with eternity,
215 Too rich for aught so fleeting!—Like a knell
Swept o'er my sense its closing words, "Farewell,

On earth we meet no more!"³—and all was gone—
The pale bright settled brow—the thrilling tone,
The still and shining eye! and never more
220 May twilight gloom or midnight hush restore
That radiant guest! One full-fraught hour of heaven,
To earthly passion's wild implorings given,
Was made my own—the ethereal fire hath shivered
The fragile censer⁴ in whose mould it quivered
225 Brightly, consumingly! What now is left?
A faded world, of glory's hues bereft—
A void, a chain!—I dwell 'midst throngs, apart,
In the cold silence of the stranger's heart;
A fixed, immortal shadow stands between
230 My spirit and life's fast receding scene;
A gift hath severed me from human ties,
A power is gone from all earth's melodies,
Which never may return: their chords are broken,
The music of another land hath spoken—
235 No after-sound is sweet!—this weary thirst!
And I have heard celestial fountains burst!—
What *here* shall quench it?
                    Dost thou not rejoice,
When the spring sends forth an awakening voice
Through the young woods?—Thou dost!—And in the birth
240 Of early leaves, and flowers, and songs of mirth,
Thousands, like thee, find gladness!—Couldst thou know
How every breeze then summons *me* to go!
How all the light of love and beauty shed
By those rich hours, but woos me to the dead!
245 The *only* beautiful that change no more—
The only loved!—the dwellers on the shore
Of spring fulfilled!—The dead!—*whom* call we so?
They that breathe purer air, that feel, that know
Things wrapt from us!—Away!—within me pent,
250 That which is barred from its own element
Still droops or struggles!—But the day *will* come—
Over the deep the free bird finds its home,
And the stream lingers 'midst the rocks, yet greets
The sea at last; and the winged flower-seed meets
255 A soil to rest in:—shall not *I*, too, be,
My spirit-love! upborne to dwell with thee?
Yes! by the power whose conquering anguish stirred
The tomb, whose cry beyond the stars was heard,
Whose agony of triumph won thee back
260 Through the dim pass no mortal step may track,
Yet shall we meet!—that glimpse of joy divine
Proved thee for ever and for ever mine!

1830

3. This is the answer to Manfred's question to the Phantom of Astarte (2.4.154): "Say, shall we meet again?" Astarte vanishes, and Nemesis says, "She's gone, and will not be recall'd." Hemans's lines also echo Endymion's renunciation of his dream god-dess at a crucial moment in Keats's *Endymion* (4.657–59): "The hour may come / When we shall meet in pure elysium. / On earth I may not love thee."
4. Container in which incense is burned.

JOHN KEATS
1795–1821

John Keats's father was head stableman at a London livery stable; he married his employer's daughter and inherited the business. The poet's mother, by all reports, was an affectionate but negligent parent to her children; remarrying almost immediately after a fall from a horse killed her first husband, she left the eight-year-old John (her firstborn), his brothers, and a sister with their grandmother and did not reenter their lives for four years. The year before his father's death, Keats had been sent to the Reverend John Clarke's private school at Enfield, famous for its progressive curriculum, where he was a noisy, high-spirited boy; despite his small stature (when full-grown, he was barely over five feet in height), he distinguished himself in sports and fistfights. Here he had the good fortune to have as a mentor Charles Cowden Clarke, son of the headmaster, who later became a writer and an editor; he encouraged Keats's passion for reading and, both at school and in the course of their later friendship, introduced him to Spenser and other poets, to music, and to the theater.

When Keats's mother returned to her children, she was already ill, and in 1810 she died of tuberculosis. Although the livery stable had prospered, and £8,000 had been left in trust to the children by Keats's grandmother, the estate remained tied up in the law courts for all of Keats's lifetime. The children's guardian, Richard Abbey, an unimaginative and practical-minded businessman, took Keats out of school at the age of fifteen and bound him apprentice to Thomas Hammond, a surgeon and apothecary at Edmonton. In 1815 Keats carried on his medical studies at Guy's Hospital, London, and the next year qualified to practice as an apothecary-surgeon—but almost immediately, over his guardian's protests, he abandoned medicine for poetry.

This decision was influenced by Keats's friendship with Leigh Hunt, then editor of the *Examiner* and a leading political radical, poet, and prolific writer of criticism and periodical essays. Hunt, the first successful author of Keats's acquaintance, added his enthusiastic encouragement of Keats's poetic efforts to that of Clarke. More important, he introduced him to writers greater than Hunt himself—William Hazlitt, Charles Lamb, and Percy Shelley—as well as to Benjamin Robert Haydon, painter of grandiose historical and religious canvases. Through Hunt, Keats also met John Hamilton Reynolds and then Charles Wentworth Dilke and Charles Brown, who became his intimate friends and provided him with an essential circumstance for a fledgling poet: a sympathetic and appreciative audience.

The rapidity and sureness of Keats's development has no match. Although he did not begin writing poetry until his eighteenth year, by 1816 in the bold sonnet "On First Looking into Chapman's Homer" he had found his voice. Later that same year he wrote "Sleep and Poetry," in which he laid out for himself a program deliberately modeled on the careers of the greatest poets, asking only

for ten years, that I may overwhelm
Myself in poesy; so I may do the deed
That my own soul has to itself decreed.

For even while his health was good, Keats felt a foreboding of early death and applied himself to his art with a desperate urgency. In 1817 he went on to compose *Endymion*, an ambitious undertaking of more than four thousand lines. It is a rich allegory of a mortal's quest for an ideal feminine counterpart and a flawless happiness beyond earthly possibility; in a number of passages, it already exhibits the sure movement and phrasing of his mature poetic style. But Keats's critical judgment and aspiration exceeded his achievement: long before he completed it, he declared impatiently that he carried on with the "slipshod" *Endymion* only as a "trial of invention" and began to block out *Hyperion*, conceived on the model of Milton's *Paradise Lost* in that most demanding of forms, the epic poem. His success in achieving the Miltonic manner is one of the reasons why Keats abandoned *Hyperion* before it was finished, for he recognized that he was uncommonly susceptible to poetic influences and regarded this as a threat to his individuality. "I will write independently," he insisted. "The Genius of Poetry must work out its own salvation in a man." He had refused the chance of intimacy with Shelley "that I might have my own unfettered scope"; he had broken away from Leigh Hunt's influence lest he get "the reputation of Hunt's *élève* [pupil]"; now he shied away from domination by Milton's powerfully infectious style.

In sentimental, later-nineteenth-century accounts of "poor Keats," 1818 was cast as the year in which this rising genius, already frail and sensitive, was mortally crushed by vicious reviews. Percy Shelley helped initiate this myth in *Adonais,* which describes Keats as "a pale flower." Byron, who did not like Keats's verse, put it unsentimentally: Keats, he wrote, was "snuffed out by an article." It is true that the critics were brutal to Keats, those associated with the Tory journals especially; for them his poetry proved an irresistible target precisely because it had been promoted by the radical Hunt. *Endymion* was mauled in the *Quarterly Review,* and one of the articles on "the Cockney School of Poetry" that appeared in *Blackwood's Magazine* condemned Keats as hopelessly vulgar, a writer who wanted to be a poet of nature but thought, as a social-climbing, undereducated Londoner would, that nature was "flowers seen in window-pots." "It is a better and wiser thing to be a starved apothecary than a starved poet," the reviewer scolded: "so back to the shop Mr John." Keats had for his own part the good sense to recognize that the attacks were motivated by political prejudice and class snobbery, and he had already passed his own severe judgment on *Endymion:* "My own domestic criticism," he said, "has given me pain without comparison beyond what *Blackwood* or the *Quarterly* could possibly inflict." More important was the financial distress of his brother George and his young bride, who emigrated to Kentucky and lost their money in an ill-advised investment. Keats, short of funds and needing to supplement the family income, had now to find ways to make money from his writing: he turned to journalism and began planning plays. His brother Tom contracted tuberculosis, and the poet, in devoted attendance, helplessly watched him waste away until his death that December. In the summer of that year, Keats had taken a strenuous walking tour in the English Lake District, Scotland, and Ireland. It was a glorious adventure but a totally exhausting one in wet, cold weather, and he returned in August with a chronically ulcerated throat made increasingly ominous by the shadow of the tuberculosis that had killed his mother and brother. And in the late fall of that same year, Keats fell unwillingly but deeply in love with Fanny Brawne, the eighteen-year-old girl next door. They became engaged, knowing, though, that Keats's poverty and worsening health might well make their marriage impossible.

In this period of turmoil, Keats achieved the culmination of his brief poetic career. Between January and September of 1819, masterpiece followed masterpiece in astonishing succession: *The Eve of St. Agnes,* "La Belle Dame sans Merci," all of the "great odes," *Lamia,* and a sufficient number of fine sonnets to make him, with Wordsworth, the major Romantic craftsman in that form. All of these poems possess the distinctive qualities of the work of Keats's maturity: a slow-paced, gracious movement; a concreteness of description in which all the senses—tactile, gustatory, kinetic, visceral, as well as visual and auditory—combine to give the total apprehension of an experience; a delight at the sheer existence of things outside himself, the poet seeming to lose his own identity in a total identification with the object he contemplates; and a concentrated felicity of phrasing that reminded his friends, as it has many critics since, of the language of Shakespeare. Under the richly sensuous surface, we find Keats's characteristic presentation of all experience as a tangle of inseparable but irreconcilable opposites. He finds melancholy in delight and pleasure in pain; he feels the highest intensity of love as an approximation to death; he inclines equally toward a life of indolence and "sensation" and toward a life of thought; he is aware both of the attraction of an imaginative dream world without "disagreeables" and the remorseless pressure of the actual; he aspires at the same time to aesthetic detachment and to social responsibility.

His letters, hardly less remarkable than his poetry, show that Keats felt on his pulses the conflicts he dramatized in his major poems. Above all, they reveal him wrestling with the problem of evil and suffering—what to make of our lives in the discovery that "the world is full of misery and heartbreak, pain, sickness and oppression." To the end of his life, he refused to seek solace for the complexity and contradictions of experience either in the abstractions of inherited philosophical doctrines or in the absolutes of a religious creed. At the close of his poetic career, in the latter part of 1819, Keats began to rework the epic *Hyperion* into the form of a dream vision that he called *The Fall of Hyperion*. In the introductory section of this fragment the poet is told by the prophetess Moneta that he has hitherto been merely a dreamer; he must know that

> The poet and the dreamer are distinct,
> Diverse, sheer opposite, antipodes,

and that the height of poetry can be reached only by

> those to whom the miseries of the world
> Are misery, and will not let them rest.

He was seemingly planning to undertake a new direction and subject matter, when illness and death intervened.

On the night of February 3, 1820, he coughed up blood. As a physician he refused to evade the truth: "I cannot be deceived in that colour; that drop of blood is my death warrant. I must die." That spring and summer a series of hemorrhages rapidly weakened him. In the autumn he allowed himself to be persuaded to seek the milder climate of Italy in the company of Joseph Severn, a young painter, but these last months were only what he called "a posthumous existence." He died in Rome on February 23, 1821, and was buried in the Protestant Cemetery, where Mary and Percy Shelley had already interred their little son William, and where Percy's ashes, too, would be deposited in 1822. At times the agony of his disease, the seeming frustration of his hopes for great poetic achievement, and the despair of his passion for Fanny Brawne compelled even Keats's brave spirit to bitterness and jealousy, but he always recovered his gallantry. His last letter, written to Charles Brown, concludes: "I can scarcely bid you good bye even in a letter. I always made an awkward bow. God bless you! John Keats."

No one can read Keats's poems and letters without an undersense of the tragic waste of an extraordinary intellect and genius cut off so early. What he might have done is beyond conjecture; what we do know is that his poetry, when he stopped writing at the age of twenty-four, exceeds the accomplishment at the same age of Chaucer, Shakespeare, and Milton.

The texts here are taken from Jack Stillinger's edition, *The Poems of John Keats* (Cambridge, Mass., 1978).

○ On First Looking into Chapman's Homer[1]

> Much have I travell'd in the realms of gold,
> And many goodly states and kingdoms seen;

---

1. Keats's mentor Charles Cowden Clarke introduced him to Homer in the robust translation by the Elizabethan poet and dramatist George Chapman. They read through the night, and Keats walked home at dawn. This sonnet reached Clarke by the ten o'clock mail that same morning. It was the gold-hunter Balboa, not Cortez, the Spanish conqueror of Mexico, who caught his first sight of the Pacific from the heights of Darien, in Panama, but none of Keats's contemporaries noticed the error.

Round many western islands have I been
Which bards in fealty to Apollo hold.
5   Oft of one wide expanse had I been told
That deep-brow'd Homer ruled as his demesne;[2]
Yet did I never breathe its pure serene[3]
Till I heard Chapman speak out loud and bold:
Then felt I like some watcher of the skies
10   When a new planet swims into his ken;°   *view*
Or like stout Cortez when with eagle eyes
He star'd at the Pacific—and all his men
Look'd at each other with a wild surmise—
Silent, upon a peak in Darien.

Oct. 1816   1816

From Sleep and Poetry[1]

[O FOR TEN YEARS]

O for ten years, that I may overwhelm
Myself in poesy; so I may do the deed
That my own soul has to itself decreed.
Then will I pass the countries that I see
100   In long perspective, and continually
Taste their pure fountains. First the realm I'll pass
Of Flora, and old Pan:[2] sleep in the grass,
Feed upon apples red, and strawberries,
And choose each pleasure that my fancy sees;
105   Catch the white-handed nymphs in shady places,
To woo sweet kisses from averted faces,—
Play with their fingers, touch their shoulders white
Into a pretty shrinking with a bite
As hard as lips can make it: till agreed,
110   A lovely tale of human life we'll read.
And one will teach a tame dove how it best
May fan the cool air gently o'er my rest;
Another, bending o'er her nimble tread,
Will set a green robe floating round her head,
115   And still will dance with ever varied ease,
Smiling upon the flowers and the trees:
Another will entice me on, and on
Through almond blossoms and rich cinnamon;
Till in the bosom of a leafy world

2. Realm, feudal possession.
3. Clear expanse of air.
1. At the age of twenty-one, Keats set himself a
regimen of poetic training modeled on the course
followed by the greatest poets. Virgil had established the pattern of beginning with pastoral writing and proceeding gradually to the point at which
he was ready to undertake the epic, and this pattern had been deliberately followed by Spenser and
Milton. Keats's version of this program, as he
describes it here, is to begin with the realm "of

Flora, and old Pan" (line 102) and, within ten
years, to climb up to the level of poetry dealing with
"the agonies, the strife / Of human hearts" (lines
124–25). The program Keats set himself is illuminated by his analysis of Wordsworth's progress
in his letter to J. H. Reynolds of May 3, 1818
(p. 945).
2. I.e., the carefree pastoral world. Flora was the
Roman goddess of flowers. Pan was the Greek god
of pastures, woods, and animal life.

120   We rest in silence, like two gems upcurl'd
       In the recesses of a pearly shell.

       And can I ever bid these joys farewell?
       Yes, I must pass them for a nobler life,
       Where I may find the agonies, the strife
125   Of human hearts: for lo! I see afar,
       O'er sailing the blue cragginess, a car³
       And steeds with streamy manes—the charioteer
       Looks out upon the winds with glorious fear:
       And now the numerous tramplings quiver lightly
130   Along a huge cloud's ridge; and now with sprightly
       Wheel downward come they into fresher skies,
       Tipt round with silver from the sun's bright eyes.
       Still downward with capacious whirl they glide;
       And now I see them on a green-hill's side
135   In breezy rest among the nodding stalks.
       The charioteer with wond'rous gesture talks
       To the trees and mountains; and there soon appear
       Shapes of delight, of mystery, and fear,
       Passing along before a dusky space
140   Made by some mighty oaks: as they would chase
       Some ever-fleeting music on they sweep.
       Lo! how they murmur, laugh, and smile, and weep:
       Some with upholden hand and mouth severe;
       Some with their faces muffled to the ear
145   Between their arms; some, clear in youthful bloom,
       Go glad and smilingly athwart° the gloom;   against
       Some looking back, and some with upward gaze;
       Yes, thousands in a thousand different ways
       Flit onward—now a lovely wreath of girls
150   Dancing their sleek hair into tangled curls;
       And now broad wings. Most awfully intent,
       The driver of those steeds is forward bent,
       And seems to listen: O that I might know
       All that he writes with such a hurrying glow.

155   The visions all are fled—the car is fled
       Into the light of heaven, and in their stead
       A sense of real things comes doubly strong,
       And, like a muddy stream, would bear along
       My soul to nothingness: but I will strive
160   Against all doubtings, and will keep alive
       The thought of that same chariot, and the strange
       Journey it went.

                     *   *   *

Oct.–Dec. 1816   1817

3. Chariot. The description that follows recalls the traditional portrayal of Apollo, god of the sun and poetry, and represents the higher poetic imagina- tion, which bodies forth the matters "of delight, of mystery, and fear" (line 138) that characterize the grander poetic genres.

On Seeing the Elgin Marbles[1]

My spirit is too weak—mortality
Weighs heavily on me like unwilling sleep,
And each imagined pinnacle and steep
Of godlike hardship tells me I must die
5 Like a sick eagle looking at the sky.
Yet 'tis a gentle luxury to weep
That I have not the cloudy winds to keep
Fresh for the opening of the morning's eye.
Such dim-conceived glories of the brain
10   Bring round the heart an undescribable feud;
So do these wonders a most dizzy pain,
That mingles Grecian grandeur with the rude
Wasting of old time—with a billowy main°—   *ocean*
A sun—a shadow of a magnitude.

Mar. 1 or 2, 1817   1817

From Endymion: A Poetic Romance[1]

"The stretched metre of an antique song"

INSCRIBED TO THE MEMORY OF THOMAS CHATTERTON

Preface

Knowing within myself the manner in which this Poem has been produced, it is not without a feeling of regret that I make it public. What manner I mean, will be quite clear to the reader, who must soon perceive great inexperience, immaturity, and every error denoting a feverish attempt, rather than a deed accomplished. The two first books, and indeed the two last, I feel sensible are not of such completion as to warrant their passing the press; nor should they if I thought a year's castigation would do them any good;—it will not: the foundations are too sandy. It is just that this youngster

---

1. Lord Elgin had brought to England in 1806 many of the marble statues and friezes that adorned the Parthenon at Athens. In 1817 Keats, along with his artist friend Haydon, viewed the marbles at the British Museum, which had just purchased them, an acquisition that was and remains controversial. Keats's sonnet first appeared on the same day in both Leigh Hunt's *Examiner* and, through Keats's friend Reynolds, *The Champion*, and then was reprinted in Haydon's magazine *Annals of the Fine Arts.*
1. This poem of more than four thousand lines (based on the classical myth of a mortal beloved by the goddess of the moon) tells of Endymion's long and agonized search for an immortal goddess whom he had seen in several visions. In the course of his wanderings, he comes upon an Indian maid who had been abandoned by the followers of Bacchus, god of wine and revelry. To his utter despair,

he succumbs to a sensual passion for her, in apparent betrayal of his love for his heavenly ideal. The conclusion to Keats's "romance" offers a way of resolving this opposition, which runs throughout the poem, between the inevitably mortal pleasures of this world and the possibility of delights that would be eternal: the Indian maid reveals that she is herself Cynthia (Diana), goddess of the moon, the celestial subject of his earlier visions.

The verse epigraph is adapted from Shakespeare's Sonnet 17, line 12: "And stretchèd metre of an antique song." Thomas Chatterton (1752–1770), to whom *Endymion* is dedicated, and who is the "marvellous Boy" of Wordsworth's "Resolution and Independence," wrote a number of brilliant pseudoarchaic poems that he attributed to an imaginary 15th-century poet, Thomas Rowley. Keats described him as "the most English of poets except Shakespeare."

should die away: a sad thought for me, if I had not some hope that while it is dwindling I may be plotting, and fitting myself for verses fit to live. This may be speaking too presumptuously, and may deserve a punishment: but no feeling man will be forward to inflict it: he will leave me alone, with the conviction that there is not a fiercer hell than the failure in a great object. This is not written with the least atom of purpose to forestall criticisms of course, but from the desire I have to conciliate men who are competent to look, and who do look with a zealous eye, to the honour of English literature.

The imagination of a boy is healthy, and the mature imagination of a man is healthy; but there is a space of life between, in which the soul is in a ferment, the character undecided, the way of life uncertain, the ambition thick-sighted: thence proceeds mawkishness, and all the thousand bitters which those men I speak of must necessarily taste in going over the following pages.

I hope I have not in too late a day touched the beautiful mythology of Greece,[2] and dulled its brightness: for I wish to try once more,[3] before I bid it farewell.

Teignmouth, April 10, 1818

From *Book 1*

[A THING OF BEAUTY]

A thing of beauty is a joy for ever:
Its loveliness increases; it will never
Pass into nothingness; but still will keep
A bower quiet for us, and a sleep
5 Full of sweet dreams, and health, and quiet breathing.
Therefore, on every morrow, are we wreathing
A flowery band to bind us to the earth,
Spite° of despondence, of the inhuman dearth   *despite*
Of noble natures, of the gloomy days,
10 Of all the unhealthy and o'er-darkened ways
Made for our searching: yes, in spite of all,
Some shape of beauty moves away the pall
From our dark spirits. Such the sun, the moon,
Trees old, and young sprouting a shady boon
15 For simple sheep; and such are daffodils
With the green world they live in; and clear rills°   *small streams*
That for themselves a cooling covert make
'Gainst the hot season; the mid forest brake,°   *thicket*
Rich with a sprinkling of fair musk-rose blooms:
20 And such too is the grandeur of the dooms°   *judgments*
We have imagined for the mighty dead;
All lovely tales that we have heard or read:

2. In 1820 an anonymous reviewer of Keats's final volume of poems cited this phrase and, in a complaint that suggests the political charge that the poetic use of classical mythology could carry at this time, wrote disparagingly of "the nonsense that Mr. Keats . . . and Mr. Percy Bysshe Shelley, and some of the poets about town, have been talking of 'the beautiful mythology of Greece' "; "To some persons . . . that mythology comes recommended chiefly by its grossness—its alliance to the sensitive pleasures which belong to the animal."
3. In *Hyperion*, which Keats was already planning.

An endless fountain of immortal drink,
Pouring unto us from the heaven's brink.

25   Nor do we merely feel these essences
For one short hour; no, even as the trees
That whisper round a temple become soon
Dear as the temple's self, so does the moon,
The passion poesy, glories infinite,
30   Haunt us till they become a cheering light
Unto our souls, and bound to us so fast,
That, whether there be shine, or gloom o'ercast,
They alway must be with us, or we die.

Therefore, 'tis with full happiness that I
35   Will trace the story of Endymion.
The very music of the name has gone
Into my being, and each pleasant scene
Is growing fresh before me as the green
Of our own vallies. * * *

[THE "PLEASURE THERMOMETER"]

"Peona!⁴ ever have I long'd to slake
770   My thirst for the world's praises: nothing base,
No merely slumberous phantasm, could unlace
The stubborn canvas for my voyage prepar'd—
Though now 'tis tatter'd; leaving my bark bar'd
And sullenly drifting: yet my higher hope
775   Is of too wide, too rainbow-large a scope,
To fret at myriads of earthly wrecks.
Wherein lies happiness? In that which becks°   beckons
Our ready minds to fellowship divine,
A fellowship with essence; till we shine,
780   Full alchemiz'd,⁵ and free of space. Behold
The clear religion of heaven! Fold
A rose leaf round thy finger's taperness,
And soothe thy lips: hist,° when the airy stress   listen
Of music's kiss impregnates the free winds,
785   And with a sympathetic touch unbinds
Eolian⁶ magic from their lucid wombs:
Then old songs waken from enclouded tombs;
Old ditties sigh above their father's grave;

4. The sister to whom Endymion confides his troubles. Of lines 769–857 Keats said to his publisher, John Taylor: "When I wrote it, it was the regular stepping of the Imagination towards a Truth. My having written that Argument will perhaps be of the greatest Service to me of anything I ever did—It set before me at once the gradations of Happiness even like a kind of Pleasure Thermometer, and is my first step towards the chief attempt in the Drama—the playing of different Natures with Joy and Sorrow." The gradations on this "Pleasure Thermometer" mark the stages on the way to what Keats calls "happiness" (line 777)—his secular version of the religious concept of "felicity" that, in the orthodox view, is to be achieved by a surrender of oneself to God. For Keats the way to happiness lies through a fusion of ourselves, first sensuously, with the lovely objects of nature and art (lines 781–97), then on a higher level, with other human beings through "love and friendship" (line 801) and, ultimately, sexual love.
5. Transformed by alchemy from a base to a precious metal.
6. From Aeolus, god of winds.

Ghosts of melodious prophecyings rave
790 Round every spot where trod Apollo's foot;
Bronze clarions awake, and faintly bruit,[7]
Where long ago a giant battle was;
And, from the turf, a lullaby doth pass
In every place where infant Orpheus[8] slept.
795 Feel we these things?—that moment have we stept
Into a sort of oneness, and our state
Is like a floating spirit's. But there are
Richer entanglements, enthralments far
More self-destroying, leading, by degrees,
800 To the chief intensity: the crown of these
Is made of love and friendship, and sits high
Upon the forehead of humanity.
All its more ponderous and bulky worth
Is friendship, whence there ever issues forth
805 A steady splendour; but at the tip-top
There hangs by unseen film, an orbed drop
Of light, and that is love: its influence,
Thrown in our eyes, genders a novel sense,
At which we start and fret; till in the end,
810 Melting into its radiance, we blend,
Mingle, and so become a part of it,—
Nor with aught else can our souls interknit
So wingedly: when we combine therewith,
Life's self is nourish'd by its proper pith,[9]
815 And we are nurtured like a pelican brood.[1]
Aye, so delicious is the unsating food,[2]
That men, who might have tower'd in the van°   forefront
Of all the congregated world, to fan
And winnow from the coming step of time
820 All chaff of custom, wipe away all slime
Left by men-slugs and human serpentry,
Have been content to let occasion die,
Whilst they did sleep in love's elysium.°   heaven
And, truly, I would rather be struck dumb,
825 Than speak against this ardent listlessness:
For I have ever thought that it might bless
The world with benefits unknowingly;
As does the nightingale, upperched high,
And cloister'd among cool and bunched leaves—
830 She sings but to her love, nor e'er conceives
How tiptoe Night holds back her dark-grey hood.[3]
Just so may love, although 'tis understood
The mere commingling of passionate breath,
Produce more than our searching witnesseth:
835 What I know not: but who, of men, can tell

---

7. Make a sound.
8. The musician of Greek legend, whose beautiful music could move even inanimate things.
9. Its own elemental substance.
1. Young pelicans were once thought to feed on their mother's flesh. In a parallel way our life is nourished by another's life, with which it fuses in love.
2. Food that never satiates, that never ceases to satisfy.
3. I.e., in order to hear better.

That flowers would bloom, or that green fruit would swell
To melting pulp, that fish would have bright mail,
The earth its dower of river, wood, and vale,
The meadows runnels, runnels pebble-stones,
840 The seed its harvest, or the lute its tones,
Tones ravishment, or ravishment its sweet,
If human souls did never kiss and greet?

"Now, if this earthly love has power to make
Men's being mortal, immortal; to shake
845 Ambition from their memories, and brim
Their measure of content; what merest whim,
Seems all this poor endeavour after fame,
To one, who keeps within his stedfast aim
A love immortal, an immortal too.
850 Look not so wilder'd; for these things are true,
And never can be born of atomies°   mites
That buzz about our slumbers, like brain-flies,
Leaving us fancy-sick. No, no, I'm sure,
My restless spirit never could endure
855 To brood so long upon one luxury,
Unless it did, though fearfully, espy
A hope beyond the shadow of a dream."

Apr.–Nov. 1817   1818

On Sitting Down to Read *King Lear* Once Again[1]

O golden-tongued Romance, with serene lute!
Fair plumed syren,[2] queen of far-away!
Leave melodizing on this wintry day,
Shut up thine olden pages, and be mute.
5 Adieu! for, once again, the fierce dispute
Betwixt damnation and impassion'd clay
Must I burn through; once more humbly assay°   test
The bitter-sweet of this Shakespearean fruit.
Chief Poet! and ye clouds of Albion,[3]
10   Begetters of our deep eternal theme!
When through the old oak forest I am gone,
Let me not wander in a barren dream:
But, when I am consumed in the fire,
Give me new phoenix[4] wings to fly at my desire.

Jan. 22, 1818   1838

1. Keats pauses, while revising *Endymion: A Poetic Romance*, to read again Shakespeare's great tragedy. The word "syren" (line 2) indicates Keats's feeling that "Romance" was enticing him from the poet's prime duty, to deal with "the agonies, the strife / Of human hearts" (*Sleep and Poetry*, lines 124–25).

2. Syrens (sirens) were sea nymphs whose singing lured listeners to their deaths.
3. Old name for England. *King Lear* is set in Celtic Britain.
4. The fabulous bird that periodically burns itself to death to rise anew from the ashes.

When I have fears that I may cease to be[1]

(handwritten margin note: Shakesperian sonnet
ab, ab, cd, cd, ee)

When I have fears that I may cease to be
    Before my pen has glean'd my teeming brain,
Before high piled books, in charactry,[2]
    Hold like rich garners the full ripen'd grain;
When I behold, upon the night's starr'd face,   5
    Huge cloudy symbols of a high romance,
And think that I may never live to trace
    Their shadows, with the magic hand of chance;
And when I feel, fair creature of an hour,
    That I shall never look upon thee more,   10
Never have relish in the fairy power
    Of unreflecting love;—then on the shore
Of the wide world I stand alone, and think
Till love and fame to nothingness do sink.

(handwritten margin note: fear to be unappriciated, to say everything and be heard before he dies.)

Jan. 1818   1848

To Homer

Standing aloof in giant ignorance,
    Of thee I hear and of the Cyclades,[1]
As one who sits ashore and longs perchance
    To visit dolphin-coral in deep seas.
So wast thou blind;—but then the veil was rent,   5
    For Jove uncurtain'd heaven to let thee live,
And Neptune made for thee a spumy tent,
    And Pan made sing for thee his forest-hive;
Aye on the shores of darkness there is light,
    And precipices show untrodden green,   10
There is a budding morrow in midnight,
    There is a triple sight in blindness keen;
Such seeing hadst thou, as it once befel
To Dian, Queen of Earth, and Heaven, and Hell.[2]

1818   1848

(handwritten margin note: 8-lines Iambic Penmeter 9-line 6 footed hexameter a,b,a,b,b,c,b,c,c Spencinian Sonnet)

The Eve of St. Agnes[1]

I

St. Agnes' Eve—Ah, bitter chill it was!
    The owl, for all his feathers, was a-cold;

---

1. The first, and one of the most successful, of Keats's attempts at the sonnet in the Shakespearean rhyme scheme.
2. Characters; printed letters of the alphabet.
1. A group of islands in the Aegean Sea, off Greece. Keats's allusion is to his ignorance of the Greek language. Schooling in Greek was a badge of gentlemanly identity in the period.
2. In late pagan cults Diana was worshiped as a

three-figured goddess, the deity of nature and of the moon as well as the queen of hell. The "triple sight" that blind Homer paradoxically commands is of these three regions and also of heaven, sea, and earth (the realms of Jove, Neptune, and Pan, lines 6–8).
1. St. Agnes, martyred ca. 303 at the age of thirteen, is the patron saint of virgins. Legend has it that if a chaste young woman performs the proper

The hare limp'd trembling through the frozen grass,
And silent was the flock in woolly fold:
5   Numb were the Beadsman's[2] fingers, while he told
His rosary, and while his frosted breath,
Like pious incense from a censer old,
Seem'd taking flight for heaven, without a death,
Past the sweet Virgin's picture, while his prayer he saith.

2

10 His prayer he saith, this patient, holy man;
Then takes his lamp, and riseth from his knees,
And back returneth, meagre,° barefoot, wan,   *lean*
Along the chapel aisle by slow degrees:
The sculptur'd dead, on each side, seem to freeze,
15 Emprison'd in black, purgatorial rails:
Knights, ladies, praying in dumb° orat'ries,°   *silent / chapels*
He passeth by; and his weak spirit fails
To think[3] how they may ache in icy hoods and mails.

3

Northward he turneth through a little door,
20 And scarce three steps, ere Music's golden tongue
Flatter'd° to tears this aged man and poor;   *beguiled*
But no—already had his deathbell rung;
The joys of all his life were said and sung:
His was harsh penance on St. Agnes' Eve:
25 Another way he went, and soon among
Rough ashes sat he for his soul's reprieve,°   *salvation*
And all night kept awake, for sinners' sake to grieve.

4

That ancient Beadsman heard the prelude soft;
And so it chanc'd, for many a door was wide,
30 From hurry to and fro. Soon, up aloft,
The silver, snarling trumpets 'gan to chide:
The level chambers, ready with their pride,°   *ostentation*
Were glowing to receive a thousand guests:
The carved angels, ever eager-eyed,
35 Star'd, where upon their heads the cornice rests,
With hair blown back, and wings put cross-wise on their breasts.

5

At length burst in the argent revelry,[4]
With plume, tiara, and all rich array,
Numerous as shadows haunting fairily
40 The brain, new stuff'd, in youth, with triumphs gay
Of old romance.° These let us wish away,   *stories*
And turn, sole-thoughted, to one Lady there,

ritual, she will dream of her future husband on the
evening before St. Agnes's Day, January 21. Keats
combines this superstition with the Romeo and
Juliet theme of young love thwarted by feuding
families and tells the story in a sequence of evolving Spenserian stanzas. The poem is Keats's first
complete success in sustained narrative romance.
For the author's revisions while composing stanzas

26 and 30 of *The Eve of St. Agnes,* see "Poems in
Process," in the appendices to this volume.
2. One who is paid to pray for his benefactor. He
"tells" (counts) the beads of his rosary to keep track
of his prayers.
3. I.e., when he thinks.
4. Silver-adorned revelers.

Whose heart had brooded, all that wintry day,
On love, and wing'd St. Agnes' saintly care,
45 As she had heard old dames full many times declare.

6

They told her how, upon St. Agnes' Eve,
Young virgins might have visions of delight,
And soft adorings from their loves receive
Upon the honey'd middle of the night,
50 If ceremonies due they did aright;
As, supperless to bed they must retire,
And couch supine their beauties, lily white;
Nor look behind, nor sideways, but require
Of heaven with upward eyes for all that they desire.

7

55 Full of this whim was thoughtful Madeline:
The music, yearning like a god in pain,
She scarcely heard: her maiden eyes divine,
Fix'd on the floor, saw many a sweeping train⁵
Pass by—she heeded not at all: in vain
60 Came many a tiptoe, amorous cavalier,
And back retir'd, not cool'd by high disdain;
But she saw not: her heart was otherwhere:
She sigh'd for Agnes' dreams, the sweetest of the year.

8

She danc'd along with vague, regardless eyes,
65 Anxious her lips, her breathing quick and short:
The hallow'd hour was near at hand: she sighs
Amid the timbrels,° and the throng'd resort   *tambourines*
Of whisperers in anger, or in sport;
'Mid looks of love, defiance, hate, and scorn,
70 Hoodwink'd with faery fancy; all amort,⁶
Save to St. Agnes⁶ and her lambs unshorn,⁷
And all the bliss to be before to-morrow morn.

9

So, purposing each moment to retire,
She linger'd still. Meantime, across the moors,
75 Had come young Porphyro, with heart on fire
For Madeline. Beside the portal doors,
Buttress'd from moonlight,⁸ stands he, and implores
All saints to give him sight of Madeline,
But for one moment in the tedious hours,
80 That he might gaze and worship all unseen;
Perchance speak, kneel, touch, kiss—in sooth such things have been.

10

He ventures in: let no buzz'd whisper tell:
All eyes be muffled, or a hundred swords

5. Skirts sweeping along the ground.
6. Entirely oblivious or dead ("amort") to everything except St. Agnes. "Hoodwinked": covered by
a hood or blindfolded.
7. On St. Agnes's Day it was the custom to offer

lambs' wool at the altar, to be made into cloth by
nuns.
8. Sheltered from the moonlight by the buttresses
(the supports projecting from the wall).

Will storm his heart, Love's fev'rous citadel:
85   For him, those chambers held barbarian hordes,
Hyena foemen, and hot-blooded lords,
Whose very dogs would execrations howl
Against his lineage: not one breast affords
Him any mercy, in that mansion foul,
90 Save one old beldame,[9] weak in body and in soul.

11

Ah, happy chance! the aged creature came,
Shuffling along with ivory-headed wand,°   *staff*
To where he stood, hid from the torch's flame,
Behind a broad hall-pillar, far beyond
95   The sound of merriment and chorus bland:°   *soft*
He startled her; but soon she knew his face,
And grasp'd his fingers in her palsied hand,
Saying, "Mercy, Porphyro! hie thee from this place;
They are all here to-night, the whole blood-thirsty race!

12

100 "Get hence! get hence! there's dwarfish Hildebrand;
He had a fever late, and in the fit
He cursed thee and thine, both house and land:
Then there's that old Lord Maurice, not a whit
More tame for his gray hairs—Alas me! flit!
105 Flit like a ghost away."—"Ah, Gossip[1] dear,
We're safe enough; here in this arm-chair sit,
And tell me how"—"Good Saints! not here, not here;
Follow me, child, or else these stones will be thy bier."°   *tomb*

13

He follow'd through a lowly arched way,
10   Brushing the cobwebs with his lofty plume,
And as she mutter'd "Well-a—well-a-day!"
He found him in a little moonlight room,
Pale, lattic'd, chill, and silent as a tomb.
"Now tell me where is Madeline," said he,
15   "O tell me, Angela, by the holy loom
Which none but secret sisterhood may see,
When they St. Agnes' wool are weaving piously."

14

"St. Agnes! Ah! it is St. Agnes' Eve—
Yet men will murder upon holy days:
20   Thou must hold water in a witch's sieve,[2]
And be liege-lord of all the Elves and Fays,
To venture so: it fills me with amaze
To see thee, Porphyro!—St. Agnes' Eve!
God's help! my lady fair the conjuror plays[3]
25   This very night: good angels her deceive!
But let me laugh awhile, I've mickle° time to grieve."   *much*

---

9. Old (and, usually, homely) woman; an ironic
development in English from the French meaning,
"lovely lady."
1. In the old sense: godmother or old friend.

2. A sieve made to hold water by witchcraft.
3. I.e., uses magic in her attempt to evoke the
vision of her lover.

15

Feebly she laugheth in the languid moon,
While Porphyro upon her face doth look,
Like puzzled urchin on an aged crone
130   Who keepeth clos'd a wond'rous riddle-book,
As spectacled she sits in chimney nook.
But soon his eyes grew brilliant, when she told
His lady's purpose; and he scarce could brook°   restrain
Tears, at the thought of those enchantments cold,
135 And Madeline asleep in lap of legends old.

16

Sudden a thought came like a full-blown rose,
Flushing his brow, and in his pained heart
Made purple riot: then doth he propose
A stratagem, that makes the beldame start:
140   "A cruel man and impious thou art:
Sweet lady, let her pray, and sleep, and dream
Alone with her good angels, far apart
From wicked men like thee. Go, go!—I deem
Thou canst not surely be the same that thou didst seem."

17

145   "I will not harm her, by all saints I swear,"
Quoth Porphyro: "O may I ne'er find grace
When my weak voice shall whisper its last prayer,
If one of her soft ringlets I displace,
Or look with ruffian passion in her face:
150   Good Angela, believe me by these tears;
Or I will, even in a moment's space,
Awake, with horrid shout, my foemen's ears,
And beard° them, though they be more fang'd than wolves and   confront
    bears."

18

"Ah! why wilt thou affright a feeble soul?
155   A poor, weak, palsy-stricken, churchyard thing,
Whose passing-bell° may ere the midnight toll;   death knell
Whose prayers for thee, each morn and evening,
Were never miss'd."—Thus plaining,° doth she bring   complaining
A gentler speech from burning Porphyro;
160   So woful, and of such deep sorrowing,
That Angela gives promise she will do
Whatever he shall wish, betide her weal or woe.[4]

19

Which was, to lead him, in close secrecy,
Even to Madeline's chamber, and there hide
165   Him in a closet, of such privacy
That he might see her beauty unespied,
And win perhaps that night a peerless bride,
While legion'd fairies pac'd the coverlet,

4. I.e., whether good or ill befalls her.

And pale enchantment held her sleepy-eyed.
70   Never on such a night have lovers met,
Since Merlin paid his Demon all the monstrous debt.[5]

20

"It shall be as thou wishest," said the Dame:
"All cates° and dainties shall be stored there   *delicacies*
Quickly on this feast-night: by the tambour frame[6]
75   Her own lute thou wilt see: no time to spare,
For I am slow and feeble, and scarce dare
On such a catering trust my dizzy head.
Wait here, my child, with patience; kneel in prayer
The while: Ah! thou must needs the lady wed,
80   Or may I never leave my grave among the dead."

21

So saying, she hobbled off with busy fear.
The lover's endless minutes slowly pass'd;
The dame return'd, and whisper'd in his ear
To follow her; with aged eyes aghast
85   From fright of dim espial. Safe at last,
Through many a dusky gallery, they gain
The maiden's chamber, silken, hush'd, and chaste;
Where Porphyro took covert, pleas'd amain.°   *mightily*
His poor guide hurried back with agues° in her brain.   *shivering*

22

90   Her falt'ring hand upon the balustrade,
Old Angela was feeling for the stair,
When Madeline, St. Agnes' charmed maid,
Rose, like a mission'd spirit,[7] unaware:
With silver taper's light, and pious care,
95   She turn'd, and down the aged gossip led
To a safe level matting. Now prepare,
Young Porphyro, for gazing on that bed;
She comes, she comes again, like ring-dove fray'd° and fled.   *frightened*

23

Out went the taper as she hurried in;
200   Its little smoke, in pallid moonshine, died:
She clos'd the door, she panted, all akin
To spirits of the air, and visions wide:
No uttered syllable, or, woe betide!
But to her heart, her heart was voluble,
205   Paining with eloquence her balmy side;
As though a tongueless nightingale[8] should swell
Her throat in vain, and die, heart-stifled, in her dell.

5. Probably the episode in the Arthurian legends in which Merlin, the magician, lost his life when the wily Vivien turned one of his own spells against him.
6. A drum-shaped embroidery frame.
7. I.e., like an angel sent on a mission.
8. An allusion to Ovid's story, in the *Metamorphoses,* of Philomel, who was raped by Tereus, her sister's husband. He cut out Philomel's tongue to prevent her from speaking of his crime, but she managed to weave her story and make herself understood to her sister, Procne. Just as Tereus was about to kill both women, Philomel and Procne were metamorphosed into a nightingale and a swallow.

24

Stain glass window [handwritten annotation]

A casement° high and triple-arch'd there was,   *window*
All garlanded with carven imag'ries
210 Of fruits, and flowers, and bunches of knot-grass,
And diamonded with panes of quaint device,
Innumerable of stains and splendid dyes,
As are the tiger-moth's deep-damask'd wings;
And in the midst, 'mong thousand heraldries,
215 And twilight saints, and dim emblazonings,
A shielded scutcheon blush'd with blood of queens and kings.⁹

25

Full on this casement shone the wintry moon,
And threw warm gules¹ on Madeline's fair breast,
As down she knelt for heaven's grace and boon;°   *gift, blessing*
220 Rose-bloom fell on her hands, together prest,
And on her silver cross soft amethyst,
And on her hair a glory,° like a saint: *halo*
She seem'd a splendid angel, newly drest,
Save wings, for heaven:—Porphyro grew faint:
225 She knelt, so pure a thing, so free from mortal taint.

26

Anon his heart revives: her vespers done,
Of all its wreathed pearls her hair she frees;²
Unclasps her warmed jewels one by one;
Loosens her fragrant boddice; by degrees
230 Her rich attire creeps rustling to her knees:
Half-hidden, like a mermaid in sea-weed,
Pensive awhile she dreams awake, and sees,
In fancy, fair St. Agnes in her bed,
But dares not look behind, or all the charm is fled.

27

235 Soon, trembling in her soft and chilly nest,
In sort of wakeful swoon, perplex'd³ she lay,
Until the poppied warmth of sleep oppress'd
Her soothed limbs, and soul fatigued away;
Flown, like a thought, until the morrow-day;
240 Blissfully haven'd both from joy and pain;
Clasp'd like a missal where swart Paynims pray;⁴
Blinded alike from sunshine and from rain,
As though a rose should shut, and be a bud again.

28

Stol'n to this paradise, and so entranced,
245 Porphyro gazed upon her empty dress,

9. I.e., among the genealogical emblems ("herald-ries") and other devices ("emblazonings"), a heral-dic shield signified by its colors that the family was of royal blood.
1. Red (heraldry).
2. The Pre-Raphaelite-inspired painter Daniel Maclise represented this moment in Keats's romance in his painting of 1868, *Madeline after Prayer*. For a reproduction of the painting, see the

color insert.
3. In a confused state between waking and sleep-ing.
4. Variously interpreted; perhaps: held tightly, cherished (or else kept shut, fastened with a clasp), like a Christian prayer book ("missal") in a land where the religion is that of dark-skinned pagans ("swart Paynims").

And listen'd to her breathing, if it chanced
To wake into a slumberous tenderness;
Which when he heard, that minute did he bless,
And breath'd himself: then from the closet crept,
50   Noiseless as fear in a wide wilderness,
And over the hush'd carpet, silent, stept,
And 'tween the curtains peep'd, where, lo!—how fast she slept.

29

Then by the bed-side, where the faded moon
Made a dim, silver twilight, soft he set
55   A table, and, half anguish'd, threw thereon
A cloth of woven crimson, gold, and jet:—
O for some drowsy Morphean amulet![5]
The boisterous, midnight, festive clarion,[6]
The kettle-drum, and far-heard clarionet,
60   Affray° his ears, though but in dying tone:—   *frighten*
The hall door shuts again, and all the noise is gone.

30

And still she slept an azure-lidded sleep,
In blanched linen, smooth, and lavender'd,
While he from forth the closet brought a heap
65   Of candied apple, quince, and plum, and gourd;°   *melon*
With jellies soother than the creamy curd,
And lucent syrops, tinct with cinnamon;
Manna and dates, in argosy transferr'd
From Fez,[7] and spiced dainties, every one,
70   From silken Samarcand to cedar'd Lebanon.

31

These delicates he heap'd with glowing hand
On golden dishes and in baskets bright
Of wreathed silver: sumptuous they stand
In the retired quiet of the night,
75   Filling the chilly room with perfume light.—
"And now, my love, my seraph[8] fair, awake!
Thou art my heaven, and I thine eremite:[9]
Open thine eyes, for meek St. Agnes' sake,
Or I shall drowse beside thee, so my soul doth ache."

32

80   Thus whispering, his warm, unnerved° arm   *unmanned, weak*
Sank in her pillow. Shaded was her dream
By the dusk curtains:—'twas a midnight charm
Impossible to melt as iced stream:
The lustrous salvers° in the moonlight gleam;   *trays*
85   Broad golden fringe upon the carpet lies:
It seem'd he never, never could redeem
From such a stedfast spell his lady's eyes;
So mus'd awhile, entoil'd in woofed phantasies.[1]

---

5. Sleep-producing charm.
6. High-pitched trumpet.
7. I.e., jellies softer ("soother") than the curds of cream, clear ("lucent") syrups tinged with cinnamon, and sweet gums ("manna") and dates transported in a great merchant ship ("argosy") from Fez, in Morocco.
8. One of the highest orders of angels.
9. Hermit, religious solitary.
1. Entangled in a weave of fantasies.

33

Awakening up, he took her hollow lute,—
290 Tumultuous,—and, in chords that tenderest be,
He play'd an ancient ditty, long since mute,
In Provence call'd, "La belle dame sans mercy":[2]
Close to her ear touching the melody;—
Wherewith disturb'd, she utter'd a soft moan:
295 He ceased—she panted quick—and suddenly
Her blue affrayed eyes wide open shone:
Upon his knees he sank, pale as smooth-sculptured stone.

34

Her eyes were open, but she still beheld,
Now wide awake, the vision of her sleep:
300 There was a painful change, that nigh° expell'd   nearly
The blisses of her dream so pure and deep:
At which fair Madeline began to weep,
And moan forth witless words with many a sigh;
While still her gaze on Porphyro would keep;
305 Who knelt, with joined hands and piteous eye,
Fearing to move or speak, she look'd so dreamingly.

[handwritten margin note: she had been dreaming of him. Dream doesn't match with reality.]

35

"Ah, Porphyro!" said she, "but even now
Thy voice was at sweet tremble in mine ear,
Made tuneable with every sweetest vow;
310 And those sad eyes were spiritual and clear:
How chang'd thou art! how pallid, chill, and drear!
Give me that voice again, my Porphyro,
Those looks immortal, those complainings dear!
Oh leave me not in this eternal woe,
315 For if thou diest, my love, I know not where to go."

36

Beyond a mortal man impassion'd far
At these voluptuous accents, he arose,
Ethereal, flush'd, and like a throbbing star
Seen mid the sapphire heaven's deep repose;
320 Into her dream he melted, as the rose
Blendeth its odour with the violet,—
Solution° sweet: meantime the frost-wind blows   fusion
Like Love's alarum pattering the sharp sleet
Against the window-panes; St. Agnes' moon hath set.

37

325 'Tis dark: quick pattereth the flaw-blown° sleet: gust-blown
"This is no dream, my bride, my Madeline!"
'Tis dark: the iced gusts still rave and beat:
"No dream, alas! alas! and woe is mine!
Porphyro will leave me here to fade and pine.—
330 Cruel! what traitor could thee hither bring?

[handwritten margin note: she's afraid he's going to leave]

2. "The Lovely Lady without Pity," title of a work by the medieval poet Alain Chartier. Keats later adopted the title for his own ballad.

I curse not, for my heart is lost in thine,
Though thou forsakest a deceived thing;—
A dove forlorn and lost with sick unpruned wing."

38

"My Madeline! sweet dreamer! lovely bride!
35 Say, may I be for aye thy vassal blest?
Thy beauty's shield, heart-shap'd and vermeil° dyed?   vermilion
Ah, silver shrine, here will I take my rest
After so many hours of toil and quest,
A famish'd pilgrim,—saved by miracle.
40 Though I have found, I will not rob thy nest
Saving of thy sweet self; if thou think'st well
To trust, fair Madeline, to no rude infidel.

39

"Hark! 'tis an elfin-storm from faery land,
Of haggard³ seeming, but a boon indeed:
45 Arise—arise! the morning is at hand;—
The bloated wassaillers⁴ will never heed:—
Let us away, my love, with happy speed;
There are no ears to hear, or eyes to see,—
Drown'd all in Rhenish and the sleepy mead:⁵
50 Awake! arise! my love, and fearless be,
For o'er the southern moors I have a home for thee."

40

She hurried at his words, beset with fears,
For there were sleeping dragons all around,
At glaring watch, perhaps, with ready spears—
55 Down the wide stairs a darkling⁶ way they found.—
In all the house was heard no human sound.
A chain-droop'd lamp was flickering by each door;
The arras,° rich with horseman, hawk, and hound,   tapestry
Flutter'd in the besieging wind's uproar;
60 And the long carpets rose along the gusty floor.

41

They glide, like phantoms, into the wide hall;
Like phantoms, to the iron porch, they glide;
Where lay the Porter, in uneasy sprawl,
With a huge empty flaggon by his side:
65 The wakeful bloodhound rose, and shook his hide,
But his sagacious eye an inmate owns:⁷
By one, and one, the bolts full easy slide:—
The chains lie silent on the footworn stones;—
The key turns, and the door upon its hinges groans.

42

70 And they are gone: ay, ages long ago
These lovers fled away into the storm.

---

3. Wild, untamed (originally, a wild hawk).   heavy fermented drink made with honey).
4. Drunken carousers.   6. In the dark.
5. Rhine wine and the sleep-producing mead (a   7. Acknowledges a member of the household.

That night the Baron dreamt of many a woe,
And all his warrior-guests, with shade and form
Of witch, and demon, and large coffin-worm,
375   Were long be-nightmar'd. Angela the old
Died palsy-twitch'd, with meagre face deform; _both_
The Beadsman, after thousand aves[8] told, _die_
For aye° unsought for slept among his ashes cold.   _ever_

Jan.–Feb. 1819   1820

Why did I laugh tonight? No voice will tell[1]

Why did I laugh tonight? No voice will tell:
No god, no demon of severe response,
Deigns to reply from heaven or from hell.
Then to my human heart I turn at once—
5   Heart! thou and I are here sad and alone;
Say, wherefore did I laugh? O mortal pain!
O darkness! darkness! ever must I moan,
To question heaven and hell and heart in vain!
Why did I laugh? I know this being's lease—
10   My fancy to its utmost blisses spreads:
Yet could I on this very midnight cease,
And the world's gaudy ensigns° see in shreds.   _banners_
Verse, fame, and beauty are intense indeed,
But death intenser—death is life's high meed.

Mar. 1819   1848

Bright star, would I were stedfast as thou art[1]

Bright star, would I were stedfast as thou art—
Not in lone splendor hung aloft the night,
And watching, with eternal lids apart,
Like nature's patient, sleepless eremite,[2]
5   The moving waters at their priestlike task
Of pure ablution[3] round earth's human shores,
Or gazing on the new soft-fallen mask
Of snow upon the mountains and the moors;
No—yet still stedfast, still unchangeable,
10   Pillow'd upon my fair love's ripening breast,
To feel for ever its soft swell and fall,

8. The prayers beginning Ave Maria ("Hail Mary").
1. In the letter to his brother and sister-in-law, George and Georgiana Keats, into which he copied this sonnet, March 19, 1819, Keats wrote: "Though the first steps to it were through my human passions, they went away, and I wrote with my Mind—and perhaps I must confess a little bit of my heart. . . . I went to bed, and enjoyed an uninterrupted sleep. Sane I went to bed and sane I arose."
1. While on a tour of the Lake District in 1818,

Keats had said that the austere scenes "refine one's sensual vision into a sort of north star which can never cease to be open lidded and steadfast over the wonders of the great Power." The thought developed into this sonnet, which Keats drafted in 1819, then copied into his volume of Shakespeare's poems at the end of September or the beginning of October 1820, while on his way to Italy, where he died.
2. Hermit, religious solitary.
3. Washing, as part of a religious rite.

Awake for ever in a sweet unrest,
Still, still to hear her tender-taken breath,
And so live ever—or else swoon to death.[4]

1819   1838

La Belle Dame sans Merci: A Ballad[1]

1

O what can ail thee, knight at arms,
    Alone and palely loitering?
The sedge° has wither'd from the lake,   *rushes*
    And no birds sing.

2

5   O what can ail thee, knight at arms,
    So haggard and so woe-begone?
The squirrel's granary is full,
    And the harvest's done.

3

I see a lily on thy brow
10   With anguish moist and fever dew,
And on thy cheeks a fading rose
    Fast withereth too.

4

I met a lady in the meads,
    Full beautiful, a fairy's child;
15   Her hair was long, her foot was light,
    And her eyes were wild.

5

I made a garland for her head,
    And bracelets too, and fragrant zone;[2]
She look'd at me as she did love,
20   And made sweet moan.

6

I set her on my pacing steed,
    And nothing else saw all day long,
For sidelong would she bend, and sing
    A fairy's song.

7

25   She found me roots of relish° sweet,   *flavor*
    And honey wild, and manna dew,

---

4. In the earlier version: "Half passionless, and so swoon on to death."
1. The title, though not the subject, was taken from a medieval poem by Alain Chartier and means "The Lovely Lady without Pity." The story of a mortal destroyed by his love for a supernatural femme fatale has been told repeatedly in myth, fairy tale, and ballad. The text printed here is

Keats's earlier version of the poem, as transcribed by Charles Brown. The version published in 1820 begins, "Ah, what can ail thee, wretched wight."
    Keats imitates a frequent procedure of folk ballads by casting the poem into the dialogue form. The first three stanzas are addressed to the knight, and the rest of the poem is his reply.
2. Belt (of flowers).

And sure in language strange she said—
I love thee true.

8

She took me to her elfin grot°   *cave*
30   And there she wept, and sigh'd full sore,
And there I shut her wild wild eyes
With kisses four.[3]

9

And there she lulled me asleep,
And there I dream'd—Ah! woe betide!
35   The latest° dream I ever dream'd   *last*
On the cold hill's side.

10

I saw pale kings, and princes too,
Pale warriors, death pale were they all;
They cried—"La belle dame sans merci
40   Hath thee in thrall!"

11

I saw their starv'd lips in the gloom°   *twilight*
With horrid warning gaped wide,
And I awoke and found me here
On the cold hill's side.

12

45   And this is why I sojourn here,
Alone and palely loitering,
Though the sedge is wither'd from the lake,
And no birds sing.

Apr. 1819   1820

Sonnet to Sleep

O soft embalmer of the still midnight,
Shutting with careful fingers and benign
Our gloom-pleas'd eyes, embower'd from the light,
Enshaded in forgetfulness divine:
5   O soothest° Sleep! if so it please thee, close,   *softest*
In midst of this thine hymn, my willing eyes,
Or wait the Amen ere thy poppy[1] throws
Around my bed its lulling charities.
Then save me or the passed day will shine
10   Upon my pillow, breeding many woes:
Save me from curious° conscience, that still hoards   *scrupulous*
Its strength for darkness, burrowing like the mole;

---

3. Keats commented in a letter to his brother and sister-in-law, "Why four kisses—you will say—why four because I wish to restrain the headlong impetuosity of my Muse—she would have fain said 'score' without hurting the rhyme—but we must temper the Imagination as the Critics say with Judgment. I was obliged to choose an even number that both eyes might have fair play."
1. Opium is made from the dried juice of the opium poppy.

Turn the key deftly in the oiled wards,[2]
And seal the hushed casket of my soul.

Apr. 1819   1838

Ode to Psyche[1]

O Goddess! hear these tuneless numbers,° wrung   *verses*
By sweet enforcement and remembrance dear,
And pardon that thy secrets should be sung
Even into thine own soft-conchèd[2] ear:
5   Surely I dreamt to-day, or did I see
The wingèd Psyche with awaken'd eyes?
I wander'd in a forest thoughtlessly,
And, on the sudden, fainting with surprise,
Saw two fair creatures, couchèd side by side
10   In deepest grass, beneath the whisp'ring roof
Of leaves and trembled blossoms, where there ran
A brooklet, scarce espied:
'Mid hush'd, cool-rooted flowers, fragrant-eyed,
Blue, silver-white, and budded Tyrian,[3]
15   They lay calm-breathing on the bedded grass;
Their arms embraced, and their pinions° too;   *wings*
Their lips touch'd not, but had not bade adieu,
As if disjoinèd by soft-handed slumber,
And ready still past kisses to outnumber
20   At tender eye-dawn of aurorean love:[4]
The wingèd boy I knew;
But who wast thou, O happy, happy dove?
His Psyche true!

O latest born and loveliest vision far
25   Of all Olympus' faded hierarchy![5]

2. The ridges in a lock that correspond to the notches of the key.

1. This poem initiated the sequence of great odes that Keats wrote in the spring of 1819. It is copied into the same journal-letter that included the "Sonnet to Sleep" and several other sonnets as well as a comment about "endeavoring to discover a better sonnet stanza than we have." It is therefore likely that Keats's experiments with sonnet schemes led to the development of the intricate and varied stanzas of his odes and also that he abandoned the sonnet on discovering the richer possibilities of the more spacious form.
Psyche, which gives us our modern term *psychology,* means mind or soul (and also butterfly) in Greek. In the story told by the Roman author Apuleius in the 2nd century, Psyche was a lovely mortal beloved by Cupid, the "winged boy" (line 21), son of Venus. To keep their love a secret from his mother, who envied Psyche's beauty, he visited his lover only in the dark of night, and had her promise never to try to discover his identity. After Psyche broke the promise, she endured various tribula-

tions as a penance and then was finally wedded to Cupid and translated to heaven as an immortal. To this goddess, added to the pantheon of pagan gods too late to have been the center of a cult, Keats in the last two stanzas promises to establish a place of worship within his own mind, with himself as poet-priest and prophet.
2. Soft and shaped like a seashell.
3. The purple dye once made in ancient Tyre.
4. Aurora was the goddess of the dawn.
5. The ranks of the gods who lived on Mount Olympus, according to the classical mythology now eclipsed (made "faded") by Christianity. "You must recollect that Psyche was not embodied as a goddess before the time of Apuleius the Platonist who lived after the Augustan age, and consequently the Goddess was never worshiped or sacrificed to with any of the ancient fervour—and perhaps never thought of in the old religion—I am more orthodox tha[n] to let a hethen Goddess be so neglected" (Keats, in a long letter written over several months to George and Georgiana Keats in America, April 30, 1819).

Fairer than Phoebe's sapphire-region'd star,[6]
Or Vesper,° amorous glow-worm of the sky;   *evening star*
Fairer than these, though temple thou hast none,
    Nor altar heap'd with flowers;
30 Nor virgin-choir to make delicious moan
      Upon the midnight hours;
No voice, no lute, no pipe, no incense sweet
    From chain-swung censer teeming;
No shrine, no grove, no oracle, no heat
35   Of pale-mouth'd prophet dreaming.

O brightest! though too late for antique vows,[7]
    Too, too late for the fond believing lyre,
When holy were the haunted° forest boughs,   *spirit-filled*
    Holy the air, the water, and the fire;
40 Yet even in these days so far retir'd
    From happy pieties, thy lucent fans,°   *shining wings*
Fluttering among the faint Olympians,
    I see, and sing, by my own eyes inspired.
So let me be thy choir, and make a moan
45   Upon the midnight hours;
Thy voice, thy lute, thy pipe, thy incense sweet
    From swinged censer teeming;
Thy shrine, thy grove, thy oracle, thy heat
    Of pale-mouth'd prophet dreaming.

50 Yes, I will be thy priest, and build a fane°   *temple*
    In some untrodden region of my mind,
Where branched thoughts, new grown with pleasant pain,
    Instead of pines shall murmur in the wind:
Far, far around shall those dark-cluster'd trees
55   Fledge the wild-ridged mountains steep by steep;[8]
And there by zephyrs, streams,° and birds, and bees,   *breezes*
    The moss-lain Dryads° shall be lull'd to sleep;   *wood nymphs*
And in the midst of this wide quietness
A rosy sanctuary will I dress
60 With the wreath'd trellis of a working brain,
    With buds, and bells, and stars without a name,
With all the gardener Fancy e'er could feign,
    Who breeding flowers, will never breed the same:
And there shall be for thee all soft delight
65   That shadowy thought can win,
A bright torch, and a casement ope at night,
    To let the warm Love[9] in!

Apr. 1819   1820

6. The moon, supervised by the goddess Phoebe
(Diana).
7. I.e., of worshipers.

8. I.e., the trees shall stand, rank against rank, like
layers of feathers.
9. I.e., Cupid, god of love.

Ode to a Nightingale[1]

1

My heart aches, and a drowsy numbness pains
  My sense, as though of hemlock[2] I had drunk,
Or emptied some dull opiate to the drains
  One minute past, and Lethe[3]-wards had sunk:
5 'Tis not through envy of thy happy lot,
  But being too happy in thine happiness,—
    That thou, light-winged Dryad of the trees,
      In some melodious plot
  Of beechen green, and shadows numberless,
10   Singest of summer in full-throated ease.

2

O, for a draught of vintage!° that hath been   *wine*
  Cool'd a long age in the deep-delved earth,
Tasting of Flora[4] and the country green,
  Dance, and Provençal song,[5] and sunburnt mirth!
15 O for a beaker full of the warm South,
  Full of the true, the blushful Hippocrene,[6]
    With beaded bubbles winking at the brim,
      And purple-stained mouth;
  That I might drink, and leave the world unseen,
20   And with thee fade away into the forest dim:

3

Fade far away, dissolve, and quite forget
  What thou among the leaves hast never known,
The weariness, the fever, and the fret
  Here, where men sit and hear each other groan;
25 Where palsy shakes a few, sad, last gray hairs,
  Where youth grows pale, and spectre-thin, and dies;[7]
    Where but to think is to be full of sorrow
      And leaden-eyed despairs,
  Where Beauty cannot keep her lustrous eyes,
30   Or new Love pine at them beyond to-morrow.

4

Away! away! for I will fly to thee,
  Not charioted by Bacchus and his pards,

---

1. Charles Brown, with whom Keats was then living in Hampstead, wrote: "In the spring of 1819 a nightingale had built her nest near my house. Keats felt a tranquil and continual joy in her song; and one morning he took his chair from the breakfast table to the grass plot under a plum tree, where he sat for two or three hours. When he came into the house, I perceived he had some scraps of paper in his hand, and these he was quietly thrusting behind the books. On inquiry, I found those scraps, four or five in number, contained his poetic feeling on the song of our nightingale."
2. A poisonous herb, not the North American evergreen tree; a sedative if taken in small doses.
3. River in Hades whose waters cause forgetfulness.
4. The Roman goddess of flowers or the flowers themselves.
5. Provence, in southern France, was in the late Middle Ages renowned for its troubadours—writers and singers of love songs.
6. Fountain of the Muses on Mount Helicon, hence the waters of inspiration, here applied metaphorically to a beaker of wine.
7. Keats's brother Tom, wasted by tuberculosis, had died the preceding winter.

But on the viewless wings of Poesy,[8]
Though the dull brain perplexes and retards:
35   Already with thee! tender is the night,
And haply the Queen-Moon is on her throne,
Cluster'd around by all her starry Fays;°   *fairies*
But here there is no light,
Save what from heaven is with the breezes blown
40   Through verdurous° glooms and winding mossy ways.   *green-foliaged*

5
I cannot see what flowers are at my feet,
Nor what soft incense hangs upon the boughs,
But, in embalmed° darkness, guess each sweet   *perfumed*
Wherewith the seasonable month endows
45   The grass, the thicket, and the fruit-tree wild;
White hawthorn, and the pastoral eglantine;[9]
Fast fading violets cover'd up in leaves;
And mid-May's eldest child,
The coming musk-rose, full of dewy wine,
50   The murmurous haunt of flies on summer eves.

6
Darkling° I listen; and, for many a time   *in darkness*
I have been half in love with easeful Death,
Call'd him soft names in many a mused° rhyme,   *meditated*
To take into the air my quiet breath;
55   Now more than ever seems it rich to die,
To cease upon the midnight with no pain,
While thou art pouring forth thy soul abroad
In such an ecstasy!
Still wouldst thou sing, and I have ears in vain—
60   To thy high requiem° become a sod.   *mass for the dead*

7
Thou wast not born for death, immortal Bird!
No hungry generations tread thee down;
The voice I hear this passing night was heard
In ancient days by emperor and clown:°   *peasant*
65   Perhaps the self-same song that found a path
Through the sad heart of Ruth,[1] when, sick for home,
She stood in tears amid the alien corn;°   *wheat*
The same that oft-times hath
Charm'd magic casements,° opening on the foam   *windows*
70   Of perilous seas, in faery lands forlorn.

8
Forlorn! the very word is like a bell
To toll me back from thee to my sole self!
Adieu! the fancy[2] cannot cheat so well

8. I.e., by getting drunk not on wine (the "vintage" of stanza 2) but on the invisible ("viewless") wings of the poetic imagination. (Bacchus, god of wine, was sometimes represented in a chariot drawn by "pards"—leopards.)
9. Sweetbrier or honeysuckle.
1. The young widow in the biblical Book of Ruth.
2. I.e., imagination, "the viewless wings of Poesy" of line 33.

As she is fam'd to do, deceiving elf.
75 Adieu! adieu! thy plaintive anthem° fades   *hymn*
    Past the near meadows, over the still stream,
    Up the hill-side; and now 'tis buried deep
    In the next valley-glades:
    Was it a vision, or a waking dream?
80 Fled is that music:—Do I wake or sleep?

May 1819   1819

Ode on a Grecian Urn[1]

1

Thou still unravish'd bride of quietness,
    Thou foster-child of silence and slow time,
    Sylvan[2] historian, who canst thus express
    A flowery tale more sweetly than our rhyme:
5 What leaf-fring'd legend haunts about thy shape
    Of deities or mortals, or of both,
        In Tempe or the dales of Arcady?[3]
    What men or gods are these? What maidens loth?
    What mad pursuit? What struggle to escape?
10   What pipes and timbrels? What wild ecstasy?

2

Heard melodies are sweet, but those unheard
    Are sweeter; therefore, ye soft pipes, play on;
    Not to the sensual ear,[4] but, more endear'd,
    Pipe to the spirit ditties of no tone:
15 Fair youth, beneath the trees, thou canst not leave
    Thy song, nor ever can those trees be bare;
        Bold lover, never, never canst thou kiss,
    Though winning near the goal—yet, do not grieve;
        She cannot fade, though thou hast not thy bliss,
20   For ever wilt thou love, and she be fair!

3

Ah, happy, happy boughs! that cannot shed
    Your leaves, nor ever bid the spring adieu;
    And, happy melodist, unwearied,

---

1. Another poem that Keats published in Haydon's *Annals of the Fine Arts*. This urn, with its sculptured reliefs of revelry and panting young lovers in chase and in flight, of a pastoral piper under spring foliage, and of the quiet procession of priest and townspeople, resembles parts of various vases, sculptures, and paintings, but it existed in all its particulars only in Keats's imagination. In the urn—which captures moments of intense experience in attitudes of grace and immobilizes them in marble—Keats found the perfect correlative for his concern with the longing for permanence in a world of change. The interpretation of the details with which he develops this concept, however, is hotly disputed. The disputes begin with the open-

ing phrase: is "still" an adverb ("as yet"), or is it an adjective ("motionless"), as the punctuation of the *Annals* version, which adds a comma after "still," suggests? And the two concluding lines have accumulated as much critical discussion as the "two-handed engine" in Milton's "Lycidas" or the most difficult cruxes in Shakespeare's plays.
2. Rustic, representing a woodland scene.
3. The valleys of Arcadia, a state in ancient Greece often used as a symbol of the pastoral ideal. "Tempe": a beautiful valley in Greece that has come to represent rural beauty.
4. The ear of sense (as opposed to that of the "spirit," or imagination).

For ever piping songs for ever new;
25 More happy love! more happy, happy love!
For ever warm and still to be enjoy'd,
For ever panting, and for ever young;
All breathing human passion far above,
That leaves a heart high-sorrowful and cloy'd,
30   A burning forehead, and a parching tongue.

4

Who are these coming to the sacrifice?
To what green altar, O mysterious priest,
Lead'st thou that heifer lowing at the skies,
And all her silken flanks with garlands drest?
35 What little town by river or sea shore,
Or mountain-built with peaceful citadel,
Is emptied of this folk, this pious morn?
And, little town, thy streets for evermore
Will silent be; and not a soul to tell
40   Why thou art desolate, can e'er return.

5

O Attic⁵ shape! Fair attitude!⁶ with brede
Of marble men and maidens overwrought,⁷
With forest branches and the trodden weed;
Thou, silent form, dost tease us out of thought
45 As doth eternity: Cold Pastoral!
When old age shall this generation waste,
Thou shalt remain, in midst of other woe
Than ours, a friend to man, to whom thou say'st,
"Beauty is truth, truth beauty,"⁸—that is all
50   Ye know on earth, and all ye need to know.

1819   1820

Ode on Melancholy

This is Keats's best-known statement of his recurrent theme of the mingled contrarieties of life. The remarkable last stanza, in which Melancholy becomes a veiled goddess worshiped in secret religious rites, implies that it is the tragic human destiny that beauty, joy, and life itself owe not only their quality but their value to the fact that they are transitory and turn into their opposites. Melancholy—a synonym for depression, involving a paralyzing self-consciousness engendered by an excess of thought—is a highly literary and even bookish ailment, as Keats knew. Shakespeare's Hamlet and Milton's speaker in "Il Penseroso" are the

5. Greek. Attica was the region of Greece in which Athens was located.
6. Probably used in its early, technical sense: the pose struck by a figure in statuary or painting.
7. Ornamented all over ("overwrought") with an interwoven pattern ("brede"). The adjective "overwrought" might also modify "maidens" and even "men" and so hint at the emotional anguish of the figures portrayed on the urn.
8. The quotation marks around this phrase are found in the volume of poems Keats published in 1820, but there are no quotation marks in the version printed in Annals of the Fine Arts that same year or in the transcripts of the poem made by

Keats's friends. This discrepancy has multiplied the diversity of critical interpretations of the last two lines. Critics disagree whether the whole of these lines is said by the urn, or "Beauty is truth, truth beauty" by the urn and the rest by the lyric speaker; whether the "ye" in the last line is addressed to the lyric speaker, to the readers, to the urn, or to the figures on the urn; whether "all ye know" is that beauty is truth, or this plus the statement in lines 46–48; and whether "beauty is truth" is a profound metaphysical proposition, an overstatement representing the limited point of view of the urn, or simply nonsensical.

disorder's most famous sufferers. Keats was also an admirer of Robert Burton's ency-clopedic *Anatomy of Melancholy* (1621).

The poem once had the following initial stanza, which Keats canceled in manuscript:

> Though you should build a bark of dead men's bones,
> And rear a phantom gibbet for a mast,
> Stitch creeds together for a sail, with groans
> To fill it out, bloodstained and aghast;
> Although your rudder be a Dragon's tail,
> Long sever'd, yet still hard with agony,
> Your cordage large uprootings from the skull
> Of bald Medusa: certes you would fail
> To find the Melancholy, whether she
> Dreameth in any isle of Lethe dull.

Ode on Melancholy

1

No, no, go not to Lethe,[1] neither twist
    Wolf's-bane, tight-rooted, for its poisonous wine;
Nor suffer thy pale forehead to be kiss'd
    By nightshade, ruby grape of Proserpine;[2]
5 Make not your rosary of yew-berries,[3]
    Nor let the beetle, nor the death-moth be
        Your mournful Psyche,[4] nor the downy owl
A partner in your sorrow's mysteries;[5]
    For shade to shade will come too drowsily,
10   And drown the wakeful anguish of the soul.[6]

2

But when the melancholy fit shall fall
    Sudden from heaven like a weeping cloud,
That fosters the droop-headed flowers all,
    And hides the green hill in an April shroud;
15 Then glut thy sorrow on a morning rose,
    Or on the rainbow of the salt sand-wave,
        Or on the wealth of globed peonies;
Or if thy mistress some rich anger shows,
    Emprison her soft hand, and let her rave,
20   And feed deep, deep upon her peerless eyes.

3

She[7] dwells with Beauty—Beauty that must die;
    And Joy, whose hand is ever at his lips
Bidding adieu; and aching Pleasure nigh,

1. The waters of forgetfulness in Hades.
2. The wife of Pluto and queen of the underworld. "Nightshade" and "wolf's-bane" (line 2) are poisonous plants.
3. A symbol of death.
4. In ancient times Psyche (the soul) was sometimes represented as a butterfly or moth, fluttering out of the mouth of a dying man. The allusion may also be to the death's-head moth, which has skull-like markings on its back. The "beetle" of line 6 refers to replicas of the large black beetle, the scarab, which were often placed by Egyptians in their tombs as a symbol of resurrection.
5. Secret rituals.
6. I.e., sorrow needs contrast to sustain its intensity.
7. Usually taken to refer to Melancholy rather than to "thy mistress" in line 18.

Turning to poison while the bee-mouth sips:
25 Ay, in the very temple of Delight
Veil'd Melancholy has her sovran shrine,
Though seen of none save him whose strenuous tongue
Can burst Joy's grape against his palate fine;[8]
His soul shall taste the sadness of her might,
30 And be among her cloudy trophies hung.[9]

1819   1820

Ode on Indolence[1]

"They toil not, neither do they spin."[2]

1

One morn before me were three figures seen,
With bowed necks, and joined hands, side-faced;
And one behind the other stepp'd serene,
In placid sandals, and in white robes graced:
5 They pass'd, like figures on a marble urn,
When shifted round to see the other side;
They came again: as when the urn once more
Is shifted round, the first seen shades return;
And they were strange to me, as may betide
10 With vases, to one deep in Phidian[3] lore.

2

How is it, shadows, that I knew ye not?
How came ye muffled in so hush a masque?
Was it a silent deep-disguised plot
To steal away, and leave without a task
15 My idle days? Ripe was the drowsy hour;
The blissful cloud of summer-indolence
Benumb'd my eyes; my pulse grew less and less;
Pain had no sting, and pleasure's wreath no flower.
O, why did ye not melt, and leave my sense
20 Unhaunted quite of all but—nothingness?

3

A third time pass'd they by, and, passing, turn'd
Each one the face a moment whiles to me;
Then faded, and to follow them I burn'd
And ached for wings, because I knew the three:
25 The first was a fair maid, and Love her name;

8. Sensitive, refined.
9. A reference to the Greek and Roman practice of hanging trophies in the temples of the gods.
1. On March 19, 1819, Keats wrote to George and Georgiana Keats: "This morning I am in a sort of temper indolent and supremely careless. . . . Neither Poetry, nor Ambition, nor Love have any alertness of countenance as they pass by me: they seem rather like three figures on a greek vase—a Man and two women—whom no one but myself could distinguish in their disguisement. This is the only

happiness; and is a rare instance of advantage in the body overpowering the Mind." The ode was probably written soon after this time, but was not published until 1848, long after the poet's death.
2. Matthew 6.28. Christ's comment on the lilies of the field—a parable justifying those who trust to God rather than worry about how they will feed or clothe themselves.
3. Phidias was the great Athenian sculptor of the 5th century B.C.E. who designed the marble sculptures for the Parthenon.

The second was Ambition, pale of cheek,
And ever watchful with fatigued eye;
The last, whom I love more, the more of blame
Is heap'd upon her, maiden most unmeek,—
30   I knew to be my demon⁴ Poesy.

4

They faded, and, forsooth! I wanted wings:
O folly! What is Love? and where is it?
And for that poor Ambition—it springs
From a man's little heart's short fever-fit;
35 For Poesy!—no,—she has not a joy,—
At least for me,—so sweet as drowsy noons,
And evenings steep'd in honied indolence;
O, for an age so shelter'd from annoy,
That I may never know how change the moons,
40   Or hear the voice of busy common-sense!

5

A third time came they by;—alas! wherefore?
My sleep had been embroider'd with dim dreams;
My soul had been a lawn besprinkled o'er
With flowers, and stirring shades, and baffled beams:
45 The morn was clouded, but no shower fell,
Though in her lids hung the sweet tears of May;
The open casement press'd a new-leaved vine,
Let in the budding warmth and throstle's lay;°   *thrush's song*
O shadows! 'twas a time to bid farewell!
50   Upon your skirts had fallen no tears of mine.

6

So, ye three ghosts, adieu! Ye cannot raise
My head cool-bedded in the flowery grass;
For I would not be dieted with praise,
A pet-lamb in a sentimental farce!⁵
55 Fade softly from my eyes, and be once more
In masque-like figures on the dreamy urn;
Farewell! I yet have visions for the night,
And for the day faint visions there is store;
Vanish, ye phantoms, from my idle spright,°   *spirit*
60   Into the clouds, and never more return!

Spring 1819   1848

Lamia   In a note printed at the end of the poem, Keats cited as his source the following story in Robert Burton's *Anatomy of Melancholy* (1621):

4. Meaning both devil and, as in Greek myth, the spirit that attends constantly on the human individual.

5. In a letter of June 9, 1819, Keats wrote: "I have been very idle lately, very averse to writing; both from the overpowering idea of our dead poets and from abatement of my love of fame. I hope I am a little more of a Philosopher than I was, consequently a little less of a versifying Pet-lamb. . . . You will judge of my 1819 temper when I tell you that the thing I have most enjoyed this year has been writing an ode to Indolence."

One Menippus Lycius, a young man twenty-five years of age, that going betwixt
Cenchreas and Corinth, met such a phantasm in the habit of a fair gentlewoman,
which, taking him by the hand, carried him home to her house, in the suburbs
of Corinth. . . . The young man, a philosopher, otherwise staid and discreet, able
to moderate his passions, though not this of love, tarried with her a while to his
great content, and at last married her, to whose wedding, amongst other guests,
came Apollonius; who, by some probable conjectures, found her out to be a
serpent, a lamia; and that all her furniture was, like Tantalus's gold, described
by Homer, no substance but mere illusions. When she saw herself descried, she
wept, and desired Apollonius to be silent, but he would not be moved, and
thereupon she, plate, house, and all that was in it, vanished in an instant: many
thousands took notice of this fact, for it was done in the midst of Greece.

In ancient demonology a "lamia" was a monster in woman's form who preyed on
human beings. There are various clues that Keats invested the ancient legend with
allegorical significance (see especially 2.229–38). Its interpretation, however, and
even the inclination of Keats's sympathies in the contest between Lamia and Apollonius, have been disputed. Perhaps Keats simply failed to make up his mind or
wavered in the course of composition. In any case the poem presents an inevitably
fatal situation, in which no one is entirely blameless or blameworthy and no character
monopolizes either our sympathy or our antipathy.

The poem, written between late June and early September 1819, is a return, after
the Spenserian stanzas of The Eve of St. Agnes, to the pentameter couplets Keats had
used in Endymion and other early poems. But Keats had in the meantime been studying John Dryden's closed and strong-paced couplets. The initial lines of Dryden's
version of Boccaccio's story Cymon and Iphigenia demonstrate the kind of narrative
model that helped Keats make the technical transition from the fluent but sprawling
gracefulness of the opening of Endymion to the vigor and economy of the opening of
Lamia:

> In that sweet isle where Venus keeps her court,
> And every grace, and all the loves, resort;
> Where either sex is formed of softer earth,
> And takes the bent of pleasure from their birth;
> There lived a Cyprian lord, above the rest
> Wise, wealthy, with a numerous issue blessed. . . .

Lamia

Part 1

Upon a time, before the faery broods
Drove Nymph and Satyr¹ from the prosperous woods,
Before King Oberon's bright diadem,
Sceptre, and mantle, clasp'd with dewy gem,
5 Frighted away the Dryads and the Fauns
From rushes green, and brakes,° and cowslip'd lawns,   *thickets*
The ever-smitten Hermes² empty left
His golden throne, bent warm on amorous theft:
From high Olympus had he stolen light,

---

1. Nymphs and satyrs—like the dryads and fauns
in line 5—were minor classical deities of the woods
and fields, said here to have been driven off by
Oberon, king of the fairies, who were supernatural
beings of the postclassical era.
2. Or Mercury; wing-footed messenger at the
summons of Jove (line 11), Hermes was notoriously amorous.

10 On this side of Jove's clouds, to escape the sight
Of his great summoner, and made retreat
Into a forest on the shores of Crete.
For somewhere in that sacred island dwelt
A nymph, to whom all hoofed Satyrs knelt;
15 At whose white feet the languid Tritons[3] poured
Pearls, while on land they wither'd and adored.
Fast by the springs where she to bathe was wont,
And in those meads where sometime she might haunt,
Were strewn rich gifts, unknown to any Muse,
20 Though Fancy's casket were unlock'd to choose.
Ah, what a world of love was at her feet!
So Hermes thought, and a celestial heat
Burnt from his winged heels to either ear,
That from a whiteness, as the lily clear,
25 Blush'd into roses 'mid his golden hair,
Fallen in jealous curls about his shoulders bare.[4]

From vale to vale, from wood to wood, he flew,
Breathing upon the flowers his passion new,
And wound with many a river to its head,
30 To find where this sweet nymph prepar'd her secret bed:
In vain; the sweet nymph might nowhere be found,
And so he rested, on the lonely ground,
Pensive, and full of painful jealousies
Of the Wood-Gods, and even the very trees.
35 There as he stood, he heard a mournful voice,
Such as once heard, in gentle heart, destroys
All pain but pity: thus the lone voice spake:
"When from this wreathed tomb shall I awake!
When move in a sweet body fit for life,
40 And love, and pleasure, and the ruddy strife
Of hearts and lips! Ah, miserable me!"
The God, dove-footed,[5] glided silently
Round bush and tree, soft-brushing, in his speed,
The taller grasses and full-flowering weed,
45 Until he found a palpitating snake,
Bright, and cirque-couchant[6] in a dusky brake.

She was a gordian[7] shape of dazzling hue,
Vermilion-spotted, golden, green, and blue;
Striped like a zebra, freckled like a pard,°   *leopard*
50 Eyed like a peacock,[8] and all crimson barr'd;
And full of silver moons, that, as she breathed,
Dissolv'd, or brighter shone, or interwreathed
Their lustres with the gloomier tapestries—
So rainbow-sided, touch'd with miseries,

3. Minor sea gods.
4. I.e., the curls clung jealously to his bare shoulders. This line is the first of a number of Alexandrines, a six-foot line, used to vary the metrical movement—a device that Keats learned from Dryden. Another such device is the triplet, occurring first in lines 61–63.
5. I.e., quietly as a dove.
6. Lying in a circular coil. Keats borrows the language of heraldry.
7. Intricately twisted, like the knot tied by King Gordius, which no one could undo.
8. Having multicolored spots, like the "eyes" in a peacock's tail.

55 She seem'd, at once, some penanced lady elf,
    Some demon's mistress, or the demon's self.
    Upon her crest she wore a wannish⁹ fire
    Sprinkled with stars, like Ariadne's tiar:¹
    Her head was serpent, but ah, bitter-sweet!
60 She had a woman's mouth with all its pearls² complete:
    And for her eyes: what could such eyes do there
    But weep, and weep, that they were born so fair?
    As Proserpine still weeps for her Sicilian air.³
    Her throat was serpent, but the words she spake
65 Came, as through bubbling honey, for Love's sake,
    And thus; while Hermes on his pinions° lay,   *wings*
    Like a stoop'd falcon⁴ ere he takes his prey.

        "Fair Hermes, crown'd with feathers, fluttering light,
    I had a splendid dream of thee last night:
70 I saw thee sitting, on a throne of gold,
    Among the Gods, upon Olympus old,
    The only sad one; for thou didst not hear
    The soft, lute-finger'd Muses chaunting clear,
    Nor even Apollo when he sang alone,
75 Deaf to his throbbing throat's long, long melodious moan.
    I dreamt I saw thee, robed in purple flakes,
    Break amorous through the clouds, as morning breaks,
    And, swiftly as a bright Phœbean dart,⁵
    Strike for the Cretan isle; and here thou art!
80 Too gentle Hermes, hast thou found the maid?"
    Whereat the star of Lethe⁶ not delay'd
    His rosy eloquence, and thus inquired:
    "Thou smooth-lipp'd serpent, surely high inspired!
    Thou beauteous wreath, with melancholy eyes,
85 Possess whatever bliss thou canst devise,
    Telling me only where my nymph is fled,—
    Where she doth breathe!" "Bright planet, thou hast said,"
    Return'd the snake, "but seal with oaths, fair God!"
    "I swear," said Hermes, "by my serpent rod,
90 And by thine eyes, and by thy starry crown!"
    Light flew his earnest words, among the blossoms blown.
    Then thus again the brilliance feminine:
    "Too frail of heart! for this lost nymph of thine,
    Free as the air, invisibly, she strays
95 About these thornless wilds; her pleasant days
    She tastes unseen; unseen her nimble feet
    Leave traces in the grass and flowers sweet;

9. Rather dark.
1. Ariadne's jeweled wedding crown, or tiara ("tiar"), was given to her by the god Bacchus, who took her as his wife after she was abandoned by her faithless mortal lover Theseus. The crown, transformed into a constellation of stars in the sky, is represented in Titian's *Bacchus and Ariadne*, which Keats had seen when the painting was exhibited in London in 1816. Keats's memories of this painting may also inform his reference to Bacchus's chariot and leopards in "Ode to a Nightingale," line 32.

2. "Pearls" had become almost a synonym for teeth in Elizabethan love poems.
3. Proserpine had been carried off to Hades by Pluto from the field of Enna, in Sicily.
4. *Stoop* is the term for the plunge of a falcon on his prey.
5. A ray of Phoebus Apollo, god of the sun.
6. Hermes, when he appeared like a star on the banks of Lethe, in the darkness of Hades. (One of Hermes' offices was to guide the souls of the dead to the lower regions.)

From weary tendrils, and bow'd branches green,
She plucks the fruit unseen, she bathes unseen:
100 And by my power is her beauty veil'd
To keep it unaffronted, unassail'd
By the love-glances of unlovely eyes,
Of Satyrs, Fauns, and blear'd Silenus'[7] sighs.
Pale grew her immortality, for woe
105 Of all these lovers, and she grieved so
I took compassion on her, bade her steep
Her hair in weïrd° syrops, that would keep   *magical*
Her loveliness invisible, yet free
To wander as she loves, in liberty.
110 Thou shalt behold her, Hermes, thou alone,
If thou wilt, as thou swearest, grant my boon!"
Then, once again, the charmed God began
An oath, and through the serpent's ears it ran
Warm, tremulous, devout, psalterian.[8]
115 Ravish'd, she lifted her Circean head,
Blush'd a live damask,[9] and swift-lisping said,
"I was a woman, let me have once more
A woman's shape, and charming as before.
I love a youth of Corinth—O the bliss!
120 Give me my woman's form, and place me where he is.
Stoop, Hermes, let me breathe upon thy brow,
And thou shalt see thy sweet nymph even now."
The God on half-shut feathers sank serene,
She breath'd upon his eyes, and swift was seen
125 Of both the guarded nymph near-smiling on the green.
It was no dream; or say a dream it was,
Real are the dreams of Gods, and smoothly pass
Their pleasures in a long immortal dream.
One warm, flush'd moment, hovering, it might seem
130 Dash'd by the wood-nymph's beauty, so he burn'd;
Then, lighting on the printless verdure, turn'd
To the swoon'd serpent, and with languid arm,
Delicate, put to proof the lythe Caducean charm.[1]
So done, upon the nymph his eyes he bent
135 Full of adoring tears and blandishment,
And towards her stept: she, like a moon in wane,
Faded before him, cower'd, nor could restrain
Her fearful sobs, self-folding like a flower
That faints into itself at evening hour:
140 But the God fostering her chilled hand,
She felt the warmth, her eyelids open'd bland,°   *softly*
And, like new flowers at morning song of bees,
Bloom'd, and gave up her honey to the lees.°   *dregs*
Into the green-recessed woods they flew;
145 Nor grew they pale, as mortal lovers do.

7. Satyr, a tutor of Bacchus, usually represented as a fat, jolly drunkard.
8. Either "like a psalm" or "like the sound of the psaltery" (an ancient stringed instrument).
9. The color of a damask rose (large and fragrant pink rose). "Circean": like that of Circe, the enchantress in the *Odyssey*.
1. I.e., put to the test the magic of the flexible Caduceus (the name given to Hermes' wand).

Left to herself, the serpent now began
To change; her elfin blood in madness ran,
Her mouth foam'd, and the grass, therewith besprent,°   sprinkled
Wither'd at dew so sweet and virulent;
150 Her eyes in torture fix'd, and anguish drear,
Hot, glaz'd, and wide, with lid-lashes all sear,
Flash'd phosphor and sharp sparks, without one cooling tear.
The colours all inflam'd throughout her train,
She writh'd about, convuls'd with scarlet pain:
155 A deep volcanian yellow took the place
Of all her milder-mooned body's grace;[2]
And, as the lava ravishes the mead,
Spoilt all her silver mail, and golden brede;[3]
Made gloom of all her frecklings, streaks and bars,
160 Eclips'd her crescents, and lick'd up her stars:
So that, in moments few, she was undrest
Of all her sapphires, greens, and amethyst,
And rubious-argent:° of all these bereft,   silvery red
Nothing but pain and ugliness were left.
165 Still shone her crown; that vanish'd, also she
Melted and disappear'd as suddenly;
And in the air, her new voice luting soft,
Cried, "Lycius! gentle Lycius!"—Borne aloft
With the bright mists about the mountains hoar°   white
170 These words dissolv'd: Crete's forests heard no more.

Whither fled Lamia, now a lady bright,
A full-born beauty new and exquisite?
She fled into that valley they pass o'er
Who go to Corinth from Cenchreas' shore;[4]
175 And rested at the foot of those wild hills,
The rugged founts of the Peæran rills,
And of that other ridge whose barren back
Stretches, with all its mist and cloudy rack,
South-westward to Cleone. There she stood
180 About a young bird's flutter from a wood,
Fair, on a sloping green of mossy tread,
By a clear pool, wherein she passioned[5]
To see herself escap'd from so sore ills,
While her robes flaunted with the daffodils.

185 Ah, happy Lycius!—for she was a maid
More beautiful than ever twisted braid,
Or sigh'd, or blush'd, or on spring-flowered lea°   meadow
Spread a green kirtle° to the minstrelsy: gown
A virgin purest lipp'd, yet in the lore
190 Of love deep learned to the red heart's core:
Not one hour old, yet of sciential brain
To unperplex bliss from its neighbour pain;

2. I.e., the yellow of sulfur (thrown up by a volcano) replaced her former silvery moon color.
3. Embroidery, interwoven pattern. "Mail": interlinked rings, as in a coat of armor.
4. Cenchrea (Keats's "Cenchreas") was a harbor of Corinth, in southern Greece.
5. Felt intense excitement.

Define their pettish limits, and estrange
Their points of contact, and swift counterchange;[6]
195 Intrigue with the specious chaos,[7] and dispart
Its most ambiguous atoms with sure art;
As though in Cupid's college she had spent
Sweet days a lovely graduate, still unshent,°   *unspoiled*
And kept his rosy terms[8] in idle languishment.

200 Why this fair creature chose so fairily
By the wayside to linger, we shall see;
But first 'tis fit to tell how she could muse
And dream, when in the serpent prison-house,
Of all she list,° strange or magnificent: *wished*
205 How, ever, where she will'd, her spirit went;
Whether to faint Elysium,[9] or where
Down through tress-lifting waves the Nereids[1] fair
Wind into Thetis' bower by many a pearly stair;
Or where God Bacchus drains his cups divine,
210 Stretch'd out, at ease, beneath a glutinous pine;
Or where in Pluto's gardens palatine°   *palatial*
Mulciber's columns gleam in far piazzian line.[2]
And sometimes into cities she would send
Her dream, with feast and rioting to blend;
215 And once, while among mortals dreaming thus,
She saw the young Corinthian Lycius
Charioting foremost in the envious race,
Like a young Jove with calm uneager face,
And fell into a swooning love of him.
220 Now on the moth-time of that evening dim
He would return that way, as well she knew,
To Corinth from the shore; for freshly blew
The eastern soft wind, and his galley now
Grated the quaystones with her brazen prow
225 In port Cenchreas, from Egina isle
Fresh anchor'd; whither he had been awhile
To sacrifice to Jove, whose temple there
Waits with high marble doors for blood and incense rare.
Jove heard his vows, and better'd his desire;
230 For by some freakful chance he made retire
From his companions, and set forth to walk,
Perhaps grown wearied of their Corinth talk:
Over the solitary hills he fared,
Thoughtless at first, but ere eve's star appeared
235 His phantasy was lost, where reason fades,
In the calm'd twilight of Platonic shades.[3]

6. I.e., of knowledgeable ("sciential") brain to dis-entangle ("unperplex") bliss from its closely related pain, to define their quarreled-over ("pettish") lim-its, and to separate out ("estrange") their points of contact and the swift changes of each condition into its opposite. Cf. Keats's "Ode on Melancholy," lines 21–26 (p. 907).
7. I.e., turn to her own artful purpose the seeming ("specious") chaos.
8. The terms spent studying in "Cupid's college."
9. Region inhabited by the virtuous after death.
1. Sea nymphs, of whom Thetis (line 208, the mother of Achilles) was one.
2. I.e., columns made by Mulciber (Vulcan, god of fire and metalworking) gleam in long lines around open courts (piazzas).
3. I.e., he was absorbed in musing about the obscurities of Plato's philosophy.

Lamia beheld him coming, near, more near—
Close to her passing, in indifference drear,
His silent sandals swept the mossy green;
240 So neighbour'd to him, and yet so unseen
She stood: he pass'd, shut up in mysteries,
His mind wrapp'd like his mantle, while her eyes
Follow'd his steps, and her neck regal white
Turn'd—syllabling thus, "Ah, Lycius bright,
245 And will you leave me on the hills alone?
Lycius, look back! and be some pity shown."
He did; not with cold wonder fearingly,
But Orpheus-like at an Eurydice;[4]
For so delicious were the words she sung,
250 It seem'd he had lov'd them a whole summer long:
And soon his eyes had drunk her beauty up,
Leaving no drop in the bewildering cup,
And still the cup was full,—while he, afraid
Lest she should vanish ere his lip had paid
255 Due adoration, thus began to adore;
Her soft look growing coy, she saw his chain so sure:
"Leave thee alone! Look back! Ah, Goddess, see
Whether my eyes can ever turn from thee!
For pity do not this sad heart belie[5]—
260 Even as thou vanishest so I shall die.
Stay! though a Naiad of the rivers, stay!
To thy far wishes will thy streams obey:
Stay! though the greenest woods be thy domain,
Alone they can drink up the morning rain:
265 Though a descended Pleiad,[6] will not one
Of thine harmonious sisters keep in tune
Thy spheres, and as thy silver proxy shine?
So sweetly to these ravish'd ears of mine
Came thy sweet greeting, that if thou shouldst fade
270 Thy memory will waste me to a shade:—
For pity do not melt!"—"If I should stay,"
Said Lamia, "here, upon this floor of clay,
And pain my steps upon these flowers too rough,
What canst thou say or do of charm enough
275 To dull the nice[7] remembrance of my home?
Thou canst not ask me with thee here to roam
Over these hills and vales, where no joy is,—
Empty of immortality and bliss!
Thou art a scholar, Lycius, and must know
280 That finer spirits cannot breathe below
In human climes, and live: Alas! poor youth,
What taste of purer air hast thou to soothe
My essence? What serener palaces,
Where I may all my many senses please,

4. As Orpheus looked at Eurydice in Hades.
Orpheus was allowed by Pluto to lead Eurydice
back to Earth on condition that he not look back
at her, but he could not resist doing so and hence
lost her once more.
5. Be false to.

6. One of the seven sisters composing the constellation Pleiades. The lines that follow allude to
the ancient belief that the planets traveled inside
crystalline spheres whose movements produced
heavenly music.
7. Detailed, minutely accurate.

285 And by mysterious sleights a hundred thirsts appease?
It cannot be—Adieu!" So said, she rose
Tiptoe with white arms spread. He, sick to lose
The amorous promise of her lone complain,
Swoon'd, murmuring of love, and pale with pain.

290 The cruel lady, without any show
Of sorrow for her tender favourite's woe,
But rather, if her eyes could brighter be,
With brighter eyes and slow amenity,°   pleasure
Put her new lips to his, and gave afresh

295 The life she had so tangled in her mesh:
And as he from one trance was wakening
Into another, she began to sing,
Happy in beauty, life, and love, and every thing,
A song of love, too sweet for earthly lyres,

300 While, like held breath, the stars drew in their panting fires.
And then she whisper'd in such trembling tone,
As those who, safe together met alone
For the first time through many anguish'd days,
Use other speech than looks; bidding him raise

305 His drooping head, and clear his soul of doubt,
For that she was a woman, and without
Any more subtle fluid in her veins
Than throbbing blood, and that the self-same pains
Inhabited her frail-strung heart as his.

310 And next she wonder'd how his eyes could miss
Her face so long in Corinth, where, she said,
She dwelt but half retir'd, and there had led
Days happy as the gold coin could invent
Without the aid of love; yet in content

315 Till she saw him, as once she pass'd him by,
Where 'gainst a column he leant thoughtfully
At Venus' temple porch, 'mid baskets heap'd
Of amorous herbs and flowers, newly reap'd
Late on that eve, as 'twas the night before

320 The Adonian feast;[8] whereof she saw no more,
But wept alone those days, for why should she adore?
Lycius from death awoke into amaze,
To see her still, and singing so sweet lays;
Then from amaze into delight he fell

325 To hear her whisper woman's lore so well;
And every word she spake entic'd him on
To unperplex'd delight[9] and pleasure known.
Let the mad poets say whate'er they please
Of the sweets of Fairies, Peris,[1] Goddesses,

330 There is not such a treat among them all,
Haunters of cavern, lake, and waterfall,
As a real woman, lineal indeed
From Pyrrha's pebbles[2] or old Adam's seed.
Thus gentle Lamia judg'd, and judg'd aright,

8. The feast of Adonis, beloved by Venus.
9. I.e., delight not mixed with its neighbor, pain
(see line 192).
1. Fairylike creatures in Persian mythology.

2. Descended from the pebbles with which, in
Greek myth, Pyrrha and Deucalion repeopled the
earth after the flood.

335　That Lycius could not love in half a fright,
　　　So threw the goddess off, and won his heart
　　　More pleasantly by playing woman's part,
　　　With no more awe than what her beauty gave,
　　　That, while it smote, still guaranteed to save.
340　Lycius to all made eloquent reply,
　　　Marrying to every word a twinborn sigh;
　　　And last, pointing to Corinth, ask'd her sweet,
　　　If 'twas too far that night for her soft feet.
　　　The way was short, for Lamia's eagerness
345　Made, by a spell, the triple league decrease
　　　To a few paces; not at all surmised
　　　By blinded Lycius, so in her comprized.[3]
　　　They pass'd the city gates, he knew not how,
　　　So noiseless, and he never thought to know.

350　　As men talk in a dream, so Corinth all,
　　　Throughout her palaces imperial,
　　　And all her populous streets and temples lewd,[4]
　　　Mutter'd, like tempest in the distance brew'd,
　　　To the wide-spreaded night above her towers.
355　Men, women, rich and poor, in the cool hours,
　　　Shuffled their sandals o'er the pavement white,
　　　Companion'd or alone; while many a light
　　　Flared, here and there, from wealthy festivals,
　　　And threw their moving shadows on the walls,
360　Or found them cluster'd in the corniced shade
　　　Of some arch'd temple door, or dusky colonnade.

　　　　Muffling his face, of greeting friends in fear,
　　　Her fingers he press'd hard, as one came near
　　　With curl'd gray beard, sharp eyes, and smooth bald crown,
365　Slow-stepp'd, and robed in philosophic gown:
　　　Lycius shrank closer, as they met and past,
　　　Into his mantle, adding wings to haste,
　　　While hurried Lamia trembled: "Ah," said he,
　　　"Why do you shudder, love, so ruefully?
370　Why does your tender palm dissolve in dew?"—
　　　"I'm wearied," said fair Lamia: "tell me who
　　　Is that old man? I cannot bring to mind
　　　His features:—Lycius! wherefore did you blind
　　　Yourself from his quick eyes?" Lycius replied,
375　" 'Tis Apollonius sage, my trusty guide
　　　And good instructor; but to-night he seems
　　　The ghost of folly haunting my sweet dreams."

　　　　While yet he spake they had arrived before
　　　A pillar'd porch, with lofty portal door,
380　Where hung a silver lamp, whose phosphor glow

3. Bound up, absorbed.
4. Temples of Venus, whose worship sometimes involved ritual prostitution. The city of Corinth was notorious in antiquity as a site of commerce and prostitution.

Reflected in the slabbed steps below,
Mild as a star in water; for so new,
And so unsullied was the marble hue,
So through the crystal polish, liquid fine,
385   Ran the dark veins, that none but feet divine
Could e'er have touch'd there. Sounds Æolian[5]
Breath'd from the hinges, as the ample span
Of the wide doors disclos'd a place unknown
Some time to any, but those two alone,
390   And a few Persian mutes, who that same year
Were seen about the markets: none knew where
They could inhabit; the most curious
Were foil'd, who watch'd to trace them to their house:
And but the flitter-winged verse must tell,
395   For truth's sake, what woe afterwards befel,
'Twould humour many a heart to leave them thus,
Shut from the busy world of more incredulous.

Part 2

Love in a hut, with water and a crust,
Is—Love, forgive us!—cinders, ashes, dust;
Love in a palace is perhaps at last
More grievous torment than a hermit's fast:—
5   That is a doubtful tale from faery land,
Hard for the non-elect to understand.
Had Lycius liv'd to hand his story down,
He might have given the moral a fresh frown,
Or clench'd it quite: but too short was their bliss
10   To breed distrust and hate, that make the soft voice hiss.
Besides, there, nightly, with terrific glare,
Love, jealous grown of so complete a pair,
Hover'd and buzz'd his wings, with fearful roar,
Above the lintel of their chamber door,
15   And down the passage cast a glow upon the floor.

For all this came a ruin: side by side
They were enthroned, in the even tide,
Upon a couch, near to a curtaining
Whose airy texture, from a golden string,
20   Floated into the room, and let appear
Unveil'd the summer heaven, blue and clear,
Betwixt two marble shafts:—there they reposed,
Where use had made it sweet, with eyelids closed,
Saving a tythe which love still open kept,
25   That they might see each other while they almost slept;
When from the slope side of a suburb hill,
Deafening the swallow's twitter, came a thrill
Of trumpets—Lycius started—the sounds fled,
But left a thought, a buzzing in his head.
30   For the first time, since first he harbour'd in

---

5. Like sounds from the wind harp (Aeolus is god of winds), which responds musically to a current of air.

That purple-lined palace of sweet sin,
His spirit pass'd beyond its golden bourn°   boundary
Into the noisy world almost forsworn.
The lady, ever watchful, penetrant,
35 Saw this with pain, so arguing a want
Of something more, more than her empery°   empire
Of joys; and she began to moan and sigh
Because he mused beyond her, knowing well
That but a moment's thought is passion's passing bell.°   death knell
40 "Why do you sigh, fair creature?" whisper'd he:
"Why do you think?" return'd she tenderly:
"You have deserted me;—where am I now?
Not in your heart while care weighs on your brow:
No, no, you have dismiss'd me; and I go
45 From your breast houseless: ay, it must be so."
He answer'd, bending to her open eyes,
Where he was mirror'd small in paradise,
"My silver planet, both of eve and morn!⁶
Why will you plead yourself so sad forlorn,
50 While I am striving how to fill my heart
With deeper crimson, and a double smart?
How to entangle, trammel up and snare
Your soul in mine, and labyrinth you there
Like the hid scent in an unbudded rose?
55 Ay, a sweet kiss—you see your mighty woes.⁷
My thoughts! shall I unveil them? Listen then!
What mortal hath a prize, that other men
May be confounded and abash'd withal,
But lets it sometimes pace abroad majestical,
60 And triumph, as in thee I should rejoice
Amid the hoarse alarm of Corinth's voice.
Let my foes choke, and my friends shout afar,
While through the thronged streets your bridal car°   chariot
Wheels round its dazzling spokes."—The lady's cheek
65 Trembled; she nothing said, but, pale and meek,
Arose and knelt before him, wept a rain
Of sorrows at his words; at last with pain
Beseeching him, the while his hand she wrung,
To change his purpose. He thereat was stung,
70 Perverse, with stronger fancy to reclaim
Her wild and timid nature to his aim:
Besides, for all his love, in self despite,
Against his better self, he took delight
Luxurious in her sorrows, soft and new.
75 His passion, cruel grown, took on a hue
Fierce and sanguineous as 'twas possible
In one whose brow had no dark veins to swell.
Fine was the mitigated fury, like
Apollo's presence when in act to strike
80 The serpent—Ha, the serpent! certes, she

6. The planet Venus, which is both the morning   7. Playfully: "You see how great your troubles
and the evening star.   were!"

Was none. She burnt, she lov'd the tyranny,
And, all subdued, consented to the hour
When to the bridal he should lead his paramour.
Whispering in midnight silence, said the youth,
85   "Sure some sweet name thou hast, though, by my truth,
I have not ask'd it, ever thinking thee
Not mortal, but of heavenly progeny,
As still I do. Hast any mortal name,
Fit appellation for this dazzling frame?
90   Or friends or kinsfolk on the citied earth,
To share our marriage feast and nuptial mirth?"
"I have no friends," said Lamia, "no, not one;
My presence in wide Corinth hardly known:
My parents' bones are in their dusty urns
95   Sepulchred, where no kindled incense burns,
Seeing all their luckless race are dead, save me,
And I neglect the holy rite for thee.
Even as you list invite your many guests;
But if, as now it seems, your vision rests
100   With any pleasure on me, do not bid
Old Apollonius—from him keep me hid."
Lycius, perplex'd at words so blind and blank,
Made close inquiry; from whose touch she shrank,
Feigning a sleep; and he to the dull shade
105   Of deep sleep in a moment was betray'd.

         It was the custom then to bring away,
The bride from home at blushing shut of day,
Veil'd, in a chariot, heralded along
By strewn flowers, torches, and a marriage song,
110   With other pageants: but this fair unknown
Had not a friend. So being left alone,
(Lycius was gone to summon all his kin)
And knowing surely she could never win
His foolish heart from its mad pompousness,
115   She set herself, high-thoughted, how to dress
The misery in fit magnificence.
She did so, but 'tis doubtful how and whence
Came, and who were her subtle servitors.
About the halls, and to and from the doors,
120   There was a noise of wings, till in short space
The glowing banquet-room shone with wide-arched grace.
A haunting music, sole perhaps and lone
Supportress of the faery-roof, made moan
Throughout, as fearful the whole charm might fade.
125   Fresh carved cedar, mimicking a glade
Of palm and plantain, met from either side,
High in the midst, in honour of the bride:
Two palms and then two plantains, and so on,
From either side their stems branch'd one to one
130   All down the aisled place; and beneath all
There ran a stream of lamps straight on from wall to wall.
So canopied, lay an untasted feast

Teeming with odours. Lamia, regal drest,
Silently paced about, and as she went,
135 In pale contented sort of discontent,
Mission'd her viewless° servants to enrich   invisible
The fretted⁸ splendour of each nook and niche.
Between the tree-stems, marbled plain at first,
Came jasper pannels; then, anon, there burst
140 Forth creeping imagery of slighter trees,
And with the larger wove in small intricacies.
Approving all, she faded at self-will,
And shut the chamber up, close, hush'd and still,
Complete and ready for the revels rude,
145 When dreadful° guests would come to spoil her solitude.   terrifying

The day appear'd, and all the gossip rout.
O senseless Lycius! Madman! wherefore flout
The silent-blessing fate, warm cloister'd hours,
And show to common eyes these secret bowers?
150 The herd approach'd; each guest, with busy brain,
Arriving at the portal, gaz'd amain,°   intently
And enter'd marveling: for they knew the street,
Remember'd it from childhood all complete
Without a gap, yet ne'er before had seen
155 That royal porch, that high-built fair demesne;°   estate
So in they hurried all, maz'd, curious and keen:
Save one, who look'd thereon with eye severe,
And with calm-planted steps walk'd in austere;
'Twas Apollonius: something too he laugh'd,
160 As though some knotty problem, that had daft°   baffled
His patient thought, had now begun to thaw,
And solve and melt:—'twas just as he foresaw.

He met within the murmurous vestibule
His young disciple. " 'Tis no common rule,
165 Lycius," said he, "for uninvited guest
To force himself upon you, and infest
With an unbidden presence the bright throng
Of younger friends; yet must I do this wrong,
And you forgive me." Lycius blush'd, and led
170 The old man through the inner doors broad-spread;
With reconciling words and courteous mien°   appearance
Turning into sweet milk the sophist's° spleen.   scholar's

Of wealthy lustre was the banquet-room,
Fill'd with pervading brilliance and perfume:
175 Before each lucid pannel fuming stood
A censer fed with myrrh and spiced wood,
Each by a sacred tripod held aloft,
Whose slender feet wide-swerv'd upon the soft
Wool-woofed° carpets: fifty wreaths of smoke   woven
180 From fifty censers their light voyage took
To the high roof, still mimick'd as they rose

8. Adorned with fretwork (interlaced patterns).

Along the mirror'd walls by twin-clouds odorous.
Twelve sphered tables, by silk seats insphered,
High as the level of a man's breast rear'd
185 On libbard's° paws, upheld the heavy gold   *leopard's*
Of cups and goblets, and the store thrice told
Of Ceres' horn,[9] and, in huge vessels, wine
Come from the gloomy tun with merry shine.
Thus loaded with a feast the tables stood,
190 Each shrining in the midst the image of a God.

  When in an antichamber every guest
Had felt the cold full sponge to pleasure press'd,
By minist'ring slaves, upon his hands and feet,
And fragrant oils with ceremony meet°   *suitable*
195 Pour'd on his hair, they all mov'd to the feast
In white robes, and themselves in order placed
Around the silken couches, wondering
Whence all this mighty cost and blaze of wealth could spring.

  Soft went the music the soft air along,
200 While fluent Greek a vowel'd undersong
Kept up among the guests, discoursing low
At first, for scarcely was the wine at flow;
But when the happy vintage touch'd their brains,
Louder they talk, and louder come the strains
205 Of powerful instruments:—the gorgeous dyes,
The space, the splendour of the draperies,
The roof of awful richness, nectarous cheer,
Beautiful slaves, and Lamia's self, appear,
Now, when the wine has done its rosy deed,
210 And every soul from human trammels freed,
No more so strange; for merry wine, sweet wine,
Will make Elysian shades not too fair, too divine.

  Soon was God Bacchus at meridian height;
Flush'd were their cheeks, and bright eyes double bright:
215 Garlands of every green, and every scent
From vales deflower'd, or forest-trees branch-rent,
In baskets of bright osier'd[1] gold were brought
High as the handles heap'd, to suit the thought
Of every guest; that each, as he did please,
220 Might fancy-fit his brows, silk-pillow'd at his ease.

  What wreath for Lamia? What for Lycius?
What for the sage, old Apollonius?
Upon her aching forehead be there hung
The leaves of willow and of adder's tongue;[2]
225 And for the youth, quick, let us strip for him
The thyrsus,[3] that his watching eyes may swim
Into forgetfulness; and, for the sage,

9. The horn of plenty, overflowing with the products of Ceres, goddess of grain.
1. Plaited. An "osier" is a strip of willow used in weaving baskets.
2. A fern whose spikes resemble a serpent's tongue.
3. The vine-covered staff of Bacchus, used to signify drunkenness.

Let spear-grass and the spiteful thistle wage
War on his temples. Do not all charms fly
230 At the mere touch of cold philosophy?[4]
There was an awful° rainbow once in heaven: awe-inspiring
We know her woof, her texture; she is given
In the dull catalogue of common things.
Philosophy will clip an Angel's wings,
235 Conquer all mysteries by rule and line,
Empty the haunted air, and gnomed mine[5]—
Unweave a rainbow, as it erewhile made
The tender-person'd Lamia melt into a shade.

By her glad Lycius sitting, in chief place,
240 Scarce saw in all the room another face,
Till, checking his love trance, a cup he took
Full brimm'd, and opposite sent forth a look
'Cross the broad table, to beseech a glance
From his old teacher's wrinkled countenance,
245 And pledge[6] him. The bald-head philosopher
Had fix'd his eye, without a twinkle or stir
Full on the alarmed beauty of the bride,
Brow-beating her fair form, and troubling her sweet pride.
Lycius then press'd her hand, with devout touch,
250 As pale it lay upon the rosy couch:
'Twas icy, and the cold ran through his veins;
Then sudden it grew hot, and all the pains
Of an unnatural heat shot to his heart.
"Lamia, what means this? Wherefore dost thou start?
255 Know'st thou that man?" Poor Lamia answer'd not.
He gaz'd into her eyes, and not a jot
Own'd° they the lovelorn piteous appeal: acknowledged
More, more he gaz'd: his human senses reel:
Some hungry spell that loveliness absorbs;
260 There was no recognition in those orbs.
"Lamia!" he cried—and no soft-toned reply.
The many heard, and the loud revelry
Grew hush; the stately music no more breathes;
The myrtle[7] sicken'd in a thousand wreaths.
265 By faint degrees, voice, lute, and pleasure ceased;
A deadly silence step by step increased,
Until it seem'd a horrid presence there,
And not a man but felt the terror in his hair.
"Lamia!" he shriek'd; and nothing but the shriek
270 With its sad echo did the silence break.
"Begone, foul dream!" he cried, gazing again
In the bride's face, where now no azure vein
Wander'd on fair-spaced temples; no soft bloom
Misted the cheek; no passion to illume

4. In the sense of "natural philosophy," or science. Benjamin Haydon tells in his *Autobiography* how, at a hard-drinking and high-spirited dinner party, Keats had agreed with Charles Lamb (to what extent jokingly, it is not clear) that Newton's *Optics* "had destroyed all the poetry of the rainbow by reducing it to the prismatic colors."
5. Gnomes were guardians of mines.
6. Drink a toast to.
7. Sacred to Venus, hence an emblem of love.

275 The deep-recessed vision:—all was blight;
    Lamia, no longer fair, there sat a deadly white.
    "Shut, shut those juggling⁸ eyes, thou ruthless man!
    Turn them aside, wretch! or the righteous ban
    Of all the Gods, whose dreadful images
280 Here represent their shadowy presences,
    May pierce them on the sudden with the thorn
    Of painful blindness; leaving thee forlorn,
    In trembling dotage to the feeblest fright
    Of conscience, for their long offended might,
285 For all thine impious proud-heart sophistries,
    Unlawful magic, and enticing lies.
    Corinthians! look upon that gray-beard wretch!
    Mark how, possess'd, his lashless eyelids stretch
    Around his demon eyes! Corinthians, see!
290 My sweet bride withers at their potency."
    "Fool!" said the sophist, in an under-tone
    Gruff with contempt; which a death-nighing moan
    From Lycius answer'd, as heart-struck and lost,
    He sank supine beside the aching ghost.
295 "Fool! Fool!" repeated he, while his eyes still
    Relented not, nor mov'd; "from every ill
    Of life have I preserv'd thee to this day,
    And shall I see thee made a serpent's prey?"
    Then Lamia breath'd death breath; the sophist's eye,
300 Like a sharp spear, went through her utterly,
    Keen, cruel, perceant,° stinging: she, as well   *piercing*
    As her weak hand could any meaning tell,
    Motion'd him to be silent; vainly so,
    He look'd and look'd again a level—No!
305 "A Serpent!" echoed he; no sooner said,
    Than with a frightful scream she vanished:
    And Lycius' arms were empty of delight,
    As were his limbs of life, from that same night.
    On the high couch he lay!—his friends came round—
310 Supported him—no pulse, or breath they found,
    And, in its marriage robe, the heavy body wound.

July–Aug. 1819   1820

To Autumn¹

I

Season of mists and mellow fruitfulness,
    Close bosom-friend of the maturing sun;
Conspiring with him how to load and bless

---

8. Deceiving, full of trickery.
1. Two days after this ode was composed, Keats wrote to J. H. Reynolds: "I never liked stubble fields so much as now—Aye, better than the chilly green of the spring. Somehow a stubble plain looks warm—in the same way that some pictures look warm—this struck me so much in my Sunday's walk that I composed upon it." For the author's revisions while composing "To Autumn," see "Poems in Process," in the appendices to this volume.

With fruit the vines that round the thatch-eves run;
5   To bend with apples the moss'd cottage-trees,
    And fill all fruit with ripeness to the core;
    To swell the gourd, and plump the hazel shells
    With a sweet kernel; to set budding more,
    And still more, later flowers for the bees,
10 Until they think warm days will never cease,
    For summer has o'er-brimm'd their clammy cells.

2

    Who hath not seen thee oft amid thy store?
    Sometimes whoever seeks abroad may find
    Thee sitting careless on a granary floor,
15 Thy hair soft-lifted by the winnowing² wind;
    Or on a half-reap'd furrow sound asleep,
    Drows'd with the fume of poppies, while thy hook°   scythe
    Spares the next swath and all its twined flowers:
    And sometimes like a gleaner thou dost keep
20 Steady thy laden head across a brook;
    Or by a cyder-press, with patient look,
    Thou watchest the last oozings hours by hours.

3

    Where are the songs of spring? Ay, where are they?
    Think not of them, thou hast thy music too,—
25 While barred clouds bloom the soft-dying day,
    And touch the stubble-plains with rosy hue;
    Then in a wailful choir the small gnats mourn
    Among the river sallows,° borne aloft   willows
    Or sinking as the light wind lives or dies;
30 And full-grown lambs loud bleat from hilly bourn;°   region
    Hedge-crickets sing; and now with treble soft
    The red-breast whistles from a garden-croft;³
    And gathering swallows twitter in the skies.

Sept. 19, 1819   1820

The Fall of Hyperion: A Dream

The Fall of Hyperion: A Dream   Late in 1818, at about the end of his twenty-third year and while he was serving as nurse to his dying brother Tom, Keats planned to undertake an epic poem, modeled on *Paradise Lost,* that he called *Hyperion.* Greek mythology gave Keats its subject—the displacement of Saturn and his fellow Titans by a new generation of gods, Zeus and the other Olympians. But in engaging this topic Keats addressed the epic question at the center of *Paradise Lost:* how did evil come into the world and why? Keats in his story set out to represent an answer, not according to any one religious creed but in terms informed by his reading in comparative religion and mythology. The Titans had been fair and benign gods, and their rule had been a golden age of happiness. Yet at the beginning of the poem all the Titans except Hyperion, god of the sun, have been dethroned; and the uncomprehending Saturn again and again raises the question of how this injustice could have come to be.

---

2. To "winnow" is to fan the chaff from the grain.   3. An enclosed plot of farmland.

In book 3 of the original *Hyperion,* the scenes among the Titans are supplemented by the experience of the Olympian Apollo, still a youth but destined to displace Hyperion as the sun god among the heavenly powers. He lives in "aching ignorance" of the universe and its processes but is aware of his ignorance and thirsts for knowledge. Suddenly Apollo reads in the face of his tutor Mnemosyne—goddess of memory, who will be mother of the Muses and so of all the arts—the silent record of the defeat of the Titans and at once soars to the knowledge that he seeks: the understanding, both intoxicating and agonizing, that life involves process, that process entails change and suffering, and that there can be no creative progress except by the defeat and destruction of the preceding stage. Apollo cries out:

> Knowledge enormous makes a God of me.
> Names, deeds, gray legends, dire events, rebellions,
> Majesties, sovran voices, agonies,
> Creations and destroyings, all at once
> Pour into the wide hollows of my brain,
> And deify me. . . .

This opening out of Apollo's awareness to the tragic nature of life is what the Titans lacked. As the fragment breaks off, Apollo is transfigured—like one who should "with fierce convulse / Die into life"—not only into one who has earned the right to displace Hyperion as god of the sun, but also into the god of the highest poetry.

Keats abandoned this extraordinary fragment in April 1819. Late that summer, however, he took up the theme again, under the title *The Fall of Hyperion: A Dream.* This time his primary model is Dante, whom he had been studying in Henry Cary's verse translation of 1814. In *The Divine Comedy* all the narrated events are represented as a vision granted to the poet at the beginning of the poem. In the same way Keats begins *The Fall of Hyperion* with a frame story whose central event is that the poet-protagonist, in a dream, falls from a paradisal landscape into a wasteland and there earns the right to a vision. That vision reincorporates the events narrated in the first *Hyperion:* Moneta (her Latin name suggests "the Admonisher"), who stands in the same relationship to the poet as, in the earlier tale, Mnemosyne stood to Apollo, permits, or challenges, this protagonist to remember, with her, her own memories of the fall of the Titans. By devising this frame story, Keats shifted his center of poetic concern from the narration of epic action to an account of the evolving consciousness of the epic poet, as he seeks to know his identity, to justify the morality of poetry, and to understand its place in the social world. The ordeal through which Apollo had become god of poetry is replaced in this second version of *Hyperion* by the ordeal of this one poet, who must prove himself able to endure the witnessing that Moneta demands of him and worthy of the power "To see as a God sees" (line 304).

A number of things caused Keats to abandon this attempt at *The Fall of Hyperion* at the sixty-first line of the second canto. (A fragment was published, against his wishes, in his 1820 volume of poems.) He wrote to Reynolds on September 21, 1819:

> I have given up Hyperion. . . . Miltonic verse cannot be written but in an artful or rather artist's humour. I wish to give myself up to other sensations. English ought to be kept up. It may be interesting to you to pick out some lines from Hyperion and put a mark X to the false beauty proceeding from art, and one ‖ to the true voice of feeling.

The two *Hyperion* fragments are impressive achievements, but as Keats with his acumen in self-criticism recognized, they have the air of artistic tours de force, written in an age in which the high artifice of the epic matter and style had ceased to be the natural voice of the poet. In the same letter Keats mentions having composed two days earlier the ode "To Autumn." In this, his last major poem, the poet had envisaged the circumstance of the cycle of life and death, and had articulated his experience in his own poetic voice.

The Fall of Hyperion: A Dream

Canto 1

Fanatics have their dreams, wherewith they weave
A paradise for a sect; the savage too
From forth the loftiest fashion of his sleep
Guesses at heaven: pity these have not
5 Trac'd upon vellum° or wild Indian leaf   *parchment*
The shadows of melodious utterance.
But bare of laurel¹ they live, dream, and die;
For Poesy alone can tell her dreams,
With the fine spell of words alone can save
10 Imagination from the sable charm
And dumb° enchantment. Who alive can say   *mute*
"Thou art no poet; may'st not tell thy dreams"?
Since every man whose soul is not a clod
Hath visions, and would speak, if he had lov'd
15 And been well nurtured in his mother tongue.
Whether the dream now purposed to rehearse
Be poet's or fanatic's will be known
When this warm scribe my hand is in the grave.

Methought I stood where trees of every clime,
20 Palm, myrtle, oak, and sycamore, and beech,
With plantane, and spice blossoms, made a screen;
In neighbourhood of fountains, by the noise
Soft showering in mine ears, and, by the touch
Of scent, not far from roses. Turning round,
25 I saw an arbour with a drooping roof
Of trellis vines, and bells, and larger blooms,
Like floral-censers swinging light in air;
Before its wreathed doorway, on a mound
Of moss, was spread a feast of summer fruits,
30 Which, nearer seen, seem'd refuse of a meal
By angel tasted, or our mother Eve;²
For empty shells were scattered on the grass,
And grape stalks but half bare, and remnants more,
Sweet smelling, whose pure kinds I could not know.
35 Still was more plenty than the fabled horn³
Thrice emptied could pour forth, at banqueting
For Proserpine return'd to her own fields,⁴
Where the white heifers low. And appetite
More yearning than on earth I ever felt
40 Growing within, I ate deliciously;
And, after not long, thirsted, for thereby
Stood a cool vessel of transparent juice,
Sipp'd by the wander'd bee, the which I took,
And, pledging all the mortals of the world,

---

1. The laurel, associated with Apollo, is the emblem of poetic fame.
2. In *Paradise Lost* 5.321ff. Eve serves the visiting angel Raphael with a meal of fruits and fruit juices.

3. The cornucopia, or horn of plenty.
4. When Proserpine each year is released by her husband, Pluto, god of the underworld, for a sojourn on Earth, it is the beginning of spring.

45 And all the dead whose names are in our lips,
   Drank. That full draught is parent of my theme.[5]
   No Asian poppy,° nor elixir fine   opium
   Of the soon fading jealous caliphat;[6]
   No poison gender'd in close monkish cell
50 To thin the scarlet conclave of old men,[7]
   Could so have rapt unwilling life away.
   Among the fragrant husks and berries crush'd,
   Upon the grass I struggled hard against
   The domineering potion; but in vain:
55 The cloudy swoon came on, and down I sunk
   Like a Silenus[8] on an antique vase.
   How long I slumber'd 'tis a chance to guess.
   When sense of life return'd, I started up
   As if with wings; but the fair trees were gone,
60 The mossy mound and arbour were no more;
   I look'd around upon the carved sides
   Of an old sanctuary with roof august,
   Builded so high, it seem'd that filmed clouds
   Might spread beneath, as o'er the stars of heaven;
65 So old the place was, I remembered none
   The like upon the earth; what I had seen
   Of grey cathedrals, buttress'd walls, rent towers,
   The superannuations° of sunk realms,   ruins
   Or nature's rocks toil'd hard in waves and winds,
70 Seem'd but the faulture° of decrepit things   defects
   To° that eternal domed monument.   compared to
   Upon the marble at my feet there lay
   Store of strange vessels, and large draperies,
   Which needs had been of dyed asbestus wove,
75 Or in that place the moth could not corrupt,[9]
   So white the linen; so, in some, distinct
   Ran imageries from a sombre loom.
   All in a mingled heap confus'd there lay
   Robes, golden tongs, censer, and chafing dish,
80 Girdles, and chains, and holy jewelries.[1]

   Turning from these with awe, once more I rais'd
   My eyes to fathom the space every way;
   The embossed roof, the silent massy range
   Of columns north and south, ending in mist
85 Of nothing, then to eastward, where black gates
   Were shut against the sunrise evermore.
   Then to the west I look'd, and saw far off
   An image, huge of feature as a cloud,
   At level of whose feet an altar slept,

5. The drink puts the poet to sleep and effects the dream within a dream that constitutes the remainder of the fragment.
6. A council of caliphs, Muslim rulers, who plot to kill each other with a poisonous drink ("elixir").
7. The College of Cardinals. This scenario of poisoning, like the preceding Orientalist reference to intrigue among the caliphs, recalls a stock setting of the period's Gothic novels.
8. An elderly satyr, usually represented as drunk.
9. Matthew 6.20: "Lay up for yourselves treasures in heaven, where neither moth nor rust doth corrupt."
1. Offerings to the gods were spread on the floor of Greek temples.

90 To be approach'd on either side by steps,
  And marble balustrade,° and patient travail   *banister*
  To count with toil the innumerable degrees.
  Towards the altar sober-pac'd I went,
  Repressing haste, as too unholy there;
95 And, coming nearer, saw beside the shrine
  One minist'ring;² and there arose a flame.
  When in mid-May the sickening east wind
  Shifts sudden to the south, the small warm rain
  Melts out the frozen incense from all flowers,
100 And fills the air with so much pleasant health
  That even the dying man forgets his shroud;
  Even so that lofty sacrificial fire,
  Sending forth Maian³ incense, spread around
  Forgetfulness of every thing but bliss,
105 And clouded all the altar with soft smoke,
  From whose white fragrant curtains thus I heard
  Language pronounc'd. "If thou canst not ascend
  These steps,⁴ die on that marble where thou art.
  Thy flesh, near cousin to the common dust,
110 Will parch for lack of nutriment—thy bones
  Will wither in few years, and vanish so
  That not the quickest eye could find a grain
  Of what thou now art on that pavement cold.
  The sands of thy short life are spent this hour,
115 And no hand in the universe can turn
  Thy hour glass, if these gummed° leaves be burnt   *aromatic*
  Ere thou canst mount up these immortal steps."
  I heard, I look'd: two senses both at once
  So fine, so subtle, felt the tyranny
120 Of that fierce threat, and the hard task proposed.
  Prodigious seem'd the toil; the leaves were yet
  Burning,—when suddenly a palsied chill
  Struck from the paved level up my limbs,
  And was ascending quick to put cold grasp
125 Upon those streams° that pulse beside the throat: *arteries*
  I shriek'd; and the sharp anguish of my shriek
  Stung my own ears—I strove hard to escape
  The numbness; strove to gain the lowest step.
  Slow, heavy, deadly was my pace: the cold
130 Grew stifling, suffocating, at the heart;
  And when I clasp'd my hands I felt them not.
  One minute before death, my iced foot touch'd
  The lowest stair; and as it touch'd, life seem'd
  To pour in at the toes: I mounted up,
135 As once fair angels on a ladder flew
  From the green turf to heaven.⁵—"Holy Power,"
  Cried I, approaching near the horned shrine,⁶

2. Who identifies herself in line 226 as Moneta.
3. Maia was one of the Pleiades, a daughter of Atlas and (by Zeus) the mother of Hermes. She was the goddess of the month of May.
4. These steps that the poet must ascend were probably suggested by the stairs going up the steep side of the purgatorial Mount in Dante's *Purga-*
torio.
5. The ladder by which, in a dream, Jacob saw angels passing between heaven and Earth (Genesis 28.12 and *Paradise Lost* 3.510–15).
6. As, e.g., in Exodus 27.2, "And thou shalt make the horns of [the altar] upon the four corners thereof." In his description of the temple and

"What am I that should so be sav'd from death?
What am I that another death come not
140 To choak my utterance sacrilegious here?"
Then said the veiled shadow—"Thou hast felt
What 'tis to die and live again before
Thy fated hour. That thou hadst power to do so
Is thy own safety; thou hast dated on
145 Thy doom."[7]—"High Prophetess," said I, "purge off
Benign, if so it please thee, my mind's film."[8]
"None can usurp this height," return'd that shade,
"But those to whom the miseries of the world
Are misery, and will not let them rest.
150 All else who find a haven in the world,
Where they may thoughtless sleep away their days,
If by a chance into this fane° they come,   temple
Rot on the pavement where thou rotted'st half."[9]—
"Are there not thousands in the world," said I,
155 Encourag'd by the sooth[1] voice of the shade,
"Who love their fellows even to the death;
Who feel the giant agony of the world;
And more, like slaves to poor humanity,
Labour for mortal good? I sure should see
160 Other men here: but I am here alone."
"They whom thou spak'st of are no vision'ries,"
Rejoin'd that voice—"They are no dreamers weak,
They seek no wonder but the human face;
No music but a happy-noted voice—
165 They come not here, they have no thought to come—
And thou art here, for thou art less than they.
What benefit canst thou do, or all thy tribe,
To the great world? Thou art a dreaming thing;
A fever of thyself—think of the earth;
170 What bliss even in hope is there° for thee?   on Earth
What haven? Every creature hath its home;
Every sole man hath days of joy and pain,
Whether his labours be sublime or low—
The pain alone; the joy alone; distinct:
175 Only the dreamer venoms all his days,
Bearing more woe than all his sins deserve.
Therefore, that happiness be somewhat shar'd,
Such things as thou art are admitted oft
Into like gardens thou didst pass erewhile,
180 And suffer'd in° these temples; for that cause   allowed to enter
Thou standest safe beneath this statue's knees."
"That I am favored for unworthiness,
By such propitious parley medicin'd
In sickness not ignoble, I rejoice,

---

its accouterments, Keats deliberately mingles Hebrew, Christian, and pagan elements to represent the poet's passage through the stage represented by all religions, which are "dreams" made into the creed for "a sect" (lines 1–18).
7. I.e., you have postponed the time when you will be judged.
8. Cf. Milton's plea, following his account of his

blindness, for a celestial light that might "Shine inward": "Irradiate, there plant eyes, all mist from thence / Purge and disperse, that I may see and tell / Of things invisible to mortal sight" (*Paradise Lost* 3.52–54).
9. I.e., where you halfway rotted.
1. Soothing, also truth-telling.

185 Aye, and could weep for love of such award."
So answer'd I, continuing, "If it please,
Majestic shadow, tell me: sure not all[2]
Those melodies sung into the world's ear
Are useless: sure a poet is a sage;
190 A humanist, physician to all men.
That I am none I feel, as vultures feel
They are no birds when eagles are abroad.
What am I then? Thou spakest of my tribe:
What tribe?"—The tall shade veil'd in drooping white
195 Then spake, so much more earnest, that the breath
Mov'd the thin linen folds that drooping hung
About a golden censer from the hand
Pendent.—"Art thou not of the dreamer tribe?
The poet and the dreamer are distinct,
200 Diverse, sheer opposite, antipodes.
The one pours out a balm upon the world,
The other vexes it." Then shouted I
Spite of myself, and with a Pythia's spleen,[3]
"Apollo! faded, far flown Apollo!
205 Where is thy misty pestilence[4] to creep
Into the dwellings, through the door crannies,
Of all mock lyrists, large self worshipers,
And careless hectorers in proud bad verse.[5]
Though I breathe death with them it will be life
210 To see them sprawl before me into graves.[6]
Majestic shadow, tell me where I am:
Whose altar this; for whom this incense curls:
What image this, whose face I cannot see,
For the broad marble knees; and who thou art,
215 Of accent feminine, so courteous."
Then the tall shade in drooping linens veil'd
Spake out, so much more earnest, that her breath
Stirr'd the thin folds of gauze that drooping hung
About a golden censer from her hand
220 Pendent; and by her voice I knew she shed
Long treasured tears. "This temple sad and lone
Is all spar'd from the thunder of a war
Foughten long since by giant hierarchy

2. Keats's friend Richard Woodhouse, whose manuscript copy of the poem is our principal source of the text, crossed out lines 187–210 with the marginal comment next to lines 197–99: "K. seems to have intended to erase this & the next 21 lines." Probably the basis for his opinion is the partial repetition of lines 187 and 194–98 in lines 211 and 216–20.
3. With the anger ("spleen") of the Pythia, the priestess who served at Delphi as the oracle of Apollo, the god of poetry.
4. Apollo was a sender of plagues, as well as the inspirer of prophecy and poetry. He was also the god of medicine. Keats's medical studies gave him special reason to be interested in this figure and the roles he combined.
5. This has been conjectured as referring to Byron, or else to several contemporaries, including

Shelley and Wordsworth. But the poetic types, not individuals, are what matter to Keats's argument.
6. In lines 147–210 we find a series of progressive distinctions: (1) between humanitarians who feel for "the miseries of the world" and people who are "thoughtless" sleepers (lines 147–53); (2) within the class of humanitarians, between those who actively "benefit . . . the great world" and the poets who are "vision'ries" and "dreamers" (lines 161–69); (3) and within the class of poets, between those who are merely dreamers and those who are sages and healers (lines 187–202). As in the colloquy between Asia and Demogorgon (see Shelley's *Prometheus Unbound* 2.4.1–128, p. 802), the interchange here may be taken to represent, in dramatized form, a process of inner analysis and self-discovery on the part of the questing poet.

Against rebellion: this old image here,
225 Whose carved features wrinkled as he fell,
Is Saturn's;[7] I, Moneta, left supreme
Sole priestess of his desolation."—
I had no words to answer; for my tongue,
Useless, could find about its roofed home
230 No syllable of a fit majesty
To make rejoinder to Moneta's mourn.
There was a silence while the altar's blaze
Was fainting for sweet food: I look'd thereon
And on the paved floor, where nigh were pil'd
235 Faggots of cinnamon, and many heaps
Of other crisped spice-wood—then again
I look'd upon the altar and its horns
Whiten'd with ashes, and its lang'rous flame,
And then upon the offerings again;
240 And so by turns—till sad Moneta cried,
"The sacrifice is done, but not the less
Will I be kind to thee for thy good will.
My power, which to me is still a curse,
Shall be to thee a wonder; for the scenes
245 Still swooning vivid through my globed brain
With an electral changing misery
Thou shalt with those dull mortal eyes behold,
Free from all pain, if wonder pain thee not."
As near as an immortal's sphered words
250 Could to a mother's soften, were these last:
But yet I had a terror of her robes,
And chiefly of the veils, that from her brow
Hung pale, and curtain'd her in mysteries
That made my heart too small to hold its blood.
255 This saw that Goddess, and with sacred hand
Parted the veils. Then saw I a wan face,
Not pin'd° by human sorrows, but bright blanch'd   *exhausted*
By an immortal sickness which kills not;
It works a constant change, which happy death
260 Can put no end to; deathwards progressing
To no death was that visage; it had pass'd
The lily and the snow; and beyond these
I must not think now, though I saw that face—
But for her eyes I should have fled away.
265 They held me back, with a benignant light,
Soft mitigated by divinest lids
Half closed, and visionless° entire they seem'd   *blind*
Of all external things—they saw me not,
But in blank splendor beam'd like the mild moon,
270 Who comforts those she sees not, who knows not
What eyes are upward cast. As I had found
A grain of gold upon a mountain's side,
And twing'd with avarice strain'd out my eyes
To search its sullen entrails rich with ore,

---

7. Cf. the "shattered visage" of the fallen statue in Shelley's "Ozymandias" (p. 768).

275 So at the view of sad Moneta's brow,
     I ached to see what things the hollow brain
     Behind enwombed: what high tragedy
     In the dark secret chambers of her skull
     Was acting, that could give so dread a stress
280 To her cold lips, and fill with such a light
     Her planetary eyes; and touch her voice
     With such a sorrow. "Shade of Memory!"
     Cried I, with act adorant at her feet,
     "By all the gloom hung round thy fallen house,
285 By this last temple, by the golden age,
     By great Apollo, thy dear foster child,
     And by thy self, forlorn divinity,
     The pale Omega⁸ of a wither'd race,
     Let me behold, according as thou said'st,
290 What in thy brain so ferments to and fro."—
     No sooner had this conjuration pass'd
     My devout lips, than side by side we stood,
     (Like a stunt bramble by a solemn pine)
     Deep in the shady sadness of a vale,⁹
295 Far sunken from the healthy breath of morn,
     Far from the fiery noon, and eve's one star.
     Onward I look'd beneath the gloomy boughs,
     And saw, what first I thought an image huge,
     Like to the image pedestal'd so high
300 In Saturn's temple. Then Moneta's voice
     Came brief upon mine ear,—"So Saturn sat
     When he had lost his realms."—Whereon there grew
     A power within me of enormous ken,°   range of vision
     To see as a God sees, and take the depth
305 Of things as nimbly as the outward eye
     Can size and shape pervade. The lofty theme
     At those few words hung vast before my mind,
     With half unravel'd web. I set myself
     Upon an eagle's watch, that I might see,
310 And seeing ne'er forget. No stir of life
     Was in this shrouded vale, not so much air
     As in the zoning° of a summer's day   course
     Robs not one light seed from the feather'd grass,
     But where the deaf leaf fell there did it rest:
315 A stream went voiceless by, still deaden'd more
     By reason of the fallen divinity
     Spreading more shade: the Naiad° mid her reeds   water nymph
     Press'd her cold finger closer to her lips.
     Along the margin sand large footmarks went
320 No farther than to where old Saturn's feet
     Had rested, and there slept, how long a sleep!
     Degraded, cold, upon the sodden ground

8. The final letter of the Greek alphabet.
9. This had been the opening line of the original
Hyperion. The rest of the poem is a revised version
of part of that first narrative, with the poet now
represented as allowed to envision the course of
events that Moneta recalls in her memory (lines
282, 289–90).

His old right hand lay nerveless, listless, dead,
Unsceptred; and his realmless[1] eyes were clos'd,
325 While his bow'd head seem'd listening to the Earth,
His antient mother,[2] for some comfort yet.

It seem'd no force could wake him from his place;
But there came one who with a kindred hand
Touch'd his wide shoulders, after bending low
330 With reverence, though to one who knew it not.
Then came the griev'd voice of Mnemosyne,[3]
And griev'd I hearken'd. "That divinity
Whom thou saw'st step from yon forlornest wood,
And with slow pace approach our fallen King,
335 Is Thea,[4] softest-natur'd of our brood."
I mark'd the goddess in fair statuary
Surpassing wan Moneta by the head,[5]
And in her sorrow nearer woman's tears.
There was a listening fear in her regard,
340 As if calamity had but begun;
As if the vanward clouds[6] of evil days
Had spent their malice, and the sullen rear
Was with its stored thunder labouring up.
One hand she press'd upon that aching spot
345 Where beats the human heart; as if just there,
Though an immortal, she felt cruel pain;
The other upon Saturn's bended neck
She laid, and to the level of his hollow ear
Leaning, with parted lips, some words she spake
350 In solemn tenor and deep organ tune;
Some mourning words, which in our feeble tongue
Would come in this-like accenting; how frail
To that large utterance of the early Gods!—
"Saturn! look up—and for what, poor lost King?[7]
355 I have no comfort for thee, no—not one:
I cannot cry, *Wherefore thus sleepest thou?*
For heaven is parted from thee, and the earth
Knows thee not, so afflicted, for a God;
And ocean too, with all its solemn noise,
360 Has from thy sceptre pass'd, and all the air
Is emptied of thine hoary majesty.
Thy thunder, captious° at the new command,   *quarrelsome*
Rumbles reluctant o'er our fallen house;
And thy sharp lightning in unpracticed hands
365 Scorches and burns our once serene domain.

---

1. Saturn's eyes, when open, express the fact that he has lost his realm.
2. Saturn and the other Titans were the children of heaven and Earth.
3. As in 2.50, Keats substitutes for "Moneta" the "Mnemosyne" of the first *Hyperion*. This may be a slip but more likely indicates an alternative name for Moneta, in her role as participant in, as well as commentator on, the tragic action.
4. Sister and wife of Hyperion.
5. I.e., Thea was a head taller than Moneta.
6. The front line of clouds.
7. Keats several times recalls King Lear in representing the condition of Saturn. Keats's contemporaries may have thought, too, of George III, mad, blind, and dethroned by his son, who had become prince regent.

With such remorseless speed still come new woes
That unbelief has not a space to breathe.[8]
Saturn, sleep on:—Me thoughtless,[9] why should I
Thus violate thy slumbrous solitude?
370 Why should I ope thy melancholy eyes?
Saturn, sleep on, while at thy feet I weep."

    As when, upon a tranced summer night,
Forests, branch-charmed by the earnest stars,[1]
Dream, and so dream all night, without a noise,
375 Save from one gradual solitary gust,
Swelling upon the silence; dying off;
As if the ebbing air had but one wave;
So came these words, and went; the while in tears
She press'd her fair large forehead to the earth,
380 Just where her fallen hair might spread in curls,
A soft and silken mat for Saturn's feet.
Long, long, those two were postured motionless,
Like sculpture builded up upon the grave
Of their own power. A long awful time
385 I look'd upon them; still they were the same;
The frozen God still bending to the earth,
And the sad Goddess weeping at his feet;
Moneta silent. Without stay or prop
But my own weak mortality, I bore
390 The load of this eternal quietude,
The unchanging gloom, and the three fixed shapes
Ponderous upon my senses a whole moon.
For by my burning brain I measured sure
Her silver seasons shedded on the night,
395 And every day by day methought I grew
More gaunt and ghostly. Oftentimes I pray'd
Intense, that death would take me from the vale
And all its burthens. Gasping with despair
Of change, hour after hour I curs'd myself:
400 Until old Saturn rais'd his faded eyes,
And look'd around, and saw his kingdom gone,
And all the gloom and sorrow of the place,
And that fair kneeling Goddess at his feet.
As the moist scent of flowers, and grass, and leaves
405 Fills forest dells with a pervading air
Known to the woodland nostril, so the words
Of Saturn fill'd the mossy glooms around,
Even to the hollows of time-eaten oaks,
And to the windings in the foxes' hole,
410 With sad low tones, while thus he spake, and sent
Strange musings to the solitary Pan.

---

8. That disbelief has not an instant to catch its
breath.
9. I.e., how thoughtless I am!
1. The grander version in the first *Hyperion*,
1.72ff., reads: "As when, upon a tranced summer-
night / Those green-rob'd senators of mighty
woods, / Tall oaks, branch-charmed by the earnest
stars, / Dream."

"Moan, brethren, moan; for we are swallow'd up
And buried from all godlike exercise
Of influence benign on planets pale,
415 And peaceful sway above man's harvesting,
And all those acts which deity supreme
Doth ease its heart of love in. Moan and wail.
Moan, brethren, moan; for lo! the rebel spheres
Spin round, the stars their antient courses keep,
420 Clouds still with shadowy moisture haunt the earth,
Still suck their fill of light from sun and moon,
Still buds the tree, and still the sea-shores murmur.
There is no death in all the universe,
No smell of death—there shall be death²—Moan, moan,
425 Moan, Cybele,³ moan, for thy pernicious babes
Have chang'd a God into a shaking palsy.
Moan, brethren, moan; for I have no strength left,
Weak as the reed—weak—feeble as my voice—
O, O, the pain, the pain of feebleness.
430 Moan, moan; for still I thaw—or give me help:
Throw down those imps⁴ and give me victory.
Let me hear other groans, and trumpets blown
Of triumph calm, and hymns of festival
From the gold peaks of heaven's high piled clouds;
435 Voices of soft proclaim,° and silver stir   proclamation
Of strings in hollow shells; and let there be
Beautiful things made new for the surprize
Of the sky children."—So he feebly ceas'd,
With such a poor and sickly sounding pause,
440 Methought I heard some old man of the earth
Bewailing earthly loss; nor could my eyes
And ears act with that pleasant unison of sense
Which marries sweet sound with the grace of form,
And dolorous accent from a tragic harp
445 With large limb'd visions.⁵ More I scrutinized:
Still fix'd he sat beneath the sable trees,
Whose arms spread straggling in wild serpent forms,
With leaves all hush'd: his awful presence there
(Now all was silent) gave a deadly lie
450 To what I erewhile heard: only his lips
Trembled amid the white curls of his beard.
They told the truth, though, round, the snowy locks
Hung nobly, as upon the face of heaven
A midday fleece of clouds. Thea arose
455 And stretch'd her white arm through the hollow dark,
Pointing some whither: whereat he too rose
Like a vast giant seen by men at sea
To grow pale from the waves at dull midnight.⁶

2. The passing of the Saturnian golden age (paralleled by Keats with the fable of the loss of Eden) has introduced suffering, and will also introduce death.
3. The wife of Saturn and mother of the Olympian gods, who have overthrown their parents.
4. I.e., his rebellious children, the Titans.
5. I.e., the narrator could not attach this speech, like that of a feebly complaining old mortal, to the visible form of the large-limbed god who uttered it.
6. I.e., like a giant who is seen at sea to emerge, pale, from the waves.

They melted from my sight into the woods:
460 Ere I could turn, Moneta cried—"These twain
Are speeding to the families of grief,
Where roof'd in by black rocks they waste in pain
And darkness for no hope."—And she spake on,
As ye may read who can unwearied pass
465 Onward from the antichamber° of this dream,   *entry room*
Where even at the open doors awhile
I must delay, and glean my memory
Of her high phrase: perhaps no further dare.

Canto 2

"Mortal, that thou may'st understand aright,
I humanize my sayings to thine ear,
Making comparisons of earthly things;[7]
Or thou might'st better listen to the wind,
5 Whose language is to thee a barren noise,
Though it blows legend-laden through the trees.
In melancholy realms big tears are shed,
More sorrow like to this, and such-like woe,
Too huge for mortal tongue, or pen of scribe.
10 The Titans fierce, self-hid, or prison-bound,
Groan for the old allegiance once more,
Listening in their doom for Saturn's voice.
But one of our whole eagle-brood still keeps
His sov'reignty, and rule, and majesty;
15 Blazing Hyperion on his orbed fire
Still sits, still snuffs the incense teeming up
From man to the Sun's God: yet unsecure;
For as upon the earth dire prodigies[8]
Fright and perplex, so also shudders he:
20 Nor at dog's howl, or gloom-bird's even screech,
Or the familiar visitings of one
Upon the first toll of his passing bell:[9]
But horrors portion'd° to a giant nerve   *proportioned*
Make great Hyperion ache. His palace bright,
25 Bastion'd with pyramids of glowing gold,
And touch'd with shade of bronzed obelisks,
Glares a blood red through all the thousand courts,
Arches, and domes, and fiery galeries:
And all its curtains of Aurorian clouds
30 Flush angerly: when he would taste the wreaths
Of incense breath'd aloft from sacred hills,
Instead of sweets, his ample palate takes
Savour of poisonous brass, and metals sick.

---

7. Cf. the angel Raphael's words as he begins to recount to Adam the history of the rebellion in heaven: "what surmounts the reach / Of human sense, I shall delineate so, / By lik'ning spiritual to corporal forms" (*Paradise Lost* 5.571–73).
8. Terrifying omens.
9. Lines 20–22 might be paraphrased: "Not, how- ever, at such portents as a dog's howl or the eve- ning screech of the owl or with the well-known feelings ['visitings'] of someone when he hears the first stroke of his own death knell." It had been the English custom to ring the church bell when a per- son was close to death, to invite hearers to pray for his departing soul.

Wherefore when harbour'd in the sleepy west,
35 After the full completion of fair day,
For rest divine upon exalted couch
And slumber in the arms of melody,
He paces through the pleasant hours of ease,
With strides colossal, on from hall to hall;
40 While, far within each aisle and deep recess,
His winged minions° in close clusters stand   *followers*
Amaz'd, and full of fear; like anxious men
Who on a wide plain gather in sad troops,
When earthquakes jar their battlements and towers.
45 Even now, while Saturn, rous'd from icy trance,
Goes, step for step, with Thea from yon woods,
Hyperion, leaving twilight in the rear,
Is sloping to the threshold of the west.
Thither we tend."—Now in clear light I stood,
50 Reliev'd from the dusk vale. Mnemosyne
Was sitting on a square edg'd polish'd stone,
That in its lucid depth reflected pure
Her priestess-garments. My quick eyes ran on
From stately nave to nave, from vault to vault,
55 Through bowers of fragrant and enwreathed light,
And diamond paved lustrous long arcades.
Anon rush'd by the bright Hyperion;
His flaming robes stream'd out beyond his heels,
And gave a roar, as if of earthly fire,
60 That scar'd away the meek ethereal hours
And made their dove-wings tremble: on he flared[1]

July–Sept. 1819   1857

This living hand, now warm and capable[1]

This living hand, now warm and capable
Of earnest grasping, would, if it were cold
And in the icy silence of the tomb,
So haunt thy days and chill thy dreaming nights
5 That thou would wish thine own heart dry of blood,
So in my veins red life might stream again,
And thou be conscience-calm'd. See, here it is—
I hold it towards you.

1819   1898

1. The manuscript breaks off at this point.
1. These lines, first published in H. B. Forman's edition of Keats's poems in 1898, were written on a sheet that later formed part of the draft of Keats's unfinished satire *The Jealousies*. They have been a key text in late-20th-century critical and theoretical discussions of interpretation. Readings range from the personal and autobiographical—Keats addressing a loved one (Fanny Brawne) or his posthumous readers (e.g., users of this Norton anthology)—to the fictionalized and dramatic (e.g., a fragment of a speech intended for the deranged Ludolph toward the end of Keats's and Charles Brown's never-produced tragedy *Otho the Great*). In their lyric character the lines are included in anthologies of love poetry. In their dramatic character they are described by critics as, for example, "ghoulishly aggressive."

Letters   Keats's letters serve as a running commentary on his life, reading, thinking, and writing. They are, in his career, the equivalent of the essays, prefaces, and defenses of poetry produced by his contemporaries. His early reputation as a poet of pure luxury, sensation, and art for art's sake has undergone a radical change since, in the twentieth century, critics began to pay close attention to the letters. For Keats thought hard and persistently about life and art, and any seed of an ethical or critical idea that he picked up from his contemporaries (in particular, Hazlitt, Coleridge, Wordsworth) instantly germinated and flourished in the rich soil of his imagination. What T. S. Eliot said about the Metaphysical poets applies to Keats in his letters: his "mode of feeling was directly and freshly altered by [his] reading and thought." And like Donne, he looked not only into the heart but, literally, "into the cerebral cortex, the nervous system, and the digestive tract." A number of Keats's casual comments on the poet and on poetry included here—especially those dealing with "negative capability" and the kind of imaginative identification with someone or something outside ourselves that we now call empathy—have become standard points of reference in aesthetic theory. But Keats regarded nothing that he said as final; each statement constituted only a stage in his continuing exploration into what he called "the mystery."

The text printed here is that of the edition of the *Letters* by Hyder E. Rollins (1958), which reproduces the original manuscripts precisely.

LETTERS

To Benjamin Bailey[1]

[THE AUTHENTICITY OF THE IMAGINATION]

[November 22, 1817]

My dear Bailey,

* * * O I wish I was as certain of the end of all your troubles as that of your momentary start about the authenticity of the Imagination. I am certain of nothing but of the holiness of the Heart's affections and the truth of Imagination—What the imagination seizes as Beauty must be truth[2]—whether it existed before or not—for I have the same Idea of all our Passions as of Love they are all in their sublime, creative of essential Beauty—In a Word, you may know my favorite Speculation by my first Book and the little song[3] I sent in my last—which is a representation from the fancy of the probable mode of operating in these Matters—The Imagination may be compared to Adam's dream[4]—he awoke and found it truth. I am the more zealous in this affair, because I have never yet been able to perceive how any thing can be known for truth by consequitive reasoning[5]—and yet it must be—Can it be that even

1. One of Keats's closest friends. Keats had stayed with him the month before at Oxford, where Bailey was an undergraduate.
2. At the close of "Ode on a Grecian Urn," Keats also grapples with these categories. Where Keats uses "truth" we might substitute the words *real* or *reality*.
3. The song was "O Sorrow," from book 4 of

Endymion.
4. In Milton's *Paradise Lost* 8.452–90 Adam dreams that Eve has been created and awakes to find her real. Adam also describes an earlier prefigurative dream in the same work, 8.283–311.
5. Consecutive reasoning—reasoning that moves by logical steps.

the greatest Philosopher ever ~~when~~ arrived at his goal without putting aside numerous objections—However it may be, O for a Life of Sensations[6] rather than of Thoughts! It is "a Vision in the form of Youth" a Shadow of reality to come—and this consideration has further conv[i]nced me for it has come as auxiliary to another favorite Speculation of mine, that we shall enjoy ourselves here after by having what we called happiness on Earth repeated in a finer tone and so repeated[7]—And yet such a fate can only befall those who delight in sensation rather than hunger as you do after Truth—Adam's dream will do here and seems to be a conviction that Imagination and its empyreal[8] reflection is the same as human Life and its spiritual repetition. But as I was saying— the simple imaginative Mind may have its rewards in the repeti[ti]on of its own silent Working coming continually on the spirit with a fine suddenness— to compare great things with small—have you never by being surprised with an old Melody—in a delicious place—by a delicious voice, fe[l]t over again your very speculations and surmises at the time it first operated on your soul— do you not remember forming to yourself the singer's face more beautiful [than] it was possible and yet with the elevation of the Moment you did not think so—even then you were mounted on the Wings of Imagination so high— that the Prototype must be here after—that delicious face you will see—What a time! I am continually running away from the subject—sure this cannot be exactly the case with a complex Mind—one that is imaginative and at the same time careful of its fruits—who would exist partly on sensation partly on thought—to whom it is necessary that years should bring the philosophic Mind[9]—such an one I consider your's and therefore it is necessary to your eternal Happiness that you not only drink this old Wine of Heaven which I shall call the redigestion of our most ethereal Musings on Earth; but also increase in knowledge and know all things. I am glad to hear you are in a fair Way for Easter—you will soon get through your unpleasant reading and then!—but the world is full of troubles and I have not much reason to think myself pesterd with many—I think Jane or Marianne has a better opinion of me than I deserve—for really and truly I do not think my Brothers illness connected with mine—you know more of the real Cause than they do—nor have I any chance of being rack'd as you have been[1]—you perhaps at one time thought there was such a thing as Worldly Happiness to be arrived at, at certain periods of time marked out—you have of necessity from your dispo- sition been thus led away—I scarcely remember counting upon any Happi- ness—I look not for it if it be not in the present hour—nothing startles me beyond the Moment. The setting sun will always set me to rights—or if a Sparrow come before my Window I take part in its existence and pick about the Gravel. The first thing that strikes me on hea[r]ing a Misfortune having befalled another is this. "Well it cannot be helped.—he will have the pleasure of trying the resourses of his spirit, and I beg now my dear Bailey that here- after should you observe any thing cold in me not to [put] it to the account of heartlessness but abstraction—for I assure you I sometimes feel not the influence of a Passion or Affection during a whole week—and so long this

6. Probably not only sense experiences but also the intuitive perceptions of truths, as opposed to truth achieved by consecutive reasoning.
7. Cf. the "Pleasure Thermometer" in *Endymion* 1.777ff. (p. 885).
8. Heavenly.
9. An echo of Wordsworth, "Ode: Intimations of Immortality," line 187.
1. Keats's friends Jane and Mariane Reynolds feared that his ill health at this time threatened tuberculosis, from which his brother Tom was suf- fering. Bailey had recently experienced pain (been "racked") because of an unsuccessful love affair.

sometimes continues I begin to suspect myself and the genuiness of my feelings at other times—thinking them a few barren Tragedy-tears. * * *
Your affectionate friend
John Keats—

To George and Thomas Keats

[NEGATIVE CAPABILITY]

[December 21, 27 (?), 1817]

My dear Brothers

I must crave your pardon for not having written ere this. * * * I spent Friday evening with Wells[1] & went the next morning to see *Death on the Pale horse.* It is a wonderful picture, when West's[2] age is considered; But there is nothing to be intense upon; no women one feels mad to kiss; no face swelling into reality. the excellence of every Art is its intensity, capable of making all disagreeables evaporate, from their being in close relationship with Beauty & Truth[3]—Examine King Lear & you will find this examplified throughout; but in this picture we have unpleasantness without any momentous depth of speculation excited, in which to bury its repulsiveness—The picture is larger than Christ rejected—I dined with Haydon[4] the sunday after you left, & had a very pleasant day, I dined too (for I have been out too much lately) with Horace Smith & met his two Brothers with Hill & Kingston & one Du Bois,[5] they only served to convince me, how superior humour is to wit in respect to enjoyment—These men say things which make one start, without making one feel, they are all alike; their manners are alike; they all know fashionables; they have a mannerism in their very eating & drinking, in their mere handling a Decanter—They talked of Kean[6] & his low company—Would I were with that company instead of yours said I to myself! I know such like acquaintance will never do for me & yet I am going to Reynolds, on wednesday—Brown & Dilke[7] walked with me & back from the Christmas pantomime.[8] I had not a dispute but a disquisition with Dilke, on various subjects; several things dovetailed in my mind, & at once it struck me, what quality went to form a Man of Achievement especially in Literature & which Shakespeare possessed so enormously—I mean *Negative Capability,*[9] that is when man is capable of being in uncer-

1. Charles Wells, a former schoolmate of Tom Keats.
2. Benjamin West (1738–1820), painter of historical pictures, was an American who moved to England and became president of the Royal Academy. The *Christ Rejected* mentioned a few sentences farther on is also by West.
3. Keats's solution to a problem at least as old as Aristotle's *Poetics*: why do we take pleasure in the aesthetic representation of a subject that in life would be ugly or painful?
4. Keats's close friend Benjamin Haydon, painter of large-scale historical and religious pictures.
5. Smith was one of the best-known literary wits of the day; the others mentioned were men of letters or of literary interests.
6. Edmund Kean, noted Shakespearean actor. His popularity in the early 19th century was contentious because he made no secret of his humble class origins. Keats had written an article on Kean

for the *Champion.*
7. Charles Armitage Brown, John Hamilton Reynolds, and Charles Wentworth Dilke were all writers and friends of Keats. Keats interrupted the writing of this letter after the dash; beginning with "Brown & Dilke" he is writing several days after the preceding sentences.
8. Christmas pantomimes were performed each year at Drury Lane and Covent Garden theaters.
9. This famous and elusive phrase has been much discussed. Keats coins it so as to distinguish between, on the one hand, a poetry that is evidently shaped by the writer's personal interests and beliefs and, on the other hand, a poetry of impersonality that records the writer's receptivity to the "uncertainties" of experience. This second kind of poetry, in which a sense of beauty overcomes considerations of truth versus falsehood, is that produced by the poet of "negative capability." Cf. Keats's dislike, in his letter to John Hamilton Reyn-

tainties, Mysteries, doubts, without any irritable reaching after fact & reason—Coleridge, for instance, would let go by a fine isolated verisimilitude caught from the Penetralium[1] of mystery, from being incapable of remaining content with half knowledge. This pursued through Volumes would perhaps take us no further than this, that with a great poet the sense of Beauty overcomes every other consideration, or rather obliterates all consideration.

Shelley's poem[2] is out & there are words about its being objected too, as much as Queen Mab was. Poor Shelley I think he has his Quota of good qualities, in sooth la!! Write soon to your most sincere friend & affectionate Brother

John

To John Hamilton Reynolds[1]

[WORDSWORTH'S POETRY]

[February 3, 1818]

My dear Reynolds,

* * * It may be said that we ought to read our Contemporaries. that Wordsworth &c should have their due from us. but for the sake of a few fine imaginative or domestic passages, are we to be bullied into a certain Philosophy engendered in the whims of an Egotist—Every man has his speculations, but every man does not brood and peacock over them till he makes a false coinage and deceives himself—Many a man can travel to the very bourne[2] of Heaven, and yet want confidence to put down his halfseeing. Sancho[3] will invent a Journey heavenward as well as any body. We hate poetry that has a palpable design upon us—and if we do not agree, seems to put its hand in its breeches pocket.[4] Poetry should be great & unobtrusive, a thing which enters into one's soul, and does not startle it or amaze it with itself but with its subject.—How beautiful are the retired flowers! how would they lose their beauty were they to throng into the highway crying out, "admire me I am a violet! dote upon me I am a primrose! Modern poets differ from the Elizabethans in this. Each of the moderns like an Elector of Hanover governs his petty state, & knows how many straws are swept daily from the Causeways in all his dominions & has a continual itching that all the Housewives should have their coppers well scoured: the antients were ~~Emperors of large~~ Emperors of vast Provinces, they had only heard of the remote ones and scarcely cared to visit them.—I will cut all this—I will have no more of Wordsworth or Hunt[5] in particular—Why should we be of the tribe of Manasseh, when we can wander with Esau?[6] why should we kick

olds, February 3, 1818, of "poetry that has a palpable design upon us" (p. 943).
1. The Latin *penetralia* signified the innermost and most secret parts of a temple.
2. *Laon and Cythna* (1817), whose treatment of incest created scandal and which had to be withdrawn by the author. Shelley revised and republished it as *The Revolt of Islam* (1818). In *Queen Mab* (1813) Shelley had presented a radical program for the achievement of a millennial earthly state through the elimination of "kings, priests, and statesmen."
1. A close friend who was at this time an insurance

clerk and also an able poet and man of letters.
2. Boundary.
3. Sancho Panza, the earthy squire in Cervantes's *Don Quixote*.
4. I.e., sulks and refuses to interact with.
5. Leigh Hunt, a poet who earlier had strongly influenced Keats's style.
6. I.e., why should we carry on a conventional way of life (as did the tribe of Manasseh in Old Testament history) when we can become adventurers (like Esau, who sold his birthright in Genesis 25.29–34 and became an outlaw).

944 / JOHN KEATS

against the Pricks, when we can walk on Roses? Why should we be owls, when we can be Eagles? Why be teased with "nice Eyed wagtails," when we have in sight "the Cherub Contemplation"?[7]—Why with Wordsworths "Matthew with a bough of wilding in his hand" when we can have Jacques "under an oak &c"[8]—The secret of the Bough of Wilding will run through your head faster than I can write it—Old Matthew spoke to him some years ago on some nothing, & because he happens in an Evening Walk to imagine the figure of the old man—he must stamp it down in black & white, and it is henceforth sacred—I don't mean to deny Wordsworth's grandeur & Hunt's merit, but I mean to say we need not be teazed with grandeur & merit—when we can have them uncontaminated & unobtrusive. Let us have the old Poets, & robin Hood[9] Your letter and its sonnets gave me more pleasure than will the 4th Book of Childe Harold[1] & the whole of any body's life & opinions. * * *

Y^r sincere friend and Coscribbler
John Keats.

To John Taylor[1]

[KEATS'S AXIOMS IN POETRY]

[February 27, 1818]

My dear Taylor,

Your alteration strikes me as being a great improvement—the page looks much better. * * * It is a sorry thing for me that any one should have to overcome Prejudices in reading my Verses—that affects me more than any hypercriticism on any particular Passage. In *Endymion* I have most likely but moved into the Go-cart from the leading strings.[2] In Poetry I have a few Axioms, and you will see how far I am from their Centre. 1st I think Poetry should surprise by a fine excess and not by Singularity—it should strike the Reader as a wording of his own highest thoughts, and appear almost a Remembrance—2nd Its touches of Beauty should never be half way therby making the reader breathless instead of content: the rise, the progress, the setting of imagery should like the Sun come natural natural too him—shine over him and set soberly although in magnificence leaving him in the Luxury of twilight—but it is easier to think what Poetry should be than to write it—and this leads me on to another axiom. That if Poetry comes not as naturally as the Leaves to a tree it had better not come at all. However it may be with me I cannot help looking into new countries with "O for a Muse of fire to ascend!"[3]—If Endymion serves me as a Pioneer perhaps I ought to be content. I have great reason to be content, for thank God I can read and perhaps

---

7. Milton, "Il Penseroso," line 54. "Nice Eyed wagtails": from Hunt's *Nymphs*.
8. Shakespeare's *As You Like It* 2.1.31. The Wordsworth phrase is from his poem "The Two April Mornings." A "wilding" is a wild apple tree.
9. A reference to two sonnets on Robin Hood, written by Reynolds, which he had sent to Keats.
1. Canto 4 of Byron's *Childe Harold's Pilgrimage* was being eagerly awaited by English readers.
1. Partner in the publishing firm of Taylor and Hessey, to whom Keats wrote this letter while

Endymion was being put through the press.
2. Go-carts were the wheeled walkers in which 19th-century toddlers learned to walk. Leading-strings were the harnesses with which they were guided and supported while they learned. Keats's point appears to be that as a poet he has not advanced and may even have regressed in *Endymion*.
3. Altered from Shakespeare's *Henry V*, Prologue, line 1.

understand Shakspeare to his depths, and I have I am sure many friends, who, if I fail, will attribute any change in my Life and Temper to Humbleness rather than to Pride—to a cowering under the Wings of great Poets rather than to a Bitterness that I am not appreciated. I am anxious to get Endymion printed that I may forget it and proceed. * * *

Your sincere and obligᵈ friend

John Keats—

P.S. You shall have a sho[r]t *Preface* in good time—

To John Hamilton Reynolds

[MILTON, WORDSWORTH, AND THE CHAMBERS OF HUMAN LIFE]

[May 3, 1818]

My dear Reynolds.

* * * Were I to study physic or rather Medicine again,—I feel it would not make the least difference in my Poetry; when the Mind is in its infancy a Bias is in reality a Bias, but when we have acquired more strength, a Bias becomes no Bias. Every department of knowledge we see excellent and calculated towards a great whole. I am so convinced of this, that I am glad at not having given away my medical Books, which I shall again look over to keep alive the little I know thitherwards; and moreover intend through you and Rice to become a sort of Pip-civilian.¹ An extensive knowledge is needful to thinking people—it takes away the heat and fever; and helps, by widening speculation, to ease the Burden of the Mystery:² a thing I begin to understand a little, and which weighed upon you in the most gloomy and true sentence in your Letter. The difference of high Sensations with and without knowledge appears to me this—in the latter case we are falling continually ten thousand fathoms deep and being blown up again without wings³ and with all [the] horror of a ~~Case~~ bare shoulderd Creature—in the former case, our shoulders are fledged⁴ and we go thro' the same ~~Fir~~ air and space without fear. * * *

You say "I fear there is little chance of any thing else in this life." You seem by that to have been going through with a more painful and acute ~~test~~ zest the same labyrinth that I have—I have come to the same conclusion thus far. My Branchings out therefrom have been numerous: one of them is the consideration of Wordsworth's genius and as a help, in the manner of gold being the meridian Line of worldly wealth,—how he differs from Milton.⁵—And here I have nothing but surmises, from an uncertainty whether Miltons apparently less anxiety for Humanity proceeds from his seeing further or no than Wordsworth: And whether Wordsworth has in truth epic passions, and martyrs himself to the human heart, the main region of his song⁶—In regard to his genius alone—we find what he says true as far as we have experienced and we can

---

1. Apparently "a small-scale layman." James Rice, a lawyer, was one of Keats's favorite friends.
2. Wordsworth, "Tintern Abbey," line 38.
3. Recalls the description of Satan's flight through Chaos (Milton, *Paradise Lost* 2.933–34).
4. Grow wings.
5. I.e., as gold is the standard of material wealth (in the way that the meridian line of Greenwich

Observatory, England, is the reference for measuring degrees of longitude), so Milton is the standard of poetic value, by which we may measure Wordsworth.
6. In the Prospectus to *The Recluse*, Wordsworth, laying out his poetic program, had identified "the Mind of Man" as "My haunt, and the main region of my song" (lines 40–41).

judge no further but by larger experience—for axioms in philosophy are not axioms until they are proved upon our pulses: We read fine——things but never feel them to [the] full until we have gone the same steps as the Author.— I know this is not plain; you will know exactly my meaning when I say, that now I shall relish Hamlet more than I ever have done—Or, better—You are sensible no man can set down Venery[7] as a bestial or joyless thing until he is sick of it and therefore all philosophizing on it would be mere wording. Until we are sick, we understand not;—in fine, as Byron says, "Knowledge is Sorrow";[8] and I go on to say that "Sorrow is Wisdom"—and further for aught we can know for certainty! "Wisdom is folly." * * *

I will return to Wordsworth—whether or no he has an extended vision or a circumscribed grandeur—whether he is an eagle in his nest, or on the wing— And to be more explicit and to show you how tall I stand by the giant, I will put down a simile of human life as far as I now perceive it; that is, to the point to which I say we both have arrived at—Well—I compare human life to a large Mansion of Many Apartments, two of which I can only describe, the doors of the rest being as yet shut upon me—The first we step into we call the infant or thoughtless Chamber, in which we remain as long as we do not think—We remain there a long while, and notwithstanding the doors of the second Chamber remain wide open, showing a bright appearance, we care not to hasten to it; but are at length imperceptibly impelled by the awakening of the thinking principle—within us—we no sooner get into the second Chamber, which I shall call the Chamber of Maiden-Thought,[9] than we become intoxicated with the light and the atmosphere, we see nothing but pleasant wonders, and think of delaying there for ever in delight: However among the effects this breathing is father of is that tremendous one of sharpening one's vision into the ~~head~~ heart and nature of Man—of convincing ones nerves that the World is full of Misery and Heartbreak, Pain, Sickness and oppression—whereby This Chamber of Maiden Thought becomes gradually darken'd and at the same time on all sides of it many doors are set open—but all dark—all leading to dark passages—We see not the ballance of good and evil. We are in a Mist—We are now in that state—We feel the "burden of the Mystery," To this point was Wordsworth come, as far as I can conceive when he wrote "Tintern Abbey" and it seems to me that his Genius is explorative of those dark Passages. Now if we live, and go on thinking, we too shall explore them. he is a Genius and superior [to] us, in so far as he can, more than we, make discoveries, and shed a light in them—Here I must think Wordsworth is deeper than Milton— though I think it has depended more upon the general and gregarious advance of intellect, than individual greatness of Mind—From the Paradise Lost and the other Works of Milton, I hope it is not too presuming, even between ourselves to say, his Philosophy, human and divine, may be tolerably understood by one not much advanced in years, In his time englishmen were just emancipated from a great superstition—and Men had got hold of certain points and resting places in reasoning which were too newly born to be doubted, and too much ~~oppressed~~ opposed by the Mass of Europe not to be thought etherial and authentically divine—who could gainsay his ideas on virtue, vice, and Chastity in Comus, just at the time of the dismissal of Codpieces[1] and a hundred other disgraces? who would not rest satisfied with his

7. Sexual indulgence.
8. *Manfred* 1.1.10: "Sorrow is knowledge."
9. I.e., innocent thought, with the implication (as

in "maiden voyage") of a first undertaking.
1. In the 15th and 16th centuries, the codpiece was a flap, often ornamental, that covered an open-

hintings at good and evil in the Paradise Lost, when just free from the inquisition and burrning in Smithfield?[2] The Reformation produced such immediate and great benefits, that Protestantism was considered under the immediate eye of heaven, and its own remaining Dogmas and superstitions, then, as it were, regenerated, constituted those resting places and seeming sure points of Reasoning—from that I have mentioned, Milton, whatever he may have thought in the sequel,[3] appears to have been content with these by his writings—He did not think into the human heart, as Wordsworth has done—Yet Milton as a Philosop[h]er, had sure as great powers as Wordsworth—What is then to be inferr'd? O many things—It proves there is really a grand march of intellect—, It proves that a mighty providence subdues the mightiest Minds to the service of the time being, whether it be in human Knowledge or Religion— * * * Tom[4] has spit a leetle blood this afternoon, and that is rather a damper—but I know—the truth is there is something real in the World Your third Chamber of Life shall be a lucky and a gentle one—stored with the wine of love—and the Bread of Friendship— * * *

Your affectionate friend
John Keats.

To Richard Woodhouse[1]

[A POET HAS NO IDENTITY]

[October 27, 1818]

My dear Woodhouse,

Your Letter gave me a great satisfaction; more on account of its friendliness, than any relish of that matter in it which is accounted so acceptable in the "genus irritabile"[2] The best answer I can give you is in a clerklike manner to make some observations on two principle points, which seem to point like indices into the midst of the whole pro and con, about genius, and views and atchievements and ambition and cœtera. 1st As to the poetical Character itself, (I mean that sort of which, if I am any thing, I am a Member; that sort distinguished from the wordsworthian or egotistical sublime; which is a thing per se and stands alone) it is not itself—it has no self—it is every thing and nothing—It has no character—it enjoys light and shade; it lives in gusto,[3] be it foul or fair, high or low, rich or poor, mean or elevated—It has as much delight in conceiving an Iago as an Imogen.[4] What shocks the virtuous philosop[h]er, delights the camelion[5] Poet. It does no harm from its relish of the dark side of things any more than from its taste for the bright one; because they both end in speculation.[6] A Poet is the most unpoetical of any thing in

ing in the front of men's breeches. In Milton's masque the chastity of a young lady is put to the proof by the evil enchanter Comus.
2. An open place northwest of the walls of the City of London where, in the 16th century, heretics were burned.
3. Later on.
4. Keats's younger brother, then eighteen, who was dying of tuberculosis.
1. A young lawyer with literary interests who early recognized Keats's talents and prepared, or preserved, manuscript copies of many of his poems

and letters.
2. "The irritable race," a phrase Horace had applied to poets (Epistles 2.2.102).
3. Hazlitt had defined gusto in his 1816 essay as "power or passion" (p. 538).
4. Iago is the villain in Shakespeare's Othello and Imogen the virtuous heroine in his Cymbeline.
5. The chameleon is a lizard that camouflages itself by changing its color to match its surroundings.
6. I.e., without affecting our practical judgment or actions. Cf. Keats's discussion of the poet of

existence; because he has no Identity—he is continually in for[7]—and filling some other Body—The Sun, the Moon, the Sea and Men and Women who are creatures of impulse are poetical and have about them an unchangeable attribute—the poet has none; no identity—he is certainly the most unpoetical of all God's Creatures. If then he has no self, and if I am a Poet, where is the Wonder that I should say I would write no more? Might I not at that very instant [have] been cogitating on the Characters of saturn and Ops?[8] It is a wretched thing to confess; but is a very fact that not one word I ever utter can be taken for granted as an opinion growing out of my identical nature—how can it, when I have no nature? When I am in a room with People if I ever am free from speculating on creations of my own brain, then not myself goes home to myself: but the identity of every one in the room begins to to press upon me[9] that, I am in a very little time an[ni]hilated—not only among Men; it would be the same in a Nursery of children: I know not whether I make myself wholly understood: I hope enough so to let you see that no dependence is to be placed on what I said that day.

In the second place I will speak of my views, and of the life I purpose to myself—I am ambitious of doing the world some good: if I should be spared that may be the work of maturer years—in the interval I will assay to reach to as high a summit in Poetry as the nerve bestowed upon me will suffer. The faint conceptions I have of Poems to come brings the blood frequently into my forehead—All I hope is that I may not lose all interest in human affairs—that the solitary indifference I feel for applause even from the finest Spirits, will not blunt any acuteness of vision I may have. I do not think it will—I feel assured I should write from the mere yearning and fondness I have for the Beautiful even if my night's labours should be burnt every morning and no eye ever shine upon them. But even now I am perhaps not speaking from myself; but from some character in whose soul I now live. I am sure however that this next sentence is from myself. I feel your anxiety, good opinion and friendliness in the highest degree, and am

Your's most sincerely
John Keats

To George and Georgiana Keats[1]

[THE VALE OF SOUL-MAKING]

[February 14–May 3, 1819]

My dear Brother & Sister—

* * * I have this moment received a note from Haslam[2] in which he expects the death of his Father who has been for some time in a state of insensibility—

"negative capability" in his letter to George and Thomas Keats begun on December 21, 1817 (p. 942).
7. Instead of "in for," Keats may have intended to write "informing."
8. Characters in Keats's *Hyperion*. Woodhouse had recently written Keats to express concern at a remark by the poet that, because former writers had preempted the best poetic materials and styles, there was nothing new left for the modern poet.

9. Perhaps "*so* to press upon me."
1. Keats's brother and his wife, who had emigrated to Louisville, Kentucky, in 1818. This is part of a long letter that Keats wrote over a period of several months, and into which he transcribed several of his poems, including "Ode to Psyche." The date of this first extract is March 19.
2. William Haslam, a young businessman and close friend.

his mother bears up he says very well—I shall go to [town] tommorrow to see him. This is the world—thus we cannot expect to give way many hours to pleasure—Circumstances are like Clouds continually gathering and bursting— While we are laughing the seed of some trouble is put into he the wide arable land of events—while we are laughing it sprouts [it] grows and suddenly bears a poison fruit which we must pluck—Even so we have leisure to reason on the misfortunes of our friends; our own touch us too nearly for words. Very few men have ever arrived at a complete disinterestedness³ of Mind: very few have been influenced by a pure desire of the benefit of others—in the greater part of the Benefactors of & to Humanity some meretricious motive has sullied their greatness—some melodramatic scenery has facinated them—From the manner in which I feel Haslam's misfortune I perceive how far I am from any humble standard of disinterestedness—Yet this feeling ought to be carried to its highest pitch, as there is no fear of its ever injuring society—which it would do I fear pushed to an extremity—For in wild nature the Hawk would loose his Breakfast of Robins and the Robin his of Worms The Lion must starve as well as the swallow—The greater part of Men make their way with the same instinctiveness, the same unwandering eye from their purposes, the same animal eagerness as the Hawk—The Hawk wants a Mate, so does the Man—look at them both they set about it and procure on[e] in the same manner—They want both a nest and they both set about one in the same manner—they get their food in the same manner—The noble animal Man for his amusement smokes his pipe—the Hawk balances about the Clouds—that is the only difference of their leisures. This it is that makes the Amusement of Life—to a speculative Mind. I go among the Feilds and catch a glimpse of a stoat⁴ or a fieldmouse peeping out of the withered grass—the creature hath a purpose and its eyes are bright with it—I go amongst the buildings of a city and I see a Man hurrying along—to what? The Creature has a purpose and his eyes are bright with it. But then as Wordsworth says, "we have all one human heart"⁵— there is an ellectric fire in human nature tending to purify—so that among these human creature[s] there is continually some birth of new heroism—The pity is that we must wonder at it: as we should at finding a pearl in rubbish—I have no doubt that thousands of people never heard of have had hearts compl[l]etely disinterested: I can remember but two—Socrates and Jesus— their Histories evince it—What I heard a little time ago, Taylor observe with respect to Socrates, may be said of Jesus—That he was so great as man that though he transmitted no writing of his own to posterity, we have his Mind and his sayings and his greatness handed to us by others. It is to be lamented that the history of the latter was written and revised by Men interested in the pious frauds of Religion. Yet through all this I see his splendour. Even here though I myself am pursueing the same instinctive course as the veriest human animal you can think of—I am however young writing at random—straining at particles of light in the midst of a great darkness—without knowing the bearing of any one assertion of any one opinion. Yet may I not in this be free from sin? May there not be superior beings amused with any graceful, though instinctive attitude my mind [may] fall into, as I am entertained with the alertness of a Stoat or the anxiety of a Deer? Though a quarrel in the streets is a thing to be hated, the energies displayed in it are fine; the commonest Man

3. Transcendence of self-interest, of one's selfish instincts.
4. A weasel.
5. "The Old Cumberland Beggar," line 153.

shows a grace in his quarrel—By a superior being our reasoning[s] may take the same tone—though erroneous they may be fine—This is the very thing in which consists poetry; and if so it is not so fine a thing as philosophy—For the same reason that an eagle is not so fine a thing as a truth—Give me this credit—Do you not think I strive—to know myself? Give me this credit—and you will not think that on my own accou[n]t I repeat Milton's lines

> "How charming is divine Philosophy
> Not harsh and crabbed as dull fools suppose
> But musical as is Apollo's lute"—[6]

No—no for myself—feeling grateful as I do to have got into a state of mind to relish them properly—Nothing ever becomes real till it is experienced—Even a Proverb is no proverb to you till your Life has illustrated it— * * * * * * I have been reading lately two very different books Robertson's America and Voltaire's Siecle De Louis xiv[7] It is like walking arm and arm between Pizarro and the great-little Monarch.[8] In How lementabl[e] a case do we see the great body of the people in both instances: in the first, where Men might seem to inherit quiet of Mind from unsophisticated senses; from uncontamination of civilisation; and especially from their being as it were estranged from the mutual helps of Society and its mutual injuries—and thereby more immediately under the Protection of Providence—even there they had mortal pains to bear as bad; or even worse than Baliffs,[9] Debts and Poverties of civilised Life—The whole appears to resolve into this—that Man is originally "a poor forked creature"[1] subject to the same mischances as the beasts of the forest, destined to hardships and disquietude of some kind or other. If he improves by degrees his bodily accommodations and comforts—at each stage, at each accent there are waiting for him a fresh set of annoyances—he is mortal and there is still a heaven with its Stars abov[e] his head. The most interesting question that can come before us is, How far by the persevering endeavours of a seldom appearing Socrates Mankind may be made happy—I can imagine such happiness carried to an extreme—but what must it end in?—Death—and who could in such a case bear with death—the whole troubles of life which are now frittered away in a series of years, would the[n] be accumulated for the last days of a being who instead of hailing its approach, would leave this world as Eve left Paradise—But in truth I do not at all believe in this sort of perfectibility—the nature of the world will not admit of it—the inhabitants of the world will correspond to itself—Let the fish philosophise the ice away from the Rivers in winter time and they shall be at continual play in the tepid delight of summer. Look at the Poles and at the sands of Africa, Whirlpools and volcanoes—Let men exterminate them and I will say that they may arrive at earthly Happiness—The point at which Man may arrive is as far as the paralel state in inanimate nature and no further—For instance suppose a rose to have sensation, it blooms on a beautiful morning it enjoys itself—but there comes a cold wind, a hot sun—it can not escape it, it cannot destroy its annoyances—they are as native to the world as itself: no more can man be happy in

---

6. *Comus,* lines 475–77.
7. Two books of history, Voltaire's *Le Siècle de Louis XIV* (1751) and William Robertson's *The History of America* (1777). In this second extract from the journal-letter, Keats is writing toward the end of April (on the 21st or 28th).
8. Francisco Pizarro, the Spanish explorer whose

exploits are described in Robertson's *America.* The "Monarch" is Louis XIV of France.
9. Bailiffs: officers of the law whose duties included making arrests for bad debts.
1. Shakespeare's *King Lear* 3.4.95–97. Lear says of "Poor Tom," "Unaccommodated man is no more but such a poor, bare, forked animal as thou art."

spite, the world[l]y elements will prey upon his nature—The common cog-
nomen of this world among the misguided and superstitious is "a vale of tears"
from which we are to be redeemed by a certain arbitrary interposition of God
and taken to Heaven—What a little circumscribe[d] straightened notion! Call
the world if you Please "The vale of Soul-making" Then you will find out the
use of the world (I am speaking now in the highest terms for human nature
admitting it to be immortal which I will here take for granted for the purpose
of showing a thought which has struck me concerning it) I say "*Soul making*"
Soul as distinguished from an Intelligence—There may be intelligences or
sparks of the divinity in millions—but they are not Souls the till they acquire
identities, till each one is personally itself. I[n]telligences are atoms of perception—they know and they see and they are pure, in short they are God—
how then are Souls to be made? How then are these sparks which are God to
have identity given them—so as ever to possess a bliss peculiar to each ones
individual existence? How, but by the medium of a world like this? This point
I sincerely wish to consider because I think it a grander system of salvation
than the chrystean religion—or rather it is a system of Spirit-creation[2]—This
is effected by three grand materials acting the one upon the other for a series
of years—These three Materials are the *Intelligence*—the *human heart* (as
distinguished from intelligence or Mind) and the *World* or *Elemental space*
suited for the proper action of *Mind and Heart* on each other for the purpose
of forming the *Soul* or *Intelligence destined to possess the sense of Identity*. I
can scarcely express what I but dimly perceive—and yet I think I perceive it—
that you may judge the more clearly I will put it in the most homely form
possible—I will call the *world* a School instituted for the purpose of teaching
little children to read—I will call the *human heart* the *horn Book*[3] used in that
School—and I will call the *Child able to read, the Soul* made from that *school*
and its *hornbook*. Do you not see how necessary a World of Pains and troubles
is to school an Intelligence and make it a soul? A Place where the heart must
feel and suffer in a thousand diverse ways! Not merely is the Heart a Hornbook, It is the Minds Bible, it is the Minds experience, it is the teat from which
the Mind or intelligence sucks its identity—As various as the Lives of Men
are—so various become their souls, and thus does God make individual beings,
Souls, Identical Souls of the sparks of his own essence—This appears to me
a faint sketch of a system of Salvation which does not affront our reason and
humanity—I am convinced that many difficulties which christians labour
under would vanish before it—There is one wh[i]ch even now Strikes me—
the Salvation of Children—In them the Spark or intelligence returns to God
without any identity—it having had no time to learn of, and be altered by, the
heart—or seat of the human Passions—It is pretty generally suspected that
the chr[i]stian scheme has been coppied from the ancient persian and greek
Philosophers. Why may they not have made this simple thing even more simple
for common apprehension by introducing Mediators and Personages in the
same manner as in the hethen mythology abstractions are personified—Seri-

2. Keats is struggling for an analogy that will
embody his solution to the ancient riddle of evil,
as an alternative to what he understands to be the
Christian view: that evil exists as a test of the individual's worthiness of salvation in heaven, and this
world is only a proving ground for a later and better
life. Keats proposes that the function of the human
experience of sorrow and pain is to feed and discipline the formless and unstocked "intelligence"
that we possess at birth and thus to shape it into a
rich and coherent "identity," or "soul." This result
provides a justification ("salvation") for our suffering in terms of our earthly life: i.e., experience is
its own reward.
3. A child's primer, which used to consist of a
sheet of paper mounted on thin wood, protected
by a sheet of transparent horn.

ously I think it probable that this System of Soul-making—may have been the Parent of all the more palpable and personal Schemes of Redemption, among the Zoroastrians the Christians and the Hindoos. For as one part of the human species must have their carved Jupiter; so another part must have the palpable and named Mediatior and saviour, their Christ their Oromanes and their Vishnu[4]—If what I have said should not be plain enough, as I fear it may not be, I will [put] you in the place where I began in this series of thoughts—I mean, I began by seeing how man was formed by circumstances—and what are circumstances?—but touchstones of his heart—? and what are touch stones?—but proovings of his hearrt?[5]—and what are proovings of his heart but fortifiers or alterers of his nature? and what is his altered nature but his soul?—and what was his soul before it came into the world and had These provings and alterations and perfectionings?—An intelligences—without Identity—and how is this Identity to be made? Through the medium of the Heart? And how is the heart to become this Medium but in a world of Circumstances?—There now I think what with Poetry and Theology you may thank your Stars that my pen is not very long winded— * * *

This is the 3d of May & every thing is in delightful forwardness; the violets are not withered, before the peeping of the first rose; You must let me know every thing, how parcels go & come, what papers you have, & what Newspapers you want, & other things—God bless you my dear Brother & Sister

Your ever Affectionate Brother
John Keats—

To Fanny Brawne

[FANNY BRAWNE AS KEATS'S "FAIR STAR"]

[July 25, 1819]

My sweet Girl,

I hope you did not blame me much for not obeying your request of a Letter on Saturday: we have had four in our small room playing at cards night and morning leaving me no undisturb'd opportunity to write. Now Rice and Martin are gone I am at liberty. Brown to my sorrow confirms the account you give of your ill health. You cannot conceive how I ache to be with you: how I would die for one hour——for what is in the world? I say you cannot conceive; it is impossible you should look with such eyes upon me as I have upon you: it cannot be. Forgive me if I wander a little this evening, for I have been all day employ'd in a very abstr[a]ct Poem[1] and I am in deep love with you—two things which must excuse me. I have, believe me, not been an age in letting you take possession of me; the very first week I knew you I wrote myself your vassal; but burnt the Letter as the very next time I saw you I thought you manifested some dislike to me. If you should ever feel for Man at the first sight what I did for you, I am lost. Yet I should not quarrel with you, but hate myself if such a thing were to happen—only I should burst if the thing were not as fine

---

4. The deity who creates and preserves the world, in Hindu belief. Oromanes (Ahriman) was the principle of evil, locked in a persisting struggle with Ormazd, the principle of good, in the Zoroastrian

religion of ancient Persia.
5. I.e., experiences by which the human heart is put to the test.
1. Probably *The Fall of Hyperion.*

as a Man as you are as a Woman. Perhaps I am too vehement, then fancy me on my knees, especially when I mention a part of you Letter which hurt me; you say speaking of Mr. Severn[2] "but you must be satisfied in knowing that I admired you much more than your friend." My dear love, I cannot believe there ever was or ever could be any thing to admire in me especially as far as sight goes—I cannot be admired, I am not a thing to be admired. You are, I love you; all I can bring you is a swooning admiration of your Beauty. I hold that place among Men which snub-nos'd brunettes with meeting eyebrows do among women—they are trash to me—unless I should find one among them with a fire in her heart like the one that burns in mine. You absorb me in spite of myself—you alone: for I look not forward with any pleasure to what is call'd being settled in the world; I tremble at domestic cares—yet for you I would meet them, though if it would leave you the happier I would rather die than do so. I have two luxuries to brood over in my walks, your Loveliness and the hour of my death. O that I could have possession of them both in the same minute. I hate the world: it batters too much the wings of my self-will, and would I could take a sweet poison from your lips to send me out of it. From no others would I take it. I am indeed astonish'd to find myself so careless of all cha[r]ms but yours—remembring as I do the time when even a bit of ribband was a matter of interest with me. What softer words can I find for you after this—what it is I will not read. Nor will I say more here, but in a Postscript answer any thing else you may have mentioned in your Letter in so many words—for I am distracted with a thousand thoughts. I will imagine you Venus tonight and pray, pray, pray to your star like a Hethen.[3]

Your's ever, fair Star,
John Keats.

To Percy Bysshe Shelley[1]

[LOAD EVERY RIFT WITH ORE]

[August 16, 1820]

My dear Shelley,

I am very much gratified that you, in a foreign country, and with a mind almost over occupied, should write to me in the strain of the Letter beside me. If I do not take advantage of your invitation it will be prevented by a circumstance I have very much at heart to prophesy[2]—There is no doubt that an english winter would put an end to me, and do so in a lingering hateful manner, therefore I must either voyage or journey to Italy as a soldier marches up to a battery. My nerves at present are the worst part of me, yet they feel soothed when I think that come what extreme may, I shall not be destined to remain in one spot long enough to take a hatred of any four particular bed-posts. I am glad you take any pleasure in my poor Poem;[3]—which I would

2. Joseph Severn, who later looked after Keats in Rome during his final illness.
3. See Keats's sonnet "Bright star" (p. 898) for parallels to this and other remarks in the present letter.
1. Written in reply to a letter urging Keats (who was ill) to spend the winter with the Shelleys in Pisa.
2. His own death.
3. Keats's Endymion, Shelley had written, contains treasures, "though treasures poured forth with indistinct profusion." Keats here responds with advice in kind.

willingly take the trouble to unwrite, if possible, did I care so much as I have done about Reputation. I received a copy of the Cenci,[4] as from yourself from Hunt. There is only one part of it I am judge of; the Poetry, and dramatic effect, which by many spirits now a days is considered the mammon. A modern work it is said must have a purpose,[5] which may be the God—*an artist* must serve Mammon—he must have "self concentration" selfishness perhaps. You I am sure will forgive me for sincerely remarking that you might curb your magnanimity and be more of an artist, and "load every rift"[6] of your subject with ore. The thought of such discipline must fall like cold chains upon you, who perhaps never sat with your wings furl'd for six Months together. And is not this extraordina[r]y talk for the writer of Endymion? whose mind was like a pack of scattered cards—I am pick'd up and sorted to a pip.[7] My Imagination is a Monastry and I am its Monk—you must explain my metap[cs][8] to yourself. I am in expectation of Prometheus[9] every day. Could I have my own wish for its interest effected you would have it still in manuscript—or be but now putting an end to the second act. I remember you advising me not to publish my first-blights, on Hampstead heath—I am returning advice upon your hands. Most of the Poems in the volume I send you[1] have been written above two years, and would never have been publish'd but from a hope of gain; so you see I am inclined enough to take your advice now. I must exp[r]ess once more my deep sense of your kindness, adding my sincere thanks and respects for M[rs] Shelley. In the hope of soon seeing you I remain

most sincerely yours,
John Keats—

To Charles Brown[1]

[KEATS'S LAST LETTER]

Rome. 30 November 1820.

My dear Brown,

'Tis the most difficult thing in the world to me to write a letter. My stomach continues so bad, that I feel it worse on opening any book,—yet I am much better than I was in Quarantine.[2] Then I am afraid to encounter the proing and conning of any thing interesting to me in England. I have an habitual feeling of my real life having past, and that I am leading a posthumous existence. God knows how it would have been—but it appears to me—however, I will not speak of that subject. I must have been at Bedhampton nearly at the time you were writing to me from Chichester[3]—how unfortunate—and to pass

---

4. Shelley's blank-verse tragedy, *The Cenci*, had been published in the spring of 1820.
5. Wordsworth had said this in his Preface to *Lyrical Ballads*. For "Mammon" see Matthew 6.24 and Luke 16.13: "Ye cannot serve God and mammon."
6. From Spenser's description of the Cave of Mammon in *The Faerie Queene* 2.7.28: "With rich metall loaded every rifte."
7. Perfectly ordered; all the suits in the deck matched up ("pips" are the conventional spots on playing cards).
8. Metaphysics.
9. *Prometheus Unbound*, of which Shelley had promised Keats a copy.

1. Keats's volume of 1820, including *Lamia, The Eve of St. Agnes*, and the odes. When Shelley drowned he had this small book open in his pocket.
1. Written to Keats's friend Charles Armitage Brown from the house on the Spanish Steps, the Piazza di Spagna, where Keats was being tended in his mortal illness by the devoted Joseph Severn.
2. When it landed at Naples, Keats's ship had been quarantined for ten miserably hot days.
3. Bedhampton and Chichester are both near the harbor town of Portsmouth, where Keats had embarked for Naples two months before.

on the river too! There was my star predominant![4] I cannot answer any thing in your letter, which followed me from Naples to Rome, because I am afraid to look it over again. I am so weak (in mind) that I cannot bear the sight of any hand writing of a friend I love so much as I do you. Yet I ride the little horse,—and, at my worst, even in Quarantine, summoned up more puns, in a sort of desperation, in one week than in any year of my life. There is one thought enough to kill me—I have been well, healthy, alert &c, walking with her[5]—and now—the knowledge of contrast, feeling for light and shade, all that information (primitive sense) necessary for a poem are great enemies to the recovery of the stomach. There, you rogue, I put you to the torture,—but you must bring your philosophy to bear—as I do mine, really—or how should I be able to live? D[r] Clarke is very attentive to me; he says, there is very little the matter with my lungs, but my stomach, he says, is very bad. I am well disappointed in hearing good news from George,—for it runs in my head we shall all die young. I have not written to x x x x x yet,[6] which he must think very neglectful; being anxious to send him a good account of my health, I have delayed it from week to week. If I recover, I will do all in my power to correct the mistakes made during sickness; and if I should not, all my faults will be forgiven. I shall write to x x x to-morrow, or next day. I will write to x x x x x in the middle of next week. Severn is very well, though he leads so dull a life with me. Remember me to all friends, and tell x x x x I should not have left London without taking leave of him, but from being so low in body and mind. Write to George as soon as you receive this, and tell him how I am, as far as you can guess;—and also a note to my sister—who walks about my imagination like a ghost—she is so like Tom.[7] I can scarcely bid you good bye even in a letter. I always made an awkward bow.

God bless you!

John Keats.

4. I.e., that was my usual luck. Cf. Shakespeare's *The Winter's Tale* 1.2.202–03: "It is a bawdy planet, that will strike / Where 'tis predominant."
5. Fanny Brawne.
6. Charles Brown, whose manuscript transcription is the only text for this letter, substituted crosses for the names of Keats's friends to conceal their identities.
7. Keats's youngest brother, whom Fanny, his only sister, closely resembled, had died of tuberculosis on December 1, 1818. George was John Keats's younger brother.

MARY WOLLSTONECRAFT SHELLEY
1797–1851

Percy Shelley wrote of his young wife, in the Dedication to *Laon and Cythna:*

> They say that thou wert lovely from thy birth,
> Of glorious parents, thou aspiring Child.

The "glorious parents" were William Godwin, the leading reformer and radical philosopher of the time, and Mary Wollstonecraft, famed as the author of *A Vindication of the Rights of Woman.* Wollstonecraft had died as the result of childbed fever incurred when she gave birth to Mary. Four years later Godwin married a widow, Mary Jane Clairmont, who soon had more than she could cope with trying to manage a family of five children of diverse parentage, amid increasing financial difficulties. Mary bitterly resented her stepmother but adored her father, who, she later said, "was my God—and I remember many childish instances of the excess of attachment I bore for him."

To ease the situation Mary was sent at the age of fourteen to live in Dundee, Scotland, with the family of William Baxter, an admirer of Godwin. After two pleasant years roaming the countryside, daydreaming, and writing stories (which have been lost), she returned in 1814 to her father's house in London. There, at the age of sixteen, she encountered the twenty-one-year-old poet Percy Bysshe Shelley, a devotee of Godwin's and an almost daily visitor, who had become estranged from his wife, Harriet. The young people fell in love; within a few months Mary was pregnant. On July 28 they ran off to Europe, taking with them her stepsister Jane Clairmont, who later changed her name to Claire. Mary described their happy though heedless wanderings through France, Switzerland, and Germany in her first book, *History of a Six Weeks' Tour*, published anonymously in 1817.

Back in England she gave premature birth to a daughter who lived only twelve days; a year later, in 1816, she bore a son, William. Shelley was usually in financial difficulties and often had to hide from his creditors to avoid arrest. Nonetheless, he contributed substantial sums (borrowed against his expectations as heir to his father, Sir Timothy) to Godwin's support, even though Godwin, despite his earlier advocacy of free love, refused to countenance Shelley's liaison with his daughter. Claire Clairmont meanwhile sought out and had a brief affair with Byron, who left her pregnant. In the spring of 1816, the Shelleys went abroad again with Claire, and at the latter's behest settled in Geneva, where Byron, accompanied by his physician and friend John William Polidori, set up residence in the nearby Villa Diodati. Mary Shelley tells us, in the introduction to *Frankenstein*, how her imagination was fired by their animated conversations during many social evenings. Encouraged and assisted by Shelley, she wrote *Frankenstein, or The Modern Prometheus*, her story of the man of science who, with catastrophic consequences, seeks to conquer nature, rival the divinity, and make new life, and who then withholds love from the life he has made. Since its anonymous publication in 1818, the novel has never been out of print. As the basis for innumerable plays (beginning in 1823) and movies (beginning in 1910), the story has become a central myth of modern Western culture.

The last six years of Mary's life with her husband, spent first in England and then in Italy, were filled with disasters. In October 1816 her sensitive and moody half-sister, Fanny Imlay, feeling herself an unloved burden on the Godwin household, committed suicide by an overdose of laudanum. Two months later Shelley's abandoned wife, Harriet, pregnant by an unknown lover, drowned herself in the Serpentine lake at Hyde Park in London. Shelley at once married Mary, but the courts denied him custody of Harriet's two children on the grounds that he was morally unfit to rear them. In September 1818 came the death of Mary's third baby, Clara, followed less than nine months later by the death from malaria, rampant in Rome at the time, of her adored son, William: "We came to Italy thinking to do Shelley's health good," Mary wrote bitterly, "but the Climate is not [by] any means warm enough to be of benefit to him & yet it is that that has destroyed my two children." These tragedies and her own ill health threw her into a depression that was only partly relieved by the birth of a second son, Percy Florence, in November 1819, and was deepened again the next spring by a miscarriage, as well as by the death of Claire's daughter, Allegra, whom Byron had placed in an Italian convent. Mary Shelley's habitual reserve, which masked the depth of her feelings, now became an apathy that caused her to withdraw, emotionally, from her husband. He became distant in turn, giving their friend Jane Williams the affection he denied his wife. When he was drowned in the Gulf of Spezia in July 1822, Mary was left with a persisting sense that she had failed her husband when he most needed her.

An impoverished widow of twenty-four, she returned to England with two ambitions. One was to disseminate the poetry and to rescue the character of Shelley, whom she idolized in memory; the other was to support by her writings her surviving son.

Her only financial assistance was a small allowance given her by Sir Timothy Shelley, which he threatened to cut off if she wrote a biography of his radical and scandal-haunted son. In the remaining quarter century of her life, Mary Shelley became a notable success as a professional woman of letters, publishing as "The Author of 'Frankenstein' " to comply with Sir Timothy's demand that she never use the Shelley name. After *Frankenstein* she wrote first a novella and then five more novels, of which the first two are the best. The novella, *Matilda*, written in 1819 but left in manuscript and not published until 1959, deals with the disastrous results of a father's incestuous passion for a daughter who resembles his dead wife. *Valperga* (1823), set in the Italian Middle Ages, is a historical romance about a quasi-Napoleonic figure who sacrifices his love and humanity to his lust for political power and about the two women whom he betrays. *The Last Man* (1826), set in the twenty-first century, tracing the progress of a plague that destroys all of humankind except for one survivor, the novel's narrator, almost equals *Frankenstein* in its analysis of human isolation. This novel also served Shelley as a forum in which to write autobiographically, for as she reflected in a diary entry, her own companions, like her ever-mourning narrator's, were gone, become "the people of the grave." She in fact arranged to endow two characters in the novel, her narrator's associates, with traits recognizably those of Percy Shelley and Byron, whose death in Greece occurred as she began writing.

Shelley all this while also contributed short stories to the gift books and literary annuals that were a publishing phenomenon during the 1820s and 1830s: deluxe volumes, gorgeously bound and lavishly illustrated, whose literary selections mingled pieces by esteemed authors—Scott, Hemans, Wordsworth, Coleridge—with contributions by the most fashionable members of the aristocracy. (All writers, however, were by the makers of gift books deemed less important than the visual artists: the stories or poems were often commissioned to accompany preexisting illustrations.) In 1835–39 she contributed to the *Cabinet Cyclopedia* five volumes of admirable biographical and critical studies of Continental authors. She also published several separate editions of her husband's writings in verse and prose. In accordance with what was then standard editorial procedure, she altered and emended Shelley's texts; she also added prefaces and notes, relating Shelley's writings to the circumstances of his life and thought, that have been an important resource for scholars of Romantic literature.

Not until old Sir Timothy died in 1844, leaving his title and estate to her son, did she find herself in comfortable circumstances. Her last years were cheered by the devotion of her son—who was an amiable man but entirely lacked the genius of his parents—and by her close friendship with Jane St. John, an admirer of Shelley's poetry, whom Sir Percy Florence married in 1848. Mary Shelley died three years later, at the age of fifty-three.

During her widowhood she craved social acceptance and status and, although she maintained liberal principles, tried hard, by adapting herself to conventional standards in her writings and her life, to work free from the onus of what her contemporaries regarded as the scandalous careers of her mother, father, and husband. In later life she wrote an apologia in her journal, dated October 21, 1838, that reveals the stresses of a life spent trying to measure up to the example, yet escape the bad reputations, of her parents and husband.

> In the first place, with regard to "the good cause"—the cause of the advancement of freedom and knowledge, of the rights of women, etc.—I am not a person of opinions. . . . Some have a passion for reforming the world; others do not cling to particular opinions. That my parents and Shelley were of the former class, makes me respect it. . . . For myself, I earnestly desire the good and enlightenment of my fellow creatures, and see all, in the present course, tending to the same, and rejoice; but I am not for violent extremes, which only brings on an injurious reaction. . . .

To hang back, as I do, brings a penalty. I was nursed and fed with a love of glory. To be something great and good was the precept given me by my father; Shelley reiterated it. . . . But Shelley died, and I was alone. . . . My total friend-lessness, my horror of pushing, and inability to put myself forward unless led, cherished and supported—all this has sunk me in a state of loneliness no other human being ever before, I believe, endured—except Robinson Crusoe. . . .

But I have never crouched to society—never sought it unworthily. If I have never written to vindicate the rights of women, I have ever defended women when oppressed. At every risk I have befriended and supported victims to the social system; but I make no boast, for in truth it is simple justice I perform; and so am I still reviled for being worldly. . . .

Such as I have written appears to me the exact truth.

From The Last Man

Introduction[1]

I visited Naples in the year 1818. On the 8th of December of that year, my companion and I crossed the Bay, to visit the antiquities which are scattered on the shores of Baiae.[2] The translucent and shining waters of the calm sea covered fragments of old Roman villas, which were interlaced by sea-weed, and received diamond tints from the chequering of the sun-beams; the blue and pellucid element was such as Galatea might have skimmed in her car of mother of pearl;[3] or Cleopatra, more fitly than the Nile, have chosen as the path of her magic ship.[4] Though it was winter, the atmosphere seemed more appropriate to early spring; and its genial warmth contributed to inspire those sensations of placid delight, which are the portion of every traveller, as he lingers, loath to quit the tranquil bays and radiant promontories of Baiae.

We visited the so called Elysian Fields and Avernus:[5] and wandered through various ruined temples, baths, and classic spots; at length we entered the gloomy cavern of the Cumaean Sibyl.[6] Our Lazzeroni[7] bore flaring torches, which shone red, and almost dusky, in the murky subterranean passages, whose darkness thirstily surrounding them, seemed eager to imbibe more and more of the element of light. We passed by a natural archway, leading to a second gallery, and enquired, if we could not enter there also. The guides pointed to the reflection of their torches on the water that paved it, leaving us

1. A contribution to Romantic-period investiga-tions of the nature of creativity, Shelley's Intro-duction to *The Last Man* (composed 1824 and published at the start of 1826) enigmatically iden-tifies the novel that follows as a strange blend of creative work, transcription, and translation, in which biography (Shelley's personal history of suf-fering) is subsumed by history and myth. Playing with the convention of Gothic romances that involves the protagonist's discovery of a decaying, all but illegible, manuscript from the past, Shelley leaves it an open question whether she is the editor or author of her "sibylline leaves."
2. Shelley begins with an actual event—the visit she and Percy paid in December 1818 to the ancient Roman resort of Baiae near Naples. See "Ode to the West Wind," lines 32–34 (p. 774).
3. Name given to a sea nymph in Greek mythol-ogy.
4. See Enobarbus's description of Cleopatra's ship

in Shakespeare's *Antony and Cleopatra* 2.2.197–203.
5. Sites near Naples named for places in mythol-ogy: the fields thought to be inhabited after death by those favored by the gods, and the entrance to the underworld, by tradition located at Lake Aver-nus.
6. The prophetess, inspired by the god Apollo, whose mad frenzies and cryptic accounts of future history are most famously described in the *Aeneid*, book 6. Other accounts describe how the sibyl wrote her prophecies on leaves, which she placed at the entrance to her cave; when the wind dis-persed them, they became unintelligible. Coleridge had titled his 1817 collection of poems *Sibylline Leaves* so as to allude, he said, "to the fragmentary and widely scattered state in which [the poems] have been long suffered to remain."
7. Generic term for the poor of Naples, here employed as guides.

to form our own conclusion; but adding it was a pity, for it led to the Sibyl's Cave. Our curiosity and enthusiasm were excited by this circumstance, and we insisted upon attempting the passage. As is usually the case in the prosecution of such enterprizes, the difficulties decreased on examination. We found, on each side of the humid pathway, "dry land for the sole of the foot."[8] At length we arrived at a large, desert, dark cavern, which the Lazzeroni assured us was the Sibyl's Cave. We were sufficiently disappointed—Yet we examined it with care, as if its blank, rocky walls could still bear trace of celestial visitant. On one side was a small opening. Whither does this lead? we asked: can we enter here?—"*Questo poi, no,*"[9]—said the wild looking savage, who held the torch; "you can advance but a short distance, and nobody visits it."

"Nevertheless, I will try it," said my companion; "it may lead to the real cavern. Shall I go alone, or will you accompany me?"

I signified my readiness to proceed, but our guides protested against such a measure. With great volubility, in their native Neapolitan dialect, with which we were not very familiar, they told us that there were spectres, that the roof would fall in, that it was too narrow to admit us, that there was a deep hole within, filled with water, and we might be drowned. My friend shortened the harangue, by taking the man's torch from him; and we proceeded alone.

The passage, which at first scarcely admitted us, quickly grew narrower and lower; we were almost bent double; yet still we persisted in making our way through it. At length we entered a wider space, and the low roof heightened; but, as we congratulated ourselves on this change, our torch was extinguished by a current of air, and we were left in utter darkness. The guides bring with them materials for renewing the light, but we had none—our only resource was to return as we came. We groped round the widened space to find the entrance, and after a time fancied that we had succeeded. This proved however to be a second passage, which evidently ascended. It terminated like the former; though something approaching to a ray, we could not tell whence, shed a very doubtful twilight in the space. By degrees, our eyes grew somewhat accustomed to this dimness, and we perceived that there was no direct passage leading us further; but that it was possible to climb one side of the cavern to a low arch at top, which promised a more easy path, from whence we now discovered that this light proceeded. With considerable difficulty we scrambled up, and came to another passage with still more of illumination, and this led to another ascent like the former.

After a succession of these, which our resolution alone permitted us to surmount, we arrived at a wide cavern with an arched dome-like roof. An aperture in the midst let in the light of heaven; but this was overgrown with brambles and underwood, which acted as a veil, obscuring the day, and giving a solemn religious hue to the apartment. It was spacious, and nearly circular, with a raised seat of stone, about the size of a Grecian couch, at one end. The only sign that life had been here, was the perfect snow-white skeleton of a goat, which had probably not perceived the opening as it grazed on the hill above, and had fallen headlong. Ages perhaps had elapsed since this catastrophe; and the ruin it had made above, had been repaired by the growth of vegetation during many hundred summers.

8. Allusion to Genesis 8.9: the dove sent by Noah from the ark finds "no rest for the sole of her foot." 9. Definitely not! (Italian).

The rest of the furniture of the cavern consisted of piles of leaves, fragments of bark, and a white filmy substance, resembling the inner part of the green hood which shelters the grain of the unripe Indian corn. We were fatigued by our struggles to attain this point, and seated ourselves on the rocky couch, while the sounds of tinkling sheep-bells, and shout of shepherd-boy, reached us from above.

At length my friend, who had taken up some of the leaves strewed about, exclaimed, "This *is* the Sibyl's cave; these are Sibylline leaves." On examination, we found that all the leaves, bark, and other substances were traced with written characters. What appeared to us more astonishing, was that these writings were expressed in various languages: some unknown to my companion, ancient Chaldee,[1] and Egyptian hieroglyphics, old as the Pyramids. Stranger still, some were in modern dialects, English and Italian. We could make out little by the dim light, but they seemed to contain prophecies, detailed relations of events but lately passed; names, now well known, but of modern date; and often exclamations of exultation or woe, of victory or defeat, were traced on their thin scant pages. This was certainly the Sibyl's Cave; not indeed exactly as Virgil describes it; but the whole of this land had been so convulsed by earthquake and volcano, that the change was not wonderful, though the traces of ruin were effaced by time; and we probably owed the preservation of these leaves, to the accident which had closed the mouth of the cavern, and the swift-growing vegetation which had rendered its sole opening impervious to the storm. We made a hasty selection of such of the leaves, whose writing one at least of us could understand; and then, laden with our treasure, we bade adieu to the dim hypaethric[2] cavern, and after much difficulty succeeded in rejoining our guides.

During our stay at Naples, we often returned to this cave, sometimes alone, skimming the sun-lit sea, and each time added to our store. Since that period, whenever the world's circumstance has not imperiously called me away, or the temper of my mind impeded such study, I have been employed in deciphering these sacred remains. Their meaning, wondrous and eloquent, has often repaid my toil, soothing me in sorrow, and exciting my imagination to daring flights, through the immensity of nature and the mind of man. For awhile my labours were not solitary; but that time is gone; and, with the selected and matchless companion of my toils, their dearest reward is also lost to me—

> Di mie tenere frondi altro lavoro
> Credea mostrarte; e qual fero pianeta
> Ne' nvidiò insieme, o mio nobil tesoro?[3]

I present the public with my latest discoveries in the slight Sibylline pages. Scattered and unconnected as they were, I have been obliged to add links, and model the work into a consistent form. But the main substance rests on the truths contained in these poetic rhapsodies, and the divine intuition which the Cumaean damsel obtained from heaven.

I have often wondered at the subject of her verses, and at the English dress of the Latin poet. Sometimes I have thought that, obscure and chaotic as they are, they owe their present form to me, their decipherer. As if we should give

---

1. Language of ancient Babylon, famed for its astronomical and astrological knowledge.
2. Open to the sky.
3. Quoted from the Italian of a sonnet by Petrarch

(1304–1374): "From my tender leaves, I thought to show you a different work, and what fierce planet ended our being together, oh, my noble treasure?"

to another artist, the painted fragments which form the mosaic copy of Raphael's Transfiguration in St. Peter's; he would put them together in a form, whose mode would be fashioned by his own peculiar mind and talent.[4] Doubtless the leaves of the Cumaean Sibyl have suffered distortion and diminution of interest and excellence in my hands. My only excuse for thus transforming them, is that they were unintelligible in their pristine condition.

My labours have cheered long hours of solitude, and taken me out of a world, which has averted its once benignant face from me, to one glowing with imagination and power. Will my readers ask how I could find solace from the narration of misery and woeful change? This is one of the mysteries of our nature, which holds full sway over me, and from whose influence I cannot escape. I confess, that I have not been unmoved by the development of the tale; and that I have been depressed, nay, agonized, at some parts of the recital, which I have faithfully transcribed from my materials. Yet such is human nature, that the excitement of mind was dear to me, and that the imagination, painter of tempest and earthquake, or, worse, the stormy and ruin-fraught passions of man, softened my real sorrows and endless regrets, by clothing these fictitious ones in that ideality, which takes the mortal sting from pain.

I hardly know whether this apology is necessary. For the merits of my adaptation and translation must decide how far I have well bestowed my time and imperfect powers, in giving form and substance to the frail and attenuated Leaves of the Sibyl.

1824   1826

The Mortal Immortal[1]

A Tale

JULY 16, 1833.—This is a memorable anniversary for me; on it I complete my three hundred and twenty-third year!

The Wandering Jew?[2]—certainly not. More than eighteen centuries have passed over his head. In comparison with him, I am a very young Immortal.

Am I, then, immortal? This is a question which I have asked myself, by day and night, for now three hundred and three years, and yet cannot answer it. I detected a gray hair amidst my brown locks this very day—that surely signifies decay. Yet it may have remained concealed there for three hundred years—for some persons have become entirely white-headed before twenty years of age.

I will tell my story, and my reader shall judge for me. I will tell my story, and so contrive to pass some few hours of a long eternity, become so wearisome to me. For ever! Can it be? to live for ever! I have heard of enchantments, in

4. The Italian Renaissance artist Raphael's painting of the transfiguration of Christ is copied in mosaic on the altarpiece of the Cappella Clementina of St. Peter's in Rome.
1. Cf. Keats's *Endymion* 1.843–44: "if this earthly love has power to make / Men's being mortal, immortal." "The Mortal Immortal" is one of the sixteen stories Shelley during her career contributed to *The Keepsake,* a gift book published annually between 1828 and 1857. This tale shares its first-person narrative form and interest in the

consequences of scientific ambition with Shelley's best-known novel. With a certain irony, given its original setting in a volume that its publisher marketed as a lasting memento of affection that might be purchased for a loved one, "The Mortal Immortal" also examines the question of whether love can survive time's ravages if beauty does not.
2. The man who, according to legend, taunted Christ on the road to the crucifixion and was therefore condemned to wander the earth until Judgment Day.

which the victims were plunged into a deep sleep, to wake, after a hundred years, as fresh as ever: I have heard of the Seven Sleepers[3]—thus to be immortal would not be so burthensome: but, oh! the weight of never-ending time— the tedious passage of the still-succeeding hours! How happy was the fabled Nourjahad![4]——But to my task.

All the world has heard of Cornelius Agrippa.[5] His memory is as immortal as his arts have made me. All the world has also heard of his scholar, who, unawares, raised the foul fiend during his master's absence, and was destroyed by him.[6] The report, true or false, of this accident, was attended with many inconveniences to the renowned philosopher. All his scholars at once deserted him—his servants disappeared. He had no one near him to put coals on his ever-burning fires while he slept, or to attend to the changeful colours of his medicines while he studied. Experiment after experiment failed, because one pair of hands was insufficient to complete them: the dark spirits laughed at him for not being able to retain a single mortal in his service.

I was then very young—very poor—and very much in love. I had been for about a year the pupil of Cornelius, though I was absent when this accident took place. On my return, my friends implored me not to return to the alchymist's abode. I trembled as I listened to the dire tale they told; I required no second warning; and when Cornelius came and offered me a purse of gold if I would remain under his roof, I felt as if Satan himself tempted me. My teeth chattered—my hair stood on end:—I ran off as fast as my trembling knees would permit.

My failing steps were directed whither for two years they had every evening been attracted,—a gently bubbling spring of pure living waters, beside which lingered a dark-haired girl, whose beaming eyes were fixed on the path I was accustomed each night to tread. I cannot remember the hour when I did not love Bertha; we had been neighbours and playmates from infancy—her parents, like mine, were of humble life, yet respectable—our attachment had been a source of pleasure to them. In an evil hour, a malignant fever carried off both her father and mother, and Bertha became an orphan. She would have found a home beneath my paternal roof, but, unfortunately, the old lady of the near castle, rich, childless, and solitary, declared her intention to adopt her. Henceforth Bertha was clad in silk—inhabited a marble palace—and was looked on as being highly favoured by fortune. But in her new situation among her new associates, Bertha remained true to the friend of her humbler days; she often visited the cottage of my father, and when forbidden to go thither, she would stray towards the neighbouring wood, and meet me beside its shady fountain.

She often declared that she owed no duty to her new protectress equal in sanctity to that which bound us. Yet still I was too poor to marry, and she grew weary of being tormented on my account. She had a haughty but an impatient

3. Legendary Christian youths who took refuge in a cave in Ephesus to escape their pagan persecutors and slept for 187 years.
4. Title character of Frances Sheridan's Oriental tale of 1767, who is tricked into believing that he has become immortal and that, when he sleeps, he does so for several years at a time. For an excerpt from *Nourjahad*, see "Romantic Orientalism" at Norton Literature Online.
5. The 16th-century German researcher of the occult and the alchemical sciences. Agrippa's

works are among the books that Victor Frankenstein reads when young and that prompt him to begin "the search of the philosopher's stone" (which had the power to transmute base metal into gold) and of "the elixir of life"; his "favourite authors" also promise to teach the "raising of ghosts or devils."
6. The story was told by Robert Southey in a 1798 poem entitled "Cornelius Agrippa: A Ballad of a Young Man That Would Read Unlawful Books."

spirit, and grew angry at the obstacles that prevented our union. We met now after an absence, and she had been sorely beset while I was away; she complained bitterly, and almost reproached me for being poor. I replied hastily,— "I am honest, if I am poor!—were I not, I might soon become rich!" This exclamation produced a thousand questions. I feared to shock her by owning the truth, but she drew it from me; and then, casting a look of disdain on me, she said—

"You pretend to love, and you fear to face the Devil for my sake!"

I protested that I had only dreaded to offend her;—while she dwelt on the magnitude of the reward that I should receive. Thus encouraged—shamed by her—led on by love and hope, laughing at my late fears, with quick steps and a light heart, I returned to accept the offers of the alchymist, and was instantly installed in my office.

A year passed away. I became possessed of no insignificant sum of money. Custom had banished my fears. In spite of the most painful vigilance, I had never detected the trace of a cloven foot; nor was the studious silence of our abode ever disturbed by demoniac howls. I still continued my stolen interviews with Bertha, and Hope dawned on me—Hope—but not perfect joy; for Bertha fancied that love and security were enemies, and her pleasure was to divide them in my bosom. Though true of heart, she was somewhat of a coquette in manner; and I was jealous as a Turk. She slighted me in a thousand ways, yet would never acknowledge herself to be in the wrong. She would drive me mad with anger, and then force me to beg her pardon. Sometimes she fancied that I was not sufficiently submissive, and then she had some story of a rival, favoured by her protectress. She was surrounded by silk-clad youths—the rich and gay—What chance had the sad-robed scholar of Cornelius compared with these?

On one occasion, the philosopher made such large demands upon my time, that I was unable to meet her as I was wont. He was engaged in some mighty work, and I was forced to remain, day and night, feeding his furnaces and watching his chemical preparations. Bertha waited for me in vain at the fountain. Her haughty spirit fired at this neglect; and when at last I stole out during the few short minutes allotted to me for slumber, and hoped to be consoled by her, she received me with disdain, dismissed me in scorn, and vowed that any man should possess her hand rather than he who could not be in two places at once for her sake. She would be revenged!—And truly she was. In my dingy retreat I heard that she had been hunting, attended by Albert Hoffer. Albert Hoffer was favoured by her protectress, and the three passed in cavalcade before my smoky window. Methought that they mentioned my name—it was followed by a laugh of derision, as her dark eyes glanced contemptuously towards my abode.

Jealousy, with all its venom, and all its misery, entered my breast. Now I shed a torrent of tears, to think that I should never call her mine; and, anon, I imprecated a thousand curses on her inconstancy. Yet, still I must stir the fires of the alchymist, still attend on the changes of his unintelligible medicines.

Cornelius had watched for three days and nights, nor closed his eyes. The progress of his alembics[7] was slower than he expected: in spite of his anxiety, sleep weighed upon his eyelids. Again and again he threw off drowsiness with

---

7. Distilling apparatuses that Agrippa uses in his alchemical investigations.

more than human energy; again and again it stole away his senses. He eyed his crucibles wistfully. "Not ready yet," he murmured; "will another night pass before the work is accomplished? Winzy,[8] you are vigilant—you are faithful—you have slept, my boy—you slept last night. Look at that glass vessel. The liquid it contains is of a soft rose-colour: the moment it begins to change its hue, awaken me—till then I may close my eyes. First, it will turn white, and then emit golden flashes; but wait not till then; when the rose-colour fades, rouse me." I scarcely heard the last words, muttered, as they were, in sleep. Even then he did not quite yield to nature. "Winzy, my boy," he again said, "do not touch the vessel—do not put it to your lips; it is a philter[9]—a philter to cure love; you would not cease to love your Bertha—beware to drink!"

And he slept. His venerable head sunk on his breast, and I scarce heard his regular breathing. For a few minutes I watched the vessel—the rosy hue of the liquid remained unchanged. Then my thoughts wandered—they visited the fountain, and dwelt on a thousand charming scenes never to be renewed—never! Serpents and adders were in my heart as the word "Never!" half formed itself on my lips. False girl!—false and cruel! Never more would she smile on me as that evening she smiled on Albert. Worthless, detested woman! I would not remain unrevenged—she should see Albert expire at her feet—she should die beneath my vengeance. She had smiled in disdain and triumph—she knew my wretchedness and her power. Yet what power had she?—the power of exciting my hate—my utter scorn—my—oh, all but indifference! Could I attain that—could I regard her with careless eyes, transferring my rejected love to one fairer and more true, that were indeed a victory!

A bright flash darted before my eyes. I had forgotten the medicine of the adept; I gazed on it with wonder: flashes of admirable beauty, more bright than those which the diamond emits when the sun's rays are on it, glanced from the surface of the liquid; an odour the most fragrant and grateful stole over my sense; the vessel seemed one globe of living radiance, lovely to the eye, and most inviting to the taste. The first thought, instinctively inspired by the grosser sense, was, I will—I must drink. I raised the vessel to my lips. "It will cure me of love—of torture!" Already I had quaffed half of the most delicious liquor ever tasted by the palate of man, when the philosopher stirred. I started—I dropped the glass—the fluid flamed and glanced along the floor, while I felt Cornelius's gripe at my throat, as he shrieked aloud, "Wretch! you have destroyed the labour of my life!"

The philosopher was totally unaware that I had drunk any portion of his drug. His idea was, and I gave a tacit assent to it, that I had raised the vessel from curiosity, and that, frighted at its brightness, and the flashes of intense light it gave forth, I had let it fall. I never undeceived him. The fire of the medicine was quenched—the fragrance died away—he grew calm, as a philosopher should under the heaviest trials, and dismissed me to rest.

I will not attempt to describe the sleep of glory and bliss which bathed my soul in paradise during the remaining hours of that memorable night. Words would be faint and shallow types of my enjoyment, or of the gladness that possessed my bosom when I woke. I trod air—my thoughts were in heaven. Earth appeared heaven, and my inheritance upon it was to be one trance of delight. "This it is to be cured of love," I thought; "I will see Bertha this day,

8. The narrator's name suggests the Scots *winze*, meaning "curse." 9. Magic potion.

and she will find her lover cold and regardless; too happy to be disdainful, yet how utterly indifferent to her!"

The hours danced away. The philosopher, secure that he had once succeeded, and believing that he might again, began to concoct the same medicine once more. He was shut up with his books and drugs, and I had a holiday. I dressed myself with care; I looked in an old but polished shield, which served me for a mirror; methought my good looks had wonderfully improved. I hurried beyond the precincts of the town, joy in my soul, the beauty of heaven and earth around me. I turned my steps towards the castle—I could look on its lofty turrets with lightness of heart, for I was cured of love. My Bertha saw me afar off, as I came up the avenue. I know not what sudden impulse animated her bosom, but at the sight, she sprung with a light fawn-like bound down the marble steps, and was hastening towards me. But I had been perceived by another person. The old high-born hag, who called herself her protectress, and was her tyrant, had seen me, also; she hobbled, panting, up the terrace; a page, as ugly as herself, held up her train, and fanned her as she hurried along, and stopped my fair girl with a "How, now, my bold mistress? whither so fast? Back to your cage—hawks are abroad!"[1]

Bertha clasped her hands—her eyes were still bent on my approaching figure. I saw the contest. How I abhorred the old crone who checked the kind impulses of my Bertha's softening heart. Hitherto, respect for her rank had caused me to avoid the lady of the castle; now I disdained such trivial considerations. I was cured of love, and lifted above all human fears; I hastened forwards, and soon reached the terrace. How lovely Bertha looked! her eyes flashing fire, her cheeks glowing with impatience and anger, she was a thousand times more graceful and charming than ever—I no longer loved—Oh! no, I adored—worshipped—idolized her!

She had that morning been persecuted, with more than usual vehemence, to consent to an immediate marriage with my rival. She was reproached with the encouragement that she had shown him—she was threatened with being turned out of doors with disgrace and shame. Her proud spirit rose in arms at the threat; but when she remembered the scorn that she had heaped upon me, and how, perhaps, she had thus lost one whom she now regarded as her only friend, she wept with remorse and rage. At that moment I appeared. "O, Winzy!" she exclaimed, "take me to your mother's cot; swiftly let me leave the detested luxuries and wretchedness of this noble dwelling—take me to poverty and happiness."

I clasped her in my arms with transport. The old lady was speechless with fury, and broke forth into invective only when we were far on our road to my natal cottage. My mother received the fair fugitive, escaped from a gilt cage to nature and liberty, with tenderness and joy; my father, who loved her, welcomed her heartily; it was a day of rejoicing, which did not need the addition of the celestial potion of the alchymist to steep me in delight.

Soon after this eventful day, I became the husband of Bertha. I ceased to be the scholar of Cornelius, but I continued his friend. I always felt grateful to him for having, unawares, procured me that delicious draught of a divine elixir, which, instead of curing me of love (sad cure! solitary and joyless remedy for evils which seem blessings to the memory), had inspired me with courage and resolution, thus winning for me an inestimable treasure in my Bertha.

1. In the *Keepsake* volume this is the scene that the artist and engraver picture.

I often called to mind that period of trance-like inebriation with wonder. The drink of Cornelius had not fulfilled the task for which he affirmed that it had been prepared, but its effects were more potent and blissful than words can express. They had faded by degrees, yet they lingered long—and painted life in hues of splendour. Bertha often wondered at my lightness of heart and unaccustomed gaiety; for, before, I had been rather serious, or even sad, in my disposition. She loved me the better for my cheerful temper, and our days were winged by joy.

Five years afterwards I was suddenly summoned to the bedside of the dying Cornelius. He had sent for me in haste, conjuring my instant presence. I found him stretched on his pallet, enfeebled even to death; all of life that yet remained animated his piercing eyes, and they were fixed on a glass vessel, full of a roseate liquid.

"Behold," he said, in a broken and inward voice, "the vanity of human wishes! a second time my hopes are about to be crowned, a second time they are destroyed. Look at that liquor—you remember five years ago I had prepared the same, with the same success;—then, as now, my thirsting lips expected to taste the immortal elixir—you dashed it from me! and at present it is too late."

He spoke with difficulty, and fell back on his pillow. I could not help saying,—

"How, revered master, can a cure for love restore you to life?"

A faint smile gleamed across his face as I listened earnestly to his scarcely intelligible answer.

"A cure for love and for all things—the Elixir of Immortality. Ah! if now I might drink, I should live for ever!"

As he spoke, a golden flash gleamed from the fluid; a well-remembered fragrance stole over the air; he raised himself, all weak as he was—strength seemed miraculously to re-enter his frame—he stretched forth his hand—a loud explosion startled me—a ray of fire shot up from the elixir, and the glass vessel which contained it was shivered to atoms! I turned my eyes towards the philosopher; he had fallen back—his eyes were glassy—his features rigid—he was dead!

But I lived, and was to live for ever! So said the unfortunate alchymist, and for a few days I believed his words. I remembered the glorious drunkenness that had followed my stolen draught. I reflected on the change I had felt in my frame—in my soul. The bounding elasticity of the one—the buoyant lightness of the other. I surveyed myself in a mirror, and could perceive no change in my features during the space of the five years which had elapsed. I remembered the radiant hues and grateful scent of that delicious beverage—worthy the gift it was capable of bestowing——I was, then, IMMORTAL!

A few days after I laughed at my credulity. The old proverb, that "a prophet is least regarded in his own country," was true with respect to me and my defunct master. I loved him as a man—I respected him as a sage—but I derided the notion that he could command the powers of darkness, and laughed at the superstitious fears with which he was regarded by the vulgar. He was a wise philosopher, but had no acquaintance with any spirits but those clad in flesh and blood. His science was simply human; and human science, I soon persuaded myself, could never conquer nature's laws so far as to imprison the soul for ever within its carnal habitation. Cornelius had brewed a soul-refreshing drink—more inebriating than wine—sweeter and more fragrant than any fruit: it possessed probably strong medicinal powers, imparting gladness to the heart and vigor to the limbs; but its effects would wear out;

already were they diminished in my frame. I was a lucky fellow to have quaffed health and joyous spirits, and perhaps long life, at my master's hands; but my good fortune ended there: longevity was far different from immortality.

I continued to entertain this belief for many years. Sometimes a thought stole across me—Was the alchymist indeed deceived? But my habitual credence was, that I should meet the fate of all the children of Adam at my appointed time—a little late, but still at a natural age. Yet it was certain that I retained a wonderfully youthful look. I was laughed at for my vanity in consulting the mirror so often, but I consulted it in vain—my brow was untrenched—my cheeks—my eyes—my whole person continued as untarnished as in my twentieth year.

I was troubled. I looked at the faded beauty of Bertha—I seemed more like her son. By degrees our neighbours began to make similar observations, and I found at last that I went by the name of the Scholar bewitched. Bertha herself grew uneasy. She became jealous and peevish, and at length she began to question me. We had no children; we were all in all to each other; and though, as she grew older, her vivacious spirit became a little allied to ill-temper, and her beauty sadly diminished, I cherished her in my heart as the mistress I had idolized, the wife I had sought and won with such perfect love.

At last our situation became intolerable: Bertha was fifty—I twenty years of age. I had, in very shame, in some measure adopted the habits of a more advanced age; I no longer mingled in the dance among the young and gay, but my heart bounded along with them while I restrained my feet; and a sorry figure I cut among the Nestors[2] of our village. But before the time I mention, things were altered—we were universally shunned; we were—at least, I was—reported to have kept up an iniquitous acquaintance with some of my former master's supposed friends. Poor Bertha was pitied, but deserted. I was regarded with horror and detestation.

What was to be done? we sat by our winter fire—poverty had made itself felt, for none would buy the produce of my farm; and often I had been forced to journey twenty miles, to some place where I was not known, to dispose of our property. It is true we had saved something for an evil day—that day was come.

We sat by our lone fireside—the old-hearted youth and his antiquated wife. Again Bertha insisted on knowing the truth; she recapitulated all she had ever heard said about me, and added her own observations. She conjured me to cast off the spell; she described how much more comely gray hairs were than my chestnut locks; she descanted on the reverence and respect due to age—how preferable to the slight regard paid to mere children: could I imagine that the despicable gifts of youth and good looks outweighed disgrace, hatred, and scorn? Nay, in the end I should be burnt as a dealer in the black art, while she, to whom I had not deigned to communicate any portion of my good fortune, might be stoned as my accomplice. At length she insinuated that I must share my secret with her, and bestow on her like benefits to those I myself enjoyed, or she would denounce me—and then she burst into tears.

Thus beset, methought it was the best way to tell the truth. I revealed it as tenderly as I could, and spoke only of a *very long life*, not of immortality—which representation, indeed, coincided best with my own ideas. When I ended, I rose and said,

"And now, my Bertha, will you denounce the lover of your youth?—You will

2. Village elders. In the *Iliad* Nestor is the old and battle-scarred advisor to the Greek army.

not, I know. But it is too hard, my poor wife, that you should suffer from my ill-luck and the accursed arts of Cornelius. I will leave you—you have wealth enough, and friends will return in my absence. I will go; young as I seem, and strong as I am, I can work and gain my bread among strangers, unsuspected and unknown. I loved you in youth; God is my witness that I would not desert you in age, but that your safety and happiness require it."

I took my cap and moved towards the door; in a moment Bertha's arms were round my neck, and her lips were pressed to mine. "No, my husband, my Winzy," she said, "you shall not go alone—take me with you; we will remove from this place, and, as you say, among strangers we shall be unsuspected and safe. I am not so very old as quite to shame you, my Winzy; and I dare say the charm will soon wear off, and, with the blessing of God, you will become more elderly-looking, as is fitting; you shall not leave me."

I returned the good soul's embrace heartily. "I will not, my Bertha; but for your sake I had not thought of such a thing. I will be your true, faithful husband while you are spared to me, and do my duty by you to the last."

The next day we prepared secretly for our emigration. We were obliged to make great pecuniary sacrifices—it could not be helped. We realised a sum sufficient, at least, to maintain us while Bertha lived; and, without saying adieu to anyone, quitted our native country to take refuge in a remote part of western France.

It was a cruel thing to transport poor Bertha from her native village, and the friends of her youth, to a new country, new language, new customs. The strange secret of my destiny rendered this removal immaterial to me; but I compassionated her deeply, and was glad to perceive that she found compensation for her misfortunes in a variety of little ridiculous circumstances. Away from all tell-tale chroniclers, she sought to decrease the apparent disparity of our ages by a thousand feminine arts—rouge, youthful dress, and assumed juvenility of manner. I could not be angry—Did not I myself wear a mask? Why quarrel with hers, because it was less successful? I grieved deeply when I remembered that this was my Bertha, whom I had loved so fondly, and won with such transport—the dark-eyed, dark-haired girl, with smiles of enchanting archness and a step like a fawn—this mincing, simpering, jealous old woman. I should have revered her gray locks and withered cheeks; but thus!— —It was my work, I knew; but I did not the less deplore this type of human weakness.

Her jealousy never slept. Her chief occupation was to discover that, in spite of outward appearances, I was myself growing old. I verily believe that the poor soul loved me truly in her heart, but never had woman so tormenting a mode of displaying fondness. She would discern wrinkles in my face and decrepitude in my walk, while I bounded along in youthful vigour, the youngest looking of twenty youths. I never dared address another woman: on one occasion, fancying that the belle of the village regarded me with favouring eyes, she bought me a gray wig. Her constant discourse among her acquaintances was, that though I looked so young, there was ruin at work within my frame; and she affirmed that the worst symptom about me was my apparent health. My youth was a disease, she said, and I ought at all times to prepare, if not for a sudden and awful death, at least to awake some morning white-headed, and bowed down with all the marks of advanced years. I let her talk—I often joined in her conjectures. Her warnings chimed in with my never-ceasing speculations concerning my state, and I took an earnest, though painful, interest in listening to all that her quick wit and excited imagination could say on the subject.

Why dwell on these minute circumstances? We lived on for many long years. Bertha became bed-rid and paralytic: I nursed her as a mother might a child. She grew peevish, and still harped upon one string—of how long I should survive her. It has ever been a source of consolation to me, that I performed my duty scrupulously towards her. She had been mine in youth, she was mine in age, and at last, when I heaped the sod over her corpse, I wept to feel that I had lost all that really bound me to humanity.

Since then how many have been my cares and woes, how few and empty my enjoyments! I pause here in my history—I will pursue it no further. A sailor without rudder or compass, tossed on a stormy sea—a traveller lost on a wide-spread heath, without landmark or star to guide him—such have I been: more lost, more hopeless than either. A nearing ship, a gleam from some far cot, may save them; but I have no beacon except the hope of death.

Death! mysterious, ill-visaged friend of weak humanity! Why alone of all mortals have you cast me from your sheltering fold? O, for the peace of the grave! the deep silence of the iron-bound tomb! that thought would cease to work in my brain, and my heart beat no more with emotions varied only by new forms of sadness!

Am I immortal? I return to my first question. In the first place, is it not more probable that the beverage of the alchymist was fraught rather with longevity than eternal life? Such is my hope. And then be it remembered, that I only drank *half* of the potion prepared by him. Was not the whole necessary to complete the charm? To have drained half the Elixir of Immortality is but to be half immortal—my For-ever is thus truncated and null.

But again, who shall number the years of the half of eternity? I often try to imagine by what rule the infinite may be divided. Sometimes I fancy age advancing upon me. One gray hair I have found. Fool! do I lament? Yes, the fear of age and death often creeps coldly into my heart; and the more I live, the more I dread death, even while I abhor life. Such an enigma is man—born to perish—when he wars, as I do, against the established laws of his nature.

But for this anomaly of feeling surely I might die: the medicine of the alchymist would not be proof against fire—sword—and the strangling waters. I have gazed upon the blue depths of many a placid lake, and the tumultuous rushing of many a mighty river, and have said, peace inhabits those waters; yet I have turned my steps away, to live yet another day. I have asked myself, whether suicide would be a crime in one to whom thus only the portals of the other world could be opened. I have done all, except presenting myself as a soldier or duellist, an object of destruction to my—no, *not* my fellow-mortals, and therefore I have shrunk away. They are not my fellows. The inextinguishable power of life in my frame, and their ephemeral existence, place us wide as the poles asunder. I could not raise a hand against the meanest or the most powerful among them.

Thus I have lived on for many a year—alone, and weary of myself—desirous of death, yet never dying—a mortal immortal. Neither ambition nor avarice can enter my mind, and the ardent love that gnaws at my heart, never to be returned—never to find an equal on which to expend itself—lives there only to torment me.

This very day I conceived a design by which I may end all—without self-slaughter, without making another man a Cain—an expedition, which mortal frame can never survive, even endued with the youth and strength that inhabits mine. Thus I shall put my immortality to the test, and rest for ever—or return, the wonder and benefactor of the human species.[3]

Before I go, a miserable vanity has caused me to pen these pages. I would not die, and leave no name behind. Three centuries have passed since I quaffed the fatal beverage: another year shall not elapse before, encountering gigantic dangers—warring with the powers of frost in their home—beset by famine, toil, and tempest—I yield this body, too tenacious a cage for a soul which thirsts for freedom, to the destructive elements of air and water—or, if I survive, my name shall be recorded as one of the most famous among the sons of men; and, my task achieved, I shall adopt more resolute means, and, by scattering and annihilating the atoms that compose my frame, set at liberty the life imprisoned within, and so cruelly prevented from soaring from this dim earth to a sphere more congenial to its immortal essence.

1833   1834

3. Cf. Walton in *Frankenstein,* who describes his expedition to the North Pole as conferring "inestimable benefit . . . on all mankind to the last gen- eration," or Frankenstein, who likewise anticipates the gratitude of posterity: "A new species would bless me as its creator and source."

LETITIA ELIZABETH LANDON
1802–1838

Letitia Elizabeth Landon, whose initials became one of the most famous literary pseudonyms of nineteenth-century Britain, was born and educated in Chelsea, London. She published her first poem in the weekly *Literary Gazette* in March 1820, when she was seventeen, and soon thereafter became a principal writer and reviewer for the magazine. Her first important collection of poems, published in 1824, was *The Improvisatrice*—a work that suggests Landon's fascination with Germaine de Staël's *Corinne* and with the Italy that she never visited but encountered in the pages of Staël, the Shelleys, and Byron. It went through six editions in its first year and was followed by *The Troubadour, Catalogue of Pictures, and Historical Sketches* (1825), which went through four. She quickly followed these with *The Golden Violet* (1827), the first of many editions of her *Poetical Works* (1827), and *The Venetian Bracelet* (1829). She also wrote essays, short fiction, children's stories, several novels, and a play; and she edited—and contributed hundreds of poems to—the albums, gift books, and annual anthologies that became a staple of British literary production of the 1820s and 1830s. All this highly remunerative work appeared from the pen of "L.E.L.," the pseudonym that she first used in the *Literary Gazette* and that attracted increasing numbers of readers and also poetic responses, as it was disclosed by stages that the author behind the initials was female, young, and a great beauty. To this day many of Landon's books continue to be catalogued under the pseudonym, and one "feminist companion" to literature in English has an entry for "L.E.L." but none for "Landon."

Landon and Felicia Hemans, as "L.E.L." and "Mrs. Hemans," were the two bestselling poets of their time—the decade and a half following the deaths of Keats, Percy Shelley, and Byron in the early 1820s—and were major inspirations to subsequent writers such as Elizabeth Barrett and Christina Rossetti. Unlike Hemans, Landon attracted scandal, partly because of her casual social relations with men and partly because of her principal subject matter, the joys and especially the sorrows of female passion. (In her preface to *The Venetian Bracelet*, she attempted wittily, but without success, to forestall this biographical reading of her poems: "With regard to the frequent application of my works to myself, considering that I sometimes pourtrayed love unrequited, then betrayed, and again destroyed by death—may I hint the conclusions are not quite logically drawn, as assuredly the same mind cannot have suffered such varied modes of misery. However, if I must have an unhappy passion, I can only console myself with my own perfect unconsciousness of so great a misfortune.") There were rumors of affairs with, among others, William Jerdan, who was editor of the *Literary Gazette*, the journalist William Maginn, and the artist Daniel Maclise. She was engaged to the editor John Forster, future biographer of Dickens, but had to break the engagement because of these rumors. In 1838 she married someone she had known for only a short time, George Maclean, governor of the British settlement at Cape Coast Castle, west Africa (in what is now Ghana). She arrived with Maclean at Cape Coast in August 1838 and two months later was dead, reportedly from an overdose of prussic acid—though whether the cause was accident, suicide, or murder has never been determined.

Landon perfected, and reviewers helped maintain, several personas in her work: the pseudonymous, therefore anonymous, writer of passionate love lyrics; the Romantic "improvisatrice" jotting down verses in the interstices of an intense social life; the renowned beauty who constantly fails in love and, in lamenting her crushed feelings, becomes the female equivalent of the Byronic hero; and an early version of the Victorian "poetess" composing songs to appeal to a burgeoning cult of domesticity. As in Hemans's poetry, some of these personas are not wholly compatible with some of the others. But their variety and vitality captivated readers and, during Landon's short life, provided her a fortune in sales and royalties.

The Proud Ladye[1]

Oh, what could the ladye's beauty match,
    An° it were not the ladye's pride?   *if*
An hundred knights from far and near
    Woo'd at that ladye's side.

5   The rose of the summer slept on her cheek,
        Its lily upon her breast,
    And her eye shone forth like the glorious star
        That rises the first in the west.

---

1. This ballad is . . . taken, with some slight change, from a legend in Russell's Germany [Landon's note]. The story, in John Russell's *A Tour in Germany* (1824), chap. 11, relates how "the fair Cunigunda, equally celebrated for her charms and her cruelty . . . would listen to no tale of love, and dreaded marriage as she did a prison. At length, to free herself from all importunities, she made a solemn vow never to give her hand but to the knight who should ride round the castle on the outer wall . . . [which] runs along the very brink of hideous precipices. . . . History has not recorded the precise number of those who actually made the attempt; it is only certain that every one of them broke his neck. . . . At length, a young and handsome knight appeared at the castle gate . . . [to] try his fortune. . . . In a short time, a shout from the

menials announced that the adventure had been achieved; and Cunigunda, exulting that she was conquered, hastened into the court. . . . But the knight stood aloof, gloomy and severe. 'I can claim you,' said he; 'but I am come, and I have risked my life, not to win your hand, but to humble your pride and punish your barbarity'—and thereupon he read her a harsh lecture on the cruelty and arrogance of her conduct towards her suitors. The spirit of chivalry weeps at recording, that he finished his oration by giving the astonished beauty a box on the ear." Landon's ballad (in the same stanza as Keats's story of another *belle dame sans merci*) was included as a separate piece within a long poem, *The Troubadour*, that she published in 1825.

There were some that woo'd for her land and gold,
10   And some for her noble name,
And more that woo'd for her loveliness;
      But her answer was still the same.

"There is a steep and lofty wall,
      Where my warders° trembling stand;   guards
15 He who at speed shall ride round its height,
      For him shall be my hand."

Many turn'd away from the deed,
      The hope of their wooing o'er;
But many a young knight mounted the steed
20   He never mounted more.

At last there came a youthful knight,
      From a strange and far countrie,
The steed that he rode was white as the foam
      Upon a stormy sea.

25 And she who had scorn'd the name of love,
      Now bow'd before its might,
And the ladye grew meek as if disdain
      Were not made for that stranger knight.

She sought at first to steal his soul
30   By dance, song, and festival;
At length on bended knee she pray'd
      He would not ride the wall.

But gaily the young knight laugh'd at her fears,
      And flung him on his steed,—
35 There was not a saint in the calendar
      That she pray'd not to in her need.

She dar'd not raise her eyes to see
      If heaven had granted her prayer,
Till she heard a light step bound to her side,—
40   The gallant knight stood there!

And took the ladye Adeline
      From her hair a jewell'd band,
But the knight repell'd the offer'd gift,
      And turn'd from the offer'd hand.

45 "And deemest thou that I dared this deed,
      Ladye, for love of thee?
The honour that guides the soldier's lance
      Is mistress enough for me.

"Enough for me to ride the ring,
50   The victor's crown to wear;
But not in honour of the eyes
      Of any ladye there.

"I had a brother whom I lost
    Through thy proud crueltie,
55 And far more was to me his love,
    Than woman's love can be.

"I came to triumph o'er the pride
    Through which that brother fell,
I laugh to scorn thy love and thee,
60   And now, proud dame, farewell!"

And from that hour the ladye pined,
    For love was in her heart,
And on her slumber there came dreams
    She could not bid depart.

65 Her eye lost all its starry light,
    Her cheek grew wan and pale,
Till she hid her faded loveliness
    Beneath the sacred veil.

And she cut off her long dark hair,
70   And bade the world farewell,
And she now dwells a veiled nun
    In Saint Marie's cell.

1825

Love's Last Lesson

"Teach it me, if you can,—forgetfulness![1]
I surely shall forget, if you can bid me;
I who have worshipp'd thee, my god on earth,
I who have bow'd me at thy lightest word.
5 Your last command, 'Forget me,' will it not
Sink deeply down within my inmost soul?
Forget thee!—ay, forgetfulness will be
A mercy to me. By the many nights
When I have wept for that I dared not sleep,—
10 A dream had made me live my woes again,
Acting my wretchedness, without the hope
My foolish heart still clings to, though that hope
Is like the opiate which may lull a while,
Then wake to double torture; by the days
15 Pass'd in lone watching and in anxious fears,
When a breath sent the crimson to my cheek,
Like the red gushing of a sudden wound;
By all the careless looks and careless words
Which have to me been like the scorpion's stinging;

1. An allusion to Byron's *Manfred* 1.1.135–36: "What wouldst thou with us, son of mortals— say?"—to which Manfred replies, "Forgetfulness." Other Byronic echoes in lines 14–15, 18–23, 85–86, and 95–98 further link Landon's speaker to the protagonists of *Childe Harold* and *Manfred*.

20   By happiness blighted, and by thee, for ever;
     By thy eternal work of wretchedness;
     By all my wither'd feelings, ruin'd health,
     Crush'd hopes, and rifled heart, I will forget thee!
     Alas! my words are vanity. Forget thee!
25   Thy work of wasting is too surely done.
     The April shower may pass and be forgotten,
     The rose fall and one fresh spring in its place,
     And thus it may be with light summer love.
     It was not thus with mine: it did not spring,
30   Like the bright colour on an evening cloud,
     Into a moment's life, brief, beautiful;
     Not amid lighted halls, when flatteries
     Steal on the ear like dew upon the rose,
     As soft, as soon dispersed, as quickly pass'd;
35   But you first call'd my woman's feelings forth,
     And taught me love ere I had dream'd love's name.
     I loved unconsciously: your name was all
     That seem'd in language, and to me the world
     Was only made for you; in solitude,
40   When passions hold their interchange together,
     Your image was the shadow of my thought;
     Never did slave, before his Eastern lord,
     Tremble as I did when I met your eye,
     And yet each look was counted as a prize;
45   I laid your words up in my heart like pearls
     Hid in the ocean's treasure-cave. At last
     I learn'd my heart's deep secret: for I hoped,
     I dream'd you loved me; wonder, fear, delight,
     Swept my heart like a storm; my soul, my life,
50   Seem'd all too little for your happiness;
     Had I been mistress of the starry worlds
     That light the midnight, they had all been yours,
     And I had deem'd such boon but poverty.
     As it was, I gave all I could—my love,
55   My deep, my true, my fervent, faithful love;
     And now you bid me learn forgetfulness:
     It is a lesson that I soon shall learn.
     There is a home of quiet for the wretched,
     A somewhat dark, and cold, and silent rest,
60   But still it is rest,—for it is the grave."

     She flung aside the scroll, as it had part
     In her great misery. Why should she write?
     What could she write? Her woman's pride forbade
     To let him look upon her heart, and see
65   It was an utter ruin;—and cold words,
     And scorn and slight, that may repay his own,
     Were as a foreign language, to whose sound
     She might not frame her utterance. Down she bent
     Her head upon an arm so white that tears
70   Seem'd but the natural melting of its snow,
     Touch'd by the flush'd cheek's crimson; yet life-blood
     Less wrings in shedding than such tears as those.

And this then is love's ending! It is like
The history of some fair southern clime.
75 Hot fires are in the bosom of the earth,
And the warm'd soil puts forth its thousand flowers,
Its fruits of gold, summer's regality,
And sleep and odours float upon the air:
At length the subterranean element
80 Breaks from its secret dwelling-place, and lays
All waste before it; the red lava stream
Sweeps like the pestilence; and that which was
A garden in its colours and its breath,
Fit for the princess of a fairy tale,
85 Is as a desert, in whose burning sands,
And ashy waters, who is there can trace
A sign, a memory of its former beauty?
It is thus with the heart; love lights it up
With hopes like young companions, and with joys
90 Dreaming deliciously of their sweet selves.

This is at first; but what is the result?
Hopes that lie mute in their own sullenness,
For they have quarrell'd even with themselves;
And joys indeed like birds of Paradise:[2]
95 And in their stead despair coils scorpion-like
Stinging itself;[3] and the heart, burnt and crush'd
With passion's earthquake, scorch'd and wither'd up,
Lies in its desolation,—this is love.

What is the tale that I would tell? Not one
100 Of strange adventure, but a common tale
Of woman's wretchedness; one to be read
Daily in many a young and blighted heart.
The lady whom I spake of rose again
From the red fever's couch, to careless eyes
105 Perchance the same as she had ever been.
But oh, how alter'd to herself! She felt
That bird-like pining for some gentle home
To which affection might attach itself,
That weariness which hath but outward part
110 In what the world calls pleasure, and that chill
Which makes life taste the bitterness of death.

And he she loved so well,—what opiate
Lull'd consciousness into its selfish sleep?—
He said he loved her not; that never vow
115 Or passionate pleading won her soul for him;
And that he guess'd not her deep tenderness.

Are words, then, only false? are there no looks,
Mute but most eloquent; no gentle cares

---

2. In Eastern tales, the bird of Paradise never rests
on the earth [Landon's note].
3. In *The Giaour: A Fragment of a Turkish Tale*

(1813), Byron had written of how "The Mind, that
broods o'er guilty woes, / Is like the Scorpion girt
by fire" (lines 423–24).

That win so much upon the fair weak things
120 They seem to guard? And had he not long read
Her heart's hush'd secret in the soft dark eye
Lighted at his approach, and on the cheek
Colouring all crimson at his lightest look?
This is the truth; his spirit wholly turn'd
125 To stern ambition's dream, to that fierce strife
Which leads to life's high places, and reck'd° not   *cared*
What lovely flowers might perish in his path.

And here at length is somewhat of revenge:
For man's most golden dreams of pride and power
130 Are vain as any woman-dreams of love;
Both end in weary brow and wither'd heart,
And the grave closes over those whose hopes
Have lain there long before.

1827

Revenge

Ay, gaze upon her rose-wreathed hair,
   And gaze upon her smile;
Seem as you drank the very air
   Her breath perfumed the while:

5 And wake for her the gifted line,
   That wild and witching lay,
And swear your heart is as a shrine,
   That only owns her sway.

'Tis well: I am revenged at last,—
10   Mark you that scornful cheek,—
The eye averted as you pass'd,
   Spoke more than words could speak.

Ay, now by all the bitter tears
   That I have shed for thee,—
15 The racking doubts, the burning fears,—
   Avenged they well may be—

By the nights pass'd in sleepless care,
   The days of endless woe;
All that you taught my heart to bear,
20   All that yourself will know.

I would not wish to see you laid
   Within an early tomb;
I should forget how you betray'd,
   And only weep your doom:

25 But this is fitting punishment,
        To live and love in vain,—
    Oh my wrung heart, be thou content,
        And feed upon his pain.

    Go thou and watch her lightest sigh,—
30   Thine own it will not be;
    And bask beneath her sunny eye,—
        It will not turn on thee.

    'Tis well: the rack, the chain, the wheel,
        Far better had'st thou proved;
35 Ev'n I could almost pity feel,
        For thou art not beloved.

                                                                1829

The Little Shroud

    She put him on a snow-white shroud,
        A chaplet° on his head;   *wreath*
    And gather'd early primroses
        To scatter o'er the dead.

5   She laid him in his little grave—
        'Twas hard to lay him there,
    When spring was putting forth its flowers,
        And every thing was fair.

    She had lost many children—now
10   The last of them was gone;
    And day and night she sat and wept
        Beside the funeral stone.

    One midnight, while her constant tears
        Were falling with the dew,
15 She heard a voice, and lo! her child
        Stood by her weeping too!

    His shroud was damp, his face was white:
        He said,—"I cannot sleep,
    Your tears have made my shroud so wet;
20   Oh, mother, do not weep!"

    Oh, love is strong!—the mother's heart
        Was filled with tender fears;
    Oh, love is strong!—and for her child
        Her grief restrained its tears.

25 One eve a light shone round her bed,
        And there she saw him stand—

Her infant, in his little shroud,
A taper in his hand.

"Lo! mother, see my shroud is dry,
30   And I can sleep once more!"
And beautiful the parting smile
The little infant wore.

And down within the silent grave
He laid his weary head;
35 And soon the early violets
Grew o'er his grassy bed.

1832

The Victorian Age
1830–1901

1832:	The First Reform Bill
1837:	Victoria becomes queen
1846:	The Corn Laws repealed
1850:	Tennyson succeeds Wordsworth as poet laureate
1851:	The Great Exhibition in London
1859:	Charles Darwin's *Origin of Species* published
1870–71:	Franco-Prussian War
1901:	Death of Victoria

In 1897 Mark Twain was visiting London during the Diamond Jubilee celebrations honoring the sixtieth anniversary of Queen Victoria's coming to the
throne. "British history is two thousand years old," Twain observed, "and yet
in a good many ways the world has moved farther ahead since the Queen was
born than it moved in all the rest of the two thousand put together." And if
the whole world had "moved" during that long lifetime and reign of Victoria's,
it was in her own country itself that the change was most marked and dramatic,
a change that brought England to its highest point of development as a world
power.

In the eighteenth century the pivotal city of Western civilization had been
Paris; by the second half of the nineteenth century this center of influence
had shifted to London, a city that expanded from about two million inhabitants
when Victoria came to the throne to six and a half million at the time of her
death. The rapid growth of London is one of the many indications of the most
important development of the age: the shift from a way of life based on the
ownership of land to a modern urban economy based on trade and manufacturing. "We have been living, as it were, the life of three hundred years in
thirty" was the impression formed by Dr. Thomas Arnold during the early
stages of England's industrialization. By the end of the century—after the
resources of steam power had been more fully exploited for fast railways and
iron ships, looms, printing presses, and farmers' combines, and after the introduction of the telegraph, intercontinental cable, photography, anesthetics, and
universal compulsory education—a late Victorian could look back with astonishment on these developments during his or her lifetime. Walter Besant, one
of these late Victorians, observed that so completely transformed were "the
mind and habits of the ordinary Englishman" by 1897, "that he would not,
could he see him, recognize his own grandfather."

Because England was the first country to become industrialized, its transformation was an especially painful one: it experienced a host of social and

economic problems consequent to rapid and unregulated industrialization. England also experienced an enormous increase in wealth. An early start enabled England to capture markets all over the globe. Cotton and other manufactured products were exported in English ships, a merchant fleet whose size was without parallel in other countries. The profits gained from trade led also to extensive capital investments in all continents. After England had become the world's workshop, London became, from 1870 on, the world's banker. England gained particular profit from the development of its own colonies, which, by 1890, comprised more than a quarter of all the territory on the surface of the earth; one in four people was a subject of Queen Victoria. By the end of the century England was the world's foremost imperial power.

The reactions of Victorian writers to the fast-paced expansion of England were various. Thomas Babington Macaulay (1800–1859) relished the spectacle with strenuous enthusiasm. During the prosperous 1850s Macaulay's essays and histories, with their recitations of the statistics of industrial growth, constituted a Hymn to Progress as well as a celebration of the superior qualities of the English people—"the greatest and most highly civilized people that ever the world saw." Other writers felt that leadership in commerce and industry was being paid for at a terrible price in human happiness, that a so-called progress had been gained only by abandoning traditional rhythms of life and traditional patterns of human relationships. The melancholy poetry of Matthew Arnold often strikes this note:

> For what wears out the life of mortal men?
> 'Tis that from change to change their being rolls;
> 'Tis that repeated shocks, again, again,
> Exhaust the energy of strongest souls.

Although many Victorians shared a sense of satisfaction in the industrial and political preeminence of England during the period, they also suffered from an anxious sense of something lost, a sense too of being displaced persons in a world made alien by technological changes that had been exploited too quickly for the adaptive powers of the human psyche.

QUEEN VICTORIA AND THE VICTORIAN TEMPER

Queen Victoria's long reign, from 1837 to 1901, defines the historical period that bears her name. The question naturally arises whether the distinctive character of those years justifies the adjective *Victorian*. In part Victoria herself encouraged her own identification with the qualities we associate with the adjective—earnestness, moral responsibility, domestic propriety. As a young wife, as the mother of nine children, and as the black-garbed Widow of Windsor in the forty years after her husband's death in 1861, Victoria represented the domestic fidelities her citizens embraced. After her death Henry James wrote, "I mourn the safe and motherly old middle-class queen, who held the nation warm under the fold of her big, hideous Scotch-plaid shawl." Changes in the reproduction of visual images aided in making her the icon she became. She is the first British monarch of whom we have photographs. These pictures, and the ease and cheapness with which they were reproduced, facilitated her representing her country's sense of itself during her reign.

Victoria came to the throne in a decade that does seem to mark a different historical consciousness among Britain's writers. In 1831 John Stuart Mill asserts, "we are living in an age of transition." In the same year Thomas Carlyle writes, "The Old has passed away, but alas, the New appears not in its stead; the Time is still in pangs of travail with the New." Although the historical changes that created the England of the 1830s had been in progress for many decades, writers of the thirties shared a sharp new sense of modernity, of a break with the past, of historical self-consciousness. They responded to their sense of the historical moment with a strenuous call to action that they self-consciously distinguished from the attitude of the previous generation.

In 1834 Carlyle urged his contemporaries, "Close thy *Byron*; open thy *Goethe*." He was saying, in effect, to abandon the introspection of the Romantics and to turn to the higher moral purpose that he found in Goethe. The popular novelist Edward Bulwer-Lytton in his *England and the English* (1833) made a similar judgment. "When Byron passed away," he wrote, ". . . we turned to the actual and practical career of life: we awoke from the morbid, the dreaming, 'the moonlight and dimness of the mind,' and by a natural reaction addressed ourselves to the active and daily objects which lay before us." This sense of historical self-consciousness, of strenuous social enterprise, and of growing national achievement led writers as early as the 1850s and 1860s to define their age as Victorian. The very fact that Victoria reigned for so long sustained the concept of a distinctive historical period that writers defined even as they lived it.

When Queen Victoria died, a reaction developed against many of the achievements of the previous century; this reinforced the sense that the Victorian age was a distinct period. In the earlier decades of the twentieth century, writers took pains to separate themselves from the Victorians. It was then the fashion for most literary critics to treat their Victorian predecessors as somewhat absurd creatures, stuffily complacent prigs with whose way of life they had little in common. Writers of the Georgian period (1911–36) took great delight in puncturing overinflated Victorian balloons, as Lytton Strachey, a member of Virginia Woolf's circle, did in *Eminent Victorians* (1918). A subtler example occurs in Woolf's *Orlando* (1928), a fictionalized survey of English literature from Elizabethan times to 1928, in which the Victorians are presented in terms of dampness, rain, and proliferating vegetation:

> Ivy grew in unparalleled profusion. Houses that had been of bare stone were smothered in greenery. . . . And just as the ivy and the evergreen rioted in the damp earth outside, so did the same fertility show itself within. The life of the average woman was a succession of childbirths. . . . Giant cauliflowers towered deck above deck till they rivaled . . . the elm trees themselves. Hens laid incessantly eggs of no special tint. . . . The whole sky itself as it spread wide above the British Isles was nothing but a vast feather bed.

This witty description not only identifies a distinguishing quality of Victorian life and literature—a superabundant energy—but reveals the author's distaste for its smothering profusion. Woolf was the daughter of Sir Leslie Stephen (1832–1904), an eminent Victorian. In her later life, when assessing her father's powerful personality, Woolf recorded in her diary that she could never have become a writer if he had not died when he did. Growing up under such towering shadows, she and her generation mocked their predecessors to make them less intimidating. In his reminiscences *Portraits from Life* (1937), the novelist Ford Madox Ford recalled his feelings of terror when he confronted the works of Carlyle and Ruskin, which he likened to an overpowering range of high mountains. The mid-Victorians, he wrote, were "a childish nightmare to me."

The Georgian reaction against the Victorians is now only a matter of the history of taste, but its aftereffects still sometimes crop up when the term *Victorian* is employed in an exclusively pejorative sense, as prudish or old-fashioned. Contemporary historians and critics find the Victorian period a richly complex example of a society struggling with the issues and problems we identify with modernism. But to give the period the single designation *Victorian* reduces its complexity. Since it is a period of almost seventy years, we can hardly expect generalizations to be uniformly applicable. It is, therefore, helpful to subdivide the age into three phases: early Victorian (1830–48), mid-Victorian (1848–70), and late Victorian (1870–1901). It is also helpful to consider the final decade, the nineties, as a bridge between two centuries.

THE EARLY PERIOD (1830–48): A TIME OF TROUBLES

In the early 1830s two historical events occurred of momentous consequence for England. In 1830 the Liverpool and Manchester Railway opened, becoming the first steam-powered, public railway line in the world. A burst of railway construction followed. By 1850 6,621 miles of railway line connected all of England's major cities. By 1900 England had 15,195 lines of track and an underground railway system beneath London. The train transformed England's landscape, supported the growth of its commerce, and shrank the distances between its cities. The opening of England's first railway coincided with the opening of the country's Reform Parliament. The railway had increased the pressure for parliamentary reform. "Parliamentary reform must follow soon after the opening of this road," a Manchester man observed in 1830. "A million of persons will pass over it in the course of this year, and see that hitherto unseen village of Newton; and they must be convinced of the absurdity of its sending two members to Parliament while Manchester sends none." Despite the growth of manufacturing cities consequent to the Industrial Revolution, England was still governed by an archaic electoral system whereby some of the new industrial cities were unrepresented in Parliament while "rotten boroughs" (communities that had become depopulated) elected the nominees of the local squire to Parliament.

By 1830 a time of economic distress had brought England close to revolution. Manufacturing interests, who refused to tolerate their exclusion from the political process any longer, led working men in agitating for reform. Fearing the kind of revolution it had seen in Europe, Parliament passed a Reform Bill in 1832 that transformed England's class structure. The Reform Bill of 1832 extended the right to vote to all males owning property worth £10 or more in annual rent. In effect the voting public thereafter included the lower middle classes but not the working classes, who did not obtain the vote until 1867, when a second Reform Bill was passed. Even more important than the extension of the franchise was the virtual abolition of the rotten boroughs and the redistribution of parliamentary representation. Because it broke up the monopoly of power that the conservative landowners had so long enjoyed (the Tory party had been in office almost continuously from 1783 to 1830), the Reform Bill represents the beginning of a new age, in which middle-class economic interests gained increasing power.

Yet even the newly constituted Parliament was unable to find legislative solutions to the problems facing the nation. The economic and social difficulties attendant on industrialization were so severe that the 1830s and 1840s became known as the Time of Troubles. After a period of prosperity from 1832 to 1836, a crash in 1837, followed by a series of bad harvests, produced a period of unemployment, desperate poverty, and rioting. Conditions in the new industrial and coal-mining areas were terrible. Workers and their families in the slums of such cities as Manchester lived in horribly crowded, unsanitary housing; and the conditions under which men, women, and children toiled in mines and factories were unimaginably brutal. Elizabeth Barrett's poem "The Cry of the Children" (1843) expresses her horrified response to an official report on child labor that described five-year-olds sitting alone in darkness to open and close ventilation doors, and twelve-year-olds dragging heavy tubs of coal through low-ceilinged mine passages for sixteen hours a day.

The owners of mines and factories regarded themselves as innocent of blame for such conditions, for they were wedded to an economic theory of laissez-faire, which assumed that unregulated working conditions would ultimately benefit everyone. A sense of the seemingly hopeless complexity of the situation during the Hungry Forties is provided by an entry for 1842 in the diary of the statesman Charles Greville, an entry written at the same time that Carlyle was making his contribution to the "Condition of England Question," *Past and Present*. Conditions in the north of England, Greville reports, were "appalling."

> There is an immense and continually increasing population, no adequate demand for labor, . . . no confidence, but a universal alarm, disquietude, and discontent. Nobody can sell anything. . . . Certainly I have never seen . . . so serious a state of things as that which now stares us in the face; and this after thirty years of uninterrupted peace, and the most ample scope afforded for the development of all our resources. . . . One remarkable feature in the present condition of affairs is that nobody can account for it, and nobody pretends to be able to point out any remedy.

In reality many remedies were proposed. One of the most striking was put forward by the Chartists, a large organization of workers. In 1838 the organization drew up a "People's Charter" advocating the extension of the right to vote, the use of secret balloting, and other legislative reforms. For ten years the Chartist leaders engaged in agitation to have their program adopted by Parliament. Their fiery speeches, delivered at conventions designed to collect signatures for petitions to Parliament, created fears of revolution. In "Locksley Hall" (1842), Alfred, Lord Tennyson seems to have had the Chartist demonstrations in mind when he wrote: "Slowly comes a hungry people, as a lion, creeping nigher, / Glares at one that nods and winks behind a slowly-dying fire." Although the Chartist movement had fallen apart by 1848, it succeeded in creating an atmosphere open to reform. One of the most important reforms was the abolition of the high tariffs on imported grains, tariffs known as the Corn Laws (the word *corn* in England refers to wheat and other grains). These high tariffs had been established to protect English farm products from having to compete with low-priced products imported from abroad. Landowners and farmers fought to keep these tariffs in force so that high prices for their wheat would be ensured; but the rest of the population suffered severely from the exorbitant price of bread or, in years of bad crops, from scarcity of food. In 1845 serious crop failures in England and the outbreak of potato blight in Ireland convinced Sir Robert Peel, the Tory prime minister, that traditional protectionism must be abandoned. In 1846 the Corn Laws were repealed by Parliament, and the way was paved for the introduction of a system of free trade whereby goods could be imported with the payment of only minimal tariff duties. Although free trade did not eradicate the slums of Manchester, it worked well for many years and helped relieve the major crisis of the Victorian economy. In 1848, when revolutions were breaking out all over Europe, England was relatively unaffected. A large Chartist demonstration in London seemed to threaten violence, but it came to nothing. The next two decades were relatively calm and prosperous.

This Time of Troubles left its mark on some early Victorian literature. "Insurrection is a most sad necessity," Carlyle writes in his *Past and Present*, "and governors who wait for that to instruct them are surely getting into the fatalest courses." A similar refrain runs through Carlyle's history *The French Revolution* (1837). Memories of the French Reign of Terror lasted longer than memories of British victories over Napoleon at Trafalgar and Waterloo, memories freshened by later outbreaks of civil strife, "the red fool-fury of the Seine" as Tennyson described one of the violent overturnings of government in France. The most marked response to the industrial and political scene, however, comes in the "Condition of England" novels of the 1840s and early 1850s. Vivid records of these times are to be found in the fiction of Charles Kingsley (1819–1875); Elizabeth Gaskell (1810–1865); and Benjamin Disraeli (1804–1881), a novelist who became prime minister. For his novel *Sybil* (1845), Disraeli chose an appropriate subtitle, *The Two Nations*—a phrase that pointed out the line dividing the England of the rich from the other nation, the England of the poor.

THE MID-VICTORIAN PERIOD (1848–70): ECONOMIC PROSPERITY, THE GROWTH OF EMPIRE, AND RELIGIOUS CONTROVERSY

In the decades following the Time of Troubles some Victorian writers, such as Charles Dickens, continued to make critical attacks on the shortcomings of the Victorian social scene. Even more critical and indignant than Dickens was John Ruskin, who turned from a purely moral and aesthetic criticism of art during this period to denounce the evils of Victorian industry, as in his *The Stones of Venice* (1851–53), which combines a history of architecture with stern prophecies about the doom of technological culture, or in his attacks on laissez-faire economics in *Unto This Last* (1862). Generally speaking, however, the realistic novels of Anthony Trollope (1815–1882), with their comfortable tolerance and equanimity, are a more characteristic reflection of the mid-Victorian attitude toward the social and political scene than are Ruskin's lamentations. Overall, this second phase of the Victorian period had many harassing problems, but it was a time of prosperity. On the whole its institutions worked well. Even the badly bungled war against Russia in the Crimea (1854–56) did not seriously affect the growing sense of satisfaction that the challenging difficulties of the 1840s had been solved or would be solved by English wisdom and energy. The monarchy was proving its worth in a modern setting. The queen and her husband, Prince Albert, were models of middle-class domesticity and devotion to duty. The aristocracy was discovering that free trade was enriching rather than impoverishing their estates; agriculture flourished together with trade and industry. And through a succession of Factory Acts in Parliament, which restricted child labor and limited hours of employment, the condition of the working classes was also being gradually improved. When we speak of Victorian complacency or stability or optimism, we are usually referring to this mid-Victorian phase—"The Age of Improvement," as the historian Asa Briggs has called it. "Of all the decades in our history," writes G. M. Young, "a wise man would choose the eighteen-fifties to be young in."

In 1851 Prince Albert opened the Great Exhibition in Hyde Park, where a gigantic glass greenhouse, the Crystal Palace, had been erected to display the exhibits of modern industry and science. The Crystal Palace was one of the first buildings constructed according to modern architectural principles in which materials such as glass and iron are employed for purely functional ends (much late Victorian furniture, on the other hand, with its fantastic and irrelevant ornamentation, was constructed according to the opposite principle). The building, as well as the exhibits, symbolized the triumphant feats of Victorian technology. As Benjamin Disraeli wrote to a friend in 1862: "It is a privilege to live in this age of rapid and brilliant events. What an error to consider it a utilitarian age. It is one of infinite romance."

England's technological progress, together with its prosperity, led to an enormous expansion of its influence around the globe. Its annual export of goods nearly trebled in value between 1850 and 1870. Not only the export of goods but that of people and capital increased. Between 1853 and 1880 2,466,000 emigrants left Britain, many bound for British colonies. By 1870 British capitalists had invested £800 million abroad; in 1850 the total had been only £300 million. This investment, of people, money, and technology, created the British Empire. Important building blocks of the empire were put in place in the mid-Victorian period. In the 1850s and 1860s there was large-scale immigration to Australia; in 1867 Parliament unified the Canadian provinces into the Dominion of Canada. In 1857 Parliament took over the government of India from the private East India Company, which had controlled the country, and started to put in place its civil service government. In 1876 Queen Victoria was named empress of India. Although the competitive scramble for African colonies did not take place until the final decades of the century, the model of empire was created earlier, made possible by technological revolution in communication and transportation. Much as Rome had built roads through Europe in the years of the Roman Empire, Britain built railways and strung telegraph wires. It also put in place a framework for education and government that preserves British influence in former colonies even today. Britain's motives, in creating its empire, were many. It sought wealth, markets for manufactured goods, sources for raw materials, and world power and influence. Many English people also saw the expansion of empire as a moral responsibility—what Rudyard Kipling, in another context, termed "the White Man's burden." Queen Victoria stated that the imperial mission was "to protect the poor natives and advance civilization." Missionary societies flourished, spreading Christianity in India, Asia, and Africa.

At the same time that the British missionary enterprise was expanding, there was increasing debate about religious belief. By the mid-Victorian period the Church of England had evolved into three major divisions: Evangelical, or Low Church; Broad Church; and High Church. The Evangelicals emphasized spiritual transformation of the individual by conversion and a strictly moral Christian life. Zealously dedicated to good causes (they were responsible for the emancipation of all slaves in the British Empire as early as 1833), advocates of a strict Puritan code of morality, and righteously censorious of worldliness in others, the Evangelicals became a powerful and active minority in the early part of the nineteenth century. Much of the power of the Evangelicals depended on the fact that their view of life and religion was virtually identical with that of a much larger group external to the Church of England: the Nonconformists, or Dissenters—that is, Baptists, Methodists, Congregationalists, and other Protestant denominations. The High Church was also associated with a group external to the Church of England; it was the "Catholic" side of the Church, emphasizing the importance of tradition, ritual, and authority. In the 1830s a High Church movement took shape, known both as "the Oxford movement," because it originated at Oxford University, and as "Tractarianism," because its leaders developed their arguments in a series of pamphlets or tracts. Led by John Henry Newman, who later converted to Roman Catholicism, Tractarians argued that the Church could maintain its power and authority only by resisting liberal tendencies and holding to its original traditions. The Broad Church resisted the doctrinal and ecclesiastical controversies that separated the High Church and Evangelical divisions. Open to modern advances in thought, its adherents emphasized the broadly inclusive nature of the Church.

Some rationalist challenges to religious belief that developed before the Victorian period maintained their influence. The most significant was Utilitarianism, also known as Benthamism or Philosophical Radicalism. Utilitarianism derived from the thought of Jeremy Bentham (1748–1832) and his disciple James Mill (1773–1836), the father of John Stuart Mill. Bentham believed that all human beings seek to maximize pleasure and minimize pain. The criterion by which we should judge a morally correct action, therefore, is the extent to which it provides the greatest pleasure to the greatest number. Measuring religion by this moral arithmetic, Benthamites concluded that it was an outmoded superstition; it did not meet the rationalist test of value. Utilitarianism was widely influential in providing a philosophical basis for political and social reforms, but it aroused considerable opposition on the part of those who felt it failed to recognize people's spiritual needs. Raised according to strict utilitarian principles by his father, John Stuart Mill came to be critical of them. In the mental and spiritual crisis portrayed in his *Autobiography* (1873), Mill describes his realization that his utilitarian upbringing had left him no power to feel. In *Sartor Resartus* (1833–34) Carlyle describes a similar spiritual crisis in which he struggles to rediscover the springs of religious feeling in the face of his despair at the specter of a universe governed only by utilitarian principles. Later both Dickens, in his portrayal of Thomas Gradgrind in *Hard Times* (1854), "a man of facts and calculations" who is "ready to weigh and measure any parcel of human nature," and Ruskin, in his *Unto This Last*, attack utilitarianism.

In mid-Victorian England, however, the challenge to religious belief gradually shifted from the Utilitarians to some of the leaders of science, in particular to Thomas Henry Huxley, who popularized the theories of Charles Darwin. Although many English scientists were themselves individuals of strong religious convictions, the impact of their scientific discoveries seemed consistently damaging to established faiths. Complaining in 1851 about the "flimsiness" of his own religious faith, Ruskin exclaimed: "If only the Geologists would let me alone, I could do very well, but those dreadful hammers! I

hear the clink of them at the end of every cadence of the Bible verses."
The damage lamented by Ruskin was effected in two ways. First the scientific attitude of mind was applied toward a study of the Bible. This kind of
investigation, developed especially in Germany, was known as the "Higher
Criticism." Instead of treating the Bible as a sacredly infallible document,
scientifically minded scholars examined it as a mere text of history and presented evidence about its composition that believers, especially in Protestant
countries, found disconcerting, to say the least. A noteworthy example of such
Higher Criticism studies was David Friedrich Strauss's *Das Leben Jesu,* which
was translated by George Eliot in 1846 as *The Life of Jesus.* The second kind
of damage was effected by the view of humanity implicit in the discoveries of
geology and astronomy, the new and "Terrible Muses" of literature, as Tennyson called them in a late poem. Geology, by extending the history of the
earth backward millions of years, reduced the stature of the human species in
time. John Tyndall, an eminent physicist, said in an address at Belfast in 1874
that in the eighteenth century people had an "unwavering trust" in the "chronology of the Old Testament" but in Victorian times they had to become accustomed to

> the idea that not for six thousand, nor for sixty thousand, nor for six
> thousand thousand, but for aeons embracing untold millions of years, this
> earth has been the theater of life and death. The riddle of the rocks has
> been read by the geologist and paleontologist, from sub-Cambrian depths
> to the deposits thickening over the sea bottoms of today. And upon the
> leaves of that stone book are . . . stamped the characters, plainer and surer
> than those formed by the ink of history, which carry the mind back into
> abysses of past time.

The discoveries of astronomers, by extending a knowledge of stellar distances
to dizzying expanses, were likewise disconcerting. Carlyle's friend John
Sterling remarked in a letter of 1837 how geology "gives one the same sort of
bewildering view of the abysmal extent of Time that Astronomy does of Space."
To Tennyson's speaker in *Maud* (1855) the stars are "innumerable" tyrants of
"iron skies." They are "Cold fires, yet with power to burn and brand / His
nothingness into man."
   In the mid-Victorian period biology reduced humankind even further into
"nothingness." Darwin's great treatise *The Origin of Species* (1859) was interpreted by the nonscientific public in a variety of ways. Some chose to assume
that evolution was synonymous with progress, but most readers recognized
that Darwin's theory of natural selection conflicted not only with the concept
of creation derived from the Bible but also with long-established assumptions
of the values attached to humanity's special role in the world. Darwin's later
treatise *The Descent of Man* (1871) raised more explicitly the haunting question of our identification with the animal kingdom. If the principle of survival
of the fittest was accepted as the key to conduct, there remained the inquiry:
fittest for what? As John Fowles writes in his 1968 novel about Victorian
England, *The French Lieutenant's Woman,* Darwin's theories made the Victorians feel "infinitely isolated." "By the 1860s the great iron structures of
their philosophies, religions, and social stratifications were already beginning
to look dangerously corroded to the more perspicacious."
   Disputes about evolutionary science, like the disputes about religion, are a
reminder that beneath the placidly prosperous surface of the mid-Victorian

age there were serious conflicts and anxieties. In the same year as the Great Exhibition, with its celebration of the triumphs of trade and industry, Charles Kingsley wrote, "The young men and women of our day are fast parting from their parents and each other; the more thoughtful are wandering either towards Rome, towards sheer materialism, or towards an unchristian and unphilosophic spiritualism."

THE LATE PERIOD (1870–1901): DECAY OF VICTORIAN VALUES

The third phase of the Victorian age is more difficult to categorize. At first glance its point of view seems merely an extension of mid-Victorianism, whose golden glow lingered on through the Jubilee years of 1887 and 1897 (years celebrating the fiftieth and sixtieth anniversaries of the queen's accession) down to 1914. For many affluent Victorians, this final phase of the century was a time of serenity and security, the age of house parties and long weekends in the country. In the amber of Henry James's prose is immortalized a sense of the comfortable pace of these pleasant, food-filled gatherings. Life in London, too, was for many an exhilarating heyday. In *My Life and Loves* the Irish-American Frank Harris (1854–1931), often a severe critic of the English scene, records his recollections of the gaiety of London in the 1880s: "London: who would give even an idea of its varied delights: London, the center of civilization, the queen city of the world without a peer in the multitude of its attractions, as superior to Paris as Paris is to New York." The exhilarating sense of London's delights reflects in part the proliferation of things: commodities, inventions, products that were changing the texture of modern life. England had become committed not only to continuing technological change but also to a culture of consumerism, generating new products for sale.

The wealth of England's empire provided the foundation on which its economy was built. The final decades of the century saw the apex of British imperialism, yet the cost of the empire became increasingly apparent in rebellions, massacres, and bungled wars, such as the Indian Mutiny in 1857; the Jamaica Rebellion in 1865; the massacre of General Gordon and his troops at Khartoum, in the Sudan, in 1885, where he had been sent to evacuate the British in the face of a religiously inspired revolt; and the Anglo-Boer War, at the end of the century, in which England engaged in a long, bloody, and unpopular struggle to annex two independent republics in the south of Africa controlled by Dutch settlers called Boers. In addition the "Irish Question," as it was called, became especially divisive in the 1880s, when home rule for Ireland became a topic of heated debate—a proposed reform that was unsuccessfully advocated by Prime Minister Gladstone and other leaders. And outside the British Empire, other developments challenged Victorian stability and security. The sudden emergence of Bismarck's Germany after the defeat of France in 1871 was progressively to confront England with powerful threats to its naval and military position and also to its preeminence in trade and industry. The recovery of the United States after the Civil War likewise provided new and serious competition not only in industry but also in agriculture. As the westward expansion of railroads in the United States and Canada opened up the vast, grain-rich prairies, the typical English farmer had to confront lower grain prices and a dramatically different scale of productivity, which England could not match. In 1873 and 1874 such severe economic depressions occurred that the rate of emigration rose to an alarming degree. Another change in the mid-Victorian balance of power was the growth of labor as a political and economic force. In 1867, under Disraeli's guidance, a second Reform Bill had been passed that extended the right to vote to sections of the working classes; and this, together with the subsequent development of trade unions, made labor a powerful political force that included a wide variety of kinds of socialism. Some labor leaders were disciples of the Tory-socialism of John Ruskin and shared his idealistic conviction that the middle-class economic and political system, with its distrust of state interference, was irresponsible and immoral. Other labor leaders had been influenced instead by the revolutionary theories of Karl Marx and Friedrich Engels as expounded in their *Communist Manifesto* of 1847 and in Marx's *Das Kapital* (1867, 1885, 1895). The first English author of note to embrace Marxism was the poet and painter William Morris, who shared with Marx a conviction that utopia could be achieved only after the working classes had, by revolution, taken control of government and industry.

In much of the literature of this final phase of Victorianism we can sense an overall change of attitudes. Some of the late Victorian writers expressed the change openly by simply attacking the major mid-Victorian idols. Samuel Butler, for example, set about demolishing Darwin, Tennyson, and Prime Minister Gladstone, figures whose aura of authority reminded him of his own father. For the more worldly and casual-mannered Prime Minister Disraeli, on the other hand, Butler could express considerable admiration: "Earnestness was his greatest danger, but if he did not quite overcome it (as who indeed can? it is the last enemy that shall be subdued), he managed to veil it with a fair amount of success." In his novel *The Way of All Flesh* (1903), much of which was written in the 1870s, Butler satirized family life, in particular the tyrannical self-righteousness of a Victorian father, his own father (a clergyman) serving as his model. In a different vein Walter Pater and his followers concluded that the striving of their predecessors was ultimately pointless, that the answers to our problems are not to be found, and that our role is to enjoy the fleeting moments of beauty in "this short day of frost and sun." It is symptomatic of this shift in point of view that Edward FitzGerald's beautiful translation (1859) of *The Rubáiyát of Omar Khayyám*, with its melancholy theme that life's problems are insoluble, went virtually unnoticed in the 1860s but became a popular favorite in subsequent decades.

THE NINETIES

The changes in attitude that had begun cropping up in the 1870s became much more conspicuous in the final decade of the century and give the nineties a special aura of notoriety. Of course the changes were not in evidence everywhere. At the empire's outposts in India and Africa, the English were building railways and administering governments with the same strenuous energy as in the mid-Victorian period. The stories of Kipling and Joseph Conrad variously record the struggles of such people. Also embodying the task of sustaining an empire were the soldiers and sailors who fought in various colonial wars, most notably in the war against the Boers in South Africa (1899–1902). But back in England, Victorian standards were breaking down on several fronts. One colorful embodiment of changing values was Victoria's son and heir, Edward, Prince of Wales, who was entering his fiftieth year as the nineties began. A pleasure-seeking easygoing person, Edward was the antithesis of his father, Prince Albert, an earnest-minded intellectual who had devoted his life to hard work and to administrative responsibilities. Edward's carryings-on were a favorite topic for newspaper articles, one of which noted how this father of five children "openly maintained scandalous relations with ballet dancers and chorus singers."

Much of the writing of the decade illustrates a breakdown of a different sort. Melancholy, not gaiety, is characteristic of its spirit. Artists of the nineties, representing the aesthetic movement, were very much aware of living at the end of a great century and often cultivated a deliberately fin de siècle ("end-of-century") pose. A studied languor, a weary sophistication, a search for new ways of titillating jaded palates can be found in both the poetry and the prose of the period. *The Yellow Book,* a periodical that ran from 1894 to 1897, is generally taken to represent the aestheticism of the nineties. The startling black-and-white drawings and designs of its art editor, Aubrey Beardsley, the prose of George Moore and Max Beerbohm, and the poetry of Ernest Dowson illustrate different aspects of the movement. In 1893 the Austrian critic Max Nordau summed up what seemed to him to be happening, in a book that was as sensational as its title: *Degeneration.*

From our perspective, however, it is easy to see in the nineties the beginning of the modernist movement in literature; a number of the great writers of the twentieth century—Yeats, Hardy, Conrad, Shaw—were already publishing.

In Dickens's *David Copperfield* (1850) the hero affirms: "I have always been thoroughly in earnest." Forty-five years later Oscar Wilde's comedy *The Importance of Being Earnest* (1895) turns the typical mid-Victorian word *earnest* into a pun, a key joke in this comic spectacle of earlier Victorian values being turned upside down. As Richard Le Gallienne (a novelist of the nineties) remarked in *The Romantic Nineties* (1926): "Wilde made dying Victorianism laugh at itself, and it may be said to have died of the laughter."

THE ROLE OF WOMEN

Political and legal reforms in the course of the Victorian period had given citizens many rights. In 1844 Friedrich Engels observed: "England is unquestionably the freest—that is the least unfree—country in the world, North America not excepted." England had indeed done much to extend its citizens' liberties, but women did not share in these freedoms. They could not vote or hold political office. (Although petitions to Parliament advocating women's suffrage were introduced as early as the 1840s, women did not get the vote until 1918.) Until the passage of the Married Women's Property Acts (1870–1908), married women could not own or handle their own property. While men could divorce their wives for adultery, wives could divorce their husbands only if adultery were combined with cruelty, bigamy, incest, or bestiality. Educational and employment opportunities for women were limited. These inequities stimulated a spirited debate about women's roles known as the "Woman Question." Some of the social changes that such discussion helped foster eventually affected the lives of all, or many, of the country's female population; nevertheless, it is important to recognize that this Victorian debate, despite the inclusive claims of its title was, with a few exceptions, conducted by the middle classes about middle-class women.

Arguments for women's rights were based on the same libertarian principles that had formed the basis of extended rights for men. In Hardy's last novel, *Jude the Obscure* (1895), his heroine justifies leaving her husband by quoting a passage from Mill's *On Liberty* (1859). She might have quoted another work by Mill, *The Subjection of Women* (1869), which, like Mary Wollstonecraft's *A Vindication of the Rights of Woman* (1792), challenges long-established assumptions about women's role in society. Legislative measures over the course of the nineteenth century gradually brought about changes in a number of areas.

The Custody Act of 1839 gave a mother the right to petition the court for access to her minor children and custody of children under seven (raised to sixteen in 1878). The Divorce and Matrimonial Causes Act of 1857 established a civil divorce court (divorce previously could be granted only by an ecclesiastical court) and provided a deserted wife the right to apply for a protection order that would allow her rights to her property. Although divorce remained so expensive as to be available only to the very rich, these changes in marriage and divorce laws, together with the Married Women's Property Acts, began to establish a basis for the rights of women in marriage.

In addition to pressuring Parliament for legal reform, feminists worked to enlarge female educational opportunities. In 1837 none of England's three universities was open to women. Tennyson's long poem *The Princess* (1847), with its fantasy of a women's college from whose precincts all males are excluded, was inspired by contemporary discussions of the need for women to obtain an education more advanced than that provided by the popular finishing schools such as Miss Pinkerton's Academy in William Makepeace Thackeray's *Vanity Fair* (1847–48). Although by the end of the poem Princess Ida has repented of her Amazonian scheme, she and the prince look forward to a future in which man will be "more of woman, she of man." The poem reflects a climate of opinion that led in 1848 to the establishment of the first women's college in London, an example later recommended by Thomas Henry Huxley, a strong advocate of advanced education for women. By the end of Victoria's reign, women could take degrees at twelve universities or university colleges and could study, although not earn a degree, at Oxford and Cambridge.

There was also agitation for improved employment opportunities for women. Writers as diverse as Charlotte Brontë, Elizabeth Barrett Browning, and Florence Nightingale complained that middle-class women were taught trivial accomplishments to fill up days in which there was nothing important to do. Had they been aware of such complaints, women from the majority lower-class population might have found it hard to show sympathy: the working lives of poor English women had always been strenuous, inside and outside the house, but industrial society brought unprecedented pressures. Although the largest proportion of working women labored as servants in the homes of the more affluent, the explosive growth of mechanized industries, especially in the textile trade, created new and grueling forms of paid employment. Hundreds of thousands of lower-class women worked at factory jobs under appalling conditions, while the need for coal to fuel England's industrial development brought women into the mines for the first time. A series of Factory Acts (1802–78) gradually regulated the conditions of labor in mines and factories, eventually reducing the sixteen-hour day and banning women from mine work altogether; but even with such changes, the lot of the country's poorest women, whether factory operatives or housemaids, seamstresses or field laborers, was undoubtedly hard. Bad working conditions and underemployment drove thousands of women into prostitution, which in the nineteenth century became increasingly professionalized—and the subject of an almost obsessive public concern, whose manifestations included frequent literary and artistic representation.

For the most part, prostitution was a trade for working-class women, but there was considerable anxiety about the possible fates of what contemporary journalists called the "surplus" or "redundant" women of the middle classes— that is, women who remained unmarried because of the imbalance in numbers between the sexes. Such women (of whom there were approximately half a million in mid-Victorian England) had few employment opportunities, none of them attractive or profitable. Emigration was frequently proposed as a solution to the problem, but the number of single female emigrants was never high enough to significantly affect the population imbalance. The only occupation at which an unmarried middle-class woman could earn a living and maintain some claim to gentility was that of a governess, but a governess could expect no security of employment, only minimal wages, and an ambiguous status, somewhere between servant and family member, that isolated her within the household. Perhaps because the governess so clearly indicated the precariousness of the unmarried middle-class woman's status in Victorian England, the governess novel, of which the most famous examples are *Jane Eyre* (1847) and *Vanity Fair*, became a popular genre through which to explore women's roles in society.

As such novels indicate, Victorian society was preoccupied not only with legal and economic limitations on women's lives but with the very nature of woman. In *The Subjection of Women*, John Stuart Mill argues that "what is now called the nature of women is eminently an artificial thing—the result of forced repression in some directions, unnatural stimulation in others." In Tennyson's *The Princess* the king voices a more traditional view of male and female roles, a view that has come to be known as the doctrine of "separate spheres":

> Man for the field and woman for the hearth:
> Man for the sword and for the needle she:
> Man with the head and woman with the heart:
> Man to command and woman to obey.

The king's relegation of women to the hearth and heart reflects an ideology that claimed that woman had a special nature peculiarly fit for her domestic role. Most aptly epitomized by the title of Coventry Patmore's immensely popular poem *The Angel in the House* (1854–62), this concept of womanhood stressed woman's purity and selflessness. Protected and enshrined within the home, her role was to create a place of peace where man could take refuge from the difficulties of modern life. In "Of Queens' Gardens" (1865), John Ruskin writes:

> This is the true nature of home—it is the place of Peace; the shelter, not only from all injury, but from all terror, doubt, and division. In so far as it is not this, it is not home; so far as the anxieties of the outer life penetrate into it, and the inconsistently-minded, unknown, unloved, or hostile society of the outer world is allowed either by husband or wife to cross the threshold, it ceases to be home; it is then only a part of that outer world which you have roofed over, and lighted fire in. But so far as it is a sacred place, a vestal temple, a temple of the hearth watched over by

Household Gods, . . . so far it vindicates the name, and fulfills the praise, of home.

Such an exalted conception of home placed great pressure on the woman who ran it to be, in Ruskin's words, "enduringly, incorruptibly good; instinctively, infallibly wise—wise, not for self-development, but for self-renunciation." It is easy to recognize the oppressive aspects of this domestic ideology. Paradoxically, however, it was used not only by antifeminists, eager to keep woman in her place, but by some feminists as well, in justifying the special contribution that woman could make to public life.

In his preface to *The Portrait of a Lady* (1881) Henry James writes: "Millions of presumptuous girls, intelligent or not intelligent, daily affront their destiny, and what is it open to their destiny to *be*, at the most, that we should make an ado about it?" Every major Victorian novelist makes the "ado" that James describes in addressing the question of woman's vocation; by the 1890s the "New Woman," an emerging form of emancipated womanhood, was endlessly debated in a wave of fiction and magazine articles. Ultimately, as Victorian texts illustrate, the basic problem was not only political, economic, and educational. It was how women were regarded, and regarded themselves, as members of a society.

LITERACY, PUBLICATION, AND READING

Literacy increased significantly during the Victorian period, although precise figures are difficult to calculate. In 1837 about half of the adult male population could read and write to some extent; by the end of the century, basic literacy was almost universal, the product in part of compulsory national education, required by 1880 to the age of ten. There was also an explosion of things to read. Because of technological changes in printing—presses powered by steam, paper made from wood pulp rather than rags, and, toward the end of the century, typesetting machines—publishers could bring out more printed material more cheaply than ever before. The number of newspapers, periodicals, and books increased exponentially during the Victorian period. Books remained fairly expensive, and most readers borrowed them from commercial lending libraries. (There were few public libraries until the final decades of the century.) After the repeal of the stamp tax and duties on advertisements just after midcentury, an extensive popular press developed.

The most significant development in publishing from the point of view of literary culture was the growth of the periodical. In the first thirty years of the Victorian period, 170 new periodicals were started in London alone. There were magazines for every taste: cheap and popular magazines that published sensational tales; religious monthlies; weekly newspapers; satiric periodicals noted for their political cartoons (the most famous of these was *Punch*); women's magazines; monthly miscellanies publishing fiction, poetry, and articles on current affairs; and reviews and quarterlies, ostensibly reviewing new books but using the reviews, which were always unsigned, as occasions for essays on the subjects in question. The chief reviews and monthly magazines had a great deal of power and influence; they defined issues in public affairs, and they made and broke literary reputations. They also published the major writers of the period: the fiction of Dickens, Thackeray, Eliot, Trollope, and Gaskell; the essays of Carlyle, Mill, Arnold, and Ruskin; and the poetry of Tennyson and the Brownings all appeared in monthly magazines. The circumstances of periodical publication exerted a shaping force on literature. Novels and long works of nonfiction prose were published in serial form. Although serial publication of works began in the late eighteenth century, it was the publication of Dickens's *Pickwick Papers* (1836–37) in individual numbers that established its popularity. All of Dickens's novels and many of those of his contemporaries were published in serial form. Readers therefore read these works in relatively short, discrete installments over a period that could extend more than a year, with time for reflection and interpretation in between. Serial publication encouraged a certain kind of plotting and pacing and allowed writers to take account of their readers' reactions as they constructed subsequent installments. Writers created a continuing world, punctuated by the ends of installments, which served to stimulate the curiosity that would keep readers buying subsequent issues. Serial publication also created a distinctive sense of a community of readers, a sense encouraged by the practice of reading aloud in family gatherings.

As the family reading of novels suggests, the middle-class reading public enjoyed a common reading culture. Poets such as Tennyson and Elizabeth Barrett Browning and anthologies such as Palgrave's *Golden Treasury* (1861) appealed to a large body of readers; prose writers such as Carlyle, Arnold, and Ruskin achieved a status as sages; and the major Victorian novelists were popular writers. Readers shared the expectation that literature would not only delight but instruct, that it would be continuous with the lived world, and that it would illuminate social problems. "Tennyson," one of his college friends warned him, "we cannot live in Art." These expectations weighed more heavily on some writers than others. Tennyson wore his public mantle with considerable ambivalence; Arnold abandoned the private mode of lyric poetry in order to speak about public issues in lectures and essays.

By the 1870s the sense of a broad readership, with a shared set of social concerns, had begun to dissolve. Writers had begun to define themselves in opposition to a general public; poets like the Pre-Raphaelites pursued art for art's sake, doing exactly what Tennyson's friend had warned against; mass publication included less and less serious literature. By the end of Victoria's reign, writers could no longer assume a unified reading public.

THE NOVEL

The novel was the dominant form in Victorian literature. Initially published, for the most part, in serial form, novels subsequently appeared in three-volume editions, or "three-deckers." "Large loose baggy monsters," Henry James called them, reflecting his dissatisfaction with their sprawling panoramic expanse. As their size suggests, Victorian novels seek to represent a large and comprehensive social world, with the variety of classes and social settings that constitute a community. They contain a multitude of characters and a number of plots, setting in motion the kinds of patterns that reveal the author's vision of the deep structures of the social world—how, in George Eliot's words, "the mysterious mixture behaves under the varying experiments of Time." They presents themselves as realistic, that is, as representing a social world that shares the features of the one we inhabit. The French novelist Stendhal (1783–1842) called the novel "a mirror wandering down a road," but the metaphor of the mirror is somewhat deceptive, since it implies that writers exert no shaping force on their material. It would be more accurate to speak not of realism but of realisms, since each novelist presents a specific vision of reality whose representational force he or she seeks to persuade us to acknowledge through a variety of techniques and conventions. The worlds of Dickens, of Trollope, of Eliot, of the Brontës hardly seem continuous with each other, but their authors share the attempt to convince us that the characters and events they imagine resemble those we experience in actual life.

The experience that Victorian novelists most frequently depict is the set of social relationships in the middle-class society developing around them. It is a society where the material conditions of life indicate social position, where money defines opportunity, where social class enforces a powerful sense of stratification, yet where chances for class mobility exist. Pip can aspire to the great expectations that provide the title for Dickens's novel; Jane Eyre can marry her employer, a landed gentleman. Most Victorian novels focus on a protagonist whose effort to define his or her place in society is the main concern of the plot. The novel thus constructs a tension between surrounding social conditions and the aspiration of the hero or heroine, whether it be for love, social position, or a life adequate to his or her imagination. This tension makes the novel the natural form to use in portraying woman's struggle for self-realization in the context of the constraints imposed upon her. For both men and women writers, the heroine is often, therefore, the representative protagonist whose search for fulfillment emblematizes the human condition. The great heroines of Victorian fiction—Jane Eyre, Maggie Tulliver, Dorothea Brooke, Isabel Archer, Tess of the d'Urbervilles, even Becky Sharp—all seem in some way to illustrate George Eliot's judgment, voiced in the Prelude to *Middlemarch* (1871–72), of "a certain spiritual grandeur ill-matched with meanness of opportunity."

From the beginning of the nineteenth century, the novel was more than a fertile medium for the portrayal of women; women writers were, for the first time, not figures on the margins but major authors. Jane Austen, the Brontës, Elizabeth Gaskell, George Eliot—all helped define the genre. When Charlotte Brontë screwed up her courage to write to the poet laureate, Robert Southey, to ask his advice about a career as a writer, he warned her, "Literature cannot be the business of a woman's life, and it ought not to be." Charlotte Brontë put this letter, with one other from Southey, in an envelope, with the inscription "Southey's advice to be kept forever. My twenty-first birthday." Brontë's ability ultimately to depart from Southey's advice derived in part from how amenable the novel was to women writers. It concerned the domestic life that women knew well—courtship, family relationships, marriage. It was a popular form whose market women could enter easily. It did not carry the burden of an august tradition as poetry did, nor did it build on the learning of a university education. In his essay "The Lady Novelists" (1852) George Henry Lewes declared, "The advent of female literature promises woman's view of life, woman's experience." His common-law wife, George Eliot, together with many of her sister novelists, fulfilled his prophecy.

Whether written by women or men, the Victorian novel was extraordinarily various. It encompassed a wealth of styles and genres from the extravagant comedy of Dickens to the Gothic romances of the Brontë sisters, from the satire of Thackeray to the probing psychological fiction of Eliot, from the social and political realism of Trollope to the sensation novels of Wilkie Collins. Later in the century a number of popular genres developed—crime, mystery,

and horror novels, as well as science fiction and detective stories. For the
Victorians the novel was both a principal form of entertainment and a spur to
social sympathy. There was not a social topic that the novel did not address.
Dickens, Gaskell, and many lesser novelists tried to stimulate efforts for social
reform through their depiction of social problems. Writing at the beginning
of the twentieth century, Joseph Conrad defined the novel in a way that could
speak for the Victorians: "What is a novel if not a conviction of our fellow-
men's existence strong enough to take upon itself a form of imagined life
clearer than reality and whose accumulated verisimilitude of selected episodes
puts to shame the pride of documentary history?"

POETRY

Victorian poetry developed in the context of the novel. As the novel emerged
as the dominant form of literature, poets sought new ways of telling stories in
verse; examples include Tennyson's *Maud*, Elizabeth Barrett Browning's
Aurora Leigh (1857), Robert Browning's *The Ring and the Book* (1868–69),
and Arthur Hugh Clough's *Amours de Voyage* (1857–58). Poets and critics
debated what the appropriate subjects of such long narrative poems should
be. Some, like Matthew Arnold, held that poets should use the heroic materials
of the past; others, like Elizabeth Barrett Browning, felt that poets should
represent "their age, not Charlemagne's." Poets also experimented with character and perspective. *Amours de Voyage* is a long epistolary poem that tells
the story of a failed romance through letters written by its various characters;
The Ring and the Book presents its plot—an old Italian murder story—through
ten different perspectives.

Victorian poetry also developed in the shadow of Romanticism. By 1837,
when Victoria ascended the throne, all the major Romantic poets, save William
Wordsworth, were dead, but they had died young, and many readers consequently still regarded them as their contemporaries. Not even twenty years
separated the birth dates of Tennyson and Browning from that of John Keats,
but they lived more than three times as long as he did. All the Victorian poets
show the strong influence of the Romantics, but they cannot sustain the confidence that the Romantics felt in the power of the imagination. The Victorians
often rewrite Romantic poems with a sense of belatedness and distance.
When, in his poem "Resignation," Arnold addresses his sister upon revisiting
a landscape, much as Wordsworth had addressed his sister in "Tintern Abbey,"
he tells her the rocks and sky "seem to bear rather than rejoice." Tennyson
frequently represents his muse as an embowered woman, cut off from the
world and doomed to death. The speakers of Browning's poems who embrace
the visions that their imaginations present are madmen. When Hardy writes
"The Darkling Thrush," in December 1900, Keats's nightingale has become
"an aged thrush, frail, gaunt, and small."

Victorian poets build upon this sense of belated Romanticism in a number
of different ways. Some poets writing in the second half of the century, like
Dante Gabriel Rossetti and Algernon Charles Swinburne, embrace an attenuated Romanticism, art pursued for its own sake. Reacting against what he
sees as the insufficiency of an allegory of the state of one's own mind as the
basis of poetry, Arnold seeks an objective basis for poetic emotion and finally
gives up writing poems altogether when he decides that the present age lacks
the culture necessary to support great poetry. The more fruitful reaction to

the subjectivity of Romantic poetry, however, was not Arnold's but Browning's. Turning from the mode of his early poetry, modeled on Percy Bysshe Shelley, Browning began writing dramatic monologues—poems, he said, that are "Lyric in expression" but "Dramatic in principle, and so many utterances of so many imaginary persons, not mine." Tennyson simultaneously developed a more lyric form of the dramatic monologue. The idea of creating a lyric poem in the voice of a speaker ironically distinct from the poet is the great achievement of Victorian poetry, one developed extensively in the twentieth century. In *Poetry and the Age* (1953), the modernist poet and critic Randall Jarrell acknowledges this fact: "The dramatic monologue, which once had depended for its effect upon being a departure from the norm of poetry, now became in one form or other the norm."

The formal experimentation of Victorian poetry, both in long narrative and in the dramatic monologue, may make it seem eclectic, but Victorian poetry shares a number of characteristics. It tends to be pictorial, using detail to construct visual images that represent the emotion or situation the poem concerns. In his review of Tennyson's first volume of poetry, Arthur Henry Hallam defines this kind of poetry as "picturesque," as combining visual impressions in such a way that they create a picture that carries the dominant emotion of the poem. This aesthetic brings poets and painters close together. Contemporary artists frequently illustrated Victorian poems, and poems themselves often present paintings. Victorian poetry also uses sound in a distinctive way. Whether it be the mellifluousness of Tennyson or Swinburne, with its emphasis on beautiful cadences, alliteration, and vowel sounds, or the roughness of Browning or Gerard Manley Hopkins, a roughness adopted in part in reaction against Tennyson, the sound of Victorian poetry reflects an attempt to use poetry as a medium with a presence almost independent of sense. The resulting style can become so syntactically elaborate that it is easy to parody, as in Hopkins's description of Browning as a man "bouncing up from table with his mouth full of bread and cheese" or T. S. Eliot's criticism of Swinburne's poetry, where "meaning is merely the hallucination of meaning." Yet it is important to recognize that these poets use sound to convey meaning, to quote Hallam's review of Tennyson once more, "where words would not." "The tone becomes the sign of the feeling." In all of these developments—the experimentation with narrative and perspective, the dramatic monologue, the use of visual detail and sound—Victorian poets seek to represent psychology in a different way. Their most distinctive achievement is a poetry of mood and character. They therefore sat in uneasy relationship to the public expectation that poets be sages with something to teach. Tennyson, Browning, and Arnold showed varying discomfort with this public role; poets beginning to write in the second half of the century distanced themselves from their public by embracing an identity as bohemian rebels. Women poets encountered a different set of difficulties in developing their poetic voice. When, in Barrett Browning's epic about the growth of a woman poet, Aurora Leigh's cousin Romney discourages her poetic ambitions by telling her that women are "weak for art" but "strong for life and duty," he articulates the prejudice of an age. Women poets view their vocation in the context of the constraints and expectations upon their sex. Perhaps because of this, their poems are less complicated by the experiments in perspective than those of their male contemporaries.

PROSE

Although Victorian poets felt ambivalent about the didactic mission the public expected of the man of letters, writers of nonfictional prose aimed specifically to instruct. Although the term *nonfictional prose* is clumsy and not quite exact (the Victorians themselves referred instead to history, biography, theology, criticism), it has its uses not only to distinguish these prose writers from the novelists but also to indicate the centrality of argument and persuasion to Victorian intellectual life. The growth of the periodical press, described earlier, provided the vehicle and marketplace for nonfictional prose. It reflects a vigorous sense of shared intellectual life and the public urgency of social and moral issues. On a wide range of controversial topics—religious, political, and aesthetic—writers seek to convince their readers to share their convictions and values. Such writers seem at times almost secular priests. Indeed, in the fifth lecture of *On Heroes, Hero-Worship, and the Heroic in History* (1841), Carlyle defines the writer precisely in these terms: "Men of Letters are a perpetual Priesthood, from age to age, teaching all Men that God is still present in their life. . . . In the true Literary Man, there is thus ever, acknowledged or not by the world, a sacredness." The modern man of letters, Carlyle argues, differs from his earlier counterpart in that he writes for money. "Never, till about a hundred years ago, was there seen any figure of a Great Soul living apart in that anomalous manner; endeavouring to speak forth the inspiration that was in him by Printed Books, and find place and subsistence by what the world would please him for doing that." This combination, of a new market position for nonfictional writing and an exalted sense of the didactic function of the writer, produces a quintessential Victorian form.

On behalf of nonfictional prose, Walter Pater argued in his essay "Style" (1889) that it was "the special and opportune art of the modern world." He believed not that it was superior to verse but that it more readily conveys the "chaotic variety and complexity" of modern life, the "incalculable" intellectual diversity of the "master currents of the present time." Pater's characterization of prose helps us understand what its writers were attempting to do. Despite the diversity of styles and subjects, Victorian prose writers were engaged in shaping belief in a bewilderingly complex and changing world. Their modes of persuasion differ. Mill and Huxley rely on clear reasoning, logical argument, and the kind of lucid style favored by essayists of the eighteenth century. Carlyle and Ruskin write a prose that is more Romantic in character, that seeks to move readers as well as convince them. Whatever the differences in their rhetorical techniques, however, they share an urgency of exposition. Not only by what they said but by how they said it, Victorian prose writers were claiming a place for literature in a scientific and materialistic culture. Arnold and Pater share this as an explicit aim. Each in his own way argues that culture—the intensely serious appreciation of great works of literature—provides the kind of immanence and meaning that people once found in religion. For Arnold this is an intensely moral experience; for Pater it is aesthetic. Together they develop the basis for the claims of modern literary criticism.

DRAMA AND THEATER

Though the Victorian age can lay claim to greatness for its poetry, its prose, and its novels, it would be difficult to make such a high claim for its plays, at least until the final decade of the century. Here we must distinguish between playwriting on the one hand and theatrical activity on the other. For the theater, throughout the period, was a flourishing and popular institution, in which were performed not merely conventional dramas but a rich variety of theatrical entertainments, many with lavish spectacular effects—burlesques, extravaganzas, highly scenic and altered versions of Shakespeare's plays, melodramas, pantomimes, and musicals. Robert Corrigan gives figures that suggest the extent of the popularity of such entertainment: "In the decade between 1850 and 1860 the number of theaters built throughout the country was doubled, and in the middle of the sixties, in London alone, 150,000 would be attending the theater on any given day. Only when we realize that the theatre was to Victorian England what television is to us today will we be able to comprehend both its wide appeal and its limited artistic achievement." The popularity of theatrical entertainment made theater a powerful influence on other genres. Dickens was devoted to the theater and composed many of the scenes of his novels with theatrical techniques. Thackeray represents himself as the puppet master of his characters in *Vanity Fair* and employs the stock gestures and expressions of melodramatic acting in his illustrations for the novel. Tennyson, Browning, and Henry James tried their hands at writing plays, though with no commercial success. Successful plays on stage were written by the lesser lights of literature such as Dion Boucicault (1820–1890), the period's most prolific and popular dramatist. The comic operas of W. S. Gilbert and Arthur Sullivan prove the exception to this judgment. Their satire of Victorian values and institutions, what Gilbert called their "topsyturvydom," and their grave and quasi-respectful treatment of the ridiculous not only make them delightful in themselves but anticipate the techniques of Shaw and Wilde. Around 1890, when the socially controversial plays of the Norwegian dramatist Henrik Ibsen (1828–1906) became known in England, Arthur Pinero (1855–1934) and Bernard Shaw began writing "problem plays," which addressed difficult social issues. In the 1890s Shaw and Oscar Wilde transformed British theater with their comic masterpieces. Although they did not like each other's work, they both created a kind of comedy that took aim at Victorian pretense and hypocrisy.

———————

Additional information about the Victorian Age, including primary texts and images, is available at Norton Literature Online (www.wwnorton.com/literature). Online topics are

- Industrialism—Progress or Decline?
- The Woman Question
- The Painterly Image in Poetry
- Victorian Imperialism

THE VICTORIAN AGE

TEXTS	CONTEXTS
1830 Alfred Lord Tennyson, *Poems, Chiefly Lyrical*	1830 Opening of Liverpool and Manchester Railway
1832 Sir Charles Lyell, *Principles of Geology*	1832 First Reform Bill
1833 Thomas Carlyle, *Sartor Resartus*	1833 Factory Act. Abolition of Slavery Act. Beginning of Oxford Movement
1836 Charles Dickens, *Pickwick Papers*	1836 First train in London
1837 Carlyle, *The French Revolution*	1837 Victoria becomes queen
	1838 "People's Charter" issued by Chartist Movement
	1840 Queen marries Prince Albert
1842 Tennyson, *Poems*. Robert Browning, *Dramatic Lyrics*	1842 Chartist Riots. Copyright Act. Mudie's Circulating Library
1843 John Ruskin, *Modern Painters* (vol. 1)	
	1845–46 Potato famine in Ireland. Mass emigration to North America
1846 George Eliot, *The Life of Jesus* (translation)	1846 Repeal of Corn Laws. Robert Browning marries Elizabeth Barrett
1847 Charlotte Brontë, *Jane Eyre*. Emily Brontë, *Wuthering Heights*	1847 Ten Hours Factory Act
1848 Elizabeth Gaskell, *Mary Barton*. William Makepeace Thackeray, *Vanity Fair*	1848 Revolution on the Continent. Second Republic established in France. Founding of Pre-Raphaelite Brotherhood
1850 Tennyson, *In Memoriam*. William Wordsworth, *The Prelude* (posthumous publication)	1850 Tennyson succeeds Wordsworth as Poet Laureate
1851 Ruskin, *Stones of Venice*	1851 Great Exhibition of science and industry at the Crystal Palace
1853 Matthew Arnold, *Poems*	
1854 Dickens, *Hard Times*	1854 Crimean War. Florence Nightingale organizes nurses to care for sick and wounded
1855 Robert Browning, *Men and Women*	
1857 Elizabeth Barrett Browning, *Aurora Leigh*	1857 Indian Mutiny. Matrimonial Causes Act
1859 Charles Darwin, *The Origin of Species*. John Stuart Mill, *On Liberty*. Tennyson, *Idylls of the King* (books 1–4)	
1860 Dickens, *Great Expectations*. Eliot, *The Mill on the Floss*	1860 Italian unification
	1861 Death of Prince Albert
	1861–65 American Civil War
1862 Christina Rossetti, *Goblin Market*	
1864 R. Browning, *Dramatis Personae*	

1000

TEXTS	CONTEXTS
1865 Lewis Carroll, *Alice's Adventures in Wonderland*	1865 Jamaica Rebellion
1866 Algernon Charles Swinburne, *Poems and Ballads*	
1867 Karl Marx, *Das Kapital*	1867 Second Reform Bill
	1868 Opening of Suez Canal
1869 Arnold, *Culture and Anarchy.* Mill, *The Subjection of Women*	
	1870 Married Women's Property Act. Victory in Franco-Prussian War makes Germany a world power. Elementary Education Act
1871 Darwin, *Descent of Man*	1871 Newnham College (first women's Oxbridge college) founded at Cambridge
1872 Eliot, *Middlemarch*	
1873 Walter Pater, *Studies in the History of the Renaissance*	
	1877 Queen Victoria made empress of India. Gerard Manley Hopkins joins Jesuit order
	1878 Electric street lighting in London
	1882 Married Women's Property Act
1885 W. S. Gilbert and Arthur Sullivan, *The Mikado*	1885 Massacre of General Gordon and his forces and fall of Khartoum
1886 Robert Louis Stevenson, *Doctor Jekyll and Mr. Hyde*	
1888 Rudyard Kipling, *Plain Tales from the Hills*	
1889 William Butler Yeats, *Crossways*	
	1890 First subway line in London
1891 Thomas Hardy, *Tess of the D'Urbervilles.* Bernard Shaw, *The Quintessence of Ibsenism.* Oscar Wilde, *The Picture of Dorian Grey.* Arthur Conan Doyle, *Adventures of Sherlock Holmes*	1891 Free elementary education
1893 Shaw, *Mrs. Warren's Profession*	1893 Independent Labour Party
1895 Wilde, *The Importance of Being Earnest.* Hardy, *Jude the Obscure*	1895 Oscar Wilde arrested and imprisoned for homosexuality
1896 A. E. Housman, *A Shropshire Lad*	
1898 Hardy, *Wessex Poems*	1898 Discovery of radium
	1899 Irish Literary Theater founded in Dublin
	1899–1902 Anglo-Boer War
1900 Joseph Conrad, *Lord Jim*	
	1901 Death of Queen Victoria; succession of Edward VII

THOMAS CARLYLE
1795–1881

W. B. Yeats once asked William Morris which writers had inspired the socialist movement of the 1880s, and Morris replied: "Oh, Ruskin and Carlyle, but somebody should have been beside Carlyle and punched his head every five minutes." Morris's mixed feelings of admiration and exasperation are typical of the response Thomas Carlyle evokes in many readers. Anyone approaching his prose for the first time should expect to be sometimes bewildered. Like Bernard Shaw, Carlyle discovered, early in life, that exaggeration can be a highly effective way of gaining the attention of an audience. But it can also be a way of distracting an audience unfamiliar with the idiosyncrasies of his rhetoric and unprepared for the distinctive enjoyments his writings can provide.

One of the idiosyncrasies of his prose is that it is meant to be read aloud. "His paragraphs," as Ralph Waldo Emerson observes, "are all a sort of splendid conversation." As a talker Carlyle was as famous in his day as Samuel Johnson in his. Charles Darwin testified that he was "the best worth listening to of any man I know." No Boswell has adequately recorded this talk, but no Boswell was needed, for Carlyle's prose adopts the rhythm, idiosyncrasy, and spontaneity of the spoken voice. It is a noisy and emphatic voice, startling on a first reading.

Carlyle was forty-one years old when Victoria became queen of England. He had been born in the same year as John Keats, yet he is rarely grouped with his contemporaries among the Romantic writers. Instead his name is linked with younger men such as Charles Dickens, Robert Browning, and John Ruskin, the early generation of Victorian writers, for whom he became (according to Elizabeth Barrett Browning) "the great teacher of the age." The classification is fitting, for it was Carlyle's role to foresee the problems that were to preoccupy the Victorians and early to report on his experiences in confronting these problems. After 1837 his loud voice began to attract an audience; and he soon became one of the most influential figures of the age, affecting the attitudes of scientists, statesmen, and especially of writers. His wife once complained that Emerson had no ideas (except mad ones) that he had not derived from Carlyle. " 'But pray, Mrs. Carlyle,' replied a friend, 'who has?' "

Carlyle was born in Ecclefechan, a village in Scotland, the eldest child of a large family. His mother, at the time of her marriage, was illiterate. His father, James Carlyle, a stonemason and later a farmer, was proudly characterized by his son as a peasant. The key to the character of James Carlyle was the Scottish Calvinism that he instilled into the members of his household. Frugality, hard work, a tender but undemonstrative family loyalty, and a peculiar blend of self-denial and self-righteousness were characteristic features of Carlyle's childhood home.

With his father's aid the young Carlyle was educated at Annan Academy and at Edinburgh University, the subject of his special interest being mathematics; he left without taking a degree. It was his parents' hope that their son would become a clergyman, but in this respect Thomas made a severe break with his ancestry. He was a prodigious reader; and his exposure to such skeptical writers as David Hume, Voltaire, and Edward Gibbon had undermined his faith. Gibbon's *Decline and Fall of the Roman Empire* (1776–88), he told Emerson, was "the splendid bridge from the old world to the new." By the time he was twenty-three Carlyle had crossed the bridge and had abandoned his Christian faith and his proposed career as a clergyman. During the period in which he was thinking through his religious position, he supported himself by teaching school in Scotland and, later, by tutoring private pupils; but from 1824 to the end of his life he relied exclusively on his writings for his livelihood. His early writings consisted of translations, biographies, and critical studies of Johann Wolfgang von Goethe and other German authors, to whose view of life he was deeply attracted. The German Romantics (loosely grouped by Carlyle under the label "Mystics") were the second most important influence on his life and character, exceeded only by his early family experiences. Aided by the writings of these German poets and philosophers, he arrived finally at a faith in life that served as a substitute for the Christian faith he had lost.

His most significant early essay, "Characteristics," appeared in *The Edinburgh Review* in 1831. A year earlier he had begun writing *Sartor Resartus*, an account of the life and opinions of an imaginary philosopher, Professor Diogenes Teufelsdröckh, a work that he had great difficulty in persuading anyone to publish. In book form *Sartor* first appeared in America in 1836, where Carlyle's follower Emerson had prepared an enthusiastic audience for this unusual work. His American following (which was later to become a vast one) did little at first, however, to relieve the poverty in which he still found himself after fifteen years of writing. In 1837 the tide at last turned when he published *The French Revolution*. "O it has been a great success, dear," his wife assured him; but her husband, embittered by the long struggle, was incredulous that the sought-for recognition had at last come to him.

It was in character for his wife, Jane Welsh Carlyle, to be less surprised by his success than he was. That Thomas Carlyle was a genius had been an article of faith to her from her first meeting with him in 1821. A witty, intelligent, and intellectually ambitious young woman, the daughter of a doctor of good family, Jane Welsh had many suitors. When in 1826 she finally accepted Carlyle, her family and friends were shocked. This peasant's son, of no fixed employment, seemed a preposterous choice. Subsequent events seemed to confirm her family's verdict. Not long after marriage Carlyle insisted on their retiring to a remote farm at Craigenputtock, where for six years (1828–34) this sociable woman was obliged to live in isolation and loneliness. After they moved to London in 1834 and settled in a house on Cheyne Walk in Chelsea, Jane Carlyle was considerably happier and enjoyed her role at the center of the intellectual and artistic circle that surrounded her husband. Her husband, however, remained a difficult man to live with. His stomach ailments, irascible nerves, and preoccupation with his writings, as well as the lionizing to which he was subjected, left him with little inclination for domestic amenities or for encouraging his wife's considerable intellectual talents. As a young girl she had wanted to be a writer; her letters, some of the most remarkable of the century, show that she had considerable literary talent.

This marriage of the Carlyles has aroused almost as much interest as that of the Brownings. Their friend the Reverend W. H. Brookfield (whose marriage was an unhappy one) once said cynically that marrying is "dipping into a pitcher of snakes for the chance of an eel," and some biographers have argued that Jane Welsh Carlyle drew a snake instead of an eel. Yet if we study her letters, it is evident that she wanted to marry a man of genius who would change the world. Despite the years she endured of comparative poverty, poor health, and loneliness, she had the satisfaction of recognizing her husband's triumph when the peasant's son she had chosen returned to Scotland to deliver his inaugural address as lord rector of Edinburgh University. While he was away, to Carlyle's great grief, she died.

During the first thirty years of his residence in London Carlyle wrote extensive historical works and many pamphlets concerning contemporary issues. After *The French Revolution* he edited, in 1845, the *Letters and Speeches of Oliver Cromwell*, a Puritan leader of heroic dimensions in Carlyle's eyes, and later wrote a full-length biography, *The History of Friedrich II of Prussia, Called Frederick the Great* (1858–65). Carlyle's pamphleteering is seen at its best in *Past and Present* (1843) and in its most violent phase in his *Latter-Day Pamphlets* (1850). Following the death of his wife, he wrote very little. For the remaining fifteen years of his life, he confined himself to reading or to talking to the stream of visitors who called at Cheyne Walk to listen to the "Sage of Chelsea," as he came to be called. In 1874 he accepted the Prussian Order of Merit from Bismarck but declined an English baronetcy offered by Disraeli. In 1881 he died and was buried near his family in Ecclefechan churchyard.

1004 / THOMAS CARLYLE

To understand Carlyle's role as historian, biographer, and social critic, it is essential to understand his attitude toward religion. Like many Victorians, Carlyle underwent a crisis of religious belief. By the time he was twenty-three, he had been shorn of his faith in Christianity. At this stage, as Carlyle observed with dismay, many people seemed content simply to stop or, worse, to adopt antispiritual ideas. A Utilitarian such as James Mill or some of his commonsensical professors at the University of Edinburgh regarded society and the universe as machines. To such thinkers the machines might sometimes seem complex, but they were not mysterious, for machines are subject to humankind's control and understanding through reason and observation. To Carlyle, and to many others, life without a sense of the divine was a meaningless nightmare. In the first part of "The Everlasting No," a chapter of *Sartor Resartus*, he memorably depicts the horrors of such a soulless world that drove him in 1822 to thoughts of suicide. The eighteenth-century Enlightenment had left him not in light but in darkness.

In developing his views of religion, Carlyle used the metaphor of the "Clothes Philosophy." The naked individual seeks clothing for protection. One solution, represented by Coleridge and his followers, was to repudiate the skepticism of Voltaire and Hume and to return to the protective beliefs and rituals of the Christian Church. To Carlyle such a return was pointless. The traditional Christian coverings were worn out—"Hebrew Old Clothes," he called them. His own solution, described in "The Everlasting Yea," was to tailor a new suit of beliefs from German philosophy, shreds of Scottish Calvinism, and his own observations. The following summarizes his basic religious attitude: "Gods die with the men who have conceived them. But the god-stuff roars eternally, like the sea. . . . Even the gods must be born again. We must be born again." Although this passage is from *The Plumed Serpent* (1926) by D. H. Lawrence (a writer who resembles Carlyle at many points), it might have come from any one of Carlyle's own books—most especially from *Sartor Resartus*, in which he describes his being born again—his "Fire-baptism"—into a new secular faith. Carlyle was thus in many ways the quintessential nineteenth-century mystic; yet at the same time, many contemporary critics note, his writings also gesture toward postmodernism. Certainly his self-aware, genre-defying, and often contradictory prose exposes the inherent difficulty of assuming that literature or philosophy can ever achieve a unified, foundational truth.

Nevertheless, Carlyle often talked like a *vitalist*; that is, as though the presence of energy in the world was, in itself, a sign of the godhead. Carlyle therefore judges everything in terms of the presence or absence of some vital spark. The minds of people, books, societies, Churches, or even landscapes are rated as alive or dead, dynamic or merely mechanical. The government of Louis XVI, for example, was obviously moribund, doomed to be swept away by the dynamic forces of the French Revolution. The government of Victorian England seemed likewise to be doomed unless infused with vital energies of leadership and an awareness of the real needs of humankind. When an editor complained that his essay "Characteristics" was "inscrutable," Carlyle remarked: "My own fear was that it might be too *scrutable*; for it indicates decisively enough that Society (in my view) is utterly condemned to destruction, and even now beginning its long travail-throes of Newbirth."

In his inquiry into the principles of government and social order, Carlyle, like many of his contemporaries, is seeking to understand a world of great social unrest and historical change. This preoccupation with revolution and the destruction of the old orders suggests that Carlyle's politics were radical, but his position is bewilderingly difficult to classify. During the Hungry Forties he was one of the most outspoken critics of middle-class bunglings and of the economic theory of laissez-faire that, in his opinion, was ultimately responsible for those bunglings. On behalf of the millions of people suffering from the miseries attendant on a major breakdown of industry and agriculture he worked strenuously. At other times, because of his insistence on strong and heroic leadership, Carlyle appears to be a violent conservative or, as some have argued, virtually a fascist. He had no confidence that democratic institutions could work efficiently. A few individuals in every age are, in his view, leaders; the rest are followers and are happy only as followers. Society should be organized so that these gifted leaders can have scope to govern effectively. Such leaders are, for Carlyle, heroes. Bernard Shaw, who learned much from Carlyle, would call them "supermen." Liberals and democrats, however, might call them dictators. Although Carlyle was aware that the Western world was committed to a faith in a system of balloting and of legislative debate, he was confident that the system would eventually break down. The democratic assumption that all voters are equally capable of choice and the assumption that people value liberty more than they value order seemed to him nonsense. Carlyle's authoritarianism intensified as he grew older. When the governor of Jamaica violently repressed a rebellion of black plantation workers, Carlyle served as chair of his defense fund, arguing that England owed the governor honor and thanks for his defense of civilization.

Carlyle's prose style reflects the intensity of his views. At the time he began to write, the essayists of the eighteenth century, Samuel Johnson in particular, were the models of good prose. Carlyle recognized that their style, however admirable an instrument for reasoning, analysis, and generalized exposition, did not suit his purposes. Like a poet, he wanted to convey the sense of experience itself. Like a preacher or prophet, he wanted to exhort or inspire his readers rather than to develop a chain of logical argument. Like a psychoanalyst, he wanted to explore the unconscious and irrational levels of human life, the hidden nine-tenths of the iceberg rather than the conscious and rational fraction above the surface. To this end he developed his highly individual manner of writing, with its vivid imagery of fire and barnyard and zoo, its mixture of biblical rhythms and explosive talk, and its inverted and unorthodox syntax. Classicists may complain, as Walter Savage Landor did, that the result is not English. Carlyle would reply that it is not eighteenth-century English, but that his style was appropriate for a Victorian who reports of revolutions in society and in thought. In reply to a friend who had protested about his stylistic experiments, Carlyle exclaimed: "Do you reckon this really a time for Purism of Style? I do not: with whole ragged battalions of Scott's Novel Scotch, with Irish, German, French, and even Newspaper Cockney . . . storming in on us, and the whole structure of our Johnsonian English breaking up from its foundations—revolution *there* as visible as anywhere else?" George Eliot wrote (in an essay of 1855) that Carlyle was "more of an artist than a philosopher." As she said: "No novelist has made his creations live for us more thoroughly." Carlyle is best regarded, that is, as a man of letters, the inventor of a distinctive and extremely effective prose medium, and one who strove tirelessly to create a new spiritual and political philosophy adequate to the age.

Sartor Resartus

Sartor Resartus is a combination of novel, autobiography, and essay. To present some of his own experiences, Carlyle invented a hero, Professor Diogenes Teufelsdröckh of Germany, whose name (meaning "God-Begotten Devil's Dreck") suggests the grotesque humor that Carlyle uses to expound a serious treatise. Teufelsdröckh tells the story of his unhappiness in love and of his difficulties in religion. He also airs his opinions on a variety of subjects. Interspersed between the professor's words (which are in quotation marks) are the remarks of an editor, also imaginary, who has the task of putting together the story from assorted documents written by Teufelsdröckh. The title, meaning "The Tailor Retailored," refers to the editor's role of patching the story together. The title also refers to Carlyle's so-called Clothes Philosophy, which is expounded by the hero in many chapters of *Sartor*. In effect this Clothes Philosophy is an attempt to demonstrate the difference between the appearances of things and their reality. The appearance of an individual depends on the costume he or she wears; the reality of that individual is the body underneath the costume. By analogy Carlyle suggests that institutions, such as churches or governments, are like clothes. They may be useful "visible emblems" of the spiritual forces that they cover, but they wear out and have to be replaced by new clothes. The Christian Church, for example, which once expressed humanity's permanent religious desires, is, in Carlyle's terms, worn out and must be discarded. But the underlying religious spirit must be recognized and kept alive at all costs. Carlyle also uses the clothes analogy to describe the relationship between the material and spiritual worlds. Clothes hide the body just as the world of nature cloaks the reality of God and as the body itself cloaks the reality of the soul. The discovery of these realities behind the appearances is, for Carlyle and for his hero, the initial stage of a solution to the dilemmas of life. As contemporary critics have pointed out, the Clothes Philosophy, as well as the unusual form of the book, suggests that Carlyle is also concerned with fundamental problems of language and representation. Implicitly, and sometimes explicitly, his text often questions whether a biographer or autobiographer can ever capture the "essence" of his or her subject.

Teufelsdröckh's religious development, as described in the following chapters, may be contrasted with J. S. Mill's account of his own crisis of spirit in his *Autobiography* (p. 1070). These selections are chapters 7 to 9 of book 2.

From Sartor Resartus

The Everlasting No

Under the strange nebulous envelopment, wherein our Professor has now shrouded himself, no doubt but his spiritual nature is nevertheless progressive, and growing: for how can the "Son of Time," in any case, stand still? We behold him, through those dim years, in a state of crisis, of transition: his mad Pilgrimings, and general solution[1] into aimless Discontinuity, what is all this but a mad Fermentation; wherefrom, the fiercer it is, the clearer product will one day evolve itself?

Such transitions are ever full of pain: thus the Eagle when he moults is sickly; and, to attain his new beak, must harshly dash-off the old one upon rocks. What Stoicism soever our Wanderer, in his individual acts and motions, may affect, it is clear that there is a hot fever of anarchy and misery raging within; coruscations of which flash out: as, indeed, how could there be other? Have we not seen him disappointed, bemocked of Destiny, through long years? All that the young heart might desire and pray for has been denied; nay, as in the last worst instance, offered and then snatched away. Ever an "excellent Passivity"; but of useful, reasonable Activity, essential to the former as Food to Hunger, nothing granted: till at length, in this wild Pilgrimage, he must forcibly seize for himself an Activity, though useless, unreasonable. Alas, his cup of bitterness, which had been filling drop by drop, ever since that first "ruddy morning" in the Hinterschlag Gymnasium, was at the very lip; and then with that poison-drop, of the Towgood-and-Blumine[2] business, it runs over, and even hisses over in a deluge of foam.

He himself says once, with more justice than originality: "Man is, properly

1. Dissolution.
2. A woman loved by Teufelsdröckh who had married his friend Towgood. His distress is pictured in the preceding chapter, titled "Sorrows of Teufels-

dröckh." "Hinterschlag Gymnasium": "Smack-bottom" grammar school, a fake German name invented by Carlyle.

speaking, based upon Hope, he has no other possession but Hope; this world of his is emphatically the Place of Hope." What, then, was our Professor's possession? We see him, for the present, quite shut-out from Hope; looking not into the golden orient, but vaguely all round into a dim copper firmament, pregnant with earthquake and tornado.

Alas, shut-out from Hope, in a deeper sense than we yet dream of! For, as he wanders wearisomely through this world, he has now lost all tidings of another and higher. Full of religion, or at least of religiosity, as our Friend has since exhibited himself, he hides not that, in those days, he was wholly irreligious: "Doubt had darkened into Unbelief," says he; "shade after shade goes grimly over your soul, till you have the fixed, starless, Tartarean[3] black." To such readers as have reflected, what can be called reflecting, on man's life, and happily discovered, in contradiction to much Profit-and-loss Philosophy, speculative and practical, that Soul is *not* synonymous with Stomach; who understand, therefore, in our Friend's words, "that, for man's well-being, Faith is properly the one thing needful;[4] how, with it, Martyrs, otherwise weak, can cheerfully endure the shame and the cross; and without it, Worldlings puke-up their sick existence, by suicide, in the midst of luxury": to such it will be clear that, for a pure moral nature, the loss of his religious Belief was the loss of everything. Unhappy young man! All wounds, the crush of long-continued Destitution, the stab of false Friendship and of false Love, all wounds in thy so genial heart, would have healed again, had not its life-warmth been withdrawn. Well might he exclaim, in his wild way: "Is there no God, then; but at best an absentee God, sitting idle, ever since the first Sabbath, at the outside of his Universe, and *seeing* it go? Has the word Duty no meaning; is what we call Duty no divine Messenger and Guide, but a false earthly Fantasm, made-up of Desire and Fear, of emanations from the Gallows and from Dr. Graham's Celestial-Bed?[5] Happiness of an approving Conscience! Did not Paul of Tarsus, whom admiring men have since named Saint, feel that *he* was 'the chief of sinners';[6] and Nero of Rome, jocund in spirit (*wohlgemuth*), spend much of his time in fiddling?[7] Foolish Word-monger and Motive-grinder, who in thy Logic-mill hast an earthly mechanism for the Godlike itself, and wouldst fain grind me out Virtue from the husks of Pleasure,[8]—I tell thee, Nay! To the unregenerate Prometheus Vinctus[9] of a man, it is ever the bitterest aggravation of his wretchedness that he is conscious of Virtue, that he feels himself the victim not of suffering only, but of injustice. What then? Is the heroic inspiration we name Virtue but some Passion; some bubble of the blood, bubbling in the direction others *profit* by? I know not; only this I know, If what thou namest Happiness be our true aim, then are we all astray. With Stupidity and sound Digestion man may front much. But what, in these dull unimaginative days, are the terrors of Conscience to the diseases of the Liver! Not on Moral-

3. Of Tartarus, the lowest region of the classical underworld, where the wicked were punished.
4. Luke 10.42.
5. James Graham (1745–1794), a quack doctor, had invented an elaborate bed that was supposed to cure sterility in couples using it. In this passage, the bed is apparently a symbol of sexual desires.
6. Paraphrase of 1 Timothy 1.15.
7. Nero (37–68 C.E.; Roman emperor, 54–68) was rumored to have recited his poems and played his lyre during a great fire in 64 C.E. that destroyed

much of Rome; thus the familiar saying "Nero fiddled while Rome burned."
8. Here, as in his earlier reference to "Profit-and-loss Philosophy," Carlyle attacks the Utilitarian concepts of Jeremy Bentham (1748–1832), who argued that the Good is whatever brings the greatest happiness (or pleasure) to the greatest number of people.
9. I.e., Prometheus Bound; this is also the title of a play by Aeschylus depicting the sufferings of a hero who defied Zeus.

ity, but on Cookery, let us build our stronghold: there brandishing our frying-pan, as censer, let us offer sweet incense to the Devil, and live at ease on the fat things *he* has provided for his Elect!"

Thus has the bewildered Wanderer to stand, as so many have done, shouting question after question into the Sibyl-cave of Destiny,[1] and receive no Answer but an Echo. It is all a grim Desert, this once-fair world of his; wherein is heard only the howling of wild-beasts, or the shrieks of despairing, hate-filled men; and no Pillar of Cloud by day, and no Pillar of Fire by night,[2] any longer guides the Pilgrim. To such length has the spirit of Inquiry carried him. "But what boots it (*was thut's*)?" cries he: "it is but the common lot in this era. Not having come to spiritual majority prior to the *Siècle de Louis Quinze*,[3] and not being born purely a Loghead (*Dummkopf*), thou hast no other outlook. The whole world is, like thee, sold to Unbelief, their old Temples of the Godhead, which for long have not been rainproof, crumble down; and men ask now: Where is the Godhead; our eyes never saw him?"

Pitiful enough were it, for all these wild utterances, to call our Diogenes wicked. Unprofitable servants as we all are,[4] perhaps at no era of his life was he more decisively the Servant of Goodness, the Servant of God, than even now when doubting God's existence. "One circumstance I note," says he: "after all the nameless woe that Inquiry, which for me, what it is not always, was genuine Love of Truth, had wrought me, I nevertheless still loved Truth, and would bate no jot[5] of my allegiance to her. 'Truth!' I cried, 'though the Heavens crush me for following her: no Falsehood! though a whole celestial Lubber-land[6] were the price of Apostasy.' In conduct it was the same. Had a divine Messenger from the clouds, or miraculous Handwriting on the wall, convincingly proclaimed to me *This thou shalt do*, with what passionate readiness, as I often thought, would I have done it, had it been leaping into the infernal Fire. Thus, in spite of all Motive-grinders, and Mechanical Profit-and-Loss Philosophies, with the sick ophthalmia and hallucination they had brought on, was the Infinite nature of Duty still dimly present to me: living without God in the world, of God's light I was not utterly bereft; if my as yet sealed eyes, with their unspeakable longing, could nowhere see Him, nevertheless in my heart He was present, and His heaven-written Law still stood legible and sacred there."

Meanwhile, under all these tribulations, and temporal and spiritual destitutions, what must the Wanderer, in his silent soul, have endured! "The painfullest feeling," writes he, "is that of your own Feebleness (*Unkraft*); ever, as the English Milton says, to be weak is the true misery.[7] And yet of your Strength there is and can be no clear feeling, save by what you have prospered in, by what you have done. Between vague wavering Capability and fixed indubitable Performance, what a difference! A certain inarticulate Self-consciousness dwells dimly in us; which only our Works can render articulate and decisively discernible. Our Works are the mirror wherein the spirit first

1. An allusion to Virgil's *Aeneid* 6.36ff.; there Aeneas questions the Cumaean Sibyl, who foretells the future.
2. Exodus 13.21.
3. The Century of Louis XV (French), allusion to *Précis du Siècle de Louis XV* (1768), Voltaire's history of the skeptical and inquiring spirit of 18th-century France during the reign of Louis XV

(1715–74).
4. An allusion to Matthew 25.20 and Luke 17.7–10.
5. Would hold back no part.
6. Land of Plenty.
7. *Paradise Lost* 1.157: "Fallen cherub, to be weak is miserable."

sees its natural lineaments. Hence, too, the folly of that impossible Precept, *Know thyself;*[8] till it be translated into this partially possible one, *Know what thou canst work at.*

"But for me, so strangely unprosperous had I been, the net-result of my Workings amounted as yet simply to—Nothing. How then could I believe in my Strength, when there was as yet no mirror to see it in? Ever did this agitating, yet, as I now perceive, quite frivolous question, remain to me insoluble: Hast thou a certain Faculty, a certain Worth, such even as the most have not; or art thou the completest Dullard of these modern times? Alas! the fearful Unbelief is unbelief in yourself; and how could I believe? Had not my first, last Faith in myself, when even to me the Heavens seemed laid open, and I dared to love, been all-too cruelly belied? The speculative Mystery of Life grew ever more mysterious to me: neither in the practical Mystery[9] had I made the slightest progress, but been everywhere buffeted, foiled, and contemptuously cast-out. A feeble unit in the middle of a threatening Infinitude, I seemed to have nothing given me but eyes, whereby to discern my own wretchedness. Invisible yet impenetrable walls, as of Enchantment, divided me from all living: was there, in the wide world, any true bosom I could press trustfully to mine? O Heaven, No, there was none! I kept a lock upon my lips: why should I speak much with that shifting variety of so-called Friends, in whose withered, vain and too-hungry souls Friendship was but an incredible tradition? In such cases, your resource is to talk little, and that little mostly from the Newspapers. Now when I look back, it was a strange isolation I then lived in. The men and women around me, even speaking with me, were but Figures; I had, practically, forgotten that they were alive, that they were not merely automatic. In midst of their crowded streets and assemblages, I walked solitary; and (except as it was my own heart, not another's, that I kept devouring) savage also, as the tiger in his jungle. Some comfort it would have been, could I, like a Faust,[1] have fancied myself tempted and tormented of the Devil; for a Hell, as I imagine, without Life, though only diabolic Life, were more frightful: but in our age of Down-pulling and Disbelief, the very Devil has been pulled down, you cannot so much as believe in a Devil. To me the Universe was all void of Life, of Purpose, of Volition, even of Hostility: it was one huge, dead, immeasurable Steam-engine, rolling on, in its dead indifference, to grind me limb from limb. O, the vast, gloomy, solitary Golgotha,[2] and Mill of Death! Why was the Living banished thither companionless, conscious? Why, if there is no Devil; nay, unless the Devil is your God?"

A prey incessantly to such corrosions, might not, moreover, as the worst aggravation to them, the iron constitution even of a Teufelsdröckh threaten to fail? We conjecture that he has known sickness; and, in spite of his locomotive habits, perhaps sickness of the chronic sort. Hear this, for example: "How beautiful to die of broken-heart, on Paper! Quite another thing in practice; every window of your Feeling, even of your Intellect, as it were, begrimed and mud-bespattered, so that no pure ray can enter; a whole Drugshop in your inwards; the fordone soul drowning slowly in quagmires of Disgust!"

---

8. This maxim was inscribed in the temple of Apollo at Delphi.
9. A profession or practical occupation.
1. Both Christopher Marlowe and Goethe wrote plays about the temptations of Johann Faust (ca.

1480–ca. 1540), a German teacher and magician who became the subject of many stories and folktales.
2. Calvary, the place where Jesus was crucified.

Putting all which external and internal miseries together, may we not find in the following sentences, quite in our Professor's still vein, significance enough? "From Suicide a certain aftershine (*Nachschein*) of Christianity withheld me: perhaps also a certain indolence of character; for, was not that a remedy I had at any time within reach? Often, however, was there a question present to me: Should some one now, at the turning of that corner, blow thee suddenly out of Space, into the other World, or other No-World, by pistol-shot,—how were it? On which ground, too, I have often, in sea-storms and sieged cities and other death-scenes, exhibited an imperturbability, which passed, falsely enough, for courage.

"So had it lasted," concludes the Wanderer, "so had it lasted, as in bitter protracted Death-agony, through long years. The heart within me, unvisited by any heavenly dewdrop, was smouldering in sulphurous, slow-consuming fire. Almost since earliest memory I had shed no tear; or once only when I, murmuring half-audibly, recited Faust's Deathsong, that wild *Selig der den er im Siegesglanze findet* (Happy whom *he* finds in Battle's splendour),[3] and thought that of this last Friend even I was not forsaken, that Destiny itself could not doom me not to die. Having no hope, neither had I any definite fear, were it of Man or of Devil: nay, I often felt as if it might be solacing, could the Arch-Devil himself, though in Tartarean terrors, but rise to me, that I might tell him a little of my mind. And yet, strangely enough, I lived in a continual, indefinite, pining fear; tremulous, pusillanimous, apprehensive of I knew not what: it seemed as if all things in the Heavens above and the Earth beneath would hurt me; as if the Heavens and the Earth were but boundless jaws of a devouring monster, wherein I, palpitating, waited to be devoured.

"Full of such humour,[4] and perhaps the miserablest man in the whole French Capital or Suburbs, was I, one sultry Dogday, after much perambulation, toiling along the dirty little *Rue Saint-Thomas de l'Enfer*,[5] among civic rubbish enough, in a close atmosphere, and over pavements hot as Nebuchadnezzar's Furnace;[6] whereby doubtless my spirits were little cheered; when, all at once, there rose a Thought in me, and I asked myself: 'What *art* thou afraid of? Wherefore, like a coward, dost thou forever pip and whimper, and go cowering and trembling? Despicable biped! what is the sum-total of the worst that lies before thee? Death? Well, Death; and say the pangs of Tophet[7] too, and all that the Devil and Man may, will or can do against thee! Hast thou not a heart; canst thou not suffer whatsoever it be; and, as a Child of Freedom, though outcast, trample Tophet itself under thy feet, while it consumes thee? Let it come, then; I will meet it and defy it!' And as I so thought, there rushed like a stream of fire over my whole soul; and I shook base Fear away from me forever. I was strong, of unknown strength; a spirit, almost a god. Ever from that time, the temper of my misery was changed: not Fear or whining Sorrow was it, but Indignation and grim fire-eyed Defiance.

"Thus had the EVERLASTING NO[8] (*das ewige Nein*) pealed authoritatively

3. Adapted from Goethe's *Faust* (1808) 1.4.1573–76.
4. State of mind.
5. St. Thomas-of-Hell Street (French). In later life Carlyle admitted that this incident was based on his own experience during a walk in Edinburgh (rather than in Paris). "Dogday": i.e., in the dog days, a hot and unwholesome summer period coinciding with the prominence of Sirius, the Dog Star.
6. Cf. Daniel 3: the Babylonian king Nebuchad-

nezzar erected a golden idol and threw those who refused to fall down and worship it into a fiery furnace.
7. Hell.
8. This phrase does not signify the hero's protest; it represents the sum of all the forces that had denied meaning to life. These negative forces, which had hitherto held the hero in bondage, are repudiated by his saying no to the "Everlasting No."

through all the recesses of my Being, of my ME; and then was it that my whole ME stood up, in native God-created majesty, and with emphasis recorded its Protest. Such a Protest, the most important transaction in Life, may that same Indignation and Defiance, in a psychological point of view, be fitly called. The Everlasting No had said: 'Behold, thou art fatherless, outcast, and the Universe is mine (the Devil's)'; to which my whole Me now made answer: '*I am not thine, but Free, and forever hate thee!*'

"It is from this hour that I incline to date my Spiritual Newbirth, or Baphometic Fire-baptism,[9] perhaps I directly thereupon began to be a Man."

Centre of Indifference

Though, after this "Baphometic Fire-baptism" of his, our Wanderer signifies that his Unrest was but increased; as indeed, "Indignation and Defiance," especially against things in general, are not the most peaceable inmates; yet can the Psychologist surmise that it was no longer a quite hopeless Unrest; that henceforth it had at least a fixed centre to revolve round. For the fire-baptised soul, long so scathed and thunder-riven, here feels its own Freedom, which feeling is its Baphometic Baptism: the citadel of its whole kingdom it has thus gained by assault, and will keep in-expugnable; outwards from which the remaining dominions, not indeed without hard battling, will doubtless by degrees be conquered and pacificated. Under another figure, we might say, if in that great moment, in the *Rue Saint-Thomas de l'Enfer,* the old inward Satanic School was not yet thrown out of doors, it received peremptory judicial notice to quit;—whereby, for the rest, its howl-chantings, Ernulphus-cursings,[1] and rebellious gnashings of teeth, might, in the meanwhile, become only the more tumultuous, and difficult to keep secret.

Accordingly, if we scrutinise these Pilgrimings well, there is perhaps discernible henceforth a certain incipient method in their madness. Not wholly as a Spectre does Teufelsdröckh now storm through the world; at worst as a spectre-fighting Man, nay who will one day be a Spectre-queller. If pilgriming restlessly to so many "Saints' Wells,"[2] and ever without quenching of his thirst, he nevertheless finds little secular wells, whereby from time to time some alleviation is ministered. In a word, he is now, if not ceasing, yet intermitting to "eat his own heart"; and clutches round him outwardly on the NOT-ME for wholesomer food. Does not the following glimpse exhibit him in a much more natural state?

"Towns also and Cities, especially the ancient, I failed not to look upon with interest. How beautiful to see thereby, as through a long vista, into the remote Time; to have as it were, an actual section of almost the earliest Past brought safe into the Present, and set before your eyes! There, in that old City, was a live ember of Culinary Fire put down, say only two-thousand years ago; and there, burning more or less triumphantly, with such fuel as the region yielded, it has burnt, and still burns, and thou thyself seest the very smoke thereof. Ah! and the far more mysterious live ember of Vital Fire was then also put

---

9. A transformation by a flash of spiritual illumination. The term may derive from Baphomet, an idol that the Knights Templar in the 14th century were accused of worshipping as part of their initiation ceremony.
1. Curse devised by Ernulf (1040–1124), bishop of Rochester, when sentencing persons to excom-

munication. "Satanic School": term coined by Robert Southey (1774–1843) to characterize the self-assertive and rebellious temper of the poetry of Byron and Shelley.
2. Holy fountains or wells, the waters of which were reputed to restore health.

down there; and still miraculously burns and spreads; and the smoke and ashes thereof (in these Judgment-Halls and Churchyards), and its bellows-engines (in these Churches), thou still seest; and its flame, looking out from every kind countenance, and every hateful one, still warms thee or scorches thee.

"Of Man's Activity and Attainment the chief results are aeriform, mystic, and preserved in Tradition only: such are his Forms of Government, with the Authority they rest on; his Customs, or Fashions both of Cloth-habits and of Soul-habits; much more his collective stock of Handicrafts, the whole Faculty he has acquired of manipulating Nature: all these things, as indispensable and priceless as they are, cannot in any way be fixed under lock and key, but must flit, spirit-like, on impalpable vehicles, from Father to Son; if you demand sight of them, they are nowhere to be met with. Visible Plowmen and Hammermen there have been, ever from Cain and Tubalcain[3] downwards: but where does your accumulated Agricultural, Metallurgic, and other Manufacturing SKILL lie warehoused? It transmits itself on the atmospheric air, on the sun's rays (by Hearing and by Vision); it is a thing aeriform, impalpable, of quite spiritual sort. In like manner, ask me not, Where are the LAWS; where is the GOVERN-MENT? In vain wilt thou go to Schönbrunn, to Downing Street, to the Palais Bourbon:[4] thou findest nothing there but brick or stone houses, and some bundles of Papers tied with tape. Where, then, is that same cunningly-devised almighty GOVERNMENT of theirs to be laid hands on? Everywhere, yet nowhere: seen only in its works, this too is a thing aeriform, invisible; or if you will, mystic and miraculous. So spiritual (geistig) is our whole daily Life: all that we do springs out of Mystery, Spirit, invisible Force; only like a little Cloud-image, or Armida's Palace,[5] air-built, does the Actual body itself forth from the great mystic Deep.

"Visible and tangible products of the Past, again, I reckon-up to the extent of three. Cities, with their Cabinets and Arsenals; then tilled Fields, to either or to both of which divisions Roads with their Bridges, may belong; and thirdly—Books. In which third truly, the last invented, lies a worth far sur-passing that of the two others. Wondrous indeed is the virtue of a true Book. Not like a dead city of stones, yearly crumbling, yearly needing repair; more like a tilled field, but then a spiritual field: like a spiritual tree, let me rather say, it stands from year to year, and from age to age (we have Books that already number some hundred-and-fifty human ages); and yearly comes its new pro-duce of leaves (Commentaries, Deductions, Philosophical, Political Systems; or were it only Sermons, Pamphlets, Journalistic Essays), every one of which is talismanic and thaumaturgic,[6] for it can persuade men. O thou who art able to write a Book, which once in the two centuries or oftener there is a man gifted to do, envy not him whom they name City-builder, and inexpressibly pity him whom they name Conqueror or City-burner! Thou too art a Con-queror and Victor; but of the true sort, namely over the Devil: thou too hast built what will outlast all marble and metal, and be a wonder-bringing City of the Mind, a Temple and Seminary and Prophetic Mount, whereto all kindreds of the Earth will pilgrim.—Fool! why journeyest thou wearisomely, in thy anti-quarian fervour, to gaze on the stone pyramids of Geeza, or the clay ones of Sacchara?[7] These stand there, as I can tell thee, idle and inert, looking over

3. Descendant of Cain, son of Adam and Eve (Genesis 4.1–22).
4. Headquarters of government in Vienna, London, and Paris, respectively.
5. The magic palace of a beautiful enchantress in Torquato Tasso's *Jerusalem Delivered* (1581).
6. Miracle-working.
7. I.e., Giza and Saqqara, near Cairo.

the Desert, foolishly enough, for the last three-thousand years: but canst thou not open thy Hebrew BIBLE, then, or even Luther's Version[8] thereof?"

No less satisfactory is his sudden appearance not in Battle, yet on some Battle-field; which, we soon gather, must be that of Wagram;[9] so that here, for once, is a certain approximation to distinctiveness of date. Omitting much, let us impart what follows:

"Horrible enough! A whole Marchfeld[1] strewed with shell-splinters, cannon-shot, ruined tumbrils, and dead men and horses; stragglers still remaining not so much as buried. And those red mould heaps: ay, there lie the Shells of Men, out of which all the Life and Virtue has been blown; and now are they swept together, and crammed-down out of sight, like blown Egg-shells!—Did Nature, when she bade the Donau bring down his mould-cargoes from the Carinthian and Carpathian Heights, and spread them out here into the softest, richest level,—intend thee, O Marchfeld, for a corn-bearing Nursery, whereon her children might be nursed; or for a Cockpit, wherein they might the more commodiously be throttled and tattered? Were thy three broad Highways, meeting here from the ends of Europe, made for Ammunition-wagons, then? Were thy Wagrams and Stillfrieds but so many ready-built Casemates,[2] wherein the house of Hapsburg might batter with artillery, and with artillery be battered? König Ottokar, amid yonder hillocks, dies under Rodolf's truncheon; here Kaiser Franz falls a-swoon under Napoleon's: within which five centuries, to omit the others, how has thy breast, fair Plain, been defaced and defiled! The greensward is torn-up and trampled-down; man's fond care of it, his fruit-trees, hedge-rows, and pleasant dwellings, blown away with gunpowder; and the kind seedfield lies a desolate, hideous Place of Sculls.[3]—Nevertheless, Nature is at work; neither shall these Powder-Devilkins with their utmost devilry gainsay[4] her: but all that gore and carnage will be shrouded-in, absorbed into manure; and next year the Marchfeld will be green, nay greener. Thrifty unwearied Nature, ever out of our great waste educing some little profit of thy own,—how dost thou, from the very carcass of the Killer, bring Life for the Living!

"What, speaking in quite unofficial language, is the net-purport and upshot of war? To my own knowledge, for example, there dwell and toil, in the British village of Dumdrudge,[5] usually some five-hundred souls. From these, by certain 'Natural Enemies'[6] of the French, there are successively selected, during the French war, say thirty able-bodied men: Dumdrudge, at her own expense, has suckled and nursed them: she has, not without difficulty and sorrow, fed them up to manhood, and even trained them to crafts, so that one can weave, another build, another hammer, and the weakest can stand under thirty stone[7] avoirdupois. Nevertheless, amid much weeping and swearing, they are selected; all dressed in red; and shipped away, at the public charges, some

8. The German translation by Martin Luther (1483–1546).
9. A village in Austria; site of Napoleon's victory over the Austrians, July 1809.
1. A fertile plain in Austria whose soil (according to Teufelsdröckh) was brought down from the Carpathian Mountains by the Danube ("Donau") River.
2. Fortified chambers. Stillfried was the site of a battle in which Ottokar, king ("König") of Bohemia, was killed by the forces of Rudolph of Haps-

burg in 1278. The Hapsburg armies at Wagram were led by Emperor Francis ("Franz") I.
3. Translation of Golgotha (Aramaic); where Jesus was crucified.
4. Contradict.
5. An imaginary location.
6. Term often used in English newspapers to account for the frequency of wars between the English and French.
7. I.e., 420 pounds.

two-thousand miles, or say only to the south of Spain;[8] and fed there till wanted. And now to that same spot, in the south of Spain, are thirty similar French artisans, from a French Dumdrudge, in like manner wending: till at length, after infinite effort, the two parties come into actual juxtaposition; and Thirty stands fronting Thirty, each with a gun in his hand. Straightway the word 'Fire!' is given: and they blow the souls out of one another; and in place of sixty brisk useful craftsmen, the world has sixty dead carcasses, which it must bury, and anew shed tears for. Had these men any quarrel? Busy as the Devil is, not the smallest! They lived far enough apart; were the entirest strangers; nay, in so wide a Universe, there was even, unconsciously, by Commerce, some mutual helpfulness between them. How then? Simpleton! their Governors had fallen-out; and, instead of shooting one another, had the cunning to make these poor blockheads shoot.—Alas, so is it in Deutschland, and hitherto in all other lands; still as of old, 'what devilry soever Kings do, the Greeks must pay the piper!'[9]—In that fiction of the English Smollett,[1] it is true, the final Cessation of War is perhaps prophetically shadowed forth; where the two Natural Enemies, in person, take each a Tobacco-pipe, filled with Brimstone; light the same, and smoke in one another's faces, till the weaker gives in: but from such predicted Peace-Era, what blood-filled trenches, and contentious centuries, may still divide us!"

Thus can the Professor, at least in lucid intervals, look away from his own sorrows, over the many-coloured world, and pertinently enough note what is passing there. We may remark, indeed, that for the matter of spiritual culture, if for nothing else, perhaps few periods of his life were richer than this. Internally, there is the most momentous instructive Course of Practical Philosophy, with Experiments, going on; towards the right comprehension of which his Peripatetic[2] habits, favourable to Meditation, might help him rather than hinder. Externally, again, as he wanders to and fro, there are, if for the longing heart little substance, yet for the seeing eye sights enough: in these so boundless Travels of his, granting that the Satanic School was even partially kept down, what an incredible knowledge of our Planet, and its Inhabitants and their Works, that is to say, of all knowable things, might not Teufelsdröckh acquire!

"I have read in most Public Libraries," says he, "including those of Constantinople and Samarcand: in most Colleges, except the Chinese Mandarin ones, I have studied, or seen that there was no studying. Unknown Languages have I oftenest gathered from their natural repertory, the Air, by my organ of Hearing; Statistics, Geographics, Topographics came, through the Eye, almost of their own accord. The ways of Man, how he seeks food, and warmth, and protection for himself, in most regions, are ocularly known to me. Like the great Hadrian, I meted-out much of the terraqueous Globe with a pair of Compasses[3] that belonged to myself only.

"Of great Scenes why speak? Three summer days, I lingered reflecting, and even composing (dichtete), by the Pine-chasms of Vaucluse; and in that clear Lakelet[4] moistened my bread. I have sat under the Palm-trees of Tadmor;[5]

8. Where British armies fought against Napoleon (1808–14).
9. Horace's Epistles 1.2.14.
1. Tobias Smollett (1721–1771), The Adventures of Ferdinand Count Fathom (1753), chap. 41.
2. Walking about, after the manner of Aristotle, who delivered his lectures while walking in the

Lyceum.
3. Legs. Hadrian (76–138 C.E.), Roman emperor, who traveled extensively throughout his empire.
4. A pool at the base of a mountain in Vaucluse in southern France, one of Petrarch's favorite haunts.
5. Palmyra in Syria.

smoked a pipe among the ruins of Babylon. The great Wall of China I have seen; and can testify that it is of gray brick, coped and covered with granite, and shows only second-rate masonry.—Great Events, also, have not I witnessed? Kings sweated-down (*ausgemergelt*) into Berlin-and-Milan Customhouse-Officers;[6] the World well won, and the World well lost oftener than once a hundred-thousand individuals shot (by each other) in one day. All kindreds and peoples and nations dashed together, and shifted and shovelled into heaps, that they might ferment there, and in time unite. The birth-pangs of Democracy,[7] wherewith convulsed Europe was groaning in cries that reached Heaven, could not escape me.

"For great Men I have ever had the warmest predilection; and can perhaps boast that few such in this era have wholly escaped me. Great Men are the inspired (speaking and acting) Texts of that divine BOOK OF REVELATION, whereof a Chapter is completed from epoch to epoch, and by some named HISTORY; to which inspired Texts your numerous talented men, and your innumerable untalented men, are the better or worse exegetic Commentaries, and wagonload of too-stupid, heretical or orthodox, weekly Sermons. For my study, the inspired Texts themselves! Thus did not I, in very early days, having disguised me as tavern-waiter, stand behind the field-chairs, under that shady Tree at Treisnitz by the Jena Highway;[8] waiting upon the great Schiller and greater Goethe; and hearing what I have not forgotten. For—"

—But at this point the Editor recalls his principle of caution, some time ago laid down, and must suppress much. Let not the sacredness of Laurelled,[9] still more, of Crowned Heads, be tampered with. Should we, at a future day, find circumstances altered, and the time come for Publication, then may these glimpses into the privacy of the Illustrious be conceded; which for the present were little better than treacherous, perhaps traitorous Eavesdroppings. Of Lord Byron, therefore, of Pope Pius, Emperor Tarakwang, and the "White Water-roses"[1] (Chinese Carbonari) with their mysteries, no notice here! Of Napoleon himself we shall only, glancing from afar, remark that Teufelsdröckh's relation to him seems to have been of very varied character. At first we find our poor Professor on the point of being shot as a spy; then taken into private conversation, even pinched on the ear, yet presented with no money; at last indignantly dismissed, almost thrown out of doors, as an "Ideologist." "He himself," says the Professor, "was among the completest Ideologists, at least Ideopraxists:[2] in the Idea (*in der Idee*) he lived, moved and fought. The man was a Divine Missionary, though unconscious of it; and preached, through the cannon's throat, that great doctrine, *La carrière ouverte aux talens*[3] (The Tools to him that can handle them), which is our ultimate Political Evangel,[4] wherein alone can liberty lie. Madly enough he preached, it is true, as Enthusiasts[5] and first Missionaries are wont, with imperfect utterance, amid

6. Napoleon reduced some of Europe's kings to the status of mere tax collectors for his regime.
7. As manifested in the revolutionary outbreaks in France (1789 and 1830) and in the agitations in England preceding the Reform Bill of 1832.
8. Where Goethe (1749–1832) and Schiller (1759–1805) met during the 1790s when they were collaborating on their writings.
9. I.e., poets, whose excellence is recognized with a crown of laurel.
1. In China a secret revolutionary society (and therefore like the early-18th-century Carbonari in

Italy, France, and Spain) during the regime of Emperor Tarakwang (Tao-kuang, 1821–50).
George Gordon, Lord Byron (1788–1824), English poet and champion of liberty. Pope Pius VII (1742–1823; pope, 1800–23) crowned Napoleon in 1804 but later came to oppose him; he also suppressed the Carbonari.
2. Those who put ideas into practice.
3. Literally, the career open to talent (French), a maxim associated with Napoleon.
4. Gospel; good news.
5. Religious fanatics.

much frothy rant; yet as articulately perhaps as the case admitted. Or call him, if you will, an American Backwoodsman, who had to fell unpenetrated forests, and battle with innumerable wolves, and did not entirely forbear strong liquor, rioting, and even theft; whom, notwithstanding, the peaceful Sower will follow, and, as he cuts the boundless harvest, bless."

More legitimate and decisively authentic is Teufelsdröckh's appearance and emergence (we know not well whence) in the solitude of the North Cape, on that June Midnight. He has a "light-blue Spanish cloak" hanging round him, as his "most commodious, principal, indeed sole upper-garment"; and stands there, on the World-promontory, looking over the infinite Brine, like a little blue Belfry (as we figure), now motionless indeed, yet ready, if stirred, to ring quaintest changes.

"Silence as of death," writes he; "for Midnight, even in the Arctic latitudes, has its character: nothing but the granite cliffs ruddy-tinged, the peaceable gurgle of that slow-heaving Polar Ocean, over which in the utmost North the great Sun hangs low and lazy, as if he too were slumbering. Yet is his cloud-couch wrought of crimson and cloth-of-gold; yet does his light stream over the mirror of waters, like a tremulous fire-pillar, shooting downwards to the abyss, and hide itself under my feet. In such moments, Solitude also is invaluable; for who would speak, or be looked on, when behind him lies all Europe and Africa, fast asleep, except the watchmen; and before him the silent Immensity, and Palace of the Eternal, whereof our Sun is but a porch-lamp?

"Nevertheless, in this solemn moment comes a man, or monster, scrambling from among the rock-hollows; and, shaggy, huge as the Hyperborean[6] Bear, hails me in Russian speech: most probably, therefore, a Russian Smuggler. With courteous brevity, I signify my indifference to contraband trade, my humane intentions, yet strong wish to be private. In vain: the monster, counting doubtless on his superior stature, and minded to make sport for himself, or perhaps profit, were it with murder, continues to advance; ever assailing me with his importunate train-oil[7] breath; and now has advanced, till we stand both on the verge of the rock, the deep Sea rippling greedily down below. What argument will avail? On the thick Hyperborean, cherubic reasoning, seraphic eloquence were lost. Prepared for such extremity, I, deftly enough, whisk aside one step; draw out, from my interior reservoirs, a sufficient Birmingham Horse-pistol, and say, 'Be so obliging as retire, Friend (Er ziehe sich zurück, Freund), and with promptitude!' This logic even the Hyperborean understands: fast enough, with apologetic, petitionary growl, he sidles off; and, except for suicidal as well as homicidal purposes, need not return.

"Such I hold to be the genuine use of Gunpowder: that it makes all men alike tall.[8] Nay, if thou be cooler, cleverer than I, if thou have more Mind, though all but no Body whatever, then canst thou kill me first, and are the taller. Hereby, at last, is the Goliath powerless, and the David resistless;[9] savage Animalism is nothing, inventive Spiritualism is all.

"With respect to Duels, indeed, I have my own ideas. Few things, in this so surprising world, strike me with more surprise. Two little visual Spectra of men, hovering with insecure enough cohesion in the midst of the UNFATH-OMABLE, and to dissolve therein, at any rate, very soon,—make pause at the distance of twelve paces asunder; whirl round; and, simultaneously by the

6. From the far North.
7. Whale oil.
8. Brave; strong.
9. For the fight between Goliath, the huge cham-

pion of the Philistines, and the young Israelite David, who killed him with a slingshot, see 1 Samuel 17.

cunningest mechanism, explode one another into Dissolution; and off-hand become Air, and Nonextant! Deuce on it (*verdammt*), the little spitfires!—Nay, I think with old Hugo von Trimberg:[1] 'God must needs laugh outright, could such a thing be, to see his wondrous Manikins here below.' "

But amid these specialties, let us not forget the great generality, which is our Chief guest here: How prospered the inner man of Teufelsdröckh under so much outward shifting? Does Legion[2] still lurk in him, though repressed; or has he exorcised that Devil's Brood? We can answer that the symptoms continue promising. Experience is the grand spiritual Doctor; and with him Teufelsdröckh has been long a patient, swallowing many a bitter bolus.[3] Unless our poor Friend belong to the numerous class of Incurables, which seems not likely, some cure will doubtless be effected. We should rather say that Legion, or the Satanic School, was now pretty well extirpated and cast out, but next to nothing introduced in its room; whereby the heart remains, for the while, in a quiet but no comfortable state.

"At length, after so much roasting," thus writes our Autobiographer, "I was what you might name calcined. Pray only that it be not rather, as is the more frequent issue, reduced to a *caputmortuum*![4] But in any case, by mere dint of practice, I had grown familiar with many things. Wretchedness was still wretched; but I could now partly see through it, and despise it. Which highest mortal, in this inane Existence, had I not found a Shadow-hunter, or Shadow-hunted; and, when I looked through his brave garnitures, miserable enough? Thy wishes have all been sniffed aside, thought I: but what, had they ever been all granted! Did not the Boy Alexander weep because he had not two Planets to conquer;[5] or a whole Solar System; or after that, a whole Universe? *Ach Gott*, when I gazed into these Stars, have they not looked-down on me as if with pity, from their serene spaces; like Eyes glistening with heavenly tears over the little lot of man! Thousands of human generations, all as noisy as our own, have been swallowed-up of[6] Time, and there remains no wreck[7] of them any more; and Arcturus and Orion and Sirius and the Pleiades are still shining in their courses, clear and young, as when the Shepherd first noted them in the plain of Shinar.[8] Pshaw! what is this paltry little Dog-cage[9] of an Earth; what art thou that sittest whining there? Thou art still Nothing, Nobody: true; but who, then, is Something, Somebody? For thee the Family of Man has no use; it rejects thee; thou art wholly as a dissevered limb: so be it; perhaps it is better so!"

Too-heavy-laden Teufelsdröckh! Yet surely his bands are loosening: one day he will hurl the burden far from him, and bound forth free and with a second youth.

The Everlasting Yea

"Temptations in the Wilderness!"[1] exclaims Teufelsdröckh: "Have we not all to be tried with such? Not so easily can the old Adam, lodged in us by birth,

---

1. Medieval poet (1260–1309).
2. Unclean spirits (Mark 5.9).
3. Large pill.
4. Death's head (Latin).
5. According to tradition, when Alexander the Great (356–323 B.C.E.) realized that he had subjugated the known world he wept because he had no worlds left to conquer.
6. By.
7. Remnant cast ashore from a shipwreck.

8. A plain in the Sumerian region (now in Iraq). "Shepherd": probably Abraham, who was commanded by the Lord to "tell the stars, if thou be able to number them" (Genesis 15.5).
9. A drum-shaped cage that turns when a dog runs inside the cylinder. This dog-powered device, attached to a kitchen spit, was used to turn roasting joints of meat.
1. Paraphrase of Matthew 4.1.

be dispossessed. Our Life is compassed round with Necessity; yet is the meaning of Life itself no other than Freedom, than Voluntary Force: thus have we a warfare; in the beginning, especially, a hard-fought battle. For the God-given mandate, *Work thou in Welldoing,* lies mysteriously written, in Promethean[2] Prophetic Characters, in our hearts; and leaves us no rest, night or day, till it be deciphered and obeyed; till it burn forth, in our conduct, a visible, acted Gospel of Freedom. And as the clay-given mandate, *Eat thou and be filled,* at the same time persuasively proclaims itself through every nerve,—must not there be a confusion, a contest, before the better Influence can become the upper?

"To me nothing seems more natural than that the Son of Man, when such God-given mandate first prophetically stirs within him, and the Clay must now be vanquished, or vanquish,—should be carried of the spirit into grim Solitudes, and there fronting the Tempter do grimmest battle with him; defiantly setting him at naught, till he yield and fly. Name it as we choose: with or without visible Devil, whether in the natural Desert of rocks and sands, or in the populous moral Desert of selfishness and baseness,—to such Temptation are we all called. Unhappy if we are not! Unhappy if we are but Half-men, in whom that divine handwriting has never blazed forth, all-subduing, in true sun-splendour; but quivers dubiously amid meaner lights: or smoulders, in dull pain, in darkness, under earthly vapours!—Our Wilderness is the wide World in an Atheistic Century; our Forty Days[3] are long years of suffering and fasting: nevertheless, to these also comes an end. Yes, to me also was given, if not Victory, yet the consciousness of Battle, and the resolve to persevere therein while life or faculty is left. To me also, entangled in the enchanted forests, demon-peopled, doleful of sight and of sound, it was given, after weariest wanderings, to work out my way into the higher sunlit slopes—of that Mountain which has no summit, or whose summit is in Heaven only!"

He says elsewhere, under a less ambitious figure; as figures are, once for all, natural to him: "Has not thy Life been that of most sufficient men (*tüchtigen Männer*) thou hast known in this generation? An outflush of foolish young Enthusiasm, like the first fallow-crop, wherein are as many weeds as valuable herbs: this all parched away, under the Droughts of practical and spiritual Unbelief, as Disappointment, in thought and act, often-repeated gave rise to Doubt, and Doubt gradually settled into Denial! If I have had a second-crop, and now see the perennial greensward, and sit under umbrageous[4] cedars, which defy all Drought (and Doubt); herein too, be the Heavens praised, I am not without examples, and even exemplars."

So that, for Teufelsdröckh also, there has been a "glorious revolution":[5] these mad shadow-hunting and shadow-hunted Pilgrimings of his were but some purifying "Temptation in the Wilderness," before his Apostolic work (such as it was) could begin; which Temptation is now happily over, and the Devil once more worsted! Was "that high moment in the *Rue de l'Enfer,*" then, properly the turning-point of the battle; when the Fiend said, *Worship me or be torn in shreds*; and was answered valiantly with an *Apage Satana?*[6]—Singular Teufelsdröckh, would thou hadst told thy singular story in plain words! But it

---

2. Fiery or fiery-spirited, an allusion to Prometheus, the defiant Titan who brought the secret of fire making to humanity.
3. The length of time that Jesus spent fasting in the wilderness (Matthew 4.2).
4. Shady.
5. The overthrow of James II of England in 1688.
6. Get thee hence, Satan (Greek; Matthew 4.10).

is fruitless to look there, in those Paper-bags,[7] for such. Nothing but innu-endoes, figurative crotchets:[8] a typical Shadow, fitfully wavering, prophetico-satiric; no clear logical Picture. "How paint to the sensual eye," asks he once, "what passes in the Holy-of-Holies of Man's Soul; in what words, known to these profane times, speak even afar-off of the unspeakable?" We ask in turn: Why perplex these times, profane as they are, with needless obscurity, by omission and by commission? Not mystical only is our Professor, but whim-sical; and involves himself, now more than ever, in eye-bewildering *chiaro-scuro*.[9] Successive glimpses, here faithfully imparted, our more gifted readers must endeavour to combine for their own behoof.

He says: "The hot Harmattan wind[1] had raged itself out; its howl went silent within me; and the long-deafened soul could now hear. I paused in my wild wanderings; and sat me down to wait, and consider; for it was as if the hour of change drew nigh. I seemed to surrender, to renounce utterly, and say: Fly, then, false shadows of Hope; I will chase you no more, I will believe you no more. And ye too, haggard spectres of Fear, I care not for you; ye too are all shadows and a lie. Let me rest here: for I am way-weary and life-weary; I will rest here, were it but to die: to die or to live is alike to me; alike insignificant."— And again: "Here, then, as I lay in that CENTRE of INDIFFERENCE; cast, doubt-less by benignant upper Influence, into a healing sleep, the heavy dreams rolled gradually away, and I awoke to a new Heaven and a new Earth.[2] The first preliminary moral Act, Annihilation of Self (*Selbsttödtung*), had been hap-pily accomplished; and my mind's eyes were now unsealed, and its hands ungyved."[3]

Might we not also conjecture that the following passage refers to his Local-ity, during this same "healing sleep"; that his Pilgrim-staff lies cast aside here, on "the high table-land"; and indeed that the repose is already taking whole-some effect on him? If it were not that the tone, in some parts, has more of riancy,[4] even of levity, than we could have expected! However, in Teufels-dröckh, there is always the strangest Dualism: light dancing, with guitar-music, will be going on in the fore-court, while by fits from within comes the faint whimpering of woe and wail. We transcribe the piece entire:

"Beautiful it was to sit there, as in my skyey Tent, musing and meditating; on the high table-land, in front of the Mountains; over me, as roof, the azure Dome, and around me, for walls, four azure-flowing curtains,—namely, of the Four azure winds, on whose bottom-fringes also I have seen gilding. And then to fancy the fair Castles that stood sheltered in these Mountain hollows; with their green flower-lawns, and white dames and damosels, lovely enough: or better still, the straw-roofed Cottages, wherein stood many a Mother baking bread, with her children round her:—all hidden and protectingly folded-up in the valley-folds; yet there and alive, as sure as if I beheld them. Or to see, as well as fancy, the nine Towns and Villages, that lay round my mountain-seat, which, in still weather, were wont to speak to me (by their steeple-bells) with metal tongue; and, in almost all weather, proclaimed their vitality by repeated Smoke-clouds; whereon, as on a culinary horologe,[5] I might read the hour of the day. For it was the smoke of cookery, as kind housewives at morning,

---

7. Bags containing documents and writings by Teufelsdröckh.
8. Perverse notions.
9. Light and shade (Italian).
1. A hot and dry wind in Africa.

2. Revelation 21.1.
3. Unfettered.
4. Gaiety.
5. Clock.

midday, eventide, were boiling their husband's kettles; and ever a blue pillar rose up into the air, successively or simultaneously, from each of the nine, saying, as plainly as smoke could say: Such and such a meal is getting ready here. Not uninteresting! For you have the whole Borough, with all its love-makings and scandal-mongeries, contentions and contentments, as in minia-ture, and could cover it all with your hat.—If, in my wide Wayfarings, I had learned to look into the business of the World in its details, here perhaps was the place for combining it into general propositions, and deducing inferences therefrom.

"Often also could I see the black Tempest marching in anger through the Distance: round some Schreckhorn,[6] as yet grim-blue, would the eddying vapour gather, and there tumultuously eddy, and flow down like a mad witch's hair; till, after a space, it vanished, and, in the clear sunbeam, your Schreck-horn stood smiling grim-white, for the vapour had held snow. How thou fer-mentest and elaboratest, in thy great fermenting-vat and laboratory of an Atmosphere, of a World, O Nature!—Or what is Nature? Ha! why do I not name thee GOD? Art not thou the 'Living Garment of God'?[7] O Heavens, is it, in very deed, HE, then, that ever speaks through thee; that lives and loves in thee, that lives and loves in me?

"Fore-shadows, call them rather fore-splendours, of that Truth, and Begin-ning of Truths, fell mysteriously over my soul. Sweeter than Dayspring to the Shipwrecked in Nova Zembla;[8] ah, like the mother's voice to her little child that strays bewildered, weeping, in unknown tumults; like soft streamings of celestial music to my too-exasperated heart, came that Evangel. The Universe is not dead and demoniacal, a charnel-house with spectres; but godlike, and my Father's!

"With other eyes, too, could I now look upon my fellow man; with an infinite Love, an infinite Pity. Poor, wandering, wayward man! Art thou not tired, and beaten with stripes, even as I am? Ever, whether thou bear the royal mantle or the beggar's gabardine, art thou not so weary, so heavy-laden; and thy Bed of Rest is but a Grave. O my Brother, my Brother, why cannot I shelter thee in my bosom, and wipe away all tears from thy eyes! Truly, the din of many-voiced Life, which, in this solitude, with the mind's organ, I could hear, was no longer a maddening discord, but a melting one; like inarticulate cries, and sobbings of a dumb creature, which in the ear of Heaven are prayers. The poor Earth, with her poor joys, was now my needy Mother, not my cruel Step-dame; man, with his so mad Wants and so mean Endeavours, had become the dearer to me; and even for his sufferings and his sins, I now first named him Brother. Thus I was standing in the porch of that 'Sanctuary of Sorrow';[9] by strange, steep ways had I too been guided thither; and ere long its sacred gates would open, and the 'Divine Depth of Sorrow' lie disclosed to me."

The Professor says, he here first got eye on the Knot that had been strangling him, and straightway could unfasten it, and was free. "A vain interminable controversy," writes he, "touching what is at present called Origin of Evil, or some such thing, arises in every soul, since the beginning of the world; and in every soul, that would pass from idle Suffering into actual Endeavouring, must first be put an end to. The most, in our time, have to go content with a

6. Peak of Terror (German); a mountain in Swit-zerland.
7. Goethe, *Faust* 1.509.
8. A Dutch sea captain, whose ship was wrecked off the island of Nova Zembla in the Arctic in 1596,

recorded in his journal his thankfulness at the coming of daylight.
9. Adapted from Goethe's *Wilhelm Meister* (1821–29).

simple, incomplete enough Suppression of this controversy; to a few some Solution of it is indispensable. In every new era, too, such Solution comes-out in different terms; and ever the Solution of the last era has become obso-lete, and is found unserviceable. For it is man's nature to change his Dialect from century to century; he cannot help it though he would. The authentic *Church-Catechism* of our present century has not yet fallen into my hands: meanwhile, for my own private behoof, I attempt to elucidate the matter so. Man's Unhappiness, as I construe, comes of his Greatness; it is because there is an Infinite in him, which with all his cunning[1] he cannot quite bury under the Finite. Will the whole Finance Ministers and Upholsterers and Confec-tions of modern Europe undertake, in joint-stock company, to make one Shoe-black HAPPY? They cannot accomplish it, above an hour or two; for the Shoeblack also has a Soul quite other than his Stomach; and would require, if you consider it, for his permanent satisfaction and saturation, simply this allotment, no more, and no less: *God's infinite Universe altogether to himself, therein to enjoy infinitely, and fill every wish as fast as it rose.* Oceans of Hochheimer, a Throat like that of Ophiuchus:[2] speak not of them; to the infinite Shoeblack they are as nothing. No sooner is your ocean filled, than he grumbles that it might have been of better vintage. Try him with half of a Universe, of an Omnipotence, he sets to quarrelling with the proprietor of the other half, and declares himself the most maltreated of men.—Always there is a black spot in our sunshine: it is even as I said, the *Shadow of Ourselves.*

"But the whim we have of Happiness is somewhat thus. By certain valua-tions, and averages, of our own striking, we come upon some sort of average terrestrial lot; this we fancy belongs to us by nature, and of indefeasible right. It is simple payment of our wages, of our deserts; requires neither thanks nor complaint; only such *overplus* as there may be do we account Happiness; any *deficit* again is Misery. Now consider that we have the valuation of our own deserts ourselves, and what a fund of Self-conceit there is in each of us,—do you wonder that the balance should so often dip the wrong way, and many a Blockhead cry: See there, what a payment; was ever worthy gentleman so used!—I tell thee, Blockhead, it all comes of thy Vanity; of what thou *fanciest* those same deserts of thine to be. Fancy that thou deservest to be hanged (as is most likely), thou wilt feel it happiness to be only shot: fancy that thou deservest to be hanged in a hair-halter, it will be a luxury to die in hemp.

"So true is it, what I then say, that *the Fraction of Life can be increased in value not so much by increasing your Numerator as by lessening your Denomi-nator.* Nay, unless my Algebra deceive me, *Unity* itself divided by *Zero* will give *Infinity.* Make thy claim of wages a zero, then; thou hast the world under thy feet. Well did the Wisest of our time write: 'It is only with Renunciation (*Ent-sagen*) that Life, properly speaking, can be said to begin.'[3]

"I asked myself: What is this that, ever since earliest years, thou hast been fretting and fuming, and lamenting and self-tormenting, on account of? Say it in a word: it is not because thou art not HAPPY? Because the THOU (sweet gentleman) is not sufficiently honoured, nourished, soft-bedded, and lovingly cared for? Foolish soul! What Act of Legislature was there that *thou* shouldst be Happy? A little while ago thou hadst no right to *be* at all. What if thou wert

1. Skill.
2. The constellation also known as the Serpent Holder. "Hochheimer": Rhine wine or hock from Hochheim.
3. Adapted from *Wilhelm Meister* by Goethe ("wisest of our time").

born and predestined not to be Happy, but to be Unhappy! Art thou nothing other than a Vulture, then, that fliest through the Universe seeking after somewhat to *eat;* and shrieking dolefully because carrion enough is not given thee? Close thy *Byron;* open thy *Goethe.*"

"*Es leuchtet mir ein,*[4] I see a glimpse of it!" cries he elsewhere: "there is in man a HIGHER than Love of Happiness: he can do without Happiness, and instead thereof find Blessedness! Was it not to preach-forth this same HIGHER that sages and martyrs, the Poet and the Priest, in all times, have spoken and suffered; bearing testimony, through life and through death, of the Godlike that is in Man, and how in the Godlike only has he Strength and Freedom? Which God-inspired Doctrine art thou also honoured to be taught; O Heavens! and broken with manifold merciful Afflictions, even till thou become contrite, and learn it! O, thank thy Destiny for these; thankfully bear what yet remain: thou hadst need of them; the Self in thee needed to be annihilated. By benignant fever-paroxysms is Life rooting out the deep-seated chronic Diseases, and triumphs over Death. On the roaring billows of Time, thou art not engulfed, but borne aloft into the azure of Eternity. Love not Pleasure; love God.[5] This is the EVERLASTING YEA wherein all contradiction is solved: wherein whoso walks and works, it is well with him."

And again: "Small is it that thou canst trample the Earth with its injuries under thy feet, as old Greek Zeno[6] trained thee: thou canst love the Earth while it injures thee, and even because it injures thee; for this a Greater than Zeno was needed, and he too was sent. Knowest thou that 'Worship of Sorrow'?[7] the Temple thereof, founded some eighteen centuries ago, now lies in ruins, overgrown with jungle, the habitation of doleful creatures:[8] nevertheless, venture forward; in a low crypt, arched out of falling fragments, thou findest the Altar still there, and its sacred Lamp perennially burning."

Without pretending to comment on which strange utterances, the Editor will only remark, that there lies beside them much of a still more questionable character; unsuited to the general apprehension; nay wherein he himself does not see his way. Nebulous disquisitions on Religion, yet not without bursts of splendour; on the "perennial continuance of Inspiration"; on Prophecy; that there are "true Priests, as well as Baal-Priests,[9] in our own day": with more of the like sort. We select some fractions, by way of finish to this farrago.

"Cease, my much-respected Herr von Voltaire,"[1] thus apostrophises the Professor: "shut thy sweet voice; for the task appointed thee seems finished. Sufficiently hast thou demonstrated this proposition, considerable or otherwise: That the Mythus of the Christian Religion looks not in the eighteenth century as it did in the eighth. Alas, were thy six-and-thirty quartos, and the six-and-thirty thousand other quartos and folios, and flying sheets or reams, printed before and since on the same subject, all needed to convince us of so little! But what next? Wilt thou help us to embody the divine Spirit of that Religion in a new Mythus, in a new vehicle and vesture, that our Souls, otherwise too like perishing, may live? What! thou hast no faculty in that kind? Only a torch for burning, no hammer for building? Take our thanks, then, and—thyself away.

---

4. An exclamation of Wilhelm Meister's (German).
5. Adapted from 2 Timothy 3.4.
6. Stoic philosopher (3rd century B.C.E.), who, after being injured in a fall, is reputed to have struck the earth with his hand as if the earth were responsible for his injury. Afterward he committed

suicide. Hence he is said to "trample the Earth."
7. Christianity.
8. Isaiah 34.13–15.
9. False priests, mentioned in 1 Kings 18.17–40.
1. French philosopher, satirist, and encyclopedist (1694–1778), famously hostile to superstition, injustice, and organized religion.

"Meanwhile what are antiquated Mythuses to me? Or is the God present, felt in my own heart, a thing which Herr von Voltaire will dispute out of me; or dispute into me? To the 'Worship of Sorrow' ascribe what origin and genesis thou pleasest, has not that Worship originated, and been generated; is it not here? Feel it in thy heart, and then say whether it is of God! This is Belief; all else is Opinion,—for which latter whoso will let him worry and be worried."

"Neither," observes he elsewhere, "shall ye tear-out one another's eyes, struggling over 'Plenary Inspiration,'[2] and suchlike: try rather to get a little even Partial Inspiration, each of you for himself. One BIBLE I know, of whose Plenary Inspiration doubt is not so much as possible; nay with my own eyes I saw God's-Hand writing it: thereof all other Bibles are but leaves,—say, in Picture-Writing to assist the weaker faculty."

Or, to give the wearied reader relief, and bring it to an end, let him take the following perhaps more intelligible passage:

"To me, in this our life," says the Professor, "which is an internecine warfare with the Time-spirit, other warfare seems questionable. Hast thou in any way a Contention with thy brother, I advise thee, think well what the meaning thereof is. If thou gauge it to the bottom, it is simply this: 'Fellow, see! thou art taking more than thy share of Happiness in the world, something from *my* share: which, by the Heavens, thou shalt not; nay I will fight thee rather.'— Alas, and the whole lot to be divided is such a beggarly matter, truly a 'feast of shells,'[3] for the substance has been spilled out: not enough to quench one Appetite; and the collective human species clutching at them!—Can we not, in all such cases, rather say: 'Take it, thou too-ravenous individual; take that pitiful additional fraction of a share, which I reckoned mine, but which thou so wantest; take it with a blessing: would to Heaven I had enough for thee!'—If Fichte's *Wissenschaftslehre*[4] be, 'to a certain extent, Applied Christianity,' surely to a still greater extent, so is this. We have here not a Whole Duty of Man,[5] yet a Half Duty, namely the Passive half: could we but do it, as we can demonstrate it!

"But indeed Conviction, were it never so excellent, is worthless till it convert itself into Conduct. Nay properly Conviction is not possible till then; inasmuch as all Speculation is by nature endless, formless, a vortex amid vortices: only by a felt indubitable certainty of Experience does it find any centre to revolve round, and so fashion itself into a system. Most true is it, as a wise man teaches us, that 'Doubt of any sort cannot be removed except by Action.' On which ground, too, let him who gropes painfully in darkness or uncertain light, and prays vehemently that the dawn may ripen into day, lay this other precept well to heart, which to me was of invaluable service: '*Do the Duty which lies nearest thee,*'[6] which thou knowest to be a Duty! Thy second Duty will already have become clearer.

"May we not say, however, that the hour of Spiritual Enfranchisement is even this: When your Ideal World, wherein the whole man has been dimly struggling and inexpressibly languishing to work, becomes revealed, and thrown open; and you discover, with amazement enough, like the Lothario in

---

2. Doctrine that all statements in the Bible are supernaturally inspired and authoritative. Voltaire had sought to demonstrate that this doctrine was absurd.
3. Empty eggshells. The phrase appears in both James Macpherson's *Fingal* (1761) and Byron's imitation of it, "The Death of Calmer and Orla" (1806).
4. The doctrine of knowledge (German); the shortened title of the 1798 work by Johann Gottlieb Fichte (1762–1814), German philosopher.
5. Title of an anonymous book of religious instruction first published in 1659. The phrase is from Ecclesiastes 12.13.
6. This and the previous quotation are from Goethe's *Wilhelm Meister*.

Wilhelm Meister, that your 'America is here or nowhere'? The Situation that has not its Duty, its Ideal, was never yet occupied by man. Yes here, in this poor, miserable, hampered, despicable Actual, wherein thou even now stand-est, here or nowhere is thy Ideal: work it out therefrom; and working, believe, live, be free. Fool! the Ideal is in thyself, the impediment too is in thyself: thy Condition is but the stuff thou art to shape that same Ideal out of: what matters whether such stuff be of this sort or that, so the Form thou give it be heroic, be poetic? O thou that pinest in the imprisonment of the Actual, and criest bitterly to the gods for a kingdom wherein to rule and create, know this of a truth: the thing thou seekest is already with thee, 'here or nowhere,' couldst thou only see!

"But it is with man's Soul as it was with Nature: the beginning of Creation is—Light.[7] Till the eye have vision, the whole members are in bonds.[8] Divine moment, when over the tempest-tost Soul, as once over the wild-weltering Chaos, it is spoken: Let there be Light! Ever to the greatest that has felt such moment, is it not miraculous and God-announcing; even as, under simpler figures, to the simplest and least. The mad primeval Discord is hushed; the rudely-jumbled conflicting elements bind themselves into separate Firma-ments: deep silent rock-foundations are built beneath; and the skyey vault with its everlasting Luminaries above: instead of a dark wasteful Chaos, we have a blooming, fertile, heaven-encompassed World.

"I too could now say to myself: Be no longer a Chaos, but a World, or even Worldkin.[9] Produce! Produce! Were it but the pitifullest infinitesimal fraction of a Product, produce it, in God's name! 'Tis the utmost thou hast in thee: out with it, then. Up, up! Whatsoever thy hand findeth to do, do it with thy whole might. Work while it is called Today; for the Night cometh, wherein no man can work."[1]

1830–31   1833–34

From Past and Present[1]

From *Democracy*

If the Serene Highnesses and Majesties do not take note of that,[2] then, as I perceive, *that* will take note of itself! The time for levity, insincerity, and idle

7. Cf. Genesis 1.3.
8. Cf. Matthew 6.22–23.
9. A little world, a microcosm.
1. Adapted from Ecclesiastes 9.10 and John 9.4.
1. In 1843 there were reputedly one and a half million unemployed in England (out of a popula-tion of eighteen million). The closing of factories and the reduction of wages led to severe rioting in the manufacturing districts. Bread-hungry mobs (as well as the Chartist mobs who demanded polit-ical reforms) caused many observers to dread that a large-scale revolution was imminent. Carlyle was so appalled by the plight of the industrial workers that he postponed his research into the life and times of Cromwell to air his views on the contem-porary crisis. *Past and Present,* a book written in seven weeks, was a call for heroic leadership. Cromwell and other historic leaders are cited, but the principal example from the past is Abbot Sam-

son, a medieval monk who established order in the monasteries under his charge. Carlyle hoped that the "Captains of Industry" might provide a com-parable leadership in 1843. He was aware that the spread of democracy was inevitable, but he had little confidence in it as a method of producing leaders. Nor did he have any confidence, at this time, in the landed aristocracy, who seemed to him preoccupied with foxhunting, preserving their game, and upholding the tariffs on grain (Corn Laws). In place of a "Do nothing Aristocracy" there was need for a "Working Aristocracy." This first selection is from book 3, chap. 13.
2. The previous chapter, "Reward," had urged that English manufacturers needed the help of every-one and that Parliament should remove the tariffs (Corn Laws) restricting the growth of trade and industry.

babble and play-acting, in all kinds, is gone by; it is a serious, grave time. Old long-vexed questions, not yet solved in logical words or parliamentary laws, are fast solving themselves in facts, somewhat unblessed to behold! This largest of questions, this question of Work and Wages, which ought, had we heeded Heaven's voice, to have begun two generations ago or more, cannot be delayed longer without hearing Earth's voice. "Labour" will verily need to be somewhat "organized," as they say,—God knows with what difficulty. Man will actually need to have his debts and earnings a little better paid by man; which, let Parliaments speak of them, or be silent of them, are eternally his due from man, and cannot, without penalty and at length not without death-penalty,[3] be withheld. How much ought to cease among us straightway; how much ought to begin straightway, while the hours yet are!

Truly they are strange results to which this of leaving all to "Cash"; of quietly shutting up the God's Temple, and gradually opening wide-open the Mammon's Temple, with "Laissez-faire, and Every man for himself,"[4]—have led us in these days! We have Upper, speaking Classes, who indeed do "speak" as never man spake before;[5] the withered flimsiness, godless baseness and barrenness of whose Speech might of itself indicate what kind of Doing and practical Governing went on under it! For Speech is the gaseous element out of which most kinds of Practice and Performance, especially all kinds of moral Performance, condense themselves, and take shape; as the one is, so will the other be. Descending, accordingly, into the Dumb Class in its Stockport Cellars and Poor-Law Bastilles,[6] have we not to announce that they are hitherto unexampled in the History of Adam's Posterity?

Life was never a May-game for men: in all times the lot of the dumb millions born to toil was defaced with manifold sufferings, injustices, heavy burdens, avoidable and unavoidable; not play at all, but hard work that made the sinews sore and the heart sore. As bond-slaves, *villani, bordarii, sochemanni,* nay indeed as dukes, earls and kings, men were oftentimes made weary of their life; and had to say, in the sweat of their brow[7] and of their soul, Behold, it is not sport, it is grim earnest, and our back can bear no more! Who knows not what massacrings and harryings there have been; grinding, long-continuing, unbearable injustices,—till the heart had to rise in madness, and some "*Eu Sachsen, nimith euer sachses,* You Saxons, out with your gully-knives, then!" You Saxons, some "arrestment," partial "arrestment of the Knaves and Dastards" has become indispensable!—The page of Dryasdust[8] is heavy with such details.

And yet I well venture to believe that in no time, since the beginnings of Society, was the lot of those same dumb millions of toilers so entirely unbearable as it is even in the days now passing over us. It is not to die, or even to die of hunger, that makes a man wretched; many men have died; all men must die,—the last exit of us all is in a Fire-Chariot of Pain.[9] But it is to live miserable we know not why; to work sore and yet gain nothing; to be heartworn, weary, yet isolated, unrelated, girt-in with a cold universal Laissez-faire: it is

3. I.e., by the outbreak of a revolution, as in France.
4. The pursuit of wealth (Mammon is the devil of covetousness) according to a noninterventionist economic policy. *Laissez-faire* literally means "let it be" (French).
5. John 7.46.
6. I.e., workhouses for the unemployed. "Stock-

port Cellars": in a cellar in the slum district of Stockport, an industrial town near Manchester, three children were poisoned by their starving parents, who wanted to collect insurance benefits from a burial society.
7. Genesis 3.19.
8. An imaginary author of dull histories.
9. 2 Kings 2.11.

to die slowly all our life long, imprisoned in a deaf, dead, Infinite Injustice, as in the accursed iron belly of a Phalaris' Bull![1] This is and remains for ever intolerable to all men whom God has made. Do we wonder at French Revolutions, Chartisms, Revolts of Three Days?[2] The times, if we will consider them, are really unexampled.

Never before did I hear of an Irish Widow reduced to "prove her sisterhood by dying of typhus-fever and infecting seventeen persons,"—saying in such undeniable way, "You *see*, I was your sister!"[3] Sisterhood, brotherhood, was often forgotten; but not till the rise of these ultimate Mammon and Shotbelt Gospels[4] did I ever see it so expressly denied. If no pious Lord or *Law-ward* would remember it, always some pious Lady (*"Hlaf-dig,"* Benefactress, *"Loaf-giveress,"* they say she is,—blessings on her beautiful heart!) was there, with mild mother-voice and hand, to remember it; some pious thoughtful *Elder*, what we now call "Prester," *Presbyter* or "Priest," was there to put all men in mind of it, in the name of the God who had made all.

Not even in Black Dahomey[5] was it ever, I think, forgotten to the typhus-fever length. Mungo Park,[6] resourceless, had sunk down to die under the Negro Village-Tree, a horrible White object in the eyes of all. But in the poor Black Woman, and her daughter who stood aghast at him, whose earthly wealth and funded capital consisted of one small calabash of rice, there lived a heart richer than *"Laissez-faire"*: they, with a royal munificence, boiled their rice for him; they sang all night to him, spinning assiduous on their cotton distaffs, as he lay to sleep: "Let us pity the poor white man; no mother has he to fetch him milk, no sister to grind him corn!" Thou poor black Noble One,— thou *Lady* too: did not a God make thee too; was there not in thee too something of a God!—

Gurth,[7] born thrall of Cedric the Saxon, has been greatly pitied by Dryasdust and others. Gurth, with the brass collar round his neck, tending Cedric's pigs in the glades of the wood, is not what I call an exemplar of human felicity: but Gurth, with the sky above him, with the free air and tinted boscage and umbrage round him, and in him at least the certainty of supper and social lodging when he came home; Gurth to me seems happy, in comparison with many a Lancashire and Buckinghamshire man, of these days, not born thrall of anybody! Gurth's brass collar did not gall him: Cedric *deserved* to be his Master. The pigs were Cedric's, but Gurth too would get his parings of them. Gurth had the inexpressible satisfaction of feeling himself related indissolubly, though in a rude brass-collar way, to his fellow-mortals in this Earth. He had superiors, inferiors, equals.—Gurth is now "emancipated" long since; has what we call "Liberty." Liberty, I am told, is a Divine thing. Liberty when it becomes the "Liberty to die by starvation" is not so divine!

Liberty? The true liberty of a man, you would say, consisted in his finding out, or being forced to find out, the right path, and to walk thereon. To learn, or to be taught, what work he actually was able for; and then by permission,

1. Phalaris was a Sicilian tyrant (6th century B.C.E.) whose victims were roasted alive by being confined inside the brass figure of a bull under which a fire was lit.
2. The 1830 revolution in France (July 27–29).
3. An incident referred to several times in *Past and Present*. Dickens in *Bleak House* (1851) also showed how indifference to the lack of sanitation in London slums led to the spread of disease to other parts of the city.
4. The attitudes of land-owning aristocracy who were committed to preserving their exclusive right to shoot game birds and animals.
5. A state in west Africa where human sacrifice and cannibalism persisted.
6. Explorer and author (1771–1806); he was killed by Africans.
7. A swineherd described in Scott's *Ivanhoe* (1819).

persuasion, and even compulsion, to set about doing of the same! That is his true blessedness, honour, "liberty" and maximum of wellbeing: if liberty be not that, I for one have small care about liberty. You do not allow a palpable madman to leap over precipices; you violate his liberty, you that are wise; and keep him, were it in strait-waistcoats, away from the precipices! Every stupid, every cowardly and foolish man is but a less palpable madman: his true liberty were that a wiser man, that any and every wiser man, could, by brass collars, or in whatever milder or sharper way, lay hold of him when he was going wrong, and order and compel him to go a little righter. O, if thou really art my *Senior,* Seigneur, my *Elder,* Presbyter or Priest,—if thou art in very deed my *Wiser,* may a beneficent instinct lead and impel thee to "conquer" me, to command me! If thou do know better than I what is good and right, I conjure[8] thee in the name of God, force me to do it; were it by never such brass collars, whips and handcuffs, leave me not to walk over precipices! That I have been called, by all the Newspapers, a "free man" will avail me little, if my pilgrimage have ended in death and wreck. O that the Newspapers had called me slave, coward, fool, or what it pleased their sweet voices to name me, and I had attained not death, but life!—Liberty requires new definitions.

A conscious abhorrence and intolerance of Folly, of Baseness, Stupidity, Poltroonery and all that brood of things, dwells deep in some men: still deeper in others an *un*conscious abhorrence and intolerance, clothed moreover by the beneficent Supreme Powers in what stout appetites, energies, egoisms so-called, are suitable to it;—these latter are your Conquerors, Romans, Normans, Russians, Indo-English; Founders of what we call Aristocracies. Which indeed have they not the most "divine right" to found;—being themselves very truly *Aristoi,* BRAVEST, BEST; and conquering generally a confused rabble of WORST, or at lowest, clearly enough, of WORSE? I think their divine right, tried, with affirmatory verdict, in the greatest Law-Court known to me, was good! A class of men who are dreadfully exclaimed against by Dryasdust; of whom nevertheless beneficent Nature has oftentimes had need; and may, alas, again have need.

When, across the hundredfold poor scepticisms, trivialisms, and constitutional cobwebberies of Dryasdust, you catch any glimpse of a William the Conqueror, a Tancred of Hauteville[9] or such like,—do you not discern veritably some rude outline of a true God-made King; whom not the Champion of England[1] cased in tin, but all Nature and the Universe were calling to the throne? It is absolutely necessary that he get thither. Nature does not mean her poor Saxon children to perish, of obesity, stupor or other malady, as yet: a stern Ruler and Line of Rulers therefore is called in,—a stern but most beneficent *perpetual House-Surgeon* is by Nature herself called in, and even the appropriate *fees* are provided for him! Dryasdust talks lamentably about Hereward and the Fen Counties; fate of earl Waltheof;[2] Yorkshire and the North reduced to ashes; all of which is undoubtedly lamentable. But even

8. Solemnly charge.
9. Norman hero of the First Crusade (1095–99). King William I of England (ca. 1028–1087; reigned 1066–87), surnamed *the Conqueror* after the Battle of Hastings in 1066. Being an illegitimate son, he also bore the surname of William the Bastard. Although some historians condemn William as a ruthless ruler, he is ranked by Carlyle as a hero because of his strong and efficient government. William fulfilled the requirements of the

kingly hero described by Carlyle in his lectures *On Heroes:* a man fittest "to *command* over us . . . to tell us what we are to *do.*"
1. An official who goes through a formality, at coronation ceremonies, of demanding whether anyone challenges the right of the monarch to ascend the throne. He wears full armor ("cased in tin") and is a symbol of outworn feudal customs.
2. His execution in 1075, on a supposedly trumped-up charge, is cited as a blot on William's

Dryasdust apprises me of one fact: "A child, in this William's reign, might have carried a purse of gold from end to end of England." My erudite friend, it is a fact which outweighs a thousand! Sweep away thy constitutional, sentimental, and other cobwebberies; look eye to eye, if thou still have any eye, in the face of this big burly William Bastard: thou wilt see a fellow of most flashing discernment, of most strong lion-heart;—in whom, as it were, within a frame of oak and iron, the gods have planted the soul of "a man of genius"! Dost thou call that nothing? I call it an immense thing!—Rage enough was in this Willelmus Conquaestor, rage enough for his occasions;—and yet the essential element of him, as of all such men, is not scorching *fire*, but shining illuminative *light*. Fire and light are strangely interchangeable; nay, at bottom, I have found them different forms of the same most godlike "elementary substance" in our world: a thing worth stating in these days. The essential element of this Conquaestor is, first of all, the most sun-eyed perception of what *is* really what on this God's-Earth;—which, thou wilt find, does mean at bottom "Justice," and "Virtues" not a few: *Conformity* to what the Maker has seen good to make; that, I suppose, will mean Justice and a Virtue or two?—

Dost thou think Willelmus Conquaestor would have tolerated ten years' jargon, one hour's jargon, on the propriety of killing Cotton-manufactures by partridge Corn-Laws?[3] I fancy, this was not the man to knock out of his night's-rest with nothing but a noisy bedlamism in your mouth![4] "Assist us still better to bush the partridges; strangle Plugson who spins the shirts?"—"*Par la Splendeur de Dieu!*"[5]—Dost thou think Willelmus Conquaestor, in this new time, with Steam-engine Captains of Industry on one hand of him, and Joe-Manton Captains of Idleness[6] on the other, would have doubted which *was* really the Best; which did deserve strangling, and which not?

I have a certain indestructible regard for Willelmus Conquaestor. A resident House-Surgeon, provided by Nature for her beloved English People, and even furnished with the requisite fees, as I said; for he by no means felt himself doing Nature's work, this Willelmus, but his own work exclusively! And his own work withal it was; informed *"par la Splendeur de Dieu."*—I say, it is necessary to get the work out of such a man, however harsh that be! When a world, not yet doomed for death, is rushing down to ever-deeper Baseness and Confusion, it is a dire necessity of Nature's to bring in her ARISTOCRACIES, her BEST, even by forcible methods. When their descendants or representatives cease entirely to *be* the Best, Nature's poor world will very soon rush down again to Baseness; and it becomes a dire necessity of Nature's to cast them out. Hence French Revolutions, Five-point Charters,[7] Democracies, and a mournful list of *Etceteras*, in these our afflicted times.

✣ ✣ ✣

record as king. Hereward the Wake was an outlaw whose exploits against William the Conqueror made him seem a romantic figure like Robin Hood.
3. See nn. 1, 2, p. 1024.
4. I.e., not the man to disturb with your mad ravings. Bedlam, the hospital of St. Mary in Bethlehem, was London's most famous lunatic asylum.
5. By the splendor of God! (French): one of William's oaths. Plugson of Undershot was Carlyle's fictive representative of the new class of industrial leaders.

6. The idle aristocracy who wasted time shooting partridges with guns made by Joseph Manton, a London gunsmith. This speech sums up the pleas of the High Tariff lobby in Parliament. "Keep the Corn Laws intact so that the aristocratic landlords may continue to enjoy shooting partridges on their estates; subdue the manufacturing leaders by preventing trade."
7. The Chartist movement for political reform called first for six, then for five major changes to the existing system of parliamentary democracy.

Democracy, the chase of Liberty in that direction, shall go its full course; unrestrained by him of Pferdefuss-Quacksalber,[8] or any of *his* household. The Toiling Millions of Mankind, in most vital need and passionate instinctive desire of Guidance, shall cast away False-Guidance; and hope, for an hour, that No-Guidance will suffice them: but it can be for an hour only. The smallest item of human Slavery is the oppression of man by his Mock-Superiors; the palpablest, but I say at bottom the smallest. Let him shake off such oppression, trample it indignantly under his feet; I blame him not, I pity and commend him. But oppression by your Mock-Superiors well shaken off, the grand problem yet remains to solve: That of finding government by your Real-Superiors! Alas, how shall we ever learn the solution of that, benighted, bewildered, sniffing, sneering, godforgetting unfortunates as we are? It is a work for centuries; to be taught us by tribulations, confusions, insurrections, obstructions; who knows if not by conflagration and despair! It is a lesson inclusive of all other lessons; the hardest of all lessons to learn.

Captains of Industry[9]

If I believed that Mammonism with its adjuncts was to continue henceforth the one serious principle of our existence, I should reckon it idle to solicit remedial measures from any Government, the disease being insusceptible of remedy. Government can do much, but it can in no wise do all. Government, as the most conspicuous object in Society, is called upon to give signal of what shall be done; and, in many ways, to preside over further, and command the doing of it. But the Government cannot do, by all its signalling and commanding, what the Society is radically indisposed to do. In the long-run every Government is the exact symbol of its People, with their wisdom and unwisdom; we have to say, Like People like Government.—The main substance of this immense Problem of Organizing Labour, and first of all of Managing the Working Classes, will, it is very clear, have to be solved by those who stand practically in the middle of it; by those who themselves work and preside over work. Of all that can be enacted by any Parliament in regard to it, the germs must already lie potentially extant in those two Classes, who are to obey such enactment. A Human Chaos *in* which there is no light, you vainly attempt to irradiate by light shed *on* it: order never can arise there.

But it is my firm conviction that the "Hell of England" will *cease* to be that of "not making money"; that we shall get a nobler Hell and a nobler Heaven! I anticipate light *in* the Human Chaos, glimmering, shining more and more; under manifold true signals from without That light shall shine. Our deity no longer being Mammon,—O Heavens, each man will then say to himself: "Why such deadly haste to make money? I shall not go to Hell, even if I do not make money! There is another Hell, I am told!" Competition, at railway-speed, in all branches of commerce and work will then abate:—good felt-hats for the head, in every sense, instead of seven-feet lath-and-plaster hats on wheels,[1] will then be discoverable! Bubble-periods,[2] with their panics and commercial crises, will again become infrequent; steady modest industry will take the place

8. Horse foot quack doctor (a fake German name invented by Carlyle).
9. From book 4, chap. 4.

1. A London hatter's mode of advertising.
2. Periods of violent fluctuation in the stock market caused by unsound speculating.

of gambling speculation. To be a noble Master, among noble Workers, will again be the first ambition with some few; to be a rich Master only the second. How the Inventive Genius of England, with the whirr of its bobbins and billy-rollers[3] shoved somewhat into the backgrounds of the brain, will contrive and devise, not cheaper produce exclusively, but fairer distribution of the produce at its present cheapness! By degrees, we shall again have a Society with something of Heroism in it, something of Heaven's Blessing on it; we shall again have, as my German friend[4] asserts, "instead of Mammon-Feudalism with unsold cotton-shirts and Preservation of the Game, noble just Industrialism and Government by the Wisest!"

It is with the hope of awakening here and there a British man to know himself for a man and divine soul, that a few words of parting admonition, to all persons to whom the Heavenly Powers have lent power of any kind in this land, may now be addressed. And first to those same Master-Workers, Leaders of Industry; who stand nearest, and in fact powerfullest, though not most prominent, being as yet in too many senses a Virtuality rather than an Actuality.

The Leaders of Industry, if Industry is ever to be led, are virtually the Captains of the World; if there be no nobleness in them, there will never be an Aristocracy more. But let the Captains of Industry consider: once again, are they born of other clay than the old Captains of Slaughter; doomed for ever to be not Chivalry, but a mere gold-plated *Doggery*,—what the French well name *Canaille*, "Doggery" with more or less gold carrion at its disposal? Captains of Industry are the true Fighters, henceforth recognizable as the only true ones: Fighters against Chaos, Necessity and the Devils and Jötuns;[5] and lead on Mankind in that great, and alone true, and universal warfare; the stars in their courses fighting for them, and all Heaven and all Earth saying audibly, Well done! Let the Captains of Industry retire into their own hearts, and ask solemnly, If there is nothing but vulturous hunger for fine wines, valet reputation and gilt carriages, discoverable there? Of hearts made by the Almighty God I will not believe such a thing. Deep-hidden under wretchedest god-forgetting Cants, Epicurisms, Dead-Sea Apisms;[6] forgotten as under foullest fat Lethe[7] mud and weeds, there is yet, in all hearts born into this God's-World, a spark of the Godlike slumbering. Awake, O nightmare sleepers; awake, arise, or be for ever fallen![8] This is not playhouse poetry; it is sober fact. Our England, our world cannot live as it is. It will connect itself with a God again, or go down with nameless throes and fire-consummation to the Devils. Thou who feelest aught of such a Godlike stirring in thee, any faintest intimation of it as through heavy-laden dreams, follow *it*, I conjure thee. Arise, save thyself, be one of those that save thy country.

Bucaniers,[9] Chactaw Indians, whose supreme aim in fighting is that they may get the scalps, the money, that they may amass scalps and money; out of such came no Chivalry, and never will! Out of such came only gore and wreck,

---

3. Machines used to prepare cotton or wool for spinning.
4. Teufelsdröckh, the hero of *Sartor Resartus* (1833–34).
5. Giants of Scandinavian mythology.
6. A reference to a Muslim story in which members of a tribe living near the Dead Sea were trans-

formed into apes because they had ignored the prophecies of Moses.
7. The river of forgetfulness in the classical underworld.
8. Satan's appeal to the devils in Milton's *Paradise Lost* 1.330.
9. Buccaneers.

infernal rage and misery; desperation quenched in annihilation. Behold it, I bid thee, behold there, and consider! What is it that thou have a hundred thousand-pound bills laid up in thy strong-room, a hundred scalps hung up in thy wigwam? I value not them or thee. Thy scalps and thy thousand-pound bills are as yet nothing, if no nobleness from within irradiate them; if no Chivalry, in action, or in embryo ever struggling towards birth and action, be there.

Love of men cannot be bought by cash-payment; and without love, men cannot endure to be together. You cannot lead a Fighting World without having it regimented, chivalried: the thing, in a day, becomes impossible; all men in it, the highest at first, the very lowest at last, discern consciously, or by a noble instinct, this necessity. And can you any more continue to lead a Working World unregimented, anarchic? I answer, and the Heavens and Earth are now answering, No! The thing becomes not "in a day" impossible; but in some two generations it does. Yes, when fathers and mothers, in Stockport hunger-cellars, begin to eat their children, and Irish widows have to prove their relationship by dying of typhus-fever; and amid Governing "Corporations of the Best and Bravest," busy to preserve their game by "bushing," dark millions of God's human creatures start up in mad Chartisms, impracticable Sacred-Months, and Manchester Insurrections;[1]—and there is a virtual Industrial Aristocracy as yet only half-alive, spell-bound amid money-bags and ledgers; and an actual Idle Aristocracy seemingly near dead in somnolent delusions, in trespasses and double-barrels,[2] "sliding," as on inclined-planes, which every new year they *soap* with new Hansard's-jargon under God's sky, and so are "sliding" ever faster, towards a "scale"[3] and balance-scale whereon is written *Thou art found Wanting;*[4]—in such days, after a generation or two, I say, it does become, even to the low and simple, very palpably impossible! No Working World, any more than a Fighting World, can be led on without a noble Chivalry of Work, and laws and fixed rules which follow out of that,— far nobler than any Chivalry of Fighting was. As an anarchic multitude on mere Supply-and-demand, it is becoming inevitable that we dwindle in horrid suicidal convulsion, and self-abrasion, frightful to the imagination, into *Chactaw* Workers. With wigwams and scalps,—with palaces and thousand-pound bills; with savagery, depopulation, chaotic desolation! Good Heavens, will not one French Revolution and Reign of Terror suffice us, but must there be two? There will be two if needed; there will be twenty if needed; there will be precisely as many as needed. The Laws of Nature will have themselves fulfilled. That is a thing certain to me.

Your gallant battle-hosts and work-hosts, as the others did, will need to be made loyally yours; they must and will be regulated, methodically secured in their just share of conquest under you;—joined with you in veritable brotherhood, sonhood, by quite other and deeper ties than those of temporary day's wages! How would mere redcoated regiments, to say nothing of chivalries,

1. In 1819 a large open-air labor meeting in Manchester was broken up by charging cavalry. Thirteen men and women were massacred, and many others were wounded. "Bushing": protecting game from poachers who use nets, by positioning bushes or branches on the grounds.
2. I.e., the only concern of the landed aristocrats is to keep trespassers off their game preserves and reserve shooting rights to themselves.
3. The "sliding scale" refers to the system of variable tariffs within the Corn Laws that benefited the aristocratic landlords. "Hansard's-jargon": parliamentary oratory, as in Hansard's printed record of debates in the Houses of Parliament.
4. The message of the miraculous writing on the wall in Daniel 5.

fight for you, if you could discharge them on the evening of the battle, on payment of the stipulated shillings,—and they discharge you on the morning of it! Chelsea Hospitals,[5] pensions, promotions, rigorous lasting covenant on the one side and on the other, are indispensable even for a hired fighter. The Feudal Baron, much more,—how could he subsist with mere temporary mercenaries round him, at sixpence a day; ready to go over to the other side, if sevenpence were offered? He could not have subsisted;—and his noble instinct saved him from the necessity of even trying! The Feudal Baron had a Man's Soul in him; to which anarchy, mutiny, and the other fruits of temporary mercenaries, were intolerable: he had never been a Baron otherwise, but had continued a Chactaw and Bucanier. He felt it precious, and at last it became habitual, and his fruitful enlarged existence included it as a necessity, to have men round him who in heart loved him; whose life he watched over with rigour yet with love; who were prepared to give their life for him, if need came. It was beautiful; it was human! Man lives not otherwise, nor can live contented, anywhere or anywhen. Isolation is the sum-total of wretchedness to man. To be cut off, to be left solitary: to have a world alien, not your world; all a hostile camp for you; not a home at all, of hearts and faces who are yours, whose you are! It is the frightfullest enchantment; too truly a work of the Evil One. To have neither superior, nor inferior, nor equal, united manlike to you. Without father, without child, without brother. Man knows no sadder destiny. "How is each of us," exclaims Jean Paul,[6] "so lonely in the wide bosom of the All!" Encased each as in his transparent "ice-palace"; our brother visible in his, making signals and gesticulations to us;—visible, but for ever unattainable: on his bosom we shall never rest, nor he on ours. It was not a God that did this; no!

Awake, ye noble Workers, warriors in the one true war: all this must be remedied. It is you who are already half-alive, whom I will welcome into life; whom I will conjure in God's name to shake off your enchanted sleep, and live wholly! Cease to count scalps, goldpurses; not in these lies your or our salvation. Even these, if you count only these, will not be left. Let bucaniering be put far from you; alter, speedily abrogate all laws of the bucaniers, if you would gain any victory that shall endure. Let God's justice, let pity, nobleness and manly valour, with more gold-purses or with fewer, testify themselves in this your brief Life-transit to all the Eternities, the Gods and Silences. It is to you I call; for ye are not dead, ye are already half-alive: there is in you a sleepless dauntless energy, the prime-matter of all nobleness in man. Honour to you in your kind. It is to you I call: ye know at least this, That the mandate of God to His creature man is: Work! The future Epic of the World rests not with those that are near dead, but with those that are alive, and those that are coming into life.

Look around you. Your world-hosts are all in mutiny, in confusion, destitution; on the eve of fiery wreck and madness! They will not march farther for you, on the sixpence a day and supply-and-demand principle; they will not; nor ought they, nor can they. Ye shall reduce them to order, begin reducing them. To order, to just subordination; noble loyalty in return for noble guidance. Their souls are driven nigh mad; let yours be sane and ever saner. Not as a bewildered bewildering mob; but as a firm regimented mass, with real

5. Homes for disabled veterans.
6. Jean Paul Richter (1763–1825), German humorist.

captains over them, will these men march any more. All human interests, combined human endeavours, and social growths in this world, have, at a certain stage of their development, required organizing: and Work, the grandest of human interests, does now require it.

God knows, the task will be hard: but no noble task was ever easy. This task will wear away your lives, and the lives of your sons and grandsons: but for what purpose, if not for tasks like this, were lives given to men? Ye shall cease to count your thousand-pound scalps, the noble of you shall cease! Nay, the very scalps, as I say, will not long be left if you count on these. Ye shall cease wholly to be barbarous vulturous Chactaws, and become noble European Nineteenth-Century Men. Ye shall know that Mammon, in never such gigs[7] and flunkey "respectabilities," is not the alone God; that of himself he is but a Devil, and even a Brute-god.

Difficult? Yes, it will be difficult. The short-fibre cotton; that too was difficult. The waste cotton-shrub, long useless, disobedient, as the thistle by the wayside,—have ye not conquered it; made it into beautiful bandana webs; white woven shirts for men; bright-tinted air-garments wherein flit goddesses? Ye have shivered mountains asunder, made the hard iron pliant to you as soft putty: the Forest-giants, Marsh-jötuns bear sheaves of golden grain; Aegir the Seademon[8] himself stretches his back for a sleek highway to you, and on Firehorses and Windhorses ye career. Ye are most strong. Thor red-bearded, with his blue sun-eyes, with his cheery heart and strong thunder-hammer, he and you have prevailed. Ye are most strong, ye Sons of the icy North, of the far East,—far marching from your rugged Eastern Wildernesses, hitherward from the grey Dawn of Time! Ye are Sons of the *Jötun-land*; the land of Difficulties Conquered. Difficult? You must try this thing. Once try it with the understanding that it will and shall have to be done. Try it as ye try the paltrier thing, making of money! I will bet on you once more, against all Jötuns, Tailor-gods,[9] Double-barrelled Law-wards, and Denizens of Chaos whatsoever.

1843   1843

---

7. Light carriages; to own one was a sign of respectability.
8. From Scandinavian mythology.
9. False gods.

JOHN HENRY CARDINAL NEWMAN
1801–1890

Like Thomas Carlyle, John Henry Newman powerfully affected the thinking of his contemporaries, whether they agreed or disagreed with him. Even today, according to Martin Svaglic, Newman attracts both "apotheosizers" and "calumniators" who praise or blame him "as an unusually compelling spokesman for what some consider eternal verities and others regressive myths." During his long lifetime Newman frequently found himself at the center of some of the most intense disputes that stirred Victorian England, disputes in which he himself emerged as a controversialist of great skill—engagingly persuasive in defense of his position and devastatingly effective in disposing of opponents. Thomas Hardy, whose position was at the opposite extreme from Newman's, paid him a high compliment when he noted in his diary: "Worked at J. H. Newman's *Apologia* which we have all been talking about lately. . . . Style charming and his logic really human, being based not on syllogisms but on converging probabilities. Only—and here comes the fatal catastrophe—there is no first link to his excellent chain of reasoning, and down you come headlong."

Newman was born in London, the son (like Robert Browning) of a banker. In his spiritual autobiography, *Apologia Pro Vita Sua* (in effect, his vindication of his life, 1864–65), he traces the principal stages of his religious development from the strongly Protestant period of his youth to his conversion to Roman Catholicism in 1845. Along the way, after being elected to a fellowship at Oriel College in Oxford and becoming an Anglican clergyman, he was attracted briefly into the orbit of religious liberalism. Gradually coming to realize, however, that liberalism, with its reliance on human reason, would be powerless to defend traditional religion from attack, Newman shifted over into the new High Church wing of the Anglican Church and soon was recognized as the leading figure of what was known as the Oxford movement. During the 1830s he built up a large and influential following by his sermons at Oxford and also by his writing of tracts—that is, appeals, in pamphlet form, on behalf of a cause. In these publications he developed arguments about the powers of church versus state and other issues of deep concern to his High Church colleagues—or Tractarians, as they were also called. Newman's own efforts to demonstrate the true catholicity of the Church of England provoked increasing opposition as his position grew closer to Roman Catholicism. Distressed by constant denunciations, he withdrew into isolation and silence. After much reflection he took the final step. At the age of forty-four he entered the Roman Catholic priesthood and moved to Birmingham, where he spent the rest of his life. In 1879 he was created cardinal. In 1991, at the instigation of Pope John Paul II, his title became The Venerable John Henry Cardinal Newman, marking the first of three stages toward sainthood.

In view of this development, Newman's response to a woman who had spoken of him as a saint is touching. In some distress he wrote to her: "Saints are not literary men, they do not love the classics, they do not write Tales."

Although the story of Newman's development seems to emphasize change, certain features remain constant. His sense of God's guidance is especially evident. Characteristic is a poem written in Italy in 1834, following a severe illness, which opens with the line "Lead, kindly light" and concludes with this stanza:

> So long Thy power hath blest me, sure it still
>   Will lead me on,
> O'er moor and fen, o'er crag and torrent, till
>   The night is gone;
> And with the morn those angel faces smile
> Which I have loved long since, and lost awhile.

Set to music, Newman's poem became one of the most popular hymns ever written.

The writing of verse, however, was a subordinate task for Newman; most of his writings are prose, and it is noteworthy that despite his mastery of prose style, Newman found the act of composition to be even more painfully difficult than most of us do. During his years at Birmingham, he was nevertheless prompted to write several books, including works of religious poetry and fiction. Of particular interest are Newman's lectures on the aims of education, which were delivered in Dublin at the newly founded Catholic University of Ireland, a university he led for a few years as rector. These lectures, published in 1852 and later titled *The Idea of a University*, are a classic statement of the value of "the disciplined intellect" that can be developed by a liberal education rather than by a technical training. Like the later lectures of Matthew Arnold and T. H. Huxley, *The Idea of a University* shows the Victorian engagement with the role of education in society. Moreover, its exploration of the qualities of the ideal gentleman (see the excerpt for *Discourse* 8 below) also speaks to a concern of his time: this classic definition is essential reading for those interested in debates about Victorian gender roles.

It should be noted that Newman's view of a liberal education is largely independent of his religious position. Such an education, he said, could form the minds of profligates and anticlericals as well as of saints and priests of the Church. In considerable measure, his view reflects his admiration for the kind of intellectual enlargement he had himself enjoyed as an undergraduate at Trinity College, Oxford. One of the most moving passages in Newman's autobiography is the account of his farewell to an Oxford friend, in February 1846, as he was preparing his final departure from the precincts of the university he loved:

> In him I took leave of my first College, Trinity, which was so dear to me. . . .
> There used to be much snapdragon growing on the walls opposite my freshman's rooms there, and I had taken it as the emblem of my perpetual residence even unto death in my University.
>   On the morning of the 23rd I left the Observatory. I have never seen Oxford since, excepting its spires, as they are seen from the railway.

From The Idea of a University

From *Discourse 5. Knowledge Its Own End*

6

Now bear with me, Gentlemen, if what I am about to say has at first sight a fanciful appearance. Philosophy, then, or Science, is related to Knowledge in this way: Knowledge is called by the name of Science or Philosophy, when it is acted upon, informed, or if I may use a strong figure, impregnated by Reason. Reason is the principle of that intrinsic fecundity of Knowledge, which, to those who possess it, is its especial value, and which dispenses with the necessity of their looking abroad for any end to rest upon external to itself. Knowledge, indeed, when thus exalted into a scientific form, is also power; not only is it excellent in itself, but whatever such excellence may be, it is something more, it has a result beyond itself. Doubtless; but that is a further consideration, with which I am not concerned. I only say that, prior to its being a power, it is a good; that it is, not only an instrument, but an end. I know well it may resolve itself into an art, and terminate in a mechanical process, and in tangible fruit; but it also may fall back upon that Reason which informs it, and resolve itself into Philosophy. In one case it is called Useful Knowledge, in the other Liberal. The same person may cultivate it in both ways at once; but this again is a matter foreign to my subject; here I do but say that there are two ways of using Knowledge, and in matter of fact those who use it in one way are not likely to use it in the other, or at least in a very limited measure. You see, then, here are two methods of Education; the end of the one is to be philosophical, of the other to be mechanical; the one rises towards general ideas, the other is exhausted upon what is particular and external. Let me not be thought to deny the necessity, or to decry the benefit, of such attention to what is particular and practical, as belongs to the useful or mechanical arts; life could not go on without them; we owe our daily welfare to them; their exercise is the duty of the many, and we owe to the many a debt of gratitude for fulfilling that duty. I only say that Knowledge, in proportion as it tends more and more to be particular, ceases to be Knowledge. It is a question whether Knowledge can in any proper sense be predicated of the brute creation; without pretending to metaphysical exactness of phraseology, which would be unsuitable to an occasion like this, I say, it seems to me improper to call that passive sensation, or perception of things, which brutes seem to possess, by the name of Knowledge. When I speak of Knowledge, I mean something intellectual, something which grasps what it perceives through the senses; something which takes a view of things; which sees more than the senses convey; which reasons upon what it sees, and while it sees; which invests it with an idea. It expresses itself, not in a mere enunciation, but by an enthymeme:[1] it is of the nature of science from the first, and in this consists its dignity. The principle of real dignity in Knowledge, its worth, its desirableness, considered irrespectively of its results, is this germ within it of a scientific or a philosophical process. This is how it comes to be an end in itself; this is why it admits of being called Liberal. Not to know the relative disposition of things is the state of slaves or children; to have mapped out the Universe is the boast, or at least the ambition, of Philosophy.

Moreover, such knowledge is not a mere extrinsic or accidental advantage, which is ours today and another's tomorrow, which may be got up from a book, and easily forgotten again, which we can command or communicate at our pleasure, which we can borrow for the occasion, carry about in our hand, and take into the market; it is an acquired illumination, it is a habit, a personal possession, and an inward endowment. And this is the reason why it is more correct, as well as more usual, to speak of a University as a place of education than of instruction, though, when knowledge is concerned, instruction would at first sight have seemed the more appropriate word. We are instructed, for instance, in manual exercises, in the fine and useful arts, in trades, and in ways of business; for these are methods, which have little or no effect upon the mind itself, are contained in rules committed to memory, to tradition, or to use, and bear upon an end external to themselves. But education is a higher word; it implies an action upon our mental nature, and the formation of a character; it is something individual and permanent, and is commonly spoken of in connection with religion and virtue. When, then, we speak of the communication of Knowledge as being Education, we thereby really imply that that Knowledge is a state or condition of mind; and since cultivation of mind is surely worth seeking for its own sake, we are thus brought once more to the conclusion, which the word "Liberal" and the word "Philosophy" have already suggested, that there is a Knowledge, which is desirable, though nothing come of it, as being of itself a treasure, and a sufficient remuneration of years of labor.

From Discourse 7. Knowledge Viewed in Relation to Professional Skill

1

I have been insisting, in my two preceding Discourses, first, on the cultivation of the intellect, as an end which may reasonably be pursued for its own sake; and next, on the nature of that cultivation, or what that cultivation consists in. Truth of whatever kind is the proper object of the intellect; its cultivation then lies in fitting it to apprehend and contemplate truth. Now the intellect in its present state, with exceptions which need not here be specified,

1. A syllogism in which one of the premises is understood but not stated.

does not discern truth intuitively, or as a whole. We know, not by a direct and simple vision, not at a glance, but, as it were, by piecemeal and accumulation, by a mental process, by going round an object, by the comparison, the combination, the mutual correction, the continual adaptation, of many partial notions, by the employment, concentration, and joint action of many faculties and exercises of mind. Such a union and concert of the intellectual powers, such an enlargement and development, such a comprehensiveness, is necessarily a matter of training. And again, such a training is a matter of rule; it is not mere application, however exemplary, which introduces the mind to truth, nor the reading many books, nor the getting up² many subjects, nor the witnessing many experiments, nor the attending many lectures. All this is short of enough; a man may have done it all, yet be lingering in the vestibule of knowledge: he may not realize what his mouth utters; he may not see with his mental eye what confronts him; he may have no grasp of things as they are; or at least he may have no power at all of advancing one step forward of himself, in consequence of what he has already acquired, no power of discriminating between truth and falsehood, of sifting out the grains of truth from the mass, of arranging things according to their real value, and, if I may use the phrase, of building up ideas. Such a power is the result of a scientific formation of mind; it is an acquired faculty of judgment, of clearsightedness, of sagacity, of wisdom, of philosophical reach of mind, and of intellectual self-possession and repose—qualities which do not come of mere acquirement. The bodily eye, the organ for apprehending material objects, is provided by nature; the eye of the mind, of which the object is truth, is the work of discipline and habit.

This process of training, by which the intellect, instead of being formed or sacrificed to some particular or accidental purpose, some specific trade or profession, or study or science, is disciplined for its own sake, for the perception of its own proper object, and for its own highest culture, is called Liberal Education; and though there is no one in whom it is carried as far as is conceivable, or whose intellect would be a pattern of what intellects should be made, yet there is scarcely anyone but may gain an idea of what real training is, and at least look towards it, and make its true scope and result, not something else, his standard of excellence; and numbers there are who may submit themselves to it, and secure it to themselves in good measure. And to set forth the right standard, and to train according to it, and to help forward all students toward it according to their various capacities, this I conceive to be the business of a University.

2

Now this is what some great men are very slow to allow; they insist that Education should be confined to some particular and narrow end, and should issue in some definite work, which can be weighed and measured. They argue as if every thing, as well as every person, had its price; and that where there has been a great outlay, they have a right to expect a return in kind. This they call making Education and Instruction "useful," and "Utility" becomes their watchword. With a fundamental principle of this nature, they very naturally go on to ask what there is to show for the expense of a University; what is the

2. Studying.

real worth in the market of the article called "a Liberal Education," on the supposition that it does not teach us definitely how to advance our manufactures, or to improve our lands, or to better our civil economy; or again, if it does not at once make this man a lawyer, that an engineer, and that a surgeon; or at least if it does not lead to discoveries in chemistry, astronomy, geology, magnetism, and science of every kind.

* * *

5

* * *

This is the obvious answer which may be made to those who urge upon us the claims of Utility in our plans of Education;[3] but I am not going to leave the subject here: I mean to take a wider view of it. Let us take "useful," as Locke[4] takes it, in its proper and popular sense, and then we enter upon a large field of thought, to which I cannot do justice in one Discourse, though today's is all the space that I can give to it. I say, let us take "useful" to mean, not what is simply good, but what *tends* to good, or is the *instrument* of good; and in this sense also, Gentlemen, I will show you how a liberal education is truly and fully a useful, though it be not a professional, education. "Good" indeed means one thing, and "useful" means another; but I lay it down as a principle, which will save us a great deal of anxiety, that, though the useful is not always good, the good is always useful. Good is not only good, but reproductive of good; this is one of its attributes; nothing is excellent, beautiful, perfect, desirable for its own sake, but it overflows, and spreads the likeness of itself all around it. Good is prolific; it is not only good to the eye, but to the taste; it not only attracts us, but it communicates itself; it excites first our admiration and love, then our desire and our gratitude, and that, in proportion to its intenseness and fullness in particular instances. A great good will impart great good. If then the intellect is so excellent a portion of us, and its cultivation so excellent, it is not only beautiful, perfect, admirable, and noble in itself, but in a true and high sense it must be useful to the possessor and to all around him; not useful in any low, mechanical, mercantile sense, but as diffusing good, or as a blessing, or a gift, or power, or a treasure, first to the owner, then through him to the world. I say then, if a liberal education be good, it must necessarily be useful too.

6

You will see what I mean by the parallel of bodily health. Health is a good in itself, though nothing came of it, and is especially worth seeking and cherishing; yet, after all, the blessings which attend its presence are so great, while they are so close to it and so redound back upon it and encircle it, that we never think of it except as useful as well as good, and praise and prize it for what it does, as well as for what it is, though at the same time we cannot point out any definite and distinct work or production which it can be said to effect. And so as regards intellectual culture, I am far from denying utility in this

3. The Utilitarians argued that a useful education would be one that trained the mind in the "habit of pushing things up to their first principles." Newman had earlier pointed out that a liberal educa-

tion does exactly that and is hence useful.
4. John Locke (1632–1704), whose treatise *Some Thoughts Concerning Education* (1693) advocated a utilitarian concept of education.

large sense as the end of Education, when I lay it down that the culture of the intellect is a good in itself and its own end; I do not exclude from the idea of intellectual culture what it cannot but be, from the very nature of things; I only deny that we must be able to point out, before we have any right to call it useful, some art, or business, or profession, or trade, or work, as resulting from it, and as its real and complete end. The parallel is exact: As the body may be sacrificed to some manual or other toil, whether moderate or oppressive, so may the intellect be devoted to some specific profession; and I do not call *this* the culture of the intellect. Again, as some member or organ of the body may be inordinately used and developed, so may memory, or imagination, or the reasoning faculty; and *this* again is not intellectual culture. On the other hand, as the body may be tended, cherished, and exercised with a simple view to its general health, so may the intellect also be generally exercised in order to its perfect state; and this *is* its cultivation.

Again, as health ought to precede labor of the body, and as a man in health can do what an unhealthy man cannot do, and as of this health the properties are strength, energy, agility, graceful carriage and action, manual dexterity, and endurance of fatigue, so in like manner general culture of mind is the best aid to professional and scientific study, and educated men can do what illiterate cannot; and the man who has learned to think and to reason and to compare and to discriminate and to analyze, who has refined his taste, and formed his judgment, and sharpened his mental vision, will not indeed at once be a lawyer, or a pleader, or an orator, or a statesman, or a physician, or a good landlord, or a man of business, or a soldier, or an engineer, or a chemist, or a geologist, or an antiquarian, but he will be placed in that state of intellect in which he can take up any one of the sciences or callings I have referred to, or any other for which he has a taste or special talent, with an ease, a grace, a versatility, and a success, to which another is a stranger. In this sense then, and as yet I have said but a very few words on a large subject, mental culture is emphatically *useful.*

If then I am arguing, and shall argue, against Professional or Scientific knowledge as the sufficient end of a University Education, let me not be supposed, Gentlemen, to be disrespectful towards particular studies, or arts, or vocations, and those who are engaged in them. In saying that Law or Medicine is not the end of a University course, I do not mean to imply that the University does not teach Law or Medicine. What indeed can it teach at all, if it does not teach something particular? It teaches *all* knowledge by teaching all *branches* of knowledge, and in no other way. I do but say that there will be this distinction as regards a Professor of Law, or of Medicine, or of Geology, or of Political Economy, in a University and out of it, that out of a University he is in danger of being absorbed and narrowed by his pursuit, and of giving Lectures which are the Lectures of nothing more than a lawyer, physician, geologist, or political economist; whereas in a University he will just know where he and his science stand, he has come to it, as it were, from a height, he has taken a survey of all knowledge, he is kept from extravagance by the very rivalry of other studies, he has gained from them a special illumination and largeness of mind and freedom and self-possession, and he treats his own in consequence with a philosophy and a resource, which belongs not to the study itself, but to his liberal education.

This then is how I should solve the fallacy, for so I must call it, by which Locke and his disciples would frighten us from cultivating the intellect, under the notion that no education is useful which does not teach us some temporal calling, or some mechanical art, or some physical secret. I say that a cultivated intellect, because it is a good in itself, brings with it a power and a grace to every work and occupation which it undertakes, and enables us to be more useful, and to a greater number. There is a duty we owe to human society as such, to the state to which we belong, to the sphere in which we move, to the individuals towards whom we are variously related, and whom we successively encounter in life; and that philosophical or liberal education, as I have called it, which is the proper function of a University, if it refuses the foremost place to professional interest, does but postpone them to the formation of the citizen, and, while it subserves the larger interests of philanthropy, prepares also for the successful prosecution of those merely personal objects which at first sight it seems to disparage.

※   ※   ※

10

But I must bring these extracts[5] to an end. Today I have confined myself to saying that that training of the intellect, which is best for the individual himself, best enables him to discharge his duties to society. The Philosopher, indeed, and the man of the world differ in their very notion, but the methods, by which they are respectively formed, are pretty much the same. The Philosopher has the same command of matters of thought, which the true citizen and gentleman has of matters of business and conduct. If then a practical end must be assigned to a University course, I say it is that of training good members of society. Its art is the art of social life, and its end is fitness for the world. It neither confines its views to particular professions on the one hand, nor creates heroes or inspires genius on the other. Works indeed of genius fall under no art; heroic minds come under no rule; a University is not a birthplace of poets or of immortal authors, of founders of schools, leaders of colonies, or conquerors of nations. It does not promise a generation of Aristotles or Newtons, of Napoleons or Washingtons, or Raphaels or Shakespeares,[6] though such miracles of nature it has before now contained within its precincts. Nor is it content on the other hand with forming the critic or the experimentalist, the economist or the engineer, though such too it includes within its scope. But a University training is the great ordinary means to a great but ordinary end; it aims at raising the intellectual tone of society, at cultivating the public mind, at purifying the national taste, at supplying true principles to popular enthusiasm and fixed aims to popular aspiration, at giving enlargement and sobriety to the ideas of the age, at facilitating the exercise of political power, and refining the intercourse of private life. It is the education which gives a man a clear conscious view of his own opinions and judgments, a truth in developing them, an eloquence in expressing them, and a force in urging them. It teaches him to see things as they are, to go right to the point, to disentangle a skein of thought, to detect what is sophistical, and to discard what is irrelevant. It prepares him to fill any post with credit, and to master any subject with facility. It shows him how to accommodate himself to others, how to

5. Quotations cited from other authorities on education.
6. That is, of natural philosophers, such as Aristotle (384–322 B.C.E.) and Sir Isaac Newton (1642–1727); of leaders of armies and nations, such as George Washington (1732–1799) and Napoleon Bonaparte (1769–1821); and of masters of the creative arts, such as Raphael (1483–1520) and William Shakespeare (1546–1616).

throw himself into their state of mind, how to bring before them his own, how to influence them, how to come to an understanding with them, how to bear with them. He is at home in any society, he has common ground with every class; he knows when to speak and when to be silent; he is able to converse, he is able to listen; he can ask a question pertinently, and gain a lesson seasonably, when he has nothing to impart himself; he is ever ready, yet never in the way; he is a pleasant companion, and a comrade you can depend upon; he knows when to be serious and when to trifle, and he has a sure tact which enables him to trifle with gracefulness and to be serious with effect. He has the repose of a mind which lives in itself, while it lives in the world, and which has resources for its happiness at home when it cannot go abroad. He has a gift which serves him in public, and supports him in retirement,[7] without which good fortune is but vulgar, and with which failure and disappointment have a charm. The art which tends to make a man all this is in the object which it pursues as useful as the art of wealth or the art of health, though it is less susceptible of method, and less tangible, less certain, less complete in its result.

From *Discourse 8. Knowledge Viewed in Relation to Religion*

10

Hence it is that it is almost a definition of a gentleman to say he is one who never inflicts pain. This description is both refined and, as far as it goes, accurate. He is mainly occupied in merely removing the obstacles which hinder the free and unembarrassed action of those about him; and he concurs with their movements rather than takes the initiative himself. His benefits may be considered as parallel to what are called comforts or conveniences in arrangements of a personal nature: like an easy chair or a good fire, which do their part in dispelling cold and fatigue, though nature provides both means of rest and animal heat without them. The true gentleman in like manner carefully avoids whatever may cause a jar or a jolt in the minds of those with whom he is cast;—all clashing of opinion, or collision of feeling, all restraint, or suspicion, or gloom, or resentment; his great concern being to make every one at their ease and at home. He has his eyes on all his company; he is tender towards the bashful, gentle towards the distant, and merciful towards the absurd; he can recollect to whom he is speaking; he guards against unseasonable allusions, or topics which may irritate; he is seldom prominent in conversation, and never wearisome. He makes light of favours while he does

---

7. In a later work, *The Grammar of Assent* (1870), Newman enlarges on this aspect of his subject in a passage describing the impact that classical literature may have on us at different ages of our lives, a passage admired by James Joyce. "Let us consider, too, how differently young and old are affected by the words of some classic author, such as Homer or Horace. Passages, which to a boy are but rhetorical commonplaces, neither better nor worse than a hundred others which any clever writer might supply, which he gets by heart and thinks very fine, and imitates, as he thinks, successfully, in his own flowing versification, at length come home to him, when long years have passed, and he has had experience of life, and pierce him, as if he had never before known them, with their sad earnestness and vivid exactness. Then he comes to understand how it is that lines, the birth of some chance morning or evening at an Ionian festival, or among the Sabine hills, have lasted generation after generation, for thousands of years, with a power over the mind, and a charm, which the current literature of his own day, with all its obvious advantages, is utterly unable to rival. Perhaps this is the reason of the medieval opinion about Virgil, as if a prophet or magician; his single words and phrases, his pathetic half lines, giving utterance, as the voice of Nature herself, to that pain and weariness, yet hope of better things, which is the experience of her children in every time."

them, and seems to be receiving when he is conferring. He never speaks of himself except when compelled, never defends himself by a mere retort, he has no ears for slander or gossip, is scrupulous in imputing motives to those who interfere with him, and interprets every thing for the best. He is never mean or little in his disputes, never takes unfair advantage, never mistakes personalities or sharp sayings for arguments, or insinuates evil which he dare not say out. From a long-sighted prudence, he observes the maxim of the ancient sage, that we should ever conduct ourselves towards our enemy as if he were one day to be our friend. He has too much good sense to be affronted at insults, he is too well employed to remember injuries, and too indolent to bear malice. He is patient, forbearing, and resigned, on philosophical principles; he submits to pain, because it is inevitable, to bereavement, because it is irreparable, and to death, because it is his destiny. If he engages in controversy of any kind, his disciplined intellect preserves him from the blundering discourtesy of better, perhaps, but less educated minds; who, like blunt weapons, tear and hack instead of cutting clean, who mistake the point in argument, waste their strength on trifles, misconceive their adversary, and leave the question more involved than they find it. He may be right or wrong in his opinion, but he is too clear-headed to be unjust; he is as simple as he is forcible, and as brief as he is decisive. Nowhere shall we find greater candour, consideration, indulgence: he throws himself into the minds of his opponents, he accounts for their mistakes. He knows the weakness of human reason as well as its strength, its province and its limits. If he be an unbeliever, he will be too profound and large-minded to ridicule religion or to act against it; he is too wise to be a dogmatist or fanatic in his infidelity. He respects piety and devotion; he even supports institutions as venerable, beautiful, or useful, to which he does not assent; he honours the ministers of religion, and it contents him to decline its mysteries without assailing or denouncing them. He is a friend of religious toleration, and that, not only because his philosophy has taught him to look on all forms of faith with an impartial eye, but also from the gentleness and effeminacy[8] of feeling, which is the attendant on civilization.

Not that he may not hold a religion too, in his own way, even when he is not a Christian. In that case his religion is one of imagination and sentiment; it is the embodiment of those ideas of the sublime, majestic, and beautiful, without which there can be no large philosophy. Sometimes he acknowledges the being of God, sometimes he invests an unknown principle or quality with the attributes of perfection. And this deduction of his reason, or creation of his fancy, he makes the occasion of such excellent thoughts, and the starting-point of so varied and systematic a teaching, that he even seems like a disciple of Christianity itself. From the very accuracy and steadiness of his logical powers, he is able to see what sentiments are consistent in those who hold any religious doctrine at all, and he appears to others to feel and to hold a whole circle of theological truths, which exist in his mind no otherwise than as a number of deductions.

1852, 1873

8. Tenderness.

JOHN STUART MILL
1806–1873

In many American colleges the writings of J. S. Mill are studied in courses in government or in philosophy, and it may therefore be asked why they should also have a
place in the study of literature. It may seem that Mill is less literary than other
Victorian prose writers. His analytic mind is preoccupied with abstractions rather
than with the concrete details that are the concern of the more typical writer; his
self-effacing manner and his relatively transparent style are the marks of an author
whose value lies in generalizations from personal experience rather than in the rendering of particular experiences for their own sake. Yet a knowledge of Mill's writings
is essential to our understanding of Victorian literature. He is one of the leading
figures in the intellectual history of his century, a thinker whose honest grappling
with the political and religious problems of his age was to have a profound influence
on writers as diverse as Matthew Arnold, Algernon Charles Swinburne, and Thomas
Hardy.

Mill was educated at home in London under the direction of his father, James Mill,
a leader of the Utilitarians. James Mill believed that ordinary schooling fails to develop
our intellectual capacities early enough, and he demonstrated his point by the extraordinary results he achieved in training his son. As a child John Stuart Mill read Greek
and Latin; and as a boy he could carry on intelligent discussions of problems in
mathematics, philosophy, and economics. By the time he was fourteen, as he reports
in his *Autobiography* (1873) his intensive education enabled him to start his career
"with an advantage of a quarter of a century" over his contemporaries.

Mill worked in the office of the East India Company for many years and also
served a term in Parliament in the 1860s; but his principal energies were devoted to
his writings on such subjects as logic and philosophy, political principles, and economics. His *System of Logic* (1843) earned him the position of the most respected
philosopher in mid-Victorian England. He began as a disciple of the Utilitarian theories of his father and of Jeremy Bentham but became gradually dissatisfied with the
narrowness of their conception of human motives. Working in the empiricist tradition, Utilitarians attempted to show that most traditional views of politics, ethics,
and psychology were based on nothing more than long-standing superstition and
habit, and that superstition and habit generally stood in the way of progress. Most
famously, they challenged the idea that human beings functioned according to God-
given intuitions and drives, arguing that the mind worked on the physical process of
the association of feelings. According to the Utilitarians, then, individuals were ultimately motivated not by an innate sense of right and wrong but by the simple desire to
find pleasure and avoid pain. Politically, the Utilitarians thus lobbied for whatever
would bring the greatest pleasure (or happiness) to the greatest number. Though Mill
was raised in this no-nonsense, reforming tradition, his honesty and open-mindedness
enabled him to appreciate the values of such anti-Utilitarians as Samuel Taylor Coleridge and Thomas Carlyle and, whenever possible, to incorporate some of these values
into the Utilitarian system. In part this sympathy was gained by the lesson he learned
through experiencing a nervous breakdown during his early twenties. This painful
event, described in a chapter of his *Autobiography,* taught him that the lack of concern
for people's affections and emotions characteristic of the Utilitarian system of thought
(and typified by his own education) was a fatal flaw in that system. His tribute to the
therapeutic value of art (because of its effect on human emotions), both in his *Autobiography* and in his early essay "What Is Poetry?" (1833) would have astonished Mill's
master, Bentham, who had equated poetry with pushpin, an idle pastime.

Mill's emotional life was also broadened by his love for Harriet Taylor, a married
woman who shared his intellectual interests and eventually became his wife, in 1851,
after the death of her husband. Mill later described her as "the inspirer, and in part

the author, of all that is best in my writings." They shared a commitment to the cause of female emancipation, one of several unpopular movements to which Mill was dedicated. Throughout human history, as he saw it, the role of a husband has always been legally that of a tyrant, and the object of his farseeing essay *The Subjection of Women* (1869) was to change law and public opinion so that half the human race might be liberated from slavery and regarded as equals. The subjection of women was, however, only one aspect of the tyranny against which he fought. His fundamental concern was to prevent the subjection of individuals in a democracy. His classic treatise *On Liberty* (1859) is not a traditional liberal attack against tyrannical kings or dictators; it is an attack against tyrannical majorities. Mill foresaw that in democracies such as the United States the pressure toward conformity might crush all individualists (intellectual individualists in particular) to the level of what he called a "collective mediocrity." Throughout all of his writings, even in his discussions of the advantages of socialism, Mill is concerned with demonstrating that the individual is more important than institutions such as church or state. In *On Liberty* we find a characteristic example of the process of his reasoning; but here, where the theme of individualism is central, his logic is charged with eloquence.

A similar eloquence is evident in a passage from his *Principles of Political Economy* (1848), a prophetic comment on the fate of the individual in an overpopulated world:

> There is room in the world, no doubt, and even in old countries, for a great increase of population, supposing the arts of life go on improving, and capital to increase. But even if innocuous, I confess I see very little reason for desiring it. . . . It is not good for a man to be kept perforce at all times in the presence of his species. A world from which solitude is extirpated, is a very poor ideal. Solitude, in the sense of being often alone, is essential to any depth of meditation or of character: and solitude in the presence of natural beauty and grandeur, is the cradle of thoughts and aspirations which are not only good for the individual, but which society could ill do without. Nor is there much satisfaction in contemplating the world with nothing left to the spontaneous activity of nature; with every rood of land brought into cultivation, which is capable of growing food for human beings; every flowery waste or natural pasture ploughed up, all quadrupeds or birds which are not domesticated for man's use exterminated as his rivals for food, every hedgerow or superfluous tree rooted out, and scarcely a place left where a wild shrub or flower could grow without being eradicated as a weed in the name of improved agriculture. If the earth must lose that great portion of its pleasantness which it owes to things that the unlimited increase of wealth and population would extirpate from it, for the mere purpose of enabling it to support a larger, but not a better or happier population, I sincerely hope, for the sake of posterity, that they will be content to be stationary, long before necessity compels them to it.

What Is Poetry?

It has often been asked, What Is Poetry? And many and various are the answers which have been returned. The vulgarest of all—one with which no person possessed of the faculties to which poetry addresses itself can ever have been satisfied—is that which confounds poetry with metrical composition; yet to this wretched mockery of a definition many have been led back by the failure of all their attempts to find any other that would distinguish what they have been accustomed to call poetry from much which they have known only under other names.

That, however, the word "poetry" imports something quite peculiar in its nature; something which may exist in what is called prose as well as in verse;

something which does not even require the instrument of words, but can speak through the other audible symbols called musical sounds, and even through the visible ones which are the language of sculpture, painting, and architecture—all this, we believe, is and must be felt, though perhaps indistinctly, by all upon whom poetry in any of its shapes produces any impression beyond that of tickling the ear. The distinction between poetry and what is not poetry, whether explained or not, is felt to be fundamental; and, where every one feels a difference, a difference there must be. All other appearances may be fallacious; but the appearance of a difference is a real difference. Appearances too, like other things, must have a cause; and that which can cause anything, even an illusion, must be a reality. And hence, while a half-philosophy disdains the classifications and distinctions indicated by popular language, philosophy carried to its highest point frames new ones, but rarely sets aside the old, content with correcting and regularizing them. It cuts fresh channels for thought, but does not fill up such as it finds ready-made: it traces, on the contrary, more deeply, broadly, and distinctly, those into which the current has spontaneously flowed.

Let us then attempt, in the way of modest inquiry, not to coerce and confine Nature within the bounds of an arbitrary definition, but rather to find the boundaries which she herself has set, and erect a barrier round them; not calling mankind to account for having misapplied the word "poetry," but attempting to clear up the conception which they already attach to it, and to bring forward as a distinct principle that which, as a vague feeling, has really guided them in their employment of the term.

The object of poetry is confessedly to act upon the emotions; and therein is poetry sufficiently distinguished from what Wordsworth affirms to be its logical opposite;[1] namely, not prose but matter of fact, or science. The one addresses itself to the belief; the other, to the feelings. The one does its work by convincing or persuading; the other, by moving. The one acts by presenting a proposition to the understanding; the other, by offering interesting objects of contemplation to the sensibilities.

This, however, leaves us very far from a definition of poetry. This distinguishes it from one thing; but we are bound to distinguish it from everything. To bring thoughts or images before the mind, for the purpose of acting upon the emotions, does not belong to poetry alone. It is equally the province (for example) of the novelist: and yet the faculty of the poet and that of the novelist are as distinct as any other two faculties; as the faculties of the novelist and of the orator, or of the poet and the metaphysician. The two characters may be united, as characters the most disparate may; but they have no natural connection.

Many of the greatest poems are in the form of fictitious narratives; and, in almost all good serious fictions, there is true poetry. But there is a radical distinction between the interest felt in a story as such, and the interest excited by poetry; for the one is derived from incident, the other from the representation of feeling. In one, the source of the emotion excited is the exhibition of a state or states of human sensibility; in the other, of a series of states of mere outward circumstances. Now, all minds are capable of being affected more or less by representations of the latter kind, and all, or almost all, by those of the former; yet the two sources of interest correspond to two distinct and (as respects their greatest development) mutually exclusive characters of mind.

1. In his "Preface" to *Lyrical Ballads* (1800).

At what age is the passion for a story, for almost any kind of story, merely as a story, the most intense? In childhood. But that also is the age at which poetry, even of the simplest description, is least relished and least understood; because the feelings with which it is especially conversant are yet undeveloped, and, not having been even in the slightest degree experienced, cannot be sympathized with. In what stage of the progress of society, again, is storytelling most valued, and the storyteller in greatest request and honor? In a rude state like that of the Tartars and Arabs at this day, and of almost all nations in the earliest ages. But, in this state of society, there is little poetry except ballads, which are mostly narrative—that is, essentially stories—and derive their principal interest from the incidents. Considered as poetry, they are of the lowest and most elementary kind: the feelings depicted, or rather indicated, are the simplest our nature has; such joys and griefs as the immediate pressure of some outward event excites in rude minds, which live wholly immersed in outward things, and have never, either from choice or a force they could not resist, turned themselves to the contemplation of the world within. Passing now from childhood, and from the childhood of society, to the grown-up men and women of this most grown-up and unchildlike age, the minds and hearts of greatest depth and elevation are commonly those which take greatest delight in poetry: the shallowest and emptiest, on the contrary, are, at all events, not those least addicted to novel-reading. This accords, too, with all analogous experience of human nature. The sort of persons whom not merely in books, but in their lives, we find perpetually engaged in hunting for excitement from without, are invariably those who do not possess, either in the vigor of their intellectual powers or in the depth of their sensibilities, that which would enable them to find ample excitement nearer home. The most idle and frivolous persons take a natural delight in fictitious narrative: the excitement it affords is of the kind which comes from without. Such persons are rarely lovers of poetry, though they may fancy themselves so because they relish novels in verse. But poetry, which is the delineation of the deeper and more secret workings of human emotion, is interesting only to those to whom it recalls what they have felt, or whose imagination it stirs up to conceive what they could feel, or what they might have been able to feel, had their outward circumstances been different.

Poetry, when it is really such, is truth; and fiction also, if it is good for anything, is truth: but they are different truths. The truth of poetry is to paint the human soul truly: the truth of fiction is to give a true picture of life. The two kinds of knowledge are different, and come by different ways, come mostly to different persons. Great poets are often proverbially ignorant of life. What they know has come by observation of themselves: they have found within them one highly delicate and sensitive specimen of human nature, on which the laws of emotion are written in large characters, such as can be read off without much study. Other knowledge of mankind, such as comes to men of the world by outward experience, is not indispensable to them as poets: but, to the novelist, such knowledge is all in all; he has to describe outward things, not the inward man; actions and events, not feelings; and it will not do for him to be numbered among those, who, as Madame Roland said of Brissot,[2] know man, but not *men.*

---

2. Jacques-Pierre Brissot (1754–1793), a leading reformer during the French Revolution, is characterized in the *Mémoires* of Jeanne-Manon Roland (1754–1793).

All this is no bar to the possibility of combining both elements, poetry and narrative or incident, in the same work, and calling it either a novel or a poem; but so may red and white combine on the same human features or on the same canvas. There is one order of composition which requires the union of poetry and incident, each in its highest kind—the dramatic. Even there, the two elements are perfectly distinguishable, and may exist of unequal quality and in the most various proportion. The incidents of a dramatic poem may be scanty and ineffective, though the delineation of passion and character may be of the highest order, as in Goethe's admirable "Torquato Tasso";[3] or, again, the story as a mere story may be well got up for effect, as is the case with some of the most trashy productions of the Minerva Press:[4] it may even be, what those are not, a coherent and probable series of events, though there be scarcely a feeling exhibited which is not represented falsely, or in a manner absolutely commonplace. The combination of the two excellences is what renders Shakespeare so generally acceptable, each sort of readers finding in him what is suitable to their faculties. To the many, he is great as a storyteller; to the few, as a poet.

In limiting poetry to the delineation of states of feeling, and denying the name where nothing is delineated but outward objects, we may be thought to have done what we promised to avoid—to have not found, but made, a definition in opposition to the usage of language, since it is established by common consent that there is a poetry called descriptive. We deny the charge. Description is not poetry because there is descriptive poetry, no more than science is poetry because there is such a thing as a didactic poem. But an object which admits of being described, or a truth which may fill a place in a scientific treatise, may also furnish an occasion for the generation of poetry, which we thereupon choose to call descriptive or didactic. The poetry is not in the object itself, nor in the scientific truth itself, but in the state of mind in which the one and the other may be contemplated. The mere delineation of the dimensions and colors of external objects is not poetry, no more than a geometrical ground-plan of St. Peter's or Westminster Abbey is painting. Descriptive poetry consists, no doubt, in description, but in description of things as they appear, not as they are; and it paints them, not in their bare and natural lineaments, but seen through the medium and arrayed in the colors of the imagination set in action by the feelings. If a poet describes a lion, he does not describe him as a naturalist would, nor even as a traveler would, who was intent upon stating the truth, the whole truth, and nothing but the truth. He describes him by imagery, that is, by suggesting the most striking likenesses and contrasts which might occur to a mind contemplating a lion, in the state of awe, wonder, or terror, which the spectacle naturally excites, or is, on the occasion, supposed to excite. Now, this is describing the lion professedly, but the state of excitement of the spectator really. The lion may be described falsely or with exaggeration and the poetry be all the better: but, if the human emotion be not painted with scrupulous truth, the poetry is bad poetry, i.e., is not poetry at all, but a failure.

Thus far, our progress towards a clear view of the essentials of poetry has brought us very close to the last two attempts at a definition of poetry which we happen to have seen in print, both of them by poets, and men of genius.

---

3. A play (1790) based on the life of this 16th-century Italian poet.

4. An early-19th-century publishing house that fostered the production of sentimental novels.

The one is by Ebenezer Elliott, the author of "Corn-law Rhymes," and other poems of still greater merit. "Poetry," says he, "is impassioned truth."[5] The other is by a writer in "Blackwood's Magazine," and comes, we think, still nearer the mark. He defines poetry, "man's thoughts tinged by his feelings." There is in either definition a near approximation to what we are in search of. Every truth which a human being can enunciate, every thought, even every outward impression, which can enter into his consciousness, may become poetry, when shown through any impassioned medium; when invested with the coloring of joy, or grief, or pity, or affection, or admiration, or reverence, or awe, or even hatred or terror; and, unless so colored, nothing, be it as interesting as it may, is poetry. But both these definitions fail to discriminate between poetry and eloquence. Eloquence, as well as poetry, is impassioned truth; eloquence, as well as poetry, is thoughts colored by the feelings. Yet common apprehension and philosophic criticism alike recognize a distinction between the two: there is much that everyone would call eloquence, which no one would think of classing as poetry. A question will sometimes arise, whether some particular author is a poet; and those who maintain the negative commonly allow, that, though not a poet, he is a highly eloquent writer. The distinction between poetry and eloquence appears to us to be equally fundamental with the distinction between poetry and narrative, or between poetry and description, while it is still farther from having been satisfactorily cleared up than either of the others.

Poetry and eloquence are both alike the expression or utterance of feeling: but, if we may be excused the antithesis, we should say that eloquence is *heard*; poetry is *over*heard. Eloquence supposes an audience. The peculiarity of poetry appears to us to lie in the poet's utter unconsciousness of a listener. Poetry is feeling confessing itself to itself in moments of solitude, and embodying itself in symbols which are the nearest possible representations of the feeling in the exact shape in which it exists in the poet's mind. Eloquence is feeling pouring itself out to other minds, courting their sympathy, or endeavoring to influence their belief, or move them to passion or to action.

All poetry is of the nature of soliloquy. It may be said that poetry which is printed on hot-pressed paper, and sold at a bookseller's shop, is a soliloquy in full dress and on the stage. It is so; but there is nothing absurd in the idea of such a mode of soliloquizing. What we have said to ourselves we may tell to others afterwards; what we have said or done in solitude we may voluntarily reproduce when we know that other eyes are upon us. But no trace of consciousness that any eyes are upon us must be visible in the work itself. The actor knows that there is an audience present: but, if he act as though he knew it, he acts ill. A poet may write poetry, not only with the intention of printing it, but for the express purpose of being paid for it. That it should *be* poetry, being written under such influences, is less probable, not, however, impossible; but no otherwise possible than if he can succeed in excluding from his work every vestige of such lookings-forth into the outward and every-day world, and can express his emotions exactly as he has felt them in solitude, or as he is conscious that he should feel them, though they were to remain for ever unuttered, or (at the lowest) as he knows that others feel them in similar circumstances of solitude. But when he turns round, and addresses himself to another person; when the act of utterance is not itself the end, but a means to an end—viz., by the feelings he himself expresses, to work upon the feelings,

5. In the "Preface" to *Corn-Law Rhymes* (1828), by Elliott (1781–1849).

or upon the belief or the will of another; when the expression of his emotions, or of his thoughts tinged by his emotions, is tinged also by that purpose, by that desire of making an impression upon another mind—then it ceases to be poetry, and becomes eloquence.

Poetry, accordingly, is the natural fruit of solitude and meditation; eloquence, of intercourse with the world. The persons who have most feeling of their own, if intellectual culture has given them a language in which to express it, have the highest faculty of poetry: those who best understand the feelings of others are the most eloquent. The persons and the nations who commonly excel in poetry are those whose character and tastes render them least dependent upon the applause or sympathy or concurrence of the world in general. Those to whom that applause, that sympathy, that concurrence, are most necessary, generally excel most in eloquence. And hence, perhaps, the French, who are the least poetical of all great and intellectual nations, are among the most eloquent; the French also being the most sociable, the vainest, and the least self-dependent.

If the above be, as we believe, the true theory of the distinction commonly admitted between eloquence and poetry, or even though it be not so, yet if, as we cannot doubt, the distinction above stated be a real bona fide distinction, it will be found to hold, not merely in the language of words, but in all other language, and to intersect the whole domain of art.

Take, for example, music. We shall find in that art, so peculiarly the expression of passion, two perfectly distinct styles—one of which may be called the poetry, the other the oratory, of music. This difference, being seized, would put an end to much musical sectarianism. There has been much contention whether the music of the modern Italian school, that of Rossini,[6] and his successors, be impassioned or not. Without doubt, the passion it expresses is not the musing, meditative tenderness or pathos or grief of Mozart or Beethoven; yet it is passion, but garrulous passion, the passion which pours itself into other ears, and therein the better calculated for dramatic effect, having a natural adaptation for dialogue. Mozart also is great in musical oratory; but his most touching compositions are in the opposite style, that of soliloquy. Who can imagine "Dove sono"[7] *heard*? We imagine it *over*heard.

Purely pathetic music commonly partakes of soliloquy. The soul is absorbed in its distress and, though there may be bystanders, it is not thinking of them. When the mind is looking within, and not without, its state does not often or rapidly vary; and hence the even, uninterrupted flow, approaching almost to monotony, which a good reader or a good singer will give to words or music of a pensive or melancholy cast. But grief, taking the form of a prayer or of a complaint, becomes oratorical: no longer low and even and subdued, it assumes a more emphatic rhythm, a more rapidly returning accent; instead of a few slow, equal notes, following one after another at regular intervals, it crowds note upon note, and often assumes a hurry and bustle like joy. Those who are familiar with some of the best of Rossini's serious compositions, such as the air "Tu che i miseri conforti,"[8] in the opera of "Tancredi," or the duet "Ebben per mia memoria,"[9] in "La Gazza Ladra," will at once understand and feel our meaning. Both are highly tragic and passionate: the passion of both

6. Gioacchino Rossini (1792–1868), composer of operas.
7. Where are fled [the lovely moments?] (Italian); soprano aria from act 3 of *The Marriage of Figaro* (1786), by the Austrian composer Wolfgang Amadeus Mozart (1756–1791).
8. You, who give comfort to the wretched (Italian); soprano aria from Rossini's *Tancredi* (1813).
9. Indeed according to my memory (Italian); soprano aria from Rossini's *La Gazza Ladra* (1817).

1050 / JOHN STUART MILL

is that of oratory, not poetry. The like may be said of that most moving invocation in Beethoven's "Fidelio,"

> "Komm, Hoffnung, lass das letzte Stern
> Der Müde nicht erbleichen"—[1]

in which Madame Schröder Devrient exhibited such consummate powers of pathetic expression. How different from Winter's beautiful "Paga fui,"[2] the very soul of melancholy exhaling itself in solitude! fuller of meaning, and therefore more profoundly poetical, than the words for which it was composed; for it seems to express, not simple melancholy, but the melancholy of remorse.

If from vocal music we now pass to instrumental, we may have a specimen of musical oratory in any fine military symphony or march; while the poetry of music seems to have attained its consummation in Beethoven's "Overture to Egmont," so wonderful in its mixed expression of grandeur and melancholy.

In the arts which speak to the eye, the same distinctions will be found to hold, not only between poetry and oratory, but between poetry, oratory, narrative, and simple imitation or description.

Pure description is exemplified in a mere portrait or a mere landscape, productions of art, it is true, but of the mechanical rather than of the fine arts; being works of simple imitation, not creation. We say, a mere portrait or a mere landscape; because it is possible for a portrait or a landscape, without ceasing to be such, to be also a picture, like Turner's landscapes, and the great portraits by Titian or Vandyke.[3]

Whatever in painting or sculpture expresses human feeling—or character, which is only a certain state of feeling grown habitual—may be called, according to circumstances, the poetry or the eloquence of the painter's or the sculptor's art: the poetry, if the feeling declares itself by such signs as escape from us when we are unconscious of being seen; the oratory, if the signs are those we use for the purpose of voluntary communication.

The narrative style answers to what is called historical painting, which it is the fashion among connoisseurs to treat as the climax of the pictorial art. That it is the most difficult branch of the art, we do not doubt, because, in its perfection, it includes the perfection of all the other branches; as, in like manner, an epic poem, though, in so far as it is epic (i.e. narrative), it is not poetry at all, is yet esteemed the greatest effort of poetic genius, because there is no kind whatever of poetry which may not appropriately find a place in it. But an historical picture as such, that is, as the representation of an incident, must necessarily, as it seems to us, be poor and ineffective. The narrative powers of painting are extremely limited. Scarcely any picture, scarcely even any series of pictures, tells its own story without the aid of an interpreter. But it is the single figures, which, to us, are the great charm even of an historical picture. It is in these that the power of the art is really seen. In the attempt to narrate, visible and permanent signs are too far behind the fugitive audible ones, which follow so fast one after another; while the faces and figures in a narrative picture, even though they be Titian's, stand still. Who would not

---

1. Come, Hope, let not the weary person's last star fade out (German); aria from *Fidelio* (1805), by the German composer Ludwig van Beethoven (1770–1827). Mill seems to be quoting from memory. The passage should read: "Komm, Hoffnung, lass den letzten Stern / Der Müden nicht erbleichen."
2. I have been contented (Italian); aria from the once-popular opera *Il Ratto di Proserpina*, by Peter

Winter (1754–1825), first performed in London in 1804.
3. Sir Anthony Van Dyck (1599–1641), Flemish painter who produced more than five hundred portraits. J.M.W. Turner (1775–1851), British landscape painter. Titian (Tiziano Vicelli, ca. 1488–1576), master painter of the Venetian school.

prefer one "Virgin and Child" of Raphael to all the pictures which Rubens,[4] with his fat, frouzy Dutch Venuses, ever painted?—though Rubens, besides excelling almost everyone in his mastery over the mechanical parts of his art, often shows real genius in *grouping* his figures, the peculiar problem of historical painting. But then, who, except a mere student of drawing and coloring, ever cared to look twice at any of the figures themselves? The power of painting lies in poetry, of which Rubens had not the slightest tincture, not in narrative, wherein he might have excelled.

The single figures, however, in an historical picture, are rather the eloquence of painting than the poetry. They mostly (unless they are quite out of place in the picture) express the feelings of one person as modified by the presence of others. Accordingly, the minds whose bent leads them rather to eloquence than to poetry rush to historical painting. The French painters, for instance, seldom attempt, because they could make nothing of, single heads, like those glorious ones of the Italian masters with which they might feed themselves day after day in their own Louvre.[5] They must all be historical; and they are, almost to a man, attitudinizers. If we wished to give any young artist the most impressive warning our imagination could devise against that kind of vice in the pictorial which corresponds to rant in the histrionic art, we would advise him to walk once up and once down the gallery of the Luxembourg.[6] Every figure in French painting or statuary seems to be showing itself off before spectators. They are not poetical, but in the worst style of corrupted eloquence.

1833, 1859

From On Liberty

From Chapter 3. Of Individuality as One of the Elements of Well-Being

* * *

Few persons, out of Germany, even comprehend the meaning of the doctrine which Wilhelm von Humboldt, so eminent both as a savant and as a politician, made the text of a treatise—that "the end of man, or that which is prescribed by the eternal or immutable dictates of reason, and not suggested by vague and transient desires, is the highest and most harmonious development of his powers to a complete and consistent whole"; that, therefore, the object "towards which every human being must ceaselessly direct his efforts, and on which especially those who design to influence their fellow men must ever keep their eyes, is the individuality of power and development"; that for this there are two requisites, "freedom, and variety of situations"; and that from the union of these arise "individual vigor and manifold diversity," which combine themselves in "originality."[1]

4. Peter Paul Rubens (1577–1640), Flemish painter (and Van Dyck's teacher). Raphael (Raffaello Sanzio, 1483–1520), Italian painter of the high Renaissance.
5. A palace in Paris, opened as a public museum in 1793; the Italian Renaissance paintings originally owned by Francis I are the core of its collection.-
6. A palace in Paris, where paintings of scenes

from French history were exhibited.
1. From *The Sphere and Duties of Government*, by Baron Wilhelm von Humboldt (1767–1835), Prussian statesman and man of letters. Originally written in 1791, the treatise was first published in Germany in 1852 and was translated into English in 1854.

Little, however, as people are accustomed to a doctrine like that of Von Humboldt, and surprising as it may be to them to find so high a value attached to individuality, the question, one must nevertheless think, can only be one of degree. No one's idea of excellence in conduct is that people should do absolutely nothing but copy one another. No one would assert that people ought not to put into their mode of life, and into the conduct of their concerns, any impress whatever of their own judgment, or of their own individual character. On the other hand, it would be absurd to pretend that people ought to live as if nothing whatever had been known in the world before they came into it; as if experience had as yet done nothing towards showing that one mode of existence, or conduct, is preferable to another. Nobody denies that people should be so taught and trained in youth, as to know and benefit by the ascertained results of human experience. But it is the privilege and proper condition of a human being, arrived at the maturity of his faculties, to use and interpret experience in his own way. It is for him to find out what part of recorded experience is properly applicable to his own circumstances and character. The traditions and customs of other people are, to a certain extent, evidence of what their experience has taught *them*; presumptive evidence, and as such, have a claim to his deference: but, in the first place, their experience may be too narrow; or they may not have interpreted it rightly. Secondly, their interpretation of experience may be correct, but unsuitable to him. Customs are made for customary circumstances, and customary characters; and his circumstances or his character may be uncustomary. Thirdly, though the customs be both good as customs, and suitable to him, yet to conform to custom, merely *as* custom, does not educate or develop in him any of the qualities which are the distinctive endowment of a human being. The human faculties of perception, judgment, discriminative feeling, mental activity, and even moral preference are exercised only in making a choice. He who does anything because it is the custom makes no choice. He gains no practice either in discerning or in desiring what is best. The mental and moral, like the muscular powers, are improved only by being used. The faculties are called into no exercise by doing a thing merely because others do it, no more than by believing a thing only because others believe it. If the grounds of an opinion are not conclusive to the person's own reason, his reason cannot be strengthened, but is likely to be weakened, by his adopting it: and if the inducements to an act are not such as are consentaneous[2] to his own feelings and character (where affection, or the rights of others, are not concerned) it is so much done towards rendering his feelings and character inert and torpid, instead of active and energetic.

He who lets the world, or his own portion of it, choose his plan of life for him has no need of any other faculty than the apelike one of imitation. He who chooses his plan for himself employs all his faculties. He must use observation to see, reasoning and judgment to foresee, activity to gather materials for decision, discrimination to decide, and when he has decided, firmness and self-control to hold to his deliberate decision. And these qualities he requires and exercises exactly in proportion as the part of his conduct which he determines according to his own judgment and feelings is a large one. It is possible that he might be guided in some good path, and kept out of harm's way,

2. Agreeable.

without any of these things. But what will be his comparative worth as a human being? It really is of importance, not only what men do, but also what manner of men they are that do it. Among the works of man, which human life is rightly employed in perfecting and beautifying, the first in importance surely is man himself. Supposing it were possible to get houses built, corn grown, battles fought, causes tried, and even churches erected and prayers said, by machinery—by automatons in human form—it would be a considerable loss to exchange for these automatons even the men and women who at present inhabit the more civilized parts of the world, and who assuredly are but starved specimens of what nature can and will produce. Human nature is not a machine to be built after a model, and set to do exactly the work prescribed for it, but a tree, which requires to grow and develop itself on all sides, according to the tendency of the inward forces which make it a living thing.

It will probably be conceded that it is desirable people should exercise their understandings, and that an intelligent following of custom, or even occasionally an intelligent deviation from custom, is better than a blind and simply mechanical adhesion to it. To a certain extent it is admitted that our understanding should be our own: but there is not the same willingness to admit that our desires and impulses should be our own likewise; or that to possess impulses of our own, and of any strength, is anything but a peril and a snare. Yet desires and impulses are as much a part of a perfect human being, as beliefs and restraints: and strong impulses are only perilous when not properly balanced; when one set of aims and inclinations is developed into strength, while others, which ought to coexist with them, remain weak and inactive. It is not because men's desires are strong that they act ill; it is because their consciences are weak. There is no natural connection between strong impulses and a weak conscience. The natural connection is the other way. To say that one person's desires and feelings are stronger and more various than those of another is merely to say that he has more of the raw material of human nature, and is therefore capable, perhaps of more evil, but certainly of more good. Strong impulses are but another name for energy. Energy may be turned to bad uses; but more good may always be made of an energetic nature than of an indolent and impassive one. Those who have most natural feeling are always those whose cultivated feelings may be made the strongest. The same strong susceptibilities which make the personal impulses vivid and powerful are also the source from whence are generated the most passionate love of virtue, and the sternest self-control. It is through the cultivation of these that society both does its duty and protects its interests: not by rejecting the stuff of which heroes are made, because it knows not how to make them. A person whose desires and impulses are his own—are the expression of his own nature, as it has been developed and modified by his own culture—is said to have a character. One whose desires and impulses are not his own, has no character, no more than a steam engine has a character. If, in addition to being his own, his impulses are strong, and are under the government of a strong will, he has an energetic character. Whoever thinks that individuality of desires and impulses should not be encouraged to unfold itself must maintain that society has no need of strong natures—is not the better for containing many persons who have much character—and that a high general average of energy is not desirable.

In some early states of society, these forces might be, and were, too much ahead of the power which society then possessed of disciplining and controlling them. There has been a time when the element of spontaneity and individuality was in excess, and the social principle had a hard struggle with it. The difficulty then was to induce men of strong bodies or minds to pay obedience to any rules which require them to control their impulses. To overcome this difficulty, law and discipline, like the Popes struggling against the Emperors, asserted a power over the whole man, claiming to control all his life in order to control his character—which society had not found any other sufficient means of binding. But society has now fairly got the better of individuality; and the danger which threatens human nature is not the excess, but the deficiency, of personal impulses and preferences. Things are vastly changed, since the passions of those who were strong by station or by personal endowment were in a state of habitual rebellion against laws and ordinances, and required to be rigorously chained up to enable the persons within their reach to enjoy any particle of security. In our times, from the highest class of society down to the lowest, everyone lives as under the eye of a hostile and dreaded censorship. Not only in what concerns others, but in what concerns only themselves, the individual or the family do not ask themselves—what do I prefer? or, what would suit my character and disposition? or, what would allow the best and highest in me to have fair play, and enable it to grow and thrive? They ask themselves, what is suitable to my position? what is usually done by persons of my station and pecuniary circumstances? or (worse still) what is usually done by persons of a station and circumstances superior to mine? I do not mean that they choose what is customary, in preference to what suits their own inclination. It does not occur to them to have any inclination, except for what is customary. Thus the mind itself is bowed to the yoke: even in what people do for pleasure, conformity is the first thing thought of; they like in crowds; they exercise choice only among things commonly done: peculiarity of taste, eccentricity of conduct, are shunned equally with crimes: until by dint of not following their own nature, they have no nature to follow: their human capacities are withered and starved: they become incapable of any strong wishes or native pleasures, and are generally without either opinions or feelings of home growth, or properly their own. Now is this, or is it not, the desirable condition of human nature?

It is so, on the Calvinistic theory. According to that, the one great offense of man is self-will. All the good of which humanity is capable is comprised in obedience. You have no choice; thus you must do, and no otherwise: "whatever is not a duty is a sin." Human nature being radically corrupt, there is no redemption for anyone until human nature is killed within him. To one holding this theory of life, crushing out any of the human faculties, capacities, and susceptibilities is no evil: man needs no capacity but that of surrendering himself to the will of God: and if he uses any of his faculties for any other purpose but to do that supposed will more effectually, he is better without them. This is the theory of Calvinism; and it is held, in a mitigated form, by many who do not consider themselves Calvinists; the mitigation consisting in giving a less ascetic interpretation to the alleged will of God; asserting it to be his will that mankind should gratify some of their inclinations; of course not in the manner they themselves prefer, but in the way of obedience, that is, in a way prescribed to them by authority; and, therefore, by the necessary conditions of the case, the same for all.

In some such insidious form there is at present a strong tendency to this narrow theory of life, and to the pinched and hidebound type of human character which it patronizes. Many persons, no doubt, sincerely think that human beings thus cramped and dwarfed are as their Maker designed them to be; just as many have thought that trees are a much finer thing when clipped into pollards,[3] or cut out into figures of animals, than as nature made them. But if it be any part of religion to believe that man was made by a good Being, it is more consistent with that faith to believe that this Being gave all human faculties that they might be cultivated and unfolded, not rooted out and consumed, and that he takes delight in every nearer approach made by his creatures to the ideal conception embodied in them, every increase in any of their capabilities of comprehension, of action, or of enjoyment. There is a different type of human excellence from the Calvinistic; a conception of humanity as having its nature bestowed on it for other purposes than merely to be abnegated. "Pagan self-assertion" is one of the elements of human worth, as well as "Christian self-denial."[4] There is a Greek ideal of self-development, which the Platonic and Christian ideal of self-government blends with, but does not supersede. It may be better to be a John Knox than an Alcibiades, but it is better to be a Pericles[5] than either, nor would a Pericles, if we had one in these days, be without anything good which belonged to John Knox.

It is not by wearing down into uniformity all that is individual in themselves, but by cultivating it and calling it forth, within the limits imposed by the rights and interests of others, that human beings become a noble and beautiful object of contemplation; and as the works partake the character of those who do them, by the same process human life also becomes rich, diversified, and animating, furnishing more abundant aliment to high thoughts and elevating feelings, and strengthening the tie which binds every individual to the race, by making the race infinitely better worth belonging to. In proportion to the development of his individuality, each person becomes more valuable to himself, and is therefore capable of being more valuable to others. There is a greater fullness of life about his own existence, and when there is more life in the units there is more in the mass which is composed of them. As much compression as is necessary to prevent the stronger specimens of human nature from encroaching on the rights of others cannot be dispensed with; but for this there is ample compensation even in the point of view of human development. The means of development which the individual loses by being prevented from gratifying his inclinations to the injury of others are chiefly obtained at the expense of the development of other people. And even to himself there is a full equivalent in the better development of the social part of his nature, rendered possible by the restraint put upon the selfish part. To be held to rigid rules of justice for the sake of others develops the feelings and capacities which have the good of others for their object. But to be restrained in things not affecting their good, by their mere displeasure, develops nothing valuable, except such force of character as may unfold itself in resisting the restraint. If acquiesced in, it dulls and blunts the whole nature. To give any fair play to the nature of each, it is essential that different persons should be allowed to lead different lives. In proportion as this latitude has been exercised in any age, has that age been noteworthy to posterity. Even despotism does not produce its worst effects, so long as individuality exists under it; and what-

3. Trees that acquire an artificial shape by being cut back to produce a mass of dense foliage.
4. From the *Essays* (1848) of John Sterling, a minor writer and friend of Carlyle's.

5. A model statesman in Athens (495–429 B.C.E.). Knox (1514–1572), a stern Scottish Calvinist reformer. Alcibiades (450–404 B.C.E.), a brilliant but dissolute Athenian commander.

ever crushes individuality is despotism, by whatever name it may be called, and whether it professes to be enforcing the will of God or the injunctions of men.

Having said that Individuality is the same thing with development, and that it is only the cultivation of individuality which produces, or can produce, well-developed human beings, I might here close the argument: for what more or better can be said of any condition of human affairs than that it brings human beings themselves nearer to the best thing they can be? or what worse can be said of any obstruction to good than that it prevents this? Doubtless, however, these considerations will not suffice to convince those who most need convincing; and it is necessary further to show that these developed human beings are of some use to the undeveloped—to point out to those who do not desire liberty, and would not avail themselves of it, that they may be in some intelligible manner rewarded for allowing other people to make use of it without hindrance.

In the first place, then, I would suggest that they might possibly learn something from them. It will not be denied by anybody, that originality is a valuable element in human affairs. There is always need of persons not only to discover new truths, and point out when what were once truths are true no longer, but also to commence new practices, and set the example of more enlightened conduct, and better taste and sense in human life. This cannot well be gainsaid by anybody who does not believe that the world has already attained perfection in all its ways and practices. It is true that this benefit is not capable of being rendered by everybody alike: there are but few persons, in comparison with the whole of mankind, whose experiments, if adopted by others, would be likely to be any improvement on established practice. But these few are the salt of the earth; without them, human life would become a stagnant pool. Not only is it they who introduce good things which did not before exist; it is they who keep the life in those which already existed. If there were nothing new to be done, would human intellect cease to be necessary? Would it be a reason why those who do the old things should forget why they are done, and do them like cattle, not like human beings? There is only too great a tendency in the best beliefs and practices to degenerate into the mechanical; and unless there were a succession of persons whose ever-recurring originality prevents the grounds of those beliefs and practices from becoming merely traditional, such dead matter would not resist the smallest shock from anything really alive, and there would be no reason why civilization should not die out, as in the Byzantine Empire. Persons of genius, it is true, are, and are always likely to be, a small minority; but in order to have them, it is necessary to preserve the soil in which they grow. Genius can only breathe freely in an *atmosphere* of freedom. Persons of genius are, *ex vi termini,*[6] *more* individual than any other people—less capable, consequently, of fitting themselves, without hurtful compression, into any of the small number of molds which society provides in order to save its members the trouble of forming their own character. If from timidity they consent to be forced into one of these molds, and to let all that part of themselves which cannot expand under the pressure remain unexpanded, society will be little the better for their genius. If they are of a strong character, and break their fetters, they become a mark for the society which has not succeeded in reducing them to commonplace, to point at with solemn

6. By force of the term (Latin); i.e., by definition.

warning as "wild," "erratic," and the like; much as if one should complain of the Niagara River for not flowing smoothly between its banks like a Dutch canal.

I insist thus emphatically on the importance of genius, and the necessity of allowing it to unfold itself freely both in thought and in practice, being well aware that no one will deny the position in theory, but knowing also that almost everyone, in reality, is totally indifferent to it. People think genius a fine thing if it enables a man to write an exciting poem, or paint a picture. But in its true sense, that of originality in thought and action, though no one says that it is not a thing to be admired, nearly all, at heart, think that they can do very well without it. Unhappily this is too natural to be wondered at. Originality is the one thing which unoriginal minds cannot feel the use of. They cannot see what it is to do for them: how should they? If they could see what it would do for them, it would not be originality. The first service which originality has to render them is that of opening their eyes: which being once fully done, they would have a chance of being themselves original. Meanwhile, recollecting that nothing was ever yet done which someone was not the first to do, and that all good things which exist are the fruits of originality, let them be modest enough to believe that there is something still left for it to accomplish, and assure themselves that they are more in need of originality, the less they are conscious of the want.

In sober truth, whatever homage may be professed, or even paid, to real or supposed mental superiority, the general tendency of things throughout the world is to render mediocrity the ascendant power among mankind. In ancient history, in the middle ages, and in a diminishing degree through the long transition from feudality to the present time, the individual was power in himself; and if he had either great talents or a high social position, he was a considerable power. At present individuals are lost in the crowd. In politics it is almost a triviality to say that public opinion now rules the world. The only power deserving the name is that of masses, and of governments while they make themselves the organ of the tendencies and instincts of masses. This is as true in the moral and social relations of private life as in public transactions. Those whose opinions go by the name of public opinion, are not always the same sort of public: in America they are the whole white population; in England, chiefly the middle class. But they are always a mass, that is to say, collective mediocrity. And what is a still greater novelty, the mass do not now take their opinions from dignitaries in Church or State, from ostensible leaders, or from books. Their thinking is done for them by men much like themselves, addressing them or speaking in their name, on the spur of the moment, through the newspapers. I am not complaining of all this. I do not assert that anything better is compatible, as a general rule, with the present low state of the human mind. But that does not hinder the government of mediocrity from being mediocre government. No government by a democracy or a numerous aristocracy, either in its political acts or in the opinions, qualities, and tone of mind which it fosters, ever did or could rise above mediocrity, except in so far as the sovereign Many have let themselves be guided (which in their best times they always have done) by the counsels and influence of a more highly gifted and instructed One or Few. The initiation of all wise or noble things, comes and must come from individuals; generally at first from some one individual. The honor and glory of the average man is that he is capable of following that initiative; that he can respond internally to wise and noble things, and be led to them with his eyes open. I am not countenancing the sort of "hero worship" which applauds the strong man of genius for forcibly seizing on the government of the world and making it do his bidding in spite of itself.[7] All he can claim is freedom to point out the way. The power of compelling others into it is not only inconsistent with the freedom and development of all the rest, but corrupting to the strong man himself. It does seem, however, that when the opinions of masses of merely average men are everywhere become or becoming the dominant power, the counterpoise and corrective to that tendency would be the more and more pronounced individuality of those who stand on the higher eminences of thought. It is in these circumstances most especially that exceptional individuals, instead of being deterred, should be encouraged in acting differently from the mass. In other times there was no advantage in their doing so, unless they acted not only differently, but better. In this age, the mere example of nonconformity, the mere refusal to bend the knee to custom, is itself a service. Precisely because the tyranny of opinion is such as to make eccentricity a reproach, it is desirable, in order to break through that tyranny, that people should be eccentric. Eccentricity has always abounded when and where strength of character has abounded; and the amount of eccentricity in a society has generally been proportional to the amount of genius, mental vigor, and moral courage which it contained. That so few now dare to be eccentric marks the chief danger of the time.

*   *   *

There is one characteristic of the present direction of public opinion, peculiarly calculated to make it intolerant of any marked demonstration of individuality. The general average of mankind are not only moderate in intellect, but also moderate in inclinations: they have no tastes or wishes strong enough to incline them to do anything unusual, and they consequently do not understand those who have, and class all such with the wild and intemperate whom they are accustomed to look down upon. Now, in addition to this fact which is general, we have only to suppose that a strong movement has set in towards the improvement of morals, and it is evident what we have to expect. In these days such a movement has set in; much has actually been effected in the way of increased regularity of conduct, and discouragement of excesses; and there is a philanthropic spirit abroad, for the exercise of which there is no more inviting field than the moral and prudential improvement of our fellow creatures. These tendencies of the times cause the public to be more disposed than at most former periods to prescribe general rules of conduct, and endeavor to make everyone conform to the approved standard. And that standard, express or tacit, is to desire nothing strongly. Its ideal of character is to be without any marked character; to maim by compression, like a Chinese lady's foot,[8] every part of human nature which stands out prominently, and tends to make the person markedly dissimilar in outline to commonplace humanity.

As is usually the case with ideals which exclude one half of what is desirable, the present standard of approbation produces only an inferior imitation of the

---

7. As advocated by Thomas Carlyle in *On Heroes, Hero-Worship, and the Heroic in History* (1841).
8. The practice of foot binding, which aimed to make women's feet only three inches long, was widespread in China from the 10th century until its formal prohibition in 1911.

other half. Instead of great energies guided by vigorous reason, and strong feelings strongly controlled by a conscientious will, its result is weak feelings and weak energies, which therefore can be kept in outward conformity to rule without any strength either of will or reason. Already energetic characters on any large scale are becoming merely traditional. There is now scarcely any outlet for energy in this country except business. The energy expended in this may still be regarded as considerable. What little is left from that employment, is expended on some hobby; which may be a useful, even a philanthropic hobby, but is always some one thing, and generally a thing of small dimensions. The greatness of England is now all collective: individually small, we only appear capable of anything great by our habit of combining; and with this our moral and religious philanthropies are perfectly contented. But it was men of another stamp than this that made England what it has been; and men of another stamp will be needed to prevent its decline.

The despotism of custom is everywhere the standing hindrance to human advancement, being in unceasing antagonism to that disposition to aim at something better than customary, which is called, according to circumstances, the spirit of liberty, or that of progress or improvement. The spirit of improvement is not always a spirit of liberty, for it may aim at forcing improvements on an unwilling people; and the spirit of liberty, in so far as it resists such attempts, may ally itself locally and temporarily with the opponents of improvement; but the only unfailing and permanent source of improvement is liberty, since by it there are as many possible independent centers of improvement as there are individuals. The progressive principle, however, in either shape, whether as the love of liberty or of improvement, is antagonistic to the sway of Custom, involving at least emancipation from that yoke; and the contest between the two constitutes the chief interest of the history of mankind. The greater part of the world has, properly speaking, no history, because the despotism of Custom is complete. This is the case over the whole East. Custom is there, in all things, the final appeal; justice and right mean conformity to custom; the argument of custom no one, unless some tyrant intoxicated with power, thinks of resisting. And we see the result. Those nations must once have had originality; they did not start out of the ground populous, lettered, and versed in many of the arts of life; they made themselves all this, and were then the greatest and most powerful nations of the world. What are they now? The subjects or dependants of tribes whose forefathers wandered in the forests when theirs had magnificent palaces and gorgeous temples, but over whom custom exercised only a divided rule with liberty and progress. A people, it appears, may be progressive for a certain length of time, and then stop: when does it stop? When it ceases to possess individuality. If a similar change should befall the nations of Europe, it will not be in exactly the same shape: the despotism of custom with which these nations are threatened is not precisely stationariness. It proscribes singularity, but it does not preclude change, provided all change together. We have discarded the fixed costumes of our forefathers; everyone must still dress like other people, but the fashion may change once or twice a year. We thus take care that when there is change it shall be for change's sake, and not from any idea of beauty or convenience; for the same idea of beauty or convenience would not strike all the world at the same moment, and be simultaneously thrown aside by all at another moment. But we are progressive as well as changeable: we continually make new inventions in mechanical things, and keep them until they are again superseded by better; we are eager for improvement in politics, in education, even in morals, though in this last our idea of improvement chiefly consists in persuading or forcing other people to be as good as ourselves. It is not progress that we object to; on the contrary, we flatter ourselves that we are the most progressive people who ever lived. It is individuality that we war against: we should think we had done wonders if we had made ourselves all alike; forgetting that the unlikeness of one person to another is generally the first thing which draws the attention of either to the imperfection of his own type, and the superiority of another, or the possibility, by combining the advantages of both, of producing something better than either. We have a warning example in China—a nation of much talent, and, in some respects, even wisdom, owing to the rare good fortune of having been provided at an early period with a particularly good set of customs, the work, in some measure, of men to whom even the most enlightened European must accord, under certain limitations, the title of sages and philosophers. They are remarkable, too, in the excellence of their apparatus for impressing, as far as possible, the best wisdom they possess upon every mind in the community, and securing that those who have appropriated most of it shall occupy the posts of honor and power. Surely the people who did this have discovered the secret of human progressiveness, and must have kept themselves steadily at the head of the movement of the world. On the contrary, they have become stationary—have remained so for thousands of years; and if they are ever to be farther improved, it must be by foreigners. They have succeeded beyond all hope in what English philanthropists are so industriously working at—in making a people all alike, all governing their thoughts and conduct by the same maxims and rules; and these are the fruits. The modern regime of public opinion is, in an unorganized form, what the Chinese educational and political systems are in an organized; and unless individuality shall be able successfully to assert itself against this yoke, Europe, notwithstanding its noble antecedents and its professed Christianity, will tend to become another China. . . .

1859

The Subjection of Women

After its 1869 publication in England and America, Mill's *The Subjection of Women* was quickly adopted by the leaders of the suffrage movement as the definitive analysis of the position of women in society. American suffragists sold copies of the book at their conventions; at the age of seventy-nine, American reformer Sarah Grimké went door to door in her hometown to sell one hundred copies.

The book had its roots in a tradition of libertarian thought and writing dating from the late eighteenth century. Out of this context came the first major work of feminist theory, Mary Wollstonecraft's *A Vindication of the Rights of Woman* (1792). (Wollstonecraft's reputation was so scandalous that Mill avoided referring to her work.) In the early decades of the century, there was much discussion of women's rights in the Unitarian and radical circles inhabited by Mill and his wife, Harriet Taylor, who wrote her own essay on women's suffrage. By the middle of the century, the "Woman Question," as the Victorians called it, had become a frequent subject of writing and debate; and an organized feminist movement had begun to develop. Early reform efforts focused on the conditions of women's work, particularly in mines and factories; access to better jobs and to higher education; and married women's property rights. Women's suffrage started attracting support in the 1860s. Mill himself introduced the first parliamentary motion extending the franchise to women in 1866.

From The Subjection of Women

From *Chapter 1*

The object of this Essay is to explain as clearly as I am able, the grounds of an opinion which I have held from the very earliest period when I had formed any opinions at all on social or political matters, and which, instead of being weakened or modified, has been constantly growing stronger by the progress of reflection and the experience of life: That the principle which regulates the existing social relations between the two sexes—the legal subordination of one sex to the other—is wrong in itself, and now one of the chief hindrances to human improvement; and that it ought to be replaced by a principle of perfect equality, admitting no power or privilege on the one side, nor disability on the other.

* * *

Some will object, that a comparison cannot fairly be made between the government of the male sex and the forms of unjust power[1] which I have adduced in illustration of it, since these are arbitrary, and the effect of mere usurpation, while it on the contrary is natural. But was there ever any domination which did not appear natural to those who possessed it? There was a time when the division of mankind into two classes, a small one of masters and a numerous one of slaves, appeared, even to the most cultivated minds, to be a natural, and the only natural, condition of the human race. No less an intellect, and one which contributed no less to the progress of human thought, than Aristotle, held this opinion without doubt or misgiving; and rested it on the same premises on which the same assertion in regard to the dominion of men over women is usually based, namely that there are different natures among mankind, free natures, and slave natures; that the Greeks were of a free nature, the barbarian races of Thracians and Asiatics of a slave nature. But why need I go back to Aristotle? Did not the slaveowners of the Southern United States maintain the same doctrine, with all the fanaticism with which men cling to the theories that justify their passions and legitimate their personal interests? Did they not call heaven and earth to witness that the dominion of the white man over the black is natural, that the black race is by nature incapable of freedom, and marked out for slavery? some even going so far as to say that the freedom of manual laborers is an unnatural order of things anywhere. Again, the theorists of absolute monarchy have always affirmed it to be the only natural form of government; issuing from the patriarchal, which was the primitive and spontaneous form of society, framed on the model of the paternal, which is anterior to society itself, and, as they contend, the most natural authority of all. Nay, for that matter, the law of force itself, to those who could not plead any other, has always seemed the most natural of all grounds for the exercise of authority. Conquering races hold it to be Nature's

---

1. As examples of unjust power Mill had cited the forceful control of slaves by slave owners or of nations by military despots.

own dictate that the conquered should obey the conquerors, or, as they eupho-
niously paraphrase it, that the feebler and more unwarlike races should submit
to the braver and manlier. The smallest acquaintance with human life in the
middle ages, shows how supremely natural the dominion of the feudal nobility
over men of low condition appeared to the nobility themselves, and how unnatural the conception seemed, of a person of the inferior class claiming equality
with them, or exercising authority over them. It hardly seemed less so to the
class held in subjection. The emancipated serfs and burgesses, even in their
most vigorous struggles, never made any pretension to a share of authority;
they only demanded more or less of limitation to the power of tyrannizing over
them. So true is it that unnatural generally means only uncustomary, and that
everything which is usual appears natural. The subjection of women to men
being a universal custom, any departure from it quite naturally appears unnatural. But how entirely, even in this case, the feeling is dependent on custom,
appears by ample experience. Nothing so much astonishes the people of distant parts of the world, when they first learn anything about England, as to be
told that it is under a queen: the thing seems to them so unnatural as to be
almost incredible. To Englishmen this does not seem in the least degree unnatural, because they are used to it; but they do feel it unnatural that women
should be soldiers or members of Parliament. In the feudal ages, on the contrary, war and politics were not thought unnatural to women, because not
unusual; it seemed natural that women of the privileged classes should be of
manly character, inferior in nothing but bodily strength to their husbands and
fathers. The independence of women seemed rather less unnatural to the
Greeks than to other ancients, on account of the fabulous Amazons[2] (whom
they believed to be historical), and the partial example afforded by the Spartan
women; who, though no less subordinate by law than in other Greek states,
were more free in fact, and being trained to bodily exercises in the same manner with men, gave ample proof that they were not naturally disqualified for
them. There can be little doubt that Spartan experience suggested to Plato,
among many other of his doctrines, that of the social and political equality of
the two sexes.[3]

But, it will be said, the rule of men over women differs from all these others
in not being a rule of force: it is accepted voluntarily; women make no complaint, and are consenting parties to it. In the first place, a great number of
women do not accept it. Ever since there have been women able to make their
sentiments known by their writings (the only mode of publicity which society
permits to them), an increasing number of them have recorded protests against
their present social condition: and recently many thousands of them, headed
by the most eminent women known to the public, have petitioned Parliament
for their admission to the Parliamentary Suffrage.[4] The claim of women to be
educated as solidly, and in the same branches of knowledge, as men, is urged
with growing intensity, and with a great prospect of success; while the demand
for their admission into professions and occupations hitherto closed against
them, becomes every year more urgent. Though there are not in this country,
as there are in the United States, periodical Conventions[5] and an organized

2. A mythical race of woman warriors.
3. Plato's *Republic*, book 5. Plato was Athenian.
4. As a member of the House of Commons, Mill
had introduced a petition for women's suffrage in
1866.

5. Such as the Women's Rights Convention held
at Worcester, Massachusetts, in October 1850,
which had occasioned an essay by Mill's wife titled
"Enfranchisement of Women" (1851).

party to agitate for the Rights of Women, there is a numerous and active Society organized and managed by women, for the more limited object of obtaining the political franchise. Nor is it only in our own country and in America that women are beginning to protest, more or less collectively, against the disabilities under which they labor. France, and Italy, and Switzerland, and Russia now afford examples of the same thing. How many more women there are who silently cherish similar aspirations, no one can possibly know; but there are abundant tokens how many *would* cherish them, were they not so strenuously taught to repress them as contrary to the proprieties of their sex. It must be remembered, also, that no enslaved class ever asked for complete liberty at once. When Simon de Montfort[6] called the deputies of the commons to sit for the first time in Parliament, did any of them dream of demanding that an assembly, elected by their constituents, should make and destroy ministries, and dictate to the king in affairs of state? No such thought entered into the imagination of the most ambitious of them. The nobility had already these pretensions; the commons pretended to nothing but to be exempt from arbitrary taxation, and from the gross individual oppression of the king's officers. It is a political law of nature that those who are under any power of ancient origin, never begin by complaining of the power itself, but only of its oppressive exercise. There is never any want of women who complain of ill usage by their husbands. There would be infinitely more, if complaint were not the greatest of all provocatives to a repetition and increase of the ill usage. It is this which frustrates all attempts to maintain the power but protect the woman against its abuses. In no other case (except that of a child) is the person who has been proved judicially to have suffered an injury, replaced under the physical power of the culprit who inflicted it. Accordingly wives, even in the most extreme and protracted cases of bodily ill usage, hardly ever dare avail themselves of the laws made for their protection: and if, in a moment of irrepressible indignation, or by the interference of neighbors, they are induced to do so, their whole effort afterward is to disclose as little as they can, and to beg off their tyrant from his merited chastisement.

All causes, social and natural, combine to make it unlikely that women should be collectively rebellious to the power of men. They are so far in a position different from all other subject classes, that their masters require something more from them than actual service. Men do not want solely the obedience of women, they want their sentiments. All men, except the most brutish, desire to have, in the woman most nearly connected with them, not a forced slave but a willing one, not a slave merely, but a favorite. They have therefore put everything in practice to enslave their minds. The masters of all other slaves rely, for maintaining obedience, on fear; either fear of themselves, or religious fears. The masters of women wanted more than simple obedience, and they turned the whole force of education to effect their purpose. All women are brought up from the very earliest years in the belief that their ideal of character is the very opposite to that of men; not self-will, and government by self-control, but submission, and yielding to the control of others. All the moralities tell them that it is the duty of women, and all the current sentimentalities that it is their nature, to live for others; to make complete abnegation of themselves, and to have no life but in their affections. And by their

6. English nobleman and statesman (ca. 1208–1265), who assembled a parliament in 1265 that has been called the basis of the modern House of Commons.

affections are meant the only ones they are allowed to have—those to the men
with whom they are connected, or to the children who constitute an additional
and indefeasible tie between them and a man. When we put together three
things—first, the natural attraction between opposite sexes; secondly, the
wife's entire dependence on the husband, every privilege or pleasure she has
being either his gift, or depending entirely on his will; and lastly, that the
principal object of human pursuit, consideration, and all objects of social
ambition, can in general be sought or obtained by her only through him, it
would be a miracle if the object of being attractive to men had not become
the polar star of feminine education and formation of character. And, this
great means of influence over the minds of women having been acquired, an
instinct of selfishness made men avail themselves of it to the utmost as a means
of holding women in subjection, by representing to them meekness, submissiveness, and resignation of all individual will into the hands of a man, as an
essential part of sexual attractiveness. Can it be doubted that any of the other
yokes which mankind have succeeded in breaking, would have subsisted till
now if the same means had existed, and had been as sedulously used, to bow
down their minds to it? If it had been made the object of the life of every young
plebeian to find personal favor in the eyes of some patrician, of every young
serf with some seigneur; if domestication with him, and a share of his personal
affections, had been held out as the prize which they all should look out for,
the most gifted and aspiring being able to reckon on the most desirable prizes;
and if, when this prize had been obtained, they had been shut out by a wall
of brass from all interests not centering in him, all feelings and desires but
those which he shared or inculcated; would not serfs and seigneurs, plebeians
and patricians, have been as broadly distinguished at this day as men and
women are? and would not all but a thinker here and there, have believed the
distinction to be a fundamental and unalterable fact in human nature?

The preceding considerations are amply sufficient to show that custom,
however universal it may be, affords in this case no presumption, and ought
not to create any prejudice, in favor of the arrangements which place women
in social and political subjection to men. But I may go farther, and maintain
that the course of history, and the tendencies of progressive human society,
afford not only no presumption in favor of this system of inequality of rights,
but a strong one against it; and that, so far as the whole course of human
improvement up to this time, the whole stream of modern tendencies, warrants
any inference on the subject, it is, that this relic of the past is discordant with
the future, and must necessarily disappear.

For, what is the peculiar character of the modern world—the difference
which chiefly distinguishes modern institutions, modern social ideas, modern
life itself, from those of times long past? It is, that human beings are no longer
born to their place in life, and chained down by an inexorable bond to the
place they are born to, but are free to employ their faculties, and such favourable chances as offer, to achieve the lot which may appear to them most
desirable.

* * *

The social subordination of women thus stands out an isolated fact in modern social institutions; a solitary breach of what has become their fundamental
law; a single relic of an old world of thought and practice exploded in everything else, but retained in the one thing of most universal interest; as if a

gigantic dolmen,[7] or a vast temple of Jupiter Olympius, occupied the site of St. Paul's and received daily worship, while the surrounding Christian churches were only resorted to on fasts and festivals. This entire discrepancy between one social fact and all those which accompany it, and the radical opposition between its nature and the progressive movement which is the boast of the modern world, and which has successively swept away everything else of an analogous character, surely affords, to a conscientious observer of human tendencies, serious matter for reflection. It raises a *primâ facie* presumption on the unfavorable side, far outweighing any which custom and usage could in such circumstances create on the favorable; and should at least suffice to make this, like the choice between republicanism and royalty, a balanced question.

The least that can be demanded is, that the question should not be considered as prejudged by existing fact and existing opinion, but open to discussion on its merits, as a question of justice and expediency: the decision on this, as on any of the other social arrangements of mankind, depending on what an enlightened estimate of tendencies and consequences may show to be most advantageous to humanity in general, without distinction of sex. And the discussion must be a real discussion, descending to foundations, and not resting satisfied with vague and general assertions. It will not do, for instance, to assert in general terms, that the experience of mankind has pronounced in favor of the existing system. Experience cannot possibly have decided between two courses, so long as there has only been experience of one. If it be said that the doctrine of the equality of the sexes rests only on theory, it must be remembered that the contrary doctrine also has only theory to rest upon. All that is proved in its favor by direct experience, is that mankind have been able to exist under it, and to attain the degree of improvement and prosperity which we now see; but whether that prosperity has been attained sooner, or is now greater, than it would have been under the other system, experience does not say. On the other hand, experience does say, that every step in improvement has been so invariably accompanied by a step made in raising the social position of women, that historians and philosophers have been led to adopt their elevation or debasement as on the whole the surest test and most correct measure of the civilization of a people or an age. Through all the progressive period of human history, the condition of women has been approaching nearer to equality with men. This does not of itself prove that the assimilation must go on to complete equality; but it assuredly affords some presumption that such is the case.

Neither does it avail anything to say that the *nature* of the two sexes adapts them to their present functions and position, and renders these appropriate to them. Standing on the ground of common sense and the constitution of the human mind, I deny that any one knows, or can know, the nature of the two sexes, as long as they have only been seen in their present relation to one another. If men had ever been found in society without women, or women without men, or if there had been a society of men and women in which the women were not under the control of the men, something might have been positively known about the mental and moral differences which may be inherent in the nature of each. What is now called the nature of women is an eminently artificial thing—the result of forced repression in some directions,

---

7. Prehistoric stone monument, here associated with pagan religious rites.

unnatural stimulation in others. It may be asserted without scruple, that no other class of dependents have had their character so entirely distorted from its natural proportions by their relation with their masters; for, if conquered and slave races have been, in some respects, more forcibly repressed, whatever in them has not been crushed down by an iron heel has generally been let alone, and if left with any liberty of development, it has developed itself according to its own laws; but in the case of women, a hot-house[8] and stove cultivation has always been carried on of some of the capabilities of their nature, for the benefit and pleasure of their masters. Then, because certain products of the general vital force sprout luxuriantly and reach a great development in this heated atmosphere and under this active nurture and watering, while other shoots from the same root, which are left outside in the wintry air, with ice purposely heaped all round them, have a stunted growth, and some are burnt off with fire and disappear; men, with that inability to recognize their own work which distinguishes the unanalytic mind, indolently believe that the tree grows of itself in the way they have made it grow, and that it would die if one half of it were not kept in a vapour bath and the other half in the snow.

Of all difficulties which impede the progress of thought, and the formation of well-grounded opinions on life and social arrangements, the greatest is now the unspeakable ignorance and inattention of mankind in respect to the influences which form human character. Whatever any portion of the human species now are, or seem to be, such, it is supposed, they have a natural tendency to be: even when the most elementary knowledge of the circumstances in which they have been placed, clearly points out the causes that made them what they are. Because a cottier[9] deeply in arrears to his landlord is not industrious, there are people who think that the Irish are naturally idle. Because constitutions can be overthrown when the authorities appointed to execute them turn their arms against them, there are people who think the French incapable of free government. Because the Greeks cheated the Turks, and the Turks only plundered the Greeks, there are persons who think that the Turks are naturally more sincere: and because women, as is often said, care nothing about politics except their personalities, it is supposed that the general good is naturally less interesting to women than to men. History, which is now so much better understood than formerly, teaches another lesson: if only by showing the extraordinary susceptibility of human nature to external influences, and the extreme variableness of those of its manifestations which are supposed to be most universal and uniform. But in history, as in traveling, men usually see only what they already had in their own minds; and few learn much from history, who do not bring much with them to its study.

Hence, in regard to that most difficult question, what are the natural differences between the two sexes—a subject on which it is impossible in the present state of society to obtain complete and correct knowledge—while almost everybody dogmatizes upon it, almost all neglect and make light of the only means by which any partial insight can be obtained into it. This is, an analytic study of the most important department of psychology, the laws of the influence of circumstances on character. For, however great and apparently ineradicable the moral and intellectual differences between men and women might be, the evidence of their being natural differences could only be negative. Those only could be inferred to be natural which could not pos-

8. A heated greenhouse.   9. Tenant cottager on a small Irish farm.

sibly be artificial—the residuum, after deducting every characteristic of either sex which can admit of being explained from education or external circumstances. The profoundest knowledge of the laws of the formation of character is indispensable to entitle any one to affirm even that there is any difference, much more what the difference is, between the two sexes considered as moral and rational beings; and since no one, as yet, has that knowledge (for there is hardly any subject which, in proportion to its importance, has been so little studied), no one is thus far entitled to any positive opinion on the subject. Conjectures are all that can at present be made; conjectures more or less probable, according as more or less authorized by such knowledge as we yet have of the laws of psychology, as applied to the formation of character.

Even the preliminary knowledge, what the differences between the sexes now are, apart from all question as to how they are made what they are, is still in the crudest[1] and most incomplete state. Medical practitioners and physiologists have ascertained, to some extent, the differences in bodily constitution; and this is an important element to the psychologist: but hardly any medical practitioner is a psychologist. Respecting the mental characteristics of women; their observations are of no more worth than those of common men. It is a subject on which nothing final can be known, so long as those who alone can really know it, women themselves, have given but little testimony, and that little, mostly suborned. It is easy to know stupid women. Stupidity is much the same all the world over. A stupid person's notions and feelings may confidently be inferred from those which prevail in the circle by which the person is surrounded. Not so with those whose opinions and feelings are an emanation from their own nature and faculties. It is only a man here and there who has any tolerable knowledge of the character even of the women of his own family. I do not mean, of their capabilities; these nobody knows, not even themselves, because most of them have never been called out. I mean their actually existing thoughts and feelings. Many a man thinks he perfectly understands women, because he has had amatory relations with several, perhaps with many of them. If he is a good observer, and his experience extends to quality as well as quantity, he may have learnt something of one narrow department of their nature—an important department, no doubt. But of all the rest of it, few persons are generally more ignorant, because there are few from whom it is so carefully hidden. The most favorable case which a man can generally have for studying the character of a woman, is that of his own wife: for the opportunities are greater, and the cases of complete sympathy not so unspeakably rare. And in fact, this is the source from which any knowledge worth having on the subject has, I believe, generally come. But most men have not had the opportunity of studying in this way more than a single case: accordingly one can, to an almost laughable degree, infer what a man's wife is like, from his opinions about women in general. To make even this one case yield any result, the woman must be worth knowing, and the man not only a competent judge, but of a character so sympathetic in itself, and so well adapted to hers, that he can either read her mind by sympathetic intuition, or has nothing in himself which makes her shy of disclosing it. Hardly anything, I believe, can be more rare than this conjunction. It often happens that there is the most complete unity of feeling and community of interests as to all external things, yet the one has as little admission

---

1. Roughest, least refined.

into the internal life of the other as if they were common acquaintance. Even
with true affection, authority on the one side and subordination on the other
prevent perfect confidence. Though nothing may be intentionally withheld,
much is not shown. In the analogous relation of parent and child, the corresponding phenomenon must have been in the observation of every one. As
between father and son, how many are the cases in which the father, in spite
of real affection on both sides, obviously to all the world does not know, nor
suspect, parts of the son's character familiar to his companions and equals.
The truth is, that the position of looking up to another is extremely unpropi-
tious to complete sincerity and openness with him. The fear of losing ground
in his opinion or in his feelings is so strong, that even in an upright character,
there is an unconscious tendency to show only the best side, or the side
which, though not the best, is that which he most likes to see: and it may be
confidently said that thorough knowledge of one another hardly ever exists,
but between persons who, besides being intimates, are equals. How much more
true, then, must all this be, when the one is not only under the authority of
the other, but has it inculcated on her as a duty to reckon everything else
subordinate to his comfort and pleasure, and to let him neither see nor feel
anything coming from her, except what is agreeable to him. All these difficulties stand in the way of a man's obtaining any thorough knowledge even of
the one woman whom alone, in general, he has sufficient opportunity of studying. When we further consider that to understand one woman is not necessarily to understand any other woman; that even if he could study many women
of one rank, or of one country, he would not thereby understand women of
other ranks or countries; and even if he did, they are still only the women
of a single period of history; we may safely assert that the knowledge which
men can acquire of women, even as they have been and are, without reference
to what they might be, is wretchedly imperfect and superficial, and always will
be so, until women themselves have told all that they have to tell.

And this time has not come; nor will it come otherwise than gradually. It is
but of yesterday that women have either been qualified by literary accomplishments, or permitted by society, to tell anything to the general public. As yet
very few of them dare tell anything, which men, on whom their literary success
depends, are unwilling to hear. Let us remember in what manner, up to a very
recent time, the expression, even by a male author, of uncustomary opinions,
or what are deemed eccentric feelings, usually was, and in some degree still
is, received; and we may form some faint conception under what impediments
a woman, who is brought up to think custom and opinion her sovereign rule,
attempts to express in books anything drawn from the depths of her own
nature. The greatest woman who has left writings behind her sufficient to give
her an eminent rank in the literature of her country, thought it necessary to
prefix as a motto to her boldest work, "Un homme peut braver l'opinion; une
femme doit s'y soumettre."[2] The greater part of what women write about
women is mere sycophancy to men. In the case of unmarried women, much
of it seems only intended to increase their chance of a husband. Many, both
married and unmarried, overstep the mark, and inculcate a servility beyond
what is desired or relished by any man, except the very vulgarest. But this is
not so often the case as, even at a quite late period, it still was. Literary women

---

2. A man can defy what is thought; a woman must submit to it (French); the epigraph to Mme de Staël's
Delphine (1802).

are becoming more freespoken, and more willing to express their real sentiments. Unfortunately, in this country especially, they are themselves such
artificial products, that their sentiments are compounded of a small element
of individual observation and consciousness, and a very large one of acquired
associations. This will be less and less the case, but it will remain true to a
great extent, as long as social institutions do not admit the same free development of originality in women which is possible to men. When that time
comes, and not before, we shall see, and not merely hear, as much as it is
necessary to know of the nature of women, and the adaptation of other things
to it.

＊　＊　＊

One thing we may be certain of—that what is contrary to women's nature
to do, they never will be made to do by simply giving their nature free play.
The anxiety of mankind to interfere in behalf of nature, for fear lest nature
should not succeed in effecting its purpose, is an altogether unnecessary solicitude. What women by nature cannot do, it is quite superfluous to forbid them
from doing. What they can do, but not so well as the men who are their
competitors, competition suffices to exclude them from; since nobody asks for
protective duties and bounties in favor of women; it is only asked that the
present bounties and protective duties in favor of men should be recalled. If
women have a greater natural inclination for some things than for others, there
is no need of laws or social inculcation to make the majority of them do the
former in preference to the latter. Whatever women's services are most wanted
for, the free play of competition will hold out the strongest inducements to
them to undertake. And, as the words imply, they are most wanted for the
things for which they are most fit; by the apportionment of which to them,
the collective faculties of the two sexes can be applied on the whole with the
greatest sum of valuable result.

The general opinion of men is supposed to be, that the natural vocation of
a woman is that of a wife and mother. I say, is supposed to be, because, judging
from acts—from the whole of the present constitution of society—one might
infer that their opinion was the direct contrary. They might be supposed to
think that the alleged natural vocation of women was of all things the most
repugnant to their nature; insomuch that if they are free to do anything else—
if any other means of living, or occupation of their time and faculties, is open,
which has any chance of appearing desirable to them—there will not be
enough of them who will be willing to accept the condition said to be natural
to them. If this is the real opinion of men in general, it would be well that it
should be spoken out. I should like to hear somebody openly enunciating the
doctrine (it is already implied in much that is written on the subject)—"It is
necessary to society that women should marry and produce children. They will
not do so unless they are compelled. Therefore it is necessary to compel them."
The merits of the case would then be clearly defined. It would be exactly that
of the slaveholders of South Carolina and Louisiana. "It is necessary that
cotton and sugar should be grown. White men cannot produce them. Negroes
will not, for any wages which we choose to give. Ergo they must be compelled."
An illustration still closer to the point is that of impressment.[3] Sailors must
absolutely be had to defend the country. It often happens that they will not

3. The practice of seizing men and forcing them into service as sailors.

voluntarily enlist. Therefore there must be the power of forcing them. How often has this logic been used! and, but for one flaw in it, without doubt it would have been successful up to this day. But it is open to the retort—First pay the sailors the honest value of their labor. When you have made it as well worth their while to serve you, as to work for other employers, you will have no more difficulty than others have in obtaining their services. To this there is no logical answer except "I will not:" and as people are now not only ashamed, but are not desirous, to rob the laborer of his hire, impressment is no longer advocated. Those who attempt to force women into marriage by closing all other doors against them, lay themselves open to a similar retort. If they mean what they say, their opinion must evidently be, that men do not render the married condition so desirable to women, as to induce them to accept it for its own recommendations. It is not a sign of one's thinking the boon one offers very attractive, when one allows only Hobson's choice,[4] "that or none." And here, I believe, is the clue to the feelings of those men, who have a real antipathy to the equal freedom of women. I believe they are afraid, not lest women should be unwilling to marry, for I do not think that any one in reality has that apprehension; but lest they should insist that marriage should be on equal conditions; lest all women of spirit and capacity should prefer doing almost anything else, not in their own eyes degrading, rather than marry, when marrying is giving themselves a master, and a master too of all their earthly possessions. And truly, if this consequence were necessarily incident to marriage, I think that the apprehension would be very well founded. I agree in thinking it probable that few women, capable of anything else, would, unless under an irresistible *entrainement*,[5] rendering them for the time insensible to anything but itself, choose such a lot, when any other means were open to them of filling a conventionally honorable place in life: and if men are determined that the law of marriage shall be a law of despotism, they are quite right, in point of mere policy, in leaving to women only Hobson's choice. But, in that case, all that has been done in the modern world to relax the chain on the minds of women, has been a mistake. They never should have been allowed to receive a literary education. Women who read, much more women who write, are, in the existing constitution of things, a contradiction and a disturbing element: and it was wrong to bring women up with any acquirements but those of an odalisque, or of a domestic servant.

1860   1869

From Autobiography

From Chapter 5. A Crisis in My Mental History.
One Stage Onward

For some years after this time[1] I wrote very little, and nothing regularly, for publication: and great were the advantages which I derived from the intermission. It was of no common importance to me, at this period, to be able to digest and mature my thoughts for my own mind only, without any immediate

---

4. A choice without an alternative, so called in reference to the practice of Thomas Hobson (1544–1630), who rented out horses and required every customer to take the horse nearest the door.

5. Rapture (French).
1. I.e., 1828. Mill had been contributing articles to the *Westminster Review*, a respected monthly periodical.

call for giving them out in print. Had I gone on writing, it would have much disturbed the important transformation in my opinions and character, which took place during those years. The origin of this transformation, or at least the process by which I was prepared for it, can only be explained by turning some distance back.

From the winter of 1821, when I first read Bentham,[2] and especially from the commencement of the *Westminster Review,* I had what might truly be called an object in life; to be a reformer of the world. My conception of my own happiness was entirely identified with this object. The personal sympathies I wished for were those of fellow laborers in this enterprise. I endeavored to pick up as many followers as I could by the way; but as a serious and permanent personal satisfaction to rest upon, my whole reliance was placed on this; and I was accustomed to felicitate myself on the certainty of a happy life which I enjoyed, through placing my happiness in something durable and distant, in which some progress might be always making, while it could never be exhausted by complete attainment. This did very well for several years, during which the general improvement going on in the world and the idea of myself as engaged with others in struggling to promote it, seemed enough to fill up an interesting and animated existence. But the time came when I awakened from this as from a dream. It was in the autumn of 1826. I was in a dull state of nerves, such as everybody is occasionally liable to; unsusceptible to enjoyment or pleasurable excitement; one of those moods when what is pleasure at other times becomes insipid or indifferent; the state, I should think, in which converts to Methodism usually are, when smitten by their first "conviction of sin." In this frame of mind it occurred to me to put the question directly to myself: "Suppose that all your objects in life were realized; that all the changes in institutions and opinions which you are looking forward to could be completely effected at this very instant: would this be a great joy and happiness to you?" And an irrepressible self-consciousness distinctly answered, "No!" At this my heart sank within me: the whole foundation on which my life was constructed fell down. All my happiness was to have been found in the continual pursuit of this end. The end had ceased to charm, and how could there ever again be any interest in the means? I seemed to have nothing left to live for.

At first I hoped that the cloud would pass away of itself; but it did not. A night's sleep, the sovereign remedy for the smaller vexations of life, had no effect on it. I awoke to a renewed consciousness of the woeful fact. I carried it with me into all companies, into all occupations. Hardly anything had power to cause me even a few minutes' oblivion of it. For some months the cloud seemed to grow thicker and thicker. The lines in Coleridge's *Dejection*—I was not then acquainted with them—exactly describe my case:

> A grief without a pang, void, dark and drear,
> A drowsy, stifled, unimpassioned grief,
> Which finds no natural outlet or relief
> In word, or sigh, or tear.[3]

In vain I sought relief from my favorite books; those memorials of past nobleness and greatness from which I had always hitherto drawn strength and animation. I read them now without feeling, or with the accustomed feeling

---

2. Jeremy Bentham (1748–1832), founder of Utilitarianism and a cofounder of the *Westminster* *Review.*
3. "Dejection: An Ode" (1802), lines 21–24.

minus all its charm; and I became persuaded that my love of mankind, and of excellence for its own sake, had worn itself out. I sought no comfort by speaking to others of what I felt. If I had loved anyone sufficiently to make confiding my griefs a necessity, I should not have been in the condition I was. I felt, too, that mine was not an interesting, or in any way respectable distress. There was nothing in it to attract sympathy. Advice, if I had known where to seek it, would have been most precious. The words of Macbeth to the physician[4] often occurred to my thoughts. But there was no one on whom I could build the faintest hope of such assistance. My father, to whom it would have been natural to me to have recourse in any practical difficulties, was the last person to whom, in such a case as this, I looked for help. Everything convinced me that he had no knowledge of any such mental state as I was suffering from, and that even if he could be made to understand it, he was not the physician who could heal it. My education, which was wholly his work, had been conducted without any regard to the possibility of its ending in this result; and I saw no use in giving him the pain of thinking that his plans had failed, when the failure was probably irremediable, and, at all events, beyond the power of *his* remedies. Of other friends, I had at that time none to whom I had any hope of making my condition intelligible. It was however abundantly intelligible to myself; and the more I dwelt upon it, the more hopeless it appeared.

My course of study had led me to believe that all mental and moral feelings and qualities, whether of a good or of a bad kind, were the results of association; that we love one thing, and hate another, take pleasure in one sort of action or contemplation, and pain in another sort, through the clinging of pleasurable or painful ideas to those things, from the effect of education or of experience. As a corollary from this, I had always heard it maintained by my father, and was myself convinced, that the object of education should be to form the strongest possible associations of the salutary class; associations of pleasure with all things beneficial to the great whole, and of pain with all things hurtful to it. This doctrine appeared inexpugnable;[5] but it now seemed to me, on retrospect, that my teachers had occupied themselves but superficially with the means of forming and keeping up these salutary associations. They seemed to have trusted altogether to the old familiar instruments, praise and blame, reward and punishment. Now, I did not doubt that by these means, begun early, and applied unremittingly, intense associations of pain and pleasure, especially of pain, might be created, and might produce desires and aversions capable of lasting undiminished to the end of life. But there must always be something artificial and casual in associations thus produced. The pains and pleasures thus forcibly associated with things are not connected with them by any natural tie; and it is therefore, I thought, essential to the durability of these associations that they should have become so intense and inveterate as to be practically indissoluble, before the habitual exercise of the power of analysis had commenced. For I now saw, or thought I saw, what I had always before received with incredulity—that the habit of analysis has a tendency to wear away the feelings: as indeed it has, when no other mental habit is cultivated, and the analyzing spirit remains without its natural complements and correctives. The very excellence of analysis (I argued) is that it tends to weaken and undermine whatever is the result of prejudice; that it enables us mentally

4. Shakespeare's *Macbeth* 5.3.42: "Canst thou not   5. Unconquerable.
minister to a mind diseased . . . ?"

to separate ideas which have only casually clung together: and no associations whatever could ultimately resist this dissolving force, were it not that we owe to analysis our clearest knowledge of the permanent sequences in nature; the real connections between Things, not dependent on our will and feelings; natural laws, by virtue of which, in many cases, one thing is inseparable from another in fact; which laws, in proportion as they are clearly perceived and imaginatively realized, cause our ideas of things which are always joined together in Nature to cohere more and more closely in our thoughts. Analytic habits may thus even strengthen the associations between causes and effects, means and ends, but tend altogether to weaken those which are, to speak familiarly, a *mere* matter of feeling. They are therefore (I thought) favorable to prudence and clear-sightedness, but a perpetual worm at the root both of the passions and of the virtues; and, above all, fearfully undermine all desires, and all pleasures, which are the effects of association, that is, according to the theory I held, all except the purely physical and organic; of the entire insufficiency of which to make life desirable, no one had a stronger conviction than I had. These were the laws of human nature, by which, as it seemed to me, I had been brought to my present state. All those to whom I looked up were of opinion that the pleasure of sympathy with human beings, and the feelings which made the good of others, and especially of mankind on a large scale, the object of existence, were the greatest and surest sources of happiness. Of the truth of this I was convinced, but to know that a feeling would make me happy if I had it, did not give me the feeling. My education, I thought, had failed to create these feelings in sufficient strength to resist the dissolving influence of analysis, while the whole course of my intellectual cultivation had made precocious and premature analysis the inveterate habit of my mind. I was thus, as I said to myself, left stranded at the commencement of my voyage, with a well-equipped ship and a rudder, but no sail; without any real desire for the ends which I had been so carefully fitted out to work for: no delight in virtue, or the general good, but also just as little in anything else. The fountains of vanity and ambition seemed to have dried up within me, as completely as those of benevolence. I had had (as I reflected) some gratification of vanity at too early an age: I had obtained some distinction, and felt myself of some importance, before the desire of distinction and of importance had grown into a passion: and little as it was which I had attained, yet having been attained too early, like all pleasures enjoyed too soon, it had made me *blasé* and indifferent to the pursuit. Thus neither selfish nor unselfish pleasures were pleasures to me. And there seemed no power in nature sufficient to begin the formation of my character anew, and create in a mind now irretrievably analytic, fresh associations of pleasure with any of the objects of human desire.

These were the thoughts which mingled with the dry heavy dejection of the melancholy winter of 1826–7. During this time I was not incapable of my usual occupations. I went on with them mechanically, by the mere force of habit. I had been so drilled in a certain sort of mental exercise that I could still carry it on when all the spirit had gone out of it. I even composed and spoke several speeches at the debating society, how, or with what degree of success, I know not. Of four years continual speaking at that society, this is the only year of which I remember next to nothing. Two lines of Coleridge, in whom alone of all writers I have found a true description of what I felt, were often in my thoughts, not at this time (for I had never read them), but in a later period of the same mental malady:

Work without hope draws nectar in a sieve,
And hope without an object cannot live.[6]

In all probability my case was by no means so peculiar as I fancied it, and I doubt not that many others have passed through a similar state; but the idiosyncrasies of my education had given to the general phenomenon a special character, which made it seem the natural effect of causes that it was hardly possible for time to remove. I frequently asked myself if I could, or if I was bound to go on living, when life must be passed in this manner. I generally answered to myself, that I did not think I could possibly bear it beyond a year. When, however, not more than half that duration of time had elapsed, a small ray of light broke in upon my gloom. I was reading, accidentally, Marmontel's *Mémoires*,[7] and came to the passage which relates his father's death, the distressed position of the family, and the sudden inspiration by which he, then a mere boy, felt and made them feel that he would be everything to them—would supply the place of all that they had lost. A vivid conception of that scene and its feelings came over me, and I was moved to tears. From this moment my burden grew lighter. The oppression of the thought that all feeling was dead within me was gone. I was no longer hopeless: I was not a stock or a stone. I had still, it seemed, some of the material out of which all worth of character, and all capacity for happiness, are made. Relieved from my ever present sense of irremediable wretchedness, I gradually found that the ordinary incidents of life could again give me some pleasure; that I could again find enjoyment, not intense, but sufficient for cheerfulness, in sunshine and sky, in books, in conversation, in public affairs; and that there was, once more, excitement, though of a moderate kind, in exerting myself for my opinions, and for the public good. Thus the cloud gradually drew off, and I again enjoyed life: and though I had several relapses, some of which lasted many months, I never again was as miserable as I had been.

The experiences of this period had two very marked effects on my opinions and character. In the first place, they led me to adopt a theory of life, very unlike that on which I had before acted, and having much in common with what at that time I certainly had never heard of, the anti-self-consciousness theory of Carlyle.[8] I never, indeed, wavered in the conviction that happiness is the test of all rules of conduct, and the end of life. But I now thought that this end was only to be attained by not making it the direct end. Those only are happy (I thought) who have their minds fixed on some object other than their own happiness; on the happiness of others, on the improvement of mankind, even on some art or pursuit, followed not as a means, but as itself an ideal end. Aiming thus at something else, they find happiness by the way. The enjoyments of life (such was now my theory) are sufficient to make it a pleasant thing, when they are taken *en passant*,[9] without being made a principal object. Once make them so, and they are immediately felt to be insufficient. They will not bear a scrutinizing examination. Ask yourself whether you are happy, and you cease to be so. The only chance is to treat, not happiness, but some end external to it, as the purpose of life. Let your self-consciousness, your scrutiny, your self-interrogation exhaust themselves on that; and if otherwise fortunately

---

6. The last two lines of Coleridge's short poem "Work without Hope" (1828).
7. Published in 1804; Jean-François Marmontel (1723–1799), French dramatist and critic.

8. See "The Everlasting Yea" (p. 1017), of Carlyle's *Sartor Resartus* (1833–34).
9. In passing (French).

circumstanced you will inhale happiness with the air you breathe, without dwelling on it or thinking about it, without either forestalling it in imagination, or putting it to flight by fatal questioning. This theory now became the basis of my philosophy of life. And I still hold to it as the best theory for all those who have but a moderate degree of sensibility[1] and of capacity for enjoyment, that is, for the great majority of mankind.

The other important change which my opinions at this time underwent was that I, for the first time, gave its proper place, among the prime necessities of human well-being, to the internal culture of the individual. I ceased to attach almost exclusive importance to the ordering of outward circumstances, and the training of the human being for speculation and for action.

I had now learnt by experience that the passive susceptibilities needed to be cultivated as well as the active capacities, and required to be nourished and enriched as well as guided. I did not, for an instant, lose sight of, or undervalue, that part of the truth which I had seen before; I never turned recreant to intellectual culture, or ceased to consider the power and practice of analysis as an essential condition both of individual and of social improvement. But I thought that it had consequences which required to be corrected, by joining other kinds of cultivation with it. The maintenance of a due balance among the faculties now seemed to me of primary importance. The cultivation of the feelings became one of the cardinal points in my ethical and philosophical creed. And my thoughts and inclinations turned in an increasing degree toward whatever seemed capable of being instrumental to that object.

I now began to find meaning in the things which I had read or heard about the importance of poetry and art as instruments of human culture. But it was some time longer before I began to know this by personal experience. The only one of the imaginative arts in which I had from childhood taken great pleasure was music; the best effect of which (and in this it surpasses perhaps every other art) consists in exciting enthusiasm; in winding up to a high pitch those feelings of an elevated kind which are already in the character, but to which this excitement gives a glow and a fervor, which, though transitory at its utmost height, is precious for sustaining them at other times. This effect of music I had often experienced; but like all my pleasurable susceptibilities it was suspended during the gloomy period. I had sought relief again and again from this quarter, but found none. After the tide had turned, and I was in process of recovery, I had been helped forward by music, but in a much less elevated manner. I at this time first became acquainted with Weber's *Oberon*,[2] and the extreme pleasure which I drew from its delicious melodies did me good, by showing me a source of pleasure to which I was as susceptible as ever. The good, however, was much impaired by the thought that the pleasure of music (as is quite true of such pleasure as this was, that of mere tune) fades with familiarity, and requires either to be revived by intermittence, or fed by continual novelty. And it is very characteristic both of my then state, and of the general tone of my mind at this period of my life, that I was seriously tormented by the thought of the exhaustibility of musical combinations. The octave consists only of five tones and two semitones, which can be put together in only a limited number of ways, of which but a small proportion are beautiful: most of these, it seemed to me, must have been already discovered, and there could

1. Sensitivity.
2. A romantic opera (1826) composed by Carl Maria von Weber (1786–1826).

not be room for a long succession of Mozarts and Webers, to strike out, as these had done, entirely new and surpassingly rich veins of musical beauty. This source of anxiety may, perhaps, be thought to resemble that of the phi-losophers of Laputa,³ who feared lest the sun should be burnt out. It was, however, connected with the best feature in my character, and the only good point to be found in my very unromantic and in no way honorable distress. For though my dejection, honestly looked at, could not be called other than egotistical, produced by the ruin, as I thought, of my fabric of happiness, yet the destiny of mankind in general was ever in my thoughts, and could not be separated from my own. I felt that the flaw in my life must be a flaw in life itself; that the question was whether, if the reformers of society and govern-ment could succeed in their objects, and every person in the community were free and in a state of physical comfort, the pleasures of life, being no longer kept up by struggle and privation, would cease to be pleasures. And I felt that unless I could see my way to some better hope than this for human happiness in general, my dejection must continue; but that if I could see such an outlet, I should then look on the world with pleasure; content as far as I was myself concerned, with any fair share of the general lot.

This state of my thoughts and feelings made the fact of my reading Words-worth for the first time (in the autumn of 1828), an important event in my life. I took up the collection of his poems from curiosity, with no expectation of mental relief from it, though I had before resorted to poetry with that hope. In the worst period of my depression, I had read through the whole of Byron (then new to me), to try whether a poet, whose peculiar department was sup-posed to be that of the intenser feelings, could rouse any feeling in me. As might be expected, I got no good from this reading, but the reverse. The poet's state of mind was too like my own. His was the lament of a man who had worn out all pleasures, and who seemed to think that life, to all who possess the good things of it, must necessarily be the vapid, uninteresting thing which I found it. His Harold and Manfred had the same burden on them which I had; and I was not in a frame of mind to derive any comfort from the vehement sensual passion of his Giaours, or the sullenness of his Laras.⁴ But while Byron was exactly what did not suit my condition, Wordsworth was exactly what did. I had looked into The Excursion⁵ two or three years before, and found little in it; and I should probably have found as little had I read it at this time. But the miscellaneous poems, in the two-volume edition of 1815 (to which little of value was added in the latter part of the author's life), proved to be the precise thing for my mental wants at that particular juncture.

In the first place, these poems addressed themselves powerfully to one of the strongest of my pleasurable susceptibilities, the love of rural objects and natural scenery; to which I had been indebted not only for much of the plea-sure of my life, but quite recently for relief from one of my longest relapses into depression. In this power of rural beauty over me, there was a foundation laid for taking pleasure in Wordsworth's poetry; the more so, as his scenery lies mostly among mountains, which, owing to my early Pyrenean excursion,⁶ were my ideal of natural beauty. But Wordsworth would never have had any

3. In part 3 of Jonathan Swift's *Gulliver's Travels* (1726).
4. The heroes of some of Byron's early poems were usually gloomy and self-preoccupied. Mill refers here to *Childe Harold's Pilgrimage* (1812–18), *Manfred* (1817), *The Giaour* (1813), and *Lara* (1814).
5. A long meditative poem by Wordsworth, pub-lished in 1814.
6. At fifteen Mill had been deeply affected by the landscape of the Pyrenees in Spain, a mountainous region that also made a strong impression on Ten-nyson.

great effect on me, if he had merely placed before me beautiful pictures of natural scenery. Scott[7] does this still better than Wordsworth, and a very second-rate landscape does it more effectually than any poet. What made Wordsworth's poems a medicine for my state of mind, was that they expressed, not mere outward beauty, but states of feeling, and of thought colored by feeling, under the excitement of beauty. They seemed to be the very culture of the feelings, which I was in quest of. In them I seemed to draw from a source of inward joy, of sympathetic and imaginative pleasure, which could be shared in by all human beings; which had no connection with struggle or imperfection, but would be made richer by every improvement in the physical or social condition of mankind. From them I seemed to learn what would be the perennial sources of happiness, when all the greater evils of life shall have been removed. And I felt myself at once better and happier as I came under their influence. There have certainly been, even in our own age, greater poets than Wordsworth; but poetry of deeper and loftier feeling could not have done for me at that time what his did. I needed to be made to feel that there was real, permanent happiness in tranquil contemplation. Wordsworth taught me this, not only without turning away from, but with a greatly increased interest in the common feelings and common destiny of human beings. And the delight which these poems gave me proved that with culture of this sort, there was nothing to dread from the most confirmed habit of analysis. At the conclusion of the Poems came the famous *Ode*, falsely called Platonic, *Intimations of Immortality*: in which, along with more than his usual sweetness of melody and rhythm, and along with the two passages of grand imagery but bad phi-losophy so often quoted, I found that he too had had similar experience to mine; that he also had felt that the first freshness of youthful enjoyment of life was not lasting; but that he had sought for compensation, and found it, in the way in which he was now teaching me to find it. The result was that I gradually, but completely, emerged from my habitual depression, and was never again subject to it. I long continued to value Wordsworth less according to his intrinsic merits than by the measure of what he had done for me. Com-pared with the greatest poets, he may be said to be the poet of unpoetical natures, possessed of quiet and contemplative tastes. But unpoetical natures are precisely those which require poetic cultivation. This cultivation Words-worth is much more fitted to give than poets who are intrinsically far more poets than he.

* * *

1873

7. Sir Walter Scott (1771–1832), Scottish poet and novelist.

ELIZABETH BARRETT BROWNING
1806–1861

During her lifetime Elizabeth Barrett Browning was one of England's most famous poets. Passionately admired by contemporaries as diverse as John Ruskin, Algernon Charles Swinburne, and Emily Dickinson for her moral and emotional ardor and her energetic engagement with the issues of her day, she was better known than her husband, Robert Browning, at the time of her death. Her work fell into disrepute with the modernist reaction against what was seen as the inappropriate didacticism and rhetorical excess of Victorian poetry; but recently scholars interested in her exploration of what it means to be a woman poet and in her response to social and political events have restored her status as a major writer.

Barrett Browning received an unusual education for a woman of her time. Availing herself of her brother's tutor, she studied Latin and Greek. She read voraciously in history, philosophy, and literature and began to write poetry from an early age—her first volume of poetry was published when she was thirteen. But as her intellectual and literary powers matured, her personal life became increasingly circumscribed both by ill health and by a tyrannically protective father, who had forbidden any of his eleven children to marry. By the age of thirty-nine, Elizabeth Barrett was a prominent woman of letters who lived in semiseclusion as an invalid in her father's house, where she occasionally received visitors in her room. One of these visitors was Robert Browning, who, moved by his admiration of her poetry, wrote to tell her "I do as I say, love these books with all my heart—and I love you too." He thereby initiated a courtship that culminated in 1846 in their secret marriage and elopement to Italy, for which her father never forgave her. In Italy Barrett Browning regained much health and strength, bearing and raising a son, Pen, to whom she was ardently devoted, and becoming deeply involved in Italian nationalist politics. She and her husband made their home in Florence, at the house called Casa Guidi, where she died in 1861.

Barrett Browning's poetry is characterized by a fervent moral sensibility. In her early work she tended to use the visionary modes of Romantic narrative poetry, but she turned increasingly to contemporary topics, particularly to liberal causes of her day. For example, in 1843, when government investigations exposed the exploitation of children employed in coal mines and factories, she wrote "The Cry of the Children," a powerful indictment of the appalling use of child labor. Like Harriet Beecher Stowe in *Uncle Tom's Cabin* (1851–52), Barrett Browning uses literature as a tool of social protest and reform, lending her voice, for example, to the cause of American abolitionism in "The Runaway Slave at Pilgrim's Point." In later poems she took up the cause of the *risorgimento*, the movement to unify Italy as a nation-state, in which Italy's struggle for freedom and identity found resonance with her own.

For many years Elizabeth Barrett Browning was best-known for her *Sonnets from the Portuguese* (1850), a sequence of forty-four sonnets presented under the guise of a translation from the Portuguese language, in which she recorded the stages of her love for Robert Browning. But increasingly, her verse novel *Aurora Leigh* (1857) has attracted critical attention. The poem depicts the growth of a woman poet and is thus, as Cora Kaplan observes, the first work in English by a woman writer in which the heroine herself is an author. When Barrett Browning first envisioned the poem, she wrote, "My chief *intention* just now is the writing of a sort of novel-poem . . . running into the midst of our conventions, and rushing into drawing-rooms and the like 'where angels fear to tread'; and so, meeting face to face and without mask the Humanity of the age, and speaking the truth as I conceive of it out plainly." The poem is a portrait of the artist as a young woman committed to a socially inclusive realist art. It is a daring work both in its presentation of social issues concerning women and in its claims for Aurora's poetic vocation; on her twentieth birthday, to pursue her career as a poet, Aurora refuses a proposal of marriage from her cousin Romney, who wants her to be his helpmate in the liberal causes he has embraced. Later in the poem, she rescues a fallen woman and takes her to Italy, where they settle together and confront a chastened Romney.

Immensely popular in its own day, *Aurora Leigh* had extravagant admirers (like Ruskin, who asserted that it was the greatest poem written in English) and critics who found fault with both its poetry and its morality. With its crowded canvas and melodramatic plot, it seems closer to the novel than to poetry, but it is important to view the poem in the context of the debate about appropriate poetic subject matter that engaged other Victorian poets. Unlike Matthew Arnold, who believed that the present age had not produced actions heroic enough to be the subject of great poetry, and unlike Alfred, Lord Tennyson, who used Arthurian legend to represent contemporary concerns, Barrett Browning felt that the present age contained the materials for an epic poetry. Virginia Woolf writes that "Elizabeth Barrett was inspired by a flash of true genius when she rushed into the drawing-room and said that here, where we live and work, is the true place for the poet." *Aurora Leigh* succeeds in giving us what Woolf describes as "a sense of life in general, of people who are unmistakably Victorian, wrestling with the problems of their own time, all brightened, intensified, and compacted by the fire of poetry. . . . Aurora Leigh, with her passionate interest in social questions, her conflict as artist and woman, her longing for knowledge and freedom, is the true daughter of her age."

The Cry of the Children[1]

"Φεῦ, φεῦ, τί προσδέρκεσθέ μ' ὄμμασιν, τέκνα;"
—*Medea*[2]

Do ye hear the children weeping, O my brothers,
　　Ere the sorrow comes with years?
They are leaning their young heads against their mothers,
　　And *that* cannot stop their tears.
5　The young lambs are bleating in the meadows,
　　The young birds are chirping in the nest,
The young fawns are playing with the shadows,
　　The young flowers are blowing toward the west—
But the young, young children, O my brothers,
10　　They are weeping bitterly!
They are weeping in the playtime of the others,
　　In the country of the free.

Do you question the young children in the sorrow
　　Why their tears are falling so?
15　The old man may weep for his to-morrow
　　Which is lost in Long Ago;
The old tree is leafless in the forest,
　　The old year is ending in the frost,
The old wound, if stricken, is the sorest,
20　　The old hope is hardest to be lost:
But the young, young children, O my brothers,
　　Do you ask them why they stand
Weeping sore° before the bosoms of their mothers,　　　*bitterly*
　　In our happy Fatherland?

1. Barrett Browning wrote "The Cry of the Children" in response to the report of a parliamentary commission, to which her friend R. H. Horne contributed, on the labor of children in mines and factories. Many of the details of Barrett Browning's poem derive from the report. See "Industrialism: Progress or Decline?" in Victorian Issues, p. 1556 below.
2. Alas, my children, why do you look at me? (Greek), from Euripides' tragedy *Medea*. Medea speaks these lines before killing her children in vengeance against her husband, who has taken a new wife. (The poem's title is spoken by the chorus.)

25 They look up with their pale and sunken faces,
   And their looks are sad to see,
  For the man's hoary anguish draws and presses
   Down the cheeks of infancy;
  "Your old earth," they say, "is very dreary,"
30 "Our young feet," they say, "are very weak;
  Few paces have we taken, yet are weary—
   Our grave-rest is very far to seek:
  Ask the aged why they weep, and not the children,
   For the outside earth is cold,
35 And we young ones stand without, in our bewildering,
   And the graves are for the old."

  "True," say the children, "it may happen
   That we die before our time:
  Little Alice died last year, her grave is shapen
40   Like a snowball, in the rime.°   *frost*
  We looked into the pit prepared to take her:
   Was no room for any work in the close clay!
  From the sleep wherein she lieth none will wake her,
   Crying, 'Get up, little Alice! it is day.'
45 If you listen by that grave, in sun and shower,
   With your ear down, little Alice never cries;
  Could we see her face, be sure we should not know her,
   For the smile has time for growing in her eyes:
  And merry go her moments, lulled and stilled in
50   The shroud by the kirk° chime.   *church*
  It is good when it happens," say the children,
   "That we die before our time."

  Alas, alas, the children! they are seeking
   Death in life, as best to have:
55 They are binding up their hearts away from breaking,
   With a ceremen° from the grave.   *shroud*
  Go out, children, from the mine and from the city,
   Sing out, children, as the little thrushes do;
  Pluck your handfuls of the meadow-cowslips pretty,
60   Laugh aloud, to feel your fingers let them through!
  But they answer, "Are your cowslips of the meadows
   Like our weeds anear the mine?[3]
  Leave us quiet in the dark of the coal-shadows,
   From your pleasures fair and fine!

65 "For oh," say the children, "we are weary,
   And we cannot run or leap;
  If we cared for any meadows, it were merely
   To drop down in them and sleep.
  Our knees tremble sorely in the stooping,
70 We fall upon our faces, trying to go;
  And, underneath our heavy eyelids drooping,

---

3. A commissioner mentions the fact of weeds being thus confounded with the idea of flowers [Barrett Browning's note].

The reddest flower would look as pale as snow.
For, all day, we drag our burden tiring
    Through the coal-dark, underground;
75 Or, all day, we drive the wheels of iron
    In the factories, round and round.

"For, all day, the wheels are droning, turning;
    Their wind comes in our faces,
Till our hearts turn, our heads with pulses burning,
80   And the walls turn in their places:
Turns the sky in the high window blank and reeling,
    Turns the long light that drops adown the wall,
Turn the black flies that crawl along the ceiling,
    All are turning, all the day, and we with all.
85 And all day, the iron wheels are droning,
    And sometimes we could pray,
'O ye wheels,' (breaking out in a mad moaning)
    'Stop! be silent for to-day!' "

Ay, be silent! Let them hear each other breathing
90   For a moment, mouth to mouth!
Let them touch each other's hands, in a fresh wreathing
    Of their tender human youth!
Let them feel that this cold metallic motion
    Is not all the life God fashions or reveals:
95 Let them prove their living souls against the notion
    That they live in you, or under you, O wheels!
Still, all day, the iron wheels go onward,
    Grinding life down from its mark;
And the children's souls, which God is calling sunward,
100   Spin on blindly in the dark.

Now tell the poor young children; O my brothers,
    To look up to Him and pray;
So the blessed One who blesseth all the others,
    Will bless them another day.
105 They answer, "Who is God that He should hear us,
    While the rushing of the iron wheels is stirred?
When we sob aloud, the human creatures near us
    Pass by, hearing not, or answer not a word.
And *we* hear not (for the wheels in their resounding)
110   Strangers speaking at the door:
Is it likely God, with angels singing round Him,
    Hears our weeping any more?

Two words, indeed, of praying we remember,
    And at midnight's hour of harm,
115 'Our Father,' looking upward in the chamber,
    We say softly for a charm.
We know no other words except 'Our Father.'
    And we think that, in some pause of angels' song,
God may pluck them with the silence sweet to gather,
120   And hold both within His right hand which is strong.

'Our Father!' If He heard us, He would surely
    (For they call Him good and mild)
Answer, smiling down the steep world very purely,
    'Come and rest with me, my child.'

125 "But, no!" say the children, weeping faster,
        "He is speechless as a stone:
And they tell us, of His image is the master
        Who commands us to work on.
Go to!" say the children,—"up in Heaven,
130   Dark, wheel-like, turning clouds are all we find.
Do not mock us; grief has made us unbelieving:
We look up for God, but tears have made us blind."
Do you hear the children weeping and disproving,
        O my brothers, what ye preach?
135 For God's possible is taught by His world's loving,[4]
        And the children doubt of each.

And well may the children weep before you!
        They are weary ere they run;
They have never seen the sunshine, nor the glory
140   Which is brighter than the sun.
They know the grief of man, without its wisdom;
    They sink in man's despair, without its calm;
Are slaves, without the liberty in Christdom,
    Are martyrs, by the pang without the palm:[5]
145 Are worn as if with age, yet unretrievingly
        The harvest of its memories cannot reap,—
Are orphans of the earthly love and heavenly.
        Let them weep! let them weep!

They look up with their pale and sunken faces,
150   And their look is dread to see,
For they mind you of their angels in high places,
        With eyes turned on Deity.
"How long," they say, "how long, O cruel nation,
    Will you stand, to move the world, on a child's heart,—
155 Stifle down with a mailed heel its palpitation,
        And tread onward to your throne amid the mart?
Our blood splashes upward, O gold-heaper,
        And your purple[6] shows your path!
But the child's sob in the silence curses deeper
160   Than the strong man in his wrath."

                                                1843

<hr />

4. I.e., we gain our sense of the possibilities of
God's love from our experience of love in the world.
5. Palm branch, symbol of victory.

6. Color associated with royalty and (in poetry)
with blood.

To George Sand[1]

A Desire

Thou large-brained woman and large-hearted man,
Self-called George Sand! whose soul, amid the lions
Of thy tumultuous senses, moans defiance
And answers roar for roar, as spirits can:
5   I would some mild miraculous thunder ran
Above the applauded circus,[2] in appliance
Of thine own nobler nature's strength and science,
Drawing two pinions, white as wings of swan,
From thy strong shoulders, to amaze the place
10   With holier light! that thou to woman's claim
And man's, mightst join beside the angel's grace
Of a pure genius sanctified from blame,
Till child and maiden pressed to thine embrace
To kiss upon thy lips a stainless fame.

1844

To George Sand

A Recognition

True genius, but true woman! dost deny
The woman's nature with a manly scorn,
And break away the gauds° and armlets worn   *ornaments*
By weaker women in captivity?
5   Ah, vain denial! that revolted cry
Is sobbed in by a woman's voice forlorn,—
Thy woman's hair, my sister, all unshorn
Floats back dishevelled strength in agony,
Disproving thy man's name: and while before
10   The world thou burnest in a poet-fire,
We see thy woman-heart beat evermore
Through the large flame. Beat purer, heart, and higher,
Till God unsex thee on the heavenly shore
Where unincarnate° spirits purely aspire!   *disembodied*

1844

---

1. Pen name of the French Romantic novelist Amandine-Aurore-Lucile Dudevant (1804–1876), famous for her unconventional ideas and behavior. Barrett Browning discovered Sand's writing while an invalid, "a prisoner," and asserts that Sand, together with Balzac, "kept the colour in my life." A defender of Sand's genius to less-sympathetic friends critical of Sand's morality, Barrett Browning writes to her friend Mary Russell Mitford (a novelist and dramatist) that Sand "is eloquent as a fallen angel . . . A true woman of genius!—but of a womanhood tired of itself, and scorned by *her,* while she bears it burning above her head."
2. A Roman spectacle that might include such entertainment as fights between humans and lions.

From Sonnets from the Portuguese

21

Say over again, and yet once over again,
That thou dost love me. Though the word repeated
Should seem "a cuckoo song,"[1] as thou dost treat it,
Remember, never to the hill or plain,
5   Valley and wood, without her cuckoo strain
Comes the fresh Spring in all her green completed.
Belovèd, I, amid the darkness greeted
By a doubtful spirit voice, in that doubt's pain
Cry, "Speak once more—thou lovest!" Who can fear
10 Too many stars, though each in heaven shall roll,
Too many flowers, though each shall crown the year?
Say thou dost love me, love me, love me—toll
The silver iterance!°—only minding, Dear,   *repetition*
To love me also in silence with thy soul.

22

When our two souls stand up erect and strong,
Face to face, silent, drawing nigh and nigher,
Until the lengthening wings break into fire
At either curvèd point—what bitter wrong
5   Can the earth do to us, that we should not long
Be here contented? Think. In mounting higher,
The angels would press on us and aspire
To drop some golden orb of perfect song
Into our deep, dear silence. Let us stay
10 Rather on earth, Belovèd,—where the unfit
Contrarious moods of men recoil away
And isolate pure spirits, and permit
A place to stand and love in for a day,
With darkness and the death-hour rounding it.

32

The first time that the sun rose on thine oath
To love me, I looked forward to the moon
To slacken all those bonds which seemed too soon
And quickly tied to make a lasting troth.
5   Quick-loving hearts, I thought, may quickly loathe;
And, looking on myself, I seemed not one
For such man's love!—more like an out-of-tune
Worn viol, a good singer would be wroth
To spoil his song with, and which, snatched in haste,
10 Is laid down at the first ill-sounding note.
I did not wrong myself so, but I placed
A wrong on *thee*. For perfect strains may float

1. The cuckoo has a repeating call.

'Neath master-hands, from instruments defaced—
And great souls, at one stroke, may do and dote.

43

How do I love thee? Let me count the ways.
I love thee to the depth and breadth and height
My soul can reach, when feeling out of sight
For the ends of Being and ideal Grace.
5   I love thee to the level of everyday's
Most quiet need, by sun and candlelight.
I love thee freely, as men strive for Right;
I love thee purely, as they turn from Praise.
I love thee with the passion put to use
10 In my old griefs, and with my childhood's faith.
I love thee with a love I seemed to lose
With my lost saints—I love thee with the breath,
Smiles, tears, of all my life!—and, if God choose,
I shall but love thee better after death.

1845–47   1850

The Runaway Slave at Pilgrim's Point[1]

I

I stand on the mark beside the shore
  Of the first white pilgrim's bended knee,
Where exile turned to ancestor,
  And God was thanked for liberty.
5 I have run through the night, my skin is as dark,
I bend my knee down on this mark:
  I look on the sky and the sea.

II

O pilgrim-souls, I speak to you!
  I see you come proud and slow
10 From the land of the spirits pale as dew
  And round me and round me ye go.
O pilgrims, I have gasped and run
All night long from the whips of one
  Who in your names works sin and woe!

III

15 And thus I thought that I would come
  And kneel here where ye knelt before,
And feel your souls around me hum
  In undertone to the ocean's roar;

1. Plymouth Rock, Massachusetts, where the Pilgrims landed in November 1620.

And lift my black face, my black hand,
20   Here, in your names, to curse this land
    Ye blessed in freedom's, evermore.

IV

I am black, I am black,
    And yet God made me, they say:
But if He did so, smiling back
25   He must have cast his work away
    Under the feet of his white creatures,
With a look of scorn, that the dusky features
    Might be trodden again to clay.

V

And yet He has made dark things
30   To be glad and merry as light:
There's a little dark bird sits and sings,
    There's a dark stream ripples out of sight,
And the dark frogs chant in the safe morass,°   *marsh*
And the sweetest stars are made to pass
35   O'er the face of the darkest night.

VI

But *we* who are dark, we are dark!
    Ah God, we have no stars!
About our souls in care and cark°   *anxiety*
    Our blackness shuts like prison-bars:
40   The poor souls crouch so far behind
    That never a comfort can they find
    By reaching through the prison-bars.

VII

Indeed we live beneath the sky,
    That great smooth Hand of God stretched out
45   On all His children fatherly,
    To save them from the dread and doubt
Which would be if, from this low place,
All opened straight up to His face
    Into the grand eternity.

VIII

50   And still God's sunshine and His frost,
    They make us hot, they make us cold,
As if we were not black and lost;
    And the beasts and birds, in wood and fold,
Do fear and take us for very men:
55   Could the whip-poor-will or the cat of the glen°   *bobcat*
    Look into my eyes and be bold?

IX

I am black, I am black!
   But, once, I laughed in girlish glee,
For one of my colour stood in the track
60   Where the drivers drove, and looked at me,
And tender and full was the look he gave—
Could a slave look *so* at another slave?—
   I look at the sky and the sea.

X

And from that hour our spirits grew
65   As free as if unsold, unbought:
Oh, strong enough, since we were two,
   To conquer the world, we thought.
The drivers drove us day by day;
We did not mind, we went one way,
70   And no better a freedom sought.

XI

In the sunny ground between the canes,°   *sugar canes*
   He said "I love you" as he passed;
When the shingle-roof rang sharp with the rains,
   I heard how he vowed it fast:
75 While others shook he smiled in the hut,
As he carved me a bowl of the cocoa-nut
   Through the roar of the hurricanes.

XII

I sang his name instead of a song,
   Over and over I sang his name,
80 Upward and downward I drew it along
   My various notes,—the same, the same!
I sang it low, that the slave-girls near
Might never guess, from aught they could hear,
   It was only a name—a name.

XIII

85 I look on the sky and the sea.
   We were two to love, and two to pray:
Yes, two, O God, who cried to Thee,
   Though nothing didst Thou say!
Coldly Thou sat'st behind the sun:
90 And now I cry who am but one,
   Thou wilt not speak to-day.

XIV

We were black, we were black,
   We had no claim to love and bliss,

What marvel if each went to wrack?°   *ruin*
95   They wrung my cold hands out of his,
They dragged him—where? I crawled to touch
His blood's mark in the dust . . . not much,
Ye pilgrim-souls, though plain as *this!*

XV

Wrong, followed by a deeper wrong!
100   Mere grief's too good for such as I:
So the white men brought the shame ere long
To strangle the sob of my agony.
They would not leave me for my dull
Wet eyes!—it was too merciful
105   To let me weep pure tears and die.

XVI

I am black, I am black!
I wore a child upon my breast,
An amulet that hung too slack,
And, in my unrest, could not rest:
110   Thus we went moaning, child and mother,
One to another, one to another,
Until all ended for the best.

XVII

For hark! I will tell you low, low,
I am black, you see,—
115   And the babe who lay on my bosom so,
Was far too white, too white for me;
As white as the ladies who scorned to pray
Beside me at church but yesterday,
Though my tears had washed a place for my knee.

XVIII

120   My own, own child! I could not bear
To look in his face, it was so white;
I covered him up with a kerchief there,
I covered his face in close and tight:
And he moaned and struggled, as well might be,
125   For the white child wanted his liberty—
Ha, ha! he wanted the master-right.

XIX

He moaned and beat with his head and feet,
His little feet that never grew;
He struck them out, as it was meet,
130   Against my heart to break it through:
I might have sung and made him mild,
But I dared not sing to the white-faced child
The only song I knew.

XX

I pulled the kerchief very close:
135   He could not see the sun, I swear,
More, then, alive, than now he does
   From between the roots of the mango . . . where?
I know where. Close! A child and mother
Do wrong to look at one another
140   When one is black and one is fair.

XXI

Why, in that single glance I had
   Of my child's face, . . . I tell you all,
I saw a look that made me mad!
   The *master's* look, that used to fall
145 On my soul like his lash . . . or worse!
And so, to save it from my curse,
   I twisted it round in my shawl.

XXII

And he moaned and trembled from foot to head,
   He shivered from head to foot;
150 Till after a time, he lay instead
   Too suddenly still and mute.
I felt, beside, a stiffening cold:
I dared to lift up just a fold,
   As in lifting a leaf of the mango-fruit.

XXIII

155 But *my* fruit . . . ha, ha!—there, had been
   (I laugh to think on 't at this hour!)
Your fine white angels (who have seen
   Nearest the secret of God's power)
And plucked my fruit to make them wine,
160 And sucked the soul of that child of mine
   As the humming-bird sucks the soul of the flower.

XXIV

Ha, ha, the trick of the angels white!
   They freed the white child's spirit so.
I said not a word, but day and night
165   I carried the body to and fro,
And it lay on my heart like a stone, as chill.
—The sun may shine out as much as he will:
   I am cold, though it happened a month ago.

XXV

From the white man's house, and the black man's hut,
170   I carried the little body on;

The forest's arms did round us shut,
  And silence through the trees did run:
They asked no question as I went,
They stood too high for astonishment,
175   They could see God sit on His throne.

XXVI

My little body, kerchiefed fast,
  I bore it on through the forest, on;
And when I felt it was tired at last,
  I scooped a hole beneath the moon:
180 Through the forest-tops the angels far,
With a white sharp finger from every star,
  Did point and mock at what was done.

XXVII

Yet when it was all done aright,—
  Earth, 'twixt me and my baby, strewed,—
185 All, changed to black earth,—nothing white,—
  A dark child in the dark!—ensued
Some comfort, and my heart grew young;
I sate down smiling there and sung
  The song I learnt in my maidenhood.

XXVIII

190 And thus we two were reconciled,
  The white child and black mother, thus;
For as I sang it soft and wild,
  The same song, more melodious,
Rose from the grave whereon I sate:
195 It was the dead child singing that,
  To join the souls of both of us.

XXIX

I look on the sea and the sky.
  Where the pilgrims' ships first anchored lay
The free sun rideth gloriously,
200   But the pilgrim-ghosts have slid away
Through the earliest streaks of the morn:
My face is black, but it glares with a scorn
  Which they dare not meet by day.

XXX

Ha!—in their stead, their hunter sons!
205   Ha, ha! they are on me—they hunt in a ring!
Keep off! I brave you all at once,
  I throw off your eyes like snakes that sting!
You have killed the black eagle at nest, I think:
Did you ever stand still in your triumph, and shrink
210   From the stroke of her wounded wing?

XXXI

(Man, drop that stone you dared to lift!—)
  I wish you who stand there five abreast,
Each, for his own wife's joy and gift,
  A little corpse as safely at rest
215 As mine in the mangoes!   Yes, but *she*
  May keep live babies on her knee,
    And sing the song she likes the best.

XXXII

I am not mad: I am black.
  I see you staring in my face—
220 I know you staring, shrinking back,
    Ye are born of the Washington-race,[2]
And this land is the free America,
  And this mark on my wrist—(I prove° what I say)   *demonstrate*
    Ropes tied me up here to the flogging-place.

XXXIII

225 You think I shrieked then?   Not a sound!
  I hung, as a gourd hangs in the sun;
I only cursed them all around
    As softly as I might have done
My very own child: from these sands
230 Up to the mountains, lift your hands,
    O slaves, and end what I begun!

XXXIV

Whips, curses; these must answer those!
  For in this UNION you have set
Two kinds of men in adverse rows,
235   Each loathing each; and all forget
The seven wounds in Christ's body fair,
  While HE sees gaping everywhere
    Our countless wounds that pay no debt.

XXXV

Our wounds are different.   Your white men
240   Are, after all, not gods indeed,
Nor able to make Christs again
    Do good with bleeding.   *We* who bleed
(Stand off!) we help not in our loss!
  We are too heavy for our cross,
245   And fall and crush you and your seed.

XXXVI

I fall, I swoon!   I look at the sky.
  The clouds are breaking on my brain;

2. I.e., the white race (the race of George Washington, the first president of the United States).

I am floated along, as if I should die
Of liberty's exquisite pain.
250   In the name of the white child waiting for me
In the death-dark where we may kiss and agree,
White men, I leave you all curse-free
In my broken heart's disdain!

1846   1848, 1850

From Aurora Leigh

From *Book 1*

[THE EDUCATION OF AURORA LEIGH][1]

Then, land!—then, England! oh, the frosty cliffs[2]
Looked cold upon me. Could I find a home
Among those mean red houses through the fog?
And when I heard my father's language first
255   From alien lips which had no kiss for mine
I wept aloud, then laughed, then wept, then wept,
And some one near me said the child was mad
Through much sea-sickness. The train swept us on:
Was this my father's England? the great isle?
260   The ground seemed cut up from the fellowship
Of verdure, field from field,[3] as man from man;
The skies themselves looked low and positive,
As almost you could touch them with a hand,
And dared to do it they were so far off
265   From God's celestial crystals;[4] all things blurred
And dull and vague. Did Shakespeare and his mates
Absorb the light here?—not a hill or stone
With heart to strike a radiant colour up
Or active outline on the indifferent air.

270   I think I see my father's sister stand
Upon the hall-step of her country-house
To give me welcome. She stood straight and calm,
Her somewhat narrow forehead braided tight
As if for taming accidental thoughts
275   From possible pulses;[5] brown hair pricked with gray
By frigid use of life (she was not old,
Although my father's elder by a year),
A nose drawn sharply, yet in delicate lines;
A close mild mouth, a little soured about
280   The ends, through speaking unrequited loves

---

1. Aurora Leigh, the only child of an Italian
mother and an English father, is raised in Italy by
her father after her mother's death when Aurora is
four years old. When she is thirteen her father also
dies, and the orphaned girl is sent to live in
England with her father's sister, who is to be
responsible for the girl's education.

2. The white chalk cliffs at Dover.
3. English fields were separated from each other
by hedgerows.
4. Perhaps a reference to the ancient notion that
the sky was composed of several crystalline spheres
orbiting the earth.
5. I.e., pulsation in her temples from excitement.

Or peradventure niggardly° half-truths;   *miserly*
Eyes of no colour,—once they might have smiled,
But never, never have forgot themselves
In smiling; cheeks, in which was yet a rose
285 Of perished summers, like a rose in a book,
Kept more for ruth° than pleasure,—if past bloom,   *remorse*
Past fading also.
                    She had lived, we'll say,
A harmless life, she called a virtuous life,
A quiet life, which was not life at all
290 (But that, she had not lived enough to know),
Between the vicar and the county squires,
The lord-lieutenant⁶ looking down sometimes
From the empyrean° to assure their souls   *highest heaven*
Against chance vulgarisms, and, in the abyss,
295 The apothecary,⁷ looked on once a year
To prove their soundness of humility.
The poor-club⁸ exercised her Christian gifts
Of knitting stockings, stitching petticoats,
Because we are of one flesh, after all,
300 And need one flannel⁹ (with a proper sense
Of difference in the quality)—and still
The book-club, guarded from your modern trick
Of shaking dangerous questions from the crease,¹
Preserved her intellectual.° She had lived   *intellectual gifts*
305 A sort of cage-bird life, born in a cage,
Accounting that to leap from perch to perch
Was act and joy enough for any bird.
Dear heaven, how silly are the things that live
In thickets, and eat berries!
                              I, alas,
310 A wild bird scarcely fledged, was brought to her cage,
And she was there to meet me. Very kind.
Bring the clean water, give out the fresh seed.

She stood upon the steps to welcome me,
Calm, in black garb. I clung about her neck,—
315 Young babes, who catch at every shred of wool
To draw the new light closer, catch and cling
Less blindly. In my ears my father's word
Hummed ignorantly, as the sea in shells,
"Love, love, my child." She, black there with my grief,
320 Might feel my love—she was his sister once—
I clung to her. A moment she seemed moved,
Kissed me with cold lips, suffered me to cling,
And drew me feebly through the hall into
The room she sat in.
                      There, with some strange spasm

6. Governor of the county.
7. Pharmacist, who in England at the time could
prescribe as well as sell medicine.
8. Club devoted to making things for the poor.
9. I.e., flannel petticoat.

1. The fold between two pages of a book, which
had to be cut to open the pages. Presumably, modern books were more apt to reveal dangerous material when the crease was cut.

325   Of pain and passion, she wrung loose my hands
     Imperiously, and held me at arm's length,
     And with two grey-steel naked-bladed eyes
     Searched through my face,—ay, stabbed it through and through,
     Through brows and cheeks and chin, as if to find
330   A wicked murderer in my innocent face,
     If not here, there perhaps. Then, drawing breath,
     She struggled for her ordinary calm—
     And missed it rather,—told me not to shrink,
     As if she had told me not to lie or swear,—
335   "She loved my father and would love me too
     As long as I deserved it." Very kind.

     I understood her meaning afterward;
     She thought to find my mother in my face,
     And questioned it for that. For she, my aunt,
340   Had loved my father truly, as she could,
     And hated, with the gall of gentle souls,
     My Tuscan[2] mother who had fooled away
     A wise man from wise courses, a good man
     From obvious duties, and, depriving her,
345   His sister, of the household precedence,
     Had wronged his tenants, robbed his native land,
     And made him mad, alike by life and death,
     In love and sorrow. She had pored° for years   *pored over*
     What sort of woman could be suitable
350   To her sort of hate, to entertain it with,
     And so, her very curiosity
     Became hate too, and all the idealism
     She ever used in life was used for hate,
     Till hate, so nourished, did exceed at last
355   The love from which it grew, in strength and heat,
     And wrinkled her smooth conscience with a sense
     Of disputable virtue (say not, sin)
     When Christian doctrine was enforced at church.

     And thus my father's sister was to me
360   My mother's hater. From that day she did
     Her duty to me (I appreciate it
     In her own word as spoken to herself),
     Her duty, in large measure, well pressed out
     But measured always. She was generous, bland,
365   More courteous than was tender, gave me still
     The first place,—as if fearful that God's saints
     Would look down suddenly and say "Herein
     You missed a point, I think, through lack of love."
     Alas, a mother never is afraid
370   Of speaking angerly to any child,
     Since love, she knows, is justified of love.
     And I, I was a good child on the whole,
     A meek and manageable child. Why not?
     I did not live, to have the faults of life:

2. From Tuscany, a region in central Italy.

375 There seemed more true life in my father's grave
Than in all England. Since *that* threw me off
Who fain would cleave (his latest will, they say,
Consigned me to his land), I only thought
Of lying quiet there where I was thrown
380 Like sea-weed on the rocks, and suffering her
To prick me to a pattern with her pin,[3]
Fibre from fibre, delicate leaf from leaf,
And dry out from my drowned anatomy
The last sea-salt left in me.
                    So it was.
385 I broke the copious curls upon my head
In braids, because she liked smooth-ordered hair.
I left off saying my sweet Tuscan words
Which still at any stirring of the heart
Came up to float across the English phrase
390 As lilies (*Bene* or *Che che*[4]), because
She liked my father's child to speak his tongue.
I learnt the collects[5] and the catechism,
The creeds, from Athanasius back to Nice,[6]
The Articles, the Tracts *against* the times[7]
395 (By no means Buonaventure's "Prick of Love"[8]),
And various popular synopses of
Inhuman doctrines never taught by John,[9]
Because she liked instructed piety.
I learnt my complement of classic French
400 (Kept pure of Balzac and neologism[1])
And German also, since she liked a range
Of liberal education,—tongues,° not books.   *languages*
I learnt a little algebra, a little
Of the mathematics,—brushed with extreme flounce[2]
405 The circle of the sciences, because
She misliked women who are frivolous.
I learnt the royal genealogies
Of Oviedo,[3] the internal laws
Of the Burmese empire,—by how many feet
410 Mount Chimborazo outsoars Teneriffe,
What navigable river joins itself
To Lara,[4] and what census of the year five
Was taken at Klagenfurt,[5]—because she liked
A general insight into useful facts.

3. As in embroidery.
4. No, no, indeed (Italian). *"Bene"*: it is well (Italian).
5. Seasonal opening prayers in the Anglican Church service.
6. Articles of Christian faith such as those proclaimed by Athanasius, an Egyptian theologian of the 4th century C.E., and at the early Church council held at Nicaea in the same era.
7. In the 1830s leaders of the conservative High Church party, such as John Henry Newman, had published *Tracts for the Times*, which expounded arguments against efforts by liberals to modernize the Anglican Church. Aurora's version of the title is hence ironic. "Articles": the thirty-nine articles are the principles of faith of the Church of England.

8. St. Bonaventure's doctrine that the power of the heart to love leads to higher illumination than the power of the mind to reason.
9. I.e., the author of the Gospel.
1. A new word or expression. Honoré de Balzac (1799–1850), a French novelist whose realism made him improper reading for a young English lady of the 19th century.
2. An ornamental edge to a skirt. "Extreme": outermost.
3. Spanish historian (16th century), who wrote a book on the genealogies of Spanish noblemen.
4. A town in Spain on the river Arlanza. Mount Chimborazo is one of the highest peaks of the Andes. Teneriffe is a mountain in the Canary Islands.
5. A town in Austria.

415   I learnt much music,—such as would have been
As quite impossible in Johnson's day[6]
As still it might be wished—fine sleights of hand
And unimagined fingering, shuffling off
The hearer's soul through hurricanes of notes
420   To a noisy Tophet;° and I drew . . . costumes   *hell*
From French engravings, nereids° neatly draped   *sea nymphs*
(With smirks of simmering godship): I washed in[7]
Landscapes from nature (rather say, washed out).
I danced the polka and Cellarius,[8]
425   Spun glass, stuffed birds, and modeled flowers in wax,
Because she liked accomplishments in girls.
I read a score of books on womanhood
To prove, if women do not think at all,
They may teach thinking (to a maiden aunt
430   Or else the author),—books that boldly assert
Their right of comprehending husband's talk
When not too deep, and even of answering
With pretty "may it please you," or "so it is,"—
Their rapid insight and fine aptitude,
435   Particular worth and general missionariness,
As long as they keep quiet by the fire
And never say "no" when the world says "ay,"
For that is fatal,—their angelic reach
Of virtue, chiefly used to sit and darn,
440   And fatten household sinners,—their, in brief,
Potential faculty in everything
Of abdicating power in it: she owned
She liked a woman to be womanly,
And English women, she thanked God and sighed
445   (Some people always sigh in thanking God),
Were models to the universe. And last
I learnt cross-stitch,[9] because she did not like
To see me wear the night with empty hands
A-doing nothing. So, my shepherdess
450   Was something after all (the pastoral saints
Be praised for't), leaning lovelorn with pink eyes
To match her shoes, when I mistook the silks;
Her head uncrushed by that round weight of hat
So strangely similar to the tortoise shell
Which slew the tragic poet.[1]
455   By the way,
The works of women are symbolical.
We sew, sew, prick our fingers, dull our sight,
Producing what? A pair of slippers, sir,
To put on when you're weary—or a stool
460   To stumble over and vex you . . . "curse that stool!"

6. Allusion to the story about Samuel Johnson (1709–1784), who, when informed of the difficulty of a piece of music a young lady was playing, replied, "I would it had been impossible."
7. As in painting with watercolors.
8. A kind of waltz.

9. I.e., embroidery.
1. According to tradition, the Greek playwright Aeschylus was killed by an eagle who, mistaking his bald head for a stone, dropped a tortoise on it to break the shell.

Or else at best, a cushion, where you lean
And sleep, and dream of something we are not
But would be for your sake. Alas, alas!
This hurts most, this—that, after all, we are paid
The worth of our work, perhaps.
465   In looking down
Those years of education (to return)
I wonder if Brinvilliers suffered more
In the water-torture[2] . . . flood succeeding flood
To drench the incapable throat and split the veins . . .
470 Than I did. Certain of your feebler souls
Go out° in such a process; many pine   *die*
To a sick, inodorous light; my own endured:
I had relations in the Unseen, and drew
The elemental nutriment and heat
475 From nature, as earth feels the sun at nights,
Or as a babe sucks surely in the dark.
I kept the life thrust on me, on the outside
Of the inner life with all its ample room
For heart and lungs, for will and intellect,
480 Inviolable by conventions. God,
I thank thee for that grace of thine!
                    At first
I felt no life which was not patience,—did
The thing she bade me, without heed to a thing
Beyond it, sat in just the chair she placed,
485 With back against the window, to exclude
The sight of the great lime-tree on the lawn,[3]
Which seemed to have come on purpose from the woods
To bring the house a message,—ay, and walked
Demurely in her carpeted low rooms,
490 As if I should not, harkening my own steps,
Misdoubt° I was alive. I read her books,   *doubt*
Was civil to her cousin, Romney Leigh,
Gave ear to her vicar, tea to her visitors,
And heard them whisper, when I changed a cup
495 (I blushed for joy at that),—"The Italian child,
For all her blue eyes and her quiet ways,
Thrives ill in England: she is paler yet
Than when we came the last time; she will die."

From *Book 2*

[AURORA'S ASPIRATIONS][4]

Times followed one another. Came a morn
I stood upon the brink of twenty years,
And looked before and after, as I stood

2. Marie Marguerite, Marquise de Brinvilliers, a celebrated criminal who was beheaded in 1676, was tortured by having water forced down her throat.
3. Cf. Coleridge's "This Lime-Tree Bower My Prison" (1800), in which the lime tree becomes the

vehicle of a realization that Nature never deserts the wise and pure even when they seem to be cut off from her most beautiful vistas.
4. Stifled by her aunt's oppressive conventionality, Aurora has found three sources of comfort and

Woman and artist,—either incomplete,
5   Both credulous of completion. There I held
The whole creation in my little cup,
And smiled with thirsty lips before I drank
"Good health to you and me, sweet neighbour mine,
And all these peoples."
                        I was glad, that day;
10   The June was in me, with its multitudes
Of nightingales all singing in the dark,
And rosebuds reddening where the calyx⁵ split.
I felt so young, so strong, so sure of God!
So glad, I could not choose be very wise!
15   And, old at twenty, was inclined to pull
My childhood backward in a childish jest
To see the face of't once more, and farewell!
In which fantastic mood I bounded forth
At early morning,—would not wait so long
20   As even to snatch my bonnet by the strings,
But, brushing a green trail across the lawn
With my gown in the dew, took will and away
Among the acacias of the shrubberies,
To fly my fancies in the open air
25   And keep° my birthday, till my aunt awoke   *observe*
To stop good dreams. Meanwhile I murmured on
As honeyed bees keep humming to themselves,
"The worthiest poets have remained uncrowned
Till death has bleached their foreheads to the bone;
30   And so with me it must be unless I prove
Unworthy of the grand adversity,
And certainly I would not fail so much.
What, therefore, if I crown myself to-day
In sport, not pride, to learn the feel of it,
35   Before my brows be numbed as Dante's own
To all the tender pricking of such leaves?
Such leaves! what leaves?"
                            I pulled the branches down
To choose from.
                "Not the bay!⁶ I choose no bay
(The fates deny us if we are overbold),
40   Nor myrtle—which means chiefly love; and love
Is something awful which one dares not touch
So early o' mornings. This verbena strains
The point of passionate fragrance; and hard by,
This guelder-rose,° at far too slight a beck   *cranberry bush*
45   Of the wind, will toss about her flower-apples.
Ah—there's my choice,—that ivy on the wall,
That headlong ivy! not a leaf will grow

---

inspiration: poetic aspirations, fostered by the discovery of her father's library; the beauty of the natural world; and the intellectual companionship of
her cousin Romney Leigh, an idealistic young man
troubled by the misery of the poor and inspired by
contemporary notions of social reform.

5. The protective outer leaves covering a flower or
bud.
6. Laurel, associated with poetry and prophecy by
the ancient Greeks, who also crowned the athletic
victors in the Pythian games with a laurel wreath.

But thinking of a wreath. Large leaves, smooth leaves,
Serrated like my vines, and half as green.
50 I like such ivy, bold to leap a height
'Twas strong to climb; as good to grow on graves
As twist about a thyrsus;[7] pretty too
(And that's not ill) when twisted round a comb."
Thus speaking to myself, half singing it,
55 Because some thoughts are fashioned like a bell
To ring with once being touched, I drew a wreath
Drenched, blinding me with dew, across my brow,
And fastening it behind so, turning faced
. . . My public!—cousin Romney—with a mouth
Twice graver than his eyes.
60   I stood there fixed,—
My arms up, like the caryatid,[8] sole
Of some abolished temple, helplessly
Persistent in a gesture which derides
A former purpose. Yet my blush was flame,
As if from flax, not stone.
65   "Aurora Leigh,
The earliest of Auroras!"[9]
                                          Hand stretched out
I clasped, as shipwrecked men will clasp a hand,
Indifferent to the sort of palm. The tide
Had caught me at my pastime, writing down
70 My foolish name too near upon the sea
Which drowned me with a blush as foolish. "You,
My cousin!"
                    The smile died out in his eyes
And dropped upon his lips, a cold dead weight,
For just a moment, "Here's a book I found!
75 No name writ on it—poems, by the form;
Some Greek upon the margin,—lady's Greek
Without the accents.[1] Read it? Not a word.
I saw at once the thing had witchcraft in't,
Whereof the reading calls up dangerous spirits:
I rather bring it to the witch."
80   "My book.
You found it" . . .
                         "In the hollow by the stream
That beech leans down into—of which you said
The Oread in it has a Naiad's[2] heart
And pines for waters."
                              "Thank you."
                                          "Thanks to *you*
85 My cousin! that I have seen you not too much
Witch, scholar, poet, dreamer, and the rest,

7. Staff twined with ivy that was carried, according to Greek myth, by Dionysus, god of wine and fertility.
8. Classical column in the form of a draped female figure.
9. Dawns; from Aurora, Roman goddess of the dawn.
1. Romney is gently mocking Aurora for her apparent ignorance of the complex rules of classical Greek accentuation.
2. Water nymph's. "Oread": tree nymph.

To be a woman also."
                    With a glance
The smile rose in his eyes again and touched
The ivy on my forehead, light as air.
90 I answered gravely "Poets needs must be
Or° men or women—more's the pity."   *either*
                    "Ah,
But men, and still less women, happily,
Scarce need be poets. Keep to the green wreath,
Since even dreaming of the stone and bronze
95 Brings headaches, pretty cousin, and defiles
The clean white morning dresses."
                    "So you judge!
Because I love the beautiful I must
Love pleasure chiefly, and be overcharged
For ease and whiteness! well, you know the world,
100 And only miss your cousin,'tis not much.
But learn this; I would rather take my part
With God's Dead, who afford to walk in white
Yet spread His glory, than keep quiet here
And gather up my feet from even a step
105 For fear to soil my gown in so much dust.
I choose to walk at all risks.—Here, if heads
That hold a rhythmic thought, must ache perforce,
For my part I choose headaches,—and to-day's
My birthday,"
                    "Dear Aurora, choose instead
To cure them. You have balsams."°   *soothing cures*
110   "I perceive.
The headache is too noble for my sex.
You think the heartache would sound decenter,
Since that's the woman's special, proper ache,
And altogether tolerable, except
115 To a woman."

[AURORA'S REJECTION OF ROMNEY]³

                    There he glowed on me
With all his face and eyes. "No other help?"
Said he—"no more than so?"
345   "What help?" I asked.
"You'd scorn my help,—as Nature's self, you say,
Has scorned to put her music in my mouth
Because a woman's. Do you now turn round
And ask for what a woman cannot give?"

350 "For what she only can, I turn and ask,"
He answered, catching up my hands in his,

3. Romney and Aurora have been arguing about whether art, particularly a young woman's poetry, is useful in a world that, according to Romney, is full of human suffering. Romney claims that women have no ability to generalize from their personal experiences and are, therefore, doomed to be trivial poets and ineffectual social reformers. Aurora is quick to agree that to be merely an inferior poet would be intolerable to her, but while she admires Romney's lofty concern for humanity, she remains untempted to join forces with him.

And dropping on me from his high-eaved brow
The full weight of his soul,—"I ask for love,
And that, she can; for life in fellowship
355 Through bitter duties—that, I know she can;
For wifehood—will she?"
                              "Now," I said, "may God
Be witness 'twixt us two!" and with the word,
Meseemed⁴ I floated into a sudden light
Above his stature,—"am I proved too weak
360 To stand alone, yet strong enough to bear
Such leaners on my shoulder? poor to think,
Yet rich enough to sympathise with thought?
Incompetent to sing, as blackbirds can,
Yet competent to love, like HIM?"
                                        I paused;
365 Perhaps I darkened, as the lighthouse will
That turns upon the sea. "It's always so.
Anything does for a wife."
                              "Aurora, dear,
And dearly honoured,"—he pressed in at once
With eager utterance,—"you translate me ill.
370 I do not contradict my thought of you
Which is most reverent, with another thought
Found less so. If your sex is weak for art
(And I, who said so, did but honour you
By using truth in courtship), it is strong
375 For life and duty. Place your fecund heart
In mine, and let us blossom for the world
That wants love's colour in the grey of time.
My talk, meanwhile, is arid to you, ay,
Since all my talk can only set you where
380 You look down coldly on the arena-heaps
Of headless bodies, shapeless, indistinct!
The Judgment-Angel scarce would find his way
Through such a heap of generalised distress
To the individual man with lips and eyes,
385 Much less Aurora. Ah, my sweet, come down,
And hand in hand we'll go where yours shall touch
These victims, one by one! till, one by one,
The formless, nameless trunk of every man
Shall seem to wear a head with hair you know,
390 And every woman catch your mother's face
To melt you into passion."
                              "I am a girl,"
I answered slowly; "you do well to name
My mother's face. Though far too early, alas,
God's hand did interpose 'twixt it and me,
395 I know so much of love as used to shine
In that face and another. Just so much;
No more indeed at all. I have not seen
So much love since, I pray you pardon me,

4. It seemed to me.

As answers even to make a marriage with
400   In this cold land of England. What you love
Is not a woman, Romney, but a cause:
You want a helpmate, not a mistress, sir,
A wife to help your ends,—in her no end.
Your cause is noble, your ends excellent,
405   But I, being most unworthy of these and that,
Do otherwise conceive of love. Farewell."

"Farewell, Aurora? you reject me thus?"
He said.
        "Sir, you were married long ago.
You have a wife already whom you love,
410   Your social theory. Bless you both, I say.
For my part, I am scarcely meek enough
To be the handmaid of a lawful spouse.
Do I look a Hagar,[5] think you?"
                    "So you jest."

"Nay, so, I speak in earnest," I replied.
415   "You treat of° marriage too much like, at least,   *talk about*
A chief apostle: you would bear with you
A wife . . . a sister . . . shall we speak it out?
A sister of charity."
                "Then, must it be
Indeed farewell? And was I so far wrong
420   In hope and in illusion, when I took
The woman to be nobler than the man,
Yourself the noblest woman, in the use
And comprehension of what love is,—love,
That generates the likeness of itself
425   Through all heroic duties? so far wrong,
In saying bluntly, venturing truth on love,
'Come, human creature, love and work with me,'—
Instead of 'Lady, thou art wondrous fair,
'And, where the Graces[6] walk before, the Muse
430   'Will follow at the lightning of their eyes,
'And where the Muse walks, lovers need to creep:
'Turn round and love me, or I die of love.' "

With quiet indignation I broke in.
"You misconceive the question like a man,
435   Who sees a woman as the complement
Of his sex merely. You forget too much
That every creature, female as the male,
Stands single in responsible act and thought
As also in birth and death. Whoever says
440   To a loyal woman, 'Love and work with me,'
Will get fair answers if the work and love,

---

5. In Genesis 16 Sarah's maidservant, who bore a child, Ishmael, by Sarah's husband, Abraham.

6. In classical mythology goddesses who personified beauty and charm.

Being good themselves, are good for her—the best *if they are given*
She was born for. Women of a softer mood, *work so ted for them*
Surprised by men when scarcely awake to life,
445 Will sometimes only hear the first word, love, *good or bad, go in for love 2*
And catch up with it any kind of work, *are given hard lives*
Indifferent, so that dear love go with it.
I do not blame such women, though, for love,
They pick much oakum;[7] earth's fanatics make
450 Too frequently heaven's saints. But *me* your work
Is not the best for,—nor your love the best,
Nor able to commend the kind of work
For love's sake merely. Ah, you force me, sir,
To be overbold in speaking of myself:
455 I too have my vocation,—work to do,
The heavens and earth have set me since I changed
My father's face for theirs, and, though your world
Were twice as wretched as you represent,
Most serious work, most necessary work
460 As any of the economists'. Reform,
Make trade a Christian possibility,
And individual right no general wrong;
Wipe out earth's furrows of the Thine and Mine,
And leave one green for men to play at bowls,[8]
465 With innings for them all! . . . What then, indeed,
If mortals are not greater by the head
Than any of their prosperities? what then,
Unless the artist keep up open roads
Betwixt the seen and unseen,—bursting through
470 The best of your conventions with his best,
The speakable, imaginable best
God bids him speak, to prove what lies beyond
Both speech and imagination? A starved man
Exceeds a fat beast: we'll not barter, sir,
475 The beautiful for barley.—And, even so,
I hold you will not compass your poor ends
Of barley-feeding and material ease,
Without a poet's individualism
To work your universal. It takes a soul,
480 To move a body: it takes a high-souled man,
To move the masses, even to a cleaner stye:
It takes the ideal, to blow a hair's-breadth off
The dust of the actual.—Ah, your Fouriers[9] failed,
Because not poets enough to understand
485 That life develops from within.——For me,
Perhaps I am not worthy, as you say,
Of work like this: perhaps a woman's soul
Aspires, and not creates: yet we aspire,
And yet I'll try out your perhaps, sir,

7. Fiber derived by untwisting (picking) old rope,
a task frequently assigned to workhouse inmates.
8. A game of skill played on a smooth lawn with
weighted wooden balls.

9. I.e., utopian thinkers; François-Marie-Charles
Fourier (1772–1837), a French political theorist
who advocated communal property as a basis for
social harmony.

490 And if I fail . . . why, burn me up my straw[1]
Like other false works—I'll not ask for grace;
Your scorn is better, cousin Romney. I
Who love my art, would never wish it lower
To suit my stature. I may love my art.
495 You'll grant that even a woman may love art,
Seeing that to waste true love on anything
Is womanly, past question."

From *Book 5*

[POETS AND THE PRESENT AGE]

The critics say that epics have died out
140 With Agamemnon and the goat-nursed gods;[2]
I'll not believe it. I could never deem,
As Payne Knight[3] did (the mythic mountaineer
Who travelled higher than he was born to live,
And showed sometimes the goitre[4] in his throat
145 Discoursing of an image seen through fog),
That Homer's heroes measured twelve feet high.
They were but men:—his Helen's hair turned grey
Like any plain Miss Smith's who wears a front;[5]
And Hector's infant whimpered at a plume[6]
150 As yours last Friday at a turkey-cock.
All actual heroes are essential men,
And all men possible heroes: every age,
Heroic in proportions, double-faced,
Looks backward and before, expects a morn
And claims an epos.°   *epic poem*
155   Ay, but every age
Appears to souls who live in't (ask Carlyle)[7]
Most unheroic. Ours, for instance, ours:
The thinkers scout it,° and the poets abound   *dismiss it scornfully*
Who scorn to touch it with a finger-tip:
160 A pewter age,[8]—mixed metal, silver-washed;
An age of scum, spooned off the richer past,
An age of patches for old gaberdines,°   *coats*
An age of mere transition,[9] meaning nought
Except that what succeeds° must shame it quite   *follows*
165 If God please. That's wrong thinking, to my mind,

1. I.e., destroy my poetry. See 1 Corinthians 3.12–15.
2. Zeus, the ruler of the ancient Greek gods, was nursed by a goat. Agamemnon: the commander of the Greeks in the Trojan War.
3. Richard Payne Knight (1750–1824), a classical philologist who claimed that Lord Elgin had wasted his labor taking the marble friezes from the Parthenon in Greece to England because the marbles were not all Greek.
4. A disease often contracted in high mountain areas because of the low iodine content of the water.
5. A piece of false hair worn over the forehead by women.

6. In the *Iliad*, book 6, the Trojan hero Hector reaches for his infant son, but the child clings to his nurse, frightened of his father's helmet and crest.
7. In *Heroes, Hero-Worship, and the Heroic in History* (1841), Carlyle argues that the present age needs a renewed perception of the heroic.
8. Allusion to the convention, which originates in Hesiod (Greek poet, ca. 8th century B.C.E), of describing civilization's decline through a succession of ages named for increasingly less precious materials: i.e., the Golden Age, the Silver Age, the Bronze Age.
9. In *The Spirit of the Age* (1831), John Stuart Mill calls the present age "an age of transition."

And wrong thoughts make poor poems.
                                        Every age,
Through being beheld too close, is ill-discerned
By those who have not lived past it. We'll suppose
Mount Athos carved, as Alexander schemed,
170   To some colossal statue of a man.[1]
The peasants, gathering brushwood in his ear,
Had guessed as little as the browsing goats
Of form or feature of humanity
Up there,—in fact, had travelled five miles off
175   Or ere the giant image broke on them,
Full human profile, nose and chin distinct,
Mouth, muttering rhythms of silence up the sky
And fed at evening with the blood of suns;
Grand torso,—hand, that flung perpetually
180   The largesse of a silver river down
To all the country pastures. 'Tis even thus
With times we live in,—evermore too great
To be apprehended near.
                                  But poets should
Exert a double vision; should have eyes
185   To see near things as comprehensively
As if afar they took their point of sight,
And distant things as intimately deep
As if they touched them. Let us strive for this.
I do distrust the poet who discerns
190   No character or glory in his times,
And trundles back his soul five hundred years,
Past moat and drawbridge, into a castle-court,
To sing—oh, not of lizard or of toad
Alive i' the ditch there,—'twere excusable,
195   But of some black chief, half knight, half sheep-lifter,°   *sheep stealer*
Some beauteous dame, half chattel and half queen,
As dead as must be, for the greater part,
The poems made on their chivalric bones;
And that's no wonder: death inherits death.

200   Nay, if there's room for poets in this world
A little overgrown (I think there is),
Their sole work is to represent the age,
Their age, not Charlemagne's,[2]—this live, throbbing age,
That brawls, cheats, maddens, calculates, aspires,
205   And spends more passion, more heroic heat,
Betwixt the mirrors of its drawing-rooms,
Than Roland[3] with his knights at Roncesvalles.
To flinch from modern varnish, coat or flounce,
Cry out for togas and the picturesque,

1. Deinocrates, a Macedonian architect (4th century B.C.E.), is said to have suggested to Alexander the Great that Mount Athos be carved into the statue of a conqueror with a city in his left hand and a basin in his right, where all the waters of the region could be collected and used to water the pasture lands below.

2. Frankish conqueror (742–814), who created a European empire.
3. Legendary medieval hero, whose adventures are told in the epic poem *Chanson de Roland* (11th century); his last battle is fought at Roncesvalles, a Spanish village.

210 Is fatal,—foolish too. King Arthur's self
Was commonplace to Lady Guenever;
And Camelot to minstrels seemed as flat
As Fleet Street⁴ to our poets.
Never flinch,
But still, unscrupulously epic, catch
215 Upon the burning lava of a song
The full-veined, heaving, double-breasted Age:
That, when the next shall come, the men of that
May touch the impress° with reverent hand, and say   *impression*
"Behold,—behold the paps° we all have sucked!   *breasts*
220 This bosom seems to beat still, or at least
It sets ours beating: this is living art,
Which thus presents and thus records true life."

1853–56   1857

Mother and Poet¹

(*Turin, After News from Gaeta, 1861*)

I

DEAD! One of them shot by the sea in the east,
And one of them shot in the west by the sea.
Dead! both my boys! When you sit at the feast
And are wanting a great song for Italy free,
5   Let none look at *me!*

2

Yet I was a poetess only last year,
And good at my art, for a woman, men said;
But *this* woman, *this,* who is agonised here,
—The east sea and west sea rhyme on in her head
10   For ever instead.

3

What art can a woman be good at? Oh, vain!
What art *is* she good at, but hurting her breast
With the milk-teeth of babes, and a smile at the pain?
Ah boys, how you hurt! you were strong as you pressed,
15   And I proud, by that test.

4

What art's for a woman? To hold on her knees
Both darlings! to feel all their arms round her throat,
Cling, strangle a little! to sew by degrees
And 'broider the long-clothes° and neat little coat;   *infant's clothing*
20   To dream and to doat.

5

To teach them . . . It stings there! *I* made them indeed
  Speak plain the word *country*. *I* taught them, no doubt,
That a country's a thing men should die for at need.
  I prated of liberty, rights, and about
25   The tyrant cast out.

6

And when their eyes flashed . . . O my beautiful eyes! . . .
  I exulted; nay, let them go forth at the wheels
Of the guns, and denied not. But then the surprise
  When one sits quite alone! Then one weeps, then one kneels!
30   God, how the house feels!

7

At first, happy news came, in gay letters moiled°   *moistened*
  With my kisses,—of camp-life and glory, and how
They both loved me; and, soon coming home to be spoiled
  In return would fan off every fly from my brow
35   With their green laurel-bough.²

8

Then was triumph at Turin: "Ancona was free!"
  And some one came out of the cheers in the street,
With a face pale as stone, to say something to me.
  My Guido was dead! I fell down at his feet,
40   While they cheered in the street.

9

I bore it; friends soothed me; my grief looked sublime
  As the ransom of Italy. One boy remained
To be leant on and walked with, recalling the time
  When the first grew immortal, while both of us strained
45   To the height he had gained.

10

And letters still came, shorter, sadder, more strong,
  Writ now but in one hand, "I was not to faint,—
One loved me for two—would be with me ere long:
  And *Viva l'Italia!*—*he* died for, our saint,
50   Who forbids our complaint."

11

My Nanni would add, "he was safe, and aware
  Of a presence that turned off the balls,°—was imprest   *cannonballs*
It was Guido himself, who knew what I could bear,
  And how 'twas impossible, quite dispossessed
55   To live on for the rest."³

12

On which, without pause, up the telegraph line
  Swept smoothly the next news from Gaeta:—*Shot.*

2. A laurel crown is the conventional mark of a poet's fame.   3. I.e., that she could survive if both sons died.

Tell his mother. Ah, ah, "his," "their" mother,—not "mine,"
No voice says *"My* mother" again to me. What!
60   You think Guido forgot?

13
Are souls straight° so happy that, dizzy with Heaven,   *immediately*
They drop earth's affections, conceive not of woe?
I think not. Themselves were too lately forgiven
Through THAT Love and Sorrow which reconciled so
65   The Above and Below.

14
O Christ of the five wounds, who look'dst through the dark
To the face of thy mother! consider, I pray,
How we common mothers stand desolate, mark,
Whose sons, not being Christs, die with eyes turned away
70   And no last word to say!

15
Both boys dead? but that's out of nature. We all
Have been patriots, yet each house must always keep one.
'Twere imbecile, hewing out roads to a wall;
And, when Italy's made, for what end is it done
75   If we have not a son?

16
Ah, ah, ah! when Gaeta's taken, what then?
When the fair wicked queen sits no more at her sport
Of the fire-balls of death crashing souls out of men?
When the guns of Cavalli[4] with final retort
80   Have cut the game short?

17
When Venice and Rome keep their new jubilee,[5]
When your flag takes all heaven for its white, green, and red,
When *you* have your country from mountain to sea,
When King Victor has Italy's crown on his head,
85   (And *I* have my Dead)—

18
What then? Do not mock me. Ah, ring your bells low,
And burn your lights faintly! *My* country is *there,*
Above the star pricked by the last peak of snow:
My Italy's THERE, with my brave civic Pair,
90   To disfranchise despair!

19
Forgive me. Some women bear children in strength,
And bite back the cry of their pain in self-scorn;
But the birth-pangs of nations will wring us at length

4. The general commanding the siege of Gaeta. "The fair wicked queen": Maria of Bavaria, wife of Francis II, the last ruler of the Neapolitan government, who retreated to Gaeta.
5. The celebration when they too will have been
united with the rest of Italy under King Victor Emmanuel II (1820–1878; reigned, 1861–78). In 1861, when the poem was written, they were the two cities that were still independent of the new state.

Into wail such as this—and we sit on forlorn
95   When the man-child is born.

20

Dead! One of them shot by the sea in the east,
And one of them shot in the west by the sea.
Both! both my boys! If in keeping the feast
You want a great song for your Italy free,
100   Let none look at *me*!

1861   1862

ALFRED, LORD TENNYSON
1809–1892

In his own lifetime Tennyson was the most popular of poets; his works, from 1850 onward, occupied a significant space on the bookshelves of almost every family of readers in England and the United States. Such popularity inevitably provoked a reaction in the decades following his death. In the course of repudiating their Victorian predecessors, the Edwardians and Georgians established the fashion of making fun of Tennyson's achievements. Samuel Butler (1835–1902), who anticipated early-twentieth-century tastes, has a characteristic entry in his *Notebooks:* "Talking it over, we agreed that Blake was no good because he learnt Italian at sixty in order to study Dante, and we knew Dante was no good because he was so fond of Virgil, and Virgil was no good because Tennyson ran [followed] him, and as for Tennyson—well, Tennyson goes without saying." Butler's flippant dismissal expresses an attitude that is no longer fashionable: Tennyson's stature as one of the major poets of the English language seems uncontroversial today.

Like his poetry, Tennyson's life and character have been reassessed in recent times. To many of his contemporaries he seemed a remote wizard secure in his laureate's robes, a man whose life had been sheltered, marred only by the loss of his best friend in youth. During much of his career Tennyson may have been isolated, but his was not a sheltered life in the real sense of the word. His childhood home, a parsonage, was a household dominated by frictions and loyalties and broodings over ancestral inheritances, in which the children showed marked strains of instability and eccentricity.

Alfred Tennyson was the fourth son in a family of twelve children. One of his brothers had to be confined to an insane asylum for life; another was long addicted to opium; another had violent quarrels with his father, the Reverend Dr. George Tennyson. This father, a man of considerable learning, had been born the eldest son of a wealthy landowner and had, therefore, expected to be heir to his family's estates. Instead he was disinherited in favor of his younger brother and had to make his own livelihood by joining the clergy, a profession that he disliked. After George Tennyson had settled in a small rectory in Somersby, his brooding sense of dissatisfaction led to increasingly violent bouts of drunkenness; he was nevertheless able to act as his sons' tutor in classical and modern languages to prepare them for entering the university.

Before leaving this strange household for Cambridge, Tennyson had already demonstrated a flair for writing verse—precocious exercises in the manner of John Milton or Byron or the Elizabethan dramatists. He had even published a volume in 1827, in collaboration with his brother Charles, *Poems by Two Brothers.* This feat drew him to the attention of a group of gifted undergraduates at Cambridge, "the Apostles," who encouraged him to devote his life to poetry. Up until that time the young man had known scarcely anyone outside the circle of his own family. Despite his massive frame and powerful physique, he was painfully shy, and the friendships he found at Cambridge as well as the intellectual and political discussions in which he participated gave him confidence and widened his horizons as a poet. The most important of these friendships was with Arthur Hallam, a leader of the Apostles, who later became engaged to Tennyson's sister Emily. Hallam's sudden death, in 1833, seemed an overwhelming calamity to his friend. Not only the long elegy *In Memoriam* (1850) but many of Tennyson's other poems are tributes to this early friendship.

Tennyson's career at Cambridge was interrupted and finally broken off in 1831 by family dissensions and financial need, and he returned home to study and practice the craft of poetry. His early volumes (1830 and 1832) were attacked as "obscure" or "affected" by some of the reviewers. Tennyson suffered acutely under hostile criticism, but he also profited from it. His 1842 volume demonstrated a remarkable leap forward, and in 1850 he at last attained fame and full critical recognition with *In Memoriam*. In the same year he became poet laureate in succession to William Wordsworth. The struggle during the previous twenty years had been made especially painful by the long postponement of his marriage to Emily Sellwood, whom he had loved since 1836 but could not marry, because of poverty, until 1850.

His life thereafter was a comfortable one. He was as popular as Byron had been, and the earnings from his poetry (sometimes exceeding £10,000 a year) enabled him to purchase a house in the country and to enjoy the kind of seclusion he liked. His notoriety was enhanced, like that of Bernard Shaw and Walt Whitman, by his colorful appearance. Huge and shaggy in cloak and broad-brimmed hat, gruff in manner, he impressed everyone as what is called a "character." The pioneering photographer Julia Cameron, who took magnificent portraits of him, called him "the most beautiful old man on earth." Like Dylan Thomas in the twentieth century, Tennyson had a booming voice that electrified listeners when he read his poetry, "mouthing out his hollow o's and a's, / Deep-chested music," as he would covertly describe himself in an early version of his Arthurian epic. Moreover, for many Victorian readers, he seemed not only a great poetical phrase maker and a striking individual but also a wise man whose occasional pronouncements on politics or world affairs represented the national voice itself. In 1884 he accepted a peerage. In 1892 he died and was buried in Westminster Abbey.

It is often said that success was bad for Tennyson and that after *In Memoriam* his poetic power seriously declined. That in his last forty-two years certain of his mannerisms became accentuated is true. One of the difficulties of his dignified blank verse was, as he said himself, that it is hard to describe commonplace objects and "at the same time to retain poetical elevation." This difficulty is evident, for example, in *Enoch Arden* (1864), a long blank verse narrative of everyday life in a fishing village, in which a basketful of fish is ornately described as "Enoch's ocean spoil / In ocean-smelling osier." In his later poems dealing with national affairs, there is also an increased shrillness of tone—a mannerism accentuated by Tennyson's realizing that he, like Charles Dickens, had a vast public behind him to back up his pronouncements.

It would be unwise, however, to ignore all of Tennyson's later productions. In 1855 he published his experimental monologue *Maud*, in which he presents an alienated hero who feels great bitterness toward society. In 1859 appeared four books of his *Idylls of the King*, a large-scale epic that occupied most of his energies in the second half of his career. The *Idylls* uses the body of Arthurian legend to construct a vision of civilization's rise and fall. In this civilization women both inspire men's highest efforts and sow the seeds of those efforts' destruction. The *Idylls* provides Tennyson's most extensive social vision, one that typifies much social thought of the age in its concern with medieval ideals of social community, heroism, and courtly love and in its despairing sense of the cycles of historical change.

W. H. Auden stated that Tennyson had "the finest ear, perhaps, of any English poet." The interesting point is that Tennyson did not "have" such an ear: he developed it. Studies of the original versions of his poems in the 1830 and 1832 volumes demonstrate how hard he worked at his craftsmanship. Like Geoffrey Chaucer or Alexander Pope or John Keats, Tennyson studied his predecessors assiduously to perfect his technique. Anyone wanting to learn the traditional craft of English verse can study profitably the various stages of revision that poems such as "The Lotos-Eaters" were subjected to by this painstaking and artful poet. Some lines written in 1988 by the American poet Karl Shapiro effectively characterize Tennyson's accomplishments in these areas:

> Long-lived, the very image of English Poet,
> Whose songs still break out tears in the generations,
> Whose poetry for practitioners still astounds,
> Who crafted his life and letters like a watch.

Tennyson's early poetry shows other skills as well. One of these was a capacity for linking scenery to states of mind. As early as 1835 J. S. Mill identified the special kind of scene painting to be found in poems such as "Mariana" (1830): "not the power of producing that rather vapid species of composition usually termed descriptive poetry . . . but the power of *creating* scenery, in keeping with some state of human feeling so fitted to it as to be the embodied symbol of it, and to summon up the state of feeling itself, with a force not to be surpassed by anything but reality."

The state of feeling to which Tennyson was most intensely drawn was a melancholy isolation, often portrayed through the consciousness of an abandoned woman, as in "Mariana." Tennyson's absorption with such emotions in his early poetry evoked considerable criticism. His friend R. C. Trench warned him, "Tennyson, we cannot live in Art," and Mill urged him to "cultivate, and with no half devotion, philosophy as well as poetry." Advice of this kind Tennyson was already predisposed to heed. The death of Hallam and the religious uncertainties that he had himself experienced, together with his own extensive study of writings by geologists, astronomers, and biologists, led him to confront many of the religious issues that bewildered his and later generations. The result was *In Memoriam*, a long elegy written over a period of seventeen years, embodying the poet's reflections on the relation of human beings to God and to nature.

Tennyson's exploration of these vast subjects prompted some readers, such as T. H. Huxley, to consider him an intellectual giant, a thinker who had mastered the scientific thought of his century and fully confronted the issues it raised. Others dismissed Tennyson, in this phase, as a lightweight. Auden went so far as to call him the "stupidest" of English poets. He added, "There was little about melancholia that he didn't know; there was little else that he did." Perhaps T. S. Eliot's evaluation of *In Memoriam* is the more thought-provoking: the poem, he wrote, is remarkable not "because of the quality of its faith but because of the quality of its doubt." Tennyson's mind was slow, ponderous, brooding; for the composition of *In Memoriam* such qualities of mind were assets, not liabilities. Very different are the poems Tennyson writes of events of the moment over which his thoughts and feelings have had no time to brood. Several of these are what he himself called "newspaper verse." They are letters to the editor in effect, with the heat we expect of such productions. "The Charge of the Light Brigade" (1854), inspired by a report in the London *Times* of a cavalry charge at Balaclava during the Crimean War, is one of the most fascinating of his productions in this category.

Tennyson's poems of contemporary events were inevitably popular in his own day. So too were those poems in which, as in "Locksley Hall" (1842), he dipped into the future. The technological changes wrought by Victorian inventors and engineers fascinated him, sometimes giving him an exultant assurance of human progress. At other times the horrors of industrialism's by-products in the slums, the persistence of barbarity and bloodshed, and the greed of the newly rich destroyed his hopes that humanity was evolving upward. In the final book of *Idylls of the King* (1869), Arthur laments that his "realm / Reels back into the beast": Tennyson was similarly haunted by the possibility of retrogression.

For despite Tennyson's fascination with technological developments, he was essentially a poet of the countryside, a man whose whole being was conditioned by the recurring rhythms of rural rather than urban life. He had the country dweller's awareness of traditional roots and sense of the past. It is appropriate that so many of his poems are about the past, not about the present or future. Tennyson said that "the words 'far, far away' had always a strange charm" for him, even in his childhood; he was haunted by what he called "the passion of the past." The past became his great theme, whether it be his own past (such as the times he shared with Hallam), his country's past (as in *Idylls of the King*), or the past of the world itself, as expressed in these lines from *In Memoriam*:

> There rolls the deep where grew the tree.
> O earth, what changes hast thou seen!
> There where the long street roars hath been
> The stillness of the central sea.

Though Tennyson more often is inspired by the recorded past of humankind, he is the first major writer to express this awareness of the vast extent of geological time that has haunted human consciousness since Victorian scientists exposed the history of the earth's crust.

Mariana[1]

"Mariana in the moated grange."
Measure for Measure

With blackest moss the flower-plots
  Were thickly crusted, one and all;
The rusted nails fell from the knots
  That held the pear to the gable wall.
5 The broken sheds looked sad and strange:
  Unlifted was the clinking latch;
Weeded° and worn the ancient thatch   *full of weeds*
  Upon the lonely moated grange.
    She only said, "My life is dreary,
10   He cometh not," she said;
    She said, "I am aweary, aweary,
      I would that I were dead!"

Her tears fell with the dews at even;
  Her tears fell ere the dews were dried;
15 She could not look on the sweet heaven,
  Either at morn or eventide.
After the flitting of the bats,
  When thickest dark did trance° the sky,   *cross*
She drew her casement curtain by,
20 And glanced athwart° the glooming flats.   *across*
    She only said, "The night is dreary,
      He cometh not," she said;

---

1. Mariana, in Shakespeare's *Measure for Measure* 3.1.255, waits in a grange (an outlying farmhouse) for her lover, who has deserted her.

She said, "I am aweary, aweary,
　　I would that I were dead!"

25　Upon the middle of the night,
　　Waking she heard the nightfowl crow;
　　The cock sung out an hour ere light;
　　From the dark fen° the oxen's low　　　　　　*marshland*
　　Came to her; without hope of change,
30　In sleep she seemed to walk forlorn,
　　Till cold winds woke the gray-eyed morn
　　About the lonely moated grange.
　　　　She only said, "The day is dreary,
　　　　He cometh not," she said;
35　　She said, "I am aweary, aweary,
　　　　I would that I were dead!"

　　About a stonecast° from the wall　　　　　　*stone's throw*
　　A sluice with blackened waters slept,
　　And o'er it many, round and small,
40　The clustered marish-mosses² crept.
　　Hard° by a poplar shook alway,　　　　　　*close*
　　All silver-green with gnarlèd bark:
　　For leagues no other tree did mark
　　The level waste, the rounding gray.
45　　She only said, "My life is dreary,
　　　　He cometh not," she said;
　　　　She said, "I am aweary, aweary,
　　　　I would that I were dead!"

　　And ever when the moon was low,
50　And the shrill winds were up and away,
　　In the white curtain, to and fro,
　　She saw the gusty shadow sway.
　　But when the moon was very low,
　　And wild winds bound within their cell,³
55　The shadow of the poplar fell
　　Upon her bed, across her brow.
　　　　She only said, "The night is dreary,
　　　　He cometh not," she said;
　　　　She said, "I am aweary, aweary,
60　　I would that I were dead!"

　　All day within the dreamy house,
　　The doors upon their hinges creaked;
　　The blue fly sung in the pane; the mouse
　　Behind the moldering wainscot° shrieked,　　*wooden paneling*
65　Or from the crevice peered about.
　　Old faces glimmered through the doors,
　　Old footsteps trod the upper floors,
　　Old voices called her from without.
　　　　She only said, "My life is dreary,

2. The little marsh-moss lumps that float on the
surface of water [Tennyson's note].

3. According to Virgil, Aeolus, god of winds, kept
the winds imprisoned in a cave (*Aeneid* 1.50–59).

70   He cometh not," she said;
         She said, "I am aweary, aweary,
             I would that I were dead!"

         The sparrow's chirrup on the roof,
             The slow clock ticking, and the sound
75   Which to the wooing wind aloof
             The poplar made, did all confound
         Her sense; but most she loathed the hour
             When the thick-moted sunbeam lay
             Athwart the chambers, and the day
80   Was sloping toward his western bower.
             Then, said she, "I am very dreary,
             He will not come," she said;
         She wept, "I am aweary, aweary,
             Oh God, that I were dead!"

                                                        1830

[handwritten margin note:] 1.
An artist, having a life outside, uncorrupted from the world, women muses, art making.

2. feminist view: women isolated, tennyson interested in women position, women in the house, isolated. if she tries to go out she will die, double bind.

The Lady of Shalott[1]

Part 1

On either side the river lie
Long fields of barley and of rye,
That clothe the wold° and meet the sky;   *rolling plain*
And through the field the road runs by
5   To many-towered Camelot;
And up and down the people go,
Gazing where the lilies blow°   *bloom*
Round an island there below,
         The island of Shalott.

10   Willows whiten, aspens quiver,
Little breezes dusk and shiver
Through the wave that runs forever
By the island in the river
         Flowing down to Camelot.

[handwritten margin note:] people say → river = time. whatev

15   Four gray walls, and four gray towers,
Overlook a space of flowers,
And the silent isle imbowers
         The Lady of Shalott.

By the margin, willow-veiled,
20   Slide the heavy barges trailed
By slow horses; and unhailed
The shallop° flitteth silken-sailed   *light open boat*

1. The story of the Lady of Shalott is a version of the tale of "Elaine the fair maid of Astolat," which appears in book 18 of Sir Thomas Malory's *Morte Darthur* (1470). Tennyson, however, claimed he did not know Malory's version when he wrote his draft in 1832, identifying his source as a 14th-century tale about "la Damigella di Scalot": "I met the story first in some Italian *novelle:* but the web, mirror, island, etc., were my own. Indeed, I doubt whether I should ever have put it in that shape if I had been aware of the Maid of Astolat in *Morte Arthur*." Tennyson subjected this poem to numerous revisions over the years.

Skimming down to Camelot:
But who hath seen her wave her hand?
25   Or at the casement seen her stand?
Or is she known in all the land,
        The Lady of Shalott?

Only reapers, reaping early
In among the bearded barley,
30   Hear a song that echoes cheerly
From the river winding clearly,
        Down to towered Camelot;
And by the moon the reaper weary,
Piling sheaves in uplands airy,
35   Listening, whispers " 'Tis the fairy
        Lady of Shalott."

Part 2

There she weaves by night and day
A magic web with colors gay.
She has heard a whisper say,
40   A curse is on her if she stay°   *pause*
        To look down to Camelot.
She knows not what the curse may be,
And so she weaveth steadily,
And little other care hath she,
45   The Lady of Shalott.

And moving through a mirror clear[2]
That hangs before her all the year,
Shadows of the world appear.
There she sees the highway near
50   Winding down to Camelot;
There the river eddy whirls,
And there the surly village churls,°   *peasants*
And the red cloaks of market girls,
        Pass onward from Shalott.

55   Sometimes a troop of damsels glad,
An abbot on an ambling pad,°   *easy-paced horse*
Sometimes a curly shepherd lad,
Or long-haired page in crimson clad,
        Goes by to towered Camelot;
60   And sometimes through the mirror blue
The knights come riding two and two:
She hath no loyal knight and true,
        The Lady of Shalott.

But in her web she still delights
65   To weave the mirror's magic sights,
For often through the silent nights

---

2. Weavers used mirrors, placed facing their looms, to see the progress of their work.

A funeral, with plumes and lights
    And music, went to Camelot;
Or when the moon was overhead,
70 Came two young lovers lately wed:
"I am half sick of shadows," said
    The Lady of Shalott.

Part 3

A bowshot from her bower eaves,
He rode between the barley sheaves,
75 The sun came dazzling through the leaves,
And flamed upon the brazen greaves[3]
    Of bold Sir Lancelot.
A red-cross knight forever kneeled
To a lady in his shield,
80 That sparkled on the yellow field,
    Beside remote Shalott.

The gemmy bridle glittered free,
Like to some branch of stars we see
Hung in the golden Galaxy.
85 The bridle bells rang merrily
    As he rode down to Camelot;
And from his blazoned baldric[4] slung
A mighty silver bugle hung,
And as he rode his armor rung,
90   Beside remote Shalott.

All in the blue unclouded weather
Thick-jeweled shone the saddle leather,
The helmet and the helmet-feather
Burned like one burning flame together,
95   As he rode down to Camelot;
As often through the purple night,
Below the starry clusters bright,
Some bearded meteor, trailing light,
    Moves over still Shalott.

100 His broad clear brow in sunlight glowed;
On burnished hooves his war horse trode;
From underneath his helmet flowed
His coal-black curls as on he rode,
    As he rode down to Camelot.
105 From the bank and from the river
He flashed into the crystal mirror,
"Tirra lirra,"[5] by the river
    Sang Sir Lancelot.

She left the web, she left the loom,
110 She made three paces through the room,

---

3. Armor protecting the leg below the knee.
4. A belt worn diagonally from one shoulder to the opposite hip, supporting a sword or bugle. "Bla-

zoned": painted with a heraldic device.
5. Cf. Autolycus's song in Shakespeare's *The Winter's Tale* 4.3.9.

She saw the water lily bloom,
She saw the helmet and the plume,
    She looked down to Camelot.
Out flew the web and floated wide;
115 The mirror cracked from side to side;
"The curse is come upon me," cried
    The Lady of Shalott.

Part 4

In the stormy east wind straining,
The pale yellow woods were waning,
120 The broad stream in his banks complaining,
Heavily the low sky raining
    Over towered Camelot;
Down she came and found a boat
Beneath a willow left afloat,
125 And round about the prow she wrote
    The Lady of Shalott.

And down the river's dim expanse
Like some bold seër in a trance,
Seeing all his own mischance—
130 With a glassy countenance
    Did she look to Camelot.
And at the closing of the day
She loosed the chain, and down she lay;
The broad stream bore her far away,
135   The Lady of Shalott.

Lying, robed in snowy white
That loosely flew to left and right—
The leaves upon her falling light—
Through the noises of the night
140   She floated down to Camelot;
And as the boat-head wound along
The willowy hills and fields among,
They heard her singing her last song,
    The Lady of Shalott.

145 Heard a carol, mournful, holy,
Chanted loudly, chanted lowly,
Till her blood was frozen slowly,
And her eyes were darkened wholly,[6]
    Turned to towered Camelot.
150 For ere she reached upon the tide
The first house by the waterside,
Singing in her song she died,
    The Lady of Shalott.

---

6. In the 1832 version this line read: "And her smooth face sharpened slowly." George Eliot informed Tennyson that she preferred the earlier version.

This 1857 engraving, created by Dante Gabriel Rossetti for publisher Edward Moxon's illustrated collection of Tennyson's poetry, shows Lancelot musing "a little space" on the Lady of Shalott in her boat.

> Under tower and balcony,
> By garden wall and gallery,
> A gleaming shape she floated by,
> Dead-pale between the houses high,
>   Silent into Camelot.
> Out upon the wharfs they came,
> Knight and burgher, lord and dame,
> And round the prow they read her name,
>   *The Lady of Shalott.*
>
> Who is this? and what is here?
> And in the lighted palace near
> Died the sound of royal cheer;
> And they crossed themselves for fear,
>   All the knights at Camelot:
> But Lancelot mused a little space;
> He said, "She has a lovely face;
> God in his mercy lend her grace,
>   The Lady of Shalott."

155

160

165

170

1831–32   1832, 1842

The Lotos-Eaters[1]

"Courage!" he[2] said, and pointed toward the land,
"This mounting wave will roll us shoreward soon."
In the afternoon they came unto a land[3]
In which it seemèd always afternoon.
5 All round the coast the languid air did swoon,
Breathing like one that hath a weary dream.
Full-faced above the valley stood the moon;
And, like a downward smoke, the slender stream
Along the cliff to fall and pause and fall did seem.

10 A land of streams! some, like a downward smoke,
Slow-dropping veils of thinnest lawn,° did go;   *fine thin linen*
And some through wavering lights and shadows broke,
Rolling a slumbrous sheet of foam below.
They saw the gleaming river seaward flow
15 From the inner land; far off, three mountaintops
Three silent pinnacles of aged snow,
Stood sunset-flushed; and, dewed with showery drops,
Up-clomb° the shadowy pine above the woven copse.   *climbed up*

The charmèd sunset lingered low adown
20 In the red West; through mountain clefts the dale
Was seen far inland, and the yellow down[4]
Bordered with palm, and many a winding vale
And meadow, set with slender galingale;[5]
A land where all things always seemed the same!
25 And round about the keel with faces pale,
Dark faces pale against that rosy flame,
The mild-eyed melancholy Lotos-eaters came.

Branches they bore of that enchanted stem,
Laden with flower and fruit, whereof they gave
30 To each, but whoso did receive of them
And taste, to him the gushing of the wave
Far far away did seem to mourn and rave
On alien shores; and if his fellow spake,
His voice was thin, as voices from the grave;

---

1. Based on a short episode from the *Odyssey* (9.82–97) in which the weary Greek veterans of the Trojan War are tempted by a desire to abandon their long voyage homeward. As Odysseus later reported: "On the tenth day we set foot on the land of the lotos-eaters who eat a flowering food. . . . I sent forth certain of my company [who] . . . mixed with the men of the lotos-eaters who gave . . . them of the lotos to taste. Now whosoever of them did eat the honey-sweet fruit of the lotos had no more wish to bring tidings nor to come back, but there he chose to abide . . . forgetful of his homeward way."
   Tennyson expands Homer's brief account into an elaborate picture of weariness and the desire for rest and death. The descriptions in the first stanzas are similar to Spenser's *The Faerie Queene* (1590) 2.6 and employ the same stanza form. The final section derives, in part, from Lucretius's conception of the gods in *De Rerum Natura* (ca. 55 B.C.E.).
2. Odysseus (or Ulysses).
3. The repetition of "land" from line 1 was deliberate; Tennyson said that this "no rhyme" was "lazier" in its effect. This technique of repeating words, phrases, and sounds continues; cf. "afternoon" (lines 3–4) and the rhyming of "adown" and "down" (lines 19 and 21).
4. An open plain on high ground.
5. A plant resembling tall coarse grass.

35 And deep-asleep he seemed, yet all awake,
And music in his ears his beating heart did make.

They sat them down upon the yellow sand,
Between the sun and moon upon the shore;
And sweet it was to dream of Fatherland,
40 Of child, and wife, and slave; but evermore
Most weary seemed the sea, weary the oar,
Weary the wandering fields of barren foam,
Then some one said, "We will return no more";
And all at once they sang, "Our island home°   Ithaca
45 Is far beyond the wave; we will no longer roam."

Choric Song[6]

I

There is sweet music here that softer falls
Than petals from blown roses on the grass,
Or night-dews on still waters between walls
Of shadowy granite, in a gleaming pass;
50 Music that gentlier on the spirit lies,
Than tired[7] eyelids upon tired eyes;
Music that brings sweet sleep down from the blissful skies.
Here are cool mosses deep,
And through the moss the ivies creep,
55 And in the stream the long-leaved flowers weep,
And from the craggy ledge the poppy hangs in sleep.

2

Why are we weighed upon with heaviness,
And utterly consumed with sharp distress,
While all things else have rest from weariness?
60 All things have rest: why should we toil alone,
We only toil, who are the first of things,
And make perpetual moan,
Still from one sorrow to another thrown;
Nor ever fold our wings,
65 And cease from wanderings,
Nor steep our brows in slumber's holy balm;
Nor harken what the inner spirit sings,
"There is no joy but calm!"—
Why should we only toil, the roof and crown of things?[8]

3

70 Lo! in the middle of the wood,
The folded leaf is wooed from out the bud
With winds upon the branch, and there
Grows green and broad, and takes no care,

6. Sung by the mariners.
7. Tennyson wanted the word to be pronounced as *tie-yerd* rather than *tier'd* or *tire-èd*, thus "making the word neither monosyllable or disyllabic, but a dreamy child of the two."

8. Cf. *The Faerie Queene* 2.6.17: "Why then dost thou, O man, that of them all / Art Lord, and eke of nature Sovereaine, / Wilfully . . . wast thy joyous houres in needlesse paine?"

Sun-steeped at noon, and in the moon
75 Nightly dew-fed; and turning yellow
Falls, and floats adown the air.
Lo! sweetened with summer light,
The full-juiced apple, waxing over-mellow,
Drops in a silent autumn night.
80 All its allotted length of days
The flower ripens in its place,
Ripens and fades, and falls, and hath no toil,
Fast-rooted in the fruitful soil.

4

Hateful is the dark blue sky,
85 Vaulted o'er the dark blue sea.
Death is the end of life; ah, why
Should life all labor be?
Let us alone. Time driveth onward fast,
And in a little while our lips are dumb.
90 Let us alone. What is it that will last?
All things are taken from us, and become
Portions and parcels of the dreadful past.
Let us alone. What pleasure can we have
To war with evil? Is there any peace
95 In ever climbing up the climbing wave?
All things have rest, and ripen toward the grave
In silence—ripen, fall, and cease:
Give us long rest or death, dark death, or dreamful ease.[9]

5

How sweet it were, hearing the downward stream,
100 With half-shut eyes ever to seem
Falling asleep in a half-dream!
To dream and dream, like yonder amber light,
Which will not leave the myrrh-bush[1] on the height;
To hear each other's whispered speech;
105 Eating the Lotos day by day,
To watch the crisping° ripples on the beach,   *curling*
And tender curving lines of creamy spray;
To lend our hearts and spirits wholly
To the influence of mild-minded melancholy;
110 To muse and brood and live again in memory,
With those old faces of our infancy
Heaped over with a mound of grass,
Two handfuls of white dust, shut in an urn of brass!

6

Dear is the memory of our wedded lives,
115 And dear the last embraces of our wives
And their warm tears; but all hath suffered change;
For surely now our household hearths are cold,

---

9. Cf. *The Faerie Queen* 1.9.40: "Sleepe after
toyle, port after stormie seas, / Ease after warre,
death after life does greatly please."

1. Myrrh, a resin used in perfume and incense, is
associated with sweetness and comfort.

Our sons inherit us,° our looks are strange,   *succeed us as our heirs*
And we should come like ghosts to trouble joy.
120 Or else the island princes² overbold
Have eat our substance, and the minstrel sings
Before them of the ten years' war in Troy,
And our great deeds, as half-forgotten things.
Is there confusion in the little isle?
125 Let what is broken so remain.
The Gods are hard to reconcile;
'Tis hard to settle order once again.
There *is* confusion worse than death,
Trouble on trouble, pain on pain,
130 Long labor unto aged breath,
Sore tasks to hearts worn out by many wars
And eyes grown dim with gazing on the pilot-stars.

7

But, propped on beds of amaranth and moly,³
How sweet—while warm airs lull us, blowing lowly—
135 With half-dropped eyelid still,
Beneath a heaven dark and holy,
To watch the long bright river drawing slowly
His waters from the purple hill—
To hear the dewy echoes calling
140 From cave to cave through the thick-twined vine—
To watch the emerald-colored water falling
Through many a woven acanthus⁴ wreath divine!
Only to hear and see the far-off sparkling brine,
Only to hear were sweet, stretched out beneath the pine.

8

145 The Lotos blooms below the barren peak,
The Lotos blows by every winding creek;
All day the wind breathes low with mellower tone;
Through every hollow cave and alley lone
Round and round the spicy downs the yellow Lotos dust is blown.
150 We have had enough of action, and of motion we,
Rolled to starboard, rolled to larboard, when the surge was seething free,
Where the wallowing monster spouted his foam-fountains in the sea.
Let us swear an oath, and keep it with an equal mind,
In the hollow Lotos land to live and lie reclined
155 On the hills like Gods together, careless of mankind.
For they lie beside their nectar, and the bolts° are hurled   *thunderbolts*
Far below them in the valleys, and the clouds are lightly curled
Round their golden houses, girdled with the gleaming world;
Where they smile in secret, looking over wasted lands,
160 Blight and famine, plague and earthquake, roaring deeps and fiery sands,
Clanging fights, and flaming towns, and sinking ships, and praying hands.
But they smile, they find a music centred in a doleful song
Steaming up, a lamentation and an ancient tale of wrong,

2. The suitors of Penelope, Odysseus's wife; during his long absence they have settled themselves as guests in his hall as they pressure her to remarry.
3. A flower with magical properties mentioned by Homer. "Amaranth": a legendary unfading flower.
4. A plant resembling a thistle. Its leaves were the model for ornaments on Corinthian columns.

Like a tale of little meaning though the words are strong;
165 Chanted from an ill-used race of men that cleave the soil,
Sow the seed, and reap the harvest with enduring toil,
Storing yearly little dues of wheat, and wine and oil;
Till they perish and they suffer—some, 'tis whispered—down in hell
Suffer endless anguish, others in Elysian valleys dwell,
170 Resting weary limbs at last on beds of asphodel.⁵
Surely, surely, slumber is more sweet than toil, the shore
Than labor in the deep mid-ocean, wind and wave and oar;
O, rest ye, brother mariners, we will not wander more.

1832, 1842

Ulysses¹

It little profits that an idle king,
By this still hearth, among these barren crags,
Matched with an aged wife, I mete and dole
Unequal laws² unto a savage race,
5 That hoard, and sleep, and feed,³ and know not me.
I cannot rest from travel; I will drink
Life to the lees. All times I have enjoyed
Greatly, have suffered greatly, both with those
That loved me, and alone; on shore, and when
10 Through scudding drifts the rainy Hyades⁴
Vexed the dim sea. I am become a name;
For always roaming with a hungry heart
Much have I seen and known—cities of men
And manners, climates, councils, governments,
15 Myself not least, but honored of them all—
And drunk delight of battle with my peers,
Far on the ringing plains of windy Troy,
I am a part of all that I have met;
Yet all experience is an arch wherethrough
20 Gleams that untraveled world whose margin fades
Forever and forever when I move.
How dull it is to pause, to make an end,
To rust unburnished, not to shine in use!⁵

5. A yellow lilylike flower supposed to grow in Elysium—in classical mythology a paradise for heroes favored by the gods.
1. According to Dante, after the fall of Troy, Ulysses never returned to his island home of Ithaca. Instead he persuaded some of his followers to seek new experiences by a voyage of exploration westward out beyond the Strait of Gibraltar. In his inspiring speech to his aging crew he said: "Consider your origin: you were not made to live as brutes, but to pursue virtue and knowledge" (*Inferno* 26). Tennyson modified Dante's 14th-century version by combining it with Homer's account (*Odyssey* 19–24). Thus Tennyson has Ulysses make his speech in Ithaca some time after he has returned home; reunited with his wife, Penelope, and his son, Telemachus; and, presumably, resumed his administrative responsibilities

involved in governing his kingdom.
Tennyson stated that this poem expressed his own "need of going forward and braving the struggle of life" after the death of Arthur Hallam.
2. Measure out rewards and punishments.
3. Cf. Shakespeare's *Hamlet* 4.4.9.23–25: "What is a man / If his chief good . . . Be but to sleep and feed?—a beast, no more."
4. A group of stars (literally, "rainy ones") in the constellation Taurus; their heliacal rising and setting generally coincided with the season of heavy rains. "Scudding drifts": driving showers of spray and rain.
5. Cf. Ulysses' speech in Shakespeare's *Troilus and Cressida* 3.3.144–47: "Perseverance, dear my lord, / Keeps honour bright. To have done is to hang / Quite out of fashion, like a rusty mail / In monumental mock'ry."

As though to breathe were life! Life piled on life
25 Were all too little, and of one to me
Little remains; but every hour is saved
From that eternal silence, something more,
A bringer of new things; and vile it were
For some three suns to store and hoard myself,
30 And this gray spirit yearning in desire
To follow knowledge like a sinking star,
Beyond the utmost bound of human thought.

This is my son, mine own Telemachus,
To whom I leave the scepter and the isle—
35 Well-loved of me, discerning to fulfill
This labor, by slow prudence to make mild
A rugged people, and through soft degrees
Subdue them to the useful and the good.
Most blameless is he, centered in the sphere
40 Of common duties, decent not to fail
In offices of tenderness, and pay
Meet° adoration to my household gods,   suitable, fitting
When I am gone. He works his work, I mine.

There lies the port; the vessel puffs her sail;
45 There gloom the dark, broad seas. My mariners,
Souls that have toiled, and wrought, and thought with me—
That ever with a frolic welcome took
The thunder and the sunshine,[6] and opposed
Free hearts, free foreheads[7]—you and I are old;
50 Old age hath yet his honor and his toil.
Death closes all; but something ere the end,
Some work of noble note, may yet be done,
Not unbecoming men that strove with Gods.
The lights begin to twinkle from the rocks;
55 The long day wanes; the slow moon climbs; the deep
Moans round with many voices. Come, my friends,
'Tis not too late to seek a newer world.
Push off, and sitting well in order smite
The sounding furrows; for my purpose holds
60 To sail beyond the sunset, and the baths[8]
Of all the western stars, until I die.
It may be that the gulfs will wash us down;
It may be we shall touch the Happy Isles,[9]
And see the great Achilles,[1] whom we knew.
65 Though much is taken, much abides; and though
We are not now that strength which in old days
Moved earth and heaven, that which we are, we are—
One equal temper of heroic hearts,

---

6. I.e., varying fortunes.
7. Confidence.
8. The outer ocean or river that the Greeks believed surrounded the flat circle of the earth; the stars descended into it.
9. In Greek myth the Islands of the Blessed, a par-

adise of perpetual summer, located in the far-western ocean, where the virtuous and heroes dwell forever after death (often identified with Elysium).
1. The greatest of the Greek warriors at Troy, where he was killed.

Made weak by time and fate, but strong in will
70 To strive, to seek, to find, and not to yield.

1833   1842

Tithonus[1]

The woods decay, the woods decay and fall,
The vapors weep their burthen to the ground,
Man comes and tills the field and lies beneath,
And after many a summer dies the swan.[2]
5   Me only cruel immortality
Consumes; I wither slowly in thine arms,[3]
Here at the quiet limit of the world,
A white-haired shadow roaming like a dream
The ever-silent spaces of the East,
10 Far-folded mists, and gleaming halls of morn.
    Alas! for this gray shadow, once a man—
So glorious in his beauty and thy choice,
Who madest him thy chosen, that he seemed
To his great heart none other than a God!
15 I asked thee, "Give me immortality."
Then didst thou grant mine asking with a smile,
Like wealthy men who care not how they give.
But thy strong Hours indignant worked their wills,
And beat me down and marred and wasted me,
20 And though they could not end me, left me maimed
To dwell in presence of immortal youth,
Immortal age beside immortal youth,
And all I was in ashes. Can thy love,
Thy beauty, make amends, though even now,
25 Close over us, the silver star,[4] thy guide,
Shines in those tremulous eyes that fill with tears
To hear me? Let me go; take back thy gift.
Why should a man desire in any way
To vary from the kindly race of men,
30 Or pass beyond the goal of ordinance[5]
Where all should pause, as is most meet for all?
    A soft air fans the cloud apart; there comes
A glimpse of that dark world where I was born.
Once more the old mysterious glimmer steals
35 From thy pure brows, and from thy shoulders pure,
And bosom beating with a heart renewed.
Thy cheek begins to redden through the gloom,
Thy sweet eyes brighten slowly close to mine,
Ere yet they blind the stars, and the wild team[6]

1. A Trojan prince loved by the goddess of the
dawn, Eos or Aurora, who obtained for him the gift
of living forever but neglected to ask for the gift of
everlasting youth.
2. Some species of swans live for at least fifty
years.

3. Aurora's arms.
4. The morning star that precedes the dawn.
5. What is decreed or ordained as human destiny.
6. The horses that draw Aurora's chariot into the
sky at daybreak.

40 Which love thee, yearning for thy yoke, arise,
And shake the darkness from their loosened manes,
And beat the twilight into flakes of fire.
Lo! ever thus thou growest beautiful
In silence, then before thine answer given
45 Departest, and thy tears are on my cheek.
Why wilt thou ever scare me with thy tears,
And make me tremble lest a saying learnt,
In days far-off, on that dark earth, be true?
"The Gods themselves cannot recall their gifts."
50 Ay me! ay me! with what another heart
In days far-off, and with what other eyes
I used to watch—if I be he that watched—
The lucid outline forming round thee; saw
The dim curls kindle into sunny rings;
55 Changed with thy mystic change, and felt my blood
Glow with the glow that slowly crimsoned all
Thy presence and thy portals, while I lay,
Mouth, forehead, eyelids, growing dewy-warm
With kisses balmier than half-opening buds
60 Of April, and could hear the lips that kissed
Whispering I knew not what of wild and sweet,
Like that strange song I heard Apollo sing,
While Ilion like a mist rose into towers.[7]
Yet hold me not forever in thine East;
65 How can my nature longer mix with thine?
Coldly thy rosy shadows bathe me, cold
Are all thy lights, and cold my wrinkled feet
Upon thy glimmering thresholds, when the steam
Floats up from those dim fields about the homes
70 Of happy men that have the power to die,
And grassy barrows° of the happier dead.   *burial mounds*
Release me, and restore me to the ground.
Thou seest all things, thou wilt see my grave;
Thou wilt renew thy beauty morn by morn,
75 I earth in earth forget these empty courts,
And thee returning on thy silver wheels.

1833, 1859   1860

Break, Break, Break

Break, break, break,
    On thy cold gray stones, O Sea!
And I would that my tongue could utter
    The thoughts that arise in me.

5   O, well for the fisherman's boy,
    That he shouts with his sister at play!

---

7. The walls of Troy ("Ilion") were supposed to have been built to the strains of the god Apollo's music.

O, well for the sailor lad,
That he sings in his boat on the bay!

And the stately ships go on
10   To their haven under the hill;
But O for the touch of a vanished hand,
And the sound of a voice that is still!

Break, break, break,
At the foot of thy crags, O Sea!
15   But the tender grace of a day that is dead
Will never come back to me.

1834   1842

The Epic [Morte d'Arthur][1]

At Francis Allen's on the Christmas eve—
The game of forfeits done—the girls all kissed
Beneath the sacred bush° and passed° away—   *mistletoe / gone*
The parson Holmes, the poet Everard Hall,
5   The host, and I sat round the wassail-bowl,
Then halfway ebbed; and there we held a talk,
How all the old honor had from Christmas gone,
Or gone or dwindled down to some odd games
In some odd nooks like this; till I, tired out
10   With cutting eights° that day upon the pond,   *figure eights*
Where, three times slipping from the outer edge,
I bumped the ice into three several stars,
Fell in a doze; and half-awake I heard
The parson taking wide and wider sweeps,
15   Now harping on the church-commissioners,[2]
Now hawking at geology and schism;
Until I woke, and found him settled down
Upon the general decay of faith
Right through the world: "at home was little left,
20   And none abroad; there was no anchor, none,
To hold by." Francis, laughing, clapped his hand
On Everard's shoulder, with "I hold by him."
"And I," quoth Everard, "by the wassail-bowl."
"Why yes," I said, "we knew your gift that way
25   At college; but another which you had—

1. At age twenty-four Tennyson proposed to write a long epic on King Arthur. Five years later he had completed one book of the twelve, the story of Arthur's death, which he published in 1842 under the title "Morte d'Arthur." In this early version the story is given a framework, "The Epic," which consists of a short introductory section (fifty-one lines) and an epilogue (thirty lines), describing a party on Christmas Eve in modern times, at which the poet ("Everard Hall") reads "Morte d'Arthur" to his friends. In 1869 Tennyson incorporated "Morte d'Arthur" into his long narrative poem *Idylls of the King*; it appears there as the twelfth book, *The Passing of Arthur*. At that time the "Epic" framework was discarded and some lines added. The 1842 version can be reconstructed from *The Passing of Arthur* (lines 170–440; only two lines are modified).

2. Commissioners appointed by the government in 1835 to regulate the finances of the Anglican Church.

I mean of verse (for so we held it then),
What came of that?" "You know," said Frank, "he burnt
His epic, his King Arthur, some twelve books"—
And then to me demanding why: "O, sir,
30   He thought that nothing new was said, or else
Something so said 'twas nothing—that a truth
Looks freshest in the fashion of the day;
God knows; he has a mint of reasons; ask.
It pleased *me* well enough." "Nay, nay," said Hall,
35   "Why take the style of those heroic times?
For nature brings not back the mastodon,
Nor we those times; and why should any man
Remodel models? these twelve books of mine
Were faint Homeric echoes,[3] nothing-worth,
40   Mere chaff and draff,° much better burnt." "But I,"   *bits of straw*
Said Francis, "picked the eleventh from this hearth,
And have it; keep a thing, its use will come.
I hoard it as a sugarplum for Holmes."
He laughed, and I, though sleepy, like a horse
45   That hears the corn-bin open, pricked my ears;
For I remembered Everard's college fame
When we were Freshmen. Then at my request
He brought it; and the poet, little urged,
But with some prelude of disparagement,
50   Read, mouthing out his hollow o's and a's,
Deep-chested music, and to this result.[4]

                    *   *   *

Here ended Hall, and our last light, that long
325   Had winked and threatened darkness, flared and fell;
At which the parson, sent to sleep with sound,
And waked with silence, grunted "Good!" but we
Sat rapt: it was the tone with which he read—
Perhaps some modern touches here and there
330   Redeemed it from the charge of nothingness—
Or else we loved the man, and prized his work;
I know not; but we sitting, as I said,
The cock crew loud, as at that time of year
The lusty bird takes every hour for dawn.[5]
335   Then Francis, muttering like a man ill-used,
"There now—that's nothing!" drew a little back,
And drove his heel into the smoldered log,
That sent a blast of sparkles up the flue.
And so to bed, where yet in sleep I seemed
340   To sail with Arthur under looming shores,
Point after point; till on to dawn, when dreams
Begin to feel the truth and stir of day,
To me, methought, who waited with the crowd,

3. After reading "Morte d'Arthur" in manuscript, Walter Savage Landor commented: "It is more Homeric than any poem of our time, and rivals some of the noblest parts of the Odyssey."
4. Here followed the 271 lines of "Morte d'Arthur" in 1842 (see *The Passing of Arthur*, lines 170–440,

pp. 1205–11). "The Epic" then continued as follows.
5. See Shakespeare's *Hamlet* 1.1.138–41, on the legend of the cock's crowing "all night long" in the season of Jesus' birth.

There came a bark° that, blowing forward, bore   *small ship*
345   King Arthur, like a modern gentleman
Of stateliest port;° and all the people cried,   *deportment*
"Arthur is come again: he cannot die."
Then those that stood upon the hills behind
Repeated—"Come again, and thrice as fair";
350   And, further inland, voices echoed—"Come
With all good things, and war shall be no more."
At this a hundred bells began to peal,
That with the sound I woke, and heard indeed
The clear church bells ring in the Christmas morn.

1833–38   1842

Locksley Hall[1]

Comrades, leave me here a little, while as yet 'tis early morn;
Leave me here, and when you want me, sound upon the bugle horn.

'Tis the place, and all around it, as of old, the curlews call,
Dreary gleams[2] about the moorland flying over Locksley Hall;

5   Locksley Hall, that in the distance overlooks the sandy tracts,
And the hollow ocean-ridges roaring into cataracts.

Many a night from yonder ivied casement, ere I went to rest,
Did I look on great Orion sloping slowly to the west.

Many a night I saw the Pleiads,[3] rising through the mellow shade,
10   Glitter like a swarm of fireflies tangled in a silver braid.

Here about the beach I wandered, nourishing a youth sublime
With the fairy tales of science, and the long result of time;

When the centuries behind me like a fruitful land reposed;
When I clung to all the present for the promise that it closed°   *enclosed*

15   When I dipped into the future far as human eye could see,
Saw the vision of the world and all the wonder that would be.—

In the spring a fuller crimson comes upon the robin's breast;
In the spring the wanton lapwing gets himself another crest;

In the spring a livelier iris changes on the burnished dove;[4]
20   In the spring a young man's fancy lightly turns to thoughts of love.

1. The situation in this poem—of a young man's being jilted by a woman who chose to marry a wealthy landowner—may have been suggested to Tennyson by the experience of his brother Frederick, a hot-tempered man who had fallen in love with his cousin Julia Tennyson and who was similarly unsuccessful. It may also have been inspired by Tennyson's own frustrated courtship of Rosa Baring, who rejected the young poet in favor of a wealthy suitor. Concerning the ranting tone of the speaker (a tone accentuated by the heavily marked trochaic meter), Tennyson said: "The whole poem represents young life, its good side, its deficiencies, and its yearnings."
2. Tennyson stated that the noun "gleams" refers not to "curlews" flying but to streaks of light.
3. Or the Pleiades, seven stars in the constellation Taurus.
4. The rainbowlike colors of a dove's throat plumage are intensified in the mating season.

Then her cheek was pale and thinner than should be for one so young,
And her eyes on all my motions with a mute observance hung.

And I said, "My cousin Amy, speak, and speak the truth to me,
Trust me, cousin, all the current of my being sets to thee."

25   On her pallid cheek and forehead came a color and a light,
As I have seen the rosy red flushing in the northern night.

And she turned—her bosom shaken with a sudden storm of sighs—
All the spirit deeply dawning in the dark of hazel eyes—

Saying, "I have hid my feelings, fearing they should do me wrong";
30   Saying, "Dost thou love me, cousin?" weeping, "I have loved thee long."

Love took up the glass of Time, and turned it in his glowing hands;
Every moment, lightly shaken, ran itself in golden sands.

Love took up the harp of Life, and smote on all the chords with might;
Smote the chord of Self, that, trembling, passed in music out of sight.

35   Many a morning on the moorland did we hear the copses ring,
And her whisper thronged my pulses with the fullness of the spring.

Many an evening by the waters did we watch the stately ships,
And our spirits rushed together at the touching of the lips.

O my cousin, shallow-hearted! O my Amy, mine no more!
40   O the dreary, dreary moorland! O the barren, barren shore!

Falser than all fancy fathoms, falser than all songs have sung,
Puppet to a father's threat, and servile to a shrewish tongue!

Is it well to wish thee happy?—having known me—to decline
On a range of lower feelings and a narrower heart than mine!

45   Yet it shall be; thou shalt lower to his level day by day,
What is fine within thee growing coarse to sympathize with clay.

As the husband is, the wife is; thou art mated with a clown,°   boor
And the grossness of his nature will have weight to drag thee down.

He will hold thee, when his passion shall have spent its novel force,
50   Something better than his dog, a little dearer than his horse.

What is this? his eyes are heavy; think not they are glazed with wine.
Go to him, it is thy duty; kiss him, take his hand in thine.

It may be my lord is weary, that his brain is overwrought;
Soothe him with thy finer fancies, touch him with thy lighter thought.

55   He will answer to the purpose, easy things to understand—
Better thou wert dead before me, though I slew thee with my hand!

Better thou and I were lying, hidden from the heart's disgrace,
Rolled in one another's arms, and silent in a last embrace.

Cursed be the social wants that sin against the strength of youth!
60 Cursed be the social lies that warp us from the living truth!

Cursed be the sickly forms that err from honest Nature's rule!
Cursed be the gold that gilds the straitened° forehead of the fool! *narrowed*

Well—'tis well that I should bluster!—Hadst thou less unworthy proved—
Would to God—for I had loved thee more than ever wife was loved.

65 Am I mad, that I should cherish that which bears but bitter fruit?
I will pluck it from my bosom, though my heart be at the root.

Never, though my mortal summers to such length of years should come
As the many-wintered crow⁵ that leads the clanging rookery home.

Where is comfort? in division of the records of the mind?
70 Can I part her from herself, and love her, as I knew her, kind?

I remember one that perished; sweetly did she speak and move;
Such a one do I remember, whom to look at was to love.

Can I think of her as dead, and love her for the love she bore?
No—she never loved me truly; love is love for evermore.

75 Comfort? comfort scorned of devils! this is truth the poet⁶ sings,
That a sorrow's crown of sorrow is remembering happier things.

Drug thy memories, lest thou learn it, lest thy heart be put to proof,
In the dead unhappy night, and when the rain is on the roof.

Like a dog, he hunts in dreams, and thou art staring at the wall,
80 Where the dying night-lamp flickers, and the shadows rise and fall.

Then a hand shall pass before thee, pointing to his drunken sleep,
To thy widowed⁷ marriage-pillows, to the tears that thou wilt weep.

Thou shalt hear the "Never, never," whispered by the phantom years.
And a song from out the distance in the ringing of thine ears;

85 And an eye shall vex thee, looking ancient kindness on thy pain.
Turn thee, turn thee on thy pillow; get thee to thy rest again.

Nay, but Nature brings thee solace; for a tender voice will cry.
'Tis a purer life than thine, a lip to drain thy trouble dry.

Baby lips will laugh me down; my latest rival brings thee rest.
90 Baby fingers, waxen touches, press me from the mother's breast.

5. A rook, a long-lived bird.
6. Dante; see *Inferno* 5.121–23.

7. Presumably figurative. Her marriage having become a mockery, she is widowed.

O, the child too clothes the father with a dearness not his due.
Half is thine and half is his; it will be worthy of the two.

O, I see thee old and formal, fitted to thy petty part,
With a little hoard of maxims preaching down a daughter's heart.

95 "They were dangerous guides the feelings—she herself was not exempt—
Truly, she herself had suffered"—Perish in thy self-contempt!

Overlive it—lower yet—be happy! wherefore should I care?
I myself must mix with action, lest I wither by despair.

What is that which I should turn to, lighting upon days like these?
100 Every door is barred with gold, and opens but to golden keys.

Every gate is thronged with suitors, all the markets overflow.
I have but an angry fancy; what is that which I should do?

I had been content to perish, falling on the foeman's ground,
When the ranks are rolled in vapor, and the winds are laid with sound.[8]

105 But the jingling of the guinea helps the hurt that Honor feels,
And the nations do but murmur, snarling at each other's heels.

Can I but relive in sadness? I will turn that earlier page.
Hide me from my deep emotion, O thou wondrous Mother-Age![9]

Make me feel the wild pulsation that I felt before the strife,
110 When I heard my days before me, and the tumult of my life;

Yearning for the large excitement that the coming years would yield,
Eager-hearted as a boy when first he leaves his father's field,

And at night along the dusky highway near and nearer drawn,
Sees in heaven the light of London flaring like a dreary dawn;

115 And his spirit leaps within him to be gone before him then,
Underneath the light he looks at, in among the throngs of men;

Men, my brothers, men the workers, ever reaping something new;
That which they have done but earnest° of the things that they
    shall do.

For I dipped into the future, far as human eye could see,
120 Saw the Vision of the world, and all the wonder that would be;

Saw the heavens fill with commerce, argosies of magic sails,[1]
Pilots of the purple twilight, dropping down with costly bales;

8. It was once believed that the firing of artillery stilled the winds.
9. A happier past at life's beginning, which generated a more confident anticipation of the future

(see also line 185).
1. Probably airships, such as balloons. "Argosies": merchant vessels.

Heard the heavens fill with shouting, and there rained a ghastly dew
From the nations' airy navies grappling in the central blue;

125 Far along the world-wide whisper of the south wind rushing warm,
With the standards of the peoples plunging through the thunderstorm;

Till the war drum throbbed no longer, and the battle flags were furled
In the Parliament of man, the Federation of the world.

There the common sense of most shall hold a fretful realm in awe,
130 And the kindly earth shall slumber, lapped in° universal law.   *encompassed by*

So I triumphed ere my passion sweeping through me left me dry,
Left me with the palsied heart, and left me with the jaundiced eye;

Eye, to which all order festers, all things here are out of joint.
Science moves, but slowly, slowly, creeping on from point to point;

135 Slowly comes a hungry people, as a lion, creeping nigher,
Glares at one that nods and winks behind a slowly-dying fire.

Yet I doubt not through the ages one increasing purpose runs,
And the thoughts of men are widened with the process of the suns.

What is that to him that reaps not harvest of his youthful joys,
140 Though the deep heart of existence beat forever like a boy's?

Knowledge comes, but wisdom lingers, and I linger on the shore,
And the individual withers, and the world is more and more.

Knowledge comes, but wisdom lingers, and he bears a laden breast,
Full of sad experience, moving toward the stillness of his rest.

145 Hark, my merry comrades call me, sounding on the bugle horn,
They to whom my foolish passion were a target for their scorn.

Shall it not be scorn to me to harp on such a moldered string?
I am shamed through all my nature to have loved so slight a thing.

Weakness to be wroth with weakness! woman's pleasure, woman's pain—
150 Nature made them blinder motions bounded in a shallower brain.

Woman is the lesser man, and all thy passions, matched with mine,
Are as moonlight unto sunlight, and as water unto wine—

Here at least, where nature sickens, nothing. Ah, for some retreat
Deep in yonder shining Orient, where my life began to beat.

155 Where in wild Mahratta-battle² fell my father evil-starred—
I was left a trampled orphan, and a selfish uncle's ward.

2. Reference to wars waged by a Hindu people against the British forces in India (1803 and 1817).

Or to burst all links of habit—there to wander far away,
On from island unto island at the gateways of the day.

Larger constellations burning, mellow moons and happy skies,
160   Breadths of tropic shade and palms in cluster, knots of Paradise.

Never comes the trader, never floats an European flag,
Slides the bird o'er lustrous woodland, swings the trailer° from the   *vine*
crag;

Droops the heavy-blossomed bower, hangs the heavy-fruited tree—
Summer isles of Eden lying in dark purple spheres of sea.

165   There methinks would be enjoyment more than in this march of mind,
In the steamship, in the railway, in the thoughts that shake mankind.

There the passions cramped no longer shall have scope and breathing space;
I will take some savage woman, she shall rear my dusky race.

Iron-jointed, supple-sinewed, they shall dive, and they shall run,
170   Catch the wild goat by the hair, and hurl their lances in the sun;

Whistle back the parrot's call, and leap the rainbows of the brooks,
Not with blinded eyesight poring over miserable books—

Fool, again the dream, the fancy! but I *know* my words are wild,
But I count the gray barbarian lower than the Christian child.

175   I, to herd with narrow foreheads, vacant of our glorious gains,
Like a beast with lower pleasures, like a beast with lower pains!

Mated with a squalid savage—what to me were sun or clime?
I the heir of all the ages, in the foremost files of time—

I that rather held it better men should perish one by one,
180   Than that earth should stand at gaze like Joshua's moon in Ajalon![3]

Not in vain the distance beacons. Forward, forward let us range,
Let the great world spin forever down the ringing grooves[4] of change.

Through the shadow of the globe we sweep into the younger day;
Better fifty years of Europe than a cycle of Cathay.[5]

185   Mother-Age—for mine I knew not—help me as when life begun;
Rift the hills, and roll the waters, flash the lightnings, weigh the sun.

3. At Joshua's command the sun and moon stood still while the Israelites completed the slaughter of their enemies in the valley of Ajalon (Joshua 10.12–13).
4. Railroad tracks. Tennyson at one time had the impression that train wheels ran in grooved rails.
5. China, regarded in the 19th century as a static, unprogressive country. Cf. Mill, *On Liberty* (1859), p. 1051.

O, I see the crescent promise of my spirit hath not set.
Ancient founts of inspiration well through all my fancy yet.

Howsoever these things be, a long farewell to Locksley Hall!
190   Now for me the woods may wither, now for me the roof-tree fall.

Comes a vapor from the margin,° blackening over heath and   *riverbank*
    holt,°   *wood*
Cramming all the blast before it, in its breast a thunderbolt.

Let it fall on Locksley Hall, with rain or hail, or fire or snow;
For the mighty wind arises, roaring seaward, and I go.

1837–38   1842

FROM THE PRINCESS[1]

Tears, Idle Tears[2]

Tears, idle tears, I know not what they mean,
Tears from the depth of some divine despair
Rise in the heart, and gather to the eyes,
In looking on the happy autumn-fields,
5   And thinking of the days that are no more.

Fresh as the first beam glittering on a sail,
That brings our friends up from the underworld,
Sad as the last which reddens over one
That sinks with all we love below the verge;
10   So sad, so fresh, the days that are no more.

Ah, sad and strange as in dark summer dawns
The earliest pipe of half-awakened birds
To dying ears, when unto dying eyes
The casement slowly grows a glimmering square;
15   So sad, so strange, the days that are no more.

Dear as remembered kisses after death,
And sweet as those by hopeless fancy feigned
On lips that are for others; deep as love,

1. *The Princess* (1847), a long narrative poem, contains interludes in which occasional songs are sung. Several of these songs, two of which are printed here, have been set to music by various 19th- and 20th-century composers.
2. Tennyson commented: "This song came to me on the yellowing autumn-tide at Tintern Abbey, full for me of its bygone memories." This locale would be for him associated both with Words- worth's "Tintern Abbey" (1798) and with memories of Arthur Hallam, who was buried across the Bristol Channel in this area. "It is what I have always felt even from a boy, and what as a boy I called the 'passion of the past.' And it is so always with me now; it is the distance that charms me in the landscape, the picture and the past, and not the immediate today in which I move."

Deep as first love, and wild with all regret;
20 O Death in Life, the days that are no more!

1847

Now Sleeps the Crimson Petal

Now sleeps the crimson petal, now the white;
Nor waves the cypress in the palace walk;
Nor winks the gold fin in the porphyry font.
The firefly wakens; waken thou with me.

5   Now droops the milk-white peacock like a ghost,
And like a ghost she glimmers on to me.

Now lies the Earth all Danaë[1] to the stars,
And all thy heart lies open unto me.

Now slides the silent meteor on, and leaves
10   A shining furrow, as thy thoughts in me.

Now folds the lily all her sweetness up,
And slips into the bosom of the lake.
So fold thyself, my dearest, thou, and slip
Into my bosom and be lost in me.

1847

["The woman's cause is man's"][1]

"Blame not thyself too much," I said, "nor blame
240   Too much the sons of men and barbarous laws;
These were the rough ways of the world till now.
Henceforth thou hast a helper, me, that know
The woman's cause is man's: they rise or sink
Together, dwarfed or godlike, bond or free:
245   For she that out of Lethe[2] scales with man
The shining steps of Nature, shares with man

---

1. A Greek princess, whose father confined her in a brazen chamber after hearing the oracle that her son would kill him. But Zeus came to her in the form of a shower of gold, and she bore the hero Perseus.

1. *The Princess* was Tennyson's attempt to address the contemporary debate over woman's proper role. It tells the story of a prince who courts the young and beautiful Princess Ida. She has vowed she will never marry and has established a women's university from which men are excluded. The prince and his two companions dress themselves up in women's clothes to gain entrance to the university. When a battle ensues—in which King Gama, the prince's father, invades the university to rescue his son and force Ida to marry him—the university is turned into a hospital and the princess is persuaded of the error of her ways. The prince's final vision, from book 7 (reprinted here), in which he imagines a future of gradual change, by which men and women adopt the strengths of the other while maintaining their distinct natures, has been a key text in discussing Victorian constructions of masculinity and femininity. In the operetta *Princess Ida* (1884), W. S Gilbert and Arthur Sullivan parody Tennyson's poem and satirize feminism.

2. In the classical underworld, the river of forgetfulness.

His nights, his days, moves with him to one goal,
Stays all the fair young planet in her hands—
If she be small, slight-natured, miserable,
250 How shall men grow? but work no more alone!
Our place is much: as far as in us lies
We two will serve them both in aiding her—
Will clear away the parasitic forms
That seem to keep her up but drag her down—
255 Will leave her space to burgeon out of all
Within her—let her make herself her own
To give or keep, to live and learn and be
All that not harms distinctive womanhood.
For woman is not undevelopt man,
260 But diverse: could we make her as the man,
Sweet Love were slain: his dearest bond is this,
Not like to like, but like in difference.
Yet in the long years liker must they grow;
The man be more of woman, she of man;
265 He gain in sweetness and in moral height,
Nor lose the wrestling thews that throw the world;
She mental breadth, nor fail in childward care,
Nor lose the childlike in the larger mind;
Till at the last she set herself to man,
270 Like perfect music unto noble words;
And so these twain, upon the skirts of Time,
Sit side by side, full-summed in all their powers,
Dispensing harvest, sowing the To-be,
Self-reverent each and reverencing each,
275 Distinct in individualities,
But like each other even as those who love.
Then comes the statelier Eden back to men:
Then reign the world's great bridals, chaste and calm:
Then springs the crowning race of humankind.
May these things be!"
280 Sighing she spoke "I fear
They will not."
"Dear, but let us type° them now   *model*
In our own lives, and this proud watchword rest
Of equal; seeing either sex alone
Is half itself, and in true marriage lies
285 Nor equal, nor unequal: each fulfils
Defect in each, and always thought in thought,
Purpose in purpose, will in will, they grow,
The single pure and perfect animal,
The two-celled heart beating, with one full stroke,
Life."
290 And again sighing she spoke: "A dream
That once was mine! what woman taught you this?"

1839–47   1847

In Memoriam A. H. H.   When Arthur Hallam died suddenly at the age of twenty-two, probably of a stroke, Tennyson felt that his life had been shattered. Hallam was not only Tennyson's closest friend, and his sister's fiancé, but a critic and champion of his poetry. Widely regarded as the most promising young man of his generation, Hallam had written a review of Tennyson's first book of poetry that is still one of the best assessments of it. When Tennyson lost Hallam's love and support, he was overwhelmed with doubts about his own life and vocation and about the meaning of the universe and humankind's place in it, doubts reinforced by his study of geology and other sciences. To express the variety of his feelings and reflections, he began to compose a series of lyrics. Tennyson later arranged these "short swallow-flights of song," as he called them, written at intervals over a period of seventeen years, into one long elegy. Although the resulting poem has many affinities with traditional elegies like Milton's "Lycidas" (1638) and Shelley's *Adonais* (1821), its structure is strikingly different. It is made up of individual lyric units that are seemingly self-contained but take their full meaning from their place in the whole. As T. S. Eliot has written, "It is unique: it is a long poem made by putting together lyrics, which have only the unity and continuity of a diary, the concentrated diary of a man confessing himself." Though intensely personal, the elegy expressed the religious doubts of his age. It is also a love poem. Like Shakespeare's sonnets, to which the poem alludes, *In Memoriam* vests its most intense emotion in male relationships.

The sections of the poem record a progressive development from despair to some sort of hope. Some of the early sections of the poem resemble traditional pastoral elegies, including those portraying the voyage during which Hallam's body was brought to England for burial (sections 9 to 15 and 19). Other early sections portraying the speaker's loneliness, in which even Christmas festivities seem joyless (sections 28 to 30), are more distinctive. The poem's internal chronology covers a span of around three years, and with the passage of time, indicated by anniversaries and by recurring changes of the seasons, the speaker comes to accept the loss and to assert his belief in life and in an afterlife. In particular the recurring Christmases (sections 28, 78, 104) indicate the stages of his development, yet the pattern of progress in the poem is not a simple unimpeded movement upward. Dramatic conflicts recur throughout. Thus the most intense expression of doubt occurs not at the beginning of *In Memoriam* but as late as sections 54, 55, and 56.

The quatrain form in which the whole poem is written is usually called the "*In Memoriam* stanza," although it had been occasionally used by earlier poets. So rigid a form taxed Tennyson's ingenuity in achieving variety, but it is one of several means by which the diverse parts of the poem are knitted together.

The introductory section, consisting of eleven stanzas, is commonly referred to as the "Prologue," although Tennyson did not assign a title to it. It was written in 1849 after the rest of the poem was complete.

---

wrote over Years & Years. Crisis of faith.

   FROM IN MEMORIAM A. H. H.

OBIIT MDCCCXXXIII[1]

Strong Son of God, immortal Love,
  Whom we, that have not seen thy face,
  By faith, and faith alone, embrace,
Believing where we cannot prove;[2]

1. He died 1833 (Latin).
2. Cf. John 20.24–29, in which Jesus rebukes Thomas for his doubts concerning the Resurrec-

tion: "Blessed are they that have not seen, and yet have believed."

5   Thine are these orbs[3] of light and shade;
      Thou madest Life in man and brute;
      Thou madest Death; and lo, thy foot
    Is on the skull which thou hast made.

    Thou wilt not leave us in the dust:
10   Thou madest man, he knows not why,
      He thinks he was not made to die;
    And thou hast made him: thou art just.

    Thou seemest human and divine,
      The highest, holiest manhood, thou.
15   Our wills are ours, we know not how;
    Our wills are ours, to make them thine.

    Our little systems[4] have their day;
      They have their day and cease to be;
      They are but broken lights of thee,
20   And thou, O Lord, art more than they.

    We have but faith: we cannot know,
      For knowledge is of things we see;
      And yet we trust it comes from thee,
    A beam in darkness: let it grow.

25   Let knowledge grow from more to more,
      But more of reverence in us dwell;
      That mind and soul, according well,
    May make one music as before,[5]

    But vaster. We are fools and slight;
30   We mock thee when we do not fear:
      But help thy foolish ones to bear;
    Help thy vain worlds to bear thy light.

    Forgive what seemed my sin in me,
      What seemed my worth since I began;
35   For merit lives from man to man,
    And not from man, O Lord, to thee.

    Forgive my grief for one removed,
      Thy creature, whom I found so fair.
      I trust he lives in thee, and there
40   I find him worthier to be loved.

    Forgive these wild and wandering cries,
      Confusions of a wasted° youth;   *desolated*
      Forgive them where they fail in truth,
    And in thy wisdom make me wise.

1849

3. The sun and moon (according to Tennyson's note).

4. Of religion and philosophy.
5. As in the days of fixed religious faith.

1

I held it truth, with him who sings
To one clear harp in divers tones,[6]
That men may rise on stepping stones
Of their dead selves to higher things.

5   But who shall so forecast the years
And find in loss a gain to match?
Or reach a hand through time to catch
The far-off interest of tears?

Let Love clasp Grief lest both be drowned,
10   Let darkness keep her raven gloss.
Ah, sweeter to be drunk with loss,
To dance with Death, to beat the ground,

Than that the victor Hours should scorn
The long result of love, and boast,
15   "Behold the man that loved and lost,
But all he was is overworn."

2

Old yew, which graspest at the stones
That name the underlying dead,
Thy fibres net the dreamless head,
Thy roots are wrapped about the bones.

5   The seasons bring the flower again,
And bring the firstling to the flock;
And in the dusk of thee the clock
Beats out the little lives of men.

O, not for thee the glow, the bloom,
10   Who changest not in any gale,
Nor branding summer suns avail
To touch thy thousand years of gloom[7]

And gazing on thee, sullen tree,
Sick for° thy stubborn hardihood,   envying
15   I seem to fail from out my blood
And grow incorporate into thee.

6. Identified by Tennyson as the German poet Johann Wolfgang von Goethe (1749–1832).
7. The ancient yew tree, growing in the grounds near the clock tower and church where Hallam was to be buried, seems neither to blossom in spring nor to change from its dark mournful color in summer. "Thousand years": cf. Book of Common Prayer, Psalm 90: "For a thousand years in Thy sight are but as yesterday when it is past, and as a watch in the night."

3

O Sorrow, cruel fellowship,
  O Priestess in the vaults of Death,
  O sweet and bitter in a breath,
What whispers from thy lying lip?

5 "The stars," she whispers, "blindly run;
  A web is woven across the sky;
  From out waste places comes a cry,
And murmurs from the dying sun;

"And all the phantom, Nature, stands—
10 With all the music in her tone,
  A hollow echo of my own—
A hollow form with empty hands."

And shall I take a thing so blind,
  Embrace her° as my natural good;   Sorrow
15 Or crush her, like a vice of blood,
Upon the threshold of the mind?

4

To Sleep I give my powers away;
  My will is bondsman to the dark;
  I sit within a helmless bark,
And with my heart I muse and say:

5 O heart, how fares it with thee now,
  That thou should fail from thy desire,
  Who scarcely darest to inquire,
"What is it makes me beat so low?"

Something it is which thou hast lost,
10 Some pleasure from thine early years.
  Break thou deep vase of chilling tears,
That grief hath shaken into frost![8]

Such clouds of nameless trouble cross
  All night below the darkened eyes;
15 With morning wakes the will, and cries,
"Thou shalt not be the fool of loss."

---

8. Water can be brought below freezing-point and not turn into ice—if it be kept still; but if it be moved suddenly it turns into ice and may break a vase [Tennyson's note].

5

I sometimes hold it half a sin
  To put in words the grief I feel;
  For words, like Nature, half reveal
And half conceal the Soul within.

5   But, for the unquiet heart and brain,
  A use in measured language lies;
  The sad mechanic exercise,
Like dull narcotics, numbing pain.

In words, like weeds,° I'll wrap me o'er,   *mourning garments*
10   Like coarsest clothes against the cold;
  But that large grief which these enfold
Is given in outline and no more.

6

One writes, that "Other friends remain,"
  That "Loss is common to the race"—
  And common is the commonplace,
And vacant chaff° well meant for grain.   *husks*

5   That loss is common would not make
  My own less bitter, rather more:
  Too common! Never morning wore
To evening, but some heart did break.

O father, wheresoe'er thou be,
10   Who pledgest° now thy gallant son;   *toasts*
  A shot, ere half thy draft be done,
Hath stilled the life that beat from thee.

O mother, praying God will save
  Thy sailor—while thy head is bowed,
15   His heavy-shotted hammock-shroud
Drops in his vast and wandering grave.[9]

Ye know no more than I who wrought
  At that last hour to please him well;[1]
  Who mused on all I had to tell,
20 And something written, something thought;

Expecting still his advent home;
  And ever met him on his way
  With wishes, thinking, "here today,"
Or "here tomorrow will he come."

9. Sailors buried at sea were often wrapped in
their own hammocks. "Heavy-shotted": heavily
weighted.

1. According to his son, Tennyson discovered that
he had been writing a letter to Hallam during the
very hour in which his friend died.

25 O somewhere, meek, the unconscious dove,
    That sittest ranging° golden hair;   *arranging*
    And glad to find thyself so fair,
    Poor child, that waitest for thy love!

    For now her father's chimney glows
30   In expectation of a guest;
    And thinking "this will please him best,"
    She takes a riband or a rose;

    For he will see them on tonight;
    And with the thought her color burns;
35   And, having left the glass, she turns
    Once more to set a ringlet right;

    And, even when she turned, the curse
    Had fallen, and her future Lord
    Was drowned in passing through the ford,
40   Or killed in falling from his horse.

    O what to her shall be the end?
    And what to me remains of good?
    To her, perpetual maidenhood,
    And unto me no second friend.

7

    Dark house,[2] by which once more I stand
        Here in the long unlovely street,
        Doors, where my heart was used to beat
    So quickly, waiting for a hand,

5   A hand that can be clasped no more—
        Behold me, for I cannot sleep,
        And like a guilty thing I creep
    At earliest morning to the door.

    He is not here; but far away
10   The noise of life begins again,
        And ghastly through the drizzling rain
    On the bald street breaks the blank day.

8

    A happy lover who has come
        To look on her that loves him well,
        Who 'lights° and rings the gateway bell,   *alights*
    And learns her gone and far from home;

2. The house on Wimpole Street, in London, where Hallam had lived.

₅ He saddens, all the magic light
    Dies off at once from bower and hall,
    And all the place is dark, and all
The chambers emptied of delight:

So find I every pleasant spot
₁₀   In which we two were wont to meet,
    The field, the chamber, and the street,
For all is dark where thou art not.

Yet as that other, wandering there
    In those deserted walks, may find
₁₅   A flower beat with rain and wind,
Which once she fostered up with care;

So seems it in my deep regret,
    O my forsaken heart, with thee
    And this poor flower of poesy
₂₀   Which little cared for fades not yet.

But since it pleased a vanished eye,[3]
    I go to plant it on his tomb,
    That if it can it there may bloom,
Or dying, there at least may die.

9

Fair ship, that from the Italian shore[4]
    Sailest the placid ocean-plains
    With my lost Arthur's loved remains,
Spread thy full wings, and waft him o'er.

₅ So draw him home to those that mourn
    In vain; a favorable speed
    Ruffle thy mirrored mast, and lead
Through prosperous floods his holy urn.

All night no ruder air perplex
₁₀   Thy sliding keel, till Phosphor,° bright   *morning star*
    As our pure love, through early light
Shall glimmer on the dewy decks.

Sphere all your lights around, above;
    Sleep, gentle heavens, before the prow;
₁₅   Sleep, gentle winds, as he sleeps now,
My friend, the brother of my love;

My Arthur, whom I shall not see
    Till all my widowed race be run;

3. Hallam expressed enthusiasm for Tennyson's
early poetry in a review written in 1831.

4. Hallam's body was conveyed back to England
by ship from Trieste, Italy.

Dear as the mother to the son,
20 More than my brothers are to me.

10

I hear the noise about thy keel;
    I hear the bell struck in the night;
    I see the cabin window bright;
    I see the sailor at the wheel.

5   Thou bring'st the sailor to his wife,
    And traveled men from foreign lands;
    And letters unto trembling hands;
    And, thy dark freight, a vanished life.

    So bring him; we have idle dreams;
10   This look of quiet flatters thus
    Our home-bred fancies. O, to us,
    The fools of habit, sweeter seems

    To rest beneath the clover sod,
    That takes the sunshine and the rains,
15   Or where the kneeling hamlet drains
    The chalice of the grapes of God;[5]

    Than if with thee the roaring wells
    Should gulf him fathom-deep in brine,
    And hands so often clasped in mine,
20 Should toss with tangle° and with shells.   seaweed

11

Calm is the morn without a sound,
    Calm as to suit a calmer grief,
    And only through the faded leaf
    The chestnut pattering to the ground;

5   Calm and deep peace on this high wold,°   open countryside
    And on these dews that drench the furze,
    And all the silvery gossamers
    That twinkle into green and gold;

    Calm and still light on yon great plain
10   That sweeps with all its autumn bowers,
    And crowded farms and lessening towers,
    To mingle with the bounding main;

5. Reference to a burial inside a church building rather than in the churchyard.

Calm and deep peace in this wide air,
    These leaves that redden to the fall,
15   And in my heart, if calm at all,
If any calm, a calm despair;

Calm on the seas, and silver sleep,
    And waves that sway themselves in rest,
    And dead calm in that noble breast
20 Which heaves but with the heaving deep.

12

Lo, as a dove when up she springs
    To bear through Heaven a tale of woe,
    Some dolorous message knit below
The wild pulsation of her wings;

5   Like her I go; I cannot stay;
    I leave this mortal ark behind,
    A weight of nerves without a mind,
And leave the cliffs, and haste away

O'er ocean-mirrors rounded large,
10   And reach the glow of southern skies,
    And see the sails at distance rise,
And linger weeping on the marge,°   shore

And saying; "Comes he thus, my friend?
    Is this the end of all my care?"
15   And circle moaning in the air:
"Is this the end? Is this the end?"

And forward dart again, and play
    About the prow, and back return
    To where the body sits, and learn
20 That I have been an hour away.

13

Tears of the widower, when he sees
    A late-lost form that sleep reveals,
    And moves his doubtful arms, and feels
Her place is empty, fall like these;

5 Which weep a loss forever new,
    A void where heart on heart reposed;
    And, where warm hands have pressed and closed,
Silence, till I be silent too;

Which weep the comrade of my choice,
10   An awful thought, a life removed,

The human-hearted man I loved,
A Spirit, not a breathing voice.

Come, Time, and teach me, many years,
  I do not suffer in a dream;
15   For now so strange do these things seem,
Mine eyes have leisure for their tears,

My fancies time to rise on wing,
  And glance about the approaching sails,
  As though they brought but merchants' bales,
20   And not the burthen that they bring.

14

If one should bring me this report,
  That thou° hadst touched the land today,   *the ship*
  And I went down unto the quay;[6]
And found thee lying in the port;

5 And standing, muffled round with woe,
  Should see thy passengers in rank
  Come stepping lightly down the plank
And beckoning unto those they know;

And if along with these should come
10   The man I held as half divine,
  Should strike a sudden hand in mine,
And ask a thousand things of home;

And I should tell him all my pain,
  And how my life had drooped of late,
15   And he should sorrow o'er my state
And marvel what possessed my brain;

And I perceived no touch of change,
  No hint of death in all his frame,
  But found him all in all the same,
20   I should not feel it to be strange.

15

Tonight the winds begin to rise
  And roar from yonder dropping day;
  The last red leaf is whirled away,
The rooks are blown about the skies;

6. By 1850 the accepted pronunciation of "quay" would rhyme with *key*, but Tennyson reverts to an earlier pronunciation, *kay*.

⁵ The forest cracked, the waters curled,
　　The cattle huddled on the lea;
　　And wildly dashed on tower and tree
　　The sunbeam strikes along the world:

　　And but for fancies, which aver
¹⁰　That all thy motions gently pass
　　Athwart a plane of molten glass,[7]
　　I scarce could brook the strain and stir

　　That makes the barren branches loud;
　　And but for fear it is not so,
¹⁵　The wild unrest that lives in woe
　　Would dote and pore on yonder cloud

　　That rises upward always higher,
　　And onward drags a laboring breast,
　　And topples round the dreary west,
²⁰　A looming bastion fringed with fire.

　　　　　　＊　＊　＊

19

　　The Danube to the Severn[8] gave
　　The darkened heart that beat no more;
　　They laid him by the pleasant shore,
　　And in the hearing of the wave.

⁵ There twice a day the Severn fills;
　　The salt sea water passes by,
　　And hushes half the babbling Wye,[9]
　　And makes a silence in the hills.

　　The Wye is hushed nor moved along,
¹⁰　And hushed my deepest grief of all,
　　When filled with tears that cannot fall,
　　I brim with sorrow drowning song.

　　The tide flows down, the wave again
　　Is vocal in its wooded walls;[1]
¹⁵　My deeper anguish also falls,
　　And I can speak a little then.

　　　　　　＊　＊　＊

---

7. I.e., a calm sea.
8. Hallam died at Vienna on the river Danube. His burial place is on the banks of the Severn, a tidal river in the southwest of England.
9. A tributary of the Severn.

1. The water of the Wye River is dammed up as the tide flows in, and its sound is silenced until, with the turn of the tide, its "wave" once more becomes "vocal"; these stanzas were written at Tintern Abbey in the Wye valley.

21

I sing to him that rests below
  And, since the grasses round me wave,
  I take the grasses of the grave,[2]
And make them pipes whereon to blow.

5 The traveler hears me now and then,
  And sometimes harshly will he speak:
  "This fellow would make weakness weak,
And melt the waxen hearts of men."

Another answers: "Let him be,
10 He loves to make parade of pain,
  That with his piping he may gain
The praise that comes to constancy."

A third is wroth: "Is this an hour
  For private sorrow's barren song,
15 When more and more the people throng
The chairs and thrones of civil power?

"A time to sicken and to swoon,
  When Science reaches forth her arms[3]
  To feel from world to world, and charms
20 Her secret from the latest moon?"[4]

Behold, ye speak an idle thing;
  Ye never knew the sacred dust.
  I do but sing because I must,
And pipe but as the linnets sing:

25 And one is glad; her note is gay,
  For now her little ones have ranged;
  And one is sad; her note is changed,
Because her brood is stolen away.

22

The path by which we twain did go,
  Which led by tracts that pleased us well,
  Through four sweet years arose and fell,
From flower to flower, from snow to snow;

5 And we with singing cheered the way,
  And, crowned with all the season lent,

2. The poet assumes that the burial was in the churchyard; in fact, on January 3, 1834, at St. Andrews in Clevedon, Somersetshire, Hallam's body was interred in a vault inside the church.

3. Astronomical instruments, such as telescopes.
4. Probably alluding to the discovery in 1846 of the planet Neptune and one of its moons.

From April on to April went,
And glad at heart from May to May.

But where the path we walked began
10   To slant the fifth autumnal slope,[5]
As we descended following Hope,
There sat the Shadow feared of man;

Who broke our fair companionship,
And spread his mantle dark and cold,
15   And wrapped thee formless in the fold,
And dulled the murmur on thy lip,

And bore thee where I could not see
Nor follow, though I walk in haste,
And think that somewhere in the waste
20   The Shadow sits and waits for me.

23

Now, sometimes in my sorrow shut,
Or breaking into song by fits,
Alone, alone, to where he sits,
The Shadow cloaked from head to foot,

5   Who keeps the keys of all the creeds,
I wander, often falling lame,
And looking back to whence I came,
Or on to where the pathway leads;

And crying, How changed from where it ran
10   Through lands where not a leaf was dumb,
But all the lavish hills would hum
The murmur of a happy Pan;[6]

When each by turns was guide to each,
And Fancy light from Fancy caught,
15   And Thought leapt out to wed with Thought
Ere Thought could wed itself with Speech;

And all we met was fair and good,
And all was good that Time could bring,
And all the secret of the Spring
20   Moved in the chambers of the blood;

And many an old philosophy
On Argive[7] heights divinely sang,

5. Hallam died just before the beginning of autumn (September 15, 1833) in the fifth year of the friendship.
6. In Greek mythology the god of woods and pas-
tures.
7. Of Argos, an ancient city-state in the north-eastern Peloponnesus; more generally, Greek.

And round us all the thicket rang
To many a flute of Arcady.[8]

24

And was the day of my delight
  As pure and perfect as I say?
  The very source and fount of day
Is dashed with wandering isles of night.[9]

5 If all was good and fair we met,
  This earth had been the Paradise
  It never looked to human eyes
Since our first sun arose and set.

And is it that the haze of grief
10   Makes former gladness loom so great?
  The lowness of the present state,
That sets the past in this relief?

Or that the past will always win
  A glory from its being far,
15   And orb into the perfect star
We saw not when we moved therein?[1]

25

I know that this was Life—the track
  Whereon with equal feet we fared;
  And then, as now, the day prepared
The daily burden for the back.

5 But this it was that made me move
  As light as carrier birds in air;
  I loved the weight I had to bear,
Because it needed help of Love;

Nor could I weary, heart or limb,
10   When mighty Love would cleave in twain
  The lading° of a single pain,   *burden*
And part it, giving half to him.

26

Still onward winds the dreary way;
  I with it, for I long to prove

---

8. A sheep-raising region in Greece associated with pastoral poetry.
9. Moving spots on the sun.
1. The poet wonders whether Earth would have the deceptive appearance of being a perfect orb if viewed from afar, on another planet.

No lapse of moons can canker Love,
Whatever fickle tongues may say.

5 And if that eye which watches guilt
And goodness, and hath power to see
Within the green the mouldered tree,
And towers fallen as soon as built—

O, if indeed that eye foresee
10   Or see—in Him is no before—
In more of life true life no more
And Love the indifference to be,

Then might I find, ere yet the morn
Breaks hither over Indian seas,
15   That Shadow waiting with the keys,
To shroud me from my proper scorn.[2]

27

I envy not in any moods
The captive void of noble rage,
The linnet born within the cage,
That never knew the summer woods;

5 I envy not the beast that takes
His license in the field of time,
Unfettered by the sense of crime,
To whom a conscience never wakes;

Nor, what may count itself as blest,
10   The heart that never plighted troth
But stagnates in the weeds of sloth;
Nor any want-begotten rest.[3]

I hold it true, whate'er befall;
I feel it, when I sorrow most;
15   'Tis better to have loved and lost
Than never to have loved at all.

28

The time draws near the birth of Christ.[4]
The moon is hid, the night is still;
The Christmas bells from hill to hill
Answer each other in the mist.

2. The Deity, being outside time, sees (rather than foresees) whether or not the rest of life ("more of life," line 11) will be pointless. If pointless, then the way for the speaker to deal with his self-scorn ("proper scorn") might be to seek death.

3. Complacency resulting from some deficiency ("want").

4. The first Christmas after Hallam's death (1833); the setting is Tennyson's family home in Lincolnshire.

5 Four voices of four hamlets round,
      From far and near, on mead and moor,
      Swell out and fail, as if a door
   Were shut between me and the sound;

   Each voice four changes[5] on the wind,
10   That now dilate, and now decrease,
      Peace and goodwill, goodwill and peace,
   Peace and goodwill, to all mankind.

   This year I slept and woke with pain,
      I almost wished no more to wake,
15   And that my hold on life would break
   Before I heard those bells again;

   But they my troubled spirit rule,
      For they controlled me when a boy;
      They bring me sorrow touched with joy,
20 The merry, merry bells of Yule.

29

   With such compelling cause to grieve
      As daily vexes household peace,
      And chains regret to his decease,
   How dare we keep our Christmas eve;

5 Which brings no more a welcome guest
      To enrich the threshold of the night
      With showered largess of delight
   In dance and song and game and jest?

   Yet go, and while the holly boughs
10   Entwine the cold baptismal font,
      Make one wreath more for Use and Wont,[6]
   That guard the portals of the house;

   Old sisters of a day gone by,
      Gray nurses, loving nothing new;
15   Why should they miss their yearly due
   Before their time? They too will die.

30

   With trembling fingers did we weave
      The holly round the Christmas hearth;

---

5. Different sequences in which church bells are pealed.
6. Personifying the spirits who expect customary observances of the Christmas season to be followed.

A rainy cloud possessed the earth,
And sadly fell our Christmas eve.

5   At our old pastimes in the hall
We gamboled, making vain pretense
Of gladness, with an awful sense
Of one mute Shadow watching all.

We paused: the winds were in the beech;
10   We heard them sweep the winter land;
And in a circle hand-in-hand
Sat silent, looking each at each.

Then echo-like our voices rang;
We sung, though every eye was dim,
15   A merry song we sang with him
Last year; impetuously we sang.

We ceased; a gentler feeling crept
Upon us: surely rest is meet.°   *proper, appropriate*
"They rest," we said, "their sleep is sweet,"
20   And silence followed, and we wept.

Our voices took a higher range;
Once more we sang: "They do not die
Nor lose their mortal sympathy,
Nor change to us, although they change;

25   "Rapt from⁷ the fickle and the frail
With gathered power, yet the same,
Pierces the keen seraphic flame
From orb to orb, from veil⁸ to veil."

Rise, happy morn, rise, holy morn,
30   Draw forth the cheerful day from night:
O Father, touch the east, and light
The light that shone when Hope was born.

✳   ✳   ✳

34

My own dim life should teach me this,
That life shall live forevermore,
Else earth is darkness at the core,
And dust and ashes all that is;

5   This round of green, this orb of flame,
Fantastic beauty; such as lurks

7. Carried away from.
8. An image representing the boundary between different worlds, especially that between Earth and heaven (cf. section 56, line 28). "From orb to orb": the angelic spirit ("flame") of the dead moves from star to star.

In some wild poet, when he works
Without a conscience or an aim.

What then were God to such as I?
10   'Twere hardly worth my while to choose
Of things all mortal, or to use
A little patience ere I die;

'Twere best at once to sink to peace,
Like birds the charming serpent⁹ draws,
15   To drop head-foremost in the jaws
Of vacant darkness and to cease.

35

Yet if some voice that man could trust
Should murmur from the narrow house,
"The cheeks drop in, the body bows;
Man dies, nor is there hope in dust";

5 Might I not say? "Yet even here,
But for one hour, O Love, I strive
To keep so sweet a thing alive."
But I should turn mine ears and hear

The moanings of the homeless sea,
10   The sound of streams that swift or slow
Draw down Aeonian¹ hills, and sow
The dust of continents to be;

And Love would answer with a sigh,
"The sound of that forgetful shore²
15   Will change my sweetness more and more,
Half-dead to know that I shall die."

O me, what profits it to put
An idle case? If Death were seen
At first as Death, Love had not been,
20 Or been in narrowest working shut,

Mere fellowship of sluggish moods,
Or in his coarsest Satyr-shape³
Had bruised the herb and crushed the grape,
And basked and battened° in the woods.⁴   *grown fat*

*   *   *

9. Some snakes are reputed to capture their prey by hypnotizing it.
1. Eons old, seemingly everlasting.
2. I.e., of Lethe, the river in the classical under-world whose water caused forgetfulness.
3. In Greek mythology satyrs were half-man, half-beast (goat or horse) in appearance, desires, and behavior.
4. Lines 18–24 may be paraphrased: if we knew death to be final and that no afterlife were possible, love could not exist except on a primitive or bestial level.

39

Old warder of these buried bones,
  And answering now my random stroke
  With fruitful cloud and living smoke,
Dark yew, that graspest at the stones

5   And dippest toward the dreamless head,
  To thee too comes the golden hour
  When flower is feeling after flower;[5]
But Sorrow—fixed upon the dead,

And darkening the dark graves of men—
10   What whispered from her lying lips?
  Thy gloom is kindled at the tips,[6]
And passes into gloom again.

                *   *   *

47

That each, who seems a separate whole,
  Should move his rounds,[7] and fusing all
  The skirts[8] of self again, should fall
Remerging in the general Soul,

5   Is faith as vague as all unsweet.
  Eternal form shall still divide
  The eternal soul from all beside;
And I shall know him when we meet;

And we shall sit at endless feast,
10   Enjoying each the other's good.
  What vaster dream can hit the mood
Of Love on earth? He seeks at least

Upon the last and sharpest height,
  Before the spirits fade away,
15   Some landing place, to clasp and say,
"Farewell! We lose ourselves in light."[9]

48

If these brief lays, of Sorrow born,
  Were taken to be such as closed

---

5. The ancient yew tree in the graveyard was described in section 2 as never changing. Now the poet discovers that in the flowering season, if the tree is struck ("my random stroke"), it gives off a cloud of golden pollen.
6. Only the tips of the yew branches are in flower.
7. I.e., go through the customary circuit of life.

8. Outer edges or fringes.
9. These lines express the hope that, as Tennyson wrote, "individuality lasts after death, and we are not utterly absorbed into the Godhead. If we are to be finally merged into the Universal Soul, Love asks to have at least one more parting before we lose ourselves."

Grave doubts and answers here proposed,
Then these were such as men might scorn.

5   Her° care is not to part and prove;   *Sorrow's*
    She takes, when harsher moods remit,
    What slender shade of doubt may flit,
    And makes it vassal unto love;

    And hence, indeed, she sports with words,
10   But better serves a wholesome law,
    And holds it sin and shame to draw
    The deepest measure from the chords;

    Nor dare she trust a larger lay,°   *song*
    But rather loosens from the lip
15   Short swallow-flights of song, that dip
    Their wings in tears, and skim away.

*   *   *

50

Be near me when my light is low,
    When the blood creeps, and the nerves prick
    And tingle; and the heart is sick,
And all the wheels of being slow.

5   Be near me when the sensuous frame
    Is racked with pangs that conquer trust;
    And Time, a maniac scattering dust,   *Iambic*
And Life, a Fury slinging flame.   *4 tetrameter*

                                               a, bb, a
Be near me when my faith is dry,
10   And men the flies of latter spring,
    That lay their eggs, and sting and sing
And weave their petty cells and die.

Be near me when I fade away,
    To point the term of human strife,
15   And on the low dark verge of life
The twilight of eternal day.

*   *   *

*England at this time!
change in traditional
thought because of
new descoveries contradicting
that.*

✗ 54

O, yet we trust that somehow good
    Will be the final goal of ill,
    To pangs of nature, sins of will,
Defects of doubt, and taints of blood;

[handwritten margin note: conflict of trusting and Knowing]

5   That nothing walks with aimless feet;
     That not one life shall be destroyed,
     Or cast as rubbish to the void,
    When God hath made the pile complete;

    That not a worm is cloven in vain;
10   That not a moth with vain desire
     Is shriveled in a fruitless fire,
    Or but° subserves another's gain.   *only*

[handwritten margin note: We trust that good will come of hardship in the end. not one life is expended without a purpose.]

    Behold, we know not anything;
     I can but trust that good shall fall
15   At last—far off—at last, to all,
    And every winter change to spring.

[handwritten margin note: undercutting of trust.]

    So runs my dream; but what am I?
     An infant crying in the night;
     An infant crying for the light, *[handwritten: → knowledge]*
20   And with no language but a cry.

[handwritten note: The wish to trust, 54]   ✗**55**

    The wish, that of the living whole
     No life may fail beyond the grave,
     Derives it not from what we have
    The likest God within the soul?[1]

5   Are God and Nature then at strife,
     That Nature lends such evil dreams?
     So careful of the type she seems,
    So careless of the single life,

    That I, considering everywhere
10   Her secret meaning in her deeds,
     And finding that of fifty seeds *[handwritten: waste]*
    She often brings but one to bear, *[handwritten: of life]*

    I falter where I firmly trod,
     And falling with my weight of cares
15   Upon the great world's altar-stairs
    That slope through darkness up to God,

    I stretch lame hands of faith, and grope,
     And gather dust and chaff, and call
     To what I feel is Lord of all,
20   And faintly trust the larger hope.[2]

[handwritten note: in response to the cruelty of Nature]

1. According to Tennyson, the "inner conscience— 2. As expressed in lines 1 and 2.
the divine in man."

X56

"So careful of the type?" but no.
From scarpèd[3] cliff and quarried stone
She° cries, "A thousand types are gone;   *Nature*
I care for nothing, all shall go.

5   "Thou makest thine appeal to me:
I bring to life, I bring to death;
The spirit does but mean the breath:
I know no more." And he, shall he,

Man, her last work, who seemed so fair,
10 Such splendid purpose in his eyes,
Who rolled the psalm to wintry skies,
Who built him fanes° of fruitless prayer,   *temples*

Who trusted God was love indeed
And love Creation's final law—
15 Though Nature, red in tooth and claw
With ravine, shrieked against his creed—

Who loved, who suffered countless ills,
Who battled for the True, the Just,
Be blown about the desert dust,
20 Or sealed within the iron hills?[4]

No more,
that is it
we are but
dust?
  No more? A monster then, a dream,
A discord. Dragons of the prime,°   *primeval age*
That tare° each other in their slime,   *tore (archaic)*
Were mellow music matched with° him.   *compared to*

25 O life as futile, then, as frail!
God O for thy voice to soothe and bless!
What hope of answer, or redress?
Behind the veil, behind the veil.

The answer, veiled
darkness, not knowing

57

Peace; come away: the song of woe
Is after all an earthly song.
Peace; come away: we do him wrong
To sing so wildly: let us go.

5 Come; let us go: your cheeks are pale;
Methinks my friend is richly shrined;
But half my life I leave behind.
But I shall pass, my work will fail.

---

3. Cut away so that the strata are exposed.   4. Preserved like fossils in rock.

Yet in these ears, till hearing dies,
10   One set slow bell will seem to toll
The passing of the sweetest soul
That ever looked with human eyes.

I hear it now, and o'er and o'er,
Eternal greetings to the dead;
15   And "Ave,° Ave, Ave," said,   *Hail (Latin)*
"Adieu, adieu," forevermore.

58

In those sad words I took farewell.
Like echoes in sepulchral halls,
As drop by drop the water falls
In vaults and catacombs, they fell;

5 And, falling, idly broke the peace
Of hearts that beat from day to day,
Half-conscious of their dying clay,
And those cold crypts where they shall cease.

The high Muse answered: "Wherefore grieve
10   Thy brethren with a fruitless tear?
Abide a little longer here,
And thou shalt take a nobler leave."

59

O Sorrow, wilt thou live with me
No casual mistress, but a wife,
My bosom friend and half of life;
As I confess it needs must be?

5 O Sorrow, wilt thou rule my blood,
Be sometimes lovely like a bride,
And put thy harsher moods aside,
If thou wilt have me wise and good?

My centered passion cannot move,
10   Nor will it lessen from today;
But I'll have leave at times to play
As with the creature of my love;

And set thee forth, for thou art mine,
With so much hope for years to come,
15   That, howsoe'er I know thee, some
Could hardly tell what name were thine.

*   *   *

64

Dost thou look back on what hath been,
  As some divinely gifted man,
  Whose life in low estate began
And on a simple village green;

5 Who breaks his birth's invidious bar,
  And grasps the skirts of happy chance,
  And breasts the blows of circumstance,
And grapples with his evil star;

Who makes by force his merit known
10 And lives to clutch the golden keys,[5]
  To mold a mighty state's decrees,
And shape the whisper of the throne;

And moving up from high to higher,
  Becomes on Fortune's crowning slope
15 The pillar of a people's hope,
The centre of a world's desire;

Yet feels, as in a pensive dream,
  When all his active powers are still,
  A distant dearness in the hill,
20 A secret sweetness in the stream,

The limit of his narrower fate,
  While yet beside its vocal springs
  He played at counselors and kings,
With one that was his earliest mate;

25 Who plows with pain his native lea
  And reaps the labour of his hands,
  Or in the furrow musing stands:
"Does my old friend remember me?"

✻ ✻ ✻

67

When on my bed the moonlight falls,
  I know that in thy place of rest
  By that broad water[6] of the west
There comes a glory on the walls:

5 Thy marble bright in dark appears,
  As slowly steals a silver flame

---

5. Badges of high public office.   6. The Severn River.

Along the letters of thy name,
And o'er the number of thy years.

The mystic glory swims away,
10   From off my bed the moonlight dies;
And closing eaves of wearied eyes
I sleep till dusk is dipped in gray;

And then I know the mist is drawn
A lucid veil from coast to coast,
15   And in the dark church like a ghost
Thy tablet glimmers to the dawn.

                    *   *   *

70

I cannot see the features right,
When on the gloom I strive to paint
The face I know; the hues are faint
And mix with hollow masks of night;

5   Cloud-towers by ghostly masons wrought,
A gulf that ever shuts and gapes,
A hand that points, and pallèd shapes
In shadowy thoroughfares of thought;

And crowds that stream from yawning doors,
10   And shoals of puckered faces drive;
Dark bulks that tumble half alive,
And lazy lengths on boundless shores;

Till all at once beyond the will
I hear a wizard music roll,
15   And through a lattice on the soul
Looks thy fair face and makes it still.

71

Sleep, kinsman thou to death and trance
And madness, thou has forged at last
A night-long present of the past
In which we went through summer France.[7]

5   Hadst thou such credit with the soul?
Then bring an opiate trebly strong,
Drug down the blindfold sense of wrong,
That so my pleasure may be whole;

---

7. In the summer of 1830 Hallam and Tennyson went through southern France en route to Spain.

While now we talk as once we talked
10   Of men and minds, the dust of change,
       The days that grow to something strange,
In walking as of old we walked

Beside the river's wooded reach,
       The fortress, and the mountain ridge,
15   The cataract flashing from the bridge,
The breaker breaking on the beach.

72

Risest thou thus, dim dawn, again,[8]
And howlest, issuing out of night,
With blasts that blow the poplar white,
And lash with storm the streaming pane?

5   Day, when my crowned estate[9] begun
       To pine in that reverse of doom,[1]
       Which sickened every living bloom,
And blurred the splendor of the sun;

Who usherest in the dolorous hour
10   With thy quick tears that make the rose
       Pull sideways, and the daisy close
Her crimson fringes to the shower;

Who mightst have heaved a windless flame
       Up the deep East, or, whispering, played
15   A checker-work of beam and shade
Along the hills, yet looked the same,

As wan, as chill, as wild as now;
       Day, marked as with some hideous crime,
       When the dark hand struck down through time,
20   And canceled nature's best: but thou,

Lift as thou mayst thy burthened brows
       Through clouds that drench the morning star,
       And whirl the ungarnered sheaf afar,
And sow the sky with flying boughs,

25   And up thy vault with roaring sound
       Climb thy thick noon, disastrous day;
       Touch thy dull goal of joyless gray,
And hide thy shame beneath the ground.

                    ☼   ☼   ☼

8. September 15, 1834, the first anniversary of
Hallam's death.
9. State of happiness.

1. The reversal or disaster that doom brought
upon him when Hallam died.

75

I leave thy praises unexpressed
In verse that brings myself relief,
And by the measure of my grief
I leave thy greatness to be guessed.

5 What practice howsoe'er expert
In fitting aptest words to things,
Or voice the richest-toned that sings,
Hath power to give thee as thou wert?

I care not in these fading days
10 To raise a cry that lasts not long,
And round thee with the breeze of song
To stir a little dust of praise.

Thy leaf has perished in the green,
And, while we breathe beneath the sun,
15 The world which credits what is done
Is cold to all that might have been.

So here shall silence guard thy fame;
But somewhere, out of human view,
Whate'er thy hands are set to do
20 Is wrought with tumult of acclaim.

*   *   *

78

Again at Christmas² did we weave
The holly round the Christmas hearth;
The silent snow possessed the earth,
And calmly fell our Christmas eve.

5 The yule clog° sparkled keen with frost,   *log*
No wing of wind the region swept,
But over all things brooding slept
The quiet sense of something lost.

As in the winters left behind,
10 Again our ancient games had place,
The mimic picture's³ breathing grace,
And dance and song and hoodman-blind.⁴

Who showed a token of distress?
No single tear, no mark of pain—
15 O sorrow, then can sorrow wane?
O grief, can grief be changed to less?

O last regret, regret can die!
No—mixed with all this mystic frame,
Her deep relations are the same,
20 But with long use her tears are dry.

* * *

82

I wage not any feud with Death
For changes wrought on form and face;
No lower life that earth's embrace
May breed with him can fright my faith.

5 Eternal process moving on,
From state to state the spirit walks;
And these are but the shattered stalks,
Or ruined chrysalis of one.

Nor blame I Death, because he bare
10 The use of virtue out of earth;
I know transplanted human worth
Will bloom to profit, otherwhere.

For this alone on Death I wreak
The wrath that garners in my heart:
15 He put our lives so far apart
We cannot hear each other speak.

83

Dip down upon the northern shore,
O sweet new-year° delaying long;   *spring 1835*
Thou doest expectant Nature wrong;
Delaying long, delay no more.

5 What stays thee from the clouded noons,
Thy sweetness from its proper place?
Can trouble live with April days,
Or sadness in the summer moons?

Bring orchis, bring the foxglove spire,
10 The little speedwell's° darling blue,   *spring flower*

Deep tulips dashed with fiery dew,
Laburnums, dropping-wells of fire.

O thou, new-year, delaying long,
Delayest the sorrow in my blood,
15   That longs to burst a frozen bud
And flood a fresher throat with song.

84

When I contemplate all alone
The life that had been thine below,
And fix my thoughts on all the glow
To which thy crescent would have grown,

5   I see thee sitting crowned with good,
A central warmth diffusing bliss
In glance and smile, and clasp and kiss,
On all the branches of thy blood;

Thy blood, my friend, and partly mine;
10   For now the day was drawing on,
When thou shouldst link thy life with one
Of mine own house, and boys of thine

Had babbled "Uncle" on my knee;
But that remorseless iron hour
15   Made cypress of her orange flower,[5]
Despair of hope, and earth of thee.

I seem to meet their least desire,
To clap their cheeks, to call them mine.
I see their unborn faces shine
20   Beside the never-lighted fire.

I see myself an honored guest,
Thy partner in the flowery walk
Of letters, genial table talk,
Or deep dispute, and graceful jest;

25   While now thy prosperous labor fills
The lips of men with honest praise,
And sun by sun the happy days
Descend below the golden hills

With promise of a morn as fair;
30   And all the train of bounteous hours
Conduct, by paths of growing powers,
To reverence and the silver hair;

5. Orange blossoms are associated with brides—here the poet's sister Emily Tennyson, to whom Hallam had been engaged. Cypress branches are associated with funerals.

Till slowly worn her earthly robe,
   Her lavish mission richly wrought,
35   Leaving great legacies of thought,
   Thy spirit should fail from off the globe;

What time mine own might also flee,
   As linked with thine in love and fate,
   And, hovering o'er the dolorous strait
40   To the other shore, involved in thee,

Arrive at last the blessed goal,
   And He that died in Holy Land
   Would reach us out the shining hand,
And take us as a single soul.

45 What reed was that on which I leant?
   Ah, backward fancy, wherefore wake
   The old bitterness again, and break
The low beginnings of content?

           *   *   *

86

Sweet after showers, ambrosial air,
   That rollest from the gorgeous gloom
   Of evening over brake° and bloom   *thicket*
And meadow, slowly breathing bare

5 The round of space,[6] and rapt below
   Through all the dewy-tasseled wood,
   And shadowing down the hornèd flood[7]
In ripples, fan my brows and blow

The fever from my cheek, and sigh
10   The full new life that feeds thy breath
   Throughout my frame, till Doubt and Death,
Ill brethren, let the fancy fly

From belt to belt of crimson seas
   On leagues of odor streaming far,
15   To where in yonder orient star
A hundred spirits whisper "Peace."

87

I passed beside the reverend walls[8]
   In which of old I wore the gown;

---

6. The "ambrosial air" is slowly clearing the clouds
from the sky.

7. Between two promontories [Tennyson's note].
8. Of Trinity College, Cambridge University.

I roved at random through the town,
And saw the tumult of the halls;

5   And heard once more in college fanes°   *chapels*
The storm their high-built organs make,
And thunder-music, rolling, shake
The prophet blazoned on the panes;

And caught once more the distant shout,
10   The measured pulse of racing oars
Among the willows; paced the shores
And many a bridge, and all about

The same gray flats again, and felt
The same, but not the same; and last
15   Up that long walk of limes I passed
To see the rooms in which he dwelt.

Another name was on the door.
I lingered; all within was noise
Of songs, and clapping hands, and boys
20   That crashed the glass and beat the floor;

Where once we held debate, a band
Of youthful friends,[9] on mind and art,
And labor, and the changing mart,
And all the framework of the land;

25   When one would aim an arrow fair,
But send it slackly from the string;
And one would pierce an outer ring,
And one an inner, here and there;

And last the master bowman, he,
30   Would cleave the mark. A willing ear
We lent him. Who but hung to hear
The rapt oration flowing free

From point to point, with power and grace
And music in the bounds of law,
35   To those conclusions when we saw
The God within him light his face,

And seem to lift the form, and glow
In azure orbits heavenly-wise;
And over those ethereal eyes
40   The bar of Michael Angelo?[1]

---

9. The Apostles, an undergraduate club to which
Tennyson and Hallam had belonged.
1. Hallam, like the Italian artist Michelangelo

(1475–1564), had a prominent ridge of bone above
his eyes.

88

Wild bird,[2] whose warble, liquid sweet,
  Rings Eden through the budded quicks,[3]
  O tell me where the senses mix,
  O tell me where the passions meet,

5 Whence radiate: fierce extremes employ
  Thy spirits in the darkening leaf,
  And in the midmost heart of grief
  Thy passion clasps a secret joy;

And I—my harp would prelude woe—
10   I cannot all command the strings;
  The glory of the sum of things
  Will flash along the chords and go.

89

Witch elms that counterchange the floor
  Of this flat lawn with dusk and bright;[4]
  And thou, with all thy breadth and height
  Of foliage, towering sycamore;

5 How often, hither wandering down,
  My Arthur found your shadows fair,
  And shook to all the liberal air
  The dust and din and steam of town!

He brought an eye for all he saw;
10   He mixed in all our simple sports;
  They pleased him, fresh from brawling courts
  And dusty purlieus° of the law.[5]   *regions*

O joy to him in this retreat,
  Immantled in ambrosial dark,
15   To drink the cooler air, and mark
  The landscape winking through the heat!

O sound to rout the brood of cares,
  The sweep of scythe in morning dew,
  The gust that round the garden flew,
20 And tumbled half the mellowing pears!

O bliss, when all in circle drawn
  About him, heart and ear were fed

2. Probably a nightingale.
3. Hawthorn hedges.
4. Shadows of the elm tree checker the lawn at

Somersby, the Tennysons' country home.
5. Hallam became a law student in London after
leaving Cambridge.

To hear him, as he lay and read
The Tuscan poets[6] on the lawn!

25 Or in the all-golden afternoon
    A guest, or happy sister, sung,
    Or here she brought the harp and flung
    A ballad to the brightening moon.

    Nor less it pleased in livelier moods,
30   Beyond the bounding hill to stray,
    And break the livelong summer day
    With banquet in the distant woods;

    Whereat we glanced from theme to theme,
    Discussed the books to love or hate,
35   Or touched the changes of the state,
    Or threaded some Socratic dream;[7]

    But if I praised the busy town,
    He loved to rail against it still,
    For "ground in yonder social mill
40 We rub each other's angles down,

    "And merge," he said, "in form and gloss
    The picturesque of man and man."
    We talked: the stream beneath us ran,
    The wine-flask lying couched in moss,

45 Or cooled within the glooming wave;
    And last, returning from afar,
    Before the crimson-circled star[8]
    Had fallen into her father's[9] grave,

    And brushing ankle-deep in flowers,
50   We heard behind the woodbine veil
    The milk that bubbled in° the pail,   *into*
    And buzzings of the honeyed hours.

                    ☆   ☆   ☆

                    91

    When rosy plumelets tuft the larch,
    And rarely° pipes the mounted thrush,   *exquisitely*
    Or underneath the barren bush
    Flits by the sea-blue bird° of March;   *kingfisher*

---

6. A group of 13th- and 14th-century poets in central Italy (Tuscany); the best-known of them are Dante and Petrarch.
7. I.e., worked our way through some discourse of Socrates (as recorded by Plato).

8. Venus, which will sink into the west as the Sun has done.
9. According to the nebular hypothesis, planets condensed out of the sun's atmosphere; in this sense the Sun is the "father" of planets.

5   Come, wear the form by which I know
    Thy spirit in time among thy peers;
    The hope of unaccomplished years
  Be large and lucid round thy brow.

  When summer's hourly-mellowing change
10   May breathe, with many roses sweet,
    Upon the thousand waves of wheat
  That ripple round the lowly grange,°   *outlying farmhouse*

  Come; not in watches of the night,
    But where the sunbeam broodeth warm,
15   Come, beauteous in thine after form,
  And like a finer light in light.

* * *

93

  I shall not see thee. Dare I say
    No spirit ever brake the band
    That stays him from the native land
  Where first he walked when clasped in clay?[1]

5   No visual shade of someone lost,
    But he, the Spirit himself, may come
    Where all the nerve of sense is numb,
  Spirit to Spirit, Ghost to Ghost.

  Oh, therefore from thy sightless° range   *invisible*
10   With gods in unconjectured bliss,
    Oh, from the distance of the abyss
  Of tenfold-complicated change,

  Descend, and touch, and enter; hear
    The wish too strong for words to name,
15   That in this blindness of the frame°   *human body*
  My Ghost may feel that thine is near.

94

  How pure at heart and sound in head,
    With what divine affections bold
    Should be the man whose thought would hold
  An hour's communion with the dead.

5   In vain shalt thou, or any, call
    The spirits from their golden day,

---

1. I.e., when he was alive and in fleshly form.

Except, like them, thou too canst say,
My spirit is at peace with all.

They haunt the silence of the breast,
10   Imaginations calm and fair,
    The memory like a cloudless air,
    The conscience as a sea at rest;

But when the heart is full of din,
    And doubt beside the portal waits,
15   They can but listen at the gates,
And hear the household jar° within.   *noise*

95

By night we lingered on the lawn,
    For underfoot the herb was dry;
    And genial warmth; and o'er the sky
The silvery haze of summer drawn;

5   And calm that let the tapers burn
    Unwavering: not a cricket chirred;
    The brook alone far off was heard,
And on the board the fluttering urn.[2]

And bats went round in fragrant skies,
10   And wheeled or lit the filmy shapes[3]
    That haunt the dusk, with ermine capes
And woolly breasts and beaded eyes;

While now we sang old songs that pealed
    From knoll to knoll, where, couched at ease,
15   The white kine° glimmered, and the trees   *cows*
Laid their dark arms[4] about the field.

But when those others, one by one,
    Withdrew themselves from me and night,
    And in the house light after light
20 Went out, and I was all alone,

A hunger seized my heart; I read
    Of that glad year which once had been,
    In those fallen leaves which kept their green,
The noble letters of the dead.

25   And strangely on the silence broke
    The silent-speaking words, and strange

2. Vessel for boiling water for tea or coffee, heated
by a fluttering flame.
3. The white-winged night moths called ermine
moths.
4. Cast the shadows of their branches.

Was love's dumb cry defying change
To test his worth; and strangely spoke

The faith, the vigor, bold to dwell
30   On doubts that drive the coward back,
And keen through wordy snares to track
Suggestion to her inmost cell.

So word by word, and line by line,
The dead man touched me from the past,
35   And all at once it seemed at last
The[5] living soul was flashed on mine.

And mine in this was wound, and whirled
About empyreal° heights of thought,   *heavenly*
And came on that which is, and caught
40   The deep pulsations of the world,

Aeonian music[6] measuring out
The steps of Time—the shocks of Chance—
The blows of Death. At length my trance
Was canceled, stricken through with doubt.[7]

45   Vague words! but ah, how hard to frame
In matter-molded forms of speech,
Or even for intellect to reach
Through memory that which I became.

Till now the doubtful dusk revealed
50   The knolls once more where, couched at ease,
The white kine glimmered, and the trees
Laid their dark arms about the field;

And sucked from out the distant gloom
A breeze began to tremble o'er
55   The large leaves of the sycamore,
And fluctuate all the still perfume,

And gathering freshlier overhead,
Rocked the full-foliaged elms, and swung
The heavy-folded rose, and flung
60   The lilies to and fro, and said,

5. "His" in the 1st edition. Also in the 1st edition, line 37 read: "And mine in his was wound."
6. Music of the universe, which has pulsated for eons.
7. In a letter of 1874, replying to an inquiry about his experience of mystical trances, Tennyson wrote: "A kind of waking trance I have frequently had, quite up from boyhood, when I have been all alone. This has generally come upon me through repeating my own name two or three times to myself silently, till all at once, as it were out of the intensity of the consciousness of individuality, the individuality itself seemed to dissolve and fade away into boundless being, and this not a confused state, but the clearest of the clearest, the surest of the surest, the weirdest of the weirdest, utterly beyond words, where death was an almost laughable impossibility, the loss of personality (if so it were) seeming no extinction but the only true life. . . . This might . . . be the state which St. Paul describes, 'Whether in the body I cannot tell, or whether out of the body I cannot tell.' . . . I am ashamed of my feeble description. Have I not said the state is utterly beyond words? But in a moment, when I come back to my normal state of 'sanity,' I am ready to fight for *mein liebes Ich* [my dear self], and hold that it will last for aeons of aeons" (*Alfred Lord Tennyson, A Memoir*, 1897, vol. 1, 320).

"The dawn, the dawn," and died away;
And East and West, without a breath,
Mixed their dim lights, like life and death,
To broaden into boundless day.

96

You say, but with no touch of scorn,
    Sweet-hearted, you,[8] whose light blue eyes
    Are tender over drowning flies,
You tell me, doubt is Devil-born.

5   I know not: one indeed I knew
    In many a subtle question versed,
    Who touched a jarring lyre at first,
But ever strove to make it true;

Perplexed in faith, but pure in deeds,
10   At last he beat his music out.
    There lives more faith in honest doubt,
Believe me, than in half the creeds.

He fought his doubts and gathered strength,
    He would not make his judgment blind,
15   He faced the specters of the mind
And laid them; thus he came at length

To find a stronger faith his own,
    And Power was with him in the night,
    Which makes the darkness and the light,
20 And dwells not in the light alone,

But in the darkness and the cloud,
    As over Sinaï's peaks of old,
    While Israel made their gods of gold,
Although the trumpet blew so loud.[9]

                 *   *   *

99

Risest thou thus, dim dawn, again,[1]
So loud with voices of the birds,
So thick with lowings of the herds,
Day, when I lost the flower of men;

8. A woman of simple faith.
9. After veiling Mount Sinai in a "thick cloud" and signifying the divine presence by "the voice of the trumpet" (Exodus 19.16), God addresses Moses from the "thick darkness" (20.21). Meanwhile Aaron made, and the Israelites worshipped, a golden calf (32.1–6).
1. September 15, 1835, the second anniversary of Hallam's death.

5   Who tremblest through thy darkling red
     On yon swollen brook that bubbles fast²
     By meadows breathing of the past,
     And woodlands holy to the dead;

     Who murmurest in the foliage eaves
10   A song that slights the coming care,³
     And Autumn laying here and there
     A fiery finger on the leaves;

     Who wakenest with thy balmy breath
     To myriads on the genial° earth,   *generative*
15   Memories of bridal, or of birth,⁴
     And unto myriads more, of death.

     Oh, wheresoever those⁵ may be,
     Betwixt the slumber of the poles,
     Today they count as kindred souls;
20   They know me not, but mourn with me.

               ※   ※   ※

103

     On that last night before we went
     From out the doors where I was bred,⁶
     I dreamed a vision of the dead,
     Which left my after-morn content.

5   Methought I dwelt within a hall,
     And maidens with me; distant hills
     From hidden summits fed with rills
     A river sliding by the wall.

     The hall with harp and carol rang.
10   They sang of what is wise and good
     And graceful. In the center stood
     A statue veiled, to which they sang;

     And which, though veiled, was known to me,
     The shape of him I loved, and love
15   Forever. Then flew in a dove
     And brought a summons from the sea;

     And when they learnt that I must go,
     They wept and wailed, but led the way

2. I.e., reflections of the clouded red light of dawn quiver on the surface of the fast-moving water.
3. I.e., that disregards future events such as death or the coming of autumn.
4. Cf. "Epilogue," lines 117–28 (p. 1187).
5. I.e., the many who remember death.

6. In 1837 Tennyson and his family moved away from their home in Lincolnshire, which had been closely associated with his friendship with Hallam. In section 104 the move seems to occur in 1835, the year of the third Christmas after Hallam's death.

To where the little shallop° lay   *light open boat*
20   At anchor in the flood below;

And on by many a level mead,°   *meadow*
And shadowing bluff that made the banks,
We glided winding under ranks
Of iris and the golden reed;

25   And still as vaster grew the shore
And rolled the floods in grander space,
The maidens gathered strength and grace
And presence, lordlier than before;

And I myself, who sat apart
30   And watched them, waxed° in every limb;   *grown*
I felt the thews of Anakim,[7]
The pulses of a Titan's[8] heart;

As one would sing the death of war,
And one would chant the history
35   Of that great race which is to be,[9]
And one the shaping of a star;

Until the forward-creeping tides
Began to foam, and we to draw
From deep to deep, to where we saw
40   A great ship lift her shining sides.[1]

The man we loved was there on deck,
But thrice as large as man he bent
To greet us. Up the side I went,
And fell in silence on his neck;

45   Whereat those maidens with one mind
Bewailed their lot; I did them wrong:
"We served thee here," they said, "so long,
And wilt thou leave us now behind?"

So rapt° I was, they could not win   *entranced*
50   An answer from my lips, but he
Replying, "Enter likewise ye
And go with us:" they entered in.

And while the wind began to sweep
A music out of sheet and shroud,

7. Plural of *Anak*; a reference to the giant sons of Anak (see Numbers 13.33).
8. Giant of Greek mythology.
9. See the account of the "crowning race" in "Epilogue," lines 128–44.
1. Cf. *The Passing of Arthur*, lines 361–469, in which Bedivere is left behind as Arthur's barge, the ship of death, sails away. In the present dream vision the speaker is taken aboard, as are his companions, who represent the creative arts of this world—"all the human powers and talents that do not pass with life but go along with it," as Tennyson said of this passage.

55   We steered her toward a crimson cloud
         That landlike slept along the deep.

104

The time draws near the birth of Christ;[2]
The moon is hid, the night is still;
A single church below the hill
Is pealing, folded in the mist.

5   A single peal of bells below,
         That wakens at this hour of rest
         A single murmur in the breast,
       That these are not the bells I know.

       Like strangers' voices here they sound,
10   In lands where not a memory strays,
          Nor landmark breathes of other days,
        But all is new unhallowed ground.

105

Tonight ungathered let us leave
This laurel, let this holly stand:[3]
We live within the stranger's land,
And strangely falls our Christmas eve.

5   Our father's dust is left alone
         And silent under other snows:
         There in due time the woodbine blows,°   blooms
       The violet comes, but we are gone.

       No more shall wayward grief abuse
10   The genial hour with mask and mime;
          For change of place, like growth of time,
        Has broke the bond of dying use.

       Let cares that petty shadows cast,
          By which our lives are chiefly proved,
15   A little spare the night I loved,
        And hold it solemn to the past.

       But let no footstep beat the floor,
          Nor bowl of wassail mantle warm;[4]

2. The third Christmas (1835) after Hallam's
death.
3. Cf. section 29, in which the family in their former home still continued to gather holly. In the
new home the customary observances lapse.
4. I.e., let no bowl of hot punch warm the mantelpiece.

For who would keep an ancient form
20   Through which the spirit breathes no more?

Be neither song, nor game, nor feast;
Nor harp be touched, nor flute be blown;
No dance, no motion, save alone
What lightens in the lucid east

25   Of rising worlds[5] by yonder wood.
Long sleeps the summer in the seed;
Run out your measured arcs, and lead
The closing cycle rich in good.

106

Ring out, wild bells, to the wild sky,
The flying cloud, the frosty light:
The year is dying in the night;
Ring out, wild bells, and let him die.

5   Ring out the old, ring in the new,
Ring, happy bells, across the snow:
The year is going, let him go;
Ring out the false, ring in the true.

Ring out the grief that saps the mind,
10   For those that here we see no more;
Ring out the feud of rich and poor,
Ring in redress to all mankind.

Ring out a slowly dying cause,
And ancient forms of party strife;
15   Ring in the nobler modes of life,
With sweeter manners, purer laws.

Ring out the want, the care, the sin,
The faithless coldness of the times:
Ring out, ring out my mournful rhymes,
20   But ring the fuller minstrel in.

Ring out false pride in place and blood,
The civic slander and the spite;
Ring in the love of truth and right,
Ring in the common love of good.

25   Ring out old shapes of foul disease;
Ring out the narrowing lust of gold;
Ring out the thousand wars of old,
Ring in the thousand years of peace.

5. The scintillating motion of the stars that rise [Tennyson's note].

Ring in the valiant man and free,
30   The larger heart, the kindlier hand;
Ring out the darkness of the land,
Ring in the Christ that is to be.[6]

107

It is the day when he was born.°   *February 1*
A bitter day that early sank
Behind a purple-frosty bank
Of vapor, leaving night forlorn.

5   The time admits not flowers or leaves
To deck the banquet. Fiercely flies
The blast of North and East, and ice
Makes daggers at the sharpened eaves,

And bristles all the brakes° and thorns   *thickets*
10   To yon hard crescent, as she hangs
Above the wood which grides[7] and clangs
Its leafless ribs and iron horns

Together, in the drifts[8] that pass
To darken on the rolling brine
15   That breaks the coast. But fetch the wine,
Arrange the board and brim the glass;

Bring in great logs and let them lie,
To make a solid core of heat;
Be cheerful-minded, talk and treat
20   Of all things even as he were by;

We keep the day. With festal cheer,
With books and music, surely we
Will drink to him, whate'er he be,
And sing the songs he loved to hear.

108

I will not shut me from my kind,
And, lest I stiffen into stone,
I will not eat my heart alone,
Nor feed with sighs a passing wind:

---

6. These allusions to the second coming of Christ and to the millennium are derived from Revelation 20, but Tennyson has interpreted the biblical account in his own way. He once told his son of his conviction that "the forms of Christian religion would alter; but that the spirit of Christ would still grow from more to more."
7. Clashes with a strident noise.
8. Either cloud drifts or clouds of snow.

5   What profit lies in barren faith,
     And vacant yearning, though with might
     To scale the heaven's highest height,
     Or dive below the wells of Death?

     What find I in the highest place,
10   But mine own phantom chanting hymns?
     And on the depths of death there swims
     The reflex of a human face.°   *his own face*

     I'll rather take what fruit may be
     Of sorrow under human skies:
15   'Tis held that sorrow makes us wise,
     Whatever wisdom sleep with thee.°   *Hallam*

109

     Heart-affluence in discursive talk
     From household fountains never dry;
     The critic clearness of an eye
     That saw through all the Muses' walk;[9]

5   Seraphic intellect and force
     To seize and throw the doubts of man;
     Impassioned logic, which outran
     The hearer in its fiery course;

     High nature amorous of the good,
10   But touched with no ascetic gloom;
     And passion pure in snowy bloom
     Through all the years of April blood;

     A love of freedom rarely felt,
     Of freedom in her regal seat
15   Of England; not the schoolboy heat,
     The blind hysterics of the Celt;[1]

     And manhood fused with female grace
     In such a sort, the child would twine
     A trustful hand, unasked, in thine,
20   And find his comfort in thy face;

     All these have been, and thee mine eyes
     Have looked on: if they looked in vain,
     My shame is greater who remain,
     Nor let thy wisdom make me wise.

                    *   *   *

9. The realm of art and literature.
1. A member or descendant of one of the groups
of peoples populating ancient Britain; cf. Arnold's
description of the Irish temperament in *On the
Study of Celtic Literature* (p. 1619).

115

Now fades the last long streak of snow,
  Now burgeons every maze of quick°   *hawthorn hedge*
  About the flowering squares,° and thick   *fields*
By ashen roots the violets blow.

5 Now rings the woodland loud and long,
  The distance takes a lovelier hue,
  And drowned in yonder living blue
The lark becomes a sightless song.

Now dance the lights on lawn and lea,
10 The flocks are whiter down the vale,
  And milkier every milky sail
On winding stream or distant sea;

Where now the seamew° pipes, or dives   *a seabird*
  In yonder greening gleam, and fly
15 The happy birds, that change their sky
To build and brood, that live their lives

From land to land; and in my breast
  Spring wakens too, and my regret
  Becomes an April violet,
20 And buds and blossoms like the rest.

*   *   *

118

Contèmplate all this work of Time,
  The giant laboring in his youth;
  Nor dream of human love and truth,
As dying Nature's earth and lime;[2]

5 But trust that those we call the dead
  Are breathers of an ampler day
  For ever nobler ends. They° say,   *Scientists*
The solid earth whereon we tread

In tracts of fluent heat began,
10 And grew to seeming-random forms,
  The seeming prey of cyclic storms,
Till at the last arose the man;

Who throve and branched from clime to clime,
  The herald of a higher race,

2. Two of the perishable organic ingredients of the human body.

15   And of himself in higher place
      If so he type³ this work of time

      Within himself, from more to more;
      Or, crowned with attributes of woe
      Like glories, move his course, and show
20   That life is not as idle ore,

      But iron dug from central gloom,
      And heated hot with burning fears,
      And dipped in baths of hissing tears,
      And battered with the shocks of doom

25   To shape and use. Arise and fly
      The reeling Faun,⁴ the sensual feast;
      Move upward, working out the beast,
      And let the ape and tiger die.

119

      Doors,⁵ where my heart was used to beat
      So quickly, not as one that weeps
      I come once more; the city sleeps;
      I smell the meadow in the street;

5   I hear a chirp of birds; I see
      Betwixt the black fronts long-withdrawn
      A light blue lane of early dawn,
      And think of early days and thee,

      And bless thee, for thy lips are bland,°   *gentle*
10   And bright the friendship of thine eye;
      And in my thoughts with scarce a sigh
      I take the pressure of thine hand.

120

      I trust I have not wasted breath:
      I think we are not wholly brain,
      Magnetic mockeries;⁶ not in vain,
      Like Paul⁷ with beasts, I fought with Death;

5   Not only cunning° casts in clay: *skillful*
      Let Science prove we are, and then

3. Emulate, prefigure as a type.
4. In Roman mythology a half-human, half-beast deity of the woods and mountains.
5. The doors of Hallam's house on London's Wim-
pole Street. Cf. section 7.
6. Mechanisms operated by responses to electrical forces.
7. 1 Corinthians 15.32.

What matters Science unto men,
At least to me? I would not stay.

Let him, the wiser man who springs
10   Hereafter, up from childhood shape
His action like the greater ape,
But I was *born* to other things.

121

Sad Hesper° o'er the buried sun   *evening star*
And ready, thou, to die with him,
Thou watchest all things ever dim
And dimmer, and a glory done.

5   The team is loosened from the wain,°   *hay wagon*
The boat is drawn upon the shore;
Thou listenest to the closing door,
And life is darkened in the brain.

Bright Phosphor,° fresher for the night,   *morning star*
10   By thee the world's great work is heard
Beginning, and the wakeful bird;
Behind thee comes the greater light.[8]

The market boat is on the stream,
And voices hail it from the brink;
15   Thou hear'st the village hammer clink,
And see'st the moving of the team.

Sweet Hesper-Phosphor, double name[9]
For what is one, the first, the last,
Thou, like my present and my past,
20   Thy place is changed; thou art the same.

*   *   *

123

There rolls the deep where grew the tree.
O earth, what changes hast thou seen!
There where the long street roars hath been
The stillness of the central sea.[1]

8. Cf. Genesis 1.16: "the greater light to rule the day."
9. The planet Venus, named for the Roman goddess of love, is both the evening star and the morning star (visible at different times in different seasons).
1. In a passage from *The Principles of Geology* (1832), a book well known to Tennyson, Sir

Charles Lyell discusses the "interchange of sea and land" that has occurred "on the surface of our globe": "In the Mediterranean alone, many flourishing inland towns and a still greater number of ports now stand where the sea rolled its waves since the era when civilized nations first grew in Europe."

5   The hills are shadows, and they flow
        From form to form, and nothing stands;
        They melt like mist, the solid lands,
    Like clouds they shape themselves and go.

    But in my spirit will I dwell,
10   And dream my dream, and hold it true;
        For though my lips may breathe adieu,
    I cannot think the thing farewell.

[margin: Individual Saving, based only on faith.]

124

    That which we dare invoke to bless;
        Our dearest faith; our ghastliest doubt;
        He, They, One, All; within, without;
    The Power in darkness whom we guess—

5   I found Him not in world or sun,
        Or eagle's wing, or insect's eye,[2]
        Nor through the questions men may try,
    The petty cobwebs we have spun.

    If e'er when faith had fallen asleep,
10   I heard a voice, "believe no more,"
        And heard an ever-breaking shore
    That tumbled in the Godless deep,

[margin: If he'd heard this then)]

    A warmth within the breast would melt
        The freezing reason's colder part,
15   And like a man in wrath the heart
    Stood up and answered, "I have felt."[3]

    No, like a child in doubt and fear:
        But that blind clamor made me wise;
        Then was I as a child that cries,
20 But, crying, knows his father near;

    And what I am beheld again
        What is, and no man understands;
        And out of darkness came the hands
    That reach through nature, molding men.

[margin: what have we but faith.]

[margin: he can't know, trust in faith.]

*   *   *

[margin: 1368 Dover Beach]

126

    Love is and was my lord and king,
        And in his presence I attend

2. He does not discover satisfactory proof of God's existence in the 18th-century argument that because objects in nature are designed there must exist a designer.
3. Cf. Carlyle's *Sartor Resartus* (1833–34), "The Everlasting No" (p. 1006).

To hear the tidings of my friend,
Which every hour his couriers bring.

5   Love is and was my king and lord,
And will be, though as yet I keep
Within the court on earth, and sleep
Encompassed by his faithful guard,

And hear at times a sentinel
10   Who moves about from place to place,
And whispers to the worlds of space,
In the deep night, that all is well.

127

And all is well, though faith and form[4]
Be sundered in the night of fear;
Well roars the storm to those that hear
A deeper voice across the storm,

5   Proclaiming social truth shall spread,
And justice, even though thrice again
The red fool-fury of the Seine
Should pile her barricades with dead.[5]

But ill for him that wears a crown,
10   And him, the lazar,[6] in his rags!
They tremble, the sustaining crags;
The spires of ice are toppled down,

And molten up, and roar in flood;
The fortress crashes from on high,
15   The brute earth lightens[7] to the sky,
And the great Aeon[8] sinks in blood,

And compassed by the fires of hell,
While thou, dear spirit, happy star,
O'erlook'st the tumult from afar,
20   And smilest, knowing all is well.

*   *   *

129

Dear friend, far off, my lost desire,
So far, so near in woe and weal,°   *happiness*

4. Traditional institutions through which faith was formerly expressed, such as the Church.
5. Reference to revolutionary uprisings in France, in each of which a king lost his throne (line 9): in 1789 against Louis XVI, in 1830 against Charles X, and in 1848 against Louis-Philippe. If, as Tennyson recollected, section 127 was finished at a date earlier than 1848, the reference to three revolutions (line 6) was prophetic. Seine: the river that runs through Paris.
6. Pauper suffering from disease.
7. Is lit up by fire.
8. A vast tract of time, here perhaps modern Western civilization.

O loved the most, when most I feel
There is a lower and a higher;

5   Known and unknown, human, divine;
Sweet human hand and lips and eye;
Dear heavenly friend that canst not die,
Mine, mine, forever, ever mine;

Strange friend, past, present, and to be;
10   Loved deeplier, darklier understood;
Behold, I dream a dream of good,
And mingle all the world with thee.

130

Thy voice is on the rolling air
I hear thee where the waters run;
Thou standest in the rising sun,
And in the setting thou art fair.

5   What art thou then? I cannot guess;
But though I seem in star and flower
To feel thee some diffusive power,
I do not therefore love thee less.

My love involves the love before;
10   My love is vaster passion now;
Tho' mix'd with God and Nature thou,
I seem to love thee more and more.

Far off thou art, but ever nigh;
I have thee still, and I rejoice;
15   I prosper, circled with thy voice;
I shall not lose thee tho' I die.

131

O living will[9] that shalt endure
When all that seems shall suffer shock,
Rise in the spiritual rock,[1]
Flow through our deeds and make them pure,

5   That we may lift from out of dust
A voice as unto him that hears,
A cry above the conquered years
To one that with us works, and trust,

9. Tennyson later commented that he meant here
the moral will of humankind.
1. Christ. Cf. 1 Corinthians 10.4: "And did all

drink the same spiritual drink; for they drank of
that spiritual Rock that followed them: and that
Rock was Christ."

With faith that comes of self-control,
10   The truths that never can be proved
Until we close with all we loved,
And all we flow from, soul in soul.

From Epilogue[2]   Epithalamion

* * *   poem celebrating
a wedding.

And rise, O moon, from yonder down,
110   Till over down and over dale
All night the shining vapor sail
And pass the silent-lighted town,

The white-faced halls, the glancing rills,
And catch at every mountain head,
115   And o'er the friths° that branch and spread   *inlets of the sea*
Their sleeping silver through the hills;

And touch with shade the bridal doors,
With tender gloom the roof, the wall;
And breaking let the splendor fall
120   To spangle all the happy shores

By which they rest, and ocean sounds,
And, star and system rolling past,
A soul shall draw from out the vast
And strike his being into bounds,

125   And, moved through life of lower phase,
Result in man,[3] be born and think,
And act and love, a closer link
Betwixt us and the crowning race

Of those that, eye to eye, shall look
130   On knowledge; under whose command
Is Earth and Earth's, and in their hand
Is Nature like an open book;

No longer half-akin to brute,
For all we thought and loved and did,
135   And hoped, and suffered, is but seed
Of what in them is flower and fruit;

Whereof the man that with me trod
This planet was a noble type°   *model, example*

2. The "Epilogue" describes the wedding day of Tennyson's sister Cecilia to Edmund Lushington. At the conclusion (printed here) the speaker reflects on the moonlit wedding night and the kind of offspring that will result from their union.

3. A child will be conceived and will develop in embryo through various stages. This development is similar to human evolution from the animal to the human level and perhaps to a future higher stage of development.

Appearing ere the times were ripe,
140 That friend of mine who lives in God,

That God, which ever lives and loves,
One God, one law, one element,
And one far-off divine event,
To which the whole creation moves.

1833–50   1850

The Charge of the Light Brigade[1]

1

Half a league,[2] half a league,
Half a league onward,
All in the valley of Death
Rode the six hundred.
5   "Forward the Light Brigade!
Charge for the guns!" he said.
Into the valley of Death
Rode the six hundred.[3]

2

"Forward, the Light Brigade!"
10   Was there a man dismayed?
Not though the soldier knew
Someone had blundered.
Theirs not to make reply,
Theirs not to reason why,
15   Theirs but to do and die.
Into the valley of Death
Rode the six hundred.

3

Cannon to right of them,
Cannon to left of them,
20   Cannon in front of them
Volleyed and thundered;
Stormed at with shot and shell,
Boldly they rode and well,
Into the jaws of Death,
25   Into the mouth of hell
Rode the six hundred.

1. During the Crimean War (1854–56), owing to confusion of orders, a brigade of British cavalry charged some entrenched batteries of Russian artillery. This blunder cost the lives of three-quarters of the six hundred horsemen engaged (see Cecil Woodham-Smith, *The Reason Why*, 1954). Tennyson rapidly composed his "ballad" (as he called the poem) after reading an account of the battle in a newspaper.
2. About a mile and a half.
3. In the recording Tennyson made of this poem, "hundred" sounds like "hunderd"—a Lincolnshire pronunciation that reinforces the rhyme with "thundered," etc. "Valley of Death": see Psalms 23.4 ("Yea, though I walk through the valley of the shadow of death").

4

Flashed all their sabers bare,
Flashed as they turned in air
Sab'ring the gunners there,
30   Charging an army, while
    All the world wondered.
Plunged in the battery smoke
Right through the line they broke;
Cossack and Russian
35   Reeled from the saber stroke
    Shattered and sundered.
Then they rode back, but not,
    Not the six hundred.

5

Cannon to right of them,
40   Cannon to left of them,
Cannon behind them
    Volleyed and thundered;
Stormed at with shot and shell,
While horse and hero fell.
45   They that had fought so well
Came through the jaws of Death,
Back from the mouth of hell,
All that was left of them,
    Left of six hundred.

6

50   When can their glory fade?
O the wild charge they made!
    All the world wondered.
Honor the charge they made!
Honor the Light Brigade,
55   Noble six hundred!

1854   1854

Idylls of the King

Idylls of the King   When John Milton was considering subjects suitable for an epic poem, one of those he entertained was the story of the British king Arthur, a semilegendary leader of about 500 C.E. who fought off the Saxon invaders who had swarmed into Britain after the withdrawal of the Roman legions. Tennyson likewise saw that the Arthurian story had epic potential and selected it for his lifework as "the greatest of all poetical subjects." At intervals, during a period of fifty years, he labored over the twelve books that make up his *Idylls of the King*, completing the work in 1888.

The principal source of Tennyson's stories of Arthur and his knights was Sir Thomas Malory's *Morte Darthur*, a version that Malory translated into English prose from French sources in 1470. As Talbot Donaldson suggested, one basis of the appeal of the Arthurian stories, like the legends of Robin Hood and stories of the American West, is that they represent the struggle of individuals to restore order when chaos

1190 / ALFRED, LORD TENNYSON

and anarchy are ascendant, a task performed in the face of seemingly overwhelming odds. The individual stories in Tennyson's *Idylls* have the same basic appeal, but the overall design of the whole poem is more ambitious and impressive. The epic represents the rise and fall of a civilization, and its underlying theme is that after two thousand years of Christianity, Western civilization may be going through a cycle in which it must confront the possibilities of a renewal in the future or an apocalyptic extinction. The first book, *The Coming of Arthur*, introduces the basic myth of a springtime hero transforming a wasteland and inspiring faith and hope in the highest values of civilized life among his devoted followers, the knights of his Round Table. Succeeding books move through summer and autumn and culminate in the bleak wintry scene of Arthur's last battle in which his order perishes in a civil war; the leader of the enemy forces is his own nephew, Sir Modred.

Throughout the later books of the *Idylls* the forces of opposition grow in strength, and discontent and resentment infect leading figures of the Round Table itself. The most glaring example is the adulterous relationship between Guinevere, Arthur's "sumptuous" queen (as Tennyson once described her), and the king's chief lieutenant and friend, Sir Lancelot. Many other fallings away subsequently come to light, such as the deceitful betrayal by Sir Gawain in the ninth book, *Pelleas and Ettarre*, and the cynical conduct of Sir Tristram, whose story is told in the bitter tenth book, *The Last Tournament*. Even Merlin, Arthur's trusted magician and counselor, becomes corrupted and can perform no further offices for the king (*Merlin and Vivien*). *The Passing of Arthur* depicts the apocalyptic end of this long process of disintegration and decay.

FROM IDYLLS OF THE KING

The Coming of Arthur

Leodogran, the King of Cameliard,
Had one fair daughter, and none other child;
And she was fairest of all flesh on earth,
Guinevere, and in her his one delight.

5   For many a petty king ere Arthur came
Ruled in this isle, and ever waging war
Each upon other, wasted all the land;
And still from time to time the heathen host
Swarm'd overseas, and harried° what was left.   *ravaged*
10   And so there grew great tracts of wilderness,
Wherein the beast was ever more and more,
But man was less and less, till Arthur came.
For first Aurelius[1] lived and fought and died,
And after him King Uther fought and died,
15   But either fail'd to make the kingdom one.
And after these King Arthur for a space,
And thro' the puissance° of his Table Round,   *power*
Drew all their petty princedoms under him,
Their king and head, and made a realm, and reign'd.

---

1. Brother of King Uther.

20   And thus the land of Cameliard was waste,
      Thick with wet woods, and many a beast therein,
      And none or few to scare or chase the beast;
      So that wild dog, and wolf and boar and bear
      Came night and day, and rooted° in the fields,   *dug for food*
25   And wallow'd in the gardens of the King.
      And ever and anon the wolf would steal
      The children and devour, but now and then,
      Her own brood lost or dead, lent her fierce teat
      To human sucklings; and the children, housed
30   In her foul den, there at their meat would growl,
      And mock their foster-mother on four feet,
      Till, straighten'd, they grew up to wolf-like men,
      Worse than the wolves. And King Leodogran
      Groan'd° for the Roman legions here again,   *yearned*
35   And Caesar's eagle:[2] then his brother king,
      Urien, assail'd him: last a heathen horde,
      Reddening the sun with smoke and earth with blood,
      And on the spike that split the mother's heart
      Spitting° the child, brake on him, till, amazed,   *impaling*
40   He knew not whither he should turn for aid.

          But—for he heard of Arthur newly crown'd,
      Tho' not without an uproar made by those
      Who cried, "He is not Uther's son"—the King
      Sent to him, saying, "Arise, and help us thou!
45   For here between the man and beast we die."

          And Arthur yet had done no deed of arms,
      But heard the call, and came: and Guinevere
      Stood by the castle walls to watch him pass;
      But since he neither wore on helm or shield
50   The golden symbol of his kinglihood,[3]
      But rode a simple knight among his knights,
      And many of these in richer arms than he,
      She saw him not, or mark'd not, if she saw,
      One among many, tho' his face was bare.
55   But Arthur, looking downward as he past,
      Felt the light of her eyes into his life
      Smite on the sudden, yet rode on, and pitch'd
      His tents beside the forest. Then he drave°   *drove away*
      The heathen; after, slew the beast, and fell'd
60   The forest, letting in the sun, and made
      Broad pathways for the hunter and the knight
      And so return'd.

                          For while he linger'd there,
      A doubt that ever smoulder'd in the hearts
      Of those great Lords and Barons of his realm
65   Flash'd forth and into war: for most of these,
      Colleaguing with a score of petty kings,

---

2. I.e., imperial protection.   3. The golden dragon [Tennyson's note].

Made head against him, crying, "Who is he
That he should rule us? who hath proven him
King Uther's son? for lo! we look at him,
70   And find nor face nor bearing, limbs nor voice,
Are like to those of Uther whom we knew.
This is the son of Gorloïs, not the King;
This is the son of Anton, not the King."

And Arthur, passing thence to battle, felt
75   Travail, and throes and agonies of the life,
Desiring to be join'd with Guinevere;
And thinking as he rode, "Her father said
That there between the man and beast they die.
Shall I not lift her from this land of beasts
80   Up to my throne, and side by side with me?
What happiness to reign a lonely king,
Vext—O ye stars that shudder over me,
O earth that soundest hollow under me,
Vext with waste dreams? for saving° I be join'd   unless
85   To her that is the fairest under heaven,
I seem as nothing in the mighty world,
And cannot will my will, nor work my work
Wholly, nor make myself in mine own realm
Victor and lord. But were I join'd with her,
90   Then might we live together as one life,
And reigning with one will in everything
Have power on this dark land to lighten it,
And power on this dead world to make it live."

Thereafter—as he speaks who tells the tale—
95   When Arthur reach'd a field-of-battle bright
With pitch'd pavilions of his foe, the world
Was all so clear about him, that he saw
The smallest rock far on the faintest hill,
And even in high day the morning star.
100   So when the King had set his banner broad,
At once from either side, with trumpet-blast,
And shouts, and clarions shrilling unto blood,
The long-lanced battle let their horses run.
And now the Barons and the kings prevail'd,
105   And now the King, as here and there that war
Went swaying; but the Powers who walk the world
Made lightnings and great thunders over him,
And dazed all eyes, till Arthur by main might,
And mightier of his hands with every blow,
110   And leading all his knighthood threw° the kings   defeated
Carádos, Urien, Cradlemont of Wales,
Claudias, and Clariance of Northumberland,
The King Brandagoras of Latangor,
With Anguisant of Erin, Morganore,
115   And Lot of Orkney. Then, before a voice
As dreadful as the shout of one who sees
To one who sins, and deems himself alone
And all the world asleep, they swerved and brake

Flying, and Arthur call'd to stay the brands°   *swords*
120 That hack'd among the flyers, "Ho! they yield!"
So like a painted battle the war stood
Silenced, the living quiet as the dead,
And in the heart of Arthur joy was lord.
He laugh'd upon his warrior° whom he loved   *Lancelot*
125 And honour'd most. "Thou dost not doubt me King,
So well thine arm hath wrought for me to-day."
"Sir and my liege," he cried, "the fire of God
Descends upon thee in the battle-field:
I know thee for my King!" Whereat the two,
130 For each had warded° either in the fight,   *guarded*
Sware on the field of death a deathless love.
And Arthur said, "Man's word is God in man:
Let chance what will, I trust thee to the death."

  Then quickly from the foughten field he sent
135 Ulfius, and Brastias, and Bedivere,
His new-made knights, to King Leodogran,
Saying, "If I in aught have served thee well,
Give me thy daughter Guinevere to wife."

  Whom when he heard, Leodogran in heart
140 Debating—"How should I that am a king,
However much he holp° me at my need,   *helped*
Give my one daughter saving to a king,
And a king's son?"—lifted his voice, and call'd
A hoary man, his chamberlain, to whom
145 He trusted all things, and of him required
His counsel: "Knowest thou aught of Arthur's birth?"

  Then spake the hoary chamberlain and said,
"Sir King, there be but two old men that know:
And each is twice as old as I; and one
150 Is Merlin, the wise man that ever served
King Uther thro' his magic art; and one
Is Merlin's master (so they call him) Bleys,
Who taught him magic; but the scholar ran
Before the master, and so far, that Bleys
155 Laid magic by, and sat him down, and wrote
All things and whatsoever Merlin did
In one great annal-book, where after-years
Will learn the secret of our Arthur's birth."

  To whom the King Leodogran replied,
160 "O friend, had I been holpen half as well
By this King Arthur as by thee to-day,
Then beast and man had had their share of me:
But summon here before us yet once more
Ulfius, and Brastias, and Bedivere."

165   Then, when they came before him, the King said,
"I have seen the cuckoo chased by lesser fowl,
And reason in the chase: but wherefore now

Do these your lords stir up the heat of war,
Some calling Arthur born of Gorloïs,
170 Others of Anton? Tell me, ye yourselves,
Hold ye this Arthur for King Uther's son?"

And Ulfius and Brastias answer'd, "Ay."
Then Bedivere, the first of all his knights
Knighted by Arthur at his crowning, spake—
175 For bold in heart and act and word was he,
Whenever slander breathed against the King—

"Sir, there be many rumours on this head:°   *subject*
For there be those who hate him in their hearts,
Call him baseborn, and since his ways are sweet,
180 And theirs are bestial, hold him less than man:
And there be those who deem him more than man,
And dream he dropt from heaven: but my belief
In all this matter—so ye care to learn—
Sir, for ye know that in King Uther's time
185 The prince and warrior Gorloïs, he that held
Tintagil castle by the Cornish sea,
Was wedded with a winsome wife, Ygerne:
And daughters had she borne him,—one whereof,
Lot's wife, the Queen of Orkney, Bellicent,
190 Hath ever like a loyal sister cleaved
To Arthur,—but a son she had not borne.
And Uther cast upon her eyes of love:
But she, a stainless wife to Gorloïs,
So loathed the bright dishonour of his love,
195 That Gorloïs and King Uther went to war:
And overthrown was Gorloïs and slain.
Then Uther in his wrath and heat besieged
Ygerne within Tintagil, where her men,
Seeing the mighty swarm about their walls,
200 Left her and fled, and Uther enter'd in,
And there was none to call to but himself.
So, compass'd by the power of the King,
Enforced she was to wed him in her tears,
And with a shameful swiftness: afterward,
205 Not many moons, King Uther died himself,
Moaning and wailing for an heir to rule
After him, lest the realm should go to wrack.°   *ruin*
And that same night, the night of the new year,
By reason of the bitterness and grief
210 That vext his mother, all before his time
Was Arthur born, and all as soon as born
Deliver'd at a secret postern-gate
To Merlin, to be holden far apart
Until his hour should come; because the lords
215 Of that fierce day were as the lords of this,
Wild beasts, and surely would have torn the child
Piecemeal among them, had they known; for each
But sought to rule for his own self and hand,

And many hated Uther for the sake
220 Of Gorloïs. Wherefore Merlin took the child,
And gave him to Sir Anton, an old knight
And ancient friend of Uther; and his wife
Nursed the young prince, and rear'd him with her own;
And no man knew. And ever since the lords
225 Have foughten like wild beasts among themselves,
So that the realm has gone to wrack: but now,
This year, when Merlin (for his hour had come)
Brought Arthur forth, and set him in the hall,
Proclaiming, 'Here is Uther's heir, your king,'
230 A hundred voices cried, 'Away with him!
No king of ours! a son of Gorloïs he,
Or else the child of Anton, and no king,
Or else baseborn.' Yet Merlin thro' his craft,
And while the people clamour'd for a king,
235 Had Arthur crown'd; but after, the great lords
Banded, and so brake out in open war."

      Then while the King debated with himself
If Arthur were the child of shamefulness,
Or born the son of Gorloïs, after death,
240 Or Uther's son, and born before his time,
Or whether there were truth in anything
Said by these three, there came to Cameliard,
With Gawain and young Modred, her two sons,
Lot's wife, the Queen of Orkney, Bellicent;
245 Whom as he could, not as he would, the King
Made feast for, saying, as they sat at meat,

      "A doubtful throne is ice on summer seas.
Ye come from Arthur's court. Victor his men
Report him! Yea, but ye—think ye this king—
250 So many those that hate him, and so strong,
So few his knights, however brave they be—
Hath body enow° to hold his foemen down?"   *enough*

      "O King," she cried, "and I will tell thee: few,
Few, but all brave, all of one mind with him;
255 For I was near him when the savage yells
Of Uther's peerage died, and Arthur sat
Crown'd on the daïs, and his warriors cried,
'Be thou the king, and we will work thy will
Who love thee.' Then the King in low deep tones,
260 And simple words of great authority,
Bound them by so strait° vows to his own self,   *strict*
That when they rose, knighted from kneeling, some
Were pale as at the passing of a ghost,
Some flush'd, and others dazed, as one who wakes
265 Half-blinded at the coming of a light.

      "But when he spake and cheer'd his Table Round
With large, divine, and comfortable words,

Beyond my tongue to tell thee—I beheld
From eye to eye thro' all their Order flash
270 A momentary likeness of the King:
And ere it left their faces, thro' the cross
And those around it and the Crucified,
Down from the casement over Arthur, smote
Flame-colour, vert° and azure, in three rays,   green
275 One falling upon each of three fair queens,
Who stood in silence near his throne, the friends
Of Arthur, gazing on him, tall, with bright
Sweet faces, who will help him at his need.

"And there I saw mage° Merlin, whose vast wit   magician
280 And hundred winters are but as the hands
Of loyal vassals toiling for their liege.

"And near him stood the Lady of the Lake,[4]
Who knows a subtler magic than his own—
Clothed in white samite,[5] mystic, wonderful.
285 She gave the King his huge cross-hilted sword,
Whereby to drive the heathen out: a mist
Of incense curl'd about her, and her face
Wellnigh was hidden in the minster° gloom;   church
But there was heard among the holy hymns
290 A voice as of the waters,[6] for she dwells
Down in a deep; calm, whatsoever storms
May shake the world, and when the surface rolls,
Hath power to walk the waters like our Lord.

"There likewise I beheld Excalibur
295 Before him at his crowning borne, the sword
That rose from out the bosom of the lake,
And Arthur row'd across and took it—rich
With jewels, elfin Urim,[7] on the hilt,
Bewildering heart and eye—the blade so bright
300 That men are blinded by it—on one side,
Graven in the oldest tongue of all this world,
'Take me,' but turn the blade and ye shall see,
And written in the speech ye speak yourself,
'Cast me away!' And sad was Arthur's face
305 Taking it, but old Merlin counsell'd him,
'Take thou and strike! the time to cast away
Is yet far-off.' So this great brand the king
Took, and by this will beat his foemen down."

Thereat Leodogran rejoiced, but thought
310 To sift his doubtings to the last, and ask'd,
Fixing full eyes of question on her face,
"The swallow and the swift are near akin,

---

4. The Lady of the Lake in the old legends is the
Church [Tennyson's note].
5. A rich silk fabric.
6. Cf. Revelation 14.2: "And I heard a voice from

heaven, as the voice of many waters."
7. Mentioned numerous times in the Old Testament, this is a device of precious stones worn by
priests and used in prophesying. "Elfin": elflike.

But thou art closer to this noble prince,
Being his own dear sister;" and she said,
315 "Daughter of Gorloïs and Ygerne am I;"
"And therefore Arthur's sister?" ask'd the King
She answer'd, "These be secret things," and sign'd
To those two sons to pass, and let them be.
And Gawain went, and breaking into song
320 Sprang out, and follow'd by his flying hair
Ran like a colt, and leapt at all he saw:
But Modred laid his ear beside the doors,
And there half-heard; the same that afterward
Struck for the throne, and striking found his doom.

325 And then the Queen made answer, "What know I?
For dark my mother was in eyes and hair,
And dark in hair and eyes am I; and dark
Was Gorloïs, yea and dark was Uther too,
Wellnigh to blackness; but this King is fair
330 Beyond the race of Britons and of men.
Moreover, always in my mind I hear
A cry from out the dawning of my life,
A mother weeping, and I hear her say,
'O that ye had some brother, pretty one,
335 To guard thee on the rough ways of the world.'

"Ay," said the King, "and hear ye such a cry?
But when did Arthur chance upon thee first?"

"O King!" she cried, "and I will tell thee true:
He found me first when yet a little maid:
340 Beaten I had been for a little fault
Whereof I was not guilty; and out I ran
And flung myself down on a bank of heath,
And hated this fair world and all therein,
And wept, and wish'd that I were dead; and he—
345 I know not whether of himself he came,
Or brought by Merlin, who, they say, can walk
Unseen at pleasure—he was at my side,
And spake sweet words, and comforted my heart,
And dried my tears, being a child with me.
350 And many a time he came, and evermore
As I grew greater grew with me; and sad
At times he seem'd, and sad with him was I,
Stern too at times, and then I loved him not,
But sweet again, and then I loved him well.
355 And now of late I see him less and less,
But those first days had golden hours for me,
For then I surely thought he would be king.

"But let me tell thee now another tale:
For Bleys, our Merlin's master, as they say,
360 Died but of late, and sent his cry to me,
To hear him speak before he left his life.

Shrunk like a fairy changeling[8] lay the mage;
And when I enter'd told me that himself
And Merlin ever served about the King,
365 Uther, before he died; and on the night
When Uther in Tintagil past away
Moaning and wailing for an heir, the two
Left the still King, and passing forth to breathe,
Then from the castle gateway by the chasm
370 Descending thro' the dismal night—a night
In which the bounds of heaven and earth were lost—
Beheld, so high upon the dreary deeps
It seem'd in heaven, a ship, the shape thereof
A dragon wing'd, and all from stem to stern
375 Bright with a shining people on the decks,
And gone as soon as seen. And then the two
Dropt to the cove, and watch'd the great sea fall,
Wave after wave, each mightier than the last,
Till last, a ninth one, gathering half the deep
380 And full of voices, slowly rose and plunged
Roaring, and all the wave was in a flame:
And down the wave and in the flame was borne
A naked babe, and rode to Merlin's feet,
Who stoopt and caught the babe, and cried 'The King!
385 Here is an heir for Uther!' And the fringe
Of that great breaker, sweeping up the strand,
Lash'd at the wizard as he spake the word,
And all at once all round him rose in fire,
So that the child and he were clothed in fire.
390 And presently thereafter follow'd calm,
Free sky and stars: 'And this same child,' he said,
'Is he who reigns; nor could I part in peace
Till this were told.' And saying this the seer
Went thro' the strait° and dreadful pass of death,   *narrow*
395 Not ever to be question'd any more
Save on the further side; but when I met
Merlin, and ask'd him if these things were truth—
The shining dragon and the naked child
Descending in the glory of the seas—
400 He laugh'd as is his wont,° and answer'd me   *custom*
In riddling triplets of old time, and said:

    " 'Rain, rain, and sun! a rainbow in the sky!
A young man will be wiser by and by;
An old man's wit may wander ere he die.
405 Rain, rain, and sun! a rainbow on the lea!
And truth is this to me, and that to thee;
And truth or clothed or naked let it be.
Rain, sun, and rain! and the free blossom blows:
Sun, rain, and sun! and where is he who knows?
410 From the great deep to the great deep he goes.'

8. Child secretly substituted for another.

"So Merlin riddling anger'd me; but thou
Fear not to give this King thine only child,
Guinevere: so great bards of him will sing
Hereafter; and dark sayings from of old
415   Ranging and ringing thro' the minds of men,
And echo'd by old folk beside their fires
For comfort after their wage-work is done,
Speak of the King; and Merlin in our time
Hath spoken also, not in jest, and sworn
420   Tho' men may wound him that he will not die,
But pass, again to come; and then or now
Utterly smite the heathen underfoot,
Till these and all men hail him for their king."

She spake and King Leodogran rejoiced,
425   But musing "Shall I answer yea or nay?"
Doubted, and drowsed, nodded and slept, and saw,
Dreaming, a slope of land that ever grew,
Field after field, up to a height, the peak
Haze-hidden, and thereon a phantom king,
430   Now looming, and now lost; and on the slope
The sword rose, the hind° fell, the herd was driven,   *peasant*
Fire glimpsed;° and all the land from roof and rick,[9]   *glimmered*
In drifts of smoke before a rolling wind,
Stream'd to the peak, and mingled with the haze
435   And made it thicker; while the phantom king
Sent out at times a voice; and here or there
Stood one who pointed toward the voice, the rest
Slew on and burnt, crying, "No king of ours,
No son of Uther, and no king of ours;"
440   Till with a wink his dream was changed, the haze
Descended, and the solid earth became
As nothing, but the King stood out in heaven,
Crown'd. And Leodogran awoke, and sent
Ulfius, and Brastias and Bedivere,
445   Back to the court of Arthur answering yea.

Then Arthur charged his warrior whom he loved
And honour'd most, Sir Lancelot, to ride forth
And bring the Queen;—and watch'd him from the gates:
And Lancelot past away among the flowers,
450   (For then was latter April) and return'd
Among the flowers, in May, with Guinevere.
To whom arrived, by Dubric the high saint,
Chief of the church in Britain, and before
The stateliest of her altar-shrines, the King
455   That morn was married, while in stainless white,
The fair beginners of a nobler time,
And glorying in their vows and him, his knights
Stood round him, and rejoicing in his joy.

9. Stacks of grain.

Far shone the fields of May thro' open door,
460 The sacred altar blossom'd white with May,
The Sun of May descended on their King,
They gazed on all earth's beauty in their Queen,
Roll'd incense, and there past along the hymns
A voice as of the waters, while the two
465 Sware at the shrine of Christ a deathless love:
And Arthur said, "Behold, thy doom° is mine.   destiny
Let chance what will, I love thee to the death!"
To whom the Queen replied with drooping eyes,
"King and my lord, I love thee to the death!"
470 And holy Dubric spread his hands and spake,
"Reign ye, and live and love, and make the world
Other, and may thy Queen be one with thee,
And all this Order of thy Table Round
Fulfil the boundless purpose of their King!"
475 So Dubric said; but when they left the shrine
Great Lords from Rome before the portal stood,
In scornful stillness gazing as they past;
Then while they paced a city all on fire
With sun and cloth of gold, the trumpets blew,
480 And Arthur's knighthood sang before the King:—

"Blow trumpet, for the world is white with May;
Blow trumpet, the long night hath roll'd away!
Blow thro' the living world—'Let the King reign.'

"Shall Rome or Heathen rule in Arthur's realm?
485 Flash brand and lance, fall battleaxe upon helm,
Fall battleaxe, and flash brand! Let the King reign.
"Strike for the King and live! his knights have heard.
That God hath told the King a secret word.
Fall battleaxe, and flash brand! Let the King reign.

490 "Blow trumpet! he will lift us from the dust.
Blow trumpet! live the strength and die the lust!
Clang battleaxe, and clash brand! Let the King reign.

"Strike for the King and die! and if thou diest,
The King is King, and ever wills the highest.
495 Clang battleaxe, and clash brand! Let the King reign.

"Blow, for our Sun is mighty in his May!
Blow, for our Sun is mightier day by day!
Clang battleaxe, and clash brand! Let the King reign.

"The King will follow Christ, and we the King
500 In whom high God hath breathed a secret thing.
Fall battleaxe, and flash brand! Let the King reign."

So sang the knighthood, moving to their hall.
There at the banquet those great Lords from Rome,
The slowly-fading mistress of the world,

505 Strode in, and claim'd their tribute as of yore.
But Arthur spake, "Behold, for these have sworn
To wage my wars, and worship me their King;
The old order changeth, yielding place to new;
And we that fight for our fair father Christ,
510 Seeing that ye be grown too weak and old
To drive the heathen from your Roman wall,
No tribute will we pay:" so those great lords
Drew back in wrath, and Arthur strove with Rome.

And Arthur and his knighthood for a space
515 Were all one will, and thro' that strength the King
Drew in the petty princedoms under him,
Fought, and in twelve great battles overcame
The heathen hordes, and made a realm and reign'd.

1869   1869

The Passing of Arthur[1]

That story which the bold Sir Bedivere,[2]
First made and latest left of all the knights,
Told, when the man was no more than a voice
In the white winter of his age, to those
5 With whom he dwelt, new faces, other minds.

For on their march to westward, Bedivere,
Who slowly paced among the slumbering host,
Heard in his tent the moanings of the King:

"I found Him in the shining of the stars,
10 I marked Him in the flowering of His fields,
But in His ways with men I find Him not.
I waged His wars, and now I pass and die.
O me! for why is all around us here
As if some lesser god had made the world,
15 But had not force to shape it as he would,
Till the High God behold it from beyond,
And enter it, and make it beautiful?
Or else as if the world were wholly fair,
But that these eyes of men are dense and dim,
20 And have not power to see it as it is:
Perchance, because we see not to the close;—
For I, being simple, thought to work His will,

---

1. On the composition of this final idyll and its relation to Tennyson's *Morte d'Arthur* of 1842, see n. 1, p. 1127. The principal source is Malory's *Morte Darthur* 21.4–5. Preceding the action of this idyll, Arthur has been in France with his nephew Gawain, fighting against the forces of Lancelot. Learning at that time of the gathering of an army against him in England, under the leadership of his nephew, Modred, Arthur returns there to engage in his last battle. Upon landing at Dover, Gawain is slain.
2. A knight who has long been close to the king, described in *The Coming of Arthur*, lines 173–74: "Bedivere, the first of all his knights / Knighted by Arthur at his crowning."

And have but stricken with the sword in vain;
And all whereon I leaned in wife and friend
25   Is traitor to my peace, and all my realm
Reels back into the beast, and is no more.
My God, thou hast forgotten me in my death:[3]
Nay—God my Christ—I pass but shall not die."

Then, ere that last weird battle in the west,
30   There came on Arthur sleeping, Gawain killed
In Lancelot's war, the ghost of Gawain blown
Along a wandering wind, and past his ear
Went shrilling. "Hollow, hollow all delight!
Hail, King! tomorrow thou shalt pass away.
35   Farewell! there is an isle of rest for thee.
And I am blown along a wandering wind,
And hollow, hollow, hollow all delight."
And fainter onward, like wild birds that change
Their season in the night and wail their way
40   From cloud to cloud, down the long wind the dream
Shrilled; but in going mingled with dim cries
Far in the moonlit haze among the hills,
As of some lonely city sacked by night,
When all is lost, and wife and child with wail
45   Pass to new lords; and Arthur woke and called,
"Who spake? A dream. O light upon the wind,
Thine, Gawain, was the voice—are these dim cries
Thine? or doth all that haunts the waste and wild
Mourn, knowing it will go along with me?"

50   This heard the bold Sir Bedivere and spake:
"O me, my King, let pass whatever will,
Elves, and the harmless glamour of the field;[4]
But in their stead thy name and glory cling
To all high places like a golden cloud
55   Forever: but as yet thou shalt not pass.
Light was Gawain in life, and light in death
Is Gawain, for the ghost is as the man;
And care not thou for dreams from him, but rise—
I hear the steps of Modred in the west,
60   And with him many of thy people, and knights
Once thine, whom thou hast loved, but grosser grown
Than heathen, spitting at their vows and thee.
Right well in heart they know thee for the King.
Arise, go forth and conquer as of old."

65   Then spake King Arthur to Sir Bedivere:
"Far other is this battle in the west
Whereto we move, than when we strove in youth,

---

3. Cf. Jesus' cry in Matthew 27.46: "My God, my
God, why hast thou forsaken me?"
4. Tennyson said the reference is to "the legends

which cluster round the King's name." One legend
told of the elves' bestowing gifts on Arthur as a
child.

And brake the petty kings, and fought with Rome,
Or thrust the heathen from the Roman wall,[5]
70 And shook him through the north. Ill doom° is mine   *destiny*
To war against my people and my knights.
The king who fights his people fights himself.
And they my knights, who loved me once, the stroke
That strikes them dead is as my death to me.
75 Yet let us hence, and find or feel a way
Through this blind haze, which ever since I saw
One lying in the dust at Almesbury,[6]
Hath folded in the passes of the world."

Then rose the King and moved his host by night,
80 And ever pushed Sir Modred, league by league,
Back to the sunset bound of Lyonnesse[7]—
A land of old upheaven from the abyss
By fire, to sink into the abyss again;
Where fragments of forgotten peoples dwelled,
85 And the long mountains ended in a coast
Of ever-shifting sand, and far away
The phantom circle of a moaning sea.
There the pursuer could pursue no more,
And he that fled no further fly the King;
90 And there, that day when the great light of heaven
Burned at his lowest in the rolling year,
On the waste sand by the waste sea they closed.
Nor ever yet had Arthur fought a fight
Like this last, dim, weird battle of the west.
95 A deathwhite mist slept over sand and sea:
Whereof the chill, to him who breathed it, drew
Down with his blood, till all his heart was cold
With formless fear; and even on Arthur fell
Confusion, since he saw not whom he fought.
100 For friend and foe were shadows in the mist,
And friend slew friend not knowing whom he slew;[8]
And some had visions out of golden youth,
And some beheld the faces of old ghosts
Look in upon the battle; and in the mist
105 Was many a noble deed, many a base,
And chance and craft and strength in single fights,
And ever and anon with host to host
Shocks, and the splintering spear, the hard mail hewn,
Shield-breakings, and the clash of brands,° the crash   *swords*
110 Of battleaxes on shattered helms, and shrieks
After the Christ, of those who falling down

5. Hadrian's Wall, built in northern Britain, by the 2nd-century Roman emperor Hadrian as a defense against invaders from the north.
6. The convent to which Guinevere withdraws in the eleventh idyll; during the king's farewell visit to her there, she lies in the dust at his feet.
7. Legendary land, extending west from Cornwall, that sank into the sea.
8. Cf. the description of a battle by the Greek writer Thucydides (ca. 455–ca. 400 B.C.E.) in his *History of the Peloponnesian War* (7.44), in which the invaders become confused by darkness and slaughter many of their own men, and Matthew Arnold's 1851 reworking of this scene in "Dover Beach," lines 35–37 (p. 1369).

Looked up for heaven, and only saw the mist;
And shouts of heathen and the traitor knights,
Oaths, insult, filth, and monstrous blasphemies,
115 Sweat, writhings, anguish, laboring of the lungs
In that close mist, and cryings for the light,
Moans of the dying, and voices of the dead.

Last, as by some one deathbed after wail
Of suffering, silence follows, or through death
120 Or deathlike swoon, thus over all that shore,
Save for some whisper of the seething seas,
A dead hush fell; but when the dolorous day
Grew drearier toward twilight falling, came
A bitter wind, clear from the North, and blew
125 The mist aside, and with that wind the tide
Rose, and the pale King glanced across the field
Of battle: but no man was moving there;
Nor any cry of Christian heard thereon,
Nor yet of heathen; only the wan wave
130 Brake in among dead faces, to and fro
Swaying the helpless hands, and up and down
Tumbling the hollow helmets of the fallen,
And shivered brands that once had fought with Rome,
And rolling far along the gloomy shores
135 The voice of days of old and days to be.

Then spake King Arthur to Sir Bedivere,
And whiter than the mist that all day long
Had held the field of battle was the King:

"Hearest thou this great voice that shakes the world,
140 And wastes the narrow realm whereon we move,
And beats upon the faces of the dead,
My dead, as though they had not died for me?—
O Bedivere, for on my heart hath fallen
Confusion, till I know not what I am,
145 Nor whence I am, nor whether I be King.
Behold, I seem but King among the dead."

Then spake the bold Sir Bedivere: "My King,
King everywhere! and so the dead have kings,
There also will I worship thee as King.
150 Yet still thy life is whole, and still I live
Who love thee; but who hates thee, he that brought
The heathen back among us, yonder stands,
Modred, unharmed, the traitor of thine house."

Then spake the King: "My house hath been my doom.
155 But call not thou this traitor of my house
Who hath but dwelled beneath one roof with me.
My house are rather they who sware my vows,
Yea, even while they brake them, owned° me King.   acknowledged
And well for thee, saying in my dark hour,

160　When all the purport of my throne hath failed,
　　　That quick or dead thou holdest me for King.
　　　King am I, whatsoever be their cry;
　　　And one last act of kinghood shalt thou see
　　　Yet, ere I pass." And uttering this the King
165　Made at the man: then Modred smote his liege
　　　Hard on that helm which many a heathen sword
　　　Had beaten thin; while Arthur at one blow,
　　　Striking the last stroke with Excalibur,
　　　Slew him, and all but slain himself, he fell.

170　　So all day long the noise of battle rolled
　　　Among the mountains by the winter sea;
　　　Until King Arthur's Table, man by man,
　　　Had fallen in Lyonnesse about their lord,
　　　King Arthur. Then, because his wound was deep,
175　The bold Sir Bedivere uplifted him,
　　　And bore him to a chapel nigh the field,
　　　A broken chancel with a broken cross,
　　　That stood on a dark strait of barren land:
　　　On one side lay the Ocean, and on one
180　Lay a great water, and the moon was full.

　　　　Then spake King Arthur to Sir Bedivere:
　　　"The sequel of today unsolders all
　　　The goodliest fellowship of famous knights
　　　Whereof this world holds record. Such a sleep
185　They sleep—the men I loved. I think that we
　　　Shall never more, at any future time,
　　　Delight our souls with talk of knightly deeds,
　　　Walking about the gardens and the halls
　　　Of Camelot, as in the days that were.
190　I perish by this people which I made,—
　　　Though Merlin sware that I should come again
　　　To rule once more;[9] but, let what will be, be,
　　　I am so deeply smitten through the helm
　　　That without help I cannot last til morn.
195　Thou therefore take my brand Excalibur,
　　　Which was my pride: for thou rememberest how
　　　In those old days, one summer noon, an arm
　　　Rose up from out the bosom of the lake,
　　　Clothed in white samite,[1] mystic, wonderful,
200　Holding the sword—and how I rowed across
　　　And took it, and have worn it, like a king;
　　　And, wheresoever I am sung or told
　　　In aftertime, this also shall be known:
　　　But now delay not: take Excalibur,
205　And fling him far into the middle mere:°　　　　*middle of the lake*
　　　Watch what thou seëst, and lightly° bring me word."　　*quickly*

9. Cf. Malory, *Morte Darthur* 21.7: "Some men
yet say in many parts of England that King Arthur
is not dead, but by the will of our Lord in another

place. And men say that he will come again."
1. A rich silk fabric.

To him replied the bold Sir Bedivere:
"It is not meet,° Sir King, to leave thee thus,   *fitting*
Aidless, alone, and smitten through the helm—
210 A little thing may harm a wounded man;
Yet I thy hest° will all perform at full,   *command*
Watch what I see, and lightly bring thee word."

So saying, from the ruined shrine he stepped,
And in the moon athwart° the place of tombs,   *across*
215 Where lay the mighty bones of ancient men,
Old knights, and over them the sea-wind sang
Shrill, chill, with flakes of foam. He, stepping down
By zigzag paths, and juts of pointed rock,
Came on the shining levels of the lake.

220 There drew he forth the brand Excalibur,
And o'er him, drawing it, the winter moon,
Brightening the skirts of a long cloud, ran forth
And sparkled keen with frost against the hilt:
For all the haft° twinkled with diamond sparks,   *hilt*
225 Myriads of topaz-lights, and jacinth°-work   *red gem*
Of subtlest jewelry. He gazed so long
That both his eyes were dazzled as he stood,
This way and that dividing the swift mind,
In act to throw: but at the last it seemed
230 Better to leave Excalibur concealed
There in the many-knotted waterflags,
That whistled stiff and dry about the marge.°   *shore*
So strode he back slow to the wounded King.

Then spake King Arthur to Sir Bedivere:
235 "Hast thou performed my mission which I gave?
What is it thou hast seen? or what hast heard?"
And answer made the bold Sir Bedivere:
"I heard the ripple washing in the reeds,
And the wild water lapping on the crag."

240 To whom replied King Arthur, faint and pale:
"Thou hast betrayed thy nature and thy name.
Not rendering true answer, as beseemed
Thy fëalty, nor like a noble knight:
For surer sign had followed, either hand,
245 Or voice, or else a motion of the mere.
This is a shameful thing for men to lie.
Yet now, I charge thee, quickly go again,
As thou art lief° and dear, and do the thing   *beloved*
I bade thee, watch, and lightly bring me word."

250 Then went Sir Bedivere the second time
Across the ridge, and paced beside the mere,
Counting the dewy pebbles, fixed in thought;
But when he saw the wonder of the hilt,

How curiously and strangely chased,[2] he smote
255 His palms together, and he cried aloud:

   "And if indeed I cast the brand away,
   Surely a precious thing, one worthy note,
   Should thus be lost forever from the earth,
   Which might have pleased the eyes of many men.
260 What good should follow this, if this were done?
   What harm, undone? Deep harm to disobey,
   Seeing obedience is the bond of rule.
   Were it well to obey then, if a king demand
   An act unprofitable, against himself?
265 The King is sick, and knows not what he does.
   What record, or what relic of my lord
   Should be to aftertime, but empty breath
   And rumors of a doubt? But were this kept,
   Stored in some treasure-house of mighty kings,
270 Some one might show it at a joust of arms,
   Saying, 'King Arthur's sword, Excalibur,
   Wrought by the lonely maiden of the Lake.
   Nine years she wrought it, sitting in the deeps
   Upon the hidden bases of the hills.'
275 So might some old man speak in the aftertime
   To all the people, winning reverence.
   But now much honor and much fame were lost."

   So spake he, clouded with his own conceit,[3]
   And hid Excalibur the second time,
280 And so strode back slow to the wounded king.

   Then spoke King Arthur, breathing heavily:
   "What is it thou hast seen? or what hast heard?"

   And answer made the bold Sir Bedivere:
   "I heard the water lapping on the crag,
285 And the long ripple washing in the reeds."

   To whom replied King Arthur, much in wrath:
   "Ah, miserable and unkind, untrue,
   Unknightly, traitor-hearted! Woe is me!
   Authority forgets a dying king,
290 Laid widowed of the power in his eye
   That bowed the will. I see thee what thou art,
   For thou, the latest-left of all my knights,
   In whom should meet the offices of all,
   Thou wouldst betray me for the precious hilt;
295 Either from lust of gold, or like a girl
   Valuing the giddy pleasure of the eyes.
   Yet, for a man may fail in duty twice,
   And the third time may prosper, get thee hence:

2. Decorated. "Curiously": skillfully.   3. Vain and foolish fancies.

But, if thou spare to fling Excalibur,
300 I will arise and slay thee with my hands."

Then quickly rose Sir Bedivere, and ran,
And, leaping down the ridges lightly, plunged
Among the bullrush beds, and clutched the sword,
And strongly wheeled and threw it. The great brand
305 Made lightnings in the splendor of the moon,
And flashing round and round and whirled in an arch,
Shot like a streamer of the northern morn,⁴
Seen where the moving isles of winter shock⁵
By night, with noises of the Northern Sea.
310 So flashed and fell the brand Excalibur:
But ere he dipped the surface, rose an arm
Clothed in white samite, mystic, wonderful,
And caught him by the hilt, and brandished him
Three times, and drew him under in the mere.
315 And lightly went the other to the King.

Then spoke King Arthur, drawing thicker breath:
"Now see I by thine eyes that this is done.
Speak out: what is it thou hast heard, or seen?"

And answer made the bold Sir Bedivere:
320 "Sir King, I closed mine eyelids, lest the gems
Should blind my purpose, for I never saw,
Nor shall see, here or elsewhere, till I die,
Not though I live three lives of mortal men,
So great a miracle as yonder hilt.
325 Then with both hands I flung him, wheeling him;
But when I looked again, behold an arm,
Clothed in white samite, mystic, wonderful,
That caught him by the hilt, and brandished him
Three times, and drew him under in the mere."

330 And answer made King Arthur, breathing hard:
"My end draws nigh; 'tis time that I were gone.
Make broad thy shoulders to receive my weight,
And bear me to the margin; yet I fear
My wound hath taken cold, and I shall die."

335 So saying, from the pavement he half rose,
Slowly, with pain, reclining on his arm,
And looking wistfully with wide blue eyes
As in a picture. Him Sir Bedivere
Remorsefully regarded through his tears,
340 And would have spoken, but he found not words;
Then took with care, and kneeling on one knee,
O'er both his shoulders drew the languid hands,
And rising bore him through the place of tombs.

4. The northern lights.   5. Where the icebergs collide.

But, as he walked, King Arthur panted hard,
345 Like one that feels a nightmare on his bed
When all the house is mute. So sighed the King,
Muttering and murmuring at his ear, "Quick, quick!
I fear it is too late, and I shall die."
But the other swiftly strode from ridge to ridge,
350 Clothed with his breath, and looking, as he walked,
Larger than human on the frozen hills.
He heard the deep behind him, and a cry
Before. His own thought drove him like a goad.
Dry clashed his harness in the icy caves
355 And barren chasms, and all to left and right
The bare black cliff clanged round him, as he based
His feet on juts of slippery crag that rang
Sharp-smitten with the dint of armèd heels—
And on a sudden, lo! the level lake,
360 And the long glories of the winter moon.

Then saw they how there hove a dusky barge,
Dark as a funeral scarf from stem to stern,
Beneath them; and descending they were ware°   aware
That all the decks were dense with stately forms,
365 Black-stoled, black-hooded, like a dream—by these
Three Queens with crowns of gold: and from them rose
A cry that shivered to the tingling stars,
And, as it were one voice, an agony
Of lamentation, like a wind that shrills
370 All night in a waste land, where no one comes,
Or hath come, since the making of the world.

Then murmured Arthur, "Place me in the barge."
So to the barge they came. There those three Queens
Put forth their hands, and took the King, and wept.
375 But she, that rose the tallest of them all
And fairest, laid his head upon her lap,
And loosed the shattered casque,° and chafed his hands,   helmet
And called him by his name, complaining loud,
And dropping bitter tears against a brow
380 Striped with dark blood: for all his face was white
And colorless, and like the withered moon
Smote by the fresh beam of the springing east;
And all his greaves and cuisses[6] dashed with drops
Of onset;[7] and the light and lustrous curls—
385 That made his forehead like a rising sun
High from the daïs-throne—were parched with dust;
Or, clotted into points and hanging loose,
Mixed with the knightly growth that fringed his lips.
So like a shattered column lay the King;
390 Not like that Arthur who, with lance in rest,

---

6. Armor to protect the front of the thighs.   7. Blood from battle.
"Greaves": armor to protect the leg below the knee.

From spur to plume a star of tournament,
Shot through the lists at Camelot, and charged
Before the eyes of ladies and of kings.

Then loudly cried the bold Sir Bedivere:
395 "Ah! my Lord Arthur, whither shall I go?
Where shall I hide my forehead and my eyes?
For now I see the true old times are dead,
When every morning brought a noble chance,
And every chance brought out a noble knight.
400 Such times have been not since the light[8] that led
The holy Elders with the gift of myrrh.
But now the whole Round Table is dissolved
Which was an image of the mighty world,
And I, the last, go forth companionless,
405 And the days darken round me, and the years,
Among new men, strange faces, other minds."

And slowly answered Arthur from the barge:
"The old order changeth, yielding place to new,
And God fulfills himself in many ways,
410 Lest one good custom should corrupt the world.
Comfort thyself: what comfort is in me?
I have lived my life, and that which I have done
May He within himself make pure! but thou,
If thou shouldst never see my face again,
415 Pray for my soul. More things are wrought by prayer
Than this world dreams of. Wherefore, let thy voice
Rise like a fountain for me night and day.
For what are men better than sheep or goats
That nourish a blind life within the brain,
420 If, knowing God, they lift not hands of prayer
Both for themselves and those who call them friend?
For so the whole round earth is every way
Bound by gold chains about the feet of God.
But now farewell. I am going a long way
425 With these thou seëst—if indeed I go
(For all my mind is clouded with a doubt)—
To the island-valley of Avilion;[9]
Where falls not hail, or rain, or any snow,
Nor ever wind blows loudly: but it lies
430 Deep-meadowed, happy, fair with orchard lawns
And bowery hollows crowned with summer sea,
Where I will heal me of my grievous wound."

So said he, and the barge with oar and sail
Moved from the brink, like some full-breasted swan
435 That, fluting a wild carol ere her death,
Ruffles her pure cold plume, and takes the flood

---

8. I.e., the star that guided the three kings ("Elders") to the infant Jesus at Bethlehem. See Matthew 2.1–12.

9. Or Avalon; in Celtic mythology and medieval romance, the Vale of the Blessed where heroes enjoyed life after death.

With swarthy webs.° Long stood Sir Bedivere   *webbed feet*
Revolving many memories, till the hull
Looked one black dot against the verge of dawn,
440 And on the mere the wailing died away.

    But when that moan had passed for evermore,
The stillness of the dead world's winter dawn
Amazed him, and he groaned, "The King is gone."
And therewithal came on him the weird rhyme,[1]
445 "From the great deep to the great deep he goes."

    Whereat he slowly turned and slowly clomb
The last hard footstep of that iron crag;
Thence marked the black hull moving yet, and cried,
"He passes to be King among the dead,
450 And after healing of his grievous wound
He comes again; but—if he come no more—
O me, be yon dark Queens in yon black boat,
Who shrieked and wailed, the three whereat we gazed
On that high day, when, clothed with living light,
455 They stood before his throne in silence, friends
Of Arthur, who should help him at his need?"[2]

    Then from the dawn it seemed there came, but faint
As from beyond the limit of the world,
Like the last echo born of a great cry,
460 Sounds, as if some fair city were one voice
Around a king returning from his wars.

    Thereat once more he moved about, and clomb
Even to the highest he could climb, and saw,
Straining his eyes beneath an arch of hand,
465 Or thought he saw, the speck that bare the King,
Down that long water opening on the deep
Somewhere far off, pass on and on, and go
From less to less and vanish into light.
And the new sun rose bringing the new year.

1833–69   1869

Crossing the Bar[1]

Sunset and evening star,
    And one clear call for me!
And may there be no moaning of the bar,[2]
    When I put out to sea,

1. In *The Coming of Arthur*, Merlin speaks a mysterious prophecy, in verse, concerning Arthur's birth; see lines 402–10 (p. 1198).
2. In *The Coming of Arthur*, Arthur's half-sister Bellicent describes his coronation. See lines 275–78 (p. 1196).

1. Although not the last poem written by Tennyson, "Crossing the Bar" appears, at his request, as the final poem in all collections of his work.
2. Mournful sound of the ocean beating on a sand bar at the mouth of a harbor.

1212 / EDWARD FITZGERALD

5   But such a tide as moving seems asleep,
     Too full for sound and foam,
     When that which drew from out the boundless deep
     Turns again home.

     Twilight and evening bell,
10   And after that the dark!
     And may there be no sadness of farewell,
     When I embark;

     For though from out our bourne° of Time and Place   boundary
     The flood may bear me far,
15   I hope to see my Pilot face to face
     When I have crossed the bar.

1889   1889

EDWARD FITZGERALD
1809–1883

Omar Khayyám was a twelfth-century mathematician, astronomer, and teacher from Nishapur in Persia. He was also the author of numerous rhymed quatrains, a verse form called in Persian *rubā'i*. Omar's four-line epigrams were subsequently brought together in collections called *Rubáiyát* and recorded in various manuscripts.

More than seven hundred years later, in 1857, an Omar manuscript came into the hands of Edward FitzGerald, who made from it one of the most popular poems of the Victorian period. FitzGerald was a scholar of comfortable means who lived in the country reading the classics and cultivating his garden. He also cultivated his friendships with writers such as Alfred, Lord Tennyson, William Makepeace Thackeray, and Thomas Carlyle, to whom he wrote charming letters. His translations from Greek and Latin were largely ignored and so too, at first, was his translation of Omar's Persian verses, which he published anonymously. In 1859 only two reviewers noticed the appearance of the *Rubáiyát of Omar Khayyám*, and the book was soon remaindered. Two years later the volume was discovered by D. G. Rossetti; enthusiasm for it gradually spread, until edition after edition was called for. FitzGerald subjected the poem to numerous revisions over the years; the first edition is printed here.

Experts have argued at great length whether FitzGerald's adaptation of Omar's poem is a faithful translation, but the question seemed unimportant to most of its original readers. Writing in 1869, the American academic Charles Eliot Norton felt that the poem "reads like the latest and freshest expression of the perplexity and of the doubt of the generation to which we ourselves belong." These nostalgic, yearning lyrics may well have spoken to the Victorians' sense of their own dislocation and paralysis, but the impressions of another place and time summoned up by the languid beauty of the verse were also captivating precisely because of their foreign aura. Certainly the highly polished stanzas of FitzGerald's *Rubáiyát* both contribute to and reflect a nineteenth-century fascination with the imagined exoticism of distant Oriental cultures.

Rubáiyát of Omar Khayyám

1

Awake! for Morning in the Bowl of Night
Has flung the Stone that puts the Stars to Flight:
And Lo! the Hunter of the East has caught
The Sultán's Turret in a Noose of Light.

2

5   Dreaming when Dawn's Left Hand was in the Sky
I heard a Voice within the Tavern cry,
    "Awake, my Little ones, and fill the Cup
"Before Life's Liquor in its Cup be dry."

3

And, as the Cock crew, those who stood before
10   The Tavern shouted—"Open then the Door!
    "You know how little while we have to stay,
"And, once departed, may return no more."

4

Now the New Year[1] reviving old Desires,
The thoughtful Soul to Solitude retires,
15   Where the WHITE HAND OF MOSES on the Bough
Puts out, and Jesus from the Ground suspires.[2]

5

Irám[3] indeed is gone with all its Rose,
And Jamshýad's[4] Sev'n-ring'd Cup where no one knows;
    But still the Vine her ancient Ruby yields,
20   And still a Garden by the Water blows.°   blooms

6

And David's Lips are lock't; but in divine
High piping Péhlevi,[5] with "Wine! Wine! Wine!
    "Red Wine!"—the Nightingale cries to the Rose
That yellow Cheek of her's to incarnadine.°   turn red

7

25   Come, fill the Cup, and in the Fire of Spring
The Winter Garment of Repentance fling:
    The Bird of Time has but a little way
To fly—and Lo! the Bird is on the Wing.

8

And look—a thousand Blossoms with the Day
30   Woke—and a thousand scatter'd into Clay:
    And this first Summer Month that brings the Rose
Shall take Jamshyd and Kaikobád[6] away.

---

1. In Persia the beginning of spring.
2. Breathes. Moses, Jesus: plants named in honor
of prophets who came before Mohammed. The
Persians believed that Jesus' healing power was in
his breath.

3. Identified by FitzGerald as a royal garden "now
sunk somewhere in the Sands of Arabia."
4. A legendary king.
5. The classical language of Persia.
6. Founder of a line of Persian kings.

9

But come with old Khayyám, and leave the Lot
Of Kaikobád and Kaikhosrú⁷ forgot!
35   Let Rustum⁸ lay about him as he will,
Or Hátim Tai⁹ cry Supper—heed them not.

10

With me along some Strip of Herbage strown
That just divides the desert from the sown,
        Where name of Slave and Sultán scarce is known,
40   And pity Sultán Máhmúd¹ on his Throne.

11

Here with a Loaf of Bread beneath the Bough,
A Flask of Wine, a Book of Verse—and Thou
        Beside me singing in the Wilderness—
And Wilderness is Paradise enow.

12

45   "How sweet is mortal Sovranty!"—think some:
Others—"How blest the Paradise to come!"
        Ah, take the Cash in hand and waive the Rest;
Oh, the brave Music of a *distant* Drum!

13

Look to the Rose that blows about us—"Lo,
50   Laughing," she says, "into the World I blow:
        "At once the silken Tassel of my Purse
Tear, and its Treasure on the Garden throw."

14

The Worldly Hope men set their Hearts upon
Turns Ashes—or it prospers; and anon,
55   Like Snow upon the Desert's dusty Face
Lighting a little Hour or two—is gone.

15

And those who husbanded the Golden Grain,
And those who flung it to the Winds like Rain,
        Alike to no such aureate Earth are turn'd
60   As, buried once, Men want dug up again.

16

Think, in this batter'd Caravanserai°   inn
Whose Doorways are alternate Night and Day,
        How Sultán after Sultán with his Pomp
Abode his Hour or two, and went his way.

17

65   They say the Lion and the Lizard keep
The Courts where Jamshýd gloried and drank deep;
        And Bahrám,² that great Hunter—the Wild Ass
Stamps o'er his Head, and he lies fast asleep.

---

7. A king.   1. A sultan who conquered India.
8. A warrior.   2. A king who was lost while hunting a wild ass.
9. A generous host.

18

I sometimes think that never blows so red
70   The Rose as where some buried Cæsar bled;
    That every Hyacinth[3] the Garden wears
  Dropt in its Lap from some once lovely Head.

19

And this delightful Herb whose tender Green
Fledges the River's Lip on which we lean—
75   Ah, lean upon it lightly! for who knows
  From what once lovely Lip it springs unseen!

20

Ah, my Belovéd, fill the Cup that clears
To-DAY of past Regrets and future Fears—
    To-morrow?—Why, To-morrow I may be
80   Myself with Yesterday's Sev'n Thousand Years.

21

Lo! some we loved, the loveliest and best
That Time and Fate of all their Vintage prest,
    Have drunk their Cup a Round or two before,
  And one by one crept silently to Rest.

22

85   And we, that now make merry in the Room
They left, and Summer dresses in new Bloom,
    Ourselves must we beneath the Couch of Earth
  Descend, ourselves to make a Couch—for whom?

23

Ah, make the most of what we yet may spend,
90   Before we too into the Dust descend;
    Dust into Dust, and under Dust, to lie,
  Sans Wine, sans Song, sans Singer, and—sans End!

24

Alike for those who for To-DAY prepare,
And those that after a To-MORROW stare,
95   A Muezzín[4] from the Tower of Darkness cries
  "Fools! your Reward is neither Here nor There!"

25

Why, all the Saints and Sages who discuss'd
Of the Two Worlds so learnedly, are thrust
    Like foolish Prophets forth; their Words to Scorn
100   Are scatter'd, and their Mouths are stopt with Dust.

26

Oh, come with old Khayyám, and leave the Wise
To talk; one thing is certain, that Life flies;

---

3. In classical myth the hyacinth was associated with grief; the plant was supposed to have sprung from the blood of Hyacinthus, a beautiful youth loved and accidentally killed by Apollo. Its petals were marked AI, the god's sorrowful cry.
4. One who calls the hour of prayer from the tower of a mosque.

One thing is certain, and the Rest is Lies;
The Flower that once has blown for ever dies.

27

105 Myself when young did eagerly frequent
Doctor and Saint, and heard great Argument
    About it and about: but evermore
Came out by the same Door as in I went.

28

With them the Seed of Wisdom did I sow,
110 And with my own hand labour'd it to grow:
    And this was all the Harvest that I reap'd—
"I came like Water, and like Wind I go."

29

Into this Universe, and *why* not knowing,
Nor *whence*, like Water willy-nilly flowing:
115   And out of it, as Wind along the Waste,
I know not *whither*, willy-nilly blowing.

30

What, without asking, hither hurried *whence?*
And, without asking, *whither* hurried hence!
    Another and another Cup to drown
120 The Memory of this Impertinence!

31

Up from Earth's Centre through the Seventh Gate
I rose, and on the Throne of Saturn[5] sate,
    And many Knots unravel'd by the Road;
But not the Knot of Human Death and Fate.

32

125 There was a Door to which I found no Key:
There was a Veil past which I could not see:
    Some little Talk awhile of ME and THEE.
There seemed—and then no more of THEE and ME.

33

Then to the rolling Heav'n itself I cried,
130 Asking, "What Lamp had Destiny to guide
    "Her little Children stumbling in the Dark?"
And—"A blind Understanding!" Heav'n replied.

34

Then to this earthen Bowl did I adjourn
My Lip the secret Well of Life to learn:
135   And Lip to Lip it murmur'd—"While you live
"Drink!—for once dead you never shall return."

35

I think the Vessel, that with fugitive
Articulation answer'd, once did live,

5. The seat of knowledge. According to a note by FitzGerald, Saturn was lord of the seventh heaven.

And merry-make; and the cold Lip I kiss'd
140   How many Kisses might it take—and give!

36

For in the Market-place, one Dusk of Day,
I watch'd the Potter thumping his wet Clay:
    And with its all obliterated Tongue
It murmur'd—"Gently, Brother, gently, pray!"

37

145   Ah, fill the Cup:—what boots it to repeat
How Time is slipping underneath our Feet:
    Unborn To-MORROW, and dead YESTERDAY,
Why fret about them if To-DAY be sweet!

38

One Moment in Annihilation's Waste,
150   One Moment, of the Well of Life to taste—
    The Stars are setting and the Caravan
Starts for the Dawn of Nothing—Oh, make haste!

39

How long, how long, in infinite Pursuit
Of This and That endeavour and dispute?
155   Better be merry with the fruitful Grape
Than sadden after none, or bitter, Fruit.

40

You know, my Friends, how long since in my House
For a new Marriage I did make Carouse:
    Divorced old barren Reason from my Bed,
160   And took the Daughter of the Vine to Spouse.

41

For "Is" and "Is-NOT" though *with* Rule and Line,
And "Up-AND-DOWN" *without*, I could define,
    I yet in all I only cared to know,
Was never deep in anything but—Wine.

42

165   And lately, by the Tavern Door agape,
Came stealing through the Dusk an Angel Shape
    Bearing a Vessel on his Shoulder; and
He bid me taste of it; and 'twas—the Grape!

43

The Grape that can with Logic absolute
170   The Two-and-Seventy jarring Sects[6] confute:
    The subtle Alchemist that in a Trice
Life's leaden Metal into Gold transmute.

44

The mighty Mahmúd, the victorious Lord,
That all the misbelieving and black Horde[7]

---

6. The 72 Sects into which Islamism so soon split
[FitzGerald's note].

7. This alludes to Mahmúd's Conquest of India
and its swarthy Idolaters [FitzGerald's note].

175   Of Fears and Sorrows that infest the Soul
      Scatters and slays with his enchanted Sword.

45

    But leave the Wise to wrangle, and with me
    The Quarrel of the Universe let be:
      And, in some corner of the Hubbub coucht,
180   Make Game of that which makes as much of Thee.

46

    For in and out, above, about, below,
    'Tis nothing but a Magic Shadow-show,[8]
      Play'd in a Box whose Candle is the Sun,
    Round which we Phantom Figures come and go.

47

185   And if the Wine you drink, the Lip you press,
    End in the Nothing all Things end in—Yes—
      Then fancy while Thou art, Thou art but what
    Thou shalt be—Nothing—Thou shalt not be less.

48

    While the Rose blows along the River Brink,
190   With old Khayyám the Ruby Vintage drink:
      And when the Angel with his darker Draught
    Draws up to Thee—take that, and do not shrink.

49

    'Tis all a Chequer-board of Nights and Days
    Where Destiny with Men for Pieces plays:
195   Hither and thither moves, and mates, and slays,
    And one by one back in the Closet lays.

50

    The Ball no Question makes of Ayes and Noes,
    But Right or Left, as strikes the Player° goes;   *polo player*
      And He that toss'd Thee down into the Field,
200   *He* knows about it all—HE knows—HE knows!

51

    The Moving Finger writes; and, having writ,
    Moves on: nor all thy Piety nor Wit
      Shall lure it back to cancel half a Line,
    Nor all thy Tears wash out a Word of it.

52

205   And that inverted Bowl we call The Sky,
    Whereunder crawling coop't we live and die,
      Lift not thy hands to *It* for help—for It
    Rolls impotently on as Thou or I.

53

    With Earth's first Clay They did the Last Man's knead,
210   And then of the Last Harvest sow'd the Seed:

---

8. A type of magic lantern, in which a cylindrical drum, its interior painted with various figures, revolves around a lighted candle.

Yea, the first Morning of Creation wrote
What the Last Dawn of Reckoning shall read.

54

I tell Thee this—When, starting from the Goal,
Over the shoulders of the flaming Foal
215   Of Heav'n Parwín and Mushtara they flung,
In my predestin'd Plot of Dust and Soul⁹

55

The Vine had struck a Fibre; which about
If clings my Being—let the Súfi° flout;   *mystic*
Of my Base Metal may be filed a Key,
220   That shall unlock the Door he howls without.

56

And this I know: whether the one True Light,
Kindle to Love, or Wrath consume me quite,
One Glimpse of It within the Tavern caught
Better than in the Temple lost outright.

57

225   Oh, Thou, who didst with Pitfall and with Gin°   *trap*
Beset the Road I was to wander in,
Thou wilt not with Predestination round
Enmesh me, and impute my Fall to Sin?

58

Oh, Thou, who Man of baser Earth didst make,
230   And who with Eden didst devise the Snake;
For all the Sin wherewith the Face of Man
Is blacken'd, Man's Forgiveness give—and take!

Kúza-Náma¹

59

Listen again. One Evening at the Close
Of Ramazán,² ere the better Moon arose,
235   In that old Potter's Shop I stood alone
With the clay Population round in Rows.

60

And, strange to tell, among that Earthen Lot
Some could articulate, while others not:
And suddenly one more impatient cried—
240   "Who *is* the Potter, pray, and who the Pot?"

61

Then said another—"Surely not in vain
"My Substance from the common Earth was ta'en,

---

9. The speaker asserts that his fate was predestined by the configuration of the stars and planets at the moment of his birth, when he "start[ed] from the Goal." His horoscope involved the Pleiades ("Parwín") and the planet Jupiter ("Mushtari"), which were "flung" by the gods into a special position in relation to the constellation Equuleus ("the Foal," or colt).
1. The Book of Pots (Persian).
2. The month of fasting (Ramadan), during which no food is eaten from sunrise to sunset.

"That He who subtly wrought me into Shape
"Should stamp me back to common Earth again."

62

245   Another said—"Why, ne'er a peevish Boy,
"Would break the Bowl from which he drank in Joy;
"Shall He that *made* the Vessel in pure Love
"And Fansy, in an after Rage destroy!"

63

None answer'd this; but after Silence spake
250   A Vessel of a more ungainly Make:
"They sneer at me for leaning all awry;
"What! did the Hand then of the Potter shake?"

64

Said one—"Folks of a surly Tapster tell,
"And daub his Visage with the Smoke of Hell;
255   "They talk of some strict Testing of us—Pish!
"He's a Good Fellow, and 'twill all be well."

65

Then said another with a long-drawn Sigh,
"My Clay with long oblivion is gone dry:
"But, fill me with the old familiar Juice,
260   "Methinks I might recover by-and-bye!"

66

So while the Vessels one by one were speaking,
One spied the little Crescent[3] all were seeking:
And then they jogg'd each other, "Brother! Brother!
"Hark to the Porter's Shoulder-knot a-creaking!"

67

265   Ah, with the Grape my fading Life provide,
And wash my Body whence the Life has died,
And in the Windingsheet of Vine-leaf wrapt,
So bury me by some sweet Garden-side.

68

That ev'n my buried Ashes such a Snare
270   Of Perfume shall fling up into the Air,
As not a True Believer passing by
But shall be overtaken unaware.

69

Indeed the Idols I have loved so long
Have done my Credit in Men's Eye much wrong:
275   Have drown'd my Honour in a shallow Cup,
And sold my Reputation for a Song.

---

3. At the Close of the Fasting Month, Ramazán . . . , the first Glimpse of the New Moon . . . is looked for
with the utmost Anxiety, and hailed with all Acclamation [FitzGerald's note].

70
Indeed, indeed, Repentance oft before
I swore—but was I sober when I swore?
And then and then came Spring, and Rose-in-hand
280 My thread-bare Penitence apieces tore.

71
And much as Wine has play'd the Infidel,
And robb'd me of my Robe of Honour—well,
I often wonder what the Vintners buy
One half so precious as the Goods they sell.

72
285 Alas, that Spring should vanish with the Rose!
That Youth's sweet-scented Manuscript should close!
The Nightingale that in the Branches sang,
Ah, whence, and whither flown again, who knows!

73
Ah Love! could thou and I with Fate conspire
290 To grasp this sorry Scheme of Things entire,
Would not we shatter it to bits—and then
Re-mould it nearer to the Heart's Desire!

74
Ah, Moon of my Delight who know'st no wane,
The Moon of Heav'n is rising once again:
295 How oft hereafter rising shall she look
Through this same Garden after me—in vain!

75
And when Thyself with shining Foot shall pass
Among the Guests Star-scatter'd on the Grass,
And in thy joyous Errand reach the Spot
300 Where I made one—turn down an empty Glass!

TAMÁM SHUD[4]

1857   1859

4. It is ended (Persian).

ELIZABETH GASKELL
1810–1865

It is ironic that the writer whom contemporaries and future generations knew as "Mrs. Gaskell" once instructed her sister-in-law that it was "a silly piece of bride-like affectation not to sign yourself by your proper name." Despite the wifely identity that the name Mrs. Gaskell connotes, Elizabeth Gaskell, as she always signed herself, wrote fiction on contemporary social topics that stimulated considerable controversy. Her first novel, *Mary Barton* (1848), presents a sympathetic picture of the hardships and the grievances of the working class. Another early novel, *Ruth* (1853), portrays the seduction and rehabilitation of an unmarried mother.

Elizabeth Cleghorn Gaskell was born in 1810 in Chelsea, on the outskirts of London, to a family that followed Unitarianism, a Christian movement that rejected the doctrine of the Trinity and advocated religious tolerance. Her mother died when Gaskell was one, and the girl was sent to rural Knutsford, in Cheshire, to be raised by her aunt. At the age of twenty-one, she met and married William Gaskell, a Unitarian minister whose chapel was in the industrial city of Manchester. For the first ten years of her marriage, she led the life of a minister's wife, bearing five children, keeping a house, and helping her husband serve his congregation. When her fourth child and only son, William, died at the age of one year, Gaskell became depressed. Her husband encouraged her to write as a way of allaying her grief, and so she produced *Mary Barton*, subtitled *A Tale of Manchester Life*. In the preface to the novel, she wrote that she was inspired by thinking "how deep might be the romance in the lives of some of those who elbowed me daily in the busy streets of the town in which I resided. I had always felt a deep sympathy with the careworn men, who looked as if doomed to struggle through their lives in strange alternations between work and want." Observing the mutual distrust of the rich and the poor, and their accompanying resentments, Gaskell hoped that her novel would help create within her middle-class readership understanding and sympathy for the working classes.

Anonymously published, the novel was widely reviewed and discussed. Gaskell was soon identified as the author; she subsequently developed a wide acquaintance in literary circles. She wrote five more novels and about thirty short stories, many of which were published in Charles Dickens's journal *Household Words* and its successor, *All the Year Round*. The contrasting experiences Gaskell's life had given her of two ways of life, of rural Knutsford and industrial Manchester, defined the poles of her fiction. Her second novel, *Cranford* (1853), presents a delicate picture of the small events of country village life, a subject to which she returns with greater range and psychological depth in her last novel, *Wives and Daughters* (1866). In *North and South* (1855), Gaskell brings together the two worlds of her fiction in the story of Margaret Hale, a young woman from a village in the south of England who moves to a factory town in the north.

One of the writers Gaskell's literary fame led her to know was Charlotte Brontë, with whom she became friends. When Brontë died in 1855, Gaskell was approached by Patrick Brontë to write the story of his daughter's life. Gaskell's *Life of Charlotte Brontë* (1857) is a masterpiece of English biography and one of her finest portrayals of character. Her focus in the *Life* on the relationship between Brontë's identity as a writer and her role as daughter, sister, and wife reflects the balance Gaskell herself sought between the stories she wove and the people she cared for. Referred to by Dickens as "my dear Scheherazade," Gaskell wrote not just to entertain but also to critique society and to promote social reform.

The Old Nurse's Story[1]

You know, my dears, that your mother was an orphan, and an only child; and I dare say you have heard that your grandfather was a clergyman up in Westmoreland, where I come from. I was just a girl in the village school, when, one day, your grandmother came in to ask the mistress if there was any scholar there who would do for a nurse-maid; and mighty proud I was, I can tell ye,

1. Originally published anonymously in the 1852 Christmas number of Dickens's journal *Household Words*; it was later republished in Gaskell's *Lizzie Leigh, and Other Tales* (1855).

when the mistress called me up, and spoke to my being a good girl at my needle, and a steady honest girl, and one whose parents were very respectable, though they might be poor. I thought I should like nothing better than to serve the pretty young lady, who was blushing as deep as I was, as she spoke of the coming baby, and what I should have to do with it. However, I see you don't care so much for this part of my story, as for what you think is to come, so I'll tell you at once I was engaged,[2] and settled at the parsonage before Miss Rosamond (that was the baby, who is now your mother) was born. To be sure, I had little enough to do with her when she came, for she was never out of her mother's arms, and slept by her all night long; and proud enough was I sometimes when missis trusted her to me. There never was such a baby before or since, though you've all of you been fine enough in your turns; but for sweet winning ways, you've none of you come up to your mother. She took after her mother, who was a real lady born; a Miss Furnivall, a granddaughter of Lord Furnivall's in Northumberland. I believe she had neither brother nor sister, and had been brought up in my lord's family till she had married your grandfather, who was just a curate, son to a shopkeeper in Carlisle—but a clever fine gentleman as ever was—and one who was a right-down hard worker in his parish, which was very wide, and scattered all abroad over the Westmoreland Fells. When your mother, little Miss Rosamond, was about four or five years old, both her parents died in a fortnight—one after the other. Ah! that was a sad time. My pretty young mistress and me was looking for another baby, when my master came home from one of his long rides, wet and tired, and took the fever he died of; and then she never held up her head again, but just lived to see her dead baby, and have it laid on her breast before she sighed away her life. My mistress had asked me, on her death-bed, never to leave Miss Rosamond; but if she had never spoken a word, I would have gone with the little child to the end of the world.

The next thing, and before we had well stilled our sobs, the executors and guardians came to settle the affairs. They were my poor young mistress's own cousin, Lord Furnivall, and Mr. Esthwaite, my master's brother, a shopkeeper in Manchester; not so well to do then, as he was afterwards, and with a large family rising about him. Well! I don't know if it were their settling, or because of a letter my mistress wrote on her death-bed to her cousin, my lord; but somehow it was settled that Miss Rosamond and me were to go to Furnivall Manor House, in Northumberland, and my lord spoke as if it had been her mother's wish that she should live with his family, and as if he had no objections, for that one or two more or less could make no difference in so grand a household. So, though that was not the way in which I should have wished the coming of my bright and pretty pet to have been looked at—who was like a sunbeam in any family, be it never so grand—I was well pleased that all the folks in the Dale should stare and admire, when they heard I was going to be young lady's maid at my Lord Furnivall's at Furnivall Manor.

But I made a mistake in thinking we were to go and live where my lord did. It turned out that the family had left Furnivall Manor House fifty years or more. I could not hear that my poor young mistress had ever been there, though she had been brought up in the family; and I was sorry for that, for I should have liked Miss Rosamond's youth to have passed where her mother's had been.

2. Hired.

My lord's gentleman, from whom I asked as many questions as I durst, said that the Manor House was at the foot of the Cumberland Fells, and a very grand place; that an old Miss Furnivall, a great-aunt of my lord's, lived there, with only a few servants; but that it was a very healthy place, and my lord had thought that it would suit Miss Rosamond very well for a few years, and that her being there might perhaps amuse his old aunt.

I was bidden by my lord to have Miss Rosamond's things ready by a certain day. He was a stern, proud man, as they say all the Lord Furnivalls were; and he never spoke a word more than was necessary. Folk did say he had loved my young mistress; but that, because she knew that his father would object, she would never listen to him, and married Mr. Esthwaite; but I don't know. He never married at any rate. But he never took much notice of Miss Rosamond; which I thought he might have done if he had cared for her dead mother. He sent his gentleman with us to the Manor House, telling him to join him at Newcastle that same evening; so there was no great length of time for him to make us known to all the strangers before he, too, shook us off; and we were left, two lonely young things (I was not eighteen), in the great old Manor House. It seems like yesterday that we drove there. We had left our own dear parsonage very early, and we had both cried as if our hearts would break, though we were travelling in my lord's carriage, which I had thought so much of once. And now it was long past noon on a September day, and we stopped to change horses for the last time at a little smoky town, all full of colliers and miners. Miss Rosamond had fallen asleep, but Mr. Henry told me to waken her, that she might see the park and the Manor House as we drove up. I thought it rather a pity; but I did what he bade me, for fear he should complain of me to my lord. We had left all signs of a town or even a village, and were then inside the gates of a large wild park—not like the parks here in the south, but with rocks, and the noise of running water, and gnarled thorn-trees, and old oaks, all white and peeled with age.

The road went up about two miles, and then we saw a great and stately house, with many trees close around it, so close that in some places their branches dragged against the walls when the wind blew; and some hung broken down; for no one seemed to take much charge of the place;—to lop the wood, or to keep the moss-covered carriage-way in order. Only in front of the house all was clear. The great oval drive was without a weed; and neither tree nor creeper was allowed to grow over the long, many-windowed front; at both sides of which a wing projected, which were each the ends of other side fronts; for the house, although it was so desolate, was even grander than I expected. Behind it rose the Fells, which seemed unenclosed and bare enough; and on the left hand of the house as you stood facing it, was a little old-fashioned flower-garden, as I found out afterwards. A door opened out upon it from the west front; it had been scooped out of the thick dark wood for some old Lady Furnivall; but the branches of the great forest trees had grown and over-shadowed it again, and there were very few flowers that would live there at that time.

When we drove up to the great front entrance, and went into the hall I thought we should be lost—it was so large, and vast, and grand. There was a chandelier all of bronze, hung down from the middle of the ceiling; and I had never seen one before, and looked at it all in amaze. Then, at one end of the hall, was a great fire-place, as large as the sides of the houses in my country, with massy andirons and dogs[3] to hold the wood; and by it were heavy old-fashioned sofas. At the opposite end of the hall, to the left as you went in—on the western side—was an organ built into the wall, and so large that it filled up the best part of that end. Beyond it, on the same side, was a door; and opposite, on each side of the fire-place, were also doors leading to the east front; but those I never went through as long as I stayed in the house, so I can't tell you what lay beyond.

The afternoon was closing in, and the hall, which had no fire lighted in it, looked dark and gloomy; but we did not stay there a moment. The old servant who had opened the door for us bowed to Mr. Henry, and took us in through the door at the further side of the great organ, and led us through several smaller halls and passages into the west drawing-room, where he said that Miss Furnivall was sitting. Poor little Miss Rosamond held very tight to me, as if she were scared and lost in that great place, and, as for myself, I was not much better. The west drawing-room was very cheerful-looking, with a warm fire in it, and plenty of good comfortable furniture about. Miss Furnivall was an old lady not far from eighty, I should think, but I do not know. She was thin and tall, and had a face as full of fine wrinkles as if they had been drawn all over it with a needle's point. Her eyes were very watchful, to make up, I suppose, for her being so deaf as to be obliged to use a trumpet.[4] Sitting with her, working at the same great piece of tapestry, was Mrs. Stark, her maid and companion, and almost as old as she was. She had lived with Miss Furnivall ever since they both were young, and now she seemed more like a friend than a servant; she looked so cold and grey, and stony, as if she had never loved or cared for any one; and I don't suppose she did care for any one, except her mistress; and, owing to the great deafness of the latter, Mrs. Stark treated her very much as if she were a child. Mr. Henry gave some message from my lord, and then he bowed good-bye to us all,—taking no notice of my sweet little Miss Rosamond's out-stretched hand—and left us standing there, being looked at by the two old ladies through their spectacles.

I was right glad when they rung for the old footman who had shown us in at first, and told him to take us to our rooms. So we went out of that great drawing-room, and into another sitting-room, and out of that, and then up a great flight of stairs, and along a broad gallery—which was something like a library, having books all down one side, and windows and writing-tables all down the other—till we came to our rooms, which I was not sorry to hear were just over the kitchens; for I began to think I should be lost in that wilderness of a house. There was an old nursery, that had been used for all the little lords and ladies long ago, with a pleasant fire burning in the grate, and the kettle boiling on the hob, and tea things spread out on the table; and out of that room was the night-nursery, with a little crib for Miss Rosamond close to my bed. And old James called up Dorothy, his wife, to bid us welcome; and both he and she were so hospitable and kind, that by-and-by Miss Rosamond and me felt quite at home; and by the time tea was over, she was sitting on Dorothy's knee, and chattering away as fast as her little tongue could go. I soon found out that Dorothy was from Westmoreland, and that bound her and me together, as it were; and I would never wish to meet with kinder people

3. Large decorative fireplace supports.
4. A horn-shaped device used by the hard of hearing to amplify sound.

than were old James and his wife. James had lived pretty nearly all his life in my lord's family, and thought there was no one so grand as they. He even looked down a little on his wife; because, till he had married her, she had never lived in any but a farmer's household. But he was very fond of her, as well he might be. They had one servant under them, to do all the rough work. Agnes they called her; and she and me, and James and Dorothy, with Miss Furnivall and Mrs. Stark, made up the family; always remembering my sweet little Miss Rosamond! I used to wonder what they had done before she came, they thought so much of her now. Kitchen and drawing-room, it was all the same. The hard, sad Miss Furnivall, and the cold Mrs. Stark, looked pleased when she came fluttering in like a bird, playing and pranking hither and thither, with a continual murmur, and pretty prattle of gladness. I am sure, they were sorry many a time when she flitted away into the kitchen, though they were too proud to ask her to stay with them, and were a little surprised at her taste; though, to be sure, as Mrs. Stark said, it was not to be wondered at, remembering what stock her father had come of. The great, old rambling house, was a famous[5] place for little Miss Rosamond. She made expeditions all over it, with me at her heels; all, except the east wing, which was never opened, and whither we never thought of going. But in the western and northern part was many a pleasant room; full of things that were curiosities to us, though they might not have been to people who had seen more. The windows were darkened by the sweeping boughs of the trees, and the ivy which had overgrown them: but, in the green gloom, we could manage to see old China jars and carved ivory boxes, and great heavy books, and, above all, the old pictures!

Once, I remember, my darling would have Dorothy go with us to tell us who they all were; for they were all portraits of some of my lord's family, though Dorothy could not tell us the names of every one. We had gone through most of the rooms, when we came to the old state drawing-room over the hall, and there was a picture of Miss Furnivall; or, as she was called in those days, Miss Grace, for she was the younger sister. Such a beauty she must have been! but with such a set, proud look, and such scorn looking out of her handsome eyes, with her eyebrows just a little raised, as if she wondered how any one could have the impertinence to look at her; and her lip curled at us, as we stood there gazing. She had a dress on, the like of which I had never seen before, but it was all the fashion when she was young; a hat of some soft white stuff like beaver, pulled a little over her brows, and a beautiful plume of feathers sweeping round it on one side; and her gown of blue satin was open in front to a quilted white stomacher.[6]

"Well, to be sure!" said I, when I had gazed my fill. "Flesh is grass,[7] they do say; but who would have thought that Miss Furnivall had been such an out-and-out beauty, to see her now?"

"Yes," said Dorothy. "Folks change sadly. But if what my master's father used to say was true, Miss Furnivall, the elder sister, was handsomer than Miss Grace. Her picture is here somewhere; but, if I show it you, you must never let on, even to James, that you have seen it. Can the little lady hold her tongue, think you?" asked she.

I was not so sure, for she was such a little sweet, bold, open-spoken child,

---

5. Exciting, wonderful.
6. Ornamental covering for the front of the body. "Beaver": felted wool.

7. Cf. 1 Peter 1.24 ("For all flesh is as grass, and all the glory of men as the flower of grass. The grass withereth, and the flower thereof falleth away").

so I set her to hide herself; and then I helped Dorothy to turn a great picture, that leaned with its face towards the wall, and was not hung up as the others were. To be sure, it beat Miss Grace for beauty; and, I think, for scornful pride, too, though in that matter it might be hard to choose. I could have looked at it an hour, but Dorothy seemed half frightened of having shown it to me, and hurried it back again, and bade me run and find Miss Rosamond, for that there were some ugly places about the house, where she should like ill for the child to go. I was a brave, high-spirited girl, and thought little of what the old woman said, for I liked hide-and-seek as well as any child in the parish; so off I ran to find my little one.

As winter drew on, and the days grew shorter, I was sometimes almost certain that I heard a noise as if some one was playing on the great organ in the hall. I did not hear it every evening; but, certainly, I did very often; usually when I was sitting with Miss Rosamond, after I had put her to bed, and keeping quite still and silent in the bedroom. Then I used to hear it booming and swelling away in the distance. The first night, when I went down to my supper, I asked Dorothy who had been playing music, and James said very shortly that I was a gowk to take the wind soughing[8] among the trees for music; but I saw Dorothy look at him very fearfully, and Bessy, the kitchen-maid, said something beneath her breath, and went quite white. I saw they did not like my question, so I held my peace till I was with Dorothy alone, when I knew I could get a good deal out of her. So, the next day, I watched my time, and I coaxed and asked her who it was that played the organ; for I knew that it was the organ and not the wind well enough, for all I had kept silence before James. But Dorothy had had her lesson, I'll warrant, and never a word could I get from her. So then I tried Bessy, though I had always held my head rather above her, as I was evened[9] to James and Dorothy, and she was little better than their servant. So she said I must never, never tell; and, if I ever told, I was never to say *she* had told me; but it was a very strange noise, and she had heard it many a time, but most of all on winter nights, and before storms; and folks did say, it was the old lord playing on the great organ in the hall, just as he used to do when he was alive; but who the old lord was, or why he played, and why he played on stormy winter evenings in particular, she either could not or would not tell me. Well! I told you I had a brave heart; and I thought it was rather pleasant to have that grand music rolling about the house, let who would be the player; for now it rose above the great gusts of wind, and wailed and triumphed just like a living creature, and then it fell to a softness most complete; only it was always music and tunes, so it was nonsense to call it the wind. I thought, at first, it might be Miss Furnivall who played, unknown to Bessy; but, one day when I was in the hall by myself, I opened the organ and peeped all about it, and around it, as I had done to the organ in Crosthwaite Church once before, and I saw it was all broken and destroyed inside, though it looked so brave[1] and fine; and then, though it was noon-day, my flesh began to creep a little, and I shut it up, and ran away pretty quickly to my own bright nursery; and I did not like hearing the music for some time after that, any more than James and Dorothy did. All this time Miss Rosamond was making herself more and more beloved. The old ladies liked her to dine with them at their early dinner; James stood behind Miss Furnivall's chair,

8. Moaning. "Shortly": curtly. "Gowk": fool.   1. Excellent.
9. Of equal status.

and I behind Miss Rosamond's, all in state; and, after dinner, she would play about in a corner of the great drawing-room, as still as any mouse, while Miss Furnivall slept, and I had my dinner in the kitchen. But she was glad enough to come to me in the nursery afterwards; for, as she said, Miss Furnivall was so sad, and Mrs. Stark so dull; but she and I were merry enough; and, by-and-by, I got not to care for that weird rolling music, which did one no harm, if we did not know where it came from.

That winter was very cold. In the middle of October the frosts began, and lasted many, many weeks. I remember, one day at dinner, Miss Furnivall lifted up her sad, heavy eyes, and said to Mrs. Stark, "I am afraid we shall have a terrible winter," in a strange kind of meaning way. But Mrs. Stark pretended not to hear, and talked very loud of something else. My little lady and I did not care for the frost;—not we! As long as it was dry we climbed up the steep brows, behind the house, and went up on the Fells, which were bleak and bare enough, and there we ran races in the fresh, sharp air; and once we came down by a new path that took us past the two old gnarled holly-trees, which grew about half-way down by the east side of the house. But the days grew shorter and shorter; and the old lord, if it was he, played away more and more stormily and sadly on the great organ. One Sunday afternoon,—it must have been towards the end of November—I asked Dorothy to take charge of little Missey when she came out of the drawing-room, after Miss Furnivall had had her nap; for it was too cold to take her with me to church, and yet I wanted to go. And Dorothy was glad enough to promise, and was so fond of the child that all seemed well; and Bessy and I set off very briskly, though the sky hung heavy and black over the white earth, as if the night had never fully gone away; and the air, though still, was very biting and keen.

"We shall have a fall of snow," said Bessy to me. And sure enough, even while we were in church, it came down thick, in great large flakes, so thick it almost darkened the windows. It had stopped snowing before we came out, but it lay soft, thick and deep beneath our feet, as we tramped home. Before we got to the hall the moon rose, and I think it was lighter then,—what with the moon, and what with the white dazzling snow—than it had been when we went to church, between two and three o'clock. I have not told you that Miss Furnivall and Mrs. Stark never went to church: they used to read the prayers together, in their quiet gloomy way; they seemed to feel the Sunday very long without their tapestry-work to be busy at. So when I went to Dorothy in the kitchen, to fetch Miss Rosamond and take her up-stairs with me, I did not much wonder when the old woman told me that the ladies had kept the child with them, and that she had never come to the kitchen, as I had bidden her, when she was tired of behaving pretty in the drawing-room. So I took off my things and went to find her, and bring her to her supper in the nursery. But when I went into the best drawing-room, there sat the two old ladies, very still and quiet, dropping out a word now and then, but looking as if nothing so bright and merry as Miss Rosamond had ever been near them. Still I thought she might be hiding from me; it was one of her pretty ways; and that she had persuaded them to look as if they knew nothing about her; so I went softly peeping under this sofa, and behind that chair, making believe I was sadly frightened at not finding her.

"What's the matter, Hester?" said Mrs. Stark sharply. I don't know if Miss Furnivall had seen me, for, as I told you, she was very deaf, and she sat quite still, idly staring into the fire, with her hopeless face. "I'm only looking for my little Rosy-Posy," replied I, still thinking that the child was there, and near me, though I could not see her.

"Miss Rosamond is not here," said Mrs. Stark. "She went away more than an hour ago to find Dorothy." And she too turned and went on looking into the fire.

My heart sank at this, and I began to wish I had never left my darling. I went back to Dorothy and told her. James was gone out for the day, but she and me and Bessy took lights, and went up into the nursery first and then we roamed over the great large house, calling and entreating Miss Rosamond to come out of her hiding place, and not frighten us to death in that way. But there was no answer; no sound.

"Oh!" said I at last, "Can she have got into the east wing and hidden there?"

But Dorothy said it was not possible, for that she herself had never been in there; that the doors were always locked, and my lord's steward had the keys, she believed; at any rate, neither she nor James had ever seen them: so, I said I would go back and see if, after all, she was not hidden in the drawing-room, unknown to the old ladies; and if I found her there, I said, I would whip her well for the fright she had given me; but I never meant to do it. Well, I went back to the west drawing-room, and I told Mrs. Stark we could not find her anywhere, and asked for leave to look all about the furniture there, for I thought now, that she might have fallen asleep in some warm hidden corner; but no! we looked, Miss Furnivall got up and looked, trembling all over, and she was no where there; then we set off again, every one in the house, and looked in all the places we had searched before, but we could not find her. Miss Furnivall shivered and shook so much, that Mrs. Stark took her back into the warm drawing-room; but not before they had made me promise to bring her to them when she was found. Well-a-day! I began to think she never would be found, when I bethought me to look out into the great front court, all covered with snow. I was up-stairs when I looked out; but, it was such clear moonlight, I could see quite plain two little footprints, which might be traced from the hall door, and round the corner of the east wing. I don't know how I got down, but I tugged open the great, stiff hall door; and, throwing the skirt of my gown over my head for a cloak, I ran out. I turned the east corner, and there a black shadow fell on the snow; but when I came again into the moon-light, there were the little footmarks going up—up to the Fells. It was bitter cold; so cold that the air almost took the skin off my face as I ran, but I ran on, crying to think how my poor little darling must be perished[2] and frightened. I was within sight of the holly-trees, when I saw a shepherd coming down the hill, bearing something in his arms wrapped in his maud.[3] He shouted to me, and asked me if I had lost a bairn;[4] and, when I could not speak for crying, he bore towards me, and I saw my wee bairnie lying still, and white, and stiff, in his arms, as if she had been dead. He told me he had been up the Fells to gather in his sheep, before the deep cold of night came on, and that under the holly-trees (black marks on the hill-side, where no other bush was for miles around) he had found my little lady—my lamb—my queen—my darling—stiff and cold, in the terrible sleep which is frost-begotten. Oh! the joy, and the tears of having her in my arms once again! for I would not let him carry her; but took her, maud and all, into my own arms, and held her near my own

2. Extremely cold.
3. Shawl of gray plaid used by shepherds in the region.
4. Child.

warm neck and heart, and felt the life stealing slowly back again into her little gentle limbs. But she was still insensible when we reached the hall, and I had no breath for speech. We went in by the kitchen door.

"Bring the warming-pan," said I; and I carried her up-stairs and began undressing her by the nursery fire, which Bessy had kept up. I called my little lammie all the sweet and playful names I could think of,—even while my eyes were blinded by my tears; and at last, oh! at length she opened her large blue eyes. Then I put her into her warm bed, and sent Dorothy down to tell Miss Furnivall that all was well; and I made up my mind to sit by my darling's bedside the live-long night. She fell away into a soft sleep as soon as her pretty head had touched the pillow, and I watched by her till morning light; when she wakened up bright and clear—or so I thought at first—and, my dears, so I think now.

She said, that she had fancied that she should like to go to Dorothy, for that both the old ladies were asleep, and it was very dull in the drawing-room; and that, as she was going through the west lobby, she saw the snow through the high window falling—falling—soft and steady; but she wanted to see it lying pretty and white on the ground; so she made her way into the great hall; and then, going to the window, she saw it bright and soft upon the drive; but while she stood there, she saw a little girl, not so old as she was, "but so pretty," said my darling, "and this little girl beckoned to me to come out; and oh, she was so pretty and so sweet, I could not choose but go." And then this other little girl had taken her by the hand, and side by side the two had gone round the east corner.

"Now you are a naughty little girl, and telling stories," said I. "What would your good mamma, that is in heaven, and never told a story in her life, say to her little Rosamond, if she heard her—and I dare say she does—telling stories!"

"Indeed, Hester," sobbed out my child; "I'm telling you true. Indeed I am."

"Don't tell me!" said I, very stern. "I tracked you by your foot-marks through the snow; there were only yours to be seen: and if you had had a little girl to go hand-in-hand with you up the hill, don't you think the foot-prints would have gone along with yours?"

"I can't help it, dear, dear Hester," said she, crying, "if they did not; I never looked at her feet, but she held my hand fast and tight in her little one, and it was very, very cold. She took me up the Fell-path, up to the holly trees; and there I saw a lady weeping and crying; but when she saw me, she hushed her weeping, and smiled very proud and grand, and took me on her knees, and began to lull me to sleep; and that's all, Hester—but that is true; and my dear mamma knows it is," said she, crying. So I thought the child was in a fever, and pretended to believe her, as she went over her story—over and over again, and always the same. At last Dorothy knocked at the door with Miss Rosamond's breakfast; and she told me the old ladies were down in the eating-parlour, and that they wanted to speak to me. They had both been into the night-nursery the evening before, but it was after Miss Rosamond was asleep; so they had only looked at her—not asked me any questions.

"I shall catch it," thought I to myself, as I went along the north gallery. "And yet," I thought, taking courage, "it was in their charge I left her; and it's they that's to blame for letting her steal away unknown and unwatched." So I went in boldly, and told my story. I told it all to Miss Furnivall, shouting it close to her ear; but when I came to the mention of the other little girl out in the snow, coaxing and tempting her out, and willing her up to the grand and beautiful lady by the Holly-tree, she threw her arms up—her old and withered arms—and cried aloud, "Oh! Heaven, forgive! Have mercy!"

Mrs. Stark took hold of her; roughly enough, I thought; but she was past Mrs. Stark's management, and spoke to me, in a kind of wild warning and authority.

"Hester! keep her from that child! It will lure her to her death! That evil child! Tell her it is a wicked, naughty child." Then, Mrs. Stark hurried me out of the room; where, indeed, I was glad enough to go; but Miss Furnivall kept shrieking out, "Oh! have mercy! Wilt Thou never forgive! It is many a long year ago——"

I was very uneasy in my mind after that. I durst never leave Miss Rosamond, night or day, for fear lest she might slip off again, after some fancy or other; and all the more, because I thought I could make out that Miss Furnivall was crazy, from their odd ways about her; and I was afraid lest something of the same kind (which might be in the family, you know) hung over my darling. And the great frost never ceased all this time; and, whenever it was a more stormy night than usual, between the gusts, and through the wind, we heard the old lord playing on the great organ. But, old lord, or not, wherever Miss Rosamond went, there I followed; for my love for her, pretty helpless orphan, was stronger than my fear for the grand and terrible sound. Besides, it rested with me to keep her cheerful and merry, as beseemed her age. So we played together, and wandered together, here and there, and everywhere; for I never dared to lose sight of her again in that large and rambling house. And so it happened, that one afternoon, not long before Christmas day, we were playing together on the billiard-table in the great hall (not that we knew the right way of playing, but she liked to roll the smooth ivory balls with her pretty hands, and I liked to do whatever she did); and, by-and-bye, without our noticing it, it grew dusk indoors, though it was still light in the open air, and I was thinking of taking her back into the nursery, when, all of a sudden, she cried out:

"Look, Hester! look! there is my poor little girl out in the snow!"

I turned towards the long narrow windows, and there, sure enough, I saw a little girl, less than my Miss Rosamond—dressed all unfit to be out-of-doors such a bitter night—crying, and beating against the window-panes, as if, she wanted to be let in. She seemed to sob and wail, till Miss Rosamond could bear it no longer, and was flying to the door to open it, when, all of a sudden, and close upon us, the great organ pealed out so loud and thundering, it fairly made me tremble; and all the more, when I remembered me that, even in the stillness of that dead-cold weather, I had heard no sound of little battering hands upon the window-glass, although the Phantom Child had seemed to put forth all its force; and, although I had seen it wail and cry, no faintest touch of sound had fallen upon my ears. Whether I remembered all this at the very moment, I do not know; the great organ sound had so stunned me into terror; but this I know, I caught up Miss Rosamond before she got the hall-door opened, and clutched her, and carried her away, kicking and scream-ing, into the large bright kitchen, where Dorothy and Agnes were busy with their mince-pies.

"What is the matter with my sweet one?" cried Dorothy, as I bore in Miss Rosamond, who was sobbing as if her heart would break.

"She won't let me open the door for my little girl to come in; and she'll die if she is out on the Fells all night. Cruel, naughty Hester," she said, slapping me; but she might have struck harder, for I had seen a look of ghastly terror on Dorothy's face, which made my very blood run cold.

"Shut the back kitchen door fast, and bolt it well," said she to Agnes. She said no more; she gave me raisins and almonds to quiet Miss Rosamond: but she sobbed about the little girl in the snow, and would not touch any of the good things. I was thankful when she cried herself to sleep in bed. Then I stole down to the kitchen, and told Dorothy I had made up my mind. I would carry my darling back to my father's house in Applethwaite; where, if we lived humbly, we lived at peace. I said I had been frightened enough with the old lord's organ-playing; but now, that I had seen for myself this little moaning child, all decked out as no child in the neighborhood could be, beating and battering to get in, yet always without any sound or noise—with the dark wound on its right shoulder; and that Miss Rosamond had known it again for the phantom that had nearly lured her to her death (which Dorothy knew was true); I would stand it no longer.

I saw Dorothy change color once or twice. When I had done, she told me she did not think I could take Miss Rosamond with me, for that she was my lord's ward, and I had no right over her; and she asked me, would I leave the child that I was so fond of, just for sounds and sights that could do me no harm; and that they had all had to get used to in their turns? I was all in a hot, trembling passion; and I said it was very well for her to talk, that knew what these sights and noises betokened, and that had, perhaps, had something to do with the Spectre-child while it was alive. And I taunted her so, that she told me all she knew, at last; and then I wished I had never been told, for it only made me more afraid than ever.

She said she had heard the tale from old neighbors, that were alive when she was first married; when folks used to come to the hall sometimes, before it had got such a bad name on the country side: it might not be true, or it might, what she had been told.

The old lord was Miss Furnivall's father—Miss Grace, as Dorothy called her, for Miss Maude was the elder, and Miss Furnivall by rights. The old lord was eaten up with pride. Such a proud man was never seen or heard of; and his daughters were like him. No one was good enough to wed them, although they had choice enough; for they were the great beauties of their day, as I had seen by their portraits, where they hung in the state drawing-room. But, as the old saying is, "Pride will have a fall;" and these two haughty beauties fell in love with the same man, and he no better than a foreign musician, whom their father had down from London to play music with him at the Manor House. For, above all things, next to his pride, the old lord loved music. He could play on nearly every instrument that ever was heard of; and it was a strange thing it did not soften him; but he was a fierce dour old man, and had broken his poor wife's heart with his cruelty, they said. He was mad after music, and would pay any money for it. So he got this foreigner to come; who made such beautiful music, that they said the very birds on the trees stopped their singing to listen. And, by degrees, this foreign gentleman got such a hold over the old lord, that nothing would serve him but that he must come every year; and it was he that had the great organ brought from Holland and built up in the hall, where it stood now. He taught the old lord to play on it; but many and many a time, when Lord Furnivall was thinking of nothing but his fine organ, and his finer music, the dark foreigner was walking abroad in the woods with one of the young ladies; now Miss Maude, and then Miss Grace.

Miss Maude won the day and carried off the prize, such as it was; and he and she were married, all unknown to any one; and before he made his next yearly visit, she had been confined of[5] a little girl at a farm-house on the Moors, while her father and Miss Grace thought she was away at Doncaster Races. But though she was a wife and a mother, she was not a bit softened, but as haughty and as passionate as ever; and perhaps more so, for she was jealous of Miss Grace, to whom her foreign husband paid a deal of court—by way of blinding her—as he told his wife. But Miss Grace triumphed over Miss Maude, and Miss Maude grew fiercer and fiercer, both with her husband and with her sister; and the former—who could easily shake off what was disagreeable, and hide himself in foreign countries—went away a month before his usual time that summer, and half threatened that he would never come back again. Meanwhile, the little girl was left at the farm-house, and her mother used to have her horse saddled and gallop wildly over the hills to see her once every week, at the very least—for where she loved, she loved; and where she hated, she hated. And the old lord went on playing—playing on his organ; and the servants thought the sweet music he made had soothed down his awful temper, of which (Dorothy said) some terrible tales could be told. He grew infirm too, and had to walk with a crutch; and his son—that was the present Lord Furnivall's father—was with the army in America, and the other son at sea; so Miss Maude had it pretty much her own way, and she and Miss Grace grew colder and bitterer to each other every day; till at last they hardly ever spoke, except when the old lord was by. The foreign musician came again the next summer, but it was for the last time; for they led him such a life with their jealousy and their passions, that he grew weary, and went away, and never was heard of again. And Miss Maude, who had always meant to have her marriage acknowledged when her father should be dead, was left now a deserted wife—whom nobody knew to have been married—with a child that she dared not own, although she loved it to distraction; living with a father whom she feared, and a sister whom she hated. When the next summer passed over and the dark foreigner never came, both Miss Maude and Miss Grace grew gloomy and sad; they had a haggard look about them, though they looked handsome as ever. But by and by Miss Maude brightened; for her father grew more and more infirm, and more than ever carried away by his music; and she and Miss Grace lived almost entirely apart, having separate rooms, the one on the west side— Miss Maude on the east—those very rooms which were now shut up. So she thought she might have her little girl with her, and no one need ever know except those who dared not speak about it, and were bound to believe that it was, as she said, a cottager's child she had taken a fancy to. All this, Dorothy said, was pretty well known; but what came afterwards no one knew, except Miss Grace, and Mrs. Stark, who was even then her maid, and much more of a friend to her than ever her sister had been. But the servants supposed, from words that were dropped, that Miss Maude had triumphed over Miss Grace, and told her that all the time the dark foreigner had been mocking her with pretended love—he was her own husband; the colour left Miss Grace's cheek and lips that very day for ever, and she was heard to say many a time that sooner or later she would have her revenge; and Mrs. Stark was for ever spying about the east rooms.

One fearful night, just after the New Year had come in, when the snow was

5. Given birth to.

lying thick and deep, and the flakes were still falling—fast enough to blind any one who might be out and abroad—there was a great and violent noise heard, and the old lord's voice above all, cursing and swearing awfully,—and the cries of a little child,—and the proud defiance of a fierce woman,—and the sound of a blow,—and a dead stillness,—and moans and wailings dying away on the hill-side! Then the old lord summoned all his servants, and told them, with terrible oaths, and words more terrible, that his daughter had disgraced herself, and that he had turned her out of doors,—her, and her child,—and that if ever they gave her help,—or food—or shelter,—he prayed that they might never enter Heaven. And, all the while, Miss Grace stood by him, white and still as any stone; and when he had ended she heaved a great sigh, as much as to say her work was done, and her end was accomplished. But the old lord never touched his organ again, and died within the year; and no wonder! for, on the morrow of that wild and fearful night, the shepherds, coming down the Fell side, found Miss Maude sitting, all crazy and smiling, under the holly-trees, nursing a dead child,—with a terrible mark on its right shoulder. "But that was not what killed it," said Dorothy; "it was the frost and the cold—every wild creature was in its hole, and every beast in its fold,—while the child and its mother were turned out to wander on the Fells! And now you know all! and I wonder if you are less frightened now?"

I was more frightened than ever; but I said I was not. I wished Miss Rosamond and myself well out of that dreadful house for ever; but I would not leave her, and I dared not take her away. But oh! how I watched her, and guarded her! We bolted the doors, and shut the window-shutters fast, an hour or more before dark, rather than leave them open five minutes too late. But my little lady still heard the weird child crying and mourning; and not all we could do or say, could keep her from wanting to go to her, and let her in from the cruel wind and the snow. All this time, I kept away from Miss Furnivall and Mrs. Stark, as much as ever I could; for I feared them—I knew no good could be about them, with their grey hard faces, and their dreamy eyes, looking back into the ghastly years that were gone. But, even in my fear, I had a kind of pity—for Miss Furnivall, at least. Those gone down to the pit[6] can hardly have a more hopeless look than that which was ever on her face. At last I even got so sorry for her—who never said a word but what was quite forced from her—that I prayed for her; and I taught Miss Rosamond to pray for one who had done a deadly sin; but often when she came to those words, she would listen, and start up from her knees, and say, "I hear my little girl plaining[7] and crying very sad—Oh! let her in, or she will die!"

One night—just after New Year's Day had come at last, and the long winter had taken a turn as I hoped—I heard the west drawing-room bell ring three times, which was the signal for me. I would not leave Miss Rosamond alone, for all she was asleep—for the old lord had been playing wilder than ever—and I feared lest my darling should waken to hear the spectre child; see her I knew she could not, I had fastened the windows too well for that. So, I took her out of her bed and wrapped her up in such outer clothes as were most handy, and carried her down to the drawing-room, where the old ladies sat at their tapestry work as usual. They looked up when I came in, and Mrs. Stark asked, quite astounded, "Why did I bring Miss Rosamond there, out of her warm bed?" I had begun to whisper, "Because I was afraid of her being tempted out while I was away, by the wild child in the snow," when she stopped me short (with a glance at Miss Furnivall) and said Miss Furnivall wanted me to undo some work she had done wrong, and which neither of them could see to unpick. So, I laid my pretty dear on the sofa, and sat down on a stool by them, and hardened my heart against them as I heard the wind rising and howling.

Miss Rosamond slept on sound, for all the wind blew so; and Miss Furnivall said never a word, nor looked round when the gusts shook the windows. All at once she started up to her full height, and put up one hand as if to bid us listen.

"I hear voices!" said she. "I hear terrible screams—I hear my father's voice!"

Just at that moment, my darling wakened with a sudden start: "My little girl is crying, oh, how she is crying!" and she tried to get up and go to her, but she got her feet entangled in the blanket, and I caught her up; for my flesh had begun to creep at these noises, which they heard while we could catch no sound. In a minute or two the noises came, and gathered fast, and filled our ears; we, too, heard voices and screams, and no longer heard the winter's wind that raged abroad. Mrs. Stark looked at me, and I at her, but we dared not speak. Suddenly Miss Furnivall went towards the door, out into the ante-room, through the west lobby, and opened the door into the great hall. Mrs. Stark followed, and I durst not be left, though my heart almost stopped beating for fear. I wrapped my darling tight in my arms, and went out with them. In the hall the screams were louder than ever; they sounded to come from the east wing—nearer and nearer—close on the other side of the locked-up doors— close behind them. Then I noticed that the great bronze chandelier seemed all alight, though the hall was dim, and that a fire was blazing in the vast hearth-place, though it gave no heat; and I shuddered up with terror, and folded my darling closer to me. But as I did so, the east door shook, and she, suddenly struggling to get free from me, cried, "Hester! I must go! My little girl is there; I hear her; she is coming! Hester, I must go!"

I held her tight with all my strength; with a set will, I held her. If I had died, my hands would have grasped her still; I was so resolved in my mind. Miss Furnivall stood listening, and paid no regard to my darling, who had got down to the ground, and whom I, upon my knees now, was holding with both my arms clasped round her neck; she still striving and crying to get free.

All at once, the east door gave way with a thundering crash, as if torn open in a violent passion, and there came into that broad and mysterious light, the figure of a tall old man, with grey hair and gleaming eyes. He drove before him, with many a relentless gesture of abhorrence, a stern and beautiful woman, with a little child clinging to her dress.

"Oh Hester! Hester!" cried Miss Rosamond. "It's the lady! the lady below the holly-trees; and my little girl is with her. Hester! Hester! let me go to her; they are drawing me to them. I feel them—I feel them. I must go!"

Again she was almost convulsed by her efforts to get away; but I held her tighter and tighter; till I feared I should do her a hurt; but rather that than let her go towards those terrible phantoms. They passed along towards the great hall-door, where the winds howled and ravened for their prey; but before they reached that, the lady turned; and I could see that she defied the old man with a fierce and proud defiance; but then she quailed—and then she threw up her arms wildly and piteously to save her child—her little child—from a blow from his uplifted crutch.

And Miss Rosamond was torn as by a power stronger than mine, and writhed in my arms, and sobbed (for by this time the poor darling was growing faint). "They want me to go with them on to the Fells—they are drawing me to them. Oh, my little girl! I would come, but cruel, wicked Hester holds me very tight." But when she saw the uplifted crutch she swooned away, and I thanked God for it. Just at this moment—when the tall old man, his hair streaming as in the blast of a furnace, was going to strike the little shrinking child—Miss Furnivall, the old woman by my side, cried out, "Oh, father! father! spare the little innocent child!" But just then I saw—we all saw—another phantom shape itself, and grow clear out of the blue and misty light that filled the hall; we had not seen her till now, for it was another lady who stood by the old man, with a look of relentless hate and triumphant scorn. That figure was very beautiful to look upon, with a soft white hat drawn down over the proud brows, and a red and curling lip. It was dressed in an open robe of blue satin. I had seen that figure before. It was the likeness of Miss Furnivall in her youth; and the terrible phantoms moved on, regardless of old Miss Furnivall's wild entreaty,—and the uplifted crutch fell on the right shoulder of the little child, and the younger sister looked on, stony and deadly serene. But at that moment, the dim lights, and the fire that gave no heat, went out of themselves, and Miss Furnivall lay at our feet stricken down by the palsy—death-stricken.

Yes! she was carried to her bed that night never to rise again. She lay with her face to the wall, muttering low but muttering alway: "Alas! alas! what is done in youth can never be undone in age! What is done in youth can never be undone in age!"

1852

CHARLES DICKENS
1812–1870

Charles Dickens was Victorian England's most beloved and distinctive novelist. In the words of the eulogy that the classicist Benjamin Jowett spoke at his funeral service, Dickens "occupied a greater space than any other writer during the last thirty-five years. We read him, talked about him, acted him; we laughed with him, we were roused by him to a consciousness of the misery of others, and to a pathetic [i.e., emotional] interest in human life."

Charles Dickens was born the second of eight children in the coastal town of Portsmouth in southern England. His father, a clerk in the Naval Pay Office, found it difficult to keep his family out of debt. Plagued by financial insecurity, the family moved from place to place, to increasingly poorer lodgings, finally ending up in London. In an effort to help the family out, a friend of his father's offered Charles a job in a shoe-blacking factory. Two days before his twelfth birthday, he began work, labeling bottles for six shillings a week. Two weeks later his father was arrested and sent to the Marshalsea Prison for debt. His family went to live in prison with him, as was the custom; but they decided that Charles should remain outside, living with a woman who took in young boarders and continuing to work.

The months in which Charles lived alone and worked in the blacking warehouse were traumatic, and the intense feeling Dickens had of humiliation and abandonment shaped his fiction in profound ways. The sense he had of himself as "a child of singular abilities: quick, eager, delicate, and soon hurt, bodily or mentally," who had been cast away to suffer unjustly, formed the basis for characters such as Oliver Twist, the young David Copperfield, and Pip in *Great Expectations* (1860–61), whose mistreatment represents Dickens's harshest indictment of society.

Dickens's father was able to leave debtors' prison after three months, upon receipt of a legacy from his mother. He removed Charles from the factory and sent him to school. At fifteen Dickens began work as a junior clerk at a law office; eighteen months later he became a freelance newspaper reporter, first reporting court proceedings and later debates in the House of Commons. Reporting led him to fiction. He began publishing literary sketches, at first anonymously and then under the pseudonym Boz. In 1836, on his twenty-fourth birthday, he published the collection *Sketches by Boz*. The success of the volume led to a commission from the publishers Chapman & Hall to publish a book in serial installments with companion illustrations. The result, *Pickwick Papers* (1836–37), brought Dickens fame and prosperity. This picaresque novel, relating the adventures of Mr. Pickwick and his friends as they travel around England, set the pattern of illustrated serial publication that was to define Dickens's writing career and to shape the reading habits of his generation. Families would wait in suspense for the next installment of a novel to be issued, which they would read aloud as an evening's entertainment. Successes followed quickly: *Oliver Twist* (1838), *Nicholas Nickleby* (1838–39), and *The Old Curiosity Shop* (1840–41).

By the time of *Pickwick*'s completion, Dickens had married Catherine Hogarth, the daughter of a fellow journalist, and had begun a family; they eventually had ten children, and household chaos would come increasingly to frustrate him. If Dickens's portrayal of women as inadequate keepers of domestic order was inspired by conditions at home, then the frequent appearance in his fiction of a very different kind of feminine character, the impossibly good and unreachable ideal, can be linked to two young women he knew in his early adulthood. Maria Beadnell, the daughter of a banker, was his first love; but his courtship was discouraged by her family, who felt he was beneath her. He was left with a painful sense that he had lost his perfect woman. Dickens was still more devastated when Mary, his seventeen-year-old sister-in-law, whom he idolized, died in his arms.

Through the 1840s and 1850s Dickens continued to write novels at an intense pace, producing *Barnaby Rudge* (1841), *Martin Chuzzlewit* (1843–44), *Dombey and Son* (1846–48), *David Copperfield* (1849–50), *Bleak House* (1852–53), *Hard Times* (1854), *Little Dorrit* (1855–57), and *A Tale of Two Cities* (1859). He also became deeply involved in a number of other activities, including traveling, working for charities, and acting. During this time he founded and edited the weekly magazine *Household Words* (incorporated in 1859 into *All the Year Round*), which published fiction by Elizabeth Gaskell, Wilkie Collins, Dickens himself, and other novelists as well as opinion pieces about political and social issues. And he began a series of Christmas books, the first of which was *A Christmas Carol* (1843).

In 1858, when Dickens separated from his wife, his life and work changed. He became involved with the actress Ellen Ternan, and he took up residence at Gad's Hill, a gentleman's house in Kent. Abandoning amateur theatricals, he embarked on a series of lucrative professional readings; they were so emotionally and physically exhausting that his doctor finally instructed him to stop. He slowed the pace of his writing, publishing only two novels in the 1860s: *Great Expectations* and *Our Mutual Friend* (1864–65). He died suddenly in 1870, leaving his last novel, *The Mystery of Edwin Drood* (1870), unfinished.

Dickens's early fiction is remarkable for its extravagance, which Franz Kafka calls "Dickens's opulence and great, careless prodigality." It marks many elements of his novels—their baggy plots, filled with incident; the constant metaphorical invention of their language; and the multitude of their characters. Anthony Trollope observed that no other writer except Shakespeare has left so many "characters which are known by their names familiarly as household words, and which bring to our minds vividly and at once, a certain well-understood set of ideas, habits, phrases and costumes, making together a man, or woman, or child, whom we know at a glance and recognize at a sound, as we do our own intimate friends."

Dickens builds character from a repeated set of gestures, phrases, and metaphors. For example, whenever Mrs. Micawber enters the story of *David Copperfield*, she repeats, "I will never desert Mr. Micawber." Having a "slit of a mouth" into which he posts his food, Wemmick in *Great Expectations* rarely appears without some reference to his "post office" mouth; Mr. Gradgrind is always identified in *Hard Times* with the squareness of each of his physical attributes. This way of creating character led the novelist E. M. Forster to use Dickens to illustrate what he means by a flat, as opposed to a round, character. Such a reductive technique of characterization might seem to have little to offer by way of depth of insight, but this is not the case. In particular, as Dickens's fiction becomes more complex in the course of his career, the repeated tics that identify his characters come to represent emotional fixations and social distortions. Dickens's early fiction exults in its comic exaggeration of human peculiarities. In his later fiction that comedy becomes grotesque, as the distortions of caricature reflect failures of humanity in his increasingly dark social vision.

Bernard Shaw wrote that "Dickens never regarded himself as a revolutionist, though he certainly was one." Dickens's early novels often concern social abuses— the workhouses in which pauper children were confined in *Oliver Twist*, abusive and fraudulent schools in *Nicholas Nickleby*. As his career progressed, Dickens felt an increasing urgency about the social criticism his novels made. He gave *Hard Times* the subtitle *For These Times* and dedicated the book to Thomas Carlyle, indicating his ambition to write a work in the tradition of Carlyle's social indictment, "Signs of the Times" (1829). In his middle novels Dickens's criticism of society becomes increasingly systemic, and he begins to use organizing metaphors to express his social vision. *Bleak House*, for example, concerns the failings of the legal system, but the obfuscation and self-interest of the law are symptomatic of a larger social ill, symbolized in the smothering fog whose description begins the novel.

Despite the bleakness of Dickens's view of society and the fierceness of his criticism of it, his novels always end with a sentimental assertion of the virtues of home and heart. Readers and critics alike in both the nineteenth and twentieth centuries often felt that this sentimentality blunted his social analysis: although Dickens tries to use fiction to stir the human heart and evoke humanitarian feelings, the domestic refuges of his novels never change the world outside. In more recent times, and in the wake of D. A. Miller's study of Victorian fiction, *The Novel and the Police* (1988), many critics now express no surprise about this narrowing of scope: according to Miller, cultural productions (such as the novel) that emanate from the heart of a bourgeois society inevitably reproduce the controlling mechanism that regulates that world as a whole, and the seemingly subversive social critique at the beginning of a Dickens novel will ultimately be contained within an idealized middle-class sitting room at its close. Such scholars throw into question the earlier view of this novelist as an energetic, if conflicted, critic of his age: Dickens is instead perceived as an unofficial spokesman of conservative ideologies. Yet there are certainly many different ways to think about unresolved tensions within Dickens's work, and the teeming pages of his fourteen novels and wide range of other writings offer endless inspiration.

The distinctive character of Dickens's fiction is so pronounced that critics often talk as if the individual worlds of all of his novels were continuous. In part Dickens's tendency to return repeatedly to the subjects that possessed his imagination supports this impression. One of those subjects is prisons. "A Visit to Newgate" is his earliest piece on the topic, to which he returns many times, as in *Great Expectations, Oliver Twist, Pickwick Papers,* and *Little Dorrit*. Prison for Dickens is a particular social abuse; the most harrowing setting in which to contemplate criminality and guilt; a metaphor for the psychological captivity his characters create for themselves; and the system through which society enforces its discipline. Throughout his fiction key elements of Victorian society, such as the prison, take on multiple layers of significance;

in this way, as the critic J. Hillis Miller observes, Dickens's creative vision in part determines the Victorian spirit itself.

A Visit to Newgate[1]

"The force of habit" is a trite phrase in everybody's mouth; and it is not a little remarkable that those who use it most as applied to others, unconsciously afford in their own persons singular examples of the power which habit and custom exercise over the minds of men, and of the little reflection they are apt to bestow on subjects with which every day's experience has rendered them familiar. If Bedlam could be suddenly removed like another Aladdin's palace,[2] and set down on the space now occupied by Newgate, scarcely one man out of a hundred, whose road to business every morning lies through Newgate-street, or the Old Bailey,[3] would pass the building without bestowing a hasty glance on its small, grated windows, and a transient thought upon the condition of the unhappy beings immured in its dismal cells; and yet these same men, day by day, and hour by hour, pass and repass this gloomy depository of the guilt and misery of London, in one perpetual stream of life and bustle, utterly unmindful of the throng of wretched creatures pent up within it—nay, not even knowing, or if they do, not heeding, the fact, that as they pass one particular angle of the massive wall with a light laugh or a merry whistle, they stand within one yard of a fellow-creature, bound and helpless, whose hours are numbered, from whom the last feeble ray of hope has fled for ever, and whose miserable career will shortly terminate in a violent and shameful death. Contact with death even in its least terrible shape, is solemn and appalling. How much more awful is it to reflect on this near vicinity to the dying—to men in full health and vigour, in the flower of youth or the prime of life, with all their faculties and perceptions as acute and perfect as your own; but dying, nevertheless—dying as surely—with the hand of death imprinted upon them as indelibly—as if mortal disease had wasted their frames to shadows, and corruption had already begun!

It was with some such thoughts as these that we determined, not many weeks since, to visit the interior of Newgate—in an amateur capacity, of course; and, having carried our intention into effect, we proceed to lay its results before our readers, in the hope—founded more upon the nature of the subject, than on any presumptuous confidence in our own descriptive powers—that this paper may not be found wholly devoid of interest. We have only to premise, that we do not intend to fatigue the reader with any statistical accounts of the prison; they will be found at length in numerous reports of numerous committees, and a variety of authorities of equal weight. We took no notes, made no memoranda, measured none of the yards, ascertained the exact number of inches in no particular room, are unable even to report of how many apartments the gaol is composed.

We saw the prison, and saw the prisoners; and what we did see, and what we thought, we will tell at once in our own way.

1. First published in *Sketches by Boz* (1836). Newgate was London's main criminal prison.
2. In *Arabian Nights*, an evil magician temporarily gets control of Aladdin's magic lamp and transports

his palace to Africa. "Bedlam": a London hospital for the insane.
3. London's criminal court.

Having delivered our credentials to the servant who answered our knock at the door of the governor's[4] house, we were ushered into the "office;" a little room, on the right-hand side as you enter, with two windows looking into the Old Bailey: fitted up like an ordinary attorney's office, or merchant's counting-house, with the usual fixtures—a wainscoted partition, a shelf or two, a desk, a couple of stools, a pair of clerks, an almanack, a clock, and a few maps. After a little delay, occasioned by sending into the interior of the prison for the officer whose duty it was to conduct us, that functionary arrived; a respectable-looking man of about two or three and fifty, in a broad-brimmed hat, and full suit of black, who, but for his keys, would have looked quite as much like a clergyman as a turnkey.[5] We were disappointed; he had not even top-boots[6] on. Following our conductor by a door opposite to that at which we had entered, we arrived at a small room, without any other furniture than a little desk, with a book for visitors' autographs, and a shelf, on which were a few boxes for papers, and casts of the heads and faces of the two notorious murderers, Bishop and Williams;[7] the former, in particular, exhibiting a style of head and set of features, which might have afforded sufficient moral grounds for his instant execution at any time, even had there been no other evidence against him. Leaving this room also, by an opposite door, we found ourself in the lodge which opens on the Old Bailey; one side of which is plentifully garnished with a choice collection of heavy sets of irons, including those worn by the redoubtable Jack Sheppard—genuine; and those *said* to have been graced by the sturdy limbs of the no less celebrated Dick Turpin[8]—doubtful. From this lodge, a heavy oaken gate, bound with iron, studded with nails of the same material, and guarded by another turnkey, opens on a few steps, if we remember right, which terminate in a narrow and dismal stone passage, running parallel with the Old Bailey, and leading to the different yards, through a number of tortuous and intricate windings, guarded in their turn by huge gates and gratings, whose appearance is sufficient to dispel at once the slightest hope of escape that any new comer may have entertained; and the very recollection of which, on eventually traversing the place again, involves one in a maze of confusion.

It is necessary to explain here, that the buildings in the prison, or in other words the different wards—form a square, of which the four sides abut respectively on the Old Bailey, the old College of Physicians (now forming a part of Newgate-market), the Sessions-house, and Newgate-street. The intermediate space is divided into several paved yards, in which the prisoners take such air and exercise as can be had in such a place. These yards, with the exception of that in which prisoners under sentence of death are confined (of which we shall presently give a more detailed description), run parallel with Newgate-street, and consequently from the Old Bailey, as it were, to Newgate-market. The women's side is in the right wing of the prison nearest the Sessions-house. As we were introduced into this part of the building first, we will adopt the same order, and introduce our readers to it also.

Turning to the right, then, down the passage to which we just now adverted, omitting any mention of intervening gates—for if we noticed every gate that was unlocked for us to pass through, and locked again as soon as we had

---

4. The head of the prison.
5. Jailer, guard.
6. High boots.
7. John Bishop and Thomas Head (aka "Wil-
liams"), notorious body snatchers who were hanged for murdering a young boy in 1831.
8. Two notorious 18th-century thieves and high-waymen. "Irons": shackles.

passed, we should require a gate at every comma—we came to a door composed of thick bars of wood, through which were discernible, passing to and fro in a narrow yard, some twenty women: the majority of whom, however, as soon as they were aware of the presence of strangers, retreated to their wards. One side of this yard is railed off at a considerable distance, and formed into a kind of iron cage, about five feet ten inches in height, roofed at the top, and defended in front by iron bars, from which the friends of the female prisoners communicate with them. In one corner of this singular-looking den, was a yellow, haggard, decrepit old woman, in a tattered gown that had once been black, and the remains of an old straw bonnet, with faded ribbon of the same hue, in earnest conversation with a young girl—a prisoner, of course—of about two-and-twenty. It is impossible to imagine a more poverty-stricken object, or a creature so borne down in soul and body, by excess of misery and destitution as the old woman. The girl was a good-looking robust female, with a profusion of hair streaming about in the wind—for she had no bonnet on—and a man's silk pocket-handkerchief loosely thrown over a most ample pair of shoulders. The old woman was talking in that low, stifled tone of voice which tells so forcibly of mental anguish; and every now and then burst into an irrepressible sharp, abrupt cry of grief, the most distressing sound that ears can hear. The girl was perfectly unmoved. Hardened beyond all hope of redemption, she listened doggedly to her mother's entreaties, whatever they were: and, beyond inquiring after "Jem," and eagerly catching at the few halfpence her miserable parent had brought her, took no more apparent interest in the conversation than the most unconcerned spectators. Heaven knows there were enough of them, in the persons of the other prisoners in the yard, who were no more concerned by what was passing before their eyes, and within their hearing, than if they were blind and deaf. Why should they be? Inside the prison, and out, such scenes were too familiar to them, to excite even a passing thought, unless of ridicule or contempt for feelings which they had long since forgotten.

A little farther on, a squalid-looking woman in a slovenly, thick-bordered cap, with her arms muffled in a large red shawl, the fringed ends of which straggled nearly to the bottom of a dirty white apron, was communicating some instructions to *her* visitor—her daughter evidently. The girl was thinly clad, and shaking with the cold. Some ordinary word of recognition passed between her and her mother when she appeared at the grating, but neither hope, condolence, regret, nor affection was expressed on either side. The mother whispered her instructions, and the girl received them with her pinched-up half-starved features twisted into an expression of careful cunning. It was some scheme for the woman's defence that she was disclosing, perhaps; and a sullen smile came over the girl's face for an instant, as if she were pleased: not so much at the probability of her mother's liberation, as at the chance of her "getting off" in spite of her prosecutors. The dialogue was soon concluded; and with the same careless indifference with which they had approached each other, the mother turned towards the inner end of the yard, and the girl to the gate at which she had entered.

The girl belonged to a class—unhappily but too extensive—the very existence of which, should make men's hearts bleed. Barely past her childhood, it required but a glance to discover that she was one of those children, born and bred in neglect and vice, who have never known what childhood is: who have never been taught to love and court a parent's smile, or to dread a parent's frown. The thousand nameless endearments of childhood, its gaiety and its innocence, are alike unknown to them. They have entered at once upon the stern realities and miseries of life, and to their better nature it is almost hopeless to appeal in aftertimes, by any of the references which will awaken, if it be only for a moment, some good feeling in ordinary bosoms, however corrupt they may have become. Talk to *them* of parental solicitude, the happy days of childhood, and the merry games of infancy! Tell them of hunger and the streets, beggary and stripes, the gin-shop, the station-house, and the pawnbroker's, and they will understand you.

Two or three women were standing at different parts of the grating, conversing with their friends, but a very large proportion of the prisoners appeared to have no friends at all, beyond such of their old companions as might happen to be within the walls. So, passing hastily down the yard, and pausing only for an instant to notice the little incidents we have just recorded, we were conducted up a clean and well-lighted flight of stone stairs to one of the wards. There are several in this part of the building, but a description of one is a description of the whole.

It was a spacious, bare, whitewashed apartment, lighted of course, by windows looking into the interior of the prison, but far more light and airy than one could reasonably expect to find in such a situation. There was a large fire with a deal table before it, round which ten or a dozen women were seated on wooden forms[9] at dinner. Along both sides of the room ran a shelf; below it, at regular intervals, a row of large hooks were fixed in the wall, on each of which was hung the sleeping mat of a prisoner: her rug and blanket being folded up, and placed on the shelf above. At night, these mats are placed on the floor, each beneath the hook on which it hangs during the day; and the ward is thus made to answer the purposes both of a day-room and sleeping apartment. Over the fireplace, was a large sheet of pasteboard, on which were displayed a variety of texts from Scripture, which were also scattered about the room in scraps about the size and shape of the copy-slips which are used in schools. On the table was a sufficient provision of a kind of stewed beef and brown bread, in pewter dishes, which are kept perfectly bright, and displayed on shelves in great order and regularity when they are not in use.

The women rose hastily, on our entrance, and retired in a hurried manner to either side of the fireplace. They were all cleanly—many of them decently—attired, and there was nothing peculiar, either in their appearance or demeanour. One or two resumed the needlework which they had probably laid aside at the commencement of their meal; others gazed at the visitors with listless curiosity; and a few retired behind their companions to the very end of the room, as if desirous to avoid even the casual observation of the strangers. Some old Irish women, both in this and other wards, to whom the thing was no novelty, appeared perfectly indifferent to our presence, and remained standing close to the seats from which they had just risen; but the general feeling among the females seemed to be one of uneasiness during the period of our stay among them: which was very brief. Not a word was uttered during the time of our remaining, unless, indeed, by the wardswoman in reply to some question which we put to the turnkey who accompanied us. In every ward on the female side, a wardswoman is appointed to preserve order, and a similar regulation is adopted among the males. The wardsmen and wardswomen are all

9. Benches.

prisoners, selected for good conduct. They alone are allowed the privilege of sleeping on bedsteads; a small stump bedstead[1] being placed in every ward for that purpose. On both sides of the gaol, is a small receiving-room, to which prisoners are conducted on their first reception, and whence they cannot be removed until they have been examined by the surgeon of the prison.[2]

Retracing our steps to the dismal passage in which we found ourselves at first (and which, by-the-bye, contains three or four dark cells for the accommodation of refractory[3] prisoners), we were led through a narrow yard to the "school"—a portion of the prison set apart for boys under fourteen years of age. In a tolerable-sized room, in which were writing-materials and some copy-books, was the school-master, with a couple of his pupils; the remainder having been fetched from an adjoining apartment, the whole were drawn up in line for our inspection. There were fourteen of them in all, some with shoes, some without; some in pinafores[4] without jackets, others in jackets without pinafores, and one in scarce anything at all. The whole number, without an exception we believe, had been committed for trial on charges of pocket-picking; and fourteen such terrible little faces we never beheld.—There was not one redeeming feature among them—not a glance of honesty—not a wink expressive of anything but the gallows and the hulks,[5] in the whole collection. As to anything like shame or contrition, that was entirely out of the question. They were evidently quite gratified at being thought worth the trouble of looking at; their idea appeared to be, that we had come to see Newgate as a grand affair, and that they were an indispensable part of the show; and every boy as he "fell in" to the line, actually seemed as pleased and important as if he had done something excessively meritorious in getting there at all. We never looked upon a more disagreeable sight, because we never saw fourteen such hopeless creatures of neglect, before.

On either side of the school-yard is a yard for men, in one of which—that towards Newgate-street—prisoners of the more respectable class are confined. Of the other, we have little description to offer, as the different wards necessarily partake of the same character. They are provided, like the wards on the women's side, with mats and rugs, which are disposed of in the same manner during the day; the only very striking difference between their appearance and that of the wards inhabited by the females, is the utter absence of any employment. Huddled together on two opposite forms, by the fireside, sit twenty men perhaps; here, a boy in livery; there, a man in a rough great-coat and top-boots; farther on, a desperate-looking fellow in his shirt sleeves, with an old Scotch cap[6] upon his shaggy head; near him again, a tall ruffian, in a smock-frock; next to him, a miserable being of distressed appearance, with his head resting on his hand;—all alike in one respect, all idle and listless. When they do leave the fire, sauntering moodily about, lounging in the window, or leaning against the wall, vacantly swinging their bodies to and fro. With the exception of a man reading an old newspaper, in two or three instances, this was the case in every ward we entered.

The only communication these men have with their friends, is through two

---

1. Bedframe that ends at the level of the mattress.
2. The regulations of the prison relative to the confinement of prisoners during the day, their sleeping at night, their taking their meals, and other matters of gaol economy, have been all altered—greatly for the better—since this sketch

was published. Even the construction of the prison itself has been changed [Dickens's note].
3. Unmanageable.
4. Aprons.
5. Prison ships.
6. Brimless woolen hat with two tails.

close iron gratings, with an intermediate space of about a yard in width between the two, so that nothing can be handed across, nor can the prisoner have any communication by touch with the person who visits him. The married men have a separate grating, at which to see their wives, but its construction is the same.

The prison chapel is situated at the back of the governor's house: the latter having no windows looking into the interior of the prison. Whether the associations connected with the place—the knowledge that here a portion of the burial service is, on some dreadful occasions, performed over the quick[7] and not upon the dead—cast over it a still more gloomy and sombre air than art has imparted to it, we know not, but its appearance is very striking. There is something in a silent and deserted place of worship, solemn and impressive at any time; and the very dissimilarity of this one from any we have been accustomed to, only enhances the impression. The meanness of its appointments—the bare and scanty pulpit, with the paltry painted pillars on either side—the women's gallery with its great heavy curtain—the men's with its unpainted benches and dingy front—the tottering little table at the altar, with the commandments on the wall above it, scarcely legible through lack of paint, and dust and damp—so unlike the velvet and gilding, the marble and wood, of a modern church—are strange and striking. There is one object, too, which rivets the attention and fascinates the gaze, and from which we may turn horror-stricken in vain, for the recollection of it will haunt us, waking and sleeping, for a long time afterwards. Immediately below the reading-desk, on the floor of the chapel, and forming the most conspicuous object in its little area, is *the condemned pew*; a huge black pen, in which the wretched people, who are singled out for death, are placed on the Sunday preceding their execution, in sight of all their fellow-prisoners, from many of whom they may have been separated but a week before, to hear prayers for their own souls, to join in the responses of their own burial service, and to listen to an address, warning their recent companions to take example by their fate, and urging themselves, while there is yet time—nearly four-and-twenty hours—to "turn, and flee from the wrath to come!"[8] Imagine what have been the feelings of the men whom that fearful pew has enclosed, and of whom, between the gallows and the knife, no mortal remnant may now remain![9] Think of the hopeless clinging to life to the last, and the wild despair, far exceeding in anguish the felon's death itself, by which they have heard the certainty of their speedy transmission to another world, with all their crimes upon their heads, rung into their ears by the officiating clergyman!

At one time—and at no distant period either—the coffins of the men about to be executed, were placed in that pew, upon the seat by their side, during the whole service. It may seem incredible, but it is true. Let us hope that the increased spirit of civilization and humanity which abolished this frightful and degrading custom, may extend itself to other usages equally barbarous; usages which have not even the plea of utility in their defense, as every year's experience has shown them to be more and more inefficacious.

7. Living.
8. Cf. Matthew 3.7 and Luke 3.7: "O generation of vipers, who hath warned you to flee from the wrath to come?"
9. Since the 16th century the corpses of hanged prisoners had been handed over to anatomists and medical schools for dissection and scientific study. This was considered an extra, postmortem punishment.

Leaving the chapel, descending to the passage so frequently alluded to, and crossing the yard before noticed as being allotted to prisoners of a more respectable description than the generality of men confined here, the visitor arrives at a thick iron gate of great size and strength. Having been admitted through it by the turnkey on duty, he turns sharp round to the left, and pauses before another gate; and, having passed this last barrier, he stands in the most terrible part of this gloomy building—the condemned ward.

The press-yard,[1] well known by name to newspaper readers, from its frequent mention in accounts of executions, is at the corner of the building, and next to the ordinary's[2] house, in Newgate-street: running from Newgate-street, towards the centre of the prison, parallel with Newgate-market. It is a long, narrow court, of which a portion of the wall in Newgate-street forms one end, and the gate the other. At the upper end, on the left-hand—that is, adjoining the wall in Newgate-street—is a cistern of water, and at the bottom a double grating (of which the gate itself forms a part) similar to that before described. Through these grates the prisoners are allowed to see their friends; a turnkey always remaining in the vacant space between, during the whole interview. Immediately on the right as you enter, is a building containing the press-room, day-room, and cells; the yard is on every side surrounded by lofty walls guarded by *chevaux de frise*;[3] and the whole is under the constant inspection of vigilant and experienced turnkeys.

In the first apartment into which we were conducted—which was at the top of a staircase, and immediately over the press-room—were five-and-twenty or thirty prisoners, all under sentence of death, awaiting the result of the recorder's report—men of all ages and appearances, from a hardened old offender with swarthy face and grizzly beard of three days' growth, to a handsome boy, not fourteen years old, and of singularly youthful appearance even for that age, who had been condemned for burglary. There was nothing remarkable in the appearance of these prisoners. One or two decently-dressed men were brooding with a dejected air over the fire; several little groups of two or three had been engaged in conversation at the upper end of the room, or in the windows; and the remainder were crowded round a young man seated at a table, who appeared to be engaged in teaching the younger ones to write. The room was large, airy, and clean. There was very little anxiety or mental suffering depicted in the countenance of any of the men;—they had all been sentenced to death, it is true, and the recorder's report had not yet been made; but, we question whether there was a man among them, notwithstanding, who did not *know* that although he had undergone the ceremony, it never was intended that his life should be sacrificed. On the table lay a Testament, but there were no tokens of its having been in recent use.

In the press-room below, were three men, the nature of whose offence rendered it necessary to separate them, even from their companions in guilt. It is a long, sombre room, with two windows sunk into the stone wall, and here the wretched men are pinioned on the morning of their execution, before moving towards the scaffold. The fate of one of these prisoners was uncertain; some mitigatory circumstances having come to light since his trial, which had been humanely represented in the proper quarter. The other two had nothing

---

1. Area from which criminals condemned to death started for the place of execution.
2. Clergyman appointed to prepare criminals for
execution.
3. Line of spikes (French).

to expect from the mercy of the crown; their doom was sealed; no plea could be urged in extenuation of their crime, and they well knew that for them there was no hope in this world. "The two short ones," the turnkey whispered, "were dead men."

The man to whom we have alluded as entertaining some hopes of escape, was lounging, at the greatest distance he could place between himself and his companions, in the window nearest to the door. He was probably aware of our approach, and had assumed an air of courageous indifference; his face was purposely averted towards the window, and he stirred not an inch while we were present. The other two men were at the upper end of the room. One of them, who was imperfectly seen in the dim light, had his back towards us, and was stooping over the fire, with his right arm on the mantel-piece, and his head sunk upon it. The other, was leaning on the sill of the farthest window. The light fell full upon him, and communicated to his pale, haggard face, and disordered hair, an appearance which, at that distance, was ghastly. His cheek rested upon his hand; and, with his face a little raised, and his eyes wildly staring before him, he seemed to be unconsciously intent on counting the chinks in the opposite wall. We passed this room again afterwards. The first man was pacing up and down the court with a firm military step—he had been a soldier in the foot-guards—and a cloth cap jauntily thrown on one side of his head. He bowed respectfully to our conductor, and the salute was returned. The other two still remained in the positions we have described, and were as motionless as statues.[4]

A few paces up the yard, and forming a continuation of the building, in which are the two rooms we have just quitted, lie the condemned cells. The entrance is by a narrow and obscure staircase leading to a dark passage, in which a charcoal stove casts a lurid tint over the objects in its immediate vicinity, and diffuses something like warmth around. From the left-hand side of this passage, the massive door of every cell on the story opens; and from it alone can they be approached. There are three of these passages, and three of these ranges of cells, one above the other; but in size, furniture and appearance, they are all precisely alike. Prior to the recorder's report being made, all the prisoners under sentence of death are removed from the day-room at five o'clock in the afternoon, and locked up in these cells, where they are allowed a candle until ten o'clock; and here they remain until seven next morning. When the warrant for a prisoner's execution arrives, he is removed to the cells and confined in one of them until he leaves it for the scaffold. He is at liberty to walk in the yard; but, both in his walks and in his cell, he is constantly attended by a turnkey who never leaves him on any pretence.

We entered the first cell. It was a stone dungeon, eight feet long by six wide, with a bench at the upper end, under which were a common rug, a bible, and prayer-book. An iron candlestick was fixed into the wall at the side; and a small high window in the back admitted as much air and light as could struggle in between a double row of heavy, crossed iron bars. It contained no other furniture of any description.

Conceive the situation of a man, spending his last night on earth in this cell. Buoyed up with some vague and undefined hope of reprieve, he knew not why—indulging in some wild and visionary idea of escaping, he knew not

---

4. These two men were executed shortly afterwards. The other was respited during his Majesty's pleasure [Dickens's note]. "His Majesty": William IV (1765–1837; reigned 1830–37).

how—hour after hour of the three preceding days allowed him for preparation, has fled with a speed which no man living would deem possible, for none but this dying man can know. He has wearied his friends with entreaties, exhausted the attendants with importunities, neglected in his feverish rest-lessness the timely warnings of his spiritual consoler; and, now that the illusion is at last dispelled, now that eternity is before him and guilt behind, now that his fears of death amount almost to madness, and an overwhelming sense of his helpless, hopeless state rushes upon him, he is lost and stupified, and has neither thoughts to turn to, nor power to call upon, the Almighty Being, from whom alone he can seek mercy and forgiveness, and before whom his repen-tance can alone avail.

Hours have glided by, and still he sits upon the same stone bench with folded arms, heedless alike of the fast decreasing time before him, and the urgent entreaties of the good man at his side. The feeble light is wasting grad-ually, and the deathlike stillness of the street without, broken only by the rumbling of some passing vehicle which echoes mournfully through the empty yards, warns him that the night is waning fast away. The deep bell of St. Paul's strikes—one! He heard it; it has roused him. Seven hours left! He paces the narrow limits of his cell with rapid strides, cold drops of terror starting on his forehead, and every muscle of his frame quivering with agony. Seven hours! He suffers himself to be led to his seat, mechanically takes the bible which is placed in his hand, and tries to read and listen. No: his thoughts will wander. The book is torn and soiled by use—and like the book he read his lessons in, at school, just forty years ago! He has never bestowed a thought upon it, perhaps, since he left it as a child: and yet the place, the time, the room— nay, the very boys he played with, crowd as vividly before him as if they were scenes of yesterday; and some forgotten phrase, some childish word, rings in his ears like the echo of one uttered but a minute since. The voice of the clergyman recalls him to himself. He is reading from the sacred book its sol-emn promises of pardon for repentance, and its awful denunciation of obdu-rate men. He falls upon his knees and clasps his hands to pray. Hush! what sound was that? He starts upon his feet. It cannot be two yet. Hark! Two quarters have struck;—the third—the fourth. It is! Six hours left. Tell him not of repentance! Six hours' repentance for eight times six years of guilt and sin! He buries his face in his hands, and throws himself on the bench.[5]

Worn with watching and excitement, he sleeps, and the same unsettled state of mind pursues him in his dreams. An insupportable load is taken from his breast; he is walking with his wife in a pleasant field, with the bright sky above them, and a fresh and boundless prospect on every side—how different from the stone walls of Newgate! She is looking—not as she did when he saw her for the last time in that dreadful place, but as she used when he loved her— long, long ago, before misery and ill-treatment had altered her looks, and vice had changed his nature, and she is leaning upon his arm, and looking up into his face with tenderness and affection—and he does *not* strike her now, nor rudely shake her from him. And oh! how glad he is to tell her all he had forgotten in that last hurried interview, and to fall on his knees before her and fervently beseech her pardon for all the unkindness and cruelty that wasted her form and broke her heart! The scene suddenly changes. He is on his trial again: there are the judge and jury, and prosecutors, and witnesses, just as

---

5. Cf. the description of Fagin's last night in the condemned cell in *Oliver Twist* (1838), chap. 52.

they were before. How full the court is—what a sea of heads—with a gallows, too, and a scaffold—and how all those people stare at *him*! Verdict, "Guilty." No matter; he will escape.

The night is dark and cold, the gates have been left open, and in an instant he is in the street, flying from the scene of his imprisonment like the wind. The streets are cleared, the open fields are gained and the broad wide country lies before him. Onward he dashes in the midst of darkness, over hedge and ditch, through mud and pool, bounding from spot to spot with a speed and lightness, astonishing even to himself. At length he pauses; he must be safe from pursuit now; he will stretch himself on that bank and sleep till sunrise.

A period of unconsciousness succeeds. He wakes, cold and wretched. The dull gray light of morning is stealing into the cell, and falls upon the form of the attendant turnkey. Confused by his dreams, he starts from his uneasy bed in momentary uncertainty. It is but momentary. Every object in the narrow cell is too frightfully real to admit of doubt or mistake. He is the condemned felon again, guilty and despairing; and in two hours more will be dead.

1835   1836

ROBERT BROWNING
1812–1889

During the years of his marriage, Robert Browning was sometimes referred to as "Mrs. Browning's husband." Elizabeth Barrett was at that time a famous poet, whereas her husband was a relatively unknown experimenter whose poems were greeted with misunderstanding or indifference. Not until the 1860s did he at last gain a public and become recognized as the rival or equal of Alfred, Lord Tennyson. In the twentieth century his reputation persisted but in an unusual way: his poetry was admired by two groups of readers widely different in tastes. To one group, among whom were the Browning societies that flourished in England and America, Browning was a wise philosopher and religious teacher who resolved the doubts that troubled Matthew Arnold and Tennyson.

The second group of readers enjoyed Browning less for his attempt to solve problems of religious doubt than for his attempt to solve the problems of how poetry should be written. Poets such as Ezra Pound and Robert Lowell recognized that more than any other nineteenth-century poet, it was Browning who energetically hacked through a trail that subsequently became the main road of twentieth-century poetry. In *Poetry and the Age* (1953) Randall Jarrell remarked that "the dramatic monologue, which once had depended for its effect upon being a departure from the norm of poetry, now became in one form or another the norm."

The dramatic monologue, as Browning uses it, separates the speaker from the poet in such a way that the reader must work through the words of the speaker to discover the meaning of the poet. For example, in the well-known early monologue "My Last Duchess" (1842), we listen to the duke as he speaks of his dead wife. From his one-sided conversation we piece together the situation, both past and present, and we infer what sort of woman the duchess really was and what sort of man the duke is. Ultimately, we may also infer what the poet himself thinks of the speaker he has created. In this poem it is fairly easy to reach such a judgment, although the pleasure of the poem results from our reconstruction of a story quite different from the one the duke thinks he is telling. Many of Browning's poems are far less stable, and it is difficult to discern the relationship of the poet to his speaker. In reading "A Grammarian's Funeral" (1855), for example, can we be sure that the central character is a hero? Or is he merely a fool? In " 'Childe Roland to the Dark Tower Came' " (1855) is the speaker describing a phantasmagoric landscape of his own paranoid imagining, or is the poem a fable of courage and defiance in a modern wasteland?

In addition to his experiments with the dramatic monologue, Browning also experimented with language and syntax. The grotesque rhymes and jaw-breaking diction that he often employs have been repugnant to some critics; George Santayana, for instance, dismissed him as a clumsy barbarian. But to those who appreciate Browning, the incongruities of language are a humorous and appropriate counterpart to an imperfect world. Ezra Pound's tribute to "Old Hippety-Hop o' the accents," as he addresses Browning, is both affectionate and memorable:

> Heart that was big as the bowels of Vesuvius
> Words that were winged as her sparks in eruption,
> Eagled and thundered as Jupiter Pluvius
> Sound in your wind past all signs o' corruption.

Robert Browning was born in Camberwell, a London suburb. His father, a bank clerk, was a learned man with an extensive library. His mother was a kindly, religious-minded woman, interested in music, whose love for her brilliant son was warmly reciprocated. Until the time of his marriage, at the age of thirty-four, Browning was rarely absent from his parents' home. He attended a boarding school near Camberwell, traveled a little (to Russia and Italy), and was a student at the University of London for a short period, but he preferred to pursue his education at home, where he was tutored in foreign languages, music, boxing, and horsemanship and where he read omnivorously. From this unusual education he acquired a store of knowledge on which to draw for the background of his poems.

The "obscurity" of which his contemporaries complained in his earlier poetry may be partly accounted for by the circumstances of Browning's education, but it also reflects his anxious desire to avoid exposing himself too explicitly before his readers. His first poem, *Pauline* (1833), published when he was twenty-one, had been modeled on the example of Percy Bysshe Shelley, the most personal of poets. When an otherwise admiring review by John Stuart Mill noted that the young author was afflicted with an "intense and morbid self-consciousness," Browning was overwhelmed with embarrassment. He resolved to avoid confessional writings thereafter.

One way of reducing the personal element in his poetry was to write plays instead of soul-searching narratives or lyrics. In 1836, encouraged by the actor W. C. Macready, Browning began work on his first play, *Strafford,* a historical tragedy that lasted only four nights when it was produced in London in 1837. For ten years the young writer struggled to write for the theater, but all his stage productions remained failures. Nevertheless, writing dialogue for actors led him to explore another form more congenial to his genius—the dramatic monologue, a form that enabled him through imaginary speakers to avoid explicit autobiography. His first collection of such monologues, *Dramatic Lyrics*, appeared in 1842; but it received no more critical enthusiasm than did his plays.

Browning's resolution to avoid the subjective manner of Shelley did not preclude his being influenced by the earlier poet in other ways. At fourteen, when he first discovered Shelley's works, he became an atheist and liberal. Although he grew away from the atheism, after a struggle, and also the extreme phases of his liberalism, he retained from Shelley's influence something permanent and more difficult to define: an ardent dedication to ideals (often undefined ideals) and an energetic striving toward goals (often undefined goals).

Browning's ardent romanticism also found expression in his love affair with Elizabeth Barrett, which had the dramatic ingredients of Browning's own favorite story of

St. George rescuing the maiden from the dragon. Few would have forecast the outcome when Browning met Elizabeth Barrett in 1845. She was six years older than he was, a semi-invalid, jealously guarded by her possessively tyrannical father. But love, as the poet was to say later, is best; and love swept aside all obstacles. After their elopement to Italy, the former semi-invalid was soon enjoying far better health and a full life. The husband likewise seemed to thrive during the years of this remarkable marriage. His most memorable volume of poems, *Men and Women* (1855), reflects his enjoyment of Italy: its picturesque landscapes and lively street scenes as well as its monuments from the past—its Renaissance past in particular.

The happy fifteen-year sojourn in Italy ended in 1861 with Elizabeth's death. The widower returned to London with his son. During the twenty-eight years remaining to him, the quantity of verse he produced did not diminish. *Dramatis Personae* (1864) is a volume containing some of his most intriguing monologues, such as "Caliban upon Setebos." And in 1868 he published his longest and most significant single poem, *The Ring and the Book,* which was inspired by his discovery of an old book of legal records concerning a murder trial in seventeenth-century Rome. His poem tells the story of a brutally sadistic husband, Count Guido Franceschini. The middle-aged Guido grows dissatisfied with his young wife, Pompilia, and accuses her of having adulterous relations with a handsome priest who, like St. George, had tried to rescue her from the appalling situation in which her husband confined her. Eventually Guido stabs his wife to death and is himself executed. In a series of twelve books, Browning retells this tale of violence, presenting it from the contrasting points of view of participants and spectators. Because of its vast scale, *The Ring and the Book* is like a Victorian novel, but in its experiments with multiple points of view it anticipates later works such as Joseph Conrad's novel *Lord Jim* (1900) and Akira Kurosawa's film *Rashōmon* (1950).

After *The Ring and the Book* several more volumes appeared. In general, Browning's writings during the last two decades of his life exhibit a certain mechanical repetition of mannerism and an excess of argumentation—tendencies into which he may have been led by the unqualified enthusiasm of his admirers, for it was during this period that he gained his great following. When he died, in 1889, he was buried in Westminster Abbey.

During the London years Browning became extremely fond of social life. He dined at the homes of friends and at clubs, where he enjoyed port wine and conversation. He would talk loudly and emphatically about many topics—except his own poetry, about which he was usually reticent. Despite his bursts of outspokenness, Browning's character seemed, in Thomas Hardy's words, "*the* literary puzzle of the nineteenth century." Like William Butler Yeats, he was a poet preoccupied with masks. On the occasion of his burial, his friend Henry James reflected that many oddities and many great writers have been buried in Westminster Abbey, "but none of the odd ones have been so great and none of the great ones been so odd."

Just as Browning's character is hard to identify so also are his poems difficult to relate to the age in which they were written. Bishops and painters of the Renaissance, physicians of the Roman Empire, musicians of eighteenth-century Germany—as we explore this gallery of talking portraits we seem to be in a world of time long past, remote from the world of steam engines and disputes about human beings' descent from the ape. Yet our first impression is misleading. Many of these portraits explore problems that confronted Browning's contemporaries, especially problems of faith and doubt, of good and evil, and of the function of the artist in modern life. "Caliban upon Setebos," for example, is a highly topical critique of Darwinism and of natural (as opposed to supernatural) religions. Browning's own attitude toward these topics is partially concealed because of his use of speakers and of settings from earlier ages, yet we do encounter certain recurrent religious assumptions that we can safely assign to the poet himself. The most recurrent is that God has created an imperfect world as a kind of testing ground, a "vale of soul-making," as John Keats had said. It followed, for Browning's purposes, that the human soul must be immortal and that heaven itself be perfect. As Abt Vogler affirms: "On the earth the broken arcs; in the heaven, a perfect round." Armed with such a faith, Browning sometimes gives the impression that he was himself untroubled by the doubts that gnawed at the hearts of Tennyson, Arnold, and other figures in the mid-Victorian period. Yet Browning's apparent optimism is consistently being tested by his bringing to light the evils of human nature. His gallery of villains—murderers, sadistic husbands, mean and petty manipulators—is an extraordinary one. Few writers, in fact, seem to have been more aware of the existence of evil.

A second aspect of Browning's poetry that separates it from the Victorian age is its style. The most representative Victorian poets such as Tennyson and Dante Gabriel Rossetti write in the manner of Keats, John Milton, and Edmund Spenser, and of classical poets such as Virgil. Theirs is the central stylistic tradition in English poetry, one that favors smoothly polished texture, elevated diction and subjects, and pleasing liquidity of sound. Browning draws from a different tradition, more colloquial and discordant, a tradition that includes the poetry of John Donne, the soliloquies of William Shakespeare, and certain features of the narrative style of Geoffrey Chaucer. Of most significance are Browning's affinities with Donne. Both poets sacrifice, on occasion, the pleasures of harmony and of a consistent elevation of tone by using a harshly discordant style and unexpected juxtapositions that startle us into an awareness of a world of everyday realities and trivialities. Readers who dislike this kind of poetry in Browning or in Donne argue that it suffers from prosiness. Oscar Wilde once described the novelist George Meredith as "a prose Browning." And so, he added, was Browning. Wilde's joke may help us to relate Browning to his contemporaries. For if Browning seems out of step with other Victorian poets, he is by no means out of step with his contemporaries in prose. The grotesque, which plays such a prominent role in the style and subject matter of Carlyle and Dickens and in the aesthetic theories of John Ruskin, is equally prominent in Browning's verse:

> Fee, faw, fum! bubble and squeak!
> Blessedest Thursday's the fat of the week.
> Rumble and tumble, sleek and rough,
> Stinking and savory, smug and gruff.

Like Thomas Carlyle's *Sartor Resartus* (1833–34), these lines from "Holy-Cross Day" (1855) present a situation of grave seriousness with noisy jocularity. It was fitting that Browning and Carlyle remained good friends, even though the elder writer kept urging Browning to give up verse in favor of prose.

The link between Browning and the Victorian prose writers is not limited to style. With the later generation of Victorian novelists, George Eliot, George Meredith, and Henry James, Browning shares a central preoccupation. Like Eliot in particular, he was interested in exposing the devious ways in which our minds work and the complexity of our motives. "My stress lay on incidents in the development of a human soul," he wrote; "little else is worth study." His psychological insights can be illustrated in poems such as "The Bishop Orders His Tomb" (1845) and "Andrea del Sarto" (1855). Although these are spoken monologues, not inner monologues in the manner of James Joyce, the insight into the workings of the mind is similarly acute. As in reading Joyce, we must be on our guard to follow the rapid shifts of the speaker's mental processes as jumps are made from one cluster of associations to another. A further challenge for the reader of Browning is to identify what has been left out. As was remarked in a letter by the 1890s poet Ernest Dowson, Browning's "masterpieces in verse" demonstrate both "subtlety" and "the tact of omission." "My Last Duchess," he added, "is pure Henry James."

But Browning's role as a forerunner of twentieth-century literature should not blind us to his essential Victorianism. Energy is the most characteristic aspect of his writing and of the man (Ivan Turgenev compared Browning's handshake to an electric shock).

Gerard Manley Hopkins described Browning as "a man bouncing up from table with his mouth full of bread and cheese and saying that he meant to stand no blasted nonsense." This buoyancy imparts a creative vitality to all of Browning's writings.

Porphyria's Lover[1]

The rain set early in tonight,
    The sullen wind was soon awake,
It tore the elm-tops down for spite,
    And did its worst to vex the lake:
5   I listened with heart fit to break.
When glided in Porphyria; straight
    She shut the cold out and the storm,
And kneeled and made the cheerless grate
    Blaze up, and all the cottage warm;
10   Which done, she rose, and from her form
Withdrew the dripping cloak and shawl,
    And laid her soiled gloves by, untied
Her hat and let the damp hair fall,
    And, last, she sat down by my side
15   And called me. When no voice replied,
She put my arm about her waist,
    And made her smooth white shoulder bare,
And all her yellow hair displaced,
    And, stooping, made my cheek lie there,
20   And spread, o'er all, her yellow hair,
Murmuring how she loved me—She
    Too weak, for all her heart's endeavor,
To set its struggling passion free
    From pride, and vainer ties dissever,
25   And give herself to me forever.
But passion sometimes would prevail,
    Nor could tonight's gay feast restrain
A sudden thought of one so pale
    For love of her, and all in vain:
30   So, she was come through wind and rain.
Be sure I looked up at her eyes
    Happy and proud; at last I knew
Porphyria worshiped me: surprise
    Made my heart swell, and still it grew
35   While I debated what to do.
That moment she was mine, mine, fair,
    Perfectly pure and good: I found
A thing to do, and all her hair
    In one long yellow string I wound
40   Three times her little throat around,
And strangled her. No pain felt she;
    I am quite sure she felt no pain.

---

1. One of a pair of monologues originally published as "Madhouse Cells," a title that emphasized the speaker's abnormal state of mind.

As a shut bud that holds a bee,
    I warily oped her lids: again
45   Laughed the blue eyes without a stain.
And I untightened next the tress
    About her neck; her cheek once more
Blushed bright beneath my burning kiss:
    I propped her head up as before,
50   Only, this time my shoulder bore
Her head, which droops upon it still:
    The smiling rosy little head,
So glad it has its utmost will,
    That all it scorned at once is fled,
55   And I, its love, am gained instead!
Porphyria's love: she guessed not how
    Her darling one wish would be heard.
And thus we sit together now,
    And all night long we have not stirred,
60   And yet God has not said a word!

1834   1836, 1842

[handwritten: He's a clueless murderous clingy guy!]

Soliloquy of the Spanish Cloister

1

Gr-r-r—there go, my heart's abhorrence!
    Water your damned flowerpots, do!
If hate killed men, Brother Lawrence,
    God's blood,[1] would not mine kill you!
5   What? your myrtle bush wants trimming?
    Oh, that rose has prior claims—
Needs its leaden vase filled brimming?
    Hell dry you up with its flames!

2

At the meal we sit together:
10   *Salve tibi!*[2] I must hear
Wise talk of the kind of weather,
    Sort of season, time of year:
Not a plenteous cork crop: scarcely
    Dare we hope oak-galls,[3] *I doubt:*
15   *What's the Latin name for "parsley"?*
    What's the Greek name for Swine's Snout?[4]

3

Whew! We'll have our platter burnished,
    Laid with care on our own shelf!
With a fire-new spoon we're furnished,
20   And a goblet for ourself,

1. An oath (archaic).
2. Hail to thee! (Latin); i.e., "your health!" This and other speeches in italics in this stanza are the words of Brother Lawrence.
3. Abnormal outgrowths on oak trees, used for tanning.
4. Dandelion (19th-century use).

Rinsed like something sacrificial
    Ere 'tis fit to touch our chaps°   *jaws*
Marked with L. for our initial!
    (He-he! There his lily snaps!)

4

25   *Saint,* forsooth! While brown Dolores
    Squats outside the Convent bank
With Sanchicha, telling stories,
    Steeping tresses in the tank,
Blue-black, lustrous, thick like horsehairs,
30   —Can't I see his dead eye glow,
Bright as 'twere a Barbary corsair's?[5]
    (That is, if he'd let it show!)

5

When he finishes refection,°   *dinner*
    Knife and fork he never lays
35   Cross-wise, to my recollection,
    As do I, in Jesu's praise.
I the Trinity illustrate,
    Drinking watered orange pulp—
In three sips the Arian[6] frustrate;
40   While he drains his at one gulp.

6

Oh, those melons? If he's able
    We're to have a feast! so nice!
One goes to the Abbot's table,
    All of us get each a slice.
45   How go on your flowers? None double?
    Not one fruit-sort can you spy?
Strange!—And I, too, at such trouble,
    Keep them close-nipped on the sly!

7

There's a great text in Galatians,[7]
50   Once you trip on it, entails
Twenty-nine distinct damnations,
    One sure, if another fails:
If I trip him just a-dying,
    Sure of heaven as sure can be,
55   Spin him round and send him flying
    Off to hell, a Manichee?[8]

8

Or, my scrofulous French novel
    On gray paper with blunt type!

---

5. Pirate of the Barbary Coast of northern Africa, renowned for fierceness and lechery.
6. Heretical follower of Arius (256–336), who denied the doctrine of the Trinity.
7. The speaker hopes to obtain Lawrence's damnation by luring him into a heresy when he may prove unable to interpret "Galatians" in an unswervingly orthodox way. In Galatians 5.15–23 St. Paul specifies an assortment of "works of the flesh" that lead to damnation, which could make up a total of "twenty-nine" (line 51).
8. A heretic, a follower of Mani (3rd century), Persian religious leader.

Simply glance at it, you grovel
60   Hand and foot in Belial's° gripe: *the devil's*
If I double down its pages
At the woeful sixteenth print,
When he gathers his greengages,
Ope a sieve and slip it in't?

9
65   Or, there's Satan!—one might venture
Pledge one's soul to him, yet leave
Such a flaw in the indenture
As he'd miss till, past retrieve,
Blasted lay that rose-acacia[9]
70   We're so proud of! *Hy, Zy, Hine*[1]
'St, there's Vespers![2] *Plena gratiâ*
Ave, Virgo![3] Gr-r-r—you swine!

ca. 1839   1842

✕ My Last Duchess[1]

Ferrara

That's my last Duchess painted on the wall,
Looking as if she were alive. I call
That piece a wonder, now: Frà Pandolf's[2] hands
Worked busily a day, and there she stands.
5   Will 't please you sit and look at her? I said
"Frà Pandolf" by design, for never read
Strangers like you that pictured countenance,
The depth and passion of its earnest glance,
But to myself they turned (since none puts by
10   The curtain I have drawn for you, but I)
And seemed as they would ask me, if they durst,
How such a glance came there; so, not the first
Are you to turn and ask thus. Sir, 'twas not
Her husband's presence only, called that spot
15   Of joy into the Duchess' cheek: perhaps
Frà Pandolf chanced to say "Her mantle laps
Over my lady's wrist too much," or "Paint
Must never hope to reproduce the faint
Half-flush that dies along her throat": such stuff
20   Was courtesy, she thought, and cause enough

9. The speaker would pledge his own soul to Satan in return for blasting Lawrence and his "rose-acacia," but the pledge would be so cleverly worded that the speaker would not have to pay his debt to Satan. There would be an escape clause ("flaw in the indenture") for himself.
1. Perhaps the opening of a mysterious curse against Lawrence.
2. Evening prayers.
3. Full of grace, Hail, Virgin! (Latin). The speaker's twisted state of mind may be reflected in his mixed-up version of the prayer to Mary: "Ave, Maria, gratia plena."
1. The poem is based on incidents in the life of Alfonso II, Duke of Ferrara in Italy, whose first wife, Lucrezia, a young woman, died in 1561 after three years of marriage. Following her death, the duke negotiated through an agent to marry a niece of the Count of Tyrol. Browning represents the duke as addressing this agent.
2. Friar Pandolf, an imaginary painter.

For calling up that spot of joy. She had
A heart—how shall I say?—too soon made glad,
Too easily impressed; she liked whate'er
She looked on, and her looks went everywhere.
25　Sir, 'twas all one! My favor at her breast,
The dropping of the daylight in the West,
The bough of cherries some officious fool
Broke in the orchard for her, the white mule
She rode with round the terrace—all and each
30　Would draw from her alike the approving speech,
Or blush, at least. She thanked men—good! but thanked
Somehow—I know not how—as if she ranked
My gift of a nine-hundred-years-old name
With anybody's gift. Who'd stoop to blame
35　This sort of trifling? Even had you skill
In speech—(which I have not)—to make your will
Quite clear to such an one, and say, "Just this
Or that in you disgusts me; here you miss,
Or there exceed the mark"—and if she let
40　Herself be lessoned so, nor plainly set
Her wits to yours, forsooth, and made excuse
—E'en then would be some stooping; and I choose
Never to stoop. Oh sir, she smiled, no doubt,
Whene'er I passed her; but who passed without
45　Much the same smile? This grew; I gave commands;
Then all smiles stopped together. There she stands
As if alive. Will 't please you rise? We'll meet
The company below, then. I repeat,
The Count your master's known munificence
50　Is ample warrant that no just pretense
Of mine for dowry will be disallowed;
Though his fair daughter's self, as I avowed
At starting, is my object. Nay, we'll go
Together down, sir. Notice Neptune, though,
55　Taming a sea horse, thought a rarity,
Which Claus of Innsbruck[3] cast in bronze for me!

1842　　　　　　　　　　　　　　　　　　　1842

The Lost Leader[1]

I

Just for a handful of silver he left us,[2]
　Just for a riband[3] to stick in his coat—
Found the one gift of which fortune bereft us,

---

3. An unidentified or imaginary sculptor. The Count of Tyrol had his capital at Innsbruck.
1. William Wordsworth, who had been an ardent liberal in his youth, had become a political conservative in later years. In old age, when he accepted a grant of money from the government and the office of poet laureate, he alienated some of his young admirers such as Browning, whose liberalism was then as passionate as Wordsworth's had once been.
2. Browning here alludes to the "thirty pieces of silver" for which Judas betrayed Jesus (Matthew 26.14–16).
3. Symbol of the office of poet laureate.

Lost all the others she lets us devote;
5 They, with the gold to give, doled him out silver,
So much was theirs who so little allowed:
How all our copper had gone for his service!
Rags—were they purple, his heart had been proud!
We that had loved him so, followed him, honored him,
10 Lived in his mild and magnificent eye,
Learned his great language, caught his clear accents,
Made him our pattern to live and to die!
Shakespeare was of us, Milton was for us,
Burns, Shelley, were with us—they watch from their graves!
15 He alone breaks from the van[4] and the freemen
—He alone sinks to the rear and the slaves!

2

We shall march prospering—not through his presence;
Songs may inspirit us—not from his lyre;
Deeds will be done—while he boasts his quiescence,
20 Still bidding crouch whom the rest bade aspire:
Blot out his name, then, record one lost soul more,
One task more declined, one more footpath untrod,
One more devils'-triumph and sorrow for angels,
One wrong more to man, one more insult to God!
25 Life's night begins: let him never come back to us!
There would be doubt, hesitation and pain,
Forced praise on our part—the glimmer of twilight,
Never glad confident morning again!
Best fight on well, for we taught him—strike gallantly,
30 Menace our heart ere we master his own;
Then let him receive the new knowledge and wait us,
Pardoned in heaven, the first by the throne!

1843   1845

How They Brought the Good News
from Ghent to Aix[1]

(16—)

I

I sprang to the stirrup, and Joris, and he;
I galloped, Dirck galloped, we galloped all three;
"Good speed!" cried the watch, as the gate-bolts undrew;
"Speed!" echoed the wall to us galloping through;
5 Behind shut the postern,° the lights sank to rest,   *side door*
And into the midnight we galloped abreast.

4. Vanguard of the army of liberalism.
1. The distance between Ghent, in Flanders, and Aix-la-Chapelle (now Aachen, in Germany) is about one hundred miles. Browning said that the incident, occurring during the wars between Flan-ders and Spain, was an imaginary one. In 1889 Thomas Edison prepared a cylinder recording of Browning's recitation of the opening lines of this poem.

2

Not a word to each other; we kept the great pace
Neck by neck, stride by stride, never changing our place;
I turned in my saddle and made its girths tight,
10   Then shortened each stirrup, and set the pique° right,   *spur or pommel*
Rebuckled the cheek-strap, chained slacker the bit,
Nor galloped less steadily Roland a whit.

3

'Twas moonset at starting; but while we drew near
Lokeren, the cocks crew and twilight dawned clear;
15   At Boom, a great yellow star came out to see;
At Düffeld, 'twas morning as plain as could be;
And from Mecheln church-steeple we heard the half-chime,
So, Joris broke silence with, "Yet there is time!"

4

At Aershot, up leaped of a sudden the sun,
20   And against him the cattle stood black every one,
To stare through the mist at us galloping past,
And I saw my stout galloper Roland at last,
With resolute shoulders, each butting away
The haze, as some bluff river headland its spray:

5

25   And his low head and crest, just one sharp ear bent back
For my voice, and the other pricked out on his track;
And one eye's black intelligence—ever that glance
O'er its white edge at me, his own master, askance!
And the thick heavy spume-flakes which ay and anon
30   His fierce lips shook upwards in galloping on.

6

By Hasselt, Dirck groaned; and cried Joris, "Stay spur!
Your Roos galloped bravely, the fault's not in her,
We'll remember at Aix"—for one heard the quick wheeze
Of her chest, saw the stretched neck and staggering knees,
35   And sunk tail, and horrible heave of the flank
As down on her haunches she shuddered and sank.

7

So, we were left galloping, Joris and I,
Past Looz and past Tongres, no cloud in the sky;
The broad sun above laughed a pitiless laugh,
40   'Neath our feet broke the brittle bright stubble like chaff;
Till over by Dalhem a dome-spire sprang white,
And "Gallop," gasped Joris, "for Aix is in sight!"

8

"How they'll greet us!"—and all in a moment his roan
Rolled neck and croup° over, lay dead as a stone;   *rump*
45   And there was my Roland to bear the whole weight
Of the news which alone could save Aix from her fate,
With his nostrils like pits full of blood to the brim,
And with circles of red for his eye-sockets' rim.

9

Then I cast loose my buffcoat, each holster let fall,
50 Shook off both my jack boots, let go belt and all,
Stood up in the stirrup, leaned, patted his ear,
Called my Roland his pet name, my horse without peer;
Clapped my hands, laughed and sang, any noise, bad or good,
Till at length into Aix Roland galloped and stood.

10

55 And all I remember is—friends flocking round
As I sat with his head 'twixt my knees on the ground;
And no voice but was praising this Roland of mine,
As I poured down his throat our last measure of wine,
Which (the burgesses voted by common consent)
60 Was no more than his due who brought good news from Ghent.

ca. 1844   1845

The Bishop Orders His Tomb at Saint Praxed's Church[1]

Rome, 15—

Vanity, saith the preacher, vanity![2]
Draw round my bed: is Anselm keeping back?
Nephews—sons mine . . . ah God, I know not! Well—
She, men would have to be your mother once,
5 Old Gandolf envied me, so fair she was!
What's done is done, and she is dead beside,
Dead long ago, and I am Bishop since,
And as she died so must we die ourselves,
And thence ye may perceive the world's a dream.
10 Life, how and what is it? As here I lie
In this state chamber, dying by degrees,
Hours and long hours in the dead night, I ask
"Do I live, am I dead?" Peace, peace seems all.
Saint Praxed's ever was the church for peace;
15 And so, about this tomb of mine. I fought
With tooth and nail to save my niche, ye know:
—Old Gandolf cozened° me, despite my care;   *cheated*

1. In "Fra Lippo Lippi" Browning represents the dawn of the Renaissance in Italy, with its fresh zest for human experiences in this world. In this monologue he portrays a later stage of the Renaissance when such worldliness, full-blown, had infected some of the leading clergy of Italy. Browning's portrait of the dying bishop is, however, not primarily a satire against corruption in the church. It is a brilliant exposition of the workings of a mind, a mind that has been conditioned by special historical circumstances. The Victorian historian of art John Ruskin said of this poem:

    I know of no other piece of modern English, prose or poetry, in which there is so much told,

as in these lines, of the Renaissance spirit—its worldliness, inconsistency, pride, hypocrisy, ignorance of itself, love of art, of luxury, and of good Latin. It is nearly all that I have said of the central Renaissance in thirty pages of the *Stones of Venice*, put into as many lines, Browning's also being the antecedent work.

    St. Praxed's Church was named in honor of St. Praxedes, a Roman virgin of the 2nd century who gave her riches to poor Christians. Both the bishop and his predecessor, Gandolf, are imaginary persons.
2. Cf. Ecclesiastes 1.2.

Shrewd was that snatch from out the corner south
He graced his carrion with,[3] God curse the same!
20   Yet still my niche is not so cramped but thence
One sees the pulpit o' the epistle side,[4]
And somewhat of the choir, those silent seats,
And up into the aery dome where live
The angels, and a sunbeam's sure to lurk:
25   And I shall fill my slab of basalt[5] there,
And 'neath my tabernacle[6] take my rest,
With those nine columns round me, two and two,
The odd one at my feet where Anselm stands:
Peach-blossom marble all, the rare, the ripe
30   As fresh-poured red wine of a mighty pulse.[7]
—Old Gandolf with his paltry onion-stone,[8]
Put me where I may look at him! True peach,
Rosy and flawless: how I earned the prize!
Draw close: that conflagration of my church
35   —What then? So much was saved if aught were missed!
My sons, ye would not be my death? Go dig
The white-grape vineyard where the oil-press stood,
Drop water gently till the surface sink,
And if ye find . . . Ah God, I know not, I! . . .
40   Bedded in store of rotten fig leaves soft,
And corded up in a tight olive-frail,[9]
Some lump, ah God, of *lapis lazuli,*[1]
Big as a jew's head cut off at the nape,[2]
Blue as a vein o'er the Madonna's breast . . .
45   Sons, all have I bequeathed you, villas, all,
That brave Frascati[3] villa with its bath,
So, let the blue lump poise between my knees,
Like God the Father's globe on both his hands
Ye worship in the Jesu Church[4] so gay,
50   For Gandolf shall not choose but see and burst!
Swift as a weaver's shuttle fleet our years:[5]
Man goeth to the grave, and where is he?
Did I say basalt for my slab, sons? Black[6]—
'Twas ever antique-black I meant! How else
55   Shall ye contrast my frieze[7] to come beneath?
The bas-relief[8] in bronze ye promised me,
Those Pans and Nymphs ye wot° of, and perchance   know

---

3. Bishop Gandolf shrewdly chose a prize spot in the southern corner of the church for his burial place. The tomb that the speaker is ordering will also be inside the church, as was common for important people in this era.
4. The Epistles of the New Testament are read from the right-hand side of the altar (as one faces it).
5. Dark-colored igneous rock.
6. Stone canopy or tentlike roof, presumably supported by the "nine columns" under which the sculptured effigy of the bishop would lie on the "slab of basalt."
7. A pulpy mash of fermented grapes from which a strong wine might be poured off.
8. An inferior marble that peels in layers.

9. Basket for holding olives.
1. Valuable bright blue stone.
2. Perhaps a reference to the head of John the Baptist, cut off at Salomé's request (Matthew 14.6–11).
3. Suburb of Rome, used as a resort by wealthy Italians.
4. Il Gesù, a Jesuit church in Rome. In a chapel in this church the figure of an angel (rather than God) holds a huge lump of lapis lazuli in his hands.
5. Cf. Job 7.6.
6. I.e., black marble.
7. Continuous band of sculpture.
8. Sculpture in which the figures do not project far from the background surface.

Some tripod, thyrsus, with a vase or so,
The Saviour at his sermon on the mount,
60 Saint Praxed in a glory, and one Pan
Ready to twitch the Nymph's last garment off,
And Moses with the tables⁹ . . . but I know
Ye mark° me not! What do they whisper thee,   heed
Child of my bowels, Anselm? Ah, ye hope
65 To revel down my villas while I gasp
Bricked o'er with beggar's moldy travertine°   Italian limestone
Which Gandolf from his tomb-top chuckles at!
Nay, boys, ye love me—all of jasper, then!
'Tis jasper ye stand pledged to, lest I grieve
70 My bath must needs be left behind, alas!
One block, pure green as a pistachio nut,
There's plenty jasper somewhere in the world—
And have I not Saint Praxed's ear to pray
Horses for ye, and brown Greek manuscripts,
75 And mistresses with great smooth marbly limbs?
—That's if ye carve my epitaph aright,
Choice Latin, picked phrase, Tully's¹ every word,
No gaudy ware like Gandolf's second line—
Tully, my masters? Ulpian² serves his need!
80 And then how I shall lie through centuries,
And hear the blessed mutter of the mass,
And see God made and eaten all day long,³
And feel the steady candle flame, and taste
Good strong thick stupefying incense-smoke!
85 For as I lie here, hours of the dead night,
Dying in state and by such slow degrees,
I fold my arms as if they clasped a crook,°   bishop's staff
And stretch my feet forth straight as stone can point,
And let the bedclothes, for a mortcloth,⁴ drop
90 Into great laps and folds of sculptor's-work:
And as yon tapers dwindle, and strange thoughts
Grow, with a certain humming in my ears,
About the life before I lived this life,
And this life too, popes, cardinals, and priests,
95 Saint Praxed at his sermon on the mount,⁵
Your tall pale mother with her talking eyes,
And new-found agate urns as fresh as day,
And marble's language, Latin pure, discreet
—Aha, ELUCESCEBAT⁶ quoth our friend?

9. The sculpture would consist of a mixture of pagan and Christian iconography. "Tripod": seat on which the Oracle of Delphi made prophecies. "Thyrsus": a staff twined with ivy that was carried, according to Greek mythology, by Dionysus, god of wine and fertility. "Glory": halo. "Tables": the stone tablets on which the Ten Commandments were written. Such intermingling of pagan and Christian traditions, characteristic of the Renaissance, had been attacked in 1841 in *Contrasts,* a book on architecture by A. W. Pugin, a Roman Catholic.
1. I.e., Marcus Tullius Cicero (106–43 B.C.E.), orator and statesman who was one of the great styl-

ists of classical Latin prose.
2. Late Latin author of legal commentaries (d. 228 C.E.); not a model of good style.
3. Reference to the doctrine of transubstantiation.
4. Rich cloth spread over a dead body or coffin.
5. The bishop is confusing St. Praxed (a woman) with Jesus—an indication that his mind is wandering.
6. He was illustrious (Latin); word from Gandolf's epitaph. The bishop considers the form of the verb to be in "gaudy" bad taste (line 78). If the epitaph had been copied from Cicero instead of from Ulpian, the word would have been *elucebat.*

100   No Tully, said I, Ulpian at the best!
      Evil and brief hath been my pilgrimage.[7]
      All *lapis*, all, sons! Else I give the Pope
      My villas! Will ye ever eat my heart?
      Ever your eyes were as a lizard's quick,
105   They glitter like your mother's for my soul,
      Or ye would heighten my impoverished frieze,
      Piece out its starved design, and fill my vase
      With grapes, and add a vizor and a Term,[8]
      And to the tripod ye would tie a lynx[9]
110   That in his struggle throws the thyrsus down,
      To comfort me on my entablature[1]
      Whereon I am to lie till I must ask
      "Do I live, am I dead?" There, leave me, there!
      For ye have stabbed me with ingratitude
115   To death—ye wish it—God, ye wish it! Stone—
      Gritstone,[2] a-crumble! Clammy squares which sweat
      As if the corpse they keep were oozing through—
      And no more *lapis* to delight the world!
      Well go! I bless ye. Fewer tapers there,
120   But in a row: and, going, turn your backs
      —Aye, like departing altar-ministrants,
      And leave me in my church, the church for peace,
      That I may watch at leisure if he leers—
      Old Gandolf, at me, from his onion-stone,
125   As still he envied me, so fair she was!

1844   1845

A Toccata of Galuppi's[1]

1

Oh, Galuppi, Baldassaro, this is very sad to find!
I can hardly misconceive you; it would prove me deaf and blind;
But although I take your meaning, 'tis with such a heavy mind!

2

Here you come with your old music, and here's all the good it brings.
5 What, they lived once thus at Venice where the merchants were the kings,
Where Saint Mark's is, where the Doges used to wed the sea with rings?[2]

7. Cf. Genesis 47.9.
8. Statue of Terminus, the Roman god of boundaries, usually represented without arms. "Vizor": part of a helmet, often represented in sculpture.
9. An animal that traditionally accompanied Bacchus.
1. Horizontal platform supporting a statue or effigy.
2. Coarse sandstone.
1. For the main speaker of this poem, Browning invents a 19th-century English scientist, who is listening to music by the Italian composer Baldassaro Galuppi (1706–1785). The music evokes for the scientist visions of 18th-century Venice, including an imaginary scene of a party at which Galuppi

performs his composition for an audience. From line 20 onward we hear snippets of conversation from members of this audience as they respond to the different moods of the piece, and then, in lines 35–43, Galuppi's own imagined musings. "Toccata": according to *Grove's Dictionary of Music*, a "touch-piece, or a composition intended to exhibit the touch and execution of the performer." The same authority states that "no particular composition was taken as the basis of the poem."
2. An annual ceremony in which the doge, the Venetian chief magistrate, threw a ring into the water to symbolize the bond between his city, with its maritime empire, and the sea.

3

Aye, because the sea's the street there; and 'tis arched by . . . what you call
. . . Shylock's bridge[3] with houses on it, where they kept the carnival:
I was never out of England—it's as if I saw it all.

4

10   Did young people take their pleasure when the sea was warm in May?
Balls and masks° begun at midnight, burning ever to midday,   *masquerades*
When they made up fresh adventures for the morrow, do you say?

5

Was a lady such a lady, cheeks so round and lips so red—
On her neck the small face buoyant, like a bellflower on its bed,
15   O'er the breast's superb abundance where a man might base his head?

6

Well, and it was graceful of them—they'd break talk off and afford
—She, to bite her mask's black velvet—he, to finger on his sword,
While you sat and played toccatas, stately at the clavichord?[4]

7

What? Those lesser thirds so plaintive, sixths diminished, sigh on sigh,
20   Told them something? Those suspensions, those solutions—"Must we die?"
Those commiserating sevenths—"Life might last! we can but try!"

8

"Were you happy?"—"Yes."—"And are you still as happy?"—"Yes. And you?"
—"Then, more kisses!"—"Did *I* stop them, when a million seemed so few?"
Hark, the dominant's persistence till it must be answered to!

9

25   So, an octave struck the answer.[5] Oh, they praised you, I dare say!
"Brave Galuppi! that was music; good alike at grave and gay!
I can always leave off talking when I hear a master play!"

10

Then they left you for their pleasure: till in due time, one by one,
Some with lives that came to nothing, some with deeds as well undone,
30   Death stepped tacitly and took them where they never see the sun.

11

But when I sit down to reason, think to take my stand nor swerve,
While I triumph o'er a secret wrung from nature's close reserve,
In you come with your cold music till I creep through every nerve.

12

Yes, you, like a ghostly cricket, creaking where a house was burned:
35   "Dust and ashes, dead and done with, Venice spent what Venice earned.
The soul, doubtless, is immortal—where a soul can be discerned.

3. The Rialto, a bridge over the Grand Canal.
4. A keyboard instrument whose strings are struck by metal hammers. Its mechanism resembles that of a piano, but its sound is more like that of a harpsichord.
5. The terms in these lines refer to the technical devices used by Galuppi to produce alternating moods in his music, conflict in each instance being resolved into harmony. Thus the "dominant" (the fifth note of the scale), after being persistently sounded, is answered by a resolving chord (lines 24–25).

13

"Yours for instance: you know physics, something of geology,
Mathematics are your pastime; souls shall rise in their degree;
Butterflies may dread extinction—you'll not die, it cannot be!

14

40 "As for Venice and her people, merely born to bloom and drop,
Here on earth they bore their fruitage, mirth and folly were the crop:
What of soul was left, I wonder, when the kissing had to stop?

15

"Dust and ashes!" So you creak it, and I want° the heart to scold.   lack
Dear dead women, with such hair, too—what's become of all the gold
45 Used to hang and brush their bosoms? I feel chilly and grown old.

ca. 1847   1855

Love among the Ruins

1

Where the quiet-colored end of evening smiles,
        Miles and miles
On the solitary pastures where our sheep
        Half-asleep
5   Tinkle homeward through the twilight, stray or stop
        As they crop—
Was the site once of a city great and gay
        (So they say),
Of our country's very capital, its prince
10   Ages since
Held his court in, gathered councils, wielding far
        Peace or war.

2

Now—the country does not even boast a tree,
        As you see,
15 To distinguish slopes of verdure, certain rills
        From the hills
Intersect and give a name to (else they run
        Into one),
Where the domed and daring palace shot its spires
20   Up like fires
O'er the hundred-gated circuit of a wall
        Bounding all,
Made of marble, men might march on nor be pressed,
        Twelve abreast.

3

25 And such plenty and perfection, see, of grass
        Never was!
Such a carpet as, this summertime, o'erspreads
        And embeds

Every vestige of the city, guessed alone,
30   Stock or stone—
Where a multitude of men breathed joy and woe
        Long ago;
Lust of glory pricked their hearts up, dread of shame
        Struck them tame;
35 And that glory and that shame alike, the gold
        Bought and sold.

4

Now—the single little turret that remains
        On the plains,
By the caper overrooted, by the gourd
40   Overscored,
While the patching houseleek's¹ head of blossom winks
        Through the chinks—
Marks the basement whence a tower in ancient time
        Sprang sublime,
45 And a burning ring, all round, the chariots traced
        As they raced,
And the monarch and his minions and his dames
        Viewed the games.

5

And I know, while thus the quiet-colored eve
50   Smiles to leave
To their folding, all our many-tinkling fleece
        In such peace,
And the slopes and rills in undistinguished gray
        Melt away—
55 That a girl with eager eyes and yellow hair
        Waits me there
In the turret whence the charioteers caught soul
        For the goal,
When the king looked, where she looks now, breathless, dumb
60   Till I come.

6

But he looked upon the city, every side,
        Far and wide,
All the mountains topped with temples, all the glades'
        Colonnades,
65 All the causeys,² bridges, aqueducts—and then,
        All the men!
When I do come, she will speak not, she will stand,
        Either hand
On my shoulder, give her eyes the first embrace
70   Of my face,
Ere we rush, ere we extinguish sight and speech
        Each on each.

---

1. Common European plant with petals clustered   2. Causeways or roads raised above low ground.
in the shape of rosettes.

7

In one year they sent a million fighters forth
    South and north,
75 And they built their gods a brazen° pillar high   *brass*
    As the sky,
Yet reserved a thousand chariots in full force—
    Gold, of course.
Oh heart! oh blood that freezes, blood that burns!
80   Earth's returns
For whole centuries of folly, noise, and sin!
    Shut them in,
With their triumphs and their glories and the rest!
    Love is best.

1853

1855

"Childe Roland to the Dark Tower Came"[1]

(See Edgar's Song in "Lear")

1

My first thought was, he lied in every word,
    That hoary cripple, with malicious eye
    Askance° to watch the working of his lie   *squinting sidewise*
On mine, and mouth scarce able to afford
5 Suppression of the glee, that pursed and scored
    Its edge, at one more victim gained thereby.

2

What else should he be set for, with his staff?
    What, save to waylay with his lies, ensnare
    All travelers who might find him posted there,
10 And ask the road? I guessed what skull-like laugh
    Would break, what crutch 'gin° write my epitaph   *would begin to*
    For pastime in the dusty thoroughfare,

3

If at his counsel I should turn aside
    Into that ominous tract which, all agree,
15   Hides the Dark Tower. Yet acquiescingly

1. Browning stated that this poem "came upon me as a kind of dream," and that it was written in one day. Although the poem was among those of his own writings that pleased him most, he was reluctant to explain what the dream (or nightmare) signified. He once agreed with a friend's suggestion that the meaning might be expressed in the statement: "He that endureth to the end shall be saved" (cf. Matthew 24.13). Most readers have responded to the poem in this way, finding in the story of Roland's quest an inspiring expression of defiance and courage. Other readers find that the poem expresses despair more than enduring hope, and it is at least true that the landscape is as grim and nightmarelike as in 20th-century writings such as T. S. Eliot's "The Hollow Men" (1925) or Franz Kafka's "In the Penal Colony" (1919).
The lines from Shakespeare's *King Lear* 3.4 (lines 158–60), from which the title is taken, are spoken when Lear is about to enter a hovel on the heath, and Edgar, feigning madness, chants the fragment of a song reminiscent of quests and challenges in fairy tales: "Child Roland to the dark tower come, / His word was still, 'Fie, fo, and fum; / I smell the blood of a British man." "Childe": a youth of gentle birth, usually a candidate for knighthood.

I did turn as he pointed: neither pride
Nor hope rekindling at the end descried,
    So much as gladness that some end might be.

4

For, what with my whole world-wide wandering,
20   What with my search drawn out through years, my hope
    Dwindled into a ghost not fit to cope
With that obstreperous joy success would bring,
I hardly tried now to rebuke the spring
    My heart made, finding failure in its scope.

5

25 As when a sick man very near to death
    Seems dead indeed, and feels begin and end
    The tears and takes the farewell of each friend,
And hears one bid the other go, draw breath
Freelier outside ("since all is o'er," he saith,
30   "And the blow fallen no grieving can amend"),

6

While some discuss if near the other graves
    Be room enough for this, and when a day
    Suits best for carrying the corpse away,
With care about the banners, scarves and staves:[2]
35 And still the man hears all, and only craves
    He may not shame such tender love and stay.

7

Thus, I had so long suffered in this quest,
    Heard failure prophesied so oft, been writ
    So many times among "The Band"—to wit,
40 The knights who to the Dark Tower's search addressed
Their steps—that just to fail as they, seemed best,
    And all the doubt was now—should I be fit?

8

So, quiet as despair, I turned from him,
    That hateful cripple, out of his highway
45   Into the path he pointed. All the day
Had been a dreary one at best, and dim
Was settling to its close, yet shot one grim
    Red leer to see the plain catch its estray.[3]

9

For mark! no sooner was I fairly found
50   Pledged to the plain, after a pace or two,
    Than, pausing to throw backward a last view
O'er the safe road, 'twas gone; gray plain all round:
Nothing but plain to the horizon's bound.
    I might go on; naught else remained to do.

2. The trappings of an imagined funeral.
3. Literally, a domestic animal that has strayed away from its home.

10

55 So, on I went. I think I never saw
     Such starved ignoble nature; nothing throve:
     For flowers—as well expect a cedar grove!
     But, cockle, spurge,[4] according to their law
     Might propagate their kind, with none to awe,
60   You'd think; a burr had been a treasure trove.

11

No! penury, inertness and grimace,
     In some strange sort, were the land's portion. "See
     Or shut your eyes," said Nature peevishly,
     "It nothing skills:[5] I cannot help my case;
65 'Tis the Last Judgment's fire must cure this place,
     Calcine[6] its clods and set my prisoners free."

12

If there pushed any ragged thistle stalk
     Above its mates, the head was chopped; the bents[7]
     Were jealous else. What made those holes and rents
70 In the dock's° harsh swarth leaves, bruised as to balk   *coarse plant*
     All hope of greenness? 'tis a brute must walk
     Pashing° their life out, with a brute's intents.   *smashing*

13

As for the grass, it grew as scant as hair
     In leprosy; thin dry blades pricked the mud
75   Which underneath looked kneaded up with blood.
     One stiff blind horse, his every bone a-stare,
     Stood stupefied, however he came there:
     Thrust out past service from the devil's stud!

14

Alive? he might be dead for aught I know,
80   With that red gaunt and colloped° neck a-strain,   *ridged*
     And shut eyes underneath the rusty mane;
     Seldom went such grotesqueness with such woe;
     I never saw a brute I hated so;
     He must be wicked to deserve such pain.

15

85 I shut my eyes and turned them on my heart.
     As a man calls for wine before he fights,
     I asked one draught of earlier, happier sights,
     Ere fitly I could hope to play my part.
     Think first, fight afterwards—the soldier's art:
90   One taste of the old time sets all to rights.

16

Not it! I fancied Cuthbert's reddening face
     Beneath its garniture of curly gold,

4. A bitter-juiced weed. "Cockle": a weed that   6. Turn to powder by heat.
bears burrs.   7. Coarse stiff grasses.
5. I.e., it is no use.

Dear fellow, till I almost felt him fold
An arm in mine to fix me to the place,
95 That way he used. Alas, one night's disgrace!
Out went my heart's new fire and left it cold.

17

Giles then, the soul of honor—there he stands
Frank as ten years ago when knighted first.
What honest man should dare (he said) he durst.
100 Good—but the scene shifts—faugh! what hangman hands
Pin to his breast a parchment? His own bands
Read it. Poor traitor, spit upon and cursed!

18

Better this present than a past like that;
Back therefore to my darkening path again!
105 No sound, no sight as far as eye could strain.
Will the night send a howlet° or a bat?   owl
I asked: when something on the dismal flat
Came to arrest my thoughts and change their train.

19

A sudden little river crossed my path
110 As unexpected as a serpent comes.
No sluggish tide congenial to the glooms;
This, as it frothed by, might have been a bath
For the fiend's glowing hoof—to see the wrath
Of its black eddy bespate° with flakes and spumes.   bespattered

20

115 So petty yet so spiteful! All along,
Low scrubby alders kneeled down over it;
Drenched willows flung them headlong in a fit
Of mute despair, a suicidal throng:
The river which had done them all the wrong,
120 Whate'er that was, rolled by, deterred no whit.

21

Which, while I forded—good saints, how I feared
To set my foot upon a dead man's cheek,
Each step, or feel the spear I thrust to seek
For hollows, tangled in his hair or beard!
125 —It may have been a water rat I speared,
But, ugh! it sounded like a baby's shriek.

22

Glad was I when I reached the other bank.
Now for a better country. Vain presage!
Who were the strugglers, what war did they wage,
130 Whose savage trample thus could pad the dank
Soil to a plash?° Toads in a poisoned tank,   puddle
Or wild cats in a red-hot iron cage—

23

The fight must so have seemed in that fell cirque.°   dreadful arena
What penned them there, with all the plain to choose?

135   No footprint leading to that horrid mews,[8]
        None out of it. Mad brewage set to work
        Their brains, no doubt, like galley slaves the Turk
        Pits for his pastime, Christians against Jews.

24

        And more than that—a furlong on—why, there!
140   What bad use was that engine for, that wheel,
        Or brake,[9] not wheel—that harrow fit to reel
        Men's bodies out like silk? with all the air
        Of Tophet's° tool, on earth left unaware,   *hell's*
        Or brought to sharpen its rusty teeth of steel.

25

145   Then came a bit of stubbed ground, once a wood,
        Next a marsh, it would seem, and now mere earth
        Desperate and done with; (so a fool finds mirth,
        Makes a thing and then mars it, till his mood
        Changes and off he goes!) within a rood[1]
150   Bog, clay and rubble, sand and stark black dearth.

26

        Now blotches rankling, colored gay and grim,
        Now patches where some leanness of the soil's
        Broke into moss or substances like boils;
        Then came some palsied oak, a cleft in him
155   Like a distorted mouth that splits its rim
        Gaping at death, and dies while it recoils.

27

        And just as far as ever from the end!
        Naught in the distance but the evening, naught
        To point my footstep further! At the thought,
160   A great black bird, Apollyon's[2] bosom friend,
        Sailed past, nor beat his wide wing dragon-penned[3]
        That brushed my cap—perchance the guide I sought.

28

        For, looking up, aware I somehow grew,
        'Spite of the dusk, the plain had given place
165   All round to mountains—with such name to grace
        Mere ugly heights and heaps now stolen in view.
        How thus they had surprised me—solve it, you!
        How to get from them was no clearer case.

29

        Yet half I seemed to recognize some trick
170   Of mischief happened to me, God knows when—
        In a bad dream perhaps. Here ended, then,
        Progress this way. When, in the very nick

8. Enclosed stable yard.
9. A toothed machine used for separating the fibers of flax or hemp; here an instrument of torture.
1. I.e., a short distance (6–8 yards).

2. In Revelation 9.11 Apollyon is "the angel of the bottomless pit." In Bunyan's *Pilgrim's Progress* (1678) he is a hideous "monster"; "he had wings like a dragon."
3. With wings or pinions like those of a dragon.

Of giving up, one time more, came a click
  As when a trap shuts—you're inside the den!

30

175 Burningly it came on me all at once,
  This was the place! those two hills on the right,
  Crouched like two bulls locked horn in horn in fight;
  While to the left, a tall scalped mountain . . . Dunce,
  Dotard, a-dozing at the very nonce,°   *moment*
180   After a life spent training for the sight!

31

What in the midst lay but the Tower itself?
  The round squat turret, blind as the fool's heart,[4]
  Built of brown stone, without a counterpart
  In the whole world. The tempest's mocking elf
185 Points to the shipman thus the unseen shelf
  He strikes on, only when the timbers start.°   *separate; come loose*

32

Not see? because of night perhaps?—why, day
  Came back again for that! before it left,
  The dying sunset kindled through a cleft:
190 The hills, like giants at a hunting, lay,
  Chin upon hand, to see the game at bay—
  "Now stab and end the creature—to the heft!"[5]

33

Not hear? when noise was everywhere! it tolled
  Increasing like a bell. Names in my ears
195 Of all the lost adventurers my peers—
  How such a one was strong, and such was bold,
  And such was fortunate, yet each of old
  Lost, lost! one moment knelled the woe of years.

34

There they stood, ranged along the hillsides, met
200 To view the last of me, a living frame
  For one more picture! in a sheet of flame
  I saw them and I knew them all. And yet
  Dauntless the slug-horn[6] to my lips I set,
  And blew. *"Childe Roland to the Dark Tower came."*

1852   1855

Fra Lippo Lippi[1]

I am poor brother Lippo, by your leave!
You need not clap your torches to my face.

4. Cf. Psalm 14.1: "The fool hath said in his heart, There is no God."
5. Handle of dagger or sword.
6. The war cry or slogan of a clan about to engage in battle (Scottish). In 1770, however, the poet Thomas Chatterton was misled into using it to mean a kind of trumpet or horn. Browning followed Chatterton's example, although the original meaning would also be relevant here.
1. This monologue portrays the dawn of the Renaissance in Italy at a point when the medieval attitude toward life and art was about to be dis-

Zooks,[2] what's to blame? you think you see a monk!
What, 'tis past midnight, and you go the rounds,
5   And here you catch me at an alley's end
Where sportive ladies leave their doors ajar?
The Carmine's[3] my cloister: hunt it up,
Do—harry out, if you must show your zeal,
Whatever rat, there, haps on his wrong hole,
10   And nip each softling of a wee white mouse,
Weke, weke, that's crept to keep him company!
Aha, you know your betters! Then, you'll take
Your hand away that's fiddling on my throat,
And please to know me likewise. Who am I?
15   Why, one, sir, who is lodging with a friend
Three streets off—he's a certain . . . how d'ye call?
Master—a . . . Cosimo of the Medici,[4]
I' the house that caps the corner. Boh! you were best!
Remember and tell me, the day you're hanged,
20   How you affected such a gullet's gripe![5]
But you,[6] sir, it concerns you that your knaves
Pick up a manner nor discredit you:
Zooks, are we pilchards,° that they sweep the streets   small fish
And count fair prize what comes into this net?
25   He's Judas to a tittle, that man is![7]
Just such a face! Why, sir, you make amends.
Lord, I'm not angry! Bid your hangdogs go
Drink out this quarter-florin[8] to the health
Of the munificent House that harbors me
30   (And many more beside, lads! more beside!)
And all's come square again. I'd like his face—
His, elbowing on his comrade in the door
With the pike and lantern—for the slave that holds
John Baptist's head a-dangle by the hair
35   With one hand ("Look you, now," as who should say)
And his weapon in the other, yet unwiped!
It's not your chance to have a bit of chalk,
A wood-coal° or the like? or you should see!   piece of charcoal
Yes, I'm the painter, since you style me so.
40   What, brother Lippo's doings, up and down,
You know them and they take you? like enough!
I saw the proper twinkle in your eye—
'Tell you, I liked your looks at very first.
Let's sit and set things straight now, hip to haunch.

placed by a fresh appreciation of earthly pleasures.
It was from Giorgio Vasari's Lives of the Painters
(1550) that Browning derived most of his information about the life of the Florentine painter and
friar Lippo Lippi (1406–1469), but the theory of
art propounded by Lippi in the poem was developed by the poet.
2. A shortened version of Gadzooks, a mild oath
now obscure in meaning but perhaps resembling a
phrase still in use: "God's truth."
3. Santa Maria del Carmine, a church and cloister
of the Carmelite order of friars to which Lippi

belonged.
4. Lippi's patron, a banker and virtual ruler of
Florence (1389–1464).
5. I.e., how you had the arrogance to choke the
gullet of someone with my connections.
6. The officer in charge of the patrol of policemen
or watchmen.
7. I.e., one of the watchmen has a face that would
serve as a model for a painting of Judas. "To a tittle": to a tee; absolutely.
8. I.e., buy a drink worth a quarter of a florin (the
florin was a gold coin first minted in Florence).

45   Here's spring come, and the nights one makes up bands
      To roam the town and sing out carnival,[9]
      And I've been three weeks shut within my mew,°   *private den*
      A-painting for the great man, saints and saints
      And saints again. I could not paint all night—
50   Ouf! I leaned out of window for fresh air.
      There came a hurry of feet and little feet,
      A sweep of lute-strings, laughs, and whifts of song—
      Flower o' the broom,
      Take away love, and our earth is a tomb!
55   *Flower o' the quince,*
      I let Lisa go, and what good in life since?[1]
      Flower o' the thyme—and so on. Round they went.
      Scarce had they turned the corner when a titter
      Like the skipping of rabbits by moonlight—three slim shapes,
60   And a face that looked up . . . zooks, sir, flesh and blood,
      That's all I'm made of! Into shreds it went,
      Curtain and counterpane and coverlet,
      All the bed-furniture—a dozen knots,
      There was a ladder! Down I let myself,
65   Hands and feet, scrambling somehow, and so dropped,
      And after them. I came up with the fun
      Hard by Saint Laurence,[2] hail fellow, well met—
      Flower o' the rose,
      If I've been merry, what matter who knows!
70   And so as I was stealing back again
      To get to bed and have a bit of sleep
      Ere I rise up tomorrow and go work
      On Jerome knocking at his poor old breast
      With his great round stone to subdue the flesh,[3]
75   You snap me of the sudden. Ah, I see!
      Though your eye twinkles still, you shake your head—
      Mine's shaved—a monk, you say—the sting's in that!
      If Master Cosimo announced himself,
      Mum's the word naturally; but a monk!
80   Come, what am I a beast for? tell us, now!
      I was a baby when my mother died
      And father died and left me in the street.
      I starved there, God knows how, a year or two
      On fig skins, melon parings, rinds and shucks,
85   Refuse and rubbish. One fine frosty day,
      My stomach being empty as your hat,
      The wind doubled me up and down I went.
      Old Aunt Lapaccia trussed me with one hand
      (Its fellow° was a stinger as I knew),   *i.e., her other hand*
90   And so along the wall, over the bridge,
      By the straight cut to the convent. Six words there,
      While I stood munching my first bread that month:

9. Season of revelry before the commencement of Lent.
1. This and other interspersed flower songs are called *stornelli* in Italy.
2. San Lorenzo, a church in Florence. "Hard by": next to.
3. A picture of Saint Jerome (ca. 340–420), whose ascetic observances were hardly a congenial subject for a painter such as Lippi.

"So, boy, you're minded," quoth the good fat father
Wiping his own mouth, 'twas refection time°—   *mealtime*
95   "To quit this very miserable world?
Will you renounce" . . . "the mouthful of bread?" thought I;
By no means! Brief, they made a monk of me;
I did renounce the world, its pride and greed,
Palace, farm, villa, shop, and banking house,
100   Trash, such as these poor devils of Medici
Have given their hearts to—all at eight years old.
Well, sir, I found in time, you may be sure,
'Twas not for nothing—the good bellyful,
The warm serge and the rope that goes all round,[4]
105   And day-long blessed idleness beside!
"Let's see what the urchin's fit for"—that came next.
Not overmuch their way, I must confess.
Such a to-do! They tried me with their books:
Lord, they'd have taught me Latin in pure waste!
110   *Flower o' the clove,*
All the Latin I construe is "amo," I love!
But, mind you, when a boy starves in the streets
Eight years together, as my fortune was,
Watching folk's faces to know who will fling
115   The bit of half-stripped grape bunch he desires,
And who will curse or kick him for his pains—
Which gentleman processional and fine,
Holding a candle to the Sacrament,
Will wink and let him lift a plate and catch
120   The droppings of the wax to sell again,
Or holla for the Eight° and have him whipped—   *Florentine magistrates*
How say I?—nay, which dog bites, which lets drop
His bone from the heap of offal in the street—
Why, soul and sense of him grow sharp alike,
125   He learns the look of things, and none the less
For admonition from the hunger-pinch.
I had a store of such remarks, be sure,
Which, after I found leisure, turned to use.
I drew men's faces on my copybooks,
130   Scrawled them within the antiphonary's marge,[5]
Joined legs and arms to the long music-notes,
Found eyes and nose and chin for A's and B's,
And made a string of pictures of the world
Betwixt the ins and outs of verb and noun,
135   On the wall, the bench, the door. The monks looked black.
"Nay," quoth the Prior,[6] "turn him out, d' ye say?
In no wise. Lose a crow and catch a lark.
What if at last we get our man of parts,°   *skill, genius*
We Carmelites, like those Camaldolese
140   And Preaching Friars,[7] to do our church up fine
And put the front on it that ought to be!"

---

4. The material ("serge") and belt ("rope") of a
monk's clothing.
5. Margin of a music book used for choral singing.

6. Head of a Carmelite convent.
7. Benedictine and Dominican religious orders,
respectively.

And hereupon he bade me daub away.
Thank you! my head being crammed, the walls a blank,
Never was such prompt disemburdening.
145 First, every sort of monk, the black and white,
I drew them, fat and lean: then, folk at church,
From good old gossips waiting to confess
Their cribs° of barrel droppings, candle ends—   *petty thefts*
To the breathless fellow at the altar-foot,
150 Fresh from his murder, safe[8] and sitting there
With the little children round him in a row
Of admiration, half for his beard and half
For that white anger of his victim's son
Shaking a fist at him with one fierce arm,
155 Signing himself with the other because of Christ
(Whose sad face on the cross sees only this
After the passion° of a thousand years)   *sufferings*
Till some poor girl, her apron o'er her head
(Which the intense eyes looked through), came at eve
160 On tiptoe, said a word, dropped in a loaf,
Her pair of earrings and a bunch of flowers
(The brute took growling), prayed, and so was gone.
I painted all, then cried " 'Tis ask and have;
Choose, for more's ready!"—laid the ladder flat,
165 And showed my covered bit of cloister wall.
The monks closed in a circle and praised loud
Till checked, taught what to see and not to see,
Being simple bodies—"That's the very man!
Look at the boy who stoops to pat the dog!
170 That woman's like the Prior's niece who comes
To care about his asthma: it's the life!"
But there my triumph's straw-fire flared and funked;[9]
Their betters took their turn to see and say:
The Prior and the learned pulled a face
175 And stopped all that in no time. "How? what's here?
Quite from the mark of painting, bless us all!
Faces, arms, legs and bodies like the true
As much as pea and pea! it's devil's game!
Your business is not to catch men with show,
180 With homage to the perishable clay,
But lift them over it, ignore it all,
Make them forget there's such a thing as flesh.
Your business is to paint the souls of men—
Man's soul, and it's a fire, smoke . . . no, it's not . . .
185 It's vapor done up like a newborn babe—
(In that shape when you die it leaves your mouth)
It's . . . well, what matters talking, it's the soul!
Give us no more of body than shows soul!
Here's Giotto,[1] with his Saint a-praising God,
190 That sets us praising—why not stop with him?

8. Having claimed sanctuary in the church.
9. Went up in smoke.
1. Great Florentine painter (1276–1337), whose

stylized pictures of religious subjects were admired
as models of pre-Renaissance art.

Why put all thoughts of praise out of our head
With wonder at lines, colors, and what not?
Paint the soul, never mind the legs and arms!
Rub all out, try at it a second time.
195 Oh, that white smallish female with the breasts,
She's just° my niece . . . Herodias,[2] I would say—   *exactly like*
Who went and danced and got men's heads cut off!
Have it all out!" Now, is this sense, I ask?
A fine way to paint soul, by painting body
200 So ill, the eye can't stop there, must go further
And can't fare worse! Thus, yellow does for white
When what you put for yellow's simply black,
And any sort of meaning looks intense
When all beside itself means and looks naught.
205 Why can't a painter lift each foot in turn,
Left foot and right foot, go a double step,
Make his flesh liker and his soul more like,
Both in their order? Take the prettiest face,
The Prior's niece . . . patron-saint—is it so pretty
210 You can't discover if it means hope, fear,
Sorrow or joy? won't beauty go with these?
Suppose I've made her eyes all right and blue,
Can't I take breath and try to add life's flash,
And then add soul and heighten them threefold?
215 Or say there's beauty with no soul at all—
(I never saw it—put the case the same—)
If you get simple beauty and naught else,
You get about the best thing God invents:
That's somewhat: and you'll find the soul you have missed,
220 Within yourself, when you return him thanks.
"Rub all out!" Well, well, there's my life, in short,
And so the thing has gone on ever since.
I'm grown a man no doubt, I've broken bounds:
You should not take a fellow eight years old
225 And make him swear to never kiss the girls.
I'm my own master, paint now as I please—
Having a friend, you see, in the Corner-house![3]
Lord, it's fast holding by the rings in front—
Those great rings serve more purposes than just
230 To plant a flag in, or tie up a horse!
And yet the old schooling sticks, the old grave eyes
Are peeping o'er my shoulder as I work,
The heads shake still—"It's art's decline, my son!
You're not of the true painters, great and old;
235 Brother Angelico's the man, you'll find;
Brother Lorenzo[4] stands his single peer:
Fag on° at flesh, you'll never make the third!"   *work hard*
Flower o' the pine,

2. I.e., Salomé (her mother was Herodias, the   3. The Medici palace.
sister-in-law of King Herod). Because John the   4. Fra Angelico (1387–1455) and Lorenzo Mon-
Baptist had aroused her mother's displeasure, Sal- aco (1370–1425), whose paintings were in the
omé asked for his head on a platter after she   approved traditional manner.
danced (Matthew 14.6–11).

You keep your mistr . . . manners, and I'll stick to mine!
240 I'm not the third, then: bless us, they must know!
Don't you think they're the likeliest to know,
They with their Latin? So, I swallow my rage,
Clench my teeth, suck my lips in tight, and paint
To please them—sometimes do and sometimes don't;
245 For, doing most, there's pretty sure to come
A turn, some warm eve finds me at my saints—
A laugh, a cry, the business of the world—
(*Flower o' the peach,*
Death for us all, and his own life for each!)
250 And my whole soul revolves, the cup runs over,
The world and life's too big to pass for a dream,
And I do these wild things in sheer despite,
And play the fooleries you catch me at,
In pure rage! The old mill-horse, out at grass
255 After hard years, throws up his stiff heels so,
Although the miller does not preach to him
The only good of grass is to make chaff.°   straw
What would men have? Do they like grass or no[5]—
May they or mayn't they? all I want's the thing
260 Settled forever one way. As it is,
You tell too many lies and hurt yourself:
You don't like what you only like too much,
You do like what, if given you at your word,
You find abundantly detestable.
265 For me, I think I speak as I was taught;
I always see the garden[6] and God there
A-making man's wife: and, my lesson learned,
The value and significance of flesh,
I can't unlearn ten minutes afterwards.

270   You understand me: I'm a beast, I know.
But see, now—why, I see as certainly
As that the morning star's about to shine,
What will hap some day. We've a youngster here
Comes to our convent, studies what I do,
275 Slouches and stares and lets no atom drop:
His name is Guidi[7]—he'll not mind the monks—
They call him Hulking Tom, he lets them talk—
He picks my practice up—he'll paint apace,
I hope so—though I never live so long,
280 I know what's sure to follow. You be judge!
You speak no Latin more than I, belike;
However, you're my man, you've seen the world
—The beauty and the wonder and the power,
The shapes of things, their colors, lights and shades,

5. I.e., while horses are allowed to enjoy playing
in the grass, human beings are taught by the
Church that physical experience is valuable only in
its relation to their future condition in the afterlife.
The biblical text "all flesh is as grass" (1 Peter 1.24)
lurks within Lippi's question.
6. I.e., Eden.

7. Guidi or Masaccio (1401–1428), a painter who
may have been Lippi's master rather than his pupil,
although Browning, in a letter to the press in 1870,
argued that Lippi had been born earlier. Like
Lippi, Masaccio was in revolt against the medieval
theory of art. His frescoes in the chapel of Santa
Maria del Carmine are considered his masterpiece.

285 Changes, surprises—and God made it all!
—For what? Do you feel thankful, aye or no,
For this fair town's face, yonder river's line,
The mountain round it and the sky above,
Much more the figures of man, woman, child,
290 These are the frame to? What's it all about?
To be passed over, despised? or dwelt upon,
Wondered at? oh, this last of course!—you say.
But why not do as well as say—paint these
Just as they are, careless what comes of it?
295 God's works—paint any one, and count it crime
To let a truth slip. Don't object, "His works
Are here already; nature is complete:
Suppose you reproduce her—(which you can't)
There's no advantage! You must beat her, then."
300 For, don't you mark?° we're made so that we love   *observe*
First when we see them painted, things we have passed
Perhaps a hundred times nor cared to see;
And so they are better, painted—better to us,
Which is the same thing. Art was given for that;
305 God uses us to help each other so,
Lending our minds out. Have you noticed, now,
Your cullion's° hanging face? A bit of chalk,   *rascal's*
And trust me but you should, though! How much more,
If I drew higher things with the same truth!
310 That were to take the Prior's pulpit-place,
Interpret God to all of you! Oh, oh,
It makes me mad to see what men shall do
And we in our graves! This world's no blot for us,
Nor blank; it means intensely, and means good:
315 To find its meaning is my meat and drink.
"Aye, but you don't so instigate to prayer!"
Strikes in the Prior: "when your meaning's plain
It does not say to folk—remember matins,
Or, mind you fast next Friday!" Why, for this
320 What need of art at all? A skull and bones,
Two bits of stick nailed crosswise, or, what's best,
A bell to chime the hour with, does as well.
I painted a Saint Laurence[8] six months since
At Prato, splashed the fresco[9] in fine style:
325 "How looks my painting, now the scaffold's down?"
I ask a brother: "Hugely," he returns—
"Already not one phiz° of your three slaves   *face*
Who turn the Deacon off his toasted side,
But it's scratched and prodded to our heart's content,
330 The pious people have so eased their own
With coming to say prayers there in a rage:
We get on fast to see the bricks beneath.
Expect another job this time next year,

8. A scene representing the fiery martyrdom of
Saint Laurence.
9. Painted on a freshly plastered surface. It must
be painted quickly before the plaster dries. Prato
is a town near Florence.

For pity and religion grow i' the crowd—
335 Your painting serves its purpose!" Hang the fools!

—That is—you'll not mistake an idle word
Spoke in a huff by a poor monk, God wot,°   knows
Tasting the air this spicy night which turns
The unaccustomed head like Chianti wine!
340 Oh, the church knows! don't misreport me, now!
It's natural a poor monk out of bounds
Should have his apt word to excuse himself:
And hearken how I plot to make amends.
I have bethought me: I shall paint a piece
345 . . . There's for you! Give me six months, then go, see
Something in Sant' Ambrogio's![1] Bless the nuns!
They want a cast o' my office.[2] I shall paint
God in the midst, Madonna and her babe,
Ringed by a bowery flowery angel brood,
350 Lilies and vestments and white faces, sweet
As puff on puff of grated orris-root[3]
When ladies crowd to Church at midsummer.
And then i' the front, of course a saint or two—
Saint John, because he saves the Florentines,
355 Saint Ambrose, who puts down in black and white
The convent's friends and gives them a long day,
And Job,[4] I must have him there past mistake,
The man of Uz (and Us without the z,
Painters who need his patience). Well, all these
360 Secured at their devotion, up shall come
Out of a corner when you least expect,
As one by a dark stair into a great light,
Music and talking, who but Lippo! I!—
Mazed,° motionless and moonstruck—I'm the man!   confused
365 Back I shrink—what is this I see and hear?
I, caught up with my monk's things by mistake,
My old serge gown and rope that goes all round,
I, in this presence, this pure company!
Where's a hole, where's a corner for escape?
370 Then steps a sweet angelic slip of a thing
Forward, puts out a soft palm—"Not so fast!"
—Addresses the celestial presence, "nay—
He made you and devised you, after all,
Though he's none of you! Could Saint John there draw—
375 His camel-hair[5] make up a painting-brush?
We come to brother Lippo for all that,
Iste perfecit opus!"[6] So, all smile—
I shuffle sideways with my blushing face

1. A convent church in Florence.
2. Sample of my work. The completed painting, which Browning saw in Florence, is Lippi's Coronation of the Virgin (1441).
3. A powder (like talcum) made from sweet-smelling roots of a flower.
4. The prosperous man who endured immense suffering without once questioning God's will (see the book of Job).
5. Cf. Mark 1.6: "And John was clothed with camel's hair."
6. This man made the work! (Latin). In this painting, as later completed, these words appear beside a figure that Browning took to be Lippi's self-portrait.

Under the cover of a hundred wings
380   Thrown like a spread of kirtles° when you're gay   *skirts*
And play hot cockles,⁷ all the doors being shut,
Till, wholly unexpected, in there pops
The hothead husband! Thus I scuttle off
To some safe bench behind, not letting go
385   The palm of her, the little lily thing
That spoke the good word for me in the nick,
Like the Prior's niece . . . Saint Lucy, I would say.
And so all's saved for me, and for the church
A pretty picture gained. Go, six months hence!
390   Your hand, sir, and good-by: no lights, no lights!
The street's hushed, and I know my own way back,
Don't fear me! There's the gray beginning. Zooks!

ca. 1853   1855

Andrea del Sarto¹

(called "The Faultless Painter")

But do not let us quarrel any more,
No, my Lucrezia; bear with me for once:
Sit down and all shall happen as you wish.
You turn your face, but does it bring your heart?
5   I'll work then for your friend's friend, never fear,
Treat his own subject after his own way,
Fix his own time, accept too his own price,
And shut the money into this small hand
When next it takes mine. Will it? tenderly?
10   Oh, I'll content him—but tomorrow, Love!
I often am much wearier than you think,
This evening more than usual, and it seems
As if—forgive now—should you let me sit
Here by the window with your hand in mine
15   And look a half-hour forth on Fiesole,²
Both of one mind, as married people use,°   *usually are*
Quietly, quietly the evening through,
I might get up tomorrow to my work
Cheerful and fresh as ever. Let us try.
20   Tomorrow, how you shall be glad for this!
Your soft hand is a woman of itself,

---

7. A game in which a player wears a blindfold.
1. This portrait of Andrea del Sarto (1486–1531) was derived from a biography written by his pupil Giorgio Vasari, author of *The Lives of the Painters* (1550). Vasari's account seeks to explain why his Florentine master, one of the most skillful painters of the Renaissance, never altogether fulfilled the promise he had shown early in his career and why he had never arrived (in Vasari's opinion) at the level of such artists as Raphael. Vasari noted that Andrea suffered from "a certain timidity of mind . . . which rendered it impossible that those evidences of ardor and animation, which are proper to the more exalted character, should ever appear in him."

Browning also follows Vasari's account of Andrea's marriage to a beautiful widow, Lucrezia, "an artful woman who made him do as she pleased in all things." Vasari reports that Andrea's "immoderate love for her soon caused him to neglect the studies demanded by his art" and that this infatuation had "more influence over him than the glory and honor towards which he had begun to make such hopeful advances."

2. A suburb on the hills overlooking Florence.

And mine the man's bared breast she curls inside.
Don't count the time lost, neither; you must serve
For each of the five pictures we require:
25   It saves° a model. So! keep looking so—   *saves the expense of*
My serpentining beauty, rounds on rounds!³
—How could you ever prick those perfect ears,
Even to put the pearl there! oh, so sweet—
My face, my moon, my everybody's moon,
30   Which everybody looks on and calls his,
And, I suppose, is looked on by in turn,
While she looks—no one's: very dear, no less.⁴
You smile? why, there's my picture ready made,
There's what we painters call our harmony!
35   A common grayness silvers everything⁵—
All in a twilight, you and I alike
—You, at the point of your first pride in me
(That's gone you know)—but I, at every point;
My youth, my hope, my art, being all toned down
40   To yonder sober pleasant Fiesole.
There's the bell clinking from the chapel top;
That length of convent wall across the way
Holds the trees safer, huddled more inside;
The last monk leaves the garden; days decrease,
45   And autumn grows, autumn in everything.
Eh? the whole seems to fall into a shape
As if I saw alike my work and self
And all that I was born to be and do,
A twilight-piece. Love, we are in God's hand.
50   How strange now, looks the life he makes us lead;
So free we seem, so fettered fast we are!
I feel he laid the fetter: let it lie!
This chamber for example—turn your head—
All that's behind us! You don't understand
55   Nor care to understand about my art,
But you can hear at least when people speak:
And that cartoon,° the second from the door   *drawing*
—It is the thing, Love! so such things should be—
Behold Madonna!—I am bold to say.
60   I can do with my pencil what I know,
What I see, what at bottom of my heart
I wish for, if I ever wish so deep—
Do easily, too—when I say, perfectly,
I do not boast, perhaps: yourself are judge,
65   Who listened to the Legate's⁶ talk last week,
And just as much they used to say in France.
At any rate 'tis easy, all of it!
No sketches first, no studies, that's long past:
I do what many dream of, all their lives,
70   —Dream? strive to do, and agonize to do,

3. Coils of hair like the coils of a serpent.
4. Her affections are centered on no one person, not even on her husband, yet she is nevertheless dear to him.
5. The predominant color in many of Andrea's paintings is silver gray.
6. A deputy of the pope.

And fail in doing. I could count twenty such
On twice your fingers, and not leave this town,
Who strive—you don't know how the others strive
To paint a little thing like that you smeared
75 Carelessly passing with your robes afloat—
Yet do much less, so much less, Someone[7] says
(I know his name, no matter)—so much less!
Well, less is more, Lucrezia: I am judged.
There burns a truer light of God in them,
80 In their vexed beating stuffed and stopped-up brain,
Heart, or whate'er else, than goes on to prompt
This low-pulsed forthright craftsman's hand of mine.
Their works drop groundward, but themselves, I know,
Reach many a time a heaven that's shut to me,
85 Enter and take their place there sure enough,
Though they come back and cannot tell the world.
My works are nearer heaven, but I sit here.
The sudden blood of these men! at a word—
Praise them, it boils, or blame them, it boils too.
90 I, painting from myself and to myself,
Know what I do, am unmoved by men's blame
Or their praise either. Somebody remarks
Morello's[8] outline there is wrongly traced,
His hue mistaken; what of that? or else,
95 Rightly traced and well ordered; what of that?
Speak as they please, what does the mountain care?
Ah, but a man's reach should exceed his grasp,
Or what's a heaven for? All is silver-gray
Placid and perfect with my art: the worse!
100 I know both what I want and what might gain,
And yet how profitless to know, to sigh
"Had I been two, another and myself,
Our head would have o'erlooked the world!" No doubt.
Yonder's a work now, of that famous youth
105 The Urbinate[9] who died five years ago.
('Tis copied,[1] George Vasari sent it me.)
Well, I can fancy how he did it all,
Pouring his soul, with kings and popes to see,
Reaching, that heaven might so replenish him,
110 Above and through his art—for it gives way;
That arm is wrongly put—and there again—
A fault to pardon in the drawing's lines,
Its body, so to speak: its soul is right,
He means right—that, a child may understand.
115 Still, what an arm! and I could alter it:
But all the play, the insight and the stretch—
Out of me, out of me! And wherefore out?
Had you enjoined them on me, given me soul,
We might have risen to Rafael, I and you!

7. Probably the artist Michelangelo (1475–1564).
8. A mountain peak outside Florence.
9. Raphael (1483–1520), or Raffaello Sanzio, born at Urbino.

1. In saying that the painting is a copy, Andrea may perhaps be concerned to prevent Lucrezia from selling it.

120 Nay, Love, you did give all I asked, I think—
     More than I merit, yes, by many times.
     But had you—oh, with the same perfect brow,
     And perfect eyes, and more than perfect mouth,
     And the low voice my soul hears, as a bird
125 The fowler's pipe,[2] and follows to the snare—
     Had you, with these the same, but brought a mind!
     Some women do so. Had the mouth there urged
     "God and the glory! never care for gain.
     The present by the future, what is that?
130 Live for fame, side by side with Agnolo!°   Michelangelo
     Rafael is waiting: up to God, all three!"
     I might have done it for you. So it seems:
     Perhaps not. All is as God overrules.
     Beside, incentives come from the soul's self;
135 The rest avail not. Why do I need you?
     What wife had Rafael, or has Agnolo?
     In this world, who can do a thing, will not;
     And who would do it, cannot, I perceive:
     Yet the will's somewhat°—somewhat, too, the power—   of some importance
140 And thus we half-men struggle. At the end,
     God, I conclude, compensates, punishes.
     'Tis safer for me, if the award be strict,
     That I am something underrated here.
     Poor this long while, despised, to speak the truth.
145 I dared not, do you know, leave home all day,
     For fear of chancing on the Paris lords.
     The best is when they pass and look aside;
     But they speak sometimes; I must bear it all.
     Well may they speak! That Francis,[3] that first time,
150 And that long festal year at Fontainebleau!
     I surely then could sometimes leave the ground,
     Put on the glory, Rafael's daily wear,
     In that humane great monarch's golden look—
     One finger in his beard or twisted curl
155 Over his mouth's good mark that made the smile,
     One arm about my shoulder, round my neck,
     The jingle of his gold chain in my ear,
     I painting proudly with his breath on me,
     All his court round him, seeing with his eyes,
160 Such frank French eyes, and such a fire of souls
     Profuse, my hand kept plying by those hearts—
     And, best of all, this, this, this face beyond,
     This in the background, waiting on my work,
     To crown the issue with a last reward!
165 A good time, was it not, my kingly days?
     And had you not grown restless . . . but I know—
     'Tis done and past; 'twas right, my instinct said;

2. Whistle or call used by hunters to lure wild fowl into range.
3. King Francis I of France (1494–1547; reigned 1515–47) had invited Andrea to his court at Fontainebleau and warmly encouraged him in his painting. On returning to Florence, however, Andrea is reputed to have stolen some funds entrusted to him by Francis; and to please Lucrezia he built a house with the money. Now he is afraid of being insulted by "Paris lords" on the streets.

Too live the life grew, golden and not gray,
And I'm the weak-eyed bat no sun should tempt
170 Out of the grange° whose four walls make his world.   *farmhouse*
How could it end in any other way?
You called me, and I came home to your heart.
The triumph was—to reach and stay there; since
I reached it ere the triumph, what is lost?
175 Let my hands frame your face in your hair's gold,
You beautiful Lucrezia that are mine!
"Rafael did this, Andrea painted that;
The Roman's is the better when you pray,
But still the other's Virgin was his wife—"
180 Men will excuse me. I am glad to judge
Both pictures in your presence; clearer grows
My better fortune, I resolve to think.
For, do you know, Lucrezia, as God lives,
Said one day Agnolo, his very self,
185 To Rafael . . . I have known it all these years . . .
(When the young man was flaming out his thoughts
Upon a palace wall for Rome to see,
Too lifted up in heart because of it)
"Friend, there's a certain sorry little scrub
190 Goes up and down our Florence, none cares how,
Who, were he set to plan and execute
As you are, pricked on by your popes and kings,
Would bring the sweat into that brow of yours!"
To Rafael's—And indeed the arm is wrong.
195 I hardly dare . . . yet, only you to see,
Give the chalk here—quick, thus the line should go!
Aye, but the soul! he's Rafael! rub it out!
Still, all I care for, if he spoke the truth,
(What he? why, who but Michel Agnolo?
200 Do you forget already words like those?)
If really there was such a chance, so lost—
Is, whether you're—not grateful—but more pleased.
Well, let me think so. And you smile indeed!
This hour has been an hour! Another smile?
205 If you would sit thus by me every night
I should work better, do you comprehend?
I mean that I should earn more, give you more.
See, it is settled dusk now; there's a star;
Morello's gone, the watch-lights show the wall,
210 The cue-owls[4] speak the name we call them by.
Come from the window, love—come in, at last,
Inside the melancholy little house
We built to be so gay with. God is just.
King Francis may forgive me: oft at nights
215 When I look up from painting, eyes tired out,
The walls become illumined, brick from brick
Distinct, instead of mortar, fierce bright gold,
That gold of his I did cement them with!

---

4. Scops owls; the term is Browning's coinage from the Italian *chiù* or *ciù*, a name that imitates their cry.

Let us but love each other. Must you go?
20 That Cousin here again? he waits outside?
Must see you—you, and not with me? Those loans?
More gaming debts to pay?⁵ you smiled for that?
Well, let smiles buy me! have you more to spend?
While hand and eye and something of a heart
25 Are left me, work's my ware, and what's it worth?
I'll pay my fancy. Only let me sit
The gray remainder of the evening out,
Idle, you call it, and muse perfectly
How I could paint, were I but back in France,
30 One picture, just one more—the Virgin's face,
Not yours this time! I want you at my side
To hear them—that is, Michel Agnolo—
Judge all I do and tell you of its worth.
Will you? Tomorrow, satisfy your friend.
35 I take the subjects for his corridor,
Finish the portrait out of hand—there, there,
And throw him in another thing or two
If he demurs; the whole should prove enough
To pay for this same Cousin's freak.° Beside,   *whim*
40 What's better and what's all I care about,
Get you the thirteen scudi° for the ruff!   *Italian coins*
Love, does that please you? Ah, but what does he,
The Cousin! What does he to please you more?

I am grown peaceful as old age tonight.
45 I regret little, I would change still less.
Since there my past life lies, why alter it?
The very wrong to Francis!—it is true
I took his coin, was tempted and complied,
And built this house and sinned, and all is said.
50 My father and my mother died of want.⁶
Well, had I riches of my own? you see
How one gets rich! Let each one bear his lot.
They were born poor, lived poor, and poor they died:
And I have labored somewhat in my time
55 And not been paid profusely. Some good son
Paint my two hundred pictures—let him try!
No doubt, there's something strikes a balance. Yes,
You loved me quite enough, it seems tonight.
This must suffice me here. What would one have?
60 In heaven, perhaps, new chances, one more chance—
Four great walls in the New Jerusalem,⁷
Meted on each side by the angel's reed,°   *measuring rod*
For Leonard,⁸ Rafael, Agnolo and me
To cover—the three first without a wife,

5. Lucrezia's "Cousin" (or lover or friend) owes gambling debts to a creditor. Andrea has already contracted (lines 5–10) to pay off these debts by painting some pictures according to the creditor's specifications. Now he agrees to pay off further debts.

6. According to Vasari, Andrea's infatuation for Lucrezia prompted him to stop supporting his poverty-stricken parents.
7. Cf. Revelation 21.10–21.
8. Leonardo da Vinci (1452–1519).

265 While I have mine! So—still they overcome
Because there's still Lucrezia—as I choose.

Again the Cousin's whistle! Go, my Love.

ca. 1853   1855

A Grammarian's Funeral[1]

Shortly after the Revival of Learning in Europe

Let us begin and carry up this corpse,
    Singing together.
Leave we the common crofts,[2] the vulgar thorpes°   *villages*
    Each in its tether[3]
5 Sleeping safe on the bosom of the plain,
    Cared for till cock-crow:
Look out if yonder be not day again
    Rimming the rock-row!
That's the appropriate country; there, man's thought,
10   Rarer, intenser,
Self-gathered for an outbreak, as it ought,
    Chafes in the censer.[4]
Leave we the unlettered plain[5] its herd and crop;
    Seek we sepulture°   *burial place*
15 On a tall mountain, citied to the top,
    Crowded with culture!
All the peaks soar, but one the rest excels;
    Clouds overcome it;
No! yonder sparkle is the citadel's
20   Circling its summit.
Thither our path lies; wind we up the heights:
    Wait ye the warning?
Our low life was the level's and the night's;
    He's for the morning.
25 Step to a tune, square chests, erect each head,
    'Ware the beholders![6]
This is our master, famous, calm, and dead,
    Borne on our shoulders.

Sleep, crop and herd! sleep, darkling thorpe and croft,
30   Safe from the weather!
He, whom we convoy to his grave aloft,
    Singing together,

1. The speaker is one of the students who are
bearing the body of their scholarly master to the
mountaintop for burial. No specific model for the
grammarian has been identified. Browning seems
to have had in mind the kind of early Renaissance
scholar whose devotion to the Greek language
made it possible for others to enjoy the more recognizably significant aspects of the revival of learning.
2. Small tracts of land farmed by peasants.
3. Restricted to a narrow sphere like an animal
tied to a stake.
4. Container in which incense is burned.
5. Flatlands at the base of the mountain that are
populated by illiterate shepherds and peasants.
6. Let the beholders beware!

He was a man born with thy face and throat,
    Lyric Apollo!⁷
35 Long he lived nameless: how should spring take note
    Winter would follow?
Till lo, the little touch, and youth was gone!
    Cramped and diminished,
Moaned he, "New measures, other feet anon!
40   My dance is finished?"
No, that's the world's way: (keep the mountain-side,
    Make for the city!)
He knew the signal, and stepped on with pride
    Over men's pity;
45 Left play for work, and grappled with the world
    Bent on escaping:
"What's in the scroll," quoth he, "thou keepest furled?
    Show me their shaping,
Theirs who most studied man, the bard and sage—
50   Give!"—So, he gowned him,⁸
Straight° got by heart that book to its last page: *immediately*
    Learned, we found him.
Yea, but we found him bald too, eyes like lead,
    Accents uncertain:
55 "Time to taste life," another would have said,
    "Up with the curtain!"
This man said rather, "Actual life comes next?
    Patience a moment!
Grant I have mastered learning's crabbed text,
60   Still there's the comment.⁹
Let me know all! Prate not of most or least,
    Painful or easy!
Even to the crumbs I'd fain° eat up the feast,   *gladly*
    Aye, nor feel queasy."
65 Oh, such a life as he resolved to live,
    When he had learned it,
When he had gathered all books had to give!
    Sooner, he spurned it.
Image the whole, then execute the parts—
70   Fancy the fabric
Quite, ere you build, ere steel strike fire from quartz,
    Ere mortar dab brick!

(Here's the town gate reached: there's the market place
    Gaping before us.)
75 Yea, this in him was the peculiar grace
    (Hearten our chorus!)
That before living he'd learn how to live—
    No end to learning:
Earn the means first—God surely will contrive
80   Use for our earning.

7. Classical god of music and poetry; the embod-   8. Dressed in academic gown; became a scholar.
iment of male beauty.   9. Commentaries or annotations on a text.

Others mistrust and say, "But time escapes:
   Live now or never!"
He said, "What's time? Leave Now for dogs and apes!
   Man has Forever."
85 Back to his book then: deeper drooped his head:
   Calculus[1] racked him:
Leaden before, his eyes grew dross of lead:
   Tussis° attacked him.   *a cough*
"Now, master, take a little rest!"—not he!
90   (Caution redoubled,
Step two abreast, the way winds narrowly!)
   Not a whit troubled
Back to his studies, fresher than at first,
   Fierce as a dragon
95 He (soul-hydroptic[2] with a sacred thirst)
   Sucked at the flagon.
Oh, if we draw a circle premature,
   Heedless of far gain,
Greedy for quick returns of profit, sure
100   Bad is our bargain!
Was it not great? did not he throw on God
   (He loves the burthen)—
God's task to make the heavenly period
   Perfect the earthen?
105 Did not he magnify the mind, show clear
   Just what it all meant?
He would not discount life, as fools do here,
   Paid by installment.
He ventured neck or nothing—heaven's success
110   Found, or earth's failure:
"Wilt thou trust death or not?" He answered "Yes:
   Hence with life's pale lure!"
That low man seeks a little thing to do,
   Sees it and does it:
115 This high man, with a great thing to pursue,
   Dies ere he knows it.
That low man goes on adding one to one,
   His hundred's soon hit:
This high man, aiming at a million,
120   Misses an unit.[3]
That, has the world here—should he need the next,
   Let the world mind him!
This, throws himself on God, and unperplexed
   Seeking shall find him.
125 So, with the throttling hands of death at strife,
   Ground he at grammar;
Still, through the rattle, parts of speech were rife:
   While he could stammer

---

1. A gallstone or other hard inorganic mass within the body.
2. Insatiably thirsty.

3. A small item, such as some trifling worldly pleasure.

He settled *Hoti's* business—let it be!—
130   Properly based *Oun*—
Gave us the doctrine of the enclitic *De*,[4]
Dead from the waist down.
Well, here's the platform, here's the proper place:
Hail to your purlieus,°   regions
135 All ye highfliers of the feathered race,
Swallows and curlews!
Here's the top peak; the multitude below
Live, for they can, there:
This man decided not to Live but Know—
140   Bury this man there?
Here—here's his place, where meteors shoot, clouds form,
Lightnings are loosened,
Stars come and go! Let joy break with the storm,
Peace let the dew send!
145 Lofty designs must close in like effects:
Loftily lying,
Leave him—still loftier than the world suspects,
Living and dying.

ca. 1854   1855

An Epistle Containing the Strange Medical Experience of Karshish, the Arab Physician[1]

Karshish, the picker-up of learning's crumbs,
The not-incurious in God's handiwork
(This man's-flesh he hath admirably made,
Blown like a bubble, kneaded like a paste,
5   To coop up and keep down on earth a space°   for a time
That puff of vapor from his mouth, man's soul[2])
—To Abib, all-sagacious in our art,
Breeder in me of what poor skill I boast,
Like me inquisitive how pricks and cracks
10 Befall the flesh through too much stress and strain,
Whereby the wily vapor fain would slip
Back and rejoin its source before the term,—
And aptest in contrivance (under God)
To baffle it by deftly stopping such:—

4. *"Hoti," "Oun,"* and *"De"*: Greek particles meaning "that," "then," and "toward." "Enclitic": in
effect (and literally, in the case of *de*) a suffix. In
an 1863 letter Browning commented to Tennyson
that he wanted his grammarian to have been working on "the biggest of the littlenesses."
1. The letter is written in 66 C.E., just before the
Romans invaded Palestine. During a journey
across the country, Karshish, whose name in Arabic means "one who gathers" (or roughly, "the
picker-up of learning's crumbs"), has been collecting information on medical and scientific

developments he has encountered. Most recently
he has been intrigued by the story of Lazarus, a Jew
who is reputed to have died and been miraculously
brought back to life by a "Nazarene physician" (as
Jesus is called here) many years earlier (cf. John
11.1–44). Karshish's letter is addressed from Bethlehem to Abib, formerly his science teacher and
now his colleague and friend. Both scientists are
imaginary characters.
2. Karshish is referring to the old belief that the
soul leaves the body with one's last breath, in the
form of a vapor.

15 The vagrant° Scholar to his Sage at home   *wandering*
Sends greeting (health and knowledge, fame with peace)
Three samples of true snakestone³—rarer still,
One of the other sort, the melon-shaped,
(But fitter, pounded fine, for charms than drugs)
20 And writeth now the twenty-second time.

My journeyings were brought to Jericho:⁴
Thus I resume. Who studious in our art
Shall count a little labor unrepaid?
I have shed sweat enough, left flesh and bone
25 On many a flinty furlong of this land.
Also, the country-side is all on fire
With rumors of a marching hitherward:
Some say Vespasian⁵ cometh, some, his son.
A black lynx snarled and pricked a tufted ear;
30 Lust of my blood inflamed his yellow balls:°   *eyeballs*
I cried and threw my staff and he was gone.
Twice have the robbers stripped and beaten me,
And once a town declared me for a spy;
But at the end, I reach Jerusalem,
35 Since this poor covert where I pass the night,
This Bethany,⁶ lies scarce the distance thence
A man with plague-sores at the third degree
Runs till he drops down dead. Thou laughest here!
'Sooth,⁷ it elates me, thus reposed and safe,
40 To void the stuffing of my travel-scrip°   *small bag*
And share with thee whatever Jewry yields.
A viscid choler is observable
In tertians,⁸ I was nearly bold to say;
And falling-sickness° hath a happier cure   *epilepsy*
45 Than our school wots° of: there's a spider here   *knows*
Weaves no web, watches on the ledge of tombs,
Sprinkled with mottles on an ash-gray back;
Take five and drop them . . . but who knows his mind,
The Syrian runagate° I trust this to?   *renegade*
50 His service payeth me a sublimate⁹
Blown up his nose to help the ailing eye.
Best wait: I reach Jerusalem at morn,
There set in order my experiences,
Gather what most deserves, and give thee all—
55 Or I might add, Judea's gum-tragacanth¹
Scales off in purer flakes, shines clearer-grained,
Cracks 'twixt the pestle and the porphyry,²
In fine° exceeds our produce. Scalp-disease   *conclusion*
Confounds me, crossing so with leprosy—

3. A stone used to treat snake bites.
4. I.e., in the last letters.
5. The Roman commander (9–79 C.E.; emperor, 69–79) who invaded Palestine in 66. His son Titus destroyed Jerusalem four years later.
6. The small village where Lazarus lives, located two miles east of Jerusalem.
7. Forsooth; in truth.
8. A sticky bile is observable in fevers occurring every other day.
9. I.e., pays me for a medicine.
1. A salve derived from a plant.
2. A hard rock against which the substance is pounded with a pestle.

60 Thou hadst admired one sort I gained at Zoar³
But zeal outruns discretion. Here I end.

Yet stay: my Syrian blinketh gratefully,
Protesteth his devotion is my price—
Suppose I write what harms not, though he steal?
65 I half resolve to tell thee, yet I blush,
What set me off a-writing first of all.
An itch I had, a sting to write, a tang!
For, be it this town's barrenness—or else
The Man° had something in the look of him—   *Lazarus*
70 His case has struck me far more than 'tis worth.
So, pardon if—(lest presently I lose
In the great press of novelty at hand
The care and pains this somehow stole from me)
I bid thee take the thing while fresh in mind,
75 Almost in sight—for, wilt thou have the truth?
The very man is gone from me but now,
Whose ailment is the subject of discourse.
Thus then, and let thy better wit help all!

'Tis but a case of mania—subinduced⁴
80 By epilepsy, at the turning-point
Of trance prolonged unduly some three days:
When, by the exhibition° of some drug   *administration*
Or spell, exorcization, stroke of art
Unknown to me and which 'twere well to know,
85 The evil thing out-breaking all at once
Left the man whole and sound of body indeed,—
But, flinging (so to speak) life's gates too wide,
Making a clear house of it too suddenly,
The first conceit° that entered might inscribe   *idea*
90 Whatever it was minded on the wall
So plainly at that vantage, as it were,
(First come, first served) that nothing subsequent
Attaineth to erase those fancy-scrawls
The just-returned and new-established soul
95 Hath gotten now so thoroughly by heart
That henceforth she will read or° these or none.   *either*
And first—the man's own firm conviction rests
That he was dead (in fact they buried him)
—That he was dead and then restored to life
100 By a Nazarene physician of his tribe:
—'Sayeth,° the same bade "Rise," and he did rise.   *he says*
"Such cases are diurnal,"⁵ thou wilt cry.
Not so this figment!—not, that such a fume,⁶
Instead of giving way to time and health,
105 Should eat itself into the life of life,
As saffron⁷ tingeth flesh, blood, bones and all!

3. Town north of the Dead Sea.
4. Brought about as a result of something else.
5. Occur every day.

6. A vapor standing for a hallucinated belief.
7. Yellow-colored dye made from the plant of the same name, also used as a spice.

For see, how he takes up the after-life.
The man—it is one Lazarus a Jew,
Sanguine,° proportioned, fifty years of age,   *robust*
110 The body's habit wholly laudable,°   *healthy*
As much, indeed, beyond the common health
As he were made and put aside to show.
Think, could we penetrate by any drug
And bathe the wearied soul and worried flesh,
115 And bring it clear and fair, by three days' sleep!
Whence has the man the balm that brightens all?
This grown man eyes the world now like a child.
Some elders of his tribe, I should premise,°   *say at first*
Led in their friend, obedient as a sheep,
120 To bear my inquisition. While they spoke,
Now sharply, now with sorrow,—told the case,—
He listened not except I spoke to him,
But folded his two hands and let them talk,
Watching the flies that buzzed: and yet no fool.
125 And that's a sample how his years must go.
Look, if a beggar, in fixed middle-life,
Should find a treasure,—can he use the same
With straitened habits and with tastes starved small,
And take at once to his impoverished brain
130 The sudden element that changes things,
That sets the undreamed-of rapture at his hand
And puts the cheap old joy in the scorned dust?
Is he not such an one as moves to mirth°—   *makes us laugh*
Warily parsimonious, when no need,
135 Wasteful as drunkenness at undue times?
All prudent counsel as to what befits
The golden mean, is lost on such an one:
The man's fantastic will is the man's law.
So here—we call the treasure knowledge, say,
140 Increased beyond the fleshly faculty—
Heaven opened to a soul while yet on earth,
Earth forced on a soul's use while seeing heaven:
The man is witless° of the size, the sum,   *unknowing*
The value in proportion of all things,
145 Or whether it be little or be much.
Discourse to him of prodigious armaments
Assembled to besiege his city now,
And of the passing of a mule with gourds—
'Tis one! Then take it on the other side,
150 Speak of some trifling fact,—he will gaze rapt
With stupor at its very littleness
(Far as I see), as if in that indeed
He caught prodigious import, whole results;
And so will turn to us the bystanders
155 In ever the same stupor (note this point)
That we too see not with his opened eyes.
Wonder and doubt come wrongly into play,
Preposterously, at cross-purposes.
Should his child sicken unto death,—why, look

160 For scarce abatement of his cheerfulness,
Or pretermission° of the daily craft!   *interruption*
While a word, gesture, glance from that same child
At play or in the school or laid asleep,
Will startle him to an agony of fear,
165 Exasperation, just as like. Demand
The reason why—" 'tis but a word," object—
"A gesture"—he regards thee as our lord[8]
Who lived there in the pyramid alone,
Looked at us (dost thou mind?) when, being young,
170 We both would unadvisedly recite
Some charm's beginning, from that book of his,
Able to bid the sun throb wide and burst
All into stars, as suns grown old are wont.
Thou and the child have each a veil alike
175 Thrown o'er your heads, from under which ye both
Stretch your blind hands and trifle with a match
Over a mine of Greek fire,[9] did ye know!
He holds on firmly to some thread of life—
(It is the life to lead perforcedly)
180 Which runs across some vast distracting orb
Of glory on either side that meager thread,
Which, conscious of, he must not enter yet—
The spiritual life around the earthly life:
The law of that is known to him as this,[1]
185 His heart and brain move there, his feet stay here.
So is the man perplexed with impulses
Sudden to start off crosswise, not straight on,
Proclaiming what is right and wrong across,
And not along, this black thread through the blaze—
190 "It should be" balked by "here it cannot be."
And oft the man's soul springs into his face
As if he saw again and heard again
His sage that bade him "Rise" and he did rise.
Something, a word, a tick o' the blood° within   *pulse beat*
195 Admonishes: then back he sinks at once
To ashes, who was very fire before,
In sedulous recurrence to his trade
Whereby he earneth him the daily bread;
And studiously the humbler for that pride,
200 Professedly the faultier that° he knows   *because*
God's secret, while he holds the thread of life.
Indeed the especial marking of the man
Is prone submission to the heavenly will—
Seeing it, what it is, and why it is.
205 'Sayeth, he will wait patient to the last
For that same death which must restore his being
To equilibrium, body loosening soul
Divorced even now by premature full growth:

8. A magician or wise man under whom Karshish   1. I.e., he knows the law of the spiritual life as well
and Abib had studied.   as that of the earthly life.
9. Weapon made of sulfur, naphtha, and saltpeter.

He will live, nay, it pleaseth him to live
210 So long as God please, and just how God please.
He even seeketh not to please God more
(Which meaneth, otherwise) than as God please.
Hence, I perceive not he affects° to preach   *aspires*
The doctrine of his sect whate'er it be,
215 Make proselytes as madmen thirst to do:
How can he give his neighbor the real ground,
His own conviction? Ardent as he is—
Call his great truth a lie, why, still the old
"Be it as God please" reassureth him.
220 I probed the sore² as thy disciple should:
"How, beast," said I, "this stolid carelessness
Sufficeth thee, when Rome is on her march
To stamp out like a little spark thy town,
Thy tribe, thy crazy tale and thee at once?"
225 He merely looked with his large eyes on me.
The man is apathetic, you deduce?
Contrariwise, he loves both old and young,
Able and weak, affects³ the very brutes
And birds—how say I? flowers of the field—
230 As a wise workman recognizes tools
In a master's workshop, loving what they make.
Thus is the man, as harmless as a lamb:
Only impatient, let him do his best,
At ignorance and carelessness and sin—
235 An indignation which is promptly curbed:
As when in certain travels I have feigned
To be an ignoramus in our art
According to some preconceived design,
And happed to hear the land's practitioners
240 Steeped in conceit sublimed⁴ by ignorance,
Prattle fantastically on disease,
Its cause and cure—and I must hold my peace!

    Thou wilt object—Why have I not ere this
Sought out the sage himself, the Nazarene
245 Who wrought this cure, inquiring at the source,
Conferring with the frankness that befits?
Alas! it grieveth me, the learnèd leech°   *doctor*
Perished in a tumult many years ago,
Accused,—our learning's fate,—of wizardry,
250 Rebellion, to the setting up a rule
And creed prodigious as described to me.
His death, which happened when the earthquake fell⁵
(Prefiguring, as soon appeared, the loss
To occult learning in our lord the sage
255 Who lived there in the pyramid alone)
Was wrought by the mad people—that's their wont!
On vain recourse, as I conjecture it,

---

2. Investigated the case.   5. The earthquake at the time of Christ's crucifix-
3. Has affection for.   ion (reported in Matthew 27.51).
4. Exalted. "Conceit": foolish fancy.

To his tried virtue, for miraculous help—
How could he stop the earthquake? That's their way!
260 The other imputations must be lies:
But take one, though I loathe to give it thee,
In mere respect for any good man's fame.
(And after all, our patient Lazarus
Is stark mad; should we count on what he says?
265 Perhaps not: though in writing to a leech
'Tis well to keep back nothing of a case.)
This man so cured regards the curer, then,
As—God forgive me! who but God himself,
Creator and sustainer of the world,
270 That came and dwelt in flesh on it awhile!
—'Sayeth that such an one was born and lived,
Taught, healed the sick, broke bread at his own house,[6]
Then died, with Lazarus by, for aught I know,
And yet was . . . what I said nor choose repeat,
275 And must have so avouched himself, in fact,
In hearing of this very Lazarus
Who saith—but why all this of what he saith?
Why write of trivial matters, things of price
Calling at every moment for remark?
280 I noticed on the margin of a pool
Blue-flowering borage, the Aleppo[7] sort,
Aboundeth, very nitrous. It is strange!

 Thy pardon for this long and tedious case,
Which, now that I review it, needs must seem
285 Unduly dwelt on, prolixly set forth!
Nor I myself discern in what is writ
Good cause for the peculiar interest
And awe indeed this man has touched me with.
Perhaps the journey's end, the weariness
290 Had wrought upon me first. I met him thus:
I crossed a ridge of short sharp broken hills
Like an old lion's cheek teeth. Out there came
A moon made like a face with certain spots
Multiform, manifold and menacing:
295 Then a wind rose behind me. So we met
In this old sleepy town at unaware,
The man and I. I send thee what is writ.
Regard it as a chance, a matter risked
To this ambiguous Syrian—he may lose,
300 Or steal, or give it thee with equal good,
Jerusalem's repose shall make amends
For time this letter wastes, thy time and mine;
Till when, once more thy pardon and farewell!

 The very God! think, Abib; dost thou think?
305 So, the All-Great, were the All-Loving too—
So, through the thunder comes a human voice

---

6. John 12.1–2.
7. Town in northern Syria. "Borage": herb used medicinally that contains potassium nitrate.

Saying, "O heart I made, a heart beats here!
Face, my hands fashioned, see it in myself!
Thou hast no power nor mayst conceive of mine,
310   But love I gave thee, with myself to love,
And thou must love me who have died for thee!"
The madman saith He said so: it is strange.

1855

Caliban upon Setebos

Caliban upon Setebos   Shakespeare's *Tempest* provided Browning with the
idea for his speaker (Caliban is Prospero's brutish slave, half-man, half-beast) and
the subject of his musings (Setebos is briefly referred to in the play as the god of
Caliban's mother, the witch Sycorax). From these beginnings Browning writes a poem
that reflects on two closely related controversies of the Victorian period. The first
concerned the nature of God and God's responsibility for the existence of pain in the
world. The second debate, stimulated by the publication of Darwin's *Origin of Species*
(1859), focused on humanity's origins and our relation to other beings.

As the poem's epigraph reveals, Browning is interested in the idea that the human
conception of the divine is conditioned by our own limitations, or by our understanding of ourselves. Caliban, a lower being, draws his notion of the god who he believes
dictates his fortunes from three main sources: his observations of life on the island,
his own character, and his experiences with Prospero, his master. The first of these,
his knowledge of the behavior and sufferings of animal life, gives rise to his "natural
theology": that is, his tendency to understand the character of his god from evidences
provided by nature rather than from the evidence of supernatural revelation. From
his perceptions of his own motivations and the conduct of his earthly ruler comes
Caliban's conception of Setebos's willful power. Caliban admires power and thinks
of his god as a being who selects at random some creatures who are to be saved and
others who are condemned to suffer. His musings thus connect in complex ways with
key and pressing issues for the religious and scientific communities of the Victorian
era: through the lens of this most unlikely philosopher, Browning raises the topics
both of eternal salvation and of natural selection. Significantly, Caliban feels the need
to posit a higher divine being, or presence, that exists "over Setebos": puzzling about
this other deity, "the Quiet," Browning's speaker delves into fundamental questions
of origin and the construction of myth.

An obstacle for the reader is Caliban's use of the third-person pronoun to refer to
himself. Thus " 'Will sprawl" means "Caliban will sprawl" (an apostrophe before the
verb usually indicates that Caliban is the implied subject). Setebos is also referred to
in the third person but with an initial capital letter ("He").

Caliban upon Setebos

Or Natural Theology in the Island

"Thou thoughtest that I was altogether such a one as thyself."[1]

['Will sprawl, now that the heat of day is best,
Flat on his belly in the pit's much mire,
With elbows wide, fists clenched to prop his chin.

---

1. Psalm 50.21. The speaker is God.

And, while he kicks both feet in the cool slush,
5   And feels about his spine small eft-things° course,   *water lizards*
Run in and out each arm, and make him laugh:
And while above his head a pompion° plant,   *pumpkin*
Coating the cave-top as a brow its eye,
Creeps down to touch and tickle hair and beard,
10   And now a flower drops with a bee inside,
And now a fruit to snap at, catch and crunch—
He looks out o'er yon sea which sunbeams cross
And recross till they weave a spider web
(Meshes of fire, some great fish breaks at times)
15   And talks to his own self, howe'er he please,
Touching that other, whom his dam° called God.   *mother*
Because to talk about Him, vexes—ha,
Could He but know! and time to vex is now,
When talk is safer than in wintertime.
20   Moreover Prosper and Miranda² sleep
In confidence he drudges at their task,
And it is good to cheat the pair, and gibe,°   *insult them*
Letting the rank tongue blossom into speech.]

Setebos, Setebos, and Setebos!
25   'Thinketh, He dwelleth i' the cold o' the moon.

'Thinketh He made it, with the sun to match,
But not the stars; the stars came otherwise;
Only made clouds, winds, meteors, such as that:
Also this isle, what lives and grows thereon,
30   And snaky sea which rounds and ends the same.

'Thinketh, it came of being ill at ease:
He hated that He cannot change His cold,
Nor cure its ache. 'Hath spied an icy fish
That longed to 'scape the rock-stream where she lived,
35   And thaw herself within the lukewarm brine
O' the lazy sea her stream thrusts far amid,
A crystal spike 'twixt two warm walls of wave;³
Only, she ever sickened, found repulse
At the other kind of water, not her life,
40   (Green-dense and dim-delicious, bred o' the sun)
Flounced back from bliss she was not born to breathe,
And in her old bounds buried her despair,
Hating and loving warmth alike: so He.

'Thinketh, He made thereat the sun, this isle,
45   Trees and the fowls here, beast and creeping thing.
Yon otter, sleek-wet, black, lithe as a leech;
Yon auk,° one fire-eye in a ball of foam,   *seabird*
That floats and feeds; a certain badger brown
He hath watched hunt with that slant white-wedge eye

2. Prospero's daughter.
3. I.e., the thin stream of cold water that is driven into the warm ocean like a spike between walls.

50 By moonlight; and the pie° with the long tongue   *magpie*
That pricks deep into oakwarts for a worm,
And says a plain word when she finds her prize,
But will not eat the ants; the ants themselves
That build a wall of seeds and settled stalks
55 About their hole—He made all these and more,
Made all we see, and us, in spite: how else?
He could not, Himself, make a second self
To be His mate; as well have made Himself:
He would not make what he mislikes or slights,
60 An eyesore to Him, or not worth His pains:
But did, in envy, listlessness, or sport,
Make what Himself would fain,° in a manner, be—   *gladly*
Weaker in most points, stronger in a few,
Worthy, and yet mere playthings all the while,
65 Things He admires and mocks too—that is it.
Because, so brave, so better though they be,
It nothing skills if He begin to plague.⁴
Look now, I melt a gourd-fruit into mash,
Add honeycomb and pods, I have perceived,
70 Which bite like finches when they bill and kiss—
Then, when froth rises bladdery,° drink up all,   *bubbly*
Quick, quick, till maggots scamper through my brain;
Last, throw me on my back i' the seeded thyme,
And wanton, wishing I were born a bird.
75 Put case, unable to be what I wish,
I yet could make a live bird out of clay:
Would not I take clay, pinch my Caliban
Able to fly?—for, there, see, he hath wings,
And great comb like the hoopoe's⁵ to admire,
80 And there, a sting to do his foes offense,
There, and I will that he begin to live,
Fly to yon rock-top, nip me off the horns
Of griggs° high up that make the merry din,   *grasshoppers*
Saucy through their veined wings, and mind me not.
85 In which feat, if his leg snapped, brittle clay,
And he lay stupid-like—why, I should laugh;
And if he, spying me, should fall to weep,
Beseech me to be good, repair his wrong,
Bid his poor leg smart less or grow again—
90 Well, as the chance were, this might take or else
Not take my fancy: I might hear his cry,
And give the mankin° three sound legs for one,   *little man*
Or pluck the other off, leave him like an egg,
And lessoned° he was mine and merely clay.   *thus taught*
95 Were this no pleasure, lying in the thyme,
Drinking the mash, with brain become alive,
Making and marring clay at will? So He.
'Thinketh, such shows nor right nor wrong in Him,
Nor kind, nor cruel: He is strong and Lord.
100 'Am strong myself compared to yonder crabs

---

4. I.e., the superior virtues of Setebos's creatures   5. Bird with bright plumage.
are no help to them if he decides to torture them.

That march now from the mountain to the sea;
'Let twenty pass, and stone the twenty-first,
Loving not, hating not, just choosing so.
'Say, the first straggler that boasts purple spots
105　Shall join the file, one pincer twisted off;
'Say, this bruised fellow shall receive a worm,
And two worms he whose nippers end in red;
As it likes me each time, I do: so He.

Well then, 'supposeth He is good i' the main,
110　Placable if His mind and ways were guessed,
But rougher than His handiwork, be sure!
Oh, He hath made things worthier than Himself,
And envieth that, so helped, such things do more
Than He who made them! What consoles but this?
115　That they, unless through Him, do naught at all,
And must submit: what other use in things?
'Hath cut a pipe of pithless elder-joint
That, blown through, gives exact the scream o' the jay
When from her wing you twitch the feathers blue:
120　Sound this, and little birds that hate the jay
Flock within stone's throw, glad their foe is hurt:
Put case such pipe could prattle and boast forsooth,
"I catch the birds, I am the crafty thing,
I make the cry my maker cannot make
125　With his great round mouth; he must blow through mine!"
Would not I smash it with my foot? So He.

But wherefore rough, why cold and ill at ease?
Aha, that is a question! Ask, for that,
What knows—the something over Setebos
130　That made Him, or He, may be, found and fought,
Worsted, drove off and did to nothing,° perchance.　　*completely overcame*
There may be something quiet o'er His head,
Out of His reach, that feels nor° joy nor grief,　　*neither*
Since both derive from weakness in some way.
135　I joy because the quails come; would not joy
Could I bring quails here when I have a mind:
This Quiet, all it hath a mind to, doth.
'Esteemeth° stars the outposts of its couch,　　*he believes*
But never spends much thought nor care that way.
140　It may look up, work up—the worse for those
It works on! 'Careth but for Setebos[6]
The many-handed as a cuttlefish,
Who, making Himself feared through what He does,
Looks up, first, and perceives he cannot soar
145　To what is quiet and hath happy life;
Next looks down here, and out of very spite
Makes this a bauble-world to ape yon real,
These good things to match those as hips[7] do grapes.
'Tis solace making baubles, aye, and sport.

6. Caliban's concern is to appease only Setebos,　　7. Hard fruits produced by wild roses.
not the other deity—the Quiet.

150 Himself peeped late, eyed Prosper at his books
Careless and lofty, lord now of the isle:
Vexed, 'stitched a book of broad leaves, arrow-shaped,
Wrote thereon, he knows what, prodigious words;
Has peeled a wand and called it by a name;
155 Weareth at whiles for an enchanter's robe
The eyed skin of a supple oncelot;[8]
And hath an ounce[9] sleeker than youngling mole,
A four-legged serpent he makes cower and couch,
Now snarl, now hold its breath and mind his eye,
160 And saith she is Miranda and my wife:
'Keeps for his Ariel[1] a tall pouch-bill crane
He bids go wade for fish and straight° disgorge;   *immediately*
Also a sea beast, lumpish, which he snared,
Blinded the eyes of, and brought somewhat tame,
165 And split its toe-webs, and now pens the drudge
In a hole o' the rock and calls him Caliban;
A bitter heart that bides its time and bites.
'Plays thus at being Prosper in a way,
Taketh his mirth with make-believes: so He.
170 His dam held that the Quiet made all things
Which Setebos vexed only: 'holds not so.
Who made them weak, meant weakness He might vex.
Had He meant other, while His hand was in,
Why not make horny eyes no thorn could prick,
175 Or plate my scalp with bone against the snow,
Or overscale my flesh 'neath joint and joint,
Like an orc's° armor? Aye—so spoil His sport!   *sea monster's*
He is the One now: only He doth all.

'Saith, He may like, perchance, what profits Him.
180 Aye, himself loves what does him good; but why?
'Gets good no otherwise. This blinded beast
Loves whoso places flesh-meat on his nose,
But, had he eyes, would want no help, but hate
Or love, just as it liked him: He hath eyes.
185 Also it pleaseth Setebos to work,
Use all His hands, and exercise much craft,
By no means for the love of what is worked.
'Tasteth, himself, no finer good i' the world
When all goes right, in this safe summertime,
190 And he wants little, hungers, aches not much,
Than trying what to do with wit and strength.
'Falls to make something: 'piled yon pile of turfs,
And squared and stuck there squares of soft white chalk,
And, with a fish-tooth, scratched a moon on each,
195 And set up endwise certain spikes of tree,
And crowned the whole with a sloth's skull a-top,
Found dead i' the woods, too hard for one to kill.

8. Browning may have invented this term from the
Spanish *oncela* or from the French *ocelot* (i.e., a
leopard or spotted wildcat).

9. A lynx or other wild feline of moderate size or
a snow leopard.
1. In *The Tempest* a spirit who serves Prospero.

No use at all i' the work, for work's sole sake;
'Shall some day knock it down again: so He.

200 'Saith He is terrible: watch His feats in proof!
One hurricane will spoil six good months' hope.
He hath a spite against me, that I know,
Just as He favors Prosper, who knows why?
So it is, all the same, as well I find.
205 'Wove wattles half the winter, fenced them firm
With stone and stake to stop she-tortoises
Crawling to lay their eggs here: well, one wave,
Feeling the foot of Him upon its neck,
Gaped as a snake does, lolled out its large tongue,
210 And licked the whole labor flat; so much for spite.
'Saw a ball° flame down late (yonder it lies)   *meteorite*
Where, half an hour before, I slept i' the shade:
Often they scatter sparkles: there is force!
'Dug up a newt He may have envied once
215 And turned to stone, shut up inside a stone.
Please Him and hinder this?—What Prosper does?[2]
Aha, if He would tell me how! Not He!
There is the sport: discover how or die!
All need not die, for of the things o' the isle
220 Some flee afar, some dive, some run up trees;
Those at His mercy—why, they please Him most
When . . . when . . . well, never try the same way twice!
Repeat what act has pleased, He may grow wroth.
You must not know His ways, and play Him off,
225 Sure of the issue.° 'Doth the like himself: *outcome*
'Spareth a squirrel that it nothing fears
But steals[3] the nut from underneath my thumb,
And when I threat, bites stoutly in defense:
'Spareth an urchin° that contrariwise   *hedgehog*
230 Curls up into a ball, pretending death
For fright at my approach: the two ways please.
But what would move my choler more than this,
That either creature counted on its life
Tomorrow and next day and all days to come,
235 Saying, forsooth, in the inmost of its heart,
"Because he did so yesterday with me,
And otherwise with such another brute,
So must he do henceforth and always."—Aye?
Would teach the reasoning couple what "must" means!
240 'Doth as he likes, or wherefore Lord? So He.

'Conceiveth all things will continue thus,
And we shall have to live in fear of Him
So long as He lives, keeps His strength: no change,
If He have done His best, make no new world
245 To please Him more, so leave off watching this—

---

2. I.e., shall I please Setebos, as Prospero does,   was punished?
and thus prevent my being punished as the newt   3. I.e., that is fearless enough to steal.

If He surprise not even the Quiet's self
Some strange day—or, suppose, grow into it
As grubs grow butterflies: else, here are we,
And there is He, and nowhere help at all.
250 'Believeth with the life, the pain shall stop.
His dam held different, that after death
He both plagued enemies and feasted friends:
Idly![4] He doth His worst in this our life,
Giving just respite lest we die through pain,
255 Saving last pain for worst—with which, an end.
Meanwhile, the best way to escape His ire
Is, not to seem too happy. 'Sees, himself,
Yonder two flies, with purple films and pink,
Bask on the pompion-bell above: kills both.
260 'Sees two black painful beetles roll their ball
On head and tail as if to save their lives:
Moves them the stick away they strive to clear.

Even so, 'would have Him misconceive, suppose
This Caliban strives hard and ails no less,
265 And always, above all else, envies Him;
Wherefore he mainly dances on dark nights,
Moans in the sun, gets under holes to laugh,
And never speaks his mind save housed as now:
Outside, 'groans, curses. If He caught me here,
270 O'erheard this speech, and asked "What chucklest at?"
'Would, to appease Him, cut a finger off,
Or of my three kid yearlings burn the best,
Or let the toothsome apples rot on tree,
Or push my tame beast for the orc to taste:
275 While myself lit a fire, and made a song
And sung it, *"What I hate, be consecrate*
To celebrate Thee and Thy state, no mate
For Thee; what see for envy in poor me?"
Hoping the while, since evils sometimes mend,
280 Warts rub away and sores are cured with slime,
That some strange day, will either the Quiet catch
And conquer Setebos, or likelier He
Decrepit may doze, doze, as good as die.

_____

[What, what? A curtain o'er the world at once!
285 Crickets stop hissing; not a bird—or, yes,
There scuds His raven[5] that has told Him all!
It was fool's play this prattling! Ha! The wind
Shoulders the pillared dust, death's house o' the move,[6]
And fast invading fires begin! White blaze—
290 A tree's head snaps—and there, there, there, there, there,
His thunder follows! Fool to gibe at Him!
Lo! 'Lieth flat and loveth Setebos!

4. I.e., Caliban thinks his mother's opinion was
wrong or idle. Setebos's sport with his creatures is
confined to this world: there is no afterlife.
5. In Norse mythology ravens brought the daily
news to Odin, the most powerful god.
6. The whirlwind stirs up a column of dust that
Caliban associates with a house of death.

'Maketh his teeth meet through his upper lip,
Will let those quails fly, will not eat this month
295   One little mess of whelks,° so he may 'scape!]   *shellfish*

ca. 1860   1864

Abt Vogler[1]

(*After He has Been Extemporizing Upon the Musical Instrument of His Invention*[2])

1

Would that the structure brave, the manifold music I build,
  Bidding my organ obey, calling its keys to their work,
Claiming each slave of the sound, at a touch, as when Solomon willed
  Armies of angels that soar, legions of demons that lurk,
5 Man, brute, reptile, fly—alien of end and of aim,
  Adverse, each from the other heaven-high, hell-deep removed—
Should rush into sight at once as he named the ineffable Name,[3]
  And pile him a palace straight,[4] to pleasure the princess[5] he loved!

2

Would it might tarry like his, the beautiful building of mine,
10   This which my keys in a crowd pressed and importuned to raise!
Ah, one and all, how they helped, would dispart° now and now   *divide*
    combine,
  Zealous to hasten the work, heighten their master his praise!
And one would bury his brow with a blind plunge down to hell,
  Burrow awhile and build, broad on the roots of things,
15 Then up again swim into sight, having based me my palace well,
  Founded it, fearless of flame, flat on the nether springs.

3

And another would mount and march, like the excellent minion he was,
  Aye, another and yet another, one crowd but with many a crest,
Raising my rampired[6] walls of gold as transparent as glass,
20   Eager to do and die, yield each his place to the rest:
For higher still and higher (as a runner tips with fire,
  When a great illumination surprises a festal night—
Outlining round and round Rome's dome from space to spire)[7]
  Up, the pinnacled glory reached, and the pride of my soul was in sight.

1. Georg Joseph Vogler (1749–1814), a German priest and musician, held the honorary title of *Abbé* or *Abt* (abbot). As a composer, teacher, and designer of musical instruments he was well known in his own day, but he was most famous as an extemporizer at the organ. Browning's soliloquy represents Vogler at the organ joyfully improvising a piece of music and then reflecting on the ephemeral existence of such a unique work of art and of its possible relation to God's purposes in heaven and on earth.
    A characteristic feature of "Abt Vogler" is the use of exceptionally long sentences, densely packed with details, which may evoke the effects of rolling organ music. The resulting movement is markedly

different from the brisk staccato rhythms of "A Toccata of Galuppi's."
2. A compact organ called the *orchestrion*.
3. According to Jewish legend, King Solomon (because he possessed a seal inscribed with the "ineffable Name" of God) had the power of compelling the demons of earth and air to perform his bidding.
4. Immediately.
5. Pharaoh's daughter (1 Kings 7.8).
6. Firmly established.
7. On festival nights the dome of Saint Peter's in Rome is illuminated by a series of lights ignited by a torchbearer.

4

25   In sight? Not half! for it seemed, it was certain, to match man's birth,
      Nature in turn conceived, obeying an impulse as I;
  And the emulous heaven yearned down, made effort to reach the earth,
      As the earth had done her best, in my passion, to scale the sky:
  Novel splendors burst forth, grew familiar and dwelt with mine,
30   Not a point nor peak but found and fixed its wandering star;
  Meteor-moons, balls of blaze: and they did not pale nor pine,
      For earth had attained to heaven, there was no more near nor far.

5

  Nay more; for there wanted not who walked in the glare and glow,
      Presences plain in the place; or, fresh from the Protoplast,[8]
35   Furnished for ages to come, when a kindlier wind should blow,
      Lured now to begin and live, in a house to their liking at last;
  Or else the wonderful Dead who have passed through the body and gone,
      But were back once more to breathe in an old world worth their new:
  What never had been, was now; what was, as it shall be anon;
40   And what is—shall I say, matched both? for I was made perfect too.

6

  All through my keys that gave their sounds to a wish of my soul,
      All through my soul that praised as its wish flowed visibly forth,
  All through music and me! For think, had I painted the whole,
      Why, there it had stood, to see, nor the process so wonderworth:
45   Had I written the same, made verse—still, effect proceeds from cause,
      Ye know why the forms are fair, ye hear how the tale is told;
  It is all triumphant art, but art in obedience to laws,
      Painter and poet are proud in the artist-list enrolled—

7

  But here is the finger of God, a flash of the will that can,
50   Existent behind all laws, that made them and, lo, they are!
  And I know not if, save in this, such gift be allowed to man,
      That out of three sounds he frame, not a fourth sound, but a star.[9]
  Consider it well: each tone of our scale in itself is naught;
      It is everywhere in the world—loud, soft, and all is said:
55   Give it to me to use! I mix it with two in my thought:
      And, there! Ye have heard and seen: consider and bow the head!

8

  Well, it is gone at last, the palace of music I reared;
      Gone! and the good tears start, the praises that come too slow;
  For one is assured at first, one scarce can say that he feared,
60   That he even gave it a thought, the gone thing was to go.
  Never to be again! But many more of the kind
      As good, nay, better perchance: is this your comfort to me?
  To me, who must be saved because I cling with my mind
      To the same, same self, same love, same God: aye, what was, shall be.

8. The original or archetypal form of a species.   9. I.e., the musician's combining of three notes
"Presences": beings of the future, not yet existing,   into a new harmonic unit is a creative act as mirac-
who are "lured" into life by the music (line 36).   ulous as the creation of a star.

9

65 Therefore to whom turn I but to thee, the ineffable Name?
Builder and maker, thou, of houses not made with hands![1]
What, have fear of change from thee who art ever the same?
Doubt that thy power can fill the heart that thy power expands?
There shall never be one lost good! What was, shall live as before;
70 The evil is null, is naught, is silence implying sound;
What was good shall be good, with, for evil, so much good more;
On the earth the broken arcs; in the heaven, a perfect round.

10

All we have willed or hoped or dreamed of good shall exist;
Not its semblance, but itself; no beauty, nor good, nor power
75 Whose voice has gone forth, but each survives for the melodist
When eternity affirms the conception of an hour.
The high that proved too high, the heroic for earth too hard,
The passion that left the ground to lose itself in the sky,
Are music sent up to God by the lover and the bard;
80 Enough that he heard it once: we shall hear it by-and-by.

11

And what is our failure here but a triumph's evidence
For the fullness of the days? Have we withered or agonized?
Why else was the pause prolonged but that singing might issue thence?
Why rushed the discords in but that harmony should be prized?
85 Sorrow is hard to bear, and doubt is slow to clear,
Each sufferer says his say, his scheme of the weal and woe:
But God has a few of us whom he whispers in the ear;
The rest may reason and welcome: 'tis we musicians know.

12

Well, it is earth with me; silence resumes her reign:
90 I will be patient and proud, and soberly acquiesce.
Give me the keys. I feel for the common chord again,
Sliding by semitones, till I sink to the minor—yes,
And I blunt it into a ninth,[2] and I stand on alien ground,
Surveying awhile the heights I rolled from into the deep;
95 Which, hark, I have dared and done, for my resting place is found,
The C Major[3] of this life: so, now I will try to sleep.

1864

Rabbi Ben Ezra[1]

1

Grow old along with me!
The best is yet to be,

1. Cf. 2 Corinthians 5.1, where Saint Paul speaks of "a building of God, a house not made with hands, eternal in the heavens."
2. A discord that requires resolution.
3. A key without sharps or flats, representing the plane of ordinary life.
1. The speaker, Abraham Ibn Ezra (ca. 1092–

1167), was an eminent biblical scholar of Spain, but Browning makes little attempt to present him as a distinct individual or to relate him to the age in which he lived. Unlike the more characteristic monologues, "Rabbi Ben Ezra" presents a meditation on a theme, not an individual in the grip of a dramatic situation.

The last of life, for which the first was made:
Our times are in His hand
5   Who saith, "A whole I planned,
Youth shows but half; trust God: see all nor be afraid!"

2

Not that, amassing flowers,
Youth sighed, "Which rose make ours,
Which lily leave and then as best recall?"
10   Not that, admiring stars,
It yearned, "Nor Jove, nor Mars;
Mine be some figured flame which blends, transcends them all!"

3

Not for such hopes and fears
Annulling youth's brief years,
15 Do I remonstrate: folly wide the mark!
Rather I prize the doubt
Low kinds exist without,
Finished and finite clods, untroubled by a spark.

4

Poor vaunt of life indeed,
20   Were man but formed to feed
On joy, to solely seek and find and feast:
Such feasting ended, then
As sure an end to men;
Irks care the crop-full bird? Frets doubt the maw-crammed beast?[2]

5

25 Rejoice we are allied
To That which doth provide
And not partake, effect and not receive!
A spark disturbs our clod;
Nearer we hold of God
30 Who gives, than of His tribes that take, I must believe.

6

Then, welcome each rebuff
That turns earth's smoothness rough,
Each sting that bids nor sit nor stand but go!
Be our joys three parts pain!
35   Strive, and hold cheap the strain;
Learn, nor account the pang; dare, never grudge the throe!°   anguish

7

For thence—a paradox
Which comforts while it mocks—
Shall life succeed in that it seems to fail:
40   What I aspired to be,
And was not, comforts me:
A brute I might have been, but would not sink i' the scale.

---

2. I.e., does care disturb a bird whose gullet ("crop") is full of food? Does doubt trouble an animal whose
stomach ("maw") is full?

8

What is he but a brute
Whose flesh has soul to suit,
45 Whose spirit works lest arms and legs want play?
To man, propose this test—
Thy body at its best,
How far can that project thy soul on its lone way?

9

Yet gifts should prove their use:
50 I own the Past profuse
Of power each side, perfection every turn:
Eyes, ears took in their dole,
Brain treasured up the whole;
Should not the heart beat once, "How good to live and learn"?

10

55 Not once beat, "Praise be Thine!
I see the whole design,
I, who saw power, see now love perfect too:
Perfect I call Thy plan:
Thanks that I was a man!
60 Maker, remake, complete—I trust what Thou shalt do!"

11

For pleasant is this flesh;
Our soul, in its rose-mesh[3]
Pulled ever to the earth, still yearns for rest;
Would we some prize might hold
65 To match those manifold
Possessions of the brute—gain most, as we did best!

12

Let us not always say,
"Spite of this flesh today
I strove, made head, gained ground upon the whole!"
70 As the bird wings and sings,
Let us cry, "All good things
Are ours, nor soul helps flesh more, now, than flesh helps soul!"

13

Therefore I summon age
To grant youth's heritage,
75 Life's struggle having so far reached its term:
Thence shall I pass, approved
A man, for aye removed
From the developed brute; a god though in the germ.

14

And I shall thereupon
80 Take rest, ere I be gone
Once more on my adventure brave and new;[4]

---

3. The body, which holds the soul in its net.   4. In the next life.

Fearless and unperplexed,
When I wage battle next,
What weapons to select, what armor to indue.°   *put on*

15

85   Youth ended, I shall try
My gain or loss thereby;
Leave the fire ashes,⁵ what survives is gold:
And I shall weigh the same,
Give life its praise or blame:
90 Young, all lay in dispute; I shall know, being old.

16

For note, when evening shuts,
A certain moment cuts
The deed off, calls the glory from the gray:
A whisper from the west
95   Shoots—"Add this to the rest,
Take it and try its worth: here dies another day."

17

So, still within this life,
Though lifted o'er its strife,
Let me discern, compare, pronounce at last,
100   "This rage was right i' the main,
That acquiescence vain:
The Future I may face now I have proved the Past."

18

For more is not reserved
To man, with soul just nerved
105 To act tomorrow what he learns today:
Here, work enough to watch
The Master work, and catch
Hints of the proper craft, tricks of the tool's true play.

19

As it was better, youth
110   Should strive, through acts uncouth,
Toward making, than repose on aught found made:
So, better, age, exempt
From strife, should know, than tempt°   *attempt*
Further. Thou waitedst age: wait death nor° be afraid!   *and do not*

20

115   Enough now, if the Right
And Good and Infinite
Be named here, as thou callest thy hand thine own,
With knowledge absolute,
Subject to no dispute
120 From fools that crowded youth, nor let thee feel alone.

5. If the fire leaves ashes.

21

Be there, for once and all,
Severed great minds from small,
Announced to each his station in the Past!
Was I, the world arraigned,[6]
125   Were they, my soul disdained,
Right? Let age speak the truth and give us peace at last![7]

22

Now, who shall arbitrate?
Ten men love what I hate,
Shun what I follow, slight what I receive;
130   Ten, who in ears and eyes
Match me: we all surmise,
They this thing, and I that: whom shall my soul believe?

23

Not on the vulgar° mass   *common*
Called "work," must sentence pass,
135   Things done, that took the eye and had the price;
O'er which, from level stand,
The low world laid its hand,
Found straightway to its mind, could value in a trice:

24

But all, the world's coarse thumb
140   And finger failed to plumb,[8]
So passed in making up the main account;
All instincts immature,
All purposes unsure,
That weighed not as his work, yet swelled the man's amount:

25

145   Thoughts hardly to be packed
Into a narrow act,
Fancies that broke through language and escaped;
All I could never be,
All, men ignored in me,
150   This, I was worth to God, whose wheel the pitcher shaped.[9]

26

Aye, note that Potter's wheel,
That metaphor! and feel
Why time spins fast, why passive lies our clay—
Thou, to whom fools propound,[1]
155   When the wine makes its round,
"Since life fleets, all is change; the Past gone, seize today!"

---

6. I.e., was I, whom the world arraigned.
7. Stanzas 20 and 21 affirm that in age we can more readily think independently than in youth. Maturity enables us to ignore the pressure of having to conform to the thinking of the crowd of small-minded people.
8. Allusion to a merchant or buyer feeling fabric to determine its price or value.

9. The speaker's highest qualities of soul were shaped on a potting wheel into an enduring "pitcher" or vessel by God. Cf. Isaiah 64.8.
1. Perhaps addressed to Omar Khayyám, whose poem, *The Rubáiyát*, urged men to eat, drink, and be merry. See FitzGerald's 1859 translation (p. 1213).

27

Fool! All that is, at all,
Lasts ever, past recall;
Earth changes, but thy soul and God stand sure:
160   What entered into thee,
That was, is, and shall be:
Time's wheel runs back or stops: Potter and clay endure.

28

He fixed thee 'mid this dance
Of plastic° circumstance,   *molded*
165 This Present, thou, forsooth, wouldst fain arrest:[2]
Machinery just meant
To give thy soul its bent,
Try thee and turn thee forth, sufficiently impressed.

29

What though the earlier grooves
170   Which ran the laughing loves
Around thy base,[3] no longer pause and press?
What though, about thy rim,
Skull-things in order grim
Grow out, in graver mood, obey the sterner stress?

30

175 Look not thou down but up!
To uses of a cup,
The festal board, lamp's flash, and trumpet's peal,
The new wine's foaming flow,
The Master's lips a-glow!
180 Thou, heaven's consummate cup, what need'st thou with earth's wheel?

31

But I need, now as then,
Thee, God, who moldest men;
And since, not even while the whirl was worst,
Did I—to the wheel of life
185   With shapes and colors rife,
Bound dizzily—mistake my end, to slake Thy thirst:

32

So, take and use Thy work:
Amend what flaws may lurk,
What strain o' the stuff, what warpings past the aim!
190 My times be in Thy hand!
Perfect the cup as planned!
Let age approve of youth, and death complete the same!

ca. 1862   1864

---

2. I.e., you would be glad to stop ("arrest") time at
this present point of your life.
3. Of the clay pitcher. "Laughing loves" may refer

to figures of cherublike boys, often featured in
Renaissance art.

EMILY BRONTË
1818–1848

Emily Brontë spent most of her life in a stone parsonage in the small village of Haworth on the wild and bleak Yorkshire moors. She was the fifth of Patrick and Maria Brontë's six children. Her father was a clergyman; her mother died when she was two. At the age of six, she was sent away to a school for the daughters of poor clergy with her three elder sisters; within a year, the two oldest girls had died, in part the result of the school's harsh and unhealthy conditions, which Charlotte Brontë was later to portray in *Jane Eyre* (1847). Mr. Brontë brought his two remaining daughters home, where, together with their brother and younger sister, he educated them himself. Emily was the most reclusive and private of the children; she shunned the company of those outside her family and suffered acutely from homesickness in her few short stays away from the parsonage.

Despite the isolation of Haworth, the Brontë family shared a rich literary life. Mr. Brontë discussed poetry, history, and politics with his children, and the children themselves created an extraordinary fantasy world together. When Mr. Brontë gave his son a box of wooden soldiers, each child excitedly seized one and named it. The soldiers became for them the centers of an increasingly elaborate set of stories that they first acted out in plays and later recorded in a series of book-length manuscripts, composed for the most part by Charlotte and her brother, Branwell. The two younger children, Emily and Anne, later started a separate series, a chronicle about an imaginary island called Gondal.

In 1850 Charlotte Brontë told the story of how she and her sisters came to write for publication. One day when she accidentally came upon a manuscript volume of verse in Emily's handwriting, she was struck by the conviction "that these were not common effusions, nor at all like the poetry women generally write." With some difficulty, Charlotte persuaded her intensely private sister to publish some of her poems in a selection of poetry by all three Brontë sisters. Averse to personal publicity and afraid that "authoresses are liable to be looked on with prejudice," Charlotte, Emily, and Anne adopted the pseudonyms of Currer, Ellis, and Acton Bell. Although the 1846 book sold only two copies, its publication inspired each of the Brontë sisters to begin work on a novel; Emily's was *Wuthering Heights* (1847). She began work on a second novel, but a year after the publication of *Wuthering Heights,* she died of tuberculosis.

Many of Emily's poems—"Remembrance" and "The Prisoner," for example—were written for the Gondal saga and express its preoccupation with political intrigue, passionate love, rebellion, war, imprisonment, and exile. Brontë also wrote personal lyrics unconnected with the Gondal stories; but both groups of poems share a drive to break through the constrictions of ordinary life, whether by the transfigurative power of the imagination, by union with another, or by death itself. Like Catherine and Heathcliff in *Wuthering Heights,* the speakers of Brontë's poems yearn for a fuller, freer world of spirit, transcending the forms and limits of mortal life. Her concern with a visionary world links her to the Romantic poets, particularly to Byron and Percy Bysshe Shelley; but her hymnlike stanzas have a haunting quality that distinguishes her individual voice.

I'm happiest when most away

I'm happiest when most away
I can bear my soul from its home of clay
On a windy night when the moon is bright
And the eye can wander through worlds of light—

5 When I am not and none beside—
Nor earth nor sea nor cloudless sky—
But only spirit wandering wide
Through infinite immensity.

1838   1910

The Night-Wind

In summer's mellow midnight,
A cloudless moon shone through
Our open parlour window
And rosetrees wet with dew.

5 I sat in silent musing,
The soft wind waved my hair:
It told me Heaven was glorious.
And sleeping Earth was fair.

I needed not its breathing
10 To bring such thoughts to me,
But still it whispered lowly,
"How dark the woods will be!

"The thick leaves in my murmur
Are rustling like a dream,
15 And all their myriad voices
Instinct° with spirit seem."   imbued

I said, "Go, gentle singer,
Thy wooing voice is kind,
But do not think its music
20 Has power to reach my mind.

"Play with the scented flower,
The young tree's supple bough,
And leave my human feelings
In their own course to flow."

25 The wanderer would not leave me;
Its kiss grew warmer still—
"O come," it sighed so sweetly,
"I'll win thee 'gainst thy will.

"Have we not been from childhood friends?
30 Have I not loved thee long?
As long as thou hast loved the night
Whose silence wakes my song.

"And when thy heart is laid at rest
Beneath the church-yard stone

35   I shall have time enough to mourn
And thou to be alone."

1840   1850

Remembrance[1]

Cold in the earth, and the deep snow piled above thee!
Far, far removed, cold in the dreary grave!
Have I forgot, my Only Love, to love thee,
Severed at last by Time's all-wearing wave?

5   Now, when alone, do my thoughts no longer hover
Over the mountains, on that northern shore;
Resting their wings where heath and fern-leaves cover
Thy noble heart for ever, ever more?

Cold in the earth, and fifteen wild Decembers
10 From those brown hills have melted into spring—
Faithful indeed is the spirit that remembers
After such years of change and suffering!

Sweet Love of youth, forgive if I forget thee
While the World's tide is bearing me along:
15 Other desires and other hopes beset me,
Hopes which obscure but cannot do thee wrong.

No later light has lightened up my heaven,
No second morn has ever shone for me:
All my life's bliss from thy dear life was given—
20 All my life's bliss is in the grave with thee.

But when the days of golden dreams had perished
And even Despair was powerless to destroy,
Then did I learn how existence could be cherished,
Strengthened and fed without the aid of joy;

25 Then did I check the tears of useless passion,
Weaned my young soul from yearning after thine;
Sternly denied its burning wish to hasten
Down to that tomb already more than mine!

And even yet, I dare not let it languish,
30 Dare not indulge in Memory's rapturous pain;
Once drinking deep of that divinest anguish,
How could I seek the empty world again?

1845   1846

---

1. Titled in manuscript "R. Alcona to J. Breznaida," this poem was originally composed as a lament by the heroine of the Gondal saga for the hero's death.

Stars

Ah! why, because the dazzling sun
Restored our earth to joy
Have you departed, every one,
And left a desert sky?

5   All through the night, your glorious eyes
Were gazing down in mine,
And with a full heart's thankful sighs
I blessed that watch divine!

I was at peace, and drank your beams
10   As they were life to me
And revelled in my changeful dreams
Like petrel° on the sea.   *small dark seabirds*

Thought followed thought—star followed star
Through boundless regions on,
15   While one sweet influence, near and far,
Thrilled through and proved us one.

Why did the morning dawn to break
So great, so pure a spell,
And scorch with fire the tranquil cheek
20   Where your cool radiance fell?

Blood-red he rose, and arrow-straight
His fierce beams struck my brow:
The soul of Nature sprang elate,
But mine sank sad and low!

25   My lids closed down—yet through their veil
I saw him blazing still;
And steep in gold the misty dale
And flash upon the hill.

I turned me to the pillow then
30   To call back Night, and see
Your worlds of solemn light, again
Throb with my heart and me!

It would not do—the pillow glowed
And glowed both roof and floor,
35   And birds sang loudly in the wood,
And fresh winds shook the door.

The curtains waved, the wakened flies
Were murmuring round my room,
Imprisoned there, till I should rise
40   And give them leave to roam.

O Stars and Dreams and Gentle Night;
O Night and Stars return!
And hide me from the hostile light
That does not warm, but burn—

45   That drains the blood of suffering men;
Drinks tears, instead of dew:
Let me sleep through his blinding reign,
And only wake with you!

1845   1846

The Prisoner. A Fragment[1]

In the dungeon crypts idly did I stray,
Reckless of the lives wasting there away;
"Draw the ponderous bars; open, Warder stern!"
He dare not say me nay—the hinges harshly turn.

5   "Our guests are darkly lodged," I whispered, gazing through
The vault whose grated eye showed heaven more grey than blue.
(This was when glad spring laughed in awaking pride.)
"Aye, darkly lodged enough!" returned my sullen guide.

Then, God forgive my youth, forgive my careless tongue!
10   I scoffed, as the chill chains on the damp flagstones rung;
"Confined in triple walls, art thou so much to fear,
That we must bind thee down and clench thy fetters here?"

The captive raised her face; it was as soft and mild
As sculptured marble saint or slumbering, unweaned child;
15   It was so soft and mild, it was so sweet and fair,
Pain could not trace a line nor grief a shadow there!

The captive raised her hand and pressed it to her brow:
"I have been struck," she said, "and I am suffering now;
Yet these are little worth, your bolts and irons strong;
20   And were they forged in steel they could not hold me long."

Hoarse laughed the jailor grim: "Shall I be won to hear;
Dost think, fond° dreaming wretch, that *I* shall grant thy prayer?   *foolish*
Or, better still, wilt melt my master's heart with groans?
Ah, sooner might the sun thaw down these granite stones!

25   "My master's voice is low, his aspect bland and kind,
But hard as hardest flint the soul that lurks behind;

---

1. An excerpt from a poem in the Gondal manuscript, "Julian M. and A. G. Rochelle," describing
an event unplaced in the story, this poem was
printed as "The Prisoner: A Fragment" in *Poems*
(1846) by the Brontë sisters. The speaker, a man,
is visiting a dungeon in his father's castle.

And I am rough and rude, yet not more rough to see
Than is the hidden ghost which has its home in me!"

About her lips there played a smile of almost scorn:
30 "My friend," she gently said, "you have not heard me mourn;
When you my kindred's lives—*my* lost life, can restore
Then may I weep and sue—but *never*, Friend, before!

"Still, let my tyrants know, I am not doomed to wear
Year after year in gloom and desolate despair;
35 A messenger of Hope comes every night to me,
And offers, for short life, eternal liberty.

"He comes with western winds, with evening's wandering airs,
With that clear dusk of heaven that brings the thickest stars;
Winds take a pensive tone, and stars a tender fire,
40 And visions rise and change that kill me with desire—

"Desire for nothing known in my maturer years
When joy grew mad with awe at counting future tears;
When, if my spirit's sky was full of flashes warm,
I knew not whence they came, from sun or thunderstorm;

45 "But first a hush of peace, a soundless calm descends;
The struggle of distress and fierce impatience ends;
Mute music soothes my breast—unuttered harmony
That I could never dream till earth was lost to me.

"Then dawns the Invisible, the Unseen its truth reveals;
50 My outward sense is gone, my inward essence feels—
Its wings are almost free, its home, its harbour found;
Measuring the gulf it stoops and dares the final bound!

"Oh, dreadful is the check—intense the agony
When the ear begins to hear and the eye begins to see;
55 When the pulse begins to throb, the brain to think again,
The soul to feel the flesh and the flesh to feel the chain!

"Yet I would lose no sting, would wish no torture less;
The more that anguish racks the earlier it will bless;
And robed in fires of Hell, or bright with heavenly shine,
60 If it but herald Death, the vision is divine."[2]

She ceased to speak, and we, unanswering turned to go—
We had no further power to work the captive woe;
Her cheek, her gleaming eye, declared that man had given
A sentence unapproved, and overruled by Heaven.

1845   1846

---

2. Cf. the words of the dying Catherine in *Wuthering Heights* (1847), chap. 15: "The thing that irks me most is this shattered prison [my body]. . . . I'm tired, tired of being enclosed here. I'm wearying to escape into that glorious world, and to be always there. . . . I shall be incomparably beyond and above you all."

No coward soul is mine[1]

No coward soul is mine
No trembler in the world's storm-troubled sphere
I see Heaven's glories shine
And Faith shines equal arming me from Fear

5   O God within my breast
Almighty ever-present Deity
Life, that in me hast rest
As I Undying Life, have power in Thee

Vain are the thousand creeds
10 That move men's hearts, unutterably vain,
Worthless as withered weeds
Or idlest froth amid the boundless main

To waken doubt in one
Holding so fast by thy infinity
15 So surely anchored on
The steadfast rock of Immortality

With wide-embracing love
Thy spirit animates eternal years
Pervades and broods above,
20 Changes, sustains, dissolves, creates and rears

Though Earth and moon were gone
And suns and universes ceased to be
And thou wert left alone
Every Existence would exist in thee

25 There is not room for Death
Nor atom that his might could render void
Since thou art Being and Breath
And what thou art may never be destroyed.

1846   1850

1. According to Charlotte Brontë, these are the last lines her sister wrote.

JOHN RUSKIN
1819–1900

John Ruskin was both the leading Victorian critic of art and an important critic of society. These two roles can be traced back to two important influences of his childhood. His father, a wealthy wine merchant, enjoyed travel, and on tours of the Continent he introduced his son to landscapes, architecture, and art. From this exposure Ruskin acquired a zest for beauty that animates even the most theoretical of his discussions of aesthetics. In his tranquil autobiography (titled *Praeterita*, 1885–89, or, as he said, "Past things"), composed in the penultimate decade of a turbulent life, Ruskin reflected on the profound experience of his first view of the Swiss Alps at sunset. For his fourteen-year-old self, he writes, "the seen walls of lost Eden could not have been more beautiful":

> It is not possible to imagine, in any time of the world, a more blessed entrance into life, for a child of such a temperament as mine. True, the temperament belonged to the age: a very few years,—within the hundred,—before that, no child could have been born to care for mountains, or for the men that lived among them, in that way. Till Rousseau's time, there had been no "sentimental" love of nature; and till Scott's, no such apprehensive love of "all sorts and conditions of men," not in the soul merely, but in the flesh . . . I went down that evening from the garden-terrace of Schaffhausen with my destiny fixed in all of it that was to be sacred and useful.

Such a rapturous response to the beauties of nature was later to be duplicated by his response to the beauties of architecture and art. During a tour of "this Holy Land of Italy" (as he called it), he visited Venice and recorded in his diary (May 6, 1841) his response to Saint Mark's cathedral square in that city: "Thank God I am here! It is the Paradise of cities and there is moon enough to make herself the sanities of earth lunatic, striking its pure flashes of light against the grey water before the window; and I am happier than I have been these five years. . . . I feel fresh and young when my foot is on these pavements."

Ruskin's choice of phrase in these accounts of how beauty affected him reflects the second influence in his life, often at odds with the first: his daily Bible readings under the direction of his mother, a devout Evangelical Christian. From this biblical indoctrination Ruskin derived some elements of his lush and highly rhythmical prose style but more especially his sense of prophecy and mission as a critic of modern society.

Ruskin's life was spent in traveling, lecturing, and writing. His prodigious literary output can be roughly divided into three phases. At first he was preoccupied with problems of art. *Modern Painters* (1843–60), which he began writing at the age of twenty-three after his graduation from Oxford, was a defense of the English landscape painter J. M. W. Turner (1775–1851). This defense (which was to extend to five volumes) involved Ruskin in problems of truth in art (as in his chapter "Pathetic Fallacy") and in the ultimate importance of imagination (as in his discussion of Turner's painting *The Slave Ship*).

During the 1850s Ruskin's principal interest shifted from art to architecture, especially to the problem of determining what kind of society is capable of producing great buildings. His enthusiasm for Gothic architecture was infectious, and he has sometimes been blamed for the prevalence of Gothic buildings on college campuses in America. A study of *The Stones of Venice* (1851–53), however (especially the chapter printed here), will show that merely to revive the Gothic style was not his concern. What he wanted to revive was the kind of society that had produced such architecture, a society in which the individual workers could express themselves and enjoy what Ruskin's disciple William Morris called "work-pleasure." A mechanized production-line society, such as Ruskin's or our own, could produce not Gothic architecture but only imitations of its mannerisms. Ruskin's concern was to change industrial society, not to decorate concrete towers with gargoyles.

This interest in the stultifying effects of industrialism led Ruskin gradually into economics. After 1860 the critic of art became (like the writer he most greatly admired, Thomas Carlyle) an outspoken critic of laissez-faire, or noninterventionist, economics. His conception of the responsibilities of employers toward their workers, as expounded in *Unto This Last* (1860), was dismissed by his contemporaries as an absurdity. What he was laboring to show was that self-seeking business relationships could be reconfigured on the principle of dedicated service, taking as a model the learned professions and the military. The soldier, however unrefined, is more highly regarded by society than the capitalist, Ruskin said, "for the soldier's trade . . . is not slaying, but being slain." Although his position was essentially conservative in the proper sense of the word (he styled himself "a violent Tory of the old school;—Walter Scott's school"), he was regarded as a radical eccentric. It was many years before his social criticism gained a following among writers as diverse as William Morris, Bernard Shaw, and D. H. Lawrence; and in particular among the founders of the British Labour Party, his influence was to be profound and lasting.

Ruskin's realization, after 1860, that despite his fame he was becoming isolated and that the world was continuing to move in directions opposite from those to which he pointed may have contributed to the recurrent mental breakdowns from which he suffered between 1870 and 1900. As he reports in *Fors Clavigera* (1880): "The doctors said I went mad, this time two years ago, from overwork," but he had not then been working harder than usual. "I went mad because nothing came of my work . . . because after I got [my manuscripts] published, nobody believed a word of them." Also contributing to his breakdowns may have been his unhappiness in his relations with women. His marriage to Effie Gray in 1848 was a disaster. After six years of living together, an annulment was arranged on the grounds that the marriage had not been consummated. Ruskin testified that he had not found his wife's person physically attractive, although by others she was considered a great beauty. One of these admirers was the Pre-Raphaelite painter John Millais, who fell in love with her at a time when he was painting her husband's portrait; shortly after the annulment he married her. (Given the spectacular failure of Ruskin's marriage and subsequent romantic relationships, it is ironic that he was to produce a highly influential, and frequently reprinted, description of the ideal characters of man and woman, husband and wife, in an 1864 lecture, "Of Queens' Gardens." See "The 'Woman Question'" below, p. 1581.) In later years Ruskin fell in love with a young Irish girl, Rose La Touche, whom he first met when he was nearly forty and she was a child of nine. They were divided not only by the gap of age but by religious differences. She was an intensely pious believer; and for several years after Ruskin proposed marriage to her, when she was eighteen, she tried unsuccessfully to persuade him to return to the Evangelical faith that he had abandoned. In 1875, after herself suffering attacks of mental illness, La Touche died at the age of twenty-five. In his autobiography Ruskin commented: "I wonder mightily what sort of creature I should have turned out, if instead of the distracting and useless pain, I had had the joy of approved love, and the untellable, incalculable motive of its sympathy and praise. It seems to me such things are not allowed in the world. The men capable of the highest imaginative passion are always tossed on fiery waves by it."

Despite both the despair that he suffered following La Touche's death and the recurring attacks of mental illness that blighted the last thirty-five years of his life, Ruskin remained active and productive up until his final silent decade of the 1890s. His publications during his active period included six volumes of his lectures on art that he had delivered as Slade Professor of Fine Arts at Oxford and his letters to laborers, *Fors Clavigera* (1871–84). One topic that becomes especially prominent in these later writings is pollution of air and water—an ideal subject for Ruskin's eloquence. In discussing it he combines his lifelong love for beautiful landscape and landscape painting with his later acquired conviction that modern industrial leadership was woefully irresponsible. A letter of A. E. Housman, who was an undergraduate at Oxford in 1877, provides a vivid record of how effective Ruskin could be:

> This afternoon Ruskin gave us a great outburst against modern times. He had got a picture of Turner's, framed and glassed, representing Leicester and the Abbey in the distance at sunset, over a river. He read the account of Wolsey's death out of *Henry VIII*. Then he pointed to the picture as representing Leicester

when Turner had drawn it. Then he said, "You, if you like, may go to Leicester to see what it is like now. I never shall. But I can make a pretty good guess." Then he caught up a paintbrush. "These stepping-stones of course have been done away with, and are replaced by a be-au-ti-ful iron bridge." Then he dashed in the iron bridge on the glass of the picture. "The color of the stream is supplied on one side by the indigo factory." Forthwith one side of the stream became indigo. "On the other side by the soap factory." Soap dashed in. "They mix in the middle—like curds," he said, working them together with a sort of malicious deliberation. "This field, over which you see the sun setting behind the abbey, is now occupied in a *proper* manner." Then there went a flame of scarlet across the picture, which developed itself into windows and roofs and red brick, and rushed up into a chimney. "The atmosphere is supplied—thus!" A puff and cloud of smoke all over Turner's sky: and then the brush thrown down, and Ruskin confronting modern civilization amidst a tempest of applause, which he always elicits now, as he has this term become immensely popular, his lectures being crowded, whereas of old he used to prophesy to empty benches.

From Modern Painters

[A DEFINITION OF GREATNESS IN ART][1]

Painting, or art generally, as such, with all its technicalities, difficulties, and particular ends, is nothing but a noble and expressive language, invaluable as the vehicle of thought, but by itself nothing. He who has learned what is commonly considered the whole art of painting, that is, the art of representing any natural object faithfully, has as yet only learned the language by which his thoughts are to be expressed. He has done just as much towards being that which we ought to respect as a great painter, as a man who has learnt how to express himself grammatically and melodiously has towards being a great poet. The language is, indeed, more difficult of acquirement in the one case than in the other, and possesses more power of delighting the sense, while it speaks to the intellect; but it is, nevertheless, nothing more than language, and all those excellences which are peculiar to the painter as such, are merely what rhythm, melody, precision, and force are in the words of the orator and the poet, necessary to their greatness, but not the tests of their greatness. It is not by the mode of representing and saying, but by what is represented and said, that the respective greatness either of the painter or the writer is to be finally determined.

※　　※　　※

※ ※ ※ So that, if I say that the greatest picture is that which conveys to the mind of the spectator the greatest number of the greatest ideas, I have a definition which will include as subjects of comparison every pleasure which art is capable of conveying. If I were to say, on the contrary, that the best picture was that which most closely imitated nature, I should assume that art could only please by imitating nature; and I should cast out of the pale[2] of criticism those parts of works of art which are not imitative, that is to say, intrinsic beauties of color and form, and those works of art wholly, which, like the Arabesques of Raffaelle in the Loggias,[3] are not imitative at all. Now, I want

---

1. From vol. 1, part 1, section 1, chap. 2.
2. Beyond the notice or attention.
3. The arabesques in the Loggia of the Vatican, designed by the Italian painter Raphael (1483–

1520), were decorative wall paintings that featured a complex pattern of leaves, animals, and human figures.

a definition of art wide enough to include all its varieties of aim. I do not say, therefore, that the art is greatest which gives most pleasure, because perhaps there is some art whose end is to teach, and not to please. I do not say that the art is greatest which teaches us most, because perhaps there is some art whose end is to please, and not to teach. I do not say that the art is greatest which imitates best, because perhaps there is some art whose end is to create and not to imitate. But I say that the art is greatest which conveys to the mind of the spectator, by any means whatsoever, the greatest number of the greatest ideas; and I call an idea great in proportion as it is received by a higher faculty of the mind, and as it more fully occupies, and in occupying, exercises and exalts, the faculty by which it is received.

If this, then, be the definition of great art, that of a great artist naturally follows. He is the greatest artist who has embodied, in the sum of his works, the greatest number of the greatest ideas.

["THE SLAVE SHIP"][4]

But I think the noblest sea that Turner has ever painted, and, if so, the noblest certainly ever painted by man, is that of "The Slave Ship," the chief Academy[5] picture of the exhibition of 1840. It is a sunset on the Atlantic after prolonged storm; but the storm is partially lulled, and the torn and streaming rain clouds are moving in scarlet lines to lose themselves in the hollow of the night. The whole surface of sea included in the picture is divided into two ridges of enormous swell, not high, nor local, but a low, broad heaving of the whole ocean, like the lifting of its bosom by deep-drawn breath after the torture of the storm. Between these two ridges the fire of the sunset falls along the trough of the sea, dyeing it with an awful but glorious light, the intense and lurid splendor which burns like gold and bathes like blood. Along this fiery path and valley the tossing waves by which the swell of the sea is restlessly divided lift themselves in dark, indefinite, fantastic forms, each casting a faint and ghastly shadow behind it along the illumined foam. They do not rise everywhere, but three or four together in wild groups, fitfully and furiously, as the under-strength of the swell compels or permits them; leaving between them treacherous spaces of level and whirling water, now lighted with green and lamplike fire, now flashing back the gold of the declining sun, now fearfully shed from above with the indistinguishable images of the burning clouds, which fall upon them in flakes of crimson and scarlet and give to the reckless waves the added motion of their own fiery being. Purple and blue, the lurid shadows of the hollow breakers are cast upon the mist of night, which gathers cold and low, advancing like the shadow of death upon the guilty ship as it labors amidst the lightning of the sea, its thin masts written upon the sky in lines of blood, girded with condemnation in that fearful hue which signs the sky with horror, and mixes its flaming flood with the sunlight, and, cast far along the desolate heave of the sepulchral waves, incarnadines the multitudinous sea.[6]

I believe, if I were reduced to rest Turner's immortality upon any single

4. From vol. 1, part 2, section 5, chap. 3. The painting is of a ship in which slaves are being transported. Victims who have died during the passage are being thrown overboard at sunset; as Ruskin noted, "the near sea is encumbered with corpses." 5. The Royal Academy of Arts, founded in London in 1768. The painting, by the great British landscapist J. M. W. Turner (1775–1851), was given to

Ruskin by his father as a New Year's present in 1844 and hung in the Ruskin household for a number of years until Ruskin decided to sell it because he found its subject "too painful to live with." The painting now hangs in the Museum of Fine Arts in Boston. 6. Cf. Shakespeare's *Macbeth* 2.2.60. "Incarnadines": reddens.

work, I should choose this. Its daring conception—ideal in the highest sense of the word—is based on the purest truth, and wrought out with the concentrated knowledge of a life; its color is absolutely perfect, not one false or morbid hue in any part or line, and so modulated that every square inch of canvas is a perfect composition; its drawing as accurate as fearless; the ship buoyant, bending, and full of motion; its tones as true as they are wonderful; and the whole picture dedicated to the most sublime of subjects and impressions—completing thus the perfect system of all truth which we have shown to be formed by Turner's works—the power, majesty, and deathfulness of the open, deep, illimitable Sea.

1843

From *Of the Pathetic Fallacy*[7]

✳   ✳   ✳

Now therefore, putting these tiresome and absurd words[8] quite out of our way, we may go on at our ease to examine the point in question—namely, the difference between the ordinary, proper, and true appearances of things to us; and the extraordinary, or false appearances, when we are under the influence of emotion, or contemplative fancy; false appearances, I say, as being entirely unconnected with any real power of character in the object, and only imputed to it by us.

For instance—

The spendthrift crocus, bursting through the mold
Naked and shivering, with his cup of gold.[9]

This is very beautiful, and yet very untrue. The crocus is not a spendthrift, but a hardy plant; its yellow is not gold, but saffron. How is it that we enjoy so much the having it put into our heads that it is anything else than a plain crocus?

It is an important question. For, throughout our past reasonings about art, we have always found that nothing could be good or useful, or ultimately pleasurable, which was untrue. But here is something pleasurable in written poetry, which is nevertheless *un*true. And what is more, if we think over our favorite poetry, we shall find it full of this kind of fallacy, and that we like it all the more for being so.

It will appear also, on consideration of the matter, that this fallacy is of two principal kinds. Either, as in this case of the crocus, it is the fallacy of willful fancy, which involves no real expectation that it will be believed; or else it is a fallacy caused by an excited state of the feelings, making us, for the time, more or less irrational. Of the cheating of the fancy we shall have to speak presently; but, in this chapter, I want to examine the nature of the other error, that which the mind admits when affected strongly by emotion. Thus, for instance, in *Alton Locke*—

7. From vol. 3, part 4, chap. 12. In this celebrated chapter Ruskin shifts from discussing problems of truth and realism in art to the same problems in literature. The term *pathetic* refers not to something feebly ineffective but to the emotion (pathos) with which a writer invests descriptions of objects and to the distortion (fallacy) that may result. Poets such as Tennyson protested that Ruskin was

being unfairly rigorous in pointing up the fallacy, and Ruskin himself falls into it often. See, e.g., his reference to "the guilty ship" in his discussion of Turner's *The Slave Ship*, above.
8. The metaphysical terms *objective* and *subjective* as applied to kinds of truth.
9. From "Astraea" (1850), a poem by Oliver Wendell Holmes.

> They rowed her in across the rolling foam—
> The cruel, crawling foam.[1]

The foam is not cruel, neither does it crawl. The state of mind which attributes to it these characters of a living creature is one in which the reason is unhinged by grief. All violent feelings have the same effect. They produce in us a falseness in all our impressions of external things, which I would generally characterize as the "pathetic fallacy."

Now we are in the habit of considering this fallacy as eminently a character of poetical description, and the temper of mind in which we allow it, as one eminently poetical, because passionate. But, I believe, if we look well into the matter, that we shall find the greatest poets do not often admit this kind of falseness—that it is only the second order of poets who much delight in it.

Thus, when Dante describes the spirits falling from the bank of Acheron "as dead leaves flutter from a bough,"[2] he gives the most perfect image possible of their utter lightness, feebleness, passiveness, and scattering agony of despair, without, however, for an instant losing his own clear perception that *these* are souls, and *those* are leaves: he makes no confusion of one with the other. But when Coleridge speaks of

> The one red leaf, the last of its clan,
> That dances as often as dance it can,[3]

he has a morbid, that is to say, a so far false, idea about the leaf: he fancies a life in it, and will, which there are not; confuses its powerlessness with choice, its fading death with merriment, and the wind that shakes it with music. Here, however, there is some beauty, even in the morbid passage; but take an instance in Homer and Pope. Without the knowledge of Ulysses, Elpenor, his youngest follower, has fallen from an upper chamber in the Circean palace, and has been left dead, unmissed by his leader or companions, in the haste of their departure. They cross the sea to the Cimmerian land; and Ulysses summons the shades from Tartarus.[4] The first which appears is that of the lost Elpenor. Ulysses, amazed, and in exactly the spirit of bitter and terrified lightness which is seen in Hamlet, addresses the spirit with the simple, startled words: "Elpenor! How camest thou under the shadowy darkness? Hast thou come faster on foot than I in my black ship?"[5] Which Pope renders thus:

> O, say, what angry power Elpenor led
> To glide in shades, and wander with the dead?
> How could thy soul, by realms and seas disjoined,
> Outfly the nimble sail, and leave the lagging wind?

I sincerely hope the reader finds no pleasure here, either in the nimbleness of the sail, or the laziness of the wind! And yet how is it that these conceits[6] are so painful now, when they have been pleasant to us in the other instances?

For a very simple reason. They are not a *pathetic* fallacy at all, for they are put into the mouth of the wrong passion—a passion which never could possibly have spoken them—agonized curiosity. Ulysses wants to know the facts

---

1. From chap. 26 of Charles Kingsley's novel *Alton Locke* (1850).
2. *Inferno* (1321), 3.112, by Dante Alighieri (1265–1321). Acheron: one river of the classical underworld.
3. *Christabel* (1816), 49–50, by Samuel Taylor Coleridge (1772–1834).
4. In classical mythology the lowest region of the underworld.
5. *Odyssey* (8th century B.C.E.), 11.51. The translation by Alexander Pope (1688–1744) was published in 1715–20.
6. Extended poetic devices.

of the matter; and the very last thing his mind could do at the moment would be to pause, or suggest in anywise what was *not* a fact. The delay in the first three lines, and conceit in the last, jar upon us instantly, like the most frightful discord in music. No poet of true imaginative power would possibly have written the passage.

Therefore, we see that the spirit of truth must guide us in some sort, even in our enjoyment of fallacy. Coleridge's fallacy has no discord in it, but Pope's has set our teeth on edge. * * *

1856

From The Stones of Venice

[THE SAVAGENESS OF GOTHIC ARCHITECTURE][1]

I am not sure when the word "Gothic" was first generically applied to the architecture of the North; but I presume that, whatever the date of its original usage, it was intended to imply reproach, and express the barbaric character of the nations among whom that architecture arose. It never implied that they were literally of Gothic lineage, far less that their architecture had been originally invented by the Goths themselves; but it did imply that they and their buildings together exhibited a degree of sternness and rudeness,[2] which, in contradistinction to the character of Southern and Eastern nations, appeared like a perpetual reflection of the contrast between the Goth and the Roman in their first encounter. And when that fallen Roman, in the utmost impotence of his luxury, and insolence of his guilt, became the model for the imitation of civilized Europe,[3] at the close of the so-called Dark Ages, the word Gothic became a term of unmitigated contempt, not unmixed with aversion. From that contempt, by the exertion of the antiquaries and architects of this century, Gothic architecture has been sufficiently vindicated; and perhaps some among us, in our admiration of the magnificent science of its structure, and sacredness of its expression, might desire that the term of ancient reproach should be withdrawn, and some other, of more apparent honorableness, adopted in its place. There is no chance, as there is no need, of such a substitution. As far as the epithet was used scornfully, it was used falsely; but there is no reproach in the word, rightly understood; on the contrary, there is a profound truth, which the instinct of mankind almost unconsciously recognizes. It is true, greatly and deeply true, that the architecture of the North is rude and wild; but it is not true that, for this reason, we are to condemn it, or despise. Far otherwise: I believe it is in this very character that it deserves our profoundest reverence.

The charts of the world which have been drawn up by modern science have thrown into a narrow space the expression of a vast amount of knowledge, but I have never yet seen any one pictorial enough to enable the spectator to

1. From vol. 2, chap. 6.
2. Lack of refinement, roughness. Goths: a Germanic people who by the 3rd century C.E. had settled north of the Black Sea.
3. Renaissance architecture, based on imitating classical buildings, was distasteful to Ruskin. He later stated that his aim in *The Stones of Venice*

had been "to show that the Gothic architecture of Venice had risen out of . . . a state of pure national faith and domestic virtue; and that its Renaissance architecture had arisen out of . . . a state of concealed national infidelity and domestic corruption."

imagine the kind of contrast in physical character which exists between Northern and Southern countries. We know the differences in detail, but we have not that broad glance and grasp which would enable us to feel them in their fullness. We know that gentians grow on the Alps, and olives on the Apennines; but we do not enough conceive for ourselves that variegated mosaic of the world's surface which a bird sees in its migration, that difference between the district of the gentian and of the olive which the stork and the swallow see far off, as they lean upon the sirocco wind.[4] Let us, for a moment, try to raise ourselves even above the level of their flight, and imagine the Mediterranean lying beneath us like an irregular lake, and all its ancient promontories sleeping in the sun: here and there an angry spot of thunder, a gray stain of storm, moving upon the burning field; and here and there a fixed wreath of white volcano smoke, surrounded by its circle of ashes; but for the most part a great peacefulness of light, Syria and Greece, Italy and Spain, laid like pieces of a golden pavement into the sea-blue, chased, as we stoop nearer to them, with bossy[5] beaten work of mountain chains, and glowing softly with terraced gardens, and flowers heavy with frankincense, mixed among masses of laurel, and orange, and plumy palm, that abate with their gray-green shadows the burning of the marble rocks, and of the ledges of porphyry sloping under lucent sand. Then let us pass farther towards the north, until we see the orient colors change gradually into a vast belt of rainy green, where the pastures of Switzerland, and poplar valleys of France, and dark forests of the Danube and Carpathians stretch from the mouths of the Loire to those of the Volga, seen through clefts in gray swirls of rain cloud and flaky veils of the mist of the brooks, spreading low along the pasture lands: and then, farther north still, to see the earth heave into mighty masses of leaden rock and heathy moor, bordering with a broad waste of gloomy purple that belt of field and wood, and splintering into irregular and grisly islands amidst the northern seas, beaten by storm, and chilled by ice drift, and tormented by furious pulses of contending tide, until the roots of the last forests fail from among the hill ravines, and the hunger of the north wind bites their peaks into barrenness; and, at last, the wall of ice, durable like iron, sets, deathlike, its white teeth against us out of the polar twilight. And, having once traversed in thought this gradation of the zoned iris of the earth in all its material vastness, let us go down nearer to it, and watch the parallel change in the belt of animal life: the multitudes of swift and brilliant creatures that glance in the air and sea, or tread the sands of the southern zone; striped zebras and spotted leopards, glistening serpents, and birds arrayed in purple and scarlet. Let us contrast their delicacy and brilliancy of color, and swiftness of motion, with the frost-cramped strength, and shaggy covering, and dusky plumage of the northern tribes; contrast the Arabian horse with the Shetland, the tiger and leopard with the wolf and bear, the antelope with the elk, the bird of paradise with the osprey: and then, submissively acknowledging the great laws by which the earth and all that it bears are ruled throughout their being, let us not condemn, but rejoice in the expression by man of his own rest in the statutes of the lands that gave him birth. Let us watch him with reverence as he sets side by side the burning gems, and smooths with soft sculpture the jasper pillars, that are to reflect a ceaseless sunshine, and rise into a cloudless sky: but not with less reverence let us stand by him, when, with rough strength and hurried stroke,

4. Hot wind from the southern Mediterranean.   5. Ornamental, or embossed. "Chased": decorated.

he smites an uncouth animation out of the rocks which he has torn from among the moss of the moorland, and heaves into the darkened air the pile of iron buttress and rugged wall, instinct with[6] work of an imagination as wild and wayward as the northern sea; creations of ungainly shape and rigid limb, but full of wolfish life; fierce as the winds that beat, and changeful as the clouds that shade them.

There is, I repeat, no degradation, no reproach in this, but all dignity and honorableness: and we should err grievously in refusing either to recognize as an essential character of the existing architecture of the North, or to admit as a desirable character in that which it yet may be, this wildness of thought, and roughness of work; this look of mountain brotherhood between the cathedral and the Alp; this magnificence of sturdy power, put forth only the more energetically because the fine finger-touch was chilled away by the frosty wind, and the eye dimmed by the moor mist, or blinded by the hail; this outspeaking of the strong spirit of men who may not gather redundant fruitage from the earth, nor bask in dreamy benignity of sunshine, but must break the rock for bread, and cleave the forest for fire, and show, even in what they did for their delight, some of the hard habits of the arm and heart that grew on them as they swung the ax or pressed the plow.

If, however, the savageness of Gothic architecture, merely as an expression of its origin among Northern nations, may be considered, in some sort, a noble character, it possesses a higher nobility still, when considered as an index, not of climate, but of religious principle.

In the 13th and 14th paragraphs of Chapter XXI of the first volume of this work, it was noticed that the systems of architectural ornament, properly so called, might be divided into three: (1) Servile ornament, in which the execution or power of the inferior workman is entirely subjected to the intellect of the higher; (2) Constitutional ornament, in which the executive inferior power is, to a certain point, emancipated and independent, having a will of its own, yet confessing its inferiority and rendering obedience to higher powers; and (3) Revolutionary ornament, in which no executive inferiority is admitted at all. I must here explain the nature of these divisions at somewhat greater length.

Of Servile ornament, the principal schools are the Greek, Ninevite, and Egyptian; but their servility is of different kinds. The Greek master-workman was far advanced in knowledge and power above the Assyrian or Egyptian. Neither he nor those for whom he worked could endure the appearance of imperfection in anything; and, therefore, what ornament he appointed to be done by those beneath him was composed of mere geometrical forms—balls, ridges, and perfectly symmetrical foliage—which could be executed with absolute precision by line and rule, and were as perfect in their way, when completed, as his own figure sculpture. The Assyrian and Egyptian, on the contrary, less cognizant of accurate form in anything, were content to allow their figure sculpture to be executed by inferior workmen, but lowered the method of its treatment to a standard which every workman could reach, and then trained him by discipline so rigid that there was no chance of his falling beneath the standard appointed. The Greek gave to the lower workman no subject which he could not perfectly execute. The Assyrian gave him subjects which he could only execute imperfectly, but fixed a legal standard for his imperfection. The workman was, in both systems, a slave.

6. Imbued with as an animating force.

But in the medieval, or especially Christian, system of ornament, this slavery is done away with altogether; Christianity having recognized, in small things as well as great, the individual value of every soul. But it not only recognizes its value; it confesses its imperfection, in only bestowing dignity upon the acknowledgment of unworthiness. That admission of lost power and fallen nature, which the Greek or Ninevite felt to be intensely painful, and, as far as might be, altogether refused, the Christian makes daily and hourly, contemplating the fact of it without fear, as tending, in the end, to God's greater glory. Therefore, to every spirit which Christianity summons to her service, her exhortation is: Do what you can, and confess frankly what you are unable to do; neither let your effort be shortened for fear of failure, nor your confession silenced for fear of shame. And it is, perhaps, the principal admirableness of the Gothic schools of architecture, that they thus receive the results of the labor of inferior minds; and out of fragments full of imperfection, and betraying that imperfection in every touch, indulgently raise up a stately and unaccusable whole.

But the modern English mind has this much in common with that of the Greek, that it intensely desires, in all things, the utmost completion or perfection compatible with their nature. This is a noble character in the abstract, but becomes ignoble when it causes us to forget the relative dignities of that nature itself, and to prefer the perfectness of the lower nature to the imperfection of the higher; not considering that as, judged by such a rule, all the brute animals would be preferable to man, because more perfect in their functions and kind, and yet are always held inferior to him, so also in the works of man, those which are more perfect in their kind are always inferior to those which are, in their nature, liable to more faults and shortcomings. For the finer the nature, the more flaws it will show through the clearness of it; and it is a law of this universe that the best things shall be seldomest seen in their best form. The wild grass grows well and strongly, one year with another; but the wheat is, according to the greater nobleness of its nature, liable to the bitterer blight. And therefore, while in all things that we see, or do, we are to desire perfection, and strive for it, we are nevertheless not to set the meaner[7] thing, in its narrow accomplishment, above the nobler thing, in its mighty progress; not to esteem smooth minuteness above shattered majesty; not to prefer mean victory to honorable defeat; not to lower the level of our aim, that we may the more surely enjoy the complacency of success. But above all, in our dealings with the souls of other men, we are to take care how we check, by severe requirement or narrow caution, efforts which might otherwise lead to a noble issue; and, still more, how we withhold our admiration from great excellencies, because they are mingled with rough faults. Now, in the make and nature of every man, however rude or simple, whom we employ in manual labor, there are some powers for better things: some tardy imagination, torpid capacity of emotion, tottering steps of thought, there are, even at the worst; and in most cases it is all our own fault that they *are* tardy or torpid. But they cannot be strengthened, unless we are content to take them in their feebleness, and unless we prize and honor them in their imperfection above the best and most perfect manual skill. And this is what we have to do with all our laborers; to look for the *thoughtful* part of them, and get that out of them, whatever we lose for it, whatever faults and errors we are obliged to take with it. For the best that is in them cannot manifest itself, but in company with

7. Lesser.

much error. Understand this clearly: You can teach a man to draw a straight line, and to cut one; to strike a curved line, and to carve it; and to copy and carve any number of given lines or forms, with admirable speed and perfect precision; and you find his work perfect of its kind: but if you ask him to think about any of those forms, to consider if he cannot find any better in his own head, he stops; his execution becomes hesitating; he thinks, and ten to one he thinks wrong; ten to one he makes a mistake in the first touch he gives to his work as a thinking being. But you have made a man of him for all that. He was only a machine before, an animated tool.

And observe, you are put to stern choice in this matter. You must either make a tool of the creature, or a man of him. You cannot make both. Men were not intended to work with the accuracy of tools, to be precise and perfect in all their actions. If you will have that precision out of them, and make their fingers measure degrees like cogwheels, and their arms strike curves like compasses, you must unhumanize them. All the energy of their spirits must be given to make cogs and compasses of themselves. All their attention and strength must go to the accomplishment of the mean act. The eye of the soul must be bent upon the finger point, and the soul's force must fill all the invisible nerves that guide it, ten hours a day, that it may not err from its steely precision, and so soul and sight be worn away, and the whole human being be lost at last—a heap of sawdust, so far as its intellectual work in this world is concerned; saved only by its Heart, which cannot go into the form of cogs and compasses, but expands, after the ten hours are over, into fireside humanity. On the other hand, if you will make a man of the working creature, you cannot make a tool. Let him but begin to imagine, to think, to try to do anything worth doing; and the engine-turned precision is lost at once. Out come all his roughness, all his dullness, all his incapability; shame upon shame, failure upon failure, pause after pause: but out comes the whole majesty of him also; and we know the height of it only, when we see the clouds settling upon him. And, whether the clouds be bright or dark, there will be transfiguration behind and within them.

And now, reader, look around this English room of yours, about which you have been proud so often, because the work of it was so good and strong, and the ornaments of it so finished. Examine again all those accurate moldings, and perfect polishings, and unerring adjustments of the seasoned wood and tempered steel. Many a time you have exulted over them, and thought how great England was, because her slightest work was done so thoroughly. Alas! if read rightly, these perfectnesses are signs of a slavery in our England a thousand times more bitter and more degrading than that of the scourged African, or helot⁸ Greek. Men may be beaten, chained, tormented, yoked like cattle, slaughtered like summer flies, and yet remain in one sense, and the best sense, free. But to smother their souls within them, to blight and hew into rotting pollards⁹ the suckling branches of their human intelligence, to make the flesh and skin which, after the worm's work on it, is to see God,¹ into leathern thongs to yoke machinery with—this it is to be slave-masters indeed; and there might be more freedom in England, though her feudal lords' lightest words were worth men's lives, and though the blood of the vexed husbandman dropped in the furrows of her fields, than there is while the animation of her multitudes is sent like fuel to feed the factory smoke, and

8. A class of serfs in ancient Sparta.
9. Trees with top branches cut back to the trunk.

1. "And though, after my skin, worms destroy this body, yet in my flesh shall I see God" (Job 19.26).

the strength of them is given daily to be wasted into the fineness of a web, or racked into the exactness of a line.

And, on the other hand, go forth again to gaze upon the old cathedral front, where you have smiled so often at the fantastic[2] ignorance of the old sculptors: examine once more those ugly goblins, and formless monsters, and stern statues, anatomiless[3] and rigid; but do not mock at them, for they are signs of the life and liberty of every workman who struck the stone; a freedom of thought, and rank in scale of being, such as no laws, no charters, no charities can secure; but which it must be the first aim of all Europe at this day to regain for her children.

Let me not be thought to speak wildly or extravagantly. It is verily this degradation of the operative into a machine, which, more than any other evil of the times, is leading the mass of the nations everywhere into vain, incoherent, destructive struggling for a freedom of which they cannot explain the nature to themselves. Their universal outcry against wealth, and against nobility, is not forced from them either by the pressure of famine, or the sting of mortified pride. These do much, and have done much in all ages; but the foundations of society were never yet shaken as they are at this day. It is not that men are ill fed, but that they have no pleasure in the work by which they make their bread, and therefore look to wealth as the only means of pleasure. It is not that men are pained by the scorn of the upper classes, but they cannot endure their own; for they feel that the kind of labor to which they are condemned is verily a degrading one, and makes them less than men. Never had the upper classes so much sympathy with the lower, or charity for them, as they have at this day, and yet never were they so much hated by them: for, of old, the separation between the noble and the poor was merely a wall built by law; now it is a veritable difference in level of standing, a precipice between upper and lower grounds in the field of humanity, and there is pestilential air at the bottom of it. I know not if a day is ever to come when the nature of right freedom will be understood, and when men will see that to obey another man, to labor for him, yield reverence to him or to his place, is not slavery. It is often the best kind of liberty—liberty from care. The man who says to one, Go, and he goeth, and to another, Come, and he cometh,[4] has, in most cases, more sense of restraint and difficulty than the man who obeys him. The movements of the one are hindered by the burden on his shoulder; of the other, by the bridle on his lips: there is no way by which the burden may be lightened; but we need not suffer from the bridle if we do not champ at it. To yield reverence to another, to hold ourselves and our lives at his disposal, is not slavery; often, it is the noblest state in which a man can live in this world. There is, indeed, a reverence which is servile, that is to say irrational or selfish: but there is also noble reverence, that is to say, reasonable and loving; and a man is never so noble as when he is reverent in this kind; nay, even if the feeling pass the bounds of mere reason, so that it be loving, a man is raised by it. Which had, in reality, most of the serf nature in him—the Irish peasant who was lying in wait yesterday for his landlord, with his musket muzzle thrust through the ragged hedge; or that old mountain servant, who, 200 years ago, at Inverkeithing, gave up his own life and the lives of his seven sons for his chief?[5]—as each fell, calling forth his brother to the death, "Another for Hec-

2. Fanciful, imaginative.
3. Devoid of anatomy (Ruskin's coinage).
4. Matthew 8.9.

5. An incident described in the preface to Sir Walter Scott's novel *The Fair Maid of Perth* (1828).

tor!" And therefore, in all ages and all countries, reverence has been paid and sacrifice made by men to each other, not only without complaint, but rejoicingly; and famine, and peril, and sword, and all evil, and all shame, have been borne willingly in the causes of masters and kings; for all these gifts of the heart ennobled the men who gave not less than the men who received them, and nature prompted, and God rewarded the sacrifice. But to feel their souls withering within them, unthanked, to find their whole being sunk into an unrecognized abyss, to be counted off into a heap of mechanism, numbered with its wheels, and weighed with its hammer strokes—this nature bade not—this God blesses not—this humanity for no long time is able to endure.

We have much studied and much perfected, of late, the great civilized invention of the division of labour; only we give it a false name. It is not, truly speaking, the labour that is divided; but the men: Divided into mere segments of men—broken into small fragments and crumbs of life; so that all the little piece of intelligence that is left in a man is not enough to make a pin, or a nail, but exhausts itself in making the point of a pin, or the head of a nail. Now it is a good and desirable thing, truly, to make many pins in a day; but if we could only see with what crystal sand their points were polished—sand of human soul, much to be magnified before it can be discerned for what it is—we should think there might be some loss in it also. And the great cry that rises from all our manufacturing cities, louder than their furnace blast, is all in very deed for this—that we manufacture everything there except men; we blanch cotton, and strengthen steel, and refine sugar, and shape pottery; but to brighten, to strengthen, to refine, or to form a single living spirit, never enters into our estimate of advantages. And all the evil to which that cry is urging our myriads can be met only in one way: not by teaching nor preaching, for to teach them is but to show them their misery, and to preach to them, if we do nothing more than preach, is to mock at it. It can be met only by a right understanding, on the part of all classes, of what kinds of labour are good for men, raising them, and making them happy; by a determined sacrifice of such convenience, or beauty, or cheapness as is to be got only by the degradation of the workman; and by equally determined demand for the products and results of healthy and ennobling labour.

And how, it will be asked, are these products to be recognized, and this demand to be regulated? Easily: by the observance of three broad and simple rules:

1. Never encourage the manufacture of any article not absolutely necessary, in the production of which *Invention* has no share.

2. Never demand an exact finish for its own sake, but only for some practical or noble end.

3. Never encourage imitation or copying of any kind, except for the sake of preserving record of great works.

The second of these principles is the only one which directly rises out of the consideration of our immediate subject; but I shall briefly explain the meaning and extent of the first also, reserving the enforcement of the third for another place.

1. Never encourage the manufacture of anything not necessary, in the production of which invention has no share.

For instance. Glass beads are utterly unnecessary, and there is no design or thought employed in their manufacture. They are formed by first drawing out the glass into rods; these rods are chopped up into fragments of the size of beads by the human hand, and the fragments are then rounded in the furnace. The men who chop up the rods sit at their work all day, their hands vibrating with a perpetual and exquisitely timed palsy, and the beads dropping beneath their vibration like hail. Neither they, nor the men who draw out the rods or fuse the fragments, have the smallest occasion for the use of any single human faculty; and every young lady, therefore, who buys glass beads is engaged in the slave trade, and in a much more cruel one than that which we have so long been endeavouring to put down.[6]

But glass cups and vessels may become the subjects of exquisite invention; and if in buying these we pay for the invention, that is to say for the beautiful form, or color, or engraving, and not for mere finish of execution, we are doing good to humanity.

So, again, the cutting of precious stones, in all ordinary cases, requires little exertion of any mental faculty; some tact and judgment in avoiding flaws, and so on, but nothing to bring out the whole mind. Every person who wears cut jewels merely for the sake of their value is, therefore, a slave driver.

But the working of the goldsmith, and the various designing of grouped jewelry and enamel-work, may become the subject of the most noble human intelligence. Therefore, money spent in the purchase of well-designed plate, of precious engraved vases, cameos, or enamels, does good to humanity; and, in work of this kind, jewels may be employed to heighten its splendor; and their cutting is then a price paid for the attainment of a noble end, and thus perfectly allowable.

I shall perhaps press this law farther elsewhere, but our immediate concern is chiefly with the second, namely, never to demand an exact finish, when it does not lead to a noble end. For observe, I have only dwelt upon the rudeness of Gothic, or any other kind of imperfectness, as admirable, where it was impossible to get design or thought without it. If you are to have the thought of a rough and untaught man, you must have it in a rough and untaught way; but from an educated man, who can without effort express his thoughts in an educated way, take the graceful expression, and be thankful. Only get the thought, and do not silence the peasant because he cannot speak good grammar, or until you have taught him his grammar. Grammar and refinement are good things, both, only be sure of the better thing first. And thus in art, delicate finish is desirable from the greatest masters, and is always given by them. In some places Michael Angelo, Leonardo, Phidias, Perugino, Turner[7] all finished with the most exquisite care; and the finish they give always leads to the fuller accomplishment of their noble purposes. But lower men than these cannot finish, for it requires consummate knowledge to finish consummately, and then we must take their thoughts as they are able to give them. So the rule is simple: Always look for invention first, and after that, for such execution as will help the invention, and as the inventor is capable of without painful effort, and no more. Above all, demand no refinement of execution where there is no thought, for that is slaves' work, unredeemed. Rather choose rough work than smooth work, so only that the practical purpose be answered, and never

6. Although the Atlantic slave trade had been outlawed early in the 18th century, transatlantic trafficking in African slaves continued until slavery was made illegal everywhere in the Americas.
7. All notable artists: Michelangelo (1475–1564), Italian sculptor, painter, and architect; Leonardo da Vinci (1452–1519), Italian painter, sculptor, and scientist; Phidias (born ca. 490 B.C.E.), an Athenian often called the greatest Greek sculptor; Perugino (Pietro di Cristoforo Vannucci, ca. 1450–1523); and J. M. W. Turner (1775–1851), British painter.

imagine there is reason to be proud of anything that may be accomplished by patience and sandpaper.

I shall only give one example, which however will show the reader what I mean, from the manufacture already alluded to, that of glass. Our modern glass is exquisitely clear in its substance, true in its form, accurate in its cutting. We are proud of this. We ought to be ashamed of it. The old Venice glass was muddy, inaccurate in all its forms, and clumsily cut, if at all. And the old Venetian was justly proud of it. For there is this difference between the English and Venetian workman, that the former thinks only of accurately matching his patterns, and getting his curves perfectly true and his edges perfectly sharp, and becomes a mere machine for rounding curves and sharpening edges, while the old Venetian cared not a whit whether his edges were sharp or not, but he invented a new design for every glass that he made, and never molded a handle or a lip without a new fancy in it. And therefore, though some Venetian glass is ugly and clumsy enough, when made by clumsy and uninventive workmen, other Venetian glass is so lovely in its forms that no price is too great for it; and we never see the same form in it twice. Now you cannot have the finish and the varied form too. If the workman is thinking about his edges, he cannot be thinking of his design; if of his design, he cannot think of his edges. Choose whether you will pay for the lovely form or the perfect finish, and choose at the same moment whether you will make the worker a man or a grindstone.

Nay, but the reader interrupts me—"If the workman can design beautifully, I would not have him kept at the furnace. Let him be taken away and made a gentleman, and have a studio, and design his glass there, and I will have it blown and cut for him by common workmen, and so I will have my design and my finish too."

All ideas of this kind are founded upon two mistaken suppositions: the first, that one man's thoughts can be, or ought to be, executed by another man's hands; the second, that manual labor is a degradation, when it is governed by intellect.

On a large scale, and in work determinable by line and rule, it is indeed both possible and necessary that the thoughts of one man should be carried out by the labor of others; in this sense I have already defined the best architecture to be the expression of the mind of manhood by the hands of childhood. But on a smaller scale, and in a design which cannot be mathematically defined, one man's thoughts can never be expressed by another: and the difference between the spirit of touch of the man who is inventing, and of the man who is obeying directions, is often all the difference between a great and a common work of art. How wide the separation is between original and secondhand execution, I shall endeavor to show elsewhere; it is not so much to our purpose here as to mark the other and more fatal error of despising manual labor when governed by intellect; for it is no less fatal an error to despise it when thus regulated by intellect, than to value it for its own sake. We are always in these days endeavoring to separate the two; we want one man to be always thinking, and another to be always working, and we call one a gentleman, and the other an operative; whereas the workman ought often to be thinking, and the thinker often to be working, and both should be gentlemen, in the best sense. As it is, we make both ungentle, the one envying, the other despising, his brother; and the mass of society is made up of morbid thinkers, and miserable workers. Now it is only by labor that thought can be made healthy, and only by thought that labor can be made happy, and the two cannot be separated with impunity. It would be well if all of us were good handi-craftsmen in some kind, and the dishonor of manual labor done away with altogether; so that though there should still be a trenchant distinction of race between nobles and commoners, there should not, among the latter, be a trenchant distinction of employment, as between idle and working men, or between men of liberal and illiberal professions. All professions should be liberal, and there should be less pride felt in peculiarity of employment, and more in excellence of achievement. And yet more, in each several[8] profession, no master should be too proud to do its hardest work. The painter should grind his own colours; the architect work in the mason's yard with his men; the master manufacturer be himself a more skillful operative than any man in his mills; and the distinction between one man and another be only in experience and skill, and the authority and wealth which these must naturally and justly obtain.

I should be led far from the matter in hand, if I were to pursue this inter-esting subject. Enough, I trust, has been said to show the reader that the rudeness or imperfection which at first rendered the term "Gothic" one of reproach is indeed, when rightly understood, one of the most noble characters of Christian architecture, and not only a noble but an *essential* one. It seems a fantastic paradox, but it is nevertheless a most important truth, that no architecture can be truly noble which is *not* imperfect. And this is easily demonstrable. For since the architect, whom we will suppose capable of doing all in perfection, cannot execute the whole with his own hands, he must either make slaves of his workmen in the old Greek, and present English fashion, and level his work to a slave's capacities, which is to degrade it; or else he must take his workmen as he finds them, and let them show their weaknesses together with their strength, which will involve the Gothic imperfection, but render the whole work as noble as the the intellect of the age can make it.

But the principle may be stated more broadly still. I have confined the illus-tration of it to architecture, but I must not leave it as if true of architecture only. Hitherto I have used the words imperfect and perfect merely to distin-guish between work grossly unskillful, and work executed with average pre-cision and science; and I have been pleading that any degree of unskillfulness should be admitted, so only that the laborer's mind had room for expression. But, accurately speaking, no good work whatever can be perfect, and *the demand for perfection is always a sign of a misunderstanding of the ends of art.* This for two reasons, both based on everlasting laws. The first, that no great man ever stops working till he has reached his point of failure; that is to say, his mind is always far in advance of his powers of execution, and the latter will now and then give way in trying to follow it; besides that he will always give to the inferior portions of his work only such inferior attention as they require; and according to his greatness he becomes so accustomed to the feeling of dissatisfaction with the best he can do, that in moments of lassitude or anger with himself he will not care though the beholder be dissatisfied also. I believe there has only been one man who would not acknowledge this neces-sity, and strove always to reach perfection, Leonardo; the end of his vain effort being merely that he would take ten years to a picture, and leave it unfinished. And therefore, if we are to have great men working at all, or less men doing

8. Different.

their best, the work will be imperfect, however beautiful. Of human work none but what is bad can be perfect, in its own bad way.[9] The second reason is that imperfection is in some sort essential to all that we know of life. It is the sign of life in a mortal body, that is to say, of a state of progress and change. Nothing that lives is, or can be, rigidly perfect; part of it is decaying, part nascent. The foxglove blossom—a third part bud, a third part past, a third part in full bloom—is a type of the life of this world. And in all things that live there are certain irregularities and deficiencies which are not only signs of life, but sources of beauty. No human face is exactly the same in its lines on each side, no leaf perfect in its lobes, no branch in its symmetry. All admit irregularity as they imply change; and to banish imperfection is to destroy expression, to check exertion, to paralyze vitality. All things are literally better, lovelier, and more beloved for the imperfections which have been divinely appointed, that the law of human life may be Effort, and the law of human judgment, Mercy.

Accept this then for a universal law, that neither architecture nor any other noble work of man can be good unless it be imperfect; and let us be prepared for the otherwise strange fact, which we shall discern clearly as we approach the period of the Renaissance, that the first cause of the fall of the arts of Europe was a relentless requirement of perfection, incapable alike either of being silenced by veneration for greatness, or softened into forgiveness of simplicity.

Thus far then of the Rudeness or Savageness, which is the first mental element of Gothic architecture. It is an element in many other healthy architectures also, as in Byzantine and Romanesque; but true Gothic cannot exist without it.

1851–53

9. The Elgin marbles are supposed by many persons to be "perfect." In the most important portions they indeed approach perfection, but only there. The draperies are unfinished, the hair and wool of the animals are unfinished, and the entire bas-reliefs of the frieze are roughly cut [Ruskin's note]. Ruskin is referring to the collection of statues and friezes brought from Athens to England by Lord Elgin, works that were considered models of perfect realism.

GEORGE ELIOT
1819–1880

Like many English novelists (Charles Dickens being an exception) George Eliot came to novel writing relatively late in life. She was forty when her first novel, *Adam Bede* (1859), an immensely popular work, was published. The lives of her characters are, therefore, viewed from the vantage point of maturity and extensive experience; and this perspective is accentuated by her practice of setting her stories back in time to the period of her own childhood, or even earlier. In most of her novels, she evokes a preindustrial rural scene or the small-town life of the English Midlands, which she views with a combination of nostalgia and candid awareness of its limitations.

The place Eliot looks back on is usually the Warwickshire countryside. There, under her real name, Marian Evans, she spent her childhood at Arbury Farm, of which her father, Robert Evans, was supervisor and land agent. The time was the 1820s and 1830s (1819, the year of her birth, was an *annus mirabilis* for the nineteenth century, for in the same year were born John Ruskin, Herman Melville, Walt Whitman, and Queen Victoria). During these decades Evans read widely in and out of school and was also strongly affected by Evangelicism; she even advocated, at one point in her girlhood, giving up novelists such as Sir Walter Scott (who was later to influence her own novel writing) on the grounds that fiction was frivolous and time wasting. Her mother's death led to her leaving school at sixteen, and in the next four or five years she seems to have experienced bouts of depression and self-doubt. In a letter of 1871, looking back to the period, she likened her state of mind to that of Mary Wollstonecraft at the time of the earlier writer's attempted suicide: "Hopelessness has been to me, all through my life, but especially in the painful years of my youth, the chief source of wasted energy with all the consequent bitterness of regret. Remember, it has happened to many to be glad they did not commit suicide, though they once ran for the final leap, or as Mary Wollstonecraft did, wetted their garments well in the rain hoping to sink the better when they plunged."

At the age of twenty-one Evans moved with her father to the town of Coventry, and in this new setting her intellectual horizons were extensively widened. As the result of her association with a group of freethinking intellectuals, and her own studies of theology, she reluctantly decided that she could no longer believe in the Christian religion. Her decision created a painful break with her father, finally resolved when she agreed to observe the formality of attending church with him and he agreed, tacitly at least, that while there she could think what she liked.

These preoccupations with theological issues led to her first book, a translation in 1846 of *The Life of Jesus* by D. F. Strauss, one of the leading figures of the Higher Criticism in Germany. This criticism was the work of a group of scholars dedicated to testing the historical authenticity of biblical narratives in the light of modern methods of research. For the rest of her life, Evans continued to read extensively in English and Continental philosophy; and when she moved to London in 1851, after her father's death, her impressive intellectual credentials led to her appointment as an assistant editor of the *Westminster Review*, a learned journal formerly edited by John Stuart Mill. In the years in which she served as editor, she wrote a number of essays, including "Margaret Fuller and Mary Wollstonecraft" and "Silly Novels by Lady Novelists," which she contributed to various periodicals in addition to the *Westminster Review*.

Her work at the *Review* brought her into contact with many important writers and thinkers. Among them was George Henry Lewes, a brilliant critic of literature and philosophy, with whom she fell in love. Lewes, a married man and father of three children, could not obtain a divorce. Evans therefore elected to live with him as a common-law wife, and what they called their "marriage" lasted happily until his death in 1878. In the last year of her life, she married an admirer and friend, J. W. Cross, who became her biographer.

Her earlier decision to live with Lewes was painfully made: "Light and easily broken ties are what I neither desire theoretically nor could live for practically. Women who are satisfied with such ties do *not* act as I have done—they obtain what they desire and are still invited to dinner." Mrs. Lewes, as she called herself, was not invited to dinner; instead, those who wanted to see her had themselves to seek her company at the house that she shared with Lewes, where she received visitors on Sunday afternoons. These Sunday afternoons became legendary occasions, over which she presided almost like a sibyl. However, her decision to live with Lewes cost her a number of social and family ties, including her relationship with her brother, Isaac, to whom she had been deeply attached since childhood. Isaac never spoke to her again after her elopement. It is reasonable to conjecture that this experience affects the stress, in all of her novels, on incidents involving choice. All of her characters are tested by situations in which they must choose, and the choices, as in *The Mill on the Floss* (1860), are often agonizingly painful.

Although she had occasionally tried her hand at fiction earlier in life, it was only after her relationship with Lewes became established that she turned her full attention to this form. *Scenes from Clerical Life* appeared in magazine installments in 1857 under the pen name that misled most of her readers (Dickens excepted) into believing the author to be a man—a "university man," it was commonly said, to Eliot's amusement and satisfaction. This work was followed by seven full-length novels in the 1860s and 1870s, most of which repeated the success of *Adam Bede* with the Victorian reading public and which, after a period of being out of favor in the early twentieth century, are now once more deeply admired by readers and critics. Virginia Woolf praised *Middlemarch* (1871–72) as "one of the few English novels written for grown-up people," and later readers have found a similar maturity combined with a powerful creative energy in other novels by Eliot such as *The Mill on the Floss* and *Daniel Deronda* (1876).

When Eliot began writing fiction, she and Lewes were reading to each other the novels of Jane Austen. Eliot's fiction owes much to Austen's with its concern with provincial society, its satire of human motives, its focus on courtship. But Eliot brings to these subjects a philosophical and psychological depth very different in character from that of the novel of manners. Eliot's fiction typically combines expansive philosophic meditation with an acute dissection of her characters' motives and feelings.

In a famous passage from *Middlemarch,* Eliot compares herself with the great eighteenth-century novelist Henry Fielding:

> A great historian, as he insisted on calling himself, who had the happiness to be dead a hundred and twenty years ago, and so to take his place among the colossi whose huge legs our living pettiness is observed to walk under, glories in his copious remarks and digressions as the least imitable part of his work. . . . But Fielding lived when the days were longer. . . . We belated historians must not linger after his example; I at least have so much to do in unravelling certain human lots, and seeing how they were woven and interwoven, that all the light I can command must be concentrated on this particular web, and not dispersed over that tempting range of relevancies called the universe.

Despite her ironic disclaimer Eliot too prides herself on her remarks and digressions— as this passage, itself a digression, suggests. As a "belated historian," however, she focuses on the intersection of a few human lives at a particular time and place in her country's history. She frequently likened herself not only to a historian but to a scientist who, with a microscope, observes and analyzes the tangled web of character and circumstance that determines human history. As both comparisons imply, Eliot strives to present her fiction as a mirror that reflects without distortion our experience of life. But her insistence on art's transparency is often troubled both by her consciousness of its fictions and by her sense of the way in which the egoism we all share distorts our perceptions. Hence she portrays this egoism with a combination of acuity and compassion. It is this distinctive compounding of realism and sympathy that makes her, according to the French critic Ferdinand Brunetière, a better realist than her famous French contemporary Gustave Flaubert, author of *Madame Bovary* (1857). Often compared with Leo Tolstoy, she is, perhaps, the greatest English realist.

Eliot's definition of herself as a historian leads us to expect her novels to offer considerable insight into contemporary issues. The Woman Question, as her essay "Margaret Fuller and Mary Wollstonecraft" suggests, held particular interest for her. She typically chooses for her heroine a young woman, like Maggie Tulliver of *The Mill on the Floss* or Dorothea Brooke of *Middlemarch,* with a powerful imagination and a yearning to be more than her society allows her to be. The prelude to *Middlemarch* speaks of the modern-day Saint Teresa, with the ardor and vision to found a religious order, caught at a historical moment that gives no outlet for her ambition. In her portrayal of the frustrations and yearnings of such a heroine, Eliot seems sympathetic to a feminist point of view. Yet her stress on the values of loyalty to one's past; of adherence to duty, despite personal desire; and of what William Wordsworth calls "little, nameless, unremembered acts of kindness and of love" suggests that her attitude toward the Woman Question is complex.

George Eliot wrote, "My function is that of the *aesthetic* not the doctrinal teacher." The largeness of vision through which Eliot enters into the consciousness of all her characters makes the perspective of her novels on many issues a complex one, for it is finally issues as they are refracted through the lens of human character that interest her.

Margaret Fuller and Mary Wollstonecraft[1]

The dearth of new books just now gives us time to recur to less recent ones which we have hitherto noticed but slightly; and among these we choose the late edition of Margaret Fuller's *Woman in the Nineteenth Century*, because we think it has been unduly thrust into the background by less comprehensive and candid productions on the same subject. Notwithstanding certain defects of taste and a sort of vague spiritualism and grandiloquence which belong to all but the very best American writers, the book is a valuable one; it has the enthusiasm of a noble and sympathetic nature, with the moderation and breadth and large allowance of a vigorous and cultivated understanding. There is no exaggeration of woman's moral excellence or intellectual capabilities; no injudicious insistence on her fitness for this or that function hitherto engrossed by men; but a calm plea for the removal of unjust laws and artificial restrictions, so that the possibilities of her nature may have room for full development, a wisely stated demand to disencumber her of the

> Parasitic forms
> That seem to keep her up, but drag her down—
> And leave her field to burgeon and to bloom
> From all within her, make herself her own
> To give or keep, to live and learn and be
> All that not harms distinctive womanhood.[2]

It is interesting to compare this essay of Margaret Fuller's published in its earliest form in 1843,[3] with a work on the position of woman, written between sixty and seventy years ago—we mean Mary Wollstonecraft's *Rights of Woman*. The latter work was not continued beyond the first volume; but so far as this carries the subject, the comparison, at least in relation to strong sense and

---

1. Published in *The Leader* in 1855, this essay is a retrospective book review of two important feminist publications—*A Vindication of the Rights of Woman* (1792), by Mary Wollstonecraft (1759–1797), and *Woman in the Nineteenth Century* (1855; published originally as *The Great Lawsuit*, 1843) by Margaret Fuller (1810–1850), an American essayist and editor whom Eliot warmly admired.

As Barbara Hardy notes, despite "her generous sympathy with Victorian feminism," George Eliot "played no active part in the movement." Eliot seems to have shared the view of women's relation to men expressed by the Prince in Alfred, Lord Tennyson's *The Princess* (1847), whose speeches she cites in this essay. As she herself wrote in 1854 in another essay, "Women in France":

Women became superior in France by being

admitted to a common fund of ideas, to common objects of interest with men; and this must ever be the essential condition at once of true womanly culture and of true social well-being. . . . Let the whole field of reality be laid open to woman as well as to man, and then that which is peculiar in the mental modification, instead of being, as it is now, a source of discord and repulsion between the sexes, will be found to be a necessary complement to the truth and beauty of life.

2. Tennyson's *The Princess* 7.253–58. As noted by Thomas Pinney, the quotation, slightly inaccurate, is from the unrevised 1847 text of the poem. See the passage containing these lines ["The woman's cause is man's"], p. 1136.

3. I.e., the original version published in *The Dial*; it was revised and expanded in 1855.

loftiness of moral tone, is not at all disadvantageous to the woman of the last century. There is in some quarters a vague prejudice against the *Rights of Woman* as in some way or other a reprehensible book, but readers who go to it with this impression will be surprised to find it eminently serious, severely moral, and withal rather heavy—the true reason, perhaps, that no edition has been published since 1796, and that it is now rather scarce. There are several points of resemblance, as well as of striking difference, between the two books. A strong understanding is present in both; but Margaret Fuller's mind was like some regions of her own American continent, where you are constantly stepping from the sunny "clearings" into the mysterious twilight of the tangled forest—she often passes in one breath from forcible reasoning to dreamy vagueness; moreover, her unusually varied culture gives her great command of illustration. Mary Wollstonecraft, on the other hand, is nothing if not rational; she has no erudition, and her grave pages are lit up by no ray of fancy. In both writers we discern, under the brave bearing of a strong and truthful nature, the beating of a loving woman's heart, which teaches them not to undervalue the smallest offices of domestic care or kindliness. But Margaret Fuller, with all her passionate sensibility, is more of the literary woman, who would not have been satisfied without intellectual production; Mary Wollstonecraft, we imagine, wrote not at all for writing's sake, but from the pressure of other motives. So far as the difference of date allows, there is a striking coincidence in their trains of thought; indeed, every important idea in the *Rights of Woman,* except the combination of home education with a common day-school for boys and girls, reappears in Margaret Fuller's essay.

One point on which they both write forcibly is the fact that, while men have a horror of such faculty or culture in the other sex as tends to place it on a level with their own, they are really in a state of subjection to ignorant and feeble-minded women. Margaret Fuller says:

> Wherever man is sufficiently raised above extreme poverty or brutal stupidity, to care for the comforts of the fireside, or the bloom and ornament of life, woman has always power enough, if she chooses to exert it, and is usually disposed to do so, in proportion to her ignorance and childish vanity. Unacquainted with the importance of life and its purposes, trained to a selfish coquetry and love of petty power, she does not look beyond the pleasure of making herself felt at the moment, and governments are shaken and commerce broken up to gratify the pique of a female favorite. The English shopkeeper's wife does not vote, but it is for her interest that the politician canvasses by the coarsest flattery.

Again:

> All wives, bad or good, loved or unloved, inevitably influence their husbands from the power their position not merely gives, but necessitates of coloring evidence and infusing feelings in hours when the—patient, shall I call him?—is off his guard.

Hear now what Mary Wollstonecraft says on the same subject:

> Women have been allowed to remain in ignorance and slavish dependence many, very many years, and still we hear of nothing but their fondness of pleasure and sway, their preference of rakes and soldiers, their childish attachment to toys, and the vanity that makes them value accom-

plishments more than virtues. History brings forward a fearful catalogue of the crimes which their cunning has produced, when the weak slaves have had sufficient address to overreach their masters. . . . When, therefore, I call women slaves, I mean in a political and civil sense; for indirectly they obtain too much power, and are debased by their exertions to obtain illicit sway. . . . The libertinism, and even the virtues of superior men, will always give women of some description great power over them; and these weak women, under the influence of childish passions and selfish vanity, *will throw a false light over the objects which the very men view with their eyes who ought to enlighten their judgment.* Men of fancy, and those sanguine characters who mostly hold the helm of human affairs in general, relax in the society of women; and surely I need not cite to the most superficial reader of history the numerous examples of vice and oppression which the private intrigues of female favorites have produced; not to dwell on the mischief that naturally arises from the blundering interposition of well-meaning folly. *For in the transactions of business it is much better to have to deal with a knave than a fool, because a knave adheres to some plan, and any plan of reason may be seen through sooner than a sudden flight of folly.* The power which vile and foolish women have had over wise men who possessed sensibility is notorious.

There is a notion commonly entertained among men that an instructed woman, capable of having opinions, is likely to prove an unpracticable yoke-fellow, always pulling one way when her husband wants to go the other, oracular in tone, and prone to give curtain lectures[4] on metaphysics. But surely, so far as obstinacy is concerned, your unreasoning animal is the most unmanageable of creatures, where you are not allowed to settle the question by a cudgel, a whip and bridle, or even a string to the leg. For our own parts, we see no consistent or commodious medium between the old plan of corporal discipline and that thorough education of women which will make them rational beings in the highest sense of the word. Wherever weakness is not harshly controlled it must *govern*, as you may see when a strong man holds a little child by the hand, how he is pulled hither and thither, and wearied in his walk by his submission to the whims and feeble movements of his companion. A really cultured woman, like a really cultured man, will be ready to yield in trifles. So far as we see, there is no indissoluble connection between infirmity of logic and infirmity of will, and a woman quite innocent of an opinion in philosophy, is as likely as not to have an indomitable opinion about the kitchen. As to airs of superiority, no woman ever had them in consequence of true culture, but only because her culture was shallow or unreal, only as a result of what Mrs. Malaprop well calls "the ineffectual qualities in a woman"[5]—mere acquisitions carried about, and not knowledge thoroughly assimilated so as to enter into the growth of the character.

To return to Margaret Fuller, some of the best things she says are on the folly of absolute definitions of woman's nature and absolute demarcations of woman's mission. "Nature," she says, "seems to delight in varying the arrangements, as if to show that she will be fettered by no rule; and we must admit

4. See Douglas Jerrold's comic sketches of a wife who delivers nightly lectures to her husband from behind their bed curtains, Mrs. *Caudle's Curtain Lectures* (1846).
5. Richard Brinsley Sheridan, *The Rivals* (1775),

3.2. In response to compliments about her "intellectual accomplishments," Mrs. Malaprop—famed for her mistaken use of words—exclaims: "Ah! few gentlemen, nowadays, know how to value the ineffectual qualities in a woman!"

the same varieties that she admits." Again: "If nature is never bound down, nor the voice of inspiration stifled, that is enough. We are pleased that women should write and speak, if they feel need of it, from having something to tell; but silence for ages would be no misfortune, if that silence be from divine command, and not from man's tradition." And here is a passage, the beginning of which has been often quoted:

> If you ask me what offices they [women] may fill, I reply—any. I do not care what case you put; let them be sea-captains if you will. I do not doubt there are women well fitted for such an office, and, if so, I should be as glad as to welcome the Maid of Saragossa, or the Maid of Missolonghi, or the Suliote heroine, or Emily Plater.[6] I think women need, especially at this juncture, a much greater range of occupation than they have, to rouse their latent powers. . . . In families that I know, some little girls like to saw wood, others to use carpenter's tools. Where these tastes are indulged, cheerfulness and good-humor are promoted. Where they are forbidden, because "such things are not proper for girls," they grow sullen and mischievous. Fourier had observed these wants of women, as no one can fail to do who watches the desires of little girls, or knows the *ennui* that haunts grown women, except where they make to themselves a serene little world by art of some kind. He, therefore, in proposing a great variety of employments, in manufactures or the care of plants and animals, allows for one-third of women as likely to have a taste for masculine pursuits, one-third of men for feminine.[7] . . . I have no doubt, however, that a large proportion of women would give themselves to the same employments as now, because there are circumstances that must lead them. Mothers will delight to make the nest soft and warm. Nature would take care of that; no need to clip the wings of any bird that wants to soar and sing, or finds in itself the strength of pinion for a migratory flight unusual to its kind. The difference would be that *all* need not be constrained to employments for which *some* are unfit.

Apropos of the same subject, we find Mary Wollstonecraft offering a suggestion which the women of the United States have already begun to carry out. She says:

> Women, in particular, all want to be ladies, which is simply to have nothing to do, but listlessly to go they scarcely care where, for they cannot tell what. But what have women to do in society? I may be asked, but to loiter with easy grace; surely you would not condemn them all to suckle fools and chronicle small beer.[8] No. *Women might certainly study the art of healing, and be physicians as well as nurses.* . . . Business of various kinds they might likewise pursue, if they were educated in a more orderly manner. . . . Women would not then marry for a support, as men accept of places under government, and neglect the implied duties.

6. A Polish patriot who became a captain in command of a company in the insurgent army fighting the Russians in 1831. "Maid of Saragossa": Maria Agustin, who fought against the French at the siege of Saragossa, in Spain, in 1808 (see Byron, *Childe Harold's Pilgrimage*, 1812, 1.54–56). "Maid of Missolonghi": an unidentified Greek, who must have made some heroic exploit during the Turkish sieges of that town in 1822 or 1826. "The Suliote

heroine": probably Moscha, who led a band of three hundred women to rout the Turks during the siege of Souli, in Albania, in 1803.
7. Charles Fourier (1772–1837), in his utopian treatise *The New Industrial World* (1829–30), develops these theories in his discussion of "the Little Hordes."
8. Iago on the role of women; Shakespeare's *Othello* 2.1.162.

Men pay a heavy price for their reluctance to encourage self-help and independent resources in women. The precious meridian years of many a man of genius have to be spent in the toil of routine, that an "establishment" may be kept up for a woman who can understand none of his secret yearnings,[9] who is fit for nothing but to sit in her drawing-room like a doll-Madonna in her shrine. No matter. Anything is more endurable than to change our established formulae about women, or to run the risk of looking up to our wives instead of looking down on them. *Sit divus, dummodo non sit vivus* (let him be a god, provided he be not living), said the Roman magnates of Romulus;[1] and so men say of women, let them be idols, useless absorbents of previous things, provided we are not obliged to admit them to be strictly fellow-beings, to be treated, one and all, with justice and sober reverence.

On one side we hear that woman's position can never be improved until women themselves are better; and, on the other, that women can never become better until their position is improved—until the laws are made more just, and a wider field opened to feminine activity. But we constantly hear the same difficulty stated about the human race in general. There is a perpetual action and reaction between individuals and institutions; we must try and mend both by little and little—the only way in which human things can be mended. Unfortunately, many over-zealous champions of women assert their actual equality with men—nay, even their moral superiority to men—as a ground for their release from oppressive laws and restrictions. They lose strength immensely by this false position. If it were true, then there would be a case in which slavery and ignorance nourished virtue, and so far we should have an argument for the continuance of bondage. But we want freedom and culture for woman, because subjection and ignorance have debased her, and with her, Man; for—

> If she be small, slight-natured, miserable,
> How shall men grow?[2]

Both Margaret Fuller and Mary Wollstonecraft have too much sagacity to fall into this sentimental exaggeration. Their ardent hopes of what women may become do not prevent them from seeing and painting women as they are. On the relative moral excellence of men and women Mary Wollstonecraft speaks with the most decision:

> Women are supposed to possess more sensibility, and even humanity, than men, and their strong attachments and instantaneous emotions of compassion are given as proofs; but the clinging affection of ignorance has seldom anything noble in it, and may mostly be resolved into selfishness, as well as the affection of children and brutes. I have known many weak women whose sensibility was entirely engrossed by their husbands; and as for their humanity, it was very faint indeed, or rather it was only a transient emotion of compassion. Humanity does not consist "in a squeamish ear," says an eminent orator.[3] "It belongs to the mind as well as to the nerves." But this kind of exclusive affection, though it degrades the individual, should not be brought forward as a proof of the inferiority of

9. Cf. Eliot's fictional representation of such a situation in her account of Dr. Lydgate's married life in *Middlemarch* (1871–72).
1. Cf. *Historia Augusta* (ca. 4th century C.E.), *Life of Geta* 2, in which the same cynical comment is made on a proposal to have a man deified. Romulus: legendary founder of Rome; after his death he was worshipped by the Romans as a god.
2. Tennyson's *The Princess* 7.249–50.
3. Perhaps Edmund Burke (1729–1797).

the sex, because it is the natural consequence of confined views; for even women of superior sense, having their attention turned to little employments and private plans, rarely rise to heroism, unless when spurred on by love! and love, as an heroic passion, like genius, appears but once in an age. I therefore agree with the moralist who asserts "that women have seldom so much generosity as men"; and that their narrow affections, to which justice and humanity are often sacrificed, render the sex apparently inferior, especially as they are commonly inspired by men; but I contend that the heart would expand as the understanding gained strength, if women were not depressed[4] from their cradles.

We had marked several other passages of Margaret Fuller's for extract, but as we do not aim at an exhaustive treatment of our subject, and are only touching a few of its points, we have, perhaps, already claimed as much of the reader's attention as he will be willing to give to such desultory material.

1855

From Silly Novels by Lady Novelists[1]

Silly Novels by Lady Novelists are a genus with many species, determined by the particular quality of silliness that predominates in them—the frothy, the prosy, the pious, or the pedantic. But it is a mixture of all these—a composite order of feminine fatuity, that produces the largest class of such novels, which we shall distinguish as the *mind-and-millinery* species. The heroine is usually an heiress, probably a peeress in her own right, with perhaps a vicious baronet, an amiable duke, and an irresistible younger son of a marquis as lovers in the foreground, a clergyman and a poet sighing for her in the middle distance, and a crowd of undefined adorers dimly indicated beyond. Her eyes and her wit are both dazzling; her nose and her morals are alike free from any tendency to irregularity; she has a superb *contralto* and a superb intellect; she is perfectly well-dressed and perfectly religious; she dances like a sylph, and reads the Bible in the original tongues. Or it may be that the heroine is not an heiress—that rank and wealth are the only things in which she is deficient; but she infallibly gets into high society, she has the triumph of refusing many matches and securing the best, and she wears some family jewels or other as a sort of crown of righteousness at the end. Rakish men either bite their lips in impotent confusion at her repartees, or are touched to penitence by her reproofs, which, on appropriate occasions, rise to a lofty strain of rhetoric; indeed, there is a general propensity in her to make speeches, and to rhapsodize at some length when she retires to her bedroom. In her recorded conversations she is amazingly eloquent, and in her unrecorded conversations, amazingly witty. She is understood to have a depth of insight that looks through and through the shallow theories of philosophers, and her superior instincts are a sort of dial by which men have only to set their clocks and watches, and all will go well. The men play a very subordinate part by her side.

4. Repressed, kept down.
1. Published anonymously in the *Westminster Review*, this review essay, satirizing a number of contemporary novels, provides a good indication of Eliot's ideas about fiction at the time she was beginning her first story, "The Sad Fortunes of the Rev. Amos Barton."

You are consoled now and then by a hint that they have affairs, which keeps you in mind that the working-day business of the world is somehow being carried on, but ostensibly the final cause of their existence is that they may accompany the heroine on her "starring" expedition through life. They see her at a ball, and are dazzled; at a flower-show, and they are fascinated; on a riding excursion, and they are witched[2] by her noble horsemanship; at church, and they are awed by the sweet solemnity of her demeanour. She is the ideal woman in feelings, faculties, and flounces. For all this, she as often as not marries the wrong person to begin with, and she suffers terribly from the plots and intrigues of the vicious baronet; but even death has a soft place in his heart for such a paragon, and remedies all mistakes for her just at the right moment. The vicious baronet is sure to be killed in a duel, and the tedious husband dies in his bed requesting his wife, as a particular favour to him, to marry the man she loves best, and having already dispatched a note to the lover informing him of the comfortable arrangement. Before matters arrive at this desirable issue our feelings are tried by seeing the noble, lovely, and gifted heroine pass through many mauvais[3] moments, but we have the satisfaction of knowing that her sorrows are wept into embroidered pocket-handkerchiefs, that her fainting form reclines on the very best upholstery, and that whatever vicissitudes she may undergo, from being dashed out of her carriage to having her head shaved in a fever, she comes out of them all with a complexion more blooming and locks more redundant[4] than ever.

We may remark, by the way, that we have been relieved from a serious scruple by discovering that silly novels by lady novelists rarely introduce us into any other than very lofty and fashionable society. We had imagined that destitute women turned novelists, as they turned governesses, because they had no other "lady-like" means of getting their bread. On this supposition, vacillating syntax and improbable incident had a certain pathos for us, like the extremely supererogatory pincushions and ill-devised nightcaps that are offered for sale by a blind man. We felt the commodity to be a nuisance, but we were glad to think that the money went to relieve the necessitous, and we pictured to ourselves lonely women struggling for a maintenance, or wives and daughters devoting themselves to the production of "copy" out of pure hero-ism,—perhaps to pay their husband's debts, or to purchase luxuries for a sick father. Under these impressions we shrank from criticising a lady's novel: her English might be faulty, but, we said to ourselves, her motives are irreproach-able; her imagination may be uninventive, but her patience is untiring. Empty writing was excused by an empty stomach, and twaddle was consecrated by tears. But no! This theory of ours, like many other pretty theories, has had to give way before observation. Women's silly novels, we are now convinced, are written under totally different circumstances. The fair writers have evidently never talked to a tradesman except from a carriage window; they have no notion of the working-classes except as "dependents;" they think five hundred a-year a miserable pittance; Belgravia[5] and "baronial halls" are their primary truths; and they have no idea of feeling interest in any man who is not at least a great landed proprietor, if not a prime minister. It is clear that they write in elegant boudoirs, with violet-colored ink and a ruby pen; that they must be

2. Bewitched.
3. Bad (French).
4. Abundant.
5. A wealthy district of London. "Five hundred a-

year": at this date an annual income of £500 would support a modest middle-class household with one or two servants.

entirely indifferent to publishers' accounts, and inexperienced in every form of poverty except poverty of brains. It is true that we are constantly struck with the want of verisimilitude in their representations of the high society in which they seem to live; but then they betray no closer acquaintance with any other form of life. If their peers and peeresses are improbable, their literary men, tradespeople, and cottagers are impossible; and their intellect seems to have the peculiar impartiality of reproducing both what they *have* seen and heard, and what they have *not* seen and heard, with equal unfaithfulness.

✻　✻　✻

Writers of the mind-and-millinery school are remarkably unanimous in their choice of diction. In their novels, there is usually a lady or gentleman who is more or less of a upas tree:[6] the lover has a manly breast; minds are redolent of various things; hearts are hollow; events are utilized; friends are consigned to the tomb; infancy is an engaging period; the sun is a luminary that goes to his western couch, or gathers the rain-drops into his refulgent bosom; life is a melancholy boon; Albion and Scotia[7] are conversational epithets. There is a striking resemblance, too, in the character of their moral comments, such, for instance, as that "It is a fact, no less true than melancholy, that all people, more or less, richer or poorer, are swayed by bad example;" that "Books, however trivial, contain some subjects from which useful information may be drawn;" that "Vice can too often borrow the language of virtue;" that "Merit and nobility of nature must exist, to be accepted, for clamour and pretension cannot impose upon those too well read in human nature to be easily deceived;" and that, "In order to forgive, we must have been injured." There is, doubtless, a class of readers to whom these remarks appear peculiarly pointed and pungent; for we often find them doubly and trebly scored with the pencil, and delicate hands giving in their determined adhesion to these hardy novelties by a distinct *très vrai*,[8] emphasized by many notes of exclamation. The colloquial style of these novels is often marked by much ingenious inversion, and a careful avoidance of such cheap phraseology as can be heard every day. Angry young gentlemen exclaim—" 'Tis ever thus, methinks;" and in the half-hour before dinner a young lady informs her next neighbour that the first day she read Shakspeare she "stole away into the park, and beneath the shadow of the greenwood tree, devoured with rapture the inspired page of the great magician." But the most remarkable efforts of the mind-and-millinery writers lie in their philosophic reflections. The authoress of "Laura Gay,"[9] for example, having married her hero and heroine, improves the event by observing that "if those sceptics, whose eyes have so long gazed on matter that they can no longer see aught else in man, could once enter with heart and soul into such bliss as this, they would come to say that the soul of man and the polypus[1] are not of common origin, or of the same texture." Lady novelists, it appears, can see something else besides matter; they are not limited to phenomena, but can relieve their eyesight by occasional glimpses of the *noumenon*,[2] and are, therefore, naturally better able than any one else to confound sceptics, even of that remarkable, but to us unknown school, which maintains that the soul of man is of the same texture as the polypus.

---

6. A Javanese tree from which an arrow poison is derived; here a figurative cliché meaning "a poisonous influence."
7. Poetic clichés for England and Scotland, respectively.
8. Very true (French).

9. The 1856 novel Eliot has just satirized in the preceding section.
1. Polyp.
2. An object of purely rational, as opposed to sensual, perception (the latter being a *phenomenon*).

The most pitiable of all silly novels by lady novelists are what we may call the *oracular* species—novels intended to expound the writer's religious, philosophical, or moral theories. There seems to be a notion abroad among women, rather akin to the superstition that the speech and actions of idiots are inspired, and that the human being most entirely exhausted of common sense is the fittest vehicle of revelation. To judge from their writings, there are certain ladies who think that an amazing ignorance, both of science and of life, is the best possible qualification for forming an opinion on the knottiest moral and speculative questions. Apparently, their recipe for solving all such difficulties is something like this:—Take a woman's head, stuff it with a smattering of philosophy and literature chopped small, and with false notions of society baked hard, let it hang over a desk a few hours every day, and serve up hot in feeble English, when not required. You will rarely meet with a lady novelist of the oracular class who is diffident of her ability to decide on theological questions,—who has any suspicion that she is not capable of discriminating with the nicest accuracy between the good and evil in all church parties,—who does not see precisely how it is that men have gone wrong hitherto,—and pity philosophers in general that they have not had the opportunity of consulting her. Great writers, who have modestly contented themselves with putting their experience into fiction, and have thought it quite a sufficient task to exhibit men and things as they are, she sighs over as deplorably deficient in the application of their powers. "They have solved no great questions"—and she is ready to remedy their omission by setting before you a complete theory of life and manual of divinity, in a love story, where ladies and gentlemen of good family go through genteel vicissitudes, to the utter confusion of Deists, Puseyites,[3] and ultra-Protestants, and to the perfect establishment of that particular view of Christianity which either condenses itself into a sentence of small caps, or explodes into a cluster of stars on the three hundred and thirtieth page. It is true, the ladies and gentlemen will probably seem to you remarkably little like any you have had the fortune or misfortune to meet with, for, as a general rule, the ability of a lady novelist to describe actual life and her fellow-men, is in inverse proportion to her confident eloquence about God and the other world, and the means by which she usually chooses to conduct you to true ideas of the invisible is a totally false picture of the visible.

✻   ✻   ✻

The epithet "silly" may seem impertinent, applied to a novel which indicates so much reading and intellectual activity as "The Enigma;"[4] but we use this epithet advisedly. If, as the world has long agreed, a very great amount of instruction will not make a wise man, still less will a very mediocre amount of instruction make a wise woman. And the most mischievous form of feminine silliness is the literary form, because it tends to confirm the popular prejudice against the more solid education of women. When men see girls wasting their time in consultations about bonnets and ball dresses, and in giggling or sentimental love-confidences, or middle-aged women mismanaging their children, and solacing themselves with acrid gossip, they can hardly help saying, "For Heaven's sake, let girls be better educated; let them have some better objects

<hr />

3. Protestants who believed in the importance of liturgical sacraments (following Edward Pusey, 1800–1882). "Deists": Protestants who believed in a personal God who created the universe but who was completely beyond human experience.
4. The 1856 novel Eliot has just satirized in the preceding section.

of thought—some more solid occupations." But after a few hours' conversation with an oracular literary woman, or a few hours' reading of her books, they are likely enough to say, "After all, when a woman gets some knowledge, see what use she makes of it! Her knowledge remains acquisition, instead of passing into culture; instead of being subdued into modesty and simplicity by a larger acquaintance with thought and fact, she has a feverish consciousness of her attainments; she keeps a sort of mental pocket-mirror, and is continually looking in it at her own 'intellectuality;' she spoils the taste of one's muffin by questions of metaphysics; 'puts down' men at a dinner table with her superior information; and seizes the opportunity of a *soirée* to catechise us on the vital question of the relation between mind and matter. And then, look at her writings! She mistakes vagueness for depth, bombast for eloquence, and affectation for originality; she struts on one page, rolls her eyes on another, grimaces in a third, and is hysterical in a fourth. She may have read many writings of great men, and a few writings of great women; but she is as unable to discern the difference between her own style and theirs as a Yorkshireman is to discern the difference between his own English and a Londoner's: rhodomontade[5] is the native accent of her intellect. No—the average nature of women is too shallow and feeble a soil to bear much tillage; it is only fit for the very lightest crops."

It is true that the men who come to such a decision on such very superficial and imperfect observation may not be among the wisest in the world; but we have not now to contest their opinion—we are only pointing out how it is unconsciously encouraged by many women who have volunteered themselves as representatives of the feminine intellect. We do not believe that a man was ever strengthened in such an opinion by associating with a woman of true culture, whose mind had absorbed her knowledge instead of being absorbed by it. A really cultured woman, like a really cultured man, is all the simpler and the less obtrusive for her knowledge; it has made her see herself and her opinions in something like just proportions; she does not make it a pedestal from which she flatters herself that she commands a complete view of men and things, but makes it a point of observation from which to form a right estimate of herself. She neither spouts poetry nor quotes Cicero[6] on slight provocation; not because she thinks that a sacrifice must be made to the prejudices of men, but because that mode of exhibiting her memory and Latinity does not present itself to her as edifying or graceful. She does not write books to confound philosophers, perhaps because she is able to write books that delight them. In conversation she is the least formidable of women, because she understands you, without wanting to make you aware that you *can't* understand her. She does not give you information, which is the raw material of culture,—she gives you sympathy, which is its subtlest essence.

A more numerous class of silly novels than the oracular, (which are generally inspired by some form of High Church, or transcendental Christianity,) is what we may call the *white neck-cloth* species, which represent the tone of thought and feeling in the Evangelical party. This species is a kind of genteel tract on a large scale, intended as a sort of medicinal sweetmeat for Low Church young ladies; an Evangelical substitute for the fashionable novel, as

---

5. Inflated diction. It is assumed a Yorkshireman cannot discern the difference between his northern dialect and the putatively more refined speech of a Londoner.
6. Roman statesman and orator (106–43 B.C.E.), and a staple of Latin instruction for centuries.

the May Meetings[7] are a substitute for the Opera. Even Quaker children, one would think, can hardly have been denied the indulgence of a doll; but it must be a doll dressed in a drab gown and a coal-scuttle bonnet—not a worldly doll, in gauze and spangles. And there are no young ladies, we imagine,—unless they belong to the Church of the United Brethren, in which people are married without any love-making[8]—who can dispense with love stories. Thus, for Evangelical young ladies there are Evangelical love stories, in which the vicissitudes of the tender passion are sanctified by saving views of Regeneration and the Atonement. These novels differ from the oracular ones, as a Low Churchwoman often differs from a High Churchwoman: they are a little less supercilious, and a great deal more ignorant, a little less correct in their syntax, and a great deal more vulgar.[9]

The Orlando[1] of Evangelical literature is the young curate, looked at from the point of view of the middle class, where cambric bands are understood to have as thrilling an effect on the hearts of young ladies as epaulettes[2] have in the classes above and below it. In the ordinary type of these novels, the hero is almost sure to be a young curate, frowned upon, perhaps, by worldly mammas, but carrying captive the hearts of their daughters, who can "never forget *that* sermon;" tender glances are seized from the pulpit stairs instead of the opera-box; *tête-à-têtes* are seasoned with quotations from Scripture, instead of quotations from the poets; and questions as to the state of the heroine's affections are mingled with anxieties as to the state of her soul. The young curate always has a background of well-dressed and wealthy, if not fashionable society;—for Evangelical silliness is as snobbish as any other kind of silliness; and the Evangelical lady novelist, while she explains to you the type of the scapegoat on one page, is ambitious on another to represent the manners and conversation of aristocratic people. Her pictures of fashionable society are often curious studies considered as efforts of the Evangelical imagination; but in one particular the novels of the White Neck-cloth School are meritoriously realistic,—their favourite hero, the Evangelical young curate is always rather an insipid personage.

* * *

But, perhaps, the least readable of silly women's novels, are the *modern-antique* species, which unfold to us the domestic life of Jannes and Jambres, the private love affairs of Sennacherib, or the mental struggles and ultimate conversion of Demetrius the silversmith.[3] From most silly novels we can at least extract a laugh; but those of the modern antique school have a ponderous, a leaden kind of fatuity, under which we groan. What can be more demonstrative of the inability of literary women to measure their own powers, than their frequent assumption of a task which can only be justified by the rarest concurrence of acquirement with genius? The finest effort to reanimate the past is of course only approximative—is always more or less an infusion of the modern spirit into the ancient form,—

7. The Church of England's Missionary Society's annual spring meetings. On the High and Low Church, see "The Victorian Age" (p. 979).
8. Courtship.
9. Common.
1. The romantic hero (in allusion to the hero of Shakespeare's *As You Like It*).
2. Attire characteristic of military men, as cambric bands (white neck-clothes) are of the clergy.

3. In Acts 19.24–27 the maker of statues of the Roman goddess Diana who denounces Paul for taking business away from him and his fellow craftsmen by converting people to Christianity. Jannes and Jambres were Egyptian magicians who opposed Moses at Pharaoh's court (2 Timothy 3.8). Sennacherib was an Assyrian king who ruled from 705 to 681 B.C.E.

Was ihr den Geist der Zeiten heisst,
Das ist im Grund der Herren eigner Geist,
In dem die Zeiten sich bespiegeln.[4]

Admitting that genius which has familiarized itself with all the relics of an ancient period can sometimes, by the force of its sympathetic divination, restore the missing notes in the "music of humanity," and reconstruct the fragments into a whole which will really bring the remote past nearer to us, and interpret it to our duller apprehension,—this form of imaginative power must always be among the very rarest, because it demands as much accurate and minute knowledge as creative vigour. Yet we find ladies constantly choosing to make their mental mediocrity more conspicuous, by clothing it in a masquerade of ancient names; by putting their feeble sentimentality into the mouths of Roman vestals or Egyptian princesses, and attributing their rhetorical arguments to Jewish high-priests and Greek philosophers. * * *

"Be not a baker if your head be made of butter," says a homely proverb, which, being interpreted, may mean, let no woman rush into print who is not prepared for the consequences. We are aware that our remarks are in a very different tone from that of the reviewers who, with a perennial recurrence of precisely similar emotions, only paralleled, we imagine, in the experience of monthly nurses,[5] tell one lady novelist after another that they "hail" her productions "with delight." We are aware that the ladies at whom our criticism is pointed are accustomed to be told, in the choicest phraseology of puffery, that their pictures of life are brilliant, their characters well drawn, their style fascinating, and their sentiments lofty. But if they are inclined to resent our plainness of speech, we ask them to reflect for a moment on the chary praise, and often captious blame, which their panegyrists give to writers whose works are on the way to become classics. No sooner does a woman show that she has genius or effective talent, than she receives the tribute of being moderately praised and severely criticised. By a peculiar thermometric adjustment, when a woman's talent is at zero, journalistic approbation is at the boiling pitch; when she attains mediocrity, it is already at no more than summer heat; and if ever she reaches excellence, critical enthusiasm drops to the freezing point. Harriet Martineau, Currer Bell, and Mrs. Gaskell[6] have been treated as cavalierly as if they had been men. And every critic who forms a high estimate of the share women may ultimately take in literature, will, on principle, abstain from any exceptional indulgence towards the productions of literary women. For it must be plain to every one who looks impartially and extensively into feminine literature, that its greatest deficiencies are due hardly more to the want of intellectual power than to the want of those moral qualities that contribute to literary excellence—patient diligence, a sense of the responsibility involved in publication, and an appreciation of the sacredness of the writer's art. In the majority of women's books you see that kind of facility which springs from the absence of any high standard; that fertility in imbecile combination or feeble imitation which a little self-criticism would check and reduce to barrenness; just as with a total want of musical ear people will sing out of

4. What they call the spirit of the age / is at the base the gentlemen's own spirit, / in which the ages are reflected (German; Goethe's *Faust I* [1808], *Nacht*, lines 577–79).
5. Women hired to look after mothers and babies in the first month after childbirth.
6. Eliot names three of the foremost British women writers of the 19th century: Martineau (1802–1876), a prolific author in a range of nonfiction genres; Charlotte Brontë (1816–1855), novelist (first published under the pseudonym Bell); and Elizabeth Gaskell (1810–1865), novelist.

tune, while a degree more melodic sensibility would suffice to render them silent. The foolish vanity of wishing to appear in print, instead of being counterbalanced by any consciousness of the intellectual or moral derogation implied in futile authorship, seems to be encouraged by the extremely false impression that to write *at all* is a proof of superiority in a woman. On this ground, we believe that the average intellect of women is unfairly represented by the mass of feminine literature, and that while the few women who write well are very far above the ordinary intellectual level of their sex, the many women who write ill are very far below it. So that, after all, the severer critics are fulfilling a chivalrous duty in depriving the mere fact of feminine authorship of any false prestige which may give it a delusive attraction, and in recommending women of mediocre faculties—as at least a negative service they can render their sex—to abstain from writing.

The standing apology for women who become writers without any special qualification is, that society shuts them out from other spheres of occupation. Society is a very culpable entity, and has to answer for the manufacture of many unwholesome commodities, from bad pickles to bad poetry. But society, like "matter," and Her Majesty's Government, and other lofty abstractions, has its share of excessive blame as well as excessive praise. Where there is one woman who writes from necessity, we believe there are three women who write from vanity; and, besides, there is something so antiseptic in the mere healthy fact of working for one's bread, that the most trashy and rotten kind of feminine literature is not likely to have been produced under such circumstances. "In all labour there is profit;"[7] but ladies' silly novels, we imagine, are less the result of labour than of busy idleness.

Happily, we are not dependent on argument to prove that Fiction is a department of literature in which women can, after their kind, fully equal men. A cluster of great names, both living and dead, rush to our memories in evidence that women can produce novels not only fine, but among the very finest;—novels, too, that have a precious speciality, lying quite apart from masculine aptitudes and experience. No educational restrictions can shut women out from the materials of fiction, and there is no species of art which is so free from rigid requirements. Like crystalline masses, it may take any form, and yet be beautiful; we have only to pour in the right elements—genuine observation, humour, and passion. But it is precisely this absence of rigid requirement which constitutes the fatal seduction of novel-writing to incompetent women. Ladies are not wont to be very grossly deceived as to their power of playing on the piano; here certain positive difficulties of execution have to be conquered, and incompetence inevitably breaks down. Every art which has its absolute *technique* is, to a certain extent, guarded from the intrusions of mere left-handed imbecility. But in novel-writing there are no barriers for incapacity to stumble against, no external criteria to prevent a writer from mistaking foolish facility for mastery. And so we have again and again the old story of La Fontaine's ass, who puts his nose to the flute, and, finding that he elicits some sound, exclaims, "Moi, aussi, je joue de la flute;"[8]—a fable which we commend, at parting, to the consideration of any feminine reader who is in danger of adding to the number of "silly novels by lady novelists."

1856   1856

---

7. Proverbs 14.23.
8. I also play the flute (French). Jean de La Fontaine (1621–1695), French author of beast fables.

MATTHEW ARNOLD
1822–1888

How is a full and enjoyable life to be lived in a modern industrial society? This was the recurrent topic in the poetry and prose of Matthew Arnold. In his poetry the question itself is raised; in his prose some answers are attempted. "The misapprehensiveness [wrongheadedness] of his age is exactly what a poet is sent to remedy," wrote Robert Browning, and yet it is to Arnold's work, not Browning's, that the statement seems more applicable. In response to rapid and potentially dislocating social changes, Arnold strove to help his contemporaries achieve a richer intellectual and emotional existence.

Matthew Arnold was born in Laleham, a village in the valley of the Thames. It seems appropriate that his childhood was spent near a river, for clear-flowing streams were later to appear in his poems as symbols of serenity. At the age of six, Arnold was moved to Rugby School, where his father, Dr. Thomas Arnold, had become headmaster. As a clergyman Dr. Arnold was a leader of the liberal or Broad Church and hence one of the principal opponents of John Henry Newman. As a headmaster he became famous as an educational reformer, a teacher who instilled in his pupils an earnest preoccupation with moral and social issues and also an awareness of the connection between liberal studies and modern life. At Rugby his eldest son, Matthew, was directly exposed to the powerful force of the father's mind and character. The son's attitude toward this force was a mixture of attraction and repulsion. That he was permanently influenced by his father is evident in his poems and in his writings on religion, education, and politics; but like many sons of clergymen, he made a determined effort in his youth to be different. As a student at Oxford he behaved like a dandy. Elegantly and colorfully dressed, alternately languid or merry in manner, he refused to be serious and irritated more solemn undergraduate friends and acquaintances with his irreverent jokes. "His manner displeases, from its seeming foppery," wrote Charlotte Brontë after talking with the young man in later years. "The shade of Dr. Arnold," she added, "seemed to me to frown on his young representative." The son of Dr. Arnold thus appeared to have no connection with Rugby School's standards of earnestness. Even his studies did not seem to occupy him seriously. By a session of cramming, he managed to earn second-class honors in his final examinations, a near disaster that was redeemed by his election to a fellowship at Oriel College.

Arnold's biographers usually dismiss his youthful frivolity of spirit as only a temporary pose or mask, but it permanently colored his prose style, brightening his most serious criticism with geniality and wit. For most readers the jauntiness of his prose is a virtue, though others find it offensive. Anyone suspicious of urbanity and irony would applaud Walt Whitman's sour comment that Arnold is "one of the dudes [dandies, or city slickers] of literature." A more appropriate estimate of his manner is provided by Arnold's own description of the French writer Charles-Augustin Sainte-Beuve: "a critic of measure, not exuberant; of the centre, not provincial . . . with gay and amiable temper, his manner as good as his matter—the 'critique souriant' [smiling critic]."

Unlike authors such as Alfred, Lord Tennyson and Thomas Carlyle who committed themselves solely to their literary pursuits, Arnold confined his writing and reading to his spare time. In 1847 he took the post of private secretary to Lord Lansdowne; and in 1851, the year of his marriage, he became an inspector of schools, a demanding and time-consuming position that he held for thirty-five years. Although his work as an inspector may have reduced his output as a writer, it had several advantages. His extensive traveling in England took him to the homes of the more ardently Protestant middle classes, and when he criticized the dullness of middle-class life (as he often did), his scorn was based on intimate knowledge. His position also led to travel on the Continent to study the schools of Europe. As a critic of English education, he was thus able to make helpful comparisons and to draw on a stock of fresh ideas in the same way as in his literary criticism he used his familiarity with French, German, Italian, and classical literatures to talk knowledgeably about the distinctive qualities of English writers. Despite the monotony of much of his work as an inspector, Arnold became convinced of its importance. It contributed to what he regarded as his century's most important need: the development of a satisfactory national system of education.

In 1849 Arnold published *The Strayed Reveler*, his first volume of poetry. Eight years later, as a tribute to his poetic achievement, he was elected to the professorship of poetry at Oxford, a part-time position that he held for ten years. Later, like Charles Dickens and William Makepeace Thackeray before him, Arnold toured America to make money by lecturing. His lectures could leave audiences indifferent, but sometimes they were highly acclaimed: thus the *Washington Post* reported that, following a two-hour address in the U.S. capital, the African American leader Frederick Douglass "moved that a tremendous vote of thanks be tendered to the speaker." A further inducement for his two visits (in 1883 and 1886) was the opportunity of seeing his daughter Lucy, who had married an American. In 1888 Arnold died of a sudden heart attack.

Arnold's career as a writer can be roughly divided into four periods. In the 1850s most of his poems appeared; in the 1860s, literary criticism and social criticism; in the 1870s, his religious and educational writings; and in the 1880s, his second set of essays in literary criticism.

Today Arnold is perhaps better known as a writer of prose than as a poet, although individual poems such as "Dover Beach" (1867) continue to be widely popular. In his own era his decision to spend hardly any time composing poetry after 1860 was considered wrongheaded by some: "Tell Mat not to write any more of those prose things like *Literature and Dogma*," Tennyson wrote in a letter, wishing that Arnold would instead "give us something like his 'Thyrsis,' 'Scholar Gypsy,' or 'Forsaken Merman.'" Others have felt that he made the right move: Arnold's poetry has been criticized, in both the nineteenth and the twentieth centuries, on numerous grounds. Some have disliked its excessive reliance on italics instead of on meter to emphasize the meaning of a line, while others object to the prosy flatness of certain passages or, conversely, to overelaborated similes in others. Yet despite these cavils, many readers find much to cherish and admire. Given Arnold's sophistication as a writer, it is perhaps surprising that his evocations of nature function so memorably in his poetry: rather than simply providing a picturesque backdrop, the setting—seashore or river or mountaintop—draws the poem's meaning together. In this respect, as in many others, Arnold displays a debt to William Wordsworth, whose poetry he greatly admired; but he also draws on his own bond with particular landscapes, especially those associated with his youth and early adulthood. The stanzas of "The Scholar Gypsy" (1853), for instance—suffused in a deep familiarity with the changing patterns of the rural scene, from the "frail-leafed, white anemone" and "dark bluebells drenched with dews" of May to the "scarlet poppies" and "pale pink convolvulus" of August—record with sensuous care the distinct seasons of the English countryside and Arnold's nostalgic memories of the rambles of his Oxford days.

Arnold's own verdict on the qualities of his poetry is interesting. In an 1869 letter to his mother, he writes:

> My poems represent, on the whole, the main movement of mind of the last quarter of a century, and thus they will probably have their day as people become conscious to themselves of what that movement of mind is, and interested in the literary productions which reflect it. It might be fairly urged that I have less poetical sentiment than Tennyson, and less intellectual vigor and abundance than Browning; yet, because I have perhaps more of a fusion of the two than either of them, and have more regularly applied that fusion to the main line of

modern development, I am likely enough to have my turn, as they have had theirs.

The emphasis in the letter on "movement of mind" suggests that Arnold's poetry and prose should be studied together. Such an approach can be fruitful provided that it does not obscure the important difference between Arnold the poet and Arnold the critic. T. S. Eliot once said of his own writings that "in one's prose reflections one may be legitimately occupied with ideals, whereas in the writing of verse, one can deal only with actuality." Arnold's writings offer a nice verification of Eliot's seeming paradox. As a poet he usually records his own experiences, his own feelings of loneliness and isolation as a lover, his longing for a serenity that he cannot find, his melancholy sense of the passing of youth (more than for many men, Arnold's thirtieth birthday was an awe-inspiring landmark after which he felt, he said, "three parts iced over"). Above all he records his despair in a universe in which humanity's role seemed an incongruous as it was later to seem to Thomas Hardy. In a memorable passage of his "Stanzas from the Grande Chartreuse" (1855), he describes himself as "Wandering between two worlds, one dead, / The other powerless to be born." And addressing the representatives of a faith that seems to him dead, he cries: "Take me, cowled forms, and fence me round, / Till I possess my soul again." As a poet, then, like T. S. Eliot and W. H. Auden, Arnold provides a record of a troubled individual in a troubled society. This was "actuality" as he experienced it—an actuality, like Eliot's and Auden's, representative of his era. As a prose writer, a formulator of "ideals," he seeks a different role—to be what Auden calls the "healer" of a diseased society, or as he himself called Goethe, the "Physician of the iron age." And in this difference we have a clue to answering the question of why Arnold virtually abandoned the writing of poetry to move into criticism. One reason was his dissatisfaction with the kind of poetry he was writing.

In one of his fascinating letters to his friend Arthur Hugh Clough in the 1850s (letters that provide the best insight we have into Arnold's mind and tastes), this note of dissatisfaction is struck: "I am glad you like the *Gypsy Scholar*—but what does it *do* for you? Homer *animates*—Shakespeare *animates*—in its poor way I think *Sohrab and Rustum animates*—the *Gypsy Scholar* at best awakens a pleasing melancholy. But this is not what we want." It is evident that early in his career Arnold had evolved a theory of what poetry should do for its readers, a theory based, in part, on his impression of what classical poetry had achieved. To help make life bearable, poetry, in Arnold's view, must bring joy. As he says in the 1853 preface to his *Poems*, it must "inspirit and rejoice the reader"; it must "convey a charm, and infuse delight." Such a demand does not exclude tragic poetry but does exclude works "in which suffering finds no vent in action; in which a continual state of mental distress is prolonged." Of Charlotte Brontë's novel *Villette* (1853) he says witheringly: "The writer's mind contains nothing but hunger, rebellion, and rage . . . No fine writing can hide this thoroughly, and it will be fatal to her in the long run." Judged by such a standard, most nineteenth-century poems, including his own long poem *Empedocles on Etna* (1852), were unsatisfactory. And when Arnold tried to write poems that would meet his own requirements—*Sohrab and Rustum* (1853) or *Balder Dead* (1855)—he felt that something was lacking. By the late 1850s he thus found himself at a dead end. Turning aside to literary criticism enabled him partially to escape the dilemma. In his prose his melancholy and "morbid" personality was subordinated to the resolutely cheerful and purposeful character he had created for himself by an effort of will.

Arnold's two volumes of *Essays in Criticism* (1865, 1888) repeatedly show how authors as different as Marcus Aurelius, Leo Tolstoy, Homer, and Wordsworth provide the virtues he sought in his reading. Among these virtues was plainness of style. Although he could on occasion recommend the richness of language of such poets as John Keats or Tennyson—their "natural magic," as he called it—Arnold usually preferred literature that was unadorned. And beyond stylistic excellences, the principal virtue he admired as a critic was the quality of "high seriousness." In a world in which the role of formal religion appeared to be shrinking, Arnold increasingly emphasized that the poet must be a serious thinker who could offer guidance to his readers. This belief perhaps caused him to undervalue other qualities in literature: in "The Study of Poetry" (1880), for instance, he displays little appreciation for Chaucer's humor and chooses instead to castigate him for his lack of high seriousness.

In "The Function of Criticism at the Present Time" (1864), Arnold makes clear that he regarded good literary criticism, like literature itself, as a potent force in producing what he conceived as a civilized society. From a close study of this essay one could forecast the third stage of his career: his excursion into the criticism of society that was to culminate in *Culture and Anarchy* (1869) and *Friendship's Garland* (1871).

Arnold's starting point as a critic of society is different from that of Carlyle and John Ruskin. The older prophets attacked the Victorian middle classes on the grounds of their materialism, their selfish indifference to the sufferings of the poor—their immorality, in effect. Arnold argued instead that the "Philistines," as he called them, were not so much wicked as ignorant, narrow-minded, and suffering from the dullness of their private lives. This novel analysis was reinforced by Arnold's conviction that the world of the future, both in England and in America, would be a middle-class world and therefore would be dominated by a class inadequately equipped either to lead or to enjoy civilized living.

To establish this point Arnold employed cajolery, satire, and even quotations from current newspapers with considerable effect. He also used memorable catch phrases (such as "sweetness and light") that sometimes pose an obstacle to understanding the complexities of his position. His view of civilization, for example, was pared down to a four-point formula of the four "powers": conduct, intellect and knowledge, beauty, and social life and manners. Applying this simple formula to a range of civilizations, Arnold had a scale by which to judge the virtues as well as the inadequacies of different countries. When he turned this instrument on his own country, he usually awarded the Victorian middle classes an A in the first category (i.e., conduct) but a failing grade in the other three categories. Unsurprisingly, he also had pronounced opinions on what he viewed as the distinct national characters of different peoples: a sample of this strain in Arnold's writing appears in the extract from his lectures *On the Study of Celtic Literature* (1867) in "Empire and National Identity" (p. 1619).

Arnold's relentless exposure of middle-class narrow-mindedness in his own country eventually led him into the arena of religious controversy. As a critic of religious institutions he was arguing, in effect, that just as the middle classes did not know how to lead full lives, neither did they know how to read the Bible intelligently or attend church intelligently. Of the Christian religion he remarked that there are two things "that surely must be clear to anybody with eyes in his head. One is, that men cannot do without it; the other that they cannot do with it as it is." His three full-length studies of the Bible, including *Literature and Dogma* (1873), are thus best considered a postscript to his social criticism. The Bible, to Arnold, was a great work of literature like the *Odyssey*, and the Church of England was a great national institution like Parliament. Both Bible and Church must be preserved not because historical Christianity was credible but because both, when properly understood, were agents of what he called "culture"—they contributed to making humanity more civilized.

Culture is perhaps Arnold's most familiar catchwood, although what he meant by it has sometimes been misunderstood. He used the term to capture the qualities of an open-minded intelligence (as described in "The Function of Criticism")—a refusal to take things on authority. In this respect Arnold appears close to T. H. Huxley and J. S. Mill. But the word also connotes a full awareness of humanity's past and a capacity to enjoy the best works of art, literature, history, and philosophy that have come down to us from that past. As a way of viewing life in all its aspects, including the social, political, and religious, culture represents for Arnold the most effective cure for the ills of a sick society. It is his principal prescription.

The attempt to define culture brings us to a final aspect of Arnold's career as a critic: his writings on education, in which he sought to make cultural values, as he said, "prevail." Most obviously these writings comprise his reply to Huxley (his admirably reasoned essay "Literature and Science," 1882) and his volumes of official reports written as an inspector of schools. Less obviously, they comprise all his prose. At their core is his belief that good education is *the* crucial need. Arnold was essentially a great teacher. He has the faults of a teacher—a tendency to repeat himself, to lean too hard on formulaic phrases—and he displays something of the lectern manner at times. He also has the great teacher's virtues, in particular the ability to skillfully convey to us the conviction on which all his arguments are based. This conviction is that the humanist tradition of which he is the expositor can enable the individual man or woman to live life more fully and to change the course of society. He believes that a democratic society can thrive only if its citizens become educated in what he saw as the great Western tradition, "the best that is known and thought." These values, which some readers find elitist, make Arnold both timely and controversial. Arnold fought for these values with the gloves on—kid gloves, his opponents used to say—and he provided a lively exhibition of footwork that is a pleasure to observe. Yet the gracefulness of the display should not obscure the fact that he lands hard blows squarely on his opponents.

Although his lifelong attacks against the inadequacies of Puritanism make Arnold one of the most anti-Victorian figures of his age, behind his attacks is a characteristically Victorian assumption: that the Puritan middle classes *can* be changed, that they are, as we would more clumsily say, educable. In 1852, writing to Clough on the subject of equality (a political objective in which he believed by conviction if not by instinct), Arnold observed: "I am more and more convinced that the world tends to become more comfortable for the mass, and more uncomfortable for those of any natural gift or distinction—and it is as well perhaps that it should be so—for hitherto the gifted have astonished and delighted the world, but not trained or inspired or in any real way changed it." Arnold's gifts as a poet and critic enabled him to do both: to delight the world and to change it.

Isolation. To Marguerite[1]

We were apart; yet, day by day,
I bade my heart more constant be.
I bade it keep the world away,
And grow a home for only thee;
5   Nor feared but thy love likewise grew,
Like mine, each day, more tried, more true.

The fault was grave! I might have known,
What far too soon, alas! I learned—
The heart can bind itself alone,
10   And faith may oft be unreturned.
Self-swayed our feelings ebb and swell—
Thou lov'st no more—Farewell! Farewell!

1. Addressed to a woman Arnold is reputed to have met in Switzerland in the 1840s. It has been commonly assumed that she was French or Swiss; but some recent biographies speculate she might have been Mary Claude, a woman Arnold knew in England at this same period who, though English, had connections with Germany and had translated German prose and verse.

Farewell!—and thou, thou lonely heart,[2]
Which never yet without remorse
15 Even for a moment didst depart
From thy remote and spherèd course
To haunt the place where passions reign—
Back to thy solitude again!

Back with the conscious thrill of shame
20 Which Luna felt, that summer night,
Flash through her pure immortal frame,
When she forsook the starry height
To hang over Endymion's sleep
Upon the pine-grown Latmian steep.[3]
25 Yet she, chaste queen, had never proved
How vain a thing is mortal love,
Wandering in Heaven, far removed.
But thou hast long had place to prove°   test
This truth—to prove, and make thine own:
30 "Thou hast been, shalt be, art, alone."

Or, if not quite alone, yet they
Which touch thee are unmating things—
Ocean and clouds and night and day;
Lorn autumns and triumphant springs;
35 And life, and others' joy and pain,
And love, if love, of happier men.

Of happier men—for they, at least,
Have *dreamed* two human hearts might blend
In one, and were through faith released
40 From isolation without end
Prolonged; nor knew, although not less
Alone than thou, their loneliness.

1849   1857

To Marguerite—Continued

Yes! in the sea of life enisled,°   encircled
With echoing straits between us thrown,
Dotting the shoreless watery wild,
We mortal millions live *alone*.
5 The islands feel the enclasping flow,
And then their endless bounds they know.

But when the moon their hollows lights,
And they are swept by balms of spring,
And in their glens, on starry nights,

2. Presumably the speaker's heart, not Marguerite's.
3. Luna (or Diana), virgin goddess of the moon,
fell in love with Endymion, a handsome shepherd
whom she discovered asleep on Mount Latmos.

10 The nightingales divinely sing;
And lovely notes, from shore to shore,
Across the sounds and channels pour—

Oh! then a longing like despair
Is to their farthest caverns sent;
15 For surely once, they feel, we were
Parts of a single continent!
Now round us spreads the watery plain—
Oh might our marges meet again!

Who ordered that their longing's fire
20 Should be, as soon as kindled, cooled?
Who renders vain their deep desire?—
A God, a God their severance ruled!
And bade betwixt their shores to be
The unplumbed, salt, estranging sea.

1849   1852

The Buried Life

Light flows our war of mocking words, and yet,
Behold, with tears mine eyes are wet!
I feel a nameless sadness o'er me roll.
Yes, yes, we know that we can jest,
5 We know, we know that we can smile!
But there's a something in this breast,
To which thy light words bring no rest,
And thy gay smiles no anodyne.
Give me thy hand, and hush awhile,
10 And turn those limpid eyes on mine,
And let me read there, love! thy inmost soul.

Alas! is even love too weak
To unlock the heart, and let it speak?
Are even lovers powerless to reveal
15 To one another what indeed they feel?
I knew the mass of men concealed
Their thoughts, for fear that if revealed
They would by other men be met
With blank indifference, or with blame reproved;
20 I knew they lived and moved
Tricked° in disguises, alien to the rest   dressed up
Of men, and alien to themselves—and yet
The same heart beats in every human breast!

But we, my love!—doth a like spell benumb
25 Our hearts, our voices?—must we too be dumb?
Ah! well for us, if even we,
Even for a moment, can get free

Our heart, and have our lips unchained;
For that which seals them hath been deep-ordained!

30 Fate, which foresaw
How frivolous a baby man would be—
By what distractions he would be possessed,
How he would pour himself in every strife,
And well-nigh change his own identity—
35 That it might keep from his capricious play
His genuine self, and force him to obey
Even in his own despite his being's law,
Bade through the deep recesses of our breast
The unregarded river of our life
40 Pursue with indiscernible flow its way;
And that we should not see
The buried stream, and seem to be
Eddying at large in blind uncertainty,
Though driving on with it eternally.

45 But often, in the world's most crowded streets,[1]
But often, in the din of strife,
There rises an unspeakable desire
After the knowledge of our buried life;
A thirst to spend our fire and restless force
50 In tracking out our true, original course;
A longing to inquire
Into the mystery of this heart which beats
So wild, so deep in us—to know
Whence our lives come and where they go.
55 And many a man in his own breast then delves,
But deep enough, alas! none ever mines.
And we have been on many thousand lines,
And we have shown, on each, spirit and power;
But hardly have we, for one little hour,
60 Been on our own line, have we been ourselves—
Hardly had skill to utter one of all
The nameless feelings that course through our breast,
But they course on forever unexpressed.
And long we try in vain to speak and act
65 Our hidden self, and what we say and do
Is eloquent, is well—but 'tis not true!
And then we will no more be racked
With inward striving, and demand
Of all the thousand nothings of the hour
70 Their stupefying power;
Ah yes, and they benumb us at our call!
Yet still, from time to time, vague and forlorn,
From the soul's subterranean depth upborne

---

1. This passage, like many others in Arnold's poetry, illustrates William Wordsworth's effect on his writings. In this instance cf. Wordsworth's "Tintern Abbey (1798), lines 25–27: "But oft, in lonely rooms, and 'mid the din / Of towns and cities, I have owed to them, / In hours of weariness, sensations sweet." Cf also The Prelude (1850) 7.626: "How oft amid those overflowing streets . . ."

As from an infinitely distant land,
75 Come airs, and floating echoes, and convey
A melancholy into all our day.[2]

Only—but this is rare—
When a beloved hand is laid in ours,
When, jaded with the rush and glare
80 Of the interminable hours,
Our eyes can in another's eyes read clear,
When our world-deafened ear
Is by the tones of a loved voice caressed—
A bolt is shot back somewhere in our breast,
85 And a lost pulse of feeling stirs again.
The eye sinks inward, and the heart lies plain,
And what we mean, we say, and what we would, we know.
A man becomes aware of his life's flow,
And hears its winding murmur; and he sees
90 The meadows where it glides, the sun, the breeze.

And there arrives a lull in the hot race
Wherein he doth forever chase
That flying and elusive shadow, rest.
An air of coolness plays upon his face,
95 And an unwonted calm pervades his breast.
And then he thinks he knows
The hills where his life rose,
And the sea where it goes.

1852

Memorial Verses[1]

April 1850

Goethe in Weimar sleeps, and Greece,
Long since, saw Byron's struggle cease.
But one such death remained to come;
The last poetic voice is dumb—
5 We stand today by Wordsworth's tomb.

When Byron's eyes were shut in death,
We bowed our head and held our breath.
He taught us little; but our soul
Had *felt* him like the thunder's roll.
10 With shivering heart the strife we saw

---

2. Cf. Wordsworth's "Ode: Intimations of Immortality" (1807), lines 149–51: "Those shadowy recollections, / Which, be they what they may, / Are yet the fountain light of all our day."
1. This elegy was written shortly after Wordsworth had died in April 1850, at the age of eighty. Arnold had known the poet as a man and deeply admired his writings—as is evident not only in this poem but in his late essay "Wordsworth" (1888). Byron,

who died in Greece in 1824, had affected Arnold profoundly in his youth, but later that strenuous "Titanic" (line 14) poetry seemed to him less satisfactory, its value limited by its lack of serenity. He gives his final verdict on Byron in his essay in *Essays in Criticism: Second Series* (1888). He regarded Goethe, who died in 1832, as a great philosophical poet and the most significant man of letters of the early 19th century.

Of passion with eternal law;
And yet with reverential awe
We watched the fount of fiery life
Which served for that Titanic strife.
15 When Goethe's death was told, we said:
Sunk, then, is Europe's sagest head.
Physician of the iron age,
Goethe has done his pilgrimage.
He took the suffering human race,
20 He read each wound, each weakness clear;
And struck his finger on the place,
And said: *Thou ailest here, and here!*
He looked on Europe's dying hour
Of fitful dream and feverish power;
25 His eye plunged down the weltering strife,
The turmoil of expiring life—
He said: *The end is everywhere,*
Art still has truth, take refuge there!
And he was happy, if to know
30 Causes of things, and far below
His feet to see the lurid flow
Of terror, and insane distress,
And headlong fate, be happiness.

And Wordsworth!—Ah, pale ghosts, rejoice!
35 For never has such soothing voice
Been to your shadowy world conveyed,
Since erst,° at morn, some wandering shade   *formerly*
Heard the clear song of Orpheus² come
Through Hades, and the mournful gloom.
40 Wordsworth has gone from us—and ye,
Ah, may ye feel his voice as we!
He too upon a wintry clime
Had fallen—on this iron time
Of doubts, disputes, distractions, fears.
45 He found us when the age had bound
Our souls in its benumbing round;
He spoke, and loosed our heart in tears.
He laid us as we lay at birth
On the cool flowery lap of earth,
50 Smiles broke from us and we had ease;
The hills were round us, and the breeze
Went o'er the sunlit fields again;
Our foreheads felt the wind and rain.
Our youth returned; for there was shed
55 On spirits that had long been dead,
Spirits dried up and closely furled,
The freshness of the early world.

Ah! since dark days still bring to light
Man's prudence and man's fiery might,

2. By means of his beautiful music, the legendary Greek singer Orpheus won his way through Hades as he searched for his dead wife, Eurydice.

60 Time may restore us in his course
Goethe's sage mind and Byron's force;
But where will Europe's latter hour
Again find Wordsworth's healing power?
Others will teach us how to dare,
65 And against fear our breast to steel;
Others will strengthen us to bear—
But who, ah! who, will make us feel?
The cloud of mortal destiny,
Others will front it fearlessly—
70 But who, like him, will put it by?

Keep fresh the grass upon his grave
O Rotha,[3] with thy living wave!
Sing him thy best! for few or none
Hears thy voice right, now he is gone.

1850   1850

Lines Written in Kensington Gardens[1]

In this lone, open glade I lie,
Screened by deep boughs on either hand;
And at its end, to stay the eye,
Those black-crowned, red-boled pine trees stand!

5 Birds here make song, each bird has his,
Across the girdling city's hum.
How green under the boughs it is!
How thick the tremulous sheep-cries come![2]

Sometimes a child will cross the glade
10 To take his nurse his broken toy;
Sometimes a thrush flit overhead
Deep in her unknown day's employ.

Here at my feet what wonders pass,
What endless, active life is here!
15 What blowing daisies, fragrant grass!
An air-stirred forest, fresh and clear.

Scarce fresher is the mountain sod
Where the tired angler lies, stretched out,
And, eased of basket and of rod,
20 Counts his day's spoil, the spotted trout.

In the huge world, which roars hard° by,   °close
Be others happy if they can!

3. A river near Wordsworth's burial place.   2. Sheep sometimes grazed in London parks.
1. A park in the heart of London.

But in my helpless cradle I
Was breathed on by the rural Pan.[3]

25   I, on men's impious uproar hurled,
Think often, as I hear them rave,
That peace has left the upper world
And now keeps only in the grave.

Yet here is peace forever new!
30   When I who watch them am away,
Still all things in this glade go through
The changes of their quiet day.

Then to their happy rest they pass!
The flowers upclose, the birds are fed,
35   The night comes down upon the grass,
The child sleeps warmly in his bed.

Calm soul of all things! make it mine
To feel, amid the city's jar,
That there abides a peace of thine,
40   Man did not make, and cannot mar.

The will to neither strive nor cry,
The power to feel with others give!
Calm, calm me more! nor let me die
Before I have begun to live.

1852

The Scholar Gypsy

The Scholar Gypsy   The story of a seventeenth-century student who left
Oxford and joined a band of gypsies had made a strong impression on Arnold. In the
poem he wistfully imagines that the spirit of this scholar is still to be encountered in
the Cumner countryside near Oxford, having achieved immortality by a serene pursuit
of the secret of human existence. Like Keats's nightingale, the scholar has escaped
"the weariness, the fever, and the fret" of modern life.

At the outset the poet addresses a shepherd who has been helping him in his search
for traces of the scholar. The shepherd is addressed as *you*. After line 61, with the
shift to *thou* and *thy*, the person addressed is the scholar, and the poet thereafter
sometimes uses the pronoun *we* to indicate he is speaking for all humanity of later
generations.

About the setting Arnold wrote to his brother Tom on May 15, 1857: "You alone
of my brothers are associated with that life at Oxford, the *freest* and most delightful
part, perhaps, of my life, when with you and Clough and Walrond I shook off all the
bonds and formalities of the place, and enjoyed the spring of life and that unforgotten
Oxfordshire and Berkshire country. Do you remember a poem of mine called 'The
Scholar Gipsy'? It was meant to fix the remembrance of those delightful wanderings
of ours in the Cumner Hills."

The passage from Joseph Glanvill's *Vanity of Dogmatizing* (1661) that inspired the
poem was included by Arnold as a note:

3. In Greek mythology the god of woods and pastures.

There was very lately a lad in the University of Oxford, who was by his poverty forced to leave his studies there; and at last to join himself to a company of vagabond gypsies. Among these extravagant people, by the insinuating subtilty of his carriage, he quickly got so much of their love and esteem as that they discovered to him their mystery. After he had been a pretty while exercised in the trade, there chanced to ride by a couple of scholars, who had formerly been of his acquaintance. They quickly spied out their old friend among the gypsies; and he gave them an account of the necessity which drove him to that kind of life, and told them that the people he went with were not such imposters as they were taken for, but that they had a traditional kind of learning among them, and could do wonders by the power of imagination, their fancy binding that of others: that himself had learned much of their art, and when he had compassed the whole secret, he intended, he said, to leave their company, and give the world an account of what he had learned.

The Scholar Gypsy

Go, for they call you, shepherd, from the hill;
Go, shepherd, and untie the wattled cotes![1]
No longer leave thy wistful flock unfed,
Nor let thy bawling fellows rack their throats,
5   Nor the cropped herbage shoot another head.
    But when the fields are still,
And the tired men and dogs all gone to rest,
And only the white sheep are sometimes seen
Cross and recross the strips of moon-blanched green,
10   Come, shepherd, and again begin the quest!

Here, where the reaper was at work of late—
In this high field's dark corner, where he leaves
His coat, his basket, and his earthen cruse,[2]
And in the sun all morning binds the sheaves,
15   Then here, at noon, comes back his stores to use—
    Here will I sit and wait,
While to my ear from uplands far away
The bleating of the folded° flocks is borne,   *penned up*
With distant cries of reapers in the corn[3]—
20   All the live murmur of a summer's day.

Screened is this nook o'er the high, half-reaped field,
And here till sundown, shepherd! will I be.
Through the thick corn the scarlet poppies peep,
And round green roots and yellowing stalks I see
25   Pale pink convolvulus in tendrils creep;
    And air-swept lindens yield
Their scent, and rustle down their perfumed showers
Of bloom on the bent grass where I am laid,
And bower me from the August sun with shade;
30   And the eye travels down to Oxford's towers.

1. Sheepfolds woven from sticks.
2. Pot or jug for carrying his drink.

3. Grain or wheat.

And near me on the grass lies Glanvill's book—
    Come, let me read the oft-read tale again!
        The story of the Oxford scholar poor,
        Of pregnant parts⁴ and quick inventive brain,
35   Who, tired of knocking at preferment's door,
            One summer morn forsook
        His friends, and went to learn the gypsy lore,
        And roamed the world with that wild brotherhood,
        And came, as most men deemed, to little good,
40   But came to Oxford and his friends no more.

But once, years after, in the country lanes,
    Two scholars, whom at college erst° he knew,   long ago
        Met him, and of his way of life inquired;
        Whereat he answered, that the gypsy crew,
45   His mates, had arts to rule as they desired
            The workings of men's brains,
        And they can bind them to what thoughts they will.
        "And I," he said, "the secret of their art,
        When fully learned, will to the world impart;
50   But it needs heaven-sent moments for this skill."

This said, he left them, and returned no more.—
    But rumors hung about the countryside,
        That the lost Scholar long was seen to stray,
        Seen by rare glimpses, pensive and tongue-tied,
55   In hat of antique shape, and cloak of grey,
            The same the gypsies wore.
        Shepherds had met him on the Hurst⁵ in spring;
        At some lone alehouse in the Berkshire moors,
        On the warm ingle-bench, the smock-frocked boors⁶
60   Had found him seated at their entering,

But, 'mid their drink and clatter, he would fly.
    And I myself seem half to know thy looks,
        And put the shepherds, wanderer! on thy trace;
        And boys who in lone wheatfields scare the rooks⁷
65   I ask if thou hast passed their quiet place;
            Or in my boat I lie
        Moored to the cool bank in the summer heats,
        'Mid wide grass meadows which the sunshine fills,
        And watch the warm, green-muffled Cumner hills,
70   And wonder if thou haunt'st their shy retreats.

For most, I know, thou lov'st retired ground!
    Thee at the ferry Oxford riders blithe,
        Returning home on summer nights, have met
        Crossing the stripling Thames at Bab-lock-hithe,⁸

4. Of rich conception, many ideas.
5. A hill near Oxford. All the place-names in the poem (except those in the final two stanzas) refer to the countryside near Oxford.
6. Rustics. "Ingle-bench": fireside bench.

7. Crows.
8. Or Bablock Hythe (a *hithe* or *hythe* is a landing place on a river). "The stripling Thames": the narrow upper reaches of the river before it broadens out to its full width.

75   Trailing in the cool stream thy fingers wet,
    As the punt's rope chops round;⁹
   And leaning backward in a pensive dream,
   And fostering in thy lap a heap of flowers
   Plucked in shy fields and distant Wychwood bowers,
80   And thine eyes resting on the moonlit stream.

   And then they land, and thou art seen no more!—
   Maidens, who from the distant hamlets come
    To dance around the Fyfield elm in May,
   Oft through the darkening fields have seen thee roam,
85   Or cross a stile into the public way.
     Oft thou hast given them store
   Of flowers—the frail-leafed, white anemone,
   Dark bluebells drenched with dews of summer eves,
   And purple orchises with spotted leaves—
90   But none hath words she can report of thee.

   And, above Godstow Bridge, when hay time's here
   In June, and many a scythe in sunshine flames,
    Men who through those wide fields of breezy grass
   Where black-winged swallows haunt the glittering Thames,
95   To bathe in the abandoned lasher¹ pass,
     Have often passed thee near
   Sitting upon the river bank o'ergrown;
   Marked thine outlandish garb, thy figure spare,
   Thy dark vague eyes, and soft abstracted air—
100   But, when they came from bathing, thou wast gone!

   At some lone homestead in the Cumner hills,
   Where at her open door the housewife darns,
    Thou hast been seen, or hanging on a gate
   To watch the threshers in the mossy barns.
105   Children, who early range these slopes and late
     For cresses from the rills,
   Have known thee eying, all an April day,
   The springing pastures and the feeding kine;°   *cattle*
   And marked thee, when the stars come out and shine,
110   Through the long dewy grass move slow away.

   In autumn, on the skirts of Bagley Wood—
   Where most the gypsies by the turf-edged way
    Pitch their smoked tents, and every bush you see
   With scarlet patches tagged and shreds of grey,
115   Above the forest ground called Thessaly—
     The blackbird, picking food,
   Sees thee, nor stops his meal, nor fears at all;
   So often has he known thee past him stray,

9. The scholar's flat-bottomed boat ("punt") is tied up by a rope at the riverbank near the ferry crossing like the speaker's boat (in the previous stanza), which was "moored to the cool bank." The motion of the boat as it is stirred by the current of the river causes the chopping sound of the rope in the water.
1. Water that spills over a dam or weir.

Rapt, twirling in thy hand a withered spray,
120   And waiting for the spark from heaven to fall.

And once, in winter, on the causeway chill
    Where home through flooded fields foot-travelers go,
    Have I not passed thee on the wooden bridge,
    Wrapped in thy cloak and battling with the snow,
125   Thy face tow'rd Hinksey and its wintry ridge?
    And thou hast climbed the hill,
    And gained the white brow of the Cumner range;
    Turned once to watch, while thick the snowflakes fall,
    The line of festal light in Christ Church hall[2]—
130   Then sought thy straw in some sequestered grange.°   *farmhouse*

But what—I dream! Two hundred years are flown
    Since first thy story ran through Oxford halls,
    And the grave Glanvill did the tale inscribe
    That thou wert wandered from the studious walls
135   To learn strange arts, and join a gypsy tribe;
    And thou from earth art gone
    Long since, and in some quiet churchyard laid—
    Some country nook, where o'er thy unknown grave
    Tall grasses and white flowering nettles wave,
140   Under a dark, red-fruited yew tree's shade.

—No, no, thou hast not felt the lapse of hours!
    For what wears out the life of mortal men?
    'Tis that from change to change their being rolls;
    'Tis that repeated shocks, again, again,
145   Exhaust the energy of strongest souls
    And numb the elastic powers.
    Till having used our nerves with bliss and teen,°   *vexation*
    And tired upon a thousand schemes our wit,
    To the just-pausing Genius[3] we remit
150   Our worn-out life, and are—what we have been.

Thou hast not lived, why should'st thou perish, so?
    Thou hadst *one* aim, *one* business, *one* desire;
    Else wert thou long since numbered with the dead!
    Else hadst thou spent, like other men, thy fire!
155   The generations of thy peers are fled,
    And we ourselves shall go;
    But thou possessest an immortal lot,
    And we imagine thee exempt from age
    And living as thou liv'st on Glanvill's page,
160   Because thou hadst—what we, alas! have not.

For early didst thou leave the world, with powers
    Fresh, undiverted to the world without,
    Firm to their mark, not spent on other things;
    Free from the sick fatigue, the languid doubt,

2. The dining hall of this Oxford college.
3. Perhaps the spirit of the universe, which pauses briefly to receive back the life given to us. (In Roman mythology a *genius* was an attendant spirit.)

165   Which much to have tried, in much been baffled, brings.
    O life unlike to ours!
    Who fluctuate idly without term or scope,
    Of whom each strives, nor knows for what he strives,
    And each half[4] lives a hundred different lives;
170   Who wait like thee, but not, like thee, in hope.

    Thou waitest for the spark from heaven! and we,
    Light half-believers of our casual creeds,
    Who never deeply felt, nor clearly willed,
    Whose insight never has borne fruit in deeds,
175   Whose vague resolves never have been fulfilled;
    For whom each year we see
    Breeds new beginnings, disappointments new;
    Who hesitate and falter life away,
    And lose tomorrow the ground won today—
180   Ah! do not we, wanderer! await it too?

    Yes, we await it!—but it still delays,
    And then we suffer! and amongst us one,[5]
    Who most has suffered, takes dejectedly
    His seat upon the intellectual throne;
185   And all his store of sad experience he
    Lays bare of wretched days;
    Tells us his misery's birth and growth and signs,
    And how the dying spark of hope was fed,
    And how the breast was soothed, and how the head,
190   And all his hourly varied anodynes.

    This for our wisest! and we others pine,
    And wish the long unhappy dream would end,
    And waive all claim to bliss, and try to bear;
    With close-lipped patience for our only friend,
195   Sad patience, too near neighbor to despair—
    But none has hope like thine!
    Thou through the fields and through the woods dost stray,
    Roaming the countryside, a truant boy,
    Nursing thy project in unclouded joy,
200   And every doubt long blown by time away.

    O born in days when wits were fresh and clear,
    And life ran gaily as the sparkling Thames;
    Before this strange disease of modern life,
    With its sick hurry, its divided aims,
205   Its heads o'ertaxed, its palsied hearts, was rife—
    Fly hence, our contact fear!
    Still fly, plunge deeper in the bowering wood!
    Averse, as Dido did with gesture stern
    From her false friend's approach in Hades turn,[6]
210   Wave us away, and keep thy solitude!

---

4. An adverb modifying "lives."
5. Probably Goethe, although possibly referring to Tennyson, whose *In Memoriam* had appeared in 1850.

6. Dido committed suicide after her lover, Aeneas, deserted her. When he later encountered her in Hades, she silently turned away from him (see Virgil's *Aeneid*, book 6).

Still nursing the unconquerable hope,
  Still clutching the inviolable shade,
    With a free, onward impulse brushing through,
  By night, the silvered branches of the glade—
215   Far on the forest skirts, where none pursue.
        On some mild pastoral slope
    Emerge, and resting on the moonlit pales
    Freshen thy flowers as in former years
    With dew, or listen with enchanted ears,
220   From the dark dingles,° to the nightingales!   *small deep valleys*

But fly our paths, our feverish contact fly!
  For strong the infection of our mental strife,
    Which, though it gives no bliss, yet spoils for rest;
  And we should win thee from thy own fair life,
225   Like us distracted, and like us unblest.
        Soon, soon thy cheer would die,
    Thy hopes grow timorous, and unfixed thy powers,
    And thy clear aims be cross and shifting made;
    And then thy glad perennial youth would fade,
230   Fade, and grow old at last, and die like ours.

Then fly our greetings, fly our speech and smiles!
  —As some grave Tyrian trader, from the sea,
    Descried at sunrise an emerging prow
  Lifting the cool-haired creepers stealthily,
235   The fringes of a southward-facing brow
        Among the Aegean isles;
    And saw the merry Grecian coaster come,
    Freighted with amber grapes, and Chian wine,
    Green, bursting figs, and tunnies° steeped in brine—   *tuna fish*
240   And knew the intruders on his ancient home,

The young lighthearted masters of the waves—
  And snatched his rudder, and shook out more sail;
    And day and night held on indignantly
  O'er the blue Midland waters with the gale,
245   Betwixt the Syrtes[7] and soft Sicily,
        To where the Atlantic raves
    Outside the western straits; and unbent sails
    There, where down cloudy cliffs, through sheets of foam,
    Shy traffickers, the dark Iberians[8] come;
250   And on the beach undid his corded bales.[9]

1853

---

7. Shoals off the coast of North Africa.
8. Dark inhabitants of Spain and Portugal—perhaps associated with gypsies.
9. The elaborate simile of the final two stanzas has been variously interpreted. The trader from Tyre (a Phoenician city, on the coast of what is now Lebanon) is disconcerted to see a new business rival, "the merry Grecian coaster," emerging from one of his habitual trading ports in the Greek islands. Like the Scholar Gypsy, when similarly intruded on by hearty extroverts, he resolves to flee and seek a less competitive sphere of life.

The reference (line 249) to the Iberians as "*shy* traffickers" (traders) is explained by Kenneth Allott as having been derived from Herodotus's *History* (4.196). Herodotus describes a distinctive method

[handwritten: Contemporary, Jump to stanzas.]

Dover Beach

[handwritten: Read it slow!]

The sea is calm tonight.
The tide is full, the moon lies fair
Upon the straits—on the French coast the light

[handwritten: Physical]

Gleams and is gone; the cliffs of England stand,
5   Glimmering and vast, out in the tranquil bay.

[handwritten: ideas]

Come to the window, sweet is the night air!
Only, from the long line of spray
Where the sea meets the moon-blanched land,
Listen! you hear the grating roar
10   Of pebbles which the waves draw back, and fling,
At their return, up the high strand,
Begin, and cease, and then again begin,
With tremulous cadence slow, and bring
The eternal note of sadness in.

15   Sophocles long ago
Heard it on the Aegean, and it brought
Into his mind the turbid ebb and flow
Of human misery;[1] we
Find also in the sound a thought,
20   Hearing it by this distant northern sea.

The Sea of Faith
Was once, too, at the full, and round earth's shore
Lay like the folds of a bright girdle furled.[2]
But now I only hear

[handwritten: Come to the window, love, look out with me.]

25   Its melancholy, long, withdrawing roar,
Retreating, to the breath
Of the night wind, down the vast edges drear
And naked shingles[3] of the world.

[handwritten: the vision is beautiful, but what you hear is misery.]

Ah, love, let us be true

[handwritten: A pretty little lie is what we see.]

30   To one another! for the world, which seems
To lie before us like a land of dreams,
So various, so beautiful, so new,
Hath really neither joy, nor love, nor light,

---

of selling goods established by merchants from Carthage who used to sail through the Strait of Gibraltar to trade with the inhabitants of the coast of West Africa. The Carthaginians would leave bales of their merchandise on display along the beaches and, without having seen their prospective customers, would return to their ships. The shy natives would then come down from their inland hiding places and set gold beside the bales they wished to buy. When the natives withdrew in their turn, the Carthaginians would return to the beach and decide whether payments were adequate, a process repeated until agreement was reached. On the Atlantic coasts this method of bargaining persisted into the 19th century. As William Beloe, a translator of the ancient Greek historian, noted in 1844: "In this manner they transact their exchange without seeing one another, or without the least

instance of dishonesty . . . on either side." For the solitary Tyrian trader such a procedure, with its avoidance of "contact" (line 221), would have been especially appropriate.

1. A reference to a chorus in *Antigone* that compares human sorrow to the sound of the waves moving the sand beneath them (lines 585–91).
2. This difficult line means, in general, that at high tide the sea envelops the land closely. Its forces are "gathered" up (to use William Wordsworth's term) like the "folds" of bright clothing ("girdle") that have been compressed ("furled"). At ebb tide, as the sea retreats, it is unfurled and spread out. It still surrounds the shoreline but not as an "enclasping flow" (as in "To Marguerite—Continued").
3. Beaches covered with pebbles.

we are living in a confused, strife world

Nor certitude, nor peace, nor help for pain;
35 And we are here as on a darkling plain *simily*
Swept with confused alarms of struggle and flight,
Where ignorant armies[4] clash by night.

ca. 1851

What do we have to believe in but each other?

1867

Stanzas from the Grande Chartreuse[1]

A crisis of what we have faith in. Nothing, but at least we have each other in this world.

Through Alpine meadows soft-suffused
With rain, where thick the crocus blows,
Past the dark forges long disused,
The mule track from Saint Laurent goes.
5 The bridge is crossed, and slow we ride,
Through forest, up the mountainside.

The autumnal evening darkens round,
The wind is up, and drives the rain;
While, hark! far down, with strangled sound
10 Doth the Dead Guier's[2] stream complain,
Where that wet smoke, among the woods,
Over his boiling cauldron broods.

Swift rush the spectral vapors white
Past limestone scars° with ragged pines,   *cliffs*
15 Showing—then blotting from our sight!—
Halt—through the cloud-drift something shines!
High in the valley, wet and drear,
The huts of Courrerie appear.

Strike leftward! cries our guide; and higher
20 Mounts up the stony forest way.
At last the encircling trees retire;
Look! through the showery twilight grey
What pointed roofs are these advance?—
A palace of the Kings of France?

25 Approach, for what we seek is here!
Alight, and sparely sup, and wait

4. Perhaps alluding to conflicts in Arnold's own time such as occurred during the revolutions of 1848 in Europe, or at the Siege of Rome by the French in 1849 (the poem's date of composition is unknown, although generally assumed to be 1851). But the passage also refers back to another battle, one that occurred more than two thousand years earlier when an Athenian army was attempting an invasion of Sicily at nighttime. As this "night battle" was described by the ancient Greek historian Thucydides in his *History of the Peloponnesian War* (7.44), the invaders became confused by darkness and slaughtered many of their own men. Hence "ignorant armies."
1. A monastery situated high in the French Alps.

It was established in 1084 by Saint Bruno, founder of the Carthusians (line 30), whose austere regimen of solitary contemplation, fasting, and religious exercises (lines 37–44) had remained virtually unchanged for centuries. Arnold visited the site on September 7, 1851, accompanied by his bride. His account may be compared with that by William Wordsworth (*Prelude* [1850] 6.414–88), who had made a similar visit in 1790.
2. The Guiers Mort River flows down from the monastery and joins the Guiers Vif in the valley below; in French, Mort and Vif mean "dead" and "alive," respectively. Wordsworth speaks of the two rivers as "the sister streams of Life and Death."

For rest in this outbuilding near;
Then cross the sward and reach that gate.
Knock; pass the wicket!° Thou art come   *gate*
30   To the Carthusians' world-famed home.

The silent courts, where night and day
Into their stone-carved basins cold
The splashing icy fountains play—
The humid corridors behold!
35   Where, ghostlike in the deepening night,
Cowled forms brush by in gleaming white.

The chapel, where no organ's peal
Invests the stern and naked prayer—
With penitential cries they kneel
40   And wrestle; rising then, with bare
And white uplifted faces stand,
Passing the Host from hand to hand;[3]

Each takes, and then his visage wan
Is buried in his cowl once more.
45   The cells!—the suffering Son of Man
Upon the wall—the knee-worn floor—
And where they sleep, that wooden bed,
Which shall their coffin be, when dead![4]

The library, where tract and tome
50   Not to feed priestly pride are there,
To hymn the conquering march of Rome,
Nor yet to amuse, as ours are!
They paint of souls the inner strife,
Their drops of blood, their death in life.

55   The garden, overgrown—yet mild,
See, fragrant herbs[5] are flowering there!
Strong children of the Alpine wild
Whose culture is the brethren's care;
Of human tasks their only one,
60   And cheerful works beneath the sun.

Those halls, too, destined to contain
Each its own pilgrim-host of old,
From England, Germany, or Spain—
All are before me! I behold
65   The House, the Brotherhood austere!
—And what am I, that I am here?

3. Arnold, during his short visit, may not actually
have witnessed Mass in the monastery. During the
service the consecrated wafer ("the Host") is not
passed from the hand of the officiating priest to
the hands of the communicant (as is the practice
in Arnold's own Anglican Church) but is placed
directly on the tongue of the communicant (who

kneels rather than stands).
4. A Carthusian is buried on a wooden plank but
does not sleep in a coffin.
5. From which the liqueur Chartreuse is manufactured. Sales of this liqueur provide the principal
revenues for the monastery's upkeep.

For rigorous teachers seized my youth,
And purged its faith, and trimmed its fire,
Showed me the high, white star of Truth,
70   There bade me gaze, and there aspire.
Even now their whispers pierce the gloom:
What dost thou in this living tomb?

Forgive me, masters of the mind![6]
At whose behest I long ago
75   So much unlearnt, so much resigned—
I come not here to be your foe!
I seek these anchorites, not in ruth,[7]
To curse and to deny your truth;

Not as their friend, or child, I speak!
80   But as, on some far northern strand,
Thinking of his own Gods, a Greek
In pity and mournful awe might stand
Before some fallen Runic stone[8]—
For both were faiths, and both are gone.

85   Wandering between two worlds, one dead,
The other powerless to be born,
With nowhere yet to rest my head,
Like these, on earth I wait forlorn.
Their faith, my tears, the world deride—
90   I come to shed them at their side.

Oh, hide me in your gloom profound,
Ye solemn seats of holy pain!
Take me, cowled forms, and fence me round,
Till I possess my soul again;
95   Till free my thoughts before me roll,
Not chafed by hourly false control!

For the world cries your faith is now
But a dead time's exploded dream;
My melancholy, sciolists[9] say,
100   Is a passed mode, an outworn theme—
As if the world had ever had
A faith, or sciolists been sad!

Ah, if it *be* passed, take away,
At least, the restlessness, the pain;
105   Be man henceforth no more a prey
To these out-dated stings again!

---

6. Writers whose insistence on testing religious beliefs in the light of fact and reason persuaded Arnold that faith in Christianity (especially in the Roman Catholic or Anglo-Catholic forms) was no longer tenable in the modern world.
7. Remorse for having adopted the rationalist view of Christianity.
8. A monument inscribed in Teutonic letters (runes), emblematic of a Nordic religion that has become extinct. The relic reminds the Greek that his own religion is likewise dying and will soon be extinct (see "Preface" to *Poems* [1853], p. 1374).
9. Superficial-minded persons who pretend to know the answers to all questions.

The nobleness of grief is gone—
Ah, leave us not the fret alone!

But—if you[1] cannot give us ease—
110   Last of the race of them who grieve
Here leave us to die out with these
Last of the people who believe!
Silent, while years engrave the brow;
Silent—the best are silent now.

115   Achilles[2] ponders in his tent,
The kings of modern thought[3] are dumb;
Silent they are, though not content,
And wait to see the future come.
They have the grief men had of yore,
120   But they contend and cry no more.

Our fathers[4] watered with their tears
This sea of time whereon we sail,
Their voices were in all men's ears
Who passed within their puissant hail.
125   Still the same ocean round us raves,
But we stand mute, and watch the waves.

For what availed it, all the noise
And outcry of the former men?—
Say, have their sons achieved more joys,
130   Say, is life lighter now than then?
The sufferers died, they left their pain—
The pangs which tortured them remain.

What helps it now, that Byron bore,
With haughty scorn which mocked the smart,
135   Through Europe to the Aetolian shore[5]
The pageant of his bleeding heart?
That thousands counted every groan,
And Europe made his woe her own?

What boots° it, Shelley! that the breeze   *avails*
140   Carried thy lovely wail away,
Musical through Italian trees
Which fringe thy soft blue Spezzian bay?[6]
Inheritors of thy distress
Have restless hearts one throb the less?

---

1. It is not clear whether the speaker has resumed addressing his "rigorous teachers" (line 67) or (as would seem more likely) a combination of the sciolists, who scorn the speaker's melancholy, and the worldly, who scorn the faith of the monks. See his address to the "sons of the world" (lines 161–68). 2. Until the death of Patroclus, he refused to participate in the Trojan War; hence he is similar to modern intellectual leaders who refuse to speak out about their frustrated sense of alienation.

3. Variously but never satisfactorily identified as John Henry Newman or Thomas Carlyle (the latter was said to have preached the gospel of silence in forty volumes). Another advocate of stoical silence was the French poet Alfred de Vigny (1797–1863). 4. Predecessors among the Romantic writers such as Byron. 5. Region in Greece where Byron died. 6. The Gulf of Spezia in Italy, where Percy Bysshe Shelley was drowned.

145 Or are we easier, to have read,
O Obermann![7] the sad, stern page,
Which tells us how thou hidd'st thy head
From the fierce tempest of thine age
In the lone brakes° of Fontainebleau,　　　　　*thickets*
150 Or chalets near the Alpine snow?

Ye slumber in your silent grave!
The world, which for an idle day
Grace to your mood of sadness gave,
Long since hath flung her weeds° away.　　　*mourning clothes*
155 The eternal trifler[8] breaks your spell;
But we—we learnt your lore too well!

Years hence, perhaps, may dawn an age,
More fortunate, alas! than we,
Which without hardness will be sage,
160 And gay without frivolity.
Sons of the world, oh, speed those years;
But, while we wait, allow our tears!

Allow them! We admire with awe
The exulting thunder of your race;
165 You give the universe your law,
You triumph over time and space!
Your pride of life, your tireless powers,
We laud them, but they are not ours.

We are like children reared in shade
170 Beneath some old-world abbey wall,
Forgotten in a forest glade,
And secret from the eyes of all.
Deep, deep the greenwood round them waves,
Their abbey, and its close° of graves!　　　*enclosure*

175 But, where the road runs near the stream,
Oft through the trees they catch a glance
Of passing troops in the sun's beam—
Pennon, and plume, and flashing lance!
Forth to the world those soldiers fare,
180 To life, to cities, and to war!

And through the wood, another way,
Faint bugle notes from far are borne,
Where hunters gather, staghounds bay,
Round some fair forest-lodge at morn.
185 Gay dames are there, in sylvan green;
Laughter and cries—those notes between!

7. Melancholy hero of *Obermann* (1804), a novel　　8. The sciolist, as in line 99.
by the French writer Étienne Sénancour.

The banners flashing through the trees
Make their blood dance and chain their eyes;
That bugle music on the breeze
190   Arrests them with a charmed surprise.
Banner by turns and bugle woo:
Ye shy recluses, follow too!

O children, what do ye reply?—
"Action and pleasure, will ye roam
195   Through these secluded dells to cry
And call us?—but too late ye come!
Too late for us your call ye blow,
Whose bent° was taken long ago.   natural inclination

"Long since we pace this shadowed nave;
200   We watch those yellow tapers shine,
Emblems of hope over the grave,
In the high altar's depth divine;
The organ carries to our ear
Its accents of another sphere.[9]

205   "Fenced early in this cloistral round
Of reverie, of shade, of prayer,
How should we grow in other ground?
How can we flower in foreign air?
—Pass, banners, pass, and bugles, cease;
210   And leave our desert to its peace!"

1852(?)   1855

Preface to *Poems* (1853)

In two small volumes of poems, published anonymously, one in 1849, the
other in 1852, many of the poems which compose the present volume have
already appeared. The rest are now published for the first time.

I have, in the present collection, omitted the poem from which the volume
published in 1852 took its title.[1] I have done so, not because the subject of it
was a Sicilian Greek born between two and three thousand years ago, although
many persons would think this a sufficient reason. Neither have I done so
because I had, in my own opinion, failed in the delineation which I intended

---

9. The organ music is from the abbey in the greenwood (line 174), as contrasted with the monastery
on the mountaintop in which there is no organ
(line 37).
1. *Empedocles on Etna*, the long poem that supplied the title for Arnold's second collection of
poems, portrays the disillusioned reflections of the
Greek philosopher and scientist Empedocles and
culminates in the speaker's suicide on Mount Etna
in Sicily, in the 5th century B.C.E. Because of his
dissatisfaction with what he calls the "morbid"
tone of *Empedocles on Etna*, Arnold continued to
exclude it from his volumes of poetry until 1867,

when he reprinted it at the request, he said, "of a
man of genius, whom it had the honor and good
fortune to interest—Mr. Robert Browning." It
should be noted that in the arguments developed
in the preface against his own poem (and against
19th-century poetry in general), Arnold is exclusively concerned with narrative and dramatic
poetry. The preface, as he remarked in 1854,
"leaves . . . untouched the question, how far, and
in what manner, the opinions there expressed
respecting the choice of subjects apply to lyric
poetry; that region of the poetical field which is
chiefly cultivated at present."

to effect. I intended to delineate the feelings of one of the last of the Greek religious philosophers, one of the family of Orpheus and Musaeus,[2] having survived his fellows, living on into a time when the habits of Greek thought and feeling had begun fast to change, character to dwindle, the influence of the Sophists[3] to prevail. Into the feelings of a man so situated there entered much that we are accustomed to consider as exclusively modern; how much, the fragments of Empedocles[4] himself which remain to us are sufficient at least to indicate. What those who are familiar only with the great monuments of early Greek genius suppose to be its exclusive characteristics, have disappeared; the calm, the cheerfulness, the disinterested objectivity have disappeared; the dialogue of the mind with itself has commenced; modern problems have presented themselves, we hear already the doubts, we witness the discouragement, of Hamlet and of Faust.[5]

The representation of such a man's feelings must be interesting, if consistently drawn. We all naturally take pleasure, says Aristotle, in any imitation or representation whatever;[6] this is the basis of our love of poetry; and we take pleasure in them, he adds, because all knowledge is naturally agreeable to us; not to the philosopher only, but to mankind at large. Every representation therefore which is consistently drawn may be supposed to be interesting, inasmuch as it gratifies this natural interest in knowledge of all kinds. What is *not* interesting is that which does not add to our knowledge of any kind; that which is vaguely conceived and loosely drawn; a representation which is general, indeterminate, and faint, instead of being particular, precise, and firm.

Any accurate representation may therefore be expected to be interesting; but, if the representation be a poetical one, more than this is demanded. It is demanded, not only that it shall interest, but also that it shall inspirit and rejoice the reader; that it shall convey a charm, and infuse delight. For the muses, as Hesiod says, were born that they might be "a forgetfulness of evils, and a truce from cares":[7] and it is not enough that the poet should add to the knowledge of men, it is required of him also that he should add to their happiness. "All art," says Schiller, "is dedicated to Joy, and there is no higher and no more serious problem, than how to make men happy. The right art is that alone, which creates the highest enjoyment."[8]

A poetical work, therefore, is not yet justified when it has been shown to be an accurate, and therefore interesting representation; it has to be shown also that it is a representation from which men can derive enjoyment. In presence of the most tragic circumstances, represented in a work of Art, the feeling of enjoyment, as is well known, may still subsist; the representation of the most utter calamity, of the liveliest anguish, is not sufficient to destroy it; the more tragic the situation, the deeper becomes the enjoyment; and the situation is more tragic in proportion as it becomes more terrible.

What then are the situations, from the representation of which, though

2. Pupil of the poet and musician Orpheus. The latter was the legendary founder of the Orphic religion that flourished in 6th-century B.C.E. Greece and later declined.
3. Greek rhetoricians, often criticized because of their reputed emphasis on winning arguments rather than on truth or knowledge.
4. Empedocles' writings (medical and scientific treatises in verse) have survived only in fragments.
5. Johann Faustus (ca. 1480–ca. 1540), a German teacher and magician who became the subject of

many stories and folktales, and later the hero of the plays by Christopher Marlowe (1604) and Goethe (1808–32).
6. See Aristotle's *Poetics*, especially 1, 2, 4, 7, 14.
7. From *Theogony* 52–56, by the Greek poet Hesiod (ca. 700 B.C.E.).
8. J. C. F. von Schiller's "On the Use of the Chorus in Tragedy," prefatory essay to *The Bride of Messina* (1803). Schiller (1759–1805) was a German poet, playwright, and critic; see *Friedrich Schiller's Works* (1903) 8.224.

accurate, no poetical enjoyment can be derived? They are those in which the suffering finds no vent in action; in which a continuous state of mental distress is prolonged, unrelieved by incident, hope, or resistance; in which there is everything to be endured, nothing to be done. In such situations there is inevitably something morbid, in the description of them something monotonous. When they occur in actual life, they are painful, not tragic; the representation of them in poetry is painful also.

To this class of situations, poetically faulty as it appears to me, that of Empedocles, as I have endeavored to represent him, belongs; and I have therefore excluded the poem from the present collection.

And why, it may be asked, have I entered into this explanation respecting a matter so unimportant as the admission or exclusion of the poem in question? I have done so, because I was anxious to avow that the sole reason for its exclusion was that which has been stated above; and that it has not been excluded in deference to the opinion which many critics of the present day appear to entertain against subjects chosen from distant times and countries: against the choice, in short, of any subjects but modern ones.

"The poet," it is said, and by an intelligent critic, "the poet who would really fix the public attention must leave the exhausted past, and draw his subjects from matters of present import, and *therefore* both of interest and novelty."[9]

Now this view I believe to be completely false. It is worth examining, inasmuch as it is a fair sample of a class of critical dicta everywhere current at the present day, having a philosophical form and air, but no real basis in fact; and which are calculated to vitiate the judgment of readers of poetry, while they exert, so far as they are adopted, a misleading influence on the practice of those who write it.

What are the eternal objects of poetry, among all nations and at all times? They are actions; human actions; possessing an inherent interest in themselves, and which are to be communicated in an interesting manner by the art of the poet.[1] Vainly will the latter imagine that he has everything in his own power; that he can make an intrinsically inferior action equally delightful with a more excellent one by his treatment of it; he may indeed compel us to admire his skill, but his work will possess, within itself, an incurable defect.

The poet, then, has in the first place to select an excellent action; and what actions are the most excellent? Those, certainly, which most powerfully appeal to the great primary human affections: to those elementary feelings which subsist permanently in the race, and which are independent of time. These feelings are permanent and the same; that which interests them is permanent and the same also. The modernness or antiquity of an action, therefore, has nothing to do with its fitness for poetical representation; this depends upon its inherent qualities. To the elementary part of our nature, to our passions, that which is great and passionate is eternally interesting; and interesting solely in proportion to its greatness and to its passion. A great human action of a thousand years ago is more interesting to it than a smaller human action of today, even though upon the representation of this last the most consummate skill may have been expended, and though it has the advantage of appealing by its modern language, familiar manners, and contemporary allusions, to all our transient feelings and interests. These, however, have no right to

---

9. In the *Spectator* of April 2nd, 1853. The words quoted were not used with reference to poems of mine [Arnold's note]. According to Arnold, the "intelligent critic" was R. S. Rintoul, editor of the *Spectator*.
1. Cf. Aristotle's *Poetics* 6.

demand of a poetical work that it shall satisfy them; their claims are to be directed elsewhere. Poetical works belong to the domain of our permanent passions; let them interest these, and the voice of all subordinate claims upon them is at once silenced.

Achilles, Prometheus, Clytemnestra, Dido—what modern poem presents personages as interesting, even to us moderns, as these personages of an "exhausted past"? We have the domestic epic dealing with the details of modern life which pass daily under our eyes;[2] we have poems representing modern personages in contact with the problems of modern life, moral, intellectual, and social; these works have been produced by poets the most distinguished of their nation and time; yet I fearlessly assert that *Hermann and Dorothea, Childe Harold, Jocelyn, The Excursion*,[3] leave the reader cold in comparison with the effect produced upon him by the latter books of the *Iliad*, by the *Oresteia*, or by the episode of Dido.[4] And why is this? Simply because in the three last-named cases the action is greater, the personages nobler, the situations more intense: and this is the true basis of the interest in a poetical work, and this alone.

It may be urged, however, that past actions may be interesting in themselves, but that they are not to be adopted by the modern poet, because it is impossible for him to have them clearly present to his own mind, and he cannot therefore feel them deeply, nor represent them forcibly. But this is not necessarily the case. The externals of a past action, indeed, he cannot know with the precision of a contemporary; but his business is with its essentials. The outward man of Oedipus or of Macbeth, the houses in which they lived, the ceremonies of their courts, he cannot accurately figure to himself; but neither do they essentially concern him. His business is with their inward man; with their feelings and behavior in certain tragic situations, which engage their passions as men; these have in them nothing local and casual; they are as accessible to the modern poet as to a contemporary.

The date of an action, then, signifies nothing: the action itself, its selection and construction, this is what is all-important. This the Greeks understood far more clearly than we do. The radical difference between their poetical theory and ours consists, as it appears to me, in this: that, with them, the poetical character of the action in itself, and the conduct of it, was the first consideration; with us, attention is fixed mainly on the value of the separate thoughts and images which occur in the treatment of an action. They regarded the whole; we regard the parts. With them, the action predominated over the expression of it; with us, the expression predominates over the action. Not that they failed in expression, or were inattentive to it; on the contrary, they are the highest models of expression, the unapproached masters of the *grand style:* but their expression is so excellent because it is so admirably kept in its right degree of prominence; because it is so simple and so well subordinated; because it draws its force directly from the pregnancy of the matter which it conveys. For what reason was the Greek tragic poet confined to so limited a range of subjects? Because there are so few actions which unite in themselves, in the highest degree, the conditions of excellence: and it was not thought that

---

2. Perhaps alluding to poems such as Tennyson's *The Princess* (1847) and Alexander Smith's *Life Drama* (1853) or to the modern novel.
3. Long poems by Goethe (1797), Byron (1818), Alphonse-Marie-Louis de Lamartine (1836), and William Wordsworth (1814), respectively.
4. See Virgil's *Aeneid,* book 4. *Oresteia:* a trilogy of plays by Aeschylus that tells the story of Agamemnon's murder by his wife, Clytemnestra, and the vengeance taken by their son, Orestes.

on any but an excellent subject could an excellent poem be constructed. A few actions, therefore, eminently adapted for tragedy, maintained almost exclusive possession of the Greek tragic stage; their significance appeared inexhaustible; they were as permanent problems, perpetually offered to the genius of every fresh poet. This too is the reason of what appears to us moderns a certain baldness of expression in Greek tragedy; of the triviality with which we often reproach the remarks of the chorus, where it takes part in the dialogue: that the action itself, the situation of Orestes, or Merope, or Alcmaeon,[5] was to stand the central point of interest, unforgotten, absorbing, principal; that no accessories were for a moment to distract the spectator's attention from this; that the tone of the parts was to be perpetually kept down, in order not to impair the grandiose effect of the whole. The terrible[6] old mythic story on which the drama was founded stood, before he entered the theater, traced in its bare outlines upon the spectator's mind; it stood in his memory, as a group of statuary, faintly seen, at the end of a long and dark vista: then came the poet, embodying outlines, developing situations, not a word wasted, not a sentiment capriciously thrown in: stroke upon stroke, the drama proceeded: the light deepened upon the group; more and more it revealed itself to the riveted gaze of the spectator: until at last, when the final words were spoken, it stood before him in broad sunlight, a model of immortal beauty.

This was what a Greek critic demanded; this was what a Greek poet endeavored to effect. It signified nothing to what time an action belonged; we do not find that the *Persae* occupied a particularly high rank among the dramas of Aeschylus, because it represented a matter of contemporary interest:[7] this was not what a cultivated Athenian required, he required that the permanent elements of his nature should be moved; and dramas of which the action, though taken from a long-distant mythic time, yet was calculated to accomplish this in a higher degree than that of the *Persae,* stood higher in his estimation accordingly. The Greeks felt, no doubt, with their exquisite sagacity of taste, that an action of present times was too near them, too much mixed up with what was accidental and passing, to form a sufficiently grand, detached, and self-subsistent object for a tragic poem: such objects belonged to the domain of the comic poet, and of the lighter kinds of poetry. For the more serious kinds, for *pragmatic* poetry, to use an excellent expression of Polybius,[8] they were more difficult and severe in the range of subjects which they permitted. Their theory and practice alike, the admirable treatise of Aristotle, and the unrivaled works of their poets, exclaim with a thousand tongues—"All depends upon the subject; choose a fitting action, penetrate yourself with the feeling of its situations; this done, everything else will follow."

But for all kinds of poetry alike there was one point on which they were rigidly exacting; the adaptability of the subject to the kind of poetry selected, and the careful construction of the poem.

How different a way of thinking from this is ours! We can hardly at the present day understand what Menander[9] meant when he told a man who inquired as to the progress of his comedy that he had finished it, not having

---

5. The son of a legendary Greek hero, who, like Orestes, avenged his father's death by killing his mother. He was the subject of several Greek plays now lost. Merope, queen of Messene in Greece, appears in plays by Euripides and in Arnold's own play *Merope* (1858).
6. Terrifying, awe-inspiring.

7. Aeschylus's *Persians* (472 B.C.E.) portrays the Greek victory over the Persian invaders, which had occurred only a few years before the play was produced.
8. Greek historian (ca. 200–ca. 118 B.C.E.).
9. Greek writer of comedies (ca. 342–ca. 292 B.C.E.).

yet written a single line, because he had constructed the action of it in his mind. A modern critic would have assured him that the merit of his piece depended on the brilliant things which arose under his pen as he went along. We have poems which seem to exist merely for the sake of single lines and passages; not for the sake of producing any total impression. We have critics who seem to direct their attention merely to detached expressions, to the language about the action, not to the action itself, I verily think that the majority of them do not in their hearts believe that there is such a thing as a total impression to be derived from a poem at all, or to be demanded from a poet; they think the term a commonplace of metaphysical criticism. They will permit the poet to select any action he pleases, and to suffer that action to go as it will, provided he gratifies them with occasional bursts of fine writing, and with a shower of isolated thoughts and images. That is, they permit him to leave their poetical sense ungratified, provided that he gratifies their rhetorical sense and their curiosity. Of his neglecting to gratify these, there is little danger. He needs rather to be warned against the danger of attempting to gratify these alone; he needs rather to be perpetually reminded to prefer his action to everything else; so to treat this, as to permit its inherent excellences to develop themselves, without interruption from the intrusion of his personal peculiarities; most fortunate, when he most entirely succeeds in effacing himself, and in enabling a noble action to subsist as it did in nature.

But the modern critic not only permits a false practice; he absolutely prescribes false aims.—"A true allegory of the state of one's own mind in a representative history," the poet is told, "is perhaps the highest thing that one can attempt in the way of poetry."[1] And accordingly he attempts it. An allegory of the state of one's own mind, the highest problem of an art which imitates actions! No assuredly, it is not, it never can be so: no great poetical work has ever been produced with such an aim. *Faust* itself, in which something of the kind is attempted, wonderful passages as it contains, and in spite of the unsurpassed beauty of the scenes which relate to Margaret, *Faust* itself, judged as a whole, and judged strictly as a poetical work, is defective: its illustrious author, the greatest poet of modern times, the greatest critic of all times, would have been the first to acknowledge it; he only defended his work, indeed, by asserting it to be "something incommensurable."[2]

The confusion of the present times is great, the multitude of voices counseling different things bewildering, the number of existing works capable of attracting a young writer's attention and of becoming his models, immense. What he wants is a hand to guide him through the confusion, a voice to prescribe to him the aim which he should keep in view, and to explain to him that the value of the literary works which offer themselves to his attention is relative to their power of helping him forward on his road towards this aim. Such a guide the English writer at the present day will nowhere find. Failing this, all that can be looked for, all indeed that can be desired is, that his attention should be fixed on excellent models; that he may reproduce, at any rate, something of their excellence, by penetrating himself with their works and by catching their spirit, if he cannot be taught to produce what is excellent independently.

1. *North British Review* 19 (Aug. 1853): 180 (U.S. edition). Arnold seems not to have noticed that Goethe (a critic he revered) had been cited earlier in the article as the authority for this critical generalization.
2. J. Eckermann's *Conversations with Goethe*, Jan. 3, 1830.

Foremost among these models for the English writer stands Shakespeare: a name the greatest perhaps of all poetical names; a name never to be mentioned without reverence. I will venture, however, to express a doubt, whether the influence of his works, excellent and fruitful for the readers of poetry, for the great majority, has been of unmixed advantage to the writers of it. Shakespeare indeed chose excellent subjects; the world could afford no better than Macbeth, or Romeo and Juliet, or Othello: he had no theory respecting the necessity of choosing subjects of present import, or the paramount interest attaching to allegories of the state of one's own mind; like all great poets, he knew well what constituted a poetical action; like them, wherever he found such an action, he took it; like them, too, he found his best in past times. But to these general characteristics of all great poets he added a special one of his own; a gift, namely, of happy, abundant, and ingenious expression, eminent and unrivaled: so eminent as irresistibly to strike the attention first in him, and even to throw into comparative shade his other excellences as a poet. Here has been the mischief. These other excellences were his fundamental excellences *as a poet*; what distinguishes the artist from the mere amateur, says Goethe, is *Architectonicè* in the highest sense;[3] that power of execution, which creates, forms, and constitutes: not the profoundness of single thoughts, not the richness of imagery, not the abundance of illustration. But these attractive accessories of a poetical work being more easily seized than the spirit of the whole, and these accessories being possessed by Shakespeare in an unequaled degree, a young writer having recourse to Shakespeare as his model runs great risk of being vanquished and absorbed by them, and, in consequence, of reproducing, according to the measure of his power, these, and these alone.[4] Of this preponderating quality of Shakespeare's genius, accordingly almost the whole of modern English poetry has, it appears to me, felt the influence. To the exclusive attention on the part of his imitators to this it is in a great degree owing, that of the majority of modern poetical works the details alone are valuable, the composition worthless. In reading them one is perpetually reminded of that terrible sentence on a modern French poet: *Il dit tout ce qu'il veut, mais malheureusement il n'a rien à dire.*[5]

Let me give an instance of what I mean. I will take it from the works of the very chief among those who seem to have been formed in the school of Shakespeare: of one whose exquisite genius and pathetic death render him forever interesting. I will take the poem of *Isabella, or the Pot of Basil*, by Keats. I choose this rather than the *Endymion*, because the latter work (which a modern critic has classed with the *Fairy Queen*!)[6] although undoubtedly there blows through it the breath of genius, is yet as a whole so utterly incoherent, as not strictly to merit the name of a poem at all. The poem of *Isabella*, then, is a perfect treasure house of graceful and felicitous words and images: almost in every stanza there occurs one of those vivid and picturesque turns of expres-

3. In the essay "Concerning the So-called Dilettantism" (1799) in his *Werke* (1833) 44.262–63.
4. Cf. Arnold's letter to Clough (Oct. 28, 1852):

> More and more I feel that the difference between a mature and a youthful age of the world compels the poetry of the former to use great plainness of speech . . . and that Keats and Shelley were on a false track when they set themselves to reproduce the exuberance of expression, the charm, the richness of images,

and the felicity, of the Elizabethan poets.
5. He says everything he wishes to, but unfortunately he has nothing to say (French). A comment about Théophile Gautier (1811–1872), whose emphasis on style was severely criticized by Arnold in his late essay "Wordsworth" (1888).
6. In the *North British Review* 19 (Aug. 1853): 172–74, John Keats's *Endymion* (1818) is twice linked with Edmund Spenser's *Faerie Queene* (1590) as "leisurely compositions of the sweet sensuous order."

sion, by which the object is made to flash upon the eye of the mind, and which thrill the reader with a sudden delight. This one short poem contains, perhaps, a greater number of happy[7] single expressions which one could quote than all the extant tragedies of Sophocles. But the action, the story? The action in itself is an excellent one; but so feebly is it conceived by the poet, so loosely constructed, that the effect produced by it, in and for itself, is absolutely null. Let the reader, after he has finished the poem of Keats, turn to the same story in the *Decameron*:[8] he will then feel how pregnant and interesting the same action has become in the hands of a great artist, who above all things delineates his object; who subordinates expression to that which it is designed to express.

I have said that the imitators of Shakespeare, fixing their attention on his wonderful gift of expression, have directed their imitation to this, neglecting his other excellences. These excellences, the fundamental excellences of poetical art, Shakespeare no doubt possessed them—possessed many of them in a splendid degree; but it may perhaps be doubted whether even he himself did not sometimes give scope to his faculty of expression to the prejudice of a higher poetical duty. For we must never forget that Shakespeare is the great poet he is from his skill in discerning and firmly conceiving an excellent action, from his power of intensely feeling a situation, of intimately associating himself with a character; not from his gift of expression, which rather even leads him astray, degenerating sometimes into a fondness for curiosity of expression, into an irritability of fancy, which seems to make it impossible for him to say a thing plainly, even when the press of the action demands the very direct language, or its level character the very simplest. Mr. Hallam, than whom it is impossible to find a saner and more judicious critic, has had the courage (for at the present day it needs courage) to remark, how extremely and faultily difficult Shakespeare's language often is.[9] It is so: you may find main scenes in some of his greatest tragedies, *King Lear* for instance, where the language is so artificial, so curiously tortured, and so difficult, that every speech has to be read two or three times before its meaning can be comprehended. This overcuriousness of expression is indeed but the excessive employment of a wonderful gift—of the power of saying a thing in a happier way than any other man; nevertheless, it is carried so far that one understands what M. Guizot meant, when he said that Shakespeare appears in his language to have tried all styles except that of simplicity.[1] He has not the severe and scrupulous self-restraint of the ancients, partly no doubt, because he had a far less cultivated and exacting audience. He has indeed a far wider range than they had, a far richer fertility of thought; in this respect he rises above them. In his strong conception of his subject, in the genuine way in which he is penetrated with it, he resembles them, and is unlike the moderns. But in the accurate limitation of it, the conscientious rejection of superfluities, the simple and rigorous development of it from the first line of his work to the last, he falls below them, and comes nearer to the moderns. In his chief works, besides what he has of his own, he has the elementary soundness of the ancients; he has their important action and their large and broad manner; but he has not their purity of method. He is therefore a less safe model; for what he has of his own is

7. Well-judged, fitting.
8. By Boccaccio (1353): fourth day, fifth story.
9. *Introduction to the Literature of Europe* (1838–39), chap. 23, by the historian Henry Hallam

(1779–1859).
1. F.P.G. Guizot (1787–1874), French historian, discusses Shakespeare's sonnets in his *Shakespeare et Son Temps* (1852) 114.

personal, and inseparable from his own rich nature; it may be imitated and exaggerated, it cannot be learned or applied as an art. He is above all suggestive; more valuable, therefore, to young writers as men than as artists. But clearness of arrangement, rigor of development, simplicity of style—these may to a certain extent be learned; and these may, I am convinced, be learned best from the ancients, who although infinitely less suggestive than Shakespeare, are thus, to the artist, more instructive.

What, then, it will be asked, are the ancients to be our sole models? the ancients with their comparatively narrow range of experience, and their widely different circumstances? Not, certainly, that which is narrow in the ancients, nor that in which we can no longer sympathize. An action like the action of the *Antigone* of Sophocles, which turns upon the conflict between the heroine's duty to her brother's corpse and that to the laws of her country, is no longer one in which it is possible that we should feel a deep interest. I am speaking too, it will be remembered, not of the best sources of intellectual stimulus for the general reader, but of the best models of instruction for the individual writer. This last may certainly learn of the ancients, better than anywhere else, three things which it is vitally important for him to know: the all-importance of the choice of a subject; the necessity of accurate construction; and the subordinate character of expression. He will learn from them how unspeakably superior is the effect of the one moral impression left by a great action treated as a whole, to the effect produced by the most striking single thought or by the happiest image. As he penetrates into the spirit of the great classical works, as he becomes gradually aware of their intense significance, their noble simplicity, and their calm pathos, he will be convinced that it is this effect, unity and profoundness of moral impression, at which the ancient poets aimed; that it is this which constitutes the grandeur of their works, and which makes them immortal. He will desire to direct his own efforts towards producing the same effect. Above all, he will deliver himself from the jargon of modern criticism, and escape the danger of producing poetical works conceived in the spirit of the passing time, and which partake of its transitoriness.

The present age makes great claims upon us; we owe it service, it will not be satisfied without our admiration. I know not how it is, but their commerce with the ancients appears to me to produce, in those who constantly practice it, a steadying and composing effect upon their judgment, not of literary works only, but of men and events in general. They are like persons who have had a very weighty and impressive experience; they are more truly than others under the empire of facts, and more independent of the language current among those with whom they live. They wish neither to applaud nor to revile their age; they wish to know what it is, what it can give them, and whether this is what they want. What they want, they know very well; they want to educe and cultivate what is best and noblest in themselves; they know, too, that this is no easy task—χαλεπόν, as Pittacus said, χαλεπὸν ἐσθλὸν ἔμμεναι[2]—and they ask themselves sincerely whether their age and its literature can assist them in the attempt. If they are endeavoring to practice any art, they remember the plain and simple proceedings of the old artists, who attained their grand results by penetrating themselves with some noble and significant action, not by inflating themselves with a belief in the pre-eminence importance and greatness of their own times. They do not talk of their mission, nor of interpreting their age, nor

2. It is hard to be good (Greek); an aphorism of the statesman and sage Pittacus (ca. 650–570 B.C.E.).

of the coming poet; all this, they know, is the mere delirium of vanity; their business is not to praise their age, but to afford to the men who live in it the highest pleasure which they are capable of feeling. If asked to afford this by means of subjects drawn from the age itself, they ask what special fitness the present age has for supplying them. They are told that it is an era of progress, an age commissioned to carry out the great ideas of industrial development and social amelioration. They reply that with all this they can do nothing; that the elements they need for the exercise of their art are great actions, calculated powerfully and delightfully to affect what is permanent in the human soul; that so far as the present age can supply such actions, they will gladly make use of them; but that an age wanting in moral grandeur can with difficulty supply such, and an age of spiritual discomfort with difficulty be powerfully and delightfully affected by them.

A host of voices will indignantly rejoin that the present age is inferior to the past neither in moral grandeur nor in spiritual health. He who possesses the discipline I speak of will content himself with remembering the judgments passed upon the present age, in this respect, by the two men, the one of strongest head, the other of widest culture, whom it has produced; by Goethe and by Niebuhr.[3] It will be sufficient for him that he knows the opinions held by these two great men respecting the present age and its literature; and that he feels assured in his own mind that their aims and demands upon life were such as he would wish, at any rate, his own to be; and their judgment as to what is impeding and disabling such as he may safely follow. He will not, however, maintain a hostile attitude towards the false pretensions of his age: he will content himself with not being overwhelmed by them. He will esteem himself fortunate if he can succeed in banishing from his mind all feelings of contradiction, and irritation, and impatience; in order to delight himself with the contemplation of some noble action of a heroic time, and to enable others, through his representation of it, to delight in it also.

I am far indeed from making any claim, for myself, that I possess this discipline; or for the following poems, that they breathe its spirit. But I say, that in the sincere endeavor to learn and practice, amid the bewildering confusion of our times, what is sound and true in poetical art, I seemed to myself to find the only sure guidance, the only solid footing, among the ancients. They, at any rate, knew what they wanted in art, and we do not. It is this uncertainty which is disheartening, and not hostile criticism. How often have I felt this when reading words of disparagement or of cavil: that it is the uncertainty as to what is really to be aimed at which makes our difficulty, not the dissatisfaction of the critic, who himself suffers from the same uncertainty. *Non me tua fervida terrent Dicta; . . . Dii me terrent, et Jupiter hostis.*[4]

Two kinds of *dilettanti*, says Goethe, there are in poetry: he who neglects the indispensable mechanical part, and thinks he has done enough if he shows spirituality and feeling; and he who seeks to arrive at poetry merely by mechanism, in which he can acquire an artisan's readiness, and is without soul and matter.[5] And he adds, that the first does most harm to art, and the last to himself. If we must be *dilettanti*; if it is impossible for us, under the circum-

---

3. B. G. Niebuhr (1776–1831), German historian. Both writers felt that their own age had added little to the store of great literature.
4. The gods frighten me, and [having] Jupiter as an enemy (Latin); from Virgil's *Aeneid* 12.894–95.

Turnus, a warrior abandoned by the gods, is replying to Aeneas, who has taunted him with being afraid.
5. See "Concerning the So-called Dilettantism" (1799) in his *Werke* (1833) 44.281.

stances amidst which we live, to think clearly, to feel nobly, and to delineate firmly; if we cannot attain to the mastery of the great artists; let us, at least, have so much respect for our art as to prefer it to ourselves. Let us not bewilder our successors; let us transmit to them the practice of poetry, with its boundaries and wholesome regulative laws, under which excellent works may again, perhaps, at some future time, be produced, not yet fallen into oblivion through our neglect, not yet condemned and canceled by the influence of their eternal enemy, caprice.

1853

From The Function of Criticism at the Present Time[1]

Many objections have been made to a proposition which, in some remarks of mine on translating Homer,[2] I ventured to put forth; a proposition about criticism, and its importance at the present day. I said: "Of the literature of France and Germany, as of the intellect of Europe in general, the main effort, for now many years, has been a critical effort; the endeavor, in all branches of knowledge, theology, philosophy, history, art, science, to see the object as in itself it really is." I added, that owing to the operation in English literature of certain causes, "almost the last thing for which one would come to English literature is just that very thing which now Europe most desires—criticism"; and that the power and value of English literature was thereby impaired. More than one rejoinder declared that the importance I here assigned to criticism was excessive, and asserted the inherent superiority of the creative effort of the human spirit over its critical effort. And the other day, having been led by a Mr. Shairp's excellent notice of Wordsworth[3] to turn again to his biography, I found, in the words of this great man, whom I, for one, must always listen to with the profoundest respect, a sentence passed on the critic's business, which seems to justify every possible disparagement of it. Wordsworth says in one of his letters:

> The writers in these publications (the Reviews), while they prosecute their inglorious employment, cannot be supposed to be in a state of mind very favorable for being affected by the finer influences of a thing so pure as genuine poetry.

And a trustworthy reporter[4] of his conversation quotes a more elaborate judgment to the same effect:

> Wordsworth holds the critical power very low, infinitely lower than the inventive; and he said today that if the quantity of time consumed in

1. This essay served as an introduction to *Essays in Criticism* (1865).
2. *On Translating Homer* (1861).
3. J. C. Shairp's essay "Wordsworth: The Man and the Poet" was published in 1864. Arnold comments in a footnote:

> I cannot help thinking that a practice, common in England during the last century, and still followed in France, of printing a notice of this kind—a notice by a competent critic—to serve as an introduction to an eminent author's works, might be revived among us with advantage. To

introduce all succeeding editions of Wordsworth, Mr. Shairp's notice might, it seems to me, excellently serve; it is written from the point of view of an admirer, nay, of a disciple, and that is right; but then the disciple must be also, as in this case he is, a critic, a man of letters, not, as too often happens, some relation or friend with no qualification for his task except affection for his author.

4. Christopher Wordsworth, *Memoirs of William Wordsworth* (1851).

writing critiques on the works of others were given to original composition, of whatever kind it might be, it would be much better employed; it would make a man find out sooner his own level, and it would do infinitely less mischief. A false or malicious criticism may do much injury to the minds of others; a stupid invention, either in prose or verse, is quite harmless.

It is almost too much to expect of poor human nature, that a man capable of producing some effect in one line of literature, should, for the greater good of society, voluntarily doom himself to impotence and obscurity in another. Still less is this to be expected from men addicted to the composition of the "false or malicious criticism" of which Wordsworth speaks. However, everybody would admit that a false or malicious criticism had better never have been written. Everybody, too, would be willing to admit, as a general proposition, that the critical faculty is lower than the inventive. But is it true that criticism is really, in itself, a baneful and injurious employment; is it true that all time given to writing critiques on the works of others would be much better employed if it were given to original composition, of whatever kind this may be? Is it true that Johnson had better have gone on producing more Irenes[5] instead of writing his Lives of the Poets; nay, is it certain that Wordsworth himself was better employed in making his Ecclesiastical Sonnets than when he made his celebrated Preface[6] so full of criticism, and criticism of the works of others? Wordsworth was himself a great critic, and it is to be sincerely regretted that he has not left us more criticism; Goethe was one of the greatest of critics, and we may sincerely congratulate ourselves that he has left us so much criticism. Without wasting time over the exaggeration which Wordsworth's judgment on criticism clearly contains, or over an attempt to trace the causes—not difficult, I think, to be traced—which may have led Wordsworth to this exaggeration, a critic may with advantage seize an occasion for trying his own conscience, and for asking himself of what real service, at any given moment, the practice of criticism either is or may be made to his own mind and spirit, and to the minds and spirits of others.

The critical power is of lower rank than the creative. True; but in assenting to this proposition, one or two things are to be kept in mind. It is undeniable that the exercise of a creative power, that a free creative activity, is the highest function of man; it is proved to be so by man's finding in it his true happiness. But it is undeniable, also, that men may have the sense of exercising this free creative activity in other ways than in producing great works of literature or art; if it were not so, all but a very few men would be shut out from the true happiness of all men. They may have it in well-doing, they may have it in learning, they may have it even in criticizing. This is one thing to be kept in mind. Another is, that the exercise of the creative power in the production of great works of literature or art, however high this exercise of it may rank, is not at all epochs and under all conditions possible; and that therefore labor may be vainly spent in attempting it, which might with more fruit be used in preparing for it, in rendering it possible. This creative power works with elements, with materials; what if it has not those materials, those elements, ready for its use? In that case it must surely wait till they are ready. Now, in literature—I will limit myself to literature, for it is about literature that the question

5. Irene (1749) is a clumsy play by Samuel Johnson (1709–1784), whose Lives of the Poets (1779–81) is a major work of criticism.

6. To Lyrical Ballads (1800). "Ecclesiastical Sonnets": a sonnet sequence (1821–22) by Wordsworth, usually regarded as minor verse.

arises—the elements with which the creative power works are ideas; the best ideas on every matter which literature touches, current at the time. At any rate we may lay it down as certain that in modern literature no manifestation of the creative power not working with these can be very important or fruitful. And I say *current* at the time, not merely accessible at the time; for creative literary genius does not principally show itself in discovering new ideas, that is rather the business of the philosopher. The grand work of literary genius is a work of synthesis and exposition, not of analysis and discovery; its gift lies in the faculty of being happily inspired by a certain intellectual and spiritual atmosphere, by a certain order of ideas, when it finds itself in them; of dealing divinely with these ideas, presenting them in the most effective and attractive combinations—making beautiful works with them, in short. But it must have the atmosphere, it must find itself amidst the order of ideas, in order to work freely; and these it is not so easy to command. This is why great creative epochs in literature are so rare, this is why there is so much that is unsatisfactory in the productions of many men of real genius; because, for the creation of a masterwork of literature two powers must concur, the power of the man and the power of the moment, and the man is not enough without the moment; the creative power has, for its happy exercise, appointed elements, and those elements are not in its own control.

Nay, they are more within the control of the critical power. It is the business of the critical power, as I said in the words already quoted, "in all branches of knowledge, theology, philosophy, history, art, science, to see the object as in itself it really is." Thus it tends, at last, to make an intellectual situation of which the creative power can profitably avail itself. It tends to establish an order of ideas, if not absolutely true, yet true by comparison with that which it displaces; to make the best ideas prevail. Presently these new ideas reach society, the touch of truth is the touch of life, and there is a stir and growth everywhere; out of this stir and growth come the creative epochs of literature.

Or, to narrow our range, and quit these considerations of the general march of genius and of society—considerations which are apt to become too abstract and impalpable—everyone can see that a poet, for instance, ought to know life and the world before dealing with them in poetry; and life and the world being in modern times very complex things, the creation of a modern poet, to be worth much, implies a great critical effort behind it; else it must be a comparatively poor, barren, and short-lived affair. This is why Byron's poetry had so little endurance in it, and Goethe's so much; both Byron and Goethe had a great productive power, but Goethe's was nourished by a great critical effort providing the true materials for it, and Byron's was not; Goethe knew life and the world, the poet's necessary subjects, much more comprehensively and thoroughly than Byron. He knew a great deal more of them, and he knew them much more as they really are.

It has long seemed to me that the burst of creative activity in our literature, through the first quarter of this century, had about it in fact something premature; and that from this cause its productions are doomed, most of them, in spite of the sanguine hopes which accompanied and do still accompany them, to prove hardly more lasting than the productions of far less splendid epochs. And this prematureness comes from its having proceeded without having its proper data, without sufficient materials to work with. In other words, the English poetry of the first quarter of this century, with plenty of energy, plenty of creative force, did not know enough. This makes Byron so empty of matter, Shelley so incoherent, Wordsworth even, profound as he is, yet so wanting in completeness and variety. Wordsworth cared little for books, and disparaged Goethe. I admire Wordsworth, as he is, so much that I cannot wish him different; and it is vain, no doubt, to imagine such a man different from what he is, to suppose that he *could* have been different. But surely the one thing wanting to make Wordsworth an even greater poet than he is—his thought richer, and his influence of wider application—was that he should have read more books, among them, no doubt, those of that Goethe whom he disparaged without reading him.

But to speak of books and reading may easily lead to a misunderstanding here. It was not really books and reading that lacked to our poetry at this epoch: Shelley had plenty of reading, Coleridge had immense reading. Pindar and Sophocles[7]—as we all say so glibly, and often with so little discernment of the real import of what we are saying—had not many books; Shakespeare was no deep reader. True; but in the Greece of Pindar and Sophocles, in the England of Shakespeare, the poet lived in a current of ideas in the highest degree animating and nourishing to the creative power; society was, in the fullest measure, permeated by fresh thought, intelligent and alive. And this state of things is the true basis for the creative power's exercise, in this it finds its data, its materials, truly ready for its hand; all the books and reading in the world are only valuable as they are helps to this. Even when this does not actually exist, books and reading may enable a man to construct a kind of semblance of it in his own mind, a world of knowledge and intelligence in which he may live and work. This is by no means an equivalent to the artist for the nationally diffused life and thought of the epochs of Sophocles or Shakespeare; but, besides that it may be a means of preparation for such epochs, it does really constitute, if many share in it, a quickening and sustaining atmosphere of great value. Such an atmosphere the many-sided learning and the long and widely combined critical effort of Germany formed for Goethe, when he lived and worked. There was no national glow of life and thought there as in the Athens of Pericles or the England of Elizabeth.[8] That was the poet's weakness. But there was a sort of equivalent for it in the complete culture and unfettered thinking of a large body of Germans. That was his strength. In the England of the first quarter of this century there was neither a national glow of life and thought, such as we had in the age of Elizabeth, nor yet a culture and a force of learning and criticism such as were to be found in Germany. Therefore the creative power of poetry wanted, for success in the highest sense, materials and a basis; a thorough interpretation of the world was necessarily denied to it.

At first sight it seems strange that out of the immense stir of the French Revolution and its age should not have come a crop of works of genius equal to that which came out of the stir of the great productive time of Greece, or out of that of the Renascence, with its powerful episode the Reformation. But the truth is that the stir of the French Revolution took a character which essentially distinguished it from such movements as these. These were, in the main, disinterestedly intellectual and spiritual movements; movements in which the human spirit looked for its satisfaction in itself and in the increased

---

7. Greek tragedian (ca. 496–406 B.C.E.). Pindar (518–438 B.C.E.), Greek lyric poet.
8. Elizabeth I (1533–1603; reigned 1558–1603). Pericles (ca. 495–429 B.C.E.), the leading states-

man of Athens during the period of the city's most outstanding achievements in art, literature, and politics.

play of its own activity. The French Revolution took a political, practical character. The movement, which went on in France under the old *régime*, from 1700 to 1789, was far more really akin than that of the Revolution itself to the movement of the Renascence; the France of Voltaire and Rousseau[9] told far more powerfully upon the mind of Europe than the France of the Revolution. Goethe reproached this last expressly with having "thrown quiet culture back."[1] Nay, and the true key to how much in our Byron, even in our Wordsworth, is this!—that they had their source in a great movement of feeling, not in a great movement of mind. The French Revolution, however—that object of so much blind love and so much blind hatred—found undoubtedly its motive power in the intelligence of men, and not in their practical sense; this is what distinguishes it from the English Revolution of Charles the First's time.[2] This is what makes it a more spiritual event than our Revolution, an event of much more powerful and worldwide interest, though practically less successful; it appeals to an order of ideas which are universal, certain, permanent. 1789 asked of a thing, Is it rational? 1642 asked of a thing, Is it legal? or, when it went furthest, Is it according to conscience? This is the English fashion, a fashion to be treated, within its own sphere, with the highest respect; for its success, within its own sphere, has been prodigious. But what is law in one place is not law in another; what is law here today is not law even here tomorrow; and as for conscience, what is binding on one man's conscience is not binding on another's. The old woman who threw her stool at the head of the surpliced minister in St. Giles's Church at Edinburgh[3] obeyed an impulse to which millions of the human race may be permitted to remain strangers. But the prescriptions of reason are absolute, unchanging, of universal validity; *to count by tens is the easiest way of counting*—that is a proposition of which everyone, from here to the Antipodes, feels the force; at least I should say so if we did not live in a country where it is not impossible that any morning we may find a letter in the *Times* declaring that a decimal coinage is an absurdity.[4] That a whole nation should have been penetrated with an enthusiasm for pure reason, and with an ardent zeal for making its prescriptions triumph, is a very remarkable thing, when we consider how little of mind, or anything so worthy and quickening as mind, comes into the motives which alone, in general, impel great masses of men. In spite of the extravagant direction given to this enthusiasm, in spite of the crimes and follies in which it lost itself, the French Revolution derives from the force, truth, and universality of the ideas which it took for its law, and from the passion with which it could inspire a multitude for these ideas, a unique and still living power; it is—it will probably long remain—the greatest, the most animating event in history. And as no sincere passion for the things of the mind, even though it turn out in many respects an unfortunate passion, is ever quite thrown away and quite barren of good, France has reaped from hers one fruit—the natural and legit-

9. Jean-Jacques Rousseau (1712–1778), Swiss-born French philosopher and political theorist. Voltaire (1694–1778), pen name of the French writer François Marie Arouet.
1. See "Vier Jahreszeiten Herbst" (1796) in his *Werke* (1887) 1.354.
2. Disputes between Charles I (1600–1649; reigned 1625–49) and Parliament led in 1642 to civil war and ultimately to the king's beheading. (Eleven years later his son, Charles II, was recalled from exile and proclaimed king.)

3. In 1637 rioting broke out in Scotland against a new kind of church service prescribed by Charles I. The riot was started by an old woman hurling a stool at a clergyman, whom she accused of saying Mass.
4. In 1863 a proposal in Parliament to introduce the French decimal system for weights and measures had provoked articles in the London *Times* defending the English system (of ounces and pounds or inches and feet) as more practical. Decimal coinage was finally instituted in 1971.

imate fruit though not precisely the grand fruit she expected: she is the country in Europe where *the people* is most alive.

But the mania for giving an immediate political and practical application to all these fine ideas of the reason was fatal. Here an Englishman is in his element: on this theme we can all go on for hours. And all we are in the habit of saying on it has undoubtedly a great deal of truth. Ideas cannot be too much prized in and for themselves, cannot be too much lived with; but to transport them abruptly into the world of politics and practice, violently to revolutionize this world to their bidding—that is quite another thing. There is the world of ideas and there is the world of practice; the French are often for suppressing the one and the English the other; but neither is to be suppressed. A member of the House of Commons said to me the other day: "That a thing is an anomaly, I consider to be no objection to it whatever." I venture to think he was wrong; that a thing is an anomaly *is* an objection to it, but absolutely and in the sphere of ideas: it is not necessarily, under such and such circumstances, or at such and such a moment, an objection to it in the sphere of politics and practice. Joubert[5] has said beautifully: *"C'est la force et le droit qui règlent toutes choses dans le monde; la force en attendant le droit."*—"Force and right are the governors of this world; force till right is ready." *Force till right is ready;* and till right is ready, force, the existing order of things, is justified, is the legitimate ruler. But right is something moral, and implies inward recognition, free assent of the will; we are not ready for right—*right*, so far as we are concerned, is *not ready*—until we have attained this sense of seeing it and willing it. The way in which for us it may change and transform force, the existing order of things, and become, in its turn, the legitimate ruler of the world, should depend on the way in which, when our time comes, we see it and will it. Therefore for other people enamored of their own newly discerned right, to attempt to impose it upon us as ours, and violently to substitute their right for our force, is an act of tyranny, and to be resisted. It sets at nought the second great half of our maxim, *force till right is ready*. This was the grand error of the French Revolution; and its movement of ideas, by quitting the intellectual sphere and rushing furiously into the political sphere, ran, indeed, a prodigious and memorable course, but produced no such intellectual fruit as the movement of ideas of the Renascence, and created, in opposition to itself, what I may call an *epoch of concentration*. The great force of that epoch of concentration was England; and the great voice of that epoch of concentration was Burke.[6] It is the fashion to treat Burke's writings on the French Revolution as superannuated and conquered by the event; as the eloquent but unphilosophical tirades of bigotry and prejudice. I will not deny that they are often disfigured by the violence and passion of the moment, and that in some directions Burke's view was bounded, and his observation therefore at fault. But on the whole, and for those who can make the needful corrections, what distinguishes these writings is their profound, permanent, fruitful, philosophical truth, They contain the true philosophy of an epoch of concentration, dissipate the heavy atmosphere which its own nature is apt to engender round it, and make its resistance rational instead of mechanical.

But Burke is so great because, almost alone in England, he brings thought

5. Joseph Joubert (1754–1824), French moralist about whom Arnold wrote in his *Essays in Criticism*.
6. Edmund Burke (1729–1797), prominent statesman and author of *Reflections on the French Revolution* (1790), which expressed the conservative opposition to revolutionary theories.

to bear upon politics, he saturates politics with thought. It is his accident[7] that his ideas were at the service of an epoch of concentration, not of an epoch of expansion; it is his characteristic that he so lived by ideas, and had such a source of them welling up within him, that he could float even an epoch of concentration and English Tory politics with them. It does not hurt him that Dr. Price[8] and the Liberals were enraged with him; it does not even hurt him that George the Third and the Tories were enchanted with him. His greatness is that he lived in a world which neither English Liberalism nor English Toryism is apt to enter—the world of ideas, not the world of catchwords and party habits. So far is it from being really true of him that he "to party gave up what was meant for mankind,"[9] that at the very end of his fierce struggle with the French Revolution, after all his invectives against its false pretensions, hollowness, and madness, with his sincere convictions of its mischievousness, he can close a memorandum on the best means of combating it, some of the last pages he ever wrote[1]—the *Thoughts on French Affairs*, in December 1791—with these striking words:

> The evil is stated, in my opinion, as it exists. The remedy must be where power, wisdom, and information, I hope, are more united with good intentions than they can be with me. I have done with this subject, I believe, forever. It has given me many anxious moments for the last two years. *If a great change is to be made in human affairs, the minds of men will be fitted to it; the general opinions and feelings will draw that way. Every fear, every hope will forward it; and then they who persist in opposing this mighty current in human affairs, will appear rather to resist the decrees of Providence itself, than the mere designs of men. They will not be resolute and firm, but perverse and obstinate.*

That return of Burke upon himself has always seemed to me one of the finest things in English literature, or indeed in any literature. That is what I call living by ideas: when one side of a question has long had your earnest support, when all your feelings are engaged, when you hear all round you no language but one, when your party talks this language like a steam engine and can imagine no other—still to be able to think, still to be irresistibly carried, if so it be, by the current of thought to the opposite side of the question, and, like Balaam, to be unable to speak anything *but what the Lord has put in your mouth.*[2] I know nothing more striking, and I must add that I know nothing more un-English.

For the Englishman in general is like my friend the Member of Parliament, and believes, point-blank, that for a thing to be an anomaly is absolutely no objection to it whatever. He is like the Lord Auckland[3] of Burke's day, who, in a memorandum on the French Revolution, talks of certain "miscreants, assuming the name of philosophers, who have presumed themselves capable of establishing a new system of society." The Englishman has been called a political animal, and he values what is political and practical so much that

7. Fortune.
8. Richard Price (1723–1791), a prorevolutionary clergyman who was an opponent of Burke's.
9. From Oliver Goldsmith's poem "Retaliation" (1774).
1. Arnold was mistaken; Burke continued to write for another six years after 1791. According to Arnold's editor, R. H. Super, the mistake was

caused by misunderstanding a passage in one of Burke's letters.
2. Balaam, a false and worldly prophet, pronounced a blessing on the Israelites instead of the curse he had intended (Numbers 22.38).
3. William Eden, first Baron Auckland (1744–1814), statesman and diplomat.

ideas easily become objects of dislike in his eyes, and thinkers, "miscreants," because ideas and thinkers have rashly meddled with politics and practice. This would be all very well if the dislike and neglect confined themselves to ideas transported out of their own sphere, and meddling rashly with practice; but they are inevitably extended to ideas as such, and to the whole life of intelligence; practice is everything, a free play of the mind is nothing. The notion of the free play of the mind upon all subjects being a pleasure in itself, being an object of desire, being an essential provider of elements without which a nation's spirit, whatever compensations it may have for them, must, in the long run, die of inanition, hardly enters into an Englishman's thoughts. It is noticeable that the word *curiosity*, which in other languages is used in a good sense, to mean, as a high and fine quality of man's nature, just this disinterested love of a free play of the mind on all subjects, for its own sake—it is noticeable, I say, that this word has in our language no sense of the kind, no sense but a rather bad and disparaging one. But criticism, real criticism, is essentially the exercise of this very quality. It obeys an instinct prompting it to try to know the best that is known and thought in the world, irrespectively of practice, politics, and everything of the kind; and to value knowledge and thought as they approach this best, without the intrusion of any other considerations whatever. This is an instinct for which there is, I think, little original sympathy in the practical English nature, and what there was of it has undergone a long benumbing period of blight and suppression in the epoch of concentration which followed the French Revolution.

But epochs of concentration cannot well endure forever; epochs of expansion, in the due course of things, follow them. Such an epoch of expansion seems to be opening in this country. In the first place all danger of a hostile forcible pressure of foreign ideas upon our practice has long disappeared; like the traveler in the fable, therefore, we begin to wear our cloak a little more loosely.[4] Then, with a long peace, the ideas of Europe steal gradually and amicably in, and mingle, though in infinitesimally small quantities at a time, with our own notions. Then, too, in spite of all that is said about the absorbing and brutalizing influence of our passionate material progress, it seems to me indisputable that this progress is likely, though not certain, to lead in the end to an apparition of intellectual life; and that man, after he has made himself perfectly comfortable and has now to determine what to do with himself next, may begin to remember that he has a mind, and that the mind may be made the source of great pleasure. I grant it is mainly the privilege of faith, at present, to discern this end to our railways, our business, and our fortune-making; but we shall see if, here as elsewhere, faith is not in the end the true prophet. Our ease, our traveling, and our unbounded liberty to hold just as hard and securely as we please to the practice to which our notions have given birth, all tend to beget an inclination to deal a little more freely with these notions themselves, to canvass them a little, to penetrate a little into their real nature. Flutterings of curiosity, in the foreign sense of the word, appear amongst us, and it is in these that criticism must look to find its account. Criticism first; a time of true creative activity, perhaps—which, as I have said, must inevitably be preceded amongst us by a time of criticism—hereafter, when criticism has done its work.

4. In Aesop's fable of the wind and the sun, the two compete to see who is more powerful. The sun wins by causing the traveler to take off his coat (the goal of both), whereas the wind can only make him hold it closely.

It is of the last importance that English criticism should clearly discern what rule for its course, in order to avail itself of the field now opening to it, and to produce fruit for the future, it ought to take. The rule may be summed up in one word—*disinterestedness*.[5] And how is criticism to show disinterestedness? By keeping aloof from what is called "the practical view of things"; by resolutely following the law of its own nature, which is to be a free play of the mind on all subjects which it touches. By steadily refusing to lend itself to any of those ulterior, political, practical considerations about ideas, which plenty of people will be sure to attach to them, which perhaps ought often to be attached to them, which in this country at any rate are certain to be attached to them quite sufficiently, but which criticism has really nothing to do with. Its business is, as I have said, simply to know the best that is known and thought in the world, and by in its turn making this known, to create a current of true and fresh ideas. Its business is to do this with inflexible honesty, with due ability; but its business is to do no more, and to leave alone all questions of practical consequences and applications, questions which will never fail to have due prominence given to them. Else criticism, besides being really false to its own nature, merely continues in the old rut which it has hitherto followed in this country, and will certainly miss the chance now given to it. For what is at present the bane of criticism in this country? It is that practical considerations cling to it and stifle it. It subserves interests not its own. Our organs of criticism are organs of men and parties having practical ends to serve, and with them those practical ends are the first thing and the play of mind the second; so much play of mind as is compatible with the prosecution of those practical ends is all that is wanted. An organ like the *Revue des Deux Mondes*,[6] having for its main function to understand and utter the best that is known and thought in the world, existing, it may be said, as just an organ for a free play of the mind, we have not. But we have the *Edinburgh Review*, existing as an organ of the old Whigs, and for as much play of mind as may suit its being that; we have the *Quarterly Review*, existing as an organ of the Tories, and for as much play of mind as may suit its being that; we have the *British Quarterly Review*, existing as an organ of the political Dissenters, and for as much play of mind as may suit its being that; we have the *Times*, existing as an organ of the common, satisfied, well-to-do Englishman, and for as much play of mind as may suit its being that. And so on through all the various fractions, political and religious, of our society; every fraction has, as such, its organ of criticism, but the notion of combining all fractions in the common pleasure of a free disinterested play of mind meets with no favor. Directly this play of mind wants to have more scope, and to forget the pressure of practical considerations a little, it is checked, it is made to feel the chain. We saw this the other day in the extinction, so much to be regretted, of the *Home and Foreign Review*.[7] Perhaps in no organ of criticism in this country was there so much knowledge, so much play of mind; but these could not save it. The *Dublin Review* subordinates play of mind to the practical business of English and Irish Catholicism, and lives. It must needs be that men should act in sects and parties, that each of these sects and parties should have its organ, and should make this organ subserve the interests of its action; but it would be well, too, that there should be a criticism, not the minister of these interests,

5. This key word in Arnold's argument connotes independence and objectivity of mind. It means not having an interest, in the sense of an ax to grind. It does not mean lack of interest.

6. An international magazine of exceptionally high quality, founded in Paris in 1829.
7. A liberal Catholic periodical, founded in 1862, which ceased publication in 1864.

not their enemy, but absolutely and entirely independent of them. No other criticism will ever attain any real authority or make any real way towards its end—the creating a current of true and fresh ideas.

It is because criticism has so little kept in the pure intellectual sphere, has so little detached itself from practice, has been so directly polemical and controversial, that it has so ill accomplished, in this country, its best spiritual work, which is to keep man from a self-satisfaction which is retarding and vulgarizing, to lead him towards perfection, by making his mind dwell upon what is excellent in itself, and the absolute beauty and fitness of things. A polemical practical criticism makes men blind even to the ideal imperfection of their practice, makes them willingly assert its ideal perfection, in order the better to secure it against attack; and clearly this is narrowing and baneful for them. If they were reassured on the practical side, speculative considerations of ideal perfection they might be brought to entertain, and their spiritual horizon would thus gradually widen. Sir Charles Adderley[8] says to the Warwickshire farmers:

> Talk of the improvement of breed! Why, the race we ourselves represent, the men and women, the old Anglo-Saxon race, are the best breed in the whole world. . . . The absence of a too enervating climate, too unclouded skies, and a too luxurious nature, has produced so vigorous a race of people, and has rendered us so superior to all the world.

Mr. Roebuck says to the Sheffield cutlers:[9]

> I look around me and ask what is the state of England? Is not property safe? Is not every man able to say what he likes? Can you not walk from one end of England to the other in perfect security? I ask you whether, the world over or in past history, there is anything like it? Nothing. I pray that our unrivaled happiness may last.

Now obviously there is a peril for poor human nature in words and thoughts of such exuberant self-satisfaction, until we find ourselves safe in the streets of the Celestial City.

> *Das wenige verschwindet leicht dem Blicke*
> *Der vorwärts sieht, wie viel noch übrig bleibt*—[1]

says Goethe; "the little that is done seems nothing when we look forward and see how much we have yet to do." Clearly this is a better line of reflection for weak humanity, so long as it remains on this earthly field of labor and trial.

But neither Sir Charles Adderley nor Mr. Roebuck is by nature inaccessible to considerations of this sort. They only lose sight of them owing to the controversial life we all lead, and the practical form which all speculation takes with us. They have in view opponents whose aim is not ideal, but practical; and in their zeal to uphold their own practice against these innovators, they go so far as even to attribute to this practice an ideal perfection. Somebody has been wanting to introduce a six-pound franchise, or to abolish church-rates,[2] or to collect agricultural statistics by force, or to diminish local self-government. How natural, in reply to such proposals, very likely improper or

8. Conservative politician and wealthy landowner (1814–1905).
9. Makers of knives and forks. John Arthur Roebuck (1801–1879), radical politician and representative in Parliament for the industrial city of Sheffield, famous for its metalworking trades.

1. Goethe's *Iphigenie auf Tauris* (1787) 1.2.91–92.
2. Taxes supporting the Church of England. "Six-pound franchise": a radical proposal to extend the right to vote to anyone owning land worth £6 annual rent.

ill-timed, to go a little beyond the mark and to say stoutly, "Such a race of people as we stand, so superior to all the world! The old Anglo-Saxon race, the best breed in the whole world! I pray that our unrivaled happiness may last! I ask you whether, the world over or in past history, there is anything like it?" And so long as criticism answers this dithyramb by insisting that the old Anglo-Saxon race would be still more superior to all others if it had no church-rates, or that our unrivaled happiness would last yet longer with a six-pound franchise, so long will the strain, "The best breed in the whole world!" swell louder and louder, everything ideal and refining will be lost out of sight, and both the assailed and their critics will remain in a sphere, to say the truth, perfectly unvital, a sphere in which spiritual progression is impossible. But let criticism leave church-rates and the franchise alone, and in the most candid spirit, without a single lurking thought of practical innovation, confront with our dithyramb this paragraph on which I stumbled in a newspaper immediately after reading Mr. Roebuck:

> A shocking child murder has just been committed at Nottingham.[3] A girl named Wragg left the workhouse there on Saturday morning with her young illegitimate child. The child was soon afterwards found dead on Mapperly Hills, having been strangled. Wragg is in custody.

Nothing but that; but, in juxtaposition with the absolute eulogies of Sir Charles Adderley and Mr. Roebuck, how eloquent, how suggestive are those few lines! "Our old Anglo-Saxon breed, the best in the whole world!"—how much that is harsh and ill-favored there is in this best! *Wragg!* If we are to talk of ideal perfection, of "the best in the whole world," has anyone reflected what a touch of grossness in our race, what an original shortcoming in the more delicate spiritual perceptions, is shown by the natural growth amongst us of such hideous names—Higginbottom, Stiggins, Bugg! In Ionia and Attica[4] they were luckier in this respect than "the best race in the world"; by the Ilissus[5] there was no Wragg, poor thing! And "our unrivaled happiness"—what an element of grimness, bareness, and hideousness mixes with it and blurs it; the workhouse, the dismal Mapperly Hills[6]—how dismal those who have seen them will remember—the gloom, the smoke, the cold, the strangled illegitimate child! "I ask you whether, the world over or in past history, there is anything like it?" Perhaps not, one is inclined to answer; but at any rate, in that case, the world is very much to be pitied. And the final touch—short, bleak and inhuman: *Wragg is in custody.* The sex lost in the confusion of our unrivaled happiness; or (shall I say?) the superfluous Christian name lopped off by the straightforward vigor of our old Anglo-Saxon breed! There is profit for the spirit in such contrasts as this; criticism serves the cause of perfection by establishing them. By eluding sterile conflict, by refusing to remain in the sphere where alone narrow and relative conceptions have any worth and validity, criticism may diminish its momentary importance, but only in this way has it a chance of gaining admittance for those wider and more perfect conceptions to which all its duty is really owed. Mr. Roebuck will have a poor opinion of an adversary who replies to his defiant songs of triumph only by murmuring under his breath, *Wragg is in custody;* but in no other way will these songs of

3. It occurred on September 10, 1864.
4. The district in Greece that includes Athens. Ionia: area of the west coast of Asia Minor where Homer was believed to have lived.

5. A stream south of Athens.
6. Adjacent to the coal-mining and industrial area of Nottingham (later associated with the writings of D. H. Lawrence).

triumph be induced gradually to moderate themselves, to get rid of what in them is excessive and offensive, and to fall into a softer and truer key.

It will be said that it is a very subtle and indirect action which I am thus prescribing for criticism, and that, by embracing in this manner the Indian[7] virtue of detachment and abandoning the sphere of practical life, it condemns itself to a slow and obscure work. Slow and obscure it may be, but it is the only proper work of criticism. The mass of mankind will never have any ardent zeal for seeing things as they are; very inadequate ideas will always satisfy them. On these inadequate ideas reposes, and must repose, the general practice of the world. That is as much as saying that whoever sets himself to see things as they are will find himself one of a very small circle; but it is only by this small circle resolutely doing its own work that adequate ideas will ever get current at all. The rush and roar of practical life will always have a dizzying and attracting effect upon the most collected spectator, and tend to draw him into its vortex; most of all will this be the case where that life is so powerful as it is in England. But it is only by remaining collected, and refusing to lend himself to the point of view of the practical man, that the critic can do the practical man any service, and it is only by the greatest sincerity in pursuing his own course, and by at last convincing even the practical man of his sincerity, that he can escape misunderstandings which perpetually threaten him.

For the practical man is not apt for fine distinctions, and yet in these distinctions truth and the highest culture greatly find their account. But it is not easy to lead a practical man—unless you reassure him as to your practical intentions, you have no chance of leading him—to see that a thing which he has always been used to look at from one side only, which he greatly values, and which, looked at from that side, quite deserves, perhaps, all the prizing and admiring which he bestows upon it—that this thing, looked at from another side, may appear much less beneficent and beautiful, and yet retain all its claims to our practical allegiance. Where shall we find language innocent enough, how shall we make the spotless purity of our intentions evident enough, to enable us to say to the political Englishman that the British Constitution itself, which, seen from the practical side, looks such a magnificent organ of progress and virtue, seen from the speculative side—with its compromises, its love of facts, its horror of theory, its studied avoidance of clear thoughts—that, seen from this side, our august Constitution sometimes looks—forgive me, shade of Lord Somers!—a colossal machine for the manufacture of Philistines?[8] How is Cobbett[9] to say this and not be misunderstood, blackened as he is with the smoke of a lifelong conflict in the field of political practice? how is Mr. Carlyle to say it and not be misunderstood, after his furious raid into this field with his *Latter-day Pamphlets?* how is Mr. Ruskin, after his pugnacious political economy?[1] I say, the critic must keep out of the region of immediate practice in the political, social, humanitarian sphere if he wants to make a beginning for that more free speculative treat-

7. I.e., Hindu.
8. The unenlightened middle classes, whose opposition to the defenders of culture is akin to that of the biblical tribe that fought against the people of Israel, "the children of light." Arnold's repeated use of this parallel has established the term in our language. John Somers (1651–1716), statesman responsible for formulating the Declaration of

Rights.
9. William Cobbett (1762–1835), vehement reformer and champion of the poor and oppressed.
1. Reference to *Unto This Last* (1862), in which John Ruskin shifted from art criticism to an attack on traditional theories of economics. In *Latter-Day Pamphlets* (1850), Thomas Carlyle expressed bitter antidemocratic views.

ment of things, which may perhaps one day make its benefits felt even in this sphere, but in a natural and thence irresistible manner.

*   *   *

If I have insisted so much on the course which criticism must take where politics and religion are concerned, it is because, where these burning matters are in question, it is most likely to go astray. I have wished, above all, to insist on the attitude which criticism should adopt towards things in general; on its right tone and temper of mind. But then comes another question as to the subject matter which literary criticism should most seek. Here, in general, its course is determined for it by the idea which is the law of its being; the idea of a disinterested endeavour to learn and propagate the best that is known and thought in the world, and thus to establish a current of fresh and true ideas. By the very nature of things, as England is not all the world, much of the best that is known and thought in the world cannot be of English growth, must be foreign; by the nature of things, again, it is just this that we are least likely to know, while English thought is streaming in upon us from all sides, and takes excellent care that we shall not be ignorant of its existence. The English critic of literature, therefore, must dwell much on foreign thought, and with particular heed on any part of it, which, while significant and fruitful in itself, is for any reason specially likely to escape him. Again, judging is often spoken of as the critic's one business, and so in some sense it is; but the judgment which almost insensibly forms itself in a fair and clear mind, along with fresh knowledge, is the valuable one; and thus knowledge, and ever fresh knowledge, must be the critic's great concern for himself. And it is by communicating fresh knowledge, and letting his own judgment pass along with it—but insensibly, and in the second place, not the first, as a sort of companion and clue, not as an abstract lawgiver—that the critic will generally do most good to his readers. Sometimes, no doubt, for the sake of establishing an author's place in literature, and his relation to a central standard (and if this is not done, how are we to get at our *best in the world?*) criticism may have to deal with a subject matter so familiar that fresh knowledge is out of the question, and then it must be all judgment; an enunciation and detailed application of principles. Here the great safeguard is never to let oneself become abstract, always to retain an intimate and lively consciousness of the truth of what one is saying, and, the moment this fails us, to be sure that something is wrong. Still under all circumstances, this mere judgment and application of principles is, in itself, not the most satisfactory work to the critic; like mathematics, it is tautological, and cannot well give us, like fresh learning, the sense of creative activity.

But stop, some one will say; all this talk is of no practical use to us whatever; this criticism of yours is not what we have in our minds when we speak of criticism; when we speak of critics and criticism, we mean critics and criticism of the current English literature of the day; when you offer to tell criticism its function, it is to this criticism that we expect you to address yourself. I am sorry for it, for I am afraid I must disappoint these expectations. I am bound by my own definition of criticism: *a disinterested endeavour to learn and propagate the best that is known and thought in the world.* How much of current English literature comes into this "best that is known and thought in the world"? Not very much I fear; certainly less, at this moment, than of the current literature of France or Germany. Well, then, am I to alter my definition of criticism, in order to meet the requirements of a number of practicing

English critics, who, after all, are free in their choice of a business? That would be making criticism lend itself just to one of those alien practical considerations, which, I have said, are so fatal to it. One may say, indeed, to those who have to deal with the mass—so much better disregarded—of current English literature, that they may at all events endeavour, in dealing with this, to try it, so far as they can, by the standard of the best that is known and thought in the world; one may say, that to get anywhere near this standard, every critic should try and possess one great literature, at least, besides his own; and the more unlike his own, the better. But, after all, the criticism I am really concerned with—the criticism which alone can much help us for the future, the criticism which, throughout Europe, is at the present day meant, when so much stress is laid on the importance of criticism and the critical spirit—is a criticism which regards Europe as being, for intellectual and spiritual purposes, one great confederation, bound to a joint action and working to a common result, and whose members have, for their proper outfit, a knowledge of Greek, Roman, and Eastern antiquity, and of one another. Special, local, and temporary advantages being put out of account, that modern nation will in the intellectual and spiritual sphere make most progress, which most thoroughly carries out this program. And what is that but saying that we too, all of us, as individuals, the more thoroughly we carry it out, shall make the more progress?

There is so much inviting us!—what are we to take? what will nourish us in growth towards perfection? That is the question which, with the immense field of life and of literature lying before him, the critic has to answer; for himself first, and afterwards for others. In this idea of the critic's business the essays brought together in the following pages have had their origin; in this idea, widely different as are their subjects, they have, perhaps, their unity.

I conclude with what I said at the beginning: to have the sense of creative activity is the great happiness and the great proof of being alive, and it is not denied to criticism to have it; but then criticism must be sincere, simple, flexible, ardent, ever widening its knowledge. Then it may have, in no contemptible measure, a joyful sense of creative activity; a sense which a man of insight and conscience will prefer to what he might derive from a poor, starved, fragmentary, inadequate creation. And at some epochs no other creation is possible.

Still, in full measure, the sense of creative activity belongs only to genuine creation; in literature we must never forget that. But what true man of letters ever can forget it? It is no such common matter for a gifted nature to come into possession of a current of true and living ideas, and to produce amidst the inspiration of them, that we are likely to underrate it. The epochs of Aeschylus[2] and Shakespeare make us feel their pre-eminence. In an epoch like those is, no doubt, the true life of literature; there is the promised land, towards which criticism can only beckon. That promised land it will not be ours to enter, and we shall die in the wilderness:[3] but to have desired to enter it, to have saluted it from afar, is already, perhaps, the best distinction among contemporaries; it will certainly be the best title to esteem with posterity.

1864, 1865

---

2. Greek tragedian (525–456 B.C.E.).
3. An allusion to the fate of rebellious Israelites (Numbers 14.26–35).

From Culture and Anarchy[1]

From Chapter 1. Sweetness and Light

The impulse of the English race towards moral development and self-conquest has nowhere so powerfully manifested itself as in Puritanism. Nowhere has Puritanism found so adequate an expression as in the religious organization of the Independents.[2] The modern Independents have a newspaper, the *Nonconformist*, written with great sincerity and ability. The motto, the standard, the profession of faith which this organ of theirs carries aloft, is: "The Dissidence of Dissent and the Protestantism of the Protestant religion." There is sweetness and light, and an ideal of complete harmonious human perfection! One need not go to culture and poetry to find language to judge it. Religion, with its instinct for perfection, supplies language to judge it, language, too, which is in our mouths every day. "Finally, be of one mind, united in feeling," says St. Peter.[3] There is an ideal which judges the Puritan ideal: "The Dissidence of Dissent and the Protestantism of the Protestant religion!" And religious organizations like this are what people believe in, rest in, would give their lives for! Such, I say, is the wonderful virtue of even the beginnings of perfection, of having conquered even the plain faults of our animality, that the religious organization which has helped us to do it can seem to us something precious, salutary, and to be propagated, even when it wears such a brand of imperfection on its forehead as this. And men have got such a habit of giving to the language of religion a special application, of making it a mere jargon, that for the condemnation which religion itself passes on the shortcomings of their religious organizations they have no ear; they are sure to cheat themselves and to explain this condemnation away. They can only be reached by the criticism which culture, like poetry, speaking of language not to be sophisticated, and resolutely testing these organizations by the ideal of a human perfection complete on all sides, applies to them.

But men of culture and poetry, it will be said, are again and again failing, and failing conspicuously, in the necessary first stage to a harmonious perfection, in the subduing of the great obvious faults of our animality, which it is the glory of these religious organizations to have helped us to subdue. True, they do often so fail. They have often been without the virtues as well as the faults of the Puritan; it has been one of their dangers that they so felt the Puritan's faults that they too much neglected the practice of his virtues. I will

1. Arnold began *Culture and Anarchy* in the context of the turbulent political debate that preceded the passage of the second Reform Bill in 1867. The political climate seemed to some to threaten anarchy, to which Arnold opposed culture. A characteristic quality of the cultured state of mind is summed up, for his purposes, in his formula "sweetness and light," a phrase suggesting reasonableness of temper and intellectual insight. Arnold derived the phrase from a fable contrasting the spider with the bee in Jonathan Swift's *The Battle of the Books* (1704). The spider (representing a narrow, self-centered, and uncultured mind) spins out of itself "nothing at all but flybane and cobweb." The bee (representing a cultured mind that has drawn nourishment from the humanist tradition) ranges far and wide and makes in its hive honey and also wax out of which candles may be made.

Therefore, the bee, Swift says, furnishes humankind "with the two noblest of things, which are sweetness and light."

The selections printed here illustrate aspects of Arnold's indictment of the middle classes for their lack of sweetness and light. The first and third expose the narrowness and dullness of middle-class Puritan religious institutions in both the 17th and 19th centuries. The second, "Doing As One Likes," shows the limitations of the middle-class political bias and the irresponsibility of laissez-faire economics. Here Arnold is most close to Thomas Carlyle and John Ruskin.

2. A 17th-century Puritan group (of which Oliver Cromwell was an adherent), allied with the Congregationalists.

3. Cf. 1 Peter 3.8.

CULTURE AND ANARCHY / 1399

not, however, exculpate them at the Puritan's expense. They have often failed in morality, and morality is indispensable. And they have been punished for their failure, as the Puritan has been rewarded for his performance. They have been punished wherein they erred; but their ideal of beauty, of sweetness and light, and a human nature complete on all its sides, remains the true ideal of perfection still; just as the Puritan's ideal of perfection remains narrow and inadequate, although for what he did well he has been richly rewarded. Notwithstanding the mighty results of the Pilgrim Fathers' voyage, they and their standard of perfection are rightly judged when we figure to ourselves Shakespeare or Virgil[4]—souls in whom sweetness and light, and all that in human nature is most humane, were eminent—accompanying them on their voyage, and think what intolerable company Shakespeare and Virgil would have found them! In the same way let us judge the religious organizations which we see all around us. Do not let us deny the good and the happiness which they have accomplished; but do not let us fail to see clearly that their idea of human perfection is narrow and inadequate, and that the Dissidence of Dissent and the Protestantism of the Protestant religion will never bring humanity to its true goal. As I said with regard to wealth: Let us look at the life of those who live in and for it—so I say with regard to the religious organizations. Look at the life imaged in such a newspaper as the *Nonconformist*—a life of jealousy of the Establishment,[5] disputes, tea-meetings, openings of chapels, sermons; and then think of it as an ideal of a human life completing itself on all sides, and aspiring with all its organs after sweetness, light, and perfection!

From Chapter 2. Doing As One Likes

* * *

When I began to speak of culture, I insisted on our bondage to machinery,[6] on our proneness to value machinery as an end in itself, without looking beyond it to the end for which alone, in truth, it is valuable. Freedom, I said, was one of those things which we thus worshiped in itself, without enough regarding the ends for which freedom is to be desired. In our common notions and talk about freedom, we eminently show our idolatry of machinery. Our prevalent notion is—and I quoted a number of instances to prove it—that it is a most happy and important thing for a man merely to be able to do as he likes. On what he is to do when he is thus free to do as he likes, we do not lay so much stress. Our familiar praise of the British Constitution under which we live, is that it is a system of checks—a system which stops and paralyzes any power in interfering with the free action of individuals. To this effect Mr. Bright,[7] who loves to walk in the old ways of the Constitution, said forcibly in one of his great speeches, what many other people are every day saying less forcibly, that the central idea of English life and politics is *the assertion of personal liberty*. Evidently this is so; but evidently, also, as feudalism, which with its ideas, and habits of subordination was for many centuries silently behind the British Constitution, dies out, and we are left with nothing but our system of checks, and our notion of its being the great right and happiness of

4. Roman poet (70–19 B.C.E.).
5. The Church of England or the Established Church.
6. Arnold uses this word to signify systems of oper-

ation and organization, not mechanized apparatus.
7. John Bright (1811–1889), self-made businessman who became a noted orator and politician.

an Englishman to do as far as possible what he likes, we are in danger of drifting towards anarchy. We have not the notion, so familiar on the Continent and to antiquity, of *the State*—the nation in its collective and corporate character, entrusted with stringent powers for the general advantage, and controlling individual wills in the name of an interest wider than that of individuals. We say, what is very true, that this notion is often made instrumental to tyranny; we say that a State is in reality made up of the individuals who compose it, and that every individual is the best judge of his own interests. Our leading class is an aristocracy, and no aristocracy likes the notion of a State-authority greater than itself, with a stringent administrative machinery superseding the decorative inutilities of lord-lieutenancy, deputy-lieutenancy, and the *posse comitatus,*[8] which are all in its own hands. Our middle class, the great representative of trade and Dissent, with its maxims of every man for himself in business, every man for himself in religion, dreads a powerful administration which might somehow interfere with it; and besides, it has its own decorative inutilities of vestrymanship[9] and guardianship, which are to this class what lord-lieutenancy and the county magistracy are to the aristocratic class, and a stringent administration might either take these functions out of its hands, or prevent its exercising them in its own comfortable, independent manner, as at present.

Then as to our working class. This class, pressed constantly by the hard daily compulsion of material wants, is naturally the very center and stronghold of our national idea, that it is man's ideal right and felicity to do as he likes. I think I have somewhere related how M. Michelet[1] said to me of the people of France, that it was "a nation of barbarians civilized by the conscription." He meant that through their military service the idea of public duty and of discipline was brought to the mind of these masses, in other respects so raw and uncultivated. Our masses are quite as raw and uncultivated as the French; and so far from their having the idea of public duty and of discipline, superior to the individual's self-will, brought to their mind by a universal obligation of military service, such as that of the conscription—so far from their having this, the very idea of a conscription is so at variance with our English notion of the prime right and blessedness of doing as one likes, that I remember the manager of the Clay Cross works in Derbyshire told me during the Crimean war,[2] when our want of soldiers was much felt and some people were talking of a conscription, that sooner than submit to a conscription the population of that district would flee to the mines, and lead a sort of Robin Hood life underground.

For a long time, as I have said, the strong feudal habits of subordination and deference continued to tell upon the working class. The modern spirit has now almost entirely dissolved those habits, and the anarchical tendency of our worship of freedom in and for itself, of our superstitious faith, as I say, in machinery, is becoming very manifest. More and more, because of this our blind faith in machinery, because of our want of light to enable us to look beyond machinery to the end for which machinery is valuable, this and that

---

8. Power of the county (Latin); a feudal method of enforcing law by local authorities instead of by agencies of the central government.
9. A vestryman is an appointed member on a local church council.

1. Jules Michelet (1798–1874), French historian.
2. A war (1854–56) in which Britain joined France, Sardinia, and Turkey in fighting against Russia in Ukraine.

man, and this and that body of men, all over the country, are beginning to assert and put in practice an Englishman's right to do what he likes; his right to march where he likes, meet where he likes, enter where he likes, hoot as he likes, threaten as he likes, smash as he likes.[3] All this, I say, tends to anarchy; and though a number of excellent people, and particularly my friends of the Liberal or progressive party, as they call themselves, are kind enough to reassure us by saying that these are trifles, that a few transient outbreaks of rowdyism signify nothing, that our system of liberty is one which itself cures all the evils which it works, that the educated and intelligent classes stand in overwhelming strength and majestic repose, ready, like our military force in riots, to act at a moment's notice—yet one finds that one's Liberal friends generally say this because they have such faith in themselves and their nostrums, when they shall return, as the public welfare requires, to place and power. But this faith of theirs one cannot exactly share, when one has so long had them and their nostrums at work, and see that they have not prevented our coming to our present embarrassed condition. And one finds, also, that the outbreaks of rowdyism tend to become less and less of trifles, to become more frequent rather than less frequent; and that meanwhile our educated and intelligent classes remain in their majestic repose, and somehow or other, whatever happens, their overwhelming strength, like our military force in riots, never does act.

How indeed, *should* their overwhelming strength act, when the man who gives an inflammatory lecture, or breaks down the park railings, or invades a Secretary of State's office, is only following an Englishman's impulse to do as he likes; and our own conscience tells us that we ourselves have always regarded this impulse as something primary and sacred? Mr. Murphy[4] lectures at Birmingham, and showers on the Catholic population of that town "words," says the Home Secretary, "only fit to be addressed to thieves or murderers." What then? Mr. Murphy has his own reasons of several kinds. He suspects the Roman Catholic Church of designs upon Mrs. Murphy; and he says if mayors and magistrates do not care for their wives and daughters, he does. But, above all, he is doing as he likes; or, in worthier language, asserting his personal liberty. "I will carry out my lectures if they walk over my body as a dead corpse, and I say to the Mayor of Birmingham that he is my servant while I am in Birmingham, and as my servant he must do his duty and protect me." Touching and beautiful words, which find a sympathetic chord in every British bosom! The moment it is plainly put before us that a man is asserting his personal liberty, we are half disarmed; because we are believers in freedom, and not in some dream of a right reason to which the assertion of our freedom is to be subordinated. Accordingly, the Secretary of State had to say that although the lecturer's language was "only fit to be addressed to thieves or murderers," yet, "I do not think he is to be deprived, I do not think that anything I have said could justify the inference that he is to be deprived, of the right of protection in a place built by him for the purpose of these lectures; because the language was not language which afforded grounds for a criminal prosecution." No, nor to be silenced by Mayor, or Home Secretary, or any

3. A reference to the riots of 1866 in which a London mob demolished the iron railings enclosing Hyde Park.
4. An orator whose inflammatory anti-Catholic public speech "The Errors of the Roman Church" led to rioting in Birmingham and other cities in 1867.

1402 / Matthew Arnold

administrative authority on earth, simply on their notion of what is discreet and reasonable! This is in perfect consonance with our public opinion, and with our national love for the assertion of personal liberty.

* * *

From *Chapter 5*. Porro Unum Est Necessarium[5]

* * *

* * * Sweetness and light evidently have to do with the bent or side in humanity which we call Hellenic. Greek intelligence has obviously for its essence the instinct for what Plato[6] calls the true, firm, intelligible law of things; the law of light, of seeing things as they are. Even in the natural sciences, where the Greeks had not time and means adequately to apply this instinct, and where we have gone a great deal further than they did, it is this instinct which is the root of the whole matter and the ground of all our success; and this instinct the world has mainly learnt of the Greeks, inasmuch as they are humanity's most signal manifestation of it. Greek art, again, Greek beauty, have their root in the same impulse to see things as they really are, inasmuch as Greek art and beauty rest on fidelity to nature—the *best* nature—and on a delicate discrimination of what this best nature is. To say we work for sweetness and light, then, is only another way of saying that we work for Hellenism. But, oh! cry many people, sweetness and light are not enough; you must put strength or energy along with them, and make a kind of trinity of strength, sweetness and light, and then, perhaps, you may do some good. That is to say, we are to join Hebraism, strictness of the moral conscience, and manful walking by the best light we have, together with Hellenism, inculcate both, and rehearse[7] the praises of both.

Or, rather, we may praise both in conjunction, but we must be careful to praise Hebraism most. "Culture," says an acute, though somewhat rigid critic, Mr. Sidgwick,[8] "diffuses sweetness and light. I do not undervalue these blessings, but religion gives fire and strength, and the world wants[9] fire and strength even more than sweetness and light." By religion, let me explain, Mr. Sidgwick here means particularly that Puritanism on the insufficiency of which I have been commenting and to which he says I am unfair. Now, no doubt, it is possible to be a fanatical partisan of light and the instincts which push us to it, a fanatical enemy of strictness of moral conscience and the instincts which push us to it. A fanaticism of this sort deforms and vulgarizes the well-known work, in some respects so remarkable, of the late Mr. Buckle.[1] Such a fanaticism carries its own mark with it, in lacking sweetness; and its own penalty, in that, lacking sweetness, it comes in the end to lack light too. And the Greeks—the great exponents of humanity's bent for sweetness and light united, of its perception that the truth of things must be at the same time beauty—singularly escaped the fanaticism which we moderns, whether we

---

5. But one thing is needful (Latin; Luke 10.42). This chapter develops a contrast established in chap. 4 between *Hebraism* (Puritan morality and energetic devotion to work) and *Hellenism* (cultivation of the aesthetic and intellectual understanding of life). The Puritan middle classes, according to Arnold, think that the "one thing needful" is the Hebraic form of virtue.

6. Greek philosopher (ca. 427–ca 347 B.C.E.).
7. Repeat.
8. Henry Sidgwick (1838–1900), philosopher whose article on Arnold appeared in *Macmillan's Magazine* (Aug. 1867).
9. Lacks.
1. Henry Thomas Buckle (1821–1862), author of *A History of Civilization* (1857–61).

Hellenize or whether we Hebraize, are so apt to show. They arrived—though failing, as has been said, to give adequate practical satisfaction to the claims of man's moral side—at the idea of a comprehensive adjustment of the claims of both the sides in man, the moral as well as the intellectual, of a full estimate of both, and of a reconciliation of both; an idea which is philosophically of the greatest value, and the best of lessons for us moderns. So we ought to have no difficulty in conceding to Mr. Sidgwick that manful walking by the best light one has—fire and strength as he calls it—has its high value as well as culture, the endeavor to see things in their truth and beauty, the pursuit of sweetness and light. But whether at this or that time, and to this or that set of persons, one ought to insist most on the praises of fire and strength, or on the praises of sweetness and light, must depend, one would think, on the circumstances and needs of that particular time and those particular persons. And all that we have been saying, and indeed any glance at the world around us, shows that with us, with the most respectable and strongest part of us, the ruling force is now, and long has been, a Puritan force—the care for fire and strength, strictness of conscience, Hebraism, rather than the care for sweetness and light, spontaneity of consciousness, Hellenism.

Well, then, what is the good of our now rehearsing the praises of fire and strength to ourselves, who dwell too exclusively on them already? When Mr. Sidgwick says so broadly, that the world wants fire and strength even more than sweetness and light, is he not carried away by a turn for broad generalization? does he not forget that the world is not all of one piece, and every piece with the same needs at the same time? It may be true that the Roman world at the beginning of our era, or Leo the Tenth's Court at the time of the Reformation, or French society in the eighteenth century,[2] needed fire and strength even more than sweetness and light. But can it be said that the Barbarians who overran the empire needed fire and strength even more than sweetness and light; or that the Puritans needed them more; or that Mr. Murphy, the Birmingham lecturer, and the Rev. W. Cattle[3] and his friends, need them more?

The Puritan's great danger is that he imagines himself in possession of a rule telling him the *unum necessarium,* or one thing needful, and that he then remains satisfied with a very crude conception of what this rule really is and what it tells him, thinks he has now knowledge and henceforth needs only to act, and, in this dangerous state of assurance and self-satisfaction, proceeds to give full swing to a number of the instincts of his ordinary self. Some of the instincts of his ordinary self he has, by the help of his rule of life, conquered; but others which he has not conquered by this help he is so far from perceiving to need subjugation, and to be instincts of an inferior self, that he even fancies it to be his right and duty, in virtue of having conquered a limited part of himself, to give unchecked swing to the remainder. He is, I say, a victim of Hebraism, of the tendency to cultivate strictness of conscience rather than spontaneity of consciousness. And what he wants is a larger conception of human nature, showing him the number of other points at which his nature must come to its best, besides the points which he himself knows and thinks of. There is no *unum necessarium,* or one thing needful, which can free human

2. Societies representing an excess of sophisticated worldliness as at the courts of a Roman emperor such as Nero (54–68 C.E.) or of Pope Leo X (1513–21) or Louis XV (1715–74), respectively.

3. A Nonconformist clergyman who was chairman of the anti-Catholic meeting addressed by Murphy in 1867 (see chapter 2, "Doing As One Likes," p. 1399).

nature from the obligation of trying to come to its best at all these points. The real *unum necessarium* for us is to come to our best at all points. Instead of our "one thing needful," justifying in us vulgarity, hideousness, ignorance, violence—our vulgarity, hideousness, ignorance, violence, are really so many touchstones[4] which try our one thing needful, and which prove that in the state, at any rate, in which we ourselves have it, it is not all we want. And as the force which encourages us to stand staunch and fast by the rule and ground we have is Hebraism, so the force which encourages us to go back upon this rule, and to try the very ground on which we appear to stand, is Hellenism—a turn for giving our consciousness free play and enlarging its range. And what I say is, not that Hellenism is always for everybody more wanted than Hebraism, but that for the Rev. W. Cattle at this particular moment, and for the great majority of us his fellow countrymen, it is more wanted.

* * *

1868, 1869

From The Study of Poetry[1]

"The future of poetry is immense, because in poetry, where it is worthy of its high destinies, our race, as time goes on, will find an ever surer and surer stay. There is not a creed which is not shaken, not an accredited dogma which is not shown to be questionable, not a received tradition which does not threaten to dissolve. Our religion has materialized itself in the fact, in the supposed fact; it has attached its emotion to the fact, and now the fact is failing it. But for poetry the idea is everything; the rest is a world of illusion, of divine illusion. Poetry attaches its emotion to the idea; the idea *is* the fact. The strongest part of our religion today is its unconscious poetry."

Let me be permitted to quote these words of my own, as uttering the thought which should, in my opinion, go with us and govern us in all our study of poetry. In the present work[2] it is the course of one great contributory stream to the world-river of poetry that we are invited to follow. We are here invited to trace the stream of English poetry. But whether we set ourselves, as here, to follow only one of the several streams that make the mighty river of poetry, or whether we seek to know them all, our governing thought should be the

4. For the importance to Arnold of the concept of the touchstone—a succinct instance or standard by which to judge other materials—see also "The Study of Poetry" (this page).
1. Aside from its vindication of the importance of literature, this essay is an interesting example of the variety of Arnold's reading. To know literature in only one language seemed to him not to know literature. His personal *Notebooks* show that throughout his active life he continued to read books in French, German, Italian, Latin, and Greek. His favorite authors in these languages are used by him as a means of testing English poetry. The testing is sometimes a severe one. Readers

may also protest that despite Arnold's wit, his essay is limited by an incomplete recognition of the values of comic literature, a shortcoming abundantly evident in the discussion of Chaucer. Nevertheless, whether we agree or disagree with some of Arnold's verdicts, we can be attracted by the combination of traditionalism and impressionism on which these verdicts are based, and we can enjoy the memorable phrasemaking in which the verdicts are expressed. "The Study of Poetry" has been extraordinarily potent in shaping literary tastes in England and in America.
2. An anthology of English poetry for which this essay served as the introduction.

same. We should conceive of poetry worthily, and more highly than it has been the custom to conceive of it. We should conceive of it as capable of higher uses, and called to higher destinies, than those which in general men have assigned to it hitherto. More and more mankind will discover that we have to turn to poetry to interpret life for us, to console us, to sustain us. Without poetry, our science will appear incomplete; and most of what now passes with us for religion and philosophy will be replaced by poetry. Science, I say, will appear incomplete without it. For finely and truly does Wordsworth call poetry "the impassioned expression which is in the countenance of all science";[3] and what is a countenance without its expression? Again, Wordsworth finely and truly calls poetry "the breath and finer spirit of all knowledge": our religion, parading evidences such as those on which the popular mind relies now; our philosophy, pluming itself on its reasonings about causation and finite and infinite being; what are they but the shadows and dreams and false shows of knowledge? The day will come when we shall wonder at ourselves for having trusted to them, for having taken them seriously; and the more we perceive their hollowness, the more we shall prize "the breath and finer spirit of knowledge" offered to us by poetry.

But if we conceive thus highly of the destinies of poetry, we must also set our standard for poetry high, since poetry, to be capable of fulfilling such high destinies, must be poetry of a high order of excellence. We must accustom ourselves to a high standard and to a strict judgment. * * *

The best poetry is what we want; the best poetry will be found to have a power of forming, sustaining, and delighting us, as nothing else can. A clearer, deeper sense of the best in poetry, and of the strength and joy to be drawn from it, is the most precious benefit which we can gather from a poetical collection such as the present. And yet in the very nature and conduct of such a collection there is inevitably something which tends to obscure in us the consciousness of what our benefit should be, and to distract us from the pursuit of it. We should therefore steadily set it before our minds at the outset, and should compel ourselves to revert constantly to the thought of it as we proceed.

Yes; constantly in reading poetry, a sense for the best, the really excellent, and of the strength and joy to be drawn from it, should be present in our minds and should govern our estimate of what we read. But this real estimate, the only true one, is liable to be superseded, if we are not watchful, by two other kinds of estimate, the historic estimate and the personal estimate, both of which are fallacious. A poet or a poem may count to us historically, they may count to us on grounds personal to ourselves, and they may count to us really. They may count to us historically. The course of development of a nation's language, thought, and poetry, is profoundly interesting; and by regarding a poet's work as a stage in this course of development we may easily bring ourselves to make it of more importance as poetry than in itself it really is, we may come to use a language of quite exaggerated praise in criticizing it; in short, to overrate it. So arises in our poetic judgments the fallacy caused by the estimate which we may call historic. Then, again, a poet or a poem may count to us on grounds personal to ourselves. Our personal affinities, likings, and circumstances, have great power to sway our estimate of this or that poet's work, and to make us attach more importance to it as poetry than in itself it

3. Preface to *Lyrical Ballads* (1800).

really possesses, because to us it is, or has been, of high importance. Here also we overrate the object of our interest, and apply to it a language of praise which is quite exaggerated. And thus we get the source of a second fallacy in our poetic judgments—the fallacy caused by an estimate which we may call personal.

* * *

* * * The historic estimate is likely in especial to affect our judgment and our language when we are dealing with ancient poets; the personal estimate when we are dealing with poets our contemporaries, or at any rate modern. The exaggerations due to the historic estimate are not in themselves, perhaps, of very much gravity. Their report hardly enters the general ear; probably they do not always impose even on the literary men who adopt them. But they lead to a dangerous abuse of language. So we hear Caedmon,[4] amongst our own poets, compared to Milton. I have already noticed the enthusiasm of one accomplished French critic for "historic origins."[5] Another eminent French critic, M. Vitet, comments upon that famous document of the early poetry of his nation, the *Chanson de Roland*.[6] It is indeed a most interesting document. The *joculator* or *jongleur*[7] Taillefer, who was with William the Conqueror's army at Hastings,[8] marched before the Norman troops, so said the tradition, singing "of Charlemagne and of Roland and of Oliver, and of the vassals who died at Roncevaux"; and it is suggested that in the *Chanson de Roland* by one Turoldus or *Theroulde*, a poem preserved in a manuscript of the twelfth century in the Bodleian Library at Oxford, we have certainly the matter, perhaps even some of the words, of the chant which Taillefer sang. The poem has vigor and freshness; it is not without pathos. But M. Vitet is not satisfied with seeing in it a document of some poetic value, and of very high historic and linguistic value; he sees in it a grand and beautiful work, a monument of epic genius. In its general design he finds the grandiose conception, in its details he finds the constant union of simplicity with greatness, which are the marks, he truly says, of the genuine epic, and distinguish it from the artificial epic of literary ages. One thinks of Homer; this is the sort of praise which is given to Homer, and justly given. Higher praise there cannot well be, and it is the praise due to epic poetry of the highest order only, and to no other. Let us try, then, the *Chanson de Roland* at its best. Roland, mortally wounded, lays himself down under a pine tree, with his face turned towards Spain and the enemy—

> De plusurs choses à remembrer li prist,
> De tantes teres cume li bers cunquist,
> De dulce France, des humes de sun lign,
> De Carlemagne sun seignor ki l'nurrit.[9]

That is primitive work, I repeat, with an undeniable poetic quality of its own. It deserves such praise, and such praise is sufficient for it. But now turn to Homer—

4. A 7th-century Old English poet.
5. Charles d'Héricault (1823–1899), a French critic cited earlier in a passage omitted here. Arnold had mildly reprimanded him for his "historical" bias in praising a 15th-century poet, Clément Marot, at the expense of classical 17th-century poets such as Racine.
6. An 11th-century epic poem in Old French that tells of the 8th-century wars of Charlemagne against the Moors in Spain and of the bravery of the French leaders Roland and Oliver. Ludovic

Vitet (1802–1873) wrote on it in his *Essais Historiques et Littéraires* (1862).
7. Jester or minstrel (French).
8. The battle in 1066 in which Harold II was killed and the English army defeated.
9. "Then began he to call many things to remembrance—all the lands which his valor conquered and pleasant France, and the men of his lineage, and Charlemagne his liege lord who nourished him." *Chanson de Roland* 3.939–42 [Arnold's note].

"Ὣς φάτο τοὺς δ' ἤδη κάτεχεν φυσίζοος αἶα
ἐν Λακεδαίμονι αὖθι, φίλῃ ἐν πατρίδι γαίῃ.¹

We are here in another world, another order of poetry altogether; here is rightly due such supreme praise as that which M. Vitet gives to the *Chanson de Roland*. If our words are to have any meaning, if our judgments are to have any solidity, we must not heap that supreme praise upon poetry of an order immeasurably inferior.

Indeed there can be no more useful help for discovering what poetry belongs to the class of the truly excellent, and can therefore do us most good, than to have always in one's mind lines and expressions of the great masters, and to apply them as a touchstone to other poetry. Of course we are not to require this other poetry to resemble them; it may be very dissimilar. But if we have any tact we shall find them, when we have lodged them well in our minds, an infallible touchstone for detecting the presence or absence of high poetic quality, and also the degree of this quality, in all other poetry which we may place beside them. Short passages, even single lines, will serve our turn quite sufficiently. Take the two lines which I have just quoted from Homer, the poet's comment on Helen's mention of her brothers—or take his

Ἆ δειλώ, τί σφῶϊ δόμεν Πηλῆϊ ἄνακτι
θνητῷ; ὑμεῖς δ' ἐστὸν ἀγήρω τ' ἀθανάτω τε.
ἦ ἵνα δυστήνοισι μετ' ἀνδράσιν ἄλγε' ἔχητον;²

the address of Zeus to the horses of Peleus—or take finally his

Καὶ σέ, γέρον, τὸ πρὶν μὲν ἀκούομεν ὄλβιον εἶναι.³

the words of Achilles to Priam, a suppliant before him. Take that incomparable line and a half of Dante, Ugolino's tremendous words—

Io no piangeva; sì dentro impietrai.
Piangevan elli . . . ⁴

take the lovely words of Beatrice to Virgil—

Io son fatta da Dio, sua mercè, tale,
Che la vostra miseria non mi tange,
Nè fiamma d'esto incendio non m'assale . . . ⁵

take the simple, but perfect, single line—

In la sua volontade è nostra pace.⁶

Take of Shakespeare a line or two of Henry the Fourth's expostulation with sleep—

Wilt thou upon the high and giddy mast
Seal up the shipboy's eyes, and rock his brains
In cradle of the rude imperious surge . . . ⁷

1. "So said she; they long since in Earth's soft arms were reposing, / There, in their own dear land, their fatherland, Lacedaemon." *Iliad* 3.243–44 (translated by Dr. Hawtrey) [Arnold's note].
2. "Ah, unhappy pair, why gave we you to King Peleus, to a mortal? but ye are without old age, and immortal. Was it that with men born to misery ye might have sorrow?" *Iliad* 17.443–45 [Arnold's note].
3. "Nay, and thou too, old man, in former days wast, as we hear, happy." *Iliad* 24.543 [Arnold's note]. Priam, king of Troy, has begged Achilles to

return the body of his son Hector, whom the Greek warrior had killed.
4. "I wailed not, so of stone I grew within; *they* wailed." *Inferno* 33.49–50 [Arnold's note].
5. "Of such sort hath God, thanked be His mercy, made me, that your misery toucheth me not, neither doth the flame of this fire strike me." *Inferno* 2.91–93 [Arnold's note]. The Roman poet Virgil is Dante's guide.
6. "In His will is our peace." *Paradiso* 3.85 [Arnold's note].
7. *2 Henry IV* 3.1.18–20.

1408 / Matthew Arnold

and take, as well, Hamlet's dying request to Horatio—

> If thou didst ever hold me in thy heart,
> Absent thee from felicity awhile,
> And in this harsh world draw thy breath in pain,
> To tell my story . . . [8]

Take of Milton that Miltonic passage—

> Darkened so, yet shone
> Above them all the archangel; but his face
> Deep scars of thunder had intrenched, and care
> Sat on his faded cheek . . . [9]

add two such lines as—

> And courage never to submit or yield
> And what is else not to be overcome . . . [1]

and finish with the exquisite close to the loss of Proserpine, the loss

> . . . which cost Ceres all that pain
> To seek her through the world.[2]

These few lines, if we have tact and can use them, are enough even of themselves to keep clear and sound our judgments about poetry, to save us from fallacious estimates of it, to conduct us to a real estimate.

The specimens I have quoted differ widely from one another, but they have in common this: the possession of the very highest poetical quality. If we are thoroughly penetrated by their power, we shall find that we have acquired a sense enabling us, whatever poetry may be laid before us, to feel the degree in which a high poetical quality is present or wanting there. Critics give themselves great labour to draw out what in the abstract constitutes the characters of a high quality of poetry. It is much better simply to have recourse to concrete examples—to take specimens of poetry of the high, the very highest quality, and to say: The characters of a high quality of poetry are what is expressed *there*. They are far better recognized by being felt in the verse of the master, than by being perused in the prose of the critic. Nevertheless if we are urgently pressed to give some critical account of them, we may safely, perhaps, venture on laying down, not indeed how and why the characters arise, but where and in what they arise. They are in the matter and substance of the poetry, and they are in its manner and style. Both of these, the substance and matter on the one hand, the style and manner on the other, have a mark, an accent, of high beauty, worth, and power. But if we are asked to define this mark and accent in the abstract, our answer must be: No, for we should thereby be darkening the question, not clearing it. The mark and accent are as given by the substance and matter of that poetry, by the style and manner of that poetry, and of all other poetry which is akin to it in quality.

Only one thing we may add as to the substance and matter of poetry, guiding ourselves by Aristotle's profound observation that the superiority of poetry over history consists in its possessing a higher truth and a higher seriousness ($\varphi\iota\lambda o\sigma o\varphi\acute{\omega}\tau\epsilon\rho o\nu$ $\kappa\alpha\grave{\iota}$ $\sigma\pi o\upsilon\delta\alpha\iota\acute{o}\tau\epsilon\rho o\nu$).[3] Let us add, therefore, to what we have

8. *Hamlet* 5.2.288–91.
9. *Paradise Lost* 1.599–602.
1. *Paradise Lost* 1.108–9.
2. *Paradise Lost* 4.271–72. Ceres, the Roman god-

dess of grain, searched for her daughter Proserpina, not knowing that she had been abducted by Pluto, the god of the underworld.
3. Aristotle's *Poetics* 9.

said, this: that the substance and matter of the best poetry acquire their special character from possessing, in an eminent degree, truth and seriousness. We may add yet further, what is in itself evident, that to the style and manner of the best poetry their special character, their accent, is given by their diction, and, even yet more, by their movement. And though we distinguish between the two characters, the two accents, of superiority, yet they are nevertheless vitally connected one with the other. The superior character of truth and seriousness, in the matter and substance of the best poetry, is inseparable from the superiority of diction and movement marking its style and manner. The two superiorities are closely related, and are in steadfast proportion one to the other. So far as high poetic truth and seriousness are wanting to a poet's matter and substance, so far also, we may be sure, will a high poetic stamp of diction and movement be wanting to his style and manner. In proportion as this high stamp of diction and movement, again, is absent from a poet's style and manner, we shall find, also, that high poetic truth and seriousness are absent from his substance and matter.

So stated, these are but dry generalities; their whole force lies in their application. And I could wish every student of poetry to make the application of them for himself. Made by himself, the application would impress itself upon his mind far more deeply than made by me. Neither will my limits allow me to make any full application of the generalities above propounded; but in the hope of bringing out, at any rate, some significance in them, and of establishing an important principle more firmly by their means, I will, in the space which remains to me, follow rapidly from the commencement the course of our English poetry with them in my view.

*　*　*

Chaucer's * * * poetical importance does not need the assistance of the historic estimate; it is real. He is a genuine source of joy and strength, which is flowing still for us and will flow always. He will be read, as time goes on, far more generally than he is read now. His language is a cause of difficulty for us; but so also, and I think in quite as great a degree, is the language of Burns.[4] In Chaucer's case, as in that of Burns, it is a difficulty to be unhesitatingly accepted and overcome.

If we ask ourselves wherein consists the immense superiority of Chaucer's poetry over the romance poetry—why it is that in passing from this to Chaucer we suddenly feel ourselves to be in another world, we shall find that his superiority is both in the substance of his poetry and in the style of his poetry. His superiority in substance is given by his large, free, simple, clear yet kindly view of human life—so unlike the total want, in the romance poets, of all intelligent command of it. Chaucer has not their helplessness; he has gained the power to survey the world from a central, a truly human point of view. We have only to call to mind the Prologue to *The Canterbury Tales*. The right comment upon it is Dryden's: "It is sufficient to say, according to the proverb, that *here is God's plenty*." And again: "He is a perpetual fountain of good sense."[5] It is by a large, free, sound representation of things, that poetry, this high criticism of life, has truth of substance; and Chaucer's poetry has truth of substance.

Of his style and manner, if we think first of the romance poetry and then of Chaucer's divine liquidness of diction, his divine fluidity of movement, it is

<hr />

4. Robert Burns (1759–1796), whose language is difficult because he frequently uses Scottish dialect.

5. Both quotations are from John Dryden's preface to his *Fables Ancient and Modern* (1700).

difficult to speak temperately. They are irresistible, and justify all the rapture with which his successors speak of his "gold dewdrops of speech."[6] Johnson misses the point entirely when he finds fault with Dryden for ascribing to Chaucer the first refinement of our numbers, and says that Gower[7] also can show smooth numbers and easy rhymes. The refinement of our numbers means something far more than this. A nation may have versifiers with smooth numbers and easy rhymes, and yet may have no real poetry at all. Chaucer is the father of our splendid English poetry; he is our "well of English undefiled,"[8] because by the lovely charm of his diction, the lovely charm of his movement, he makes an epoch and founds a tradition. In Spenser, Shakespeare, Milton, Keats, we can follow the tradition of the liquid diction, the fluid movement, of Chaucer; at one time it is his liquid diction of which in these poets we feel the virtue, and at another time it is his fluid movement. And the virtue is irresistible.

Bounded as is my space, I must yet find room for an example of Chaucer's virtue, as I have given examples to show the virtue of the great classics. I feel disposed to say that a single line is enough to show the charm of Chaucer's verse; that merely one line like this—

O martyr souded[9] in virginitee!

has a virtue of manner and movement such as we shall not find in all the verse of romance poetry—but this is saying nothing. The virtue is such as we shall not find, perhaps, in all English poetry, outside the poets whom I have named as the special inheritors of Chaucer's tradition. A single line, however, is too little if we have not the strain of Chaucer's verse well in our memory; let us take a stanza. It is from *The Prioress's Tale,* the story of the Christian child murdered in a Jewry—[1]

My throte is cut unto my nekke-bone
Saidè this child, and as by way of kinde
I should have deyd, yea, longè time agone;
But Jesu Christ, as ye in bookès finde,
Will that his glory last and be in minde,
And for the worship of his mother dere
Yet may I sing O *Alma* loud and clere.

Wordsworth has modernized this Tale, and to feel how delicate and evanescent is the charm of verse, we have only to read Wordsworth's first three lines of this stanza after Chaucer's—

My throat is cut unto the bone, I trow,
Said this young child, and by the law of kind
I should have died, yea, many hours ago.

The charm is departed. It is often said that the power of liquidness and fluidity in Chaucer's verse was dependent upon a free, a licentious dealing with language, such as is now impossible; upon a liberty, such as Burns too enjoyed,

6. "The Life of Our Lady," a poem by John Lydgate (ca. 1370–ca.1451).
7. John Gower (ca. 1325–1408), friend of Chaucer and author of the *Confessio Amantis,* a long poem in octosyllabic couplets. Samuel Johnson (1709–1784), critic, essayist, and poet.
8. Said of Chaucer by Edmund Spenser in The

Faerie Queene (1590) 4.2.32.
9. The French *soudé:* soldered, fixed fast [Arnold's note]. From *The Canterbury Tales, The Prioress's Tale* (line 127); Chaucer wrote "souded to" rather than "souded in."
1. Jewish ghetto.

of making words like *neck, bird,* into a dissyllable by adding to them, and words like *cause, rhyme,* into a dissyllable by sounding the *e* mute. It is true that Chaucer's fluidity is conjoined with this liberty, and is admirably served by it; but we ought not to say that it was dependent upon it. It was dependent upon his talent. Other poets with a like liberty do not attain to the fluidity of Chaucer; Burns himself does not attain to it. Poets, again, who have a talent akin to Chaucer's, such as Shakespeare or Keats, have known how to attain to his fluidity without the like liberty.

And yet Chaucer is not one of the great classics. His poetry transcends and effaces, easily and without effort, all the romance poetry of Catholic Christendom; it transcends and effaces all the English poetry contemporary with it, it transcends and effaces all the English poetry subsequent to it down to the age of Elizabeth. Of such avail is poetic truth of substance, in its natural and necessary union with poetic truth of style. And yet, I say, Chaucer is not one of the great classics. He has not their accent. What is wanting to him is suggested by the mere mention of the name of the first great classic of Christendom, the immortal poet who died eighty years before Chaucer—Dante. The accent of such verse as

In la sua volontade è nostra pace . . .

is altogether beyond Chaucer's reach; we praise him, but we feel that this accent is out of the question for him. It may be said that it was necessarily out of the reach of any poet in the England of that stage of growth. Possibly; but we are to adopt a real, not a historic, estimate of poetry. However we may account for its absence, something is wanting, then, to the poetry of Chaucer, which poetry must have before it can be placed in the glorious class of the best. And there is no doubt what that something is. It is the σπουδαιότης, the high and excellent seriousness, which Aristotle assigns as one of the grand virtues of poetry. The substance of Chaucer's poetry, his view of things and his criticism of life, has largeness, freedom, shrewdness, benignity; but it has not this high seriousness. Homer's criticism of life has it, Dante's has it, Shakespeare's has it. It is this chiefly which gives to our spirits what they can rest upon; and with the increasing demands of our modern ages upon poetry, this virtue of giving us what we can rest upon will be more and more highly esteemed. A voice from the slums of Paris, fifty or sixty years after Chaucer, the voice of poor Villon out of his life of riot and crime, has at its happy moments (as, for instance, in the last stanza of *La Belle Heaulmière*)[2] more of this important poetic virtue of seriousness than all the productions of Chaucer. But its apparition[3] in Villon, and in men like Villon, is fitful; the greatness of the great poets, the power of their criticism of life, is that their virtue is sustained.

To our praise, therefore, of Chaucer as a poet there must be this limitation: he lacks the high seriousness of the great classics, and therewith an important

2. The name *Heaulmière* is said to be derived from a headdress (helm) worn as a mask by courtesans. In Villon's ballad a poor old creature of this class laments her days of youth and beauty. The last stanza of the ballad runs thus—"*Ainsi le bon temps regretons / Entrenous, pauvres vieilles sottes, / Assises bas, à croppetons, / Tost en ung tas comme pelottes; / A petit feu de chenevottes / Tost allumeés, tost estaincles, / Et jadis fusmes si mignottes! / Ainsi en prend à maintz et maintes.*" [It may be translated:] "Thus amongst ourselves we regret the good time, poor silly old things, low-seated on our heels, all in a heap like so many balls; by a little fire of hemp stalks, soon lighted, soon spent. And once we were such darlings! So fares it with many and many a one" [Arnold's note]. François Villon (1431–1484), French poet and vagabond.
3. Appearance.

part of their virtue. Still, the main fact for us to bear in mind about Chaucer is his sterling value according to that real estimate which we firmly adopt for all poets. He has poetic truth of substance, though he has not high poetic seriousness, and corresponding to his truth of substance he has an exquisite virtue of style and manner. With him is born our real poetry.

For my present purpose I need not dwell on our Elizabethan poetry, or on the continuation and close of this poetry in Milton. We all of us profess to be agreed in the estimate of this poetry; we all of us recognize it as great poetry, our greatest, and Shakespeare and Milton as our poetical classics. The real estimate, here, has universal currency. With the next age of our poetry divergency and difficulty begin. An historic estimate of that poetry has established itself; and the question is, whether it will be found to coincide with the real estimate.

The age of Dryden, together with our whole eighteenth century which followed it, sincerely believed itself to have produced poetical classics of its own, and even to have made advance, in poetry, beyond all its predecessors. Dryden regards as not seriously disputable the opinion "that the sweetness of English verse was never understood or practiced by our fathers."[4] Cowley[5] could see nothing at all in Chaucer's poetry. Dryden heartily admired it, and, as we have seen, praised its matter admirably; but of its exquisite manner and movement all he can find to say is that "there is the rude sweetness of a Scotch tune in it, which is natural and pleasing, though not perfect."[6] Addison,[7] wishing to praise Chaucer's numbers, compares them with Dryden's own. And all through the eighteenth century, and down even into our own times, the stereotyped phrase of approbation for good verse found in our early poetry has been, that it even approached the verse of Dryden, Addison, Pope, and Johnson.

Are Dryden and Pope poetical classics? Is the historic estimate, which represents them as such, and which has been so long established that it cannot easily give way, the real estimate? Wordsworth and Coleridge, as is well known, denied it; but the authority of Wordsworth and Coleridge does not weigh much with the young generation, and there are many signs to show that the eighteenth century and its judgments are coming into favor again. Are the favorite poets of the eighteenth century classics?

It is impossible within my present limits to discuss the question fully. And what man of letters would not shrink from seeming to dispose dictatorially of the claims of two men who are, at any rate, such masters in letters as Dryden and Pope; two men of such admirable talent, both of them, and one of them, Dryden, a man, on all sides, of such energetic and genial power? And yet, if we are to gain the full benefit from poetry, we must have the real estimate of it. I cast about for some mode of arriving, in the present case, at such an estimate without offense. And perhaps the best way is to begin, as it is easy to begin, with cordial praise.

When we find Chapman,[8] the Elizabethan translator of Homer, expressing himself in his preface thus: "Though truth in her very nakedness sits in so deep a pit, that from Gades to Aurora and Ganges few eyes can sound her, I hope yet those few here will so discover and confirm that, the date being out of her darkness in this morning of our poet, he shall now gird his temples with

4. *Essay on Dramatic Poesy* (1668).
5. Abraham Cowley (1618–1667), English poet.
6. Preface to his *Fables*.
7. Joseph Addison (1672–1719), essayist and

poet.
8. George Chapman (ca. 1559–1634), poet and dramatist; the quotation is from his translation (1598–1611) of the *Iliad*.

THE STUDY OF POETRY / 1413

the sun," we pronounce that such a prose is intolerable. When we find Milton writing: "And long it was not after, when I was confirmed in this opinion, that he, who would not be frustrate of his hope to write well hereafter in laudable things, ought himself to be a true poem"[9]—we pronounce that such a prose has its own grandeur, but that it is obsolete and inconvenient. But when we find Dryden telling us: "What Virgil wrote in the vigor of his age, in plenty and at ease, I have undertaken to translate in my declining years; struggling with wants, oppressed with sickness, curbed in my genius, liable to be misconstrued in all I write"[1]—then we exclaim that here at last we have the true English prose, a prose such as we would all gladly use if we only knew how. Yet Dryden was Milton's contemporary.

But after the Restoration the time had come when our nation felt the imperious need of a fit prose. So, too, the time had likewise come when our nation felt the imperious need of freeing itself from the absorbing preoccupation which religion in the Puritan age had exercised. It was impossible that this freedom should be brought about without some negative excess, without some neglect and impairment of the religious life of the soul; and the spiritual history of the eighteenth century shows us that the freedom was not achieved without them. Still, the freedom was achieved; the preoccupation, an undoubtedly baneful and retarding one if it had continued, was got rid of. And as with religion amongst us at that period, so it was also with letters. A fit prose was a necessity; but it was impossible that a fit prose should establish itself amongst us without some touch of frost to the imaginative life of the soul. The needful qualities for a fit prose are regularity, uniformity, precision, balance. The men of letters, whose destiny it may be to bring their nation to the attainment of a fit prose, must of necessity, whether they work in prose or in verse, give a predominating, an almost exclusive attention to the qualities of regularity, uniformity, precision, balance. But an almost exclusive attention to these qualities involves some repression and silencing of poetry.

We are to regard Dryden as the puissant and glorious founder, Pope as the splendid high priest, of our age of prose and reason, of our excellent and indispensable eighteenth century. For the purposes of their mission and destiny their poetry, like their prose, is admirable. Do you ask me whether Dryden's verse, take it almost where you will, is not good?

A milk-white Hind, immortal and unchanged,
Fed on the lawns and in the forest ranged.[2]

I answer: Admirable for the purposes of the inaugurator of an age of prose and reason. Do you ask me whether Pope's verse, take it almost where you will, is not good?

To Hounslow Heath I point, and Banstead Down;
Thence comes your mutton, and these chicks my own.[3]

I answer: Admirable for the purposes of the high priest of an age of prose and reason. But do you ask me whether such verse proceeds from men with an adequate poetic criticism of life, from men whose criticism of life has a high seriousness, or even, without that high seriousness, has poetic largeness, freedom, insight, benignity? Do you ask me whether the application of ideas to

9. "Apology for Smectymnuus" (1642).
1. "Postscript to the Reader" (1698) in his translation of Virgil.
2. *The Hind and the Panther* (1687) 1.1–2.
3. *Imitations of Horace* (1737), Satire 2.2.143–44.

life in the verse of these men, often a powerful application, no doubt, is a powerful *poetic* application? Do you ask me whether the poetry of these men has either the matter or the inseparable manner of such an adequate poetic criticism; whether it has the accent of

Absent thee from felicity awhile . . .

or of

And what is else not to be overcome . . .

or of

O martyr souded in virginitee!

I answer: It has not and cannot have them; it is the poetry of the builders of an age of prose and reason. Though they may write in verse, though they may in a certain sense be masters of the art of versification, Dryden and Pope are not classics of our poetry, they are classics of our prose.

Gray[4] is our poetical classic of that literature and age; the position of Gray is singular, and demands a word of notice here. He has not the volume or the power of poets who, coming in times more favorable, have attained to an independent criticism of life. But he lived with the great poets, he lived, above all, with the Greeks, through perpetually studying and enjoying them; and he caught their poetic point of view for regarding life, caught their poetic manner. The point of view and the manner are not self-sprung in him, he caught them of others; and he had not the free and abundant use of them. But whereas Addison and Pope never had the use of them, Gray had the use of them at times. He is the scantiest and frailest of classics in our poetry, but he is a classic.[5]

* * *

At any rate the end to which the method and the estimate are designed to lead, and from leading to which, if they do lead to it, they get their whole value—the benefit of being able clearly to feel and deeply to enjoy the best, the truly classic, in poetry—is an end, let me say it once more at parting, of supreme importance. We are often told that an era is opening in which we are to see multitudes of a common sort of readers, and masses of a common sort of literature; that such readers do not want and could not relish anything better than such literature, and that to provide it is becoming a vast and profitable industry. Even if good literature entirely lost currency with the world, it would still be abundantly worth while to continue to enjoy it by oneself. But it never will lose currency with the world, in spite of momentary appearances; it never will lose supremacy. Currency and supremacy are insured to it, not indeed by the world's deliberate and conscious choice, but by something far deeper—by the instinct of self-preservation in humanity.

1880

4. Thomas Gray (1716–1771), British poet.
5. After Gray, the only other poet discussed by Arnold is Burns (not printed here). Arnold con-

cludes that "Burns, like Chaucer, comes short of the high seriousness of the great classics."

Literature and Science[1]

Practical people talk with a smile of Plato and of his absolute ideas: and it is impossible to deny that Plato's ideas do often seem unpractical and unpracticable, and especially when one views them in connection with the life of a great work-a-day world like the United States. The necessary staple of the life of such a world Plato regards with disdain; handicraft and trade and the working professions he regards with disdain; but what becomes of the life of an industrial modern community if you take handicraft and trade and the working professions out of it? The base mechanic arts and handicrafts, says Plato, bring about a natural weakness in the principle of excellence in a man, so that he cannot govern the ignoble growths in him, but nurses them, and cannot understand fostering any other. Those who exercise such arts and trades, as they have their bodies, he says, marred by their vulgar businesses, so they have their souls, too, bowed and broken by them. And if one of these uncomely people has a mind to seek self-culture and philosophy, Plato compares him to a bald little tinker, who has scraped together money, and has got his release from service, and has had a bath, and bought a new coat, and is rigged out like a bridegroom about to marry the daughter of his master who has fallen into poor and helpless estate.[2]

Nor do the working professions fare any better than trade at the hands of Plato. He draws for us an inimitable picture of the working lawyer, and of his life of bondage; he shows how this bondage from his youth up has stunted and warped him, and made him small and crooked of soul, encompassing him with difficulties which he is not man enough to rely on justice and truth as means to encounter, but has recourse, for help out of them, to falsehood and wrong. And so, says Plato, this poor creature is bent and broken, and grows up from boy to man without a particle of soundness in him, although exceedingly smart and clever in his own esteem.[3]

One cannot refuse to admire the artist who draws these pictures. But we say to ourselves that his ideas show the influence of a primitive and obsolete order of things, when the warrior caste and the priestly caste were alone in honor, and the humble work of the world was done by slaves. We have now changed all that; the modern majesty consists in work, as Emerson declares;[4] and in work, we may add, principally of such plain and dusty kind as the work of cultivators of the ground, handicraftsmen, men of trade and business, men of the working professions. Above all is this true in a great industrious community such as that of the United States.

Now education, many people go on to say, is still mainly governed by the ideas of men like Plato, who lived when the warrior caste and the priestly or philosophical class were alone in honor, and the really useful part of the community were slaves. It is an education fitted for persons of leisure in such a community. This education passed from Greece and Rome to the feudal com-

1. Delivered as a lecture during Arnold's tour of the United States in 1883 and published in *Discourses in America* (1885), this essay has become a classic contribution to a subject endlessly debated. Its main argument was summed up by Stuart P. Sherman: "If Arnold had said outright that the study of letters helps us to *bear* the grand results of science, he would not have been guilty

of a superficial epigram; he would have spoken from the depths of his experience."
2. *Republic* 6.495.
3. *Republic* 3.405.
4. See Ralph Waldo Emerson's "Literary Ethics," an address delivered at Dartmouth College in 1838.

munities of Europe, where also the warrior caste and the priestly caste were alone held in honor, and where the really useful and working part of the community, though not nominally slaves as in the pagan world, were practically not much better off than slaves, and not more seriously regarded. And how absurd it is, people end by saying, to inflict this education upon an industrious modern community, where very few indeed are persons of leisure, and the mass to be considered has not leisure, but is bound, for its own great good, and for the great good of the world at large, to plain labor and to industrial pursuits, and the education in question tends necessarily to make men dissatisfied with these pursuits and unfitted for them!

That is what is said. So far I must defend Plato, as to plead that his view of education and studies is in the general, as it seems to me, sound enough, and fitted for all sorts and conditions of men, whatever their pursuits may be. "An intelligent man," says Plato, "will prize those studies which result in his soul getting soberness, righteousness, and wisdom, and will less value the others."[5] I cannot consider *that* a bad description of the aim of education, and of the motives which should govern us in the choice of studies, whether we are preparing ourselves for a hereditary seat in the English House of Lords or for the pork trade in Chicago.

Still I admit that Plato's world was not ours, that his scorn of trade and handicraft is fantastic,[6] that he had no conception of a great industrial community such as that of the United States, and that such a community must and will shape its education to suit its own needs. If the usual education handed down to it from the past does not suit it, it will certainly before long drop this and try another. The usual education in the past has been mainly literary. The question is whether the studies which were long supposed to be the best for all of us are practically the best now; whether others are not better. The tyranny of the past, many think, weighs on us injuriously in the predominance given to letters in education. The question is raised whether, to meet the needs of our modern life, the predominance ought not now to pass from letters to science; and naturally the question is nowhere raised with more energy than here in the United States. The design of abasing what is called "mere literary instruction and education," and of exalting what is called "sound, extensive, and practical scientific knowledge," is, in this intensely modern world of the United States, even more perhaps than in Europe, a very popular design, and makes great and rapid progress.

I am going to ask whether the present movement for ousting letters from their old predominance in education, and for transferring the predominance in education to the natural sciences, whether this brisk and flourishing movement ought to prevail, and whether it is likely that in the end it really will prevail. An objection may be raised which I will anticipate. My own studies have been almost wholly in letters, and my visits to the field of the natural sciences have been very slight and inadequate, although those sciences have always strongly moved my curiosity. A man of letters, it will perhaps be said, is not competent to discuss the comparative merits of letters and natural science as means of education. To this objection I reply, first of all, that his incompetence, if he attempts the discussion but is really incompetent for it, will be abundantly visible; nobody will be taken in; he will have plenty of sharp observers and critics to save mankind from that danger. But the line I am going to follow is, as you will soon discover, so extremely simple, that perhaps

<hr />

5. *Republic* 9.591.   6. Unconvincing, fanciful.

it may be followed without failure even by one who for a more ambitious line of discussion would be quite incompetent.

Some of you may possibly remember a phrase of mine which has been the object of a good deal of comment; an observation to the effect that in our culture, the aim being *to know ourselves and the world*, we have, as the means to this end, *to know the best which has been thought and said in the world*.[7] A man of science, who is also an excellent writer and the very prince of debaters, Professor Huxley, in a discourse at the opening of Sir Josiah Mason's college at Birmingham,[8] laying hold of this phrase, expanded it by quoting some more words of mine, which are these: "The civilized world is to be regarded as now being, for intellectual and spiritual purposes, one great confederation, bound to a joint action and working to a common result; and whose members have for their proper outfit a knowledge of Greek, Roman, and Eastern antiquity, and of one another. Special local and temporary advantages being put out of account, that modern nation will in the intellectual and spiritual sphere make most progress, which most thoroughly carries out this program."

Now on my phrase, thus enlarged, Professor Huxley remarks that when I speak of the above-mentioned knowledge as enabling us to know ourselves and the world, I assert *literature* to contain the materials which suffice for thus making us know ourselves and the world. But it is not by any means clear, says he, that after having learnt all which ancient and modern literatures have to tell us, we have laid a sufficiently broad and deep foundation for that criticism of life, that knowledge of ourselves and the world, which constitutes culture. On the contrary, Professor Huxley declares that he finds himself "wholly unable to admit that either nations or individuals will really advance, if their outfit draws nothing from the stores of physical science. An army without weapons of precision, and with no particular base of operations, might more hopefully enter upon a campaign on the Rhine, than a man, devoid of a knowledge of what physical science has done in the last century, upon a criticism of life."

This shows how needful it is for those who are to discuss any matter together, to have a common understanding as to the sense of the terms they employ—how needful, and how difficult. What Professor Huxley says, implies just the reproach which is so often brought against the study of belles-lettres, as they are called: that the study is an elegant one, but slight and ineffectual; a smattering of Greek and Latin and other ornamental things, of little use for anyone whose object is to get at truth, and to be a practical man. So, too, M. Renan[9] talks of the "superficial humanism" of a school course which treats us as if we were all going to be poets, writers, preachers, orators, and he opposes this humanism to positive science, or the critical search after truth. And there is always a tendency in those who are remonstrating against the predominance of letters in education, to understand by letters belles-lettres, and by belles-lettres a superficial humanism, the opposite of science or true knowledge.

But when we talk of knowing Greek and Roman antiquity, for instance, which is the knowledge people have called the humanities, I for my part mean a knowledge which is something more than a superficial humanism, mainly decorative. "I call all teaching *scientific*," says Wolf,[1] the critic of Homer, "which is systematically laid out and followed up to its original sources. For

7. See "The Function of Criticism at the Present Time" (p. 1384).
8. See "Science and Culture" (p. 1429).
9. Ernest Renan (1823–1892), French religious philosopher and archaeologist.
1. Friedrich August Wolf (1759–1824), German scholar.

example: a knowledge of classical antiquity is scientific when the remains of classical antiquity are correctly studied in the original languages." There can be no doubt that Wolf is perfectly right; that all learning is scientific which is systematically laid out and followed up to its original sources, and that a genuine humanism is scientific.

When I speak of knowing Greek and Roman antiquity, therefore, as a help to knowing ourselves and the world, I mean more than a knowledge of so much vocabulary, so much grammar, so many portions of authors in the Greek and Latin languages, I mean knowing the Greeks and Romans, and their life and genius,[2] and what they were and did in the world; what we get from them, and what is its value. That, at least, is the ideal; and when we talk of endeavoring to know Greek and Roman antiquity, as a help to knowing ourselves and the world, we mean endeavoring so to know them as to satisfy this ideal, however much we may still fall short of it.

The same also as to knowing our own and other modern nations, with the like aim of getting to understand ourselves and the world. To know the best that has been thought and said by the modern nations, is to know, says Professor Huxley, "only what modern *literatures* have to tell us; it is the criticism of life contained in modern literature." And yet "the distinctive character of our times," he urges, "lies in the vast and constantly increasing part which is played by natural knowledge." And how, therefore, can a man, devoid of knowledge of what physical science has done in the last century, enter hopefully upon a criticism of modern life?

Let us, I say, be agreed about the meaning of the terms we are using. I talk of knowing the best which has been thought and uttered in the world; Professor Huxley says this means knowing *literature*. Literature is a large word; it may mean everything written with letters or printed in a book. Euclid's *Elements* and Newton's *Principia*[3] are thus literature. All knowledge that reaches us through books is literature. But by literature Professor Huxley means belles-lettres. He means to make me say, that knowing the best which has been thought and said by the modern nations is knowing their belles-lettres and no more. And this is no sufficient equipment, he argues, for a criticism of modern life. But as I do not mean, by knowing ancient Rome, knowing merely more or less of Latin belles-lettres, and taking no account of Rome's military, and political, and legal, and administrative work in the world; and as, by knowing ancient Greece, I understand knowing her as the giver of Greek art, and the guide to a free and right use of reason and to scientific method, and the founder of our mathematics and physics and astronomy and biology—I understand knowing her as all this, and not merely knowing certain Greek poems, and histories, and treatises, and speeches—so as to the knowledge of modern nations also. By knowing modern nations, I mean not merely knowing their belles-lettres, but knowing also what has been done by such men as Copernicus, Galileo, Newton, Darwin. "Our ancestors learned," says Professor Huxley, "that the earth is the center of the visible universe, and that man is the cynosure of things terrestrial; and more especially was it inculcated that the course of nature had no fixed order, but that it could be, and constantly was, altered." "But for us now," continues Professor Huxley, "the notions of

2. Characteristic spirit or excellence.
3. A comprehensive treatise on mathematics (ca. 300 B.C.E.) and a foundational work of modern

physics (*The Mathematical Principles of Natural Philosophy*, 1687), respectively.

the beginning and the end of the world entertained by our forefathers are no longer credible. It is very certain that the earth is not the chief body in the material universe, and that the world is not subordinated to man's use. It is even more certain that nature is the expression of a definite order, with which nothing interferes." "And yet," he cries, "the purely classical education advocated by the representatives of the humanists in our day gives no inkling of all this."

In due place and time I will just touch upon that vexed question of classical education; but at present the question is as to what is meant by knowing the best which modern nations have thought and said. It is not knowing their belles-lettres merely which is meant. To know Italian belles-lettres is not to know Italy, and to know English belles-lettres is not to know England. Into knowing Italy and England there comes a great deal more, Galileo and Newton amongst it. The reproach of being a superficial humanism, a tincture of belles-lettres, may attach rightly enough to some other disciplines; but to the particular discipline recommended when I proposed knowing the best that has been thought and said in the world, it does not apply. In that best I certainly include what in modern times has been thought and said by the great observers and knowers of nature.

There is, therefore, really no question between Professor Huxley and me as to whether knowing the great results of the modern scientific study of nature is not required as a part of our culture, as well as knowing the products of literature and art. But to follow the processes by which those results are reached, ought, say the friends of physical science, to be made the staple of education for the bulk of mankind. And here there does arise a question between those whom Professor Huxley calls with playful sarcasm "the Levites of culture," and those whom the poor humanist is sometimes apt to regard as its Nebuchadnezzars.[4]

The great results of the scientific investigation of nature we are agreed upon knowing, but how much of our study are we bound to give to the processes by which those results are reached? The results have their visible bearing on human life. But all the processes, too, all the items of fact, by which those results are reached and established, are interesting. All knowledge is interesting to a wise man, and the knowledge of nature is interesting to all men. It is very interesting to know, that, from the albuminous white of the egg, the chick in the egg gets the materials for its flesh, bones, blood, and feathers; while, from the fatty yolk of the egg, it gets the heat and energy which enable it at length to break its shell and begin the world. It is less interesting, perhaps, but still it is interesting, to know that when a taper burns, the wax is converted into carbonic acid and water. Moreover, it is quite true that the habit of dealing with facts, which is given by the study of nature, is, as the friends of physical science praise it for being, an excellent discipline. The appeal, in the study of nature, is constantly to observation and experiment; not only is it said that the thing is so, but we can be made to see that it is so. Not only does a man tell us that when a taper burns the wax is converted into carbonic acid and water, as a man may tell us, if he likes, that Charon[5] is punting his ferry boat on the

4. Huxley implies that the humanists are hidebound conservatives like the Levites, priests who were preoccupied with traditional ritual observances. Arnold implies that the scientists may be like Nebuchadnezzar, a Babylonian king who destroyed the temple of Jerusalem.
5. In Greek mythology the boatman who conducted the souls of the dead across the river Styx.

river Styx, or that Victor Hugo is a sublime poet, or Mr. Gladstone[6] the most admirable of statesmen; but we are made to see that the conversion into carbonic acid and water does actually happen. This reality of natural knowledge it is, which makes the friends of physical science contrast it, as a knowledge of things, with the humanist's knowledge, which is, say they, a knowledge of words. And hence Professor Huxley is moved to lay it down that, "for the purpose of attaining real culture, an exclusively scientific education is at least as effectual as an exclusively literary education." And a certain President of the Section for Mechanical Science in the British Association is, in Scripture phrase, "very bold,"[7] and declares that if a man, in his mental training, "has substituted literature and history for natural science, he has chosen the less useful alternative." But whether we go these lengths or not, we must all admit that in natural science the habit gained of dealing with facts is a most valuable discipline, and that everyone should have some experience of it.

More than this, however, is demanded by the reformers. It is proposed to make the training in natural science the main part of education, for the great majority of mankind at any rate. And here, I confess, I part company with the friends of physical science, with whom up to this point I have been agreeing. In differing from them, however, I wish to proceed with the utmost caution and diffidence. The smallness of my own acquaintance with the disciplines of natural science is ever before my mind, and I am fearful of doing these disciplines an injustice. The ability and pugnacity of the partisans of natural science make them formidable persons to contradict. The tone of tentative inquiry, which befits a being of dim faculties and bounded knowledge, is the tone I would wish to take and not to depart from. At present it seems to me, that those who are for giving to natural knowledge, as they call it, the chief place in the education of the majority of mankind, leave one important thing out of their account: the constitution of human nature. But I put this forward on the strength of some facts not at all recondite, very far from it; facts capable of being stated in the simplest possible fashion, and to which, if I so state them, the man of science will, I am sure, be willing to allow their due weight.

Deny the facts altogether, I think, he hardly can. He can hardly deny, that when we set ourselves to enumerate the powers which go to the building up of human life, and say that they are the power of conduct, the power of intellect and knowledge, the power of beauty, and the power of social life and manners—he can hardly deny that this scheme, though drawn in rough and plain lines enough, and not pretending to scientific exactness, does yet give a fairly true representation of the matter. Human nature is built up by these powers; we have the need for them all. When we have rightly met and adjusted the claims of them all, we shall then be in a fair way for getting soberness and righteousness, with wisdom. This is evident enough, and the friends of physical science would admit it.

But perhaps they may not have sufficiently observed another thing: namely, that the several powers just mentioned are not isolated, but there is, in the generality of mankind, a perpetual tendency to relate them one to another in divers ways. With one such way of relating them I am particularly concerned now. Following our instinct for intellect and knowledge, we acquire pieces of

6. William Ewart Gladstone (1809–1898), leader of the Liberal Party from 1868 to 1875 and from 1880 to 1894 and prime minister four times. Hugo

(1802–1885), French poet and novelist.
7. Romans 10.20.

knowledge; and presently, in the generality of men, there arises the desire to relate these pieces of knowledge to our sense for conduct, to our sense for beauty—and there is weariness and dissatisfaction if the desire is balked. Now in this desire lies, I think, the strength of that hold which letters have upon us.

All knowledge is, as I said just now, interesting; and even items of knowledge which from the nature of the case cannot well be related, but must stand isolated in our thoughts, have their interest. Even lists of exceptions have their interest. If we are studying Greek accents, it is interesting to know that *pais* and *pas*, and some other monosyllables of the same form of declension, do not take the circumflex upon the last syllable of the genitive plural, but vary, in this respect, from the common rule. If we are studying physiology, it is interesting to know that the pulmonary artery carries dark blood and the pulmonary vein carries bright blood, departing in this respect from the common rule for the division of labor between the veins and the arteries. But everyone knows how we seek naturally to combine the pieces of our knowledge together, to bring them under general rules, to relate them to principles; and how unsatisfactory and tiresome it would be to go on forever learning lists of exceptions, or accumulating items of fact which must stand isolated.

Well, that same need of relating our knowledge, which operates here within the sphere of our knowledge itself, we shall find operating, also, outside that sphere. We experience, as we go on learning and knowing—the vast majority of us experience—the need of relating what we have learnt and known to the sense which we have in us for conduct, to the sense which we have in us for beauty.

A certain Greek prophetess of Mantineia in Arcadia, Diotima by name, once explained to the philosopher Socrates that love, and impulse, and bent of all kinds, is, in fact, nothing else but the desire in men that good should forever be present to them. This desire for good, Diotima assured Socrates, is our fundamental desire, of which fundamental desire every impulse in us is only some one particular form.[8] And therefore this fundamental desire it is, I suppose—this desire in men that good should be forever present to them—which acts in us when we feel the impulse for relating our knowledge to our sense for conduct and to our sense for beauty. At any rate, with men in general the instinct exists. Such is human nature. And the instinct, it will be admitted, is innocent, and human nature is preserved by our following the lead of its innocent instincts. Therefore, in seeking to gratify this instinct in question, we are following the instinct of self-preservation in humanity.

But, no doubt, some kinds of knowledge cannot be made to directly serve the instinct in question, cannot be directly related to the sense for beauty, to the sense for conduct. These are instrument knowledges; they lead on to other knowledges, which can. A man who passes his life in instrument knowledges is a specialist. They may be invaluable as instruments to something beyond, for those who have the gift thus to employ them; and they may be disciplines in themselves wherein it is useful for everyone to have some schooling. But it is inconceivable that the generality of men should pass all their mental life with Greek accents or with formal logic. My friend Professor Sylvester, who is one of the first[9] mathematicians in the world, holds transcendental

---

8. Plato's *Symposium* 201–7.
9. Foremost. James J. Sylvester (1814–1897), pro-

fessor of mathematics at Johns Hopkins University and at Oxford.

doctrines as to the virtue of mathematics, but those doctrines are not for common men. In the very Senate House and heart of our English Cambridge[1] I once ventured, though not without an apology for my profaneness, to hazard the opinion that for the majority of mankind a little of mathematics, even, goes a long way. Of course this is quite consistent with their being of immense importance as an instrument to something else; but it is the few who have the aptitude for thus using them, not the bulk of mankind.

The natural sciences do not, however, stand on the same footing with these instrument knowledges. Experience shows us that the generality of men will find more interest in learning that, when a taper burns, the wax is converted into carbonic acid and water, or in learning the explanation of the phenomenon of dew, or in learning how the circulation of the blood is carried on, than they find in learning that the genitive plural of *pais* and *pas* does not take the circumflex on the termination. And one piece of natural knowledge is added to another, and others are added to that, and at last we come to propositions so interesting as Mr. Darwin's famous proposition that "our ancestor was a hairy quadruped furnished with a tail and pointed ears, probably arboreal in his habits."[2] Or we come to propositions of such reach and magnitude as those which Professor Huxley delivers, when he says that the notions of our forefathers about the beginning and the end of the world were all wrong, and that nature is the expression of a definite order with which nothing interferes.

Interesting, indeed, these results of science are, important they are, and we should all of us be acquainted with them. But what I now wish you to mark is, that we are still, when they are propounded to us and we receive them, we are still in the sphere of intellect and knowledge. And for the generality of men there will be found, I say, to arise, when they have duly taken in the proposition that their ancestor was "a hairy quadruped furnished with a tail and pointed ears, probably arboreal in his habits," there will be found to arise an invincible desire to relate this proposition to the sense in us for conduct, and to the sense in us for beauty. But this the men of science will not do for us, and will hardly even profess to do. They will give us other pieces of knowledge, other facts, about other animals and their ancestors, or about plants, or about stones, or about stars; and they may finally bring us to those great "general conceptions of the universe, which are forced upon us all," says Professor Huxley, "by the progress of physical science." But still it will be *knowledge* only which they give us; knowledge not put for us into relation with our sense for conduct, our sense for beauty, and touched with emotion by being so put; not thus put for us, and therefore, to the majority of mankind, after a certain while, unsatisfying, wearying.

Not to the born naturalist, I admit. But what do we mean by a born naturalist? We mean a man in whom the zeal for observing nature is so uncommonly strong and eminent, that it marks him off from the bulk of mankind. Such a man will pass his life happily in collecting natural knowledge and reasoning upon it, and will ask for nothing, or hardly anything, more. I have heard it said that the sagacious and admirable naturalist whom we lost not very long ago, Mr. Darwin, once owned to a friend that for his part he did not experience the necessity for two things which most men find so necessary to

1. In its original form "Literature and Science" had been delivered as a lecture at Cambridge University, where mathematics traditionally has been emphasized.
2. *The Descent of Man* (1871), chap. 21 (see below, p. 1546).

them—religion and poetry; science and the domestic affections, he thought, were enough. To a born naturalist, I can well understand that this should seem so. So absorbing is his occupation with nature, so strong his love for his occupation, that he goes on acquiring natural knowledge and reasoning upon it, and has little time or inclination for thinking about getting it related to the desire in man for conduct, the desire in man for beauty. He relates it to them for himself as he goes along, so far as he feels the need; and he draws from the domestic affections all the additional solace necessary. But then Darwins are extremely rare. Another great and admirable master of natural knowledge, Faraday,[3] was a Sandemanian. That is to say, he related his knowledge to his instinct for conduct and to his instinct for beauty, by the aid of that respectable Scottish sectary, Robert Sandeman.[4] And so strong, in general, is the demand of religion and poetry to have their share in a man, to associate themselves with his knowing, and to relieve and rejoice it, that, probably, for one man amongst us with the disposition to do as Darwin did in this respect, there are at least fifty with the disposition to do as Faraday.

Education lays hold upon us, in fact, by satisfying this demand. Professor Huxley holds up to scorn medieval education, with its neglect of the knowledge of nature, its poverty even of literary studies, its formal logic devoted to "show-ing how and why that which the Church said was true must be true." But the great medieval Universities were not brought into being, we may be sure, by the zeal for giving a jejune and contemptible education. Kings have been their nursing fathers, and queens have been their nursing mothers,[5] but not for this. The medieval Universities came into being, because the supposed knowledge, delivered by Scripture and the Church, so deeply engaged men's hearts, by so simply, easily, and powerfully relating itself to their desire for conduct, their desire for beauty. All other knowledge was dominated by this supposed knowl-edge and was subordinated to it, because of the surpassing strength of the hold which it gained upon the affections of men, by allying itself profoundly with their sense for conduct, their sense for beauty.

But now, says Professor Huxley, conceptions of the universe fatal to the notions held by our forefathers have been forced upon us by physical science. Grant to him that they are thus fatal, that the new conceptions must and will soon become current everywhere, and that everyone will finally perceive them to be fatal to the beliefs of our forefathers. The need of humane letters, as they are truly called, because they serve the paramount desire in men that good should be forever present to them—the need of humane letters, to estab-lish a relation between the new conceptions, and our instinct for beauty, our instinct for conduct, is only the more visible. The Middle Age could do without humane letters, as it could do without the study of nature, because its sup-posed knowledge was made to engage its emotions so powerfully. Grant that the supposed knowledge disappears, its power of being made to engage the emotions will of course disappear along with it—but the emotions themselves, and their claim to be engaged and satisfied, will remain. Now if we find by experience that humane letters have an undeniable power of engaging the emotions, the importance of humane letters in a man's training becomes not

---

3. Michael Faraday (1791–1867), British chemist.
4. Founder of a Scottish sect bearing his name

(1718–1771). "Sectary": zealous member of a sect.
5. Isaiah 49.23.

less, but greater, in proportion to the success of modern science in extirpating what it calls "medieval thinking."

Have humane letters, then, have poetry and eloquence, the power here attributed to them of engaging the emotions, and do they exercise it? And if they have it and exercise it, *how* do they exercise it, so as to exert an influence upon man's sense for conduct, his sense for beauty? Finally, even if they both can and do exert an influence upon the senses in question, how are they to relate to them the results—the modern results—of natural science? All these questions may be asked. First, have poetry and eloquence the power of calling out the emotions? The appeal is to experience. Experience shows that for the vast majority of men, for mankind in general, they have the power. Next, do they exercise it? They do. But then, *how* do they exercise it so as to affect man's sense for conduct, his sense for beauty? And this is perhaps a case for applying the Preacher's words: "Though a man labour to seek it out, yet he shall not find it; yea, farther, though a wise man think to know it, yet shall he not be able to find it."[6] Why should it be one thing, in its effect upon the emotions, to say, "Patience is a virtue," and quite another thing, in its effect upon the emotions, to say with Homer,

$$\tau\lambda\eta\tau\grave{o}\nu\ \gamma\grave{a}\rho\ Mo\hat{\imath}\rho\alpha\iota\ \theta\upsilon\mu\grave{o}\nu\ \theta\acute{\epsilon}\sigma\alpha\nu\ \grave{a}\nu\theta\rho\acute{\omega}\pi\sigma\iota\sigma\iota\nu^7—$$

"for an enduring heart have the destinies appointed to the children of men"? Why should it be one thing, in its effect upon the emotions, to say with the philosopher Spinoza, *Felicitas in eo consistit quod homo suum esse conservare potest*—"Man's happiness consists in his being able to preserve his own essence,"[8] and quite another thing, in its effect upon the emotions, to say with the Gospel, "What is a man advantaged, if he gain the whole world, and lose himself, forfeit himself?"[9] How does this difference of effect arise? I cannot tell, and I am not much concerned to know; the important thing is that it does arise, and that we can profit by it. But how, finally, are poetry and eloquence to exercise the power of relating the modern results of natural science to man's instinct for conduct, his instinct for beauty? And here again I answer that I do not know *how* they will exercise it, but that they can and will exercise it I am sure. I do not mean that modern philosophical poets and modern philosophical moralists are to come and relate for us, in express terms, the results of modern scientific research to our instinct for conduct, our instinct for beauty. But I mean that we shall find, as a matter of experience, if we know the best that has been thought and uttered in the world, we shall find that the art and poetry and eloquence of men who lived, perhaps, long ago, who had the most limited natural knowledge, who had the most erroneous conceptions about many important matters, we shall find that this art, and poetry, and eloquence, have in fact not only the power of refreshing and delighting us, they have also the power—such is the strength and worth, in essentials, of their authors' criticism of life—they have a fortifying, and elevating, and quickening, and suggestive power, capable of wonderfully helping us to relate the results of modern science to our need for conduct, our need for beauty. Homer's conceptions of the physical universe were, I imagine, grotesque; but really, under the shock of hearing from modern science that "the world is not subordinated to man's use, and that man is not the cynosure of things terres-

---

6. Ecclesiastes 8.17 [Arnold's note].
7. *Iliad* 24.49 [Arnold's note].

8. *Ethics* (1677) 4.18.
9. Cf. Luke 9.25.

trial," I could, for my own part, desire no better comfort than Homer's line which I quoted just now,

τλητὸν γὰρ Μοῖραι θυμὸν θέσαν ἀνθρώποισιν—

"for an enduring heart have the destinies appointed to the children of men"!

And the more that men's minds are cleared, the more that the results of science are frankly accepted, the more that poetry and eloquence come to be received and studied as what in truth they really are—the criticism of life by gifted men, alive and active with extraordinary power at an unusual number of points—so much the more will the value of humane letters, and of art also, which is an utterance having a like kind of power with theirs, be felt and acknowledged, and their place in education be secured.

Let us therefore, all of us, avoid indeed as much as possible any invidious comparison between the merits of humane letters, as means of education, and the merits of the natural sciences. But when some President of a Section for Mechanical Science insists on making the comparison, and tells us that "he who in his training has substituted literature and history for natural science has chosen the less useful alternative," let us make answer to him that the student of humane letters only, will, at least, know also the great general conceptions brought in by modern physical science; for science, as Professor Huxley says, forces them upon us all. But the student of the natural sciences only, will, by our very hypothesis, know nothing of humane letters; not to mention that in setting himself to be perpetually accumulating natural knowledge, he sets himself to do what only specialists have in general the gift for doing genially. And so he will probably be unsatisfied, or at any rate incomplete, and even more incomplete than the student of humane letters only.

I once mentioned in a school report, how a young man in one of our English training colleges having to paraphrase the passage in *Macbeth* beginning,

Can'st thou not minister to a mind diseased?[1]

turned this line into, "Can you not wait upon the lunatic?" And I remarked what a curious state of things it would be, if every pupil of our national schools knew, let us say, that the moon is two thousand one hundred and sixty miles in diameter, and thought at the same time that a good paraphrase for

Can'st thou not minister to a mind diseased?

was, "Can you not wait upon the lunatic?" If one is driven to choose, I think I would rather have a young person ignorant about the moon's diameter, but aware that "Can you not wait upon the lunatic?" is bad, than a young person whose education had been such as to manage things the other way.

Or to go higher than the pupils of our national schools. I have in my mind's eye a member of our British Parliament who comes to travel here in America, who afterwards relates his travels, and who shows a really masterly knowledge of the geology of this great country and of its mining capabilities, but who ends by gravely suggesting that the United States should borrow a prince from our Royal Family, and should make him their king, and should create a House of Lords of great landed proprietors after the pattern of ours; and then America, he thinks, would have her future happily and perfectly secured. Surely, in this case, the President of the Section for Mechanical Science would himself

1. Shakespeare's *Macbeth* 5.3.42.

hardly say that our member of Parliament, by concentrating himself upon geology and mineralogy, and so on, and not attending to literature and history, had "chosen the more useful alternative."

If then there is to be separation and option between humane letters on the one hand, and the natural sciences on the other, the great majority of mankind, all who have not exceptional and overpowering aptitudes for the study of nature, would do well, I cannot but think, to choose to be educated in humane letters rather than in the natural sciences. Letters will call out their being at more points, will make them live more.

I said that before I ended I would just touch on the question of classical education, and I will keep my word. Even if literature is to retain a large place in our education, yet Latin and Greek, say the friends of progress, will certainly have to go. Greek is the grand offender in the eyes of these gentlemen. The attackers of the established course of study think that against Greek, at any rate, they have irresistible arguments. Literature may perhaps be needed in education, they say; but why on earth should it be Greek literature? Why not French or German? Nay, "has not an Englishman models in his own literature of every kind of excellence?"[2] As before, it is not on any weak pleadings of my own that I rely for convincing the gainsayers; it is on the constitution of human nature itself, and on the instinct of self-preservation in humanity. The instinct for beauty is set in human nature, as surely as the instinct for knowledge is set there, or the instinct for conduct. If the instinct for beauty is served by Greek literature and art as it is served by no other literature and art, we may trust to the instinct of self-preservation in humanity for keeping Greek as part of our culture. We may trust to it for even making the study of Greek more prevalent than it is now. Greek will come, I hope, some day to be studied more rationally than at present; but it will be increasingly studied as men increasingly feel the need in them for beauty, and how powerfully Greek art and Greek literature can serve this need. Women will again study Greek, as Lady Jane Grey[3] did; I believe that in that chain of forts, with which the fair host of the Amazons are now engirdling our English universities,[4] I find that here in America, in colleges like Smith College in Massachusetts, and Vassar College in the State of New York, and in the happy families of the mixed universities out West, they are studying it already.

Defuit una mihi symmetria prisca—"The antique symmetry was the one thing wanting to me," said Leonardo da Vinci; and he was an Italian. I will not presume to speak for the Americans, but I am sure that, in the Englishman, the want of this admirable symmetry of the Greeks is a thousand times more great and crying than in any Italian. The results of the want show themselves most glaringly, perhaps, in our architecture, but they show themselves, also, in all our art. *Fit details strictly combined, in view of a large general result nobly conceived;* that is just the beautiful *symmetria prisca* of the Greeks, and it is just where we English fail, where all our art fails. Striking ideas we have, and well-executed details we have; but that high symmetry which, with satisfying and delightful effect, combines them, we seldom or never have. The glorious beauty of the Acropolis at Athens did not come from single fine things stuck about on that hill, a statue here, a gateway there—no, it arose from all things

2. Cf. Huxley's "Science and Culture." (p. 1429).
3. Reputed to be a learned scholar in Greek. Grey (1537–1554) was proclaimed queen of England in 1553 but was forced to abdicate the throne nine

days later. She was executed by order of Queen Mary.
4. Colleges for women at Oxford and Cambridge.

being perfectly combined for a supreme total effect. What must not an Englishman feel about our deficiencies in this respect, as the sense for beauty, whereof this symmetry is an essential element, awakens and strengthens within him! what will not one day be his respect and desire for Greece and its *symmetria prisca*, when the scales drop from his eyes as he walks the London streets, and he sees such a lesson in meanness as the Strand, for instance, in its true deformity! But here we are coming to our friend Mr. Ruskin's province,[5] and I will not intrude upon it, for he is its very sufficient guardian.

And so we at last find, it seems, we find flowing in favor of the humanities the natural and necessary stream of things, which seemed against them when we started. The "hairy quadruped furnished with a tail and pointed ears, probably arboreal in his habits," this good fellow carried hidden in his nature, apparently, something destined to develop into a necessity for humane letters. Nay, more; we seem finally to be even led to the further conclusion that our hairy ancestor carried in his nature, also, a necessity for Greek.

And therefore, to say the truth, I cannot really think that humane letters are in much actual danger of being thrust out from their leading place in education, in spite of the array of authorities against them at this moment. So long as human nature is what it is, their attractions will remain irresistible. As with Greek, so with letters generally: they will some day come, we may hope, to be studied more rationally, but they will not lose their place. What will happen will rather be that there will be crowded into education other matters besides, far too many; there will be, perhaps, a period of unsettlement and confusion and false tendency; but letters will not in the end lose their leading place. If they lose it for a time, they will get it back again. We shall be brought back to them by our wants and aspirations. And a poor humanist may possess his soul in patience, neither strive nor cry,[6] admit the energy and brilliancy of the partisans of physical science, and their present favor with the public, to be far greater than his own, and still have a happy faith that the nature of things works silently on behalf of the studies which he loves, and that, while we shall all have to acquaint ourselves with the great results reached by modern science, and to give ourselves as much training in its disciplines as we can conveniently carry, yet the majority of men will always require humane letters; and so much the more, as they have the more and the greater results of science to relate to the need in man for conduct, and to the need in him for beauty.

1882, 1885

5. In books such as *The Stones of Venice* (1851–53), John Ruskin had criticized the "meanness" of Victorian architecture.

6. Matthew 12.19; "possess his soul in patience," Luke 21.19.

THOMAS HENRY HUXLEY
1825–1895

In Victorian controversies over religion and education, one of the most distinctive participants was Thomas Henry Huxley, a scientist who wrote clear, readable, and very persuasive English prose. Huxley's literary skill was responsible for his being lured out of his laboratory onto the platforms of public debate where his role was to champion, as he said, "the application of scientific methods of investigation to all the problems of life."

Huxley, a schoolmaster's son, was born in a London suburb. Until beginning the study of medicine, at seventeen, he had had little formal education, having taught himself classical and modern languages and the rudiments of scientific theory. In 1846, after receiving his degree in medicine, he embarked on a long voyage to the South Seas during which he studied the marine life of the tropical oceans and established a considerable reputation as a zoologist. Later he made investigations in geology and physiology, completing a total of 250 research papers during his lifetime. He also held teaching positions and served on public committees, but it was as a popularizer of science that he made his real mark. His popularizing was of two kinds. The first was to make the results of scientific investigations intelligible to a large audience. Such lectures as "On a Piece of Chalk" (not included here) are models of clear, vivid exposition that can be studied with profit by anyone interested in the art of teaching. His second kind of popularizing consisted of expounding the values of scientific education or of the application of scientific thinking to problems in religion. Here Huxley excels not so much as a teacher as a debater. In 1860 he demonstrated his argumentative skill when, as Darwin's defender or "bulldog," he demolished Bishop Wilberforce in a battle over *The Origin of Species* (an account of the confrontation, written by Huxley's son Leonard, appears in the "Evolution" cluster). In the 1870s, in such lectures as "Science and Culture" (1880), he engaged in more genial fencing with Matthew Arnold concerning the relative importance of the study of science or the humanities in education. And in the 1880s he debated with William Gladstone on the topic of interpreting the Bible. His essay "Agnosticism and Christianity" (1889) indicates his premises in this controversy.

Summing up his own career in his "Autobiography" (1890), Huxley noted that he had subordinated his ambition for scientific fame to other ends: "to the popularization of science; to the development and organization of scientific education; to the endless series of battles and skirmishes over evolution; and to untiring opposition to that ecclesiastical spirit, that clericalism, which . . . to whatever denomination it may belong, is the deadly enemy of science." In fighting these "battles" Huxley operated from different bases. Most of the time he wrote as a biologist engaged in assessing all assumptions by the tests of laboratory science. In this role he argued that humans are merely animals and that traditional religion is a tissue of superstitions and lies. For some recent critics Huxley comes close to setting up his own religion of sorts, so fervent and sweeping is his rhetoric in defense of scientific naturalism. Further, it has been argued that the emphasis he and other like-minded writers placed on the inevitability of English technological progress significantly affected Britain's expansionist imperial policies in the last quarter of the nineteenth century. Nevertheless, Huxley's vision was broader than that of most of his comrades in the science and religion debates. In fact, he often wrote as a humanist and even as a follower of Thomas Carlyle. As he stated in a letter: "*Sartor Resartus* led me to know that a deep sense of religion was compatible with the entire absence of theology." In this second role he argued that humans are a very special kind of animal whose great distinction is that they are endowed with a moral sense and with freedom of the will; creatures who are admirable not for following nature but for departing from nature. The humanistic streak muddies the seemingly clear current of Huxley's thinking yet makes him a more interesting figure than he might otherwise have been. It is noteworthy that in the writings of his grandsons—Julian Huxley, a biologist, and Aldous Huxley, a novelist—a similar division of mind can once more be detected.

Even in his dying, T. H. Huxley continued his role as controversialist. The words he asked to be engraved on his tomb are typical of his view of life and typical, also, in the effect they had on his contemporaries, some of whom found the epitaph to be shocking:

Be not afraid, ye waiting hearts that weep
For still he giveth His beloved sleep,
And if an endless sleep He wills, so best.

From Science and Culture[1]

[THE VALUES OF EDUCATION IN THE SCIENCES]

From the time that the first suggestion to introduce physical science into ordinary education was timidly whispered, until now, the advocates of scientific education have met with opposition of two kinds. On the one hand, they have been pooh-poohed by the men of business who pride themselves on being the representatives of practicality; while, on the other hand, they have been excommunicated by the classical scholars, in their capacity of Levites in charge of the ark of culture[2] and monopolists of liberal education.

The practical men believed that the idol whom they worship—rule of thumb—has been the source of the past prosperity, and will suffice for the future welfare of the arts and manufactures. They are of opinion that science is speculative rubbish; that theory and practice have nothing to do with one another; and that the scientific habit of mind is an impediment, rather than an aid, in the conduct of ordinary affairs.

I have used the past tense in speaking of the practical men—for although they were very formidable thirty years ago, I am not sure that the pure species has not been extirpated. In fact, so far as mere argument goes, they have been subjected to such a *feu d'enfer*[3] that it is a miracle if any have escaped. But I have remarked that your typical practical man has an unexpected resemblance to one of Milton's angels. His spiritual wounds, such as are inflicted by logical weapons, may be as deep as a well and as wide as a church door,[4] but beyond shedding a few drops of ichor,[5] celestial or otherwise, he is no whit the worse. So, if any of these opponents be left, I will not waste time in vain repetition of the demonstrative evidence of the practical value of science; but knowing that a parable will sometimes penetrate where syllogisms fail to effect an entrance, I will offer a story for their consideration.

Once upon a time, a boy, with nothing to depend upon but his own vigorous nature, was thrown into the thick of the struggle for existence in the midst of a great manufacturing population. He seems to have had a hard fight, inasmuch as, by the time he was thirty years of age, his total disposable funds amounted to twenty pounds. Nevertheless, middle life found him giving proof of his comprehension of the practical problems he had been roughly called upon to solve, by a career of remarkable prosperity.

Finally, having reached old age with its well-earned surroundings of "honour, troops of friends,"[6] the hero of my story bethought himself of those who

1. This essay was first delivered as an address in 1880. The occasion had been the opening of a new Scientific College at Birmingham, which had been endowed by Sir Josiah Mason (1795–1881), a self-made businessman. For Matthew Arnold's reply to Huxley's argument, see his essay "Literature and Science" (p. 1415).
2. In the Old Testament the whole tribe of Levi was entrusted with Israel's ritual observances (Numbers 3.1–13); in Joshua 6 priests carried the Ark of the Covenant.
3. Hellfire (French).
4. Cf. Shakespeare's *Romeo and Juliet* 3.1.92–93.
5. Ethereal fluid that supposedly flows through the veins of the gods. On angels' wounds see Milton's *Paradise Lost* 6.320–56.
6. Cf. Shakespeare's *Macbeth* 5.3.26.

were making a like start in life, and how he could stretch out a helping hand to them.

After long and anxious reflection this successful practical man of business could devise nothing better than to provide them with the means of obtaining "sound, extensive, and practical scientific knowledge." And he devoted a large part of his wealth and five years of incessant work to this end.

I need not point the moral of a tale which, as the solid and spacious fabric of the Scientific College assures us, is no fable, nor can anything which I could say intensify the force of this practical answer to practical objections.

We may take it for granted then, that, in the opinion of those best qualified to judge, the diffusion of thorough scientific education is an absolutely essential condition of industrial progress; and that the College which has been opened today will confer an inestimable boon upon those whose livelihood is to be gained by the practice of the arts and manufactures of the district.

The only question worth discussion is whether the conditions under which the work of the College is to be carried out are such as to give it the best possible chance of achieving permanent success.

Sir Josiah Mason, without doubt most wisely, has left very large freedom of action to the trustees, to whom he proposes ultimately to commit the administration of the College, so that they may be able to adjust its arrangements in accordance with the changing conditions of the future. But, with respect to three points, he has laid most explicit injunctions upon both administrators and teachers.

Party politics are forbidden to enter into the minds of either, so far as the work of the College is concerned; theology is as sternly banished from its precincts; and finally, it is especially declared that the College shall make no provision for "mere literary instruction and education."

It does not concern me at present to dwell upon the first two injunctions any longer than may be needful to express my full conviction of their wisdom. But the third prohibition brings us face to face with those other opponents of scientific education, who are by no means in the moribund condition of the practical man, but alive, alert, and formidable.

It is not impossible that we shall hear this express exclusion of "literary instruction and education" from a College which, nevertheless, professes to give a high and efficient education, sharply criticized. Certainly the time was that the Levites of culture would have sounded their trumpets against its walls as against an educational Jericho.[7]

How often have we not been told that the study of physical science is incompetent to confer culture; that it touches none of the higher problems of life; and, what is worse, that the continual devotion to scientific studies tends to generate a narrow and bigoted belief in the applicability of scientific methods to the search after truth of all kinds? How frequently one has reason to observe that no reply to a troublesome argument tells so well as calling its author a "mere scientific specialist." And, as I am afraid it is not permissible to speak of this form of opposition to scientific education in the past tense; may we not expect to be told that this, not only omission, but prohibition, of "mere literary instruction and education" is a patent example of scientific narrowmindedness?

7. Seven priests blew their trumpets before the city walls of Jericho to bring the walls down (Joshua 6.6–20).

I am not acquainted with Sir Josiah Mason's reasons for the action which he has taken; but if, as I apprehend is the case, he refers to the ordinary classical course of our schools and universities by the name of "mere literary instruction and education," I venture to offer sundry reasons of my own in support of that action.

For I hold very strongly by two convictions: The first is that neither the discipline nor the subject matter of classical education is of such direct value to the student of physical science as to justify the expenditure of valuable time upon either; and the second is that for the purpose of attaining real culture, an exclusively scientific education is at least as effectual as an exclusively literary education.

I need hardly point out to you that these opinions, especially the latter, are diametrically opposed to those of the great majority of educated Englishmen, influenced as they are by school and university traditions. In their belief, culture is obtainable only by a liberal education; and a liberal education is synonymous, not merely with education and instruction in literature, but in one particular form of literature, namely, that of Greek and Roman antiquity. They hold that the man who has learned Latin and Greek, however little, is educated; while he who is versed in other branches of knowledge, however deeply, is a more or less respectable specialist, not admissible into the cultured caste. The stamp of the educated man, the University degree, is not for him.

I am too well acquainted with the generous catholicity of spirit, the true sympathy with scientific thought, which pervades the writings of our chief apostle of culture[8] to identify him with these opinions; and yet one may cull from one and another of those epistles to the Philistines, which so much delight all who do not answer to that name, sentences which lend them some support.

Mr. Arnold tells us that the meaning of culture is "to know the best that has been thought and said in the world." It is the criticism of life contained in literature. That criticism regards "Europe as being, for intellectual and spiritual purposes, one great confederation, bound to a joint action and working to a common result; and whose members have, for their common outfit, a knowledge of Greek, Roman, and Eastern antiquity, and of one another. Special, local, and temporary advantages being put out of account, that modern nation will in the intellectual and spiritual sphere make most progress, which most thoroughly carries out this program. And what is that but saying that we too, all of us, as individuals, the more thoroughly we carry it out, shall make the more progress?"[9]

We have here to deal with two distinct propositions. The first, that a criticism of life is the essence of culture; the second, that literature contains the materials which suffice for the construction of such criticism.

I think that we must all assent to the first proposition. For culture certainly means something quite different from learning or technical skill. It implies the possession of an ideal, and the habit of critically estimating the value of things by comparison with a theoretic standard. Perfect culture should supply a complete theory of life, based upon a clear knowledge alike of its possibilities and of its limitations.

But we may agree to all this, and yet strongly dissent from the assumption that literature alone is competent to supply this knowledge. After having learnt all that Greek, Roman, and Eastern antiquity have thought and said, and all that modern literature have to tell us, it is not self-evident that we have laid a sufficiently broad and deep foundation for that criticism of life which constitutes culture.

Indeed, to anyone acquainted with the scope of physical science, it is not at all evident. Considering progress only in the "intellectual and spiritual sphere," I find myself wholly unable to admit that either nations or individuals will really advance, if their common outfit draws nothing from the stores of physical science. I should say that an army, without weapons of precision and with no particular base of operations, might more hopefully enter upon a campaign on the Rhine than a man, devoid of a knowledge of what physical science has done in the last century, upon a criticism of life.

When a biologist meets with an anomaly, he instinctively turns to the study of development to clear it up. The rationale of contradictory opinions may with equal confidence be sought in history.

It is, happily, no new thing that Englishmen should employ their wealth in building and endowing institutions for educational purposes. But, five or six hundred years ago, deeds of foundation expressed or implied conditions as nearly as possible contrary to those which have been thought expedient by Sir Josiah Mason. That is to say, physical science was practically ignored, while a certain literary training was enjoined as a means to the acquirement of knowledge which was essentially theological.

The reason of this singular contradiction between the actions of men alike animated by a strong and disinterested desire to promote the welfare of their fellows, is easily discovered.

At that time, in fact, if anyone desired knowledge beyond such as could be obtained by his own observation, or by common conversation, his first necessity was to learn the Latin language, inasmuch as all the higher knowledge of the western world was contained in words written in that language. Hence, Latin grammar, with logic and rhetoric, studied through Latin, were the fundamentals of education. With respect to the substance of the knowledge imparted through this channel, the Jewish and Christian Scriptures, as interpreted and supplemented by the Romish Church, were held to contain a complete and infallibly true body of information.

Theological dicta were, to the thinkers of those days, that which the axioms and definitions of Euclid[1] are to the geometers of these. The business of the philosophers of the Middle Ages was to deduce from the data furnished by the theologians, conclusions in accordance with ecclesiastical decrees. They were allowed the high privilege of showing, by logical process, how and why that which the Church said was true, must be true. And if their demonstrations fell short of or exceeded this limit, the Church was maternally ready to check their aberrations; if need were, by the help of the secular arm.

Between the two, our ancestors were furnished with a compact and complete criticism of life. They were told how the world began and how it would end; they learned that all material existence was but a base and insignificant blot upon the fair face of the spiritual world, and that nature was, to all intents and purposes, the playground of the devil; they learned that the earth is the

1. Greek mathematician (active ca. 300 B.C.E.). His *Elements* remained a standard text of geometrical reasoning through the 19th century.

center of the visible universe, and that man is the cynosure of things terrestrial, and more especially was it inculcated that the course of nature had no fixed order, but that it could be, and constantly was, altered by the agency of innumerable spiritual beings, good and bad, according as they were moved by the deeds and prayers of men. The sum and substance of the whole doctrine was to produce the conviction that the only thing really worth knowing in this world was how to secure that place in a better which, under certain conditions, the Church promised.

Our ancestors had a living belief in this theory of life, and acted upon it in their dealings with education, as in all other matters. Culture meant saintliness—after the fashion of the saints of those days; the education that led to it was, of necessity, theological; and the way to theology lay through Latin.

That the study of nature—further than was requisite for the satisfaction of everyday wants—should have any bearing on human life was far from the thoughts of men thus trained. Indeed, as nature had been cursed for man's sake, it was an obvious conclusion that those who meddled with nature were likely to come into pretty close contact with Satan. And, if any born scientific investigator followed his instincts, he might safely reckon upon earning the reputation, and probably upon suffering the fate, of a sorcerer.

Had the western world been left to itself in Chinese isolation, there is no saying how long this state of things might have endured. But, happily, it was not left to itself. Even earlier than the thirteenth century, the development of Moorish civilization in Spain and the great movement of the Crusades had introduced the leaven which, from that day to this, has never ceased to work. At first, through the intermediation of Arabic translations, afterwards by the study of the originals, the western nations of Europe became acquainted with the writings of the ancient philosophers and poets, and, in time, with the whole of the vast literature of antiquity.

Whatever there was of high intellectual aspiration or dominant capacity in Italy, France, Germany, and England, spent itself for centuries in taking possession of the rich inheritance left by the dead civilizations of Greece and Rome. Marvelously aided by the invention of printing,[2] classical learning spread and flourished. Those who possessed it prided themselves on having attained the highest culture then within the reach of mankind.

And justly. For, saving Dante on his solitary pinnacle, there was no figure in modern literature at the time of the Renaissance to compare with the men of antiquity; there was no art to compete with their sculpture; there was no physical science but that which Greece had created. Above all, there was no other example of perfect intellectual freedom—of the unhesitating acceptance of reason as the sole guide to truth and the supreme arbiter of conduct.

The new learning necessarily soon exerted a profound influence upon education. The language of the monks and schoolmen[3] seemed little better than gibberish to scholars fresh from Virgil and Cicero,[4] and the study of Latin was placed upon a new foundation. Moreover, Latin itself ceased to afford the sole key to knowledge. The student who sought the highest thought of antiquity found only a secondhand reflection of it in Roman literature, and turned his face to the full light of the Greeks. And after a battle, not altogether dissimilar to that which is at present being fought over the teaching of physical science,

---

2. In the mid-15th century.
3. Exponents of the theology, philosophy, and logic of the medieval period in Europe.

4. The two Roman writers generally viewed as the masters of, respectively, Latin poetry and Latin prose.

the study of Greek was recognized as an essential element of all higher education.

Then the Humanists, as they were called, won the day; and the great reform which they effected was of incalculable service to mankind. But the nemesis of all reformers is finality; and the reformers of education, like those of religion, fell into the profound, however common, error of mistaking the beginning for the end of the work of reformation.

The representatives of the Humanists, in the nineteenth century, take their stand upon classical education as the sole avenue to culture as firmly as if we were still in the age of Renaissance. Yet, surely, the present intellectual relations of the modern and the ancient worlds are profoundly different from those which obtained three centuries ago. Leaving aside the existence of a great and characteristically modern literature, of modern painting, and, especially, of modern music, there is one feature of the present state of the civilized world which separates it more widely from the Renaissance than the Renaissance was separated from the Middle Ages.

This distinctive character of our own times lies in the vast and constantly increasing part which is played by natural knowledge. Not only is our daily life shaped by it; not only does the prosperity of millions of men depend upon it, but our whole theory of life has long been influenced, consciously or unconsciously, by the general conceptions of the universe which have been forced upon us by physical science.

In fact, the most elementary acquaintance with the results of scientific investigation shows us that they offer a broad and striking contradiction to the opinion so implicitly credited and taught in the Middle Ages.

The notions of the beginning and the end of the world entertained by our forefathers are no longer credible. It is very certain that the earth is not the chief body in the material universe, and that the world is not subordinated to man's use. It is even more certain that nature is the expression of a definite order with which nothing interferes, and that the chief business of mankind is to learn that order and govern themselves accordingly. Moreover this scientific "criticism of life" presents itself to us with different credentials from any other. It appeals not to authority, nor to what anybody may have thought or said, but to nature. It admits that all our interpretations of natural fact are more or less imperfect and symbolic, and bids the learner seek for truth not among words but among things. It warns us that the assertion which outstrips evidence is not only a blunder but a crime.

The purely classical education advocated by the representatives of the Humanists in our day gives no inkling of all this. A man may be a better scholar than Erasmus,[5] and know no more of the chief causes of the present intellectual fermentation than Erasmus did. Scholarly and pious persons, worthy of all respect, favor us with allocutions upon the sadness of the antagonism of science to their medieval way of thinking, which betray an ignorance of the first principles of scientific investigation, an incapacity for understanding what a man of science means by veracity, and an unconsciousness of the weight of established scientific truths, which is almost comical.

* * *

5. Eminent Dutch humanist and scholar (1466–1536).

Thus I venture to think that the pretensions of our modern Humanists to the possession of the monopoly of culture and to the exclusive inheritance of the spirit of antiquity must be abated, if not abandoned. But I should be very sorry that anything I have said should be taken to imply a desire on my part to depreciate the value of classical education, as it might be and as it sometimes is. The native capacities of mankind vary no less than their opportunities; and while culture is one, the road by which one man may best reach it is widely different from that which is most advantageous to another. Again, while scientific education is yet inchoate and tentative, classical education is thoroughly well organized upon the practical experience of generations of teachers. So that, given ample time for learning and estimation for ordinary life, or for a literary career, I do not think that a young Englishman in search of culture can do better than follow the course usually marked out for him, supplementing its deficiencies by his own efforts.

But for those who mean to make science their serious occupation; or who intend to follow the profession of medicine; or who have to enter early upon the business of life; for all these, in my opinion, classical education is a mistake; and it is for this reason that I am glad to see "mere literary education and instruction" shut out from the curriculum of Sir Josiah Mason's College, seeing that its inclusion would probably lead to the introduction of the ordinary smattering of Latin and Greek.

Nevertheless, I am the last person to question the importance of genuine literary education, or to suppose that intellectual culture can be complete without it. An exclusively scientific training will bring about a mental twist as surely as an exclusively literary training. The value of the cargo does not compensate for a ship's being out of trim; and I should be very sorry to think that the Scientific College would turn out none but lopsided men.

There is no need, however, that such a catastrophe should happen. Instruction in English, French, and German is provided, and thus the three greatest literatures of the modern world are made accessible to the student.

French and German, and especially the latter language, are absolutely indispensable to those who desire full knowledge in any department of science. But even supposing that the knowledge of these languages acquired is not more than sufficient for purely scientific purposes, every Englishman has, in his native tongue, an almost perfect instrument of literary expression; and, in his own literature, models of every kind of literary excellence. If an Englishman cannot get literary culture out of his Bible, his Shakespeare, his Milton, neither, in my belief, will the profoundest study of Homer and Sophocles, Virgil and Horace, give it to him.

Thus, since the constitution of the College makes sufficient provision for literary as well as for scientific education, and since artistic instruction is also contemplated, it seems to me that a fairly complete culture is offered to all who are willing to take advantage of it.

1880, 1881

From Agnosticism and Christianity[1]

[AGNOSTICISM DEFINED]

Nemo ergo ex me scire quaerat, quod me nescire scio, nisi forte ut nescire discat.
—AUGUSTINUS, *De Civ. Dei*, XII.7.[2]

The present discussion has arisen out of the use, which has become general in the last few years, of the terms "Agnostic"[3] and "Agnosticism." The people who call themselves "Agnostics" have been charged with doing so because they have not the courage to declare themselves "Infidels." It has been insinuated that they have adopted a new name in order to escape the unpleasantness which attaches to their proper denomination. To this wholly erroneous imputation I have replied by showing that the term "Agnostic" did, as a matter of fact, arise in a manner which negatives it; and my statement has not been, and cannot be, refuted. Moreover, speaking for myself, and without impugning the right of any other person to use the term in another sense, I further say that Agnosticism is not properly described as a "negative" creed, nor indeed as a creed of any kind, except in so far as it expresses absolute faith in the validity of a principle, which is as much ethical as intellectual. This principle may be stated in various ways, but they all amount to this: that it is wrong for a man to say that he is certain of the objective truth of any proposition unless he can produce evidence which logically justifies that certainty. This is what Agnosticism asserts; and, in my opinion, it is all that is essential to Agnosticism. That which Agnostics deny and repudiate, as immoral, is the contrary doctrine, that there are propositions which men ought to believe, without logically satisfactory evidence; and that reprobation ought to attach to the profession of disbelief in such inadequately supported propositions. The justification of the Agnostic principles lies in the success which follows upon its application, whether in the field of natural, or in that of civil, history; and in the fact that, so far as these topics are concerned, no sane man thinks of denying its validity.

Still speaking for myself, I add that though Agnosticism is not, and cannot be, a creed, except in so far as its general principle is concerned; yet that the application of that principle results in the denial of, or the suspension of judgment concerning, a number of propositions respecting which our contemporary ecclesiastical "gnostics" profess entire certainty. And, in so far as these eccelesiastical persons can be justified in their old-established custom (which many nowadays think more honored in the breach than the observance) of using opprobrious names to those who differ from them, I fully admit their right to call me and those who think with me "Infidels"; all I have ventured to urge is that they must not expect us to speak of ourselves by that title.

The extent of the region of the uncertain, the number of the problems the investigation of which ends in a verdict of not proven, will vary according to the knowledge and the intellectual habits of the individual Agnostic. I do not very much care to speak of anything as "unknowable." What I am sure about

---

1. This essay appeared in a magazine in 1889 as a reply to critics who had argued that agnostics were simply infidels under a new name. It was later included in Huxley's volume *Essays on Some Controverted Questions* (1892).

2. No one, therefore, should seek to learn knowledge from me, for I know that I do not know—unless indeed he wishes to learn that he does not know (Latin); Saint Augustine, *City of God* 12.7.
3. The term *agnostic* was coined by Huxley.

is that there are many topics about which I know nothing; and which, so far as I can see, are out of reach of my faculties. But whether these things are knowable by anyone else is exactly one of those matters which is beyond my knowledge, though I may have a tolerably strong opinion as to the probabilities of the case. Relatively to myself, I am quite sure that the region of uncertainty—the nebulous country in which words play the part of realities—is far more extensive than I could wish. Materialism and Idealism; Theism and Atheism; the doctrine of the soul and its mortality or immortality—appear in the history of philosophy like the shades of Scandinavian heroes, eternally slaying one another and eternally coming to life again in a metaphysical "Nifelheim."[4] It is getting on for twenty-five centuries, at least, since mankind began seriously to give their minds to these topics. Generation after generation, philosophy has been doomed to roll the stone uphill; and, just as all the world swore it was at the top, down it has rolled to the bottom again.[5] All this is written in innumerable books; and he who will toil through them will discover that the stone is just where it was when the work began. Hume saw this; Kant[6] saw it; since their time, more and more eyes have been cleansed of the films which prevented them from seeing it; until now the weight and number of those who refuse to be the prey of verbal mystifications has begun to tell in practical life.

It was inevitable that a conflict should arise between Agnosticism and Theology; or rather, I ought to say, between Agnosticism and Ecclesiasticism. For Theology, the science, is one thing; and Ecclesiasticism, the championship of a foregone conclusion[7] as to the truth of a particular form of Theology, is another. With scientific Theology, Agnosticism has no quarrel. On the contrary, the Agnostic, knowing too well the influence of prejudice and idiosyncrasy, even on those who desire most earnestly to be impartial, can wish for nothing more urgently than that the scientific theologian should not only be at perfect liberty to thresh out the matter in his own fashion; but that he should, if he can, find flaws in the Agnostic position; and, even if demonstration is not to be had, that he should put, in their full force, the grounds of the conclusions he thinks probable. The scientific theologian admits the Agnostic principle, however widely his results may differ from those reached by the majority of Agnostics.

But, as between Agnosticism and Ecclesiasticism, or, as our neighbors across the Channel call it, Clericalism, there can be neither peace nor truce. The Cleric asserts that it is morally wrong not to believe certain propositions, whatever the results of a strict scientific investigation of the evidence of these propositions. He tells us "that religious error is, in itself, of an immoral nature."[8] He declares that he has prejudged certain conclusions, and looks upon those who show cause for arrest of judgment as emissaries of Satan. It necessarily follows that, for him, the attainment of faith, not the ascertainment of truth, is the highest aim of mental life. And, on careful analysis of the nature of this faith, it will too often be found to be, not the mystic process of unity with the Divine, understood by the religious enthusiast; but that which the

4. In Norse mythology realms of cold and darkness.
5. Cf. the Greek story of Sisyphus, who was in Hades, condemned to keep rolling a stone uphill, which always rolled downhill again before it reached the summit.
6. Immanuel Kant (1724–1804), German philosopher who focused in large part on defining the limits of human knowledge; the writings of the

Scottish empiricist David Hume (1711–1776) were a major influence on his work.
7. Let us maintain, before we have proved. This seeming paradox is the secret of happiness. (Dr. Newman, "Tract 85") [Huxley's note]. For John Henry Newman, see p. 1033.
8. Dr. Newman, Essay on Development [Huxley's note]. See An Essay on the Development of Christian Doctrine (1845).

candid simplicity of a Sunday scholar once defined it to be. "Faith," said this unconscious plagiarist of Tertullian,[9] "is the power of saying you believe things which are incredible."

Now I, and many other Agnostics, believe that faith, in this sense, is an abomination; and though we do not indulge in the luxury of self-righteousness so far as to call those who are not of our way of thinking hard names, we do feel that the disagreement between ourselves and those who hold this doctrine is even more moral than intellectual. It is desirable there should be an end of any mistakes on this topic. If our clerical opponents were clearly aware of the real state of the case, there would be an end of the curious delusion, which often appears between the lines of their writings, that those whom they are so fond of calling "Infidels" are people who not only ought to be, but in their hearts are, ashamed of themselves. It would be discourteous to do more than hint the antipodal opposition of this pleasant dream of theirs to facts.

The clerics and their lay allies commonly tell us that if we refuse to admit that there is good ground for expressing definite convictions about certain topics, the bonds of human society will dissolve and mankind lapse into savagery. There are several answers to this assertion. One is that the bonds of human society were formed without the aid of their theology; and, in the opinion of not a few competent judges, have been weakened rather than strengthened by a good deal of it. Greek science, Greek art, the ethics of old Israel, the social organization of old Rome, contrived to come into being, without the help of anyone who believed in a single distinctive article of the simplest of the Christian creeds. The science, the art, the jurisprudence, the chief political and social theories, of the modern world have grown out of those of Greece and Rome—not by favor of, but in the teeth of, the fundamental teachings of early Christianity, to which science, art, and any serious occupation with the things of this world, were alike despicable.

Again, all that is best in the ethics of the modern world, in so far as it has not grown out of Greek thought, or Barbarian manhood, is the direct development of the ethics of old Israel. There is no code of legislation, ancient or modern, at once so just and so merciful, so tender to the weak and poor, as the Jewish law; and, if the Gospels are to be trusted, Jesus of Nazareth himself declared that he taught nothing but that which lay implicitly, or explicitly, in the religious and ethical system of his people.

> And the scribe said unto him, Of a truth, Teacher, thou hast well said that he is one; and there is none other but he and to love him with all the heart, and with all the understanding, and with all the strength, and to love his neighbour as himself, is much more than all whole burnt offerings and sacrifices. (Mark xii.32–33)

Here is the briefest of summaries of the teaching of the prophets of Israel of the eighth century;[1] does the Teacher, whose doctrine is thus set forth in his presence, repudiate the exposition? Nay; we are told, on the contrary, that Jesus saw that he "answered discreetly," and replied, "Thou are not far from the kingdom of God."

So that I think that even if the creeds, from the so-called "Apostles' " to the so-called "Athanasian,"[2] were swept into oblivion; and even if the human race

9. Latin author and Church father (ca. 155–ca. 222). Tertullian wrote of Christ's resurrection, "It is certain because it is impossible" (De Carne Christi 5).
1. See Deuteronomy 6.4–5; 1 Samuel 15.22.

2. Two important summaries of Christian doctrine. The Athanasian creed dates back to ca. 361; the Apostles' baptismal creed developed between the 2nd and 9th centuries.

should arrive at the conclusion that, whether a bishop washes a cup or leaves it unwashed, is not a matter of the least consequence, it will get on very well. The causes which have led to the development of morality in mankind, which have guided or impelled us all the way from the savage to the civilized state, will not cease to operate because a number of ecclesiastical hypotheses turn out to be baseless. And, even if the absurd notion that morality is more the child of speculation than of practical necessity and inherited instinct, had any foundation; if all the world is going to thieve, murder, and otherwise misconduct itself as soon as it discovers that certain portions of ancient history are mythical; what is the relevance of such arguments to any one who holds by the Agnostic principle?

Surely, the attempt to cast out Beelzebub by the aid of Beelzebub[3] is a hopeful procedure as compared to that of preserving morality by the aid of immorality. For I suppose it is admitted that an Agnostic may be perfectly sincere, may be competent, and may have studied the question at issue with as much care as his clerical opponents. But, if the Agnostic really believes what he says, the "dreadful consequence" argufier (consistently, I admit, with his own principles) virtually asks him to abstain from telling the truth, or to say what he believes to be untrue, because of the supposed injurious consequences to morality. "Beloved brethren, that we may be spotlessly moral, before all things let us lie," is the sum total of many an exhortation addressed to the "Infidel." Now, as I have already pointed out, we cannot oblige our exhorters. We leave the practical application of the convenient doctrines of "Reserve" and "Non-natural interpretation" to those who invented them.[4]

I trust that I have now made amends for any ambiguity, or want of fullness, in my previous exposition of that which I hold to be the essence of the Agnostic doctrine. Henceforward, I might hope to hear no more of the assertion that we are necessarily Materialists, Idealists, Atheists, Theists, or any other ists, if experience had led me to think that the proved falsity of a statement was any guarantee against its repetition. And those who appreciate the nature of our position will see, at once, that when Ecclesiasticism declares that we ought to believe this, that, and the other, and are very wicked if we don't, it is impossible for us to give any answer but this: We have not the slightest objection to believe anything you like, if you will give us good grounds for belief; but, if you cannot, we must respectfully refuse, even if that refusal should wreck morality and insure our own damnation several times over. We are quite content to leave that to the decision of the future. The course of the past has impressed us with the firm conviction that no good ever comes of falsehood, and we feel warranted in refusing even to experiment in that direction.

✻   ✻   ✻

1889, 1892

---

3. Mark 3.22–27.
4. A way of maintaining assent to a Scriptural passage without accepting its literal or obvious sense; a device here stigmatized as intellectually dishon-

est. "Reserve": "an intentional suppression of truth in cases where it might lead to inconvenience" (OED).

GEORGE MEREDITH
1828–1909

Like Thomas Hardy, George Meredith preferred writing poetry to writing novels, but it was as the author of *The Ordeal of Richard Feverel* (1859), *The Egoist* (1879), and other novels that he made his mark. His poems nevertheless deserve more attention than they have yet received, especially *Modern Love* (1862), a fascinating narrative poem that was greeted by the *Saturday Review* as "a grave moral mistake." This sequence of fifty sixteen-line sonnets is a kind of novel in verse that analyzes the sufferings of a husband and wife whose marriage is breaking up. The story is told, for the most part, by the husband speaking in the first person, but the opening and closing sections are narrated in the third person. *Modern Love* was probably derived, in part, from Meredith's experiences. At twenty-one, at the outset of his career as a writer in London, he married a daughter of the satirist Thomas Love Peacock (1785–1866). Nine years later, after a series of quarrels, his wife eloped to Europe with another artist. The Merediths were never reconciled, and in 1861 she died.

From Modern Love

1

By this he knew she wept with waking eyes:
That, at his hand's light quiver by her head,
The strange low sobs that shook their common bed
Were called into her with a sharp surprise,
5   And strangled mute, like little gaping snakes,
Dreadfully venomous to him. She lay
Stone-still, and the long darkness flowed away
With muffled pulses. Then, as midnight makes
Her giant heart of Memory and Tears
10 Drink the pale drug of silence, and so beat
Sleep's heavy measure, they from head to feet
Were moveless, looking through their dead black years
By vain regret scrawled over the blank wall.
Like sculptured effigies they might be seen
15 Upon their marriage tomb, the sword between;[1]
Each wishing for the sword that severs all.

2

It ended, and the morrow brought the task.
Her eyes were guilty gates, that let him in
By shutting all too zealous for their sin:
Each sucked a secret, and each wore a mask.
5   But, oh, the bitter taste her beauty had!
He sickened as at breath of poison-flowers:
A languid humor stole among the hours,
And if their smiles encountered, he went mad,
And raged deep inward, till the light was brown
10 Before his vision, and the world, forgot,

---

1. In medieval legend a naked sword between lovers ensured chastity.

Looked wicked as some old dull murder spot.
A star with lurid beams, she seemed to crown
The pit of infamy: and then again
He fainted on his vengefulness, and strove
15 To ape the magnanimity of love,
And smote himself, a shuddering heap of pain.

17

At dinner, she is hostess, I am host.
Went the feast ever cheerfuller? She keeps
The Topic over intellectual deeps
In buoyancy afloat. They see no ghost.
5 With sparkling surface-eyes we ply the ball:
It is in truth a most contagious game:
HIDING THE SKELETON, shall be its name.
Such play as this the devils might appall!
But here's the greater wonder: in that we,
10 Enamored of an acting naught can tire.
Each other, like true hypocrites, admire;
Warm-lighted looks, Love's ephemeridae,[2]
Shoot gaily o'er the dishes and the wine.
We waken envy of our happy lot.
15 Fast, sweet, and golden, shows the marriage knot.
Dear guests, you now have seen Love's corpse-light[3] shine.

49

He found her by the ocean's moaning verge,
Nor any wicked change in her discerned;
And she believed his old love had returned,
Which was her exultation, and her scourge.
5 She took his hand, and walked with him, and seemed
The wife he sought, though shadowlike and dry.
She had one terror, lest her heart should sigh,
And tell her loudly she no longer dreamed.
She dared not say, "This is my breast: look in."
10 But there's a strength to help the desperate weak.
That night he learned how silence best can speak
The awful things when Pity pleads for Sin.
About the middle of the night her call
Was heard, and he came wondering to the bed.
15 "Now kiss me, dear! it may be, now!" she said.
Lethe[4] had passed those lips, and he knew all.

50

Thus piteously Love closed what he begat:
The union of this ever diverse pair!
These two were rapid falcons in a snare,

---

2. Insects that live for one day only.
3. Phosphorescent light such as that seen in marshes. When appearing in a cemetery it was believed to portend a funeral.
4. River of forgetfulness in Hades, the Greek underworld.

Condemned to do the flitting of the bat.
5 Lovers beneath the singing sky of May,
They wandered once; clear as the dew on flowers:
But they fed not on the advancing hours:
Their hearts held cravings for the buried day.
Then each applied to each that fatal knife,
10 Deep questioning, which probes to endless dole.°   grief
Ah, what a dusty answer gets the soul
When hot for certainties in this our life!—
In tragic hints here see what evermore
Moves dark as yonder midnight ocean's force,
15 Thundering like ramping hosts of warrior horse,
To throw that faint thin line upon the shore!

1862

DANTE GABRIEL ROSSETTI
1828–1882

Dante Gabriel Rossetti was the son of an Italian patriot and scholar whose political activities had led to his being exiled to England. The Rossetti household in London was one in which liberal politics and artistic topics were hotly debated; all four children—Maria Francesca, Dante Gabriel, William Michael, and Christina Georgina—wrote, drew, or engaged in scholarly pursuits from a young age. Displaying extraordinary early promise both as a painter and as a poet, Dante Gabriel luxuriated in colors and textures, and was especially drawn to feminine beauty. His view of life and art, derived in part from his close study of John Keats's poems and letters, anticipated by many years the aesthetic movement later to be represented by men such as Walter Pater, Oscar Wilde, and the painter James McNeill Whistler, who insisted that art must be exclusively concerned with the beautiful, not with the useful or didactic.

The beauty that Rossetti admired in the faces of women was of a distinctive kind. In at least two of his models he found what he sought. The first was his wife, Elizabeth Siddal, whose suicide in 1862 haunted him with a sense of guilt for the rest of his life. The other was Jane Morris, the wife of his friend William Morris. In Rossetti's paintings both of these models are shown with dreamy stares, as if they were breathless from visions of heaven; but counteracting this impression is an emphasis on parted lips and voluptuous curves suggesting a more earthly kind of ecstasy. Similar combinations of spirituality and physicality, or mind and body, are to be found in many of Rossetti's poems. For instance, the central figure of "The Blessed Damozel" (1850), a poem begun when Rossetti was eighteen and was heavily influenced by the work of Dante Alighieri, leans upon "the gold bar of heaven" and makes it "warm" with her bosom. In Jenny (1870), another work started in Rossetti's early adulthood, a male speaker muses about the life and thoughts of the young prostitute whose head rests upon his knee as she sleeps: his speculations thus replace, or stand in for, more overt sexual acts between them. And The House of Life (1870), his sonnet sequence, undertakes to explore the relationship of spirit to body in love. Some Victorian readers found little Dante-like spirituality in The House of Life; the critic Robert Buchanan, for example, saw only lewd sensuality, and his 1871 pamphlet, "The Fleshly School of Poetry," treated Rossetti's poetry to the most severe abuse. Buchanan's attack hurt the poet profoundly and contributed to the recurring bouts of nervous depression from which he suffered in the remaining years of his life.

Rossetti and his artist friends called women such as Jane Morris "stunners." The epithet can also be applied to Rossetti's poetry, especially his later writings. In his maturity he used stunning polysyllabic diction to convey opulence and density. Earlier poems such as "My Sister's Sleep" (1850) are usually much less elaborate in manner and reflect the original aesthetic values of the Pre-Raphaelite movement in which Rossetti played a central and founding role. In 1848 a group of young artists and writers came together in what they called the Pre-Raphaelite Brotherhood. The most prominent members were painters, notably John Everett Millais, William Holman Hunt, and Rossetti. Their principal object was to reform English painting by repudiating the established academic style in favor of a revival of the simplicity and pure colors of pre-Renaissance art. Because each artist preferred to develop his own individual manner, the Brotherhood did not cohere for more than a few years. Rossetti grew away from the Pre-Raphaelite manner and his early choice of religious subjects, cultivating instead a more richly ornate style of painting. In both the early and the late phases of his art, however, many have viewed him as essentially a poet in his painting and a painter in his poetry. "Colour and meter," he once said, "these are the true patents of nobility in painting and poetry, taking precedence of all intellectual claims."

For images of some Rossetti paintings, see "The Painterly Image in Poetry" at Norton Literature Online.

The Blessed Damozel[1]

The blessed damozel leaned out
　　From the gold bar of heaven;
Her eyes were deeper than the depth
　　Of waters stilled at even;
5　She had three lilies in her hand,
　　And the stars in her hair were seven.

Her robe, ungirt from clasp to hem,
　　No wrought flowers did adorn,
But a white rose of Mary's gift,
10　　For service meetly° worn;　　　　　　　　　　　*fittingly*
Her hair that lay along her back
　　Was yellow like ripe corn.°　　　　　　　　　　*grain*

Herseemed[2] she scarce had been a day
　　One of God's choristers;
15　The wonder was not yet quite gone
　　From that still look of hers;
Albeit, to them she left, her day
　　Had counted as ten years.

(To one it is ten years of years.
20　　. . . Yet now, and in this place,
Surely she leaned o'er me—her hair
　　Fell all about my face. . . .

1. A poetic version of "damsel," signifying a young unmarried lady. Rossetti once explained that "Blessed Damozel" is related to Edgar Allan Poe's "The Raven" (1845), a poem he admired. "I saw that Poe had done the utmost it was possible to do with the grief of the lover on earth, and so I deter-

mined to reverse the conditions, and give utterance to the yearning of the loved one in heaven." The thoughts of the damozel's still-living lover appear in the poem in parentheses.
2. It seemed to her.

Nothing: the autumn-fall of leaves.
The whole year sets apace.)

25 It was the rampart of God's house
    That she was standing on;
    By God built over the sheer depth
    The which is Space begun;
    So high, that looking downward thence
30   She scarce could see the sun.

    It lies in heaven, across the flood
    Of ether, as a bridge.
    Beneath the tides of day and night
    With flame and darkness ridge
35 The void, as low as where this earth
    Spins like a fretful midge.

    Around her, lovers, newly met
    'Mid deathless love's acclaims,
    Spoke evermore among themselves
40   Their heart-remembered names;
    And the souls mounting up to God
    Went by her like thin flames.

    And still she bowed herself and stooped
    Out of the circling charm;
45 Until her bosom must have made
    The bar she leaned on warm,

A detail from *The Blessed Damozel* (1875–78). In the second phase of his painting career, Rossetti turned from the religious and literary subjects of his early work (see, for instance, his illustration for "The Lady of Shalott," p. 1118) to huge sensual portraits of women, often designed as companion pieces to his poems. For another example of Rossetti's visual art, see the frontispiece he drew for his sister Christina's first volume of poems, p. 1470.

And the lilies lay as if asleep
    Along her bended arm.

From the fixed place of heaven she saw
50   Time like a pulse shake fierce
Through all the worlds. Her gaze still strove
    Within the gulf to pierce
Its path; and now she spoke as when
    The stars sang in their spheres.

55 The sun was gone now; the curled moon
    Was like a little feather
Fluttering far down the gulf; and now
    She spoke through the still weather.
Her voice was like the voice the stars
60   Had when they sang together.[3]

(Ah, sweet! Even now, in that bird's song,
    Strove not her accents there,
Fain to be harkened? When those bells
    Possessed the midday air,
65 Strove not her steps to reach my side
    Down all the echoing stair?)

"I wish that he were come to me,
    For he will come," she said.
"Have I not prayed in heaven?—on earth,
70   Lord, Lord, has he not prayed?
Are not two prayers a perfect strength?
    And shall I feel afraid?

"When round his head the aureole° clings,   *halo*
    And he is clothed in white,
75 I'll take his hand and go with him
    To the deep wells of light;
As unto a stream we will step down,
    And bathe there in God's sight.

"We two will stand beside that shrine,
80   Occult,° withheld, untrod,   *hidden, mysterious*
Whose lamps are stirred continually
    With prayer sent up to God;
And see our old prayers, granted, melt
    Each like a little cloud.

85 "We two will lie i' the shadow of
    That living mystic tree[4]
Within whose secret growth the Dove[5]
    Is sometimes felt to be,

---

3. Job 38.7.
4. A tangible manifestation of the Holy Spirit (Mark 1.10), frequent in Christian art.
5. The tree of life, as described in an apocalyptic vision in the Bible (Revelation 22.2).

While every leaf that His plumes touch
90   Saith His Name audibly.

"And I myself will teach to him,
      I myself, lying so,
The songs I sing here; which his voice
      Shall pause in, hushed and slow,
95 And find some knowledge at each pause,
      Or some new thing to know."

(Alas! We two, we two, thou say'st!
      Yea, one wast thou with me
That once of old. But shall God lift
100   To endless unity
The soul whose likeness with thy soul
      Was but its love for thee?)

"We two," she said, "will seek the groves
      Where the lady Mary is,
105 With her five handmaidens, whose names
      Are five sweet symphonies,
Cecily, Gertrude, Magdalen,
      Margaret, and Rosalys.[6]

"Circlewise sit they, with bound locks
110   And foreheads garlanded;
Into the fine cloth white like flame
      Weaving the golden thread,
To fashion the birth-robes for them
      Who are just born, being dead.

115 "He shall fear, haply,° and be dumb;   perhaps
      Then will I lay my cheek
To his, and tell about our love,
      Not once abashed or weak;
And the dear Mother will approve
120   My pride, and let me speak.

"Herself shall bring us, hand in hand,
      To Him round whom all souls
Kneel, the clear-ranged unnumbered heads
      Bowed with their aureoles;
125 And angels meeting us shall sing
      To their citherns and citoles.[7]

"There will I ask of Christ the Lord
      Thus much for him and me—
Only to live as once on earth
130   With Love—only to be,
As then awhile, forever now,
      Together, I and he."

6. Rossetti creates this list of Mary's handmaidens   ical characters.
from various saints, historical figures, and allegor-   7. Guitarlike instruments.

She gazed and listened and then said,
　　Less sad of speech than mild—
135　"All this is when he comes." She ceased.
　　The light thrilled toward her, filled
With angels in strong, level flight.
　　Her eyes prayed, and she smiled.

(I saw her smile.) But soon their path
140　Was vague in distant spheres;
And then she cast her arms along
　　The golden barriers,
And laid her face between her hands,
　　And wept. (I heard her tears.)

1846　　　　　　　　　　　　　　　　　　　　1850

My Sister's Sleep[1]

She fell asleep on Christmas Eve.
　　At length the long-ungranted shade
　　Of weary eyelids overweighed
The pain nought else might yet relieve.

5　Our mother, who had leaned all day
　　Over the bed from chime to chime,
　　Then raised herself for the first time,
And as she sat her down, did pray.

Her little worktable was spread
10　With work to finish. For° the glare　　　　　*because of*
　　Made by her candle, she had care
To work some distance from the bed.

Without, there was a cold moon up,
　　Of winter radiance sheer and thin;
15　The hollow halo it was in
Was like an icy crystal cup.

Through the small room, with subtle sound
　　Of flame, by vents the fireshine drove
　　And reddened. In its dim alcove
20　The mirror shed a clearness round.

I had been sitting up some nights,
　　And my tired mind felt weak and blank;
　　Like a sharp strengthening wine it drank
The stillness and the broken lights.

---

1. The incident in this poem is imaginary, not autobiographical.

25 Twelve struck. That sound, by dwindling years
   Heard in each hour, crept off; and then
   The ruffled silence spread again,
Like water that a pebble stirs.

   Our mother rose from where she sat;
30 Her needles, as she laid them down,
   Met lightly, and her silken gown
Settled—no other noise than that.

   "Glory unto the Newly Born!"
   So, as said angels, she did say,
35 Because we were in Christmas Day,
Though it would still be long till morn.

   Just then in the room over us
   There was a pushing back of chairs,
   As some who had sat unawares
40 So late, now heard the hour, and rose.

   With anxious softly-stepping haste
   Our mother went where Margaret lay,
   Fearing the sounds o'erhead—should they
Have broken her long watched-for rest!

45 She stooped an instant, calm, and turned,
   But suddenly turned back again;
   And all her features seemed in pain
With woe, and her eyes gazed and yearned.

   For my part, I but hid my face,
50 And held my breath, and spoke no word.
   There was none spoken; but I heard
The silence for a little space.

   Our mother bowed herself and wept;
   And both my arms fell, and I said,
55 "God knows I knew that she was dead."
And there, all white, my sister slept.

   Then kneeling, upon Christmas morn
   A little after twelve o'clock,
   We said, ere the first quarter struck,
60 "Christ's blessing on the newly born!"

1847   1850

Jenny

Vengeance of Jenny's case! Fie on her! Never name her, child!—(Mrs. Quickly.)[1]

Lazy laughing languid Jenny,
Fond of a kiss and fond of a guinea,[2]
Whose head upon my knee to-night
Rests for a while, as if grown light
5   With all our dances and the sound
To which the wild tunes spun you round:
Fair Jenny mine, the thoughtless queen
Of kisses which the blush between
Could hardly make much daintier;
10   Whose eyes are as blue skies, whose hair
Is countless gold incomparable:
Fresh flower, scarce touched with signs that tell
Of Love's exuberant hotbed:—Nay,
Poor flower left torn since yesterday
15   Until to-morrow leave you bare;
Poor handful of bright spring-water
Flung in the whirlpool's shrieking face;
Poor shameful Jenny, full of grace[3]
Thus with your head upon my knee;—
20   Whose person or whose purse may be
The lodestar° of your reverie?   guiding star

This room of yours, my Jenny, looks
A change from mine so full of books,
Whose serried[4] ranks hold fast, forsooth,
25   So many captive hours of youth,—
The hours they thieve from day and night
To make one's cherished work come right,
And leave it wrong for all their theft,
Even as to-night my work was left:
30   Until I vowed that since my brain
And eyes of dancing seemed so fain,°   desirous
My feet should have some dancing too:—
And thus it was I met with you.
Well, I suppose 'twas hard to part,
35   For here I am. And now, sweetheart,
You seem too tired to get to bed.

It was a careless life I led
When rooms like this were scarce so strange
Not long ago. What breeds the change,—
40   The many aims or the few years?
Because to-night it all appears
Something I do not know again.

---

1. Shakespeare, *The Merry Wives of Windsor*
4.1.53–54. Mistress Quickly continues: "if she be
a whore."
2. English gold coin worth twenty-one shillings.

3. Allusion to the first line of the prayer to the
Virgin Mary: "Hail Mary, full of grace."
4. Pressed close together.

The cloud's not danced out of my brain—
The cloud that made it turn and swim
45 While hour by hour the books grew dim.
Why, Jenny, as I watch you there,—
For all your wealth of loosened hair,
Your silk ungirdled and unlac'd
And warm sweets open to the waist.
50 All golden in the lamplight's gleam,—
You know not what a book you seem,
Half-read by lightning in a dream!
How should you know, my Jenny? Nay,
And I should be ashamed to say:—
55 Poor beauty, so well worth a kiss!
But while my thought runs on like this
With wasteful whims more than enough,
I wonder what you're thinking of.

If of myself you think at all,
60 What is the thought?—conjectural
On sorry matters best unsolved?—
Or inly° is each grace revolved   *inwardly*
To fit me with a lure?—or (sad
To think!) perhaps you're merely glad
65 That I'm not drunk or ruffianly
And let you rest upon my knee.

For sometimes, were the truth confess'd,
You're thankful for a little rest,—
Glad from the crush to rest within,
70 From the heart-sickness and the din
Where envy's voice at virtue's pitch
Mocks you because your gown is rich;
And from the pale girl's dumb rebuke,
Whose ill-clad grace and toil-worn look
75 Proclaim the strength that keeps her weak,
And other nights than yours bespeak;
And from the wise unchildish elf,
To schoolmate lesser than himself
Pointing you out, what thing you are:—
80 Yes, from the daily jeer and jar,
From shame and shame's outbraving too,
Is rest not sometimes sweet to you?—
But most from the hatefulness of man,
Who spares not to end what he began,
85 Whose acts are ill and his speech ill,
Who, having used you at his will,
Thrusts you aside, as when I dine
I serve° the dishes and the wine.   *treat*

Well, handsome Jenny mine, sit up:
90 I've filled our glasses, let us sup,
And do not let me think of you,
Lest shame of yours suffice for two.

What, still so tired? Well, well then, keep
Your head there, so you do not sleep;
95   But that the weariness may pass
And leave you merry, take this glass.
Ah! lazy lily hand, more bless'd
If ne'er in rings it had been dress'd
Nor ever by a glove conceal'd!

100   Behold the lilies of the field,
They toil not neither do they spin;
(So doth the ancient text[5] begin,—
Not of such rest as one of these
Can share.) Another rest and ease
105   Along each summer-sated path
From its new lord the garden hath,
Than that whose spring in blessings ran
Which praised the bounteous husbandman,°   *farmer*
Ere yet, in days of hankering breath,
110   The lilies sickened unto death.

What, Jenny, are your lilies dead?
Aye, and the snow-white leaves are spread
Like winter on the garden-bed.
But you had roses left in May,—
115   They were not gone too. Jenny, nay,
But must your roses die, and those
Their purfled[6] buds that should unclose?
Even so; the leaves are curled apart,
Still red as from the broken heart,
120   And here's the naked stem of thorns.

Nay, nay, mere words. Here nothing warns
As yet of winter. Sickness here
Or want alone could waken fear,—
Nothing but passion wrings a tear.
125   Except when there may rise unsought
Haply at times a passing thought
Of the old days which seem to be
Much older than any history
That is written in any book;
130   When she would lie in fields and look
Along the ground through the blown grass
And wonder where the city was,
Far out of sight, whose broil and bale°   *turmoil and evil*
They told her then for a child's tale.

135   Jenny, you know the city now.
A child can tell the tale there, how
Some things which are not yet enroll'd
In market-lists are bought and sold
Even till the early Sunday light,

5. Matthew 6.28.   6. With a decorative edging.

140 When Saturday night is market-night
Everywhere, be it dry or wet,
And market-night in the Haymarket.⁷
Our learned London children know,
Poor Jenny, all your pride and woe;
145 Have seen your lifted silken skirt
Advertise dainties through the dirt;
Have seen your coach-wheels splash rebuke
On virtue; and have learned your look
When, wealth and health slipped past, you stare
150 Along the streets alone, and there,
Round the long park, across the bridge,
The cold lamps at the pavement's edge
Wind on together and apart,
A fiery serpent for your heart.

155 Let the thoughts pass, an empty cloud I
Suppose I were to think aloud,—
What if to her all this were said?
Why, as a volume seldom read
Being opened halfway shuts again,
160 So might the pages of her brain
Be parted at such words, and thence
Close back upon the dusty sense.
For is there hue or shape defin'd
In Jenny's desecrated mind,
165 Where all contagious currents meet,
A Lethe⁸ of the middle street?
Nay, it reflects not any face,
Nor sound is in its sluggish pace,
But as they coil those eddies° clot,   small whirlpools
170 And night and day remember not.

Why, Jenny, you're asleep at last!—
Asleep, poor Jenny, hard and fast,—
So young and soft and tired; so fair,
With chin thus nestled in your hair,
175 Mouth quiet, eyelids almost blue
As if some sky of dreams shone through!

Just as another woman sleeps!
Enough to throw one's thoughts in heaps
Of doubt and horror,—what to say
180 Or think,—this awful secret sway,
The potter's power over the clay!
Of the same lump (it has been said)
For honour and dishonour made,⁹
Two sister vessels. Here is one.

---

7. Street in London frequented by prostitutes.
8. The river of forgetfulness in the Greek underworld. Gutters in London often ran through the middle of the street.

9. Romans 9.21: "Hath not the potter power over the clay, of the same lump to make one vessel unto honor, and another unto dishonor?"

185   My cousin Nell is fond of fun,
And fond of dress, and change, and praise,
So mere a woman in her ways:
And if her sweet eyes rich in youth
Are like her lips that tell the truth,
190   My cousin Nell is fond of love.
And she's the girl I'm proudest of.
Who does not prize her, guard her well?
The love of change, in cousin Nell,
Shall find the best and hold it dear:
195   The unconquered mirth turn quieter
Not through her own, through others' woe:
The conscious pride of beauty glow
Beside another's pride in her,
One little part of all they share.
200   For Love himself shall ripen these
In a kind soil to just increase
Through years of fertilizing peace.

    Of the same lump (as it is said)
For honour and dishonour made,
205   Two sister vessels. Here is one.

    It makes a goblin[1] of the sun.

    So pure,—so fall'n! How dare to think
Of the first common kindred link?
Yet, Jenny, till the world shall burn
210   It seems that all things take their turn;
And who shall say but this fair tree
May need, in changes that may be,
Your children's children's charity?
Scorned then, no doubt, as you are scorn'd!
215   Shall no man hold his pride forewarn'd
Till in the end, the Day of Days,
At Judgment, one of his own race,
As frail and lost as you, shall rise,—
His daughter, with his mother's eyes?

220   How Jenny's clock ticks on the shelf!
Might not the dial scorn itself
That has such hours to register?
Yet as to me, even so to her
Are golden sun and silver moon,
225   In daily largesse of earth's boon,
Counted for life-coins to one tune.
And if, as blindfold fates are toss'd,
Through some one man this life be lost,
Shall soul not somehow pay for soul?

230   Fair shines the gilded aureole°   *halo*
In which our highest painters place

1. A gold coin (slang).

Some living woman's simple face.
And the stilled features thus descried
As Jenny's long throat droops aside,—
235 The shadows where the cheeks are thin,
And pure wide curve from ear to chin,—
With Raffael's, Leonardo's[2] hand
To show them to men's souls, might stand,
Whole ages long, the whole world through,
240 For preachings of what God can do.
What has man done here? How atone,
Great God, for this which man has done?
And for the body and soul which by
Man's pitiless doom must now comply
245 With lifelong hell, what lullaby
Of sweet forgetful second birth
Remains? All dark. No sign on earth
What measure of God's rest endows
The many mansions of his house.[3]

250 If but a woman's heart might see
Such erring heart unerringly
For once! But that can never be.

Like a rose shut in a book
In which pure women may not look,
255 For its base pages claim control
To crush the flower within the soul;
Where through each dead rose-leaf that clings,
Pale as transparent Psyche-wings,[4]
To the vile text, are traced such things
260 As might make lady's cheek indeed
More than a living rose to read;
So nought save foolish foulness may
Watch with hard eyes the sure decay:
And so the life-blood of this rose,
265 Puddled with shameful knowledge, flows
Through leaves no chaste hand may unclose;
Yet still it keeps such faded show
Of when 'twas gathered long ago,
That the crushed petals' lovely grain,
270 The sweetness of the sanguine° stain,   blood-red
Seen of a woman's eyes, must make
Her pitiful heart, so prone to ache,
Love roses better for its sake:—
Only that this can never be:—
275 Even so unto her sex is she.

Yet, Jenny, looking long at you,
The woman almost fades from view.

2. The painters Raphael (Raffaello Sanzio, 1483–1520) and Leonardo da Vinci (1452–1519).
3. Cf. John 14.2: "In my Father's house are many mansions."
4. The soul, often symbolized by a butterfly that escaped the body after death. Also, in the well-known story told by Apuleius (*The Golden Ass*, 2nd century C.E.), Psyche was a maiden beloved by Cupid.

A cipher of man's changeless sum
Of lust, past, present, and to come,
280   Is left. A riddle that one shrinks
To challenge from the scornful sphinx.⁵

Like a toad within a stone
Seated while Time crumbles on;
Which sits there since the earth was curs'd
285   For Man's transgression at the first;
Which, living through all centuries,
Not once has seen the sun arise;
Whose life, to its cold circle charmed,
The earth's whole summers have not warmed;
290   Which always—whitherso the stone
Be flung—sits there, deaf, blind, alone;—
Aye, and shall not be driven out
Till that which shuts him round about
Break at the very Master's stroke,
295   And the dust thereof vanish as smoke,
And the seed of Man vanish as dust:—
Even so within this world is Lust.

Come, come, what use in thoughts like this?
Poor little Jenny, good to kiss,—
300   You'd not believe by what strange roads
Thought travels, when your beauty goads
A man to-night to think of toads!
Jenny, wake up . . . Why, there's the dawn!

And there's an early waggon drawn
305   To market, and some sheep that jog
Bleating before a barking dog;
And the old streets come peering through
Another night that London knew;
And all as ghostlike as the lamps.

310   So on the wings of day decamps
My last night's frolic. Glooms begin
To shiver off as lights creep in
Past the gauze curtains half drawn-to,
And the lamp's doubled shade grows blue,—
315   Your lamp, my Jenny, kept alight,
Like a wise virgin's, all one night!⁶
And in the alcove coolly spread
Glimmers with dawn your empty bed;
And yonder your fair face I see
320   Reflected lying on my knee,
Where teems with first foreshadowings
Your pier-glass⁷ scrawled with diamond rings:

---

5. In Greek mythology a monster with a lion's
body, bird's wings, and woman's face. The answer
to her riddle—what walks on four legs in the morning, three at noon, and three in the evening?—is
man, at different ages.

6. Cf. Matthew 25.1–13. In the parable of the
wise and foolish virgins, the wise virgins took sufficient oil to keep their lamps burning all night.
7. A mirror. Lovers would scratch their names on
it with the diamonds in their rings.

And on your bosom all night worn
Yesterday's rose now droops forlorn,
325   But dies not yet this summer morn.

And now without, as if some word
Had called upon them that they heard,
The London sparrows far and nigh
Clamour together suddenly;
330   And Jenny's cage-bird grown awake
Here in their song his part must take,
Because here too the day doth break.

And somehow in myself the dawn
Among stirred clouds and veils withdrawn
335   Strikes greyly on her. Let her sleep.
But will it wake her if I heap
These cushions thus beneath her head
Where my knee was? No,—there's your bed,
My Jenny, while you dream. And there
340   I lay among your golden hair,
Perhaps the subject of your dreams,
These golden coins.
                             For still one deems
That Jenny's flattering sleep confers
New magic on the magic purse,—
345   Grim web, how clogged with shrivelled flies!
Between the threads fine fumes arise
And shape their pictures in the brain.
There roll no streets in glare and rain.
Nor flagrant man-swine whets his tusk;
350   But delicately sighs in musk
The homage of the dim boudoir;
Or like a palpitating star
Thrilled into song, the opera-night
Breathes faint in the quick pulse of light;
355   Or at the carriage-window shine
Rich wares for choice; or, free to dine,
Whirls through its hour of health (divine
For her) the concourse of the Park.
And though in the discounted dark
360   Her functions there and here are one,
Beneath the lamps and in the sun
There reigns at least the acknowledged belle
Apparelled beyond parallel.
Ah Jenny, yes, we know your dreams.

365   For even the Paphian[8] Venus seems
A goddess o'er the realms of love,
When silver-shrined in shadowy grove:
Aye, or let offerings nicely plac'd

---

8. Of Paphos, a city on Cyprus that was the site of a famous temple of Aphrodite (the Roman Venus).
Also, a term for prostitute.

But hide Priapus⁹ to the waist,
370   And whoso looks on him shall see
An eligible deity.

Why, Jenny, waking here alone
May help you to remember one,
Though all the memory's long outworn
375   Of many a double-pillowed morn.
I think I see you when you wake,
And rub your eyes for me, and shake
My gold, in rising, from your hair,
A Danaë¹ for a moment there.

380   Jenny, my love rang true! for still
Love at first sight is vague, until
That tinkling makes him audible.

And must I mock you to the last,
Ashamed of my own shame,—aghast
385   Because some thoughts not born amiss
Rose at a poor fair face like this?
Well, of such thoughts so much I know:
In my life, as in hers, they show,
By a far gleam which I may near,
390   A dark path I can strive to clear.

Only one kiss.   Good-bye, my dear.

1848   1870

From The House of Life

The Sonnet

A Sonnet is a moment's monument—
Memorial from the Soul's eternity
To one dead deathless hour. Look that it be,
Whether for lustral° rite or dire portent,   *purificatory*
5   Of its own arduous fullness reverent;
Carve it in ivory or in ebony,
As Day or Night may rule; and let Time see
Its flowering crest impearled and orient.

A Sonnet is a coin; its face reveals
10   The soul—its converse, to what Power 'tis due—
Whether for tribute to the august appeals
Of Life, or dower in Love's high retinue,
It serve; or, 'mid the dark wharf's cavernous breath,
In Charon's¹ palm it pay the toll to Death.

---

9. A Greek fertility god, whose symbol was the phallus.
1. In Greek mythology a maiden whom Zeus visited in the form of a shower of gold.

1. In classical mythology the ferryman who, for a fee, rowed the souls of the dead across the river Styx.

Nuptial Sleep[2]

At length their long kiss severed, with sweet smart:
And as the last slow sudden drops are shed
From sparkling eaves when all the storm has fled,
So singly flagged the pulses of each heart.
5 Their bosoms sundered, with the opening start
Of married flowers to either side outspread
From the knit stem; yet still their mouths, burnt red,
Fawned on each other where they lay apart.

Sleep sank them lower than the tide of dreams,
10 And their dreams watched them sink, and slid away.
Slowly their souls swam up again, through gleams
Of watered light and dull drowned waifs of day;
Till from some wonder of new woods and streams
He woke, and wondered more: for there she lay.

19. Silent Noon

Your hands lie open in the long fresh grass—
The finger-points look through like rosy blooms;
Your eyes smile peace. The pasture gleams and glooms
'Neath billowing skies that scatter and amass.
5 All round our nest, far as the eye can pass,
Are golden kingcup-fields with silver edge
Where the cow-parsley skirts the hawthorn hedge.
'Tis visible silence, still as the hourglass.

Deep in the sun-searched growths the dragonfly
10 Hangs like a blue thread loosened from the sky—
So this winged hour is dropped to us from above.
Oh! clasp we to our hearts, for deathless dower,
This close-companioned inarticulate hour
When twofold silence was the song of love.

77. Soul's Beauty[3]

Under the arch of Life, where love and death,
Terror and mystery, guard her shrine, I saw
Beauty enthroned; and though her gaze struck awe,
I drew it in as simply as my breath.
5 Hers are the eyes which, over and beneath,
The sky and sea bend on thee,—which can draw,

By sea or sky or woman, to one law,
The allotted bondman° of her palm and wreath.   *slave*

This is that Lady Beauty, in whose praise
10   Thy voice and hand shake still,—long known to thee
By flying hair and fluttering hem,—the beat
Following her daily of thy heart and feet,
How passionately and irretrievably,
In what fond flight, how many ways and days!

78. Body's Beauty

Of Adams's first wife, Lilith, it is told
(The witch he loved before the gift of Eve,)
That, ere the snake's, her sweet tongue could deceive,
And her enchanted hair was the first gold.
5   And still she sits, young while the earth is old,
And subtly of herself contemplative,
Draws men to watch the bright web she can weave,
Till heart and body and life are in its hold.

The rose and poppy are her flowers; for where
10   Is he not found, O Lilith, whom shed scent
And soft-shed kisses and soft sleep shall snare?
Lo! as that youth's eyes burned at thine, so went
Thy spell through him, and left his straight neck bent
And round his heart one strangling golden hair.

1848–80   1870, 1881

CHRISTINA ROSSETTI
1830–1894

Referring to the title of George Gissing's 1893 novel about women who choose not to marry, the critic Jerome McGann calls Christina Rossetti "one of nineteenth-century England's greatest 'Odd Women.' " Her life had little apparent incident. She was the youngest child in the Rossetti family. Her father was an exiled Italian patriot who wrote poetry and commentaries on Dante that tried to find evidence in his poems of mysterious ancient conspiracies; her mother was an Anglo-Italian who had worked as a governess. Their household was a lively gathering place for Italian exiles, full of conversation of politics and culture; and Christina, like her brothers Dante Gabriel and William Michael, was encouraged to develop an early love for art and literature and to draw and write poetry from a very early age. When she was an adolescent, her life changed dramatically: her father became a permanent invalid, the family's economic situation worsened, and her own health deteriorated. Subsequently she, her mother, and her sister became intensely involved with the Anglo-Catholic movement within the Church of England. For the rest of her life, Rossetti governed herself by strict religious principles, giving up theater, opera, and chess; on two occasions she canceled plans for marriage because of religious scruples, breaking her first engagement when her fiancé reverted to Roman Catholicism and ultimately refusing to marry a second suitor because he seemed insufficiently concerned with religion. She lived a quiet life, occupying herself with charitable work—including ten years of volunteer service at a penitentiary for fallen women—with caring for her family, and with writing poetry.

Rossetti's first volume of poetry, *Goblin Market and Other Poems* (1862), contains all the different poetic modes that mark her achievement—pure lyric, narrative fable, ballad, and the devotional verse to which she increasingly turned in her later years. The most remarkable poem in the book is the title piece, which early established its popularity as a seemingly simple moral fable for children. Later readers have likened it to S. T. Coleridge's *The Rime of the Ancient Mariner* (1798) and have detected in it a complex representation of the religious themes of temptation and sin, and of redemption by vicarious suffering; the fruit that tempts Laura, however, clearly is not from the tree of knowledge but from the orchard of sensual delights. In its deceptively simple style *Goblin Market*, like many of Rossetti's poems, demonstrates her affinity with the early aims of the Pre-Raphaelite group, though her work as a whole resists this classification. A consciousness of gender often leads her to criticize the conventional representation of women in Pre-Raphaelite art, as in her sonnet "In an Artist's Studio" (1896), and a stern religious vision controls the sensuous impulses typical of Pre-Raphaelite poetry and painting. Virginia Woolf has described the distinctive combination of sensuousness and religious severity in Rossetti's work:

> Your poems are full of gold dust and "sweet geraniums' varied brightness"; your eye noted incessantly how rushes are "velvet headed," and lizards have a "strange metallic mail"—your eye, indeed, observed with a sensual pre-Raphaelite intensity that must have surprised Christina the Anglo-Catholic. But to her you owed perhaps the fixity and sadness of your muse. . . . No sooner have you feasted on beauty with your eyes than your mind tells you that beauty is vain and beauty passes. Death, oblivion, and rest lap round your songs with their dark wave.

William Michael Rossetti wrote of his sister, "She was replete with the spirit of self-postponement." Christina Rossetti was a poet who created, in Sandra M. Gilbert and Susan Gubar's phrase, "an aesthetics of renunciation." She writes a poetry of deferral, of deflection, of negation, whose very denials and constraints give her a powerful way to articulate a poetic self in critical relationship to the little that the world offers. Like Emily Dickinson, she often, as in "Winter: My Secret" (1862) uses a coy playfulness and sardonic wit to reduce the self but at the same time to preserve for it a secret inner space. And like Dickinson, she wrote many poems of an extraordinarily pure lyric beauty that made Virginia Woolf compare Rossetti's work to that of classical composers: "Your instinct was so sure, so direct, so intense that it produced poems that sing like music in one's ears—like a melody by Mozart or an air by Gluck."

Song

She sat and sang alway
   By the green margin of a stream,
Watching the fishes leap and play
   Beneath the glad sunbeam.

5   I sat and wept alway
   Beneath the moon's most shadowy beam,
Watching the blossoms of the May
   Weep leaves into the stream.

    I wept for memory;
10   She sang for hope that is so fair:
    My tears were swallowed by the sea;
    Her songs died on the air.

1848   1862

Song

    When I am dead, my dearest,
      Sing no sad songs for me;
    Plant thou no roses at my head,
      Nor shady cypress tree:[1]
5   Be the green grass above me
      With showers and dewdrops wet;
    And if thou wilt, remember,
      And if thou wilt, forget.

    I shall not see the shadows,
10   I shall not feel the rain;
    I shall not hear the nightingale
      Sing on, as if in pain:
    And dreaming through the twilight
      That doth not rise nor set,
15   Haply° I may remember,   *perhaps*
      And haply may forget.

1848   1862

After Death

    The curtains were half drawn, the floor was swept
    And strewn with rushes, rosemary and may[1]
    Lay thick upon the bed on which I lay,
    Where thro' the lattice ivy-shadows crept.
5   He leaned above me, thinking that I slept
    And could not hear him; but I heard him say:
    "Poor child, poor child": and as he turned away
    Came a deep silence, and I knew he wept.
    He did not touch the shroud, or raise the fold
10   That hid my face, or take my hand in his,
      Or ruffle the smooth pillows for my head:
    He did not love me living; but once dead
    He pitied me; and very sweet it is
    To know he still is warm tho' I am cold.

1849   1862

---

1. The cypress tree is associated with mourning.   1. Flowers associated with death.

Dead before Death

Ah! changed and cold, how changed and very cold!
With stiffened smiling lips and cold calm eyes:
Changed, yet the same; much knowing, little wise;
This was the promise of the days of old!
5 Grown hard and stubborn in the ancient mould,
Grown rigid in the sham of lifelong lies:
We hoped for better things as years would rise,
But it is over as a tale once told.
All fallen the blossom that no fruitage bore,
10 All lost the present and the future time,
All lost, all lost, the lapse that went before:
So lost till death shut-to the opened door,
So lost from chime to everlasting chime,
So cold and lost for ever evermore.

1854   1862

Cobwebs

It is a land with neither night nor day,
Nor heat nor cold, nor any wind, nor rain,
Nor hills nor valleys; but one even plain
Stretches thro' long unbroken miles away:
5 While thro' the sluggish air a twilight grey
Broodeth; no moons or seasons wax and wane,
No ebb and flow are there along the main,°   ocean
No bud-time no leaf-falling, there for aye:°—   forever
No ripple on the sea, no shifting sand,
10 No beat of wings to stir the stagnant space,
No pulse of life thro' all the loveless land:
And loveless sea; no trace of days before,
No guarded home, no toil-won resting place,
No future hope no fear for evermore.

1855   1896

A Triad

Three sang of love together: one with lips
Crimson, with cheeks and bosom in a glow,
Flushed to the yellow hair and finger tips;
And one there sang who soft and smooth as snow
5 Bloomed like a tinted hyacinth at a show;
And one was blue with famine after love,
Who like a harpstring snapped rang harsh and low
The burden of what those were singing of.
One shamed herself in love; one temperately
10 Grew gross in soulless love, a sluggish wife;

One famished died for love. Thus two of three
Took death for love and won him after strife;
One droned in sweetness like a fattened bee:
All on the threshold, yet all short of life.

1856   1862

In an Artist's Studio[1]

One face looks out from all his canvases,
    One selfsame figure sits or walks or leans;
    We found her hidden just behind those screens,
That mirror gave back all her loveliness.
5   A queen in opal or in ruby dress,
    A nameless girl in freshest summer-greens,
    A saint, an angel;—every canvas means
The same one meaning, neither more nor less.
He feeds upon her face by day and night,
10   And she with true kind eyes looks back on him
Fair as the moon and joyful as the light:
    Not wan with waiting, not with sorrow dim;
Not as she is, but was when hope shone bright;
Not as she is, but as she fills his dream.

1856   1896

A Birthday

My heart is like a singing bird
    Whose nest is in a watered shoot;°   *slim branch*
My heart is like an apple tree
    Whose boughs are bent with thickset fruit;
5   My heart is like a rainbow shell
    That paddles in a halcyon° sea;   *tranquil*
My heart is gladder than all these
    Because my love is come to me.

Raise me a dais of silk and down;
10   Hang it with vair° and purple dyes;   *squirrel fur*
Carve it in doves and pomegranates,
    And peacocks with a hundred eyes;
Work it in gold and silver grapes,
    In leaves and silver fleurs-de-lys;
15 Because the birthday of my life
    Is come, my love is come to me.

1857   1862

---

1. According to Christina's brother William Michael, this poem focuses on the work of their older brother, Dante Gabriel: "The reference is apparently to our brother's studio, and to his constantly repeated heads of the lady whom he afterwards married, Miss Siddal."

An Apple-Gathering

I plucked pink blossoms from mine apple tree
    And wore them all that evening in my hair:
Then in due season when I went to see
    I found no apples there.

5 With dangling basket all along the grass
    As I had come I went the selfsame track:
My neighbours mocked me while they saw me pass
    So empty-handed back.

Lilian and Lilias smiled in trudging by,
10   Their heaped-up basket teazed me like a jeer;
Sweet-voiced they sang beneath the sunset sky,
    Their mother's home was near.

Plump Gertrude passed me with her basket full,
    A stronger hand than hers helped it along;
15 A voice talked with her thro' the shadows cool
    More sweet to me than song.

Ah Willie, Willie, was my love less worth
    Than apples with their green leaves piled above?
I counted rosiest apples on the earth
20   Of far less worth than love.

So once it was with me you stooped to talk
    Laughing and listening in this very lane:
To think that by this way we used to walk
    We shall not walk again!

25 I let my neighbours pass me, ones and twos
    And groups; the latest said the night grew chill,
And hastened: but I loitered, while the dews
    Fell fast I loitered still.

1857   1862

Winter: My Secret

I tell my secret? No indeed, not I:
Perhaps some day, who knows?
But not today; it froze, and blows, and snows,
And you're too curious: fie!
5 You want to hear it? well:
Only, my secret's mine, and I won't tell.

Or, after all, perhaps there's none:
Suppose there is no secret after all,
But only just my fun.

10 Today's a nipping day, a biting day;
In which one wants a shawl,
A veil, a cloak, and other wraps:
I cannot ope to every one who taps,
And let the draughts come whistling thro' my hall;
15 Come bounding and surrounding me,
Come buffeting, astounding me,
Nipping and clipping thro' my wraps and all.
I wear my mask for warmth: who ever shows
His nose to Russian snows
20 To be pecked at by every wind that blows?
You would not peck? I thank you for good will,
Believe, but leave that truth untested still.

Spring's an expansive time: yet I don't trust
March with its peck of dust,
25 Nor April with its rainbow-crowned brief showers,
Nor even May, whose flowers
One frost may wither thro' the sunless hours.

Perhaps some languid summer day,
When drowsy birds sing less and less,
30 And golden fruit is ripening to excess,
If there's not too much sun nor too much cloud,
And the warm wind is neither still nor loud,
Perhaps my secret I may say,
Or you may guess.

1857   1862

Up-Hill

Does the road wind up-hill all the way?
    Yes, to the very end.
Will the day's journey take the whole long day?
    From morn to night, my friend.

5   But is there for the night a resting-place?
    A roof for when the slow dark hours begin.
May not the darkness hide it from my face?
    You cannot miss that inn.

Shall I meet other wayfarers at night?
10   Those who have gone before.
Then must I knock, or call when just in sight?
    They will not keep you standing at that door.

Shall I find comfort, travel-sore and weak?
    Of labour you shall find the sum.
15 Will there be beds for me and all who seek?
    Yea, beds for all who come.

1858   1862

Goblin Market

Morning and evening
Maids heard the goblins cry:
"Come buy our orchard fruits,
Come buy, come buy:
5   Apples and quinces,
Lemons and oranges,
Plump unpecked cherries,
Melons and raspberries,
Bloom-down-cheeked peaches,
10 Swart-headed mulberries,
Wild free-born cranberries,
Crab-apples, dewberries,
Pine-apples, blackberries,
Apricots, strawberries;—
15 All ripe together
In summer weather,—
Morns that pass by,
Fair eves that fly;
Come buy, come buy:
20 Our grapes fresh from the vine,
Pomegranates full and fine,
Dates and sharp bullaces,
Rare pears and greengages,
Damsons¹ and bilberries,
25 Taste them and try:
Currants and gooseberries,
Bright-fire-like barberries,
Figs to fill your mouth,
Citrons from the South,
30 Sweet to tongue and sound to eye;
Come buy, come buy."

Evening by evening
Among the brookside rushes,
Laura bowed her head to hear,
35 Lizzie veiled her blushes:
Crouching close together
In the cooling weather,
With clasping arms and cautioning lips,
With tingling cheeks and finger tips.
40 "Lie close," Laura said,
Pricking up her golden head:
"We must not look at goblin men,
We must not buy their fruits:
Who knows upon what soil they fed
45 Their hungry thirsty roots?"
"Come buy," call the goblins
Hobbling down the glen.

---

1. Bullaces, greengages, and damsons are varieties of plums.

"Oh," cried Lizzie, "Laura, Laura,
You should not peep at goblin men."
50 Lizzie covered up her eyes,
Covered close lest they should look;
Laura reared her glossy head,
And whispered like the restless brook:
"Look, Lizzie, look, Lizzie,
55 Down the glen tramp little men.
One hauls a basket,
One bears a plate,
One lugs a golden dish
Of many pounds weight.
60 How fair the vine must grow
Whose grapes are so luscious;
How warm the wind must blow
Thro' those fruit bushes."
"No," said Lizzie: "No, no, no;
65 Their offers should not charm us,
Their evil gifts would harm us."
She thrust a dimpled finger
In each ear, shut eyes and ran:
Curious Laura chose to linger
70 Wondering at each merchant man.
One had a cat's face,
One whisked a tail,
One tramped at a rat's pace,
One crawled like a snail,
75 One like a wombat prowled obtuse and furry,
One like a ratel[2] tumbled hurry skurry.
She heard a voice like voice of doves
Cooing all together:
They sounded kind and full of loves
80 In the pleasant weather.

Laura stretched her gleaming neck
Like a rush-imbedded swan,
Like a lily from the beck,°   *small brook*
Like a moonlit poplar branch,
85 Like a vessel at the launch
When its last restraint is gone.

Backwards up the mossy glen
Turned and trooped the goblin men,
With their shrill repeated cry,
90 "Come buy, come buy."
When they reached where Laura was
They stood stock still upon the moss,
Leering at each other,
Brother with queer brother;
95 Signalling each other,
Brother with sly brother.

2. South African mammal resembling a badger (pronounced *ray-tell*).

One set his basket down,
One reared° his plate;   *raised*
One began to weave a crown
100   Of tendrils, leaves and rough nuts brown
(Men sell not such in any town);
One heaved the golden weight
Of dish and fruit to offer her:
"Come buy, come buy," was still their cry.
105   Laura stared but did not stir,
Longed but had no money:
The whisk-tailed merchant bade her taste
In tones as smooth as honey,
The cat-faced purr'd,
110   The rat-paced spoke a word
Of welcome, and the snail-paced even was heard;
One parrot-voiced and jolly
Cried "Pretty Goblin" still° for "Pretty Polly;"—   *always*
One whistled like a bird.

115   But sweet-tooth Laura spoke in haste:
"Good folk, I have no coin;
To take were to purloin:
I have no copper in my purse,
I have no silver either,
120   And all my gold is on the furze
That shakes in windy weather
Above the rusty heather."
"You have much gold upon your head,"
They answered all together:
125   "Buy from us with a golden curl."
She clipped a precious golden lock,
She dropped a tear more rare than pearl,
Then sucked their fruit globes fair or red:
Sweeter than honey from the rock.
130   Stronger than man-rejoicing wine,[3]
Clearer than water flowed that juice;
She never tasted such before,
How should it cloy with length of use?
She sucked and sucked and sucked the more
135   Fruits which that unknown orchard bore;
She sucked until her lips were sore;
Then flung the emptied rinds away
But gathered up one kernel-stone,
And knew not was it night or day
140   As she turned home alone.

Lizzie met her at the gate
Full of wise upbraidings:
"Dear, you should not stay so late,
Twilight is not good for maidens;

3. Psalm 104.15. "Sweeter . . . rock," Psalm 81.16.

145 Should not loiter in the glen
In the haunts of goblin men.
Do you not remember Jeanie,
How she met them in the moonlight,
Took their gifts both choice and many,
150 Ate their fruits and wore their flowers
Plucked from bowers
Where summer ripens at all hours?
But ever in the noonlight
She pined and pined away;
155 Sought them by night and day,
Found them no more but dwindled and grew grey;
Then fell with the first snow,
While to this day no grass will grow
Where she lies low:
160 I planted daisies there a year ago
That never blow.°   *bloom*
You should not loiter so."
"Nay, hush," said Laura:
"Nay, hush, my sister:
165 I ate and ate my fill,
Yet my mouth waters still;
Tomorrow night I will
Buy more:" and kissed her:
"Have done with sorrow;
170 I'll bring you plums tomorrow
Fresh on their mother twigs,
Cherries worth getting;
You cannot think what figs
My teeth have met in,
175 What melons icy-cold
Piled on a dish of gold
Too huge for me to hold,
What peaches with a velvet nap,
Pellucid grapes without one seed:
180 Odorous indeed must be the mead
Whereon they grow, and pure the wave they drink
With lilies at the brink,
And sugar-sweet their sap."

Golden head by golden head,
185 Like two pigeons in one nest
Folded in each other's wings,
They lay down in their curtained bed:
Like two blossoms on one stem,
Like two flakes of new-fall'n snow,
190 Like two wands of ivory
Tipped with gold for awful° kings.   *awe-inspiring*
Moon and stars gazed in at them,
Wind sang to them lullaby,
Lumbering owls forbore to fly,
195 Not a bat flapped to and fro
Round their rest:

GOBLIN MARKET
and other poems
by Chriſtina Roſſetti

"Golden head by golden head"

London and Cambridge
Macmillan and Co. 1862

This frontispiece is one of the two illustrations that Dante Gabriel Rossetti provided for his sister's first volume of poetry in 1862.

Cheek to cheek and breast to breast
Locked together in one nest.

Early in the morning
200 When the first cock crowed his warning,
Neat like bees, as sweet and busy,
Laura rose with Lizzie:
Fetched in honey, milked the cows,
Aired and set to rights the house,
205 Kneaded cakes of whitest wheat,
Cakes for dainty mouths to eat,
Next churned butter, whipped up cream,
Fed their poultry, sat and sewed;
Talked as modest maidens should:
210 Lizzie with an open heart,
Laura in an absent dream,
One content, one sick in part;
One warbling for the mere bright day's delight,
One longing for the night.

215 At length slow evening came:
They went with pitchers to the reedy brook;

Lizzie most placid in her look,
Laura most like a leaping flame.
They drew the gurgling water from its deep;
220 Lizzie plucked purple and rich golden flags,°   *irises*
Then turning homewards said: "The sunset flushes
Those furthest loftiest crags;
Come, Laura, not another maiden lags,
No wilful squirrel wags,
225 The beasts and birds are fast asleep."
But Laura loitered still among the rushes
And said the bank was steep.

And said the hour was early still,
The dew not fall'n, the wind not chill:
230 Listening ever, but not catching
The customary cry,
"Come buy, come buy,"
With its iterated jingle
Of sugar-baited words:
235 Not for all her watching
Once discerning even one goblin
Racing, whisking, tumbling, hobbling;
Let alone the herds
That used to tramp along the glen,
240 In groups or single,
Of brisk fruit-merchant men.

Till Lizzie urged, "O Laura, come;
I hear the fruit-call but I dare not look:
You should not loiter longer at this brook:
245 Come with me home.
The stars rise, the moon bends her arc,
Each glowworm winks her spark,
Let us get home before the night grows dark:
For clouds may gather
250 Tho' this is summer weather,
Put out the lights and drench us thro';
Then if we lost our way what should we do?"

Laura turned cold as stone
To find her sister heard that cry alone,
255 That goblin cry,
"Come buy our fruits, come buy."
Must she then buy no more such dainty fruit?
Must she no more such succous° pasture find, *juicy, succulent*
Gone deaf and blind?
260 Her tree of life drooped from the root:
She said not one word in her heart's sore ache;
But peering thro' the dimness, nought discerning,
Trudged home, her pitcher dripping all the way;
So crept to bed, and lay
265 Silent till Lizzie slept;
Then sat up in a passionate yearning,

And gnashed her teeth for baulked desire, and wept
As if her heart would break.

Day after day, night after night,
270 Laura kept watch in vain
In sullen silence of exceeding pain.
She never caught again the goblin cry:
"Come buy, come buy;"—
She never spied the goblin men
275 Hawking their fruits along the glen:
But when the noon waxed bright
Her hair grew thin and gray;
She dwindled, as the fair full moon doth turn
To swift decay and burn
280 Her fire away.

One day remembering her kernel-stone
She set it by a wall that faced the south;
Dewed it with tears, hoped for a root,
Watched for a waxing shoot,
285 But there came none;
It never saw the sun,
It never felt the trickling moisture run:
While with sunk eyes and faded mouth
She dreamed of melons, as a traveller sees
290 False waves in desert drouth
With shade of leaf-crowned trees,
And burns the thirstier in the sandful breeze.

She no more swept the house,
Tended the fowls or cows,
295 Fetched honey, kneaded cakes of wheat,
Brought water from the brook:
But sat down listless in the chimney-nook
And would not eat.

Tender Lizzie could not bear
300 To watch her sister's cankerous care
Yet not to share.
She night and morning
Caught the goblins' cry:
"Come buy our orchard fruits,
305 Come buy, come buy:"—
Beside the brook, along the glen,
She heard the tramp of goblin men,
The voice and stir
Poor Laura could not hear;
310 Longed to buy fruit to comfort her,
But feared to pay too dear.
She thought of Jeanie in her grave,
Who should have been a bride;
But who for joys brides hope to have
315 Fell sick and died
In her gay prime,

In earliest Winter time,
With the first glazing rime,
With the first snow-fall of crisp Winter time.

320 Till Laura dwindling
Seemed knocking at Death's door:
Then Lizzie weighed° no more   *evaluated, considered*
Better and worse;
But put a silver penny in her purse,
325 Kissed Laura, crossed the heath with clumps of furze
At twilight, halted by the brook:
And for the first time in her life
Began to listen and look.

    Laughed every goblin
330 When they spied her peeping:
Came towards her hobbling,
Flying, running, leaping,
Puffing and blowing,
Chuckling, clapping, crowing,
335 Clucking and gobbling,
Mopping and mowing,[4]
Full of airs and graces,
Pulling wry faces,

    Demure grimaces,
340 Cat-like and rat-like,
Ratel-and wombat-like,
Snail-paced in a hurry,
Parrot-voiced and whistler,
Helter skelter, hurry skurry,
345 Chattering like magpies,
Fluttering like pigeons,
Gliding like fishes,—
Hugged her and kissed her,
Squeezed and caressed her:
350 Stretched up their dishes,
Panniers, and plates:
"Look at our apples
Russet and dun,
Bob at our cherries,
355 Bite at our peaches,
Citrons and dates,
Grapes for the asking,
Pears red with basking
Out in the sun,
360 Plums on their twigs;
Pluck them and suck them,
Pomegranates, figs."—

    "Good folk," said Lizzie,
Mindful of Jeanie:

4. Grimacing, making faces.

365   "Give me much and many:"—
Held out her apron,
Tossed them her penny.
"Nay, take a seat with us,
Honour and eat with us,"
370   They answered grinning:
"Our feast is but beginning.
Night yet is early,
Warm and dew-pearly,
Wakeful and starry:
375   Such fruits as these
No man can carry;
Half their bloom would fly,
Half their dew would dry,
Half their flavour would pass by.
380   Sit down and feast with us,
Be welcome guest with us,
Cheer you and rest with us."—
"Thank you," said Lizzie: "But one waits
At home alone for me:
385   So without further parleying,
If you will not sell me any
Of your fruits tho' much and many,
Give me back my silver penny
I tossed you for a fee."—

390   They began to scratch their pates,
No longer wagging, purring,
But visibly demurring,
Grunting and snarling.
One called her proud,
395   Cross-grained, uncivil;
Their tones waxed loud,
Their looks were evil.
Lashing their tails
They trod and hustled her,
400   Elbowed and jostled her,
Clawed with their nails,
Barking, mewing, hissing, mocking,
Tore her gown and soiled her stocking,
Twitched her hair out by the roots,
405   Stamped upon her tender feet,
Held her hands and squeezed their fruits
Against her mouth to make her eat.

White and golden Lizzie stood,
Like a lily in a flood,—
410   Like a rock of blue-veined stone
Lashed by tides obstreperously,—
Like a beacon left alone
In a hoary roaring sea,
Sending up a golden fire,—
415   Like a fruit-crowned orange-tree

White with blossoms honey-sweet
Sore beset by wasp and bee,—
Like a royal virgin town
Topped with gilded dome and spire
420 Close beleaguered by a fleet
Mad to tug her standard down.

One may lead a horse to water,
Twenty cannot make him drink.
Tho' the goblins cuffed and caught her,
425 Coaxed and fought her,
Bullied and besought her,
Scratched her, pinched her black as ink,
Kicked and knocked her,
Mauled and mocked her,
430 Lizzie uttered not a word;
Would not open lip from lip
Lest they should cram a mouthful in:
But laughed in heart to feel the drip
Of juice that syruped all her face,
435 And lodged in dimples of her chin,
And streaked her neck which quaked like curd.
At last the evil people
Worn out by her resistance
Flung back her penny, kicked their fruit
440 Along whichever road they took,
Not leaving root or stone or shoot;
Some writhed into the ground,
Some dived into the brook
With ring and ripple,
445 Some scudded on the gale without a sound,
Some vanished in the distance.

In a smart, ache, tingle,
Lizzie went her way;
Knew not was it night or day;
450 Sprang up the bank, tore thro' the furze,
Threaded copse and dingle,
And heard her penny jingle
Bouncing in her purse,
Its bounce was music to her ear.
455 She ran and ran
As if she feared some goblin man
Dogged her with gibe or curse
Or something worse:
But not one goblin skurried after,
460 Nor was she pricked by fear;
The kind heart made her windy-paced
That urged her home quite out of breath with haste
And inward laughter.

She cried "Laura," up the garden,
465 "Did you miss me?

Come and kiss me.
Never mind my bruises,
Hug me, kiss me, suck my juices
Squeezed from goblin fruits for you,
470   Goblin pulp and goblin dew.
Eat me, drink me, love me;
Laura, make much of me:
For your sake I have braved the glen
And had to do with goblin merchant men."

475   Laura started from her chair,
Flung her arms up in the air,
Clutched her hair:
"Lizzie, Lizzie, have you tasted
For my sake the fruit forbidden?
480   Must your light like mine be hidden,
Your young life like mine be wasted,
Undone in mine undoing
And ruined in my ruin,
Thirsty, cankered, goblin-ridden?"—
485   She clung about her sister,
Kissed and kissed and kissed her:
Tears once again
Refreshed her shrunken eyes,
Dropping like rain
490   After long sultry drouth;
Shaking with aguish° fear, and pain,   feverish
She kissed and kissed her with a hungry mouth.

Her lips began to scorch,
That juice was wormwood to her tongue,
495   She loathed the feast:
Writhing as one possessed she leaped and sung,
Rent all her robe, and wrung
Her hands in lamentable haste,
And beat her breast.
500   Her locks streamed like the torch
Borne by a racer at full speed,
Or like the mane of horses in their flight,
Or like an eagle when she stems⁵ the light
Straight toward the sun,
505   Or like a caged thing freed,
Or like a flying flag when armies run.

Swift fire spread thro' her veins, knocked at her heart,
Met the fire smouldering there
And overbore its lesser flame;
510   She gorged on bitterness without a name:
Ah! fool, to choose such part
Of soul-consuming care!
Sense failed in the mortal strife:

5. Makes headway against.

Like the watch-tower of a town
515 Which an earthquake shatters down,
Like a lightning-stricken mast,
Like a wind-uprooted tree
Spun about,
Like a foam-topped waterspout
520 Cast down headlong in the sea,
She fell at last;
Pleasure past and anguish past,
Is it death or is it life?

Life out of death.
525 That night long Lizzie watched by her,
Counted her pulse's flagging stir,
Felt for her breath,
Held water to her lips, and cooled her face
With tears and fanning leaves:
530 But when the first birds chirped about their eaves,
And early reapers plodded to the place
Of golden sheaves,
And dew-wet grass
Bowed in the morning winds so brisk to pass,
535 And new buds with new day
Opened of cup-like lilies on the stream,
Laura awoke as from a dream,
Laughed in the innocent old way,
Hugged Lizzie but not° twice or thrice;   *not only*
540 Her gleaming locks showed not one thread of grey,
Her breath was sweet as May
And light danced in her eyes.

Days, weeks, months, years
Afterwards, when both were wives
545 With children of their own;
Their mother-hearts beset with fears,
Their lives bound up in tender lives;
Laura would call the little ones
And tell them of her early prime,
550 Those pleasant days long gone
Of not-returning time:
Would talk about the haunted glen,
The wicked, quaint° fruit-merchant men,   *strange*
Their fruits like honey to the throat
555 But poison in the blood;
(Men sell not such in any town:)
Would tell them how her sister stood
In deadly peril to do her good,
And win the fiery antidote:
560 Then joining hands to little hands
Would bid them cling together,
"For there is no friend like a sister
In calm or stormy weather;
To cheer one on the tedious way,

565 To fetch one if one goes astray,
     To lift one if one totters down,
     To strengthen whilst one stands."

1859   1862

"No, Thank You, John"

I never said I loved you, John:
   Why will you teaze me day by day,
And wax a weariness to think upon
   With always "do" and "pray"?

5 You know I never loved you, John;
      No fault of mine made me your toast:
   Why will you haunt me with a face as wan
      As shows an hour-old ghost?

   I dare say Meg or Moll would take
10   Pity upon you, if you'd ask:
   And pray don't remain single for my sake
      Who can't perform that task.

   I have no heart?—Perhaps I have not;
      But then you're mad to take offence
15 That I don't give you what I have not got:
      Use your own common sense.

   Let bygones be bygones:
      Don't call me false, who owed not to be true:
   I'd rather answer "No" to fifty Johns
20   Than answer "Yes" to you.

   Let's mar our pleasant days no more,
      Song-birds of passage, days of youth:
   Catch at today, forget the days before:
      I'll wink° at your untrue.   close (both) eyes

25 Let us strike hands as hearty friends;
      No more, no less; and friendship's good:
   Only don't keep in view ulterior ends,
      And points not understood

   In open treaty. Rise above
30   Quibbles and shuffling off and on:
   Here's friendship for you if you like; but love,—
      No, thank you, John.

1860   1862

Promises Like Pie-Crust

Promise me no promises,
　　So will I not promise you:
Keep we both our liberties,
　　Never false and never true:
5　Let us hold the die uncast,
　　Free to come as free to go:
For I cannot know your past,
　　And of mine what can you know?

You, so warm, may once have been
10　　Warmer towards another one:
I, so cold, may once have seen
　　Sunlight, once have felt the sun:
Who shall show us if it was
　　Thus indeed in time of old?
15　Fades the image from the glass,
　　And the fortune is not told.

If you promised, you might grieve
　　For lost liberty again:
If I promised, I believe
20　　I should fret to break the chain.
Let us be the friends we were,
　　Nothing more but nothing less:
Many thrive on frugal fare
　　Who would perish of excess.

1861   1896

In Progress

Ten years ago it seemed impossible
　　That she should ever grow so calm as this,
　　With self-remembrance in her warmest kiss
And dim dried eyes like an exhausted well.
5　Slow-speaking when she has some fact to tell,
　　Silent with long-unbroken silences,
　　Centred in self yet not unpleased to please,
Gravely monotonous like a passing bell.[1]
Mindful of drudging daily common things,
10　Patient at pastime, patient at her work,
　　Wearied perhaps but strenuous certainly.
　　Sometimes I fancy we may one day see
Her head shoot forth seven stars from where they lurk
And her eyes lightnings and her shoulders wings.

1862   1896

1. Bell rung during or after a person's death, a death bell.

A Life's Parallels

Never on this side of the grave again,
    On this side of the river,
On this side of the garner of the grain,
    Never,—

5 Ever while time flows on and on and on,
    That narrow noiseless river,
Ever while corn bows heavy-headed, wan,
    Ever,—

Never despairing, often fainting, rueing,
10   But looking back, ah never!
Faint yet pursuing, faint yet still pursuing
    Ever.

                                              1881

From Later Life

17

Something this foggy day, a something which
Is neither of this fog nor of today,
Has set me dreaming of the winds that play
Past certain cliffs, along one certain beach,
5 And turn the topmost edge of waves to spray:
Ah pleasant pebbly strand so far away,
So out of reach while quite within my reach,
As out of reach as India or Cathay!°   China (poetic)
I am sick of where I am and where I am not,
10 I am sick of foresight and of memory,
I am sick of all I have and all I see,
    I am sick of self, and there is nothing new;
Oh weary impatient patience of my lot!—
Thus with myself: how fares it, Friends, with you?

                                              1881

Cardinal Newman[1]

In the grave, whither thou goest[2]

O weary Champion of the Cross, lie still:
Sleep thou at length the all-embracing sleep:
Long was thy sowing-day, rest now and reap:

---

1. Written on the occasion of the death of John   2. Ecclesiastes 9.10.
Henry Newman (1801–1890).

Thy fast was long, feast now thy spirit's fill.
5   Yea, take thy fill of love, because thy will
    Chose love not in the shallows but the deep:
    Thy tides were springtides, set against the neap[3]
    Of calmer souls: thy flood rebuked their rill.°   small stream
    Now night has come to thee—please God, of rest:
10 So some time must it come to every man;
    To first and last, where many last are first.[4]
    Now fixed and finished thine eternal plan,
    Thy best has done its best, thy worst its worst:
    Thy best its best, Please God, thy best its best.

1890

Sleeping at Last

Sleeping at last, the trouble & tumult over,
Sleeping at last, the struggle & horror past,
Cold & white out of sight of friend & of lover
    Sleeping at last.

5   No more a tired heart downcast or overcast,
No more pangs that wring or shifting fears that hover,
Sleeping at last in a dreamless sleep locked fast.

Fast asleep. Singing birds in their leafy cover
Cannot wake her, nor shake her the gusty blast.
10 Under the purple thyme and the purple clover
    Sleeping at last.

1896

3. Tides that do not rise to the high-water mark of the spring tides.
4. Rossetti alludes to the parable of the vineyard,
in which "the last shall be first." See Matthew 20.16, Luke 13.30.

WILLIAM MORRIS
1834–1896

In his autobiography William Butler Yeats observes that if some angel offered him the choice, he would rather live William Morris's life than his own or any other man's. Morris's career was more multifaceted than that of any other Victorian writer. He was a poet, a writer of prose romances, a painter, a designer of furniture, a businessman, a printer, and a leader of the British socialist movement.

    Born of wealthy parents and brought up in the Essex countryside, he went to Oxford with the intention of becoming a clergyman. However, art for him soon displaced religion. At Oxford he discovered the work of John Ruskin, which was, in his words, "a revelation." Later in life he wrote, "It was through him that I learned to give form to my discontent. . . . Apart from the desire to produce beautiful things, the leading passion of my life has been and is hatred of modern civilization." Morris's career in many ways realized Ruskin's views. In 1861 Morris and several friends founded a company to design and produce furniture, wallpaper, textiles, stained glass, tapestries, and carpets, objects still prized today as masterpieces of decorative art. Morris's aim was not only to make beautiful things but to restore creativity to modern manufacture, much as Ruskin had urged in "The Nature of Gothic," a chapter in *The Stones of Venice* (1851–53). The minor arts, he believed, were in a state of complete degradation; through his firm he wanted to restore beauty of design and individual craftsmanship.

In his design work Morris developed close ties with the Pre-Raphaelite Brotherhood, a society of artists that had been cofounded by Dante Gabriel Rossetti, who became a particular friend. In 1858 Morris published a remarkable book of poetry, *The Defence of Guenevere, and other Poems*, which some critics regard as the finest book of Pre-Raphaelite verse. Using medieval materials, the poems plunge the reader into the middle of dramatic situations with little sense of larger narrative context or even right and wrong, where little is clear but the vividness of the characters' perceptions. After *The Defence of Guenevere*, Morris turned from lyric to narrative, publishing *The Life and Death of Jason* (1867) and *The Earthly Paradise* (1868–70), a series of twenty-four classical and medieval tales. He then discovered the Icelandic sagas. He cotranslated the *Volsunga Saga* and wrote a poem based on it, *The Story of Sigurd the Volsung* (1876). In 1877 he founded the Society for the Protection of Ancient Buildings.

In the late 1870s, after Morris came to the conclusion that art could not have real life and growth under the commercialism of modern society, he turned to socialism. In 1883 he joined the Socialist Democratic Federation; the next year he led the secession of a large faction to found the Socialist League. He was at the center of socialist activity in England through the rest of the decade. At the famous debates held on Sunday evenings at Morris's house, political and literary figures regularly gathered, including Yeats and Bernard Shaw. Morris lectured and wrote tirelessly for the cause, producing essays, columns, and a series of socialist literary works, including *A Dream of John Ball* (1887) and *News from Nowhere* (1890), a utopian vision of life under communism in twenty-first-century England.

In 1890 Morris's health failed and factionalism brought his leadership of the Socialist League to an end. In 1891 he cofounded the Kelmscott Press, the first fine art press in England, whose masterpiece was the Kelmscott Chaucer, an edition of *The Canterbury Tales* with illustrations by the Pre-Raphaelite painter Edward Burne Jones and designs by Morris himself.

In the obituary he published after Morris's death, Shaw wrote, "He was ultra-modern—not merely up-to-date, but far ahead of it: his wall papers, his hangings, his tapestries, and his printed books have the twentieth century in every touch of them." Not only did Morris develop design principles that remained important in the twentieth century, but he also had a radical vision of the relationship of aesthetics to politics. He was, as Shaw said, "a complete artist."

The Defence of Guenevere

For this poem Morris created strikingly original adaptations of episodes from one of his favorite books, Thomas Malory's *Morte Darthur* (1470). In Malory's narrative, Arthur's kingdom is eventually destroyed by dissension among his followers; especially damaging to the king's reign are rumors of an adulterous relationship between Queen Guenevere and Arthur's chief knight, Launcelot. Morris's poem alludes to two occasions in Mallory's work when Guenevere is discovered in apparently compromising circumstances that lead to public accusations of adultery. On the first occasion (described in lines 167–220), her accuser, Sir Mellyagraunce, is challenged by Launcelot to a trial of battle. After Mellyagraunce is slain, the queen's honor is temporarily restored, though in Morris's telling this earlier scandal is revived by Sir Gauwaine in his accusations against her. The second occasion, which occurs just before Morris's poem opens, is more seriously incriminating. Thirteen knights plot successfully to trap Launcelot when he is visiting the queen's chamber at night at her invitation (events described in lines 242–76). In his escape Launcelot kills all but one of the knights—an event that later leads to civil war. In Malory's version there is no formal trial of the queen after Launcelot's escape; she is simply told of her sentence—she will be burned at the stake—and is thereafter rescued by Launcelot, who takes her away to safety in his castle. In inventing his trial scene Morris probably drew from a different episode in Malory (book 18, chapter 3), which ends with Sir Gauwaine accusing Guenevere of murder and treason in the presence of many other knights.

According to Morris's daughter, this poem originally opened with a long introductory passage of description and background. Because Morris subsequently decided to omit it, we are plunged at once into a dramatic scene much like those that begin some of the poems of Robert Browning (the Victorian poet whom Morris most admired). Also reminiscent of Browning's work are the constant shifts in Guenevere's speech from an awareness of her present situation to the recollection of moments in her past, such as the spring day early in her marriage to Arthur when Launcelot first kissed her.

The year after Morris's poem appeared, four books of Tennyson's *Idylls of the King*, including one that focused on Guenevere, were published. It is interesting to compare the two portraits of the queen, especially their pictoral qualities, but Morris's powerful depiction of an eloquent Guenevere is very different from Tennyson's subdued representation of a guilt-ridden wife. Equally fascinating is a comparison of the two poems with Morris's painting *Queen Guenevere* (1858). Despite his copious production of visual artifacts, this is the only full-size oil painting Morris ever finished. His model for Guenevere, who stands pensively in front of a rumpled bed, was Jane Burden, who became his wife the following year.

The Defence of Guenevere

But, knowing now that they would have her speak,
She threw her wet hair backward from her brow,
Her hand close to her mouth touching her cheek,

As though she had had there a shameful blow,
5   And feeling it shameful to feel aught° but shame   anything
All through her heart, yet felt her cheek burned so,

She must a little touch it; like one lame
She walked away from Gauwaine, with her head
Still lifted up; and on her cheek of flame

10 The tears dried quick; she stopped at last and said:
"O knights and lords, it seems but little skill°   use
To talk of well-known things past now and dead.

"God wot° I ought to say, I have done ill,   knows
And pray you all forgiveness heartily!
15 Because you must be right, such great lords—still

"Listen, suppose your time were come to die,
And you were quite alone and very weak;
Yea, laid a dying while very mightily

"The wind was ruffling up the narrow streak
20   Of river through your broad lands running well:
Suppose a hush should come, then someone speak:

" 'One of these cloths is heaven, and one is hell,
Now choose one cloth forever, which they be,
I will not tell you, you must somehow tell

25   " 'Of your own strength and mightiness; here, see!'
Yea, yea, my lord, and you to ope your eyes,
At foot of your familiar bed to see

"A great God's angel standing, with such dyes,
Not known on earth, on his great wings, and hands,
30   Held out two ways, light from the inner skies

"Showing him well, and making his commands
Seem to be God's commands, moreover, too,
Holding within his hands the cloths on wands;

"And one of these strange choosing cloths was blue,
35   Wavy and long, and one cut short and red;
No man could tell the better of the two.

"After a shivering half hour you said,
'God help! heaven's color, the blue'; and he said, 'hell.'
Perhaps you then would roll upon your bed,

40   "And cry to all good men that loved you well,
'Ah Christ! if only I had known, known, known';
Launcelot went away, then I could tell,

"Like wisest man how all things would be, moan,
And roll and hurt myself, and long to die,
45   And yet fear much to die for what was sown.

"Nevertheless you, O Sir Gauwaine, lie,
Whatever may have happened through these years,
God knows I speak truth, saying that you lie."

Her voice was low at first, being full of tears,
50   But as it cleared, it grew full loud and shrill,
Growing a windy shriek in all men's ears,

A ringing in their startled brains, until
She said that Gauwaine lied, then her voice sunk,
And her great eyes began again to fill,

55 Though still she stood right up, and never shrunk,
But spoke on bravely, glorious lady fair!
Whatever tears her full lips may have drunk,

She stood, and seemed to think, and wrung her hair,
Spoke out at last with no more trace of shame,
60 With passionate twisting of her body there:

"It chanced upon a day that Launcelot came
To dwell at Arthur's court: at Christmas time
This happened; when the heralds sung his name,

" 'Son of King Ban[1] of Benwick,' seemed to chime
65 Along with all the bells that rang that day,
O'er the white roofs, with little change of rhyme.

"Christmas and whitened winter passed away,
And over me the April sunshine came,
Made very awful with black hail-clouds, yea.

70 "And in Summer I grew white with flame,
And bowed my head down—Autumn, and the sick
Sure knowledge things would never be the same,

"However often Spring might be most thick
Of blossoms and buds, smote on me, and I grew
75 Careless of most things, let the clock tick, tick,

"To my unhappy pulse, that beat right through
My eager body; while I laughed out loud,
And let my lips curl up at false or true,

"Seemed cold and shallow without any cloud.
80 Behold my judges, then the cloths were brought:
While I was dizzied thus, old thoughts would crowd,

"Belonging to the time ere I was bought
By Arthur's great name and his little love,
Must I give up forever then, I thought,

85 "That which I deemed would ever round me move
Glorifying all things; for a little word,[2]
Scarce ever meant at all, must I now prove

"Stone-cold for ever? Pray you, does the Lord
Will that all folks should be quite happy and good?
90 I love God now a little, if this cord[3]

---

1. Launcelot's father, a king of Brittany.   3. Her bond with Launcelot.
2. Her marriage vow.

"Were broken, once for all what striving could
Make me love anything in earth or heaven.
So day by day it grew, as if one should

"Slip slowly down some path worn smooth and even,
95   Down to a cool sea on a summer day;
Yet still in slipping there was some small leaven

"Of stretched hands catching small stones by the way,
Until one surely reached the sea at last,
And felt strange new joy as the worn head lay

100 "Back, with the hair like seaweed; yea all past
Sweat of the forehead, dryness of the lips,
Washed utterly out by the dear waves o'ercast,

"In the lone sea, far off from any ships!
Do I not know now of a day in Spring?
105 No minute of that wild day ever slips

"From out my memory; I hear thrushes sing,
And wheresoever I may be, straightway
Thoughts of it all come up with most fresh sting:

"I was half mad with beauty on that day,
110 And went without my ladies all alone,
In a quiet garden walled round every way;

"I was right joyful of that wall of stone,
That shut the flowers and trees up with the sky,
And trebled all the beauty: to the bone,

115 "Yea right through to my heart, grown very shy
With weary thoughts, it pierced, and made me glad;
Exceedingly glad, and I knew verily,

"A little thing just then had° made me mad;   would have
I dared not think, as I was wont to do,
120 Sometimes, upon my beauty; if I had

"Held out my long hand up against the blue,
And, looking on the tenderly darkened fingers,
Thought that by rights one ought to see quite through,

"There, see you, where the soft still light yet lingers,
125 Round by the edges; what should I have done,
If this had joined with yellow spotted singers,

"And startling green drawn upward by the sun?
But shouting, loosed out, see now! all my hair,
And trancedly stood watching the west wind run

130   "With faintest half-heard breathing sound—why there
      I lose my head e'en now in doing this;
      But shortly listen—In that garden fair

      "Came Launcelot walking; this is true, the kiss
      Wherewith we kissed in meeting that spring day,
135   I scarce dare talk of the remembered bliss,

      "When both our mouths went wandering in one way,
      And aching sorely, met among the leaves;
      Our hands being left behind strained far away.

      "Never within a yard of my bright sleeves
140   Had Launcelot come before—and now, so nigh!
      After that day why is it Guenevere grieves?

      "Nevertheless you, O Sir Gauwaine, lie,
      Whatever happened on through all those years,
      God knows I speak truth, saying that you lie.

145   "Being such a lady could I weep these tears
      If this were true? A great queen such as I
      Having sinned this way, straight her conscience sears;

      "And afterwards she liveth hatefully,
      Slaying and poisoning, certes° never weeps—   *certainly*
150   Gauwaine, be friends now, speak me lovingly.

      "Do I not see how God's dear pity creeps
      All through your frame, and trembles in your mouth?
      Remember in what grave your mother sleeps,

      "Buried in some place far down in the south,
155   Men are forgetting as I speak to you;
      By her head severed in that awful drouth

      "Of pity that drew Agravaine's fell blow,[4]
      I pray your pity! let me not scream out
      Forever after, when the shrill winds blow

160   "Through half your castle-locks! let me not shout
      Forever after in the winter night
      When you ride out alone! in battle rout

      "Let not my rusting tears make your sword light!°   *weak*
      Ah! God of mercy how he turns away!
165   So, ever must I dress me to the fight,

---

4. In Morris's version Gauwaine's brother, Agravaine, beheads their mother, Morgan Le Fay, after she is accused of adultery. In Malory's narrative another brother, Gaheris, kills her (book 10, chap. 24). "Fell": cruel.

"So—let God's justice work! Gauwaine, I say,
See me hew down your proofs: yea all men know
Even as you said how Mellyagraunce one day,

"One bitter day in *la Fausse Garde*,[5] for so
170 All good knights held it after, saw—
Yea, sirs, by cursed unknightly outrage; though

"You, Gauwaine, held his word without a flaw,
This Mellyagraunce saw blood upon my bed[6]—
Whose blood then pray you? is there any law

175 "To make a queen say why some spots of red
Lie on her coverlet? or will you say,
'Your hands are white, lady, as when you wed,

" 'Where did you bleed?' and must I stammer out—'Nay,
I blush indeed, fair lord, only to rend
180 My sleeve up to my shoulder, where there lay

" 'A knife-point last night': so must I defend
The honor of the lady Guenevere?
Not so, fair lords, even if the world should end

"This very day, and you were judges here
185 Instead of God. Did you see Mellyagraunce
When Launcelot stood by him? what white fear

"Curdled his blood, and how his teeth did dance,
His side sink in? as my knight cried and said,
'Slayer of unarmed men, here is a chance!

190 " 'Setter of traps, I pray you guard your head,
By God I am so glad to fight with you,
Stripper of ladies,[7] that my hand feels lead

" 'For driving weight; hurrah now! draw and do,
For all my wounds are moving in my breast,
195 And I am getting mad with waiting so.'

"He struck his hands together o'er the beast,
Who fell down flat, and groveled at his feet,
And groaned at being slain so young—'at least.'

5. The False Castle (French); a term expressing her contempt. Launcelot's castle is named the Joyous Garde.
6. In an earlier episode in Malory's narrative, Guenevere and some of her young knights who have been wounded in a skirmish are confined for a night in a room in Mellyagraunce's castle. Discovering bloodstains on her bedclothes the following morning, Mellyagraunce accuses her of adulterous relations with one of the wounded knights. Actually her visiting bedfellow had been Launcelot, who had cut his hand on the window bars as he climbed into her room.
7. Mellyagraunce discovers the bloodstains on Guenevere's bedclothes by pulling open her bed-curtains; he had intended to rape the queen. "Setter of traps": Mellyagraunce tried to prevent Launcelot from coming to defend the queen's honor by making him fall through a trapdoor into a dungeon.

The Romantic Period
(1785–1830)

La Prise de la Bastille, le 14 Juillet 1789, Claude Cholat, 1789

This amateur painting (in gouache on cardboard) was made "on the spot" by one of the participants in the five-hour siege, a local wine merchant, and presented to the French National Assembly two years later. The storming of the Bastille—the fortress and state prison in Paris, a hated symbol of absolutism—marked the entry of the lower classes ("the people") into the Revolution. The anniversary of the event, July 14, is the principal French national holiday. RÉUNION DES MUSÉES NATIONAUX/ART RESOURCE, NY.

Plate 1 of *The Marriage of Heaven and Hell*, William Blake, 1790–93

This title page of a work composed in the early years of the French Revolution (see p. 110) juxtaposes lighthearted activities (birds and humans soaring, strolling, playing music, dancing, embracing) with bleak and ominous surroundings (the leaflessness of the trees, the intensity of the flames). The larger reclining figures at the bottom of the page, sexy but genderless, are usually read as a devil and an angel whose embrace symbolizes the union ("marriage") of contraries running throughout the work. LIBRARY OF CONGRESS, WASHINGTON DC, USA/BRIDGEMAN ART LIBRARY.

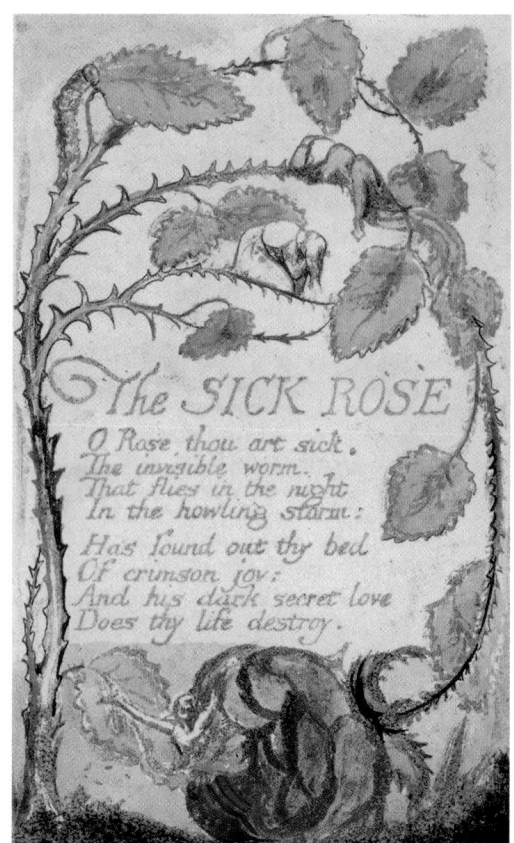

The Sick Rose, William Blake, 1794

Blake's "illumination" (the poem is plate 39 of *Songs of Innocence and of Experience*; see p. 91) further complicates an already highly ambiguous poetic text. In the picture are two worms—one eating a leaf in the upper left corner, the other coming out of the fallen blossom at the bottom—and three female figures, two of which, situated on the thorny stems above the engraved text, appear to be in postures of despair. The third female figure, emerging from the blossom, has arms flung forward in an expression of either ecstasy or terror. LIBRARY OF CONGRESS, WASHINGTON DC, USA/BRIDGEMAN ART LIBRARY.

Glad Day, or *The Dance of Albion,*
William Blake, ca. 1793

Blake kept returning to this image of liberation. He first designed it in 1780, shortly
after finishing his apprenticeship as an engraver, when the vision of a rising sun and a
radiant human body may have expressed his
own youthful sense of freedom. But later,
in an age of revolution, he identified the
figure as Albion—"Albion rose from where
he labourd at the Mill with Slaves." For
Blake the giant Albion represents the ancient form of Britain, a universal man who
has fallen on evil, repressive times but is destined to awake and to unite all people in a dance of liberty,
both political and spiritual. Eventually, in *Jerusalem* (ca. 1820), Blake's last great prophetic work, the
figure of Albion merged with Jesus, risen from the tomb as an embodiment of "the human form divine"—immortal and perpetually creative. BRITISH MUSEUM, LONDON, UK/BRIDGEMAN ART LIBRARY.

First draft of *The Eve of St.
Agnes,* John Keats, 1819

The extant holograph of *The Eve
of St. Agnes*—here a part of the
page containing stanza 30 (see p.
895)—is possibly the messiest
and most fragile manuscript in all
of English poetry. The poem's
Spenserian stanzas require an
elaborate calculation of rhymes
ahead of time to line up the
quadruple b-rhymes and triple c-
rhymes needed for each stanza.
In page after page of this first
draft, Keats's final wording varies
in only a phrase or two (if that
much) from the version that was
published in 1820, still the standard text. THE HARVARD KEATS
COLLECTION, HOUGHTON LIBRARY,
HARVARD UNIVERSITY, CAMBRIDGE.

Interior of Tintern Abbey, J. M. W. Turner, 1794

Turner painted this watercolor at the age of nineteen, a year after Wordsworth made his first visit to the abbey (1793) and four years before the poet returned for a second visit (1798), as recorded in the famous "Lines . . ." pondering the changes that have taken place in both the speaker and the scene in the interim (see p. 258). In Turner's version—as, in a different way, in Wordsworth's—the ruined symbol of religion, towering above two tiny human figures, presumably tourists, in the lower left, is in the process of being taken over (allegorically superseded) by the more powerful force of nature. VICTORIA & ALBERT MUSEUM, LONDON/ART RESOURCE, NY.

Lord Byron, by Thomas Phillips, 1835 (after an original of 1813)

Garbed theatrically in an Albanian soldier's dress that he had purchased while on his travels, Byron appears in this portrait as one of his own exotic heroes. The profits from his "Eastern" tales *Lara* and *The Corsair* in fact helped pay the painter's fees for the portrait, which Byron commissioned in 1813, choosing to be pictured not as a member of the British Establishment but as an outsider. The archives of London's National Portrait Gallery record more than forty portraits of Byron done during his lifetime, as well as a waxwork model from life made by Madame Tussaud in 1816: a statistic that suggests the poet's keen awareness of the magnetism and marketability of his image. NATIONAL PORTRAIT GALLERY, LONDON, UK/BRIDGEMAN ART LIBRARY.

Grasmere Lake from the northwest shore

Wordsworth saw the vale and lake of Grasmere for the first time when he was a teenager, in the 1780s, hiking over from Hawkshead, a few miles to the south, where he was in school, and coming through the cleft in the top center of the picture. He returned in 1799 and lived and wrote his poems there—in a succession of houses called Dove Cottage, Allan Bank, the Rectory, and Rydal Mount—for the next fifty years. PATRICK WARD/CORBIS.

Manfred on the Jungfrau,
John Martin, 1837

Manfred, about to throw himself off the cliff, is seized and held back by a passing chamois hunter (see p. 644). Martin's watercolor (based on his oil painting of 1826, no longer extant) emphasizes the sublimity and dramatic intensity of the Alpine setting and presents another version of the "deep romantic chasm" central to the imagery of Coleridge's "Kubla Khan" (see p. 446). BIRMINGHAM MUSEUMS AND ART GALLERY, UK/BRIDGEMAN ART LIBRARY.

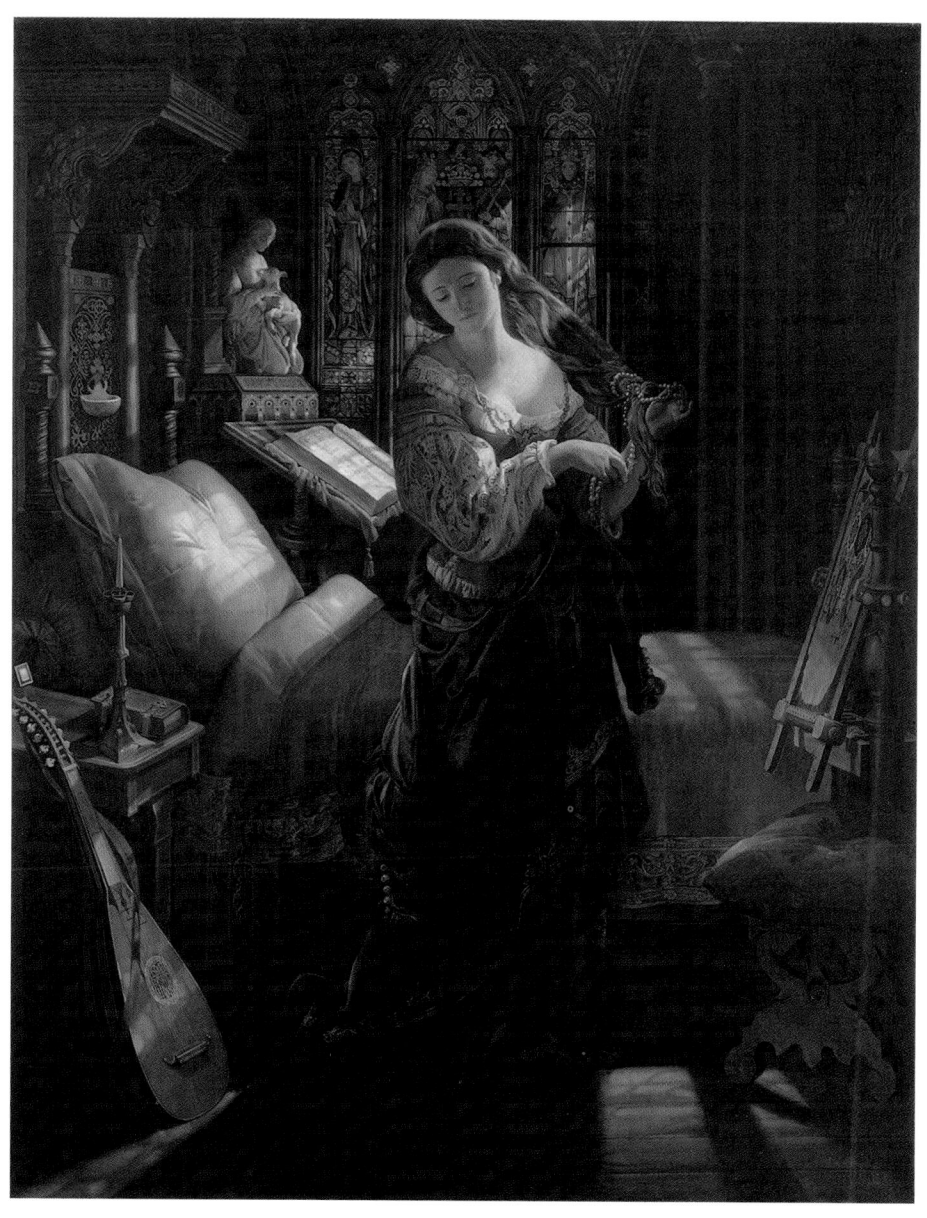

Madeline after Prayer, Daniel Maclise, 1868

Maclise's painting illustrates the particulars of Madeline's freeing her hair "of all its wreathed pearls" (*The Eve of St. Agnes,* line 227; see p. 894) and more generally the stanzas describing the "casement high and triple-arch'd" and other furnishings of her bedroom. The pre-Raphaelite-influenced picture captures the rich colors and textures of the situation, but Keats's *words* actually provide many more details than the painting, including the hidden observer of this scene, Madeline's lover, Porphyro, who grows faint on seeing Madeline's appearance as a "splendid angel."

The Nightmare, by Henry Fuseli, ca. 1783–1791

The first version of this painting created a sensation when the Swiss-born artist Fuseli exhibited it at London's Royal Academy in 1781. Even Horace Walpole, who had used his own nightmare of "a gigantic hand in armour" when composing his Gothic novel, *The Castle of Otranto,* found Fuseli's trademark blend of violence, eroticism, and the irrational excessively disturbing: "shockingly mad, madder than ever; quite mad" was Walpole's verdict on the witchcraft scene that Fuseli exhibited four years later. It is no surprise to learn that during the 1920s Sigmund Freud kept an engraving of *The Nightmare* on display. SNARK/ART RESOURCE, NY.

Illustration of *The Rime of the Ancient Mariner,* Gustave Doré, 1876

Coleridge's poems—especially *The Ancient Mariner* and "Kubla Khan," with their abundance of color, texture, and mysterious detail—have been illustrated many times. Doré's elaborate engravings, originally published in an edition of the poem in 1876, are perhaps the best known of all, "darkly brooding, richly detailed, almost symphonic in their comprehensiveness and complexity," as one critic has described them. This plate illustrates lines 59–60, "The ice was here, the ice was there, / The ice was all around" (see p. 432). FROM *THE RIME OF THE ANCIENT MARINER,* DOVER PUBLICATIONS, INC.

The Victorian Age
(1830–1901)

Slave Ship (Slavers Throwing Overboard the Dead and Dying—Typhoon Coming On),
J. M. W. Turner, 1840

The subject of Turner's painting—slaves thrown overboard, still in chains, as a storm approaches—is the occasion for apocalyptic use of light and color. For several years John Ruskin owned this painting, a gift from his father; but he later sold it, finding the subject "too painful to live with." While many contemporaries criticized the painting for what they saw as its extravagance, Ruskin praised it as Turner's noblest work, in a passage from *Modern Painters* (see p. 1321) that is one of Ruskin's own finest passages of prose painting. BURSTEIN COLLECTION/CORBIS.

Ophelia, John Everett Millais, 1851–52

Millais's painting illustrates the lines from *Hamlet* (4.7.137–54) in which Gertrude describes Ophelia's drowning herself. Many of the individual plants and flowers—the pansies on her dress, the violets around her neck—derive from the queen's speech and Ophelia's mad scene (4.5.163–94). Like much Pre-Raphaelite art, the painting sets an erotic subject in the midst of photographically precise, symbolic detail. The model for the painting was Elizabeth Siddal (later to become Dante Gabriel Rossetti's wife), who posed for the picture in a warm bath. Erich Lessing/Art Resource, NY.

Work, Ford Madox Brown, 1852, 1856–63

Brown's painting constructs a comprehensive picture of Victorian society through the relationships of various classes of the population to work. The excavators at the center represent work in its essential, physical form; the leisured gentry on horseback at the top of the painting have no need to work; the ragged girl in the foreground cares for her orphaned brothers and sisters. Under the trees are vagrants and distressed haymakers. Thomas Carlyle and F. D. Maurice, "brain workers" whose social ideas influenced the painting, stand on the right. MANCHESTER CITY ART GALLERY, MANCHESTER, UK.

The Awakening Conscience, William Holman Hunt, 1853–54

Every detail of Hunt's painting of a fallen woman, hearing the voice of conscience while in the arms of her lover, has symbolic resonance—the soiled glove on the carpet, the bird that has escaped the cat, the songs on the piano ("Oft in the Stilly Night") and on the floor ("Tears, Idle Tears"—see p. 1135), the window through which the woman gazes, reflected in the mirror behind the couple. Like Millais's *Ophelia*, the painting surrounds and interprets its subject with a crowded canvas of discrete, photographically rendered objects. TATE GALLERY, LONDON/ART RESOURCE, NY.

ul's Beauty, Dante Gabriel
ssetti, 1864–70

o titled *Sibylla Palmifera*
e palm-bearing sibyl),
ul's Beauty represents the
attainable ideal that
pires the artist. Painted as
ompanion to the sonnet of
e same name (see p. 1458),
e picture strives to represent
d evoke the erotic and aes-
tic absorption the poem al-
orizes. Rossetti devoted the
t fifteen years of his paint-
g career to these looming
ntal portraits with richly
corated backgrounds, the
tails of which carry sym-
ic significance (in this
inting, the arch of life, the
pid, the poppies, the skull,
e butterflies).

Body's Beauty, Dante Gabriel
Rossetti, 1864–73

Also titled *Lady Lilith* (after
Adam's first wife, who ran
away to become a witch),
Body's Beauty represents sensual absorption. Paired with
the sonnet of the same name
(see p. 1459), the painting associates the sexual allure of
the woman at the center with
the golden hair that represents her value, and her narcissistic contemplation of herself with the art that she
embodies. Like the Lady of
Shalott, Lady Lilith is a
weaver, but a deadly one—the
poppies and roses surrounding
her link death and sexuality.

The Beguiling of Merlin, Edward Burne-Jones, 1870–74

Burne-Jones draws on a medieval version of the Arthurian legend for this painting, in which Merlin's pupil, Nimuë (also called Nimiane, Vivian, or Vivien), uses one of Merlin's own spells to imprison him in a hawthorn tree. The winding branches of the tree, echoed in the Medusa-like snakes of Nimuë's hair, create a flat decorative surface. Although the Nimuë of the story is a femme fatale enchanting the helpless Merlin, her posture and expression and the similarity of the two faces make the painting ambiguous.

The Passing of Arthur, Julia Margaret Cameron, 1875

Using photography in the way that earlier artists had used engravings to illustrate literary texts, Cameron produced a set of tableaux vivants to illustrate Tennyson's *Idylls of the King,* posing family and friends in costume in a combination of reality and fantasy that recalls the Pre-Raphaelites. This photograph illustrates lines 361–93 of *The Passing of Arthur* (see p. 1209), where the three queens attend the dying king in the barge that takes him to Avalon.

Nocturne in Black and Gold, the Falling Rocket, James A. M. Whistler, 1875

Whistler's impressionist painting of fireworks approaches the abstraction suggested in his title. He emphatically rejected the precise depiction of objects in earlier Victorian painting. When the critic John Ruskin saw the painting in Grosvenor Gallery, he wrote in *Fors Clavigera* that he "never expected to hear a coxcomb ask two hundred guineas for flinging a pot of paint in the public's face." Whistler sued Ruskin for libel and won; but he was awarded damages of only one farthing, and the trial left him financially ruined. THE DETROIT INSTITUTE OF ARTS, USA/BRIDGEMAN ART LIBRARY. GIFT OF DEXTER M. FERRY, JR.

Climax, Aubrey Beardsley, 1893

After seeing a drawing in *Studio* magazine of Salome holding the head of John the Baptist, Oscar Wilde asked the artist, Aubrey Beardsley, to illustrate the English translation of his play *Salome*. The engraving makes the sexuality of the two figures ambiguous, and links them through the likeness of their faces and their Medusa-like hair. The decorative surface of the drawing absorbs its morbid, erotic subject in aesthetic pattern. FROM *BEST WORKS OF AUBREY BEARDSLEY*, DOVER PUBLICATIONS, INC.

The Twentieth Century and After

Les Demoiselles d'Avignon, Pablo Picasso, 1907

This masterpiece by Spanish expatriate painter Pablo Picasso helped unleash the experimental energies of modern art. The painting breaks with formal traditions of one-point perspective and human modeling, violently fracturing space in jagged planes. At the same time it defies conventions of sexual decorum in the visual arts, confronting the viewer with five naked prostitutes in a brothel. The masklike faces, particularly of the women to the right, echo African art; they suggest the crucial role non-Western art will play in the development of modernism. The abstract faces, angular forms, and formally fragmented bodies intimate the revolutionary techniques of analytic cubism that Picasso and his French collaborator Georges Braque would develop in Paris from 1907 to 1914. THE MUSEUM OF MODERN ART/SCALA/ART RESOURCE, NY.

The Merry-Go-Round, Mark Gertler, 1916

Painted in the midst of World War I, *The Merry-Go-Round* explores the insufferable condition of life on the home front and on the battlefields. Its circularity describes the frustration of the deadlock on the Western Front, while its mingling of automatized soldiers and women conveys the sense of psychological menace pervading civilian society. The grinning puppet-like figures and the fun-fair setting convey an atmosphere of ghastly levity, in which war becomes a game. Glaring artificial colors contribute to the impression of a violent and confined world, where even nature is mechanical. TATE GALLERY, LONDON/ART RESOURCE, NY.

Over the Top, 1st Artists' Rifles at Marcoing, 30th December 1917,
John Northcote Nash, 1918

John Nash enlisted in the Artists' Rifles in 1916 and survived several attempts at going "over the top" before his appointment as a War Artist two years later. In this painting he powerfully recollects the futile danger of an attack near Cambrai in 1917. A line of soldiers clambers out of a crude, wound-red trench to trudge through snow toward an unseen enemy. Several men are killed immediately, then fall prostrate or fall back into the ready-made grave of their recent refuge. Years later Nash recalled that the advance had from the outset been doomed, "was in fact pure murder," designed to divert attention from a bombing raid elsewhere. Of the eighty men who set out, only twelve, including Nash, returned. IMPERIAL WAR MUSEUM, LONDON, UK/BRIDGEMAN ART LIBRARY.

Tube Shelter Perspective (1941) and *Family Group* (1947), Henry Moore

In their disparate treatments of space and community, these works powerfully demonstrate the antithetic atmospheres of war and peace. Moore took up sketching during World War I because of a scarcity of sculpting material. His impression of crowds sheltering in the London Underground during an air raid, ranged in parallel lines down a seemingly endless tunnel, evokes the involuntary intimacy of strangers—forced into proximity, yet still isolated and anonymous. *Family Group,* by contrast, expresses a postwar moment of relative security, when the birth of Moore's only daughter coincided with the government's promotion of traditional family values, and Moore's return to sculpture found a ready market for large-scale public art. Two parents, infants on their knees, sit in a cozy circle, their bodies merging in a physical expression of unity. The holes within the sculpture recall the wartime tunnel, transforming it from a void that swallows masses of people to a harmonious space controlled by the bodies. *Family Group:* Christie's Images/Corbis; *Tube Shelter Perspective:* Henry Moore Foundation; Tate Gallery, London/Art Resource, NY.

Painting, Francis Bacon, 1946

Bacon's nightmarish association of the slaughterhouse with the emblems of political and religious power conjures both the suffering and the hypocrisy of the twentieth century. The bust of a man, his face overshadowed by an open umbrella, surrounded by microphones, the whole superimposed upon a butcher's display, evokes the discrepancy between rhetoric and means of power. While the umbrella offers a ludicrous symbol of respectability, the visual parallels between man and meat draw attention to the brutal foundations of political influence. The man's broad shoulders resemble the squared outline of the carcass behind him. The red and white of his face, and his exposed teeth, suggest the flesh and bone of the beef. Incongruous religious references, in the cruciform spread of the carcass and the churchlike decorations on the walls, augment the painting's insinuations of corruption. The Estate of Francis Bacon/ARS, NY/DACS, London; Digital Image; The Museum of Modern Art/Scala/Art Resource, NY.

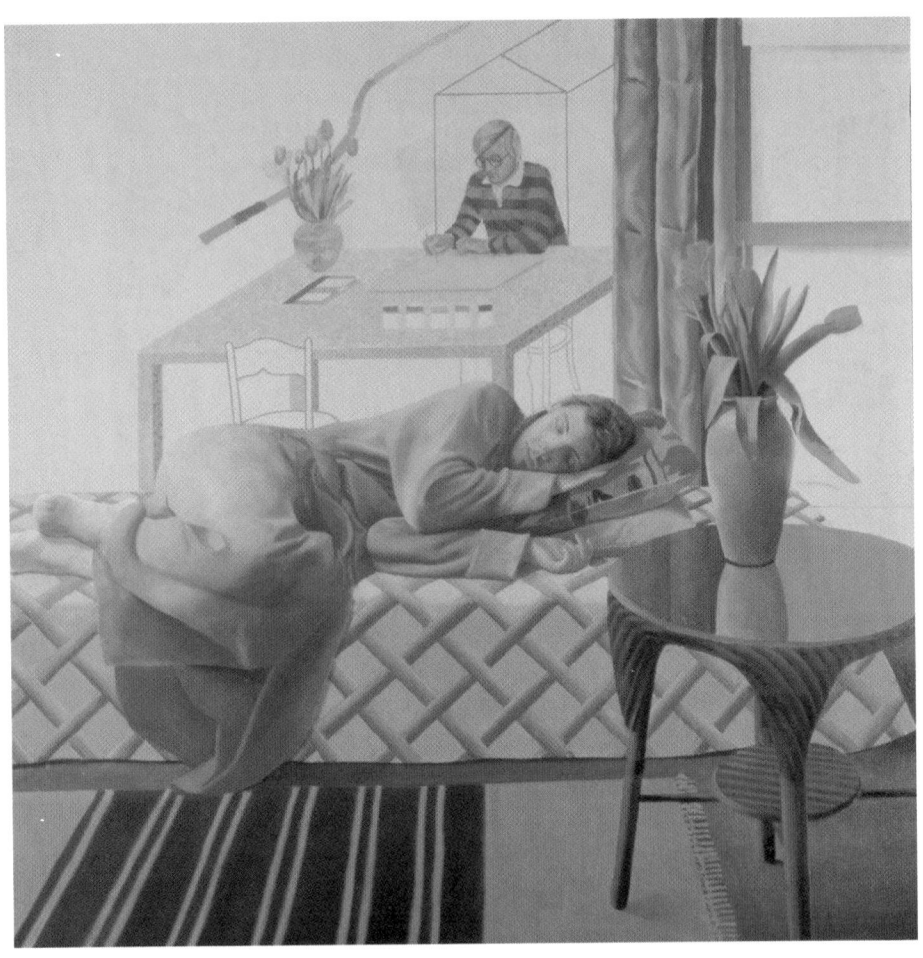

Model with Unfinished Self-Portrait, David Hockney, 1977

In *Model with Unfinished Self-Portrait* layers of illusion, realism undermined by artifice, and pictures within pictures draw our attention to the deceptive nature of painting. At first we seem to see in mirror image a model (Gregory Evans, Hockney's lover) sleeping while the artist paints; but as the title implies, the figure in fact lies in front of *Self-Portrait with Blue Guitar*, a painting developed concurrently with *Model*, depicting Hockney as Picasso, drawing a guitar. Hockney used the relationship between the canvases to reinforce his persona: *Model* invokes Picasso's technique of combining naturalistic with stylized or unfinished elements; while *Self-Portrait*, which eventually incorporated a bust of Dora Maar, Picasso's mistress, encourages an analogy between Picasso, Hockney, and their respective muses. PRIVATE COLLECTION/BRIDGEMAN ART LIBRARY.

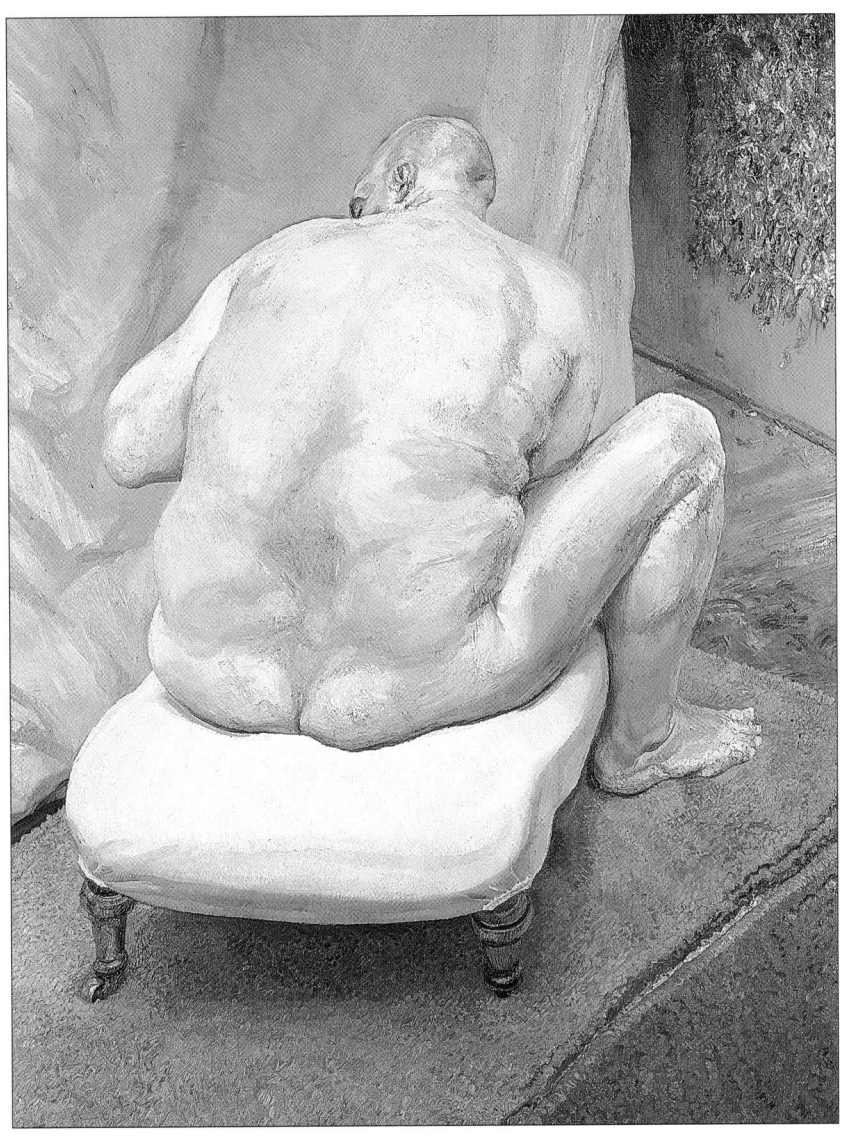

Naked Man, Back View, Lucian Freud, 1993

Freud's nudes study the details of the human body with an unflinching fascination that is modern in its refusal to censor or sentimentalize. Bowery, Freud's model, was a two-hundred-pound nightclub performer, famous for the gorgeous and outrageous costumes he used to reinvent himself in public. Yet Freud, recalling their first encounter, remembered the shape of his lower limbs rather than his outfit, observing that "his calves went right down to his feet, almost avoiding the whole business of ankles altogether." His depiction of Bowery in the nude strongly evokes the magnificence and the vulnerability of a body better known for its sartorial transformations. COURTESY OF ACQUAVELLA GALLERIES, INC. © 1993 THE METROPOLITAN MUSEUM OF ART, PURCHASE LILA ACHESON WALLACE GIFT (1993.71).

Marsyas, Anish Kapoor, October 9, 2002–April 6, 2003

Designed as a temporary installation to fill the vast central Turbine Hall at London's Tate Modern, *Marsyas* consists of a dark-red plastic membrane joining together three steel rings, two positioned vertically at either end and the third hung horizontally between. Its title refers to Marsyas, the satyr whom, in Greek mythology, Apollo flayed alive, and the membrane's color and contortions evoke flesh, even mutilated flesh. Yet the whole structure also has an ethereal quality, opening around each ring like the throat of an enormous flower. Suspended in the air, its intense, monochromatic surface resisting spatial recession, it seeks, as Kapoor has commented, "to make body into sky." COPYRIGHT 2002 ANISH KAPOOR; TATE GALLERY, LONDON/ART RESOURCE, NY.

"My knight said, 'Rise you, sir, who are so fleet
200 At catching ladies, half-armed will I fight,
My left side all uncovered!' then I weet,°   *know*

"Up sprang Sir Mellyagraunce with great delight
Upon his knave's face; not until just then
Did I quite hate him, as I saw my knight

205 "Along the lists look to my stake and pen°   *prison*
With such a joyous smile, it made me sigh
From agony beneath my waist-chain,[8] when

"The fight began, and to me they drew nigh;
Ever Sir Launcelot kept him on the right,
210 And traversed warily, and ever high

"And fast leaped caitiff's sword, until my knight
Sudden threw up his sword to his left hand,
Caught it, and swung it; that was all the fight.

"Except a spout of blood on the hot land;
215 For it was hottest summer; and I know
I wondered how the fire, while I should stand,

"And burn, against the heat, would quiver so,
Yards above my head; thus these matters went:
Which things were only warnings of the woe

220 "That fell on me. Yet Mellyagraunce was shent,°   *destroyed*
For Mellyagraunce had fought against the Lord;
Therefore, my lords, take heed lest you be blent°   *blinded*

"With all this wickedness; say no rash word
Against me, being so beautiful; my eyes,
225 Wept all away to gray, may bring some sword

"To drown you in your blood; see my breast rise,
Like waves of purple sea, as here I stand;
And how my arms are moved in wonderful wise,

"Yea also at my full heart's strong command,
230 See through my long throat how the words go up
In ripples to my mouth; how in my hand

"The shadow lies like wine within a cup
Of marvelously colored gold; yea now
This little wind is rising, look you up,

235 "And wonder how the light is falling so
Within my moving tresses: will you dare,
When you have looked a little on my brow,

---

8. She is chained to a stake, at which she will be burned if Launcelot fails to overcome her accuser.

"To say this thing is vile? or will you care
For any plausible lies of cunning woof,[9]
240 When you can see my face with no lie there

"Forever? am I not a gracious proof—
'But in your chamber Launcelot was found'—
Is there a good knight then would stand aloof,

"When a queen says with gentle queenly sound:
245 'O true as steel come now and talk with me,
I love to see your step upon the ground

" 'Unwavering, also well I love to see
That gracious smile light up your face, and hear
Your wonderful words, that all mean verily

250 " 'The thing they seem to mean: good friend, so dear
To me in everything, come here tonight,
Or else the hours will pass most dull and drear;

" 'If you come not, I fear this time I might
Get thinking over much of times gone by,
255 When I was young, and green hope was in sight:

" 'For no man cares now to know why I sigh;
And no man comes to sing me pleasant songs,
Nor any brings me the sweet flowers that lie

" 'So thick in the gardens; therefore one so longs
260 To see you, Launcelot; that we may be
Like children once again, free from all wrongs

" 'Just for one night.' Did he not come to me?
What thing could keep true Launcelot away
If I said 'Come?' there was one less than three

265 "In my quiet room that night, and we were gay;
Till sudden I rose up, weak, pale, and sick,
Because a bawling broke our dream up, yea

"I looked at Launcelot's face and could not speak,
For he looked helpless too, for a little while;
270 Then I remember how I tried to shriek,

"And could not, but fell down; from tile to tile
The stones they threw up rattled o'er my head
And made me dizzier; till within a while

"My maids were all about me, and my head
275 On Launcelot's breast was being soothed away
From its white chattering, until Launcelot said—

9. Guenevere imagines these lies as being woven on a loom. "Woof": the threads woven across the threads stretched lengthwise on a loom (the warp).

"By God! I will not tell you more today,
Judge any way you will—what matters it?
You know quite well the story of that fray,

280 "How Launcelot stilled their bawling, the mad fit
That caught up Gauwaine—all, all, verily,
But just that which would save me; these things flit.

"Nevertheless you, O Sir Gauwaine, lie,
Whatever may have happened these long years,
285 God knows I speak truth, saying that you lie!

"All I have said is truth, by Christ's dear tears."
She would not speak another word, but stood,
Turned sideways; listening, like a man who hears

His brother's trumpet sounding through the wood
290 Of his foes' lances. She leaned eagerly,
And gave a slight spring sometimes, as she could

At last hear something really; joyfully
Her cheek grew crimson, as the headlong speed
Of the roan charger drew all men to see,
295 The knight who came was Launcelot at good need.

1858

How I Became a Socialist[1]

I am asked by the Editor to give some sort of a history of the above conversion, and I feel that it may be of some use to do so, if my readers will look
upon me as a type of a certain group of people, but not so easy to do clearly,
briefly and truly. Let me, however, try. But first, I will say what I mean by
being a Socialist, since I am told that the word no longer expresses definitely
and with certainty what it did ten years ago. Well, what I mean by Socialism
is a condition of society in which there should be neither rich nor poor, neither
master nor master's man, neither idle nor overworked, neither brain-sick brain
workers, nor heart-sick hand workers, in a word, in which all men would be
living in equality of condition, and would manage their affairs unwastefully,
and with the full consciousness that harm to one would mean harm to all—
the realization at last of the meaning of the word COMMONWEALTH.

Now this view of Socialism which I hold to-day, and hope to die holding, is
what I began with; I had no transitional period, unless you may call such a
brief period of political radicalism during which I saw my ideal clear enough,
but had no hope of any realization of it. That came to an end some months
before I joined the (then) Democratic Federation,[2] and the meaning of my
joining that body was that I had conceived a hope of the realization of my
ideal. If you ask me how much of a hope, or what I thought we Socialists then
living and working would accomplish towards it, or when there would be

---

1. Written for the socialist magazine *Justice* in
1894.

2. The first socialist organization in London,
founded in 1881.

effected any change in the face of society, I must say, I do not know. I can only say that I did not measure my hope, nor the joy that it brought me at the time. For the rest, when I took that step I was blankly ignorant of economics; I had never so much as opened Adam Smith, or heard of Ricardo, or of Karl Marx.[3] Oddly enough, I *had* read some of Mill,[4] to wit, those posthumous papers of his (published, was it in the *Westminster Review* or the *Fortnightly?*) in which he attacks Socialism in its Fourierist[5] guise. In those papers he put the arguments, as far as they go, clearly and honestly, and the result, so far as I was concerned, was to convince me that Socialism was a necessary change, and that it was possible to bring it about in our own days. Those papers put the finishing touch to my conversion to Socialism. Well, having joined a Socialist body (for the Federation soon became definitely Socialist), I put some conscience into trying to learn the economical side of Socialism, and even tackled Marx, though I must confess that, whereas I thoroughly enjoyed the historical part of "Capital," I suffered agonies of confusion of the brain over reading the pure economics of that great work. Anyhow, I read what I could, and will hope that some information stuck to me from my reading; but more, I must think, from continuous conversation with such friends as Bax and Hyndman and Scheu,[6] and the brisk course of propaganda meetings which were going on at the time, and in which I took my share. Such finish to what of education in practical Socialism as I am capable of I received afterwards from some of my Anarchist friends, from whom I learned, quite against their intention, that Anarchism was impossible, much as I learned from Mill against *his* intention that Socialism was necessary.

But in this telling how I fell into *practical* Socialism I have begun, as I perceive, in the middle, for in my position of a well-to-do man, not suffering from the disabilities which oppress a working-man at every step, I feel that I might never have been drawn into the practical side of the question if an ideal had not forced me to seek towards it. For politics as politics, *i.e.*, not regarded as a necessary if cumbersome and disgustful means to an end, would never have attracted me, nor when I had become conscious of the wrongs of society as it now is, and the oppression of poor people, could I have ever believed in the possibility of a *partial* setting right of those wrongs. In other words, I could never have been such a fool as to believe in the happy and "respectable" poor.

If, therefore, my ideal forced me to look for practical Socialism, what was it that forced me to conceive of an ideal? Now, here comes in what I said (in this paper) of my being a type of a certain group of mind.

Before the uprising of *modern* Socialism almost all intelligent people either were, or professed themselves to be, quite contented with the civilization of this century. Again, almost all of these really were thus contented, and saw nothing to do but to perfect the said civilization by getting rid of a few ridiculous survivals of the barbarous ages. To be short, this was the *Whig*[7] frame

3. German political philosopher (1818–1883), who developed the concept of communism; his *Capital* (1867–94) is an analysis of capitalism. Smith (1723–1790), Scottish economist who argued that natural laws of production and exchange govern economies and produce wealth. Smith's work was an important justification of capitalism and laissez-faire (noninterventionist) economics. David Ricardo (1772–1823), English economist whose labor theory of value influenced Marx.
4. James Mill (1773–1836), philosopher, political economist, and historian, and the father of John

Stuart Mill.
5. Characteristic of a political philosophy, developed by Charles Fourier (1772–1837), that advocated a social reorganization to equalize wealth.
6. Ernest Belfort Bax (1854–1926), H. M. Hyndman (1842–1921), and Andreas Scheu (1844–1927), leaders in the early English socialist movement.
7. From the monarchical crisis of 1678–81 onward, the term *Whig* (from *whiggamore*, a Scottish name for a cattle driver) designated a member of one of the two major parliamentary alliances (the Tories being the opposing group). Originally

of mind, natural to the modern prosperous middle-class men, who, in fact, as far as mechanical progress is concerned, have nothing to ask for, if only Socialism would leave them alone to enjoy their plentiful style.

But besides these contented ones there were others who were not really contented, but had a vague sentiment of repulsion to the triumph of civilization, but were coerced into silence by the measureless power of Whiggery. Lastly, there were a few who were in open rebellion against the said Whiggery—a few, say two, Carlyle and Ruskin. The latter, before my days of practical Socialism, was my master towards the ideal aforesaid, and, looking backward, I cannot help saying, by the way, how deadly dull the world would have been twenty years ago but for Ruskin! It was through him that I learned to give form to my discontent, which I must say was not by any means vague. Apart from the desire to produce beautiful things, the leading passion of my life has been and is hatred of modern civilization. What shall I say of it now, when the words are put into my mouth, my hope of its destruction—what shall I say of its supplanting by Socialism?

What shall I say concerning its mastery of and its waste of mechanical power, its commonwealth so poor, its enemies of the commonwealth so rich, its stupendous organization—for the misery of life! Its contempt of simple pleasures which everyone could enjoy but for its folly? Its eyeless vulgarity which has destroyed art, the one certain solace of labour? All this I felt then as now, but I did not know why it was so. The hope of the past times was gone, the struggles of mankind for many ages had produced nothing but this sordid, aimless, ugly confusion; the immediate future seemed to me likely to intensify all the present evils by sweeping away the last survivals of the days before the dull squalor of civilization had settled down on the world. This was a bad lookout indeed, and, if I may mention myself as a personality and not as a mere type, especially so to a man of my disposition, careless of metaphysics and religion, as well as of scientific analysis, but with a deep love of the earth and the life on it, and a passion for the history of the past of mankind. Think of it! Was it all to end in a counting-house on the top of a cinder-heap, with Podsnap's[8] drawing-room in the offing, and a Whig committee dealing out champagne to the rich and margarine to the poor in such convenient proportions as would make all men contented together, though the pleasure of the eyes was gone from the world, and the place of Homer was to be taken by Huxley?[9] Yet, believe me, in my heart, when I really forced myself to look towards the future, that is what I saw in it, and, as far as I could tell, scarce anyone seemed to think it worth while to struggle against such a consummation of civilization. So there I was in for a fine pessimistic end of life, if it had not somehow dawned on me that amidst all this filth of civilization the seeds of a great chance, what we others call Social-Revolution, were beginning to germinate. The whole face of things was changed to me by that discovery, and

an aristocratic faction interested in reducing the power of the Crown, the Whigs became progressively associated with reform, and thus formed important bonds with other groups and individuals, such as moneyed industrialists, champions of free trade, and religious dissenters. This Whig-Radical coalition was known colloquially as the Liberal Party from 1839 onward; it adopted the name officially when it assumed the form of a modern political party in the 1860s. The term *Whig* remained in informal use, often in connection with a self-congratulatory state of mind most famously promulgated by Thomas Babington Macaulay (1800–1859). His writings presented all English history as leading up to the parliamentary Reform Bill of 1832, and celebrated contemporary English life as the pinnacle of human achievement and civilization (see the first extract in "Industrialism," p. 1156 below).

8. Character in Charles Dickens's *Our Mutual Friend* (1865), who represents the epitome of pretentious middle-class respectability.

9. T. H. Huxley (1825–1895), writer on science, education, and philosophy. See p. 1427.

all I had to do then in order to become a Socialist was to hook myself on to the practical movement, which, as before said, I have tried to do as well as I could.

To sum up, then, the study of history and the love and practice of art forced me into a hatred of the civilization which, if things were to stop as they are, would turn history into inconsequent nonsense, and make art a collection of the curiosities of the past which would have no serious relation to the life of the present.

But the consciousness of revolution stirring amidst our hateful modern society prevented me, luckier than many others of artistic perceptions, from crystallizing into a mere railer against "progress" on the one hand, and on the other from wasting time and energy in any of the numerous schemes by which the quasi-artistic of the middle classes hope to make art grow when it has no longer any root, and thus I became a practical Socialist.

A last word or two. Perhaps some of our friends will say, what have we to do with these matters of history and art? We want by means of Social-Democracy to win a decent livelihood, we want in some sort to live, and that at once. Surely any one who professes to think that the question of art and cultivation must go before that of the knife and fork (and there are some who do propose that) does not understand what art means, or how that its roots must have a soil of a thriving and unanxious life. Yet it must be remembered that civilization has reduced the workman to such a skinny and pitiful existence, that he scarcely knows how to frame a desire for any life much better than that which he now endures perforce. It is the province of art to set the true ideal of a full and reasonable life before him, a life to which the perception and creation of beauty, the enjoyment of real pleasure that is, shall be felt to be as necessary to man as his daily bread, and that no man, and no set of men, can be deprived of this except by mere opposition, which should be resisted to the utmost.

1894   1894

ALGERNON CHARLES SWINBURNE
1837–1909

In a review of Charles Baudelaire's *Les Fleurs du Mal* (1857), Algernon Charles Swinburne remarks that "the mass of readers seem actually to think that a poem is the better for containing a moral lesson." He goes on to praise the courage and sense of a man who acts on the conviction "that the art of poetry has nothing to do with didactic matter at all." Certainly Swinburne's poems are not didactic in the sense of containing traditional moral values. As John Morley commented while reviewing Swinburne's first volume of poems, "He is so firmly and avowedly fixed in an attitude of revolt against the current notions of decency and dignity and social duty that to beg of him to be a little more decent, to fly a little less persistently and gleefully to the animal side of human nature, is simply to beg him to be something different from Mr. Swinburne." Swinburne set about shocking his elders by a variety of rebellious gestures. In religion he appeared to be a pagan; in politics, a liberal republican dedicated to the overthrow of established governments. On the subjects of love and sex, he was similarly unconventional. Frequently preoccupied with the pleasures of the lover who inflicts or accepts pain (particularly with the excitement of flagellation), Swinburne also often turns in his poetry to the theme of homoerotic desire, a taboo topic for his Victorian audience. As Arnold Bennett said of "Anactoria" (1866), a dramatic monologue in which the poet Sappho addresses a woman with whom she is madly in love, Swinburne played "a rare trick" on England by "enshrining in the topmost heights of its literature a lovely poem that cannot be discussed."

To a more limited extent, Swinburne also expressed his rebellion against established codes by his personal behavior. He came from a distinguished family and attended Eton and Oxford, but sought the company of the bohemians of Paris and of London, where he became temporarily associated with Dante Gabriel Rossetti and other Pre-Raphaelites. By 1879 his alcoholism had profoundly affected his frail physique, and he was obliged to put himself into the protective custody of a friend, Theodore Watts-Dunton, who took him to the countryside and kept him alive although sobered and tamed.

Swinburne continued to write voluminously and sometimes memorably, but his most fascinating poetry appeared in his early publications. He described his early play *Atalanta in Calydon* (1865) as "pure Greek," and his command of classical allusions here, as well as in other poems, is indeed impressive. Yet the kind of spirit that he found in Greek literature was not the traditional quality of classic serenity admired by Matthew Arnold. Like Percy Bysshe Shelley (the poet he most closely resembles), Swinburne loved Greece as a land of liberty in which men had expressed themselves with the fewest restraints. To call such an ardently romantic poet "classical" requires a series of qualifying clauses that makes the term meaningless.

In his play and in the volume that followed it, *Poems and Ballads* (1866), Swinburne demonstrated a metrical virtuosity that dazzled his early readers and is still dazzling. Those who demand that poetry should make sense, first and foremost, may find that much of his poetry is not to their taste. What he offers, instead, are heady rhythmical patterns in which words are relished as much for their sound as for their sense.

> There lived a singer in France of old
> By the tideless dolorous midland sea.
> In a land of sand and ruin and gold
> here shone one woman, and none but she.

These lines from *The Triumph of Time* have often been cited to illustrate Swinburne's qualities. Like some poems of the later French symbolists, such passages defy traditional kinds of critical analysis and oblige us to reconsider the variety of ways in which poetry may achieve its effects.

Another noteworthy aspect of these poems is their recurring preoccupation with death, as in the memorable re-creations of Proserpina's underworld garden, frozen in timelessness. And as the critic Jerome McGann notes: "No English poet has composed more elegies than Swinburne." The death of any prominent figure, such as Robert Browning, almost always prompted Swinburne to compose a poem for the occasion. "Ave atque Vale" (1868), his farewell to Baudelaire, is an especially moving tribute, and shows Swinburne focusing on a subject extremely close to his heart. For Swinburne the work of his beloved French poet possessed a "languid, lurid beauty"; to us the phrase may seem equally applicable to Swinburne's poetry.

Hymn to Proserpine

(After the Proclamation in Rome of the Christian Faith)

Vicisti, Galilaee[1]

I have lived long enough, having seen one thing, that love hath an end;
Goddess and maiden and queen, be near me now and befriend.
Thou art more than the day or the morrow, the seasons that laugh or that
    weep;
For these give joy and sorrow; but thou, Proserpina, sleep.
5 Sweet is the treading of wine, and sweet the feet of the dove;
But a goodlier gift is thine than foam of the grapes or love.
Yea, is not even Apollo,[2] with hair and harpstring of gold,
A bitter god to follow, a beautiful god to behold?
I am sick of singing; the bays[3] burn deep and chafe. I am fain°   *glad*
10 To rest a little from praise and grievous pleasure and pain.
For the gods we know not of, who give us our daily breath,
We know they are cruel as love or life, and lovely as death.

O gods dethroned and deceased, cast forth, wiped out in a day!
From your wrath is the world released, redeemed from your chains, men
    say.
15 New gods are crowned in the city; their flowers have broken your rods;
They are merciful, clothed with pity, the young compassionate gods.
But for me their new device is barren, the days are bare;
Things long past over suffice, and men forgotten that were.
Time and the gods are at strife; ye dwell in the midst thereof,
20 Draining a little life from the barren breasts of love.
I say to you, cease, take rest; yea, I say to you all, be at peace,
Till the bitter milk of her breast and the barren bosom shall cease.
Wilt thou yet take all, Galilean? But these thou shalt not take—
The laurel, the palms, and the paean, the breasts of the nymphs in the
    brake,°   *thicket*
25 Breasts more soft than a dove's, that tremble with tenderer breath;
And all the wings of the Loves, and all the joy before death;
All the feet of the hours that sound as a single lyre,
Dropped and deep in the flowers, with strings that flicker like fire.
More than these wilt thou give, things fairer than all these things?
30 Nay, for a little we live, and life hath mutable wings.
A little while and we die; shall life not thrive as it may?

1. Thou hast conquered, O Galilean (Latin); words supposedly addressed to Jesus, who grew up in Galilee, by the Roman emperor Julian the Apostate on his deathbed in 363. Julian had tried to revive paganism and to discourage Christianity, which, after a proclamation in 313, had been tolerated from then on. His efforts were unsuccessful. The speaker of the poem, a Roman patrician and also a poet (line 9), is like Emperor Julian: he prefers the old order of pagan gods. His hymn is addressed to the goddess Proserpina (the Greek Persephone), who was carried off by Pluto (Hades) to be queen of the underworld. In this role she is addressed in the poem as goddess of death and of sleep. The speaker also associates her with the earth (line 93) because she was the daughter of Ceres (or Demeter), goddess of agriculture, whose Greek name means "Earth Mother." Swinburne may have derived some details here from the 4th-century Latin poet Claudian, whose long narrative *The Rape of Proserpina* provides helpful background for this hymn.
2. Classical god of poetry, and in art the ideal of young male beauty.
3. Laurel leaves of a poet's crown.

For no man under the sky lives twice, outliving his day.
And grief is a grievous thing, and a man hath enough of his tears;
Why should he labor, and bring fresh grief to blacken his years?

35   Thou hast conquered, O pale Galilean; the world has grown gray from thy
      breath;
We have drunken of things Lethean,[4] and fed on the fullness of death.
Laurel is green for a season, and love is sweet for a day;
But love grows bitter with treason, and laurel outlives not May.
Sleep, shall we sleep after all? for the world is not sweet in the end;
40   For the old faiths loosen and fall, the new years ruin and rend.
Fate is a sea without shore, and the soul is a rock that abides;
But her ears are vexed with the roar and her face with the foam of the
      tides.
O lips that the live blood faints in, the leavings of racks and rods!
O ghastly glories of saints, dead limbs of gibbeted gods!
45   Though all men abase them before you in spirit, and all knees bend,
I kneel not, neither adore you, but standing look to the end.

All delicate days and pleasant, all spirits and sorrows are cast
Far out with the foam of the present that sweeps to the surf of the past;
Where beyond the extreme sea wall, and between the remote sea gates,
50   Waste water washes, and tall ships founder, and deep death waits;
Where, mighty with deepening sides, clad about with the seas as with
      wings,
And impelled of invisible tides, and fulfilled of unspeakable things,
White-eyed and poisonous-finned, shark-toothed and serpentine-curled,
Rolls, under the whitening wind of the future, the wave of the world.
55   The depths stand naked in sunder behind it, the storms flee away;
In the hollow before it the thunder is taken and snared as a prey;
In its sides is the north wind bound; and its salt is of all men's tears,
With light of ruin, and sound of changes, and pulse of years;
With travail of day after day, and with trouble of hour upon hour.
60   And bitter as blood is the spray; and the crests are as fangs that devour;
And its vapor and storm of its steam as the sighing of spirits to be;
And its noise as the noise in a dream; and its depths as the roots of the sea;
And the height of its heads as the height of the utmost stars of the air;
And the ends of the earth at the might thereof tremble, and time is made
      bare.
65   Will ye bridle the deep sea with reins, will ye chasten the high sea with
      rods?[5]
Will ye take her to chain her with chains, who is older than all ye gods?
All ye as a wind shall go by, as a fire shall ye pass and be past;
Ye are gods, and behold, ye shall die, and the waves be upon you at last.
In the darkness of time, in the deeps of the years, in the changes of things,
70   Ye shall sleep as a slain man sleeps, and the world shall forget you or kings.
Though the feet of thine high priests tread where thy lords and our
      forefathers trod,

4. I.e., of Lethe (literally, "Forgetfulness"), a river in the underworld.
5. According to the ancient Greek historian Herodotus, after storm waves destroyed his bridge the enraged Xerxes, king of the Persians, ordered that the Hellespont be whipped; see *History* 7.33–34.

Though these that were gods are dead, and thou being dead art a god,
Though before thee the throned Cytherean[6] be fallen, and hidden her head,
Yet thy kingdom shall pass, Galilean, thy dead shall go down to thee dead.

75 Of the maiden thy mother men sing as a goddess with grace clad around;
Thou art throned where another was king; where another was queen she is
crowned.
Yea, once we had sight of another; but now she is queen, say these.
Not as thine, not as thine was our mother, a blossom of flowering seas,
Clothed round with the world's desire as with raiment, and fair as the foam.
80 And fleeter than kindled fire, and a goddess, and mother of Rome.[7]
For thine came pale and a maiden, and sister to sorrow; but ours,
Her deep hair heavily laden with odour and colour of flowers,
White rose of the rose-white water, a silver splendour, a flame,
Bent down unto us that besought her, and earth grew sweet with her name.
85 For thine came weeping, a slave among slaves, and rejected; but she
Came flushed from the full-flushed wave, and imperial, her foot on the sea.
And the wonderful waters knew her, the winds and the viewless ways,
And the roses grew rosier, and bluer the sea-blue stream of the bays.

Ye are fallen, our lords, by what token? we wist that ye should not fall.
90 Ye were all so fair that are broken; and one more fair than ye all.
But I turn to her° still, having seen she shall surely abide in   *Proserpina*
the end.
Goddess and maiden and queen, be near me now and befriend.
O daughter of earth, of my mother, her crown and blossom of birth,
I am also, I also, thy brother; I go as I came unto earth.
95 In the night where thine eyes are as moons are in heaven, the night where
thou art,
Where the silence is more than all tunes, where sleep overflows from the
heart,
Where the poppies are sweet as the rose in our world, and the red rose is
white,
And the wind falls faint as it blows with the fume of the flowers of the
night,
And the murmur of spirits that sleep in the shadow of gods from afar
100 Grows dim in thine ears and deep as the deep dim soul of a star,
In the sweet low light of thy face, under heavens untrod by the sun,
Let my soul with their souls find place, and forget what is done and
undone.
Thou art more than the gods who number the days of our temporal breath;
For these give labor and slumber; but thou, Proserpina, death.
105 Therefore now at thy feet I abide for a season in silence. I know
I shall die as my fathers died, and sleep as they sleep; even so.
For the glass° of the years is brittle wherein we gaze for a span.   *mirror*
A little soul for a little bears up this corpse which is man.
So long I endure, no longer; and laugh not again, neither weep.
110 For there is no god found stronger than death; and death is a sleep.

1866

6. Venus (or Aphrodite), who was born from the waves near the island of Cythera.
7. Romans traced their legendary origins back to Aeneas, a Trojan prince who was the son of Aphrodite.

Hermaphroditus[1]

1

Lift up thy lips, turn round, look back for love,
   Blind love that comes by night and casts out rest
   Of all things tired thy lips look weariest,
Save the long smile that they are wearied of.
5 Ah sweet, albeit no love be sweet enough,
   Choose of two loves and cleave unto the best;
   Two loves at either blossom of thy breast
Strive until one be under and one above.
Their breath is fire upon the amorous air,
10 Fire in thine eyes and where thy lips suspire:°   *breathe out*
And whosoever hath seen thee, being so fair,
   Two things turn all his life and blood to fire;
A strong desire begot on great despair,
   A great despair cast out by strong desire.

2

15 Where between sleep and life some brief space is,
   With love like gold bound round about the head,
   Sex to sweet sex with lips and limbs is wed,
Turning the fruitful feud of hers and his
To the waste wedlock of a sterile kiss;
20 Yet from them something like as fire is shed
   That shall not be assuaged till death be dead,
Though neither life nor sleep can find out this.
Love made himself of flesh that perisheth
   A pleasure-house for all the loves his kin;
25 But on the one side sat a man like death,
   And on the other a woman sat like sin.
So with veiled eyes and sobs between his breath
   Love turned himself and would not enter in.

3

Love, is it love or sleep or shadow or light
30 That lies between thine eyelids and thine eyes?
   Like a flower laid upon a flower it lies,
Or like the night's dew laid upon the night.
Love stands upon thy left hand and thy right,
   Yet by no sunset and by no moonrise
35 Shall make thee man and ease a woman's sighs,
Or make thee woman for a man's delight.
To what strange end hath some strange god made fair
   The double blossom of two fruitless flowers?
Hid love in all the folds of all thy hair,
40 Fed thee on summers, watered thee with showers,

1. Son of Hermes and Aphrodite. One day as he bathed in a spring, Salmacis, the nymph of the spring, fell in love with him. When he rejected her, she clung to him, praying that their bodies never be separated. The gods answered her prayer, making their bodies one. The statue in the Louvre that inspired this poem, a Roman copy of a Greek original, shows the god lying on his side, with the breasts of a woman and the genitals of a man.

Given all the gold that all the seasons wear
To thee that art a thing of barren hours?

4

Yea, love, I see; it is not love but fear.
    Nay, sweet, it is not fear but love, I know;
45   Or wherefore should thy body's blossom blow
So sweetly, or thine eyelids leave so clear
Thy gracious eyes that never made a tear—
    Though for their love our tears like blood should flow,
    Though love and life and death should come and go,
45   So dreadful, so desirable, so dear?
Yea, sweet, I know; I saw in what swift wise°   *how swiftly*
    Beneath the woman's and the water's kiss
    Thy moist limbs melted into Salmacis,
And the large light turned tender in thine eyes,
50   And all thy boy's breath softened into sighs;
    But Love being blind,² how should he know of this?

AU MUSÉE DU LOUVRE, *Mars* 1863.³

1863   1866

Ave atque Vale¹

In Memory of Charles Baudelaire

Nous devrions pourtant lui porter quelques fleurs;
Les morts, les pauvres morts, ont de grandes douleurs,
Et quand Octobre souffle, émondeur des vieux arbres,
Son vent mélancolique à l'entour de leurs marbres,
Certe, ils doivent trouver les vivants bien ingrats.
                            —"*Les Fleurs du Mal.*"²

I

Shall I strew on thee rose or rue or laurel,³
    Brother, on this that was the veil⁴ of thee?
    Or quiet sea-flower molded by the sea,
Or simplest growth of meadow-sweet or sorrel,

2. Love, personified in classical mythology as Eros or Cupid, is often represented as blindfolded or blind.
3. At the Museum of the Louvre, March 1863 (French).
1. Hail and farewell (Latin); a line from an elegy by Catullus occasioned by a farewell visit to the grave of his brother, to whom he brought gifts, a situation closely echoed in Swinburne's final stanza. Swinburne's elegy likewise begins with a visit to the grave of a man whom the poet regards as a brother but had never met. Charles Baudelaire (1821–1867) had impressed Swinburne as one of the "most perfect poets of the century." In 1861, in an essay on the 2nd edition of Baudelaire's collection *Les Fleurs du Mal* (*Flowers of Evil*, 1857), Swinburne had commented on the French poet's preoccupation with "sad and strange things"—"the sharp and cruel enjoyments of pain, the acrid relish

of suffering felt or inflicted"; "it has the languid, lurid beauty of close and threatening weather—a heavy, heated temperature, with dangerous hot-house scents in it." These qualities are also celebrated in Swinburne's elegy, into which are woven many allusions to Baudelaire's poems, especially his "Litanies de Satan," which Swinburne regarded as the keynote poem of *Les Fleurs du Mal*.
2. From "La Servante au Grand Coeur" ("The Great-hearted Servant"): We must nevertheless bring some flowers to her [or him]. / The dead, the poor dead, have great sadnesses, / And when October, the pruner of old trees, blows, / Its melancholy wind in the vicinity of their marble tombs, / Then indeed they must find the living highly ungrateful (French).
3. Respectively, symbols of love, mourning, and poetic fame.
4. I.e., the body as a veil for the soul.

5   Such as the summer-sleepy Dryads° weave,   *wood nymphs*
     Waked up by snow-soft sudden rains at eve?
     Or wilt thou rather, as on earth before,
     Half-faded fiery blossoms, pale with heat
     And full of bitter summer, but more sweet
10   To thee than gleanings of a northern shore
     Trod by no tropic feet?[5]

2

     For always thee the fervid languid glories
     Allured of heavier suns in mightier skies;
     Thine ears knew all the wandering watery sighs
15   Where the sea sobs round Lesbian promontories,
     The barren kiss of piteous wave to wave
     That knows not where is that Leucadian grave[6]
     Which hides too deep the supreme head of song.
     Ah, salt and sterile as her kisses were,
20   The wild sea winds her and the green gulfs bear
     Hither and thither, and vex and work her wrong,
     Blind gods that cannot spare.

3

     Thou sawest, in thine old singing season, brother,
     Secrets and sorrows unbeheld of us:
25   Fierce loves, and lovely leaf-buds poisonous,
     Bare to thy subtler eye, but for none other
     Blowing by night in some unbreathed-in clime;
     The hidden harvest of luxurious time,
     Sin without shape, and pleasure without speech;
30   And where strange dreams in a tumultuous sleep
     Make the shut eyes of stricken spirits weep;
     And with each face thou sawest the shadow on each,
     Seeing as men sow men reap.[7]

4

     O sleepless heart and sombre soul unsleeping,
35   That were athirst for sleep and no more life
     And no more love, for peace and no more strife!
     Now the dim gods of death have in their keeping
     Spirit and body and all the springs of song,
     Is it well now where love can do no wrong,
40   Where stingless pleasure has no foam or fang
     Behind the unopening closure of her lips?
     Is it not well where soul from body slips
     And flesh from bone divides without a pang
     As dew from flower-bell drips?

5

45   It is enough; the end and the beginning
     Are one thing to thee, who art past the end.

---

5. A voyage to the tropics in Baudelaire's youth made a lasting impact on his poetry.
6. According to legend, the poet Sappho, who was born on the island of Lesbos, killed herself by leaping from the rock of Leucas into the Ionian Sea.

In this section Swinburne makes allusions to Baudelaire's "Lesbos."
7. Cf. Galatians 6.7: "Whatsoever a man soweth, that shall he also reap."

O hand unclasped of unbeholden friend,
For thee no fruits to pluck, no palms for winning,
No triumph and no labour and no lust,
50   Only dead yew-leaves and a little dust.
O quiet eyes wherein the light saith naught,
Whereto the day is dumb, nor any night
With obscure finger silences your sight,
Nor in your speech the sudden soul speaks thought,
55   Sleep, and have sleep for light.

6

Now all strange hours and all strange loves are over,
Dreams and desires and sombre songs and sweet,
Hast thou found place at the great knees and feet
Of some pale Titan-woman like a lover,
60   Such as thy vision here solicited,[8]
Under the shadow of her fair vast head,
The deep division of prodigious breasts,
The solemn slope of mighty limbs asleep,
The weight of awful tresses that still keep
65   The savor and shade of old-world pine forests
Where the wet hill-winds weep?

7

Hast thou found any likeness for thy vision?
O gardener of strange flowers, what bud, what bloom,
Hast thou found sown, what gathered in the gloom?
70   What of despair, of rapture, of derision,
What of life is there, what of ill or good?
Are the fruits grey like dust or bright like blood?
Does the dim ground grow any seed of ours,
The faint fields quicken any terrene° root,   *earthly*
75   In low lands where the sun and moon are mute
And all the stars keep silence? Are there flowers
At all, or any fruit?

8

Alas, but though my flying song flies after,
O sweet strange elder singer, thy more fleet
80   Singing, and footprints of thy fleeter feet,
Some dim derision of mysterious laughter
From the blind tongueless warders of the dead,
Some gainless glimpse of Proserpine's[9] veiled head,
Some little sound of unregarded tears
85   Wept by effaced unprofitable eyes,
And from pale mouths some cadence of dead sighs—
These only, these the hearkening spirit hears,
Sees only such things rise.

9

Thou art far too far for wings of words to follow,
90   Far too far off for thought or any prayer.

8. An allusion to Baudelaire's "La Géante" ("The   9. Queen of the underworld.
Giantess").

What ails us with thee, who are wind and air?
What ails us gazing where all seen is hollow?
Yet with some fancy, yet with some desire,
Dreams pursue death as winds a flying fire,
95   Our dreams pursue our dead and do not find.
Still, and more swift than they, the thin flame flies,
The low light fails us in elusive skies,
Still the foiled earnest ear is deaf, and blind
Are still the eluded eyes.

10

100   Not thee, O never thee, in all time's changes,
Not thee, but this the sound of thy sad soul,
The shadow of thy swift spirit, this shut scroll
I lay my hand on, and not death estranges
My spirit from communion of thy song—
105   These memories and these melodies that throng
Veiled porches of a Muse funereal[1]—
These I salute, these touch, these clasp and fold
As though a hand were in my hand to hold,
Or through mine ears a mourning musical[2]
110   Of many mourners rolled.

11

I among these, I also, in such station
As when the pyre was charred, and piled the sods,
And offering to the dead made, and their gods,
The old mourners had, standing to make libation,
115   I stand, and to the gods and to the dead
Do reverence without prayer or praise, and shed
Offering to these unknown, the gods of gloom,
And what of honey and spice my seedlands bear,
And what I may of fruits in this chilled air,
120   And lay, Orestes-like, across the tomb
A curl of severed hair.[3]

12

But by no hand nor any treason stricken,
Not like the low-lying head of Him, the King,
The flame that made of Troy a ruinous thing,
125   Thou liest, and on this dust no tears could quicken
There fall no tears like theirs[4] that all men hear
Fall tear by sweet imperishable tear
Down the opening leaves of holy poets' pages.
Thee not Orestes, not Electra mourns;
130   But bending us-ward with memorial urns

1. According to Jerome McGann, Swinburne associates Baudelaire's distinctive kind of poetry with a tenth muse, one who inspires songs of lamentation ("funereal"). What is meant by this muse's "veiled porches" seems tantalizingly obscure.
2. I.e., a musical mourning.
3. For lines 120–29 see Aeschylus's *The Libation Bearers* 4–8. King Agamemnon, after returning home from Troy, had been treacherously slain, an event that made "a ruinous thing" of the Greek victory. His son, Orestes, visits Agamemnon's grave and dedicates on it a lock of his own hair; it is discovered soon thereafter by his sister, Electra, who visits her father's grave to offer mourning libations.
4. Referring to the muses and holy poets, not to Orestes and Electra [noted by Jerome McGann].

1504 / ALGERNON CHARLES SWINBURNE

The most high Muses that fulfill all ages
Weep, and our God's heart yearns.

13

For, sparing of his sacred strength, not often
Among us darkling here the lord of light[5]
135   Makes manifest his music and his might
In hearts that open and in lips that soften
With the soft flame and heat of songs that shine.
Thy lips indeed he touched with bitter wine,
And nourished them indeed with bitter bread;
140   Yet surely from his hand thy soul's food came;
The fire that scarred thy spirit at his flame
Was lighted, and thine hungering heart he fed
Who feeds our hearts with fame.

14

Therefore he too now at thy soul's sunsetting,
145   God of all suns and songs he too bends down
To mix his laurel with thy cypress[6] crown.
And save thy dust from blame and from forgetting,
Therefore he too, seeing all thou wert and art,
Compassionate, with sad and sacred heart,
150   Mourns thee of many his children the last dead,
And hallows with strange tears and alien sighs
Thine unmelodious mouth and sunless eyes,
And over thine irrevocable head
Sheds light from the under skies.[7]

15

155   And one weeps with him in the ways Lethean,[8]
And stains with tears her changing bosom chill;
That obscure Venus of the hollow hill,
That thing transformed which was the Cytherean,
With lips that lost their Grecian laugh divine
160   Long since, and face no more called Erycine;[9]
A ghost, a bitter and luxurious god.
Thee also with fair flesh and singing spell
Did she, a sad and second prey,[1] compel
Into the footless places once more trod,
165   And shadows hot from hell.

16

And now no sacred staff shall break in blossom,[2]
No choral salutation lure to light

5. Apollo, god of light and poetry.
6. Associated with mourning. "Laurel": the crown of Apollo, a wreath honoring poets.
7. I.e., flickering light of the underworld.
8. Of Lethe, the river of forgetfulness in Hades.
9. The Venus of medieval legends held her court inside a mountain in Germany (the Hörselberg). This later Venus is a transformed version of the joyous foam-born goddess associated with the island of Cythera and also worshipped in Sicily at a shrine on Mount Eryx (hence "Erycine"). The Roman poet Horace described her as "blithe goddess of Eryx, about whom hover mirth and desire"

(Odes 1.2.33–34).
1. The first "prey" of Venus had been Tannhäuser, whom she had lured into the "footless places" of her cave. Baudelaire is her "second prey." Swinburne, after reading Baudelaire's 1861 pamphlet on Wagner's Tannhäuser (1845), described this Venus as "the queen of evil, the lady of lust."
2. Such a miraculous event occurred when Tannhäuser made a pilgrimage to Rome to seek absolution for having lived in sin with Venus. Previously the pope had denied absolution until the day his staff should bloom.

A spirit sick with perfume and sweet night
And love's tired eyes and hands and barren bosom.
170   There is no help for these things; none to mend
And none to mar; not all our songs, O friend,
Will make death clear or make life durable.
Howbeit with rose and ivy and wild vine
And with wild notes about this dust of thine
175   At least I fill the place where white dreams dwell[3]
And wreathe an unseen shrine.

17

Sleep; and if life was bitter to thee, pardon,
If sweet, give thanks; thou hast no more to live;
And to give thanks is good, and to forgive.
180   Out of the mystic and the mournful garden
Where all day through thine hands in barren braid
Wove the sick flowers of secrecy and shade,
Green buds of sorrow and sin, and remnants grey,
Sweet-smelling, pale with poison, sanguine-hearted,
185   Passions that sprang from sleep and thoughts that started,
Shall death not bring us all as thee one day
Among the days departed?

18

For thee, O now a silent soul, my brother,
Take at my hands this garland, and farewell.
190   Thin is the leaf, and chill the wintry smell,
And chill the solemn earth, a fatal mother,
With sadder than the Niobean womb,[4]
And in the hollow of her breasts a tomb.
Content thee, howsoe'er, whose days are done;
195   There lies not any troublous thing before,
Nor sight nor sound to war against thee more,
For whom all winds are quiet as the sun,
All waters as the shore.

1866–67   1868

3. Presumably the abode of the ghosts of the dead.   than the goddess Leto, the goddess's children—
4. After Niobe boasted of having more children   Apollo and Diana (Artemis)—killed them all.

WALTER PATER
1839–1894

Studies in the History of the Renaissance, a collection of essays published in 1873, was the first of several volumes that established Walter Pater as one of the most influential writers of the late Victorian period. His flair for critical writing may have first been sparked when he was an undergraduate at Oxford (1858–62), where he heard and enjoyed the lectures of Matthew Arnold, who was then professor of poetry. After graduation Pater remained at Oxford, a shy bachelor who spent his life teaching classics (for the story of his earlier years see "The Child in the House" [1895], an autobiographical sketch that provides a helpful introduction to all of his writings). In view of his quiet disposition Pater was surprised and even alarmed by the impact made by his books on young readers of the 1870s and 1880s. Some of his younger followers such as Oscar Wilde and George Moore may have misread him. As T. S. Eliot wrote somewhat primly, "[Pater's] view of art, as expressed in *The Renaissance*, impressed itself upon a number of writers in the nineties, and propagated some confusion between life and art which is not wholly irresponsible for some untidy lives." It can be demonstrated that Pater's writings (especially his historical novel *Marius the Epicurean*, 1885) have much in common with the works of his earnest-minded mid-Victorian predecessors, but his disciples overlooked these similarities. To them his work seemed strikingly different and, in its quiet way, more subversive than the head-on attacks against traditional Victorianism made by Algernon Charles Swinburne or Samuel Butler. Instead of recommending a continuation of the painful quest for Truth that had dominated Oxford in the days of John Henry Newman, Pater assured his readers that the quest was pointless. Truth, he said, is relative. And instead of echoing Thomas Carlyle's call to duty and social responsibilities, Pater reminded his readers that life passes quickly and that our only responsibility is to enjoy fully "this short day of frost and sun"—to relish its sensations, especially those sensations provoked by works of art.

This epicurean gospel was conveyed in a highly wrought prose style that baffles anyone who likes to read quickly. Pater believed that prose was as difficult an art as poetry, and he expected his own elaborate sentences to be savored. Like Gustave Flaubert (1821–1880), the French novelist whom he admired, Pater painstakingly revised his sentences with special attention to their rhythms, seeking always the right word, *le mot juste*, as Flaubert called it. For many years Pater's day would begin with his making a careful study of a dictionary. What Pater said of Dante is an apt description of his own polished style: "He is one of those artists whose general effect largely depends on vocabulary, on the minute particles of which his work is wrought, on the colour and outline of single words and phrases." An additional characteristic of his highly wrought style is its relative absence of humor. Pater was valued among his friends for his flashes of wit and for his lively and irreverent conversation, but in his writings such traits are suppressed. As Michael Levey observed in *The Case of Walter Pater* (1978), "Even for irony the mood of his writing is almost too intense."

In addition to being a key figure in the transition from mid-Victorianism to the "decadence" of the 1890s, Pater commands our attention as the writer of exemplary impressionistic criticism. In each of his essays he seeks to communicate what he called the "special unique impression of pleasure" made on him by the works of some artist or writer. His range of subjects included the dialogues of Plato, the paintings of Leonardo da Vinci, the plays of Shakespeare, and the writings of the French Romantic school of the nineteenth century. Of particular value to students of English literature are his discriminating studies of William Wordsworth, Samuel Taylor Coleridge, Charles Lamb, and Sir Thomas Browne in his volume of *Appreciations* (1889) and his essay on the poetry of William Morris titled "Aesthetic Poetry" (1868). These and other essays by Pater were praised by Oscar Wilde in a review in 1890 as "absolutely modern, in the true meaning of the term modernity. For he to whom the present is the only thing that is present, knows nothing of the age in which he lives. . . . The true critic is he who bears within himself the dreams and ideas and feelings of myriad generations, and to whom no form of thought is alien, no emotional impulse obscure."

The final sentences of his *Appreciations* volume are a revealing indication of Pater's critical position. After having attempted to show the differences between the classical and romantic schools of art, he concludes that most great artists combine the qualities of both. "To discriminate schools, of art, of literature," he writes, "is, of course, part of the obvious business of literary criticism: but, in the work of literary production, it is easy to be overmuch occupied concerning them. For, in truth, the legitimate contention is, not of one age or school of literary art against another, but of all successive schools alike, against the stupidity which is dead to the substance, and the vulgarity which is dead to form."

From Studies in the History of the Renaissance

Preface

Many attempts have been made by writers on art and poetry to define beauty in the abstract, to express it in the most general terms, to find some universal formula for it. The value of these attempts has most often been in the suggestive and penetrating things said by the way. Such discussions help us very little to enjoy what has been well done in art or poetry, to discriminate between what is more and what is less excellent in them, or to use words like beauty, excellence, art, poetry, with a more precise meaning than they would otherwise have. Beauty, like all other qualities presented to human experience, is relative; and the definition of it becomes unmeaning and useless in proportion to its abstractness. To define beauty, not in the most abstract but in the most concrete terms possible, to find not its universal formula, but the formula which expresses most adequately this or that special manifestation of it, is the aim of the true student of aesthetics.

"To see the object as in itself it really is,"[1] has been justly said to be the aim of all true criticism whatever; and in aesthetic criticism the first step towards seeing one's object as it really is, is to know one's own impression as it really is, to discriminate it, to realize it distinctly. The objects with which aesthetic criticism deals—music, poetry, artistic and accomplished forms of human life—are indeed receptacles of so many powers or forces: they possess, like the products of nature, so many virtues or qualities. What is this song or picture, this engaging personality presented in life or in a book, to me? What effect does it really produce on me? Does it give me pleasure? and if so, what sort or degree of pleasure? How is my nature modified by its presence, and under its influence? The answers to these questions are the original facts with which the aesthetic critic has to do; and, as in the study of light, of morals, of number, one must realize such primary data for one's self, or not at all. And he who experiences these impressions strongly, and drives directly at the discrimination and analysis of them, has no need to trouble himself with the abstract question what beauty is in itself, or what its exact relation to truth or experience—metaphysical questions, as unprofitable as metaphysical questions elsewhere. He may pass them all by as being, answerable or not, of no interest to him.

The aesthetic critic, then, regards all the objects with which he has to do, all works of art, and the fairer forms of nature and human life, as powers or forces producing pleasurable sensations, each of a more or less peculiar or unique kind. This influence he feels, and wishes to explain, by analyzing and reducing it to its elements. To him, the picture, the landscape, the engaging personality in life or in a book, "La Gioconda," the hills of Carrara, Pico of Mirandola,[2] are valuable for their virtues, as we say, in speaking of a herb, a

---

1. Matthew Arnold, "The Function of Criticism at the Present Time" (1864; p. 1384).
2. Pico della Mirandola (1463–1494), Italian philosopher and classical scholar, subject of an essay by Pater that was included in *Studies in the History* of the Renaissance. "La Gioconda": another name for Leonardo da Vinci's painting the *Mona Lisa* (1503–6; see below). "The hills of Carrara": marble quarries in Italy, particularly associated with Michelangelo.

wine, a gem; for the property each has of affecting one with a special, a unique, impression of pleasure. Our education becomes complete in proportion as our susceptibility to these impressions increases in depth and variety. And the function of the aesthetic critic is to distinguish, to analyze, and separate from its adjuncts, the virtue by which a picture, a landscape, a fair personality in life or in a book, produces this special impression of beauty or pleasure, to indicate what the source of that impression is, and under what conditions it is experienced. His end is reached when he has disengaged that virtue, and noted it, as a chemist notes some natural element, for himself and others; and the rule for those who would reach this end is stated with great exactness in the words of a recent critic of Sainte-Beuve: *De se borner à connaître de près les belles choses, et à s'en nourrir en exquis amateurs, en humanistes accomplis.*[3]

What is important, then, is not that the critic should possess a correct abstract definition of beauty for the intellect, but a certain kind of tempera-ment, the power of being deeply moved by the presence of beautiful objects. He will remember always that beauty exists in many forms. To him all periods, types, schools of taste, are in themselves equal. In all ages there have been some excellent workmen, and some excellent work done. The question he asks is always: In whom did the stir, the genius, the sentiment of the period find itself? where was the receptacle of its refinement, its elevation, its taste? "The ages are all equal," says William Blake, "but genius is always above its age."[4]

Often it will require great nicety to disengage this virtue from the commoner elements with which it may be found in combination. Few artists, not Goethe or Byron even, work quite cleanly, casting off all debris, and leaving us only what the heat of their imagination has wholly fused and transformed. Take, for instance, the writings of Wordsworth. The heat of his genius, entering into the substance of his work, has crystallized a part, but only a part, of it; and in that great mass of verse there is much which might well be forgotten. But scattered up and down it, sometimes fusing and transforming entire compo-sitions, like the stanzas on *Resolution and Independence,* or the *Ode on the Recollections of Childhood,*[5] sometimes, as if at random, depositing a fine crys-tal here or there, in a matter it does not wholly search through and transmute, we trace the action of his unique, incommunicable faculty, that strange, mys-tical sense of a life in natural things, and of man's life as a part of nature, drawing strength and color and character from local influences, from the hills and streams, and from natural sights and sounds. Well! that is the *virtue,* the active principle in Wordsworth's poetry; and then the function of the critic of Wordsworth is to follow up that active principle, to disengage it, to mark the degree in which it penetrates his verse.

The subjects of the following studies are taken from the history of the *Renaissance,* and touch what I think the chief points in that complex, many-sided movement. I have explained in the first of them what I understand by the word, giving it a much wider scope than was intended by those who orig-inally used it to denote that revival of classical antiquity in the fifteenth century which was only one of many results of a general excitement and enlightening

3. To confine themselves to knowing beautiful things intimately, and to sustain themselves by these, as sensitive amateurs and accomplished humanists do (French). In 1980 the editor Donald J. Hill discovered that this quotation is *by* the French man of letters Charles-Augustin Sainte-Beuve (1804–1869) rather than about him; therefore, Hill conjectures that "a recent critic"

ought to be "a recent critique."
4. From Blake's annotations to *The Works of Sir Joshua Reynolds* (1778). The "genius" was the German artist Albrecht Dürer (1471–1528).
5. Wordsworth's ode is actually titled "Intimations of Immortality from Recollections of Early Child-hood"; both poems were published in 1807.

of the human mind, but of which the great aim and achievements of what, as Christian art, is often falsely opposed to the Renaissance, were another result. This outbreak of the human spirit may be traced far into the Middle Age itself, with its motives already clearly pronounced, the care for physical beauty, the worship of the body, the breaking down of those limits which the religious system of the Middle Age imposed on the heart and the imagination. I have taken as an example of this movement, this earlier Renaissance within the Middle Age itself, and as an expression of its qualities, two little compositions in early French; not because they constitute the best possible expression of them, but because they help the unity of my series, inasmuch as the Renaissance ends also in France, in French poetry, in a phase of which the writings of Joachim du Bellay[6] are in many ways the most perfect illustration. The Renaissance, in truth, put forth in France an aftermath, a wonderful later growth, the products of which have to the full that subtle and delicate sweetness which belongs to a refined and comely decadence, just as its earliest phases have the freshness which belongs to all periods of growth in art, the charm of *ascêsis*,[7] of the austere and serious girding of the loins in youth.

But it is in Italy, in the fifteenth century, that the interest of the Renaissance mainly lies—in that solemn fifteenth century which can hardly be studied too much, not merely for its positive results in the things of the intellect and the imagination, its concrete works of art, its special and prominent personalities, with their profound aesthetic charm, but for its general spirit and character, for the ethical qualities of which it is a consummate type.

The various forms of intellectual activity which together make up the culture of an age, move for the most part from different starting points, and by unconnected roads. As products of the same generation they partake indeed of a common character, and unconsciously illustrate each other; but of the producers themselves, each group is solitary, gaining what advantage or disadvantage there may be in intellectual isolation. Art and poetry, philosophy and the religious life, and that other life of refined pleasure and action in the conspicuous places of the world, are each of them confined to its own circle of ideas, and those who prosecute either of them are generally little curious of the thoughts of others. There come, however, from time to time, eras of more favorable conditions, in which the thoughts of men draw nearer together than is their wont, and the many interests of the intellectual world combine in one complete type of general culture. The fifteenth century in Italy is one of these happier eras, and what is sometimes said of the age of Pericles is true of that of Lorenzo:[8] it is an age productive in personalities, many-sided, centralized, complete. Here, artists and philosophers and those whom the action of the world has elevated and made keen, do not live in isolation, but breathe a common air, and catch light and heat from each other's thoughts. There is a spirit of general elevation and enlightenment in which all alike communicate. The unity of this spirit gives unity to all the various products of the Renaissance; and it is to this intimate alliance with mind, this participation in the best thoughts which that age produced, that the art of Italy in the fifteenth century owes much of its grave dignity and influence.

I have added an essay on Winckelmann,[9] as not incongruous with the stud-

---

6. French poet and critic (ca.1522–1560), subject of another essay in *Studies of the History of the Renaissance*.
7. Asceticism (Greek).
8. Lorenzo de Medici (1449–1492, also known as Lorenzo the Magnificent), ruler of Florence and

patron of the arts. Pericles (ca. 495–429 B.C.E.), a statesman who led Athens during its period of greatest political and cultural dominance.
9. Johann Joachim Winckelmann (1717–1768), German classicist.

ies which precede it, because Winckelmann, coming in the eighteenth century, really belongs in spirit to an earlier age. By his enthusiasm for the things of the intellect and the imagination for their own sake, by his Hellenism, his lifelong struggle to attain to the Greek spirit, he is in sympathy with the humanists of a previous century. He is the last fruit of the Renaissance, and explains in a striking way its motive and tendencies.

["LA GIOCONDA"][1]

"La Gioconda" is, in the truest sense, Leonardo's masterpiece, the revealing instance of his mode of thought and work. In suggestiveness, only the "Melancholia" of Dürer is comparable to it; and no crude symbolism disturbs the effect of its subdued and graceful mystery. We all know the face and hands of the figure, set in its marble chair, in that circle of fantastic rocks, as in some faint light under sea. Perhaps of all ancient pictures time has chilled it least. As often happens with works in which invention seems to reach its limit, there is an element in it given to, not invented by, the master. In that inestimable folio of drawings, once in the possession of Vasari, were certain designs by Verrocchio,[2] faces of such impressive beauty that Leonardo in his boyhood copied them many times. It is hard not to connect with these designs of the elder, by-past master, as with its germinal principle, the unfathomable smile, always with a touch of something sinister in it, which plays over all Leonardo's work. Besides, the picture is a portrait. From childhood we see this image defining itself on the fabric of his dreams, and but for express historical testimony, we might fancy that this was but his ideal lady, embodied and beheld at last. What was the relationship of a living Florentine to this creature of his thought? By what strange affinities had the dream and the person grown up thus apart, and yet so closely together? Present from the first incorporeally in Leonardo's brain, dimly traced in the designs of Verrocchio, she is found present at last in Il Giocondo's house. That there is much of mere portraiture in the picture is attested by the legend that by artificial means, the presence of mimes[3] and flute-players, that subtle expression was protracted on the face. Again, was it in four years and by renewed labor never really completed, or in four months and as by stroke of magic, that the image was projected?

The presence that rose thus so strangely beside the waters, is expressive of what in the ways of a thousand years men had come to desire. Hers is the head upon which all "the ends of the world are come,"[4] and the eyelids are a little weary. It is a beauty wrought out from within upon the flesh, the deposit, little cell by cell, of strange thoughts and fantastic reveries and exquisite passions. Set it for a moment beside one of those white Greek goddesses or beautiful women of antiquity, and how would they be troubled by this beauty, into which the soul with all its maladies has passed! All the thoughts and experience of the world have etched and molded there, in that which they have of power to refine and make expressive the outward form, the animalism of Greece, the lust of Rome, the mysticism of the Middle Age with its spiritual ambition and

1. Or *Mona Lisa*, the famous painting by Leonardo da Vinci (1452–1519) that now hangs in the Louvre in Paris. The sitter for the portrait may have been Lisa, the third wife of the Florentine Francesco del Giocondo (to whom Pater refers as "Il Giocondo")—hence her title, La Gioconda. *Mona* (more correctly *Monna*) *Lisa* means "Madonna Lisa" or "My Lady Lisa." This selection is drawn from the essay on Leonardo.
2. Andrea del Verrocchio (1435–1488), Florentine painter and sculptor. Giorgio Vasari (1511–1574), author of *Lives of the Most Excellent Italian Painters* (1550).
3. Mimics or clowns.
4. 1 Corinthians 10.11.

imaginative loves, the return of the Pagan world, the sins of the Borgias.[5] She is older than the rocks among which she sits; like the vampire, she has been dead many times, and learned the secrets of the grave; and has been a diver in deep seas, and keeps their fallen day about her; and trafficked for strange webs with Eastern merchants, and, as Leda, was the mother of Helen of Troy,[6] and, as Saint Anne, the mother of Mary; and all this has been to her but as the sound of lyres and flutes, and lives only in the delicacy with which it has molded the changing lineaments, and tinged the eyelids and the hands. The fancy of a perpetual life, sweeping together ten thousand experiences, is an old one; and modern philosophy has conceived the idea of humanity as wrought upon by, and summing up in itself, all modes of thought and life. Certainly Lady Lisa might stand as the embodiment of the old fancy, the symbol of the modern idea.

Conclusion[7]

Λέγει που Ἡράκλειτος ὅτι πάντα χωρεῖ καὶ οὐδὲν μένει[8]

To regard all things and principles of things as inconstant modes or fashions has more and more become the tendency of modern thought. Let us begin with that which is without—our physical life. Fix upon it in one of its more exquisite intervals, the moment, for instance, of delicious recoil from the flood of water in summer heat. What is the whole physical life in that moment but a combination of natural elements to which science gives their names? But those elements, phosphorus and lime and delicate fibers, are present not in the human body alone: we detect them in places most remote from it. Our physical life is a perpetual motion of them—the passage of the blood, the waste and repairing of the lenses of the eye, the modification of the tissues of the brain under every ray of light and sound—processes which science reduces to simpler and more elementary forces. Like the elements of which we are composed, the action of these forces extends beyond us: it rusts iron and ripens corn.[9] Far out on every side of us those elements are broadcast, driven in many currents; and birth and gesture and death and the springing of violets from the grave are but a few out of ten thousand resultant combinations. That clear, perpetual outline of face and limb is but an image of ours, under which we group them—a design in a web, the actual threads of which pass out beyond it. This at least of flamelike our life has, that it is but the concurrence, renewed from moment to moment, of forces parting sooner or later on their ways.

Or, if we begin with the inward world of thought and feeling, the whirlpool is still more rapid, the flame more eager and devouring. There it is no longer the gradual darkening of the eye, the gradual fading of color from the wall— movements of the shore-side, where the water flows down indeed, though in apparent rest—but the race of the midstream, a drift of momentary acts of sight and passion and thought. At first sight experience seems to bury us under

5. A powerful Italian family during the Renaissance, notorious for scandalous conduct.
6. Helen's father was Zeus (who approached Leda in the form of a swan).
7. This brief "Conclusion" was omitted in the second edition of this book, as I conceived it might possibly mislead some of those young men into whose hands it might fall. On the whole, I have thought it best to reprint it here, with some slight changes which bring it closer to my original meaning. I have dealt more fully in *Marius the Epicurean* with the thoughts suggested by it [Pater's note to the 3rd edition, 1888].
8. Heraclitus says, "All things give way; nothing remaineth" [Pater's translation]. The Greek philosopher was active ca. 500 B.C.E.
9. Grain.

a flood of external objects, pressing upon us with a sharp and importunate reality, calling us out of ourselves in a thousand forms of action. But when reflection begins to play upon those objects they are dissipated under its influence; the cohesive force seems suspended like some trick of magic; each object is loosed into a group of impressions—colour, odour, texture—in the mind of the observer. And if we continue to dwell in thought on this world, not of objects in the solidity with which language invests them, but of impressions, unstable, flickering, inconsistent, which burn and are extinguished with our consciousness of them, it contracts still further: the whole scope of observation is dwarfed into the narrow chamber of the individual mind. Experience, already reduced to a group of impressions, is ringed round for each one of us by that thick wall of personality through which no real voice has ever pierced on its way to us, or from us to that which we can only conjecture to be without. Every one of those impressions is the impression of the individual in his isolation, each mind keeping as a solitary prisoner its own dream of a world. Analysis goes a step farther still, and assures us that those impressions of the individual mind to which, for each one of us, experience dwindles down, are in perpetual flight; that each of them is limited by time, and that as time is infinitely divisible, each of them is infinitely divisible also; all that is actual in it being a single moment, gone while we try to apprehend it, of which it may ever be more truly said that it has ceased to be than that it is. To such a tremulous wisp constantly reforming itself on the stream, to a single sharp impression, with a sense in it, a relic more or less fleeting, of such moments gone by, what is real in our life fines itself down. It is with this movement, with the passage and dissolution of impressions, images, sensations, that analysis leaves off—that continual vanishing away, that strange, perpetual weaving and unweaving of ourselves.

Philosophiren, says Novalis, *ist dephlegmatisiren, vivificiren.*[1] The service of philosophy, of speculative culture, towards the human spirit is to rouse, to startle it to a life of constant and eager observation. Every moment some form grows perfect in hand or face; some tone on the hills or the sea is choicer than the rest; some mood of passion or insight or intellectual excitement is irresistibly real and attractive to us—for that moment only. Not the fruit of experience, but experience itself, is the end. A counted number of pulses only is given to us of a variegated, dramatic life. How may we see in them all that is to be seen in them by the finest senses? How shall we pass most swiftly from point to point, and be present always at the focus where the greatest number of vital forces unite in their purest energy?

To burn always with this hard, gemlike flame, to maintain this ecstasy, is success in life. In a sense it might even be said that our failure is to form habits: for, after all, habit is relative to a stereotyped world, and meantime it is only the roughness of the eye that makes any two persons, things, situations, seem alike. While all melts under our feet, we may well grasp at any exquisite passion, or any contribution to knowledge that seems by a lifted horizon to set the spirit free for a moment, or any stirring of the senses, strange dyes, strange colours, and curious odours, or work of the artist's hands, or the face of one's friend. Not to discriminate every moment some passionate attitude in those about us, and in the very brilliancy of their gifts some tragic dividing of forces on their ways, is, on this short day of frost and sun, to sleep before evening.

1. To philosophize is to cast off inertia, to make oneself alive (German). "Novalis" was the pseudonym of Friedrich von Hardenberg (1772–1801), German Romantic writer.

With this sense of the splendour of our experience and of its awful[2] brevity, gathering all we are into one desperate effort to see and touch, we shall hardly have time to make theories about the things we see and touch. What we have to do is to be forever curiously testing new opinions and courting new impressions, never acquiescing in a facile orthodoxy of Comte, or of Hegel,[3] or of our own. Philosophical theories or ideas, as points of view, instruments of criticism, may help us to gather up what might otherwise pass unregarded by us. "Philosophy is the microscope of thought." The theory or idea or system which requires of us the sacrifice of any part of this experience, in consideration of some interest into which we cannot enter, or some abstract theory we have not identified with ourselves, or of what is only conventional, has no real claim upon us.

One of the most beautiful passages of Rousseau[4] is that in the sixth book of the *Confessions*, where he describes the awakening in him of the literary sense. An undefinable taint of death had clung always about him, and now in early manhood he believed himself smitten by mortal disease. He asked himself how he might make as much as possible of the interval that remained; and he was not biased by anything in his previous life when he decided that it must be by intellectual excitement, which he found just then in the clear, fresh writings of Voltaire. Well! we are all *condamnés* as Victor Hugo[5] says: we are all under sentence of death but with a sort of indefinite reprieve—*les hommes sont tous condamnés à mort avec des sursis indéfinis:* we have an interval, and then our place knows us no more. Some spend this interval in listlessness, some in high passions, the wisest, at least among "the children of this world,"[6] in art and song. For our one chance lies in expanding that interval, in getting as many pulsations as possible into the given time. Great passions may give us this quickened sense of life, ecstasy and sorrow of love, the various forms of enthusiastic activity, disinterested or otherwise, which come naturally to many of us. Only be sure it is passion—that it does yield you this fruit of a quickened, multiplied consciousness. Of such wisdom, the poetic passion, the desire of beauty, the love of art for its own sake, has most. For art comes to you proposing frankly to give nothing but the highest quality to your moments as they pass, and simply for those moments' sake.

1868

1873

2. Awe-inspiring.
3. Georg W. F. Hegel (1770–1831), German idealistic philosopher. Auguste Comte (1798–1857), French founder of positivism.
4. Jean-Jacques Rousseau (1712–1778), Swiss-born French political theorist and philosopher; his *Confessions* were published in 1781 and 1788.

5. French novelist and poet (1802–1885). The quotation is taken from his work *Le Dernier Jour d'un Condamné* (*The Last Day of a Condemned Man*, 1832). "Voltaire" was the pen name of the French author and philosopher François-Marie Arouet (1694–1778).
6. Luke 16.8.

GERARD MANLEY HOPKINS
1844–1889

It has been said that the most important date in Gerard Manley Hopkins's career was 1918, twenty-nine years after his death, for it was then that the first publication of his poems made them accessible to the world of readers. During his lifetime these remarkable poems, most of them celebrating the wonders of God's creation, had been known only to a small circle of friends, including his literary executor, the poet Robert Bridges, who waited until 1918 before releasing them to a publisher. Partly because his work was first made public in a twentieth-century volume, but especially because of his striking experiments in meter and diction, Hopkins was widely hailed as a pioneering figure of "modern" literature, miraculously unconnected with his fellow Victorian poets (who during the 1920s and 1930s were largely out of fashion among critical readers). And this way of classifying and evaluating his writings has long persisted. In 1936 a substantial selection of his poems led off *The Faber Book of Modern Verse*, one of the most influential anthologies of the century, featuring poets such as W. H. Auden, Dylan Thomas, and T. S. Eliot (the only one whose selections occupy more pages than those allotted to Hopkins). And the first four editions of *The Norton Anthology of English Literature* (1962–79) grouped Hopkins with these twentieth-century poets. To reclassify him is not to repudiate his earlier reputation as a "modern" but rather to suggest that his work can be better understood and appreciated if it is restored to the Victorian world out of which it developed.

Hopkins was born near London into a large and cultivated family in comfortable circumstances. After a brilliant career at Highgate School, he entered Oxford in 1863, where he was exposed to a variety of Victorian ways of thinking, both secular and religious. Among the influential leaders at Oxford was Matthew Arnold, professor of poetry; but more important for Hopkins was his tutor, Walter Pater, an aesthetician whose emphasis on the intense apprehension of sensuous beauty struck a responsive chord in Hopkins. At Oxford he was also exposed to the Broad Church theology of one of the tutors at his college (Balliol), Benjamin Jowett. But Hopkins became increasingly attracted first to the High Church movement represented at Oxford by Edward Pusey, and then to Roman Catholicism. Profoundly influenced by John Henry Newman's conversion to Rome and by subsequent conversations with Newman, Hopkins entered the Roman Catholic Church in 1866. The estrangement from his family that resulted from his conversion was very painful for him; his parents' letters to him were so "terrible" (he reported to Newman) that he could not bear to "read them twice." And this alienation was heightened by his decision not only to become a Roman Catholic but to become a priest and, in particular, a Jesuit priest, for many Victorian Protestants regarded the Jesuit order with a special distrust. For the rest of his life, Hopkins served as a priest and teacher in various places, among them Oxford, Liverpool, and Lancashire. In 1884 he was appointed professor of classics at University College in Dublin.

At school and at Oxford in the early 1860s, Hopkins had written poems in the vein of John Keats. He burned most of these early writings after his conversion (although drafts survive), for he believed that his vocation must require renouncing such personal satisfactions as the writing of poems. Only after his superiors in the church encouraged him to do so did he resume writing poetry. Yet during the seven years of silence, as his letters show, he had been thinking about experimenting with what he called a "new rhythm." The result, in 1876, was his rhapsodic lyric-narrative, "The Wreck of the Deutschland," a long ode about the wreck of a ship in which five Franciscan nuns were drowned. The style of the poem was so distinctive that the editor of the Jesuit magazine to which he had submitted it "dared not print it," as Hopkins reported. During the remaining fourteen years of his life, Hopkins wrote poems but seldom submitted them for publication, partly because he was convinced that poetic fame was incompatible with his religious vocation but also because of a fear that readers would be discouraged by the eccentricity of his work.

Hopkins's sense of his own uniqueness is in accord with the larger philosophy that informs his poetry. Drawing on the theology of Duns Scotus, a medieval philosopher, he felt that everything in the universe was characterized by what he called *inscape*, the distinctive design that constitutes individual identity. This identity is not static but dynamic. Each being in the universe "selves," that is, enacts its identity. And the human being, the most highly selved, the most individually distinctive being in the universe, recognizes the inscape of other beings in an act that Hopkins calls *instress,* the apprehension of an object in an intense thrust of energy toward it that enables one to realize its specific distinctiveness. Ultimately, the instress of inscape leads one to Christ, for the individual identity of any object is the stamp of divine creation on it. In the act of instress, therefore, the human being becomes a celebrant of the divine, at once recognizing God's creation and enacting his or her own God-given identity within it.

Poetry for Hopkins enacts this celebration. It is instress, and it realizes the inscape of its subject in its own distinctive design. Hopkins wrote, "But as air, melody, is what strikes me most of all in music and design in painting, so design, pattern or what I am in the habit of calling 'inscape' is what I above all aim at in poetry." To create inscape, Hopkins seeks to give each poem a unique design that captures the initial inspiration when he is "caught" by his subject. Many of the characteristics of Hopkins's style—his disruption of conventional syntax, his coining and compounding of words, his use of ellipsis and repetition—can be understood as ways of representing the stress and action of the brain in moments of inspiration. He creates compounds to represent the unique interlocking of the characteristics of an object—"piece-bright," "dapple-dawn-drawn," "blue-bleak." He omits syntactical connections to fuse qualities more intensely—"the dearest freshness deep down things." He creates puns to suggest how God's creation rhymes and chimes in a divine patterning. He violates conventional syntactic order to represent the shape of mental experience. In the act of imaginative apprehension, a language particular to the moment generates itself.

Hopkins also uses a new rhythm to give each poem its distinctive design. In the new metric system he created, which he called *sprung rhythm,* lines have a given number of stresses, but the number and placement of unstressed syllables is highly variable. Hopkins rarely marks all the intended stresses, only those that readers might not anticipate. To indicate stressed syllables, Hopkins often uses both the stress (´) and the "great stress" (˝). A curved line marks an "outride"—one or more syllables added to a foot but not counted in the scansion of the line; they indicate a stronger stress on the preceding syllable and a short pause after the outride. Here, for example, is the scansion for the first three lines of "The Windhover":

> I caúght this mórning mórning's mínion, kíng-
> dom of dáylight's daúphin, dapple-dawn-drawn Fálcon, in his ríding
> Of the rólling level underneáth him steady aír, and stríding

Hopkins argued that sprung rhythm was the natural rhythm of common speech and written prose, as well as of music. He found a model for it in Old English poetry and in nursery rhymes, but he claimed that it had not been used in English poetry since the Elizabethan age.

The density and difficulty that result from Hopkins's unconventional rhythm and syntax make his poetry seem modern, but his concern with the imagination's shaping of the natural world puts him very much in the Romantic tradition; and his creation of a rough and difficult style, designed to capture the mind's own motion, resembles the style of Robert Browning. "A horrible thing has happened to me," Hopkins wrote in 1864, "I have begun to *doubt* Tennyson." He criticizes Tennyson for using the grand style as a smooth and habitual poetic speech. Like Algernon Charles Swinburne, Walter Pater, and Henry James as well as Browning, Hopkins displays a new mannerism, characteristic of the latter part of the nineteenth century, which paradoxically combines an elaborate aestheticism with a more complex representation of consciousness.

In Hopkins's early poetry his singular apprehension of the beauty of individual objects always brings him to an ecstatic illumination of the presence of God. But in his late poems, the so-called terrible sonnets, his distinctive individuality comes to isolate him from the God who made him thus. Hopkins wrote, "To me there is no resemblance: searching nature, I taste *self* but at one tankard, that of my own being."

In the terrible sonnets Hopkins confronts the solipsism to which his own stress on individuality seems to lead him. Like the mad speakers of so many Victorian dramatic monologues, he cannot escape a world solely of his own imagining. Yet even these poems of despair, which simultaneously echo the bleaker side of the Romantic tradition and anticipate more modern attitudes, reflect a traditional religious vision: the dark night of the soul as described by the Spanish mystic Saint John of the Cross.

In his introduction to *The Oxford Book of Modern Verse*, Yeats calls Hopkins's poetry "a last development of poetical diction." Yeats's remark indicates the anomaly that Hopkins's work poses. Perhaps it is only appropriate for a writer who stressed the uniqueness of inscape to strike us with the individuality of his achievement.

God's Grandeur

The world is charged with the grandeur of God.
It will flame out, like shining from shook foil;[1]
It gathers to a greatness, like the ooze of oil
Crushed.[2] Why do men then now not reck his rod?
5 Generations have trod, have trod, have trod;
And all is seared with trade; bleared, smeared with toil;
And wears man's smudge and shares man's smell: the soil
Is bare now, nor can foot feel, being shod.

And for° all this, nature is never spent;   *despite*
10   There lives the dearest freshness deep down things;
And though the last lights off the black West went
Oh, morning, at the brown brink eastward, springs—
Because the Holy Ghost over the bent
World broods with warm breast and with ah! bright wings.

1877   1918

The Starlight Night

Look at the stars! look, look up at the skies!
O look at all the fire-folk sitting in the air!
The bright boroughs, the circle-citadels there!
Down in dim woods the diamond delves!° the elves'-eyes!   *quarries*
5 The grey lawns cold where gold, where quickgold;[1] lies!
Wind-beat whitebeam! airy abeles° set on a flare!   *white poplars*
Flake-doves sent floating forth at a farmyard scare!—
Ah well! it is all a purchase, all is a prize.

Buy then! bid then!—What?—Prayer, patience, alms, vows.
10   Look, look: a May-mess,[2] like on orchard boughs!

---

1. Hopkins explained this image in a letter: "I mean foil in its sense of leaf or tinsel. . . . Shaken goldfoil gives off broad glares like sheet lightning and also, and this is true of nothing else, owing to its zigzag dints and creasings and network of small many cornered facets, a sort of fork lightning too."

2. I.e., from the crushing of olives.
1. Coined by analogy with quicksilver. The starlight night resembles the lawns below it, where the dew, reflecting the starlight, looks like gold.
2. A profusion of growing things such as May blossoms.

Look! March-bloom, like on mealed-with-yellow sallows![3]
These are indeed the barn; withindoors house
The shocks. This piece-bright paling[4] shuts the spouse
Christ home, Christ and his mother and all his hallows.° saints

1877   1918

As Kingfishers Catch Fire

As kingfishers catch fire, dragonflies draw flame;
  As tumbled over rim in roundy wells
  Stones ring; like each tucked° string tells, each hung bell's plucked
Bow swung finds tongue to fling out broad its name;
5 Each mortal thing does one thing and the same:
  Deals out that being indoors° each one dwells; within
  Selves[1]—goes itself; *myself* it speaks and spells,
Crying *What I do is me: for that I came.*

I say more: the just man justices;[2]
10   Keeps gráce: thát keeps all his goings graces;
Acts in God's eye what in God's eye he is—
  Chríst. For Christ plays in ten thousand places,
Lovely in limbs, and lovely in eyes not his
  To the Father through the features of men's faces.

1877   1918

Spring

Nothing is so beautiful as Spring—
  When weeds, in wheels, shoot long and lovely and lush;
  Thrush's eggs look little low heavens, and thrush
Through the echoing timber does so rinse and wring
5 The ear, it strikes like lightnings to hear him sing;
  The glassy peartree leaves and blooms, they brush
  The descending blue; that blue is all in a rush
With richness; the racing lambs too have fair their fling.

What is all this juice and all this joy?
10   A strain of the earth's sweet being in the beginning
In Eden garden.—Have, get, before it cloy,
  Before it cloud, Christ, lord, and sour with sinning,
Innocent mind and Mayday in girl and boy,
  Most, O maid's child,[1] thy choice and worthy the winning.

1877   1918

3. Willows, here with yellow spots like meal.
4. Picket fence. "Shocks": sheaves of grain.
1. Fulfills its individuality.

2. Acts in a just manner.
1. Jesus, son of the Virgin Mary.

The Windhover[1]

To Christ our Lord

I caught this morning morning's minion,° king-   *darling*
   dom of daylight's dauphin,[2] dapple-dawn-drawn Falcon, in his riding
   Of the rolling level underneath him steady air, and striding
High there, how he rung upon the rein of a wimpling[3] wing
5   In his ecstasy! then off, off forth on swing,
   As a skate's heel sweeps smooth on a bow-bend: the hurl and gliding
   Rebuffed the big wind. My heart in hiding
Stirred for a bird,—the achieve of, the mastery of the thing!

Brute beauty and valour and act, oh, air, pride, plume, here
10   Buckle![4] AND the fire that breaks from thee then, a billion
Times told lovelier, more dangerous, O my chevalier!°   *knight*

No wonder of it: shéer plód makes plough down sillion[5]
Shine, and blue-bleak embers, ah my dear,
Fall, gall[6] themselves, and gash gold-vermilion.

1877   1918

Pied[1] Beauty

Glory be to God for dappled things—
   For skies of couple-colour as a brinded[2] cow;
      For rose-moles all in stipple upon trout that swim;
Fresh-firecoal chestnut-falls,[3] finches' wings;
5   Landscape plotted and pieced—fold, fallow, and plough;[4]
      And áll trádes, their gear and tackle and trim.°   *equipment*

All things counter, original, spare,[5] strange;
   Whatever is fickle, freckled (who knows how?)
      With swift, slow; sweet, sour; adazzle, dim;
10   He fathers-forth whose beauty is past change:
              Praise him.

1877   1918

1. Kestrel, a small falcon noted for hovering in the air.
2. A prince who is heir to the French throne.
3. Rippling. "Rung upon the rein": circled at the end of a rein.
4. The verb can be read as imperative or indicative. All three meanings are relevant: to prepare for action, to fasten together, to collapse.
5. The ridge between two furrows of a plowed field.
6. Break the surface of.
1. Of two or more colors in blotches, variegated.
2. Brownish orange in color with streaks of gray.
3. I.e., freshly fallen chestnuts, bright as coals.
4. Divided into fields used as pastures ("fold"), lying fallow, or plowed for cultivation. The landscape thus appears like patches of different colors.
5. Rare. "Counter": contrary.

Hurrahing in Harvest

Summer ends now; now, barbarous in beauty, the stooks[1] rise
Around; up above, what wind-walks! what lovely behaviour
Of silk-sack clouds! has wilder, wilful-wavier
Meal-drift moulded ever and melted across skies?

5   I walk, I lift up, I lift up heart, eyes,
Down all that glory in the heavens to glean our Saviour;
And, éyes, heárt, what looks, what lips yet gave you a
Rapturous love's greeting of realer, of rounder replies?

And the azurous hung hills are his world-wielding shoulder
10   Majestic—as a stallion stalwart, very-violet-sweet!—
These things, these things were here and but the beholder
Wanting; which two when they once meet,
The heart rears wings bold and bolder
And hurls for him, O half hurls earth for him off under his feet.

1877   1918

Binsey Poplars

felled 1879

My aspens dear, whose airy cages quelled,
Quelled or quenched in leaves the leaping sun,
All felled, felled, are all felled;
       Of a fresh and following folded rank
5   Not spared, not one
             That dandled a sandalled
       Shadow that swam or sank
On meadow and river and wind-wandering
       weed-winding bank.

10   O if we but knew what we do
       When we delve° or hew—   *dig*
     Hack and rack° the growing green!   *torture*
       Since country is so tender
       To touch, her being só slender,
15   That, like this sleek and seeing ball°   *the eye*
     But a prick will make no eye at all,

       Where we, even where we mean
         To mend her we end her,
         When we hew or delve:
20   After-comers cannot guess the beauty been.
       Ten or twelve, only ten or twelve
       Strokes of havoc únselve°   *rob of self*

1. Sheaves of grain.

The sweet especial scene,
Rural scene, a rural scene,
25   Sweet especial rural scene.

1879   1918

Duns Scotus's Oxford[1]

Towery city and branchy between towers;
Cuckoo-echoing, bell-swarmèd, lark-charmèd, rook-racked, river-rounded;
The dapple-eared lily below thee; that country and town did
Once encounter in, here coped and poisèd powers;

5   Thou hast a base and brickish skirt there, sours
That neighbour-nature thy grey beauty is grounded
Best in;[2] graceless growth, thou hast confounded
Rural rural keeping—folk, flocks, and flowers.

Yet ah! this air I gather and I release
10 He lived on; these weeds and waters, these walls are what
He haunted who of all men most sways my spirits to peace;

Of realty° the rarest-veinèd unraveller; a not   *reality*
Rivalled insight, be rival Italy or Greece;
Who fired France for Mary without spot.[3]

1879   1918

Felix Randal

Felix Randal the farrier,° O is he dead then? my duty   *blacksmith*
    all ended,
Who have watched his mould of man, big-boned and hardy-handsome
Pining, pining, till time when reason rambled in it and some
Fatal four disorders, fleshed there, all contended?

5   Sickness broke him. Impatient, he cursed at first, but mended
Being anointed[1] and all; though a heavenlier heart began some
Months earlier, since I had our sweet reprieve and ransom[2]
Tendered to him. Ah well, God rest him all road ever[3] he offended!

1. Duns Scotus, the medieval theologian, lectured at Oxford about 1301. His idea that individuality is the final perfection of any creature influenced Hopkins's conception of inscape. When Hopkins came on two of Scotus's commentaries in 1872, he wrote that he was immediately "flush with a new stroke of enthusiasm . . . when I took in any inscape of the sky or sea I thought of Scotus."
2. Hopkins contrasts the "here" of the "grey beauty" of the medieval city of Oxford, where country and town are both protected ("coped," as within a priest's cloak) and in equilibrium ("poisèd powers"), with the "there" of its new surburban "brickish skirt": housing developments and industrial complexes that were built around the perimeter of the city in the 19th century.
3. In Paris, Scotus was influential in defending the doctrine of the Immaculate Conception—i.e., that Mary was born without original sin.
1. In Extreme Unction (the sacrament for the dying.)
2. Holy Communion preceded by confession and absolution.
3. In whatever way.

This seeing the sick endears them to us, us too it endears.
10 My tongue had taught thee comfort, touch had quenched thy tears,
Thy tears that touched my heart, child, Felix, poor Felix Randal;
How far from then forethought of, all thy more boisterous years,
When thou at the random⁴ grim forge, powerful amidst peers,
Didst fettle° for the great grey drayhorse his bright and battering   *prepare*
sandal!

1880   1918

Spring and Fall:¹

to a young child

Márgarét, áre you gríeving
Over Goldengrove unleaving?
Leáves, líke the things of man, you
With your fresh thoughts care for, can you?
5 Áh! ás the heart grows older
It will come to such sights colder
By and by, nor spare a sigh
Though worlds of wanwood leafmeal² lie;
And yet you *will* weep and know why.
10 Now no matter, child, the name:
Sórrow's spríngs áre the same.
Nor mouth had, no nor mind, expressed
What heart heard of, ghost° guessed: *spirit*
It ís the blight man was born for,
15 It is Margaret you mourn for.

1880   1918

[Carrion Comfort]¹

Not, I'll not, carrion comfort, Despair, not feast on thee,²
Not untwist—slack they may be—these last strands of man
In me ór, most weary, cry *I can no more*. I can;
Can something, hope, wish day come, not choose not to be.

5 But ah, but O thou terrible, why wouldst thou rude on me
Thy wring-world right foot rock?³ lay a lionlimb against me?
scan

4. Built with stones of irregular size and shape.
1. This deceptively simple poem is deeply informed by Christian theology: according to Catholic doctrine, the fall of Adam and Eve brought into the world both mortality and the legacy of Original Sin for all human beings ("the blight man was born for").
2. Coined by analogy with piecemeal. "Wanwood": pale or dim; the forest may be pale because of light-colored autumn leaves or dim because light is filtered through the leaves.

1. This title was supplied by Bridges. The poem is one of the "terrible sonnets," as are the three following poems.
2. The satisfaction of giving in to despair as a kind of "comfort" is implicitly likened to a vulture's satisfaction in feasting on dead flesh.
3. I.e., why would you roughly rock me with your world-wringing right foot?

With darksome devouring eyes my bruisèd bones? and fan,
O in turns of tempest, me heaped there; me frantic to avoid
    thee and flee?

Why? That my chaff might fly; my grain lie,[4] sheer and clear.
10 Nay in all that toil, that coil,° since (seems) I kissed the rod,   *tumult*
Hand rather,[5] my heart lo! lapped strength, stole joy, would
    laugh, chéer.
Cheer whom though? The Hero whose heaven-handling
    flung me, fóot tród
Me? or me that fought him? O which one? is it each one?
    That night, that year
Of now done darkness I wretch lay wrestling with (my God!)
    my God.

1885   1918

No worst, there is none

No worst, there is none. Pitched past pitch of grief,
More pangs will, schooled at forepangs, wilder wring.
Comforter, where, where is your comforting?
Mary, mother of us, where is your relief?

5   My cries heave, herds-long;[1] huddle in a main, a chief-
woe, world-sorrow; on an age-old anvil wince and sing—
Then lull, then leave off. Fury had shrieked "No ling-
ering! Let me be fell: force[2] I must be brief."
O the mind, mind has mountains; cliffs of fall
10 Frightful, sheer, no-man-fathomed. Hold them cheap
May who ne'er hung there. Nor does long our small
Durance° deal with that steep or deep. Here! creep,   *endurance*
Wretch, under a comfort serves in a whirlwind: all
Life death does end and each day dies with sleep.

1885   1918

I wake and feel the fell of dark, not day

I wake and feel the fell° of dark, not day.   *bitterness*
What hours, O what black hoúrs we have spent
This night! what sights you, heart, saw; ways you went!
And more must, in yet longer light's delay.

5   With witness I speak this. But where I say
Hours I mean years, mean life. And my lament

4. Metaphors of winnowing, or removing the empty husks ("chaff") that are blown away from the valuable grain that remains, appear frequently in the Bible to represent the separation of virtue from wickedness. See, e.g., Psalm 1.4, Luke 3.16–17.
5. I.e., the hand that wields the rod.
1. Like the succession of cries made by cattle that have been following one another in a long line.
2. Necessarily, inevitably. "Fell": fierce.

Is cries countless, cries like dead letters[1] sent
To dearest him that lives alas! away.

I am gall, I am heartburn. God's most deep decree
10 Bitter would have me taste: my taste was me;
Bones built in me, flesh filled, blood brimmed the curse.

Selfyeast of spirit a dull dough sours. I see
The lost are like this, and their scourge to be
As I am mine, their sweating selves; but worse.

1885   1918

That Nature Is a Heraclitean Fire[1] and of the Comfort of the Resurrection

Cloud-puffball, torn tufts, tossed pillows | flaunt forth, then chevy°   *race*
    on an air-
built thoroughfare: heaven-roysterers,° in gay-gangs | they   *swaggerers*
    throng; they glitter in marches.
Down roughcast, down dazzling whitewash, | wherever an elm arches.
Shivelights and shadowtackle[2] in long | lashes lace, lance, and pair.
5 Delightfully the bright wind boisterous | ropes, wrestles, beats earth bare
Of yestertempest's creases; in pool and rut peel parches[3]
Squandering ooze to squeezed | dough, crust, dust; stanches, starches
Squadroned masks and manmarks[4] | treadmire toil there
Footfretted in it. Million-fuelèd, | nature's bonfire burns on.
10 But quench her bonniest, dearest | to her, her clearest-selvèd°   *most individual*
    spark
Man, how fast his firedint | his mark on mind, is gone!
Both are in an unfathomable, all is in an enormous dark
Drowned. O pity and indig | nation! Manshape, that shone
Sheer off, disseveral,° a star, | death blots black out; nor mark   *separate*
15   Is any of him at all so stark
But vastness blurs and time | beats level. Enough! the Resurrection,
A heart's-clarion! Away grief's gasping, | joyless days, dejection.
        Across my foundering deck shone
A beacon, an eternal beam. | Flesh fade, and mortal trash
20 Fall to the residuary worm; | world's wildfire, leave but ash:
        In a flash, at a trumpet crash,
I am all at once what Christ is, | since he was what I am, and
This Jack, joke, poor potsherd, | patch, matchwood,[5] immortal diamond,
        Is immortal diamond.

1888   1918

---

1. Letters undelivered or returned to the sender by the post office.
1. The Greek philosopher Heraclitus (fl. ca. 500 B.C.E.) taught that all things are in flux and that they ultimately return to the basic principle of fire.
2. Branches imagined as the shadows of a ship's

rigging. "Shivelights": strips of light.
3. Ruts described as peeled places. "Parches" is a verb whose subject is *wind*.
4. The marks that people have made on the earth by walking ("footfretted") on it.
5. Kindling. "Jack": ordinary man.

Thou art indeed just, Lord

*Justus quidem tu es, Domine, si disputem tecum; verumtamen justa
loquar ad te: Quare via impiorum prosperatur? &c.*[1]

Thou art indeed just, Lord, if I contend
With thee; but, sir, so what I plead is just.
Why do sinners' ways prosper? and why must
Disappointment all I endeavour end?

5 Wert thou my enemy, O thou my friend,
How wouldst thou worse, I wonder, than thou dost
Defeat, thwart me? Oh, the sots and thralls of lust
Do in spare hours more thrive than I that spend,

Sir, life upon thy cause. See, banks and brakes°   *thickets*
10 Now, leavèd how thick! lacèd they are again
With fretty chervil,[2] look, and fresh wind shakes

Them; birds build—but not I build; no, but strain,
Time's eunuch, and not breed one work that wakes.
Mine, O thou lord of life, send my roots rain.

1889   1918

From Journal[1]

May 3 [1866]. Cold. Morning raw and wet, afternoon fine. Walked then
with Addis, crossing Bablock Hythe, round by Skinner's Weir[2] through many
fields into the Witney road. Sky sleepy blue without liquidity. From Cumnor
Hill saw St. Philip's and the other spires through blue haze rising pale in a
pink light. On further side of the Witney road hills, just fleeced with grain or
other green growth, by their dips and waves foreshortened here and there and
so differenced in brightness and opacity the green on them, with delicate
effect. On left, brow of the near hill glistening with very bright newly turned
sods and a scarf of vivid green slanting away beyond the skyline, against which
the clouds shewed the slightest tinge of rose or purple. Copses in grey-red or
grey-yellow—the tinges immediately forerunning the opening of full leaf.
Meadows skirting Seven-bridge road voluptuous green. Some oaks are out in
small leaf. Ashes not out, only tufted with their fringy blooms. Hedges
springing richly. Elms in small leaf, with more or less opacity. White poplars
most beautiful in small grey crisp spray-like leaf. Cowslips capriciously colouring meadows in creamy drifts. Bluebells, purple orchis. Over the green

1. "Righteous art thou, O Lord, when I plead with
thee: yet let me talk with thee of thy judgments:
Wherefore doth the way of the wicked prosper?"
(Jeremiah 12.1). The Latin was Hopkins's title.
2. A kind of herb, related to parsley.
1. With the exception of one year, Hopkins kept a
journal from May 1866 to Feb. 1875. Its most
interesting entries are minutely observed descriptions of natural phenomena, which reveal the char-

acter of his imagination. The brackets and
abbreviations are Hopkins's.
2. Dam. William E. Addis (1844–1917), friend of
Hopkins at Oxford; like him he became a Catholic
convert and priest. The places mentioned are
around Oxford. Compare Matthew Arnold's evocation of this same landscape in "The Scholar
Gypsy" (p. 1361).

water of the river passing the slums of the town and under its bridges swallows shooting, blue and purple above and shewing their amber-tinged breasts reflected in the water, their flight unsteady with wagging wings and leaning first to one side then the other. Peewits flying. Towards sunset the sky partly swept, as often, with moist white cloud, tailing off across which are morsels of grey-black woolly clouds. Sun seemed to make a bright liquid hole in this, its texture had an upward northerly sweep or drift from the W, marked softly in grey. Dog violets. Eastward after sunset range of clouds rising in bulky heads moulded softly in tufts or bunches of snow—so it looks—and membered somewhat elaborately, rose-coloured. Notice often imperfect fairy rings. Apple and other fruit trees blossomed beautifully.

✻   ✻   ✻

Feb.—1870. One day in the Long Retreat (which ended on Xmas Day) they were reading in the refectory Sister Emmerich's account[3] of the Agony in the Garden[4] and I suddenly began to cry and sob and could not stop. I put it down for this reason, that if I had been asked a minute beforehand I should have said that nothing of the sort was going to happen and even when it did I stood in a manner wondering at myself not seeing in my reason the traces of an adequate cause for such strong emotion—the traces of it I say because of course the cause in itself is adequate for the sorrow of a lifetime. I remember much the same thing on Maundy Thursday when the presanctified Host[5] was carried to the sacristy. But neither the weight nor the stress of sorrow, that is to say of the thing which should cause sorrow, by themselves move us or bring the tears as a sharp knife does not cut for being pressed as long as it is pressed without any shaking of the hand but there is always one touch, something striking sideways and unlooked for, which in both cases undoes resistance and pierces, and this may be so delicate that the pathos seems to have gone directly to the body and cleared the understanding in its passage. On the other hand the pathetic touch by itself, as in dramatic pathos, will only draw slight tears if its matter is not important or not of import to us, the strong emotion coming from a force which was gathered before it was discharged: in this way a knife may pierce the flesh which it had happened only to graze and only grazing will go no deeper.

✻   ✻   ✻

May 18 [1870].—Great brilliancy and projection: the eye seemed to fall perpendicular from level to level along our trees, the nearer and further Park; all things hitting the sense with double but direct instress. ✻ ✻ ✻

This was later. One day when the bluebells were in bloom I wrote the following. I do not think I have ever seen anything more beautiful than the bluebell I have been looking at. I know the beauty of our Lord by it. It[s inscape] is [mixed of] strength and grace, like an ash [tree]. The head is strongly drawn over [backwards] and arched down like a cutwater[6] [drawing itself back from the line of the keel.] The lines of the bells strike and overlie this, rayed but not symmetrically, some lie parallel. They look steely against [the] paper, the shades lying between the bells and behind the cockled petal-

3. *The Dolorous Passion of Our Lord Jesus Christ; from the Meditations of Anne Catherine Emmerich*, an Augustinian nun (1774–1824).
4. Luke 22.39–44.

5. The bread wafer sanctified for Holy Communion. "Maundy Thursday": the Thursday before Easter, day of the Last Supper.
6. The forward edge of a ship's prow.

ends and nursing up the precision of their distinctness, the petal-ends themselves being delicately lit. Then there is the straightness of the trumpets in the
bells softened by the slight entasis⁷ and [by] the square splay of the mouth.
One bell, the lowest, some way detached and carried on a longer footstalk,
touched out with the tips of the petals on oval / not like the rest in a plane
perpendicular of the axis of the bell but a little atilt, and so with [the] square-
in-rounding turns of the petals.

*   *   *

Aug. 10 [1872].—I was looking at high waves. The breakers always are
parallel to the coast and shape themselves to it except where the curve is sharp
however the wind blows. They are rolled out by the shallowing shore just as a
piece of putty between the palms whatever its shape runs into a long roll. The
slant ruck⁸ or crease one sees in them shows the way of the wind. The regularity of the barrels surprised and charmed the eye; the edge behind the comb
or crest was as smooth and bright as glass. It may be noticed to be green behind
and silver white in front: the silver marks where the air begins, the pure white
is foam, the green / solid water. Then looked at to the right or left they are
scrolled over like mouldboards⁹ or feathers or jibsails seen by the edge. It is
pretty to see the hollow of the barrel disappearing as the white combs on each
side run along the wave gaining ground till the two meet at a pitch and crush
and overlap each other.
About all the turns of the scaping from the break and flooding of wave to
its run out again I have not yet satisfied myself. The shores are swimming and
the eyes have before them a region of milky surf but it is hard for them to
unpack the huddling and gnarls of the water and law out the shapes and the
sequence of the running: I catch however the looped or forked wisp made by
every big pebble the backwater runs over—if it were clear and smooth there
would be a network from their overlapping, such as can in fact be seen on
smooth sand after the tide is out—; then I saw it run browner, the foam
dwindling and twitched into long chains of suds, while the strength of the
back-draught shrugged the stones together and clocked them one against
another.

1959

---

7. Outward curvature.   9. Curved iron plates attached to plowshares.
8. Fold or crease.

Light Verse

The Victorian era produced a remarkable outburst of humorous prose and verse from the time of Charles Dickens's *Pickwick Papers* (1836–37) at the beginning of the period to the operas of W.S. Gilbert and Sir Arthur Sullivan near the end. The following selections provide examples of two varieties of Victorian light verse. One, represented by Gilbert, makes lighthearted mockery of institutions such as the Court of Chancery and marriage, as well as prevalent cultural trends and styles. This burlesque mode, employed to poke fun at a host of social and political issues and figures, can also be found in the pages of *Punch*, a humorous and satirical magazine that began publication in 1841. Although exaggeration and absurdity are important ingredients in these writings, the comic worlds they create are still recognizably related to the ordinary world.

The other variety is a more distinctive Victorian specialty, nonsense writing, represented here by compositions by Edward Lear and Lewis Carroll. Originally intended for children, these playful writings have often been equally relished by adults. In the twentieth century Carroll's *Alice* books in particular proved especially attractive to psychoanalytically minded readers; those interested in literary parody, philosophical speculation, and linguistic and mathematical puzzles also found them an absorbing, as well as an amusing, study. Whatever critical approach we choose for our readings, the great popularity of these works in their own era encourages us to question the Victorians' reputation for somber and stuffy humorlessness.

EDWARD LEAR
1812–1888

Edward Lear was a landscape painter who spent much of his life in Mediterranean countries. In 1846 he published his first *Book of Nonsense*, a collection of limericks for children. The form of the limerick was not invented by Lear, but his use of it helped establish its popularity. In later volumes of the *Book of Nonsense*, he used other verse forms, some of them modeled on rhythms developed by his close friend Tennyson. Best-remembered as the author of "The Owl and the Pussy-Cat" (1870), Lear classified his own poems as "nonsense pure and absolute."

Limerick

There was an Old Man who supposed
That the street door was partially closed;
But some very large rats ate his coats and his hats,
While that futile old gentleman dozed.

1846

The Jumblies

They went to sea in a sieve, they did;
  In a sieve they went to sea;
In spite of all their friends could say,
On a winter's morn, on a stormy day,
5   In a sieve they went to sea.
And when the sieve turned round and round,
And everyone cried, "You'll be drowned!"
They called aloud, "Our sieve ain't big,
But we don't care a button; we don't care a fig—
10   In a sieve we'll go to sea!"
    Far and few, far and few,
     Are the lands where the Jumblies live.
     Their heads are green, and their hands are blue;
     And they went to sea in a sieve.

15 They sailed away in a sieve, they did,
  In a sieve they sailed so fast,
With only a beautiful pea-green veil
Tied with a ribbon, by way of a sail,
  To a small tobacco-pipe mast.
20 And everyone said who saw them go,
"Oh! won't they be soon upset, you know,
For the sky is dark, and the voyage is long;
And, happen what may, it's extremely wrong
  In a sieve to sail so fast."

25 The water it soon came in, it did;
  The water it soon came in.
So, to keep them dry, they wrapped their feet
In a pinky° paper all folded neat;   *tiny*
  And they fastened it down with a pin.
30 And they passed the night in a crockery-jar;
And each of them said, "How wise we are!
Though the sky be dark, and the voyage be long,
Yet we never can think we were rash or wrong,
  While round in our sieve we spin."

35 And all night long they sailed away;
  And, when the sun went down,
They whistled and warbled a moony song

To the echoing sound of a coppery gong,
In the shade of the mountains brown,
40   "O Timballoo! how happy we are
When we live in a sieve and a crockery-jar!
And all night long, in the moonlight pale,
We sail away with a pea-green sail
In the shade of the mountains brown."

45   They sailed to the Western Sea, they did—
To a land all covered with trees;
And they bought an owl, and a useful cart,
And a pound of rice, and a cranberry tart,
And a hive of silvery bees;
50   And they bought a pig, and some green jackdaws,
And a lovely monkey with lollipop paws,
And seventeen bags of edelweiss tea,
And forty bottles of ring-bo-ree,
And no end of Stilton cheese.

55   And in twenty years they all came back—
In twenty years or more;
And everyone said, "How tall they've grown!
For they've been to the Lakes, and the Torrible Zone,
And the hills of the Chankly Bore."[1]
60   And they drank their health, and gave them a feast
Of dumplings made of beautiful yeast;
And everyone said, "If we only live,
We, too, will go to sea in a sieve,
To the hills of the Chankly Bore."
65   Far and few, far and few,
Are the lands where the Jumblies live.
Their heads are green, and their hands are blue;
And they went to sea in a sieve.

1871

1. Lear here invents names that are half plausible because they resemble the real names of geographical features: a *bore* is a surge wave that rises regularly in estuaries or when two tides meet, while "the Torrible Zone" is a play on the Torrid Zone, the region along the equator between the Tropics of Cancer and Capricorn.

LEWIS CARROLL
1832–1898

Charles Lutwidge Dodgson was a deacon in the Anglican Church and a lecturer in mathematics at Oxford as well as a pioneer in the art of portrait photography. Most of his publications were mathematical treatises, but his fame rests on the strange pair of books he wrote for children: *Alice in Wonderland* (1865) and *Through the Looking-Glass* (1871), both published under the pseudonym Lewis Carroll. The various songs and poems scattered throughout the stories are frequently parodies of ditties such as "Twinkle, Twinkle Little Star" and "How doth the little busy bee," nursery classics that a child like Alice would have been able to recite. Others, like "The Mouse's Tale," whose text is set out in the form of a long and twisting tail, are playful in different ways. "Jabberwocky," provided here and followed by the discussion that Alice and Humpty Dumpty conduct about its meaning, is a particularly good example of Carroll's fondness for word games. It is an indication of the poem's popularity that the invented word *chortle*, formed by blending *chuckle* and *snort*, has passed into English.

Jabberwocky[1]

'Twas brillig, and the slithy toves
  Did gyre and gimble in the wabe;
All mimsy were the borogoves,
  And the mome raths outgrabe.

5 "Beware the Jabberwock, my son!
  The jaws that bite, the claws that catch!
Beware the Jubjub bird, and shun
  The frumious Bandersnatch!"

He took his vorpal sword in hand;
10 Long time the manxome foe he sought—
So rested he by the Tumtum tree,
  And stood awhile in thought.

And, as in uffish thought he stood,
  The Jabberwock, with eyes of flame,
15 Came whiffling through the tulgey wood,
  And burbled as it came!

One, two! One, two! And through and through
  The vorpal blade went snicker-snack!
He left it dead, and with its head
20 He went galumphing back.

"And hast thou slain the Jabberwock?
  Come to my arms, my beamish boy!
O frabjous day! Callooh! Callay!"
  He chortled in his joy.

25 'Twas brillig, and the slithy toves
  Did gyre and gimble in the wabe;
All mimsy were the borogoves,
  And the mome raths outgrabe.

1855   1871

[Humpty Dumpty's Explication of "Jabberwocky"][1]

"You seem very clever at explaining words, Sir," said Alice. "Would you kindly tell me the meaning of the poem 'Jabberwocky'?"

---

1. From *Through the Looking-Glass*, chap. 1.   1. From *Through the Looking-Glass*, chap. 6.

"Let's hear it," said Humpty Dumpty. "I can explain all the poems that ever were invented—and a good many that haven't been invented just yet."

This sounded very hopeful, so Alice repeated the first verse:

> " 'Twas brillig, and the slithy toves
> Did gyre and gimble in the wabe;
> All mimsy were the borogoves,
> And the mome raths outgrabe."

"That's enough to begin with," Humpty Dumpty interrupted: "there are plenty of hard words there. 'Brillig' means four o'clock in the afternoon—the time when you begin *broiling* things for dinner."

"That'll do very well," said Alice: "and 'slithy'?"[2]

"Well, 'slithy' means 'lithe and slimy.' 'Lithe' is the same as 'active.' You see it's like a portmanteau[3]—there are two meanings packed up into one word."

"I see it now," Alice remarked thoughtfully: "and what are 'toves'?"

"Well, 'toves' are something like badgers—they're something like lizards— and they're something like corkscrews."

"They must be very curious creatures."

"They are that," said Humpty Dumpty: "also they make their nests under sundials—also they live on cheese."

"And what's to 'gyre' and to 'gimble'?"

"To 'gyre' is to go round and round like a gyroscope. To 'gimble' is to make holes like a gimlet."

"And the 'wabe' is the grass plot round a sundial, I suppose?" said Alice, surprised at her own ingenuity.

"Of course it is. It's called 'wabe,' you know, because it goes a long way before it, and a long way behind it——"

"And a long way beyond it on each side," Alice added.

"Exactly so. Well then, 'mimsy' is 'flimsy and miserable' (there's another portmanteau for you). And a 'borogove' is a thin shabby-looking bird with its feathers sticking out all round—something like a live mop."

"And then 'mome raths'?" said Alice. "If I'm not giving you too much trouble."

"Well, a 'rath' is a sort of green pig: but 'mome' I'm not certain about. I think it's short for 'from home'—meaning that they'd lost their way, you know."

"And what does 'outgrabe' mean?"

"Well, 'outgribing' is something between bellowing and whistling, with a kind of sneeze in the middle: however, you'll hear it done, maybe—down in the wood yonder—and when you've once heard it you'll be *quite* content. Who's been repeating all that hard stuff to you?"

"I read it in a book," said Alice.

1871

---

2. Concerning the pronunciation of these words, Carroll later said: "The 'i' in 'slithy' is long, as in 'writhe'; and 'toves' is pronounced so as to rhyme with 'groves.' Again, the first 'o' in 'borogoves' is pronounced like the 'o' in 'borrow.' I have heard people try to give it the sound of the 'o' in 'worry.' Such is Human Perversity."

3. Large suitcase.

The White Knight's Song[1]

I'll tell thee everything I can;
　　There's little to relate.
I saw an aged, aged man,
　　A-sitting on a gate.
5　"Who are you, aged man?" I said.
　　"And how is it you live?"
And his answer trickled through my head
　　Like water through a sieve.

He said "I look for butterflies
10　　That sleep among the wheat;
I make them into mutton-pies,
　　And sell them in the street.
I sell them unto men," he said,
　　"Who sail on stormy seas;
15　And that's the way I get my bread—
　　A trifle, if you please."

But I was thinking of a plan
　　To dye one's whiskers green,
And always use so large a fan
20　　That they could not be seen.
So, having no reply to give
　　To what the old man said,
I cried, "Come, tell me how you live!"
　　And thumped him on the head.

25　His accents mild took up the tale;
　　He said, "I go my ways,
And when I find a mountain-rill,
　　I set it in a blaze;
And thence they make a stuff they call
30　　Rowland's Macassar Oil[2]—
Yet twopence-halfpenny is all
　　They give me for my toil."

But I was thinking of a way
　　To feed oneself on batter,
35　And so go on from day to day
　　Getting a little fatter.
I shook him well from side to side,
　　Until his face was blue;
"Come, tell me how you live," I cried
40　　"And what it is you do!"

He said, "I hunt for haddocks' eyes
　　Among the heather bright,

---

1. From *Through the Looking-Glass*, chap. 8. Carroll's "Song" is a parodic version of William Wordsworth's poem concerning an aged leech gatherer: "Resolution and Independence" (1807).
2. Brand of hair oil, much used in the 19th century.

And work them into waistcoat-buttons
   In the silent night.
45 And these I do not sell for gold
   Or coin of silvery shine,
But for a copper halfpenny,
   And that will purchase nine.

"I sometimes dig for buttered rolls,
50   Or set limed twigs[3] for crabs;
I sometimes search the grassy knolls
   For wheels of hansom-cabs.
And that's the way" (he gave a wink)
   "By which I get my wealth—
55 And very gladly will I drink
   Your Honor's noble health."

I heard him then, for I had just
   Completed my design
To keep the Menai bridge[4] from rust
60   By boiling it in wine.
I thanked him much for telling me
   The way he got his wealth,
But chiefly for his wish that he
   Might drink my noble health.

65 And now, if e'er by chance I put
   My fingers into glue,
Or madly squeeze a right-hand foot
   Into a left-hand shoe,
Or if I drop upon my toe
70   A very heavy weight,
I weep, for it reminds me so
   Of that old man I used to know—
Whose look was mild, whose speech was slow,
   Whose hair was whiter than the snow,
75 Whose face was very like a crow,
   With eyes, like cinders, all aglow,
Who seemed distracted with his woe,
   Who rocked his body to and fro,
And muttered mumblingly and low,
80 As if his mouth were full of dough,
   Who snorted like a buffalo—
That summer evening long ago
   A-sitting on a gate.

1856   1871

---

3. A method of catching small birds, which become caught on birdlime, a sticky substance.

4. Suspension bridge in Wales (completed in 1826).

W. S. GILBERT
1836–1911

Before becoming a full-time writer, William Schwenck Gilbert worked in the civil service and as a lawyer. In 1869 he published *Bab Ballads*, a collection of narrative verses he had first contributed to a magazine called *Fun*. These ballads are indeed funny but also curiously macabre in their imperturbable accounts of disasters, cannibalism, and murders. Gilbert's skills as a writer of light verse, together with his experience in devising plays for the London theater, contributed to his triumphant success as a librettist in a series of light operas that he composed in collaboration with the eminent musician Sir Arthur Sullivan. For twenty-five years (1871–96). Gilbert and Sullivan captivated audiences in London and New York with productions such as *H.M.S. Pinafore* (1878), *The Pirates of Penzance* (1879), *Princess Ida* (1884)—a comedic response to Tennyson's poem *The Princess* (1847)—and *The Mikado* (1885). Most of these operas exhibit Gilbert's satirical flair; gentle fun is poked at the pretentious ineffectuality of the House of Lords and of corner-cutting lawyers and politicians as well as of bumbling admirals and generals. The good-hearted quality is especially evident in the happy endings of the operas: the satire is usually blunted in the finale by a jovial-spirited acceptance of characters who in earlier scenes were exposed as foolish or inept.

In recognition of his work, Gilbert was knighted by King Edward VII in 1907 (some twenty-five years after Sullivan was knighted in token of Queen Victoria's interest in his "serious" music). Gilbert died on May 29, 1911, while attempting to save a young woman from drowning.

When I, Good Friends, Was Called to the Bar[1]

When I, good friends, was called to the bar,
  I'd an appetite fresh and hearty,
But I was, as many young barristers are,
  An impecunious party.°   *penniless individual*
5 I'd a swallow-tail coat of a beautiful blue—
  A brief which I bought of a booby[2]—
A couple of shirts and a collar or two,
  And a ring that looked like a ruby!

CHORUS.   A couple of shirts, etc.

In Westminster Hall[3] I danced a dance,
10 Like a semidespondent fury;[4]
For I thought I should never hit on a chance
  Of addressing a British jury—
But I soon got tired of third-class journeys,[5]
  And dinners of bread and water;

1. Before a breach of promise suit begins in *Trial by Jury*, the singer of this piece, the judge presiding over the case, tells the court how he "came to be a judge."
2. A fool or dunce. "Brief": a summary of the facts of a case that is prepared (usually by a solicitor) to assist a barrister in presenting the case in court.
3. Courtrooms of the Court of Chancery in London.
4. The Furies are the avenging goddesses in Greek mythology.
5. British passenger trains had first-, second-, and third-class sections.

15 So I fell in love with a rich attorney's
        Elderly, ugly daughter.

CHORUS.   So he fell in love, etc.

     The rich attorney, he jumped with joy,
        And replied to my fond professions:
     "You shall reap the reward of your pluck, my boy,
20   At the Bailey and Middlesex Sessions.⁶
     You'll soon get used to her looks," said he,
        "And a very nice girl you'll find her!
     She may very well pass for forty-three
        In the dusk, with a light behind her!"

CHORUS.   She may very well, etc.

25 The rich attorney was good as his word;
        The briefs came trooping gaily,
     And every day my voice was heard
        At the Sessions or Ancient Bailey.
     All thieves who could my fees afford
30   Relied on my orations,
     And many a burglar I've restored
        To his friends and his relations.

CHORUS.   And many a burglar, etc.

     At length I became as rich as the Gurneys⁷—
        An incubus⁸ then I thought her,
35 So I threw over that rich attorney's
        Elderly, ugly daughter.
     The rich attorney my character high
        Tried vainly to disparage—
     And now, if you please, I'm ready to try
40   This Breach of Promise of Marriage!

                                              1875

If You're Anxious for to Shine in the High Aesthetic Line¹

     Am I alone,
        And unobserved? I am!
     Then let me own
        I'm an aesthetic sham!

---

6. Meetings of the county court of Middlesex (which includes London). "Bailey": the Old Bailey was a court where criminals were tried.
7. A wealthy banking family.
8. Evil spirit (usually male) that descends on persons in their sleep.
1. Sung in *Patience* (Act 1) by Reginald Bunthorne, a caricature of contemporary poets of the "aesthetic school" such as Oscar Wilde.

5   This air severe
         Is but a mere
             Veneer!

       This cynic smile
         Is but a wile
10   Of guile!

       This costume chaste
         Is but good taste
             Misplaced!

       Let me confess!
15   A languid love for lilies does *not* blight me!
     Lank limbs and haggard cheeks do *not* delight me!
       I do *not* care for dirty greens
         By any means.
       I do *not* long for all one sees
20   That's Japanese.[2]
       I am *not* fond of uttering platitudes
         In stained-glass attitudes.
     In short, my medievalism's affectation,
     Born of a morbid love of admiration!
25   If you're anxious for to shine in the high aesthetic line as a man of
         culture rare,
     You must get up all the germs of the transcendental terms, and plant
         them everywhere.
     You must lie upon the daisies and discourse in novel phrases of your
         complicated state of mind,
     The meaning doesn't matter if it's only idle chatter of a transcendental
         kind.
                       And everyone will say,
30   As you walk your mystic way,
     "If this young man expresses himself in terms too deep for *me*,
     Why, what a very singularly deep young man this deep young man
         must be!"

     Be eloquent in praise of the very dull old days which have long since
         passed away,
     And convince 'em, if you can, that the reign of good Queen Anne was
         Culture's palmiest[3] day.
35   Of course you will pooh-pooh whatever's fresh and new, and declare
         it's crude and mean,
     For Art stopped short in the cultivated court of the Empress
         Josephine.[4]

---

2. Admiring Japanese vases and paintings had become a cult practice among aesthetes like the painter James McNeill Whistler (1834–1903). Bunthorne's other references are probably to Pre-Raphaelite paintings such as Dante Gabriel Rossetti's portraits of languidly gazing women (sometimes in green dresses) in which the subject might be posed in a cramped posture recalling that of a figure in a stained-glass window.
3. Most prosperous. Queen Anne (1665–1714) ruled from 1702 to 1714.
4. Napoleon's wife (1763–1814), empress of France from 1804 to 1811.

And everyone will say,
As you walk your mystic way,
"If that's not good enough for him which is good enough for *me,*
40 Why, what a very cultivated kind of youth this kind of youth must be!"

Then a sentimental passion of a vegetable fashion[5] must excite
    your languid spleen,°   *melancholy*
An attachment *à la* Plato[6] for a bashful young potato, or a not-
    too-French French bean!
Though the Philistines[7] may jostle, you will rank as an apostle in the
    high aesthetic band,
If you walk down Piccadilly with a poppy or a lily in your medieval
    hand.[8]
45   And everyone will say,
                  As you walk your flowery way,
"If he's content with a vegetable love which would certainly not suit
    me,
Why, what a most particularly pure young man this pure young man
    must be!"

1881

---

5. Gilbert here begins to play with the concept of "vegetable love," a phrase taken from Andrew Marvell's poem "To His Coy Mistress" (1681).
6. Platonic love denotes a spiritual relationship, devoid of sexual desire.
7. A term used by Matthew Arnold to describe the respectable middle classes, who predictably disapproved of the aesthetes' flamboyant behavior.
8. Another reference to frequently repeated motifs in Pre-Raphaelite art. Piccadilly: a busy street in central London.

Victorian Issues

EVOLUTION

One of the most dramatic controversies in the Victorian age concerned theories of evolution. This controversy exploded into prominence in 1859 when Charles Darwin's *Origin of Species* was published, but it had been rumbling for many years previously. Sir Charles Lyell's *Principles of Geology* (1830) and Robert Chambers's popular book *Vestiges of Creation* (1843–46) had already raised issues that Tennyson aired in his *In Memoriam A.H.H.* (1850). It was Darwin, however, with his monumental marshaling of evidence to establish his theory of natural selection, who finally brought the topic fully into the open, and the public, as well as the experts, took sides.

The opposition aroused by Darwin's treatise came from two different quarters. The first consisted of some of his fellow scientists, who affirmed that his theory was unsound. The second consisted of religious leaders who attacked his theory because it seemed to contradict a literal interpretation of the Bible. Sometimes the two kinds of opposition combined forces, as in 1860 when his scientific opponents selected Bishop Wilberforce to be their spokesman in spearheading their attack on *The Origin of Species*. In replying to such attacks, Darwin had the good fortune to be supported by two of the ablest popularizers of science in his day, T. H. Huxley and John Tyndall. Moreover, although shy by temperament, Darwin was himself (as Tyndall affirms and the selections printed here will illustrate) an exceptionally effective expositor of his own theories.

Darwin rightly saw himself as a scientist and for the most part restricted his attention to observations about the natural world; the applications of his concept of "the survival of the fittest" to activities within and between human societies and cultures, which came to be known in the late nineteenth century as "Social Darwinism," were primarily conducted by other writers, most notably Herbert Spencer. Nevertheless, the shock that Darwin felt as a young man when he first saw the "savages" of South America's Tierra del Fuego (described in the extract provided from *The Descent of Man,* 1871) stayed with him all his life, and was probably one of the factors that caused him to speculate about social behaviors and systems in evolutionary terms.

It is instructive to compare the selections here with Tennyson's *In Memoriam*, Robert Browning's "Caliban upon Setebos" (1864), and the extracts from the writings of Huxley.

CHARLES DARWIN

Charles Darwin (1809–1882) developed an interest in geology and biology at Cambridge, where he was studying to become a clergyman. Aided by a private income, he resolved to devote the rest of his life to scientific research. The observations he made during a long voyage to the South Seas on the HMS *Beagle* (on which he served as a naturalist) led Darwin to construct hypotheses about evolution. In 1858, more than twenty years after his return to England from his voyage, he ventured to submit a paper developing his theory of the origin of species. A year later, when his theory appeared in book form, as *The Origin of Species*, Darwin emerged as a famous and controversial figure.

From The Origin of Species

From *Chapter 3. Struggle for Existence*

We will now discuss in a little more detail the struggle for existence. Nothing is easier than to admit in words the truth of the universal struggle for life, or more difficult—at least I have found it so—than constantly to bear this conclusion in mind. Yet unless it be thoroughly engrained in the mind, the whole economy of nature, with every fact on distribution, rarity, abundance, extinction, and variation, will be dimly seen or quite misunderstood. We behold the face of nature bright with gladness, we often see superabundance of food; we do not see or we forget, that the birds which are idly singing round us mostly live on insects or seeds, and are thus constantly destroying life; or we forget how largely these songsters, or their eggs, or their nestlings, are destroyed by birds and beasts of prey; we do not always bear in mind, that, though food may be now superabundant, it is not so at all seasons of each recurring year.

[THE TERM, STRUGGLE FOR EXISTENCE, USED IN A LARGE SENSE]

I should premise that I use this term in a large and metaphorical sense including dependence of one being on another, and including (which is more important) not only the life of the individual, but success in leaving progeny. Two canine animals, in a time of dearth, may be truly said to struggle with each other which shall get food and live. But a plant on the edge of a desert is said to struggle for life against the drought, though more properly it should be said to be dependent on the moisture. A plant which annually produces a thousand seeds, of which only one of an average comes to maturity, may be more truly said to struggle with the plants of the same and other kinds which already clothe the ground. The mistletoe is dependent on the apple and a few other trees, but can only in a farfetched sense be said to struggle with these trees, for, if too many of these parasites grow on the same tree, it languishes and dies. But several seedling mistletoes, growing close together on the same branch, may more truly be said to struggle with each other. As the mistletoe is disseminated by birds, its existence depends on them; and it may methodically be said to struggle with other fruit-bearing plants, in tempting the birds to devour and thus disseminate its seeds. In these several senses, which pass into each other, I use for convenience' sake the general term of Struggle for Existence.

[GEOMETRICAL RATIO OF INCREASE]

A struggle for existence inevitably follows from the high rate at which all organic beings tend to increase. Every being, which during its natural lifetime produces several eggs or seeds, must suffer destruction during some period of its life, and during some season or occasional year, otherwise, on the principle of geometrical increase, its numbers would quickly become so inordinately great that no country could support the product. Hence, as more individuals are produced than can possibly survive, there must in every case be a struggle for existence, either one individual with another of the same species, or with the individuals of distinct species, or with the physical conditions of life. It is the doctrine of Malthus[1] applied with manifold force to the whole animal and vegetable kingdoms; for in this case there can be no artificial increase of food, and no prudential restraint from marriage. Although some species may be now increasing, more or less rapidly, in numbers, all cannot do so, for the world would not hold them.

There is no exception to the rule that every organic being naturally increases at so high a rate, that, if not destroyed, the earth would soon be covered by the progeny of a single pair. Even slow-breeding man has doubled in twenty-five years, and at this rate, in less than a thousand years, there would literally not be standing-room for his progeny. Linnæus[2] has calculated that if an annual plant produced only two seeds—and there is no plant so unproductive as this—and their seedlings next year produced two, and so on, then in twenty years there should be a million plants. The elephant is reckoned the slowest breeder of all known animals, and I have taken some pains to estimate its probable minimum rate of natural increase; it will be safest to assume that it begins breeding when thirty years old, and goes on breeding till ninety years old, bringing forth six young in the interval, and surviving till one hundred years old; if this be so, after a period of from 740 to 750 years there would be nearly nineteen million elephants alive, descended from the first pair.

※　※　※

[COMPLEX RELATIONS OF ALL ANIMALS AND PLANTS TO EACH OTHER IN THE STRUGGLE FOR EXISTENCE]

Many cases are on record showing how complex and unexpected are the checks and relations between organic beings, which have to struggle together in the same country.

※　※　※

Nearly all our orchidaceous plants absolutely require the visits of insects to remove their pollen-masses and thus to fertilise them. I find from experiments that humble-bees[3] are almost indispensable to the fertilisation of the hearts-ease (Viola tricolor), for other bees do not visit this flower. I have also found that the visits of bees are necessary for the fertilisation of some kinds of clover; for instance, 20 heads of Dutch clover (Trifolium repens) yielded 2,290 seeds, but 20 other heads protected from bees produced not one. Again, 100 heads

1. Thomas Robert Malthus (1766–1834), British social theorist who argued that the population, increasing geometrically, would grow beyond the means of subsistence, which increased arithmetically, without the necessary natural checks of poverty, disease, and starvation.

2. Carl Linnaeus (1707–1778), Swedish naturalist who developed the binomial system—genus plus species name—for naming plants and animals (e.g., Viola tricolor, below).
3. Bumblebees.

of red clover (T. pratense) produced 2,700 seeds, but the same number of protected heads produced not a single seed. Humble-bees alone visit red clover, as other bees cannot reach the nectar. It has been suggested that moths may fertilise the clovers; but I doubt whether they could do so in the case of the red clover, from their weight not being sufficient to depress the wing petals. Hence we may infer as highly probable that, if the whole genus of humble-bees became extinct or very rare in England, the heartsease and red clover would become very rare, or wholly disappear. The number of humble-bees in any district depends in a great measure upon the number of field-mice, which destroy their combs and nests; and Col. Newman,[4] who has long attended to the habits of humble-bees, believes that "more than two-thirds of them are thus destroyed all over England." Now the number of mice is largely dependent, as every one knows, on the number of cats; and Col. Newman says, "Near villages and small towns I have found the nests of humble-bees more numerous than elsewhere, which I attribute to the number of cats that destroy the mice." Hence it is quite credible that the presence of a feline animal in large numbers in a district might determine, through the intervention first of mice and then of bees, the frequency of certain flowers in that district!

In the case of every species, many different checks, acting at different periods of life, and during different seasons or years, probably come into play; some one check or some few being generally the most potent; but all will concur in determining the average number or even the existence of the species. In some cases it can be shown that widely-different checks act on the same species in different districts. When we look at the plants and bushes clothing an entangled bank, we are tempted to attribute their proportional numbers and kinds to what we call chance. But how false a view is this! Every one has heard that when an American forest is cut down a very different vegetation springs up; but it has been observed that ancient Indian ruins in the Southern United States, which must formerly have been cleared of trees, now display the same beautiful diversity and proportion of kinds as in the surrounding virgin forest. What a struggle must have gone on during long centuries between the several kinds of trees each annually scattering its seeds by the thousand; what war between insect and insect—between insects, snails, and other animals with birds and beasts of prey—all striving to increase, all feeding on each other, or on the trees, their seeds and seedlings, or on the other plants which first clothed the ground and thus checked the growth of the trees! Throw up a handful of feathers, and all fall to the ground according to definite laws; but how simple is the problem where each shall fall compared to that of the action and reaction of the innumerable plants and animals which have determined, in the course of centuries, the proportional numbers and kinds of trees now growing on the old Indian ruins!

From *Chapter 15. Recapitulation and Conclusion*

I see no good reason why the views given in this volume should shock the religious feelings of any one. It is satisfactory, as showing how transient such impressions are, to remember that the greatest discovery ever made by man, namely, the law of the attraction of gravity, was also attacked by Leibnitz,[5] "as

4. Henry Wenman Newman (1788–1865), British army officer who succeeded to his father's estates in 1829.
5. Gottfried Wilhelm Leibniz (1646–1716),

German philosopher and mathematician; he was a contemporary of Isaac Newton, who set forth the law of universal gravitation.

subversive of natural, and inferentially of revealed, religion." A celebrated author and divine has written to me that "he has gradually learnt to see that it is just as noble a conception of the Deity to believe that He created a few original forms capable of self-development into other and needful forms, as to believe that He required a fresh act of creation to supply the voids caused by the action of His laws."

Why, it may be asked, until recently did nearly all the most eminent living naturalists and geologists disbelieve in the mutability of species? It cannot be asserted that organic beings in a state of nature are subject to no variation; it cannot be proved that the amount of variation in the course of long ages is a limited quality; no clear distinction has been, or can be, drawn between species and well-marked varieties. It cannot be maintained that species when inter-crossed are invariably sterile, and varieties invariably fertile; or that sterility is a special endowment and sign of creation. The belief that species were immutable productions was almost unavoidable as long as the history of the world was thought to be of short duration;[6] and now that we have acquired some idea of the lapse of time, we are too apt to assume, without proof, that the geological record is so perfect that it would have afforded us plain evidence of the mutation of species, if they had undergone mutation.

But the chief cause of our natural unwillingness to admit that one species has given birth to clear and distinct species, is that we are always slow in admitting great changes of which we do not see the steps. The difficulty is the same as that felt by so many geologists, when Lyell[7] first insisted that long lines of inland cliffs had been formed, and great valleys excavated, by the agencies which we see still at work. The mind cannot possibly grasp the full meaning of the term of even a million years; it cannot add up and perceive the full effects of many slight variations, accumulated during an almost infinite number of generations.

Although I am fully convinced of the truth of the views given in this volume under the form of an abstract, I by no means expect to convince experienced naturalists whose minds are stocked with a multitude of facts all viewed, during a long course of years, from a point of view directly opposite to mine. It is so easy to hide our ignorance under such expressions as the "plan of creation," "unity of design," &c., and to think that we give an explanation when we only re-state a fact. Any one whose disposition leads him to attach more weight to unexplained difficulties than to the explanation of a certain number of facts will certainly reject the theory. A few naturalists, endowed with much flexibility of mind, and who have already begun to doubt the immutability of species, may be influenced by this volume; but I look with confidence to the future,—to young and rising naturalists, who will be able to view both sides of the question with impartiality.[8] Whoever is led to believe that species are mutable will do good service by conscientiously expressing his conviction; for

6. Calculations based on the genealogies within the Bible put the age of the world at no more than six thousand years.
7. Charles Lyell (1797–1875), geologist whose book *Principles of Geology* (1830–33) was important in dissociating geological theory from the Bible and in establishing nature as the record of the earth's history, which he saw as a process of lengthy and gradual change rather than swift catastrophic events.
8. Despite the initial theological resistance to Darwin's theory, his ideas were swiftly accepted by his fellow scientists, and intellectual elites, even in the Church, soon followed suit. It would take much longer for the larger public to come around, although Darwin's burial in Westminster Abbey—a great civic honor—suggests he had won over many of his fellow citizens.

thus only can the load of prejudice by which this subject is overwhelmed be removed.

* * *

It may be asked how far I extend the doctrine of the modification of species. The question is difficult to answer, because the more distinct the forms are which we consider, by so much the arguments in favour of community of descent become fewer in number and less in force. But some arguments of the greatest weight extend very far. All the members of whole classes are connected together by a chain of affinities, and all can be classed on the same principle, in groups subordinate to groups. Fossil remains sometimes tend to fill up very wide intervals between existing orders.

Organs in a rudimentary condition plainly show that an early progenitor had the organ in a fully developed condition; and this in some cases implies an enormous amount of modification in the descendants. Throughout whole classes various structures are formed on the same pattern, and at a very early age the embryos closely resemble each other. Therefore I cannot doubt that the theory of descent with modification embraces all the members of the same great class or kingdom. I believe that animals are descended from at most only four or five progenitors, and plants from an equal or lesser number.

Analogy would lead me one step farther, namely, to the belief that all animals and plants are descended from some one prototype. But analogy may be a deceitful guide. Nevertheless all living things have much in common, in their chemical composition, their cellular structure, their laws of growth, and their liability to injurious influences. We see this even in so trifling a fact as that the same poison often similarly affects plants and animals; or that the poison secreted by the gall-fly produces monstrous growths on the wild rose or oak-tree. With all organic beings excepting perhaps some of the very lowest, sexual production seems to be essentially similar. With all, as far as is at present known the germinal vesicle is the same; so that all organisms start from a common origin. If we look even to the two main divisions—namely, to the animal and vegetable kingdoms—certain low forms are so far intermediate in character that naturalists have disputed to which kingdom they should be referred. As Professor Asa Gray[9] has remarked, "the spores and other reproductive bodies of many of the lower algae may claim to have first a characteristically animal, and then an unequivocally vegetable existence." Therefore, on the principle of natural selection with divergence of character, it does not seem incredible that, from such low and intermediate form, both animals and plants may have been developed; and, if we admit this, we must likewise admit that all the organic beings which have ever lived on this earth may be descended from some one primordial form.

* * *

When we feel assured that all the individuals of the same species, and all the closely allied species of most genera, have within a not very remote period descended from one parent, and have migrated from some one birth-place; and when we better know the many means of migration, then, by the light which geology now throws, and will continue to throw, on former changes of

---

9. American botanist (1810–1888).

climate and of the level of the land, we shall surely be enabled to trace in an admirable manner the former migrations of the inhabitants of the whole world. Even at present, by comparing the differences between the inhabitants of the sea on the opposite sides of a continent, and the nature of the various inhabitants on that continent, in relation to their apparent means of immigration, some light can be thrown on ancient geography.

The noble science of Geology loses glory from the extreme imperfection of the record.[1] The crust of the earth with its imbedded remains must not be looked at as a well-filled museum, but as a poor collection made at hazard and at rare intervals. The accumulation of each great fossiliferous formation will be recognised as having depended on an unusual concurrence of favourable circumstances, and the blank intervals between the successive stages as having been of vast duration. But we shall be able to gauge with some security the duration of these intervals by a comparison of the preceding and succeeding organic forms. We must be cautious in attempting to correlate as strictly contemporaneous two formations, which do not include many identical species, by the general succession of the forms of life. As species are produced and exterminated by slowly acting and still existing causes, and not by miraculous acts of creation; and as the most important of all causes of organic change is one which is almost independent of altered and perhaps suddenly altered physical conditions, namely, the mutual relation of organism to organism,—the improvement of one organism entailing the improvement or the extermination of others; it follows, that the amount of organic change in the fossils of consecutive formations probably serves as a fair measure of the relative though not actual lapse of time. A number of species, however, keeping in a body might remain for a long period unchanged, whilst within the same period several of these species by migrating into new countries and coming into competition with foreign associates, might become modified; so that we must not overrate the accuracy of organic change as a measure of time.

In the future I see open fields for far more important researches. Psychology will be securely based on the foundation already well laid by Mr. Herbert Spencer,[2] that of the necessary acquirement of each mental power and capacity by gradation. Much light will be thrown on the origin of man and his history.

Authors of the highest eminence seem to be fully satisfied with the view that each species has been independently created. To my mind it accords better with what we know of the laws impressed on matter by the Creator, that the production and extinction of the past and present inhabitants of the world should have been due to secondary causes, like those determining the birth and death of the individual. When I view all beings not as special creations, but as the lineal descendants of some few beings which lived long before the first bed of the Cambrian system was deposited,[3] they seem to me to

1. Geology had captured the early Victorian imagination, largely thanks to the radical theories of Charles Lyell and to mounting interest in dinosaurs (a term coined in 1842 by the pioneering comparative anatomist Sir Richard Owen, who was the first to classify "dinosauria" as a suborder of large extinct reptiles). Perhaps Darwin here forecasts one reason why popular interest would shift in the later part of the century; after his *Origin* was published, biology, not geology, became the focal point of public debate.
2. British social theorist (1820–1903), who developed the concept of social Darwinism.
3. I.e., before the earliest geological period of the Paleozoic (now dated at more than 544 million years ago).

become ennobled. Judging from the past, we may safely infer that not one living species will transmit its unaltered likeness to a distant futurity. And of the species now living very few will transmit progeny of any kind to a far distant futurity; for the manner in which all organic beings are grouped, shows that the greater number of species in each genus, and all the species in many genera, have left no descendants, but have become utterly extinct. We can so far take a prophetic glance into futurity as to foretell that it will be the common and widely-spread species, belonging to the larger and dominant groups within each class, which will ultimately prevail and procreate new and dominant species. As all the living forms of life are the lineal descendants of those which lived long before the Cambrian epoch, we may feel certain that the ordinary succession by generation has never once been broken, and that no cataclysm has desolated the whole world. Hence we may look with some confidence to a secure future of great length. And as natural selection works solely by and for the good of each being, all corporeal and mental endowments will tend to progress towards perfection.

It is interesting to contemplate a tangled bank, clothed with many plants of many kinds, with birds singing on the bushes, with various insects flitting about, and with worms crawling through the damp earth, and to reflect that these elaborately constructed forms, so different from each other, and dependent upon each other in so complex a manner, have all been produced by laws acting around us. These laws, taken in the largest sense, being Growth with Reproduction; Inheritance which is almost implied by reproduction; Variability from the indirect and direct action of the conditions of life, and from use and disuse: a Ratio of Increase so high as to lead to a Struggle for Life, and as a consequence to Natural Selection, entailing Divergence of Character and the Extinction of less-improved forms. Thus, from the war of nature, from famine and death, the most exalted object which we are capable of conceiving, namely, the production of the higher animals, directly follows. There is grandeur in this view of life, with its several powers, having been originally breathed by the Creator into a few forms or into one; and that, whilst this planet has gone cycling on according to the fixed law of gravity, from so simple a beginning endless forms most beautiful and most wonderful have been, and are being evolved.

1859

CHARLES DARWIN

After he published *The Origin of Species*, Darwin wrote several treatises, some of which develop and clarify the theory of *The Origin of Species*. One of these works, *The Descent of Man* (1871), was especially provocative in its stress on the similarities between humans and animals and in its naturalistic explanations of the beautiful colorings of birds, insects, and flowers.

From The Descent of Man

[NATURAL SELECTION AND SEXUAL SELECTION][1]

A brief summary will here be sufficient to recall to the reader's mind the more salient points in this work. Many of the views which have been advanced are highly speculative, and some no doubt will prove erroneous; but I have in every case given the reasons which have led me to one view rather than to another. It seemed worth while to try how far the principle of evolution would throw light on some of the more complex problems in the natural history of man. False facts are highly injurious to the progress of science, for they often long endure; but false views, if supported by some evidence, do little harm, as everyone takes a salutary pleasure in proving their falseness; and when this is done, one path towards error is closed and the road to truth is often at the same time opened.

The main conclusion arrived at in this work, and now held by many naturalists who are well competent to form a sound judgment, is that man is descended from some less highly organized form. The grounds upon which this conclusion rests will never be shaken, for the close similarity between man and the lower animals in embryonic development, as well as in innumerable points of structure and constitution, both of high and of the most trifling importance—the rudiments which he retains, and the abnormal reversions to which he is occasionally liable—are facts which cannot be disputed. They have long been known, but until recently they told us nothing with respect to the origin of man. Now when viewed by the light of our knowledge of the whole organic world, their meaning is unmistakable. The great principle of evolution stands up clear and firm, when these groups of facts are considered in connection with others, such as the mutual affinities of the members of the same group, their geographical distribution in past and present times, and their geological succession. It is incredible that all these facts should speak falsely. He who is not content to look, like a savage, at the phenomena of nature as disconnected cannot any longer believe that man is the work of a separate act of creation. He will be forced to admit that the close resemblance of the embryo of man to that, for instance, of a dog—the construction of his skull, limbs, and whole frame, independently of the uses to which the parts may be put, on the same plan with that of other mammals—the occasional reappearance of various structures, for instance of several distinct muscles, which man does not normally possess, but which are common to the Quadrumana[2]—and a crowd of analogous facts—all point in the plainest manner to the conclusion that man is the codescendant with other mammals of a common progenitor.

※　　※　　※

By considering the embryological structure of man—the homologies which he presents with the lower animals, the rudiments which he retains, and the reversions to which he is liable—we can partly recall in imagination the former condition of our early progenitors; and can approximately place them in their

---

1. From chap. 21.
2. Animals, such as monkeys, whose hind feet and forefeet can be used as hands—hence "four-handed."

proper position in the zoological series. We thus learn that man is descended from a hairy quadruped, furnished with a tail and pointed ears, probably arboreal in its habits, and an inhabitant of the Old World. This creature, if its whole structure had been examined by a naturalist, would have been classed amongst the Quadrumana, as surely as would the common and still more ancient progenitor of the Old and New World monkeys. The Quadrumana and all the higher mammals are probably derived from an ancient marsupial animal, and this through a long line of diversified forms, either from some reptilelike or some amphibianlike creature, and this again from some fishlike animal. In the dim obscurity of the past we can see that the early progenitor of all the Vertebrata must have been an aquatic animal, provided with branchiae,[3] with the two sexes united in the same individual, and with the most important organs of the body (such as the brain and heart) imperfectly developed. This animal seems to have been more like the larvae of our existing marine ascidians[4] than any other known form.

✳ ✳ ✳

Sexual selection has been treated at great length in these volumes; for, as I have attempted to show, it has played an important part in the history of the organic world.

✳ ✳ ✳

The belief in the power of sexual selection rests chiefly on the following considerations. The characters which we have the best reason for supposing to have been thus acquired are confined to one sex; and this alone renders it probable that they are in some way connected with the act of reproduction. These characters in innumerable instances are fully developed only at maturity; and often during only a part of the year, which is always the breeding season. The males (passing over a few exceptional cases) are the most active in courtship; they are the best armed, and are rendered the most attractive in various ways. It is to be especially observed that the males display their attractions with elaborate care in the presence of the females; and that they rarely or never display them excepting during the season of love. It is incredible that all this display should be purposeless. Lastly we have distinct evidence with some quadrupeds and birds that the individuals of the one sex are capable of feeling a strong antipathy or preference for certain individuals of the opposite sex.

Bearing these facts in mind, and not forgetting the marked results of man's unconscious selection, it seems to me almost certain that if the individuals of one sex were during a long series of generations to prefer pairing with certain individuals of the other sex, characterized in some peculiar manner, the offspring would slowly but surely become modified in this same manner. I have not attempted to conceal that, excepting when the males are more numerous than the females, or when polygamy prevails, it is doubtful how the more attractive males succeed in leaving a larger number of offspring to inherit their superiority in ornaments or other charms than the less attractive males; but I have shown that this would probably follow from the females—especially the

3. Gills.
4. Part of a group of marine animals called tuni-

cata, or popularly "sea squirts," sometimes assumed to be ancestors of the vertebrate animals.

more vigorous females which would be the first to breed, preferring not only the more attractive but at the same time the more vigorous and victorious males.

Although we have some positive evidence that birds appreciate bright and beautiful objects, as with the bowerbirds of Australia, and although they certainly appreciate the power of song, yet I fully admit that it is an astonishing fact that the females of many birds and some mammals should be endowed with sufficient taste for what has apparently been effected through sexual selection; and this is even more astonishing in the case of reptiles, fish, and insects. But we really know very little about the minds of the lower animals. It cannot be supposed that male birds of paradise or peacocks, for instance, should take so much pains in erecting, spreading, and vibrating their beautiful plumes before the females for no purpose. We should remember the fact given on excellent authority in a former chapter, namely that several peahens, when debarred from an admired male, remained widows during a whole season rather than pair with another bird.

Nevertheless I know of no fact in natural history more wonderful than that the female argus pheasant should be able to appreciate the exquisite shading of the ball-and-socket ornaments and the elegant patterns on the wing feathers of the male. He who thinks that the male was created as he now exists must admit that the great plumes, which prevent the wings from being used for flight, and which, as well as the primary feathers, are displayed in a manner quite peculiar to this one species during the act of courtship, and at no other time, were given to him as an ornament. If so, he must likewise admit that the female was created and endowed with the capacity of appreciating such ornaments. I differ only in the conviction that the male argus pheasant acquired his beauty gradually, through the females having preferred during many generations the more highly ornamented males; the aesthetic capacity of the females having been advanced through exercise or habit in the same manner as our own taste is gradually improved. In the male, through the fortunate chance of a few feathers not having been modified, we can distinctly see how simple spots with a little fulvous⁵ shading on one side might have been developed by small and graduated steps into the wonderful ball-and-socket ornaments; and it is probable that they were actually thus developed.

✳   ✳   ✳

He who admits the principle of sexual selection will be led to the remarkable conclusion that the cerebral system not only regulates most of the existing functions of the body, but has indirectly influenced the progressive development of various bodily structures and of certain mental qualities. Courage, pugnacity, perseverance, strength and size of body, weapons of all kinds, musical organs, both vocal and instrumental, bright colours, stripes and marks, and ornamental appendages have all been indirectly gained by the one sex or the other, through the influence of love and jealousy, through the appreciation of the beautiful in sound, color or form, and through the exertion of a choice; and these powers of the mind manifestly depend on the development of the cerebral system.

✳   ✳   ✳

5. Dull yellow.

The main conclusion arrived at in this work, namely that man is descended from some lowly-organized form, will, I regret to think, be highly distasteful to many persons. But there can hardly be a doubt that we are descended from barbarians. The astonishment which I felt on first seeing a party of Fuegians[6] on a wild and broken shore will never be forgotten by me, for the reflection at once rushed into my mind—such were our ancestors. These men were absolutely naked and bedaubed with paint, their long hair was tangled, their mouths frothed with excitement, and their expression was wild, startled, and distrustful. They possessed hardly any arts,[7] and like wild animals lived on what they could catch; they had no government, and were merciless to everyone not of their own small tribe. He who has seen a savage in his native land will not feel much shame, if forced to acknowledge that the blood of some more humble creature flows in his veins. For my own part I would as soon be descended from that heroic little monkey, who braved his dreaded enemy in order to save the life of his keeper; or from that old baboon, who, descending from the mountains, carried away in triumph his young comrade from a crowd of astonished dogs[8]—as from a savage who delights to torture his enemies, offers up bloody sacrifices, practices infanticide without remorse, treats his wives like slaves, knows no decency, and is haunted by the grossest superstitions.

Man may be excused for feeling some pride at having risen, though not through his own exertions, to the very summit of the organic scale; and the fact of his having thus risen, instead of having been aboriginally placed there, may give him hopes for a still higher destiny in the distant future. But we are not here concerned with hopes or fears, only with the truth as far as our reason allows us to discover it. I have given the evidence to the best of my ability; and we must acknowledge, as it seems to me, that man with all his noble qualities, with sympathy which feels for the most debased, with benevolence which extends not only to other men but to the humblest living creature, with his godlike intellect which has penetrated into the movements and constitution of the solar system—with all these exalted powers—Man still bears in his bodily frame the indelible stamp of his lowly origin.

1871

6. Natives inhabiting the islands off the southern tip of South America, Tierra del Fuego, which Darwin had visited in 1832. See his *Voyage of the Beagle* (1839), chap. 10.

7. Crafts and skills.
8. Incidents described in chap. 4 to demonstrate that animals may be endowed with a moral sense.

LEONARD HUXLEY

At meetings of the British Association for the Advancement of Science, the reading of a paper is followed by a discussion. In 1860, at Oxford, this discussion developed into a debate between Thomas Henry Huxley (1825–1895), a defender of Charles Darwin's theories, and Bishop Samuel Wilberforce (1805–1873). Although he had studied mathematics as an undergraduate, Wilberforce could hardly lay claim to be a scientist. He was willing, nevertheless, to speak on behalf of those scientists who disagreed with *The Origin of Species* (1859), and he reportedly came to the meeting ready to "smash Darwin." The bishop's principal qualifications for this role were his great powers as a smoothly persuasive orator (he was commonly known by his detractors as "Soapy Sam"), but he met more than his match in Huxley.

Because no complete transcript of this celebrated debate was made at the time, Huxley's son Leonard (1860–1933), in writing his father's biography, had to reconstruct the scene by combining quotations from reports made by magazine writers and other witnesses. The account given here is from chapter 14.

From The Life and Letters of Thomas Henry Huxley

[THE HUXLEY-WILBERFORCE DEBATE AT OXFORD]

The famous Oxford Meeting of 1860 was of no small importance in Huxley's career. It was not merely that he helped to save a great cause from being stifled under misrepresentation and ridicule—that he helped to extort for it a fair hearing; it was now that he first made himself known in popular estimation as a dangerous adversary in debate—a personal force in the world of science which could not be neglected. From this moment he entered the front fighting line in the most exposed quarter of the field. * * *

It was the merest chance, as I have already said, that Huxley attended the meeting of the section that morning. Dr. Draper[1] of New York was to read a paper on the *Intellectual Development of Europe considered with reference to the views of Mr. Darwin.* "I can still hear," writes one who was present, "the American accents of Dr. Draper's opening address when he asked 'Air we a fortuitous concourse of atoms?' " However, it was not to hear him, but the eloquence of the Bishop, that the members of the Association crowded in such numbers into the Lecture Room of the Museum, that this, the appointed meeting place of the section, had to be abandoned for the long west room, since cut in two by a partition for the purposes of the library. It was not term time, nor were the general public admitted; nevertheless the room was crowded to suffocation long before the protagonists appeared on the scene, 700 persons or more managing to find places. The very windows by which the room was lighted down the length of its west side were packed with ladies, whose white handkerchiefs, waving and fluttering in the air at the end of the Bishop's speech, were an unforgettable factor in the acclamation of the crowd.

On the east side between the two doors was the platform. Professor Henslow, the President of the section, took his seat in the center; upon his right was the Bishop, and beyond him again Dr. Draper; on his extreme left was Mr. Dingle, a clergyman from Lanchester, near Durham, with Sir J. Hooker and Sir J. Lubbock in front of him, and nearer the center, Professor Beale of King's College, London, and Huxley.[2]

The clergy, who shouted lustily for the Bishop, were massed in the middle of the room; behind them in the northwest corner a knot of undergraduates (one of these was T. H. Green,[3] who listened but took no part in the cheering) had gathered together beside Professor Brodie,[4] ready to lift their voices, poor

---

1. John W. Draper (1811–1882), British-born chemist, photographer, and historian who was a professor at the University of the City of New York.
2. Except for the clergyman Dingle, all those named are scientists of some repute: John Stevens Henslow (1796–1861), professor of botany at Cambridge; Sir Joseph Dalton Hooker (1817–1911), botanist (and Henslow's son-in-law); Sir

John Lubbock (1834–1913), banker, statesman, naturalist, and Darwin's neighbor; and Lionel Smith Beale (1828–1905), professor of medicine.
3. Later a prominent British philosopher (1836–1882).
4. Sir Benjamin Brodie (1783–1862), physiologist and surgeon.

minority though they were, for the opposite party. Close to them stood one of the few men among the audience already in Holy orders, who joined in—and indeed led—the cheers for the Darwinians.

So "Dr. Draper droned out his paper, turning first to the right hand and then to the left, of course bringing in a reference to the *Origin of Species* which set the ball rolling."

An hour or more that paper lasted, and then discussion began. The President "wisely announced *in limine*[5] that none who had not valid arguments to bring forward on one side or the other would be allowed to address the meeting; a caution that proved necessary, for no fewer than four combatants had their utterances burked[6] by him, because of their indulgence in vague declamation."

First spoke (writes Professor Farrar[7]) a layman from Brompton, who gave his name as being one of the Committee of the (newly formed) Economic section of the Association. He, in a stentorian voice, let off his theological venom. Then jumped up Richard Greswell[8] with a thin voice, saying much the same, but speaking as a scholar; but we did not merely want any theological discussion, so we shouted them down. Then a Mr. Dingle got up and tried to show that Darwin would have done much better if he had taken him into consultation. He used the blackboard and began a mathematical demonstration on the question—"Let this point A be man, and let that point B be the mawnkey." He got no further; he was shouted down with cries of "mawnkey." None of these had spoken more than three minutes. It was when these were shouted down that Henslow said he must demand that the discussion should rest on *scientific* grounds only.

Then there were calls for the Bishop, but he rose and said he understood his friend Professor Beale had something to say first. Beale, who was an excellent histologist,[9] spoke to the effect that the new theory ought to meet with fair discussion, but added, with great modesty, that he himself had not sufficient knowledge to discuss the subject adequately. Then the Bishop spoke the speech that you know, and the question about his mother being an ape, or his grandmother.

From the scientific point of view, the speech was of small value. It was evident from his mode of handling the subject that he had been "crammed up to the throat," and knew nothing at first hand; he used no argument beyond those to be found in his *Quarterly* article, which appeared a few days later, and is now admitted to have been inspired by Owen.[1] "He ridiculed Darwin badly and Huxley savagely; but," confesses one of his strongest opponents, "all in such dulcet tones, so persuasive a manner, and in such well turned periods, that I who had been inclined to blame the President for allowing a discussion that could serve no scientific purpose, now forgave him from the bottom of my heart."

The Bishop spoke thus "for full half an hour with inimitable spirit, emptiness and unfairness." "In a light, scoffing tone, florid and fluent, he assured us there was nothing in the idea of evolution; rock pigeons were what rock

5. As a starting point (Latin).
6. Suppressed, hushed.
7. Adam Storey Farrar (1826–1905), canon of Durham and professor of divinity at Durham University.
8. A clergyman who was a tutor of Worcester College, Oxford.

9. A biologist specializing in the study of the minute structure of the tissues of plants and animals.
1. Sir Richard Owen (1804–1892), a leading zoologist and paleontologist who was opposed to Darwin's theories. Wilberforce's review of Darwin's *The Origin of Species* (1859) appeared in the July 1860 issue of the *Quarterly Review*.

pigeons had always been. Then, turning to his antagonist with a smiling insolence, he begged to know, was it through his grandfather or his grandmother
that he claimed his descent from a monkey?"
This was the fatal mistake of his speech. Huxley instantly grasped the tac-
tical advantage which the descent to personalities gave him. He turned to Sir
Benjamin Brodie, who was sitting beside him, and emphatically striking his
hand upon his knee, exclaimed, "The Lord hath delivered him into mine
hands."[2] The bearing of the exclamation did not dawn upon Sir Benjamin until
after Huxley had completed his "forcible and eloquent" answer to the scientific
part of the Bishop's argument, and proceeded to make his famous retort.

> On this (continues the writer in *Macmillan's Magazine*) Mr. Huxley
> slowly and deliberately arose. A slight tall figure, stern and pale, very quiet
> and very grave, he stood before us and spoke those tremendous words—
> words which no one seems sure of now, nor, I think, could remember just
> after they were spoken, for their meaning took away our breath, though
> it left us in no doubt as to what it was. He was not ashamed to have a
> monkey for his ancestor; but he would be ashamed to be connected with
> a man who used great gifts to obscure the truth. No one doubted his
> meaning, and the effect was tremendous. One lady fainted and had to be
> carried out; I, for one, jumped out of my seat.

The fullest and probably most accurate account of these concluding words is
the following, from a letter of the late John Richard Green, then an undergraduate, to his friend, afterwards Professor Boyd Dawkins:[3]

> I asserted—and I repeat—that a man has no reason to be ashamed of
> having an ape for his grandfather. If there were an ancestor whom I should
> feel shame in recalling it would rather be a man—a man of restless and
> versatile intellect—who, not content with an equivocal success in his own
> sphere of activity, plunges into scientific questions with which he has no
> real acquaintance, only to obscure them by an aimless rhetoric, and dis-
> tract the attention of his hearers from the real point at issue by eloquent
> digressions and skilled appeals to religious prejudice.

The result of this encounter, though a check to the other side, cannot, of
course, be represented as an immediate and complete triumph for evolutionary
doctrine. This was precluded by the character and temper of the audience,
most of whom were less capable of being convinced by the arguments than
shocked by the boldness of the retort, although, being gentlefolk, as Professor
Farrar remarks, they were disposed to admit on reflection that the Bishop had
erred on the score of taste and good manners. Nevertheless, it was a noticeable
feature of the occasion, Sir M. Foster[4] tells me, that when Huxley rose he was
received coldly, just a cheer of encouragement from his friends, the audience
as a whole not joining in it. But as he made his points the applause grew and
widened, until, when he sat down, the cheering was not very much less than
that given to the Bishop. To that extent he carried an unwilling audience with
him by the force of his speech. The debate on the ape question, however, was
continued elsewhere during the next two years, and the evidence was com-

---

2. Cf. 2 Samuel 5.19 (where the Lord promises to
deliver the Philistines into David's hands).
3. William Boyd Dawkins (1838–1929), British
geologist and archaeologist. Green (1837–1883),

British historian.
4. Sir Michael Foster (1836–1907), British physiologist and educator.

pleted by the unanswerable demonstrations of Sir W. H. Flower[5] at the Cambridge meeting of the Association in 1862.

The importance of the Oxford meeting lay in the open resistance that was made to authority, at a moment when even a drawn battle was hardly less effectual than acknowledged victory. Instead of being crushed under ridicule, the new theories secured a hearing, all the wider, indeed, for the startling nature of their defense.

1901

5. Sir William Henry Flower (1831–1899), British zoologist.

SIR EDMUND GOSSE

Philip Henry Gosse (1810–1888) was a zoologist of some repute and also an ardent adherent of a strict Protestant sect, the Plymouth Brethren. In an attempt to reconcile his scientific knowledge with his fundamentalist religious position, Gosse published in 1857 a work called *Omphalos,* the Greek word for "navel." The term is of central significance in the book's primary assertion that the earth carries the marks of a past that did not actually happen: just as Adam and Eve were created with navels even though they had not been born to a mother, Gosse argues, so had God created the world with what appear to be millions of years' worth of accumulated rock strata. The book pleased no one. Gosse's agonized experience is described by his son, the literary critic Sir Edmund Gosse (1849–1928), in an autobiography published in 1907. This selection is from chapter 5.

From Father and Son

So, through my Father's brain, in that year of scientific crisis, 1857, there rushed two kinds of thought, each absorbing, each convincing, yet totally irreconcilable. There is a peculiar agony in the paradox that truth has two forms, each of them indisputable, yet each antagonistic to the other. It was this discovery, that there were two theories of physical life, each of which was true, but the truth of each incompatible with the truth of the other, which shook the spirit of my Father with perturbation. It was not, really, a paradox, it was a fallacy, if he could only have known it, but he allowed the turbid volume of superstition to drown the delicate stream of reason. He took one step in the service of truth, and then he drew back in an agony, and accepted the servitude of error.

This was the great moment in the history of thought when the theory of the mutability of species was preparing to throw a flood of light upon all departments of human speculation and action. It was becoming necessary to stand emphatically in one army or the other. Lyell[1] was surrounding himself with disciples, who were making strides in the direction of discovery. Darwin had long been collecting facts with regard to the variation of animals and plants.

1. Sir Charles Lyell (1797–1875), British geologist.

Hooker and Wallace, Asa Gray and even Agassiz,[2] each in his own sphere, were coming closer and closer to a perception of that secret which was first to reveal itself clearly to the patient and humble genius of Darwin. In the year before, in 1856, Darwin, under pressure from Lyell, had begun that modest statement of the new revelation, that "abstract of an essay," which developed so mightily into *The Origin of Species.* Wollaston's *Variation of Species*[3] had just appeared, and had been a nine days' wonder in the wilderness.

On the other side, the reactionaries, although never dreaming of the fate which hung over them, had not been idle. In 1857 the astounding question had for the first time been propounded with contumely,[4] "What, then, did we come from orangoutang?" The famous *Vestiges of Creation*[5] had been supplying a sugar-and-water panacea for those who could not escape from the trend of evidence, and who yet clung to revelation. Owen[6] was encouraging reaction by resisting, with all the strength of his prestige, the theory of the mutability of species.

In this period of intellectual ferment, as when a great political revolution is being planned, many possible adherents were confidentially tested with hints and encouraged to reveal their bias in a whisper. It was the notion of Lyell, himself a great mover of men, that, before the doctrine of natural selection was given to a world which would be sure to lift up at it a howl of execration, a certain bodyguard of sound and experienced naturalists, expert in the description of species, should be privately made aware of its tenor. Among those who were thus initiated, or approached with a view towards possible illumination, was my Father. He was spoken to by Hooker, and later on by Darwin, after meetings of the Royal Society[7] in the summer of 1857.

My Father's attitude towards the theory of natural selection was critical in his career, and oddly enough, it exercised an immense influence on my own experience as a child. Let it be admitted at once, mournful as the admission is, that every instinct in his intelligence went out at first to greet the new light. It had hardly done so, when a recollection of the opening chapter of Genesis checked it at the outset. He consulted with Carpenter,[8] a great investigator, but one who was fully as incapable as himself of remodeling his ideas with regard to the old, accepted hypotheses. They both determined, on various grounds, to have nothing to do with the terrible theory, but to hold steadily to the law of the fixity of species.* * *

My Father had never admired Sir Charles Lyell. I think that the famous Lord Chancellor manner of the geologist intimidated him, and we undervalue the intelligence of those whose conversation puts us at a disadvantage. For Darwin and Hooker, on the other hand, he had a profound esteem, and I know not whether this had anything to do with the fact that he chose, for his impetuous experiment in reaction, the field of geology, rather than that of zoology

---

2. Noted scientists: Sir Joseph Dalton Hooker (1817–1911), British botanist and explorer; Alfred Russel Wallace (1823–1913), British naturalist; Asa Gray (1810–1888), American botanist; and Louis Agassiz (1807–1873), Swiss geologist and comparative anatomist.
3. *On the Variation of Species, with Especial Reference to Insecta* (1856), by the British entomologist Thomas V. Wollaston (1822–1878).
4. Insolent or insulting language or treatment.
5. This popular work of 1843–46 by Robert Chambers claimed to be "the first attempt to connect the natural sciences into a history of creation"; it asserted that all parts of nature were evolving onward and upward toward a greater state of perfection under God's direction.
6. Sir Richard Owen (1804–1892), a leading British zoologist and paleontologist who was opposed to Darwin's theories.
7. The Royal Society of London for the Promotion of Natural Knowledge; founded in 1660, it was an important meeting place for independent scientists.
8. William B. Carpenter (1813–1885), British naturalist.

or botany. Lyell had been threatening to publish a book on the geological history of Man, which was to be a bombshell flung into the camp of the catastrophists. My Father, after long reflection, prepared a theory of his own, which, as he fondly hoped, would take the wind out of Lyell's sails, and justify geology to godly readers of Genesis. It was, very briefly, that there had been no gradual modification of the surface of the earth, or slow development of organic forms, but that when the catastrophic act of creation took place, the world presented, instantly, the structural appearance of a planet on which life had long existed.

The theory, coarsely enough, and to my Father's great indignation, was defined by a hasty press as being this—that God hid the fossils in the rocks in order to tempt geologists into infidelity. In truth, it was the logical and inevitable conclusion of accepting, literally, the doctrine of a sudden act of creation; it emphasized the fact that any breach in the circular course of nature could be conceived only on the supposition that the object created bore false witness to past processes, which had never taken place.

Never was a book cast upon the waters with greater anticipations of success than was this curious, this obstinate, this fanatical volume. My Father lived in a fever of suspense, waiting for the tremendous issue. This *Omphalos* of his, he thought, was to bring all the turmoil of scientific speculation to a close, fling geology into the arms of Scripture, and make the lion eat grass with the lamb.[9] It was not surprising, he admitted, that there had been experienced an ever-increasing discord between the facts which geology brings to light and the direct statements of the early chapters of Genesis. Nobody was to blame for that. My Father, and my Father alone, possessed the secret of the enigma; he alone held the key which could smoothly open the lock of geological mystery. He offered it, with a glowing gesture, to atheists and Christians alike. This was to be the universal panacea; this the system of intellectual therapeutics which could not but heal all the maladies of the age. But, alas! atheists and Christians alike looked at it, and laughed, and threw it away.

In the course of that dismal winter, as the post began to bring in private letters, few and chilly, and public reviews, many and scornful, my Father looked in vain for the approval of the churches, and in vain for the acquiescence of the scientific societies, and in vain for the gratitude of those "thousands of thinking persons," which he had rashly assured himself of receiving. As his reconciliation of Scripture statements and geological deductions was welcomed nowhere; as Darwin continued silent, and the youthful Huxley was scornful, and even Charles Kingsley,[1] from whom my Father had expected the most instant appreciation, wrote that he could not "give up the painful and slow conclusion of five and twenty years' study of geology, and believe that God has written on the rocks one enormous and superfluous lie"— as all this happened or failed to happen, a gloom, cold and dismal, descended upon our morning teacups.* * *

1907

9. Allusion to the biblical prophecy of a new world order in which "the wolf also shall dwell with the lamb . . . and the lion shall eat straw like the ox" (Isaiah 11.6–7).
1. Clergyman and novelist (1819–1875).

INDUSTRIALISM: PROGRESS OR DECLINE?

In 1835 the French statesman and author Alexis de Tocqueville wrote of Manchester: "From this foul drain, the greatest stream of human industry flows out to fertilize the whole world. From this filthy sewer pure gold flows. Here humanity attains its most complete development and its most brutish, here civilization works its miracles and civilized man is turned almost into a savage." De Tocqueville's graphic sense of the wealth and the wretchedness that the Industrial Revolution had created epitomized contemporary responses to the way in which manufacturing had transformed nineteenth-century England. Victorians debated whether the machine age was a blessing or a curse, whether the economic system was making humanity happier or more miserable. Did the Industrial Revolution represent progress, and how, in fact, was progress to be defined?

The Industrial Revolution was the result of a complex set of causes, none of which, by itself, could have given rise to the phenomenon: the crucial technological innovations would have meant little without notable population growth, an increase in agricultural efficiency that released much of the workforce from field labor, and key economic changes, such as greater mobility of capital. Transformations in the production of textiles led to the first and most dramatic break with age-old practices. First powered by hand, or sometimes by water, machinery to speed up spinning and weaving processes was developed in England in the eighteenth century; by the 1780s manufacturers were installing steam engines, newly improved by James Watt, in large buildings called mills or factories. Mill towns, producing cotton or woollen cloth for the world's markets, grew quickly in northern England; the population of the city of Manchester, for example, increased tenfold in the years between 1760 and 1830. The development of the railways in the 1830s initiated a new phase in the industrial age, marked by an enormous expansion in the production of iron and coal. By the beginning of the Victorian period, the Industrial Revolution had already created profound economic and social changes. Hundreds of thousands of workers had migrated to the industrial towns, where they lived in horribly crowded, unsanitary housing and labored very long hours—fourteen a day or more—at very low wages. Employers often preferred to hire women and children, who worked for even less money than men.

Moved by the terrible suffering of the workers, which was intensified by a severe depression in the early 1840s, writers and legislators drew increasingly urgent attention to the condition of the working class. A number of parliamentary committees and commissions in the 1830s and 1840s introduced testimony about working conditions in mines and factories that led to the beginning of government regulation and inspection, particularly of the working conditions of women and children. Other eyewitness accounts created a growing consciousness of the plight of the workers. In *The Condition of the Working Class* (1845), Friedrich Engels described the conclusions he drew in the twenty months he spent observing industrial conditions in Manchester. In a series of interviews written for the *Morning Chronicle* (1849–52), later published as *London Labour and the London Poor* (1861–62), the journalist Henry Mayhew created a portrait of working London by collecting scores of interviews with workers. Novels portraying the painful consequences of industrialism, such as Elizabeth Gaskell's *Mary Barton* (1848) and *North and South* (1855) and Charles Dickens's *Hard Times* (1854), began to appear.

The terrible living and working conditions of industrial laborers led a number of writers to see the Industrial Revolution as an appalling retrogression. Thomas Carlyle and John Ruskin both lamented the changed conditions of labor, the loss of craftsmanship and individual creativity, and the disappearance of what Karl Marx called the "feudal, patriarchal, idyllic relations" between employer and employee that they believed had existed in earlier economies. They criticized industrial manufacture not only for the misery of the conditions it created but also for its regimentation of minds and hearts as well as bodies and resources. In works such as *Past and Present* (1843) and *Unto This Last* (1860), Carlyle and Ruskin advocated a nostalgic and conservative ideal, in which employers and workers returned to a medieval relationship to craft and to authority and responsibility. Other writers drew more radical conclusions. William Morris's perception of the workers' plight led him to socialism, though a socialism with a medieval ideal; and Marx, in collaboration with Engels, based *The Communist Manifesto* of 1848 in part on Engels's observation of Manchester in *The Condition of the Working Class*. The outrage expressed by these authors is very different from the satisfaction evident in the writings of the historian Thomas Babington Macaulay, who congratulated England on the progress that industrialism had enabled.

It is instructive to compare the selections in this section with Carlyle's chapter "Captains of Industry" from *Past and Present*; Elizabeth Barrett Browning's poem about child labor, "The Cry of the Children" (1843); Ruskin's arguments about manufacture in *The Stones of Venice* (1851–53); and William Morris's explanation in "How I Became a Socialist" (1894).

For additional texts concerning industrialism, see "Industrialism: Progress or Decline?" at Norton Literature Online.

THOMAS BABINGTON MACAULAY

In a book titled *Colloquies on the Progress and Prospects of Society* (1829), the poet Robert Southey (1774–1843) had sought to expose the evils of industrialism and to assert the superiority of the traditional feudal and agricultural way of life of England's past. His romantic conservatism provoked Macaulay (1800–1859) to review the book in a long and characteristic essay, published in the *Edinburgh Review* (1830). As in his popular *History of England* (1849–61), Macaulay seeks here to demolish his opponent with a bombardment of facts and figures, demonstrating that industrialism and middle-class government have resulted in progress and increased comforts for humankind.

From A Review of Southey's *Colloquies*

[EVIDENCE OF PROGRESS]

* * * Perhaps we could not select a better instance of the spirit which pervades the whole book than the passages in which Mr. Southey gives his opinion of the manufacturing system. There is nothing which he hates so bitterly. It is, according to him, a system more tyrannical than that of the feudal ages, a system of actual servitude, a system which destroys the bodies and degrades the minds of those who are engaged in it. He expresses a hope that the competition of other nations may drive us out of the field; that our foreign trade may decline; and that we may thus enjoy a restoration of national sanity and strength. But he seems to think that the extermination of the whole manufacturing population would be a blessing, if the evil could be removed in no other way.

Mr. Southey does not bring forward a single fact in support of these views; and, as it seems to us, there are facts which lead to a very different conclusion.

In the first place, the poor rate[1] is very decidedly lower in the manufacturing than in the agricultural districts. If Mr. Southey will look over the Parliamentary returns on this subject, he will find that the amount of parochial relief required by the laborers in the different counties of England is almost exactly in inverse proportion to the degree in which the manufacturing system has been introduced into those counties. The returns for the years ending in March, 1825, and in March, 1828, are now before us. In the former year we find the poor rate highest in Sussex,[2] about twenty shillings to every inhabitant. Then come Buckinghamshire, Essex, Suffolk, Bedfordshire, Huntingdonshire, Kent, and Norfolk. In all these the rate is above fifteen shillings a head. We will not go through the whole. Even in Westmoreland and the North Riding of Yorkshire, the rate is at more than eight shillings. In Cumberland and Monmouthshire, the most fortunate of all the agricultural districts, it is at six shillings. But in the West Riding of Yorkshire,[3] it is as low as five shillings: and when we come to Lancashire, we find it at four shillings, one-fifth of what it is in Sussex. The returns of the year ending in March, 1828, are a little, and but a little, more unfavourable to the manufacturing districts. Lancashire, even in that season of distress, required a smaller poor rate than any other district, and little more than one-fourth of the poor rate raised in Sussex. Cumberland alone, of the agricultural districts, was as well off as the West Riding of Yorkshire. These facts seem to indicate that the manufacturer[4] is both in a more comfortable and in a less dependent situation than the agricultural laborer.

As to the effect of the manufacturing system on the bodily health, we must beg leave to estimate it by a standard far too low and vulgar for a mind so imaginative as that of Mr. Southey, the proportion of births and deaths. We know that, during the growth of this atrocious system, this new misery, to use the phrases of Mr. Southey, this new enormity, this birth of a portentous age, this pest which no man can approve whose heart is not seared or whose understanding has not been darkened, there has been a great diminution of mortality, and that this diminution has been greater in the manufacturing towns than anywhere else. The mortality still is, as it always was, greater in towns than in the country. But the difference has diminished in an extraordinary degree. There is the best reason to believe that the annual mortality of Manchester, about the middle of the last century, was one in twenty-eight. It is now reckoned at one in forty-five. In Glasgow and Leeds a similar improvement has taken place. Nay, the rate of mortality in those three great capitals of the manufacturing districts is now considerably less than it was, fifty years ago, over England and Wales, taken together, open country and all. We might with some plausibility maintain that the people live longer because they are better fed, better lodged, better clothed, and better attended in sickness, and that these improvements are owing to that increase of national wealth which the manufacturing system has produced.

Much more might be said on this subject. But to what end? It is not from bills of mortality and statistical tables that Mr. Southey has learned his political creed. He cannot stoop to study the history of the system which he abuses, to strike the balance between the good and evil which it has produced, to

1. Taxes on property, to provide food and lodging for the unemployed or unemployable. The amount or rate of such taxes varied from district to district in England, depending on local conditions of unemployment.
2. A predominantly agricultural district.
3. A manufacturing district.
4. I.e., factory worker.

compare district with district, or generation with generation. We will give his own reason for his opinion, the only reason which he gives for it, in his own words:

> We remained a while in silence looking upon the assemblage of dwellings below. Here, and in the adjoining hamlet of Millbeck, the effects of manufacturer and of agriculture may be seen and compared. The old cottages are such as the poet and the painter equally delight in beholding. Substantially built of the native stone without mortar, dirtied with no white lime, and their long low roofs covered with slate, if they had been raised by the magic of some indigenous Amphion's music,[5] the materials could not have adjusted themselves more beautifully in accord with the surrounding scene; and time has still further harmonized them with weather stains, lichens, and moss, short grasses, and short fern, and stoneplants of various kinds. The ornamented chimneys, round or square, less adorned than those which, like little turrets, crest the houses of the Portuguese peasantry, and yet not less happily suited to their place; the hedge of clipped box beneath the windows, the rose bushes beside the door, the little patch of flower ground, with its tall hollyhocks in front; the garden beside, the beehives, and the orchard with its bank of daffodils and snowdrops, the earliest and the profusest in these parts, indicate in the owners some portion of ease and leisure, some regard to neatness and comfort, some sense of natural, and innocent, and healthful enjoyment. The new cottages of the manufacturers are upon the manufacturing pattern—naked, and in a row.
>
> "How is it," said I, "that everything which is connected with manufactures presents such features of unqualified deformity? From the largest of Mammon's temples down to the poorest hovel in which his helotry[6] are stalled, these edifices have all one character. Time will not mellow them; nature will neither clothe nor conceal them; and they will remain always as offensive to the eye as to the mind."

Here is wisdom. Here are the principles on which nations are to be governed. Rosebushes and poor rates, rather than steam engines and independence. Mortality and cottages with weather stains, rather than health and long life with edifices which time cannot mellow. We are told that our age has invented atrocities beyond the imagination of our fathers; that society has been brought into a state compared with which extermination would be a blessing; and all because the dwellings of cotton-spinners are naked and rectangular. Mr. Southey has found out a way, he tells us, in which the effects of manufactures and agriculture may be compared. And what is this way? To stand on a hill, to look at a cottage and a factory, and to see which is the prettier. Does Mr. Southey think that the body of the English peasantry live, or ever lived, in substantial or ornamented cottages, with boxhedges, flower gardens, beehives, and orchards? If not, what is his parallel worth? We despise those mock philosophers,[7] who think that they serve the cause of science by depreciating

---

5. According to Greek mythology, Amphion's magical skill as a harp player caused the walls of Thebes to be erected without human aid.
6. I.e., slaves (helots were a class of serfs in ancient Sparta). Mammon: the devil of covetousness.
7. Presumably such Utilitarian philosophers as

Jeremy Bentham, who had equated poetry with pushpin, an idle pastime. It should be noted, however, that although Macaulay often attacked the Utilitarians for their narrow preoccupation with theory, his own position had much in common with theirs.

literature and the fine arts. But if anything could excuse their narrowness of mind, it would be such a book as this. It is not strange that, when one enthusiast makes the picturesque the test of political good, another should feel inclined to proscribe altogether the pleasures of taste and imagination.

* * *

It is not strange that, differing so widely from Mr. Southey as to the past progress of society, we should differ from him also as to its probable destiny. He thinks, that to all outward appearance, the country is hastening to destruction; but he relies firmly on the goodness of God. We do not see either the piety or the rationality of thus confidently expecting that the Supreme Being will interfere to disturb the common succession of causes and effects. We, too, rely on his goodness, on his goodness as manifested, not in extraordinary interpositions, but in those general laws which it has pleased him to establish in the physical and in the moral world. We rely on the natural tendency of the human intellect to truth, and on the natural tendency of society to improvement. We know no well-authenticated instance of a people which has decidedly retrograded in civilization and prosperity, except from the influence of violent and terrible calamities, such as those which laid the Roman Empire in ruins, or those which, about the beginning of the sixteenth century, desolated Italy.[8] We know of no country which, at the end of fifty years of peace and tolerably good government, has been less prosperous than at the beginning of that period. The political importance of a state may decline, as the balance of power is disturbed by the introduction of new forces. Thus the influence of Holland and of Spain is much diminished. But are Holland and Spain poorer than formerly? We doubt it. Other countries have outrun them. But we suspect that they have been positively, though not relatively, advancing. We suspect that Holland is richer than when she sent her navies up the Thames,[9] that Spain is richer than when a French king was brought captive to the footstool of Charles the Fifth.[1]

History is full of the signs of this natural progress of society. We see in almost every part of the annals of mankind how the industry of individuals, struggling up against wars, taxes, famines, conflagrations, mischievous prohibitions, and more mischievous protections, creates faster than governments can squander, and repairs whatever invaders can destroy. We see the wealth of nations increasing, and all the arts of life approaching nearer and nearer to perfection, in spite of the grossest corruption and the wildest profusion on the part of rulers.

The present moment is one of great distress. But how small will that distress appear when we think over the history of the last forty years; a war,[2] compared with which all other wars sink into insignificance; taxation, such as the most heavily taxed people of former times could not have conceived; a debt larger than all the public debts that ever existed in the world added together; the food of the people studiously rendered dear;[3] the currency imprudently

8. These "calamities" were invasions by outside powers: in 410 the Visigoths sacked Rome, and the French and Spanish fought for control of the Italian states in the early 16th century.
9. In 1667 a Dutch fleet displayed its power by sailing up the river Thames without being challenged by the English navy.
1. Charles V, Holy Roman emperor (and king of Spain as Charles I), captured the king of France, Francis I, in the battle of Pavia (1525).

2. The wars against France and Napoleon, extending, with some interruptions, from 1792 to 1815. During the war years England lost one in six men of fighting age and had to endure the pressure of Napoleon's trade boycotts; the historian Derek Beales claims that the resulting economic disruption was comparable to that experienced in World War I.
3. Expensive.

debased, and imprudently restored. Yet is the country poorer than in 1790? We firmly believe that, in spite of all the misgovernment of her rulers, she has been almost constantly becoming richer and richer. Now and then there has been a stoppage, now and then a short retrogression; but as to the general tendency there can be no doubt. A single breaker may recede; but the tide is evidently coming in.

If we were to prophesy that in the year 1930 a population of fifty millions, better fed, clad, and lodged than the English of our time, will cover these islands, that Sussex and Huntingdonshire will be wealthier than the wealthiest parts of the West Riding of Yorkshire now are, that cultivation, rich as that of a flower garden, will be carried up to the very tops of Ben Nevis and Helvellyn,[4] that machines constructed on principles yet undiscovered will be in every house, that there will be no highways but railroads, no traveling but by steam, that our debt, vast as it seems to us, will appear to our great-grandchildren a trifling encumbrance, which might easily be paid off in a year or two, many people would think us insane. We prophesy nothing; but this we say: If any person had told the Parliament which met in perplexity and terror after the crash in 1720[5] that in 1830 the wealth of England would surpass all their wildest dreams, that the annual revenue would equal the principal of that debt which they considered as an intolerable burden, that for one man of ten thousand pounds then living there would be five men of fifty thousand pounds, that London would be twice as large and twice as populous, and that nevertheless the rate of mortality would have diminished to one-half of what it then was, that the post office would bring more into the exchequer than the excise and customs had brought in together under Charles the Second, that stage coaches would run from London to York in twenty-four hours, that men would be in the habit of sailing without wind, and would be beginning to ride without horses, our ancestors would have given as much credit to the prediction as they gave to *Gulliver's Travels*.[6] Yet the prediction would have been true; and they would have perceived that it was not altogether absurd, if they had considered that the country was then raising every year a sum which would have purchased the fee-simple of the revenue of the Plantagenets,[7] ten times what supported the Government of Elizabeth, three times what, in the time of Cromwell,[8] had been thought intolerably oppressive. To almost all men the state of things under which they have been used to live seems to be the necessary state of things. We have heard it said that five per cent is the natural interest of money, that twelve is the natural number of a jury, that forty shillings is the natural qualification of a county voter. Hence it is that, though in every age everybody knows that up to his own time progressive improvement has been taking place, nobody seems to reckon on any improvement during the next generation. We cannot absolutely prove that those are in error who tell us that society has reached a turning point, that we have seen our best days. But so said all who came before us, and with just as much apparent reason. "A million a year will beggar us," said the patriots of 1640. "Two millions a year will grind the country to powder," was the cry in 1660. "Six millions a year, and a debt of fifty millions!" exclaimed Swift, "the high allies have been

---

4. Mountains in Scotland and in the English Lake District, respectively.
5. The first great stock market crash, commonly known as the South Sea Bubble.
6. The 1726 novel by the Irish churchman, satirist, and poet Jonathan Swift (1667–1745). Charles II reigned from 1660 to 1685.

7. The Plantagenet family provided the monarchs of England from 1145 to 1485. "Fee-simple": absolute ownership of their estates.
8. Oliver Cromwell effectively ruled England from the beheading of Charles I in 1651 until his own death in 1658. Elizabeth I reigned from 1558 to 1603.

the ruin of us." "A hundred and forty millions of debt!" said Junius;[9] "well may we say that we owe Lord Chatham more than we shall ever pay, if we owe him such a load as this." "Two hundred and forty millions of debt!" cried all the statesmen of 1783 in chorus; "what abilities, or what economy on the part of a minister, can save a country so burdened?" We know that if, since 1783, no fresh debt had been incurred, the increased resources of the country would have enabled us to defray that debt at which Pitt, Fox, and Burke[1] stood aghast, nay, to defray it over and over again, and that with much lighter taxation than what we have actually borne. On what principle is it that, when we see nothing but improvement behind us, we are to expect nothing but deterioration before us?

It is not by the intermeddling of Mr. Southey's idol, the omniscient and omnipotent State, but by the prudence and energy of the people, that England has hitherto been carried forward in civilization; and it is to the same prudence and the same energy that we now look with comfort and good hope. Our rulers will best promote the improvement of the nation by strictly confining them- selves to their own legitimate duties, by leaving capital to find its most lucrative course, commodities their fair price, industry and intelligence their natural reward, idleness and folly their natural punishment, by maintaining peace, by defending property, by diminishing the price of law, and by observing strict economy in every department of the State. Let the Government do this: the People will assuredly do the rest.

1830

9. Pseudonym of a political commentator whose letters (1769–72) usually praised William Pitt, earl of Chatham (1708–1778). Pitt, as leader of the war against France, which gained Canada for England, could have been blamed for running his country into debt.
1. Noted statesmen and members of Parliament in Great Britain: William Pitt the Younger (1759– 1806), Charles James Fox (1749–1806), and Edmund Burke (1729–1797).

THE CHILDREN'S EMPLOYMENT COMMISSION

Although official attempts to regulate child labor began in 1788, when Parliament passed the Chimney Sweepers Act, the more general problem was not addressed until well into the nineteenth century. Government investigations (Select Committees and Royal Commissions) took place in 1816 and the early 1830s and led to numerous legislative measures, but most of their provisions were meaningless because they were not enforced. The Factories Regulation Act of 1833 marks the first significant point of successful intervention: the act both established a minimum age for all workers in textile mills (nine years old) and set limits to the hours that children in different age groups and women could work in a week. More broadly, a Royal Commission was convened in 1842–43 to examine "the mines and collieries of the United Kingdom and all trades and manufactures whatever in which children work together in num- bers." The reports of the commission, from which this extract and two illustrations are taken, caused dismay and disbelief when they were made generally available; Elizabeth Barrett Browning's poem "The Cry of the Children" (1843) was one of the many public responses to the scandal. In the legislation that followed, girls and women were banned from mine work; although the authors of the bill had also hoped to prohibit the employment of boys under thirteen years of age, parliamentary debate knocked the age down to ten.

The first illustration shows a hurrier, a worker who dragged a loaded corve, or wagon; these weighed between two hundred and five hundred pounds and were attached to the hurrier by a chain. The passageways in the mine (or pit) were sometimes only sixteen inches high. The second illustration presents a thruster, who pushed a corve. The child on the left is a trapper: the youngest workers of all, these five- or six-year-olds sat alone in darkness to open and close the doors that controlled the mine's ventilation system. The extract comes from the evidence collected by Commissioner S. S. Scriven, who visited the mines in the West Riding of Yorkshire in the company of a local doctor and lawyer, and interviewed the child laborers there.

From First Report of the Commissioners, Mines

[CHILD MINE-WORKER IN YORKSHIRE]

Margaret Gomley, living at Lindley Moor, aged 9. May 7:

They call me Peggy for my nick-name down here, but my right name is Margaret; I am about nine years, or going nine; I have been at work in the pit thrusting corves above a year; come in the morning sometimes at seven o'clock, sometimes half-past seven, and I go sometimes home at six o'clock, sometimes at seven when I do over-work. I get my breakfast of porridge before I come, and bring a piece of muffin, which I eat on coming to pit; I get my dinner at 12 o'clock, which is a dry muffin, and sometimes butter on, but have no time allowed to stop to eat it, I eat it while I am thrusting the load; I get no tea, but get some supper when I get home, and then go to bed when I have washed me; and am very tired. I worked in pit last winter; I don't know at what hour I went down, as we have no clock, but it was day-light; it was six o'clock when we came up, but not always. They flog us down in the pit, sometimes with their hand upon my bottom, which hurts me very much; Thomas Copeland flogs me more than once in a day, which makes me cry. There are two other girls working with me, and there was four, but one left because she had the bellyache; I am poorly myself sometimes with bellyache, and sometimes headache. I had rather lake than go into the pit; I get 5*d.* a-day, but I had rather set cards[1] for 5*d.* a-day than go into the pit. The men often swear at me; many times they say Damn thee, and other times God damn thee (and such like), Peggy.

[Commissioner Scriven's commentary]

I descended this pit accompanied by one of the banksmen,[2] and, on alighting at the bottom, found the entrance to the mainway 2 feet 10 inches, and, which extended 500 yards. The bottom was deep in mire, and, as I had no corves low enough to convey me to the workings, waited some time under the dripping shaft the arrival of the hurriers, as I had reason to suspect there were some very young children labouring there. At length three girls arrived, with as many boys. It was impossible in the dark to distinguish the sexes. They were all naked excepting their shifts or shirts. Having placed one into the corve, I gave the signal, and ascended. On alighting on the pit's bank I discovered that it was a girl. I could not have believed that I should have found human nature so

---

1. I.e., work in a textile factory, where workers programmed looms to weave patterns with a series of punched cards. "Lake": play truant, or hookey

(Yorkshire dialect). "5*d.*": five pence (*d.* abbreviates *denarius,* "penny" in Latin).
2. Colliery supervisors who worked above ground.

An illustration of a "hurrier" in a Yorkshire coalmine, taken from the 1842–43 Children's Employment Commission report.

An illustration of a "trapper" and a "thruster" in a Lancashire coalmine, taken from the 1842–43 Children's Employment Commission report.

degraded. There is nothing that I can conceive amidst all the misery and wretchedness in the worst of factories equal to this. Mr. Holroyd, solicitor, and Mr. Brook, surgeon, practising in Stainland, were present, who confessed that, although living within a few miles, they could not have believed that such a system of unchristian cruelty could have existed.

1842–43

FRIEDRICH ENGELS

These eyewitness accounts from *The Condition of the Working Class* (1845) describe conditions of 1844, when Engels (1820–1895), the son of a successful German industrialist, had been living in England, chiefly in Manchester. The book was first translated from the German into English in 1892; this translation is by W. O. Henderson

and W. H. Chaloner (1958). The first two paragraphs are the conclusion of chapter
2, *The Industrial Proletariat*; the balance is from chapter 3.

From The Great Towns

Industry and commerce attain their highest stage of development in the big
towns, so that it is here that the effects of industrialization on the wage earners
can be most clearly seen. It is in these big towns that the concentration of
property has reached its highest point. Here the manners and customs of the
good old days have been most effectively destroyed. Here the very name of
"Merry England" has long since been forgotten, because the inhabitants of
the great manufacturing centers have never even heard from their grandparents what life was like in those days. In these towns there are only rich and
poor, because the lower middle classes are fast disappearing. At one time this
section of the middle classes was the most stable social group, but now it has
become the least stable. It is represented in the big factory towns today partly
by a few survivors from a bygone age and partly by a group of people who are
anxious to get rich as quickly as possible. Of these shady speculators and
dubious traders one becomes rich while ninety-nine go bankrupt. Indeed, for
more than half of those who have failed, bankruptcy has become a habit.

The vast majority of the inhabitants of these towns are the workers. We
propose to discuss their condition and to discover how they have been influenced by life and work in the great factory towns.

✷ ✷ ✷

London is unique, because it is a city in which one can roam for hours
without leaving the built-up area and without seeing the slightest sign of the
approach of open country. This enormous agglomeration of population on a
single spot has multiplied a hundred-fold the economic strength of the two
and a half million inhabitants concentrated there. This great population has
made London the commercial capital of the world and has created the gigantic
docks in which are assembled the thousands of ships which always cover the
River Thames. I know nothing more imposing than the view one obtains of
the river when sailing from the sea up to London Bridge. Especially above
Woolwich the houses and docks are packed tightly together on both banks of
the river. The further one goes up the river the thicker becomes the concentration of ships lying at anchor, so that eventually only a narrow shipping lane
is left free in midstream. Here hundreds of steamships dart rapidly to and fro.
All this is so magnificent and impressive that one is lost in admiration. The
traveler has good reason to marvel at England's greatness even before he steps
on English soil.

It is only later that the traveler appreciates the human suffering which has
made all this possible. He can only realize the price that has been paid for all
this magnificence after he has tramped the pavements of the main streets of
London for some days and has tired himself out by jostling his way through
the crowds and dodging the endless stream of coaches and carts which fills
the streets. It is only when he has visited the slums of this great city that it
dawns upon him that the inhabitants of modern London have had to sacrifice
so much that is best in human nature in order to create those wonders of

civilization with which their city teems. The vast majority of Londoners have had to let so many of their potential creative faculties lie dormant, stunted and unused in order that a small, closely-knit group of their fellow citizens could develop to the full the qualities with which nature has endowed them. The restless and noisy activity of the crowded streets is highly distasteful, and it is surely abhorrent to human nature itself. Hundreds of thousands of men and women drawn from all classes and ranks of society pack the streets of London. Are they not all human beings with the same innate characteristics and potentialities? Are they not all equally interested in the pursuit of happiness? And do they not all aim at happiness by following similar methods? Yet they rush past each other as if they had nothing in common. They are tacitly agreed on one thing only—that everyone should keep to the right of the pavement so as not to collide with the stream of people moving in the opposite direction. No one even thinks of sparing a glance for his neighbor in the streets. The more that Londoners are packed into a tiny space, the more repulsive and disgraceful becomes the brutal indifference with which they ignore their neighbors and selfishly concentrate upon their private affairs. We know well enough that this isolation of the individual—this narrow-minded egotism—is everywhere the fundamental principle of modern society. But nowhere is this selfish egotism so blatantly evident as in the frantic bustle of the great city. The disintegration of society into individuals, each guided by his private principles and each pursuing his own aims has been pushed to its furthest limits in London. Here indeed human society has been split into its component atoms.

From this it follows that the social conflict—the war of all against all—is fought in the open. * * * Here men regard their fellows not as human beings, but as pawns in the struggle for existence. Everyone exploits his neighbor with the result that the stronger tramples the weaker under foot. The strongest of all, a tiny group of capitalists, monopolize everything, while the weakest, who are in the vast majority, succumb to the most abject poverty.

What is true of London is true also of all the great towns, such as Manchester, Birmingham, and Leeds. Everywhere one finds on the one hand the most barbarous indifference and selfish egotism and on the other the most distressing scenes of misery and poverty. Signs of social conflict are to be found everywhere. Everyone turns his house into a fortress to defend himself—under the protection of the law—from the depredations of his neighbors. Class warfare is so open and shameless that it has to be seen to be believed. The observer of such an appalling state of affairs must shudder at the consequences of such feverish activity and can only marvel that so crazy a social and economic structure should survive at all.

* * *

Every great town has one or more slum areas into which the working classes are packed. Sometimes, of course, poverty is to be found hidden away in alleys close to the stately homes of the wealthy. Generally, however, the workers are segregated in separate districts where they struggle through life as best they can out of sight of the more fortunate classes of society. The slums of the English towns have much in common—the worst houses in a town being found in the worst districts. They are generally unplanned wildernesses of one- or two-storied terrace houses[1] built of brick. Wherever possible these have

---

1. Row houses.

cellars which are also used as dwellings. These little houses of three or four rooms and a kitchen are called cottages, and throughout England, except for some parts of London, are where the working classes normally live. These streets themselves are usually unpaved and full of holes. They are filthy and strewn with animal and vegetable refuse. Since they have neither gutters nor drains the refuse accumulates in stagnant, stinking puddles. Ventilation in the slums is inadequate owing to the hopelessly unplanned nature of these areas. A great many people live huddled together in a very small area, and so it is easy to imagine the nature of the air in these workers' quarters. However, in fine weather the streets are used for the drying of washing, and clothes lines are stretched across the streets from house to house and wet garments are hung out on them.

We propose to describe some of these slums in detail.

*　*　*

If we cross Blackstone Edge on foot or take the train we reach Manchester, the regional capital of South Lancashire, and enter the classic home of English industry. This is the masterpiece of the Industrial Revolution and at the same time the mainspring of all the workers' movements. Once more we are in a beautiful hilly countryside. The land slopes gently down toward the Irish Sea, intersected by the charming green valleys of the Ribble, the Irwell, the Mersey, and their tributaries. A hundred years ago this region was to a great extent thinly populated marshland. Now it is covered with towns and villages and is the most densely populated part of England. In Lancashire—particularly in Manchester—is to be found not only the origin but the heart of the industry of the United Kingdom. Manchester Exchange is the thermometer which records all the fluctuations of industrial and commercial activity. The evolution of the modern system of manufacture has reached its climax in Manchester. It was in the South Lancashire cotton industry that water and steam power first replaced hand machines. It was here that such machines as the power-loom and the self-acting mule[2] replaced the old hand-loom and spinning wheel. It is here that the division of labor has been pushed to its furthest limits. These three factors are the essence of modern industry. In all three of them the cotton industry was the pioneer and remains ahead in all branches of industry. In the circumstances it is to be expected that it is in this region that the inevitable consequences of industrialization in so far as they affect the working classes are most strikingly evident. Nowhere else can the life and conditions of the industrial proletariat be studied in all their aspects as in South Lancashire. Here can be seen most clearly the degradation into which the worker sinks owing to the introduction of steam power, machinery, and the division of labor. Here, too, can be seen most the strenuous efforts of the proletariat to raise themselves from their degraded situation. I propose to examine conditions in Manchester in greater detail for two reasons. In the first place, Manchester is the classic type of modern industrial town. Secondly, I know Manchester as well as I know my native town and I know more about it than most of its inhabitants.

*　*　*

*　*　* Owing to the curious lay-out of the town it is quite possible for someone to live for years in Manchester and to travel daily to and from his work

2. A machine that automatically winds spun yarn directly onto spindles.

without ever seeing a working-class quarter or coming into contact with an artisan. He who visits Manchester simply on business or for pleasure need never see the slums, mainly because the working-class districts and the middle-class districts are quite distinct. This division is due partly to deliberate policy and partly to instinctive and tacit agreement between the two social groups. In those areas where the two social groups happen to come into contact with each other the middle classes sanctimoniously ignore the existence of their less fortunate neighbors. In the center of Manchester there is a fairly large commercial district, which is about half a mile long and half a mile broad. This district is almost entirely given over to offices and warehouses. Nearly the whole of this district has no permanent residents and is deserted at night, when only policemen patrol its dark, narrow thoroughfares with their bull's-eye lanterns.[3] This district is intersected by certain main streets which carry an enormous volume of traffic. The lower floors of the buildings are occupied by shops of dazzling splendor. A few of the upper stories on these premises are used as dwellings and the streets present a relatively busy appearance until late in the evening. Around this commercial quarter there is a belt of built-up areas on the average one and a half miles in width, which is occupied entirely by working-class dwellings. This area of workers' houses includes all Manchester proper, except the center, all Salford and Hulme, an important part of Pendleton and Chorlton, two-thirds of Ardwick, and certain small areas of Cheetham Hill and Broughton. Beyond this belt of working-class houses or dwellings lie the districts inhabited by the middle classes and the upper classes. The former are to be found in regularly laid out streets near the working-class districts—in Chorlton and in the remoter parts of Cheetham Hill. The villas of the upper classes are surrounded by gardens and lie in the higher and remoter parts of Chorlton and Ardwick or on the breezy heights of Cheetham Hill, Broughton, and Pendleton. The upper class enjoy healthy country air and live in luxurious and comfortable dwellings which are linked to the center of Manchester by omnibuses which run every fifteen or thirty minutes. To such an extent has the convenience of the rich been considered in the planning of Manchester that these plutocrats can travel from their houses to their places of business in the center of the town by the shortest routes, which run entirely through working-class districts, without even realizing how close they are to the misery and filth which lie on both sides of the road.

* * *

* * * I will now give a description of the working-class districts of Manchester. The first of them is the Old Town, which lies between the northern limit of the commercial quarter and the River Irk. Here even the better streets, such Todd Street, Long Millgate, Withy Grove, and Shudehill are narrow and tortuous. The houses are dirty, old, and tumble-down. The sidestreets have been built in a disgraceful fashion. If one enters the district near the "Old Church" and goes down Long Millgate, one sees immediately on the right hand side a row of antiquated houses where not a single front wall is standing upright. This is a remnant of the old Manchester of the days before the town became industrialized. The original inhabitants and their children have left for better houses in other districts, while the houses in Long Millgate, which no longer satisfied them, were left to a tribe of workers containing a strong

---

3. Lanterns that have a hemispherical lens.

Irish element. Here one is really and truly in a district which is quite obviously given over entirely to the working classes, because even the shopkeepers and the publicans of Long Millgate make no effort to give their establishments a semblance of cleanliness. The condition of this street may be deplorable, but it is by no means as bad as the alleys and courts which lie behind it, and which can be approached only by covered passages so narrow that two people cannot pass. Anyone who has never visited these courts and alleys can have no idea of the fantastic[4] way in which the houses have been packed together in disorderly confusion in impudent defiance of all reasonable principles of town planning. And the fault lies not merely in the survival of old property from earlier periods in Manchester's history. Only in quite modern times has the policy of cramming as many houses as possible on to such space as was not utilized in earlier periods reached its climax. The result is that today not an inch of space remains between the houses and any further building is now physically impossible. To prove my point I reproduce a small section of a plan of Manchester.[5] It is by no means the worst slum in Manchester and it does not cover one-tenth of the area of Manchester.

This sketch will be sufficient to illustrate the crazy layout of the whole district lying near the River Irk. There is a very sharp drop of some 15 to 30 feet down to the south bank of the Irk at this point. As many as three rows of houses have generally been squeezed onto this precipitous slope. The lowest row of houses stands directly on the bank of the river while the front walls of the highest row stand on the crest of the ridge in Long Millgate. Moreover, factory buildings are also to be found on the banks of the river. In short the layout of the upper part of Long Millgate at the top of the rise is just as disorderly and congested as the lower part of the street. To the right and left a number of covered passages from Long Millgate give access to several courts. On reaching them one meets with a degree of dirt and revolting filth the like of which is not to be found elsewhere. The worst courts are those leading down to the Irk, which contain unquestionably the most dreadful dwellings I have ever seen. In one of these courts, just at the entrance where the covered passage ends, there is a privy without a door. This privy is so dirty that the inhabitants of the court can only enter or leave the court if they are prepared to wade through puddles of stale urine and excrement. Anyone who wishes to confirm this description should go to the first court on the bank of the Irk above Ducie Bridge. Several tanneries are situated on the bank of the river and they fill the neighborhood with the stench of animal putrefaction. The only way of getting to the courts below Ducie Bridge is by going down flights of narrow dirty steps and one can only reach the houses by treading over heaps of dirt and filth. The first court below Ducie Bridge is called Allen's Court. At the time of the cholera [1832] this court was in such a disgraceful state that the sanitary inspectors [of the local Board of Health] evacuated the inhabitants. The court was then swept and fumigated with chlorine. In his pamphlet[6] Dr. Kay gives a horrifying description of conditions in this court at that time. Since Kay wrote this pamphlet, this court appears to have been at any rate partly demolished and rebuilt. If one looks down the river from Ducie Bridge one does at least see several ruined walls and high piles of rubble, side by side

4. Confused, haphazard.
5. Not reprinted here.
6. *The Moral and Physical Conditions of the Working Classes Employed in the Cotton Manufacture in*

Manchester (1832), by the British doctor and public health and education reformer James Phillips Kay-Shuttleworth (1804–1877).

with some recently built houses. The view from this bridge, which is mercifully concealed by a high parapet from all but the tallest mortals, is quite characteristic of the whole district. At the bottom the Irk flows, or rather, stagnates. It is a narrow, coal-black, stinking river full of filth and rubbish which it deposits on the more low-lying right bank. In dry weather this bank presents the spectacle of a series of the most revolting blackish-green puddles of slime from the depths of which bubbles of miasmatic gases constantly rise and create a stench which is unbearable even to those standing on the bridge forty or fifty feet above the level of the water. Moreover, the flow of the river is continually interrupted by numerous high weirs, behind which large quantities of slime and refuse collect and putrefy. Above Ducie Bridge there are some tall tannery buildings, and further up there are dye-works, bone mills, and gasworks. All the filth, both liquid and solid, discharged by these works finds its way into the River Irk, which also receives the contents of the adjacent sewers and privies. The nature of the filth deposited by this river may well be imagined. If one looks at the heaps of garbage below Ducie Bridge one can gauge the extent to which accumulated dirt, filth, and decay permeate the courts on the steep left bank of the river. The houses are packed very closely together and since the bank of the river is very steep it is possible to see a part of every house. All of them have been blackened by soot, all of them are crumbling with age and all have broken window panes and window frames. In the background there are old factory buildings which look like barracks. On the opposite, low-lying bank of the river, one sees a long row of houses and factories. The second house is a roofless ruin, filled with refuse, and the third is built in such a low situation that the ground floor is uninhabitable and has neither doors nor windows. In the background one sees the paupers' cemetery, and the stations of the railways to Liverpool and Leeds. Behind these buildings is situated the workhouse, Manchester's "Poor Law Bastille."[7] The workhouse is built on a hill and from behind its high walls and battlements seems to threaten the whole adjacent working-class quarter like a fortress.

Above Ducie Bridge the left bank of the Irk becomes flatter and the right bank of the Irk becomes steeper and so the condition of the houses on both sides of the river becomes worse rather than better. Turning left from the main street which is still Long Millgate, the visitor can easily lose his way. He wanders aimlessly from one court to another. He turns one corner after another through innumerable narrow dirty alleyways and passages, and in only a few minutes he has lost all sense of direction and does not know which way to turn. The area is full of ruined or half-ruined buildings. Some of them are actually uninhabited and that means a great deal in this quarter of the town. In the houses one seldom sees a wooden or a stone floor, while the doors and windows are nearly always broken and badly fitting. And as for the dirt! Everywhere one sees heaps of refuse, garbage, and filth. There are stagnant pools instead of gutters and the stench alone is so overpowering that no human being, even partially civilized, would find it bearable to live in such a district.[8]

7. The workhouses established by the Poor Laws of the 1830s, because of the strict regimens enforced on inmates, were commonly likened to prisons such as the Bastille in Paris.
8. Cf. another account of Manchester slums of the same decade in Elizabeth Gaskell's novel *Mary Barton* (1848), chap. 6:

Women from their doors tossed household slops of *every* description into the gutter; they ran into the next pool, which overflowed and stagnated. Heaps of ashes were stepping-stones, on which the passer-by, who cared in the least for cleanliness, took care not to put his foot. Our friends [two factory workers] were not dainty, but even

The recently constructed extension of the Leeds railway which crosses the Irk at this point has swept away some of these courts and alleys, but it has thrown open to public gaze some of the others. So it comes about that there is to be found immediately under the railway bridge a court which is even filthier and more revolting than all the others. This is simply because it was formerly so hidden and secluded that it could only be reached with considerable difficulty, [but is now exposed to the human eye]. I thought I knew this district well, but even I would never have found it had not the railway viaduct made a breach in the slums at this point. One walks along a very rough path on the river bank, in between clothes-posts and washing lines to reach a chaotic group of little, one-storied, one-roomed cabins. Most of them have earth floors, and working, living, and sleeping all take place in the one room. In such a hole, barely six feet long and five feet wide, I saw two beds—and what beds and bedding!—which filled the room, except for the fireplace and the doorstep. Several of these huts, as far as I could see, were completely empty, although the door was open and the inhabitants were leaning against the door posts. In front of the doors filth and garbage abounded. I could not see the pavement, but from time to time, I felt it was there because my feet scraped it. This whole collection of cattle sheds for human beings was surrounded on two sides by houses and a factory and on a third side by the river. [It was possible to get to this slum by only two routes]. One was the narrow path along the river bank, while the other was a narrow gateway which led to another human rabbit warren which was nearly as badly built and was nearly in such a bad condition as the one I have just described.

Enough of this! All along the Irk slums of this type abound. There is an unplanned and chaotic conglomeration of houses, most of which are more or less unhabitable. The dirtiness of the interiors of these premises is fully in keeping with the filth that surrounds them. How can people dwelling in such places keep clean! There are not even adequate facilities for satisfying the most natural daily needs. There are so few privies that they are either filled up everyday or are too far away for those who need to use them. How can these people wash when all that is available is the dirty water of the Irk? Pumps and piped water are to be found only in the better-class districts of the town. Indeed no one can blame these helots[9] of modern civilization if their homes are no cleaner than the occasional pigsties which are a feature of these slums. There are actually some property owners who are not ashamed to let[1] dwellings such as those which are to be found below Scotland Bridge. Here on the quayside a mere six feet from the water's edge is to be found a row of six or seven cellars, the bottoms of which are at least two feet beneath the low-water level of the Irk. [What can one say of the owner of] the corner house—situated on the opposite bank of the river above Scotland Bridge—who actually lets the upper floor although the premises downstairs are quite uninhabitable and no attempt has been made to board up the gaps left by the

---

they picked their way, till they got to some steps leading down . . . into the cellar in which a family of human beings lived. . . . After the account I have given of the state of the street, no one can be surprised that on going into the cellar inhabited by Davenport, the smell was so foetid as almost to knock the two men down. Quickly recovering themselves, as those inured to such things do, they began to penetrate the thick darkness of the place, and to see three or four children rolling on the damp, nay wet brick floor, through which the stagnant, filthy moisture of the street oozed up; the fireplace was empty and black; the wife sat on her husband's lair [couch], and cried in the dank loneliness.

9. I.e., slaves (helots were a class of serfs in ancient Sparta).

1. Rent.

disappearance of doors and windows? This sort of thing is by no means uncommon in this part of Manchester, where, owing to the lack of conveniences, such deserted ground floors are often used by the whole neighborhood as privies.

1845

CHARLES KINGSLEY

The following selection is from chapter 8 of *Alton Locke,* a novel by Kingsley (1819–1875). Under the influence of Thomas Carlyle's writings and also as a result of his own observations, Kingsley, a clergyman, became deeply concerned with the sufferings of the working classes. The speaker here, a young tailor, is accompanied by an elderly Scottish bookseller, Sandy Mackaye.

From Alton Locke

[A LONDON SLUM]

It was a foul, chilly, foggy Saturday night. From the butchers' and greengrocers' shops the gaslights flared and flickered, wild and ghastly, over haggard groups of slipshod dirty women, bargaining for scraps of stale meat and frost-bitten vegetables, wrangling about short weight and bad quality. Fish stalls and fruit stalls lined the edge of the greasy pavement, sending up odors as foul as the language of sellers and buyers. Blood and sewer water crawled from under doors and out of spouts, and reeked down the gutters among offal, animal and vegetable, in every stage of putrefaction. Foul vapours rose from cow sheds and slaughterhouses, and the doorways of undrained alleys, where the inhabitants carried the filth out on their shoes from the backyard into the court, and from the court up into the main street; while above, hanging like cliffs over the streets—those narrow, brawling torrents of filth, and poverty, and sin—the houses with their teeming load of life were piled up into the dingy, choking night. A ghastly, deafening, sickening sight it was. Go, scented Belgravian![1] and see what London is! and then go to the library which God has given thee—one often fears in vain—and see what science says this London might be!

✻   ✻   ✻

We went on through a back street or two, and then into a huge, miserable house, which, a hundred years ago, perhaps, had witnessed the luxury, and rung to the laughter of some one great fashionable family, alone there in their glory. Now every room of it held its family, or its group of families—a phalanstery[2] of all the fiends—its grand staircase, with the carved balustrades rotting and crumbling away piecemeal, converted into a common sewer for all its inmates. Up stair after stair we went, while wails of children, and curses

---

1. Inhabitant of Belgravia, a wealthy residential district of London.
2. A kind of model cooperative community pro-

posed by the French socialist Charles Fourier (1772–1837).

of men, steamed out upon the hot stifling rush of air from every doorway, till, at the topmost story, we knocked at a garret door. We entered. Bare it was of furniture, comfortless, and freezing cold; but, with the exception of the plaster dropping from the roof, and the broken windows, patched with rags and paper, there was a scrupulous neatness about the whole, which contrasted strangely with the filth and slovenliness outside. There was no bed in the room—no table. On a broken chair by the chimney sat a miserable old woman, fancying that she was warming her hands over embers which had long been cold, shaking her head, and muttering to herself, with palsied lips, about the guardians[3] and the workhouse; while upon a few rags on the floor lay a girl, ugly, small-pox-marked, hollow-eyed, emaciated, her only bedclothes the skirt of a large handsome new riding habit, at which two other girls, wan and tawdry, were astitching busily, as they sat right and left of her on the floor. The old woman took no notice of us as we entered; but one of the girls looked up, and, with a pleased gesture of recognition, put her finger up to her lips, and whispered, "Ellen's asleep."

"I'm not asleep, dears," answered a faint unearthly voice; "I was only praying. Is that Mr. Mackaye?"

"Aye, my lassies; but ha' ye gotten na fire the nicht?"

"No," said one of them, bitterly, "we've earned no fire tonight, by fair trade or foul either."

1850

3. Members of the local Board of Guardians, the body that supervised the workhouse.

CHARLES DICKENS

The following selection is from chapter 5 of *Hard Times,* a novel by Dickens (1812–1870). The picture of Coketown was based on his impressions of the raw industrial towns of central and northern England such as Manchester and, in particular, Preston, a cotton-manufacturing center in Lancashire.

From Hard Times

[COKETOWN]

It was a town of red brick, or of brick that would have been red if the smoke and ashes had allowed it; but as matters stood it was a town of unnatural red and black like the painted face of a savage. It was a town of machinery and tall chimneys, out of which interminable serpents of smoke trailed themselves forever and ever, and never got uncoiled. It had a black canal in it, and a river that ran purple with ill-smelling dye, and vast piles of buildings full of windows where there was a rattling and a trembling all day long, and where the piston of the steam engine worked monotonously up and down like the head of an elephant in a state of melancholy madness. It contained several large streets all very like one another, and many small streets still more like one another, inhabited by people equally like one another, who all went in and out at the same hours, with the same sound upon the same pavements, to do the same work, and to whom every day was the same as yesterday and tomorrow, and every year the counterpart of the last and the next.

These attributes of Coketown were in the main inseparable from the work by which it was sustained; against them were to be set off, comforts of life which found their way all over the world, and elegancies of life which made, we will not ask how much of the fine lady, who could scarcely bear to hear the place mentioned. The rest of its features were voluntary, and they were these.

You saw nothing in Coketown but what was severely workful. If the members of a religious persuasion built a chapel there—as the members of eighteen religious persuasions had done—they made it a pious warehouse of red brick, with sometimes (but this is only in highly ornamented examples) a bell in a birdcage on the top of it. The solitary exception was the New Church; a stuccoed edifice with a square steeple over the door terminating in four short pinnacles like florid wooden legs. All the public inscriptions in the town were painted alike, in severe characters of black and white. The jail might have been the infirmary, the infirmary might have been the jail, the town hall might have been either, or both, or anything else, for anything that appeared to the contrary in the graces of their construction. Fact, fact, fact, everywhere in the material aspect of the town; fact, fact, fact, everywhere in the immaterial. The M'Choakumchild school was all fact, and the school of design was all fact, and the relations between master and man were all fact, and everything was fact between the lying-in hospital[1] and the cemetery, and what you couldn't state in figures, or show to be purchasable in the cheapest market and salable in the dearest, was not, and never should be, world without end, Amen.

1854

1. Maternity hospital.

ANONYMOUS

In 1965 A. L. Lloyd, a collector of British folk songs, heard "Poverty Knock" from a weaver who had learned it sixty years earlier. The song dates from before that.

Poverty Knock[1]

REFRAIN[2]

Poverty, poverty knock!
Me loom is a-sayin' all day.
Poverty, poverty knock!
Gaffer's° too skinny° to pay.   *the foreman's / stingy*

1. The sound of a 19th-century loom.   2. Repeated after each stanza.

Poverty, poverty knock!
Keepin' one eye on the clock.
Ah know ah can guttle°   *eat*
When ah hear me shuttle
Go: Poverty, poverty knock!

Up every mornin' at five.
Ah wonder that we keep alive.
Tired an' yawnin' on the cold mornin',
It's back to the dreary old drive.

5   Oh dear, we're goin' to be late.
Gaffer is stood at the gate.
We're out o' pocket, our wages they're docket°   *docked*
We'll 'a' to buy grub on the slate.³

An' when our wages they'll bring,
10   We're often short of a string.⁴
While we are fratchin' wi' gaffer for snatchin',⁵
We know to his brass° he will cling.   *money*

We've got to wet our own yarn
By dippin' it into the tarn.°   *pool*
15   It's wet an' soggy an' makes us feel groggy,
An' there's mice in that dirty old barn.

Oh dear, me poor 'ead it sings.
Ah should have woven three strings,
But threads are breakin' and my back is achin'.
20   Oh dear, ah wish ah had wings.

Sometimes a shuttle flies out,
Gives some poor woman a clout.
Ther she lies bleedin', but nobody's 'eedin'.
Who's goin' t'carry her out?

25   Tuner⁶ should tackle me loom.
'E'd rather sit on his bum.
'E's far too busy a-courtin' our Lizzie,
An' ah cannat get 'im to come.

Lizzie is so easy led.
30   Ah think that 'e teks her to bed.
She allus was skinny, now look at her pinny.°   *pinafore*
It's just about time they was wed.

1967

3. On credit, as recorded on a piece of slate.   5. Cheating. "Fratchin' ": quarreling.
4. Not paid for all our work. "String": a piece of   6. The man who maintains the loom.
cloth.

HENRY MAYHEW

In 1849 Mayhew (1812–1887) was asked by the *Morning Chronicle* to be the metropolitan correspondent for its series "Labour and the Poor." His interviews of workers and of street folk, later published as a book, convey a vivid sense of the lives of London's poor.

From London Labour and the London Poor

[BOY INMATE OF THE CASUAL WARDS][1]

I am now seventeen. My father was a cotton-spinner in Manchester, but has been dead ten years; and soon after that my mother went into the workhouse, leaving me with an aunt; and I had to work in a cotton factory. As young as I was, I earned 2s. 2d.[2] a-week at first. I can read well, and write a little. I worked at the factory two years, and was then earning 7s. a-week. I then ran away, for I had always a roving mind; but I should have stayed if my master hadn't knocked me about so. I thought I should make my fortune in London—I'd heard it was such a grand place. I had read in novels and romances,—halfpenny and penny books,—about such things, but I've met with nothing of the kind. I started without money, and begged my way from Manchester to London, saying I was going up to look for work. I wanted to see the place more than anything else. I suffered very much on the road, having to be out all night often; and the nights were cold, though it was summer. When I got to London all my hopes were blighted. I could get no further. I never tried for work in London, for I believe there are no cotton factories in it; besides, I wanted to see life. I begged, and slept in the unions.[3] I got acquainted with plenty of boys like myself. We met at the casual wards, both in London and the country. I have now been five years at this life. We were merry enough in the wards, we boys, singing and telling stories.

✳ ✳ ✳

I live a roving life, at first, being my own master. I was fond of going to plays, and such-like, when I got money; but now I'm getting tired of it, and wish for something else. I have tried for work at cotton factories in Lancashire and Yorkshire, but never could get any. I'm sure I could settle now. I couldn't have done that two years ago, the roving spirit was so strong upon me and the company I kept got a strong hold on me. Two winters back, there was a regular gang of us boys in London. After sleeping at a union, we would fix where to meet at night to get into another union to sleep. There were thirty of us that way, all boys; besides forty young men, and thirty young women. Sometimes we walked the streets all night. We didn't rob, at least I never saw any robbing. We had pleasure in chaffing[4] the policemen, and some of us got taken up. I always escaped. We got broken up in time,—some's dead, some's gone to sea, some into the country, some home, and some lagged.[5] Among them were many

---

1. Short-term poor shelters.
2. Two shillings, two pence (*s.* for *solidus* and *d.* for *denarius*, Latin for "shilling" and "penny," respectively).
3. Shelters for the poor maintained by two or more parishes.
4. Making fun of.
5. Were transported to one of Britain's penal colonies or were arrested (slang).

young lads very expert in reading, writing, and arithmetic. One young man—
he was only twenty-five—could speak several languages: he had been to sea.
He was then begging, though a strong young man. I suppose he liked that life:
some soon got tired of it.

I often have suffered from cold and hunger. I never made more than 3d. a-
day in money, take the year round, by begging; some make more than 6d. . . .
but then, I've had meat and bread given besides. I say nothing when I beg,
but that I am a poor boy out of work and starving. I never stole anything
in my life. I've often been asked to do so by my mates. I never would. The
young women steal the most. I know, least, I did know, two that kept young
men, their partners, going about the country with them, chiefly by their stealing. Some do so by their prostitution. Those go as partners are all prostitutes.
There is a great deal of sickness among the young men and women, but I never
was ill these last seven years. Fevers, colds, and venereal diseases, are very
common.

1851

ANNIE BESANT

In 1873 Besant (1847–1933) left the Church and her marriage to an Anglican clergyman to become active in feminist and socialist causes. When she heard about the
high dividends and low wages at the match factory of Bryant and May, she wrote a
series of articles, including this one published in the magazine *Link,* that led to
a public boycott and a strike of fourteen hundred match workers.

The "White Slavery" of London Match Workers

Bryant and May, now a limited liability company, paid last year a dividend
of 23 per cent to its shareholders; two years ago it paid a dividend of 25 per
cent, and the original £5 shares were then quoted for sale at £18 7s . 6d.[1] The
highest dividend paid has been 38 per cent.

Let us see how the money is made with which these monstrous dividends
are paid.* * *

The hour for commencing work is 6.30 in summer and 8 in winter; work
concludes at 6 P.M. Half-an-hour is allowed for breakfast and an hour for
dinner. This long day of work is performed by young girls, who have to stand
the whole of the time. A typical case is that of a girl of 16, a piece-worker; she
earns 4s. a week, and lives with a sister, employed by the same firm, who "earns
good money, as much as 8s. or 9s. per week." Out of the earnings 2s. is paid
for the rent of one room; the child lives on only bread-and-butter and tea,
alike for breakfast and dinner, but related with dancing eyes that once a month
she went to a meal where "you get coffee, and bread and butter, and jam, and
marmalade, and lots of it." . . . The splendid salary of 4s. is subject to deduc-

---

1. Eighteen pounds, seven shillings, six pence (*s.* for *solidus* and *d.* for *denarius,* Latin for "shilling" and
"penny," respectively).

tions in the shape of fines; if the feet are dirty, or the ground under the bench is left untidy, a fine of 3*d.* is inflicted; for putting "burnts"—matches that have caught fire during the work—on the bench 1*s.* has been forfeited, and one unhappy girl was once fined 2*s.* 6*d.* for some unknown crime. If a girl leaves four or five matches on her bench when she goes for a fresh "frame" she is fined 3*d.*, and in some departments a fine of 3*d.* is inflicted for talking. If a girl is late she is shut out for "half the day," that is for the morning six hours, and 5*d.* is deducted out of her day's 8*d.* One girl was fined 1*s.* for letting the web twist around a machine in the endeavour to save her fingers from being cut, and was sharply told to take care of the machine, "never mind your fingers." Another, who carried out the instructions and lost a finger thereby, was left unsupported while she was helpless. The wage covers the duty of submitting to an occasional blow from a foreman; one, who appears to be a gentleman of variable temper, "clouts" them "when he is mad."

One department of the work consists in taking matches out of a frame and putting them into boxes; about three frames can be done in an hour, and ½*d.* is paid for each frame emptied; only one frame is given out at a time, and the girls have to run downstairs and upstairs each time to fetch the frame, thus much increasing their fatigue. One of the delights of the frame work is the accidental firing of the matches: when this happens the worker loses the work, and if the frame is injured she is fined or "sacked." 5*s.* a week had been earned at this by one girl I talked to.

The "fillers" get ¾*d.* a gross for filling boxes; at "boxing," *i.e.* wrapping papers round the boxes, they can earn from 4*s.* 6*d.* to 5*s.* a week. A very rapid "filler" has been known to earn once "as much as 9*s.*" in a week, and 6*s.* a week "sometimes." The making of boxes is not done in the factory; for these 2¼*d.* a gross is paid to people who work in their own homes, and "find your own paste." Daywork is a little better paid than piecework, and is done chiefly by married women, who earn as much sometimes as 10*s.* a week, the piecework falling to the girls. Four women day workers, spoken of with reverent awe, earn—13*s.* a week.

A very bitter memory survives in the factory. Mr. Theodore Bryant, to show his admiration of Mr. Gladstone[2] and the greatness of his own public spirit, bethought him to erect a statue to that eminent statesman. In order that his workgirls might have the privilege of contributing, he stopped 1*s.* each out of their wages, and further deprived them of half-a-day's work by closing the factory, "giving them a holiday." ("We don't want no holidays," said one of the girls pathetically, for—needless to say—the poorer employees of such a firm lose their wages when a holiday is "given.") So furious were the girls at this cruel plundering, that many went to the unveiling of the statue with stones and bricks in their pockets, and I was conscious of a wish that some of those bricks had made an impression on Mr. Bryant's conscience. Later on they surrounded the statue—"we paid for it" they cried savagely—shouting and yelling, and a gruesome story is told that some cut their arms and let their blood trickle on the marble paid for, in very truth, by their blood. . . .

Such is a bald account of one form of white slavery as it exists in London. With chattel slaves Mr. Bryant could not have made his huge fortune, for he could not have fed, clothed, and housed them for 4*s.* a week each, and they

---

2. William Ewart Gladstone (1809–1898), leader of the Liberal Party from 1868 to 1875 and from 1880 to 1894 and prime minister four times.

would have had a definite money value which would have served as a protection. But who cares for the fate of these white wage slaves? Born in slums, driven to work while still children, undersized because underfed, oppressed because helpless, flung aside as soon as worked out, who cares if they die or go on the streets,[3] provided only that the Bryant and May shareholders get their 23 per cent, and Mr. Theodore Bryant can erect statues and buy parks? Oh if we had but a people's Dante, to make a special circle in the Inferno for those who live on this misery,[4] and suck wealth out of the starvation of helpless girls.

   Failing a poet to hold up their conduct to the execration of posterity, enshrined in deathless verse, let us strive to touch their consciences, *i.e.* their pockets, and let us at least avoid being "partakers of their sins," by abstaining from using their commodities.

1888

3. Become prostitutes.
4. In his *Inferno* the Italian poet Dante Alighieri (1265–1321) describes hell as divided into differ-

ent levels, or circles, for different kinds of sinners, with each sin carrying its own specific punishments.

ADA NIELD CHEW

Born on a farm in North Staffordshire, Chew (1870–1945) left school at the age of eleven to help her mother with taking care of house and family. In her early twenties she worked as a tailor in a factory in Crewe. She wrote a series of letters to the *Crewe Chronicle* about working conditions in the factory. When her identity was discovered, an uproar ensued, and she was fired. She became active in politics and continued to write for political causes.

A Living Wage for Factory Girls at Crewe, 5 May 1894

Sir,

   —Will you grant me space in your sensible and widely read paper to complain of a great grievance of the class—that of tailoresses in some of the Crewe factories—to which I belong? I have hoped against hope that some influential man (or woman) would take up our cause and put us in the right way to remedy—for of course there is a remedy—for the evils we are suffering from. But although one cannot open a newspaper without seeing what all sorts and conditions of men are constantly agitating for and slowly but surely obtaining—as in the miners' eight hour bill[1]—only very vague mention is ever made of the under-paid, over-worked "Factory Girl." And I have come to the conclusion, sir, that as long as we are silent ourselves and apparently content with our lot, so long shall we be left in the enjoyment [?] of that lot.

   The rates paid for the work done by us are so fearfully low as to be totally

1. Bill limiting miners' work shifts to eight hours.

inadequate to—I had almost said keep body and soul together. Well, sir, it is a fact which I could prove, if necessary, that we are compelled, not by our employers, but by stern necessity, in order to keep ourselves in independence, which self-respecting girls even in our class of life like to do, to work so many hours—I would rather not say how many—that life loses its savour, and our toil, which in moderation and at a fair rate of remuneration would be pleasurable, becomes drudgery of the most wearisome kind.

To take what may be considered a good week's wage the work has to be so close and unremitting that we cannot be said to "live"—we merely exist. We eat, we sleep, we work, endlessly, ceaselessly work, from Monday morning till Saturday night, without remission. Cultivation of the mind? How is it possible? Reading? Those of us who are determined to live like human beings and require food for mind as well as body are obliged to take time which is necessary for sleep to gratify this desire. As for recreation and enjoying the beauties of nature, the seasons come and go, and we have barely time to notice whether it is spring or summer.

Certainly we have Sundays: but Sunday is to many of us, after our week of slavery, a day of exhaustion. It has frequently been so in my case, and I am not delicate. This, you will understand, sir, is when work is plentiful. Of course we have slack times, of which the present is one (otherwise I should not have time to write to you). It may be said that we should utilise these slack times for recruiting our bodies and cultivating our minds. Many of us do so, as far as is possible in the anxious state we are necessarily in, knowing that we are not earning our "keep," for it is not possible, absolutely not possible, for the average ordinary "hand" to earn enough in busy seasons, even with the overtime I have mentioned, to make up for slack ones.

"A living wage!" Ours is a lingering, dying wage. Who reaps the benefit of our toil? I read sometimes of a different state of things in other factories, and if in others, why not those in Crewe? I have just read the report of the Royal Commission on Labour. Very good, but while Royal Commissions are enquiring and reporting and making suggestions, some of the workers are being hurried to their graves.

I am afraid I am trespassing a great deal on your space, sir, but my subject has such serious interest for me—I sometimes wax very warm as I sit stitching and thinking over our wrongs—that they, and the knowledge that your columns are always open to the needy, however humble, must be my excuse.

I am, sir, yours sincerely,
A CREWE FACTORY GIRL
Crewe, 1 May 1894

Editor's note: Our correspondent writes a most intelligent letter; and if she is a specimen of the factory girl, then Crewe factory proprietors should be proud of their "hands." We shall be glad to hear further from our correspondent as to the wages paid, the numbers of hours worked, and the conditions of their employment. *Crewe Chronicle*, 5 May 1894

1894

THE "WOMAN QUESTION": THE VICTORIAN DEBATE ABOUT GENDER

"The greatest social difficulty in England today is the relationship between men and women. The principal difference between ourselves and our ancestors is that they took society as they found it while we are self-conscious and perplexed. The institution of marriage might almost seem just now to be upon trial." This assertion by Justin M'Carthy, appearing in an essay on novels in the *Westminster Review* (July 1864), could be further extended, for on trial throughout the Victorian period was not only the institution of marriage but the family itself and, most particularly, the traditional roles of women as wives, mothers, and daughters. The "Woman Question," as it was called, engaged many Victorians, both male and female.

As indicated in our introduction to the Victorian age, the Woman Question encompassed not one question but many. The mixed opinions of Queen Victoria illustrate some of its different aspects. Believing in education for her sex, she gave support and encouragement to the founding of a college for women in 1847. On the other hand, she opposed the concept of votes for women, which she described in a letter as "this mad folly." Equally thought-provoking are her comments on women and marriage. Happily married herself until the death of Prince Albert in 1861, Victoria was nevertheless aware of some of the sacrifices marriage imposed on women. Writing in 1858 to her recently married daughter, she remarked: "There is great happiness . . . in devoting oneself to another who is worthy of one's affection; still, men are very selfish and the woman's devotion is always one of submission which makes our poor sex so very unenviable. This you will feel hereafter—I know; though it cannot be otherwise as God has willed it so."

Many of the queen's female subjects shared her assumptions that woman's role was to be accepted as divinely willed—as illustrated in the selections from Sarah Ellis's popular work of 1839, *The Women of England,* a manual of inspirational advice now usually classified with more practical books like Mrs. Beeton's *Book of Household Management* (1861) as "domestic conduct literature." The required "submission" of which the queen wrote was justified in many quarters on the grounds of the supposed intellectual inferiority of women. As popularly accepted lore expressed it: "Average Weight of Man's Brain 3½ lbs; Woman's 2 lbs, 11 ozs." In the minds of many, then, the possessors of the "shallower brain" (to borrow a phrase from the speaker of Tennyson's "Locksley Hall," 1842), naturally deserved a dependent role. In reminding wives of their range of duties, another nineteenth-century conduct book available in many editions, *The Female Instructor,* recommended that a wife always wear her wedding ring so that whenever she felt "ruffled," she might "cast [her] eyes upon it, and call to mind who gave it to [her]." In this climate it would follow that a woman who tried to cultivate her intellect beyond drawing-room accomplishments was violating the order of Nature and of religious tradition. Woman was to be valued, instead, for other qualities considered especially characteristic of her sex: tenderness of understanding, unworldliness and innocence, domestic affection, and, in various degrees, submissiveness.

By virtue of these qualities, woman became an object to be worshipped—an "angel in the house," as Coventry Patmore described her in the title of his popular poem (1854–62). In a similar vein John Ruskin insisted in his highly influential and much-reprinted essay "Of Queens' Gardens" (1865) that men and women "are in nothing alike, and the happiness and perfection of both depends on each asking and receiving from the other what the other can only give": the powers of "a true wife," he felt, made the home "a sacred place." A number of feminists as well as more traditional thinkers held this ideal view of woman's character, but, as George Eliot argues in her essay on Mary Wollstonecraft (see above), the exalted pedestal on which women were placed was one of the principal obstacles to their achieving any alteration in status.

That woman's position in society and in marriage was taken as a natural, and thus inevitable, state also stood in the way of change. Echoing the arguments of Wollstonecraft and John Stuart Mill, the feminist writer Mona Caird contended in 1888 that the institution of marriage was socially constructed and had a specific history: far from being a relationship ordained by God, marriage was an association that could and ought to be reinvented to promote freedom and equality for both partners.

Caird recognizes that the type of marriage she envisions is a distant ideal: to move toward it, she calls for a "gradual alteration of opinion which will rebuild [established institutions] from the very foundation." Earlier in the century those established institutions appear to have left some women, married and unmarried alike, dissatisfied and unfulfilled. It is commonly said that boredom was a particular problem for Victorian women, but generalizations about underoccupied females in this era need to be severely qualified. In the mid-Victorian period, one-quarter of England's female population had jobs, most of them onerous and low paying. At the same time other women earned their livings by working as prostitutes (the existence of this "Great Social Evil," as the Victorians regarded it, being one indication that the "angel in the house" was not always able to exert her moralizing influence on her mate or her male children). While the millions of women employed as domestics, seamstresses, factory workers, farm laborers, or prostitutes had many problems, excessive leisure was not chief among them. To be bored was the privilege of wives and daughters in upper- and middle-class homes, establishments in which feminine idleness was treasured as a status symbol. Among this small and influential segment of the population, as the novelist Dinah Maria Mulock emphasizes, comfortably well-off wives and daughters found that there was "nothing to do," because in such households the servants ran everything, even taking over the principal role in rearing children. Freed from demanding domestic duties, such women could not then devote their unoccupied time to other labors, for there were few sanctioned opportunities for interesting and challenging work, and little support or encouragement for serious study or artistic endeavor. If family finances failed and they were called on "to do" something, women from these classes faced considerable difficulties: their severely limited choice of respectable paid occupations meant that many sought employment as governesses. Frequently taken up as a topic in novels of the period, the complex and compromised social position of the governess is, for instance, a notable feature of Charlotte Brontë's *Jane Eyre* (1847). Brontë's character, however, does not limit her criticism to her own impoverished plight when she expresses her frustration with the social attitudes that governed the behavior of women of her class more broadly:

> Women are supposed to be very calm generally: but women feel just as men feel; they need exercise for their faculties and a field for their efforts as much as their brothers do; they suffer from too rigid a restraint, too absolute a stagnation, precisely as men would suffer; and it is narrow-minded in their more privileged fellow-creatures to say that they ought to confine themselves to making puddings and knitting stockings, to playing on the piano and embroidering bags. It is thoughtless to condemn them, or laugh at them, if they seek to do more or learn more than custom has pronounced necessary for their sex.

George Meredith, in his *Essay on Comedy* (1873), develops the same argument; the test of a civilization, he writes, is whether men "consent to talk on equal terms with their women, and to listen to them." Yet at least two reviewers of *Jane Eyre*, both women, regarded such proposals as tantamount to sedition. Margaret Oliphant called the novel "A wild declaration of the 'Rights of Women' in a new aspect," and Elizabeth Rigby attacked its "pervading tone of ungodly discontent."

In some households such discontent, whether godly or ungodly, led to a daughter's open rebellion. One remarkable rebel was Florence Nightingale, who found family life in the 1850s intolerably pointless and, despite parental opposition, cut loose from home to carve out a career for herself in nursing and in hospital administration.

As chronicled by Sir Walter Besant, similar drives for independence produced extraordinary changes for women during the late Victorian period, making a wide variety of professional opportunities available to them. The era also witnessed the arrival of the much-debated phenomenon of the "New Woman": frequently satirized as simply a bicycle-riding, cigarette-smoking, mannish creature, this confident and assertive figure burst onto the scene in the 1890s, often becoming the focus of attention in articles, stories, and plays (the character of Vivie in Bernard Shaw's *Mrs. Warren's Profession* [1898] is a good example of the type), and, indeed, the author of literary works herself. Women of course had begun to be published before Victoria's reign, and many women became successful novelists. And yet embarking on such a career was never an easy choice. The selections from Harriet Martineau's autobiography included here suggest some of the obstacles, internal and external, against which the aspiring woman writer struggled. Inevitably, some female writers were hacks, and they provide George Eliot with easy targets for ridicule in her essay "Silly Novels by Lady Novelists" (1856). Nonetheless, women emerge as major novelists during the period, as illustrated in the careers of the Brontë sisters and Eliot herself.

It is instructive to compare the texts collected below with Eliot's judicious essay on the Woman Question, inspired by her rereading of Mary Wollstonecraft—and with her fiction. For these issues engaged Eliot's attention in her novels as well, as is demonstrated in her highly complex portrait of Maggie Tulliver, the bookish early-Victorian heroine of *The Mill on the Floss* (1860). To be sure, not all her female characters are frustrated and discontented; as a realist Eliot recognized that many upper- and middle-class women apparently found their leisurely lives fully enjoyable. In *Middlemarch* (1871–72), for example, Celia Brooke Chetham rejoices in her comfortable life as wife and mother on a country estate. Yet to her sister Dorothea (whom Celia regards with affectionate indulgence as an eccentric misfit), the traditional womanly lot in life is as painfully frustrating as Florence Nightingale had found it. It was on behalf of such women as Dorothea that John Stuart Mill developed his argument in *The Subjection of Women* (1869), a classic essay that should be read in conjunction with the selections in this section. Also revealing in this context are some of the extracts above from Tennyson's 1847 poem *The Princess* ("The woman's cause is man's") and from Elizabeth Barrett Browning's *Aurora Leigh* (1857), a novel in verse that portrays the life of a woman poet (book 1 describes how the typical girl's education constricts a woman's mind, and book 2 features Aurora's defense of her vocation as a poet).

For additional texts on the Woman Question, go to Norton Literature Online.

SARAH STICKNEY ELLIS

In 1837 the essayist Sarah Stickney (1812?–1872) married William Ellis, a missionary, and began to work with him for the temperance movement and other evangelical causes. Ellis's 1839 book on women's education and domestic roles became a best seller, going through sixteen editions in two years. In the 1840s she founded a girls' school that put into practice her belief that feminine education should cultivate what she called "the heart" rather than the intellectual faculties of her pupils.

From The Women of England: Their Social Duties and Domestic Habits

[DISINTERESTED KINDNESS]

To men belongs the potent—(I had almost said the *omnipotent*) consideration of worldly aggrandizement; and it is constantly misleading their steps, closing their ears against the voice of conscience, and beguiling them with the promise of peace, where peace was never found.

* * *

How often has man returned to his home with a mind confused by the many voices, which in the mart, the exchange, or the public assembly, have addressed themselves to his inborn selfishness, or his worldly pride; and while his integrity was shaken, and his resolution gave way beneath the pressure of apparent necessity, or the insidious pretenses of expediency, he has stood corrected before the clear eye of woman, as it looked directly to the naked truth, and detected the lurking evil of the specious act he was about to commit. Nay, so potent may have become this secret influence, that he may have borne it about with him like a kind of second conscience, for mental reference, and spiritual counsel, in moments of trial; and when the snares of the world were around him, and temptations from within and without have bribed over the witness in his own bosom, he has thought of the humble monitress[1] who sat alone, guarding the fireside comforts of his distant home; and the remembrance of her character, clothed in moral beauty, has scattered the clouds before his mental vision, and sent him back to that beloved home, a wiser and a better man.

The women of England, possessing the grand privilege of being better instructed than those of any other country, in the minutiae of domestic comfort, have obtained a degree of importance in society far beyond what their unobtrusive virtues would appear to claim. The long-established customs of their country have placed in their hands the high and holy duty of cherishing and protecting the minor morals of life, from whence springs all that is elevated in purpose, and glorious in action. The sphere of their direct personal influence is central, and consequently small; but its extreme operations are as widely extended as the range of human feeling. They may be less striking in society than some of the women of other countries, and may feel themselves, on brilliant and stirring occasions, as simple, rude, and unsophisticated in the popular science of excitement; but as far as the noble daring of Britain has sent forth her adventurous sons, and that is to every point of danger on the habitable globe, they have borne along with them a generosity, a disinterestedness, and a moral courage, derived in no small measure from the female influence of their native country.

It is a fact well worthy of our serious attention, and one which bears immediately upon the subject under consideration, that the present state of our national affairs is such as to indicate that the influence of woman in counteracting the growing evils of society is about to be more needed than ever.

* * *

---

1. Female advisor or mentor.

In order to ascertain what kind of education is most effective in making woman what she ought to be, the best method is to inquire into the character, station, and peculiar duties of woman throughout the largest portion of her earthly career; and then ask, for what she is most valued, admired, and beloved?

In answer to this, I have little hesitation in saying—for her disinterested[2] kindness. Look at all the heroines, whether of romance or reality—at all the female characters that are held up to universal admiration—at all who have gone down to honored graves, amongst the tears and lamentations of their survivors. Have these been the learned, the accomplished women; the women who could solve problems, and elucidate systems of philosophy? No: or if they have, they have also been women who were dignified with the majesty of moral greatness.

*   *   *

Let us single out from any particular seminary[3] a child who has been there from the years of ten to fifteen, and reckon, if it can be reckoned, the pains that have been spent in making that child proficient in Latin. Have the same pains been spent in making her disinterestedly kind? And yet what man is there in existence who would not rather his wife should be free from selfishness, than be able to read Virgil without the use of a dictionary?

*   *   *

I still cling fondly to the hope that some system of female instruction will be discovered, by which the young women of England may be sent from school to the homes of their parents, habituated to be on the watch for every opportunity of doing good to others; making it the first and the last inquiry of every day, "What can I do to make my parents, my brothers, or my sisters, more happy? I am but a feeble instrument in the hands of Providence, but as He will give me strength, I hope to pursue the plan to which I have been accustomed, of seeking my own happiness only in the happiness of others."

1839

2. I.e., independent, impartial.
3. School (in the early 19th century, often specifically a private school for girls).

COVENTRY PATMORE

Originally published between 1854 and 1862, *The Angel in the House*, a long poem about courtship and marriage by Coventry Patmore (1823–1896), became a best seller in the United States and later in Britain. Dedicated to the author's first wife, Emily Augusta Andrews, the poem celebrates their fifteen years of married life. (She died in 1862, and Patmore, who lived another three decades, remarried twice.) The poem, popular among Patmore's contemporaries (including Gerard Manley Hopkins and John Ruskin), fell out of favor in later years. Feminist critics such as Virginia Woolf criticized *The Angel in the House* both for the sentimentality of its ideal of woman and for the oppressive effect of this ideal on women's lives. Since Woolf, the phrase "the angel in the house" has often been used to encapsulate a patronizing Victorian attitude toward women, for which the poem is cited as prime evidence.

From The Angel in the House

The Paragon

When I behold the skies aloft
   Passing the pageantry of dreams,
The cloud whose bosom, cygnet-soft,
   A couch for nuptial Juno[1] seems,
5 The ocean broad, the mountains bright,
   The shadowy vales with feeding herds,
I from my lyre the music smite,
   Nor want for justly matching words.
All forces of the sea and air,
10   All interests of hill and plain,
I so can sing, in seasons fair,
   That who hath felt may feel again.
Elated oft by such free songs,
   I think with utterance free to raise
15 That hymn for which the whole world longs,
   A worthy hymn in woman's praise;
   A hymn bright-noted like a bird's,
   Arousing these song-sleepy times
With rhapsodies of perfect words,
20   Ruled by returning kiss of rhymes.
But when I look on her and hope
   To tell with joy what I admire,
My thoughts lie cramp'd in narrow scope,
   Or in the feeble birth expire;
25 No mystery of well-woven speech,
   No simplest phrase of tenderest fall,
No liken'd excellence can reach
   Her, the most excellent of all,
The best half of creation's best,
30   Its heart to feel, its eye to see,
The crown and complex of the rest,
   Its aim and its epitome.
Nay, might I utter my conceit,°   *fancy, idea*
   'Twere after all a vulgar song,
35 For she's so simply, subtly sweet,
   My deepest rapture does her wrong.
Yet is it now my chosen task
   To sing her worth as Maid and Wife;
Nor happier post than this I ask,
40   To live her laureate[2] all my life.
On wings of love uplifted free,
   And by her gentleness made great,
I'll teach how noble man should be
   To match with such a lovely mate;
45 And then in her may move the more
   The woman's wish to be desired,

1. In Roman mythology the wife of the chief god (Jupiter) and a goddess presiding especially over the married life of women.
2. I.e., to be the one who celebrates her in poetry.

(By praise increased,) till both shall soar,
 With blissful emulations fired.
 And, as geranium, pink,° or rose   *type of flower*
50 Is thrice itself through power of art,
 So may my happy skill disclose
 New fairness even in her fair heart;
 Until that churl shall nowhere be
 Who bends not, awed, before the throne
55 Of her affecting majesty,
 So meek, so far unlike our own;
 Until (for who may hope too much
 From her who wields the powers of love?)
 Our lifted lives at last shall touch
60 That happy goal to which they move;
 Until we find, as darkness rolls
 Away, and evil mists dissolve,
 The nuptial contrasts are the poles
 On which the heavenly spheres revolve.

Victorean ideal wife mother selflessly devoted 1854–62

JOHN RUSKIN

Ruskin (1819–1900) began his career writing about art but eventually became one of England's fiercest social critics. In 1864 he delivered two lectures in the industrial city of Manchester—the first, "Of Kings' Treasuries," supporting the development of public libraries in the name of "noble education" and the second, "Of Queens' Gardens," on the special powers and duties of women. Published together the following year as *Sesame and Lilies*, the essays were considered ideal reading matter for middle-class young women and enjoyed exceptional sales for the remainder of the nineteenth century. In recent years "Of Queens' Gardens," with its assertions about the distinct differences between men and women, and their respective roles in the two separate spheres of public and private life, has become a classic text for the examination of Victorian ideology.

From Of Queens' Gardens

Now their separate characters are briefly these. The man's power is active, progressive, defensive. He is eminently the doer, the creator, the discoverer, the defender. His intellect is for speculation and invention; his energy for adventure, for war, and for conquest, wherever war is just, wherever conquest necessary. But the woman's power is for rule, not for battle,—and her intellect is not for invention or creation, but for sweet ordering, arrangement, and decision. She sees the qualities of things, their claims, and their places. Her great function is Praise; she enters into no contest, but infallibly adjudges the crown of contest. By her office, and place, she is protected from all danger and temptation, The man, in his rough work in open world, must encounter all peril and trial;—to him, therefore, must be the failure, the offence, the inevitable error: often he must be wounded, or subdued; often misled; and *always* hardened. But he guards the woman from all this; within his house, as ruled by her, unless she herself has sought it, need enter no danger, no temptation, no cause of error or offence. This is the true nature of home—it is the place of Peace; the shelter, not only from all injury, but from all terror, doubt, and division. In so far as it is not this, it is not home; so far as the anxieties of the outer life penetrate into it, and the inconsistently-minded, unknown, unloved, or hostile society of the outer world is allowed by either husband or wife to cross the threshold, it ceases to be home; it is then only a part of that outer world which you have roofed over, and lighted fire in. But so far as it is a sacred place, a vestal temple, a temple of the hearth watched over by Household Gods, before whose faces none may come but those whom they can receive with love,—so far as it is this, and roof and fire are types only of a nobler shade and light,—shade as of the rock in a weary land, and light as of the Pharos[1] in the stormy sea;—so far it vindicates the name, and fulfils the praise, of Home.

And wherever a true wife comes, this home is always round her. The stars only may be over her head; the glowworm in the night-cold grass may be the only fire at her foot; but home is yet wherever she is; and for a noble woman it stretches far round her, better than ceiled with cedar, or painted with vermilion,[2] shedding its quiet light far, for those who else were homeless.

This, then, I believe to be,—will you not admit it to be?—the woman's true place and power. But do not you see that, to fulfil this, she must—as far as one can use such terms of a human creature—be incapable of error? So far as she rules, all must be right, or nothing is. She must be enduringly, incorruptibly good; instinctively, infallibly wise—wise, not for self-development, but for self-renunciation: wise, not that she may set herself above her husband, but that she may never fail from his side: wise, not with the narrowness of insolent and loveless pride, but with the passionate gentleness of an infinitely variable, because infinitely applicable, modesty of service—the true changefulness of woman. In that great sense—"La donna è mobile," not "Qual piúm' al vento";[3] no, nor yet "Variable as the shade, by the light quivering aspen made";[4] but variable as the *light,* manifold in fair and serene division, that it may take the colour of all that it falls upon, and exalt it.

✳ ✳ ✳

1864   1865

---

1. A lighthouse that was one of the Seven Wonders of the Ancient World (its island is now part of the city of Alexandria). The phrase "rock in a weary land" alludes to Isaiah 32.2.
2. Cf. Jeremiah 22.14. "Ceiled": roofed over.

3. "Women are as fickle as feathers in the wind," the first two lines of the famous aria by the womanizing Duke in Giuseppe Verdi's *Rigoletto* (1851).
4. Sir Walter Scott, *Marmion* (1808) 6.30.

HARRIET MARTINEAU

Martineau (1802–1876), who grew up in the town of Norwich, suffered a painfully unhappy childhood and adolescence both because of recurring illnesses and because of the strict and narrow lifestyle of her middle-class Unitarian family. A prolific author, she produced many kinds of books—history, political and economic theory, travel narratives, fiction, translation. She was best-known for her collection of instructive stories, *Illustrations of Political Economy* (1832–34); but she also dealt with a wide variety of other issues, such as slavery in the United States (she was an early supporter of the abolitionists). Her *Autobiography*, written in 1855, was published in 1877. In the first selection she is eighteen years old.

From Autobiography

When I was young, it was not thought proper for young ladies to study very conspicuously; and especially with pen in hand. Young ladies (at least in provincial towns) were expected to sit down in the parlour to sew,—during which reading aloud was permitted,—or to practice their music; but so as to be fit to receive callers, without any signs of bluestockingism[1] which could be reported abroad. Jane Austen herself, the Queen of novelists, the immortal creator of Anne Elliott, Mr. Knightley,[2] and a score or two more of unrivalled intimate friends of the whole public, was compelled by the feelings of her family to cover up her manuscripts with a large piece of muslin work, kept on the table for the purpose, whenever any genteel people came in. So it was with other young ladies, for some time after Jane Austen was in her grave; and thus my first studies in philosophy were carried on with great care and reserve. I was at the work table regularly after breakfast,—making my own clothes, or the shirts of the household, or about some fancy work: I went out walking with the rest,—before dinner in winter, and after tea in summer: and if ever I shut myself into my own room for an hour of solitude, I knew it was at the risk of being sent for to join the sewing-circle, or to read aloud,—I being the reader, on account of my growing deafness.[3] But I won time for what my heart was set upon, nevertheless,—either in the early morning, or late at night. I had a strange passion for translating, in those days; and a good preparation it proved for the subsequent work of my life. Now, it was meeting James at seven in the morning to read Lowth's Prelections[4] in the Latin, after having been busy since five about something else, in my own room. Now it was translating Tacitus,[5] in order to try what was the utmost compression of style that I could attain.—About this I may mention an incident while it occurs. We had all grown up with a great reverence for Mrs. Barbauld[6] (which she fully deserved from much wiser people than ourselves) and, reflectively, for Dr. Aikin,[7] her

1. Female intellectualism or literary activity (from the so-called bluestocking clubs of the 18th century—informal gatherings of women with literary interests and select men of letters; as the derisive name implies, some of the men attending habitually wore unconventional blue worsted rather than silk stockings).
2. Major characters from, respectively, the novels *Persuasion* (1817) and *Emma* (1815) by Austen (1775–1817).
3. Martineau's hearing problems worsened in adolescence, and she became almost entirely deaf.
4. *Praelectiones de Sacra Poesi Herbraeorum* (Lec-

tures on Hebrew Poetry, 1753–70), by Robert Lowth (1710–1787), an English bishop and scholar. "James": James Martineau (1805–1900), Harriet's younger brother, who later became a renowned Unitarian preacher and moral philosopher.
5. Roman historian (ca. 55–ca. 120), whose writings offer a model of concise prose.
6. Anna Laetitia Barbauld (1743–1825), poet and writer of prose for children.
7. John Aikin (1747–1822), English physician, author, and biographer; he collaborated with his sister in some publications.

brother,—also able in his way, and far more industrious, but without her genius. Among a multitude of other labours, Dr. Aikin had translated the Agricola[8] of Tacitus. I went into such an enthusiasm over the original, and especially over the celebrated concluding passage, that I thought I would translate it, and correct it by Dr. Aikin's, which I could procure from our public library. I did it, and found my own translation unquestionably the best of the two. I had spent an infinity of pains over it,—word by word; and I am confident I was not wrong in my judgment. I stood pained and mortified before my desk, I remember, thinking how strange and small a matter was human achievement, if Dr. Aikin's fame was to be taken as a testimony of literary desert. I had beaten him whom I had taken for my master. I need not point out that, in the first place, Dr. Aikin's fame did not hang on this particular work; nor that, in the second place, I had exaggerated his fame by our sectarian estimate of him.[9] I give the incident as a curious little piece of personal experience, and one which helped to make me like literary labour more for its own sake, and less for its rewards, than I might otherwise have done.—Well: to return to my translating propensities. Our cousin J. M. L., then studying for his profession in Norwich, used to read Italian with Rachel[1] and me,—also before breakfast. We made some considerable progress, through the usual course of prose authors and poets; and out of this grew a fit which Rachel and I at one time took, in concert with our companions and neighbours, the C.'s, to translate Petrarch.[2] Nothing could be better as an exercise in composition than translating Petrarch's sonnets into English of the same limits. It was putting ourselves under compulsion to do with the Italian what I had set myself voluntarily to do with the Latin author. I believe we really succeeded pretty well; and I am sure that all these exercises were a singularly apt preparation for my after work. At the same time, I went on studying Blair's Rhetoric[3] (for want of a better guide) and inclining mightily to every kind of book or process which could improve my literary skill,—really as if I had foreseen how I was to spend my life.

* * *

At this time,—(I think it must have been in 1821,) was my first appearance in print. * * * My brother James, then my idolized companion, discovered how wretched I was when he left me for his college, after the vacation; and he told me that I must not permit myself to be so miserable. He advised me to take refuge, on each occasion, in a new pursuit; and on that particular occasion, in an attempt at authorship. I said, as usual, that I would if he would: to which he answered that it would never do for him, a young student, to rush into print before the eyes of his tutors; but he desired me to write something that was in my head, and try my chance with it in the "Monthly Repository,"—the poor little Unitarian periodical in which I have mentioned that Talfourd[4] tried his young powers. What James desired, I always did, as of course; and after he had left me to my widowhood soon after six o'clock, one bright September morning, I was at my desk before seven, beginning a letter to the Editor of the "Monthly Repository,"—that editor being the formidable prime minister of his sect,—Rev. Robert Aspland.[5] I suppose I must tell what that first paper was,

8. A biography of Julius Agricola (40–93 C.E.), Tacitus's father-in-law and a Roman senator and general. Aikin's translation, which went into several editions, was first published in 1774.
9. Aikin, like Martineau, was a Unitarian.
1. Martineau's younger sister.
2. Italian poet (Francesco Petrarca, 1304–1374).

3. *Lectures on Rhetoric and Belles Lettres* (1784), by Hugh Blair (1718–1800), a Scottish divine and professor of rhetoric, which expressed 18th-century ideals of prose style.
4. Sir Thomas Noon Talfourd (1795–1854), English lawyer and author.
5. A Unitarian divine (1782–1845).

though I had much rather not; for I am so heartily ashamed of the whole business as never to have looked at the article since the first flutter of it went off. It was on Female Writers on Practical Divinity. I wrote away, in my abominable scrawl of those days, on foolscap paper,[6] feeling mightily like a fool all the time. I told no one, and carried my expensive packet to the post-office myself, to pay the postage. I took the letter V for my signature,—I cannot at all remember why. The time was very near the end of the month: I had no definite expectation that I should ever hear any thing of my paper; and certainly did not suppose it could be in the forthcoming number. That number was sent in before service-time on a Sunday morning. My heart may have been beating when I laid hands on it; but it thumped prodigiously when I saw my article there, and, in the Notices to Correspondents, a request to hear more from V. of Norwich. There is certainly something entirely peculiar in the sensation of seeing oneself in print for the first time:—the lines burn themselves in upon the brain in a way of which black ink is incapable, in any other mode. So I felt that day, when I went about with my secret.—I have said what my eldest brother was to us,—in what reverence we held him. He was just married, and he and his bride asked me to return from chapel with them to tea. After tea he said, "Come now, we have had plenty of talk; I will read you something; " and he held out his hand for the new "Repository." After glancing at it, he exclaimed, "They have got a new hand here. Listen." After a paragraph, he repeated, "Ah! this is a new hand; they have had nothing so good as this for a long while." (It would be impossible to convey to any who do not know the "Monthly Repository" of that day, how very small a compliment this was.) I was silent, of course. At the end of the first column, he exclaimed about the style, looking at me in some wonder at my being as still as a mouse. Next (and well I remember his tone, and thrill to it still) his words were—"What a fine sentence that is! Why, do you not think so?" I mumbled out, sillily enough, that it did not seem any thing particular. "Then," said he, "you were not listening. I will read it again. There now!" As he still got nothing out of me, he turned round upon me, as we sat side by side on the sofa, with "Harriet, what is the matter with you? I never knew you so slow to praise any thing before." I replied, in utter confusion,—"I never could baffle any body. The truth is, that paper is mine." He made no reply; read on in silence, and spoke no more till I was on my feet to come away. He then laid his hand on my shoulder, and said gravely (calling me 'dear' for the first time) "Now, dear, leave it to other women to make shirts and darn stockings; and do you devote yourself to this." I went home in a sort of dream, so that the squares of the pavement seemed to float before my eyes. That evening made me an authoress.

✻   ✻   ✻

While I was at Newcastle [1829], a change, which turned out a very happy one, was made in our domestic arrangements. ✻ ✻ ✻ I call it a misfortune, because in common parlance it would be so treated; but I believe that my mother and all her other daughters would have joined heartily, if asked, in my conviction that it was one of the best things that ever happened to us. My mother and her daughters lost, at a stroke, nearly all they had in the world by the failure of the house,—the old manufactory,—in which their money was placed. We never recovered more than the merest pittance; and at the time, I, for one, was left destitute;—that is to say, with precisely one shilling in my

6. A thirteen-by-sixteen-inch sheet of paper.

purse. The effect upon me of this new "calamity," as people called it, was like that of a blister upon a dull, weary pain, or series of pains. I rather enjoyed it, even at the time; for there was scope for action; whereas, in the long, dreary series of preceding trials, there was nothing possible but endurance. In a very short time, my two sisters at home and I began to feel the blessing of a wholly new freedom. I, who had been obliged to write before breakfast, or in some private way, had henceforth liberty to do my own work in my own way; for we had lost our gentility. Many and many a time since have we said that, but for that loss of money, we might have lived on in the ordinary provincial method of ladies with small means, sewing, and economizing, and growing narrower every year; whereas, by being thrown, while it was yet time, on our own resources, we have worked hard and usefully, won friends, reputation and independence, seen the world abundantly, abroad and at home, and, in short, have truly lived instead of vegetated.

1855   1877

ANONYMOUS

In early January 1858 a letter appeared in the London *Times* above the signature "One More Unfortunate." This individual, who claimed to be a prostitute, described her respectable upbringing and her experience as a governess, lamented her disgrace, and called on men to be more compassionate in their reform efforts. Responding in part to this piece, another letter, also apparently from a prostitute and titled "The Great Social Evil," was then published on February 24, 1858. Although it is impossible to establish definitively whether the letter writers were genuinely who they said they were, the story of how the second correspondent came to be a prostitute, which appears in the following extract, would have seemed extremely plausible to contemporary readers. It is instructive to compare this selection with Dante Gabriel Rossetti's poem *Jenny* (1870), in which a speaker muses on the life and thoughts of a young prostitute, and the account of the early days of Mrs. Warren's profession in Bernard Shaw's 1898 play of that name.

The Great Social Evil

To the Editor of the Times

Sir,—another "Unfortunate," but of a class entirely different from the one who has already instructed the public in your columns, presumes to address you.

I am a stranger to all the fine sentiments which still linger in the bosom of your correspondent. I have none of those youthful recollections which, contrasting her early days with her present life, aggravate the misery of the latter. My parents did not give me any education; they did not instil into my mind virtuous precepts nor set me a good example. All my experiences in early life were gleaned among associates who knew nothing of the laws of God but by

dim tradition and faint report, and whose chiefest triumphs of wisdom consisted in picking their way through the paths of destitution in which they were
cast by cunning evasion or in open defiance of the laws of man.

        *   *   *

Let me tell you something of my parents. My father's most profitable occupation was brickmaking. When not employed at this he did anything he could
get to do. My mother worked with him in the brickfield, and so did I and a
progeny of brothers and sisters; for, somehow or other, although my parents
occupied a very unimportant space in the world, it pleased God to make them
fruitful. We all slept in the same room. There were few privacies, few family
secrets in our house.

        *   *   *

I was a very pretty child, and had a sweet voice; of course I used to sing.
Most London boys and girls of the lower classes sing. "My face is my fortune,
kind Sir, she said" was the ditty on which I bestowed most pains, and my
father and mother would wink knowingly as I sang it. The latter would also
tell me how pretty she was when young, and how she sang, and what a fool
she had been, and how well she might have done had she been wise.

Frequently we had quite a stir in our colony.[1] Some young lady who had
quitted the paternal restraints, or perhaps, been started off, none knew whither
or how, to seek her fortune, would reappear among us with a profusion of
ribands, fine clothes, and lots of cash. Visiting the neighbours, treating indiscriminately, was the order of the day on such occasions, without any more
definite information of the means by which the dazzling transformation had
been effected than could be conveyed by knowing winks and the words "luck"
and "friends." Then she would disappear and leave us in our dirt, penury, and
obscurity. You cannot conceive, Sir, how our young ambition was stirred by
these visitations.

Now commences an important era in my life. I was a fine, robust, healthy
girl, 13 years of age. I had larked with the boys of my own age. I had huddled
with them, boys and girls together, all night long in our common haunts. I
had seen much and heard abundantly of the mysteries of the sexes. To me
such things had been matters of common sight and common talk. For some
time I had trembled and coquetted on the verge of a strong curiosity, and a
natural desire, and without a particle of affection, scarce a partiality, I lost
what? not my virtue, for I never had any. That which is commonly, but untruly
called virtue, I gave away.

You reverend Mr. Philanthropist—what call you virtue? Is it not the principle, the essence, which keeps watch and ward over the conduct, over the
substance, the materiality? No such principle ever kept watch and ward over
me, and I repeat that I never lost that which I never had—my virtue.

According to my own ideas at the time I only extended my rightful enjoyments. Opportunity was not long wanting to put my newly-acquired knowledge
to profitable use. In the commencement of my fifteenth year one of our be-
ribanded visitors took me off, and introduced me to the great world, and thus
commenced my career as what you better classes call a prostitute. I cannot
say that I felt any other shame than the bashfulness of a noviciate introduced

1. I.e., neighborhood, group of streets.

to strange society. Remarkable for good looks, and no less so for good temper, I gained money, dressed gaily, and soon agreeably astonished my parents and old neighbours by making a descent upon them.

Passing over the vicissitudes of my course, alternating between reckless gaiety and extreme destitution, I improved myself greatly; and at the age of 18 was living partly under the protection of one who thought he discovered that I had talent, and some good qualities as well as beauty, who treated me more kindly and considerately than I had ever before been treated, and thus drew from me something like a feeling of regard, but not sufficiently strong to lift me to that sense of my position which the so-called virtuous and respectable members of society seem to entertain. Under the protection of this gentleman, and encouraged by him, I commenced the work of my education; that portion of education which is comprised in some knowledge of my own language and the ordinary accomplishments of my sex;—moral science, as I believe it is called, has always been an enigma to me, and is so to this day.

*   *   *

Now, what if I am a prostitute, what business has society to abuse me? Have I received any favours at the hands of society? If I am a hideous cancer in society, are not the causes of the disease to be sought in the rottenness of the carcass? Am I not its legitimate child; no bastard, Sir? Why does my unnatural parent repudiate me, and what has society ever done for me, that I should do anything for it, and what have I ever done against society that it should drive me into a corner and crush me to the earth? I have neither stolen (at least not since I was a child), nor murdered, nor defrauded. I earn my money and pay my way, and try to do good with it, according to my ideas of good. I do not get drunk, nor fight, nor create uproar in the streets or out of them. I do not use bad language. I do not offend the public eye by open indecencies. I go to the Opera, I go to Almack's,[2] I go to the theatres, I go to quiet, well-conducted casinos, I go to all places of public amusement, behaving myself with as much propriety as society can exact. I pay business visits to my tradespeople, the most fashionable of the West-end.[3] My milliners, my silk-mercers,[4] my boot-maker know, all of them, who I am and how I live, and they solicit my patronage as earnestly and cringingly as if I were Madam, the lady of the right rev. patron of the Society for the Suppression of Vice.[5] They find my money as good and my pay better (for we are robbed on every hand) than that of Madam, my Lady; and, if all the circumstances and conditions of our lives had been reversed, would Madam, my Lady, have done better or been better than I?

I speak for others as well as for myself, for the very great majority, nearly all of the real undisguised prostitutes in London, spring from my class, and are made by and under pretty much such conditions of life as I have narrated, and particularly by untutored and unrestrained intercourse of the sexes in early life. We come from the dregs of society, as our so-called betters term it. What business has society to have dregs—such dregs as we? You railers of the Society for the Suppression of Vice, you the pious, the moral, the respectable, as you call yourselves, who stand on your smooth and pleasant side of the great gulf you have dug and keep between yourselves and the dregs, why don't you

2. Assembly rooms, the scene of social functions.
3. The affluent area of central London and location of fashionable shops and theaters.
4. Dealers in textiles.
5. A society founded in 1802.

bridge it over, or fill it up, and by some humane and generous process absorb us into your leavened mass, until we become interpenetrated with goodness like yourselves? Why stand on your eminence shouting that we should be ashamed of ourselves? What have we to be ashamed of, we who do not know what shame is—the shame you mean? I conduct myself prudently, and defy you and your policemen too. Why stand you there mouthing with sleek face about morality? What is morality? Will you make us responsible for what we never knew? Teach us what is right and tutor us in good before you punish us for doing wrong. We who are the real prostitutes of the true natural growth of society, and no impostors, will not be judged by "One more Unfortunate," nor measured by any standard of her setting up. She is a mere chance intruder in our ranks, and has no business there.

*　*　*

Hurling big figures at us, it is said that there are 80,000 of us in London alone—which is a monstrous falsehood—and of this 80,000, poor hard-working sewing girls, sewing women, are numbered in by thousands and called indiscriminately prostitutes; writing, preaching, speechifying, that they have lost their virtue too.

It is a cruel calumny to call them in mass prostitutes; and, as for their virtue, they lose it as one loses his watch who is robbed by the highway thief. Their virtue is the watch, and society is the thief. These poor women toiling on starvation wages, while penury, misery, and famine clutch them by the throat and say, "Render up your body or die."

*　*　*

Admire this magnificent shop in this fashionable street; its front, fittings, and decorations cost not less than a thousand pounds. The respectable master of the establishment keeps his carriage, and lives in his countryhouse. He has daughters too; his patronesses are fine ladies, the choicest impersonations of society. Do they think, as they admire the taste and elegance of that trades-man's show, of the poor creatures who wrought it, and of what they were paid for it? Do they reflect on the weary toiling fingers, on the eyes dim with watch-ing, on the bowels yearning with hunger, on the bended frames, on the broken constitutions, on poor human nature driven to its coldest corner and reduced to its narrowest means in the production of these luxuries and adornments? This is an old story! Would it not be truer and more charitable to call these poor souls "victims?"—some gentler, some more humane name than prosti-tute—to soften by some Christian expression, if you cannot better the un-Christian system, the opprobrium of a fate to which society has itself driven them by the direst straits? What business has society to point its finger in scorn, and to raise its voice in reprobation of them? Are they not its children, born of its cold indifference, of its callous selfishness, of its cruel pride?

Sir, I have trespassed on your patience beyond limit, and yet much remains to be said, which I leave for further communication if you think proper to insert this. The difficulty of dealing with the evil is not so great as society considers it. Setting aside "the sin," we are not so bad as we are thought to be. The difficulty is for society to set itself, with the necessary earnestness, self-humiliation, and self-denial to the work. But of this hereafter. To deprive us of proper and harmless amusements, to subject us in mass to the pressure of force—of force wielded, for the most part, by ignorant, and often by brutal men—is only to add the cruelty of active persecution to the cruelty of the passive indifference which made us as we are.

I remain your humble servant,
ANOTHER UNFORTUNATE

1858

DINAH MARIA MULOCK

In 1857 Mulock (1826–1887) published her best-known novel, the Victorian best seller *John Halifax, Gentleman*. This work was followed the year after by *A Woman's Thoughts on Women* and subsequently by other, sometimes more overtly feminist, novels. In 1864 she married George Craik, a partner in the publishing firm Macmillan; her works often appear under the name Dinah Maria Craik.

From A Woman's Thoughts about Women

[SOMETHING TO DO]

Man and woman were made for, and not like one another. Only one "right" we have to assert in common with mankind—and that is as much in our hands as theirs—the right of having something to do.

✻ ✻ ✻

But how few parents ever consider this! Tom, Dick, and Harry, aforesaid, leave school and plunge into life; "the girls" likewise finish their education, come home, and stay at home. That is enough. Nobody thinks it needful to waste a care upon them. Bless them, pretty dears, how sweet they are! papa's nosegay[1] of beauty to adorn his drawing-room. He delights to give them all they can desire—clothes, amusements, society; he and mamma together take every domestic care off their hands; they have abundance of time and nothing to occupy it; plenty of money, and little use for it; pleasure without end, but not one definite object of interest or employment; flattery and flummery[2] enough, but no solid food whatever to satisfy mind or heart—if they happen to possess either—at the very emptiest and most craving season[3] of both. They have literally nothing whatever to do. ✻ ✻ ✻

✻ ✻ ✻

And so their whole energies are devoted to the massacre of old Time. They prick him to death with crochet and embroidery needles; strum him deaf with piano and harp playing—*not* music; cut him up with morning visitors, or leave his carcass in ten-minute parcels at every "friend's" house they can think of. Finally, they dance him defunct at all sort of unnatural hours; and then, rejoicing in the excellent excuse, smother him in sleep for a third of the following day. Thus he dies, a slow, inoffensive, perfectly natural death; and they will

---

1. Posy: small bouquet of flowers.
2. Nonsense (literally, a sweet and insubstantial

dessert).
3. Seasoning, salt and pepper.

never recognize his murder till, on the confines of this world, or from the unknown shores of the next, the question meets them: "What have you done with Time?"—Time, the only mortal gift bestowed equally on every living soul, and excepting the soul, the only mortal loss which is totally irretrievable.

             *   *   *

But "what am I to do with my life?" as once asked me one girl out of the numbers who begin to feel aware that, whether marrying or not, each possesses an individual life, to spend, to use, or to lose. And herein lies the momentous question.

             *   *   *

A definite answer to this question is simply impossible. Generally—and this is the best and safest guide—she will find her work lying very near at hand: some desultory tastes to condense into regular studies, some faulty household quietly to remodel, some child to teach, or parent to watch over. All these being needless or unattainable, she may extend her service out of the home into the world, which perhaps never at any time so much needed the help of us women. And hardly one of its charities and duties can be done so thoroughly as by a wise and tender woman's hand.

             *   *   *

These are they who are little spoken of in the world at large. * * * They have made for themselves a place in the world: the harsh, practical, yet not ill-meaning world, where all find their level soon or late, and where a frivolous young maid sunk into a helpless old one, can no more expect to keep her pristine position than a last year's leaf to flutter upon a spring bough. But an old maid who deserves well of this same world, by her ceaseless work therein, having won her position, keeps it to the end.

Not an ill position either, or unkindly; often higher and more honourable than that of many a mother of ten sons. In households, where "Auntie" is the universal referee, nurse, playmate, comforter, and counselor: in society, where "that nice Miss So-and-so," though neither clever, handsome, nor young, is yet such a person as can neither be omitted nor overlooked: in charitable works, where she is "such a practical body—always knows exactly what to do, and how to do it": or perhaps, in her own house, solitary indeed, as every single woman's home must be, yet neither dull nor unhappy in itself, and the nucleus of cheerfulness and happiness to many another home besides.

             *   *   *

Published or unpublished, this woman's life is a goodly chronicle, the title page of which you may read in her quiet countenance; her manner, settled, cheerful, and at ease; her unfailing interest in all things and all people. You will rarely find she thinks much about herself; she has never had time for it. And this her life-chronicle, which, out of its very fullness, has taught her that the more one does, the more one finds to do—she will never flourish in your face, or the face of Heaven, as something uncommonly virtuous and extraordinary. She knows that, after all, she has simply done what it was her duty to do.

But—and when her place is vacant on earth, this will be said of her assuredly, both here and Otherwhere—"*She hath done what she could.*"

1858

FLORENCE NIGHTINGALE

In 1854 Nightingale (1820–1910) became famous for organizing a contingent of nurses to care for sick and wounded soldiers during the Crimean War, an event that provided an outlet for her passionate desire to change the world of hospital treatment. But Nightingale achieved her dream of an active and productive life only after many years of waiting; at the age of thirty-two she was still living at home, unmarried (having declined several proposals). Some members of her well-to-do family, in particular her mother, strongly opposed her nursing ambitions and pressured her to remain at home. In 1852, so bored with family and social life that she thought of suicide, she began writing *Cassandra*, which she called her "family manuscript"; it records her frustrations before she escaped into a professional world where there was "something to do." In 1859 she revised the manuscript, and a few copies were privately printed that year, but it was not published until 1928. The title refers to the Trojan princess whose true prophecies went unheeded by those around her because she was judged insane.

From Cassandra

[NOTHING TO DO]

Why have women passion, intellect, moral activity—these three—and a place in society where no one of the three can be exercised? Men say that God punishes for complaining. No, but men are angry with misery. They are irritated with women for not being happy. They take it as a personal offense. To God alone may women complain without insulting Him!

*　*　*

Is discontent a privilege?

Yes, it is a privilege for you to suffer for your race—a privilege not reserved to the Redeemer, and the martyrs alone, but one enjoyed by numbers in every age.

The commonplace life of thousands; and in that is its only interest—its only merit as a history; viz., that it *is* the type of common sufferings—the story of one who has not the courage to resist nor to submit to the civilization of her time—is this.

Poetry and imagination begin life. A child will fall on its knees on the gravel walk at the sight of a pink hawthorn in full flower, when it is by itself, to praise God for it.

Then comes intellect. It wishes to satisfy the wants which intellect creates for it. But there is a physical, not moral, impossibility of supplying the wants of the intellect in the state of civilization at which we have arrived. The stimulus, the training, the time, are all three wanting to us; or, in other words, the means and inducements are not there.

Look at the poor lives we lead. It is a wonder that we are so good as we are, not that we are so bad. In looking round we are struck with the power of the organizations[1] we see, not with their want of power. Now and then, it is true, we are conscious that *there* is an inferior organization, but, in general, just the contrary. Mrs A. has the imagination, the poetry of a Murillo,[2] and has suffi-

---

1. Beings, organisms.
2. Bartolomé Murillo (1617–1682), Spanish painter.

cient power of execution to show that she might have had a great deal more. Why is she not a Murillo? From a material difficulty, not a mental one. If she has a knife and fork in her hands for three hours of the day, she cannot have a pencil or brush. Dinner is the great sacred ceremony of this day, the great sacrament. To be absent from dinner is equivalent to being ill. Nothing else will excuse us from it. Bodily incapacity is the only apology valid. If she has a pen and ink in her hands during other three hours, writing answers for the penny post,[3] again, she cannot have her pencil, and so *ad infinitum* through life. People have no type before them in their lives, neither fathers nor mothers, nor the children themselves. They look at things in detail. They say, "It is very desirable that A., my daughter, should go to such a party, should know such a lady, should sit by such a person." It is true. But what standard have they before them of the nature and destination of man? The very words are rejected as pedantic. But might they not, at least, have a type in their minds that such an one might be a discoverer through her intellect, such another through her art, a third through her moral power?

Women often try one branch of intellect after another in their youth, e.g., mathematics. But that, least of all, is compatible with the life of "society." It is impossible to follow up anything systematically. Women often long to enter some man's profession where they would find direction, competition (or rather opportunity of measuring the intellect with others) and, above all, time.

In those wise institutions, mixed as they are with many follies, which will last as long as the human race lasts, because they are adapted to the wants of the human race; those institutions which we call monasteries, and which, embracing much that is contrary to the laws of nature, are yet better adapted to the union of the life of action and that of thought than any other mode of life with which we are acquainted; in many such, four and a half hours, at least, are daily set aside for thought, rules are given for thought, training and opportunity afforded. Among us there is *no* time appointed for this purpose, and the difficulty is that, in our social life, we must be always doubtful whether we ought not to be with somebody else or be doing something else.

Are men better off than women in this?

If one calls upon a friend in London and sees her son in the drawing room, it strikes one as odd to find a young man sitting idle in his mother's drawing room in the morning. For men, who are seen much in those haunts, there is no end of the epithets we have: "knights of the carpet," "drawing-room heroes," "ladies' men." But suppose we were to see a number of men in the morning sitting round a table in the drawing-room, looking at prints, doing worsted work,[4] and reading little books, how we should laugh! A member of the House of Commons was once known to do worsted work. Of another man was said, "His only fault is that he is too good; he drives out with his mother every day in the carriage, and if he is asked anywhere he answers that he must dine with his mother, but, if she can spare him, he will come in to tea, and he does not come."

Now, why is it more ridiculous for a man than for a woman to do worsted work and drive out every day in the carriage? Why should we laugh if we were

3. Replying (to social correspondence and invitations) in letters, which would then be mailed; a uniform rate of a penny for each letter was insti-tuted in 1840.
4. Embroidery or other needlework with fine woollen yarn.

to see a parcel of men sitting round a drawing room table in the morning, and think it all right if they were women?

Is man's time more valuable than woman's? or is the difference between man and woman this, that woman has confessedly nothing to do?

Women are never supposed to have any occupation of sufficient importance *not* to be interrupted, except "suckling their fools";[5] and women themselves have accepted this, have written books to support it, and have trained themselves so as to consider whatever they do as *not* of such value to the world or to others, but that they can throw it up at the first "claim of social life." They have accustomed themselves to consider intellectual occupation as a merely selfish amusement, which it is their "duty" to give up for every trifler more selfish than themselves.

✻ ✻ ✻

Women have no means given them, whereby they *can* resist the "claims of social life." They are taught from their infancy upwards that it is a wrong, ill-tempered, and a misunderstanding of "woman's mission" (with a great M) if they do not allow themselves *willingly* to be interrupted at all hours. If a woman has once put in a claim to be treated as a man by some work of science or art or literature, which she can *show* as the "fruit of her leisure," then she will be considered justified in *having* leisure (hardly, perhaps, even then). But if not, not. If she has nothing to show, she must resign herself to her fate.

"I like riding about this beautiful place, why don't you? I like walking about the garden, why don't you?" is the common expostulation—as if we were children, whose spirits rise during a fortnight's holiday, who think that they will last forever—and look neither backwards nor forwards.

Society triumphs over many. They wish to regenerate the world with their institutions, with their moral philosophy, with their love. Then they sink to living from breakfast till dinner, from dinner till tea, with a little worsted work, and to looking forward to nothing but bed.

When shall we see a life full of steady enthusiasm, walking straight to its aim, flying home, as that bird is now, against the wind—with the calmness and the confidence of one who knows the laws of God and can apply them?

✻ ✻ ✻

When shall we see a woman making a *study* of what she does? Married women cannot; for a man would think, if his wife undertook any great work with the intention of carrying it out—of making anything but a sham of it—that she would "suckle his fools and chronicle his small beer" less well for it—that he would not have so good a dinner—that she would destroy, as it is called, his domestic life.

The intercourse of[6] man and woman—how frivolous, how unworthy it is! Can we call *that* the true vocation of woman—her high career? Look round at the marriages which you know. The true marriage—that noble union, by which a man and woman become together the one perfect being—probably does not exist at present upon earth.

It is not surprising that husbands and wives seem so little part of one another. It is surprising that there is so much love as there is. For there is no

---

5. See Iago's cynical comments on the role of women in Shakespeare's *Othello* 2.1.162: "To suckle fools, and chronicle small beer." "Small

bear" colloquially means "unimportant matters."
6. Social communication between.

food for it. What does it live upon—what nourishes it? Husbands and wives never seem to have anything to say to one another. What do they talk about? Not about any great religious, social, political questions or feelings. They talk about who shall come to dinner, who is to live in this lodge and who in that, about the improvement of the place, or when they shall go to London. If there are children, they form a common subject of some nourishment. But, even then, the case is oftenest thus—the husband is to think of how they are to get on in life; the wife of bringing them up at home.

But any real communion between husband and wife—any descending into the depths of their being, and drawing out thence what they find and comparing it—do we ever dream of such a thing? Yes, we may dream of it during the season of "passion," but we shall not find it afterwards. We even expect it to go off, and lay our account that it will. If the husband has, by chance, gone into the depths of *his* being, and found there anything unorthodox, he, oftenest, conceals it carefully from his wife—he is afraid of "unsettling her opinions."

✳ ✳ ✳

✳ ✳ ✳ For a woman is "by birth a Tory"[7]—has often been said—by education a "Tory," we mean.

Women dream till they have no longer the strength to dream; those dreams against which they so struggle, so honestly, vigorously, and conscientiously, and so in vain, yet which are their life, without which they could not have lived; those dreams go at last. All their plans and visions seem vanished, and they know not where; gone, and they cannot recall them. They do not even remember them. And they are left without the food of reality or of hope.

Later in life, they neither desire nor dream, neither of activity, nor of love, nor of intellect. The last often survives the longest. They wish, if their experiences would benefit anybody, to give them to someone. But they never find an hour free in which to collect their thoughts, and so discouragement becomes ever deeper and deeper, and they less and less capable of undertaking anything.

It seems as if the female spirit of the world were mourning everlastingly over blessings, not *lost*, but which she has never had, and which, in her discouragement she feels that she never will have, they are so far off.

The more complete a woman's organization, the more she will feel it, till at last there shall arise a woman, who will resume, in her own soul, all the sufferings of her race, and that woman will be the Saviour of her race.

1852–59   1928

7. Nickname for a member or supporter of the British Conservative Party, which generally sought to preserve the established religious and political order.

MONA CAIRD

In several novels and many essays, the feminist writer Caird (1854–1932) explored the position of women in Victorian society. *The Daughters of Danaus* (1894) features a heroine whose desire to pursue a musical career conflicts with her family ties and responsibilities. Caird's article "Marriage," which appeared in the *Westminster Review* in 1888, inspired a heated exchange in the journals of the 1890s. Her essays on the subject of marriage were later collected and published as *The Morality of Marriage, and Other Essays on the Status and Destiny of Woman* (1897).

From Marriage

We come then to the conclusion that the present form of marriage—exactly in proportion to its conformity with orthodox ideas—is a vexatious failure. If certain people have made it a success by ignoring those orthodox ideas, such instances afford no argument in favour of the institution as it stands. We are also led to conclude that modern "Respectability" draws its life-blood from the degradation of womanhood in marriage and in prostitution. But what is to be done to remedy these manifold evils? how is marriage to be rescued from a mercenary society, torn from the arms of "Respectability," and established on a footing which will make it no longer an insult to human dignity?

First of all we must set up an ideal, undismayed by what will seem its Utopian impossibility. Every good thing that we enjoy to-day was once the dream of a "crazy enthusiast" mad enough to believe in the power of ideas and in the power of man to have things as he wills. The ideal marriage then, despite all dangers and difficulties, should be *free*. So long as love and trust and friendship remain, no bonds are necessary to bind two people together; life apart will be empty and colourless; but whenever these cease the tie becomes false and iniquitous, and no one ought to have power to enforce it. The matter is one in which any interposition, whether of law or of society, is an impertinence. Even the idea of "duty" ought to be excluded from the most perfect marriage, because the intense attraction of one being for another, the intense desire for one another's happiness, would make interchanges of whatever kind the outcome of a feeling far more passionate than that of duty. It need scarcely be said that there must be a full understanding and acknowledgment of the obvious right of the woman to *possess herself* body and soul, to give or withhold herself body and soul exactly as she wills. The moral right here is so palpable, and its denial implies ideas so low and offensive to human dignity, that no fear of consequences ought to deter us from making this liberty an element of our ideal, in fact its fundamental principle. Without it, no ideal could hold up its head. Moreover, "consequences" in the long run are never beneficent, where obvious moral rights are disregarded. The idea of a perfectly free marriage would imply the possibility of any form of contract being entered into between the two persons, the State and society standing aside, and recognizing the entirely private character of the transaction.

The economical independence of woman is the first condition of free marriage. She ought not to be tempted to marry, or to remain married, for the sake of bread and butter. But the condition is a very hard one to secure. Our present competitive system, with the daily increasing ferocity of the struggle for existence, is fast reducing itself to an absurdity, woman's labour helping to make the struggle only the fiercer. The problem now offered to the mind and conscience of humanity is to readjust its industrial organization in such a way as to gradually reduce this absurd and useless competition within reasonable limits, and to bring about in its place some form of cooperation, in which no man's interest will depend on the misfortune of his neighbour, but rather on his neighbour's happiness and welfare. It is idle to say that this cannot be done; the state of society shows quite clearly that it *must* be done sooner or later; otherwise some violent catastrophe will put an end to a condition of things which is hurrying towards impossibility. Under improved economical conditions the difficult problem of securing the real independence of women, and thence of the readjustment of their position in relation to men and to society would find easy solution.

When girls and boys are educated together, when the unwholesome atmosphere of social life becomes fresher and nobler, when the pressure of existence slackens (as it will and *must* do), and when the whole nature has thus a chance to expand, such additions to the scope and interest of life will cease to be thought marvellous or "unnatural." "Human nature" has more variety of powers and is more responsive to conditions than we imagine. It is hard to believe in things for which we feel no capacity in ourselves, but fortunately such things exist in spite of our placid unconsciousness. Give room for the development of individuality, and individuality develops, to the amazement of spectators! Give freedom in marriage, and each pair will enter upon their union after their own particular fashion, creating a refreshing diversity in modes of life, and consequently of character. Infinitely preferable will this be to our own gloomy uniformity, the offspring of our passion to be in all things exactly like our neighbours.

The proposed freedom in marriage would of course have to go hand-in-hand with the co-education of the sexes. It is our present absurd interference with the natural civilizing influences of one sex upon the other, that creates half the dangers and difficulties of our social life, and gives colour to the fears of those who would hedge round marriage with a thousand restraints or so-called safeguards, ruinous to happiness, and certainly not productive of a satisfactory social condition. Already the good results of this method of co-education have been proved by experiment in America, but we ought to go farther in this direction than our go-ahead cousins have yet gone. Meeting freely in their working-hours as well as at times of recreation, men and women would have opportunity for forming reasonable judgments of character, for making friendships irrespective of sex, and for giving and receiving that inspiring influence which apparently can only be given by one sex to the other.[1] There would also be a chance of forming genuine attachments founded on friendship; marriage would cease to be the haphazard thing it is now; girls would no longer fancy themselves in love with a man because they had met none other on terms equally intimate, and they would not be tempted to marry for the sake of freedom and a place in life, for existence would be free and full from the beginning.

The general rise in health, physical and moral, following the improvement in birth, surroundings, and training, would rapidly tell upon the whole state of society. Any one who has observed carefully knows how grateful a response the human organism gives to improved conditions, if only these remain constant. We should have to deal with healthier, better equipped, more reasonable men and women, possessing well-developed minds, and hearts kindly disposed

1. Mr. Henry Stanton, in his work on *The Woman Question in Europe*, speaks of the main idea conveyed in Legouvé's *Histoire des Femmes* as follows: —"Equality in difference is its key-note. The question is not to make woman a man, but to complete man by woman" [Caird's note]. Caird is prob- ably imperfectly recalling the name of Theodore Stanton (1851–1925), the editor of *The Woman Question in Europe: A Series of Original Essays* (1884). *Histoire Morale des Femmes* (*Moral History of Women*), by Ernest Legouvé (1807–1903), was published in Paris in 1849.

towards their fellow-creatures. Are such people more likely to enter into a union frivolously and ignorantly than are the average men and women of to-day? Surely not. If the number of divorces did not actually decrease there would be the certainty that no couple remained united against their will, and that no lives were sacrificed to a mere convention. With the social changes which would go hand in hand with changes in the status of marriage, would come inevitably many fresh forms of human power, and thus all sorts of new and stimulating influences would be brought to bear upon society. No man has a right to consider himself educated until he has been under the influence of cultivated women, and the same may be said of women as regards men.[2] Development involves an increase of complexity. It is so in all forms of existence, vegetable and animal; it is so in human life. It will be found that men and women as they increase in complexity can enter into a numberless variety of relationships, abandoning no good gift that they now possess, but adding to their powers indefinitely, and thence to their emotions and experiences. The action of the man's nature upon the woman's and of the woman's upon the man's, is now only known in a few instances; there is a whole world yet to explore in this direction, and it is more than probable that the future holds a discovery in the domain of spirit as great as that of Columbus in the domain of matter.

With regard to the dangers attending these readjustments, there is no doubt much to be said. The evils that hedge around marriage are linked with other evils, so that movement is difficult and perilous indeed. Nevertheless, we have to remember that we now live in the midst of dangers, and that human happiness is cruelly murdered by our systems of legalized injustice. By sitting still circumspectly and treating our social system as if it were a card-house which would tumble down at a breath, we merely wait to see it fall from its own internal rottenness, and *then* we shall have dangers to encounter indeed! The time has come, not for violent overturning of established institutions before people admit that they are evil, but for a gradual alteration of opinion which will rebuild them from the very foundation. The method of the most enlightened reformer is to crowd out old evil by new good, and to seek to sow the seed of the nobler future where alone it can take root and grow to its full height: in the souls of men and women. Far-seeing we ought to be, but we know in our hearts right well that fear will never lead us to the height of our ever-growing possibility. Evolution has ceased to be a power driving us like dead leaves on a gale; thanks to science, we are no longer entirely blind, and we aspire to direct that mighty force for the good of humanity. We see a limitless field of possibility opening out before us; the adventurous spirit in us might leap up at the wonderful romance of life! We recognize that no power, however trivial, fails to count in the general sum of things which moves this way or that—towards heaven or hell, according to the preponderating motives of individual units. We shall begin, slowly but surely, to see the folly of permitting the forces of one sex to pull against and neutralize the workings of the other, to the confusion of our efforts and the checking of our progress. We shall see, in the relations of men and women to one another, the source of all good or of all evil, precisely as those relations are true and noble and equal,

2. Mrs. Cady Stanton believes that there is a sex in mind, and that men can only be inspired to their highest achievements by women, while women are stimulated to their utmost only by men [Caird's note]. Elizabeth Cady Stanton (1815–1902), prominent American women's suffragist.

or false and low and unjust. With this belief we shall seek to move opinion in all the directions that may bring us to this "consummation devoutly to be wished,"[3] and we look forward steadily, hoping and working for the day when men and women shall be comrades and fellow-workers as well as lovers and husbands and wives, when the rich and many-sided happiness which they have the power to bestow one on another shall no longer be enjoyed in tantalizing snatches, but shall gladden and give new life to all humanity. That will be the day prophesied by Lewis Morris[4] in *The New Order*—

> "When man and woman in an equal union
> Shall merge, and marriage be a true communion."

1888

3. Cf. Shakespeare's *Hamlet* 3.1.65–66.   4. Welsh poet (1833–1907).

WALTER BESANT

Besant (1836–1901) was a literary critic, historian, and novelist. His history *The Queen's Reign* (1897) celebrated the improvements that he felt he had witnessed during his lifetime.

From The Queen's Reign

[THE TRANSFORMATION OF WOMEN'S STATUS BETWEEN 1837 AND 1897]

Let me present to you, first, an early Victorian girl, born about the Waterloo year;[1] next, her granddaughter, born about 1875. * * *

The young lady of 1837 * * * cannot reason on any subject whatever because of her ignorance—as she herself would say, because she is a woman. In her presence, and indeed in the presence of ladies generally, men talk trivialities. * * * It has often been charged against Thackeray[2] that his good women were insipid. Thackeray, like most artists, could only draw the women of his own time, and at that time they were undoubtedly insipid. Men, I suppose, liked them so. To be childishly ignorant; to carry shrinking modesty so far as to find the point of a shoe projecting beyond the folds of a frock indelicate; to confess that serious subjects were beyond a woman's grasp; never even to pretend to form an independent judgment; to know nothing of Art, History, Science, Literature, Politics, Sociology, Manners—men liked these things; women yielded to please the men; her very ignorance formed a subject of laudable pride with the Englishwoman of the Forties. * * * There was something Oriental in the seclusion of women in the home, and their exclusion from active and practical life.

1. I.e., 1815, the year Napoleon Bonaparte was defeated by British and Prussian forces at the Battle of Waterloo.
2. William Makepeace Thackeray (1811–1863), British novelist. The character of Amelia Sedley, in his novel *Vanity Fair* (1848), is cited by Besant as typical of the "insipid" women of the 1840s.

* * *

Let us turn to the Englishwoman—the young Englishwoman—of 1897. She is educated. Whatever things are taught to the young man are taught to the young woman. If she wants to explore the wickedness of the world she can do so, for it is all in the books. The secrets of Nature are not closed to her; she can learn the structure of the body if she wishes. At school, at college, she studies just as the young man studies, but harder and with greater concentration. * * * She has invaded the professions. She cannot become a priest, because the Oriental prejudice against women still prevails, so that women in High Church places are not allowed to sing in the choir, or to play the organ, not to speak of preaching. * * * In the same way she cannot enter the Law. Some day she will get over this restriction, but not yet. For a long time she was kept out of medicine. That restriction is now removed; she can, and she does, practice as a physician or a surgeon, generally the former.[3] I believe that she has shown in this profession, as in her university studies, she can stand, *inter pares*,[4] among her equals and her peers, not her superiors. There is no branch of literature in which women have not distinguished themselves. * * * In music they compose, but not greatly; they play and sing divinely. The acting of the best among them is equal to that of any living man. They have become journalists, in some cases of remarkable ability; in fact, there are thousands of women who now make their livelihood by writing in all its branches. As for the less common professions—the accountants, architects, actuaries, agents—they are rapidly being taken over by women.

It is no longer a question of necessity; women do not ask themselves whether they must earn their own bread, or live a life of dependence. Necessity or no necessity they demand work, with independence and personal liberty. Whether they will take upon them the duties and responsibilities of marriage, they postpone for further consideration. I believe that, although in the first eager running there are many who profess to despise marriage, the voice of nature and the instinctive yearning for love will prevail.

Personal independence: that is the keynote of the situation. Mothers no longer attempt the old control over their daughters: they would find it impossible. The girls go off by themselves on their bicycles;[5] they go about as they please; they neither compromise themselves nor get talked about. For the first time in man's history it is regarded as a right and proper thing to trust a girl as a boy insists upon being trusted. Out of this personal freedom will come, I daresay, a change in the old feelings of young man to maiden. He will not see in her a frail, tender plant which must be protected from cold winds; she can protect herself perfectly well. He will not see in her any longer a creature of sweet emotions and pure aspirations, coupled with a complete ignorance of the world, because she already knows all that she wants to know. Nor will he see in her a companion whose mind is a blank, and whose conversation is insipid, because she already knows as much as he knows himself. Nor, again, will he see in her a housewife whose whole time will be occupied in superintending servants or in making, brewing, confecting things with her own hand.

1897

---

3. The first woman to have her name placed on the British Medical Register was Elizabeth Blackwell (who earned her degree in the United States), in 1859; it took another two decades for women to gain the right to study and take the required examinations in medicine in Great Britain.

4. Among equals (Latin).
5. Modern bicycles (with wheels of equal size and pneumatic tires) began to be manufactured in the late 1880s and became extremely popular in Europe and the United States.

EMPIRE AND NATIONAL IDENTITY

Great Britain during Victoria's reign was not just a powerful island nation. It was the center of a global empire that brought the British into contact with a wide variety of other cultures, though the exchange was usually an unequal one. By the end of the nineteenth century, nearly one-quarter of the earth's land surface was part of the British Empire, and more than four hundred million people were governed (however nominally) from Great Britain. Queen Victoria's far-flung empire was a truly heterogeneous entity, controlled by heterogeneous practices. It included Crown Colonies such as Jamaica, ruled from Britain, and protectorates such as Uganda, which had relinquished only partial sovereignty to Britain. Ireland was a kind of internal colony whose demands for home rule were alternately entertained and discounted. India had started the century under the control of a private entity, the East India Company, but was ruled directly from Britain after the 1857 Indian Mutiny (the first war of Indian independence), and Victoria was crowned empress of India in 1877. Canada, with its substantial European population, had been virtually self-governing from the middle of the nineteenth century onward and was increasingly considered a near-equal partner in the imperial project; Australia enjoyed a parallel status, despite its inauspicious earlier history as the site of British penal colonies. By contrast, colonies and protectorates with large indigenous populations, such as Sierra Leone, or with large transplanted populations of ex-slaves and non-European laborers, such as Trinidad, would not gain autonomy until the twentieth century.

The scope of imperial enterprise at the close of the Victorian era is especially astounding given Britain's catastrophic loss of its American colonies (historians generally view the American Revolution of 1776 as marking the end of the first British Empire). But although empire was never a central preoccupation of the government during the first half of the nineteenth century, the second empire had continued to grow; Britain acquired a number of new territories, greatly expanded its colonies in Australia and Canada (which saw large-scale British emigration), and steadily pushed its way across the Indian subcontinent. A far more rapid expansion took place between 1870 and 1900, three decades that witnessed "the new imperialism"—a significantly different British mode of empire building that would continue until World War I (1914–18). Britain's rivalry with its European neighbors was an instrumental factor: the balance of power in Europe had shifted in the wake of the Franco-Prussian War (1870–71), leading to competition for new territories. Particularly fierce was "the scramble for Africa," as the partitioning of that continent was called. Expansion did not go unchallenged—the British fought both with indigenous peoples and with other European powers or settlers in numerous conflicts—but it progressed at an astonishing pace nonetheless.

To summarize Britain's attitude toward its imperial activities over the centuries is no easy task. The historian Sir John Seeley famously remarked in *The Expansion of England* (1883) that "we seem, as it were, to have conquered and peopled half the world in a fit of absence of mind," but many would now argue that economic motives were always present, and that Britain was driven to claim territories outside its national borders primarily by the urge to obtain raw materials such as sugar, spices, tea, tin, and rubber; to procure markets for its own goods; and to secure trade routes. From this perspective Britain's enhanced national pride in its expanding physical size, and thus ever-increasing political and military clout, was an important side effect of commercial growth but did not instigate its exploits overseas. To look at the British Empire in this way is to see it at its most naked, and to confront head-on the desire for financial profit that occasioned the physical violence and cultural devastation that so often accompanied its arrival in, and occupation of, another land. As Marlow comments in Joseph Conrad's *Heart of Darkness* (1902), "The conquest of the earth, which mostly means the taking it away from those who have a different complexion or slightly flatter noses than ourselves, is not a pretty thing when you look into it too much." But Conrad's storyteller cannot leave it at that, adding, "What redeems it is the idea only." As we try to understand, if not redeem, the British Empire, we must investigate some of the principal ideas that collected around this huge and diverse phenomenon, and that underwent significant shifts over the decades of Victoria's reign.

Joseph Chamberlain asserts in "The True Conception of Empire" (1897) that the balance sheet dictated what early-nineteenth-century Britons thought about their relationship with the colonies: having in the previous century "appeared rather in the light of a grasping and absentee landlord desiring to take from his tenants the utmost rents he could exact," Britain, shaken by its American losses, worried that some of its overseas enterprises would prove a financial drain. Yet India was another story, and by 1800 the importance to British prosperity of the trading opportunities in that continent was already viewed as axiomatic. In managing its businesses, however, the East India Company grew progressively more entangled with issues of Indian administration and politics; in its turn the British government became increasingly concerned with overseeing, and ultimately taking over, these functions. From this state of affairs a notion of trusteeship began to emerge—a belief that Britain had the responsibility to provide good government for the Indian people. Underlying this conviction was the assumption that Britain would thereby bestow the benefits of its culturally and morally superior civilization upon a lesser people (Thomas Babington Macaulay's confident pronouncements in his 1835 "Minute on Indian Education" evince this sentiment with particular succinctness). Evangelical Christianity played a contributory role as well, and not just through the missionaries who worked in India beginning in the early nineteenth century. More broadly, for the majority of Britons who believed that Protestantism was the one true faith, and that it was their religious duty to bring the potential for salvation to as many souls as possible, the imposition of British rule was divinely sanctioned. But there was still no widespread popular or governmental enthusiasm for the idea of imperialism as Britain's special destiny, and various factors, not least England's long and troubled relationship with Ireland, ensured that many viewed the project of colonial rule with suspicion throughout the middle years of the century. With the rise of the new imperialism, however, preexisting ideas about Britain's superiority, now bolstered by supposedly "scientific" theories supporting the notion of its evolutionary advancement, were channeled into a romantic vision of the British Empire as a tremendous force for the good not only of the residents of Great Britain or those overseas of traditionally "British" descent but of the whole world. In the last three decades of Victoria's rule (and well into the twentieth century), a large proportion of British people took pride simultaneously in the global supremacy of their empire and in what they perceived to be their generous and selfless willingness to pick up the thankless, but necessary, task of imperial rule ("the white man's burden," as Rudyard Kipling would call it in another context). Only if we appreciate just how genuinely many Britons believed that they and their country were performing a noble duty can we begin to make sense of the feelings of outraged surprise and betrayal (often accompanied by virulent racism and vicious reprisals) that erupted when subjugated peoples periodically rose up against British control.

The British Empire had an incalculable physical and psychological impact on the individuals and cultures it colonized, but it also significantly changed the colonizers themselves, both at home and abroad. The need to concentrate on the imperial mission affected in theoretical and practical ways the consolidation of a specifically *British* identity: the conflicted relations and characteristic differences between people from the various parts of the British Isles (politically dominant England and long-conquered Wales, Scotland, and Ireland) appeared less significant when set against the much more obvious inequities of power and greater cultural, racial, religious, and linguistic differences across the globe. A number of similar processes worked to solidify nationhood more generally. For instance, members of the working class in Great Britain only rarely connected their subordination to the English ruling class with that suffered by colonized peoples: they were much more likely to understand their identity through those "ties of kindred, of religion, of history, and of language," as Chamberlain puts it, that bound them to other historically British citizens, however privileged. Intensified competition with the empire-building powers of continental Europe after the Franco-Prussian War also played an important role, as did the mounting stridency of other nationalist movements abroad. In the last quarter of the century, the patriotic fervor celebrating the achievements of the British nation as a whole increased dramatically—a phenomenon undoubtedly assisted by the growth both in the size of the reading public (literacy was practically universal in Britain by 1900, thanks to the progressive extension of elementary education) and in the number of flag-waving newspapers, periodicals, and books available for it to consume.

The citizens of Great Britain were thus welded into a more cohesive whole. But few of them were ready to accept the peoples of the colonies (and especially indigenous nonwhite populations) as truly "British," despite the inclusive rhetoric of empire (the "one imperial whole" that Alfred, Lord Tennyson salutes in his poem on the opening of the Indian and Colonial Exhibition of 1886). Of course, there were exceptions: recounting his experiences on a visit to Britain for that same exhibition, the Indian T. N. Mukharji remembers that on one occasion in London, "somebody called me a foreigner. 'He is no foreigner!' cried several voices, 'He is a British subject as you and I.' " To J. A. Hobson, the author of the influential *Imperialism: A Study* (1902), the importance of this casual affirmation of shared subjecthood was negligible, given that "not five per cent of the population of our Empire are possessed of any appreciable portion of the political and civil liberties which are the basis of British civilisation." Writing after Britain's imperial confidence had been severely damaged by the unanticipated length and difficulty of the Anglo-Boer War of 1899–1902 in South Africa, Hobson in his meticulous analysis aimed not only to cast serious doubt on imperialism's putative financial benefit to Britain but also to demonstrate the overall falsity of the empire's claim to support the extension of self-government in its territories. In exposing the repeated misrepresentations and self-serving justifications at the heart of the British Empire, Hobson joined voices with others around the globe, such as the West Indian intellectual J. J. Thomas, and entered a tradition of anti-imperial critique that was to grow exponentially in the twentieth century.

It is instructive to consider the following discussions of Britain's relationship with other parts of the world, and its understanding of its own identity, in the context of a number of other selections. The popularity of Edward FitzGerald's translation of the *Rubáiyát of Omar Khayyám* (1859) testifies to the Victorians' fascination with what they saw as the exotic appeal of distant cultures; Tennyson's poem "Locksley Hall" (1842) also reflects on "yonder shining Orient." Matthew Arnold's prose writings frequently address the issue of national character, while John Henry Newman sets forth an ideal of English manliness in his "definition of a gentleman" in Discourse 8 of *The Idea of a University* (1852). Versions of this ideal from the apex of Great Britain's period of national pride appear in two highly popular poems, W. E. Henley's "Invictus" (1888) and Kipling's "If" (1910); Kipling's other poems and his novella *The Man Who Would Be King* (1888) are also essential reading for those interested in the intensification of imperial enthusiasm at the end of Victoria's reign. At the same time we should heed the warning of the postcolonial critic Gayatri Spivak against limiting any investigation of empire and national identity only to those writings that seem overtly concerned with the topic. "It should not be possible to read nineteenth-century British literature," she insists at the beginning of an analysis of Charlotte Brontë's *Jane Eyre* (1847), "without remembering that imperialism, understood as England's social mission, was a crucial part of the cultural representation of England to the English." In other words, images, explanations, and justifications of this massive enterprise were continually created and reflected throughout the pages of a wide range of Victorian texts.

For additional texts on the subject of empire, see "Victorian Imperialism" at Norton Literature Online.

THOMAS BABINGTON MACAULAY

The historian, essayist, and parliamentarian Macaulay (1800–1859) served as a member of the supreme council of the East India Company from 1834 to 1838, and in that capacity he oversaw major educational and legal reforms. His "Minute," or official memorandum, was written to rebut those council members who believed that Indian students should continue to be educated in Sanskrit and Persian as well as in English; Macaulay's party carried the argument.

From Minute on Indian Education

We now come to the gist of the matter. We have a fund to be employed as Government shall direct for the intellectual improvement of the people of this country. The simple question is, what is the most useful way of employing it?

All parties seem to be agreed on one point, that the dialects commonly spoken among the natives of this part of India contain neither literary or scientific information, and are, moreover, so poor and rude that, until they are enriched from some other quarter, it will not be easy to translate any valuable work into them. It seems to be admitted on all sides that the intellectual improvement of those classes of the people who have the means of pursuing higher studies can at present be effected only by means of some language not vernacular amongst them.

What, then, shall that language be? One half of the Committee maintain that it should be the English. The other half strongly recommend the Arabic[1] and Sanscrit. The whole question seems to me to be, which language is the best worth knowing?

I have no knowledge of either Sanscrit or Arabic.—But I have done what I could to form a correct estimate of their value. I have read translations of the most celebrated Arabic and Sanscrit works. I have conversed both here and at home with men distinguished by their proficiency in the Eastern tongues. I am quite ready to take the Oriental learning at the valuation of the Orientalists themselves. I have never found one among them who could deny that a single shelf of a good European library was worth the whole native literature of India and Arabia. The intrinsic superiority of the Western literature is, indeed, fully admitted by those members of the Committee who support the Oriental plan of education.

It will hardly be disputed, I suppose, that the department of literature in which the Eastern writers stand highest is poetry. And I certainly never met with any Orientalist who ventured to maintain that the Arabic and Sanscrit poetry could be compared to that of the great European nations. But, when we pass from works of imagination to works in which facts are recorded and general principles investigated, the superiority of the Europeans becomes absolutely immeasurable. It is, I believe, no exaggeration to say, that all the historical information which has been collected from all the books written in the Sanscrit language is less valuable than what may be found in the most paltry abridgments used at preparatory schools in England. In every branch of

---

1. Actually Persian, the language (written in Arabic script) of the Mogul dynasty that had ruled much of India since the 16th century.

physical or moral philosophy the relative position of the two nations is nearly the same.

How, then, stands the case? We have to educate a people who cannot at present be educated by means of their mother-tongue. We must teach them some foreign language. The claims of our own language it is hardly necessarily to recapitulate. It stands pre-eminent even among the languages of the West. It abounds with works of imagination not inferior to the noblest which Greece has bequeathed to us; with models of every species of eloquence; with historical compositions, which, considered merely as narratives, have seldom been surpassed, and which, considered as vehicles of ethical and political instruction, have never been equalled; with just and lively representations of human life and human nature; with the most profound speculations on metaphysics, morals, government, jurisprudence, and trade; with full and correct information respecting every experimental science which tends to preserve the health, to increase the comfort, or to expand the intellect of man. Whoever knows that language, has ready access to all the vast intellectual wealth, which all the wisest nations of the earth have created and hoarded in the course of ninety generations. It may safely be said that the literature now extant in that language is of far greater value than all the literature which three hundred years ago was extant in all the languages of the world spoken together. Nor is this all. In India, English is the language spoken by the ruling class. It is spoken by the higher class of natives at the seats of Government. It is likely to become the language of commerce throughout the seas of the East. It is the language of two great European communities which are rising, the one in the south of Africa, the other in Australasia; communities which are every year becoming more important, and more closely connected with our Indian empire. Whether we look at the intrinsic value of our literature or at the particular situation of this country, we shall see the strongest reason to think that, of all foreign tongues, the English tongue is that which would be the most useful to our native subjects.

✻ ✻ ✻

✻ ✻ ✻ It is said that the Sanscrit and Arabic are the languages in which the sacred books of a hundred millions of people are written, and that they are, on that account, entitled to peculiar[2] encouragement. Assuredly it is the duty of the British Government in India to be not only tolerant, but neutral on all religious questions. But to encourage the study of a literature admitted to be of small intrinsic value only because that literature inculcates the most serious errors on the most important subjects, is a course hardly reconcilable with reason, with morality, or even with that very neutrality which ought, as we all agree, to be sacredly preserved. It is confessed that a language is barren of useful knowledge. We are told to teach it because it is fruitful of monstrous superstitions. We are to teach false history, false astronomy, false medicine, because we find them in company with a false religion.

✻ ✻ ✻

In one point I fully agree with the gentlemen to whose general views I am opposed. I feel, with them, that it is impossible for us, with our limited means, to attempt to educate the body of the people. We must at present do our best to

2. Special.

form a class who may be interpreters between us and the millions whom we govern; a class of persons, Indian in blood and colour, but English in taste, in opinions, in morals, and in intellect. To that class we may leave it to refine the vernacular dialects of the country, to enrich those dialects with terms of science borrowed from the Western nomenclature, and to render them by degrees fit vehicles for conveying knowledge to the great mass of the population.

*　*　*

1835   1835

WILLIAM HOWARD RUSSELL

One of the first war correspondents, the Irish-born Russell (1820–1907) became famous for his dispatches to the London *Times* during the Crimean War (1854–56) and later reported on the American Civil War (1861–65). After the outbreak of the Indian Mutiny (1857–59), a rebellion of native troops and peasantry, later referred to in India as the First War of Indian Independence, Russell traveled to northern India to report on the revolt's suppression by British troops. More sympathetic toward the Indians than most Victorians, Russell debunked many of the most shocking rumors about the rape, torture, and killing of British people and criticized the cruelty of indiscriminate British reprisals. In the following excerpts he reflects on the fate of the British community at Cawnpore, which surrendered to the Indian rebels and was subsequently massacred.

From My Diary in India, In the Year 1858–9

[CAWNPORE]

February 12th.—* * * The scenes where great crimes have been perpetrated ever possess an interest, which I would not undertake to stigmatise as morbid; and surely among the sites rendered infamous for all time, Cawnpore will be pre-eminent as the magnitude of the atrocities with which it is connected. But, though pre-eminent among crimes, the massacre of Cawnpore is by no means singular or unprecedented in any of the circumstances which mark turpitude and profundity of guilt. We who suffered from it think that there never was such wickedness in the world, and the incessant efforts of a gang of forgers and utterers of lies have surrounded it with horrors needlessly invented in the hope of adding to the indignation and burning desire for vengeance which the naked facts aroused. Helpless garrisons, surrendering under capitulation, have been massacred ere now; men, women, and children have been ruthlessly butchered by the enemies of their race ere now; risings, such as that of the people of Pontus under Mithridates, of the Irish Roman Catholics against the Protestant settlers in 1641, of the actors in the Sicilian vespers, of the assassins who smote and spared none on the eve of St. Bartholomew,[1] have taken place before, and have been over and over again

1. All incidents in which culturally or religiously distinct minorities were attacked by members of a dominant population. Mithradates VI, the ruler of Pontus, a kingdom of northeast Asia Minor, led his

attended by inhuman cruelty, violation, and torture. The history of mediæval Europe affords many instances of crimes as great as those of Cawnpore; the history of civilized nations could afford some parallel to them even in modern times. In fact, the peculiar[2] aggravation of the Cawnpore massacres was this, that the deed was done by a subject race—by black men who dared to shed the blood of their masters and mistresses, and to butcher poor helpless ladies and children, who were the women and offspring of the dominant and conquering people. Here we had not only a servile war and a sort of Jacquerie[3] combined, but we had a war of religion, a war of race, a war of revenge, mingled together in a contest in which the insurgents were also actuated by some national promptings to shake off the yoke of a stranger, and to reestablish the full power of native chiefs, and the full sway of native religions. There is a kind of God's revenge against murder in the unsuccessful issue of all enterprises commenced in massacre, and carried on by cruelty and bloodshed. Whatever the causes of the mutiny and the revolt, it is clear enough that one of the modes by which the leaders, as if by common instinct, determined to effect their end was, the destruction of every white man, woman, or child who fell into their hands—a design which the kindliness of the people, or motives of policy, frustrated on many remarkable occasions. It must be remembered that the punishments of the Hindoo are cruel, and whether he be mild or not, he certainly is not, any more than the Mussulman,[4] distinguished for clemency towards his enemies. But philosophize and theorize as we may, Cawnpore will be a name ever heard by English ears with horror long after the present generation has passed away.

*　　*　　*

February 13th.—* * * The difficulty, in my mind, was to believe that it [Cawnpore] could ever have been defended at all. Make every allowance for the effects of weather, for circumstances, it is still the most wretched defensive position that could be imagined. Honour to those who defended it! Pity for their fate! Above all, pity for the lot of those whom the strong arms and brave hearts failed to save from the unknown dangers of that foul treachery! It was a horrible spot! Inside the shattered rooms, which had been the scene of such devotion and suffering, are heaps of rubbish and filth. The intrenchment is used as a *cloaca maxima*[5] by the natives, camp-followers, coolies, and others who bivouac in the sandy plains around it. The smells are revolting. Rows of gorged vultures sit with outspread wings on the mouldering parapets, or perch in clusters on the two or three leafless trees at the angle of the works by which we enter. I shot one with my revolver; and as the revolting creature disgorged its meal, twisting its bare black snake-like neck to and fro, I made a vow I would never incur the risk of beholding such a disgusting sight again.

*　　*　　*

armies to massacre Roman and Italian residents in Asia in 88 B.C.E. In 1641 in Ulster, a county in northern Ireland, dispossessed native Irish Catholics rose up against English and Scottish Protestant settlers. Sicilians rebelled in 1282 against Charles I, the French-born king of Naples (son of Louis VIII and brother of Louis IX of France). In 1572, on the evening before the feast day of St. Bartholomew (August 24), some Catholic nobles in the French royal court began a massacre of Huguenots (French Protestants), giving new impetus to a lengthy religious civil war.
2. Particular.
3. Peasant rebellion; the term derives from the 1358 uprising of peasants, known derisively as "Jacques," against nobles in northern France.
4. Muslim.
5. Largest sewer (Latin), after the main sewer draining northeast Rome (which even in the classical period was covered).

February 14th.—* * * All the country about Cawnpore is covered with the finest powdered dust, two or three inches deep, which rises into the air on the smallest provocation. It is composed of sand, pulverized earth, and the brick powder and mortar of the dilapidated houses; whatever, in fact, can turn into dust. As the natives shuffle along, their pointed slippers fling up suffocating clouds of this unpleasant compound, and when these slippers are multiplied by thousands, the air is filled with a floating stratum of it, fifteen or eighteen feet high, and extending over the whole of the station. Even in the old days, when the roads were watered, the station of Cawnpore had a bad notoriety for dust. What an earthquake to shake to pieces, what a volcano to smother with lava and ashes, has this mutiny been! Not alone cities, but confidence and trust have gone, never more to be restored!

Among those heaps of dust and ashes, those arid mounds of brick, those new-made trenches, I try in vain to realize what was once this station of Cawnpore. The solemn etiquette, the visits to the Brigadier and the General *en grande tenue*, the invitations to dinner, the white kid-gloves, the balls, the liveries, the affectation of the *plus haut des hauts tons,* the millinery anxieties of the ladies, the ices, and champagne, and supper, the golden-robed Nana Sahib,⁶ moving about amid haughty stares and ill-concealed dislike. "What the deuce does the General ask that nigger here for?" The little and big flirtations, the drives on the road—a dull, ceremonious pleasure—the faded fun of the private theatricals, the exotic absurdities of the masonic revels, the marryings and givings in marriage, the little bills done by the rich bunneahs,⁷ the small and great pecuniary relations between the station and the bazaar, the sense of security—and then on all this exaggerated relief of an English garrison-town and watering-place, the deep gloom of apprehension—at first "a shave of old Smith's,"⁸ then a well-authenticated report, then a certainty of disaffection—rolling like thunder-clouds, and darkening the glassy surface of the gay society till it burst on it in stormy and cruel reality. But I cannot.

"Ah! you should have seen Cawnpore in its palmy days, when there were two cavalry regiments here, a lot of artillery, and three regiments of infantry in the cantonments.⁹ Chock full of pretty women! The private theatricals every week; balls, and picnics, and dinners every evening. By Jove! it's too horrible to look at it now!" And so, indeed, it was. But one is tempted to ask if there is not some lesson and some warning given to our race in reference to India by the tremendous catastrophe of Cawnpore? I am deeply impressed by the difficulty of ruling India, as it is now governed by force, exercised by a few who are obliged to employ natives as the instruments of coercion. That force is the base of our rule I have no doubt; for I see nothing else but force employed in our relations with the governed. The efforts to improve the condition of the people are made by bodies or individuals who have no connection with the Government. The action of the Government in matters of improvement is only excited by considerations of revenue. Does it—as the great instructor of the people, the exponent of our superior morality and civilization—does it observe treaties, keep faith, pursue a fixed and equitable policy, and follow the precepts of Christianity in its conduct towards states and peoples? Are not our courts of law con-

6. A dispossessed Hindu ruler who took at least nominal charge of the rebel forces at Cawnpore and who was seen by many British as the mastermind behind the massacres. "*En grande tenue*": in full military dress (French). "*Plus haut des hauts tons*": the highest of high fashions (French).
7. The receipts written up by wealthy merchants.

8. An unconfirmed report (military slang) of an incident from Lieutenant Colonel George Acklom Smith at his post at Fatehgarh, sixty miles from Cawnpore.
9. Permanent military stations in British India. "Palmy": prosperous.

demned by ourselves? Are not our police admitted to be a curse and a blight upon the country? In effect, the grave, unhappy doubt which settles on my mind is, whether India is the better for our rule, so far as regards the social condition of the great mass of the people. We have put down widow-burning,[1] we have sought to check infanticide; but I have travelled hundreds of miles through a country peopled with beggars and covered with wigwam villages.

1858–59   1860

1. Suttee, the custom of a Hindu widow willingly immolating herself on her husband's funeral pyre; it was outlawed by the British in 1829.

ELIZA COOK

A mainly self-educated poet of working-class origins, Cook (1818–1889) published her first collection of verse when she was seventeen; many of her poems, such as "The Englishman" (1851), were widely popular. Beginning in 1849, Cook edited her own periodical, *Eliza Cook's Journal,* which proved a great success with her middle-class audience. Poor health forced her to discontinue publication of the journal in 1854, and in later life she produced far fewer poems than in her prolific youth.

The Englishman

There's a land that bears a world-known name,
    Though it is but a little spot;
I say 'tis first on the scroll of fame,
    And who shall aver it is not.
5   Of the deathless ones who shine and live
    In arms, in arts, or song,
The brightest the whole wide world can give
    To that little land belong.
'Tis the star of earth, deny it who can,
10   The island home of an Englishman.

There's a flag that waves o'er every sea,
    No matter when or where;
And to treat that flag as aught but the free
    Is more than the strongest dare.
15   For the lion spirits that tread the deck
    Have carried the palm[1] of the brave;
And that flag *may* sink with a shot-torn wreck,
    But never float over a slave.
Its honour is stainless, deny it who can,
20   And this is the flag of an Englishman.

There's a heart that leaps with burning glow,
    The wronged and the weak to defend;
And strikes as soon for a trampled foe

1. Palm branch, symbol of victory. "Lion spirits": the lion is the national emblem of Britain.

As it does for a soul-bound friend.
25 It nurtures a deep and honest love,
The passions of faith and pride,
And yearns with the fondness of a dove
To the light of its own fireside.
'Tis a rich rough gem, deny it who can,
30 And this is the heart of an Englishman.

The Briton may traverse the pole or the zone
And boldly claim his right;
For he calls such a vast domain his own,
That the sun never sets on his might.
35 Let the haughty stranger seek to know
The place of his home and birth;
And a flush will pour from cheek to brow
While he tells his native earth.
For a glorious charter,° deny it who can,   privilege
40 Is breathed in the words "I'm an Englishman."

1851

CHARLES MACKAY

A successful journalist and poet, Mackay (1814–1889) also served for several years as the editor of the *Illustrated London News*. In the song collection *The Emigrants,* issued as a musical supplement to that periodical and frequently reprinted, Mackay focuses on emigration from Britain to Canada, a colony that had achieved self-governing status by the 1850s. During that decade, on average more than three hundred thousand people a year left the British Isles; these emigrants, large numbers of whom were fleeing poverty, hunger, and political upheaval in Ireland and Scotland, headed overwhelmingly to the United States and Canada.

From The Emigrants

A Series of Songs for a Musical Entertainment

II.—CHEER, BOYS! CHEER!

I

Cheer, boys! cheer! no more of idle sorrow,
Courage, true hearts, shall bear us on our way!
Hope points before, and shows the bright to-morrow,
Let us forget the darkness of to-day!
5 So farewell, England! Much as we may love thee,
We'll dry the tears that we have shed before;
Why should we weep to sail in search of fortune?
So farewell, England! farewell evermore!
Cheer, boys! cheer! for England, mother England!
10 Cheer, boys! cheer! the willing strong right hand,
Cheer, boys! cheer! there's work for honest labour—
Cheer, boys! cheer!—in the new and happy land!

II

Cheer, boys! cheer! the steady breeze is blowing,
   To float us freely o'er the ocean's breast;
The world shall follow in the track we're going,
   The star of empire glitters in the west.
5 Here we had toil and little to reward it,
   But there shall plenty smile upon our pain,
And ours shall be the mountain and the forest,
   And boundless prairies ripe with golden grain.
      Cheer, boys! cheer! for England, mother England!
10   Cheer, boys! cheer! united heart and hand!—
      Cheer, boys! cheer! there's wealth for honest labour—
      Cheer, boys! cheer!—in the new and happy land!

III.—FAR, FAR UPON THE SEA.

I

    Far, far upon the sea,
    The good ship speeding free,
Upon the deck we gather young and old;
    And view the flapping sail,
5   Spreading out before the gale,
Full and round without a wrinkle or a fold:
    Or watch the waves that glide
    By the stately vessel's side,
And the wild sea-birds that follow through the air.
10   Or we gather in a ring,
    And with cheerful voices sing,
'Oh! gaily goes the ship when the wind blows fair.'

II

    Far, far upon the sea,
    With the sunshine on our lee,°   *sheltered side*
We talk of pleasant days when we were young,
    And remember, though we roam,
5   The sweet melodies of home—
The songs of happy childhood which we sung.
    And though we quit her shore,
    To return to it no more,
Sound the glories that Britannia yet shall bear;
10   That 'Britons rule the waves,'
    'And never shall be slaves.'[1]
'Oh! gaily goes the ship when the wind blows fair.'

III

    Far, far upon the sea,
    Whate'er our country be,
The thought of it shall cheer us as we go.
    And Scotland's sons shall join,
5   In the song of 'Auld lang Syne,'[2]
With voice by memory soften'd, clear and low,

1. Allusion to the refrain of "Rule, Britannia" (1740), a song with words by James Thomson and music by Thomas Arne.   2. Long ago (Scots); the title of a famous Scottish song whose lyrics were composed or given standard form in 1796 by Robert Burns.

And the men of Erin's Isle,°   *Ireland*
Battling sorrow with a smile,
Shall sing 'St Patrick's Morning,'[3] void of care;
10   And thus we pass the day
As we journey on the way;—
'Oh! gaily goes the ship when the wind blows fair.'

1855

3. A title shared by a number of traditional Irish folk songs.

ANONYMOUS

In 1845 potato blight severely damaged the crop in Ireland. Its return over the next several years caused widespread famine and disease, killing 1.5 million people and leading another million to emigrate. The British government's wholly inadequate response to the famine, which included exporting grain from Ireland while Irish people starved, contributed to the long-standing bitterness against British rule. Some came together in 1858 to advocate the use of force to liberate Ireland; taking their name from a group of legendary Irish warriors, they called themselves the Fenians, or Irish Republican Brotherhood, forerunners of the Irish Republican Army. Often thwarted by British infiltration of their ranks, the Fenians organized a rebellion in March 1867 that the British easily quelled. *The Nation,* a newspaper established in 1842 to promote Irish self-government, published the following statement around the time of that uprising.

[Proclamation of an Irish Republic]

The Irish People to the World

We have suffered centuries of outrage, enforced poverty, and bitter misery. Our rights and liberties have been trampled on by an alien aristocracy, who, treating us as foes, usurped our lands, and drew away from our unfortunate country all material riches. The real owners of the soil were removed to make room for cattle, and driven across the ocean to seek the means of living, and the political rights denied to them at home, while our men of thought and action were condemned to loss of life and liberty. But we never lost the memory and hope of a national existence. We appealed in vain to the reason and sense of justice of the dominant powers.

Our mildest remonstrances were met with sneers and contempt. Our appeals to arms were always unsuccessful.

To-day, having no honourable alternative left, we again appeal to force as our last resource. We accept the conditions of appeal, manfully deeming it better to die in the struggle for freedom than to continue an existence of utter serfdom.

All men are born with equal rights, and in associating to protect one another and share public burthens, justice demands that such associations should rest upon a basis which maintains equality instead of destroying it.

We therefore declare that, unable longer to endure the curse of Monarchical

Government, we aim at founding a Republic based on universal suffrage, which shall secure to all the intrinsic value of their labour.

The soil of Ireland, at present in the possession of an oligarchy, belongs to us, the Irish people, and to us it must be restored.

We declare, also, in favour of absolute liberty of conscience, and the complete separation of Church and State.

We appeal to the Highest Tribunal for evidence of the justness of our cause. History bears testimony to the intensity of our sufferings, and we declare, in the face of our brethren, that we intend no war against the people of England—our war is against the aristocratic locusts, whether English or Irish, who have eaten the verdure of our fields—against the aristocratic leeches who drain alike our fields and theirs.

Republicans of the entire world, our cause is your cause. Our enemy is your enemy. Let your hearts be with us. As for you, workmen of England, it is not only your hearts we wish, but your arms. Remember the starvation and degradation brought to your firesides by the oppression of labour. Remember the past, look well to the future, and avenge yourselves by giving liberty to your children in the coming struggle for human liberty.

Herewith we proclaim the Irish Republic,
        THE PROVISIONAL GOVERNMENT.

1867

MATTHEW ARNOLD

The following selection comes from a series of lectures on Celtic literature delivered by Arnold (1822–1888) in his capacity as professor of poetry at Oxford. Historically, the Celts were an ancient people who settled in Europe; their linguistic descendants survived in Scotland, Wales, and Ireland. Like many of his contemporaries, Arnold thought that national character was determined by "race"; as the critic Lionel Trilling remarks in his 1949 study of the British writer, "Arnold was at pains to show that the English are an amalgam of several 'bloods'—German, Norman, Celtic," each of which carried its own special characteristics and required the balance of the other components that made up English identity. At the end of his lectures, Arnold called on Oxford University to create a professorship of Celtic "to send . . . a message of peace to Ireland."

From On the Study of Celtic Literature

And as in material civilisation he has been ineffectual, so has the Celt been ineffectual in politics. This colossal, impetuous, adventurous wanderer, the Titan of the early world, who in primitive times fills so large a place on earth's scene, dwindles and dwindles as history goes on, and at last is shrunk to what we now see him. For ages and ages the world has been constantly slipping, ever more and more, out of the Celt's grasp. "They went forth to the war," Ossian says most truly, *"but they always fell."*[1]

---

1. A quotation from the poem "Cath-Loda," one of the works that the Scottish poet James Macpherson

And yet, if one sets about constituting an ideal genius, what a great deal of the Celt does one find oneself drawn to put into it! Of an ideal genius one does not want the elements, any of them, to be in a state of weakness; on the contrary, one wants all of them to be in the highest state of power; but with a law of measure, of harmony, presiding over the whole. So the sensibility[2] of the Celt, if everything else were not sacrificed to it, is a beautiful and admirable force. For sensibility, the power of quick and strong perception and emotion, is one of the very prime constituents of genius, perhaps its most positive constituent; it is to the soul what good senses are to the body, the grand natural condition of successful activity. Sensibility gives genius its materials; one cannot have too much of it, if one can but keep its master and not be its slave. Do not let us wish that the Celt had had less sensibility, but that he had been more master of it. Even as it is, if his sensibility has been a source of weakness to him, it has been a source of power too, and a source of happiness. Some people have found in the Celtic nature and its sensibility the main root out of which chivalry and romance and the glorification of a feminine ideal spring; this is a great question, with which I cannot deal here. Let me notice in passing, however, that there is, in truth, a Celtic air about the extravagance of chivalry, its reaction against the despotism of fact, its straining human nature further than it will stand. But putting all this question of chivalry and its origin on one side, no doubt the sensibility of the Celtic nature, its nervous exaltation, have something feminine in them, and the Celt is thus peculiarly[3] disposed to feel the spell of the feminine idiosyncrasy; he has an affinity to it; he is not far from its secret. Again, his sensibility gives him a peculiarly near and intimate feeling of nature and the life of nature; here, too, he seems in a special way attracted by the secret before him, the secret of natural beauty and natural magic, and to be close to it, to half-divine it. In the productions of the Celtic genius, nothing, perhaps, is so interesting as the evidences of this power: I shall have occasion to give specimens of them by-and-by. The same sensibility made the Celts full of reverence and enthusiasm for genius, learning, and the things of the mind; *to be a bard, freed a man,*—that is a characteristic stroke of this generous and ennobling ardour of theirs, which no race has ever shown more strongly. Even the extravagance and exaggeration of the sentimental Celtic nature has often something romantic and attractive about it, something which has a sort of smack of misdirected good. The Celt, undisciplinable, anarchical, and turbulent by nature, but out of affection and admiration giving himself body and soul to some leader, that is not a promising political temperament, it is just the opposite of the Anglo-Saxon temperament, disciplinable and steadily obedient within certain limits, but retaining an inalienable part of freedom and self-dependence; but it is a temperament for which one has a kind of sympathy notwithstanding. And very often, for the gay defiant reaction against fact of the lively Celtic nature one has more than sympathy; one feels, in spite of the extravagance, in spite of good sense disapproving, magnetised and exhilarated by it. The Gauls[4] had a rule inflicting a fine on every warrior who, when he appeared on parade, was found to stick out too much in front,—to be corpulent, in short. Such a rule is surely the maddest article of war ever framed, and to people to whom nature has assigned a large

---

(1736–1796) claimed to have translated from the Gaelic writings of Ossian, a 3rd-century poet-warrior figure in traditional Irish folklore. A committee of scholars appointed in 1797 determined that the prose poems were largely composed by Macpherson.

2. Susceptibility to emotional influence.
3. Especially.
4. The name given by the Romans to a Celtic people living in modern-day France.

volume of intestines, must appear, no doubt, horrible; but yet has it not an udacious, sparkling, immaterial manner with it, which lifts one out of routine, and sets one's spirits in a glow?

All tendencies of human nature are in themselves vital and profitable; when they are blamed, they are only to be blamed relatively, not absolutely. This holds true of the Saxon's phlegm as well as of the Celt's sentiment. Out of the steady humdrum habit of the creeping Saxon, as the Celt calls him,—out of his way of going near the ground,—has come, no doubt, Philistinism,[5] that plant of essentially Germanic growth, flourishing with its genuine marks only in the German fatherland, Great Britain and her colonies, and the United States of America; but what a soul of goodness there is in Philistinism itself! and this soul of goodness I, who am often supposed to be Philistinism's mortal enemy merely because I do not wish it to have things all its own way, cherish as much as anybody. This steady-going habit leads at last, as I have said, up to science, up to the comprehension and interpretation of the world. With us in Great Britain, it is true, it does not seem to lead so far as that; it is in Germany, where the habit is more unmixed, that it can lead to science. Here with us it seems at a certain point to meet with a conflicting force, which checks it and prevents its pushing on to science; but before reaching this point what conquests has it not won! and all the more, perhaps, for stopping short at this point, for spending its exertions within a bounded field, the field of plain sense, of direct practical utility. How it has augmented the comforts and conveniences of life for us! Doors that open, windows that shut, locks that turn, razors that shave, coats that wear, watches that go, and a thousand more such good things, are the invention of the Philistines.

*   *   *

1867

5. A label Arnold repeatedly used for the attitude of the unenlightened middle classes of his time, in whose opposition to the defenders of culture he sees a resemblance to the biblical tribe who fought against the people of Israel, "the children of light."

JAMES ANTHONY FROUDE

The historian Froude (1818–1894) came to fame as the author of a twelve-volume *History of England* (1856–70) and the biography of his mentor, Thomas Carlyle (1882–1884). Inspired by his visits to South Africa to explore other parts of the empire, he toured British possessions in the Caribbean in the winter of 1886–87 and there gathered information for *The English in the West Indies* (1888), in which he expressed his belief that the colonies populated by nonwhite people were not suited to self-rule. In the following selection he focuses on his travels in Trinidad, a Caribbean island that passed from Spanish to British control near the end of the eighteenth century.

From The English in the West Indies

Trinidad is not one of our oldest possessions, but we had held it long enough for the old planter civilisation to take root and grow, and our road led us through jungles of flowering shrubs which were running wild over what had been once cultivated estates. Stranger still (for one associates colonial life instinctively with what is new and modern), we came at one place on an avenue of vast trees, at the end of which stood the ruins of a mansion of some great man of the departed order. Great man he must have been, for there was a gateway half crumbled away on which were his crest and shield in stone, with supporters on either side, like the Baron of Bradwardine's Bears;[1] fallen now like them, but unlike them never, I fear, to be set up again. The Anglo-West Indians, like the English gentry in Ireland, were a fine race of men in their day, and perhaps the improving them off the earth has been a less beneficial process in either case than we are in the habit of supposing.

Entering among the hills we came on their successors. In Trinidad there are 18,000 freeholders, most of them negroes and representatives of the old slaves. Their cabins are spread along the road on either side, overhung with bread-fruit trees, tamarinds, calabash trees, out of which they make their cups and water jugs. The luscious granadilla climbs among the branches; plantains throw their cool shade over the doors; oranges and limes and citrons perfume the air, and droop their boughs under the weight of their golden burdens. There were yams in the gardens and cows in the paddocks, and cocoa bushes loaded with purple or yellow pods. Children played about in swarms, in happy idleness and abundance, with schools, too, at intervals, and an occasional Catholic chapel, for the old religion prevails in Trinidad, never having been disturbed. What form could human life assume more charming than that which we were now looking on? Once more, the earth does not contain any peasantry so well off, so well cared for, so happy, so sleek and contented as the sons and daughters of the emancipated slaves in the English West Indian Islands. Sugar may fail the planter, but cocoa, which each peasant can grow with small effort for himself, does not fail and will not. He may 'better his condition,' if he has any such ambition, without stirring beyond his own ground, and so far, perhaps, his ambition may extend, if it is not turned off upon politics. Even the necessary evils of the tropics are not many or serious. His skin is proof against mosquitoes. There are snakes in Trinidad as there were snakes in Eden. 'Plenty snakes,' said one of them who was at work in his garden, 'plenty snakes, but no bitee.' As to costume, he would prefer the costume of innocence if he was allowed. Clothes in such a climate are superfluous for warmth, and to the minds of the negroes, unconscious as they are of shame, superfluous for decency.

✳   ✳   ✳

We made several similar small expeditions into the settled parts of the neighbourhood, seeing always (whatever else we saw) the boundless happiness of the black race. Under the rule of England in these islands the two million of these poor brothers-in-law of ours are the most perfectly contented specimens of the human race to be found upon the planet. Even Schopenhauer,[2] could he have known them, would have admitted that there were some of us who were not hopelessly wretched. If happiness be the satisfaction of every conscious desire, theirs is a condition which admits of no improvement: were they

---

1. A reference to Sir Walter Scott's novel *Waverley* (1814). The baron's battlements are adorned with carved stone bears that are torn down during the course of the novel and restored to their original position by its end.
2. Arthur Schopenhauer (1788–1860), German philosopher who emphasized the tragedy of life.

independent, they might quarrel among themselves, and the weaker become the bondmen[3] of the stronger; under the beneficent despotism of the English Government, which knows no difference of colour and permits no oppression, they can sleep, lounge, and laugh away their lives as they please, fearing no danger. If they want money, work and wages are waiting for them. No one can say what may be before them hereafter. The powers which envy human beings too perfect felicity may find ways one day of disturbing the West Indian negro; but so long as the English rule continues, he may be assured of the same tranquil existence.

As life goes he has been a lucky mortal. He was taken away from Dahomey and Ashantee[4]—to be a slave indeed, but a slave to a less cruel master than he would have found at home. He had a bad time of it occasionally, and the plantation whip and the branding irons are not all dreams, yet his owner cared for him at least as much as he cared for his cows and his horses. Kind usage to animals is more economical than barbarity, and Englishmen in the West Indies were rarely inhuman. Lord Rodney[5] says:

'I have been often in all the West India Islands, and I have often made my observations on the treatment of the negro slaves, and can aver that I never knew the least cruelty inflicted on them, but that in general they lived better than the honest day-labouring man in England, without doing a fourth part of his work in a day, and I am fully convinced that the negroes in our islands are better provided for and live better than when in Guinea.'[6]

Rodney, it is true, was a man of facts and was defective in sentiment. Let us suppose him wrong, let us believe the worst horrors of the slave trade or slave usage as fluent tongue of missionary or demagogue has described them, yet nevertheless, when we consider what the lot of common humanity has been and is, we shall be dishonest if we deny that the balance has been more than redressed; and the negroes who were taken away out of Africa, as compared with those who were left at home, were as the 'elect to salvation,'[7] who after a brief purgatory are secured an eternity of blessedness. The one condition is the maintenance of the authority of the English crown. The whites of the islands cannot equitably rule them. They have not shaken off the old traditions. If, for the sake of theory or to shirk responsibility, we force them to govern them-selves, the state of Hayti[8] stands as a ghastly example of the condition into which they will then inevitably fall. If we persist, we shall be sinning against light—the clearest light that was ever given in such affairs. The most hardened believers in the regenerating effects of political liberty cannot be completely blind to the ruin which the infliction of it would necessarily bring upon the race for whose interests they pretend particularly to care.

* * *

1886–87   1888

---

3. Bondsmen, slaves.
4. Also Asante, Ashanti (now part of Ghana), like Dahomey an area of western Africa that prospered in the 18th and 19th centuries and engaged in the slave trade.
5. George Brydges Rodney (1719–1792), British admiral who commanded several naval campaigns against Britain's rival colonial powers in the West Indies.
6. Region of western Africa involved in the slave trade until the middle of the 19th century (the

transatlantic slave trade had been outlawed by Britain and the United States in 1807 and 1808, respectively).
7. Cf. 2 Thessalonians 2.13. In Calvinist Protestantism, the "elect" are those people chosen by God to be saved from eternal damnation.
8. Haiti, which gained its independence following a slave revolt that began in 1791. Through much of the 19th century, it experienced rapid and sometimes violent changes of leadership.

JOHN JACOB THOMAS

Thomas (ca. 1840–1889), a descendant of slaves, was born into poverty on the Caribbean island of Trinidad. Primarily a self-educated intellectual, he became a linguist, folklorist, teacher, civil servant, editor, and author. His *Froudacity* (1889) is a spirited book-length rebuttal of James Anthony Froude's *English in the West Indies* (1888), challenging its assumptions about the inferiority of nonwhite people and exposing its mistakes and its misrepresentations of his native land.

From Froudacity

From *Social Revolution*

Never was the Knight of La Mancha[1] more convinced of his imaginary mission to redress the wrongs of the world than Mr. James Anthony Froude seems to be of his ability to alter the course of events, especially those bearing on the destinies of the Negro in the British West Indies. The doctrinaire style of his utterances, his sublime indifference as to what Negro opinion and feelings may be, on account of his revelations, are uniquely charming. In that portion of his book headed "Social Revolution" our author, with that mixture of frankness and cynicism which is so dear to the soul of the British *esprit fort*[2] of today, has challenged a comparison between British Colonial policy on the one hand, and the Colonial policy of France and Spain on the other. This he does with an evident recklessness that his approval of Spain and France involves a definite condemnation of his own country. However, let us hear him:—

"The English West Indies, like other parts of the world, are going through a silent revolution. Elsewhere the revolution, as we hope, is a transition state, a new birth; a passing away of what is old and worn out, that a fresh and healthier order may rise in its place. In the West Indies the most sanguine of mortals will find it difficult to entertain any such *hope at all.*"

As Mr. Froude is speaking dogmatically here of *his*, or rather *our*, West Indies, let us hear him as he proceeds:—

"We have been a ruling power there for two hundred and fifty years; the *whites whom we planted as our representatives* are drifting into ruin, and they regard England and England's policy as the principal cause of it. The *blacks whom, in a fit of virtuous benevolence,* we emancipated, do not feel *particularly obliged to us.* They think, if they think at all, that they were ill-treated originally, and have received no more than was due to them."

Thus far. Now, as to "the *whites* whom we planted as our *representatives,*" and who, Mr. Froude avers, are drifting into ruin, we confess to a total ignorance of their whereabouts in these islands in this jubilee year of Negro Emancipation.[3] Of the *representatives* of Britain immediately before and after Emancipation we happen to know something, which, on the testimony of Englishmen, Mr. Froude will be made quite welcome to before our task is ended. With respect to Mr. Froude's statement as to the ingratitude of the emanci-

---

1. Don Quixote, the title character of Miguel de Cervantes's novel (1605, 1615), whose name became synonymous with foolish, self-deluded idealism.
2. Freethinker (French).

3. The fifty-year anniversary of the freeing of slaves in the British West Indies. Slavery was abolished in British colonial possessions in 1833, but ex-slaves working on plantations were apprenticed to their former owners until 1838.

pated Blacks, if it is aimed at the slaves who were actually set free, it is utterly untrue; for no class of persons, in their humble and artless way, are more attached to the Queen's majesty, whom they regard as incarnating in her gracious person the benevolence which Mr. Froude so jauntily scoffs at. But if our censor's remark under this head is intended for the present generation of Blacks, it is a pure and simple absurdity. What are *we* Negroes of the present day to be grateful for to the US, personified by Mr. Froude and the Colonial Office exportations? We really believe, from what we know of Englishmen, that very few indeed would regard Mr. Froude's reproach otherwise than as a palpable adding of insult to injury. Obliged to "us," indeed! Why, Mr. Froude, who speaks of us as dogs and horses, suggests that the same kindliness of treatment that secures the attachment of those noble brutes would have the same result in our case. With the same consistency that marks his utterances throughout his book, he tells his readers "that there is no original or congenital difference between the capacity of the White and the Negro races." He adds, too, significantly: "With the *same chances* and with the same *treatment,* I believe that distinguished men would be produced *equally* from *both* races." After this truthful testimony, which Pelion upon Ossa[4] of evidence has confirmed, does Mr. Froude, in the fatuity of his skin-pride, believe that educated men, worthy of the name, would be otherwise than resentful, if not disgusted, at being shunted out of bread in their own native land, which their parents' labours and taxes have made desirable, in order to afford room to blockheads, vulgarians, or worse, imported from beyond the seas? Does Mr. Froude's scorn of the Negroes' skin extend, inconsistently on his part, to their intelligence and feelings also? And if so, what has the Negro to care—if let alone and not wantonly thwarted in his aspirations? It sounds queer, not to say unnatural and scandalous, that Englishmen should in these days of light be the champions of injustice towards their fellow-subjects, not for any intellectual or moral disqualification, but on the simple account of the darker skin of those who are to be assailed and thwarted in their life's career and aspirations. Really, are we to be grateful that the colour difference should be made the basis and justification of the dastardly denials of justice, social, intellectual, and moral, which have characterized the *régime* of those who Mr. Froude boasts were left to be the representatives of Britain's morality and fair play?

✣   ✣   ✣

1889

---

4. I.e., mountains. The proverbial phrase "to heap Ossa upon Pelion" derives from Greek mythology and the unsuccessful attempt of the giants to scale Olympus and threaten the gods by stacking one mountain on top of the other.

ALFRED, LORD TENNYSON

In his capacity as poet laureate, Tennyson (1809–1892) was invited by Albert Edward, the Prince of Wales and Queen Victoria's eldest son, to write a poem for the opening of the Indian and Colonial Exhibition of 1886. It was one of numerous elaborately staged and popular events—hosted by London after the success of the Great Exhibition in 1851—that made a spectacle of colonial products, crafts, and peoples for the British public. Tennyson's verses were set to music by Sir Arthur Sullivan (1842–1900) and sung at the inaugural ceremony at the Albert Hall in the presence of the queen.

Opening of the Indian and Colonial Exhibition by the Queen

Written at the Request of the Prince of Wales

I

Welcome, welcome with one voice!
In your welfare we rejoice,
Sons and brothers that have sent,
From isle and cape and continent,
5   Produce of your field and flood,
Mount and mine, and primal wood;
Works of subtle brain and hand,
And splendours of the morning land,°   *the East*
Gifts from every British zone;
10   Britons, hold your own![1]

II

May we find, as ages run,
The mother featured in the son;
And may yours for ever be
That old strength and constancy
15   Which has made your fathers great
In our ancient island State,
And wherever her flag fly,
Glorying between sea and sky,
Makes the might of Britain known;
20   Britons, hold your own!

III

Britain fought her sons of yore—
Britain fail'd; and never more,
Careless of our growing kin,
Shall we sin our fathers' sin,
25   Men that in a narrower day—
Unprophetic rulers they—
Drove from out the mother's nest
That young eagle of the West°   *United States*
To forage for herself alone;
30   Britons, hold your own!

IV

Sharers of our glorious past,
Brothers, must we part at last?
Shall we not thro' good and ill
Cleave to one another still?

---

1. A phrase reminiscent of Tennyson's earlier "Britons, Guard Your Own" (1852), a poem that supported the formation of a militia against the threat of French forces.

35   Britain's myriad voices call,
     'Sons, be welded each and all,
     Into one imperial whole,
     One with Britain, heart and soul!
     One life, one flag, one fleet, one Throne!'
40   Britons, hold your own!

1886

T. N. MUKHARJI

Trailokya Nath Mukharji, a government official and Brahman (a member of the highest Hindu caste), traveled to England with the Indian delegation for the Indian and Colonial Exhibition of 1886. On his return home his impressions of the trip were serialized in a weekly Indian newspaper, and then reprinted in a book published in London and Calcutta. In the following selection Mukharji describes his experiences with, and observations of, the British.

From A Visit to Europe

[THE INDIAN AND COLONIAL EXHIBITION]

Another place of considerable interest to the natives of England was the Indian Bazar where Hindu and Muhammadan artisans carried on their avocations, to witness which men, women and children flocked from all parts of the kingdom. A dense crowd always stood there, looking at our men as they wove the gold brocade, sang the patterns of the carpet[1] and printed the calico with the hand. They were as much astonished to see the Indians produce works of art with the aid of rude apparatus they themselves had discarded long ago, as a Hindu would be to see a chimpanzee officiating as a priest in a funeral ceremony and reading out Sanskrit texts from a palm leaf book spread before him. We were very interesting beings no doubt, so were the Zulus before us, and so is the Sioux chief at the present time (1887). Human nature everywhere thirsts for novelty, and measures out its favours in proportion to the rarity and oddity of a thing. It was from the ladies that we received the largest amount of patronage. We were pierced through and through by stares from eyes of all colours—green, gray, blue and black—and every movement and act of ours, walking, sitting, eating, reading, received its full share of "O, I, never!" The number of wives we left behind at home was also a constant theme of speculation among them, and shrewd guesses were sometimes made on this point, 250 being a favourite number. You could tell any amount of stories on this subject without exciting the slightest suspicion. Once, one of our number told a pretty waitress—"I am awfully pleased with you, and I want to marry you. Will you accept the fortieth wifeship in my household which became vacant just before I left my country?" She asked—"How many wives have you altogether?" "Two hundred and fifty, the usual number," was the ready answer.

---

1. When carpets are produced on handlooms, overseers sometimes sing out the number and color of each thread needed for the pattern; the weavers then repeat back the instructions in a chorus.

"What became of your wife, number 40?" "I killed her, because one morning she could not cook my porridge well." The poor girl was horrified, and exclaimed—"O you monster, O you wretch!" Then she narrated the sad fate of a friend of hers. She was a sweet little child, when an African student studying in Edinburgh came and wooed her. They got married in England and fondly loved each other. Everything went well as long as the pair lived in England, but after a short time he took his fair wife to his desert home in Liberia. Not a single white man or woman could she see there, and she felt very lonely. But the sight of her mother-in-law, who dressed in feathers and skins came dancing into the house half-tipsy, was more than she could bear. She pined for a short time and died.

Of course, every nation in the world considers other nations as savages or at least much inferior to itself. It was so from the beginning and it will be so as long as human nature will retain its present character. We did not therefore wonder that the common people should take us for barbarians, awkward as we were in every respect. They have very strict notions of dress, manners and the general bearing of a man, any deviation from which is seriously noticed. Utmost indulgence was however shewn to us everywhere. Her Majesty was graciously pleased to lay aside the usual rules, and this favour was shewn us wherever we went. Gentlemen and ladies of high education and culture, however, honoured us as the representatives of the most ancient nation now existing on the face of the earth. They would frequently ask us home, get up private parties and arrange for all sorts of amusements. In other houses we grew more intimate and formed part of the family party. To these we were always welcome, and could go and come whenever we liked. We got some friends among them, and these gentlemen would often come and fetch us home if we absented ourselves for more than the ordinary length of time. I fondly remember the happy days I passed with them, and feel thankful for the kindness they shewed me during my sojourn in their country.

In public matters non-official gentlemen were also very partial to us. "We want to hear the turbanned gentleman" was the wish often and often expressed. But we ceased not to be a prodigious wonder to strangers and to the common people. Would they discuss us so freely if they knew that we understood their language? It was very amusing to hear what they said about us. Often when fatigued with work, or when cares and anxieties cast a gloom upon our mind, we found such talks about us more refreshing than a glass of port wine. I wish I had the ability to do justice to the discussing power of these ladies and gentlemen exercised in their kind notice of us, for in that case I could produce one of the most interesting books ever published. Or if I had known that I would be required to write an account of my visit to Europe, I would have taken notes of at least some of the remarkable hits on truth unconsciously made by ignorant people from the country, which are applicable to all nations and which set one to philosophise on the material difference that exists between our own estimate of ourselves and the estimate which others form of us.

If we were interesting beings in the eyes of the Londoners, who had oftener opportunities of seeing their fellow subjects from the far East, how much more would we be so to the simple villagers who came by thousands to see the wonders of the Exhibition. Their conduct towards us was always kind and respectful. They liked to talk to us, and whenever convenient we tried to satisfy their curiosity. Men, women and children, whose relations are in India serving as soldiers or in any other capacity, would come through the crowd, all panting,

to shake hands with us and ask about their friends. Many queer incidents happened in this way. "Do you know Jim,—James Robinson you know of——
——Regiment?" asked a fat elderly woman, who one day came bustling through the crowd and took me by storm, without any of those preliminary manœuvres usually adopted to open a conversation with a stranger. I expressed my regret in not having the honour of Jim's acquaintance. The good old lady then explained to me that she was Jim's aunt, and gave me a long history of her nephew, and the circumstances which led to his enlistment as a soldier. If the truant nephew lost the golden opportunity of sending through us his dutiful message to his aunt, she on her part was not wanting in her affectionate remembrances of him. Among other things, most of which I did not understand, for she did not speak the English we ordinarily hear nor was her language quite coherent at the time, she begged me to carry to Jim the important intelligence that Mrs. Jones' fat pig obtained a prize at the Smithfield Agricultural Show.[2] I shewed my alacrity to carry the message right off to Jim in the wilds of Upper Burma by immediately taking leave of the lady, who joined her friends and explained to them that I was a bosom friend of her nephew.

Once, I was sitting in one of the swellish[3] restaurants at the Exhibition, glancing over a newspaper which I had no time to read in the morning. At a neighbouring table sat a respectable-looking family group evidently from the country, from which furtive glances were occasionally thrown in my direction. I thought I might do worse than having a little fun, if any could be made out of the notice that was being taken of me. I seemed to be suddenly aware that I was being looked at, which immediately scared away half a dozen eyes from my table. It took fully five minutes' deep undivided attention to my paper again to reassure and tempt out those eyes from the plates where they took refuge, and the glances from them, which at first flashed and flickered like lightning, became steadier the more my mind seemed to get absorbed in the subject I was reading. The closer inspection to which I submitted ended in my favour. Perhaps, no symptom being visible in my external appearance of the cannibalistic tendencies of my heart, or owing probably to the notion that I must have by that time got over my partiality for human flesh, or knowing at least that the place was safe enough against any treacherous spring which I might take into my head to make upon them, or owing to whatever other cause, the party gradually grew bolder, began to talk in whispers and actually tried to attract my attention towards them. The latter duty ultimately devolved upon the beauty of the party, a pretty girl of about seventeen. Of course it was not intended for my ears, but somehow I heard her say—"Oh, how I wish to speak to him?" Could I withstand such an appeal? I rose and approaching the little Curiosity asked—"Did you speak to me, young lady?" She blushed and hung down her head. Her papa came to the rescue. "My daughter, Sir, is delighted with the magnificent things brought from your country to this Exhibition. She saw some writing in your language on a few plates and shields, and is anxious to know its meaning. We did not know whom to ask, when we saw you. Will you take a seat here, and do me the honour to take a glass of something with me? What will it be? Sparkling moselle?[4] I find is good here; or shall it be champagne or anything stronger?" He said. The proferred glass was declined with thanks, but I took a chair and explained the meaning of some of the

2. Britain's most important agricultural event, held annually in London since 1799.
3. Stylish.
4. A white wine.

verses damascened on the Koftgari ware.[5] The young lady soon got over her bashfulness, and talked with a vivacity which I did not expect from her. She was delighted with everything I said, expressed her astonishment at my knowledge of English, and complimented me for the performance of the band brought from *my country, viz.*, the West Indian band composed of Negroes and Mulattos, which compliment made me wince a little, but nevertheless I went on chattering for a quarter of an hour and furnishing her with sufficient means to annihilate her friend Minnie, Jane or Lizzy or whoever she might be, and to brag among her less fortunate relations for six months to come of her having actually seen and talked to a genuine "Blackie."

☆   ☆   ☆

1887   1889

5. Steel merchandise of Indian manufacture with an inlaid pattern in gold.

JOSEPH CHAMBERLAIN

Chamberlain (1836–1914) was a manufacturer who made his fortune at the age of thirty-eight; he spent the rest of his life in politics, generally allying himself with radical causes. An enthusiastic promoter of imperial expansion and consolidation, he was appointed colonial secretary in 1895. The following selection is taken from a speech Chamberlain delivered in 1897 at the Royal Colonial Institute's annual dinner; published later that year in his *Foreign and Colonial Speeches*, the text records the frequent "cheers" and "laughter" and expressions of agreement ("hear, hear") that greeted his performance.

From The True Conception of Empire

It seems to me that there are three distinct stages in our Imperial history. We began to be, and we ultimately became, a great Imperial Power in the eighteenth century, but, during the greater part of that time, the colonies were regarded, not only by us, but by every European Power that possessed them, as possessions valuable in proportion to the pecuniary advantage which they brought to the mother country which, under that order of ideas, was not truly a mother at all, but appeared rather in the light of a grasping and absentee landlord desiring to take from his tenants the utmost rents he could exact. The colonies were valued and maintained because it was thought that they would be a source of profit—of direct profit—to the mother country.

That was the first stage, and when we were rudely awakened by the War of Independence in America from this dream, that the colonies could be held for our profit alone, the second chapter was entered upon, and public opinion seems then to have drifted to the opposite extreme; and, because the colonies were no longer a source of revenue, it seems to have been believed and argued by many people that their separation from us was only a matter of time, and that that separation should be desired and encouraged lest haply they might prove an encumbrance and a source of weakness.

It was while those views were still entertained, while the little Englanders[1]—(laughter)—were in their full career, that this Institute was founded to protest against doctrines so injurious to our interests—(cheers)—and so derogatory to our honour; and I rejoice that what was then, as it were, "a voice crying in the wilderness"[2] is now the expressed and determined will of the overwhelming majority of the British people. (Loud cheers.) Partly by the efforts of this Institute and similar organisations, partly by the writings of such men as Froude and Seeley[3]—(hear, hear)—but mainly by the instinctive good sense and patriotism of the people at large, we have now reached the third stage in our history, and the true conception of our Empire. (Cheers.)

What is that conception? As regards the self-governing colonies[4] we no longer talk of them as dependencies. The sense of possession has given place to the sentiment of kinship. We think and speak of them as part of ourselves—(cheers)—as part of the British Empire, united to us, although they may be dispersed throughout the world, by ties of kindred, of religion, of history, and of language, and joined to us by the seas that formerly seemed to divide us. (Cheers.)

But the British Empire is not confined to the self-governing colonies and the United Kingdom. It includes a much greater area, a much more numerous population in tropical climes, where no considerable European settlement is possible, and where the native population must always vastly outnumber the white inhabitants; and in these cases also the same change has come over the Imperial idea. Here also the sense of possession has given place to a different sentiment—the sense of obligation. We feel now that our rule over these territories can only be justified if we can show that it adds to the happiness and prosperity of the people—(cheers)—and I maintain that our rule does, and has, brought security and peace and comparative prosperity to countries that never knew these blessings before. (Cheers.)

In carrying out this work of civilisation we are fulfilling what I believe to be our national mission, and we are finding scope for the exercise of those faculties and qualities which have made of us a great governing race. (Cheers.) I do not say that our success has been perfect in every case, I do not say that all our methods have been beyond reproach; but I do say that in almost every instance in which the rule of the Queen has been established and the great *Pax Britannica*[5] has been enforced, there has come with it greater security to life and property, and a material improvement in the condition of the bulk of the population. (Cheers.) No doubt, in the first instance, when these conquests have been made, there has been bloodshed, there has been loss of life among the native populations, loss of still more precious lives among those who have been sent out to bring these countries into some kind of disciplined order, but it must be remembered that that is the condition of the mission we have to fulfil.

✳   ✳   ✳

✳ ✳ ✳ You cannot have omelettes without breaking eggs; you cannot destroy the practices of barbarism, of slavery, of superstition, which for centuries have

1. Critics of imperial expansion who advocated sharply limiting the scope and responsibilities of the British Empire.
2. Allusion to the Gospels, especially Matthew 3.3; the phrase is usually interpreted as referring to John the Baptist's prophecies of the coming of Jesus.
3. Sir John Robert Seeley (1834–1895), English historian, essayist, and author of *The Expansion of England* (1883), which portrays the growth of the British Empire as a natural process. James Anthony Froude (1818–1894), English author and historian (see p. 1621).
4. Canada, New Zealand, Australia, and South Africa.
5. British peace (Latin), which the British Empire supposedly imposed on its colonial possessions (by analogy with the *pax Romana* of the Roman Empire).

desolated the interior of Africa, without the use of force; but if you will fairly contrast the gain to humanity with the price which we are bound to pay for it, I think you may well rejoice in the result of such expeditions as those which have recently been conducted with such signal success—(cheers)—in Nyassa-land, Ashanti, Benin, and Nupé[6]—expeditions which may have, and indeed have, cost valuable lives, but as to which we may rest assured that for one life lost a hundred will be gained, and the cause of civilisation and the prosperity of the people will in the long run be eminently advanced. (Cheers.) But no doubt such a state of things, such a mission as I have described, involve heavy responsibility. In the wide dominions of the Queen the doors of the temple of Janus[7] are never closed—(hear, hear)—and it is a gigantic task that we have undertaken when we have determined to wield the sceptre of empire. Great is the task, great is the responsibility, but great is the honour—(cheers); and I am convinced that the conscience and the spirit of the country will rise to the height of its obligations, and that we shall have the strength to fulfil the mission which our history and our national character have imposed upon us. (Cheers.)

* * *

1897　　　　　　　　　　　　　　　　　　　　　　　　　　1897

6. All areas of British exploration on the African continent during the last decades of the 19th century: Nyassaland (or Nyasaland), a region of south-eastern Africa that constitutes modern-day Malawï; Ashanti (also Asante, Ashantee), a western African state located in the territory of present-day Ghana; Benin, a state in western Africa later incorporated into Nigeria; and Nupé, an area of western Africa that is now part of Nigeria.
7. Twin-faced Roman god of doorways. The doors to his temple near the Roman Forum were kept open during wartime and closed during times of peace.

J. A. HOBSON

John Atkinson Hobson (1858–1940), the distinguished Liberal economist and author, first taught classics and then worked as a lecturer in English literature and economics for the Oxford University Extension Delegacy and for the London Society for the Extension of University Teaching, before becoming a freelance writer. His many books include *Problems of Poverty* (1891), *The Evolution of Modern Capitalism* (1894), *The Problem of the Unemployed* (1896), and *John Ruskin, Social Reformer* (1898).

From Imperialism: A Study

[THE POLITICAL SIGNIFICANCE OF IMPERIALISM]

The curious ignorance which prevails regarding the political character and tendencies of Imperialism cannot be better illustrated than by the following passage from a learned work upon "The History of Colonisation":[1] "The extent of British dominion may perhaps be better imagined than described, when the fact is appreciated that, of the entire land surface of the globe, approximately

1. H. C. Morris, *The History of Colonization* (1900), vol. 2, p. 80 [Hobson's note]. The work's full title is *The History of Colonization from the Earliest Times to the Present Day.*

one-fifth is actually or theoretically under that flag, while more than one-sixth of all the human beings living in this planet reside under one or the other type of English colonisation. The names by which authority is exerted are numerous, and processes are distinct, but the goals to which this manifold mechanism is working are very similar. According to the climate, the natural conditions and the inhabitants of the regions affected, procedure and practice differ. The means are adapted to the situation; there is not any irrevocable, immutable line of policy: from time to time, from decade to decade, English statesmen have applied different treatments to the same territory. Only one fixed rule of action seems to exist; it is to promote the interests of the colony to the utmost, to develop its scheme of government as rapidly as possible, and eventually to elevate it from the position of inferiority to that of association. Under the charm of this beneficent spirit the chief colonial establishments of Great Britain have already achieved substantial freedom, without dissolving nominal ties; the other subordinate possessions are aspiring to it, while, on the other hand, this privilege of local independence has enabled England to assimilate with ease many feudatory States[2] into the body politic of her system." Here then is the theory that Britons are a race endowed, like the Romans, with a genius for government, that our colonial and imperial policy is animated by a resolve to spread throughout the world the arts of free self-government which we enjoy at home,[3] and that in truth we are accomplishing this work.

Now, without discussing here the excellencies or the defects of the British theory and practice of representative self-government, to assert that our "fixed rule of action" has been to educate our dependencies in this theory and practice is quite the largest misstatement of the facts of our colonial and imperial policy that is possible. Upon the vast majority of the populations throughout our Empire we have bestowed no real powers of self-government, nor have we any serious intention of doing so, or any serious belief that it is possible for us to do so.

Of the three hundred and sixty-seven millions of British subjects outside these isles, not more than ten millions, or one in thirty-seven, have any real self-government for purposes of legislation and administration.

Political freedom, and civil freedom, so far as it rests upon the other, are simply non-existent for the over-whelming majority of British subjects. In the self-governing colonies of Australasia and North America alone is responsible representative government a reality, and even there considerable populations of outlanders,[4] as in West Australia, or servile labour, as in Queensland, temper the genuineness of democracy. In Cape Colony and Natal recent events[5] testify how feebly the forms and even the spirit of the free British institutions have taken root in States where the great majority of the population were always excluded from political rights. The franchise and the rights it carries will remain virtually a white monopoly in so-called self-governing colonies, where the coloured population is to the white as four to one and ten to one respectively.

In certain of our older Crown colonies there exists a representative element in the government. While the administration is entirely vested in a governor

2. Feudally subject states.
3. "The British Empire is a galaxy of free States," said Sir W. Laurier in a speech, 8 July 1902 [Hobson's note]. Sir Wilfred Laurier (1841–1919), Canadian political leader.
4. Foreigners denied full citizenship.
5. The Anglo-Boer War of 1899–1902, fought

between the British and the Dutch Afrikaners, or Boers, who had settled in regions of South Africa. Cape Colony and Natal, former British colonies now part of modern-day South Africa, were sites of long-standing friction between the British and the Boers.

appointed by the Crown, assisted by a council nominated by him, the colonists elect a portion of the legislative assembly. The following colonies belong to this order: Jamaica, Barbados, Trinidad, Bahamas, British Guiana, Windward Islands, Bermudas, Malta, Mauritius, Ceylon.

The representative element differs considerably in size and influence in these colonies, but nowhere does it outnumber the non-elected element. It thus becomes an advisory rather than a really legislative factor. Not merely is the elected always dominated in numbers by the non-elected element, but in all cases the veto of the Colonial Office is freely exercised upon measures passed by the assemblies. To this it should be added that in nearly all cases a fairly high property qualification is attached to the franchise, precluding the coloured people from exercising an elective power proportionate to their numbers and their stake in the country.

The entire population of these modified Crown colonies amounted to 5,700,000 in 1898.[6]

The overwhelming majority of the subjects of the British Empire are under Crown colony government, or under protectorates. In neither case do they enjoy any of the important political rights of British citizens: in neither case are they being trained in the arts of free British institutions. In the Crown colony the population exercises no political privileges. The governor, appointed by the Colonial Office, is absolute, alike for legislation and administration; he is aided by a council of local residents usually chosen by himself or by home authority, but its function is merely advisory, and its advice can be and frequently is ignored. In the vast protectorates we have assumed in Africa and Asia there is no tincture of British representative government; the British factor consists in arbitrary acts of irregular interference with native government. Exceptions to this exist in the case of districts assigned to Chartered Companies, where business men, animated avowedly by business ends, are permitted to exercise arbitrary powers of government over native populations under the imperfect check of some British Imperial Commissioner.

Again, in certain native and feudatory States of India our Empire is virtually confined to government of foreign relations, military protection, and a veto upon grave internal disorder, the real administration of the countries being left in the hands of native princes or headmen. However excellent this arrangement may be, it lends little support to the general theory of the British Empire as an educator of free political institutions.

Where British government is real, it does not carry freedom or self-government; where it does carry a certain amount of freedom and self-government, it is not real. Not five per cent. of the population of our Empire are possessed of any appreciable portion of the political and civil liberties which are the basis of British civilisation. Outside the ten millions of British subjects in Canada, Australia, and New Zealand, no considerable body is endowed with full self-government in the more vital matters, or is being "elevated from the position of inferiority to that of association."

This is the most important of all facts for students of the present and probable future of the British Empire. We have taken upon ourselves in these little islands the responsibility of governing huge aggregations of lower races in all parts of the world by methods which are antithetic to the methods of government which we most value for ourselves.

1902

6. In all essential features, India and Egypt are to be classed as Crown colonies [Hobson's note].

Late Victorians

The state of mind prevailing during the final decades of the nineteenth century was characterized previously (in the introduction to the Victorian age) as typical neither of the earlier Victorians nor of the twentieth century. As a result of their between-centuries role, writers of the 1880s and 1890s are sometimes styled "Late Victorians"—a perfectly legitimate label, chronologically speaking—and sometimes (more ambiguously) "the first of the 'moderns.'" In this anthology, we retain as Late Victorians those writers who made their chief contribution before 1900. And we reserve for the twentieth century a number of writers already on the scene in the last two decades of Victoria's reign whose work achieved particular prominence in the twentieth century: these are William Butler Yeats, Joseph Conrad, A. E. Housman, and Thomas Hardy. The treatment of Hardy's writings exemplifies this principle. He was born fifteen to twenty years before most of the writers of the eighties and nineties, and his last two great novels, *Tess of the D'Urbervilles* and *Jude the Obscure,* were published in 1891 and 1896 respectively. But since it was only after 1900 that Hardy made his name as a poet, we include him in the twentieth century, even though many of the attitudes toward life and literature in his poetry are recognizably Victorian and his writings can be considered as having contributed, in part, to the overall accomplishments of Victorian literature. To be sure, the same generalizations might be made about Gerard Manley Hopkins, whom we include in the Victorian section because he wrote during the Victorian period—even though his work was not published until 1918, when it had a great effect on modernist poets and critics. That such placements can be problematic is a striking reminder that literary history, like all history, resists being divided into the time categories we set up for convenient reference.

The writers most closely identified with the fin de siècle (the French for, literally, "end of the century"), a phrase often used in connection with this period, were proponents of "art for art's sake": they believed that art should be restricted to celebrating beauty in a highly polished style, unconcerned with controversial issues such as politics. These tenets are perhaps most frequently associated with Oscar Wilde, but the "aesthetes," as these artists and writers were called, included painters such as James McNeill Whistler, critics such as Arthur Symons, and the young Yeats. In 1936, when Yeats in old age was compiling an anthology of "modern verse," he looked back, as he often did, to the group of poets of the 1890s to which he had once been attached. They styled themselves the Rhymers' Club, and they met at a restaurant in London to read their poems aloud to each other. Yeats recalled that an admiration for the writings of Walter Pater was a badge of membership. Indeed, the first "poem" in his anthology is a passage of Pater's prose that Yeats prints as verse—the passage about the *Mona Lisa* in *Studies in the History of the Renaissance* (1873) that begins "She is older than the rocks among which she sits."

The Rhymers' Club poets liked to think of themselves as anti-Victorians, and they had some cause to do so—they consciously revolted against the moral earnestness of early Victorian prophets such as Thomas Carlyle and against a large set of middle-class opinions that they enjoyed mocking. Even Matthew Arnold, although appreciated for his ridicule of middle-class Philistines, was suspect in the eyes of the aesthetes because he had attacked, in his essay on William Wordsworth, the French poet Théophile Gautier, whom they viewed as a chief progenitor of the aesthetic movement. What Alfred, Lord Tennyson called in 1873 "poisonous honey stolen from France" was, in the 1890s, favored fare. Yet the credo of art for art's sake also had roots in the writings of earlier nineteenth-century British writers. The poets of the aesthetic movement were in a sense the last heirs of the Romantics; the appeal to sensation in their imagery goes back through Dante Gabriel Rossetti and Tennyson to John Keats. They developed this sensationalism much more histrionically than did their predecessors, however, seeking compensation for the drabness of ordinary life in melancholy suggestiveness, antibourgeois outrageousness, heady ritualism, world weariness, or mere emotional debauchery—qualities that led some critics to denounce the fin de siècle as a time of decadence and degeneration. But the importance of this era of English literary history does not lie in its writers' sensationalism and desire to shock. Their strongly held belief in the independence of art, their view that a work of art has its own unique kind of value—that, in T. S. Eliot's phrase, poetry must be judged "as poetry and not another thing"—is what most strongly influenced later generations. Not only did the aesthetic movement nurse the young Yeats and provide him with his lifelong belief in poetry as poetry rather than as a means to some moral or other end; it also provided some of the principal schools of twentieth-century criticism with their basic assumptions. "Art for art's sake" was in the nineties a provocative slogan; in the modern period many leading critics (usually associated with the tenets of New Criticism in North America, and Practical Criticism in Great Britain) were largely concerned with demonstrating the uniqueness of the literary use of language. They sought to train readers to see works of literary art as possessing a special kind of form, a special kind of meaning, and hence a special kind of value. In this regard the later critics were the heirs of the nineties, however much they modified or enriched the legacy. It was the poets of the fin de siècle, too, who first absorbed the influence of the French symboliste poets, an influence that became pervasive in the twentieth century and is especially strong (in different ways) in the poetry of Yeats and Eliot.

Though this era is characterized as "decadent," the poetry of the period was more various than that label suggests. Much as Wilde and Aubrey Beardsley expanded the range of male literary identity through their dandyism and effeminacy, women writers of the aesthetic movement such as the pseudonymous Michael Field (Katharine Harris Bradley and her niece Edith Emma Cooper) and Mary Elizabeth Coleridge made equally untraditional claims for women's experience, as Field translated and elaborated on Sappho's poems and Coleridge took on the witch's voice. There were also poets, such as William Ernest Henley and Rudyard Kipling, whose tone was strenuously masculine. They embraced the values not of languid contemplation but of a life of action, and they shared a commitment to realism that links them to naturalist novelists of the decade such as George Gissing and George Moore. Henley's realism appears in his grim sketches of hospital experiences, and Kipling's in his distinctive re-creation of the lives of common soldiers in the British Army in India and Africa.

Realism of another brand is evident in the tightly crafted dramas of the playwright Bernard Shaw. Works such as *Mrs Warren's Profession* (1898) reveal that some late-century artists wanted to engage with the pressing social, moral, and political issues of the day, and strove to challenge their audiences with thorny problems. Readers were unsettled, too, by one of the best-selling novellas of the period, *The Strange Case of Dr. Jekyll and Mr. Hyde* (1886). Although this horror story owes its allegiance to Gothicism rather than realism, many critics suggest that Robert Louis Stevenson's tale of a man split between his respectable public identity and an amoral secret self captures key anxieties of the fin de siècle. Within Wilde's oeuvre this theme is most closely embodied in the novel *The Picture of Dorian Gray* (1891), but it also has an important place, in a very different mode, within *The Importance of Being Earnest* (performed 1895). In this light, bright, and sparkling drama, the concept of the double life is central to the two principal male characters, who have both invented fictitious characters (Algernon's Bunbury and Jack's brother Ernest) that enable them to indulge their desires.

In its variety of literary expressions, the fin de siècle manifests something akin to a split personality. Sometimes that division appears within the work of a single writer. Kipling has often been seen primarily as the spokesman of the British Empire, the poet who coined the phrase "the white man's burden" to describe the northern races' necessary shouldering of the heavy weight of imperial rule. Yet Kipling also created the short story "The Man Who Would Be King" (1888), a highly ambivalent allegory of empire, and wrote "Recessional" for Queen Victoria's Diamond Jubilee in 1897. Instead of offering a complacent celebration of her sixty-year reign, this hymn delivers a haunting elegy: by placing the achievements of his country and his century in the vaster perspectives of human history, Kipling makes us fully aware of their fragility.

MICHAEL FIELD
Katharine Bradley (1846–1914)
Edith Cooper (1862–1913)

Michael Field was the pseudonym adopted by Katharine Bradley and her niece Edith Cooper; together they published twenty-seven verse plays and eight volumes of poems. When Robert Browning wrote to Michael Field to praise a volume of plays, Cooper responded by comparing her collaborative relationship with Bradley to that of two famous Jacobean playwrights: "My Aunt and I work together after the fashion of Beaumont and Fletcher. She is my senior, by but fifteen years. She has lived with me, taught me, encouraged me and joined me to her poetic life." When Browning let slip the secret of their authorship, Bradley begged him to maintain the disguise. The revelation of their secret, she pleaded, "would indeed be utter ruin to us," adding, "We have many things to say that the world will not tolerate from a woman's lips."

Katharine Harris Bradley lost her father, a tobacco manufacturer, when she was two and her mother when she was twenty-two. After her mother's death Bradley attended Newnham College, the newly established women's college at Cambridge, and the Collège de France in Paris. On her return home she joined John Ruskin's Guild of Saint George, a small utopian society. When Bradley wrote to Ruskin telling him that she had lost God and found a Skye terrier, he angrily ended their friendship. Shortly thereafter she began attending classes at Bristol University with her niece,

Edith Emma Cooper, whom she had adopted and raised after Edith's mother became ill. The two became lovers and began a life of writing and traveling together. Their first joint volume of poetry, *Long Ago* (1889), was inspired by Henry Wharton's 1885 edition of the writings of the ancient Greek poet Sappho, the first English translation to represent the object of Sappho's love poems as a woman. The preface to *Long Ago* explains their attempt to create poems elaborating on Sappho's fragments: "Devoutly as the fiery-bosomed Greek turned in her anguish to Aphrodite to accomplish her heart's desires, I have turned to the one woman who has dared to speak unfalteringly of the fearful mastery of love."

Bradley and Cooper knew most of the literary figures of the nineties, including Walter Pater, Oscar Wilde, and William Butler Yeats, although their relationship to the decadent movement was complex. The eroticism of their early poetry, with its frank expression of love between women, seems consistent with the spirit of the decade; but Bradley and Cooper sharply criticized the work of the artist Aubrey Beardsley for its depravity and withdrew one of their poems from publication in *The Yellow Book* to protest its style (Beardsley was the journal's art editor). In 1906 they converted to Roman Catholicism when their beloved chow dog died, thus reversing the substitution of dog for God that Bradley had flippantly described to Ruskin three decades earlier. In 1911 Cooper was diagnosed with cancer. Suffering too from cancer, which she kept a secret from Cooper to spare her pain, Bradley survived her niece by only eight months.

[Maids, not to you my mind doth change]

Ταῖς κάλαις ἴμμιν [τὸ] νόημα τῶμον οὐ διάμειπτον.[1]

Maids, not to you my mind doth change;
Men I defy, allure, estrange,
Prostrate, make bond or free:
Soft as the stream beneath the plane°   tree
5   To you I sing my love's refrain;
Between us is no thought of pain,
Peril, satiety.

Soon doth a lover's patience tire,
But ye to manifold desire
10 Can yield response, ye know
When for long, museful days I pine,
The presage at my heart divine;
To you I never breathe a sign
Of inward want or woe.

15 When injuries my spirit bruise,
Allaying virtue ye infuse
With unobtrusive skill:
And if care frets ye come to me
As fresh as nymph from stream or tree,
20 And with your soft vitality
My weary bosom fill.

1889

1. A fragment from the works of the Greek poet Sappho (born ca. 612 B.C.E.); the epigraph is translated in the first line of the poem.

[A girl]

A girl,
Her soul a deep-wave pearl
Dim, lucent of all lovely mysteries;
A face flowered for heart's ease,
5   A brow's grace soft as seas
Seen through faint forest-trees:
A mouth, the lips apart,
Like aspen-leaflets trembling in the breeze
From her tempestuous heart.
10   Such: and our souls so knit,
I leave a page half-writ—
    The work begun
Will be to heaven's conception done,
    If she come to it.

1893

Unbosoming

The love that breeds
In my heart for thee!
As the iris is full, brimful of seeds,
And all that it flowered for among the reeds
5   Is packed in a thousand vermilion-beads
That push, and riot, and squeeze, and clip,°   *clutch*
Till they burst the sides of the silver scrip,°   *purse*
And at last we see
What the bloom, with its tremulous, bowery fold
10   Of zephyr-petal at heart did hold:
So my breast is rent
With the burthen and strain of its great content;
For the summer of fragrance and sighs is dead,
The harvest-secret is burning red,
15   And I would give thee, after my kind,
The final issues of heart and mind.

1893

[It was deep April, and the morn]

It was deep April, and the morn
    Shakspere was born;[1]
The world was on us, pressing sore;
My Love and I took hands and swore,
5   Against the world, to be

---

1. Shakespeare's birthday conventionally is given as April 23, 1564.

Poets and lovers evermore,
To laugh and dream on Lethe's[2] shore,
To sing to Charon[3] in his boat,
Heartening the timid souls afloat;
10   Of judgment never to take heed,
But to those fast-locked souls to speed,
Who never from Apollo[4] fled,
Who spent no hour among the dead;
Continually
15   With them to dwell,
Indifferent to heaven and hell.

1893

To Christina Rossetti

Lady, we would behold thee moving bright
As Beatrice or Matilda[1] mid the trees,
Alas! thy moan was as a moan for ease
And passage through cool shadows to the night:
5   Fleeing from love, hadst thou not poet's right
To slip into the universe? The seas
Are fathomless to rivers drowned in these,
And sorrow is secure in leafy light.
Ah, had this secret touched thee, in a tomb
10   Thou hadst not buried thy enchanting self,
As happy Syrinx[2] murmuring with the wind,
Or Daphne,[3] thrilled through all her mystic bloom,
From safe recess as genius[4] or as elf,
Thou hadst breathed joy in earth and in thy kind.

1896

Nests in Elms

The rooks are cawing up and down the trees!
Among their nests they caw. O sound I treasure,
Ripe as old music is, the summer's measure,
Sleep at her gossip, sylvan mysteries,
5   With prate and clamour to give zest of these—
In rune I trace the ancient law of pleasure,

2. The river of forgetfulness in the underworld (a reference, like those that follow, to classical mythology).
3. The ferryman who rows the dead across the river Styx to the underworld.
4. God of poetry and of the sun.
1. An idealized virgin in Dante's *Purgatorio* (28, 30), who explains to the poet that he is in the Garden of Eden. Beatrice, Dante's idealized beloved, appears to the poet in the Earthly Paradise at the

top of the mountain of Purgatory.
2. A nymph who, when pursued by Pan, prayed to the river nymphs to save her; she was transformed into reeds, from which Pan made his flute (in Greek, *syrinx* literally means "Panpipe").
3. A nymph who, to escape Apollo's pursuit, was transformed into a laurel tree (the literal meaning of *daphnē* in Greek).
4. The spirit of a place.

Of love, of all the busy-ness of leisure,
With dream on dream of never-thwarted ease.
O homely birds, whose cry is harbinger
10   Of nothing sad, who know not anything
Of sea-birds' loneliness, of Procne's[1] strife,
Rock round me when I die! So sweet it were
To die by open doors, with you on wing
Humming the deep security of life.

1908

Eros[1]

O Eros of the mountains, of the earth,
One thing I know of thee that thou art old,
Far, sovereign, lonesome tyrant of the dearth
Of chaos, ruler of the primal cold!
5   None gave thee nurture: chaos' icy rings
Pressed on thy plenitude. O fostering power,
Thine the first voice, first warmth, first golden wings,
First blowing zephyr, earliest opened flower,
Thine the first smile of Time: thou hast no mate,
10   Thou art alone forever, giving all:
After thine image, Love, thou did'st create
Man to be poor, man to be prodigal;
And thus, O awful° god, he is endued   awe-inspiring
With the raw hungers of thy solitude.

1908

1. In Greek mythology Procne's husband, King Tereus, raped her sister, Philomela. Tereus then ripped out Philomela's tongue to keep her from revealing the crime, but she wove the story into a tapestry. In revenge Procne killed their son and served him to Tereus in a stew. When the sisters fled Tereus, all three were changed into birds: Tereus, into a hoopoe; Procne, a nightingale; and Philomela, a swallow.
1. Love (Greek); in Greek mythology the god of love.

WILLIAM ERNEST HENLEY
1849–1903

During the 1880s and 1890s William Ernest Henley edited the *National Observer* and other periodicals in London, where he became a powerful figure in literary circles. The affectionate regard in which he was held by his contemporaries was enhanced by his courageously confronting long years of crippling physical pain caused by tuberculosis of the bone. William Butler Yeats said of him: "I disagreed with him about everything, but I admired him beyond words."

Most of Henley's poems, such as his vivid accounts of his hospital experiences, are realistic sketches of city life, often in free verse. Also characteristic, but in a different vein, are his hearty affirmations of faith in the indomitable human spirit, as in "Invictus" (1888), and his patriotic verses expressing his pride in England's imperial role and her shouldering the responsibility for a world order. In "Pro Rege Nostro" (Latin for "For Our Kingdom"; 1892) he writes

> They call you proud and hard,
>   England, my England:
> You with worlds to watch and ward,
>   England, my own!
> You whose mailed hand keeps the keys
>   Of such teeming destinies
> You could know nor dread nor ease
>   Were the Song on your bugles blown,
>   England
>   Round the Pit on your bugles blown!

The spirit in poems such as these links Henley's writings to those of his friend Rudyard Kipling, and is also to be found throughout a highly influential anthology that Henley edited for use in schools. First published in 1892 and subtitled "A Book of Verse for Boys," *Lyra Heroica* (Latin for *The Heroic Lyre*, or harp) is filled with poetic accounts of selfless and noble deeds that often involve dying for one's country in battle.

In Hospital

Waiting

A square, squat room (a cellar on promotion),
Drab to the soul, drab to the very daylight;
Plasters[1] astray in unnatural-looking tinware;
Scissors and lint and apothecary's jars.

5 Here, on a bench a skeleton would writhe from,
Angry and sore, I wait to be admitted;
Wait till my heart is lead upon my stomach,
While at their ease two dressers do their chores.

One has a probe—it feels to me a crowbar.
10 A small boy sniffs and shudders after bluestone.[2]
A poor old tramp explains his poor old ulcers.
Life is (I think) a blunder and a shame.

1875

Invictus[1]

Out of the night that covers me,
  Black as the Pit from pole to pole,
I thank whatever gods may be
  For my unconquerable soul.

---

1. Medicated bandages.
2. Hydrated copper sulfate, commonly used in emergency wards as an emetic for patients who have taken poison.
1. Unconquered (Latin).

5 In the fell° clutch of circumstance   *cruel*
   I have not winced nor cried aloud.
   Under the bludgeonings of chance
   My head is bloody, but unbowed.

   Beyond this place of wrath and tears
10 Looms but the Horror of the shade,
   And yet the menace of the years
   Finds, and shall find, me unafraid.

   It matters not how strait° the gate,   *narrow*
   How charged with punishments the scroll,
15 I am the master of my fate;
   I am the captain of my soul.

1875   1888

ROBERT LOUIS STEVENSON
1850–1894

Robert Louis (originally Lewis) Balfour Stevenson was born in Edinburgh on November 13, 1850, the only child of Margaret Balfour and Thomas Stevenson, a well-known marine engineer and designer of lighthouses. His family was part of the respectable Scottish middle classes, a membership that would both benefit Stevenson—although there were difficult stretches in his relationship with his father, he generally did not have to worry about money—and leave him with a restlessness for adventure and excitement. Driven at the same time by a quest for a climate that would ease his chronically diseased lungs, Stevenson traveled more broadly than any other prominent Victorian writer. And yet it could be argued that although he was constantly on the move in far-flung lands, Stevenson returned again and again in his creative fiction, explicitly or implicitly, to the tensions of his own personal and national heritage—to the pronounced conflicts of his upbringing and of Scotland's somber, religiously oppressive society.

An awkward sensitive boy, Stevenson was subjected to the disciplinary strictures of his stern Presbyterian father and to the more affectionate, although also deeply devout, care of his mother and his nurse. Plagued by night terrors and bouts of sickness, the young Stevenson seemed "in body . . . assuredly badly set up," as a schoolmate said in later years; "his limbs were long, lean, and spidery, and his chest flat, so as almost to suggest some malnutrition." This constitutional weakness was to afflict Stevenson throughout his life, and he enjoyed only short periods of reasonable health. As a student at Edinburgh University, Stevenson soon began to avoid the engineering classes that would have enabled him to follow in his father's footsteps, and embarked instead on a course of reading—"an extensive and highly rational system of truancy," as he called it—to learn how to become a writer. In time, as a compromise to placate his father, he switched to the study of law; although he never practiced as a lawyer, he did pass the Scottish bar examination in 1875. But his interests clearly lay elsewhere: in this period Stevenson began dressing like a bohemian, reading scandalous French poetry, and hanging around brothels, where the prostitutes nicknamed him "Velvet Jack." By all accounts he was a witty and attentive conversationalist; his friend the folklorist and writer Andrew Lang later described him in verse as a "Buffoon and lover, poet and sensualist: / A deal of Ariel, just a streak of Puck, / Much Antony, of Hamlet most of all."

At the age of twenty-two, Stevenson further distanced himself from his father by confessing that he had turned both socialist and agnostic; he subsequently began to spend increasingly longer periods in France, partly because of respiratory troubles but also to be in the company of painters and writers. Back in Britain he developed important and useful friendships with artistic and literary figures, including Sidney Colvin, a professor of art, and the poet and editor W. E. Henley; with their support Stevenson started to publish essays and books of travel writing. As if to complete his breach with bourgeois Scottish respectability, Stevenson then fell in love with Fanny Osbourne, an American woman ten years his senior, who was estranged from her husband but not yet divorced.

In 1879 Stevenson's global wanderings began in earnest, starting with a trip to California to marry the newly divorced Fanny. Despite constant travel and recurrent illness, Stevenson found the time and energy to write. *Treasure Island,* begun as an amusement for his stepson, was his first popular success: serialized in 1881 and published in book form in 1883, the story of the cabin boy Jim Hawkins's adventures includes a covert portrait of Stevenson's one-legged friend Henley in the figure of the pirate Long John Silver. Soon thereafter he published another children's classic: *A Child's Garden of Verses* (1885), a collection of poems dedicated to his former nurse. In the years to come, Stevenson worked in numerous genres, including short fiction, swashbuckling romances, historical adventures (*Kidnapped,* 1886, a story set in Scotland just after the Jacobite rebellion of 1745, and its sequel, *Catriona,* 1893), and more gothic undertakings, such as the bleak and brooding novel *The Master of Ballantrae* (1889).

The work that first established Stevenson's critical reputation, however, was a horror story that prefigured *The Master of Ballantrae*'s fascination with the darker side of human nature and reflected his long-standing interest in the idea of a double life: *The Strange Case of Dr. Jekyll and Mr. Hyde,* written in 1885 and published the following year. The novella rapidly became a best seller in both Britain and America, and like Mary Shelley's *Frankenstein* of 1818 (to which *Jekyll and Hyde* pays homage at various moments) and Bram Stoker's *Dracula* (1897), the story has enjoyed a continuous and lively presence in popular culture up to the present day. Yet our familiarity with the outline of the tale may not prepare us for the psychological and ethical complexity of the original. Certainly the novelist's friends found *Jekyll and Hyde* genuinely unnerving: the writer and historian J. A. Symonds wrote to Stevenson that the story "has left such a deeply painful impression on my heart that I do not know how I am ever to turn to it again," while Lang commented that "we would welcome a spectre, a ghoul, or even a vampire, rather than meet Mr. Edward Hyde." For some, many aspects of the novella have seemed markedly Scottish in flavor: the novelist G. K. Chesterton insisted that its London is really Edinburgh, its Englishmen actually Scotsmen—"No modern English lawyer," he protested of the character Mr. Utterson, "ever read a book of dry divinity in the evening, merely because it was Sunday." Nevertheless, the distinctive tone and theme of *Jekyll and Hyde* have led many critics to characterize it—often together with another work that shares its preoccupation with the divided self, Oscar Wilde's *Picture of Dorian Gray* (1891)—as an expression of quintessentially fin de siècle anxieties.

From 1888 onward the Stevensons embarked on a series of journeys in the South Seas, once again in the hope that the climate would benefit Robert's health. They eventually settled in Samoa, where Stevenson became a favorite with the locals (who called him Tusitala, or "teller of tales") before he died of a cerebral hemorrhage in 1894. At the time of his death, Stevenson was only forty-four years old and still furiously at work, this time on a historical novel titled *Weir of Hermiston.*

The Strange Case of Dr. Jekyll and Mr. Hyde

Story of the Door

Mr. Utterson the lawyer was a man of a rugged countenance, that was never lighted by a smile; cold, scanty and embarrassed in discourse; backward in sentiment; lean, long, dusty, dreary and yet somehow lovable. At friendly meetings, and when the wine was to his taste, something eminently human beaconed from his eye; something indeed which never found its way into his talk, but which spoke not only in these silent symbols of the after-dinner face, but more often and loudly in the acts of his life. He was austere with himself; drank gin when he was alone, to mortify a taste for vintages; and though he enjoyed the theatre, had not crossed the doors of one for twenty years. But he had an approved[1] tolerance for others; sometimes wondering, almost with envy, at the high pressure of spirits involved in their misdeeds; and in any extremity inclined to help rather than to reprove. "I incline to Cain's heresy,"[2] he used to say quaintly: "I let my brother go to the devil in his own way." In this character, it was frequently his fortune to be the last reputable acquaintance and the last good influence in the lives of down-going men. And to such as these, so long as they came about his chambers, he never marked a shade of change in his demeanour.

No doubt the feat was easy to Mr. Utterson; for he was undemonstrative at the best, and even his friendship seemed to be founded in a similar catholicity[3] of good-nature. It is the mark of a modest man to accept his friendly circle ready-made from the hands of opportunity; and that was the lawyer's way. His friends were those of his own blood or those whom he had known the longest; his affections, like ivy, were the growth of time, they implied no aptness in the object. Hence, no doubt, the bond that united him to Mr. Richard Enfield, his distant kinsman, the well-known man about town. It was a nut to crack for many, what these two could see in each other, or what subject they could find in common. It was reported by those who encountered them in their Sunday walks, that they said nothing, looked singularly dull, and would hail with obvious relief the appearance of a friend. For all that, the two men put the greatest store by these excursions, counted them the chief jewel of each week, and not only set aside occasions of pleasure, but even resisted the calls of business, that they might enjoy them uninterrupted.

It chanced on one of these rambles that their way led them down a by-street in a busy quarter of London. The street was small and what is called quiet, but it drove a thriving trade on the week-days. The inhabitants were all doing well, it seemed, and all emulously hoping to do better still, and laying out the surplus of their gains in coquetry;[4] so that the shop fronts stood along that thoroughfare with an air of invitation, like rows of smiling saleswomen. Even on Sunday, when it veiled its more florid charms and lay comparatively empty of passage, the street shone out in contrast to its dingy neighbourhood, like a fire in a forest; and with its freshly painted shutters, well-polished brasses, and general cleanliness and gaiety of note, instantly caught and pleased the eye of the passenger.[5]

---

1. Proved.
2. Refusal of responsibility for one's fellow man. After Cain kills his brother, Abel, and God asks where Abel is, Cain responds, "Am I my brother's keeper?" (Genesis 4.9).
3. Universality.
4. Attractive display.
5. Passerby.

Two doors from one corner, on the left hand going east, the line was broken by the entry of a court; and just at that point, a certain sinister block of building thrust forward its gable on the street. It was two storeys high; showed no window, nothing but a door on the lower storey and a blind forehead of discoloured wall on the upper; and bore in every feature, the marks of prolonged and sordid negligence. The door, which was equipped with neither bell nor knocker, was blistered and distained.[6] Tramps slouched into the recess and struck matches on the panels; children kept shop upon the steps; the schoolboy had tried his knife on the mouldings; and for close on a generation, no one had appeared to drive away these random visitors or to repair their ravages.

Mr. Enfield and the lawyer were on the other side of the by-street; but when they came abreast of the entry, the former lifted up his cane and pointed.

"Did you ever remark that door?" he asked; and when his companion had replied in the affirmative, "It is connected in my mind," added he, "with a very odd story."

"Indeed?" said Mr. Utterson, with a slight change of voice, "and what was that?"

"Well, it was this way," returned Mr. Enfield: "I was coming home from some place at the end of the world, about three o'clock of a black winter morning, and my way lay through a part of town where there was literally nothing to be seen but lamps. Street after street, and all the folks asleep—street after street, all lighted up as if for a procession and all as empty as a church—till at last I got into that state of mind when a man listens and listens and begins to long for the sight of a policeman. All at once, I saw two figures: one a little man who was stumping along eastward at a good walk, and the other a girl of maybe eight or ten who was running as hard as she was able down a cross street. Well, sir, the two ran into one another naturally enough at the corner; and then came the horrible part of the thing; for the man trampled calmly over the child's body and left her screaming on the ground. It sounds nothing to hear, but it was hellish to see. It wasn't like a man; it was like some damned Juggernaut.[7] I gave a view halloa,[8] took to my heels, collared my gentleman, and brought him back to where there was already quite a group about the screaming child. He was perfectly cool and made no resistance, but gave me one look, so ugly that it brought out the sweat on me like running. The people who had turned out were the girl's own family; and pretty soon, the doctor, for whom she had been sent, put in his appearance. Well, the child was not much the worse, more frightened, according to the Sawbones;[9] and there you might have supposed would be an end to it. But there was one curious circumstance. I had taken a loathing to my gentleman at first sight. So had the child's family, which was only natural. But the doctor's case was what struck me. He was the usual cut and dry apothecary, of no particular age and colour, with a strong Edinburgh accent, and about as emotional as a bagpipe. Well, sir, he was like the rest of us; every time he looked at my prisoner, I saw that Sawbones turn sick and white with the desire to kill him. I knew what was in his mind, just as he knew what was in mine; and killing being out of the question, we did the next best. We told the man we could

6. Discolored.
7. A relentless force that crushes individuals in its path. Originally a title of Krishna (an avatar of the Hindu god Vishnu); at an annual festival his statue was drawn on an enormous cart, under whose

wheels many worshippers threw themselves to be crushed.
8. Shout.
9. Doctor (slang).

and would make such a scandal out of this, as should make his name stink from one end of London to the other. If he had any friends or any credit,[1] we undertook that he should lose them. And all the time, as we were pitching it in red hot, we were keeping the women off him as best we could, for they were as wild as harpies.[2] I never saw a circle of such hateful faces; and there was the man in the middle, with a kind of black, sneering coolness—frightened too, I could see that—but carrying it off, sir, really like Satan. 'If you choose to make capital out of this accident,' said he, 'I am naturally helpless. No gentleman but wishes to avoid a scene,' says he. 'Name your figure.' Well, we screwed him up to a hundred pounds for the child's family; he would have clearly liked to stick out; but there was something about the lot of us that meant mischief, and at last he struck.[3] The next thing was to get the money; and where do you think he carried us but to that place with the door?— whipped out a key, went in, and presently came back with the matter of ten pounds in gold and a cheque for the balance on Coutts's,[4] drawn payable to bearer and signed with a name that I can't mention, though it's one of the points of my story, but it was a name at least very well known and often printed. The figure was stiff; but the signature was good for more than that, if it was only genuine. I took the liberty of pointing out to my gentleman that the whole business looked apocryphal, and that a man does not, in real life, walk into a cellar door at four in the morning and come out of it with another man's cheque for close upon a hundred pounds. But he was quite easy and sneering. 'Set your mind at rest,' says he, 'I will stay with you till the banks open and cash the cheque myself.' So we all set off, the doctor, and the child's father, and our friend and myself, and passed the rest of the night in my chambers; and next day, when we had breakfasted, went in a body to the bank. I gave in the check myself, and said I had every reason to believe it was a forgery. Not a bit of it. The cheque was genuine."

"Tut-tut," said Mr. Utterson.

"I see you feel as I do," said Mr. Enfield. "Yes, it's a bad story. For my man was a fellow that nobody could have to do with, a really damnable man; and the person that drew the cheque is the very pink of the proprieties, celebrated too, and (what makes it worse) one of your fellows who do what they call good. Black mail, I suppose; an honest man paying through the nose for some of the capers of his youth. Black Mail House is what I call that place with the door, in consequence. Though even that, you know, is far from explaining all," he added, and with the words fell into a vein of musing.

From this he was recalled by Mr. Utterson asking rather suddenly: "And you don't know if the drawer of the cheque lives there?"

"A likely place, isn't it?" returned Mr. Enfield. "But I happen to have noticed his address; he lives in some square or other."

"And you never asked about the—place with the door?" said Mr. Utterson.

"No, sir: I had a delicacy," was the reply. "I feel very strongly about putting questions; it partakes too much of the style of the day of judgment. You start a question, and it's like starting a stone. You sit quietly on the top of a hill; and away the stone goes, starting others; and presently some bland old bird (the last you would have thought of) is knocked on the head in his own back

---

1. Good name.
2. In classical mythology monsters with women's faces and bodies and birds' wings and claws.
3. Gave in.
4. A prestigious London bank.

garden and the family have to change their name. No, sir, I make it a rule of mine: the more it looks like Queer Street,[5] the less I ask."

"A very good rule, too," said the lawyer.

"But I have studied the place for myself," continued Mr. Enfield. "It seems scarcely a house. There is no other door, and nobody goes in or out of that one but, once in a great while, the gentleman of my adventure. There are three windows looking on the court on the first floor;[6] none below; the windows are always shut but they're clean. And then there is a chimney which is generally smoking; so somebody must live there. And yet it's not so sure; for the buildings are so packed together about that court, that it's hard to say where one ends and another begins."

The pair walked on again for a while in silence; and then "Enfield," said Mr. Utterson, "that's a good rule of yours."

"Yes, I think it is," returned Enfield.

"But for all that," continued the lawyer, "there's one point I want to ask: I want to ask the name of that man who walked over the child."

"Well," said Mr. Enfield, "I can't see what harm it would do. It was a man of the name of Hyde."

"H'm," said Mr. Utterson. "What sort of a man is he to see?"

"He is not easy to describe. There is something wrong with his appearance; something displeasing, something downright detestable. I never saw a man I so disliked, and yet I scarce know why. He must be deformed somewhere; he gives a strong feeling of deformity, although I couldn't specify the point. He's an extraordinary looking man, and yet I really can name nothing out of the way. No, sir; I can make no hand of it; I can't describe him. And it's not want of memory; for I declare I can see him this moment."

Mr. Utterson again walked some way in silence and obviously under a weight of consideration. "You are sure he used a key?" he inquired at last.

"My dear sir . . ." began Enfield, surprised out of himself.

"Yes, I know," said Utterson; "I know it must seem strange. The fact is, if I do not ask you the name of the other party, it is because I know it already. You see, Richard, your tale has gone home. If you have been inexact in any point, you had better correct it."

"I think you might have warned me," returned the other with a touch of sullenness. "But I have been pedantically exact, as you call it. The fellow had a key; and what's more, he has it still. I saw him use it, not a week ago."

Mr. Utterson sighed deeply but said never a word; and the young man presently resumed. "Here is another lesson to say nothing," said he. "I am ashamed of my long tongue. Let us make a bargain never to refer to this again."

"With all my heart," said the lawyer. "I shake hands on that, Richard."

Search for Mr. Hyde

That evening Mr. Utterson came home to his bachelor house in sombre spirits and sat down to dinner without relish. It was his custom of a Sunday, when this meal was over, to sit close by the fire, a volume of some dry divinity[7] on his reading desk, until the clock of the neighbouring church rang out the

5. I.e., looks like someone is in trouble or a bad fix (slang).
6. I.e., the first floor above the ground floor (what Americans call the second floor).
7. Theology.

hour of twelve, when he would go soberly and gratefully to bed. On this night, however, as soon as the cloth was taken away, he took up a candle and went into his business room. There he opened his safe, took from the most private part of it a document endorsed on the envelope as Dr. Jekyll's Will, and sat down with a clouded brow to study its contents. The will was holograph,[8] for Mr. Utterson, though he took charge of it now that it was made, had refused to lend the least assistance in the making of it; it provided not only that, in case of the decease of Henry Jekyll, M.D., D.C.L., LL.D., F.R.S.,[9] etc., all his possessions were to pass into the hands of his "friend and benefactor Edward Hyde," but that in case of Dr. Jekyll's "disappearance or unexplained absence for any period exceeding three calendar months," the said Edward Hyde should step into the said Henry Jekyll's shoes without further delay and free from any burthen or obligation, beyond the payment of a few small sums to the members of the doctor's household. This document had long been the lawyer's eyesore. It offended him both as a lawyer and as a lover of the sane and customary sides of life, to whom the fanciful was the immodest. And hitherto it was his ignorance of Mr. Hyde that had swelled his indignation; now, by a sudden turn, it was his knowledge. It was already bad enough when the name was but a name of which he could learn no more. It was worse when it began to be clothed upon with detestable attributes; and out of the shifting, insubstantial mists that had so long baffled his eye, there leaped up the sudden, definite presentment[1] of a fiend.

"I thought it was madness," he said, as he replaced the obnoxious paper in the safe, "and now I begin to fear it is disgrace."

With that he blew out his candle, put on a greatcoat, and set forth in the direction of Cavendish Square, that citadel of medicine,[2] where his friend, the great Dr. Lanyon, had his house and received his crowding patients. "If anyone knows, it will be Lanyon," he had thought.

The solemn butler knew and welcomed him; he was subjected to no stage of delay, but ushered direct from the door to the dining-room where Dr. Lanyon sat alone over his wine. This was a hearty, healthy, dapper, red-faced gentleman, with a shock of hair prematurely white, and a boisterous and decided manner. At sight of Mr. Utterson, he sprang up from his chair and welcomed him with both hands. The geniality, as was the way of the man, was somewhat theatrical to the eye; but it reposed on genuine feeling. For these two were old friends, old mates both at school and college, both thorough respecters of themselves and of each other, and, what does not always follow, men who thoroughly enjoyed each other's company.

After a little rambling talk, the lawyer led up to the subject which so disagreeably preoccupied his mind.

"I suppose, Lanyon," said he, "you and I must be the two oldest friends that Henry Jekyll has?"

"I wish the friends were younger," chuckled Dr. Lanyon. "But I suppose we are. And what of that? I see little of him now."

"Indeed?" said Utterson. "I thought you had a bond of common interest."

"We had," was the reply. "But it is more than ten years since Henry Jekyll became too fanciful for me. He began to go wrong, wrong in mind; and though

---

8. In the author's handwriting.
9. Doctor of Medicine, Doctor of Civil Law, Doctor of Laws, and Fellow of the Royal Society.

1. Image.
2. A once-aristocratic neighborhood where fashionable doctors had their offices.

of course I continue to take an interest in him for old sake's sake, as they say, I see and I have seen devilish little of the man. Such unscientific balderdash," added the doctor, flushing suddenly purple, "would have estranged Damon and Pythias."[3]

This little spirit of temper was somewhat of a relief to Mr. Utterson. "They have only differed on some point of science," he thought; and being a man of no scientific passions (except in the matter of conveyancing,[4]) he even added: "It is nothing worse than that!" He gave his friend a few seconds to recover his composure, and then approached the question he had come to put. "Did you ever come across a protégé of his—one Hyde?" he asked.

"Hyde?" repeated Lanyon. "No. Never heard of him. Since my time."

That was the amount of information that the lawyer carried back with him to the great, dark bed on which he tossed to and fro, until the small hours of the morning began to grow large. It was a night of little ease to his toiling mind, toiling in mere[5] darkness and besieged by questions.

Six o'clock struck on the bells of the church that was so conveniently near to Mr. Utterson's dwelling, and still he was digging at the problem. Hitherto it had touched him on the intellectual side alone; but now his imagination also was engaged, or rather enslaved; and as he lay and tossed in the gross darkness of the night and the curtained room, Mr. Enfield's tale went by before his mind in a scroll of lighted pictures. He would be aware of the great field of lamps of a nocturnal city; then of the figure of a man walking swiftly; then of a child running from the doctor's; and then these met, and that human Juggernaut trod the child down and passed on regardless of her screams. Or else he would see a room in a rich house, where his friend lay asleep, dreaming and smiling at his dreams; and then the door of that room would be opened, the curtains of the bed plucked apart, and the sleeper recalled,[6] and lo! there would stand by his side a figure to whom power was given, and even at that dead hour, he must rise and do its bidding. The figure in these two phases haunted the lawyer all night; and if at any time he dozed over, it was but to see it glide more stealthily through sleeping houses, or move the more swiftly and still the more swiftly, even to dizziness, through wider labyrinths of lamp-lighted city, and at every street corner crush a child and leave her screaming. And still the figure had no face by which he might know it; even in his dreams, it had no face, or one that baffled him and melted before his eyes; and thus it was that there sprang up and grew apace in the lawyer's mind a singularly strong, almost an inordinate, curiosity to behold the features of the real Mr. Hyde. If he could but once set eyes on him, he thought the mystery would lighten and perhaps roll altogether away, as was the habit of mysterious things when well examined. He might see a reason for his friend's strange preference or bondage (call it which you please) and even for the startling clause of the will. At least it would be a face worth seeing: the face of a man who was without bowels of mercy:[7] a face which had but to show itself to raise up, in the mind of the unimpressionable Enfield, a spirit of enduring hatred.

From that time forward, Mr. Utterson began to haunt the door in the by-street of shops. In the morning before office hours, at noon when business was plenty, and time scarce, at night under the face of the fogged city moon,

3. Two inseparable youths in Greek legend whose willingness to die for each other symbolizes true friendship.
4. Legal transfer of property by writing deeds.
5. Pure.
6. Revived, awakened.
7. Compassion.

by all lights and at all hours of solitude or concourse, the lawyer was to be found on his chosen post.

"If he be Mr. Hyde," he had thought, "I shall be Mr. Seek."

And at last his patience was rewarded. It was a fine dry night; frost in the air; the streets as clean as a ballroom floor; the lamps, unshaken by any wind, drawing a regular pattern of light and shadow. By ten o'clock, when the shops were closed, the by-street was very solitary and, in spite of the low growl of London from all round, very silent. Small sounds carried far; domestic sounds out of the houses were clearly audible on either side of the roadway; and the rumour[8] of the approach of any passenger preceded him by a long time. Mr. Utterson had been some minutes at his post, when he was aware of an odd, light footstep drawing near. In the course of his nightly patrols, he had long grown accustomed to the quaint effect with which the footfalls of a single person, while he is still a great way off, suddenly spring out distinct from the vast hum and clatter of the city. Yet his attention had never before been so sharply and decisively arrested; and it was with a strong, superstitious prevision of success that he withdrew into the entry of the court.

The steps drew swiftly nearer, and swelled out suddenly louder as they turned the end of the street. The lawyer, looking forth from the entry, could soon see what manner of man he had to deal with. He was small and very plainly dressed, and the look of him, even at that distance, went somehow strongly against the watcher's inclination. But he made straight for the door, crossing the roadway to save time; and as he came, he drew a key from his pocket like one approaching home.

Mr. Utterson stepped out and touched him on the shoulder as he passed. "Mr. Hyde, I think?"

Mr. Hyde shrank back with a hissing intake of the breath. But his fear was only momentary; and though he did not look the lawyer in the face, he answered coolly enough: "That is my name. What do you want?"

"I see you are going in," returned the lawyer. "I am an old friend of Dr. Jekyll's—Mr. Utterson of Gaunt Street—you must have heard my name; and meeting you so conveniently, I thought you might admit me."

"You will not find Dr. Jekyll; he is from home," replied Mr. Hyde, blowing in the key. And then suddenly, but still without looking up, "How did you know me?" he asked.

"On your side," said Mr. Utterson, "will you do me a favour?"

"With pleasure," replied the other. "What shall it be?"

"Will you let me see your face?" asked the lawyer.

Mr. Hyde appeared to hesitate, and then, as if upon some sudden reflection, fronted about with an air of defiance; and the pair stared at each other pretty fixedly for a few seconds. "Now I shall know you again," said Mr. Utterson. "It may be useful."

"Yes," returned Mr. Hyde, "it is as well we have met; and à propos, you should have my address." And he gave a number of a street in Soho.[9]

"Good God!" thought Mr. Utterson, "can he, too, have been thinking of the will?" But he kept his feelings to himself and only grunted in acknowledgment of the address.

"And now," said the other, "how did you know me?"

---

8. Noise.
9. Seedy district in central London. "À propos": by the way (French).

"By description," was the reply.

"Whose description?"

"We have common friends," said Mr. Utterson.

"Common friends?" echoed Mr. Hyde, a little hoarsely. "Who are they?"

"Jekyll, for instance," said the lawyer.

"He never told you," cried Mr. Hyde, with a flush of anger. "I did not think you would have lied."

"Come," said Mr. Utterson, "that is not fitting language."

The other snarled aloud into a savage laugh; and the next moment, with extraordinary quickness, he had unlocked the door and disappeared into the house.

The lawyer stood awhile when Mr. Hyde had left him, the picture of disquietude. Then he began slowly to mount the street, pausing every step or two and putting his hand to his brow like a man in mental perplexity. The problem he was thus debating as he walked, was one of a class that is rarely solved. Mr. Hyde was pale and dwarfish, he gave an impression of deformity without any nameable malformation, he had a displeasing smile, he had borne himself to the lawyer with a sort of murderous mixture of timidity and boldness, and he spoke with a husky, whispering and somewhat broken voice; all these were points against him, but not all of these together could explain the hitherto unknown disgust, loathing and fear with which Mr. Utterson regarded him. "There must be something else," said the perplexed gentleman. "There *is* something more, if I could find a name for it. God bless me, the man seems hardly human! Something troglodytic, shall we say? or can it be the old story of Dr. Fell? or is it the mere radiance of a foul soul that thus transpires through, and transfigures, its clay continent?[1] The last, I think; for, O my poor old Harry Jekyll, if ever I read Satan's signature upon a face, it is on that of your new friend."

Round the corner from the by-street, there was a square of ancient, handsome houses, now for the most part decayed from their high estate and let in flats and chambers to all sorts and conditions of men: map-engravers, architects, shady lawyers and the agents of obscure enterprises. One house, however, second from the corner, was still occupied entire; and at the door of this, which wore a great air of wealth and comfort, though it was now plunged in darkness except for the fanlight, Mr. Utterson stopped and knocked. A well-dressed, elderly servant opened the door.

"Is Dr. Jekyll at home, Poole?" asked the lawyer.

"I will see, Mr. Utterson," said Poole, admitting the visitor, as he spoke, into a large, low-roofed, comfortable hall, paved with flags,[2] warmed (after the fashion of a country house) by a bright, open fire, and furnished with costly cabinets of oak. "Will you wait here by the fire, sir? or shall I give you a light in the dining-room?"

"Here, thank you," said the lawyer, and he drew near and leaned on the tall fender.[3] This hall, in which he was now left alone, was a pet fancy of his friend the doctor's; and Utterson himself was wont to speak of it as the pleasantest room in London. But to-night there was a shudder in his blood; the face of Hyde sat heavy on his memory; he felt (what was rare with him) a nausea and

---

1. Container. "Troglodytic": like a prehistoric cave dweller or apelike. Dr. Fell: figure from the nursery rhyme "I do not like thee Dr. Fell; / The reason why I cannot tell."
2. Flagstones.
3. Metal frame in front of a fireplace.

distaste of life; and in the gloom of his spirits, he seemed to read a menace in the flickering of the firelight on the polished cabinets and the uneasy starting of the shadow on the roof. He was ashamed of his relief, when Poole presently returned to announce that Dr. Jekyll was gone out.

"I saw Mr. Hyde go in by the old dissecting-room door, Poole," he said. "Is that right, when Dr. Jekyll is from home?"

"Quite right, Mr. Utterson, sir," replied the servant. "Mr. Hyde has a key."

"Your master seems to repose a great deal of trust in that young man, Poole," resumed the other musingly.

"Yes, sir, he do indeed," said Poole. "We have all orders to obey him."

"I do not think I ever met Mr. Hyde?" asked Utterson.

"O, dear no, sir. He never *dines* here," replied the butler. "Indeed we see very little of him on this side of the house; he mostly comes and goes by the laboratory."

"Well, good-night, Poole."

"Good-night, Mr. Utterson."

And the lawyer set out homeward with a very heavy heart. "Poor Harry Jekyll," he thought, "my mind misgives me he is in deep waters! He was wild when he was young; a long while ago to be sure; but in the law of God, there is no statute of limitations. Ay, it must be that; the ghost of some old sin, the cancer of some concealed disgrace: punishment coming, *pede claudo*,[4] years after memory has forgotten and self-love condoned the fault." And the lawyer, scared by the thought, brooded awhile on his own past, groping in all the corners of memory, lest by chance some Jack-in-the-Box of an old iniquity should leap to light there. His past was fairly blameless; few men could read the rolls of their life with less apprehension; yet he was humbled to the dust by the many ill things he had done, and raised up again into a sober and fearful gratitude by the many that he had come so near to doing, yet avoided. And then by a return on his former subject, he conceived a spark of hope. "This Master Hyde, if he were studied," thought he, "must have secrets of his own; black secrets, by the look of him; secrets compared to which poor Jekyll's worst would be like sunshine. Things cannot continue as they are. It turns me cold to think of this creature stealing like a thief to Harry's bedside; poor Harry, what a wakening! And the danger of it; for if this Hyde suspects the existence of the will, he may grow impatient to inherit. Ay, I must put my shoulder to the wheel—if Jekyll will but let me," he added, "if Jekyll will only let me." For once more he saw before his mind's eye, as clear as a transparency, the strange clauses of the will.

Dr. Jekyll Was Quite at Ease

A fortnight later, by excellent good fortune, the doctor gave one of his pleasant dinners to some five or six old cronies, all intelligent, reputable men and all judges of good wine; and Mr. Utterson so contrived that he remained behind after the others had departed. This was no new arrangement, but a thing that had befallen many scores of times. Where Utterson was liked, he was liked well. Hosts loved to detain the dry lawyer, when the light-hearted and the loose-tongued had already their foot on the threshold; they liked to

---

4. With lame foot (Latin). From the Roman poet Horace's *Odes* 3.2.32: "Rarely has Vengeance with her lame foot abandoned the wicked man with a head start on her."

sit awhile in his unobtrusive company, practising for solitude, sobering their minds in the man's rich silence after the expense and strain of gaiety. To this rule, Dr. Jekyll was no exception; and as he now sat on the opposite side of the fire—a large, well-made, smooth-faced man of fifty, with something of a slyish cast perhaps, but every mark of capacity and kindness—you could see by his looks that he cherished for Mr. Utterson a sincere and warm affection.

"I have been wanting to speak to you, Jekyll," began the latter. "You know that will of yours?"

A close observer might have gathered that the topic was distasteful; but the doctor carried it off gaily. "My poor Utterson," said he, "you are unfortunate in such a client. I never saw a man so distressed as you were by my will; unless it were that hide-bound pedant, Lanyon, at what he called my scientific heresies. O, I know he's a good fellow—you needn't frown—an excellent fellow, and I always mean to see more of him; but a hide-bound pedant for all that; an ignorant, blatant pedant. I was never more disappointed in any man than Lanyon."

"You know I never approved of it," pursued Utterson, ruthlessly disregarding the fresh topic.

"My will? Yes, certainly, I know that," said the doctor, a trifle sharply. "You have told me so."

"Well, I tell you so again," continued the lawyer. "I have been learning something of young Hyde."

The large handsome face of Dr. Jekyll grew pale to the very lips, and there came a blackness about his eyes. "I do not care to hear more," said he. "This is a matter I thought we had agreed to drop."

"What I heard was abominable," said Utterson.

"It can make no change. You do not understand my position," returned the doctor, with a certain incoherency of manner. "I am painfully situated, Utterson; my position is a very strange—a very strange one. It is one of those affairs that cannot be mended by talking."

"Jekyll," said Utterson, "you know me: I am a man to be trusted. Make a clean breast of this in confidence; and I make no doubt I can get you out of it."

"My good Utterson," said the doctor, "this is very good of you, this is downright good of you, and I cannot find words to thank you in. I believe you fully; I would trust you before any man alive, ay, before myself, if I could make the choice; but indeed it isn't what you fancy; it is not so bad as that; and just to put your good heart at rest, I will tell you one thing: the moment I choose, I can be rid of Mr. Hyde. I give you my hand upon that; and I thank you again and again; and I will just add one little word, Utterson, that I'm sure you'll take in good part: this is a private matter, and I beg of you to let it sleep."

Utterson reflected a little, looking in the fire.

"I have no doubt you are perfectly right," he said at last, getting to his feet.

"Well, but since we have touched upon this business, and for the last time I hope," continued the doctor, "there is one point I should like you to understand. I have really a very great interest in poor Hyde. I know you have seen him; he told me so; and I fear he was rude. But I do sincerely take a great, a very great interest in that young man; and if I am taken away, Utterson, I wish you to promise me that you will bear with him and get his rights for him. I think you would, if you knew all; and it would be a weight off my mind if you would promise."

"I can't pretend that I shall ever like him," said the lawyer.

"I don't ask that," pleaded Jekyll, laying his hand upon the other's arm; "I only ask for justice; I only ask you to help him for my sake, when I am no longer here."

Utterson heaved an irrepressible sigh. "Well," said he, "I promise."

The Carew Murder Case

Nearly a year later, in the month of October, 18—, London was startled by a crime of singular ferocity and rendered all the more notable by the high position of the victim. The details were few and startling. A maid servant living alone in a house not far from the river, had gone upstairs to bed about eleven. Although a fog rolled over the city in the small hours, the early part of the night was cloudless, and the lane, which the maid's window overlooked, was brilliantly lit by the full moon. It seems she was romantically given, for she sat down upon her box, which stood immediately under the window, and fell into a dream of musing. Never (she used to say, with streaming tears, when she narrated that experience), never had she felt more at peace with all men or thought more kindly of the world. And as she so sat she became aware of an aged and beautiful gentleman with white hair, drawing near along the lane; and advancing to meet him, another and very small gentleman, to whom at first she paid less attention. When they had come within speech (which was just under the maid's eyes) the older man bowed and accosted the other with a very pretty manner of politeness. It did not seem as if the subject of his address were of great importance; indeed, from his pointing, it sometimes appeared as if he were only inquiring his way; but the moon shone on his face as he spoke, and the girl was pleased to watch it, it seemed to breathe such an innocent and old-world kindness of disposition, yet with something high too, as of a well-founded self-content. Presently her eye wandered to the other, and she was surprised to recognise in him a certain Mr. Hyde, who had once visited her master and for whom she had conceived a dislike. He had in his hand a heavy cane, with which he was trifling; but he answered never a word, and seemed to listen with an ill-contained impatience. And then all of a sudden he broke out in a great flame of anger, stamping with his foot, brandishing the cane, and carrying on (as the maid described it) like a madman. The old gentleman took a step back, with the air of one very much surprised and a trifle hurt; and at that Mr. Hyde broke out of all bounds and clubbed him to the earth. And next moment, with ape-like fury, he was trampling his victim under foot and hailing down a storm of blows, under which the bones were audibly shattered and the body jumped upon the roadway. At the horror of these sights and sounds, the maid fainted.

It was two o'clock when she came to herself and called for the police. The murderer was gone long ago; but there lay his victim in the middle of the lane, incredibly mangled. The stick with which the deed had been done, although it was of some rare and very tough and heavy wood, had broken in the middle under the stress of this insensate cruelty; and one splintered half had rolled in the neighbouring gutter—the other, without doubt, had been carried away by the murderer. A purse and a gold watch were found upon the victim; but no cards or papers, except a sealed and stamped envelope, which he had been probably carrying to the post,[5] and which bore the name and address of Mr. Utterson.

5. I.e., postal letter box.

This was brought to the lawyer the next morning, before he was out of bed; and he had no sooner seen it and been told the circumstances, than he shot out a solemn lip. "I shall say nothing till I have seen the body," said he; "this may be very serious. Have the kindness to wait while I dress." And with the same grave countenance he hurried through his breakfast and drove to the police station, whither the body had been carried. As soon as he came into the cell, he nodded.

"Yes," said he, "I recognise him. I am sorry to say that this is Sir Danvers Carew."

"Good God, sir," exclaimed the officer, "is it possible?" And the next moment his eye lighted up with professional ambition. "This will make a deal of noise," he said. "And perhaps you can help us to the man." And he briefly narrated what the maid had seen, and showed the broken stick.

Mr. Utterson had already quailed at the name of Hyde; but when the stick was laid before him, he could doubt no longer; broken and battered as it was, he recognised it for one that he had himself presented many years before to Henry Jekyll.

"Is this Mr. Hyde a person of small stature?" he inquired.

"Particularly small and particularly wicked-looking, is what the maid calls him," said the officer.

Mr. Utterson reflected; and then, raising his head, "If you will come with me in my cab," he said, "I think I can take you to his house."

It was by this time about nine in the morning, and the first fog of the season. A great chocolate-coloured pall lowered[6] over heaven, but the wind was continually charging and routing these embattled vapours; so that as the cab crawled from street to street, Mr. Utterson beheld a marvellous number of degrees and hues of twilight; for here it would be dark like the back-end of evening; and there would be a glow of a rich, lurid brown, like the light of some strange conflagration; and here, for a moment, the fog would be quite broken up, and a haggard shaft of daylight would glance in between the swirling wreaths. The dismal quarter of Soho seen under these changing glimpses, with its muddy ways, and slatternly passengers, and its lamps, which had never been extinguished or had been kindled afresh to combat this mournful reinvasion of darkness, seemed, in the lawyer's eyes, like a district of some city in a nightmare. The thoughts of his mind, besides, were of the gloomiest dye; and when he glanced at the companion of his drive, he was conscious of some touch of that terror of the law and the law's officers, which may at times assail the most honest.

As the cab drew up before the address indicated, the fog lifted a little and showed him a dingy street, a gin palace, a low French eating house, a shop for the retail of penny numbers[7] and twopenny salads, many ragged children huddled in the doorways, and many women of many different nationalities passing out, key in hand, to have a morning glass; and the next moment the fog settled down again upon that part, as brown as umber, and cut him off from his blackguardly surroundings. This was the home of Henry Jekyll's favourite; of a man who was heir to quarter of a million sterling.[8]

An ivory-faced and silvery-haired old woman opened the door. She had an evil face, smoothed by hypocrisy; but her manners were excellent. Yes, she

6. Was gloomy and threatening.
7. Cheap serial installments of popular fiction.
"Gin palace:" cheap bar.
8. I.e., pounds sterling.

said, this was Mr. Hyde's, but he was not at home; he had been in that night very late, but had gone away again in less than an hour; there was nothing strange in that; his habits were very irregular, and he was often absent; for instance, it was nearly two months since she had seen him till yesterday.

"Very well, then, we wish to see his rooms," said the lawyer; and when the woman began to declare it was impossible, "I had better tell you who this person is," he added. "This is Inspector Newcomen of Scotland Yard."

A flash of odious joy appeared upon the woman's face. "Ah!" said she, "he is in trouble! What has he done?"

Mr. Utterson and the inspector exchanged glances. "He don't seem a very popular character," observed the latter. "And now, my good woman, just let me and this gentleman have a look about us."

In the whole extent of the house, which but for the old woman remained otherwise empty, Mr. Hyde had only used a couple of rooms; but these were furnished with luxury and good taste. A closet was filled with wine; the plate was of silver, the napery[9] elegant; a good picture hung upon the walls, a gift (as Utterson supposed) from Henry Jekyll, who was much of a connoisseur; and the carpets were of many piles and agreeable in colour. At this moment, however, the rooms bore every mark of having been recently and hurriedly ransacked; clothes lay about the floor, with their pockets inside out; lock-fast drawers stood open; and on the hearth there lay a pile of gray ashes, as though many papers had been burned. From these embers the inspector disinterred the butt end of a green cheque book, which had resisted the action of the fire; the other half of the stick was found behind the door; and as this clinched his suspicions, the officer declared himself delighted. A visit to the bank, where several thousand pounds were found to be lying to the murderer's credit, completed his gratification.

"You may depend upon it, sir," he told Mr. Utterson: "I have him in my hand. He must have lost his head, or he never would have left the stick or, above all, burned the cheque book. Why, money's life to the man. We have nothing to do but wait for him at the bank, and get out the handbills."

This last, however, was not so easy of accomplishment; for Mr. Hyde had numbered few familiars—even the master of the servant maid had only seen him twice; his family could nowhere be traced; he had never been photographed; and the few who could describe him differed widely, as common observers will. Only on one point, were they agreed; and that was the haunting sense of unexpressed deformity with which the fugitive impressed his beholders.

Incident of the Letter

It was late in the afternoon, when Mr. Utterson found his way to Dr. Jekyll's door, where he was at once admitted by Poole, and carried down by the kitchen offices and across a yard which had once been a garden, to the building which was indifferently[1] known as the laboratory or the dissecting rooms. The doctor had bought the house from the heirs of a celebrated surgeon; and his own tastes being rather chemical than anatomical, had changed the destination[2] of the block at the bottom of the garden. It was the first time that the lawyer

9. Table linen.   2. Purpose.
1. Without distinction.

had been received in that part of his friend's quarters; and he eyed the dingy, windowless structure with curiosity, and gazed round with a distasteful sense of strangeness as he crossed the theatre,[3] once crowded with eager students and now lying gaunt and silent, the tables laden with chemical apparatus, the floor strewn with crates and littered with packing straw, and the light falling dimly through the foggy cupola. At the further end, a flight of stairs mounted to a door covered with red baize; and through this, Mr. Utterson was at last received into the doctor's cabinet.[4] It was a large room, fitted round with glass presses, furnished, among other things, with a cheval-glass[5] and a business table, and looking out upon the court by three dusty windows barred with iron. A fire burned in the grate; a lamp was set lighted on the chimney shelf, for even in the houses the fog began to lie thickly; and there, close up to the warmth, sat Dr. Jekyll, looking deadly sick. He did not rise to meet his visitor, but held out a cold hand and bade him welcome in a changed voice.

"And now," said Mr. Utterson, as soon as Poole had left them, "you have heard the news?"

The doctor shuddered. "They were crying it in the square," he said. "I heard them in my dining-room."

"One word," said the lawyer. "Carew was my client, but so are you, and I want to know what I am doing. You have not been mad enough to hide this fellow?"

"Utterson, I swear to God," cried the doctor, "I swear to God I will never set eyes on him again. I bind my honour to you that I am done with him in this world. It is all at an end. And indeed he does not want my help; you do not know him as I do; he is safe, he is quite safe; mark my words, he will never more be heard of."

The lawyer listened gloomily; he did not like his friend's feverish manner. "You seem pretty sure of him," said he; "and for your sake, I hope you may be right. If it came to a trial, your name might appear."

"I am quite sure of him," replied Jekyll; "I have grounds for certainty that I cannot share with anyone. But there is one thing on which you may advise me. I have—I have received a letter; and I am at a loss whether I should show it to the police. I should like to leave it in your hands, Utterson; you would judge wisely, I am sure; I have so great a trust in you."

"You fear, I suppose, that it might lead to his detection?" asked the lawyer.

"No," said the other. "I cannot say that I care what becomes of Hyde; I am quite done with him. I was thinking of my own character, which this hateful business has rather exposed."

Utterson ruminated awhile; he was surprised at his friend's selfishness, and yet relieved by it. "Well," said he, at last, "let me see the letter."

The letter was written in an odd, upright hand and signed "Edward Hyde": and it signified, briefly enough, that the writer's benefactor, Dr. Jekyll, whom he had long so unworthily repaid for a thousand generosities, need labour under no alarm for his safety, as he had means of escape on which he placed a sure dependence. The lawyer liked this letter well enough; it put a better colour on the intimacy than he had looked for; and he blamed himself for some of his past suspicions.

---

3. Room with tiers of rising seats surrounding a central platform, used for lectures and medical demonstrations.
4. Small private room. "Baize": coarse woolen material.
5. Large freestanding mirror, hinged on a frame. "Presses": cupboards with glass doors.

"Have you the envelope?" he asked.

"I burned it," replied Jekyll, "before I thought what I was about. But it bore no postmark. The note was handed in."

"Shall I keep this and sleep upon it?" asked Utterson.

"I wish you to judge for me entirely," was the reply. "I have lost confidence in myself."

"Well, I shall consider," returned the lawyer. "And now one word more: it was Hyde who dictated the terms in your will about that disappearance?"

The doctor seemed seized with a qualm of faintness; he shut his mouth tight and nodded.

"I knew it," said Utterson. "He meant to murder you. You have had a fine escape."

"I have had what is far more to the purpose," returned the doctor solemnly: "I have had a lesson—O God, Utterson, what a lesson I have had!" And he covered his face for a moment with his hands.

On his way out, the lawyer stopped and had a word or two with Poole. "By the bye," said he, "there was a letter handed in to-day: what was the messenger like?" But Poole was positive nothing had come except by post; "and only circulars by that," he added.

This news sent off the visitor with his fears renewed. Plainly the letter had come by the laboratory door; possibly, indeed, it had been written in the cabinet; and if that were so, it must be differently judged, and handled with the more caution. The newsboys, as he went, were crying themselves hoarse along the footways: "Special edition. Shocking murder of an M.P."[6] That was the funeral oration of one friend and client; and he could not help a certain apprehension lest the good name of another should be sucked down in the eddy of the scandal. It was, at least, a ticklish decision that he had to make; and self-reliant as he was by habit, he began to cherish a longing for advice. It was not to be had directly; but perhaps, he thought, it might be fished for.

Presently after, he sat on one side of his own hearth, with Mr. Guest, his head clerk, upon the other, and midway between, at a nicely calculated distance from the fire, a bottle of a particular old wine that had long dwelt unsunned in the foundations of his house. The fog still slept on the wing above the drowned city, where the lamps glimmered like carbuncles;[7] and through the muffle and smother of these fallen clouds, the procession of the town's life was still rolling in through the great arteries with a sound as of a mighty wind. But the room was gay with firelight. In the bottle the acids were long ago resolved; the imperial dye[8] had softened with time, as the colour grows richer in stained windows; and the glow of hot autumn afternoons on hillside vineyards, was ready to be set free and to disperse the fogs of London. Insensibly the lawyer melted. There was no man from whom he kept fewer secrets than Mr. Guest; and he was not always sure that he kept as many as he meant. Guest had often been on business to the doctor's; he knew Poole; he could scarce have failed to hear of Mr. Hyde's familiarity about the house; he might draw conclusions: was it not as well, then, that he should see a letter which put that mystery to rights? and above all since Guest, being a great student and critic of handwriting, would consider the step natural and obliging? The clerk, besides, was a man of counsel; he would scarce read so strange a doc-

6. Member of Parliament.
7. Precious fiery-red stones.
8. Purple.

ument without dropping a remark; and by that remark Mr. Utterson might shape his future course.

"This is a sad business about Sir Danvers," he said.

"Yes, sir, indeed. It has elicited a great deal of public feeling," returned Guest. "The man, of course, was mad."

"I should like to hear your views on that," replied Utterson. "I have a document here in his handwriting; it is between ourselves, for I scarce know what to do about it; it is an ugly business at the best. But there it is; quite in your way: a murderer's autograph."

Guest's eyes brightened, and he sat down at once and studied it with passion. "No, sir," he said: "not mad; but it is an odd hand."

"And by all accounts a very odd writer," added the lawyer.

Just then the servant entered with a note.

"Is that from Dr. Jekyll, sir?" inquired the clerk. "I thought I knew the writing. Anything private, Mr. Utterson?"

"Only an invitation to dinner. Why? Do you want to see it?"

"One moment. I thank you, sir;" and the clerk laid the two sheets of paper alongside and sedulously compared their contents. "Thank you, sir," he said at last, returning both; "it's a very interesting autograph."

There was a pause, during which Mr. Utterson struggled with himself. "Why did you compare them, Guest?" he inquired suddenly.

"Well, sir," returned the clerk, "there's a rather singular resemblance; the two hands are in many points identical: only differently sloped."

"Rather quaint,"[9] said Utterson.

"It is, as you say, rather quaint," returned Guest.

"I wouldn't speak of this note, you know," said the master.

"No, sir," said the clerk. "I understand."

But no sooner was Mr. Utterson alone that night than he locked the note into his safe, where it reposed from that time forward. "What!" he thought. "Henry Jekyll forge for a murderer!" And his blood ran cold in his veins.

Remarkable Incident of Dr. Lanyon

Time ran on; thousands of pounds were offered in reward, for the death of Sir Danvers was resented as a public injury; but Mr. Hyde had disappeared out of the ken of the police as though he had never existed. Much of his past was unearthed, indeed, and all disreputable: tales came out of the man's cruelty, at once so callous and violent; of his vile life, of his strange associates, of the hatred that seemed to have surrounded his career; but of his present whereabouts, not a whisper. From the time he had left the house in Soho on the morning of the murder, he was simply blotted out; and gradually, as time drew on, Mr. Utterson began to recover from the hotness of his alarm, and to grow more at quiet with himself. The death of Sir Danvers was, to his way of thinking, more than paid for by the disappearance of Mr. Hyde. Now that that evil influence had been withdrawn, a new life began for Dr. Jekyll. He came out of his seclusion, renewed relations with his friends, became once more their familiar guest and entertainer; and whilst he had always been known for charities, he was now no less distinguished for religion. He was busy, he was much in the open air, he did good; his face seemed to open and brighten, as

9. Odd, unusual.

if with an inward consciousness of service; and for more than two months, the doctor was at peace.

On the 8th of January Utterson had dined at the doctor's with a small party; Lanyon had been there; and the face of the host had looked from one to the other as in the old days when the trio were inseparable friends. On the 12th, and again on the 14th, the door was shut against the lawyer. "The doctor was confined to the house," Poole said, "and saw no one." On the 15th, he tried again, and was again refused; and having now been used for the last two months to see his friend almost daily, he found this return of solitude to weigh upon his spirits. The fifth night he had in Guest to dine with him; and the sixth he betook himself to Dr. Lanyon's.

There at least he was not denied admittance; but when he came in, he was shocked at the change which had taken place in the doctor's appearance. He had his death-warrant written legibly upon his face. The rosy man had grown pale; his flesh had fallen away; he was visibly balder and older; and yet it was not so much these tokens of a swift physical decay that arrested the lawyer's notice, as a look in the eye and quality of manner that seemed to testify to some deep-seated terror of the mind. It was unlikely that the doctor should fear death; and yet that was what Utterson was tempted to suspect. "Yes," he thought; "he is a doctor, he must know his own state and that his days are counted; and the knowledge is more than he can bear." And yet when Utterson remarked on his ill-looks, it was with an air of great firmness that Lanyon declared himself a doomed man.

"I have had a shock," he said, "and I shall never recover. It is a question of weeks. Well, life has been pleasant; I liked it; yes, sir, I used to like it. I sometimes think if we knew all, we should be more glad to get away."

"Jekyll is ill, too," observed Utterson. "Have you seen him?"

But Lanyon's face changed, and he held up a trembling hand. "I wish to see or hear no more of Dr. Jekyll," he said in a loud, unsteady voice. "I am quite done with that person; and I beg that you will spare me any allusion to one whom I regard as dead."

"Tut-tut," said Mr. Utterson; and then after a considerable pause, "Can't I do anything?" he inquired. "We are three very old friends, Lanyon; we shall not live to make others."

"Nothing can be done," returned Lanyon; "ask himself."

"He will not see me," said the lawyer.

"I am not surprised at that," was the reply. "Some day, Utterson, after I am dead, you may perhaps come to learn the right and wrong of this. I cannot tell you. And in the meantime, if you can sit and talk with me of other things, for God's sake, stay and do so; but if you cannot keep clear of this accursed topic, then, in God's name, go, for I cannot bear it."

As soon as he got home, Utterson sat down and wrote to Jekyll, complaining of his exclusion from the house, and asking the cause of this unhappy break with Lanyon; and the next day brought him a long answer, often very pathetically worded, and sometimes darkly mysterious in drift. The quarrel with Lanyon was incurable. "I do not blame our old friend," Jekyll wrote, "but I share his view that we must never meet. I mean from henceforth to lead a life of extreme seclusion; you must not be surprised, nor must you doubt my friendship, if my door is often shut even to you. You must suffer me to go my own dark way. I have brought on myself a punishment and a danger that I cannot name. If I am the chief of sinners, I am the chief of sufferers also. I could not think that this earth contained a place for sufferings and terrors so unmanning; and you can do but one thing, Utterson, to lighten this destiny, and that is to respect my silence." Utterson was amazed; the dark influence of Hyde had been withdrawn, the doctor had returned to his old tasks and amities; a week ago, the prospect had smiled with every promise of a cheerful and an honoured age; and now in a moment, friendship, and peace of mind, and the whole tenor of his life were wrecked. So great and unprepared a change pointed to madness; but in view of Lanyon's manner and words, there must lie for it some deeper ground.

A week afterwards Dr. Lanyon took to his bed, and in something less than a fortnight he was dead. The night after the funeral, at which he had been sadly affected, Utterson locked the door of his business room, and sitting there by the light of a melancholy candle, drew out and set before him an envelope addressed by the hand and sealed with the seal of his dead friend. "PRIVATE: for the hands of G. J. Utterson ALONE, and in case of his predecease *to be destroyed unread*," so it was emphatically superscribed; and the lawyer dreaded to behold the contents. "I have buried one friend today," he thought: "what if this should cost me another?" And then he condemned the fear as a disloyalty, and broke the seal. Within there was another enclosure, likewise sealed, and marked upon the cover as "not to be opened till the death or disappearance of Dr. Henry Jekyll." Utterson could not trust his eyes. Yes, it was disappearance; here again, as in the mad will which he had long ago restored to its author, here again were the idea of a disappearance and the name of Henry Jekyll bracketted. But in the will, that idea had sprung from the sinister suggestion of the man Hyde; it was set there with a purpose all too plain and horrible. Written by the hand of Lanyon, what should it mean? A great curiosity came on the trustee, to disregard the prohibition and dive at once to the bottom of these mysteries; but professional honour and faith to his dead friend were stringent obligations; and the packet slept in the inmost corner of his private safe.

It is one thing to mortify curiosity, another to conquer it; and it may be doubted if, from that day forth, Utterson desired the society of his surviving friend with the same eagerness. He thought of him kindly; but his thoughts were disquieted and fearful. He went to call indeed; but he was perhaps relieved to be denied admittance; perhaps, in his heart, he preferred to speak with Poole upon the doorstep and surrounded by the air and sounds of the open city, rather than to be admitted into that house of voluntary bondage, and to sit and speak with its inscrutable recluse. Poole had, indeed, no very pleasant news to communicate. The doctor, it appeared, now more than ever confined himself to the cabinet over the laboratory, where he would sometimes even sleep; he was out of spirits, he had grown very silent, he did not read; it seemed as if he had something on his mind. Utterson became so used to the unvarying character of these reports, that he fell off little by little in the frequency of his visits.

Incident at the Window

It chanced on Sunday, when Mr. Utterson was on his usual walk with Mr. Enfield, that their way lay once again through the by-street; and that when they came in front of the door, both stopped to gaze on it.

"Well," said Enfield, "that story's at an end at least. We shall never see more of Mr. Hyde."

"I hope not," said Utterson. "Did I ever tell you that I once saw him, and shared your feeling of repulsion?"

"It was impossible to do the one without the other," returned Enfield. "And by the way, what an ass you must have thought me, not to know that this was a back way to Dr. Jekyll's! It was partly your own fault that I found it out, even when I did."

"So you found it out, did you?" said Utterson. "But if that be so, we may step into the court and take a look at the windows. To tell you the truth, I am uneasy about poor Jekyll; and even outside, I feel as if the presence of a friend might do him good."

The court was very cool and a little damp, and full of premature twilight, although the sky, high up overhead, was still bright with sunset. The middle one of the three windows was half way open; and sitting close beside it, taking the air with an infinite sadness of mien, like some disconsolate prisoner, Utterson saw Dr. Jekyll.

"What! Jekyll!" he cried. "I trust you are better."

"I am very low, Utterson," replied the doctor, drearily, "very low. It will not last long, thank God."

"You stay too much indoors," said the lawyer. "You should be out, whipping up the circulation like Mr. Enfield and me. (This is my cousin—Mr. Enfield—Dr. Jekyll.) Come now; get your hat and take a quick turn with us."

"You are very good," sighed the other. "I should like to very much; but no, no, no, it is quite impossible; I dare not. But indeed, Utterson, I am very glad to see you; this is really a great pleasure; I would ask you and Mr. Enfield up, but the place is really not fit."

"Why then," said the lawyer, good-naturedly, "the best thing we can do is to stay down here and speak with you from where we are."

"That is just what I was about to venture to propose," returned the doctor with a smile. But the words were hardly uttered, before the smile was struck out of his face and succeeded by an expression of such abject terror and despair, as froze the very blood of the two gentlemen below. They saw it but for a glimpse, for the window was instantly thrust down; but that glimpse had been sufficient, and they turned and left the court without a word. In silence, too, they traversed the by-street; and it was not until they had come into a neighbouring thoroughfare, where even upon a Sunday there were still some stirrings of life, that Mr. Utterson at last turned and looked at his companion. They were both pale; and there was an answering horror in their eyes.

"God forgive us, God forgive us," said Mr. Utterson.

But Mr. Enfield only nodded his head very seriously, and walked on once more in silence.

The Last Night

Mr. Utterson was sitting by his fireside one evening after dinner, when he was surprised to receive a visit from Poole.

"Bless me, Poole, what brings you here?" he cried; and then taking a second look at him, "What ails you?" he added; "is the doctor ill?"

"Mr. Utterson," said the man, "there is something wrong."

"Take a seat, and here is a glass of wine for you," said the lawyer. "Now, take your time, and tell me plainly what you want."

"You know the doctor's ways, sir," replied Poole, "and how he shuts himself up. Well, he's shut up again in the cabinet; and I don't like it, sir—I wish I may die if I like it. Mr. Utterson, sir, I'm afraid."

"Now, my good man," said the lawyer, "be explicit. What are you afraid of?"

"I've been afraid for about a week," returned Poole, doggedly disregarding the question, "and I can bear it no more."

The man's appearance amply bore out his words; his manner was altered for the worse; and except for the moment when he had first announced his terror, he had not once looked the lawyer in the face. Even now, he sat with the glass of wine untasted on his knee, and his eyes directed to a corner of the floor. "I can bear it no more," he repeated.

"Come," said the lawyer, "I see you have some good reason, Poole; I see there is something seriously amiss. Try to tell me what it is."

"I think there's been foul play," said Poole, hoarsely.

"Foul play!" cried the lawyer, a good deal frightened and rather inclined to be irritated in consequence. "What foul play? What does the man mean?"

"I daren't say, sir," was the answer; "but will you come along with me and see for yourself?"

Mr. Utterson's only answer was to rise and get his hat and great coat; but he observed with wonder the greatness of the relief that appeared upon the butler's face, and perhaps with no less, that the wine was still untasted when he set it down to follow.

It was a wild, cold, seasonable night of March, with a pale moon, lying on her back as though the wind had tilted her, and a flying wrack of the most diaphanous and lawny[1] texture. The wind made talking difficult, and flecked the blood into the face. It seemed to have swept the streets unusually bare of passengers, besides; for Mr. Utterson thought he had never seen that part of London so deserted. He could have wished it otherwise; never in his life had he been conscious of so sharp a wish to see and touch his fellow-creatures; for struggle as he might, there was born in upon his mind a crushing antici-pation of calamity. The square, when they got there, was all full of wind and dust, and the thin trees in the garden were lashing themselves along the railing. Poole, who had kept all the way a pace or two ahead, now pulled up in the middle of the pavement, and in spite of the biting weather, took off his hat and mopped his brow with a red pocket-handkerchief. But for all the hurry of his coming, these were not the dews of exertion that he wiped away, but the moisture of some strangling anguish; for his face was white and his voice, when he spoke, harsh and broken.

"Well, sir," he said, "here we are, and God grant there be nothing wrong."

"Amen, Poole," said the lawyer.

Thereupon the servant knocked in a very guarded manner; the door was opened on the chain; and a voice asked from within, "Is that you, Poole?"

"It's all right," said Poole. "Open the door."

The hall, when they entered it, was brightly lighted up; the fire was built high; and about the hearth the whole of the servants, men and women, stood huddled together like a flock of sheep. At the sight of Mr. Utterson, the house-maid broke into hysterical whimpering; and the cook, crying out "Bless God!

---

1. Of fine linen. "Wrack": i.e., rack, a mass of high clouds driven by the wind.

it's Mr. Utterson," ran forward as if to take him in her arms.

"What, what? Are you all here?" said the lawyer peevishly. "Very irregular, very unseemly; your master would be far from pleased."

"They're all afraid," said Poole.

Blank silence followed, no one protesting; only the maid lifted up her voice and now wept loudly.

"Hold your tongue!" Poole said to her, with a ferocity of accent that testified to his own jangled nerves; and indeed, when the girl had so suddenly raised the note of her lamentation, they had all started and turned towards the inner door with faces of dreadful expectation. "And now," continued the butler, addressing the knife-boy, "reach me a candle, and we'll get this through hands² at once." And then he begged Mr. Utterson to follow him, and led the way to the back garden.

"Now, sir," said he, "you come as gently as you can. I want you to hear, and I don't want you to be heard. And see here, sir, if by any chance he was to ask you in, don't go."

Mr. Utterson's nerves, at this unlooked-for termination, gave a jerk that nearly threw him from his balance; but he recollected his courage and followed the butler into the laboratory building and through the surgical theatre, with its lumber³ of crates and bottles, to the foot of the stair. Here Poole motioned him to stand on one side and listen; while he himself, setting down the candle and making a great and obvious call on his resolution, mounted the steps and knocked with a somewhat uncertain hand on the red baize of the cabinet door.

"Mr. Utterson, sir, asking to see you," he called; and even as he did so, once more violently signed to the lawyer to give ear.

A voice answered from within: "Tell him I cannot see anyone," it said complainingly.

"Thank you, sir," said Poole, with a note of something like triumph in his voice; and taking up his candle, he led Mr. Utterson back across the yard and into the great kitchen, where the fire was out and the beetles were leaping on the floor.

"Sir," he said, looking Mr. Utterson in the eyes, "was that my master's voice?"

"It seems much changed," replied the lawyer, very pale, but giving look for look.

"Changed? Well, yes, I think so," said the butler. "Have I been twenty years in this man's house, to be deceived about his voice? No, sir; master's made away with; he was made away with, eight days ago, when we heard him cry out upon the name of God; and *who's* in there instead of him, and *why* it stays there, is a thing that cries to Heaven, Mr. Utterson!"

"This is a very strange tale, Poole; this is rather a wild tale, my man," said Mr. Utterson, biting his finger. "Suppose it were as you suppose, supposing Dr. Jekyll to have been—well, murdered, what could induce the murderer to stay? That won't hold water; it doesn't commend itself to reason."

"Well, Mr. Utterson, you are a hard man to satisfy, but I'll do it yet," said Poole. "All this last week (you must know) him, or it, or whatever it is that lives in that cabinet, has been crying night and day for some sort of medicine and cannot get it to his mind. It was sometimes his way—the master's, that is—to write his orders on a sheet of paper and throw it on the stair. We've

2. We'll deal with this.   3. Stored accumulation.

had nothing else this week back; nothing but papers, and a closed door, and the very meals left there to be smuggled in when nobody was looking. Well, sir, every day, ay, and twice and thrice in the same day, there have been orders and complaints, and I have been sent flying to all the wholesale chemists in town. Every time I brought the stuff back, there would be another paper telling me to return it, because it was not pure, and another order to a different firm. This drug is wanted bitter bad, sir, whatever for."

"Have you any of these papers?" asked Mr. Utterson.

Poole felt in his pocket and handed out a crumpled note, which the lawyer, bending nearer to the candle, carefully examined. Its contents ran thus: "Dr. Jekyll presents his compliments to Messrs. Maw. He assures them that their last sample is impure and quite useless for his present purpose. In the year 18—, Dr. J. purchased a somewhat large quantity from Messrs. M. He now begs them to search with the most sedulous care, and should any of the same quality be left, to forward it to him at once. Expense is no consideration. The importance of this to Dr. J. can hardly be exaggerated." So far the letter had run composedly enough, but here with a sudden splutter of the pen, the writer's emotion had broken loose. "For God's sake," he had added, "find me some of the old."

"This is a strange note," said Mr. Utterson; and then sharply, "How do you come to have it open?"

"The man at Maw's was main angry, sir, and he threw it back to me like so much dirt," returned Poole.

"This is unquestionably the doctor's hand, do you know?" resumed the lawyer.

"I thought it looked like it," said the servant rather sulkily; and then, with another voice, "But what matters hand of write?" he said. "I've seen him!"

"Seen him?" repeated Mr. Utterson. "Well?"

"That's it!" said Poole. "It was this way. I came suddenly into the theatre from the garden. It seems he had slipped out to look for this drug or whatever it is; for the cabinet door was open, and there he was at the far end of the room digging among the crates. He looked up when I came in, gave a kind of cry, and whipped upstairs into the cabinet. It was but for one minute that I saw him, but the hair stood upon my head like quills. Sir, if that was my master, why had he a mask upon his face? If it was my master, why did he cry out like a rat, and run from me? I have served him long enough. And then . . ." The man paused and passed his hand over his face.

"These are all very strange circumstances," said Mr. Utterson, "but I think I begin to see daylight. Your master, Poole, is plainly seized with one of those maladies that both torture and deform the sufferer; hence, for aught I know, the alteration of his voice; hence the mask and the avoidance of his friends; hence his eagerness to find this drug, by means of which the poor soul retains some hope of ultimate recovery—God grant that he be not deceived! There is my explanation; it is sad enough, Poole, ay, and appalling to consider; but it is plain and natural, hangs well together, and delivers us from all exorbitant alarms."

"Sir," said the butler, turning to a sort of mottled pallor, "that thing was not my master, and there's the truth. My master"—here he looked round him and began to whisper—"is a tall, fine build of a man, and this was more of a dwarf." Utterson attempted to protest. "O, sir," cried Poole, "do you think I do not know my master after twenty years? Do you think I do not know where his head comes to in the cabinet door, where I saw him every morning of my life? No, sir, that thing in the mask was never Dr. Jekyll—God knows what it was, but it was never Dr. Jekyll; and it is the belief of my heart that there was murder done."

"Poole," replied the lawyer, "if you say that, it will become my duty to make certain. Much as I desire to spare your master's feelings, much as I am puzzled by this note which seems to prove him to be still alive, I shall consider it my duty to break in that door."

"Ah, Mr. Utterson, that's talking!" cried the butler.

"And now comes the second question," resumed Utterson: "Who is going to do it?"

"Why, you and me," was the undaunted reply.

"That's very well said," returned the lawyer; "and whatever comes of it, I shall make it my business to see you are no loser."

"There is an axe in the theatre," continued Poole; "and you might take the kitchen poker for yourself."

The lawyer took that rude but weighty instrument into his hand, and balanced it. "Do you know, Poole," he said, looking up, "that you and I are about to place ourselves in a position of some peril?"

"You may say so, sir, indeed," returned the butler.

"It is well, then, that we should be frank," said the other. "We both think more than we have said; let us make a clean breast. This masked figure that you saw, did you recognise it?"

"Well, sir, it went so quick, and the creature was so doubled up, that I could hardly swear to that," was the answer. "But if you mean, was it Mr. Hyde?— why, yes, I think it was! You see, it was much of the same bigness; and it had the same quick, light way with it; and then who else could have got in by the laboratory door? You have not forgot, sir, that at the time of the murder he had still the key with him? But that's not all. I don't know, Mr. Utterson, if ever you met this Mr. Hyde?"

"Yes," said the lawyer, "I once spoke with him."

"Then you must know as well as the rest of us that there was something queer about that gentleman—something that gave a man a turn—I don't know rightly how to say it, sir, beyond this: that you felt it in your marrow kind of cold and thin."

"I own I felt something of what you describe," said Mr. Utterson.

"Quite so, sir," returned Poole. "Well, when that masked thing like a monkey jumped from among the chemicals and whipped into the cabinet, it went down my spine like ice. O, I know it's not evidence, Mr. Utterson; I'm book-learned enough for that; but a man has his feelings, and I give you my bible-word it was Mr. Hyde!"

"Ay, ay," said the lawyer. "My fears incline to the same point. Evil, I fear, founded—evil was sure to come—of that connection. Ay, truly, I believe you; I believe poor Harry is killed; and I believe his murderer (for what purpose, God alone can tell) is still lurking in his victim's room. Well, let our name be vengeance. Call Bradshaw."

The footman came at the summons, very white and nervous.

"Pull yourself together, Bradshaw," said the lawyer. "This suspense, I know, is telling upon all of you; but it is now our intention to make an end of it. Poole, here, and I are going to force our way into the cabinet. If all is well, my shoulders are broad enough to bear the blame. Meanwhile, lest anything should really be amiss, or any malefactor seek to escape by the back, you and the boy must go round the corner with a pair of good sticks and take your post at the laboratory door. We give you ten minutes, to get to your stations."

As Bradshaw left, the lawyer looked at his watch. "And now, Poole, let us get to ours," he said; and taking the poker under his arm, led the way into the yard. The scud[4] had banked over the moon, and it was now quite dark. The wind, which only broke in puffs and draughts into that deep well of building, tossed the light of the candle to and fro about their steps, until they came into the shelter of the theatre, where they sat down silently to wait. London hummed solemnly all around; but nearer at hand, the stillness was only broken by the sounds of a footfall moving to and fro along the cabinet floor.

"So it will walk all day, sir," whispered Poole; "ay, and the better part of the night. Only when a new sample comes from the chemist, there's a bit of a break. Ah, it's an ill-conscience that's such an enemy to rest! Ah, sir, there's blood foully shed in every step of it! But hark again, a little closer—put your heart in your ears, Mr. Utterson, and tell me, is that the doctor's foot?"

The steps fell lightly and oddly, with a certain swing, for all they went so slowly; it was different indeed from the heavy creaking tread of Henry Jekyll. Utterson sighed. "Is there never anything else?" he asked.

Poole nodded. "Once," he said. "Once I heard it weeping!"

"Weeping? how that?" said the lawyer, conscious of a sudden chill of horror.

"Weeping like a woman or a lost soul," said the butler. "I came away with that upon my heart, that I could have wept too."

But now the ten minutes drew to an end. Poole disinterred the axe from under a stack of packing straw; the candle was set upon the nearest table to light them to the attack; and they drew near with bated breath to where that patient foot was still going up and down, up and down, in the quiet of the night.

"Jekyll," cried Utterson, with a loud voice, "I demand to see you." He paused a moment, but there came no reply. "I give you fair warning, our suspicions are aroused, and I must and shall see you," he resumed; "if not by fair means, then by foul—if not of your consent, then by brute force!"

"Utterson," said the voice, "for God's sake, have mercy!"

"Ah, that's not Jekyll's voice—it's Hyde's!" cried Utterson. "Down with the door, Poole!"

Poole swung the axe over his shoulder; the blow shook the building, and the red baize door leaped against the lock and hinges. A dismal screech, as of mere animal terror, rang from the cabinet. Up went the axe again, and again the panels crashed and the frame bounded; four times the blow fell; but the wood was tough and the fittings were of excellent workmanship; and it was not until the fifth, that the lock burst in sunder and the wreck of the door fell inwards on the carpet.

The besiegers, appalled by their own riot and the stillness that had succeeded, stood back a little and peered in. There lay the cabinet before their eyes in the quiet lamplight, a good fire glowing and chattering on the hearth, the kettle singing its thin strain, a drawer or two open, papers neatly set forth on the business table, and nearer the fire, the things laid out for tea: the quietest room, you would have said, and, but for the glazed presses full of chemicals, the most commonplace that night in London.

4. Loose clouds driven rapidly before the wind.

Right in the midst there lay the body of a man sorely contorted and still twitching. They drew near on tip-toe, turned it on its back and beheld the face of Edward Hyde. He was dressed in clothes far too large for him, clothes of the doctor's bigness; the cords of his face still moved with a semblance of life, but life was quite gone: and by the crushed phial in the hand and the strong smell of kernels[5] that hung upon the air, Utterson knew that he was looking on the body of a self-destroyer.

"We have come too late," he said sternly, "whether to save or punish. Hyde is gone to his account; and it only remains for us to find the body of your master."

The far greater proportion of the building was occupied by the theatre, which filled almost the whole ground story and was lighted from above, and by the cabinet, which formed an upper story at one end and looked upon the court. A corridor joined the theatre to the door on the by-street; and with this the cabinet communicated separately by a second flight of stairs. There were besides a few dark closets and a spacious cellar. All these they now thoroughly examined. Each closet needed but a glance, for all were empty, and all, by the dust that fell from their doors, had stood long unopened. The cellar, indeed, was filled with crazy lumber, mostly dating from the times of the surgeon who was Jekyll's predecessor; but even as they opened the door they were advertised of the uselessness of further search, by the fall of a perfect mat of cobweb which had for years sealed up the entrance. Nowhere was there any trace of Henry Jekyll, dead or alive.

Poole stamped on the flags of the corridor. "He must be buried here," he said, hearkening to the sound.

"Or he may have fled," said Utterson, and he turned to examine the door in the by-street. It was locked; and lying near by on the flags, they found the key, already stained with rust.

"This does not look like use," observed the lawyer.

"Use!" echoed Poole. "Do you not see, sir, it is broken? much as if a man had stamped on it."

"Ay," continued Utterson, "and the fractures, too, are rusty." The two men looked at each other with a scare. "This is beyond me, Poole," said the lawyer. "Let us go back to the cabinet."

They mounted the stair in silence, and still with an occasional awestruck glance at the dead body, proceeded more thoroughly to examine the contents of the cabinet. At one table, there were traces of chemical work, various measured heaps of some white salt being laid on glass saucers, as though for an experiment in which the unhappy man had been prevented.

"That is the same drug that I was always bringing him," said Poole; and even as he spoke, the kettle with a startling noise boiled over.

This brought them to the fireside, where the easy-chair was drawn cosily up, and the tea things stood ready to the sitter's elbow, the very sugar in the cup. There were several books on a shelf; one lay beside the tea things open, and Utterson was amazed to find it a copy of a pious work, for which Jekyll had several times expressed a great esteem, annotated, in his own hand, with startling blasphemies.

Next, in the course of their review of the chamber, the searchers came to the cheval glass, into whose depths they looked with an involuntary horror.

---

5. I.e., pits: cyanide smells of bitter almond or of peach pits.

But it was so turned as to show them nothing but the rosy glow playing on the roof, the fire sparkling in a hundred repetitions along the glazed front of the presses, and their own pale and fearful countenances stooping to look in.

"This glass have seen some strange things, sir," whispered Poole.

"And surely none stranger than itself," echoed the lawyer in the same tones. "For what did Jekyll"—he caught himself up at the word with a start, and then conquering the weakness—"what could Jekyll want with it?" he said.

"You may say that!" said Poole.

Next they turned to the business table. On the desk, among the neat array of papers, a large envelope was uppermost, and bore, in the doctor's hand, the name of Mr. Utterson. The lawyer unsealed it, and several enclosures fell to the floor. The first was a will, drawn in the same eccentric terms as the one which he had returned six months before, to serve as a testament in case of death and as a deed of gift in case of disappearance; but in place of the name of Edward Hyde, the lawyer, with indescribable amazement, read the name of Gabriel John Utterson. He looked at Poole, and then back at the paper, and last of all at the dead malefactor stretched upon the carpet.

"My head goes round," he said. "He has been all these days in possession; he had no cause to like me; he must have raged to see himself displaced; and he has not destroyed this document."

He caught up the next paper; it was a brief note in the doctor's hand and dated at the top. "O Poole!" the lawyer cried, "he was alive and here this day. He cannot have been disposed of in so short a space; he must be still alive, he must have fled! And then, why fled? and how? and in that case, can we venture to declare this suicide? O, we must be careful. I foresee that we may yet involve your master in some dire catastrophe."

"Why don't you read it, sir?" asked Poole.

"Because I fear," replied the lawyer solemnly. "God grant I have no cause for it!" And with that he brought the paper to his eyes and read as follows:

"MY DEAR UTTERSON,—When this shall fall into your hands, I shall have disappeared, under what circumstances I have not the penetration to foresee, but my instinct and all the circumstances of my nameless situation tell me that the end is sure and must be early. Go then, and first read the narrative which Lanyon warned me he was to place in your hands; and if you care to hear more, turn to the confession of

"Your unworthy and unhappy friend,
                                                    "HENRY JEKYLL."

"There was a third enclosure?" asked Utterson.

"Here, sir," said Poole, and gave into his hands a considerable packet sealed in several places.

The lawyer put it in his pocket. "I would say nothing of this paper. If your master has fled or is dead, we may at least save his credit. It is now ten; I must go home and read these documents in quiet; but I shall be back before midnight, when we shall send for the police."

They went out, locking the door of the theatre behind them; and Utterson, once more leaving the servants gathered about the fire in the hall, trudged back to his office to read the two narratives in which this mystery was now to be explained.

Dr. Lanyon's Narrative

On the ninth of January, now four days ago, I received by the evening delivery a registered envelope, addressed in the hand of my colleague and old school-companion, Henry Jekyll. I was a good deal surprised by this; for we were by no means in the habit of correspondence; I had seen the man, dined with him, indeed, the night before; and I could imagine nothing in our intercourse that should justify formality of registration. The contents increased my wonder; for this is how the letter ran:

"10th December, 18—

"DEAR LANYON,—You are one of my oldest friends; and although we may have differed at times on scientific questions, I cannot remember, at least on my side, any break in our affection. There was never a day when, if you had said to me, 'Jekyll, my life, my honour, my reason, depend upon you,' I would not have sacrificed my left hand to help you. Lanyon, my life, my honour, my reason, are all at your mercy; if you fail me to-night I am lost. You might suppose, after this preface, that I am going to ask you for something dishonourable to grant. Judge for yourself.

"I want you to postpone all other engagements for to-night—ay, even if you were summoned to the bedside of an emperor; to take a cab, unless your carriage should be actually at the door; and with this letter in your hand for consultation, to drive straight to my house. Poole, my butler, has his orders; you will find him waiting your arrival with a locksmith. The door of my cabinet is then to be forced: and you are to go in alone; to open the glazed press (letter E) on the left hand, breaking the lock if it be shut; and to draw out, *with all its contents as they stand*, the fourth drawer from the top or (which is the same thing) the third from the bottom. In my extreme distress of mind, I have a morbid fear of misdirecting you; but even if I am in error, you may know the right drawer by its contents: some powders, a phial and a paper book. This drawer I beg of you to carry back with you to Cavendish Square exactly as it stands.

"That is the first part of the service: now for the second. You should be back, if you set out at once on the receipt of this, long before midnight; but I will leave you that amount of margin, not only in the fear of one of those obstacles that can neither be prevented nor foreseen, but because an hour when your servants are in bed is to be preferred for what will then remain to do. At midnight, then, I have to ask you to be alone in your consulting room, to admit with your own hand into the house a man who will present himself in my name, and to place in his hands the drawer that you will have brought with you from my cabinet. Then you will have played your part and earned my gratitude completely. Five minutes afterwards, if you insist upon an explanation, you will have understood that these arrangements are of capital importance; and that by the neglect of one of them, fantastic as they must appear, you might have charged your conscience with my death or the shipwreck of my reason.

"Confident as I am that you will not trifle with this appeal, my heart sinks and my hand trembles at the bare thought of such a possibility. Think of me at this hour, in a strange place, labouring under a blackness of distress that no fancy can exaggerate, and yet well aware that, if you will but punctually serve me, my troubles will roll away like a story that is told. Serve me, my dear Lanyon, and save

"Your friend,
H. J."

"P. S.—I had already sealed this up when a fresh terror struck upon my soul. It is possible that the post-office may fail me, and this letter not come into your hands until to-morrow morning. In that case, dear Lanyon, do my errand when it shall be most convenient for you in the course of the day; and once more expect my messenger at midnight. It may then already be too late; and if that night passes without event, you will know that you have seen the last of Henry Jekyll."

Upon the reading of this letter, I made sure my colleague was insane; but till that was proved beyond the possibility of doubt, I felt bound to do as he requested. The less I understood of this farrago,[6] the less I was in a position to judge of its importance; and an appeal so worded could not be set aside without a grave responsibility. I rose accordingly from table, got into a hansom, and drove straight to Jekyll's house. The butler was awaiting my arrival; he had received by the same post as mine a registered letter of instruction, and had sent at once for a locksmith and a carpenter. The tradesmen came while we were yet speaking; and we moved in a body to old Dr. Denman's surgical theatre, from which (as you are doubtless aware) Jekyll's private cabinet is most conveniently entered. The door was very strong, the lock excellent; the carpenter avowed he would have great trouble and have to do much damage, if force were to be used; and the locksmith was near despair. But this last was a handy fellow, and after two hours' work, the door stood open. The press marked E was unlocked; and I took out the drawer, had it filled up with straw and tied in a sheet, and returned with it to Cavendish Square.

Here I proceeded to examine its contents. The powders were neatly enough made up, but not with the nicety of the dispensing chemist; so that it was plain they were of Jekyll's private manufacture: and when I opened one of the wrappers I found what seemed to me a simple crystalline salt of a white colour. The phial, to which I next turned my attention, might have been about half full of a blood-red liquor, which was highly pungent to the sense of smell and seemed to me to contain phosphorus and some volatile ether. At the other ingredients I could make no guess. The book was an ordinary version book[7] and contained little but a series of dates. These covered a period of many years, but I observed that the entries ceased nearly a year ago and quite abruptly. Here and there a brief remark was appended to a date, usually no more than a single word: "double" occurring perhaps six times in a total of several hundred entries; and once very early in the list and followed by several marks of exclamation, "total failure!!!" All this, though it whetted my curiosity, told me little that was definite. Here were a phial of some tincture, a paper of some salt, and the record of a series of experiments that had led (like too many of Jekyll's investigations) to no end of practical usefulness. How could the presence of these articles in my house affect either the honour, the sanity, or the life of my flighty colleague? If his messenger could go to one place, why could he not go to another? And even granting some impediment, why was

---

6. Mixture.

7. School notebook used to record translations.

this gentleman to be received by me in secret? The more I reflected the more convinced I grew that I was dealing with a case of cerebral disease; and though I dismissed my servants to bed, I loaded an old revolver, that I might be found in some posture of self-defence.

Twelve o'clock had scarce rung out over London, ere the knocker sounded very gently on the door. I went myself at the summons, and found a small man crouching against the pillars of the portico.

"Are you come from Dr. Jekyll?" I asked.

He told me "yes" by a constrained gesture; and when I had bidden him enter, he did not obey me without a searching backward glance into the darkness of the square. There was a policeman not far off, advancing with his bull's eye[8] open; and at the sight, I thought my visitor started and made greater haste.

These particulars struck me, I confess, disagreeably; and as I followed him into the bright light of the consulting room, I kept my hand ready on my weapon. Here, at last, I had a chance of clearly seeing him. I had never set eyes on him before, so much was certain. He was small, as I have said; I was struck besides with the shocking expression of his face, with his remarkable combination of great muscular activity and great apparent debility of constitution, and—last but not least—with the odd, subjective disturbance caused by his neighbourhood. This bore some resemblance to incipient rigour,[9] and was accompanied by a marked sinking of the pulse. At the time, I set it down to some idiosyncratic, personal distaste, and merely wondered at the acuteness of the symptoms; but I have since had reason to believe the cause to lie much deeper in the nature of man, and to turn on some nobler hinge than the principle of hatred.

This person (who had thus, from the first moment of his entrance, struck in me what I can only describe as a disgustful curiosity) was dressed in a fashion that would have made an ordinary person laughable; his clothes, that is to say, although they were of rich and sober fabric, were enormously too large for him in every measurement—the trousers hanging on his legs and rolled up to keep them from the ground, the waist of the coat below his haunches, and the collar sprawling wide upon his shoulders. Strange to relate, this ludicrous accoutrement was far from moving me to laughter. Rather, as there was something abnormal and misbegotten in the very essence of the creature that now faced me—something seizing,[1] surprising and revolting—this fresh disparity seemed but to fit in with and to reinforce it; so that to my interest in the man's nature and character, there was added a curiosity as to his origin, his life, his fortune and status in the world.

These observations, though they have taken so great a space to be set down in, were yet the work of a few seconds. My visitor was, indeed, on fire with sombre excitement.

"Have you got it?" he cried. "Have you got it?" And so lively was his impatience that he even laid his hand upon my arm and sought to shake me.

I put him back, conscious at his touch of a certain icy pang along my blood. "Come, sir," said I. "You forget that I have not yet the pleasure of your acquaintance. Be seated, if you please." And I showed him an example, and sat down myself in my customary seat and with as fair an imitation of my ordinary manner to a patient, as the lateness of the hour, the nature of my preoccu-

8. Sliding door of his lantern.
9. Sudden chill.
1. Powerfully impressive.

pations, and the horror I had of my visitor, would suffer me to muster.

"I beg your pardon, Dr. Lanyon," he replied civilly enough. "What you say is very well founded; and my impatience has shown its heels to my politeness. I come here at the instance[2] of your colleague, Dr. Henry Jekyll, on a piece of business of some moment; and I understood . . ." He paused and put his hand to his throat, and I could see, in spite of his collected manner, that he was wrestling against the approaches of the hysteria—"I understood, a drawer . . ."

But here I took pity on my visitor's suspense, and some perhaps on my own growing curiosity.

"There it is, sir," said I, pointing to the drawer, where it lay on the floor behind a table and still covered with the sheet.

He sprang to it, and then paused, and laid his hand upon his heart: I could hear his teeth grate with the convulsive action of his jaws; and his face was so ghastly to see that I grew alarmed both for his life and reason.

"Compose yourself," said I.

He turned a dreadful smile to me, and as if with the decision of despair, plucked away the sheet. At sight of the contents, he uttered one loud sob of such immense relief that I sat petrified. And the next moment, in a voice that was already fairly well under control, "Have you a graduated[3] glass?" he asked.

I rose from my place with something of an effort and gave him what he asked.

He thanked me with a smiling nod, measured out a few minims[4] of the red tincture and added one of the powders. The mixture, which was at first of a reddish hue, began, in proportion as the crystals melted, to brighten in colour, to effervesce audibly, and to throw off small fumes of vapour. Suddenly and at the same moment, the ebullition[5] ceased and the compound changed to a dark purple, which faded again more slowly to a watery green. My visitor, who had watched these metamorphoses with a keen eye, smiled, set down the glass upon the table, and then turned and looked upon me with an air of scrutiny.

"And now," said he, "to settle what remains. Will you be wise? will you be guided? will you suffer me to take this glass in my hand and to go forth from your house without further parley? or has the greed of curiosity too much command of you? Think before you answer, for it shall be done as you decide. As you decide, you shall be left as you were before, and neither richer nor wiser, unless the sense of service rendered to a man in mortal distress may be counted as a kind of riches of the soul. Or, if you shall so prefer to choose, a new province of knowledge and new avenues to fame and power shall be laid open to you, here, in this room, upon the instant; and your sight shall be blasted by a prodigy to stagger the unbelief of Satan."

"Sir," said I, affecting a coolness that I was far from truly possessing, "you speak enigmas, and you will perhaps not wonder that I hear you with no very strong impression of belief. But I have gone too far in the way of inexplicable services to pause before I see the end."

"It is well," replied my visitor. "Lanyon, you remember your vows: what follows is under the seal of our profession. And now, you who have so long been bound to the most narrow and material views, you who have denied the virtue of transcendental medicine, you who have derided your superiors—behold!"

2. Request.
3. Marked with lines to indicate quantities.
4. Drops (a minim is a liquid measure equal to

$\frac{1}{480}$th of an ounce).
5. Bubbling.

He put the glass to his lips and drank at one gulp. A cry followed; he reeled, staggered, clutched at the table and held on, staring with injected[6] eyes, gasping with open mouth; and as I looked there came, I thought, a change—he seemed to swell—his face became suddenly black and the features seemed to melt and alter—and the next moment, I had sprung to my feet and leaped back against the wall, my arm raised to shield me from that prodigy, my mind submerged in terror.

"O God!" I screamed, and "O God!" again and again; for there before my eyes—pale and shaken, and half fainting, and groping before him with his hands, like a man restored from death—there stood Henry Jekyll!

What he told me in the next hour, I cannot bring my mind to set on paper. I saw what I saw, I heard what I heard, and my soul sickened at it; and yet now when that sight has faded from my eyes, I ask myself if I believe it, and I cannot answer. My life is shaken to its roots; sleep has left me; the deadliest terror sits by me at all hours of the day and night; I feel that my days are numbered, and that I must die; and yet I shall die incredulous. As for the moral turpitude that man unveiled to me, even with tears of penitence, I cannot, even in memory, dwell on it without a start of horror. I will say but one thing, Utterson, and that (if you can bring your mind to credit it) will be more than enough. The creature who crept into my house that night was, on Jekyll's own confession, known by the name of Hyde and hunted for in every corner of the land as the murderer of Carew.

HASTIE LANYON.

Henry Jekyll's Full Statement of the Case

I was born in the year 18— to a large fortune, endowed besides with excellent parts,[7] inclined by nature to industry, fond of the respect of the wise and good among my fellow-men, and thus, as might have been supposed, with every guarantee of an honourable and distinguished future. And indeed the worst of my faults was a certain impatient gaiety of disposition, such as has made the happiness of many, but such as I found it hard to reconcile with my imperious desire to carry my head high, and wear a more than commonly grave countenance before the public. Hence it came about that I concealed my pleasures; and that when I reached years of reflection, and began to look round me and take stock of my progress and position in the world, I stood already committed to a profound duplicity of life. Many a man would have even blazoned such irregularities as I was guilty of; but from the high views that I had set before me, I regarded and hid them with an almost morbid sense of shame. It was thus rather the exacting nature of my aspirations than any particular degradation in my faults, that made me what I was, and, with even a deeper trench than in the majority of men, severed in me those provinces of good and ill which divide and compound man's dual nature. In this case, I was driven to reflect deeply and inveterately on that hard law of life, which lies at the root of religion and is one of the most plentiful springs of distress. Though so profound a double-dealer, I was in no sense a hypocrite; both sides of me were in dead earnest; I was no more myself when I laid aside restraint and plunged

---

6. Swollen.   7. Abilities.

in shame, than when I laboured, in the eye of day, at the furtherance of knowledge or the relief of sorrow and suffering. And it chanced that the direction of my scientific studies, which led wholly towards the mystic and the transcendental, reacted and shed a strong light on this consciousness of the perennial war among my members. With every day, and from both sides of my intelligence, the moral and the intellectual, I thus drew steadily nearer to that truth, by whose partial discovery I have been doomed to such a dreadful shipwreck: that man is not truly one, but truly two. I say two, because the state of my own knowledge does not pass beyond that point. Others will follow, others will outstrip me on the same lines; and I hazard the guess that man will be ultimately known for a mere polity of multifarious, incongruous and independent denizens. I for my part, from the nature of my life, advanced infallibly in one direction and in one direction only. It was on the moral side, and in my own person, that I learned to recognise the thorough and primitive duality of man; I saw that, of the two natures that contended in the field of my consciousness, even if I could rightly be said to be either, it was only because I was radically both; and from an early date, even before the course of my scientific discoveries had begun to suggest the most naked possibility of such a miracle, I had learned to dwell with pleasure, as a beloved day-dream, on the thought of the separation of these elements. If each, I told myself, could but be housed in separate identities, life would be relieved of all that was unbearable; the unjust might go his way, delivered from the aspirations and remorse of his more upright twin; and the just could walk steadfastly and securely on his upward path, doing the good things in which he found his pleasure, and no longer exposed to disgrace and penitence by the hands of this extraneous evil. It was the curse of mankind that these incongruous faggots[8] were thus bound together—that in the agonised womb of consciousness, these polar twins should be continuously struggling. How, then, were they dissociated?

I was so far in my reflections when, as I have said, a side light began to shine upon the subject from the laboratory table. I began to perceive more deeply than it has ever yet been stated, the trembling immateriality, the mist-like transience, of this seemingly so solid body in which we walk attired. Certain agents I found to have the power to shake and to pluck back that fleshly vestment, even as a wind might toss the curtains of a pavilion. For two good reasons, I will not enter deeply into this scientific branch of my confession. First, because I have been made to learn that the doom and burthen of our life is bound forever on man's shoulders, and when the attempt is made to cast it off, it but returns upon us with more unfamiliar and more awful pressure. Second, because, as my narrative will make, alas! too evident, my discoveries were incomplete. Enough, then, that I not only recognised my natural body for the mere aura and effulgence of certain of the powers that made up my spirit, but managed to compound a drug by which these powers should be dethroned from their supremacy, and a second form and countenance substituted, none the less natural to me because they were the expression, and bore the stamp, of lower elements in my soul.

I hesitated long before I put this theory to the test of practice. I knew well that I risked death; for any drug that so potently controlled and shook the very fortress of identity, might by the least scruple[9] of an overdose or at the least

8. Bundles of sticks used for fuel.
9. A minute amount (literally, an apothecaries' weight equal to about 1.3 grams).

inopportunity in the moment of exhibition, utterly blot out that immaterial tabernacle which I looked to it to change. But the temptation of a discovery so singular and profound, at last overcame the suggestions of alarm. I had long since prepared my tincture; I purchased at once, from a firm of wholesale chemists, a large quantity of a particular salt which I knew, from my experiments, to be the last ingredient required; and late one accursed night, I compounded the elements, watched them boil and smoke together in the glass, and when the ebullition had subsided, with a strong glow of courage, drank off the potion.

The most racking pangs succeeded: a grinding in the bones, deadly nausea, and a horror of the spirit that cannot be exceeded at the hour of birth or death. Then these agonies began swiftly to subside, and I came to myself as if out of a great sickness. There was something strange in my sensations, something indescribably new and, from its very novelty, incredibly sweet. I felt younger, lighter, happier in body; within I was conscious of a heady recklessness, a current of disordered sensual images running like a mill race[1] in my fancy, a solution of the bonds of obligation, an unknown but not an innocent freedom of the soul. I knew myself, at the first breath of this new life, to be more wicked, tenfold more wicked, sold a slave to my original evil; and the thought, in that moment, braced and delighted me like wine. I stretched out my hands, exulting in the freshness of these sensations; and in the act, I was suddenly aware that I had lost in stature.

There was no mirror, at that date, in my room; that which stands beside me as I write, was brought there later on and for the very purpose of these transformations. The night, however, was far gone into the morning—the morning, black as it was, was nearly ripe for the conception of the day—the inmates of my house were locked in the most rigorous hours of slumber; and I determined, flushed as I was with hope and triumph, to venture in my new shape as far as to my bedroom. I crossed the yard, wherein the constellations looked down upon me, I could have thought, with wonder, the first creature of that sort that their unsleeping vigilance had yet disclosed to them; I stole through the corridors, a stranger in my own house; and coming to my room, I saw for the first time the appearance of Edward Hyde.

I must here speak by theory alone, saying not that which I know, but that which I suppose to be most probable. The evil side of my nature, to which I had now transferred the stamping efficacy, was less robust and less developed than the good which I had just deposed. Again, in the course of my life, which had been, after all, nine-tenths a life of effort, virtue and control, it had been much less exercised and much less exhausted. And hence, as I think, it came about that Edward Hyde was so much smaller, slighter and younger than Henry Jekyll. Even as good shone upon the countenance of the one, evil was written broadly and plainly on the face of the other. Evil besides (which I must still believe to be the lethal side of man) had left on that body an imprint of deformity and decay. And yet when I looked upon that ugly idol in the glass, I was conscious of no repugnance, rather of a leap of welcome. This, too, was myself. It seemed natural and human. In my eyes it bore a livelier image of the spirit, it seemed more express and single, than the imperfect and divided countenance I had been hitherto accustomed to call mine. And in so far I was

1. Water current that drives a mill wheel.

doubtless right. I have observed that when I wore the semblance of Edward Hyde, none could come near to me at first without a visible misgiving of the flesh. This, as I take it, was because all human beings, as we meet them, are commingled out of good and evil: and Edward Hyde, alone in the ranks of mankind, was pure evil.

I lingered but a moment at the mirror: the second and conclusive experiment had yet to be attempted; it yet remained to be seen if I had lost my identity beyond redemption and must flee before daylight from a house that was no longer mine; and hurrying back to my cabinet, I once more prepared and drank the cup, once more suffered the pangs of dissolution, and came to myself once more with the character, the stature and the face of Henry Jekyll.

That night I had come to the fatal cross roads. Had I approached my discovery in a more noble spirit, had I risked the experiment while under the empire of generous or pious aspirations, all must have been otherwise, and from these agonies of death and birth, I had come forth an angel instead of a fiend. The drug had no discriminating action; it was neither diabolical nor divine; it but shook the doors of the prison-house of my disposition; and like the captives of Philippi, that which stood within ran forth.[2] At that time my virtue slumbered; my evil, kept awake by ambition, was alert and swift to seize the occasion; and the thing that was projected was Edward Hyde. Hence, although I had now two characters as well as two appearances, one was wholly evil, and the other was still the old Henry Jekyll, that incongruous compound of whose reformation and improvement I had already learned to despair. The movement was thus wholly towards the worse.

Even at that time, I had not yet conquered my aversion to the dryness of a life of study. I would still be merrily disposed at times; and as my pleasures were (to say the least) undignified, and I was not only well known and highly considered, but growing towards the elderly man, this incoherency of my life was daily growing more unwelcome. It was on this side that my new power tempted me until I fell in slavery. I had but to drink the cup, to doff at once the body of the noted professor, and to assume, like a thick cloak, that of Edward Hyde. I smiled at the notion; it seemed to me at the time to be humorous; and I made my preparations with the most studious care. I took and furnished that house in Soho, to which Hyde was tracked by the police; and engaged as housekeeper a creature whom I well knew to be silent and unscrupulous. On the other side, I announced to my servants that a Mr. Hyde (whom I described) was to have full liberty and power about my house in the square; and to parry mishaps, I even called and made myself a familiar object, in my second character. I next drew up that will to which you so much objected; so that if anything befell me in the person of Dr. Jekyll, I could enter on that of Edward Hyde without pecuniary loss. And thus fortified, as I supposed, on every side, I began to profit by the strange immunities of my position.

Men have before hired bravos[3] to transact their crimes, while their own person and reputation sat under shelter. I was the first that ever did so for his pleasures. I was the first that could thus plod in the public eye with a load of genial respectability, and in a moment, like a schoolboy, strip off these lendings[4] and spring headlong into the sea of liberty. But for me, in my impenetrable mantle, the safety was complete. Think of it—I did not even exist! Let

2. Cf. Acts 16.26: when the apostle Paul and his friend Silas were imprisoned at Philippi, a city in eastern Macedonia, an earthquake freed all the prisoners (none of whom fled).

3. Thugs.
4. Borrowed clothing; a reference to King Lear's cry on the heath "Off, off you lendings!" (Shakespeare, *King Lear* 3.4.97).

me but escape into my laboratory door, give me but a second or two to mix and swallow the draught that I had always standing ready; and whatever he had done, Edward Hyde would pass away like the stain of breath upon a mirror; and there in his stead, quietly at home, trimming the midnight lamp in his study, a man who could afford to laugh at suspicion, would be Henry Jekyll.

The pleasures which I made haste to seek in my disguise were, as I have said, undignified; I would scarce use a harder term. But in the hands of Edward Hyde, they soon began to turn towards the monstrous. When I would come back from these excursions, I was often plunged into a kind of wonder at my vicarious depravity. This familiar[5] that I called out of my own soul, and sent forth alone to do his good pleasure, was a being inherently malign and villainous; his every act and thought centered on self; drinking pleasure with bestial avidity from any degree of torture to another; relentless like a man of stone. Henry Jekyll stood at times aghast before the acts of Edward Hyde; but the situation was apart from ordinary laws, and insidiously relaxed the grasp of conscience. It was Hyde, after all, and Hyde alone, that was guilty. Jekyll was no worse; he woke again to his good qualities seemingly unimpaired; he would even make haste, where it was possible, to undo the evil done by Hyde. And thus his conscience slumbered.

Into the details of the infamy at which I thus connived (for even now I can scarce grant that I committed it) I have no design of entering; I mean but to point out the warnings and the successive steps with which my chastisement approached. I met with one accident which, as it brought on no consequence, I shall no more than mention. An act of cruelty to a child aroused against me the anger of a passer-by, whom I recognised the other day in the person of your kinsman; the doctor and the child's family joined him; there were moments when I feared for my life; and at last, in order to pacify their too just resentment, Edward Hyde had to bring them to the door, and pay them in a cheque drawn in the name of Henry Jekyll. But this danger was easily eliminated from the future, by opening an account at another bank in the name of Edward Hyde himself; and when, by sloping my own hand backward, I had supplied my double with a signature, I thought I sat beyond the reach of fate.

Some two months before the murder of Sir Danvers, I had been out for one of my adventures, had returned at a late hour, and woke the next day in bed with somewhat odd sensations. It was in vain I looked about me; in vain I saw the decent furniture and tall proportions of my room in the square; in vain that I recognised the pattern of the bed curtains and the design of the mahogany frame; something still kept insisting that I was not where I was, that I had not wakened where I seemed to be, but in the little room in Soho where I was accustomed to sleep in the body of Edward Hyde. I smiled to myself, and, in my psychological way began lazily to inquire into the elements of this illusion, occasionally, even as I did so, dropping back into a comfortable morning doze. I was still so engaged when, in one of my more wakeful moments, my eyes fell upon my hand. Now the hand of Henry Jekyll (as you have often remarked) was professional in shape and size: it was large, firm, white and comely. But the hand which I now saw, clearly enough, in the yellow light of a mid-London morning, lying half shut on the bed clothes, was lean, corded, knuckly, of a dusky pallor and thickly shaded with a swart[6] growth of hair. It was the hand of Edward Hyde.

I must have stared upon it for near half a minute, sunk as I was in the mere

5. Spirit or demon. 6. Dark.

stupidity of wonder, before terror woke up in my breast as sudden and startling as the crash of cymbals; and bounding from my bed, I rushed to the mirror. At the sight that met my eyes, my blood was changed into something exquisitely thin and icy. Yes, I had gone to bed Henry Jekyll, I had awakened Edward Hyde. How was this to be explained? I asked myself; and then, with another bound of terror—how was it to be remedied? It was well on in the morning; the servants were up; all my drugs were in the cabinet—a long journey down two pair of stairs, through the back passage, across the open court and through the anatomical theatre, from where I was then standing horror-struck. It might indeed be possible to cover my face; but of what use was that, when I was unable to conceal the alteration in my stature? And then with an overpowering sweetness of relief, it came back upon my mind that the servants were already used to the coming and going of my second self. I had soon dressed, as well as I was able, in clothes of my own size: had soon passed through the house, where Bradshaw stared and drew back at seeing Mr. Hyde at such an hour and in such a strange array; and ten minutes later, Dr. Jekyll had returned to his own shape and was sitting down, with a darkened brow, to make a feint of breakfasting.

Small indeed was my appetite. This inexplicable incident, this reversal of my previous experience, seemed, like the Babylonian finger on the wall,[7] to be spelling out the letters of my judgment; and I began to reflect more seriously than ever before on the issues and possibilities of my double existence. That part of me which I had the power of projecting, had lately been much exercised and nourished; it had seemed to me of late as though the body of Edward Hyde had grown in stature, as though (when I wore that form) I were conscious of a more generous tide of blood; and I began to spy a danger that, if this were much prolonged, the balance of my nature might be permanently overthrown, the power of voluntary change be forfeited, and the character of Edward Hyde become irrevocably mine. The power of the drug had not been always equally displayed. Once, very early in my career, it had totally failed me; since then I had been obliged on more than one occasion to double, and once, with infinite risk of death, to treble the amount; and these rare uncertainties had cast hitherto the sole shadow on my contentment. Now, however, and in the light of that morning's accident, I was led to remark that whereas, in the beginning, the difficulty had been to throw off the body of Jekyll, it had of late gradually but decidedly transferred itself to the other side. All things therefore seemed to point to this: that I was slowly losing hold of my original and better self, and becoming slowly incorporated with my second and worse.

Between these two, I now felt I had to choose. My two natures had memory in common, but all other faculties were most unequally shared between them. Jekyll (who was composite) now with the most sensitive apprehensions, now with a greedy gusto, projected and shared in the pleasures and adventures of Hyde; but Hyde was indifferent to Jekyll, or but remembered him as the mountain bandit remembers the cavern in which he conceals himself from pursuit. Jekyll had more than a father's interest; Hyde had more than a son's indifference. To cast in my lot with Jekyll, was to die to those appetites which I had long secretly indulged and had of late begun to pamper. To cast it in with Hyde, was to die to a thousand interests and aspirations, and to become, at a

7. In Daniel 5.5–31; the writing foretold the overthrow of Belshazzar, the Babylonian king, because of his transgressions against the Lord.

blow and forever, despised and friendless. The bargain might appear unequal; but there was still another consideration in the scales; for while Jekyll would suffer smartingly in the fires of abstinence, Hyde would be not even conscious of all that he had lost. Strange as my circumstances were, the terms of this debate are as old and commonplace as man; much the same inducements and alarms cast the die for any tempted and trembling sinner; and it fell out with me, as it falls with so vast a majority of my fellows, that I chose the better part and was found wanting in the strength to keep to it.

Yes, I preferred the elderly and discontented doctor, surrounded by friends and cherishing honest hopes; and bade a resolute farewell to the liberty, the comparative youth, the light step, leaping impulses and secret pleasures, that I had enjoyed in the disguise of Hyde. I made this choice perhaps with some unconscious reservation, for I neither gave up the house in Soho, nor destroyed the clothes of Edward Hyde, which still lay ready in my cabinet. For two months, however, I was true to my determination; for two months I led a life of such severity as I had never before attained to, and enjoyed the compensations of an approving conscience. But time began at last to obliterate the freshness of my alarm; the praises of conscience began to grow into a thing of course; I began to be tortured with throes and longings, as of Hyde struggling after freedom; and at last, in an hour of moral weakness, I once again compounded and swallowed the transforming draught.

I do not suppose that, when a drunkard reasons with himself upon his vice, he is once out of five hundred times affected by the dangers that he runs through his brutish, physical insensibility; neither had I, long as I had considered my position, made enough allowance for the complete moral insensibility and insensate readiness to evil, which were the leading characters of Edward Hyde. Yet it was by these that I was punished. My devil had been long caged, he came out roaring. I was conscious, even when I took the draught, of a more unbridled, a more furious propensity to ill. It must have been this, I suppose, that stirred in my soul that tempest of impatience with which I listened to the civilities of my unhappy victim; I declare, at least, before God, no man morally sane could have been guilty of that crime upon so pitiful a provocation; and that I struck in no more reasonable spirit than that in which a sick child may break a plaything. But I had voluntarily stripped myself of all those balancing instincts by which even the worst of us continues to walk with some degree of steadiness among temptations; and in my case, to be tempted, however slightly, was to fall.

Instantly the spirit of hell awoke in me and raged. With a transport of glee, I mauled the unresisting body, tasting delight from every blow; and it was not till weariness had begun to succeed, that I was suddenly, in the top fit of my delirium, struck through the heart by a cold thrill of terror. A mist dispersed; I saw my life to be forfeit; and fled from the scene of these excesses, at once glorifying and trembling, my lust of evil gratified and stimulated, my love of life screwed to the topmost peg.[8] I ran to the house in Soho, and (to make assurance doubly sure) destroyed my papers; thence I set out through the lamplit streets, in the same divided ecstasy of mind, gloating on my crime, light-headedly devising others in the future, and yet still hastening and still hearkening in my wake for the steps of the avenger. Hyde had a song upon his lips as he compounded the draught, and as he drank it, pledged[9] the dead

8. Strained to the highest point.   9. Drank a toast to.

man. The pangs of transformation had not done tearing him, before Henry Jekyll, with streaming tears of gratitude and remorse, had fallen upon his knees and lifted his clasped hands to God. The veil of self-indulgence was rent from head to foot.[1] I saw my life as a whole: I followed it up from the days of childhood, when I had walked with my father's hand, and through the self-denying toils of my professional life, to arrive again and again, with the same sense of unreality, at the damned horrors of the evening. I could have screamed aloud; I sought with tears and prayers to smother down the crowd of hideous images and sounds with which my memory swarmed against me; and still, between the petitions, the ugly face of my iniquity stared into my soul. As the acuteness of this remorse began to die away, it was succeeded by a sense of joy. The problem of my conduct was solved. Hyde was thenceforth impossible; whether I would or not, I was now confined to the better part of my existence; and O, how I rejoiced to think it! with what willing humility, I embraced anew the restrictions of natural life! with what sincere renunciation, I locked the door by which I had so often gone and come, and ground the key under my heel!

The next day, came the news that the murder had been overlooked,[2] that the guilt of Hyde was patent to the world, and that the victim was a man high in public estimation. It was not only a crime, it had been a tragic folly. I think I was glad to know it; I think I was glad to have my better impulses thus buttressed and guarded by the terrors of the scaffold. Jekyll was now my city of refuge; let but Hyde peep out an instant, and the hands of all men would be raised to take and slay him.

I resolved in my future conduct to redeem the past; and I can say with honesty that my resolve was fruitful of some good. You know yourself how earnestly in the last months of last year, I laboured to relieve suffering; you know that much was done for others, and that the days passed quietly, almost happily for myself. Nor can I truly say that I wearied of this beneficent and innocent life; I think instead that I daily enjoyed it more completely; but I was still cursed with my duality of purpose; and as the first edge of my penitence wore off, the lower side of me, so long indulged, so recently chained down, began to growl for license. Not that I dreamed of resuscitating Hyde; the bare idea of that would startle me to frenzy: no, it was in my own person, that I was once more tempted to trifle with my conscience; and it was as an ordinary secret sinner, that I at last fell before the assaults of temptation.

There comes an end to all things; the most capacious measure is filled at last; and this brief condescension to my evil finally destroyed the balance of my soul. And yet I was not alarmed; the fall seemed natural, like a return to the old days before I had made my discovery. It was a fine, clear, January day, wet under foot where the frost had melted, but cloudless overhead; and the Regent's Park[3] was full of winter chirrupings and sweet with spring odours. I sat in the sun on a bench; the animal within me licking the chops of memory; the spiritual side a little drowsed, promising subsequent penitence, but not yet moved to begin. After all, I reflected, I was like my neighbours; and then I smiled, comparing myself with other men, comparing my active goodwill with the lazy cruelty of their neglect. And at the very moment of that vain-glorious thought, a qualm came over me, a horrid nausea and the most deadly shud-

1. See Matthew 27.51: "the veil of the temple was rent in twain, from the top to the bottom."
2. Seen from above.
3. A large park in northwest London.

dering. These passed away, and left me faint; and then as in its turn the faintness subsided, I began to be aware of a change in the temper of my thoughts, a greater boldness, a contempt of danger, a solution of the bonds of obligation. I looked down; my clothes hung formlessly on my shrunken limbs; the hand that lay on my knee was corded and hairy. I was once more Edward Hyde. A moment before I had been safe of all men's respect, wealthy, beloved—the cloth laying for me in the dining-room at home; and now I was the common quarry of mankind, hunted, houseless, a known murderer, thrall to the gallows.

My reason wavered, but it did not fail me utterly. I have more than once observed that, in my second character, my faculties seemed sharpened to a point and my spirits more tensely elastic; thus it came about that, where Jekyll perhaps might have succumbed, Hyde rose to the importance of the moment. My drugs were in one of the presses of my cabinet; how was I to reach them? That was the problem that (crushing my temples in my hands) I set myself to solve. The laboratory door I had closed. If I sought to enter by the house, my own servants would consign me to the gallows. I saw I must employ another hand, and thought of Lanyon. How was he to be reached? how persuaded? Supposing that I escaped capture in the streets, how was I to make my way into his presence? and how should I, an unknown and displeasing visitor, prevail on the famous physician to rifle the study of his colleague, Dr. Jekyll? Then I remembered that of my original character, one part remained to me: I could write my own hand; and once I had conceived that kindling spark, the way that I must follow became lighted up from end to end.

Thereupon, I arranged my clothes as best I could, and summoning a passing hansom, drove to an hotel in Portland Street, the name of which I chanced to remember. At my appearance (which was indeed comical enough, however tragic a fate these garments covered) the driver could not conceal his mirth. I gnashed my teeth upon him with a gust of devilish fury; and the smile withered from his face—happily for him—yet more happily for myself, for in another instant I had certainly dragged him from his perch. At the inn, as I entered, I looked about me with so black a countenance as made the attendants tremble; not a look did they exchange in my presence; but obsequiously took my orders, led me to a private room, and brought me wherewithal to write. Hyde in danger of his life was a creature new to me; shaken with inordinate anger, strung to the pitch of murder, lusting to inflict pain. Yet the creature was astute; mastered his fury with a great effort of the will; composed his two important letters, one to Lanyon and one to Poole; and that he might receive actual evidence of their being posted, sent them out with directions that they should be registered.

Thenceforward, he sat all day over the fire in the private room, gnawing his nails; there he dined, sitting alone with his fears, the waiter visibly quailing before his eye; and thence, when the night was fully come, he set forth in the corner of a closed cab, and was driven to and fro about the streets of the city. He, I say—I cannot say, I. That child of Hell had nothing human; nothing lived in him but fear and hatred. And when at last, thinking the driver had begun to grow suspicious, he discharged the cab and ventured on foot, attired in his misfitting clothes, an object marked out for observation, into the midst of the nocturnal passengers, these two base passions raged within him like a tempest. He walked fast, hunted by his fears, chattering to himself, skulking through the less frequented thoroughfares, counting the minutes that still divided him from midnight. Once a woman spoke to him, offering, I think, a box of lights.[4] He smote her in the face, and she fled.

When I came to myself at Lanyon's, the horror of my old friend perhaps affected me somewhat: I do not know; it was at least but a drop in the sea to the abhorrence with which I looked back upon these hours. A change had come over me. It was no longer the fear of the gallows, it was the horror of being Hyde that racked me. I received Lanyon's condemnation partly in a dream; it was partly in a dream that I came home to my own house and got into bed. I slept after the prostration of the day, with a stringent and profound slumber which not even the nightmares that wrung me could avail to break. I awoke in the morning shaken, weakened, but refreshed. I still hated and feared the thought of the brute that slept within me, and I had not of course forgotten the appalling dangers of the day before; but I was once more at home, in my own house and close to my drugs; and gratitude for my escape shone so strong in my soul that it almost rivalled the brightness of hope.

I was stepping leisurely across the court after breakfast, drinking the chill of the air with pleasure, when I was seized again with those indescribable sensations that heralded the change; and I had but the time to gain the shelter of my cabinet, before I was once again raging and freezing with the passions of Hyde. It took on this occasion a double dose to recall me to myself; and alas! six hours after, as I sat looking sadly in the fire, the pangs returned, and the drug had to be re-administered. In short, from that day forth it seemed only by a great effort as of gymnastics, and only under the immediate stimulation of the drug, that I was able to wear the countenance of Jekyll. At all hours of the day and night, I would be taken with the premonitory shudder; above all, if I slept, or even dozed for a moment in my chair, it was always as Hyde that I awakened. Under the strain of this continually impending doom and by the sleeplessness to which I now condemned myself, ay, even beyond what I had thought possible to man, I became, in my own person, a creature eaten up and emptied by fever, languidly weak both in body and mind, and solely occupied by one thought: the horror of my other self. But when I slept, or when the virtue of the medicine wore off, I would leap almost without transition (for the pangs of transformation grew daily less marked) into the possession of a fancy brimming with images of terror, a soul boiling with causeless hatreds, and a body that seemed not strong enough to contain the raging energies of life. The powers of Hyde seemed to have grown with the sickliness of Jekyll. And certainly the hate that now divided them was equal on each side. With Jekyll, it was a thing of vital instinct. He had now seen the full deformity of that creature that shared with him some of the phenomena of consciousness, and was co-heir with him to death: and beyond these links of community, which in themselves made the most poignant part of his distress, he thought of Hyde, for all his energy of life, as of something not only hellish but inorganic. This was the shocking thing; that the slime of the pit seemed to utter cries and voices; that the amorphous dust gesticulated and sinned; that what was dead, and had no shape, should usurp the offices of life. And this again, that that insurgent horror was knit to him closer than a wife, closer than an eye; lay caged in his flesh, where he heard it mutter and felt it struggle to be born; and at every hour of weakness, and in the confidence of slumber, prevailed against him, and deposed him out of life. The hatred of

4. Matches.

Hyde for Jekyll, was of a different order. His terror of the gallows drove him continually to commit temporary suicide, and return to his subordinate station of a part instead of a person; but he loathed the necessity, he loathed the despondency into which Jekyll was now fallen, and he resented the dislike with which he was himself regarded. Hence the apelike tricks that he would play me, scrawling in my own hand blasphemies on the pages of my books, burning the letters and destroying the portrait of my father; and indeed, had it not been for his fear of death, he would long ago have ruined himself in order to involve me in the ruin. But his love of life is wonderful; I go further: I, who sicken and freeze at the mere thought of him, when I recall the abjection and passion of this attachment, and when I know how he fears my power to cut him off by suicide, I find it in my heart to pity him.

It is useless, and the time awfully fails me, to prolong this description; no one has ever suffered such torments, let that suffice; and yet even to these, habit brought—no, not alleviation—but a certain callousness of soul, a certain acquiescence of despair; and my punishment might have gone on for years, but for the last calamity which has now fallen, and which has finally severed me from my own face and nature. My provision of the salt, which had never been renewed since the date of the first experiment, began to run low. I sent out for a fresh supply, and mixed the draught; the ebullition followed, and the first change of colour, not the second; I drank it and it was without efficiency. You will learn from Poole how I have had London ransacked; it was in vain; and I am now persuaded that my first supply was impure, and that it was that unknown impurity which lent efficacy to the draught.

About a week has passed, and I am now finishing this statement under the influence of the last of the old powders. This, then, is the last time, short of a miracle, that Henry Jekyll can think his own thoughts or see his own face (now how sadly altered!) in the glass. Nor must I delay too long to bring my writing to an end; for if my narrative has hitherto escaped destruction, it has been by a combination of great prudence and great good luck. Should the throes of change take me in the act of writing it, Hyde will tear it in pieces; but if some time shall have elapsed after I have laid it by, his wonderful self-ishness and circumscription to the moment will probably save it once again from the action of his apelike spite. And indeed the doom that is closing on us both, has already changed and crushed him. Half an hour from now, when I shall again and forever reindue[5] that hated personality, I know how I shall sit shuddering and weeping in my chair, or continue, with the most strained and fearstruck ecstasy of listening, to pace up and down this room (my last earthly refuge) and give ear to every sound of menace. Will Hyde die upon the scaffold? or will he find courage to release himself at the last moment? God knows; I am careless;[6] this is my true hour of death, and what is to follow concerns another than myself. Here then, as I lay down the pen and proceed to seal up my confession, I bring the life of that unhappy Henry Jekyll to an end.

1885   1886

5. Put on again.   6. Indifferent.

OSCAR WILDE
1854–1900

In Oscar Wilde's comedy *The Importance of Being Earnest* (1895) there is an account of a rakish character, Ernest Worthing, whose death in a Paris hotel is reported by the manager. Five years later Wilde died in Paris (where he was living in exile) attended by a hotel manager. The coincidence seems a curious paradigm of Wilde's career, for the connections between his life and his art were unusually close. Indeed, in his last years he told André Gide that he seemed to have put his genius into his life and only his talent into his writings.

His father, Sir William, was a distinguished surgeon in Dublin, where Wilde was born and grew up. After studying classics at Trinity College, Dublin, he won a scholarship to Oxford and there established a brilliant academic record. At Oxford he came under the influence of the aesthetic theories of John Ruskin (who was at the time professor of fine arts) and, more important, of Walter Pater. With characteristic hyperbole Wilde affirmed of Pater's *Studies in the History of the Renaissance* (1873): "It is my golden book; I never travel anywhere without it. But it is the very flower of decadence; the last trumpet should have sounded the moment it was written."

After graduating in 1878, Wilde moved to London, where his fellow Irishmen Bernard Shaw and William Butler Yeats were also to settle. Here Wilde quickly established himself both as a writer and as a spokesperson for the school of "art for art's sake." In Wilde's view this school included not only French poets and critics but also a line of English poets going back through Dante Gabriel Rossetti and the Pre-Raphaelites to John Keats. In 1882 he visited America for a long (and successful) lecture tour, during which he startled audiences by airing the gospel of the "aesthetic movement." In one of these lectures, he asserted that "to disagree with three fourths of all England on all points of view is one of the first elements of sanity."

For his role as a spokesperson for aestheticism, Wilde had many gifts. From all accounts he was a dazzling conversationalist. Yeats reported, after first listening to him: "I never before heard a man talking with perfect sentences, as if he had written them all overnight with labour and yet all spontaneous." Wilde delighted his listeners not only by his polished wordplay but also by uttering opinions that were both outrageous and incongruous—for example, his solemn affirmation that Queen Victoria was one of the three women he most admired and whom he would have married "with pleasure" (the other two were the actress Sarah Bernhardt and Lillie Langtry, reputedly a mistress of Victoria's son Edward, Prince of Wales).

In addition to his mastery of witty conversation, Wilde had the gifts of an actor who delights in gaining attention. Pater had been a very shy and reticent man, but there was nothing reticent about his disciple, who had early discovered that a flamboyant style of dress was one of the most effective means of gaining attention. Like the dandies of the earlier decades of the nineteenth century (including Benjamin Disraeli and Charles Dickens), Wilde favored colorful costumes in marked contrast to the sober black suits of the late-Victorian middle classes. A green carnation in his buttonhole and velvet knee breeches became for Wilde badges of his youthful iconoclasm; and even when he approached middle age, he continued to emphasize the gap between generations. In a letter written when he was forty-two years old, he remarks: "The opinions of the old on matters of Art are, of course, of no value whatever."

Wilde's campaign quickly gained an amused response from middle-class quarters. In 1881 W. S. Gilbert and Sir Arthur Sullivan staged their comic opera *Patience*, which mocked the affectations of the aesthetes in the character of Bunthorne, especially in his song "If You're Anxious for to Shine in the High Aesthetic Line."

Wilde's successes for seventeen years in England and America were, of course, not limited to his self-advertising stunts as a dandy. In his writings he excelled in a variety of genres: as a critic of literature and of society (*The Decay of Lying*, 1889, and *The*

Soul of Man under Socialism, 1891) and also as a novelist, poet, and dramatist. Much of his prose, including *The Critic as Artist* (1890), develops Pater's aestheticism, particularly its sense of the superiority of art to life and its lack of obligation to any standards of mimesis. His novel *The Picture of Dorian Gray,* which created a sensation when it was published in 1891, takes a somewhat different perspective. The novel is a strikingly ingenious story of a handsome young man and his selfish pursuit of sensual pleasures. Until the end of the book he remains fresh and healthy in appearance while his portrait mysteriously changes into a horrible image of his corrupted soul. Although the preface to the novel (reprinted here) emphasizes that art and morality are totally separate, in the novel, at least in its later chapters, Wilde seems to be portraying the evils of self-regarding hedonism.

As a poet Wilde felt overshadowed by the Victorian predecessors whom he admired—Robert Browning, D. G. Rossetti, and Algernon Charles Swinburne—and had trouble finding his own voice. Many of the poems in his first volume (1881) are highly derivative, but pieces such as "Impression du Matin" (1885) and "The Harlot's House" (1881) offer a distinctive perspective on city streets that seems to anticipate early poems by T. S. Eliot. His most outstanding success, however, was as a writer of comedies; staged in London and New York from 1892 through 1895, these included *Lady Windermere's Fan, A Woman of No Importance, An Ideal Husband,* and *The Importance of Being Earnest.*

In the spring of 1895 this triumphant success suddenly crumbled when Wilde was arrested and sentenced to prison, with hard labor, for two years. Although Wilde was married and the father of two children, he did not hide his relationships with men, and in fact ended up shaping, to his personal cost, a long-standing public image of "the homosexual." When he began a romance (in 1891) with the handsome young poet Lord Alfred Douglas, he set in motion the events that brought about his ruin. In 1895 Lord Alfred's father, the marquess of Queensberry, accused Wilde of homosexuality; Wilde recklessly sued for libel, lost the case, and was thereupon arrested and convicted for what had only recently come onto the statute books as a serious offense. (A late addition to the Criminal Law Amendment Act of 1885, known as the Labouchère Amendment after the member of Parliament who had proposed it, effectively criminalized all forms of sexual relations between men.) The revulsion of feeling against him in Britain and America was violent, and the aesthetic movement suffered a severe setback not only with the public but among writers as well.

His two years in jail led Wilde to write two sober and emotionally high-pitched works, his poem *The Ballad of Reading Gaol* (1898) and his prose confession *De Profundis* (1905). After leaving prison, Wilde, a ruined man, emigrated to France, where he lived out the last three years of his life under an assumed name. Before his departure from England he had been divorced and declared a bankrupt, and in France he had to rely on friends for financial support. Wilde is buried in Paris in the Père Lachaise cemetery.

Impression du Matin[1]

The Thames nocturne of blue and gold[2]
Changed to a harmony in grey;
A barge with ochre-colored hay
Dropped from the wharf:[3] and chill and cold

1. Impression of the morning (French).
2. Cf. the "Nocturnes" (paintings of nighttime scenes) by James McNeill Whistler in the 1870s. *Nocturne in Blue and Gold: Old Battersea Bridge* was one of this series; it was painted by 1875 but given its present title in 1892. In the next line

Wilde may be referring to an earlier painting by Whistler, *Harmony in Gray and Green: Miss Cicely Alexander* (1872–74).
3. I.e., left the wharf and went down river with the ebb tide.

5   The yellow fog came creeping down
     The bridges, till the houses' walls
     Seemed changed to shadows, and St. Paul's
     Loomed like a bubble o'er the town.[4]

     Then suddenly arose the clang
10   Of waking life; the streets were stirred
     With country wagons; and a bird
     Flew to the glistening roofs and sang.

     But one pale woman all alone,
     The daylight kissing her wan hair,
15   Loitered beneath the gas lamps' flare,
     With lips of flame and heart of stone.

1881

The Harlot's House

     We caught the tread of dancing feet,
     We loitered down the moonlit street,
     And stopped beneath the Harlot's house.

     Inside, above the din and fray,
5   We heard the loud musicians play
     The "Treues Liebes Herz" of Strauss.[1]

     Like strange mechanical grotesques,
     Making fantastic arabesques,
     The shadows raced across the blind.

10   We watched the ghostly dancers spin
     To sound of horn and violin,
     Like black leaves wheeling in the wind.

     Like wire-pulled automatons,
     Slim silhouetted skeletons
15   Went sidling through the slow quadrille,[2]

     Then took each other by the hand,
     And danced a stately saraband;[3]
     Their laughter echoed thin and shrill.

     Sometimes a clockwork puppet pressed
20   A phantom lover to her breast,
     Sometimes they seemed to try to sing,

---

4. I.e., the large dome of St. Paul's Cathedral in London.

1. *Heart of True Love*, a waltz by the Austrian composer and "Waltz King" Johann Strauss (1825–1899).

2. An intricate dance involving four couples facing each other in a square.

3. A slow and stately dance, originating in Spain.

Sometimes a horrible marionette
Came out, and smoked its cigarette
Upon the steps like a live thing.[4]

25 Then turning to my love I said,
"The dead are dancing with the dead,
The dust is whirling with the dust."

But she, she heard the violin,
And left my side, and entered in;
30 Love passed into the house of Lust.

Then suddenly the tune went false,
The dancers wearied of the waltz,
The shadows ceased to wheel and whirl,

And down the long and silent street,
35 The dawn, with silver-sandaled feet,
Crept like a frightened girl.

1885, 1908

From The Critic as Artist[1]

[CRITICISM ITSELF AN ART]

ERNEST   Gilbert, you sound too harsh a note. Let us go back to the more
gracious fields of literature. What was it you said? That it was more difficult
to talk about a thing than to do it?
GILBERT [After a pause.]   Yes: I believe I ventured upon that simple truth.
Surely you see now that I am right? When man acts he is a puppet. When he
describes he is a poet. The whole secret lies in that. It was easy enough on
the sandy plains by windy Ilion[2] to send the notched arrow from the painted
bow, or to hurl against the shield of hide and flamelike brass the long ash-
handled spear. It was easy for the adulterous queen to spread the Tyrian
carpets for her lord,[3] and then, as he lay couched in the marble bath, to
throw over his head the purple net, and call to her smooth-faced lover to stab
through the meshes at the heart that should have broken at Aulis.[4] For

4. In an illustration for the poem by Althea Gyles
(approved by Wilde), the marionette is pictured as
a man in evening dress.
1. In "the library of a house in Piccadilly," Gilbert
and Ernest, two sophisticated young men, are talking about the use and function of criticism. Earlier
in the dialogue Ernest had complained that criticism is officious and useless: "Why should the artist be troubled by the shrill clamour of criticism?
Why should those who cannot create take upon
themselves to estimate the value of creative work?"
Gilbert, in his reply, argues that criticism is creative in its own right. He digresses to compare the
life of action unfavorably with the life of art:
actions are dangerous and their results unpredictable; "if we lived long enough to see the results of

our actions it may be that those who call themselves good would be sickened by a dull remorse,
and those whom the world calls evil stirred by a
noble joy." The excerpt printed here begins immediately following this digression.
2. Troy. Gilbert is referring to Homer's *Iliad*.
3. Agamemnon, king of Mycenae. Aeschylus's
tragedy of that name tells how his wife, Clytemnestra ("the adulterous queen"), and his cousin
Aegisthus ("her smooth-faced lover") conspired to
murder him. He hubristically walked on carpets
dyed purple, a color derived from shellfish off Tyre
(a city located in what is today Lebanon).
4. Where Agamemnon sacrificed his daughter
Iphigenia (so that the Greek fleet could sail for
Troy), thus incurring Clytemnestra's wrath.

Antigone[5] even, with Death waiting for her as her bridegroom, it was easy to pass through the tainted air at noon, and climb the hill, and strew with kindly earth the wretched naked corse that had no tomb. But what of those who wrote about these things? What of those who gave them reality, and made them live forever? Are they not greater than the men and women they sing of? "Hector that sweet knight is dead."[6] And Lucian[7] tells us how in the dim underworld Menippus saw the bleaching skull of Helen, and marveled that it was for so grim a favour that all those horned ships were launched, those beautiful mailed men laid low, those towered cities brought to dust. Yet, every day the swanlike daughter of Leda comes out on the battlements, and looks down at the tide of war. The greybeards wonder at her loveliness, and she stands by the side of the king.[8] In his chamber of stained ivory lies her leman.[9] He is polishing his dainty armour, and combing the scarlet plume. With squire and page, her husband passes from tent to tent. She can see his bright hair, and hears, or fancies that she hears, that clear cold voice. In the courtyard below, the son of Priam is buckling on his brazen cuirass. The white arms of Andromache[1] are around his neck. He sets his helmet on the ground, lest their babe should be frightened. Behind the embroidered curtains of his pavilion sits Achilles,[2] in perfumed raiment, while in harness of gilt and silver the friend of his soul[3] arrays himself to go forth to fight. From a curiously carven chest that his mother Thetis had brought to his shipside, the Lord of the Myrmidons[4] takes out that mystic chalice that the lip of man had never touched, and cleanses it with brimstone, and with fresh water cools it, and, having washed his hands, fills with black wine its burnished hollow, and spills the thick grape-blood upon the ground in honor of Him whom at Dodona[5] barefooted prophets worshipped, and prays to Him, and knows not that he prays in vain, and that by the hands of two knights from Troy, Panthous' son, Euphorbus, whose love-locks were looped with gold, and the Priamid,[6] the lion-hearted, Patroclus, the comrade of comrades, must meet his doom. Phantoms, are they? Heroes of mist and mountain? Shadows in a song? No: they are real. Action! What is action? It dies at the moment of its energy. It is a base concession to fact. The world is made by the singer for the dreamer.

ERNEST While you talk it seems to me to be so.

GILBERT It is so in truth. On the mouldering citadel of Troy lies the lizard like a thing of green bronze. The owl has built her nest in the palace of Priam. Over the empty plain wander shepherd and goatherd with their flocks, and where, on the wine-surfaced, oily sea, οἶνοψ πόντος,[7] as Homer

5. Antigone defied Creon, king of Thebes, by sprinkling earth on the body of her brother whose burial Creon had forbidden, and was punished by death; see Sophocles' play *Antigone* (ca. 441 B.C.E.).
6. Cf. Shakespeare's *Love's Labour's Lost* 5.2.647: "The sweet war-man [Hector] is dead and rotten."
7. Greek satirist (b. ca. 120 C.E.), one of whose main influences was Menippus (early 3rd century B.C.E.), a Greek philosopher who was the first to express his views in a seriocomic style. The reference is to Lucian's *Dialogues of the Dead*.
8. Priam. Homer in *Iliad* 3.156–58 describes the old men of Troy admiring the beauty of Helen, daughter of Leda and of Zeus (who came to Leda in the form of a swan).
9. Lover (i.e., Paris).
1. Wife of Hector, one of the sons of Priam and the finest Trojan warrior.
2. Son of Peleus and of the sea nymph Thetis; Achilles was the greatest Greek warrior fighting in the Trojan War. The scene set here is a tissue of recollections from the *Iliad*.
3. I.e., Patroclus.
4. Warriors who accompanied Achilles to Troy.
5. Seat of a very ancient oracle of Zeus.
6. The son of Priam, i.e., Hector. With Euphorbus's help he killed Patroclus, and in turn he was slain by Achilles.
7. Wine-dark sea (Greek).

calls it, copper-prowed and streaked with vermilion, the great galleys of the Danaoi[8] came in their gleaming crescent, the lonely tunny-fisher[9] sits in his little boat and watches the bobbing corks of his net. Yet, every morning the doors of the city are thrown open, and on foot, or in horse-drawn chariot, the warriors go forth to battle, and mock their enemies from behind their iron masks. All day long the fight rages, and when night comes the torches gleam by the tents, and the cresset[1] burns in the hall. Those who live in marble or on painted panel know of life but a single exquisite instant, eternal indeed in its beauty, but limited to one note of passion or one mood of calm. Those whom the poet makes live have their myriad emotions of joy and terror, of courage and despair, of pleasure and of suffering. The seasons come and go in glad or saddening pageant, and with winged or leaden feet the years pass by before them. They have their youth and their manhood, they are children, and they grow old. It is always dawn for St. Helena, as Veronese saw her at the window.[2] Through the still morning air the angels bring her the symbol of God's pain.[3] The cool breezes of the morning lift the gilt threads from her brow. On that little hill by the city of Florence, where the lovers of Giorgione[4] are lying, it is always the solstice of noon, made so languorous by summer suns that hardly can the slim naked girl dip into the marble tank the round bubble of clear glass, and the long fingers of the lute player rest idly upon the chords. It is twilight always for the dancing nymphs whom Corot[5] set free among the silver poplars of France. In eternal twilight they move, those frail diaphanous figures, whose tremulous white feet seem not to touch the dew-drenched grass they tread on. But those who walk in epos,[6] drama, or romance, see through the labouring months the young moons wax and wane, and watch the night from evening unto morning star, and from sunrise unto sunsetting can note the shifting day with all its gold and shadow. For them, as for us, the flowers bloom and wither, and the Earth, that Green-tressed Goddess as Coleridge calls her,[7] alters her raiment for their pleasure. The statue is concentrated to one moment of perfection. The image stained upon the canvas possesses no spiritual element of growth or change. If they know nothing of death, it is because they know little of life, for the secrets of life and death belong to those, and those only, whom the sequence of time affects, and who possess not merely the present but the future, and can rise or fall from a past of glory or of shame. Movement, that problem of the visible arts, can be truly realized by Literature alone. It is Literature that shows us the body in its swiftness and the soul in its unrest.

ERNEST   Yes; I see now what you mean. But, surely, the higher you place the creative artist, the lower must the critic rank.

GILBERT   Why so?

ERNEST   Because the best that he can give us will be but an echo of rich

---

8. Greeks.
9. Tuna-fishers.
1. Metal basket holding fuel burned for illumination, often hung from the ceiling.
2. One of the best-known works of the Italian painter Paolo Veronese (Paolo Caliari, 1528–1588) is *Helena's Vision*.
3. I.e., the cross.
4. Italian painter (ca. 1477–1511), the most bril-

liant colorist of his time. The painting is *The Concert*.
5. Jean-Baptiste-Camille Corot (1796–1875), French painter best-known for his shimmering trees.
6. Epic poetry.
7. Cf. S. T. Coleridge's "Hymn to the Earth" (1834), line 10, where Earth is called "Green-haired Goddess."

music, a dim shadow of clear-outlined form. It may, indeed, be that life is chaos, as you tell me that it is; that its martyrdoms are mean and its heroisms ignoble; and that it is the function of Literature to create, from the rough material of actual existence, a new world that will be more marvellous, more enduring, and more true than the world that common eyes look upon, and through which common natures seek to realize their perfection. But surely, if this new world has been made by the spirit and touch of a great artist, it will be a thing so complete and perfect that there will be nothing left for the critic to do. I quite understand now, and indeed admit most readily, that it is far more difficult to talk about a thing than to do it. But it seems to me that this sound and sensible maxim, which is really extremely soothing to one's feelings, and should be adopted as its motto by every Academy of Literature all over the world, applies only to the relations that exist between Art and Life, and not to any relations that there may be between Art and Criticism.

GILBERT   But, surely, Criticism is itself an art. And just as artistic creation implies the working of the critical faculty, and, indeed, without it cannot be said to exist at all, so Criticism is really creative in the highest sense of the word. Criticism is, in fact, both creative and independent.

ERNEST   Independent?

GILBERT   Yes; independent. Criticism is no more to be judged by any low standard of imitation or resemblance than is the work of poet or sculptor. The critic occupies the same relation to the work of art that he criticizes as the artist does to the visible world of form and colour, or the unseen world of passion and of thought. He does not even require for the perfection of his art the finest materials. Anything will serve his purpose. And just as out of the sordid and sentimental amours of the silly wife of a small country doctor in the squalid village of Yonville-l'Abbaye, near Rouen, Gustave Flaubert[8] was able to create a classic, and make a masterpiece of style, so, from subjects of little or of no importance, such as the pictures in this year's Royal Academy,[9] or in any year's Royal Academy for that matter, Mr. Lewis Morris's poems, M. Ohnet's novels, or the plays of Mr. Henry Arthur Jones,[1] the true critic can, if it be his pleasure so to direct or waste his faculty of contemplation, produce work that will be flawless in beauty and instinct with intellectual subtlety. Why not? Dullness is always an irresistible temptation for brilliancy, and stupidity is the permanent *Bestia Trionfans*[2] that calls wisdom from its cave. To an artist so creative as the critic, what does subject matter signify? No more and no less than it does to the novelist and the painter. Like them, he can find his motives everywhere. Treatment is the test. There is nothing that has not in it suggestion or challenge.

ERNEST   But is Criticism really a creative art?

GILBERT   Why should it not be? It works with materials, and puts them into a form that is at once new and delightful. What more can one say of poetry? Indeed, I would call criticism a creation within a creation. For just as the

8. French novelist (1821–1880); the reference is to his novel *Madame Bovary* (1857).
9. The Royal Academy of Arts, founded in 1768, holds an annual summer exhibition of new work.
1. Wilde is mischievously suggesting his low opinion of the contemporary writers just named. Morris (1833–1907) was a popular Welsh poet and essayist often ridiculed by the critics; Georges Ohnet (1848–1918) was a French novelist and dramatist; and Jones (1851–1929) was one of the leading English playwrights of his time.
2. Triumphant beast (Wilde's mixture of Italian and Latin); a reference to *Spaccio della Bestia Trionfante* (*Expulsion of the Triumphant Beast*, 1584), a philosophical allegory by the Italian philosopher Giordano Bruno.

great artists, from Homer and Aeschylus, down to Shakespeare and Keats, did not go directly to life for their subject matter, but sought for it in myth, and legend, and ancient tale, so the critic deals with materials that others have, as it were, purified for him, and to which imaginative form and colour have been already added. Nay, more, I would say that the highest Criticism, being the purest form of personal impression, is in its way more creative than creation, as it has least reference to any standard external to itself, and is, in fact, its own reason for existing, and, as the Greeks would put it, in itself, and to itself, an end. Certainly, it is never trammeled by any shackles of verisimilitude. No ignoble considerations of probability, that cowardly concession to the tedious repetitions of domestic or public life, affect it ever. One may appeal from fiction unto fact. But from the soul there is no appeal.

ERNEST   From the soul?

GILBERT   Yes, from the soul. That is what the highest criticism really is, the record of one's own soul. It is more fascinating than history, as it is concerned simply with oneself. It is more delightful than philosophy, as its subject is concrete and not abstract, real and not vague. It is the only civilized form of autobiography, as it deals not with the events, but with the thoughts of one's life, not with life's physical accidents of deed or circumstance, but with the spiritual moods and imaginative passions of the mind. I am always amused by the silly vanity of those writers and artists of our day who seem to imagine that the primary function of the critic is to chatter about their second-rate work. The best that one can say of most modern creative art is that it is just a little less vulgar than reality, and so the critic, with his fine sense of distinction and sure instinct of delicate refinement, will prefer to look into the silver mirror or through the woven veil, and will turn his eyes away from the chaos and clamour of actual existence, though the mirror be tarnished and the veil be torn. His sole aim is to chronicle his own impressions. It is for him that pictures are painted, books written, and marble hewn into form.

ERNEST   I seem to have heard another theory of Criticism.

GILBERT   Yes: it has been said by one whose gracious memory we all revere,[3] and the music of whose pipe once lured Proserpina from her Sicilian fields, and made those white feet stir, and not in vain, the Cumnor cowslips, that the proper aim of Criticism is to see the object as in itself it really is. But this is a very serious error, and takes no cognizance of Criticism's most perfect form, which is in its essence purely subjective, and seeks to reveal its own secret and not the secret of another. For the highest Criticism deals with art not as expressive but as impressive purely.

ERNEST   But is that really so?

GILBERT   Of course it is. Who cares whether Mr. Ruskin's views on Turner[4] are sound or not? What does it matter? That mighty and majestic prose of his, so fervid and so fiery-colored in its noble eloquence, so rich in its elaborate symphonic music, so sure and certain, at its best, in subtle choice of

---

3. I.e., Matthew Arnold, whose poem "Thyrsis" (1866; lines 91–100) evokes the legend of Proserpina, a goddess associated with the pastoral landscapes of Sicily. Arnold believed that it would be "in vain" to summon Proserpina to visit the Cumnor hills landscape (near Oxford), but Wilde's speaker here flatters Arnold that the summons was so beautiful that it was "not in vain." For the prose

passage about the "aim of Criticism," see Arnold's "The Function of Criticism at the Present Time" (1864; p. 1384).

4. For John Ruskin's defense of the paintings of J. M. W. Turner, see Modern Painters (1843), especially his praise of Turner's The Slave Ship (p. 1321).

word and epithet, is at least as great a work of art as any of those wonderful sunsets that bleach or rot on their corrupted canvases in England's Gallery; greater indeed, one is apt to think at times, not merely because its equal beauty is more enduring, but on account of the fuller variety of its appeal, soul speaking to soul in those long-cadenced lines, not through form and colour alone, though through these, indeed, completely and without loss, but with intellectual and emotional utterance, with lofty passion and with loftier thought, with imaginative insight, and with poetic aim; greater, I always think, even as Literature is the greater art. Who, again, cares whether Mr. Pater has put into the portrait of Mona Lisa[5] something that Leonardo never dreamed of? The painter may have been merely the slave of an archaic smile, as some have fancied, but whenever I pass into the cool galleries of the Palace of the Louvre, and stand before that strange figure "set in its marble chair in that cirque of fantastic rocks, as in some faint light under sea," I murmur to myself, "She is older than the rocks among which she sits; like the vampire, she has been dead many times, and learned the secrets of the grave; and has been a diver in deep seas, and keeps their fallen day about her: and trafficked for strange webs with Eastern merchants; and, as Leda, was the mother of Helen of Troy, and, as St. Anne, the mother of Mary; and all this has been to her but as the sound of lyres and flutes, and lives only in the delicacy with which it has moulded the changing lineaments, and tinged the eyelids and the hands." And I say to my friend, "The presence that thus so strangely rose beside the waters is expressive of what in the ways of a thousand years man had come to desire"; and he answers me, "Hers is the head upon which all 'the ends of the world are come,' and the eyelids are a little weary."

And so the picture becomes more wonderful to us than it really is, and reveals to us a secret of which, in truth, it knows nothing, and the music of the mystical prose is as sweet in our ears as was that flute-player's music that lent to the lips of La Gioconda[6] those subtle and poisonous curves. Do you ask me what Leonardo would have said had any one told him of this picture that "all the thoughts and experience of the world had etched and moulded therein that which they had of power to refine and make expressive the outward form, the animalism of Greece, the lust of Rome, the reverie of the Middle Age with its spiritual ambition and imaginative loves, the return of the Pagan world, the sins of the Borgias?" He would probably have answered that he had contemplated none of these things, but had concerned himself simply with certain arrangements of lines and masses, and with new and curious colour-harmonies of blue and green. And it is for this very reason that the criticism which I have quoted is criticism of the highest kind. It treats the work of art simply as a starting point for a new creation. It does not confine itself—let us at least suppose so for the moment—to discovering the real intention of the artist and accepting that as final. And in this it is right, for the meaning of any beautiful created thing is, at least, as much in the soul of him who looks at it, as it was in his soul who wrought it. Nay, it is rather the beholder who lends to the beautiful thing its myriad meanings, and makes it marvelous for us, and sets it in some new relation

5. All remaining references in this paragraph and the first in the next are to Walter Pater's *Studies in the History of the Renaissance* (p. 1507).

6. I.e., the *Mona Lisa* (the portrait was of the wife of Francesco del Gioconda—hence "La Gioconda").

to the age, so that it becomes a vital portion of our lives, and symbol of what we pray for, or perhaps of what, having prayed for, we fear that we may receive. The longer I study, Ernest, the more clearly I see that the beauty of the visible arts is, as the beauty of music, impressive[7] primarily, and that it may be marred, and indeed often is so, by any excess of intellectual intention on the part of the artist. For when the work is finished it has, as it were, an independent life of its own, and may deliver a message far other than that which was put into its lips to say. Sometimes, when I listen to the overture to *Tannhäuser*,[8] I seem indeed to see that comely knight treading delicately on the flower-strewn grass, and to hear the voice of Venus calling to him from the caverned hill. But at other times it speaks to me of a thousand different things, of myself, it may be, and my own life, or of the lives of others whom one has loved and grown weary of loving, or of the passions that man has known, or of the passions that man has not known, and so has sought for. Tonight it may fill one with that ΕΡΩΣ ΤΩΝ ΑΔΥΝΑΤΩΝ, that *amour de l'impossible*,[9] which falls like a madness on many who think they live securely and out of reach of harm, so that they sicken suddenly with the poison of unlimited desire, and, in the infinite pursuit of what they may not obtain, grow faint and swoon or stumble. Tomorrow, like the music of which Aristotle and Plato tell us, the noble Dorian music of the Greek,[1] it may perform the office of a physician, and give us an anodyne against pain, and heal the spirit that is wounded, and "bring the soul into harmony with all right things." And what is true about music is true about all the arts. Beauty has as many meanings as man has moods. Beauty is the symbol of symbols. Beauty reveals everything, because it expresses nothing. When it shows us itself, it shows us the whole fiery-coloured world.

ERNEST   But is such work as you have talked about really criticism?

GILBERT   It is the highest Criticism, for it criticizes not merely the individual work of art, but Beauty itself, and fills with wonder a form which the artist may have left void, or not understood, or understood incompletely.

ERNEST   The highest Criticism, then, is more creative than creation, and the primary aim of the critic is to see the object as in itself it really is not; that is your theory, I believe?

GILBERT   Yes, that is my theory. To the critic the work of art is simply a suggestion for a new work of his own, that need not necessarily bear any obvious resemblance to the thing it criticizes. The one characteristic of a beautiful form is that one can put into it whatever one wishes, and see in it whatever one chooses to see; and the Beauty, that gives to creation its universal and aesthetic element, makes the critic a creator in his turn, and whispers of a thousand different things which were not present in the mind of him who carved the statue or painted the panel or graved the gem.

It is sometimes said by those who understand neither the nature of the highest Criticism nor the charm of the highest Art, that the pictures that the critic loves most to write about are those that belong to the anecdotage

7. I.e., designed to create an impression of the senses.
8. The 1845 opera by Richard Wagner, based on the legend of a 14th-century German poet who fell under the spell of Venus and lived with her in a mountain, Hörselberg.
9. Love of the impossible, in Greek (in capital letters, perhaps to give the effect of an inscription)

and in French.
1. Both Plato (*Republic* 3) and Aristotle (*Politics* 8) praise the educational appropriateness of the Dorian mode (Aristotle calls it especially steady and manly), as opposed to eastern music; the Dorians were a people of ancient Greece, the last of the northern invaders (ca. 1100–950 B.C.E.).

of painting, and that deal with scenes taken out of literature or history. But this is not so. Indeed, pictures of this kind are far too intelligible. As a class, they rank with illustrations, and even considered from this point of view are failures, as they do not stir the imagination, but set definite bounds to it. For the domain of the painter is, as I suggested before, widely different from that of the poet. To the latter belongs life in its full and absolute entirety; not merely the beauty that men look at, but the beauty that men listen to also; not merely the momentary grace of form or the transient gladness of colour, but the whole sphere of feeling, the perfect cycle of thought. The painter is so far limited that it is only through the mask of the body that he can show us the mystery of the soul; only through conventional images that he can handle ideas; only through its physical equivalents that he can deal with psychology. And how inadequately does he do it then, asking us to accept the torn turban of the Moor for the noble rage of Othello, or a dotard in a storm for the wild madness of Lear! Yet it seems as if nothing could stop him. Most of our elderly English painters spend their wicked and wasted lives in poaching upon the domain of the poets, marring their motives by clumsy treatment, and striving to render, by visible form or colour, the marvel of what is invisible, the splendour of what is not seen. Their pictures are, as a natural consequence, insufferably tedious. They have degraded the invisible arts into the obvious arts, and the one thing not worth looking at is the obvious. I do not say that poet and painter may not treat of the same subject. They have always done so, and will always do so. But while the poet can be pictorial or not, as he chooses, the painter must be pictorial always. For a painter is limited, not to what he sees in nature, but to what upon canvas may be seen.

And so, my dear Ernest, pictures of this kind will not really fascinate the critic. He will turn from them to such works as make him brood and dream and fancy, to works that possess the subtle quality of suggestion, and seem to tell one that even from them there is an escape into a wider world. It is sometimes said that the tragedy of an artist's life is that he cannot realize his ideal. But the true tragedy that dogs the steps of most artists is that they realize their ideal too absolutely. For, when the ideal is realized, it is robbed of its wonder and its mystery, and becomes simply a new starting point for an ideal that is other than itself. This is the reason why music is the perfect type of art. Music can never reveal its ultimate secret. This, also, is the explanation of the value of limitations in art. The sculptor gladly surrenders imitative colour, and the painter the actual dimensions of form, because by such renunciations they are able to avoid too definite a presentation of the Real, which would be mere imitation, and too definite a realization of the Ideal, which would be too purely intellectual. It is through its very incompleteness that Art becomes complete in beauty, and so addresses itself, not to the faculty of recognition nor to the faculty of reason, but to the aesthetic sense alone, which, while accepting both reason and recognition as stages of apprehension, subordinates them both to a pure synthetic impression of the work of art as a whole, and, taking whatever alien emotional elements the work may possess, uses their very complexity as a means by which a richer unity may be added to the ultimate impression itself. You see, then, how it is that the aesthetic critic rejects these obvious modes of art that have but one message to deliver, and having delivered it become dumb and sterile, and seeks rather for such modes as suggest reverie and mood, and by their imaginative beauty make all interpretations true, and no interpretation final. Some resemblance, no doubt, the creative work of the critic will have to the work that has stirred him to creation, but it will be such resemblance as exists, not between Nature and the mirror that the painter of landscape or figure may be supposed to hold up to her, but between Nature and the work of the decorative artist. Just as on the flowerless carpets of Persia, tulip and rose blossom indeed and are lovely to look on, though they are not reproduced in visible shape or line; just as the pearl and purple of the sea shell is echoed in the church of St. Mark at Venice; just as the vaulted ceiling of the wondrous chapel at Ravenna is made gorgeous by the gold and green and sapphire of the peacock's tail, though the birds of Juno[2] fly not across it; so the critic reproduces the work that he criticizes in a mode that is never imitative, and part of whose charm may really consist in the rejection of resemblance, and shows us in this way not merely the meaning but also the mystery of Beauty, and, by transforming each art into literature, solves once for all the problem of Art's unity.

But I see it is time for supper. After we have discussed some Chambertin and a few ortolans,[3] we will pass on to the question of the critic considered in the light of the interpreter.

ERNEST   Ah! you admit, then, that the critic may occasionally be allowed to see the object as in itself it really is.

GILBERT   I am not quite sure. Perhaps I may admit it after supper. There is a subtle influence in supper.

1890, 1891

 Preface to *The Picture of Dorian Gray*

The artist is the creator of beautiful things.
To reveal art and conceal the artist is art's aim.
The critic is he who can translate into another manner or a new material his impression of beautiful things.
 The highest, as the lowest, form of criticism is a mode of autobiography.
Those who find ugly meanings in beautiful things are corrupt without being charming. This is a fault.
 Those who find beautiful meanings in beautiful things are the cultivated. For these there is hope.
They are the elect to whom beautiful things mean only Beauty.
 There is no such thing as a moral or an immoral book.
 Books are well written, or badly written. That is all.
The nineteenth-century dislike of Realism is the rage of Caliban[1] seeing his own face in a glass.
 The nineteenth-century dislike of Romanticism is the rage of Caliban not seeing his own face in a glass.

---

2. Peacocks, associated in classical mythology with the goddess Juno (in Greek, Hera) because she is said to have set in the bird's tail the eyes of hundred-eyed Argus, who died in her service.
3. Small birds esteemed by epicures for their del-

icate flavor. "Chambertin": one of the finest wines of Burgundy.
1. The character in Shakespeare's *The Tempest* who is half-human, half-monster.

The moral life of man forms part of the subject matter of the artist, but the morality of art consists in the perfect use of an imperfect medium. No artist desires to prove anything. Even things that are true can be proved.

No artist has ethical sympathies. An ethical sympathy in an artist is an unpardonable mannerism of style.

No artist is ever morbid. The artist can express everything.

Thought and language are to the artist instruments of an art.

Vice and Virtue are to the artist materials for an art.

From the point of view of form, the type of all the arts is the art of the musician. From the point of view of feeling, the actor's craft is the type.

All art is at once surface and symbol.

Those who go beneath the surface do so at their peril.

Those who read the symbol do so at their peril.

It is the spectator, and not life, that art really mirrors.

Diversity of opinion about a work of art shows that the work is new, complex, and vital.

When critics disagree the artist is in accord with himself. We can forgive a man for making a useful thing as long as he does not admire it. The only excuse for making a useless thing is that one admires it intensely.

All art is quite useless.

1891

The Importance of Being Earnest

Of the four stage comedies by Wilde, his last, *The Importance of Being Earnest*, is generally regarded as his masterpiece. It was first staged in February 1895 and was an immediate hit. Only one critic failed to find it delightful; curiously, this was Wilde's fellow playwright from Ireland, Bernard Shaw, who, though amused, found Wilde's wit "hateful" and "sinister," and thought the play exhibited "real degeneracy." Despite Shaw's complaints, the first London production ran for eighty-six performances; but when Wilde was sentenced to prison, production ceased for several years. Shortly before his death it was revived in London and New York, and it has subsequently become a classic.

In its original version the play was in four acts. At the request of the stage producer, Wilde reduced it to three acts—the version almost always used in performances and therefore the version reprinted here. A few of the notes in the text cite passages from the four-act version.

The play was first published in 1899. Earlier, in an interview, Wilde had described his overall aim in writing it: "It has as its philosophy . . . that we should treat all the trivial things of life seriously, and all the serious things of life with sincere and studied triviality." Just before his death he remarked that although he was pleased with the "bright and happy" tone and temper of his play, he wished it might have had a "higher seriousness of intent." Later critics have found this seriousness of intent in the play's deconstruction of Victorian moral and social values. Like another Victorian masterpiece of the absurd, *Alice's Adventures in Wonderland* (1865), *The Importance of Being Earnest* empties manners and morals of their underlying sense to create a nominalist world where earnest is not a quality of character but a name, where words, to paraphrase Humpty Dumpty in *Through the Looking-Glass* (1871), mean what you choose them to mean, neither more nor less.

The literary ancestry of Wilde's play has been variously identified. In its witty wordplay and worldly attitudes it has been likened to comedies of the Restoration period such as William Congreve's *Love for Love* (1695). In its genial and lighthearted tone, it has some affinities with the festive comedies of Shakespeare, such as *Twelfth Night* (ca. 1601), and with Oliver Goldsmith's *She Stoops to Conquer* (1773). A more immediate predecessor was *Engaged* (1877), a comic play by W. S. Gilbert that anticipated some of the burlesque effects exploited by Wilde, such as the inviolable imperturbability of the speakers and the interrupting of sentimental scenes by the consumption of food. Gilbert's advice to the actors who were putting on his *Engaged* is worth citing as a clue to how *The Importance of Being Earnest* may be most effectively imagined as a stage representation:

> It is absolutely essential to the success of this piece that it should be played with the most perfect earnestness and gravity throughout. . . . Directly the actors show that they are conscious of the absurdity of their utterances the piece begins to drag.

The Importance of Being Earnest

First Act

SCENE—*Morning room in* ALGERNON's *flat in Half-Moon Street.*[1]

The room is luxuriously and artistically furnished. The sound of a piano is heard in the adjoining room.

> [LANE *is arranging afternoon tea on the table, and after the music has ceased,* ALGERNON *enters.*]

ALGERNON Did you hear what I was playing, Lane?

LANE I didn't think it polite to listen, sir.

ALGERNON I'm sorry for that, for your sake. I don't play accurately—anyone can play accurately—but I play with wonderful expression. As far as the piano is concerned, sentiment is my forte. I keep science for Life.

LANE Yes, sir.

ALGERNON And, speaking of the science of Life, have you got the cucumber sandwiches cut for Lady Bracknell?[2]

LANE Yes, sir. [*Hands them on a salver.*]

ALGERNON [*Inspects them, takes two, and sits down on the sofa.*] Oh! . . . by the way, Lane, I see from your book[3] that on Thursday night, when Lord Shoreham and Mr. Worthing were dining with me, eight bottles of champagne are entered as having been consumed.

LANE Yes, sir; eight bottles and a pint.

ALGERNON Why is it that at a bachelor's establishment the servants invariably drink the champagne? I ask merely for information.

LANE I attribute it to the superior quality of the wine, sir. I have often observed that in married households the champagne is rarely of a first-rate brand.

ALGERNON Good Heavens! Is marriage so demoralizing as that?

LANE I believe it *is* a very pleasant state, sir. I have had very little experience of it myself up to the present. I have only been married once. That was in

---

1. A highly fashionable location (at the time of the play) in the West End of London.
2. Bracknell is the name of a place in Berkshire where the mother of Lord Alfred Douglas had her

summer home, which Wilde had visited.
3. Cellar book, in which records were kept of wines.

consequence of a misunderstanding between myself and a young person.

ALGERNON [*Languidly.*] I don't know that I am much interested in your family life, Lane.

LANE No, sir; it is not a very interesting subject. I never think of it myself.

ALGERNON Very natural, I am sure. That will do, Lane, thank you.

LANE Thank you, sir. [LANE *goes out.*]

ALGERNON Lane's views on marriage seem somewhat lax. Really, if the lower orders don't set us a good example, what on earth is the use of them? They seem, as a class, to have absolutely no sense of moral responsibility.

[*Enter* LANE.]

LANE Mr. Ernest Worthing.

[*Enter* JACK.] [LANE *goes out.*]

ALGERNON How are you, my dear Ernest? What brings you up to town?

JACK Oh, pleasure, pleasure! What else should bring one anywhere? Eating as usual, I see, Algy!

ALGERNON [*Stiffly.*] I believe it is customary in good society to take some slight refreshment at five o'clock. Where have you been since last Thursday?

JACK [*Sitting down on the sofa.*] In the country.

ALGERNON What on earth do you do there?

JACK [*Pulling off his gloves.*] When one is in town one amuses oneself. When one is in the country one amuses other people. It is excessively boring.

ALGERNON And who are the people you amuse?

JACK [*Airily.*] Oh, neighbours, neighbours.

ALGERNON Got nice neighbours in your part of Shropshire?

JACK Perfectly horrid! Never speak to one of them.

ALGERNON How immensely you must amuse them! [*Goes over and takes sandwich.*] By the way, Shropshire is your county, is it not?

JACK Eh? Shropshire?[4] Yes, of course. Hallo! Why all these cups? Why cucumber sandwiches? Why such reckless extravagance in one so young? Who is coming to tea?

ALGERNON Oh! merely Aunt Augusta and Gwendolen.

JACK How perfectly delightful!

ALGERNON Yes, that is all very well; but I am afraid Aunt Augusta won't quite approve of your being here.

JACK May I ask why?

ALGERNON My dear fellow, the way you flirt with Gwendolen is perfectly disgraceful. It is almost as bad as the way Gwendolen flirts with you.

JACK I am in love with Gwendolen. I have come up to town expressly to propose to her.

ALGERNON I thought you had come up for pleasure? . . . I call that business.

JACK How utterly unromantic you are!

ALGERNON I really don't see anything romantic in proposing. It is very romantic to be in love. But there is nothing romantic about a definite proposal. Why, one may be accepted. One usually is, I believe. Then the excitement is all over. The very essence of romance is uncertainty. If ever I get married, I'll certainly try to forget the fact.

---

4. As we learn later, the estate is in Hertfordshire, a long distance from Shropshire. In the four-act version of the play, when this discrepancy is pointed out by Algernon, Jack replies: "My dear fellow! Surely you don't expect me to be accurate about geography? No gentleman is accurate about geography. Why, I got a prize for geography when I was at school. I can't be expected to know anything about it now."

JACK   I have no doubt about that, dear Algy. The Divorce Court was specially invented for people whose memories are so curiously constituted.

ALGERNON   Oh! there is no use speculating on that subject. Divorces are made in Heaven—[JACK *puts out his hand to take a sandwich.* ALGERNON *at once interferes.*] Please don't touch the cucumber sandwiches. They are ordered specially for Aunt Augusta. [*Takes one and eats it.*]

JACK   Well, you have been eating them all the time.

ALGERNON   That is quite a different matter. She is my aunt. [*Takes plate from below.*] Have some bread and butter. The bread and butter is for Gwendolen. Gwendolen is devoted to bread and butter.

JACK [*Advancing to table and helping himself.*]   And very good bread and butter it is too.

ALGERNON   Well, my dear fellow, you need not eat as if you were going to eat it all. You behave as if you were married to her already. You are not married to her already, and I don't think you ever will be.

JACK   Why on earth do you say that?

ALGERNON   Well, in the first place, girls never marry the men they flirt with. Girls don't think it right.

JACK   Oh, that is nonsense!

ALGERNON   It isn't. It is a great truth. It accounts for the extraordinary number of bachelors that one sees all over the place. In the second place, I don't give my consent.

JACK   Your consent!

ALGERNON   My dear fellow, Gwendolen is my first cousin. And before I allow you to marry her, you will have to clear up the whole question of Cecily. [*Rings bell.*]

JACK   Cecily! What on earth do you mean? What do you mean, Algy, by Cecily? I don't know anyone of the name of Cecily.
       [*Enter* LANE.]

ALGERNON   Bring me that cigarette case Mr. Worthing left in the smoking-room the last time he dined here.

LANE   Yes, sir.   [LANE *goes out.*]

JACK   Do you mean to say you have had my cigarette case all this time? I wish to goodness you had let me know. I have been writing frantic letters to Scotland Yard[5] about it. I was very nearly offering a large reward.

ALGERNON   Well, I wish you would offer one. I happen to be more than usually hard up.[6]

JACK   There is no good offering a large reward now that the thing is found.
       [*Enter* LANE *with the cigarette case on a salver.* ALGERNON *takes it at once.* LANE *goes out.*]

ALGERNON   I think that is rather mean of you, Ernest, I must say. [*Opens case and examines it.*] However, it makes no matter, for, now that I look at the inscription inside, I find that the thing isn't yours after all.

JACK   Of course it's mine. [*Moving to him.*] You have seen me with it a hundred times, and you have no right whatsoever to read what is written inside. It is a very ungentlemanly thing to read a private cigarette case.

ALGERNON   Oh! it is absurd to have a hard-and-fast rule about what one should read and what one shouldn't. More than half of modern culture depends on what one shouldn't read.

---

5. Police headquarters in London.   6. Short of money.

JACK I am quite aware of the fact, and I don't propose to discuss modern culture. It isn't the sort of thing one should talk of in private. I simply want my cigarette case back.

ALGERNON Yes; but this isn't your cigarette case. This cigarette case is a present from someone of the name of Cecily, and you said you didn't know anyone of that name.

JACK Well, if you want to know, Cecily happens to be my aunt.

ALGERNON Your aunt!

JACK Yes. Charming old lady she is, too. Lives at Tunbridge Wells.⁷ Just give it back to me, Algy.

ALGERNON [*retreating to back of sofa.*] But why does she call herself little Cecily if she is your aunt and lives at Tunbridge Wells? [*Reading.*] "From little Cecily with her fondest love."

JACK [*Moving to sofa and kneeling upon it.*] My dear fellow, what on earth is there in that? Some aunts are tall, some aunts are not tall. That is a matter that surely an aunt may be allowed to decide for herself. You seem to think that every aunt should be exactly like your aunt! That is absurd! For Heaven's sake give me back my cigarette case. [*Follows Algy round the room.*]

ALGERNON Yes. But why does your aunt call you her uncle? "From little Cecily, with her fondest love to her dear Uncle Jack." There is no objection, I admit, to an aunt being a small aunt, but why an aunt, no matter what her size may be, should call her own nephew her uncle, I can't quite make out. Besides, your name isn't Jack at all; it is Ernest.

JACK It isn't Ernest; it's Jack.

ALGERNON You have always told me it was Ernest. I have introduced you to everyone as Ernest. You answer to the name of Ernest. You look as if your name was Ernest. You are the most earnest looking person I ever saw in my life. It is perfectly absurd your saying that your name isn't Ernest. It's on your cards. Here is one of them. [*Taking it from case.*] "Mr. Ernest Worthing, B. 4, The Albany."⁸ I'll keep this as a proof that your name is Ernest if ever you attempt to deny it to me, or to Gwendolen, or to anyone else. [*Puts the card in his pocket.*]

JACK Well, my name is Ernest in town and Jack in the country, and the cigarette case was given to me in the country.

ALGERNON Yes, but that does not account for the fact that your small Aunt Cecily, who lives at Tunbridge Wells, calls you her dear uncle. Come, old boy, you had much better have the thing out at once.

JACK My dear Algy, you talk exactly as if you were a dentist. It is very vulgar to talk like a dentist when one isn't a dentist. It produces a false impression.

ALGERNON Well, that is exactly what dentists always do. Now, go on! Tell me the whole thing. I may mention that I have always suspected you of being a confirmed and secret Bunburyist; and I am quite sure of it now.

JACK Bunburyist? What on earth do you mean by a Bunburyist?

ALGERNON I'll reveal to you the meaning of that incomparable expression as soon as you are kind enough to inform me why you are Ernest in town and Jack in the country.

JACK Well, produce my cigarette case first.

ALGERNON Here it is. [*Hands cigarette case.*] Now produce your explanation, and pray make it improbable. [*Sits on sofa.*]

7. A fashionable resort town south of London.
8. A former residence of the duke of Albany

(brother of George IV) near Piccadilly that had been converted into elegant apartments.

JACK   My dear fellow, there is nothing improbable about my explanation at all. In fact it's perfectly ordinary. Old Mr. Thomas Cardew, who adopted me when I was a little boy, made me in his will guardian to his granddaughter, Miss Cecily Cardew. Cecily, who addresses me as her uncle from motives of respect that you could not possibly appreciate, lives at my place in the country under the charge of her admirable governess, Miss Prism.

ALGERNON   Where is that place in the country, by the way?

JACK   That is nothing to you, dear boy. You are not going to be invited. . . . I may tell you candidly that the place is not in Shropshire.

ALGERNON   I suspected that, my dear fellow! I have Bunburyed all over Shropshire on two separate occasions. Now, go on. Why are you Ernest in town and Jack in the country?

JACK   My dear Algy, I don't know whether you will be able to understand my real motives. You are hardly serious enough. When one is placed in the position of guardian, one has to adopt a very high moral tone on all subjects. It's one's duty to do so. And as a high moral tone can hardly be said to conduce very much to either one's health or one's happiness, in order to get up to town I have always pretended to have a younger brother of the name of Ernest, who lives in the Albany, and gets into the most dreadful scrapes. That, my dear Algy, is the whole truth pure and simple.

ALGERNON   The truth is rarely pure and never simple. Modern life would be very tedious if it were either, and modern literature a complete impossibility!

JACK   That wouldn't be at all a bad thing.

ALGERNON   Literary criticism is not your forte, my dear fellow. Don't try it. You should leave that to people who haven't been at a University. They do it so well in the daily papers. What you really are is a Bunburyist. I was quite right in saying you were a Bunburyist. You are one of the most advanced Bunburyists I know.

JACK   What on earth do you mean?

ALGERNON   You have invented a very useful young brother called Ernest, in order that you may be able to come up to town as often as you like. I have invented an invaluable permanent invalid called Bunbury, in order that I may be able to go down into the country whenever I choose. Bunbury is perfectly invaluable. If it wasn't for Bunbury's extraordinary bad health, for instance, I wouldn't be able to dine with you at Willis's tonight, for I have been really engaged[9] to Aunt Augusta for more than a week.

JACK   I haven't asked you to dine with me anywhere tonight.

ALGERNON   I know. You are absurdly careless about sending out invitations. It is very foolish of you. Nothing annoys people so much as not receiving invitations.

JACK   You had much better dine with your Aunt Augusta.

ALGERNON   I haven't the smallest intention of doing anything of the kind. To begin with, I dined there on Monday, and once a week is quite enough to dine with one's own relations. In the second place, whenever I do dine there I am always treated as a member of the family, and sent down with[1] either no woman at all, or two. In the third place, I know perfectly well whom she will place me next to, tonight. She will place me next Mary Farquhar, who always flirts with her own husband across the dinner table. That is not very pleasant. Indeed, it is not even decent . . . and that sort of thing is enor-

9. I.e., committed to attend her dinner party. "Willis's": a first-class restaurant in the vicinity of

St. James's Street, in the center of London.
1. I.e., required to escort, as a dinner partner.

mously on the increase. The amount of women in London who flirt with their own husbands is perfectly scandalous. It looks so bad. It is simply washing one's clean linen in public. Besides, now that I know you to be a confirmed Bunburyist, I naturally want to talk to you about Bunburying. I want to tell you the rules.

JACK   I'm not a Bunburyist at all. If Gwendolen accepts me, I am going to kill my brother, indeed I think I'll kill him in any case. Cecily is a little too much interested in him. It is rather a bore. So I am going to get rid of Ernest. And I strongly advise you to do the same with Mr. . . . with your invalid friend who has the absurd name.

ALGERNON   Nothing will induce me to part with Bunbury, and if you ever get married, which seems to me extremely problematic, you will be very glad to know Bunbury. A man who marries without knowing Bunbury has a very tedious time of it.

JACK   That is nonsense. If I marry a charming girl like Gwendolen, and she is the only girl I ever saw in my life that I would marry, I certainly won't want to know Bunbury.

ALGERNON   Then your wife will. You don't seem to realize, that in married life three is company and two is none.

JACK   [*Sententiously.*]   That, my dear young friend, is the theory that the corrupt French Drama has been propounding for the last fifty years.[2]

ALGERNON   Yes; and that the happy English home has proved in half the time.

JACK   For heaven's sake, don't try to be cynical. It's perfectly easy to be cynical.

ALGERNON   My dear fellow, it isn't easy to be anything nowadays. There's such a lot of beastly competition about. [*The sound of an electric bell is heard.*] Ah! that must be Aunt Augusta. Only relatives, or creditors, ever ring in that Wagnerian manner.[3] Now, if I get her out of the way for ten minutes, so that you can have an opportunity for proposing to Gwendolen, may I dine with you tonight at Willis's?

JACK   I suppose so, if you want to.

ALGERNON   Yes, but you must be serious about it. I hate people who are not serious about meals. It is so shallow of them.
        [*Enter* LANE.]

LANE   Lady Bracknell and Miss Fairfax.
        [ALGERNON *goes forward to meet them. Enter* LADY BRACKNELL *and* GWENDOLEN.]

LADY BRACKNELL   Good afternoon, dear Algernon, I hope you are behaving very well.

ALGERNON   I'm feeling very well, Aunt Augusta.

LADY BRACKNELL   That's not quite the same thing. In fact the two things rarely go together. [*Sees* JACK *and bows to him with icy coldness.*]

ALGERNON [*To* GWENDOLEN.]   Dear me, you are smart![4]

GWENDOLEN   I am always smart! Aren't I, Mr. Worthing?

JACK   You're quite perfect, Miss Fairfax.

GWENDOLEN   Oh! I hope I am not that. It would leave no room for develop-

---

2. Almost all the plays by the leading French playwrights of the second half of the 19th century (Alexandre Dumas *fils*, Émile Augier, and Victorien Sardou) focus on marital infidelity. As Brander Matthews, an American critic, noted in 1882, "the trio—husband, wife, and lover" had become "almost universal" in the French theater.

3. Insistently loud, like some of the music in the large-scale operas of Richard Wagner (1813–1883).

4. Elegantly fashionable.

ments, and I intend to develop in many directions. [GWENDOLEN *and* JACK *sit down together in the corner.*]

LADY BRACKNELL   I'm sorry if we are a little late, Algernon, but I was obliged to call on dear Lady Harbury. I hadn't been there since her poor husband's death. I never saw a woman so altered; she looks quite twenty years younger. And now I'll have a cup of tea, and one of those nice cucumber sandwiches you promised me.

ALGERNON   Certainly, Aunt Augusta. [*Goes over to tea-table.*]

LADY BRACKNELL   Won't you come and sit here, Gwendolen?

GWENDOLEN   Thanks, mamma,[5] I'm quite comfortable where I am.

ALGERNON   [*Picking up empty plate in horror.*]   Good heavens! Lane! Why are there no cucumber sandwiches? I ordered them specially.

LANE   [*Gravely.*]   There were no cucumbers in the market this morning, sir. I went down twice.

ALGERNON   No cucumbers!

LANE   No, sir. Not even for ready money.[6]

ALGERNON   That will do, Lane, thank you.

LANE   Thank you, sir.

ALGERNON   I am greatly distressed, Aunt Augusta, about there being no cucumbers, not even for ready money.

LADY BRACKNELL   It really makes no matter, Algernon. I had some crumpets[7] with Lady Harbury, who seems to me to be living entirely for pleasure now.

ALGERNON   I hear her hair has turned quite gold from grief.

LADY BRACKNELL   It certainly has changed its colour. From what cause I, of course, cannot say. [ALGERNON *crosses and hands tea.*] Thank you. I've quite a treat for you tonight, Algernon. I am going to send you down with Mary Farquhar. She is such a nice woman, and so attentive to her husband. It's delightful to watch them.

ALGERNON   I am afraid, Aunt Augusta, I shall have to give up the pleasure of dining with you tonight after all.

LADY BRACKNELL   [*Frowning.*]   I hope not, Algernon. It would put my table completely out. Your uncle would have to dine upstairs.[8] Fortunately he is accustomed to that.

ALGERNON   It is a great bore, and, I need hardly say, a terrible disappointment to me, but the fact is I have just had a telegram to say that my poor friend Bunbury is very ill again. [*Exchanges glances with* JACK.] They seem to think I should be with him.

LADY BRACKNELL   It is very strange. This Mr. Bunbury seems to suffer from curiously bad health.

ALGERNON   Yes; poor Bunbury is a dreadful invalid.

LADY BRACKNELL   Well, I must say, Algernon, that I think it is high time that Mr. Bunbury made up his mind whether he was going to live or to die. This shilly-shallying with the question is absurd. Nor do I in any way approve of the modern sympathy with invalids. I consider it morbid. Illness of any kind is hardly a thing to be encouraged in others. Health is the primary duty of life. I am always telling that to your poor uncle, but he never seems to take much notice . . . as far as any improvement in his ailments goes. I should

---

5. Pronounced with the accent on the second syllable.
6. Immediate payment in cash (rather than on credit).

7. Round griddle breads, served toasted.
8. Because otherwise she would have more women than men at the table.

be obliged if you would ask Mr. Bunbury, from me, to be kind enough not to have a relapse on Saturday, for I rely on you to arrange my music for me. It is my last reception, and one wants something that will encourage conversation, particularly at the end of the season[9] when everyone has practically said whatever they had to say, which, in most cases, was probably not much.

ALGERNON   I'll speak to Bunbury, Aunt Augusta, if he is still conscious, and I think I can promise you he'll be all right by Saturday. Of course the music is a great difficulty. You see, if one plays good music, people don't listen, and if one plays bad music, people don't talk. But I'll run over the program I've drawn out, if you will kindly come into the next room for a moment.

LADY BRACKNELL   Thank you, Algernon. It is very thoughtful of you. [*Rising, and following* ALGERNON.] I'm sure the program will be delightful, after a few expurgations. French songs I cannot possibly allow. People always seem to think that they are improper, and either look shocked, which is vulgar, or laugh, which is worse. But German sounds a thoroughly respectable language, and indeed, I believe is so. Gwendolen, you will accompany me.

GWENDOLEN   Certainly, mamma.

[LADY BRACKNELL *and* ALGERNON *go into the music room,* GWENDOLEN *remains behind.*]

JACK   Charming day it has been, Miss Fairfax.

GWENDOLEN   Pray don't talk to me about the weather, Mr. Worthing. Whenever people talk to me about the weather, I always feel quite certain that they mean something else. And that makes me so nervous.

JACK   I do mean something else.

GWENDOLEN   I thought so. In fact, I am never wrong.

JACK   And I would like to be allowed to take advantage of Lady Bracknell's temporary absence . . .

GWENDOLEN   I would certainly advise you to do so. Mamma has a way of coming back suddenly into a room that I have often had to speak to her about.

JACK [*Nervously.*]   Miss Fairfax, ever since I met you I have admired you more than any girl . . . I have ever met since . . . I met you.

GWENDOLEN   Yes, I am quite aware of the fact. And I often wish that in public, at any rate, you had been more demonstrative. For me you have always had an irresistible fascination. Even before I met you I was far from indifferent to you. [JACK *looks at her in amazement.*] We live, as I hope you know, Mr. Worthing, in an age of ideals. The fact is constantly mentioned in the more expensive monthly magazines, and has reached the provincial pulpits, I am told: and my ideal has always been to love someone of the name of Ernest. There is something in that name that inspires absolute confidence. The moment Algernon first mentioned to me that he had a friend called Ernest, I knew I was destined to love you.

JACK   You really love me, Gwendolen?

GWENDOLEN   Passionately!

JACK   Darling! You don't know how happy you've made me.

GWENDOLEN   My own Ernest!

JACK   But you don't really mean to say that you couldn't love me if my name wasn't Ernest?

9. The social season, extending from May through July, when people of fashion came into London from their country estates for entertainments and parties.

GWENDOLEN   But your name is Ernest.

JACK   Yes, I know it is. But supposing it was something else? Do you mean to say you couldn't love me then?

GWENDOLEN [*Glibly.*]   Ah! that is clearly a metaphysical speculation, and like most metaphysical speculations has very little reference at all to the actual facts of real life, as we know them.

JACK   Personally, darling, to speak quite candidly, I don't much care about the name of Ernest . . . I don't think the name suits me at all.

GWENDOLEN   It suits you perfectly. It is a divine name. It has a music of its own. It produces vibrations.

JACK   Well, really, Gwendolen, I must say that I think there are lots of other much nicer names. I think Jack, for instance, a charming name.

GWENDOLEN   Jack? . . . No, there is very little music in the name Jack, if any at all, indeed. It does not thrill. It produces absolutely no vibrations. . . . I have known several Jacks, and they all, without exception, were more than usually plain. Besides, Jack is a notorious domesticity for John! And I pity any woman who is married to a man called John. She would probably never be allowed to know the entrancing pleasure of a single moment's solitude. The only really safe name is Ernest.

JACK   Gwendolen, I must get christened at once—I mean we must get married at once. There is no time to be lost.

GWENDOLEN   Married, Mr. Worthing?

JACK [*Astounded.*]   Well . . . surely. You know that I love you, and you led me to believe, Miss Fairfax, that you were not absolutely indifferent to me.

GWENDOLEN   I adore you. But you haven't proposed to me yet. Nothing has been said at all about marriage. The subject has not even been touched on.

JACK   Well . . . may I propose to you now?

GWENDOLEN   I think it would be an admirable opportunity. And to spare you any possible disappointment, Mr. Worthing, I think it only fair to tell you quite frankly beforehand that I am fully determined to accept you.

JACK   Gwendolen!

GWENDOLEN   Yes, Mr. Worthing, what have you got to say to me?

JACK   You know what I have got to say to you.

GWENDOLEN   Yes, but you don't say it.

JACK   Gwendolen, will you marry me? [*Goes on his knees.*]

GWENDOLEN   Of course I will, darling. How long you have been about it! I am afraid you have had very little experience in how to propose.

JACK   My own one, I have never loved anyone in the world but you.

GWENDOLEN   Yes, but men often propose for practice. I know my brother Gerald does. All my girlfriends tell me so. What wonderfully blue eyes you have, Ernest! They are quite, quite blue. I hope you will always look at me just like that, especially when there are other people present.

[*Enter* LADY BRACKNELL.]

LADY BRACKNELL   Mr. Worthing! Rise, sir, from this semi-recumbent posture. It is most indecorous.

GWENDOLEN   Mamma! [*He tries to rise; she restrains him.*] I must beg you to retire. This is no place for you. Besides, Mr. Worthing has not quite finished yet.

LADY BRACKNELL   Finished what, may I ask?

GWENDOLEN   I am engaged to Mr. Worthing, mamma.

[*They rise together.*]

LADY BRACKNELL   Pardon me, you are not engaged to anyone. When you do become engaged to someone, I, or your father, should his health permit him, will inform you of the fact. An engagement should come on a young girl as a surprise, pleasant or unpleasant, as the case may be. It is hardly a matter that she could be allowed to arrange for herself. . . . And now I have a few questions to put to you, Mr. Worthing. While I am making these inquiries, you, Gwendolen, will wait for me below in the carriage.

GWENDOLEN [*Reproachfully.*]   Mamma!

LADY BRACKNELL   In the carriage, Gwendolen! [GWENDOLEN *goes to the door. She and* JACK *blow kisses to each other behind* LADY BRACKNELL'*s back.* LADY BRACKNELL *looks vaguely about as if she could not understand what the noise was. Finally turns round.*] Gwendolen, the carriage!

GWENDOLEN   Yes, mamma. [*Goes out, looking back at* JACK.]

LADY BRACKNELL [*Sitting down.*]   You can take a seat, Mr. Worthing.
    [*Looks in her pocket for notebook and pencil.*]

JACK   Thank you, Lady Bracknell, I prefer standing.

LADY BRACKNELL [*Pencil and notebook in hand.*]   I feel bound to tell you that you are not down on my list of eligible young men, although I have the same list as the dear Duchess of Bolton has. We work together, in fact. However, I am quite ready to enter your name, should your answers be what a really affectionate mother requires. Do you smoke?

JACK   Well, yes, I must admit I smoke.

LADY BRACKNELL   I am glad to hear it. A man should always have an occupation of some kind. There are far too many idle men in London as it is. How old are you?

JACK   Twenty-nine.

LADY BRACKNELL   A very good age to be married at. I have always been of opinion that a man who desires to get married should know either everything or nothing. Which do you know?

JACK [*After some hesitation.*]   I know nothing, Lady Bracknell.

LADY BRACKNELL   I am pleased to hear it. I do not approve of anything that tampers with natural ignorance. Ignorance is like a delicate exotic fruit; touch it and the bloom is gone. The whole theory of modern education is radically unsound. Fortunately in England, at any rate, education produces no effect whatsoever. If it did, it would prove a serious danger to the upper classes, and probably lead to acts of violence in Grosvenor Square.[1] What is your income?

JACK   Between seven and eight thousand a year.

LADY BRACKNELL [*Makes a note in her book.*]   In land, or in investments?

JACK   In investments, chiefly.

LADY BRACKNELL   That is satisfactory. What between the duties expected of one during one's lifetime, and the duties exacted from one after one's death,[2] land has ceased to be either a profit or a pleasure. It gives one position, and prevents one from keeping it up. That's all that can be said about land.

JACK   I have a country house with some land, of course, attached to it, about fifteen hundred acres, I believe; but I don't depend on that for my real income. In fact, as far as I can make out, the poachers are the only people who make anything out of it.

LADY BRACKNELL   A country house! How many bedrooms? Well, that point

---

1. A fashionable residential area in the West End of London.

2. The wordplay is on "death duties"—i.e., inheritance taxes.

can be cleared up afterwards. You have a town house, I hope? A girl with a simple, unspoiled nature, like Gwendolen, could hardly be expected to reside in the country.

JACK   Well, I own a house in Belgrave Square,[3] but it is let by the year to Lady Bloxham. Of course, I can get it back whenever I like, at six months' notice.

LADY BRACKNELL   Lady Bloxham? I don't know her.

JACK   Oh, she goes about very little. She is a lady considerably advanced in years.

LADY BRACKNELL   Ah, nowadays that is no guarantee of respectability of character. What number in Belgrave Square?

JACK   149.

LADY BRACKNELL [*Shaking her head.*]   The unfashionable side. I thought there was something. However, that could easily be altered.

JACK   Do you mean the fashion, or the side?

LADY BRACKNELL [*Sternly.*]   Both, if necessary, I presume. What are your politics?

JACK   Well, I am afraid I really have none. I am a Liberal Unionist.[4]

LADY BRACKNELL   Oh, they count as Tories. They dine with us. Or come in the evening, at any rate. Now to minor matters. Are your parents living?

JACK   I have lost both my parents.

LADY BRACKNELL   Both? To lose one parent may be regarded as a misfortune—to lose *both* seems like carelessness. Who was your father? He was evidently a man of some wealth. Was he born in what the Radical papers call the purple of commerce, or did he rise from the ranks of aristocracy?

JACK   I am afraid I really don't know. The fact is, Lady Bracknell, I said I had lost my parents. It would be nearer the truth to say that my parents seem to have lost me. . . . I don't actually know who I am by birth. I was . . . well, I was found.

LADY BRACKNELL   Found!

JACK   The late Mr. Thomas Cardew, an old gentleman of a very charitable and kindly disposition, found me, and gave me the name of Worthing, because he happened to have a first-class ticket for Worthing in his pocket at the time. Worthing is a place in Sussex. It is a seaside resort.

LADY BRACKNELL   Where did the charitable gentleman who had a first-class ticket for this seaside resort find you?

JACK [*Gravely.*]   In a handbag.

LADY BRACKNELL   A handbag?

JACK [*Very seriously.*]   Yes, Lady Bracknell. I was in a handbag—a somewhat large, black leather handbag, with handles to it—an ordinary handbag, in fact.

LADY BRACKNELL   In what locality did this Mr. James, or Thomas, Cardew come across this ordinary handbag?

JACK   In the cloak room at Victoria Station. It was given to him in mistake for his own.[5]

LADY BRACKNELL   The cloak room at Victoria Station?

---

3. Another fashionable residential area in the West End.
4. A splinter group of members of the Liberal Party who in 1886, led by Joseph Chamberlain, joined forces with the Conservative Party (the "Tories") in opposing home rule for Ireland.

5. In the four-act version of the play, Jack explains further what happened to Mr. Cardew: "He did not discover the error till he arrived at his own house. All subsequent efforts to ascertain who I was were unavailing."

JACK   Yes. The Brighton line.

LADY BRACKNELL   The line is immaterial. Mr. Worthing, I confess I feel some-what bewildered by what you have just told me. To be born, or at any rate, bred in a handbag, whether it had handles or not, seems to me to display a contempt for the ordinary decencies of family life that reminds one of the worst excesses of the French Revolution. And I presume you know what that unfortunate movement led to? As for the particular locality in which the handbag was found, a cloak room at a railway station might serve to conceal a social indiscretion—has probably, indeed, been used for that purpose before now—but it could hardly be regarded as an assured basis for a recognized position in good society.

JACK   May I ask you then what you would advise me to do? I need hardly say I would do anything in the world to ensure Gwendolen's happiness.

LADY BRACKNELL   I would strongly advise you, Mr. Worthing, to try and acquire some relations as soon as possible, and to make a definite effort to produce at any rate one parent, of either sex, before the season is quite over.[6]

JACK   Well, I don't see how I could possibly manage to do that. I can produce the handbag at any moment, it is in my dressing room at home. I really think that should satisfy you, Lady Bracknell.

LADY BRACKNELL   Me, sir! What has it to do with me? You can hardly imagine that I and Lord Bracknell would dream of allowing our only daughter—a girl brought up with the utmost care—to marry into a cloak room, and form an alliance with a parcel? Good morning, Mr. Worthing!

[LADY BRACKNELL *sweeps out in majestic indignation.*]

JACK   Good morning! [ALGERNON, *from the other room, strikes up the Wedding March.* JACK *looks perfectly furious, and goes to the door.*] For goodness' sake don't play that ghastly tune, Algy! How idiotic you are!

[*The music stops, and* ALGERNON *enters cheerily.*]

ALGERNON   Didn't it go off all right, old boy? You don't mean to say Gwendolen refused you? I know it is a way she has. She is always refusing people. I think it is most ill-natured of her.

JACK   Oh, Gwendolen is as right as a trivet.[7] As far as she is concerned, we are engaged. Her mother is perfectly unbearable. Never met such a Gorgon[8] . . . I don't really know what a Gorgon is like, but I am quite sure that Lady Bracknell is one. In any case, she is a monster, without being a myth, which is rather unfair . . . I beg your pardon, Algy, I suppose I shouldn't talk about your own aunt in that way before you.

ALGERNON   My dear boy, I love hearing my relations abused. It is the only thing that makes me put up with them at all. Relations are simply a tedious pack of people who haven't got the remotest knowledge of how to live, nor the smallest instinct about when to die.

JACK   Oh, that is nonsense!

6. In the four-act version of the play, Jack later comments to Algernon about Lady Bracknell's demands about locating parents: "After all what does it matter whether a man has ever had a father and mother or not? Mothers, of course, are all right. They pay a chap's bills and don't bother him. But fathers bother a chap and never pay his bills. I don't know a single chap at the club who speaks to his father." And Algernon remarks: "Yes. Fathers are certainly not popular just at present. . . . They are like these chaps, the minor poets. They are never quoted."
7. Proverbial expression meaning reliably steady, like a tripod ("trivet") used to support pots over a fire.
8. In classical mythology a snake-haired female monster; at the sight of her, other creatures turned to stone.

ALGERNON It isn't!

JACK Well, I won't argue about the matter. You always want to argue about things.

ALGERNON That is exactly what things were originally made for.

JACK Upon my word, if I thought that, I'd shoot myself . . . [A pause.] You don't think there is any chance of Gwendolen becoming like her mother in about a hundred and fifty years, do you, Algy?

ALGERNON All women become like their mothers. That is their tragedy. No man does. That's his.

JACK Is that clever?

ALGERNON It is perfectly phrased! and quite as true as any observation in civilized life should be.

JACK I am sick to death of cleverness. Everybody is clever nowadays. You can't go anywhere without meeting clever people. The thing has become an absolute public nuisance. I wish to goodness we had a few fools left.

ALGERNON We have.

JACK I should extremely like to meet them. What do they talk about?

ALGERNON The fools? Oh! about the clever people, of course.

JACK What fools!

ALGERNON By the way, did you tell Gwendolen the truth about your being Ernest in town, and Jack in the country?

JACK [In a very patronizing manner.] My dear fellow, the truth isn't quite the sort of thing one tells to a nice sweet refined girl. What extraordinary ideas you have about the way to behave to a woman!

ALGERNON The only way to behave to a woman is to make love to[9] her, if she is pretty, and to someone else if she is plain.

JACK Oh, that is nonsense.

ALGERNON What about your brother? What about the profligate Ernest?

JACK Oh, before the end of the week I shall have got rid of him. I'll say he died in Paris of apoplexy. Lots of people die of apoplexy, quite suddenly, don't they?

ALGERNON Yes, but it's hereditary, my dear fellow. It's a sort of thing that runs in families. You had much better say a severe chill.

JACK You are sure a severe chill isn't hereditary, or anything of that kind?

ALGERNON Of course it isn't!

JACK Very well, then. My poor brother Ernest is carried off suddenly in Paris, by a severe chill. That gets rid of him.[1]

ALGERNON But I thought you said that . . . Miss Cardew was a little too much interested in your poor brother Ernest? Won't she feel his loss a good deal?

JACK Oh, that is all right. Cecily is not a silly romantic girl, I am glad to say. She has got a capital appetite, goes on long walks, and pays no attention at all to her lessons.

ALGERNON I would rather like to see Cecily.

JACK I will take very good care you never do. She is excessively pretty, and she is only just eighteen.

ALGERNON Have you told Gwendolen yet that you have an excessively pretty ward who is only just eighteen?

9. Woo, court.
1. In the four-act version of the play, Jack explains further: "I'll wear mourning for him, of course; that would be only decent. I don't at all mind wearing mourning. I think that all black, with a good pearl pin, rather smart. Then I'll go down home and break the news to my household."

JACK   Oh! one doesn't blurt these things out to people. Cecily and Gwendolen are perfectly certain to be extremely great friends. I'll bet you anything you like that half an hour after they have met, they will be calling each other sister.

ALGERNON   Women only do that when they have called each other a lot of other things first. Now, my dear boy, if we want to get a good table at Willis's, we really must go and dress. Do you know it is nearly seven?

JACK   [Irritably.]   Oh! it always is nearly seven.

ALGERNON   Well, I'm hungry.

JACK   I never knew you when you weren't. . . .

ALGERNON   What shall we do after dinner? Go to the theatre?

JACK   Oh no! I loathe listening.

ALGERNON   Well, let us go to the club?

JACK   Oh, no! I hate talking.

ALGERNON   Well, we might trot around to the Empire² at ten?

JACK   Oh no! I can't bear looking at things. It is so silly.

ALGERNON   Well, what shall we do?

JACK   Nothing!

ALGERNON   It is awfully hard work doing nothing. However, I don't mind hard work where there is no definite object of any kind.

[Enter LANE.]

LANE   Miss Fairfax.

[Enter GWENDOLEN. LANE goes out.]

ALGERNON   Gwendolen, upon my word!

GWENDOLEN   Algy, kindly turn your back. I have something very particular to say to Mr. Worthing.

ALGERNON   Really, Gwendolen, I don't think I can allow this at all.

GWENDOLEN   Algy, you always adopt a strictly immoral attitude towards life. You are not quite old enough to do that. [ALGERNON retires to the fireplace.]

JACK   My own darling!

GWENDOLEN   Ernest, we may never be married. From the expression on mamma's face I fear we never shall. Few parents nowadays pay any regard to what their children say to them. The old-fashioned respect for the young is fast dying out. Whatever influence I ever had over mamma, I lost at the age of three. But although she may prevent us from becoming man and wife, and I may marry someone else, and marry often, nothing that she can possibly do can alter my eternal devotion to you.

JACK   Dear Gwendolen!

GWENDOLEN   The story of your romantic origin, as related to me by mamma, with unpleasing comments, has naturally stirred the deeper fibres of my nature. Your Christian name has an irresistible fascination. The simplicity of your character makes you exquisitely incomprehensible to me. Your town address at the Albany I have. What is your address in the country?

JACK   The Manor House, Woolton, Hertfordshire.

[ALGERNON, who has been carefully listening, smiles to himself, and writes the address on his shirt-cuff.³ Then picks up the Railway Guide.]

GWENDOLEN   There is a good postal service, I suppose? It may be necessary to do something desperate. That of course will require serious consideration. I will communicate with you daily.

2. A music hall in Leicester Square that featured light entertainment.

3. Because shirt cuffs were heavily starched they provided a good surface on which to make notes.

JACK   My own one!
GWENDOLEN   How long do you remain in town?
JACK   Till Monday.
GWENDOLEN   Good! Algy, you may turn round now.
ALGERNON   Thanks, I've turned round already.
GWENDOLEN   You may also ring the bell.
JACK   You will let me see you to your carriage, my own darling?
GWENDOLEN   Certainly.
JACK [To LANE, who now enters.]   I will see Miss Fairfax out.
LANE   Yes, sir. [JACK and GWENDOLEN go off.]
            [LANE presents several letters on a salver to ALGERNON. It is to be sur-
            mised that they are bills, as ALGERNON after looking at the envelopes,
            tears them up.]
ALGERNON   A glass of sherry, Lane.
LANE   Yes, sir.
ALGERNON   Tomorrow, Lane, I'm going Bunburying.
LANE   Yes, sir.
ALGERNON   I shall probably not be back till Monday. You can put up my dress
            clothes, my smoking jacket,⁴ and all the Bunbury suits . . .
LANE   Yes, sir. [Handing sherry.]
ALGERNON   I hope tomorrow will be a fine day, Lane.
LANE   It never is, sir.
ALGERNON   Lane, you're a perfect pessimist.
LANE   I do my best to give satisfaction, sir.
            [Enter JACK. LANE goes off.]
JACK   There's a sensible, intellectual girl! the only girl I ever cared for in my
            life. [ALGERNON is laughing immoderately.] What on earth are you so amused
            at?
ALGERNON   Oh, I'm a little anxious about poor Bunbury, that is all.
JACK   If you don't take care, your friend Bunbury will get you into a serious
            scrape some day.
ALGERNON   I love scrapes. They are the only things that are never serious.
JACK   Oh, that's nonsense, Algy. You never talk anything but nonsense.
ALGERNON   Nobody ever does.
            [JACK looks indignantly at him, and leaves the room. ALGERNON lights a
            cigarette, reads his shirt-cuff, and smiles.]
                                    ACT-DROP⁵

                                Second Act

SCENE—*Garden at the Manor House. A flight of grey stone steps leads
up to the house. The garden, an old-fashioned one, full of roses. Time
of year, July. Basket chairs, and a table covered with books, are set under
a large yew tree.*

[MISS PRISM⁶ *discovered seated at the table.* CECILY *is at the back watering flowers.*]

---

4. Coat worn when gentlemen assembled in a
room designated for smoking. The object was to
avoid contaminating their regular clothing with the
smell of cigars or pipes, which was considered
offensive to ladies. "Put up": pack up.
5. A special curtain lowered during theatrical performances to denote intervals between acts or
scenes.
6. The name recalls Charles Dickens's *Little Dorrit* (1855–57), in which Mrs. General, a prim and
proper teacher of manners for young ladies, trains
them to repeat "prunes and prism" aloud because
this exercise "gives a pretty form to the lips."

MISS PRISM [*Calling.*]   Cecily, Cecily! Surely such a utilitarian occupation as the watering of flowers is rather Moulton's duty than yours? Especially at a moment when intellectual pleasures await you. Your German grammar is on the table. Pray open it at page fifteen. We will repeat yesterday's lesson.

CECILY [*Coming over very slowly.*]   But I don't like German. It isn't at all a becoming language. I know perfectly well that I look quite plain after my German lesson.

MISS PRISM   Child, you know how anxious your guardian is that you should improve yourself in every way. He laid particular stress on your German, as he was leaving for town yesterday. Indeed, he always lays stress on your German when he is leaving for town.

CECILY   Dear Uncle Jack is so very serious! Sometime he is so serious that I think he cannot be quite well.

MISS PRISM [*Drawing herself up.*]   Your guardian enjoys the best of health, and his gravity of demeanour is especially to be commended in one so comparatively young as he is. I know no one who has a higher sense of duty and responsibility.

CECILY   I suppose that is why he often looks a little bored when we three are together.

MISS PRISM   Cecily! I am surprised at you. Mr. Worthing has many troubles in his life. Idle merriment and triviality would be out of place in his conversation. You must remember his constant anxiety about that unfortunate young man his brother.

CECILY   I wish Uncle Jack would allow that unfortunate young man, his brother, to come down here sometimes. We might have a good influence over him, Miss Prism. I am sure you certainly would. You know German, and geology, and things of that kind influence a man very much. [CECILY *begins to write in her diary.*]

MISS PRISM [*Shaking her head.*]   I do not think that even I could produce any effect on a character that according to his own brother's admission is irretrievably weak and vacillating. Indeed I am not sure that I would desire to reclaim him. I am not in favor of this modern mania for turning bad people into good people at a moment's notice. As a man sows so let him reap.[7] You must put away your diary, Cecily. I really don't see why you should keep a diary at all.

CECILY   I keep a diary in order to enter the wonderful secrets of my life. If I didn't write them down I should probably forget all about them.

MISS PRISM   Memory, my dear Cecily, is the diary that we all carry about with us.

CECILY   Yes, but it usually chronicles the things that have never happened, and couldn't possibly have happened. I believe that Memory is responsible for nearly all the three-volume novels that Mudie[8] sends us.

MISS PRISM   Do not speak slightingly of the three-volume novel, Cecily. I wrote one myself in earlier days.

CECILY   Did you really, Miss Prism? How wonderfully clever you are! I hope it did not end happily? I don't like novels that end happily. They depress me so much.

7. Cf. Galatians 6.7.
8. Mudie's Circulating Library, which lent copies of new three-volume novels (usually sentimental tales) to subscribers for a moderate fee. Mudie's power in controlling the book market, especially for novels, was on the wane by 1895.

MISS PRISM   The good ended happily, and the bad unhappily. That is what Fiction means.

CECILY   I suppose so. But it seems very unfair. And was your novel ever published?

MISS PRISM   Alas! no. The manuscript unfortunately was abandoned. I use the word in the sense of lost or mislaid. To your work, child, these speculations are profitless.

CECILY   [Smiling.]   But I see dear Dr. Chasuble⁹ coming up through the garden.

MISS PRISM   [Rising and advancing.]   Dr. Chasuble! This is indeed a pleasure.

[Enter CANON CHASUBLE.]

CHASUBLE   And how are we this morning? Miss Prism, you are, I trust, well?

CECILY   Miss Prism has just been complaining of a slight headache. I think it would do her so much good to have a short stroll with you in the Park, Dr. Chasuble.

MISS PRISM   Cecily, I have not mentioned anything about a headache.

CECILY   No, dear Miss Prism, I know that, but I felt instinctively that you had a headache. Indeed I was thinking about that, and not about my German lesson, when the Rector came in.

CHASUBLE   I hope, Cecily, you are not inattentive.

CECILY   Oh, I am afraid I am.

CHASUBLE   That is strange. Were I fortunate enough to be Miss Prism's pupil, I would hang upon her lips. [MISS PRISM glares.] I spoke metaphorically.—My metaphor was drawn from bees. Ahem! Mr. Worthing, I suppose, has not returned from town yet?

MISS PRISM   We do not expect him till Monday afternoon.

CHASUBLE   Ah yes, he usually likes to spend his Sunday in London. He is not one of those whose sole aim is enjoyment, as, by all accounts, that unfortunate young man his brother seems to be. But I must not disturb Egeria¹ and her pupil any longer.

MISS PRISM   Egeria? My name is Laetitia, Doctor.

CHASUBLE   [Bowing.]   A classical allusion merely, drawn from the Pagan authors. I shall see you both no doubt at Evensong?²

MISS PRISM   I think, dear Doctor, I will have a stroll with you. I find I have a headache after all, and a walk might do it good.

CHASUBLE   With pleasure, Miss Prism, with pleasure. We might go as far as the schools and back.

MISS PRISM   That would be delightful. Cecily, you will read your Political Economy³ in my absence. The chapter on the Fall of the Rupee⁴ you may omit. It is somewhat too sensational. Even these metallic problems have their melodramatic side. [Goes down the garden with DR. CHASUBLE.]

CECILY   [Picks up books and throws them back on table.]   Horrid Political Economy! Horrid Geography! Horrid, horrid German!

[Enter MERRIMAN with a card on a salver.]

MERRIMAN   Mr. Ernest Worthing has just driven over from the station. He has brought his luggage with him.

9. A chasuble is an ornate garment worn by a priest.
1. In Roman legend a nymph who gave counsel to the second king of Rome. Her name was therefore also used as an epithet for a woman who provides guidance.
2. Evening church services.
3. I.e., book about economics.
4. The basic unit of currency in India. British civil servants who worked in India were paid in rupees and would suffer from its fall in value.

CECILY [*Takes the card and reads it.*] "Mr. Ernest Worthing, B. 4, The Albany, W." Uncle Jack's brother! Did you tell him Mr. Worthing was in town?

MERRIMAN Yes, Miss. He seemed very much disappointed. I mentioned that you and Miss Prism were in the garden. He said he was anxious to speak to you privately for a moment.

CECILY. Ask Mr. Ernest Worthing to come here. I suppose you had better talk to the housekeeper about a room for him.

MERRIMAN Yes, Miss.   [MERRIMAN *goes off.*]

CECILY I have never met any really wicked person before. I feel rather frightened. I am so afraid he will look just like everyone else. [*Enter* ALGERNON, *very gay and debonair.*] He does!

ALGERNON [*Raising his hat.*] You are my little cousin Cecily, I'm sure.

CECILY You are under some strange mistake. I am not little. In fact, I believe I am more than usually tall for my age. [ALGERNON *is rather taken aback.*] But I am your cousin Cecily. You, I see from your card, are Uncle Jack's brother, my cousin Ernest, my wicked cousin Ernest.

ALGERNON Oh! I am not really wicked at all, cousin Cecily. You mustn't think that I am wicked.

CECILY If you are not, then you have certainly been deceiving us all in a very inexcusable manner. I hope you have not been leading a double life, pretending to be wicked and being really good all the time. That would be hypocrisy.

ALGERNON [*Looks at her in amazement.*] Oh! Of course I have been rather reckless.

CECILY I am glad to hear it.

ALGERNON In fact, now you mention the subject, I have been very bad in my own small way.

CECILY I don't think you should be so proud of that, though I am sure it must have been very pleasant.

ALGERNON It is much pleasanter being here with you.

CECILY I can't understand how you are here at all. Uncle Jack won't be back till Monday afternoon.

ALGERNON That is a great disappointment. I am obliged to go up by the first train on Monday morning. I have a business appointment that I am anxious . . . to miss.

CECILY Couldn't you miss it anywhere but in London?

ALGERNON No: the appointment is in London.

CECILY Well, I know, of course, how important it is not to keep a business engagement, if one wants to retain any sense of the beauty of life, but still I think you had better wait till Uncle Jack arrives. I know he wants to speak to you about your emigrating.

ALGERNON About my what?

CECILY Your emigrating. He has gone up to buy your outfit.

ALGERNON I certainly wouldn't let Jack buy my outfit. He has no taste in neckties at all.

CECILY I don't think you will require neckties. Uncle Jack is sending you to Australia.[5]

***

5. The British had originally viewed Australia as a place to which they banished their criminals. By this time, however, it was perceived in some quarters as a place, like Canada, to which families might send harmless but useless members, who would be paid an allowance to remain abroad.

ALGERNON   Australia? I'd sooner die.

CECILY   Well, he said at dinner on Wednesday night, that you would have to choose between this world, the next world, and Australia.

ALGERNON   Oh, well! The accounts I have received of Australia and the next world are not particularly encouraging. This world is good enough for me, cousin Cecily.

CECILY   Yes, but are you good enough for it?

ALGERNON   I'm afraid I'm not that. That is why I want you to reform me. You might make that your mission, if you don't mind, cousin Cecily.

CECILY   I'm afraid I've no time, this afternoon.

ALGERNON   Well, would you mind my reforming myself this afternoon?

CECILY   It is rather Quixotic of you. But I think you should try.

ALGERNON   I will. I feel better already.

CECILY   You are looking a little worse.

ALGERNON   That is because I am hungry.

CECILY   How thoughtless of me. I should have remembered that when one is going to lead an entirely new life, one requires regular and wholesome meals. Won't you come in?

ALGERNON   Thank you. Might I have a buttonhole[6] first? I never have any appetite unless I have a buttonhole first.

CECILY   A Maréchal Niel?[7] [*Picks up scissors.*]

ALGERNON   No, I'd sooner have a pink rose.

CECILY   Why? [*Cuts a flower.*]

ALGERNON   Because you are like a pink rose, cousin Cecily.

CECILY   I don't think it can be right for you to talk to me like that. Miss Prism never says such things to me.

ALGERNON   Then Miss Prism is a shortsighted old lady. [CECILY *puts the rose in his buttonhole.*] You are the prettiest girl I ever saw.

CECILY   Miss Prism says that all good looks are a snare.

ALGERNON   They are a snare that every sensible man would like to be caught in.

CECILY   Oh! I don't think I would care to catch a sensible man. I shouldn't know what to talk to him about.

[*They pass into the house.* MISS PRISM *and* DR. CHASUBLE *return.*]

MISS PRISM   You are too much alone, dear Dr. Chasuble. You should get married. A misanthrope I can understand—a womanthrope, never!

CHASUBLE [*With a scholar's shudder.*][8]   Believe me, I do not deserve so neologistic a phrase. The precept as well as the practice of the Primitive Church[9] was distinctly against matrimony.

MISS PRISM [*Sententiously.*]   That is obviously the reason why the Primitive Church has not lasted up to the present day. And you do not seem to realize, dear Doctor, that by persistently remaining single, a man converts himself into a permanent public temptation. Men should be more careful; this very celibacy leads weaker vessels astray.

---

6. I.e., a flower to wear in the buttonhole of his coat lapel.
7. A chrome-yellow variety of rose named after Adolphe Niel (1802–1869), one of the generals of Napoleon III.
8. He shudders because instead of using the cor-

rect word for woman hater, *misogynist,* she has coined her own term, one that is etymologically nonsensical.
9. The early Christian Church, of the 1st to 4th centuries.

CHASUBLE But is a man not equally attractive when married?
MISS PRISM No married man is ever attractive except to his wife.
CHASUBLE And often, I've been told, not even to her.
MISS PRISM That depends on the intellectual sympathies of the woman. Maturity can always be depended on. Ripeness can be trusted. Young women are green. [DR. CHASUBLE *starts.*] I spoke horticulturally. My metaphor was drawn from fruits. But where is Cecily?
CHASUBLE Perhaps she followed us to the schools.
    [*Enter* JACK *slowly from the back of the garden. He is dressed in the deepest mourning, with crape hat-band and black gloves.*]
MISS PRISM Mr. Worthing!
CHASUBLE Mr. Worthing?
MISS PRISM This is indeed a surprise. We did not look for you till Monday afternoon.
JACK [*Shakes* MISS PRISM's *hand in a tragic manner.*] I have returned sooner than I expected. Dr. Chasuble, I hope you are well?
CHASUBLE Dear Mr. Worthing, I trust this garb of woe does not betoken some terrible calamity?
JACK My brother.
MISS PRISM More shameful debts and extravagance?
CHASUBLE Still leading his life of pleasure?
JACK [*Shaking his head.*] Dead!
CHASUBLE Your brother Ernest dead?
JACK Quite dead.
MISS PRISM What a lesson for him! I trust he will profit by it.
CHASUBLE Mr. Worthing, I offer you my sincere condolence. You have at least the consolation of knowing that you were always the most generous and forgiving of brothers.
JACK Poor Ernest! He had many faults, but it is a sad, sad blow.
CHASUBLE Very sad indeed. Were you with him at the end?
JACK No. He died abroad; in Paris, in fact. I had a telegram last night from the manager of the Grand Hotel.
CHASUBLE Was the cause of death mentioned?
JACK A severe chill, it seems.
MISS PRISM As a man sows, so shall he reap.
CHASUBLE [*Raising his hand.*] Charity, dear Miss Prism, charity! None of us are perfect. I myself am peculiarly susceptible to drafts. Will the interment take place here?
JACK No. He seemed to have expressed a desire to be buried in Paris.
CHASUBLE In Paris! [*Shakes his head.*] I fear that hardly points to any very serious state of mind at the last. You would no doubt wish me to make some slight allusion to this tragic domestic affliction next Sunday. [JACK *presses his hand convulsively.*] My sermon on the meaning of the manna in the wilderness can be adapted to almost any occasion, joyful, or, as in the present case, distressing. [*All sigh.*] I have preached it at harvest celebrations, christenings, confirmations, on days of humiliation and festal days. The last time I delivered it was in the Cathedral, as a charity sermon on behalf of the Society for the Prevention of Discontent among the Upper Orders. The Bishop, who was present, was much struck by some of the analogies I drew.

JACK   Ah! That reminds me, you mentioned christenings, I think, Dr. Chasuble? I suppose you know how to christen all right? [DR. CHASUBLE *looks astounded.*] I mean, of course, you are continually christening, aren't you?

MISS PRISM   It is, I regret to say, one of the Rector's most constant duties in this parish. I have often spoken to the poorer classes on the subject. But they don't seem to know what thrift is.

CHASUBLE   But is there any particular infant in whom you are interested, Mr. Worthing? Your brother was, I believe, unmarried, was he not?

JACK   Oh yes.

MISS PRISM   [*Bitterly.*]   People who live entirely for pleasure usually are.

JACK   But it is not for any child, dear Doctor. I am very fond of children. No! the fact is, I would like to be christened myself, this afternoon, if you have nothing better to do.

CHASUBLE   But surely, Mr. Worthing, you have been christened already?

JACK   I don't remember anything about it.

CHASUBLE   But have you any grave doubts on the subject?

JACK   I certainly intend to have. Of course I don't know if the thing would bother you in any way, or if you think I am a little too old now.

CHASUBLE   Not at all. The sprinkling, and, indeed, the immersion of adults is a perfectly canonical practice.

JACK   Immersion!

CHASUBLE   You need have no apprehensions. Sprinkling is all that is necessary, or indeed I think advisable. Our weather is so changeable. At what hour would you wish the ceremony performed?

JACK   Oh, I might trot round about five if that would suit you.

CHASUBLE   Perfectly, perfectly! In fact I have two similar ceremonies to perform at that time. A case of twins that occurred recently in one of the outlying cottages on your own estate. Poor Jenkins the carter, a most hardworking man.

JACK   Oh! I don't see much fun in being christened along with other babies. It would be childish. Would half-past five do?

CHASUBLE   Admirably! Admirably! [*Takes out watch.*] And now, dear Mr. Worthing, I will not intrude any longer into a house of sorrow. I would merely beg you not to be too much bowed down by grief. What seem to us bitter trials are often blessings in disguise.

MISS PRISM   This seems to me a blessing of an extremely obvious kind.
        [*Enter* CECILY *from the house.*]

CECILY   Uncle Jack! Oh, I am pleased to see you back. But what horrid clothes you have got on! Do go and change them.

MISS PRISM   Cecily!

CHASUBLE   My child! my child! [CECILY *goes towards* JACK; *he kisses her brow in a melancholy manner.*]

CECILY   What is the matter, Uncle Jack? Do look happy! You look as if you had toothache, and I have got such a surprise for you. Who do you think is in the dining room? Your brother!

JACK   Who?

CECILY   Your brother Ernest. He arrived about half an hour ago.

JACK   What nonsense! I haven't got a brother!

CECILY   Oh, don't say that. However badly he may have behaved to you in the past he is still your brother. You couldn't be so heartless as to disown him.

I'll tell him to come out. And you will shake hands with him, won't you, Uncle Jack? [*Runs back into the house.*]

CHASUBLE   These are very joyful tidings.

MISS PRISM   After we had all been resigned to his loss, his sudden return seems to me peculiarly distressing.

JACK   My brother is in the dining room? I don't know what it all means. I think it is perfectly absurd.

> [*Enter* ALGERNON *and* CECILY *hand in hand. They come slowly up to* JACK.]

JACK   Good heavens! [*Motions* ALGERNON *away.*]

ALGERNON   Brother John, I have come down from town to tell you that I am very sorry for all the trouble I have given you, and that I intend to lead a better life in the future. [JACK *glares at him and does not take his hand.*]

CECILY   Uncle Jack, you are not going to refuse your own brother's hand?

JACK   Nothing will induce me to take his hand. I think his coming down here disgraceful. He knows perfectly well why.

CECILY   Uncle Jack, do be nice. There is some good in everyone. Ernest has just been telling me about his poor invalid friend Mr. Bunbury whom he goes to visit so often. And surely there must be much good in one who is kind to an invalid, and leaves the pleasures of London to sit by a bed of pain.

JACK   Oh! he has been talking about Bunbury, has he?

CECILY   Yes, he has told me all about poor Mr. Bunbury, and his terrible state of health.

JACK   Bunbury! Well, I won't have him talk to you about Bunbury or about anything else. It is enough to drive one perfectly frantic.

ALGERNON   Of course I admit that the faults were all on my side. But I must say that I think that Brother John's coldness to me is peculiarly painful. I expected a more enthusiastic welcome, especially considering it is the first time I have come here.

CECILY   Uncle Jack, if you don't shake hands with Ernest, I will never forgive you.

JACK   Never forgive me?

CECILY   Never, never, never!

JACK   Well, this is the last time I shall ever do it. [*Shakes hands with* ALGERNON *and glares.*]

CHASUBLE   It's pleasant, is it not, to see so perfect a reconciliation? I think we might leave the two brothers together.

MISS PRISM   Cecily, you will come with us.

CECILY   Certainly, Miss Prism. My little task of reconciliation is over.

CHASUBLE   You have done a beautiful action today, dear child.

MISS PRISM   We must not be premature in our judgments.

CECILY   I feel very happy. [*They all go off.*]

JACK   You young scoundrel, Algy, you must get out of this place as soon as possible. I don't allow any Bunburying here.

> [*Enter* MERRIMAN.]

MERRIMAN   I have put Mr. Ernest's things in the room next to yours, sir. I suppose that is all right?

JACK   What?

MERRIMAN   Mr. Ernest's luggage, sir. I have unpacked it and put it in the room next to your own.

JACK   His luggage?

MERRIMAN   Yes, sir. Three portmanteaus, a dressing case, two hat-boxes, and a large luncheon basket.[1]

ALGERNON   I am afraid I can't stay more than a week this time.

JACK   Merriman, order the dogcart[2] at once. Mr. Ernest has been suddenly called back to town.

MERRIMAN   Yes, sir.   [*Goes back into the house.*]

ALGERNON   What a fearful liar you are, Jack. I have not been called back to town at all.

JACK   Yes, you have.

ALGERNON   I haven't heard anyone call me.

JACK   Your duty as a gentleman calls you back.

ALGERNON   My duty as a gentleman has never interfered with my pleasures in the smallest degree.

JACK   I can quite understand that.

ALGERNON   Well, Cecily is a darling.

JACK   You are not to talk of Miss Cardew like that. I don't like it.

ALGERNON   Well, I don't like your clothes. You look perfectly ridiculous in them. Why on earth don't you go up and change? It is perfectly childish to be in deep mourning for a man who is actually staying for a whole week with you in your house as a guest. I call it grotesque.

JACK   You are certainly not staying with me for a whole week as a guest or anything else. You have got to leave . . . by the four-five train.

ALGERNON   I certainly won't leave you so long as you are in mourning. It would be most unfriendly. If I were in mourning you would stay with me, I suppose. I should think it very unkind if you didn't.

JACK   Well, will you go if I change my clothes?

ALGERNON   Yes, if you are not too long. I never saw anybody take so long to dress, and with such little result.

JACK   Well, at any rate, that is better than being always overdressed as you are.

ALGERNON   If I am occasionally a little overdressed, I make up for it by being always immensely overeducated.

JACK   Your vanity is ridiculous, your conduct an outrage, and your presence in my garden utterly absurd. However, you have got to catch the four-five, and I hope you will have a pleasant journey back to town. This Bunburying, as you call it, has not been a great success for you. [*Goes into the house.*]

ALGERNON   I think it has been a great success. I'm in love with Cecily, and that is everything.

    [*Enter* CECILY *at the back of the garden. She picks up the can and begins to water the flowers.*]

But I must see her before I go, and make arrangements for another Bunbury. Ah, there she is.

---

1. According to *Cassell's Domestic Dictionary* (1877–79), "a convenient little receptacle in which gentlemen who are going out shooting for the day, or artists who wish to sketch, can carry their luncheon with them." "Portmanteaus": large leather suitcases. A "dressing case" (also according to *Cassell's*) was "ordinarily made of rosewood, mahogany or coromandel wood." It was supposed to include "scent bottles, jars for pomade and tooth-powders, hair brushes and combs, shaving, nail and tooth brushes, razors and strop, nail scissors, button-hook, tweezer, nail file and penknife" [noted by Russell Jackson].
2. A horse-drawn cart with seats, originally designed to carry hunters and their hunting dogs.

CECILY   Oh, I merely came back to water the roses. I thought you were with Uncle Jack.

ALGERNON   He's gone to order the dogcart for me.

CECILY   Oh, is he going to take you for a nice drive?

ALGERNON   He's going to send me away.

CECILY   Then have we got to part?

ALGERNON   I am afraid so. It's very painful parting.

CECILY   It is always painful to part from people whom one has known for a very brief space of time. The absence of old friends one can endure with equanimity. But even a momentary separation from anyone to whom one has just been introduced is almost unbearable.

ALGERNON   Thank you.

[*Enter* MERRIMAN.]

MERRIMAN   The dogcart is at the door, sir. [ALGERNON *looks appealingly at* CECILY.]

CECILY   It can wait, Merriman . . . for . . . five minutes.

MERRIMAN   Yes, Miss.   [*Exit* MERRIMAN.]

ALGERNON   I hope, Cecily, I shall not offend you if I state quite frankly and openly that you seem to me to be in every way the visible personification of absolute perfection.

CECILY   I think your frankness does you great credit, Ernest. If you will allow me I will copy your remarks into my diary. [*Goes over to table and begins writing in diary.*]

ALGERNON   Do you really keep a diary? I'd give anything to look at it. May I?

CECILY   Oh no. [*Puts her hand over it.*] You see, it is simply a very young girl's record of her own thoughts and impressions, and consequently meant for publication. When it appears in volume form I hope you will order a copy. But pray, Ernest, don't stop. I delight in taking down from dictation. I have reached "absolute perfection." You can go on. I am quite ready for more.

ALGERNON [*Somewhat taken aback.*]   Ahem! Ahem!

CECILY   Oh, don't cough, Ernest. When one is dictating one should speak fluently and not cough. Besides, I don't know how to spell a cough. [*Writes as* ALGERNON *speaks.*]

ALGERNON [*Speaking very rapidly.*]   Cecily, ever since I first looked upon your wonderful and incomparable beauty, I have dared to love you wildly, passionately, devotedly, hopelessly.

CECILY   I don't think that you should tell me that you love me wildly, passionately, devotedly, hopelessly. Hopelessly doesn't seem to make much sense, does it?

ALGERNON   Cecily!

[*Enter* MERRIMAN.]

MERRIMAN   The dogcart is waiting, sir.

ALGERNON   Tell it to come round next week, at the same hour.

MERRIMAN [*Looks at* CECILY, *who makes no sign.*]   Yes, sir.

[MERRIMAN *retires.*]

CECILY   Uncle Jack would be very much annoyed if he knew you were staying on till next week, at the same hour.

ALGERNON   Oh, I don't care about Jack. I don't care for anybody in the whole world but you. I love you, Cecily. You will marry me, won't you?

CECILY   You silly boy! Of course. Why, we have been engaged for the last three months.

ALGERNON   For the last three months?

CECILY   Yes, it will be exactly three months on Thursday.

ALGERNON   But how did we become engaged?

CECILY   Well, ever since dear Uncle Jack first confessed to us that he had a younger brother who was very wicked and bad, you of course have formed the chief topic of conversation between myself and Miss Prism. And of course a man who is much talked about is always very attractive. One feels there must be something in him after all. I daresay it was foolish of me, but I fell in love with you, Ernest.

ALGERNON   Darling! And when was the engagement actually settled?

CECILY   On the 14th of February last. Worn out by your entire ignorance of my existence, I determined to end the matter one way or the other, and after a long struggle with myself I accepted you under this dear old tree here. The next day I bought this little ring in your name, and this is the little bangle with the true lovers' knot I promised you always to wear.

ALGERNON   Did I give you this? It's very pretty, isn't it?

CECILY   Yes, you've wonderfully good taste, Ernest. It's the excuse I've always given for your leading such a bad life. And this is the box in which I keep all your dear letters. [*Kneels at table, opens box, and produces letters tied up with blue ribbon.*]

ALGERNON   My letters! But my own sweet Cecily, I have never written you any letters.

CECILY   You need hardly remind me of that, Ernest. I remember only too well that I was forced to write your letters for you. I always wrote three times a week, and sometimes oftener.

ALGERNON   Oh, do let me read them, Cecily?

CECILY   Oh, I couldn't possibly. They would make you far too conceited. [*Replaces box.*] The three you wrote me after I had broken off the engagement are so beautiful, and so badly spelled, that even now I can hardly read them without crying a little.

ALGERNON   But was our engagement ever broken off?

CECILY   Of course it was. On the 22nd of last March. You can see the entry if you like. [*Shows diary.*] "Today I broke off my engagement with Ernest. I feel it is better to do so. The weather still continues charming."

ALGERNON   But why on earth did you break it off? What had I done? I had done nothing at all. Cecily, I am very much hurt indeed to hear you broke it off. Particularly when the weather was so charming.

CECILY   It would hardly have been a really serious engagement if it hadn't been broken off at least once. But I forgave you before the week was out.

ALGERNON   [*Crossing to her, and kneeling.*]   What a perfect angel you are, Cecily.

CECILY   You dear romantic boy. [*He kisses her, she puts her fingers through his hair.*] I hope your hair curls naturally, does it?

ALGERNON   Yes, darling, with a little help from others.

CECILY   I am so glad.

ALGERNON   You'll never break off our engagement again, Cecily?

CECILY   I don't think I could break it off now that I have actually met you. Besides, of course, there is the question of your name.

ALGERNON   Yes, of course. [*Nervously.*]

CECILY   You must not laugh at me, darling, but it had always been a girlish dream of mine to love someone whose name was Ernest. [ALGERNON *rises,*

CECILY *also.*] There is something in that name that seems to inspire absolute confidence. I pity any poor married woman whose husband is not called Ernest.

ALGERNON   But, my dear child, do you mean to say you could not love me if I had some other name?

CECILY   But what name?

ALGERNON   Oh, any name you like—Algernon—for instance . . .

CECILY   But I don't like the name of Algernon.

ALGERNON   Well, my own dear, sweet, loving little darling, I really can't see why you should object to the name of Algernon. It is not at all a bad name. In fact, it is rather an aristocratic name. Half of the chaps who get into the Bankruptcy Court are called Algernon. But seriously, Cecily . . . [*Moving to her.*] . . . if my name was Algy, couldn't you love me?

CECILY [*Rising.*]   I might respect you, Ernest, I might admire your character, but I fear that I should not be able to give you my undivided attention.

ALGERNON   Ahem! Cecily! [*Picking up hat.*] Your Rector here is, I suppose, thoroughly experienced in the practice of all the rites and ceremonials of the Church?

CECILY   Oh, yes. Dr. Chasuble is a most learned man. He has never written a single book, so you can imagine how much he knows.

ALGERNON   I must see him at once on a most important christening—I mean on most important business.

CECILY   Oh!

ALGERNON   I shan't be away more than half an hour.

CECILY   Considering that we have been engaged since February the 14th, and that I only met you today for the first time, I think it is rather hard that you should leave me for so long a period as half an hour. Couldn't you make it twenty minutes?

ALGERNON   I'll be back in no time. [*Kisses her and rushes down the garden.*]

CECILY   What an impetuous boy he is! I like his hair so much. I must enter his proposal in my diary.

[*Enter* MERRIMAN.]

MERRIMAN   A Miss Fairfax has just called to see Mr. Worthing. On very important business, Miss Fairfax states.

CECILY   Isn't Mr. Worthing in his library?

MERRIMAN   Mr. Worthing went over in the direction of the Rectory some time ago.

CECILY   Pray ask the lady to come out here; Mr. Worthing is sure to be back soon. And you can bring tea.

MERRIMAN   Yes, Miss.   [*Goes out.*]

CECILY   Miss Fairfax! I suppose one of the many good elderly women who are associated with Uncle Jack in some of his philanthropic work in London. I don't quite like women who are interested in philanthropic work. I think it is so forward of them.

[*Enter* MERRIMAN.]

MERRIMAN   Miss Fairfax.

[*Enter* GWENDOLEN.]   [*Exit* MERRIMAN.]

CECILY [*Advancing to meet her.*]   Pray let me introduce myself to you. My name is Cecily Cardew.

GWENDOLEN   Cecily Cardew? [*Moving to her and shaking hands.*] What a very sweet name! Something tells me that we are going to be great friends. I like you already more than I can say. My first impressions of people are never wrong.

CECILY   How nice of you to like me so much after we have known each other such a comparatively short time. Pray sit down.

GWENDOLEN [Still standing up.]   I may call you Cecily, may I not?

CECILY   With pleasure!

GWENDOLEN   And you will always call me Gwendolen, won't you?

CECILY   If you wish.

GWENDOLEN   Then that is all quite settled, is it not?

CECILY   I hope so. [A pause. They both sit down together.]

GWENDOLEN   Perhaps this might be a favorable opportunity for my mentioning who I am. My father is Lord Bracknell. You have never heard of papa, I suppose?

CECILY   I don't think so.

GWENDOLEN   Outside the family circle, papa, I am glad to say, is entirely unknown. I think that is quite as it should be. The home seems to me to be the proper sphere for the man. And certainly once a man begins to neglect his domestic duties he becomes painfully effeminate, does he not? And I don't like that. It makes men so very attractive. Cecily, mamma, whose views on education are remarkably strict, has brought me up to be extremely short-sighted; it is part of her system; so do you mind my looking at you through my glasses?

CECILY   Oh! not at all, Gwendolen. I am very fond of being looked at.

GWENDOLEN [After examining CECILY carefully through a lorgnette.]   You are here on a short visit, I suppose.

CECILY   Oh no! I live here.

GWENDOLEN [Severely.]   Really? Your mother, no doubt, or some female relative of advanced years, resides here also?

CECILY   Oh no! I have no mother, nor, in fact, any relations.

GWENDOLEN   Indeed?

CECILY   My dear guardian, with the assistance of Miss Prism, has the arduous task of looking after me.

GWENDOLEN   Your guardian?

CECILY   Yes, I am Mr. Worthing's ward.

GWENDOLEN   Oh! It is strange he never mentioned to me that he had a ward. How secretive of him! He grows more interesting hourly. I am not sure, however, that the news inspires me with feelings of unmixed delight. [Rising and going to her.] I am very fond of you, Cecily; I have liked you ever since I met you! But I am bound to state that now that I know that you are Mr. Worthing's ward, I cannot help expressing a wish you were—well just a little older than you seem to be—and not quite so very alluring in appearance. In fact, if I may speak candidly——

CECILY   Pray do! I think that whenever one has anything unpleasant to say, one should always be quite candid.

GWENDOLEN   Well, to speak with perfect candour, Cecily, I wish that you were fully forty-two, and more than usually plain for your age. Ernest has a strong upright nature. He is the very soul of truth and honour. Disloyalty would be as impossible to him as deception. But even men of the noblest possible moral character are extremely susceptible to the influence of the physical charms of others. Modern, no less than Ancient History, supplies us with many most painful examples of what I refer to. If it were not so, indeed, History would be quite unreadable.

CECILY I beg your pardon, Gwendolen, did you say Ernest?

GWENDOLEN Yes.

CECILY Oh, but it is not Mr. Ernest Worthing who is my guardian. It is his brother—his elder brother.

GWENDOLEN [Sitting down again.] Ernest never mentioned to me that he had a brother.

CECILY I am sorry to say they have not been on good terms for a long time.

GWENDOLEN Ah! that accounts for it. And now that I think of it I have never heard any man mention his brother. The subject seems distasteful to most men. Cecily, you have lifted a load from my mind. I was growing almost anxious. It would have been terrible if any cloud had come across a friendship like ours, would it not? Of course you are quite, quite sure that it is not Mr. Ernest Worthing who is your guardian?

CECILY Quite sure. [A pause.] In fact, I am going to be his.

GWENDOLEN [Inquiringly.] I beg your pardon?

CECILY [Rather shy and confidingly.] Dearest Gwendolen, there is no reason why I should make a secret of it to you. Our little county newspaper is sure to chronicle the fact next week. Mr. Ernest Worthing and I are engaged to be married.

GWENDOLEN [Quite politely, rising.] My darling Cecily, I think there must be some slight error. Mr. Ernest Worthing is engaged to me. The announcement will appear in the Morning Post[3] on Saturday at the latest.

CECILY [Very politely, rising.] I am afraid you must be under some misconception. Ernest proposed to me exactly ten minutes ago. [Shows diary.]

GWENDOLEN [Examines diary through her lorgnette carefully.] It is certainly very curious, for he asked me to be his wife yesterday afternoon at 5:30. If you would care to verify the incident, pray do so. [Produces diary of her own.] I never travel without my diary. One should always have something sensational to read in the train. I am so sorry, dear Cecily, if it is any disappointment to you, but I am afraid I have the prior claim.

CECILY It would distress me more than I can tell you, dear Gwendolen, if it caused you any mental or physical anguish, but I feel bound to point out that since Ernest proposed to you he clearly has changed his mind.

GWENDOLEN [Meditatively.] If the poor fellow has been entrapped into any foolish promise I shall consider it my duty to rescue him at once, and with a firm hand.

CECILY [Thoughtfully and sadly.] Whatever unfortunate entanglement my dear boy may have got into, I will never reproach him with it after we are married.

GWENDOLEN Do you allude to me, Miss Cardew, as an entanglement? You are presumptuous. On an occasion of this kind it becomes more than a moral duty to speak one's mind. It becomes a pleasure.

CECILY Do you suggest, Miss Fairfax, that I entrapped Ernest into an engagement? How dare you? This is no time for wearing the shallow mask of manners. When I see a spade I call it a spade.

GWENDOLEN [Satirically.] I am glad to say that I have never seen a spade. It

3. A popular journal featuring society gossip and also announcements of engagements and marriages.

is obvious that our social spheres have been widely different.

[*Enter* MERRIMAN, *followed by the footman. He carries a salver, table-cloth, and plate stand.* CECILY *is about to retort. The presence of the servants exercises a restraining influence, under which both girls chafe.*]

MERRIMAN Shall I lay tea here as usual, Miss?

CECILY [*Sternly, in a calm voice.*] Yes, as usual.

[MERRIMAN *begins to clear table and lay cloth. A long pause.* CECILY *and* GWENDOLEN *glare at each other.*]

GWENDOLEN Are there many interesting walks in the vicinity, Miss Cardew?

CECILY Oh! yes! a great many. From the top of one of the hills quite close one can see five counties.

GWENDOLEN Five counties! I don't think I should like that. I hate crowds.

CECILY [*Sweetly.*] I suppose that is why you live in town?

[GWENDOLEN *bites her lip, and beats her foot nervously with her parasol.*]

GWENDOLEN [*Looking round.*] Quite a well-kept garden this is, Miss Cardew.

CECILY So glad you like it, Miss Fairfax.

GWENDOLEN I had no idea there were any flowers in the country.

CECILY Oh, flowers are as common here, Miss Fairfax, as people are in London.

GWENDOLEN Personally I cannot understand how anybody manages to exist in the country, if anybody who is anybody does. The country always bores me to death.

CECILY Ah! This is what the newspapers call agricultural depression, is it not? I believe the aristocracy are suffering very much from it just at present.[4] It is almost an epidemic amongst them, I have been told. May I offer you some tea, Miss Fairfax?

GWENDOLEN [*With elaborate politeness.*] Thank you. [*Aside.*] Detestable girl! But I require tea!

CECILY [*Sweetly.*] Sugar?

GWENDOLEN [*Superciliously.*] No, thank you. Sugar is not fashionable any more. [CECILY *looks angrily at her, takes up the tongs and puts four lumps of sugar into the cup.*]

CECILY [*Severely.*] Cake or bread and butter?

GWENDOLEN [*In a bored manner.*] Bread and butter, please. Cake is rarely seen at the best houses nowadays.

CECILY [*Cuts a very large slice of cake, and puts it on the tray.*] Hand that to Miss Fairfax.

[MERRIMAN *does so, and goes out with footman.* GWENDOLEN *drinks the tea and makes a grimace. Puts down cup at once, reaches out her hand to the bread and butter, looks at it, and finds it is cake. Rises in indignation.*]

GWENDOLEN You have filled my tea with lumps of sugar, and though I asked most distinctly for bread and butter, you have given me cake. I am known for the gentleness of my disposition, and the extraordinary sweetness of my nature, but I warn you, Miss Cardew, you may go too far.

CECILY [*Rising.*] To save my poor, innocent, trusting boy from the machinations of any other girl there are no lengths to which I would not go.

---

4. From the 1870s on, landowners (including aristocrats) had been suffering severe losses because of adverse economic conditions.

GWENDOLEN   From the moment I saw you I distrusted you. I felt that you were false and deceitful. I am never deceived in such matters. My first impressions of people are invariably right.

CECILY   It seems to me, Miss Fairfax, that I am trespassing on your valuable time. No doubt you have many other calls of a similar character to make in the neighborhood.

[*Enter* JACK.]

GWENDOLEN [*Catching sight of him.*]   Ernest! My own Ernest!

JACK   Gwendolen! Darling! [*Offers to kiss her.*]

GWENDOLEN [*Drawing back.*]   A moment! May I ask if you are engaged to be married to this young lady? [*Points to* CECILY.]

JACK [*Laughing.*]   To dear little Cecily! Of course not! What could have put such an idea into your pretty little head?

GWENDOLEN   Thank you. You may! [*Offers her cheek.*]

CECILY [*Very sweetly.*]   I knew there must be some misunderstanding, Miss Fairfax. The gentleman whose arm is at present round your waist is my dear guardian, Mr. John Worthing.

GWENDOLEN   I beg your pardon?

CECILY   This is Uncle Jack.

GWENDOLEN [*Receding.*]   Jack! Oh!

[*Enter* ALGERNON.]

CECILY   Here is Ernest.

ALGERNON [*Goes straight over to* CECILY *without noticing anyone else.*]   My own love! [*Offers to kiss her.*]

CECILY [*Drawing back.*]   A moment, Ernest! May I ask you—are you engaged to be married to this young lady?

ALGERNON [*Looking round.*]   To what young lady? Good heavens! Gwendolen!

CECILY   Yes! to good heavens, Gwendolen, I mean to Gwendolen.

ALGERNON [*Laughing.*]   Of course not! What could have put such an idea into your pretty little head?

CECILY   Thank you. [*Presenting her cheek to be kissed.*] You may. [ALGERNON *kisses her.*]

GWENDOLEN   I felt there was some slight error, Miss Cardew. The gentleman who is now embracing you is my cousin, Mr. Algernon Moncrieff.

CECILY. [*Breaking away from* ALGERNON.]   Algernon Moncrieff! Oh! [*The two girls move towards each other and put their arms round each other's waists as if for protection.*]

CECILY   Are you called Algernon?

ALGERNON   I cannot deny it.

CECILY   Oh!

GWENDOLEN   Is your name really John?

JACK [*Standing rather proudly.*]   I could deny it if I liked, I could deny anything if I liked. But my name certainly is John. It has been John for years.

CECILY [*To* GWENDOLEN.]   A gross deception has been practiced on both of us.

GWENDOLEN   My poor wounded Cecily!

CECILY   My sweet wronged Gwendolen!

GWENDOLEN [*Slowly and seriously.*]   You will call me sister, will you not? [*They embrace.* JACK *and* ALGERNON *groan and walk up and down.*]

CECILY [*Rather brightly.*]   There is just one question I would like to be allowed to ask my guardian.

GWENDOLEN   An admirable idea! Mr. Worthing, there is just one question I would like to be permitted to put to you. Where is your brother Ernest? We are both engaged to be married to your brother Ernest, so it is a matter of some importance to us to know where your brother Ernest is at present.

JACK [*Slowly and hesitatingly.*] Gwendolen—Cecily—it is very painful for me to be forced to speak the truth. It is the first time in my life that I have ever been reduced to such a painful position, and I am really quite inexperienced in doing anything of the kind. However I will tell you quite frankly that I have no brother Ernest. I have no brother at all. I never had a brother in my life, and I certainly have not the smallest intention of ever having one in the future.

CECILY [*Surprised.*] No brother at all?

JACK [*Cheerily.*] None!

GWENDOLEN [*Severely.*] Had you never a brother of any kind?

JACK [*Pleasantly.*] Never. Not even of any kind.

GWENDOLEN I am afraid it is quite clear, Cecily, that neither of us is engaged to be married to anyone.

CECILY It is not a very pleasant position for a young girl suddenly to find herself in. Is it?

GWENDOLEN Let us go into the house. They will hardly venture to come after us there.

CECILY No, men are so cowardly, aren't they?

[*They retire into the house with scornful looks.*]

JACK This ghastly state of things is what you call Bunburying, I suppose?

ALGERNON Yes, and a perfectly wonderful Bunbury it is. The most wonderful Bunbury I have ever had in my life.

JACK Well, you've no right whatsoever to Bunbury here.

ALGERNON That is absurd. One has a right to Bunbury anywhere one chooses. Every serious Bunburyist knows that.

JACK Serious Bunburyist! Good heavens!

ALGERNON Well, one must be serious about something, if one wants to have any amusement in life. I happen to be serious about Bunburying. What on earth you are serious about I haven't got the remotest idea. About everything, I should fancy. You have such an absolutely trivial nature.

JACK Well, the only small satisfaction I have in the whole of this wretched business is that your friend Bunbury is quite exploded. You won't be able to run down to the country quite so often as you used to do, dear Algy. And a very good thing too.

ALGERNON Your brother is a little off-colour, isn't he, dear Jack? You won't be able to disappear to London quite so frequently as your wicked custom was. And not a bad thing either.

JACK As for your conduct towards Miss Cardew, I must say that your taking in a sweet, simple, innocent girl like that is quite inexcusable. To say nothing of the fact that she is my ward.

ALGERNON I can see no possible defence at all for your deceiving a brilliant, clever, thoroughly experienced young lady like Miss Fairfax. To say nothing of the fact that she is my cousin.

JACK I wanted to be engaged to Gwendolen, that is all. I love her.

ALGERNON Well, I simply wanted to be engaged to Cecily. I adore her.

JACK There is certainly no chance of your marrying Miss Cardew.

ALGERNON I don't think there is much likelihood, Jack, of you and Miss Fairfax being united.

JACK Well, that is no business of yours.

ALGERNON   If it was my business, I wouldn't talk about it. [*Begins to eat muffins.*] It is very vulgar to talk about one's business. Only people like stockbrokers do that, and then merely at dinner parties.

JACK   How can you sit there, calmly eating muffins when we are in this horrible trouble, I can't make out. You seem to me to be perfectly heartless.

ALGERNON   Well, I can't eat muffins in an agitated manner. The butter would probably get on my cuffs. One should always eat muffins quite calmly. It is the only way to eat them.

JACK   I say it's perfectly heartless your eating muffins at all, under the circumstances.

ALGERNON   When I am in trouble, eating is the only thing that consoles me. Indeed, when I am in really great trouble, as anyone who knows me intimately will tell you, I refuse everything except food and drink. At the present moment I am eating muffins because I am unhappy. Besides, I am particularly fond of muffins. [*Rising.*]

JACK [*Rising.*]   Well, that is no reason why you should eat them all in that greedy way. [*Takes muffins from* ALGERNON.]

ALGERNON [*Offering tea cake.*]   I wish you would have tea cake instead. I don't like tea cake.

JACK   Good heavens! I suppose a man may eat his own muffins in his own garden.

ALGERNON   But you have just said it was perfectly heartless to eat muffins.

JACK   I said it was perfectly heartless of you, under the circumstances. That is a very different thing.

ALGERNON   That may be. But the muffins are the same. [*He seizes the muffin dish from* JACK.]

JACK   Algy, I wish to goodness you would go.

ALGERNON   You can't possibly ask me to go without having some dinner. It's absurd. I never go without my dinner. No one ever does, except vegetarians and people like that. Besides I have just made arrangements with Dr. Chasuble to be christened at a quarter to six under the name of Ernest.

JACK   My dear fellow, the sooner you give up that nonsense the better. I made arrangements this morning with Dr. Chasuble to be christened myself at 5: 30, and I naturally will take the name of Ernest. Gwendolen would wish it. We can't both be christened Ernest. It's absurd. Besides, I have a perfect right to be christened if I like. There is no evidence at all that I ever have been christened by anybody. I should think it extremely probable I never was, and so does Dr. Chasuble. It is entirely different in your case. You have been christened already.

ALGERNON   Yes, but I have not been christened for years.

JACK   Yes, but you have been christened. That is the important thing.

ALGERNON   Quite so. So I know my constitution can stand it. If you are not quite sure about your ever having been christened, I must say I think it rather dangerous your venturing on it now. It might make you very unwell. You can hardly have forgotten that someone very closely connected with you was very nearly carried off this week in Paris by a severe chill.

JACK   Yes, but you said yourself that a severe chill was not hereditary.

ALGERNON   It usen't to be, I know—but I daresay it is now. Science is always making wonderful improvements in things.

JACK [*Picking up the muffin dish.*]   Oh, that is nonsense; you are always talking nonsense.

ALGERNON   Jack, you are at the muffins again! I wish you wouldn't. There are only two left. [*Takes them.*] I told you I was particularly fond of muffins.

JACK   But I hate tea cake.

ALGERNON   Why on earth then do you allow tea cake to be served up for your guests? What ideas you have of hospitality!

JACK   Algernon! I have already told you to go. I don't want you here. Why don't you go!

ALGERNON   I haven't quite finished my tea yet! and there is still one muffin left. [*Jack groans, and sinks into a chair.* ALGERNON *still continues eating.*]

ACT-DROP

Third Act

SCENE—*Morning room*[5] *at the Manor House.*

[GWENDOLEN *and* CECILY *are at the window, looking out into the garden.*]

GWENDOLEN   The fact that they did not follow us at once into the house, as anyone else would have done, seems to me to show that they have some sense of shame left.

CECILY   They have been eating muffins. That looks like repentance.

GWENDOLEN [*After a pause.*]   They don't seem to notice us at all. Couldn't you cough?

CECILY   But I haven't got a cough.

GWENDOLEN   They're looking at us. What effrontery!

CECILY   They're approaching. That's very forward of them.

GWENDOLEN   Let us preserve a dignified silence.

CECILY   Certainly. It's the only thing to do now.

[*Enter* JACK *followed by* ALGERNON. *They whistle some dreadful popular air from a British Opera.*[6]]

GWENDOLEN   This dignified silence seems to produce an unpleasant effect.

CECILY   A most distasteful one.

GWENDOLEN   But we will not be the first to speak.

CECILY   Certainly not.

GWENDOLEN   Mr. Worthing, I have something very particular to ask you. Much depends on your reply.

CECILY   Gwendolen, your common sense is invaluable. Mr. Moncrieff, kindly answer me the following question. Why did you pretend to be my guardian's brother?

ALGERNON   In order that I might have an opportunity of meeting you.

CECILY [*To* GWENDOLEN.]   That certainly seems a satisfactory explanation, does it not?

GWENDOLEN   Yes, dear, if you can believe him.

CECILY   I don't. But that does not affect the wonderful beauty of his answer.

GWENDOLEN   True. In matters of grave importance, style, not sincerity is the vital thing. Mr. Worthing, what explanation can you offer to me for pretending to have a brother? Was it in order that you might have an oppor-

5. A relatively informally furnished room for receiving visitors making morning calls (usually close friends of the host or hostess). Afternoon visitors, on the other hand, would be received in the drawing room, a much more formal and elegant setting.
6. Probably a reference to one of the operas of W. S. Gilbert and Sir Arthur Sullivan.

tunity of coming up to town to see me as often as possible?

JACK Can you doubt it, Miss Fairfax?

GWENDOLEN I have the gravest doubts upon the subject. But I intend to crush them. This is not the moment for German scepticism.[7] [*Moving to* CECILY.] Their explanations appear to be quite satisfactory, especially Mr. Worthing's. That seems to me to have the stamp of truth upon it.

CECILY I am more than content with what Mr. Moncrieff said. His voice alone inspires one with absolute credulity.

GWENDOLEN Then you think we should forgive them?

CECILY Yes. I mean no.

GWENDOLEN True! I had forgotten. There are principles at stake that one cannot surrender. Which of us should tell them? The task is not a pleasant one.

CECILY Could we not both speak at the same time?

GWENDOLEN An excellent idea! I nearly always speak at the same time as other people. Will you take the time from me?

CECILY Certainly. [GWENDOLEN *beats time with uplifted finger.*]

GWENDOLEN AND CECILY [*Speaking together.*] Your Christian names are still an insuperable barrier. That is all!

JACK AND ALGERNON [*Speaking together.*] Our Christian names! Is that all? But we are going to be christened this afternoon.

GWENDOLEN [*To* JACK.] For my sake you are prepared to do this terrible thing?

JACK I am.

CECILY [*To* ALGERNON.] To please me you are ready to face this fearful ordeal?

ALGERNON I am!

GWENDOLEN How absurd to talk of the equality of the sexes! Where questions of self-sacrifice are concerned, men are infinitely beyond us.

JACK We are. [*Clasps hands with* ALGERNON.]

CECILY They have moments of physical courage of which we women know absolutely nothing.

GWENDOLEN [*To* JACK.] Darling!

ALGERNON [*To* CECILY.] Darling. [*They fall into each other's arms.*]

[*Enter* MERRIMAN. *When he enters he coughs loudly, seeing the situation.*]

MERRIMAN Ahem! Ahem! Lady Bracknell!

JACK Good heavens!

[*Enter* LADY BRACKNELL. *The couples separate in alarm. Exit* MERRIMAN.]

LADY BRACKNELL Gwendolen! What does this mean?

GWENDOLEN Merely that I am engaged to be married to Mr. Worthing, mamma.

LADY BRACKNELL Come here. Sit down. Sit down immediately. Hesitation of any kind is a sign of mental decay in the young, of physical weakness in the old. [*Turns to* JACK.] Apprised, sir, of my daughter's sudden flight by her trusty maid, whose confidence I purchased by means of a small coin, I followed her at once by a luggage train.[8] Her unhappy father is, I am glad to say, under the impression that she is attending a more than usually

7. Many 19th-century German scholars (e.g., D. F. Strauss) were notorious among the British for being skeptical in their analyses of religious texts.

8. Freight train.

lengthy lecture by the University Extension Scheme on the Influence of a Permanent Income on Thought. I do not propose to undeceive him. Indeed I have never undeceived him on any question. I would consider it wrong. But of course, you will clearly understand that all communication between yourself and my daughter must cease immediately from this moment. On this point, as indeed on all points, I am firm.

JACK   I am engaged to be married to Gwendolen, Lady Bracknell!

LADY BRACKNELL   You are nothing of the kind, sir. And now, as regards Algernon! . . . Algernon!

ALGERNON   Yes, Aunt Augusta.

LADY BRACKNELL   May I ask if it is in this house that your invalid friend Mr. Bunbury resides?

ALGERNON   [Stammering.]   Oh! No! Bunbury doesn't live here. Bunbury is somewhere else at present. In fact, Bunbury is dead.

LADY BRACKNELL   Dead! When did Mr. Bunbury die? His death must have been extremely sudden.

ALGERNON [Airily.]   Oh! I killed Bunbury this afternoon. I mean poor Bunbury died this afternoon.

LADY BRACKNELL   What did he die of?

ALGERNON   Bunbury? Oh, he was quite exploded.

LADY BRACKNELL   Exploded! Was he the victim of a revolutionary outrage? I was not aware that Mr. Bunbury was interested in social legislation. If so, he is well punished for his morbidity.

ALGERNON   My dear Aunt Augusta, I mean he was found out! The doctors found out that Bunbury could not live, that is what I mean—so Bunbury died.

LADY BRACKNELL   He seems to have had great confidence in the opinion of his physicians. I am glad, however, that he made up his mind at the last to some definite course of action, and acted under proper medical advice. And now that we have finally got rid of this Mr. Bunbury, may I ask, Mr. Worthing, who is that young person whose hand my nephew Algernon is now holding in what seems to me a peculiarly unnecessary manner?

JACK   That lady is Miss Cecily Cardew, my ward.

[LADY BRACKNELL bows coldly to CECILY.]

ALGERNON   I am engaged to be married to Cecily, Aunt Augusta.

LADY BRACKNELL   I beg your pardon?

CECILY   Mr. Moncrieff and I are engaged to be married, Lady Bracknell.

LADY BRACKNELL [With a shiver, crossing to the sofa and sitting down.]   I do not know whether there is anything peculiarly exciting in the air of this particular part of Hertfordshire, but the number of engagements that go on seems to me considerably above the proper average that statistics have laid down for our guidance. I think some preliminary inquiry on my part would not be out of place. Mr. Worthing, is Miss Cardew at all connected with any of the larger railway stations in London? I merely desire information. Until yesterday I had no idea that there were any families or persons whose origin was a Terminus.[9] [JACK looks perfectly furious, but restrains himself.]

JACK [In a clear, cold voice.]   Miss Cardew is the granddaughter of the late Mr. Thomas Cardew of 149, Belgrave Square, S.W.; Gervase Park, Dorking, Surrey; and the Sporran, Fifeshire, N.B.[1]

---

9. Station at the end of a railway line.   1. Presumably North Britain, i.e., Scotland.

LADY BRACKNELL   That sounds not unsatisfactory. Three addresses always inspire confidence, even in tradesmen. But what proof have I of their authenticity?

JACK   I have carefully preserved the Court Guides[2] of the period. They are open to your inspection, Lady Bracknell.

LADY BRACKNELL [Grimly.]   I have known strange errors in that publication.

JACK   Miss Cardew's family solicitors are Messrs. Markby, Markby, and Markby.

LADY BRACKNELL   Markby, Markby, and Markby? A firm of the very highest position in their profession. Indeed I am told that one of the Mr. Markbys is occasionally to be seen at dinner parties. So far I am satisfied.

JACK [Very irritably.]   How extremely kind of you, Lady Bracknell! I have also in my possession, you will be pleased to hear, certificates of Miss Cardew's birth, baptism, whooping cough, registration, vaccination, confirmation, and the measles; both the German and the English variety.

LADY BRACKNELL   Ah! A life crowded with incident, I see; though perhaps somewhat too exciting for a young girl. I am not myself in favor of premature experiences. [Rises, looks at her watch.] Gwendolen! the time approaches for our departure. We have not a moment to lose. As a matter of form, Mr. Worthing, I had better ask you if Miss Cardew has any little fortune?

JACK   Oh! about a hundred and thirty thousand pounds in the Funds.[3] That is all. Good-bye, Lady Bracknell. So pleased to have seen you.

LADY BRACKNELL [Sitting down again.]   A moment, Mr. Worthing. A hundred and thirty thousand pounds! And in the Funds! Miss Cardew seems to me a most attractive young lady, now that I look at her. Few girls of the present day have any really solid qualities, any of the qualities that last, and improve with time. We live, I regret to say, in an age of surfaces. [To CECILY.] Come over here, dear. [CECILY goes across.] Pretty child! your dress is sadly simple, and your hair seems almost as Nature might have left it. But we can soon alter all that. A thoroughly experienced French maid produces a really marvellous result in a very brief space of time. I remember recommending one to young Lady Lancing, and after three months her own husband did not know her.

JACK [Aside.]   And after six months nobody knew her.[4]

LADY BRACKNELL [Glares at JACK for a few moments. Then bends, with a practiced smile, to CECILY.]   Kindly turn round, sweet child. [CECILY turns completely round.] No, the side view is what I want. [CECILY presents her profile.] Yes, quite as I expected. There are distinct social possibilities in your profile. The two weak points in our age are its want of principle and its want of profile. The chin a little higher, dear. Style largely depends on the way the chin is worn. They are worn very high, just at present. Algernon!

ALGERNON   Yes, Aunt Augusta!

LADY BRACKNELL   There are distinct social possibilities in Miss Cardew's profile.

ALGERNON   Cecily is the sweetest, dearest, prettiest girl in the whole world. And I don't care twopence about social possibilities.

LADY BRACKNELL   Never speak disrespectfully of Society, Algernon. Only peo-

2. Directories commonly used in this era.
3. Interest-bearing government bonds.

4. I.e., she became socially unacceptable because of her scandalous behavior.

ple who can't get into it do that. [*To* CECILY.] Dear child, of course you know that Algernon has nothing but his debts to depend upon. But I do not approve of mercenary marriages. When I married Lord Bracknell I had no fortune of any kind. But I never dreamed for a moment of allowing that to stand in my way. Well, I suppose I must give my consent.

ALGERNON   Thank you, Aunt Augusta.

LADY BRACKNELL   Cecily, you may kiss me!

CECILY [*Kisses her.*]   Thank you, Lady Bracknell.

LADY BRACKNELL   You may also address me as Aunt Augusta for the future.

CECILY   Thank you, Aunt Augusta.

LADY BRACKNELL   The marriage, I think, had better take place quite soon.

ALGERNON   Thank you, Aunt Augusta.

CECILY   Thank you, Aunt Augusta.

LADY BRACKNELL   To speak frankly, I am not in favour of long engagements. They give people the opportunity of finding out each other's character before marriage, which I think is never advisable.

JACK   I beg your pardon for interrupting you, Lady Bracknell, but this engagement is quite out of the question. I am Miss Cardew's guardian, and she cannot marry without my consent until she comes of age. That consent I absolutely decline to give.

LADY BRACKNELL   Upon what grounds may I ask? Algernon is an extremely, I may almost say an ostentatiously, eligible young man. He has nothing, but he looks everything. What more can one desire?

JACK   It pains me very much to have to speak frankly to you, Lady Bracknell, about your nephew, but the fact is that I do not approve at all of his moral character. I suspect him of being untruthful. [ALGERNON *and* CECILY *look at him in indignant amazement.*]

LADY BRACKNELL   Untruthful! My nephew Algernon? Impossible! He is an Oxonian.[5]

JACK   I fear there can be no possible doubt about the matter. This afternoon, during my temporary absence in London on an important question of romance, he obtained admission to my house by means of the false pretence of being my brother. Under an assumed name he drank, I've just been informed by my butler, an entire pint bottle of my Perrier-Jouet, Brut, '89;[6] a wine I was specially reserving for myself. Continuing his disgraceful deception, he succeeded in the course of the afternoon in alienating the affections of my only ward. He subsequently stayed to tea, and devoured every single muffin. And what makes his conduct all the more heartless is, that he was perfectly well aware from the first that I have no brother, that I never had a brother, and that I don't intend to have a brother, not even of any kind. I distinctly told him so myself yesterday afternoon.

LADY BRACKNELL   Ahem! Mr. Worthing, after careful consideration I have decided entirely to overlook my nephew's conduct to you.

JACK   That is very generous of you, Lady Bracknell. My own decision, however, is unalterable. I decline to give my consent.

LADY BRACKNELL [*To* CECILY.]   Come here, sweet child. [CECILY *goes over.*] How old are you, dear?

---

5. I.e., he had been a student at Oxford (in medieval Latin, *Oxonia*).

6. An outstanding brand and year of dry champagne.

CECILY   Well, I am really only eighteen, but I always admit to twenty when I go to evening parties.

LADY BRACKNELL   You are perfectly right in making some slight alteration. Indeed, no woman should ever be quite accurate about her age. It looks so calculating. . . . [*In a meditative manner.*] Eighteen, but admitting to twenty at evening parties. Well, it will not be very long before you are of age and free from the restraints of tutelage. So I don't think your guardian's consent is, after all, a matter of any importance.

JACK   Pray excuse me, Lady Bracknell, for interrupting you again, but it is only fair to tell you that according to the terms of her grandfather's will Miss Cardew does not come legally of age till she is thirty-five.

LADY BRACKNELL   That does not seem to me to be a grave objection. Thirty-five is a very attractive age. London society is full of women of the very highest birth who have, of their own free choice, remained thirty-five for years. Lady Dumbleton is an instance in point. To my own knowledge she has been thirty-five ever since she arrived at the age of forty, which was many years ago now. I see no reason why our dear Cecily should not be even still more attractive at the age you mention than she is at present. There will be a large accumulation of property.

CECILY   Algy, could you wait for me till I was thirty-five?

ALGERNON   Of course I could, Cecily. You know I could.

CECILY   Yes, I felt it instinctively, but I couldn't wait all that time. I hate waiting even five minutes for anybody. It always makes me rather cross. I am not punctual myself, I know, but I do like punctuality in others, and waiting, even to be married, is quite out of the question.

ALGERNON   Then what is to be done, Cecily?

CECILY   I don't know, Mr. Moncrieff.

LADY BRACKNELL   My dear Mr. Worthing, as Miss Cardew states positively that she cannot wait till she is thirty-five—a remark which I am bound to say seems to me to show a somewhat impatient nature—I would beg of you to reconsider your decision.

JACK   But my dear Lady Bracknell, the matter is entirely in your own hands. The moment you consent to my marriage with Gwendolen, I will most gladly allow your nephew to form an alliance with my ward.

LADY BRACKNELL   [*Rising and drawing herself up.*] You must be quite aware that what you propose is out of the question.

JACK   Then a passionate celibacy is all that any of us can look forward to.

LADY BRACKNELL   This is not the destiny I propose for Gwendolen. Algernon, of course, can choose for himself. [*Pulls out her watch.*] Come, dear; [GWENDOLEN *rises.*] we have already missed five, if not six, trains. To miss any more might expose us to comment on the platform.

[*Enter* DR. CHASUBLE.]

CHASUBLE   Everything is quite ready for the christenings.

LADY BRACKNELL   The christenings, sir! Is not that somewhat premature!

CHASUBLE [*Looking rather puzzled, and pointing to* JACK *and* ALGERNON.] Both these gentlemen have expressed a desire for immediate baptism.

LADY BRACKNELL   At their age? The idea is grotesque and irreligious! Algernon, I forbid you to be baptized. I will not hear of such excesses. Lord Bracknell would be highly displeased if he learned that that was the way in which you wasted your time and money.

CHASUBLE   Am I to understand then that there are to be no christenings at all this afternoon?

JACK   I don't think that, as things are now, it would be of much practical value to either of us, Dr. Chasuble.

CHASUBLE   I am grieved to hear such sentiments from you, Mr. Worthing. They savour of the heretical views of the Anabaptists,[7] views that I have completely refuted in four of my unpublished sermons. However, as your present mood seems to be one peculiarly secular, I will return to the church at once. Indeed, I have just been informed by the pew-opener[8] that for the last hour and a half Miss Prism has been waiting for me in the vestry.

LADY BRACKNELL   [Starting.]   Miss Prism! Did I hear you mention a Miss Prism?

CHASUBLE   Yes, Lady Bracknell. I am on my way to join her.

LADY BRACKNELL   Pray allow me to detain you for a moment. This matter may prove to be one of vital importance to Lord Bracknell and myself. Is this Miss Prism a female of repellent aspect, remotely connected with education?

CHASUBLE   [Somewhat indignantly.]   She is the most cultivated of ladies, and the very picture of respectability.

LADY BRACKNELL   It is obviously the same person. May I ask what position she holds in your household?

CHASUBLE   [Severely.]   I am a celibate, madam.

JACK   [Interposing.]   Miss Prism, Lady Bracknell, has been for the last three years Miss Cardew's esteemed governess and valued companion.

LADY BRACKNELL   In spite of what I hear of her, I must see her at once. Let her be sent for.

CHASUBLE   [Looking off.]   She approaches; she is nigh.

[Enter MISS PRISM hurriedly.]

MISS PRISM   I was told you expected me in the vestry, dear Canon. I have been waiting for you there for an hour and three quarters. [Catches sight of ADY BRACKNELL who has fixed her with a stony glare. MISS PRISM grows pale and quails. She looks anxiously round as if desirous to escape.]

LADY BRACKNELL   [In a severe, judicial voice.]   Prism! [MISS PRISM bows her head in shame.] Come here, Prism! [MISS PRISM approaches in a humble manner.] Prism! Where is that baby? [General consternation. THE CANON starts back in horror. ALGERNON and JACK pretend to be anxious to shield CECILY and GWENDOLEN from hearing the details of a terrible public scandal.] Twenty-eight years ago, Prism, you left Lord Bracknell's house, Number 104, Upper Grosvenor Street, in charge of a perambulator that contained a baby, of the male sex. You never returned. A few weeks later, through the elaborate investigations of the Metropolitan police, the perambulator was discovered at midnight, standing by itself in a remote corner of Bayswater.[9] It contained the manuscript of a three-volume novel of more than usually revolting sentimentality. [MISS PRISM starts in involuntary indignation.] But the baby was not there! [Everyone looks at MISS PRISM.] Prism! Where is that baby? [A pause.]

7. A radical Protestant sect of the 17th century, whose repudiation of infant baptism was regarded as heretical by Anglicans.
8. A person employed at church services to usher worshippers to their pews and open the doors for them.
9. A once fashionable locality in the West End near Kensington Gardens.

MISS PRISM   Lady Bracknell, I admit with shame that I do not know. I only wish I did. The plain facts of the case are these. On the morning of the day you mention, a day that is forever branded on my memory, I prepared as usual to take the baby out in its perambulator. I had also with me a somewhat old, but capacious handbag, in which I had intended to place the manuscript of a work of fiction that I had written during my few unoccupied hours. In a moment of mental abstraction, for which I never can forgive myself, I deposited the manuscript in the bassinette, and placed the baby in the handbag.

JACK   [*Who has been listening attentively.*]   But where did you deposit the handbag?

MISS PRISM   Do not ask me, Mr. Worthing.

JACK   Miss Prism, this is a matter of no small importance to me. I insist on knowing where you deposited the handbag that contained that infant.

MISS PRISM   I left it in the cloak room of one of the larger railway stations in London.

JACK   What railway station?

MISS PRISM   [*Quite crushed.*]   Victoria. The Brighton line. [*Sinks into a chair.*]

JACK   I must retire to my room for a moment. Gwendolen, wait here for me.

GWENDOLEN   If you are not too long, I will wait here for you all my life.

[*Exit* JACK *in great excitement.*]

CHASUBLE   What do you think this means, Lady Bracknell?

LADY BRACKNELL   I dare not even suspect, Dr. Chasuble. I need hardly tell you that in families of high position strange coincidences are not supposed to occur. They are hardly considered the thing.

[*Noises heard overhead as if someone was throwing trunks about. Everyone looks up.*]

CECILY   Uncle Jack seems strangely agitated.

CHASUBLE   Your guardian has a very emotional nature.

LADY BRACKNELL   This noise is extremely unpleasant. It sounds as if he was having an argument. I dislike arguments of any kind. They are always vulgar, and often convincing.

CHASUBLE   [*Looking up.*]   It has stopped now. [*The noise is redoubled.*]

LADY BRACKNELL   I wish he would arrive at some conclusion.

GWENDOLEN   This suspense is terrible. I hope it will last.

[*Enter* JACK *with a handbag of black leather in his hand.*]

JACK   [*Rushing over to* MISS PRISM.]   Is this the handbag, Miss Prism? Examine it carefully before you speak. The happiness of more than one life depends on your answer.

MISS PRISM   [*Calmly.*]   It seems to be mine. Yes, here is the injury it received through the upsetting of a Gower Street omnibus in younger and happier days. Here is the stain on the lining caused by the explosion of a temperance beverage, an incident that occurred at Leamington. And here, on the lock, are my initials. I had forgotten that in an extravagant mood I had had them placed there. The bag is undoubtedly mine. I am delighted to have it so unexpectedly restored to me. It has been a great inconvenience being without it all these years.

JACK   [*In a pathetic voice.*]   Miss Prism, more is restored to you than this handbag. I was the baby you placed in it.

MISS PRISM   [*Amazed.*]   You!

JACK   [*Embracing her.*]   Yes . . . mother!

MISS PRISM [*Recoiling in indignant astonishment.*] Mr. Worthing! I am unmarried!

JACK Unmarried! I do not deny that is a serious blow. But after all, who has the right to cast a stone[1] against one who has suffered? Cannot repentance wipe out an act of folly? Why should there be one law for men, and another for women? Mother, I forgive you. [*Tries to embrace her again.*]

MISS PRISM [*Still more indignant.*] Mr. Worthing, there is some error. [*Pointing to* LADY BRACKNELL.] There is the lady who can tell you who you really are.

JACK [*After a pause.*] Lady Bracknell, I hate to seem inquisitive, but would you kindly inform me who I am?

LADY BRACKNELL I am afraid that the news I have to give you will not altogether please you. You are the son of my poor sister, Mrs. Moncrieff, and consequently Algernon's elder brother.

JACK Algy's elder brother! Then I have a brother after all. I knew I had a brother! I always said I had a brother! Cecily—how could you have ever doubted that I had a brother? [*Seizes hold of* ALGERNON.] Dr. Chasuble, my unfortunate brother. Miss Prism, my unfortunate brother. Gwendolen, my unfortunate brother. Algy, you young scoundrel, you will have to treat me with more respect in the future. You have never behaved to me like a brother in all your life.

ALGERNON Well, not till today, old boy, I admit. I did my best, however, though I was out of practice. [*Shakes hands.*]

GWENDOLEN [*To* JACK.] My own! But what own are you? What is your Christian name, now that you have become someone else?

JACK Good heavens! . . . I had quite forgotten that point. Your decision on the subject of my name is irrevocable, I suppose?

GWENDOLEN I never change, except in my affections.

CECILY What a noble nature you have, Gwendolen!

JACK Then the question had better be cleared up at once. Aunt Augusta, a moment. At the time when Miss Prism left me in the handbag, had I been christened already?

LADY BRACKNELL Every luxury that money could buy, including christening, had been lavished on you by your fond and doting parents.

JACK Then I was christened! That is settled. Now, what name was I given? Let me know the worst.

LADY BRACKNELL Being the eldest son you were naturally christened after your father.

JACK [*Irritably.*] Yes, but what was my father's Christian name?

LADY BRACKNELL [*Meditatively.*] I cannot at the present moment recall what the General's Christian name was. But I have no doubt he had one. He was eccentric, I admit. But only in later years. And that was the result of the Indian climate, and marriage, and indigestion, and other things of that kind.

JACK Algy! Can't you recollect what our father's Christian name was?

ALGERNON My dear boy, we were never even on speaking terms. He died before I was a year old.

---

1. When the scribes and Pharisees brought to Jesus an adulterous woman with the reminder that the law of Moses required her to be stoned, he answered: "He that is without sin among you, let him first cast a stone at her" (John 8.7).

JACK His name would appear in the Army Lists of the period, I suppose, Aunt Augusta?

LADY BRACKNELL The General was essentially a man of peace, except in his domestic life. But I have no doubt his name would appear in any military directory.

JACK The Army Lists of the last forty years are here. These delightful records should have been my constant study. [*Rushes to bookcase and tears the books out.*] M. Generals . . . Mallam, Maxbohm,² Magley, what ghastly names they have—Markby, Migsby, Mobbs, Moncrieff! Lieutenant 1840, Captain, Lieutenant Colonel, Colonel, General 1869, Christian names, Ernest John. [*Puts book very quietly down and speaks quite calmly.*] I always told you, Gwendolen, my name was Ernest, didn't I? Well it is Ernest after all. I mean it naturally is Ernest.

LADY BRACKNELL Yes, I remember now that the General was called Ernest. I knew I had some particular reason for disliking the name.

GWENDOLEN Ernest! My own Ernest! I felt from the first that you could have no other name!

JACK Gwendolen, it is a terrible thing for a man to find out suddenly that all his life he has been speaking nothing but the truth. Can you forgive me?

GWENDOLEN I can. For I feel that you are sure to change.

JACK My own one!

CHASUBLE [*To* MISS PRISM.] Laetitia! [*Embraces her.*]

MISS PRISM [*Enthusiastically.*] Frederick! At last!

ALGERNON Cecily! [*Embraces her.*] At last!

JACK Gwendolen! [*Embraces her.*] At last!

LADY BRACKNELL My nephew, you seem to be displaying signs of triviality.

JACK On the contrary, Aunt Augusta, I've now realized for the first time in my life the vital Importance of Being Earnest.

CURTAIN

performed 1895   1899

From De Profundis¹

And the end of it all is that I have got to forgive you. I must do so. I don't write this letter to put bitterness into your heart, but to pluck it out of mine. For my own sake I must forgive you. One cannot always keep an adder in one's breast to feed on one, nor rise up every night to sow thorns in the garden of one's soul. It will not be difficult at all for me to do so, if you help me a little. Whatever you did to me in old days I always readily forgave. It did you no good

---

2. A play on the name of Max Beerbohm (1872–1956), English essayist, caricaturist, and parodist.
1. Out of the depths (Latin); Psalm 130.1: "Out of the depths have I cried unto thee, O Lord." While in prison in Reading Gaol, Wilde was allowed a pen and paper only to write letters. Given one sheet of paper at a time, which was taken away after it was filled, Wilde wrote this work as a letter to Lord Alfred Douglas, whose nickname was Bosie. Wilde titled it *Epistola: In Carcere et Vin-*

culis (*Letter: In Prison and in Chains*). He was given the manuscript on his release and turned it over to a friend, Robert Ross, who gave it its current title and published it in an abridged version in 1905, after Wilde's death. After Douglas's death in 1945, a fuller text was published by Wilde's son, Vyvyan Holland; but only in 1962, when scholars could consult the original manuscript, did a complete version appear.

then. Only one whose life is without stain of any kind can forgive sins. But now when I sit in humiliation and disgrace it is different. My forgiveness should mean a great deal to you now. Some day you will realise it. Whether you do so early or late, soon or not at all, my way is clear before me. I cannot allow you to go through life bearing in your heart the burden of having ruined a man like me. The thought might make you callously indifferent, or morbidly sad. I must take the burden from you and put it on my own shoulders.

I must say to myself that neither you nor your father, multiplied a thousand times over, could possibly have ruined a man like me: that I ruined myself: and that nobody, great or small, can be ruined except by his own hand. I am quite ready to do so. I am trying to do so, though you may not think it at the present moment. If I have brought this pitiless indictment against you, think what an indictment I bring without pity against myself. Terrible as what you did to me was, what I did to myself was far more terrible still.

I was a man who stood in symbolic relations to the art and culture of my age. I had realised this for myself at the very dawn of my manhood, and had forced my age to realise it afterwards. Few men hold such a position in their own lifetime and have it so acknowledged. It is usually discerned, if discerned at all, by the historian, or the critic, long after both the man and his age have passed away. With me it was different. I felt it myself, and made others feel it. Byron[2] was a symbolic figure, but his relations were to the passion of his age and its weariness of passion. Mine were to something more noble, more permanent, of more vital issue, of larger scope.

The gods had given me almost everything. I had genius, a distinguished name, high social position, brilliancy, intellectual daring: I made art a philosophy, and philosophy an art: I altered the minds of men and the colours of things: there was nothing I said or did that did not make people wonder: I took the drama, the most objective form known to art, and made it as personal a mode of expression as the lyric or the sonnet, at the same time that I widened its range and enriched its characterization: drama, novel, poem in rhyme, poem in prose, subtle or fantastic dialogue, whatever I touched I made beautiful in a new mode of beauty: to truth itself I gave what is false no less than what is true as its rightful province, and showed that the false and the true are merely forms of intellectual existence. I treated Art as the supreme reality, and life as a mere mode of fiction: I awoke the imagination of my century so that it created myth and legend around me: I summed up all systems in a phrase, and all existence in an epigram.

Along with these things, I had things that were different. I let myself be lured into long spells of senseless and sensual ease. I amused myself with being a *flâneur*,[3] a dandy, a man of fashion. I surrounded myself with the smaller natures and the meaner[4] minds. I became the spendthrift of my own genius, and to waste an eternal youth gave me a curious joy. Tired of being on the heights I deliberately went to the depths in the search for new sensations. What the paradox was to me in the sphere of thought, perversity became to me in the sphere of passion. Desire, at the end, was a malady, or a madness, or both. I grew careless of the lives of others. I took pleasure where it pleased me and passed on. I forgot that every little action of the common day makes

---

2. George Gordon, Lord Byron (1788–1824), Romantic poet.

3. Idle stroller (French).

4. More shallow or more trivial.

or unmakes character, and that therefore what one has done in the secret chamber one has some day to cry aloud on the housetops. I ceased to be Lord over myself. I was no longer the Captain of my Soul,[5] and did not know it. I allowed you to dominate me, and your father to frighten me. I ended in horrible disgrace. There is only one thing for me now, absolute Humility: just as there is only one thing for you, absolute Humility also. You had better come down into the dust and learn it beside me.

I have lain in prison for nearly two years. Out of my nature has come wild despair; an abandonment to grief that was piteous even to look at: terrible and impotent rage: bitterness and scorn: anguish that wept aloud: misery that could find no voice: sorrow that was dumb. I have passed through every possible mood of suffering. Better than Wordsworth himself I know what Wordsworth meant when he said:

> Suffering is permanent, obscure, and dark
> And has the nature of Infinity.[6]

But while there were times when I rejoiced in the idea that my sufferings were to be endless, I could not bear them to be without meaning. Now I find hidden away in my nature something that tells me that nothing in the whole world is meaningless, and suffering least of all. That something hidden away in my nature, like a treasure in a field, is Humility.

It is the last thing left in me, and the best: the ultimate discovery at which I have arrived: the starting-point for a fresh development. It has come to me right out of myself, so I know that it has come at the proper time. It could not have come before, nor later. Had anyone told me of it, I would have rejected it. Had it been brought to me, I would have refused it. As I found it, I want to keep it. I must do so. It is the one thing that has in it the elements of life, of a new life, a *Vita Nuova*[7] for me.

*   *   *

Morality does not help me. I am a born antinomian.[8] I am one of those who are made for exceptions, not for laws. But while I see that there is nothing wrong in what one does, I see that there is something wrong in what one becomes. It is well to have learned that.

Religion does not help me. The faith that others give to what is unseen, I give to what one can touch, and look at. My Gods dwell in temples made with hands, and within the circle of actual experience is my creed made perfect and complete: too complete it may be, for like many or all of those who have placed their Heaven in this earth, I have found in it not merely the beauty of Heaven, but the horror of Hell also. When I think about Religion at all, I feel as if I would like to found an order for those who cannot believe: the Confraternity of the Fatherless one might call it, where on an altar, on which no taper burned, a priest, in whose heart peace had no dwelling, might celebrate with unblessed bread and a chalice empty of wine. Everything to be true must become a religion. And agnosticism should have its ritual no less than faith. It has sown its martyrs, it should reap its saints, and praise God daily for having hidden Himself from man. But whether it be faith or agnosticism, it must be nothing external to me. Its symbols must be of my own creating. Only that is

---

5. See W. E. Henley's "Invictus" (1888), line 16.
6. From *The Borderers* (written 1796–97), lines 1543–44.
7. New life (Italian); here Dante's earliest work (1292–94) about his love for Beatrice.
8. Rejecter of moral law.

spiritual which makes its own form. If I may not find its secret within myself, I shall never find it. If I have not got it already, it will never come to me.

Reason does not help me. It tells me that the laws under which I am convicted are wrong and unjust laws, and the system under which I have suffered a wrong and unjust system. But, somehow, I have got to make both of these things just and right to me. And exactly as in Art one is only concerned with what a particular thing is at a particular moment to oneself, so it is also in the ethical evolution of one's character. I have got to make everything that has happened to me good for me. The plank-bed, the loathsome food, the hard ropes shredded into oakum till one's fingertips grow dull with pain, the menial offices[9] with which each day begins and finishes, the harsh orders that routine seems to necessitate, the dreadful dress that makes sorrow grotesque to look at, the silence, the solitude, the shame—each and all of these things I have to transform into a spiritual experience. There is not a single degradation of the body which I must not try and make into a spiritualizing of the soul.

I want to get to the point when I shall be able to say, quite simply and without affectation, that the two great turning-points of my life were when my father sent me to Oxford, and when society sent me to prison. I will not say that it is the best thing that could have happened to me, for that phrase would savour of too great bitterness towards myself. I would sooner say, or hear it said of me, that I was so typical a child of my age that in my perversity,[1] and for that perversity's sake, I turned the good things of my life to evil, and the evil things of my life to good. What is said, however, by myself or by others matters little. The important thing, the thing that lies before me, the thing that I have to do, or be for the brief remainder of my days one maimed, marred, and incomplete, is to absorb into my nature all that has been done to me, to make it part of me, to accept it without complaint, fear, or reluctance. The supreme vice is shallowness. Whatever is realized is right.

1897   1962

9. Duties. "Oakum": loose fiber from old hemp ropes, which prisoners were often made to shred.   1. I.e., obstinate desire to behave unconventionally.

BERNARD SHAW
1856–1950

Winston Churchill described Bernard Shaw as a "bright, nimble, fierce, and comprehending being, Jack Frost dancing bespangled in the sunshine." Born and raised in the Victorian period, this extraordinary character was an important and engaged public intellectual. His experience encompassed the momentous historical changes of the last half of the nineteenth century and the first half of the twentieth, and he made it his business to pronounce on them all in the witty epigrammatic style that characterizes his plays.

Like Oscar Wilde, the other playwright whose work changed the course of British drama, Shaw was an Irishman. Born in Dublin, he was, in his own words, "the fruit of an unsuitable marriage between two quite amiable people who finally separated in the friendliest fashion." His mother, an aspiring singer, went to London to pursue her musical career; Shaw followed five years later, in 1876, quitting the job he had held since the age of fifteen at a land agent's office. He intended to become a novelist. He spent much of his time in the Reading Room of the British Museum, where a young journalist named William Archer introduced himself because he was so intrigued by the combination of things Shaw was studying—Karl Marx's *Das Kapital* (vol. 1, 1867) and the score of Richard Wagner's opera *Tristan and Isolde* (1859).

These two works indicate the main involvements of Shaw's life in London. *Das Kapital* convinced him that socialism was the answer to society's problems. With the socialist economist Sidney Webb and his wife, also a socialist economist, Beatrice Webb, Shaw joined the Fabian Society, a socialist organization that had committed itself to gradual reform rather than revolution. Shaw quickly became a leader in the group and its principal spokesperson. His pronouncements and tracts had a wit absent from most political writing. In *Fabian Tract No. 2* (1884), for example, he argued that nineteenth-century capitalism had divided society "into hostile classes, with large appetites and no dinners at one extreme and large dinners and no appetites at the other." Though painfully shy, he disciplined himself to become an accomplished public speaker. Accepting fees from no one, he spoke everywhere, stipulating only that he could speak on whatever subject he liked.

Meanwhile, his acquaintance with William Archer led him to journalism. He worked first as an art critic, then as a music critic, championing Wagner's operas and introducing a new standard of wit and judgment to music reviewing, writing for example of a hapless soprano who "fell fearlessly on Mozart and was defeated with heavy loss to the hearers," of a corps de ballet that "wandered about in the prompt corner as if some vivisector had removed from their heads that portion of the brain which enables us to find our way out the door," and of Schubert's "Death and the Maiden" quartet, which makes one "reconciled to Death and indifferent to the Maiden." Shaw then turned to drama criticism, where he later described his work as "a siege laid to the theatre of the XIXth Century by an author who had to cut his own way into it at the point of the pen, and throw some of its defenders into the moat." Just as he had championed Wagner's music, he now championed the plays of the Norwegian dramatist, Henrik Ibsen. In 1891 he published *The Quintessence of Ibsenism,* in which, in setting out the reasons for his admiration of Ibsen, he defined the kind of drama he wanted to write.

In the first ten years of his life in London, Shaw had written five unsuccessful novels. When he turned to drama in the 1890s, he found his medium. Shaw's first play, *Widowers' Houses* (1892), dealt with the problem of slum landlords. Though it ran for only two performances, Shaw's career as a dramatist was launched. In the course of his career he wrote more than fifty plays. Among the most famous are *Mrs Warren's Profession* (1893), *Arms and the Man* (1894), *Candida* (1894), *The Devil's Disciple* (1896), *Caesar and Cleopatra* (1898), *Man and Superman* (1903), *Major Barbara* (1905), *Androcles and the Lion* (1912), *Pygmalion* (1912; later the basis of the musical *My Fair Lady), Heartbreak House* (1919), *Back to Methuselah* (1920), and *Saint Joan* (1923). (Because the production and publication history of Shaw's plays is so complex, this list gives the date of composition for each.) Shaw at first had difficulty getting his plays performed. Therefore, in 1898 he decided to publish them in book form as *Plays Pleasant and Unpleasant,* for which he wrote a didactic preface— the first of many that he provided for his plays. Then, in 1904, the producer and Shakespearean scholar Harley Granville-Barker put on *Candida* at the Royal Court Theatre, which he was managing. The play was a success, and Shaw went on to work with Barker in creating the Royal Court's long-standing reputation as the center for avant-garde drama in London.

In *The Quintessence of Ibsenism,* Shaw defines the elements of the kind of theater he aspired to create:

first, the introduction of the discussion and its development until it so overspreads and interpenetrates the action that it finally assimilates it, making play and discussion practically identical; and second, as a consequence of making the spectators themselves the persons of the drama, and the incidents of their own lives its incidents, the disuse of the old stage tricks by which audiences had to be induced to take an interest in unreal people and improbable circumstances.

Instead of these "tricks," Shaw wished to pioneer "a forensic technique of recrimination, disillusion, and penetration through ideals to the truth, with a free use of all the rhetorical and lyrical arts of the orator, the preacher, the pleader, and the rhapsodist." He created a drama of ideas, in which his characters strenuously argue points of view that justify their social positions—whether that of the prostitute in *Mrs Warren's Profession* or of the munitions manufacturer in *Major Barbara*. His object is to attack the complacencies and conventional moralism of his audience. By the rhetorical brilliance of his dialogue and by surprising reversals of plot conventions, Shaw manipulates his audience into a position of uncomfortable sympathy with points of view and characters that violate traditional assumptions.

By the end of the first decade of the twentieth century, as a result of the success of his plays at the Royal Court Theatre, Shaw had become a literary celebrity. Like Oscar Wilde, he had worked to develop a public persona, but with a substantial difference in aim. Whereas Wilde used his public image to define an aesthetic point of view, Shaw used his public personality—iconoclastic, clownish, argumentative— to advocate social ideas. He was radical in many respects. He was a vegetarian, a nonsmoker, and a nondrinker. He was courageous enough to be a pacifist in World War I. He championed the reform of English spelling and punctuation. He believed in women's rights and the abolition of private property. He also believed in the Life Force and progressive evolution, driven by the power of the human will, a point of view that led him to sympathize with Mussolini and other dictators before World War II. Shaw's insistent rationality made some of his contemporaries view him as bloodless. After seeing *Arms and the Man*, William Butler Yeats described a nightmare in which he was haunted by a sewing machine "that clicked and shone, but the incredible thing was that the machine smiled, smiled perpetually." However, Yeats goes on to say, "Yet I delighted in Shaw the formidable man. He could hit my enemies and the enemies of all I loved, as I could never hit, as no living author that was dear to me could ever hit."

Shaw wrote *Mrs Warren's Profession* in 1893; though it was published in *Plays Pleasant and Unpleasant* in 1898, its public performance was long prohibited by British censors. In 1902 the Stage Society, technically a private club and so not under the jurisdiction of the censors, gave performances for its own members. The play was produced in New York in 1905; but it was closed down by the police, and the producer and his company were arrested. They were eventually acquitted, and the play was allowed to continue. No legal public performance took place in England until 1926, the year after Shaw won the Nobel Prize.

Shaw's preface to the play attacks the confusions and contradictions involved in the censorship of plays and contains an eloquent plea for the recognition of the seriousness and morality of *Mrs Warren's Profession*. The play was written, he tells us, "to draw attention to the truth that prostitution is caused, not by female depravity and male licentiousness, but simply by underpaying, undervaluing, and overworking women so shamefully that the poorest of them are forced to resort to prostitution to keep body and soul together." He argues that Mrs. Warren's defense of herself in the play is "valid and unanswerable." (It is interesting to compare Mrs. Warren's defense with that of the correspondent to the London *Times* who, claiming to be a prostitute, wrote "The Great Social Evil" [p. 1592].) Shaw's discussion of Mrs. Warren's self-justification continues:

> But it is no defence at all of the vice which she organizes. It is no defence of an immoral life to say that the alternative offered by society collectively to poor women is a miserable life, starved, overworked, fetid, ailing, ugly. Though it is

quite natural and *right* for Mrs Warren to choose what is, according to her lights, the least immoral alternative, it is none the less infamous of society to offer such alternatives. For the alternatives offered are not morality and immorality but two sorts of immorality. The man who cannot see that starvation, overwork, dirt, and disease are as anti-social as prostitution—that they are the vices and crimes of a nation, and not merely its misfortunes—is (to put it as politely as possible) a hopelessly Private Person.

This is Shaw's way of saying that such a man is a hopeless idiot; the word *idiot* comes from the Greek *idiōtēs*, "a private person," as distinct from one interested in public affairs.

Shaw's belief in spelling reform led him to introduce simplifications in his own texts that he insisted on his publishers using. These simplifications (omission of the apostrophe in a number of contractions, and the use of widely spaced letters rather than italics to indicate emphasis, for example) are retained in the selection reprinted here.

Mrs Warren's Profession

Act 1

Summer afternoon in a cottage garden on the eastern slope of a hill a little south of Haslemere in Surrey.[1] Looking up the hill, the cottage is seen in the left hand corner of the garden, with its thatched roof and porch, and a large latticed window to the left of the porch. A paling[2] completely shuts in the garden, except for a gate on the right. The common[3] rises uphill beyond the paling to the sky line. Some folded canvas garden chairs are leaning against the side bench in the porch. A lady's bicycle is propped against the wall, under the window. A little to the right of the porch a hammock is slung from two posts. A big canvas umbrella, stuck in the ground, keeps the sun off the hammock, in which a young lady lies reading and making notes, her head towards the cottage and her feet towards the gate. In front of the hammock, and within reach of her hand, is a common kitchen chair, with a pile of serious-looking books and a supply of writing paper on it.

A gentleman walking on the common comes into sight from behind the cottage. He is hardly past middle age, with something of the artist about him, unconventionally but carefully dressed, and clean-shaven except for a moustache, with an eager susceptible face and very amiable and considerate manners. He has silky black hair, with waves of grey and white in it. His eyebrows are white, his moustache black. He seems not certain of his way. He looks over the paling; takes stock of the place; and sees the young lady.

THE GENTLEMAN [*Taking off his hat.*] I beg your pardon. Can you direct me to Hindhead View—Mrs Alison's?
THE YOUNG LADY [*Glancing up from her book.*] This is Mrs Alison's. [*She resumes her work.*]
THE GENTLEMAN Indeed! Perhaps—may I ask are you Miss Vivie Warren?
THE YOUNG LADY [*Sharply, as she turns on her elbow to get a good look at him.*] Yes.
THE GENTLEMAN [*Daunted and conciliatory.*] I'm afraid I appear intrusive. My name is Praed. [VIVIE *at once throws her books upon the chair, and gets out of the hammock.*] Oh, pray dont let me disturb you.

1. County southeast of London.
2. Picket fence.
3. Area of open land for public use.

VIVIE [*Striding to the gate and opening it for him.*] Come in, Mr Praed. [*He comes in.*] Glad to see you. [*She proffers her hand and takes his with a resolute and hearty grip. She is an attractive specimen of the sensible, able, highly-educated young middle-class Englishwoman. Age 22. Prompt, strong, confident, self-possessed. Plain business-like dress, but not dowdy. She wears a chatelaine*⁴ *at her belt, with a fountain pen and a paper knife among its pendants.*]

PRAED Very kind of you indeed, Miss Warren. [*She shuts the gate with a vigorous slam. He passes in to the middle of the garden, exercising his fingers, which are slightly numbed by her greeting.*] Has your mother arrived?

VIVIE [*Quickly, evidently scenting aggression.*] Is she coming?

PRAED [*Surprised.*] Didnt you expect us?

VIVIE No.

PRAED Now, goodness me, I hope Ive not mistaken the day. That would be just like me, you know. Your mother arranged that she was to come down from London and that I was to come over from Horsham to be introduced to you.

VIVIE [*Not at all pleased.*] Did she? Hm! My mother has rather a trick of taking me by surprise—to see how I behave myself when she's away, I suppose. I fancy I shall take my mother very much by surprise one of these days, if she makes arrangements that concern me without consulting me beforehand. She hasnt come.

PRAED [*Embarrassed.*] I'm really very sorry.

VIVIE [*Throwing off her displeasure.*] It's not your fault, Mr Praed, is it? And I'm very glad youve come. You are the only one of my mother's friends I have ever asked her to bring to see me.

PRAED [*Relieved and delighted.*] Oh, now this is really very good of you, Miss Warren!

VIVIE Will you come indoors; or would you rather sit out here and talk?

PRAED It will be nicer out here, dont you think?

VIVIE Then I'll go and get you a chair. [*She goes to the porch for a garden chair.*]

PRAED [*Following her.*] Oh, pray, pray! Allow me. [*He lays hands on the chair.*]

VIVIE [*Letting him take it.*] Take care of your fingers: theyre rather dodgy things, those chairs. [*She goes across to the chair with the books on it; pitches them into the hammock; and brings the chair forward with one swing.*]

PRAED [*Who has just unfolded his chair.*] Oh, now d o let me take that hard chair. I like hard chairs.

VIVIE So do I. Sit down, Mr Praed. [*This invitation she gives with genial peremptoriness, his anxiety to please her clearly striking her as a sign of weakness of character on his part. But he does not immediately obey.*]

PRAED By the way, though, hadnt we better go to the station to meet your mother?

VIVIE [*Coolly.*] Why? She knows the way.

PRAED [*Disconcerted.*] Er—I suppose she does. [*He sits down.*]

VIVIE Do you know, you are just like what I expected. I hope you are disposed to be friends with me.

PRAED [*Again beaming.*] Thank you, my d e a r Miss Warren: thank you. Dear me! I'm glad your mother hasnt spoilt you!

---

4. A decorative clasp or hook on a girdle or belt, to which a number of short chains are attached bearing household implements or ornaments.

VIVIE   How?

PRAED   Well, in making you too conventional. You know, my dear Miss Warren, I am a born anarchist. I hate authority. It spoils the relations between parent and child: even between mother and daughter. Now I was always afraid that your mother would strain her authority to make you very conventional. It's such a relief to find that she hasnt.

VIVIE   Oh! have I been behaving unconventionally?

PRAED   Oh no; oh dear no. At least not conventionally unconventionally, you understand. [*She nods and sits down. He goes on, with a cordial outburst.*] But it was so charming of you to say that you were disposed to be friends with me! You modern young ladies are splendid: perfectly splendid!

VIVIE   [*Dubiously.*]   Eh? [*Watching him with dawning disappointment as to the quality of his brains and character.*]

PRAED   When I was your age, young men and women were afraid of each other: there was no good fellowship. Nothing real. Only gallantry copied out of novels, and as vulgar and affected as it could be. Maidenly reserve! gentlemanly chivalry! always saying no when you meant yes! simple purgatory for shy and sincere souls.

VIVIE   Yes, I imagine there must have been a frightful waste of time. Especially women's time.

PRAED   Oh, waste of life, waste of everything. But things are improving. Do you know, I have been in a positive state of excitement about meeting you ever since your magnificent achievements at Cambridge: a thing unheard of in my day. It was perfectly splendid, you tieing with the third wrangler.[5] Just the right place, you know. The first wrangler is always a dreamy, morbid fellow, in whom the thing is pushed to the length of a disease.

VIVIE   It doesnt pay. I wouldnt do it again for the same money.

PRAED   [*Aghast.*]   The same money!

VIVIE   I did it for £50.

PRAED   Fifty pounds!

VIVIE   Yes. Fifty pounds. Perhaps you dont know how it was. Mrs. Latham, my tutor at Newnham,[6] told my mother that I could distinguish myself in the mathematical tripos if I went in for it in earnest. The papers were full just then of Phillipa Summers beating the senior wrangler.[7] You remember about it, of course.

PRAED   [*Shakes his head energetically.*]!!!

VIVIE   Well anyhow she did; and nothing would please my mother but that I should do the same thing. I said flatly it was not worth my while to face the grind since I was not going in for teaching; but I offered to try for fourth wrangler, or thereabouts, for £50. She closed with me at that, after a little grumbling; and I was better than my bargain. But I wouldn't do it again for that. Two hundred pounds would have been nearer the mark.

PRAED   [*Much damped.*]   Lord bless me! Thats a very practical way of looking at it.

VIVIE   Did you expect to find me an unpractical person?

---

5. A term unique to Cambridge, denoting distinction in the final honors examination (known as the tripos) leading to a B.A. in mathematics. The person who achieved the top mark was the senior wrangler, followed by the junior wrangler and then the third wrangler.

6. Women's college at Cambridge University.
7. In 1890 Philippa Fawcett was placed above the senior wrangler (although women began taking examinations in 1882, they were not admitted to the university until 1921 and gained full status only in 1947).

PRAED   But surely it's practical to consider not only the work these honors cost, but also the culture they bring.

VIVIE   Culture! My dear Mr Praed: do you know what the mathematical tripos means? It means grind, grind, grind for six to eight hours a day at mathematics, and nothing but mathematics. I'm supposed to know something about science; but I know nothing except the mathematics it involves. I can make calculations for engineers, electricians, insurance companies, and so on; but I know next to nothing about engineering or electricity or insurance. I dont even know arithmetic well. Outside mathematics, lawn-tennis, eating, sleeping, cycling, and walking, I'm a more ignorant barbarian than any woman could possibly be who hadnt gone in for the tripos.

PRAED   [Revolted.] What a monstrous, wicked, rascally system! I knew it! I felt at once that it meant destroying all that makes womanhood beautiful.

VIVIE   I dont object to it on that score in the least. I shall turn it to very good account, I assure you.

PRAED   Pooh! In what way?

VIVIE   I shall set up in chambers in the City, and work at actuarial calculations and conveyancing. Under cover of that I shall do some law, with one eye on the Stock Exchange all the time. Ive come down here by myself to read law: not for a holiday, as my mother imagines. I hate holidays.

PRAED   You make my blood run cold. Are you to have no romance, no beauty in your life?

VIVIE   I don't care for either, I assure you.

PRAED   You cant mean that.

VIVIE   Oh yes I do. I like working and getting paid for it. When I'm tired of working, I like a comfortable chair, a cigar, a little whisky, and a novel with a good detective story in it.

PRAED   [Rising in a frenzy of repudiation.] I dont believe it. I am an artist; and I cant believe it: I refuse to believe it. It's only that you havnt discovered yet what a wonderful world art can open up to you.

VIVIE   Yes I have. Last May I spent six weeks in London with Honoria Fraser. Mamma thought we were doing a round of sightseeing together; but I was really at Honoria's chambers in Chancery Lane[8] every day, working away at actuarial calculations for her, and helping her as well as a greenhorn could. In the evenings we smoked and talked, and never dreamt of going out except for exercise. And I never enjoyed myself more in my life. I cleared all my expenses, and got initiated into the business without a fee into the bargain.

PRAED   But bless my heart and soul, Miss Warren, do you call that discovering art?

VIVIE   Wait a bit. That wasnt the beginning. I went up to town on an invitation from some artistic people in Fitzjohn's Avenue:[9] one of the girls was a Newnham chum. They took me to the National Gallery[1]—

PRAED   [Approving.] Ah!! [He sits down, much relieved.]

VIVIE   [Continuing.] —to the Opera—

PRAED   [Still more pleased.] Good!

VIVIE   —and to a concert where the band played all the evening: Beethoven and Wagner and so on. I wouldnt go through that experience again for anything

8. I.e., office in the legal quarter of London.
9. A road in Hampstead (northwest London).
1. In Trafalgar Square; it contains one of the finest

collections of western European paintings in the world.

you could offer me. I held out for civility's sake until the third day; and then I said, plump out,[2] that I couldnt stand any more of it, and went off to Chancery Lane. N o w you know the sort of perfectly splendid modern young lady I am. How do you think I shall get on with my mother?

PRAED [*Startled.*] Well, I hope—er—

VIVIE It's not so much what you hope as what you believe, that I want to know.

PRAED Well, frankly, I am afraid your mother will be a little disappointed. Not from any shortcoming on your part, you know: I dont mean that. But you are so different from her ideal.

VIVIE Her what?!

PRAED Her ideal.

VIVIE Do you mean her ideal of ME?

PRAED Yes.

VIVIE What on earth is it like?

PRAED Well, you must have observed, Miss Warren, that people who are dissatisfied with their own bringing-up generally think that the world would be all right if everybody were to be brought up quite differently. Now your mother's life has been—er—I suppose you know—

VIVIE Dont suppose anything, Mr Praed. I hardly know my mother. Since I was a child I have lived in England, at school or college, or with people paid to take charge of me. I have been boarded out all my life. My mother has lived in Brussels or Vienna and never let me go to her. I only see her when she visits England for a few days. I dont complain: it's been very pleasant; for people have been very good to me; and there has always been plenty of money to make things smooth. But dont imagine I know anything about my mother. I know far less than you do.

PRAED [*Very ill at ease.*] In that case—[*He stops, quite at a loss. Then, with a forced attempt at gaiety*] But what nonsense we are talking! Of course you and your mother will get on capitally. [*He rises, and looks abroad at the view.*] What a charming little place you have here!

VIVIE [*Unmoved.*] Rather a violent change of subject, Mr Praed. Why wont my mother's life bear being talked about?

PRAED Oh, you really mustnt say that. Isnt it natural that I should have a certain delicacy in talking to my old friend's daughter about her behind her back? You and she will have plenty of opportunity of talking about it when she comes.

VIVIE No: s h e wont talk about it either. [*Rising.*] However, I daresay you have good reasons for telling me nothing. Only, mind this, Mr Praed. I expect there will be a battle royal[3] when my mother hears of my Chancery Lane project.

PRAED [*Ruefully.*] I'm afraid there will.

VIVIE Well, I shall win, because I want nothing but my fare to London to start there to-morrow earning my own living by devilling[4] for Honoria. Besides, I have no mysteries to keep up; and it seems she has. I shall use that advantage over her if necessary.

PRAED [*Greatly shocked.*] Oh no! No, pray. Youd not do such a thing.

2. Straight out, without hesitation.
3. A fierce fight.

4. Acting as assistant to a barrister (trial lawyer) as a way of gaining legal experience.

VIVIE   Then tell me why not.

PRAED   I really cannot. I appeal to your good feeling. [*She smiles at his sen-timentality.*] Besides you may be too bold. Your mother is not to be trifled with when she's angry.

VIVIE   You cant frighten me, Mr Praed. In that month at Chancery Lane I had opportunities of taking the measure of one or two women v e r y like my mother. You may back me to win. But if I hit harder in my ignorance than I need, remember that it is you who refuse to enlighten me. Now, let us drop the subject. [*She takes her chair and replaces it near the hammock with the same vigorous swing as before.*]

PRAED   [*Taking a desperate resolution.*]   One word, Miss Warren. I had better tell you. It's very difficult; but—

[MRS WARREN *and* SIR GEORGE CROFTS *arrive at the gate.* MRS WARREN *is between 40 and 50, formerly pretty, showily dressed in a brilliant hat and a gay blouse fitting tightly over her bust and flanked by fashionable sleeves. Rather spoilt and domineering, and decidedly vulgar, but, on the whole, a genial and fairly presentable old blackguard[5] of a woman.*

CROFTS *is a tall powerfully-built man of about 50, fashionably dressed in the style of a young man. Nasal voice, reedier than might be expected from his strong frame. Clean-shaven bulldog jaws, large flat ears, and thick neck: gentlemanly combination of the most brutal types of city man, sporting man, and man about town.*]

VIVIE   Here they are. [*Coming to them as they enter the garden.*] How do, mater?[6] Mr Praed's been here this half hour waiting for you.

MRS WARREN   Well, if youve been waiting, Praddy, it's your own fault: I thought youd have the gumption[7] to know I was coming by the 3.10 train. Vivie: put your hat on, dear: youll get sunburnt. Oh, I forgot to introduce you. Sir George Crofts: my little Vivie.

[CROFTS *advances to* VIVIE *with his most courtly manner. She nods, but makes no motion to shake hands.*]

CROFTS   May I shake hands with a young lady whom I have known by repu-tation very long as the daughter of one of my oldest friends?

VIVIE   [*Who has been looking him up and down sharply.*]   If you like. [*She takes his tenderly proffered hand and gives it a squeeze that makes him open his eyes; then turns away, and says to her mother*] Will you come in, or shall I get a couple more chairs? [*She goes into the porch for the chairs.*]

MRS WARREN   Well George, what do you think of her?

CROFTS   [*Ruefully.*]   She has a powerful fist. Did you shake hands with her, Praed?

PRAED   Yes: it will pass off presently.

CROFTS   I hope so. [VIVIE *reappears with two more chairs. He hurries to her assistance.*] Allow me.

MRS WARREN   [*Patronizingly.*]   Let Sir George help you with the chairs, dear.

VIVIE   [*Pitching them into his arms.*]   Here you are. [*She dusts her hands and turns to* MRS WARREN.] Youd like some tea, wouldnt you?

MRS WARREN   [*Sitting in* PRAED's *chair and fanning herself.*]   I'm dying for a drop to drink.

VIVIE   I'll see about it. [*She goes into the cottage.*]

5. Rogue.   7. Here common sense.
6. Mother (Latin).

[SIR GEORGE *has by this time managed to unfold a chair and plant it beside* MRS WARREN, *on her left. He throws the other on the grass and sits down, looking dejected and rather foolish, with the handle of his stick in his mouth.* PRAED, *still very uneasy, fidgets about the garden on their right.*]

MRS WARREN [*To* PRAED, *looking at* CROFTS.] Just look at him, Praddy: he looks cheerful, dont he? He's been worrying my life out these three years to have that little girl of mine shewn to him; and now that Ive done it, he's quite out of countenance. [*Briskly.*] Come! sit up, George; and take your stick out of your mouth. [CROFTS *sulkily obeys.*]

PRAED I think, you know—if you dont mind my saying so—that we had better get out of the habit of thinking of her as a little girl. You see she has really distinguished herself; and I'm not sure, from what I have seen of her, that she is not older than any of us.

MRS WARREN [*Greatly amused.*] Only listen to him, George! Older than any of us! Well, she has been stuffing you nicely with her importance.

PRAED But young people are particularly sensitive about being treated in that way.

MRS WARREN Yes; and young people have to get all that nonsense taken out of them, and a good deal more besides. Dont you interfere, Praddy: I know how to treat my own child as well as you do. [PRAED, *with a grave shake of his head, walks up the garden with his hands behind his back.* MRS WARREN *pretends to laugh, but looks after him with perceptible concern. Then she whispers to* CROFTS] Whats the matter with him? What does he take it like that for?

CROFTS [*Morosely.*] Youre afraid of Praed.

MRS WARREN What! Me! Afraid of dear old Praddy! Why, a fly wouldnt be afraid of him.

CROFTS Y o u r e afraid of him.

MRS WARREN [*Angry.*] I'll trouble you to mind your own business, and not try any of your sulks on me. I'm not afraid of y o u, anyhow. If you cant make yourself agreeable, youd better go home. [*She gets up, and turning her back on him, finds herself face to face with* PRAED.] Come, Praddy, I know it was only your tender-heartedness. Youre afraid I'll bully her.

PRAED My dear Kitty: you think I'm offended. Dont imagine that: pray dont. But you know I often notice things that escape you; and though you never take my advice, you sometimes admit afterwards that you ought to have taken it.

MRS WARREN Well, what do you notice now?

PRAED Only that Vivie is a grown woman. Pray, Kitty, treat her with every respect.

MRS WARREN [*With genuine amazement.*] Respect! Treat my own daughter with respect! What next, pray!

VIVIE [*Appearing at the cottage door and calling to* MRS WARREN.] Mother: will you come to my room before tea?

MRS WARREN Yes, dearie. [*She laughs indulgently at* PRAED's *gravity, and pats him on the cheek as she passes him on her way to the porch.*] Dont be cross, Praddy. [*She follows* VIVIE *into the cottage.*]

CROFTS [*Furtively.*] I say, Praed.

PRAED Yes.

CROFTS I want to ask you a rather particular question.

PRAED   Certainly. [*He takes* MRS WARREN's *chair and sits close to* CROFTS.]
CROFTS   Thats right: they might hear us from the window. Look here: did
Kitty ever tell you who that girl's father is?
PRAED   Never.
CROFTS   Have you any suspicion of who it might be?
PRAED   None.
CROFTS [*Not believing him.*]   I know, of course, that you perhaps might feel
bound not to tell if she had said anything to you. But it's very awkward to
be uncertain about it now that we shall be meeting the girl every day. We
dont exactly know how we ought to feel towards her.
PRAED   What difference can that make? We take her on her own merits. What
does it matter who her father was?
CROFTS [*Suspiciously.*]   Then you know who he was?
PRAED [*With a touch of temper.*]   I said no just now. Did you not hear me?
CROFTS   Look here, Praed. I ask you as a particular favor. If you do know
[*Movement of protest from* PRAED.]—I only say, if you know you might at
least set my mind at rest about her. The fact is, I feel attracted.
PRAED [*Sternly.*]   What do you mean?
CROFTS   Oh, dont be alarmed: it's quite an innocent feeling. Thats what puz-
zles me about it. Why, for all I know, *I* might be her father.
PRAED   You! Impossible!
CROFTS [*Catching him up cunningly.*]   You know for certain that I'm not?
PRAED   I know nothing about it, I tell you, any more than you. But really,
Crofts—oh no, it's out of the question. Theres not the least resemblance.
CROFTS   As to that, theres no resemblance between her and her mother that
I can see. I suppose she's not y o u r daughter, is she?
PRAED [*Rising indignantly.*]   Really, Crofts—!
CROFTS   No offence, Praed. Quite allowable as between two men of the world.
PRAED [*Recovering himself with an effort and speaking gently and gravely.*]
Now listen to me, my dear Crofts. [*He sits down again.*] I have nothing to
do with that side of Mrs Warren's life, and never had. She has never spoken
to me about it; and of course I have never spoken to her about it. Your
delicacy[8] will tell you that a handsome woman needs s o m e friends who
are not—well, not on that footing with her. The effect of her own beauty
would become a torment to her if she could not escape from it occasionally.
You are probably on much more confidential terms with Kitty than I am.
Surely you can ask her the question yourself.
CROFTS   I have asked her, often enough. But she's so determined to keep the
child all to herself that she would deny that it ever had a father if she could.
[*Rising.*] I'm thoroughly uncomfortable about it, Praed.
PRAED [*Rising also.*]   Well, as you are, at all events, old enough to be her dont
mind agreeing that we both regard Miss Vivie in a parental way, as a young
girl whom we are bound to protect and help. What do you say?
CROFTS [*Aggressively.*]   I'm no older than you, if you come to that.
PRAED   Yes you are, my dear fellow: you were born old. I was born a boy: Ive
never been able to feel the assurance of a grown-up man in my life. [*He
folds his chair and carries it to the porch.*]
MRS WARREN [*Calling from within the cottage.*]   Prad-dee! George! Tea-ea-ea-
ea!

---

8. Sensitivity, tact.

CROFTS [*Hastily.*]   She's calling us. [*He hurries in.*]
   [PRAED *shakes his head bodingly, and is following* CROFTS *when he is hailed by a young gentleman who has just appeared on the common, and is making for the gate. He is pleasant, pretty, smartly dressed, cleverly good-for-nothing, not long turned 20, with a charming voice and agreeably disrespectful manners. He carries a light sporting magazine rifle.*]
THE YOUNG GENTLEMAN   Hallo! Praed!
PRAED   Why, Frank Gardner! [FRANK *comes in and shakes hands cordially.*] What on earth are you doing here?
FRANK   Staying with my father.
PRAED   The Roman father?[9]
FRANK   He's rector here. I'm living with my people this autumn for the sake of economy. Things came to a crisis in July: the Roman father had to pay my debts. He's stony broke in consequence; and so am I. What are you up to in these parts? Do you know the people here?
PRAED   Yes: I'm spending the day with a Miss Warren.
FRANK [*Enthusiastically.*]   What! Do you know Vivie? Isnt she a jolly girl? I'm teaching her to shoot with this. [*Putting down the rifle.*] I'm so glad she knows you: youre just the sort of fellow she ought to know. [*He smiles, and raises the charming voice almost to a singing tone as he exclaims*] It's e v e r so jolly to find you here, Praed.
PRAED   I'm an old friend of her mother. Mrs Warren brought me over to make her daughter's acquaintance.
FRANK   The mother! Is s h e here?
PRAED   Yes: inside, at tea.
MRS WARREN [*Calling from within.*]   Prad-dee-ee-ee-eee! The tea-cake'll be cold.
PRAED [*Calling.*]   Yes, Mrs Warren. In a moment. Ive just met a friend here.
MRS WARREN   A what?
PRAED [*Louder.*]   A friend.
MRS WARREN   Bring him in.
PRAED   All right. [*to* FRANK] Will you accept the invitation?
FRANK [*Incredulous, but immensely amused.*]   Is that Vivie's mother?
PRAED   Yes.
FRANK   By jove! What a lark! Do you think she'll like me?
PRAED   Ive no doubt youll make yourself popular, as usual. Come in and try. [*Moving towards the house.*]
FRANK   Stop a bit. [*Seriously.*] I want to take you into my confidence.
PRAED   Pray dont. It's only some fresh folly, like the barmaid at Redhill.[1]
FRANK   It's ever so much more serious than that. You say youve only just met Vivie for the first time?
PRAED   Yes.
FRANK [*Rhapsodically.*]   Then you can have no idea what a girl she is. Such character! Such sense! And her cleverness! Oh, my eye, Praed, but I can tell you she is clever! And—need I add?—she loves me.

9. I.e., a father with a Roman (strong) sense of duty, not a Roman Catholic priest. We learn in the next line that Frank's father is a clergyman in the   Church of England.
1. A nearby town.

CROFTS [*Putting his head out of the window.*] I say, Praed: what are you about? D o come along. [*He disappears.*]

FRANK Hallo! Sort of chap that would take a prize at a dog show, aint he? Who's he?

PRAED Sir George Crofts, an old friend of Mrs Warren's. I think we had better come in.
[*On their way to the porch they are interrupted by a call from the gate. Turning, they see an elderly clergyman looking over it.*]

THE CLERGYMAN [*Calling.*] Frank!

FRANK Hallo! [*To* PRAED.] The Roman father. [*To the clergyman.*] Yes, gov'nor:[2] all right: presently. [*To* PRAED.] Look here, Praed: youd better go in to tea. I'll join you directly.

PRAED Very good. [*He goes into the cottage.*]
[*The clergyman remains outside the gate, with his hands on the top of it. The* REV. SAMUEL GARDNER, *a beneficed clergyman*[3] *of the Established Church, is over 50. Externally he is pretentious, booming, noisy, important. Really he is that obsolescent social phenomenon the fool of the family dumped on the Church by his father, the patron, clamorously asserting himself as father and clergyman without being able to command respect in either capacity.*]

REV. SAMUEL Well, sir. Who are your friends here, if I may ask?

FRANK Oh, it's all right, gov'nor! Come in.

REV. SAMUEL No sir; not until I know whose garden I am entering.

FRANK It's all right. It's Miss Warren's.

REV. SAMUEL I have not seen her at church since she came.

FRANK Of course not: she's a third wrangler. Ever so intellectual. Took a higher degree than you did; so why should she go to hear you preach?

REV. SAMUEL Dont be disrespectful, sir.

FRANK Oh, it dont matter: nobody hears us. Come in. [*He opens the gate, unceremoniously pulling his father with it into the garden.*] I want to introduce you to her. Do you remember the advice you gave me last July, gov'nor?

REV. SAMUEL [*Severely.*] Yes, I advised you to conquer your idleness and flippancy, and to work your way into an honorable profession and live on it and not upon me.

FRANK No; thats what you thought of afterwards. What you actually said was that since I had neither brains nor money, I'd better turn my good looks to account by marrying somebody with both. Well, look here. Miss Warren has brains: you cant deny that.

REV. SAMUEL Brains are not everything.

FRANK No, of course not: theres the money—

REV. SAMUEL [*Interrupting him austerely.*] I was not thinking of money, sir. I was speaking of higher things. Social position, for instance.

FRANK I dont care a rap about that.

REV. SAMUEL But I do, sir.

FRANK Well, nobody wants you to marry her. Anyhow, she has what amounts to a high Cambridge degree; and she seems to have as much money as she wants.

---

2. I.e., governor, a common nickname given to a father or other male authority figure.
3. I.e., the recipient of an endowed Church office from which he receives income. Such positions were generally controlled by major landowners.

REV. SAMUEL [*Sinking into a feeble vein of humor.*] I greatly doubt whether she has as much money as y o u will want.

FRANK Oh, come; I havnt been so very extravagant. I live ever so quietly; I dont drink; I dont bet much; and I never go regularly on the razzle-dazzle[4] as you did when you were my age.

REV. SAMUEL [*Booming hollowly.*] Silence, sir.

FRANK Well, you told me yourself, when I was making ever such an ass of myself about the barmaid at Redhill, that you once offered a woman £50 for the letters you wrote to her when—

REV. SAMUEL [*Terrified.*] Sh-sh-sh, Frank, for heaven's sake! [*He looks round apprehensively. Seeing no one within earshot he plucks up courage to boom again, but more subduedly.*] You are taking an ungentlemanly advantage of what I confided to you for your own good, to save you from an error you would have repented all your life long. Take warning by your father's follies, sir; and dont make them an excuse for your own.

FRANK Did you ever hear the story of the Duke of Wellington[5] and his letters?

REV. SAMUEL No, sir; and I dont want to hear it.

FRANK The old Iron Duke didnt throw away £50: not he. He just wrote: "Dear Jenny: publish and be damned! Yours affectionately, Wellington." Thats what you should have done.

REV. SAMUEL [*Piteously.*] Frank, my boy: when I wrote those letters I put myself into that woman's power. When I told you about them I put myself, to some extent, I am sorry to say, in your power. She refused my money with these words, which I shall never forget. "Knowledge is power" she said; "and I never sell power." Thats more than twenty years ago; and she has never made use of her power or caused me a moment's uneasiness. You are behaving worse to me than she did, Frank.

FRANK Oh yes I dare say! Did you ever preach at her the way you preach at me every day?

REV. SAMUEL [*Wounded almost to tears.*] I leave you sir. You are incorrigible. [*He turns towards the gate.*]

FRANK [*Utterly unmoved.*] Tell them I shant be home to tea, will you, gov'nor, like a good fellow? [*He moves towards the cottage door and is met by* PRAED *and* VIVIE *coming out.*]

VIVIE. [*To* FRANK.] Is that your father, Frank? I do so want to meet him.

FRANK Certainly. [*Calling after his father.*] Gov'nor. Youre wanted. [*The parson turns at the gate, fumbling nervously at his hat.* PRAED *crosses the garden to the opposite side, beaming in anticipation of civilities.*] My father: Miss Warren.

VIVIE [*Going to the clergyman and shaking his hand.*] Very glad to see you here, Mr Gardner. [*Calling to the cottage.*] Mother: come along: youre wanted.

[MRS WARREN *appears on the threshold, and is immediately transfixed recognizing the clergyman.*]

VIVIE [*Continuing.*] Let me introduce—

MRS WARREN [*Swooping on the* REVEREND SAMUEL.] Why, it's Sam Gardner, gone into the Church! Well, I never! Dont you know us, Sam? This is George Crofts, as large as life and twice as natural. Dont you remember me?

---

4. I.e., out on the town.
5. Arthur Wellesley (1769–1852), military hero and statesmen.

REV. SAMUEL [*Very red.*]   I really—er—
MRS WARREN   Of course you do. Why, I have a whole album of your letters still: I came across them only the other day.
REV. SAMUEL [*Miserably confused.*]   Miss Vavasour, I believe.
MRS WARREN [*Correcting him quickly in a loud whisper.*]   Tch! Nonsense! Mrs Warren: dont you see my daughter there?

Act 2

Inside the cottage after nightfall. Looking eastward from within instead of westward from without, the latticed window, with its curtains drawn, is now seen in the middle of the front wall of the cottage, with the porch door to the left of it. In the left-hand side wall is the door leading to the kitchen. Farther back against the same wall is a dresser with a candle and matches on it, and FRANK's *rifle standing beside them, with the barrel resting in the plate-rack. In the centre a table stands with a lighted lamp on it.* VIVIE's *books and writing materials are on a table to the right of the window, against the wall. The fireplace is on the right, with a settle:*[6] *there is no fire. Two of the chairs are set right and left of the table. The cottage door opens, shewing a fine starlit night without; and* MRS WARREN, *her shoulders wrapped in a shawl borrowed from* VIVIE, *enters, followed by* FRANK, *who throws his cap on the window seat. She has had enough of walking, and gives a gasp of relief as she unpins her hat; takes it off; sticks the pin through the crown; and puts it on the table.*

MRS WARREN   O Lord! I dont know which is the worst of the country, the walking or the sitting at home with nothing to do. I could do with a whisky and soda now very well, if only they had such a thing in this place.
FRANK   Perhaps Vivie's got some.
MRS WARREN   Nonsense! What would a young girl like her be doing with such things! Never mind: it dont matter. I wonder how she passes her time here! I'd a good deal rather be in Vienna.
FRANK   Let me take you there. [*He helps her to take off her shawl, gallantly giving her shoulders a very perceptible squeeze as he does so.*]
MRS WARREN   Ah! would you? I'm beginning to think youre a chip of the old block.
FRANK   Like the gov'nor, eh? [*He hangs the shawl on the nearest chair, and sits down.*]
MRS WARREN   Never you mind. What do you know about such things? Youre only a boy. [*She goes to the hearth, to be farther from temptation.*]
FRANK   Do come to Vienna with me? It'd be ever such larks.
MRS WARREN   No, thank you. Vienna is no place for you—at least not until youre a little older. [*She nods at him to emphasize this piece of advice. He makes a mock-piteous face, belied by his laughing eyes. She looks at him; then comes back to him.*] Now, look here, little boy [*taking his face in her hands and turning it up to her*]; I know you through and through by your likeness to your father, better than you know yourself. Dont you go taking any silly ideas into your head about me. Do you hear?
FRANK [*Gallantly wooing her with his voice.*]   Cant help it, my dear Mrs Warren: it runs in the family.
        [*She pretends to box his ears; then looks at the pretty laughing upturned*

6. A high-backed wooden bench.

*face for a moment, tempted. At last she kisses him, and immediately
turns away, out of patience with herself.*]
MRS WARREN   There! I shouldnt have done that. I am wicked. Never you mind,
my dear: it's only a motherly kiss. Go and make love to[7] Vivie.
FRANK   So I have.
MRS WARREN   [*Turning on him with a sharp note of alarm in her voice.*]   What!
FRANK   Vivie and I are ever such chums.
MRS WARREN   What do you mean? Now see here: I wont have any young
scamp tampering with my little girl. Do you hear? I wont have it.
FRANK   [*Quite unabashed.*]   My dear Mrs Warren: dont you be alarmed. My
intentions are honorable: ever so honorable; and your little girl is jolly well
able to take care of herself. She dont need looking after half so much as her
mother. She aint so handsome, you know.
MRS WARREN   [*Taken aback by his assurance.*]   Well, you have got a nice
healthy two inches thick of cheek all over you.[8] I dont know where you got
it. Not from your father, anyhow.
CROFTS   [*In the garden.*]   The gipsies, I suppose?
REV. SAMUEL   [*Replying.*]   The broomsquires[9] are far worse.
MRS WARREN   [*To FRANK.*]   S-sh! Remember! youve had your warning.
      [CROFTS *and the* REVEREND SAMUEL *come in from the garden, the clergy-
      man continuing his conversation as he enters.*]
REV. SAMUEL   The perjury at the Winchester assizes[1] is deplorable.
MRS WARREN   Well? What became of you two? And wheres Praddy and Vivie?
CROFTS   [*Putting his hat on the settle and his stick in the chimney corner.*]   They
went up the hill. We went to the village. I wanted a drink. [*He sits down on
the settle, putting his legs up along the seat.*]
MRS WARREN   Well, she oughtnt to go off like that without telling me. [*To
FRANK.*] Get your father a chair, Frank: where are your manners? [FRANK
*springs up and gracefully offers his father his chair; and then takes another
from the wall and sits down at the table, in the middle, with his father on his
right and* MRS WARREN *on his left.*] George: where are you going to stay to-
night? You cant stay here. And whats Praddy going to do?
CROFTS   Gardner'll put me up.
MRS WARREN   Oh no doubt youve taken care of yourself! But what about
Praddy?
CROFTS   Dont know. I suppose he can sleep at the inn.
MRS WARREN   Havnt you room for him, Sam?
REV. SAMUEL   Well—er—you see, as rector here, I am not free to do as I like.
Er—what is Mr Praed's social position?
MRS. WARREN   Oh, he's all right: he's an architect. What an old stick-in-the-
mud you are, Sam!
FRANK   Yes, it's all right, gov'nor. He built that place down in Wales for the
Duke. Caernarvon Castle[2] they call it. You must have heard of it. [*He winks
with lightning smartness at* MRS WARREN, *and regards his father blandly.*]
REV. SAMUEL   Oh, in that case, of course we shall only be too happy. I suppose
he knows the Duke personally.
FRANK   Oh, ever so intimately! We can stick him in Georgina's old room.

---

7. Woo, court.
8. I.e., you are very cheeky (presumptuous).
9. Minor country landowners.

1. Law courts.
2. Frank here plays on his father's ignorance and
snobbery: the castle was built in the 13th century.

MRS WARREN   Well, thats settled. Now if those two would only come in and let us have supper. Theyve no right to stay out after dark like this.

CROFTS [*Aggressively.*]   What harm are they doing you?

MRS WARREN   Well, harm or not, I dont like it.

FRANK   Better not wait for them, Mrs Warren. Praed will stay out as long as possible. He has never known before what it is to stray over the heath on a summer night with my Vivie.

CROFTS [*Sitting up in some consternation.*]   I say, you know! Come!

REV. SAMUEL [*Rising, startled out of his professional manner into real force and sincerity.*]   Frank, once for all, it's out of the question. Mrs Warren will tell you that it's not to be thought of.

CROFTS   Of course not.

FRANK [*With enchanting placidity.*]   Is that so, Mrs Warren?

MRS WARREN [*Reflectively.*]   Well, Sam, I dont know. If the girl wants to get married, no good can come of keeping her unmarried.

REV. SAMUEL [*Astounded.*]   But married to him!—your daughter to my son! Only think: it's impossible.

CROFTS   Of course it's impossible. Dont be a fool, Kitty.

MRS WARREN [*Nettled.*]   Why not? Isnt my daughter good enough for your son?

REV. SAMUEL   But surely, my dear Mrs Warren, you know the reasons—

MRS WARREN [*Defiantly.*]   I know no reasons. If you know any, you can tell them to the lad, or to the girl, or to your congregation, if you like.

REV. SAMUEL [*Collapsing helplessly into his chair.*]   You know very well that I couldnt tell anyone the reasons. But my boy will believe me when I tell him there a r e reasons.

FRANK   Quite right, Dad: he will. But has your boy's conduct ever been influenced by your reasons?

CROFTS   You cant marry her: and thats all about it. [*He gets up and stands on the hearth, with his back to the fireplace, frowning determinedly.*]

MRS WARREN [*Turning on him sharply.*]   What have you got to do with it, pray?

FRANK [*With his prettiest lyrical cadence.*]   Precisely what I was going to ask, myself, in my own graceful fashion.

CROFTS [*To MRS WARREN.*]   I suppose you dont want to marry the girl to a man younger than herself and without either a profession or twopence to keep her on. Ask Sam, if you dont believe me. [*To the parson.*] How much more money are you going to give him?

REV. SAMUEL   Not another penny. He has had his patrimony; and he spent the last of it in July. [MRS WARREN's *face falls.*]

CROFTS [*Watching her.*]   There! I told you. [*He resumes his place on the settle up his legs on the seat again, as if the matter were finally disposed of.*]

FRANK [*Plaintively.*]   This is ever so mercenary. Do you suppose Miss Warren's going to marry for money? If we love one another—

MRS WARREN   Thank you. Your love's a pretty cheap commodity, my lad. If you have no means of keeping a wife, that settles it: you cant have Vivie.

FRANK [*Much amused.*]   What do y o u say, gov'nor, eh?

REV. SAMUEL   I agree with Mrs Warren.

FRANK   And good old Crofts has already expressed his opinion.

CROFTS [*Turning angrily on his elbow.*]   Look here: I want none of y o u r cheek.

FRANK [*Pointedly.*]   I'm ever so sorry to surprise you, Crofts, but you allowed yourself the liberty of speaking to me like a father a moment ago. One father is enough, thank you.

CROFTS [*Contemptuously.*]   Yah! [*He turns away again.*]

FRANK [*Rising.*]   Mrs Warren: I cannot give my Vivie up, even for your sake.

MRS WARREN [*Muttering.*]   Young scamp!

FRANK [*Continuing.*]   And as you no doubt intend to hold out other prospects to her, I shall lose no time in placing my case before her. [*They stare at him; and he begins to declaim gracefully.*]

> He either fears his fate too much,
> Or his deserts are small,
> That dares not put it to the touch
> To gain or lose it all.[3]

[*The cottage door opens whilst he is reciting; and* VIVIE *and* PRAED *come in. He breaks off.* PRAED *puts his hat on the dresser. There is an immediate improvement in the company's behavior.* CROFTS *takes down his legs from the settle and pulls himself together as* PRAED *joins him at the fireplace.* MRS WARREN *loses her ease of manner and takes refuge in querulousness.*]

MRS WARREN   Wherever have you been, Vivie?

VIVIE [*Taking off her hat and throwing it carelessly on the table.*]   On the hill.

MRS WARREN   Well, you shouldnt go off like that without letting me know. How could I tell what had become of you? And night coming on too!

VIVIE [*Going to the door of the kitchen and opening it, ignoring her mother.*]   Now, about supper? [*All rise except* MRS WARREN.] We shall be rather crowded in here, I'm afraid.

MRS WARREN   Did you hear what I said, Vivie?

VIVIE [*Quietly.*]   Yes, mother. [*Reverting to the supper difficulty.*] How many are we? [*Counting.*] One, two, three, four, five, six. Well, two will have to wait until the rest are done: Mrs Alison has only plates and knives for four.

PRAED   Oh, it doesnt matter about me. I—

VIVIE   You have had a long walk and are hungry, Mr Praed: you shall have your supper at once. I can wait myself. I want one person to wait with me. Frank: are you hungry?

FRANK   Not the least in the world. Completely off my peck,[4] in fact.

MRS WARREN [*To* CROFTS.]   Neither are you, George. You can wait.

CROFTS   Oh, hang it. Ive eaten nothing since tea-time. Cant Sam do it?

FRANK   Would you starve my poor father?

REV. SAMUEL [*Testily.*]   Allow me to speak for myself, sir. I am perfectly willing to wait.

VIVIE [*Decisively.*]   Theres no need. Only two are wanted. [*She opens the door of the kitchen.*] Will you take my mother in, Mr Gardner. [*The parson takes* MRS WARREN; *and they pass into the kitchen.* PRAED *and* CROFTS *follow. All except* PRAED *clearly disapprove of the arrangement, but do not know how to resist it.* VIVIE *stands at the door looking in at them.*] Can you squeeze past to that corner, Mr Praed: it's rather a tight fit. Take care of your coat against the white-wash: thats right. Now, are you all comfortable?

---

3. From the poem "My Dear and Only Love," by the marquess of Montrose (1612–1650).   4. Food (slang).

PRAED [*Within.*]   Quite, thank you.

MRS WARREN [*Within.*]   Leave the door open, dearie. [VIVIE *frowns; but* FRANK *checks her with a gesture, and steals to the cottage door, which he softly sets wide open.*] Oh Lor, what a draught! Youd better shut it, dear.

> [VIVIE *shuts it with a slam, and then, noting with disgust that her mother's hat and shawl are lying about, takes them tidily to the window seat, whilst* FRANK *noiselessly shuts the cottage door.*]

FRANK [*Exulting.*]   Aha! Got rid of em. Well, Vivvums: what do you think of my governor?

VIVIE [*Preoccupied and serious.*]   Ive hardly spoken to him. He doesnt strike me as being a particularly able person.

FRANK   Well, you know, the old man is not altogether such a fool as he looks. You see, he was shoved into the Church rather; and in trying to live up to it he makes a much bigger ass of himself than he really is. I dont dislike him as much as you might expect. He means well. How do you think youll get on with him?

VIVIE [*Rather grimly.*]   I dont think my future life will be much concerned with him, or with any of that old circle of my mother's, except perhaps Praed. [*She sits down on the settle.*] What do you think of my mother?

FRANK   Really and truly?

VIVIE   Yes, really and truly.

FRANK   Well, she's ever so jolly. But she's rather a caution, isn't she? And Crofts! Oh my eye, Crofts! [*He sits beside her.*]

VIVIE   What a lot, Frank!

FRANK   What a crew!

VIVIE [*With intense contempt for them.*]   If I thought that *I* was like that— that I was going to be a waster, shifting along from one meal to another with no purpose, and no character, and no grit in me, I'd open an artery and bleed to death without one moment's hesitation.

FRANK   Oh no, you wouldnt. Why should they take any grind when they can afford not to? I wish I had their luck. No: what I object to is their form. It isnt the thing: it's slovenly, ever so slovenly.

VIVIE   Do you think your form will be any better when youre as old as Crofts, if you dont work?

FRANK   Of course I do. Ever so much better. Vivvums mustnt lecture: her little boy's incorrigible. [*He attempts to take her face caressingly in his hands.*]

VIVIE [*Striking his hands down sharply.*]   Off with you: Vivvums is not in a humor for petting her little boy this evening. [*She rises and comes forward to the other side of the room.*]

FRANK [*Following her.*]   How unkind!

VIVIE [*Stamping at him.*]   Be serious. I'm serious.

FRANK   Good. Let us talk learnedly. Miss Warren: do you know that all the most advanced thinkers are agreed that half the diseases of modern civilization are due to starvation of the affections in the young. Now, I—

VIVIE [*Cutting him short.*]   You are very tiresome. [*She opens the inner door.*] Have you room for Frank there? He's complaining of starvation.

MRS WARREN [*Within.*]   Of course there is. [*Clatter of knives and glasses as she moves the things on the table.*] Here! theres room now beside me. Come along, Mr Frank.

FRANK   Her little boy will be ever so even with his Vivvums for this. [*He passes into the kitchen.*]

MRS WARREN [*Within.*] Here, Vivie: come on you too, child. You must be famished. [*She enters, followed by* CROFTS, *who holds the door open for* VIVIE *with marked deference. She goes out without looking at him; and he shuts the door after her.*] Why, George, you cant be done: youve eaten nothing. Is there anything wrong with you?

CROFTS Oh, all I wanted was a drink. [*He thrusts his hands in his pockets, and begins prowling about the room, restless and sulky.*]

MRS WARREN Well, I like enough to eat. But a little of that cold beef and cheese and lettuce goes a long way. [*With a sigh of only half repletion she sits down lazily on the settle.*]

CROFTS What do you go encouraging that young pup for?

MRS WARREN [*On the alert at once.*] Now see here, George: what are you up to about that girl? Ive been watching your way of looking at her. Remember: I know you and what your looks mean.

CROFTS Theres no harm in looking at her, is there?

MRS WARREN I'd put you out and pack you back to London pretty soon if I saw any of your nonsense. My girl's little finger is more to me than your whole body and soul. [CROFTS *receives this with a sneering grin.* MRS WARREN, *flushing a little at her failure to impose on him in the character of a theatrically devoted mother, adds in a lower key*] Make your mind easy: the young pup has no more chance than you have.

CROFTS Maynt a man take an interest in a girl?

MRS WARREN Not a man like you.

CROFTS How old is she?

MRS WARREN Never you mind how old she is.

CROFTS Why do you make such a secret of it?

MRS WARREN Because I choose.

CROFTS Well, I'm not fifty yet; and my property is as good as ever it was—

MRS WARREN [*Interrupting him.*] Yes; because youre as stingy as youre vicious.

CROFTS [*Continuing.*] And a baronet isnt to be picked up every day. No other man in my position would put up with you for a mother-in-law. Why shouldnt she marry me?

MRS WARREN You!

CROFTS We three could live together quite comfortably. I'd die before her and leave her a bouncing widow with plenty of money. Why not? It's been growing in my mind all the time Ive been walking with that fool inside there.

MRS WARREN [*Revolted.*] Yes; it's the sort of thing that would grow in your mind.

[*He halts in his prowling; and the two look at one another, she steadfastly, with a sort of awe behind her contemptuous disgust: he stealthily, with a carnal gleam in his eye and a loose grin.*]

CROFTS [*Suddenly becoming anxious and urgent as he sees no sign of sympathy in her.*] Look here, Kitty: youre a sensible woman: you neednt put on any moral airs. I'll ask no more questions; and you need answer none. I'll settle the whole property on her; and if you want a cheque for yourself on the wedding day, you can name any figure you like—in reason.

MRS WARREN So it's come to that with you, George, like all the other worn-out old creatures!

CROFTS [*Savagely.*] Damn you!

[*Before she can retort the door of the kitchen is opened; and the voices*] *of the others are heard returning.* CROFTS, *unable to recover his presence of mind, hurries out of the cottage. The clergyman appears at the kitchen door.*]

REV. SAMUEL [*Looking around.*] Where is Sir George?

MRS WARREN Gone out to have a pipe. [*The clergyman takes his hat from the table, and joins* MRS WARREN *at the fireside. Meanwhile* VIVIE *comes in, followed by* FRANK, *who collapses into the nearest chair with an air of extreme exhaustion.* MRS WARREN *looks round at* VIVIE *and says, with her affectation of maternal patronage even more forced than usual*] Well, dearie: have you had a good supper?

VIVIE You know what Mrs Alison's suppers are. [*She turns to* FRANK *and pets him.*] Poor Frank! was all the beef gone? did it get nothing but bread and cheese and ginger beer? [*Seriously, as if she had done quite enough trifling for one evening.*] Her butter is really awful. I must get some down from the stores.

FRANK Do, in heaven's name!

[VIVIE *goes to the writing-table and makes a memorandum to order the butter.* PRAED *comes in from the kitchen, putting up his handkerchief, which he has been using as a napkin.*]

REV. SAMUEL Frank, my boy: it is time for us to be thinking of home. Your mother does not know yet that we have visitors.

PRAED I'm afraid we're giving trouble.

FRANK [*Rising.*] Not the least in the world; my mother will be delighted to see you. She's a genuinely intellectual artistic woman; and she sees nobody here from one year's end to another except the gov'nor; so you can imagine how jolly dull it pans out for her. [*To his father.*] Y o u r e not intellectual or artistic are you, pater?[5] So take Praed home at once; and I'll stay here and entertain Mrs Warren. Youll pick up Crofts in the garden. He'll be excellent company for the bull-pup.

PRAED [*Taking his hat from the dresser, and coming close to* FRANK.] Come with us, Frank. Mrs Warren has not seen Miss Vivie for a long time; and we have prevented them from having a moment together yet.

FRANK [*Quite softened, and looking at* PRAED *with romantic admiration.*] Of course. I forgot. Ever so thanks for reminding me. Perfect gentleman, Praddy. Always were. My ideal through life. [*He rises to go, but pauses a moment between the two older men, and puts his hand on* PRAED's *shoulder.*] Ah, if you had only been my father instead of this unworthy old man! [*He puts his other hand on his father's shoulder.*]

REV. SAMUEL [*Blustering.*] Silence, sir, silence; you are profane.

MRS WARREN [*Laughing heartily.*] You should keep him in better order, Sam. Goodnight. Here: take George his hat and stick with my compliments.

REV. SAMUEL [*Taking them.*] Goodnight. [*They shake hands. As he passes* VIVIE *he shakes hands with her also and bids her goodnight. Then, in booming command, to* FRANK.] Come along, sir, at once. [*He goes out.*]

MRS WARREN Byebye, Praddy.

PRAED Byebye, Kitty.

[*They shake hands affectionately and go out together, she accompanying him to the garden gate.*]

FRANK [*To* VIVIE.] Kissums?

---

5. Father (Latin).

VIVIE [*Fiercely.*] No. I hate you. [*She takes a couple of books and some paper from the writing-table, and sits down with them at the middle table, at the end next the fireplace.*]

FRANK [*Grimacing.*] Sorry. [*He goes for his cap and rifle.* MRS WARREN *returns. He takes her hand.*] Goodnight, d e a r Mrs Warren. [*He kisses her hand. She snatches it away, her lips tightening, and looks more than half disposed to box his ears. He laughs mischievously and runs off, clapping-to the door behind him.*]

MRS WARREN [*Resigning herself to an evening of boredom now that the men are gone.*] Did you ever in your life hear anyone rattle on so? Isnt he a tease? [*She sits at the table.*] Now that I think of it, dearie, dont you go on encouraging him. I'm sure he's a regular good-for-nothing.

VIVIE [*Rising to fetch more books.*] I'm afraid so. Poor Frank! I shall have to get rid of him; but I shall feel sorry for him, though he's not worth it. That man Crofts does not seem to me to be good for much either: is he? [*She throws the books on the table rather roughly.*]

MRS WARREN [*Galled by* VIVIE's *indifference.*] What do you know of men, child, to talk that way about them? Youll have to make up your mind to see a good deal of Sir George Crofts, as he's a friend of mine.

VIVIE [*Quite unmoved.*] Why? [*She sits down and opens a book.*] Do you expect that we shall be much together? You and I, I mean?

MRS WARREN [*Staring at her.*] Of course: until youre married. Youre not going back to college again.

VIVIE Do you think my way of life would suit you? I doubt it.

MRS WARREN Y o u r way of life! What do you mean?

VIVIE [*Cutting a page of her book with the paper knife on her chatelaine.*] Has it really never occurred to you, mother, that I have a way of life like other people?

MRS WARREN What nonsense is this youre trying to talk? Do you want to shew your independence, now that youre a great little person at school? Dont be a fool, child.

VIVIE [*Indulgently.*] Thats all you have to say on the subject, is it, mother?

MRS WARREN [*Puzzled, then angry.*] Dont you keep on asking me questions like that. [*Violently.*] Hold your tongue. [VIVIE *works on, losing no time, and saying nothing.*] You and your way of life, indeed! What next? [*She looks at* VIVIE *again. No reply.*] Your way of life will be what I please, so it will. [*Another pause.*] Ive been noticing these airs in you ever since you got that tripos or whatever you call it. If you think I'm going to put up with them youre mistaken; and the sooner you find it out, the better. [*Muttering.*] All I have to say on the subject, indeed! [*Again raising her voice angrily.*] Do you know who youre speaking to, Miss?

VIVIE [*Looking across at her without raising her head from her book.*] No. Who are you? What are you?

MRS WARREN [*Rising breathless.*] You young imp!

VIVIE Everybody knows my reputation, my social standing, and the profession I intend to pursue. I know nothing about you. What is that way of life which you invite me to share with you and Sir George Crofts, pray?

MRS WARREN Take care. I shall do something I'll be sorry for after, and you too.

VIVIE [*Putting aside her books with cool decision.*] Well, let us drop the subject until you are better able to face it. [*Looking critically at her mother.*] You want some good walks and a little lawn tennis to set you up. You are shockingly out of condition: you were not able to manage twenty yards uphill today without stopping to pant; and your wrists are mere rolls of fat. Look at mine. [*She holds out her wrists.*]

MRS WARREN [*After looking at her helplessly, begins to whimper.*]   Vivie—

VIVIE [*Springing up sharply.*]   Now pray dont begin to cry. Anything but that. I really cannot stand whimpering. I will go out of the room if you do.

MRS WARREN [*Piteously.*]   Oh, my darling, how can you be so hard on me? Have I no rights over you as your mother?

VIVIE   Are you my mother?

MRS WARREN [*Appalled.*]   Am I your mother! Oh, Vivie!

VIVIE   Then where are our relatives? my father? our family friends? You claim the rights of a mother: the right to call me fool and child; to speak to me as no woman in authority over me at college dare speak to me; to dictate my way of life; and to force on me the acquaintance of a brute whom anyone can see to be the most vicious sort of London man about town. Before I give myself the trouble to resist such claims, I may as well find out whether they have any real existence.

MRS WARREN [*Distracted, throwing herself on her knees.*]   Oh no, no. Stop, stop. I am your mother: I swear it. Oh, you cant mean to turn on me—my own child! It's not natural. You believe me, dont you? Say you believe me.

VIVIE   Who was my father?

MRS WARREN   You dont know what youre asking. I cant tell you.

VIVIE [*Determinedly.*]   Oh yes you can, if you like. I have a right to know; and you know very well that I have that right. You can refuse to tell me, if you please; but if you do, you will see the last of me tomorrow morning.

MRS WARREN   Oh, it's too horrible to hear you talk like that. You wouldnt— you c o u l d n t leave me.

VIVIE [*Ruthlessly.*]   Yes, without a moment's hesitation, if you trifle with me about this. [*Shivering with disgust.*] How can I feel sure that I may not have the contaminated blood of that brutal waster in my veins?

MRS WARREN   No, no. On my oath it's not he, nor any of the rest that you have ever met. I'm certain of that, at least.

[VIVIE*'s eyes fasten sternly on her mother as the significance of this flashes on her.*]

VIVIE [*Slowly.*]   You are certain of that, a t l e a s t. Ah! You mean that that is all you are certain of. [*Thoughtfully.*] I see. [MRS WARREN *buries her face in her hands.*] Dont do that, mother: you know you dont feel it a bit. [MRS WARREN *takes down her hands and looks up deplorably at* VIVIE, *who takes out her watch and says*] Well, that is enough for tonight. At what hour would you like breakfast? Is half-past eight too early for you?

MRS WARREN [*Wildly.*]   My God, what sort of woman are you?

VIVIE [*Coolly.*]   The sort the world is mostly made of, I should hope. Otherwise I dont understand how it gets its business done. Come [*taking her mother by the wrist, and pulling her up pretty resolutely*]: pull yourself together. Thats right.

MRS WARREN [*Querulously.*]   Youre very rough with me, Vivie.

VIVIE   Nonsense. What about bed? It's past ten.

MRS WARREN [*Passionately.*]   Whats the use of my going to bed? Do you think I could sleep?

VIVIE   Why not? I shall.

MRS WARREN   You! youve no heart. [*She suddenly breaks out vehemently in her natural tongue—the dialect of a woman of the people—with all her affectations of maternal authority and conventional manners gone, and an overwhelming inspiration of true conviction and scorn in her.*] Oh, I wont bear it: I wont put up with the injustice of it. What right have you to set yourself up above me like this? You boast of what you are to me—to m e, who gave you the chance of being what you are. What chance had I! Shame on you for a bad daughter and a stuck-up prude!

VIVIE   [*Sitting down with a shrug, no longer confident; for her replies, which have sounded sensible and strong to her so far, now begin to ring rather woodenly and even priggishly against the new tone of her mother.*] Dont think for a moment I set myself above you in any way. You attacked me with the conventional authority of a mother: I defended myself with the conventional superiority of a respectable woman. Frankly, I am not going to stand any of your nonsense; and when you drop it I shall not expect you to stand any of mine. I shall always respect your right to your own opinions and your own way of life.

MRS WARREN   My own opinions and my own way of life! Listen to her talking! Do you think I was brought up like you? able to pick and choose my own way of life? Do you think I did what I did because I liked it, or thought it right, or wouldnt rather have gone to college and been a lady if I'd had the chance?

VIVIE   Everybody has some choice, mother. The poorest girl alive may not be able to choose between being Queen of England or Principal of Newnham; but she can choose between ragpicking and flower-selling, according to her taste. People are always blaming their circumstances for what they are. I dont believe in circumstances. The people who get on in this world are the people who get up and look for the circumstances they want, and, if they cant find them, make them.

MRS WARREN   Oh, it's easy to talk, very easy, isnt it? Here! would you like to know what my circumstances were?

VIVIE   Yes: you had better tell me. Wont you sit down?

MRS WARREN   Oh, I'll sit down: dont you be afraid. [*She plants her chair farther forward with brazen energy, and sits down.* VIVIE *is impressed in spite of herself.*] D'you know what your gran'mother was?

VIVIE   No.

MRS WARREN   No you dont. I do. She called herself a widow and had a fried-fish shop down by the Mint,[6] and kept herself and four daughters out of it. Two of us were sisters: that was me and Liz; and we were both good-looking and well made. I suppose our father was a well-fed man: mother pretended he was a gentleman; but I dont know. The other two were only half sisters: undersized, ugly, starved looking, hard working, honest poor creatures: Liz and I would have half-murdered them if mother hadnt half-murdered us to keep our hands off them. They were the respectable ones. Well, what did they get by their respectability? I'll tell you. One of them worked in a whitelead[7] factory twelve hours a day for nine shillings a week until she died of lead poisoning. She only expected to get her hands a little paralyzed; but she died. The other was always held up to us as a model because she married

---

6. The Royal Mint (where coins were produced) was close to the Tower in the east of London, at this time a poor area of the city.
7. A pigment used in paints.

a Government laborer in the Deptford victualling yard, and kept his room and the three children neat and tidy on eighteen shillings a week—until he took to drink. That was worth being respectable for, wasnt it?

VIVIE [*Now thoughtfully attentive.*] Did you and your sister think so?

MRS WARREN Liz didnt, I can tell you: she had more spirit. We both went to a church school—that was part of the ladylike airs we gave ourselves to be superior to the children that knew nothing and went nowhere—and we stayed there until Liz went out one night and never came back. I know the school-mistress thought I'd soon follow her example; for the clergyman was always warning me that Lizzie'd end by jumping off Waterloo Bridge.[8] Poor fool: that was all he knew about it! But I was more afraid of the whitelead factory than I was of the river; and so would you have been in my place. That clergyman got me a situation as a scullery maid in a temperance restaurant where they sent out for anything you liked. Then I was waitress; and then I went to the bar at Waterloo station: fourteen hours a day serving drinks and washing glasses for four shillings a week and my board. That was considered a great promotion for me. Well, one cold, wretched night, when I was so tired I could hardly keep myself awake, who should come up for a half of Scotch but Lizzie, in a long fur cloak, elegant and comfortable, with a lot of sovereigns[9] in her purse.

VIVIE [*Grimly.*] My aunt Lizzie!

MRS WARREN. Yes; and a very good aunt to have, too. She's living down at Winchester now, close to the cathedral, one of the most respectable ladies there. Chaperones girls at the county ball, if you please. No river for Liz, thank you! You remind me of Liz a little: she was a first-rate business woman—saved money from the beginning—never let herself look too like what she was—never lost her head or threw away a chance. When she saw I'd grown up good-looking she said to me across the bar "What are you doing there, you little fool? wearing out your health and your appearance for other people's profit!" Liz was saving money then to take a house for herself in Brussels; and she thought we two could save faster than one. So she lent me some money and gave me a start; and I saved steadily and first paid her back, and then went into business with her as her partner. Why shouldnt I have done it? The house in Brussels was real high class: a much better place for a woman to be in than the factory where Anne Jane got poisoned. None of our girls were ever treated as I was treated in the scullery of that temperance place, or at the Waterloo bar, or at home. Would you have had me stay in them and become a worn out old drudge before I was forty?

VIVIE [*Intensely interested by this time.*] No; but why did you choose that business? Saving money and good management will succeed in any business.

MRS WARREN Yes, saving money. But where can a woman get the money to save in any other business? Could you save out of four shillings a week and keep yourself dressed as well? Not you. Of course, if youre a plain woman and cant earn anything more; or if you have a turn for music, or the stage, or newspaper writing; thats different. But neither Liz nor I had any turn for

---

8. I.e., become a prostitute, and then throw herself into the river Thames (traditionally presented as the fate of fallen women).

9. Gold coins, each worth one pound. "A half": a half gill (two fluid ounces).

such things: all we had was our appearance and our turn for pleasing men. Do you think we were such fools as to let other people trade in our good looks by employing us as shopgirls, or barmaids, or waitresses, when we could trade in them ourselves and get all the profits instead of starvation wages? Not likely.

VIVIE   You were certainly quite justified—from the business point of view.

MRS WARREN   Yes; or any other point of view. What is any respectable girl brought up to do but to catch some rich man's fancy and get the benefit of his money by marrying him?—as if a marriage ceremony could make any difference in the right or wrong of the thing! Oh! the hypocrisy of the world makes me sick! Liz and I had to work and save and calculate just like other people; elseways we should be as poor as any good-for-nothing drunken waster of a woman that thinks her luck will last for ever. [With great energy.] I despise such people: theyve no character; and if theres a thing I hate in a woman, it's want of character.

VIVIE   Come now, mother: frankly! Isnt it part of what you call character in a woman that she should greatly dislike such a way of making money?

MRS WARREN   Why, of course. Everybody dislikes having to work and make money; but they have to do it all the same. I'm sure Ive often pitied a poor girl; tired out and in low spirits, having to try to please some man that she doesnt care two straws for—some half-drunken fool that thinks he's making himself agreeable when he's teasing and worrying and disgusting a woman so that hardly any money could pay her for putting up with it. But she has to bear with disagreeables and take the rough with the smooth, just like a nurse in a hospital or anyone else. It's not work that any woman would do for pleasure, goodness knows; though to hear the pious people talk you would suppose it was a bed of roses.

VIVIE   Still, you consider it worth while. It pays.

MRS WARREN   Of course it's worth while to a poor girl, if she can resist temptation and is good-looking and well conducted and sensible. It's far better than any other employment open to her. I always thought that oughtnt to be. It c a n t be right, Vivie, that there shouldnt be better opportunities for women. I stick to that: it's wrong. But it's so, right or wrong; and a girl must make the best of it. But of course it's not worth while for a lady. If you took to it youd be a fool; but I should have been a fool if I'd taken to anything else.

VIVIE   [More and more deeply moved.]   Mother; suppose we were both as poor as you were in those wretched old days, are you quite sure that you wouldnt advise me to try the Waterloo bar, or marry a laborer, or even go into the factory?

MRS WARREN   [Indignantly.]   Of course not. What sort of mother do you take me for! How could you keep your self-respect in such starvation and slavery? And whats a woman worth? whats life worth? without self-respect! Why am I independent and able to give my daughter a first-rate education, when other women that had just as good opportunities are in the gutter? Because I always knew how to respect myself and control myself. Why is Liz looked up to in a cathedral town? The same reason. Where would we be now if we'd minded the clergyman's foolishness? Scrubbing floors for one and six-pence[1] a day and nothing to look forward to but the workhouse infirmary.

_____

1. I.e., one and a half shillings.

Dont you be led astray by people who dont know the world, my girl. The only way for a woman to provide for herself decently is for her to be good to some man that can afford to be good to her. If she's in his own station of life, let her make him marry her; but if she's far beneath him she cant expect it: why should she? it wouldn't be for her own happiness. Ask any lady in London society that has daughters; and she'll tell you the same, except that I tell you straight and she'll tell you crooked. Thats all the difference.

VIVIE [*Fascinated, gazing at her.*] My dear mother; you are a wonderful woman: you are stronger than all England. And are you really and truly not one wee bit doubtful—or—or—ashamed?

MRS WARREN Well, of course, dearie, it's only good manners to be ashamed of it; it's expected from a woman. Women have to pretend to feel a great deal that they dont feel. Liz used to be angry with me for plumping out the truth about it. She used to say that when every woman could learn enough from what was going on in the world before her eyes, there was no need to talk about it to her. But then Liz was such a perfect lady! She had the true instinct of it; while I was always a bit of a vulgarian. I used to be so pleased when you sent me your photos to see that you were growing up like Liz: youve just her ladylike, determined way. But I cant stand saying one thing when everyone knows I mean another. Whats the use in such hypocrisy? If people arrange the world that way for women, theres no good pretending it's arranged the other way. No: I never was a bit ashamed really. I consider I had a right to be proud of how we managed everything so respectably, and never had a word against us, and how the girls were so well taken care of. Some of them did very well: one of them married an ambassador. But of course now I darent talk about such things: whatever would they think of us! [*She yawns.*] Oh dear! I do believe I'm getting sleepy after all. [*She stretches herself lazily, thoroughly relieved by her explosion, and placidly ready for her night's rest.*]

VIVIE I believe it is I who will not be able to sleep now. [*She goes to the dresser and lights the candle. Then she extinguishes the lamp, darkening the room a good deal.*] Better let in some fresh air before locking up. [*She opens the cottage door, and finds that it is broad moonlight.*] What a beautiful night! Look! [*She draws aside the curtains of the window. The landscape is seen bathed in the radiance of the harvest moon rising over Blackdown.*[2]]

MRS WARREN [*With a perfunctory glance at the scene.*] Yes, dear; but take care you dont catch your death of cold from the night air.

VIVIE [*Contemptuously.*] Nonsense.

MRS WARREN [*Querulously.*] Oh yes: everything I say is nonsense, according to you.

VIVIE [*Turning to her quickly.*] No: really that is not so, mother. You have got completely the better of me tonight, though I intended it to be the other way. Let us be good friends now.

MRS WARREN [*Shaking her head a little ruefully.*] So it has been the other way. But I suppose I must give in to it. I always got the worst of it from Liz; and now I suppose it'll be the same with you.

VIVIE Well, never mind. Come: goodnight, dear old mother. [*She takes her mother in her arms.*]

2. A hill near Haslemere.

MRS WARREN [*Fondly.*]   I brought you up well, didnt I, dearie?
VIVIE   You did.
MRS WARREN   And youll be good to your poor old mother for it, wont you?
VIVIE   I will, dear. [*Kissing her.*] Goodnight.
MRS WARREN [*With unction.*]   Blessings on my own dearie darling! a mother's blessing!
   [*She embraces her daughter protectingly, instinctively looking upward for divine sanction.*]

Act 3

In the Rectory garden next morning, with the sun shining from a cloudless sky. The garden wall has a five-barred wooden gate, wide enough to admit a carriage, in the middle. Beside the gate hangs a bell on a coiled spring, communicating with a pull outside. The carriage drive comes down the middle of the garden and then swerves to its left, where it ends in a little gravelled circus³ opposite the Rectory porch. Beyond the gate is seen the dusty high road, parallel with the wall, bounded on the farther side by a strip of turf and an unfenced pine wood. On the lawn, between the house and the drive, is a clipped yew tree, with a garden bench in its shade. On the opposite side the garden is shut in by a box hedge; and there is a sundial on the turf, with an iron chair near it. A little path leads off through the box hedge, behind the sundial.

FRANK seated on the chair near the sundial, on which he has placed the morning papers, is reading The Standard. His father comes from the house, red-eyed and shivery, and meets FRANK's eye with misgiving.

FRANK [*Looking at his watch.*]   Half-past eleven. Nice hour for a rector to come down to breakfast!
REV. SAMUEL   Dont mock, Frank: dont mock. I am a little—er—[*Shivering.*]—
FRANK   Off color?
REV. SAMUEL [*Repudiating the expression.*]   No, sir: unwell this morning. Wheres your mother?
FRANK   Dont be alarmed: she's not here. Gone to town by the 11.13 with Bessie. She left several messages for you. Do you feel equal to receiving them now, or shall I wait til youve breakfasted?
REV. SAMUEL   I h a v e breakfasted, sir. I am surprised at your mother going to town when we have people staying with us. Theyll think it very strange.
FRANK   Possibly she has considered that. At all events, if Crofts is going to stay here, and you are going to sit up every night with him until four, recalling the incidents of your fiery youth, it is clearly my mother's duty, as a prudent housekeeper, to go up to the stores and order a barrel of whisky and few hundred siphons.
REV. SAMUEL   I did not observe that Sir George drank excessively.
FRANK   You were not in a condition to, gov'nor.
REV. SAMUEL   Do you mean to say that I—?
FRANK [*Calmly.*]   I never saw a beneficed clergyman less sober. The anecdotes you told about your past career were so awful that I really dont think Praed

3. A round open space.

would have passed the night under your roof if it hadnt been for the way my mother and he took to one another.

REV. SAMUEL   Nonsense, sir. I am Sir George Crofts' host. I must talk to him about something; and he has only one subject. Where is Mr Praed now?

FRANK   He is driving my mother and Bessie to the station.

REV. SAMUEL   Is Crofts up yet?

FRANK   Oh, long ago. He hasnt turned a hair: he's in much better practice than you. Has kept it up ever since, probably. He's taken himself off somewhere to smoke.

[FRANK *resumes his paper. The parson turns disconsolately towards the gate; then comes back irresolutely.*]

REV. SAMUEL   Er—Frank.

FRANK   Yes.

REV. SAMUEL   Do you think the Warrens will expect to be asked here after yesterday afternoon?

FRANK   Theyve been asked already.

REV. SAMUEL   [*Appalled.*]   What!!!

FRANK   Crofts informed us at breakfast that you told him to bring Mrs Warren and Vivie over here today, and to invite them to make this house their home. My mother then found she must go to town by the 11.13 train.

REV. SAMUEL   [*With despairing vehemence.*]   I never gave any such invitation. I never thought of such a thing.

FRANK   [*Compassionately.*]   How do you know, gov'nor, what you said and thought last night?

PRAED   [*Coming in through the hedge.*]   Good morning.

REV. SAMUEL   Good morning. I must apologize for not having met you at breakfast. I have a touch of—of—

FRANK   Clergyman's sore throat, Praed. Fortunately not chronic.

PRAED   [*Changing the subject.*]   Well, I must say your house is in a charming spot here. Really most charming.

REV. SAMUEL   Yes: it is indeed. Frank will take you for a walk, Mr Praed, if you like. I'll ask you to excuse me: I must take the opportunity to write my sermon while Mrs Gardner is away and you are all amusing yourselves. You wont mind, will you?

PRAED   Certainly not. Dont stand on the slightest ceremony with me.

REV. SAMUEL   Thank you. I'll—er—er—[*He stammers his way to the porch and vanishes into the house.*]

PRAED   Curious thing it must be writing a sermon every week.

FRANK   Ever so curious, if he did it. He buys em. He's gone for some soda water.

PRAED   My dear boy: I wish you would be more respectful to your father. You know you can be so nice when you like.

FRANK   My dear Praddy: you forget that I have to live with the governor. When two people live together—it doesnt matter whether theyre father and son or husband and wife or brother and sister—they cant keep up the polite humbug thats so easy for ten minutes on an afternoon call. Now the governor, who unites to many admirable domestic qualities the irresoluteness of a sheep and the pompousness and aggressiveness of a jackass—

PRAED   No, pray, pray, my dear Frank, remember! He is your father.

FRANK   I give him due credit for that. [*Rising and flinging down his paper.*]

But just imagine his telling Crofts to bring the Warrens over here! He must have been ever so drunk. You know, my dear Praddy, my mother wouldnt stand Mrs Warren for a moment. Vivie mustnt come here until she's gone back to town.

PRAED   But your mother doesnt know anything about Mrs Warren, does she? [*He picks up the paper and sits down to read it.*]

FRANK   I don't know. Her journey to town looks as if she did. Not that my mother would mind in the ordinary way: she has stuck like a brick to lots of women who had got into trouble. But they were all nice women. Thats what makes the real difference. Mrs Warren, no doubt, has her merits; but she's ever so rowdy; and my mother simply wouldnt put up with her. So— hallo! [*This exclamation is provoked by the reappearance of the clergyman, who comes out of the house in haste and dismay.*]

REV. SAMUEL   Frank: Mrs Warren and her daughter are coming across the heath with Crofts: I saw them from the study windows. What am I to say about your mother?

FRANK   Stick on your hat and go out and say how delighted you are to see them; and that Frank's in the garden; and that mother and Bessie have been called to the bedside of a sick relative, and were ever so sorry they couldnt stop; and that you hope Mrs Warren slept well; and—and—say any blessed thing except the truth, and leave the rest to Providence.

REV. SAMUEL   But how are we to get rid of them afterwards?

FRANK   Theres no time to think of that now. Here! [*He bounds into the house.*]

REV. SAMUEL   He's so impetuous. I dont know what to do with him, Mr Praed.

FRANK [*Returning with a clerical felt hat, which he claps on his father's head.*] Now: off with you. [*Rushing him through the gate.*] Praed and I'll wait here, to give the thing an unpremeditated air. [*The clergyman, dazed but obedient, hurries off.*]

FRANK   We must get the old girl back to town somehow, Praed. Come! Honestly, dear Praddy, do you like seeing them together?

PRAED   Oh, why not?

FRANK [*His teeth on edge.*]   Dont it make your flesh creep ever so little? that wicked old devil, up to every villainy under the sun, I'll swear, and Vivie— ugh!

PRAED   Hush, pray. Theyre coming.

[*The clergyman and* CROFTS *are seen coming along the road, followed by* MRS WARREN *and* VIVIE *walking affectionately together.*]

FRANK   Look: she actually has her arm round the old woman's waist. It's her right arm: she began it. She's gone sentimental, by God! Ugh! ugh! Now do you feel the creeps? [*The clergyman opens the gate; and* MRS WARREN *and* VIVIE *pass him and stand in the middle of the garden looking at the house.* FRANK, *in an ecstasy of dissimulation, turns gaily to* MRS WARREN, *exclaiming*] Ever so delighted to see you, Mrs Warren. This quiet old rectory garden becomes you perfectly.

MRS WARREN   Well, I never! Did you hear that, George? He says I look well in a quiet old rectory garden.

REV. SAMUEL [*Still holding the gate for* CROFTS, *who loafs through it, heavily bored.*]   You look well everywhere, Mrs Warren.

FRANK   Bravo, gov'nor! Now look here: lets have a treat before lunch. First lets see the church. Everyone has to do that. It's a regular old thirteenth century church, you know: the gov'nor's ever so fond of it, because he got up a restoration fund and had it completely rebuilt six years ago. Praed will be able to shew its points.

PRAED [*Rising.*]   Certainly, if the restoration has left any to shew.

REV. SAMUEL [*Mooning hospitably at them.*]   I shall be pleased, I'm sure, if Sir George and Mrs Warren really care about it.

MRS WARREN   Oh, come along and get it over.

CROFTS [*Turning back towards the gate.*]   Ive no objection.

REV. SAMUEL   Not that way. We go through the fields, if you dont mind. Round here. [*He leads the way by the little path through the box hedge.*]

CROFTS   Oh, all right. [*He goes with the parson.*]

[PRAED *follows with* MRS WARREN. VIVIE *does not stir: she watches them until they have gone, with all the lines of purpose in her face marking it strongly.*]

FRANK   Aint you coming?

VIVIE   No. I want to give you a warning, Frank. You were making fun of my mother just now when you said that about the rectory garden. That is barred in future. Please treat my mother with as much respect as you treat your own.

FRANK   My dear Viv: she wouldnt appreciate it: the two cases require different treatment. But what on earth has happened to you? Last night we were perfectly agreed as to your mother and her set. This morning I find you attitudinizing sentimentally with your arm round your parent's waist.

VIVIE [*Flushing.*]   Attitudinizing!

FRANK   That was how it struck me. First time I ever saw you do a second-rate thing.

VIVIE [*Controlling herself.*]   Yes, Frank: there has been a change; but I dont think it a change for the worse. Yesterday I was a little prig.

FRANK   And today?

VIVIE [*Wincing; then looking at him steadily.*]   Today I know my mother better than you do.

FRANK   Heaven forbid!

VIVIE   What do you mean?

FRANK   Viv: theres a freemasonry[4] among thoroughly immoral people that you know nothing of. Youve too much character. Thats the bond between your mother and me: thats why I know her better than youll ever know her.

VIVIE   You are wrong: you know nothing about her. If you knew the circumstances against which my mother had to struggle—

FRANK [*Adroitly finishing the sentence for her.*]   I should know why she is what she is, shouldnt I? What difference would that make? Circumstances or no circumstances, Viv, you wont be able to stand your mother.

VIVIE [*Very angrily.*]   Why not?

FRANK   Because she's an old wretch, Viv. If you ever put your arm round her waist in my presence again, I'll shoot myself there and then as a protest against an exhibition which revolts me.

VIVIE   Must I choose between dropping your acquaintance and dropping my mother's?

FRANK [*Gracefully.*]   That would put the old lady at ever such a disadvantage. No, Viv: your infatuated little boy will have to stick to you in any case. But he's all the more anxious that you shouldnt make mistakes. It's no use, Viv:

---

4. A secret understanding.

your mother's impossible. She may be a good sort; but she's a bad lot, a very bad lot.

VIVIE [*Hotly.*] Frank—! [*He stands his ground. She turns away and sits down on the bench under the yew tree, struggling to recover her self-command. Then she says*] Is she to be deserted by all the world because she's what you call a bad lot? Has she no right to live?

FRANK No fear of that, Viv: she wont ever be deserted. [*He sits on the bench beside her.*]

VIVIE But I am to desert her, I suppose.

FRANK [*Babyishly, lulling her and making love to her with his voice.*] Mustnt go live with her. Little family group of mother and daughter wouldnt be a success. Spoil our little group.

VIVIE [*Falling under the spell.*] What little group?

FRANK The babes in the wood:[5] Vivie and little Frank. [*He nestles against her like a weary child.*] Lets go and get covered up with leaves.

VIVIE [*Rhythmically, rocking him like a nurse.*] Fast asleep, hand in hand, under the trees.

FRANK The wise little girl with her silly little boy.

VIVIE The dear little boy with his dowdy little girl.

FRANK Ever so peaceful, and relieved from the imbecility of the little boy's father and the questionableness of the little girl's—

VIVIE [*Smothering the word against her breast.*] Sh-sh-sh-sh! little girl wants to forget all about her mother. [*They are silent for some moments, rocking one another. Then VIVIE wakes up with a shock, exclaiming*] What a pair of fools we are! Come: sit up. Gracious! your hair. [*She smoothes it.*] I wonder do all grown up people play in that childish way when nobody is looking. I never did it when I was a child.

FRANK Neither did I. You are my first playmate. [*He catches her hand to kiss it, but checks himself to look round first. Very unexpectedly, he sees CROFTS emerging from the box hedge.*] Oh damn!

VIVIE Why damn, dear?

FRANK [*Whispering.*] Sh! Here's this brute Crofts. [*He sits farther away from her with an unconcerned air.*]

CROFTS. Could I have a few words with you, Miss Vivie?

VIVIE Certainly.

CROFTS [*To FRANK.*] Youll excuse me, Gardner. Theyre waiting for you in the church, if you don't mind.

FRANK [*Rising.*] Anything to oblige you, Crofts—except church. If you should happen to want me, Vivvums, ring the gate bell. [*He goes into the house with unruffled suavity.*]

CROFTS [*Watching him with a crafty air as he disappears, and speaking to VIVIE with an assumption of being on privileged terms with her.*] Pleasant young fellow that, Miss Vivie. Pity he has no money, isnt it?

VIVIE Do you think so?

CROFTS Well, whats he to do? No profession. No property. Whats he good for?

VIVIE I realize his disadvantages, Sir George.

CROFTS [*A little taken aback at being so precisely interpreted.*] Oh, it's not that. But while we're in this world we're in it; and money's money. [*Vivie does not answer.*] Nice day, isnt it?

VIVIE [*With scarcely veiled contempt for this effort at conversation.*] Very.

CROFTS [*With brutal good humor, as if he liked her pluck.*] Well, thats not what I came to say. [*Sitting down beside her.*] Now listen, Miss Vivie. I'm quite aware that I'm not a young lady's man.

VIVIE Indeed, Sir George?

CROFTS No; and to tell you the honest truth I dont want to be either. But when I say a thing I mean it; when I feel a sentiment I feel it in earnest; and what I value I pay hard money for. Thats the sort of man I am.

VIVIE It does you great credit, I'm sure.

CROFTS Oh, I dont mean to praise myself. I have my faults, Heaven knows: no man is more sensible of that than I am. I know I'm not perfect: thats one of the disadvantages of being a middle-aged man; for I'm not a young man, and I know it. But my code is a simple one, and, I think, a good one. Honor between man and man; fidelity between man and woman; and no cant about this religion or that religion, but an honest belief that things are making for good on the whole.

VIVIE [*With biting irony.*] "A power, not ourselves, that makes for righteousness," eh?[6]

CROFTS [*Taking her seriously.*] Oh certainly. Not ourselves, of course. You understand what I mean. Well, now as to practical matters. You may have an idea that Ive flung my money about; but I havnt: I'm richer today than when I first came into the property. Ive used my knowledge of the world to invest my money in ways that other men have overlooked; and whatever else I may be, I'm a safe man from the money point of view.

VIVIE It's very kind of you to tell me all this.

CROFTS Oh well, come, Miss Vivie: you neednt pretend you dont see what I'm driving at. I want to settle down with a Lady Crofts. I suppose you think me very blunt, eh?

VIVIE Not at all: I am much obliged to you for being so definite and business-like. I quite appreciate the offer: the money, the position, L a d y C r o f t s, and so on. But I think I will say no, if you dont mind. I'd rather not. [*She rises, and strolls across to the sundial to get out of his immediate neighborhood.*]

CROFTS [*Not at all discouraged, and taking advantage of the additional room left him on the seat to spread himself comfortably, as if a few preliminary refusals were part of the inevitable routine of courtship.*] I'm in no hurry. It was only just to let you know in case young Gardner should try to trap you. Leave the question open.

VIVIE [*Sharply.*] My no is final. I wont go back from it.

[CROFTS *is not impressed. He grins; leans forward with his elbows on his knees to prod with his stick at some unfortunate insect in the grass; and looks cunningly at her. She turns away impatiently.*]

CROFTS I'm a good deal older than you. Twenty-five years; quarter of a century. I shant live for ever; and I'll take care that you shall be well off when I'm gone.

---

6. Vivie refers to Matthew Arnold's much-quoted words: "an abstract, an eternal power, or only a stream of tendency, not ourselves, and making for righteousness" (*Literature and Dogma* [1873], chap. 1).

VIVIE   I am proof against even that inducement, Sir George. Dont you think youd better take your answer? There is not the slightest chance of my altering it.

CROFTS [*Rising after a final slash at a daisy, and coming nearer to her.*] Well, no matter. I could tell you some things that would change your mind fast enough; but I wont, because I'd rather win you by honest affection. I was a good friend to your mother: ask her whether I wasnt. She'd never have made the money that paid for your education if it hadnt been for my advice and help, not to mention the money I advanced her. There are not many men would have stood by her as I have. I put not less than £40,000 into it, from first to last.

VIVIE [*Staring at him.*] Do you mean to say you were my mother's business partner?

CROFTS   Yes. Now just think of all the trouble and the explanations it would save if we were to keep the whole thing in the family, so to speak. Ask your mother whether she'd like to have to explain all her affairs to a perfect stranger.

VIVIE   I see no difficulty, since I understand that the business is wound up, and the money invested.

CROFTS [*Stopping short, amazed.*] Wound up! Wind up a business thats paying 35 per cent in the worst years! Not likely. Who told you that?

VIVIE [*Her color quite gone.*] Do you mean that it is still—? [*She stops abruptly, and puts her hand on the sundial to support herself. Then she gets quickly to the iron chair and sits down.*] What business are you talking about?

CROFTS   Well, the fact is it's not what would be considered exactly a high-class business in my set—the county set, you know—our set it will be if you think better of my offer. Not that theres any mystery about it: dont think that. Of course you know by your mother's being in it that it's perfectly straight and honest. Ive known her for many years; and I can say of her that she'd cut off her hands sooner than touch anything that was not what it ought to be. I'll tell you all about it if you like. I dont know whether youve found in travelling how hard it is to find a really comfortable private hotel.

VIVIE [*Sickened, averting her face.*] Yes: go on.

CROFTS   Well, thats all it is. Your mother has a genius for managing such things. We've got two in Brussels, one in Ostend, one in Vienna, and two in Budapest. Of course there are others besides ourselves in it; but we hold most of the capital; and your mother's indispensable as managing director. Youve noticed, I daresay, that she travels a good deal. But you see you cant mention such things in society. Once let out the word hotel and everybody says you keep a public-house.[7] You wouldnt like people to say that of your mother, would you? Thats why we're so reserved about it. By the way, youll keep it to yourself, wont you? Since it's been a secret so long, it had better remain so.

VIVIE   And this is the business you invite me to join you in?

CROFTS   Oh, no. My wife shant be troubled with business. Youll not be in it more than youve always been.

VIVIE   I always been! What do you mean?

CROFTS   Only that youve always lived on it. It paid for your education and the

---

7. I.e., a bar.

dress you have on your back. Dont turn up your nose at business, Miss
Vivie: where would your Newnhams and Girtons[8] be without it?

VIVIE [*Rising, almost beside herself.*]   Take care. I know what this business is.

CROFTS [*Staring, with a suppressed oath.*]   Who told you?

VIVIE   Your partner. My mother.

CROFTS [*Black with rage.*]   The old—

VIVIE   Just so.

[*He swallows the epithet and stands for a moment swearing and raging
foully to himself. But he knows that his cue is to be sympathetic. He
takes refuge in generous indignation.*]

CROFTS   She ought to have had more consideration for you. I'd never have
told you.

VIVIE   I think you would probably have told me when we were married; it
would have been a convenient weapon to break me in with.

CROFTS [*Quite sincerely.*]   I never intended that. On my word as a gentleman
I didnt.

[VIVIE *wonders at him. Her sense of the irony of his protest cools and
braces her. She replies with contemptuous self-possession.*]

VIVIE   It does not matter. I suppose you understand that when we leave here
today our acquaintance ceases.

CROFTS   Why? Is it for helping your mother?

VIVIE   My mother was a very poor woman who had no reasonable choice but
to do as she did. You were a rich gentleman; and you did the same for the
sake of 35 per cent. You are a pretty common sort of scoundrel, I think.
That is my opinion of you.

CROFTS [*After a stare: not at all displeased, and much more at ease on these frank
terms than on their former ceremonious ones.*]   Ha! ha! ha! ha! Go it, little
missie, go it: it doesnt hurt me and it amuses you. Why the devil shouldnt
I invest my money that way? I take the interest on my capital like other
people: I hope you dont think I dirty my own hands with the work. Come!
you wouldnt refuse the acquaintance of my mother's cousin the Duke of
Belgravia because some of the rents he gets are earned in queer ways. You
wouldnt cut[9] the Archbishop of Canterbury, I suppose, because the Ecclesiastical Commissioners have a few publicans and sinners among their tenants. Do you remember your Crofts scholarship at Newnham? Well, that
was founded by my brother the M.P.[1] He gets his 22 per cent out of a factory
with 600 girls in it, and not one of them getting wages enough to live on.
How d'ye suppose they manage when they have no family to fall back on?
Ask your mother. And do you expect me to turn my back on 35 per cent
when all the rest are pocketing what they can, like sensible men? No such
fool! If youre going to pick and choose your acquaintants on moral principles, youd better clear out of this country, unless you want to cut yourself
out of all decent society.

VIVIE [*Conscience stricken.*]   You might go on to point out that I myself never
asked where the money I spent came from. I believe I am just as bad as you.

CROFTS [*Greatly reassured.*]   Of course you are; and a very good thing too!
What harm does it do after all? [*Rallying her jocularly.*] So you dont think

---

8. Girton, like Newnham, is a women's college at
Cambridge University.

9. Break off acquaintance with.
1. Member of Parliament.

me such a scoundrel now you come to think it over. Eh?

VIVIE I have shared profits with you; and I admitted you just now to the familiarity of knowing what I think of you.

CROFTS [*With serious friendliness.*] To be sure you did. You wont find me a bad sort: I dont go in for being superfine intellectually; but Ive plenty of honest human feeling; and the old Crofts breed comes out in a sort of instinctive hatred of anything low, in which I'm sure youll sympathize with me. Believe me, Miss Vivie, the world isnt such a bad place as the croakers[2] make out. As long as you dont fly openly in the face of society, society doesnt ask any inconvenient questions; and it makes precious short work of the cads who do. There are no secrets better kept than the secrets everybody guesses. In the class of people I can introduce you to, no lady or gentleman would so far forget themselves as to discuss my business affairs or your mother's. No man can offer you a safer position.

VIVIE [*Studying him curiously.*] I suppose you really think youre getting on famously with me.

CROFTS Well, I hope I may flatter myself that you think better of me than you did at first.

VIVIE [*Quietly.*] I hardly find you worth thinking about at all now. When I think of the society that tolerates you, and the laws that protect you! when I think of how helpless nine out of ten young girls would be in the hands of you and my mother! the unmentionable woman and her capitalist bully—

CROFTS [*Livid.*] Damn you!

VIVIE You need not. I feel among the damned already.

[*She raises the latch of the gate to open it and go out. He follows her and puts his hand heavily on the top bar to prevent its opening.*]

CROFTS [*Panting with fury.*] Do you think I'll put up with this from you, you young devil?

VIVIE [*Unmoved.*] Be quiet. Some one will answer the bell. [*Without flinching a step she strikes the bell with the back of her hand. It clangs harshly; and he starts back involuntarily. Almost immediately* FRANK *appears at the porch with his rifle.*]

FRANK [*With cheerful politeness.*] Will you have the rifle, Viv; or shall I operate?

VIVIE Frank: have you been listening?

FRANK [*Coming down into the garden.*] Only for the bell, I assure you; so that you shouldn't have to wait. I think I shewed great insight into your character, Crofts.

CROFTS For two pins I'd take that gun from you and break it across your head.

FRANK [*Stalking him cautiously.*] Pray dont. I'm ever so careless in handling firearms. Sure to be a fatal accident, with a reprimand from the coroner's jury for my negligence.

VIVIE Put the rifle away, Frank: it's quite unnecessary.

FRANK Quite right, Viv. Much more sportsmanlike to catch him in a trap. [*CROFTS, understanding the insult, makes a threatening movement.*] Crofts: there are fifteen cartridges in the magazine here; and I am a dead shot at the present distance and at an object of your size.

CROFTS Oh, you neednt be afraid. I'm not going to touch you.

2. Those that prophesy doom.

FRANK   Ever so magnanimous of you under the circumstances! Thank you!

CROFTS   I'll tell you this before I go. It may interest you, since youre so fond of one another. Allow me, Mister Frank, to introduce you to your half-sister, the eldest daughter of the Reverend Samuel Gardner. Miss Vivie: your half-brother. Good morning. [*He goes out through the gate and along the road.*]

FRANK [*After a pause of stupefaction, raising the rifle.*]   Youll testify before the coroner that it's an accident, Viv. [*He takes aim at the retreating figure of* CROFTS. VIVIE *seizes the muzzle and pulls it round against her breast.*]

VIVIE   Fire now. You may.

FRANK [*Dropping his end of the rifle hastily.*]   Stop! take care. [*She lets go. It falls on the turf.*] Oh, youve given your little boy such a turn. Suppose it had gone off! ugh! [*He sinks on the garden seat, overcome.*]

VIVIE   Suppose it had: do you think it would not have been a relief to have some sharp physical pain tearing through me?

FRANK [*Coaxingly.*]   Take it ever so easy, dear Viv. Remember; even if the rifle scared that fellow into telling the truth for the first time in his life, that only makes us the babes in the wood in earnest. [*He holds out his arms to her.*] Come and be covered up with leaves again.

VIVIE [*With a cry of disgust.*]   Ah, not that, not that. You make all my flesh creep.

FRANK   Why, whats the matter?

VIVIE   Goodbye. [*She makes for the gate.*]

FRANK [*Jumping up.*]   Hallo! Stop! Viv! Viv! [*She turns in the gateway.*] Where are you going to? Where shall we find you?

VIVIE   At Honoria Fraser's chambers, 67 Chancery Lane, for the rest of my life. [*She goes off quickly in the opposite direction to that taken by* CROFTS.]

FRANK   But I say—wait—dash it! [*He runs after her.*]

Act 4

HONORIA FRASER's *chambers in Chancery Lane. An office at the top of New Stone Buildings, with a plate-glass window, distempered walls, electric light, and a patent stove. Saturday afternoon. The chimneys of Lincoln's Inn[3] and the western sky beyond are seen through the window. There is a double writing table in the middle of the room, with a cigar box, ash pans, and a portable electric reading lamp almost snowed up in heaps of papers and books. This table has knee holes and chairs right and left and is very untidy. The clerk's desk, closed and tidy, with its high stool, is against the wall, near a door communicating with the inner rooms. In the opposite wall is the door leading to the public corridor. Its upper panel is of opaque glass, lettered in black on the outside,* FRASER AND WARREN. *A baize screen hides the corner between this door and the window.*

FRANK, *in a fashionable light-colored coaching suit, with his stick, gloves, and white hat in his hands, is pacing up and down the office. Somebody tries the door with a key.*

FRANK [*Calling.*]   Come in. It's not locked.

[VIVIE *comes in, in her hat and jacket. She stops and stares at him.*]

VIVIE [*Sternly.*]   What are you doing here?

FRANK   Waiting to see you. I've been here for hours. Is this the way you attend

---

3. One of the four legal societies in London collectively known as the Inns of Court, which alone have the right to admit candidates to the English bar, thereby allowing them to practice law.

to your business? [*He puts his hat and stick on the table, and perches himself with a vault on the clerk's stool, looking at her with every appearance of being in a specially restless, teasing flippant mood.*]

VIVIE Ive been away exactly twenty minutes for a cup of tea. [*She takes off her hat and jacket and hangs them up behind the screen.*] How did you get in?

FRANK The staff had not left when I arrived. He's gone to play cricket on Primrose Hill.⁴ Why dont you employ a woman, and give your sex a chance?

VIVIE What have you come for?

FRANK [*Springing off the stool and coming close to her.*] Viv: lets go and enjoy the Saturday half-holiday somewhere, like the staff. What do you say to Richmond,⁵ and then a music hall, and a jolly supper?

VIVIE Cant afford it. I shall put in another six hours work before I go to bed.

FRANK Cant afford it, cant we? Aha! Look here. [*He takes out a handful of sovereigns and makes them chink.*] Gold, Viv: gold!

VIVIE Where did you get it?

FRANK Gambling, Viv: gambling. Poker.

VIVIE Pah! It's meaner⁶ than stealing it. No: I'm not coming. [*She sits down to work at the table, with her back to the glass door, and begins turning over the papers.*]

FRANK [*Remonstrating piteously.*] But, my dear Viv, I want to talk to you ever so seriously.

VIVIE Very well: sit down in Honoria's chair and talk here. I like ten minutes chat after tea. [*He murmurs.*] No use groaning: I'm inexorable. [*He takes the opposite seat disconsolately.*] Pass that cigar box, will you?

FRANK [*Pushing the cigar box across.*] Nasty womanly habit. Nice men dont do it any longer.

VIVIE Yes: they object to the smell in the office; and weve had to take to cigarets. See! [*She opens the box and takes out a cigaret, which she lights. She offers him one; but he shakes his head with a wry face. She settles herself comfortably in her chair, smoking.*] Go ahead.

FRANK Well, I want to know what youve done—what arrangements youve made.

VIVIE Everything was settled twenty minutes after I arrived here. Honoria has found the business too much for her this year; and she was on the point of sending for me and proposing a partnership when I walked in and told her I hadnt a farthing⁷ in the world. So I installed myself and packed her off for a fortnight's holiday. What happened at Haslemere when I left?

FRANK Nothing at all. I said youd gone to town on particular business.

VIVIE Well?

FRANK Well, either they were too flabbergasted to say anything, or else Crofts had prepared your mother. Anyhow, she didnt say anything; and Crofts didnt say anything; and Praddy only stared. After tea they got up and went; and Ive not seen them since.

VIVIE [*Nodding placidly with one eye on a wreath of smoke.*] Thats all right.

FRANK [*Looking round disparagingly.*] Do you intend to stick in this confounded place?

VIVIE [*Blowing the wreath decisively away, and sitting straight up.*] Yes. These

4. A park in northwest London.
5. A residential suburb in southwest London; there were beautiful views from Richmond Hill,

but Frank might be proposing a riverside walk.
6. Lower, more degenerate.
7. A quarter of a penny.

two days have given me back all my strength and self-possession. I will never take a holiday again as long as I live.

FRANK [*With a very wry face.*] Mps! You look quite happy. And as hard as nails.

VIVIE [*Grimly.*] Well for me that I am!

FRANK [*Rising.*] Look here, Viv: we must have an explanation. We parted the other day under a complete misunderstanding. [*He sits on the table, close to her.*]

VIVIE [*Putting away the cigaret.*] Well: clear it up.

FRANK You remember what Crofts said?

VIVIE Yes.

FRANK That revelation was supposed to bring about a complete change in the nature of our feeling for one another. It placed us on the footing of brother and sister.

VIVIE Yes.

FRANK Have you ever had a brother?

VIVIE No.

FRANK Then you dont know what being brother and sister feels like? Now I have lots of sisters; and the fraternal feeling is quite familiar to me. I assure you my feeling for you is not the least in the world like it. The girls will go their way; I will go mine; and we shant care if we never see one another again. Thats brother and sister. But as to you, I cant be easy if I have to pass a week without seeing you. Thats not brother and sister. It's exactly what I felt an hour before Crofts made his revelation. In short, dear Viv, it's love's young dream.

VIVIE [*Bitingly.*] The same feeling, Frank, that brought your father to my mother's feet. Is that it?

FRANK [*So revolted that he slips off the table for a moment.*] I very strongly object, Viv, to have my feelings compared to any which the Reverend Samuel is capable of harboring; and I object still more to a comparison of you to your mother. [*Resuming his perch.*] Besides, I dont believe the story. I have taxed my father with it, and obtained from him what I consider tantamount to a denial.

VIVIE What did he say?

FRANK He said he was sure there must be some mistake.

VIVIE Do you believe him?

FRANK I am prepared to take his word as against Crofts'.

VIVIE Does it make any difference? I mean in your imagination or conscience; for of course it makes no real difference.

FRANK [*Shaking his head.*] None whatever to me.

VIVIE Nor to me.

FRANK [*Staring.*] But this is ever so surprising! [*He goes back to his chair.*] I thought our whole relations were altered in your imagination and conscience, as you put it, the moment those words were out of the brute's muzzle.

VIVIE No: it was not that. I didnt believe him. I only wish I could.

FRANK Eh?

VIVIE I think brother and sister would be a very suitable relation for us.

FRANK You really mean that?

VIVIE Yes. It's the only relation I care for, even if we could afford any other. I mean that.

FRANK [*Raising his eyebrows like one on whom a new light has dawned, and rising with quite an effusion of chivalrous sentiment.*] My dear Viv: why didnt you say so before? I am ever so sorry for persecuting you. I understand, of course.

VIVIE [*Puzzled.*] Understand what?

FRANK Oh, I'm not a fool in the ordinary sense: only in the Scriptural sense of doing all the things the wise man declared to be folly, after trying them himself on the most extensive scale.[8] I see I am no longer Vivvum's little boy. Dont be alarmed: I shall never call you Vivvums again—at least unless you get tired of your new little boy, whoever he may be.

VIVIE My new little boy!

FRANK [*With conviction.*] Must be a new little boy. Always happens that way. No other way, in fact.

VIVIE None that you know of, fortunately for you.
[*Someone knocks at the door.*]

FRANK My curse upon yon caller, whoe'er he be!

VIVIE It's Praed. He's going to Italy and wants to say goodbye. I asked him to call this afternoon. Go and let him in.

FRANK We can continue our conversation after his departure for Italy. I'll stay him out. [*He goes to the door and opens it.*] How are you, Praddy? Delighted to see you. Come in.
[PRAED, *dressed for travelling, comes in, in high spirits.*]

PRAED How do you do, Miss Warren? [*She presses his hand cordially, though a certain sentimentality in his high spirits jars on her.*] I start in an hour from Holborn Viaduct.[9] I wish I could persuade you to try Italy.

VIVIE What for?

PRAED Why, to saturate yourself with beauty and romance, of course.
[VIVIE, *with a shudder, turns her chair to the table, as if the work waiting for her were a support to her.* PRAED *sits opposite to her.* FRANK *places a chair near* VIVIE, *and drops lazily and carelessly into it, talking at her over his shoulder.*]

FRANK No use, Praddy. Viv is a little Philistine.[1] She is indifferent to my romance, and insensible to my beauty.

VIVIE Mr Praed: once for all, there is no beauty and no romance in life for me. Life is what it is; and I am prepared to take it as it is.

PRAED [*Enthusiastically.*] You will not say that if you come with me to Verona and on to Venice. You will cry with delight at living in such a beautiful world.

FRANK This is most eloquent, Praddy. Keep it up.

PRAED Oh, I assure you *I* have cried—I shall cry again, I hope—at fifty! At your age, Miss Warren, you would not need to go so far as Verona. Your spirits would absolutely fly up at the mere sight of Ostend. You would be charmed with the gaiety, the vivacity, the happy air of Brussels.

VIVIE [*Springing up with an exclamation of loathing.*] Agh!

PRAED [*Rising.*] Whats the matter?

FRANK[*Rising.*] Hallo, Viv!

---

8. Cf. Ecclesiastes 2.13: "Then I saw that wisdom excelleth folly."
9. A railway station in the City of London.
1. Matthew Arnold's term for a member of the dull and unenlightened middle classes; in his view their opposition to the defenders of culture makes them akin to the biblical tribe that fought against the people of Israel, "the people of light."

VIVIE [*To* PRAED, *with deep reproach.*] Can you find no better example of your beauty and romance than Brussels to talk to me about?

PRAED [*Puzzled.*] Of course it's very different from Verona. I dont suggest for a moment that—

VIVIE [*Bitterly.*] Probably the beauty and romance come to much the same in both places.

PRAED [*Completely sobered and much concerned.*] My dear Miss Warren: I— [*Looking inquiringly at* FRANK.] Is anything the matter?

FRANK She thinks your enthusiasm frivolous, Praddy. She's had ever such a serious call.

VIVIE [*Sharply.*] Hold your tongue, Frank. Dont be silly.

FRANK [*Sitting down.*] Do you call this good manners, Praed?

PRAED [*Anxious and considerate.*] Shall I take him away, Miss Warren? I feel sure we have disturbed you at your work.

VIVIE Sit down: I'm not ready to go back to work yet. [PRAED *sits.*] You both think I have an attack of nerves. Not a bit of it. But there are two subjects I want dropped, if you dont mind. One of them [*To* FRANK.] is love's young dream in any shape or form: the other [*To* PRAED.] is the romance and beauty of life, especially Ostend and the gaiety of Brussels. You are welcome to any illusions you may have left on these subjects: I have none. If we three are to remain friends, I must be treated as a woman of business, permanently single [*To* FRANK.] and permanently unromantic.[*To* PRAED.]

FRANK I also shall remain permanently single until you change your mind. Praddy: change the subject. Be eloquent about something else.

PRAED [*Diffidently.*] I'm afraid theres nothing else in the world that I can talk about. The Gospel of Art is the only one I can preach. I know Miss Warren is a great devotee of the Gospel of Getting On; but we cant discuss that without hurting your feelings, Frank, since you are determined not to get on.

FRANK Oh, dont mind my feelings. Give me some improving advice by all means: it does me ever so much good. Have another try to make a successful man of me, Viv. Come; lets have it all: energy, thrift, foresight, self-respect, character. Dont you hate people who have no character, Viv?

VIVIE [*Wincing.*] Oh, stop, stop: let us have no more of that horrible cant. Mr Praed: if there are really only those two gospels in the world, we had better all kill ourselves; for the same taint is in both, through and through.

FRANK [*Looking critically at her.*] There is a touch of poetry about you today, Viv, which has hitherto been lacking.

PRAED [*Remonstrating.*] My dear Frank: arnt you a little unsympathetic?

VIVIE [*Merciless to herself.*] No: it's good for me. It keeps me from being sentimental.

FRANK [*Bantering her.*] Checks your strong natural propensity that way, dont it?

VIVIE [*Almost hysterically.*] Oh yes; go on: dont spare me. I was sentimental for one moment in my life—beautifully sentimental—by moonlight; and now—

FRANK [*Quickly.*] I say, Viv: take care. Dont give yourself away.

VIVIE Oh, do you think Mr Praed does not know all about my mother? [*Turning on* PRAED.] You had better have told me that morning, Mr Praed. You are very old fashioned in your delicacies, after all.

PRAED Surely it is you who are a little old fashioned in your prejudices, Miss

Warren, I feel bound to tell you, speaking as an artist, and believing that the most intimate human relationships are far beyond and above the scope of the law, that though I know that your mother is an unmarried woman, I do not respect her the less on that account. I respect her more.

FRANK [*Airily.*] Hear! Hear!

VIVIE [*Staring at him.*] Is that all you know?

PRAED Certainly that is all.

VIVIE Then you neither of you know anything. Your guesses are innocence itself compared to the truth.

PRAED [*Rising, startled and indignant, and preserving his politeness with an effort.*] I hope not. [*More emphatically.*] I hope not, Miss Warren.

FRANK [*Whistles.*] Whew!

VIVIE You are not making it easy for me to tell you, Mr Praed.

PRAED [*His chivalry drooping before their conviction.*] If there is anything worse—that is, anything else—are you sure you are right to tell us, Miss Warren?

VIVIE I am sure that if I had the courage I should spend the rest of my life in telling everybody—stamping and branding it into them until they all felt their part in its abomination as I feel mine. There is nothing I despise more than the wicked convention that protects these things by forbidding a woman to mention them. And yet I cant tell you. The two infamous words that describe what my mother is are ringing in my ears and struggling on my tongue; but I cant utter them: the shame of them is too horrible for me. [*She buries her face in her hands. The two men, astonished, stare at one another and then at her. She raises her head again desperately and snatches a sheet of paper and a pen.*] Here: let me draft you a prospectus.

FRANK Oh, she's mad. Do you hear, Viv? mad. Come! pull yourself together.

VIVIE You shall see. [*She writes.*] "Paid up capital: not less than £40,000 standing in the name of Sir George Crofts, Baronet, the chief shareholder. Premises at Brussels, Ostend, Vienna and Budapest. Managing director: Mrs Warren"; and now dont let us forget her qualifications: the two words. [*She writes the words and pushes the paper to them.*] There! Oh no: dont read it: dont! [*She snatches it back and tears it to pieces; then seizes her head in her hands and hides her face on the table.*]

> [FRANK, *who has watched the writing over his shoulder, and opened his eyes very widely at it, takes a card from his pocket; scribbles the two words on it; and silently hands it to* PRAED, *who reads it with amazement, and hides it hastily in his pocket.*]

FRANK [*Whispering tenderly.*] Viv, dear: thats all right. I read what you wrote: so did Praddy. We understand. And we remain, as this leaves us at present, yours ever so devotedly.

PRAED We do indeed, Miss Warren. I declare you are the most splendidly courageous woman I ever met.

> [*This sentimental compliment braces* VIVIE. *She throws it away from her with an impatient shake, and forces herself to stand up, though not without some support from the table.*]

FRANK Dont stir, Viv, if you dont want to. Take it easy.

VIVIE Thank you. You can always depend on me for two things: not to cry and not to faint. [*She moves a few steps towards the door of the inner room, and stops close to* PRAED *to say.*] I shall need much more courage than that when I tell my mother that we have come to the parting of the ways. Now

I must go into the next room for a moment to make myself neat again, if you dont mind.

PRAED   Shall we go away?

VIVIE   No; I shall be back presently. Only for a moment. [*She goes into the other room,* PRAED *opening the door for her.*]

PRAED   What an amazing revelation! I'm extremely disappointed in Crofts: I am indeed.

FRANK   I'm not in the least. I feel he's perfectly accounted for at last. But what a facer for me, Praddy! I cant marry her now.

PRAED [*Sternly.*]   Frank! [*The two look at one another,* FRANK *unruffled,* PRAED *deeply indignant.*] Let me tell you, Gardner, that if you desert her now you will behave very despicably.

FRANK   Good old Praddy! Ever chivalrous! But you mistake: it's not the moral aspect of the case: it's the money aspect. I really cant bring myself to touch the old woman's money now.

PRAED   And was that what you were going to marry on?

FRANK   What else? *I* havnt any money, nor the smallest turn for making it. If I married Viv now she would have to support me; and I should cost her more than I am worth.

PRAED   But surely a clever bright fellow like you can make something by your own brains.

FRANK   Oh yes, a little. [*He takes out his money again.*] I made all that yesterday in an hour and a half. But I made it in a highly speculative business. No, dear Praddy: even if Bessie and Georgina marry millionaires and the governor dies after cutting them off with a shilling, I shall have only four hundred a year. And he wont die until he's three score and ten: he hasnt originality enough. I shall be on short allowance for the next twenty years. No short allowance for Viv, if I can help it. I withdraw gracefully and leave the field to the gilded youth of England. So thats settled. I shant worry her about it: I'll just send her a little note after we're gone. She'll understand.

PRAED [*Grasping his hand.*]   Good fellow, Frank! I heartily beg your pardon. But must you never see her again?

FRANK   Never see her again! Hang it all, be reasonable. I shall come along as often as possible, and be her brother. I cannot understand the absurd consequences you romantic people expect from the most ordinary transactions. [*A knock at the door.*] I wonder who this is. Would you mind opening the door? If it's a client it will look more respectable than if I appeared.

PRAED   Certainly. [*He goes to the door and opens it.* FRANK *sits down in* VIVIE's *chair to scribble a note.*] My dear Kitty: come in: come in.

[MRS WARREN *comes in, looking apprehensively round for* VIVIE. *She has done her best to make herself matronly and dignified. The brilliant hat is replaced by a sober bonnet, and the gay blouse covered by a costly black silk mantle. She is pitiably anxious and ill at ease: evidently panic-stricken.*]

MRS WARREN [*To* FRANK.]   What! Y o u r e here, are you?

FRANK [*Turning in his chair from his writing, but not rising.*]   Here, and charmed to see you. You come like a breath of spring.

MRS WARREN   Oh, get out with your nonsense. [*In a low voice.*] Wheres Vivie?

[FRANK *points expressively to the door of the inner room, but says nothing.*]

MRS WARREN [*Sitting down suddenly and almost beginning to cry.*] Praddy: wont she see me, dont you think?

PRAED My dear Kitty: dont distress yourself. Why should she not?

MRS WARREN Oh, you never can see why not: youre too innocent. Mr Frank: did she say anything to you?

FRANK [*Folding his note.*] She must see you, if [*very expressively*] you wait til she comes in.

MRS WARREN [*Frightened.*] Why shouldnt I wait?

[FRANK *looks quizzically at her; puts his note carefully on the inkbottle, so that* VIVIE *cannot fail to find it when next she dips her pen; then rises and devotes his attention entirely to her.*]

FRANK My dear Mrs Warren: suppose you were a sparrow—ever so tiny and pretty a sparrow hopping in the roadway—and you saw a steam roller coming in your direction, would you wait for it?

MRS WARREN Oh, dont bother me with your sparrows. What did she run away from Haslemere like that for?

FRANK I'm afraid she'll tell you if you rashly await her return.

MRS WARREN Do you want me to go away?

FRANK No: I always want you to stay. But I advise you to go away.

MRS WARREN What! and never see her again!

FRANK Precisely.

MRS WARREN [*Crying again.*] Praddy: dont let him be cruel to me. [*She hastily checks her tears and wipes her eyes.*] She'll be so angry if she sees Ive been crying.

FRANK [*With a touch of real compassion in his airy tenderness.*] You know that Praddy is the soul of kindness, Mrs Warren. Praddy: what do you say? Go or stay?

PRAED [*To* MRS WARREN.] I really should be very sorry to cause you unnecessary pain; but I think perhaps you had better not wait. The fact is—[VIVIE *is heard at the inner door.*]

FRANK Sh! Too late. She's coming.

MRS WARREN Dont tell her I was crying. [VIVIE *comes in. She stops gravely on seeing* MRS WARREN, *who greets her with hysterical cheerfulness.*] Well, dearie. So here you are at last.

VIVIE I am glad you have come: I want to speak to you. You said you were going, Frank, I think.

FRANK Yes. Will you come with me, Mrs Warren? What do you say to a trip to Richmond, and the theatre in the evening? There is safety in Richmond. No steam roller there.

VIVIE Nonsense, Frank. My mother will stay here.

MRS WARREN [*Scared.*] I dont know: perhaps I'd better go. We're disturbing you at your work.

VIVIE [*With quiet decision.*] Mr. Praed: please take Frank away. Sit down, mother. [MRS WARREN *obeys helplessly.*]

PRAED Come, Frank. Goodbye, Miss Vivie.

VIVIE [*Shaking hands.*] Goodbye. A pleasant trip.

PRAED Thank you: thank you. I hope so.

FRANK [*To* MRS WARREN.] Goodbye: youd ever so much better have taken my advice. [*He shakes hands with her. Then airily to* VIVIE] Byebye, Viv.

VIVIE Goodbye. [*He goes out gaily without shaking hands with her.*]

PRAED [*Sadly.*] Goodbye, Kitty.

MRS WARREN [*Sniveling.*] —oobye!

[PRAED *goes.* VIVIE, *composed and extremely grave, sits down in Honoria's chair, and waits for her mother to speak.* MRS WARREN, *dreading a pause, loses no time in beginning.*]

MRS WARREN   Well, Vivie, what did you go away like that for without saying a word to me? How could you do such a thing! And what have you done to poor George? I wanted him to come with me; but he shuffled out of it. I could see that he was quite afraid of you. Only fancy: he wanted me not to come. As if [*Trembling.*] I should be afraid of you, dearie. [VIVIE'S *gravity deepens.*] But of course I told him it was all settled and comfortable between us, and that we were on the best of terms. [*She breaks down.*] Vivie: whats the meaning of this? [*She produces a commercial envelope, and fumbles at the enclosure with trembling fingers.*] I got it from the bank this morning.

VIVIE   It is my month's allowance. They sent it to me as usual the other day. I simply sent it back to be placed to your credit, and asked them to send you the lodgment receipt.[2] In future I shall support myself.

MRS WARREN [*Not daring to understand.*]   Wasnt it enough? Why didnt you tell me? [*With a cunning gleam in her eye.*] I'll double it: I was intending to double it. Only let me know how much you want.

VIVIE   You know very well that that has nothing to do with it. From this time I go my own way in my own business and among my own friends. And you will go yours. [*She rises.*] Goodbye.

MRS WARREN [*Rising, appalled.*]   Goodbye?

VIVIE   Yes: Goodbye. Come: dont let us make a useless scene: you understand perfectly well. Sir George Crofts has told me the whole business.

MRS WARREN [*Angrily.*]   Silly old—[*She swallows an epithet, and turns white at the narrowness of her escape from uttering it.*]

VIVIE   Just so.

MRS WARREN   He ought to have his tongue cut out. But I thought it was ended: you said you didnt mind.

VIVIE [*Steadfastly.*]   Excuse me: I d o mind.

MRS WARREN   But I explained—

VIVIE   You explained how it came about. You did not tell me that it is still going on. [*She sits.*]

[MRS WARREN, *silenced for a moment, looks forlornly at* VIVIE, *who waits, secretly hoping that the combat is over. But the cunning expression comes back into* MRS WARREN'S *face; and she bends across the table, sly and urgent, half whispering.*]

MRS WARREN   Vivie: do you know how rich I am?

VIVIE   I have no doubt you are very rich.

MRS WARREN   But you dont know all that that means: youre too young. It means a new dress every day; it means theatres and balls every night; it means having the pick of all the gentlemen in Europe at your feet; it means a lovely house and plenty of servants; it means the choicest of eating and drinking; it means everything you like, everything you want, everything you can think of. And what are you here? A mere drudge, toiling and moiling[3] early and late for your bare living and two cheap dresses a year. Think over it. [*Soothingly.*] Youre shocked, I know. I can enter into your feelings; and I think they do you credit; but trust me, nobody will blame you: you may

2. Deposit slip.   3. Drudging.

take my word for that. I know what young girls are; and I know youll think better of it when youve turned it over in your mind.

VIVIE   So thats how it's done, is it? You must have said all that to many a woman, mother, to have it so pat.

MRS WARREN [*Passionately.*] What harm am I asking you to do? [VIVIE *turns away contemptuously.* MRS WARREN *continues desperately.*] Vivie: listen to me: you dont understand: youve been taught wrong on purpose: you dont know what the world is really like.

VIVIE [*Arrested.*] Taught wrong on purpose! What do you mean?

MRS WARREN   I mean that youre throwing away all your chances for nothing. You think that people are what they pretend to be: that the way you were taught at school and college to think right and proper is the way things really are. But it's not: it's all only a pretence, to keep the cowardly slavish common run of people quiet. Do you want to find that out, like other women, at forty, when youve thrown yourself away and lost your chances; or wont you take it in good time now from your own mother, that loves you and swears to you that it's truth: gospel truth? [*Urgently*] Vivie: the big people, the clever people, the managing people, all know it. They do as I do, and think what I think. I know plenty of them. I know them to speak to, to introduce you to, to make friends of for you. I dont mean anything wrong; thats what you dont understand: your head is full of ignorant ideas about me. What do the people that taught you know about life or about people like me? When did they ever meet me, or speak to me, or let anyone tell them about me? the fools! Would they ever have done anything for you if I hadnt paid them? Havnt I told you that I want you to be respectable? Havnt I brought you up to be respectable? And how can you keep it up without my money and my influence and Lizzie's friends? Cant you see that youre cutting your own throat as well as breaking my heart in turning your back on me?

VIVIE   I recognize the Crofts philosophy of life, mother. I heard it all from him that day at the Gardners'.

MRS WARREN   You think I want to force that played-out old sot on you! I dont, Vivie: on my oath I dont.

VIVIE   It would not matter if you did: you would not succeed. [MRS WARREN *winces, deeply hurt by the implied indifference towards her affectionate intention.* VIVIE, *neither understanding this nor concerning herself about it, goes on calmly.*] Mother: you dont at all know the sort of person I am. I dont object to Crofts more than to any other coarsely built man of his class. To tell you the truth, I rather admire him for being strong-minded enough to enjoy himself in his own way and make plenty of money instead of living the usual shooting, hunting, dining-out, tailoring, loafing life of his set merely because all the rest do it. And I'm perfectly aware that if I'd been in the same circumstances as my aunt Liz, I'd have done exactly what she did. I dont think I'm more prejudiced or straitlaced than you: I think I'm less. I'm certain I'm less sentimental. I know very well that fashionable morality is all a pretence, and that if I took your money and devoted the rest of my life to spending it fashionably, I might be as worthless and vicious as the silliest woman could possibly want to be without having a word said to me about it. But I dont want to be worthless. I shouldnt enjoy trotting about the park to advertize my dressmaker and carriage builder, or being bored at the opera to shew off a shopwindowful of diamonds.

MRS WARREN [*Bewildered.*] But—

VIVIE   Wait a moment: Ive not done. Tell me why you continue your business now that you are independent of it. Your sister, you told me, has left all that behind her. Why dont you do the same?

MRS WARREN   Oh, it's all very easy for Liz: she likes good society, and has the air of being a lady. Imagine me in a cathedral town! Why, the very rooks in the trees would find me out even if I could stand the dulness of it. I must have work and excitement, or I should go melancholy mad. And what else is there for me to do? The life suits me: I'm fit for it and not for anything else. If I didnt do it somebody else would; so I dont do any real harm by it. And then it brings in money; and I like making money. No; it's no use: I cant give it up—not for anybody. But what need you know about it? I'll never mention it. I'll keep Crofts away. I'll not trouble you much: you see I have to be constantly running about from one place to another. Youll be quit of me altogether when I die.

VIVIE   No: I am my mother's daughter. I am like you: I must have work, and must make more money than I spend. But my work is not your work, and my way not your way. We must part. It will not make much difference to us: instead of meeting one another for perhaps a few months in twenty years we shall never meet: thats all.

MRS WARREN   [Her voice stifled in tears.]   Vivie: I meant to have been more with you: I did indeed.

VIVIE   It's no use, mother: I am not to be changed by a few cheap tears and entreaties any more than you are, I daresay.

MRS WARREN   [Wildly.]   Oh, you call a mother's tears cheap.

VIVIE   They cost you nothing; and you ask me to give you the peace and quietness of my whole life in exchange for them. What use would my company be to you if you could get it? What have we two in common that could make either of us happy together?

MRS WARREN   [Lapsing recklessly into her dialect.]   We're mother and daughter. I want my daughter. Ive a right to you. Who is to care for me when I'm old? Plenty of girls have taken to me like daughters and cried at leaving me; but I let them all go because I had you to look forward to. I kept myself lonely for you. Youve no right to turn on me now and refuse to do your duty as a daughter.

VIVIE   [Jarred and antagonized by the echo of the slums in her mother's voice.]   My duty as a daughter! I thought we should come to that presently. Now once for all, mother, you want a daughter and Frank wants a wife. I dont want a mother; and I dont want a husband. I have spared neither Frank nor myself in sending him about his business. Do you think I will spare y o u ?

MRS WARREN   [Violently.]   Oh, I know the sort you are: no mercy for yourself or anyone else. I know. My experience has done that for me anyhow: I can tell the pious, canting, hard, selfish woman when I meet her. Well, keep yourself to yourself: I dont want you. But listen to this. Do you know what I would do with you if you were a baby again? aye, as sure as there's a Heaven above us.

VIVIE   Strangle me, perhaps.

MRS WARREN   No: I'd bring you up to be a real daughter to me, and not what you are now, with your pride and your prejudices and the college education you stole from me: yes, stole: deny it if you can: what was it but stealing? I'd bring you up in my own house, I would.

VIVIE   [Quietly.]   In one of your own houses.

MRS WARREN [*Screaming.*] Listen to her! listen to how she spits on her mother's grey hairs! Oh, may you live to have your own daughter tear and trample on you as you have trampled on me. And you will: you will. No woman ever had luck with a mother's curse on her.

VIVIE I wish you wouldnt rant, mother. It only hardens me. Come: I suppose I am the only young woman you ever had in your power that you did good to. Dont spoil it all now.

MRS WARREN Yes, Heaven forgive me, it's true; and you are the only one that ever turned on me. Oh, the injustice of it! the injustice! the injustice! I always wanted to be a good woman. I tried honest work; and I was slave-driven until I cursed the day I ever heard of honest work. I was a good mother; and because I made my daughter a good woman she turns me out as if I was a leper. Oh, if I only had my life to live over again! I'd talk to that lying clergyman in the school. From this time forth, so help me Heaven in my last hour, I'll do wrong and nothing but wrong. And I'll prosper on it.

VIVIE Yes: it's better to choose your line and go through with it. If I had been you, mother, I might have done as you did; but I should not have lived one life and believed in another. You are a conventional woman at heart. That is why I am bidding you goodbye now. I am right, am I not?

MRS WARREN [*Taken aback.*] Right to throw away all my money?

VIVIE No: right to get rid of you? I should be a fool not to! Isnt that so?

MRS WARREN [*Sulkily.*] Oh well, yes, if you come to that, I suppose you are. But Lord help the world if everybody took to doing the right thing! And now I'd better go than stay where I'm not wanted. [*She turns to the door.*]

VIVIE [*Kindly.*] Wont you shake hands?

MRS WARREN [*After looking at her fiercely for a moment with a savage impulse to strike her.*] No, thank you. Goodbye.

VIVIE [*Matter-of-factly.*] Goodbye. [MRS WARREN *goes out, slamming the door behind her. The strain on* VIVIE's *face relaxes; her grave expression breaks up into one of joyous content; her breath goes out in a half sob, half laugh of intense relief. She goes buoyantly to her place at the writing-table; pushes the electric lamp out of the way; pulls over a great sheaf of papers; and is in the act of dipping her pen in the ink when she finds* FRANK's *note. She opens it unconcernedly and reads it quickly, giving a little laugh at some quaint turn of expression in it.*] And goodbye, Frank. [*She tears the note up and tosses the pieces into the wastepaper basket without a second thought. Then she goes at her work with a plunge, and soon becomes absorbed in its figures.*]

1893   1898

MARY ELIZABETH COLERIDGE
1861–1907

The great-great-niece of Samuel Taylor Coleridge, Mary Elizabeth Coleridge, once wrote: "I have no fairy god-mother, but lay claim to a fairy great-great uncle, which is perhaps the reason that I am condemned to wander restlessly around the Gates of Fairyland, although I have never yet passed them." Born in London to a literary and musical family that regularly entertained guests such as Alfred, Lord Tennyson and

Robert Browning, Coleridge lived her whole life at home with her parents and one sister. She was unusually well educated, under the supervision of a tutor, William Cory, a scholar and poet, who had been forced by scandal to leave his teaching position at Eton. Coleridge thus received an education usually reserved for boys. She knew six languages, including Greek, and studied philosophy. In the 1890s she began giving lessons in English literature to working girls; in 1895 she started to teach at the Working Woman's College, an activity she continued for the rest of her life. She died suddenly of appendicitis at the age of forty-six.

Coleridge's tutor, Cory, encouraged her to write poetry and short stories. When Henry Newbolt, a poet and family friend, joined her reading group (then composed of five women), the Quintette, he urged her to publish her first two novels. She later published three more, in addition to a number of stories and essays. Although she wrote poetry continuously, she published little of it during her life. When a manuscript of her poems was given to Robert Bridges, a family friend who was also close to Gerard Manley Hopkins and was responsible for the posthumous publication of Hopkins's poetry, Bridges recognized her talent. He made suggestions for revisions and encouraged her to publish a volume. She allowed two small volumes to be privately printed in the nineties, under the pseudonym *Anodos*, or "The Wanderer"; most of her poetry was published after her death.

Although Coleridge did not participate in the feminist debates of her time, her poems contain a subversive sense of anarchic female energy. She believed women had a spiritual identity distinct from men's; she wrote, "I don't think we are separate only in body and in mind, I think we are separate in soul too." Some of her poems rewrite earlier texts. Sandra Gilbert and Susan Gubar have speculated that "The Other Side of a Mirror" (1896) portrays the mad Bertha Mason from Charlotte të's *Jane Eyre* (1847); Angela Leighton and Margaret Reynolds have argued that "The Witch" (1907) reimagines Samuel Taylor Coleridge's visionary poem *Christabel* (1816). Both of these poems demonstrate another characteristic of her writing—presentation of a luminous narrative fragment with little sense of surrounding context. The effect, in the words of Newbolt, her friend, is one of "very deep shadows filled with strange shapes."

The Other Side of a Mirror

I sat before my glass one day,
    And conjured up a vision bare,
Unlike the aspects glad and gay,
    That erst° were found reflected there—   *formerly*
5   The vision of a woman, wild
    With more than womanly despair.

Her hair stood back on either side
    A face bereft of loveliness.
It had no envy now to hide
10   What once no man on earth could guess.
It formed the thorny aureole°   *halo*
    Of hard unsanctified distress.

Her lips were open—not a sound
    Came through the parted lines of red.
15   Whate'er it was, the hideous wound
    In silence and in secret bled.

No sigh relieved her speechless woe,
  She had no voice to speak her dread.

  And in her lurid eyes there shone
20   The dying flame of life's desire,
  Made mad because its hope was gone,
  And kindled at the leaping fire
  Of jealousy, and fierce revenge,
  And strength that could not change nor tire.

25 Shade of a shadow in the glass,
  O set the crystal surface free!
  Pass—as the fairer visions pass—
  Nor ever more return, to be
  The ghost of a distracted hour,
30   That heard me whisper, "I am she!"

1882   1896

The Witch

  I have walked a great while over the snow,
  And I am not tall nor strong.
  My clothes are wet, and my teeth are set,
  And the way was hard and long.
5 I have wandered over the fruitful earth,
  But I never came here before.
  Oh, lift me over the threshold, and let me in at the door!

  The cutting wind is a cruel foe.
  I dare not stand in the blast.
10 My hands are stone, and my voice a groan,
  And the worst of death is past.
  I am but a little maiden still,
  My little white feet are sore.
  Oh, lift me over the threshold, and let me in at the door!

15 Her voice was the voice that women have,
  Who plead for their heart's desire.
  She came—she came—and the quivering flame
  Sank and died in the fire.
  It never was lit again on my hearth
20 Since I hurried across the floor,
  To lift her over the threshold, and let her in at the door.

1892   1907

RUDYARD KIPLING
1865–1936

Like many children born to upper- or middle-class Britons living in India in the
Victorian era, Rudyard Kipling was sent to Great Britain at the age of six to begin his
education. For the next six years in England, he was desperately unhappy; his parents
had chosen to board him in a rigidly Calvinistic foster home, and he was treated with
considerable cruelty. His parents finally removed him when he was twelve and sent
him to a private school, where his experience was far better. His views in later life
were deeply affected by the English schoolboy code of honor and duty, especially
when it involved loyalty to a group or team. At seventeen he rejoined his parents in
India, where his father taught sculpture at the Bombay School of Art. By the time he
returned to England seven years later, the poems and stories he had written while
working as a newspaper reporter in India had brought him early fame. In 1892 he
married an American woman; they lived in Brattleboro, Vermont, until a fierce quarrel
with his brother-in-law drove him back to England in 1896. Kipling settled on a
country estate and purchased, at the turn of the century, an expensive early-model
automobile. He seems to have been the first English author to own an automobile—an
appropriate distinction, because he was intrigued by all kinds of machinery and feats
of engineering. In this keen interest, as in many tastes, he differed markedly from his
contemporaries in the nineties, the aesthetes. Kipling was also the first English author
to receive the Nobel Prize for Literature (1907).

In the final decades of the nineteenth century, India was the most important colony
of Britain's empire—the "Jewel in the Crown," as Prime Minister Benjamin Disraeli
had dubbed it. The English were consequently curious about the world of India, a
world that Kipling's stories and poems helped them envision. Indeed, Leonard Woolf,
Virginia Woolf's husband, wrote of his own experience in India in the early years of
the twentieth century: "I could never make up my mind whether Kipling had moulded
his characters accurately in the image of Anglo-Indian society or whether we were
moulding our characters accurately in the image of a Kipling story." During his seven
years in India in the 1880s, Kipling gained a rich experience of colonial life, which
he presented in his stories and poems. His first volume of stories, *Plain Tales from
the Hills* (1888), explores some of the psychological and moral problems of the Anglo-
Indians and their relationship with the people they had colonized. In his two volumes
of the *Jungle Book* (1894, 1895) he draws on the Indian scene to create a world of
jungle animals. Capable, on occasion, of constructing offensive stereotypes, Kipling
at other times demonstrates a remarkably detailed and intelligent interest in Indian
culture, as in his complex novel *Kim* (1901): amid a welter of representations of
different modes of existence, the contemplative and religious way of life of the Indian
lama, or monk, is treated with no less respect and sympathy than the active and
worldly way of life of the Victorian English governing classes.

In his poems Kipling also draws on the Indian scene, most commonly as it is viewed
through the eyes of the men sent out from England to garrison the country and fight
off invaders on the northwest frontiers. Kipling is usually thought of as the poet of
British imperialism, as indeed he often was; but these poems about ordinary British
soldiers in India contain little by way of flag-waving celebrations of the triumph of
empire. The soldier who speaks in "The Widow at Windsor" (1892) is simply bewildered by the events in which he has taken part. As one of the soldiers of the queen
(one of "Missis Victorier's sons"), he has done his duty, but he does not see the empire
as a divine design to which he has contributed. Kipling develops a new subject in the
working-class imperial soldier (a subject, we should note, who frequently gives voice
to deeply racist attitudes), and thus a new way to portray modern social experience.

The common man's perspective, expressed in the accent of the London cockney,
was one of the qualities that gained Kipling an immediate audience for his *Barrack-*

Room Ballads (1890, 1892). For many years Kipling was extremely popular. What attracted his vast audience was not just the novelty of his subjects but also his mastery of swinging verse rhythms. To some degree Kipling's literary ancestry helps explain his success. In part he learned his craft as a poet from traditional sources. His own family had connections with the Pre-Raphaelites, and he was considerably influenced by such immediate literary predecessors as Robert Browning and Algernon Charles Swinburne. But two of the forces strongly influencing his style and rhythms were not traditional. One of these was the Protestant hymn. Both his parents were children of Methodist clergymen, and chapel singing, as well as preaching, affected him profoundly. "Three generations of Wesleyan ministers . . . lie behind me," he noted; the family tradition can be heard in such secular sermons as "If" (1910) and the elegiac hymn "Recessional" (1897). The second influence came from what seems an antithetical secular quarter: the songs of the music hall. As a teenager in London, Kipling had enjoyed music hall entertainments, which were to reach their peak of popularity in the 1890s. Like Tennyson, Kipling knew how to make poems that call to be set to music, verses such as "Mandalay" (1890) or "Gentlemen-Rankers" (1892), with its memorable refrain: "We're poor little lambs who've lost our way, / Baa! Baa! Baa!" Much of Kipling's poetry is best appreciated with the melodies and ambience of the music hall in mind.

In recent years Kipling's stories have received more attention than his poems. By portraying the British community in India and its relationship with the people it ruled, Kipling created a rich and various fictional world that reflects on England's imperialism as lived by the officers of the empire in all their peculiar social relationships. "The Man Who Would Be King" (1888) presents an intriguing approach to the topic. The narrator, a newspaper editor, tells us of his dealings with a couple of "Loafers." Peachey Carnehan and Daniel Dravot have no official positions in India but are quick to exploit any opportunities their European status may afford them; this pair of rogues heads out to the mountainous region of Kafiristan, intent on establishing their own dynasty. An action-packed tale of adventure in faraway places with strange-sounding names, the story also invites us to think critically about the general project of empire—about the assumptions it holds, the methods it employs, and the human cost of its endeavors.

After leaving India, Kipling gradually turned to English subjects in his fiction, but the cataclysm of World War I did much to diminish his output. As chair of the Imperial War Graves Commission, he played a difficult and important public role, responsible for (among other things) choosing the words to be inscribed on countless monuments and memorials across the globe. Kipling's task was all the more poignant because the body of his only son, who had died in the battle of Loos (1915), was never found. A deeply melancholy autobiography, *Something of Myself,* was published in 1937, the year after Kipling's death.

The Man Who Would Be King[1]

"Brother to a Prince and fellow to a beggar if he be found worthy."[2]

The law, as quoted, lays down a fair conduct of life, and one not easy to follow. I have been fellow to a beggar again and again under circumstances

1. Kipling based his story on the true-life exploits of an American adventurer, Josiah Harlan, who awarded himself the title of prince after occupying a region in the Hindu Kush in the late 1830s.
2. Meant to suggest the principles of Freemasonry, a secret fraternal society that developed from the masons' guild in medieval Britain. By Victorian times it had grown to a prominent national organization, whose members were bound to help each other in times of distress. Kipling was a member.

which prevented either of us finding out whether the other was worthy. I have still to be brother to a Prince, though I once came near to kinship with what might have been a veritable King and was promised the reversion of[3] a Kingdom—army, law-courts, revenue and policy all complete. But, to-day, I greatly fear that my King is dead, and if I want a crown I must go and hunt it for myself.

The beginning of everything was in a railway train upon the road to Mhow from Ajmir.[4] There had been a Deficit in the Budget, which necessitated traveling, not Second-class, which is only half as dear as First-class, but by Intermediate, which is very awful indeed. There are no cushions in the Intermediate class, and the population are either Intermediate, which is Eurasian, or native, which for a long night journey is nasty, or Loafer,[5] which is amusing though intoxicated. Intermediates do not patronize refreshment-rooms. They carry their food in bundles and pots, and buy sweets from the native sweetmeat-sellers, and drink the roadside water. That is why in the hot weather Intermediates are taken out of the carriages dead, and in all weathers are most properly looked down upon.

My particular Intermediate happened to be empty till I reached Nasirabad, when a huge gentleman in shirt-sleeves entered, and, following the custom of Intermediates, passed the time of day. He was a wanderer and a vagabond like myself, but with an educated taste for whiskey. He told tales of things he had seen and done, of out-of-the-way corners of the Empire into which he had penetrated, and of adventures in which he risked his life for a few days' food. "If India was filled with men like you and me, not knowing more than the crows where they'd get their next day's rations, it isn't seventy millions of revenue the land would be paying—it's seven hundred millions," said he; and as I looked at his mouth and chin I was disposed to agree with him. We talked politics—the politics of Loaferdom that sees things from the underside where the lath and plaster is not smoothed off[6]—and we talked postal arrangements because my friend wanted to send a telegram back from the next station to Ajmir, which is the turning-off place from the Bombay to the Mhow line as you travel westward. My friend had no money beyond eight annas which he wanted[7] for dinner, and I had no money at all, owing to the hitch in the Budget before mentioned. Further, I was going into a wilderness where, though I should resume touch with the Treasury, there were no telegraph offices. I was, therefore, unable to help him in any way.

"We might threaten a Station-master, and make him send a wire on tick,"[8] said my friend, "but that'd mean inquiries for you and for me, and I've got my hands full these days. Did you say you are traveling back along this line within any days?"

"Within ten," I said.

"Can't you make it eight?" said he. "Mine is rather urgent business."

"I can send your telegram within ten days if that will serve you," I said.

"I couldn't trust the wire to fetch him now I think of it. It's this way. He leaves Delhi on the 23d for Bombay. That means he'll be running through Ajmir about the night of the 23d."

3. Right to inherit.
4. These, and the other places mentioned at the beginning of the story, are in northern India.
5. A European in India with no official attachment or position.

6. I.e., the unfinished side of a wall.
7. Needed. "Annas": there are sixteen annas in a rupee, the basic monetary unit of India.
8. On credit.

"But I'm going into the Indian Desert," I explained.

"Well *and* good," said he. "You'll be changing at Marwar Junction to get into Jodhpore territory—you must do that—and he'll be coming through Marwar Junction in the early morning of the 24th by the Bombay Mail. Can you be at Marwar Junction on that time? 'Twon't be inconveniencing you because I know that there's precious few pickings to be got out of these Central India States—even though you pretend to be correspondent of the *Backwoodsman*."[9]

"Have you ever tried that trick?" I asked.

"Again and again, but the Residents[1] find you out, and then you get escorted to the Border before you've time to get your knife into them. But about my friend here. I *must* give him a word o' mouth to tell him what's come to me or else he won't know where to go. I would take it more than kind of you if you was to come out of Central India in time to catch him at Marwar Junction, and say to him:—'He has gone South for the week.' He'll know what that means. He's a big man with a red beard, and a great swell[2] he is. You'll find him sleeping like a gentleman with all his luggage round him in a Second-class compartment. But don't you be afraid. Slip down the window, and say:—'He has gone South for the week,' and he'll tumble.[3] It's only cutting your time of stay in those parts by two days. I ask you as a stranger—going to the West,"[4] he said, with emphasis.

"Where have *you* come from?" said I.

"From the East," said he, "and I am hoping that you will give him the message on the Square[5]—for the sake of my Mother as well as your own."

Englishmen are not usually softened by appeals to the memory of their mothers, but for certain reasons, which will be fully apparent, I saw fit to agree.

"It's more than a little matter," said he, "and that's why I ask you to do it— and now I know that I can depend on you doing it. A Second-class carriage at Marwar Junction, and a red-haired man asleep in it. You'll be sure to remember. I get out at the next station, and I must hold on there till he comes or sends me what I want."

"I'll give the message if I catch him," I said, "and for the sake of your Mother as well as mine I'll give you a word of advice. Don't try to run the Central India States just now as the correspondent of the *Backwoodsman*. There's a real one knocking about here, and it might lead to trouble."

"Thank you," said he, simply, "and when will the swine be gone? I can't starve because he's ruining my work. I wanted to get hold of the Degumber Rajah down here about his father's widow, and give him a jump."

"What did he do to his father's widow, then?"

"Filled her up with red pepper and slippered her to death as she hung from a beam. I found that out myself, and I'm the only man that would dare going into the State to get hush-money for it. They'll try to poison me, same as they did in Chortumna when I went on the loot there. But you'll give the man at Marwar Junction my message?"

He got out at a little roadside station, and I reflected. I had heard, more than once, of men personating correspondents of newspapers and bleeding

9. This fictitious newspaper appears to be based on the Allahabad *Pioneer*, for which Kipling worked as a roving correspondent. "Central India States": quasi-independent "Native States," as they were also known, presided over by Indian royalty.
1. British political officers appointed to oversee affairs at the courts of Indian rulers.
2. Fashionable fellow.
3. Catch on, understand.
4. This phrase and the following one are from the code of the Freemasons.
5. Honestly.

small Native States with threats of exposure, but I had never met any of the caste before. They lead a hard life, and generally die with great suddenness. The Native States have a wholesome horror of English newspapers, which may throw light on their peculiar methods of government, and do their best to choke correspondents with champagne, or drive them out of their mind with four-in-hand barouches.[6] They do not understand that nobody cares a straw for the internal administration of Native States so long as oppression and crime are kept within decent limits, and the ruler is not drugged, drunk, or diseased from one end of the year to the other. Native States were created by Providence in order to supply picturesque scenery, tigers, and tall-writing.[7] They are the dark places of the earth, full of unimaginable cruelty, touching the Railway and the Telegraph on one side, and, on the other, the days of Harun-al-Raschid.[8] When I left the train I did business with divers Kings, and in eight days passed through many changes of life. Sometimes I wore dress-clothes and consorted with Princes and Politicals,[9] drinking from crystal and eating from silver. Sometimes I lay out upon the ground and devoured what I could get, from a plate made of a flapjack, and drank the running water, and slept under the same rug as my servant. It was all in the day's work.

Then I headed for the Great Indian Desert upon the proper date, as I had promised, and the night Mail set me down at Marwar Junction, where a funny little, happy-go-lucky, native-managed railway runs to Jodhpore. The Bombay Mail from Delhi makes a short halt at Marwar. She arrived as I got in, and I had just time to hurry to her platform and go down the carriages. There was only one Second-class on the train. I slipped the window, and looked down upon a flaming red beard, half covered by a railway rug. That was my man, fast asleep, and I dug him gently in the ribs. He woke with a grunt, and I saw his face in the light of the lamps. It was a great and shining face.

"Tickets again?" said he.

"No," said I. "I am to tell you that he is gone South for the week. He is gone South for the week!"

The train had begun to move out. The red man rubbed his eyes. "He has gone South for the week," he repeated. "Now that's just like his impidence. Did he say that I was to give you anything?—'Cause I won't."

"He didn't," I said, and dropped away, and watched the red lights die out in the dark. It was horribly cold, because the wind was blowing off the sands. I climbed into my own train—not an Intermediate Carriage this time—and went to sleep.

If the man with the beard had given me a rupee I should have kept it as a memento of a rather curious affair. But the consciousness of having done my duty was my only reward.

Later on I reflected that two gentlemen like my friends could not do any good if they foregathered and personated correspondents of newspapers, and might, if they "stuck up"[1] one of the little rat-trap states of Central India or Southern Rajputana, get themselves into serious difficulties. I therefore took some trouble to describe them as accurately as I could remember to people who would be interested in deporting them; and succeeded, so I was later informed, in having them headed back from Degumber borders.

6. Fashionable four-wheeled carriages.
7. Tall tales.
8. The caliph of Baghdad (763–809), who figures in many tales of the *Arabian Nights*.

9. I.e., Residents.
1. Fraudulently extorted money from. "Foregathered": met.

Then I became respectable, and returned to an Office where there were no Kings and no incidents except the daily manufacture of a newspaper. A newspaper office seems to attract every conceivable sort of person, to the prejudice of discipline. Zenana-mission ladies[2] arrive, and beg that the Editor will instantly abandon all his duties to describe a Christian prize-giving in a back-slum of a perfectly inaccessible village; Colonels who have been overpassed for commands sit down and sketch the outline of a series of ten, twelve, or twenty-four leading articles on Seniority *versus* Selection; missionaries wish to know why they have not been permitted to escape from their regular vehicles of abuse and swear at a brother missionary under special patronage of the editorial We; stranded theatrical companies troop up to explain that they cannot pay for their advertisements, but on their return from New Zealand or Tahiti will do so with interest; inventors of patent punkah[3]-pulling machines, carriage couplings and unbreakable swords and axle-trees call with specifications in their pockets and hours at their disposal; tea-companies enter and elaborate their prospectuses with the office pens; secretaries of ball-committees clamour to have the glories of their last dance more fully expounded; strange ladies rustle in and say:—"I want a hundred lady's cards printed *at once*, please," which is manifestly part of an Editor's duty; and every dissolute ruffian that ever tramped the Grand Trunk Road[4] makes it his business to ask for employment as a proof-reader. And, all the time, the telephone-bell is ringing madly, and Kings are being killed on the Continent, and Empires are saying—"You're another," and Mister Gladstone is calling down brimstone upon the British Dominions,[5] and the little black copy-boys are whining, *"kaa-pi chay-ha-yeh"* (copy wanted) like tired bees, and most of the paper is as blank as Modred's shield.[6]

But that is the amusing part of the year. There are other six months wherein none ever come to call, and the thermometer walks inch by inch up to the top of the glass, and the office is darkened to just above reading-light, and the press machines are red-hot of touch, and nobody writes anything but accounts of amusements in the Hill-stations[7] or obituary notices. Then the telephone becomes a tinkling terror, because it tells you of the sudden deaths of men and women that you knew intimately, and the prickly-heat covers you as with a garment, and you sit down and write:—"A slight increase of sickness is reported from the Khuda Janta Khan[8] District. The outbreak is purely sporadic in its nature, and, thanks to the energetic efforts of the District authorities, is now almost at an end. It is, however, with deep regret we record the death, etc."

Then the sickness really breaks out, and the less recording and reporting the better for the peace of the subscribers. But the Empires and the Kings continue to divert themselves as selfishly as before, and the Foreman thinks that a daily paper really ought to come out once in twenty-four hours, and all the people at the Hill-stations in the middle of their amusements say:—"Good gracious! Why can't the paper be sparkling? I'm sure there's plenty going on up here."

2. Female missionaries doing work among Indian women, who were customarily confined to a part of the house called the *Zenana*.
3. Large swinging fan, usually worked by hand.
4. Major road connecting Calcutta and Delhi.
5. Places under British control. William Ewart Gladstone (1809–1898), leader of the Liberal Party from 1868 to 1875 and 1880 to 1894, and four times prime minister; he strongly opposed

overseas expansion. "Brimstone": i.e., fire and brimstone, the supposed torments of hell.
6. In British legend the shield of King Arthur's traitorous nephew was blank because he had done no deeds of valor.
7. Official outposts in the northern hills, to which many British people in India would retire during the hottest months.
8. "God Knows Town"; i.e., Nowheresville.

That is the dark half of the moon, and, as the advertisements say, "must be experienced to be appreciated."

It was in that season, and a remarkably evil season, that the paper began running the last issue of the week on Saturday night, which is to say, Sunday morning, after the custom of a London paper. This was a great convenience, for immediately after the paper was put to bed,[9] the dawn would lower the thermometer from 96° to almost 84° for half an hour, and in that chill—you have no idea how cold is 84° on the grass until you begin to pray for it—a very tired man could set off to sleep ere the heat roused him.

One Saturday night it was my pleasant duty to put the paper to bed alone. A King or courtier or a courtesan or a community was going to die or get a new Constitution, or do something that was important on the other side of the world, and the paper was to be held open till the latest possible minute in order to catch the telegram. It was a pitchy black night, as stifling as a June night can be, and the *loo*, the red-hot wind from the westward, was booming among the tinder-dry trees and pretending that the rain was on its heels. Now and again a spot of almost boiling water would fall on the dust with the flop of a frog, but all our weary world knew that was only pretence. It was a shade cooler in the press-room than the office, so I sat there, while the type clicked and clicked and the night-jars hooted at the windows, and the all but naked compositors wiped the sweat from their foreheads and called for water. The thing that was keeping us back, whatever it was, would not come off, though the *loo* dropped and the last type was set, and the whole round earth stood still in the choking heat, with its finger on its lip, to wait the event. I drowsed, and wondered whether the telegraph was a blessing, and whether this dying man, or struggling people, was aware of the inconvenience the delay was causing. There was no special reason beyond the heat and worry to make tension, but, as the clock hands crept up to three o'clock and the machines spun their fly-wheels two and three times to see that all was in order, before I said the word that would set them off, I could have shrieked aloud.

Then the roar and rattle of the wheels shivered the quiet into little bits. I rose to go away, but two men in white clothes stood in front of me. The first one said:—"It's him!" The second said:—"So it is!" And they both laughed almost as loudly as the machinery roared, and mopped their foreheads. "We see there was a light burning across the road and we were sleeping in that ditch there for coolness, and I said to my friend here, 'The office is open. Let's come along and speak to him as turned us back from the Degumber State,' " said the smaller of the two. He was the man I had met in the Mhow train, and his fellow was the red-bearded man of Marwar Junction. There was no mistaking the eyebrows of the one or the beard of the other.

I was not pleased, because I wished to go to sleep, not to squabble with loafers. "What do you want?" I asked.

"Half an hour's talk with you cool and comfortable, in the office," said the red-bearded man. "We'd *like* some drink—the Contrack doesn't begin yet, Peachey, so you needn't look—but what we really want is advice. We don't want money. We ask you as a favour, because you did us a bad turn about Degumber."

I led from the press-room to the stifling office with the maps on the walls, and the red-haired man rubbed his hands. "That's something like," said he.

9. The final preparations were made for printing the newspaper.

"This was the proper shop to come to. Now, Sir, let me introduce to you Brother[1] Peachey Carnehan, that's him, and Brother Daniel Dravot, that is *me*, and the less said about our professions the better, for we have been most things in our time. Soldier, sailor, compositor, photographer, proof-reader, street-preacher, and correspondents of the *Backwoodsman* when we thought the paper wanted one. Carnehan is sober, and so am I. Look at us first and see that's sure. It will save you cutting into my talk. We'll take one of your cigars apiece, and you shall see us light."

I watched the test. The men were absolutely sober, so I gave them each a tepid peg.[2]

"Well *and* good," said Carnehan of the eyebrows, wiping the froth from his moustache. "Let me talk now, Dan. We have been all over India, mostly on foot. We have been boiler-fitters, engine-drivers, petty contractors, and all that, and we have decided that India isn't big enough for such as us."

They certainly were too big for the office. Dravot's beard seemed to fill half the room and Carnehan's shoulders the other half, as they sat on the big table. Carnehan continued: "The country isn't half worked out because they that governs it won't let you touch it. They spend all their blessed time in governing it, and you can't lift a spade, nor chip a rock, nor look for oil, nor anything like that without all the Government saying—'Leave it alone and let us govern.' Therefore, such as it is, we will let it alone, and go away to some other place where a man isn't crowded and can come to his own. We are not little men, and there is nothing that we are afraid of except Drink, and we have signed a Contrack on that. *Therefore*, we are going away to be Kings."

"Kings in our own right," muttered Dravot.

"Yes, of course," I said. "You've been tramping in the sun, and it's a very warm night, and hadn't you better sleep over the notion? Come to-morrow."

"Neither drunk nor sunstruck," said Dravot. "We have slept over the notion half a year, and require to see Books and Atlases, and we have decided that there is only one place now in the world that two strong men can Sar-a-*whack*.[3] They call it Kafiristan.[4] By my reckoning it's the top right-hand corner of Afghanistan, not more than three hundred miles from Pesha-wur. They have two and thirty heathen idols there, and we'll be the thirty-third. It's a mountainous country, and the women of those parts are very beautiful."

"But that is provided against in the Contrack," said Carnehan. "Neither Women nor Liquor, Daniel."

"And that's all we know, except that no one has gone there, and they fight, and in any place where they fight, a man who knows how to drill men can always be a King. We shall go to those parts and say to any King we find— 'D'you want to vanquish your foes?' and we will show him how to drill men; for that we know better than anything else. Then we will subvert that King and seize his Throne and establish a Dy-nasty."

"You'll be cut to pieces before you're fifty miles across the Border," I said. "You have to travel through Afghanistan to get to that country. It's one mass of mountains and peaks and glaciers, and no Englishman has been through

1. A title meant to recall the Freemason connection.
2. A drink.
3. A reference to Sir James Brooke (1803–1868), "the White Rajah of Sarawak," who, in return for helping the rajah of Sarawak, in Borneo, put down a rebellion, succeeded him after his death and established a dynasty.
4. A real place, in the Hindu Kush.

it. The people are utter brutes, and even if you reached them you couldn't do anything."

"That's more like," said Carnehan: "If you could think us a little more mad we would be more pleased. We have come to you to know about this country, to read a book about it, and to be shown maps. We want you to tell us that we are fools and to show us your books." He turned to the bookcases.

"Are you at all in earnest?" I said.

"A little," said Dravot, sweetly. "As big a map as you have got, even if it's all blank where Kafiristan is, and any books you've got. We can read, though we aren't very educated."

I uncased the big thirty-two-miles-to-the-inch map of India, and two smaller Frontier maps, hauled down volume INF-KAN of the *Encyclopaedia Britannica*, and the men consulted them.

"See here!" said Dravot, his thumb on the map. "Up to Jagdallak, Peachey and me know the road. We was there with Roberts's Army.[5] We'll have to turn off to the right at Jagdallak through Laghmann territory. Then we get among the hills—fourteen thousand feet—fifteen thousand—it will be cold work there, but it don't look very far on the map."

I handed him Wood on the *Sources of the Oxus*.[6] Carnehan was deep in the *Encyclopaedia*.

"They're a mixed lot," said Dravot, reflectively; "and it won't help us to know the names of their tribes. The more tribes the more they'll fight, and the better for us. From Jagdallak to Ashang. H'mm!"

"But all the information about the country is as sketchy and inaccurate as can be," I protested. "No one knows anything about it really. Here's the file of the *United Services' Institute*. Read what Bellew says."

"Blow Bellew!" said Carnehan. "Dan, they're an all-fired lot of heathens, but this book here says they think they're related to us English."

I smoked while the men pored over Raverty, Wood, the maps, and the *Encyclopaedia*.

"There is no use your waiting," said Dravot, politely. "It's about four o'clock now. We'll go before six o'clock if you want to sleep, and we won't steal any of the papers. Don't you sit up. We're two harmless lunatics and if you come, to-morrow evening, down to the Serai[7] we'll say good-bye to you."

"You *are* two fools," I answered. "You'll be turned back at the Frontier or cut up the minute you set foot in Afghanistan. Do you want any money or a recommendation downcountry? I can help you to the chance of work next week."

"Next week we shall be hard at work ourselves, thank you," said Dravot. "It isn't so easy being a King as it looks. When we've got our Kingdom in going order we'll let you know, and you can come up and help us to govern it."

"Would two lunatics make a Contrack like that?" said Carnehan, with subdued pride, showing me a greasy half-sheet of note-paper on which was written the following. I copied it, then and there, as a curiosity:

This Contract between me and you persuing witnesseth in the name of God— Amen and so forth.

---

5. In the Second Afghan War (1878–80), a force under the command of General Frederick Roberts made a three-hundred-mile forced march through the area.

6. The Oxus is a river whose sources are in the area.

7. Place or building for the accommodation of travelers and their pack animals.

(One) That me and you will settle this matter together: i. e., to be Kings of Kafiristan.

(Two) That you and me will not, while this matter is being settled, look at any Liquor, nor any Woman, black, white or brown, so as to get mixed up with one or the other harmful.

(Three) That we conduct ourselves with dignity and discretion and if one of us gets into trouble the other will stay by him.

Signed by you and me this day.
Peachey Taliaferro Carnehan.
Daniel Dravot.
Both Gentlemen at Large.

"There was no need for the last article," said Carnehan, blushing modestly; "but it looks regular. Now you know the sort of men that loafers are—we are loafers, Dan, until we get out of India—and do you think that we would sign a Contrack like that unless we was in earnest? We have kept away from the two things that make life worth having."

"You won't enjoy your lives much longer if you are going to try this idiotic adventure. Don't set the office on fire," I said, "and go away before nine o'clock."

I left them still poring over the maps and making notes on the back of the "Contrack." "Be sure to come down to the Serai to-morrow," were their parting words.

The Kumharsen Serai is the great foursquare sink of humanity where the strings of camels and horses from the North load and unload. All the nationalities of Central Asia may be found there, and most of the folk of India proper. Balkh and Bokhara there meet Bengal and Bombay, and try to draw eye-teeth. You can buy ponies, turquoises, Persian pussy-cats, saddle-bags, fat-tailed sheep and musk in the Kumharsen Serai, and get many strange things for nothing. In the afternoon I went down there to see whether my friends intended to keep their word or were lying about drunk.

A priest attired in fragments of ribbons and rags stalked up to me, gravely twisting a child's paper whirligig.[8] Behind was his servant bending under the load of a crate of mud toys. The two were loading up two camels, and the inhabitants of the Serai watched them with shrieks of laughter.

"The priest is mad," said a horse-dealer to me. "He is going up to Kabul to sell toys to the Amir.[9] He will either be raised to honor or have his head cut off. He came in here this morning and has been behaving madly ever since."

"The witless are under the protection of God," stammered a flat-cheeked Usbeg[1] in broken Hindi. "They foretell future events."

"Would they could have foretold that my caravan would have been cut up by the Shinwaris almost within shadow of the Pass!"[2] grunted the Eusufzai agent of a Rajputana trading-house whose goods had been feloniously diverted into the hands of other robbers just across the Border, and whose misfortunes were the laughing-stock of the bazar. "Ohé, priest, whence come you and whither do you go?"

"From Roum[3] have I come," shouted the priest, waving his whirligig; "from

---

8. Pinwheel.
9. The ruler of Afghanistan, based in the city of Kabul.
1. Person from Uzbekistan.
2. The Khyber or Khaiber Pass, running thirty-

three miles through the mountains. Then on the northwest frontier of British India, it now links Afghanistan and Pakistan.
3. Turkey.

Roum, blown by the breath of a hundred devils across the sea! O thieves, robbers, liars, the blessing of Pir Khan on pigs, dogs, and perjurers! Who will take the Protected of God to the North to sell charms that are never still to the Amir? The camels shall not gall,[4] the sons shall not fall sick, and the wives shall remain faithful while they are away, of the men who give me place in their caravan. Who will assist me to slipper the King of the Roos[5] with a golden slipper with a silver heel? The protection of Pir Khan be upon his labors!" He spread out the skirts of his gaberdine and pirouetted between the lines of tethered horses.

"There starts a caravan from Peshawur to Kabul in twenty days, *Huzrut*,"[6] said the Eusufzai trader. "My camels go therewith. Do thou also go and bring us good-luck."

"I will go even now!" shouted the priest. "I will depart upon my winged camels, and be at Peshawur in a day! Ho! Hazar[7] Mir Khan," he yelled to his servant, "drive out the camels, but let me first mount my own."

He leaped on the back of his beast as it knelt, and, turning round to me, cried:—"Come thou also, Sahib, a little along the road, and I will sell thee a charm—an amulet that shall make thee King of Kafiristan."

Then the light broke upon me, and I followed the two camels out of the Serai till we reached open road and the priest halted.

"What d' you think o' that?" said he in English. "Carnehan can't talk their patter, so I've made him my servant. He makes a handsome servant. 'Tisn't for nothing that I've been knocking about the country for fourteen years. Didn't I do that talk neat? We'll hitch on to a caravan at Peshawur till we get to Jagdallak, and then we'll see if we can get donkeys for our camels, and strike into Kafiristan. Whirligigs for the Amir, O Lor! Put your hand under the camel-bags and tell me what you feel."

I felt the butt of a Martini,[8] and another and another.

"Twenty of 'em," said Dravot, placidly. "Twenty of 'em, and ammunition to correspond, under the whirligigs and the mud dolls."

"Heaven help you if you are caught with those things!" I said. "A Martini is worth her weight in silver among the Pathans."[9]

"Fifteen hundred rupees of capital—every rupee we could beg, borrow, or steal—are invested on these two camels," said Dravot. "We won't get caught. We're going through the Khaiber with a regular caravan. Who'd touch a poor mad priest?"

"Have you got everything you want?" I asked, overcome with astonishment.

"Not yet, but we shall soon. Give us a memento of your kindness, *Brother*. You did me a service yesterday, and that time in Marwar. Half my Kingdom shall you have, as the saying is." I slipped a small charm compass from my watch-chain and handed it up to the priest.

"Good-bye," said Dravot, giving me hand cautiously. "It's the last time we'll shake hands with an Englishman these many days. Shake hands with him, Carnehan," he cried, as the second camel passed me.

Carnehan leaned down and shook hands. Then the camels passed away along the dusty road, and I was left alone to wonder. My eye could detect no failure in the disguises. The scene in Serai attested that they were complete

---

4. Become sore.
5. Czar of Russia.
6. Presence (an honorary form of address).

7. Get ready.
8. Rifle issued to British infantry.
9. The principal tribe in Afghanistan.

to the native mind. There was just the chance, therefore, that Carnehan and Dravot would be able to wander through Afghanistan without detection. But, beyond, they would find death, certain and awful death.

Ten days later a native friend of mine, giving me the news of the day from Peshawur, wound up his letter with:—"There has been much laughter here on account of a certain mad priest who is going in his estimation to sell petty gauds and insignificant trinkets which he ascribes as great charms to H. H.[1] the Amir of Bokhara. He passed through Peshawur and associated himself to the Second Summer caravan that goes to Kabul. The merchants are pleased, because through superstition they imagine that such mad fellows bring good-fortune."

The two, then, were beyond the Border. I would have prayed for them, but, that night, a real King died in Europe, and demanded an obituary notice.

The wheel of the world swings through the same phases again and again. Summer passed and winter thereafter, and came and passed again. The daily paper continued and I with it, and upon the third summer there fell a hot night, a night-issue, and a strained waiting for something to be telegraphed from the other side of the world, exactly as had happened before. A few great men had died in the past two years, the machines worked with more clatter, and some of the trees in the Office garden were a few feet taller. But that was all the difference.

I passed over to the press-room, and went through just such a scene as I have already described. The nervous tension was stronger than it had been two years before, and I felt the heat more acutely. At three o'clock I cried, "Print off," and turned to go, when there crept to my chair what was left of a man. He was bent into a circle, his head was sunk between his shoulders, and he moved his feet one over the other like a bear. I could hardly see whether he walked or crawled—this rag-wrapped, whining cripple who addressed me by name, crying that he was come back. "Can you give me a drink?" he whimpered. "For the Lord's sake, give me a drink!"

I went back to the office, the man following with groans of pain, and I turned up the lamp.

"Don't you know me?" he gasped, dropping into a chair, and he turned his drawn face, surmounted by a shock of grey hair, to the light.

I looked at him intently. Once before had I seen eyebrows that met over the nose in an inch-broad black band, but for the life of me I could not tell where.

"I don't know you," I said, handing him the whiskey. "What can I do for you?"

He took a gulp of the spirit raw, and shivered in spite of the suffocating heat.

"I've come back," he repeated; "and I was the King of Kafiristan—me and Dravot—crowned Kings we was! In this office we settled it—you setting there and giving us the books. I am Peachey—Peachey Taliaferro Carnehan, and you've been setting here ever since—O Lord!"

I was more than a little astonished, and expressed my feelings accordingly.

"It's true," said Carnehan, with a dry cackle, nursing his feet, which were wrapped in rags. "True as gospel. Kings we were, with crowns upon our heads—me and Dravot—poor Dan—oh, poor, poor Dan, that would never take advice, not though I begged of him!"

1. His Highness.

"Take the whiskey," I said, "and take your own time. Tell me all you can recollect of everything from beginning to end. You got across the border on your camels, Dravot dressed as a mad priest and you his servant. Do you remember that?"

"I ain't mad—yet, but I shall be that way soon. Of course I remember. Keep looking at me, or maybe my words will go all to pieces. Keep looking at me in my eyes and don't say anything."

I leaned forward and looked into his face as steadily as I could. He dropped one hand upon the table and I grasped it by the wrist. It was twisted like a bird's claw, and upon the back was a ragged, red, diamond-shaped scar.

"No, don't look there. Look at *me*," said Carnehan.

"That comes afterward, but for the Lord's sake don't distrack me. We left with that caravan, me and Dravot playing all sorts of antics to amuse the people we were with. Dravot used to make us laugh in the evenings when all the people was cooking their dinners—cooking their dinners, and . . . what did they do then? They lit little fires with sparks that went into Dravot's beard, and we all laughed—fit to die. Little red fires they was, going into Dravot's big red beard—so funny." His eyes left mine and he smiled foolishly.

"You went as far as Jagdallak with that caravan," I said, at a venture, "after you had lit those fires. To Jagdallak, where you turned off to try to get into Kafiristan."

"No, we didn't neither. What are you talking about? We turned off before Jagdallak, because we heard the roads was good. But they wasn't good enough for our two camels—mine and Dravot's. When we left the caravan, Dravot took off all his clothes and mine too, and said we would be heathen, because the Kafirs[2] didn't allow Mohammedans to talk to them. So we dressed betwixt and between, and such a sight as Daniel Dravot I never saw yet nor expect to see again. He burned half his beard, and slung a sheep-skin over his shoulder, and shaved his head into patterns. He shaved mine, too, and made me wear outrageous things to look like a heathen. That was in a most mountaineous country, and our camels couldn't go along any more because of the mountains. They were tall and black, and coming home I saw them fight like wild goats—there are lots of goats in Kafiristan. And these mountains, they never keep still, no more than goats. Always fighting they are, and don't let you sleep at night."

"Take some more whiskey," I said, very slowly. "What did you and Daniel Dravot do when the camels could go no further because of the rough roads that led into Kafiristan?"

"What did which do? There was a party called Peachey Taliaferro Carnehan that was with Dravot. Shall I tell you about him? He died out there in the cold. Slap from the bridge fell old Peachey, turning and twisting in the air like a penny whirligig that you can sell to the Amir—No; they was two for three ha'pence, those whirligigs, or I am much mistaken and woful sore. And then these camels were no use, and Peachey said to Dravot—'For the Lord's sake, let's get out of this before our heads are chopped off,' and with that they killed the camels all among the mountains, not having anything in particular to eat, but first they took off the boxes with the guns and the ammunition, till two men came along driving four mules. Dravot up and dances in front of them, singing,—'Sell me four mules.' Says the first man,—'If you are rich enough to buy, you are rich enough to rob;' but before ever he could put his hand to his

2. Non-Muslims.

knife, Dravot breaks his neck over his knee, and the other party runs away. So Carnehan loaded the mules with the rifles that was taken off the camels, and together we starts forward into those bitter cold mountaineous parts, and never a road broader than the back of your hand."

He paused for a moment, while I asked him if he could remember the nature of the country through which he had journeyed.

"I am telling you as straight as I can, but my head isn't as good as it might be. They drove nails through it to make me hear better how Dravot died. The country was mountaineous and the mules were most contrary, and the inhabitants was dispersed and solitary. They went up and up, and down and down, and that other party, Carnehan, was imploring of Dravot not to sing and whistle so loud, for fear of bringing down the tremenjus avalanches. But Dravot says that if a King couldn't sing it wasn't worth being King, and whacked the mules over the rump, and never took no heed for ten cold days. We came to a big level valley all among the mountains, and the mules were near dead, so we killed them, not having anything in special for them or us to eat. We sat upon the boxes, and played odd and even[3] with the cartridges that was jolted out.

"Then ten men with bows and arrows ran down that valley, chasing twenty men with bows and arrows, and the row was tremenjus. They was fair men—fairer than you or me—with yellow hair and remarkable well built.[4] Says Dravot, unpacking the guns—'This is the beginning of the business. We'll fight for the ten men,' and with that he fires two rifles at the twenty men, and drops one of them at two hundred yards from the rock where we was sitting. The other men began to run, but Carnehan and Dravot sits on the boxes picking them off at all ranges, up and down the valley. Then we goes up to the ten men that had run across the snow too, and they fires a footy[5] little arrow at us. Dravot he shoots above their heads and they all falls down flat. Then he walks over and kicks them, and then he lifts them up and shakes hands all round to make them friendly like. He calls them and gives them the boxes to carry, and waves his hand for all the world as though he was King already. They takes the boxes and him across the valley and up the hill into a pine wood on the top, where there was half a dozen big stone idols. Dravot he goes to the biggest—a fellow they call Imbra—and lays a rifle and a cartridge at his feet, rubbing his nose respectful with his own nose, patting him on the head, and saluting in front of it. He turns round to the men and nods his head, and says,—'That's all right. I'm in the know too, and all these old jim-jams[6] are my friends.' Then he opens his mouth and points down it, and when the first man brings him food, he says—'No;' and when the second man brings him food, he says—'No;' but when one of the old priests and the boss of the village brings him food, he says—'Yes;' very haughty, and eats it slow. That was how we came to our first village, without any trouble, just as though we had tumbled from the skies. But we tumbled from one of those damned rope-bridges, you see, and you couldn't expect a man to laugh much after that."

"Take some more whiskey and go on," I said. "That was the first village you came into. How did you get to be King?"

"I wasn't King," said Carnehan. "Dravot he was the King, and a handsome

3. A game in which a player guesses the number of objects that another player is holding.
4. There was a legend that Alexander the Great had left a Greek colony in the area in the 4th cen-

tury B.C.E.
5. Paltry, insignificant.
6. Knickknacks.

man he looked with the gold crown on his head and all. Him and the other party stayed in that village, and every morning Dravot sat by the side of old Imbra, and the people came and worshipped. That was Dravot's order. Then a lot of men came into the valley, and Carnehan and Dravot picks them off with the rifles before they knew where they was, and runs down into the valley and up again the other side, and finds another village, same as the first one, and the people all falls down flat on their faces, and Dravot says,—'Now what is the trouble between you two villages?' and the people points to a woman, as fair as you or me, that was carried off, and Dravot takes her back to the first village and counts up the dead—eight there was. For each dead man Dravot pours a little milk on the ground and waves his arms like a whirligig and 'That's all right,' says he. Then he and Carnehan takes the big boss of each village by the arm and walks them down into the valley, and shows them how to scratch a line with a spear right down the valley, and gives each a sod of turf from both sides o' the line. Then all the people comes down and shouts like the devil and all, and Dravot says,—'Go and dig the land, and be fruitful and multiply,'[7] which they did, though they didn't understand. Then we asks the names of things in their lingo—bread and water and fire and idols and such, and Dravot leads the priest of each village up to the idol, and says he must sit there and judge the people, and if anything goes wrong he is to be shot.

"Next week they was all turning up the land in the valley as quiet as bees and much prettier, and the priests heard all the complaints and told Dravot in dumb show what it was about. 'That's just the beginning,' says Dravot. 'They think we're Gods.' He and Carnehan picks out twenty good men and shows them how to click off a rifle, and form fours, and advance in line, and they was very pleased to do so, and clever to see the hang of it. Then he takes out his pipe and his baccy-pouch and leaves one at one village and one at the other, and off we two goes to see what was to be done in the next valley. That was all rock, and there was a little village there, and Carnehan says,—'Send 'em to the old valley to plant,' and takes 'em there and gives 'em some land that wasn't took before. They were a poor lot, and we blooded 'em with a kid[8] before letting 'em into the new Kingdom. That was to impress the people, and then they settled down quiet, and Carnehan went back to Dravot, who had got into another valley, all snow and ice and most mountaineous. There was no people there, and the Army got afraid, so Dravot shoots one of them, and goes on till he finds some people in a village, and the Army explains that unless the people wants to be killed they had better not shoot their little matchlocks;[9] for they had matchlocks. We makes friends with the priest and I stays there alone with two of the Army, teaching the men how to drill, and a thundering big Chief comes across the snow with kettle-drums and horns twanging, because he heard there was a new God kicking about. Carnehan sights for the brown[1] of the men half a mile across the snow and wings one of them. Then he sends a message to the Chief that, unless he wished to be killed, he must come and shake hands with me and leave his arms behind. The Chief comes alone first, and Carnehan shakes hands with him and whirls his arms about, same as Dravot used, and very much surprised that Chief was, and strokes my

7. God's command to Adam and Eve (Genesis 1.28).
8. I.e., a kid goat, a fake religious ritual.
9. Primitive muskets.

1. A hunting term, meaning to fire into the middle of a group of game birds rather than aiming at a particular one.

eyebrows. Then Carnehan goes alone to the Chief, and asks him in dumb show if he had an enemy he hated. 'I have,' says the Chief. So Carnehan weeds out the pick of his men, and sets the two of the Army to show them drill, and at the end of two weeks the men can manoeuvre about as well as Volunteers. So he marches with the Chief to a great big plain on the top of a mountain, and the Chief's men rushes into a village and takes it; we three Martinis firing into the brown of the enemy. So we took that village too, and I gives the Chief a rag from my coat and says, 'Occupy till I come;'[2] which was scriptural. By way of a reminder, when me and the Army was eighteen hundred yards away, I drops a bullet near him standing on the snow, and all the people falls flat on their faces. Then I sends a letter to Dravot, wherever he be by land or by sea."

At the risk of throwing the creature out of train I interrupted,—"How could you write a letter up yonder?"

"The letter?—Oh!—The letter! Keep looking at me between the eyes, please. It was a string-talk letter, that we'd learned the way of it from a blind beggar in the Punjab."

I remember that there had once come to the office a blind man with a knotted twig and a piece of string which he wound round the twig according to some cipher of his own. He could, after the lapse of days or hours, repeat the sentence which he had reeled up. He had reduced the alphabet to eleven primitive sounds; and tried to teach me his method, but failed.

"I sent that letter to Dravot," said Carnehan; "and told him to come back because this Kingdom was growing too big for me to handle, and then I struck for the first valley, to see how the priests were working. They called the village we took along with the Chief, Bashkai, and the first village we took, Er-Heb. The priests at Er-Heb was doing all right, but they had a lot of pending cases about land to show me, and some men from another village had been firing arrows at night. I went out and looked for that village and fired four rounds at it from a thousand yards. That used all the cartridges I cared to spend, and I waited for Dravot, who had been away two or three months, and I kept my people quiet.

"One morning I heard the devil's own noise of drums and horns, and Dan Dravot marches down the hill with his Army and a tail of hundreds of men, and, which was the most amazing—a great gold crown on his head. 'My Gord, Carnehan,' says Daniel, 'this is a tremenjus business, and we've got the whole country as far as it's worth having. I am the son of Alexander by Queen Semiramis,[3] and you're my younger brother and a God too! It's the biggest thing we've ever seen. I've been marching and fighting for six weeks with the Army, and every footy[4] little village for fifty miles has come in rejoiceful; and more than that, I've got the key of the whole show, as you'll see, and I've got a crown for you! I told 'em to make two of 'em at a place called Shu, where the gold lies in the rock like suet in mutton. Gold I've seen, and turquoise I've kicked out of the cliffs, and there's garnets in the sands of the river, and here's a chunk of amber that a man brought me. Call up all the priests and, here, take your crown.'

"One of the men opens a black hair bag and I slips the crown on. It was too small and too heavy, but I wore it for the glory. Hammered gold it was—five pound weight, like a hoop of a barrel.

---

2. In Jesus' parable of the talents, a nobleman gives each of his servants a coin to invest with those instructions (Luke 19.13).

3. Legendary Assyrian queen.
4. Worthless.

" 'Peachey,' says Dravot, 'we don't want to fight no more. The Craft's[5] the trick, so help me!' and he brings forward that same Chief that I left at Bashkai—Billy Fish we called him afterward, because he was so like Billy Fish that drove the big tank-engine at Mach on the Bolan[6] in the old days. 'Shake hands with him,' says Dravot, and I shook hands and nearly dropped, for Billy Fish gave me the Grip.[7] I said nothing, but tried him with the Fellow Craft Grip. He answers, all right, and I tried the Master's Grip, but that was a slip. 'A Fellow Craft he is!' I says to Dan. 'Does he know the word?' 'He does,' says Dan, 'and all the priests know. It's a miracle! The Chiefs and the priests can work a Fellow Craft Lodge in a way that's very like ours, and they've cut the marks on the rocks, but they don't know the Third Degree, and they've come to find out. It's Gord's Truth. I've known these long years that the Afghans knew up to the Fellow Craft Degree, but this is a miracle. A God and a Grand-Master of the Craft am I, and a Lodge in the Third Degree I will open, and we'll raise the head priests and the Chiefs of the villages.'

" 'It's against all the law,' I says, 'holding a Lodge without warrant from any one; and we never held office in any Lodge.'

" 'It's a master-stroke of policy,' says Dravot. 'It means running the country as easy as a four-wheeled bogy[8] on a down grade. We can't stop to inquire now, or they'll turn against us. I've forty Chiefs at my heel, and passed and raised according to their merit they shall be. Billet these men on the villages and see that we run up a Lodge of some kind. The temple of Imbra will do for the Lodge-room. The women must make aprons as you show them. I'll hold a levee[9] of Chiefs to-night and Lodge to-morrow.'

"I was fair run off my legs, but I wasn't such a fool as not to see what a pull this Craft business gave us. I showed the priests' families how to make aprons of the degrees, but for Dravot's apron the blue border and marks was made of turquoise lumps on white hide, not cloth. We took a great square stone in the temple for the Master's chair, and little stones for the officers' chairs, and painted the black pavement with white squares, and did what we could to make things regular.

"At the levee which was held that night on the hillside with big bonfires, Dravot gives out that him and me were Gods and sons of Alexander, and Past Grand-Masters in the Craft, and was come to make Kafiristan a country where every man should eat in peace and drink in quiet, and specially obey us. Then the Chiefs come round to shake hands, and they was so hairy and white and fair it was just shaking hands with old friends. We gave them names according as they was like men we had known in India—Billy Fish, Holly Wilworth, Pikky Kergan that was Bazar-master when I was at Mhow, and so on and so on.

"*The* most amazing miracle was at Lodge next night. One of the old priests was watching us continuous, and I felt uneasy, for I knew we'd have to fudge the Ritual, and I didn't know what the men knew. The old priest was a stranger come in from beyond the village of Bashkai. The minute Dravot puts on the Master's apron that the girls had made for him, the priest fetches a whoop and a howl, and tries to overturn the stone that Dravot was sitting on. 'It's all up now,' I says. 'That comes of meddling with the Craft without warrant!'

5. Freemasonry.
6. The Bolan Pass, which was brought under British control in 1879 during the Second Afghan War.
7. Freemason handshake.
8. Railway truck.
9. Gathering.

Dravot never winked an eye, not when ten priests took and tilted over the Grand-Master's chair—which was to say the stone of Imbra. The priest begins rubbing the bottom end of it to clear away the black dirt, and presently he shows all the other priests the Master's Mark, same as was on Dravot's apron, cut into the stone. Not even the priests of the temple of Imbra knew it was there. The old chap falls flat on his face at Dravot's feet and kisses 'em. 'Luck again,' says Dravot, across the Lodge to me, 'they say it's the missing Mark that no one could understand the why of. We're more than safe now.' Then he bangs the butt of his gun for a gavel and says:—'By virtue of the authority vested in me by my own right hand and the help of Peachey, I declare myself Grand-Master of all Freemasonry in Kafiristan in this the Mother Lodge o' the country, and King of Kafiristan equally with Peachey!' At that he puts on his crown and I puts on mine—I was doing Senior Warden—and we opens the Lodge in most ample form. It was a amazing miracle! The priests moved in Lodge through the first two degrees almost without telling, as if the memory was coming back to them. After that, Peachey and Dravot raised such as was worthy—high priests and Chiefs of far-off villages. Billy Fish was the first, and I can tell you we scared the soul out of him. It was not in any way according to Ritual, but it served our turn. We didn't raise more than ten of the biggest men, because we didn't want to make the Degree common. And they was clamoring to be raised.

" 'In another six months,' says Dravot, 'we'll hold another Communication[1] and see how you are working.' Then he asks them about their villages, and learns that they was fighting one against the other and were fair sick and tired of it. And when they wasn't doing that they was fighting with the Moham-medans. 'You can fight those when they come into our country,' says Dravot. 'Tell off[2] every tenth man of your tribes for a Frontier guard, and send two hundred at a time to this valley to be drilled. Nobody is going to be shot or speared any more so long as he does well, and I know that you won't cheat me because you're white people—sons of Alexander—and not like common, black Mohammedans. You are *my* people and by God,' says he, running off into English at the end—'I'll make a damned fine Nation of you, or I'll die in the making!'

"I can't tell all we did for the next six months because Dravot did a lot I couldn't see the hang off, and he learned their lingo in a way I never could. My work was to help the people plough, and now and again go out with some of the Army and see what the other villages were doing, and make 'em throw rope-bridges across the ravines which cut up the country horrid. Dravot was very kind to me, but when he walked up and down in the pine wood pulling that bloody red beard of his with both fists I knew he was thinking plans I could not advise him about, and I just waited for orders.

"But Dravot never showed me disrespect before the people. They were afraid of me and the Army, but they loved Dan. He was the best of friends with the priests and the Chiefs; but any one could come across the hills with a com-plaint and Dravot would hear him out fair, and call four priests together and say what was to be done. He used to call in Billy Fish from Bashkai, and Pikky Kergan from Shu, and an old Chief we called Kafuzelum—it was like enough to his real name—and hold councils with 'em when there was any fighting to

1. In Freemasonry an official Lodge meeting, in which all members have a part.   2. Count off.

be done in small villages. That was his Council of War, and the four priests of Bashkai, Shu, Khawak, and Madora was his Privy Council. Between the lot of 'em they sent me, with forty men and twenty rifles, and sixty men carrying turquoises, into the Ghorband country to buy those hand-made Martini rifles, that come out of the Amir's workshops at Kabul, from one of the Amir's Herati regiments that would have sold the very teeth out of their mouths for turquoises.

"I stayed in Ghorband a month, and gave the Governor there the pick of my baskets for hush-money, and bribed the Colonel of the regiment some more, and, between the two and the tribes-people, we got more than a hundred hand-made Martinis, a hundred good Kohat Jezails[3] that'll throw to six hundred yards, and forty man-loads of very bad ammunition for the rifles. I came back with what I had, and distributed 'em among the men that the Chiefs sent to me to drill. Dravot was too busy to attend to those things, but the old Army that we first made helped me, and we turned out five hundred men that could drill, and two hundred that knew how to hold arms pretty straight. Even those cork-screwed, hand-made guns was a miracle to them. Dravot talked big about powder-shops and factories, walking up and down in the pine wood when the winter was coming on.

" 'I won't make a Nation,' says he. 'I'll make an Empire! These men aren't niggers; they're English! Look at their eyes—look at their mouths. Look at the way they stand up. They sit, on chairs in their own houses. They're the Lost Tribes,[4] or something like it, and they've grown to be English. I'll take a census in the spring if the priests don't get frightened. There must be a fair two million of 'em in these hills. The villages are full o' little children. Two million people—two hundred and fifty thousand fighting men—and all English! They only want the rifles and a little drilling. Two hundred and fifty thousand men, ready to cut in on Russia's right flank when she tries for India! Peachey, man,' he says, chewing his beard in great hunks, 'we shall be Emperors—Emperors of the Earth! Rajah Brooke will be a suckling to us. I'll treat with the Viceroy[5] on equal terms. I'll ask him to send me twelve picked English—twelve that I know of—to help us govern a bit. There's Mackray, Sergeant-pensioner at Segowli—many's the good dinner he's given me, and his wife a pair of trousers. There's Donkin, the Warder of Tounghoo Jail; there's hundreds that I could lay my hand on if I was in India. The Viceroy shall do it for me. I'll send a man through in the spring for those men, and I'll write for a dispensation from the Grand-Lodge for what I've done as Grand-Master. That—and all the Sniders[6] that'll be thrown out when the native troops in India take up the Martini. They'll be worn smooth, but they'll do for fighting in these hills. Twelve English, a hundred thousand Sniders run through the Amir's country in driblets—I'd be content with twenty thousand in one year—and we'd be an Empire. When everything was shipshape, I'd hand over the crown—this crown I'm wearing now—to Queen Victoria on my knees, and she'd say: "Rise up, Sir Daniel Dravot." Oh, it's big! It's big, I tell you! But there's so much to be done in every place—Bashkai, Khawak, Shu, and everywhere else.'

" 'What is it?' I says. 'There are no more men coming in to be drilled this autumn. Look at those fat, black clouds. They're bringing the snow.'

3. Afghan muskets.
4. Of the twelve original Hebrew tribes mentioned in the Bible, ten were lost by assimilating with neighboring peoples.

5. Head of the British administration in India. Rajah Brooke: see n. 3, p. 1800. "Suckling": infant.
6. Older rifles being replaced by Martinis.

" 'It isn't that,' says Daniel, putting his hand very hard on my shoulder; 'and I don't wish to say anything that's against you, for no other living man would have followed me and made me what I am as you have done. You're a first-class Commander-in-Chief, and the people know you; but—it's a big country, and somehow you can't help me, Peachey, in the way I want to be helped.'

" 'Go to your blasted priests, then!' I said, and I was sorry when I made that remark, but it did hurt me sore to find Daniel talking so superior when I'd drilled all the men, and done all he told me.

" 'Don't let's quarrel, Peachey,' says Daniel, without cursing. 'You're a King, too, and the half of this Kingdom is yours; but can't you see, Peachey, we want cleverer men than us now—three or four of 'em, that we can scatter about for our Deputies. It's a hugeous great State, and I can't always tell the right thing to do, and I haven't time for all I want to do, and here's the winter coming on and all.' He put half his beard into his mouth, and it was as red as the gold of his crown.

" 'I'm sorry, Daniel,' says I. 'I've done all I could. I've drilled the men and shown the people how to stack their oats better; and I've brought in those tinware rifles from Ghorband—but I know what you're driving at. I take it Kings always feel oppressed that way.'

" 'There's another thing too,' says Dravot, walking up and down. 'The winter's coming and these people won't be giving much trouble and if they do we can't move about. I want a wife.'

" 'For Gord's sake leave the women alone!' I says. 'We've both got all the work we can, though I *am* a fool. Remember the Contrack, and keep clear o' women.'

" 'The Contrack only lasted till such time as we was Kings; and Kings we have been these months past,' says Dravot, weighing his crown in his hand. 'You go get a wife too, Peachey—a nice, strappin', plump girl that'll keep you warm in the winter. They're prettier than English girls, and we can take the pick of 'em. Boil 'em once or twice in hot water, and they'll come as fair as chicken and ham.'

" 'Don't tempt me!' I says. 'I will not have any dealings with a woman not till we are a dam' side more settled than we are now. I've been doing the work o' two men, and you've been doing the work o' three. Let's lie off a bit, and see if we can get some better tobacco from Afghan country and run in some good liquor; but no women.'

" 'Who's talking o' *women*?' says Dravot. 'I said *wife*—a Queen to breed a King's son for the King. A Queen out of the strongest tribe, that'll make them your blood-brothers, and that'll lie by your side and tell you all the people thinks about you and their own affairs. That's what I want.'

" 'Do you remember that Bengali woman I kept at Mogul Serai when I was a plate-layer?'[7] says I. 'A fat lot o' good she was to me. She taught me the lingo and one or two other things; but what happened? She ran away with the Station-master's servant and half my month's pay. Then she turned up at Dadur Junction in tow of a half-caste, and had the impidence to say I was her husband—all among the drivers in the running-shed!'

" 'We've done with that,' says Dravot. 'These women are whiter than you or me, and a Queen I will have for the winter months.'

" 'For the last time o' asking, Dan, do *not*,' I says. 'It'll only bring us harm.

7. Layer of railway track.

The Bible says that Kings ain't to waste their strength on women,[8] 'specially when they've got a new raw Kingdom to work over.'

" 'For the last time of answering, I will,' said Dravot, and he went away through the pine-trees looking like a big red devil. The low sun hit his crown and beard on one side and the two blazed like hot coals.

"But getting a wife was not as easy as Dan thought. He put it before the Council, and there was no answer till Billy Fish said that he'd better ask the girls. Dravot damned them all round. 'What's wrong with me?' he shouts, standing by the idol Imbra. 'Am I a dog or am I not enough of a man for your wenches? Haven't I put the shadow of my hand over this country? Who stopped the last Afghan raid?' It was me really, but Dravot was too angry to remember. 'Who brought your guns? Who repaired the bridges? Who's the Grand-Master of the sign cut in the stone?' and he thumped his hand on the block that he used to sit on in Lodge, and at Council, which opened like Lodge always. Billy Fish said nothing, and no more did the others. 'Keep your hair on, Dan,' said I; 'and ask the girls. That's how it's done at Home, and these people are quite English.'

" 'The marriage of the King is a matter of State,' says Dan, in a white-hot rage, for he could feel, I hope, that he was going against his better mind. He walked out of the Council-room, and the others sat still, looking at the ground.

" 'Billy Fish,' says I to the Chief of Bashkai, 'what's the difficulty here? A straight answer to a true friend,' 'You know,' says Billy Fish. 'How should a man tell you who know everything? How can daughters of men marry Gods or Devils? It's not proper.'

"I remembered something like that in the Bible;[9] but if, after seeing us as long as they had, they still believed we were Gods, it wasn't for me to undeceive them.

" 'A God can do anything,' says I. 'If the King is fond of a girl he'll not let her die.' 'She'll have to,' said Billy Fish. 'There are all sorts of Gods and Devils in these mountains, and now and again a girl marries one of them and isn't seen any more. Besides, you two know the Mark cut in the stone. Only the Gods know that. We thought you were men till you showed the sign of the Master.'

"I wished then that we had explained about the loss of the genuine secrets of a Master-Mason at the first go-off; but I said nothing. All that night there was a blowing of horns in a little dark temple half-way down the hill, and I heard a girl crying fit to die. One of the priests told us that she was being prepared to marry the King.

" 'I'll have no nonsense of that kind,' says Dan. 'I don't want to interfere with your customs, but I'll take my own wife.' 'The girl's a little bit afraid,' says the priest. 'She thinks she's going to die, and they are a-heartening of her up down in the temple.'

" 'Hearten her very tender, then,' says Dravot, 'or I'll hearten you with the butt of a gun so that you'll never want to be heartened again.' He licked his lips, did Dan, and stayed up walking about more than half the night, thinking of the wife that he was going to get in the morning. I wasn't any means comfortable, for I knew that dealings with a woman in foreign parts, though you

---

8. "Give not thy strength unto women, nor thy ways to that which destroyeth kings" (Proverbs 31.3).

9. "That the sons of God saw the daughters of men that they were fair; and they took them wives of all which they chose" (Genesis 6.2).

was a crowned King twenty times over, could not but be risky. I got up very early in the morning while Dravot was asleep, and I saw the priests talking together in whispers, and the Chiefs talking together too, and they looked at me out of the corners of their eyes.

" 'What is up, Fish?' I says to the Bashkai man, who was wrapped up in his furs and looking splendid to behold.

" 'I can't rightly say,' says he; 'but if you can induce the King to drop all this nonsense about marriage, you'll be doing him and me and yourself a great service.'

" 'That I do believe,' says I. 'But sure, you know, Billy, as well as me, having fought against and for us, that the King and me are nothing more than two of the finest men that God Almighty ever made. Nothing more, I do assure you.'

" 'That may be,' says Billy Fish, 'and yet I should be sorry if it was.' He sinks his head upon his great fur cloak for a minute and thinks. 'King,' says he, 'be you man or God or Devil, I'll stick by you to-day. I have twenty of my men with me, and they will follow me. We'll go to Bashkai until the storm blows over.'

"A little snow had fallen in the night, and everything was white except the greasy fat clouds that blew down and down from the north. Dravot came out with his crown on his head, swinging his arms and stamping his feet, and looking more pleased than Punch.[1]

" 'For the last time, drop it, Dan,' says I, in a whisper. 'Billy Fish here says that there will be a row.'

" 'A row among my people!' says Dravot. 'Not much. Peachey, you're a fool not to get a wife too. Where's the girl?' says he, with a voice as loud as the braying of a jackass. 'Call up all the Chiefs and priests, and let the Emperor see if his wife suits him.'

"There was no need to call any one. They were all there leaning on their guns and spears round the clearing in the centre of the pine wood. A deputation of priests went down to the little temple to bring up the girl, and the horns blew up fit to wake the dead. Billy Fish saunters round and gets as close to Daniel as he could, and behind him stood his twenty men with matchlocks. Not a man of them under six feet. I was next to Dravot, and behind me was twenty men of the regular Army. Up comes the girl, and a strapping wench she was, covered with silver and turquoises, but white as death, and looking back every minute at the priests.

" 'She'll do,' said Dan, looking her over. 'What's to be afraid of, lass? Come and kiss me.' He puts his arm round her. She shuts her eyes, gives a bit of a squeak, and down goes her face in the side of Dan's flaming red beard.

" 'The slut's bitten me!' says he, clapping his hand to his neck, and, sure enough, his hand was red with blood. Billy Fish and two of his matchlockmen catches hold of Dan by the shoulders and drags him into the Bashkai lot, while the priests howl in their lingo,—'Neither God nor Devil, but a man!' I was all taken aback, for a priest cut at me in front, and the Army behind began firing into the Bashkai men.

" 'God A-mighty!' says Dan. 'What is the meaning o' this?'

" 'Come back! Come away!' says Billy Fish. 'Ruin and Mutiny is the matter. We'll break for Bashkai if we can.'

---

1. Common expression: the character in the Punch-and-Judy puppet show has a fixed grin and is delighted with his evil deeds.

"I tried to give some sort of orders to my men—the men o' the regular Army—but it was no use, so I fired into the brown of 'em with an English Martini and drilled three beggars in a line. The valley was full of shouting, howling creatures, and every soul was shrieking, 'Not a God nor a Devil, but only a man!' The Bashkai troops stuck to Billy Fish all they were worth, but their matchlocks wasn't half as good as the Kabul breech-loaders, and four of them dropped. Dan was bellowing like a bull, for he was very wrathy; and Billy Fish had a hard job to prevent him running out at the crowd.

" 'We can't stand,' says Billy Fish. 'Make a run for it down the valley! The whole place is against us.' The matchlock-men ran, and we went down the valley in spite of Dravot's protestations. He was swearing horribly and crying out that he was a King. The priests rolled great stones on us, and the regular Army fired hard, and there wasn't more than six men, not counting Dan, Billy Fish, and Me, that came down to the bottom of the valley alive.

"Then they stopped firing and the horns in the temple blew again. 'Come away—for Gord's sake come away!' says Billy Fish. 'They'll send runners out to all the villages before ever we get to Bashkai. I can protect you there, but I can't do anything now.'

"My own notion is that Dan began to go mad in his head from that hour. He stared up and down like a stuck pig. Then he was all for walking back alone and killing the priests with his bare hands; which he could have done. 'An Emperor am I,' says Daniel, 'and next year I shall be a Knight of the Queen.'

" 'All right, Dan,' says I; 'but come along now while there's time.'

" 'It's your fault,' says he, 'for not looking after your Army better. There was mutiny in the midst and you didn't know—you damned engine-driving, plate-laying, missionary's-pass-hunting hound!' He sat upon a rock and called me every foul name he could lay tongue to. I was too heart-sick to care, though it was all his foolishness that brought the smash.

" 'I'm sorry, Dan,' says I, 'but there's no accounting for natives. This business is our Fifty-Seven.[2] Maybe we'll make something out of it yet, when we've got to Bashkai.'

" 'Let's get to Bashkai, then,' says Dan, 'and, by God, when I come back here again I'll sweep the valley so there isn't a bug in a blanket left!'

"We walked all that day, and all that night Dan was stumping up and down on the snow, chewing his beard and muttering to himself.

" 'There's no hope o' getting clear,' said Billy Fish. 'The priests will have sent runners to the villages to say that you are only men. Why didn't you stick on as Gods till things was more settled? I'm a dead man,' says Billy Fish, and he throws himself down on the snow and begins to pray to his Gods.

"Next morning we was in a cruel bad country—all up and down, no level ground at all, and no food either. The six Bashkai men looked at Billy Fish hungry-wise as if they wanted to ask something, but they said never a word. At noon we came to the top of a flat mountain all covered with snow, and when we climbed up into it, behold, there was an Army in position waiting in the middle!

" 'The runners have been very quick,' says Billy Fish, with a little bit of a laugh. 'They are waiting for us.'

"Three or four men began to fire from the enemy's side, and a chance shot

2. Mutiny of 1857, when regiments of the Bengal army rebelled against their British officers.

took Daniel in the calf of the leg. That brought him to his senses. He looks across the snow at the Army, and sees the rifles that we had brought into the country.

" 'We're done for,' says he. 'They are Englishmen, these people,—and it's my blasted nonsense that has brought you to this. Get back, Billy Fish, and take your men away; you've done what you could, and now cut for it. Carnehan,' says he, 'shake hands with me and go along with Billy. Maybe they won't kill you. I'll go and meet 'em alone. It's me that did it. Me, the King!'

" 'Go!' says I. 'Go to Hell, Dan. I'm with you here. Billy Fish, you clear out, and we two will meet those folk.'

" 'I'm a Chief,' says Billy Fish, quite quiet. 'I stay with you. My men can go.'

"The Bashkai fellows didn't wait for a second word, but ran off, and Dan and me and Billy Fish walked across to where the drums were drumming and the horns were horning. It was cold—awful cold. I've got that cold in the back of my head now. There's a lump of it there."

The punkah-coolies[3] had gone to sleep. Two kerosene lamps were blazing in the office, and the perspiration poured down my face and splashed on the blotter as I leaned forward. Carnehan was shivering, and I feared that his mind might go. I wiped my face, took a fresh grip of the piteously mangled hands, and said: "What happened after that?"

The momentary shift of my eyes had broken the clear current.

"What was you pleased to say?" whined Carnehan. "They took them without any sound. Not a little whisper all along the snow, not though the King knocked down the first man that set hand on him—not though old Peachey fired his last cartridge into the brown of 'em. Not a single solitary sound did those swines make. They just closed up tight, and I tell you their furs stunk. There was a man called Billy Fish, a good friend of us all, and they cut his throat, Sir, then and there, like a pig; and the King kicks up the bloody snow and says:—'We've had a dashed fine run for our money. What's coming next?' But Peachey, Peachey Taliaferro, I tell you, Sir, in confidence as betwixt two friends, he lost his head, Sir. No, he didn't neither. The King lost his head, so he did, all along o' one of those cunning rope-bridges. Kindly let me have the paper-cutter, Sir. It tilted this way. They marched him a mile across that snow to a rope-bridge over a ravine with a river at the bottom. You may have seen such. They prodded him behind like an ox. 'Damn your eyes!' says the King. 'D'you suppose I can't die like a gentleman?' He turns to Peachey—Peachey that was crying like a child. 'I've brought you to this, Peachey,' says he. 'Brought you out of your happy life to be killed in Kafiristan, where you was late Commander-in-Chief of the Emperor's forces. Say you forgive me, Peachey.' 'I do,' says Peachey. 'Fully and freely do I forgive you, Dan.' 'Shake hands, Peachey,' says he. 'I'm going now. Out he goes, looking neither right nor left, and when he was plumb in the middle of those dizzy dancing ropes, 'Cut, you beggars,' he shouts; and they cut, and old Dan fell, turning round and round and round twenty thousand miles, for he took half an hour to fall till he struck the water, and I could see his body caught on a rock with the gold crown close beside.

"But do you know what they did to Peachey between two pine trees? They crucified him, Sir, as Peachey's hand will show. They used wooden pegs for his hands and his feet; and he didn't die. He hung there and screamed, and

---

3. Servants who operate punkahs, or fans.

they took him down next day, and said it was a miracle that he wasn't dead. They took him down—poor old Peachey that hadn't done them any harm—that hadn't done them any . . ."

He rocked to and fro and wept bitterly, wiping his eyes with the back of his scarred hands and moaning like a child for some ten minutes.

"They was cruel enough to feed him up in the temple, because they said he was more of a God than old Daniel that was a man. Then they turned him out on the snow, and told him to go home, and Peachey came home in about a year, begging along the roads quite safe; for Daniel Dravot he walked before and said:—'Come along, Peachey. It's a big thing we're doing.' The mountains they danced at night, and the mountains they tried to fall on Peachey's head, but Dan he held up his hand, and Peachey came along bent double. He never let go of Dan's hand, and he never let go of Dan's head. They gave it to him as a present in the temple, to remind him not to come again, and though the crown was pure gold, and Peachey was starving, never would Peachey sell the same. You knew Dravot, Sir! You knew Right Worshipful Brother Dravot! Look at him now!"

He fumbled in the mass of rags round his bent waist; brought out a black horsehair bag embroidered with silver thread; and shook therefrom on to my table—the dried, withered head of Daniel Dravot! The morning sun that had long been paling the lamps struck the red beard and blind, sunken eyes; struck, too, a heavy circlet of gold studded with raw turquoises, that Carnehan placed tenderly on the battered temples.

"You behold now," said Carnehan, "the Emperor in his habit as he lived[4]—the King of Kafiristan with his crown upon his head. Poor old Daniel that was a monarch once!"

I shuddered, for, in spite of defacements manifold, I recognized the head of the man of Marwar Junction. Carnehan rose to go. I attempted to stop him. He was not fit to walk abroad. "Let me take away the whiskey, and give me a little money," he gasped. "I was a King once. I'll go to the Deputy Commissioner and ask to set in the Poorhouse till I get my health. No, thank you, I can't wait till you get a carriage for me. I've urgent private affairs—in the south—at Marwar."

He shambled out of the office and departed in the direction of the Deputy Commissioner's house. That day at noon I had occasion to go down the blinding hot Mall, and I saw a crooked man crawling along the white dust of the roadside, his hat in his hand, quavering dolorously after the fashion of street-singers at Home. There was not a soul in sight, and he was out of all possible earshot of the houses. And he sang through his nose, turning his head from right to left:

> "The Son of Man goes forth to war,
>   A golden crown to gain;
>   His blood-red banner streams afar—
>   Who follows in his train?"[5]

I waited to hear no more, but put the poor wretch into my carriage and drove him off to the nearest missionary for eventual transfer to the Asylum.

---

4. Allusion to Hamlet's description of his father's ghost: "My father, in his habit as he lived" (Shakespeare, *Hamlet* 3.4.126).
5. A well-known hymn, by Reginald Heber (1783–

1826), corrected in later editions to the actual words of the first line: "The Son of God goes forth to war."

He repeated the hymn twice while he was with me, whom he did not in the least recognize, and I left him singing it to the missionary.

Two days later I inquired after his welfare of the Superintendent of the Asylum.

"He was admitted suffering from sunstroke. He died early yesterday morning," said the Superintendent. "Is it true that he was half an hour bareheaded in the sun at midday?"

"Yes," said I, "but do you happen to know if he had anything upon him by any chance when he died?"

"Not to my knowledge," said the Superintendent.

And there the matter rests.

1888

Danny Deever

"What are the bugles blowin' for?" said Files-on-Parade.[1]
"To turn you out, to turn you out," the Colour-Sergeant[2] said.
"What makes you look so white, so white?" said Files-on-Parade.
"I'm dreadin' what I've got to watch," the Colour-Sergeant said.
5   For they're hangin' Danny Deever, you can hear the Dead March play,
The regiment's in 'ollow square[3]—they're hangin' him today;
They've taken of his buttons off an' cut his stripes[4] away,
An they're hangin' Danny Deever in the mornin'.

"What makes the rear rank breathe so 'ard?" said Files-on-Parade.
10 "It's bitter cold, it's bitter cold," the Colour-Sergeant said.
"What makes that front-rank man fall down?" said Files-on-Parade.
"A touch o' sun, a touch o' sun," the Colour-Sergeant said.
They are hangin' Danny Deever, they are marchin' of 'im round,
They 'ave 'alted Danny Deever by 'is coffin on the ground;
15 An' 'e'll swing in 'arf a minute for a sneakin' shootin' hound—
O they're hangin' Danny Deever in the mornin'!

" 'Is cot was right-'and cot to mine," said Files-on-Parade.
" 'E's sleepin' out an' far tonight," the Colour-Sergeant said.
"I've drunk 'is beer a score o' times," said Files-on-Parade.
20 " 'E's drinkin bitter beer[5] alone," the Colour-Sergeant said.
They are hangin' Danny Deever, you must mark 'im to 'is place,
For 'e shot a comrade sleepin'—you must look 'im in the face;
Nine 'undred of 'is county[6] an' the Regiment's disgrace,
While they're hangin' Danny Deever in the mornin'.

25 "What's that so black agin the sun?" said Files-on-Parade.
"It's Danny fightin' 'ard for life," the Colour-Sergeant said.

1. Army private. "Files" here should be spoken as two syllables (fy-ulls).
2. High-ranking noncommissioned officer.
3. Ceremonial formation: the troops line four sides of a parade square, facing inward.
4. Chevrons denoting rank, worn by corporals and sergeants on the sleeves of their tunics.
5. Or simply "bitter," a favorite variety of beer drunk in English pubs. The word bitter thus becomes a grim pun.
6. English regiments often bear the name of a particular county from which most of its members have been recruited (e.g., the Lancashire Fusiliers).

"What's that that whimpers over'ead?" said Files-on-Parade.
"It's Danny's soul that's passin' now," the Colour-Sergeant said.
   For they're done with Danny Deever, you can 'ear the quickstep play,
30   The regiment's in column, an' they're marchin' us away;
   Ho! the young recruits are shakin', an' they'll want their beer today,
   After hangin' Danny Deever in the mornin'.

1890

The Widow at Windsor

   'Ave you 'eard o' the Widow at Windsor
     With a hairy[1] gold crown on 'er 'ead?
   She 'as ships on the foam—she 'as millions at 'ome,
     An' she pays us poor beggars in red.[2]
5   (Ow, poor beggars in red!)
   There's 'er nick[3] on the cavalry 'orses,
     There's 'er mark[4] on the medical stores—
   An' 'er troopers° you'll find with a fair wind be'ind   *troopships*
     That takes us to various wars.
10   (Poor beggars!—barbarious wars!)
       Then 'ere's to the Widow at Windsor,
        An' 'ere's to the stores an' the guns,
       The men an' the 'orses what makes up the forces
        O' Missis Victorier's sons.
15   (Poor beggars! Victorier's sons!)

   Walk wide o' the Widow at Windsor,
     For 'alf o' Creation she owns:
   We 'ave bought 'er the same with the sword an' the flame,
     An' we've salted it down with our bones.
20   (Poor beggars!—it's blue with our bones!)
   Hands off o' the sons o' the widow,
     Hands off o' the goods in 'er shop,
   For the kings must come down an' the emperors frown
     When the Widow at Windsor says "Stop!"
25   (Poor beggars!—we're sent to say "Stop!")
       Then 'ere's to the Lodge o' the Widow,
        From the Pole to the Tropics it runs—
       To the Lodge that we tile with the rank an' the file,
        An' open in form with the guns.[5]
30   (Poor beggars!—it's always they guns!)

1. Airy, lofty. London Cockney speech traditionally drops the *h*s from words that start with this letter, and sometimes adds an *h* to the beginning of words that start with a vowel.
2. British military uniforms were bright red.
3. A nick on one of their hoofs identified army horses as property of the Crown.
4. The queen's mark: "V.R.I." (*Victoria Regina et Imperatrix*, "Victoria Queen and Empress").

5. Here, as in "The Man Who Would Be King," Kipling employs terms and concepts from Freemasonry (see n. 2, p. 1794). Victoria's "Lodge" (her Masonic branch, or district) traverses the globe ("From the Pole to the Tropics"); the soldiers patrol its perimeters (to "tile" is to guard the door of a Masonic lodge), and gunfire stands in for the Masons' formal opening ceremonies.

We 'ave 'eard o' the Widow at Windsor,
    It's safest to leave 'er alone:
For 'er sentries we stand by the sea an' the land
    Wherever the bugles are blown.[6]
35   (Poor beggars!—an' don't we get blown!)
Take 'old o' the Wings o' the Mornin',[7]
    An' flop round the earth till you're dead;
But you won't get away from the tune that they play
    To the bloomin' old rag° over'ead.   *i.e., the flag*
40   (Poor beggars!—it's 'ot over'ead!)
Then 'ere's to the sons o' the Widow,
    Wherever, 'owever they roam.
'Ere's all they desire, an' if they require
    A speedy return to their 'ome.
45   (Poor beggars!—they'll never see 'ome!)

                                                    1892

Recessional[1]

1897

God of our fathers, known of old—
    Lord of our far-flung battle-line—
Beneath whose awful Hand we hold
    Dominion over palm and pine—
5 Lord God of Hosts, be with us yet
Lest we forget—lest we forget!

The tumult and the shouting dies—
    The Captains and the Kings depart—
Still stands Thine ancient Sacrifice,
10   An humble and a contrite heart.[2]
Lord God of Hosts, be with us yet,
Lest we forget—lest we forget!

Far-called, our navies melt away—
    On dune and headland sinks the fire[3]—
15 Lo, all our pomp of yesterday
Is one with Nineveh and Tyre![4]
Judge of the Nations, spare us yet,
Lest we forget—lest we forget!

6. Allusion to W. E. Henley's poem "Pro Rege Nostro" (1892; see p. 1642).
7. Psalm 139.9.
1. A hymn sung as the clergy and choir leave a church in procession at the end of a service. Kipling's hymn was written on the occasion of the Jubilee celebrations honoring the sixtieth anniversary of Queen Victoria's reign, celebrations that had prompted a good deal of boasting in the press about the greatness of her empire. "Recessional" was first published in the London *Times,* and Kipling refused to accept any payment for its publication, then or later. After World War I the poem's

refrain—"Lest we forget"—gained additional poignancy: it was employed as an epitaph on countless war memorials.
2. Cf. Psalm 51.17: "The sacrifices of God are a broken spirit: a broken and a contrite heart, O God, thou wilt not despise."
3. Bonfires were lit on high ground all over Britain on the night of the Jubilee.
4. Once capitals of great empires. The ruins of Nineveh, in Assyria, were discovered buried in desert sands by British archaeologists in the 1850s. Tyre, in Phoenicia, had dwindled into a small Lebanese town.

If, drunk with sight of power, we loose
20   Wild tongues that have not Thee in awe—
Such boasting as the Gentiles use
    Or lesser breeds without the Law[5]—
Lord God of Hosts, be with us yet,
Lest we forget—lest we forget!

25   For heathen heart that puts her trust
    In reeking tube° and iron shard—[6]   cannon, rifle
All valiant dust that builds on dust,
    And guarding calls not Thee to guard—
For frantic boast and foolish word,
30   Thy mercy on Thy People, Lord!

1897   1897, 1899

The White Man's Burden[1]

Take up the White Man's burden—
    Send forth the best ye breed—
Go bind your sons to exile
    To serve your captives' need;
5   To wait in heavy harness,
    On fluttered folk and wild—
Your new-caught, sullen peoples,
    Half-devil and half-child.

Take up the White Man's burden—
10   In patience to abide,
To veil the threat of terror
    And check the show of pride;
By open speech and simple,
    An hundred times made plain,
15   To seek another's profit,
    And work another's gain.

Take up the White Man's burden—
    The savage wars of peace—
Fill full the mouth of Famine
20   And bid the sickness cease;
And when your goal is nearest
    The end for others sought,
Watch Sloth and heathen Folly
    Bring all your hope to nought.

5. Cf. Romans 2.14: "For when the Gentiles, which have not the law, do by nature the things contained in the law, these, having not the law, are a law unto themselves."
6. Cf. Psalms 20.7: "Some trust in chariots, and some in horses, but we will remember the name of the Lord our God."
1. This poem was conceived for Queen Victoria's Jubilee in 1897, but Kipling abandoned it in favor of "Recessional." He returned to the poem when disagreements between Spain and the United States over Spanish colonial rule in Cuba and elsewhere sparked the Spanish-American War in 1898. In its revised form the poem reacts to resistance in the Philippines to the United States' assumption of colonial power.

25 Take up the White Man's burden—
    No tawdry rule of kings,
But toil of serf and sweeper[2]—
    The tale of common things.
The ports ye shall not enter,
30   The roads ye shall not tread,
Go make them with your living,
    And mark them with your dead.

Take up the White Man's burden—
    And reap his old reward:
35 The blame of those ye better,
    The hate of those ye guard—
The cry of hosts ye humour
    (Ah, slowly!) toward the light:—
'Why brought ye us from bondage,
40   Our loved Egyptian night?'[3]

Take up the White Man's burden—
    Ye dare not stoop to less—
Nor call too loud on Freedom
    To cloak your weariness;
45 By all ye cry or whisper,
    By all ye leave or do,
The silent, sullen peoples
    Shall weigh your Gods and you.

Take up the White Man's burden—
50   Have done with childish days—
The lightly proffered laurel,[4]
    The easy, ungrudged praise.
Comes now, to search your manhood
    Through all the thankless years,
55 Cold, edged with dear-bought wisdom,
    The judgment of your peers!

1899

If—

If you can keep your head when all about you
    Are losing theirs and blaming it on you;
If you can trust yourself when all men doubt you,
    But make allowance for their doubting too;
5 If you can wait and not be tired by waiting,
    Or being lied about, don't deal in lies,

2. Street sweeper, who in India would belong to the lowest caste.
3. Cf. Exodus 16.2–3. When the Israelites were suffering from hunger in the wilderness, they criticized Moses and Aaron for taking them from what they saw as the relative comfort of Egyptian slavery.
4. A symbol of military distinction in the triumphs celebrated by victorious Roman generals (later, Roman emperors wore a laurel crown as part of their official regalia).

Or being hated don't give way to hating,
And yet don't look too good, nor talk too wise:

If you can dream—and not make dreams your master;
10   If you can think—and not make thoughts your aim,
If you can meet with Triumph and Disaster
And treat those two impostors just the same;
If you can bear to hear the truth you've spoken
Twisted by knaves to make a trap for fools,
15   Or watch the things you gave your life to, broken,
And stoop and build 'em up with worn-out tools:

If you can make one heap of all your winnings
And risk it on one turn of pitch-and-toss,[1]
And lose, and start again at your beginnings
20   And never breathe a word about your loss;
If you can force your heart and nerve and sinew
To serve your turn long after they are gone,
And so hold on when there is nothing in you
Except the Will which says to them: 'Hold on!'

25   If you can talk with crowds and keep your virtue,
Or walk with Kings—nor° lose the common touch,   *and not*
If neither foes nor loving friends can hurt you,
If all men count with you, but none too much;
If you can fill the unforgiving minute
30   With sixty seconds' worth of distance run,
Yours is the Earth and everything that's in it,
And—which is more—you'll be a Man, my son!

1910

1. A game, played with coins, that combines skill (tossing a coin as close as possible to a fixed mark) and luck (flipping coins and keeping those that come up heads).

ERNEST DOWSON
1867–1900

Ernest Christopher Dowson spent much of his childhood traveling with his father on the Continent, mostly in France. His education was thus irregular and informal, but he acquired a thorough knowledge of French and of his favorite French writers—Gustave Flaubert, Honoré de Balzac, and Paul Verlaine—and a good knowledge of Latin poetry, especially Catullus, Propertius, and Horace. Dowson went to Oxford in 1886, but he did not take to regular academic instruction and left after a year. Though nominally assisting his father to manage a dock in the London district of Limehouse, Dowson spent most of his time writing poetry, stories, and essays and talking with Lionel Johnson, W. B. Yeats, and other members of the Rhymers' Club, in which he played a prominent part. Between 1890 and 1894 Dowson, though leading the irregular life of so many of the nineties poets, produced his best work, and his volume *Verses* came out in 1896. Late nights and excessive drinking impaired a constitution already threatened by tuberculosis. He moved to France in 1894, making a living by translating from the French for an English publisher though his health was steadily worsening. After his return to England, he was discovered near death by a friend, who took the poet to his home and nursed Dowson until he died six weeks later.

Dowson was a member of what Yeats called "the tragic generation" of poets in the nineties who seemed to be driven by their own restless energies to dissipation and premature death. As a poet he was considerably influenced by Algernon Charles Swinburne (whose feverish emotional tone he often captures very skillfully). Dowson experimented with a variety of meters, and in "Cynara" (1891) he used the twelve-syllable alexandrine as the normal line of a six-line stanza in a manner more common in French than in English poetry. He was also especially interested in the work of the French symbolist poets and in their theories of verbal suggestiveness and of poetry as incantation: he believed (as he once wrote in a letter) that a finer poetry could sometimes be achieved by "mere sound and music, with just a suggestion of sense."

Cynara

Non sum qualis eram bonae sub regno Cynarae[1]

Last night, ah, yesternight, betwixt her lips and mine
There fell thy shadow, Cynara! thy breath was shed
Upon my soul between the kisses and the wine;
And I was desolate and sick of an old passion,
5 Yea, I was desolate and bowed my head:
I have been faithful to thee, Cynara! in my fashion.

All night upon mine heart I felt her warm heart beat,
Night-long within mine arms in love and sleep she lay;
Surely the kisses of her bought red mouth were sweet;
10 But I was desolate and sick of an old passion,
  When I awoke and found the dawn was grey:
I have been faithful to thee, Cynara! in my fashion.

I have forgot much, Cynara! gone with the wind,
Flung roses, roses riotously with the throng,
15 Dancing, to put thy pale, lost lilies out of mind;
But I was desolate and sick of an old passion,
  Yea, all the time, because the dance was long:
I have been faithful to thee, Cynara! in my fashion.

I cried for madder music and for stronger wine,
20 But when the feast is finished and the lamps expire,
Then falls thy shadow, Cynara! the night is thine;
And I am desolate and sick of an old passion,
  Yea, hungry for the lips of my desire:
I have been faithful to thee, Cynara! in my fashion.

1891, 1896

1. I am not as I was under the reign of the good Cynara (Latin; Horace, *Odes* 4.1.3–4). In this poem the poet pleads with Venus to stop tormenting him with love, since he is growing old and is no longer what he was when under the sway of Cynara *(Sin-ah-rah),* the girl he used to love. Of Dowson's "Cynara" W. B. Yeats later wrote: "Dow- son, who seemed to drink so little and had so much dignity and reserve, was breaking his heart for the daughter of the keeper of an Italian eating house, in dissipation and drink." Dowson's "Cynara" was, in fact, a Polish girl by the name of Adelaide Fol- tinowicz; he fell in love with her when she was eleven and he was twenty-two years of age.

They Are Not Long

Vitae summa brevis spem nos vetat incohare longam.[1]

They are not long, the weeping and the laughter,
    Love and desire and hate:
I think they have no portion in us after
    We pass the gate.

5   They are not long, the days of wine and roses:
    Out of a misty dream
Our path emerges for a while, then closes
    Within a dream.

1896

---

1. The shortness of life prevents us from entertaining far-off hopes (Latin; Horace, *Odes* 1.4.15).

The Twentieth Century and After

1914–18:   World War I
1922:   James Joyce's *Ulysses*; T. S. Eliot's *The Waste Land*
1929:   Stock market crash; Great Depression begins
1939–45:   World War II
1947:   India and Pakistan become independent nations
1953:   Premiere of Samuel Beckett's *Waiting for Godot*
1957–62:   Ghana, Nigeria, Uganda, Jamaica, and Trinidad and Tobago
            become independent nations
1958:   Chinua Achebe's *Things Fall Apart*
1991:   Collapse of the Soviet Union
2001:   Attacks destroy World Trade Center

HISTORICAL BACKGROUND

The roots of modern literature are in the late nineteenth century. The aesthetic movement, with its insistence on "art for art's sake," assaulted middle-class assumptions about the nature and function of art. Rejecting Victorian notions of the artist's moral and educational duties, aestheticism helped widen the breach between writers and the general public, resulting in the "alienation" of the modern artist from society. This alienation is evident in the lives and work of the French symbolists and other late-nineteenth-century bohemians who repudiated conventional notions of respectability, and it underlies key works of modern literature, such as James Joyce's *Portrait of the Artist as a Young Man* and T. S. Eliot's *Waste Land*.

The growth of public education in England as a result of the Education Act of 1870, which finally made elementary schooling compulsory and universal, led to the rapid emergence of a mass literate population, at whom a new mass-produced popular literature and new cheap journalism (the "yellow press") were directed. The audience for literature split up into "highbrows," "middle-brows," and "lowbrows," and the segmentation of the reading public, developing with unprecedented speed and to an unprecedented degree, helped widen the gap between popular art and art esteemed only by the sophisticated and the expert. This breach yawned ever wider with the twentieth-century emergence of modernist iconoclasm and avant-garde experiment in literature, music, and the visual arts.

Queen Victoria's contemporaries felt her Jubilee in 1887 and, even more, her Diamond Jubilee in 1897 marked the end of an era. The reaction against middle-class Victorian attitudes that is central to modernism was already under way in the two decades before the queen's death in 1901. Samuel Butler savagely attacked the Victorian conceptions of the family, education, and religion in his novel *The Way of All Flesh* (completed in 1884, posthumously published in 1903), the bitterest indictment in English literature of the Victorian way of life. And the high tide of anti-Victorianism was marked by the publication in 1918 of a classic of ironic debunking, Lytton Strachey's collection of biographical essays *Eminent Victorians*.

A pivotal figure between Victorianism and modernism, Thomas Hardy marked the end of the Victorian period and the dawn of the new age in "The Darkling Thrush," a poem originally titled "By the Century's Deathbed" and postdated December 31, 1900, the last day of the nineteenth century. The poem marks the demise of a century of relative conviction and optimism, and it intimates the beginnings of a new era in its skeptical irresolution, its bleak sense of the modern world as "hard and dry"—favorite adjectives of later writers such as Ezra Pound and T. E. Hulme:

> The land's sharp features seemed to be
> The Century's corpse outleant,
> His crypt the cloudy canopy,
> The wind his death-lament.
> The ancient pulse of germ and birth
> Was shrunken hard and dry,
> And every spirit upon earth
> Seemed fervourless as I.

This poem and other works by Hardy, A. E. Housman, and Joseph Conrad exemplify the pessimism of imaginative writing in the last decade of the nineteenth century and the first decade of the twentieth. Stoicism—a stiff-upper-lip determination to endure whatever fate may bring—also characterizes the literature written in the transitional period between the Victorian era and modernism, including the work of minor authors such as Robert Louis Stevenson and Rudyard Kipling.

By the dawn of the twentieth century, traditional stabilities of society, religion, and culture seemed to have weakened, the pace of change to be accelerating. The unsettling force of modernity profoundly challenged traditional ways of structuring and making sense of human experience. Because of the rapid pace of social and technological change, because of the mass dislocation of populations by war, empire, and economic migration, because of the mixing in close quarters of cultures and classes in rapidly expanding cities, modernity disrupted the old order, upended ethical and social codes, cast into doubt previously stable assumptions about self, community, the world, and the divine.

Early-twentieth-century writers were keenly aware that powerful concepts and vocabularies were emerging in anthropology, psychology, philosophy, and the visual arts that reimagined human identity in radically new ways. Sigmund Freud's seminal *Interpretation of Dreams* was published in 1900, and soon psychoanalysis was changing how people saw and described rationality, the self, and personal development. In his prose and poetry D. H. Lawrence adapted the Oedipus complex to interpret and present his relationships with his parents, though rejecting Freud's negative definition of the unconscious. By the time of his death in 1939, Freud had become, as W. H. Auden wrote in an elegy for him, "a whole climate of opinion / / under whom we conduct our different lives." Also in the early twentieth century, Sir James Frazer's

Golden Bough (1890–1915) and other works of anthropology were altering basic conceptions of culture, religion, and myth. Eliot observed that Frazer's work "influenced our generation profoundly," and the critic Lionel Trilling suggested that "perhaps no book has had so decisive an effect upon modern literature as Frazer's." For both anthropologists and modern writers, Western religion was now decentered by being placed in a comparative context as one of numerous related mythologies, with Jesus Christ linked to "primitive" fertility gods thought to die and revive in concert with the seasons. Furthering this challenge to religious doctrine were the writings of Friedrich Nietzsche, the nineteenth-century German philosopher who declared the death of God, repudiated Christianity, and offered instead a harshly tragic conception of life: people look "deeply into the true nature of things" and realize "that no action of theirs can work any change," but they nevertheless laugh and stoically affirm their fate. W. B. Yeats, who remarks in a 1902 letter that his eyes are exhausted from reading "that strong enchanter," greets death and destruction in a Nietzschean spirit of tragic exultation.

These profound changes in modern intellectual history coincided with changes of a more mundane sort, for everyday life was also undergoing rapid transformation during the first years of the twentieth century. Electricity was spreading, cinema and radio were proliferating, and new pharmaceuticals such as aspirin were being developed. As labor was increasingly managed and rationalized, as more and more people crowded into cities, as communications and transportation globalized space and accelerated time, literature could not stand still, and modern writers sought to create new forms that could register these profound alterations in human experience. This was a period of scientific revolution, as exemplified in German physics by Max Planck's quantum theory (1900) and Albert Einstein's theory of relativity (1905), and T. S. Eliot reflects the increasing dominance of science when he argues that the poet surrenders to tradition and thus extinguishes rather than expresses personality: "It is in this depersonalization that art may be said to approach the condition of science," he claims, adding that "the mind of the poet is the shred of platinum" that catalyzes change but itself remains "inert, neutral, and unchanged" ("Tradition and the Individual Talent").

The early twentieth century also brought countless advances in technology: the first wireless communication across the Atlantic occurred in 1901, the Wright Brothers flew the first airplane in 1903, and Henry Ford introduced the first mass-produced car, the Model T or "Tin Lizzie," in 1913. Not that modern writers univocally embraced such changes. Although some were more sanguine, many modern writers were paradoxically repulsed by aspects of modernization. Mass-produced appliances and products, such as the "gramophone" and canned goods ("tins"), are objects of revulsion in Eliot's *Waste Land*, for example. Because scientific materialism and positivism, according to which empirical explanations could be found for everything, were weakening the influence of organized religion, many writers looked to literature as an alternative. His "simple-minded" Protestantism spoiled by science, Yeats says in his autobiography, he "made a new religion, almost an infallible church of poetic tradition." Whether or not they welcomed the demise of tradition, habit, and certitude in favor of the new, modern writers articulated the effects of modernity's relentless change, loss, and destabilization. "Things fall apart," Yeats wrote, "the centre cannot hold." Eliot describes in *Four Quartets* his quest for the "still point of the turning world." The modernist drive to "make it new"—in

Ezra Pound's famous slogan—thus arises in part out of an often ambivalent consciousness of the relentless mutations brought by modernization.

The position of women, too, was rapidly changing during this period. The Married Woman's Property Act of 1882 allowed married women to own property in their own right, and women were admitted to universities at different times during the latter part of the century. Since the days of Mary Wollstonecraft, women in Great Britain had been arguing and lobbying for the right to vote, but in the first decades of the twentieth century, Emmeline Pankhurst and her daughter Christabel encouraged suffragettes, as they were known, to take a more militant approach, which included boycotts, bombings, and hunger strikes. The long fight for women's suffrage was finally won in 1918 for women thirty and over, and in 1928 for women twenty-one and over. These shifts in attitudes toward women, in the roles women played in the national life, and in the relations between the sexes are reflected in a variety of ways in the literature of the period.

Britain's modern political history begins with the Anglo-Boer War (1899–1902), fought by the British to establish political and economic control over the Boer republics (self-governing states) of South Africa. It was an imperial war against which many British intellectuals protested and one that the British in the end were slightly ashamed of having won. The war spanned the reign of Queen Victoria, who died in 1901, and Edward VII, who held the throne from 1901 to 1910. This latter decade is known as the Edwardian period, and the king stamped his extrovert and self-indulgent character upon it. The wealthy made it a vulgar age of conspicuous enjoyment, but most writers and artists kept well away from involvement in high society: in general this period had no equivalent to Queen Victoria's friendship with Tennyson. The alienation of artists and intellectuals from political rulers and middle-class society was proceeding apace. From 1910 (when George V came to the throne) until World War I broke out in August 1914, Britain achieved a temporary equilibrium between Victorian earnestness and Edwardian flashiness; in retrospect the Georgian period seems peculiarly golden, the last phase of assurance and stability before the old order throughout Europe broke up in violence. Yet even then, under the surface, there was restlessness and experimentation. The age of Rupert Brooke's idyllic sonnets on the English countryside was also the age of T. S. Eliot's first experiments in a radically new kind of poetry, James Joyce's and Virginia Woolf's in radically new forms of fiction.

Edwardian as a term applied to English cultural history suggests a period in which the social and economic stabilities of the Victorian age—country houses with numerous servants, a flourishing and confident middle class, a strict hierarchy of social classes—remained unimpaired, though on the level of ideas a sense of change and liberation existed. *Georgian* refers largely to the lull before the storm of World War I. That war, as the bitterly skeptical and antiheroic work of Wilfred Owen, Siegfried Sassoon, Isaac Rosenberg, and other war poets makes clear, produced major shifts in attitude toward Western myths of progress and civilization. The postwar disillusion of the 1920s resulted, in part, from the sense of utter social and political collapse during a war in which unprecedented millions were killed.

By the beginning of World War I, nearly a quarter of the earth's surface and more than a quarter of the world's population were under British dominion, including the vast African territories acquired in the preceding hundred years. Some of the colonies in the empire were settler nations with large European populations, such as Canada, Australia, and New Zealand, and in 1907 the empire granted them the new status of dominions, recognizing their relative control over internal affairs. Over time these largely independent nations came to be known as the British Commonwealth, an association of self-governing countries. The twentieth century witnessed the emergence of internationally acclaimed literary voices from these dominions, from the early-century New Zealander Katherine Mansfield to the late-century Australian Les Murray and Canadians Alice Munro and Anne Carson. The rest of the colonies in the British Empire consisted primarily of indigenous populations that had little or no political power, but nationalist movements were gaining strength in the early years of the century—as when, in 1906, the Congress movement in India first demanded *swaraj* ("self-rule") soon to become the mantra of Indian nationalism. In Britain imperialist and anti-imperialist sentiments often met head on in Parliament and the press, the debate involving writers as far apart as Rudyard Kipling and E. M. Forster.

A steadily rising Irish nationalism resulted in increasingly violent protests against the cultural, economic, and political subordination of Ireland to the British Crown and government. During the Easter Rising of 1916, Irish rebels in Dublin staged a revolt against British rule, and by executing fifteen Irish leaders, the British inadvertently intensified the drive for independence, finally achieved in 1921–22 when the southern counties were declared the Irish Free State. (The six counties of Northern Ireland remained, however, part of Great Britain.) No one can fully understand Yeats or Joyce without some awareness of the Irish struggle for independence, and the way in which the Irish literary revival of the late nineteenth and early twentieth centuries (with Yeats at the forefront) reflected a determination to achieve a vigorous national life cultur-ally even if the road seemed blocked politically.

Depression and unemployment in the early 1930s, followed by the rise of Hitler and the shadow of Fascism and Nazism over Europe, with its threat of another war, deeply affected the emerging poets and novelists of the time. While Eliot, Lawrence, Wyndham Lewis, Yeats, Pound, and others of the older generation turned to the political right, the impotence of capitalist govern-ments in the face of Fascism combined with economic dislocation to turn the majority of young intellectuals (and not only intellectuals) in the 1930s to the political left. The 1930s were the so-called red decade, because only the left seemed to offer any solution in various forms of socialism, communism, and left liberalism. The early poetry of W. H. Auden and his contemporaries cried out for "the death of the old gang" (in Auden's phrase) and a clean sweep politically and economically, while the right-wing army's rebellion against the left-wing republican government in Spain, which started in the summer of 1936 and soon led to full-scale civil war, was regarded as a rehearsal for an inevitable second world war and thus further emphasized the inadequacy of politicians. Yet though the younger writers of the period expressed the up-to-date, radical political views of the left, they were less technically inventive than the first-generation modernists, such as Eliot, Joyce, and Woolf. The outbreak of World War II in September 1939—following shortly on Hitler's pact with the Soviet Union, which so shocked and disillusioned many of the young left-wing writers that they subsequently moved politically to the cen-ter—marked the sudden end of the red decade. What was from the beginning expected to be a long and costly war brought inevitable exhaustion. The dim-inution of British political power, its secondary status in relation to the United

States as a player in the Cold War, brought about a painful reappraisal of Britain's place in the world, even as countries that had lost the war—West Germany and Japan—were, in economic terms, winning the peace that followed.

In winning a war, Great Britain lost an empire. The largest, most powerful, best organized of the modern European empires, it had expropriated enormous quantities of land, raw materials, and labor from its widely scattered overseas territories. India, long the jewel in the imperial Crown, won its independence in 1947, along with the newly formed Muslim state of Pakistan. The postwar wave of decolonization that began in South Asia spread to Africa and the Caribbean: in 1957 Ghana was the first nation in sub-Saharan Africa to become independent, unleashing an unstoppable wave of liberation from British rule that freed Nigeria in 1960, Sierra Leone in 1961, Uganda in 1962, Kenya in 1963; in the Caribbean, Jamaica and Trinidad and Tobago in 1962, Barbados and Guyana in 1966, and Saint Lucia in 1979. India and Pakistan elected to remain within a newly expanded and reconceived British Commonwealth, but other former colonies did not. The Irish Republic withdrew from the Commonwealth in 1949; the Republic of South Africa, in 1961. Postwar decolonization coincided with and encouraged the efflorescence of postcolonial writing that would bring about the most dramatic geographic shift in literature in English since its inception. Writers from Britain's former colonies published influential and innovative novels, plays, and poems, hybridizing their local traditions and varieties of English with those of the empire. The names of the Nobel Prize winners Wole Soyinka, Nadine Gordimer, Derek Walcott, V. S. Naipaul, and J. M. Coetzee were added to the annals of literature in English.

While Britain was decolonizing its empire, the former empire was colonizing Britain, as Louise Bennett wryly suggests in her poem "Colonization in Reverse." Encouraged by the postwar labor shortage in England and the scarcity of work at home, waves of Caribbean migrants journeyed to and settled in "the motherland," the first group on the *Empire Windrush* that sailed from Jamaica to Tilbury Docks in 1948. Migrants followed from India, Pakistan, Bangladesh, Africa, and other regions of the "New Commonwealth." Even as immigration laws became more restrictive in the 1960s, relatives of earlier migrants and refugees from these and other nations continued to arrive, transforming Britain into an increasingly multiracial society and infusing energy into British arts and literature. But people of Caribbean, African, and South Asian origin, who brought distinctive vernaculars and cultural traditions with them, painfully discovered that their official status as British subjects often did not translate into their being welcomed as full-fledged members of British society. The friction between color-blind and ethnically specific notions of Englishness prompted a large-scale and ongoing rethinking of national identity in Britain. Among the arrivals in England were many who journeyed there to study in the late 1940s and 1950s and eventually became prominent writers, such as Bennett, Soyinka, Kamau (then Edward) Brathwaite, and Chinua Achebe. In the 1970s and 1980s a younger generation of black and Asian British writers emerged—some born in the U.K., some in the ex-empire—including Salman Rushdie, Hanif Kureishi, John Agard, and Caryl Phillips, and in the 1990s and the first decade of the new millennium, still younger writers including Jackie Kay and Zadie Smith.

London, as the capital of the empire, had long dominated the culture as well as the politics and the economy of the British Isles. London spoke for Britain in the impeccable southern English intonations of the radio announcers of the state-owned British Broadcasting Corporation (known as the BBC), but from the end of World War II this changed. Regional dialects and multicultural accents were admitted to the airwaves. Regional radio and television stations sprang up. In the 1940s and 1950s the BBC produced a weekly program called "Caribbean Voices," which proved an important stimulus to anglophone writing in the West Indies. The Arts Council, which had subsidized the nation's drama, literature, music, painting, and plastic arts from London, delegated much of its grant-giving responsibility to regional arts councils. This gave a new confidence to writers and artists outside London—the Beatles were launched from Liverpool—and has since contributed to a notable renaissance of regional literature.

From the 1960s London ceased to be essentially the sole cultural stage of the United Kingdom, and though its Parliament remained the sole political stage until 1999, successive governments came under increasing pressure from the regions and the wider world. After decades of predominantly Labour governments, Margaret Thatcher led the Conservatives to power in the general election of 1979, becoming thereby the country's first woman to hold the office of prime minister, an office she was to hold for an unprecedented twelve years. Pursuing a vision of a "new," more productive Britain, she curbed the power of the unions and began to dismantle the "welfare state," privatizing nationalized industries and utilities in the interests of an aggressive free-market economy. Initially her policies seemed to have a bracing effect on a nation still sunk in postwar, postimperial torpor, but writers such as Ian McEwan and Caryl Churchill and filmmakers such as Derek Jarman protested that Conservative reforms widened the gap between rich and poor, black and white, north and south, and between the constituent parts of the United Kingdom.

Thatcher was deposed by her own party in 1990, and the Conservatives were routed in the election of 1997. The electorate's message was clear, and Tony Blair, the new Labour prime minister, moved to restore the rundown Health Service and system of state education. Honoring other of his campaign pledges, he offered Scotland its own parliament and Wales its own assembly, each with tax-raising powers and a substantial budget for the operation of its social services, and each holding its first elections in 1999. Though a commanding figure in British politics, Blair faced increasing skepticism over his justification for joining forces with the U.S.-led invasion and occupation of Iraq in 2003.

Meanwhile the Labour government made significant progress toward solving the bitter and bloody problems of Northern Ireland, where, since the late 1960s, the Irish Republican Army (IRA) had waged a violent campaign for a united Ireland and against British rule, met by violent suppression by the British Army and reprisals by Protestant Unionists, who sought to keep Northern Ireland a part of the United Kingdom. In the 1990s politics finally took precedence over armed struggle in the Republican movement. In 1998 the Good Friday Agreement, also known as the Belfast Agreement, led to elections to a Northern Ireland Assembly, which met for the first time in 1999, and the leaders of the main Roman Catholic and Protestant parties were jointly awarded the Nobel Peace Prize. Although hope persisted that peaceful coexistence and substantial self-governance in Ulster could continue, disagreements between the parties over IRA weapons and alleged spying led to the suspension of the Northern Ireland Assembly and Executive Committee in 2002.

POETRY

The years leading up to World War I saw the start of a poetic revolution. The imagist movement, influenced by the philosopher poet T. E. Hulme's insistence on hard, clear, precise images, arose in reaction to what it saw as Romantic fuzziness and facile emotionalism in poetry. (Like other modernists, the imagists somewhat oversimplified the nineteenth-century aesthetic against which they defined their own artistic ideal, while scanting underlying continuities.) The movement developed initially in London, where the modernist American poet Ezra Pound was living, and quickly migrated across the Atlantic, and its early members included Hulme, Pound, H. D. (Hilda Doolittle), Amy Lowell, Richard Aldington, John Gould Fletcher, and F. S. Flint. As Flint explained in an article in March 1913, partly dictated by Pound, imagists insisted on "direct treatment of the 'thing,' whether subjective or objective," on the avoidance of all words "that did not contribute to the presentation," and on a freer metrical movement than a strict adherence to the "sequence of a metronome" could allow. Inveighing in manifestos against Victorian discursiveness, the imagists wrote short, sharply etched, descriptive lyrics, but they lacked a technique for the production of longer and more complex poems.

Other new ideas about poetry helped provide this technique, many of them associated with another American in London, T. S. Eliot. Sir Herbert Grierson's 1912 edition of John Donne's poems both reflected and encouraged a new enthusiasm for seventeenth-century Metaphysical poetry. The revived interest in Metaphysical "wit" brought with it a desire on the part of pioneering poets to introduce into their work a much higher degree of intellectual complexity than had been found among the Victorians or the Georgians. The full subtlety of French symbolist poetry also now came to be appreciated; it had been admired in the 1890s, but more for its dreamy suggestiveness than for its imagistic precision and complexity. At the same time modernist writers wanted to bring poetic language and rhythms closer to those of conversation, or at least to spice the formalities of poetic utterance with echoes of the colloquial and even the slangy. Irony, which made possible several levels of discourse simultaneously, and wit, with the use of puns (banished from serious poetry for more than two hundred years), helped achieve that union of thought and passion that Eliot, in his review of Grierson's anthology of Metaphysical poetry (1921), saw as characteristic of the Metaphysicals and wished to bring back into poetry. A new critical movement and a new creative movement in poetry went hand in hand, with Eliot the high priest of both. He extended the scope of imagism by bringing the English Metaphysicals and the French symbolists (as well as the English Jacobean dramatists) to the rescue, thus adding new criteria of complexity and allusiveness to the criteria of concreteness and precision stressed by the imagists. Eliot also introduced into modern English and American poetry the kind of irony achieved by shifting suddenly from the formal to the colloquial, or by oblique allusions to objects or ideas that contrasted sharply with the surface meaning of the poem. Nor were Eliot and the imagists alone in their efforts to reinvent poetry. From 1912 D. H. Lawrence began writing poems freer in form and emotion, wanting to unshackle verse from the constraints of the "gem-like" lyric and approach even the "insurgent naked throb of the instant moment." Thus between, say, 1911 (the first year covered by Edward Marsh's anthologies of Georgian poetry) and 1922 (the year of the publication of *The Waste Land*), a major revolution occurred in English—and for that matter American—poetic theory and practice, one that determined the way in which many poets now think about their art.

This modernist revolution was by no means an isolated literary phenomenon. Writers on both sides of the English Channel were influenced by the French impressionist, postimpressionist, and cubist painters' radical reexamination of the nature of reality. The influence of Italian futurism was likewise strong on the painter and writer Wyndham Lewis, whose short-lived journal *Blast* was meant to be as shocking in its visual design as in its violent rhetoric. The poet Mina Loy shared the futurist fascination with modernity and speed, while repudiating its misogyny and jingoism, as evidenced by her "Feminist Manifesto." Pound wrote books about the French sculptor Henri Gaudier-Brzeska and the American composer George Antheil, and indeed the jagged rhythms and wrenching dissonances of modern music influenced a range of writers. Wilfred Owen wrote in 1918: "I suppose I am doing in poetry what the advanced composers are doing in music"; and Eliot, while writing *The Waste Land* three years later, was so impressed by a performance of the composer Igor Stravinsky's *Le Sacre du Printemps* (*The Rite of Spring*) that he stood up at the end and cheered.

The posthumous 1918 publication by Robert Bridges of Gerard Manley Hopkins's poetry encouraged experimentation in language and rhythms, as evidenced by the verse's influence on Eliot, Auden, and the Welshman Dylan Thomas. Hopkins combined precision of the individual image with a complex ordering of images and a new kind of metrical patterning he named "sprung rhythm," in which the stresses of a line could be more freely distributed.

Meanwhile Yeats's remarkable oeuvre, stretching across the whole modern period, reflected varying developments of the age yet maintained an unmistakably individual accent. Beginning with the ideas of the aesthetes, turning to a tougher and sparer ironic language without losing its characteristic verbal magic, working out its author's idiosyncratic notions of symbolism, developing in its full maturity into a rich symbolic and Metaphysical poetry with its own curiously haunting cadences and with imagery both shockingly realistic and movingly suggestive, Yeats's work encapsulates a history of English poetry between 1890 and 1939.

In his poem "Remembering the 'Thirties," Donald Davie declared: "A neutral tone is nowadays preferred." That tone—Auden's coolly clinical tone—dominated the poetry of the decade. The young poets of the early 1930s—Auden, Stephen Spender, C. Day Lewis, Louis MacNeice—were the first generation to grow up in the shadow of the first-generation modern poets. Hopkins's attention to sonorities, Hardy's experiments in stanzaic patterns, Yeats's ambivalent meditations on public themes, Eliot's satiric treatment of a mechanized and urbanized world, and Owen's pararhymed enactments of pity influenced Auden and the other poets in his circle. But these younger poets also had to distinguish themselves from the still-living eminences in poetry, and they did so by writing poems more low-pitched and ironic than Yeats's, for example, or more individually responsive to and active in the social world than Eliot's.

As World War II began, the neutral tone gave way to, as in Auden's work, an increasingly direct and humane voice and to the vehemence of what came to be known as the New Apocalypse. The poets of this movement, most notably Dylan Thomas, owed something of their imagistic audacity and rhetorical violence to the French surrealists, whose poetry was introduced to English readers in translations and in *A Short Survey of Surrealism* (1936) by David Gascoyne, one of the New Apocalypse poets. Many of the surrealists, such as Salvador Dalí and André Breton, were both poets and painters, and in their verbal as well as their visual art they sought to express, often by free association, the operation of the unconscious mind.

With the coming of the 1950s, however, the pendulum swung back. A new generation of poets, including Donald Davie, Thom Gunn, and Philip Larkin, reacted against what seemed to them the verbal excesses and extravagances of Dylan Thomas and Edith Sitwell, as well as the arcane myths and knotty allusiveness of Yeats, Eliot, and Pound. "The Movement," as this new group came to be called, aimed once again for a neutral tone, a purity of diction, in which to render an unpretentious fidelity to mundane experience. Larkin, its most notable exponent, rejected the intimidating gestures of an imported modernism in favor of a more civil and accessible "native" tradition that went back to Hardy, Housman, and the Georgian pastoralists of the 1910s.

Not everyone in England followed the lead of Larkin and the Movement, some rejecting the Movement's notion of a limited, rationalist, polished poetics. In the late 1950s and the 1960s Ted Hughes began to write poems in which predators and victims in the natural world suggest the violence and irrationality of modern history, including the carnage of World War I, in which his father had fought. Geoffrey Hill also saw a rationalist humanism as inadequate to the ethical and religious challenges of twentieth-century war, genocide, and atrocity, which he evoked in a strenuous language built on the traditions of high modernism and Metaphysical poetry.

Since the 1980s the spectrum of Britain's poets has become more diverse in class, ethnicity, gender, and region than ever before, bringing new voices into the English literary tradition. Born in the northern industrial city of Leeds, Tony Harrison brings the local vernacular, the oral energy and resonance of Yorkshire idiom and rhythms, into contact with traditional English and classical verse. Born in Scotland to an Irish mother in a left-wing, working-class Catholic family, Carol Ann Duffy grew up amid Irish, Scottish, and Standard varieties of English, and this youthful experience helped equip her to speak in different voices in her feminist monologues.

Post–World War II Ireland—both North and South—was among the most productive spaces for poetry in the second half of the twentieth century. Born just two and a half weeks after Yeats died, Seamus Heaney, his most celebrated successor, responds to the horrors of sectarian bloodshed in Northern Ireland with subtlety and acute ethical sensitivity in poems that draw on both Irish genres and sonorities and the English literary tradition of Wordsworth, Hopkins, and Ted Hughes. Paul Muldoon, one of Heaney's former students in Belfast, also writes about the Troubles in Northern Ireland but through eerily distorted fixed forms and multiple screens of irony, combining experimental zaniness with formal reserve. Born in the Irish Republic, Eavan Boland has made a space within the largely male tradition of Irish verse—with its standard, mythical emblems of femininity—for Irish women's historical experiences of suffering and survival.

The massive postwar change in the geographical contours of poetry written in English involved, in part, the emergence of new voices and styles from the "Old Commonwealth," or dominions, such as Canada and Australia. Self-conscious about being at the margins of the former empire, Les Murray fashions a brash, playful, overbrimming poetry that mines the British and classical traditions while remaking them in what he styles his "redneck" Australian manner. Anne Carson continues Canadian poetry's dialogue with its British literary origins, imaginatively transporting, for example, the Victorian writers Charlotte and Emily Brontë into a Canadian landscape, but she also illustrates a heightened interest in U.S. poetry and popular culture, bringing into the literary mix influences that range from ancient Greek poetry to Ezra Pound and Sylvia Plath, television and video.

From the former colonies of the British Empire in the so-called Third World came some of the most important innovations in the language and thematic reach of poetry in English. Born under British rule, students of colonial educations that repressed or denigrated native languages and traditions, these postcolonial poets grew up with an acute awareness of the riches of their own cultural inheritances, as well as a deep knowledge of the British literary canon. They expanded the range of possibilities in English-language poetry by hybridizing traditions of the British Isles with their indigenous images and speech rhythms, creoles and genres. Some of these writers, such as the Nobel laureate Derek Walcott, the most eminent West Indian poet, have drawn largely on British, American, and classical European models, though Walcott creolizes the rhythms, diction, and sensibility of English-language poetry. "I have Dutch, nigger, and English in me," declares the mulatto hero of "The Schooner *Flight*, "and either I'm nobody, or I'm a nation." Other poets have emphasized even more strongly Afro-Caribbean inheritances in speech and culture. When colonial prejudices still branded West Indian English, or Creole, a backward language, a "corruption" of English, the Afro-Jamaican poets Claude McKay and Louise Bennett claimed its wit, vibrancy, and proverbial richness for poetry. In the late 1960s the Barbadian Kamau (then Edward) Brathwaite revalued the linguistic, musical, and mythic survivals of Africa in the Caribbean—resources long repressed because of colonial attitudes. In poetry as well as fiction, Nigeria was the most prolific anglophone African nation around the time of independence, said to be the "golden age" of letters in sub-Saharan Africa. Wole Soyinka, later the first black African to win the Nobel Prize, stretched English syntax and figurative language in poems dense with Yoruba-inspired wordplay and myth. At the same time poets from India were bringing its great variety of indigenous cultures into English-language poetry. A. K. Ramanujan's sharply etched poems interfuse Anglo-modernist principles with the south Indian legacies of Tamil and Kannada poetry. All of these poets respond with emotional ambivalence and linguistic versatility to the experience of living after colonialism, between non-Western traditions and modernity, in a period of explosive change in the relation between Western and "native" cultures.

A century that began with a springtime of poetic innovation drew to its close with the full flowering of older poets such as Walcott, Hill, and Heaney, and the twenty-first century opened with welcome signs of fresh growth in English-language poetry, including new books by Paul Muldoon, Anne Carson, and Carol Ann Duffy.

FICTION

Novels—"loose baggy monsters," in Henry James's phrase—can be, can do, can include anything at all. The form defies prescriptions and limits. Yet its variety converges on persistent issues such as the construction of the self within society, the reproduction of the real world, and the temporality of human experience and of narrative. The novel's flexibility and porousness, its omnivorousness and multivoicedness have enabled writers to take advantage of modernity's global dislocation and mixture of peoples, while meeting the challenges to the imagination of mass death and world war, of the relentless and rapid mutations in modern cultures and societies, in evolving knowledge and belief.

The twentieth century's novels may be divided roughly into three main subperiods: high modernism through the 1920s, celebrating personal and textual inwardness, complexity, and difficulty; the reaction against modernism, involving a return to social realism, moralism, and assorted documentary endeavors, in the 1930s, 1940s, and 1950s; and the period after the collapse of the British Empire (especially from the time of the countercultural revolution of the 1960s), in which the fictional claims of various realisms—urban, proletarian, provincial English (e.g., northern), regional (e.g., Scottish and Irish), immigrant, postcolonial, feminist, gay—are asserted alongside, but also through, a continuing self-consciousness about language and form and meaning that is, in effect, the enduring legacy of modernism. By the end of the century, modernism had given way to the striking pluralism of postmodernism and postcolonialism. Yet the roots of the late-century panoramic mix of voices and styles lay in the early part of the century, when writers on the margins of "Englishness"—a Pole, Joseph Conrad; an Irishman, James Joyce; an American, Henry James; an Englishwoman, Virginia Woolf; and a working-class Englishman, D. H. Lawrence—were the most instrumental inventors of the modernist "English" novel.

The high modernists wrote in the wake of the shattering of confidence in the old certainties about the deity and the Christian faith, about the person, knowledge, materialism, history, the old grand narratives, which had, more or less, sustained the Western novel through the nineteenth century. They boldly ventured into this general shaking of belief in the novel's founding assumptions—that the world, things, and selves were knowable, that language was a reliably revelatory instrument, that the author's story gave history meaning and moral shape, that narratives should fall into ethically instructive beginnings, middles, and endings. Trying to be true to the new skepticisms and hesitations, the modernists also attempted to construct credible new alternatives to the old belief systems.

The once-prevailing nineteenth-century notions of ordinary reality came under serious attack. In her famous 1919 essay "Modern Fiction," Virginia Woolf explicitly assaulted the "materialism" of the realistic Edwardian heirs of Victorian naturalist confidence, Arnold Bennett, H. G. Wells, and John Galsworthy. For Woolf, as for other modernists, what was knowable, and thus representable, was not out there as some given, fixed, transcribable essence. Reality existed, rather, only as it was perceived. Hence the introduction of the impressionistic, flawed, even utterly unreliable narrator—a substitute for the classic nineteenth-century authoritative narrating voice, usually the voice of the author or some close substitute. Even a relatively reliable narrator, such as Conrad's Marlow, the main narrating voice of *Heart of Darkness*, as of *Lord Jim*, dramatized the struggle to know, penetrate, and interpret reality, with his large rhetoric of the invisible, inaudible, impossible, unintelligible, and so unsayable. The real was offered, thus, as refracted and reflected in the novel's representative consciousness. "Look within," Woolf urged the novelist. Reality and its truth had gone inward.

Woolf's subject would be "an ordinary mind on an ordinary day." The life that mattered most would now be mental life. And so the modernist novel turned resolutely inward, its concern being now with consciousness—a flow of reflections, momentary impressions, disjunctive bits of recall and half-memory, simultaneously revealing both the past and the way the past is repressed. Psychoanalysis partly enabled this concentration: to narrate the reality of persons as the life of the mind in all its complexity and inner tumult—consciousness, unconsciousness, id, libido, and so on. And the apparent truths of this inward life were, of course, utterly tricky, scattered, fragmentary, spotty, now illuminated, now twilit, now quite occluded. For Woolf, Joyce's *Ulysses* was a prime expression of this desired impressionistic agenda: "he is concerned at all costs to reveal the flickerings of that innermost flame which flashes its messages through the brain."

The characters of Joyce and Woolf are caught, then, as they are immersed in the so-called stream of consciousness; and some version of an interior flow of thought becomes the main modernist access to "character." The reader overhears the characters speaking, so to say, from within their particular consciousnesses, but not always directly. The modernists felt free also to enter their characters' minds, to speak as it were on their behalf, in the technique known as "free indirect style" (*style indirect libre* in French).

A marked feature of the new fictional selfhood was a fraught condition of existential loneliness. Conrad's Lord Jim, Joyce's Leopold Bloom and Stephen Dedalus, Lawrence's Paul Morel and Birkin, and Woolf's Mrs. Dalloway were people on their own, individuals bereft of the old props, Church, Bible, ideological consensus, and so doomed to make their own puzzled way through life's labyrinths without much confidence in belief, in the knowable solidity of the world, above all in language as a tool of knowledge about self and other. Jacob of Woolf's *Jacob's Room* remains stubbornly unknowable to his closest friends and loved ones, above all to his novelist. The walls and cupboards of Rhoda's room in *The Waves,* also by Woolf, bend disconcertingly around her bed; she tries in vain to restore her sense of the solidity of things by touching the bottom bed rail with her toes; her mind "pours" out of her; the very boundaries of her self soften, slip, dissolve. The old conclusive plots—everything resolved on the novel's last page, on the model of the detective story—gave place to irresolute open endings: the unending vista of the last paragraph in Lawrence's *Sons and Lovers;* the circularity by which the last sentence of Joyce's *Finnegans Wake* hooks back to be completed in the novel's first word, so that reading simply starts over.

Novelists built modern myths on the dry bones of the old Christian ones. In his review of *Ulysses* ("*Ulysses*, Order, and Myth," 1923), T. S. Eliot famously praised the novel for replacing the old "narrative method" by a new "mythical method": Joyce's Irish Jew, Bloom, is mythicized as a modern Ulysses, his day's odyssey often ironically reviving episodes in Homer's *Odyssey*. This manipulation of "a continuous parallel between contemporaneity and antiquity" was, Eliot thought, "a step toward making the modern world possible for art," much in keeping with the new anthropology and psychology as well as with what Yeats was doing in verse. Such private myth-making could, of course, take worrying turns. The "religion of the blood" that D. H. Lawrence celebrated led directly to the fascist sympathies of his *Aaron's Rod* and the revived Aztec blood cult of *The Plumed Serpent*.

Language and textuality, reading and writing were now central to these highly metafictional novels, which are often about writers and artists, and surrogates for artists, such as Woolf's Mrs. Ramsay with her dinners and Mrs. Dalloway with her party, producers of what Woolf called the "unpublished works of women." But this self-reflexivity was not necessarily consoling—Mrs. Flanders's vision blurs and an inkblot spreads across the postcard we find her writing in the opening page of *Jacob's Room*. Perhaps the greatest modernist example of language gone rampant, *Finnegans Wake* taxes even its most dedicated readers and verges on unreadability for others.

The skeptical modernist linguistic turn, the rejection of materialist externality and of the Victorians' realist project, left ineradicable traces on later fiction, but modernism's revolutions were not absolute or permanent. *Ulysses* and *Finnegans Wake* were influential but unrepeatable. And even within the greatest modernist fictions the worldly and the material, political and moral questions never dried up. Woolf and Joyce, for example, celebrate the perplexities of urban life in London and Dublin, and, indeed, modernist fiction is largely an art of the great city. Lawrence was preoccupied with the condition of England, industrialism, provincial life. Satire was one of modernism's recurrent notes. So it was not odd for the right-wing novelists who came through in the 1920s, such as Wyndham Lewis and Evelyn Waugh, to resort to the social subject and the satiric stance, nor for their left-leaning contemporaries—who came to be seen as even more characteristic of the red decade of the 1930s—such as Graham Greene and George Orwell, to engage with the human condition in ways that Dickens or Balzac, let alone Bennett-Wells-Galsworthy, would have recognized as not all that distant from their own spirit.

Despite the turn to documentary realism in the 1930s, the modernist emphasis on linguistic self-consciousness did not disappear. Instead the new writers politicized the modern novel's linguistic self-consciousness: they deployed the discourse of the unemployed or of the West Midlands' proletariat, for example, for political ends. The comically chaotic meeting of English and German languages in Christopher Isherwood's Berlin stories is central to the fiction's dire warning about Anglo-German politics; Newspeak in George Orwell's *Nineteen-Eighty-Four* is the culmination of the author's nearly two decades of politically motivated engagement with the ways of English speakers at home and abroad. In this politicized aftermath of the modernist experiment, novelists such as Aldous Huxley in *Brave New World* satirically engage the socio-politico-moral matter of the 1930s in part through reflections on the corruptions of language.

Where World War I was a great engine of modernism, endorsing the chaos of shattered belief, the fragility of language and of the human subject, the Spanish Civil War and then World War II confirmed the English novel in its return to registering the social scene and the historical event. World War II provoked whole series of more or less realist fictions, including Evelyn Waugh's *Sword of Honour* trilogy, as well as powerful singletons such as Graham Greene's *Ministry of Fear* and Waugh's *Brideshead Revisited*. The new fictions of the post–World War II period speak with the satirical energies of the young demobilized officer class (Kingsley Amis's *Lucky Jim* set the disgruntled tone), and of the ordinary provincial citizen finding a fictional voice yet again in the new Welfare State atmosphere of the 1950s, as in Alan Sillitoe's proletarian Nottingham novel *Saturday Night and Sunday Morning.*

Questing for new moral bases for the post-Holocaust nuclear age, William Golding published the first of many intense post-Christian moral fables with *The Lord of the Flies,* and Iris Murdoch the first of many novels of moral philosophy with *Under the Net,* both in 1954. Murdoch espoused the "sovereignty of good" and the importance of the novel's loving devotion to "the otherness of the other person." Murdoch and Golding were consciously retrospective (as were the contemporary Roman Catholic novelists Greene, Waugh, and Muriel Spark) in their investment in moral form. But even such firmly grounded determinations could not calm the anxieties of belatedness. As the century drew on, British fiction struggled with a disconcertingly pervasive sense of posteriority—postwar flatness, postimperial diminutions of power and influence, and the sense of the grand narratives now losing their force as never before.

Some younger novelists, such as Ian McEwan and Martin Amis (son of Kingsley), became obsessed with Germany (the now accusingly prosperous old foe), and with the still haunting ghosts of the *Hitlerzeit*—and not least after 1989, when the Berlin Wall came down and wartime European horrors stirred into vivid focus. The dereliction of the once-grand imperial center, London, became a main topic for McEwan and for Amis, as well as for the later Kingsley Amis and the ex-Rhodesian Doris Lessing. Whereas Conrad, E. M. Forster (*A Passage to India*), and Jean Rhys (*Wide Sargasso Sea*) had been harshly accusatory about Britain's overseas behavior, now nostalgia for old imperial days shrouded the pages of Lawrence Durrell's *Alexandria Quartet* and Paul Scott's *Raj Quartet* and *Staying On.* Observers of English fiction worried that the only tasks left for it were to ruminate over past history and rehash old stories. The modernist Joycean strategy of resurrecting ancient narratives to revitalize present consciousness had given way to a fear that the postmodern novelist was condemned to a disabled career of parroting old stuff. *On est parlé,* "one is spoken," rather than speaking for oneself, thinks the main character of Julian Barnes's *Flaubert's Parrot,* reflecting in some dismay on this dilemma. Ventriloquial reproduction of old voices became Peter Ackroyd's trademark. Worries about being merely possessed by the past came to seem central to late-twentieth-century English fiction, as in A. S. Byatt's *Possession,* which is about the magnetism of past (Victorian) writers and writings.

Yet this was also a time for the spectacular emergence of many robust new voices, particularly from assorted margins—writers for whom the enervation at the English center represented an opportunity for telling their untold stories. After a sensational trial in 1960, the ban on D. H. Lawrence's erotically explicit *Lady Chatterley's Lover* was finally lifted, ensuring greater freedom in the narrative exploration of sexuality. Relaxing views on gender roles, the influx of women into the workplace, and the collapse of the grand patriarchal narratives also gave impetus to feminist revisionary narratives of history, and the remaking of narrative technique as more fluid and free. In the 1980s and 1990s prominent and inventive women's voices included those of Jeanette Winterson, celebrator of women's arts and bodiliness, and Angela Carter, feminist neomythographer, reviser of fairy tales, rewriter of the Marquis de Sade, espouser of raucous and rebellious heroines. Among the chorus of voices seeking to express with new intimacy and vividness experiences once held taboo were those of uncloseted gay writers, such as Alan Hollinghurst, pioneer of the openly male-homosexual literary novel of the post–World War II period, and Adam Mars-Jones, short-story chronicler of the HIV/AIDS crisis. The literary counterpart for political decolonization and devolution within the British Isles was the emergence of a multitude of regional and national voices outside the south of England, many deploying a vigorously local idiom, such as the Scottish novelist Irvine Welsh and the Irish writer Roddy Doyle, who reached mass international audiences through 1990s film versions of their novels *Trainspotting* (Welsh) and *The Commitments* (Doyle).

While postimperial anxieties and exhaustion seemed to beset many postwar English writers, postcolonial novelists were energetically claiming for literature in English untold histories, hybrid identities, and vibrantly creolized vocabularies. A major phase in the huge geographic shift in the center of gravity of English-language fiction occurred during the postwar decolonization of much of South Asia, Africa, and the Caribbean, when Chinua Achebe's *Things Fall Apart* (1958) was published, just two years before Nigerian independence. Retelling the story of colonial incursion from an indigenous viewpoint, Achebe's influential novel intricately represents an African community before and after the arrival of whites, in a language made up of English and Igbo words, encompassed by a narrative that enmeshes African proverbs and oral tales with English realism and modernist reflexivity. A few years later and on the eve of his natal island's independence, the Trinidad-born writer V. S. Naipaul published his first major novel, *A House for Mr. Biswas* (1961), one of many works that brilliantly develop the potential of a translucent realist fiction to explore issues such as migrant identities, cross-cultural mimicry, and the spaces of colonialism. The Indian-born Salman Rushdie, more restive than Naipaul in relation to Englishness and English literary traditions, has exuberantly championed hybrid narrative forms made out of the fresh convergence of modern European fiction and "Third World" orality, magical realism, and polyglossia, his novels, such as *Midnight's Children* (1981) and *The Satanic Verses* (1988), wryly offering a "chutnification of history" in South Asia and in an Asianized England. The colonies where English literature had once been used to impose imperial models of "civilization" now gave rise to novelists who, ironically, outstripped in imaginative freshness, cultural energy, and narrative inventiveness their counterparts from the seat of the empire.

White fiction writers from the colonies and dominions, many of them women, and many of them resident in England, such as Katherine Mansfield, Doris Lessing, and Jean Rhys, had long brought fresh perspectives to the novel from the outposts of empire, each of these eminent writers sharply etching a feminist critique of women's lives diminished by subordination to the colonial order. South Africa, not least because of its fraught racial and political history, can count among its progeny some of the most celebrated fiction writers of the late twentieth century. Nadine Gordimer has extended the potential of an ethical narrative realism to probe the fierce moral challenges of apartheid and its aftermath, whereas J. M. Coetzee has used self-reflexively postmodern and allegorical forms to inquire into the tangled complexities and vexed complicities of white South African experience.

Late-twentieth-century and early-twenty-first-century "English" fiction would have looked startlingly thin and poverty-stricken were it not for the large presence in Britain of writers of non-European origin. Like the first modern novelists, many of the novelists who have most enriched English-language fiction in recent decades are migrants, émigrés, and expatriates, such as Naipaul and Rushdie, and such as the delicately ironic realist Kazuo Ishiguro, from Japan, and the postsurreal fabulist Wilson Harris, from Guyana. Still others are the sons and daughters of non-European immigrants to Britain, such as two of the most visible exemplars of the often comically cross-cultural fiction of a new multiracial England, Hanif Kureishi and Zadie Smith, both born on the peripheries of London, Kureishi to a Pakistani father and English mother, Smith to a Jamaican mother and English father. These and other "British" novelists of color, giving voice to new and emergent experiences of immigration, hybridization, and cross-racial encounter, take advantage of the novel's fecund polymorphousness with little anxiety about belatedness, no fright over parroting, and no neomodernist worries about attempting realistic encounters with the world.

DRAMA

Late Victorians from one perspective, Oscar Wilde and Bernard Shaw can also be seen as early moderns, forerunners of the twentieth century's renovators of dramatic form. The wit of Wilde's drawing-room comedies is combative and generative of paradoxes, but beneath the glitter of his verbal play are serious— if heavily coded—reflections on social, political, and feminist issues. Shaw brought still another kind of wit into drama—not Wilde's lighthearted sparkle but the provocative paradox that was meant to tease and disturb, to challenge the complacency of the audience. Over time the desire to unsettle, to shock, even to alienate the audience became one hallmark of modern drama.

Wilde and Shaw were both born in Ireland, and it was in Dublin that the century's first major theatrical movement originated. To nourish Irish poetic drama and foster the Irish literary renaissance, Yeats and Lady Augusta Gregory founded the Irish Literary Theatre in 1899, with Yeats's early nationalist play The Countess Cathleen as its first production. In 1902 the Irish Literary Theatre was able to maintain a permanent all-Irish company and changed its name to the Irish National Theatre, which moved in 1904 to the Abbey Theatre, by which name it has been known ever since. J. M. Synge brought the speech and imagination of Irish country people into theater, but the Abbey's 1907 staging of his play The Playboy of the Western World so offended orthodox religious and nationalist sentiment that the audience rioted. While defending Synge and other pioneers of Irish drama, Yeats also continued to write his own plays, which drew themes from old Irish legend and which, after 1913, stylized and ritualized theatrical performance on the model of Japanese Noh drama. In the 1920s Sean O'Casey brought new vitality to the Abbey Theatre, using the Easter Rising and Irish civil war as a background for controversial plays (one of which again sparked riots) that combined tragic melodrama, humor of character, and irony of circumstance. In England T. S. Eliot attempted with considerable success to revive a ritual poetic drama with his Murder in the Cathedral (1935), though his later attempts to combine religious symbolism with the chatter of entertaining society comedy, as in The Cocktail Party (1950), were uneven.

Despite the achievements of Yeats, Synge, O'Casey, and Eliot, it cannot be said of Irish and British drama, as it can of poetry and fiction in the first half of the century, that a technical revolution changed the whole course of literary

1844 / THE TWENTIETH CENTURY AND AFTER

history. The major innovations in the first half of the twentieth century were on the Continent. German expressionist drama developed out of the dark, psychological focus of the later plays of the Swedish dramatist August Strindberg (1849–1912). Another worldwide influence was the "epic" drama of the leftist German dramatist Bertolt Brecht (1898–1956): to foster ideological awareness, he rejected the idea that the audience should identify with a play's characters and become engrossed in its plot; the playwright should break the illusion of reality through the alienation effect (*Verfremdungseffekt*) and foreground the play's theatrical constructedness and historical specificity. The French dramatist Antonin Artaud (1896–1948) also defied realism and rationalism, but unlike Brecht, his theory of the theater of cruelty sought a transformative, mystical communion with the audience through incantations and sounds, physical gestures and strange scenery. Another French dramatist, the Romanian-born Eugène Ionesco (1909–1994), helped inaugurate the theater of the absurd just after World War II, in plays that enact people's hopeless efforts to communicate and that comically intimate a tragic vision of life devoid of meaning or purpose. In such Continental drama the influences of symbolism (on the later Strindberg), Marxism (on Brecht), and surrealism (on Artaud and Ionesco) contributed to the shattering of naturalistic convention in drama, making the theater a space where linear plot gave way to fractured scenes and circular action, transparent conversation was displaced by misunderstanding and verbal opacity, a predictable and knowable universe was unsettled by eruptions of the irrational and the absurd.

In Britain the impact of these Continental innovations was delayed by a conservative theater establishment until the late 1950s and 1960s, when they converged with the countercultural revolution to transform the nature of English-language theater. Meanwhile the person who played the most significant role in the anglophone absorption of modernist experiment was the Irishman Samuel Beckett. He changed the history of drama with his first produced play, written in French in 1948 and translated by the author as *Waiting for Godot* (premiered in Paris in 1953, in London in 1955). The play astonishingly did away with plot ("Nothing happens—twice," as one critic put it), as did *Endgame* (1958) and Beckett's later plays, such as *Not I* (1973) and *That Time* (1976). In the shadow of the mass death of World War II, the plotlessness, the minimal characterization and setting, the absurdist intimation of an existential darkness without redemption, the tragicomic melding of anxiety, circular wordplay, and slapstick action in Beckett's plays gave impetus to a seismic shift in British writing for the theater.

The epicenter of the new developments in British drama was the Royal Court Theatre, symbolically located a little away from London's West End "theater land" (the rough equivalent of Broadway in New York). From 1956 the Royal Court was the home of the English Stage Company. Together they provided a venue and a vision that provoked and enabled a new wave of writers. John Osborne's *Look Back in Anger* (1956), the hit of the ESC's first season (significantly helped by the play's television broadcast), offered the audience "lessons in feeling" through a searing depiction of class-based indignation, emotional cruelty, and directionless angst, all in a surprisingly nonmetropolitan setting. At the Royal Court the working-class naturalism of the so-called "kitchen sink" dramatists and other "angry young men" of the 1950s, such as Arnold Wesker, author of the trilogy *Chicken Soup with Barley* (1958), also broke with the genteel proprieties and narrowly upper-class set designs that, in one unadventurous drawing-room comedy after another, had dominated the British stage for decades. The political consciousness of the new theater was still more evident in John Arden's plays produced for the Royal Court, such as *Sergeant Musgrave's Dance* (1959), which explores colonial oppression, communal guilt for wartime atrocities, and pacifism in the stylized setting of an isolated mining town. By the later 1960s the influence of the counterculture on British theater was unavoidable. Joe Orton challenged bourgeois sentiment in a series of classically precise, blackly comic, and sexually ambiguous parodies, such as his farce *What the Butler Saw* (1969).

While plays of social and political critique were one response to the postwar period, Beckett and the theater of the absurd inspired another group of Royal Court writers to refocus theater on language, symbolism, and existential realities. Informed by kitchen-sink naturalism and absurdism, Harold Pinter's "comedies of menace" map out a social trajectory from his early study of working-class stress and inarticulate anxiety, *The Room* (1957), through the film-noirish black farce of *The Dumb Waiter* (1960) and the emotional power plays of *The Caretaker* (1960), to the savagely comic study of middle-class escape from working-class mores in *The Homecoming* (1965). Later plays reflect on patrician suspicion and betrayal, though in the 1980s his work acquired a more overtly political voice. Though less bleak than Pinter, Tom Stoppard is no less indebted to Beckett's wordplay, skewed conversations, and theatrical technique, as evidenced by *Rosencrantz and Guildenstern Are Dead* (1967) and other plays, many of which embed within themselves earlier literary works (such as *Godot* and *Hamlet*) and thus offer virtuoso postmodernist reflections on art, language, and performance. This enjoyment and exploitation of self-conscious theatricality arises partly out of the desire to show theater as different from film and television and is also apparent in the 1970s productions of another playwright: the liturgical stylization of Peter Shaffer's *Equus* (1973) and the bleak mental landscape of his Antonio Salieri in *Amadeus* (1979) emphasize the stage as battleground and site of struggle (an effect lost in their naturalistic film versions). Stoppard's time shifts and memory lapses in *Travesties* (1974) allow a nonnaturalistic study of the role of memory and imagination in the creative process, a theme he returns to in *Arcadia* (1993), a stunning double-exposure account of a Romantic poet and his modern critical commentators occupying the same physical space but never reaching intellectual common ground.

Legal reform intensified the postwar ferment in British theater. Since the Theatres Act of 1843, writers for the public stage had been required to submit their playscripts to the Lord Chamberlain's office for state censorship, but in 1968 a new Theatres Act abolished that office. With this new freedom from conservative mores and taste, Howard Brenton, Howard Barker, Edward Bond, and David Hare were able to write challenging studies of violence, social deprivation, and political and sexual aggression, often using mythical settings and epic stories to construct austere tableaux of power and oppression. Bond's *Lear* (1971) typifies his ambitious combination of soaring lyrical language and alienatingly realistic violence. Directors such as Peter Brook took advantage of the new freedom in plays that emphasized, as had Artaud's theater of cruelty, physical gesture, bodily movement, and ritualized spectacle. The post-1968 liberalization also encouraged the emergence of new theater groups addressing specific political agendas, many of them inspired by Brecht's "epic" theater's distancing, discontinuous, and socially critical style. Companies such

as Monstrous Regiment, Gay Sweatshop, Joint Stock, and John McGrath's 7:
84 worked collaboratively with dramatists who were invited to help devise and
develop shows. Increasingly in the 1970s published plays were either transcriptions of the first production or "blueprints for the alchemy of live performance" (Micheline Wandor). In Ireland the founding of the Field Day Theatre
Company in 1980 by the well-established playwright Brian Friel and actor
Stephen Rea had similar motives of collaborative cultural catalysis. Their first
production, Friel's *Translations* (1980), exploring linguistic colonialism and
the fragility of cultural identity in nineteenth-century Ireland, achieved huge
international success.

This ethos of collaboration and group development helped foster the first
major cohort of women dramatists to break through onto mainstream stages.
Working with Joint Stock and Monstrous Regiment in the late 1970s on plays
such as the gender-bending anticolonial *Cloud Nine* (1979), Caryl Churchill
developed plays out of workshops exploring gender, class, and colonialism.
She carefully transcribes and overlaps the speech of her characters to create
a seamlessly interlocking web of discourse, a streamlined version of the ebb
and flow of normal speech. In *Top Girls* (1982) and *Serious Money* (1987),
plays that anatomize the market-driven ethos of the 1980s, she explores modern society with the wit and detachment of Restoration comedy. Pam Gems
studies the social and sexual politics of misogyny and feminism in her campy
theatrical explorations of strong women—*Queen Cristina* (1977), *Piaf* (1978),
Camille (1984)—while Sarah Daniels reinterprets the naturalism of kitchen-
sink drama by adding to it the linguistic stylization of Churchill.

Massive strides in the diversification of English-language theater occurred
during the era of decolonization, when two eminent poets, Derek Walcott and
Wole Soyinka, helped breathe new life into anglophone drama. As early as the
1950s Derek Walcott was writing and directing plays about Caribbean history
and experience, re-creating in his drama a West Indian "oral culture, of chants,
jokes, folk-songs, and fables," at a time when theater in the Caribbean tended
to imitate European themes and styles. After moving to Trinidad in 1958, he
founded what came to be known as the Trinidad Theatre Workshop, and for
much of the next twenty years devoted himself to directing and writing plays
that included *Dream on Monkey Mountain*, first produced in 1967, in which
Eurocentric and Afrocentric visions of Caribbean identity collide. Since then,
a notable breakthrough in Caribbean theater has been the collaborative work
of the Sistren Theatre Collective in Jamaica, which, following the lead of
Louise Bennett and other West Indian poets, draws on women's personal histories in dramatic performances that make vivid use of Jamaican speech,
expression, and rhythm. Meanwhile in Africa, Wole Soyinka, who had been
involved with the Royal Court Theatre in the late 1950s when Brecht's influence was first being absorbed, returned to Nigeria in the year of its independence to write and direct plays that fused Euromodernist dramatic techniques
with conventions from Yoruba popular and traditional drama. His play *Death
and the King's Horseman*, premiered in Nigeria in 1976, represents a tragic
confrontation between colonial officials and the guardians of Yoruba rituals
and beliefs. While Soyinka has been a towering presence in sub-Saharan
Africa, other playwrights, such as the fellow Nigerian Femi Osofisan and the
South African Athol Fugard, have used the stage to probe issues of class, race,
and the often violent legacy of colonialism. In England playwrights of Caribbean, African, and Asian origin or descent, such as Mustapha Matura, Caryl

Phillips, and Hanif Kureishi, the latter of whom is best-known internationally for his screenplays for *My Beautiful Laundrette* (1985), *Sammy and Rosie Get Laid* (1988), *My Son the Fanatic* (1998), and *The Mother* (2004), have revitalized British drama with a host of new vocabularies, new techniques, new visions of identity in an increasingly cross-ethnic and transnational world. The century that began with its first great dramatic movement in Ireland was followed by a century that began with English-language drama more diverse in its accents and styles, more international in its bearings and vision than ever before.

Additional information about the Twentieth Century and After, including primary texts and images, is available at Norton Literature Online (www .wwnorton.literature). Online topics are

- Representing the Great War
- Modernist Experiment
- Imagining Ireland

TEXTS	CONTEXTS
1899, 1902 Joseph Conrad, *Heart of Darkness*	
	1900 Max Planck, quantum theory
	1901 First wireless communication across the Atlantic
	1901–10 Reign of Edward VII
	1902 End of the Anglo-Boer War
	1903 Henry Ford introduces the first mass-produced car. Wright Brothers make the first successful airplane flight
	1905 Albert Einstein, theory of special relativity. Impressionist exhibition, London
1910 Bernard Shaw, *Pygmalion*	**1910** Postimpressionist exhibition, London
	1910–36 Reign of George V
1913 Ezra Pound, "A Few Don'ts by an Imagiste"	
1914 James Joyce, *Dubliners.* Thomas Hardy, *Satires of Circumstance*	**1914–18** World War I
1914–15 *Blast*	
1916 Joyce, *A Portrait of the Artist as a Young Man*	**1916** Easter Rising in Dublin
1917 T. S. Eliot, "The Love Song of J. Alfred Prufrock"	
1918 Gerard Manley Hopkins, *Poems*	**1918** Armistice. Franchise Act grants vote to women thirty and over
1920 D. H. Lawrence, *Women in Love.* Wilfred Owen, *Poems*	**1920** Treaty of Versailles. League of Nations formed
1921 William Butler Yeats, *Michael Robartes and the Dancer*	**1921–22** Formation of Irish Free State with Northern Ireland (Ulster) remaining part of Great Britain
1922 Katherine Mansfield, *The Garden Party and Other Stories.* Joyce, *Ulysses.* Eliot, *The Waste Land.*	
1924 Forster, *A Passage to India*	
1927 Virginia Woolf, *To the Lighthouse*	
1928 Yeats, *The Tower*	**1928** Women twenty-one and over granted voting rights
1929 Woolf, *A Room of One's Own.* Robert Graves, *Goodbye to All That*	**1929** Stock market crash; Great Depression begins
	1933 Hitler comes to power in Germany
1935 Eliot, *Murder in the Cathedral*	

TEXTS	CONTEXTS
	1936–39 Spanish Civil War
	1936 Edward VIII succeeds George V, but abdicates in favor of his brother, crowned as George VI
1937 David Jones, *In Parenthesis*	
1939 Joyce, *Finnegans Wake*. Yeats, *Last Poems and Two Plays*	1939–45 World War II
1940 W. H. Auden, *Another Time*	1940 Fall of France. Battle of Britain
	1941–45 The Holocaust
1943 Eliot, *Four Quartets*	
1945 Auden, *Collected Poems*. George Orwell, *Animal Farm*	1945 First atomic bombs dropped, on Japan
1946 Dylan Thomas, *Deaths and Entrances*	
	1947 India and Pakistan become independent nations
	1948 *Empire Windrush* brings West Indians to U.K.
1949 Orwell, *Nineteen-Eighty-Four*	
	1950 Apartheid laws passed in South Africa
1953 Premiere of Samuel Beckett's *Waiting for Godot*	
	1956 Suez Crisis
	1957 Ghana becomes independent
1958 Chinua Achebe, *Things Fall Apart*	
	1960 Nigeria becomes independent
	1961 Berlin Wall erected
1962 Doris Lessing, *The Golden Notebook*	1962 Cuban missile crisis. Uganda, Jamaica, Trinidad and Tobago become independent
1964 Philip Larkin, *The Whitsun Weddings*	
	1965 U.S. troops land in South Vietnam
1966 Nadine Gordimer, *The Late Bourgeois World*. Tom Stoppard, *Rosencrantz and Guildenstern Are Dead*. Jean Rhys, *Wide Sargasso Sea*	1966 Barbados and Guyana become independent
	1969 Apollo moon landing
1971 V. S. Naipaul, *In a Free State*	1971 Indo-Pakistan War, leading to creation of Bangladesh
	1972 Britain enters European Common Market
	1973 U.S. troops leave Vietnam
1975 Seamus Heaney, *North*	

TEXTS	CONTEXTS
1979 Caryl Churchill, *Cloud 9*	1979 Islamic Revolution in Iran; the Shah flees. Soviets invade Afghanistan
	1979–90 Margaret Thatcher is British prime minister
1980 J. M. Coetzee, *Waiting for the Barbarians*	1980–88 Iran-Iraq War
1981 Salman Rushdie, *Midnight's Children*. Brian Friel, *Translations*	
	1982 Falklands War
1985 Production of Hanif Kureishi's *My Beautiful Laundrette*	
1988 Rushdie, *The Satanic Verses*	
1989 Kazuo Ishiguro, *The Remains of the Day*	1989 Fall of the Berlin Wall. Tiananmen Square, Beijing, demonstration and massacre
1990 Derek Walcott, *Omeros*	
	1991 Collapse of the Soviet Union
1992 Thom Gunn, *The Man with Night Sweats*	
1993 Tom Stoppard, *Arcadia*	
	1994 Democracy comes to South Africa
1997 Arundhati Roy, *The God of Small Things*	1997 Labour Party victory in the U.K. ends eighteen years of Conservative government
	1998 British handover of Hong Kong to China. Northern Ireland Assembly established
1999 Carol Ann Duffy, *The World's Wife*	
2000 Zadie Smith, *White Teeth*	
	2001 September 11 attacks destroy World Trade Center
2002 Paul Muldoon, *Moy Sand and Gravel*	2002 Euro becomes sole currency in most of European Union
	2003 Invasion of Iraq led by U.S. and U.K.

THOMAS HARDY
1840–1928

Thomas Hardy was born near Dorchester, in that area of southwest England that he was to make the "Wessex" of his novels. He attended local schools until the age of fifteen, when he was apprenticed to a Dorchester architect with whom he worked for six years. In 1861 he went to London to continue his studies and to practice as an architect. Meanwhile he was completing his general education informally through his own erratic reading and was becoming more and more interested in both fiction and poetry. After some early attempts at writing both short stories and poems, he decided to concentrate on fiction. His first novel was rejected by the publishers in 1868 on the recommendation of George Meredith, who nevertheless advised Hardy to write another. The result was *Desperate Remedies,* published anonymously in 1871, followed the next year by his first real success (also published anonymously), *Under the Greenwood Tree.* His career as a novelist was now well launched; Hardy gave up his architectural work and produced a series of novels that ended with *Jude the Obscure* in 1895. The hostile reception of this novel—lambasted as *Jude the Obscene*—sent him back to poetry. Straddling the Victorian and modern periods, he published all his novels in the nineteenth century, all but the first of his poetry collections, *Wessex and Other Verses* (1898), in the twentieth. His remarkable epic-drama of the Napoleonic Wars, *The Dynasts,* came out in three parts between 1903 and 1908; after this he wrote mostly lyric poetry.

Hardy's novels, set in a predominantly rural "Wessex," show the forces of nature outside and inside individuals combining to shape human destiny. Against a background of immemorial agricultural labor, with ancient monuments such as Stonehenge or an old Roman amphitheater reminding us of the human past, he presents characters at the mercy of their own passions or finding temporary salvation in the age-old rhythms of rural work or rural recreation. Men and women in Hardy's fiction are not masters of their fates; they are at the mercy of the indifferent forces that manipulate their behavior and their relations with others, but they can achieve dignity through endurance, heroism, or simple strength of character. The characteristic Victorian novelist—e.g., Dickens or Thackeray—was concerned with the behavior and problems of people in a given social milieu, which were described in detail; Hardy preferred to go directly for the elemental in human behavior with a minimum of contemporary social detail. Most of his novels are tragic, exploring the bitter ironies of life with an almost malevolent staging of coincidence to emphasize the disparity between human desire and ambition on the one hand and what fate has in store for the characters on the other. But fate is not a wholly external force. Men and women are driven by the demands of their own nature as much as by anything outside them. Perhaps the darkest of Hardy's novels, *Tess of the D'Urbervilles* (1891) is the story of an intelligent and sensitive young woman, daughter of a poor family, driven to murder and so to death by hanging, by a painfully ironic concatenation of events and circumstances. Published in the same year as *Tess,* the story anthologized here, "On the Western Circuit," similarly has at its center a young country woman seduced by a sophisticated city man; her "ruin" (see also Hardy's poem "The Ruined Maid") leads—contrary to the good intentions of the three protagonists, and again as the result of bitter irony—to *his* ruin and a lifetime of misery for all concerned.

Hardy denied that he was a pessimist, calling himself a "meliorist"—that is, one who believes that the world can be made better by human effort. But there is little sign of meliorism in either his most important novels or his lyric poetry. A number of his poems, such as the one he wrote about the *Titanic* disaster, "The Convergence of the Twain," illustrate the perversity of fate, the disastrous or ironic coincidence. Other poems go beyond this mood to present with quiet gravity and a carefully controlled elegiac feeling some aspect of human sorrow or loss or frustration or regret, always grounded in a particular, fully realized situation. "Hap" shows Hardy in the characteristic mood of complaining about the irony of human destiny in a universe ruled by chance, but a poem such as "The Walk" (one of a group of poems written after the death of his first wife in 1912) gives, with remarkable power, concrete embodiment to a sense of loss.

Hardy's poetry, like his prose, often has a self-taught air about it; both can seem, on first reading, roughly hewn. He said he wanted to avoid "the jewelled line," and like many modern and contemporary poets, he sought instead what he called "dissonances, and other irregularities" in his art, because these convey more authenticity and spontaneity. "Art is a disproportioning . . . of realities," he declared. Though he adheres to the metered line, Hardy roughens prosody and contorts syntax, and he creates irregular and complex stanza forms. His diction includes archaisms and deliberately awkward coinages (e.g., "Powerfuller" and "unblooms" in "Hap"). He distorts many conventions of traditional genres such as the sonnet, the love poem, the war poem, and the elegy. Though rooted in the Victorian period, Hardy thus looks ahead to the dislocations of poetic form carried out by subsequent poets of the twentieth century.

The sadness in Hardy—his inability to believe in the government of the world by a benevolent God, his sense of the waste and frustration involved in human life, his insistent irony when faced with moral or metaphysical questions—is part of the late-Victorian mood, found also, say, in A. E. Housman's poetry and, earlier, in Edward FitzGerald's *Rubáiyát of Omar Khayyám*, published when Hardy was nineteen. What has been termed "the disappearance of God" affected him more deeply than it did many of his contemporaries, because until he was twenty-five he seriously considered becoming an Anglican priest. Yet his characteristic themes and attitudes cannot be related simply to the reaction to new scientific and philosophical ideas (Darwin's theory of evolution, for example) that we see in many forms in late-nineteenth-century literature. The favorite poetic mood of both Tennyson and Arnold was also an elegiac one (e.g., in Tennyson's "Break, Break, Break" and Arnold's "Dover Beach"), but the mood of Hardy's poetry differs from Victorian sorrow; it is sterner, more skeptical, as though braced by a long look at the worst. It is this sternness, this ruggedness of his poetry, together with its verbal and emotional integrity, its formal variety and tonal complexity, its quietly searching individual accent, that helped bring about the steady rise in Hardy's reputation as a poet. Ezra Pound remarked in a 1934 letter: "Nobody has taught me anything about writing since Thomas Hardy died." W. H. Auden begins an essay with this testament to the effect of Hardy's verse: "I cannot write objectively about Thomas Hardy because I was once in love with him." And Hardy appears as the major figure—with more poems than either Yeats or Eliot—in Philip Larkin's influential *Oxford Book of Twentieth-Century English Verse* (1973).

On the Western Circuit[1]

I

The man who played the disturbing part in the two quiet feminine lives hereunder depicted—no great man, in any sense, by the way—first had knowledge of them on an October evening, in the city of Melchester. He had been standing in the Close,[2] vainly endeavouring to gain amid the darkness a

---

1. When first published in magazine form in England and America in 1891, "On the Western Circuit" was altered to minimize its illicit sexuality. References to Anna's seduction and pregnancy were eliminated, and Mrs. Harnham was made a widow rather than a wife. When Hardy published the story in his collection *Life's Little Ironies*

(1894), he restored it to its original form. The Western Circuit was the subdivision of England's High Court of Justice with jurisdiction over the southwestern counties. In Hardy's literary landscape Melchester is Salisbury, which has a particularly beautiful cathedral.
2. Closed yard surrounding a church.

glimpse of the most homogeneous pile of mediæval architecture in England, which towered and tapered from the damp and level sward[3] in front of him. While he stood the presence of the Cathedral walls was revealed rather by the ear than by the eyes; he could not see them, but they reflected sharply a roar of sound which entered the Close by a street leading from the city square, and, falling upon the building, was flung back upon him.

He postponed till the morrow his attempt to examine the deserted edifice, and turned his attention to the noise. It was compounded of steam barrel-organs, the clanging of gongs, the ringing of hand-bells, the clack of rattles, and the undistinguishable shouts of men. A lurid light hung in the air in the direction of the tumult. Thitherward he went, passing under the arched gateway, along a straight street, and into the square.

He might have searched Europe over for a greater contrast between juxtaposed scenes. The spectacle was that of the eighth chasm of the Inferno as to colour and flame, and, as to mirth, a development of the Homeric heaven. A smoky glare, of the complexion of brass-filings, ascended from the fiery tongues of innumerable naphtha lamps affixed to booths, stalls, and other temporary erections which crowded the spacious market-square. In front of this irradiation scores of human figures, more or less in profile, were darting athwart and across, up, down, and around, like gnats against a sunset.

Their motions were so rhythmical that they seemed to be moved by machinery. And it presently appeared that they were moved by machinery indeed; the figures being those of the patrons of swings, see-saws, flying-leaps, above all of the three steam roundabouts[4] which occupied the centre of the position. It was from the latter that the din of steam-organs came.

Throbbing humanity in full light was, on second thoughts, better than architecture in the dark. The young man, lighting a short pipe, and putting his hat on one side and one hand in his pocket, to throw himself into harmony with his new environment, drew near to the largest and most patronized of the steam circuses, as the roundabouts were called by their owners. This was one of brilliant finish, and it was now in full revolution. The musical instrument around which and to whose tones the riders revolved, directed its trumpet-mouths of brass upon the young man, and the long plate-glass mirrors set at angles, which revolved with the machine, flashed the gyrating personages and hobby-horses kaleidoscopically into his eyes.

It could now be seen that he was unlike the majority of the crowd. A gentlemanly young fellow, one of the species found in large towns only, and London particularly, built on delicate lines, well, though not fashionably dressed, he appeared to belong to the professional class; he had nothing square or practical about his look, much that was curvilinear and sensuous. Indeed, some would have called him a man not altogether typical of the middle-class male of a century wherein sordid ambition is the master-passion that seems to be taking the time-honoured place of love.

The revolving figures passed before his eyes with an unexpected and quiet grace in a throng whose natural movements did not suggest gracefulness or quietude as a rule. By some contrivance there was imparted to each of the hobby-horses a motion which was really the triumph and perfection of roundabout inventiveness—a galloping rise and fall, so timed that, of each pair of steeds, one was on the spring while the other was on the pitch. The riders were quite fascinated by these equine undulations in this most delightful

---

3. Grassy surface of ground.   4. Carousels.

holiday-game of our times. There were riders as young as six, and as old as sixty years, with every age between. At first it was difficult to catch a personality, but by and by the observer's eyes centred on the prettiest girl out of the several pretty ones revolving.

It was not that one with the light frock and light hat whom he had been at first attracted by; no, it was the one with the black cape, grey skirt, light gloves and—no, not even she, but the one behind her; she with the crimson skirt, dark jacket, brown hat and brown gloves. Unmistakably that was the prettiest girl.

Having finally selected her, this idle spectator studied her as well as he was able during each of her brief transits across his visual field. She was absolutely unconscious of everything save the act of riding: her features were rapt in an ecstatic dreaminess; for the moment she did not know her age or her history or her lineaments, much less her troubles. He himself was full of vague latter-day glooms and popular melancholies, and it was a refreshing sensation to behold this young thing then and there, absolutely as happy as if she were in a Paradise.

Dreading the moment when the inexorable stoker, grimily lurking behind the glittering rococo-work,[5] should decide that this set of riders had had their pennyworth, and bring the whole concern of steam-engine, horses, mirrors, trumpets, drums, cymbals, and such-like to pause and silence, he waited for her every reappearance, glancing indifferently over the intervening forms, including the two plainer girls, the old woman and child, the two youngsters, the newly-married couple, the old man with a clay pipe, the sparkish youth with a ring, the young ladies in the chariot, the pair of journeyman[6]-carpenters, and others, till his select country beauty followed on again in her place. He had never seen a fairer product of nature, and at each round she made a deeper mark in his sentiments. The stoppage then came, and the sighs of the riders were audible.

He moved round to the place at which he reckoned she would alight; but she retained her seat. The empty saddles began to refill, and she plainly was deciding to have another turn. The young man drew up to the side of her steed, and pleasantly asked her if she had enjoyed her ride.

'O yes!' she said, with dancing eyes. 'It has been quite unlike anything I have ever felt in my life before!'

It was not difficult to fall into conversation with her. Unreserved—too unreserved—by nature, she was not experienced enough to be reserved by art, and after a little coaxing she answered his remarks readily. She had come to live in Melchester from a village on the Great Plain,[7] and this was the first time that she had ever seen a steam-circus; she could not understand how such wonderful machines were made. She had come to the city on the invitation of Mrs Harnham, who had taken her into her household to train her as a servant, if she showed any aptitude. Mrs Harnham was a young lady who before she married had been Miss Edith White, living in the country near the speaker's cottage; she was now very kind to her through knowing her in childhood so well. She was even taking the trouble to educate her. Mrs Harnham was the only friend she had in the world, and being without children had wished to

5. Florid ornamentation. "Stoker": man who stokes the furnace powering the "steam circus."
6. Craftsman who has completed an apprenticeship but not yet attained mastership of his craft or

guild.
7. In Hardy's Wessex the Salisbury Plain, a large plateau on which stands Stonehenge.

have her near her in preference to anybody else, though she had only lately come; allowed her to do almost as she liked, and to have a holiday whenever she asked for it. The husband of this kind young lady was a rich wine-merchant of the town, but Mrs Harnham did not care much about him. In the daytime you could see the house from where they were talking. She, the speaker, liked Melchester better than the lonely country, and she was going to have a new hat for next Sunday that was to cost fifteen and ninepence.[8]

Then she inquired of her acquaintance where he lived, and he told her in London, that ancient and smoky city, where everybody lived who lived at all, and died because they could not live there. He came into Wessex two or three times a year for professional reasons; he had arrived from Wintoncester yesterday, and was going on into the next county in a day or two. For one thing he did like the country better than the town, and it was because it contained such girls as herself.

Then the pleasure-machine started again, and, to the light-hearted girl, the figure of the handsome young man, the market-square with its lights and crowd, the houses beyond, and the world at large, began moving round as before, countermoving in the revolving mirrors on her right hand, she being as it were the fixed point in an undulating, dazzling, lurid universe, in which loomed forward most prominently of all the form of her late interlocutor. Each time that she approached the half of her orbit that lay nearest him they gazed at each other with smiles, and with that unmistakable expression which means so little at the moment, yet so often leads up to passion, heart-ache, union, disunion, devotion, overpopulation, drudgery, content, resignation, despair.

When the horses slowed anew he stepped to her side and proposed another heat. 'Hang the expense for once,' he said. 'I'll pay!'

She laughed till the tears came.

'Why do you laugh, dear?' said he.

'Because—you are so genteel that you must have plenty of money, and only say that for fun!' she returned.

'Ha-ha!' laughed the young man in unison, and gallantly producing his money she was enabled to whirl on again.

As he stood smiling there in the motley crowd, with his pipe in his hand, and clad in the rough pea-jacket and wideawake[9] that he had put on for his stroll, who would have supposed him to be Charles Bradford Raye, Esquire, stuff-gownsman,[1] educated at Wintoncester, called to the Bar at Lincoln's-Inn,[2] now going the Western Circuit, merely detained in Melchester by a small arbitration after his brethren had moved on to the next county-town?

II

The square was overlooked from its remoter corner by the house of which the young girl had spoken, a dignified residence of considerable size, having several windows on each floor. Inside one of these, on the first floor, the apartment being a large drawing-room, sat a lady, in appearance from twenty-

8. Approximately one dollar.
9. Soft felt hat.
1. A junior counsel, who wears a gown of "stuff" rather than silk; qualified to plead cases in court but not appointed to a senior position.
2. One of the four London Inns of Court, at which lawyers must be trained to qualify for the bar and to which they afterward must belong to practice law. "Wintoncester": Winchester College, the oldest English public school (the equivalent in the American system of an elite private secondary boarding school).

eight to thirty years of age. The blinds were still undrawn, and the lady was absently surveying the weird scene without, her cheek resting on her hand. The room was unlit from within, but enough of the glare from the market-place entered it to reveal the lady's face. She was what is called an interesting creature rather than a handsome woman; dark-eyed, thoughtful, and with sensitive lips.

A man sauntered into the room from behind and came forward.

'O, Edith, I didn't see you,' he said. 'Why are you sitting here in the dark?'

'I am looking at the fair,' replied the lady in a languid voice.

'Oh? Horrid nuisance every year! I wish it could be put a stop to.'

'I like it.'

'H'm. There's no accounting for taste.'

For a moment he gazed from the window with her, for politeness sake, and then went out again.

In a few minutes she rang.

'Hasn't Anna come in?' asked Mrs Harnham.

'No m'm.'

'She ought to be in by this time. I meant her to go for ten minutes only.'

'Shall I go and look for her, m'm?' said the house-maid alertly.

'No. It is not necessary: she is a good girl and will come soon.'

However, when the servant had gone Mrs Harnham arose, went up to her room, cloaked and bonneted herself, and proceeded downstairs, where she found her husband.

'I want to see the fair,' she said; 'and I am going to look for Anna. I have made myself responsible for her, and must see she comes to no harm. She ought to be indoors. Will you come with me?'

'Oh, she's all right. I saw her on one of those whirligig things, talking to her young man as I came in. But I'll go if you wish, though I'd rather go a hundred miles the other way.'

'Then please do so. I shall come to no harm alone.'

She left the house and entered the crowd which thronged the market-place, where she soon discovered Anna, seated on the revolving horse. As soon as it stopped Mrs Harnham advanced and said severely, 'Anna, how can you be such a wild girl? You were only to be out for ten minutes.'

Anna looked blank, and the young man, who had dropped into the background, came to help her alight.

'Please don't blame her,' he said politely. 'It is my fault that she has stayed. She looked so graceful on the horse that I induced her to go round again. I assure you that she has been quite safe.'

'In that case I'll leave her in your hands,' said Mrs Harnham, turning to retrace her steps.

But this for the moment it was not so easy to do. Something had attracted the crowd to a spot in their rear, and the wine-merchant's wife, caught by its sway, found herself pressed against Anna's acquaintance without power to move away. Their faces were within a few inches of each other, his breath fanned her cheek as well as Anna's. They could do no other than smile at the accident; but neither spoke, and each waited passively. Mrs Harnham then felt a man's hand clasping her fingers, and from the look of consciousness on the young fellow's face she knew the hand to be his: she also knew that from the position of the girl he had no other thought than that the imprisoned hand was Anna's. What prompted her to refrain from undeceiving him she could hardly tell. Not content with holding the hand, he playfully slipped two of his fingers inside her glove, against her palm. Thus matters continued till the pressure lessened; but several minutes passed before the crowd thinned sufficiently to allow Mrs Harnham to withdraw.

'How did they get to know each other, I wonder?' she mused as she retreated. 'Anna is really very forward—and he very wicked and nice.'

She was so gently stirred with the stranger's manner and voice, with the tenderness of his idle touch, that instead of re-entering the house she turned back again and observed the pair from a screened nook. Really she argued (being little less impulsive than Anna herself) it was very excusable in Anna to encourage him, however she might have contrived to make his acquaintance; he was so gentlemanly, so fascinating, had such beautiful eyes. The thought that he was several years her junior produced a reasonless sigh.

At length the couple turned from the roundabout towards the door of Mrs Harnham's house, and the young man could be heard saying that he would accompany her home. Anna, then, had found a lover, apparently a very devoted one. Mrs Harnham was quite interested in him. When they drew near the door of the wine-merchant's house, a comparatively deserted spot by this time, they stood invisible for a little while in the shadow of a wall, where they separated, Anna going on to the entrance, and her acquaintance returning across the square.

'Anna,' said Mrs Harnham, coming up. 'I've been looking at you! That young man kissed you at parting, I am almost sure.'

'Well,' stammered Anna; 'he said, if I didn't mind—it would do me no harm, and, and, him a great deal of good!'

'Ah, I thought so! And he was a stranger till tonight?'

'Yes ma'am.'

'Yet I warrant you told him your name and everything about yourself?'

'He asked me.'

'But he didn't tell you his?'

'Yes ma'am, he did!' cried Anna victoriously. 'It is Charles Bradford, of London.'

'Well, if he's respectable, of course I've nothing to say against your knowing him,' remarked her mistress, prepossessed, in spite of general principles, in the young man's favour. 'But I must reconsider all that, if he attempts to renew your acquaintance. A country-bred girl like you, who has never lived in Melchester till this month, who had hardly ever seen a black-coated man till you came here, to be so sharp as to capture a young Londoner like him!'

'I didn't capture him. I didn't do anything,' said Anna, in confusion.

When she was indoors and alone Mrs Harnham thought what a well-bred and chivalrous young man Anna's companion had seemed. There had been a magic in his wooing touch of her hand; and she wondered how he had come to be attracted by the girl.

The next morning the emotional Edith Harnham went to the usual week-day service in Melchester cathedral. In crossing the Close through the fog she again perceived him who had interested her the previous evening, gazing up thoughtfully at the high-piled architecture of the nave: and as soon as she had taken her seat he entered and sat down in a stall opposite hers.

He did not particularly heed her; but Mrs Harnham was continually occupying her eyes with him, and wondered more than ever what had attracted him in her unfledged maid-servant. The mistress was almost as unaccustomed as the maiden herself to the end-of-the-age young man, or she might have wondered less. Raye, having looked about him awhile, left abruptly, without regard to the service that was proceeding; and Mrs Harnham—lonely, impressionable creature that she was—took no further interest in praising the Lord. She wished she had married a London man who knew the subtleties of love-making as they were evidently known to him who had mistakenly caressed her hand.

III

The calendar at Melchester had been light, occupying the court only a few hours; and the assizes[3] at Casterbridge, the next county-town on the Western Circuit, having no business for Raye, he had not gone thither. At the next town after that they did not open till the following Monday, trials to begin on Tuesday morning. In the natural order of things Raye would have arrived at the latter place on Monday afternoon; but it was not till the middle of Wednesday that his gown and grey wig, curled in tiers, in the best fashion of Assyrian bas-reliefs, were seen blowing and bobbing behind him as he hastily walked up the High Street from his lodgings. But though he entered the assize building there was nothing for him to do, and sitting at the blue baize table in the well of the court, he mended pens with a mind far away from the case in progress. Thoughts of unpremeditated conduct, of which a week earlier he would not have believed himself capable, threw him into a mood of dissatisfied depression.

He had contrived to see again the pretty rural maiden Anna, the day after the fair, had walked out of the city with her to the earthworks[4] of Old Melchester, and feeling a violent fancy for her, had remained in Melchester all Sunday, Monday, and Tuesday; by persuasion obtaining walks and meetings with the girl six or seven times during the interval; had in brief won her, body and soul.

He supposed it must have been owing to the seclusion in which he had lived of late in town that he had given way so unrestrainedly to a passion for an artless creature whose inexperience had, from the first, led her to place herself unreservedly in his hands. Much he deplored trifling with her feelings for the sake of a passing desire; and he could only hope that she might not live to suffer on his account.

She had begged him to come to her again; entreated him; wept. He had promised that he would do so, and he meant to carry out that promise. He could not desert her now. Awkward as such unintentional connections were, the interspace of a hundred miles—which to a girl of her limited capabilities was like a thousand—would effectually hinder this summer fancy from greatly encumbering his life; while thought of her simple love might do him the negative good of keeping him from idle pleasures in town when he wished to work hard. His circuit journeys would take him to Melchester three or four times a year; and then he could always see her.

The pseudonym, or rather partial name, that he had given her as his before knowing how far the acquaintance was going to carry him, had been spoken

3. Sessions of the superior court. "Calendar": list of cases to be tried.

4. Banks of earth constructed as fortifications in ancient times.

on the spur of the moment, without any ulterior intention whatever. He had not afterwards disturbed Anna's error, but on leaving her he had felt bound to give her an address at a stationer's not far from his chambers, at which she might write to him under the initials 'C. B'.

In due time Raye returned to his London abode, having called at Melchester on his way and spent a few additional hours with his fascinating child of nature. In town he lived monotonously every day. Often he and his rooms were enclosed by a tawny fog from all the world besides, and when he lighted the gas to read or write by, his situation seemed so unnatural that he would look into the fire and think of that trusting girl at Melchester again and again. Often, oppressed by absurd fondness for her, he would enter the dim religious nave of the Law Courts by the north door, elbow other juniors habited like himself, and like him unretained; edge himself into this or that crowded court where a sensational case was going on, just as if he were in it, though the police officers at the door knew as well as he knew himself that he had no more concern with the business in hand than the patient idlers at the gallery-door outside, who had waited to enter since eight in the morning because, like him, they belonged to the classes that live on expectation. But he would do these things to no purpose, and think how greatly the characters in such scenes contrasted with the pink and breezy Anna.

An unexpected feature in that peasant maiden's conduct was that she had not as yet written to him, though he had told her she might do so if she wished. Surely a young creature had never before been so reticent in such circumstances. At length he sent her a brief line, positively requesting her to write. There was no answer by the return post, but the day after a letter in a neat feminine hand, and bearing the Melchester post-mark, was handed to him by the stationer.

The fact alone of its arrival was sufficient to satisfy his imaginative sentiment. He was not anxious to open the epistle, and in truth did not begin to read it for nearly half-an-hour, anticipating readily its terms of passionate retrospect and tender adjuration. When at last he turned his feet to the fireplace and unfolded the sheet, he was surprised and pleased to find that neither extravagance nor vulgarity was there. It was the most charming little missive he had ever received from woman. To be sure the language was simple and the ideas were slight; but it was so self-possessed; so purely that of a young girl who felt her womanhood to be enough for her dignity that he read it through twice. Four sides were filled, and a few lines written across, after the fashion of former days; the paper, too, was common, and not of the latest shade and surface. But what of those things? He had received letters from women who were fairly called ladies, but never so sensible, so human a letter as this. He could not single out any one sentence and say it was at all remarkable or clever; the *ensemble* of the letter it was which won him; and beyond the one request that he would write or come to her again soon there was nothing to show her sense of a claim upon him.

To write again and develop a correspondence was the last thing Raye would have preconceived as his conduct in such a situation; yet he did send a short, encouraging line or two, signed with his pseudonym, in which he asked for another letter, and cheeringly promised that he would try to see her again on some near day, and would never forget how much they had been to each other during their short acquaintance.

IV

To return now to the moment at which Anna, at Melchester, had received Raye's letter.

It had been put into her own hand by the postman on his morning rounds. She flushed down to her neck on receipt of it, and turned it over and over. 'It is mine?' she said.

'Why, yes, can't you see it is?' said the postman, smiling as he guessed the nature of the document and the cause of the confusion.

'O yes, of course!' replied Anna, looking at the letter, forcedly tittering, and blushing still more.

Her look of embarrassment did not leave her with the postman's departure. She opened the envelope, kissed its contents, put away the letter in her pocket, and remained musing till her eyes filled with tears.

A few minutes later she carried up a cup of tea to Mrs Harnham in her bed-chamber. Anna's mistress looked at her, and said: 'How dismal you seem this morning, Anna. What's the matter?'

'I'm not dismal, I'm glad; only I—' She stopped to stifle a sob.

'Well?'

'I've got a letter—and what good is it to me, if I can't read a word in it!'

'Why, I'll read it, child, if necessary.'

'But this is from somebody—I don't want anybody to read it but myself!' Anna murmured.

'I shall not tell anybody. Is it from that young man?'

'I think so.' Anna slowly produced the letter, saying: 'Then will you read it to me, ma'am?'

This was the secret of Anna's embarrassment and flutterings. She could neither read nor write. She had grown up under the care of an aunt by marriage, at one of the lonely hamlets on the Great Mid-Wessex Plain where, even in days of national education, there had been no school within a distance of two miles. Her aunt was an ignorant woman; there had been nobody to investigate Anna's circumstances, nobody to care about her learning the rudiments; though, as often in such cases, she had been well fed and clothed and not unkindly treated. Since she had come to live at Melchester with Mrs Harnham, the latter, who took a kindly interest in the girl, had taught her to speak correctly, in which accomplishment Anna showed considerable readiness, as is not unusual with the illiterate; and soon became quite fluent in the use of her mistress's phraseology. Mrs Harnham also insisted upon her getting a spelling and copy book, and beginning to practise in these. Anna was slower in this branch of her education, and meanwhile here was the letter.

Edith Harnham's large dark eyes expressed some interest in the contents, though, in her character of mere interpreter, she threw into her tone as much as she could of mechanical passiveness. She read the short epistle on to its concluding sentence, which idly requested Anna to send him a tender answer.

'Now—you'll do it for me, won't you, dear mistress?' said Anna eagerly. 'And you'll do it as well as ever you can, please? Because I couldn't bear him to think I am not able to do it myself. I should sink into the earth with shame if he knew that!'

From some words in the letter Mrs Harnham was led to ask questions, and the answers she received confirmed her suspicions. Deep concern filled Edith's heart at perceiving how the girl had committed her happiness to the issue of this new-sprung attachment. She blamed herself for not interfering in a flirtation which had resulted so seriously for the poor little creature in her charge; though at the time of seeing the pair together she had a feeling that it was hardly within her province to nip young affection in the bud. However, what was done could not be undone, and it behoved her now, as Anna's only protector, to help her as much as she could. To Anna's eager request that she, Mrs Harnham, should compose and write the answer to this young London man's letter, she felt bound to accede, to keep alive his attachment to the girl if possible; though in other circumstances she might have suggested the cook as an amanuensis.[5]

A tender reply was thereupon concocted, and set down in Edith Harnham's hand. This letter it had been which Raye had received and delighted in. Written in the presence of Anna it certainly was, and on Anna's humble notepaper, and in a measure indited by the young girl; but the life, the spirit, the individuality, were Edith Harnham's.

'Won't you at least put your name yourself?' she said. 'You can manage to write that by this time?'

'No, no,' said Anna, shrinking back. 'I should do it so bad. He'd be ashamed of me, and never see me again!'

The note, so prettily requesting another from him, had, as we have seen, power enough in its pages to bring one. He declared it to be such a pleasure to hear from her that she must write every week. The same process of manufacture was accordingly repeated by Anna and her mistress, and continued for several weeks in succession; each letter being penned and suggested by Edith, the girl standing by; the answer read and commented on by Edith, Anna standing by and listening again.

Late on a winter evening, after the dispatch of the sixth letter, Mrs Harnham was sitting alone by the remains of her fire. Her husband had retired to bed, and she had fallen into that fixity of musing which takes no count of hour or temperature. The state of mind had been brought about in Edith by a strange thing which she had done that day. For the first time since Raye's visit Anna had gone to stay over a night or two with her cottage friends on the Plain, and in her absence had arrived, out of its time, a letter from Raye. To this Edith had replied on her own responsibility, from the depths of her own heart, without waiting for her maid's collaboration. The luxury of writing to him what would be known to no consciousness but his was great, and she had indulged herself therein.

Why was it a luxury?

Edith Harnham led a lonely life. Influenced by the belief of the British parent that a bad marriage with its aversions is better than free womanhood with its interests, dignity, and leisure, she had consented to marry the elderly wine-merchant as a *pis aller,*[6] at the age of seven-and-twenty—some three years before this date—to find afterwards that she had made a mistake. That contract had left her still a woman whose deeper nature had never been stirred.

She was now clearly realising that she had become possessed to the bottom of her soul with the image of a man to whom she was hardly so much as a name. From the first he had attracted her by his looks and voice; by his tender touch; and, with these as generators, the writing of letter after letter and the reading of their soft answers had insensibly developed on her side an emotion which fanned his; till there had resulted a magnetic reciprocity between the correspondents, notwithstanding that one of them wrote in a character not her own. That he had been able to seduce another woman in two days was his crowning though unrecognised fascination for her as the she-animal.

They were her own impassioned and pent-up ideas—lowered to monosyllabic phraseology in order to keep up the disguise—that Edith put into letters signed with another name, much to the shallow Anna's delight, who, unassisted, could not for the world have conceived such pretty fancies for winning him, even had she been able to write them. Edith found that it was these, her own foisted-in sentiments, to which the young barrister mainly responded. The few sentences occasionally added from Anna's own lips made apparently no impression upon him.

The letter-writing in her absence Anna never discovered; but on her return the next morning she declared she wished to see her lover about something at once, and begged Mrs Harnham to ask him to come.

There was a strange anxiety in her manner which did not escape Mrs Harnham, and ultimately resolved itself into a flood of tears. Sinking down at Edith's knees, she made confession that the result of her relations with her lover it would soon become necessary to disclose.

Edith Harnham was generous enough to be very far from inclined to cast Anna adrift at this conjuncture. No true woman ever is so inclined from her own personal point of view, however prompt she may be in taking such steps to safeguard those dear to her. Although she had written to Raye so short a time previously, she instantly penned another Anna-note hinting clearly though delicately the state of affairs.

Raye replied by a hasty line to say how much he was concerned at her news: he felt that he must run down to see her almost immediately.

But a week later the girl came to her mistress's room with another note, which on being read informed her that after all he could not find time for the journey. Anna was broken with grief; but by Mrs Harnham's counsel strictly refrained from hurling at him the reproaches and bitterness customary from young women so situated. One thing was imperative: to keep the young man's romantic interest in her alive. Rather therefore did Edith, in the name of her protégée, request him on no account to be distressed about the looming event, and not to inconvenience himself to hasten down. She desired above everything to be no weight upon him in his career, no clog upon his high activities. She had wished him to know what had befallen: he was to dismiss it again from his mind. Only he must write tenderly as ever, and when he should come again on the spring circuit it would be soon enough to discuss what had better be done.

It may well be supposed that Anna's own feelings had not been quite in accord with these generous expressions; but the mistress's judgment had ruled, and Anna had acquiesced. 'All I want is that niceness you can so well put into your letters, my dear, dear mistress, and that I can't for the life o' me make up out of my own head; though I mean the same thing and feel it exactly when you've written it down!'

When the letter had been sent off, and Edith Harnham was left alone, she bowed herself on the back of her chair and wept.

'I wish his child was mine—I wish it was!' she murmured. 'Yet how can I say such a wicked thing!'

V

The letter moved Raye considerably when it reached him. The intelligence itself had affected him less than her unexpected manner of treating him in relation to it. The absence of any word of reproach, the devotion to his interests, the self-sacrifice apparent in every line, all made up a nobility of character that he had never dreamt of finding in womankind.

'God forgive me!' he said tremulously. 'I have been a wicked wretch. I did not know she was such a treasure as this!'

He reassured her instantly; declaring that he would not of course desert her, that he would provide a home for her somewhere. Meanwhile she was to stay where she was as long as her mistress would allow her.

But a misfortune supervened in this direction. Whether an inkling of Anna's circumstances reached the knowledge of Mrs Harnham's husband or not cannot be said, but the girl was compelled, in spite of Edith's entreaties, to leave the house. By her own choice she decided to go back for a while to the cottage on the Plain. This arrangement led to a consultation as to how the correspondence should be carried on; and in the girl's inability to continue personally what had been begun in her name, and in the difficulty of their acting in concert as heretofore, she requested Mrs Harnham—the only well-to-do friend she had in the world—to receive the letters and reply to them off-hand, sending them on afterwards to herself on the Plain, where she might at least get some neighbour to read them to her, if a trustworthy one could be met with. Anna and her box then departed for the Plain.

Thus it befell that Edith Harnham found herself in the strange position of having to correspond, under no supervision by the real woman, with a man not her husband, in terms which were virtually those of a wife, concerning a corporeal condition that was not Edith's at all; the man being one for whom, mainly through the sympathies involved in playing this part, she secretly cherished a predilection, subtle and imaginative truly, but strong and absorbing. She opened each letter, read it as if intended for herself, and replied from the promptings of her own heart and no other.

Throughout this correspondence, carried on in the girl's absence, the highstrung Edith Harnham lived in the ecstasy of fancy; the vicarious intimacy engendered such a flow of passionateness as was never exceeded. For conscience' sake Edith at first sent on each of his letters to Anna, and even rough copies of her replies; but later on these so-called copies were much abridged, and many letters on both sides were not sent on at all.

Though sensuous, and, superficially at least, infested with the self-indulgent vices of artificial society, there was a substratum of honesty and fairness in Raye's character. He had really a tender regard for the country girl, and it grew more tender than ever when he found her apparently capable of expressing the deepest sensibilities in the simplest words. He meditated, he wavered; and finally resolved to consult his sister, a maiden lady much older than himself, of lively sympathies and good intent. In making this confidence he showed her some of the letters.

'She seems fairly educated,' Miss Raye observed. 'And bright in ideas. She expresses herself with a taste that must be innate.'

'Yes. She writes very prettily, doesn't she, thanks to these elementary schools?'

'One is drawn out towards her, in spite of one's self, poor thing.'

The upshot of the discussion was that though he had not been directly advised to do it, Raye wrote, in his real name, what he would never have decided to write on his own responsibility; namely that he could not live without her, and would come down in the spring and shelve her looming difficulty by marrying her.

This bold acceptance of the situation was made known to Anna by Mrs Harnham driving out immediately to the cottage on the Plain. Anna jumped for joy like a little child. And poor, crude directions for answering appropriately were given to Edith Harnham, who on her return to the city carried them out with warm intensifications.

'O!' she groaned, as she threw down the pen. 'Anna—poor good little fool— hasn't intelligence enough to appreciate him! How should she? While I—don't bear his child!'

It was now February. The correspondence had continued altogether for four months; and the next letter from Raye contained incidentally a statement of his position and prospects. He said that in offering to wed her he had, at first, contemplated the step of retiring from a profession which hitherto had brought him very slight emolument, and which, to speak plainly, he had thought might be difficult of practice after his union with her. But the unexpected mines of brightness and warmth that her letters had disclosed to be lurking in her sweet nature had led him to abandon that somewhat sad prospect. He felt sure that, with her powers of development, after a little private training in the social forms of London under his supervision, and a little help from a governess if necessary, she would make as good a professional man's wife as could be desired, even if he should rise to the woolsack.[7] Many a Lord Chancellor's wife had been less intuitively a lady than she had shown herself to be in her lines to him.

'O—poor fellow, poor fellow!' mourned Edith Harnham.

Her distress now raged as high as her infatuation. It was she who had wrought him to this pitch—to a marriage which meant his ruin; yet she could not, in mercy to her maid, do anything to hinder his plan. Anna was coming to Melchester that week, but she could hardly show the girl this last reply from the young man; it told too much of the second individuality that had usurped the place of the first.

Anna came, and her mistress took her into her own room for privacy. Anna began by saying with some anxiety that she was glad the wedding was so near.

'O Anna!' replied Mrs Harnham. 'I think we must tell him all—that I have been doing your writing for you?—lest he should not know it till after you become his wife, and it might lead to dissension and recriminations—'

'O mis'ess, dear mis'ess—please don't tell him now!' cried Anna in distress. 'If you were to do it, perhaps he would not marry me; and what should I do then? It would be terrible what would come to me! And I am getting on with my writing, too. I have brought with me the copybook you were so good as to give me, and I practise every day, and though it is so, so hard, I shall do it well at last, I believe, if I keep on trying.'

Edith looked at the copybook. The copies had been set by herself, and such progress as the girl had made was in the way of grotesque facsimile of her mistress's hand. But even if Edith's flowing calligraphy were reproduced the inspiration would be another thing.

'You do it so beautifully,' continued Anna, 'and say all that I want to say so much better than I could say it, that I do hope you won't leave me in the lurch just now!'

'Very well,' replied the other. 'But I—but I thought I ought not to go on!'

'Why?'

Her strong desire to confide her sentiments led Edith to answer truly: 'Because of its effect upon me.'

'But it *can't* have any!'

'Why, child?'

'Because you are married already!' said Anna with lucid simplicity.

'Of course it can't,' said her mistress hastily; yet glad, despite her conscience, that two or three out-pourings still remained to her. 'But you must concentrate your attention on writing your name as I write it here.'

VI

Soon Raye wrote about the wedding. Having decided to make the best of what he feared was a piece of romantic folly, he had acquired more zest for the grand experiment. He wished the ceremony to be in London, for greater privacy. Edith Harnham would have preferred it at Melchester; Anna was passive. His reasoning prevailed, and Mrs Harnham threw herself with mournful zeal into the preparations for Anna's departure. In a last desperate feeling that she must at every hazard be in at the death of her dream, and see once again the man who by a species of telepathy had exercised such an influence on her, she offered to go up with Anna and be with her through the ceremony—'to see the end of her,' as her mistress put it with forced gaiety; an offer which the girl gratefully accepted; for she had no other friend capable of playing the part of companion and witness, in the presence of a gentlemanly bridegroom, in such a way as not to hasten an opinion that he had made an irremediable social blunder.

It was a muddy morning in March when Raye alighted from a four-wheel cab at the door of a registry-office in the S.W. district of London, and carefully handed down Anna and her companion Mrs Harnham. Anna looked attractive in the somewhat fashionable clothes which Mrs Harnham had helped her to buy, though not quite so attractive as, an innocent child, she had appeared in her country gown on the back of the wooden horse at Melchester Fair.

Mrs Harnham had come up this morning by an early train, and a young man—a friend of Raye's—having met them at the door, all four entered the registry-office together. Till an hour before this time Raye had never known the wine-merchant's wife, except at that first casual encounter, and in the flutter of the performance before them he had little opportunity for more than a brief acquaintance. The contract of marriage at a registry is soon got through; but somehow, during its progress, Raye discovered a strange and secret gravitation between himself and Anna's friend.

The formalities of the wedding—or rather ratification of a previous union—being concluded, the four went in one cab to Raye's lodgings, newly taken in a new suburb in preference to a house, the rent of which he could ill afford just then. Here Anna cut the little cake which Raye had bought at a pastry-

1866 / Thomas Hardy

cook's on his way home from Lincoln's Inn the night before. But she did not do much besides. Raye's friend was obliged to depart almost immediately, and when he had left the only ones virtually present were Edith and Raye, who exchanged ideas with much animation. The conversation was indeed theirs only, Anna being as a domestic animal who humbly heard but understood not. Raye seemed startled in awakening to this fact, and began to feel dissatisfied with her inadequacy.

At last, more disappointed than he cared to own, he said, 'Mrs Harnham, my darling is so flurried that she doesn't know what she is doing or saying. I see that after this event a little quietude will be necessary before she gives tongue to that tender philosophy which she used to treat me to in her letters.'

They had planned to start early that afternoon for Knollsea, to spend the few opening days of their married life there, and as the hour for departure was drawing near Raye asked his wife if she would go to the writing-desk in the next room and scribble a little note to his sister, who had been unable to attend through indisposition, informing her that the ceremony was over, thanking her for her little present, and hoping to know her well now that she was the writer's sister as well as Charles's.

'Say it in the pretty poetical way you know so well how to adopt,' he added, 'for I want you particularly to win her, and both of you to be dear friends.'

Anna looked uneasy, but departed to her task, Raye remaining to talk to their guest. Anna was a long while absent, and her husband suddenly rose and went to her.

He found her still bending over the writing-table, with tears brimming up in her eyes; and he looked down upon the sheet of note-paper with some interest, to discover with what tact she had expressed her good-will in the delicate circumstances. To his surprise she had progressed but a few lines, in the characters and spelling of a child of eight, and with the ideas of a goose.

'Anna,' he said, staring; 'what's this?'

'It only means—that I can't do it any better!' she answered, through her tears.

'Eh? Nonsense!'

'I can't!' she insisted, with miserable, sobbing hardihood. 'I—I—didn't write those letters, Charles! I only told *her* what to write! And not always that! But I am learning, O so fast, my dear, dear husband! And you'll forgive me, won't you, for not telling you before?' She slid to her knees, abjectly clasped his waist and laid her face against him.

He stood a few moments, raised her, abruptly turned, and shut the door upon her, rejoining Edith in the drawing-room. She saw that something untoward had been discovered, and their eyes remained fixed on each other.

'Do I guess rightly?' he asked, with wan quietude. '*You* were her scribe through all this?'

'It was necessary,' said Edith.

'Did she dictate every word you ever wrote to me?'

'Not every word.'

'In fact, very little?'

'Very little.'

'You wrote a great part of those pages every week from your own conceptions, though in her name!'

'Yes.'

'Perhaps you wrote many of the letters when you were alone, without communication with her?'

'I did.'

He turned to the bookcase, and leant with his hand over his face; and Edith, seeing his distress, became white as a sheet.

'You have deceived me—ruined me!' he murmured.

'O, don't say it!' she cried in her anguish, jumping up and putting her hand on his shoulder. 'I can't bear that!'

'Delighting me deceptively! Why did you do it—*why* did you!'

'I began doing it in kindness to her! How could I do otherwise than try to save such a simple girl from misery? But I admit that I continued it for pleasure to myself.'

Raye looked up. 'Why did it give you pleasure?' he asked.

'I must not tell,' said she.

He continued to regard her, and saw that her lips suddenly began to quiver under his scrutiny, and her eyes to fill and droop. She started aside, and said that she must go to the station to catch the return train: could a cab be called immediately?

But Raye went up to her, and took her unresisting hand. 'Well, to think of such a thing as this!' he said. 'Why, you and I are friends—lovers—devoted lovers—by correspondence!'

'Yes; I suppose.'

'More.'

'More?'

'Plainly more. It is no use blinking that. Legally I have married her—God help us both!—in soul and spirit I have married you, and no other woman in the world!'

'Hush!'

'But I will not hush! Why should you try to disguise the full truth, when you have already owned half of it? Yes, it is between you and me that the bond is—not between me and her! Now I'll say no more. But, O my cruel one, I think I have one claim upon you!'

She did not say what, and he drew her towards him, and bent over her. 'If it was all pure invention in those letters,' he said emphatically, 'give me your cheek only. If you meant what you said, let it be lips. It is for the first and last time, remember!'

She put up her mouth, and he kissed her long. 'You forgive me?' she said, crying.

'Yes.'

'But you are ruined!'

'What matter!' he said, shrugging his shoulders. 'It serves me right!'

She withdrew, wiped her eyes, entered and bade good-bye to Anna, who had not expected her to go so soon, and was still wrestling with the letter. Raye followed Edith downstairs, and in three minutes she was in a hansom driving to the Waterloo station.

He went back to his wife. 'Never mind the letter, Anna, to-day,' he said gently. 'Put on your things. We, too, must be off shortly.'

The simple girl, upheld by the sense that she was indeed married, showed her delight at finding that he was as kind as ever after the disclosure. She did not know that before his eyes he beheld as it were a galley, in which he, the fastidious urban, was chained to work for the remainder of his life, with her, the unlettered peasant, chained to his side.

Edith travelled back to Melchester that day with a face that showed the very stupor of grief, her lips still tingling from the desperate pressure of his kiss. The end of her impassioned dream had come. When at dusk she reached the Melchester station her husband was there to meet her, but in his perfunctoriness and her preoccupation they did not see each other, and she went out of the station alone.

She walked mechanically homewards without calling a fly.[8] Entering, she could not bear the silence of the house, and went up in the dark to where Anna had slept, where she remained thinking awhile. She then returned to the drawing-room, and not knowing what she did, crouched down upon the floor.

'I have ruined him!' she kept repeating. 'I have ruined him; because I would not deal treacherously towards her!'

In the course of half an hour a figure opened the door of the apartment.

'Ah—who's that?' she said, starting up, for it was dark.

'Your husband—who should it be?' said the worthy merchant.

'Ah—my husband!—I forgot I had a husband!' she whispered to herself.

'I missed you at the station,' he continued. 'Did you see Anna safely tied up? I hope so, for 'twas time.'

'Yes—Anna is married.'

Simultaneously with Edith's journey home Anna and her husband were sitting at the opposite windows of a second-class carriage which sped along to Knollsea. In his hand was a pocket-book full of creased sheets closely written over. Unfolding them one after another he read them in silence, and sighed.

'What are you doing, dear Charles?' she said timidly from the other window, and drew nearer to him as if he were a god.

'Reading over all those sweet letters to me signed "Anna," ' he replied with dreary resignation.

1891

Hap[1]

If but some vengeful god would call to me
From up the sky, and laugh: 'Thou suffering thing,
Know that thy sorrow is my ecstasy,
That thy love's loss is my hate's profiting!'

5 Then would I bear it, clench myself, and die,
Steeled by the sense of ire° unmerited;   *anger*
Half-eased in that a Powerfuller than I
Had willed and meted° me the tears I shed.   *allotted, given*

But not so. How arrives it joy lies slain,
10 And why unblooms the best hope ever sown?
—Crass Casualty obstructs the sun and rain,

---

8. Carriage.

1. I.e., chance (as also "Casualty," line 11).

And dicing Time for gladness casts a moan. . . .
These purblind Doomsters[2] had as readily strown
Blisses about my pilgrimage as pain.

1866   1898

Neutral Tones

We stood by a pond that winter day,
And the sun was white, as though chidden of° God,   *rebuked by*
And a few leaves lay on the starving sod;°   *turf*
—They had fallen from an ash, and were gray.

5   Your eyes on me were as eyes that rove
Over tedious riddles of years ago;
And some words played between us to and fro
On which lost the more by our love.

The smile on your mouth was the deadest thing
10   Alive enough to have strength to die;
And a grin of bitterness swept thereby
Like an ominous bird a-wing . . .

Since then, keen lessons that love deceives,
And wrings with wrong, have shaped to me
15   Your face, and the God-curst sun, and a tree,
And a pond edged with grayish leaves.

1867   1898

I Look into My Glass[1]

I look into my glass,
And view my wasting skin,
And say, 'Would God it came to pass
My heart had shrunk as thin!'

5   For then, I, undistrest
By hearts grown cold to me,
Could lonely wait my endless rest
With equanimity.

But Time, to make me grieve,
10   Part steals, lets part abide;
And shakes this fragile frame at eve
With throbbings of noontide.

1898

2. Half-blind judges.   1. Mirror.

A Broken Appointment

You did not come.
And marching Time drew on, and wore me numb.—
Yet less for loss of your dear presence there
Than that I thus found lacking in your make
5 That high compassion which can overbear
Reluctance for pure lovingkindness' sake
Grieved I, when, as the hope-hour stroked its sum,
You did not come.

You love not me,
10 And love alone can lend you loyalty;
—I know and knew it. But, unto the store
Of human deeds divine in all but name,
Was it not worth a little hour or more
To add yet this: Once you, a woman, came
15 To soothe a time-torn man; even though it be
You love not me?

                                                      1901

Drummer Hodge

1
They throw in Drummer Hodge, to rest
    Uncoffined—just as found:
His landmark is a kopje-crest
    That breaks the veldt[1] around;
5 And foreign constellations[2] west°   set
    Each night above his mound.

2
Young Hodge the Drummer never knew—
    Fresh from his Wessex home—
The meaning of the broad Karoo,[3]
10   The Bush,[4] the dusty loam,
And why uprose to nightly view
    Strange stars amid the gloam.

3
Yet portion of that unknown plain
    Will Hodge for ever be;
15 His homely Northern breast and brain

---

1. South African Dutch (Afrikaans) word for a plain or prairie. "Kopje-crest": Afrikaans for a small hill. The poem is a lament for an English soldier killed in the Anglo-Boer War (1899–1902).
2. Those visible only in the Southern Hemisphere.

3. A dry tableland region in South Africa (usually spelled "Karroo").
4. British colonial word for an uncleared area of land.

Grow to some Southern tree,
And strange-eyed constellations reign
His stars eternally.

1899, 1901

The Darkling[1] Thrush

I leant upon a coppice gate[2]
    When Frost was spectre-gray,
And Winter's dregs made desolate
    The weakening eye of day.
5 The tangled bine-stems[3] scored the sky
    Like strings of broken lyres,
And all mankind that haunted nigh°   *near*
    Had sought their household fires.

The land's sharp features seemed to be
10   The Century's corpse outleant,[4]
His crypt the cloudy canopy,
    The wind his death-lament.
The ancient pulse of germ and birth
    Was shrunken hard and dry,
15 And every spirit upon earth
    Seemed fervourless as I.

At once a voice arose among
    The bleak twigs overhead
In a full-hearted evensong
20   Of joy illimited;
An aged thrush, frail, gaunt, and small,
    In blast-beruffled plume,
Had chosen thus to fling his soul
    Upon the growing gloom.

25 So little cause for carolings
    Of such ecstatic sound
Was written on terrestrial things
    Afar or nigh around,
That I could think there trembled through
30   His happy good-night air
Some blessed Hope, whereof he knew
    And I was unaware.

1900, 1901

1. In the dark.
2. Gate leading to a small wood or thicket.
3. Twining stems of shrubs.

4. Leaning out (of its coffin); i.e., the 19th century was dead. This poem was dated December 31, 1900.

The Ruined Maid

'O 'Melia,[1] my dear, this does everything crown!
Who could have supposed I should meet you in Town?
And whence such fair garments, such prosperi-ty?'—
'O didn't you know I'd been ruined?' said she.

5   —'You left us in tatters, without shoes or socks,
Tired of digging potatoes, and spudding up docks;[2]
And now you've gay bracelets and bright feathers three!'—
'Yes: that's how we dress when we're ruined,' said she.

    —'At home in the barton° you said "thee" and "thou",   *farmyard*
10 And "thik oon", and "theäs oon", and "t'other"; but now
Your talking quite fits 'ee for high compa-ny!'—
'Some polish is gained with one's ruin,' said she.

    —'Your hands were like paws then, your face blue and bleak
But now I'm bewitched by your delicate cheek,
15 And your little gloves fit as on any la-dy!'—
'We never do work when we're ruined,' said she.

    —'You used to call home-life a hag-ridden dream,
And you'd sigh, and you'd sock;° but at present you seem   *sigh*
To know not of megrims° or melancho-ly!'—   *low spirits*
20 'True. One's pretty lively when ruined,' said she.

    —'I wish I had feathers, a fine sweeping gown,
And a delicate face, and could strut about Town!'—
'My dear—a raw country girl, such as you be,
Cannot quite expect that. You ain't ruined,' said she.

1866   1901

A Trampwoman's Tragedy

(182–)

I

From Wynyard's Gap[1] the livelong day,
    The livelong day,
We beat afoot the northward way
    We had travelled times before.
5 The sun-blaze burning on our backs,
    Our shoulders sticking to our packs,

---

1. Diminutive form of Amelia.
2. Digging up a species of thick-rooted weed.
1. The places named are in Somerset, in south-west England on the northern edge of the area that Hardy called "Wessex" and of which his native Dorset, the county south and southwest of Somerset, reaching to the English Channel, was the major part.

By fosseway,² fields, and turnpike tracks
    We skirted sad Sedge-Moor.³

2
    Full twenty miles we jaunted on,
10   We jaunted on,—
    My fancy-man, and jeering John,
        And Mother Lee, and I.
    And, as the sun drew down to west,
    We climbed the toilsome Poldon crest,
15 And saw, of landskip° sights the best,   *landscape*
        The inn that beamed thereby.

3
    For months we had padded side by side,
        Ay, side by side
    Through the Great Forest, Blackmoor wide,
20   And where the Parret ran,
    We'd faced the gusts on Mendip ridge,
    Had crossed the Yeo unhelped by bridge,
    Been stung by every Marshwood midge,
        I and my fancy-man.

4
25 Lone inns we loved, my man and I,
        My man and I;
    'King's Stag', 'Windwhistle'⁴ high and dry,
        'The Horse' on Hintock Green,
    The cozy house at Wynyard's Gap,
30 'The Hut' renowned on Bredy Knap,
    And many another wayside tap°   *taproom, inn*
        Where folk might sit unseen.

5
    Now as we trudged—O deadly day,
        O deadly day!—
35 I teased my fancy-man in play
        And wanton idleness.
    I walked alongside jeering John,
    I laid his hand my waist upon;
    I would not bend my glances on
40   My lover's dark distress.

6
    Thus Poldon top at last we won,
        At last we won,

2. Path running along a ditch.
3. Sad because of the Battle of Sedgemoor (1685), when the rebellion of the duke of Monmouth against James II was crushed with excessive cruelty.
4. The highness and dryness of Windwhistle Inn was impressed upon the writer two or three years ago, when, after climbing on a hot afternoon to the beautiful spot near which it stands and entering the inn for tea, he was informed by the landlady that none could be had, unless he would fetch water from a valley half a mile off, the house containing not a drop, owing to its situation. However, a tantalizing row of full barrels behind her back testified to a wetness of a certain sort, which was not at that time desired [Hardy's note].

And gained the inn at sink of sun
Far-famed as 'Marshal's Elm'.[5]
45 Beneath us figured tor and lea,[6]
From Mendip to the western sea—
I doubt if finer sight there be
Within this royal realm.

7

Inside the settle all a-row—
50   All four a-row
We sat, I next to John, to show
That he had wooed and won.
And then he took me on his knee,
And swore it was his turn to be
55 My favoured mate, and Mother Lee
Passed to my former one.

8

Then in a voice I had never heard,
    I had never heard,
My only Love to me: 'One word,
60   My lady, if you please!
Whose is the child you are like to bear?—
His? After all my months o' care?'
God knows 'twas not! But, O despair!
I nodded—still to tease.

9

65 Then up he sprung, and with his knife—
    And with his knife
He let out jeering Johnny's life,
    Yes; there, at set of sun.
The slant ray through the window nigh
70 Gilded John's blood and glazing eye,
Ere scarcely Mother Lee and I
    Knew that the deed was done.

10

The taverns tell the gloomy tale,
    The gloomy tale,
75 How that at Ivel-chester jail
    My Love, my sweetheart swung;
Though stained till now by no misdeed
Save one horse ta'en in time o' need;
(Blue Jimmy stole right many a steed
80   Ere his last fling he flung).[7]

11

Thereaft I walked the world alone,
    Alone, alone!

5. "Marshal's Elm," so picturesquely situated, is no longer an inn, though the house, or part of it, still remains. It used to exhibit a fine old swinging sign [Hardy's note].
6. Rocky hill and tract of open ground.

7. "Blue Jimmy" was a notorious horse stealer of Wessex in those days, who appropriated more than a hundred horses before he was caught, among others one belonging to a neighbor of the writer's grandfather. He was hanged at the now demol-

On his death-day I gave my groan
    And dropt his dead-born child.
85 'Twas nigh° the jail, beneath a tree,   *near*
None tending me; for Mother Lee
Had died at Glaston, leaving me
    Unfriended on the wild.

12

And in the night as I lay weak,
90   As I lay weak,
The leaves a-falling on my cheek,
    The red moon low declined—
The ghost of him I'd die to kiss
Rose up and said: 'Ah, tell me this!
95 Was the child mine, or was it his?
    Speak, that I rest may find!'

13

O doubt not but I told him then,
    I told him then,
That I had kept me from all men
100   Since we joined lips and swore.
Whereat he smiled, and thinned away
As the wind stirred to call up day . . .
—'Tis past! And here alone I stray
    Haunting the Western Moor.

Apr. 1902   1909

One We Knew

(M. H.[1] 1772–1857)

She told how they used to form for the country dances—
    'The Triumph,' 'The New-rigged Ship'—
To the light of the guttering wax in the panelled manses,
    And in cots to the blink of a dip.[2]

5 She spoke of the wild 'poussetting' and 'allemanding'[3]
    On carpet, on oak, and on sod;°   *turf*
And the two long rows of ladies and gentlemen standing,
    And the figures the couples trod.

She showed us the spot where the maypole was yearly planted,
10   And where the bandsmen stood
While breeched and kerchiefed partners whirled, and panted
    To choose each other for good.[4]

---

ished Ivel-chester or Ilchester jail above mentioned—that building formerly of so many sinister
associations in the minds of the local peasantry,
and the continual haunt of fever, which at last led
to its condemnation. Its site is now an innocent-
looking green meadow [Hardy's note].
1. Hardy's grandmother.
2. I.e., in cottages by the light of a candle.

3. Allemande is the name of a dance originating
in Germany. To pousette is to dance round with
hands joined.
4. A tall pole, gaily painted and decorated with
flowers and ribbons ("the maypole"), was danced
around on May 1 by men (wearing "breeches," or
trousers) and women (wearing "kerchiefs," or
headscarves).

She told of that far-back day when they learnt astounded
    Of the death of the King of France:
15 Of the Terror; and then of Bonaparte's unbounded
    Ambition and arrogance.

Of how his threats woke warlike preparations
    Along the southern strand,
And how each night brought tremors and trepidations
20   Lest morning should see him land.

She said she had often heard the gibbet creaking
    As it swayed in the lightning flash,
Had caught from the neighbouring town a small child's shrieking
    At the cart-tail under the lash. . . .

25 With cap-framed face and long gaze into the embers—
    We seated around her knees—
She would dwell on such dead themes, not as one who remembers,
    But rather as one who sees.

She seemed one left behind of a band gone distant
30   So far that no tongue could hail:
Past things retold were to her as things existent,
    Things present but as a tale.

May 20, 1902   1909

She Hears the Storm

There was a time in former years—
    While my roof-tree was his—
When I should have been distressed by fears
    At such a night as this.

5 I should have murmured anxiously,
    'The pricking rain strikes cold;
His road is bare of hedge or tree,
    And he is getting old.'

But now the fitful chimney-roar,
10   The drone of Thorncombe trees,
The Froom in flood upon the moor,
    The mud of Mellstock Leaze,[1]

The candle slanting sooty wick'd,
    The thuds upon the thatch,
15 The eaves-drops on the window flicked,
    The clacking garden-hatch,°   *gate*

---

1. The place-names in Hardy's fictional "Wessex" were often invented ("Thorncombe," "Mellstock Leaze"), but he also used the names of real locations, as in "A Trampwoman's Tragedy." "The Froom" is presumably the river Frome, flowing through Dorset and Somerset.

And what they mean to wayfarers,
    I scarcely heed or mind;
He has won that storm-tight roof of hers
20   Which Earth grants all her kind.

1909

Channel Firing[1]

That night your great guns, unawares,
Shook all our coffins as we lay,
And broke the chancel[2] window-squares,
We thought it was the Judgement-day

5   And sat upright. While drearisome
Arose the howl of wakened hounds:
The mouse let fall the altar-crumb,
The worms drew back into the mounds,

The glebe cow[3] drooled. Till God called, 'No;
10   It's gunnery practise out at sea
Just as before you went below;
The world is as it used to be:

'All nations striving strong to make
Red war yet redder. Mad as hatters[4]
15   They do no more for Christès[5] sake
Than you who are helpless in such matters.

'That this is not the judgement-hour
For some of them's a blessed thing,
For if it were they'd have to scour
20   Hell's floor for so much threatening. . . .

'Ha, ha. It will be warmer when
I blow the trumpet (if indeed
I ever do; for you are men,
And rest eternal sorely need).'

25   So down we lay again. 'I wonder,
Will the world ever saner be,'
Said one, 'than when He sent us under
In our indifferent century!'

And many a skeleton shook his head.
30   'Instead of preaching forty year,'

1. Written in April 1914, when Anglo-German naval rivalry was growing steadily more acute; the title refers to gunnery practice in the English Channel. Four months later (August 4), World War I broke out.
2. Part of church nearest to the altar.
3. I.e., cow on a small plot of land belonging to a church (a "glebe" is a small field).
4. Cf. the Mad Hatter in Lewis Carroll's *Alice's Adventures in Wonderland* (1865).
5. The archaic spelling and pronunciation suggest a ballad note of doom.

My neighbour Parson Thirdly said,
'I wish I had stuck to pipes and beer.'

Again the guns disturbed the hour,
Roaring their readiness to avenge,
35 As far inland as Stourton Tower,
And Camelot, and starlit Stonehenge.[6]

1914   1914

The Convergence of the Twain

(Lines on the loss of the Titanic)[1]

I

In a solitude of the sea
Deep from human vanity,
And the Pride of Life that planned her, stilly couches she.

2

Steel chambers, late the pyres
5 Of her salamandrine[2] fires,
Cold currents thrid,[3] and turn to rhythmic tidal lyres.

3

Over the mirrors meant
To glass the opulent
The sea-worm crawls—grotesque, slimed, dumb, indifferent.

4

10 Jewels in joy designed
To ravish the sensuous mind
Lie lightless, all their sparkles bleared and black and blind.

5

Dim moon-eyed fishes near
Gaze at the gilded gear
15 And query: 'What does this vaingloriousness down here?' . . .

6

Well: while was fashioning
This creature of cleaving wing,
The Immanent Will[4] that stirs and urges everything

---

6. The sound of guns preparing for war across the Channel reaches Alfred's ("Stourton") Tower (near Stourton in Dorset), commemorating King Alfred's defeat of a Danish invasion in 878; also the site of King Arthur's court at Camelot (supposedly near Glastonbury) and the famous prehistoric stone circle of Stonehenge on Salisbury Plain.
1. The *Titanic* was the largest and most luxurious ocean liner of the day. Considered unsinkable, it sank with great loss of life on April 15, 1912, on the ship's maiden voyage, from Southampton to the United States, after colliding with an iceberg. "Twain": two.
2. I.e., destructive. The salamander was supposed to be able to survive fire.
3. A variant form of the verb *thread*.
4. The force (blind, but slowly gaining consciousness throughout history) that drives the world, according to Hardy's philosophy.

7

Prepared a sinister mate
20   For her—so gaily great—
A Shape of Ice, for the time far and dissociate.

8

And as the smart ship grew
In stature, grace, and hue,
In shadowy silent distance grew the Iceberg too.

9

25   Alien they seemed to be:
No mortal eye could see
The intimate welding of their later history,

10

Or sign that they were bent
By paths coincident
30 On being anon° twin halves of one august° event,   *soon / important*

11

Till the Spinner of the Years
Said 'Now!' And each one hears,
And consummation comes, and jars two hemispheres.

1912   1912, 1914

Ah, Are You Digging on My Grave?

'Ah, are you digging on my grave
    My loved one?—planting rue?'[1]
—'No: yesterday he went to wed
One of the brightest wealth has bred.
5   'It cannot hurt her now,' he said,
    "That I should not be true." '

'Then who is digging on my grave?
    My nearest dearest kin?'
—'Ah, no; they sit and think, "What use!
10 What good will planting flowers produce?
No tendance of her mound can loose
    Her spirit from Death's gin." '°   *trap*

'But some one digs upon my grave?
    My enemy?—prodding sly?'
15 —'Nay: when she heard you had passed the Gate
That shuts on all flesh soon or late,
She thought you no more worth her hate,
    And cares not where you lie.'

---

1. A yellow-flowered herb, traditionally an emblem of sorrow (*rue* is also an archaic word for "sorrow").

'Then, who is digging on my grave?
20   Say—since I have not guessed!'
—'O it is I, my mistress dear,
Your little dog, who still lives near,
And much I hope my movements here
    Have not disturbed your rest?'

25 'Ah, yes! *You* dig upon my grave . . .
    Why flashed it not on me
That one true heart was left behind!
What feeling do we ever find
To equal among human kind
30   A dog's fidelity!'

'Mistress, I dug upon your grave
    To bury a bone, in case
I should be hungry near this spot
When passing on my daily trot.
35 I am sorry, but I quite forgot
    It was your resting-place.'

1914

Under the Waterfall

'Whenever I plunge my arm, like this,
In a basin of water, I never miss
The sweet sharp sense of a fugitive day
Fetched back from its thickening shroud of gray.
5   Hence the only prime
      And real love-rhyme
      That I know by heart,
      And that leaves no smart,
Is the purl° of a little valley fall   *rippling flow*
10 About three spans wide and two spans tall
Over a table of solid rock,
And into a scoop of the self-same block;
The purl of a runlet that never ceases
In stir of kingdoms, in wars, in peaces;
15 With a hollow boiling voice it speaks
And has spoken since hills were turfless peaks.'

'And why gives this the only prime
Idea to you of a real love-rhyme?
And why does plunging your arm in a bowl
20 Full of spring water, bring throbs to your soul?'

'Well, under the fall, in a crease of the stone,
Though where precisely none ever has known,
Jammed darkly, nothing to show how prized,
And by now with its smoothness opalized,
25   Is a drinking-glass:

For, down that pass
My lover and I
Walked under a sky
Of blue with a leaf-wove awning of green,
30 In the burn of August, to paint the scene,
And we placed our basket of fruit and wine
By the runlet's rim, where we sat to dine;
And when we had drunk from the glass together,
Arched by the oak-copse from the weather,
35 I held the vessel to rinse in the fall,
Where it slipped, and sank, and was past recall,
Though we stooped and plumbed the little abyss
With long bared arms. There the glass still is.
And, as said, if I thrust my arm below
40 Cold water in basin or bowl, a throe°   *violent pang*
From the past awakens a sense of that time,
And the glass we used, and the cascade's rhyme.
The basin seems the pool, and its edge
The hard smooth face of the brook-side ledge,
45 And the leafy pattern of china-ware
The hanging plants that were bathing there.

'By night, by day, when it shines or lours,
There lies intact that chalice of ours,
And its presence adds to the rhyme of love
50 Persistently sung by the fall above.
No lip has touched it since his and mine
In turns therefrom sipped lovers' wine.'

1914

The Walk

You did not walk with me
Of late to the hill-top tree
    By the gated ways,
    As in earlier days;
5   You were weak and lame,
      So you never came,
And I went alone, and I did not mind,
Not thinking of you as left behind.

I walked up there to-day
10 Just in the former way:
    Surveyed around
    The familiar ground
    By myself again:
    What difference, then?
15 Only that underlying sense
Of the look of a room on returning thence.

1912–13   1914

The Voice

Woman much missed, how you call to me, call to me,
Saying that now you are not as you were
When you had changed from the one who was all to me,
But as at first, when our day was fair.

5 Can it be you that I hear? Let me view you, then,
Standing as when I drew near to the town
Where you would wait for me: yes, as I knew you then,
Even to the original air-blue gown!

Or is it only the breeze, in its listlessness
10 Travelling across the wet mead° to me here,   meadow
You being ever dissolved to wan wistlessness,°   inattention
Heard no more again far or near?

Thus I; faltering forward,
Leaves around me falling,
15 Wind oozing thin through the thorn from norward,°   northward
And the woman calling.

Dec. 1912   1914

The Workbox

'See, here's the workbox, little wife,
That I made of polished oak.'
He was a joiner,° of village life;   carpenter
She came of borough folk.°   townspeople

5 He holds the present up to her
As with a smile she nears
And answers to the profferer,
' 'Twill last all my sewing years!'

'I warrant it will. And longer too.
10 'Tis a scantling° that I got   small piece of wood
Off poor John Wayward's coffin, who
Died of they knew not what.

'The shingled pattern that seems to cease
Against your box's rim
15 Continues right on in the piece
That's underground with him.

'And while I worked it made me think
Of timber's varied doom;
One inch where people eat and drink,
20 The next inch in a tomb.

'But why do you look so white, my dear,
   And turn aside your face?
You knew not that good lad, I fear,
   Though he came from your native place?'

25 'How could I know that good young man,
   Though he came from my native town,
When he must have left far earlier than
   I was a woman grown?'

'Ah, no. I should have understood!
30   It shocked you that I gave
To you one end of a piece of wood
   Whose other is in a grave?'

'Don't, dear, despise my intellect,
   Mere accidental things
35 Of that sort never have effect
   On my imaginings.'

Yet still her lips were limp and wan,
   Her face still held aside,
As if she had known not only John,
40   But known of what he died.

1914

During Wind and Rain

They sing their dearest songs—
He, she, all of them—yea,
Treble and tenor and bass,
   And one to play;
5 With the candles mooning° each face. . . .   *lighting*
   Ah, no; the years O!
How the sick leaves reel down in throngs!

They clear the creeping moss—
Elders and juniors—aye,
10 Making the pathways neat
   And the garden gay;
And they build a shady seat. . . .
   Ah, no; the years, the years;
See, the white storm-birds wing across.

15 They are blithely breakfasting all—
Men and maidens—yea,
Under the summer tree,
   With a glimpse of the bay,
While pet fowl come to the knee. . . .

20   Ah, no; the years O!
     And the rotten rose is ript from the wall.

        They change to a high new house,
        He, she, all of them—aye,
        Clocks and carpets and chairs
25   On the lawn all day,
        And brightest things that are theirs. . . .
        Ah, no; the years, the years;
     Down their carved names the rain-drop ploughs.

                                                        1917

In Time of 'The Breaking of Nations'[1]

                        I
        Only a man harrowing clods
        In a slow silent walk
        With an old horse that stumbles and nods
        Half asleep as they stalk.

                        2
5   Only thin smoke without flame
        From the heaps of couch-grass;
        Yet this will go onward the same
        Though Dynasties pass.

                        3
        Yonder a maid and her wight°   man
10   Come whispering by:
        War's annals will cloud into night
        Ere their story die.

1915   1916, 1917

He Never Expected Much

                    [or]
            A CONSIDERATION
    (A reflection) On my Eighty-Sixth Birthday

        Well, World, you have kept faith with me,
            Kept faith with me;
        Upon the whole you have proved to be
            Much as you said you were.
5   Since as a child I used to lie
        Upon the leaze° and watch the sky,   pasture
        Never, I own, expected I
            That life would all be fair.

---

1. Cf. "Thou art my battle axe and weapon of war: for with thee will I break in pieces the nations" (Jeremiah 51.20). The poem was written during World War I.

'Twas then you said, and since have said,
10   Times since have said,
In that mysterious voice you shed
From clouds and hills around:
'Many have loved me desperately,
Many with smooth serenity,
15   While some have shown contempt of me
Till they dropped underground.

'I do not promise overmuch,
Child; overmuch;
Just neutral-tinted haps° and such,'   *happenings*
20   You said to minds like mine.
Wise warning for your credit's sake!
Which I for one failed not to take,
And hence could stem such strain and ache
As each year might assign.

1926   1928

JOSEPH CONRAD
1857–1924

Joseph Conrad was born Józef Teodor Konrad Korzeniowski in Poland (then under Russian rule), son of a Polish patriot who suffered exile in Russia for his Polish nationalist activities and died in 1869, leaving Conrad to be brought up by a maternal uncle. At the age of fifteen he amazed his family and friends by announcing his passionate desire to go to sea; he was eventually allowed to go to Marseilles, France, in 1874, and from there he made a number of voyages on French merchant ships to Martinique and other islands in the Caribbean. In 1878 he signed on an English ship that brought him to the east coast English port of Lowestoft, where (still as an ordinary seaman) he joined the crew of a small coasting vessel plying between Lowestoft and Newcastle. In six voyages between these two ports he learned English. Thus launched on a career in the British merchant service, Conrad sailed on a variety of British ships to East Asia, Australia, India, South America, and Africa, eventually gaining his master's certificate in 1886, the year he became a naturalized British subject. He received his first command in 1888, and in 1890 took a steamboat up the Congo River in nightmarish circumstances (described in *Heart of Darkness*, 1899) that permanently afflicted his health and his imagination.

In the early 1890s he was already thinking of turning some of his Malayan experiences into English fiction, and in 1892–93, when serving as first mate on the *Torrens* sailing from London to Adelaide, he revealed to a sympathetic passenger that he had begun a novel (*Almayer's Folly*), while on the return journey he impressed the young novelist John Galsworthy, who was on board, with his conversation. Conrad found it difficult to obtain a command, and this difficulty, together with the interest aroused by *Almayer's Folly* when it was published in 1895, helped turn him away from the sea to a career as a writer. He settled in London and in 1896 married an Englishwoman. This son of a Polish patriot turned merchant seaman turned writer was henceforth—after twenty years at sea—an English novelist.

In his travels through Asian, African, and Caribbean landscapes that eventually made their way into his fiction, Conrad witnessed at close range the workings of

European empires, including the British, French, Belgian, Dutch, and German, that at the time controlled most of the earth's surface and were extracting from it vast quantities of raw materials and profiting from forced or cheap labor. In the essay "Geography and Some Explorers," Conrad describes the imperial exploitation he observed in Africa as "the vilest scramble for loot that ever disfigured the history of human conscience and geographical exploration." What he saw of the uses and abuses of imperial power helped make him deeply skeptical. Marlow, the intermediate narrator of *Heart of Darkness*, reflects: "The conquest of the earth, which mostly means the taking it away from those who have a different complexion or slightly flatter noses than ourselves, is not a pretty thing when you look into it too much. What redeems it is the idea only. An idea at the back of it. . . ." And yet in this novella, the ideas at the back of colonialism's ruthless greed and violence are hardly shown to redeem anything at all.

Conrad's questioning of the ethics of empire, perhaps harkening back to his childhood experience as a Pole under Russian occupation, is part of his many-faceted exploration of the ethical ambiguities in human experience. In his great novel *Lord Jim* (1900), which like *Heart of Darkness* uses the device of an intermediate narrator, he probes the meaning of a gross failure of duty on the part of a romantic and idealistic young sailor, and by presenting the hero's history from a series of different points of view sustains the ethical questioning to the end. By deploying intermediate narrators and multiple points of view in his fiction, he suggests the complexity of experience and the difficulty of judging human actions.

Although Conrad's plots and exotic settings recall imperial romance and Victorian tales of adventure, he helped develop modern narrative strategies—frame narration, fragmented perspective, flashbacks and flash-forwards, psychologically laden symbolism—that disrupt chronology, render meaning indeterminate, reveal unconscious drives, blur boundaries between civilization and barbarism, and radically cast in doubt epistemological and ethical certainties. Another indication of Conrad's modernist proclivities is the alienation of his characters. Many of his works expose the difficulty of true communion, while also paradoxically exposing how communion is sometimes unexpectedly forced on us, often with someone who may be on the surface our moral opposite, so that we are compelled into a mysterious recognition of our opposite as our true self. Other stories and novels—and Conrad wrote prolifically despite his late start—explore the ways in which the codes we live by are tested in moments of crisis, revealing either their inadequacy or our own. Imagination can corrupt (as with Lord Jim) or save (as in *The Shadow-Line*, 1917), and a total lack of it can either see a person through (Captain MacWhirr in *Typhoon*, 1902) or render a person comically ridiculous (Captain Mitchell in *Nostromo*, 1904). Set in an imaginary Latin American republic, *Nostromo* subtly studies the corrupting effects of politics and "material interests" on personal relationships. Conrad wrote two other political novels—*The Secret Agent* (1906) and *Under Western Eyes* (1911). The latter is a story of Dostoyevskian power about a Russian student who becomes involuntarily associated with anti-government violence in czarist Russia and is maneuvered by circumstances into a position where, although a government spy, he has to pretend to be a revolutionary among revolutionaries. Having to pretend consistently to be the opposite of what he is, this character, like others in Conrad's fiction, is alienated, trapped, unable to communicate. Conrad was as much a pessimist as Hardy, but Conrad aesthetically embodied his pessimism in subtler ways.

He was also a great master of English prose, an astonishing fact given that English was his third language after Polish and French, that he was twenty-one before he learned English, and that to the end of his life he spoke English with a strong foreign accent. He approached English's linguistic and literary conventions aslant, but the seeming handicap of his foreignness helped him bring to the English novel a fresh geopolitical understanding, a formal seriousness, and a psychological depth, all of which opened up new possibilities for imaginative literature in English, as indicated by his profound, if vexed, influence on later writers as different from himself as the Nigerian Chinua Achebe and the Anglo-Trinidadian V. S. Naipaul.

Preface to *The Nigger of the "Narcissus"*[1]

[THE TASK OF THE ARTIST]

A work that aspires, however humbly, to the condition of art should carry its justification in every line. And art itself may be defined as a single-minded attempt to render the highest kind of justice to the visible universe, by bringing to light the truth, manifold and one, underlying its every aspect. It is an attempt to find in its forms, in its colours, in its light, in its shadows, in the aspects of matter and in the facts of life what of each is fundamental, what is enduring and essential—their one illuminating and convincing quality—the very truth of their existence. The artist, then, like the thinker or the scientist, seeks the truth and makes his appeal. Impressed by the aspect of the world the thinker plunges into ideas, the scientist into facts—whence, presently, emerging they make their appeal to those qualities of our being that fit us best for the hazardous enterprise of living. They speak authoritatively to our common-sense, to our intelligence, to our desire of peace or to our desire of unrest; not seldom to our prejudices, sometimes to our fears, often to our egoism—but always to our credulity. And their words are heard with reverence, for their concern is with weighty matters: with the cultivation of our minds and the proper care of our bodies, with the attainment of our ambitions, with the perfection of the means and the glorification of our precious aims.

It is otherwise with the artist.

Confronted by the same enigmatical spectacle the artist descends within himself, and in that lonely region of stress and strife, if he be deserving and fortunate, he finds the terms of his appeal. His appeal is made to our less obvious capacities: to that part of our nature which, because of the warlike conditions of existence, is necessarily kept out of sight within the more resisting and hard qualities—like the vulnerable body within a steel armour. His appeal is less loud, more profound, less distinct, more stirring—and sooner forgotten. Yet its effect endures forever. The changing wisdom of successive generations discards ideas, questions facts, demolishes theories. But the artist appeals to that part of our being which is not dependent on wisdom; to that in us which is a gift and not an acquisition—and, therefore, more permanently enduring. He speaks to our capacity for delight and wonder, to the sense of mystery surrounding our lives; to our sense of pity, and beauty, and pain; to the latent feeling of fellowship with all creation—and to the subtle but invincible conviction of solidarity that knits together the loneliness of innumerable hearts, to the solidarity in dreams, in joy, in sorrow, in aspirations, in illusions, in hope, in fear, which binds men to each other, which binds together all humanity—the dead to the living and the living to the unborn.

---

1. Conrad wrote *The Nigger of the "Narcissus"* in 1896–97, shortly after his marriage; it was published first in *The New Review*, August–December 1897, and then in book form in 1898. Conrad took particular pleasure in writing the novel and later called it "the story by which, as a creative artist, I stand or fall." A few months after finishing it, feeling that he was now wholly dedicated to writing and had "done with the sea," he wrote this preface, which first appeared in the 1898 edition.

It is only some such train of thought, or rather of feeling, that can in a measure explain the aim of the attempt, made in the tale which follows,[2] to present an unrestful episode in the obscure lives of a few individuals out of all the disregarded multitude of the bewildered, the simple and the voiceless. For, if any part of truth dwells in the belief confessed above, it becomes evident that there is not a place of splendour or a dark corner of the earth that does not deserve, if only a passing glance of wonder and pity. The motive then, may be held to justify the matter of the work; but this preface, which is simply an avowal of endeavour, cannot end here—for the avowal is not yet complete.

Fiction—if it at all aspires to be art—appeals to temperament. And in truth it must be, like painting, like music, like all art, the appeal of one temperament to all the other innumerable temperaments whose subtle and resistless power endows passing events with their true meaning, and creates the moral, the emotional atmosphere of the place and time. Such an appeal to be effective must be an impression conveyed through the senses; and, in fact, it cannot be made in any other way, because temperament, whether individual or collective, is not amenable to persuasion. All art, therefore, appeals primarily to the senses, and the artistic aim when expressing itself in written words must also make its appeal through the senses, if its high desire is to reach the secret spring of responsive emotions. It must strenuously aspire to the plasticity of sculpture, to the colour of painting, and to the magic suggestiveness of music—which is the art of arts. And it is only through complete, unswerving devotion to the perfect blending of form and substance; it is only through an unremitting never-discouraged care for the shape and ring of sentences that an approach can be made to plasticity, to colour, and that the light of magic suggestiveness may be brought to play for an evanescent instant over the commonplace surface of words: of the old, old words, worn thin, defaced by ages of careless usage.

The sincere endeavour to accomplish that creative task, to go as far on that road as his strength will carry him, to go undeterred by faltering, weariness or reproach, is the only valid justification for the worker in prose. And if his conscience is clear, his answer to those who in the fulness of a wisdom which looks for immediate profit, demand specifically to be edified, consoled, amused; who demand to be promptly improved, or encouraged, or frightened, or shocked, or charmed, must run thus:—My task which I am trying to achieve is, by the power of the written word to make you hear, to make you feel—it is, before all, to make you *see*. That—and no more, and it is everything. If I succeed, you shall find there according to your deserts: encouragement, consolation, fear, charm—all you demand—and, perhaps, also that glimpse of truth for which you have forgotten to ask.

To snatch in a moment of courage, from the remorseless rush of time, a passing phase of life, is only the beginning of the task. The task approached in tenderness and faith is to hold up unquestioningly, without choice and without fear, the rescued fragment before all eyes in the light of a sincere mood. It is to show its vibration, its colour, its form; and through its movement, its form, and its colour, reveal the substance of its truth—disclose its inspiring secret: the stress and passion within the core of each convincing moment. In a single-minded attempt of that kind, if one be deserving and fortunate, one may perchance attain to such clearness of sincerity that at last the presented vision of regret or pity, of terror or mirth, shall awaken in the hearts of the

2. *The Nigger of the "Narcissus."*

beholders that feeling of unavoidable solidarity; of the solidarity in mysterious origin, in toil, in joy, in hope, in uncertain fate, which binds men to each other and all mankind to the visible world.

It is evident that he who, rightly or wrongly, holds by the convictions expressed above cannot be faithful to any one of the temporary formulas of his craft. The enduring part of them—the truth which each only imperfectly veils—should abide with him as the most precious of his possessions, but they all: Realism, Romanticism, Naturalism, even the unofficial sentimentalism (which like the poor, is exceedingly difficult to get rid of),[3] all these gods must, after a short period of fellowship, abandon him—even on the very threshold of the temple—to the stammerings of his conscience and to the outspoken consciousness of the difficulties of his work. In that uneasy solitude the supreme cry of Art for Art itself, loses the exciting ring of its apparent immorality. It sounds far off. It has ceased to be a cry, and is heard only as a whisper, often incomprehensible, but at times and faintly encouraging.

Sometimes, stretched at ease in the shade of a roadside tree, we watch the motions of a labourer in a distant field, and after a time, begin to wonder languidly as to what the fellow may be at. We watch the movements of his body, the waving of his arms, we see him bend down, stand up, hesitate, begin again. It may add to the charm of an idle hour to be told the purpose of his exertions. If we know he is trying to lift a stone, to dig a ditch, to uproot a stump, we look with a more real interest at his efforts; we are disposed to condone the jar of his agitation upon the restfulness of the landscape; and even, if in a brotherly frame of mind, we may bring ourselves to forgive his failure. We understood his object, and, after all, the fellow has tried, and perhaps he had not the strength—and perhaps he had not the knowledge. We forgive, go on our way—and forget.

And so it is with the workman of art. Art is long and life is short,[4] and success is very far off. And thus, doubtful of strength to travel so far, we talk a little about the aim—the aim of art, which, like life itself, is inspiring, difficult— obscured by mists. It is not in the clear logic of a triumphant conclusion; it is not in the unveiling of one of those heartless secrets which are called the Laws of Nature. It is not less great, but only more difficult.

To arrest, for the space of a breath, the hands busy about the work of the earth, and compel men entranced by the sight of distant goals to glance for a moment at the surrounding vision of form and colour, of sunshine and shadows; to make them pause for a look, for a sigh, for a smile—such is the aim, difficult and evanescent, and reserved only for a very few to achieve. But sometimes, by the deserving and the fortunate, even that task is accomplished. And when it is accomplished—behold!—all the truth of life is there: a moment of vision, a sigh, a smile—and the return to an eternal rest.

1897   1898

---

3. "For the poor always ye have with you" (John 12.8).

4. *Ars longa, vita brevis:* a Latin proverb, deriving from a dictum of the Greek physician Hippocrates.

Heart of Darkness   This story is derived from Conrad's experience in the Congo in 1890. Like Marlow, the narrator of the story, Conrad had as a child determined one day to visit the heart of Africa. "It was in 1868, when nine years old or thereabouts, that while looking at a map of Africa at the time and putting my finger on the blank space then representing the unsolved mystery of that continent, I said to myself with absolute assurance and an amazing audacity which are no longer in my character now: 'When I grow up I shall go there' " (A Personal Record, 1912).

Conrad was promised a job as a Congo River pilot through the influence of his distant cousin Marguerite Poradowska, who lived in Brussels and knew important officials of the Belgian company that exploited the Congo. At this time the Congo, although nominally an independent state, the Congo Free State (État Indépendent du Congo), was virtually the personal property of Leopold II, king of Belgium, who made a fortune out of it. Later, the appalling abuses involved in the naked colonial exploitation that went on in the Congo were exposed to public view, and international criticism compelled the setting up of a committee of inquiry in 1904. From 1885 to 1908 masses of Congolese men were worked to death, women were raped, hands were cut off, villages were looted and burned. What Conrad saw in 1890 shocked him profoundly and shook his view of the moral basis of colonialism, of exploration and trade in newly discovered countries, indeed of civilization in general. "Heart of Darkness is experience, too," Conrad wrote in his 1917 "Author's Note," "but it is experience pushed a little (and only very little) beyond the actual facts of the case for the perfectly legitimate, I believe, purpose of bringing it home to the minds and bosoms of the readers." And later he told Edward Garnett: "Before the Congo I was just a mere animal."

Conrad arrived in Africa in May 1890 and made his way up the Congo River very much as described in Heart of Darkness. At Kinshasa (which Conrad spells Kinchassa) on Stanley Pool, which he reached after an exhausting two-hundred-mile trek from Matadi, near the mouth of the river, Conrad was taken aback to learn that the steamer of which he was to be captain had been damaged and was undergoing repairs. He was sent as supernumerary on another steamer to learn the river. This steamer was sent to Stanley Falls to collect and bring back to Kinshasa one Georges Antoine Klein, an agent of the company who had fallen so gravely ill that he died on board. Conrad then fell seriously ill and eventually returned to London in January 1891 without ever having served as a Congo River pilot. The Congo experience permanently impaired his health; it also permanently haunted his imagination. The nightmare atmosphere of Heart of Darkness is an accurate reflection of Conrad's response to his traumatic experience.

The theme of the story is partly the "choice of nightmares" facing whites in the Congo—either to become like the commercially minded manager, who sees Africa, its people, and its resources solely as instruments of financial gain, or to become like Kurtz, the self-tortured and corrupted idealist (inspired by Klein). The manager is a "hollow man" (T. S. Eliot used a quotation from this story as one epigraph for his poem "The Hollow Men"); his only objections to Kurtz are commercial, not moral: Kurtz's methods are "unsound" and would therefore lose the company money. At the last Kurtz seems to recognize the moral horror of his having succumbed to the dark temptations that African life posed for the European. "He had summed up—he had judged." But the story also has other levels of meaning, and the counterpointing of Western civilization in Europe with what that civilization has done in Africa (see the concluding interview between Marlow and Kurtz's "intended"—based on an interview between Conrad and the dead Klein's fiancée) throws out several of these. The story first appeared in Blackwood's Magazine in 1899 and was revised for book publication in 1902 as part of Youth: A Narrative, and Two Other Stories. See also the extract from Chinua Achebe's essay "An Image of Africa: Racism in Conrad's Heart of Darkness" (p. 2709).

Heart of Darkness

1

The *Nellie*, a cruising yawl,[1] swung to her anchor without a flutter of the sails, and was at rest. The flood had made, the wind was nearly calm, and being bound down the river, the only thing for it was to come to and wait for the turn of the tide.

The sea-reach of the Thames stretched before us like the beginning of an interminable waterway. In the offing the sea and the sky were welded together without a joint, and in the luminous space the tanned sails of the barges drifting up with the tide seemed to stand still in red clusters of canvas sharply peaked, with gleams of varnished sprits. A haze rested on the low shores that ran out to sea in vanishing flatness. The air was dark above Gravesend,[2] and farther back still seemed condensed into a mournful gloom, brooding motionless over the biggest, and the greatest, town on earth.

The Director of Companies was our captain and our host. We four affectionately watched his back as he stood in the bows looking to seaward. On the whole river there was nothing that looked half so nautical. He resembled a pilot, which to a seaman is trustworthiness personified. It was difficult to realise his work was not out there in the luminous estuary, but behind him, within the brooding gloom.

Between us there was, as I have already said somewhere, the bond of the sea. Besides holding our hearts together through long periods of separation, it had the effect of making us tolerant of each other's yarns—and even convictions. The Lawyer—the best of old fellows—had, because of his many years and many virtues, the only cushion on deck, and was lying on the only rug. The Accountant had brought out already a box of dominoes, and was toying architecturally with the bones. Marlow sat cross-legged right aft, leaning against the mizzenmast. He had sunken cheeks, a yellow complexion, a straight back, an ascetic aspect, and, with his arms dropped, the palms of hands outwards, resembled an idol. The Director, satisfied the anchor had good hold, made his way aft and sat down amongst us. We exchanged a few words lazily. Afterwards there was silence on board the yacht. For some reason or other we did not begin that game of dominoes. We felt meditative, and fit for nothing but placid staring. The day was ending in a serenity of still and exquisite brilliance. The water shone pacifically; the sky, without a speck, was a benign immensity of unstained light; the very mist on the Essex marshes was like a gauzy and radiant fabric, hung from the wooded rises inland, and draping the low shores in diaphanous folds. Only the gloom to the west, brooding over the upper reaches, became more sombre every minute, as if angered by the approach of the sun.

And at last, in its curved and imperceptible fall, the sun sank low, and from glowing white changed to a dull red without rays and without heat, as if about to go out suddenly, stricken to death by the touch of that gloom brooding over a crowd of men.

Forthwith a change came over the waters, and the serenity became less brilliant but more profound. The old river in its broad reach rested unruffled

1. Two-masted boat.
2. River port on the south bank of the Thames twenty-four miles east (downriver) of London.

at the decline of day, after ages of good service done to the race that peopled its banks, spread out in the tranquil dignity of a waterway leading to the uttermost ends of the earth. We looked at the venerable stream not in the vivid flush of a short day that comes and departs for ever, but in the august light of abiding memories. And indeed nothing is easier for a man who has, as the phrase goes, "followed the sea" with reverence and affection, than to evoke the great spirit of the past upon the lower reaches of the Thames. The tidal current runs to and fro in its unceasing service, crowded with memories of men and ships it has borne to the rest of home or to the battles of the sea. It had known and served all the men of whom the nation is proud, from Sir Francis Drake to Sir John Franklin,[3] knights all, titled and untitled—the great knights-errant of the sea. It had borne all the ships whose names are like jewels flashing in the night of time, from the *Golden Hind* returning with her round flanks full of treasure, to be visited by the Queen's Highness and thus pass out of the gigantic tale, to the *Erebus* and *Terror*, bound on other conquests— and that never returned. It had known the ships and the men. They had sailed from Deptford, from Greenwich, from Erith—the adventurers and the settlers; kings' ships and the ships of men on 'Change; captains, admirals, the dark "interlopers"[4] of the Eastern trade, and the commissioned "generals" of East India fleets. Hunters for gold or pursuers of fame, they all had gone out on that stream, bearing the sword, and often the torch, messengers of the might within the land, bearers of a spark from the sacred fire. What greatness had not floated on the ebb of that river into the mystery of an unknown earth! . . . The dreams of men, the seed of commonwealths, the germs of empires.

The sun set; the dusk fell on the stream, and lights began to appear along the shore. The Chapman lighthouse, a three-legged thing erect on a mud-flat, shone strongly. Lights of ships moved in the fairway[5]—a great stir of lights going up and going down. And farther west on the upper reaches the place of the monstrous town was still marked ominously on the sky, a brooding gloom in sunshine, a lurid glare under the stars.

"And this also," said Marlow suddenly, "has been one of the dark places of the earth."

He was the only man of us who still "followed the sea." The worst that could be said of him was that he did not represent his class. He was a seaman, but he was a wanderer too, while most seamen lead, if one may so express it, a sedentary life. Their minds are of the stay-at-home order, and their home is always with them—the ship; and so is their country—the sea. One ship is very much like another, and the sea is always the same. In the immutability of their surroundings the foreign shores, the foreign faces, the changing immensity of life, glide past, veiled not by a sense of mystery but by a slightly disdainful ignorance; for there is nothing mysterious to a seaman unless it be the sea itself, which is the mistress of his existence and as inscrutable as Destiny. For

---

3. Sir John Franklin (1786–1847), Arctic explorer who in 1845 commanded an expedition consisting of the ships *Erebus* and *Terror* in search of the Northwest Passage. The ships never returned. Sir Francis Drake (ca. 1540–1596), Elizabethan naval hero and explorer, sailed around the world on his ship *The Golden Hind*. Queen Elizabeth knighted Drake aboard his ship, loaded with captured Spanish treasure, on his return.
4. Private ships muscling in on the monopoly of the East India Company, which was founded in

1600, lost its trading monopoly in 1813, and transferred its governmental functions to the Crown in 1858. Deptford, on the south bank of the Thames, on the eastern edge of London, was once an important dockyard. Greenwich is on the south bank of the Thames immediately east of Deptford. Erith is eight miles farther east. " 'Change": the Stock Exchange.
5. Navigable part of a river, through which ships enter and depart.

the rest, after his hours of work, a casual stroll or a casual spree on shore suffices to unfold for him the secret of a whole continent, and generally he finds the secret not worth knowing. The yarns of seamen have a direct simplicity, the whole meaning of which lies within the shell of a cracked nut. But Marlow was not typical (if his propensity to spin yarns be excepted), and to him the meaning of an episode was not inside like a kernel but outside, enveloping the tale which brought it out only as a glow brings out a haze, in the likeness of one of these misty halos that sometimes are made visible by the spectral illumination of moonshine.

His remark did not seem at all surprising. It was just like Marlow. It was accepted in silence. No one took the trouble to grunt even; and presently he said, very slow:

"I was thinking of very old times, when the Romans first came here, nineteen hundred years ago—the other day. . . . Light came out of this river since—you say Knights? Yes; but it is like a running blaze on a plain, like a flash of lightning in the clouds. We live in the flicker—may it last as long as the old earth keeps rolling! But darkness was here yesterday. Imagine the feelings of a commander of a fine—what d'ye call 'em?—trireme[6] in the Mediterranean, ordered suddenly to the north; run overland across the Gauls in a hurry; put in charge of one of these craft the legionaries—a wonderful lot of handy men they must have been too—used to build, apparently by the hundred, in a month or two, if we may believe what we read. Imagine him here—the very end of the world, a sea the colour of lead, a sky the colour of smoke, a kind of ship about as rigid as a concertina—and going up this river with stores, or orders, or what you like. Sandbanks, marshes, forests, savages—precious little to eat fit for a civilised man, nothing but Thames water to drink. No Falernian wine[7] here, no going ashore. Here and there a military camp lost in a wilderness, like a needle in a bundle of hay—cold, fog, tempests, disease, exile, and death—death skulking in the air, in the water, in the bush. They must have been dying like flies here. Oh yes—he did it. Did it very well, too, no doubt, and without thinking much about it either, except afterwards to brag of what he had gone through in his time, perhaps. They were men enough to face the darkness. And perhaps he was cheered by keeping his eye on a chance of promotion to the fleet at Ravenna[8] by and by, if he had good friends in Rome and survived the awful climate. Or think of a decent young citizen in a toga—perhaps too much dice, you know—coming out here in the train of some prefect, or tax-gatherer, or trader, even, to mend his fortunes. Land in a swamp, march through the woods, and in some inland post feel the savagery, the utter savagery, had closed round him—all that mysterious life of the wilderness that stirs in the forest, in the jungles, in the hearts of wild men. There's no initiation either into such mysteries. He has to live in the midst of the incomprehensible, which is also detestable. And it has a fascination, too, that goes to work upon him. The fascination of the abomination—you know. Imagine the growing regrets, the longing to escape, the powerless disgust, the surrender, the hate."

He paused.

"Mind," he began again, lifting one arm from the elbow, the palm of the

6. Ancient Greek and Roman galley with three ranks of oars.
7. Wine from a famed wine-making district in Campania (Italy).

8. A city in northern Italy once directly on the Adriatic Sea and an important naval station in Roman times. It is now about six miles from the sea, connected with it by a canal.

hand outwards, so that, with his legs folded before him, he had the pose of a Buddha preaching in European clothes and without a lotus-flower—"Mind, none of us would feel exactly like this. What saves us is efficiency—the devotion to efficiency. But these chaps were not much account, really. They were no colonists; their administration was merely a squeeze, and nothing more, I suspect. They were conquerors, and for that you want only brute force—nothing to boast of, when you have it, since your strength is just an accident arising from the weakness of others. They grabbed what they could get for the sake of what was to be got. It was just robbery with violence, aggravated murder on a great scale, and men going at it blind—as is very proper for those who tackle a darkness. The conquest of the earth, which mostly means the taking it away from those who have a different complexion or slightly flatter noses than ourselves, is not a pretty thing when you look into it too much. What redeems it is the idea only. An idea at the back of it; not a sentimental pretence but an idea; and an unselfish belief in the idea—something you can set up, and bow down before, and offer a sacrifice to. . . ."

He broke off. Flames glided in the river, small green flames, red flames, white flames, pursuing, overtaking, joining, crossing each other—then separating slowly or hastily. The traffic of the great city went on in the deepening night upon the sleepless river. We looked on, waiting patiently—there was nothing else to do till the end of the flood; but it was only after a long silence, when he said, in a hesitating voice, "I suppose you fellows remember I did once turn fresh-water sailor for a bit," that we knew we were fated, before the ebb began to run, to hear about one of Marlow's inconclusive experiences.

"I don't want to bother you much with what happened to me personally," he began, showing in this remark the weakness of many tellers of tales who seem so often unaware of what their audience would best like to hear; "yet to understand the effect of it on me you ought to know how I got out there, what I saw, how I went up that river to the place where I first met the poor chap. It was the farthest point of navigation and the culminating point of my experience. It seemed somehow to throw a kind of light on everything about me—and into my thoughts. It was sombre enough too—and pitiful—not extraordinary in any way—not very clear either. No, not very clear. And yet it seemed to throw a kind of light.

"I had then, as you remember, just returned to London after a lot of Indian Ocean, Pacific, China Seas—a regular dose of the East—six years or so, and I was loafing about, hindering you fellows in your work and invading your homes, just as though I had got a heavenly mission to civilise you. It was very fine for a time, but after a bit I did get tired of resting. Then I began to look for a ship—I should think the hardest work on earth. But the ships wouldn't even look at me. And I got tired of that game too.

"Now when I was a little chap I had a passion for maps. I would look for hours at South America, or Africa, or Australia, and lose myself in all the glories of exploration. At that time there were many blank spaces on the earth, and when I saw one that looked particularly inviting on a map (but they all look that) I would put my finger on it and say, When I grow up I will go there. The North Pole was one of these places, I remember. Well, I haven't been there yet, and shall not try now. The glamour's off. Other places were scattered about the Equator, and in every sort of latitude all over the two hemispheres. I have been in some of them, and . . . well, we won't talk about that. But there was one yet—the biggest, the most blank, so to speak—that I had a hankering after.

"True, by this time it was not a blank space any more. It had got filled since my boyhood with rivers and lakes and names. It had ceased to be a blank space of delightful mystery—a white patch for a boy to dream gloriously over. It had become a place of darkness. But there was in it one river especially, a mighty big river, that you could see on the map, resembling an immense snake uncoiled, with its head in the sea, its body at rest curving afar over a vast country, and its tail lost in the depths of the land. And as I looked at the map of it in a shop-window, it fascinated me as a snake would a bird—a silly little bird. Then I remembered there was a big concern, a Company for trade on that river. Dash it all! I thought to myself, they can't trade without using some kind of craft on that lot of fresh water—steamboats! Why shouldn't I try to get charge of one? I went on along Fleet Street,[9] but could not shake off the idea. The snake had charmed me.

"You understand it was a Continental concern, that Trading Society; but I have a lot of relations living on the Continent, because it's cheap and not so nasty as it looks, they say.

"I am sorry to own I began to worry them. This was already a fresh departure for me. I was not used to get things that way, you know. I always went my own road and on my own legs where I had a mind to go. I wouldn't have believed it of myself; but, then—you see—I felt somehow I must get there by hook or by crook. So I worried them. The men said, 'My dear fellow,' and did nothing. Then—would you believe it?—I tried the women. I, Charlie Marlow, set the women to work—to get a job. Heavens! Well, you see, the notion drove me. I had an aunt, a dear enthusiastic soul. She wrote: 'It will be delightful. I am ready to do anything, anything for you. It is a glorious idea. I know the wife of a very high personage in the Administration, and also a man who has lots of influence with,' etc. etc. She was determined to make no end of fuss to get me appointed skipper of a river steamboat, if such was my fancy.

"I got my appointment—of course; and I got it very quick. It appears the Company had received news that one of their captains had been killed in a scuffle with the natives. This was my chance, and it made me the more anxious to go. It was only months and months afterwards, when I made the attempt to recover what was left of the body, that I heard the original quarrel arose from a misunderstanding about some hens. Yes, two black hens. Fresleven— that was the fellow's name, a Dane—thought himself wronged somehow in the bargain, so he went ashore and started to hammer the chief of the village with a stick. Oh, it didn't surprise me in the least to hear this, and at the same time to be told that Fresleven was the gentlest, quietest creature that ever walked on two legs. No doubt he was; but he had been a couple of years already out there engaged in the noble cause, you know, and he probably felt the need at last of asserting his self-respect in some way. Therefore he whacked the old nigger mercilessly, while a big crowd of his people watched him, thunder- struck, till some man—I was told the chief's son—in desperation at hearing the old chap yell, made a tentative jab with a spear at the white man—and of course it went quite easy between the shoulder-blades. Then the whole pop- ulation cleared into the forest, expecting all kinds of calamities to happen, while, on the other hand, the steamer Fresleven commanded left also in a bad panic, in charge of the engineer, I believe. Afterwards nobody seemed to trou- ble much about Fresleven's remains, till I got out and stepped into his shoes. I couldn't let it rest, though; but when an opportunity offered at last to meet

9. Street in central London.

1896 / JOSEPH CONRAD

my predecessor, the grass growing through his ribs was tall enough to hide his bones. They were all there. The supernatural being had not been touched after he fell. And the village was deserted, the huts gaped black, rotting, all askew within the fallen enclosures. A calamity had come to it, sure enough. The people had vanished. Mad terror had scattered them, men, women, and children, through the bush, and they had never returned. What became of the hens I don't know either. I should think the cause of progress got them, anyhow. However, through this glorious affair I got my appointment, before I had fairly begun to hope for it.

"I flew around like mad to get ready, and before forty-eight hours I was crossing the Channel to show myself to my employers, and sign the contract. In a very few hours I arrived in a city that always makes me think of a whited sepulchre. Prejudice no doubt. I had no difficulty in finding the Company's offices. It was the biggest thing in the town, and everybody I met was full of it. They were going to run an over-sea empire, and make no end of coin by trade.

"A narrow and deserted street in deep shadow, high houses, innumerable windows with venetian blinds, a dead silence, grass sprouting between the stones, imposing carriage archways right and left, immense double doors standing ponderously ajar. I slipped through one of these cracks, went up a swept and ungarnished staircase, as arid as a desert, and opened the first door I came to. Two women, one fat and the other slim, sat on straw-bottomed chairs, knitting black wool. The slim one got up and walked straight at me— still knitting with downcast eyes—and only just as I began to think of getting out of her way, as you would for a somnambulist, stood still, and looked up. Her dress was as plain as an umbrella-cover, and she turned round without a word and preceded me into a waiting-room. I gave my name, and looked about. Deal table in the middle, plain chairs all round the walls, on one end a large shining map, marked with all the colours of a rainbow. There was a vast amount of red—good to see at any time, because one knows that some real work is done in there, a deuce of a lot of blue, a little green, smears of orange, and, on the East Coast, a purple patch, to show where the jolly pioneers of progress drink the jolly lager-beer. However, I wasn't going into any of these. I was going into the yellow. Dead in the centre. And the river was there— fascinating—deadly—like a snake. Ough! A door opened, a white-haired secretarial head, but wearing a compassionate expression, appeared, and a skinny forefinger beckoned me into the sanctuary. Its light was dim, and a heavy writing desk squatted in the middle. From behind that structure came out an impression of pale plumpness in a frockcoat. The great man himself. He was five feet six, I should judge, and had his grip on the handle-end of ever so many millions. He shook hands, I fancy, murmured vaguely, was satisfied with my French. *Bon voyage.*

"In about forty-five seconds I found myself again in the waiting-room with the compassionate secretary, who, full of desolation and sympathy, made me sign some document. I believe I undertook amongst other things not to disclose any trade secrets. Well, I am not going to.

"I began to feel slightly uneasy. You know I am not used to such ceremonies, and there was something ominous in the atmosphere. It was just as though I had been let into some conspiracy—I don't know—something not quite right; and I was glad to get out. In the outer room the two women knitted black wool feverishly. People were arriving, and the younger one was walking back and forth introducing them. The old one sat on her chair. Her flat cloth slippers were propped up on a foot-warmer, and a cat reposed on her lap. She wore a starched white affair on her head, had a wart on one cheek, and silver-rimmed spectacles hung on the tip of her nose. She glanced at me above the glasses. The swift and indifferent placidity of that look troubled me. Two youths with foolish and cheery countenances were being piloted over, and she threw at them the same quick glance of unconcerned wisdom. She seemed to know all about them and about me too. An eerie feeling came over me. She seemed uncanny and fateful. Often far away there I thought of these two, guarding the door of Darkness, knitting black wool as for a warm pall, one introducing, introducing continuously to the unknown, the other scrutinising the cheery and foolish faces with unconcerned old eyes. *Ave!* Old knitter of black wool. *Morituri te salutant.*[1] Not many of those she looked at ever saw her again— not half, by a long way.

"There was yet a visit to the doctor. 'A simple formality,' assured me the secretary, with an air of taking an immense part in all my sorrows. Accordingly a young chap wearing his hat over the left eyebrow, some clerk I suppose— there must have been clerks in the business, though the house was as still as a house in a city of the dead—came from somewhere upstairs, and led me forth. He was shabby and careless, with ink-stains on the sleeves of his jacket, and his cravat was large and billowy, under a chin shaped like the toe of an old boot. It was a little too early for the doctor, so I proposed a drink, and thereupon he developed a vein of joviality. As we sat over our vermuths he glorified the Company's business, and by and by I expressed casually my surprise at him not going out there. He became very cool and collected all at once. 'I am not such a fool as I look, quoth Plato to his disciples,' he said sententiously, emptied his glass with great resolution, and we rose.

"The old doctor felt my pulse, evidently thinking of something else the while. 'Good, good for there,' he mumbled, and then with a certain eagerness asked me whether I would let him measure my head. Rather surprised, I said Yes, when he produced a thing like callipers and got the dimensions back and front and every way, taking notes carefully. He was an unshaven little man in a threadbare coat like a gaberdine, with his feet in slippers, and I thought him a harmless fool. 'I always ask leave, in the interests of science, to measure the crania of those going out there,' he said. 'And when they come back too?' I asked. 'Oh, I never see them,' he remarked; 'and, moreover, the changes take place inside, you know.' He smiled, as if at some quiet joke. 'So you are going out there. Famous. Interesting too.' He gave me a searching glance, and made another note. 'Ever any madness in your family?' he asked, in a matter-of-fact tone. I felt very annoyed. 'Is that question in the interests of science too?' 'It would be,' he said, without taking notice of my irritation, 'interesting for science to watch the mental changes of individuals, on the spot, but . . . ' 'Are you an alienist?'[2] I interrupted. 'Every doctor should be—a little,' answered that original[3] imperturbably. 'I have a little theory which you Messieurs who go out there must help me to prove. This is my share in the advantages my country shall reap from the possession of such a magnificent dependency. The mere wealth I leave to others. Pardon my questions, but you are the first

1. "Hail! . . . Those who are about to die salute you" (Latin). The Roman gladiators' salute to the emperor on entering the arena.
2. Doctor who treats mental diseases. (The term has now been replaced by *psychiatrist*.)
3. Eccentric person.

Englishman coming under my observation . . . ' I hastened to assure him I was not in the least typical. 'If I were,' said I, 'I wouldn't be talking like this with you.' 'What you say is rather profound, and probably erroneous,' he said, with a laugh. 'Avoid irritation more than exposure to the sun. Adieu. How do you English say, eh? Good-bye. Ah! Good-bye. Adieu. In the tropics one must before everything keep calm.' . . . He lifted a warning forefinger. . . . '*Du calme, du calme. Adieu.*'

"One thing more remained to do—say good-bye to my excellent aunt. I found her triumphant. I had a cup of tea—the last decent cup of tea for many days—and in a room that most soothingly looked just as you would expect a lady's drawing-room to look, we had a long quiet chat by the fireside. In the course of these confidences it became quite plain to me I had been represented to the wife of the high dignitary, and goodness knows to how many more people besides, as an exceptional and gifted creature—a piece of good fortune for the Company—a man you don't get hold of every day. Good heavens! and I was going to take charge of a two-penny-halfpenny river-steamboat with a penny whistle attached! It appeared, however, I was also one of the Workers, with a capital—you know. Something like an emissary of light, something like a lower sort of apostle. There had been a lot of such rot let loose in print and talk just about that time, and the excellent woman, living right in the rush of all that humbug, got carried off her feet. She talked about 'weaning those ignorant millions from their horrid ways,' till, upon my word, she made me quite uncomfortable. I ventured to hint that the Company was run for profit.

" 'You forget, dear Charlie, that the labourer is worthy of his hire,' she said brightly. It's queer how out of touch with truth women are. They live in a world of their own, and there had never been anything like it, and never can be. It is too beautiful altogether, and if they were to set it up it would go to pieces before the first sunset. Some confounded fact we men have been living contentedly with ever since the day of creation would start up and knock the whole thing over.

"After this I got embraced, told to wear flannel, be sure to write often, and so on—and I left. In the street—I don't know why—a queer feeling came to me that I was an impostor. Odd thing that I, who used to clear out for any part of the world at twenty-four hours' notice, with less thought than most men give to the crossing of a street, had a moment—I won't say of hesitation, but of startled pause, before this commonplace affair. The best way I can explain it to you is by saying that, for a second or two, I felt as though, instead of going to the centre of a continent, I were about to set off for the centre of the earth.

"I left in a French steamer, and she called in every blamed port they have out there, for, as far as I could see, the sole purpose of landing soldiers and custom-house officers. I watched the coast. Watching a coast as it slips by the ship is like thinking about an enigma. There it is before you—smiling, frowning, inviting, grand, mean, insipid, or savage, and always mute with an air of whispering, Come and find out. This one was almost featureless, as if still in the making, with an aspect of monotonous grimness. The edge of a colossal jungle, so dark green as to be almost black, fringed with white surf, ran straight, like a ruled line, far, far away along a blue sea whose glitter was blurred by a creeping mist. The sun was fierce, the land seemed to glisten and drip with steam. Here and there greyish-whitish specks showed up clustered inside the white surf, with a flag flying above them perhaps—settlements some centuries old, and still no bigger than pin-heads on the untouched expanse of their background. We pounded along, stopped, landed soldiers; went on, landed custom-house clerks to levy toll in what looked like a God-forsaken wilderness, with a tin shed and a flag-pole lost in it; landed more soldiers—to take care of the custom-house clerks presumably. Some, I heard, got drowned in the surf; but whether they did or not, nobody seemed particularly to care. They were just flung out there, and on we went. Every day the coast looked the same, as though we had not moved; but we passed various places—trading places—with names like Gran' Bassam, Little Popo; names that seemed to belong to some sordid farce acted in front of a sinister back-cloth. The idleness of a passenger, my isolation amongst all these men with whom I had no point of contact, the oily and languid sea, the uniform sombreness of the coast, seemed to keep me away from the truth of things, within the toil of a mournful and senseless delusion. The voice of the surf heard now and then was a positive pleasure, like the speech of a brother. It was something natural, that had its reason, that had a meaning. Now and then a boat from the shore gave one a momentary contact with reality. It was paddled by black fellows. You could see from afar the white of their eyeballs glistening. They shouted, sang; their bodies streamed with perspiration; they had faces like grotesque masks—these chaps; but they had bone, muscle, a wild vitality, an intense energy of move-ment, that was as natural and true as the surf along their coast. They wanted no excuse for being there. They were a great comfort to look at. For a time I would feel I belonged still to a world of straightforward facts; but the feeling would not last long. Something would turn up to scare it away. Once, I remem-ber, we came upon a man-of-war anchored off the coast. There wasn't even a shed there, and she was shelling the bush. It appears the French had one of their wars going on thereabouts. Her ensign dropped limp like a rag; the muz-zles of the long six-inch guns stuck out all over the low hull; the greasy, slimy swell swung her up lazily and let her down, swaying her thin masts. In the empty immensity of earth, sky, and water, there she was, incomprehensible, firing into a continent. Pop, would go one of the six-inch guns; a small flame would dart and vanish, a little white smoke would disappear, a tiny projectile would give a feeble screech—and nothing happened. Nothing could happen. There was a touch of insanity in the proceeding, a sense of lugubrious drollery in the sight; and it was not dissipated by somebody on board assuring me earnestly there was a camp of natives—he called them enemies!—hidden out of sight somewhere.

"We gave her her letters (I heard the men in that lonely ship were dying of fever at the rate of three a day) and went on. We called at some more places with farcical names, where the merry dance of death and trade goes on in a still and earthy atmosphere as of an overheated catacomb; all along the form-less coast bordered by dangerous surf, as if Nature herself had tried to ward off intruders; in and out of rivers, streams of death in life, whose banks were rotting into mud, whose waters, thickened into slime, invaded the contorted mangroves,[4] that seemed to writhe at us in the extremity of an impotent despair. Nowhere did we stop long enough to get a particularised impression, but the general sense of vague and oppressive wonder grew upon me. It was like a weary pilgrimage amongst hints for nightmares.

"It was upward of thirty days before I saw the mouth of the big river. We

4. Tropical evergreen trees or shrubs with roots and stems forming dense thickets.

anchored off the seat of the government. But my work would not begin till some two hundred miles farther on. So as soon as I could I made a start for a place thirty miles higher up.

"I had my passage on a little sea-going steamer. Her captain was a Swede, and knowing me for a seaman, invited me on the bridge. He was a young man, lean, fair, and morose, with lanky hair and a shuffling gait. As we left the miserable little wharf, he tossed his head contemptuously at the shore. 'Been living there?' he asked. I said, 'Yes.' 'Fine lot these government chaps—are they not?' he went on, speaking English with great precision and considerable bitterness. 'It is funny what some people will do for a few francs a month. I wonder what becomes of that kind when it goes up country?' I said to him I expected to see that soon. 'So-o-o!' he exclaimed. He shuffled athwart, keeping one eye ahead vigilantly. 'Don't be too sure,' he continued. 'The other day I took up a man who hanged himself on the road. He was a Swede, too.' 'Hanged himself! Why, in God's name?' I cried. He kept on looking out watchfully. 'Who knows? The sun too much for him, or the country perhaps.'

"At last we opened a reach. A rocky cliff appeared, mounds of turned-up earth by the shore, houses on a hill, others with iron roofs, amongst a waste of excavations, or hanging to the declivity. A continuous noise of the rapids above hovered over this scene of inhabited devastation. A lot of people, mostly black and naked, moved about like ants. A jetty[5] projected into the river. A blinding sunlight drowned all this at times in a sudden recrudescence of glare. 'There's your Company's station,' said the Swede, pointing to three wooden barrack-like structures on the rocky slope. 'I will send your things up. Four boxes did you say? So. Farewell.'

"I came upon a boiler wallowing in the grass, then found a path leading up the hill. It turned aside for the boulders, and also for an undersized railway truck lying there on its back with its wheels in the air. One was off. The thing looked as dead as the carcass of some animal. I came upon more pieces of decaying machinery, a stack of rusty nails. To the left a clump of trees made a shady spot, where dark things seemed to stir feebly. I blinked, the path was steep. A horn tooted to the right, and I saw the black people run. A heavy and dull detonation shook the ground, a puff of smoke came out of the cliff, and that was all. No change appeared on the face of the rock. They were building a railway. The cliff was not in the way or anything; but this objectless blasting was all the work going on.

"A slight clinking behind me made me turn my head. Six black men advanced in a file, toiling up the path. They walked erect and slow, balancing small baskets full of earth on their heads, and the clink kept time with their footsteps. Black rags were wound round their loins, and the short ends behind waggled to and fro like tails. I could see every rib, the joints of their limbs were like knots in a rope; each had an iron collar on his neck, and all were connected together with a chain whose bights swung between them, rhythmically clinking. Another report from the cliff made me think suddenly of that ship of war I had seen firing into a continent. It was the same kind of ominous voice; but these men could by no stretch of imagination be called enemies. They were called criminals, and the outraged law, like the bursting shells, had come to them, an insoluble mystery from the sea. All their meagre breasts panted together, the violently dilated nostrils quivered, the eyes stared stonily uphill.

5. Wharf or pier.

They passed me within six inches, without a glance, with that complete, death-like indifference of unhappy savages. Behind this raw matter one of the reclaimed, the product of the new forces at work, strolled despondently, carrying a rifle by its middle. He had a uniform jacket with one button off, and seeing a white man on the path, hoisted his weapon to his shoulder with alacrity. This was simple prudence, white men being so much alike at a distance that he could not tell who I might be. He was speedily reassured, and with a large, white, rascally grin, and a glance at his charge, seemed to take me into partnership in his exalted trust. After all, I also was a part of the great cause of these high and just proceedings.

"Instead of going up, I turned and descended to the left. My idea was to let that chain-gang get out of sight before I climbed the hill. You know I am not particularly tender; I've had to strike and to fend off. I've had to resist and to attack sometimes—that's only one way of resisting—without counting the exact cost, according to the demands of such sort of life as I had blundered into. I've seen the devil of violence, and the devil of greed, and the devil of hot desire; but, by all the stars! these were strong, lusty, red-eyed devils, that swayed and drove men—men, I tell you. But as I stood on this hillside, I foresaw that in the blinding sunshine of that land I would become acquainted with a flabby, pretending, weak-eyed devil of a rapacious and pitiless folly. How insidious he could be, too, I was only to find out several months later and a thousand miles farther. For a moment I stood appalled, as though by a warning. Finally I descended the hill, obliquely, towards the trees I had seen.

"I avoided a vast artificial hole somebody had been digging on the slope, the purpose of which I found it impossible to divine. It wasn't a quarry or a sandpit, anyhow. It was just a hole. It might have been connected with the philanthropic desire of giving the criminals something to do. I don't know. Then I nearly fell into a very narrow ravine, almost no more than a scar in the hillside. I discovered that a lot of imported drainage-pipes for the settlement had been tumbled in there. There wasn't one that was not broken. It was a wanton smash-up. At last I got under the trees. My purpose was to stroll into the shade for a moment; but no sooner within than it seemed to me I had stepped into the gloomy circle of some Inferno. The rapids were near, and an uninterrupted, uniform, headlong, rushing noise filled the mournful stillness of the grove, where not a breath stirred, not a leaf moved, with a mysterious sound—as though the tearing pace of the launched earth had suddenly become audible.

"Black shapes crouched, lay, sat between the trees, leaning against the trunks, clinging to the earth, half coming out, half effaced within the dim light, in all the attitudes of pain, abandonment, and despair. Another mine on the cliff went off, followed by a slight shudder of the soil under my feet. The work was going on. The work! And this was the place where some of the helpers had withdrawn to die.

"They were dying slowly—it was very clear. They were not enemies, they were not criminals, they were nothing earthly now—nothing but black shadows of disease and starvation, lying confusedly in the greenish gloom. Brought from all the recesses of the coast in all the legality of time contracts, lost in uncongenial surroundings, fed on unfamiliar food, they sickened, became inefficient, and were then allowed to crawl away and rest. These moribund shapes were free as air—and nearly as thin. I began to distinguish the gleam of eyes under the trees. Then, glancing down, I saw a face near my hand. The black bones reclined at full length with one shoulder against the tree, and slowly the eyelids rose and the sunken eyes looked up at me, enormous and vacant, a kind of blind, white flicker in the depths of the orbs, which died out slowly. The man seemed young—almost a boy—but you know with them it's hard to tell. I found nothing else to do but to offer him one of my good Swede's ship's biscuits I had in my pocket. The fingers closed slowly on it and held— there was no other movement and no other glance. He had tied a bit of white worsted[6] round his neck—Why? Where did he get it? Was it a badge—an ornament—a charm—a propitiatory act? Was there any idea at all connected with it? It looked startling round his black neck, this bit of white thread from beyond the seas.

"Near the same tree two more bundles of acute angles sat with their legs drawn up. One, with his chin propped on his knees, stared at nothing, in an intolerable and appalling manner: his brother phantom rested its forehead, as if overcome with a great weariness; and all about others were scattered in every pose of contorted collapse, as in some picture of a massacre or a pestilence. While I stood horror-struck, one of these creatures rose to his hands and knees, and went off on all-fours towards the river to drink. He lapped out of his hand, then sat up in the sunlight, crossing his shins in front of him, and after a time let his woolly head fall on his breastbone.

"I didn't want any more loitering in the shade, and I made haste towards the station. When near the buildings I met a white man, in such an unexpected elegance of get-up that in the first moment I took him for a sort of vision. I saw a high starched collar, white cuffs, a light alpaca[7] jacket, snowy trousers, a clear necktie, and varnished boots. No hat. Hair parted, brushed, oiled, under a green-lined parasol held in a big white hand. He was amazing, and had a penholder behind his ear.

"I shook hands with this miracle, and I learned he was the Company's chief accountant, and that all the book-keeping was done at this station. He had come out for a moment, he said, 'to get a breath of fresh air.' The expression sounded wonderfully odd, with its suggestion of sedentary desk-life. I wouldn't have mentioned the fellow to you at all, only it was from his lips that I first heard the name of the man who is so indissolubly connected with the memories of that time. Moreover, I respected the fellow. Yes; I respected his collars, his vast cuffs, his brushed hair. His appearance was certainly that of a hairdresser's dummy; but in the great demoralisation of the land he kept up his appearance. That's backbone. His starched collars and got-up shirt-fronts were achievements of character. He had been out nearly three years; and, later, I could not help asking him how he managed to sport such linen. He had just the faintest blush, and said modestly, 'I've been teaching one of the native women about the station. It was difficult. She had a distaste for the work.' Thus this man had verily accomplished something. And he was devoted to his books, which were in apple-pie order.

"Everything else in the station was in a muddle,—heads, things, buildings. Strings of dusty niggers with splay feet arrived and departed; a stream of manufactured goods, rubbishy cottons, beads, and brass-wire sent into the depths of darkness, and in return came a precious trickle of ivory.

"I had to wait in the station for ten days—an eternity. I lived in a hut in the

6. Fine wool fabric.
7. Made from the wool of a South American animal by that name.

yard, but to be out of the chaos I would sometimes get into the accountant's office. It was built of horizontal planks, and so badly put together that, as he bent over his high desk, he was barred from neck to heels with narrow strips of sunlight. There was no need to open the big shutter to see. It was hot there too; big flies buzzed fiendishly, and did not sting, but stabbed. I sat generally on the floor, while, of faultless appearance (and even slightly scented), perching on a high stool, he wrote, he wrote. Sometimes he stood up for exercise. When a truckle-bed with a sick man (some invalided agent from up country) was put in there, he exhibited a gentle annoyance. 'The groans of this sick person' he said, 'distract my attention. And without that it is extremely difficult to guard against clerical errors in this climate.'

"One day he remarked, without lifting his head, 'In the interior you will no doubt meet Mr Kurtz.' On my asking who Mr Kurtz was, he said he was a first-class agent; and seeing my disappointment at this information, he added slowly, laying down his pen, 'He is a very remarkable person.' Further questions elicited from him that Mr Kurtz was at present in charge of a trading-post, a very important one, in the true ivory-country, at 'the very bottom of there. Sends in as much ivory as all the others put together . . .' He began to write again. The sick man was too ill to groan. The flies buzzed in a great peace.

"Suddenly there was a growing murmur of voices and a great tramping of feet. A caravan had come in. A violent babble of uncouth sounds burst out on the other side of the planks. All the carriers were speaking together, and in the midst of the uproar the lamentable voice of the chief agent was heard 'giving it up' tearfully for the twentieth time that day. . . . He rose slowly. 'What a frightful row,' he said. He crossed the room gently to look at the sick man, and returning, said to me, 'He does not hear.' 'What! Dead?' I asked, startled. 'No, not yet,' he answered, with great composure. Then, alluding with a toss of the head to the tumult in the station-yard, 'When one has got to make correct entries, one comes to hate those savages—hate them to the death.' He remained thoughtful for a moment. 'When you see Mr Kurtz,' he went on, 'tell him from me that everything here'—he glanced at the desk—'is very satisfactory. I don't like to write to him—with those messengers of ours you never know who may get hold of your letter—at that Central Station.' He stared at me for a moment with his mild, bulging eyes. 'Oh, he will go far, very far,' he began again. 'He will be a somebody in the Administration before long. They, above—the Council in Europe, you know—mean him to be.'

"He turned to his work. The noise outside had ceased, and presently in going out I stopped at the door. In the steady buzz of flies the homeward-bound agent was lying flushed and insensible; the other, bent over his books, was making correct entries of perfectly correct transactions; and fifty feet below the doorstep I could see the still tree-tops of the grove of death.

"Next day I left that station at last, with a caravan of sixty men, for a two-hundred-mile tramp.

"No use telling you much about that. Paths, paths, everywhere; a stamped-in network of paths spreading over the empty land, through long grass, through burnt grass, through thickets, down and up chilly ravines, up and down stony hills ablaze with heat; and a solitude, a solitude, nobody, not a hut. The population had cleared out a long time ago. Well, if a lot of mysterious niggers armed with all kinds of fearful weapons suddenly took to travelling on the road between Deal and Gravesend, catching the yokels right and left to carry heavy loads for them, I fancy every farm and cottage thereabouts would get empty very soon. Only here the dwellings were gone too. Still, I passed through several abandoned villages. There's something pathetically childish in the ruins of grass walls. Day after day, with the stamp and shuffle of sixty pair of bare feet behind me, each pair under a 60-lb. load. Camp, cook, sleep, strike camp, march. Now and then a carrier dead in harness, at rest in the long grass near the path, with an empty water-gourd and his long staff lying by his side. A great silence around and above. Perhaps on some quiet night the tremor of far-off drums, sinking, swelling, a tremor vast, faint; a sound weird, appealing, suggestive, and wild—and perhaps with as profound a meaning as the sound of bells in a Christian country. Once a white man in an unbuttoned uniform, camping on the path with an armed escort of lank Zanzibaris,[8] very hospitable and festive—not to say drunk. Was looking after the upkeep of the road, he declared. Can't say I saw any road or any upkeep, unless the body of a middle-aged negro, with a bullet-hole in the forehead, upon which I absolutely stumbled three miles farther on, may be considered as a permanent improvement. I had a white companion too, not a bad chap, but rather too fleshy and with the exasperating habit of fainting on the hot hillsides, miles away from the least bit of shade and water. Annoying, you know, to hold your own coat like a parasol over a man's head while he is coming-to. I couldn't help asking him once what he meant by coming there at all. 'To make money, of course. What do you think?' he said scornfully. Then he got fever, and had to be carried in a hammock slung under a pole. As he weighed sixteen stone[9] I had no end of rows with the carriers. They jibbed, ran away, sneaked off with their loads in the night—quite a mutiny. So, one evening, I made a speech in English with gestures, not one of which was lost to the sixty pairs of eyes before me, and the next morning I started the hammock off in front all right. An hour afterwards I came upon the whole concern wrecked in a bush—man, hammock, groans, blankets, horrors. The heavy pole had skinned his poor nose. He was very anxious for me to kill somebody, but there wasn't the shadow of a carrier near. I remembered the old doctor—'It would be interesting for science to watch the mental changes of individuals, on the spot.' I felt I was becoming scientifically interesting. However, all that is to no purpose. On the fifteenth day I came in sight of the big river again, and hobbled into the Central Station. It was on a back water surrounded by scrub and forest, with a pretty border of smelly mud on one side, and on the three others enclosed by a crazy fence of rushes. A neglected gap was all the gate it had, and the first glance at the place was enough to let you see the flabby devil was running that show. White men with long staves in their hands appeared languidly from amongst the buildings, strolling up to take a look at me, and then retired out of sight somewhere. One of them, a stout, excitable chap with black moustaches, informed me with great volubility and many digressions, as soon as I told him who I was, that my steamer was at the bottom of the river. I was thunderstruck. What, how, why? Oh, it was 'all right.' The 'manager himself' was there. All quite correct. 'Everybody had behaved splendidly! splendidly!'—'You must,' he said in agitation, 'go and see the general manager at once. He is waiting!'

"I did not see the real significance of that wreck at once. I fancy I see it

8. Natives of Zanzibar, an island off the east coast of Africa, once part of the sultanate of Zanzibar and a British protectorate, now part of the independent state of Tanzania. Zanzibaris were used as mercenaries throughout Africa.
9. One stone equals 14 pounds. The man weighed 224 pounds.

now, but I am not sure—not at all. Certainly the affair was too stupid—when I think of it—to be altogether natural. Still . . . But at the moment it presented itself simply as a confounded nuisance. The steamer was sunk. They had started two days before in a sudden hurry up the river with the manager on board, in charge of some volunteer skipper, and before they had been out three hours they tore the bottom out of her on stones, and she sank near the south bank. I asked myself what I was to do there, now my boat was lost. As a matter of fact, I had plenty to do in fishing my command out of the river. I had to set about it the very next day. That, and the repairs when I brought the pieces to the station, took some months.

"My first interview with the manager was curious. He did not ask me to sit down after my twenty-mile walk that morning. He was commonplace in complexion, in feature, in manners, and in voice. He was of middle size and of ordinary build. His eyes, of the usual blue, were perhaps remarkably cold, and he certainly could make his glance fall on one as trenchant and heavy as an axe. But even at these times the rest of his person seemed to disclaim the intention. Otherwise there was only an indefinable, faint expression of his lips, something stealthy—a smile—not a smile—I remember it, but I can't explain. It was unconscious, this smile was, though just after he had said something it got intensified for an instant. It came at the end of his speeches like a seal applied on the words to make the meaning of the commonest phrase appear absolutely inscrutable. He was a common trader, from his youth up employed in these parts—nothing more. He was obeyed, yet he inspired neither love nor fear, nor even respect. He inspired uneasiness. That was it! Uneasiness. Not a definite mistrust—just uneasiness—nothing more. You have no idea how effective such a . . . a . . . faculty can be. He had no genius for organising, for initiative, or for order even. That was evident in such things as the deplorable state of the station. He had no learning, and no intelligence. His position had come to him—why? Perhaps because he was never ill . . . He had served three terms of three years out there . . . Because triumphant health in the general rout of constitutions is a kind of power in itself. When he went home on leave he rioted on a large scale—pompously. Jack ashore—with a difference—in externals only. This one could gather from his casual talk. He originated nothing, he could keep the routine going—that's all. But he was great. He was great by this little thing that it was impossible to tell what could control such a man. He never gave that secret away. Perhaps there was nothing within him. Such a suspicion made one pause—for out there there were no external checks. Once when various tropical diseases had laid low almost every 'agent' in the station, he was heard to say, 'Men who come out here should have no entrails.' He sealed the utterance with that smile of his, as though it had been a door opening into a darkness he had in his keeping. You fancied you had seen things—but the seal was on. When annoyed at meal-times by the constant quarrels of the white men about precedence, he ordered an immense round table to be made, for which a special house had to be built. This was the station's mess-room. Where he sat was the first place—the rest were nowhere. One felt this to be his unalterable conviction. He was neither civil nor uncivil. He was quiet. He allowed his 'boy'—an overfed young negro from the coast—to treat the white men, under his very eyes, with provoking insolence.

"He began to speak as soon as he saw me. I had been very long on the road. He could not wait. Had to start without me. The up-river stations had to be relieved. There had been so many delays already that he did not know who was dead and who was alive, and how they got on—and so on, and so on. He paid no attention to my explanations, and, playing with a stick of sealing-wax, repeated several times that the situation was 'very grave, very grave.' There were rumours that a very important station was in jeopardy, and its chief, Mr Kurtz, was ill. Hoped it was not true. Mr Kurtz was . . . I felt weary and irritable. Hang Kurtz, I thought. I interrupted him by saying I had heard of Mr Kurtz on the coast. 'Ah! So they talk of him down there,' he murmured to himself. Then he began again, assuring me Mr Kurtz was the best agent he had, an exceptional man, of the greatest importance to the Company; therefore I could understand his anxiety. He was, he said, 'very, very uneasy.' Certainly he fidgeted on his chair a good deal, exclaimed, 'Ah, Mr Kurtz!' broke the stick of sealing-wax and seemed dumbfounded by the accident. Next thing he wanted to know 'how long it would take to' . . . I interrupted him again. Being hungry, you know, and kept on my feet too, I was getting savage. 'How can I tell?' I said, 'I haven't even seen the wreck yet—some months, no doubt.' All this talk seemed to me so futile. 'Some months,' he said. 'Well, let us say three months before we can make a start. Yes. That ought to do the affair.' I flung out of his hut (he lived all alone in a clay hut with a sort of verandah) muttering to myself my opinion of him. He was a chattering idiot. Afterwards I took it back when it was borne in upon me startlingly with what extreme nicety he had estimated the time requisite for the 'affair.'

"I went to work the next day, turning, so to speak, my back on that station. In that way only it seemed to me I could keep my hold on the redeeming facts of life. Still, one must look about sometimes; and then I saw this station, these men strolling aimlessly about in the sunshine of the yard. I asked myself sometimes what it all meant. They wandered here and there with their absurd long staves in their hands, like a lot of faithless pilgrims bewitched inside a rotten fence. The word 'ivory' rang in the air, was whispered, was sighed. You would think they were praying to it. A taint of imbecile rapacity blew through it all, like a whiff from some corpse. By Jove! I've never seen anything so unreal in my life. And outside, the silent wilderness surrounding this cleared speck on the earth struck me as something great and invincible, like evil or truth, waiting patiently for the passing away of this fantastic invasion.

"Oh, these months! Well, never mind. Various things happened. One evening a grass shed full of calico, cotton prints, beads, and I don't know what else, burst into a blaze so suddenly that you would have thought the earth had opened to let an avenging fire consume all that trash. I was smoking my pipe quietly by my dismantled steamer, and saw them all cutting capers in the light, with their arms lifted high, when the stout man with moustaches came tearing down to the river, a tin pail in his hand, assured me that everybody was 'behaving splendidly, splendidly,' dipped about a quart of water and tore back again. I noticed there was a hole in the bottom of his pail.

"I strolled up. There was no hurry. You see the thing had gone off like a box of matches. It had been hopeless from the very first. The flame had leaped high, driven everybody back, lighted up everything—and collapsed. The shed was already a heap of embers glowing fiercely. A nigger was being beaten near by. They said he had caused the fire in some way; be that as it may, he was screeching most horribly. I saw him, later, for several days, sitting in a bit of shade looking very sick and trying to recover himself: afterwards he arose and went out—and the wilderness without a sound took him into its bosom again.

As I approached the glow from the dark I found myself at the back of two men, talking. I heard the name of Kurtz pronounced, then the words, 'take advantage of this unfortunate accident.' One of the men was the manager. I wished him a good evening. 'Did you ever see anything like it—eh? it is incredible,' he said, and walked off. The other man remained. He was a first-class agent, young, gentlemanly, a bit reserved, with a forked little beard and a hooked nose. He was standoffish with the other agents, and they on their side said he was the manager's spy upon them. As to me, I had hardly ever spoken to him before. We got into talk, and by and by we strolled away from the hissing ruins. Then he asked me to his room, which was in the main building of the station. He struck a match, and I perceived that this young aristocrat had not only a silver-mounted dressing-case but also a whole candle all to himself. Just at that time the manager was the only man supposed to have any right to candles. Native mats covered the clay walls; a collection of spears, assegais,¹ shields, knives, was hung up in trophies. The business entrusted to this fellow was the making of bricks—so I had been informed; but there wasn't a fragment of a brick anywhere in the station, and he had been there more than a year—waiting. It seems he could not make bricks without something, I don't know what—straw maybe. Anyway, it could not be found there, and as it was not likely to be sent from Europe, it did not appear clear to me what he was waiting for. An act of special creation perhaps. However, they were all waiting—all the sixteen or twenty pilgrims of them—for something; and upon my word it did not seem an uncongenial occupation, from the way they took it, though the only thing that ever came to them was disease—as far as I could see. They beguiled the time by backbiting and intriguing against each other in a foolish kind of way. There was an air of plotting about that station, but nothing came of it, of course. It was as unreal as everything else—as the philanthropic pretence of the whole concern, as their talk, as their government, as their show of work. The only real feeling was a desire to get appointed to a trading-post where ivory was to be had, so that they could earn percentages. They intrigued and slandered and hated each other only on that account—but as to effectually lifting a little finger—oh no. By heavens! there is something after all in the world allowing one man to steal a horse while another must not look at a halter. Steal a horse straight out. Very well. He has done it. Perhaps he can ride. But there is a way of looking at a halter that would provoke the most charitable of saints into a kick.

"I had no idea why he wanted to be sociable, but as we chatted in there it suddenly occurred to me the fellow was trying to get at something—in fact, pumping me. He alluded constantly to Europe, to the people I was supposed to know there—putting leading questions as to my acquaintances in the sepulchral city, and so on. His little eyes glittered like mica² discs—with curiosity—though he tried to keep up a bit of superciliousness. At first I was astonished, but very soon I became awfully curious to see what he would find out from me. I couldn't possibly imagine what I had in me to make it worth his while. It was very pretty to see how he baffled himself, for in truth my body was full only of chills, and my head had nothing in it but that wretched steamboat business. It was evident he took me for a perfectly shameless prevaricator. At last he got angry, and, to conceal a movement of furious annoyance, he yawned. I rose. Then I noticed a small sketch in oils, on a panel, representing

1. Slender iron-tipped spears.   2. Glassy mineral.

a woman, draped and blindfolded, carrying a lighted torch. The background was sombre—almost black. The movement of the woman was stately, and the effect of the torchlight on the face was sinister.

"It arrested me, and he stood by civilly, holding an empty half-pint champagne bottle (medical comforts) with the candle stuck in it. To my question he said Mr Kurtz had painted this—in this very station more than a year ago—while waiting for means to go to his trading-post. 'Tell me, pray,' said I, 'who is this Mr Kurtz?'

" 'The chief of the Inner Station,' he answered in a short tone, looking away. 'Much obliged,' I said, laughing. 'And you are the brickmaker of the Central Station. Every one knows that.' He was silent for a while. 'He is a prodigy,' he said at last. 'He is an emissary of pity, and science, and progress, and devil knows what else. We want,' he began to declaim suddenly, 'for the guidance of the cause entrusted to us by Europe, so to speak, higher intelligence, wide sympathies, a singleness of purpose.' 'Who says that?' I asked. 'Lots of them,' he replied. 'Some even write that; and so *he* comes here, a special being, as you ought to know.' 'Why ought I to know?' I interrupted, really surprised. He paid no attention. 'Yes. To-day he is chief of the best station, next year he will be assistant-manager, two years more and . . . but I daresay you know what he will be in two years' time. You are of the new gang—the gang of virtue. The same people who sent him specially also recommended you. Oh, don't say no. I've my own eyes to trust.' Light dawned upon me. My dear aunt's influential acquaintances were producing an unexpected effect upon that young man. I nearly burst into a laugh. 'Do you read the Company's confidential correspondence?' I asked. He hadn't a word to say. It was great fun. 'When Mr Kurtz,' I continued severely, 'is General Manager, you won't have the opportunity.'

"He blew the candle out suddenly, and we went outside. The moon had risen. Black figures strolled about listlessly, pouring water on the glow, whence proceeded a sound of hissing; steam ascended in the moonlight; the beaten nigger groaned somewhere. 'What a row the brute makes!' said the indefatigable man with the moustaches, appearing near us. 'Serve him right. Transgression—punishment—bang! Pitiless, pitiless. That's the only way. This will prevent all conflagrations for the future. I was just telling the manager . . .' He noticed my companion, and became crestfallen all at once. 'Not in bed yet,' he said, with a kind of servile heartiness; 'it's so natural. Ha! Danger—agitation.' He vanished. I went on to the river-side, and the other followed me. I heard a scathing murmur at my ear, 'Heap of muffs—go to.' The pilgrims could be seen in knots gesticulating, discussing. Several had still their staves in their hands. I verily believe they took these sticks to bed with them. Beyond the fence the forest stood up spectrally in the moonlight, and through the dim stir, through the faint sounds of that lamentable courtyard, the silence of the land went home to one's very heart—its mystery, its greatness, the amazing reality of its concealed life. The hurt nigger moaned feebly somewhere near by, and then fetched a deep sigh that made me mend my pace away from there. I felt a hand introducing itself under my arm. 'My dear sir,' said the fellow, 'I don't want to be misunderstood, and especially by you, who will see Mr Kurtz long before I can have that pleasure. I wouldn't like him to get a false idea of my disposition. . . .'

"I let him run on, this papier-mâché Mephistopheles, and it seemed to me that if I tried I could poke my forefinger through him, and would find nothing inside but a little loose dirt, maybe. He, don't you see, had been planning to be assistant-manager by and by under the present man, and I could see that the coming of that Kurtz had upset them both not a little. He talked precipitately, and I did not try to stop him. I had my shoulders against the wreck of my steamer, hauled up on the slope like a carcass of some big river animal. The smell of mud, of primeval mud, by Jove! was in my nostrils, the high stillness of primeval forest was before my eyes; there were shiny patches on the black creek. The moon had spread over everything a thin layer of silver—over the rank grass, over the mud, upon the wall of matted vegetation standing higher than the wall of a temple, over the great river I could see through a sombre gap glittering, glittering, as it flowed broadly by without a murmur. All this was great, expectant, mute, while the man jabbered about himself. I wondered whether the stillness on the face of the immensity looking at us two were meant as an appeal or as a menace. What were we who had strayed in here? Could we handle that dumb thing, or would it handle us? I felt how big, how confoundedly big, was that thing that couldn't talk and perhaps was deaf as well. What was in there? I could see a little ivory coming out from there, and I had heard Mr Kurtz was in there. I had heard enough about it too—God knows! Yet somehow it didn't bring any image with it—no more than if I had been told an angel or a fiend was in there. I believed it in the same way one of you might believe there are inhabitants in the planet Mars. I knew once a Scotch sailmaker who was certain, dead sure, there were people in Mars. If you asked him for some idea how they looked and behaved, he would get shy and mutter something about 'walking on all-fours.' If you as much as smiled, he would—though a man of sixty—offer to fight you. I would not have gone so far as to fight for Kurtz, but I went for him near enough to a lie. You know I hate, detest, and can't bear a lie, not because I am straighter than the rest of us, but simply because it appals me. There is a taint of death, a flavour of mortality in lies—which is exactly what I hate and detest in the world—what I want to forget. It makes me miserable and sick, like biting something rotten would do. Temperament, I suppose. Well, I went near enough to it by letting the young fool there believe anything he liked to imagine as to my influence in Europe. I became in an instant as much of a pretence as the rest of the bewitched pilgrims. This simply because I had a notion it somehow would be of help to that Kurtz whom at the time I did not see—you understand. He was just a word for me. I did not see the man in the name any more than you do. Do you see him? Do you see the story? Do you see anything? It seems to me I am trying to tell you a dream—making a vain attempt, because no relation of a dream can convey the dream-sensation, that commingling of absurdity, surprise, and bewilderment in a tremor of struggling revolt, that notion of being captured by the incredible which is of the very essence of dreams. . . ."

He was silent for a while.

". . . No, it is impossible; it is impossible to convey the life-sensation of any given epoch of one's existence—that which makes its truth, its meaning—its subtle and penetrating essence. It is impossible. We live, as we dream—alone. . . ."

He paused again as if reflecting, then added:

"Of course in this you fellows see more than I could then. You see me, whom you know. . . ."

It had become so pitch dark that we listeners could hardly see one another. For a long time already he, sitting apart, had been no more to us than a voice. There was not a word from anybody. The others might have been asleep, but

I was awake. I listened, I listened on the watch for the sentence, for the word, that would give me the clue to the faint uneasiness inspired by this narrative that seemed to shape itself without human lips in the heavy night-air of the river.

". . . Yes—I let him run on," Marlow began again, "and think what he pleased about the powers that were behind me. I did! And there was nothing behind me! There was nothing but that wretched, old, mangled steamboat I was leaning against, while he talked fluently about 'the necessity for every man to get on.' 'And when one comes out here, you conceive, it is not to gaze at the moon.' Mr Kurtz was a 'universal genius,' but even a genius would find it easier to work with 'adequate tools—intelligent men.' He did not make bricks—why, there was a physical impossibility in the way—as I was well aware; and if he did secretarial work for the manager, it was because 'no sensible man rejects wantonly the confidence of his superiors.' Did I see it? I saw it. What more did I want? What I really wanted was rivets, by heaven! Rivets. To get on with the work—to stop the hole. Rivets I wanted. There were cases of them down at the coast—cases—piled up—burst—split! You kicked a loose rivet at every second step in that station yard on the hillside. Rivets had rolled into the grove of death. You could fill your pockets with rivets for the trouble of stooping down—and there wasn't one rivet to be found where it was wanted. We had plates that would do, but nothing to fasten them with. And every week the messenger, a lone negro, letter-bag on shoulder and staff in hand, left our station for the coast. And several times a week a coast caravan came in with trade goods—ghastly glazed calico that made you shudder only to look at it, glass beads value about a penny a quart, confounded spotted cotton handkerchiefs. And no rivets. Three carriers could have brought all that was wanted to set that steamboat afloat.

"He was becoming confidential now, but I fancy my unresponsive attitude must have exasperated him at last, for he judged it necessary to inform me he feared neither God nor devil, let alone any mere man. I said I could see that very well, but what I wanted was a certain quantity of rivets—and rivets were what really Mr Kurtz wanted, if he had only known it. Now letters went to the coast every week. . . . 'My dear sir,' he cried, 'I write from dictation.' I demanded rivets. There was a way—for an intelligent man. He changed his manner; became very cold, and suddenly began to talk about a hippopotamus; wondered whether sleeping on board the steamer (I stuck to my salvage night and day) I wasn't disturbed. There was an old hippo that had the bad habit of getting out on the bank and roaming at night over the station grounds. The pilgrims used to turn out in a body and empty every rifle they could lay hands on at him. Some even had sat up o' nights for him. All this energy was wasted, though. 'That animal has a charmed life,' he said; 'but you can say this only of brutes in this country. No man—you apprehend me?—no man here bears a charmed life.' He stood there for a moment in the moonlight with his delicate hooked nose set a little askew, and his mica eyes glittering without a wink, then, with a curt Good-night, he strode off. I could see he was disturbed and considerably puzzled, which made me feel more hopeful than I had been for days. It was a great comfort to turn from that chap to my influential friend, the battered, twisted, ruined, tinpot steamboat. I clambered on board. She rang under my feet like an empty Huntley & Palmer biscuit-tin kicked along a gutter; she was nothing so solid in make, and rather less pretty in shape, but I had expended enough hard work on her to make me love her. No influential friend would have served me better. She had given me a chance to come out a bit—to find out what I could do. No, I don't like work. I had rather laze about and think of all the fine things that can be done. I don't like work—no man does—but I like what is in the work—the chance to find yourself. Your own reality—for yourself, not for others—what no other man can ever know. They can only see the mere show, and never can tell what it really means.

"I was not surprised to see somebody sitting aft, on the deck, with his legs dangling over the mud. You see I rather chummed with the few mechanics there were in that station, whom the other pilgrims naturally despised—on account of their imperfect manners, I suppose. This was the foreman—a boiler-maker by trade—a good worker. He was a lank, bony, yellow-faced man, with big intense eyes. His aspect was worried, and his head was as bald as the palm of my hand; but his hair in falling seemed to have stuck to his chin, and had prospered in the new locality, for his beard hung down to his waist. He was a widower with six young children (he had left them in charge of a sister of his to come out there), and the passion of his life was pigeon-flying. He was an enthusiast and a connoisseur. He would rave about pigeons. After work hours he used sometimes to come over from his hut for a talk about his children and his pigeons; at work, when he had to crawl in the mud under the bottom of the steamboat, he would tie up that beard of his in a kind of white serviette[3] he brought for the purpose. It had loops to go over his ears. In the evening he could be seen squatted on the bank rinsing that wrapper in the creek with great care, then spreading it solemnly on a bush to dry.

"I slapped him on the back and shouted 'We shall have rivets!' He scrambled to his feet exclaiming 'No! Rivets!' as though he couldn't believe his ears. Then in a low voice, 'You . . . eh?' I don't know why we behaved like lunatics. I put my finger to the side of my nose and nodded mysteriously. 'Good for you!' he cried, snapped his fingers above his head, lifting one foot. I tried a jig. We capered on the iron deck. A frightful clatter came out of that hulk, and the virgin forest on the other bank of the creek sent it back in a thundering roll upon the sleeping station. It must have made some of the pilgrims sit up in their hovels. A dark figure obscured the lighted doorway of the manager's hut, vanished, then, a second or so after, the doorway itself vanished too. We stopped, and the silence driven away by the stamping of our feet flowed back again from the recesses of the land. The great wall of vegetation, an exuberant and entangled mass of trunks, branches, leaves, boughs, festoons, motionless in the moonlight, was like a rioting invasion of soundless life, a rolling wave of plants, piled up, crested, ready to topple over the creek, to sweep every little man of us out of his little existence. And it moved not. A deadened burst of mighty splashes and snorts reached us from afar, as though an ichthyosaurus[4] had been taking a bath of glitter in the great river. 'After all,' said the boiler-maker in a reasonable tone, 'why shouldn't we get the rivets?' Why not, indeed! I did not know of any reason why we shouldn't. 'They'll come in three weeks,' I said confidently.

"But they didn't. Instead of rivets there came an invasion, an infliction, a visitation. It came in sections during the next three weeks, each section headed by a donkey carrying a white man in new clothes and tan shoes, bowing from that elevation right and left to the impressed pilgrims. A quarrelsome band of footsore sulky niggers trod on the heels of the donkey; a lot of tents, camp-

3. Table napkin.   4. Large prehistoric marine creature.

stools, tin boxes, white cases, brown bales would be shot down in the courtyard, and the air of mystery would deepen a little over the muddle of the
station. Five such instalments came, with their absurd air of disorderly flight
with the loot of innumerable outfit shops and provision stores, that, one would
think, they were lugging, after a raid, into the wilderness for equitable division.
It was an inextricable mess of things decent in themselves but that human
folly made look like the spoils of thieving.

"This devoted band called itself the Eldorado[5] Exploring Expedition, and I
believe they were sworn to secrecy. Their talk, however, was the talk of sordid
buccaneers: it was reckless without hardihood, greedy without audacity, and
cruel without courage; there was not an atom of foresight or of serious intention in the whole batch of them, and they did not seem aware these things are
wanted for the work of the world. To tear treasure out of the bowels of the
land was their desire, with no more moral purpose at the back of it than there
is in burglars breaking into a safe. Who paid the expenses of the noble enterprise I don't know; but the uncle of our manager was leader of that lot.

"In exterior he resembled a butcher in a poor neighbourhood, and his eyes
had a look of sleepy cunning. He carried his fat paunch with ostentation on
his short legs, and during the time his gang infested the station spoke to no
one but his nephew. You could see these two roaming about all day long with
their heads close together in an everlasting confab.[6]

"I had given up worrying myself about the rivets. One's capacity for that
kind of folly is more limited than you would suppose. I said Hang!—and let
things slide. I had plenty of time for meditation, and now and then I would
give some thought to Kurtz. I wasn't very interested in him. No. Still, I was
curious to see whether this man, who had come out equipped with moral ideas
of some sort, would climb to the top after all, and how he would set about his
work when there."

2

"One evening as I was lying flat on the deck of my steamboat, I heard voices
approaching—and there were the nephew and the uncle strolling along the
bank. I laid my head on my arm again, and had nearly lost myself in a doze,
when somebody said in my ear, as it were: 'I am as harmless as a little child,
but I don't like to be dictated to. Am I the manager—or am I not? I was ordered
to send him there. It's incredible.' . . . I became aware that the two were standing on the shore alongside the forepart of the steamboat, just below my head.
I did not move; it did not occur to me to move: I was sleepy. 'It *is* unpleasant,'
grunted the uncle. 'He has asked the Administration to be sent there,' said the
other, 'with the idea of showing what he could do; and I was instructed accordingly. Look at the influence that man must have. Is it not frightful?' They both
agreed it was frightful, then made several bizarre remarks: 'Make rain and fine
weather—one man—the Council—by the nose'—bits of absurd sentences that
got the better of my drowsiness, so that I had pretty near the whole of my wits
about me when the uncle said, 'The climate may do away with this difficulty
for you. Is he alone there?' 'Yes,' answered the manager; 'he sent his assistant
down the river with a note to me in these terms: "Clear this poor devil out of

5. Fabled land of gold (*el dorado,* Spanish for "the
gilded") imagined by the Spanish conquistadors to
exist in South America.
6. Confabulation, talk.

the country, and don't bother sending more of that sort. I had rather be alone than have the kind of men you can dispose of with me." It was more than a year ago. Can you imagine such impudence?' 'Anything since then?' asked the other hoarsely. 'Ivory,' jerked the nephew; 'lots of it—prime sort—lots—most annoying, from him.' 'And with that?' questioned the heavy rumble. 'Invoice,' was the reply fired out, so to speak. Then silence. They had been talking about Kurtz.

"I was broad awake by this time, but, lying perfectly at ease, remained still, having no inducement to change my position. 'How did that ivory come all this way?' growled the elder man, who seemed very vexed. The other explained that it had come with a fleet of canoes in charge of an English half-caste clerk Kurtz had with him; that Kurtz had apparently intended to return himself, the station being by that time bare of goods and stores, but after coming three hundred miles, had suddenly decided to go back, which he started to do alone in a small dugout with four paddlers, leaving the half-caste to continue down the river with the ivory. The two fellows there seemed astounded at anybody attempting such a thing. They were at a loss for an adequate motive. As for me, I seemed to see Kurtz for the first time. It was a distinct glimpse: the dugout, four paddling savages, and the lone white man turning his back suddenly on the headquarters, on relief, on thoughts of home—perhaps; setting his face towards the depths of the wilderness, towards his empty and desolate station. I did not know the motive. Perhaps he was just simply a fine fellow who stuck to his work for its own sake. His name, you understand, had not been pronounced once. He was 'that man.' The half-caste, who, as far as I could see, had conducted a difficult trip with great prudence and pluck, was invariably alluded to as 'that scoundrel.' The 'scoundrel' had reported that the 'man' had been very ill—had recovered imperfectly. . . . The two below me moved away then a few paces, and strolled back and forth at some little distance. I heard: 'Military post—doctor—two hundred miles—quite alone now—unavoidable delays—nine months—no news—strange rumours.' They approached again, just as the manager was saying, 'No one, as far as I know, unless a species of wandering trader—a pestilential fellow, snapping ivory from the natives.' Who was it they were talking about now? I gathered in snatches that this was some man supposed to be in Kurtz's district, and of whom the manager did not approve. 'We will not be free from unfair competition till one of these fellows is hanged for an example,' he said. 'Certainly,' grunted the other; 'get him hanged! Why not? Anything—anything can be done in this country. That's what I say; nobody here, you understand, *here*, can endanger your position. And why? You stand the climate—you outlast them all. The danger is in Europe; but there before I left I took care to—' They moved off and whispered, then their voices rose again. 'The extraordinary series of delays is not my fault. I did my possible.'[7] The fat man sighed, 'Very sad.' 'And the pestiferous absurdity of his talk,' continued the other; 'he bothered me enough when he was here. "Each station should be like a beacon on the road towards better things, a centre for trade of course, but also for humanising, improving, instructing." Conceive you—that ass! And he wants to be manager! No, it's—' Here he got choked by excessive indignation, and I lifted

7. Literal rendering of the French *J'ai fait mon possible* (I have done all I could). Conrad sprinkles the conversation of his Belgian characters with Gallicisms to remind us that their words, though reported in English, were spoken in French. Other examples are "a species of wandering trader" (above), "Conceive you" (below), "I would be desolated" (p. 1921).

my head the least bit. I was surprised to see how near they were—right under me. I could have spat upon their hats. They were looking on the ground, absorbed in thought. The manager was switching his leg with a slender twig: his sagacious relative lifted his head. 'You have been well since you came out this time?' he asked. The other gave a start. 'Who? I? Oh! Like a charm—like a charm. But the rest—oh, my goodness! All sick. They die so quick, too, that I haven't the time to send them out of the country—it's incredible!' 'H'm. Just so,' grunted the uncle. 'Ah! my boy, trust to this—I say, trust to this.' I saw him extend his short flipper of an arm for a gesture that took in the forest, the creek, the mud, the river—seemed to beckon with a dishonouring flourish before the sunlit face of the land a treacherous appeal to the lurking death, to the hidden evil, to the profound darkness of its heart. It was so startling that I leaped to my feet and looked back at the edge of the forest, as though I had expected an answer of some sort to that black display of confidence. You know the foolish notions that come to one sometimes. The high stillness confronted these two figures with its ominous patience, waiting for the passing away of a fantastic invasion.

"They swore aloud together—out of sheer fright, I believe—then, pretending not to know anything of my existence, turned back to the station. The sun was low; and leaning forward side by side, they seemed to be tugging painfully uphill their two ridiculous shadows of unequal length, that trailed behind them slowly over the tall grass without bending a single blade.

"In a few days the Eldorado Expedition went into the patient wilderness, that closed upon it as the sea closes over a diver. Long afterwards the news came that all the donkeys were dead. I know nothing as to the fate of the less valuable animals. They, no doubt, like the rest of us, found what they deserved. I did not inquire. I was then rather excited at the prospect of meeting Kurtz very soon. When I say very soon I mean it comparatively. It was just two months from the day we left the creek when we came to the bank below Kurtz's station.

"Going up that river was like travelling back to the earliest beginnings of the world, when vegetation rioted on the earth and the big trees were kings. An empty stream, a great silence, an impenetrable forest. The air was warm, thick, heavy, sluggish. There was no joy in the brilliance of sunshine. The long stretches of the waterway ran on, deserted, into the gloom of overshadowed distances. On silvery sandbanks hippos and alligators sunned themselves side by side. The broadening waters flowed through a mob of wooded islands; you lost your way on that river as you would in a desert, and butted all day long against shoals, trying to find the channel, till you thought yourself bewitched and cut off for ever from everything you had known once—somewhere—far away—in another existence perhaps. There were moments when one's past came back to one, as it will sometimes when you have not a moment to spare to yourself; but it came in the shape of an unrestful and noisy dream, remembered with wonder amongst the overwhelming realities of this strange world of plants, and water, and silence. And this stillness of life did not in the least resemble a peace. It was the stillness of an implacable force brooding over an inscrutable intention. It looked at you with a vengeful aspect. I got used to it afterwards; I did not see it any more; I had no time. I had to keep guessing at the channel; I had to discern, mostly by inspiration, the signs of hidden banks; I watched for sunken stones; I was learning to clap my teeth smartly before my heart flew out, when I shaved by a fluke some infernal sly old snag that would have ripped the life out of the tin-pot steamboat and drowned all the pilgrims; I had to keep a look-out for the signs of dead wood we could cut up in the night for next day's steaming. When you have to attend to things of that sort, to the mere incidents of the surface, the reality—the reality, I tell you— fades. The inner truth is hidden—luckily, luckily. But I felt it all the same; I felt often its mysterious stillness watching me at my monkey tricks, just as it watches you fellows performing on your respective tight-ropes for—what is it? half a crown a tumble—"

"Try to be civil, Marlow," growled a voice, and I knew there was at least one listener awake besides myself.

"I beg your pardon. I forgot the heartache which makes up the rest of the price. And indeed what does the price matter, if the trick be well done? You do your tricks very well. And I didn't do badly either, since I managed not to sink that steamboat on my first trip. It's a wonder to me yet. Imagine a blind-folded man set to drive a van over a bad road. I sweated and shivered over that business considerably, I can tell you. After all, for a seaman, to scrape the bottom of the thing that's supposed to float all the time under his care is the unpardonable sin. No one may know of it, but you never forget the thump— eh? A blow on the very heart. You remember it, you dream of it, you wake up at night and think of it—years after—and go hot and cold all over. I don't pretend to say that steamboat floated all the time. More than once she had to wade for a bit, with twenty cannibals splashing around and pushing. We had enlisted some of these chaps on the way for a crew. Fine fellows—cannibals— in their place. They were men one could work with, and I am grateful to them. And, after all, they did not eat each other before my face: they had brought along a provision of hippo-meat which went rotten, and made the mystery of the wilderness stink in my nostrils. Phoo! I can sniff it now. I had the manager on board and three or four pilgrims with their staves—all complete. Sometimes we came upon a station close by the bank, clinging to the skirts of the unknown, and the white men rushing out of a tumble-down hovel, with great gestures of joy and surprise and welcome, seemed very strange—had the appearance of being held there captive by a spell. The word 'ivory' would ring in the air for a while—and on we went again into the silence, along empty reaches, round the still bends, between the high walls of our winding way, reverberating in hollow claps the ponderous beat of the stern-wheel. Trees, trees, millions of trees, massive, immense, running up high; and at their foot, hugging the bank against the stream, crept the little begrimed steamboat, like a sluggish beetle crawling on the floor of a lofty portico. It made you feel very small, very lost, and yet it was not altogether depressing, that feeling. After all, if you were small, the grimy beetle crawled on—which was just what you wanted it to do. Where the pilgrims imagined it crawled to I don't know. To some place where they expected to get something, I bet! For me it crawled towards Kurtz—exclusively; but when the steam-pipes started leaking we crawled very slow. The reaches opened before us and closed behind, as if the forest had stepped leisurely across the water to bar the way for our return. We penetrated deeper and deeper into the heart of darkness. It was very quiet there. At night sometimes the roll of drums behind the curtain of trees would run up the river and remain sustained faintly, as if hovering in the air high over our heads, till the first break of day. Whether it meant war, peace, or prayer we could not tell. The dawns were heralded by the descent of a chill stillness; the woodcutters slept, their fires burned low; the snapping of a twig would make you start. We were wanderers on a prehistoric earth, on an earth that wore the aspect of an unknown planet. We could have fancied ourselves the first of men taking possession of an accursed inheritance, to be subdued at the cost of profound anguish and of excessive toil. But suddenly, as we struggled round a bend, there would be a glimpse of rush walls, of peaked grass-roofs, a burst of yells, a whirl of black limbs, a mass of hands clapping, of feet stamping, of bodies swaying, of eyes rolling, under the droop of heavy and motionless foliage. The steamer toiled along slowly on the edge of a black and incomprehensible frenzy. The prehistoric man was cursing us, praying to us, welcoming us—who could tell? We were cut off from the comprehension of our surroundings; we glided past like phantoms, wondering and secretly appalled, as sane men would be before an enthusiastic outbreak in a mad-house. We could not understand because we were too far and could not remember, because we were travelling in the night of first ages, of those ages that are gone, leaving hardly a sign—and no memories.

"The earth seemed unearthly. We are accustomed to look upon the shackled form of a conquered monster, but there—there you could look at a thing monstrous and free. It was unearthly, and the men were—No, they were not inhuman. Well, you know, that was the worst of it—this suspicion of their not being inhuman. It would come slowly to one. They howled and leaped, and spun, and made horrid faces; but what thrilled you was just the thought of their humanity—like yours—the thought of your remote kinship with this wild and passionate uproar. Ugly. Yes, it was ugly enough; but if you were man enough you would admit to yourself that there was in you just the faintest trace of a response to the terrible frankness of that noise, a dim suspicion of there being a meaning in it which you—you so remote from the night of first ages—could comprehend. And why not? The mind of man is capable of any-thing—because everything is in it, all the past as well as all the future. What was there after all? Joy, fear, sorrow, devotion, valour, rage—who can tell?—but truth—truth stripped of its cloak of time. Let the fool gape and shudder—the man knows, and can look on without a wink. But he must at least be as much of a man as these on the shore. He must meet that truth with his own true stuff—with his own inborn strength. Principles? Principles won't do. Acquisitions, clothes, pretty rags—rags that would fly off at the first good shake. No; you want a deliberate belief. An appeal to me in this fiendish row—is there? Very well; I hear; I admit, but I have a voice too, and for good or evil mine is the speech that cannot be silenced. Of course, a fool, what with sheer fright and fine sentiments, is always safe. Who's that grunting? You wonder I didn't go ashore for a howl and a dance? Well, no—I didn't. Fine sentiments, you say? Fine sentiments be hanged! I had no time. I had to mess about with white-lead and strips of woollen blanket helping to put bandages on those leaky steam-pipes—I tell you. I had to watch the steering, and circumvent those snags, and get the tin-pot along by hook or by crook. There was surface-truth enough in these things to save a wiser man. And between whiles I had to look after the savage who was fireman. He was an improved specimen; he could fire up a vertical boiler. He was there below me, and, upon my word, to look at him was as edifying as seeing a dog in a parody of breeches and a feather hat, walking on his hind legs. A few months of training had done for that really fine chap. He squinted at the steam-gauge and at the water-gauge with an evident effort of intrepidity—and he had filed teeth too, the poor devil, and the wool of his pate shaved into queer patterns, and three ornamental scars on each of his cheeks. He ought to have been clapping his hands and stamping his feet on the bank, instead of which he was hard at work, a thrall to strange witchcraft, full of improving knowledge. He was useful because he had been instructed; and what he knew was this—that should the water in that transparent thing disappear, the evil spirit inside the boiler would get angry through the greatness of his thirst, and take a terrible vengeance. So he sweated and fired up and watched the glass fearfully (with an impromptu charm, made of rags, tied to his arm, and a piece of polished bone, as big as a watch, stuck flatways through his lower lip), while the wooded banks slipped past us slowly, the short noise was left behind, the interminable miles of silence—and we crept on, towards Kurtz. But the snags were thick, the water was treacherous and shallow, the boiler seemed indeed to have a sulky devil in it, and thus neither that fireman nor I had any time to peer into our creepy thoughts.

"Some fifty miles below the Inner Station we came upon a hut of reeds, an inclined and melancholy pole, with the unrecognisable tatters of what had been a flag of some sort flying from it, and a neatly stacked wood-pile. This was unexpected. We came to the bank, and on the stack of firewood found a flat piece of board with some faded pencil-writing on it. When deciphered it said: 'Wood for you. Hurry up. Approach cautiously.' There was a signature, but it was illegible—not Kurtz—a much longer word. Hurry up. Where? Up the river? 'Approach cautiously.' We had not done so. But the warning could not have been meant for the place where it could be only found after approach. Something was wrong above. But what—and how much? That was the question. We commented adversely upon the imbecility of that telegraphic style. The bush around said nothing, and would not let us look very far, either. A torn curtain of red twill hung in the doorway of the hut, and flapped sadly in our faces. The dwelling was dismantled; but we could see a white man had lived there not very long ago. There remained a rude table—a plank on two posts; a heap of rubbish reposed in a dark corner, and by the door I picked up a book. It had lost its covers, and the pages had been thumbed into a state of extremely dirty softness; but the back had been lovingly stitched afresh with white cotton thread, which looked clean yet. It was an extraordinary find. Its title was, *An Inquiry into some Points of Seamanship*, by a man Towser, Towson—some such name—Master in His Majesty's Navy. The matter looked dreary reading enough, with illustrative diagrams and repulsive tables of figures, and the copy was sixty years old. I handled this amazing antiquity with the greatest possible tenderness, lest it should dissolve in my hands. Within, Towson or Towser was inquiring earnestly into the breaking strain of ships' chains and tackle, and other such matters. Not a very enthralling book; but at the first glance you could see there a singleness of intention, an honest concern for the right way of going to work, which made these humble pages, thought out so many years ago, luminous with another than a professional light. The simple old sailor, with his talk of chains and purchases, made me forget the jungle and the pilgrims in a delicious sensation of having come upon something unmistakably real. Such a book being there was wonderful enough; but still more astounding were the notes pencilled in the margin, and plainly referring to the text. I couldn't believe my eyes! They were in cipher! Yes, it looked like cipher. Fancy a man lugging with him a book of that description into this nowhere and studying it—and making notes—in cipher at that! It was an extravagant mystery.

"I had been dimly aware for some time of a worrying noise, and when I lifted my eyes I saw the wood-pile was gone, and the manager, aided by all the pilgrims, was shouting at me from the river-side. I slipped the book into my pocket. I assure you to leave off reading was like tearing myself away from the shelter of an old and solid friendship.

"I started the lame engine ahead. 'It must be this miserable trader—this intruder,' exclaimed the manager, looking back malevolently at the place we had left. 'He must be English,' I said. 'It will not save him from getting into trouble if he is not careful,' muttered the manager darkly. I observed with assumed innocence that no man was safe from trouble in this world.

"The current was more rapid now, the steamer seemed at her last gasp, the stern-wheel flopped languidly, and I caught myself listening on tiptoe for the next beat of the float,[8] for in sober truth I expected the wretched thing to give up every moment. It was like watching the last flickers of a life. But still we crawled. Sometimes I would pick out a tree a little way ahead to measure our progress towards Kurtz by, but I lost it invariably before we got abreast. To keep the eyes so long on one thing was too much for human patience. The manager displayed a beautiful resignation. I fretted and fumed and took to arguing with myself whether or no I would talk openly with Kurtz; but before I could come to any conclusion it occurred to me that my speech or my silence, indeed any action of mine, would be a mere futility. What did it matter what any one knew or ignored? What did it matter who was manager? One gets sometimes such a flash of insight. The essentials of this affair lay deep under the surface, beyond my reach, and beyond my power of meddling.

"Towards the evening of the second day we judged ourselves about eight miles from Kurtz's station. I wanted to push on; but the manager looked grave, and told me the navigation up there was so dangerous that it would be advisable, the sun being very low already, to wait where we were till next morning. Moreover, he pointed out that if the warning to approach cautiously were to be followed, we must approach in daylight—not at dusk, or in the dark. This was sensible enough. Eight miles meant nearly three hours' steaming for us, and I could also see suspicious ripples at the upper end of the reach. Nevertheless, I was annoyed beyond expression at the delay, and most unreasonably too, since one night more could not matter much after so many months. As we had plenty of wood, and caution was the word, I brought up in the middle of the stream. The reach was narrow, straight, with high sides like a railway cutting. The dusk came gliding into it long before the sun had set. The current ran smooth and swift, but a dumb immobility sat on the banks. The living trees, lashed together by the creepers and every living bush of the undergrowth, might have been changed into stone, even to the slenderest twig, to the lightest leaf. It was not sleep—it seemed unnatural, like a state of trance. Not the faintest sound of any kind could be heard. You looked on amazed, and began to suspect yourself of being deaf—then the night came suddenly, and struck you blind as well. About three in the morning some large fish leaped, and the loud splash made me jump as though a gun had been fired. When the sun rose there was a white fog, very warm and clammy, and more blinding than the night. It did not shift or drive; it was just there, standing all round you like something solid. At eight or nine, perhaps, it lifted as a shutter lifts. We had a glimpse of the towering multitude of trees, of the immense

8. Automatic water-level regulator opening and closing a water-supply valve.

matted jungle, with the blazing little ball of the sun hanging over it—all per-fectly still—and then the white shutter came down again, smoothly, as if slid-ing in greased grooves. I ordered the chain, which we had begun to heave in, to be paid out again. Before it stopped running with a muffled rattle, a cry, a very loud cry, as of infinite desolation, soared slowly in the opaque air. It ceased. A complaining clamour, modulated in savage discords, filled our ears. The sheer unexpectedness of it made my hair stir under my cap. I don't know how it struck the others: to me it seemed as though the mist itself had screamed, so suddenly, and apparently from all sides at once, did this tumul-tuous and mournful uproar arise. It culminated in a hurried outbreak of almost intolerably excessive shrieking, which stopped short, leaving us stiffened in a variety of silly attitudes, and obstinately listening to the nearly as appalling and excessive silence. 'Good God! What is the meaning—?' stammered at my elbow one of the pilgrims—a little fat man, with sandy hair and red whiskers, who wore side-spring boots, and pink pyjamas tucked into his socks. Two others remained open-mouthed a whole minute, then dashed into the little cabin, to rush out incontinently and stand darting scared glances, with Win-chesters at 'ready' in their hands. What we could see was just the steamer we were on, her outlines blurred as though she had been on the point of dissolv-ing, and a misty strip of water, perhaps two feet broad, around her—and that was all. The rest of the world was nowhere, as far as our eyes and ears were concerned. Just nowhere. Gone, disappeared; swept off without leaving a whis-per or a shadow behind.

"I went forward, and ordered the chain to be hauled in short, so as to be ready to trip the anchor and move the steamboat at once if necessary. 'Will they attack?' whispered an awed voice. 'We will all be butchered in this fog,' murmured another. The faces twitched with the strain, the hands trembled slightly, the eyes forgot to wink. It was very curious to see the contrast of expressions of the white men and of the black fellows of our crew, who were as much strangers to that part of the river as we, though their homes were only eight hundred miles away. The whites, of course greatly discomposed, had besides a curious look of being painfully shocked by such an outrageous row. The others had an alert, naturally interested expression; but their faces were essentially quiet, even those of the one or two who grinned as they hauled at the chain. Several exchanged short, grunting phrases, which seemed to settle the matter to their satisfaction. Their headman, a young, broad-chested black, severely draped in dark-blue fringed cloths, with fierce nostrils and his hair all done up artfully in oily ringlets, stood near me. 'Aha!' I said, just for good fellowship's sake. 'Catch 'im,' he snapped, with a bloodshot widening of his eyes and a flash of sharp teeth—'catch 'im. Give 'im to us.' 'To you, eh?' I asked; 'what would you do with them?' 'Eat 'im!' he said curtly, and, leaning his elbow on the rail, looked out into the fog in a dignified and profoundly pensive attitude. I would no doubt have been properly horrified, had it not occurred to me that he and his chaps must be very hungry: that they must have been growing increasingly hungry for at least this month past. They had been engaged for six months (I don't think a single one of them had any clear idea of time, as we at the end of countless ages have. They still belonged to the beginnings of time—had no inherited experience to teach them, as it were), and of course, as long as there was a piece of paper written over in accordance with some farcical law or other made down the river, it didn't enter anybody's head to trouble how they would live. Certainly they had brought with them some rotten hippo-meat, which couldn't have lasted very long, anyway, even if the pilgrims hadn't, in the midst of a shocking hullabaloo, thrown a considerable quantity of it overboard. It looked like a high-handed proceeding; but it was really a case of legitimate self-defence. You can't breathe dead hippo waking, sleeping, and eating, and at the same time keep your precarious grip on existence. Besides that, they had given them every week three pieces of brass wire, each about nine inches long; and the theory was they were to buy their provisions with that currency in river-side villages. You can see how *that* worked. There were either no villages, or the people were hostile, or the director, who like the rest of us fed out of tins, with an occasional old he-goat thrown in, didn't want to stop the steamer for some more or less recondite reasons. So, unless they swallowed the wire itself, or made loops of it to snare the fishes with, I don't see what good their extravagant salary could be to them. I must say it was paid with a regularity worthy of a large and honourable trading company. For the rest, the only thing to eat—though it didn't look eatable in the least—I saw in their possession was a few lumps of some stuff like half-cooked dough, of a dirty lavender colour, they kept wrapped in leaves, and now and then swallowed a piece of, but so small that it seemed done more for the look of the thing than for any serious purpose of sustenance. Why in the name of all the gnawing devils of hunger they didn't go for us—they were thirty to five—and have a good tuck-in for once, amazes me now when I think of it. They were big powerful men, with not much capacity to weigh the consequences, with courage, with strength, even yet, though their skins were no longer glossy and their muscles no longer hard. And I saw that something restraining, one of those human secrets that baffle probability, had come into play there. I looked at them with a swift quickening of interest—not because it occurred to me I might be eaten by them before very long, though I own to you that just then I perceived—in a new light, as it were—how unwholesome the pilgrims looked, and I hoped, yes, I positively hoped, that my aspect was not so—what shall I say?—so—unappetising: a touch of fantastic vanity which fitted well with the dream-sensation that pervaded all my days at that time. Perhaps I had a little fever too. One can't live with one's finger everlastingly on one's pulse. I had often 'a little fever,' or a little touch of other things—the playful paw-strokes of the wilderness, the preliminary trifling before the more serious onslaught which came in due course. Yes; I looked at them as you would on any human being, with a curiosity of their impulses, motives, capacities, weaknesses, when brought to the test of an inexorable physical necessity. Restraint! What possible restraint? Was it superstition, disgust, patience, fear—or some kind of primitive honour? No fear can stand up to hunger, no patience can wear it out, disgust simply does not exist where hunger is; and as to superstition, beliefs, and what you may call principles, they are less than chaff in a breeze. Don't you know the devilry of lingering starvation, its exasperating torment, its black thoughts, its sombre and brooding ferocity? Well, I do. It takes a man all his inborn strength to fight hunger properly. It's really easier to face bereavement, dishonour, and the perdition of one's soul—than this kind of prolonged hunger. Sad, but true. And these chaps too had no earthly reason for any kind of scruple. Restraint! I would just as soon have expected restraint from a hyena prowling amongst the corpses of a battlefield. But there was the fact facing me—the fact dazzling, to be seen, like the foam on the depths of the sea, like a ripple on an unfathomable enigma, a mystery greater—when I thought of it—than the curious, inexplicable note of desperate grief in this savage clamour that had swept by us on the river-bank, behind the blind whiteness of the fog.

"Two pilgrims were quarrelling in hurried whispers as to which bank. 'Left.' 'No, no; how can you? Right, right, of course.' 'It is very serious,' said the manager's voice behind me; 'I would be desolated if anything should happen to Mr Kurtz before we came up.' I looked at him, and had not the slightest doubt he was sincere. He was just the kind of man who would wish to preserve appearances. That was his restraint. But when he muttered something about going on at once, I did not even take the trouble to answer him. I knew, and he knew, that it was impossible. Were we to let go our hold of the bottom, we would be absolutely in the air—in space. We wouldn't be able to tell where we were going to—whether up or down stream, or across—till we fetched against one bank or the other—and then we wouldn't know at first which it was. Of course I made no move. I had no mind for a smash-up. You couldn't imagine a more deadly place for a shipwreck. Whether drowned at once or not, we were sure to perish speedily in one way or another. 'I authorise you to take all the risks,' he said, after a short silence. 'I refuse to take any,' I said shortly; which was just the answer he expected, though its tone might have surprised him. 'Well, I must defer to your judgment. You are captain,' he said, with marked civility. I turned my shoulder to him in sign of my appreciation, and looked into the fog. How long would it last? It was the most hopeless look-out. The approach to this Kurtz grubbing for ivory in the wretched bush was beset by as many dangers as though he had been an enchanted princess sleeping in a fabulous castle. 'Will they attack, do you think?' asked the manager, in a confidential tone.

"I did not think they would attack, for several obvious reasons. The thick fog was one. If they left the bank in their canoes they would get lost in it, as we would be if we attempted to move. Still, I had also judged the jungle of both banks quite impenetrable—and yet eyes were in it, eyes that had seen us. The river-side bushes were certainly very thick; but the undergrowth behind was evidently penetrable. However, during the short lift I had seen no canoes anywhere in the reach—certainly not abreast of the steamer. But what made the idea of attack inconceivable to me was the nature of the noise—of the cries we had heard. They had not the fierce character boding of immediate hostile intention. Unexpected, wild, and violent as they had been, they had given me an irresistible impression of sorrow. The glimpse of the steamboat had for some reason filled those savages with unrestrained grief. The danger, if any, I expounded, was from our proximity to a great human passion let loose. Even extreme grief may ultimately vent itself in violence—but more generally takes the form of apathy. . . .

"You should have seen the pilgrims stare! They had no heart to grin, or even to revile me; but I believe they thought me gone mad—with fright, maybe. I delivered a regular lecture. My dear boys, it was no good bothering. Keep a look-out? Well, you may guess I watched the fog for the signs of lifting as a cat watches a mouse; but for anything else our eyes were of no more use to us than if we had been buried miles deep in a heap of cotton-wool. It felt like it too—choking, warm, stifling. Besides, all I said, though it sounded extravagant, was absolutely true to fact. What we afterwards alluded to as an attack was really an attempt at repulse. The action was very far from being aggressive—it was not even defensive, in the usual sense: it was undertaken under the stress of desperation, and in its essence was purely protective.

"It developed itself, I should say, two hours after the fog lifted, and its commencement was at a spot, roughly speaking, about a mile and a half below Kurtz's station. We had just floundered and flopped round a bend, when I saw an islet, a mere grassy hummock of bright green, in the middle of the stream. It was the only thing of the kind; but as we opened the reach more, I perceived it was the head of a long sandbank, or rather of a chain of shallow patches stretching down the middle of the river. They were discoloured, just awash, and the whole lot was seen just under the water, exactly as a man's backbone is seen running down the middle of his back under the skin. Now, as far as I did see, I could go to the right or to the left of this. I didn't know either channel, of course. The banks looked pretty well alike, the depth appeared the same; but as I had been informed the station was on the west side, I naturally headed for the western passage.

"No sooner had we fairly entered it than I became aware it was much narrower than I had supposed. To the left of us there was the long uninterrupted shoal,[9] and to the right a high steep bank heavily overgrown with bushes. Above the bush the trees stood in serried ranks. The twigs overhung the current thickly, and from distance to distance a large limb of some tree projected rigidly over the stream. It was then well on in the afternoon, the face of the forest was gloomy, and a broad strip of shadow had already fallen on the water. In this shadow we steamed up—very slowly, as you may imagine. I sheered her well inshore—the water being deepest near the bank, as the sounding-pole informed me.

"One of my hungry and forbearing friends was sounding in the bows just below me. This steamboat was exactly like a decked scow. On the deck there were two little teak-wood houses, with doors and windows. The boiler was in the fore-end, and the machinery right astern. Over the whole there was a light roof, supported on stanchions. The funnel projected through that roof, and in front of the funnel a small cabin built of light planks served for a pilot-house. It contained a couch, two camp-stools, a loaded Martini-Henry[1] leaning in one corner, a tiny table, and the steering-wheel. It had a wide door in front and a broad shutter at each side. All these were always thrown open, of course. I spent my days perched up there on the extreme fore-end of that roof, before the door. At night I slept, or tried to, on the couch. An athletic black belonging to some coast tribe, and educated by my poor predecessor, was the helmsman. He sported a pair of brass earrings, wore a blue cloth wrapper from the waist to the ankles, and thought all the world of himself. He was the most unstable kind of fool I had ever seen. He steered with no end of a swagger while you were by; but if he lost sight of you, he became instantly the prey of an abject funk, and would let that cripple of a steamboat get the upper hand of him in a minute.

"I was looking down at the sounding-pole, and feeling much annoyed to see at each try a little more of it stick out of that river, when I saw my poleman give up the business suddenly, and stretch himself flat on the deck, without even taking the trouble to haul his pole in. He kept hold on it though, and it trailed in the water. At the same time the fireman, whom I could also see below me, sat down abruptly before his furnace and ducked his head. I was

9. Sandbank.
1. Rifle combining the seven-grooved barrel of the Scottish gun maker A. Henry with the block-action breech mechanism introduced by the Swiss inventor F. Martini.

amazed. Then I had to look at the river mighty quick, because there was a snag in the fairway. Sticks, little sticks, were flying about—thick; they were whizzing before my nose, dropping below me, striking behind me against my pilot-house. All this time the river, the shore, the woods, were very quiet—perfectly quiet. I could only hear the heavy splashing thump of the stern-wheel and the patter of these things. We cleared the snag clumsily. Arrows, by Jove! We were being shot at! I stepped in quickly to close the shutter on the land-side. That fool-helmsman, his hands on the spokes, was lifting his knees high, stamping his feet, champing his mouth, like a reined-in horse. Confound him! And we were staggering within ten feet of the bank. I had to lean right out to swing the heavy shutter, and I saw a face amongst the leaves on the level with my own, looking at me very fierce and steady; and then suddenly, as though a veil had been removed from my eyes, I made out, deep in the tangled gloom, naked breasts, arms, legs, glaring eyes—the bush was swarming with human limbs in movement, glistening, of bronze colour. The twigs shook, swayed, and rustled, the arrows flew out of them, and then the shutter came to. 'Steer her straight,' I said to the helmsman. He held his head rigid, face forward; but his eyes rolled, he kept on lifting and setting down his feet gently, his mouth foamed a little. 'Keep quiet!' I said in a fury. I might just as well have ordered a tree not to sway in the wind. I darted out. Below me there was a great scuffle of feet on the iron deck; confused exclamations; a voice screamed, 'Can you turn back?' I caught sight of a V-shaped ripple on the water ahead. What? Another snag! A fusillade burst out under my feet. The pilgrims had opened with their Winchesters, and were simply squirting lead into that bush. A deuce of a lot of smoke came up and drove slowly forward. I swore at it. Now I couldn't see the ripple or the snag either. I stood in the doorway, peering, and the arrows came in swarms. They might have been poisoned, but they looked as though they wouldn't kill a cat. The bush began to howl. Our wood-cutters raised a warlike whoop; the report of a rifle just at my back deafened me. I glanced over my shoulder, and the pilot-house was yet full of noise and smoke when I made a dash at the wheel. The fool-nigger had dropped everything, to throw the shutter open and let off that Martini-Henry. He stood before the wide opening, glaring, and I yelled at him to come back, while I straightened the sudden twist out of that steamboat. There was no room to turn even if I had wanted to, the snag was somewhere very near ahead in that confounded smoke, there was no time to lose, so I just crowded her into the bank—right into the bank, where I knew the water was deep.

"We tore slowly along the overhanging bushes in a whirl of broken twigs and flying leaves. The fusillade below stopped short, as I had foreseen it would when the squirts got empty. I threw my head back to a glinting whizz that traversed the pilot-house, in at one shutter-hole and out at the other. Looking past that mad helmsman, who was shaking the empty rifle and yelling at the shore, I saw vague forms of men running bent double, leaping, gliding, distinct, incomplete, evanescent. Something big appeared in the air before the shutter, the rifle went overboard, and the man stepped back swiftly, looked at me over his shoulder in an extraordinary, profound, familiar manner, and fell upon my feet. The side of his head hit the wheel twice, and the end of what appeared a long cane clattered round and knocked over a little camp-stool. It looked as though after wrenching that thing from somebody ashore he had lost his balance in the effort. The thin smoke had blown away, we were clear of the snag, and looking ahead I could see that in another hundred yards or so I would be free to sheer off, away from the bank; but my feet felt so very warm and wet that I had to look down. The man had rolled on his back and stared straight up at me; both his hands clutched that cane. It was the shaft of a spear that, either thrown or lunged through the opening, had caught him in the side just below the ribs; the blade had gone in out of sight, after making a frightful gash; my shoes were full; a pool of blood lay very still, gleaming dark-red under the wheel; his eyes shone with an amazing lustre. The fusillade burst out again. He looked at me anxiously, gripping the spear like something precious, with an air of being afraid I would try to take it away from him. I had to make an effort to free my eyes from his gaze and attend to the steering. With one hand I felt above my head for the line of the steam whistle, and jerked out screech after screech hurriedly. The tumult of angry and warlike yells was checked instantly, and then from the depths of the woods went out such a tremulous and prolonged wail of mournful fear and utter despair as may be imagined to follow the flight of the last hope from the earth. There was a great commotion in the bush; the shower of arrows stopped, a few dropping shots rang out sharply—then silence, in which the languid beat of the stern-wheel came plainly to my ears. I put the helm hard a-starboard at the moment when the pilgrim in pink pyjamas, very hot and agitated, appeared in the doorway. 'The manager sends me—' he began in an official tone, and stopped short. 'Good God!' he said, glaring at the wounded man.

"We two whites stood over him, and his lustrous and inquiring glance enveloped us both. I declare it looked as though he would presently put to us some question in an understandable language; but he died without uttering a sound, without moving a limb, without twitching a muscle. Only in the very last moment, as though in response to some sign we could not see, to some whisper we could not hear, he frowned heavily, and that frown gave to his black death-mask an inconceivably sombre, brooding, and menacing expression. The lustre of inquiring glance faded swiftly into vacant glassiness. 'Can you steer?' I asked the agent eagerly. He looked very dubious; but I made a grab at his arm, and he understood at once I meant him to steer whether or no. To tell you the truth, I was morbidly anxious to change my shoes and socks. 'He is dead,' murmured the fellow, immensely impressed. 'No doubt about it,' said I, tugging like mad at the shoe-laces. 'And by the way, I suppose Mr Kurtz is dead as well by this time.'

"For the moment that was the dominant thought. There was a sense of extreme disappointment, as though I had found out I had been striving after something altogether without a substance. I couldn't have been more disgusted if I had travelled all this way for the sole purpose of talking with Mr Kurtz. Talking with . . . I flung one shoe overboard, and became aware that that was exactly what I had been looking forward to—a talk with Kurtz. I made the strange discovery that I had never imagined him as doing, you know, but as discoursing. I didn't say to myself, 'Now I will never see him,' or 'Now I will never shake him by the hand,' but, 'Now I will never hear him.' The man presented himself as a voice. Not of course that I did not connect him with some sort of action. Hadn't I been told in all the tones of jealousy and admiration that he had collected, bartered, swindled, or stolen more ivory than all the other agents together? That was not the point. The point was in his being a gifted creature, and that of all his gifts the one that stood out pre-eminently, that carried with it a sense of real presence, was his ability to talk, his words—the gift of expression, the bewildering, the illuminating, the most exalted and the most contemptible, the pulsating stream of light, or the deceitful flow from the heart of an impenetrable darkness.

"The other shoe went flying unto the devil-god of that river. I thought, By Jove! it's all over. We are too late; he has vanished—the gift has vanished, by means of some spear, arrow, or club. I will never hear that chap speak after all—and my sorrow had a startling extravagance of emotion, even such as I had noticed in the howling sorrow of these savages in the bush. I couldn't have felt more of lonely desolation somehow, had I been robbed of a belief or had missed my destiny in life. . . . Why do you sigh in this beastly way, somebody? Absurd? Well, absurd. Good Lord! mustn't a man ever— Here, give me some tobacco." . . .

There was a pause of profound stillness, then a match flared, and Marlow's lean face appeared, worn, hollow, with downward folds and dropped eyelids, with an aspect of concentrated attention; and as he took vigorous draws at his pipe, it seemed to retreat and advance out of the night in the regular flicker of the tiny flame. The match went out.

"Absurd!" he cried. "This is the worst of trying to tell . . . Here you all are, each moored with two good addresses, like a hulk with two anchors, a butcher round one corner, a policeman round another, excellent appetites, and temperature normal—you hear—normal from year's end to year's end. And you say, Absurd! Absurd be—exploded! Absurd! My dear boys, what can you expect from a man who out of sheer nervousness had just flung overboard a pair of new shoes? Now I think of it, it is amazing I did not shed tears. I am, upon the whole, proud of my fortitude. I was cut to the quick at the idea of having lost the inestimable privilege of listening to the gifted Kurtz. Of course I was wrong. The privilege was waiting for me. Oh yes, I heard more than enough. And I was right, too. A voice. He was very little more than a voice. And I heard—him—it—this voice—other voices—all of them were so little more than voices—and the memory of that time itself lingers around me, impalpable, like a dying vibration of one immense jabber, silly, atrocious, sordid, savage, or simply mean, without any kind of sense. Voices, voices—even the girl herself—now—"

He was silent for a long time.

"I laid the ghost of his gifts at last with a lie," he began suddenly. "Girl! What? Did I mention a girl? Oh, she is out of it—completely. They—the women I mean—are out of it—should be out of it. We must help them to stay in that beautiful world of their own, lest ours gets worse. Oh, she had to be out of it. You should have heard the disinterred body of Mr Kurtz saying, 'My Intended.' You would have perceived directly then how completely she was out of it. And the lofty frontal bone of Mr Kurtz! They say the hair goes on growing sometimes, but this—ah—specimen was impressively bald. The wilderness had patted him on the head, and, behold, it was like a ball—an ivory ball; it had caressed him, and—lo!—he had withered; it had taken him, loved him, embraced him, got into his veins, consumed his flesh, and sealed his soul to its own by the inconceivable ceremonies of some devilish initiation. He was its spoiled and pampered favourite. Ivory? I should think so. Heaps of it, stacks of it. The old mud shanty was bursting with it. You would think there was not a single tusk left either above or below the ground in the whole country. 'Mostly fossil,' the manager had remarked disparagingly. It was no more fossil than I am; but they call it fossil when it is dug up. It appears these niggers do bury the tusks sometimes—but evidently they couldn't bury this parcel deep enough to save the gifted Mr Kurtz from his fate. We filled the steamboat with it, and had to pile a lot on the deck. Thus he could see and enjoy as long as he could see, because the appreciation of this favour had remained with him to the last. You should have heard him say, 'My ivory.' Oh yes, I heard him. 'My Intended, my ivory, my station, my river, my—' everything belonged to him. It made me hold my breath in expectation of hearing the wilderness burst into a prodigious peal of laughter that would shake the fixed stars in their places. Everything belonged to him—but that was a trifle. The thing was to know what he belonged to, how many powers of darkness claimed him for their own. That was the reflection that made you creepy all over. It was impossible—it was not good for one either—trying to imagine. He had taken a high seat amongst the devils of the land—I mean literally. You can't understand. How could you?—with solid pavement under your feet, surrounded by kind neighbours ready to cheer you or to fall on you, stepping delicately between the butcher and the policeman, in the holy terror of scandal and gallows and lunatic asylums—how can you imagine what particular region of the first ages a man's untrammelled feet may take him into by the way of solitude—utter solitude without a policeman—by the way of silence—utter silence, where no warning voice of a kind neighbour can be heard whispering of public opinion? These little things make all the great difference. When they are gone you must fall back upon your own innate strength, upon your own capacity for faithfulness. Of course you may be too much of a fool to go wrong—too dull even to know you are being assaulted by the powers of darkness. I take it, no fool ever made a bargain for his soul with the devil: the fool is too much of a fool, or the devil too much of a devil—I don't know which. Or you may be such a thunderingly exalted creature as to be altogether deaf and blind to anything but heavenly sights and sounds. Then the earth for you is only a standing place—and whether to be like this is your loss or your gain I won't pretend to say. But most of us are neither one nor the other. The earth for us is a place to live in, where we must put up with sights, with sounds, with smells, too, by Jove!—breathe dead hippo, so to speak, and not be contaminated. And there, don't you see? your strength comes in, the faith in your ability for the digging of unostentatious holes to bury the stuff in—your power of devotion, not to yourself, but to an obscure, back-breaking business. And that's difficult enough. Mind, I am not trying to excuse or even explain—I am trying to account to myself for—for—Mr Kurtz—for the shade of Mr Kurtz. This initiated wraith from the back of Nowhere honoured me with its amazing confidence before it vanished altogether. This was because it could speak English to me. The original Kurtz had been educated partly in England, and—as he was good enough to say himself—his sympathies were in the right place. His mother was half-English, his father was half-French. All Europe contributed to the making of Kurtz; and by and by I learned that, most appropriately, the International Society for the Suppression of Savage Customs had entrusted him with the making of a report, for its future guidance. And he had written it too. I've seen it. I've read it. It was eloquent, vibrating with eloquence, but too high-strung, I think. Seventeen pages of close writing he had found time for! But this must have been before his—let us say—nerves went wrong, and caused him to preside at certain midnight dances ending with unspeakable rites, which—as far as I reluctantly gathered from what I heard at various times—were offered up to him—do you understand?—to Mr Kurtz himself. But it was a beautiful piece of writing. The opening paragraph, however, in the light of later information, strikes me now as ominous. He began with the argument that we whites, from the point of development we had arrived at, 'must necessarily appear to them [savages] in the nature of supernatural beings—we approach them with the might as of a deity,' and so on, and so on. 'By the simple exercise of our will we can exert a power for good practically unbounded,' etc. etc. From that point he soared and took me with him. The peroration was magnificent, though difficult to remember, you know. It gave me the notion of an exotic Immensity ruled by an august Benevolence. It made me tingle with enthusiasm. This was the unbounded power of eloquence—of words—of burning noble words. There were no practical hints to interrupt the magic current of phrases, unless a kind of note at the foot of the last page, scrawled evidently much later, in an unsteady hand, may be regarded as the exposition of a method. It was very simple, and at the end of that moving appeal to every altruistic sentiment it blazed at you, luminous and terrifying, like a flash of lightning in a serene sky: 'Exterminate all the brutes!' The curious part was that he had apparently forgotten all about that valuable postscriptum, because, later on, when he in a sense came to himself, he repeatedly entreated me to take good care of 'my pamphlet' (he called it), as it was sure to have in the future a good influence upon his career. I had full information about all these things, and, besides, as it turned out, I was to have the care of his memory. I've done enough for it to give me the indisputable right to lay it, if I choose, for an everlasting rest in the dust-bin of progress, amongst all the sweepings and, figuratively speaking, all the dead cats of civilisation. But then, you see, I can't choose. He won't be forgotten. Whatever he was, he was not common. He had the power to charm or frighten rudimentary souls into an aggravated witchdance in his honour; he could also fill the small souls of the pilgrims with bitter misgivings: he had one devoted friend at least, and he had conquered one soul in the world that was neither rudimentary nor tainted with self-seeking. No; I can't forget him, though I am not prepared to affirm the fellow was exactly worth the life we lost in getting to him. I missed my late helmsman awfully—I missed him even while his body was still lying in the pilot-house. Perhaps you will think it passing strange this regret for a savage who was no more account than a grain of sand in a black Sahara. Well, don't you see, he had done something, he had steered; for months I had him at my back—a help—an instrument. It was a kind of partnership. He steered for me—I had to look after him, I worried about his deficiencies, and thus a subtle bond had been created, of which I only became aware when it was suddenly broken. And the intimate profundity of that look he gave me when he received his hurt remains to this day in my memory—like a claim of distant kinship affirmed in a supreme moment.

"Poor fool! If he had only left that shutter alone. He had no restraint, no restraint—just like Kurtz—a tree swayed by the wind. As soon as I had put on a dry pair of slippers, I dragged him out, after first jerking the spear out of his side, which operation I confess I performed with my eyes shut tight. His heels leaped together over the little doorstep; his shoulders were pressed to my breast; I hugged him from behind desperately. Oh! he was heavy, heavy; heavier than any man on earth, I should imagine. Then without more ado I tipped him overboard. The current snatched him as though he had been a wisp of grass, and I saw the body roll over twice before I lost sight of it for ever. All the pilgrims and the manager were then congregated on the awning-deck about the pilot-house, chattering at each other like a flock of excited magpies, and there was a scandalised murmur at my heartless promptitude. What they wanted to keep that body hanging about for I can't guess. Embalm it, maybe. But I had also heard another, and a very ominous, murmur on the deck below. My friends the wood-cutters were likewise scandalised, and with a better show of reason—though I admit that the reason itself was quite inadmissible. Oh, quite! I had made up my mind that if my late helmsman was to be eaten, the fishes alone should have him. He had been a very second-rate helmsman while alive, but now he was dead he might have become a first-class temptation, and possibly cause some startling trouble. Besides, I was anxious to take the wheel, the man in pink pyjamas showing himself a hopeless duffer at the business.

"This I did directly the simple funeral was over. We were going half-speed, keeping right in the middle of the stream, and I listened to the talk about me. They had given up Kurtz, they had given up the station; Kurtz was dead, and the station had been burnt—and so on—and so on. The red-haired pilgrim was beside himself with the thought that at least this poor Kurtz had been properly revenged. 'Say! We must have made a glorious slaughter of them in the bush. Eh? What do you think? Say?' He positively danced, the bloodthirsty little gingery beggar.[2] And he had nearly fainted when he saw the wounded man! I could not help saying, 'You made a glorious lot of smoke, anyhow.' I had seen, from the way the tops of the bushes rustled and flew, that almost all the shots had gone too high. You can't hit anything unless you take aim and fire from the shoulder; but these chaps fired from the hip with their eyes shut. The retreat, I maintained—and I was right—was caused by the screeching of the steam-whistle. Upon this they forgot Kurtz, and began to howl at me with indignant protests.

"The manager stood by the wheel murmuring confidentially about the necessity of getting well away down the river before dark at all events, when I saw in the distance a clearing on the river-side and the outlines of some sort of building. 'What's this?' I asked. He clapped his hands in wonder. 'The station!' he cried. I edged in at once, still going half-speed.

"Through my glasses I saw the slope of a hill interspersed with rare trees and perfectly free from undergrowth. A long decaying building on the summit was half buried in the high grass; the large holes in the peaked roof gaped black from afar; the jungle and the woods made a background. There was no enclosure or fence of any kind; but there had been one apparently, for near the house half a dozen slim posts remained in a row, roughly trimmed, and with their upper ends ornamented with round carved balls. The rails, or whatever there had been between, had disappeared. Of course the forest surrounded all that. The river-bank was clear, and on the water side I saw a white man under a hat like a cart-wheel beckoning persistently with his whole arm. Examining the edge of the forest above and below, I was almost certain I could see movements—human forms gliding here and there. I steamed past prudently, then stopped the engines and let her drift down. The man on the shore began to shout, urging us to land. 'We have been attacked,' screamed the manager. 'I know—I know. It's all right,' yelled back the other, as cheerful as you please. 'Come along. It's all right. I am glad.'

"His aspect reminded me of something I had seen—something funny I had seen somewhere. As I manœuvred to get alongside, I was asking myself, 'What

2. Little redheaded rascal.

does this fellow look like?' Suddenly I got it. He looked like a harlequin.[3] His clothes had been made of some stuff that was brown holland[4] probably, but it was covered with patches all over, with bright patches, blue, red, and yellow—patches on the back, patches on the front, patches on elbows, on knees; coloured binding round his jacket, scarlet edging at the bottom of his trousers; and the sunshine made him look extremely gay and wonderfully neat withal, because you could see how beautifully all this patching had been done. A beardless, boyish face, very fair, no features to speak of, nose peeling, little blue eyes, smiles and frowns chasing each other over that open countenance like sunshine and shadow on a wind-swept plain. 'Look out, captain!' he cried; 'there's a snag lodged in here last night.' What! Another snag? I confess I swore shamefully. I had nearly holed my cripple, to finish off that charming trip. The harlequin on the bank turned his little pug nose up to me. 'You English?' he asked, all smiles. 'Are you?' I shouted from the wheel. The smiles vanished, and he shook his head as if sorry for my disappointment. Then he brightened up. 'Never mind!' he cried encouragingly. 'Are we in time?' I asked. 'He is up there,' he replied, with a toss of the head up the hill, and becoming gloomy all of a sudden. His face was like the autumn sky, overcast one moment and bright the next.

"When the manager, escorted by the pilgrims, all of them armed to the teeth, had gone to the house, this chap came on board. 'I say, I don't like this. These natives are in the bush,' I said. He assured me earnestly it was all right. 'They are simple people,' he added; 'well, I am glad you came. It took me all my time to keep them off.' 'But you said it was all right,' I cried. 'Oh, they meant no harm,' he said; and as I stared he corrected himself, 'Not exactly.' Then vivaciously, 'My faith, your pilot-house wants a clean up!' In the next breath he advised me to keep enough steam on the boiler to blow the whistle in case of any trouble. 'One good screech will do more for you than all your rifles. They are simple people,' he repeated. He rattled away at such a rate he quite overwhelmed me. He seemed to be trying to make up for lots of silence, and actually hinted, laughing, that such was the case. 'Don't you talk with Mr Kurtz?' I said. 'You don't talk with that man—you listen to him,' he exclaimed with severe exaltation. 'But now—' He waved his arm, and in the twinkling of an eye was in the uttermost depths of despondency. In a moment he came up again with a jump, possessed himself of both my hands, shook them continuously, while he gabbled: 'Brother sailor . . . honour . . . pleasure . . . delight . . . introduce myself . . . Russian . . . son of an arch-priest . . . Government of Tambov . . . What? Tobacco! English tobacco; the excellent English tobacco! Now, that's brotherly. Smoke? Where's a sailor that does not smoke?'

"The pipe soothed him, and gradually I made out he had run away from school, had gone to sea in a Russian ship; ran away again; served some time in English ships; was now reconciled with the arch-priest. He made a point of that. 'But when one is young one must see things, gather experience, ideas; enlarge the mind.' 'Here!' I interrupted. 'You can never tell! Here I met Mr Kurtz,' he said, youthfully solemn and reproachful. I held my tongue after that. It appears he had persuaded a Dutch trading-house on the coast to fit him out with stores and goods, and had started for the interior with a light heart, and no more idea of what would happen to him than a baby. He had

---

3. Character from Italian comedy traditionally dressed in multicolored clothes.

4. Coarse linen fabric.

been wandering about that river for nearly two years alone, cut off from every-body and everything. 'I am not so young as I look. I am twenty-five,' he said. 'At first old Van Shuyten would tell me to go to the devil,' he narrated with keen enjoyment; 'but I stuck to him, and talked and talked, till at last he got afraid I would talk the hind-leg off his favourite dog, so he gave me some cheap things and a few guns, and told me he hoped he would never see my face again. Good old Dutchman, Van Shuyten. I sent him one small lot of ivory a year ago, so that he can't call me a little thief when I get back. I hope he got it. And for the rest I don't care. I had some wood stacked for you. That was my old house. Did you see?'

"I gave him Towson's book. He made as though he would kiss me, but restrained himself. 'The only book I had left, and I thought I had lost it,' he said, looking at it ecstatically. 'So many accidents happen to a man going about alone, you know. Canoes get upset sometimes—and sometimes you've got to clear out so quick when the people get angry.' He thumbed the pages. 'You made notes in Russian?' I asked. He nodded. 'I thought they were written in cipher,' I said. He laughed, then became serious. 'I had lots of trouble to keep these people off,' he said. 'Did they want to kill you?' I asked. 'Oh no!' he cried, and checked himself. 'Why did they attack us?' I pursued. He hesitated, then said shamefacedly, 'They don't want him to go.' 'Don't they?' I said curiously. He nodded a nod full of mystery and wisdom. 'I tell you,' he cried, 'this man has enlarged my mind.' He opened his arms wide, staring at me with his little blue eyes that were perfectly round."

3

"I looked at him, lost in astonishment. There he was before me, in motley, as though he had absconded from a troupe of mimes, enthusiastic, fabulous. His very existence was improbable, inexplicable, and altogether bewildering. He was an insoluble problem. It was inconceivable how he had existed, how he had succeeded in getting so far, how he had managed to remain—why he did not instantly disappear. 'I went a little farther,' he said, 'then still a little farther—till I had gone so far that I don't know how I'll ever get back. Never mind. Plenty time. I can manage. You take Kurtz away quick—quick—I tell you.' The glamour of youth enveloped his particoloured rags, his destitution, his loneliness, the essential desolation of his futile wanderings. For months—for years—his life hadn't been worth a day's purchase; and there he was gal-lantly, thoughtlessly alive, to all appearance indestructible solely by the virtue of his few years and of his unreflecting audacity. I was seduced into something like admiration—like envy. Glamour urged him on, glamour kept him unscathed. He surely wanted nothing from the wilderness but space to breathe in and to push on through. His need was to exist, and to move onwards at the greatest possible risk, and with a maximum of privation. If the absolutely pure, uncalculating, unpractical spirit of adventure had ever ruled a human being, it ruled this be-patched youth. I almost envied him the possession of this modest and clear flame. It seemed to have consumed all thought of self so completely, that, even while he was talking to you, you forgot that it was he—the man before your eyes—who had gone through these things. I did not envy him his devotion to Kurtz, though. He had not meditated over it. It came to him, and he accepted it with a sort of eager fatalism. I must say that to me it appeared about the most dangerous thing in every way he had come upon so far.

"They had come together unavoidably, like two ships becalmed near each other, and lay rubbing sides at last. I suppose Kurtz wanted an audience, because on a certain occasion, when encamped in the forest, they had talked all night, or more probably Kurtz had talked. 'We talked of everything,' he said, quite transported at the recollection. 'I forgot there was such a thing as sleep. The night did not seem to last an hour. Everything! Everything! . . . Of love too.' 'Ah, he talked to you of love!' I said, much amused. 'It isn't what you think,' he cried, almost passionately. 'It was in general. He made me see things—things.'

"He threw his arms up. We were on deck at the time, and the head-man of my wood-cutters, lounging near by, turned upon him his heavy and glittering eyes. I looked around, and I don't know why, but I assure you that never, never before, did this land, this river, this jungle, the very arch of this blazing sky, appear to me so hopeless and so dark, so impenetrable to human thought, so pitiless to human weakness. 'And, ever since, you have been with him, of course?' I said.

"On the contrary. It appears their intercourse had been very much broken by various causes. He had, as he informed me proudly, managed to nurse Kurtz through two illnesses (he alluded to it as you would to some risky feat), but as a rule Kurtz wandered alone, far in the depths of the forest. 'Very often coming to this station, I had to wait days and days before he would turn up,' he said. 'Ah, it was worth waiting for!—sometimes.' 'What was he doing? exploring or what?' I asked. 'Oh yes, of course'; he had discovered lots of villages, a lake too—he did not know exactly in what direction; it was dangerous to inquire too much—but mostly his expeditions had been for ivory. 'But he had no goods to trade with by that time,' I objected. 'There's a good lot of cartridges left even yet,' he answered, looking away. 'To speak plainly, he raided the country,' I said. He nodded. 'Not alone, surely!' He muttered something about the villages round that lake. 'Kurtz got the tribe to follow him, did he?' I suggested. He fidgeted a little. 'They adored him,' he said. The tone of these words was so extraordinary that I looked at him searchingly. It was curious to see his mingled eagerness and reluctance to speak of Kurtz. The man filled his life, occupied his thoughts, swayed his emotions. 'What can you expect?' he burst out; 'he came to them with thunder and lightning, you know—and they had never seen anything like it—and very terrible. He could be very terrible. You can't judge Mr Kurtz as you would an ordinary man. No, no, no! Now—just to give you an idea—I don't mind telling you, he wanted to shoot me too one day—but I don't judge him.' 'Shoot you!' I cried. 'What for?' 'Well, I had a small lot of ivory the chief of that village near my house gave me. You see I used to shoot game for them. Well, he wanted it, and wouldn't hear reason. He declared he would shoot me unless I gave him the ivory and then cleared out of the country, because he could do so, and had a fancy for it, and there was nothing on earth to prevent him killing whom he jolly well pleased. And it was true too. I gave him the ivory. What did I care! But I didn't clear out. No, no. I couldn't leave him. I had to be careful, of course, till we got friendly again for a time. He had his second illness then. Afterwards I had to keep out of the way; but I didn't mind. He was living for the most part in those villages on the lake. When he came down to the river, sometimes he would take to me, and sometimes it was better for me to be careful. This man suffered too much. He hated all this, and somehow he couldn't get away. When I had a chance I begged him to try and leave while there was time; I offered to go back with him. And he would say yes, and then he would remain; go off on another ivory hunt; disappear for weeks; forget himself amongst these people—forget himself—you know.' 'Why! he's mad,' I said. He protested indignantly. Mr Kurtz couldn't be mad. If I had heard him talk, only two days ago, I wouldn't dare hint at such a thing. . . . I had taken up my binoculars while we talked, and was looking at the shore, sweeping the limit of the forest at each side and at the back of the house. The consciousness of there being people in that bush, so silent, so quiet—as silent and quiet as the ruined house on the hill—made me uneasy. There was no sign on the face of nature of this amazing tale that was not so much told as suggested to me in desolate exclamations, completed by shrugs, in interrupted phrases, in hints ending in deep sighs. The woods were unmoved, like a mask—heavy, like the closed door of a prison—they looked with their air of hidden knowledge, of patient expectation, of unapproachable silence. The Russian was explaining to me that it was only lately that Mr Kurtz had come down to the river, bringing along with him all the fighting men of that lake tribe. He had been absent for several months—getting himself adored, I suppose—and had come down unexpectedly, with the intention to all appearance of making a raid either across the river or down stream. Evidently the appetite for more ivory had got the better of the—what shall I say?—less material aspirations. However, he had got much worse suddenly. 'I heard he was lying helpless, and so I came up—took my chance,' said the Russian. 'Oh, he is bad, very bad.' I directed my glass to the house. There were no signs of life, but there was the ruined roof, the long mud wall peeping above the grass, with three little square window-holes, no two of the same size; all this brought within reach of my hand, as it were. And then I made a brusque movement, and one of the remaining posts of that vanished fence leaped up in the field of my glass. You remember I told you I had been struck at the distance by certain attempts at ornamentation, rather remarkable in the ruinous aspect of the place. Now I had suddenly a nearer view, and its first result was to make me throw my head back as if before a blow. Then I went carefully from post to post with my glass, and I saw my mistake. These round knobs were not ornamental but symbolic; they were expressive and puzzling, striking and disturbing—food for thought and also for the vultures if there had been any looking down from the sky; but at all events for such ants as were industrious enough to ascend the pole. They would have been even more impressive, those heads on the stakes, if their faces had not been turned to the house. Only one, the first I had made out, was facing my way. I was not so shocked as you may think. The start back I had given was really nothing but a movement of surprise. I had expected to see a knob of wood there, you know. I returned deliberately to the first I had seen—and there it was, black, dried, sunken, with closed eyelids—a head that seemed to sleep at the top of that pole, and, with the shrunken dry lips showing a narrow white line of the teeth, was smiling too, smiling continuously at some endless and jocose dream of that eternal slumber.

"I am not disclosing any trade secrets. In fact the manager said afterwards that Mr Kurtz's methods had ruined the district. I have no opinion on that point, but I want you clearly to understand that there was nothing exactly profitable in these heads being there. They only show that Mr Kurtz lacked restraint in the gratification of his various lusts, that there was something wanting in him—some small matter which, when the pressing need arose, could not be found under his magnificent eloquence. Whether he knew of this deficiency himself I can't say. I think the knowledge came to him at last—

only at the very last. But the wilderness had found him out early, and had taken on him a terrible vengeance for the fantastic invasion. I think it had whispered to him things about himself which he did not know, things of which he had no conception till he took counsel with this great solitude—and the whisper had proved irresistibly fascinating. It echoed loudly within him because he was hollow at the core. . . . I put down the glass, and the head that had appeared near enough to be spoken to seemed at once to have leaped away from me into inaccessible distance.

"The admirer of Mr Kurtz was a bit crestfallen. In a hurried, indistinct voice he began to assure me he had not dared to take these—say, symbols—down. He was not afraid of the natives; they would not stir till Mr Kurtz gave the word. His ascendancy was extraordinary. The camps of these people surrounded the place, and the chiefs came every day to see him. They would crawl . . . 'I don't want to know anything of the ceremonies used when approaching Mr Kurtz,' I shouted. Curious, this feeling that came over me that such details would be more intolerable than those heads drying on the stakes under Mr Kurtz's windows. After all, that was only a savage sight, while I seemed at one bound to have been transported into some lightless region of subtle horrors, where pure, uncomplicated savagery was a positive relief, being something that had a right to exist—obviously—in the sunshine. The young man looked at me with surprise. I suppose it did not occur to him that Mr Kurtz was no idol of mine. He forgot I hadn't heard any of these splendid monologues on, what was it? on love, justice, conduct of life—or what not. If it had come to crawling before Mr Kurtz, he crawled as much as the veriest savage of them all. I had no idea of the conditions, he said: these heads were the heads of rebels. I shocked him excessively by laughing. Rebels! What would be the next definition I was to hear? There had been enemies, criminals, workers—and these were rebels. Those rebellious heads looked very subdued to me on their sticks. 'You don't know how such a life tries a man like Kurtz,' cried Kurtz's last disciple. 'Well, and you?' I said. 'I! I! I am a simple man. I have no great thoughts. I want nothing from anybody. How can you compare me to . . . ?' His feelings were too much for speech, and suddenly he broke down. 'I don't understand,' he groaned. 'I've been doing my best to keep him alive, and that's enough. I had no hand in all this. I have no abilities. There hasn't been a drop of medicine or a mouthful of invalid food for months here. He was shamefully abandoned. A man like this, with such ideas. Shamefully! Shamefully! I—I—haven't slept for the last ten nights. . . . '

"His voice lost itself in the calm of the evening. The long shadows of the forest had slipped down hill while we talked, had gone far beyond the ruined hovel, beyond the symbolic row of stakes. All this was in the gloom, while we down there were yet in the sunshine, and the stretch of the river abreast of the clearing glittered in a still and dazzling splendour, with a murky and overshadowed bend above and below. Not a living soul was seen on the shore. The bushes did not rustle.

"Suddenly round the corner of the house a group of men appeared, as though they had come up from the ground. They waded waist-deep in the grass, in a compact body, bearing an improvised stretcher in their midst. Instantly, in the emptiness of the landscape, a cry arose whose shrillness pierced the still air like a sharp arrow flying straight to the very heart of the land; and, as if by enchantment, streams of human beings—of naked human beings—with spears in their hands, with bows, with shields, with wild glances and savage movements, were poured into the clearing by the dark-faced and pensive forest. The bushes shook, the grass swayed for a time, and then everything stood still in attentive immobility.

" 'Now, if he does not say the right thing to them we are all done for,' said the Russian at my elbow. The knot of men with the stretcher had stopped too, half-way to the steamer, as if petrified. I saw the man on the stretcher sit up, lank and with an uplifted arm, above the shoulders of the bearers. 'Let us hope that the man who can talk so well of love in general will find some particular reason to spare us this time,' I said. I resented bitterly the absurd danger of our situation, as if to be at the mercy of that atrocious phantom had been a dishonouring necessity. I could not hear a sound, but through my glasses I saw the thin arm extended commandingly, the lower jaw moving, the eyes of that apparition shining darkly far in its bony head that nodded with grotesque jerks. Kurtz—Kurtz—that means 'short' in German—don't it? Well, the name was as true as everything else in his life—and death. He looked at least seven feet long. His covering had fallen off, and his body emerged from it pitiful and appalling as from a winding-sheet. I could see the cage of his ribs all astir, the bones of his arm waving. It was as though an animated image of death carved out of old ivory had been shaking its hand with menaces at a motionless crowd of men made of dark and glittering bronze. I saw him open his mouth wide—it gave him a weirdly voracious aspect, as though he had wanted to swallow all the air, all the earth, all the men before him. A deep voice reached me faintly. He must have been shouting. He fell back suddenly. The stretcher shook as the bearers staggered forward again, and almost at the same time I noticed that the crowd of savages was vanishing without any perceptible movement of retreat, as if the forest that had ejected these beings so suddenly had drawn them in again as the breath is drawn in a long aspiration.

"Some of the pilgrims behind the stretcher carried his arms—two shot-guns, a heavy rifle, and a light revolver-carbine—the thunderbolts of that pitiful Jupiter. The manager bent over him murmuring as he walked beside his head. They laid him down in one of the little cabins—just a room for a bedplace and a camp-stool or two, you know. We had brought his belated correspondence, and a lot of torn envelopes and open letters littered his bed. His hand roamed feebly amongst these papers. I was struck by the fire of his eyes and the composed languor of his expression. It was not so much the exhaustion of disease. He did not seem in pain. This shadow looked satiated and calm, as though for the moment it had had its fill of all the emotions.

"He rustled one of the letters, and looking straight in my face said, 'I am glad.' Somebody had been writing to him about me. These special recommendations were turning up again. The volume of tone he emitted without effort, almost without the trouble of moving his lips, amazed me. A voice! a voice! It was grave, profound, vibrating, while the man did not seem capable of a whisper. However, he had enough strength in him—factitious no doubt—to very nearly make an end of us, as you shall hear directly.

"The manager appeared silently in the doorway; I stepped out at once and he drew the curtain after me. The Russian, eyed curiously by the pilgrims, was staring at the shore. I followed the direction of his glance.

"Dark human shapes could be made out in the distance, flitting indistinctly against the gloomy border of the forest, and near the river two bronze figures, leaning on tall spears, stood in the sunlight under fantastic head-dresses of spotted skins, warlike and still in statuesque repose. And from right to left along the lighted shore moved a wild and gorgeous apparition of a woman.

"She walked with measured steps, draped in striped and fringed cloths, treading the earth proudly, with a slight jingle and flash of barbarous ornaments. She carried her head high; her hair was done in the shape of a helmet; she had brass leggings to the knee, brass wire gauntlets to the elbow, a crimson spot on her tawny cheek, innumerable necklaces of glass beads on her neck; bizarre things, charms, gifts of witch-men, that hung about her, glittered and trembled at every step. She must have had the value of several elephant tusks upon her. She was savage and superb, wild-eyed and magnificent; there was something ominous and stately in her deliberate progress. And in the hush that had fallen suddenly upon the whole sorrowful land, the immense wilderness, the colossal body of the fecund and mysterious life seemed to look at her, pensive, as though it had been looking at the image of its own tenebrous and passionate soul.

"She came abreast of the steamer, stood still, and faced us. Her long shadow fell to the water's edge. Her face had a tragic and fierce aspect of wild sorrow and of dumb pain mingled with the fear of some struggling, half-shaped resolve. She stood looking at us without a stir, and like the wilderness itself, with an air of brooding over an inscrutable purpose. A whole minute passed, and then she made a step forward. There was a low jingle, a glint of yellow metal, a sway of fringed draperies, and she stopped as if her heart had failed her. The young fellow by my side growled. The pilgrims murmured at my back. She looked at us all as if her life had depended upon the unswerving steadiness of her glance. Suddenly she opened her bared arms and threw them up rigid above her head, as though in an uncontrollable desire to touch the sky, and at the same time the swift shadows darted out on the earth, swept around on the river, gathering the steamer into a shadowy embrace. A formidable silence hung over the scene.

"She turned away slowly, walked on, following the bank, and passed into the bushes to the left. Once only her eyes gleamed back at us in the dusk of the thickets before she disappeared.

" 'If she had offered to come aboard I really think I would have tried to shoot her,' said the man of patches nervously. 'I had been risking my life every day for the last fortnight to keep her out of the house. She got in one day and kicked up a row about those miserable rags I picked up in the storeroom to mend my clothes with. I wasn't decent. At least it must have been that, for she talked like a fury to Kurtz for an hour, pointing at me now and then. I don't understand the dialect of this tribe. Luckily for me, I fancy Kurtz felt too ill that day to care, or there would have been mischief. I don't understand. . . . No—it's too much for me. Ah, well, it's all over now.'

"At this moment I heard Kurtz's deep voice behind the curtain: 'Save me!— save the ivory, you mean. Don't tell me. Save me! Why, I've had to save you. You are interrupting my plans now. Sick! Sick! Not so sick as you would like to believe. Never mind. I'll carry my ideas out yet—I will return. I'll show you what can be done. You with your little peddling notions—you are interfering with me. I will return. I . . . '

"The manager came out. He did me the honour to take me under the arm and lead me aside. 'He is very low, very low,' he said. He considered it necessary to sigh, but neglected to be consistently sorrowful. 'We have done all we could for him—haven't we? But there is no disguising the fact, Mr Kurtz has done more harm than good to the Company. He did not see the time was not ripe for vigorous action. Cautiously, cautiously—that's my principle. We must be cautious yet. The district is closed to us for a time. Deplorable! Upon the whole, the trade will suffer. I don't deny there is a remarkable quantity of ivory—mostly fossil. We must save it, at all events—but look how precarious the position is—and why? Because the method is unsound.' 'Do you,' said I, looking at the shore, 'call it "unsound method"?' 'Without doubt,' he exclaimed hotly, 'Don't you?' . . . 'No method at all,' I murmured after a while. 'Exactly,' he exulted. 'I anticipated this. Shows a complete want of judgment. It is my duty to point it out in the proper quarter.' 'Oh,' said I, 'that fellow—what's his name?—the brickmaker, will make a readable report for you.' He appeared confounded for a moment. It seemed to me I had never breathed an atmosphere so vile, and I turned mentally to Kurtz for relief—positively for relief. 'Nevertheless, I think Mr Kurtz is a remarkable man,' I said with emphasis. He started, dropped on me a cold heavy glance, said very quietly, 'He *was*,' and turned his back on me. My hour of favour was over; I found myself lumped along with Kurtz as a partisan of methods for which the time was not ripe: I was unsound! Ah! but it was something to have at least a choice of nightmares.

"I had turned to the wilderness really, not to Mr Kurtz, who, I was ready to admit, was as good as buried. And for a moment it seemed to me as if I also were buried in a vast grave full of unspeakable secrets. I felt an intolerable weight oppressing my breast, the smell of the damp earth, the unseen presence of victorious corruption, the darkness of an impenetrable night. . . . The Russian tapped me on the shoulder. I heard him mumbling and stammering something about 'brother seaman—couldn't conceal—knowledge of matters that would affect Mr Kurtz's reputation.' I waited. For him evidently Mr Kurtz was not in his grave; I suspect that for him Mr Kurtz was one of the immortals. 'Well!' said I at last, 'speak out. As it happens, I am Mr Kurtz's friend—in a way.'

"He stated with a good deal of formality that had we not been 'of the same profession,' he would have kept the matter to himself without regard to consequences. He suspected 'there was an active ill-will towards him on the part of these white men that—' 'You are right,' I said, remembering a certain conversation I had overheard. 'The manager thinks you ought to be hanged.' He showed a concern at this intelligence which amused me at first. 'I had better get out of the way quietly,' he said earnestly. 'I can do no more for Kurtz now, and they would soon find some excuse. What's to stop them? There's a military post three hundred miles from here.' 'Well, upon my word,' said I, 'perhaps you had better go if you have any friends amongst the savages near by.' 'Plenty,' he said. 'They are simple people—and I want nothing, you know.' He stood biting his lip, then: 'I don't want any harm to happen to these whites here, but of course I was thinking of Mr Kurtz's reputation—but you are a brother seaman and—' 'All right,' said I, after a time. 'Mr Kurtz's reputation is safe with me.' I did not know how truly I spoke.

"He informed me, lowering his voice, that it was Kurtz who had ordered the attack to be made on the steamer. 'He hated sometimes the idea of being taken away—and then again . . . But I don't understand these matters. I am a simple man. He thought it would scare you away—that you would give it up, thinking him dead. I could not stop him. Oh, I had an awful time of it this last month.' 'Very well,' I said. 'He is all right now.' 'Ye-e-es,' he muttered, not very convinced apparently. 'Thanks,' said I; 'I shall keep my eyes open.' 'But quiet—eh?' he urged anxiously. 'It would be awful for his reputation if anybody here—' I promised a complete discretion with great gravity. 'I have a canoe and three black fellows waiting not very far. I am off. Could you give me a few Martini-Henry cartridges?' I could, and did, with proper secrecy. He helped himself, with a wink at me, to a handful of my tobacco. 'Between sailors—you know—good English tobacco.' At the door of the pilot-house he turned round—'I say, haven't you a pair of shoes you could spare?' He raised one leg. 'Look.' The soles were tied with knotted strings sandal-wise under his bare feet. I rooted out an old pair, at which he looked with admiration before tucking it under his left arm. One of his pockets (bright red) was bulging with cartridges, from the other (dark blue) peeped 'Towson's Inquiry,' etc. etc. He seemed to think himself excellently well equipped for a renewed encounter with the wilderness. 'Ah! I'll never, never meet such a man again. You ought to have heard him recite poetry—his own too it was, he told me. Poetry!' He rolled his eyes at the recollection of these delights. 'Oh, he enlarged my mind!' 'Good-bye,' said I. He shook hands and vanished in the night. Sometimes I ask myself whether I had ever really seen him—whether it was possible to meet such a phenomenon! . . .

"When I woke up shortly after midnight his warning came to my mind with its hint of danger that seemed, in the starred darkness, real enough to make me get up for the purpose of having a look round. On the hill a big fire burned, illuminating fitfully a crooked corner of the station-house. One of the agents with a picket of a few of our blacks, armed for the purpose, was keeping guard over the ivory; but deep within the forest, red gleams that wavered, that seemed to sink and rise from the ground amongst confused columnar shapes of intense blackness, showed the exact position of the camp where Mr Kurtz's adorers were keeping their uneasy vigil. The monotonous beating of a big drum filled the air with muffled shocks and a lingering vibration. A steady droning sound of many men chanting each to himself some weird incantation came out from the black, flat wall of the woods as the humming of bees comes out of a hive, and had a strange narcotic effect upon my half-awake senses. I believe I dozed off leaning over the rail, till an abrupt burst of yells, an overwhelming outbreak of a pent-up and mysterious frenzy, woke me up in a bewildered wonder. It was cut short all at once, and the low droning went on with an effect of audible and soothing silence. I glanced casually into the little cabin. A light was burning within, but Mr Kurtz was not there.

"I think I would have raised an outcry if I had believed my eyes. But I didn't believe them at first—the thing seemed so impossible. The fact is I was completely unnerved by a sheer blank fright, pure abstract terror, unconnected with any distinct shape of physical danger. What made this emotion so overpowering was—how shall I define it?—the moral shock I received, as if something altogether monstrous, intolerable to thought and odious to the soul, had been thrust upon me unexpectedly. This lasted of course the merest fraction of a second, and then the usual sense of commonplace, deadly danger, the possibility of a sudden onslaught and massacre, or something of the kind, which I saw impending, was positively welcome and composing. It pacified me, in fact, so much, that I did not raise an alarm.

"There was an agent buttoned up inside an ulster[5] and sleeping on a chair on deck within three feet of me. The yells had not awakened him; he snored very slightly; I left him to his slumbers and leaped ashore. I did not betray Mr

5. Long overcoat.

Kurtz—it was ordered I should never betray him—it was written I should be loyal to the nightmare of my choice. I was anxious to deal with this shadow by myself alone—and to this day I don't know why I was so jealous of sharing with any one the peculiar blackness of that experience.

"As soon as I got on the bank I saw a trail—a broad trail through the grass. I remember the exultation with which I said to myself, 'He can't walk—he is crawling on all-fours—I've got him.' The grass was wet with dew. I strode rapidly with clenched fists. I fancy I had some vague notion of falling upon him and giving him a drubbing. I don't know. I had some imbecile thoughts. The knitting old woman with the cat obtruded herself upon my memory as a most improper person to be sitting at the other end of such an affair. I saw a row of pilgrims squirting lead in the air out of Winchesters held to the hip. I thought I would never get back to the steamer, and imagined myself living alone and unarmed in the woods to an advanced age. Such silly things—you know. And I remember I confounded the beat of the drum with the beating of my heart, and was pleased at its calm regularity.

"I kept to the track though—then stopped to listen. The night was very clear; a dark blue space, sparkling with dew and starlight, in which black things stood very still. I thought I could see a kind of motion ahead of me. I was strangely cocksure of everything that night. I actually left the track and ran in a wide semicircle (I verily believe chuckling to myself) so as to get in front of that stir, of that motion I had seen—if indeed I had seen anything. I was circumventing Kurtz as though it had been a boyish game.

"I came upon him, and, if he had not heard me coming, I would have fallen over him too, but he got up in time. He rose, unsteady, long, pale, indistinct, like a vapour exhaled by the earth, and swayed slightly, misty and silent before me; while at my back the fires loomed between the trees, and the murmur of many voices issued from the forest. I had cut him off cleverly; but when actually confronting him I seemed to come to my senses, I saw the danger in its right proportion. It was by no means over yet. Suppose he began to shout? Though he could hardly stand, there was still plenty of vigour in his voice. 'Go away—hide yourself,' he said, in that profound tone. It was very awful. I glanced back. We were within thirty yards of the nearest fire. A black figure stood up, strode on long black legs, waving long black arms, across the glow. It had horns—antelope horns, I think—on its head. Some sorcerer, some witch-man no doubt: it looked fiend-like enough. 'Do you know what you are doing?' I whispered. 'Perfectly,' he answered, raising his voice for that single word: it sounded to me far off and yet loud, like a hail through a speaking-trumpet. If he makes a row we are lost, I thought to myself. This clearly was not a case for fisticuffs, even apart from the very natural aversion I had to beat that Shadow—this wandering and tormented thing. 'You will be lost,' I said—'utterly lost.' One gets sometimes such a flash of inspiration, you know. I did say the right thing, though indeed he could not have been more irretrievably lost than he was at this very moment, when the foundations of our intimacy were being laid—to endure—to endure—even to the end—even beyond.

" 'I had immense plans,' he muttered irresolutely. 'Yes,' said I; 'but if you try to shout I'll smash your head with—' There was not a stick or a stone near. 'I will throttle you for good,' I corrected myself. 'I was on the threshold of great things,' he pleaded, in a voice of longing, with a wistfulness of tone that made my blood run cold. 'And now for this stupid scoundrel—' 'Your success in Europe is assured in any case,' I affirmed steadily. I did not want to have the throttling of him, you understand—and indeed it would have been very little use for any practical purpose. I tried to break the spell—the heavy, mute spell of the wilderness—that seemed to draw him to its pitiless breast by the awakening of forgotten and brutal instincts, by the memory of gratified and monstrous passions. This alone, I was convinced, had driven him out to the edge of the forest, to the bush, towards the gleam of fires, the throb of drums, the drone of weird incantations; this alone had beguiled his unlawful soul beyond the bounds of permitted aspirations. And, don't you see, the terror of the position was not in being knocked on the head—though I had a very lively sense of that danger too—but in this, that I had to deal with a being to whom I could not appeal in the name of anything high or low. I had, even like the niggers, to invoke him—himself—his own exalted and incredible degradation. There was nothing either above or below him, and I knew it. He had kicked himself loose of the earth. Confound the man! he had kicked the very earth to pieces. He was alone, and I before him did not know whether I stood on the ground or floated in the air. I've been telling you what we said—repeating the phrases we pronounced—but what's the good? They were common everyday words—the familiar, vague sounds exchanged on every waking day of life. But what of that? They had behind them, to my mind, the terrific suggestiveness of words heard in dreams, of phrases spoken in nightmares. Soul! If anybody had ever struggled with a soul, I am the man. And I wasn't arguing with a lunatic either. Believe me or not, his intelligence was perfectly clear—concentrated, it is true, upon himself with horrible intensity, yet clear; and therein was my only chance—barring, of course, the killing him there and then, which wasn't so good, on account of unavoidable noise. But his soul was mad. Being alone in the wilderness, it had looked within itself, and, by heavens! I tell you, it had gone mad. I had—for my sins, I suppose, to go through the ordeal of looking into it myself. No eloquence could have been so withering to one's belief in mankind as his final burst of sincerity. He struggled with himself too. I saw it—I heard it. I saw the inconceivable mystery of a soul that knew no restraint, no faith, and no fear, yet struggling blindly with itself. I kept my head pretty well; but when I had him at last stretched on the couch, I wiped my forehead, while my legs shook under me as though I had carried half a ton on my back down that hill. And yet I had only supported him, his bony arm clasped round my neck—and he was not much heavier than a child.

"When next day we left at noon, the crowd, of whose presence behind the curtain of trees I had been acutely conscious all the time, flowed out of the woods again, filled the clearing, covered the slope with a mass of naked, breathing, quivering, bronze bodies. I steamed up a bit, then swung downstream, and two thousand eyes followed the evolutions of the splashing, thumping, fierce river-demon beating the water with its terrible tail and breathing black smoke into the air. In front of the first rank, along the river, three men, plastered with bright red earth from head to foot, strutted to and fro restlessly. When we came abreast again, they faced the river, stamped their feet, nodded their horned heads, swayed their scarlet bodies; they shook towards the fierce river-demon a bunch of black feathers, a mangy skin with a pendent tail—something that looked like a dried gourd; they shouted periodically together strings of amazing words that resembled no sounds of human language; and the deep murmurs of the crowd, interrupted suddenly, were like the responses of some satanic litany.

"We had carried Kurtz into the pilot-house: there was more air there. Lying on the couch, he stared through the open shutter. There was an eddy in the mass of human bodies, and the woman with helmeted head and tawny cheeks rushed out to the very brink of the stream. She put out her hands, shouted something, and all that wild mob took up the shout in a roaring chorus of articulated, rapid, breathless utterance.

" 'Do you understand this?' I asked.

"He kept on looking out past me with fiery, longing eyes, with a mingled expression of wistfulness and hate. He made no answer, but I saw a smile, a smile of indefinable meaning, appear on his colourless lips that a moment after twitched convulsively. 'Do I not?' he said slowly, gasping, as if the words had been torn out of him by a supernatural power.

"I pulled the string of the whistle, and I did this because I saw the pilgrims on deck getting out their rifles with an air of anticipating a jolly lark. At the sudden screech there was a movement of abject terror through that wedged mass of bodies. 'Don't! don't you frighten them away,' cried some one on deck disconsolately. I pulled the string time after time. They broke and ran, they leaped, they crouched, they swerved, they dodged the flying terror of the sound. The three red chaps had fallen flat, face down on the shore, as though they had been shot dead. Only the barbarous and superb woman did not so much as flinch, and stretched tragically her bare arms after us over the sombre and glittering river.

"And then that imbecile crowd down on the deck started their little fun, and I could see nothing more for smoke.

"The brown current ran swiftly out of the heart of darkness, bearing us down towards the sea with twice the speed of our upward progress; and Kurtz's life was running swiftly too, ebbing, ebbing out of his heart into the sea of inexorable time. The manager was very placid, he had no vital anxieties now, he took us both in with a comprehensive and satisfied glance: the 'affair' had come off as well as could be wished. I saw the time approaching when I would be left alone of the party of 'unsound method.' The pilgrims looked upon me with disfavour. I was, so to speak, numbered with the dead. It is strange how I accepted this unforeseen partnership, this choice of nightmares forced upon me in the tenebrous land invaded by these mean and greedy phantoms.

"Kurtz discoursed. A voice! a voice! It rang deep to the very last. It survived his strength to hide in the magnificent folds of eloquence the barren darkness of his heart. Oh, he struggled! he struggled! The wastes of his weary brain were haunted by shadowy images now—images of wealth and fame revolving obsequiously round his unextinguishable gift of noble and lofty expression. My Intended, my station, my career, my ideas—these were the subjects for the occasional utterances of elevated sentiments. The shade of the original Kurtz frequented the bedside of the hollow sham, whose fate it was to be buried presently in the mould of primeval earth. But both the diabolic love and the unearthly hate of the mysteries it had penetrated fought for the possession of that soul satiated with primitive emotions, avid of lying fame, of sham distinction, of all the appearances of success and power.

"Sometimes he was contemptibly childish. He desired to have kings meet him at railway stations on his return from some ghastly Nowhere, where he intended to accomplish great things. 'You show them you have in you something that is really profitable, and then there will be no limits to the recognition of your ability,' he would say. 'Of course you must take care of the motives— right motives—always.' The long reaches that were like one and the same reach, monotonous bends that were exactly alike, slipped past the steamer with their multitude of secular[6] trees looking patiently after this grimy fragment of another world, the forerunner of change, of conquest, of trade, of massacres, of blessings. I looked ahead—piloting. 'Close the shutter,' said Kurtz suddenly one day; 'I can't bear to look at this.' I did so. There was a silence. 'Oh, but I will wring your heart yet!' he cried at the invisible wilderness.

"We broke down—as I had expected—and had to lie up for repairs at the head of an island. This delay was the first thing that shook Kurtz's confidence. One morning he gave me a packet of papers and a photograph—the lot tied together with a shoe-string. 'Keep this for me,' he said. 'This noxious fool' (meaning the manager) 'is capable of prying into my boxes when I am not looking.' In the afternoon I saw him. He was lying on his back with closed eyes, and I withdrew quietly, but I heard him mutter, 'Live rightly, die, die . . .' I listened. There was nothing more. Was he rehearsing some speech in his sleep, or was it a fragment of a phrase from some newspaper article? He had been writing for the papers and meant to do so again, 'for the furthering of my ideas. It's a duty.'

"His was an impenetrable darkness. I looked at him as you peer down at a man who is lying at the bottom of a precipice where the sun never shines. But I had not much time to give him, because I was helping the engine-driver to take to pieces the leaky cylinders, to straighten a bent connecting-rod, and in other such matters. I lived in an infernal mess of rust, filings, nuts, bolts, spanners, hammers, ratchet-drills—things I abominate, because I don't get on with them. I tended the little forge we fortunately had aboard; I toiled wearily in a wretched scrap-heap—unless I had the shakes too bad to stand.

"One evening coming in with a candle I was startled to hear him say a little tremulously, 'I am lying here in the dark waiting for death.' The light was within a foot of his eyes. I forced myself to murmur, 'Oh, nonsense!' and stood over him as if transfixed.

"Anything approaching the change that came over his features I have never seen before, and hope never to see again. Oh, I wasn't touched. I was fasci-nated. It was as though a veil had been rent. I saw on that ivory face the expression of sombre pride, of ruthless power, of craven terror—of an intense and hopeless despair. Did he live his life again in every detail of desire, temp-tation, and surrender during that supreme moment of complete knowledge? He cried in a whisper at some image, at some vision—he cried out twice, a cry that was no more than a breath:

" 'The horror! The horror!'

"I blew the candle out and left the cabin. The pilgrims were dining in the mess-room, and I took my place opposite the manager, who lifted his eyes to give me a questioning glance, which I successfully ignored. He leaned back, serene, with that peculiar smile of his sealing the unexpressed depths of his meanness. A continuous shower of small flies streamed upon the lamp, upon the cloth, upon our hands and faces. Suddenly the manager's boy put his insolent black head in the doorway, and said in a tone of scathing contempt:

" 'Mistah Kurtz—he dead.'

"All the pilgrims rushed out to see. I remained, and went on with my dinner. I believe I was considered brutally callous. However, I did not eat much. There was a lamp in there—light, don't you know—and outside it was so beastly,

---

6. Centuries old.

beastly dark. I went no more near the remarkable man who had pronounced a judgement upon the adventures of his soul on this earth. The voice was gone. What else had been there? But I am of course aware that next day the pilgrims buried something in a muddy hole.

"And then they very nearly buried me.

"However, as you see, I did not go to join Kurtz there and then. I did not. I remained to dream the nightmare out to the end, and to show my loyalty to Kurtz once more. Destiny. My destiny! Droll thing life is—that mysterious arrangement of merciless logic for a futile purpose. The most you can hope from it is some knowledge of yourself—that comes too late—a crop of unextinguishable regrets. I have wrestled with death. It is the most unexciting contest you can imagine. It takes place in an impalpable greyness, with nothing underfoot, with nothing around, without spectators, without clamour, without glory, without the great desire of victory, without the great fear of defeat, in a sickly atmosphere of tepid scepticism, without much belief in your own right, and still less in that of your adversary. If such is the form of ultimate wisdom, then life is a greater riddle than some of us think it to be. I was within a hair's-breadth of the last opportunity for pronouncement, and I found with humiliation that probably I would have nothing to say. This is the reason why I affirm that Kurtz was a remarkable man. He had something to say. He said it. Since I had peeped over the edge myself, I understand better the meaning of his stare, that could not see the flame of the candle, but was wide enough to embrace the whole universe, piercing enough to penetrate all the hearts that beat in the darkness. He had summed up—he had judged. 'The horror!' He was a remarkable man. After all, this was the expression of some sort of belief; it had candour, it had conviction, it had a vibrating note of revolt in its whisper, it had the appalling face of a glimpsed truth—the strange commingling of desire and hate. And it is not my own extremity I remember best—a vision of greyness without form filled with physical pain, and a careless contempt for the evanescence of all things—even of this pain itself. No! It is his extremity that I seem to have lived through. True, he had made that last stride, he had stepped over the edge, while I had been permitted to draw back my hesitating foot. And perhaps in this is the whole difference; perhaps all the wisdom, and all truth, and all sincerity, are just compressed into that inappreciable moment of time in which we step over the threshold of the invisible. Perhaps! I like to think my summing-up would not have been a word of careless contempt. Better his cry—much better. It was an affirmation, a moral victory paid for by innumerable defeats, by abominable terrors, by abominable satisfactions. But it was a victory! That is why I have remained loyal to Kurtz to the last, and even beyond, when a long time after I heard once more, not his own voice, but the echo of his magnificent eloquence thrown to me from a soul as translucently pure as a cliff of crystal.

"No, they did not bury me, though there is a period of time which I remember mistily, with a shuddering wonder, like a passage through some inconceivable world that had no hope in it and no desire. I found myself back in the sepulchral city resenting the sight of people hurrying through the streets to filch a little money from each other, to devour their infamous cookery, to gulp their unwholesome beer, to dream their insignificant and silly dreams. They trespassed upon my thoughts. They were intruders whose knowledge of life was to me an irritating pretence, because I felt so sure they could not possibly know the things I knew. Their bearing, which was simply the bearing of commonplace individuals going about their business in the assurance of perfect safety, was offensive to me like the outrageous flauntings of folly in the face of a danger it is unable to comprehend. I had no particular desire to enlighten them, but I had some difficulty in restraining myself from laughing in their faces, so full of stupid importance. I daresay I was not very well at that time. I tottered about the streets—there were various affairs to settle—grinning bitterly at perfectly respectable persons. I admit my behaviour was inexcusable, but then my temperature was seldom normal in these days. My dear aunt's endeavours to 'nurse up my strength' seemed altogether beside the mark. It was not my strength that wanted nursing, it was my imagination that wanted soothing. I kept the bundle of papers given me by Kurtz, not knowing exactly what to do with it. His mother had died lately, watched over, as I was told, by his Intended. A clean-shaven man, with an official manner and wearing gold-rimmed spectacles, called on me one day and made inquiries, at first circuitous, afterwards suavely pressing, about what he was pleased to denominate certain 'documents.' I was not surprised, because I had had two rows with the manager on the subject out there. I had refused to give up the smallest scrap out of that package, and I took the same attitude with the spectacled man. He became darkly menacing at last, and with much heat argued that the Company had the right to every bit of information about its 'territories.' And, said he, 'Mr Kurtz's knowledge of unexplored regions must have been necessarily extensive and peculiar—owing to his great abilities and to the deplorable circumstances in which he had been placed: therefore—' I assured him Mr Kurtz's knowledge, however extensive, did not bear upon the problems of commerce or administration. He invoked then the name of science. 'It would be an incalculable loss if,' etc. etc. I offered him the report on the 'Suppression of Savage Customs,' with the postscriptum torn off. He took it up eagerly, but ended by sniffing at it with an air of contempt. 'This is not what we had a right to expect,' he remarked. 'Expect nothing else,' I said. 'There are only private letters.' He withdrew upon some threat of legal proceedings, and I saw him no more; but another fellow, calling himself Kurtz's cousin, appeared two days later, and was anxious to hear all the details about his dear relative's last moments. Incidentally he gave me to understand that Kurtz had been essentially a great musician. 'There was the making of an immense success,' said the man, who was an organist, I believe, with lank grey hair flowing over a greasy coat-collar. I had no reason to doubt his statement; and to this day I am unable to say what was Kurtz's profession, whether he ever had any—which was the greatest of his talents. I had taken him for a painter who wrote for the papers, or else for a journalist who could paint—but even the cousin (who took snuff during the interview) could not tell me what he had been—exactly. He was a universal genius—on that point I agreed with the old chap, who thereupon blew his nose noisily into a large cotton handkerchief and withdrew in senile agitation, bearing off some family letters and memoranda without importance. Ultimately a journalist anxious to know something of the fate of his 'dear colleague' turned up. This visitor informed me Kurtz's proper sphere ought to have been politics 'on the popular side.' He had furry straight eyebrows, bristly hair cropped short, an eyeglass on a broad ribbon, and, becoming expansive, confessed his opinion that Kurtz really couldn't write a bit—'but heavens! how that man could talk! He electrified large meetings. He had faith—don't you see?—he had the faith. He could get himself to believe anything—anything. He would have been a splendid leader of an extreme party.' 'What party?' I asked. 'Any party,' answered the other. 'He was an—an—extremist.' Did I not think so? I assented. Did I know, he asked, with a sudden flash of curiosity, 'what it was that had induced him to go out there?' 'Yes,' said I, and forthwith handed him the famous Report for publication, if he thought fit. He glanced through it hurriedly, mumbling all the time, judged 'it would do,' and took himself off with this plunder.

"Thus I was left at last with a slim packet of letters and the girl's portrait. She struck me as beautiful—I mean she had a beautiful expression. I know that the sunlight can be made to lie too, yet one felt that no manipulation of light and pose could have conveyed the delicate shade of truthfulness upon those features. She seemed ready to listen without mental reservation, without suspicion, without a thought for herself. I concluded I would go and give her back her portrait and those letters myself. Curiosity? Yes; and also some other feeling perhaps. All that had been Kurtz's had passed out of my hands: his soul, his body, his station, his plans, his ivory, his career. There remained only his memory and his Intended—and I wanted to give that up too to the past, in a way—to surrender personally all that remained of him with me to that oblivion which is the last word of our common fate. I don't defend myself. I had no clear perception of what it was I really wanted. Perhaps it was an impulse of unconscious loyalty, or the fulfilment of one of those ironic necessities that lurk in the facts of human existence. I don't know. I can't tell. But I went.

"I thought his memory was like the other memories of the dead that accumulate in every man's life—a vague impress on the brain of shadows that had fallen on it in their swift and final passage; but before the high and ponderous door, between the tall houses of a street as still and decorous as a well-kept alley in a cemetery, I had a vision of him on the stretcher, opening his mouth voraciously, as if to devour all the earth with all its mankind. He lived then before me; he lived as much as he had ever lived—a shadow insatiable of splendid appearances, of frightful realities; a shadow darker than the shadow of the night, and draped nobly in the folds of a gorgeous eloquence. The vision seemed to enter the house with me—the stretcher, the phantom-bearers, the wild crowd of obedient worshippers, the gloom of the forests, the glitter of the reach between the murky bends, the beat of the drum, regular and muffled like the beating of a heart—the heart of a conquering darkness. It was a moment of triumph for the wilderness, an invading and vengeful rush which, it seemed to me, I would have to keep back alone for the salvation of another soul. And the memory of what I had heard him say afar there, with the horned shapes stirring at my back, in the glow of fires, within the patient woods, those broken phrases came back to me, were heard again in their ominous and terrifying simplicity. I remembered his abject pleading, his abject threats, the colossal scale of his vile desires, the meanness, the torment, the tempestuous anguish of his soul. And later on I seemed to see his collected languid manner, when he said one day, 'This lot of ivory now is really mine. The Company did not pay for it. I collected it myself at a very great personal risk. I am afraid they will try to claim it as theirs though. H'm. It is a difficult case. What do you think I ought to do—resist? Eh? I want no more than justice.' . . . He wanted no more than justice—no more than justice. I rang the bell before a mahogany door on the first floor, and while I waited he seemed to stare at me out of the glossy panel—stare with that wide and immense stare embracing, condemning, loathing all the universe. I seemed to hear the whispered cry, 'The horror! The horror!'

"The dusk was falling. I had to wait in a lofty drawing-room with three long windows from floor to ceiling that were like three luminous and bedraped columns. The bent gilt legs and backs of the furniture shone in indistinct curves. The tall marble fireplace had a cold and monumental whiteness. A grand piano stood massively in a corner; with dark gleams on the flat surfaces like a sombre and polished sarcophagus. A high door opened—closed. I rose.

"She came forward, all in black, with a pale head, floating towards me in the dusk. She was in mourning. It was more than a year since his death, more than a year since the news came; she seemed as though she would remember and mourn for ever. She took both my hands in hers and murmured, 'I had heard you were coming.' I noticed she was not very young—I mean not girlish. She had a mature capacity for fidelity, for belief, for suffering. The room seemed to have grown darker, as if all the sad light of the cloudy evening had taken refuge on her forehead. This fair hair, this pale visage, this pure brow, seemed surrounded by an ashy halo from which the dark eyes looked out at me. Their glance was guileless, profound, confident, and trustful. She carried her sorrowful head as though she were proud of that sorrow, as though she would say, I—I alone know how to mourn for him as he deserves. But while we were still shaking hands, such a look of awful desolation came upon her face that I perceived she was one of those creatures that are not the playthings of Time. For her he had died only yesterday. And, by Jove! the impression was so powerful that for me too he seemed to have died only yesterday—nay, this very minute. I saw her and him in the same instant of time—his death and her sorrow—I saw her sorrow in the very moment of his death. Do you understand? I saw them together—I heard them together. She had said, with a deep catch of the breath, 'I have survived'; while my strained ears seemed to hear distinctly, mingled with her tone of despairing regret, the summing-up whisper of his eternal condemnation. I asked myself what I was doing there, with a sensation of panic in my heart as though I had blundered into a place of cruel and absurd mysteries not fit for a human being to behold. She motioned me to a chair. We sat down. I laid the packet gently on the little table, and she put her hand over it. . . . 'You knew him well,' she murmured, after a moment of mourning silence.

" 'Intimacy grows quickly out there,' I said. 'I knew him as well as it is possible for one man to know another.'

" 'And you admired him,' she said. 'It was impossible to know him and not to admire him. Was it?'

" 'He was a remarkable man,' I said unsteadily. Then before the appealing fixity of her gaze, that seemed to watch for more words on my lips, I went on, 'It was impossible not to—'

" 'Love him,' she finished eagerly, silencing me into an appalled dumbness. 'How true! how true! But when you think that no one knew him so well as I! I had all his noble confidence. I knew him best.'

" 'You knew him best,' I repeated. And perhaps she did. But with every word spoken the room was growing darker, and only her forehead, smooth and white, remained illumined by the unextinguishable light of belief and love.

" 'You were his friend,' she went on. 'His friend,' she repeated, a little louder. 'You must have been, if he had given you this, and sent you to me. I feel I can speak to you—and oh! I must speak. I want you—you who have heard his last words—to know I have been worthy of him. . . . It is not pride. . . . Yes! I am proud to know I understood him better than any one on earth—he told me so himself. And since his mother died I have had no one—no one—to—to—'

1946 / Joseph Conrad

"I listened. The darkness deepened. I was not even sure whether he had given me the right bundle. I rather suspect he wanted me to take care of another batch of his papers which, after his death, I saw the manager examining under the lamp. And the girl talked, easing her pain in the certitude of my sympathy; she talked as thirsty men drink. I had heard that her engagement with Kurtz had been disapproved by her people. He wasn't rich enough or something. And indeed I don't know whether he had not been a pauper all his life. He had given me some reason to infer that it was his impatience of comparative poverty that drove him out there.

" ' . . . Who was not his friend who had heard him speak once?' she was saying. 'He drew men towards him by what was best in them.' She looked at me with intensity. 'It is the gift of the great,' she went on, and the sound of her low voice seemed to have the accompaniment of all the other sounds, full of mystery, desolation, and sorrow, I had ever heard—the ripple of the river, the soughing of the trees swayed by the wind, the murmurs of the crowds, the faint ring of incomprehensible words cried from afar, the whisper of a voice speaking from beyond the threshold of an eternal darkness. 'But you have heard him! You know!' she cried.

" 'Yes, I know,' I said with something like despair in my heart, but bowing my head before the faith that was in her, before that great and saving illusion that shone with an unearthly glow in the darkness, in the triumphant darkness from which I could not have defended her—from which I could not even defend myself.

" 'What a loss to me—to us!'—she corrected herself with beautiful generosity; then added in a murmur, 'To the world.' By the last gleams of twilight I could see the glitter of her eyes, full of tears—of tears that would not fall.

" 'I have been very happy—very fortunate—very proud,' she went on. 'Too fortunate. Too happy for a little while. And now I am unhappy for—for life.'

"She stood up; her fair hair seemed to catch all the remaining light in a glimmer of gold. I rose too.

" 'And of all this,' she went on mournfully, 'of all his promise, and of all his greatness, of his generous mind, of his noble heart, nothing remains—nothing but a memory. You and I—'

" 'We shall always remember him,' I said hastily.

" 'No!' she cried. 'It is impossible that all this should be lost—that such a life should be sacrificed to leave nothing—but sorrow. You know what vast plans he had. I knew of them too—I could not perhaps understand—but others knew of them. Something must remain. His words, at least, have not died.'

" 'His words will remain,' I said.

" 'And his example,' she whispered to herself. 'Men looked up to him—his goodness shone in every act. His example—'

" 'True,' I said; 'his example too. Yes, his example. I forgot that.'

" 'But I do not. I cannot—I cannot believe—not yet. I cannot believe that I shall never see him again, that nobody will see him again, never, never, never.'

"She put out her arms as if after a retreating figure, stretching them black and with clasped pale hands across the fading and narrow sheen of the window. Never see him! I saw him clearly enough then. I shall see this eloquent phantom as long as I live, and I shall see her too, a tragic and familiar Shade, resembling in this gesture another one, tragic also, and bedecked with powerless charms, stretching bare brown arms over the glitter of the infernal stream, the stream of darkness. She said suddenly very low, 'He died as he lived.'

" 'His end,' said I, with dull anger stirring in me, 'was in every way worthy of his life.'

" 'And I was not with him,' she murmured. My anger subsided before a feeling of infinite pity.

" 'Everything that could be done—' I mumbled.

" 'Ah, but I believed in him more than any one on earth—more than his own mother, more than—himself. He needed me! Me! I would have treasured every sigh, every word, every sign, every glance.'

"I felt like a chill grip on my chest. 'Don't,' I said, in a muffled voice.

" 'Forgive me. I—I—have mourned so long in silence—in silence. . . . You were with him—to the last? I think of his loneliness. Nobody near to understand him as I would have understood. Perhaps no one to hear. . . . '

" 'To the very end,' I said shakily. 'I heard his very last words. . . . ' I stopped in a fright.

" 'Repeat them,' she murmured in a heart-broken tone. 'I want—I want—something—something—to—to live with.'

"I was on the point of crying at her, 'Don't you hear them?' The dusk was repeating them in a persistent whisper all around us, in a whisper that seemed to swell menacingly like the first whisper of a rising wind. 'The horror! The horror!'

" 'His last word—to live with,' she insisted. 'Don't you understand I loved him—I loved him—I loved him!'

"I pulled myself together and spoke slowly.

" 'The last word he pronounced was—your name.'

"I heard a light sigh and then my heart stood still, stopped dead short by an exulting and terrible cry, by the cry of inconceivable triumph and of unspeakable pain. 'I knew it—I was sure!' . . . She knew. She was sure. I heard her weeping; she had hidden her face in her hands. It seemed to me that the house would collapse before I could escape, that the heavens would fall upon my head. But nothing happened. The heavens do not fall for such a trifle. Would they have fallen, I wonder, if I had rendered Kurtz that justice which was his due? Hadn't he said he wanted only justice? But I couldn't. I could not tell her. It would have been too dark—too dark altogether. . . ."[7]

Marlow ceased, and sat apart, indistinct and silent, in the pose of a meditating Buddha. Nobody moved for a time. "We have lost the first of the ebb," said the Director suddenly. I raised my head. The offing was barred by a black bank of clouds, and the tranquil waterway leading to the uttermost ends of the earth flowed sombre under an overcast sky—seemed to lead into the heart of an immense darkness.

1898–99   1899, 1902

---

7. Writing to William Blackwood (editor of *Blackwood's Magazine*, where the story first appeared) in May 1902, Conrad referred to "the last pages of Heart of Darkness where the interview of the man and the girl locks in—as it were—the whole 30,000 words of narrative description into one suggestive view of a whole phase of life, and makes of that story something quite on another plane than an anecdote of a man who went mad in the Centre of Africa" (Joseph Conrad, *Letters to William Blackwood and David S. Meldrum*, ed. William Blackburn, 1958).

A. E. HOUSMAN
1859–1936

Alfred Edward Housman was born in Fockbury, Worcestershire (close to the Shropshire border), and attended school at the nearby town of Bromsgrove. He studied classics and philosophy at Oxford and in 1881 shocked his friends and teachers by failing his final examinations (he was at the time in a state of psychological turmoil resulting from his suppressed homosexual love for a fellow student). He obtained a civil service job and pursued his classical studies alone, gradually building up a reputation as a great textual critic of Latin literature. In 1892 he was appointed to the chair of Latin at University College, London, and from 1911 until his death he was professor of Latin at Cambridge.

Housman's classical studies consisted of meticulous, impersonal textual investigations; both his scholarship and his life were reserved and solitary. Yet his feeling for literature ran strong and deep, and in his lecture "The Name and Nature of Poetry" (1933) he says that poetry should be "more physical than intellectual," having a skin-bristling, spine-shivering effect on the reader. His own poetry was limited both in quantity and in range, but—stark, lucid, elegant—it exemplifies the "superior terseness" he prized in verse. Two "slim volumes"—*A Shropshire Lad* (1896) and *Last Poems* (1922)—were all that appeared during his lifetime, and after his death his brother Laurence brought out another small book, *More Poems* (1936).

As a poet Housman aimed not to expand or develop the resources of English poetry but by limitation and concentration to achieve an utterance both compact and moving. He was influenced by Greek and Latin lyric poetry, by the traditional ballad, and by the lyrics of the early-nineteenth-century German poet Heinrich Heine. His favorite theme is that of the doomed youth acting out the tragedy of his brief life; the context is agricultural activity in England, with the land bearing visual reminders of humanity's long history. Nature is beautiful but indifferent and is to be enjoyed while we are still able to enjoy it. Love, friendship, and conviviality cannot last and may well result in betrayal or death, but are likewise to be relished while there is time. Wryly ironic in tone, stoic in temperament, Housman sounds a note of resigned wisdom with quiet poignancy. He avoids self-pity by projecting emotion through an imagined character, notably the "Shropshire lad," so that even the first-person poems seem to be distanced in some degree. At the same time the poems are distinguished from the "gather ye rosebuds" (or carpe diem) tradition by the undertones of fatalism and even doom.

Loveliest of Trees

Loveliest of trees, the cherry now
Is hung with bloom along the bough,
And stands about the woodland ride
Wearing white for Eastertide.

5   Now, of my threescore years and ten,
Twenty will not come again,
And take from seventy springs a score,
It only leaves me fifty more.

And since to look at things in bloom
10   Fifty springs are little room,
About the woodlands I will go
To see the cherry hung with snow.

1896

When I Was One-and-Twenty

When I was one-and-twenty
I heard a wise man say,
"Give crowns and pounds and guineas
But not your heart away;
5   Give pearls away and rubies
But keep your fancy free."
But I was one-and-twenty,
No use to talk to me.

When I was one-and-twenty
10   I heard him say again,
"The heart out of the bosom
Was never given in vain;
'Tis paid with sighs a plenty
And sold for endless rue."°   *repentance*
15   And I am two-and-twenty,
And oh, 'tis true, 'tis true.

1896

To an Athlete Dying Young

The time you won your town the race
We chaired you through the market-place;
Man and boy stood cheering by,
And home we brought you shoulder-high.

5   Today, the road all runners come,
Shoulder-high we bring you home,
And set you at your threshold down,
Townsman of a stiller town.

Smart lad, to slip betimes away
10   From fields where glory does not stay,
And early though the laurel¹ grows
It withers quicker than the rose.

Eyes the shady night has shut
Cannot see the record cut,°   *broken*

1. In ancient Greece and Rome victorious athletes were crowned with laurel wreaths.

15 And silence sounds no worse than cheers
After earth has stopped the ears:

Now you will not swell the rout°   crowd
Of lads that wore their honours out,
Runners whom renown outran
20 And the name died before the man.

So set, before its echoes fade,
The fleet foot on the sill of shade,
And hold to the low lintel up
The still-defended challenge-cup.

25 And round that early laurelled head
Will flock to gaze the strengthless dead
And find unwithered on its curls
The garland briefer than a girl's.

1896

Terence,[1] This Is Stupid Stuff

"Terence, this is stupid stuff:
You eat your victuals fast enough;
There can't be much amiss, 'tis clear,
To see the rate you drink your beer.
5 But oh, good Lord, the verse you make,
It gives a chap the belly-ache.
The cow, the old cow, she is dead;
It sleeps well, the hornèd head:
We poor lads, 'tis our turn now
10 To hear such tunes as killed the cow.
Pretty friendship 'tis to rhyme
Your friends to death before their time
Moping melancholy mad:
Come, pipe a tune to dance to, lad."

15 Why, if 'tis dancing you would be,
There's brisker pipes than poetry.
Say, for what were hop-yards meant,
Or why was Burton built on Trent?[2]
Oh many a peer[3] of England brews
20 Livelier liquor than the Muse,
And malt does more than Milton can
To justify God's ways to man.[4]
Ale, man, ale's the stuff to drink
For fellows whom it hurts to think:

1. *The Poems of Terence Hearsay* was Housman's intended title for *The Shropshire Lad*.
2. Burton-on-Trent is the most famous of all English brewing towns.
3. A reference to the "beer barons," brewery magnates raised to the peerage (i.e., made nobles).
4. Cf. Milton's promise in *Paradise Lost* (1.17–26) to "justify the ways of God to men."

25 Look into the pewter pot
    To see the world as the world's not.
    And faith, 'tis pleasant till 'tis past:
    The mischief is that 'twill not last.
    Oh I have been to Ludlow⁵ fair
30 And left my necktie God knows where,
    And carried half-way home, or near,
    Pints and quarts of Ludlow beer:
    Then the world seemed none so bad,
    And I myself a sterling lad;
35 And down in lovely muck I've lain,
    Happy till I woke again.
    Then I saw the morning sky:
    Heigho, the tale was all a lie;
    The world, it was the old world yet,
40 I was I, my things were wet,
    And nothing now remained to do
    But begin the game anew.

        Therefore, since the world has still
    Much good, but much less good than ill,
45 And while the sun and moon endure
    Luck's a chance, but trouble's sure,
    I'd face it as a wise man would,
    And train for ill and not for good.
    'Tis true the stuff I bring for sale
50 Is not so brisk a brew as ale:
    Out of a stem that scored° the hand   *cut*
    I wrung it in a weary land.
    But take it: if the smack is sour,
    The better for the embittered hour;
55 It should do good to heart and head
    When your soul is in my soul's stead;
    And I will friend you, if I may,
    In the dark and cloudy day.

        There was a king reigned in the East:
60 There, when kings will sit to feast,
    They get their fill before they think
    With poisoned meat and poisoned drink.
    He gathered all that springs to birth
    From the many-venomed earth;
65 First a little, thence to more,
    He sampled all her killing store;
    And easy, smiling, seasoned sound,
    Sate the king when healths went round.
    They put arsenic in his meat
70 And stared aghast to watch him eat;
    They poured strychnine in his cup
    And shook to see him drink it up:
    They shook, they stared as white's their shirt:

5. A market town in Shropshire.

Them it was their poison hurt.
75 —I tell the tale that I heard told.
Mithridates, he died old.⁶

1896

The Chestnut Casts His Flambeaux¹

The chestnut casts his flambeaux, and the flowers
Stream from the hawthorn in the wind away,
The doors clap to, the pane is blind with showers.
Pass me the can,° lad; there's an end of May.   *tankard*

5   There's one spoilt spring to scant our mortal lot,
One season ruined of our little store.
May will be fine next year as like as not:
Oh ay, but then we shall be twenty-four.

We for a certainty are not the first
10   Have sat in taverns while the tempest hurled
Their hopeful plans to emptiness, and cursed
Whatever brute and blackguard made the world.

It is in truth iniquity on high
To cheat our sentenced souls of aught they crave,
15 And mar the merriment as you and I
Fare on our long fool's-errand to the grave.

Iniquity it is; but pass the can.
My lad, no pair of kings our mothers bore;
Our only portion is the estate of man:
20   We want the moon, but we shall get no more.

If here today the cloud of thunder lours°   *looks threatening*
Tomorrow it will hie° on far behests;°   *go quickly / commands*
The flesh will grieve on other bones than ours
Soon, and the soul will mourn in other breasts.

25   The troubles of our proud and angry dust
Are from eternity, and shall not fail.
Bear them we can, and if we can we must.
Shoulder the sky, my lad, and drink your ale.

1922

---

6. The story of Mithridates, king of Pontus, who made himself immune to poison by taking small doses daily, is told in Pliny's *Natural History*.

1. Literally, torches. Housman here refers to the erect flower clusters (white, dashed with red and yellow) of the horse chestnut tree.

Epitaph on an Army of Mercenaries[1]

These, in the day when heaven was falling,
The hour when earth's foundations fled,
Followed their mercenary calling
And took their wages and are dead.

5   Their shoulders held the sky suspended;
They stood, and earth's foundations stay;
What God abandoned, these defended,
And saved the sum of things for pay.

1922

---

1. To honor the heroism of the professional soldiers of the British Regular Army in the First Battle
of Ypres (1914), Housman published this poem in
The Times on the third anniversary of the turning
point of that battle, October 31, 1917. See Hugh
MacDiarmid's angry response, "Another Epitaph
on an Army of Mercenaries" (p. 2468).

Voices from World War I

The original spark that set off what proved to be the bloodiest and most widespread war that had yet been fought was the murder of the Archduke Ferdinand of Austria in the Balkan state of Serbia on June 28, 1914. Austria, supported by Germany, used the murder as a reason for declaring war on Serbia, which in turn was supported by its fellow-Slav country Russia. Because Russia was bound by a treaty obligation to both France and Britain, Russia and France were soon at war with Germany and Austria. The most effective way for Germany to attack France was to go through Belgium, though all the powers had guaranteed Belgian neutrality. The attack on Belgium impelled Britain to declare war on Germany on August 4, but rival imperialisms, an international armaments race, France's desire to regain Alsace-Lorraine, which it had lost to Germany in 1870, and German and Austrian ambitions in the Balkans were some of the many other factors that brought about the four-year struggle, a struggle that shook the world. Turkey sided with Germany and Austria in October 1914, and Bulgaria allied itself with them the following year. Britain and France were joined by Japan late in August 1914, by Italy (although Italy had in 1882 joined the "Triple Alliance" with Germany and Austria directed against France and Russia) in May 1915, and by the United States in April 1917.

Before the collapse of Germany followed by the armistice of November 11, 1918, some 8,700,000 lives had been lost (including 780,000 British—virtually a whole generation of young men) and the prolonged horrors of trench warfare had seared themselves into the minds of the survivors. For three years the battle line, "the Western Front," was stabilized between northwest France and Switzerland, with both sides dug in and making repeated, costly, and generally useless attempts to advance. The German use of poison gas at the Second Battle of Ypres in 1915, the massive German attack at Verdun in 1916, and the British introduction of tanks on the Somme in the same year failed to produce the breakthrough each side desired. Desolate, war-scarred landscapes with blasted trees and mud everywhere, trenches half-filled with water and infested with rats, miles of protective barbed wire requiring individual "volunteers" to crawl through machine-gun fire and cut it so an advance could begin, long-continued massive bombardments by heavy artillery, and a sense of stalemate that suggested to the soldiers involved that this living hell could go on forever—all this was long kept from the knowledge of the civilians at home, who continued to use the old patriotic slogans and write in old-fashioned romantic terms about glorious cavalry charges and the noble pursuit of heroic ideals. But those poets who were involved on the front, however romantically they may have felt about the cause when they first joined up, soon realized the full horror of war, and this realization affected both their imaginations and their poetic techniques. They had to find a way of expressing the terrible truths they had experienced, and even when they did not express them directly, the underlying knowledge affected the way they wrote.

The poetry that was in vogue when war broke out, and that some poets continued to write for some years afterward, was named "Georgian" in honor of King George V, who had succeeded Edward VII in 1910. The term was first used of poets when Edward Marsh brought out in 1912 the first of a series of five anthologies called *Georgian Poetry*. The work therein represented an attempt to wall in the garden of English poetry against the disruptive forces of modern civilization. Cultured meditations of the English countryside ("I love the mossy quietness / That grows upon the great stone flags") alternated with self-conscious exercises in the exotic ("When I was

1954

but thirteen or so / I went into a golden land, / Chimporazo, Cotopaxi / Took me by the hand"). Sometimes the magical note was authentic, as in many of Walter de la Mare's poems, and sometimes the meditative strain was original and impressive, as in Edward Thomas's poetry. But as World War I went on, with more and more poets killed and the survivors increasingly disillusioned, the whole world on which the Georgian imagination rested came to appear unreal. A patriotic poem such as Rupert Brooke's "The Soldier" became a ridiculous anachronism in the face of the realities of trench warfare, and the even more blatantly patriotic note sounded by other Georgian poems (as in John Freeman's "Happy Is England Now," which claimed that "there's not a nobleness of heart, hand, brain / But shines the purer; happiest is England now / In those that fight") seemed obscene. The savage ironies of Siegfried Sassoon's war poems and the combination of pity and irony in Wilfred Owen's work portrayed a world undreamed of in the golden years from 1910 to 1914.

World War I left throughout Europe a sense that the bases of civilization had been destroyed, that all traditional values had been wiped out. We see this sense reflected in the years immediately after the war in different ways in, for example, T. S. Eliot's *Waste Land* and Aldous Huxley's early fiction. But the poets who wrote during the war most directly reflected the impact of the war experience.

For more documents, images, and contexts related to this subject, see "Representing the Great War" at Norton Literature Online.

RUPERT BROOKE
1887–1915

Rupert Brooke was educated at Rugby School and at King's College, Cambridge. When World War I began he was commissioned as an officer into the Royal Naval Division and took part in its brief and abortive expedition to Antwerp. On leave in December 1914 he wrote the "war sonnets" that were to make him famous; five months later he died of dysentery and blood poisoning on a troopship destined for Gallipoli.

Brooke was the most popular of the Georgians, pastoral poets who infused nature with nationalist feeling. His early death symbolized the death of a whole generation of patriotic Englishmen. Shortly before then the dean of St. Paul's read "The Soldier" in a sermon from the Cathedral pulpit, and in a 1915 valediction in the London *Times,* Winston Churchill sounded a note that swelled over the following months and years: "Joyous, fearless, versatile, deeply instructed, with classic symmetry of mind and body, he was all that one would wish England's noblest sons to be in days when no sacrifice but the most precious is acceptable, and the most precious is that which is most freely proffered." Brooke's *1914 and Other Poems* was published in June 1915, and during the next decade this and his *Collected Poems* sold three hundred thousand copies.

The Soldier

If I should die, think only this of me:
   That there's some corner of a foreign field
That is forever England. There shall be
   In that rich earth a richer dust concealed;

5   A dust whom England bore, shaped, made aware,
    Gave, once, her flowers to love, her ways to roam,
    A body of England's, breathing English air,
    Washed by the rivers, blest by suns of home.

    And think, this heart, all evil shed away,
10   A pulse in the Eternal mind, no less
        Gives somewhere back the thoughts by England given,
    Her sights and sounds; dreams happy as her day;
    And laughter, learnt of friends; and gentleness,
        In hearts at peace, under an English heaven.

1914   1915

EDWARD THOMAS
1878–1917

Edward Thomas was born of Welsh parents in London and was educated there and
at Lincoln College, Oxford, which he left with a wife, a baby, and high literary ambitions. Despite his chronic depression, which became more marked over the difficult
years that followed, he reviewed up to fifteen books a week, published thirty books
between 1897 and 1917, and during those twenty years edited sixteen anthologies
and editions. His great gifts as a literary critic appeared to best advantage in his
reviewing of poetry, and he was the first to salute new stars in the literary firmament
such as Robert Frost and Ezra Pound.

   Although he had long been conscientiously reviewing poetry, which he regarded as
the highest form of literature, he apparently made no serious attempt to write poems
until the autumn of 1914. Then, under the stress of deciding whether or not to enlist,
poems began to pour out of him: five between December 3 and 7, and ten more
before the end of the month. His friend Frost offered to find him work in the United
States, but feelings of patriotism, and the attraction of a salary that would support
his growing family, led him to enlist in July 1915. His awareness of the natural world,
its richness and beauty, was then intensified by a sense of impending loss and the
certainty of death—his own and others'. In the long sentences that make up his verse,
he ruminates with great delicacy on beauty and nature, but he also demonstrates an
unsentimental toughness. In "Rain," for example, he compares the dead to "Myriads
of broken reeds all still and stiff." As violence to the natural order of things, war
indirectly but persistently shadows Thomas's poems. In January 1917 he was sent to
the Western Front and, on Easter Monday, was killed by a shell blast.

Adlestrop[1]

   Yes, I remember Adlestrop—
   The name, because one afternoon
   Of heat the express-train drew up there
   Unwontedly. It was late June.

---

1. A village in Gloucestershire.

5   The steam hissed. Someone cleared his throat.
No one left and no one came
On the bare platform. What I saw
Was Adlestrop—only the name

And willows, willow-herb, and grass,
10 And meadowsweet, and haycocks dry,
No whit less still and lonely fair
Than the high cloudlets in the sky.

And for that minute a blackbird sang
Close by, and round him, mistier,
15 Farther and farther, all the birds
Of Oxfordshire and Gloucestershire.

Jan. 1915   1917

Tears

It seems I have no tears left. They should have fallen—
Their ghosts, if tears have ghosts, did fall—that day
When twenty hounds streamed by me, not yet combed out
But still all equals in their rage of gladness
5 Upon the scent, made one, like a great dragon
In Blooming Meadow that bends towards the sun
And once bore hops: and on that other day
When I stepped out from the double-shadowed Tower
Into an April morning, stirring and sweet
10 And warm. Strange solitude was there and silence.
A mightier charm than any in the Tower
Possessed the courtyard. They were changing guard,
Soldiers in line, young English countrymen,
Fair-haired and ruddy, in white tunics. Drums
15 And fifes were playing "The British Grenadiers."[1]
The men, the music piercing that solitude
And silence, told me truths I had not dreamed,
And have forgotten since their beauty passed.

Jan. 1915   1917

The Owl

Downhill I came, hungry, and yet not starved;
Cold, yet had heat within me that was proof
Against the North wind; tired, yet so that rest
Had seemed the sweetest thing under a roof.

1. Famous British marching song about the Brigade of Guards, an elite infantry unit.

5   Then at the inn I had food, fire, and rest,
Knowing how hungry, cold, and tired was I.
All of the night was quite barred out except
An owl's cry, a most melancholy cry

Shaken out long and clear upon the hill,
10 No merry note, nor cause of merriment,
But one telling me plain what I escaped
And others could not, that night, as in I went.

And salted° was my food, and my repose,   *flavored (as with salt)*
Salted and sobered, too, by the bird's voice
15 Speaking for all who lay under the stars,
Soldiers and poor, unable to rejoice.

Feb. 1915   1917

Rain[1]

Rain, midnight rain, nothing but the wild rain
On this bleak hut, and solitude, and me
Remembering again that I shall die
And neither hear the rain nor give it thanks
5   For washing me cleaner than I have been
Since I was born into this solitude.
Blessed are the dead that the rain rains upon:
But here I pray that none whom once I loved
Is dying tonight or lying still awake
10 Solitary, listening to the rain,
Either in pain or thus in sympathy
Helpless among the living and the dead,
Like a cold water among broken reeds,
Myriads of broken reeds all still and stiff,
15 Like me who have no love which this wild rain
Has not dissolved except the love of death,
If love it be towards what is perfect and
Cannot, the tempest tells me, disappoint.

Jan. 1916   1917

The Cherry Trees

The cherry trees bend over and are shedding
On the old road where all that passed are dead,

1. Cf. Thomas's account of an English walking tour, *The Icknield Way* (1913): "In the heavy, black rain falling straight from invisible, dark sky to invisible, dark earth the heat of summer is annihilated, the splendour is dead, the summer is gone. The midnight rain buries it away where it has buried all sound but its own. I am alone in the dark still night, and my ear listens to the rain piping in the gutters and roaring softly in the trees of the world. Even so will the rain fall darkly upon the grass over the grave when my ears can hear it no more. . . . Black and monotonously sounding is the midnight and solitude of the rain. In a little while or in an age— for it is all one—I shall know the full truth of the words I used to love, I knew not why, in my days of nature, in the days before the rain: 'Blessed are the dead that the rain rains on.'"

Their petals, strewing the grass as for a wedding
This early May morn when there is none to wed.

May 1916   1917

As the Team's Head Brass[1]

As the team's head brass flashed out on the turn
The lovers disappeared into the wood.
I sat among the boughs of the fallen elm
That strewed an angle of the fallow,[2] and
5   Watched the plough narrowing a yellow square
Of charlock.° Every time the horses turned   *wild mustard*
Instead of treading me down, the ploughman leaned
Upon the handles to say or ask a word,
About the weather, next about the war.
10 Scraping the share he faced towards the wood,
And screwed along the furrow till the brass flashed
Once more.
                    The blizzard felled the elm whose crest
I sat in, by a woodpecker's round hole,
The ploughman said. "When will they take it away?"
15 "When the war's over." So the talk began—
One minute and an interval of ten,
A minute more and the same interval.
"Have you been out?" "No." "And don't want to, perhaps?"
"If I could only come back again, I should.
20 I could spare an arm. I shouldn't want to lose
A leg. If I should lose my head, why, so,
I should want nothing more. . . . Have many gone
From here?" "Yes." "Many lost?" "Yes, a good few.
Only two teams work on the farm this year.
25 One of my mates is dead. The second day
In France they killed him. It was back in March,
The very night of the blizzard, too. Now if
He had stayed here we should have moved the tree."
"And I should not have sat here. Everything
30 Would have been different. For it would have been
Another world." "Ay, and a better, though
If we could see all all might seem good." Then
The lovers came out of the wood again:
The horses started and for the last time
35 I watched the clods crumble and topple over
After the ploughshare and the stumbling team.

May 1916   1917

1. Also known as horse brass: a decorative brass
medallion or emblem attached to a horse's harness.

2. Ground plowed and harrowed but left uncrop-
ped for a year or more.

SIEGFRIED SASSOON
1886–1967

Siegfried Sassoon was educated at Marlborough College and Clare College, Cambridge (which he left without taking a degree). His father came from a prosperous family of Sephardic Jews, his mother from Anglican English gentry. As a young man he divided his time between literary London and the life of a country gentleman. These worlds and the brutally different one of the trenches, in which he found himself in 1914, are memorably described in his classic *Memoirs of a Fox-Hunting Man* (1928) and its sequel, *Memoirs of an Infantry Officer* (1930).

He fought at Mametz Wood and in the Somme Offensive of July 1916 with such conspicuous courage that he acquired the Military Cross and the nickname Mad Jack. After a sniper's bullet went through his chest, however, he was sent back to England at the beginning of April 1917, and he began to take a different view of the war. Eventually, with courage equal to any he had shown in action, he made public a letter he sent to his commanding officer: "I am making this statement as an act of wilful defiance of military authority, because I believe that the war is being deliberately prolonged by those who have the power to end it." Sassoon continued: "I am a soldier, convinced that I am acting on behalf of soldiers. I believe that this war, upon which I entered as a war of defence and liberation, has now become a war of aggression and conquest." (For the full text, see "Representing the Great War" at Norton Literature Online.) The military authorities, rather than make a martyr of him, announced that he was suffering from shell shock and sent him to a hospital near Edinburgh, where he met and befriended Wilfred Owen.

Sassoon's public protest may have been smothered, but his poems, with their shock tactics, bitter irony, and masterly use of direct speech (learned from Thomas Hardy), continued to attack the old men of the army, Church, and government, whom he held responsible for the miseries and murder of the young. His poems satirically play on contrasts between the romanticization of war and the grim realities. They angrily flaunt the grisly effects of violence: in "The Rear-Guard" a corpse is "a soft unanswering heap" whose "fists of fingers clutched a blackening wound."

Sassoon returned to the Western Front in 1918, was wounded again, and was again sent home. An increasingly reclusive country gentleman, he continued to write poetry, but his style never regained the satiric pungency of the war poems that made him famous. His 1933 marriage failed because of his homosexuality; and after he became a Roman Catholic in 1957, he wrote mainly devotional poems.

'They'

The Bishop tells us: "When the boys come back
They will not be the same; for they'll have fought
In a just cause: they lead the last attack
On Anti-Christ; their comrades' blood has bought
5   New right to breed an honourable race,
They have challenged Death and dared him face to face.'

'We're none of us the same!' the boys reply.
'For George lost both his legs; and Bill's stone blind;
Poor Jim's shot through the lungs and like to die;
10   And Bert's gone syphilitic: you'll not find

A chap who's served that hasn't found *some* change.'
And the Bishop said: 'The ways of God are strange!'

Oct. 31, 1916   1917

The Rear-Guard

(Hindenburg Line, April 1917)[1]

Groping along the tunnel, step by step,
He winked his prying torch with patching glare
From side to side, and sniffed the unwholesome air.
Tins, boxes, bottles, shapes too vague to know;
5   A mirror smashed, the mattress from a bed;
And he, exploring fifty feet below
The rosy gloom of battle overhead.

Tripping, he grabbed the wall; saw some one lie
Humped at his feet, half-hidden by a rug,
10   And stooped to give the sleeper's arm a tug.
'I'm looking for headquarters.' No reply.
'God blast your neck!' (For days he'd had no sleep)
'Get up and guide me through this stinking place.'
Savage, he kicked a soft unanswering heap,
15   And flashed his beam across the livid face
Terribly glaring up, whose eyes yet wore
Agony dying hard ten days before;
And fists of fingers clutched a blackening wound.

Alone he staggered on until he found
20   Dawn's ghost that filtered down a shafted stair
To the dazed, muttering creatures underground
Who hear the boom of shells in muffled sound.
At last, with sweat of horror in his hair,
He climbed through darkness to the twilight air,
25   Unloading hell behind him step by step.

Apr. 22, 1917   1918

The General

'Good-morning; good-morning!' the General said
When we met him last week on our way to the line.
Now the soldiers he smiled at are most of 'em dead,
And we're cursing his staff for incompetent swine.

---

1. In 1916 Field Marshal Paul von Hindenburg (1847–1934) became commander in chief of the German armies and, for a time, blocked the Allied advance in western France with the massive defen-sive "line" named after him. Its barbed-wire entan-glements, deep trenches, and gun emplacements ran from Lens to Rheims.

5   'He's a cheery old card,' grunted Harry to Jack
     As they slogged up to Arras[1] with rifle and pack.

                    • • •

     But he did for them both by his plan of attack.

Apr. 1917   1918

Glory of Women

     You love us when we're heroes, home on leave,
     Or wounded in a mentionable place.
     You worship decorations; you believe
     That chivalry redeems the war's disgrace.
5   You make us shells.[1] You listen with delight,
     By tales of dirt and danger fondly thrilled.
     You crown our distant ardours while we fight,
     And mourn our laurelled[2] memories when we're killed.
     You can't believe that British troops 'retire'
10   When hell's last horror breaks them, and they run,
     Trampling the terrible corpses—blind with blood.
        O German mother dreaming by the fire,
     While you are knitting socks to send your son
     His face is trodden deeper in the mud.

1917   1918

Everyone Sang

     Everyone suddenly burst out singing;
     And I was filled with such delight
     As prisoned birds must find in freedom,
     Winging wildly across the white
5   Orchards and dark-green fields; on—on—and out of sight.

     Everyone's voice was suddenly lifted;
     And beauty came like the setting sun:
     My heart was shaken with tears; and horror
     Drifted away . . . O, but Everyone
10   Was a bird; and the song was wordless; the singing will never be done.

Apr. 1919   1919

1. A city in northern France, in the front line through much of the war. The British assault on the Western Front that began on April 9, 1917, was known as the Battle of Arras.

1. Many women were recruited into munitions factories during the war.
2. In ancient Greece and Rome, victorious generals were crowned with laurel wreaths.

On Passing the New Menin Gate[1]

Who will remember, passing through this Gate,
The unheroic Dead who fed the guns?
Who shall absolve the foulness of their fate,—
Those doomed, conscripted, unvictorious ones?
5   Crudely renewed, the Salient[2] holds its own.
Paid are its dim defenders by this pomp;
Paid, with a pile of peace-complacent stone,
The armies who endured that sullen swamp.

Here was the world's worst wound. And here with pride
10   'Their name liveth for ever,' the Gateway claims.
Was ever an immolation so belied
As these intolerably nameless names?
Well might the Dead who struggled in the slime
Rise and deride this sepulchre° of crime.   *tomb*

1927–28   1928

From Memoirs of an Infantry Officer

[THE OPENING OF THE BATTLE OF THE SOMME]

On July [1916] the first the weather, after an early morning mist, was of the kind commonly called heavenly. Down in our frowsty cellar we breakfasted at six, unwashed and apprehensive. Our table, appropriately enough, was an empty ammunition box. At six-forty-five the final bombardment began, and there was nothing for us to do except sit round our candle until the tornado ended. For more than forty minutes the air vibrated and the earth rocked and shuddered. Through the sustained uproar the tap and rattle of machine-guns could be identified; but except for the whistle of bullets no retaliation came our way until a few 5.9[1] shells shook the roof of our dug-out. Barton and I sat speechless, deafened and stupefied by the seismic state of affairs, and when he lit a cigarette the match flame staggered crazily. Afterwards I asked him what he had been thinking about. His reply was 'Carpet slippers and Kettle-holders'. My own mind had been working in much the same style, for during that cannonading cataclysm the following refrain was running in my head:

> *They come as a boon and a blessing to men,*
> *The Something, the Owl, and the Waverley Pen.*

For the life of me I couldn't remember what the first one was called. Was it the Shakespeare? Was it the Dickens? Anyhow it was an advertisement which I'd often seen in smoky railway stations. Then the bombardment lifted and lessened, our vertigo abated, and we looked at one another in dazed relief. Two Brigades of our Division were now going over the top on our right. Our

---

1. The names of 54,889 men are engraved on this war memorial outside Brussels.
2. Protruding part of fortifications or, as here, line of defensive trenches. Salients are particularly vul-

nerable, being exposed to enemy fire from the front and both sides.
1. I.e., 5.9-caliber.

Brigade was to attack 'when the main assault had reached its final objective'. In our fortunate rôle of privileged spectators Barton and I went up the stairs to see what we could from Kingston Road Trench. We left Jenkins crouching in a corner, where he remained most of the day. His haggard blinking face haunts my memory. He was an example of the paralysing effect which such an experience could produce on a nervous system sensitive to noise, for he was a good officer both before and afterwards. I felt no sympathy for him at the time, but I do now. From the support-trench, which Barton called 'our opera box', I observed as much of the battle as the formation of the country allowed, the rising ground on the right making it impossible to see anything of the attack towards Mametz. A small shiny black note-book contains my pencilled particulars, and nothing will be gained by embroidering them with afterthoughts. I cannot turn my field-glasses on to the past.[2]

7.45. The barrage is now working to the right of Fricourt and beyond. I can see the 21st Division advancing about three-quarters of a mile away on the left and a few Germans coming to meet them, apparently surrendering. Our men in small parties (not extended in line) go steadily on to the German front-line. Brilliant sunshine and a haze of smoke drifting along the landscape. Some Yorkshires[3] a little way below on the left, watching the show and cheering as if at a football match. The noise almost as bad as ever.

9.30. Came back to dug-out and had a shave. 21st Division still going across the open, apparently without casualties. The sunlight flashes on bayonets as the tiny figures move quietly forward and disappear beyond mounds of trench debris. A few runners come back and ammunition parties go across. Trench-mortars are knocking hell out of Sunken Road trench and the ground where the Manchesters[4] will attack soon. Noise not so bad now and very little retaliation.

9.50. Fricourt half-hidden by clouds of drifting smoke, blue, pinkish and grey. Shrapnel bursting in small bluish-white puffs with tiny flashes. The birds seem bewildered; a lark begins to go up and then flies feebly along, thinking better of it. Others flutter above the trench with querulous cries, weak on the wing. I can see seven of our balloons,[5] on the right. On the left our men still filing across in twenties and thirties. Another huge explosion in Fricourt and a cloud of brown-pink smoke. Some bursts are yellowish.

10.5. I can see the Manchesters down in New Trench, getting ready to go over. Figures filing down the trench. Two of them have gone out to look at our wire gaps![6] Have just eaten my last orange. . . . I am staring at a sunlit picture of Hell, and still the breeze shakes the yellow weeds, and the poppies glow under Crawley Ridge where some shells fell a few minutes ago. Manchesters are sending forward some scouts. A bayonet glitters. A runner comes back across the open to their Battalion Headquarters, close here on the right. 21st Division still trotting along the sky line toward La Boisselle. Barrage going strong to the right of Contalmaison Ridge. Heavy shelling toward Mametz.

1916   1930

---

2. The extracts that follow are edited versions of the actual entries in Sassoon's diary. (See *Siegfried Sassoon: Diaries 1915–1918*, ed. Rupert Hart-Davis, 1983, pp. 82–83.)
3. Men of a Yorkshire regiment.

4. Men of the Manchester regiment.
5. Long cables, tethering such balloons, prevented attacks by low-flying aircraft.
6. Holes, made by shell fire, in the long coils of barbed wire protecting the trenches.

IVOR GURNEY
1890–1937

Ivor Bertie Gurney was born in Gloucester and showed an early aptitude for music. After five years at the King's School, Gloucester, he won a scholarship to the Royal College of Music. He first acquired a modest reputation as a composer. After war broke out in August 1914, he enlisted; his battalion was sent to France the following year, and Gurney experienced the horrors of the Western Front. He was wounded in April 1917, and when in the hospital in Rouen, he sent some of his poems to friends in London. The resultant volume, *Severn and Somme*, was published that year. (The Severn is the English river at the head of whose estuary Gloucester is situated; it appears often in his poetry. The Somme is the northern French river that was the scene of some of the most murderous fighting in the war.) Gurney was returned to the front in time to take part in the grim Paschendale offensive of the summer of 1917. He suffered the effects of a poison-gas attack on August 22 and was sent home, where he moved from hospital to hospital. He returned to the Royal College of Music to study under the composer Ralph Vaughan Williams (1872–1958) and continued also to write poetry. His second book of poems, *War's Embers*, appeared in 1919. Gurney, now believed to have been schizophrenic, spent the last fifteen years of his life in mental asylums.

Gurney was a mere private in the war, unlike officers such as Wilfred Owen and Siegfried Sassoon, and his poems recapture with immediacy particular scenes and moments in the trenches. He was influenced by the poetry of Edward Thomas, with whom he shares a limpid directness, and Gerard Manley Hopkins, whose "terrible" sonnets are racked by despair. Though ruminating on traditional subjects such as landscape, nature, and mortality, Gurney dislocates these Georgian conventions through the compression, disharmony, and unredemptive language of his poetry. His "modern" techniques include syntactic contortions, colloquial diction, shifting rhythms and rhymes, and enjambments that accentuate the jarring experience of war (a body described as "that red wet / Thing" in "To His Love").

To His Love

He's gone, and all our plans
  Are useless indeed.
We'll walk no more on Cotswold[1]
  Where the sheep feed
5   Quietly and take no heed.

His body that was so quick
  Is not as you
Knew it, on Severn river°   *a British river*
  Under the blue
10   Driving our small boat through.

You would not know him now . . .
  But still he died
Nobly, so cover him over
  With violets of pride
15   Purple from Severn side.

1. Range of hills in Gloucestershire, in western England.

Cover him, cover him soon!
And with thick-set
Masses of memoried flowers—
Hide that red wet
20   Thing I must somehow forget.

1919

The Silent One

Who died on the wires,[1] and hung there, one of two—
Who for his hours of life had chattered through
Infinite lovely chatter of Bucks[2] accent:
Yet faced unbroken wires; stepped over, and went
5   A noble fool, faithful to his stripes—and ended.
But I weak, hungry, and willing only for the chance
Of line—to fight in the line, lay down under unbroken
Wires, and saw the flashes and kept unshaken,
Till the politest voice—a finicking accent, said:
10   "Do you think you might crawl through there: there's a hole."
Darkness, shot at: I smiled, as politely replied—
"I'm afraid not, Sir." There was no hole no way to be seen
Nothing but chance of death, after tearing of clothes.
Kept flat, and watched the darkness, hearing bullets whizzing—
15   And thought of music—and swore deep heart's deep oaths
(Polite to God) and retreated and came on again,
Again retreated—and a second time faced the screen.

1954

1. The barbed wire protecting the front from   2. Buckinghamshire, in southern England.
infantry attack.

ISAAC ROSENBERG
1890–1918

Isaac Rosenberg was born in Bristol to a poor Jewish family that moved to London
in 1897. There, at Stepney, he attended elementary schools until the age of fourteen,
when he became apprenticed as an engraver in a firm of art publishers and attended
evening classes at the Art School of Birkbeck College. His first ambition was to be a
painter, and in 1911, when his apprenticeship was over, a group of three Jewish
women provided the means for his studying at the Slade School of Art. His interest
in writing poetry steadily developed, and with his sister's encouragement he circulated
copies of his poems among members of London's literary set and gained a certain
reputation, though neither his poetry nor his painting won him any material success.
In 1912 he published *Night and Day*, the first of three pamphlets of poetry at his own
expense. The other two were *Youth* (1915) and *Moses, A Play* (1916).
   In 1915 Rosenberg enlisted in the army, and he was killed in action on April 1,

1918. After his death his reputation steadily grew as an unusually interesting and original poet, who, though he did not live to maturity, nevertheless broke new ground in imagery, rhythms, and the handling of dramatic effects. His poetry strangely amalgamates acerbic irony (the sardonic grin of a rat in "Break of Day in the Trenches") with lush, resonant, even biblical diction and imagery ("shrieking iron and flame / Hurled through still heavens"). The fierce apprehension of the physical reality of war, the exclamatory directness of the language, and the vivid sense of involvement distinguish his poems. Perhaps Rosenberg's working-class background had something to do with this vividness: like Ivor Gurney and David Jones, he served in the ranks.

Break of Day in the Trenches

The darkness crumbles away.
It is the same old druid[1] Time as ever,
Only a live thing leaps my hand,
A queer sardonic rat,
5   As I pull the parapet's[2] poppy
To stick behind my ear.
Droll rat, they would shoot you if they knew
Your cosmopolitan sympathies.
Now you have touched this English hand
10   You will do the same to a German
Soon, no doubt, if it be your pleasure
To cross the sleeping green between.
It seems you inwardly grin as you pass
Strong eyes, fine limbs, haughty athletes,
15   Less chanced than you for life,
Bonds to the whims of murder,
Sprawled in the bowels of the earth,
The torn fields of France.
What do you see in our eyes
20   At the shrieking iron and flame
Hurled through still heavens?
What quaver—what heart aghast?
Poppies whose roots are in man's veins
Drop, and are ever dropping;
25   But mine in my ear is safe—
Just a little white with the dust.

June 1916   1922

Louse Hunting

Nudes—stark and glistening,
Yelling in lurid glee. Grinning faces
And raging limbs
Whirl over the floor one fire.
5   For a shirt verminously busy

1. Ancient Celtic priest.   2. Wall protecting a trench.

Yon soldier tore from his throat, with oaths
Godhead might shrink at, but not the lice.
And soon the shirt was aflare
Over the candle he'd lit while we lay.

10 Then we all sprang up and stript
To hunt the verminous brood.
Soon like a demons' pantomime
The place was raging.
See the silhouettes agape,
15 See the gibbering shadows
Mixed with the battled arms on the wall.
See gargantuan hooked fingers
Pluck in supreme flesh
To smutch° supreme littleness.   blacken, besmirch
20 See the merry limbs in hot Highland fling[1]
Because some wizard vermin
Charmed from the quiet this revel
When our ears were half lulled
By the dark music
25 Blown from Sleep's trumpet.

1917   1922

Returning, We Hear the Larks

Sombre the night is.
And though we have our lives, we know
What sinister threat lurks there.

Dragging these anguished limbs, we only know
5 This poison-blasted track opens on our camp—
On a little safe sleep.

But hark! joy—joy—strange joy.
Lo! heights of night ringing with unseen larks.
Music showering on our upturned list'ning faces.

10 Death could drop from the dark
As easily as song—
But song only dropped,
Like a blind man's dreams on the sand
By dangerous tides,
15 Like a girl's dark hair for she dreams no ruin lies there,
Or her kisses where a serpent hides.

1917   1922

1. In wild Scottish dance.

Dead Man's Dump

The plunging limbers[1] over the shattered track
Racketed with their rusty freight,
Stuck out like many crowns of thorns,
And the rusty stakes like sceptres old
5   To stay the flood of brutish men
Upon our brothers dear.

The wheels lurched over sprawled dead
But pained them not, though their bones crunched,
Their shut mouths made no moan.
10   They lie there huddled, friend and foeman,
Man born of man, and born of woman,
And shells go crying over them
From night till night and now.

Earth has waited for them,
15   All the time of their growth
Fretting for their decay:
Now she has them at last!
In the strength of their strength
Suspended—stopped and held.

20   What fierce imaginings their dark souls lit?
Earth! have they gone into you?
Somewhere they must have gone,
And flung on your hard back
Is their soul's sack,
25   Emptied of God-ancestralled essences.
Who hurled them out? Who hurled?

None saw their spirits' shadow shake the grass,
Or stood aside for the half-used life to pass
Out of those doomed nostrils and the doomed mouth,
30   When the swift iron burning bee
Drained the wild honey of their youth.

What of us who, flung on the shrieking pyre,
Walk, our usual thoughts untouched,
Our lucky limbs as on ichor[2] fed,
35   Immortal seeming ever?
Perhaps when the flames beat loud on us,
A fear may choke in our veins
And the startled blood may stop.

1. Two-wheeled carts, here carrying barbed wire.
2. In Greek mythology the ethereal fluid that flowed in the veins of the gods.

The air is loud with death,
40   The dark air spurts with fire,
The explosions ceaseless are.
Timelessly now, some minutes past,
These dead strode time with vigorous life,
Till the shrapnel called "An end!"
45   But not to all. In bleeding pangs
Some borne on stretchers dreamed of home,
Dear things, war-blotted from their hearts.

A man's brains splattered on
A stretcher-bearer's face;
50   His shook shoulders slipped their load,
But when they bent to look again
The drowning soul was sunk too deep
For human tenderness.

They left this dead with the older dead,
55   Stretched at the crossroads.

Burnt black by strange decay
Their sinister faces lie;
The lid over each eye,
The grass and coloured clay
60   More motion have than they,
Joined to the great sunk silences.

Here is one not long dead;
His dark hearing caught our far wheels,
And the choked soul stretched weak hands
65   To reach the living word the far wheels said,
The blood-dazed intelligence beating for light,
Crying through the suspense of the far torturing wheels
Swift for the end to break,
Or the wheels to break,
70   Cried as the tide of the world broke over his sight.

Will they come? Will they ever come?
Even as the mixed hoofs of the mules,
The quivering-bellied mules,
And the rushing wheels all mixed
75   With his tortured upturned sight.
So we crashed round the bend,
We heard his weak scream,
We heard his very last sound,
And our wheels grazed his dead face.

1917   1922

WILFRED OWEN
1893–1918

Wilfred Owen was brought up in the backstreets of Birkenhead and Shrewsbury, and on leaving school he took up a post as lay assistant to a country vicar. Removed from the influence of a devout mother, he became increasingly critical of the Church's role in society. His letters and poems of this period show an emerging awareness of the poor's sufferings and the first stirrings of the compassion that was to characterize his later poems about the Western Front. In 1913 he broke with the vicar and went to teach English in France.

For more than a year after the outbreak of war, Owen could not decide whether he ought to enlist. Finally he did, and from January to May 1917 he fought as an officer in the Battle of the Somme. Then, suffering from shell shock, he was sent to a hospital near Edinburgh, where he had the good fortune to meet Siegfried Sassoon, whose first fiercely realistic war poems had just appeared. The influence of Sassoon's satiric realism was a useful tonic to Owen's lush, Keatsian Romanticism. Throughout his months in the hospital, Owen suffered from the horrendous nightmares symptomatic of shell shock. The experience of battle, banished from his waking mind, erupted into his dreams and then into poems haunted with obsessive images of blinded eyes ("Dulce et Decorum Est") and the mouth of hell ("Miners" and "Strange Meeting"). The distinctive music of such later poems owes much of its power to Owen's mastery of alliteration, onomatopoeia, assonance, half-rhyme, and the pararhyme that he pioneered. This last technique, the rhyming of two words with identical or similar consonants but differing, stressed vowels (such as *groined / groaned, killed / cold, hall / hell*), of which the second is usually the lower in pitch, produces effects of dissonance, failure, and unfulfillment that subtly reinforce his themes.

Echoing Dante, Shakespeare, Shelley, Keats, and the Bible, Owen puts literary and religious language into jarring new relationships with the absurdities of modern war experience. He recuperates but distorts the conventions of pastoral elegy, relocating them to scenes of terror, extreme pain, and irredeemable mass death.

In the year of life left to him after leaving the hospital in November 1917, Owen matured rapidly. Success as a soldier, marked by the award of the Military Cross, and as a poet, which had won him the recognition of his peers, gave him a new confidence. He wrote eloquently of the tragedy of young men killed in battle. In his later elegies a disciplined sensuality and a passionate intelligence find their fullest, most moving, and most memorable expression.

Owen was killed in action a week before the war ended.

Anthem for Doomed Youth

What passing-bells for these who die as cattle?
  —Only the monstrous anger of the guns.
  Only the stuttering rifles' rapid rattle
Can patter out their hasty orisons.°   *prayers*
5   No mockeries now for them; no prayers nor bells;
    Nor any voice of mourning save the choirs,—
  The shrill, demented choirs of wailing shells;
    And bugles calling for them from sad shires.°   *counties*

  What candles may be held to speed them all?
10   Not in the hands of boys but in their eyes

Shall shine the holy glimmers of goodbyes.
The pallor of girls' brows shall be their pall;
Their flowers the tenderness of patient minds,
And each slow dusk a drawing-down of blinds.

Sept.–Oct. 1917   1920

Apologia Pro Poemate Meo[1]

I, too, saw God through mud,—
    The mud that cracked on cheeks when wretches smiled.
    War brought more glory to their eyes than blood,
    And gave their laughs more glee than shakes a child.

5 Merry it was to laugh there—
    Where death becomes absurd and life absurder.
    For power was on us as we slashed bones bare
    Not to feel sickness or remorse of murder.

I, too, have dropped off Fear—
10   Behind the barrage, dead as my platoon,
    And sailed my spirit surging light and clear
    Past the entanglement where hopes lay strewn;

And witnessed exultation—[2]
    Faces that used to curse me, scowl for scowl,
15   Shine and lift up with passion of oblation,[3]
    Seraphic° for an hour; though they were foul.   *ecstatic*

I have made fellowships—
    Untold of happy lovers in old song.
    For love is not the binding of fair lips
20   With the soft silk of eyes that look and long,

By Joy, whose ribbon slips,—
    But wound with war's hard wire whose stakes are strong;
    Bound with the bandage of the arm that drips;
    Knit in the webbing of the rifle-thong.

25 I have perceived much beauty
    In the hoarse oaths that kept our courage straight;
    Heard music in the silentness of duty;
    Found peace where shell-storms spouted reddest spate.

Nevertheless, except you share
30   With them in hell the sorrowful dark of hell,

---

1. This Latin title, meaning "Apology for My Poem," may have been prompted by that of Cardinal Newman's *Apologia Pro Vita Sua,* "Apology for His Life." Here an apology is a written vindication rather than a remorseful account.
2. Cf. Shelley, *A Defence of Poetry:* "Poetry is a mirror which makes beautiful that which is distorted. . . . It exalts the beauty of that which is most beautiful, and it adds beauty to that which is most deformed; it marries exultation and horror."
3. Sacrifice offered to God.

Whose world is but the trembling of a flare
And heaven but as the highway for a shell,

You shall not hear their mirth:
You shall not come to think them well content
35   By any jest of mine. These men are worth
Your tears. You are not worth their merriment.

Nov.–Dec. 1917   1920

Miners[1]

There was a whispering in my hearth,
    A sigh of the coal,
Grown wistful of a former earth
    It might recall.

5   I listened for a tale of leaves
    And smothered ferns,
Frond-forests, and the low sly lives
    Before the fauns.

My fire might show steam-phantoms simmer
10   From Time's old cauldron,
Before the birds made nests in summer,
    Or men had children.

But the coals were murmuring of their mine,
    And moans down there
15 Of boys that slept wry sleep, and men
    Writhing for air.

And I saw white bones in the cinder-shard,
    Bones without number.
Many the muscled bodies charred,
20   And few remember.

I thought of all that worked dark pits
    Of war,[2] and died
Digging the rock where Death reputes
    Peace lies indeed.

25 Comforted years will sit soft-chaired,
    In rooms of amber;
The years will stretch their hands, well-cheered
    By our life's ember;

---

1. Wrote a poem on the Colliery Disaster [of Jan. 12, 1918, at Halmerend]: but I get mixed up with the War at the end. It is short, but oh! sour [Owen's Jan. 14 letter to his mother]. The explosion killed about 150 miners.
2. Miners who dug tunnels under no-man's-land in which to detonate mines beneath the enemy trenches.

The centuries will burn rich loads
30   With which we groaned,
Whose warmth shall lull their dreaming lids,
    While songs are crooned;
But they will not dream of us poor lads,
    Left in the ground.

Jan. 1918   1931

Dulce Et Decorum Est[1]

Bent double, like old beggars under sacks,
Knock-kneed, coughing like hags, we cursed through sludge,
Till on the haunting flares we turned our backs
And towards our distant rest began to trudge.
5   Men marched asleep. Many had lost their boots
But limped on, blood-shod. All went lame; all blind;
Drunk with fatigue; deaf even to the hoots
Of tired, outstripped Five-Nines[2] that dropped behind.

Gas! Gas! Quick, boys!—An ecstasy of fumbling,
10   Fitting the clumsy helmets just in time;
But someone still was yelling out and stumbling,
And flound'ring like a man in fire or lime . . .
Dim, through the misty panes[3] and thick green light,
As under a green sea, I saw him drowning.

15   In all my dreams, before my helpless sight,
He plunges at me, guttering, choking, drowning.

If in some smothering dreams you too could pace
Behind the wagon that we flung him in,
And watch the white eyes writhing in his face,
20   His hanging face, like a devil's sick of sin;
If you could hear, at every jolt, the blood
Come gargling from the froth-corrupted lungs,
Obscene as cancer, bitter as the cud
Of vile, incurable sores on innocent tongues,—
25   My friend,[4] you would not tell with such high zest
To children ardent for some desperate glory,
The old Lie: Dulce et decorum est
Pro patria mori.

Oct. 1917–Mar. 1918   1920

1. The famous Latin tag [from Horace, *Odes* 3.2.13] means, of course, *It is sweet and meet to die for one's country. Sweet! And decorous!* [Owen's Oct. 16, 1917, letter to his mother].
2. I.e., 5.9-caliber shells.
3. Of the gas mask's celluloid window.

4. Jessie Pope, to whom the poem was originally to have been dedicated, published jingoistic war poems urging young men to enlist. See her poems in "Representing the Great War" at Norton Literature Online.

Strange Meeting[1]

It seemed that out of battle I escaped
Down some profound dull tunnel,[2] long since scooped
Through granites which titanic wars had groined.°   grooved

Yet also there encumbered sleepers groaned,
5   Too fast in thought or death to be bestirred.
Then, as I probed them, one sprang up, and stared
With piteous recognition in fixed eyes,
Lifting distressful hands, as if to bless.
And by his smile, I knew that sullen hall,—
10   By his dead smile I knew we stood in Hell.

With a thousand pains that vision's face was grained;
Yet no blood reached there from the upper ground,
And no guns thumped, or down the flues made moan.
"Strange friend," I said, "here is no cause to mourn."
15   "None," said that other, "save the undone years,
The hopelessness. Whatever hope is yours,
Was my life also; I went hunting wild
After the wildest beauty in the world,
Which lies not calm in eyes, or braided hair,
20   But mocks the steady running of the hour,
And if it grieves, grieves richlier than here.
For by my glee might many men have laughed,
And of my weeping something had been left,
Which must die now. I mean the truth untold,
25   The pity of war, the pity war distilled.[3]
Now men will go content with what we spoiled,
Or, discontent, boil bloody, and be spilled.
They will be swift with swiftness of the tigress.
None will break ranks, though nations trek from progress.
30   Courage was mine, and I had mystery,
Wisdom was mine, and I had mastery:
To miss the march of this retreating world
Into vain citadels that are not walled.
Then, when much blood had clogged their chariot-wheels,
35   I would go up and wash them from sweet wells,
Even with truths that lie too deep for taint.[4]
I would have poured my spirit without stint
But not through wounds; not on the cess[5] of war.
Foreheads of men have bled where no wounds were.

---

1. Cf. Shelley, *The Revolt of Islam*, lines 1828–32:

And one whose spear had pierced me, leaned
   beside,
   With quivering lips and humid eyes;—and all
Seemed like some brothers on a journey wide
Gone forth, whom now strange meeting did
   befall
   In a strange land.

The speaker of Owen's poem imagines his victim a
poet like himself.

2. Cf. Sassoon's "The Rear-Guard" (p. 1961).
3. My subject is War, and the pity of War. The
Poetry is in the pity [Owen's draft preface to his
poems].
4. Cf. "Thoughts that do often lie too deep for
tears," line 203 of William Wordsworth's "Ode:
Intimations of Immortality" (1807).
5. Luck, as in the phrase *bad cess to you* (may evil
befall you), and muck or excrement, as in the word
cesspool.

40 "I am the enemy you killed, my friend.
I knew you in this dark: for so you frowned
Yesterday through me as you jabbed and killed.
I parried; but my hands were loath and cold.
Let us sleep now. . . ."

May [?] 1918   1920

Futility

Move him into the sun—
Gently its touch awoke him once,
At home, whispering of fields half-sown.
Always it woke him, even in France,
5   Until this morning and this snow.
If anything might rouse him now
The kind old sun will know.

Think how it wakes the seeds—
Woke once the clays of a cold star.
10 Are limbs, so dear achieved, are sides
Full-nerved, still warm, too hard to stir?
Was it for this the clay grew tall?
—O what made fatuous sunbeams toil
To break earth's sleep at all?

May 1918   1920

S.I.W.[1]

I will to the King,
And offer him consolation in his trouble,
For that man there has set his teeth to die,
And being one that hates obedience,
Discipline, and orderliness of life,
I cannot mourn him.
                                    W. B. YEATS[2]

I. The Prologue

Patting goodbye, doubtless they told the lad
He'd always show the Hun[3] a brave man's face;
Father would sooner him dead than in disgrace,—
Was proud to see him going, aye, and glad.
5   Perhaps his mother whimpered how she'd fret
Until he got a nice safe wound to nurse.
Sisters would wish girls too could shoot, charge, curse . . .

1. Military abbreviation for self-inflicted wound.
2. Irish poet and playwright (1865–1939). The
passage from the play The King's Threshold (1906)

describes the poet Seanchan's heroic resolve to die.
3. German soldier; in the fourth century a
nomadic people feared for their military prowess.

Brothers—would send his favourite cigarette.
Each week, month after month, they wrote the same,
10 Thinking him sheltered in some Y.M. Hut,[4]
Because he said so, writing on his butt°   *rifle's stock*
Where once an hour a bullet missed its aim.
And misses teased the hunger of his brain.
His eyes grew old with wincing, and his hand
15 Reckless with ague.° Courage leaked, as sand   *fever*
From the best sandbags after years of rain.
But never leave, wound, fever, trench-foot, shock,
Untrapped the wretch. And death seemed still withheld
For torture of lying machinally shelled,
20 At the pleasure of this world's Powers who'd run amok.

He'd seen men shoot their hands, on night patrol.
Their people never knew. Yet they were vile.
'Death sooner than dishonour, that's the style!'
So Father said.

II. The Action

One dawn, our wire patrol
25 Carried him. This time, Death had not missed.
We could do nothing but wipe his bleeding cough.
Could it be accident?—Rifles go off . . .
Not sniped? No. (Later they found the English ball.)

III. The Poem

It was the reasoned crisis of his soul
30 Against more days of inescapable thrall,
Against infrangibly° wired and blind trench wall   *unbreakably*
Curtained with fire, roofed in with creeping fire,
Slow grazing fire, that would not burn him whole
But kept him for death's promises and scoff,
35 And life's half-promising, and both their riling.

IV. The Epilogue

With him they buried the muzzle his teeth had kissed,
And truthfully wrote the mother, 'Tim died smiling.'

Sept. 1917, May 1918   1920

Disabled

He sat in a wheeled chair, waiting for dark,
And shivered in his ghastly suit of grey,
Legless, sewn short at elbow. Through the park

---

4. Hostel of the Young Men's Christian Association.

Voices of boys rang saddening like a hymn,
5 Voices of play and pleasure after day,
Till gathering sleep had mothered them from him.

• • •

About this time Town used to swing so gay
When glow-lamps budded in the light blue trees,
And girls glanced lovelier as the air grew dim,—
10 In the old times, before he threw away his knees.
Now he will never feel again how slim
Girls' waists are, or how warm their subtle hands.
All of them touch him like some queer disease.

• • •

There was an artist silly for his face,
15 For it was younger than his youth, last year.
Now, he is old; his back will never brace;
He's lost his colour very far from here,
Poured it down shell-holes till the veins ran dry,
And half his lifetime lapsed in the hot race
20 And leap of purple spurted from his thigh.

• • •

One time he liked a blood-smear down his leg,
After the matches, carried shoulder-high.[1]
It was after football, when he'd drunk a peg,[2]
He thought he'd better join.—He wonders why.
25 Someone had said he'd look a god in kilts,
That's why; and maybe, too, to please his Meg,
Aye, that was it, to please the giddy jilts[3]
He asked to join. He didn't have to beg;
Smiling they wrote his lie: aged nineteen years.[4]
30 Germans he scarcely thought of; all their guilt,
And Austria's, did not move him. And no fears
Of Fear came yet. He thought of jewelled hilts
For daggers in plaid socks;[5] of smart salutes;
And care of arms; and leave; and pay arrears;
35 Esprit de corps;[6] and hints for young recruits.
And soon, he was drafted out with drums and cheers.

• • •

Some cheered him home, but not as crowds cheer Goal.
Only a solemn man who brought him fruits
Thanked him; and then enquired about his soul.

• • •

40 Now, he will spend a few sick years in institutes,
And do what things the rules consider wise,

---

1. Cf. Housman's "To an Athlete Dying Young"
(p. 1949, lines 1–4).
2. Slang for a drink, usually brandy and soda.
3. Capricious women.
4. The recruiting officers entered on his enlistment form his lie that he was nineteen years old
and, therefore, above the minimum age for military
service.
5. Kilted Scottish Highlanders used to carry a
small ornamental dagger in the top of a stocking.
6. Regard for the honor and interests of an organization or, as here, a military unit. "Pay arrears":
back pay.

And take whatever pity they may dole.
Tonight he noticed how the women's eyes
Passed from him to the strong men that were whole.
45   How cold and late it is! Why don't they come
And put him into bed? Why don't they come?

Oct. 1917–July 1918   1920

From Owen's Letters to His Mother

16 January 1917

*   *   *

I can see no excuse for deceiving you about these last 4 days. I have suffered seventh hell.
I have not been at the front.
I have been in front of it.
I held an advanced post, that is, a 'dug-out' in the middle of No Man's Land.
We had a march of 3 miles over shelled road then nearly 3 along a flooded trench. After that we came to where the trenches had been blown flat out and had to go over the top. It was of course dark, too dark, and the ground was not mud, not sloppy mud, but an octopus of sucking clay, 3, 4, and 5 feet deep, relieved only by craters full of water. Men have been known to drown in them. Many stuck in the mud & only got on by leaving their waders, equipment, and in some cases their clothes.
High explosives were dropping all around out, and machine guns spluttered every few minutes. But it was so dark that even the German flares did not reveal us.
Three quarters dead, I mean each of us ¾ dead, we reached the dug-out, and relieved the wretches therein. I then had to go forth and find another dug-out for a still more advanced post where I left 18 bombers. I was responsible for other posts on the left but there was a junior officer in charge.
My dug-out held 25 men tight packed. Water filled it to a depth of 1 or 2 feet, leaving say 4 feet of air.
One entrance had been blown in & blocked.
So far, the other remained.
The Germans knew we were staying there and decided we shouldn't.
Those fifty hours were the agony of my happy life.
Every ten minutes on Sunday afternoon seemed an hour.
I nearly broke down and let myself drown in the water that was now slowly rising over my knees.
Towards 6 o'clock, when, I suppose, you would be going to church, the shelling grew less intense and less accurate: so that I was mercifully helped to do my duty and crawl, wade, climb and flounder over No Man's Land to visit my other post. It took me half an hour to move about 150 yards.
I was chiefly annoyed by our own machine guns from behind. The seeng-seeng-seeng of the bullets reminded me of Mary's canary. On the whole I can support[1] the canary better.

---

1. Tolerate. Mary: Owen's sister.

In the Platoon on my left the sentries over the dug-out were blown to nothing. One of these poor fellows was my first servant whom I rejected. If I had kept him he would have lived, for servants don't do Sentry Duty. I kept my own sentries half way down the stairs during the more terrific bombardment. In spite of this one lad was blown down and, I am afraid, blinded.[2]

31 December 1917

Last year, at this time, (it is just midnight, and now is the intolerable instant of the Change) last year I lay awake in a windy tent in the middle of a vast, dreadful encampment. It seemed neither France nor England, but a kind of paddock where the beasts are kept a few days before the shambles. I heard the revelling of the Scotch troops, who are now dead, and who knew they would be dead. I thought of this present night, and whether I should indeed—whether we should indeed—whether you would indeed—but I thought neither long nor deeply, for I am a master of elision.

But chiefly I thought of the very strange look on all faces in that camp; an incomprehensible look, which a man will never see in England, though wars should be in England; nor can it be seen in any battle. But only in Étaples.[3]

It was not despair, or terror, it was more terrible than terror, for it was a blindfold look, and without expression, like a dead rabbit's.

It will never be painted, and no actor will ever seize it. And to describe it, I think I must go back and be with them.

Preface[1]

This book is not about heroes. English poetry is not yet fit to speak of them.

Nor is it about deeds, or lands, nor anything about glory, honour, might, majesty, dominion, or power, except War.

Above all I am not concerned with Poetry.

My subject is War, and the pity of War.[2]

The Poetry is in the pity.

Yet these elegies are to this generation in no sense consolatory. They may be to the next. All a poet can do today is warn. That is why the true Poets must be truthful.

(If I thought the letter of this book would last, I might have used proper names; but if the spirit of it survives—survives Prussia[3]—my ambition and those names will have achieved fresher fields than Flanders.[4] . . .)

1918   1920

---

2. This incident prompted Owen's poem "The Sentry."
3. Until 1914, a fishing port of 5,800 inhabitants, Étaples and its surrounding hills housed 100,000 soldiers on their way to and from the front in 1917.
1. In May 1918 Wilfred Owen was posted in Ripon, North Yorkshire, England, and was preparing a book of his war poems. Around this time he drafted this unfinished preface, which was published posthumously, along with most of his poems, in *Poems* (1920), edited by his friend the poet Siegfried Sassoon. The text is reprinted from

The Poems of Wilfred Owen (1985), ed. Jon Stallworthy.
2. Cf. Jude 1.25: "To the only wise God our Saviour, be glory and majesty, dominion and power, both now and ever."
3. Dominant region of the German Empire until the end of World War I.
4. In western Belgium, site of the front line. The Canadian poet John McCrae (1872–1918) memorialized one devastating 1915 battle in his famous poem "In Flanders Fields."

MAY WEDDERBURN CANNAN
1893–1973

Born and educated in Oxford, May Wedderburn Cannan was the daughter of the secretary to the delegates (or chief executive) of the Oxford University Press. At eighteen, she joined the Red Cross Voluntary Aid Detachment, and when England entered the war three years later, she was active in the Red Cross mobilization, setting up a hospital in a local school. During the early part of the war, she worked at Oxford University Press, continued her volunteer nursing, and spent a month as a volunteer worker in a soldiers' canteen in Rouen, France. In 1918 she joined the War Office in Paris to work in intelligence. Her fiancé, Bevil Quiller-Couch, survived the devastating Battle of the Somme and the remainder of the war, only to die of pneumonia several months after the armistice. Canaan later worked at King's College, London, and at the Athenaeum Club as assistant librarian. She wrote three books of poems—*In War Time* (1917), *The Splendid Days* (1919), and *The House of Hope* (1923)—and a novel, *The Lonely Generation* (1934). Her unfinished autobiography, *Grey Ghosts and Voices,* was published posthumously in 1976.

"Rouen," with its echoes of G. K. Chesterton's incantatory "Tarantella" (beginning "Do you remember an Inn, / Miranda?"), voices emotions closer to those of Rupert Brooke's "The Soldier" than to any given expression by the other soldier poets in this section. In 1917, however, Cannan and Brooke spoke for what was then the majority. As she wrote in her autobiography: "Siegfried Sassoon wrote to the Press from France saying that the war was now a war of conquest and without justification, and declared himself to be a conscientious objector. . . . A saying went round, 'Went to the war with Rupert Brooke and came home with Siegfried Sassoon.' " Her own poems pose an alternative to protest and despair: "I had much admired some of Sassoon's verse but I was not coming home with him. Someone must go on writing for those who were still convinced of the right of the cause for which they had taken up arms."

Rouen

26 April–25 May 1915

Early morning over Rouen, hopeful, high, courageous morning,
And the laughter of adventure and the steepness of the stair,
And the dawn across the river, and the wind across the bridges,
And the empty littered station and the tired people there.

5   Can you recall those mornings and the hurry of awakening,
And the long-forgotten wonder if we should miss the way,
And the unfamiliar faces, and the coming of provisions,
And the freshness and the glory of the labour of the day?

Hot noontide over Rouen, and the sun upon the city,
10 Sun and dust unceasing, and the glare of cloudless skies,
And the voices of the Indians and the endless stream of soldiers,
And the clicking of the tatties,[1] and the buzzing of the flies.

Can you recall those noontides and the reek of steam and coffee,
Heavy-laden noontides with the evening's peace to win,

---

1. Screens or mats hung in a doorway and kept wet to cool and freshen the air.

15 And the little piles of Woodbines,[2] and the sticky soda bottles,
And the crushes[3] in the "Parlour," and the letters coming in?

Quiet night-time over Rouen, and the station full of soldiers,
All the youth and pride of England from the ends of all the earth;
And the rifles piled together, and the creaking of the sword-belts,
20 And the faces bent above them, and the gay, heart-breaking mirth.

Can I forget the passage from the cool white-bedded Aid Post
Past the long sun-blistered coaches of the khaki Red Cross train
To the truck train full of wounded, and the weariness and laughter,
And "Good-bye, and thank-you, Sister,"[4] and the empty yards again?

25 Can you recall the parcels that we made them for the railroad,
Crammed and bulging parcels held together by their string,
And the voices of the sergeants who called the Drafts[5] together,
And the agony and splendour when they stood to save the King?[6]

Can you forget their passing, the cheering and the waving,
30 The little group of people at the doorway of the shed,
The sudden awful silence when the last train swung to darkness,
And the lonely desolation, and the mocking stars o'erhead?

Can you recall the midnights, and the footsteps of night watchers,
Men who came from darkness and went back to dark again,
35 And the shadows on the rail-lines and the all-inglorious labour,
And the promise of the daylight firing blue the window-pane?

Can you recall the passing through the kitchen door to morning,
Morning very still and solemn breaking slowly on the town,
And the early coastways engines that had met the ships at daybreak,
40 And the Drafts just out from England, and the day shift coming down?

Can you forget returning slowly, stumbling on the cobbles,
And the white-decked Red Cross barges dropping seawards for the tide,
And the search for English papers, and the blessed cool of water,
And the peace of half-closed shutters that shut out the world outside?

45 Can I forget the evenings and the sunsets on the island,
And the tall black ships at anchor far below our balcony,
And the distant call of bugles, and the white wine in the glasses,
And the long line of the street lamps, stretching Eastwards to the sea?

. . . When the world slips slow to darkness, when the office fire burns lower,
50 My heart goes out to Rouen, Rouen all the world away;
When other men remember I remember our Adventure
And the trains that go from Rouen at the ending of the day.

1916

---

2. Popular brand of cheap cigarette.   5. Groups of soldiers.
3. Crowded social gatherings.   6. I.e., to sing the British National Anthem, "God
4. Nurse.   Save the King."

From Grey Ghosts and Voices

I suppose it is difficult for anyone to realise now what "France" meant to us. In the second war I met a young man of the Left who assured me that Rupert Brooke's verse was of no account, phoney, because it was "impossible that anyone should have thought like that." I turned and rent him, saying that he was entitled to his own opinion of Rupert Brooke's verse, but *not* entitled to say that no one could have thought like that. How could he know how we had thought?—All our hopes and all our loves, and God knew, all our fears, were in France; to get to France, if only to stand on her soil, was something; to share, in however small a way, in what was done there was Heart's Desire.

I asked my Father¹ could I take all my holidays in one and go for four weeks to France—I did not want holidays, I said, but I did want France. It was dark and we were walking home through the confines of Little Clarendon Street; my voice, I knew, shook; he took his pipe out of his mouth, halted his step for a moment and looked down at me. "Ah! France," he said, "France, yes I think you should go. We'll manage." I stammered thanks and we walked home in silence, understanding each other.

The Canteen was started at Rouen because Lord Brassey's yacht, *The Sunbeam*, had made two or three journeys there during the shortage of hospital ships bringing wounded home. Lady Mabelle Egerton, his daughter, looking round the desolate railway yards beyond the quays asked the R[ail]. T[ransport]. O[fficer]. if there was anything that could be done for the troops; drafts going up the line to Railhead, who had to spend a long day there, and sometimes a long night.

He said that the men brought their rations, including tea, but that there was no means of making hot water. (It was long before the days of another war when motorised infantry "brewed up" with their petrol cans)—Could she find some philanthropic person to take on the job? She could find no one— and decided to do it herself, and so the canteen, later known affectionately to thousands of the B[ritish]. E[xpeditionary]. F[orce]. and the New Armies, as "the Coffee Shop" was born.

I had a passport. I packed. Left as little urgent work behind me as I could, and met Lucie, who I adored, in London. We travelled to Southampton and Hilary, who after sick leave had been posted to a home battalion of his regiment in Hampshire, came to dinner and we sat far into the night talking. He had been in France; I was going, and generously he treated me as if I was one of the fraternity. . . .

I had done nothing about a berth, and there was none to be had so I spent the night curled up, blissfully happy, on a coil of rope in the bow where no one noticed me, and woke in the early morning as we came into Le Havre. There were English soldiers in the streets, and in the cold spring sunshine a battery clattered by. We went up by train to Rouen. Someone had got us a couple of rooms in a small hotel with a restaurant below that overlooked the quays; those same broad quays where Bevil had disembarked. I fell into bed too happy to worry or to dream and went on duty after breakfast next morning.

Along the length of railway line ran a row of sheds with huge sliding doors.

---

1. Chief executive of the Oxford University Press, for which his daughter then worked.

In the first, and smaller one, was established a boiler room where enormous vats of hot water forever boiled. * * *

When the big trains were due in we opened the sliding doors of the sheds, the train doors banged and banged down the long line of the corridors and some 2,000 men would surge in. Barricaded behind our heavy table, and thankful for it when the pressure was heavy or a draft[2] had somehow got hold of some drink, we handed out bowls of coffee and sandwiches, washed dirty bowls till the water in the tall vats was chocolate brown, and served again.

Someone would play the piano; Annie Laurie; Loch Lomond.[3] Blurred lanterns lit the scene as best they might when it rained and our candles in the tills under the tables guttered in the wind. One was hot or horrid cold, harried, dirty, and one's feet ached with the stone floors. When the smaller drafts came one could distinguish faces, and regimental badges; have a word or two. * * *

When the whistle blew they stood to save the King[4] and the roof came off the sheds. Two thousand men, maybe, singing—it was the most moving thing I knew. Then there'd be the thunder of seats pushed back, the stamp of army boots on the pavé, and as the train went out they sang Tipperary.[5]

1976

2. Group of soldiers.
3. Two Scottish songs.
4. I.e., to sing the British National Anthem, "God
Save the King."
5. The Irish song "It's a Long Way to Tipperary."

ROBERT GRAVES
1895–1985

Robert von Ranke Graves was born in London of partly Anglo-Irish and partly German descent—his great-uncle was the distinguished German historian Leopold von Ranke. He left Charterhouse School to go immediately into the army, serving in World War I until he was invalided out in 1917. After the war he went to Oxford, took a B.Litt. degree, and in 1929 published *Goodbye to All That*, a vivid account of his experiences in the war, including his almost dying from severe chest wounds. His autobiography, as he put it, "paid my debts and enabled me to set up in Majorca as a writer." He lived on that Spanish island with the American poet Laura Riding—his muse and mentor—until in 1936 the outbreak of the Spanish Civil War forced them to leave. Their relationship soon ended, and after World War II he returned to Majorca, where he remained for the rest of his life.

Graves began as a Georgian poet, but he was a Georgian with a difference. The mingling of the colloquial and the visionary in his vocabulary, the accent of conversation underlying the regular rhythms of his stanzas, the tension between a Romantic indulgence in emotion and a cool appraisal of its significance—these are qualities found even in his early poetry. His best work combines the ironic and the imaginative in a highly individual manner, and he is also capable of a down-to-earth poetry, often mocking in tone and dealing with simple domestic facts or even the more annoying of personal relationships. He admired Thomas Hardy but chided Yeats, Pound, and Eliot for their obscurity and slovenliness, preferring that poetry be lucid, orderly, and civil.

Graves made his living by his prose, which is extensive and varied and includes, in addition to *Goodbye to All That*, a number of historical novels in which characters and events from the classical or biblical past are reconstructed in a modern idiom: the most notable of his historical novels are *I, Claudius* (1934), *Claudius the God* (1934), and *King Jesus* (1946). In *The White Goddess* (1948), a study of mythology drawn from a great variety of sources and devoted to what he considered the great female inspirational principle, Graves argued that only a return to goddess worship and an abandonment of patriarchal for matriarchal society could help modern poetry recover its lost force, clarity, and mythic wisdom.

From Goodbye to All That

[THE ATTACK ON HIGH WOOD]

Next evening, July 19th, we were relieved and told that we would be attacking High Wood,[1] which could be seen a thousand yards away to the right at the top of a slope. High Wood, which the French called 'Raven Wood', formed part of the main German battle-line that ran along the ridge, with Delville Wood not far off on the German left. Two British brigades had already attempted it; in both cases a counter-attack drove them out again. The Royal Welch[2] were now reduced by casualties to about four hundred strong, including transport, stretcher-bearers, cooks and other non-combatants. I took command of 'B' Company.

The German batteries were handing out heavy stuff, six- and eight-inch, and so much of it that we decided to move back fifty yards at a rush. As we did so, an eight-inch shell burst three paces behind me. I heard the explosion, and felt as though I had been punched rather hard between the shoulder-blades, but without any pain. I took the punch merely for the shock of the explosion; but blood trickled into my eye and, turning faint, I called to Moodie: 'I've been hit.' Then I fell. A minute or two before I had got two very small wounds on my left hand; and in exactly the same position as the two that drew blood from my right hand during the preliminary bombardment at Loos.[3] This I took as a lucky sign, and for further security repeated to myself a line of Nietzsche's, in French translation:

> *Non, tu ne me peus pas tuer!*[4]

One piece of shell went through my left thigh, high up, near the groin; I must have been at the full stretch of my stride to escape emasculation. The wound over the eye was made by a little chip of marble, possibly from one of the Bazentin[5] cemetery headstones. [Later, I had it cut out, but a smaller piece has since risen to the surface under my right eyebrow, where I keep it for a souvenir.] This, and a finger-wound which split the bone, probably came from another shell bursting in front of me. But a piece of shell had also gone in two inches below the point of my right shoulder-blade and came out through my chest two inches above the right nipple.

1. The battle for High Wood, one of the bloodiest fights of the Somme Offensive, began on July 14, 1916, and was won by the British on September 15, 1916.
2. Royal Welch Fusiliers.
3. The Battle of Loos, September 1915.
4. No, you cannot kill me. Friedrich Nietzsche (1844–1900), German philosopher.
5. The Battle of Bazentin Ridge, July 14–17, 1916, part of the Somme Offensive.

My memory of what happened then is vague. Apparently Dr Dunn came up through the barrage with a stretcher-party, dressed my wound, and got me down to the old German dressing-station at the north end of Mametz Wood.[6] I remember being put on the stretcher, and winking at the stretcher-bearer sergeant who had just said: 'Old Gravy's got it, all right!' They laid my stretcher in a corner of the dressing-station, where I remained unconscious for more than twenty-four hours.

Late that night, Colonel Crawshay came back from High Wood and visited the dressing-station; he saw me lying in the corner, and they told him I was done for. The next morning, July 21st, clearing away the dead, they found me still breathing and put me on an ambulance for Heilly, the nearest field hospital. The pain of being jolted down the Happy Valley, with a shell hole at every three or four yards of the road, woke me up. I remember screaming. But back on the better roads I became unconscious again. That morning, Crawshay wrote the usual formal letters of condolence to the next-of-kin of the six or seven officers who had been killed. This was his letter to my mother:

22.7.16

Dear Mrs Graves,

I very much regret to have to write and tell you your son has died of wounds. He was very gallant, and was doing so well and is a great loss.

He was hit by a shell and very badly wounded, and died on the way down to the base I believe. He was not in bad pain, and our doctor managed to get across and attend to him at once.

We have had a very hard time, and our casualties have been large. Believe me you have all our sympathy in your loss, and we have lost a very gallant soldier.

Please write to me if I can tell you or do anything.

Yours sincerely,
C. Crawshay, Lt.-Col.

Then he made out the official casualty list—a long one, because only eighty men were left in the battalion—and reported me 'died of wounds'. Heilly lay on the railway; close to the station stood the hospital tents with the red cross prominently painted on the roofs, to discourage air-bombing. Fine July weather made the tents insufferably hot. I was semi-conscious now, and aware of my lung-wound through a shortness of breath. It amused me to watch the little bubbles of blood, like scarlet soap-bubbles, which my breath made in escaping through the opening of the wound. The doctor came over to my bed. I felt sorry for him; he looked as though he had not slept for days.

I asked him: 'Can I have a drink?'

'Would you like some tea?'

I whispered: 'Not with condensed milk.'

He said, most apologetically: 'I'm afraid there's no fresh milk.'

Tears of disappointment pricked my eyes; I expected better of a hospital behind the lines.

'Will you have some water?'

___

6. Recently captured by the British.

'Not if it's boiled.'

'It is boiled. And I'm afraid I can't give you anything alcoholic in your present condition.'

'Some fruit then?'

'I have seen no fruit for days.'

Yet a few minutes later he returned with two rather unripe greengages.[7] In whispers I promised him a whole orchard when I recovered.

The nights of the 22nd and 23rd were horrible. Early on the morning of the 24th, when the doctor came round the ward, I said: 'You must send me away from here. This heat will kill me.' It was beating on my head through the canvas.

'Stick it out. Your best chance is to lie here and not to be moved. You'd not reach the Base alive.'

'Let me risk the move. I'll be all right, you'll see.'

Half an hour later he returned. 'Well, you're having it your way. I've just got orders to evacuate every case in the hospital. Apparently the Guards have been in it up at Delville Wood, and they'll all be coming down tonight.' I did not fear that I would die, now—it was enough to be honourably wounded and bound for home.

A brigade-major, wounded in the leg, who lay in the next bed, gave me news of the battalion. He looked at my label and said: 'I see you're in the Second Royal Welch. I watched your High Wood show through field-glasses. The way your battalion shook out into artillery formation, company by company—with each section of four or five men in file at fifty yards interval and distance—going down into the hollow and up the slope through the barrage, was the most beautiful bit of parade-ground drill I've ever seen. Your company officers must have been superb.' Yet one company at least had started without a single officer. When I asked whether they had held the wood, he told me: 'They hung on to the near end. I believe what happened was that the Public Schools Battalion came away at dark; and so did most of the Scotsmen. Your chaps were left there more or less alone for some time. They steadied themselves by singing. Afterwards the chaplain—R. C.[8] of course—Father McCabe, brought the Scotsmen back. Being Glasgow Catholics, they would follow a priest where they wouldn't follow an officer. The centre of the wood was impossible for either the Germans or your fellows to hold—a terrific concentration of artillery on it. The trees were splintered to matchwood. Late that night a brigade of the Seventh Division relieved the survivors; it included your First Battalion.'

1929, 1957

The Dead Fox Hunter

(In memory of Captain A. L. Samson, 2nd Battalion Royal Welch Fusiliers, killed near Cuinchy,[1] Sept. 25th, 1915)

We found the little captain at the head;
    His men lay well-aligned.
We touched his hand—stone cold—and he was dead,

---

7. Type of plum.
8. Roman Catholic.

1. Village in northern France.

And they, all dead behind,
5   Had never reached their goal, but they died well;
They charged in line, and in the same line fell.

The well-known rosy colours of his face
    Were almost lost in grey.
We saw that, dying and in hopeless case,
10   For others' sake that day
He'd smothered all rebellious groans: in death
His fingers were tight clenched between his teeth.

For those who live uprightly and die true
    Heaven has no bars or locks,
15   And serves all taste . . . or what's for him to do
    Up there, but hunt the fox?
Angelic choirs? No, Justice must provide
For one who rode straight and in hunting died.

So if Heaven had no Hunt before he came,
20   Why, it must find one now:
If any shirk and doubt they know the game,
    There's one to teach them how:
And the whole host of Seraphim° complete   *angels*
Must jog in scarlet to his opening Meet.

1916

Recalling War

Entrance and exit wounds are silvered clean,
The track aches only when the rain reminds.
The one-legged man forgets his leg of wood,
The one-armed man his jointed wooden arm.
5   The blinded man sees with his ears and hands
As much or more than once with both his eyes.
Their war was fought these twenty years ago
And now assumes the nature-look of time,
As when the morning traveller turns and views
10   His wild night-stumbling carved into a hill.

What, then, was war? No mere discord of flags
But an infection of the common sky
That sagged ominously upon the earth
Even when the season was the airiest May.
15   Down pressed the sky, and we, oppressed, thrust out
Boastful tongue, clenched fist and valiant yard.
Natural infirmities were out of mode,
For Death was young again: patron alone
Of healthy dying, premature fate-spasm.

20 Fear made fine bed-fellows. Sick with delight
    At life's discovered transitoriness,
    Our youth became all-flesh and waived the mind.
    Never was such antiqueness of romance,
    Such tasty honey oozing from the heart.
25 And old importances came swimming back—
    Wine, meat, log-fires, a roof over the head,
    A weapon at the thigh, surgeons at call.
    Even there was a use again for God—
    A word of rage in lack of meat, wine, fire,
30 In ache of wounds beyond all surgeoning.

    War was return of earth to ugly earth,
    War was foundering° of sublimities,   *collapsing*
    Extinction of each happy art and faith
    By which the world had still kept head in air,
35 Protesting logic or protesting love,
    Until the unendurable moment struck—
    The inward scream, the duty to run mad.

    And we recall the merry ways of guns—
    Nibbling the walls of factory and church
40 Like a child, piecrust; felling groves of trees
    Like a child, dandelions with a switch.
    Machine-guns rattle toy-like from a hill,
    Down in a row the brave tin-soldiers fall:
    A sight to be recalled in elder days
45 When learnedly the future we devote
    To yet more boastful visions of despair.

1935   1938

DAVID JONES
1895–1974

David Jones was born in Brockley, Kent, son of a Welsh father and an English mother, and studied at the Camberwell School of Art before joining the army in January 1915 to serve as a private soldier until the end of World War I—service that provided the material for his modern epic of war, *In Parenthesis*. He attended Westminster Art School after the war and subsequently made a name for himself as an illustrator, engraver, and watercolorist. In 1921 he joined the Roman Catholic Church and a few months later began working with the Catholic stone carver and engraver Eric Gill. Jones's Welsh and English origins, his visual sensitivity as an artist, and his interest in Catholic liturgy and ritual can be seen in his literary work, which includes the obscure but powerful long religious poem *The Anathémata* (1952) and *The Sleeping Lord and Other Fragments* (1973).

In Parenthesis, Jones's first literary work, was published in 1937 and won the Hawthornden Prize. Its seven parts, combining prose and poetry, evoke the activities of a

British infantry unit from its training in England to its participation in the Somme Offensive of July 1916. The work proceeds chronologically, beginning with a battalion parade in England before embarkation for France, moving to the preparation for the offensive, and concluding when the protagonist Private John Ball's platoon is destroyed. Far from a straightforward narrative, since every contemporary detail is associated with the heroic past, the poem echoes in carefully patterned moments Shakespeare's history plays, Malory's accounts of Arthurian quests, Welsh epics of heroic and futile battles, the Bible, and Catholic liturgy. Even so, *In Parenthesis* avoids the traditional epic concentration on high-ranking heroes and builds its narrative around ordinary characters, both English and Welsh. Identified with historical or mythological figures, they—Mr. Jenkins, Sergeant Snell, Corporal Quilter, Lance-Corporal Lewis, and John Ball, who is wounded in the leg, as Jones was at the First Battle of the Somme—are presented in vivid silhouettes and sudden stabs of personal memory.

Begun a decade after the armistice, *In Parenthesis* could not have been written when Wilfred Owen and Siegfried Sassoon wrote their war poems. Jones profits from the ways in which James Joyce's *Ulysses* and T. S. Eliot's *Waste Land* drew on mythology and ritual and thus gained depth and scope. He has combined the pity for and irony of the soldier that we see in Owen with the distanced, more elaborately illustrated, less immediately personal style of Eliot's long poem. And like Eliot, he introduces notes to help the reader follow the mythological and literary references. Unique among the soldier poets, Jones combines the immediacy of war poetry with high modernism's strategies of formal discontinuity and rich allusiveness. The poem conveys the texture of war experience through comic or sardonic references to popular soldiers' songs, to follies and vices and vanities and every kind of trivial behavior. At the same time the poem is multilayered and densely textured, its complex allusions to history, ritual, and heroic myth infusing the characters and the war with mysterious meaning.

The extracts printed here are, first, from Jones's preface, in which he explains his intention and method, and, second, from part 7, describing events during and after the attack. At the beginning of the last section quoted, Ball is wounded and crawling toward the rear through the mingled bodies of British and German soldiers. In his fevered imagination he sees the Queen of the Woods distributing flowers to the dead. He wonders whether he can continue carrying his rifle, which he finally leaves under an oak tree. (At the end of the medieval French epic *Chanson de Roland [Song of Roland]*, the dying Roland tries in vain to shatter his sword, Durendal, to prevent its being taken as a trophy by the Saracens; he finally puts it under his body.) In the end Ball lies still under the oak beside a dead German and a dead Englishman, hearing the reserves coming forward to continue the battle.

FROM IN PARENTHESIS

From Preface

This writing has to do with some things I saw, felt, & was part of. The period covered begins early in December 1915 and ends early in July 1916. The first date corresponds to my going to France. The latter roughly marks a change in the character of our lives in the Infantry on the West Front. From then onward things hardened into a more relentless, mechanical affair, took on a more sinister aspect. The wholesale slaughter of the later years, the conscripted levies filling the gaps in every file of four, knocked the bottom out of the intimate, continuing, domestic life of small contingents of men, within whose structure Roland could find, and, for a reasonable while, enjoy, his Oliver.[1] In the earlier months there was a certain attractive amateurishness, and elbow-room for idiosyncrasy that connected one with a less exacting past. The period of the individual rifle-man, of the "old sweat" of the Boer campaign, the "Bairns-father"[2] war, seemed to terminate with the Somme battle. There were, of course, glimpses of it long after—all through in fact—but it seemed never quite the same. * * *

My companions in the war were mostly Londoners with an admixture of Welshmen, so that the mind and folk-life of those two differing racial groups are an essential ingredient to my theme. Nothing could be more representative. These came from London. Those from Wales. Together they bore in their bodies the genuine tradition of the Island of Britain, from Bendigeid Vran to Jingle and Marie Lloyd. These were the children of Doll Tearsheet. Those are before Caractacus[3] was. Both speak in parables, the wit of both is quick, both are natural poets; yet no two groups could well be more dissimilar. It was curious to know them harnessed together, and together caught in the toils of "good order and military discipline"; to see them shape together to the remains of an antique regimental tradition, to see them react to the few things that united us—the same jargon, the same prejudice against "other arms" and against the Staff, the same discomforts, the same grievances, the same maims, the same deep fears, the same pathetic jokes; to watch them, oneself part of them, respond to the war landscape; for I think the day by day in the Waste Land, the sudden violences and the long stillnesses, the sharp contours and unformed voids of that mysterious existence, profoundly affected the imaginations of those who suffered it. It was a place of enchantment. It is perhaps best described in Malory,[4] book iv, chapter 15—that landscape spoke "with a grimly voice."

I suppose at no time did one so much live with a consciousness of the past, the very remote, and the more immediate and trivial past, both superficially and more subtly. No one, I suppose, however much not given to association, could see infantry in tin-hats, with ground-sheets over their shoulders, with sharpened pine-stakes in their hands, and not recall

> . . . or may we cram,
> Within this wooden O . . . [5]

But there were deeper complexities of sight and sound to make ever present

the pibble pabble in Pompey's camp.[6]

Every man's speech and habit of mind were a perpetual showing: now of Napier's expedition, now of the Legions at the Wall, now of "train-band captain," now of Jack Cade, of John Ball, of the commons in arms. Now of *High*

1. Roland's close friend and companion-at-arms in the medieval French epic *Chanson de Roland* (*Song of Roland*).
2. Bruce Bairnsfather (1888–1959), English cartoonist and journalist, best-known for his sketches of life in the trenches during World War I.
3. Caractacus or Caradoc, king of the Silures in the west of Britain during the reign of Roman emperor Claudius. He was taken to Rome as a prisoner in 51 C.E., but was pardoned by Claudius,

who was impressed by his nobility of spirit. Bendigeid Vran, hero in Welsh heroic legend. Alfred Jingle, character in Dickens's *Pickwick Papers*. Marie Lloyd (real name Matilda Alice Victoria Wood), English music-hall comedienne. Doll Tearsheet, prostitute in Shakespeare's *2 Henry IV*.
4. Sir Thomas Malory, author of *Morte Darthur*.
5. Shakespeare's *Henry V*, prologue, lines 12–13. The "wooden O" is the stage of the theater.
6. Cf. *Henry V* 4.1.71.

Germany, of *Dolly Gray,* of Bullcalf, Wart and Poins; of Jingo largenesses, of things as small as the Kingdom of Elmet; of Wellington's raw shire recruits, of ancient border antipathies, of our contemporary, less intimate, larger unities, of *John Barleycorn,* of "sweet Sally Frampton." Now of Coel Hên—of the Celtic cycle that lies, a subterranean influence as a deep water troubling, under every tump[7] in this Island, like Merlin[8] complaining under his big rock.[9] * * *

* * *

This writing is called *In Parenthesis* because I have written it in a kind of space between—I don't know between quite what—but as you turn aside to do something; and because for us amateur soldiers (and especially for the writer, who was not only amateur, but grotesquely incompetent, a knocker-over of piles, a parade's despair) the war itself was a parenthesis—how glad we thought we were to step outside its brackets at the end of '18—and also because our curious type of existence here is altogether in parenthesis.

D. J.

From Part 7: The Five Unmistakeable Marks[1]

> Gododdin I demand thy support.
> It is our duty to sing: a meeting
> place has been found.[2]

* * *

The gentle slopes are green to remind you
of South English places, only far wider and flatter spread and grooved and
harrowed criss-cross whitely and the disturbed subsoil heaped up albescent.[3]

Across upon this undulated board of verdure[4] chequered bright
when you look to left and right
small, drab, bundled pawns severally make effort
moved in tenuous line
and if you looked behind—the next wave came slowly, as successive surfs creep
in to dissipate on flat shore;
and to your front, stretched long laterally,

---

7. Mound or tumulus.
8. The powerful enchanter of the Arthurian legends.
9. The mass of references here provide a wide area of historical and literary association, beginning with *Henry V* and going on to refer to Sir William Napier, who fought in the Peninsular War and later wrote a famous history of that campaign; to the Roman legions who manned the Great Wall built by the Romans in Britain; to Jack Cade, who led an unsuccessful popular revolt against the misrule of Henry VI in 1450, and John Ball, a leader of the Peasants' Revolt of 1381; to a number of English ballads and popular songs and to characters in *Henry IV*; to the ancient British kingdom of Elmet in southwest Yorkshire, finally overthrown by Anglo-Saxon invaders early in the 7th century; to Wellington's "raw shire recruits," who helped win the Battle of Waterloo; and concluding with a reference to the old Celtic British myths that lie

beneath everything.
1. Carroll's *Hunting of the Snark,* Fit the 2nd verse 15 [Jones's note]. Lewis Carroll's mock-heroic nonsense poem concerns the hunting of the elusive animal Snark, which may be known by "five unmistakable marks." A reference to the five wounds of the crucified Christ may also be intended.
2. From *Y Gododdin,* early Welsh epical poem attributed to Aneirin (6th century); commemorates raid of 300 Welsh of Gododdin (the territory of the Otadini located near the Firth of Forth) into English kingdom of Deira. Describes the ruin of this 300 in battle at Catraeth (perhaps Catterick in Yorkshire). Three men alone escaped death, including the poet, who laments his friends [Jones's note].
3. Becoming white.
4. Green vegetation.

and receded deeply,
the dark wood.

And now the gradient runs more flatly toward the separate scarred saplings,
where they make fringe for the interior thicket and you take notice.
      There between the thinning uprights
at the margin
straggle tangled oak and flayed sheeny beech-bole, and fragile birch
      whose silver queenery is draggled and ungraced
and June shoots lopt
and fresh stalks bled
            runs the Jerry[5] trench.
And cork-screw stapled trip-wire
to snare among the briars
and iron warp with bramble weft[6]
with meadow-sweet and lady-smock
for a fair camouflage.

Mr Jenkins half inclined his head to them—he walked just barely in advance
of his platoon and immediately to the left of Private Ball.
      He makes the conventional sign
and there is the deeply inward effort of spent men who would make response
for him,
and take it at the double.
He sinks on one knee
and now on the other,
his upper body tilts in rigid inclination
this way and back;
weighted lanyard[7] runs out to full tether,
            swings like a pendulum
            and the clock run down.
Lurched over, jerked iron saucer over tilted brow,
clampt unkindly over lip and chin
nor no ventaille[8] to this darkening
            and masked face lifts to grope the air
and so disconsolate;
enfeebled fingering at a paltry strap—
buckle holds,
holds him blind against the morning.
      Then stretch still where weeds pattern the chalk predella[9]—
where it rises to his wire[1]—and Sergeant T. Quilter takes over.

                        *   *   *

It's difficult with the weight of the rifle.
Leave it—under the oak.
Leave it for a salvage-bloke[2]
let it lie bruised for a monument

---

5. British army slang for "German" in both world wars.
6. Warp and weft are the horizontal and vertical threads of woven cloth.
7. Short cord (here "weighted" by a whistle).
8. Hinged visor of a helmet.
9. A platform or shelf below or behind an altar.
1. The approach to the German trenches here rose slightly, in low chalk ridges [Jones's note].
2. Man (slang).

dispense the authenticated fragments to the faithful.
It's the thunder-besom for us
it's the bright bough borne
it's the tensioned yew for a Genoese jammed arbalest[3] and a scarlet square for
a mounted *mareschal*,[4] it's that county-mob back to back.[5] Majuba mountain
and Mons Cherubim[6] and spreaded mats for Sydney Street East,[7] and come
to Bisley for a Silver Dish.[8] It's R.S.M. O'Grady[9] says, it's the soldier's best
friend if you care for the working parts and let us be 'aving those springs
released smartly in Company billets on wet forenoons and clickerty-click and
one up the spout and you men must really cultivate the habit of treating this
weapon with the very greatest care and there should be a healthy rivalry among
you—it should be a matter of very proper pride and
    Marry it man! Marry it!
Cherish her, she's your very own.
    Coax it man coax it—it's delicately and ingeniously made—it's an instru-
ment of precision—it costs us tax-payers, money—I want you men to remember that.
    Fondle it like a granny—talk to it—consider it as you would a friend—
and when you ground these arms she's not a rooky's gas-pipe for greenhorns
to tarnish.[1]
You've known her hot and cold.
You would choose her from among many.
You know her by her bias, and by her exact error at 300, and by the deep scar
at the small, by the fair flaw in the grain, above the lower sling-swivel—
but leave it under the oak.

                ✳   ✳   ✳

The secret princes between the leaning trees have diadems given them.
    Life the leveller hugs her impudent equality—she may proceed at once
to less discriminating zones.

The Queen of the Woods has cut bright boughs of various flowering.
    These knew her influential eyes. Her awarding hands can pluck for each
their fragile prize.
    She speaks to them according to precedence. She knows what's due to
this elect society. She can choose twelve gentle-men. She knows who is most
lord between the high trees and on the open down.
    Some she gives white berries
        some she gives brown

3. A powerful medieval crossbow.
4. Marshal (French).
5. The Gloucestershire Regiment, during an action near Alexandria, in 1801, about-turned their rear rank and engaged the enemy back to back [Jones's note].
6. The British were defeated by the Boers on Majuba Hill on February 27, 1881. The "Angels of Mons" were angels (varying in number from two to a platoon) widely believed to have helped the British repel an attack at Mons by superior German forces on August 23, 1914.
7. In what became known as the Siege or Battle of Sydney Street, Winston Churchill, when he was home secretary in 1911, directed military operations in London against a group of anarchists. "It

is said that in 'The Battle of Sydney Street' under Mr. Churchill's Home Secretaryship mats were spread on the pavement for troops firing from the prone position" [Jones's note].
8. At Bisley marksmen compete annually in rifle shooting for trophies such as "a Silver Dish."
9. "R.S.M.": regimental sergeant major. "R.S.M. O'Grady," according to Jones's note, "refers to mythological personage figuring in Army exercises, the precise describing of which would be tedious. Anyway these exercises were supposed to foster alertness in dull minds—and were a curious blend of the parlour game and military drill."
1. I have employed here only such ideas as were common to the form of speech affected by Instructors in Musketry [Jones's note].

Emil has a curious crown it's
   made of golden saxifrage.
Fatty wears sweet-briar,
he will reign with her for a thousand years.
For Balder she reaches high to fetch his.
Ulrich smiles for his myrtle wand.
That swine Lillywhite has daisies to his chain—you'd hardly credit it.
She plaits torques[2] of equal splendour for Mr Jenkins and Billy Crower.
Hansel with Gronwy share dog-violets for a palm, where they lie in serious embrace beneath the twisted tripod.
Siôn gets St John's Wort—that's fair enough.
Dai Great-coat,[3] she can't find him anywhere—she calls both high and low, she had a very special one for him.
Among this July noblesse she is mindful of December wood—when the trees of the forest beat against each other because of him.
She carries to Aneirin-in-the-nullah[4] a rowan[5] sprig, or the glory of Guenedota.[6] You couldn't hear what she said to him, because she was careful for the Disciplines of the Wars.

At the gate of the wood you try a last adjustment, but slung so, it's an impediment, it's of detriment to your hopes, you had best be rid of it—the sagging webbing and all and what's left of your two fifty[7]—but it were wise to hold on to your mask.

You're clumsy in your feebleness, you implicate your tin-hat rim with the slack sling of it.
   Let it lie for the dews to rust it, or ought you to decently cover the working parts.
   Its dark barrel, where you leave it under the oak, reflects the solemn star that rises urgently from Cliff Trench.
   It's a beautiful doll for us
it's the Last Reputable Arm.
   But leave it—under the oak.
leave it for a Cook's tourist to the Devastated Areas and crawl as far
   as you can and wait for the bearers.[8]

1937

2. Collars, like those of gold worn by warriors of *Y Gododdin*.
3. Character whose first name is the familiar Welsh form of David, alluding to a figure in Malory's *Morte Darthur*.
4. A river, stream, or riverbed.
5. Also called mountain ash, a tree with magical properties in Celtic folklore.
6. The northwest parts of Wales. The last king of Wales, Llywelyn, was killed there in 1282. Jones refers to his death in another note on this part of Wales. He adds: "His [Llywelyn's] contemporary, Gruffydd ap yr Ynad Côch, sang of his death: 'The voice of lamentation is heard in every place . . . the course of nature is changed . . . the trees of the forest furiously rush against each other.' "
7. Two hundred and fifty rounds of ammunition.
8. This may appear to be an anachronism, but I remember in 1917 discussing with a friend the possibilities of tourist activity if peace ever came. I remember we went into details and wondered if the unexploded projectile lying near us would go up under a holiday-maker, and how people would stand up to be photographed on our parapets. I recall feeling very angry about this, as you do if you think of strangers ever occupying a house you live in, and which has, for you, particular associations [Jones's note].

Modernist Manifestos

At the beginning of the twentieth century, traditions and boundaries of many kinds were under assault across the Western world. Rapid developments in science and technology were transforming the texture of everyday life and conceptions of the universe; psychology, anthropology, and philosophy were challenging old ways of conceiving the human mind and religion; empire, migration, and city life were forcing together peoples of diverse origins. This dizzying pace of change, this break with tradition, this eruption of modernity can also be seen in the cutting-edge art and literature of the time. Avant-garde modernism caught fire in Europe in the decade before World War I. The Spanish expatriate artist Pablo Picasso's landmark cubist painting of 1907, *Les Demoiselles d'Avignon* (see the color insert), shattered centuries of artistic convention. Two years later the Italian poet F. T. Marinetti published his first futurist manifesto in the French journal *Le Figaro,* blasting the dead weight of "museums, libraries, and academies," glorifying "the beauty of speed." Written from 1911 to 1913, the Russian-born composer Igor Stravinsky's ballet *Le Sacre du Printemps* (*The Rite of Spring*) marked such a daring departure from harmonic and rhythmic traditions in Western classical music that its first performance, in Paris, sparked a riot. Like Picasso, Marinetti, and Stravinsky, other avant-garde modernists—advocates of radical newness in the arts—exploded conventions in music, painting, fiction, poetry, and other genres, opening up new formal and thematic possibilities for the twentieth century.

In just a few years the rebellious energies and convention-defying activities of avant-garde modernism swept through the major European cities, from Moscow and Milan to Munich, Paris, and London. Some of the leading figures of avant-garde modernism published manifestos, public declarations explaining, justifying, and promoting their ambitions and revolutionary views. The modernists were not the first artists to adapt the manifesto from the political sphere, but they used manifestos widely and vociferously, trumpeting iconoclastic ideas in terms that were meant not only to rally but also, in some cases, to shock. These documents were so influential that they have become an integral part of the history of modernism.

London, where the startling impact of cubism and futurism was felt almost immediately, became a central site in the formation of anglophone modernism. London's publishing opportunities and literary ferment attracted an array of visiting and expatriate writers. The American poet Ezra Pound arrived there in 1908, at twenty-three, and soon ignited London's literary avant-garde, his apartment in Kensington a magnet for like-minded innovators. He befriended the English philosopher poet T. E. Hulme, who led an avant-garde literary group. Like the cubists and futurists, these modernists advocated a radical break with artistic convention. In lectures Hulme influentially denounced Romanticism as so much moaning and whining and proposed a "hard, dry" literature in its stead—a notion Pound echoed in his call for "harder and saner" verse, "like granite." After T. S. Eliot came to England in 1914, astonishing Pound by his having "modernized himself *on his own,*" he also composed essays marked by Hulme's influence. Aggressively asserting new form and subject matter while holding up the standard of classic texts, the modernists repudiated what they saw as the slushy, self-indulgent literature of the nineteenth century—"blurry, messy," and "sentimentalistic," in Pound's words. This desire to break decisively with Romanticism and Victorianism—often realized more in theory than in practice— became a recurrent feature in their public declarations. The 1914 manifesto of the journal *Blast* thunders, "**BLAST** / years 1837 to 1900": like other avant-garde manifestos, this one damns the middle class for perpetuating Victorian taste and conventional mores. The agitations, declarations, and poetic experiments of Hulme, Pound, and others resulted in the formation of imagism. Leaders of this London-born movement advocated clear and immediate images, exact and efficient diction, inventive and musical rhythms. The imagist poem was to be brief and stripped down, presenting an image in as few words as possible without commenting on it. In his lecture "Romanticism and Classicism" Hulme said the poet must render "the exact curve of what he sees whether it be an object or an idea in the mind." Having arranged for the nascent movement to be announced by the English poet and critic F. S. Flint in a brief article/interview entitled "Imagisme" (spelled in the French manner), Pound demanded, through Flint's introductory synopsis of imagism's precepts, "Direct treatment of the 'thing,' whether subjective or objective." The principles of imagism and Pound's further recommendations in "A Few Don'ts by an Imagiste" had a profound transatlantic influence long after the movement had petered out.

The American poet H. D. (then called Hilda Doolittle) arrived in London in 1911, just in time to become a major figure in the imagist movement. Her poems, written under the influence of ancient Greek lyrical fragments, so impressed Pound that he sent them, signed "H. D. Imagiste" at his insistence, to Harriet Monroe, the founding editor of *Poetry*, a Chicago clearinghouse for modern verse. He told Monroe that H. D.'s poems were "modern" and "laconic," though classical in subject: "Objective—no slither; direct—no excessive use of adjectives, no metaphors that won't permit examination. It's straight talk, straight as the Greek!" Eventually H. D. and Pound wrote ambitious long poems that broke the mold of the imagist lyric, but even in their more capacious work, imagist compression, immediacy, and juxtaposition remained generative principles.

As early as 1914 Pound was tiring of imagism as too static and insufficiently rigorous. Together with the London-based English painter and writer Wyndham Lewis, he helped found a new modernist movement in the arts, vorticism, which emphasized dynamism of content. Pound conceived the vortex—an image of whirling, intensifying, encompassing energy—as the movement's emblem. Like imagism, vorticism lasted for only a few years. Its most raucous embodiment was the 1914 vorticist manifesto in Wyndham Lewis's journal *Blast,* and its main aesthetic achievements were Lewis's paintings and the London-based French artist Henri Gaudier-Brzeska's sculptures.

The *Blast* manifesto is clearly influenced by continental modernism, most visibly Italian futurism in the experimental layout and the fire-breathing rhetoric of destruction: the vorticists blast conventions, dull people, and middle-class attitudes. The English-born poet Mina Loy became closely involved with the leaders of the futurist movement, including Marinetti, while in Florence from 1906 to 1916. She was excited by futurism's embrace of modernity and its violent rebuke of tradition, but her typographically experimental "Feminist Manifesto" also marks a break with the movement's misogyny and jingoism. Marinetti, Pound, and Lewis—despite their progressive prewar views on many social and artistic matters—later embraced fascism, believing it would help advance their cultural ideals.

Modernist manifestos take on a variety of different forms. Some are individual statements, such as Hulme's lecture "Romanticism and Classicism." Others are meant to be declarations on behalf of an emergent group or movement, such as "A Few Don'ts by an Imagiste" or the *Blast* manifesto. Occasionally, and paradoxically, a manifesto is a nonpublic declaration, unpublished in the author's lifetime, as in the case of Loy's "Feminist Manifesto." Although the manifesto is not an art form in the same sense as a poem or painting is, manifestos became an important literary genre in the modernist era, and some are more than mere declarations of doctrine. The vorticist manifesto and Loy's "Feminist Manifesto," for example, cross poetry with poster art, creatively manipulating words on the page for maximum effect. In their jagged typography, wild energy, and radical individualism turned to a collective purpose, these modernist manifestos helped advance and now exemplify elements of innovative art through the twentieth century.

For more documents, images, and contexts related to this subject, see "Modernist Experiment" at Norton Literature Online.

T. E. HULME

Although he published only six poems during his brief life, T. E. Hulme (1883–1917), English poet, philosopher, and critic, was one of the strongest intellectual forces behind the development of modernism. In this essay, probably composed in either 1911 or 1912 and probably delivered as a lecture in 1912, Hulme prophesies a "dry, hard, classical verse" that exhibits precision, clarity, and freshness. He sharply repudiates the "spilt religion" of Romanticism, responsible for vagueness in the arts. Hulme sees human beings as limited and capable of improvement only through the influence of tradition. These ideas were an important influence on the thought and poetry of T. S. Eliot. Hulme's views of conventional language, the visual image, and verbal exactitude also shaped the imagism and vorticism of Ezra Pound and others.

Hulme was born in Staffordshire, England, and attended St. John's College, Cambridge, from which he was expelled for rebellious behavior in 1904 without finishing his degree. He lived mainly in London, where, befriending Pound and other poets and artists, he became a central figure of the prewar avant-garde. A critic of pacifism, Hulme enlisted as a private in the army when World War I broke out in 1914, and was killed in battle in 1917. First published posthumously in *Speculations* (1924), this essay is excerpted from *The Collected Writings of T. E. Hulme* (1994), ed. Karen Csengeri.

From Romanticism and Classicism

I want to maintain that after a hundred years of romanticism, we are in for a classical revival, and that the particular weapon of this new classical spirit, when it works in verse, will be fancy. * * *

I know that in using the words 'classic' and 'romantic' I am doing a dangerous thing. They represent five or six different kinds of antitheses, and while I may be using them in one sense you may be interpreting them in another. In this present connection I am using them in a perfectly precise and limited sense. I ought really to have coined a couple of new words, but I prefer to use the ones I have used, as I then conform to the practice of the group of polemical writers who make most use of them at the present day, and have almost succeeded in making them political catchwords. I mean Maurras, Lasserre and all the group connected with *L'Action Française*.[1]

At the present time this is the particular group with which the distinction is most vital. Because it has become a party symbol. If you asked a man of a

1. Charles Maurras (1868–1952) and Pierre Lasserre (1867–1930) were intellectuals associated with *l'Action Française*, a reactionary political movement that denigrated Romanticism and supported the Catholic Church as a force for order. (T. S. Eliot also fell under the movement's influence.)

certain set whether he preferred the classics or the romantics, you could deduce from that what his politics were.

The best way of gliding into a proper definition of my terms would be to start with a set of people who are prepared to fight about it—for in them you will have no vagueness. (Other people take the infamous attitude of the person with catholic tastes who says he likes both.)

About a year ago, a man whose name I think was Fauchois gave a lecture at the Odéon on Racine,[2] in the course of which he made some disparaging remarks about his dullness, lack of invention and the rest of it. This caused an immediate riot: fights took place all over the house; several people were arrested and imprisoned, and the rest of the series of lectures took place with hundreds of gendarmes[3] and detectives scattered all over the place. These people interrupted because the classical ideal is a living thing to them and Racine is the great classic. That is what I call a real vital interest in literature. They regard romanticism as an awful disease from which France had just recovered.

The thing is complicated in their case by the fact that it was romanticism that made the revolution.[4] They hate the revolution, so they hate romanticism.

I make no apology for dragging in politics here; romanticism both in England and France is associated with certain political views, and it is in taking a concrete example of the working out of a principle in action that you can get its best definition.

What was the positive principle behind all the other principles of '89? I am talking here of the revolution in as far as it was an idea; I leave out material causes—they only produce the forces. The barriers which could easily have resisted or guided these forces had been previously rotted away by ideas. This always seems to be the case in successful changes; the privileged class is beaten only when it has lost faith in itself, when it has itself been penetrated with the ideas which are working against it.

It was not the rights of man—that was a good solid practical war-cry. The thing which created enthusiasm, which made the revolution practically a new religion, was something more positive than that. People of all classes, people who stood to lose by it, were in a positive ferment about the idea of liberty. There must have been some idea which enabled them to think that something positive could come out of so essentially negative a thing. There was, and here I get my definition of romanticism. They had been taught by Rousseau[5] that man was by nature good, that it was only bad laws and customs that had suppressed him. Remove all these and the infinite possibilities of man would have a chance. This is what made them think that something positive could come out of disorder, this is what created the religious enthusiasm. Here is the root of all romanticism: that man, the individual, is an infinite reservoir of possibilities; and if you can so rearrange society by the destruction of oppressive order then these possibilities will have a chance and you will get Progress.

One can define the classical quite clearly as the exact opposite to this. Man is an extraordinarily fixed and limited animal whose nature is absolutely con-

---

2. Jean Racine (1639–1699), French tragic playwright associated with classicism. The riot occurred at a lecture delivered by French playwright René Fauchois (1882–1962) at the Odéon Theater, Paris, on November 3, 1910.
3. Police officers (French).

4. The French Revolution (1789–99).
5. Jean-Jacques Rousseau (1712–1778), Swiss-born French writer and philosopher whose ideas greatly influenced the leaders of the French Revolution and the development of Romanticism.

stant. It is only by tradition and organisation that anything decent can be got out of him.

✻   ✻   ✻

Put shortly, these are the two views, then. One, that man is intrinsically good, spoilt by circumstance; and the other that he is intrinsically limited, but disciplined by order and tradition to something fairly decent. To the one party man's nature is like a well, to the other like a bucket. The view which regards man as a well, a reservoir full of possibilities, I call the romantic; the one which regards him as a very finite and fixed creature, I call the classical.

One may note here that the Church has always taken the classical view since the defeat of the Pelagian heresy[6] and the adoption of the sane classical dogma of original sin.

It would be a mistake to identify the classical view with that of materialism. On the contrary it is absolutely identical with the normal religious attitude. I should put it in this way: That part of the fixed nature of man is the belief in the Deity. This should be as fixed and true for every man as belief in the existence of matter and in the objective world. It is parallel to appetite, the instinct of sex, and all the other fixed qualities. Now at certain times, by the use of either force or rhetoric, these instincts have been suppressed—in Florence under Savonarola, in Geneva under Calvin, and here under the Roundheads.[7] The inevitable result of such a process is that the repressed instinct bursts out in some abnormal direction. So with religion. By the perverted rhetoric of Rationalism, your natural instincts are suppressed and you are converted into an agnostic. Just as in the case of the other instincts, Nature has her revenge. The instincts that find their right and proper outlet in religion must come out in some other way. You don't believe in a God, so you begin to believe that man is a god. You don't believe in Heaven, so you begin to believe in a heaven on earth. In other words, you get romanticism. The concepts that are right and proper in their own sphere are spread over, and so mess up, falsify and blur the clear outlines of human experience. It is like pouring a pot of treacle[8] over the dinner table. Romanticism then, and this is the best definition I can give of it, is spilt religion.

I must now shirk the difficulty of saying exactly what I mean by romantic and classical in verse. I can only say that it means the result of these two attitudes towards the cosmos, towards man, in so far as it gets reflected in verse. The romantic, because he thinks man infinite, must always be talking about the infinite; and as there is always the bitter contrast between what you think you ought to be able to do and what man actually can, it always tends, in its later stages at any rate, to be gloomy. I really can't go any further than to say it is the reflection of these two temperaments, and point out examples of the different spirits. On the one hand I would take such diverse people as Horace, most of the Elizabethans and the writers of the Augustan age, and on the other side Lamartine, Hugo, parts of Keats, Coleridge, Byron, Shelley and Swinburne.[9]

---

6. Controversial Church doctrine denying the transmission of original sin, named after the theologian Pelagius (ca. 354–after 418).
7. Puritan members of the Parliamentary Party during the English Civil War (1642–51), named for their short haircuts. Girolamo Savonarola (1452–1498), Dominican monk who denounced the extravagance of the Renaissance. John Calvin

(1509–1564), Protestant theologian who stressed the predestination and the depravity of humankind.
8. Molasses (British).
9. Horace (65–8 B.C.E.), Roman poet. "The Elizabethans": English poets and playwrights (such as Shakespeare) writing during the reign of Queen Elizabeth I (1558–1603). "The Augustan age": the

* * *

What I mean by classical in verse, then, is this. That even in the most imaginative flights there is always a holding back, a reservation. The classical poet never forgets this finiteness, this limit of man. He remembers always that he is mixed up with earth. He may jump, but he always returns back; he never flies away into the circumambient gas.

You might say if you wished that the whole of the romantic attitude seems to crystallise in verse round metaphors of flight. Hugo is always flying, flying over abysses, flying up into the eternal gases. The word infinite in every other line.

In the classical attitude you never seem to swing right along to the infinite nothing. If you say an extravagant thing which does exceed the limits inside which you know man to be fastened, yet there is always conveyed in some way at the end an impression of yourself standing outside it, and not quite believing it, or consciously putting it forward as a flourish. You never go blindly into an atmosphere more than the truth, an atmosphere too rarefied for man to breathe for long. You are always faithful to the conception of a limit. It is a question of pitch; in romantic verse you move at a certain pitch of rhetoric which you know, man being what he is, to be a little high-falutin. The kind of thing you get in Hugo or Swinburne. In the coming classical reaction that will feel just wrong. * * *

* * *

I object even to the best of the romantics. I object still more to the receptive attitude.[1] I object to the sloppiness which doesn't consider that a poem is a poem unless it is moaning or whining about something or other. I always think in this connection of the last line of a poem of John Webster's which ends with a request I cordially endorse:

'End your moan and come away.'[2]

The thing has got so bad now that a poem which is all dry and hard, a properly classical poem, would not be considered poetry at all. How many people now can lay their hands on their hearts and say they like either Horace or Pope? They feel a kind of chill when they read them.

The dry hardness which you get in the classics is absolutely repugnant to them. Poetry that isn't damp isn't poetry at all. They cannot see that accurate description is a legitimate object of verse. Verse to them always means a bringing in of some of the emotions that are grouped round the word infinite.

The essence of poetry to most people is that it must lead them to a beyond of some kind. Verse strictly confined to the earthly and the definite (Keats is full of it) might seem to them to be excellent writing, excellent craftsmanship, but not poetry. So much has romanticism debauched us, that, without some form of vagueness, we deny the highest.

In the classic it is always the light of ordinary day, never the light that never

---

late seventeenth and early eighteenth centuries, when English writers such as John Dryden (1631–1700) and Alexander Pope (1688–1744) embraced a classicism likened to the Augustan Age of Rome. Alphonse Lamartine (1790–1869), French poet and politician. Victor Hugo (1802–1885), French poet and novelist. John Keats (1795–1821), Samuel Taylor Coleridge (1772–1834), George Gordon (Lord) Byron (1788–1824), Percy Bysshe Shelley (1792–1822), Algernon Charles Swinburne (1837–1909), English poets.

1. Elsewhere in the essay, Hulme claims that every sort of verse has an accompanying receptive attitude by which readers come to expect certain qualities from poetry. These receptive attitudes, he explains, sometimes outlast the poetry from which they develop.

2. From *The Duchess of Malfi* (1623) 4.2, by the English dramatist John Webster (ca. 1580–ca. 1625).

was on land or sea. It is always perfectly human and never exaggerated: man is always man and never a god.

But the awful result of romanticism is that, accustomed to this strange light, you can never live without it. Its effect on you is that of a drug.

✳   ✳   ✳

✳ ✳ ✳ It is essential to prove that beauty may be in small, dry things.

The great aim is accurate, precise and definite description. The first thing is to recognise how extraordinarily difficult this is. It is no mere matter of carefulness; you have to use language, and language is by its very nature a communal thing; that is, it expresses never the exact thing but a compromise—that which is common to you, me and everybody. But each man sees a little differently, and to get out clearly and exactly what he does see, he must have a terrific struggle with language, whether it be with words or the technique of other arts. Language has its own special nature, its own conventions and communal ideas. It is only by a concentrated effort of the mind that you can hold it fixed to your own purpose. I always think that the fundamental process at the back of all the arts might be represented by the following metaphor. You know what I call architect's curves—flat pieces of wood with all different kinds of curvature. By a suitable selection from these you can draw approximately any curve you like. The artist I take to be the man who simply can't bear the idea of that 'approximately'. He will get the exact curve of what he sees whether it be an object or an idea in the mind. I shall here have to change my metaphor a little to get the process in his mind. Suppose that instead of your curved pieces of wood you have a springy piece of steel of the same types of curvature as the wood. Now the state of tension or concentration of mind, if he is doing anything really good in this struggle against the ingrained habit of the technique, may be represented by a man employing all his fingers to bend the steel out of its own curve and into the exact curve which you want. Something different to what it would assume naturally.

✳   ✳   ✳

This is the point I aim at, then, in my argument. I prophesy that a period of dry, hard, classical verse is coming. I have met the preliminary objection founded on the bad romantic æsthetic that in such verse, from which the infinite is excluded, you cannot have the essence of poetry at all.

✳   ✳   ✳

✳ ✳ ✳ Poetry ✳ ✳ ✳ is a compromise for a language of intuition which would hand over sensations bodily. It always endeavours to arrest you, and to make you continuously see a physical thing, to prevent you gliding through an abstract process. It chooses fresh epithets and fresh metaphors, not so much because they are new, and we are tired of the old, but because the old cease to convey a physical thing and become abstract counters. A poet says a ship 'coursed the seas' to get a physical image, instead of the counter word 'sailed'. Visual meanings can only be transferred by the new bowl of metaphor; prose is an old pot that lets them leak out. Images in verse are not mere decoration, but the very essence of an intuitive language. Verse is a pedestrian taking you over the ground, prose—a train which delivers you at a destination.

✳   ✳   ✳

* * * The point is that exactly the same activity is at work as in the highest verse. That is the avoidance of conventional language in order to get the exact curve of the thing.

*　*　*

* * * A powerfully imaginative mind seizes and combines at the same instant all the important ideas of its poem or picture, and while it works with one of them, it is at the same instant working with and modifying all in their relation to it and never losing sight of their bearings on each other—as the motion of a snake's body goes through all parts at once and its volition acts at the same instant in coils which go contrary ways.

A romantic movement must have an end of the very nature of the thing. It may be deplored, but it can't be helped—wonder must cease to be wonder.

I guard myself here from all the consequences of the analogy, but it expresses at any rate the inevitableness of the process. A literature of wonder must have an end as inevitably as a strange land loses its strangeness when one lives in it. Think of the lost ecstasy of the Elizabethans. 'Oh my America, my new found land,'[3] think of what it meant to them and of what it means to us. Wonder can only be the attitude of a man passing from one stage to another, it can never be a permanently fixed thing.

1911–12   1924

3. Line 27 of John Donne's "To His Mistress Going to Bed."

F. S. FLINT AND EZRA POUND

In the March 1913 issue of *Poetry* magazine, the English poet and translator F. S. Flint published an article summarizing an interview with an unidentified "imagiste"— surely Ezra Pound. The article, partly dictated and rewritten by Pound, famously states the three principles of imagism—directness, economy, musical rhythm—which Pound later said he and the poets H. D. and Richard Aldington had agreed on in 1912. Flint's prefatory piece was followed in the same issue by Pound's manifesto, "A Few Don'ts by an Imagiste." There Pound defines the image and issues injunctions and admonitions to help poets strip their verse of unnecessary rhetoric and abstraction. Poets, he argues, should write direct, musically cadenced, image-grounded verse.

Born in London, F. S. Flint (1885–1960) worked in the British civil service, translated poetry (mostly French), and eventually published volumes of his own imagist poetry. Ezra Pound (1885–1972) was born in Hailey, Idaho, and was educated at the University of Pennsylvania and Hamilton College. During his twelve years in London, from 1908 to 1920, where he became closely associated with W. B. Yeats and T. E. Hulme, he was the most vigorous entrepreneur of literary modernism, helping James Joyce, T. S. Eliot, and other writers launch their careers. In London he also began working on material for his major work, the massive poem *The Cantos*. Living briefly in Paris and then for twenty years in Italy as an ardent supporter of the Fascist regime, he was arrested for treason in 1945, having made Rome Radio broadcasts against the U.S. war effort. He spent twelve years, from 1946 to 1958, in a Washington, D.C., asylum for the criminally insane before returning to Italy, where he fell into an almost complete silence until the end of his life.

Imagisme[1]

Some curiosity has been aroused concerning *Imagisme*, and as I was unable to find anything definite about it in print, I sought out an *imagiste*, with intent to discover whether the group itself knew anything about the "movement." I gleaned these facts.

The *imagistes* admitted that they were contemporaries of the Post Impressionists and the Futurists; but they had nothing in common with these schools. They had not published a manifesto. They were not a revolutionary school; their only endeavor was to write in accordance with the best tradition, as they found it in the best writers of all time,—in Sappho, Catullus, Villon.[2] They seemed to be absolutely intolerant of all poetry that was not written in such endeavor, ignorance of the best tradition forming no excuse. They had a few rules, drawn up for their own satisfaction only, and they had not published them. They were:

1. Direct treatment of the "thing," whether subjective or objective.

2. To use absolutely no word that did not contribute to the presentation.

3. As regarding rhythm: to compose in sequence of the musical phrase, not in sequence of a metronome.

By these standards they judged all poetry, and found most of it wanting. They held also a certain 'Doctrine of the Image,' which they had not committed to writing; they said that it did not concern the public, and would provoke useless discussion.

The devices whereby they persuaded approaching poetasters to attend their instruction were:

1. They showed him his own thought already splendidly expressed in some classic (and the school musters altogether a most formidable erudition).

2. They re-wrote his verses before his eyes, using about ten words to his fifty.

Even their opponents admit of them—ruefully—"At least they do keep bad poets from writing!"

I found among them an earnestness that is amazing to one accustomed to the usual London air of poetic dilettantism. They consider that Art is all science, all religion, philosophy and metaphysic. It is true that *snobisme* may be urged against them; but it is at least *snobisme* in its most dynamic form, with a great deal of sound sense and energy behind it; and they are stricter with themselves than with any outsider.

F. S. Flint

A Few Don'ts by an Imagiste

An "Image" is that which presents an intellectual and emotional complex in an instant of time. I use the term "complex" rather in the technical sense

---

1. In response to many requests for information regarding *Imagism* and the *Imagistes*, we publish this note by Mr. Flint, supplementing it with further exemplification by Mr. Pound. It will be seen from these that *Imagism* is not necessarily associated with Hellenic subjects, or with *vers libre* as a

prescribed form ["Editor's Note" from original]. "*Vers libre*": free verse (French).
2. François Villon (1431–after 1463), French poet. Sappho (fl. ca. 610–ca. 580 B.C.E.), Greek poet. Catullus (ca. 84–ca. 54 B.C.E.), Roman poet.

employed by the newer psychologists, such as Hart,[1] though we might not agree absolutely in our application.

It is the presentation of such a "complex" instantaneously which gives that sense of sudden liberation; that sense of freedom from time limits and space limits; that sense of sudden growth, which we experience in the presence of the greatest works of art.

It is better to present one Image in a lifetime than to produce voluminous works.

All this, however, some may consider open to debate. The immediate necessity is to tabulate A LIST OF DONT's for those beginning to write verses. But I can not put all of them into Mosaic negative.[2]

To begin with, consider the three rules recorded by Mr. Flint, not as dogma—never consider anything as dogma—but as the result of long contemplation, which, even if it is some one else's contemplation, may be worth consideration.

Pay no attention to the criticism of men who have never themselves written a notable work. Consider the discrepancies between the actual writing of the Greek poets and dramatists, and the theories of the Graeco-Roman grammarians, concocted to explain their metres.

Language

Use no superfluous word, no adjective, which does not reveal something. Don't use such an expression as "dim lands of *peace*." It dulls the image. It mixes an abstraction with the concrete. It comes from the writer's not realizing that the natural object is always the *adequate* symbol.

Go in fear of abstractions. Don't retell in mediocre verse what has already been done in good prose. Don't think any intelligent person is going to be deceived when you try to shirk all the difficulties of the unspeakably difficult art of good prose by chopping your composition into line lengths.

What the expert is tired of today the public will be tired of tomorrow.

Don't imagine that the art of poetry is any simpler than the art of music, or that you can please the expert before you have spent at least as much effort on the art of verse as the average piano teacher spends on the art of music.

Be influenced by as many great artists as you can, but have the decency either to acknowledge the debt outright, or to try to conceal it.

Don't allow "influence" to mean merely that you mop up the particular decorative vocabulary of some one or two poets whom you happen to admire. A Turkish war correspondent was recently caught red-handed babbling in his dispatches of "dove-gray" hills, or else it was "pearl-pale," I can not remember.

Use either no ornament or good ornament.

Rhythm and Rhyme

Let the candidate fill his mind with the finest cadences he can discover, preferably in a foreign language so that the meaning of the words may be less likely to divert his attention from the movement; e.g., Saxon charms, Hebri-

1. British psychologist Bernard Hart (1879–1966) discusses "the complex" in *The Psychology of Insanity* (1912), a book that helped popularize psycho-analysis.
2. Reference to the Ten Commandments delivered to Moses (Exodus 20).

dean Folk Songs, the verse of Dante, and the lyrics of Shakespeare—if he can dissociate the vocabulary from the cadence. Let him dissect the lyrics of Goethe[3] coldly into their component sound values, syllables long and short, stressed and unstressed, into vowels and consonants.

It is not necessary that a poem should rely on its music, but if it does rely on its music that music must be such as will delight the expert.

Let the neophyte know assonance and alliteration, rhyme immediate and delayed, simple and polyphonic, as a musician would expect to know harmony and counterpoint and all the minutiae of his craft. No time is too great to give to these matters or to any one of them, even if the artist seldom have need of them.

Don't imagine that a thing will "go" in verse just because it's too dull to go in prose.

Don't be "viewy"—leave that to the writers of pretty little philosophic essays. Don't be descriptive; remember that the painter can describe a landscape much better than you can, and that he has to know a deal more about it.

When Shakespeare talks of the "Dawn in russet mantle clad"[4] he presents something which the painter does not present. There is in this line of his nothing that one can call description; he presents.

Consider the way of the scientists rather than the way of an advertising agent for a new soap.

The scientist does not expect to be acclaimed as a great scientist until he has *discovered* something. He begins by learning what has been discovered already. He goes from that point onward. He does not bank on being a charming fellow personally. He does not expect his friends to applaud the results of his freshman class work. Freshmen in poetry are unfortunately not confined to a definite and recognizable class room. They are "all over the shop." Is it any wonder "the public is indifferent to poetry?"

Don't chop your stuff into separate *iambs*. Don't make each line stop dead at the end, and then begin every next line with a heave. Let the beginning of the next line catch the rise of the rhythm wave, unless you want a definite longish pause.

In short, behave as a musician, a good musician, when dealing with that phase of your art which has exact parallels in music. The same laws govern, and you are bound by no others.

Naturally, your rhythmic structure should not destroy the shape of your words, or their natural sound, or their meaning. It is improbable that, at the start, you will be able to get a rhythm-structure strong enough to affect them very much, though you may fall a victim to all sorts of false stopping due to line ends and caesurae.

The musician can rely on pitch and the volume of the orchestra. You can not. The term harmony is misapplied to poetry; it refers to simultaneous sounds of different pitch. There is, however, in the best verse a sort of residue of sound which remains in the ear of the hearer and acts more or less as an organ-base. A rhyme must have in it some slight element of surprise if it is to give pleasure; it need not be bizarre or curious, but it must be well used if used at all.

---

3. Johann Wolfgang von Goethe (1749–1832), German Romantic poet, playwright, and novelist.
4. From Horatio's speech in the opening scene of

Shakespeare's *Hamlet*: "But look, the morn in russet mantle clad / Walks o'er the dew of yon high eastern hill" (1.1.147–48).

Vide further Vildrac and Duhamel's notes on rhyme in *"Technique Poetique."*[5]

That part of your poetry which strikes upon the imaginative *eye* of the reader will lose nothing by translation into a foreign tongue; that which appeals to the ear can reach only those who take it in the original.

Consider the definiteness of Dante's presentation, as compared with Milton's rhetoric. Read as much of Wordsworth[6] as does not seem too unutterably dull.

If you want the gist of the matter go to Sappho, Catullus, Villon, Heine when he is in the vein, Gautier when he is not too frigid; or, if you have not the tongues, seek out the leisurely Chaucer.[7] Good prose will do you no harm, and there is good discipline to be had by trying to write it.

Translation is likewise good training, if you find that your original matter "wobbles" when you try to rewrite it. The meaning of the poem to be translated can not "wobble."

If you are using a symmetrical form, don't put in what you want to say and then fill up the remaining vacuums with slush.

Don't mess up the perception of one sense by trying to define it in terms of another. This is usually only the result of being too lazy to find the exact word. To this clause there are possibly exceptions.

The first three simple proscriptions[8] will throw out nine-tenths of all the bad poetry now accepted as standard and classic; and will prevent you from many a crime of production.

". . . *Mais d'abord il faut etre un poete,*"[9] as MM. Duhamel and Vildrac have said at the end of their little book, *"Notes sur la Technique Poetique"*; but in an American one takes that at least for granted, otherwise why does one get born upon that august continent!

Ezra Pound

5. Charles Vildrac (1882–1971), French poet, playwright, and critic, and Georges Duhamel (1884–1966), French novelist and critic, cowrote *Notes sur la Technique Poétique* (1910). *"Vide"*: consider.
6. John Milton (1608–1674) and William Words-worth (1770–1850), English poets.
7. Geoffrey Chaucer (ca. 1342–1400), English poet. Heinrich Heine (1797–1856), German poet. Théophile Gautier (1811–1872), French poet.
8. Noted by Mr. Flint [Pound's note].
9. But first it is necessary to be a poet (French).

AN IMAGIST CLUSTER:
T. E. HULME, EZRA POUND, H. D.

At the inception of imagism in London, the key imagists included the English poet philosopher T. E. Hulme and the expatriate American poets Ezra Pound and H. D. The paths of these three writers were densely interconnected at this juncture. In his poetry volume *Ripostes* (1912), Pound published an appendix of five poems, "The Complete Poetical Works of T. E. Hulme," prefaced by a note that printed the term *imagistes* for the first time. That year, in a London teashop, Pound had announced to the English poet Richard Aldington and the American poet H. D. that they were "imagistes," and two years later he included their and his work in the first imagist anthology, *Des Imagistes*. Although imagism began in London, with a French-styled name, the American poet Amy Lowell (1874–1925), derided by Pound for watering down imagism's principles, helped disseminate its ideas in the United States, where she publicized and promoted imagism in anthologies, lectures, and readings.

In spare, hard-edged poems the imagists sought to turn verse away from what they saw as the slack sentimentality and fuzzy abstraction, the explanatory excess and metrical predictability of Victorian poetry. Imagism owed a debt to the symbolism of Yeats and nineteenth-century French poets, but it shifted the emphasis from the musical to the visual, the mysterious to the actual, the ambiguously suggestive symbol to the clear-cut natural image. The imagists looked to models from East Asia (haiku for Pound's "In a Station in the Metro") and classical Europe (Greek verse for H. D.'s "Oread"). Their poetry is compressed, achieving a maximum effect with a minimum of words. It is often centered in a single figurative juxtaposition, conjoining tenor and vehicle without explanation. And it typically relies not on strict meters but on informal rhythms or cadences.

H. D. (1886–1961) was born Hilda Doolittle in Bethlehem, Pennsylvania, and educated at Bryn Mawr College. In 1911 she went to Europe for what she thought would be a brief visit but became a lifelong stay, mainly in England and in Switzerland. After her initial imagist phase she wrote more expansive works, including the three long, meditative poems that make up *Trilogy* (1973), precipitated by the experience of the London bombings in World War II.

T. E. HULME: Autumn

A touch of cold in the Autumn night—
I walked abroad,
And saw the ruddy moon lean over a hedge
Like a red-faced farmer.
5   I did not stop to speak, but nodded,
And round about were the wistful stars
With white faces like town children.

1912

EZRA POUND: In a Station of the Metro

The apparition of these faces in the crowd;
Petals on a wet, black bough.[1]

1913, 1916

1. Pound describes this poem's genesis in *Gaudier-Brzeska* (1916): "Three years ago in Paris I got out of a 'metro' train at La Concorde, and saw suddenly a beautiful face, and then another and another, and then a beautiful child's face, and then another beautiful woman, and I tried all that day to find words for what this had meant to me, and I could not find any words that seemed to me worthy, or as lovely as that sudden emotion. And that evening . . . I was still trying and I found, suddenly, the expression. I do not mean that I found words, but there came an equation . . . not in speech, but in little splotches of colour. . . . The 'one-image poem' is a form of super-position, that is to say, it is one idea getting out of the impasse in which I had been left by my metro emotion. I wrote a thirty-line poem, and destroyed it. . . . Six months later I made a poem half that length; a year later I made the following *hokku*-like sentence." "*Hokku*": another term for haiku.

H. D.: Oread[1]

Whirl up, sea—
Whirl your pointed pines,
Splash your great pines
On our rocks,
5   Hurl your green over us,
Cover us with your pools of fir.

1914

H. D.: Sea Rose

Rose, harsh rose,
marred and with stint of petals,
meagre flower, thin,
sparse of leaf,

5   more precious
than a wet rose,
single on a stem—
you are caught in the drift.

Stunted, with small leaf,
10 you are flung on the sands,
you are lifted
in the crisp sand
that drives in the wind.

Can the spice-rose
15 drip such acrid fragrance
hardened in a leaf?

1916

1. Greek nymph of the mountains.

BLAST

The journal *Blast* was published only twice—on June 20, 1914, though released on July 2, one month before Great Britain entered World War I, and a year later, during the war that would bring its short life to an end. But its initial preface and two-part manifesto, printed in the first pages of the first number and excerpted below, are among the most important documents in the history of modernism. They rhetorically and typographically embody the violent iconoclasm of vorticism, an avant-garde movement in the literary and visual arts centered in London. The English writer and painter Wyndham Lewis founded and edited *Blast*, whose title he said, "means the blowing away of dead ideas and worn-out notions" (it also suggests *fire, explosion,* and *damn!*). He drafted much of the vorticist manifesto and fashioned its shocking visual design, likening *Blast* to a "battering ram." Ezra Pound became a vorticist after abandoning imagism, because he felt that the *vortex,* "the point of maximum energy," offered a more dynamic model for art than the static image of the imagists. The French sculptor Henri Gaudier-Brzeska (1891–1915), killed in World War I and memorialized both in the "War Number" of *Blast* and in Pound's book named for him, was another key vorticist leader. In the pages of *Blast* 1 and 2, artworks by Lewis, Gaudier-Brzeska, and other visual artists appeared alongside writings by Lewis, Pound, T. S. Eliot, and other avant-gardists.

The vorticist manifesto, signed by Lewis, Pound, and Gaudier-Brzeska, among others, reflects the London modernists' competitive anxiety about European avant-gardes such as cubism and especially futurism. Under the charismatic leadership of F. T. Marinetti, the futurists celebrated speed, modernization, and the machine, while calling for the destruction of the museums, the libraries, all such bastions of the past. The vorticists—in lists of things and people to "**BLAST**" and "**BLESS**" compiled at group meetings—similarly blast convention, standardization, the middle class, even the "years 1837 to 1900." And yet despite their cosmopolitan enthusiasms, the vorticists also assert their independence, repeatedly criticizing the futurists. For all their antipathy toward England, they also "**BLESS**" it, revaluing, for example, English mobility (via the sea) and inventiveness (as the engine of the Industrial Revolution).

Wyndham Lewis (1882–1957) studied for several years at London's Slade School of Art before exploring the avant-garde visual arts in Paris. On returning to London in 1909, he began to write fiction and exhibit his paintings. During World War I he served as an artillery officer and then as a war artist, and afterward he continued to paint and publish essays, poetry, and fiction, including his first novel, *Tarr* (1918). Like Ezra Pound, he alienated many friends because of his subsequent support of fascism.

The excerpts below are taken from *Blast: Review of the Great English Vortex,* No. 1 (1914). For the complete two-part *Blast* manifesto and more on futurism and cubism, see "Modernist Experiment" at Norton Literature Online.

Long Live the Vortex!

Long live the great art vortex sprung up in the centre of this town![1]

We stand for the Reality of the Present—not for the sentimental Future, or the sacripant[2] Past.

We want to leave Nature and Men alone.

We do not want to make people wear Futurist Patches, or fuss men to take to pink and sky-blue trousers.[3]

---

1. London
2. Boastful of valor.
3. The futurists celebrated the technology, power, and dynamism of the modern age and sought to break with the past and traditional forms.

We are not their wives or tailors.

The only way Humanity can help artists is to remain independent and work unconsciously.

WE NEED THE UNCONSCIOUSNESS OF HUMANITY—Their stupidity, animalism and dreams.

We believe in no perfectibility except our own.

Intrinsic beauty is in the Interpreter and Seer, not in the object or content.

We do not want to change the appearance of the world, because we are not Naturalists, Impressionists or Futurists (the latest form of Impressionism),[4] and do not depend on the appearance of the world for our art.

WE ONLY WANT THE WORLD TO LIVE, and to feel it's crude energy flowing through us.

It may be said that great artists in England are always revolutionary, just as in France any really great artist had a strong traditional vein.

Blast sets out to be an avenue for all those vivid and violent ideas that could reach the Public in no other way.

Blast will be popular, essentially. It will not appeal to any particular class, but to the fundamental and popular instincts in every class and description of people, TO THE INDIVIDUAL. The moment a man feels or realizes himself as an artist, he ceases to belong to any milieu or time. Blast is created for this timeless, fundamental Artist that exists in everybody.

The Man in the Street and the Gentleman are equally ignored.

Popular art does not mean the art of the poor people, as it is usually supposed to. It means the art of the individuals.

Education (art education and general education) tends to destroy the creative instinct. Therefore it is in times when education has been non-existant that art chiefly flourished.

But it is nothing to do with "the People."

It is a mere accident that that is the most favourable time for the individual to appear.

To make the rich of the community shed their education skin, to destroy politeness, standardization and academic, that is civilized, vision, is the task we have set ourselves.

We want to make in England not a popular art, not a revival of lost folk art, or a romantic fostering of such unactual conditions, but to make individuals, wherever found.

We will convert the King[5] if possible.

A VORTICIST KING! WHY NOT?

DO YOU THINK LLOYD GEORGE[6] HAS THE VORTEX IN HIM?

MAY WE HOPE FOR ART FROM LADY MOND?[7]

4. Naturalism, a late-nineteenth-century school of realism, claimed all human life was governed by natural laws. Impressionism emphasized the subjectivity of perspective over any inherent quality in a represented object.
5. George V ascended the British throne in 1910 and remained the king until 1936.
6. David Lloyd George (1863–1945), British politician, prime minister 1916–22.
7. Wife of wealthy industrialist Sir Robert Mond, and a prominent member of fashionable London society.

We are against the glorification of "the People," as we are against snobbery. It is not necessary to be an outcast bohemian, to be unkempt or poor, any more than it is necessary to be rich or handsome, to be an artist. Art is nothing to do with the coat you wear. A top-hat can well hold the Sixtine. A cheap cap could hide the image of Kephren.[8]

AUTOMOBILISM (Marinetteism)[9] bores us. We don't want to go about making a hullo-bulloo about motor cars, anymore than about knives and forks, elephants or gas-pipes.

Elephants are VERY BIG. Motor cars go quickly.

Wilde gushed twenty years ago about the beauty of machinery. Gissing,[1] in his romantic delight with modern lodging houses was futurist in this sense.

The futurist is a sensational and sentimental mixture of the aesthete of 1890 and the realist of 1870.

The "Poor" are detestable animals! They are only picturesque and amusing for the sentimentalist or the romantic! The "Rich" are bores without a single exception, *en tant que riches!*[2]

We want those simple and great people found everywhere.

Blast presents an art of Individuals.

6

BLAST
years 1837 to 1900[1]
Curse abysmal inexcusable middle-class
(also Aristocracy and Proletariat).

BLAST
pasty shadow cast by gigantic Boehm[2]
(Imagined at introduction of BOURGEOIS VICTORIAN VISTAS).

8. Ancient Egyptian pharaoh buried in one of the great pyramids at Giza. "The Sixtine": the Sistine Chapel, in the Vatican.
9. Filippo Tommaso Marinetti (1876–1944), Italian writer and founder of Futurism, glorified war and technology and invented a "drama of objects" in which human actors play no parts.
1. George Gissing (1837–1903), naturalist English novelist. Oscar Wilde (1854–1900), Irish writer and critic; in his 1891 essay "The Soul of Man under Socialism," he writes: "All unintellectual

labour, all monotonous, dull labour, all labour that deals with dreadful things, and involves unpleasant conditions, must be done by machinery. . . . At *present machinery competes against man. Under proper conditions machinery will serve man.*"
2. Insofar as they are rich (French).
1. Queen Victoria reigned from 1837 to 1901. This sixth list of items in the "BLAST" section comes last, before the "BLESS" section.
2. Joseph Edgar Boehm (1834–1890) sculpted a colossal marble statue of Queen Victoria.

WRING THE NECK OF All sick inventions born in that progressive white wake.

BLAST their weeping whiskers—hirsute[3]

RHETORIC of EUNUCH and STYLIST—

SENTIMENTAL HYGIENICS

ROUSSEAUISMS[4] (Wild Nature cranks)

FRATERNIZING WITH MONKEYS

DIABOLICS—Raptures and roses
of the erotic bookshelves
culminating in

PURGATORY OF PUTNEY.[5]

CHAOS OF ENOCH ARDENS

> laughing Jennys
> Ladies with Pains
> good-for-nothing Guineveres.[6]

SNOBBISH BORROVIAN running after

GIPSY KINGS and ESPADAS[7]

bowing the knee to
wild Mother Nature,
her feminine contours,
Unimaginative insult to
MAN.

DAMN

all those to-day who have taken on that Rotten Menagerie,
and still crack their whips and tumble in Piccadilly Circus,
as though London were a provincial town.

---

3. Hairy.
4. Jean-Jacques Rousseau (1712–1778), French philosopher who argued that humans are good and noble in their natural state, before society and civilization corrupt them.
5. A middle-class London suburb.
6. In late-medieval romance, King Arthur's queen in Camelot; also, the title character in two narrative poems by the English poet Alfred, Lord Ten-nyson (1809–1892). "Enoch Arden" (1864) is another narrative poem by Tennyson, rejected here for its sentimentalism. Jenny is the title character of another sentimental poem (1870), by the English poet Dante Gabriel Rossetti (1828–1882).
7. Swords (Spanish). "Borrovian": from George Henry Borrow (1803–1881), English writer of popular gypsy romances, such as *The Zincali: An Account of the Gypsies of Spain* (1843).

WE WHISPER IN YOUR EAR A GREAT SECRET.

LONDON IS NOT A PROVINCIAL TOWN.

We will allow Wonder Zoos. But we do not want the

GLOOMY VICTORIAN CIRCUS[8] in Piccadilly Circus.

IT IS PICCADILLY'S CIRCUS!

NOT MEANT FOR MENAGERIES trundling out of Sixties DICKENSIAN CLOWNS, CORELLI LADY RIDERS,[9] TROUPS OF PERFORMING GIPSIES (who complain besides that 1/6 a night does not pay fare back to Clapham).[1]

BLAST[2]

The Post Office   Frank Brangwyn   Robertson Nicol

Rev. Pennyfeather   Galloway Kyle

(Bells)   (Cluster of Grapes)

Bishop of London and all his posterity

Galsworthy   Dean Inge   Croce   Matthews

Rev Meyer   Seymour Hicks

8. "Circus": here traveling entertainment act with animals and acrobats; also British traffic circle. "Wonder Zoos": traveling exhibition of exotic animals.

9. Marie Corelli, pseudonym of Mary Mackay (1855–1924), best-selling (and royal favorite) English writer of romances and religious novels in which she aimed to reform social ills. "Dickensian clowns": from the novels of English writer Charles Dickens (1812–1870).

1. Suburban district of London. "1/6": 18d, or a shilling and sixpence, then equivalent to about thirty-five cents.

2. Those blasted here range from individuals, such as Charles Burgess Fry, England's star cricket player and a tireless self-promoter, to things blasted seemingly for the thrill of doing so, such as codliver oil. Blasted, too, are institutions or members of the national, literary, or cultural establishment (e.g., the post office, a much-lauded model of Victorian efficiency, and the British Academy, established in 1902 by Royal Charter as the

Lionel Cust   C. B. Fry   Bergson   Abdul Bahai
Hawtrey   Edward Elgar   Sardlea
Filson Young   Marie Corelli   Geddes
Codliver Oil   St. Loe Strachey   Lyceum Club
Rhabindraneth Tagore   Lord Glenconner of Glen
Weiniger   Norman Angel   Ad. Mahon
Mr. and Mrs. Dearmer   Beecham   Ella
A. C. Benson   (Pills, Opera, Thomas)   Sydney Webb
British Academy   Messrs. Chapell
Countess of Warwick   George Edwards
Willie Ferraro   Captain Cook   R. J. Campbell
Clan Thesiger   Martin Harvey   William Archer
George Grossmith   R. H. Benson
Annie Besant   Chenil   Clan Meynell
Father Vaughan   Joseph Holbrooke   Clan Strachey

1914

national academy for humanities and social sciences), including various clergy and public leaders (e.g., Bishop of London; William Ralph Inge, dean of St. Paul's Cathedral; the Reverends Pennyfeather and Meyer; R. J. Campbell, English Congregationalist minister in the City Temple of London, and a Pantheist; Cardinal Herbert Vaughan, archbishop of Westminster and superior of the Catholic Missionary Society; Norman Angell, pacifist British economist; Arthur Christopher Benson, schoolmaster at Eton College, author of Edward VII's coronation ode). Critics unfriendly to the avant-garde are also included (e.g., William Archer, drama critic for the Nation; Sir William Robertson Nicoll, biblical editor and sometime literary critic; Lionel Cust, director of the National Portrait Gallery and contributor to the *Dictionary of National Biography*, etc.). Also blasted are artists and writers whom the Vorticists believed were meager talents in spite of their popularity (e.g., painter Frank Brangwyn, poet Ella Wheeler Wilcox, actors George Grossmith and Seymour Hicks, composers Joseph Holbrooke and Edward Elgar, etc.), as well as those associated with fads (e.g., Sir Abdul Baha Bahai, leader of the Bahai faith) or idealistic social reform (e.g., author Marie Corelli; Sidney Webb, a leader of the Fabian Socialist organization; Annie Besant, theosophist and suffragist). Some names (e.g., Indian poet Rabindranath Tagore) are misspelled. For a detailed discussion of the cursing and blessing in *Blast*, see William C. Wees, *Vorticism and the English Avant-Garde* (1972).

MINA LOY

Mina Loy (1882–1966) was born in London to a Protestant mother and a Jewish father. She began her artistic career in the visual arts, but she later became an experimental poet, writing lyrics and long poems that created a stir because of their poetic, linguistic, and sexual iconoclasm. From 1899 to 1916 she lived and worked mostly in Munich, Paris, and especially Florence. She moved to New York in 1916 and to Paris in 1923, then settled in the United States in 1936.

Loy composed this manifesto, which she considered a rough draft and never published, in November 1914 and sent it to her friend Mabel Dodge (1879–1962), American author and celebrated patron of the arts. In the decade before she wrote it, feminist activism had intensified in England, particularly the militant civil disobedience of Christabel Pankhurst and other suffragettes in the Women's Social and Political Union. Loy's piece, which bears fruitful comparison with the masculine *Blast* manifesto published a few months earlier, was partly the result of Loy's quarrels with the Italian futurists, with whom she was closely associated despite the movement's misogyny. In the manifesto Loy tries to harness for feminism the radicalism and individualism of the avant-garde, calling for a complete revolution of gender relations. She abandons the suffragette movement's central issue of equality and insists instead on an adversarial model of gender, claiming that women should not look to men for a standard of value but should find it within themselves. First published in *The Last Lunar Baedeker* (1982), the manifesto is reprinted from *The Lost Lunar Baedeker* (1996); both volumes were edited by Roger L. Conover.

For a sample of Loy's poetry, see "Modernist Experiment" at Norton Literature Online.

Feminist Manifesto

The feminist movement as at present instituted is

Inadequate

Women if you want to realise yourselves—you are on the eve of a devastating psychological upheaval—all your pet illusions must be unmasked—the lies of centuries have got to go— are you prepared for the **Wrench**—? There is no half-measure—NO scratching on the surface of the rubbish heap of tradition, will bring about **Reform**, the only method is

Absolute Demolition

Cease to place your confidence in economic legislation, vice-crusades & uniform education—you are glossing over

Reality.

Professional & commercial careers are opening up for you—

Is that all you want ?

And if you honestly desire to find your level without prejudice—be **Brave** & deny at the outset—that pathetic clap-trap war cry **Woman** **is** **the**
equal **of** **man**—

She is **NOT!** for

The man who lives a life in which his activities conform to a
social code which is a protectorate of the feminine element—
——is no longer **masculine**
The women who adapt themselves to a theoretical valuation of
their sex as a **relative** **impersonality** , are not yet
Feminine
Leave off looking to men to find out what you are **not** —seek
within yourselves to find out what you **are**
As conditions are at present constituted—you have the choice
between **Parasitism,** **& Prostitu-**
tion —or **Negation**

Men & women are enemies, with the enmity of the exploited
for the parasite, the parasite for the exploited—at present they
are at the mercy of the advantage that each can take of the
others sexual dependence—. The only point at which the
interests of the sexes merge—is the sexual embrace.

The first illusion it is to your interest to demolish is the
division of women into two classes   **the mistress,**
& the mother every well-balanced & developed woman
knows that is not true, Nature has endowed the complete
woman with a faculty for expressing herself through all her
functions—there are **no restrictions** the woman who is
so incompletely evolved as to be un-self-conscious in sex, will
prove a restrictive influence on the temperamental expansion
of the next generation; the woman who is a poor mistress will
be an incompetent mother—an inferior mentality—& will
enjoy an inadequate apprehension of **Life** .

To obtain results you must make sacrifices & the first &
greatest sacrifice you have to make is of your "virtue"
The fictitious value of woman as identified with her physical
purity—is too easy a stand-by——rendering her lethargic in
the acquisition of intrinsic merits of character by which she
could obtain a concrete value— therefore, the first self-
enforced law for the female sex, as a protection against the
man made bogey of virtue—which is the principle instrument
of her subjection, would be the unconditional surgical
destruction of virginity through-out the female population at
puberty—.

The value of man is assessed entirely according to his use or
interest to the community, the value of woman, depends
entirely on chance, her success or insuccess in manoeuvering
a man into taking the life-long responsibility of her—
The advantages of marriage of too ridiculously ample—
compared to all other trades—for under modern conditions a
woman can accept preposterously luxurious support from a
man (with-out return of any sort—even offspring)—as a thank
offering for her virginity
The woman who has not succeeded in striking that
advantageous bargain—is prohibited from any but
surreptitious re-action to Life-stimuli—& entirely
debarred maternity.
Every woman has a right to maternity—
Every woman of superior intelligence should realize her race-
responsibility, in producing children in adequate proportion to
the unfit or degenerate members of her sex—

Each child of a superior woman should be the result of a
definite period of psychic development in her life—& not
necessarily of a possibly irksome & outworn continuance of an
alliance—spontaneously adapted for vital creation in the
beginning but not necessarily harmoniously balanced as the
parties to it—follow their individual lines of personal
evolution—

For the harmony of the race, each individual should be the
expression of an easy & ample interpenetration of the male &
female temperaments—free of stress
Woman must become more responsible for the child than
man—
Women must destroy in themselves, the desire to be loved—

The feeling that it is a personal insult when a man transfers
his attentions from her to another woman
The desire for comfortable protection instead of an intelligent
curiosity & courage in meeting & resisting the pressure of life
sex or so called love must be reduced to its initial element,
honour, grief, sentimentality, pride & consequently jealousy
must be detached from it.
Woman for her happiness must retain her deceptive fragility of
appearance, combined with indomitable will, irreducible
courage, & abundant health the outcome of sound nerves—
Another great illusion that woman must use all her
introspective clear-sightedness & unbiassed bravery to
destroy—for the sake of her self respect is the impurity of sex
the realisation in defiance of superstition that there is nothing
impure in sex—except in the mental attitude to it—will
constitute an incalculable & wider social regeneration than it
is possible for our generation to imagine.

1914   1982

WILLIAM BUTLER YEATS
1865–1939

William Butler Yeats was born to an Anglo-Irish family in Dublin. His father, J. B.
Yeats, had abandoned law to take up painting, at which he made a somewhat precarious living. His mother came from the Pollexfen family that lived near Sligo, in the
west of Ireland, where Yeats spent much of his childhood. The Yeatses moved to
London in 1874, then returned to Dublin in 1880. Yeats attended first high school
and then art school, which he soon left to concentrate on poetry.

Yeats's father was a religious skeptic, but he believed in the "religion of art." Yeats,
religious by temperament but unable to believe in Christian orthodoxy, sought all his
life to compensate for his lost religion. This search led him to various kinds of mysticism, to folklore, theosophy, spiritualism, and neoplatonism. He said he "made a
new religion, almost an infallible church of poetic tradition."

Yeats's childhood and young manhood were spent between Dublin, London, and Sligo, and each of these places contributed something to his poetic development. In London in the 1890s he met the important poets of the day, founded the Irish Literary Society, and acquired late-Romantic, Pre-Raphaelite ideas of poetry: he believed, in this early stage of his career, that a poet's language should be dreamy, evocative, and ethereal. From the countryside around Sligo he gained a knowledge of the life of the peasantry and of their folklore. In Dublin, where he founded the National Literary Society, he was influenced by Irish nationalism and, although often disagreeing with those who wished to use literature for political ends, he nevertheless came to see his poetry as contributing to the rejuvenation of Irish culture.

Yeats's poetry began in the tradition of self-conscious Romanticism, strongly influenced by the English poets Edmund Spenser, Percy Shelley, and, a little later, William Blake, whose works he edited. About the same time he was writing poems (e.g., "The Stolen Child") deriving from his Sligo experience, with quietly precise nature imagery, Irish place-names, and themes from Irish folklore. A little later he drew on the great stories of the heroic age of Irish history and translations of Gaelic poetry into "that dialect which gets from Gaelic its syntax and keeps its still partly Tudor vocabulary." The heroic legends of ancient Ireland and the folk traditions of the modern Irish countryside helped brace his early dreamlike imagery. "The Lake Isle of Innisfree"— "my first lyric with anything in its rhythm of my own music," said Yeats—is both a Romantic evocation of escape into dream, art, and the imagination, and a specifically Irish reverie on freedom and self-reliance.

Yeats vigorously hybridizes Irish and English traditions, and eventually draws into this potent intercultural mix East and South Asian cultural resources, including Japanese Noh theater and Indian meditative practices. Resolutely Irish, he imaginatively reclaims a land colonized by the British; imposes Irish rhythms, images, genres, and syntax on English-language poetry; and revives native myths, place-names, and consciousness. Yet he is also cosmopolitan, insisting on the transnationalism of the collective storehouse of images he calls "Spiritus Mundi" or "Anima Mundi," spending much of his life in England, and cross-pollinating forms, ideas, and images from Ireland and England, Europe and Asia.

Irish nationalism first sent Yeats in search of a consistently simpler and more popular style, to express the elemental facts about Irish life and aspirations. This led him to the concrete image, as did translations from Gaelic folk songs, in which "nothing . . . was abstract, nothing worn-out." But other forces were also working on him. In 1902 a friend gave him the works of the German philosopher Friedrich Nietzsche, to which he responded with great excitement, and it would seem that, in persuading the passive love-poet to get off his knees, Nietzsche's books intensified his search for a more active stance, a more vigorous style. At the start of the twentieth century, Yeats wearied of his early languid aesthetic, declaring his intentions, in a 1901 letter, to make "everything hard and clear" and, in another of 1904, to leave behind "sentiment and sentimental sadness." He wished for poems not of disembodied beauty but that could "carry the normal, passionate, reasoning self, the personality as a whole." In poems of his middle period, such as "Adam's Curse" and "A Coat," Yeats combines the colloquial with the formal, enacting in his more austere diction, casual rhythms, and passionate syntax his will to leave behind the poetic "embroideries" of his youth and walk "naked." The American poet Ezra Pound, who spent winters from 1913 to 1916 with Yeats in a stone cottage in Sussex, strengthened Yeats's resolve to develop a less mannered, more stripped down style.

In 1889 Yeats had met the beautiful actor and Irish nationalist Maud Gonne, with whom he was desperately in love for many years, but who persistently refused to marry him. She became the subject of many of his early love poems, and in later poems, such as "No Second Troy" and "A Prayer for My Daughter," he expresses anger over her self-sacrifice to political activism. He had also met Lady Gregory, Anglo-Irish writer and promoter of Irish literature, in 1896, and Yeats spent many holidays at her aristocratic country house, Coole Park. Disliking the moneygrubbing and prudery of the middle classes, as indicated in "September 1913," he looked for his ideal characters either below them, to peasants and beggars, or above them, to the aristocracy, for each of these had their own traditions and lived according to them. Under Lady Gregory's influence Yeats began to organize the Irish dramatic movement in 1899 and, with her help, founded the Abbey Theater in 1904. His active participation in theatrical production—confronting political censorship, economic problems of paying carpenters and actors, and other aspects of "theatre business, management of men"—also helped toughen his style, as he demonstrates in "The Fascination of What's Difficult." Yeats's long-cherished hope had been to "bring the halves together"—Protestant and Catholic—through a literature infused with Ireland's ancient myths and cultural riches before the divisions between rival Christianities. But in a string of national controversies, he ran afoul of both the Roman Catholic middle class and the Anglo-Irish Protestant ascendancy, and at last, bitterly turning his back on Ireland, moved to England.

Then came the Easter Rising of 1916, led by men and women he had long known, some of whom were executed or imprisoned by the British. Persuaded by Gonne (whose estranged husband was one of the executed leaders) that "tragic dignity had returned to Ireland," Yeats returned. His culturally nationalist work had helped inspire the poet revolutionaries, and so he asked himself, as he put it in the late poem "Man and the Echo," did his work "send out / Certain men the English shot?" Yeats's nationalism and antinationalism, his divided loyalties to Ireland and to England, find powerfully ambivalent expression in "Easter, 1916" and other poems. Throughout his poetry he brilliantly mediates between contending aspects of himself—late-Romantic visionary and astringent modern skeptic, Irish patriot and irreverent antinationalist, shrewd man of action and esoteric dreamer. As he said: "We make out of the quarrel with others, rhetoric, but of the quarrel with ourselves, poetry." Conceiving consciousness as conflict, he fashioned a kind of poetry that could embody the contradictory feelings and ideas of his endless inner debate.

To mark his recommitment to Ireland, Yeats refurbished and renamed Thoor (Castle) Ballylee, the Norman tower on Lady Gregory's land, in which he lived off and on, and which became, along with its inner winding stair, a central symbol in his later poetry. In 1922 he was appointed a senator of the recently established Irish Free State, and he served until 1928, playing an active part not only in promoting the arts but also in general political affairs, in which he supported the views of the minority Protestant landed class. At the same time he was continuing his esoteric studies. He married Georgie (changed by Yeats to George) Hyde Lees in 1917, when he was fifty-two, and she proved so sympathetic to his imaginative needs that the automatic writing she produced for several years (believed by Yeats to have been dictated by spirits) gave him the elements of a symbolic system that he later worked out in his book *A Vision* (1925, 1937). The system was a theory of the movements of history and of the different types of personality, each movement and type being related to a different phase of the moon. At the center of the symbolic system were the interpenetrating cones, or "gyres," that represented the movement through major cycles of history and across antitheses of human personality.

He compressed and embodied his personal mythology in visionary poems of great scope, linguistic force, and incantatory power, such as "The Second Coming" and "Leda and the Swan." In poems of the 1920s and 1930s, winding stairs, spinning tops, "gyres," spirals of all kinds, are important symbols, serving as a means of resolving some of the contraries that had arrested him from the beginning—paradoxes of time and eternity, change and continuity, spirit and the body, life and art. If his earliest poetry was sometimes static, a beautifully stitched tapestry laden with symbols of inner states, his late poetry became more dynamic, its propulsive syntax and muscular rhythms more suited to his themes of lust, rage, and the body. He had once screened these out of his verse as unpoetic, along with war, violence, "the mire of human veins." Now he embraced the mortal world intensely. In "A Dialogue of Self and Soul," the self defies the soul's injunction to leave the world behind: "I am content to live it all again / And yet again, if it be life to pitch / Into the frog-spawn of a blind man's ditch." Yeats no longer sought transcendence of the human, but instead aimed for the active interpenetration of the corporeal and the visionary. In his Nietzsche-inspired poems of "tragic joy," such as "Lapis Lazuli," he affirmed ruin and destruction as necessary to imaginative creation.

One key to Yeats's greatness is that there are many different Yeatses: a hard-nosed skeptic and an esoteric idealist, a nativist and a cosmopolitan, an Irish nationalist and an ironic antinationalist, a Romantic brooding on loss and unrequited desire and a modernist mocking idealism, nostalgia, and contemporary society. Similarly, in his poetic innovations and consolidations, he is both a conservative and a radical. That is, he is a literary traditionalist, working within such inherited genres as love poetry, the elegy, the self-elegy, the sonnet, and the occasional poem on public themes. But he is also a restless innovator who disrupts generic conventions, breaking up the coherence of the sonnet, de-idealizing the dead mourned in elegies, and bringing into public poems an intense personal ambivalence. In matters of form, too, he rhymes but often in off-rhyme, uses standard meters but bunches or scatters their stresses, employs an elegant syntax that nevertheless has the passionate urgency of colloquial speech; his diction, tone, enjambments, and stanzas intermix ceremony with contortion, controlled artifice with wayward unpredictability. A difficulty in reading Yeats—but also one of the great rewards—is comprehending his manysidedness.

Like Pound, T. S. Eliot, and Windham Lewis, Yeats was attracted to right-wing politics, and in the 1930s he was briefly drawn to fascism. His late interest in authoritarian politics arose in part from his desire for a feudal, aristocratic society that, unlike middle-class culture, in his view, might allow the imagination to flourish, and in part from his anticolonialism, since he thought a fascist Spain, for example, would "weaken the British Empire." But eventually he was appalled by all political ideologies, and the grim prophecy of "The Second Coming" seemed to him increasingly apt.

Written in a rugged, colloquial, and concrete language, Yeats's last poems have a controlled yet startling wildness. His return to life, to "the foul rag-and-bone shop of the heart," is one of the most impressive final phases of any poet's career. In one of his last letters he wrote: "When I try to put all into a phrase I say, 'Man can embody truth but he cannot know it.' . . . The abstract is not life and everywhere draws out its contradictions. You can refute Hegel but not the Saint or the Song of Sixpence." He died in southern France just before the beginning of World War II. His grave is, as his poem directed, near Sligo, "under Ben Bulben." He left behind a body of verse that, in variety and power, has been an enduring influence for English-language poets around the globe, from W. H. Auden and Seamus Heaney to Derek Walcott and A. K. Ramanujan.

The Stolen Child[1]

Where dips the rocky highland
Of Sleuth Wood[2] in the lake,
There lies a leafy island
Where flapping herons wake
5   The drowsy water-rats;
There we've hid our faery vats,

---

1. I.e., a child stolen by fairies to be their companion, as in Irish folklore.
2. This and other places mentioned in the poem are in County Sligo, in the west of Ireland, where Yeats spent much of his childhood.

Full of berries
And of reddest stolen cherries.
Come away, O human child!
10 *To the waters and the wild*
With a faery, hand in hand,
For the world's more full of weeping than you can understand.

Where the wave of moonlight glosses
The dim grey sands with light,
15 Far off by furthest Rosses
We foot it all the night,
Weaving olden dances,
Mingling hands and mingling glances
Till the moon has taken flight;
20 To and fro we leap
And chase the frothy bubbles,
While the world is full of troubles
And is anxious in its sleep.
Come away, O human child!
25 *To the waters and the wild*
With a faery, hand in hand,
For the world's more full of weeping than you can understand.

Where the wandering water gushes
From the hills above Glen-Car,
30 In pools among the rushes
That scarce could bathe a star,
We seek for slumbering trout
And whispering in their ears
Give them unquiet dreams;
35 Leaning softly out
From ferns that drop their tears
Over the young streams.
Come away, O human child!
To the waters and the wild
40 *With a faery, hand in hand,*
For the world's more full of weeping than you can understand.

Away with us he's going,
The solemn-eyed:
He'll hear no more the lowing
45 Of the calves on the warm hillside
Or the kettle on the hob
Sing peace into his breast,
Or see the brown mice bob
Round and round the oatmeal-chest.
50 *For he comes, the human child,*
To the waters and the wild
With a faery, hand in hand,
From a world more full of weeping than he can understand.

1886, 1889

Down by the Salley Gardens[1]

Down by the salley gardens my love and I did meet;
She passed the salley gardens with little snow-white feet.
She bid me take love easy, as the leaves grow on the tree;
But I, being young and foolish, with her would not agree.

5 In a field by the river my love and I did stand,
And on my leaning shoulder she laid her snow-white hand.
She bid me take life easy, as the grass grows on the weirs;°   *dams*
But I was young and foolish, and now am full of tears.

1889

The Rose of the World[1]

Who dreamed that beauty passes like a dream?
For these red lips, with all their mournful pride,
Mournful that no new wonder may betide,
Troy[2] passed away in one high funeral gleam,
5 And Usna's children died.[3]

We and the labouring world are passing by:
Amid men's souls, that waver and give place
Like the pale waters in their wintry race,
Under the passing stars, foam of the sky,
10 Lives on this lonely face.

Bow down, archangels, in your dim abode:
Before you were, or any hearts to beat,
Weary and kind one lingered by His seat;
He made the world to be a grassy road
15 Before her wandering feet.

1892, 1895

1. Originally titled "An Old Song Resung," with Yeats's footnote: "This is an attempt to reconstruct an old song from three lines imperfectly remembered by an old peasant woman in the village of Ballysodare, Sligo, who often sings them to herself." "Salley": a variant of *sallow*, a species of willow tree.
1. The Platonic idea of eternal beauty. "I notice upon reading these poems for the first time for several years that the quality symbolized as The Rose differs from the Intellectual Beauty of Shelley and of Spenser in that I have imagined it as suffering with man and not as something pursued and seen from afar" [Yeats, in 1925]. Yeats wrote this poem to Maud Gonne.
2. Ancient city destroyed by the Greeks, according to legend, after the abduction of the beautiful Helen.
3. In Old Irish legend the Ulster warrior Naiose, son of Usna or Usnach (pronounced *Úskna*) carried off the beautiful Deirdre, whom King Conchubar of Ulster had intended to marry, and with his two brothers took her to Scotland. Eventually Conchubar lured the four of them back to Ireland and killed the three brothers.

The Lake Isle of Innisfree[1]

[handwritten annotation: 1 real line, split / 4 or 5 beats]

I will arise and go now, and go to Innisfree,
And a small cabin build there, of clay and wattles[2] made:
Nine bean-rows will I have there, a hive for the honey-bee,
And live alone in the bee-loud glade.

5   And I shall have some peace there, for peace comes dropping slow,
Dropping from the veils of the morning to where the cricket sings;
There midnight's all a glimmer, and noon a purple glow,
And evening full of the linnet's wings.

I will arise and go now, for always night and day
10 I hear lake water lapping with low sounds by the shore;
While I stand on the roadway, or on the pavements grey,
I hear it in the deep heart's core.

[handwritten annotation: its imagery has to do with sound]

1890   1890, 1892

The Sorrow of Love[1]

The brawling of a sparrow in the eaves,
The brilliant moon and all the milky sky,
And all that famous harmony of leaves,
Had blotted out man's image and his cry.

5   A girl arose that had red mournful lips
And seemed the greatness of the world in tears,
Doomed like Odysseus and the labouring ships
And proud as Priam murdered with his peers;[2]

Arose, and on the instant clamorous eaves,
10 A climbing moon upon an empty sky,
And all that lamentation of the leaves,
Could but compose man's image and his cry.

1891   1892, 1925

1. Inis Fraoigh (Heather Island) is a small island in Lough Gill, near Sligo, in the west of Ireland. In his autobiography Yeats writes: "I had still the ambition, formed in Sligo in my teens, of living in imitation of Thoreau on Innisfree . . . and when walking through Fleet Street [in London] very homesick I heard a little tinkle of water and saw a fountain in a shop-window which balanced a little ball upon its jet, and began to remember lake water. From the sudden remembrance came my poem *Innisfree,* my first lyric with anything in its rhythm of my own music."
2. Stakes interwoven with twigs or branches.
1. For earlier versions of this poem, see "Poems in Process," in the appendices to this volume.
2. Odysseus (whom the Romans called Ulysses) is the hero of Homer's *Odyssey,* which describes how, after having fought in the siege of Troy, he wandered for ten years before reaching his home, the Greek island of Ithaca. Priam was king of Troy at the time of the siege and was killed when the Greeks captured the city.

When You Are Old[1]

When you are old and grey and full of sleep,
And nodding by the fire, take down this book,
And slowly read, and dream of the soft look
Your eyes had once, and of their shadows deep;

5 How many loved your moments of glad grace,
And loved your beauty with love false or true,
But one man loved the pilgrim soul in you,
And loved the sorrows of your changing face;

And bending down beside the glowing bars,[2]
10 Murmur, a little sadly, how Love fled
And paced upon the mountains overhead
And hid his face amid a crowd of stars.

1891   1892, 1899

Who Goes with Fergus?[1]

Who will go drive with Fergus now,
And pierce the deep wood's woven shade,
And dance upon the level shore?
Young man, lift up your russet brow,
5 And lift your tender eyelids, maid,
And brood on hopes and fear no more.

And no more turn aside and brood
Upon love's bitter mystery;
For Fergus rules the brazen cars,°   *bronze chariots*
10 And rules the shadows of the wood,
And the white breast of the dim sea
And all dishevelled wandering stars.

1893

The Man Who Dreamed of Faeryland

He stood among a crowd at Drumahair;[1]
His heart hung all upon a silken dress,

1. A poem suggested by a sonnet by the French poet Pierre de Ronsard (1524–1585); it begins: "Quand vous serez bien vieille, au soir, à la chandelle" (When you are quite old, in the evening by candlelight).
2. I.e., of the grate.
1. In a late version of this Irish heroic legend, Fergus, "king of the proud Red Branch Kings," gave up his throne voluntarily to King Conchubar of Ulster to learn by dreaming and meditating the bitter wisdom of the poet and philosopher.
1. This and other place-names in the poem refer to places in County Sligo.

And he had known at last some tenderness,
Before earth took him to her stony care;
5   But when a man poured fish into a pile,
It seemed they raised their little silver heads,
And sang what gold morning or evening sheds
Upon a woven world-forgotten isle
Where people love beside the ravelled[2] seas;
10   That Time can never mar a lover's vows
Under that woven changeless roof of boughs:
The singing shook him out of his new ease.

He wandered by the sands of Lissadell;
His mind ran all on money cares and fears,
15   And he had known at last some prudent years
Before they heaped his grave under the hill;
But while he passed before a plashy place,
A lug-worm with its grey and muddy mouth
Sang that somewhere to north or west or south
20   There dwelt a gay, exulting, gentle race
Under the golden or the silver skies;
That if a dancer stayed his hungry foot
It seemed the sun and moon were in the fruit:
And at that singing he was no more wise.

25   He mused beside the well of Scanavin,
He mused upon his mockers: without fail
His sudden vengeance were a country tale,
When earthy night had drunk his body in;
But one small knot-grass growing by the pool
30   Sang where—unnecessary cruel voice—
Old silence bids its chosen race rejoice,
Whatever ravelled waters rise and fall
Or stormy silver fret the gold of day,
And midnight there enfold them like a fleece
35   And lover there by lover be at peace.
The tale drove his fine angry mood away.

He slept under the hill of Lugnagall;
And might have known at last unhaunted sleep
Under that cold and vapour-turbaned steep,
40   Now that the earth had taken man and all:
Did not the worms that spired about his bones
Proclaim with that unwearied, reedy cry
That God has laid His fingers on the sky,
That from those fingers glittering summer runs
45   Upon the dancer by the dreamless wave.
Why should those lovers that no lovers miss
Dream, until God burn Nature with a kiss?
The man has found no comfort in the grave.

1891, 1930

2. Tangled; here turbulent.

Antinomies

Adam's Curse[1]

Rhyming couplets, but messed up with droplines and no exact rhymes. Enough to monotony to break up and couplets.

We sat together at one summer's end,
That beautiful mild woman, your close friend,
And you and I,[2] and talked of poetry.
I said, "A line will take us hours maybe;
Yet if it does not seem a moment's thought,   5
Our stitching and unstitching has been naught.
Better go down upon your marrow-bones
And scrub a kitchen pavement, or break stones   *Art*
Like an old pauper, in all kinds of weather;
For to articulate sweet sounds together   10
Is to work harder than all these, and yet
Be thought an idler by the noisy set
Of bankers, schoolmasters, and clergymen
The martyrs call the world."   *drop line*

                                    And thereupon

Work heard. Ought to appear effortless

That beautiful mild woman for whose sake   15
There's many a one shall find out all heartache   *Beauty*
On finding that her voice is sweet and low
Replied, "To be born woman is to know—
Although they do not talk of it at school—
That we must labour to be beautiful."   20

I said, "It's certain there is no fine thing
Since Adam's fall but needs much labouring.   *work*
There have been lovers who thought love should be
So much compounded of high courtesy
That they would sigh and quote with learned looks   25
Precedents out of beautiful old books;   *Love*
Yet now it seems an idle trade enough."

We sat grown quiet at the name of love;
We saw the last embers of daylight die,
And in the trembling blue-green of the sky   30
A moon, worn as if it had been a shell
Washed by time's waters as they rose and fell
About the stars and broke in days and years.

I had a thought for no one's but your ears:
That you were beautiful, and that I strove   35
To love you in the old high way of love;
That it had all seemed happy, and yet we'd grown
As weary-hearted as that hollow moon.

Nov. 1902   1902, 1922

---

1. When Adam was evicted from the Garden of Eden, God cursed him with a life of toil and labor (Genesis 3.17–19).   2. The two women in the poem are modeled on Maud Gonne and her sister, Kathleen Pilcher (1868–1919).

No Second Troy

Why should I blame her[1] that she filled my days
With misery, or that she would of late
Have taught to ignorant men most violent ways,
Or hurled the little streets upon the great,
5   Had they but courage equal to desire?
What could have made her peaceful with a mind
That nobleness made simple as a fire,
With beauty like a tightened bow, a kind
That is not natural in an age like this,
10 Being high and solitary and most stern?
Why, what could she have done, being what she is?
Was there another Troy for her to burn?[2]

Dec. 1908   1910

The Fascination of What's Difficult[1]

The fascination of what's difficult
Has dried the sap out of my veins, and rent
Spontaneous joy and natural content
Out of my heart. There's something ails our colt[2]
5   That must, as if it had not holy blood
Nor on Olympus[3] leaped from cloud to cloud,
Shiver under the lash, strain, sweat and jolt
As though it dragged road metal. My curse on plays
That have to be set up in fifty ways,
10 On the day's war with every knave and dolt,
Theatre business, management of men.
I swear before the dawn comes round again
I'll find the stable and pull out the bolt.

Sept. 1909–Mar. 1910   1910

A Coat

I made my song a coat
Covered with embroideries
Out of old mythologies
From heel to throat;

1. Maud Gonne, whose revolutionary activities are at issue in the poem.
2. Helen of Troy was the legendary cause of the Trojan War and thus of Troy's destruction.
1. Written when Yeats was director-manager of the Abbey Theatre. "Subject. To complain of the fascination of what's difficult. It spoils spontaneity and pleasure, and wastes time. Repeat the line ending difficult three times and rhyme on bolt, exalt, colt, jolt" [Yeats's diary for September 1909].
2. Pegasus, in Greek mythology a winged horse associated with poetry.
3. A mountain in Greece; the home of the gods.

5 But the fools caught it,
Wore it in the world's eyes
As though they'd wrought it.
Song, let them take it,
For there's more enterprise
10 In walking naked.

1912   1914

September 1913

What need you,[1] being come to sense,
But fumble in a greasy till°   cash register
And add the halfpence to the pence
And prayer to shivering prayer, until
5 You have dried the marrow from the bone;
For men were born to pray and save:
Romantic Ireland's dead and gone,
It's with O'Leary[2] in the grave.

Yet they were of a different kind,
10 The names that stilled your childish play,
They have gone about the world like wind,
But little time had they to pray
For whom the hangman's rope was spun,
And what, God help us, could they save?
15 Romantic Ireland's dead and gone,
It's with O'Leary in the grave.

Was it for this the wild geese[3] spread
The grey wing upon every tide;
For this that all that blood was shed,
20 For this Edward Fitzgerald died,
And Robert Emmet and Wolfe Tone,[4]
All that delirium of the brave?
Romantic Ireland's dead and gone,
It's with O'Leary in the grave.

25 Yet could we turn the years again,
And call those exiles as they were

1. Members of the new, largely Roman Catholic middle class. When the art dealer Hugh Lane (d. 1915) offered to give his collection of French impressionist paintings to the city of Dublin, provided they were permanently housed in a suitable gallery, Yeats became angry over fierce public opposition to funding the project.
2. John O'Leary (1830–1907), Irish nationalist, who, after five years' imprisonment and fifteen years' exile, returned to Dublin in 1885; he rallied the young Yeats to the cause of literary nationalism.
3. Popular name for the Irish who, because of the penal laws against Catholics (1695–1727), were forced to flee to the Continent.
4. Theobald Wolfe Tone (1763–1798), one of the chief founders of the United Irishmen (an Irish nationalist organization) and leader of the 1798 Irish Rising, committed suicide in prison. Lord Edward Fitzgerald (1763–1798), British officer who, after being dismissed from the army for disloyal activities, joined the United Irishmen, helped lead the 1798 Irish Rising, and died in prison. Robert Emmet (1778–1803), a leader of the abortive 1803 Irish Nationalist Revolt, was hanged for treason.

In all their loneliness and pain,
You'd cry, "Some woman's yellow hair
Has maddened every mother's son":
30   They weighed so lightly what they gave.
But let them be, they're dead and gone,
They're with O'Leary in the grave.

Sept. 1913   1913

Easter, 1916[1]

I have met them at close of day
Coming with vivid faces
From counter or desk among grey
Eighteenth-century houses.
5   I have passed with a nod of the head
Or polite meaningless words,
Or have lingered awhile and said
Polite meaningless words,
And thought before I had done
10   Of a mocking tale or a gibe
To please a companion
Around the fire at the club,
Being certain that they and I
But lived where motley[2] is worn:
15   All changed, changed utterly:
A terrible beauty is born.

That woman's days were spent
In ignorant good-will,
Her nights in argument
20   Until her voice grew shrill.
What voice more sweet than hers
When, young and beautiful,
She rode to harriers?[3]
This man had kept a school
25   And rode our wingèd horse;[4]
This other his helper and friend[5]
Was coming into his force;
He might have won fame in the end,
So sensitive his nature seemed,
30   So daring and sweet his thought.

1. During the Easter Rising of 1916, Irish nationalists revolted against the British government and
proclaimed an Irish Republic. Nearly sixteen hundred Irish Volunteers and two hundred members
of the Citizen Army seized buildings and a park in
Dublin. The rebellion began on Easter Monday,
April 24, 1916, and was crushed in six days. Over
the next two weeks fifteen of the leaders were executed by firing squad. Yeats knew the chief nationalist leaders personally. For more on the Easter
Rising, see "Imagining Ireland" at Norton Literature Online.

2. The multicolored clothes of a jester.
3. Constance Gore-Booth (1868–1927), afterward Countess Markievicz, took a prominent role
in the uprising. Her death sentence was reduced
to imprisonment. The other rebel leaders to whom
Yeats refers were executed.
4. Padraic Pearse (1879–1916), founder of a boys'
school in Dublin and poet—hence the "winged
horse," or Pegasus, the horse of the Muses.
5. Thomas MacDonagh (1878–1916), poet and
dramatist.

This other man I had dreamed
A drunken, vainglorious lout.[6]
He had done most bitter wrong
To some who are near my heart,
35　Yet I number him in the song;
He, too, has resigned his part
In the casual comedy;
He, too, has been changed in his turn,
Transformed utterly:
40　A terrible beauty is born.

Hearts with one purpose alone
Through summer and winter seem
Enchanted to a stone
To trouble the living stream.
45　The horse that comes from the road,
The rider, the birds that range
From cloud to tumbling cloud,
Minute by minute they change;
A shadow of cloud on the stream
50　Changes minute by minute;
A horse-hoof slides on the brim,
And a horse plashes within it;
The long-legged moor-hens dive,
And hens to moor-cocks call;
55　Minute by minute they live:
The stone's in the midst of all.

Too long a sacrifice
Can make a stone of the heart.
O when may it suffice?
60　That is Heaven's part, our part
To murmur name upon name,
As a mother names her child
When sleep at last has come
On limbs that had run wild.
65　What is it but nightfall?
No, no, not night but death;
Was it needless death after all?
For England may keep faith
For all that is done and said.[7]
70　We know their dream; enough
To know they dreamed and are dead;
And what if excess of love
Bewildered them till they died?
I write it out in a verse—
75　MacDonagh and MacBride
And Connolly[8] and Pearse

6. Major John MacBride (1865–1916), Irish revolutionary and estranged husband of Maud Gonne.
7. In 1914 the English government had passed Home Rule for Ireland into law, but because of

World War I had suspended it, promising to implement it later.
8. James Connolly (1870–1916), a trade-union organizer and military commander of the rebellion.

Now and in time to be,
Wherever green is worn,
Are changed, changed utterly:
80   A terrible beauty is born.

May–Sept. 1916   1916, 1920

The Wild Swans at Coole[1]

The trees are in their autumn beauty,
The woodland paths are dry,
Under the October twilight the water
Mirrors a still sky;
5   Upon the brimming water among the stones
Are nine-and-fifty swans.

The nineteenth autumn has come upon me
Since I first made my count;[2]
I saw, before I had well finished,
10   All suddenly mount
And scatter wheeling in great broken rings
Upon their clamorous wings.

I have looked upon those brilliant creatures,
And now my heart is sore.
15   All's changed since I, hearing at twilight,
The first time on this shore,
The bell-beat of their wings above my head,
Trod with a lighter tread.

Unwearied still, lover by lover,
20   They paddle in the cold
Companionable streams or climb the air;
Their hearts have not grown old;
Passion or conquest, wander where they will,
Attend upon them still.

25   But now they drift on the still water,
Mysterious, beautiful;
Among what rushes will they build,
By what lake's edge or pool
Delight men's eyes when I awake some day
30   To find they have flown away?

Oct. 1916   1917

1. Coole Park, in County Galway, was the estate of the Irish playwright Lady Augusta Gregory (1852–1932).

2. Yeats made his first long visit to Coole in 1897; from then on he spent summers there, often staying into the fall.

In Memory of Major Robert Gregory[1]

1

Now that we're almost settled in our house
I'll name the friends that cannot sup with us
Beside a fire of turf° in th' ancient tower,[2]   peat
And having talked to some late hour
5   Climb up the narrow winding stair to bed:
Discoverers of forgotten truth
Or mere companions of my youth,
All, all are in my thoughts to-night being dead.

2

Always we'd have the new friend meet the old
10   And we are hurt if either friend seem cold,
And there is salt to lengthen out the smart
In the affections of our heart,
And quarrels are blown up upon that head;
But not a friend that I would bring
15   This night can set us quarrelling,
For all that come into my mind are dead.

3

Lionel Johnson[3] comes the first to mind,
That loved his learning better than mankind,
Though courteous to the worst; much falling he
20   Brooded upon sanctity
Till all his Greek and Latin learning seemed
A long blast upon the horn that brought
A little nearer to his thought
A measureless consummation that he dreamed.

4

25   And that enquiring man John Synge[4] comes next,
That dying chose the living world for text
And never could have rested in the tomb
But that, long travelling, he had come
Towards nightfall upon certain set apart
30   In a most desolate stony place,
Towards nightfall upon a race
Passionate and simple like his heart.

1. Robert Gregory (1881–1918) was the only child of Lady Augusta Gregory. The first printing of this elegy included the following note: "(Major Robert Gregory, R.F.C. [Royal Flying Corps], M.C. [Military Cross], Legion of Honour, was killed in action on the Italian Front, January 23, 1918)." For another of Yeats's poems on Gregory's death, see "Representing the Great War" at Norton Literature Online.
2. In 1917 Yeats purchased the Norman tower Thor Ballylee, near Lady Gregory's home in Coole Park. While that residence was being renovated, Yeats and his wife were living in a house that Lady Gregory had lent them.
3. English poet and scholar (1867–1902); he was "much falling" (line 19) because of his drinking.
4. Irish playwright (1871–1909), associated with the Irish literary renaissance and the Abbey Theatre. When Yeats first met Synge, in 1896, he encouraged him to travel to the Aran Islands ("a most desolate and stony place") and write about its rural residents.

5

And then I think of old George Pollexfen,[5]
In muscular youth well known to Mayo[6] men
35   For horsemanship at meets or at racecourses,
That could have shown how pure-bred horses
And solid men, for all their passion, live
But as the outrageous stars incline
By opposition, square and trine;[7]
40   Having grown sluggish and contemplative.

6

They were my close companions many a year,
A portion of my mind and life, as it were,
And now their breathless faces seem to look
Out of some old picture-book;
45   I am accustomed to their lack of breath,
But not that my dear friend's dear son,
Our Sidney[8] and our perfect man,
Could share in that discourtesy of death.

7

For all things the delighted eye now sees
50   Were loved by him;[9] the old storm-broken trees
That cast their shadows upon road and bridge;
The tower set on the stream's edge;
The ford where drinking cattle make a stir
Nightly, and startled by that sound
55   The water-hen must change her ground;
He might have been your heartiest welcomer.

8

When with the Galway foxhounds he would ride
From Castle Taylor to the Roxborough side[1]
Or Esserkelly plain, few kept his pace;
60   At Mooneen he had leaped a place
So perilous that half the astonished meet
Had shut their eyes; and where was it
He rode a race without a bit?
And yet his mind outran the horses' feet.

9

65   We dreamed that a great painter had been born[2]
To cold Clare[3] rock and Galway rock and thorn,
To that stern colour and that delicate line
That are our secret discipline

---

5. Yeats's maternal uncle (1839–1910), with whom he had spent holidays in Sligo as a young man.
6. County in western Ireland.
7. Terms from astrology, in which both Yeats and his uncle were interested.
8. Sir Philip Sidney (1554–1586), English poet and exemplar of the "Renaissance man"; like Gregory, he was killed in battle.

9. Robert Gregory encouraged Yeats to buy the tower.
1. Big country houses in County Galway. Roxborough was Lady Gregory's childhood home.
2. "Robert Gregory painted the Burren Hills and thereby found what promised to grow into a great style, but he had hardly found it before he was killed" (Yeats, "Ireland and the Arts").
3. County south of Galway.

Wherein the gazing heart doubles her might.
70 Soldier, scholar, horseman, he,
And yet he had the intensity
To have published all to be a world's delight.

10

What other could so well have counselled us
In all lovely intricacies of a house
75 As he that practised or that understood
All work in metal or in wood,
In moulded plaster or in carven stone?
Soldier, scholar, horseman, he,
And all he did done perfectly
80 As though he had but that one trade alone.

11

Some burn damp faggots,[4] others may consume
The entire combustible world in one small room
As though dried straw, and if we turn about
The bare chimney is gone black out
85 Because the work had finished in that flare.
Soldier, scholar, horseman, he,
As 'twere all life's epitome,
What made us dream that he could comb grey hair?

12

I had thought, seeing how bitter is that wind
90 That shakes the shutter, to have brought to mind
All those that manhood tried, or childhood loved
Or boyish intellect approved,
With some appropriate commentary on each;
Until imagination brought
95 A fitter welcome; but a thought
Of that late death took all my heart for speech.

June 1918   1918

The Second Coming

Turning and turning in the widening gyre[1]
The falcon cannot hear the falconer;
Things fall apart; the centre cannot hold;
Mere anarchy is loosed upon the world,
5 The blood-dimmed tide is loosed, and everywhere
The ceremony of innocence is drowned;
The best lack all conviction, while the worst
Are full of passionate intensity.[2]

---

4. Bundles of sticks.
1. Yeats's term (pronounced with a hard g) for a spiraling motion in the shape of a cone. He envisions the two-thousand-year cycle of the Christian age as spiraling toward its end and the next historical cycle as beginning after a violent reversal: "the end of an age, which always receives the revelation

of the character of the next age, is represented by the coming of one gyre to its place of greatest expansion and of the other to that of its greatest contraction" [Yeats's note].
2. The poem was written in January 1919, in the aftermath of World War I and the Russian Revolution and on the eve of the Anglo-Irish War.

Surely some revelation is at hand;
10   Surely the Second Coming is at hand.
The Second Coming![3] Hardly are those words out
When a vast image out of *Spiritus Mundi*[4]
Troubles my sight: somewhere in sands of the desert
A shape with lion body and the head of a man,
15   A gaze blank and pitiless as the sun,
Is moving its slow thighs, while all about it
Reel shadows of the indignant desert birds.
The darkness drops again; but now I know
That twenty centuries of stony sleep
20   Were vexed to nightmare by a rocking cradle,
And what rough beast, its hour come round at last,
Slouches towards Bethlehem[5] to be born?

Jan. 1919   1920, 1921

A Prayer for My Daughter

Once more the storm is howling, and half hid
Under this cradle-hood and coverlid
My child sleeps on.[1] There is no obstacle
But Gregory's wood[2] and one bare hill
5   Whereby the haystack- and roof-levelling wind,
Bred on the Atlantic, can be stayed;
And for an hour I have walked and prayed
Because of the great gloom that is in my mind.

I have walked and prayed for this young child an hour
10   And heard the sea-wind scream upon the tower,
And under the arches of the bridge, and scream
In the elms above the flooded stream;
Imagining in excited reverie
That the future years had come,
15   Dancing to a frenzied drum,
Out of the murderous innocence of the sea.

May she be granted beauty and yet not
Beauty to make a stranger's eye distraught,
Or hers before a looking-glass, for such,
20   Being made beautiful overmuch,
Consider beauty a sufficient end,
Lose natural kindness and maybe
The heart-revealing intimacy
That chooses right, and never find a friend.

3. Christ's second coming is heralded by the coming of the Beast of the Apocalypse, or Antichrist (1 John 2.18).
4. The spirit of the universe (Latin); i.e., Yeats said, "a general storehouse of images," a collective unconscious or memory, in which the human race preserves its past memories.

5. Jesus' birthplace.
1. Yeats's daughter and first child, Anne Butler Yeats, was born on February 26, 1919, in Dublin and brought home to Yeats's refitted Norman tower of Thoor Ballylee in Galway.
2. Lady Gregory's wood at Coole, only a few miles from Thoor Ballylee.

25 Helen being chosen found life flat and dull
    And later had much trouble from a fool,³
    While that great Queen, that rose out of the spray,⁴
    Being fatherless could have her way
    Yet chose a bandy-leggèd smith for man.
30 It's certain that fine women eat
    A crazy salad with their meat
    Whereby the Horn of Plenty⁵ is undone.

    In courtesy I'd have her chiefly learned;
    Hearts are not had as a gift but hearts are earned
35 By those that are not entirely beautiful;
    Yet many, that have played the fool
    For beauty's very self, has charm made wise,
    And many a poor man that has roved,
    Loved and thought himself beloved,
40 From a glad kindness cannot take his eyes.

    May she become a flourishing hidden tree
    That all her thoughts may like the linnet° be,   small songbird
    And have no business but dispensing round
    Their magnanimities of sound,
45 Not but in merriment begin a chase,
    Nor but in merriment a quarrel.
    O may she live like some green laurel
    Rooted in one dear perpetual place.

    My mind, because the minds that I have loved,
50 The sort of beauty that I have approved,
    Prosper but little, has dried up of late,
    Yet knows that to be choked with hate
    May well be of all evil chances chief.
    If there's no hatred in a mind
55 Assault and battery of the wind
    Can never tear the linnet from the leaf.

    An intellectual hatred is the worst,
    So let her think opinions are accursed.
    Have I not seen the loveliest woman⁶ born
60 Out of the mouth of Plenty's horn,
    Because of her opinionated mind
    Barter that horn and every good
    By quiet natures understood
    For an old bellows full of angry wind?

65 Considering that, all hatred driven hence,
    The soul recovers radical innocence
    And learns at last that it is self-delighting,

---

3. Menelaus, Helen's husband. Her abduction by
Paris precipitated the Trojan War.
4. Venus, born from the sea, was the Roman goddess of love; her husband, Vulcan, was the lame
god of fire and metalwork (line 29).

5. In Greek mythology the goat's horn that suckled the god Zeus flowed with nectar and ambrosia;
the cornucopia thus became a symbol of plenty.
6. Maud Gonne.

Self-appeasing, self-affrighting,
And that its own sweet will is Heaven's will;
70 She can, though every face should scowl
And every windy quarter howl
Or every bellows burst, be happy still.

And may her bridegroom bring her to a house
Where all's accustomed, ceremonious;
75 For arrogance and hatred are the wares
Peddled in the thoroughfares.
How but in custom and in ceremony
Are innocence and beauty born?
Ceremony's a name for the rich horn,
80 And custom for the spreading laurel tree.

Feb.–June 1919   1919, 1921

✗ Leda and the Swan[1]   *14 lines = Sonnet*

A sudden blow: the great wings beating still
Above the staggering girl, her thighs caressed
By the dark webs, her nape caught in his bill,
He holds her helpless breast upon his breast. *can't fight it*

5 How can those terrified vague fingers push
The feathered glory from her loosening thighs?
And how can body, laid in that white rush,   *Shakesperian rhyme*
But feel the strange heart beating where it lies?

this one event has large consequences. Fall of Troy / inevitability. Civilization.

A shudder in the loins engenders there *e*
10 The broken wall, the burning roof and tower[2] *f*
And Agamemnon dead. *drop line*
                        Being so caught up, *G*
So mastered by the brute blood of the air, *e*
Did she put on his knowledge with his power *f*
Before the indifferent beak could let her drop? *G*   *Petrarchian rhyme*

Sept. 1923   1924, 1928

---

1. In Greek mythology the god Zeus, in the form of a swan, raped Leda, a mortal. Helen, Clytemnestra, Castor, and Pollux were the children of this union. Yeats saw Leda's rape as the beginning of a new age, analogous with the dove's annunciation to Mary of Jesus' conception: "I imagine the annunciation that founded Greece as made to Leda, remembering that they showed in a Spartan temple, strung up to the roof as a holy relic, an unhatched egg of hers, and that from one of her eggs came love and from the other war" (*A Vision*). For the author's revisions while composing the poem, see "Poems in Process," in the appendices to this volume.

2. I.e., the destruction of Troy, caused by Helen's abduction by Paris. Agamemnon, the leader of the Greek army that besieged Troy, was murdered by his wife, Clytemnestra, the other daughter of Leda and the swan. *for good reason!*

✦ Sailing to Byzantium[1]

1

That is no country for old men. The young
In one another's arms, birds in the trees,
—Those dying generations—at their song,
The salmon-falls, the mackerel-crowded seas,
5 Fish, flesh, or fowl, commend all summer long
Whatever is begotten, born, and dies.
Caught in that sensual music all neglect
Monuments of unageing intellect.

2

An aged man is but a paltry thing,
10 A tattered coat upon a stick, unless
Soul clap its hands and sing,[2] and louder sing
For every tatter in its mortal dress,
Nor is there singing school but studying
Monuments of its own magnificence;
15 And therefore I have sailed the seas and come
To the holy city of Byzantium.

3

O sages standing in God's holy fire
As in the gold mosaic of a wall,[3]
Come from the holy fire, perne in a gyre,[4]
20 And be the singing-masters of my soul.
Consume my heart away; sick with desire
And fastened to a dying animal
It knows not what it is; and gather me
Into the artifice of eternity.

4

25 Once out of nature I shall never take
My bodily form from any natural thing,
But such a form as Grecian goldsmiths make
Of hammered gold and gold enamelling
To keep a drowsy Emperor awake;[5]
30 Or set upon a golden bough to sing
To lords and ladies of Byzantium
Of what is past, or passing, or to come.

Sept. 1926   1927

---

1. Yeats wrote in *A Vision:* "I think that if I could be given a month of Antiquity and leave to spend it where I chose, I would spend it in Byzantium [now Istanbul] a little before Justinian opened St. Sophia and closed the Academy of Plato [in the 6th century C.E.]. . . . I think that in early Byzantium, maybe never before or since in recorded history, religious, aesthetic and practical life were one, that architect and artificers . . . spoke to the multitude and the few alike. The painter, the mosaic worker, the worker in gold and silver, the illuminator of sacred books, were almost impersonal, almost perhaps without the consciousness of individual design, absorbed in their subject-matter and that the vision of a whole people."
2. The poet William Blake (1757–1827) saw the soul of his dead brother rising to heaven, "clapping his hands for joy."
3. The mosaics in San Apollinaire Nuovo, in Ravenna, Italy, depict rows of Christian saints on a gold background; Yeats saw them in 1907.
4. I.e., whirl in a spiral.
5. I have read somewhere that in the Emperor's palace at Byzantium was a tree made of gold and silver, and artificial birds that sang [Yeats's note].

Among School Children

1

I walk through the long schoolroom questioning;
A kind old nun in a white hood replies;
The children learn to cipher° and to sing,   *do arithmetic*
To study reading-books and history,
5   To cut and sew, be neat in everything
In the best modern way—the children's eyes
In momentary wonder stare upon
A sixty-year-old smiling public man.[1]

2

I dream of a Ledaean[2] body, bent
10   Above a sinking fire, a tale that she
Told of a harsh reproof, or trivial event
That changed some childish day to tragedy—
Told, and it seemed that our two natures blent
Into a sphere from youthful sympathy,
15   Or else, to alter Plato's parable,
Into the yolk and white of the one shell.[3]

3

And thinking of that fit of grief or rage
I look upon one child or t'other there
And wonder if she stood so at that age—
20   For even daughters of the swan can share
Something of every paddler's heritage—
And had that colour upon cheek or hair,
And thereupon my heart is driven wild:
She stands before me as a living child.

4

25   Her present image floats into the mind—
Did Quattrocento[4] finger fashion it
Hollow of cheek as though it drank the wind
And took a mess of shadows for its meat?
And I though never of Ledaean kind
30   Had pretty plumage once—enough of that,
Better to smile on all that smile, and show
There is a comfortable kind of old scarecrow.

5

What youthful mother, a shape upon her lap
Honey of generation had betrayed,
35   And that must sleep, shriek, struggle to escape
As recollection or the drug decide,[5]

1. Yeats, as part of his work in the Irish Senate, visited a Montessori school in Waterford in 1926.
2. A body like Leda's. Yeats associated her daughter, Helen of Troy, with Maud Gonne.
3. In the *Symposium*, by the Greek philosopher Plato (ca. 428–ca. 348 B.C.E.), Aristophanes argues that "the primeval man" was both male and female but was divided (like an egg separated into yoke and white); the resulting two beings come together in love to become one again.
4. I.e., the skill of a 15th-century Italian painter.
5. I have taken the "honey of generation" from Porphyry's essay on "The Cave of Nymphs" [Yeats's note]. Porphyry (ca. 234–ca. 305 C.E.) was a Neoplatonic philosopher.

Would think her son, did she but see that shape
With sixty or more winters on its head,
A compensation for the pang of his birth,
40   Or the uncertainty of his setting forth?

6

Plato thought nature but a spume that plays
Upon a ghostly paradigm of things;[6]
Solider Aristotle played the taws
Upon the bottom of a king of kings;[7]
45   World-famous golden-thighed Pythagoras[8]
Fingered upon a fiddle-stick or strings
What a star sang and careless Muses heard:
Old clothes upon old sticks to scare a bird.

7

Both nuns and mothers worship images,
50   But those the candles light are not as those
That animate a mother's reveries,
But keep a marble or a bronze repose.
And yet they too break hearts—O Presences
That passion, piety or affection knows,
55   And that all heavenly glory symbolise—
O self-born mockers of man's enterprise;

8

Labour is blossoming or dancing where
The body is not bruised to pleasure soul,
Nor beauty born out of its own despair,
60   Nor blear-eyed wisdom out of midnight oil.
O chestnut tree, great-rooted blossomer,
Are you the leaf, the blossom or the bole?°   *trunk*
O body swayed to music, O brightening glance,
How can we know the dancer from the dance?

June 1926   1927

A Dialogue of Self and Soul[1]

1

My Soul. I summon to the winding ancient stair;
Set all your mind upon the steep ascent,
Upon the broken, crumbling battlement,
Upon the breathless starlit air,
5   Upon the star that marks the hidden pole;

---

6. Plato thought nature merely an image of an ideal world that exists elsewhere.
7. Plato's student Aristotle (384–322 B.C.E.) was "solider" because he regarded this world as the authentic one. He tutored Alexander the Great (356–323 B.C.E.), the "king of kings," and disciplined him with the "taws," or leather strap.
8. Greek philosopher (ca. 580–500 B.C.E), known for his doctrine of the harmony of the spheres and

his discovery of the mathematical basis of musical intervals. His disciples, the Pythagoreans, venerated their master as a god with a golden thigh.
1. In a letter of October 2, 1923, Yeats wrote: "I am writing a new tower poem 'Sword and Tower,' which is a choice of rebirth rather than deliverance from birth. I make my Japanese sword and its silk covering my symbol of life." Junzo Sato, a friend, had given him the ceremonial sword in 1920.

Fix every wandering thought upon
That quarter where all thought is done:
Who can distinguish darkness from the soul?

My Self. The consecrated blade upon my knees
10   Is Sato's ancient blade, still as it was,
Still razor-keen, still like a looking-glass
Unspotted by the centuries;
That flowering, silken, old embroidery, torn
From some court-lady's dress and round
15   The wooden scabbard bound and wound,
Can, tattered, still protect, faded adorn.

My Soul. Why should the imagination of a man
Long past his prime remember things that are
Emblematical of love and war?
20   Think of ancestral night that can,
If but imagination scorn the earth
And intellect its wandering
To this and that and t'other thing,
Deliver from the crime of death and birth.

25   *My Self.* Montashigi, third of his family, fashioned it
Five hundred years ago, about it lie
Flowers from I know not what embroidery—
Heart's purple—and all these I set
For emblems of the day against the tower
30   Emblematical of the night,
And claim as by a soldier's right
A charter to commit the crime once more.

My Soul. Such fullness in that quarter overflows
And falls into the basin of the mind
35   That man is stricken deaf and dumb and blind,
For intellect no longer knows
Is from the *Ought,* or *Knower* from the *Known*—
That is to say, ascends to Heaven;
Only the dead can be forgiven;
40   But when I think of that my tongue's a stone.

2

My Self. A living man is blind and drinks his drop.
What matter if the ditches are impure?
What matter if I live it all once more?
Endure that toil of growing up;
45   The ignominy of boyhood; the distress
Of boyhood changing into man;
The unfinished man and his pain
Brought face to face with his own clumsiness;

The finished man among his enemies?—
50   How in the name of Heaven can he escape
That defiling and disfigured shape

The mirror of malicious eyes
Casts upon his eyes until at last
He thinks that shape must be his shape?
55   And what's the good of an escape
If honour find him in the wintry blast?

I am content to live it all again
And yet again, if it be life to pitch
Into the frog-spawn of a blind man's ditch,
60   A blind man battering blind men;
Or into that most fecund ditch of all,
The folly that man does
Or must suffer, if he woos
A proud woman not kindred of his soul.

65   I am content to follow to its source
Every event in action or in thought;
Measure the lot; forgive myself the lot!
When such as I cast out remorse
So great a sweetness flows into the breast
70   We must laugh and we must sing,
We are blest by everything,
Everything we look upon is blest.

July–Dec. 1927   1929

Byzantium[1]

The unpurged images of day recede;
The Emperor's drunken soldiery are abed;
Night resonance recedes, night-walkers' song
After great cathedral gong;
5   A starlit or a moonlit dome[2] disdains
All that man is,
All mere complexities,
The fury and the mire° of human veins.   deep mud

Before me floats an image, man or shade,
10   Shade more than man, more image than a shade;
For Hades' bobbin[3] bound in mummy-cloth
May unwind the winding path;[4]
A mouth that has no moisture and no breath

---

1. On October 4, 1930, Yeats sent his friend Sturge Moore a copy of this poem, saying: "The poem originates from a criticism of yours. You objected to the last verse of 'Sailing to Byzantium' because a bird made by a goldsmith was just as natural as anything else. That showed me that the idea needed exposition." The previous April, Yeats had noted in his diary: "Subject for a poem": "Describe Byzantium as it is in the system towards the end of the first Christian millennium. A walking mummy. Flames at the street corners where the soul is purified, birds of hammered gold singing in the golden trees, in the harbour [dolphins] offering their backs to the wailing dead that they may carry them to Paradise."
2. Of the great church of St. Sophia.
3. Spool. Hades was the Greek god of the underworld, the realm of the dead.
4. I.e., the spool of people's fate, which spins their destiny and which is wound like a mummy, may be unwound and lead to the timeless world of pure spirit.

Breathless mouths may summon;
15 I hail the superhuman;
I call it death-in-life and life-in-death.⁵

Miracle, bird or golden handiwork,
More miracle than bird or handiwork,
Planted on the starlit golden bough,
20 Can like the cocks of Hades crow,
Or, by the moon embittered, scorn aloud
In glory of changeless metal
Common bird or petal
And all complexities of mire or blood.

25 At midnight on the Emperor's pavement flit
Flames that no faggot° feeds, nor steel has lit,   *bundle of sticks*
Nor storm disturbs, flames begotten of flame,
Where blood-begotten spirits come
And all complexities of fury leave,
30 Dying into a dance,
An agony of trance,
An agony of flame that cannot singe a sleeve.

Astraddle on the dolphin's mire and blood,⁶
Spirit after spirit! The smithies break the flood,
35 The golden smithies of the Emperor!
Marbles of the dancing floor
Break bitter furies of complexity,
Those images that yet
Fresh images beget,
40 That dolphin-torn, that gong-tormented sea.

Sept. 1930   1932

Crazy Jane Talks with the Bishop¹

I met the Bishop on the road
And much said he and I.
"Those breasts are flat and fallen now
Those veins must soon be dry;
5 Live in a heavenly mansion,
Not in some foul sty."

"Fair and foul are near of kin,
And fair needs foul," I cried.
"My friends are gone, but that's a truth
10 Nor grave nor bed denied,

5. On Roman tombstones the cock is a herald of rebirth, thus of the continuing cycle of human life.
6. In ancient mythology dolphins were thought to carry the souls of the dead to the Isles of the Blessed.
1. One of a series of poems about an old woman partly modeled on Cracked Mary, an old woman who lived near Lady Gregory.

Learned in bodily lowliness
And in the heart's pride.

"A woman can be proud and stiff
When on love intent;
15   But Love has pitched his mansion in
The place of excrement;
For nothing can be sole or whole
That has not been rent."

Nov. 1931   1932

Lapis Lazuli

(For Harry Clifton)[1]

I have heard that hysterical women say
They are sick of the palette and fiddle-bow,
Of poets that are always gay,
For everybody knows or else should know
5   That if nothing drastic is done[2]
Aeroplane and Zeppelin[3] will come out,
Pitch like King Billy[4] bomb-balls in
Until the town lie beaten flat.

All perform their tragic play,
10   There struts Hamlet, there is Lear,
That's Ophelia, that Cordelia;
Yet they, should the last scene be there,
The great stage curtain about to drop,
If worthy their prominent part in the play,
15   Do not break up their lines to weep.
They know that Hamlet and Lear are gay;
Gaiety transfiguring all that dread.
All men have aimed at, found and lost;
Black out; Heaven blazing into the head:
20   Tragedy wrought to its uttermost.
Though Hamlet rambles and Lear rages,
And all the drop scenes drop at once
Upon a hundred thousand stages,
It cannot grow by an inch or an ounce.

25   On their own feet they came, or on shipboard,
Camel-back, horse-back, ass-back, mule-back,

1. The English writer Harry Clifton (1908–1978) gave Yeats for his seventieth birthday a piece of lapis lazuli, a deep blue stone, "carved by some Chinese sculptor into the semblance of a mountain with temple, trees, paths, and an ascetic and pupil about to climb the mountain. Ascetic, pupil, hard stone, eternal theme of the sensual east. The heroic cry in the midst of despair. But no, I am wrong, the east has its solutions always and therefore knows nothing of tragedy. It is we, not the east, that must raise the heroic cry" [Yeats to Dorothy Wellesley, July 6, 1935].
2. Because Europe was (in 1936) close to war.
3. German zeppelins, or airships, bombed London during World War I.
4. King William III (William of Orange), who defeated the army of King James II at the Battle of the Boyne, in Ireland, in 1690. In a popular ballad, "King William he threw his bomb-balls in, / And set them on fire."

Old civilisations put to the sword.
Then they and their wisdom went to rack:
No handiwork of Callimachus,[5]   *culture had been destroyed*
30 Who handled marble as if it were bronze,
Made draperies that seemed to rise
When sea-wind swept the corner, stands;
His long lamp chimney shaped like the stem
Of a slender palm, stood but a day;
35 All things fall and are built again
And those that build them again are gay.

Two Chinamen, behind them a third,
Are carved in Lapis Lazuli,
Over them flies a long-legged bird
40 A symbol of longevity;
The third, doubtless a serving-man,
Carries a musical instrument.

Every discolouration of the stone,   *expanding, imagining a scene, creating a world of Art in that Art. An object of Art*
Every accidental crack or dent
45 Seems a water-course or an avalanche,
Or lofty slope where it still snows
Though doubtless plum or cherry-branch
Sweetens the little half-way house
Those Chinamen climb towards, and I
50 Delight to imagine them seated there;
There, on the mountain and the sky,
On all the tragic scene they stare. *tragedy of the world.*
One asks for mournful melodies;
Accomplished fingers begin to play.
55 Their eyes mid many wrinkles, their eyes,
Their ancient, glittering eyes, are gay.

July 1936   *answer to despair: Art for art's sake, impulse to create lives through the worst*   *The importance of Art making. Art survives*   1938

Under Ben Bulben[1]

1

Swear by what the Sages spoke
Round the Mareotic Lake[2]
That the Witch of Atlas knew,
Spoke and set the cocks a-crow.

5. Athenian sculptor (5th century B.C.E.), supposedly the originator of the Corinthian column and of the use of the running drill to imitate folds in drapery in statues. Yeats wrote of him: "With Callimachus pure Ionic revives again . . . and upon the only example of his work known to us, a marble chair, a Persian is represented, and may one not discover a Persian symbol in that bronze lamp, shaped like a palm . . . ? But he was an archaistic workman, and those who set him to work brought back public life to an older form" (*A Vision*).
1. A mountain near Sligo; Yeats's grave is in sight of it, in Drumcliff churchyard.
2. Lake Mareotis, near Alexandria, Egypt, was an ancient center of Christian Neoplatonism and of neo-Pythagorean philosophy. The lake is mentioned in Percy Bysshe Shelley's poem "The Witch of Atlas." In an essay on Shelley, Yeats interprets the witch as a symbol of timeless, absolute beauty; passing in a boat by this and another lake, she "sees all human life shadowed upon its waters . . . and because she can see the reality of things she is described as journeying 'in the calm depths' of 'the wide lake' we journey over unpiloted."

5   Swear by those horsemen, by those women,
Complexion and form prove superhuman,[3]
That pale, long visaged company
That airs an immortality
Completeness of their passions won;
10   Now they ride the wintry dawn
Where Ben Bulben sets the scene.

Here's the gist of what they mean.

2

Many times man lives and dies
Between his two eternities,
15   That of race and that of soul,
And ancient Ireland knew it all.
Whether man dies in his bed
Or the rifle knocks him dead,
A brief parting from those dear
20   Is the worst man has to fear.
Though grave-diggers' toil is long,
Sharp their spades, their muscle strong,
They but thrust their buried men
Back in the human mind again.

3

25   You that Mitchel's prayer have heard
"Send war in our time, O Lord!"[4]
Know that when all words are said
And a man is fighting mad,
Something drops from eyes long blind
30   He completes his partial mind,
For an instant stands at ease,
Laughs aloud, his heart at peace,
Even the wisest man grows tense
With some sort of violence
35   Before he can accomplish fate
Know his work or choose his mate.

4

Poet and sculptor do the work
Nor let the modish painter shirk
What his great forefathers did,
40   Bring the soul of man to God,
Make him fill the cradles right.

---

3. Superhuman beings or fairies, like the Sidhe, believed to ride through the countryside near Ben Bulben.

4. From *Jail Journal*, by the Irish nationalist John Mitchel (1815–1875).

Measurement began our might:
Forms a stark Egyptian thought,
Forms that gentler Phidias[5] wrought.

45 Michael Angelo left a proof
On the Sistine Chapel roof,
Where but half-awakened Adam
Can disturb globe-trotting Madam
Till her bowels are in heat,
50 Proof that there's a purpose set
Before the secret working mind:
Profane perfection of mankind.

Quattrocento[6] put in paint,
On backgrounds for a God or Saint,
55 Gardens where a soul's at ease;
Where everything that meets the eye
Flowers and grass and cloudless sky
Resemble forms that are, or seem
When sleepers wake and yet still dream,
60 And when it's vanished still declare,
With only bed and bedstead there,
That Heavens had opened.

                              Gyres[7] run on;
When that greater dream had gone
Calvert and Wilson, Blake and Claude[8]
65 Prepared a rest for the people of God,
Palmer's[9] phrase, but after that
Confusion fell upon our thought.

                    5

Irish poets learn your trade
Sing whatever is well made,
70 Scorn the sort now growing up
All out of shape from toe to top,
Their unremembering hearts and heads
Base-born products of base beds.
Sing the peasantry, and then
75 Hard-riding country gentlemen,
The holiness of monks, and after
Porter-drinkers'[1] randy laughter;
Sing the lords and ladies gay
That were beaten into the clay

---

5. Greek sculptor (fl. ca. 490–430 B.C.E.).
6. 15th-century Italian art.
7. Yeats's term for conelike spirals or cycles of history.
8. Edward Calvert (1799–1883), English visionary artist and follower of William Blake (1757–1827), English mystical poet and artist. Richard

Wilson (1714–1782), English landscape painter and disciple of Claude Lorraine (1600–1682), French artist.
9. Samuel Palmer (1805–1881), English landscape painter who admired Blake.
1. Drinkers of dark brown bitter beer.

80 Through seven heroic centuries;[2]
    Cast your mind on other days
    That we in coming days may be
    Still the indomitable Irishry.

                        6

    Under bare Ben Bulben's head
85 In Drumcliff churchyard Yeats is laid,
    An ancestor was rector there[3]
    Long years ago; a church stands near,
    By the road an ancient Cross.
    No marble, no conventional phrase,
90 On limestone quarried near the spot
    By his command these words are cut:

            Cast a cold eye
            On life, on death.
            Horseman, pass by!

Sept. 1938   1939

                Man and the Echo

    Man. In a cleft that's christened Alt
        Under broken stone I halt
        At the bottom of a pit
        That broad noon has never lit,
5   And shout a secret to the stone.
        All that I have said and done,
        Now that I am old and ill,
        Turns into a question till
        I lie awake night after night
10   And never get the answers right.
        Did that play of mine[1] send out
        Certain men the English shot?
        Did words of mine put too great strain
        On that woman's reeling brain?[2]
15   Could my spoken words have checked
        That whereby a house[3] lay wrecked?
        And all seems evil until I
        Sleepless would lie down and die.

    Echo. Lie down and die.

---

2. Since the Norman conquest of Ireland, in the 12th century.
3. Yeats's great-grandfather, the Reverend John Yeats (1774–1846), was rector of Drumcliff Church, Sligo.
1. *Cathleen ni Houlihan*, a nationalist play Yeats wrote with Lady Gregory and in which Maud Gonne played the title role in 1902. It helped inspire the Easter Rising of 1916.
2. Margot Ruddock (1907–1951), a young poet with whom Yeats had a brief affair in the 1930s and to whom he offered financial support when she suffered a nervous breakdown.
3. Coole Park, Lady Gregory's home, in disrepair since her death in 1932.

Man.   That were to shirk
20   The spiritual intellect's great work
      And shirk it in vain. There is no release
      In a bodkin[4] or disease,
      Nor can there be a work so great
      As that which cleans man's dirty slate.
25   While man can still his body keep
      Wine or love drug him to sleep,
      Waking he thanks the Lord that he
      Has body and its stupidity,
      But body gone he sleeps no more
30   And till his intellect grows sure
      That all's arranged in one clear view
      Pursues the thoughts that I pursue,
      Then stands in judgment on his soul,
      And, all work done, dismisses all
35   Out of intellect and sight
      And sinks at last into the night.

Echo. Into the night.

Man.   O rocky voice
      Shall we in that great night rejoice?
      What do we know but that we face
40   One another in this place?
      But hush, for I have lost the theme
      Its joy or night seem but a dream;
      Up there some hawk or owl has struck
      Dropping out of sky or rock,
45   A stricken rabbit is crying out
      And its cry distracts my thought.

1938   1939

The Circus Animals' Desertion

1

      I sought a theme and sought for it in vain,
      I sought it daily for six weeks or so.
      Maybe at last being but a broken man,
      I must be satisfied with my heart, although
5   Winter and summer till old age began
      My circus animals were all on show,
      Those stilted boys, that burnished chariot,
      Lion and woman and the Lord knows what.[1]

---

4. Dagger. Cf. *Hamlet* 3.1.77–78: "When he himself might his quietus make / With a bare bodkin."
1. Yeats refers to the ancient Irish heroes of his early work ("Those stilted boys"), the gilded carriage of his play *The Unicorn from the Stars* (1908), and the lion in several of his poems, including "The Second Coming."

2

What can I but enumerate old themes,
10   First that sea-rider Oisin[2] led by the nose
Through three enchanted islands, allegorical dreams,
Vain gaiety, vain battle, vain repose,
Themes of the embittered heart, or so it seems,
That might adorn old songs or courtly shows;
15   But what cared I that set him on to ride,
I, starved for the bosom of his fairy bride.

And then a counter-truth filled out its play,
"The Countess Cathleen"[3] was the name I gave it,
She, pity-crazed, had given her soul away,
20   But masterful Heaven had intervened to save it.
I thought my dear must her own soul destroy
So did fanaticism and hate enslave it,
And this brought forth a dream and soon enough
This dream itself had all my thought and love.

25   And when the Fool and Blind Man stole the bread
Cuchulain fought the ungovernable sea;[4]
Heart mysteries there, and yet when all is said
It was the dream itself enchanted me:
Character isolated by a deed
30   To engross the present and dominate memory.
Players and painted stage took all my love
And not those things that they were emblems of.

3

Those masterful images because complete
Grew in pure mind but out of what began?
35   A mound of refuse or the sweepings of a street,
Old kettles, old bottles, and a broken can,
Old iron, old bones, old rags, that raving slut
Who keeps the till. Now that my ladder's gone
I must lie down where all the ladders start
40   In the foul rag and bone shop of the heart.

1939

2. In the long title-poem of Yeats's first successful book, *The Wanderings of Oisin and Other Poems* (1889), the legendary poet warrior Oisin (pronounced *Ushēēn*) is enchanted by the beautiful fairy woman Niamh (pronounced *Neeve*), who leads him to the Islands of Delight, of Many Fears, and of Forgetfulness.
3. A play (published in 1892) about an Irish countess (an idealized version of Maud Gonne) who sells her soul to the devil to buy food for the starving Irish poor but is taken up to heaven (for God "Looks always on the motive, not the deed").
4. In Yeats's play *On Baile's Strand* (1904), the legendary warrior Cuchulain (pronounced *Cu-HOOlin* by Yeats, *KooHULLin* in Irish), crazed by his discovery that he has killed his son, fights with the sea.

From Introduction
[A General Introduction for My Work][1]

I. The First Principle

A poet writes always of his personal life, in his finest work out of its tragedies, whatever it be, remorse, lost love or mere loneliness; he never speaks directly as to someone at the breakfast table, there is always a phantasmagoria. Dante and Milton had mythologies, Shakespeare the characters of English history, of traditional romance; even when the poet seems most himself, when Raleigh and gives potentates the lie,[2] or Shelley 'a nerve o'er which do creep the else unfelt oppressions of mankind',[3] or Byron when 'the heart wears out the breast as the sword wears out the sheath',[4] he is never the bundle of accident and incoherence that sits down to breakfast; he has been re-born as an idea, something intended, complete. A novelist might describe his accidence, his incoherence, he must not, he is more type than man, more passion than type. He is Lear, Romeo, Oedipus, Tiresias; he has stepped out of a play and even the woman he loves is Rosalind, Cleopatra, never The Dark Lady.[5] He is part of his own phantasmagoria and we adore him because nature has grown intelligible, and by so doing a part of our creative power. 'When mind is lost in the light of the Self', says the Prashna Upanishad,[6] 'it dreams no more; still in the body it is lost in happiness.' 'A wise man seeks in Self', says the Chāndôgya Upanishad, 'those that are alive and those that are dead and gets what the world cannot give.' The world knows nothing because it has made nothing, we know everything because we have made everything.

II. Subject-Matter

* * *

* * *I am convinced that in two or three generations it will become generally known that the mechanical theory[7] has no reality, that the natural and supernatural are knit together, that to escape a dangerous fanaticism we must study a new science; at that moment Europeans may find something attractive in a Christ posed against a background not of Judaism but of Druidism, not shut off in dead history, but flowing, concrete, phenomenal.

I was born into this faith, have lived in it, and shall die in it; my Christ, a legitimate deduction from the Creed of St Patrick[8] as I think, is that Unity of Being Dante compared to a perfectly proportioned human body, Blake's 'Imag-

---

1. Written in 1937 and originally printed as "A General Introduction for My Work" in *Essays and Introductions* (1961), the text is excerpted from *Later Essays*, ed. William H. O'Donnell (1994), vol. 5 of *The Collected Works of W. B. Yeats*.
2. From "The Lie," by the English writer and explorer Sir Walter Ralegh (1552–1618): "Tell potentates, they live / Acting by others' action; / Not loved unless they give, / Not strong but by a faction: / If potentates reply, / Give potentates the lie."
3. From "Julian and Maddalo," by the English poet Percy Bysshe Shelley (1792–1822).
4. Cf. "So, we'll go no more a roving," by the English poet George Gordon, Lord Byron (p. 616,

lines 5–6).
5. The woman to whom many of Shakespeare's de-idealizing sonnets are addressed. The rest of the names refer to characters in Shakespeare's plays and in Sophocles' ancient Greek drama *Oedipus the King*.
6. One of a series of ancient philosophical dialogues in Sanskrit. From *Ten Principal Upanishads* (1937), translated by Yeats and the Indian monk Shri Purohit Swami (1882–1941).
7. Theory explaining the universe in strictly naturalistic, Newtonian terms.
8. From the second paragraph of "The Confession of St. Patrick, or His Epistle to the Irish," by the fifth-century saint, the apostle of Ireland.

ination',[9] what the Upanishads have named 'Self': nor is this unity distant and therefore intellectually understandable, but imminent,[1] differing from man to man and age to age, taking upon itself pain and ugliness, 'eye of newt, and leg of frog'.[2]

Subconscious preoccupation with this theme brought me A Vision,[3] its harsh geometry an incomplete interpretation. The 'Irishry' have preserved their ancient 'deposit' through wars which, during the sixteenth and seventeenth centuries, became wars of extermination; no people, Lecky said at the opening of his Ireland in the Eighteenth Century,[4] have undergone greater persecution, nor did that persecution altogether cease up to our own day. No people hate as we do in whom that past is always alive; there are moments when hatred poisons my life and I accuse myself of effeminacy because I have not given it adequate expression. It is not enough to have put it into the mouth of a rambling peasant poet. Then I remind myself that, though mine is the first English marriage I know of in the direct line, all my family names are English and that I owe my soul to Shakespeare, to Spenser and to Blake, perhaps to William Morris,[5] and to the English language in which I think, speak and write, that everything I love has come to me through English; my hatred tortures me with love, my love with hate. I am like the Tibetan monk who dreams at his initiation that he is eaten by a wild beast and learns on waking that he himself is eater and eaten. This is Irish hatred and solitude, the hatred of human life that made Swift write Gulliver[6] and the epitaph upon his tomb, that can still make us wag between extremes and doubt our sanity.

Again and again I am asked why I do not write in Gaelic; some four or five years ago I was invited to dinner by a London society and found myself among London journalists, Indian students and foreign political refugees. An Indian paper says it was a dinner in my honour, I hope not; I have forgotten though I have a clear memory of my own angry mind. I should have spoken as men are expected to speak at public dinners; I should have paid and been paid conventional compliments; then they would speak of the refugees, from that on all would be lively and topical, foreign tyranny would be arraigned, England seem even to those confused Indians the protector of liberty; I grew angrier and angrier; Wordsworth, that typical Englishman, had published his famous sonnet to François Dominique Toussaint, a Santo Domingo negro:

> There's not a breathing of the common wind
> That will forget thee[7]

in the year when Emmet conspired and died, and he remembered that rebellion as little as the half hanging and the pitch cap that preceded it by half a

---

9. In Jerusalem the English poet William Blake (1757–1827) describes imagination as the "Divine body of the lord Jesus." Yeats's ideas about the Unity of Being are drawn from his reading of Dante's Il Convito.
1. In manuscript Yeats wrote "imanent" (a misspelling of "immanent"), but he allowed "immi-nent" to stand in the typescript.
2. Ingredients of the witches' cauldron in Shakespeare's Macbeth 4.1.
3. Yeats's mystical writings (1925, 1937), in which he sketches out and schematizes many of his theories.
4. A History of Ireland in the Eighteenth Century, by the Irish historian William Edward Hartpole Lecky (1838–1903).

5. English poet and designer (1834–1896). Edmund Spenser (1552–1599), English poet who, in addition to poetic works such as The Faerie Queene, wrote a treatise proposing the extermination of the Irish.
6. Gulliver's Travels, by the Irish satirist Jonathan Swift (1667–1745). Yeats's poem "Swift's Epitaph," a loose translation of the Latin on Swift's tomb, claims that "Swift has sailed into his rest; / Savage indignation there / Cannot lacerate his breast."
7. From "To Toussaint L'Ouverture," by the English poet William Wordsworth (1770–1850). L'Ouverture (1743–1803) died in prison after rebelling against France's rule in Haiti.

dozen years.[8] That there might be no topical speeches I denounced the oppression of the people of India; being a man of letters, not a politician, I told how they had been forced to learn everything, even their own Sanscrit, through the vehicle of English till the first discoverers of wisdom had become bywords for vague abstract facility. I begged the Indian writers present to remember that no man can think or write with music and vigour except in his mother tongue. I turned a friendly audience hostile, yet when I think of that scene I am unrepentant and angry.

I could no more have written in Gaelic than can those Indians write in English; Gaelic is my national language, but it is not my mother tongue.

III. Style and Attitude

Style is almost unconscious. I know what I have tried to do, little what I have done. Contemporary lyric poems, even those that moved me—'The Stream's Secret', 'Dolores'[9]—seemed too long, but an Irish preference for a swift current might be mere indolence, yet Burns may have felt the same when he read Thomson and Cowper.[1] The English mind is meditative, rich, deliberate; it may remember the Thames[2] valley. I planned to write short lyrics or poetic drama where every speech [would] be short and concentrated, knit by dramatic tension, and I did so with more confidence because young English poets were at that time writing out of emotion at the moment of crisis, though their old slow-moving meditation returned almost at once. Then, and in this English poetry has followed my lead, I tried to make the language of poetry coincide with that of passionate, normal speech. I wanted to write in whatever language comes most naturally when we soliloquise, as I do all day long, upon the events of our own lives or of any life where we can see ourselves for the moment. I sometimes compare myself with the mad old slum women I hear denouncing and remembering; 'how dare you,' I heard one say of some imaginary suitor, 'and you without health or a home'. If I spoke my thoughts aloud they might be as angry and as wild. It was a long time before I had made a language to my liking; I began to make it when I discovered some twenty years ago that I must seek, not as Wordsworth thought words in common use,[3] but a powerful and passionate syntax, and a complete coincidence between period and stanza. Because I need a passionate syntax for passionate subject-matter I compel myself to accept those traditional metres that have developed with the language. Ezra Pound, Turner, Lawrence, wrote admirable free verse, I could not.[4] I would lose myself, become joyless like those mad old women. The translators of the Bible, Sir Thomas Browne,[5] certain translators from the Greek when translators still bothered about rhythm, created a form midway between prose and verse that seems natural to impersonal meditation; but all

8. Paper caps filled with burning pitch were used for torture during the martial law preceding and following the Irish Rising of 1798. Robert Emmet (1778–1803), Irish nationalist executed after the Irish rebellion of 1803.
9. Long poems by Dante Gabriel Rossetti (1828–1882) and Algernon Charles Swinburne (1837–1909), respectively.
1. James Thomson (1700–1748) and William Cowper (1731–1800), poets most famous for their long poems. Robert Burns (1759–1796), Scottish poet of short lyrics.

2. English river that runs through London.
3. In the preface to Lyrical Ballads (1800), Wordsworth says that poetry should be written in "language really used by men."
4. In his Oxford Book of Modern Verse (1936), Yeats included free verse by the American poet Ezra Pound (1885–1972), the English poet Walter Turner (1889–1946), and the English poet and novelist D. H. Lawrence (1885–1930).
5. English physician and author (1605–1682) with an elaborate prose style.

that is personal soon rots; it must be packed in ice or salt. Once when I was in delirium from pneumonia I dictated a letter to George Moore[6] telling him to eat salt because it was a symbol of eternity; the delirium passed, I had no memory of that letter, but I must have meant what I now mean. If I wrote of personal love or sorrow in free verse, or in any rhythm that left it unchanged, amid all its accident, I would be full of self-contempt because of my egotism and indiscretion, and I foresee the boredom of my reader. I must choose a traditional stanza, even what I alter must seem traditional. I commit my emotion to shepherds, herdsmen, camel-drivers, learned men, Milton's or Shelley's Platonist, that tower Palmer drew.[7] Talk to me of originality and I will turn on you with rage. I am a crowd, I am a lonely man, I am nothing. Ancient salt is best packing. The heroes of Shakespeare convey to us through their looks, or through the metaphorical patterns of their speech, the sudden enlargement of their vision, their ecstasy at the approach of death, 'She should have died hereafter', 'Of many million kisses, the poor last', 'Absent thee from felicity awhile'; they have become God or Mother Goddess, the pelican, 'My baby at my breast',[8] but all must be cold; no actress has ever sobbed when she played Cleopatra, even the shallow brain of a producer has never thought of such a thing. The supernatural is present, cold winds blow across our hands, upon our faces, the thermometer falls, and because of that cold we are hated by journalists and groundlings. There may be in this or that detail painful tragedy, but in the whole work none. I have heard Lady Gregory say, rejecting some play in the modern manner sent to the Abbey Theatre, 'Tragedy must be a joy to the man who dies.' Nor is it any different with lyrics, songs, narrative poems; neither scholars nor the populace have sung or read anything generation after generation because of its pain. The maid of honour whose tragedy they sing must be lifted out of history with timeless pattern, she is one of the four Maries,[9] the rhythm is old and familiar, imagination must dance, must be carried beyond feeling into the aboriginal ice. Is ice the correct word? I once boasted, copying the phrase from a letter of my father's, that I would write a poem 'cold and passionate as the dawn'.[1]

When I wrote in blank verse I was dissatisfied; my vaguely mediaeval *Countess Cathleen* fitted the measure, but our Heroic Age went better, or so I fancied, in the ballad metre of *The Green Helmet*.[2] There was something in what I felt about Deirdre, about Cuchulain,[3] that rejected the Renaissance and its characteristic metres, and this was a principal reason why I created in dance plays the form that varies blank verse with lyric metres. When I speak blank verse and analyse my feelings I stand at a moment of history when instinct, its traditional songs and dances, its general agreement, is of the past. I have

---

6. Irish novelist (1852–1933).
7. The English artist Samuel Palmer (1805–1881) drew "The Lonely Tower" (1879) as an illustration of Milton's poem about the pensive man, "Il Penseroso" (1645), in which a scholar in a "high lonely tower" is dedicated to uncovering Plato's insights in Shelley's "Prince Athanase," the idealistic hero searches for love.
8. From *Macbeth* 5.4, *Anthony and Cleopatra* 4.15, *Hamlet* 5.2, respectively. "Pelican": thought to feed its babies with its blood and thus often a symbol of self-sacrifice.
9. Mary, Queen of Scots (1542–1587) was served by four women named Mary.

1. From "The Fisherman" (1916): "Before I am old / I shall have written him one / Poem maybe as cold / And passionate as the dawn."
2. *The Countess Cathleen* (1892, later revised) is written in blank verse; *The Green Helmet* (1910), in iambic heptameter, which resembles the meter of a ballad (alternating between four- and three-stress lines).
3. The warrior hero of the Irish mythological Ulster Cycle; he also appears in Yeats's "dance" plays, derived from Japanese Noh drama. "Deirdre": in the Ulster Cycle, woman chosen to be queen of Ulster before she elopes with Naoise (pronounced *Neesha*).

been cast up out of the whale's belly though I still remember the sound and sway that came from beyond its ribs,[4] and, like the Queen in Paul Fort's ballad,[5] I smell of the fish of the sea. The contrapuntal structure of the verse, to employ a term adopted by Robert Bridges,[6] combines the past and present. If I repeat the first line of *Paradise Lost* so as to emphasise its five feet I am among the folk singers, 'Of mán's first dísobédience ánd the frúit', but speak it as I should I cross it with another emphasis, that of passionate prose, 'Of mán's first disobédience and the frúit', or 'Of mán's fírst dísobedience and the frúit', the folk song is still there, but a ghostly voice, an unvariable possibility, an unconscious norm. What moves me and my hearer is a vivid speech that has no laws except that it must not exorcise the ghostly voice. I am awake and asleep, at my moment of revelation, self-possessed in self-surrender; there is no rhyme, no echo of the beaten drum, the dancing foot, that would overset my balance. When I was a boy I wrote a poem upon dancing that had one good line: 'They snatch with their hands at the sleep of the skies.' If I sat down and thought for a year I would discover that but for certain syllabic limitations, a rejection or acceptance of certain elisions, I must wake or sleep.

The Countess Cathleen could speak a blank verse which I had loosened, almost put out of joint, for her need, because I thought of her as mediaeval and thereby connected her with the general European movement. For Deirdre and Cuchulain and all the other figures of Irish legend are still in the whale's belly.

IV. Whither?

The young English poets reject dream and personal emotion; they have thought out opinions that join them to this or that political party; they employ an intricate psychology, action in character, not as in the ballads character in action, and all consider that they have a right to the same close attention that men pay to the mathematician and the metaphysician. One of the more distinguished has just explained that man has hitherto slept but must now awake.[7] They are determined to express the factory, the metropolis, that they may be modern. Young men teaching school in some picturesque cathedral town, or settled for life in Capri or in Sicily, defend their type of metaphor by saying that it comes naturally to a man who travels to his work by Tube.[8] I am indebted to a man of this school who went through my work at my request, crossing out all conventional metaphors,[9] but they seem to me to have rejected also those dream associations which were the whole art of Mallarmé.[1] He had topped a previous wave. As they express not what the Upanishads call 'that ancient Self' but individual intellect, they have the right to choose the man in the Tube because of his objective importance. They attempt to kill the whale, push the Renaissance higher yet, out-think Leonardo;[2] their verse kills the folk

4. Cf. Jonah 2.10: "And the Lord spake unto the fish, and it vomited out Jonah upon the dry land."
5. "La Reine à la Mer" ("The Queen of the Sea," 1894–96), by the French poet Paul Fort (1872–1960).
6. English poet (1844–1930), who stressed the poetic tension of the counterpoint between regular meters and the rhythm of poetry as actually spoken.
7. Perhaps W. H. Auden (1907–1973) or C. Day

Lewis (1904–1972).
8. London's underground railway. Lewis taught in the spa town of Cheltenham in the early 1930s. D. H. Lawrence lived in Capri and Sicily in the early 1920s.
9. Ezra Pound did this circa 1910.
1. Stéphane Mallarmé (1842–1898), French poet.
2. Leonardo da Vinci (1452–1519), Italian artist and inventor.

ghost and yet would remain verse. I am joined to the 'Irishry' and I expect a counter-Renaissance. No doubt it is part of the game to push that Renaissance; I make no complaint; I am accustomed to the geometrical arrangement of history in *A Vision*, but I go deeper than 'custom' for my convictions. When I stand upon O'Connell Bridge[3] in the half-light and notice that discordant architecture, all those electric signs, where modern heterogeneity has taken physical form, a vague hatred comes up out of my own dark and I am certain that wherever in Europe there are minds strong enough to lead others the same vague hatred rises; in four or five or in less generations this hatred will have issued in violence and imposed some kind of rule of kindred. I cannot know the nature of that rule, for its opposite fills the light; all I can do to bring it nearer is to intensify my hatred. I am no Nationalist, except in Ireland for passing reasons; State and Nation are the work of intellect, and when you consider what comes before and after them they are, as Victor Hugo said of something or other, not worth the blade of grass God gives for the nest of the linnet.[4]

1937   1961

3. Over Dublin's river Liffey.
4. Small finch. Victor Hugo (1802–1885), French writer.

E. M. FORSTER
1879–1970

Born in London, Edward Morgan Forster was an infant when his father, an architect of Welsh extraction, died of consumption. An only child, Forster was raised by his paternal great-aunt and his mother, a member of a family distinguished over several generations for its evangelical religion and its philanthropic reformist activities. He was educated at Tonbridge School (the "Sawston" of his novel *The Longest Journey*), where he suffered from the cruelty of his classmates and other tribulations of being a day boy at a boarding school. As a student at King's College, Cambridge, he found an intellectual companionship that influenced his entire life. The friends he made were to become, with Forster, members of the "Bloomsbury Group"—so called because some of its prominent figures lived in the Bloomsbury district of London—which included the writers Lytton Strachey and Virginia Woolf, the art historians Clive Bell and Roger Fry, and the economist John Maynard Keynes. Forster's main interest was always in personal relations, the "little society" we make for ourselves with our friends. He cast a wary eye on society at large, his point of view being always that of the independent liberal, suspicious of political slogans and catchwords, critical of Victorian attitudes and British imperialism.

After graduation from Cambridge, Forster visited Greece and spent some time in Italy in 1901, and this experience influenced him permanently; throughout his life he tended to set Greek and Italian peasant life in symbolic contrast to the stuffy and repressed life of middle-class England. Both Greek mythology and Italian Renaissance art opened up to him a world of vital exuberance, and most of his work is concerned with ways of discovering such a quality in personal relationships amid the complexities and distortions of modern life. He began writing as a contributor to the newly founded liberal *Independent Review* in 1903, and in 1905 published his first novel, *Where*

Angels Fear to Tread, a tragicomic projection of conflicts between refined English gentility and coarse Italian vitality.

Forster's second novel, *The Longest Journey* (1907), examines the differences between living and dead relationships with much incidental satire of English public-school education and English notions of respectability. *A Room with a View* (1908) explores the nature of love with a great deal of subtlety, using (as with his first novel) Italy as a liberating agent for the British tourists whom he also satirizes. *Howards End* (1910) involves a conflict between two families, one interested in art and literature and the other only in money and business, and probes the relation between inward feeling and outward action, between the kinds of reality in which people live. "Only connect!" exclaims one of the characters. "Only connect the prose and the passion, and both will be exalted, and human love will soon be at its height." But no one knew better than Forster that this is more easily said than done and that false or premature connections, connections made by rule and not achieved through total realization of the personality, can destroy and corrupt.

A pacifist, Forster refused to fight in World War I and instead served in the International Red Cross in Egypt. In Alexandria he had his first significant sexual relationship, with Mohammed el Adl, an Egyptian tram conductor; he feared social disapproval less there than in England, where, not long after Oscar Wilde's infamous prosecution for homosexual offenses, he hid his personal life from public scrutiny.

He traveled to India in 1912 and 1922, and in his last (for Forster published no more fiction during his life) and best-known novel, *A Passage to India* (1924), he takes the fraught relations between British and colonized Indians in the subcontinent as a background for the most searching and complex of all his explorations of the possibilities and limitations, the promises and pitfalls, of human relationships. Published posthumously was another novel, *Maurice*, written more than fifty years before and circulated privately during his life, in which he tried to define and do justice to homosexual love, which had played an important part in his life. In addition to fiction Forster also wrote critical, autobiographical, and descriptive prose, notably *Aspects of the Novel* (1927), which, as a discussion of the techniques of fiction by a practicing novelist, has become a minor classic of criticism.

"The Other Boat," which concerns cross-ethnic homosexual attraction that collides with the sexual taboos and racial hierarchies of empire, is an unusually long and rich short story that Forster originally intended to turn into a novel, beginning it around 1913 but not completing it until 1957–58, and it was not published until after his death, first appearing in *The Life to Come and Other Stories* (1972). The first part of the story tells of a British family's journey by ship from India to England, and the rest of the story, set some years later, reverses direction, the journey into the Mediterranean and on toward India becoming the backdrop for the loosening—and then drastic reassertion—of British imperial norms of order, discipline, racial superiority, and heterosexuality. As in other of Forster's works, the passage into another cultural geography calls into question British middle-class values, which exact a high price in repression, tragically conflict with the protagonist's sensual and emotional desires, and ultimately explode into violence.

The Other Boat

I

'Cocoanut, come and play at soldiers.'
'I cannot, I am beesy.'
'But you must, Lion wants you.'

2060 / E. M. FORSTER

'Yes, come along, man,' said Lionel, running up with some paper cocked hats[1] and a sash. It was long long ago, and little boys still went to their deaths stiffly, and dressed in as many clothes as they could find.

'I cannot, I am beesy,' repeated Cocoanut.

'But man, what are you busy about?'

'I have soh many things to arrange, man.'

'Let's leave him and play by ourselves,' said Olive. 'We've Joan and Noel and Baby and Lieutenant Bodkin. Who wants Cocoanut?'

'Oh, shut up! *I* want him. We must have him. He's the only one who falls down when he's killed. All you others go on fighting long too long. The battle this morning was a perfect fast. Mother said so.'

'Well, I'll die.'

'So you say beforehand, but when it comes to the point you won't. Noel won't. Joan won't. Baby doesn't do anything properly—of course he's too little—and you can't expect Lieutenant Bodkin to fall down. Cocoanut, man, do.'

'I—weel—not.'

'Cocoanut cocoanut cocoanut cocoanut cocoanut cocoanut,' said Baby.

The little boy rolled on the deck screaming happily. He liked to be pressed by these handsome good-natured children. 'I must go and see the m'm m'm m'm,' he said.

'The what?'

'The m'm m'm m'm. They live—oh, so many of them—in the thin part of the ship.'

'He means the bow,'[2] said Olive. 'Oh, come along, Lion. He's hopeless.'

'What are m'm m'm m'm?'

'M'm.' He whirled his arms about, and chalked some marks on the planks.

'What are those?'

'M'm.'

'What's their name?'

'They have no name.'

'What do they do?'

'They just go so and oh! and so—ever—always——'

'Flying fish? . . . Fairies? . . . Noughts and crosses?'[3]

'They have no name.'

'Mother!' said Olive to a lady who was promenading with a gentleman, 'hasn't everything a name?'

'I suppose so.'

'Who's this?' asked the lady's companion.

'He's always hanging on to my children. I don't know.'

'Touch of the tar-brush,[4] eh?'

'Yes, but it doesn't matter on a voyage home. I would never allow it going to India.' They passed on, Mrs March calling back, 'Shout as much as you like, boys, but don't scream, don't scream.'

'They must have a name,' said Lionel, recollecting, 'because Adam named all the animals when the Bible was beginning.'

'They weren't in the Bible, m'm m'm m'm; they were all the time up in the

---

1. Triangular hats worn in navy and army.
2. Forward part of the ship.
3. Tic-tac-toe.

4. Appearance of having non-European ancestry, i.e., of having brown skin.

thin part of the sheep, and when you pop out they pop in, so how could Adam have?'

'Noah's ark is what he's got to now.'

Baby said 'Noah's ark, Noah's ark, Noah's ark,' and they all bounced up and down and roared. Then, without any compact, they drifted from the saloon[5] deck on to the lower, and from the lower down the staircase that led to the forecastle,[6] much as the weeds and jellies were drifting about outside in the tropical sea. Soldiering was forgotten, though Lionel said, 'We may as well wear our cocked hats.' They played with a fox-terrier, who was in the charge of a sailor, and asked the sailor himself if a roving life was a happy one. Then drifting forward again, they climbed into the bows, where the m'm m'm m'm were said to be.

Here opened a glorious country, much the best in the boat. None of the March children had explored there before, but Cocoanut, having few domesticities, knew it well. That bell that hung in the very peak—it was the ship's bell and if you rang it the ship would stop. Those big ropes were tied into knots—twelve knots an hour. This paint was wet, but only as far as there. Up that hole was coming a Lascar.[7] But of the m'm m'm m'm he said nothing until asked. Then he explained in offhand tones that if you popped out they popped in, so that you couldn't expect to see them.

What treachery! How disappointing! Yet so ill-balanced were the children's minds that they never complained. Olive, in whom the instincts of a lady were already awaking, might have said a few well-chosen words, but when she saw her brothers happy she forgot too, and lifted Baby up on to a bollard[8] because he asked her to. They all screamed. Into their midst came the Lascar and laid down a mat for his three-o'clock prayer. He prayed as if he was still in India, facing westward, not knowing that the ship had rounded Arabia so that his holy places now lay behind him.[9] They continued to scream.

Mrs March and her escort remained on the saloon deck, inspecting the approach to Suez.[1] Two continents were converging with great magnificence of mountains and plain. At their junction, nobly placed, could be seen the smoke and the trees of the town. In addition to her more personal problems, she had become anxious about Pharaoh. 'Where exactly was Pharaoh drowned?'[2] she asked Captain Armstrong. 'I shall have to show my boys.' Captain Armstrong did not know, but he offered to ask Mr Hotblack, the Moravian[3] missionary. Mr Hotblack knew—in fact he knew too much. Somewhat snubbed by the military element in the earlier part of the voyage, he now bounced to the surface, became authoritative and officious, and undertook to wake Mrs March's little ones when they were passing the exact spot. He spoke of the origins of Christianity in a way that made her look down her nose, saying that the Canal was one long genuine Bible picture gallery, that donkeys could still be seen going down into Egypt carrying Holy Families,[4] and naked Arabs

---

5. Deck with large cabin(s) for passenger use.
6. Raised deck at the forward part of the ship.
7. An Indian sailor.
8. A thick post for securing ropes to.
9. Muslims pray facing Mecca.
1. Egyptian city at the south end of the Suez Canal (the shortest maritime route between Europe and India; it separates Asia from Africa).
2. In Exodus 14.21–23 Moses parts the Red Sea,

but after the Israelites have passed, the sea closes, drowning Pharoah and his army.
3. Member of a Protestant denomination, originally from a 15th-century reform religious movement in Moravia and Bohemia.
4. In Matthew 2.13–15 the family of the baby Jesus, fleeing from King Herod, travels from Bethlehem into Egypt; the journey is often depicted as taking place by donkey.

wading into the water to fish; 'Peter and Andrew by Galilee's shore, why, it hits the truth plumb.'[5] A clergyman's daughter and a soldier's wife, she could not admit that Christianity had ever been oriental. What good thing can come out of the Levant,[6] and is it likely that the apostles[7] ever had a touch of the tar-brush? Still, she thanked Mr Hotblack (for, having asked a favour of him, she had contracted an obligation towards him), and she resigned herself to greeting him daily until Southampton,[8] when their paths would part.

Then she observed, against the advancing land, her children playing in the bows without their topis[9] on. The sun in those far-off days was a mighty power and hostile to the Ruling Race.[1] Officers staggered at a touch of it, Tommies[2] collapsed. When the regiment was under canvas, it wore helmets at tiffin,[3] lest the rays penetrated the tent. She shouted at her doomed offspring, she gesticulated, Captain Armstrong and Mr Hotblack shouted, but the wind blew their cries backwards. Refusing company, she hurried forward alone; the children were far too excited and covered with paint.

'Lionel! Olive! Olive! What are you doing?'

'M'm m'm m'm, mummy—it's a new game.'

'Go back and play properly under the awning at once—it's far too hot. You'll have sunstroke every one of you. Come, Baby!'

'M'm m'm m'm.'

'Now, you won't want me to carry a great boy like you, surely.'

Baby flung himself round the bollard and burst into tears.

'It always ends like this,' said Mrs March as she detached him. 'You all behave foolishly and selfishly and then Baby cries. No, Olive—don't help me. Mother would rather do everything herself.'

'Sorry,' said Lionel gruffly. Baby's shrieks rent the air. Thoroughly naughty, he remained clasping an invisible bollard.[4] As she bent him into a portable shape, another mishap occurred. A sailor—an Englishman—leapt out of the hatchway with a piece of chalk and drew a little circle round her where she stood. Cocoanut screamed, 'He's caught you. He's come.'

'You're on dangerous ground, lady,' said the sailor respectfully. 'Men's quarters. Of course we leave it to your generosity.'

Tired with the voyage and the noise of the children, worried by what she had left in India and might find in England, Mrs March fell into a sort of trance. She stared at the circle stupidly, unable to move out of it, while Cocoanut danced round her and gibbered.

'Men's quarters—just to keep up the old custom.'

'I don't understand.'

'Passengers are often kind enough to pay their footing,' he said, feeling awkward; though rapacious he was independent. 'But of course there's no compulsion, lady. Ladies and gentlemen do as they feel.'

'I will certainly do what is customary—Baby, *be* quiet.'

'Thank you, lady. We divide whatever you give among the crew. Of course not those chaps.' He indicated the Lascar.

'The money shall be sent to you. I have no purse.'

5. Peter and Andrew, Jesus' disciples, were fishermen on the Sea of Galilee.
6. Historical term for region of the eastern Mediterranean.
7. Jesus' disciples.
8. Major port on the English Channel.
9. Pith helmets worn for protection from sun and heat.
1. I.e., the British.
2. Nickname for British soldiers.
3. Lunch (Anglo-Indian).
4. Post on a ship for securing ropes to.

He touched his forelock[5] cynically. He did not believe her. She stepped out of the circle and as she did so Cocoanut sprang into it and squatted grinning. 'You're a silly little boy and I shall complain to the stewardess about you,' she told him with unusual heat. 'You never will play any game properly and you stop the others. You're a silly idle useless unmanly little boy.'

II

S. S. Normannia
Red Sea
October, 191–

Hullo the Mater!

You may be thinking it is about time I wrote you a line, so here goes, however you should have got my wire sent before leaving Tilbury[6] with the glad news that I got a last minute passage on this boat when it seemed quite impossible I should do so. The Arbuthnots are on it too all right, so is a Lady Manning who claims acquaintance with Olive, not to mention several remarkably cheery subalterns,[7] poor devils, don't know what they are in for in the tropics. We make up two Bridge tables every night besides hanging together at other times, and get called the Big Eight, which I suppose must be regarded as a compliment. How I got my passage is curious. I was coming away from the S.S.[8] office after my final try in absolute despair when I ran into an individual whom you may or may not remember—he was a kid on that other boat when we cleared all out of India on that unlikely occasion over ten years ago—got called Cocoanut because of his peculiar shaped head. He has now turned into an equally weird youth, who has however managed to become influential in shipping circles, I can't think how some people manage to do things. He duly recognized me—dagoes[9] sometimes have marvellous memories—and on learning my sad plight fixed me up with a (single berth) cabin, so all is well. He is on board too, but our paths seldom cross. He has more than a touch of the tar-brush, so consorts with his own dusky fraternity, no doubt to their mutual satisfaction.

The heat is awful and I fear this is but a dull letter in consequence. Bridge I have already mentioned, and there are the usual deck games, betting on the ship's log, etc., still I think everyone will be glad to reach Bombay and get into harness.[1] Colonel and Mrs Arbuthnot are very friendly, and speaking confidentially I don't think it will do my prospects any harm having got to know them better. Well I will now conclude this screed[2] and I will write again when I have rejoined the regiment and contacted Isabel. Best love to all which naturally includes yourself from

Your affectionate first born,
Lionel March

PS. Lady Manning asks to be remembered to Olive, nearly forgot.

---

5. Lock of hair growing from the front of the head.
6. Port on the river Thames estuary.
7. Junior officers.
8. Steamship.

9. Disparaging term for foreigners.
1. Get to work, especially with military undertakings.
2. Gossipy letter.

When Captain March had posted this epistle he rejoined the Big Eight. Although he had spent the entire day with them they were happy to see him, for he exactly suited them. He was what any rising young officer ought to be— clean-cut, athletic, good-looking without being conspicuous. He had had wonderful professional luck, which no one grudged him: he had got into one of the little desert wars that were becoming too rare, had displayed dash and decision, had been wounded, and had been mentioned in despatches and got his captaincy early. Success had not spoiled him, nor was he vain of his personal appearance, although he must have known that thick fairish hair, blue eyes, glowing cheeks and strong white teeth constitute, when broad shoulders support them, a combination irresistible to the fair sex. His hands were clumsier than the rest of him, but bespoke hard honest work, and the springy gleaming hairs on them suggested virility. His voice was quiet, his demeanour assured, his temper equable. Like his brother officers he wore a mess[3] uniform slightly too small for him, which accentuated his physique—the ladies accentuating theirs by wearing their second best frocks and reserving their best ones for India.

Bridge proceeded without a hitch, as his mother had been given to understand it might. She had not been told that on either side of the players, violet darkening into black, rushed the sea, nor would she have been interested. Her son gazed at it occasionally, his forehead furrowed. For despite his outstanding advantages he was a miserable card-player, and he was having wretched luck. As soon as the Normannia entered the Mediterranean he had begun to lose, and the 'better luck after Port Said,[4] always the case' that had been humorously promised him had never arrived. Here in the Red Sea he had lost the maximum the Big Eight's moderate stakes allowed. He couldn't afford it, he had no private means and he ought to be saving up for the future, also it was humiliating to let down his partner: Lady Manning herself. So he was thankful when play terminated and the usual drinks circulated. They sipped and gulped while the lighthouses on the Arabian coast winked at them and slid northwards. 'Bedfordshire!'[5] fell pregnantly from the lips of Mrs Arbuthnot. And they dispersed, with the certainty that the day which was approaching would exactly resemble the one that had died.

In this they were wrong.

Captain March waited until all was quiet, still frowning at the sea. Then with something alert and predatory about him, something disturbing and disturbed, he went down to his cabin.

'Come een,' said a sing-song voice.

For it was not a single cabin, as he had given his mother to understand. There were two berths, and the lower one contained Cocoanut. Who was naked. A brightly coloured scarf lay across him and contrasted with his blackish-grayish skin, and an aromatic smell came off him, not at all unpleasant. In ten years he had developed into a personable adolescent, but still had the same funny-shaped head. He had been doing his accounts and now he laid them down and gazed at the British officer adoringly.

'Man, I thought you was never coming,' he said, and his eyes filled with tears.

---

3. Mealtime.
4. Egyptian city at the northern entrance to the Suez Canal.

5. County in the southeastern Midlands of England.

'It's only those bloody Arbuthnots and their blasted bridge,' replied Lionel and closed the cabin door.

'I thought you was dead.'

'Well, I'm not.'

'I thought I should die.'

'So you will.' He sat down on the berth, heavily and with deliberate heaviness. The end of the chase was in sight. It had not been a long one. He had always liked the kid, even on that other boat, and now he liked him more than ever. Champagne in an ice-bucket too. An excellent kid. They couldn't associate on deck with that touch of the tar-brush, but it was a very different business down here, or soon would be. Lowering his voice, he said: 'The trouble is we're not supposed to do this sort of thing under any circumstances whatsoever, which you never seem to understand. If we got caught there'd be absolute bloody hell to pay, yourself as well as me, so for God's sake don't make a noise.'

'Lionel, O Lion of the Night, love me.'

'All right. Stay where you are.' Then he confronted the magic that had been worrying him on and off the whole evening and had made him inattentive at cards. A tang of sweat spread as he stripped and a muscle thickened up out of gold. When he was ready he shook off old Cocoanut, who was now climbing about like a monkey, and put him where he had to be, and manhandled him, gently, for he feared his own strength and was always gentle, and closed on him, and they did what they both wanted to do.

Wonderful, wonnerful . . .

They lay entwined, Nordic warrior and subtle supple boy, who belonged to no race and always got what he wanted. All his life he had wanted a toy that would not break, and now he was planning how he would play with Lionel for ever. He had longed for him ever since their first meeting, embraced him in dreams when only that was possible, met him again as the omens foretold, and marked him down, spent money to catch him and lime[6] him, and here he lay, caught, and did not know it.

There they lay caught, both of them, and did not know it, while the ship carried them inexorably towards Bombay.

III

It had not always been so wonderful, wonnerful. Indeed the start of the affair had been grotesque and nearly catastrophic. Lionel had stepped on board at Tilbury entirely the simple soldier man, without an inkling of his fate. He had thought it decent of a youth whom he had only known as a child to fix him up with a cabin, but had not expected to find the fellow on board too— still less to have to share the cabin with him. This gave him a nasty shock. British officers are never stabled with dagoes, never, it was too damn awkward for words. However, he could not very well protest under the circumstances, nor did he in his heart want to, for his colour-prejudices were tribal rather than personal, and only worked when an observer was present. The first half-hour together went most pleasantly, they were unpacking and sorting things out before the ship started, he found his childhood's acquaintance friendly

6. Ensnare.

and quaint, exchanged reminiscences, and even started teasing and bossing him as in the old days, and got him giggling delightedly. He sprang up to his berth and sat on its edge, swinging his legs. A hand touched them, and he thought no harm until it approached their junction. Then he became puzzled, scared and disgusted in quick succession, leapt down with a coarse barrack-room oath and a brow of thunder and went straight to the Master at Arms[7] to report an offence against decency. Here he showed the dash and decision that had so advantaged him in desert warfare: in other words he did not know what he was doing.

The Master at Arms could not be found, and during the delay Lionel's rage abated somewhat, and he reflected that if he lodged a formal complaint he would have to prove it, which he could not do, and might have to answer questions, at which he was never good. So he went to the Purser[8] instead, and he demanded to be given alternative accommodation, without stating any reason for the change. The Purser stared: the boat was chockablock full already, as Captain March must have known. 'Don't speak to me like that,' Lionel stormed, and shouldered his way to the gunwale[9] to see England recede. Here was the worst thing in the world, the thing for which Tommies got given the maximum, and here was he bottled up with it for a fortnight. What the hell was he to do? Go forward with the charge or blow his own brains out or what?

On to him thus desperately situated the Arbuthnots descended. They were slight acquaintances, their presence calmed him, and before long his light military guffaw rang out as if nothing had happened. They were pleased to see him, for they were hurriedly forming a group of sahibs[1] who would hang together during the voyage and exclude outsiders. With his help the Big Eight came into being, soon to be the envy of less happy passengers; introductions; drinks; jokes; difficulties of securing a berth. At this point Lionel made a shrewd move: everything gets known on a boat and he had better anticipate discovery. 'I got a passage all right,' he brayed, 'but at the cost of sharing my cabin with a wog.'[2] All condoled, and Colonel Arbuthnot in the merriest of moods exclaimed, 'Let's hope the blacks don't come off on the sheets,' and Mrs Arbuthnot, wittier still, cried, 'Of course they won't, dear, if it's a wog it'll be the coffees.' Everyone shouted with laughter, the good lady basked in the applause, and Lionel could not understand why he suddenly wanted to throw himself into the sea. It was so unfair, he was the aggrieved party, yet he felt himself in the wrong and almost a cad. If only he had found out the fellow's tastes in England he would never have touched him, no, not with tongs. But could he have found out? You couldn't tell by just looking. Or could you? Dimly, after ten years' forgetfulness, something stirred in that faraway boat of his childhood and he saw his mother . . . Well, she was always objecting to something or other, the poor Mater. No, he couldn't possibly have known.

The Big Eight promptly reserved tables for lunch and all future meals, and Cocoanut and his set were relegated to a second sitting—for it became evident that he too was in a set: the tagrag and coloured bobtail[3] stuff that accumulates in corners and titters and whispers, and may well be influential, but who cares?

---

7. Officer in charge of enforcing discipline on a ship.
8. Ship's officer who keeps accounts and manages provisions.
9. Upper edge of a ship's side.

1. Respectful term for Europeans in colonial India.
2. Offensive term for a foreign person of color.
3. "Tagrag and bobtail" is another version of "rag, tag, and bobtail," meaning the riffraff, or rabble.

Lionel regarded it with distaste and looked for a touch of the hangdog[4] in his unspeakable cabin-mate, but he was skipping and gibbering on the promenade deck as if nothing had occurred. He himself was safe for the moment, eating curry by the side of Lady Manning, and amusing her by his joke about the various names which the cook would give the same curry on successive days. Again something stabbed him and he thought: 'But what shall I do, *do*, when night comes? There will have to be some sort of showdown.' After lunch the weather deteriorated. England said farewell to her children with her choppiest seas, her gustiest winds, and the banging of invisible pots and pans in the empyrean.[5] Lady Manning thought she might do better in a deckchair. He squired her to it and then collapsed and re-entered his cabin as rapidly as he had left it a couple of hours earlier.

It now seemed full of darkies, who rose to their feet as he retched,[6] assisted him up to his berth and loosened his collar, after which the gong summoned them to their lunch. Presently Cocoanut and his elderly Parsee[7] secretary looked in to inquire and were civil and helpful and he could not but thank them. The showdown must be postponed. Later in the day he felt better and less inclined for it, and the night did not bring its dreaded perils or indeed anything at all. It was almost as if nothing had happened—almost but not quite. Master Cocoanut had learned his lesson, for he pestered no more, yet he skilfully implied that the lesson was an unimportant one. He was like someone who has been refused a loan and indicates that he will not apply again. He seemed positively not to mind his disgrace—incomprehensibly to Lionel, who expected either repentance or terror. Could it be that he himself had made too much fuss?

In this uneventful atmosphere the voyage across the Bay of Biscay[8] proceeded. It was clear that his favours would not again be asked, and he could not help wondering what would have happened if he had granted them. Propriety was re-established, almost monotonously; if he and Cocoanut ever overlapped in the cabin and had to settle (for instance) who should wash first, they solved the problem with mutual tact.

And then the ship entered the Mediterranean.

Resistance weakened under the balmier sky, curiosity increased. It was an exquisite afternoon—their first decent weather. Cocoanut was leaning out of the porthole to see the sunlit rock of Gibraltar.[9] Lionel leant against him to look too and permitted a slight, a very slight familiarity with his person. The ship did not sink nor did the heavens fall. The contact started something whirling about inside his head and all over him, he could not concentrate on after-dinner bridge, he felt excited, frightened and powerful all at once and kept looking at the stars. Cocoa, who said weird things sometimes, declared that the stars were moving into a good place and could be kept there.

That night champagne appeared in the cabin, and he was seduced. He never could resist champagne. Curse, oh curse! How on earth had it happened? Never again. More happened off the coast of Sicily, more, much more at Port Said, and here in the Red Sea they slept together as a matter of course.

---

4. Sneaky or despicable person.
5. Sky.
6. Stretched.
7. Indian follower of Zoroastrianism, an ancient religion originating in Iran.

8. Arm of the Atlantic bordered by the west coast of France and the north coast of Spain.
9. Limestone promontory at the southern tip of Spain.

IV

And this particular night they lay motionless for longer than usual, as though something in the fall of their bodies had enchanted them. They had never been so content with each other before, and only one of them realized that nothing lasts, that they might be more happy or less happy in the future, but would never again be exactly thus. He tried not to stir, not to breathe, not to live even, but life was too strong for him and he sighed.

'All right?' whispered Lionel.

'Yes.'

'Did I hurt?'

'Yes.'

'Sorry.'

'Why?'

'Can I have a drink?'

'You can have the whole world.'

'Lie still and I'll get you one too, not that you deserve it after making such a noise.'

'Was I again a noise?'

'You were indeed. Never mind, you shall have a nice drink.' Half Ganymede, half Goth,[1] he jerked a bottle out of the ice-bucket. Pop went a cork and hit the partition wall. Sounds of feminine protest became audible, and they both laughed. 'Here, hurry up, scuttle up and drink.' He offered the goblet, received it back, drained it, refilled. His eyes shone, any depths through which he might have passed were forgotten. 'Let's make a night of it,' he suggested. For he was of the conventional type who once the conventions are broken breaks them into little pieces, and for an hour or two there was nothing he wouldn't say or do.

Meanwhile the other one, the deep one, watched. To him the moment of ecstasy was sometimes the moment of vision, and his cry of delight when they closed had wavered into fear. The fear passed before he could understand what it meant or against what it warned him, against nothing perhaps. Still, it seemed wiser to watch. As in business, so in love, precautions are desirable, insurances must be effected. 'Man, shall we now perhaps have our cigarette?' he asked.

This was an established ritual, an assertion deeper than speech that they belonged to each other and in their own way. Lionel assented and lit the thing, pushed it between dusky lips, pulled it out, pulled at it, replaced it, and they smoked it alternately with their faces touching. When it was finished Cocoa refused to extinguish the butt in an ashtray but consigned it through the porthole into the flying waters with incomprehensible words. He thought the words might protect them, though he could not explain how, or what they were.

'That reminds me . . .' said Lionel, and stopped. He had been reminded, and for no reason, of his mother. He did not want to mention her in his present state, the poor old Mater, especially after all the lies she had been told.

'Yes, of what did it remind you, our cigarette? Yes and please? I should know.'

---

1. An uncouth or uncivilized person. "Ganymede": in Greek mythology a Trojan boy whom Zeus, attracted by his great beauty, carried away to be the gods' cupbearer.

'Nothing.' And he stretched himself, flawless except for a scar down in the groin.

'Who gave you that?'

'One of your fuzzy-wuzzy cousins.'

'Does it hurt?'

'No.' It was a trophy from the little desert war. An assegai[2] had nearly unmanned him, nearly but not quite, which Cocoa said was a good thing. A dervish,[3] a very holy man, had once told him that what nearly destroys may bring strength and can be summoned in the hour of revenge. 'I've no use for revenge,' Lionel said.

'Oh Lion, why not when it can be so sweet?'

He shook his head and reached up for his pyjamas, a sultan's gift. It was presents all the time in these days. His gambling debts were settled through the secretary, and if he needed anything, or was thought to need it, something or other appeared. He had ceased to protest and now accepted indiscriminately. He could trade away the worst of the junk later on—some impossible jewelry for instance which one couldn't be seen dead in. He did wish, though, that he could have given presents in return, for he was anything but a sponger. He had made an attempt two nights previously, with dubious results. 'I seem always taking and never giving,' he had said. 'Is there nothing of mine you'd fancy? I'd be so glad if there was.' To receive the reply: 'Yes. Your hairbrush'— 'My *hairbrush*?'—and he was not keen on parting with this particular object, for it had been a coming-of-age gift from Isabel. His hesitation brought tears to the eyes, so he had to give in. 'You're welcome to my humble brush if you want it, of course. I'll just comb it out for you first'—'No, no, as it is uncombed,' and it was snatched away fanatically. Almost like a vulture snatching. Odd little things like this did happen occasionally, m'm m'm m'ms he called them, for they reminded him of oddities on the other boat. They did no one any harm, so why worry? Enjoy yourself while you can. He lolled at his ease and let the gifts rain on him as they would—a Viking at a Byzantine court, spoiled, adored and not yet bored.

This was certainly the life, and sitting on one chair with his feet on another he prepared for their usual talk, which might be long or short but was certainly the life. When Cocoanut got going it was fascinating. For all the day he had slipped around the ship, discovering people's weaknesses. More than that, he and his cronies were cognizant of financial possibilities that do not appear in the City columns,[4] and could teach one how to get rich if one thought it worth while. More than that, he had a vein of fantasy. In the midst of something ribald and scandalous—the discovery of Lady Manning, for instance: Lady Manning of all people in the cabin of the Second Engineer—he imagined the discovery being made by a flying fish who had popped through the Engineer's porthole, and he indicated the expression on the fish's face.

Yes, this was the life, and one that he had never experienced in his austere apprenticeship: luxury, gaiety, kindness, unusualness, and delicacy that did not exclude brutal pleasure. Hitherto he had been ashamed of being built like a brute: his preceptors had condemned carnality or had dismissed it as a waste

---

2. Slender spear.
3. Member of any of various Muslim ascetic orders.
4. Newspapers of the City of London, the financial district.

of time, and his mother had ignored its existence in him and all her children; being hers, they had to be pure.

What to talk about this pleasurable evening? How about the passport scandal? For Cocoanut possessed two passports, not one like most people, and they confirmed a growing suspicion that he might not be altogether straight. In England Lionel would have sheered off at once from such a subject, but since Gibraltar they had become so intimate and morally so relaxed that he experienced nothing but friendly curiosity. The information on the passports was conflicting, so that it was impossible to tell the twister's[5] age, or where he had been born or indeed what his name was. 'You could get into serious trouble over this,' Lionel had warned him, to be answered by irresponsible giggles. 'You could, you know. However, you're no better than a monkey, and I suppose a monkey can't be expected to know it's own name.' To which the reply had been 'Lion, he don't know nothing at all. Monkey's got to come along to tell a Lion he's alive.' It was never easy to score. He had picked up his education, if that was the word for it, in London, and his financial beginnings in Amsterdam, one of the passports was Portuguese, the other Danish, and half the blood must be Asiatic, unless a drop was Negro.

'Now come along, tell me the truth and nothing but the truth for a change,' he began. 'Ah, that reminds me I've at last got off that letter to the Mater. She adores news. It was a bit difficult to think of anything to interest her, however I filled it up with tripe about the Arbuthnots, and threw you in at the end as a sort of makeweight.'

'To make what sort of weight?'

'Well, naturally I didn't say what we do. I'm not stark staring raving mad. I merely mentioned I'd run into you in the London office, and got a cabin through you, that is to say single-berth one. I threw dust in her eyes all right.'

'Dear Lionel, you don't know how to throw dust or even where it is. Of mud you know a little, good, but not dust. Why bring me into the matter at all?'

'Oh, for the sake of something to say.'

'Did you say I too was on board?'

'I did in passing,' he said irritably, for he now realized he had better not have. 'I was writing that damned epistle, not you, and I had to fill it up. Don't worry—she's forgotten your very existence by this time.'

The other was certain she hadn't. If he had foreseen this meeting and had worked towards it through dreams, why should not an anxious parent have foreseen it too? She had valid reasons for anxiety, for things had actually started on that other boat. A trivial collision between children had alerted them towards each other as men. Thence had their present happiness sprung, thither might it wither, for the children had been disturbed. That vengeful onswishing of skirts . . . ! 'What trick can I think of this time that will keep him from her? I love him, I am clever, I have money. I will try.' The first step was to contrive his exit from the Army. The second step was to dispose of that English girl in India, called Isabel, about whom too little was known. Marriage or virginity or concubinage for Isabel? He had no scruples at perverting Lionel's instincts in order to gratify his own, or at endangering his prospects of paternity. All that mattered was their happiness, and he thought he knew what that was. Much depended on the next few days: he had to work hard and to work with the stars. His mind played round approaching problems,

5. One who speaks or acts to evade the truth.

combining them, retreating from them, and aware all the time of a further problem, of something in the beloved which he did not understand. He half-closed his eyes and watched, and listened through half-closed ears. By not being too much on the spot and sacrificing shrewdness to vision he sometimes opened a door. And sure enough Lionel said, 'As a matter of fact the Mater never liked you,' and a door opened, slowly.

'Man, how should she? Oh, when the chalk went from the hand of the sailor round the feet of the lady and she could not move and we all knew it, and oh man how we mocked her.'

'I don't remember—well, I do a little. It begins to come back to me and does sound like the sort of thing that would put her off. She certainly went on about you after we landed, and complained that you made things interesting when they weren't, funny thing to say, still the Mater is pretty funny. So we put our heads together as children sometimes do——'

'Do they? Oh yes.'

'—and Olive who's pretty bossy herself decreed we shouldn't mention you again as it seemed to worry her extra and she had just had a lot of worry. He actually—I hadn't meant to tell you this, it's a dead secret.'

'It shall be. I swear. By all that is without me and within me I swear.' He became incomprehensible in his excitement and uttered words in that unknown tongue. Nearly all tongues were unknown to Lionel, and he was impressed.

'Well, he actually——'

'Man, of whom do you now speak?'

'Oh yes, the Mater's husband, my Dad. He was in the Army too, in fact he attained the rank of major, but a quite unspeakable thing happened—he went native somewhere out East and got cashiered[6]—deserted his wife and left her with five young children to bring up, and no money. She was taking us all away from him when you met us and still had a faint hope that he might pull himself together and follow her. Not he. He never even wrote—remember, this is absolutely secret.'

'Yes, yes,' but he thought the secret a very tame one: how else should a middle-aged husband behave? 'But, Lionel, one question to you the more. For whom did the Major desert the Mater?'

'He went native.'

'With a girl or with a boy?'

'A boy? Good God! Well, I mean to say, with a girl, naturally—I mean, it was somewhere right away in the depths of Burma.'

'Even in Burma there are boys. At least I once heard so. But the Dad went native with a girl. Ver' well. Might not therefore there be offspring?'

'If there were, they'd be half-castes.[7] Pretty depressing prospect. Well, you know what I mean. My family—Dad's, that's to say—can trace itself back nearly two hundred years, and the Mater's goes back to the War of the Roses. It's really pretty awful, Cocoa.'

The half-caste smiled as the warrior floundered. Indeed he valued him most when he fell full length. And the whole conversation—so unimportant in itself—gave him a sense of approaching victory which he had not so far entertained. He had a feeling that Lionel knew that he was in the net or almost in

6. Dishonorably discharged.
7. Offensive term for people of mixed racial descent.

it, and did not mind. Cross-question him further! Quick! Rattle him! 'Is Dad dead?' he snapped.

'I couldn't very well come East if he wasn't. He has made our name stink in these parts. As it is I've had to change my name, or rather drop half of it. He called himself Major Corrie March. We were all proud of the "Corrie" and had reason to be. Try saying "Corrie March" to the Big Eight here, and watch the effect.'

'You must get two passports, must you not, one with and one without a "Corrie" on it. I will fix it, yes? At Bombay?'

'So as I can cheat like you? No, thank you. My name is Lionel March and that's my name.' He poured out some more champagne.

'Are you like him?'

'I should hope not. I hope I'm not cruel and remorseless and selfish and self-indulgent and a liar as he was.'

'I don't mean unimportant things like that. I mean are you like him to look at?'

'You have the strangest ideas of what is important.'

'Was his body like yours?'

'How should I know?'—and he was suddenly shy. 'I was only a kid and the Mater's torn up every photograph of him she could lay her hands on. He was a hundred per cent Aryan all right and there was plenty of him as there certainly is of me—indeed there'll be too much of me if I continue swilling at this rate. Suppose we talk about your passports for a change.'

'Was he one in whom those who sought rest found fire, and fire rest?'

'I've not the least idea what you're talking about. Do you mean I'm such a one myself?'

'I do.'

'I've not the least idea——' Then he hesitated. 'Unless . . . no, you're daft[8] as usual, and in any case we've spent more than enough time in dissecting my unfortunate parent. I brought him up to show you how much the Mater has to put up with, one has to make endless allowances for her and you mustn't take it amiss if she's unreasonable about you. She'd probably like you if she got the chance. There was something else that upset her at the time . . . I seem to be bringing out all the family skeletons in a bunch, still they won't go any further, and I feel like chattering to someone about everything, once in a way. I've never had anyone to talk to like you. Never, and don't suppose I ever shall. Do you happen to remember the youngest of us all, the one we called Baby?'

'Ah, that pretty Baby!'

'Well, a fortnight after we landed and while we were up at my grandfather's looking for a house, that poor kid died.'

'Die what of?' he exclaimed, suddenly agitated. He raised his knees and rested his chin on them. With his nudity and his polished duskiness and his strange-shaped head, he suggested an image crouched outside a tomb.

'Influenza, quite straightforward. It was going through the parish and he caught it. But the worst of it was the Mater wouldn't be reasonable. She would insist that it was sunstroke, and that he got it running about with no topi on when she wasn't looking after him properly in this very same Red Sea.'

'Her poor pretty Baby. So I killed him for her.'

'Cocoa! How ever did you guess that? It's exactly what she twisted it round to. We had quite a time with her. Olive argued, grandfather prayed . . . and I could only hang around and do the wrong thing, as I generally do.'

'But she—she saw me only, running in the sun with my devil's head, and m'm m'm m'm all you follow me till the last one the tiny one dies, and she, she talking to an officer, a handsome one, oh to sleep in his arms as I shall in yours, so she forgets the sun and it strikes the tiny one. I see.'

'Yes, you see in a wrong sort of way'; every now and then came these outbursts which ought to be rubbish yet weren't. Wrong of course about his mother, who was the very soul of purity, and over Captain Armstrong, who had become their valued family adviser. But right over Baby's death: she actually had declared that the idle unmanly imp had killed him, and designedly. Of recent years she had not referred to the disaster, and might have forgotten it. He was more than ever vexed with himself for mentioning Cocoanut in the letter he had recently posted to her.

'Did I kill him for you also?'

'For me? Of course not. I know the difference between influenza and sunstroke, and you don't develop the last-named after a three weeks' interval.'

'Did I kill him for anyone—or for anything?'

Lionel gazed into eyes that gazed through him and through cabin walls into the sea. A few days ago he would have ridiculed the question, but tonight he was respectful. This was because his affection, having struck earthward, was just trying to flower. 'Something's worrying you? Why not tell me about it?' he said.

'Did you love pretty Baby?'

'No, I was accustomed to see him around but he was too small to get interested in and I haven't given him a thought for years. So all's well.'

'There is nothing between us then?'

'Why should there be?'

'Lionel—dare I ask you one more question?'

'Yes, of course.'

'It is about blood. It is the last of all the questions. Have you ever shed blood?'

'No—oh, sorry, I should have said yes. I forgot that little war of mine. It goes clean out of my head between times. A battle's such a mess-up, you wouldn't believe, and this one had a miniature sandstorm raging to make confusion more confounded. Yes, I shed blood all right, or so the official report says. I didn't know at the time.' He was suddenly silent. Vividly and unexpectedly the desert surged up, and he saw it as a cameo,[9] from outside. The central figure—a grotesque one—was himself going berserk, and close to him was a dying savage who had managed to wound him and was trying to speak.

'I hope I never shed blood,' the other said. 'I do not blame others, but for me never.'

'I don't expect you ever will. You're not exactly cut out for a man of war. All the same, I've fallen for you.'

He had not expected to say this, and it was the unexpectedness that so delighted the boy. He turned away his face. It was distorted with joy and suffused with the odd purplish tint that denoted violent emotion. Everything had gone fairly right for a long time. Each step in the stumbling confession had brought him nearer to knowing what the beloved was like. But an open

9. Vividly carved stone.

avowal—he had not hoped for so much. 'Before morning I shall have enslaved him,' he thought, 'and he will begin doing whatever I put into his mind.' Even now he did not exult, for he knew by experience that though he always got what he wanted he seldom kept it, also that too much adoration can develop a flaw in the jewel. He remained impassive, crouched like a statue, chin on knees, hands round ankles, waiting for words to which he could safely reply.

'It seemed just a bit of foolery at first,' he went on. 'I woke up properly ashamed of myself after Gib, I don't mind telling you. Since then it's been getting so different, and now it's nothing but us. I tell you one thing though, one silly mistake I've made. I ought never to have mentioned you in that letter to the Mater. There's no advantage in putting her on the scent of something she can't understand; it's all right what we do, I don't mean that.'

'So you want the letter back?'

'But it's posted! Not much use wanting it.'

'Posted?' He was back to his normal and laughed gaily, his sharp teeth gleaming. 'What is posting? Nothing at all, even in a red English pillar-box. Even thence you can get most things out, and here is a boat. No! My secretary comes to you tomorrow morning: 'Excuse me, Captain March, sir, did you perhaps drop this unposted letter upon the deck?' You thank secretary, you take letter, you write Mater a better letter. Does anything trouble you now?'

'Not really. Except——'

'Except what?'

'Except I'm—I don't know. I'm fonder of you than I know how to say.'

'Should that trouble you?'

O calm mutual night, to one of them triumphant and promising both of them peace! O silence except for the boat throbbing gently! Lionel sighed, with a happiness he couldn't understand. 'You ought to have someone to look after you,' he said tenderly. Had he said this before to a woman and had she responded? No such recollection disturbed him, he did not even know that he was falling in love. 'I wish I could stay with you myself, but of course that's out of the question. If only things were a little different I——Come along, let's get our sleep.'

'You shall sleep and you shall awake.' For the moment was upon them at last, the flower opened to receive them, the appointed star mounted the sky, the beloved leaned against him to switch off the light over by the door. He closed his eyes to anticipate divine darkness. He was going to win. All was happening as he had planned, and when morning came and practical life had to be re-entered he would have won.

'Damn!'

The ugly stupid little word rattled out. 'Damn and blast,' Lionel muttered. As he stretched towards the switch, he had noticed the bolt close to it, and he discovered that he had left the door unbolted. The consequences could have been awkward. 'Pretty careless of me,' he reflected, suddenly wide awake. He looked round the cabin as a general might at a battlefield nearly lost by his own folly. The crouched figure was only a unit in it, and no longer the centre of desire. 'Cocoa, I'm awfully sorry,' he went on. 'As a rule it's you who take the risks, this time it's me. I apologize.'

The other roused himself from the twilight where he had hoped to be joined, and tried to follow the meaningless words. Something must have miscarried, but what? The sound of an apology was odious. He had always loathed the English trick of saying 'It's all my fault'; and if he encountered it in business it provided an extra incentive to cheat, and it was contemptible on the lips of a hero. When he grasped what the little trouble was and what the empty 'damns' signified, he closed his eyes again and said, 'Bolt the door therefore.'

'I have.'

'Turn out the light therefore.'

'I will. But a mistake like this makes one feel all insecure. It could have meant a courtmartial.'

'Could it, man?' he said sadly—sad because the moment towards which they were moving might be passing, because the chances of their convergence might be lost. What could he safely say? 'You was not to blame over the door, dear Lion,' he said. 'I mean we was both to blame. I knew it was unlocked all the time.' He said this hoping to console the beloved and to recall him to the entrance of night. He could not have made a more disastrous remark.

'You knew. But why didn't you say?'

'I had not the time.'

'Not the time to say "Bolt the door"?'

'No, I had not the time. I did not speak because there was no moment for such a speech.'

'No moment when I've been here for ages?'

'And when in that hour? When you come in first? Then? When you embrace me and summon my heart's blood. Is that the moment to speak? When I rest in your arms and you in mine, when your cigarette burns us, when we drink from one glass? When you are smiling? Do I interrupt then? Do I then say, "Captain March, sir, you have however forgotten to bolt the cabin door?" And when we talk of our faraway boat and of poor pretty Baby whom I never killed and I did not want to kill, and I never dreamt to kill—of what should we talk but of things far away? Lionel, no, no. Lion of the Night, come back to me before our hearts cool. Here is our place and we have so far no other and only we can guard each other. The door shut, the door unshut, is nothing, and is the same.'

'It wouldn't be nothing if the steward had come in,' said Lionel grimly.

'What harm if he did come in?'

'Give him the shock of his life, to say the least of it.'

'No shock at all. Such men are accustomed to far worse. He would be sure of a larger tip and therefore pleased. "Excuse me, gentlemen . . ." Then he goes and tomorrow my secretary tips him.'

'Cocoa, for God's sake, the things you sometimes say . . .' The cynicism repelled him. He noticed that it sometimes came after a bout of high faluting. It was a sort of backwash.[1] 'You never seem to realize the risks we run, either. Suppose I got fired from the Army through this.'

'Yes, suppose?'

'Well, what else could I do?'

'You could be my assistant manager at Basra.'[2]

'Not a very attractive alternative.' He was not sure whether he was being laughed at or not, which always rattled him, and the incident of the unbolted door increased in importance. He apologized again 'for my share in it' and added, 'You've not told that scruffy Parsee of yours about us, I do trust.'

'No. Oh no no no no and oh no. Satisfied?'

---

1. Motion of a receding wave.   2. City in what is now southeast Iraq.

'Nor the Goanese[3] steward?'
'Not told. Only tipped. Tip all. Of what other use is money?'
'I shall think you've tipped me next.'
'So I have.'
'That's not a pretty thing to say.'
'I am not pretty. I am not like you.' And he burst into tears. Lionel knew
that nerves were on edge, but the suggestion that he was a hireling hurt him
badly. He whose pride and duty it was to be independent and command! Had
he been regarded as a male prostitute? 'What's upset you?' he said as kindly
as possible. 'Don't take on so, Cocoa, there's no occasion for it.'
The sobs continued. He was weeping because he had planned wrongly. Rage
rather than grief convulsed him. The bolt unbolted, the little snake not driven
back into its hole—he had foreseen everything else and ignored the enemy at
the gate. Bolt and double-bolt now—they would never complete the movement
of love. As sometimes happened to him when he was unhinged, he could
foretell the immediate future, and he knew before Lionel spoke exactly what
he was going to say.
'I think I'll go on deck for a smoke.'
'Go.'
'I've a bit of a headache with this stupid misunderstanding, plus too much
booze. I want a breath of fresh air. Then I'll come back.'
'When you come back you will not be you. And I may not be I.'
Further tears. Snivellings. 'We're both to blame,' said Lionel patiently, taking up the cigarette-case. 'I'm not letting myself off. I was careless. But why
you didn't tell me at once I shall never understand, not if you talk till you're
blue. I've explained to you repeatedly that this game we've been playing's a
risky one, and honestly I think we'd better never have started it. However, we'll
talk about that when you're not so upset.' Here he remembered that the
cigarette-case was one of his patron's presents to him, so he substituted for it
a favourite old pipe. The change was observed and it caused a fresh paroxysm.
Like many men of the warm-blooded type, he was sympathetic to a few tears
but exasperated when they persisted. Fellow crying and not trying to stop.
Fellow crying as if he had the right to cry. Repeating 'I'll come back' as cordially
as he could, he went up on deck to think the whole situation over. For there
were several things about it he didn't like at all.
Cocoanut stopped weeping as soon as he was alone. Tears were a method
of appeal which had failed, and he must seek comfort for his misery and
desolation elsewhere. What he longed to do was to climb up into Lionel's berth
above him and snuggle down there and dream that he might be joined. He
dared not. Whatever else he ventured, it must not be that. It was forbidden to
him, although nothing had ever been said. It was the secret place, the sacred
place whence strength issued, as he had learned during the first half-hour of
the voyage. It was the lair of a beast who might retaliate. So he remained down
in his own berth, the safe one, where his lover would certainly never return.
It was wiser to work and make money, and he did so for a time. It was still
wiser to sleep, and presently he put his ledger aside and lay motionless. His
eyes closed. His nostrils occasionally twitched as if responding to something
which the rest of his body ignored. The scarf covered him. For it was one of

3. From Goa, India.

his many superstitions that it is dangerous to lie unclad when alone. Jealous of what she sees, the hag comes with her scimitar,[4] and she . . . Or she lifts up a man when he feels lighter than air.

V

Up on deck, alone with his pipe, Lionel began to recover his poise and his sense of leadership. Not that he and his pipe were really alone, for the deck was covered with passengers who had had their bedding carried up and now slept under the stars. They lay prone in every direction, and he had to step carefully between them on his way to the railing. He had forgotten that this migration happened nightly as soon as a boat entered the Red Sea; his nights had passed otherwise and elsewhere. Here lay a guileless subaltern, cherry-cheeked; there lay Colonel Arbuthnot, his bottom turned. Mrs Arbuthnot lay parted from her lord in the ladies' section. In the morning, very early, the Goanese stewards would awake the sahibs and carry their bedding back to their cabins. It was an old ritual—not practised in the English Channel or the Bay of Biscay or even in the Mediterranean—and on previous voyages he had taken part in it.

How decent and reliable they looked, the folk to whom he belonged! He had been born one of them, he had his work with them, he meant to marry into their caste. If he forfeited their companionship he would become nobody and nothing. The widened expanse of the sea, the winking lighthouse, helped to compose him, but what really recalled him to sanity was this quiet sleeping company of his peers. He liked his profession, and was rising in it thanks to that little war; it would be mad to jeopardize it, which he had been doing ever since he drank too much champagne at Gibraltar.

Not that he had ever been a saint. No—he had occasionally joined a brothel expedition, so as not to seem better than his fellow officers. But he had not been so much bothered by sex as were some of them. He hadn't had the time, what with his soldiering duties and his obligations at home as eldest son, and the doc said an occasional wet dream was nothing to worry about. Don't sleep on your back, though. On this simple routine he had proceeded since puberty. And during the past few months he had proceeded even further. Learning that he was to be posted to India, where he would contact Isabel, he had disciplined himself more severely and practised chastity even in thought. It was the least he could do for the girl he hoped to marry. Sex had entirely receded—only to come charging back like a bull. That infernal Cocoa—the mischief he had done. He had woken up so much that might have slept.

For Isabel's sake, as for his profession's, their foolish relationship must stop at once. He could not think how he had yielded to it, or why it had involved him so deeply. It would have ended at Bombay, it would have to end now, and Cocoanut must cry his eyes out if he thought it worth while. So far all was clear. But behind Isabel, behind the Army, was another power, whom he could not consider calmly; his mother, blind-eyed in the midst of the enormous web she had spun—filaments drifting everywhere, strands catching. There was no reasoning with her or about her, she understood nothing and controlled everything. She had suffered too much and was too high-minded to be judged like

4. Curved Asian sword.

other people, she was outside carnality and incapable of pardoning it. Earlier in the evening, when Cocoa mentioned her, he had tried to imagine her with his father, enjoying the sensations he was beginning to find so pleasant, but the attempt was sacrilegious and he was shocked at himself. From the great blank country she inhabited came a voice condemning him and all her children for sin, but condemning him most. There was no parleying[5] with her—she was a voice. God had not granted her ears—nor could she see, mercifully: the sight of him stripping[6] would have killed her. He, her first-born, set apart for the redemption of the family name. His surviving brother was too much a bookworm to be of any use, and the other two were girls.

He spat into the sea. He promised her 'Never again'. The words went out into the night like other enchantments. He said them aloud, and Colonel Arbuthnot, who was a light sleeper, woke up and switched on his torch.

'Hullo, who's that, what's there?'

'March, sir, Lionel March. I'm afraid I've disturbed you.'

'No, no, Lionel, that's all right, I wasn't asleep. Ye gods, what gorgeous pyjamas the fellow's wearing. What's he going about like a lone wolf for? Eh?'

'Too hot in my cabin, sir. Nothing sinister.'

'How goes the resident wog?'

'The resident wog he sleeps.'

'By the way, what's his name?'

'Moraes, I believe.'

'Exactly. Mr Moraes is in for trouble.'

'Oh. What for, sir?'

'For being on board. Lady Manning has just heard the story. It turns out that he gave someone in the London office a fat bribe to get him a passage though the boat was full, and as an easy way out they put him into your cabin. I don't care who gives or takes bribes. Doesn't interest me. But if the Company thinks it can treat a British officer like that it's very much mistaken. I'm going to raise hell at Bombay.'

'He's not been any particular nuisance,' said Lionel after a pause.

'I daresay not. It's the question of our prestige in the East, and it is also very hard luck on you, very hard. Why don't you come and sleep on deck like the rest of the gang?'

'Sound idea, I will.'

'We've managed to cordon off this section of the deck, and woe betide anything black that walks this way, if it's only a beetle. Good night.'

'Good night, sir.' Then something snapped and he heard himself shouting, 'Bloody rubbish, leave the kid alone.'

'Wh—what's that, didn't catch,' said the puzzled Colonel.

'Nothing sir, sorry sir.' And he was back in the cabin.

Why on earth had he nearly betrayed himself just as everything was going right? There seemed a sort of devil around. At the beginning of the voyage he had tempted him to throw himself overboard for no reason, but this was something more serious. 'When you come back to the cabin you will not be you,' Cocoa had said; and was it so?

However, the lower berth was empty, that was something, the boy must have gone to the lav, and he slipped out of his effeminate pyjamas and prepared

---

5. Mutual conversation.
6. Forster's substitution for his original phrase, "topping a dago." "Topping": copulating with.

to finish the night where he belonged—a good sleep there would steady him. His forearm was already along the rail, his foot poised for the upspring, when he saw what had happened.

'Hullo, Cocoanut, up in my berth for a change?' he said in clipped officer-tones, for it was dangerous to get angry. 'Stay there if you want to, I've just decided to sleep on deck.' There was no reply, but his own remarks pleased him and he decided to go further. 'As a matter of fact I shan't be using our cabin again except when it is absolutely necessary,' he continued. 'It's scarcely three days to Bombay, so I can easily manage, and I shan't, we shan't be meeting again after disembarkation. As I said earlier on, the whole thing has been a bit of a mistake. I wish we . . . ' He stopped. If only it wasn't so difficult to be kind! But his talk with the Colonel and his communion with the Mater prevented it. He must keep with his own people, or he would perish. He added, 'Sorry to have to say all this.'

'Kiss me.'

The words fell quietly after his brassiness and vulgarity and he could not answer them. The face was close to his now, the body curved away seductively into darkness.

'Kiss me.'

'No.'

'Noah? No? Then I kiss you.' And he lowered his mouth on to the muscular forearm and bit it.

Lionel yelped with the pain.

'Bloody bitch, wait till I . . . ' Blood oozed between the gold-bright hairs. 'You wait . . . ' And the scar in his groin reopened. The cabin vanished. He was back in a desert fighting savages. One of them asked for mercy, stumbled, and found none.

The sweet act of vengeance followed, sweeter than ever for both of them, and as ecstasy hardened into agony his hands twisted the throat. Neither of them knew when the end came, and he when he realized it felt no sadness, no remorse. It was part of a curve that had long been declining, and had nothing to do with death. He covered again with his warmth and kissed the closed eyelids tenderly and spread the bright-coloured scarf. Then he burst out of the stupid cabin on to the deck, and naked and with the seeds of love on him he dived into the sea.

The scandal was appalling. The Big Eight did their best, but it was soon all over the boat that a British officer had committed suicide after murdering a half-caste. Some of the passengers recoiled from such news. Others snuffled for more. The secretary of Moraes was induced to gossip and hint at procliv-ities, the cabin steward proved to have been overtipped, the Master at Arms had had complaints which he had managed to stifle, the Purser had been suspicious throughout, and the doctor who examined the injuries divulged that strangulation was only one of them, and that March had been a monster in human form, of whom the earth was well rid. The cabin was sealed up for further examination later, and the place where the two boys had made love and the tokens they had exchanged in their love went on without them to Bombay. For Lionel had been only a boy.

His body was never recovered—the blood on it quickly attracted the sharks. The body of his victim was consigned to the deep with all possible speed. There was a slight disturbance at the funeral. The native crew had become interested in it, no one understood why, and when the corpse was lowered were heard betting which way it would float. It moved northwards—contrary to the prevailing current—and there were clappings of hands and some smiles.

Finally Mrs March had to be informed. Colonel Arbuthnot and Lady Manning were deputed for the thankless task. Colonel Arbuthnot assured her that her son's death had been accidental, whatever she heard to the contrary; that he had stumbled overboard in the darkness during a friendly talk they had had together on deck. Lady Manning spoke with warmth and affection of his good looks and good manners and his patience 'with us old fogies at our Bridge.' Mrs March thanked them for writing but made no comment. She also received a letter from Lionel himself—the one that should have been intercepted in the post—and she never mentioned his name again.

1913–58   1972

VIRGINIA WOOLF
1882–1941

Virginia Woolf was born in London, daughter of Julia Jackson Duckworth, a member of the Duckworth publishing family, and Leslie (later Sir Leslie) Stephen, the Victorian critic, philosopher, biographer, and scholar. She grew up within a large and talented family, educating herself in her father's magnificent library, meeting in childhood many eminent Victorians, and learning Greek from the essayist and critic Walter Pater's sister. Writing and the intellectual life thus came naturally to her. But her youth was shadowed by suffering: her older half-brother sexually abused her; her mother died in 1895, precipitating the first of her mental breakdowns; a beloved half-sister died in childbirth two years later; her father died of cancer in 1904; and a brother died of typhoid in 1906.

After her father's death she settled with her sister and two brothers in Bloomsbury, the district of London that later became associated with the group among whom she moved. The "Bloomsbury Group" was an intellectual coterie frequented at various times by the biographer Lytton Strachey, the economist John Maynard Keynes, the art critic Roger Fry, and the novelist E. M. Forster. When her sister, Vanessa, a notable painter, married Clive Bell, an art critic, in 1907, Woolf and her brother Adrian took another house in Bloomsbury, and there they entertained their literary and artistic friends at evening gatherings, where the conversation sparkled. The Bloomsbury Group thrived at the center of the middle-class and upper-middle-class London intelligentsia. Their intelligence was equaled by their frankness, notably on sexual topics, and the sexual life of Bloomsbury provided ample material for discussion and contributed to Woolf's freedom of thinking about gender relations. The painter Duncan Grant, for example, was at different times the lover of Keynes, Woolf's brother Adrian, and her sister, whose daughter, Angelica, he fathered. Woolf too was bisexual; and thirteen years after her marriage to the journalist and essayist Leonard Woolf, she fell passionately in love with the poet Vita [Victoria] Sackville-West, wife of the bisexual diplomat and author Harold Nicolson. Woolf's relationship with this aristocratic lesbian inspired the most lighthearted and scintillating of her books, *Orlando* (1928), a novel about a transhistorical androgynous protagonist, whose identity shifts from masculine to feminine over centuries.

Underneath Woolf's liveliness and wit—qualities so well known among the Bloomsbury Group—lay psychological tensions created partly by her childhood wounds and partly by her perfectionism, she being her own most exacting critic. The public was unaware until her death that she had been subject to periods of severe depression, particularly after finishing a book. In March 1941 she drowned herself in a river, an act influenced by her dread of World War II (she and Leonard would have been arrested by the Gestapo had the Nazis invaded England) and her fear that she was about to lose her mind and become a burden on her husband, who had supported her emotionally and intellectually. (In 1917 the Woolfs had founded the Hogarth Press, which published some of the most interesting literature of their time, including T. S. Eliot's *Poems* [1919], fiction by Maxim Gorky, Katherine Mansfield, and E. M. Forster, the English translations of Freud, and Virginia's novels.)

As a fiction writer Woolf rebelled against what she called the "materialism" of novelists such as her contemporaries Arnold Bennett and John Galsworthy, who depicted suffering and social injustice through gritty realism, and she sought to render more delicately those aspects of consciousness in which she felt the truth of human experience lay. In her essay "Modern Fiction" she defines the task of the novelist as looking within, as conveying the mind receiving "a myriad impressions," as representing the "luminous halo" or "semi-transparent envelope surrounding us from the beginning of consciousness to the end." In her novels she abandoned linear narratives in favor of interior monologues and stream of consciousness narration, exploring with great subtlety problems of personal identity and personal relationships as well as the significance of time, change, loss, and memory for human personality. After two conventionally realistic novels, *The Voyage Out* (1915) and *Night and Day* (1919), she developed her own style, a carefully modulated flow that brought into prose fiction something of the rhythms and imagery of lyric poetry. While intensely psychological and interior, her novels also found inspiration and material in the physical realities of the body and in the heavily trafficked and populated streets of London. In *Monday or Tuesday* (1921), a series of sketches, she explored the possibilities of moving between action and contemplation, between retrospection and anticipation, between specific external events and delicate tracings of the flow of consciousness. These technical experiments made possible those later novels in which her characteristic method is fully developed—the elegiac *Jacob's Room* (1922); *Mrs. Dalloway* (1925), the first completely successful realization of her style; *To the Lighthouse* (1927), which in part memorializes her parents; *The Waves* (1931), the most experimental and difficult of her novels; and *Between the Acts* (1941), which includes a discontinuous pageant of English history and was published after her death.

Woolf was also a prodigious reviewer and essayist. She began to write criticism in 1905 for the *Times Literary Supplement* and published some five hundred reviews and essays for it and other periodicals, collected in *The Common Reader* (1925) and *The Second Common Reader* (1932); her prose presents itself as suggestive rather than authoritative and has an engaging air of spontaneity. In marked contrast to the formal language of the lecture hall or philosophical treatise, arenas and forms of learning from which women were historically barred, she writes in an informal, personal, playfully polemical tone, which is implicitly linked to her identity as a female writer. In her essays she is equally concerned with her own craft as a writer and with what it was like to be a quite different person living in a different age. At once more informal and more revealing are the six volumes of her *Letters* (1975–80) and five volumes of her *Diary* (1977–84), which she began to write in 1917. These, with their running commentary on her life and work, resemble a painter's sketchbooks and serve as a reminder that her writings, for all their variety, have the coherence found only in the work of the greatest literary artists.

Over the course of her career, Woolf grew increasingly concerned with the position of women, especially professional women, and the constrictions under which they suffered. She wrote several cogent essays on the subject, and women's social subjection also arises in her fiction. Her novel *The Years* (1937) was originally to have reflections on the position of women interspersed amid the action, but she later decided to publish them as a separate book, *Three Guineas* (1938). In *A Room of*

One's Own (1929), an essay based on two lectures on "Women and Fiction" delivered to female students at Cambridge, Woolf discusses various male institutions that historically either were denied to or oppressed women. Refused access to education, wealth, and property ownership, women lacked the conditions necessary to write and were unable to develop a literature of their own. Woolf advocated the creation of a literature that would include women's experience and ways of thinking, but instead of encouraging an exclusively female perspective, she proposed literature that would be "androgynous in mind" and resonate equally with men and women.

The Mark on the Wall

Perhaps it was the middle of January in the present year that I first looked up and saw the mark on the wall. In order to fix a date it is necessary to remember what one saw. So now I think of the fire; the steady film of yellow light upon the page of my book; the three chrysanthemums in the round glass bowl on the mantelpiece. Yes, it must have been the winter time, and we had just finished our tea, for I remember that I was smoking a cigarette when I looked up and saw the mark on the wall for the first time. I looked up through the smoke of my cigarette and my eye lodged for a moment upon the burning coals, and that old fancy of the crimson flag flapping from the castle tower came into my mind, and I thought of the cavalcade of red knights riding up the side of the black rock. Rather to my relief the sight of the mark interrupted the fancy, for it is an old fancy, an automatic fancy, made as a child perhaps. The mark was a small round mark, black upon the white wall, about six or seven inches above the mantelpiece.

How readily our thoughts swarm upon a new object, lifting it a little way, as ants carry a blade of straw so feverishly, and then leave it. . . . If that mark was made by a nail, it can't have been for a picture, it must have been for a miniature—the miniature of a lady with white powdered curls, powder-dusted cheeks, and lips like red carnations. A fraud of course, for the people who had this house before us would have chosen pictures in that way—an old picture for an old room. That is the sort of people they were—very interesting people, and I think of them so often, in such queer places, because one will never see them again, never know what happened next. They wanted to leave this house because they wanted to change their style of furniture, so he said, and he was in process of saying that in his opinion art should have ideas behind it when we were torn asunder, as one is torn from the old lady about to pour out tea and the young man about to hit the tennis ball in the back garden of the suburban villa as one rushes past in the train.

But for that mark, I'm not sure about it; I don't believe it was made by a nail after all; it's too big, too round, for that. I might get up, but if I got up and looked at it, ten to one I shouldn't be able to say for certain; because once a thing's done, no one ever knows how it happened. Oh! dear me, the mystery of life; the inaccuracy of thought! The ignorance of humanity! To show how very little control of our possessions we have—what an accidental affair this living is after all our civilisation—let me just count over a few of the things lost in one lifetime, beginning, for that seems always the most mysterious of losses—what cat would gnaw, what rat would nibble—three pale blue canisters of book-binding tools? Then there were the bird cages, the iron hoops, the steel skates, the Queen Anne coal-scuttle, the bagatelle[1] board, the hand organ—all gone, and jewels, too. Opals and emeralds, they lie about the roots of turnips. What a scraping paring affair it is to be sure! The wonder is that I've any clothes on my back, that I sit surrounded by solid furniture at this moment. Why, if one wants to compare life to anything, one must liken it to being blown through the Tube[2] at fifty miles an hour—landing at the other end without a single hairpin in one's hair! Shot out at the feet of God entirely naked! Tumbling head over heels in the asphodel meadows[3] like brown paper parcels pitched down a shoot in the post office! With one's hair flying back like the tail of a race-horse. Yes, that seems to express the rapidity of life, the perpetual waste and repair; all so casual, all so haphazard. . . .

But after life. The slow pulling down of thick green stalks so that the cup of the flower, as it turns over, deluges one with purple and red light. Why, after all, should one not be born there as one is born here, helpless, speechless, unable to focus one's eyesight, groping at the roots of the grass, at the toes of the Giants? As for saying which are trees, and which are men and women, or whether there are such things, that one won't be in a condition to do for fifty years or so. There will be nothing but spaces of light and dark, intersected by thick stalks, and rather higher up perhaps, rose-shaped blots of an indistinct colour—dim pinks and blues—which will, as time goes on, become more definite, become—I don't know what. . . .

And yet that mark on the wall is not a hole at all. It may even be caused by some round black substance, such as a small rose leaf, left over from the summer, and I, not being a very vigilant housekeeper—look at the dust on the mantelpiece, for example, the dust which, so they say, buried Troy[4] three times over, only fragments of pots utterly refusing annihilation, as one can believe.

The tree outside the window taps very gently on the pane. . . . I want to think quietly, calmly, spaciously, never to be interrupted, never to have to rise from my chair, to slip easily from one thing to another, without any sense of hostility, or obstacle. I want to sink deeper and deeper, away from the surface, with its hard separate facts. To steady myself, let me catch hold of the first idea that passes . . . Shakespeare. . . . Well, he will do as well as another. A man who sat himself solidly in an arm-chair, and looked into the fire, so— A shower of ideas fell perpetually from some very high Heaven down through his mind. He leant his forehead on his hand, and people, looking in through the open door—for this scene is supposed to take place on a summer's evening— But how dull this is, this historical fiction! It doesn't interest me at all. I wish I could hit upon a pleasant track of thought, a track indirectly reflecting credit upon myself, for those are the pleasantest thoughts, and very frequent even in the minds of modest mouse-coloured people, who believe genuinely that they dislike to hear their own praises. They are not thoughts directly praising oneself; that is the beauty of them; they are thoughts like this:

"And then I came into the room. They were discussing botany. I said how I'd seen a flower growing on a dust heap on the site of an old house in Kingsway.[5] The seed, I said, must have been sown in the reign of Charles the First. What flowers grew in the reign of Charles the First?" I asked—(but I don't

---

1. Game played on oblong table with cue and balls. "Coal-scuttle": metal pail for carrying coal.
2. The London underground railway, or subway.
3. I.e., heaven, the next world (in Greek mythology asphodel flowers grow in the Elysian fields).
4. Legendary site of ancient war chronicled in Homer's Greek epic *The Iliad*.
5. Street in London.

2084 / VIRGINIA WOOLF

remember the answer). Tall flowers with purple tassels to them perhaps. And so it goes on. All the time I'm dressing up the figure of myself in my own mind, lovingly, stealthily, not openly adoring it, for if I did that, I should catch myself out, and stretch my hand at once for a book in self-protection. Indeed, it is curious how instinctively one protects the image of oneself from idolatry or any other handling that could make it ridiculous, or too unlike the original to be believed in any longer. Or is it not so very curious after all? It is a matter of great importance. Suppose the looking-glass smashes, the image disappears, and the romantic figure with the green of forest depths all about it is there no longer, but only that shell of a person which is seen by other people—what an airless, shallow, bald, prominent world it becomes! A world not to be lived in. As we face each other in omnibuses and underground railways we are looking into the mirror; that accounts for the vagueness, the gleam of glassiness, in our eyes. And the novelists in future will realise more and more the importance of these reflections, for of course there is not one reflection but an almost infinite number; those are the depths they will explore, those the phantoms they will pursue, leaving the description of reality more and more out of their stories, taking a knowledge of it for granted, as the Greeks did and Shakespeare perhaps—but these generalisations are very worthless. The military sound of the word is enough. It recalls leading articles, cabinet ministers—a whole class of things indeed which, as a child, one thought the thing itself, the standard thing, the real thing, from which one could not depart save at the risk of nameless damnation. Generalisations bring back somehow Sunday in London, Sunday afternoon walks, Sunday luncheons, and also ways of speaking of the dead, clothes, and habits—like the habit of sitting all together in one room until a certain hour, although nobody liked it. There was a rule for everything. The rule for tablecloths at that particular period was that they should be made of tapestry with little yellow compartments marked upon them, such as you may see in photographs of the carpets in the corridors of the royal palaces. Tablecloths of a different kind were not real tablecloths. How shocking, and yet how wonderful it was to discover that these real things, Sunday luncheons, Sunday walks, country houses, and tablecloths were not entirely real, were indeed half phantoms, and the damnation which visited the disbeliever in them was only a sense of illegitimate freedom. What now takes the place of those things I wonder, those real standard things? Men perhaps, should you be a woman; the masculine point of view which governs our lives, which sets the standard, which establishes Whitaker's Table of Precedency,[6] which has become, I suppose, since the war, half a phantom to many men and women, which soon, one may hope, will be laughed into the dustbin where the phantoms go, the mahogany sideboards and the Landseer[7] prints, Gods and Devils, Hell and so forth, leaving us all with an intoxicating sense of illegitimate freedom—if freedom exists. . . .

In certain lights that mark on the wall seems actually to project from the wall. Nor is it entirely circular. I cannot be sure, but it seems to cast a perceptible shadow, suggesting that if I ran my finger down that strip of the wall it would, at a certain point, mount and descend a small tumulus, a smooth

---

6. *Whitaker's Almanack,* an annual compendium of information, prints a "Table of Precedency," which shows the order in which the various ranks in public life and society proceed on formal occasions.

7. Sir Edwin Henry Landseer (1802–1873), English painter, reproductions of whose *Stag at Bay, Monarch of the Glen,* and similar animal paintings were often found in Victorian homes.

THE MARK ON THE WALL / 2085

tumulus like those barrows on the South Downs[8] which are, they say, either tombs or camps. Of the two I should prefer them to be tombs, desiring melancholy like most English people, and finding it natural at the end of a walk to think of the bones stretched beneath the turf. . . . There must be some book about it. Some antiquary must have dug up those bones and given them a name. . . . What sort of a man is an antiquary, I wonder? Retired Colonels for the most part, I daresay, leading parties of aged labourers to the top here, examining clods of earth and stone, and getting into correspondence with the neighbouring clergy, which, being opened at breakfast time, gives them a feeling of importance, and the comparison of arrow-heads necessitates cross-country journeys to the country towns, an agreeable necessity both to them and to their elderly wives, who wish to make plum jam or to clean out the study, and have every reason for keeping that great question of the camp or the tomb in perpetual suspension, while the Colonel himself feels agreeably philosophic in accumulating evidence on both sides of the question. It is true that he does finally incline to believe in the camp; and, being opposed, indites a pamphlet which he is about to read at the quarterly meeting of the local society when a stroke lays him low, and his last conscious thoughts are not of wife or child, but of the camp and that arrowhead there, which is now in the case at the local museum, together with the foot of a Chinese murderess, a handful of Elizabethan nails, a great many Tudor clay pipes, a piece of Roman pottery, and the wineglass that Nelson[9] drank out of—proving I really don't know what.

No, no, nothing is proved, nothing is known. And if I were to get up at this very moment and ascertain that the mark on the wall is really—what shall we say?—the head of a gigantic old nail, driven in two hundred years ago, which has now, owing to the patient attrition of many generations of housemaids, revealed its head above the coat of paint, and is taking its first view of modern life in the sight of a white-walled fire-lit room, what should I gain?— Knowledge? Matter for further speculation? I can think sitting still as well as standing up. And what is knowledge? What are our learned men save the descendants of witches and hermits who crouched in caves and in woods brewing herbs, interrogating shrew-mice and writing down the language of the stars? And the less we honour them as our superstitions dwindle and our respect for beauty and health of mind increases. . . . Yes, one could imagine a very pleasant world. A quiet, spacious world, with the flowers so red and blue in the open fields. A world without professors or specialists or house-keepers with the profiles of policemen, a world which one could slice with one's thought as a fish slices the water with his fin, grazing the stems of the water-lilies, hanging suspended over nests of white sea eggs. . . . How peaceful it is down here, rooted in the centre of the world and gazing up through the grey waters, with their sudden gleams of light, and their reflections—if it were not for Whitaker's Almanack—if it were not for the Table of Precedency!

I must jump up and see for myself what that mark on the wall really is—a nail, a rose-leaf, a crack in the wood?

Here is Nature once more at her old game of self-preservation. This train of thought, she perceives, is threatening mere waste of energy, even some

8. A range of low hills in southeastern England. "Barrows": mounds of earth or stones erected by prehistoric peoples, usually as burial places.

9. Horatio Nelson (1758–1805), British admiral. "Tudor": 15th-century English.

2086 / Virginia Woolf

collision with reality, for who will ever be able to lift a finger against Whitaker's Table of Precedency? The Archbishop of Canterbury is followed by the Lord High Chancellor; the Lord High Chancellor is followed by the Archbishop of York. Everybody follows somebody, such is the philosophy of Whitaker; and the great thing is to know who follows whom. Whitaker knows, and let that, so Nature counsels, comfort you, instead of enraging you; and if you can't be comforted, if you must shatter this hour of peace, think of the mark on the wall.

I understand Nature's game—her prompting to take action as a way of ending any thought that threatens to excite or to pain. Hence, I suppose, comes our slight contempt for men of action—men, we assume, who don't think. Still, there's no harm in putting a full stop to one's disagreeable thoughts by looking at a mark on the wall.

Indeed, now that I have fixed my eyes upon it, I feel that I have grasped a plank in the sea; I feel a satisfying sense of reality which at once turns the two Archbishops and the Lord High Chancellor to the shadows of shades. Here is something definite, something real. Thus, waking from a midnight dream of horror, one hastily turns on the light and lies quiescent, worshipping the chest of drawers, worshipping solidity, worshipping reality, worshipping the impersonal world which is a proof of some existence other than ours. That is what one wants to be sure of. . . . Wood is a pleasant thing to think about. It comes from a tree; and trees grow, and we don't know how they grow. For years and years they grow, without paying any attention to us, in meadows, in forests, and by the side of rivers—all things one likes to think about. The cows swish their tails beneath them on hot afternoons; they paint rivers so green that when a moorhen dives one expects to see its feathers all green when it comes up again. I like to think of the fish balanced against the stream like flags blown out; and of water-beetles slowly raising domes of mud upon the bed of the river. I like to think of the tree itself: first of the close dry sensation of being wood; then the grinding of the storm; then the slow, delicious ooze of sap; I like to think of it, too, on winter's nights standing in the empty field with all leaves close-furled, nothing tender exposed to the iron bullets of the moon, a naked mast upon an earth that goes tumbling, tumbling, all night long. The song of birds must sound very loud and strange in June; and how cold the feet of insects must feel upon it, as they make laborious progresses up the creases of the bark, or sun themselves upon the thin green awning of the leaves, and look straight in front of them with diamond-cut red eyes. . . . One by one the fibres snap beneath the immense cold pressure of the earth, then the last storm comes and, falling, the highest branches drive deep into the ground again. Even so, life isn't done with; there are a million patient, watchful lives still for a tree, all over the world, in bedrooms, in ships, on the pavement, living rooms, where men and women sit after tea, smoking cigarettes. It is full of peaceful thoughts, happy thoughts, this tree. I should like to take each one separately—but something is getting in the way. . . . Where was I? What has it all been about? A tree? A river? The Downs?[1] Whitaker's Almanack? The fields of asphodel? I can't remember a thing. Everything's moving, falling, slipping, vanishing. . . . There is a vast upheaval of matter. Someone is standing over me and saying:

"I'm going out to buy a newspaper."

1. Part of the sea off the east coast of Kent.

MODERN FICTION / 2087

"Yes?"
"Though it's no good buying newspapers. . . . Nothing ever happens. Curse this war; God damn this war! . . . All the same, I don't see why we should have a snail on our wall."
Ah, the mark on the wall! It was a snail.

1921

Modern Fiction

In making any survey, even the freest and loosest, of modern fiction, it is difficult not to take it for granted that the modern practice of the art is somehow an improvement upon the old. With their simple tools and primitive materials, it might be said, Fielding[1] did well and Jane Austen even better, but compare their opportunities with ours! Their masterpieces certainly have a strange air of simplicity. And yet the analogy between literature and the process, to choose an example, of making motor cars scarcely holds good beyond the first glance. It is doubtful whether in the course of the centuries, though we have learnt much about making machines, we have learnt anything about making literature. We do not come to write better; all that we can be said to do is to keep moving, now a little in this direction, now in that, but with a circular tendency should the whole course of the track be viewed from a sufficiently lofty pinnacle. It need scarcely be said that we make no claim to stand, even momentarily, upon that vantage-ground. On the flat, in the crowd, half blind with dust, we look back with envy to those happier warriors, whose battle is won and whose achievements wear so serene an air of accomplishment that we can scarcely refrain from whispering that the fight was not so fierce for them as for us. It is for the historian of literature to decide; for him to say if we are now beginning or ending or standing in the middle of a great period of prose fiction, for down in the plain little is visible. We only know that certain gratitudes and hostilities inspire us; that certain paths seem to lead to fertile land, others to the dust and the desert; and of this perhaps it may be worth while to attempt some account.

Our quarrel, then, is not with the classics, and if we speak of quarrelling with Mr Wells, Mr Bennett, and Mr Galsworthy;[2] it is partly that by the mere fact of their existence in the flesh their work has a living, breathing, everyday imperfection which bids us take what liberties with it we choose. But it is also true, that, while we thank them for a thousand gifts, we reserve our unconditional gratitude for Mr Hardy, for Mr Conrad, and in much lesser degree for the Mr Hudson of *The Purple Land, Green Mansions,* and *Far Away and Long Ago.*[3] Mr Wells, Mr Bennett, and Mr Galsworthy have excited so many hopes and disappointed them so persistently that our gratitude largely takes the form of thanking them for having shown us what they might have done but have not done; what we certainly could not do, but as certainly, perhaps, do not wish to do. No single phrase will sum up the charge or grievance which

1. Henry Fielding (1707–1754), English novelist.
2. H. G. Wells (1866–1946), Arnold Bennett (1867–1931), John Galsworthy (1867–1933), English novelists.
3. W. H. Hudson (1841–1922), naturalist and

writer, was born in Argentina, although he later lived in London. *The Purple Land* (1885) is about South America; *Green Mansions* (1904), a novel set in South America, was his first real success.

we have to bring against a mass of work so large in its volume and embodying so many qualities, both admirable and the reverse. If we tried to formulate our meaning in one word we should say that these three writers are materialists. It is because they are concerned not with the spirit but with the body that they have disappointed us, and left us with the feeling that the sooner English fiction turns its back upon them, as politely as may be, and marches, if only into the desert, the better for its soul. Naturally, no single word reaches the centre of three separate targets. In the case of Mr Wells it falls notably wide of the mark. And yet even with him it indicates to our thinking the fatal alloy in his genius, the great clod of clay that has got itself mixed up with the purity of his inspiration. But Mr Bennett is perhaps the worst culprit of the three, inasmuch as he is by far the best workman. He can make a book so well constructed and solid in its craftsmanship that it is difficult for the most exacting of critics to see through what chink or crevice decay can creep in. There is not so much as a draught between the frames of the windows, or a crack in the boards. And yet—if life should refuse to live there? That is a risk which the creator of *The Old Wives' Tale*, George Cannon, Edwin Clayhanger,[4] and hosts of other figures, may well claim to have surmounted. His characters live abundantly, even unexpectedly, but it remains to ask how do they live, and what do they live for? More and more they seem to us, deserting even the well-built villa in the Five Towns,[5] to spend their time in some softly padded first-class railway carriage, pressing bells and buttons innumerable; and the destiny to which they travel so luxuriously becomes more and more unquestionably an eternity of bliss spent in the very best hotel in Brighton.[6] It can scarcely be said of Mr Wells that he is a materialist in the sense that he takes too much delight in the solidity of his fabric. His mind is too generous in its sympathies to allow him to spend much time in making things shipshape and substantial. He is a materialist from sheer goodness of heart, taking upon his shoulders the work that ought to have been discharged by Government officials, and in the plethora of his ideas and facts scarcely having leisure to realize, or forgetting to think important, the crudity and coarseness of his human beings. Yet what more damaging criticism can there be both of his earth and of his Heaven than that they are to be inhabited here and hereafter by his Joans and his Peters?[7] Does not the inferiority of their natures tarnish whatever institutions and ideals may be provided for them by the generosity of their creator? Nor, profoundly though we respect the integrity and humanity of Mr Galsworthy, shall we find what we seek in his pages.

If we fasten, then, one label on all these books, on which is one word, materialists, we mean by it that they write of unimportant things; that they spend immense skill and immense industry making the trivial and the transitory appear the true and the enduring.

We have to admit that we are exacting, and, further, that we find it difficult to justify our discontent by explaining what it is that we exact. We frame our question differently at different times. But it reappears most persistently as we drop the finished novel on the crest of a sigh—Is it worth while? What is the point of it all? Can it be that, owing to one of those little deviations which

---

4. Characters in Arnold Bennett's novels; *The Old Wives' Tale* (1908) is the best-known.
5. The pottery towns of Staffordshire in which much of Bennett's fiction was set.
6. Once-fashionable seaside resort on the south-

west coast of England.
7. In his novel *Joan and Peter: The Story of an Education* (1918), Wells advocates education to address social problems.

the human spirit seems to make from time to time, Mr Bennett has come down with his magnificent apparatus for catching life just an inch or two on the wrong side? Life escapes; and perhaps without life nothing else is worth while. It is a confession of vagueness to have to make use of such a figure as this, but we scarcely better the matter by speaking, as critics are prone to do, of reality. Admitting the vagueness which afflicts all criticism of novels, let us hazard the opinion that for us at this moment the form of fiction most in vogue more often misses than secures the thing we seek. Whether we call it life or spirit, truth or reality, this, the essential thing, has moved off, or on, and refuses to be contained any longer in such ill-fitting vestments as we provide. Nevertheless, we go on perseveringly, conscientiously, constructing our two and thirty chapters after a design which more and more ceases to resemble the vision in our minds. So much of the enormous labour of proving the solidity, the likeness to life, of the story is not merely labour thrown away but labour misplaced to the extent of obscuring and blotting out the light of the conception. The writer seems constrained, not by his own free will but by some powerful and unscrupulous tyrant who has him in thrall, to provide a plot, to provide comedy, tragedy, love interest, and an air of probability embalming the whole so impeccable that if all his figures were to come to life they would find themselves dressed down to the last button of their coats in the fashion of the hour. The tyrant is obeyed; the novel is done to a turn. But sometimes, more and more often as time goes by, we suspect a momentary doubt, a spasm of rebellion, as the pages fill themselves in the customary way. Is life like this? Must novels be like this?

Look within and life, it seems, is very far from being "like this." Examine for a moment an ordinary mind on an ordinary day. The mind receives a myriad impressions—trivial, fantastic, evanescent, or engraved with the sharpness of steel. From all sides they come, an incessant shower of innumerable atoms; and as they fall, as they shape themselves into the life of Monday or Tuesday,[8] the accent falls differently from of old; the moment of importance came not here but there; so that, if a writer were a free man and not a slave, if he could write what he chose, not what he must, if he could base his work upon his own feeling and not upon convention, there would be no plot, no comedy, no tragedy, no love interest or catastrophe in the accepted style, and perhaps not a single button sewn on as the Bond Street[9] tailors would have it. Life is not a series of gig-lamps[1] symmetrically arranged; life is a luminous halo, a semi-transparent envelope surrounding us from the beginning of consciousness to the end. Is it not the task of the novelist to convey this varying, this unknown and uncircumscribed spirit, whatever aberration or complexity it may display, with as little mixture of the alien and external as possible? We are not pleading merely for courage and sincerity; we are suggesting that the proper stuff of fiction is a little other than custom would have us believe it.

It is, at any rate, in some such fashion as this that we seek to define the quality which distinguishes the work of several young writers, among whom Mr James Joyce is the most notable, from that of their predecessors. They attempt to come closer to life, and to preserve more sincerely and exactly what interests and moves them, even if to do so they must discard most of the conventions which are commonly observed by the novelist. Let us record the

8. *Monday or Tuesday* was Woolf's 1921 collection of experimental stories and sketches.
9. Fashionable shopping street in London.
1. Carriage lamps.

atoms as they fall upon the mind in the order in which they fall, let us trace the pattern, however disconnected and incoherent in appearance, which each sight or incident scores upon the consciousness. Let us not take it for granted that life exists more fully in what is commonly thought big than in what is commonly thought small. Anyone who has read *The Portrait of the Artist as a Young Man* or, what promises to be a far more interesting work, *Ulysses*,[2] now appearing in the *Little Review*, will have hazarded some theory of this nature as to Mr Joyce's intention. On our part, with such a fragment before us, it is hazarded rather than affirmed; but whatever the intention of the whole, there can be no question but that it is of the utmost sincerity and that the result, difficult or unpleasant as we may judge it, is undeniably important. In contrast with those whom we have called materialists, Mr Joyce is spiritual; he is con-cerned at all costs to reveal the flickerings of that innermost flame which flashes its messages through the brain, and in order to preserve it he disregards with complete courage whatever seems to him adventitious, whether it be probability, or coherence, or any other of these signposts which for generations have served to support the imagination of a reader when called upon to imag-ine what he can neither touch nor see. The scene in the cemetery,[3] for instance, with its brilliancy, its sordidity, its incoherence, its sudden lightning flashes of significance, does undoubtedly come so close to the quick of the mind that, on a first reading at any rate, it is difficult not to acclaim a mas-terpiece. If we want life itself, here surely we have it. Indeed, we find ourselves fumbling rather awkwardly if we try to say what else we wish, and for what reason a work of such originality yet fails to compare, for we must take high examples, with *Youth* or *The Mayor of Casterbridge*.[4] It fails because of the comparative poverty of the writer's mind, we might say simply and have done with it. But it is possible to press a little further and wonder whether we may not refer our sense of being in a bright yet narrow room, confined and shut in, rather than enlarged and set free, to some limitation imposed by the method as well as by the mind. Is it the method that inhibits the creative power? Is it due to the method that we feel neither jovial nor magnanimous, but centred in a self which, in spite of its tremor of susceptibility, never embraces or creates what is outside itself and beyond? Does the emphasis laid, perhaps didactically, upon indecency contribute to the effect of something angular and isolated? Or is it merely that in any effort of such originality it is much easier, for contemporaries especially, to feel what it lacks than to name what it gives? In any case it is a mistake to stand outside examining "methods". Any method is right, every method is right, that expresses what we wish to express, if we are writers; that brings us closer to the novelist's intention if we are readers. This method has the merit of bringing us closer to what we were prepared to call life itself; did not the reading of *Ulysses* suggest how much of life is excluded or ignored, and did it not come with a shock to open *Tristram Shandy* or even *Pendennis*[5] and be by them convinced that there are not only other aspects of life, but more important ones into the bargain.

However this may be, the problem before the novelist at present, as we suppose it to have been in the past, is to contrive means of being free to set down what he chooses. He has to have the courage to say that what interests

<hr>

2. Written April, 1919 [Woolf's note].
3. The sixth episode ("Hades") of *Ulysses*, where Bloom goes to Paddy Dignam's funeral.
4. A story and a novel by, respectively, Joseph

Conrad and Thomas Hardy.
5. Novels by, respectively, the English writers Laurence Sterne (1713–1768) and William Make-peace Thackeray (1811–1863).

him is no longer "this" but "that": out of "that" alone must he construct his work. For the moderns "that", the point of interest, lies very likely in the dark places of psychology. At once, therefore, the accent falls a little differently; the emphasis is upon something hitherto ignored; at once a different outline of form becomes necessary, difficult for us to grasp, incomprehensible to our predecessors. No one but a modern, no one perhaps but a Russian, would have felt the interest of the situation which Tchekov has made into the short story which he calls "Gusev."[6] Some Russian soldiers lie ill on board a ship which is taking them back to Russia. We are given a few scraps of their talk and some of their thoughts; then one of them dies and is carried away; the talk goes on among the others for a time, until Gusev himself dies, and looking "like a carrot or a radish" is thrown overboard. The emphasis is laid upon such unexpected places that at first it seems as if there were no emphasis at all; and then, as the eyes accustom themselves to twilight and discern the shapes of things in a room we see how complete the story is, how profound, and how truly in obedience to his vision Tchekov has chosen this, that, and the other, and placed them together to compose something new. But it is impossible to say "this is comic," or "that is tragic," nor are we certain, since short stories, we have been taught, should be brief and conclusive, whether this, which is vague and inconclusive, should be called a short story at all.

The most elementary remarks upon modern English fiction can hardly avoid some mention of the Russian influence, and if the Russians are mentioned one runs the risk of feeling that to write of any fiction save theirs is waste of time. If we want understanding of the soul and heart where else shall we find it of comparable profundity? If we are sick of our own materialism the least considerable of their novelists has by right of birth a natural reverence for the human spirit. "Learn to make yourself akin to people. . . . But let this sympathy be not with the mind—for it is easy with the mind—but with the heart, with love towards them." In every great Russian writer we seem to discern the features of a saint, if sympathy for the sufferings of others, love towards them, endeavour to reach some goal worthy of the most exacting demands of the spirit constitute saintliness. It is the saint in them which confounds us with a feeling of our own irreligious triviality, and turns so many of our famous novels to tinsel and trickery. The conclusions of the Russian mind, thus comprehensive and compassionate, are inevitably, perhaps, of the utmost sadness. More accurately indeed we might speak of the inconclusiveness of the Russian mind. It is the sense that there is no answer, that if honestly examined life presents question after question which must be left to sound on and on after the story is over in hopeless interrogation that fills us with a deep, and finally it may be with a resentful, despair. They are right perhaps; unquestionably they see further than we do and without our gross impediments of vision. But perhaps we see something that escapes them, or why should this voice of protest mix itself with our gloom? The voice of protest is the voice of another and an ancient civilisation which seems to have bred in us the instinct to enjoy and fight rather than to suffer and understand. English fiction from Sterne to Meredith[7] bears witness to our natural delight in humour and comedy, in the beauty of earth, in the activities of the intellect, and in the splendour of the body. But any deductions that we may draw from the comparison of two fic-

6. 1890 story by the Russian writer Anton Pavlovich Chekhov (1860–1904).

7. George Meredith (1828–1909), English novelist.

tions so immeasurably far apart are futile save indeed as they flood us with a view of the infinite possibilities of the art and remind us that there is no limit to the horizon, and that nothing—no "method," no experiment, even of the wildest—is forbidden, but only falsity and pretence. "The proper stuff of fiction" does not exist; everything is the proper stuff of fiction, every feeling, every thought; every quality of brain and spirit is drawn upon; no perception comes amiss. And if we can imagine the art of fiction come alive and standing in our midst, she would undoubtedly bid us break her and bully her, as well as honour and love her, for so her youth is renewed and her sovereignty assured.

1925

A Room of One's Own[1]

Chapter One

But, you may say, we asked you to speak about women and fiction—what has that got to do with a room of one's own? I will try to explain. When you asked me to speak about women and fiction I sat down on the banks of a river and began to wonder what the words meant. They might mean simply a few remarks about Fanny Burney; a few more about Jane Austen; a tribute to the Brontës and a sketch of Haworth Parsonage under snow; some witticisms if possible about Miss Mitford; a respectful allusion to George Eliot; a reference to Mrs. Gaskell[2] and one would have done. But at second sight the words seemed not so simple. The title women and fiction might mean, and you may have meant it to mean, women and what they are like; or it might mean women and the fiction that they write; or it might mean women and the fiction that is written about them; or it might mean that somehow all three are inextricably mixed together and you want me to consider them in that light. But when I began to consider the subject in this last way, which seemed the most interesting, I soon saw that it had one fatal drawback. I should never be able to come to a conclusion. I should never be able to fulfil what is, I understand, the first duty of a lecturer—to hand you after an hour's discourse a nugget of pure truth to wrap up between the pages of your notebooks and keep on the mantelpiece for ever. All I could do was to offer you an opinion upon one minor point—a woman must have money and a room of her own if she is to write fiction; and that, as you will see, leaves the great problem of the true nature of woman and the true nature of fiction unsolved. I have shirked the duty of coming to a conclusion upon these two questions—women and fiction remain, so far as I am concerned, unsolved problems. But in order to make some amends I am going to do what I can to show you how I arrived at this opinion about the room and the money. I am going to develop in your presence as fully and freely as I can the train of thought which led me to think this. Perhaps if I lay bare the ideas, the prejudices, that lie behind this statement

1. This essay is based upon two papers read to the Arts Society at Newnham and the Odtaa at Girton in October 1928. The papers were too long to be read in full, and have since been altered and expanded [Woolf's note]. Newnham and Girton are women's colleges at Cambridge. Odtaa, or "One Damn Thing After Another," was an elite literary society.

2. All English writers: Frances Burney (1752–1840); Jane Austen (1775–1817); Charlotte (1816–1855), Emily (1818–1848), and Anne (1820–1849) Brontë, who grew up in the parsonage in Haworth (Yorkshire), where their father was curate; Mary Russell Mitford (1787–1855); George Eliot (pseudonym of Marian Evans, 1819–1880); and Elizabeth Gaskell (1810–1865).

you will find that they have some bearing upon women and some upon fiction. At any rate, when a subject is highly controversial—and any question about sex is that—one cannot hope to tell the truth. One can only show how one came to hold whatever opinion one does hold. One can only give one's audience the chance of drawing their own conclusions as they observe the limitations, the prejudices, the idiosyncrasies of the speaker. Fiction here is likely to contain more truth than fact. Therefore I propose, making use of all the liberties and licences of a novelist, to tell you the story of the two days that preceded my coming here—how, bowed down by the weight of the subject which you have laid upon my shoulders, I pondered it, and made it work in and out of my daily life. I need not say that what I am about to describe has no existence; Oxbridge[3] is an invention; so is Fernham; "I" is only a convenient term for somebody who has no real being. Lies will flow from my lips, but there may perhaps be some truth mixed up with them; it is for you to seek out this truth and to decide whether any part of it is worth keeping. If not, you will of course throw the whole of it into the wastepaper basket and forget all about it.

Here then was I (call me Mary Beton, Mary Seton, Mary Carmichael[4] or by any name you please—it is not a matter of any importance) sitting on the banks of a river a week or two ago in fine October weather, lost in thought. That collar I have spoken of, women and fiction, the need of coming to some conclusion on a subject that raises all sorts of prejudices and passions, bowed my head to the ground. To the right and left bushes of some sort, golden and crimson, glowed with the colour, even it seemed burnt with the heat, of fire. On the further bank the willows wept in perpetual lamentation, their hair about their shoulders. The river reflected whatever it chose of sky and bridge and burning tree, and when the undergraduate had oared his boat through the reflections they closed again, completely, as if he had never been. There one might have sat the clock round lost in thought. Thought—to call it by a prouder name than it deserved—had let its line down into the stream. It swayed, minute after minute, hither and thither among the reflections and the weeds, letting the water lift it and sink it, until—you know the little tug—the sudden conglomeration of an idea at the end of one's line: and then the cautious hauling of it in, and the careful laying of it out? Alas, laid on the grass how small, how insignificant this thought of mine looked; the sort of fish that a good fisherman puts back into the water so that it may grow fatter and be one day worth cooking and eating. I will not trouble you with that thought now, though if you look carefully you may find it for yourselves in the course of what I am going to say.

But however small it was, it had, nevertheless, the mysterious property of its kind—put back into the mind, it became at once very exciting, and important; and as it darted and sank, and flashed hither and thither, set up such a wash and tumult of ideas that it was impossible to sit still. It was thus that I found myself walking with extreme rapidity across a grass plot. Instantly a man's figure rose to intercept me. Nor did I at first understand that the gesticulations of a curious-looking object, in a cut-away coat and evening shirt, were aimed at me. His face expressed horror and indignation. Instinct rather than reason came to my help; he was a Beadle;[5] I was a woman. This was the

3. A common term blending Oxford and Cambridge.
4. Reference to the "Scottish Ballad of the Queen's Marys," also called "The Four Marys" (ca.

1563), a ballad about ladies-in-waiting to Mary, Queen of Scots.
5. Officer in a university who precedes public processions.

turf; there was the path. Only the Fellows and Scholars are allowed here; the gravel is the place for me. Such thoughts were the work of a moment. As I regained the path the arms of the Beadle sank, his face assumed its usual repose, and though turf is better walking than gravel, no very great harm was done. The only charge I could bring against the Fellows and Scholars of whatever the college might happen to be was that in protection of their turf, which has been rolled for 300 years in succession, they had sent my little fish into hiding.

What idea it had been that had sent me so audaciously trespassing I could not now remember. The spirit of peace descended like a cloud from heaven, for if the spirit of peace dwells anywhere, it is in the courts and quadrangles of Oxbridge on a fine October morning. Strolling through those colleges past those ancient halls the roughness of the present seemed smoothed away; the body seemed contained in a miraculous glass cabinet through which no sound could penetrate, and the mind, freed from any contact with facts (unless one trespassed on the turf again), was at liberty to settle down upon whatever meditation was in harmony with the moment. As chance would have it, some stray memory of some old essay about revisiting Oxbridge in the long vacation brought Charles Lamb to mind—Saint Charles, said Thackeray,[6] putting a letter of Lamb's to his forehead. Indeed, among all the dead (I give you my thoughts as they came to me), Lamb is one of the most congenial; one to whom one would have liked to say, Tell me then how you wrote your essays? For his essays are superior even to Max Beerbohm's,[7] I thought, with all their perfection, because of that wild flash of imagination, that lightning crack of genius in the middle of them which leaves them flawed and imperfect, but starred with poetry. Lamb then came to Oxbridge perhaps a hundred years ago. Certainly he wrote an essay—the name escapes me[8]—about the manuscript of one of Milton's poems which he saw here. It was *Lycidas* perhaps, and Lamb wrote how it shocked him to think it possible that any word in *Lycidas* could have been different from what it is. To think of Milton changing the words in that poem seemed to him a sort of sacrilege. This led me to remember what I could of *Lycidas* and to amuse myself with guessing which word it could have been that Milton had altered, and why. It then occurred to me that the very manuscript itself which Lamb had looked at was only a few hundred yards away, so that one could follow Lamb's footsteps across the quadrangle to that famous library[9] where the treasure is kept. Moreover, I recollected, as I put this plan into execution, it is in this famous library that the manuscript of Thackeray's *Esmond* is also preserved. The critics often say that *Esmond* is Thackeray's most perfect novel. But the affectation of the style, with its imitation of the eighteenth century, hampers one, so far as I remember; unless indeed the eighteenth-century style was natural to Thackeray—a fact that one might prove by looking at the manuscript and seeing whether the alterations were for the benefit of the style or of the sense. But then one would have to decide what is style and what is meaning, a question which— but here I was actually at the door which leads into the library itself. I must have opened it, for instantly there issued, like a guardian angel barring the way with a flutter of black gown instead of white wings, a deprecating, silvery,

6. William Makepeace Thackeray (1811–1863), English novelist, wrote *The History of Henry Esmond, Esquire* (1852), mentioned later. Charles Lamb (1775–1834), English critic and essayist.

7. English essayist and parodist (1872–1956).
8. "Oxford in the Vacation" (1823).
9. The library at Trinity College, Cambridge.

kindly gentleman, who regretted in a low voice as he waved me back that ladies are only admitted to the library if accompanied by a Fellow of the College or furnished with a letter of introduction.

That a famous library has been cursed by a woman is a matter of complete indifference to a famous library. Venerable and calm, with all its treasures safe locked within its breast, it sleeps complacently and will, so far as I am concerned, so sleep for ever. Never will I wake those echoes, never will I ask for that hospitality again, I vowed as I descended the steps in anger. Still an hour remained before luncheon, and what was one to do? Stroll on the meadows? sit by the river? Certainly it was a lovely autumn morning; the leaves were fluttering red to the ground; there was no great hardship in doing either. But the sound of music reached my ear. Some service or celebration was going forward. The organ complained magnificently as I passed the chapel door. Even the sorrow of Christianity sounded in that serene air more like the recollection of sorrow than sorrow itself; even the groanings of the ancient organ seemed lapped in peace. I had no wish to enter had I the right, and this time the verger might have stopped me, demanding perhaps my baptismal certificate, or a letter of introduction from the Dean. But the outside of these magnificent buildings is often as beautiful as the inside. Moreover, it was amusing enough to watch the congregation assembling, coming in and going out again, busying themselves at the door of the chapel like bees at the mouth of a hive. Many were in cap and gown; some had tufts of fur on their shoulders; others were wheeled in bath-chairs; others, though not past middle age, seemed creased and crushed into shapes so singular that one was reminded of those giant crabs and crayfish who heave with difficulty across the sand of an aquarium. As I leant against the wall the University indeed seemed a sanctuary in which are preserved rare types which would soon be obsolete if left to fight for existence on the pavement of the Strand.[1] Old stories of old deans and old dons came back to mind, but before I had summoned up courage to whistle—it used to be said that at the sound of a whistle old Professor ———— instantly broke into a gallop—the venerable congregation had gone inside. The outside of the chapel remained. As you know, its high domes and pinnacles can be seen, like a sailing-ship always voyaging never arriving, lit up at night and visible for miles, far away across the hills. Once, presumably, this quadrangle with its smooth lawns, its massive buildings, and the chapel itself was marsh too, where the grasses waved and the swine rooted. Teams of horses and oxen, I thought, must have hauled the stone in wagons from far countries, and then with infinite labour the grey blocks in whose shade I was now standing were poised in order one on top of another, and then the painters brought their glass for the windows, and the masons were busy for centuries up on that roof with putty and cement, spade and trowel.[2] Every Saturday somebody must have poured gold and silver out of a leathern purse into their ancient fists, for they had their beer and skittles presumably of an evening. An unending stream of gold and silver, I thought, must have flowed into this court perpetually to keep the stones coming and the masons working; to level, to ditch, to dig and to drain. But it was then the age of faith, and money was poured liberally to set these stones on a deep foundation, and when the stones were raised, still more money was poured in from the coffers of kings and queens and great

1. A busy thoroughfare in London.
2. King's College Chapel, Cambridge, was built from 1446 to 1547.

nobles to ensure that hymns should be sung here and scholars taught. Lands were granted; tithes were paid. And when the age of faith was over and the age of reason had come, still the same flow of gold and silver went on; fellowships were founded; lectureships endowed; only the gold and silver flowed now, not from the coffers of the king, but from the chests of merchants and manufacturers, from the purses of men who had made, say, a fortune from industry, and returned, in their wills, a bounteous share of it to endow more chairs, more lectureships, more fellowships in the university where they had learnt their craft. Hence the libraries and laboratories; the observatories; the splendid equipment of costly and delicate instruments which now stands on glass shelves, where centuries ago the grasses waved and the swine rootled. Certainly, as I strolled round the court, the foundation of gold and silver seemed deep enough; the pavement laid solidly over the wild grasses. Men with trays on their heads went busily from staircase to staircase. Gaudy blossoms flowered in window-boxes. The strains of the gramophone blared out from the rooms within. It was impossible not to reflect—the reflection whatever it may have been was cut short. The clock struck. It was time to find one's way to luncheon.

It is a curious fact that novelists have a way of making us believe that luncheon parties are invariably memorable for something very witty that was said, or for something very wise that was done. But they seldom spare a word for what was eaten. It is part of the novelist's convention not to mention soup and salmon and ducklings, as if soup and salmon and ducklings were of no importance whatsoever, as if nobody ever smoked a cigar or drank a glass of wine. Here, however, I shall take the liberty to defy that convention and to tell you that the lunch on this occasion began with soles, sunk in a deep dish, over which the college cook had spread a counterpane of the whitest cream, save that it was branded here and there with brown spots like the spots on the flanks of a doe. After that came the partridges, but if this suggests a couple of bald, brown birds on a plate you are mistaken. The partridges, many and various, came with all their retinue of sauces and salads, the sharp and the sweet, each in its order; their potatoes, thin as coins but not so hard; their sprouts, foliated as rosebuds but more succulent. And no sooner had the roast and its retinue been done with than the silent serving-man, the Beadle himself perhaps in a milder manifestation, set before us, wreathed in napkins, a confection which rose all sugar from the waves. To call it pudding and so relate it to rice and tapioca would be an insult. Meanwhile the wineglasses had flushed yellow and flushed crimson; had been emptied; had been filled. And thus by degrees was lit, halfway down the spine, which is the seat of the soul, not that hard little electric light which we call brilliance, as it pops in and out upon our lips, but the more profound, subtle and subterranean glow, which is the rich yellow flame of rational intercourse. No need to hurry. No need to sparkle. No need to be anybody but oneself. We are all going to heaven and Vandyck[3] is of the company—in other words, how good life seemed, how sweet its rewards, how trivial this grudge or that grievance, how admirable friendship and the society of one's kind, as, lighting a good cigarette, one sunk among the cushions in the window-seat.

If by good luck there had been an ash-tray handy, if one had not knocked

---

3. Sir Anthony Van Dyck (1599–1641), born in Antwerp but lived for some years in England. He painted many grand portraits of the English royal family and court.

the ash out of the window in default, if things had been a little different from what they were, one would not have seen, presumably, a cat without a tail. The sight of that abrupt and truncated animal padding softly across the quadrangle changed by some fluke of the subconscious intelligence the emotional light for me. It was as if some one had let fall a shade. Perhaps the excellent hock[4] was relinquishing its hold. Certainly, as I watched the Manx cat pause in the middle of the lawn as if it too questioned the universe, something seemed lacking, something seemed different. But what was lacking, what was different, I asked myself, listening to the talk. And to answer that question I had to think myself out of the room, back into the past, before the war indeed, and to set before my eyes the model of another luncheon party held in rooms not very far distant from these; but different. Everything was different. Meanwhile the talk went on among the guests, who were many and young, some of this sex, some of that; it went on swimmingly, it went on agreeably, freely, amusingly. And as it went on I set it against the background of that other talk, and as I matched the two together I had no doubt that one was the descendant, the legitimate heir of the other. Nothing was changed; nothing was different save only—here I listened with all my ears not entirely to what was being said, but to the murmur or current behind it. Yes, that was it—the change was there. Before the war at a luncheon party like this people would have said precisely the same things but they would have sounded different, because in those days they were accompanied by a sort of humming noise, not articulate, but musical, exciting, which changed the value of the words themselves. Could one set that humming noise to words? Perhaps with the help of the poets one could. A book lay beside me and, opening it, I turned casually enough to Tennyson. And here I found Tennyson was singing:

> There has fallen a splendid tear
>   From the passion-flower at the gate.
> She is coming, my dove, my dear;
>   She is coming, my life, my fate;
> The red rose cries, "She is near, she is near";
>   And the white rose weeps, "She is late";
> The larkspur listens, "I hear, I hear";
>   And the lily whispers, "I wait."[5]

Was that what men hummed at luncheon parties before the war? And the women?

> My heart is like a singing bird
>   Whose nest is in a water'd shoot;
> My heart is like an apple tree
>   Whose boughs are bent with thick-set fruit;
> My heart is like a rainbow shell
>   That paddles in a halcyon sea;
> My heart is gladder than all these
>   Because my love is come to me.[6]

Was that what women hummed at luncheon parties before the war?

There was something so ludicrous in thinking of people humming such things even under their breath at luncheon parties before the war that I burst

4. Rhine wine.   6. Christina Rossetti's *A Birthday*, first stanza.
5. *Maud* 1.22.10.

out laughing, and had to explain my laughter by pointing at the Manx cat, who did look a little absurd, poor beast, without a tail, in the middle of the lawn. Was he really born so, or had he lost his tail in an accident? The tailless cat, though some are said to exist in the Isle of Man,[7] is rarer than one thinks. It is a queer animal, quaint rather than beautiful. It is strange what a difference a tail makes—you know the sort of things one says as a lunch party breaks up and people are finding their coats and hats.

This one, thanks to the hospitality of the host, had lasted far into the afternoon. The beautiful October day was fading and the leaves were falling from the trees in the avenue as I walked through it. Gate after gate seemed to close with gentle finality behind me. Innumerable beadles were fitting innumerable keys into well-oiled locks; the treasure-house was being made secure for another night. After the avenue one comes out upon a road—I forget its name—which leads you, if you take the right turning, along to Fernham. But there was plenty of time. Dinner was not till half-past seven. One could almost do without dinner after such a luncheon. It is strange how a scrap of poetry works in the mind and makes the legs move in time to it along the road. Those words—

> There has fallen a splendid tear
> From the passion-flower at the gate.
> She is coming, my dove, my dear—

sang in my blood as I stepped quickly along towards Headingley. And then, switching off into the other measure, I sang, where the waters are churned up by the weir:

> My heart is like a singing bird
> Whose nest is in a water'd shoot;
> My heart is like an apple tree . . .

What poets, I cried aloud, as one does in the dusk, what poets they were!

In a sort of jealousy, I suppose, for our own age, silly and absurd though these comparisons are, I went on to wonder if honestly one could name two living poets now as great as Tennyson and Christina Rossetti were then. Obviously it is impossible, I thought, looking into those foaming waters, to compare them. The very reason why the poetry excites one to such abandonment, such rapture, is that it celebrates some feeling that one used to have (at luncheon parties before the war perhaps), so that one responds easily, familiarly, without troubling to check the feeling, or to compare it with any that one has now. But the living poets express a feeling that is actually being made and torn out of us at the moment. One does not recognize it in the first place; often for some reason one fears it; one watches it with keenness and compares it jealously and suspiciously with the old feeling that one knew. Hence the difficulty of modern poetry; and it is because of this difficulty that one cannot remember more than two consecutive lines of any good modern poet. For this reason—that my memory failed me—the argument flagged for want of material. But why, I continued, moving on towards Headingley, have we stopped humming under our breath at luncheon parties? Why has Alfred ceased to sing

> She is coming, my dove, my dear?

7. One of the British Isles in the Irish Sea.

Why has Christina ceased to respond

> My heart is gladder than all these
> Because my love is come to me?

Shall we lay the blame on the war? When the guns fired in August 1914, did the faces of men and women show so plain in each other's eyes that romance was killed? Certainly it was a shock (to women in particular with their illusions about education, and so on) to see the faces of our rulers in the light of the shell-fire. So ugly they looked—German, English, French—so stupid. But lay the blame where one will, on whom one will, the illusion which inspired Tennyson and Christina Rossetti to sing so passionately about the coming of their loves is far rarer now than then. One has only to read, to look, to listen, to remember. But why say "blame"? Why, if it was an illusion, not praise the catastrophe, whatever it was, that destroyed illusion and put truth in its place? For truth . . . those dots mark the spot where, in search of truth, I missed the turning up to Fernham. Yes indeed, which was truth and which was illusion, I asked myself. What was the truth about these houses, for example, dim and festive now with their red windows in the dusk, but raw and red and squalid, with their sweets and their boot-laces, at nine o'clock in the morning? And the willows and the river and the gardens that run down to the river, vague now with the mist stealing over them, but gold and red in the sunlight—which was the truth, which was the illusion about them? I spare you the twists and turns of my cogitations, for no conclusion was found on the road to Headingley, and I ask you to suppose that I soon found out my mistake about the turning and retraced my steps to Fernham.

As I have said already that it was an October day, I dare not forfeit your respect and imperil the fair name of fiction by changing the season and describing lilacs hanging over garden walls, crocuses, tulips and other flowers of spring. Fiction must stick to facts, and the truer the facts the better the fiction—so we are told. Therefore it was still autumn and the leaves were still yellow and falling, if anything, a little faster than before, because it was now evening (seven twenty-three to be precise) and a breeze (from the southwest to be exact) had risen. But for all that there was something odd at work:

> My heart is like a singing bird
> Whose nest is in a water'd shoot;
> My heart is like an apple tree
> Whose boughs are bent with thick-set fruit—

perhaps the words of Christina Rossetti were partly responsible for the folly of the fancy—it was nothing of course but a fancy—that the lilac was shaking its flowers over the garden walls, and the brimstone butterflies were scudding hither and thither, and the dust of the pollen was in the air. A wind blew, from what quarter I know not, but it lifted the half-grown leaves so that there was a flash of silver grey in the air. It was the time between the lights when colours undergo their intensification and purples and golds burn in window-panes like the beat of an excitable heart; when for some reason the beauty of the world revealed and yet soon to perish (here I pushed into the garden, for, unwisely, the door was left open and no beadles seemed about), the beauty of the world which is so soon to perish, has two edges, one of laughter, one of anguish, cutting the heart asunder. The gardens of Fernham lay before me in the spring twilight, wild and open, and in the long grass, sprinkled and carelessly flung, were daffodils and bluebells, not orderly perhaps at the best of times, and now wind-blown and waving as they tugged at their roots. The windows of the building, curved like ships' windows among generous waves of red brick, changed from lemon to silver under the flight of the quick spring clouds. Somebody was in a hammock, somebody, but in this light they were phantoms only, half guessed, half seen, raced across the grass—would no one stop her?—and then on the terrace, as if popping out to breathe the air, to glance at the garden, came a bent figure, formidable yet humble, with her great forehead and her shabby dress—could it be the famous scholar, could it be J—— H—— herself?[8] All was dim, yet intense too, as if the scarf which the dusk had flung over the garden were torn asunder by star or sword—the flash of some terrible reality leaping, as its way is, out of the heart of the spring. For youth——

Here was my soup. Dinner was being served in the great dining-hall. Far from being spring it was in fact an evening in October. Everybody was assembled in the big dining-room. Dinner was ready. Here was the soup. It was a plain gravy soup. There was nothing to stir the fancy in that. One could have seen through the transparent liquid any pattern that there might have been on the plate itself. But there was no pattern. The plate was plain. Next came beef with its attendant greens and potatoes—a homely trinity, suggesting the rumps of cattle in a muddy market, and sprouts curled and yellowed at the edge, and bargaining and cheapening, and women with string bags on Monday morning. There was no reason to complain of human nature's daily food, seeing that the supply was sufficient and coal-miners doubtless were sitting down to less. Prunes and custard followed. And if any one complains that prunes, even when mitigated by custard, are an uncharitable vegetable (fruit they are not), stringy as a miser's heart and exuding a fluid such as might run in misers' veins who have denied themselves wine and warmth for eighty years and yet not given to the poor, he should reflect that there are people whose charity embraces even the prune. Biscuits and cheese came next, and here the water-jug was liberally passed round, for it is the nature of biscuits to be dry, and these were biscuits to the core. That was all. The meal was over. Everybody scraped their chairs back; the swing-doors swung violently to and fro; soon the hall was emptied of every sign of food and made ready no doubt for breakfast next morning. Down corridors and up staircases the youth of England went banging and singing. And was it for a guest, a stranger (for I had no more right here in Fernham than in Trinity or Somerville or Girton or Newnham or Christchurch),[9] to say, "The dinner was not good," or to say (we were now, Mary Seton and I, in her sitting-room), "Could we not have dined up here alone?" for if I had said anything of the kind I should have been prying and searching into the secret economies of a house which to the stranger wears so fine a front of gaiety and courage. No, one could say nothing of the sort. Indeed, conversation for a moment flagged. The human frame being what it is, heart, body and brain all mixed together, and not contained in separate compartments as they will be no doubt in another million years, a good dinner is of great importance to good talk. One cannot think well, love well, sleep well, if one has not dined well. The lamp in the spine does not light on beef and prunes. We are all *probably* going to heaven, and Vandyck is, we *hope*, to

8. Jane Harrison (1850–1928), fellow and lecturer in classical archaeology at Newnham College, Cambridge; author of *Ancient Art and Ritual* (1913) and other influential books.
9. Oxford college. Somerville is a women's college at Oxford.

meet us round the next corner—that is the dubious and qualifying state of mind that beef and prunes at the end of the day's work breed between them. Happily my friend, who taught science, had a cupboard where there was a squat bottle and little glasses—(but there should have been sole and partridge to begin with)—so that we were able to draw up to the fire and repair some of the damages of the day's living. In a minute or so we were slipping freely in and out among all those objects of curiosity and interest which form in the mind in the absence of a particular person, and are naturally to be discussed on coming together again—how somebody has married, another has not; one thinks this, another that; one has improved out of all knowledge, the other most amazingly gone to the bad—with all those speculations upon human nature and the character of the amazing world we live in which spring naturally from such beginnings. While these things were being said, however, I became shamefacedly aware of a current setting in of its own accord and carrying everything forward to an end of its own. One might be talking of Spain or Portugal, of book or racehorse, but the real interest of whatever was said was none of those things, but a scene of masons on a high roof some five centuries ago. Kings and nobles brought treasure in huge sacks and poured it under the earth. This scene was for ever coming alive in my mind and placing itself by another of lean cows and a muddy market and withered greens and the stringy hearts of old men—these two pictures, disjointed and disconnected and non-sensical as they were, were for ever coming together and combating each other and had me entirely at their mercy. The best course, unless the whole talk was to be distorted, was to expose what was in my mind to the air, when with good luck it would fade and crumble like the head of the dead king when they opened the coffin at Windsor.[1] Briefly, then, I told Miss Seton about the masons who had been all those years on the roof of the chapel, and about the kings and queens and nobles bearing sacks of gold and silver on their shoulders, which they shovelled into the earth; and then how the great financial magnates of our own time came and laid cheques and bonds, I suppose, where the others had laid ingots and rough lumps of gold. All that lies beneath the colleges down there, I said; but this college, where we are now sitting, what lies beneath its gallant red brick and the wild unkempt grasses of the garden? What force is behind the plain china off which we dined, and (here it popped out of my mouth before I could stop it) the beef, the custard and the prunes?

Well, said Mary Seton, about the year 1860—Oh, but you know the story, she said, bored, I suppose, by the recital. And she told me—rooms were hired. Committees met. Envelopes were addressed. Circulars were drawn up. Meetings were held; letters were read out; so-and-so has promised so much; on the contrary, Mr ——— won't give a penny. The *Saturday Review* has been very rude. How can we raise a fund to pay for offices? Shall we hold a bazaar? Can't we find a pretty girl to sit in the front row? Let us look up what John Stuart Mill[2] said on the subject. Can any one persuade the editor of the ——— to print a letter? Can we get Lady ——— to sign it? Lady ——— is out of town. That was the way it was done, presumably, sixty years ago, and it was a prodigious effort, and a great deal of time was spent on it. And it was only after a long struggle and with the utmost difficulty that they got thirty thousand

---

1. Windsor Castle.
2. English philosopher and economist (1806–1873).

pounds together.[3] So obviously we cannot have wine and partridges and servants carrying tin dishes on their heads, she said. We cannot have sofas and separate rooms. "The amenities," she said, quoting from some book or other, "will have to wait."[4]

At the thought of all those women working year after year and finding it hard to get two thousand pounds together, and as much as they could do to get thirty thousand pounds, we burst out in scorn at the reprehensible poverty of our sex. What had our mothers been doing then that they had no wealth to leave us? Powdering their noses? Looking in at shop windows? Flaunting in the sun at Monte Carlo?[5] There were some photographs on the mantel-piece. Mary's mother—if that was her picture—may have been a wastrel in her spare time (she had thirteen children by a minister of the church), but if so her gay and dissipated life had left too few traces of its pleasures on her face. She was a homely body; an old lady in a plaid shawl which was fastened by a large cameo;[6] and she sat in a basket-chair, encouraging a spaniel to look at the camera, with the amused, yet strained expression of one who is sure that the dog will move directly the bulb is pressed. Now if she had gone into business; had become a manufacturer of artificial silk or a magnate on the Stock Exchange; if she had left two or three hundred thousand pounds to Fernham, we could have been sitting at our ease tonight and the subject of our talk might have been archaeology, botany, anthropology, physics, the nature of the atom, mathematics, astronomy, relativity, geography. If only Mrs Seton and her mother and her mother before her had learnt the great art of making money and had left their money, like their fathers and their grandfathers before them, to found fellowships and lectureships and prizes and scholarships appropriated to the use of their own sex, we might have dined very tolerably up here alone off a bird and a bottle of wine; we might have looked forward without undue confidence to a pleasant and honourable lifetime spent in the shelter of one of the liberally endowed professions. We might have been exploring or writing; mooning about the venerable places of the earth; sitting contemplative on the steps of the Parthenon, or going at ten to an office and coming home comfortably at half-past four to write a little poetry. Only, if Mrs Seton and her like had gone into business at the age of fifteen, there would have been—that was the snag in the argument—no Mary. What, I asked, did Mary think of that? There between the curtains was the October night, calm and lovely, with a star or two caught in the yellowing trees. Was she ready to resign her share of it and her memories (for they had been a happy family, though a large one) of games and quarrels up in Scotland, which she is never tired of praising for the fineness of its air and the quality of its cakes, in order that Fernham might have been endowed with fifty thousand pounds or so by a stroke of the pen? For, to endow a college would necessitate the suppression of families altogether. Making a fortune and bearing thirteen children—no human being could stand it. Consider the facts, we said. First there are nine months before

3. "We are told that we ought to ask for £30,000 at least. . . . It is not a large sum, considering that there is to be but one college of this sort for Great Britain, Ireland and the Colonies, and considering how easy it is to raise immense sums for boys' schools. But considering how few people really wish women to be educated, it is a good deal."— Lady Stephen, *Life of Miss Emily Davies* [Woolf's note]. Emily Davies (1830–1921), English educa-tor, who established what was to become Girton College.
4. "Every penny which could be scraped together was set aside for building, and the amenities had to be postponed."—R. Strachey, *The Cause* [Woolf's note].
5. Resort town in Monaco, on the French Riviera.
6. Vividly carved stone.

the baby is born. Then the baby is born. Then there are three or four months spent in feeding the baby. After the baby is fed there are certainly five years spent in playing with the baby. You cannot, it seems, let children run about the streets. People who have seen them running wild in Russia say that the sight is not a pleasant one. People say, too, that human nature takes its shape in the years between one and five. If Mrs Seton, I said, had been making money, what sort of memories would you have had of games and quarrels? What would you have known of Scotland, and its fine air and cakes and all the rest of it? But it is useless to ask these questions, because you would never have come into existence at all. Moreover, it is equally useless to ask what might have happened if Mrs Seton and her mother and her mother before her had amassed great wealth and laid it under the foundations of college and library, because, in the first place, to earn money was impossible for them, and in the second, had it been possible, the law denied them the right to possess what money they earned. It is only for the last forty-eight years that Mrs Seton has had a penny of her own. For all the centuries before that it would have been her husband's property—a thought which, perhaps, may have had its share in keeping Mrs Seton and her mothers off the Stock Exchange. Every penny I earn, they may have said, will be taken from me and disposed of according to my husband's wisdom—perhaps to found a scholarship or to endow a fellowship in Balliol or Kings,[7] so that to earn money, even if I could earn money, is not a matter that interests me very greatly. I had better leave it to my husband.

At any rate, whether or not the blame rested on the old lady who was looking at the spaniel, there could be no doubt that for some reason or other our mothers had mismanaged their affairs very gravely. Not a penny could be spared for "amenities"; for partridges and wine, beadles and turf, books and cigars, libraries and leisure. To raise bare walls out of the bare earth was the utmost they could do.

So we talked standing at the window and looking, as so many thousands look every night, down on the domes and towers of the famous city beneath us. It was very beautiful, very mysterious in the autumn moonlight. The old stone looked very white and venerable. One thought of all the books that were assembled down there; of the pictures of old prelates and worthies hanging in the panelled rooms; of the painted windows that would be throwing strange globes and crescents on the pavement; of the tablets and memorials and inscriptions; of the fountains and the grass; of the quiet rooms looking across the quiet quadrangles. And (pardon me the thought) I thought, too, of the admirable smoke and drink and the deep armchairs and the pleasant carpets: of the urbanity, the geniality, the dignity which are the offspring of luxury and privacy and space. Certainly our mothers had not provided us with anything comparable to all this—our mothers who found it difficult to scrape together thirty thousand pounds, our mothers who bore thirteen children to ministers of religion at St Andrews.[8]

So I went back to my inn, and as I walked through the dark streets I pondered this and that, as one does at the end of the day's work. I pondered why it was that Mrs Seton had no money to leave us; and what effect poverty has

---

7. Colleges at Oxford and Cambridge, respectively.
8. Perhaps St. Andrew Holborn, a church in London designed by Sir Christopher Wren (1632–1723).

on the mind; and what effect wealth has on the mind; and I thought of the queer old gentlemen I had seen that morning with tufts of fur upon their shoulders; and I remembered how if one whistled one of them ran; and I thought of the organ booming in the chapel and of the shut doors of the library; and I thought how unpleasant it is to be locked out; and I thought how it is worse perhaps to be locked in; and, thinking of the safety and prosperity of the one sex and of the poverty and insecurity of the other and of the effect of tradition and of the lack of tradition upon the mind of a writer, I thought at last that it was time to roll up the crumpled skin of the day, with its arguments and its impressions and its anger and its laughter, and cast it into the hedge. A thousand stars were flashing across the blue wastes of the sky. One seemed alone with an inscrutable society. All human beings were laid asleep—prone, horizontal, dumb. Nobody seemed stirring in the streets of Oxbridge. Even the door of the hotel sprang open at the touch of an invisible hand—not a boots was sitting up to light me to bed, it was so late.

Chapter Two

The scene, if I may ask you to follow me, was now changed. The leaves were still falling, but in London now, not Oxbridge; and I must ask you to imagine a room, like many thousands, with a window looking across people's hats and vans and motor-cars to other windows, and on the table inside the room a blank sheet of paper on which was written in large letters WOMEN AND FICTION, but no more. The inevitable sequel to lunching and dining at Oxbridge seemed, unfortunately, to be a visit to the British Museum. One must strain off what was personal and accidental in all these impressions and so reach the pure fluid, the essential oil of truth. For that visit to Oxbridge and the luncheon and the dinner had started a swarm of questions. Why did men drink wine and women water? Why was one sex so prosperous and the other so poor? What effect has poverty on fiction? What conditions are necessary for the creation of works of art?—a thousand questions at once suggested themselves. But one needed answers, not questions; and an answer was only to be had by consulting the learned and the unprejudiced, who have removed themselves above the strife of tongue and the confusion of body and issued the result of their reasoning and research in books which are to be found in the British Museum. If truth is not to be found on the shelves of the British Museum, where, I asked myself, picking up a notebook and a pencil, is truth?

Thus provided, thus confident and enquiring, I set out in the pursuit of truth. The day, though not actually wet, was dismal, and the streets in the neighbourhood of the Museum were full of open coal-holes, down which sacks were showering; four-wheeled cabs were drawing up and depositing on the pavement corded boxes containing, presumably, the entire wardrobe of some Swiss or Italian family seeking fortune or refuge or some other desirable commodity which is to be found in the boarding-houses of Bloomsbury in the winter. The usual hoarse-voiced men paraded the streets with plants on barrows. Some shouted; others sang. London was like a workshop. London was like a machine. We were all being shot backwards and forwards on this plain foundation to make some pattern. The British Museum was another department of the factory. The swing-doors swung open; and there one stood under the vast dome, as if one were a thought in the huge bald forehead which is so splendidly encircled by a band of famous names. One went to the counter;

one took a slip of paper; one opened a volume of the catalogue, and . . . . . the five dots here indicate five separate minutes of stupefaction, wonder and bewilderment. Have you any notion how many books are written about women in the course of one year? Have you any notion how many are written by men? Are you aware that you are, perhaps, the most discussed animal in the universe? Here had I come with a notebook and a pencil proposing to spend a morning reading, supposing that at the end of the morning I should have transferred the truth to my notebook. But I should need to be a herd of elephants, I thought, and a wilderness of spiders, desperately referring to the animals that are reputed longest lived and most multitudinously eyed, to cope with all this. I should need claws of steel and beak of brass even to penetrate the husk. How shall I ever find the grains of truth embedded in all this mass of paper, I asked myself, and in despair began running my eye up and down the long list of titles. Even the names of the books gave me food for thought. Sex and its nature might well attract doctors and biologists; but what was surprising and difficult of explanation was the fact that sex—woman, that is to say—also attracts agreeable essayists, light-fingered novelists, young men who have taken the M.A. degree; men who have taken no degree; men who have no apparent qualification save that they are not women. Some of these books were, on the face of it, frivolous and facetious; but many, on the other hand, were serious and prophetic, moral and hortatory. Merely to read the titles suggested innumerable schoolmasters, innumerable clergymen mounting their platforms and pulpits and holding forth with a loquacity which far exceeded the hour usually allotted to such discourse on this one subject. It was a most strange phenomenon; and apparently—here I consulted the letter M—one confined to male sex. Women do not write books about men—a fact that I could not help welcoming with relief, for if I had first to read all that men have written about women, then all that women have written about men, the aloe that flowers once in a hundred years would flower twice before I could set pen to paper. So, making a perfectly arbitrary choice of a dozen volumes or so, I sent my slips of paper to lie in the wire tray, and waited in my stall, among the other seekers for the essential oil of truth.

What could be the reason, then, of this curious disparity, I wondered, drawing cart-wheels on the slips of paper provided by the British taxpayer for other purposes. Why are women, judging from this catalogue, so much more interesting to men than men are to women? A very curious fact it seemed, and my mind wandered to picture the lives of men who spend their time in writing books about women; whether they were old or young, married or unmarried, red-nosed or hump-backed—anyhow, it was flattering, vaguely, to feel oneself the object of such attention, provided that it was not entirely bestowed by the crippled and the infirm—so I pondered until all such frivolous thoughts were ended by an avalanche of books sliding down on to the desk in front of me. Now the trouble began. The student who has been trained in research at Oxbridge has no doubt some method of shepherding his question past all distractions till it runs into its answer as a sheep runs into its pen. The student by my side, for instance, who was copying assiduously from a scientific manual was, I felt sure, extracting pure nuggets of the essential ore every ten minutes or so. His little grunts of satisfaction indicated so much. But if, unfortunately, one has had no training in a university, the question far from being shepherded to its pen flies like a frightened flock hither and thither, helter-skelter, pursued by a whole pack of hounds. Professors, schoolmasters, sociologists, clergymen, novelists, essayists, journalists, men who had no qualification save that they were not women, chased my simple and single question—Why are women poor?—until it became fifty questions; until the fifty questions leapt frantically into mid-stream and were carried away. Every page in my notebook was scribbled over with notes. To show the state of mind I was in, I will read you a few of them, explaining that the page was headed quite simply, WOMEN AND POVERTY, in block letters; but what followed was something like this:

> Condition in Middle Ages of,
> Habits in the Fiji Islands of,
> Worshipped as goddesses by,
> Weaker in moral sense than,
> Idealism of,
> Greater conscientiousness of,
> South Sea Islanders, age of puberty among,
> Attractiveness of,
> Offered as sacrifice to,
> Small size of brain of,
> Profounder sub-consciousness of,
> Less hair on the body of,
> Mental, moral and physical inferiority of,
> Love of children of,
> Greater length of life of,
> Weaker muscles of,
> Strength of affections of,
> Vanity of,
> Higher education of,
> Shakespeare's opinion of,
> Lord Birkenhead's opinion of,
> Dean Inge's opinion of,
> La Bruyère's opinion of,
> Dr Johnson's opinion of,
> Mr Oscar Browning's[9] opinion of, . . .

Here I drew breath and added, indeed, in the margin, Why does Samuel Butler[1] say, "Wise men never say what they think of women"? Wise men never say anything else apparently. But, I continued, leaning back in my chair and looking at the vast dome in which I was a single but by now somewhat harassed thought, what is so unfortunate is that wise men never think the same thing about women. Here is Pope:

> Most women have no character at all.[2]

And here is La Bruyère:

> Les femmes sont extrêmes; elles sont meilleures ou pires que les hommes—[3]

9. Famous history lecturer (1837–1923) at King's College, Cambridge. F. E. Smith, earl of Birkenhead (1872–1930), was lord chancellor (1919–22) and an opponent of women's suffrage. William Ralph Inge (1860–1954) was dean of St. Paul's Cathedral in London (1911–34). Woolf quotes the opinions of the French moralist Jean de La Bruyère

(1645–1696) and of the English writer Samuel Johnson (1609–1784) below.
1. English writer (1835–1902).
2. From "Epistle to a Lady," by the English poet Alexander Pope (1688–1744).
3. Women are extreme: they are better or worse than men (French).

a direct contradiction by keen observers who were contemporary. Are they capable of education or incapable? Napoleon thought them incapable. Dr Johnson thought the opposite.[4] Have they souls or have they not souls? Some savages say they have none. Others, on the contrary, maintain that women are half divine and worship them on that account.[5] Some sages hold that they are shallower in the brain; others that they are deeper in the consciousness. Goethe honoured them; Mussolini[6] despises them. Wherever one looked men thought about women and thought differently. It was impossible to make head or tail of it all, I decided, glancing with envy at the reader next door who was making the neatest abstracts, headed often with an A or a B or a C, while my own notebook rioted with the wildest scribble of contradictory jottings. It was distressing, it was bewildering, it was humiliating. Truth had run through my fingers. Every drop had escaped.

I could not possibly go home, I reflected, and add as a serious contribution to the study of women and fiction that women have less hair on their bodies than men, or that the age of puberty among the South Sea Islanders is nine— or is it ninety?—even the handwriting had become in its distraction indecipherable. It was disgraceful to have nothing more weighty or respectable to show after a whole morning's work. And if I could not grasp the truth about W. (as for brevity's sake I had come to call her) in the past, why bother about W. in the future? It seemed pure waste of time to consult all those gentlemen who specialise in woman and her effect on whatever it may be—politics, children, wages, morality—numerous and learned as they are. One might as well leave their books unopened.

But while I pondered I had unconsciously, in my listlessness, in my desperation, been drawing a picture where I should, like my neighbour, have been writing a conclusion. I had been drawing a face, a figure. It was the face and the figure of Professor von X. engaged in writing his monumental work entitled *The Mental, Moral, and Physical Inferiority of the Female Sex.* He was not in my picture a man attractive to women. He was heavily built; he had a great jowl; to balance that he had very small eyes; he was very red in the face. His expression suggested that he was labouring under some emotion that made him jab his pen on the paper as if he were killing some noxious insect as he wrote, but even when he had killed it that did not satisfy him; he must go on killing it; and even so, some cause for anger and irritation remained. Could it be his wife, I asked, looking at my picture. Was she in love with a cavalry officer? Was the cavalry officer slim and elegant and dressed in astrachan? Had he been laughed at, to adopt the Freudian theory, in his cradle by a pretty girl? For even in his cradle the professor, I thought, could not have been an attractive child. Whatever the reason, the professor was made to look very angry and very ugly in my sketch, as he wrote his great book upon the mental, moral and physical inferiority of women. Drawing pictures was an idle way of

4. " 'Men know that women are an overmatch for them, and therefore they choose the weakest or the most ignorant. If they did not think so, they never could be afraid of women knowing as much as themselves.' . . . In justice to the sex, I think it but candid to acknowledge that, in a subsequent conversation, he told me that he was serious in what he said."—Boswell, *The Journal of a Tour to the Hebrides* [Woolf's note]. James Boswell (1740– 1795), Scottish lawyer, diarist, and writer,

renowned for his biography of Samuel Johnson.
5. "The ancient Germans believed that there was something holy in women, and accordingly consulted them as oracles."—Frazer, *Golden Bough* [Woolf's note]. Sir James Frazer (1854–1941), Scottish anthropologist.
6. Italian Fascist dictator (1883–1945). Johann Wolfgang von Goethe (1749–1832), German poet, novelist, and playwright.

finishing an unprofitable morning's work. Yet it is in our idleness, in our dreams, that the submerged truth sometimes comes to the top. A very elementary exercise in psychology, not to be dignified by the name of psychoanalysis, showed me, on looking at my notebook, that the sketch of the angry professor had been made in anger. Anger had snatched my pencil while I dreamt. But what was anger doing there? Interest, confusion, amusement, boredom—all these emotions I could trace and name as they succeeded each other throughout the morning. Had anger, the black snake, been lurking among them? Yes, said the sketch, anger had. It referred me unmistakably to the one book, to the one phrase, which had roused the demon; it was the professor's statement about the mental, moral and physical inferiority of women. My heart had leapt. My cheeks had burnt. I had flushed with anger. There was nothing specially remarkable, however foolish, in that. One does not like to be told that one is naturally the inferior of a little man—I looked at the student next me—who breathes hard, wears a ready-made tie, and has not shaved this fortnight. One has certain foolish vanities. It is only human nature, I reflected, and began drawing cartwheels and circles over the angry professor's face till he looked like a burning bush or a flaming comet—anyhow, an apparition without human semblance or significance. The professor was nothing now but a faggot burning on the top of Hampstead Heath.[7] Soon my own anger was explained and done with; but curiosity remained. How explain the anger of the professors? Why were they angry? For when it came to analysing the impression left by these books there was always an element of heat. This heat took many forms; it showed itself in satire, in sentiment, in curiosity, in reprobation. But there was another element which was often present and could not immediately be identified. Anger, I called it. But it was anger that had gone underground and mixed itself with all kinds of other emotions. To judge from its odd effects, it was anger disguised and complex, not anger simple and open.

Whatever the reason, all these books, I thought, surveying the pile on the desk, are worthless for my purposes. They were worthless scientifically, that is to say, though humanly they were full of instruction, interest, boredom, and very queer facts about the habits of the Fiji Islanders. They had been written in the red light of emotion and not in the white light of truth. Therefore they must be returned to the central desk and restored each to his own cell in the enormous honeycomb. All that I had retrieved from that morning's work had been the one fact of anger. The professors—I lumped them together thus—were angry. But why, I asked myself, having returned the books, why, I repeated, standing under the colonnade among the pigeons and the prehistoric canoes, why are they angry? And, asking myself this question, I strolled off to find a place for luncheon. What is the real nature of what I call for the moment their anger? I asked. Here was a puzzle that would last all the time that it takes to be served with food in a small restaurant somewhere near the British Museum. Some previous luncher had left the lunch edition of the evening paper on a chair, and, waiting to be served, I began idly reading the headlines. A ribbon of very large letters ran across the page. Somebody had made a big score in South Africa. Lesser ribbons announced that Sir Austen Chamberlain was at Geneva.[8] A meat axe with human hair on it had been found in a cellar.

---

7. An extensive area of open land on a hill overlooking London. "Faggot": a bundle of sticks.

8. Headquarters of the League of Nations. Chamberlain (1863–1937) was a British statesman and

Mr Justice ———— commented in the Divorce Courts upon the Shamelessness of Women. Sprinkled about the paper were other pieces of news. A film actress had been lowered from a peak in California and hung suspended in mid-air. The weather was going to be foggy. The most transient visitor to this planet, I thought, who picked up this paper could not fail to be aware, even from this scattered testimony, that England is under the rule of a patriarchy. Nobody in their senses could fail to detect the dominance of the professor. His was the power and the money and the influence. He was the proprietor of the paper and its editor and sub-editor. He was the Foreign Secretary and the Judge. He was the cricketer; he owned the racehorses and the yachts. He was the director of the company that pays two hundred per cent to its shareholders. He left millions to charities and colleges that were ruled by himself. He suspended the film actress in mid-air. He will decide if the hair on the meat axe is human; he it is who will acquit or convict the murderer, and hang him, or let him go free. With the exception of the fog he seemed to control everything. Yet he was angry. I knew that he was angry by this token. When I read what he wrote about women I thought, not of what he was saying, but of himself. When an arguer argues dispassionately he thinks only of the argument; and the reader cannot help thinking of the argument too. If he had written dispassionately about women, had used indisputable proofs to establish his argument and had shown no trace of wishing that the result should be one thing rather than another, one would not have been angry either. One would have accepted the fact, as one accepts the fact that a pea is green or a canary yellow. So be it, I should have said. But I had been angry because he was angry. Yet it seemed absurd, I thought, turning over the evening paper, that a man with all this power should be angry. Or is anger, I wondered, somehow, the familiar, the attendant sprite[9] on power? Rich people, for example, are often angry because they suspect that the poor want to seize their wealth. The professors, or patriarchs, as it might be more accurate to call them, might be angry for that reason partly, but partly for one that lies a little less obviously on the surface. Possibly they were not "angry" at all; often, indeed, they were admiring, devoted, exemplary in the relations of private life. Possibly when the professor insisted a little too emphatically upon the inferiority of women, he was concerned not with their inferiority, but with his own superiority. That was what he was protecting rather hot-headedly and with too much emphasis, because it was a jewel to him of the rarest price. Life for both sexes—and I looked at them, shouldering their way along the pavement—is arduous, difficult, a perpetual struggle. It calls for gigantic courage and strength. More than anything, perhaps, creatures of illusion as we are, it calls for confidence in oneself. Without self-confidence we are as babes in the cradle. And how can we generate this imponderable quality, which is yet so invaluable, most quickly? By thinking that other people are inferior to oneself. By feeling that one has some innate superiority—it may be wealth, or rank, a straight nose, or the portrait of a grandfather by Romney[1]—for there is no end to the pathetic devices of the human imagination—over other people. Hence the enormous importance to a patriarch who has to conquer, who has to rule, of feeling that great numbers of people, half the human race indeed, are by nature inferior to himself. It

brother of Neville Chamberlain, British prime minister (1937–40).
9. Spirit.

1. George Romney (1734–1802), fashionable English portrait painter.

must indeed be one of the chief sources of his power. But let me turn the light of this observation on to real life, I thought. Does it help to explain some of those psychological puzzles that one notes in the margin of daily life? Does it explain my astonishment the other day when Z, most humane, most modest of men, taking up some book by Rebecca West[2] and reading a passage in it, exclaimed, "The arrant feminist! She says that men are snobs!" The exclamation, to me so surprising—for why was Miss West an arrant feminist for making a possibly true if uncomplimentary statement about the other sex?—was not merely the cry of wounded vanity; it was a protest against some infringement of his power to believe in himself. Women have served all these centuries as looking-glasses possessing the magic and delicious power of reflecting the figure of man at twice its natural size. Without that power probably the earth would still be swamp and jungle. The glories of all our wars would be unknown. We should still be scratching the outlines of deer on the remains of mutton bones and bartering flints for sheepskins or whatever simple ornament took our unsophisticated taste. Supermen and Fingers of Destiny would never have existed. The Czar and the Kaiser[3] would never have worn their crowns or lost them. Whatever may be their use in civilised societies, mirrors are essential to all violent and heroic action. That is why Napoleon and Mussolini[4] both insist so emphatically upon the inferiority of women, for if they were not inferior, they would cease to enlarge. That serves to explain in part the necessity that women so often are to men. And it serves to explain how restless they are under her criticism; how impossible it is for her to say to them this book is bad, this picture is feeble, or whatever it may be, without giving far more pain and rousing far more anger than a man would do who gave the same criticism. For if she begins to tell the truth, the figure in the looking-glass shrinks; his fitness for life is diminished. How is he to go on giving judgement, civilising natives, making laws, writing books, dressing up and speechifying at banquets, unless he can see himself at breakfast and at dinner at least twice the size he really is? So I reflected, crumbling my bread and stirring my coffee and now and again looking at the people in the street. The looking-glass vision is of supreme importance because it charges the vitality; it stimulates the nervous system. Take it away and man may die, like the drug fiend deprived of his cocaine. Under the spell of that illusion, I thought, looking out of the window, half the people on the pavement are striding to work. They put on their hats and coats in the morning under its agreeable rays. They start the day confident, braced, believing themselves desired at Miss Smith's tea party; they say to themselves as they go into the room, I am the superior of half the people here, and it is thus that they speak with that self-confidence, that self-assurance, which have had such profound consequences in public life and lead to such curious notes in the margin of the private mind.

But these contributions to the dangerous and fascinating subject of the psychology of the other sex—it is one, I hope, that you will investigate when you have five hundred a year of your own—were interrupted by the necessity of paying the bill. It came to five shillings and ninepence. I gave the waiter a ten-shilling note and he went to bring me change. There was another ten-shilling note in my purse; I noticed it, because it is a fact that still takes my breath away—the power of my purse to breed ten-shillings notes automati-

<hr>

2. Adopted name of Cicily Isabel Fairfield (1892– 1983), English feminist, journalist, and novelist.

3. Rulers of Russia and Germany, respectively.
4. I.e., dictators.

cally. I open it and there they are. Society gives me chicken and coffee, bed and lodging, in return for a certain number of pieces of paper which were left me by an aunt, for no other reason than that I share her name.

My aunt, Mary Beton, I must tell you, died by a fall from her horse when she was riding out to take the air in Bombay. The news of my legacy reached me one night about the same time that the act was passed that gave votes to women. A solicitor's letter fell into the post-box and when I opened it I found that she had left me five hundred pounds a year for ever. Of the two—the vote and the money—the money, I own, seemed infinitely the more important. Before that I had made my living by cadging odd jobs from newspapers, by reporting a donkey show here or a wedding there; I had earned a few pounds by addressing envelopes, reading to old ladies, making artificial flowers, teaching the alphabet to small children in a kindergarten. Such were the chief occupations that were open to women before 1918. I need not, I am afraid, describe in any detail the hardness of the work, for you know perhaps women who have done it; nor the difficulty of living on the money when it was earned, for you may have tried. But what still remains with me as a worse infliction than either was the poison of fear and bitterness which those days bred in me. To begin with, always to be doing work that one did not wish to do, and to do it like a slave, flattering and fawning, not always necessarily perhaps, but it seemed necessary and the stakes were too great to run risks; and then the thought of that one gift which it was death to hide—a small one but dear to the possessor—perishing and with it myself, my soul—all this became like a rust eating away the bloom of the spring, destroying the tree at its heart. However, as I say, my aunt died; and whenever I change a ten-shilling note a little of that rust and corrosion is rubbed off; fear and bitterness go. Indeed, I thought, slipping the silver into my purse, it is remarkable, remembering the bitterness of those days, what a change of temper a fixed income will bring about. No force in the world can take from me my five hundred pounds. Food, house and clothing are mine for ever. Therefore not merely do effort and labour cease, but also hatred and bitterness. I need not hate any man; he cannot hurt me. I need not flatter any man; he has nothing to give me. So imperceptibly I found myself adopting a new attitude towards the other half of the human race. It was absurd to blame any class or any sex, as a whole. Great bodies of people are never responsible for what they do. They are driven by instincts which are not within their control. They too, the patriarchs, the professors, had endless difficulties, terrible drawbacks to contend with. Their education had been in some ways as faulty as my own. It had bred in them defects as great. True, they had money and power, but only at the cost of harbouring in their breasts an eagle, a vulture, for ever tearing the liver out and plucking at the lungs—the instinct for possession, the rage for acquisition which drives them to desire other people's fields and goods perpetually; to make frontiers and flags; battleships and poison gas; to offer up their own lives and their children's lives. Walk through the Admiralty Arch⁵ (I had reached that monument), or any other avenue given up to trophies and cannon, and reflect upon the kind of glory celebrated there. Or watch in the spring sunshine the stockbroker and the great barrister going indoors to make money and more money and more money when it is a fact that five hundred pounds a year will

5. Between the Mall and Trafalgar Square in London, constructed 1906–11 to commemorate Britain's imperial successes.

keep one alive in the sunshine. These are unpleasant instincts to harbour, I reflected. They are bred of the conditions of life; of the lack of civilisation, I thought, looking at the statue of the Duke of Cambridge,[6] and in particular at the feathers in his cocked hat, with a fixity that they have scarcely ever received before. And, as I realised these drawbacks, by degrees fear and bitterness modified themselves into pity and toleration; and then in a year or two, pity and toleration went, and the greatest release of all came, which is freedom to think of things in themselves. That building, for example, do I like it or not? Is that picture beautiful or not? Is that in my opinion a good book or a bad? Indeed my aunt's legacy unveiled the sky to me, and substituted for the large and imposing figure of a gentleman, which Milton recommended for my perpetual adoration, a view of the open sky.

So thinking, so speculating, I found my way back to my house by the river. Lamps were being lit and an indescribable change had come over London since the morning hour. It was as if the great machine after labouring all day had made with our help a few yards of something very exciting and beautiful—a fiery fabric flashing with red eyes, a tawny monster roaring with hot breath. Even the wind seemed flung like a flag as it lashed the houses and rattled the hoardings.

In my little street, however, domesticity prevailed. The house painter was descending his ladder; the nursemaid was wheeling the perambulator carefully in and out back to nursery tea; the coal-heaver was folding his empty sacks on top of each other; the woman who keeps the green-grocer's shop was adding up the day's takings with her hands in red mittens. But so engrossed was I with the problem you have laid upon my shoulders that I could not see even these usual sights without referring them to one centre. I thought how much harder it is now than it must have been even a century ago to say which of these employments is the higher, the more necessary. Is it better to be a coal-heaver or a nursemaid; is the charwoman[7] who has brought up eight children of less value to the world than the barrister who has made a hundred thousand pounds? It is useless to ask such questions; for nobody can answer them. Not only do the comparative values of charwomen and lawyers rise and fall from decade to decade, but we have no rods with which to measure them even as they are at the moment. I had been foolish to ask my professor to furnish me with "indisputable proofs" of this or that in his argument about women. Even if one could state the value of any one gift at the moment, those values will change; in a century's time very possibly they will have changed completely. Moreover, in a hundred years, I thought, reaching my own doorstep, women will have ceased to be the protected sex. Logically they will take part in all the activities and exertions that were once denied them. The nursemaid will heave coal. The shop-woman will drive an engine. All assumptions founded on the facts observed when women were the protected sex will have disappeared—as, for example (here a squad of soldiers marched down the street), that women and clergymen and gardeners live longer than other people. Remove that protection, expose them to the same exertions and activities, make them soldiers and sailors and engine-drivers and dock labourers, and will not women die off so much younger, so much quicker, than men that one will say, "I saw a woman today," as one used to say, "I saw an aeroplane." Anything may happen when

6. On Whitehall Lane, directly off Trafalgar Square.

7. Household worker.

womanhood has ceased to be a protected occupation, I thought, opening the door. But what bearing has all this upon the subject of my paper, Women and Fiction? I asked, going indoors.

Chapter Three

It was disappointing not to have brought back in the evening some important statement, some authentic fact. Women are poorer than men because—this or that. Perhaps now it would be better to give up seeking for the truth, and receiving on one's head an avalanche of opinion hot as lava, discoloured as dish-water. It would be better to draw the curtains; to shut out distractions; to light the lamp; to narrow the enquiry and to ask the historian, who records not opinions but facts, to describe under what conditions women lived, not throughout the ages, but in England, say in the time of Elizabeth.[8]

For it is a perennial puzzle why no woman wrote a word of that extraordinary literature when every other man, it seemed, was capable of song or sonnet. What were the conditions in which women lived, I asked myself; for fiction, imaginative work that is, is not dropped like a pebble upon the ground, as science may be; fiction is like a spider's web, attached ever so lightly perhaps, but still attached to life at all four corners. Often the attachment is scarcely perceptible; Shakespeare's plays, for instance, seem to hang there complete by themselves. But when the web is pulled askew, hooked up at the edge, torn in the middle, one remembers that these webs are not spun in midair by incorporeal creatures, but are the work of suffering human beings, and are attached to grossly material things, like health and money and the houses we live in.

I went, therefore, to the shelf where the histories stand and took down one of the latest, Professor Trevelyan's *History of England*.[9] Once more I looked up Women, found "position of," and turned to the pages indicated. "Wife-beating," I read, "was a recognised right of man, and was practised without shame by high as well as low. . . . Similarly," the historian goes on, "the daughter who refused to marry the gentleman of her parents' choice was liable to be locked up, beaten and flung about the room, without any shock being inflicted on public opinion. Marriage was not an affair of personal affection, but of family avarice, particularly in the 'chivalrous' upper classes. . . . Betrothal often took place while one or both of the parties was in the cradle, and marriage when they were scarcely out of the nurses' charge." That was about 1470, soon after Chaucer's time. The next reference to the position of women is some two hundred years later, in the time of the Stuarts.[1] "It was still the exception for women of the upper and middle class to choose their own husbands, and when the husband had been assigned, he was lord and master, so far at least as law and custom could make him. Yet even so," Professor Trevelyan concludes, "neither Shakespeare's women nor those of authentic seventeenth-century memoirs, like the Verneys and the Hutchinsons,[2] seem wanting in personality and character." Certainly, if we consider

---

8. She reigned from 1558 to 1603.
9. G. M. Trevelyan's *History of England* (1926) long held its place as the standard one-volume history of the country.
1. I.e., during the reign of the British house of Stuart (1603–49, 1660–1714).
2. "The ideal family life of the period [1640–50]

that ended in such tragic political division has been recorded once for all in the *Memoirs of the Verney Family*" (Trevelyan, *History of England*). Lucy Hutchinson (1620–after 1675) wrote the biography of her husband, Col. John Hutchinson (1615–1664); it was first published in 1806.

it, Cleopatra must have had a way with her; Lady Macbeth, one would suppose, had a will of her own; Rosalind,[3] one might conclude, was an attractive girl. Professor Trevelyan is speaking no more than the truth when he remarks that Shakespeare's women do not seem wanting in personality and character. Not being a historian, one might go even further and say that women have burnt like beacons in all the works of all the poets from the beginning of time—Clytemnestra, Antigone, Cleopatra, Lady Macbeth, Phèdre, Cressida, Rosalind, Desdemona, the Duchess of Malfi, among the dramatists; then among the prose writers: Millamant, Clarissa, Becky Sharp, Anna Karenina, Emma Bovary, Madame de Guermantes[4]—the names flock to mind, nor do they recall women "lacking in personality and character." Indeed, if woman had no existence save in the fiction written by men, one would imagine her a person of the utmost importance, very various; heroic and mean; splendid and sordid; infinitely beautiful and hideous in the extreme; as great as a man, some think even greater.[5] But this is woman in fiction. In fact, as Professor Trevelyan points out, she was locked up, beaten and flung about the room.

A very queer, composite being thus emerges. Imaginatively she is of the highest importance; practically she is completely insignificant. She pervades poetry from cover to cover; she is all but absent from history. She dominates the lives of kings and conquerors in fiction; in fact she was the slave of any boy whose parents forced a ring upon her finger. Some of the most inspired words, some of the most profound thoughts in literature fall from her lips; in real life she could hardly read, could scarcely spell, and was the property of her husband.

It was certainly an odd monster that one made up by reading the historians first and the poets afterwards—a worm winged like an eagle; the spirit of life and beauty in a kitchen chopping up suet. But these monsters, however amusing to the imagination, have no existence in fact. What one must do to bring her to life was to think poetically and prosaically at one and the same moment, thus keeping in touch with fact—that she is Mrs Martin, aged thirty-six, dressed in blue, wearing a black hat and brown shoes; but not losing sight of fiction either—that she is a vessel in which all sorts of spirits and forces are coursing and flashing perpetually. The moment, however, that one tries this method with the Elizabethan woman, one branch of illumination fails; one is held up by the scarcity of facts. One knows nothing detailed, nothing perfectly true and substantial about her. History scarcely mentions her. And I turned

3. These three Shakespearean heroines are, respectively, in *Antony and Cleopatra, Macbeth,* and *As You Like It.*
4. Characters in, respectively, Aeschylus's *Agamemnon;* Sophocles' *Antigone;* Shakespeare's *Antony and Cleopatra* and *Macbeth;* Racine's *Phèdre;* Shakespeare's *Troilus and Cressida, As You Like It,* and *Othello;* Webster's *The Duchess of Malfi;* Congreve's *Way of the World;* Richardson's *Clarissa;* Thackeray's *Vanity Fair;* Tolstoy's *Anna Karenina;* Flaubert's *Madame Bovary;* and Proust's *A la Recherche du Temps Perdu (In Search of Lost Time).*
5. "It remains a strange and almost inexplicable fact that in Athena's city, where women were kept in almost Oriental suppression as odalisques or drudges, the stage should yet have produced figures like Clytemnestra and Cassandra, Atossa and Antigone, Phèdre and Medea, and all the other

heroines who dominate play after play of the 'misogynist' Euripides. But the paradox of this world where in real life a respectable woman could hardly show her face alone in the street, and yet on the stage woman equals or surpasses man, has never been satisfactorily explained. In modern tragedy the same predominance exists. At all events, a very cursory survey of Shakespeare's work (similarly with Webster, though not with Marlowe or Jonson) suffices to reveal how this dominance, this initiative of women, persists from Rosalind to Lady Macbeth. So too in Racine; six of his tragedies bear their heroines' names; and what male characters of his shall we set against Hermione and Andromaque, Bérénice and Roxane, Phèdre and Athalie? So again with Ibsen; what men shall we match with Solveig and Nora, Hedda and Hilda Wangel and Rebecca West?"—F. L. Lucas, *Tragedy,* pp. 114–15 [Woolf's note].

to Professor Trevelyan again to see what history meant to him. I found by looking at his chapter headings that it meant—
"The Manor Court and the Methods of Open-field Agriculture . . . The Cistercians and Sheep-farming . . . The Crusades . . . The University . . . The House of Commons . . . The Hundred Years' War . . . The Wars of the Roses . . . The Renaissance Scholars . . . The Dissolution of the Monasteries . . . Agrarian and Religious Strife . . . The Origin of English Sea-power . . . The Armada . . ." and so on. Occasionally an individual woman is mentioned, an Elizabeth, or a Mary; a queen or a great lady. But by no possible means could middle-class women with nothing but brains and character at their command have taken part in any one of the great movements which, brought together, constitute the historian's view of the past. Nor shall we find her in any collection of anecdotes. Aubrey[6] hardly mentions her. She never writes her own life and scarcely keeps a diary; there are only a handful of her letters in existence. She left no plays or poems by which we can judge her. What one wants, I thought—and why does not some brilliant student at Newnham or Girton supply it?—is a mass of information; at what age did she marry; how many children had she as a rule; what was her house like; had she a room to herself; did she do the cooking; would she be likely to have a servant? All these facts lie somewhere, presumably, in parish registers and account books; the life of the average Elizabethan woman must be scattered about somewhere, could one collect it and make a book of it. It would be ambitious beyond my daring, I thought, looking about the shelves for books that were not there, to suggest to the students of those famous colleges that they should re-write history, though I own that it often seems a little queer as it is, unreal, lop-sided; but why should they not add a supplement to history? calling it, of course, by some inconspicuous name so that women might figure there without impropriety? For one often catches a glimpse of them in the lives of the great, whisking away into the background, concealing, I sometimes think, a wink, a laugh, perhaps a tear. And, after all, we have lives enough of Jane Austen; it scarcely seems necessary to consider again the influence of the tragedies of Joanna Baillie[7] upon the poetry of Edgar Allan Poe; as for myself, I should not mind if the homes and haunts of Mary Russell Mitford[8] were closed to the public for a century at least. But what I find deplorable, I continued, looking about the bookshelves again, is that nothing is known about women before the eighteenth century. I have no model in my mind to turn about this way and that. Here am I asking why women did not write poetry in the Elizabethan age, and I am not sure how they were educated; whether they were taught to write; whether they had sitting-rooms to themselves; how many women had children before they were twenty-one; what, in short, they did from eight in the morning till eight at night. They had no money evidently; according to Professor Trevelyan they were married whether they liked it or not before they were out of the nursery, at fifteen or sixteen very likely. It would have been extremely odd, even upon this showing, had one of them suddenly written the plays of Shakespeare, I concluded, and I thought of that old gentleman, who is dead now, but was a bishop, I think, who declared that it was impossible for any woman, past, present, or to come, to have the genius of Shakespeare. He wrote to the

6. John Aubrey (1626–1697), English writer, especially of short biographies.
7. English poet and dramatist (1762–1851).
8. Poet and novelist (1787–1855), best-known for sketches of country life.

papers about it. He also told a lady who applied to him for information that cats do not as a matter of fact go to heaven, though they have, he added, souls of a sort. How much thinking those old gentlemen used to save one! How the borders of ignorance shrank back at their approach! Cats do not go to heaven. Women cannot write the plays of Shakespeare.

Be that as it may, I could not help thinking, as I looked at the works of Shakespeare on the shelf, that the bishop was right at least in this; it would have been impossible, completely and entirely, for any woman to have written the plays of Shakespeare in the age of Shakespeare. Let me imagine, since facts are so hard to come by, what would have happened had Shakespeare had a wonderfully gifted sister, called Judith,[9] let us say. Shakespeare himself went, very probably—his mother was an heiress—to the grammar school, where he may have learnt Latin—Ovid, Virgil and Horace—and the elements of grammar and logic. He was, it is well known, a wild boy who poached rabbits, perhaps shot a deer, and had, rather sooner than he should have done, to marry a woman in the neighbourhood, who bore him a child rather quicker than was right. That escapade sent him to seek his fortune in London. He had, it seemed, a taste for the theatre; he began by holding horses at the stage door. Very soon he got work in the theatre, became a successful actor, and lived at the hub of the universe, meeting everybody, knowing everybody, practising his art on the boards, exercising his wits in the streets, and even getting access to the palace of the queen. Meanwhile his extraordinarily gifted sister, let us suppose, remained at home. She was as adventurous, as imaginative, as agog to see the world as he was. But she was not sent to school. She had no chance of learning grammar and logic, let alone of reading Horace and Virgil. She picked up a book now and then, one of her brother's perhaps, and read a few pages. But then her parents came in and told her to mend the stockings or mind the stew and not moon about with books and papers. They would have spoken sharply but kindly, for they were substantial people who knew the conditions of life for a woman and loved their daughter—indeed, more likely than not she was the apple of her father's eye. Perhaps she scribbled some pages up in an apple loft on the sly, but was careful to hide them or set fire to them. Soon, however, before she was out of her teens, she was to be betrothed to the son of a neighbouring wool-stapler.[1] She cried out that marriage was hateful to her, and for that she was severely beaten by her father. Then he ceased to scold her. He begged her instead not to hurt him, not to shame him in this matter of her marriage. He would give her a chain of beads or a fine petticoat, he said; and there were tears in his eyes. How could she disobey him? How could she break his heart? The force of her own gift alone drove her to it. She made up a small parcel of her belongings, let herself down by a rope one summer's night and took the road to London. She was not seventeen. The birds that sang in the hedge were not more musical than she was. She had the quickest fancy, a gift like her brother's, for the tune of words. Like him, she had a taste for the theatre. She stood at the stage door; she wanted to act, she said. Men laughed in her face. The manager—a fat, loose-lipped man—guffawed. He bellowed something about poodles dancing and women acting—no woman, he said, could possibly be an actress. He hinted—

9. Shakespeare had a daughter named Judith.
1. A stapler is a dealer in staple goods (i.e., established goods in trade and marketing); hence a

wool-stapler is a dealer in wool (one of the "staple" products of 16th-century England).

you can imagine what. She could get no training in her craft. Could she even seek her dinner in a tavern or roam the streets at midnight? Yet her genius was for fiction and lusted to feed abundantly upon the lives of men and women and the study of their ways. At last—for she was very young, oddly like Shakespeare the poet in her face, with the same grey eyes and rounded brows—at last Nick Greene the actor-manager took pity on her; she found herself with child by that gentleman and so—who shall measure the heat and violence of the poet's heart when caught and tangled in a woman's body?—killed herself one winter's night and lies buried at some cross-roads where the omnibuses now stop outside the Elephant and Castle.[2]

That, more or less, is how the story would run, I think, if a woman in Shakespeare's day had had Shakespeare's genius. But for my part, I agree with the deceased bishop, if such he was—it is unthinkable that any woman in Shakespeare's day should have had Shakespeare's genius. For genius like Shakespeare's is not born among labouring, uneducated, servile people. It was not born in England among the Saxons and the Britons. It is not born today among the working classes. How, then, could it have been born among women whose work began, according to Professor Trevelyan, almost before they were out of the nursery, who were forced to it by their parents and held to it by all the power of law and custom? Yet genius of a sort must have existed among women as it must have existed among the working classes. Now and again an Emily Brontë or a Robert Burns[3] blazes out and proves its presence. But certainly it never got itself on to paper. When, however, one reads of a witch being ducked, of a woman possessed by devils, of a wise woman selling herbs, or even of a very remarkable man who had a mother, then I think we are on the track of a lost novelist, a suppressed poet, of some mute and inglorious[4] Jane Austen, some Emily Brontë who dashed her brains out on the moor or mopped and mowed about the highways crazed with the torture that her gift had put her to. Indeed, I would venture to guess that Anon, who wrote so many poems without signing them, was often a woman. It was a woman Edward Fitzgerald,[5] I think, suggested who made the ballads and the folk-songs, crooning them to her children, beguiling her spinning with them, or the length of the winter's night.

This may be true or it may be false—who can say?—but what is true in it, so it seemed to me, reviewing the story of Shakespeare's sister as I had made it, is that any woman born with a great gift in the sixteenth century would certainly have gone crazed, shot herself, or ended her days in some lonely cottage outside the village, half witch, half wizard, feared and mocked at. For it needs little skill in psychology to be sure that a highly gifted girl who had tried to use her gift for poetry would have been so thwarted and hindered by other people, so tortured and pulled asunder by her own contrary instincts, that she must have lost her health and sanity to a certainty. No girl could have walked to London and stood at a stage door and forced her way into the presence of actor-managers without doing herself a violence and suffering an anguish which may have been irrational—for chastity may be a fetish invented by certain societies for unknown reasons—but were none the less inevitable.

2. Suicides were buried at crossroads. The Elephant and Castle was a tavern south of the river Thames, where roads went off to different parts of southern England.
3. Scottish poet (1759–1796).

4. An echo of Thomas Gray's "Elegy Written in a Country Churchyard" (1751), line 59: "Some mute inglorious Milton here may rest."
5. Poet and translator (1809–1883).

2118 / Virginia Woolf

Chastity had then, it has even now, a religious importance in a woman's life, and has so wrapped itself round with nerves and instincts that to cut it free and bring it to the light of day demands courage of the rarest. To have lived a free life in London in the sixteenth century would have meant for a woman who was poet and playwright a nervous stress and dilemma which might well have killed her. Had she survived, whatever she had written would have been twisted and deformed, issuing from a strained and morbid imagination. And undoubtedly, I thought, looking at the shelf where there are no plays by women, her work would have gone unsigned. That refuge she would have sought certainly. It was the relic of the sense of chastity that dictated anonymity to women even so late as the nineteenth century. Currer Bell, George Eliot, George Sand,[6] all the victims of inner strife as their writings prove, sought ineffectively to veil themselves by using the name of a man. Thus they did homage to the convention, which if not implanted by the other sex was liberally encouraged by them (the chief glory of a woman is not to be talked of, said Pericles,[7] himself a much-talked-of man), that publicity in women is detestable. Anonymity runs in their blood. The desire to be veiled still possesses them. They are not even now as concerned about the health of their fame as men are, and, speaking generally, will pass a tombstone or a signpost without feeling an irresistible desire to cut their names on it, as Alf, Bert or Chas. must do in obedience to their instinct, which murmurs if it sees a fine woman go by, or even a dog, Ce chien est à moi.[8] And, of course, it may not be a dog, I thought, remembering Parliament Square, the Sieges Allee[9] and other avenues; it may be a piece of land or a man with curly black hair. It is one of the great advantages of being a woman that one can pass even a very fine negress without wishing to make an Englishwoman of her.

That woman, then, who was born with a gift of poetry in the sixteenth century, was an unhappy woman, a woman at strife against herself. All the conditions of her life, all her own instincts, were hostile to the state of mind which is needed to set free whatever is in the brain. But what is the state of mind that is most propitious to the act of creation, I asked. Can one come by any notion of the state that furthers and makes possible that strange activity? Here I opened the volume containing the Tragedies of Shakespeare. What was Shakespeare's state of mind, for instance, when he wrote *Lear* and *Antony and Cleopatra*? It was certainly the state of mind most favourable to poetry that there has ever existed. But Shakespeare himself said nothing about it. We only know casually and by chance that he "never blotted a line."[1] Nothing indeed was ever said by the artist himself about his state of mind until the eighteenth century perhaps. Rousseau[2] perhaps began it. At any rate, by the nineteenth century self-consciousness had developed so far that it was the habit for men of letters to describe their minds in confessions and autobiographies. Their lives also were written, and their letters were printed after their deaths. Thus, though we do not know what Shakespeare went through when he wrote *Lear*, we do know what Carlyle went through when he wrote the *French Revolution;* what Flaubert went through when he wrote *Madame Bovary;* what Keats was

---

6. Male pseudonyms, respectively, of Charlotte Brontë, Marian Evans, and Amandine-Aurore-Lucie Dupin (1804–1876).
7. Athenian statesman (ca. 495–429 B.C.E.).
8. This dog is mine (French).
9. Avenue of Victory, a busy thoroughfare in Berlin. "Parliament Square": London intersection.

1. Ben Jonson, *Timber* (1640): "I remember, the players have often mentioned it as an honour to Shakespeare that in his writing (whatsoever he penned) he never blotted out a line."
2. Jean-Jacques Rousseau (1712–1778), early-Romantic French philosopher and memoirist.

going through when he tried to write poetry against the coming of death and the indifference of the world.

And one gathers from this enormous modern literature of confession and self-analysis that to write a work of genius is almost always a feat of prodigious difficulty. Everything is against the likelihood that it will come from the writer's mind whole and entire. Generally material circumstances are against it. Dogs will bark; people will interrupt; money must be made; health will break down. Further, accentuating all these difficulties and making them harder to bear is the world's notorious indifference. It does not ask people to write poems and novels and histories; it does not need them. It does not care whether Flaubert finds the right word or whether Carlyle scrupulously verifies this or that fact. Naturally, it will not pay for what it does not want. And so the writer, Keats, Flaubert, Carlyle, suffers, especially in the creative years of youth, every form of distraction and discouragement. A curse, a cry of agony, rises from those books of analysis and confession. "Mighty poets in their misery dead"³—that is the burden of their song. If anything comes through in spite of all this, it is a miracle, and probably no book is born entire and uncrippled as it was conceived.

But for women, I thought, looking at the empty shelves, these difficulties were infinitely more formidable. In the first place, to have a room of her own, let alone a quiet room or a sound-proof room, was out of the question, unless her parents were exceptionally rich or very noble, even up to the beginning of the nineteenth century. Since her pin money, which depended on the good will of her father, was only enough to keep her clothed, she was debarred from such alleviations as came even to Keats or Tennyson or Carlyle, all poor men, from a walking tour, a little journey to France, from the separate lodging which, even if it were miserable enough, sheltered them from the claims and tyrannies of their families. Such material difficulties were formidable; but much worse were the immaterial. The indifference of the world which Keats and Flaubert and other men of genius have found so hard to bear was in her case not indifference but hostility. The world did not say to her as it said to them, Write if you choose; it makes no difference to me. The world said with a guffaw, Write? What's the good of your writing? Here the psychologists of Newnham and Girton might come to our help, I thought, looking again at the blank spaces on the shelves. For surely it is time that the effect of discouragement upon the mind of the artist should be measured, as I have seen a dairy company measure the effect of ordinary milk and Grade A milk upon the body of the rat. They set two rats in cages side by side, and of the two one was furtive, timid and small, and the other was glossy, bold and big. Now what food do we feed women as artists upon? I asked, remembering, I suppose, that dinner of prunes and custard. To answer that question I had only to open the evening paper and to read that Lord Birkenhead is of opinion—but really I am not going to trouble to copy out Lord Birkenhead's opinion upon the writing of women. What Dean Inge says I will leave in peace. The Harley Street specialist⁴ may be allowed to rouse the echoes of Harley Street with his vociferations without raising a hair on my head. I will quote, however, Mr Oscar Browning, because Mr Oscar Browning was a great figure in Cambridge at one time, and used to examine the students at Girton and Newnham. Mr Oscar

3. From Wordsworth's "Resolution and Independence" (1807), line 116.

4. On Harley Street in London many medical specialists have their consulting rooms.

Browning was wont to declare "that the impression left on his mind, after looking over any set of examination papers, was that, irrespective of the marks he might give, the best woman was intellectually the inferior of the worst man." After saying that Mr Browning went back to his rooms—and it is this sequel that endears him and makes him a human figure of some bulk and majesty—he went back to his rooms and found a stable-boy lying on the sofa—"a mere skeleton, his cheeks were cavernous and sallow, his teeth were black, and he did not appear to have the full use of his limbs. . . . 'That's Arthur' [said Mr Browning]. 'He's a dear boy really and most high-minded.' " The two pictures always seem to me to complete each other. And happily in this age of biography the two pictures often do complete each other, so that we are able to interpret the opinions of great men not only by what they say, but by what they do.

But though this is possible now, such opinions coming from the lips of important people must have been formidable enough even fifty years ago. Let us suppose that a father from the highest motives did not wish his daughter to leave home and become writer, painter or scholar. "See what Mr Oscar Browning says," he would say; and there was not only Mr Oscar Browning; there was the *Saturday Review*; there was Mr Greg[5]—the "essentials of a woman's being," said Mr Greg emphatically, "are that *they are supported by, and they minister to, men*"—there was an enormous body of masculine opinion to the effect that nothing could be expected of women intellectually. Even if her father did not read out loud these opinions, any girl could read them for herself; and the reading, even in the nineteenth century, must have lowered her vitality, and told profoundly upon her work. There would always have been that assertion—you cannot do this, you are incapable of doing that—to protest against, to overcome. Probably for a novelist this germ is no longer of much effect; for there have been women novelists of merit. But for painters it must still have some sting in it; and for musicians, I imagine, is even now active and poisonous in the extreme. The woman composer stands where the actress stood in the time of Shakespeare. Nick Greene, I thought, remembering the story I had made about Shakespeare's sister, said that a woman acting put him in mind of a dog dancing. Johnson repeated the phrase two hundred years later of women preaching. And here, I said, opening a book about music, we have the very words used again in this year of grace, 1928, of women who try to write music. "Of Mlle Germaine Tailleferre one can only repeat Dr Johnson's dictum concerning a woman preacher, transposed into terms of music. 'Sir, a woman's composing is like a dog's walking on his hind legs. It is not done well, but you are surprised to find it done at all.' "[6] So accurately does history repeat itself.

Thus, I concluded, shutting Mr Oscar Browning's life and pushing away the rest, it is fairly evident that even in the nineteenth century a woman was not encouraged to be an artist. On the contrary, she was snubbed, slapped, lectured and exhorted. Her mind must have been strained and her vitality lowered by the need of opposing this, of disproving that. For here again we come within range of that very interesting and obscure masculine complex which has had so much influence upon the woman's movement; that deepseated desire, not so much that *she* shall be inferior as that *he* shall be superior, which plants him wherever one looks, not only in front of the arts, but barring the way to

5. Sir W. W. Greg (1875–1959), bibliographer and literary scholar.

6. *A Survey of Contemporary Music*, Cecil Gray, p. 246 [Woolf's note].

politics too, even when the risk to himself seems infinitesimal and the suppliant humble and devoted. Even Lady Bessborough, I remembered, with all her passion for politics, must humbly bow herself and write to Lord Granville Leveson-Gower:[7] ". . . notwithstanding all my violence in politics and talking so much on that subject, I perfectly agree with you that no woman has any business to meddle with that or any other serious business, farther than giving her opinion (if she is ask'd)." And so she goes on to spend her enthusiasm where it meets with no obstacle whatsoever upon that immensely important subject, Lord Granville's maiden speech in the House of Commons. The spectacle is certainly a strange one, I thought. The history of men's opposition to women's emancipation is more interesting perhaps than the story of that emancipation itself. An amusing book might be made of it if some young student at Girton or Newnham would collect examples and deduce a theory— but she would need thick gloves on her hands, and bars to protect her of solid gold.

But what is amusing now, I recollected, shutting Lady Bessborough, had to be taken in desperate earnest once. Opinions that one now pastes in a book labelled cock-a-doodle-dum and keeps for reading to select audiences on summer nights once drew tears, I can assure you. Among your grandmothers and great-grandmothers there were many that wept their eyes out. Florence Nightingale shrieked loud in her agony.[8] Moreover, it is all very well for you, who have got yourselves to college and enjoy sitting-rooms—or is it only bed-sitting-rooms?—of your own to say that genius should disregard such opinions; that genius should be above caring what is said of it. Unfortunately, it is precisely the men or women of genius who mind most what is said of them. Remember Keats. Remember the words he had cut on his tombstone.[9] Think of Tennyson; think—but I need hardly multiply instances of the undeniable, if very unfortunate, fact that it is the nature of the artist to mind excessively what is said about him. Literature is strewn with the wreckage of men who have minded beyond reason the opinions of others.

And this susceptibility of theirs is doubly unfortunate, I thought, returning again to my original enquiry into what state of mind is most propitious for creative work, because the mind of an artist, in order to achieve the prodigious effort of freeing whole and entire the work that is in him, must be incandescent, like Shakespeare's mind, I conjectured, looking at the book which lay open at *Antony and Cleopatra*. There must be no obstacle in it, no foreign matter unconsumed.

For though we say that we know nothing about Shakespeare's state of mind, even as we say that, we are saying something about Shakespeare's state of mind. The reason perhaps why we know so little of Shakespeare—compared with Donne or Ben Jonson or Milton—is that his grudges and spites and antipathies are hidden from us. We are not held up by some "revelation" which reminds us of the writer. All desire to protest, to preach, to proclaim an injury, to pay off a score, to make the world the witness of some hardship or grievance was fired out of him and consumed. Therefore his poetry flows from him free and unimpeded. If ever a human being got his work expressed completely, it

7. English statesman (1773–1846). Lady Bessborough is Henrietta, countess of Bessborough (1761–1821).
8. See *Cassandra,* by Florence Nightingale, printed in *The Cause,* by R. Strachey [Woolf's note]. Florence Nightingale (1820–1910), English nurse, who originated and directed a group of field nurses during the Crimean War and is considered the founder of modern nursing.
9. "Here lies one whose name was writ in water."

was Shakespeare. If ever a mind was incandescent, unimpeded, I thought, turning again to the bookcase, it was Shakespeare's mind.

Chapter Four

That one would find any woman in that state of mind in the sixteenth century was obviously impossible. One has only to think of the Elizabethan tombstones with all those children kneeling with clasped hands; and their early deaths; and to see their houses with their dark, cramped rooms, to realise that no woman could have written poetry then. What one would expect to find would be that rather later perhaps some great lady would take advantage of her comparative freedom and comfort to publish something with her name to it and risk being thought a monster. Men, of course, are not snobs, I continued, carefully eschewing "the arrant feminism" of Miss Rebecca West; but they appreciate with sympathy for the most part the efforts of a countess to write verse. One would expect to find a lady of title meeting with far greater encouragement than an unknown Miss Austen or a Miss Brontë at that time would have met with. But one would also expect to find that her mind was disturbed by alien emotions like fear and hatred and that her poems showed traces of that disturbance. Here is Lady Winchilsea,[1] for example, I thought, taking down her poems. She was born in the year 1661; she was noble both by birth and by marriage; she was childless; she wrote poetry, and one has only to open her poetry to find her bursting out in indignation against the position of women:

> How are we fallen! fallen by mistaken rules,
> And Education's more than Nature's fools;
> Debarred from all improvements of the mind,
> And to be dull, expected and designed;
> And if some one would soar above the rest,
> With warmer fancy, and ambition pressed,
> So strong the opposing faction still appears,
> The hopes to thrive can ne'er outweigh the fears.

Clearly her mind has by no means "consumed all impediments and become incandescent." On the contrary, it is harrassed and distracted with hates and grievances. The human race is split up for her into two parties. Men are the "opposing faction"; men are hated and feared, because they have the power to bar her way to what she wants to do—which is to write.

> Alas! a woman that attempts the pen,
> Such a presumptuous creature is esteemed,
> The fault can by no virtue be redeemed.
> They tell us we mistake our sex and way;
> Good breeding, fashion, dancing, dressing, play,
> Are the accomplishments we should desire;
> To write, or read, or think, or to enquire,
> Would cloud our beauty, and exhaust our time,
> And interrupt the conquests of our prime,
> Whilst the dull manage of a servile house
> Is held by some our utmost art and use.

---

1. Anne Finch, countess of Winchilsea (1661–1720); the quotations are from her poem "The Introduction."

Indeed she has to encourage herself to write by supposing that what she writes will never be published; to soothe herself with the sad chant:

> To some few friends, and to thy sorrows sing,
> For groves of laurel thou wert never meant;
> Be dark enough thy shades, and be thou there content.

Yet it is clear that could she have freed her mind from hate and fear and not heaped it with bitterness and resentment, the fire was hot within her. Now and again words issue of pure poetry:

> Nor will in fading silks compose,
> Faintly the inimitable rose.

—they are rightly praised by Mr Murry,[2] and Pope, it is thought, remembered and appropriated those others:

> Now the jonquille o'ercomes the feeble brain;
> We faint beneath the aromatic pain.

It was a thousand pities that the woman who could write like that, whose mind was turned to nature and reflection, should have been forced to anger and bitterness. But how could she have helped herself? I asked, imagining the sneers and the laughter, the adulation of the toadies,[3] the scepticism of the professional poet. She must have shut herself up in a room in the country to write, and been torn asunder by bitterness and scruples perhaps, though her husband was of the kindest, and their married life perfection. She "must have," I say, because when one comes to seek out the facts about Lady Winchilsea, one finds, as usual, that almost nothing is known about her. She suffered terribly from melancholy, which we can explain at least to some extent when we find her telling us how in the grip of it she would imagine:

> My lines decried, and my employment thought,
> An useless folly or presumptuous fault:

The employment, which was thus censured, was, as far as one can see, the harmless one of rambling about the fields and dreaming:

> My hand delights to trace unusual things,
> And deviates from the known and common way,
> Nor will in fading silks compose,
> Faintly the inimitable rose.

Naturally, if that was her habit and that was her delight, she could only expect to be laughed at; and, accordingly, Pope or Gay[4] is said to have satirised her "as a blue-stocking with an itch for scribbling." Also it is thought that she offended Gay by laughing at him. She said that his *Trivia* showed that "he was more proper to walk before a chair than to ride in one." But this is all "dubious gossip" and, says Mr Murry, "uninteresting." But there I do not agree with him, for I should have liked to have had more even of dubious gossip so that I might have found out or made up some image of this melancholy lady, who loved wandering in the fields and thinking about unusual things and scorned, so rashly, so unwisely, "the dull manage of a servile house." But she became

2. John Middleton Murry (1889–1957), English literary critic.
3. Sycophants.
4. John Gay (1685–1732), English poet and play-wright, author of the poem "Trivia, or The Art of Walking the Streets of London" (1716), mentioned below.

diffuse, Mr Murry says. Her gift is all grown about with weeds and bound with briars. It had no chance of showing itself for the fine distinguished gift it was. And so, putting her back on the shelf, I turned to the other great lady, the Duchess whom Lamb loved, hare-brained, fantastical Margaret of Newcastle,[5] her elder, but her contemporary. They were very different, but alike in this that both were noble and both childless, and both were married to the best of husbands. In both burnt the same passion for poetry and both are disfigured and deformed by the same causes. Open the Duchess and one finds the same outburst of rage, "Women live like Bats or Owls, labour like Beasts, and die like Worms. . . ." Margaret too might have been a poet; in our day all that activity would have turned a wheel of some sort. As it was, what could bind, tame or civilise for human use that wild, generous, untutored intelligence? It poured itself out, higgledy-piggledy, in torrents of rhyme and prose, poetry and philosophy which stand congealed in quartos and folios that nobody ever reads. She should have had a microscope put in her hand. She should have been taught to look at the stars and reason scientifically. Her wits were turned with solitude and freedom. No one checked her. No one taught her. The professors fawned on her. At Court they jeered at her. Sir Egerton Brydges[6] complained of her coarseness—"as flowing from a female of high rank brought up in the Courts." She shut herself up at Welbeck[7] alone.

What a vision of loneliness and riot the thought of Margaret Cavendish brings to mind! as if some giant cucumber had spread itself over all the roses and carnations in the garden and choked them to death. What a waste that the woman who wrote "the best bred women are those whose minds are civilest" should have frittered her time away scribbling nonsense and plunging ever deeper into obscurity and folly till the people crowded round her coach when she issued out. Evidently the crazy Duchess became a bogey to frighten clever girls with. Here, I remembered, putting away the Duchess and opening Dorothy Osborne's[8] letters, is Dorothy writing to Temple about the Duchess's new book. "Sure the poore woman is a little distracted, shee could never bee soe rediculous else as to venture at writeing book's and in verse too, if I should not sleep this fortnight I should not come to that."

And so, since no woman of sense and modesty could write books, Dorothy, who was sensitive and melancholy, the very opposite of the Duchess in temper, wrote nothing. Letters did not count. A woman might write letters while she was sitting by her father's sick-bed. She could write them by the fire whilst the men talked without disturbing them. The strange thing is, I thought, turning over the pages of Dorothy's letters, what a gift that untaught and solitary girl had for the framing of a sentence, for the fashioning of a scene. Listen to her running on:

"After dinner wee sitt and talk till Mr B. com's in question and then I am gon. the heat of the day is spent in reading or working and about six or seven a Clock, I walke out into a Common that lyes hard by the house where a great many young wenches keep Sheep and Cow's and sitt in the shades singing of Ballads; I goe to them and compare their voyces and Beauty's to some Ancient Shepherdesses that I have read of and finde a vaste difference there, but trust mee I think these are as innocent as those could bee. I talke to them, and

---

5. Margaret Lucas Cavendish, duchess of New-castle (1623–1673), author of "Female Orations," quoted below.
6. English writer (1762–1837).

7. Estate of Margaret's husband, in Nottingham-shire.
8. Later, Lady Temple (1627–1695), famous for her letters to her future husband.

finde they want nothing to make them the happiest People in the world, but the knoledge that they are soe. most commonly when we are in the middest of our discourse one looks aboute her and spyes her Cow's goeing into the Corne and then away they all run, as if they had wing's at theire heels. I that am not soe nimble stay behinde, and when I see them driveing home theire Cattle I think tis time for mee to retyre too. when I have supped I goe into the Garden and soe to the syde of a small River that runs by it where I sitt downe and wish you with mee. . . ."

One could have sworn that she had the makings of a writer in her. But "if I should not sleep this fortnight I should not come to that"—one can measure the opposition that was in the air to a woman writing when one finds that even a woman with a great turn for writing has brought herself to believe that to write a book was to be ridiculous, even to show oneself distracted. And so we come, I continued, replacing the single short volume of Dorothy Osborne's letters upon the shelf, to Mrs Behn.[9]

And with Mrs Behn we turn a very important corner on the road. We leave behind, shut up in their parks among their folios, those solitary great ladies who wrote without audience or criticism, for their own delight alone. We come to town and rub shoulders with ordinary people in the streets. Mrs Behn was a middle-class woman with all the plebeian virtues of humour, vitality and courage; a woman forced by the death of her husband and some unfortunate adventures of her own to make her living by her wits. She had to work on equal terms with men. She made, by working very hard, enough to live on. The importance of that fact outweighs anything that she actually wrote, even the splendid "A Thousand Martyrs I have made," or "Love in Fantastic Triumph sat," for here begins the freedom of the mind, or rather the possibility that in the course of time the mind will be free to write what it likes. For now that Aphra Behn had done it, girls could go to their parents and say, You need not give me an allowance; I can make money by my pen. Of course the answer for many years to come was, Yes, by living the life of Aphra Behn! Death would be better! and the door was slammed faster than ever. That profoundly interesting subject, the value that men set upon women's chastity and its effect upon their education, here suggests itself for discussion, and might provide an interesting book if any student at Girton or Newnham cared to go into the matter. Lady Dudley, sitting in diamonds among the midges of a Scottish moor, might serve for frontispiece. Lord Dudley, *The Times* said when Lady Dudley died the other day, "a man of cultivated taste and many accomplishments, was benevolent and bountiful, but whimsically despotic. He insisted upon his wife's wearing full dress, even at the remotest shooting-lodge in the Highlands; he loaded her with gorgeous jewels," and so on, "he gave her everything—always excepting any measure of responsibility." Then Lord Dudley had a stroke and she nursed him and ruled his estates with supreme competence for ever after. That whimsical despotism was in the nineteenth century too.

But to return. Aphra Behn proved that money could be made by writing at the sacrifice, perhaps, of certain agreeable qualities; and so by degrees writing became not merely a sign of folly and a distracted mind, but was of practical importance. A husband might die, or some disaster overtake the family. Hundreds of women began as the eighteenth century drew on to add to their pin

9. Aphra Behn (ca. 1640–1689), English poet and playwright, and author of *Oroonoko*.

money, or to come to the rescue of their families by making translations or writing the innumerable bad novels which have ceased to be recorded even in text-books, but are to be picked up in the fourpenny boxes in the Charing Cross Road.[1] The extreme activity of mind which showed itself in the later eighteenth century among women—the talking, and the meeting, the writing of essays on Shakespeare, the translating of the classics—was founded on the solid fact that women could make money by writing. Money dignifies what is frivolous if unpaid for. It might still be well to sneer at "blue stockings with an itch for scribbling," but it could not be denied that they could put money in their purses. Thus, towards the end of the eighteenth century a change came about which, if I were rewriting history, I should describe more fully and think of greater importance than the Crusades or the Wars of the Roses. The middle-class woman began to write. For if *Pride and Prejudice* matters, and *Middlemarch* and *Villette* and *Wuthering Heights*[2] matter, then it matters far more than I can prove in an hour's discourse that women generally, and not merely the lonely aristocrat shut up in her country house among her folios and her flatterers, took to writing. Without those forerunners, Jane Austen and the Brontës and George Eliot could no more have written than Shakespeare could have written without Marlowe, or Marlowe without Chaucer, or Chaucer without those forgotten poets who paved the ways and tamed the natural savagery of the tongue. For masterpieces are not single and solitary births; they are the outcome of many years of thinking in common, of thinking by the body of the people, so that the experience of the mass is behind the single voice. Jane Austen should have laid a wreath upon the grave of Fanny Burney, and George Eliot done homage to the robust shade of Eliza Carter[3]— the valiant old woman who tied a bell to her bedstead in order that she might wake early and learn Greek. All women together ought to let flowers fall upon the tomb of Alphra Behn which is, most scandalously but rather appropriately, in Westminster Abbey,[4] for it was she who earned them the right to speak their minds. It is she—shady and amorous as she was—who makes it not quite fantastic for me to say to you tonight: Earn five hundred a year by your wits.

Here, then, one had reached the early nineteenth century. And here, for the first time, I found several shelves given up entirely to the works of women. But why, I could not help asking, as I ran my eyes over them, were they, with very few exceptions, all novels? The original impulse was to poetry. The "supreme head of song" was a poetess. Both in France and in England the women poets precede the women novelists. Moreover, I thought, looking at the four famous names, what had George Eliot in common with Emily Brontë? Did not Charlotte Brontë fail entirely to understand Jane Austen? Save for the possibly relevant fact that not one of them had a child, four more incongruous characters could not have met together in a room—so much so that it is tempting to invent a meeting and a dialogue between them. Yet by some strange force they were all compelled, when they wrote, to write novels. Had it something to do with being born of the middle class, I asked; and with the fact, which Miss Emily Davies[5] a little later was so strikingly to demonstrate, that the middle-class family in the early nineteenth century was possessed only of a single sitting-room between them? If a woman wrote, she would have to

1. A street in London famed for its bookshops.
2. Novels by, respectively, Jane Austen, George Eliot, Charlotte Brontë, and Emily Brontë. *Emma*, mentioned below, is by Austen.
3. English poet and translator (1717–1806).
4. Site of Poet's Corner, which contains the tombs of many notable authors.
5. See n. 3, p. 2102.

write in the common sitting-room. And, as Miss Nightingale was so vehemently to complain,—"women never have an half hour . . . that they can call their own"—she was always interrupted. Still it would be easier to write prose and fiction there than to write poetry or a play. Less concentration is required. Jane Austen wrote like that to the end of her days. "How she was able to effect all this," her nephew writes in his Memoir, "is surprising, for she had no separate study to repair to, and most of the work must have been done in the general sitting-room, subject to all kinds of casual interruptions. She was careful that her occupation should not be suspected by servants or visitors or any persons beyond her own family party."[6] Jane Austen hid her manuscripts or covered them with a piece of blotting-paper. Then, again, all the literary training that a woman had in the early nineteenth century was training in the observation of character, in the analysis of emotion. Her sensibility had been educated for centuries by the influences of the common sitting-room. People's feelings were impressed on her; personal relations were always before her eyes. Therefore, when the middle-class woman took to writing, she naturally wrote novels, even though, as seems evident enough, two of the four famous women here named were not by nature novelists. Emily Brontë should have written poetic plays; the overflow of George Eliot's capacious mind should have spread itself when the creative impulse was spent upon history or biography. They wrote novels, however; one may even go further, I said, taking *Pride and Prejudice* from the shelf, and say that they wrote good novels. Without boasting or giving pain to the opposite sex, one may say that *Pride and Prejudice* is a good book. At any rate, one would not have been ashamed to have been caught in the act of writing *Pride and Prejudice*. Yet Jane Austen was glad that a hinge creaked, so that she might hide her manuscript before any one came in. To Jane Austen there was something discreditable in writing *Pride and Prejudice*. And, I wondered, would *Pride and Prejudice* have been a better novel if Jane Austen had not thought it necessary to hide her manuscript from visitors? I read a page or two to see; but I could not find any signs that her circumstances had harmed her work in the slightest. That, perhaps, was the chief miracle about it. Here was a woman about the year 1800 writing without hate, without bitterness, without fear, without protest, without preaching. That was how Shakespeare wrote, I thought, looking at *Antony and Cleopatra*; and when people compare Shakespeare and Jane Austen, they may mean that the minds of both had consumed all impediments; and for that reason we do not know Jane Austen and we do not know Shakespeare, and for that reason Jane Austen pervades every word that she wrote, and so does Shakespeare. If Jane Austen suffered in any way from her circumstances it was in the narrowness of life that was imposed upon her. It was impossible for a woman to go about alone. She never travelled; she never drove through London in an omnibus or had luncheon in a shop by herself. But perhaps it was the nature of Jane Austen not to want what she had not. Her gift and her circumstances matched each other completely. But I doubt whether that was true of Charlotte Brontë, I said, opening *Jane Eyre* and laying it beside *Pride and Prejudice*.

I opened it at chapter twelve and my eye was caught by the phrase, "Anybody may blame me who likes." What were they blaming Charlotte Brontë for, I wondered? And I read how Jane Eyre used to go up on to the roof when Mrs. Fairfax was making jellies and looked over the fields at the distant view. And

---

6. *Memoir of Jane Austen,* by her nephew, James Edward Austen-Leigh [Woolf's note].

then she longed—and it was for this that they blamed her—that "then I longed for a power of vision which might overpass that limit; which might reach the busy world, towns, regions full of life I had heard of but never seen: that then I desired more of practical experience than I possessed; more of intercourse with my kind, of acquaintance with variety of character than was here within my reach. I valued what was good in Mrs. Fairfax, and what was good in Adèle; but I believed in the existence of other and more vivid kinds of goodness, and what I believed in I wished to behold.

"Who blames me? Many, no doubt, and I shall be called discontented. I could not help it: the restlessness was in my nature; it agitated me to pain sometimes. . . .

"It is vain to say human beings ought to be satisfied with tranquillity: they must have action; and they will make it if they cannot find it. Millions are condemned to a stiller doom than mine, and millions are in silent revolt against their lot. Nobody knows how many rebellions ferment in the masses of life which people earth. Women are supposed to be very calm generally: but women feel just as men feel; they need exercise for their faculties and a field for their efforts as much as their brothers do; they suffer from too rigid a restraint, too absolute a stagnation, precisely as men would suffer; and it is narrow-minded in their more privileged fellow-creatures to say that they ought to confine themselves to making puddings and knitting stockings, to playing on the piano and embroidering bags. It is thoughtless to condemn them, or laugh at them, if they seek to do more or learn more than custom has pronounced necessary for their sex.

"When thus alone I not unfrequently heard Grace Poole's laugh. . . ."

That is an awkward break, I thought. It is upsetting to come upon Grace Poole all of a sudden. The continuity is disturbed. One might say, I continued, laying the book down beside *Pride and Prejudice*, that the woman who wrote those pages had more genius in her than Jane Austen; but if one reads them over and marks that jerk in them, that indignation, one sees that she will never get her genius expressed whole and entire. Her books will be deformed and twisted. She will write in a rage where she should write calmly. She will write foolishly where she should write wisely. She will write of herself where she should write of her characters. She is at war with her lot. How could she help but die young, cramped and thwarted?

One could not but play for a moment with the thought of what might have happened if Charlotte Brontë had possessed say three hundred a year—but the foolish woman sold the copyright of her novels outright for fifteen hundred pounds; had somehow possessed more knowledge of the busy world, and towns and regions full of life; more practical experience, and intercourse with her kind and acquaintance with a variety of character. In those words she puts her finger exactly not only upon her own defects as a novelist but upon those of her sex at that time. She knew, no one better, how enormously her genius would have profited if it had not spent itself in solitary visions over distant fields; if experience and intercourse and travel had been granted her. But they were not granted; they were withheld; and we must accept the fact that all those good novels, *Villette, Emma, Wuthering Heights, Middlemarch,* were written by women without more experience of life than could enter the house of a respectable clergyman; written too in the common sitting-room of that respectable house and by women so poor that they could not afford to buy more than a few quires of paper at a time upon which to write *Wuthering*

Heights or *Jane Eyre.* One of them, it is true, George Eliot, escaped after much tribulation, but only to a secluded villa in St John's Wood.[7] And there she settled down in the shadow of the world's disapproval. "I wish it to be understood," she wrote, "that I should never invite any one to come and see me who did not ask for the invitation"; for was she not living in sin with a married man and might not the sight of her damage the chastity of Mrs Smith or whoever it might be that chanced to call? One must submit to the social convention, and be "cut off from what is called the world." At the same time, on the other side of Europe, there was a young man living freely with this gipsy or with that great lady; going to the wars; picking up unhindered and uncensored all that varied experience of human life which served him so splendidly later when he came to write his books. Had Tolstoi[8] lived at the Priory in seclusion with a married lady "cut off from what is called the world," however edifying the moral lesson, he could scarcely, I thought, have written *War and Peace.*

But one could perhaps go a little deeper into the question of novel-writing and the effect of sex upon the novelist. If one shuts one's eyes and thinks of the novel as a whole, it would seem to be a creation owning a certain looking-glass likeness to life, though of course with simplifications and distortions innumerable. At any rate, it is a structure leaving a shape on the mind's eye, built now in squares, now pagoda shaped, now throwing out wings and arcades, now solidly compact and domed like the Cathedral of Saint Sofia at Constantinople. This shape, I thought, thinking back over certain famous novels, starts in one the kind of emotion that is appropriate to it. But that emotion at once blends itself with others, for the "shape" is not made by the relation of stone to stone, but by the relation of human being to human being. Thus a novel starts in us all sorts of antagonistic and opposed emotions. Life conflicts with something that is not life. Hence the difficulty of coming to any agreement about novels, and the immense sway that our private prejudices have upon us. On the one hand, we feel You—John the hero—must live, or I shall be in the depths of despair. On the other, we feel, Alas, John, you must die, because the shape of the book requires it. Life conflicts with something that is not life. Then since life it is in part, we judge it as life. James is the sort of man I most detest, one says. Or, This is a farrago of absurdity. I could never feel anything of the sort myself. The whole structure, it is obvious, thinking back on any famous novel, is one of infinite complexity, because it is thus made up of so many different judgments, of so many different kinds of emotion. The wonder is that any book so composed holds together for more than a year or two, or can possibly mean to the English reader what it means for the Russian or the Chinese. But they do hold together occasionally very remarkably. And what holds them together in these rare instances of survival (I was thinking of *War and Peace*) is something that one calls integrity, though it has nothing to do with paying one's bills or behaving honourably in an emergency. What one means by integrity, in the case of the novelist, is the conviction that he gives one that this is the truth. Yes, one feels, I should never have thought that this could be so; I have never known people behaving like that. But you have convinced me that so it is, so it happens. One holds every phrase, every scene to the light as one reads—for Nature seems, very oddly, to have provided us with an inner light by which to judge of the novelist's

---

7. A suburb in northwest London that developed in the 1840s.

8. Leo Tolstoy (1828–1910), Russian novelist.

integrity or disintegrity. Or perhaps it is rather that Nature, in her most irrational mood, has traced in invisible ink on the walls of the mind a premonition which these great artists confirm; a sketch which only needs to be held to the fire of genius to become visible. When one so exposes it and sees it come to life one exclaims in rapture, But this is what I have always felt and known and desired! And one boils over with excitement, and, shutting the book even with a kind of reverence as if it were something very precious, a stand-by to return to as long as one lives, one puts it back on the shelf, I said, taking *War and Peace* and putting it back in its place. If, on the other hand, these poor sentences that one takes and tests rouse first a quick and eager response with their bright colouring and their dashing gestures but there they stop: something seems to check them in their development: or if they bring to light only a faint scribble in that corner and a blot over there, and nothing appears whole and entire, then one heaves a sigh of disappointment and says, Another failure. This novel has come to grief somewhere.

And for the most part, of course, novels do come to grief somewhere. The imagination falters under the enormous strain. The insight is confused; it can no longer distinguish between the true and the false; it has no longer the strength to go on with the vast labour that calls at every moment for the use of so many different faculties. But how would all this be affected by the sex of the novelist, I wondered, looking at *Jane Eyre* and the others. Would the fact of her sex in any way interfere with the integrity of a woman novelist—that integrity which I take to be the backbone of the writer? Now, in the passages I have quoted from *Jane Eyre*, it is clear that anger was tampering with the integrity of Charlotte Brontë the novelist. She left her story, to which her entire devotion was due, to attend to some personal grievance. She remembered that she had been starved of her proper due of experience—she had been made to stagnate in a parsonage mending stockings when she wanted to wander free over the world. Her imagination swerved from indignation and we feel it swerve. But there were many more influences than anger tugging at her imagination and deflecting it from its path. Ignorance, for instance. The portrait of Rochester is drawn in the dark. We feel the influence of fear in it; just as we constantly feel an acidity which is the result of oppression, a buried suffering smouldering beneath her passion, a rancour which contracts those books, splendid as they are, with a spasm of pain.

And since a novel has this correspondence to real life, its values are to some extent those of real life. But it is obvious that the values of women differ very often from the values which have been made by the other sex; naturally, this is so. Yet it is the masculine values that prevail. Speaking crudely, football and sport are "important"; the worship of fashion, the buying of clothes "trivial." And these values are inevitably transferred from life to fiction. This is an important book, the critic assumes, because it deals with war. This is an insignificant book because it deals with the feelings of women in a drawing-room. A scene in a battlefield is more important than a scene in a shop—everywhere and much more subtly the difference of value persists. The whole structure, therefore, of the early nineteenth-century novel was raised, if one was a woman, by a mind which was slightly pulled from the straight, and made to alter its clear vision in deference to external authority. One has only to skim those old forgotten novels and listen to the tone of voice in which they are written to divine that the writer was meeting criticism; she was saying this by way of aggression, or that by way of conciliation. She was admitting that she was "only a woman," or protesting that she was "as good as a man." She met that criticism as her temperament dictated, with docility and diffidence, or with anger and emphasis. It does not matter which it was; she was thinking of something other than the thing itself. Down comes her book upon our heads. There was a flaw in the centre of it. And I thought of all the women's novels that lie scattered, like small pock-marked apples in an orchard, about the secondhand book shops of London. It was the flaw in the centre that had rotted them. She had altered her values in deference to the opinion of others.

But how impossible it must have been for them not to budge either to the right or to the left. What genius, what integrity it must have required in face of all that criticism, in the midst of that purely patriarchal society, to hold fast to the thing as they saw it without shrinking. Only Jane Austen did it and Emily Brontë. It is another feather, perhaps the finest, in their caps. They wrote as women write, not as men write. Of all the thousand women who wrote novels then, they alone entirely ignored the perpetual admonitions of the eternal pedagogue—write this, think that. They alone were deaf to that persistent voice, now grumbling, now patronising, now domineering, now grieved, now shocked, now angry, now avuncular, that voice which cannot let women alone, but must be at them, like some too conscientious governess, adjuring them, like Sir Egerton Brydges, to be refined; dragging even into the criticism of poetry criticism of sex;[9] admonishing them, if they would be good and win, as I suppose, some shiny prize, to keep within certain limits which the gentleman in question thinks suitable: ". . . female novelists should only aspire to excellence by courageously acknowledging the limitations of their sex."[1] That puts the matter in a nutshell, and when I tell you, rather to your surprise, that this sentence was written not in August 1828 but in August 1928, you will agree, I think, that however delightful it is to us now, it represents a vast body of opinion—I am not going to stir those old pools, I take only what chance has floated to my feet—that was far more vigorous and far more vocal a century ago. It would have needed a very stalwart young woman in 1828 to disregard all those snubs and chidings and promises of prizes. One must have been something of a firebrand to say to oneself, Oh, but they can't buy literature too. Literature is open to everybody. I refuse to allow you, Beadle though you are, to turn me off the grass. Lock up your libraries if you like; but there is no gate, no lock, no bolt that you can set upon the freedom of my mind.

But whatever effect discouragement and criticism had upon their writing— and I believe that they had a very great effect—that was unimportant compared with the other difficulty which faced them (I was still considering those early nineteenth-century novelists) when they came to set their thoughts on paper—that is that they had no tradition behind them, or one so short and partial that it was of little help. For we think back through our mothers if we are women. It is useless to go to the great men writers for help, however much one may go to them for pleasure. Lamb, Browne, Thackeray, Newman, Sterne, Dickens, De Quincey—whoever it may be—never helped a woman yet, though

---

9. "[She] has a metaphysical purpose, and that is a dangerous obsession, especially with a woman, for women rarely possess men's healthy love of rhetoric. It is a strange lack in the sex which is in other things more primitive and more materialistic."—*New Criterion*, June 1928 [Woolf's note].

1. "If, like the reporter, you believe that female novelists should only aspire to excellence by courageously acknowledging the limitations of their sex (Jane Austen [has] demonstrated how gracefully this gesture can be accomplished). . . ."—*Life and Letters*, August 1928 [Woolf's note].

2132 / VIRGINIA WOOLF

she may have learnt a few tricks of them and adapted them to her use. The weight, the pace, the stride of a man's mind are too unlike her own for her to lift anything substantial from him successfully. The ape is too distant to be sedulous. Perhaps the first thing she would find, setting pen to paper, was that there was no common sentence ready for her use. All the great novelists like Thackeray and Dickens and Balzac have written a natural prose, swift but not slovenly, expressive but not precious, taking their own tint without ceasing to be common property. They have based it on the sentence that was current at the time. The sentence that was current at the beginning of the nineteenth century ran something like this perhaps: "The grandeur of their works was an argument with them, not to stop short, but to proceed. They could have no higher excitement or satisfaction than in the exercise of their art and endless generations of truth and beauty. Success prompts to exertion; and habit facilitates success." That is a man's sentence; behind it one can see Johnson, Gibbon[2] and the rest. It was a sentence that was unsuited for a woman's use. Charlotte Brontë, with all her splendid gift for prose, stumbled and fell with that clumsy weapon in her hands. George Eliot committed atrocities with it that beggar description. Jane Austen looked at it and laughed at it and devised a perfectly natural, shapely sentence proper for her own use and never departed from it. Thus, with less genius for writing than Charlotte Brontë, she got infinitely more said. Indeed, since freedom and fullness of expression are of the essence of the art, such a lack of tradition, such a scarcity and inadequacy of tools, must have told enormously upon the writing of women. Moreover, a book is not made of sentences laid end to end, but of sentences built, if an image helps, into arcades or domes. And this shape too has been made by men out of their own needs for their own uses. There is no reason to think that the form of the epic or of the poetic play suits a woman any more than the sentence suits her. But all the older forms of literature were hardened and set by the time she became a writer. The novel alone was young enough to be soft in her hands—another reason, perhaps, why she wrote novels. Yet who shall say that even now "the novel" (I give it inverted commas to mark my sense of the words' inadequacy), who shall say that even this most pliable of all forms is rightly shaped for her use? No doubt we shall find her knocking that into shape for herself when she has the free use of her limbs; and providing some new vehicle, not necessarily in verse, for the poetry in her. For it is the poetry that is still denied outlet. And I went on to ponder how a woman nowadays would write a poetic tragedy in five acts—would she use verse—would she not use prose rather?

But these are difficult questions which lie in the twilight of the future. I must leave them, if only because they stimulate me to wander from my subject into trackless forests where I shall be lost and, very likely, devoured by wild beasts. I do not want, and I am sure that you do not want me, to broach that very dismal subject, the future of fiction, so that I will only pause here one moment to draw your attention to the great part which must be played in that future so far as women are concerned by physical conditions. The book has somehow to be adapted to the body, and at a venture one would say that women's books should be shorter, more concentrated, than those of men, and framed so that they do not need long hours of steady and uninterrupted work.

2. Edward Gibbon (1737–1794), English historian, author of *The History of the Decline and Fall of the Roman Empire.*

For interruptions there will always be. Again, the nerves that feed the brain would seem to differ in men and women, and if you are going to make them work their best and hardest, you must find out what treatment suits them— whether these hours of lectures, for instance, which the monks devised, pre- sumably, hundreds of years ago, suit them—what alternations of work and rest they need, interpreting rest not as doing nothing but as doing something but something that is different; and what should that difference be? All this should be discussed and discovered; all this is part of the question of women and fiction. And yet, I continued, approaching the bookcase again, where shall I find that elaborate study of the psychology of women by a woman? If through their incapacity to play football women are not going to be allowed to practise medicine——

Happily my thoughts were now given another turn.

Chapter Five

I had come at last, in the course of this rambling, to the shelves which hold books by the living; by women and by men; for there are almost as many books written by women now as by men. Or if that is not yet quite true, if the male is still the voluble sex, it is certainly true that women no longer write novels solely. There are Jane Harrison's books on Greek archaeology; Vernon Lee's books on aesthetics; Gertrude Bell's[3] books on Persia. There are books on all sorts of subjects which a generation ago no woman could have touched. There are poems and plays and criticism; there are histories and biographies, books of travel and books of scholarship and research; there are even a few philosophies and books about science and economics. And though novels predominate, nov- els themselves may very well have changed from association with books of a different feather. The natural simplicity, the epic age of women's writing, may have gone. Reading and criticism may have given her a wider range, a greater subtlety. The impulse towards autobiography may be spent. She may be begin- ning to use writing as an art, not as a method of self-expression. Among these new novels one might find an answer to several such questions.

I took down one of them at random. It stood at the very end of the shelf, was called *Life's Adventure*, or some such title, by Mary Carmichael,[4] and was published in this very month of October. It seems to be her first book, I said to myself, but one must read it as if it were the last volume in a fairly long series, continuing all those other books that I have been glancing at—Lady Winchilsea's poems and Aphra Behn's plays and the novels of the four great novelists. For books continue each other, in spite of our habit of judging them separately. And I must also consider her—this unknown woman—as the descendant of all those other women whose circumstances I have been glanc- ing at and see what she inherits of their characteristics and restrictions. So, with a sigh, because novels so often provide an anodyne and not an antidote, glide one into torpid slumbers instead of rousing one with a burning brand, I settled down with a notebook and a pencil to make what I could of Mary Carmichael's first novel, *Life's Adventure*.

3. English archaeologist and writer (1868–1926). Harrison (1850–1928), scholar and lecturer at Cambridge. Lee (1856–1935), essayist and art critic.
4. The novel *Love's Creation* was published in

London in 1928 under the name Marie Carmi- chael, the pseudonym for Marie Stopes, a crusader for birth control. The plot and characters resemble those mentioned by Woolf.

To begin with, I ran my eye up and down the page. I am going to get the hang of her sentences first, I said, before I load my memory with blue eyes and brown and the relationship that there may be between Chloe and Roger. There will be time for that when I have decided whether she has a pen in her hand or a pickaxe. So I tried a sentence or two on my tongue. Soon it was obvious that something was not quite in order. The smooth gliding of sentence after sentence was interrupted. Something tore, something scratched; a single word here and there flashed its torch in my eyes. She was "unhanding" herself as they say in the old plays. She is like a person striking a match that will not light, I thought. But why, I asked her as if she were present, are Jane Austen's sentences not of the right shape for you? Must they all be scrapped because Emma and Mr Woodhouse are dead? Alas, I sighed, that it should be so. For while Jane Austen breaks from melody to melody as Mozart from song to song, to read this writing was like being out at sea in an open boat. Up one went, down one sank. This terseness, this shortwindedness, might mean that she was afraid of something; afraid of being called "sentimental" perhaps; or she remembers that women's writing has been called flowery and so provides a superfluity of thorns; but until I have read a scene with some care, I cannot be sure whether she is being herself or some one else. At any rate, she does not lower one's vitality, I thought, reading more carefully. But she is heaping up too many facts. She will not be able to use half of them in a book of this size. (It was about half the length of *Jane Eyre*.) However, by some means or other she succeeded in getting us all—Roger, Chloe, Olivia, Tony and Mr Bigham—in a canoe up the river. Wait a moment, I said, leaning back in my chair, I must consider the whole thing more carefully before I go any further.

I am almost sure, I said to myself, that Mary Carmichael is playing a trick on us. For I feel as one feels on a switchback railway when the car, instead of sinking, as one has been led to expect, swerves up again. Mary is tampering with the expected sequence. First she broke the sentence; now she has broken the sequence. Very well, she has every right to do both these things if she does them not for the sake of breaking, but for the sake of creating. Which of the two it is I cannot be sure until she has faced herself with a situation. I will give her every liberty, I said, to choose what that situation shall be; she shall make it of tin cans and old kettles if she likes; but she must convince me that she believes it to be a situation; and then when she has made it she must face it. She must jump. And, determined to do my duty by her as reader if she would do her duty by me as writer, I turned the page and read . . . I am sorry to break off so abruptly. Are there no men present? Do you promise me that behind that red curtain over there the figure of Sir Chartres Biron[5] is not concealed? We are all women, you assure me? Then I may tell you that the very next words I read were these—"Chloe liked Olivia . . ." Do not start. Do not blush. Let us admit in the privacy of our own society that these things sometimes happen. Sometimes women do like women.

"Chloe liked Olivia," I read. And then it struck me how immense a change was there. Chloe liked Olivia perhaps for the first time in literature. Cleopatra did not like Octavia. And how completely *Antony and Cleopatra* would have been altered had she done so! As it is, I thought, letting my mind, I am afraid, wander a little from *Life's Adventure*, the whole thing is simplified, conven-

5. Chief magistrate of London who in 1928 judged that the novel *The Well of Loneliness*, by the lesbian writer Radclyffe Hall, was an "obscene libel" and ordered all copies destroyed.

tionalised, if one dared say it, absurdly. Cleopatra's only feeling about Octavia is one of jealousy. Is she taller than I am? How does she do her hair? The play, perhaps, required no more. But how interesting it would have been if the relationship between the two women had been more complicated. All these relationships between women, I thought, rapidly recalling the splendid gallery of fictitious women, are too simple. So much has been left out, unattempted. And I tried to remember any case in the course of my reading where two women are represented as friends. There is an attempt at it in *Diana of the Crossways*. They are confidantes, of course, in Racine[6] and the Greek tragedies. They are now and then mothers and daughters. But almost without exception they are shown in their relation to men. It was strange to think that all the great women of fiction were, until Jane Austen's day, not only seen by the other sex, but seen only in relation to the other sex. And how small a part of a woman's life is that; and how little can a man know even of that when he observes it through the black or rosy spectacles which sex puts upon his nose. Hence, perhaps, the peculiar nature of woman in fiction; the astonishing extremes of her beauty and horror; her alternations between heavenly goodness and hellish depravity—for so a lover would see her as his love rose or sank, was prosperous or unhappy. This is not so true of the nineteenth-century novelists, of course. Woman becomes much more various and complicated there. Indeed it was the desire to write about women perhaps that led men by degrees to abandon the poetic drama which, with its violence, could make so little use of them, and to devise the novel as a more fitting receptacle. Even so it remains obvious, even in the writing of Proust,[7] that a man is terribly hampered and partial in his knowledge of women, as a woman in her knowledge of men.

Also, I continued, looking down at the page again, it is becoming evident that women, like men, have other interests besides the perennial interests of domesticity. "Chloe liked Olivia. They shared a laboratory together. . . ." I read on and discovered that these two young women were engaged in mincing liver, which is, it seems, a cure for pernicious anaemia: although one of them was married and had—I think I am right in stating—two small children. Now all that, of course, has had to be left out, and thus the splendid portrait of the fictitious woman is much too simple and much too monotonous. Suppose, for instance, that men were only represented in literature as the lovers of women, and were never the friends of men, soldiers, thinkers, dreamers; how few parts in the plays of Shakespeare could be allotted to them; how literature would suffer! We might perhaps have most of Othello; and a good deal of Antony; but no Caesar, no Brutus, no Hamlet, no Lear, no Jaques—literature would be incredibly impoverished, as indeed literature is impoverished beyond our counting by the doors that have been shut upon women. Married against their will, kept in one room, and to one occupation, how could a dramatist give a full or interesting or truthful account of them? Love was the only possible interpreter. The poet was forced to be passionate or bitter, unless indeed he chose to "hate women," which meant more often than not that he was unattractive to them.

Now if Chloe likes Olivia and they share a laboratory, which of itself will

---

6. Jean Racine (1639–1699), French dramatist. "*Diana of the Crossways*": 1885 novel by the English author George Meredith (1828–1909).

7. Marcel Proust (1871–1922), French novelist and author of the seven-volume *A la Recherche du Temps Perdu* (1913–27).

make their friendship more varied and lasting because it will be less personal; if Mary Carmichael knows how to write, and I was beginning to enjoy some quality in her style; if she has a room to herself, of which I am not quite sure; if she has five hundred a year of her own—but that remains to be proved— then I think that something of great importance has happened.

For if Chloe likes Olivia and Mary Carmichael knows how to express it she will light a torch in that vast chamber where nobody has yet been. It is all half lights and profound shadows like those serpentine caves where one goes with a candle peering up and down, not knowing where one is stepping. And I began to read the book again, and read how Chloe watched Olivia put a jar on a shelf and say how it was time to go home to her children. That is a sight that has never been seen since the world began, I exclaimed. And I watched too, very curiously. For I wanted to see how Mary Carmichael set to work to catch those unrecorded gestures, those unsaid or half-said words, which form themselves, no more palpably than the shadows of moths on the ceiling, when women are alone, unlit by the capricious and coloured light of the other sex. She will need to hold her breath, I said, reading on, if she is to do it; for women are so suspicious of any interest that has not some obvious motive behind it, so terribly accustomed to concealment and suppression, that they are off at the flicker of an eye turned observingly in their direction. The only way for you to do it, I thought, addressing Mary Carmichael as if she were there, would be to talk of something else, looking steadily out of the window, and thus note, not with a pencil in a notebook, but in the shortest of shorthand, in words that are hardly syllabled yet, what happens when Olivia—this organism that has been under the shadow of the rock these million years—feels the light fall on it, and sees coming her way a piece of strange food—knowledge, adventure, art. And she reaches out for it, I thought, again raising my eyes from the page, and has to devise some entirely new combination of her resources, so highly developed for their purposes, so as to absorb the new into the old without disturbing the infinitely intricate and elaborate balance of the whole.

But, alas, I had done what I had determined not to do; I had slipped unthinkingly into praise of my own sex. "Highly developed"—"infinitely intricate"— such are undeniably terms of praise, and to praise one's own sex is always suspect, often silly; moreover, in this case, how could one justify it? One could not go to the map and say Columbus discovered America and Columbus was a woman; or take an apple and remark, Newton discovered the laws of gravitation and Newton was a woman; or look into the sky and say aeroplanes are flying overhead and aeroplanes were invented by women. There is no mark on the wall to measure the precise height of women. There are no yard measures, neatly divided into the fractions of an inch, that one can lay against the qualities of a good mother or the devotion of a daughter, or the fidelity of a sister, or the capacity of a housekeeper. Few women even now have been graded at the universities; the great trials of the professions, army and navy, trade, politics and diplomacy have hardly tested them. They remain even at this moment almost unclassified. But if I want to know all that a human being can tell me about Sir Hawley Butts, for instance, I have only to open Burke or Debrett[8] and I shall find that he took such and such a degree; owns a hall; has an heir; was Secretary to a Board; represented Great Britain in Canada; and has

8. Annual reference works of genealogy and the peerage. Sir Hawley Butts, however, seems to be Woolf's invention.

received a certain number of degrees, offices, medals and other distinctions by which his merits are stamped upon him indelibly. Only Providence can know more about Sir Hawley Butts than that.

When, therefore, I say "highly developed," "infinitely intricate," of women, I am unable to verify my words either in Whitaker, Debrett or the University Calendar. In this predicament what can I do? And I looked at the bookcase again. There were the biographies: Johnson and Goethe and Carlyle and Sterne and Cowper and Shelley and Voltaire and Browning and many others. And I began thinking of all those great men who have for one reason or another admired, sought out, lived with, confided in, made love to, written of, trusted in, and shown what can only be described as some need of and dependence upon certain persons of the opposite sex. That all these relationships were absolutely Platonic I would not affirm, and Sir William Joynson Hicks[9] would probably deny. But we should wrong these illustrious men very greatly if we insisted that they got nothing from these alliances but comfort, flattery and the pleasures of the body. What they got, it is obvious, was something that their own sex was unable to supply; and it would not be rash, perhaps, to define it further, without quoting the doubtless rhapsodical words of the poets, as some stimulus, some renewal of creative power which is in the gift only of the opposite sex to bestow. He would open the door of drawing-room or nursery, I thought, and find her among her children perhaps, or with a piece of embroidery on her knee—at any rate, the centre of some different order and system of life, and the contrast between this world and his own, which might be the law courts or the House of Commons, would at once refresh and invigorate; and there would follow, even in the simplest talk, such a natural difference of opinion that the dried ideas in him would be fertilised anew; and the sight of her creating in a different medium from his own would so quicken his creative power that insensibly his sterile mind would begin to plot again, and he would find the phrase or the scene which was lacking when he put on his hat to visit her. Every Johnson has his Thrale,[1] and holds fast to her for some such reasons as these, and when the Thrale marries her Italian music master Johnson goes half mad with rage and disgust, not merely that he will miss his pleasant evenings at Streatham, but that the light of his life will be "as if gone out."

And without being Dr Johnson or Goethe or Carlyle or Voltaire, one may feel, though very differently from these great men, the nature of this intricacy and the power of this highly developed creative faculty among women. One goes into the room—but the resources of the English language would be much put to the stretch, and whole flights of words would need to wing their way illegitimately into existence before a woman could say what happens when she goes into a room. The rooms differ so completely; they are calm or thunderous; open on to the sea, or, on the contrary, give on to a prison yard; are hung with washing; or alive with opals and silks; are hard as horsehair or soft as feathers—one has only to go into any room in any street for the whole of that extremely complex force of femininity to fly in one's face. How should it be otherwise? For women have sat indoors all these millions of years, so that by this time the very walls are permeated by their creative force, which has,

9. English Conservative politician and evangelical religious figure (1865–1932).
1. Hester Lynch Thrale (1741–1821), who with her husband, Henry, was for many years friend and hostess to Samuel Johnson at their home in Streatham Place. After Henry's death she married an Italian musician, much to Johnson's distress; his reaction helped end their friendship.

indeed, so overcharged the capacity of bricks and mortar that it must needs harness itself to pens and brushes and business and politics. But this creative power differs greatly from the creative power of men. And one must conclude that it would be a thousand pities if it were hindered or wasted, for it was won by centuries of the most drastic discipline, and there is nothing to take its place. It would be a thousand pities if women wrote like men, or lived like men, or looked like men, for if two sexes are quite inadequate, considering the vastness and variety of the world, how should we manage with one only? Ought not education to bring out and fortify the differences rather than the similarities? For we have too much likeness as it is, and if an explorer should come back and bring word of other sexes looking through the branches of other trees at other skies, nothing would be of greater service to humanity; and we should have the immense pleasure into the bargain of watching Professor X rush for his measuring-rods to prove himself "superior."

Mary Carmichael, I thought, still hovering at a little distance above the page, will have her work cut out for her merely as an observer. I am afraid indeed that she will be tempted to become, what I think the less interesting branch of the species—the naturalist-novelist, and not the contemplative. There are so many new facts for her to observe. She will not need to limit herself any longer to the respectable houses of the upper middle classes. She will go without kindness or condescension, but in the spirit of fellowship into those small, scented rooms where sit the courtesan, the harlot and the lady with the pug dog. There they still sit in the rough and ready-made clothes that the male writer has had perforce to clap upon their shoulders. But Mary Carmichael will have out her scissors and fit them close to every hollow and angle. It will be a curious sight, when it comes, to see these women as they are, but we must wait a little, for Mary Carmichael will still be encumbered with that self-consciousness in the presence of "sin" which is the legacy of our sexual barbarity. She will still wear the shoddy old fetters of class on her feet.

However, the majority of women are neither harlots nor courtesans; nor do they sit clasping pug dogs to dusty velvet all through the summer afternoon. But what do they do then? and there came to my mind's eye one of those long streets somewhere south of the river whose infinite rows are innumerably populated. With the eye of the imagination I saw a very ancient lady crossing the street on the arm of a middle-aged woman, her daughter, perhaps, both so respectably booted and furred that their dressing in the afternoon must be a ritual, and the clothes themselves put away in cupboards with camphor, year after year, throughout the summer months. They cross the road when the lamps are being lit (for the dusk is their favourite hour), as they must have done year after year. The elder is close on eighty; but if one asked her what her life has meant to her, she would say that she remembered the streets lit for the battle of Balaclava, or had heard the guns fire in Hyde Park for the birth of King Edward the Seventh.[2] And if one asked her, longing to pin down the moment with date and season, but what were you doing on the fifth of April 1868, or the second of November 1875, she would look vague and say that she could remember nothing. For all the dinners are cooked; the plates and cups washed; the children set to school and gone out into the world.

2. In 1841 (since Woolf is writing in 1928, Edward's birth would actually have been before the birth of a woman "close on eighty"). The "battle of Balaclava," famous for the Charge of the Light Brigade, occurred in 1854.

Nothing remains of it all. All has vanished. No biography or history has a word to say about it. And the novels, without meaning to, inevitably lie.

All these infinitely obscure lives remain to be recorded, I said, addressing Mary Carmichael as if she were present; and went on in thought through the streets of London feeling in imagination the pressure of dumbness, the accumulation of unrecorded life, whether from the women at the street corners with their arms akimbo, and the rings embedded in their fat swollen fingers, talking with a gesticulation like the swing of Shakespeare's words; or from the violet-sellers and match-sellers and old crones stationed under doorways; or from drifting girls whose faces, like waves in sun and cloud, signal the coming of men and women and the flickering lights of shop windows. All that you will have to explore, I said to Mary Carmichael, holding your torch firm in your hand. Above all, you must illumine your own soul with its profundities and its shallows, and its vanities and its generosities, and say what your beauty means to you or your plainness, and what is your relation to the everchanging and turning world of gloves and shoes and stuffs swaying up and down among the faint scents that come through chemists' bottles down arcades of dress material over a floor of pseudo-marble. For in imagination I had gone into a shop; it was laid with black and white paving; it was hung, astonishingly beautifully, with coloured ribbons. Mary Carmichael might well have a look at that in passing, I thought, for it is a sight that would lend itself to the pen as fittingly as any snowy peak or rocky gorge in the Andes. And there is the girl behind the counter too—I would as soon have her true history as the hundred and fiftieth life of Napoleon or seventieth study of Keats and his use of Miltonic inversion which old Professor Z and his like are now inditing. And then I went on very warily, on the very tips of my toes (so cowardly am I, so afraid of the lash that was once almost laid on my own shoulders), to murmur that she should also learn to laugh, without bitterness, at the vanities—say rather at the peculiarities, for it is a less offensive word—of the other sex. For there is a spot the size of a shilling at the back of the head which one can never see for oneself. It is one of the good offices that sex can discharge for sex—to describe that spot the size of a shilling at the back of the head. Think how much women have profited by the comments of Juvenal; by the criticism of Strindberg.[3] Think with what humanity and brilliancy men, from the earliest ages, have pointed out to women that dark place at the back of the head! And if Mary were very brave and very honest, she would go behind the other sex and tell us what she found there. A true picture of man as a whole can never be painted until a woman has described that spot the size of a shilling. Mr Woodhouse and Mr Casaubon[4] are spots of that size and nature. Not of course that any one in their senses would counsel her to hold up to scorn and ridicule of set purpose—literature shows the futility of what is written in that spirit. Be truthful, one would say, and the result is bound to be amazingly interesting. Comedy is bound to be enriched. New facts are bound to be discovered.

However, it was high time to lower my eyes to the page again. It would be better, instead of speculating what Mary Carmichael might write and should write, to see what in fact Mary Carmichael did write. So I began to read again. I remembered that I had certain grievances against her. She had broken up

3. August Strindberg (1849–1912), Swedish playwright. Juvenal (55 to 60–ca. 127), Roman satirist.
4. The husband of the heroine in George Eliot's *Middlemarch*. Woodhouse is the father of the heroine in Jane Austen's *Emma*.

Jane Austen's sentence, and thus given me no chance of pluming myself upon my impeccable taste, my fastidious ear. For it was useless to say, "Yes, yes, this is very nice; but Jane Austen wrote much better than you do," when I had to admit that there was no point of likeness between them. Then she had gone further and broken the sequence—the expected order. Perhaps she had done this unconsciously, merely giving things their natural order, as a woman would, if she wrote like a woman. But the effect was somehow baffling; one could not see a wave heaping itself, a crisis coming round the next corner. Therefore I could not plume myself either upon the depths of my feelings and my profound knowledge of the human heart. For whenever I was about to feel the usual things in the usual places, about love, about death, the annoying creature twitched me away, as if the important point were just a little further on. And thus she made it impossible for me to roll out my sonorous phrases about "elemental feelings," the "common stuff of humanity," "depths of the human heart," and all those other phrases which support us in our belief that, however clever we may be on top, we are very serious, very profound and very humane underneath. She made me feel, on the contrary, that instead of being serious and profound and humane, one might be—and the thought was far less seductive—merely lazy minded and conventional into the bargain.

But I read on, and noted certain other facts. She was no "genius"—that was evident. She had nothing like the love of Nature, the fiery imagination, the wild poetry, the brilliant wit, the brooding wisdom of her great predecessors, Lady Winchilsea, Charlotte Brontë, Jane Austen and George Eliot; she could not write with the melody and the dignity of Dorothy Osborne—indeed she was no more than a clever girl whose books will no doubt be pulped by the publishers in ten years' time. But, nevertheless, she had certain advantages which women of far greater gift lacked even half a century ago. Men were no longer to her "the opposing faction"; she need not waste her time railing against them; she need not climb on to the roof and ruin her peace of mind longing for travel, experience and a knowledge of the world and character that were denied her. Fear and hatred were almost gone, or traces of them showed only in a slight exaggeration of the joy of freedom, a tendency to the caustic and satirical, rather than to the romantic, in her treatment of the other sex. Then there could be no doubt that as a novelist she enjoyed some natural advantages of a high order. She had a sensibility that was very wide, eager and free. It responded to an almost imperceptible touch on it. It feasted like a plant newly stood in the air on every sight and sound that came its way. It ranged, too, very subtly and curiously, among almost unknown or unrecorded things; it lighted on small things and showed that perhaps they were not small after all. It brought buried things to light and made one wonder what need there had been to bury them. Awkward though she was and without the unconscious bearing of long descent which makes the least turn of the pen of a Thackeray or a Lamb delightful to the ear, she had—I began to think—mastered the first great lesson; she wrote as a woman, but as a woman who has forgotten that she is a woman, so that her pages were full of that curious sexual quality which comes only when sex is unconscious of itself.

All this was to the good. But no abundance of sensation or fineness of perception would avail unless she could build up out of the fleeting and the personal the lasting edifice which remains unthrown. I had said that I would wait until she faced herself with "a situation." And I meant by that until she proved by summoning, beckoning and getting together that she was not a skimmer of surfaces merely, but had looked beneath into the depths. Now is the time, she would say to herself at a certain moment, when without doing anything violent I can show the meaning of all this. And she would begin—how unmistakable that quickening is!—beckoning and summoning, and there would rise up in memory, half forgotten, perhaps quite trivial things in other chapters dropped by the way. And she would make their presence felt while some one sewed or smoked a pipe as naturally as possible, and one would feel, as she went on writing, as if one had gone to the top of the world and seen it laid out, very majestically, beneath.

At any rate, she was making the attempt. And as I watched her lengthening out for the test, I saw, but hoped that she did not see, the bishops and the deans, the doctors and the professors, the patriarchs and the pedagogues all at her shouting warning and advice. You can't do this and you shan't do that! Fellows and scholars only allowed on the grass! Ladies not admitted without a letter of introduction! Aspiring and graceful female novelists this way! So they kept at her like the crowd at a fence on the race-course, and it was her trial to take her fence without looking to right or left. If you stop to curse you are lost, I said to her; equally, if you stop to laugh. Hesitate or fumble and you are done for. Think only of the jump, I implored her, as if I had put the whole of my money on her back; and she went over it like a bird. But there was a fence beyond that and a fence beyond that. Whether she had the staying power I was doubtful, for the clapping and the crying were fraying to the nerves. But she did her best. Considering that Mary Carmichael was no genius, but an unknown girl writing her first novel in a bed-sitting-room, without enough of those desirable things, time, money and idleness, she did not do so badly, I thought.

Give her another hundred years, I concluded, reading the last chapter—people's noses and bare shoulders showed naked against a starry sky, for some one had twitched the curtain in the drawing-room—give her a room of her own and five hundred a year, let her speak her mind and leave out half that she now puts in, and she will write a better book one of these days. She will be a poet, I said, putting *Life's Adventure*, by Mary Carmichael, at the end of the shelf, in another hundred years' time.

Chapter Six

Next day the light of the October morning was falling in dusty shafts through the uncurtained windows, and the hum of traffic rose from the street. London then was winding itself up again; the factory was astir; the machines were beginning. It was tempting, after all this reading, to look out of the window and see what London was doing on the morning of the twenty-sixth of October 1928. And what was London doing? Nobody, it seemed, was reading *Antony and Cleopatra*. London was wholly indifferent, it appeared, to Shakespeare's plays. Nobody cared a straw—and I do not blame them—for the future of fiction, the death of poetry or the development by the average woman of a prose style completely expressive of her mind. If opinions upon any of these matters had been chalked on the pavement, nobody would have stooped to read them. The nonchalance of the hurrying feet would have rubbed them out in half an hour. Here came an errand-boy; here a woman with a dog on a lead. The fascination of the London street is that no two people are ever alike; each seems bound on some private affair of his own. There were the business-like, with their little bags; there were the drifters rattling sticks upon area railings; there were affable characters to whom the streets serve for clubroom, hailing men in carts and giving information without being asked for it. Also there were funerals to which men, thus suddenly reminded of the passing of their own bodies, lifted their hats. And then a very distinguished gentleman came slowly down a doorstep and paused to avoid collision with a bustling lady who had, by some means or other, acquired a splendid fur coat and a bunch of Parma violets. They all seemed separate, self-absorbed, on business of their own.

At this moment, as so often happens in London, there was a complete lull and suspension of traffic. Nothing came down the street; nobody passed. A single leaf detached itself from the plane tree at the end of the street, and in that pause and suspension fell. Somehow it was like a signal falling, a signal pointing to a force in things which one had overlooked. It seemed to point to a river, which flowed past, invisibly, round the corner, down the street, and took people and eddied them along, as the stream at Oxbridge had taken the undergraduate in his boat and the dead leaves. Now it was bringing from one side of the street to the other diagonally a girl in patent leather boots, and then a young man in a maroon overcoat; it was also bringing a taxi-cab; and it brought all three together at a point directly beneath my window; where the taxi stopped; and the girl and the young man stopped; and they got into the taxi; and then the cab glided off as if it were swept on by the current elsewhere.

The sight was ordinary enough; what was strange was the rhythmical order with which my imagination had invested it; and the fact that the ordinary sight of two people getting into a cab had the power to communicate something of their own seeming satisfaction. The sight of two people coming down the street and meeting at the corner seems to ease the mind of some strain, I thought, watching the taxi turn and make off. Perhaps to think, as I had been thinking these two days, of one sex as distinct from the other is an effort. It interferes with the unity of the mind. Now that effort had ceased and that unity had been restored by seeing two people come together and get into a taxi-cab. The mind is certainly a very mysterious organ, I reflected, drawing my head in from the window, about which nothing whatever is known, though we depend upon it so completely. Why do I feel that there are severances and oppositions in the mind, as there are strains from obvious causes on the body? What does one mean by "the unity of the mind," I pondered, for clearly the mind has so great a power of concentrating at any point at any moment that it seems to have no single state of being. It can separate itself from the people in the street, for example, and think of itself as apart from them, at an upper window looking down on them. Or it can think with other people spontaneously, as, for instance, in a crowd waiting to hear some piece of news read out. It can think back through its fathers or through its mothers, as I have said that a woman writing thinks back through her mothers. Again if one is a woman one is often surprised by a sudden splitting off of consciousness, say in walking down Whitehall,[5] when from being the natural inheritor of that civilisation, she becomes, on the contrary, outside of it, alien and critical. Clearly the mind is always altering its focus, and bringing the world into different perspectives. But some of these states of mind seem, even if adopted spontaneously, to be less comfortable than others. In order to keep oneself continuing in them one is unconsciously holding something back, and gradually the repression

5. London thoroughfare along which are located the chief offices of the British government.

becomes an effort. But there may be some state of mind in which one could continue without effort because nothing is required to be held back. And this perhaps, I thought, coming in from the window, is one of them. For certainly when I saw the couple get into the taxi-cab the mind felt as if, after being divided, it had come together again in a natural fusion. The obvious reason would be that it is natural for the sexes to co-operate. One has a profound, if irrational, instinct in favour of the theory that the union of man and woman makes for the greatest satisfaction, the most complete happiness. But the sight of the two people getting into the taxi and the satisfaction it gave me made me also ask whether there are two sexes in the mind corresponding to the two sexes in the body, and whether they also require to be united in order to get complete satisfaction and happiness. And I went on amateurishly to sketch a plan of the soul so that in each of us two powers preside, one male, one female; and in the man's brain, the man predominates over the woman, and in the woman's brain, the woman predominates over the man. The normal and comfortable state of being is that when the two live in harmony together, spiritually cooperating. If one is a man, still the woman part of the brain must have effect; and a woman also must have intercourse with the man in her. Coleridge perhaps meant this when he said that a great mind is androgynous. It is when this fusion takes place that the mind is fully fertilised and uses all its faculties. Perhaps a mind that is purely masculine cannot create, any more than a mind that is purely feminine, I thought. But it would be well to test what one meant by man-womanly, and conversely by woman-manly, by pausing and looking at a book or two.

Coleridge certainly did not mean, when he said that a great mind is androgynous, that it is a mind that has any special sympathy with women; a mind that takes up their cause or devotes itself to their interpretation. Perhaps the androgynous mind is less apt to make these distinctions than the single-sexed mind. He meant, perhaps, that the androgynous mind is resonant and porous; that it transmits emotion without impediment; that it is naturally creative, incandescent and undivided. In fact one goes back to Shakespeare's mind as the type of the androgynous, of the man-womanly mind, though it would be impossible to say what Shakespeare thought of women. And if it be true that it is one of the tokens of the fully developed mind that it does not think specially or separately of sex, how much harder it is to attain that condition now than ever before. Here I came to the books by living writers, and there paused and wondered if this fact were not at the root of something that had long puzzled me. No age can ever have been as stridently sex-conscious as our own; those innumerable books by men about women in the British Museum are a proof of it. The Suffrage campaign[6] was no doubt to blame. It must have roused in men an extraordinary desire for self-assertion; it must have made them lay an emphasis upon their own sex and its characteristics which they would not have troubled to think about had they not been challenged. And when one is challenged, even by a few women in black bonnets, one retaliates, if one has never been challenged before, rather excessively. That perhaps accounts for some of the characteristics that I remember to have found here, I thought, taking down a new novel by Mr A, who is in the prime of life and very well thought of, apparently, by the reviewers. I opened it. Indeed, it was delightful to read a man's writing again. It was so direct, so straightforward

6. Movement of the 19th and early-20th centuries seeking the right for women to vote.

after the writing of women. It indicated such freedom of mind, such liberty of person, such confidence in himself. One had a sense of physical well-being in the presence of this well-nourished, well-educated, free mind, which had never been thwarted or opposed, but had had full liberty from birth to stretch itself in whatever way it liked. All this was admirable. But after reading a chapter or two a shadow seemed to lie across the page. It was a straight dark bar, a shadow shaped something like the letter "I." One began dodging this way and that to catch a glimpse of the landscape behind it. Whether that was indeed a tree or a woman walking I was not quite sure. Back one was always hailed to the letter "I." One began to be tired of "I." Not but what this "I" was a most respectable "I"; honest and logical; as hard as a nut, and polished for centuries by good teaching and good feeding. I respect and admire that "I" from the bottom of my heart. But—here I turned a page or two, looking for something or other—the worst of it is that in the shadow of the letter "I" all is shapeless as mist. Is that a tree? No, it is a woman. But . . . she has not a bone in her body, I thought, watching Phoebe, for that was her name, coming across the beach. Then Alan got up and the shadow of Alan at once obliterated Phoebe. For Alan had views and Phoebe was quenched in the flood of his views. And then Alan, I thought, had passions; and here I turned page after page very fast, feeling that the crisis was approaching, and so it was. It took place on the beach under the sun. It was done very openly. It was done very vigorously. Nothing could have been more indecent. But . . . I had said "but" too often. One cannot go on saying "but." One must finish the sentence some-how, I rebuked myself. Shall I finish it, "But—I am bored!" But why was I bored? Partly because of the dominance of the letter "I" and the aridity, which, like the giant beech tree, it casts within its shade. Nothing will grow there. And partly for some more obscure reason. There seemed to be some obstacle, some impediment of Mr A's mind which blocked the fountain of creative energy and shored it within narrow limits. And remembering the lunch party at Oxbridge, and the cigarette ash and the Manx cat and Tennyson and Chris-tina Rossetti all in a bunch, it seemed possible that the impediment lay there. As he no longer hums under his breath, "There has fallen a splendid tear from the passion-flower at the gate," when Phoebe crosses the beach, and she no longer replies, "My heart is like a singing bird whose nest is in a water'd shoot," when Alan approaches what can he do? Being honest as the day and logical as the sun, there is only one thing he can do. And that he does, to do him justice, over and over (I said, turning the pages) and over again. And that, I added, aware of the awful nature of the confession, seems somehow dull. Shakespeare's indecency uproots a thousand other things in one's mind, and is far from being dull. But Shakespeare does it for pleasure; Mr A, as the nurses say, does it on purpose. He does it in protest. He is protesting against the equality of the other sex by asserting his own superiority. He is therefore impeded and inhibited and self-conscious as Shakespeare might have been if he too had known Miss Clough[7] and Miss Davies. Doubtless Elizabethan lit-erature would have been very different from what it is if the woman's move-ment had begun in the sixteenth century and not in the nineteenth.

What, then, it amounts to, if this theory of the two sides of the mind holds good, is that virility has now become self-conscious—men, that is to say, are

7. Anne Jemima Clough (1820–1892), first principal of Newnham College, Cambridge, and advocate for women's suffrage and higher education.

now writing only with the male side of their brains. It is a mistake for a woman to read them, for she will inevitably look for something that she will not find. It is the power of suggestion that one most misses, I thought, taking Mr B the critic in my hand and reading, very carefully and very dutifully, his remarks upon the art of poetry. Very able they were, acute and full of learning; but the trouble was, that his feelings no longer communicated; his mind seemed separated into different chambers; not a sound carried from one to the other. Thus, when one takes a sentence of Mr B into the mind it falls plump to the ground—dead; but when one takes a sentence of Coleridge into the mind, it explodes and gives birth to all kinds of other ideas, and that is the only sort of writing of which one can say that it has the secret of perpetual life.

But whatever the reason may be, it is a fact that one must deplore. For it means—here I had come to rows of books by Mr Galsworthy and Mr Kipling[8] —that some of the finest works of our greatest living writers fall upon deaf ears. Do what she will a woman cannot find in them that fountain of perpetual life which the critics assure her is there. It is not only that they celebrate male virtues, enforce male values and describe the world of men; it is that the emotion with which these books are permeated is to a woman incomprehensible. It is coming, it is gathering, it is about to burst on one's head, one begins saying long before the end. That picture will fall on old Jolyon's head;[9] he will die of the shock; the old clerk will speak over him two or three obituary words; and all the swans on the Thames will simultaneously burst out singing. But one will rush away before that happens and hide in the gooseberry bushes, for the emotion which is so deep, so subtle, so symbolical to a man moves a woman to wonder. So with Mr Kipling's officers who turn their backs; and his Sowers who sow the Seed; and his Men who are alone with their Work; and the Flag— one blushes at all these capital letters as if one had been caught eavesdropping at some purely masculine orgy. The fact is that neither Mr Galsworthy nor Mr Kipling has a spark of the woman in him. Thus all their qualities seem to a woman, if one may generalise, crude and immature. They lack suggestive power. And when a book lacks suggestive power, however hard it hits the surface of the mind it cannot penetrate within.

And in that restless mood in which one takes books out and puts them back again without looking at them I began to envisage an age to come of pure, of self-assertive virility, such as the letters of professors (take Sir Walter Raleigh's letters, for instance) seem to forebode, and the rulers of Italy have already brought into being. For one can hardly fail to be impressed in Rome by the sense of unmitigated masculinity; and whatever the value of unmitigated masculinity upon the state, one may question the effect of it upon the art of poetry. At any rate, according to the newspapers, there is a certain anxiety about fiction in Italy. There has been a meeting of academicians whose object it is "to develop the Italian novel." "Men famous by birth, or in finance, industry or the Fascist corporations" came together the other day and discussed the matter, and a telegram was sent to the Duce[1] expressing the hope "that the Fascist era would soon give birth to a poet worthy of it." We may all join in that pious hope, but it is doubtful whether poetry can come out of an incubator. Poetry ought to have a mother as well as a father. The Fascist poem,

8. John Galsworthy (1867–1933) and Rudyard Kipling (1865–1936), English novelists.
9. A reference to an event in John Galsworthy's

popular fictional series *The Forsyte Saga* (1922).
1. "The leader," i.e., Mussolini.

one may fear, will be a horrid little abortion such as one sees in a glass jar in the museum of some county town. Such monsters never live long, it is said; one has never seen a prodigy of that sort cropping grass in a field. Two heads on one body do not make for length of life.

However, the blame for all this, if one is anxious to lay blame, rests no more upon one sex than upon the other. All seducers and reformers are responsible, Lady Bessborough when she lied to Lord Granville; Miss Davies when she told the truth to Mr Greg. All who have brought about a state of sex-consciousness are to blame, and it is they who drive me, when I want to stretch my faculties on a book, to seek it in that happy age, before Miss Davies and Miss Clough were born, when the writer used both sides of his mind equally. One must turn back to Shakespeare then, for Shakespeare was androgynous; and so was Keats and Sterne and Cowper and Lamb and Coleridge. Shelley perhaps was sexless. Milton and Ben Jonson had a dash too much of the male in them. So had Wordsworth and Tolstoi. In our time Proust was wholly androgynous, if not perhaps a little too much of a woman. But that failing is too rare for one to complain of it, since without some mixture of the kind the intellect seems to predominate and the other faculties of the mind harden and become barren. However, I consoled myself with the reflection that this is perhaps a passing phase; much of what I have said in obedience to my promise to give you the course of my thoughts will seem out of date; much of what flames in my eyes will seem dubious to you who have not yet come of age.

Even so, the very first sentence that I would write here, I said, crossing over to the writing-table and taking up the page headed Women and Fiction, is that it is fatal for any one who writes to think of their sex. It is fatal to be a man or woman pure and simple; one must be woman-manly or man-womanly. It is fatal for a woman to lay the least stress on any grievance; to plead even with justice any cause; in any way to speak consciously as a woman. And fatal is no figure of speech; for anything written with that conscious bias is doomed to death. It ceases to be fertilised. Brilliant and effective, powerful and masterly, as it may appear for a day or two, it must wither at nightfall; it cannot grow in the minds of others. Some collaboration has to take place in the mind between the woman and the man before the act of creation can be accomplished. Some marriage of opposites has to be consummated. The whole of the mind must lie wide open if we are to get the sense that the writer is communicating his experience with perfect fullness. There must be freedom and there must be peace. Not a wheel must grate, not a light glimmer. The curtains must be close drawn. The writer, I thought, once his experience is over, must lie back and let his mind celebrate its nuptials in darkness. He must not look or question what is being done. Rather, he must pluck the petals from a rose or watch the swans float calmly down the river. And I saw again the current which took the boat and the undergraduate and the dead leaves; and the taxi took the man and the woman, I thought, seeing them come together across the street, and the current swept them away, I thought, hearing far off the roar of London's traffic, into that tremendous stream.

Here, then, Mary Beton ceases to speak. She has told you how she reached the conclusion—the prosaic conclusion—that it is necessary to have five hundred a year and a room with a lock on the door if you are to write fiction or poetry. She has tried to lay bare the thoughts and impressions that led her to think this. She has asked you to follow her flying into the arms of a Beadle, lunching here, dining there, drawing pictures in the British Museum, taking books from the shelf, looking out of the window. While she has been doing all these things, you no doubt have been observing her failings and foibles and deciding what effect they have had on her opinions. You have been contradicting her and making whatever additions and deductions seem good to you. That is all as it should be, for in a question like this truth is only to be had by laying together many varieties of error. And I will end now in my own person by anticipating two criticisms, so obvious that you can hardly fail to make them.

No opinion has been expressed, you may say, upon the comparative merits of the sexes even as writers. That was done purposely, because, even if the time had come for such a valuation—and it is far more important at the moment to know how much money women had and how many rooms than to theorise about their capacities—even if the time had come I do not believe that gifts, whether of mind or character, can be weighed like sugar and butter, not even in Cambridge, where they are so adept at putting people into classes and fixing caps on their heads and letters after their names. I do not believe that even the Table of Precedency which you will find in Whitaker's *Almanac* represents a final order of values, or that there is any sound reason to suppose that a Commander of the Bath will ultimately walk in to dinner behind a Master in Lunacy. All this pitting of sex against sex, of quality against quality; all this claiming of superiority and imputing of inferiority, belong to the private-school stage of human existence where there are "sides," and it is necessary for one side to beat another side, and of the utmost importance to walk up to a platform and receive from the hands of the Headmaster himself a highly ornamental pot. As people mature they cease to believe in sides or in Headmasters or in highly ornamental pots. At any rate, where books are concerned, it is notoriously difficult to fix labels of merit in such a way that they do not come off. Are not reviews of current literature a perpetual illustration of the difficulty of judgement? "This great book," "this worthless book," the same book is called by both names. Praise and blame alike mean nothing. No, delightful as the pastime of measuring may be, it is the most futile of all occupations, and to submit to the decrees of the measurers the most servile of attitudes. So long as you write what you wish to write, that is all that matters; and whether it matters for ages or only for hours, nobody can say. But to sacrifice a hair of the head of your vision, a shade of its colour, in deference to some Headmaster with a silver pot in his hand or to some professor with a measuring-rod up his sleeve, is the most abject treachery, and the sacrifice of wealth and chastity which used to be said to be the greatest of human disasters, a mere flea-bite in comparison.

Next I think that you may object that in all this I have made too much of the importance of material things. Even allowing a generous margin for symbolism, that five hundred a year stands for the power to contemplate, that a lock on the door means the power to think for oneself, still you may say that the mind should rise above such things; and that great poets have often been poor men. Let me then quote to you the words of your own Professor of Literature, who knows better than I do what goes to the making of a poet. Sir Arthur Quiller-Couch writes:[2]

"What are the great poetical names of the last hundred years or so? Cole-

2. *The Art of Writing*, by Sir Arthur Quiller-Couch [Woolf's note].

ridge, Wordsworth, Byron, Shelley, Landor, Keats, Tennyson, Browning, Arnold, Morris, Rossetti, Swinburne—we may stop there. Of these, all but Keats, Browning, Rossetti were University men; and of these three, Keats, who died young, cut off in his prime, was the only one not fairly well to do. It may seem a brutal thing to say, and it is a sad thing to say: but, as a matter of hard fact, the theory that poetical genius bloweth where it listeth, and equally in poor and rich, holds little truth. As a matter of hard fact, nine out of those twelve were University men: which means that somehow or other they pro- cured the means to get the best education England can give. As a matter of hard fact, of the remaining three you know that Browning was well to do, and I challenge you that, if he had not been well to do, he would no more have attained to write *Saul* or *The Ring and the Book* than Ruskin would have attained to writing *Modern Painters* if his father had not dealt prosperously in business. Rossetti had a small private income; and, moreover, he painted. There remains but Keats; whom Atropos slew young, as she slew John Clare in a mad-house, and James Thomson[3] by the laudanum he took to drug dis- appointment. These are dreadful facts, but let us face them. It is—however dishonouring to us as a nation—certain that, by some fault in our common- wealth, the poor poet has not in these days, nor has had for two hundred years, a dog's chance. Believe me—and I have spent a great part of ten years in watching some three hundred and twenty elementary schools—we may prate of democracy, but actually, a poor child in England has little more hope than had the son of an Athenian slave to be emancipated into that intellectual freedom of which great writings are born."

Nobody could put the point more plainly. "The poor poet has not in these days, nor has had for two hundred years, a dog's chance . . . a poor child in England has little more hope than had the son of an Athenian slave to be emancipated into that intellectual freedom of which great writings are born." That is it. Intellectual freedom depends upon material things. Poetry depends upon intellectual freedom. And women have always been poor, not for two hundred years merely, but from the beginning of time. Women have had less intellectual freedom than the sons of Athenian slaves. Women, then, have not had a dog's chance of writing poetry. That is why I have laid so much stress on money and a room of one's own. However, thanks to the toils of those obscure women in the past, of whom I wish we knew more, thanks, curiously enough, to two wars, the Crimean which let Florence Nightingale out of her drawing-room, and the European War which opened the doors to the average woman some sixty years later, these evils are in the way to be bettered. Oth- erwise you would not be here tonight, and your chance of earning five hundred pounds a year, precarious as I am afraid that it still is, would be minute in the extreme.

Still, you may object, why do you attach so much importance to this writing of books by women when, according to you, it requires so much effort, leads perhaps to the murder of one's aunts, will make one almost certainly late for luncheon, and may bring one into very grave disputes with certain very good fellows? My motives, let me admit, are partly selfish. Like most uneducated Englishwomen, I like reading—I like reading books in the bulk. Lately my diet has become a trifle monotonous; history is too much about wars; biography

3. Scottish pre-Romantic poet (1700–1748). Atropos: in Greek mythology the Fate who cut the thread of life. Clare (1793–1864), English Romantic poet.

too much about great men; poetry has shown, I think, a tendency to sterility, and fiction—but I have sufficiently exposed my disabilities as a critic of modern fiction and will say no more about it. Therefore I would ask you to write all kinds of books, hesitating at no subject however trivial or however vast. By hook or by crook, I hope that you will possess yourselves of money enough to travel and to idle, to contemplate the future or the past of the world, to dream over books and loiter at street corners and let the line of thought dip deep into the stream. For I am by no means confining you to fiction. If you would please me—and there are thousands like me—you would write books of travel and adventure, and research and scholarship, and history and biography, and criticism and philosophy and science. By so doing you will certainly profit the art of fiction. For books have a way of influencing each other. Fiction will be much the better for standing cheek by jowl with poetry and philosophy. Moreover, if you consider any great figure of the past, like Sappho, like the Lady Murasaki,[4] like Emily Brontë, you will find that she is an inheritor as well as an originator, and has come into existence because women have come to have the habit of writing naturally; so that even as a prelude to poetry such activity on your part would be invaluable.

But when I look back through these notes and criticise my own train of thought as I made them, I find that my motives were not altogether selfish. There runs through these comments and discursions the conviction—or is it the instinct?—that good books are desirable and that good writers, even if they show every variety of human depravity, are still good human beings. Thus when I ask you to write more books I am urging you to do what will be for your good and for the good of the world at large. How to justify this instinct or belief I do not know, for philosophic words, if one has not been educated at a university, are apt to play one false. What is meant by "reality"? It would seem to be something very erratic, very undependable—now to be found in a dusty road, now in a scrap of newspaper in the street, now in a daffodil in the sun. It lights up a group in a room and stamps some casual saying. It overwhelms one walking home beneath the stars and makes the silent world more real than the world of speech—and then there it is again in an omnibus in the uproar of Piccadilly.[5] Sometimes, too, it seems to dwell in shapes too far away for us to discern what their nature is. But whatever it touches, it fixes and makes permanent. That is what remains over when the skin of the day has been cast into the hedge; that is what is left of past time and of our loves and hates. Now the writer, as I think, has the chance to live more than other people in the presence of this reality. It is his business to find it and collect it and communicate it to the rest of us. So at least I infer from reading *Lear* or *Emma* or *La Recherche du Temps Perdu*. For the reading of these books seems to perform a curious couching operation on the senses; one sees more intensely afterwards; the world seems bared of its covering and given an intenser life. Those are the enviable people who live at enmity with unreality; and those are the pitiable who are knocked on the head by the thing done without knowing or caring. So that when I ask you to earn money and have a room of your own, I am asking you to live in the presence of reality, an invigorating life, it would appear, whether one can impart it or not.

---

4. Shikibu Murasaki (978?–?1026), Japanese court lady, author of *The Tale of Genji*. Sappho (fl. ca. 610–ca. 580 B.C.E.), Greek lyric poet, who lived on the island of Lesbos.
5. London street that ends in the bustling intersection of Piccadilly Circus.

Here I would stop, but the pressure of convention decrees that every speech must end with a peroration. And a peroration addressed to women should have something, you will agree, particularly exalting and ennobling about it. I should implore you to remember your responsibilities, to be higher, more spiritual; I should remind you how much depends upon you, and what an influence you can exert upon the future. But those exhortations can safely, I think, be left to the other sex, who will put them, and indeed have put them, with far greater eloquence than I can compass. When I rummage in my own mind I find no noble sentiments about being companions and equals and influencing the world to higher ends. I find myself saying briefly and prosaically that it is much more important to be oneself than anything else. Do not dream of influencing other people, I would say, if I knew how to make it sound exalted. Think of things in themselves.

And again I am reminded by dipping into newspapers and novels and biographies that when a woman speaks to women she should have something very unpleasant up her sleeve. Women are hard on women. Women dislike women. Women—but are you not sick to death of the word? I can assure you that I am. Let us agree, then, that a paper read by a woman to women should end with something particularly disagreeable.

But how does it go? What can I think of? The truth is, I often like women. I like their unconventionality. I like their subtlety. I like their anonymity. I like—but I must not run on in this way. That cupboard there,—you say it holds clean table-napkins only; but what if Sir Archibald Bodkin[6] were concealed among them? Let me then adopt a sterner tone. Have I, in the preceding words, conveyed to you sufficiently the warnings and reprobation of mankind? I have told you the very low opinion in which you were held by Mr Oscar Browning. I have indicated what Napoleon once thought of you and what Mussolini thinks now. Then, in case any of you aspire to fiction, I have copied out for your benefit the advice of the critic about courageously acknowledging the limitations of your sex. I have referred to Professor X and given prominence to his statement that women are intellectually, morally and physically inferior to men. I have handed on all that has come my way without going in search of it, and here is a final warning—from Mr John Langdon Davies.[7] Mr John Langdon Davies warns women "that when children cease to be altogether desirable, women cease to be altogether necessary." I hope you will make a note of it.

How can I further encourage you to go about the business of life? Young women, I would say, and please attend, for the peroration is beginning, you are, in my opinion, disgracefully ignorant. You have never made a discovery of any sort of importance. You have never shaken an empire or led an army into battle. The plays of Shakespeare are not by you, and you have never introduced a barbarous race to the blessings of civilisation. What is your excuse? It is all very well for you to say, pointing to the streets and squares and forests of the globe swarming with black and white and coffee-coloured inhabitants, all busily engaged in traffic and enterprise and love-making, we have had other work on our hands. Without our doing, those seas would be unsailed and those fertile lands a desert. We have borne and bred and washed

6. British director of public prosecutions who decided to ban James Joyces's *Ulysses* for obscenity in 1922.

7. *A Short History of Women*, by John Langdon Davies [Woolf's note].

and taught, perhaps to the age of six or seven years, the one thousand six hundred and twenty-three million human beings who are, according to statistics, at present in existence, and that, allowing that some had help, takes time. There is truth in what you say—I will not deny it. But at the same time may I remind you that there have been at least two colleges for women in existence in England since the year 1866; that after the year 1880 a married woman was allowed by law to possess her own property; and that in 1919—which is a whole nine years ago—she was given a vote? May I also remind you that the most of the professions have been open to you for close on ten years now? When you reflect upon these immense privileges and the length of time during which they have been enjoyed, and the fact that there must be at this moment some two thousand women capable of earning over five hundred a year in one way or another, you will agree that the excuse of lack of opportunity, training, encouragement, leisure and money no longer holds good. Moreover, the economists are telling us that Mrs Seton has had too many children. You must, of course, go on bearing children, but, so they say, in twos and threes, not in tens and twelves.

Thus, with some time on your hands and with some book learning in your brains—you have had enough of the other kind, and are sent to college partly, I suspect, to be uneducated—surely you should embark upon another stage of your very long, very laborious and highly obscure career. A thousand pens are ready to suggest what you should do and what effect you will have. My own suggestion is a little fantastic, I admit; I prefer, therefore, to put it in the form of fiction.

I told you in the course of this paper that Shakespeare had a sister; but do not look for her in Sir Sidney Lee's[8] life of the poet. She died young—alas, she never wrote a word. She lies buried where the omnibuses now stop, opposite the Elephant and Castle. Now my belief is that this poet who never wrote a word and was buried at the crossroads still lives. She lives in you and in me, and in many other women who are not here tonight, for they are washing up the dishes and putting the children to bed. But she lives; for great poets do not die; they are continuing presences; they need only the opportunity to walk among us in the flesh. This opportunity, as I think, it is now coming within your power to give her. For my belief is that if we live another century or so—I am talking of the common life which is the real life and not of the little separate lives which we live as individuals—and have five hundred a year each of us and rooms of our own; if we have the habit of freedom and the courage to write exactly what we think; if we escape a little from the common sitting-room and see human beings not always in their relation to each other but in relation to reality; and the sky, too, and the trees or whatever it may be in themselves; if we look past Milton's bogey,[9] for no human being should shut out the view; if we face the fact, for it is a fact, that there is no arm to cling to, but that we go alone and that our relation is to the world of reality and not only to the world of men and women, then the opportunity will come and the dead poet who was Shakespeare's sister will put on the body which she has so often laid down. Drawing her life from the lives of the unknown who were her

---

8. Biographer and Shakespeare scholar (1859–1926), author of *Life of William Shakespeare* (1898).
9. Milton, with his unhappy first marriage, his campaign for freedom of divorce, and his deliber-

ate subordination of Eve to Adam in *Paradise Lost*, was and often still is held to be (not altogether accurately) what the present age calls a male chauvinist.

forerunners, as her brother did before her, she will be born. As for her coming without that preparation, without that effort on our part, without that determination that when she is born again she shall find it possible to live and write her poetry, that we cannot expect, for that would be impossible. But I maintain that she would come if we worked for her, and that so to work, even in poverty and obscurity, is worth while.

1929

Professions for Women[1]

When your secretary invited me to come here, she told me that your Society is concerned with the employment of women and she suggested that I might tell you something about my own professional experiences. It is true I am a woman; it is true I am employed; but what professional experiences have I had? It is difficult to say. My profession is literature; and in that profession there are fewer experiences for women than in any other, with the exception of the stage—fewer, I mean, that are peculiar to women. For the road was cut many years ago—by Fanny Burney, by Aphra Behn, by Harriet Martineau,[2] by Jane Austen, by George Eliot—many famous women, and many more unknown and forgotten, have been before me, making the path smooth, and regulating my steps. Thus, when I came to write, there were very few material obstacles in my way. Writing was a reputable and harmless occupation. The family peace was not broken by the scratching of a pen. No demand was made upon the family purse. For ten and sixpence one can buy paper enough to write all the plays of Shakespeare—if one has a mind that way. Pianos and models, Paris, Vienna, and Berlin, masters and mistresses, are not needed by a writer. The cheapness of writing paper is, of course, the reason why women have succeeded as writers before they have succeeded in the other professions.

But to tell you my story—it is a simple one. You have only got to figure to yourselves a girl in a bedroom with a pen in her hand. She had only to move that pen from left to right—from ten o'clock to one. Then it occurred to her to do what is simple and cheap enough after all—to slip a few of those pages into an envelope, fix a penny stamp in the corner, and drop the envelope into the red box at the corner. It was thus that I became a journalist; and my effort was rewarded on the first day of the following month—a very glorious day it was for me—by a letter from an editor containing a cheque for one pound ten shillings and sixpence. But to show you how little I deserve to be called a professional woman, how little I know of the struggles and difficulties of such lives, I have to admit that instead of spending that sum upon bread and butter, rent, shoes and stockings, or butcher's bills, I went out and bought a cat—a beautiful cat, a Persian cat, which very soon involved me in bitter disputes with my neighbours.

What could be easier than to write articles and to buy Persian cats with the profits? But wait a moment. Articles have to be about something. Mine, I seem to remember, was about a novel by a famous man. And while I was writ-

1. A paper read to the Women's Service League [Woolf's note]. Woolf here echoes her points in *A Room of One's Own* about a woman's needing money (specifically, five hundred British pounds) and a room in which to write.

2. Economist, moralist, journalist, and novelist (1802–1876). Burney (1752–1840), author of *Evelina* and other novels. Behn (1640–1689), writer of romances and plays.

ing this review, I discovered that if I were going to review books I should need to do battle with a certain phantom. And the phantom was a woman, and when I came to know her better I called her after the heroine of a famous poem, The Angel in the House.[3] It was she who used to come between me and my paper when I was writing reviews. It was she who bothered and wasted my time and so tormented me that at last I killed her. You who come of a younger and happier generation may not have heard of her—you may not know what I mean by The Angel in the House. I will describe her as shortly as I can. She was intensely sympathetic. She was immensely charming. She was utterly unselfish. She excelled in the difficult arts of family life. She sacrificed herself daily. If there was chicken, she took the leg; if there was a draught she sat in it—in short she was so constituted that she never had a mind or a wish of her own, but preferred to sympathise always with the minds and wishes of others. Above all—I need not say it—she was pure. Her purity was supposed to be her chief beauty—her blushes, her great grace. In those days—the last of Queen Victoria—every house had its Angel. And when I came to write I encountered her with the very first words. The shadow of her wings fell on my page; I heard the rustling of her skirts in the room. Directly, that is to say, I took my pen in my hand to review that novel by a famous man, she slipped behind me and whispered: 'My dear, you are a young woman. You are writing about a book that has been written by a man. Be sympathetic; be tender; flatter; deceive; use all the arts and wiles of our sex. Never let anybody guess that you have a mind of your own. Above all, be pure.' And she made as if to guide my pen. I now record the one act for which I take some credit to myself, though the credit rightly belongs to some excellent ancestors of mine who left me a certain sum of money—shall we say five hundred pounds a year?—so that it was not necessary for me to depend solely on charm for my living. I turned upon her and caught her by the throat. I did my best to kill her. My excuse, if I were to be had up in a court of law, would be that I acted in self-defence. Had I not killed her she would have killed me. She would have plucked the heart out of my writing. For, as I found, directly I put pen to paper, you cannot review even a novel without having a mind of your own, without expressing what you think to be the truth about human relations, morality, sex. And all these questions, according to the Angel of the House, cannot be dealt with freely and openly by women; they must charm, they must conciliate, they must—to put it bluntly—tell lies if they are to succeed. Thus, whenever I felt the shadow of her wing or the radiance of her halo upon my page, I took up the inkpot and flung it at her. She died hard. Her fictitious nature was of great assistance to her. It is far harder to kill a phantom than a reality. She was always creeping back when I thought I had despatched her. Though I flatter myself that I killed her in the end, the struggle was severe; it took much time that had better have been spent upon learning Greek grammar; or in roaming the world in search of adventures. But it was a real experience; it was an experience that was bound to befall all women writers at that time. Killing the Angel in the House was part of the occupation of a woman writer.

But to continue my story. The Angel was dead; what then remained? You may say that what remained was a simple and common object—a young woman in a bedroom with an inkpot. In other words, now that she had rid herself of falsehood, that young woman had only to be herself. Ah, but what

3. By Coventry Patmore (1823–1896), published 1854–62.

is 'herself'? I mean, what is a woman? I assure you, I do not know. I do not believe that you know. I do not believe that anybody can know until she has expressed herself in all the arts and professions open to human skill. That indeed is one of the reasons why I have come here—out of respect for you, who are in process of showing us by your experiments what a woman is, who are in process of providing us, by your failures and successes, with that extremely important piece of information.

But to continue the story of my professional experiences. I made one pound ten and six by my first review; and I bought a Persian cat with the proceeds. Then I grew ambitious. A Persian cat is all very well, I said; but a Persian cat is not enough. I must have a motor-car. And it was thus that I became a novelist—for it is a very strange thing that people will give you a motor-car if you will tell them a story. It is a still stranger thing that there is nothing so delightful in the world as telling stories. It is far pleasanter than writing reviews of famous novels. And yet, if I am to obey your secretary and tell you my professional experiences as a novelist, I must tell you about a very strange experience that befell me as a novelist. And to understand it you must try first to imagine a novelist's state of mind. I hope I am not giving away professional secrets if I say that a novelist's chief desire is to be as unconscious as possible. He has to induce in himself a state of perpetual lethargy. He wants life to proceed with the utmost quiet and regularity. He wants to see the same faces, to read the same books, to do the same things day after day, month after month, while he is writing, so that nothing may break the illusion in which he is living—so that nothing may disturb or disquiet the mysterious nosings about, feelings round, darts, dashes, and sudden discoveries of that very shy and illusive spirit, the imagination. I suspect that this state is the same both for men and women. Be that as it may, I want you to imagine me writing a novel in a state of trance. I want you to figure to yourselves a girl sitting with a pen in her hand, which for minutes, and indeed for hours, she never dips into the inkpot. The image that comes to my mind when I think of this girl is the image of a fisherman lying sunk in dreams on the verge of a deep lake with a rod held out over the water. She was letting her imagination sweep unchecked round every rock and cranny of the world that lies submerged in the depths of our unconscious being. Now came the experience that I believe to be far commoner with women writers than with men. The line raced through the girl's fingers. Her imagination had rushed away. It had sought the pools, the depths, the dark places where the largest fish slumber. And then there was a smash. There was an explosion. There was foam and confusion. The imagination had dashed itself against something hard. The girl was roused from her dream. She was indeed in a state of the most acute and difficult distress. To speak without figure, she had thought of something, something about the body, about the passions which it was unfitting for her as a woman to say. Men, her reason told her, would be shocked. The consciousness of what men will say of a woman who speaks the truth about her passions had roused her from her artist's state of unconsciousness. She could write no more. The trance was over. Her imagination could work no longer. This I believe to be a very common experience with women writers—they are impeded by the extreme conventionality of the other sex. For though men sensibly allow themselves great freedom in these respects, I doubt that they realize or can control the extreme severity with which they condemn such freedom in women.

These then were two very genuine experiences of my own. These were two of the adventures of my professional life. The first—killing the Angel in the House—I think I solved. She died. But the second, telling the truth about my own experiences as a body, I do not think I solved. I doubt that any woman has solved it yet. The obstacles against her are still immensely powerful—and yet they are very difficult to define. Outwardly, what is simpler than to write books? Outwardly, what obstacles are there for a woman rather than for a man? Inwardly, I think, the case is very different; she has still many ghosts to fight, many prejudices to overcome. Indeed it will be a long time still, I think, before a woman can sit down to write a book without finding a phantom to be slain, a rock to be dashed against. And if this is so in literature, the freest of all professions for women, how is it in the new professions which you are now for the first time entering?

Those are the questions that I should like, had I time, to ask you. And indeed, if I have laid stress upon these professional experiences of mine, it is because I believe that they are, though in different forms, yours also. Even when the path is nominally open—when there is nothing to prevent a woman from being a doctor, a lawyer, a civil servant—there are many phantoms and obstacles, as I believe, looming in her way. To discuss and define them is I think of great value and importance; for thus only can the labour be shared, the difficulties be solved. But besides this, it is necessary also to discuss the ends and the aims for which we are fighting, for which we are doing battle with these formidable obstacles. Those aims cannot be taken for granted; they must be perpetually questioned and examined. The whole position, as I see it—here in this hall surrounded by women practising for the first time in history I know not how many different professions—is one of extraordinary interest and importance. You have won rooms of your own in the house hitherto exclusively owned by men. You are able, though not without great labour and effort, to pay the rent. You are earning your five hundred pounds a year. But this freedom is only a beginning; the room is your own, but it is still bare. It has to be furnished; it has to be decorated; it has to be shared. How are you going to furnish it, how are you going to decorate it? With whom are you going to share it, and upon what terms? These, I think are questions of the utmost importance and interest. For the first time in history you are able to ask them; for the first time you are able to decide for yourselves what the answers should be. Willingly would I stay and discuss those questions and answers—but not tonight. My time is up; and I must cease.

1942

From A Sketch of the Past[1]

[MOMENTS OF BEING AND NON-BEING]

—I begin: the first memory.

This was of red and purple flowers on a black ground—my mother's dress; and she was sitting either in a train or in an omnibus, and I was on her lap. I

1. The autobiographical essay from which this extract is taken was published in *Moments of Being*, ed. Jeanne Schulkind (1976). Woolf began it on April 18, 1939, as a relief from the labor of writing *Roger Fry: A Biography* (1940). The last date entered in the manuscript is November 17, 1940, some four months before her death. Under the shadow of approaching war, she gropes back for the bright memories of childhood, especially those associated with the Stephens' summer home, Talland House, at St. Ives in Cornwall, the setting for her novel *To the Lighthouse* (1927).

therefore saw the flowers she was wearing very close; and can still see purple and red and blue, I think, against the black; they must have been anemones, I suppose. Perhaps we were going to St Ives; more probably, for from the light it must have been evening, we were coming back to London. But it is more convenient artistically to suppose that we were going to St Ives, for that will lead to my other memory, which also seems to be my first memory, and in fact it is the most important of all my memories. If life has a base that it stands upon, if it is a bowl that one fills and fills and fills—then my bowl without a doubt stands upon this memory. It is of lying half asleep, half awake, in bed in the nursery at St Ives. It is of hearing the waves breaking, one, two, one, two, and sending a splash of water over the beach; and then breaking, one, two, one, two, behind a yellow blind. It is of hearing the blind draw its little acorn[2] across the floor as the wind blew the blind out. It is of lying and hearing this splash and seeing this light, and feeling, it is almost impossible that I should be here; of feeling the purest ecstasy I can conceive.

I could spend hours trying to write that as it should be written, in order to give the feeling which is even at this moment very strong in me. But I should fail (unless I had some wonderful luck); I dare say I should only succeed in having the luck if I had begun by describing Virginia herself.

Here I come to one of the memoir writer's difficulties—one of the reasons why, though I read so many, so many are failures. They leave out the person to whom things happened. The reason is that it is so difficult to describe any human being. So they say: "This is what happened"; but they do not say what the person was like to whom it happened. And the events mean very little unless we know first to whom they happened. Who was I then? Adeline Virginia Stephen, the second daughter of Leslie and Julia Prinsep Stephen, born on 25th January 1882, descended from a great many people, some famous, others obscure; born into a large connection, born not of rich parents, but of well-to-do parents, born into a very communicative, literate, letter writing, visiting, articulate, late nineteenth century world; so that I could if I liked to take the trouble, write a great deal here not only about my mother and father but about uncles and aunts, cousins and friends. But I do not know how much of this, or what part of this, made me feel what I felt in the nursery at St Ives. I do not know how far I differ from other people. That is another memoir writer's difficulty. Yet to describe oneself truly one must have some standard of comparison; was I clever, stupid, good looking, ugly, passionate, cold—? Owing partly to the fact that I was never at school, never competed in any way with children of my own age, I have never been able to compare my gifts and defects with other people's. But of course there was one external reason for the intensity of this first impression: the impression of the waves and the acorn on the blind; the feeling, as I describe it sometimes to myself, of lying in a grape and seeing through a film of semi-transparent yellow—it was due partly to the many months we spent in London. The change of nursery was a great change. And there was the long train journey; and the excitement. I remember the dark; the lights; the stir of the going up to bed.

But to fix my mind upon the nursery—it had a balcony; there was a partition, but it joined the balcony of my father's and mother's bedroom. My mother would come out onto her balcony in a white dressing gown. There were passion

---

2. I.e., the acorn-shaped button on the end of the blind cord.

flowers growing on the wall; they were great starry blossoms, with purple streaks, and large green buds, part empty, part full.

If I were a painter I should paint these first impressions in pale yellow, silver, and green. There was the pale yellow blind; the green sea; and the silver of the passion flowers. I should make a picture that was globular; semi-transparent. I should make a picture of curved petals; of shells; of things that were semi-transparent; I should make curved shapes, showing the light through, but not giving a clear outline. Everything would be large and dim; and what was seen would at the same time be heard; sounds would come through this petal or leaf—sounds indistinguishable from sights. Sound and sight seem to make equal parts of these first impressions. When I think of the early morning in bed I also hear the caw of rooks[3] falling from a great height. The sound seems to fall through an elastic, gummy air; which holds it up; which prevents it from being sharp and distinct. The quality of the air above Talland House seemed to suspend sound, to let it sink down slowly, as if it were caught in a blue gummy veil. The rooks cawing is part of the waves breaking—one, two, one, two—and the splash as the wave drew back and then it gathered again, and I lay there half awake, half asleep, drawing in such ecstasy as I cannot describe.

The next memory—all these colour-and-sound memories hang together at St Ives—was much more robust; it was highly sensual. It was later. It still makes me feel warm; as if everything were ripe; humming; sunny; smelling so many smells at once; and all making a whole that even now makes me stop—as I stopped then going down to the beach; I stopped at the top to look down at the gardens. They were sunk beneath the road. The apples were on a level with one's head. The gardens gave off a murmur of bees; the apples were red and gold; there were also pink flowers; and grey and silver leaves. The buzz, the croon, the smell, all seemed to press voluptuously against some membrane; not to burst it; but to hum round one such a complete rapture of pleasure that I stopped, smelt; looked. But again I cannot describe that rapture. It was rapture rather than ecstasy.

The strength of these pictures—but sight was always then so much mixed with sound that picture is not the right word—the strength anyhow of these impressions makes me again digress. Those moments—in the nursery, on the road to the beach—can still be more real than the present moment. This I have just tested. For I got up and crossed the garden. Percy was digging the asparagus bed; Louie[4] was shaking a mat in front of the bedroom door. But I was seeing them through the sight I saw here—the nursery and the road to the beach. At times I can go back to St Ives more completely than I can this morning. I can reach a state where I seem to be watching things happen as if I were there. That is, I suppose, that my memory supplies what I had forgotten, so that it seems as if it were happening independently, though I am really making it happen. In certain favourable moods, memories—what one has forgotten—come to the top. Now if this is so, is it not possible—I often wonder—that things we have felt with great intensity have an existence independent of our minds; are in fact still in existence? And if so, will it not be possible, in time, that some device will be invented by which we can tap them? I see it—the past—as an avenue lying behind; a long ribbon of scenes, emotions. There at

3. Black crows.
4. The gardener and "daily help," respectively, at   Monks House, the Woolfs' country home in Rod-
mell, Sussex.

2158 / VIRGINIA WOOLF

the end of the avenue still, are the garden and the nursery. Instead of remembering here a scene and there a sound, I shall fit a plug into the wall;[5] and listen in to the past. I shall turn up August 1890. I feel that strong emotion must leave its trace; and it is only a question of discovering how we can get ourselves again attached to it, so that we shall be able to live our lives through from the start.

But the peculiarity of these two strong memories is that each was very simple. I am hardly aware of myself, but only of the sensation. I am only the container of the feeling of ecstasy, of the feeling of rapture. Perhaps this is characteristic of all childhood memories; perhaps it accounts for their strength. Later we add to feelings much that makes them more complex; and therefore less strong; or if not less strong, less isolated, less complete. But instead of analysing this, here is an instance of what I mean—my feeling about the looking-glass in the hall.

There was a small looking-glass in the hall at Talland House. It had, I remember, a ledge with a brush on it. By standing on tiptoe I could see my face in the glass. When I was six or seven perhaps, I got into the habit of looking at my face in the glass. But I only did this if I was sure that I was alone. I was ashamed of it. A strong feeling of guilt seemed naturally attached to it. But why was this so? One obvious reason occurs to me—Vanessa and I were both what was called tomboys; that is, we played cricket, scrambled over rocks, climbed trees, were said not to care for clothes and so on. Perhaps therefore to have been found looking in the glass would have been against our tomboy code. But I think that my feeling of shame went a great deal deeper. I am almost inclined to drag in my grandfather—Sir James, who once smoked a cigar, liked it, and so threw away his cigar and never smoked another. I am almost inclined to think that I inherited a streak of the puritan, of the Clapham Sect.[6] At any rate, the looking-glass shame has lasted all my life, long after the tomboy phase was over. I cannot now powder my nose in public. Everything to do with dress—to be fitted, to come into a room wearing a new dress—still frightens me; at least makes me shy, self-conscious, uncomfortable. "Oh to be able to run, like Julian Morrell,[7] all over the garden in a new dress", I thought not many years ago at Garsington; when Julian undid a parcel and put on a new dress and scampered round and round like a hare. Yet femininity was very strong in our family. We were famous for our beauty—my mother's beauty, Stella's beauty, gave me as early as I can remember, pride and pleasure. What then gave me this feeling of shame, unless it were that I inherited some opposite instinct? My father was spartan, ascetic, puritanical. He had I think no feeling for pictures; no ear for music; no sense of the sound of words. This leads me to think that my—I would say 'our' if I knew enough about Vanessa, Thoby and Adrian[8]—but how little we know even about brothers and sisters—this leads me to think that my natural love for beauty was checked by some ancestral dread. Yet this did not prevent me from feeling ecstasies and raptures spontaneously and intensely and without any shame or the least sense of guilt, so long as they were disconnected with my own body. I thus detect another

5. I.e., as if plugging in a radio.
6. In marrying Jane Catherine Venn, Woolf's grandfather, James Stephen, had allied himself with the heart of the so-called Clapham sect. John and Henry Venn, respectively rector and curate of Clapham in south London, were prominent members of this evangelical society, which, in the early

19th century, was instrumental in bringing about the abolition of the slave trade.
7. Daughter of Philip Morrell, member of Parliament, and his wife, Ottoline, the celebrated literary hostess. Garsington Manor was their house in Oxfordshire.
8. Woolf's brothers and sister.

element in the shame which I had in being caught looking at myself in the glass in the hall. I must have been ashamed or afraid of my own body. Another memory, also of the hall, may help to explain this. There was a slab outside the dining room door for standing dishes upon. Once when I was very small George Duckworth[9] lifted me onto this, and as I sat there he began to explore my body. I can remember the feel of his hand going under my clothes; going firmly and steadily lower and lower. I remember how I hoped that he would stop; how I stiffened and wriggled as his hand approached my private parts. But it did not stop. His hand explored my private parts too. I remember resenting, disliking it—what is the word for so dumb and mixed a feeling? It must have been strong, since I still recall it. This seems to show that a feeling about certain parts of the body; how they must not be touched; how it is wrong to allow them to be touched; must be instinctive. It proves that Virginia Stephen was not born on the 25th January 1882, but was born many thousands of years ago; and had from the very first to encounter instincts already acquired by thousands of ancestresses in the past.

And this throws light not merely on my own case, but upon the problem that I touched on the first page; why it is so difficult to give any account of the person to whom things happen. The person is evidently immensely complicated. Witness the incident of the looking-glass. Though I have done my best to explain why I was ashamed of looking at my own face I have only been able to discover some possible reasons; there may be others; I do not suppose that I have got at the truth; yet this is a simple incident; and it happened to me personally; and I have no motive for lying about it. In spite of all this, people write what they call "lives" of other people; that is, they collect a number of events, and leave the person to whom it happened unknown. Let me add a dream; for it may refer to the incident of the looking-glass. I dreamt that I was looking in a glass when a horrible face—the face of an animal—suddenly showed over my shoulder. I cannot be sure if this was a dream, or if it happened. Was I looking in the glass one day when something in the background moved, and seemed to me alive? I cannot be sure. But I have always remembered the other face in the glass, whether it was a dream or a fact, and that it frightened me.

These then are some of my first memories. But of course as an account of my life they are misleading, because the things one does not remember are as important; perhaps they are more important. If I could remember one whole day I should be able to describe, superficially at least, what life was like as a child. Unfortunately, one only remembers what is exceptional. And there seems to be no reason why one thing is exceptional and another not. Why have I forgotten so many things that must have been, one would have thought, more memorable than what I do remember? Why remember the hum of bees in the garden going down to the beach, and forget completely being thrown naked by father into the sea? (Mrs Swanwick says she saw that happen.)[1]

This leads to a digression, which perhaps may explain a little of my own psychology; even of other people's. Often when I have been writing one of my so-called novels I have been baffled by this same problem; that is, how to

9. Woolf's half-brother and the subject of her autobiographical essay "22 Hyde Park Gate," written in 1920 and published in *Moments of Being* (1978).
1. In Mrs. Swanwick's autobiography, *I Have Been Young* (1935), she recalls having known Leslie Stephen at St. Ives: "We watched with delight his naked babies running about the beach or being towed into the sea between his legs, and their beautiful mother."

describe what I call in my private shorthand—"non-being." Every day includes much more non-being than being. Yesterday for example, Tuesday the 18th of April, was [as] it happened a good day; above the average in "being." It was fine; I enjoyed writing these first pages; my head was relieved of the pressure of writing about Roger; I walked over Mount Misery[2] and along the river; and save that the tide was out, the country, which I notice very closely always, was coloured and shaded as I like—there were the willows, I remember, all plumy and soft green and purple against the blue. I also read Chaucer with pleasure; and began a book—the memoirs of Madame de la Fayette[3]—which interested me. These separate moments of being were however embedded in many more moments of non-being. I have already forgotten what Leonard[4] and I talked about at lunch; and at tea; although it was a good day the goodness was embedded in a kind of nondescript cotton wool. This is always so. A great part of every day is not lived consciously. One walks, eats, sees things, deals with what has to be done; the broken vacuum cleaner; ordering dinner; writing orders to Mabel;[5] washing; cooking dinner; bookbinding. When it is a bad day the proportion of non-being is much larger. I had a slight temperature last week; almost the whole day was non-being. The real novelist can somehow convey both sorts of being. I think Jane Austen can; and Trollope; perhaps Thackeray and Dickens and Tolstoy. I have never been able to do both. I tried—in *Night and Day*; and in *The Years*.[6] But I will leave the literary side alone for the moment.

As a child then, my days, just as they do now, contained a large proportion of this cotton wool, this non-being. Week after week passed at St Ives and nothing made any dint upon me. Then, for no reason that I know about, there was a sudden violent shock; something happened so violently that I have remembered it all my life. I will give a few instances. The first: I was fighting with Thoby on the lawn. We were pommelling each other with our fists. Just as I raised my fist to hit him, I felt: why hurt another person? I dropped my hand instantly, and stood there, and let him beat me. I remember the feeling. It was a feeling of hopeless sadness. It was as if I became aware of something terrible; and of my own powerlessness. I slunk off alone, feeling horribly depressed. The second instance was also in the garden at St Ives. I was looking at the flower bed by the front door; "That is the whole," I said. I was looking at a plant with a spread of leaves; and it seemed suddenly plain that the flower itself was a part of the earth; that a ring enclosed what was the flower; and that was the real flower; part earth; part flower. It was a thought I put away as being likely to be very useful to me later. The third case was also at St Ives. Some people called Valpy had been staying at St Ives, and had left. We were waiting at dinner one night, when somehow I overheard my father or my mother say that Mr Valpy had killed himself. The next thing I remember is being in the garden at night and walking on the path by the apple tree. It seemed to me that the apple tree was connected with the horror of Mr Valpy's suicide. I could not pass it. I stood there looking at the grey-green creases of the bark—it was a moonlit night—in a trance of horror. I seemed to be dragged

2. Two cottages on the hillside between Southease and Piddinghoe known locally as Mount Misery.
3. French novelist (1634–1693).
4. Her husband, the English writer Leonard Woolf (1880–1969). In 1917 the Woolfs founded the Hogarth Press, a literary publisher.

5. Instructions to the Woolfs' maid.
6. Novels published in 1919 and 1938, respectively. Anthony Trollope (1815–1882), English novelist. William Makepeace Thackeray (1811–1863), English novelist. Leo Tolstoy (1828–1910), Russian novelist.

down, hopelessly, into some pit of absolute despair from which I could not escape. My body seemed paralysed.

These are three instances of exceptional moments. I often tell them over, or rather they come to the surface unexpectedly. But now that for the first time I have written them down, I realise something that I have never realised before. Two of these moments ended in a state of despair. The other ended, on the contrary, in a state of satisfaction. When I said about the flower "That is the whole," I felt that I had made a discovery. I felt that I had put away in my mind something that I should go back [to], to turn over and explore. It strikes me now that this was a profound difference. It was the difference in the first place between despair and satisfaction. This difference I think arose from the fact that I was quite unable to deal with the pain of discovering that people hurt each other; that a man I had seen had killed himself. The sense of horror held me powerless. But in the case of the flower I found a reason; and was thus able to deal with the sensation. I was not powerless. I was conscious—if only at a distance—that I should in time explain it. I do not know if I was older when I saw the flower than I was when I had the other two experiences. I only know that many of these exceptional moments brought with them a peculiar horror and a physical collapse; they seemed dominant; myself passive. This suggests that as one gets older one has a greater power through reason to provide an explanation; and that this explanation blunts the sledge-hammer force of the blow. I think this is true, because though I still have the peculiarity that I receive these sudden shocks, they are now always welcome; after the first surprise, I always feel instantly that they are particularly valuable. And so I go on to suppose that the shock-receiving capacity is what makes me a writer. I hazard the explanation that a shock is at once in my case followed by the desire to explain it. I feel that I have had a blow; but it is not, as I thought as a child, simply a blow from an enemy hidden behind the cotton wool of daily life; it is or will become a revelation of some order; it is a token of some real thing behind appearances; and I make it real by putting it into words. It is only by putting it into words that I make it whole; this wholeness means that it has lost its power to hurt me; it gives me, perhaps because by doing so I take away the pain, a great delight to put the severed parts together. Perhaps this is the strongest pleasure known to me. It is the rapture I get when in writing I seem to be discovering what belongs to what; making a scene come right; making a character come together. From this I reach what I might call a philosophy; at any rate it is a constant idea of mine; that behind the cotton wool is hidden a pattern; that we—I mean all human beings—are connected with this; that the whole world is a work of art; that we are parts of the work of art. *Hamlet* or a Beethoven quartet is the truth about this vast mass that we call the world. But there is no Shakespeare, there is no Beethoven; certainly and emphatically there is no God; we are the words; we are the music; we are the thing itself. And I see this when I have a shock.

This intuition of mine—it is so instinctive that it seems given to me, not made by me—has certainly given its scale to my life ever since I saw the flower in the bed by the front door at St Ives. If I were painting myself I should have to find some—rod, shall I say—something that would stand for the conception. It proves that one's life is not confined to one's body and what one says and does; one is living all the time in relation to certain background rods or conceptions. Mine is that there is a pattern hid behind the cotton wool. And this conception affects me every day. I prove this, now, by spending the morning writing, when I might be walking, running a shop, or learning to do something that will be useful if war comes. I feel that by writing I am doing what is far more necessary than anything else.

All artists I suppose feel something like this. It is one of the obscure elements in life that has never been much discussed. It is left out in almost all biographies and autobiographies, even of artists. Why did Dickens spend his entire life writing stories? What was his conception? I bring in Dickens partly because I am reading *Nicholas Nickleby* at the moment; also partly because it struck me, on my walk yesterday, that these moments of being of mine were scaffolding in the background; were the invisible and silent part of my life as a child. But in the foreground there were of course people; and these people were very like characters in Dickens. They were caricatures; they were very simple; they were immensely alive. They could be made with three strokes of the pen, if I could do it. Dickens owes his astonishing power to make characters alive to the fact that he saw them as a child sees them; as I saw Mr Wolstenholme; C. B. Clarke, and Mr Gibbs.

I name these three people because they all died when I was a child. Therefore they have never been altered. I see them exactly as I saw them then. Mr Wolstenholme was a very old gentleman who came every summer to stay with us. He was brown; he had a beard and very small eyes in fat cheeks; and he fitted into a brown wicker beehive chair as if it had been his nest. He used to sit in this beehive chair smoking and reading. He had only one characteristic—that when he ate plum tart he spurted the juice through his nose so that it made a purple stain on his grey moustache. This seemed enough to cause us perpetual delight. We called him "The Woolly One." By way of shading him a little I remember that we had to be kind to him because he was not happy at home; that he was very poor, yet once gave Thoby half a crown; that he had a son who was drowned in Australia; and I know too that he was a great mathematician. He never said a word all the time I knew him. But he still seems to me a complete character; and whenever I think of him I begin to laugh.

Mr Gibbs was perhaps less simple. He wore a tie ring; had a bald, benevolent head; was dry; neat; precise; and had folds of skin under his chin. He made father groan—"why can't you go—why can't you go?" And he gave Vanessa and myself two ermine skins, with slits down the middle out of which poured endless wealth—streams of silver. I also remember him lying in bed, dying; husky; in a night shirt; and showing us drawings by Retzsch.[7] The character of Mr Gibbs also seems to me complete and amuses me very much.

As for C. B. Clarke, he was an old botanist; and he said to my father "All you young botanists like Osmunda."[8] He had an aunt aged eighty who went for a walking tour in the New Forest. That is all—that is all I have to say about these three old gentlemen. But how real they were! How we laughed at them! What an immense part they played in our lives!

One more caricature comes into my mind; though pity entered into this one. I am thinking of Justine Nonon. She was immensely old. Little hairs sprouted on her long bony chin. She was a hunchback; and walked like a spider, feeling her way with her long dry fingers from one chair to another. Most of the time she sat in the arm-chair beside the fire. I used to sit on her knee; and her knee

---

7. Friedrich Retzsch (1779–1857), German engraver. 8. Flowering ferns.

jogged up and down; and she sang in a hoarse cracked voice "Ron ron ron—
et plon plon plon—" and then her knee gave and I was tumbled onto the floor.
She was French; she had been with the Thackerays. She only came to us on
visits. She lived by herself at Shepherd's Bush; and used to bring Adrian a
glass jar of honey. I got the notion that she was extremely poor; and it made
me uncomfortable that she brought this honey, because I felt she did it by
way of making her visit acceptable. She said too: "I have come in my carriage
and pair"—which meant the red omnibus. For this too I pitied her; also
because she began to wheeze; and the nurses said she would not live much
longer; and soon she died. That is all I know about her; but I remember her
as if she were a completely real person, with nothing left out, like the three
old men.

Apr. 1939–Nov. 1940   1978

JAMES JOYCE
1882–1941

James Joyce was born in Dublin, son of a talented but feckless father, who is accurately described in Joyce's novel *A Portrait of the Artist as a Young Man* (1916) as
having been "a medical student, an oarsman, a tenor, an amateur actor, a shouting
politician, a small landlord, a small investor, a drinker, a good fellow, a storyteller,
somebody's secretary, something in a distillery, a tax-gatherer, a bankrupt, and at
present a praiser of his own past." The elder Joyce drifted steadily down the financial
and social scale, his family moving from house to house, each one less genteel and
more shabby than the previous. James Joyce's primary education was Catholic, from
the age of six to the age of nine at Clongowes Wood College and from eleven to
sixteen at Belvedere College. Both were Jesuit institutions and were normal roads to
the priesthood. He then studied modern languages at University College, Dublin.

From a comparatively young age Joyce regarded himself as a rebel against the
shabbiness and philistinism of Dublin. In his last year of school at Belvedere he began
to reject his Catholic faith in favor of a literary mission that he saw as involving
rebellion and exile. He refused to play any part in the nationalist or other popular
activities of his fellow students, and he created some stir by his outspoken articles,
one of which, on the Norwegian playwright Henrik Ibsen, appeared in London's *Fortnightly Review* when Joyce was eighteen. He taught himself Dano-Norwegian in order
to read Ibsen and to write to him. When an article by Joyce, significantly titled "The
Day of the Rabblement," was refused, on instructions of the faculty adviser, by the
student magazine that had commissioned it, he had it printed privately. By 1902,
when he received his A.B. degree, he was already committed to a career as exile and
writer. For Joyce, as for his character Stephen Dedalus, the latter implied the former.
To preserve his integrity, to avoid involvement in popular causes, to devote himself
to the life of the artist, he felt that he had to go abroad.

Joyce went to Paris after graduation, was recalled to Dublin by his mother's fatal
illness, had a short spell there as a schoolteacher, then returned to the Continent in
1904 to teach English at Trieste and then at Zurich. He took with him Nora Barnacle,
a woman from Galway with no interest in literature; her vivacity and wit charmed
Joyce, and the two lived in devoted companionship until his death, although they
were not married until 1931. In 1920 Joyce and Barnacle settled in Paris, where they

lived until December 1940, when the war forced them to take refuge in Switzerland; he died in Zurich a few weeks later.

Proud, obstinate, absolutely convinced of his genius, given to fits of sudden gaiety and of sudden silence, Joyce was not always an easy person to get along with, yet he never lacked friends, and throughout his thirty-six years on the Continent he was always the center of a literary circle. Life was hard at first. In Trieste he had very little money, and he did not improve matters by drinking heavily, a habit checked somewhat by his brother Stanislaus, who came out from Dublin to act (as Stanislaus put it much later) as his "brother's keeper." Joyce also suffered from eye diseases and, blind for brief periods, underwent twenty-five operations. In 1917 Edith Rockefeller McCormick and then the lawyer John Quinn, steered in Joyce's direction by Ezra Pound, helped out financially, but a more permanent benefactor was the English feminist and editor Harriet Shaw Weaver, who not only subsidized Joyce generously from 1917 to the end of his life but also occupied herself indefatigably with arrangements for publishing his work.

In spite of doing most of his writing in Trieste, Zurich, and Paris, Joyce paradoxically wrote only and always about Dublin. No writer has ever been more soaked in Dublin, its atmosphere, its history, its topography. He devised ways of expanding his accounts of Dublin, however, so that they became microcosms of human history, geography, and experience.

Joyce began his career by writing a series of stories etching with extraordinary clarity aspects of Dublin life. These stories—published as *Dubliners* in 1914—are sharp realistic sketches of what Joyce called the "paralysis" that beset the lives of people in then-provincial Ireland. The language is crisp, lucid, and detached, and the details are chosen and organized so that carefully interacting symbolic meanings are set up. Some of the stories, such as "Araby," are built around what Joyce called an "epiphany," a dramatic but fleeting moment of revelation about the self or the world. Many end abruptly, without conventional narrative closure, or they lack overt connectives and transitions, leaving multiple possibilities in suspension. The last story in *Dubliners*, "The Dead," was not part of the original draft of the book but was added later, when Joyce was preoccupied with the nature of artistic objectivity. At a festive event, attended by guests whose portraits Joyce draws with precision and economy, a series of jolting events frees the protagonist, Gabriel, from his possessiveness and egotism. The view he attains at the end is the mood of supreme neutrality that Joyce saw as the beginning of artistic awareness. It is the view of art developed by Stephen Dedalus in *A Portrait of the Artist as a Young Man*.

Dubliners represents Joyce's first phase: he had to come to terms with the life he had rejected. Next he had to come to terms with the meaning of his own growth as a man dedicated to imaginative writing, and he did so by writing a novel about the youth and development of an artist, a kind of novel known by the German term *Künstlerroman* (a variation on the *Bildungsroman*). The book's narrative style changes to evoke developments in Stephen's consciousness, from the bare record of a child's tactile experiences to the ironically lush descriptions of artistic illumination to the self-sufficiency of the final diary entries. Joyce wove his autobiography into a novel so finely chiseled and carefully organized, so stripped of everything superfluous, that each word contributes to the presentation of the theme: the parallel movement toward art and toward exile. A part of his first draft was published posthumously under the original title, *Stephen Hero* (1944), and a comparison between it and the final version, *Portrait of the Artist*, shows how carefully Joyce reworked and compressed his material for maximum effect.

In *Portrait* Stephen works out a theory in which art moves from the lyrical form (the simplest, the personal expression of an instant of emotion) through the narrative form (no longer purely personal) to the dramatic (the highest and most nearly perfect form, where "the artist, like the God of creation, remains within or behind or beyond or above his handiwork, invisible, refined out of existence, indifferent, paring his fingernails"). This view of art, which involves the objectivity, even the exile, of the artist—even though the artist uses only the materials provided for him or her by his or her own life—overlaps with the emphasis on masks, impersonality, and ironic detachment in the work of other modernist writers, such as Pound, W. B. Yeats, and T. S. Eliot. Joyce's next novel, *Ulysses* (1922), and his last, *Finnegans Wake* (1939), represent the most consummate craftsmanship, put at the service of a humanely comic vision. His innovations in organization, style, and narrative technique have influenced countless other writers, but these books are unique.

From the beginning Joyce had trouble getting into print. Publication of *Dubliners* was held up for many years while he fought with both English and Irish publishers about words and phrases that they wished to eliminate. *Ulysses* was banned in Britain and America on publication; its earlier serialization in an American magazine, *The Little Review* (March 1918–December 1920), had been stopped abruptly when the U.S. Post Office brought a charge of obscenity against the work. Fortunately Judge John Woolsey's history-making decision in a U.S. district court on December 6, 1933, resulted in the lifting of the ban and the free circulation of *Ulysses* first in America and soon afterward in Britain.

ULYSSES

Ulysses is an account of one day in the lives of Dubliners; it thus describes a limited number of events involving a limited number of people in a limited environment. Yet Joyce's ambition—which took him seven years to realize—is to present the events in such a manner that depth and implication are given to them and they become symbolic. The episodes in *Ulysses* correspond to episodes in Homer's ancient Greek epic *Odyssey*. Joyce regarded Homer's Odysseus, or Ulysses, as the most "complete" man in literature, shown in all his aspects—coward and hero, cautious and reckless, weak and strong, husband and philanderer, father and son, dignified and ridiculous; so he makes his hero, Leopold Bloom, an Irish Jew, into a modern Ulysses. The parallels between the Homeric archetypes and the modern-day characters and events create a host of interpretive complexities. They can seem tight or loose, deflating or ennobling, ironic or heroic, epic or mock-epic, depending on their specific use in different episodes and, to some extent, on the propensities of the reader.

Ulysses opens at eight o'clock on the morning of June 16, 1904. Stephen Dedalus (the same character as in *Portrait,* but two years after the last glimpse of him there) had been summoned back to Dublin by his mother's fatal illness and now lives in an old military tower on the shore with Buck Mulligan, a rollicking medical student, and an Englishman called Haines. In the first three episodes of *Ulysses,* which concentrate on Stephen, he is built up as an aloof, uncompromising artist, rejecting all advances by representatives of the normal world, the incomplete man, to be contrasted later with the complete Leopold Bloom, who is much more "normal" and conciliatory. After tracing Stephen through his early-morning activities and learning the main currents of his mind, we go, in the fourth episode, to the home of Bloom. We follow closely his every activity: attending a funeral, transacting business, eating lunch, walking through the Dublin streets, worrying about his wife's infidelity with Blazes Boylan—and at each point the contents of his mind, including retrospect and anticipation, are presented to us, until his past history is revealed. Finally Bloom and Stephen, who have been just missing each other all day, get together. By this time it is late, and Stephen, who has been drinking with some medical students, is the worse for liquor. Bloom, moved by a paternal feeling toward Stephen (his own son had died in infancy and in a symbolic way Stephen takes his place), follows him during subsequent adventures in the role of protector. The climax of the book comes when Stephen, far gone in drink, and Bloom, worn out with fatigue, succumb to a series of hallucinations, where their unconscious minds surface in dramatic form and their personalities are revealed with a completeness and a frankness unique in literature. Then Bloom takes the unresponsive Stephen home and gives him a meal. After Stephen's departure Bloom retires to bed—it is now two in the morning, June 17—while his wife, Molly, lying in bed, closes the book with a long monologue in which she recalls her romantic and other experiences. Her monologue unfolds in eight flowing, unpunctuated paragraphs, which culminate in the book's final, resonant affirmation, a memory of her response to Bloom's marriage proposal: "and yes I said yes I will Yes."

On the level of realistic description, *Ulysses* pulses with life and can be enjoyed for its evocation of early-twentieth-century Dublin. On the level of psychological exploration, it gives a profound and moving presentation of the personalities and consciousnesses of Leopold Bloom, Stephen Dedalus, and Molly Bloom. On the level of style, it exhibits the most fascinating linguistic virtuosity, many an episode written in a distinctive way that reflects its subject—e.g., newspaper headlines intruding in a chapter set in a newspaper office (the "Aeolus" episode), the sentimental language of women's magazines dominating a chapter set on a beach where girls are playing ("Nausicaa"), and the pastiche of styles of English literature from its Anglo-Saxon birth to the twentieth century taking over in a chapter set in a maternity hospital ("Oxen of the Sun"). On a deeper symbolic level, the novel explores the paradoxes of human loneliness and sociability (for Bloom is both Jew and Dubliner, both exile and citizen), and it explores the problems posed by the relations between parent and child, between the generations, and between the sexes. At the same time, through its use of themes from Homer, Dante, and Shakespeare and from literature, philosophy, and history, the book weaves a subtle pattern of allusion and suggestion. The more one reads *Ulysses* the more one finds in it, but at the same time one does not need to probe into the symbolic meaning to relish both its literary artistry and its emotional richness. At the forefront stands Bloom, from one point of view a frustrated and confused outsider in the society in which he moves, from another a champion of kindness and justice whose humane curiosity about his fellows redeems him from mere vulgarity and gives the book its positive human foundation.

Readers who come to *Ulysses* with expectations about the way the story is to be presented derived from their reading of Victorian novels or even of twentieth-century novelists such as Conrad and Lawrence will find much that is at first puzzling. Joyce presents the consciousness of his characters directly, without any explanatory comment that tells the reader whose consciousness is being rendered (this is the stream of consciousness method, also known as interior monologue). He may move, in the same paragraph and without any sign that he is making such a transition, from a description of a character's action—e.g., Stephen walking along the shore or Bloom entering a restaurant—to an evocation of the character's mental response to this action. That response is always multiple: it derives partly from the character's immediate situation and partly from the whole complex of attitudes created by a personal past history. To suggest this multiplicity, Joyce may vary his style, from the flippant to the serious or from a realistic description to a suggestive set of images that indicate what might be called the general tone of the character's consciousness. Past and present mingle in the texture of the prose because they mingle in the texture of consciousness, and this mingling can be indicated by puns, by sudden breaks into a new kind of style or a new kind of subject matter, or by some other device for keeping the reader constantly in sight of the shifting, kaleidoscopic nature of human awareness. With a little experience the reader learns to follow the implications of Joyce's shifts in manner and content—even to follow that initially bewildering passage in the "Proteus" episode in which Stephen does not go to visit his uncle and aunt but, passing the road that leads to their house, imagines the kind of conversation that would take place in his home *if* he had gone to visit his uncle and had then returned home and reported that he had done so. *Ulysses* must not be approached as though it were a traditional novel; we must set aside our preconceptions, follow wherever the author leads us, and let the language tell us what it has to say.

Joyce's final work, *Finnegans Wake* took more than fourteen years to write, and Joyce considered it his masterpiece. In *Ulysses* he had made the symbolic aspect of the novel at least as important as the realistic aspect, but in *Finnegans Wake* he gave up realism altogether. This vast story of a symbolic Irishman's cosmic dream develops by enormous reverberating puns a continuous expansion of meaning, the elements in the puns deriving from every conceivable source in history, literature, mythology, and Joyce's personal experience. The whole book being (on one level at least) a dream, Joyce invents his own dream language, in which words are combined, distorted, created by fitting together bits of other words, used with several different meanings at once, often drawn from several different languages at once, and fused in all sorts of ways to achieve whole clusters of meaning simultaneously. In fact, so many echoing suggestions can be found in every word or phrase that a full annotation of even a few pages would require a large book. Over time, readers and critics of *Finnegans Wake* have sorted out the complex interactions of the multiple puns and pun clusters through which the ideas are projected, and every rereading reveals new meanings. Many readers find the efforts of explication too arduous, but the book has great beauty and fascination even for the casual reader. Newcomers are advised to read aloud— or to listen to the recording of Joyce reading aloud—the extract printed here to appreciate the degree to which the rhythms of the prose assist in conveying the meaning.

To an even greater extent than *Ulysses*, *Finnegans Wake* aims to embrace all of human history. The title comes from an Irish American ballad about Tom Finnegan, a hod carrier who falls off a ladder when drunk and is apparently killed, but who revives when during the wake (the watch by his dead body) someone spills whiskey on him. The theme of death and resurrection, of cycles of change coming round in the course of history, is central to *Finnegans Wake,* which derives one of its main principles of organization from the cyclical theory of history put forward in 1725 by the Italian philosopher Giambattista Vico. Vico held that history passes through four phases: the divine, or theocratic, when people are governed by their awe of the supernatural; the aristocratic (the "heroic age" reflected in Homer and in *Beowulf*); the democratic and individualistic; and the final stage of chaos, a fall into confusion that startles humanity back into supernatural reverence and starts the process once again. Joyce, like Yeats, saw his own generation as in the final stage awaiting the shock that will bring humans back to the first.

A mere account of the narrative line of *Finnegans Wake* cannot give any idea of the content of the work. If one explains that it opens with Finnegan's fall, then introduces his successor, Humphrey Chimpden Earwicker, who keeps a pub in Chapelizod, a Dublin suburb on the river Liffey, near Phoenix Park; that HCE is feeling guilty about an indecency he committed (or may have committed) in Phoenix Park; that his dream constitutes the novel; that his wife, Anna Livia Plurabelle, or ALP (who is also Eve, Iseult, Ireland, the Liffey), changes her role just as he does; that HCE and ALP have two sons, Shem and Shaun (or Jerry and Kevin), who represent introvert and extrovert, artist and practical man, creator and popularizer, and who symbolize this dichotomy in human nature by all kinds of metamorphoses; and if one adds that, in the four books into which *Finnegans Wake* is divided (after Vico's pattern), actions comic or grotesque or sad or tender or desperate or passionate or terribly ordinary (and very often several of these things at the same time) take place with all the shifting meanings of a dream, so that characters change into others or into inanimate objects and the setting keeps shifting—still one has said very little about what makes *Finnegans Wake* what it is. The dreamer is at once a particular person and a universal figure, his initials also standing for "Here Comes Everybody." His mysterious misdemeanor in Phoenix Park is in a sense Original Sin: Earwicker is Adam as well as a primeval giant, the Hill of Howth, the Great Parent ("Haveth Childers Everywhere" is another expansion of HCE), and Man in History. Other characters who flit and change through the book, such as the Twelve Customers (who are also twelve jurymen and public opinion) and the Four Old Men (who are also judges, the authors of the four Gospels, and the four elements), help weave the texture of multiple significance so characteristic of the work. But always it is the punning language, extending significance downward—rather than the plot, developing it lengthwise—that bears the main load of meaning.

Araby[1]

North Richmond Street, being blind, was a quiet street except at the hour when the Christian Brothers' School[2] set the boys free. An uninhabited house of two storeys stood at the blind end, detached from its neighbours in a square ground. The other houses of the street, conscious of decent lives within them, gazed at one another with brown imperturbable faces.

The former tenant of our house, a priest, had died in the back drawing-room. Air, musty from having been long enclosed, hung in all the rooms, and the waste room behind the kitchen was littered with old useless papers. Among these I found a few paper-covered books, the pages of which were curled and damp: *The Abbot*, by Walter Scott, *The Devout Communicant* and *The Memoirs of Vidocq*.[3] I liked the last best because its leaves were yellow. The wild garden behind the house contained a central apple-tree and a few straggling bushes under one of which I found the late tenant's rusty bicycle-pump. He had been a very charitable priest; in his will he had left all his money to institutions and the furniture of his house to his sister.

When the short days of winter came dusk fell before we had well eaten our dinners. When we met in the street the houses had grown sombre. The space of sky above us was the colour of ever-changing violet and towards it the lamps of the street lifted their feeble lanterns. The cold air stung us and we played till our bodies glowed. Our shouts echoed in the silent street. The career of our play brought us through the dark muddy lanes behind the houses where we ran the gantlet of the rough tribes from the cottages, to the back doors of the dark dripping gardens where odours arose from the ashpits, to the dark odorous stables where a coachman smoothed and combed the horse or shook music from the buckled harness. When we returned to the street light from the kitchen windows had filled the areas. If my uncle was seen turning the corner we hid in the shadow until we had seen him safely housed. Or if Mangan's sister came out on the doorstep to call her brother in to his tea we watched her from our shadow peer up and down the street. We waited to see

1. The third of the fifteen stories in *Dubliners*. This tale of the frustrated quest for beauty in the midst of drabness is both meticulously realistic in its handling of details of Dublin life and the Dublin scene and highly symbolic in that almost every image and incident suggests some particular aspect of the theme (e.g., the suggestion of the Holy Grail in the image of the chalice, mentioned in the fifth paragraph). Joyce was drawing on his own childhood recollections, and the uncle in the story is a reminiscence of Joyce's father. But in all the stories in *Dubliners* dealing with childhood, the child lives not with his parents but with an uncle and aunt—a symbol of that isolation and lack of proper relation between "consubstantial" (in the flesh) parents

and children that is a major theme in Joyce's work.
2. The Joyce family moved to 17 North Richmond Street, Dublin, in 1894; and Joyce had earlier briefly attended the Christian Brothers' school a few doors away (the Christian Brothers are a Catholic religious community). The details of the house described here correspond exactly to those of number 17.
3. François Eugéne Vidocq (1775–1857) had an extraordinary career as soldier, thief, chief of the French detective force, and private detective. *The Abbot* is a historical novel dealing with Mary, Queen of Scots. *The Devout Communicant* is a Catholic religious manual.

whether she would remain or go in and, if she remained, we left our shadow and walked up to Mangan's steps resignedly. She was waiting for us, her figure defined by the light from the half-opened door. Her brother always teased her before he obeyed and I stood by the railings looking at her. Her dress swung as she moved her body and the soft rope of her hair tossed from side to side.

Every morning I lay on the floor in the front parlour watching her door. The blind was pulled down to within an inch of the sash so that I could not be seen. When she came out on the doorstep my heart leaped. I ran to the hall, seized my books and followed her. I kept her brown figure always in my eye and, when we came near the point at which our ways diverged, I quickened my pace and passed her. This happened morning after morning. I had never spoken to her, except for a few casual words, and yet her name was like a summons to all my foolish blood.

Her image accompanied me even in places the most hostile to romance. On Saturday evenings when my aunt went marketing I had to go to carry some of the parcels. We walked through the flaring streets, jostled by drunken men and bargaining women, amid the curses of labourers, the shrill litanies of shop-boys who stood on guard by the barrels of pigs' cheeks, the nasal chanting of street-singers, who sang a *come-all-you*[4] about O'Donovan Rossa, or a ballad about the troubles in our native land. These noises converged in a single sensation of life for me: I imagined that I bore my chalice safely through a throng of foes. Her name sprang to my lips at moments in strange prayers and praises which I myself did not understand. My eyes were often full of tears (I could not tell why) and at times a flood from my heart seemed to pour itself out into my bosom. I thought little of the future. I did not know whether I would ever speak to her or not or, if I spoke to her, how I could tell her of my confused adoration. But my body was like a harp and her words and gestures were like fingers running upon the wires.

One evening I went into the back drawing-room in which the priest had died. It was a dark rainy evening and there was no sound in the house. Through one of the broken panes I heard the rain impinge upon the earth, the fine incessant needles of water playing in the sodden beds. Some distant lamp or lighted window gleamed below me. I was thankful that I could see so little. All my senses seemed to desire to veil themselves and, feeling that I was about to slip from them, I pressed the palms of my hands together until they trembled, murmuring: *O love! O love!* many times.

At last she spoke to me. When she addressed the first words to me I was so confused that I did not know what to answer. She asked me was I going to *Araby*.[5] I forgot whether I answered yes or no. It would be a splendid bazaar, she said; she would love to go.

—And why can't you? I asked.

While she spoke she turned a silver bracelet round and round her wrist. She could not go, she said, because there would be a retreat that week in her convent.[6] Her brother and two other boys were fighting for their caps and I was alone at the railings. She held one of the spikes, bowing her head towards me. The light from the lamp opposite our door caught the white curve of her

4. Street ballad, so called from its opening words. This one was about the 19th-century Irish nationalist Jeremiah Donovan, popularly known as O'Donovan Rossa.
5. The bazaar, described by its "official catalogue" as a "Grand Oriental Fête," was actually held in Dublin on May 14–19, 1894.
6. I.e., her convent school. "Retreat": period of seclusion from ordinary activities devoted to religious exercises.

neck, lit up her hair that rested there and, falling, lit up the hand upon the railing. It fell over one side of her dress and caught the white border of a petticoat, just visible as she stood at ease.

—It's well for you, she said.

—If I go, I said, I will bring you something.

What innumerable follies laid waste my waking and sleeping thoughts after that evening! I wished to annihilate the tedious intervening days. I chafed against the work of school. At night in my bedroom and by day in the classroom her image came between me and the page I strove to read. The syllables of the word *Araby* were called to me through the silence in which my soul luxuriated and cast an Eastern enchantment over me. I asked for leave to go to the bazaar on Saturday night. My aunt was surprised and hoped it was not some Freemason affair.[7] I answered few questions in class. I watched my master's face pass from amiability to sternness; he hoped I was not beginning to idle. I could not call my wandering thoughts together. I had hardly any patience with the serious work of life which, now that it stood between me and my desire, seemed to me child's play, ugly monotonous child's play.

On Saturday morning I reminded my uncle that I wished to go to the bazaar in the evening. He was fussing at the hallstand, looking for the hat-brush, and answered me curtly:

—Yes, boy, I know.

As he was in the hall I could not go into the front parlour and lie at the window. I left the house in bad humour and walked slowly towards the school. The air was pitilessly raw and already my heart misgave me.

When I came home to dinner my uncle had not yet been home. Still it was early. I sat staring at the clock for some time and, when its ticking began to irritate me, I left the room. I mounted the staircase and gained the upper part of the house. The high cold empty gloomy rooms liberated me and I went from room to room singing. From the front window I saw my companions playing below in the street. Their cries reached me weakened and indistinct and, leaning my forehead against the cool glass, I looked over at the dark house where she lived. I may have stood there for an hour, seeing nothing but the brown-clad figure cast by my imagination, touched discreetly by the lamplight at the curved neck, at the hand upon the railings and at the border below the dress.

When I came downstairs again I found Mrs Mercer sitting at the fire. She was an old garrulous woman, a pawn-broker's widow, who collected used stamps for some pious purpose. I had to endure the gossip of the tea-table. The meal was prolonged beyond an hour and still my uncle did not come. Mrs Mercer stood up to go: she was sorry she couldn't wait any longer, but it was after eight o'clock and she did not like to be out late, as the night air was bad for her. When she had gone I began to walk up and down the room, clenching my fists. My aunt said:

—I'm afraid you may put off your bazaar for this night of Our Lord.

At nine o'clock I heard my uncle's latchkey in the halldoor. I heard him talking to himself and heard the hallstand rocking when it had received the weight of his overcoat. I could interpret these signs. When he was midway through his dinner I asked him to give me the money to go to the bazaar. He had forgotten.

—The people are in bed and after their first sleep now, he said.

I did not smile. My aunt said to him energetically:

—Can't you give him the money and let him go? You've kept him late enough as it is.

My uncle said he was very sorry he had forgotten. He said he believed in the old saying: *All work and no play makes Jack a dull boy*. He asked me where I was going and, when I had told him a second time he asked me did I know *The Arab's Farewell to his Steed*.[8] When I left the kitchen he was about to recite the opening lines of the piece to my aunt.

I held a florin[9] tightly in my hand as I strode down Buckingham Street towards the station. The sight of the streets thronged with buyers and glaring with gas recalled to me the purpose of my journey. I took my seat in a third-class carriage of a deserted train. After an intolerable delay the train moved out of the station slowly. It crept onward among ruinous houses and over the twinkling river. At Westland Row Station a crowd of people pressed to the carriage doors; but the porters moved them back, saying that it was a special train for the bazaar. I remained alone in the bare carriage. In a few minutes the train drew up beside an improvised wooden platform. I passed out on to the road and saw by the lighted dial of a clock that it was ten minutes to ten. In front of me was a large building which displayed the magical name.

I could not find any sixpenny entrance and, fearing that the bazaar would be closed, I passed in quickly through a turnstile, handing a shilling to a weary-looking man. I found myself in a big hall girdled at half its height by a gallery. Nearly all the stalls were closed and the greater part of the hall was in darkness. I recognized a silence like that which pervades a church after a service. I walked into the centre of the bazaar timidly. A few people were gathered about the stalls which were still open. Before a curtain, over which the words *Café Chantant*[1] were written in coloured lamps, two men were counting money on a salver. I listened to the fall of the coins.

Remembering with difficulty why I had come I went over to one of the stalls and examined porcelain vases and flowered tea-sets. At the door of the stall a young lady was talking and laughing with two young gentlemen. I remarked their English accents and listened vaguely to their conversation.

—O, I never said such a thing!

—O, but you did!

—O, but I didn't!

—Didn't she say that?

—Yes. I heard her.

—O, there's a . . . fib!

Observing me the young lady came over and asked me did I wish to buy anything. The tone of her voice was not encouraging; she seemed to have spoken to me out of a sense of duty. I looked humbly at the great jars that stood like eastern guards at either side of the dark entrance to the stall and murmured:

—No, thank you.

The young lady changed the position of one of the vases and went back to the two young men. They began to talk of the same subject. Once or twice the young lady glanced at me over her shoulder.

---

8. Once-popular sentimental poem by Caroline Norton.

9. A silver coin, now obsolete, worth two shillings.

1. Singing café (French; literal trans.); a café that provided musical entertainment, popular early in the 20th century.

I lingered before her stall, though I knew my stay was useless, to make my interest in her wares seem the more real. Then I turned away slowly and walked down the middle of the bazaar. I allowed the two pennies to fall against the sixpence in my pocket. I heard a voice call from one end of the gallery that the light was out. The upper part of the hall was now completely dark.

Gazing up into the darkness I saw myself as a creature driven and derided by vanity; and my eyes burned with anguish and anger.

1905   1914

The Dead

Lily, the caretaker's daughter, was literally run off her feet. Hardly had she brought one gentleman into the little pantry behind the office on the ground floor and helped him off with his overcoat than the wheezy hall-door bell clanged again and she had to scamper along the bare hallway to let in another guest. It was well for her she had not to attend to the ladies also. But Miss Kate and Miss Julia had thought of that and had converted the bathroom upstairs into a ladies' dressing-room. Miss Kate and Miss Julia were there, gossiping and laughing and fussing, walking after each other to the head of the stairs, peering down over the banisters and calling down to Lily to ask her who had come.

It was always a great affair, the Misses Morkan's annual dance. Everybody who knew them came to it, members of the family, old friends of the family, the members of Julia's choir, any of Kate's pupils that were grown up enough and even some of Mary Jane's pupils too. Never once had it fallen flat. For years and years it had gone off in splendid style as long as anyone could remember; ever since Kate and Julia, after the death of their brother Pat, had left the house in Stoney Batter and taken Mary Jane, their only niece, to live with them in the dark gaunt house on Usher's Island, the upper part of which they had rented from Mr Fulham, the cornfactor[1] on the ground floor. That was a good thirty years ago if it was a day. Mary Jane, who was then a little girl in short clothes, was now the main prop of the household for she had the organ in Haddington Road.[2] She had been through the Academy and gave a pupils' concert every year in the upper room of the Antient Concert Rooms.[3] Many of her pupils belonged to better-class families on the Kingstown and Dalkey line. Old as they were, her aunts also did their share. Julia, though she was quite grey, was still the leading soprano in Adam and Eve's, and Kate, being too feeble to go about much, gave music lessons to beginners on the old square piano in the back room. Lily, the caretaker's daughter, did housemaid's work for them. Though their life was modest they believed in eating well; the best of everything: diamond-bone sirloins, three-shilling tea and the best bottled stout.[4] But Lily seldom made a mistake in the orders so that she got on well with her three mistresses. They were fussy, that was all. But the only thing they would not stand was back answers.

Of course they had good reason to be fussy on such a night. And then it

1. Grain merchant.
2. Haddington Road, like Adam and Eve's below, is a church.
3. Concert hall in Dublin. The academy was the Royal Irish Academy of Music.
4. A dark brown malt liquor, akin to beer.

was long after ten o'clock and yet there was no sign of Gabriel and his wife. Besides they were dreadfully afraid that Freddy Malins might turn up screwed.[5] They would not wish for worlds that any of Mary Jane's pupils should see him under the influence; and when he was like that it was sometimes very hard to manage him. Freddy Malins always came late but they wondered what could be keeping Gabriel: and that was what brought them every two minutes to the banisters to ask Lily had Gabriel or Freddy come.

—O, Mr Conroy, said Lily to Gabriel when she opened the door for him, Miss Kate and Miss Julia thought you were never coming. Good-night, Mrs Conroy.

—I'll engage[6] they did, said Gabriel, but they forget that my wife here takes three mortal hours to dress herself.

He stood on the mat, scraping the snow from his goloshes, while Lily led his wife to the foot of the stairs and called out:

—Miss Kate, here's Mrs Conroy.

Kate and Julia came toddling down the dark stairs at once. Both of them kissed Gabriel's wife, said she must be perished alive and asked was Gabriel with her.

—Here I am as right as the mail, Aunt Kate! Go on up. I'll follow, called out Gabriel from the dark.

He continued scraping his feet vigorously while the three women went upstairs, laughing, to the ladies' dressing-room. A light fringe of snow lay like a cape on the shoulders of his overcoat and like toecaps on the toes of his goloshes; and, as the buttons of his overcoat slipped with a squeaking noise through the snow-stiffened frieze,[7] a cold fragrant air from out-of-doors escaped from crevices and folds.

—Is it snowing again, Mr Conroy? asked Lily.

She had preceded him into the pantry to help him off with his overcoat. Gabriel smiled at the three syllables she had given his surname and glanced at her. She was a slim, growing girl, pale in complexion and with hay-coloured hair. The gas in the pantry made her look still paler. Gabriel had known her when she was a child and used to sit on the lowest step nursing a rag doll.

—Yes, Lily, he answered, and I think we're in for a night of it.

He looked up at the pantry ceiling, which was shaking with the stamping and shuffling of feet on the floor above, listened for a moment to the piano and then glanced at the girl, who was folding his overcoat carefully at the end of a shelf.

—Tell me, Lily, he said in a friendly tone, do you still go to school?

—O no, sir, she answered. I'm done schooling this year and more.

—O, then, said Gabriel gaily, I suppose we'll be going to your wedding one of these fine days with your young man, eh?

The girl glanced back at him over her shoulder and said with great bitterness:

—The men that is now is only all palaver[8] and what they can get out of you.

Gabriel coloured as if he felt he had made a mistake and, without looking at her, kicked off his goloshes and flicked actively with his muffler at his patent-leather shoes.

He was a stout tallish young man. The high colour of his cheeks pushed upwards even to his forehead where it scattered itself in a few formless patches of pale red; and on his hairless face there scintillated restlessly the polished lenses and the bright gilt rims of the glasses which screened his delicate and restless eyes. His glossy black hair was parted in the middle and brushed in a long curve behind his ears where it curled slightly beneath the groove left by his hat.

When he had flicked lustre into his shoes he stood up and pulled his waist-coat down more tightly on his plump body. Then he took a coin rapidly from his pocket.

—O Lily, he said, thrusting it into her hands, it's Christmas-time, isn't it? Just . . . here's a little. . . .

He walked rapidly towards the door.

—O no, sir! cried the girl, following him. Really, sir, I wouldn't take it.

—Christmas-time! Christmas-time! said Gabriel, almost trotting to the stairs and waving his hand to her in deprecation.

The girl, seeing that he had gained the stairs, called out after him:

—Well, thank you, sir.

He waited outside the drawing-room door until the waltz should finish, listening to the skirts that swept against it and to the shuffling of feet. He was still discomposed by the girl's bitter and sudden retort. It had cast a gloom over him which he tried to dispel by arranging his cuffs and the bows of his tie. Then he took from his waistcoat pocket a little paper and glanced at the headings he had made for his speech. He was undecided about the lines from Robert Browning for he feared they would be above the heads of his hearers. Some quotation that they could recognise from Shakespeare or from the Melodies[9] would be better. The indelicate clacking of the men's heels and the shuffling of their soles reminded him that their grade of culture differed from his. He would only make himself ridiculous by quoting poetry to them which they could not understand. They would think that he was airing his superior education. He would fail with them just as he had failed with the girl in the pantry. He had taken up a wrong tone. His whole speech was a mistake from first to last, an utter failure.

Just then his aunts and his wife came out of the ladies' dressing-room. His aunts were two small plainly dressed old women. Aunt Julia was an inch or so the taller. Her hair, drawn low over the tops of her ears, was grey; and grey also, with darker shadows, was her large flaccid face. Though she was stout in build and stood erect her slow eyes and parted lips gave her the appearance of a woman who did not know where she was or where she was going. Aunt Kate was more vivacious. Her face, healthier than her sister's, was all puckers and creases, like a shrivelled red apple, and her hair, braided in the same old-fashioned way, had not lost its ripe nut colour.

They both kissed Gabriel frankly. He was their favourite nephew, the son of their dead elder sister, Ellen, who had married T. J. Conroy of the Port and Docks.[1]

—Gretta tells me you're not going to take a cab back to Monkstown tonight, Gabriel, said Aunt Kate.

—No, said Gabriel, turning to his wife, we had quite enough of that last year, hadn't we? Don't you remember, Aunt Kate, what a cold Gretta got out

9. *Irish Melodies* by Dublin-born Thomas Moore (1779–1852), a collection of songs—including one called "O Ye Dead"—that was extremely popular

in late-19th- and early-20th-century Ireland.
1. Board managing the Port of Dublin.

of it? Cab windows rattling all the way, and the east wind blowing in after we passed Merrion. Very jolly it was. Gretta caught a dreadful cold.

Aunt Kate frowned severely and nodded her head at every word.

—Quite right, Gabriel, quite right, she said. You can't be too careful.

—But as for Gretta there, said Gabriel, she'd walk home in the snow if she were let.

Mrs Conroy laughed.

—Don't mind him, Aunt Kate, she said. He's really an awful bother, what with green shades for Tom's eyes at night and making him do the dumb-bells, and forcing Eva to eat the stirabout.[2] The poor child! And she simply hates the sight of it! . . . O, but you'll never guess what he makes me wear now!

She broke out into a peal of laughter and glanced at her husband, whose admiring and happy eyes had been wandering from her dress to her face and hair. The two aunts laughed heartily too, for Gabriel's solicitude was a standing joke with them.

—Goloshes! said Mrs Conroy. That's the latest. Whenever it's wet underfoot I must put on my goloshes. To-night even he wanted me to put them on, but I wouldn't. The next thing he'll buy me will be a diving suit.

Gabriel laughed nervously and patted his tie reassuringly while Aunt Kate nearly doubled herself, so heartily did she enjoy the joke. The smile soon faded from Aunt Julia's face and her mirthless eyes were directed towards her nephew's face. After a pause she asked:

—And what are goloshes, Gabriel?

—Goloshes, Julia! exclaimed her sister. Goodness me, don't you know what goloshes are? You wear them over your . . . over your boots, Gretta, isn't it?

—Yes, said Mrs Conroy. Guttapercha things. We both have a pair now. Gabriel says everyone wears them on the continent.

—O, on the continent, murmured Aunt Julia, nodding her head slowly.

Gabriel knitted his brows and said, as if he were slightly angered:

—It's nothing very wonderful but Gretta thinks it very funny because she says the word reminds her of Christy Minstrels.[3]

—But tell me, Gabriel, said Aunt Kate, with brisk tact. Of course, you've seen about the room. Gretta was saying . . .

—O, the room is all right, replied Gabriel. I've taken one in the Gresham.[4]

—To be sure, said Aunt Kate, by far the best thing to do. And the children, Gretta, you're not anxious about them?

—O, for one night, said Mrs Conroy. Besides, Bessie will look after them.

—To be sure, said Aunt Kate again. What a comfort it is to have a girl like that, one you can depend on! There's that Lily, I'm sure I don't know what has come over her lately. She's not the girl she was at all.

Gabriel was about to ask his aunt some questions on this point but she broke off suddenly to gaze after her sister who had wandered down the stairs and was craning her neck over the banisters.

—Now, I ask you, she said, almost testily, where is Julia going? Julia! Julia! Where are you going?

2. Porridge made by stirring oatmeal in boiling milk or water.
3. Originally the name of a troupe of entertainers imitating African Americans, founded by George Christy of New York. By Joyce's time the meaning had become extended to any group with blackened faces who sang what were known as Negro melodies to banjo accompaniment, interspersed with jokes.
4. The Gresham Hotel, still one of the best hotels in Dublin.

Julia, who had gone halfway down one flight, came back and announced blandly:

—Here's Freddy.

At the same moment a clapping of hands and a final flourish of the pianist told that the waltz had ended. The drawing-room door was opened from within and some couples came out. Aunt Kate drew Gabriel aside hurriedly and whispered into his ear:

—Slip down, Gabriel, like a good fellow and see if he's all right, and don't let him up if he's screwed. I'm sure he's screwed. I'm sure he is.

Gabriel went to the stairs and listened over the banisters. He could hear two persons talking in the pantry. Then he recognised Freddy Malins' laugh. He went down the stairs noisily.

—It's such a relief, said Aunt Kate to Mrs Conroy, that Gabriel is here. I always feel easier in my mind when he's here. . . . Julia, there's Miss Daly and Miss Power will take some refreshment. Thanks for your beautiful waltz, Miss Daly. It made lovely time.

A tall wizen-faced man, with a stiff grizzled moustache and swarthy skin, who was passing out with his partner said:

—And may we have some refreshment, too, Miss Morkan?

—Julia, said Aunt Kate summarily, and here's Mr Browne and Miss Furlong. Take them in, Julia, with Miss Daly and Miss Power.

—I'm the man for the ladies, said Mr Browne, pursing his lips until his moustache bristled and smiling in all his wrinkles. You know, Miss Morkan, the reason they are so fond of me is—

He did not finish his sentence, but, seeing that Aunt Kate was out of earshot, at once led the three young ladies into the back room. The middle of the room was occupied by two square tables placed end to end, and on these Aunt Julia and the caretaker were straightening and smoothing a large cloth. On the sideboard were arrayed dishes and plates, and glasses and bundles of knives and forks and spoons. The top of the closed square piano served also as a sideboard for viands and sweets. At a smaller sideboard in one corner two young men were standing, drinking hop-bitters.

Mr Browne led his charges thither and invited them all, in jest, to some ladies' punch, hot, strong and sweet. As they said they never took anything strong he opened three bottles of lemonade for them. Then he asked one of the young men to move aside, and, taking hold of the decanter, filled out for himself a goodly measure of whisky. The young men eyed him respectfully while he took a trial sip.

—God help me, he said, smiling, it's the doctor's orders.

His wizened face broke into a broader smile, and the three young ladies laughed in musical echo to his pleasantry, swaying their bodies to and fro, with nervous jerks of their shoulders. The boldest said:

—O, now, Mr Browne, I'm sure the doctor never ordered anything of the kind.

Mr Browne took another sip of his whisky and said, with sidling mimicry:

—Well, you see, I'm like the famous Mrs Cassidy, who is reported to have said: *Now, Mary Grimes, if I don't take it, make me take it, for I feel I want it.*

His hot face had leaned forward a little too confidentially and he had assumed a very low Dublin accent so that the young ladies, with one instinct, received his speech in silence. Miss Furlong, who was one of Mary Jane's pupils, asked Miss Daly what was the name of the pretty waltz she had played;

and Mr Browne, seeing that he was ignored, turned promptly to the two young men who were more appreciative.

A red-faced young woman, dressed in pansy, came into the room, excitedly clapping her hands and crying:

—Quadrilles![5] Quadrilles!

Close on her heels came Aunt Kate, crying:

—Two gentlemen and three ladies, Mary Jane!

—O, here's Mr Bergin and Mr Kerrigan, said Mary Jane. Mr Kerrigan, will you take Miss Power? Miss Furlong, may I get you a partner, Mr Bergin. O, that'll just do now.

—Three ladies, Mary Jane, said Aunt Kate.

The two young gentlemen asked the ladies if they might have the pleasure, and Mary Jane turned to Miss Daly.

—O, Miss Daly, you're really awfully good, after playing for the last two dances, but really we're so short of ladies to-night.

—I don't mind in the least, Miss Morkan.

—But I've a nice partner for you, Mr Bartell D'Arcy, the tenor. I'll get him to sing later on. All Dublin is raving about him.

—Lovely voice, lovely voice! said Aunt Kate.

As the piano had twice begun the prelude to the first figure Mary Jane led her recruits quickly from the room. They had hardly gone when Aunt Julia wandered slowly into the room, looking behind her at something.

—What is the matter, Julia? asked Aunt Kate anxiously. Who is it?

Julia, who was carrying in a column of table-napkins, turned to her sister and said, simply, as if the question had surprised her:

—It's only Freddy, Kate, and Gabriel with him.

In fact right behind her Gabriel could be seen piloting Freddy Malins across the landing. The latter, a young man of about forty, was of Gabriel's size and build, with very round shoulders. His face was fleshy and pallid, touched with colour only at the thick hanging lobes of his ears and at the wide wings of his nose. He had coarse features, a blunt nose, a convex and receding brow, tumid and protruded lips. His heavy-lidded eyes and the disorder of his scanty hair made him look sleepy. He was laughing heartily in a high key at a story which he had been telling Gabriel on the stairs and at the same time rubbing the knuckles of his left fist backwards and forwards into his left eye.

—Good-evening, Freddy, said Aunt Julia.

Freddy Malins bade the Misses Morkan good-evening in what seemed an offhand fashion by reason of the habitual catch in his voice and then, seeing that Mr Browne was grinning at him from the sideboard, crossed the room on rather shaky legs and began to repeat in an undertone the story he had just told to Gabriel.

—He's not so bad, is he? said Aunt Kate to Gabriel.

Gabriel's brows were dark but he raised them quickly and answered:

—O no, hardly noticeable.

—Now, isn't he a terrible fellow! she said. And his poor mother made him take the pledge[6] on New Year's Eve. But come on, Gabriel, into the drawing-room.

Before leaving the room with Gabriel she signalled to Mr Browne by frown-

---

5. A square dance usually performed by four couples.

6. Sign a solemn promise not to drink alcohol.

2178 / JAMES JOYCE

ing and shaking her forefinger in warning to and fro. Mr Browne nodded in
answer and, when she had gone, said to Freddy Malins:

—Now, then, Teddy, I'm going to fill you out a good glass of lemonade just
to buck you up.

Freddy Malins, who was nearing the climax of his story, waved the offer
aside impatiently but Mr Browne, having first called Freddy Malins' attention
to a disarray in his dress, filled out and handed him a full glass of lemonade.
Freddy Malins' left hand accepted the glass mechanically, his right hand being
engaged in the mechanical readjustment of his dress. Mr Browne, whose face
was once more wrinkling with mirth, poured out for himself a glass of whisky
while Freddy Malins exploded, before he had well reached the climax of his
story, in a kink of high-pitched bronchitic laughter and, setting down his
untasted and overflowing glass, began to rub the knuckles of his left fist backwards and forwards into his left eye, repeating words of his last phrase as well
as his fit of laughter would allow him.

Gabriel could not listen while Mary Jane was playing her Academy piece,
full of runs and difficult passages, to the hushed drawing-room. He liked music
but the piece she was playing had no melody for him and he doubted whether
it had any melody for the other listeners, though they had begged Mary Jane
to play something. Four young men, who had come from the refreshment-
room to stand in the door-way at the sound of the piano, had gone away quietly
in couples after a few minutes. The only persons who seemed to follow the
music were Mary Jane herself, her hands racing along the key-board or lifted
from it at the pauses like those of a priestess in momentary imprecation, and
Aunt Kate standing at her elbow to turn the page.

Gabriel's eyes, irritated by the floor, which glittered with beeswax under the
heavy chandelier, wandered to the wall above the piano. A picture of the balcony scene in *Romeo and Juliet* hung there and beside it was a picture of the
two murdered princes in the Tower[7] which Aunt Julia had worked in red, blue
and brown wools when she was a girl. Probably in the school they had gone
to as girls that kind of work had been taught, for one year his mother had
worked for him as a birthday present a waistcoat of purple tabinet,[8] with little
foxes' heads upon it, lined with brown satin and having round mulberry buttons. It was strange that his mother had had no musical talent though Aunt
Kate used to call her the brains carrier of the Morkan family. Both she and
Julia had always seemed a little proud of their serious and matronly sister. Her
photograph stood before the pierglass.[9] She held an open book on her knees
and was pointing out something in it to Constantine who, dressed in a man-
o'-war suit,[1] lay at her feet. It was she who had chosen the names for her sons
for she was very sensible of the dignity of family life. Thanks to her, Constantine was now senior curate[2] in Balbriggan and, thanks to her, Gabriel himself
had taken his degree in the Royal University. A shadow passed over his face
as he remembered her sullen opposition to his marriage. Some slighting
phrases she had used still rankled in his memory; she had once spoken of
Gretta as being country cute and that was not true of Gretta at all. It was

---

7. Probably Edward V and his brother Richard,
duke of York, reputedly murdered in 1483 by their
uncle and successor, Richard III.
8. Silk and wool fabric made chiefly in Ireland.

9. Large tall mirror.
1. Sailor suit, favorite wear for children of both
sexes early in the 20th century.
2. Clergyman appointed to assist a parish priest.

Gretta who had nursed her during all her last long illness in their house at Monkstown.

He knew that Mary Jane must be near the end of her piece for she was playing again the opening melody with runs of scales after every bar and while he waited for the end the resentment died down in his heart. The piece ended with a trill of octaves in the treble and a final deep octave in the bass. Great applause greeted Mary Jane as, blushing and rolling up her music nervously, she escaped from the room. The most vigorous clapping came from the four young men in the doorway who had gone away to the refreshment-room at the beginning of the piece but had come back when the piano had stopped.

Lancers[3] were arranged. Gabriel found himself partnered with Miss Ivors. She was a frank-mannered talkative young lady, with a freckled face and prominent brown eyes. She did not wear a low-cut bodice and the large brooch which was fixed in the front of her collar bore on it an Irish device.

When they had taken their places she said abruptly:

—I have a crow to pluck with you.

—With me? said Gabriel.

She nodded her head gravely.

—What is it? asked Gabriel, smiling at her solemn manner.

—Who is G. C.? answered Miss Ivors, turning her eyes upon him.

Gabriel coloured and was about to knit his brows, as if he did not understand, when she said bluntly:

—O, innocent Amy! I have found out that you write for *The Daily Express*. Now, aren't you ashamed of yourself?

—Why should I be ashamed of myself? asked Gabriel, blinking his eyes and trying to smile.

—Well, I'm ashamed of you, said Miss Ivors frankly. To say you'd write for a rag like that. I didn't think you were a West Briton.[4]

A look of perplexity appeared on Gabriel's face. It was true that he wrote a literary column every Wednesday in *The Daily Express*, for which he was paid fifteen shillings. But that did not make him a West Briton surely. The books he received for review were almost more welcome than the paltry cheque. He loved to feel the covers and turn over the pages of newly printed books. Nearly every day when his teaching in the college was ended he used to wander down the quays to the second-hand booksellers, to Hickey's on Bachelor's Walk, to Webb's, or Massey's on Aston's Quay, or to O'Clohissey's in the by-street. He did not know how to meet her charge. He wanted to say that literature was above politics. But they were friends of many years' standing and their careers had been parallel, first at the University and then as teachers: he could not risk a grandiose phrase with her. He continued blinking his eyes and trying to smile and murmured lamely that he saw nothing political in writing reviews of books.

When their turn to cross had come he was still perplexed and inattentive. Miss Ivors promptly took his hand in a warm grasp and said in a soft friendly tone:

—Of course, I was only joking. Come, we cross now.

When they were together again she spoke of the University question[5] and

---

3. A square dance for four or more couples.
4. A pejorative term for one who denies a separate Irish nationality and sees Ireland as simply a western extension of Great Britain.
5. Namely, whether Ireland's elite Protestant universities should be open to Catholics.

2180 / JAMES JOYCE

Gabriel felt more at ease. A friend of hers had shown her his review of Browning's poems. That was how she had found out the secret: but she liked the review immensely. Then she said suddenly:

—O, Mr Conroy, will you come for an excursion to the Aran Isles[6] this summer? We're going to stay there a whole month. It will be splendid out in the Atlantic. You ought to come. Mr Clancy is coming, and Mr Kilkelly and Kathleen Kearney. It would be splendid for Gretta too if she'd come. She's from Connacht,[7] isn't she?

—Her people are, said Gabriel shortly.

—But you will come, won't you? said Miss Ivors, laying her warm hand eagerly on his arm.

—The fact is, said Gabriel, I have already arranged to go—

—Go where? asked Miss Ivors.

—Well, you know, every year I go for a cycling tour with some fellows and so—

—But where? asked Miss Ivors.

—Well, we usually go to France or Belgium or perhaps Germany, said Gabriel awkwardly.

—And why do you go to France and Belgium, said Miss Ivors, instead of visiting your own land?

—Well, said Gabriel, it's partly to keep in touch with the languages and partly for a change.

—And haven't you your own language to keep in touch with—Irish? asked Miss Ivors.

—Well, said Gabriel, if it comes to that, you know, Irish is not my language.

Their neighbours had turned to listen to the cross-examination. Gabriel glanced right and left nervously and tried to keep his good humour under the ordeal which was making a blush invade his forehead.

—And haven't you your own land to visit, continued Miss Ivors, that you know nothing of, your own people, and your own country?

—O, to tell you the truth, retorted Gabriel suddenly, I'm sick of my own country, sick of it!

—Why? asked Miss Ivors.

Gabriel did not answer for his retort had heated him.

—Why? repeated Miss Ivors.

They had to go visiting together and, as he had not answered her, Miss Ivors said warmly:

—Of course, you've no answer.

Gabriel tried to cover his agitation by taking part in the dance with great energy. He avoided her eyes for he had seen a sour expression on her face. But when they met in the long chain he was surprised to feel his hand firmly pressed. She looked at him from under her brows for a moment quizzically[8] until he smiled. Then, just as the chain was about to start again, she stood on tiptoe and whispered into his ear:

—West Briton!

When the lancers were over Gabriel went away to a remote corner of the room where Freddy Malins' mother was sitting. She was a stout feeble old woman with white hair. Her voice had a catch in it like her son's and she

---

6. Three small islands lying across the entrance to Galway Bay, on the west coast of Ireland.
7. Or Connaught, a rural region on the west coast

of Ireland.
8. Teasingly.

stuttered slightly. She had been told that Freddy had come and that he was nearly all right. Gabriel asked her whether she had had a good crossing. She lived with her married daughter in Glasgow and came to Dublin on a visit once a year. She answered placidly that she had had a beautiful crossing and that the captain had been most attentive to her. She spoke also of the beautiful house her daughter kept in Glasgow, and of all the nice friends they had there. While her tongue rambled on Gabriel tried to banish from his mind all memory of the unpleasant incident with Miss Ivors. Of course the girl or woman, or whatever she was, was an enthusiast but there was a time for all things. Perhaps he ought not to have answered her like that. But she had no right to call him a West Briton before people, even in joke. She had tried to make him ridiculous before people, heckling him and staring at him with her rabbit's eyes.

He saw his wife making her way towards him through the waltzing couples. When she reached him she said into his ear:

—Gabriel, Aunt Kate wants to know won't you carve the goose as usual. Miss Daly will carve the ham and I'll do the pudding.

—All right, said Gabriel.

—She's sending in the younger ones first as soon as this waltz is over so that we'll have the table to ourselves.

—Were you dancing? asked Gabriel.

—Of course I was. Didn't you see me? What words had you with Molly Ivors?

—No words. Why? Did she say so?

—Something like that. I'm trying to get that Mr D'Arcy to sing. He's full of conceit, I think.

—There were no words, said Gabriel moodily, only she wanted me to go for a trip to the west of Ireland and I said I wouldn't.

His wife clasped her hands excitedly and gave a little jump.

—O, do go, Gabriel, she cried. I'd love to see Galway again.

—You can go if you like, said Gabriel coldly.

She looked at him for a moment, then turned to Mrs Malins and said:

—There's a nice husband for you, Mrs Malins.

While she was threading her way back across the room Mrs Malins, without adverting to the interruption, went on to tell Gabriel what beautiful places there were in Scotland and beautiful scenery. Her son-in-law brought them every year to the lakes and they used to go fishing. Her son-in-law was a splendid fisher. One day he caught a fish, a beautiful big big fish, and the man in the hotel boiled it for their dinner.

Gabriel hardly heard what she said. Now that supper was coming near he began to think again about his speech and about the quotation. When he saw Freddy Malins coming across the room to visit his mother Gabriel left the chair free for him and retired into the embrasure[9] of the window. The room had already cleared and from the back room came the clatter of plates and knives. Those who still remained in the drawing-room seemed tired of dancing and were conversing quietly in little groups. Gabriel's warm trembling fingers tapped the cold pane of the window. How cool it must be outside! How pleasant it would be to walk out alone, first along by the river and then through the park! The snow would be lying on the branches of the trees and forming a

9. Opening for a window in a thick wall.

bright cap on the top of the Wellington Monument.[1] How much more pleasant it would be there than at the supper-table!

He ran over the headings of his speech: Irish hospitality, sad memories, the Three Graces, Paris,[2] the quotation from Browning. He repeated to himself a phrase he had written in his review: *One feels that one is listening to a thought-tormented music.* Miss Ivors had praised the review. Was she sincere? Had she really any life of her own behind all her propagandism? There had never been any ill-feeling between them until that night. It unnerved him to think that she would be at the supper-table, looking up at him while he spoke with her critical quizzing eyes. Perhaps she would not be sorry to see him fail in his speech. An idea came into his mind and gave him courage. He would say, alluding to Aunt Kate and Aunt Julia: *Ladies and Gentlemen, the generation which is now on the wane among us may have had its faults but for my part I think it had certain qualities of hospitality, of humour, of humanity, which the new and very serious and hypereducated generation that is growing up around us seems to me to lack.* Very good: that was one for Miss Ivors. What did he care that his aunts were only two ignorant old women?

A murmur in the room attracted his attention. Mr Browne was advancing from the door, gallantly escorting Aunt Julia, who leaned upon his arm, smiling and hanging her head. An irregular musketry of applause escorted her also as far as the piano and then, as Mary Jane seated herself on the stool, and Aunt Julia, no longer smiling, half turned so as to pitch her voice fairly into the room, gradually ceased. Gabriel recognised the prelude. It was that of an old song of Aunt Julia's—*Arrayed for the Bridal.*[3] Her voice, strong and clear in tone, attacked with great spirit the runs which embellish the air and though she sang very rapidly she did not miss even the smallest of the grace notes. To follow the voice, without looking at the singer's face, was to feel and share the excitement of swift and secure flight. Gabriel applauded loudly with all the others at the close of the song and loud applause was borne in from the invisible supper-table. It sounded so genuine that a little colour struggled into Aunt Julia's face as she bent to replace in the music-stand the old leather-bound song-book that had her initials on the cover. Freddy Malins, who had listened with his head perched sideways to hear her better, was still applauding when everyone else had ceased and talking animatedly to his mother who nodded her head gravely and slowly in acquiescence. At last, when he could clap no more, he stood up suddenly and hurried across the room to Aunt Julia whose hand he seized and held in both his hands, shaking it when words failed him or the catch in his voice proved too much for him.

—I was just telling my mother, he said, I never heard you sing so well, never. No, I never heard your voice so good as it is to-night. Now! Would you believe that now? That's the truth. Upon my word and honour that's the truth. I never heard your voice sound so fresh and so . . . so clear and fresh, never.

Aunt Julia smiled broadly and murmured something about compliments as

---

1. Tribute to Arthur Wellesley (1769–1852), 1st duke of Wellington, Dublin-born hero of the British army. The obelisk stands in Dublin's Phoenix Park.
2. In Greek mythology Paris was selected by Zeus to choose which of three goddesses was the most beautiful. The Graces were three sister-goddesses—Aglaia, splendor; Euphrosyne, festivity; and Thalia, rejoicing—who together represented loveliness

and joy. Gabriel is making a mental note to refer to his two aunts and Mary Jane in a complimentary way.
3. This old song (beginning "Arrayed for the bridal, in beauty behold her") "is replete with long and complicated runs, requiring a sophisticated and gifted singer" (Bowen, *Musical Allusions in the Works of James Joyce,* 1974); the suggestion is that Aunt Julia was a really accomplished singer.

she released her hand from his grasp. Mr Browne extended his open hand towards her and said to those who were near him in the manner of a showman introducing a prodigy to an audience:

—Miss Julia Morkan, my latest discovery!

He was laughing very heartily at this himself when Freddy Malins turned to him and said:

—Well, Browne, if you're serious you might make a worse discovery. All I can say is I never heard her sing half so well as long as I am coming here. And that's the honest truth.

—Neither did I, said Mr Browne. I think her voice has greatly improved.

Aunt Julia shrugged her shoulders and said with meek pride:

—Thirty years ago I hadn't a bad voice as voices go.

—I often told Julia, said Aunt Kate emphatically, that she was simply thrown away in that choir. But she never would be said by me.

She turned as if to appeal to the good sense of the others against a refractory child while Aunt Julia gazed in front of her, a vague smile of reminiscence playing on her face.

—No, continued Aunt Kate, she wouldn't be said or led by anyone, slaving there in that choir night and day, night and day. Six o'clock on Christmas morning! And all for what?

—Well, isn't it for the honour of God, Aunt Kate? asked Mary Jane, twisting round on the piano-stool and smiling.

Aunt Kate turned fiercely on her niece and said:

—I know all about the honour of God, Mary Jane, but I think it's not at all honourable for the pope to turn out the women out of the choirs that have slaved there all their lives and put little whipper-snappers of boys over their heads. I suppose it is for the good of the Church if the pope does it. But it's not just, Mary Jane, and it's not right.

She had worked herself into a passion and would have continued in defence of her sister for it was a sore subject with her but Mary Jane, seeing that all the dancers had come back, intervened pacifically:

—Now, Aunt Kate, you're giving scandal to Mr Browne who is of the other persuasion.[4]

Aunt Kate turned to Mr Browne, who was grinning at this allusion to his religion, and said hastily:

—O, I don't question the pope's being right. I'm only a stupid old woman and I wouldn't presume to do such a thing. But there's such a thing as common everyday politeness and gratitude. And if I were in Julia's place I'd tell that Father Healy straight up to his face . . .

—And besides, Aunt Kate, said Mary Jane, we really are all hungry and when we are hungry we are all very quarrelsome.

—And when we are thirsty we are also quarrelsome, added Mr Browne.

—So that we had better go to supper, said Mary Jane, and finish the discussion afterwards.

On the landing outside the drawing-room Gabriel found his wife and Mary Jane trying to persuade Miss Ivors to stay for supper. But Miss Ivors, who had put on her hat and was buttoning her cloak, would not stay. She did not feel in the least hungry and she had already overstayed her time.

—But only for ten minutes, Molly, said Mrs Conroy. That won't delay you.

---

4. I.e., Protestant.

—To take a pick itself, said Mary Jane, after all your dancing.

—I really couldn't, said Miss Ivors.

—I am afraid you didn't enjoy yourself at all, said Mary Jane hopelessly.

—Ever so much, I assure you, said Miss Ivors, but you really must let me run off now.

—But how can you get home? asked Mrs Conroy.

—O, it's only two steps up the quay.

Gabriel hesitated a moment and said:

—If you will allow me, Miss Ivors, I'll see you home if you really are obliged to go.

But Miss Ivors broke away from them.

—I won't hear of it, she cried. For goodness sake go in to your suppers and don't mind me. I'm quite well able to take care of myself.

—Well, you're the comical girl, Molly, said Mrs Conroy frankly.

—*Beannacht libh,*[5] cried Miss Ivors, with a laugh, as she ran down the staircase.

Mary Jane gazed after her, a moody puzzled expression on her face, while Mrs Conroy leaned over the banisters to listen for the hall-door. Gabriel asked himself was he the cause of her abrupt departure. But she did not seem to be in ill humour: she had gone away laughing. He stared blankly down the staircase.

At that moment Aunt Kate came toddling out of the supper-room, almost wringing her hands in despair.

—Where is Gabriel? she cried. Where on earth is Gabriel? There's everyone waiting in there, stage to let, and nobody to carve the goose!

—Here I am, Aunt Kate! cried Gabriel, with sudden animation, ready to carve a flock of geese, if necessary.

A fat brown goose lay at one end of the table and at the other end, on a bed of creased paper strewn with sprigs of parsley, lay a great ham, stripped of its outer skin and peppered over with crust crumbs, a neat paper frill round its shin and beside this was a round of spiced beef. Between these rival ends ran parallel lines of side-dishes: two little minsters of jelly, red and yellow; a shallow dish full of blocks of blancmange[6] and red jam, a large green leaf-shaped dish with a stalk-shaped handle, on which lay bunches of purple raisins and peeled almonds, a companion dish on which lay a solid rectangle of Smyrna figs, a dish of custard topped with grated nutmeg, a small bowl full of chocolates and sweets wrapped in gold and silver papers and a glass vase in which stood some tall celery stalks. In the centre of the table there stood, as sentries to a fruit-stand which upheld a pyramid of oranges and American apples, two squat old-fashioned decanters of cut glass, one containing port and the other dark sherry. On the closed square piano a pudding in a huge yellow dish lay in waiting and behind it were three squads of bottles of stout and ale and minerals, drawn up according to the colours of their uniforms, the first two black, with brown and red labels, the third and smallest squad white, with transverse green sashes.

Gabriel took his seat boldly at the head of the table and, having looked to the edge of the carver, plunged his fork firmly into the goose. He felt quite at ease now for he was an expert carver and liked nothing better than to find himself at the head of a well-laden table.

---

5. Blessing on you (Gaelic; literal trans.); goodbye.   6. Sweet almond-flavored pudding.

—Miss Furlong, what shall I send you? he asked. A wing or a slice of the breast?

—Just a small slice of the breast.

—Miss Higgins, what for you?

—O, anything at all, Mr Conroy.

While Gabriel and Miss Daly exchanged plates of goose and plates of ham and spiced beef Lily went from guest to guest with a dish of hot floury potatoes wrapped in a white napkin. This was Mary Jane's idea and she had also suggested apple sauce for the goose but Aunt Kate had said that plain roast goose without apple sauce had always been good enough for her and she hoped she might never eat worse. Mary Jane waited on her pupils and saw that they got the best slices and Aunt Kate and Aunt Julia opened and carried across from the piano bottles of stout and ale for the gentlemen and bottles of minerals for the ladies. There was a great deal of confusion and laughter and noise, the noise of orders and counter-orders, of knives and forks, of corks and glass-stoppers. Gabriel began to carve second helpings as soon as he had finished the first round without serving himself. Everyone protested loudly so that he compromised by taking a long draught of stout for he had found the carving hot work. Mary Jane settled down quietly to her supper but Aunt Kate and Aunt Julia were still toddling round the table, walking on each other's heels, getting in each other's way and giving each other unheeded orders. Mr Browne begged of them to sit down and eat their suppers and so did Gabriel but they said there was time enough so that, at last, Freddy Malins stood up and, capturing Aunt Kate, plumped her down on her chair amid general laughter.

When everyone had been well served Gabriel said, smiling:

—Now, if anyone wants a little more of what vulgar people call stuffing let him or her speak.

A chorus of voices invited him to begin his own supper and Lily came forward with three potatoes which she had reserved for him.

—Very well, said Gabriel amiably, as he took another preparatory draught, kindly forget my existence, ladies and gentlemen, for a few minutes.

He set to his supper and took no part in the conversation with which the table covered Lily's removal of the plates. The subject of talk was the opera company which was then at the Theatre Royal. Mr Bartell D'Arcy, the tenor, a dark-complexioned young man with a smart moustache, praised very highly the leading contralto of the company but Miss Furlong thought she had a rather vulgar style of production. Freddy Malins said there was a negro chieftain singing in the second part of the Gaiety pantomime who had one of the finest tenor voices he had every heard.

—Have you heard him? he asked Mr Bartell D'Arcy across the table.

—No, answered Mr Bartell D'Arcy carelessly.

—Because, Freddy Malins explained, now I'd be curious to hear your opinion of him. I think he has a grand voice.

—It takes Teddy to find out the really good things, said Mr Browne familiarly to the table.

—And why couldn't he have a voice too? asked Freddy Malins sharply. Is it because he's only a black?

Nobody answered this question and Mary Jane led the table back to the legitimate opera. One of her pupils had given her a pass for *Mignon*.[7] Of course it was very fine, she said, but it made her think of poor Georgina Burns. Mr

---

7. Opera by Ambroise Thomas first produced in Paris in 1866 and in London in 1870.

Browne could go back farther still, to the old Italian companies that used to come to Dublin—Tietjens, Ilma de Murzka, Campanini, the great Trebelli, Giuglini, Ravelli, Aramburo. Those were the days, he said, when there was something like singing to be heard in Dublin. He told too of how the top gallery of the old Royal used to be packed night after night, of how one night an Italian tenor had sung five encores to Let Me Like a Soldier Fall,[8] introducing a high C every time, and of how the gallery boys would sometimes in their enthusiasm unyoke the horses from the carriage of some great *prima donna* and pull her themselves through the streets to her hotel. Why did they never play the grand old operas now, he asked, *Dinorah, Lucrezia Borgia?*[9] Because they could not get the voices to sing them: that was why.

—O, well, said Mr Bartell D'Arcy, I presume there are as good singers to-day as there were then.

—Where are they? asked Mr Browne defiantly.

—In London, Paris, Milan, said Mr Bartell d'Arcy warmly. I suppose Caruso,[1] for example, is quite as good, if not better than any of the men you have mentioned.

—Maybe so, said Mr Browne. But I may tell you I doubt it strongly.

—O, I'd give anything to hear Caruso sing, said Mary Jane.

—For me, said Aunt Kate, who had been picking a bone, there was only one tenor. To please me, I mean. But I suppose none of you ever heard of him.

—Who was he, Miss Morkan? asked Mr Bartell D'Arcy politely.

—His name, said Aunt Kate, was Parkinson. I heard him when he was in his prime and I think he had then the purest tenor voice that was ever put into a man's throat.

—Strange, said Mr Bartell d'Arcy. I never even heard of him.

—Yes, yes, Miss Morkan is right, said Mr Browne. I remember hearing of old Parkinson but he's too far back for me.

—A beautiful pure sweet mellow English tenor, said Aunt Kate with enthusiasm.

Gabriel having finished, the huge pudding was transferred to the table. The clatter of forks and spoons began again. Gabriel's wife served out spoonfuls of the pudding and passed the plates down the table. Midway down they were held up by Mary Jane, who replenished them with raspberry or orange jelly or with blancmange and jam. The pudding was of Aunt Julia's making and she received praises for it from all quarters. She herself said that it was not quite brown enough.

—Well, I hope, Miss Morkan, said Mr Browne, that I'm brown enough for you because, you know, I'm all brown.

All the gentlemen, except Gabriel, ate some of the pudding out of compliment to Aunt Julia. As Gabriel never ate sweets the celery had been left for him. Freddy Malins also took a stalk of celery and ate it with his pudding. He had been told that celery was a capital thing for the blood and he was just then under doctor's care. Mrs Malins, who had been silent all through the

8. This song, from the opera *Maritana* by W. Wallace (it actually begins "Yes! let me like a soldier fall"), ends on middle C; it would be a piece of exhibitionism to end on a high C, as Joyce's father, who had a good voice, used to do. Joyce's brother Stanislaus remembered the song as insufferable rubbish. Mr. Browne is not to be taken seriously as a music critic.
9. An opera by Donizetti, first produced at La Scala, Milan, in 1833. *Dinorah* is an opera by Meyerbeer, first produced in Paris in 1859.
1. Enrico Caruso (1873–1921), the great Italian dramatic tenor.

supper, said that her son was going down to Mount Melleray in a week or so. The table then spoke of Mount Melleray, how bracing the air was down there, how hospitable the monks were and how they never asked for a penny-piece from their guests.

—And do you mean to say, asked Mr Browne incredulously, that a chap can go down there and put up there as if it were a hotel and live on the fat of the land and then come away without paying a farthing?

—O, most people give some donation to the monastery when they leave, said Mary Jane.

—I wish we had an institution like that in our Church, said Mr Browne candidly.

He was astonished to hear that the monks never spoke, got up at two in the morning and slept in their coffins. He asked what they did it for.

—That's the rule of the order, said Aunt Kate firmly.

—Yes, but why? asked Mr Browne.

Aunt Kate repeated that it was the rule, that was all. Mr Browne still seemed not to understand. Freddy Malins explained to him, as best he could, that the monks were trying to make up for the sins committed by all the sinners in the outside world. The explanation was not very clear for Mr Browne grinned and said:

—I like that idea very much but wouldn't a comfortable spring bed do them as well as a coffin?

—The coffin, said Mary Jane, is to remind them of their last end.

As the subject had grown lugubrious it was buried in a silence of the table during which Mrs Malins could be heard saying to her neighbour in an indistinct undertone:

—They are very good men, the monks, very pious men.

The raisins and almonds and figs and apples and oranges and chocolates and sweets were now passed about the table and Aunt Julia invited all the guests to have either port or sherry. At first Mr Bartell D'Arcy refused to take either but one of his neighbours nudged him and whispered something to him upon which he allowed his glass to be filled. Gradually as the last glasses were being filled the conversation ceased. A pause followed, broken only by the noise of the wine and by unsettlings of chairs. The Misses Morkan, all three, looked down at the tablecloth. Someone coughed once or twice and then a few gentlemen patted the table gently as a signal for silence. The silence came and Gabriel pushed back his chair and stood up.

The patting at once grew louder in encouragement and then ceased altogether. Gabriel leaned his ten trembling fingers on the tablecloth and smiled nervously at the company. Meeting a row of upturned faces he raised his eyes to the chandelier. The piano was playing a waltz tune and he could hear the skirts sweeping against the drawing-room door. People, perhaps, were standing in the snow on the quay outside, gazing up at the lighted windows and listening to the waltz music. The air was pure there. In the distance lay the park where the trees were weighted with snow. The Wellington Monument wore a gleaming cap of snow that flashed westward over the white field of Fifteen Acres.

He began:

—Ladies and Gentlemen.

—It has fallen to my lot this evening, as in years past, to perform a very pleasing task but a task for which I am afraid my poor powers as a speaker are all too inadequate.

—No, no! said Mr Browne.

—But, however that may be, I can only ask you to-night to take the will for the deed and to lend me your attention for a few moments while I endeavour to express to you in words what my feelings are on this occasion.

—Ladies and Gentlemen. It is not the first time that we have gathered together under this hospitable roof, around this hospitable board. It is not the first time that we have been the recipients—or perhaps, I had better say, the victims—of the hospitality of certain good ladies.

He made a circle in the air with his arm and paused. Everyone laughed or smiled at Aunt Kate and Aunt Julia and Mary Jane who all turned crimson with pleasure. Gabriel went on more boldly:

—I feel more strongly with every recurring year that our country has no tradition which does it so much honour and which it should guard so jealously as that of its hospitality. It is a tradition that is unique as far as my experience goes (and I have visited not a few places abroad) among the modern nations. Some would say, perhaps, that with us it is rather a failing than anything to be boasted of. But granted even that, it is, to my mind, a princely failing, and one that I trust will long be cultivated among us. Of one thing, at least, I am sure. As long as this one roof shelters the good ladies aforesaid—and I wish from my heart it may do so for many and many a long year to come—the tradition of genuine warm-hearted courteous Irish hospitality, which our fore-fathers have handed down to us and which we in turn must hand down to our descendants, is still alive among us.

A hearty murmur of assent ran round the table. It shot through Gabriel's mind that Miss Ivors was not there and that she had gone away discourteously: and he said with confidence in himself:

—Ladies and Gentlemen.

—A new generation is growing up in our midst, a generation actuated by new ideas and new principles. It is serious and enthusiastic for these new ideas and its enthusiasm, even when it is misdirected, is, I believe, in the main sincere. But we are living in a sceptical and, if I may use the phrase, a thought-tormented age: and sometimes I fear that this new generation, educated or hypereducated as it is, will lack those qualities of humanity, of hospitality, of kindly humour which belonged to an older day. Listening to-night to the names of all those great singers of the past it seemed to me, I must confess, that we were living in a less spacious age. Those days might, without exaggeration, be called spacious days: and if they are gone beyond recall let us hope, at least, that in gatherings such as this we shall still speak of them with pride and affection, still cherish in our hearts the memory of those dead and gone great ones whose fame the world will not willingly let die.

—Hear, hear! said Mr Browne loudly.

—But yet, continued Gabriel, his voice falling into a softer inflection, there are always in gatherings such as this sadder thoughts that will recur to our minds: thoughts of the past, of youth, of changes, of absent faces that we miss here to-night. Our path through life is strewn with many such sad memories: and were we to brood upon them always we could not find the heart to go on bravely with our work among the living. We have all of us living duties and living affections which claim, and rightly claim, our strenuous endeavours.

—Therefore, I will not linger on the past. I will not let any gloomy moralising intrude upon us here to-night. Here we are gathered together for a brief moment from the bustle and rush of our everyday routine. We are met here as friends, in the spirit of good-fellowship, as colleagues, also to a certain extent, in the true spirit of *camaraderie*, and as the guests of—what shall I call them?—the Three Graces of the Dublin musical world.

The table burst into applause and laughter at this sally. Aunt Julia vainly asked each of her neighbours in turn to tell her what Gabriel had said.

—He says we are the Three Graces,[2] Aunt Julia, said Mary Jane.

Aunt Julia did not understand but she looked up, smiling, at Gabriel, who continued in the same vein:

—Ladies and Gentlemen.

—I will not attempt to play to-night the part that Paris played on another occasion. I will not attempt to choose between them. The task would be an invidious one and one beyond my poor powers. For when I view them in turn, whether it be our chief hostess herself, whose good heart, whose too good heart, has become a byword with all who know her, or her sister, who seems to be gifted with perennial youth and whose singing must have been a surprise and a revelation to us all to-night, or, last but not least, when I consider our youngest hostess, talented, cheerful, hard-working and the best of nieces, I confess, Ladies and Gentlemen, that I do not know to which of them I should award the prize.

Gabriel glanced down at his aunts and, seeing the large smile on Aunt Julia's face and the tears which had risen to Aunt Kate's eyes, hastened to his close. He raised his glass of port gallantly, while every member of the company fingered a glass expectantly, and said loudly:

—Let us toast them all three together. Let us drink to their health, wealth, long life, happiness and prosperity and may they long continue to hold the proud and self-won position which they hold in their profession and the position of honour and affection which they hold in our hearts.

All the guests stood up, glass in hand, and, turning towards the three seated ladies, sang in unison, with Mr Browne as leader:

> *For they are jolly gay fellows,*
> *For they are jolly gay fellows,*
> *For they are jolly gay fellows,*
> *Which nobody can deny.*

Aunt Kate was making frank use of her handkerchief and even Aunt Julia seemed moved. Freddy Malins beat time with his pudding-fork and the singers turned towards one another, as if in melodious conference, while they sang, with emphasis:

> *Unless he tells a lie,*
> *Unless he tells a lie.*

Then, turning once more towards their hostesses, they sang:

> *For they are jolly gay fellows,*
> *For they are jolly gay fellows,*
> *For they are jolly gay fellows,*
> *Which nobody can deny.*

The acclamation which followed was taken up beyond the door of the supper-room by many of the other guests and renewed time after time, Freddy Malins acting as officer with his fork on high.

---

2. See n. 2, p. 2182.

The piercing morning air came into the hall where they were standing so that Aunt Kate said:

—Close the door, somebody. Mrs Malins will get her death of cold.

—Browne is out there, Aunt Kate, said Mary Jane.

—Browne is everywhere, said Aunt Kate, lowering her voice.

Mary Jane laughed at her tone.

—Really, she said archly, he is very attentive.

—He has been laid on here like the gas, said Aunt Kate in the same tone, all during the Christmas.

She laughed herself this time good-humouredly and then added quickly:

—But tell him to come in, Mary Jane, and close the door. I hope to goodness he didn't hear me.

At that moment the hall-door was opened and Mr Browne came in from the doorstep, laughing as if his heart would break. He was dressed in a long green overcoat with mock astrakhan cuffs and collar and wore on his head an oval fur cap. He pointed down the snow-covered quay from where the sound of shrill prolonged whistling was borne in.

—Teddy will have all the cabs in Dublin out, he said.

Gabriel advanced from the little pantry behind the office, struggling into his overcoat and, looking round the hall, said:

—Gretta not down yet?

—She's getting on her things, Gabriel, said Aunt Kate.

—Who's playing up there? asked Gabriel.

—Nobody. They're all gone.

—O no, Aunt Kate, said Mary Jane. Bartell D'Arcy and Miss O'Callaghan aren't gone yet.

—Someone is strumming at the piano, anyhow, said Gabriel.

Mary Jane glanced at Gabriel and Mr Browne and said with a shiver:

—It makes me feel cold to look at you two gentlemen muffled up like that. I wouldn't like to face your journey home at this hour.

—I'd like nothing better this minute, said Mr Browne stoutly, than a rattling fine walk in the country or a fast drive with a good spanking goer between the shafts.

—We used to have a very good horse and trap[3] at home, said Aunt Julia sadly.

—The never-to-be-forgotten Johnny, said Mary Jane, laughing.

Aunt Kate and Gabriel laughed too.

—Why, what was wonderful about Johnny? asked Mr Browne.

—The late lamented Patrick Morkan, our grandfather, that is, explained Gabriel, commonly known in his later years as the old gentleman, was a glue-boiler.[4]

—O, now, Gabriel, said Aunt Kate, laughing, he had a starch mill.

—Well, glue or starch, said Gabriel, the old gentleman had a horse by the name of Johnny. And Johnny used to work in the old gentleman's mill, walking round and round in order to drive the mill. That was all very well; but now comes the tragic part about Johnny. One fine day the old gentleman thought he'd like to drive out with the quality[5] to a military review in the park.

—The Lord have mercy on his soul, said Aunt Kate compassionately.

3. A two-wheeled horse-drawn carriage on springs.
4. Glue was made by boiling animal hides and hoofs.
5. People of rank or high social position.

—Amen, said Gabriel. So the old gentleman, as I said, harnessed Johnny and put on his very best tall hat and his very best stock collar and drove out in grand style from his ancestral mansion somewhere near Back Lane, I think.

Everyone laughed, even Mrs Malins, at Gabriel's manner and Aunt Kate said:

—O now, Gabriel, he didn't live in Back Lane, really. Only the mill was there.

—Out from the mansion of his forefathers, continued Gabriel, he drove with Johnny. And everything went on beautifully until Johnny came in sight of King Billy's statue:[6] and whether he fell in love with the horse King Billy sits on or whether he thought he was back again in the mill, anyhow he began to walk round the statue.

Gabriel paced in a circle round the hall in his goloshes amid the laughter of the others.

—Round and round he went, said Gabriel, and the old gentleman, who was a very pompous old gentleman, was highly indignant. *Go on, sir! What do you mean, sir? Johnny! Johnny! Most extraordinary conduct! Can't understand the horse!*

The peals of laughter which followed Gabriel's imitation of the incident were interrupted by a resounding knock at the hall-door. Mary Jane ran to open it and let in Freddy Malins. Freddy Malins, with his hat well back on his head and his shoulders humped with cold, was puffing and steaming after his exertions.

—I could only get one cab, he said.

—O, we'll find another along the quay, said Gabriel.

—Yes, said Aunt Kate. Better not keep Mrs Malins standing in the draught.

Mrs Malins was helped down the front steps by her son and Mr Browne and, after many manœuvres, hoisted into the cab. Freddy Malins clambered in after her and spent a long time settling her on the seat, Mr Browne helping him with advice. At last she was settled comfortably and Freddy Malins invited Mr Browne into the cab. There was a good deal of confused talk, and then Mr Browne got into the cab. The cabman settled his rug over his knees, and bent down for the address. The confusion grew greater and the cabman was directed differently by Freddy Malins and Mr Browne, each of whom had his head out through a window of the cab. The difficulty was to know where to drop Mr Browne along the route and Aunt Kate, Aunt Julia and Mary Jane helped the discussion from the doorstep with cross-directions and contradictions and abundance of laughter. As for Freddy Malins he was speechless with laughter. He popped his head in and out of the window every moment, to the great danger of his hat, and told his mother how the discussion was progressing till at last Mr Browne shouted to the bewildered cabman above the din of everybody's laughter:

—Do you know Trinity College?

—Yes, sir, said the cabman.

—Well, drive bang up against Trinity College gates, said Mr Browne, and then we'll tell you where to go. You understand now?

—Yes, sir, said the cabman.

—Make like a bird for Trinity College.

—Right, sir, cried the cabman.

6. Statue of King William III of England in front of Trinity College, Dublin. He defeated predominantly Irish Catholic forces in the 1690 Battle of the Boyne.

The horse was whipped up and the cab rattled off along the quay amid a chorus of laughter and adieus.

Gabriel had not gone to the door with the others. He was in a dark part of the hall gazing up the staircase. A woman was standing near the top of the first flight, in the shadow also. He could not see her face but he could see the terracotta and salmonpink panels of her skirt which the shadow made appear black and white. It was his wife. She was leaning on the banisters, listening to something. Gabriel was surprised at her stillness and strained his ear to listen also. But he could hear little save the noise of laughter and dispute on the front steps, a few chords struck on the piano and a few notes of a man's voice singing.

He stood still in the gloom of the hall, trying to catch the air that the voice was singing and gazing up at his wife. There was grace and mystery in her attitude as if she were a symbol of something. He asked himself what is a woman standing on the stairs in the shadow, listening to distant music, a symbol of. If he were a painter he would paint her in that attitude. Her blue felt hat would show off the bronze of her hair against the darkness and the dark panels of her skirt would show off the light ones. *Distant Music* he would call the picture if he were a painter.

The hall-door was closed; and Aunt Kate, Aunt Julia and Mary Jane came down the hall, still laughing.

—Well, isn't Freddy terrible? said Mary Jane. He's really terrible.

Gabriel said nothing but pointed up the stairs towards where his wife was standing. Now that the hall-door was closed the voice and the piano could be heard more clearly. Gabriel held up his hand for them to be silent. The song seemed to be in the old Irish tonality and the singer seemed uncertain both of his words and of his voice. The voice, made plaintive by distance and by the singer's hoarseness, faintly illuminated the cadence of the air with words expressing grief:

> *O, the rain falls on my heavy locks*
> *And the dew wets my skin,*
> *My babe lies cold . . .*

—O, exclaimed Mary Jane. It's Bartell D'Arcy singing and he wouldn't sing all the night. O, I'll get him to sing a song before he goes.

—O do, Mary Jane, said Aunt Kate.

Mary Jane brushed past the others and ran to the staircase but before she reached it the singing stopped and the piano was closed abruptly.

—O, what a pity! she cried. Is he coming down, Gretta?

Gabriel heard his wife answer yes and saw her come down towards them. A few steps behind her were Mr Bartell D'Arcy and Miss O'Callaghan.

—O, Mr D'Arcy, cried Mary Jane, it's downright mean of you to break off like that when we were all in raptures listening to you.

—I have been at him all the evening, said Miss O'Callaghan, and Mrs Conroy too and he told us he had a dreadful cold and couldn't sing.

—O, Mr D'Arcy, said Aunt Kate, now that was a great fib to tell.

—Can't you see that I'm as hoarse as a crow? said Mr D'Arcy roughly.

He went into the pantry hastily and put on his overcoat. The others, taken aback by his rude speech, could find nothing to say. Aunt Kate wrinkled her brows and made signs to the others to drop the subject. Mr D'Arcy stood swathing his neck carefully and frowning.

—It's the weather, said Aunt Julia, after a pause.

—Yes, everybody has colds, said Aunt Kate readily, everybody.

—They say, said Mary Jane, we haven't had snow like it for thirty years; and I read this morning in the newspapers that the snow is general all over Ireland.

—I love the look of snow, said Aunt Julia sadly.

—So do I, said Miss O'Callaghan. I think Christmas is never really Christmas unless we have the snow on the ground.

—But poor Mr D'Arcy doesn't like the snow, said Aunt Kate, smiling.

Mr D'Arcy came from the pantry, full swathed and buttoned, and in a repentant tone told them the history of his cold. Everyone gave him advice and said it was a great pity and urged him to be very careful of his throat in the night air. Gabriel watched his wife who did not join in the conversation. She was standing right under the dusty fanlight and the flame of the gas lit up the rich bronze of her hair which he had seen her drying at the fire a few days before. She was in the same attitude and seemed unaware of the talk about her. At last she turned towards them and Gabriel saw that there was colour on her cheeks and that her eyes were shining. A sudden tide of joy went leaping out of his heart.

—Mr D'Arcy, she said, what is the name of that song you were singing?

—It's called *The Lass of Aughrim*,[7] said Mr D'Arcy, but I couldn't remember it properly. Why? Do you know it?

—*The Lass of Aughrim*, she repeated. I couldn't think of the name.

—It's a very nice air, said Mary Jane. I'm sorry you were not in voice tonight.

—Now, Mary Jane, said Aunt Kate, don't annoy Mr D'Arcy. I won't have him annoyed.

Seeing that all were ready to start she shepherded them to the door where good-night was said:

—Well, good-night, Aunt Kate, and thanks for the pleasant evening.

—Good-night, Gabriel. Good-night, Gretta!

—Good-night, Aunt Kate, and thanks ever so much. Good-night, Aunt Julia.

—O, good-night, Gretta, I didn't see you.

—Good-night, Mr D'Arcy. Good-night, Miss O'Callaghan.

—Good-night, Miss Morkan.

—Good-night, again.

—Good-night, all. Safe home.

—Good-night. Good-night.

The morning was still dark. A dull yellow light brooded over the houses and the river; and the sky seemed to be descending. It was slushy underfoot; and only streaks and patches of snow lay on the roofs, on the parapets of the quay and on the area railings. The lamps were still burning redly in the murky air and, across the river, the palace of the Four Courts stood out menacingly against the heavy sky.

She was walking on before him with Mr Bartell D'Arcy, her shoes in a brown parcel tucked under one arm and her hands holding her skirt up from the slush. She had no longer any grace of attitude but Gabriel's eyes were still bright with happiness. The blood went bounding along his veins; and the thoughts went rioting through his brain, proud, joyful, tender, valorous.

7. An Irish version of a ballad about a girl deserted by her lover, whom she later tries to find, bringing the baby she had by him. Other versions are called "Love Gregory" and "Lord Gregory" (the name of the deserting lover), "The Lass of Lochryan," and "The Lass of Ocram."

She was walking on before him so lightly and so erect that he longed to run after her noiselessly, catch her by the shoulders and say something foolish and affectionate into her ear. She seemed to him so frail that he longed to defend her against something and then to be alone with her. Moments of their secret life together burst like stars upon his memory. A heliotrope[8] envelope was lying beside his breakfast-cup and he was caressing it with his hand. Birds were twittering in the ivy and the sunny web of the curtain was shimmering along the floor: he could not eat for happiness. They were standing on the crowded platform and he was placing a ticket inside the warm palm of her glove. He was standing with her in the cold, looking in through a grated window at a man making bottles in a roaring furnace. It was very cold. Her face, fragrant in the cold air, was quite close to his; and suddenly she called out to the man at the furnace:

—Is the fire hot, sir?

But the man could not hear her with the noise of the furnace. It was just as well. He might have answered rudely.

A wave of yet more tender joy escaped from his heart and went coursing in warm flood along his arteries. Like the tender fires of stars moments of their life together, that no one knew of or would ever know of, broke upon and illumined his memory. He longed to recall to her those moments, to make her forget the years of their dull existence together and remember only their moments of ecstasy. For the years, he felt, had not quenched his soul or hers. Their children, his writing, her household cares had not quenched all their souls' tender fire. In one letter that he had written to her then he had said: *Why is it that words like these seem to me so dull and cold? Is it because there is no word tender enough to be your name?*

Like distant music these words that he had written years before were borne towards him from the past. He longed to be alone with her. When the others had gone away, when he and she were in their room in the hotel, then they would be alone together. He would call her softly:

—Gretta!

Perhaps she would not hear at once: she would be undressing. Then something in his voice would strike her. She would turn and look at him. . . .

At the corner of Winetavern Street they met a cab. He was glad of its rattling noise as it saved him from conversation. She was looking out of the window and seemed tired. The others spoke only a few words, pointing out some building or street. The horse galloped along wearily under the murky morning sky, dragging his old rattling box after his heels, and Gabriel was again in a cab with her, galloping to catch the boat, galloping to their honeymoon.

As the cab drove across O'Connell[9] Bridge Miss O'Callaghan said:

—They say you never cross O'Connell Bridge without seeing a white horse.

—I see a white man this time, said Gabriel.

—Where? asked Mr Bartell D'Arcy.

Gabriel pointed to the statue, on which lay patches of snow. Then he nodded familiarly to it and waved his hand.

—Good-night, Dan, he said gaily.

When the cab drew up before the hotel Gabriel jumped out and, in spite of Mr Bartell D'Arcy's protest, paid the driver. He gave the man a shilling over his fare. The man saluted and said:

8. Grayish purple.
9. Daniel O'Connell (1775–1847), Irish nation-
alist, statesman, and orator. His statue stands by O'Connell Bridge in Dublin.

—A prosperous New Year to you, sir.

—The same to you, said Gabriel cordially.

She leaned for a moment on his arm in getting out of the cab and while standing at the curbstone, bidding the others good-night. She leaned lightly on his arm, as lightly as when she had danced with him a few hours before. He had felt proud and happy then, happy that she was his, proud of her grace and wifely carriage. But now, after the kindling again of so many memories, the first touch of her body, musical and strange and perfumed, sent through him a keen pang of lust. Under cover of her silence he pressed her arm closely to his side; and, as they stood at the hotel door, he felt that they had escaped from their lives and duties, escaped from home and friends and run away together with wild and radiant hearts to a new adventure.

An old man was dozing in a great hooded chair in the hall. He lit a candle in the office and went before them to the stairs. They followed him in silence, their feet falling in soft thuds on the thickly carpeted stairs. She mounted the stairs behind the porter, her head bowed in the ascent, her frail shoulders curved as with a burden, her skirt girt tightly about her. He could have flung his arms about her hips and held her still for his arms were trembling with desire to seize her and only the stress of his nails against the palms of his hands held the wild impulse of his body in check. The porter halted on the stairs to settle his guttering candle. They halted too on the steps below him. In the silence Gabriel could hear the falling of the molten wax into the tray and the thumping of his own heart against his ribs.

The porter led them along a corridor and opened a door. Then he set his unstable candle down on a toilet-table and asked at what hour they were to be called in the morning.

—Eight, said Gabriel.

The porter pointed to the tap of the electric-light and began a muttered apology but Gabriel cut him short.

—We don't want any light. We have light enough from the street. And I say, he added, pointing to the candle, you might remove that handsome article, like a good man.

The porter took up his candle again, but slowly for he was surprised by such a novel idea. Then he mumbled good-night and went out. Gabriel shot the lock to.

A ghostly light from the street lamp lay in a long shaft from one window to the door. Gabriel threw his overcoat and hat on a couch and crossed the room towards the window. He looked down into the street in order that his emotion might calm a little. Then he turned and leaned against a chest of drawers with his back to the light. She had taken off her hat and cloak and was standing before a large swinging mirror, unhooking her waist.[1] Gabriel paused for a few moments, watching her, and then said:

—Gretta!

She turned away from the mirror slowly and walked along the shaft of light towards him. Her face looked so serious and weary that the words would not pass Gabriel's lips. No, it was not the moment yet.

—You looked tired, he said.

—I am a little, she answered.

—You don't feel ill or weak?

—No, tired: that's all.

1. Shirtwaist; a tailored blouse.

She went on to the window and stood there, looking out. Gabriel waited again and then, fearing that diffidence was about to conquer him, he said abruptly:

—By the way, Gretta!

—What is it?

—You know that poor fellow Malins? he said quickly.

—Yes. What about him?

—Well, poor fellow, he's a decent sort of chap after all, continued Gabriel in a false voice. He gave me back that sovereign I lent him and I didn't expect it really. It's a pity he wouldn't keep away from that Browne, because he's not a bad fellow at heart.

He was trembling now with annoyance. Why did she seem so abstracted? He did not know how he could begin. Was she annoyed, too, about something? If she would only turn to him or come to him of her own accord! To take her as she was would be brutal. No, he must see some ardour in her eyes first. He longed to be master of her strange mood.

—When did you lend him the pound? she asked, after a pause.

Gabriel strove to restrain himself from breaking out into brutal language about the sottish Malins and his pound. He longed to cry to her from his soul, to crush her body against his, to overmaster her. But he said:

—O, at Christmas, when he opened that little Christmas-card shop in Henry Street.

He was in such a fever of rage and desire that he did not hear her come from the window. She stood before him for an instant, looking at him strangely. Then, suddenly raising herself on tiptoe and resting her hands lightly on his shoulders, she kissed him.

—You are a very generous person, Gabriel, she said.

Gabriel, trembling with delight at her sudden kiss and at the quaintness of her phrase, put his hands on her hair and began smoothing it back, scarcely touching with his fingers. The washing had made it fine and brilliant. His heart was brimming over with happiness. Just when he was wishing for it she had come to him of her own accord. Perhaps her thoughts had been running with his. Perhaps she had felt the impetuous desire that was in him and then the yielding mood had come upon her. Now that she had fallen to him so easily he wondered why he had been so diffident.

He stood, holding her head between his hands. Then, slipping one arm swiftly about her body and drawing her towards him, he said softly:

—Gretta dear, what are you thinking about?

She did not answer nor yield wholly to his arm. He said again, softly:

—Tell me what it is, Gretta. I think I know what is the matter. Do I know?

She did not answer at once. Then she said in an outburst of tears:

—O, I am thinking about that song, *The Lass of Aughrim*.

She broke loose from him and ran to the bed and, throwing her arms across the bed-rail, hid her face. Gabriel stood stock-still for a moment in astonishment and then followed her. As he passed in the way of the cheval-glass[2] he caught sight of himself in full length, his broad, well-filled shirt-front, the face whose expression always puzzled him when he saw it in a mirror and his glimmering gilt-rimmed eyeglasses. He halted a few paces from her and said:

—What about the song? Why does that make you cry?

2. Full-length mirror that can be tilted.

She raised her head from her arms and dried her eyes with the back of her hand like a child. A kinder note than he had intended went into his voice.

—Why, Gretta? he asked.

—I am thinking about a person long ago who used to sing that song.

—And who was the person long ago? asked Gabriel, smiling.

—It was a person I used to know in Galway when I was living with my grandmother, she said.

The smile passed away from Gabriel's face. A dull anger began to gather again at the back of his mind and the dull fires of his lust began to glow angrily in his veins.

—Someone you were in love with? he asked ironically.

—It was a young boy I used to know, she answered, named Michael Furey. He used to sing that song, *The Lass of Aughrim.* He was very delicate.

Gabriel was silent. He did not wish her to think that he was interested in this delicate boy.

—I can see him so plainly, she said after a moment. Such eyes as he had: big dark eyes! And such an expression in them—an expression!

—O then, you were in love with him? said Gabriel.

—I used to go out walking with him, she said, when I was in Galway.

A thought flew across Gabriel's mind.

—Perhaps that was why you wanted to go to Galway with that Ivors girl? he said coldly.

She looked at him and asked in surprise:

—What for?

Her eyes made Gabriel feel awkward. He shrugged his shoulders and said:

—How do I know! To see him perhaps.

She looked away from him along the shaft of light towards the window in silence.

—He is dead, she said at length. He died when he was only seventeen. Isn't it a terrible thing to die so young as that?

—What was he? asked Gabriel, still ironically.

—He was in the gasworks,[3] she said.

Gabriel felt humiliated by the failure of his irony and by the evocation of this figure from the dead, a boy in the gasworks. While he had been full of memories of their secret life together, full of tenderness and joy and desire, she had been comparing him in her mind with another. A shameful consciousness of his own person assailed him. He saw himself as a ludicrous figure, acting as a pennyboy for his aunts, a nervous well-meaning sentimentalist, orating to vulgarians and idealising his own clownish lusts, the pitiable fatuous fellow he had caught a glimpse of in the mirror. Instinctively he turned his back more to the light lest she might see the shame that burned upon his forehead.

He tried to keep up his tone of cold interrogation but his voice when he spoke was humble and indifferent.

—I suppose you were in love with this Michael Furey, Gretta, he said.

—I was great with him at that time, she said.

Her voice was veiled and sad. Gabriel, feeling now how vain it would be to try to lead her whither he had purposed, caressed one of her hands and said, also sadly:

3. Factory where coal gas for heating and lighting is produced.

—And what did he die of so young, Gretta? Consumption, was it?

—I think he died for me, she answered.

A vague terror seized Gabriel at this answer as if, at that hour when he had hoped to triumph, some impalpable and vindictive being was coming against him, gathering forces against him in its vague world. But he shook himself free of it with an effort of reason and continued to caress her hand. He did not question her again for he felt that she would tell him of herself. Her hand was warm and moist: it did not respond to his touch but he continued to caress it just as he had caressed her first letter to him that spring morning.

—It was in the winter, she said, about the beginning of the winter when I was going to leave my grandmother's and come up here to the convent. And he was ill at the time in his lodgings in Galway and wouldn't be let out and his people in Oughterard were written to. He was in decline, they said, or something like that. I never knew rightly.

She paused for a moment and sighed.

—Poor fellow, she said. He was very fond of me and he was such a gentle boy. We used to go out together, walking, you know, Gabriel, like the way they do in the country. He was going to study singing only for his health. He had a very good voice, poor Michael Furey.

—Well; and then? asked Gabriel.

—And then when it came to the time for me to leave Galway and come up to the convent he was much worse and I wouldn't be let see him so I wrote a letter saying I was going up to Dublin and would be back in the summer and hoping he would be better then.

She paused for a moment to get her voice under control and then went on:

—Then the night before I left I was in my grandmother's house in Nuns' Island, packing up, and I heard gravel thrown up against the window. The window was so wet I couldn't see so I ran downstairs as I was and slipped out the back into the garden and there was the poor fellow at the end of the garden, shivering.

—And did you not tell him to go back? asked Gabriel.

—I implored him to go home at once and told him he would get his death in the rain. But he said he did not want to live. I can see his eyes as well as well! He was standing at the end of the wall where there was a tree.

—And did he go home? asked Gabriel.

—Yes, he went home. And when I was only a week in the convent he died and he was buried in Oughterard where his people came from. O, the day I heard that, that he was dead!

She stopped, choking with sobs, and overcome by emotion, flung herself face downward on the bed, sobbing in the quilt. Gabriel held her hand for a moment longer, irresolutely, and then, shy of intruding on her grief, let it fall gently and walked quietly to the window.

She was fast asleep.

Gabriel, leaning on his elbow, looked for a few moments unresentfully on her tangled hair and half-open mouth, listening to her deep-drawn breath. So she had had that romance in her life: a man had died for her sake. It hardly pained him now to think how poor a part he, her husband, had played in her life. He watched her while she slept as though he and she had never lived together as man and wife. His curious eyes rested long upon her face and on her hair: and, as he thought of what she must have been then, in that time of her first girlish beauty, a strange friendly pity for her entered his soul. He did not like to say even to himself that her face was no longer beautiful but he knew that it was no longer the face for which Michael Furey had braved death.

Perhaps she had not told him all the story. His eyes moved to the chair over which she had thrown some of her clothes. A petticoat string dangled to the floor. One boot stood upright, its limp upper fallen down: the fellow of it lay upon its side. He wondered at his riot of emotions of an hour before. From what had it proceeded? From his aunt's supper, from his own foolish speech, from the wine and dancing, the merry-making when saying good-night in the hall, the pleasure of the walk along the river in the snow. Poor Aunt Julia! She, too, would soon be a shade with the shade of Patrick Morkan and his horse. He had caught that haggard look upon her face for a moment when she was singing *Arrayed for the Bridal*. Soon, perhaps, he would be sitting in that same drawing-room, dressed in black, his silk hat on his knees. The blinds would be drawn down and Aunt Kate would be sitting beside him, crying and blowing her nose and telling him how Julia had died. He would cast about in his mind for some words that might console her, and would find only lame and useless ones. Yes, yes: that would happen very soon.

The air of the room chilled his shoulders. He stretched himself cautiously along under the sheets and lay down beside his wife. One by one they were all becoming shades. Better pass boldly into that other world, in the full glory of some passion, than fade and wither dismally with age. He thought of how she who lay beside him had locked in her heart for so many years that image of her lover's eyes when he had told her that he did not wish to live.

Generous tears filled Gabriel's eyes. He had never felt like that himself towards any woman but he knew that such a feeling must be love. The tears gathered more thickly in his eyes and in the partial darkness he imagined he saw the form of a young man standing under a dripping tree. Other forms were near. His soul had approached that region where dwell the vast hosts of the dead. He was conscious of, but could not apprehend, their wayward and flickering existence. His own identity was fading out into a grey impalpable world: the solid world itself which these dead had one time reared and lived in was dissolving and dwindling.

A few light taps upon the pane made him turn to the window. It had begun to snow again. He watched sleepily the flakes, silver and dark, falling obliquely against the lamplight. The time had come for him to set out on his journey westward. Yes, the newspapers were right: snow was general all over Ireland. It was falling on every part of the dark central plain, on the treeless hills, falling softly upon the Bog of Allen[4] and, farther westward, softly falling into the dark mutinous Shannon waves. It was falling, too, upon every part of the lonely churchyard on the hill where Michael Furey lay buried. It lay thickly drifted on the crooked crosses and headstones, on the spears of the little gate, on the barren thorns. His soul swooned slowly as he heard the snow falling faintly through the universe and faintly falling, like the descent of their last end, upon all the living and the dead.

1914

---

4. The name given to many separate peat bogs between the rivers Liffey (which runs through Dublin) and Shannon (which runs through the central plain of Ireland).

From Ulysses[1]

[PROTEUS][2]

Ineluctable modality of the visible: at least that if no more, thought through my eyes.[3] Signatures of all things[4] I am here to read, seaspawn and seawrack, the nearing tide, that rusty boot. Snotgreen, bluesilver, rust: coloured signs. Limits of the diaphane.[5] But he adds: in bodies. Then he was aware of them bodies before of them coloured. How? By knocking his sconce against them, sure. Go easy. Bald he was and a millionaire, *maestro di color che sanno.*[6] Limit of the diaphane in. Why in? Diaphane, adiaphane.[7] If you can put your five fingers through it, it is a gate, if not a door. Shut your eyes and see.

Stephen closed his eyes to hear his boots crush crackling wrack and shells. You are walking through it howsomever. I am, a stride at a time. A very short space of time through very short times of space. Five, six: the *Nacheinander.*[8] Exactly: and that is the ineluctable modality of the audible. Open your eyes. No. Jesus! If I fell over a cliff that beetles o'er his base,[9] fell through the *Nebeneinander*[1] ineluctably. I am getting on nicely in the dark. My ash sword hangs at my side. Tap with it: they do.[2] My two feet in his boots[3] are at the

1. *Ulysses* was first published in book form on Feb. 2, 1922, Joyce's fortieth birthday. The text given here has been collated with the 1932 Odyssey Press edition.
2. "Proteus," the third of the novel's eigtheen episodes, is so titled because of the deliberate analogies that exist between it and the description of Proteus in Homer's *Odyssey* 4. (Joyce did not title any of the episodes in *Ulysses*, but the names are his; he used them in correspondence and in talk with friends.)

In the *Odyssey* Proteus is the sea god, who continually alters his shape: when Telemachus, Ulysses' son, asks Menelaus for help in finding his father, Menelaus tells him that he encountered Proteus by the seashore on the island of Pharos "in front of Égypt," and that, by holding on to him while he changed from one shape to another, he was able to force him to tell what had happened to Ulysses and the other Greek heroes of the Trojan War. In Joyce's narrative Stephen Dedalus (who, like Homer's Telemachus, is looking for a father, but not in the literal "consubstantial" sense) is walking alone by the Dublin shore, "along Sandymount strand," speculating on the shifting shapes of things and the possibility of knowing truth by appearances.

Stephen meditates first on the "modality of the visible" and on the mystical notion that the Demiurge, God's subordinate, writes his signature on all things; then on the "modality of the audible," closing his eyes and trying to know reality through the sense of hearing. As he continues his walk, the people and objects he sees mingle in his thoughts with memories of his past relations with his family, of his schooldays, of his residence in Paris (from where he was recalled by his mother's fatal illness), of his feeling guilty about his mother's death (he had refused to kneel down and pray at her bedside, because he considered it a betrayal of his integrity as an unbeliever), and also with a variety of speculations about life and reality often derived from mystical works he had read "in the stagnant bay of

Marsh's library" (in Dublin). Stephen's highly theoretical, inquiring, musing mind contrasts sharply with the practical, humane, sensual, concrete imagination of the book's real hero, Leopold Bloom, but significant parallels exist between the streams of consciousness of the two. Some of the more important themes that emerge in Stephen's reverie are pointed out in the footnotes.
3. I.e., the sense of sight provides an unavoidable way ("ineluctable modality") of knowing reality, the knowledge thus provided being a kind of "thought through [the] eyes."
4. From Jakob Böhme (1575–1624), German mystic.
5. Transparency. Stephen is speculating on Aristotle's view of perception as developed in his *De Anima*.
6. One tradition held that Aristotle was bald, with thin legs, small eyes, and a lisp. Aristotle is also traditionally supposed to have inherited considerable wealth and to have been presented with a fortune by his former pupil Alexander the Great. The Italian phrase, Dante's description of Aristotle in the *Inferno*, means "the master of them that know."
7. What is not transparent (opposite of "diaphane").
8. After one another (German). Stephen, with eyes shut, is now sensing reality through the sense of sound only: unlike sight, sound falls on the sense of hearing in chronological sequence, one sound after another.
9. "What if it tempt you toward the flood, my lord, / Or to the dreadful summit of the cliff / That beetles o'er his base into the sea" (*Hamlet* 1.4.50–52). Allusions to *Hamlet* occur often in *Ulysses*.
1. Beside one another (German).
2. Stephen is still walking with his eyes shut, tapping with his "ash sword" (the ash-wood walking stick he carries), as "they" (i.e., blind people) do.
3. I.e., his friend Buck Mulligan's. Stephen, lacking boots of his own, had borrowed a cast-off pair of Mulligan's.

ends of my legs, *nebeneinander*. Sounds solid: made by the mallet of *Los demiurgos*.[4] Am I walking into eternity along Sandymount strand? Crush, crack, crik, crick. Wild sea money. Dominie Deasy kens them a'.[5]

> *Won't you come to Sandymount,*
> *Madeline the mare?*

Rhythm begins, you see. I hear. A catalectic tetrameter[6] of iambs marching. No, agallop: *deline the mare*.

Open your eyes now. I will. One moment. Has all vanished since? If I open and am for ever in the black adiaphane. *Basta!*[7] I will see if I can see.

See now. There all the time without you: and ever shall be, world without end.

They came down the steps from Leahy's terrace prudently, *Frauenzimmer*:[8] and down the shelving shore flabbily, their splayed feet sinking in the silted sand. Like me, like Algy,[9] coming down to our mighty mother. Number one swung lourdily[1] her midwife's bag, the other's gamp[2] poked in the beach. From the liberties, out for the day. Mrs Florence MacCabe, relict of the late Patk MacCabe,[3] deeply lamented, of Bride Street. One of her sisterhood lugged me squealing into life. Creation from nothing. What has she in the bag? A misbirth with a trailing navelcord, hushed in ruddy wool. The cords of all link back, strandentwining cable of all flesh. That is why mystic monks. Will you be as gods? Gaze in your *omphalos*. Hello. Kinch here. Put me on to Edenville. Aleph, alpha: nought, nought, one.[4]

Spouse and helpmate of Adam Kadmon: Heva,[5] naked Eve. She had no navel. Gaze. Belly without blemish, bulging big, a buckler of taut vellum, no, whiteheaped corn, orient and immortal, standing from everlasting to everlasting. Womb of sin.[6]

---

4. The Demiurge, or demiurgos, supernatural being who, according to Gnostic philosophy, made the world in subordination to God. The mystical notion of the Demiurge, whose mallet fashioned all things and who writes his signature on them, haunts Stephen's mind. The world, sensed by the ear only, "sounds solid," as though made by the Demiurge's hammer. The ending *-os* gives the word the appearance of a Spanish plural, so Joyce whimsically writes *"Los demiurgos,"* which in Spanish would be "the demiurges."
5. "Dominie": schoolmaster. Mr. Deasy was the headmaster of the school where Stephen taught (the previous episode has shown Stephen teaching). "Kens them a' ": knows them all; Stephen is putting Deasy into a mock-Scottish folk song.
6. The first of the two lines of popular verse that have come into Stephen's head consists metrically of four iambic feet ("tetrameter") with the last foot unlike the first, not defective ("catalectic").
7. Enough! (Italian).
8. Dames, wenches (German). Here, midwives. Stephen sees them coming from Leahy's Terrace, which runs by the beach.
9. Algernon Charles Swinburne, who wrote: "I will go back to the great sweet mother, / Mother and lover of men, the sea. / I will go down to her, I and none other" ("The Triumph of Time," lines 1–3).
1. Heavily (coined by Stephen from the French *lourd*). Stephen, like Joyce, had studied modern languages at University College, Dublin, and his preoccupation with words and languages is part of his character as potential literary artist.

2. Umbrella; and perhaps reference to Mrs. Gamp, the nurse in Dickens's *Martin Chuzzlewit*.
3. Stephen imagines the first midwife is called Mrs. MacCabe. "Relict": widow.
4. Stephen is speculating on the mystical significance of the navel cord, seeing it as linking the generations, the combined navel cords stretching back to Adam and Eve. A mystic gazed in his *omphalos* (navel) to make contact with the first man. Stephen thinks of himself ("Kinch," his nickname) calling up Adam in "Edenville" through his navel, using the line of linked navel cords as a telephone line. Adam's telephone number, "Aleph, alpha: nought, nought, one," begins with the first letters of the Hebrew and of the Greek alphabet to suggest the great primeval number.
5. Hebrew for Eve. Because she was not born in the regular way, but created from Adam's rib, she had no navel. "Adam Kadmon": Adam the Beginner, so called in Hebrew cabalistic literature of the Middle Ages.
6. Stephen is led, through reflection on Eve's navel-less "belly without blemish," to a recollection of the description of the original Eden (Paradise) by Thomas Traherne (ca. 1637–1674), from whose prose *Centuries of Meditation* he quotes: "The corn was orient and immortal wheat, which should never be reaped, nor was ever sown. I thought it had stood from everlasting to everlasting." But immediately afterward Stephen reflects that such language is inappropriate to Eve's body, as hers was the "womb of sin"—i.e., she first ate the fatal apple and brought forth sin.

Wombed in sin darkness I was too, made not begotten. By them, the man with my voice and my eyes and a ghostwoman with ashes on her breath.[7] They clasped and sundered, did the coupler's will. From before the ages He willed me and now may not will me away or ever. A *lex eterna*[8] stays about Him. Is that then the divine substance wherein Father and Son are consubstantial? Where is poor dear Arius[9] to try conclusions? Warring his life long on the contransmagnificandjewbangtantiality.[1] Illstarred heresiarch.[2] In a Greek watercloset he breathed his last: *euthanasia*. With beaded mitre and with crozier, stalled upon his throne, widower of a widowed see, with upstiffed omophorion, with clotted hinderparts.

Airs romped round him, nipping and eager airs. They are coming, waves. The whitemaned seahorses, champing, brightwindbridled, the steeds of Mananaan.[3]

I mustn't forget his letter for the press. And after? The Ship, half twelve. By the way go easy with that money like a good young imbecile. Yes, I must.[4]

His pace slackened. Here. Am I going to aunt Sara's or not? My consubstantial father's voice. Did you see anything of your artist brother Stephen lately? No? Sure he's not down in Strasburg terrace with his aunt Sally? Couldn't he fly a bit higher than that, eh? And and and and tell us Stephen, how is uncle Si? O weeping God, the things I married into. De boys up in de hayloft. The drunken little costdrawer and his brother, the cornet player. Highly respectable gondoliers. And skeweyed Walter sirring his father, no less. Sir. Yes, sir. No, sir. Jesus wept: and no wonder, by Christ.[5]

I pull the wheezy bell of their shuttered cottage: and wait. They take me for a dun, peer out from a coign of vantage.[6]

—It's Stephen, sir.

—Let him in. Let Stephen in.

A bolt drawn back and Walter welcomes me.

—We thought you were someone else.

In his broad bed nuncle Richie, pillowed and blanketed, extends over the

---

7. Stephen is haunted by thoughts of his mother in this guise.
8. Eternal law (Latin). God's eternal law, Stephen reflects, willed his birth from the beginning. He then goes on to speculate on the nature of the divine substance and whether God the Father and God the Son are of the same substance ("consubstantial").
9. Third-century theologian who "tried conclusions" on this matter, maintaining that Christ was less divine than God (Arius's views were condemned as heretical by the Council of Nicaea in 325).
1. Ironic "portmanteau word" made up of terms connected with the Arian controversy—"consubstantial," "transubstantial" (of a substance that changes into another)—and with the facts of Christ's nature (e.g., "Jew"; Jesus was a Jew, as Leopold Bloom in a later episode reminds an anti-Semitic Irishman).
2. Arch-heretic. Arius died suddenly in Constantinople in 336. He was never a bishop, and Stephen's image of him at the moment of death in full episcopal attire seems to combine recollections of other early "heresiarchs." In an earlier reverie Stephen had conjured up in his mind "a horde of heresies fleeing with mitres awry." These heretics

are connected in Stephen's mind with argument about the relation between God the Father and God the Son and so with the problem of the true nature of paternity, which haunts him constantly.
3. Mananaan MacLir, Celtic sea god; his steeds are the "whitemaned seahorses." ("White horses" is still the name in Britain for the white foam atop waves.)
4. Mr. Deasy had given Stephen a letter to the press to be taken to the newspaper office. After that he has an appointment with Mulligan at The Ship, a tavern. "That money" is Mr. Deasy's last payment to him.
5. Stephen has been wondering whether to call on his uncle and aunt, Richie and Sara Goulding. He imagines his father interrogating him about the visit as if he had gone; he then pictures his cousins asking after his father, Simon Dedalus (his cousins' "uncle Si"). Simon is contemptuous of his wife's relations (Sara Goulding is his wife's sister). Stephen knows that any mention of them will bring on the familiar abuse of "the things I married into"—at best "highly respectable gondoliers" (from Gilbert and Sullivan's opera *The Gondoliers*). The scene that follows is also Stephen's purely imaginary picture of what the visit would be like.
6. Favorable corner.

hillock of his knees a sturdy forearm. Cleanchested. He has washed the upper moiety.

—Morrow, nephew.

He lays aside the lapboard whereon he drafts his bills of costs for the eyes of master Goff and master Shapland Tandy, filing consents and common searches and a writ of *Duces Tecum*.[7] A bogoak frame over his bald head: Wilde's *Requiescat*.[8] The drone of his misleading whistle brings Walter back.

—Yes, sir?

—Malt[9] for Richie and Stephen, tell mother. Where is she?

—Bathing Crissie, sir.

Papa's little bedpal. Lump of love.

—No, uncle Richie . . .

—Call me Richie. Damn your lithia water.[1] It lowers. Whusky!

—Uncle Richie, really. . . .

—Sit down or by the law Harry I'll knock you down.

Walter squints vainly for a chair.

—He has nothing to sit down on, sir.

—He has nowhere to put it, you mug. Bring in our chippendale chair. Would you like a bite of something? None of your damned lawdeedaw air here: the rich of a rasher fried with a herring? Sure? So much the better. We have nothing in the house but backache pills.

All'erta![2] He drones bars of Ferrando's *aria di sortita*. The grandest number, Stephen, in the whole opera. Listen.

His tuneful whistle sounds again, finely shaded, with rushes of the air, his fists bigdrumming on his padded knees.

This wind is sweeter.

Houses of decay, mine, his and all. You told the Clongowes gentry you had an uncle a judge and an uncle a general in the army.[3] Come out of them, Stephen. Beauty is not there. Nor in the stagnant bay of Marsh's library where you read the fading prophecies of Joachim Abbas.[4] For whom? The hundred-headed rabble of the cathedral close.[5] A hater of his kind ran from them to the wood of madness, his mane foaming in the moon, his eyeballs stars. Houyhnhnm, horsenostrilled.[6] The oval equine faces, Temple, Buck Mulligan, Foxy Campbell. Lantern jaws. Abbas[7] father, furious dean, what offence laid fire to their brains? Paff! *Descende, calve, ut nimium decalveris.*[8] A garland of

7. You shall take with you (Latin); opening words of a search warrant. Goulding was a law clerk with Messrs. Goff and Tandy.
8. Poem by Oscar Wilde.
9. Whiskey.
1. Mineral water containing lithium salts, often used therapeutically.
2. Look out! (Italian); the first words of the *aria di sortita* (aria sung by a character about to leave the stage) sung by Ferrando, captain of the guard, in Verdi's opera *Il Trovatore*.
3. Stephen, reflecting on the steady social decline of his family, is remembering that, while at school at Clongowes Wood College, he had pretended to have important relations.
4. Abbot Joachim of Floris (the monastery of San Giovanni in Fiore, Italy), 12th-century mystic and theologian, whose prophetic work *Expositio in Apocalypsin* Stephen (like Joyce) had read in Marsh's Library.

5. I.e., the precinct of a cathedral (Marsh's Library is in the close of St. Patrick's Cathedral).
6. St. Patrick's Close has recalled Jonathan Swift, who was dean of St. Patrick's. Stephen remembers Swift's misanthropy (he was "a hater of his kind") and his creation of the Houyhnhnms (noble horses) in book 4 of *Gulliver's Travels*. Then he thinks of people he knew who have horse faces.
7. Literally: father.
8. Go down, bald-head, lest you become even balder (Latin). This sentence, from Joachim's *Concordia* of the Old and New Testaments, is based on the mocking cry of the children to the prophet Elisha (2 Kings 2.23: "Go up, thou bald head"); Joachim saw Elisha as a forerunner of St. Benedict—both had shaven or baldish heads. Stephen goes on to imagine the "comminated" (threatened) head of Joachim descending, clutching a "monstrance" (receptacle in which the Host [consecrated bread or wafer] is exposed for adoration), in

2204 / JAMES JOYCE

grey hair on his comminated head see him me clambering down to the footpace
(*descende*), clutching a monstrance, basiliskeyed. Get down, bald poll! A choir
gives back menace and echo, assisting about the altar's horns, the snorted
Latin of jackpriests moving burly in their albs, tonsured and oiled and gelded,
fat with the fat of kidneys of wheat.

And at the same instant perhaps a priest round the corner is elevating it.
Dringdring! And two streets off another locking it into a pyx.[9] Dringadring!
And in a ladychapel another taking housel all to his own cheek. Dringdring!
Down, up, forward, back. Dan Occam[1] thought of that, invincible doctor. A
misty English morning the imp hypostasis tickled his brain. Bringing his host
down and kneeling he heard twine with his second bell the first bell in the
transept (he is lifting his) and, rising, heard (now I am lifting) their two bells
(he is kneeling) twang in diphthong.

Cousin Stephen, you will never be a saint.[2] Isle of saints.[3] You were awfully
holy, weren't you? You prayed to the Blessed Virgin that you might not have
a red nose. You prayed to the devil in Serpentine avenue that the fubsy widow
in front might lift her clothes still more from the wet street. O si, certo![4] Sell
your soul for that, do, dyed rags pinned round a squaw. More tell me, more
still! On the top of the Howth tram alone crying to the rain: *Naked women!*
What about that, eh?

What about what? What else were they invented for?

Reading two pages apiece of seven books every night, eh? I was young. You
bowed to yourself in the mirror, stepping forward to applause earnestly, striking face. Hurray for the Goddamned idiot! Hray! No-one saw: tell no-one.
Books you were going to write with letters for titles. Have you read his F? O
yes, but I prefer Q. Yes, but W is wonderful. O yes, W. Remember your epiph-
anies[5] on green oval leaves, deeply deep, copies to be sent if you died to all
the great libraries of the world, including Alexandria? Someone was to read
them there after a few thousand years, a mahamanvantara.[6] Pico della Mirandola[7] like. Ay, very like a whale.[8] When one reads these strange pages of one
long gone one feels that one is at one with one who once . . .

The grainy sand had gone from under his feet. His boots trod again a damp
crackling mast, razorshells, squeaking pebbles, that on the unnumbered pebbles beats, wood sieved by the shipworm, lost Armada. Unwholesome sandflats
waited to suck his treading soles, breathing upward sewage breath. He coasted

---

the midst of a nightmare church service.
9. Vessel in which the Host is kept. Stephen is
imagining such a service, with himself officiating
(he almost became a priest).
1. William of Occam or Ockham ("Dan" means
"master"), 14th-century English theologian, who
held that the individual thing is the reality and its
name, the universal, an abstraction; he was concerned with hypostasis—the essential part of a
thing as distinct from its attributes.
2. A parody of the words of Dryden to his distant
relative Swift: "Cousin, you will never make a
poet."
3. Ireland was called "*insula sanctorum*" (isle of
saints) in the Middle Ages.
4. Oh yes, certainly! (Italian).
5. Joyce's term for the prose poems he wrote as a
young man. An epiphany, he said, was the sudden
"revelation of the whatness of a thing"—of a gesture, a phrase, or a thought he had experienced;

he attempted to express, in the writing, the
moment at which "the soul of the commonest
object . . . seems to us radiant." Stephen's recollection of early and exotic literary ambitions is drawn
directly from Joyce's ambitions at the same age.
6. Cycle of change and recurrence, in Indian mystical thought. It is connected in Stephen's mind
with the constant ebb and flow of the sea by which
he is walking.
7. 15-century mystical philosopher; his *Heptaplus*
is a mystical account of the Creation, much influenced by Jewish cabalistic thought.
8. Polonius to Hamlet (*Hamlet* 3.2.351) with reference to the changing shape of a cloud. The Protean theme of constant change, of ebb and flow,
and of metempsychosis (i.e., transmigration of
souls), is a major theme in *Ulysses*, is working in Stephen's mind. The following sentence is a parody of
an elegant, condescending modern essay on Pico
or some other early mystic.

them, walking warily. A porterbottle stood up, stogged to its waist, in the cakey sand dough. A sentinel: isle of dreadful thirst.⁹ Broken hoops on the shore; at the land a maze of dark cunning nets; farther away chalkscrawled backdoors and on the higher beach a dryingline with two crucified shirts. Ringsend: wigwams of brown steersmen and master mariners. Human shells.

He halted. I have passed the way to aunt Sara's. Am I not going there? Seems not. No-one about. He turned northeast and crossed the firmer sand towards the Pigeonhouse.¹

—*Qui vous a mis dans cette fichue position?*

—*C'est le pigeon, Joseph.*

Patrice, home on furlough, lapped warm milk with me in the bar Mac-Mahon. Son of the wild goose, Kevin Egan of Paris. My father's a bird, he lapped the sweet *lait chaud* with pink young tongue, plump bunny's face. Lap, *lapin*. He hopes to win in the *gros lots*. About the nature of women he read in Michelet. But he must send me *La Vie de Jésus* by M. Léo Taxil. Lent it to his friend.²

—*C'est tordant, vous savez. Moi, je suis socialiste. Je ne crois pas en l'existence de Dieu. Faut pas le dire à mon père.*

—*Il croit?*

—*Mon père, oui.*

*Schluss.*³ He laps.

My Latin quarter hat. God, we simply must dress the character. I want puce gloves. You were a student, weren't you? Of what in the other devil's name? Paysayenn. P. C. N., you know: *physiques, chimiques et naturelles.*⁴ Aha. Eating your groatsworth of *mou en civet,*⁵ fleshpots of Egypt, elbowed by belching cabmen. Just say in the most natural tone: when I was in Paris, *boul'Mich',*⁶ I used to. Yes, used to carry punched tickets to prove an alibi if they arrested you for murder somewhere. Justice. On the night of the seventeenth of February 1904 the prisoner was seen by two witnesses. Other fellow did it: other me. Hat, tie, overcoat, nose. *Lui, c'est moi.*⁷ You seem to have enjoyed yourself.

Proudly walking. Whom were you trying to walk like? Forget: a dispossessed. With mother's money order, eight shillings, the banging door of the post office slammed in your face by the usher. Hunger toothache. *Encore deux minutes.*

9. The atmosphere of the sandflats reminds Stephen of a desert island where people die of thirst. (The island of Pharos, where Menelaus found Proteus, was an "island of dreadful hunger.")
1. The Pigeon House in Ringsend, an old structure built on a breakwater in Dublin Bay and which in the course of time has served a great variety of purposes, suggests to Stephen the Dove, which is the symbol of the Holy Spirit, and this in turn suggests an irreverent dialogue (supposedly between Joseph and Mary when Mary is found to be pregnant: "Who has got you into this wretched condition?" "It was the pigeon [i.e., the Holy Dove], Joseph"). This he had picked up in Paris from the blasphemous M. Léo Taxil, whose book *La Vie de Jésus* ("The Life of Jesus") is mentioned in the next paragraph.
2. Stephen had first met Léo Taxil through Patrice, the son of "Kevin Egan of Paris," who in real life was the exiled nationalist Joseph Casey. The phrase "my father's a bird" comes from *The Song of the Cheerful Jesus,* a blasphemous poem by Buck Mulligan (based on Joyce's friend Oliver

Gogarty, who really wrote the poem); Stephen recalls Patrice reciting it as he drank warm milk ("*lait chaud*"), lapping it like a "*lapin*" (rabbit), and expressing the hope that he would win something substantial in the French national lottery (*gros lot:* "first prize"). Jules Michelet (1798–1874), French historian.
3. End (German). Conversation in French between Stephen and Patrice: "It's screamingly funny, you know. I'm a socialist myself. I don't believe in the existence of God. Mustn't tell my father." "He is a believer?" "My father, yes."
4. I.e., the faculty of physics, chemistry, and biology at the École de Médecine in Paris, where Stephen, like Joyce, took a premedical course for a short time. The faculty was popularly known as "P.C.N." (pronounced "Paysayenn").
5. Stew.
6. Popular Parisian abbreviation for the Boulevard Saint Michel.
7. "He is me"—a parody of Louis XIV's remark "*L'état c'est moi*" (I am the state).

Look clock. Must get. *Fermé.* Hired dog! Shoot him to bloody bits with a bang shotgun, bits man spattered walls all brass buttons. Bits all khrrrrklak in place clack back. Not hurt? O, that's all right. Shake hands. See what I meant, see? O, that's all right. Shake a shake. O, that's all only all right.[8]

You were going to do wonders, what? Missionary to Europe after fiery Columbanus. Fiacre and Scotus on their creepystools[9] in heaven spilt from their pintpots, loudlatinlaughing: *Euge!*[1] *Euge!* Pretending to speak broken English as you dragged your valise, porter threepence, across the slimy pier at Newhaven. *Comment?* Rich booty you brought back; *Le Tutu,* five tattered numbers of *Pantalon Blanc et Culotte Rouge,*[2] a blue French telegram, curiosity to show:

—Mother dying come home father.[3]

The aunt thinks you killed your mother. That's why she won't.[4]

> *Then here's a health to Mulligan's aunt*
> *And I'll tell you the reason why.*
> *She always kept things decent in*
> *The Hannigan famileye.*

His feet marched in sudden proud rhythm over the sand furrows, along by the boulders of the south wall. He stared at them proudly, piled stone mammoth skulls. Gold light on sea, on sand, on boulders. The sun is there, the slender trees, the lemon houses.

Paris rawly waking, crude sunlight on her lemon streets. Moist pith of farls[5] of bread, the froggreen wormwood, her matin incense, court the air. Belluomo rises from the bed of his wife's lover's wife, the kerchiefed housewife is astir, a saucer of acetic acid in her hand. In Rodot's Yvonne and Madeleine newmake their tumbled beauties, shattering with gold teeth *chaussons* of pastry, their mouths yellowed with the *pus of flan breton.*[6] Faces of Paris men go by, their wellpleased pleasers, curled *conquistadores.*[7]

Noon slumbers. Kevin Egan rolls gunpowder cigarettes through fingers smeared with printer's ink,[8] sipping his green fairy as Patrice his white. About us gobblers fork spiced beans down their gullets. *Un demi setier!*[9] A jet of coffee steam from the burnished caldron. She serves me at his beck. *Il est irlandais. Hollandais? Non fromage. Deux irlandais, nous, Irlande, vous savez? Ah, oui!*[1] She thought you wanted a cheese *hollandais.* Your postprandial, do you know

8. A recollection of the occasion when, desperate for money, Stephen had received a money order for eight shillings from his mother. Afflicted with both hunger and toothache, he had gone to cash it at the post office—which was closed, even though, as he expostulated with the man at the door, there were still two minutes (*"encore deux minutes"*) until the official closing time. In his retrospective rage he imagines himself shooting the "hired dog" to bits, and then in a revulsion of feeling has a mental reconciliation with him.
9. Low stools. "Columbanus": 6th-century Irish missionary on the Continent. Fiacre was a 6th-century Irish saint. John Duns Scotus (1266–1308), Scottish scholastic theologian and philosopher.
1. Well done!
2. Like *Le Tutu,* the name of a French popular periodical.
3. This telegram was actually received by Joyce in Paris.

4. Stephen recalls Buck Mulligan's telling him that his (Mulligan's) aunt disapproved of Stephen because, by refusing to pray at his dying mother's bedside, he had hastened her death. Stephen then tries to laugh away his guilty feeling by quoting mentally a (slightly parodied) verse of a popular song.
5. Thin circular cakes.
6. Memories of a restaurant in Paris. "Chaussons": pastry turnovers. "Flan breton": pastry filled with custard.
7. Conquerors (Spanish).
8. Egan (i.e., Joseph Casey) became a typesetter for the Parisian edition of the *New York Herald.*
9. Abusive Parisian slang for a liquid measure (about one-fourth of a liter)—here, presumably, of wine or beer. "Green Fairy": absinthe, a strong green liqueur.
1. He is Irish. Dutch? Not cheese. We are two Irishmen, Ireland, you understand? Oh, yes!

that word? Postprandial. There was a fellow I knew once in Barcelona, queer fellow, used to call it his postprandial. Well: *slainte!*[2] Around the slabbed tables the tangle of wined breaths and grumbling gorges. His breath hangs over our saucestained plates, the green fairy's fang thrusting between his lips. Of Ireland, the Dalcassians, of hopes, conspiracies, of Arthur Griffith now.[3] To yoke me as his yokefellow, our crimes our common cause. You're your father's son. I know the voice. His fustian shirt, sanguineflowered, trembles its Spanish tassels at his secrets. M. Drumont,[4] famous journalist, Drumont, know what he called queen Victoria? Old hag with the yellow teeth. *Vieille ogresse* with the *dents jaunes.* Maud Gonne, beautiful woman, *la Patrie,* M. Millevoye, Félix Faure,[5] know how he died? Licentious men. The *froeken, bonne à tout faire,*[6] who rubs male nakedness in the bath at Upsala. *Moi faire,* she said, *tous les messieurs.*[7] Not this *monsieur,* I said. Most licentious custom. Bath a most private thing. I wouldn't let my brother, not even my own brother, most lascivious thing. Green eyes, I see you. Fang, I feel. Lascivious people.

The blue fuse burns deadly between hands and burns clear. Loose tobacco shreds catch fire: a flame and acrid smoke light our corner. Raw facebones under his peep of day boy's hat. How the head centre got away, authentic version. Got up as a young bride, man, veil, orangeblossoms, drove out the road to Malahide. Did, faith. Of lost leaders, the betrayed, wild escapes. Disguises, clutched at, gone not here.[8]

Spurned lover. I was a strapping young gossoon[9] at that time, I tell you. I'll show you my likeness one day. I was, faith. Lover, for her love he prowled with colonel Richard Burke, tanist of his sept,[1] under the walls of Clerkenwell[2] and, crouching, saw a flame of vengeance hurl them upward in the fog. Shattered glass and toppling masonry. In gay Paree he hides, Egan of Paris, unsought by any save by me. Making his day's stations, the dingy printing-case, his three taverns, the Montmartre lair he sleeps short night in, *rue de la Goutte-d'Or,* damascened with flyblown faces of the gone. Loveless, landless, wifeless. She is quite nicey comfy without her outcast man,[3] madame in *rue Gît-le-Cœur,* canary and two buck lodgers. Peachy cheeks, a zebra skirt, frisky as a young thing's. Spurned and undespairing. Tell Pat[4] you saw me, won't you? I wanted to get poor Pat a job one time. *Mon fils,* soldier of France. I taught him to sing *The boys of Kilkenny are stout roaring blades.* Know that old lay? I taught Patrice that. Old Kilkenny: saint Canice, Strongbow's castle on the Nore.[5] Goes like this. O, O. He takes me, Napper Tandy,[6] by the hand.

2. Your health! (Gaelic).
3. Two extremes of Irish history. From the Dalcassian line came the early kings of Munster (from 300 C.E. on). Arthur Griffith (1872–1922) was an Irish revolutionary leader, founder of the Sinn Fein ("Ourselves Alone") movement.
4. Edouard Drumont (1844–1917), French politician and bitter anti-Semite.
5. 19th-century French statesman. "Maud Gonne," the beautiful actress and violent Irish nationalist whom W. B. Yeats loved. "La Patrie": journal edited by Lucien Millevoye, French nationalist deputy and Maud Gonne's lover.
6. Maid-of-all-work (French). "Froeken": fröken, unmarried woman or Miss (Swedish).
7. I do all the gentlemen (in broken French).
8. Another Protean theme of change. Egan had told Stephen of his cousin James Stephens's escape from prison disguised as a bride.

9. Boy.
1. Clan. "Tanist": successor-apparent to a Celtic chief.
2. District in east-central London. Stephen is recalling Egan's conversation about the Fenian violence in London that necessitated his fleeing to France.
3. I.e., Egan's wife, who is "quite nicey comfy" in the metaphorical "*rue Gît-le-Cœur*" (i.e., the street where the heart lies dead) back home in Ireland.
4. Patrice, Egan's son.
5. Kilkenny is called after the Irish Saint Canice (its Irish name is Cill Chainnigh), on the river Nore, where Strongbow (the second earl of Pembroke, who invaded Ireland in the 12th century), had his stronghold.
6. James Napper Tandy (1740–1803), Irish revolutionary hero of the song "The Wearing of the Green."

O, O the boys of
Kilkenny . . .

Weak wasting hand on mine. They have forgotten Kevin Egan, not he them.
Remembering thee, O Sion.[7] He had come nearer the edge of the sea and wet sand slapped his boots.
The new air greeted him, harping in wild nerves, wind of wild air of seeds of
brightness. Here, I am not walking out to the Kish lightship, am I? He stood
suddenly, his feet beginning to sink slowly in the quaking soil. Turn back.
Turning, he scanned the shore south, his feet sinking again slowly in new
sockets. The cold domed room of the tower[8] waits. Through the barbicans[9]
the shafts of light are moving ever, slowly ever as my feet are sinking, creeping
duskward over the dial floor. Blue dusk, nightfall, deep blue night. In the
darkness of the dome they wait, their pushedback chairs, my obelisk valise,
around a board of abandoned platters. Who to clear it? He has the key.[1] I will
not sleep there when this night comes. A shut door of a silent tower, entombing
their blind bodies, the panthersahib and his pointer.[2] Call: no answer. He lifted
his feet up from the suck and turned back by the mole of boulders. Take all,
keep all. My soul walks with me, form of forms. So in the moon's midwatches
I pace the path above the rocks, in sable silvered, hearing Elsinore's tempting
flood.[3]

The flood is following me. I can watch it flow past from here. Get back then
by the Poolbeg road to the strand there. He climbed over the sedge and eely
oarweeds and sat on a stool of rock, resting his ashplant in a grike.[4]

A bloated carcass of a dog lay lolled on bladderwrack. Before him the gunwale of a boat, sunk in sand. *Un coche ensablé*[5] Louis Veuillot called Gautier's[6]
prose. These heavy sands are language tide and wind have silted here. And
there, the stoneheaps of dead builders, a warren of weasel rats. Hide gold
there. Try it. You have some. Sands and stones. Heavy of the past. Sir Lout's
toys. Mind you don't get one bang on the ear. I'm the bloody well gigant rolls
all them bloody well boulders, bones for my steppingstones. Feefawfum. I
zmellz de bloodz oldz an Iridzman.[7]

A point, live dog, grew into sight running across the sweep of sand. Lord,
is he going to attack me? Respect his liberty. You will not be master of others
or their slave. I have my stick. Sit tight. From farther away, walking shoreward
across from the crested tide, figures, two. The two maries. They have tucked
it safe mong the bulrushes. Peekaboo. I see you. No, the dog. He is running
back to them. Who?

Galleys of the Lochlanns[8] ran here to beach, in quest of prey, their blood-
beaked prows riding low on a molten pewter surf. Dane vikings, torcs of toma-

---

7. Cf. Psalm 137.1 (in the King James Bible): "we
wept, when we remembered Zion." But "Zion" in
the Douay (Roman Catholic) Bible, is spelled
"Sion," and the Book of Common Prayer has
"When we remembered thee, O Sion."
8. Where Stephen lived with Buck Mulligan.
9. Outworks of a castle.
1. In the preceding episode Mulligan asked for
and got the key of the tower from Stephen.
2. I.e., Mulligan and the Englishman Haines, who
lived with Stephen in the tower. Stephen thinks of
them as calling for him in vain, because he has
decided not to return.
3. Cf. *Hamlet* 1.2.241, where the ghost of Hamlet's murdered father is described as having a beard
of "sable silver'd."

4. Chink, crevice.
5. A coach embedded in the sand (French).
6. Théophile Gautier, 19th-century French poet,
novelist, and critic. Veuillot, 19th-century French
journalist.
7. Stephen is thinking of the boulders on the
shore as the work of a large but clumsy giant ("Sir
Lout"). "They [Sir Lout and his family] were giants
right enough. . . . My Sir Lout has rocks in his
mouth instead of teeth. He articulates badly"
(Joyce to Frank Budgen, reported in Budgen's
James Joyce and the Making of Ulysses, 1934).
8. Scandinavians (Gaelic). Stephen is meditating
on the Vikings who settled Dublin; it was here that
they came ashore, he thinks. Malachi (below), king
of Meath, had their first leader drowned.

hawks aglitter on their breasts when Malachi wore the collar of gold. A school of turlehide whales stranded in hot noon, spouting, hobbling in the shallows. Then from the starving cagework city a horde of jerkined dwarfs, my people, with flayers' knives, running, scaling, hacking in green blubbery whalemeat. Famine, plague and slaughters. Their blood is in me, their lusts my waves. I moved among them on the frozen Liffey, that I, a changeling, among the spluttering resin fires. I spoke to no-one: none to me.

The dog's bark ran towards him, stopped, ran back. Dog of my enemy. I just simply stood pale, silent, bayed about. *Terribilia meditans.*[9] A primrose doublet, fortune's knave, smiled on my fear. For that are you pining, the bark of their applause? Pretenders: live their lives. The Bruce's brother, Thomas Fitzgerald, silken knight, Perkin Warbeck, York's false scion, in breeches of silk of whiterose ivory, wonder of a day, and Lambert Simnel, with a tail of nans and sutlers, a scullion crowned.[1] All kings' sons. Paradise of pretenders then and now. He saved men from drowning[2] and you shake at a cur's yelping. But the courtiers who mocked Guido in Or san Michele were in their own house. House of . . . We don't want any of your medieval abstrusiosities. Would you do what he did? A boat would be near, a lifebuoy. *Natürlich,*[3] put there for you. Would you or would you not? The man that was drowned nine days ago off Maiden's rock. They are waiting for him now. The truth, spit it out. I would want to. I would try. I am not a strong swimmer. Water cold soft. When I put my face into it in the basin at Clongowes. Can't see! Who's behind me? Out quickly, quickly! Do you see the tide flowing quickly in on all sides, sheeting the lows of sands quickly, shellcocoacoloured? If I had land under my feet. I want his life still to be his, mine to be mine. A drowning man. His human eyes scream to me out of horror of his death. I . . . With him together down . . . I could not save her.[4] Waters: bitter death: lost.

A woman and a man. I see her skirties. Pinned up, I bet.

Their dog ambled about a bank of dwindling sand, trotting, sniffing on all sides. Looking for something lost in a past life. Suddenly he made off like a bounding hare, ears flung back, chasing the shadow of a lowskimming gull. The man's shrieked whistle struck his limp ears. He turned, bounded back, came nearer, trotted on twinkling shanks. On a field tenney a buck, trippant, proper, unattired.[5] At the lacefringe of the tide he halted with stiff forehoofs, seawardpointed ears. His snout lifted barked at the wavenoise, herds of seamorse.[6] They serpented towards his feet, curling, unfurling many crests, every ninth, breaking, plashing, from far, from farther out, waves and waves.

Cocklepickers.[7] They waded a little way in the water and, stooping, soused their bags, and, lifting them again, waded out. The dog yelped running to them, reared up and pawed them, dropping on all fours, again reared up at them with mute bearish fawning. Unheeded he kept by them as they came towards the drier sand, a rag of wolf's tongue redpanting from his jaws. His speckled body ambled ahead of them and then loped off at a calf's gallop. The carcass

---

9. Meditating terrible things (Latin).
1. Stephen is meditating on pretenders (i.e., false claimants): the names here are those of pretenders who have figured in English history.
2. Mulligan had saved a man from drowning.
3. Of course (German).
4. A man had been drowned off the coast, and his body had not yet been recovered. As Stephen thinks of the horror of drowning, he recalls once

again his mother's death.
5. The dog is described in the language of heraldry. "On an orange-brown (tawny) background, a buck, tripping, in natural colors, without horns."
6. Seahorses, with a pun on Morse code.
7. Stephen recognizes the man and woman on the beach as gypsy cockle pickers (cockles are edible shellfish, like mussels).

lay on his path. He stopped, sniffed, stalked round it, brother, nosing closer, went round it, sniffing rapidly like a dog all over the dead dog's bedraggled fell. Dogskull, dogsniff, eyes on the ground, moves to one great goal. Ah, poor dogsbody. Here lies poor dogsbody's body.

—Tatters! Outofthat, you mongrel.

The cry brought him skulking back to his master and a blunt bootless kick sent him unscathed across a spit of sand, crouched in flight. He slunk back in a curve. Doesn't see me. Along by the edge of the mole he lolloped, dawdled, smelt a rock and from under a cocked hindleg pissed against it. He trotted forward and, lifting his hindleg, pissed quick short at an unsmelt rock. The simple pleasures of the poor. His hindpaws then scattered sand: then his forepaws dabbled and delved. Something he buried there, his grandmother.[8] He rooted in the sand, dabbling, delving and stopped to listen to the air, scraped up the sand again with a fury of his claws, soon ceasing, a pard,[9] a panther, got in spousebreach,[1] vulturing the dead.

After he woke me last night same dream or was it? Wait. Open hallway. Street of harlots. Remember. Haroun al Raschid.[2] I am almosting it. That man led me, spoke. I was not afraid. The melon he had he held against my face. Smiled: creamfruit smell. That was the rule, said. In. Come. Red carpet spread. You will see who.

Shouldering their bags they trudged, the red Egyptians.[3] His blued feet out of turnedup trousers slapped the clammy sand, a dull brick muffler strangling his unshaven neck. With woman steps she followed: the ruffian and his strolling mort. Spoils[4] slung at her back. Loose sand and shellgrit crusted her bare feet. About her windraw face her hair trailed. Behind her lord his helpmate, bing awast, to Romeville.[5] When night hides her body's flaws calling under her brown shawl from an archway where dogs have mired. Her fancyman is treating two Royal Dublins in O'Loughlin's of Blackpitts. Buss her, wap in rogues' rum lingo, for, O, my dimber wapping dell.[6] A shefiend's whiteness under her rancid rags. Fumbally's lane that night: the tanyard smells.

> White thy fambles, red thy gan
> And thy quarrons dainty is.
> Couch a hogshead with me then.
> In the darkmans clip and kiss.[7]

Morose delectation Aquinas tunbelly calls this, *frate porcospino.*[8] Unfallen Adam rode and not rutted. Call away let him:[9] *thy quarrons dainty is.* Language no whit worse than his. Monkwords, marybeads jabber on their girdles: roguewords, tough nuggets patter in their pockets.

---

8. Reference to a joke Stephen had made to his pupils in school that morning about "the fox burying his grandmother under a hollybush."
9. Leopard or panther.
1. I.e., begotten in adultery.
2. Stephen's dream of the famous Caliph of Baghdad, of the "street of harlots," and of his meeting a man with a melon foreshadows his meeting later in the day with Leopold Bloom and his visit to the brothel area of Dublin.
3. I.e., gypsies. As Stephen watches the gypsy cockle pickers with their dog he imagines their vagabond life and recalls fragments of gypsy speech and of thieves' slang.
4. The association of gypsy ("mort": free gypsy woman; harlot) with Egyptian reminds Stephen of the Israelites "spoiling the Egyptians" (Exodus

12.36).
5. Go away to London.
6. 17th-century thieves' slang. "Buss": kiss. "Wap": copulate with. "Rum": good. "Dimber": pretty. "Wapping dell": whore.
7. More thieves' slang. "Fambles": hands. "Gan": mouth. "Quarrons": body. "Couch a hogshead": come to bed. "Darkmans": night. "Clip": kiss. These four lines and some of the phrases in the preceding paragraph are quoted from a song of the period, "The Rogue's Delight in Praise of His Strolling Mort" (cf. n. 3 and n. 4, this page).
8. Brother porcupine (Italian), a reference to the fat ("tunbelly") but prickly 13-century philosopher, St. Thomas Aquinas.
9. The gypsy is calling his dog.

Passing now.

A side-eye at my Hamlet hat. If I were suddenly naked here as I sit? I am not. Across the sands of all the world, followed by the sun's flaming sword, to the west, trekking to evening lands. She trudges, schlepps, trains, drags, trascines her load.[1] A tide westering, moondrawn, in her wake. Tides, myriadislanded, within her, blood not mine, *oinopa ponton*,[2] a winedark sea. Behold the handmaid of the moon. In sleep the wet sign calls her hour, bids her rise. Bridebed, childbed, bed of death, ghostcandled.[3] *Omnis caro ad te veniet.* He comes, pale vampire, through storm his eyes, his bat sails bloodying the sea, mouth to her mouth's kiss.[4]

Here. Put a pin in that chap, will you? My tablets.[5] Mouth to her kiss. No. Must be two of em. Glue em well. Mouth to her mouth's kiss.

His lips lipped and mouthed fleshless lips of air: mouth to her womb. Oomb, allwombing tomb.[6] His mouth moulded issuing breath, unspeeched: ooeeehah: roar of cataractic planets, globed, blazing, roaring wayawayawayawayaway. Paper. The banknotes, blast them. Old Deasy's letter. Here. Thanking you for the hospitality tear the blank end off. Turning his back to the sun he bent over far to a table of rock and scribbled words.[7] That's twice I forgot to take slips from the library counter.

His shadow lay over the rocks as he bent, ending. Why not endless till the farthest star? Darkly they are there behind this light, darkness shining in the brightness, delta of Cassiopeia, worlds. Me sits there with his augur's rod of ash, in borrowed sandals, by day beside a livid sea, unbeheld, in violet night walking beneath a reign of uncouth stars.[8] I throw this ended shadow from me, manshape ineluctable, call it back. Endless, would it be mine, form of my form? Who watches me here? Who ever anywhere will read these written words? Signs on a white field. Somewhere to someone in your flutiest voice. The good bishop of Cloyne[9] took the veil of the temple out of his shovel hat: veil of space with coloured emblems hatched on its field. Hold hard. Coloured on a flat: yes, that's right. Flat I see, then think distance, near, far, flat I see, east, back. Ah, see now. Falls back suddenly, frozen in stereoscope. Click does the trick. You find my words dark. Darkness is in our souls, do you not think? Flutier. Our souls, shamewounded by our sins, cling to us yet more, a woman to her lover clinging, the more the more.

She trusts me, her hand gentle, the longlashed eyes. Now where the blue hell am I bringing her beyond the veil?[1] Into the ineluctable modality of the ineluctable visuality. She, she, she. What she? The virgin at Hodges Figgis' window on Monday looking in for one of the alphabet books you were going

---

1. All words suggesting moving or dragging. " 'I like that crescendo of verbs,' he [Joyce] said. 'The irresistible tug of the tides' " (Budgen).
2. Winedark sea (Homer).
3. He is thinking of his mother again. The following Latin (from the burial service) means: All flesh will come to thee.
4. Death comes like the Flying Dutchman in a phantom ship to give the fatal kiss.
5. Cf. *Hamlet* 1.5.107: "My tablets."
6. Cf. Blake's poem "The Gates of Paradise," esp. the lines "The door of death I open found / And the worm weaving in the ground: / Thou'rt my mother from the womb, / Wife, sister, daughter, to the tomb." Cf. also *Romeo and Juliet* 2.2.9–10: "the earth, that's nature's mother, is her tomb. / What is her burying grave, that is her womb."
7. Stephen tears off the blank end of Mr. Deasy's

letter to the press and writes a poem, which is quoted later in the novel.
8. He imagines himself as the constellation Cassiopeia, supposed to represent the wife of Cepheus (an Ethiopian king) seated in a chair and holding up her arms. His ash walking stick he thinks of as an "augur's [Roman soothsayer's] rod of ash."
9. George Berkeley (1685–1753), bishop of Cloyne (in Ireland), who argued that the external world has no objective reality but exists only in the mind of the perceiver. Stephen (as at the opening of this episode) is experimenting again with ways of sensing reality.
1. "She" is Psyche, the soul, whom he is bringing from "beyond the veil." But from metaphysical speculations on reality and the soul Stephen is led (by the Psyche association) to think of "the virgin at Hodges Figgis' [a bookseller's] window."

to write. Keen glance you gave her. Wrist through the braided jess of her sunshade. She lives in Leeson park with a grief and kickshaws, a lady of letters. Talk that to some else, Stevie: a pickmeup. Bet she wears those curse of God stays suspenders and yellow stockings, darned with lumpy wool. Talk about apple dumplings, *piuttosto*.[2] Where are your wits?

Touch me. Soft eyes. Soft soft soft hand. I am lonely here. O, touch me soon, now. What is that word known to all men? I am quiet here alone. Sad too. Touch, touch me.

He lay back at full stretch over the sharp rocks, cramming the scribbled note and pencil into a pocket, his hat tilted down on his eyes. That is Kevin Egan's movement I made, nodding for his nap, sabbath sleep. *Et vidit Deus. Et erant valde bona.*[3] Alo! *Bonjour.* Welcome as the flowers in May. Under its leaf he watched through peacocktwittering lashes the southing sun. I am caught in this burning scene. Pan's hour, the faunal noon. Among gumheavy serpentplants, milkoozing fruits, where on the tawny waters leaves lie wide. Pain is far.

And no more turn aside and brood.[4]

His gaze brooded on his broadtoed boots, a buck's castoffs, *nebeneinander.* He counted the creases of rucked leather wherein another's foot had nested warm. The foot that beat the ground in tripudium, foot I dislove. But you were delighted when Esther Osvalt's shoe went on you: girl I knew in Paris. *Tiens, quel petit pied!*[5] Staunch friend, a brother soul: Wilde's love that dare not speak its name.[6] He now will leave me. And the blame? As I am. As I am. All or not at all.

In long lassoes from the Cock lake the water flowed full, covering green-goldenly lagoons of sand, rising, flowing. My ashplant will float away. I shall wait. No, they will pass on, passing chafing against the low rocks, swirling, passing. Better get this job over quick. Listen: a fourworded wavespeech: seesoo, hrss, rsseeiss ooos. Vehement breath of waters amid seasnakes, rearing horses, rocks. In cups of rocks it slops: flop, slop, slap: bounded in barrels. And, spent, its speech ceases. It flows purling, widely flowing, floating foampool, flower unfurling.

Under the upswelling tide he saw the writhing weeds lift languidly and sway reluctant arms, hising up their petticoats,[7] in whispering water swaying and upturning coy silver fronds. Day by day: night by night: lifted, flooded and let fall. Lord, they are weary: and, whispered to, they sigh. Saint Ambrose heard it, sigh of leaves and waves, waiting, awaiting the fullness of their times, *diebus ac noctibus iniurias patiens ingemiscit.*[8] To no end gathered; vainly then released, forthflowing, wending back: loom of the moon. Weary too in sight of lovers, lascivious men, a naked woman shining in her courts, she draws a toil of waters.

Five fathoms out there. Full fathom five thy father lies.[9] At one he said.

2. Rather, sooner (Italian).
3. Connecting two phrases from the Vulgate (Latin Bible): "And God saw" (Genesis 1.4) and "And they were very good" (Genesis 1.31).
4. The first line of the second (and last) stanza of Yeats's poem "Who Goes with Fergus?" which is often in Stephen's mind. The line expresses for him the mood, of noontide stillness and of lotos eating in a lush Asian scene, that overcomes him momentarily when he realizes that it is twelve o'clock, the hour of the Greek nature god Pan, "faunal noon." This Asian lotos-eating theme, which is associated

also with Bloom, is important in the *Odyssey.*
5. Look, what a little foot! (French).
6. Asked at his 1895 trial for homosexuality what this line meant, Oscar Wilde defined it as the great spiritual affection of an elder man for a younger man.
7. A phrase from a vulgar song sung by Mulligan earlier that morning.
8. Night and day he patiently groaned forth his wrongs (St. Ambrose).
9. From Ariel's song (*The Tempest* 1.2.400).

Found drowned. High water at Dublin bar. Driving before it a loose drift of rubble, fanshoals of fishes, silly shells. A corpse rising salt-white from the undertow, bobbing landward a pace a pace a porpoise. There he is. Hook it quick. Sunk though he be beneath the watery floor. We have him. Easy now. Bag of corpsegas sopping in foul brine. A quiver of minnows, fat of a spongy titbit, flash through the slits of his buttoned trouserfly. God becomes man becomes fish becomes barnacle goose becomes featherbed mountain. Dead breaths I living breathe, tread dead dust, devour a urinous offal from all dead. Hauled stark over the gunwhale he breathes upward the stench of his green grave, his leprous nosehole snoring to the sun.

A seachange[1] this, brown eyes saltblue. Seadeath, mildest of all deaths known to man. Old Father Ocean. *Prix de Paris:*[2] beware of imitations. Just you give it a fair trial. We enjoyed ourselves immensely.

Come. I thirst. Clouding over. No black clouds anywhere, are there? Thunderstorm. Allbright he falls, proud lightning of the intellect, *Lucifer, dico, qui nescit occasum.*[3] No. My cockle hat and staff and hismy sandal shoon.[4] Where? To evening lands. Evening will find itself.

He took the hilt of his ashplant, lunging with it softly, dallying still. Yes, evening will find itself in me, without me. All days make their end. By the way next when is it? Tuesday will be the longest day. Of all the glad new year, mother,[5] the rum tum tiddledy tum. Lawn Tennyson,[6] gentleman poet. *Già.*[7] For the old hag with the yellow teeth. And Monsieur Drumont, gentleman journalist. *Già.* My teeth are very bad. Why, I wonder? Feel. That one is going too. Shells. Ought I go to a dentist, I wonder, with what money? That one. Toothless Kinch, the superman. Why is that, I wonder, or does it mean something perhaps?

My handkerchief. He threw it. I remember. Did I not take it up?

His hand groped vainly in his pockets. No, I didn't. Better buy one.

He laid the dry snot picked from his nostril on a ledge of rock, carefully. For the rest let look who will.

Behind. Perhaps there is someone.

He turned his face over a shoulder, rere regardant.[8] Moving through the air high spars of a threemaster, her sails brailed up on the crosstrees, homing, upstream, silently moving, a silent ship.

[LESTRYGONIANS][9]

Pineapple rock, lemon platt, butter scotch. A sugarsticky girl shovelling scoopfuls of creams for a christian brother. Some school treat. Bad for their

1. Another quotation from Ariel's song (1.2.404).
2. Prize of Paris. The reference is probably to the Paris Exposition of 1889, where prizes were awarded in various categories of food and other commodities; the winners bore the seal of the prize on the label (hence, "beware of imitations"). Stephen mentally awards the prize to death by drowning.
3. Lucifer, I say, who knows not his fall (Latin). Thunder and lightning recall the fall of Lucifer.
4. From Ophelia's mad song (*Hamlet* 4.5.23–26): "How should I your true love know / From another one?— / By his cockle hat and staff, / And his sandal shoon." Ophelia, too, was drowned.
5. Cf. Alfred, Lord Tennyson, "The May Queen": "You must wake and call me early, call me early, mother dear; / Tomorrow 'ill be the happiest time of all the glad New Year."
6. A parody of the poet's name, punning on "lawn

tennis," attributed to W. B. Yeats.
7. Let's go (Italian).
8. Looking behind him (heraldic terminology). Stephen, as we leave him sitting by the shore, is described in a highly stylized, heraldic language.
9. The eighth of the novel's eighteen episodes. It is lunchtime in Dublin, and Leopold Bloom, as he walks through the city in no great hurry (for he likes to linger and watch what goes on around him), thinks of food. The Lestrygonians in book 10 of the *Odyssey* are cannibals, and throughout this episode there are suggestions of the slaughter of living creatures for food or of food as something disgusting, which make somewhat tenuous contact with Homer's description of the cannibals spearing Ulysses' men for food. This episode shows us Bloom's consciousness responding to the sights and sounds of Dublin. His humane curiosity, his desire to learn and to improve the human lot, his

tummies. Lozenge and comfit manufacturer to His Majesty the King. God.
Save. Our. Sitting on his throne sucking red jujubes white.

A sombre Y. M. C. A. young man, watchful among the warm sweet fumes
of Graham Lemon's, placed a throwaway in a hand of Mr Bloom.

Heart to heart talks.

Bloo . . . Me? No.

Blood of the Lamb.[1]

His slow feet walked him riverward, reading. Are you saved? All are washed
in the blood of the lamb. God wants blood victim. Birth, hymen, martyr, war,
foundation of a building, sacrifice, kidney burntoffering, druids' altars. Elijah
is coming. Dr John Alexander Dowie,[2] restorer of the church in Zion, is
coming.

Is coming! Is coming!! Is coming!!!
All heartily welcome.

Paying game. Torry and Alexander last year. Polygamy. His wife will put the
stopper on that. Where was that ad some Birmingham firm the luminous crucifix. Our Saviour. Wake up in the dead of night and see him on the wall,
hanging. Pepper's ghost idea.[3] Iron Nails Ran In.

Phosphorus it must be done with. If you leave a bit of codfish for instance.
I could see the bluey silver over it. Night I went down to the pantry in the
kitchen. Don't like all the smells in it waiting to rush out. What was it she[4]
wanted? The Malaga raisins. Thinking of Spain. Before Rudy[5] was born. The
phosphorescence, that bluey greeny. Very good for the brain.

From Butler's monument house corner he glanced along Bachelor's walk.
Dedalus' daughter there still outside Dillon's auctionrooms. Must be selling
off some old furniture. Knew her eyes at once from the father. Lobbing about
waiting for him. Home always breaks up when the mother goes. Fifteen children he had. Birth every year almost. That's in their theology or the priest
won't give the poor woman the confession, the absolution. Increase and multiply. Did you ever hear such an idea? Eat you out of house and home. No
families themselves to feed. Living on the fat of the land. Their butteries and
larders. I'd like to see them do the black fast Yom Kippur.[6] Crossbuns. One
meal and a collation for fear he'd collapse on the altar. A housekeeper of one
of those fellows if you could pick it out of her. Never pick it out of her. Like
getting L s. d.[7] out of him. Does himself well. No guests. All for number one.
Watching his water. Bring your own bread and butter. His reverence. Mum's
the word.

sympathetic concern for Mrs. Breen and Mrs.
Purefoy, his feeding the gulls, his recollections of
a happier time when his daughter was a baby and
his relations with his wife were thoroughly satisfactory, his interest in opera, his continuous shying
away from thoughts of his wife's rendezvous with
the dashing Blazes Boylan—all this helps to build
up his character in depth and to differentiate him
sharply from Stephen. Unlike Stephen, Bloom's
interest in language is confined to simple puns and
translations; his interest in poetry is obvious and
sentimental; his interest in the nature of reality
takes the form of half-forgotten fragments of science remaining in his mind from school days.
Everything about him is concrete, practical, sensual, and middlebrow or lowbrow, as distinct from
the abstract, theoretical, esoteric speculations of
Stephen in the "Proteus" episode.
1. Bloom has been handed a religious leaflet

("throwaway") containing the phrase "Blood of the
Lamb." He at first mistakes "Blood" for "Bloom."
2. Scottish American evangelist (1847–1907),
who established the "Christian Catholic Apostolic
Church in Zion" in 1896 and founded Zion City,
IL, in 1901.
3. A dramatic troupe advertising as "The original
Pepper's Ghost! and Spectral Opera Company"
was popular in the late-19th century; it seems to
have specialized in ghostly special effects, possibly
achieved through the use of phosphorescent material on its costumes.
4. I.e., Bloom's wife, Molly, born in Gibraltar.
5. Their son, who had died in infancy eleven years
before.
6. Jewish Day of Atonement.
7. I.e., cash: L, s., d. are the abbreviations, respectively, for pounds, shillings, and pence.

Good Lord, that poor child's dress is in flitters. Underfed she looks too. Potatoes and marge, marge and potatoes. It's after they feel it. Proof of the pudding. Undermines the constitution.

As he set foot on O'Connell bridge a puffball of smoke plumed up from the parapet. Brewery barge with export stout. England. Sea air sours it, I heard. Be interesting some day get a pass through Hancock to see the brewery. Regular world in itself. Vats of porter, wonderful. Rats get in too. Drink themselves bloated as big as a collie floating. Dead drunk on the porter. Drink till they puke again like christians. Imagine drinking that! Rats: vats. Well of course if we knew all the things.

Looking down he saw flapping strongly, wheeling between the gaunt quaywalls, gulls. Rough weather outside. If I threw myself down? Reuben J's son must have swallowed a good bellyful of that sewage.[8] One and eightpence too much. Hhhhm. It's the droll way he comes out with the things. Knows how to tell a story too.

They wheeled lower. Looking for grub. Wait.

He threw down among them a crumpled paper ball. Elijah thirtytwo feet per sec is com.[9] Not a bit. The ball bobbed unheeded on the wake of swells, floated under by the bridgepiers. Not such damn fools. Also the day I threw that stale cake out of the Erin's King picked it up in the wake fifty yards astern. Live by their wits. They wheeled, flapping.

> *The hungry famished gull*
> *Flaps o'er the waters dull.*

That is how poets write, the similar sounds. But then Shakespeare has no rhymes: blank verse. The flow of the language it is. The thoughts. Solemn.

> *Hamlet, I am thy father's spirit*
> *Doomed for a certain time to walk the earth.*[1]

—Two apples a penny! Two for a penny!

His gaze passed over the glazed apples serried on her stand. Australians they must be this time of year. Shiny peels: polishes them up with a rag or a handkerchief.

Wait. Those poor birds.

He halted again and bought from the old applewoman two Banbury cakes for a penny and broke the brittle paste and threw its fragments down into the Liffey. See that? The gulls swooped silently two, then all from their heights, pouncing on prey. Gone. Every morsel.

Aware of their greed and cunning he shook the powdery crumb from his hands. They never expected that. Manna.[2] Live on fishy flesh they have to, all seabirds, gulls, seagoose. Swans from Anna Liffey[3] swim down here sometimes to preen themselves. No accounting for tastes. Wonder what kind is swanmeat. Robinson Crusoe had to live on them.

They wheeled, flapping weakly. I'm not going to throw any more. Penny quite enough. Lot of thanks I get. Not even a caw. They spread foot and mouth

8. The son of Reuben J. Dodd, Dublin solicitor (lawyer), had been rescued from the river Liffey by a man to whom Reuben J. had given two shillings as a reward—"one and eightpence too much," as Simon Dedalus had remarked to Bloom earlier that morning when they were discussing the incident. In the following sentences Bloom is thinking of Dedalus's comment.
9. I.e., Elijah is coming, accelerating at the rate of

thirty-two feet per second per second, the acceleration rate of falling bodies. ("Elijah is coming" is the legend on the handbill Bloom is tossing away).
1. *Hamlet* 1.5.9–10 (slightly misquoted).
2. The divine food (small, round, and white) that the children of Israel ate in the wilderness (Exodus 16.14–15).
3. The Liffey flows from the Wicklow Mountains northeast and east to Dublin Bay.

disease too. If you cram a turkey, say, on chestnutmeal it tastes like that. Eat pig like pig. But then why is it that saltwater fish are not salty? How is that?

His eyes sought answer from the river and saw a rowboat rock at anchor on the treacly swells lazily its plastered board.

Kino's
11 / -
Trousers[4]

Good idea that. Wonder if he pays rent to the corporation. How can you own water really? It's always flowing in a stream, never the same, which in the stream of life we trace. Because life is a stream. All kinds of places are good for ads. That quack doctor for the clap used to be stuck up in all the greenhouses. Never see it now. Strictly confidential. Dr Hy Franks. Didn't cost him a red like Maginni the dancing master self advertisement. Got fellows to stick them up or stick them up himself for that matter on the q.t. running in to loosen a button. Flybynight. Just the place too. POST NO BILLS. POST NO PILLS.[5] Some chap with a dose burning him.

If he . . .

O!

Eh?

No . . . No.

No, no. I don't believe it. He wouldn't surely?

No, no.[6]

Mr Bloom moved forward, raising his troubled eyes. Think no more about that. After one. Timeball on the ballastoffice is down. Dunsink time. Fascinating little book that is of Sir Robert Ball's. Parallax. I never exactly understood.[7] There's a priest. Could ask him. Par it's Greek: parallel, parallax. Met him pike hoses[8] she called it till I told her about the transmigration. O rocks!

Mr Bloom smiled O rocks at two windows of the ballastoffice. She's right after all. Only big words for ordinary things on account of the sound. She's not exactly witty. Can be rude too. Blurt out what I was thinking. Still I don't know. She used to say Ben Dollard had a base barreltone voice. He has legs like barrels and you'd think he was singing into a barrel. Now isn't that wit? They used to call him big Ben. Not half as witty as calling him base barreltone. Appetite like an albatross. Get outside of a baron of beef. Powerful man he was at stowing away number one Bass.[9] Barrel of Bass. See? It all works out.

A procession of whitesmocked men marched slowly towards him along the gutter, scarlet sashes across their boards. Bargains. Like that priest they are this morning: we have sinned: we have suffered. He read the scarlet letters on

---

4. I.e., eleven shillings ("11 / -") for Kino's Trousers. Bloom is a canvasser for advertisements: he receives commissions from newspapers for getting tradesmen to place advertisements with them.
5. The revised text edited by John Kidd (1993) reads, POST NO BILLS. POST 110 PILLS. "Post no bills" can mean either "do not affix any posters" or "mail no accounts." Bloom is punning to himself on the quack doctor's advertising (by posting bills), collecting his money (by mailing accounts), and sending pills to patients by mail.
6. Blazes Boylan, flashy philanderer, is due to call on Molly Bloom that afternoon, to discuss the program of a concert that he is managing for her (Molly is a singer). Bloom knows that Boylan and his wife will commit adultery together. Here it suddenly occurs to him that Boylan might give Molly

a "dose" of veneral disease, but he puts the thought from him as incredible.
7. The "timeball on the ballastoffice" registers the official time of the observatory at Dunsink (Dublin). Noticing that the timeball is down, which means that it is after one o'clock, Bloom is reminded of the observatory, then of the Irish astronomer Sir Robert Ball's popular book on astronomy, *The Story of the Heavens* (1886), and of the astronomical term *parallax*, which he found in the book but "never exactly understood."
8. Molly's way of pronouncing *metempsychosis*. When Bloom had explained metempsychosis to her that morning, she had exclaimed "O rocks!" at the pretentious term. He now mentally repeats "O rocks!" at the thought of the word *parallax*.
9. A popular British ale.

their five tall white hats: H. E. L. Y. S. Wisdom Hely's. Y lagging behind drew a chunk of bread from under his foreboard, crammed it into his mouth and munched as he walked. Our staple food. Three bob a day, walking along the gutters, street after street. Just keep skin and bone together, bread and skilly. They are not Boyl: no: M'Glade's men. Doesn't bring in any business either. I suggested to him about a transparent showcart with two smart girls sitting inside writing letters, copybooks, envelopes, blottingpaper. I bet that would have caught on. Smart girls writing something catch the eye at once. Everyone dying to know what she's writing. Get twenty of them round you if you stare at nothing. Have a finger in the pie. Women too. Curiosity. Pillar of salt.[1] Wouldn't have it of course because he didn't think of it himself first. Or the inkbottle I suggested with a false stain of black celluloid. His ideas for ads like Plumtree's potted under the obituaries, cold meat department. You can't lick 'em. What? Our envelopes. Hello! Jones, where are you going? Can't stop, Robinson, I am hastening to purchase the only reliable inkeraser *Kansell*, sold by Hely's Ltd, 85 Dame street. Well out of that ruck I am. Devil of a job it was collecting accounts of those convents. Tranquilla convent. That was a nice nun there, really sweet face. Wimple suited her small head. Sister? Sister? I am sure she was crossed in love by her eyes. Very hard to bargain with that sort of a woman. I disturbed her at her devotions that morning. But glad to communicate with the outside world. Our great day, she said. Feast of Our Lady of Mount Carmel. Sweet name too: caramel. She knew, I think she knew by the way she. If she had married she would have changed. I suppose they really were short of money. Fried everything in the best butter all the same. No lard for them. My heart's broke eating dripping. They like buttering themselves in and out. Molly tasting it, her veil up. Sister? Pat Claffey, the pawnbroker's daughter. It was a nun they say invented barbed wire.

He crossed Westmoreland street when apostrophe S had plodded by. Rover cycleshop. Those races are on today. How long ago is that? Year Phil Gilligan died. We were in Lombard street west. Wait, was in Thom's. Got the job in Wisdom Hely's year we married. Six years. Ten years ago: ninetyfour he died, yes that's right the big fire at Arnott's. Val Dillon was lord mayor. The Glencree dinner. Alderman Robert O'Reilly emptying the port into his soup before the flag fell, Bobbob lapping it for the inner alderman. Couldn't hear what the band played. For what we have already received may the Lord make us. Milly[2] was a kiddy then. Molly had that elephantgrey dress with the braided frogs. Mantailored with selfcovered buttons. She didn't like it because I sprained my ankle first day she wore choir picnic at the Sugarloaf. As if that. Old Goodwin's tall hat done up with some sticky stuff. Flies' picnic too. Never put a dress on her back like it. Fitted her like a glove, shoulder and hips. Just beginning to plump it out well. Rabbitpie we had that day. People looking after her.

Happy. Happier then. Snug little room that was with the red wallpaper, Dockrell's, one and ninepence a dozen. Milly's tubbing night. American soap I bought: elderflower. Cosy smell of her bathwater. Funny she looked soaped all over. Shapely too. Now photography.[3] Poor papa's daguerreotype atelier he told me of. Hereditary taste.

He walked along the curbstone.

1. Cf. Genesis 19. 1–26, where Lot's wife defies God's order to "look not behind thee" and is turned into "a pillar of salt."

2. Bloom's fifteen-year-old daughter. "For . . . us": cf. the Lord's Prayer, often said before meals.
3. Milly is working at a photographer's.

2218 / James Joyce

Stream of life. What was the name of that priestlylooking chap was always squinting in when he passed? Weak eyes, woman. Stopped in Citron's saint Kevin's parade. Pen something. Pendennis? My memory is getting. Pen . . . ? Of course it's years ago. Noise of the trams probably. Well, if he couldn't remember the dayfather's name that he sees every day.

Bartell d'Arcy was the tenor, just coming out then. Seeing her home after practice. Conceited fellow with his waxedup moustache. Gave her that song *Winds that blow from the south.*

Windy night that was I went to fetch her there was that lodge meeting on about those lottery tickets after Goodwin's concert in the supperroom or oakroom of the Mansion house. He and I behind. Sheet of her music blew out of my hand against the High school railings. Lucky it didn't. Thing like that spoils the effect of a night for her. Professor Goodwin linking her in front. Shaky on his pins, poor old sot. His farewell concerts. Positively last appearance on any stage. May be for months and may be for never. Remember her laughing at the wind, her blizzard collar up. Corner of Harcourt road remember that gust. Brrfoo! Blew up all her skirts and her boa nearly smothered old Goodwin. She did get flushed in the wind. Remember when we got home raking up the fire and frying up those pieces of lap of mutton for her supper with the Chutney sauce she liked. And the mulled rum. Could see her in the bedroom from the hearth unclamping the busk of her stays: white.

Swish and soft flop her stays made on the bed. Always warm from her. Always liked to let her self out. Sitting there after till near two taking out her hairpins. Milly tucked up in beddyhouse. Happy. Happy. That was the night . . .

—O, Mr Bloom, how do you do?

—O, how do you do, Mrs Breen?[4]

—No use complaining. How is Molly those times? Haven't seen her for ages.

—In the pink, Mr Bloom said gaily, Milly has a position down in Mullingar, you know.

—Go away! Isn't that grand for her?

—Yes, in a photographer's there. Getting on like a house on fire. How are all your charges?

—All on the baker's list, Mrs Breen said.

How many has she? No other in sight.

—You're in black I see. You have no . . .

—No, Mr. Bloom said. I have just come from a funeral.

Going to crop up all day, I foresee. Who's dead, when and what did he die of? Turn up like a bad penny.

—O dear me, Mrs Breen said, I hope it wasn't any near relation.

May as well get her sympathy.

—Dignam, Mr Bloom said. An old friend of mine. He died quite suddenly, poor fellow. Heart trouble, I believe. Funeral was this morning.

> Your funeral's tomorrow
> While you're coming through the rye.
> Diddlediddle dumdum
> Diddlediddle . . .

—Sad to lose the old friends, Mrs Breen's womaneyes said melancholily.

Now that's quite enough about that. Just quietly: husband.

4. Mrs. Breen had been an old sweetheart of Bloom's.

—And your lord and master?

Mrs Breen turned up her two large eyes. Hasn't lost them anyhow.

—O, don't be talking, she said. He's a caution to rattlesnakes. He's in there now with his lawbooks finding out the law of libel. He has me heartscalded. Wait till I show you.

Hot mockturtle vapour and steam of newbaked jampuffs rolypoly poured out from Harrison's. The heavy noonreek tickled the top of Mr Bloom's gullet. Want to make good pastry, butter, best flour, Demerara sugar, or they'd taste it with the hot tea. Or is it from her? A barefoot arab stood over the grating, breathing in the fumes. Deaden the gnaw of hunger that way. Pleasure or pain is it? Penny dinner. Knife and fork chained to the table.

Opening her handbag, chipped leather, hatpin: ought to have a guard on those things. Stick it in a chap's eye in the tram. Rummaging. Open. Money. Please take one. Devils if they lose sixpence. Raise Cain. Husband barging. Where's the ten shillings I gave you on Monday? Are you feeding your little brother's family? Soiled handkerchief: medicinebottle. Pastille that was fell. What is she? . . .

—There must be a new moon out, she said. He's always bad then.[5] Do you know what he did last night?

Her hand ceased to rummage. Her eyes fixed themselves on him, wide in alarm, yet smiling.

—What? Mr. Bloom asked.

Let her speak. Look straight in her eyes. I believe you. Trust me.

—Woke me up in the night, she said. Dream he had, a nightmare. Indiges.[6]

—Said the ace of spades[7] was walking up the stairs.

—The ace of spades! Mr Bloom said.

She took a folded postcard from her handbag.

—Read that, she said. He got it this morning.

—What is it? Mr Bloom asked, taking the card. U. P.?[8]

—U.p.: up, she said. Someone taking a rise out of him. It's a great shame for them whoever he is.

—Indeed it is, Mr Bloom said.

She took back the card, sighing.

—And now he's going round to Mr Menton's office. He's going to take an action for ten thousand pounds, he says.

She folded the card into her untidy bag and snapped the catch.

Same blue serge dress she had two years ago, the nap bleaching. Seen its best days. Wispish hair over her ears. And that dowdy toque: three old grapes to take the harm out of it. Shabby genteel. She used to be a tasty dresser. Lines round her mouth. Only a year or so older than Molly.

See the eye that woman gave her, passing. Cruel. The unfair sex.

He looked still at her, holding back behind his look his discontent. Pungent mockturtle oxtail mulligatawny. I'm hungry too. Flakes of pastry on the gusset of her dress: daub of sugary flour stuck to her cheek. Rhubarb tart with liberal fillings, rich fruit interior. Josie Powell that was. In Luke Doyle's long ago, Dolphin's Barn, the charades. U.p.: up.

Change the subject.

---

5. Mr. Breen is mentally disturbed.

6. I.e., indigestion, which Bloom thinks caused Mr. Breen's nightmare.

7. A symbol of death.

8. Expression used in Charles Dickens's *Oliver Twist* (1838) to announce the approaching death of an old woman. It also suggests "you're crazy" or "you've been screwed."

—Do you ever see anything of Mrs Beaufoy, Mr Bloom asked.

—Mina Purefoy? she said.

Philip Beaufoy I was thinking. Playgoers' Club[9] Matcham often thinks of the masterstroke. Did I pull the chain? Yes. The last act.

—Yes.

—I just called to ask on the way in is she over it. She's in the lying-in hospital in Holles street. Dr Horne got her in. She's three days bad now.

—O, Mr Bloom said. I'm sorry to hear that.

—Yes, Mrs Breen said. And a houseful of kids at home. It's a very stiff birth, the nurse told me.

—O, Mr Bloom said.

His heavy pitying gaze absorbed her news. His tongue clacked in compassion. Dth! Dth!

—I'm sorry to hear that, he said. Poor thing! Three days! That's terrible for her.

Mrs Breen nodded

—She was taken bad on the Tuesday . . .

Mr Bloom touched her funnybone gently, warning her.

—Mind! Let this man pass.

A bony form strode along the curbstone from the river, staring with a rapt gaze into the sunlight through a heavystringed glass. Tight as a skullpiece a tiny hat gripped his head. From his arm a folded dustcoat, a stick and an umbrella dangled to his stride.

—Watch him, Mr Bloom said. He always walks outside the lampposts. Watch!

—Who is he if it's a fair question? Mrs Breen asked. Is he dotty?

—His name is Cashel Boyle O'Connor Fitzmaurice Tisdall Farrell, Mr Bloom said smiling. Watch!

—He has enough of them, she said. Denis will be like that one of these days.

She broke off suddenly.

—There he is, she said. I must go after him. Goodbye. Remember me to Molly, won't you?

—I will, Mr Bloom said.

He watched her dodge through passers towards the shopfronts. Denis Breen in skimpy frockcoat and blue canvas shoes shuffled out of Harrison's hugging two heavy tomes to his ribs. Blown in from the bay. Like old times. He suffered her to overtake him without surprise and thrust his dull grey beard towards her, his loose jaw wagging as he spoke earnestly.

Meshuggah.[1] Off his chump.

Mr Bloom walked on again easily, seeing ahead of him in sunlight the tight skullpiece, the dangling stick, umbrella, dustcoat. Going the two days. Watch him! Out he goes again. One way of getting on in the world. And that other old mosey lunatic in those duds. Hard time she must have with him.

U.p.: up. I'll take my oath that's Alf Bergan or Richie Goulding. Wrote it for a lark in the Scotch house, I bet anything. Round to Menton's office. His oyster eyes staring at the postcard. Be a feast for the gods.

9. Bloom is thinking of the story "Matcham's Masterstroke," by "Mr. Philip Beaufoy, Playgoers' Club, London," which he had read on the toilet that morning. He then mentally quotes the opening sentence.

1. Mad (Yiddish).

He passed the *Irish Times*. There might be other answers lying there. Like to answer them all. Good system for criminals. Code. At their lunch now. Clerk with the glasses there doesn't know me. O, leave them there to simmer. Enough bother wading through fortyfour of them. Wanted smart lady typist to aid gentleman in literary work. I called you naughty darling because I do not like that other world. Please tell me what is the meaning. Please tell me what perfume does your wife. Tell me who made the world.[2] The way they spring those questions on you. And the other one Lizzie Twigg.[3] My literary efforts have had the good fortune to meet with the approval of the eminent poet A. E. (Mr Geo. Russell).[4] No time to do her hair drinking sloppy tea with a book of poetry.

Best paper by long chalks for a small ad. Got the provinces now. Cook and general, exc cuisine, housemaid kept. Wanted live man for spirit counter. Resp. girl (R. C.) wishes to hear of post in fruit or pork shop. James Carlisle made that. Six and a half per cent dividend. Made a big deal on Coates's shares. Ca' canny. Cunning old Scotch hunks. All the toady news. Our gracious and popular vicereine.[5] Bought the *Irish Field* now. Lady Mountcashel has quite recovered after her confinement and rode out with the Ward Union staghounds at the enlargement yesterday at Rathoath. Uneatable fox. Pothunters too. Fear injects juices make it tender enough for them. Riding astride. Sit her horse like a man. Weightcarrying huntress. No sidesaddle or pillion for her, not for Joe. First to the meet and in at the death. Strong as a broodmare some of those horsey women. Swagger around livery stables. Toss off a glass of brandy neat while you'd say knife. That one at the Grosvenor this morning. Up with her on the car: wishswish. Stonewall or fivebarred gate put her mount to it. Think that pugnosed driver did it out of spite. Who is this she was like? O yes! Mrs Miriam Dandrade that sold me her old wraps and black underclothes in the Shelbourne hotel. Divorced Spanish American. Didn't take a feather out of her my handling them. As if I was her clotheshorse. Saw her in the viceregal party when Stubbs the park ranger got me in with Whelan of the *Express*. Scavenging what the quality left. High tea. Mayonnaise I poured on the plums thinking it was custard. Her ears ought to have tingled for a few weeks after. Want to be a bull for her. Born courtesan. No nursery work for her, thanks.

Poor Mrs Purefoy! Methodist husband. Method in his madness. Saffron bun and milk and soda lunch in the educational dairy. Eating with a stopwatch, thirtytwo chews to the minute. Still his muttonchop whiskers grew. Supposed to be well connected. Theodore's cousin in Dublin Castle. One tony relative in every family. Hardy annuals he presents her with. Saw him out at the Three Jolly Topers marching along bareheaded and his eldest boy carrying one in a marketnet. The squallers. Poor thing! Then having to give the breast year after

2. Cf. Marlowe's *The Tragical History of Doctor Faustus* 5, lines 237–44:

FAUSTUS . . . Tell me who made the world?
MEPHASTOPHILIS I will not.
. . . Think on hell Faustus, for thou art damned.
FAUSTUS Think, Faustus, upon God, that made the world.

3. Bloom is mentally quoting a letter written to him by the typist Martha Clifford, with whom he is carrying on a purely epistolary love affair (she

had misspelled *word* as *world*: "I do not like that other world"). Lizzie Twigg was one of the other typists who had answered his advertisement for a secretary "to aid gentleman in literary work" (Bloom's pretext for beginning such an affair).
4. Æ (George Russell, 1867–1935), the Irish poet mentioned as a reference by Lizzie Twigg when she answered Bloom's advertisement, is later encountered by Bloom with a woman who Bloom speculates might be Lizzie.
5. Wife of the viceroy, who represented the British Crown in Ireland; Bloom is thinking of the society column in the *Irish Times*.

2222 / JAMES JOYCE

year all hours of the night. Selfish those t.t's[6] are. Dog in the manger. Only one lump of sugar in my tea, if you please.

He stood at Fleet street crossing. Luncheon interval a sixpenny at Rowe's? Must look up that ad in the national library.[7] An eightpenny in the Burton. Better. On my way.

He walked on past Bolton's Westmoreland house. Tea. Tea. Tea. I forgot to tap Tom Kernan.[8]

Sss. Dth, dth, dth! Three days imagine groaning on a bed with a vinegared handkerchief round her forehead, her belly swollen out. Phew! Dreadful simply! Child's head too big: forceps. Doubled up inside her trying to butt its way out blindly, groping for the way out. Kill me that would. Lucky Molly got over hers lightly. They ought to invent something to stop that. Life with hard labour. Twilightsleep idea: queen Victoria was given that. Nine she had. A good layer. Old woman that lived in a shoe she had so many children. Suppose he was consumptive. Time someone thought about it instead of gassing about the what was it the pensive bosom of the silver effulgence.[9] Flapdoddle to feed fools on. They could easily have big establishments. Whole thing quite painless out of all the taxes give every child born five quid at compound interest up to twentyone, five per cent is a hundred shillings and five tiresome pounds, multiply by twenty decimal system, encourage people to put by money save hundred and ten and a bit twentyone years want to work it out on paper come to a tidy sum, more than you think.

Not stillborn of course. They are not even registered. Trouble for nothing.

Funny sight two of them together, their bellies out. Molly and Mrs Moisel. Mothers' meeting. Phthisis retires for the time being, then returns. How flat they look after all of a sudden! Peaceful eyes. Weight off their mind. Old Mrs Thornton was a jolly old soul. All my babies, she said. The spoon of pap in her mouth before she fed them. O, that's nyumyum. Got her hand crushed by old Tom Wall's son. His first bow to the public. Head like a prize pumpkin. Snuffy Dr Murren. People knocking them up at all hours. For God's sake doctor. Wife in her throes. Then keep them waiting months for their fee. To attendance on your wife. No gratitude in people. Humane doctors, most of them.

Before the huge high door of the Irish house of parliament a flock of pigeons flew. Their little frolic after meals. Who will we do it on? I pick the fellow in black. Here goes. Here's good luck. Must be thrilling from the air. Apjohn, myself and Owen Goldberg up in the trees near Goose green playing the monkeys. Mackerel they called me.

A squad of constables debouched from College street, marching in Indian file. Goosestep. Foodheated faces, sweating helmets, patting their truncheons. After their feed with a good load of fat soup under their belts. Policeman's lot is oft a happy one.[1] They split up into groups and scattered, saluting towards their beats. Let out to graze. Best moment to attack one in pudding time. A punch in his dinner. A squad of others, marching irregularly, rounded Trinity[2] railings, making for the station. Bound for their troughs. Prepare to receive cavalry. Prepare to receive soup.

6. Abbreviation of *teetotalers*, total abstainers from alcohol.
7. Bloom's goal, on his walk through Dublin, is the National Library, where he wants to look up an advertisement in a back number of the *Kilkenny People*.
8. A Dublin tea merchant and friend of Bloom's, whom Bloom had earlier intended to ask ("tap")

for some tea.
9. "Pensive bosom" and "silver effulgence": Bloom recalls two phrases from a public speech that is quoted (via a newspaper account) in "Aeolus," the novel's seventh episode.
1. Cf. W. S. Gilbert, *Pirates of Penzance*: "The policeman's lot is not a happy one."
2. Trinity College, Dublin.

He crossed under Tommy Moore's roguish finger. They did right to put him up over a urinal: meeting of the waters.[3] Ought to be places for women. Running into cakeshops. Settle my hat straight. *There is not in this wide world a vallee.* Great song of Julia Morkan's. Kept her voice up to the very last. Pupil of Michael Balfe's wasn't she?

He gazed after the last broad tunic. Nasty customers to tackle. Jack Power could a tale unfold: father a G man. If a fellow gave them trouble being lagged they let him have it hot and heavy in the bridewell.[4] Can't blame them after all with the job they have especially the young hornies. That horsepoliceman the day Joe Chamberlain was given his degree in Trinity he got a run for his money.[5] My word he did! His horse's hoofs clattering after us down Abbey street. Luck I had the presence of mind to dive into Manning's or I was souped. He did come a wallop, by George. Must have cracked his skull on the cobblestones. I oughtn't to have got myself swept along with those medicals. And the Trinity jibs[6] in their mortarboards. Looking for trouble. Still I got to know that young Dixon who dressed that sting for me in the Mater and now he's in Holles street where Mrs Purefoy. Wheels within wheels. Police whistle in my ears still. All skedaddled. Why he fixed on me. Give me in charge. Right here it began.

—Up the Boers!

—Three cheers for De Wet![7]

—We'll hang Joe Chamberlain on a sourapple tree.

Silly billies: mob of young cubs yelling their guts out. Vinegar hill. The Butter exchange band. Few years' time half of them magistrates and civil servants. War comes on: into the army helterskelter: same fellows used to. Whether on the scaffold high.

Never know who you're talking to. Corny Kelleher he has Harvey Duff in his eye. Like that Peter or Denis or James Carey that blew the gaff on the invincibles. Member of the corporation too. Egging raw youths on to get in the know. All the time drawing secret service pay from the castle.[8] Drop him like a hot potato. Why those plainclothes men are always courting slaveys. Easily twig a man used to uniform. Squarepushing up against a backdoor. Maul her a bit. Then the next thing on the menu. And who is the gentleman does be visiting there? Was the young master saying anything? Peeping Tom through the keyhole. Decoy duck. Hotblooded young student fooling round her fat arms ironing.

—Are those yours, Mary?

—I don't wear such things . . . Stop or I'll tell the missus on you. Out half the night.

—There are great times coming, Mary. Wait till you see.

—Ah, get along with your great times coming.

Barmaids too. Tobaccoshopgirls.

James Stephens'[9] idea was the best. He knew them. Circles of ten so that a fellow couldn't round on more than his own ring. Sinn Fein.[1] Back out you

3. "The Meeting of the Waters" was a famous poem by the much-loved Irish poet Thomas Moore (1779–1852), whose statue Bloom now passes.
4. Prison.
5. When Joseph Chamberlain, the British colonial secretary, came to Dublin to receive an honorary degree from Trinity College, a group of medical students rioted against him and against the Anglo-Boer War (1899–1902), in which the Boers, or

Afrikaners, fought and lost to the British Empire.
6. Trinity College students.
7. Boer general. "Up" here as in "up with."
8. I.e., from the British government, whose representative lived at Dublin Castle.
9. Irish nationalist revolutionary.
1. Ourselves Alone (Gaelic); Irish revolutionary movement.

get the knife. Hidden hand. Stay in. The firing squad. Turnkey's daughter got
him out of Richmond, off from Lusk. Putting up in the Buckingham Palace
hotel under their very noses. Garibaldi.[2]
 You must have a certain fascination: Parnell. Arthur Griffith[3] is a square-
headed fellow but he has no go in him for the mob. Want to gas about our
lovely land. Gammon[4] and spinach. Dublin Bakery Company's tearoom.
Debating societies. That republicanism is the best form of government. That
the language question should take precedence of the economic question. Have
your daughters inveigling them to your house. Stuff them up with meat and
drink. Michaelmas goose. Here's a good lump of thyme seasoning under the
apron for you. Have another quart of goosegrease before it gets too cold. Half-
fed enthusiasts. Penny roll and a walk with the band. No grace for the carver.
The thought that the other chap pays best sauce in the world. Make themselves
thoroughly at home. Show us over those apricots, meaning peaches. The not
far distant day. Home Rule sun rising up in the northwest.[5]
 His smile faded as he walked, a heavy cloud hiding the sun slowly, shadowing Trinity's surly front. Trams passed one another, ingoing, outgoing,
clanging. Useless words. Things go on same; day after day: squads of police
marching out, back: trams in, out. Those two loonies mooching about. Dignam
carted off. Mina Purefoy swollen belly on a bed groaning to have a child tugged
out of her. One born every second somewhere. Other dying every second.
Since I fed the birds five minutes. Three hundred kicked the bucket. Other
three hundred born, washing the blood off, all are washed in the blood of the
lamb, bawling maaaaaa.
 Cityful passing away, other cityful coming, passing away too: other coming
on, passing on. Houses, lines of houses, streets, miles of pavements, piledup
bricks, stones. Changing hands. This owner, that. Landlord never dies they
say. Other steps into his shoes when he gets his notice to quit. They buy the
place up with gold and still they have all the gold. Swindle in it somewhere.
Piled up in cities, worn away age after age. Pyramids in sand. Built on bread
and onions. Slaves Chinese wall. Babylon. Big stones left. Round towers. Rest
rubble, sprawling suburbs, jerrybuilt, Kerwan's mushroom houses built of
breeze. Shelter for the night.
 No-one is anything.
 This is the very worst hour of the day. Vitality. Dull, gloomy: hate this hour.
Feel as if I had been eaten and spewed.
 Provost's house. The reverend Dr Salmon: tinned salmon. Well tinned in
there. Wouldn't live in it if they paid me. Hope they have liver and bacon
today. Nature abhors a vacuum.
 The sun freed itself slowly and lit glints of light among the silverware in
Walter Sexton's window opposite by which John Howard Parnell[6] passed,
unseeing.
 There he is: the brother. Image of him. Haunting face. Now that's a coin-
cidence. Course hundreds of times you think of a person and don't meet him.
Like a man walking in his sleep. No-one knows him. Must be a corporation

2. Bloom is thinking of a variety of nationalist conspirators who escaped from danger, among them
the 19th-century Italian patriot and general Giuseppe Garibaldi.
3. Founder of Sinn Fein (1872–1922). Charles
Stewart Parnell (1846–1891), Irish nationalist
political leader.
4. Ham, bacon.
5. Reference to Griffith's comment on the *Freeman's Journal* masthead, which showed the sun rising in the northwest from behind the Bank of
Ireland. Bloom has a *Freeman* in his pocket.
6. Charles Parnell's brother.

meeting today. They say he never put on the city marshal's uniform since he got the job. Charley Beulger used to come out on his high horse, cocked hat, puffed, powdered and shaved. Look at the woebegone walk of him. Eaten a bad egg. Poached eyes on ghost. I have a pain. Great man's brother: his brother's brother. He'd look nice on the city charger. Drop into the D. B. C. probably for his coffee, play chess there. His brother used men as pawns. Let them all go to pot. Afraid to pass a remark on him. Freeze them up with that eye of his. That's the fascination: the name. All a bit touched. Mad Fanny and his other sister Mrs Dickinson driving about with scarlet harness. Bolt upright like surgeon M'Ardle. Still David Sheehy beat him for south Meath. Apply for the Chiltern Hundreds[7] and retire into public life. The patriot's banquet. Eating orangepeels in the park. Simon Dedalus said when they put him in parliament that Parnell would come back from the grave and lead him out of the House of Commons by the arm.

—Of the twoheaded octopus, one of whose heads is the head upon which the ends of the world have forgotten to come while the other speaks with a Scotch accent. The tentacles . . .

They passed from behind Mr Bloom along the curbstone. Beard and bicycle. Young woman.

And there he is too. Now that's really a coincidence: second time. Coming events cast their shadows before. With the approval of the eminent poet, Mr Geo Russell. That might be Lizzie Twigg with him.[8] A. E.: what does that mean? Initials perhaps. Albert Edward, Arthur Edmund, Alphonsus Eb Ed El Esquire. What was he saying? The ends of the world with a Scotch accent. Tentacles: octopus. Something occult: symbolism. Holding forth. She's taking it all in. Not saying a word. To aid gentleman in literary work.

His eyes followed the high figure in homespun, beard and bicycle, a listening woman at his side. Coming from the vegetarian. Only weggebobbles and fruit. Don't eat a beefsteak. If you do the eyes of that cow will pursue you through all eternity. They say it's healthier. Wind and watery though. Tried it. Keep you on the run all day. Bad as a bloater. Dreams all night. Why do they call that thing they gave me nutsteak? Nutarians. Fruitarians. To give you the idea you are eating rumpsteak. Absurd. Salty too. They cook in soda. Keep you sitting by the tap all night.

Her stockings are loose over her ankles. I detest that: so tasteless. Those literary etherial people they are all. Dreamy, cloudy, symbolistic. Esthetes they are. I wouldn't be surprised if it was that kind of food you see produces the like waves of the brain the poetical. For example one of those policemen sweating Irish stew into their shirts; you couldn't squeeze a line of poetry out of him. Don't know what poetry is even. Must be in a certain mood.

> The dreamy cloudy gull
> Waves o'er the waters dull.

He crossed at Nassau street corner and stood before the window of Yeates and Son, pricing the fieldglasses. Or will I drop into old Harris's and have a chat with young Sinclair? Wellmannered fellow. Probably at his lunch. Must

7. The stewardship of the Chiltern Hundreds (a tract of land in central England owned by the British Crown) is by a legal figment held to be an office of profit under the Crown and is conferred on members of Parliament wishing to resign, which by law they cannot do. Members of Parliament who accept an office of profit under the Crown must vacate their seats.
8. Bloom wonders whether the woman with A. E. might be Lizzie Twigg and then goes on to speculate on the meaning of "A. E." and on Russell's mystical ideas.

get those old glasses of mine set right. Gœrz lenses six guineas. Germans making their way everywhere. Sell on easy terms to capture trade. Undercutting. Might chance on a pair in the railway lost property office. Astonishing the things people leave behind them in trains and cloakrooms. What do they be thinking about? Women too. Incredible. Last year travelling to Ennis had to pick up that farmer's daughter's bag and hand it to her at Limerick junction. Unclaimed money too. There's a little watch up there on the roof of the bank to test those glasses by.

His lids came down on the lower rims of his irides. Can't see it. If you imagine it's there you can almost see it. Can't see it.

He faced about and, standing between the awnings, held out his right hand at arm's length towards the sun. Wanted to try that often. Yes: completely. The tip of his little finger blotted out the sun's disk. Must be the focus where the rays cross. If I had black glasses. Interesting. There was a lot of talk about those sunspots when we were in Lombard street west. Terrific explosions they are. There will be a total eclipse this year: autumn some time.

Now that I come to think of it, that ball falls at Greenwich time. It's the clock is worked by an electric wire from Dunsink. Must go out there some first Saturday of the month. If I could get an introduction to professor Joly or learn up something about his family. That would do to: man always feels complimented. Flattery where least expected. Nobleman proud to be descended from some king's mistress. His foremother. Lay it on with a trowel. Cap in hand goes through the land. Not go in and blurt out what you know you're not to: what's parallax? Show this gentleman the door.

Ah.

His hand fell again to his side.

Never know anything about it. Waste of time. Gasballs spinning about, crossing each other, passing. Same old dingdong always. Gas, then solid, then world, then cold, then dead shell drifting around, frozen rock like that pineapple rock. The moon. Must be a new moon out, she said. I believe there is.

He went on by la maison Claire.

Wait. The full moon was the night we were Sunday fortnight exactly there is a new moon. Walking down by the Tolka. Not bad for a Fairview moon. She was humming. The young May moon she's beaming, love. He other side of her. Elbow, arm. He. Glowworm's la-amp is gleaming, love. Touch. Fingers. Asking. Answer. Yes.

Stop. Stop. If it was it was.[9] Must.

Mr Bloom, quickbreathing, slowlier walking passed Adam court.

With deep quiet relief, his eyes took note: this is street here middle of the day Bob Doran's bottle shoulders. On his annual bend, M'Coy said. They drink in order to say or do something or *cherchez la femme*.[1] Up in the Coombe with chummies and streetwalkers and then the rest of the year as sober as a judge.

Yes. Thought so. Sloping into the Empire. Gone. Plain soda would do him good. Where Pat Kinsella had his Harp theatre before Whitbread ran the Queen's.[2] Broth of a boy. Dion Boucicault[3] business with his harvestmoon face in a poky bonnet. Three Purty Maids from School. How time flies eh? Showing long red pantaloons under his skirts. Drinkers, drinking, laughed spluttering, their drink against their breath. More power, Pat. Coarse red: fun

9. Bloom is thinking again of his wife's infidelity.
1. Look for the woman, i.e., in the case (French).
2. The Queen's Theatre.

3. Irish-born American dramatist, manager, and actor.

for drunkards: guffaw and smoke. Take off that white hat. His parboiled eyes. Where is he now? Beggar somewhere. The harp that once did starve us all.[4] I was happier then. Or was that I? Or am I now I? Twentyeight I was. She twentythree when we left Lombard street west something changed. Could never like it again after Rudy. Can't bring back time. Like holding water in your hand. Would you go back to then? Just beginning then. Would you? Are you not happy in your home, you poor little naughty boy? Wants to sew on buttons for me. I must answer. Write it in the library.

Grafton street gay with housed awnings lured his senses. Muslin prints silk, dames and dowagers, jingle of harnesses, hoofthuds lowringing in the baking causeway. Thick feet that woman has in the white stockings. Hope the rain mucks them up on her. Countrybred chawbacon. All the beef to the heels were in. Always gives a woman clumsy feet. Molly looks out of plumb.

He passed, dallying, the windows of Brown Thomas, silk mercers. Cascades of ribbons. Flimsy China silks. A tilted urn poured from its mouth a flood of bloodhued poplin: lustrous blood. The huguenots brought that here. *La causa è santa!*[5] *Tara tara.* Great chorus that. *Tara.* Must be washed in rainwater. Meyerbeer. *Tara: bom bom bom.*

Pincushions. I'm a long time threatening to buy one. Stick them all over the place. Needles in window curtains.

He bared slightly his left forearm. Scrape: nearly gone. Not today anyhow. Must go back for that lotion. For her birthday perhaps. Junejuly augseptember eighth. Nearly three months off. Then she mightn't like it. Women won't pick up pins. Say it cuts lo.

Gleaming silks, petticoats on slim brass rails, rays of flat silk stockings. Useless to go back. Had to be. Tell me all.

High voices. Sunwarm silk. Jingling harnesses. All for a woman, home and houses, silkwebs, silver, rich fruits, spicy from Jaffa. Agendath Netaim.[6] Wealth of the world.

A warm human plumpness settled down on his brain. His brain yielded. Perfume of embraces all him assailed. With hungered flesh obscurely, he mutely craved to adore.

Duke street. Here we are. Must eat. The Burton. Feel better then.

He turned Combridge's corner, still pursued. Jingling hoofthuds. Perfumed bodies, warm, full. All kissed, yielded: in deep summer fields, tangled pressed grass, in trickling hallways of tenements, along sofas, creaking beds.

—Jack, love!

—Darling!

—Kiss me, Reggy!

—My boy!

—Love![7]

---

4. A reference to the lack of financial success of the Harp Theatre through a punning reworking of Moore's famous "Harp That Once Through Tara's Halls."

5. "The cause is sacred," chorus from Meyerbeer's opera *Les Huguenots,* which Bloom is recalling. The Huguenots were 16th- and 17th-century French Protestants, many of whom fled to Britain to escape persecution.

6. Planters' Company (Hebrew). Bloom recalls a leaflet, which he had seen that morning and is still carrying in his pocket, advertising an early Zionist settlement

7. Sensual images are leading Bloom to imagine love scenes from a sentimental novel as he enters Burton's restaurant. In the *Odyssey,* the Lestrygonians had used "the handsome daughter of Lestrygonian Antiphates" as a decoy to lure Ulysses' men to her father.

His heart astir he pushed in the door of the Burton restaurant. Stink gripped his trembling breath: pungent meatjuice, slop of greens. See the animals feed. Men, men, men.

Perched on high stools by the bar, hats shoved back, at the tables calling for more bread no charge, swilling, wolfing gobfuls of sloppy food, their eyes bulging, wiping wetted moustaches. A pallid suetfaced young man polished his tumbler knife fork and spoon with his napkin. New set of microbes. A man with an infant's saucestained napkin tucked round him shovelled gurgling soup down his gullet. A man spitting back on his plate: halfmasticated gristle: no teeth to chewchewchew it. Chump chop from the grill. Bolting to get it over. Sad booser's eyes. Bitten off more than he can chew. Am I like that? See ourselves as others see us. Hungry man is an angry man. Working tooth and jaw. Don't! O! A bone! That last pagan king of Ireland Cormac in the schoolpoem choked himself at Sletty southward of the Boyne.[8] Wonder what he was eating. Something galoptious.[9] Saint Patrick converted him to Christianity. Couldn't swallow it all however.

—Roast beef and cabbage.

—One stew.

Smells of men. His gorge rose. Spaton sawdust, sweetish warmish cigarettesmoke, reek of plug, spilt beer, men's beery piss, the stale of ferment.

Couldn't eat a morsel here. Fellow sharpening knife and fork, to eat all before him, old chap picking his tootles. Slight spasm, full, chewing the cud. Before and after. Grace after meals. Look on this picture then on that. Scoffing up stewgravy with sopping sippets of bread. Lick it off the plate, man! Get out of this.

He gazed round the stooled and tabled eaters, tightening the wings of his nose.

—Two stouts here.

—One corned and cabbage.

That fellow ramming a knifeful of cabbage down as if his life depended on it. Good stroke. Give me the fidgets to look. Safer to eat from his three hands. Tear it limb from limb. Second nature to him. Born with a silver knife in his mouth. That's witty, I think. Or no. Silver means born rich. Born with a knife. But then the allusion is lost.

An illgirt server gathered sticky clattering plates. Rock, the bailiff, standing at the bar blew the foamy crown from his tankard. Well up: it splashed yellow near his boot. A diner, knife and fork upright, elbows on table, ready for a second helping stared towards the food-lift across his stained square of newspaper. Other chap telling him something with his mouth full. Sympathetic listener. Table talk. I munched hum un thu Unchster Bunk un Munchday. Ha? Did you, faith?

Mr Bloom raised two fingers doubtfully to his lips. His eyes said:

—Not here. Don't see him.[1]

Out. I hate dirty eaters.

He backed towards the door. Get a light snack in Davy Byrne's. Stopgap. Keep me going. Had a good breakfast.

—Roast and mashed here.

---

8. Bloom is recalling a "schoolpoem" about a legendary incident in Irish history.
9. I.e., "goluptious," slang for delicious.

1. He pretends he is looking for someone he cannot see, so that he has an excuse to leave without eating.

—Pint of stout.

Every fellow for his own, tooth and nail. Gulp. Grub. Gulp. Gobstuff.

He came out into clearer air and turned back towards Grafton street. Eat or be eaten. Kill! Kill!

Suppose that communal kitchen years to come perhaps. All trotting down with porringers and tommycans to be filled. Devour contents in the street. John Howard Parnell example the provost of Trinity every mother's son don't talk of your provosts and provost of Trinity women and children, cabmen, priests, parsons, fieldmarshals, archbishops. From Ailesbury road, Clyde road, artisans' dwellings north Dublin union, lord mayor in his gingerbread coach, old queen in a bathchair. My plate's empty. After you with our incorporated drinking cup. Like sir Philip Crampton's fountain. Rub off the microbes with your handkerchief. Next chap rubs on a new batch with his. Father O'Flynn would make hares of them all. Have rows all the same. All for number one. Children fighting for the scrapings of the pot. Want a souppot as big as the Phoenix park. Harpooning flitches and hindquarters out of it. Hate people all round you. City Arms hotel *table d'hôte* she called it. Soup, joint and sweet. Never know whose thoughts you're chewing. Then who'd wash up all the plates and forks? Might be all feeding on tabloids that time. Teeth getting worse and worse.

After all there's a lot in that vegetarian fine flavour of things from the earth garlic, of course, it stinks Italian organgrinders crisp of onions mushrooms truffles. Pain to animal too. Pluck and draw fowl. Wretched brutes there at the cattlemarket waiting for the poleaxe to split their skulls open. Moo. Poor trembling calves. Meh. Staggering bob. Bubble and squeak. Butchers' buckets wobble lights. Give us that brisket off the hook. Plup. Rawhead and bloody bones. Flayed glasseyed sheep hung from their haunches, sheepsnouts bloody-papered snivelling nosejam on sawdust. Top and lashers going out. Don't maul them pieces, young one.

Hot fresh blood they prescribe for decline. Blood always needed. Insidious. Lick it up smokinghot, thick sugary. Famished ghosts.

Ah, I'm hungry.

He entered Davy Byrne's. Moral pub. He doesn't chat. Stands a drink now and then. But in leapyear once in four. Cashed a cheque for me once.

What will I take now? He drew his watch. Let me see now. Shandygaff?

—Hello, Bloom, Nosey Flynn said from his nook.

—Hello, Flynn.

—How's things?

—Tiptop . . . Let me see. I'll take a glass of burgundy and . . . let me see.

Sardines on the shelves. Almost taste them by looking. Sandwich? Ham and his descendants mustered and bred there. Potted meats. What is home without Plumtree's potted meat? Incomplete. What a stupid ad! Under the obituary notices they stuck it. All up a plumtree. Dignam's potted mat. Cannibals would with lemon and rice. White missionary too salty. Like pickled pork. Expect the chief consumes the parts of honour. Ought to be tough from exercise. His wives in a row to watch the effect. *There was a right royal old nigger. Who ate or something the somethings of the reverend Mr MacTrigger.* With it an abode of bliss. Lord knows what concoction. Cauls mouldy tripes windpipes faked and minced up. Puzzle find the meat. Kosher. No meat and milk together. Hygiene that was what they call now, Yom Kippur fast spring cleaning of inside. Peace and war depend on some fellow's digestion. Religions. Christmas turkeys and

2230 / JAMES JOYCE

geese. Slaughter of innocents.[2] Eat, drink and be merry. Then casual wards full after. Heads bandaged. Cheese digests all but itself. Mighty cheese.

—Have you a cheese sandwich?

—Yes, sir.

Like a few olives too if they had them. Italian I prefer. Good glass of burgundy; take away that. Lubricate. A nice salad, cool as a cucumber. Tom Kernan can dress. Puts gusto into it. Pure olive oil. Milly served me that cutlet with a sprig of parsley. Take one Spanish onion. God made food, the devil the cooks. Devilled crab.

—Wife well?

—Quite well, thanks . . . A cheese sandwich, then. Gorgonzola, have you?

—Yes, sir.

Nosey Flynn sipped his grog.

—Doing any singing those times?

Look at his mouth. Could whistle in his own ear. Flap ears to match. Music. Knows as much about it as my coachman. Still better tell him. Does no harm. Free ad.

—She's engaged for a big tour end of this month. You may have heard perhaps.

—No. O, that's the style. Who's getting it up?

The curate[3] served.

—How much is that?

—Seven d., sir . . . Thank you, sir.

Mr Bloom cut his sandwich into slender strips. *Mr MacTrigger.* Easier than the dreamy creamy stuff. *His five hundred wives. Had the time of their lives.*

—Mustard, sir?

—Thank you.

He studded under each lifted strip yellow blobs. *Their lives.* I have it. *It grew bigger and bigger and bigger.*

—Getting it up? he said. Well, it's like a company idea, you see. Part shares and part profits.

—Ay, now I remember, Nosey Flynn said, putting his hand in his pocket to scratch his groin. Who is this was telling me? Isn't Blazes Boylan mixed up in it?

A warm shock of air heat of mustard hanched on Mr Bloom's heart. He raised his eyes and met the stare of a bilious clock. Two. Pub clock five minutes fast. Time going on. Hands moving. Two. Not yet.[4]

His midriff yearned then upward, sank within him, yearned more longly, longingly.

Wine.

He smellsipped the cordial juice and, bidding his throat strongly to speed it, set his wineglass delicately down.

—Yes, he said. He's the organiser in point of fact.

No fear: no brains.

Nosey Flynn snuffled and scratched. Flea having a good square meal.

—He had a good slice of luck, Jack Mooney was telling me, over that boxing match Myler Keogh won again that soldier in the Portobello barracks. By God, he had the little kipper down in the country Carlow he was telling me. . . .

<hr/>

2. Cf. Herod's massacre of innocent children after hearing prophecies of Jesus' birth (Matthew 2.16).
3. Bartender.
4. I.e., not yet time for Boylan to visit Molly.

Hope that dewdrop doesn't come down into his glass. No, snuffled it up.

—For near a month, man, before it came off. Sucking duck eggs by God till further orders. Keep him off the boose, see? O, by God, Blazes is a hairy chap.

Davy Byrne came forward from the hindbar in tuckstitched shirtsleeves, cleaning his lips with two wipes of his napkin. Herring's blush. Whose smile upon each feature plays with such and such replete. Too much fat on the parsnips.

—And here's himself and pepper on him, Nosey Flynn said. Can you give us a good one for the Gold cup?

—I'm off that, Mr Flynn, Davy Byrne answered. I never put anything on a horse.

—You're right there, Nosey Flynn said.

Mr Bloom ate his strips of sandwich, fresh clean bread, with relish of disgust, pungent mustard, the feety savour of green cheese. Sips of his wine soothed his palate. Not logwood that. Tastes fuller this weather with the chill off.

Nice quiet bar. Nice piece of wood in that counter. Nicely planed. Like the way it curves there.

—I wouldn't do anything at all in that line, Davy Byrne said. It ruined many a man, the same horses.

Vintners' sweepstake. Licensed for the sale of beer, wine and spirits for consumption on the premises. Heads I win tails you lose.

—True for you, Nosey Flynn said. Unless you're in the know. There's no straight sport going now. Lenehan gets some good ones. He's giving Sceptre today. Zinfandel's the favourite, lord Howard de Walden's, won at Epsom. Morny Cannon is riding him. I could have got seven to one against Saint Amant a fortnight before.

—That so? Davy Byrne said. . . .

He went towards the window and, taking up the petty cash book, scanned its pages.

—I could, faith, Nosey Flynn said, snuffling. That was a rare bit of horseflesh. Saint Frusquin was her sire. She won in a thunderstorm, Rothschild's filly, with wadding in her ears. Blue jacket and yellow cap. Bad luck to big Ben Dollard and his John O'Gaunt. He put me off it. Ay.

He drank resignedly from his tumbler, running his fingers down the flutes.

—Ay, he said, sighing.

Mr Bloom, champing standing, looked upon his sigh. Nosey numbskull. Will I tell him that horse Lenehan?[5] He knows already. Better let him forget. Go and lose more. Fool and his money. Dewdrop coming down again. Cold nose he'd have kissing a woman. Still they might like. Prickly beards they like. Dogs' cold noses. Old Mrs Riordan with the rumbling stomach's Skye terrier in the City Arms hotel. Molly fondling him in her lap. O, the big doggybowwowsywowsy!

Wine soaked and softened rolled pith of bread mustard a moment mawkish cheese. Nice wine it is. Taste it better because I'm not thirsty. Bath of course does that. Just a bite or two. Then about six o'clock I can. Six. Six. Time will be gone then. She . . .

Mild fire of wine kindled his veins. I wanted that badly. Felt so off colour. His eyes unhungrily saw shelves of tins, sardines, gaudy lobsters' claws. All

5. Bloom is wondering whether to pass on a tip from Lenehan, who wrote for the racing paper *Sport*.

the odd things people pick up for food. Out of shells, periwinkles with a pin, off trees, snails out of the ground the French eat, out of the sea with bait on a hook. Silly fish learn nothing in a thousand years. If you didn't know risky putting anything into your mouth. Poisonous berries. Johnny Magories. Roundness you think good. Gaudy colour warns you off. One fellow told another and so on. Try it on the dog first. Led on by the smell or the look. Tempting fruit. Ice cones. Cream. Instinct. Orangegroves for instance. Need artificial irrigation. Bleibtreustrasse.[6] Yes but what about oysters. Unsightly like a clot of phlegm. Filthy shells. Devil to open them too. Who found them out? Garbage, sewage they feed on. Fizz and Red bank oysters. Effect on the sexual. Aphrodis. He was in the Red bank this morning. Was he oyster old fish at table. Perhaps he young flesh in bed. No. June has no ar no oysters. But there are people like tainted game. Jugged hare. First catch your hare. Chinese eating eggs fifty years old, blue and green again. Dinner of thirty courses. Each dish harmless might mix inside. Idea for a poison mystery. That archduke Leopold was it. No. Yes, or was it Otto one of those Habsburgs? Or who was it used to eat the scruff off his own head? Cheapest lunch in town. Of course, aristocrats, then the others copy to be in the fashion. Milly too rock oil and flour. Raw pastry I like myself. Half the catch of oysters they throw back in the sea to keep up the price. Cheap. No-one would buy. Caviare. Do the grand. Hock in green glasses. Swell blowout. Lady this. Powdered bosom pearls. The *élite. Crème de la crème.*[7] They want special dishes to pretend they're. Hermit with a platter of pulse keep down the stings of the flesh. Know me come eat with me. Royal sturgeon. High sheriff, Coffey, the butcher, right to venisons of the forest from his ex.[8] Send him back the half of a cow. Spread I saw down in the Master of the Rolls' kitchen area. Whitehatted *Chef* like a rabbi. Combustible duck. Curly cabbage *à la duchesse de Parme.* Just as well to write it on the bill of fare so you can know what you've eaten too many drugs spoil the broth. I know it myself. Dosing it with Edwards' desicated soup. Geese stuffed silly for them. Lobsters boiled alive. Do ptake some ptarmigan. Wouldn't mind being a waiter in a swell hotel. Tips, evening dress, halfnaked ladies. May I tempt you to a little more filleted lemon sole, miss Dubedat? Yes, do bedad. And she did bedad. Huguenot name I expect that. A miss Dubedat lived in Killiney, I remember. *Du, de la,* French. Still it's the same fish, perhaps old Micky Hanlon of Moore street ripped the guts out of making money, hand over fist, finger in fishes' gills, can't write his name on a cheque, think he was painting the landscape with his mouth twisted. Moooikill A Aitcha Ha. Ignorant as a kish of brogues,[9] worth fifty thousand pounds.

Stuck on the pane two flies buzzed, stuck.

Glowing wine on his palate lingered swallowed. Crushing in the winepress grapes of Burgundy. Sun's heat it is. Seems to a secret touch telling me memory. Touched his sense moistened remembered. Hidden under wild ferns on Howth. Below us bay sleeping sky. No sound. The sky. The bay purple by the Lion's head. Green by Drumleck. Yellowgreen towards Sutton. Fields of undersea, the lines faint brown in grass, buried cities. Pillowed on my coat

6. The Berlin street that contained the offices of the "Planters' Company" (see n. 6, p. 2227).
7. Cream of the cream (i.e., the very best, socially).
8. All sturgeon caught in or off Britain were the property of the king, according to the ancient traditional rights to certain kinds of fish or game. Bloom goes on to imagine a Dublin butcher having a "right to venisons of the forest from his ex[cellency]"—i.e., the viceroy.
9. A basket of shoes.

she had her hair, earwigs in the heather scrub my hand under her nape, you'll toss me all. O wonder! Coolsoft with ointments her hand touched me, caressed: her eyes upon me did not turn away. Ravished over her I lay, full lips full open, kissed her mouth. Yum. Softly she gave me in my mouth the seedcake warm and chewed. Mawkish pulp her mouth had mumbled sweet and sour with spittle. Joy: I ate it: joy. Young life, her lips that gave me pouting. Soft, warm, sticky gumjelly lips. Flowers her eyes were, take me, willing eyes. Pebbles fell. She lay still. A goat. No-one. High on Ben Howth rhododendrons a nannygoat walking surefooted, dropping currants. Screened under ferns she laughed warmfolded. Wildly I lay on her, kissed her, eyes, her lips, her stretched neck, beating, woman's breasts full in her blouse of nun's veiling, fat nipples upright. Hot I tongued her. She kissed me. I was kissed. All yielding she tossed my hair. Kissed, she kissed me.[1]

Me. And me now.

Stuck, the flies buzzed.

His downcast eyes followed the silent veining of the oaken slab. Beauty: it curves: curves are beauty. Shapely goddesses, Venus, Juno: curves the world admires. Can see them library museum standing in the round hall, naked goddesses. Aids to digestion. They don't care what man looks. All to see. Never speaking, I mean to say to fellows like Flynn. Suppose she did Pygmalion and Galatea[2] what would she say first? Mortal! Put you in your proper place. Quaffing nectar at mess with gods, golden dishes, all ambrosial. Not like a tanner lunch we have, boiled mutton, carrots and turnips, bottle of Allsop. Nectar, imagine it drinking electricity: god's food. Lovely forms of women sculped Junonian. Immortal lovely. And we stuffing food in one hole and out behind: food, chyle, blood, dung, earth, food: have to feed it like stoking an engine. They have no. Never looked. I'll look today. Keeper won't see. Bend down let something see if she.

Dribbling a quiet message from his bladder came to go to do not to do there to do. A man and ready he drained his glass to the lees and walked, to men too they gave themselves, manly conscious, lay with men lovers, a youth enjoyed her, to the yard.

When the sound of his boots had ceased Davy Byrne said from his book:

—What is this he is? Isn't he in the insurance line?

—He's out of that long ago, Nosey Flynn said. He does canvassing for the *Freeman*.

—I know him well to see, Davy Byrne said. Is he in trouble?

—Trouble? Nosey Flynn said. Not that I heard of. Why?

—I noticed he was in mourning.

—Was he? Nosey Flynn said. So he was, faith. I asked him how was all at home. You're right, by God. So he was.

—I never broach the subject, Davy Byrne said humanely, if I see a gentleman is in trouble that way. It only brings it up fresh in their minds.

—It's not the wife anyhow, Nosey Flynn said. I met him the day before yesterday and he coming out of that Irish farm dairy John Wyse Nolan's wife

1. Bloom is remembering when he first proposed to Molly, on the Hill of Howth, near Dublin. Molly also recalls this in the final episode ("Penelope"), which is her soliloquy: "we were lying among the rhododendrons on Howth head in the gray tweed suit and his straw hat the day I got him to propose to me yes . . . my God after that long kiss I near lost my breath . . . I saw he understood or felt what a woman is and I knew I could always get round him and I gave him all the pleasure I could leading him on."

2. In Greek mythology Pygmalion, king of Cyprus, sculpted a statue of the goddess Aphrodite that became a mortal woman, Galatea.

has in Henry street with a jar of cream in his hand taking it home to his better half. She's well nourished, I tell you. Plovers on toast.

—And is he doing for the *Freeman?* Davy Byrne said.

Nosey Flynn pursed his lips.

—He doesn't buy cream on the ads he picks up. You can make bacon of that.

—How so? Davy Byrne asked, coming from his book.

Nosey Flynn made swift passes in the air with juggling fingers. He winked.

—He's in the craft,[3] he said.

—Do you tell me so? Davy Byrne said.

—Very much so, Nosey Flynn said. Ancient free and accepted order. Light, life and love, by God. They give him a leg up. I was told that by a, well, I won't say who.

—Is that a fact?

—O, it's a fine order, Nosey Flynn said. They stick to you when you're down. I know a fellow was trying to get into it, but they're as close as damn it. By God they did right to keep the women out of it.

Davy Byrne smiledyawnednodded all in one:

—Iiiiiichaaaaaaach!

—There was one woman, Nosey Flynn said, hid herself in a clock to find out what they do be doing. But be damned but they smelt her out and swore her in on the spot a master mason. That was one of the Saint Legers of Doneraile.

Davy Byrne, sated after his yawn, said with tearwashed eyes:

—And is that a fact? Decent quiet man he is. I often saw him in here and I never once saw him, you know, over the line.

—God Almighty couldn't make him drunk, Nosey Flynn said firmly. Slips off when the fun gets too hot. Didn't you see him look at his watch? Ah, you weren't there. If you ask him to have a drink first thing he does he outs with the watch to see what he ought to imbibe. Declare to God he does.

—There are some like that, Davy Byrne said. He's a safe man, I'd say.

—He's not too bad, Nosey Flynn said, snuffling it up. He has been known to put his hand down too to help a fellow. Give the devil his due. O, Bloom has his good points. But there's one thing he'll never do.

His hand scrawled a dry pen signature beside his grog.

—I know, Davy Byrne said.

—Nothing in black and white, Nosey Flynn said.

Paddy Leonard and Bantam Lyons came in. Tom Rochford followed frowning, a plaining hand on his claret waistcoat.

—Day, Mr Byrne.

—Day, gentlemen.

They paused at the counter.

—Who's standing? Paddy Leonard asked.

—I'm sitting anyhow, Nosey Flynn answered.

—Well, what'll it be? Paddy Leonard asked.

—I'll take a stone ginger, Bantam Lyons said.

—How much? Paddy Leonard cried. Since when, for God's sake? What's yours, Tom?

—How is the main drainage? Nosey Flynn asked, sipping.

---

3. I.e., in the "free and accepted order" of Freemasons, one of the oldest European secret societies; it was not in good repute in predominantly Roman Catholic countries like Ireland.

For answer Tom Rochford pressed his hand to his breastbone and hiccupped.

—Would I trouble you for a glass of fresh water, Mr Byrne? he said.

—Certainly, sir.

Paddy Leonard eyed his alemates.

—Lord love a duck, he said, look at what I'm standing drinks to! Cold water and gingerpop! Two fellows that would suck whisky off a sore leg. He has some bloody horse up his sleeve for the Gold cup. A dead snip.

—Zinfandel is it? Nosey Flynn asked.

Tom Rochford spilt powder from a twisted paper into the water set before him.

—That cursed dyspepsia, he said before drinking.

—Breadsoda is very good, Davy Byrne said.

Tom Rochford nodded and drank.

—Is it Zinfandel?

—Say nothing, Bantam Lyons winked. I'm going to plunge five bob on my own.

—Tell us if you're worth your salt and be damned to you, Paddy Leonard said. Who gave it to you?

Mr Bloom on his way out raised three fingers in greeting.

—So long, Nosey Flynn said.

The others turned.

—That's the man now that gave it to me, Bantam Lyons whispered.

—Prrwht! Paddy Leonard said with scorn. Mr Byrne, sir, we'll take two of your small Jamesons[4] after that and a . . .

—Stone ginger, Davy Byrne added civilly.

—Ay, Paddy Leonard said. A suckingbottle for the baby.

Mr Bloom walked towards Dawson street, his tongue brushing his teeth smooth. Something green it would have to be: spinach say. Then with those Röntgen rays[5] searchlight you could.

At Duke lane a ravenous terrier choked up a sick knuckly cud on the cobblestones and lapped it with new zest. Surfeit. Returned with thanks having fully digested the contents. First sweet then savoury. Mr Bloom coasted warily. Ruminants. His second course. Their upper jaw they move. Wonder if Tom Rochford will do anything with that invention of his. Wasting time explaining it to Flynn's mouth. Lean people long mouths. Ought to be a hall or a place where inventors could go in and invent free. Course then you'd have all the cranks pestering.

He hummed, prolonging in solemn echo, the closes of the bars:

> *Don Giovanni, a cenar teco*
> *M'invitasti.*[6]

Feel better. Burgundy. Good pick me up. Who distilled first? Some chap in the blues. Dutch courage. That *Kilkenny People* in the national library now I must.

Bare clean closestools, waiting, in the window of William Miller, plumber,

---

4. Brand of Irish whiskey.
5. X-rays.
6. Because Molly is a singer, Bloom is familiar with opera. Here he recalls the song sung by the Commendatore's statue in Mozart's *Don Giovanni* and below he translates accurately the Italian words he quotes, except for *"teco"* (with thee). This opera supplies some of the key themes in *Ulysses*, and the famous duet between Don Giovanni and Zerlina, *"Là ci darèm la mano"* (There we will join hands), haunts Bloom's mind throughout the day. It is on the program of Molly's concert that she is discussing with Boylan that afternoon, and Bloom associates it with her adultery with Boylan.

turned back his thoughts. They could: and watch it all the way down, swallow a pin sometimes come out of the ribs years after, tour round the body, changing biliary duct, spleen squirting liver, gastric juice coils of intestines like pipes. But the poor buffer would have to stand all the time with his insides entrails on show. Science.

—*A cenar teco.*
What does that *teco* mean? Tonight perhaps.

> *Don Giovanni, thou hast me invited*
> *To come to supper tonight,*
> *The rum the rumdum.*

Doesn't go properly.

Keyes: two months if I get Nannetti[7] to. That'll be two pounds ten, about two pounds eight. Three Hynes owes me. Two eleven. Prescott's ad. Two fifteen. Five guineas about. On the pig's back.

Could buy one of those silk petticoats for Molly, colour of her new garters. Today. Today. Not think.[8]

Tour the south then. What about English wateringplaces? Brighton, Margate. Piers by moonlight. Her voice floating out. Those lovely seaside girls. Against John Long's a drowsing loafer lounged in heavy thought, gnawing a crusted knuckle. Handy man wants job. Small wages. Will eat anything.

Mr Bloom turned at Gray's confectioner's window of unbought tarts and passed the reverend Thomas Connellan's bookstore. *Why I left the church of Rome? Birds' Nest.* Women run him. They say they used to give pauper children soup to change to protestants in the time of the potato blight. Society over the way papa went to for the conversion of poor jews. Same bait. *Why we left the church of Rome?*

A blind stripling stood tapping the curbstone with his slender cane. No tram in sight. Wants to cross.

—Do you want to cross? Mr Bloom asked.

The blind stripling did not answer. His wallface frowned weakly. He moved his head uncertainly.

—You're in Dawson street, Mr Bloom said. Molesworth street is opposite. Do you want to cross? There's nothing in the way.

The cane moved out trembling to the left. Mr Bloom's eye followed its line and saw again the dyeworks' van drawn up before Drago's. Where I saw his brillantined hair just when I was. Horse drooping. Driver in John Long's. Slaking his drouth.

—There's a van there, Mr Bloom said, but it's not moving. I'll see you across. Do you want to go to Molesworth street?

—Yes, the stripling answered. South Frederick street.

—Come, Mr Bloom said.

He touched the thin elbow gently: then took the limp seeing hand to guide it forward.

Say something to him. Better not do the condescending. They mistrust what you tell them. Pass a common remark.

—The rain kept off.

7. Proofreader and business manager of the *Freeman's Journal* and in charge of the advertising Bloom is trying to get for the paper. If he will add a complimentary reference to Keyes, a grocer, in a gossip column, Keyes promises to renew his advertisement, which means a commission for Bloom.
8. I.e., of Molly and Boylan.

No answer.

Stains on his coat. Slobbers his food, I suppose. Tastes all different for him. Have to be spoonfed first. Like a child's hand, his hand. Like Milly's was. Sensitive. Sizing me up I daresay from my hand. Wonder if he has a name. Van. Keep his cane clear of the horse's legs tired drudge get his doze. That's right. Clear. Behind a bull: in front of a horse.

—Thanks, sir.

Knows I'm a man. Voice.

—Right now? First turn to the left.

The blind stripling tapped the curbstone and went on his way, drawing his cane back, feeling again.

Mr Bloom walked behind the eyeless feet, a flatcut suit of herringbone tweed. Poor young fellow! How on earth did he know that van was there? Must have felt it. See things in their foreheads perhaps. Kind of sense of volume. Weight would he feel it if something was removed. Feel a gap. Queer idea of Dublin he must have, tapping his way round by the stones. Could he walk in a beeline if he hadn't that cane? Bloodless pious face like a fellow going in to be a priest.

Penrose! That was that chap's name.

Look at all the things they can learn to do. Read with their fingers. Tune pianos. Or we are surprised they have any brains. Why we think a deformed person or a hunchback clever if he says something we might say. Of course the other senses are more. Embroider. Plait baskets. People ought to help. Workbasket I could buy Molly's birthday. Hates sewing. Might take an objection. Dark men they call them.

Sense of smell must be stronger too. Smells on all sides bunched together. Each person too. Then the spring, the summer: smells. Tastes. They say you can't taste wines with your eyes shut or a cold in the head. Also smoke in the dark they say get no pleasure.

And with a woman, for instance. More shameless not seeing. That girl passing the Stewart institution, head in the air. Look at me. I have them all on. Must be strange not to see her. Kind of a form in his mind's eye. The voice temperature when he touches her with fingers must almost see the lines, the curves. His hands on her hair, for instance. Say it was black for instance. Good. We call it black. Then passing over her white skin. Different feel perhaps. Feeling of white.

Postoffice. Must answer.[9] Fag[1] today. Send her a postal order two shillings half a crown. Accept my little present. Stationer's just here too. Wait. Think over it.

With a gentle finger he felt ever so slowly the hair combed back above his ears. Again. Fibres of fine fine straw. Then gently his finger felt the skin of his right cheek. Downy hair there too. Not smooth enough. The belly is the smoothest. No-one about. There he goes into Frederick street. Perhaps to Levenston's dancing academy piano. Might be settling my braces.

Walking by Doran's public house he slid his hand between waistcoat and trousers and, pulling aside his shirt gently, felt a slack fold of his belly. But I know it's whitey yellow. Want to try in the dark to see.

He withdrew his hand and pulled his dress to.

Poor fellow! Quite a boy. Terrible. Really terrible. What dreams would he

---

9. Martha Clifford's letter.   1. Nuisance.

have, not seeing. Life a dream for him. Where is the justice being born that way. All those women and children excursion beanfeast burned and drowned in New York.[2] Holocaust. Karma they call that transmigration for sins you did in a past life the reincarnation met him pike hoses.[3] Dear, dear, dear. Pity of course: but somehow you can't cotton on to them someway.

Sir Frederick Falkiner going into the freemasons' hall. Solemn as Troy. After his good lunch in Earlsfort terrace. Old legal cronies cracking a magnum. Tales of the bench and assizes and annals of the bluecoat school.[4] I sentenced him to ten years. I suppose he'd turn up his nose at that stuff I drank. Vintage wine for them, the year marked on a dusty bottle. Has his own ideas of justice in the recorder's court. Wellmeaning old man. Police charge sheets crammed with cases get their percentage manufacturing crime. Sends them to the rightabout. The devil on moneylenders. Gave Reuben J. a great strawcalling. Now he's really what they call a dirty jew. Power those judges have. Crusty old topers in wigs. Bear with a sore paw. And may the Lord have mercy on your soul.

Hello, placard. Mirus bazaar. His excellency the lord lieutenant. Sixteenth today it is. In aid of funds for Mercer's hospital. The *Messiah* was first given for that. Yes. Handel. What about going out there. Ballsbridge. Drop in on Keyes. No use sticking to him like a leech. Wear out my welcome. Sure to know someone on the gate.

Mr Bloom came to Kildare street. First I must. Library.

Straw hat in sunlight. Tan shoes. Turnedup trousers. It is. It is.[5]

His heart quopped[6] softly. To the right. Museum. Goddesses. He swerved to the right.

Is it? Almost certain. Won't look. Wine in my face. Why did I? Too heady. Yes, it is. The walk. Not see. Not see. Get on.

Making for the museum gate with long windy strides he lifted his eyes. Handsome building. Sir Thomas Deane designed. Not following me?

Didn't see me perhaps. Light in his eyes.

The flutter of his breath came forth in short sighs. Quick. Cold statues: quiet there. Safe in a minute.

No, didn't see me. After two. Just at the gate.

My heart!

His eyes beating looked steadfastly at cream curves of stone. Sir Thomas Deane was the Greek architecture.

Look for something I.

His hasty hand went quick into a pocket, took out, read unfolded Agendath Netaim. Where did I?

Busy looking for.

He thrust back quickly Agendath.

Afternoon she said.

I am looking for that. Yes, that. Try all pockets. Handker. *Freeman*. Where did I? Ah, yes. Trousers. Purse. Potato. Where did I?

Hurry. Walk quietly. Moment more. My heart.

2. This terrible disaster on an excursion steamer on a New York City river took place on June 15, 1904, and was reported in the Dublin papers on June 16.
3. I.e., metempsychosis. Bloom is remembering again their morning conversation on this subject, when Molly exclaimed, "O rocks!"
4. Sir Frederick Falkiner wrote the history of the "bluecoat school," in Oxmantown, Dublin, founded by Charles II for poor children.
5. Bloom catches a glimpse of Boylan and tries to avoid an encounter.
6. Throbbed, quivered (dialect, now obsolete).

His hand looking for the where did I put found in his hip pocket soap lotion have to call tepid paper stuck. Ah, soap there! Yes. Gate.[7]
Safe!

1914–21   1922

Finnegans Wake   Because the meanings in *Finnegans Wake* are developed not by action but by language—a great network of multiple puns that echo themes back and forth throughout the book—the careful reading of a single passage, even out of context, will convey more than any summary of the "plot" (some discussion of the general plan of the work is given in the Joyce headnote). The passage printed here was one of Joyce's favorites, and there exists an audio recording of it made by him. It consists of the closing pages of chapter 8 of book 1; the chapter was published separately as "Anna Livia Plurabelle" in 1928 and 1930, although the finished book omits this title.

The entire chapter is a dialogue, and the scene is the river Liffey: two washerwomen are washing in public the dirty linen of HCE and ALP (the "hero" and "heroine") and gossiping as they work. As this excerpt opens, it is growing dark; things become gradually less and less distinct, so that the washerwomen cannot be sure what the objects seen in the dusk really are. As it grows darker, the river becomes wider (we get nearer its mouth) and the wind rises, so that the women have more and more difficulty hearing each other. At last, as night falls, they become part of the landscape, an elm tree and a stone on the river bank. Toward the end of the dialogue they ask to hear a tale of Shem and Shaun (the two sons of HCE and ALP), and this question points the way to book 2, which opens with the boys (metamorphosed for the moment into Glugg and Chuff) playing in front of the tavern in the evening.

A complete annotation of even this brief passage is, of course, a physical impossibility in this anthology. The notes that are provided are intended to indicate the nature of what Joyce does with language and to enable the reader to see some of what is going on. But all sorts of suggestions built up in the language are not referred to in the notes; all readers will find some for themselves.

From Finnegans Wake

From *Anna Livia Plurabelle*

* * * Well, you know or don't you kennet[1] or haven't I told you every telling has a taling and that's the he and the she of it. Look, look, the dusk is growing! My branches lofty are taking root. And my cold cher's gone ashley.[2] Fieluhr?

---

7. Anxious to avoid Boylan, Bloom pretends to admire the architecture of the Museum and National Library building and then pretends to be looking for something in his pockets, where he finds the "Agendath Netaim" leaflet. He continues to search desperately in his pockets to avoid looking up and seeing Boylan, discovers the potato he carries as a remedy against rheumatism and a cake of soap he had bought that morning (the soap reminds him that he must call at the chemist's to collect a face lotion he had ordered for Molly). At last he goes through the National Library gate and feels safe.
1. Ken it ("know it") + Kennet (river in England). Rivers in *Finnegans Wake* symbolize the flow of life, and thousands of river names are suggested throughout the book in allusive pun combinations, as here.
2. "Cold cher": cold cheer (i.e., cold comfort) + cold chair + (perhaps) culture. "Gone ashley": gone to ashes. Going to ashes suggests the fiery death and rebirth of the mythical bird called the phoenix: from the ashes of the dead phoenix rises a new one. Modern culture, which can provide only cold cheer, is in the state of decay, the "going to ashes," which precedes the stage of rebirth into a new cultural cycle (according to Giambattista Vico's cyclical theory of history, which is important to *Finnegans Wake*). "Gone ashley" also means "turned into an ash tree" (i.e., it is so cold that speaker feels herself turning into a tree).

Filou![3] What age is at? It saon[4] is late. 'Tis endless now senne[5] eye or erewone[6] last saw Waterhouse's clogh.[7] They took it asunder, I hurd thum sigh. When will they reassemble it? O, my back, my back, my bach![8] I'd want to go to Aches-les-Pains.[9] Pingpong! There's the Belle for Sexaloitez![10] And Concepta de Send-us-pray! Pang! Wring out the Clothes! Wring in the dew![11] Godavari,[12] vert the showers![13] And grant thaya grace! Aman. Will we spread them here now? Ay, we will. Flip! Spread on your bank and I'll spread mine on mine. Flep! It's what I'm doing. Spread! It's churning chill. Der went[14] is rising. I'll lay a few stones on the hostel sheets. A man and his bride embraced between them. Else I'd have sprinkled and folded them only. And I'll tie my butcher's apron here. It's suety yet. The strollers will pass it by. Six shifts, ten kerchiefs, nine to hold to the fire and this for the code,[15] the convent napkins, twelve, one baby's shawl. Good mother Jossiph[16] knows, she said. Whose head? Mutter snores? Deataceas![17] Wharnow are alle her childer, say? In kingdome gone or power to come or gloria be to them farther? Allalivial, allalluvial![18] Some here, more no more, more again lost alla stranger.[19] I've heard tell that same brooch of the Shannons[20] was married into a family in Spain. And all the Dunders de Dunnes[21] in Markland's[22] Vineland beyond the Brendan's herring pool[23] takes number nine in yangsee's[24] hats. And one of Biddy's[25] beads went bobbing till she rounded up lost histereve[26] with a marigold and a cobbler's candle in a side strain of a main drain of a manzinahurries[27] off Bachelor's Walk. But all that's left to the last of the Meaghers[28] in the loup[29] of the years prefixed and between is one kneebuckle and two hooks in the front. Do you tell me that now? I do in troth. Orara por Orbe and poor Las Animals![30] Ussa, Ulla, we're

3. Pickpocket; thief (French). "Fieluhr": Viel Uhr? (What's the time?; German). From an old anecdote of a German soldier and a French soldier shouting at each other across the Rhine. They mishear each other as the washerwomen will later.
4. Soon + Saône (river in France).
5. Since + Senne (river in Belgium).
6. E'er a one + Erewhon (novel by Samuel Butler—an anagram for Nowhere).
7. Waterhouse's clock, a well-known clock on Dame Street, Dublin.
8. "Brook" (German) + "dear" (Welsh).
9. Cf. Aix-les-Bains, France.
10. "Sachselüte," a Zurich fertility rite (literally, the ringing of six o'clock), which celebrates the burial of winter.
11. Tennyson, In Memoriam: "Ring out the old, ring in the new."
12. God of Eire + the name of a river in India.
13. "Vert": avert + vert (green; French), for "the showers" make grass green.
14. Der Wind (the wind; German) + Derwent (river in England).
15. Cold + code (i.e., the code in which the book is written). The numbers in this sentence have special meanings indicated in other episodes.
16. Joseph + joss (God; pidgin English) + gossip (which derives from "god-sib," Middle English, "godparent").
17. A play on Deo gratias ("thanks be to God") and on Dea Tacita ("silent-goddess"), a name from Roman mythology.
18. Multiple punning—Anna Livia + all alive + la lluvia (rain; Spanish) + alluvial—suggesting the mother-river-fertility associations of ALP. At least two other meanings are also present: All alive O! (street cry of shellfish vendors) + Alleluia (Vulgate Latin form of Hallelujah).
19. Cf. à l'étranger (abroad; French).
20. Same ornament and branch of the Shannons

(family and river).
21. The form of the name suggests an aristocratic Anglo-Norman family. "Dunder" suggests thunder. Dun is an Irish word meaning "hill," "fort on a hill."
22. Borderland + land of the mark (i.e., land of money, or America; Markland's Vineland was one of Leif Eriksson's names for America). Both King Mark of Cornwall (a character in the Tristan and Iseult story) and Mark of the Gospels are primary symbolic characters in Finnegans Wake.
23. The Atlantic Ocean. St. Brendan was an Irish monk who sailed out into the Atlantic to find the terrestrial paradise.
24. Yankees' + Yangtze (river in China). The de Dunnes have swollen heads now that they have emigrated to America.
25. Diminutive form of the name Bridget. St. Brigid (or Bridget) is a patron saint of Ireland. "Biddy" is also a term for an Irish maidservant.
26. Yester eve (last night) + eve of history. The sentence may be paraphrased: "Irish history got lost when she went off in a side branch of the main Roman Catholic Church, and Biddy (i.e., Ireland) landed herself in the dirt." Also, hysteria + eve.
27. A urinal + Manzanares (river in Spain). Also, man's in a hurry.
28. Thomas Francis Meagher, Irish patriot and revolutionary, who was transported to Van Diemen's Land in 1849 and escaped to America in 1852.
29. Loop + loup ("wolf" and also "solitary man"; French). Cf. Wolfe Tone, the ill-fated Irish revolutionist.
30. Souls (Spanish) + the name of a river in Colorado. Ora pro nobis (pray for us; Latin) + Orara (river in New South Wales) + pro orbe (for the world; Latin) + Orbe (river in France). The entire sentence may be read: "Pray for us and for all souls."

umbas[31] all! Mezha, didn't you hear it a deluge of times, ufer[32] and ufer, respund to spond?[33] You deed, you deed! I need, I need! It's that irrawaddyng[34] I've stoke in my aars. It all but husheth the lethest zswound. Oronoko![35] What's your trouble? Is that the great Finnleader[36] himself in his joakimono[37] on his statue riding the high horse there forehengist?[38] Father of Otters,[39] it is himself! Yonne there! Isset that? On Fallareen Common? You're thinking of Astley's Amphitheayter where the bobby restrained you making sugarstuck pouts to the ghostwhite horse of the Peppers.[40] Throw the cobwebs from your eyes, woman, and spread your washing proper! It's well I know your sort of slop. Flap! Ireland sober is Ireland stiff.[41] Lord help you, Maria, full of grease, the load is with me! Your prayers. I sonht zo![42] Madammangut! Were you lifting your elbow, tell us, glazy cheeks, in Conway's Carrigacurra canteen? Was I what, hobbledyhips?[43] Flop! Your rere gait's creakorheuman bitts your butts disagrees.[44] Amn't I up since the damp dawn, marthared mary allacook, with Corrigan's pulse and varicoarse veins, my pramaxle smashed, Alice Jane in decline and my oneeyed mongrel twice run over, soaking and bleaching boiler rags, and sweating cold, a widow like me, for to deck my tennis champion son, the laundryman with the lavandier flannels? You won your limpopo[45] limp from the husky[46] hussars when Collars and Cuffs was heir to the town and your slur gave the stink to Carlow.[47] Holy Scamander,[48] I sar[49] it again! Near the golden falls. Icis on us! Seints of light! Zezere![50] Subdue your noise, you hamble creature! What is it but a blackburry growth or the dwyergray ass them four old codgers[51] owns. Are you meanam[52] Tarpey and Lyons and Gregory?[53] I meyne now, thank all, the four of them, and the roar of them, that draves[54] that stray in the mist and old Johnny MacDougal along with them. Is that the Poolbeg flasher beyant,[55] pharphar, or a fireboat coasting nyar[56] the Kishtna[57] or a glow I behold within a hedge or my Garry come back from the Indes? Wait till the honeying of the lune,[58] love! Die eve, little eve, die![59] We see that

31. *Umbra* (shade; Latin) + Umba (river in Africa). "Ussa," "Ulla," and "Mezha" are also river names; each contains a number of other meanings.
32. Bank (of river).
33. *Spund* (bung; German).
34. A multiple pun: Irrawady (river in Burma) + irritating + wadding. This and the following sentence may be paraphrased: "It's that wadding I've stuck in my ears. It hushes the least sound."
35. *Oroonoko* (novel by Aphra Behn about a "noble savage," published ca. 1678) + Orinoco (river in Venezuela).
36. Fionn mac Cumhail (Finn MacCool), legendary hero of ancient Ireland.
37. Comic kimono. *Joki* is the Finnish word for river; the name Joachim is perhaps also implied.
38. According to tradition, Hengist was the Jute invader of England (with Horsa), ca. 449; he founded the kingdom of Kent.
39. Father of Waters (i.e., the Mississippi) + Father of Orders (i.e., Saint Patrick).
40. Philip Astley's Royal Amphitheatre was a famous late-18th-century English circus, specializing in trained horses. "Pepper's Ghost" was a popular circus act. One of the washerwomen has been reproving the other, who thought she saw the great Finn himself riding his high horse, by telling her that once before she had to be restrained by a policeman for making "sugarstuck pouts" at a circus horse.
41. The temperance reformer Father Matthew had as his slogan "Ireland sober is Ireland free."
42. I thought so + Izonzo (river in Italy).

43. Hobbledehoy + wobbly hips.
44. The sentence is a punning discussion of her hard work and ailments.
45. A river in south Africa.
46. Cf. *uisge* (whiskey, but literally "water [of life]"; Gaelic).
47. I.e., "You got a slur on your reputation carrying on with soldiers in the Age of Elegance, and the scandal was all over Ireland" (ALP is being addressed and some of her many lovers are mentioned). "Carlow": a county in Ireland.
48. River near Troy, famous in classical legend.
49. I saw + Isar (river in Germany).
50. See there + Zezere (river in Portugal).
51. The Four Old Men, who represent, among other things, the authors of the Gospels, and the four elements.
52. Meaning + Menam (river in Thailand).
53. Tarpey, Lyons, Gregory, and MacDougal (next sentence) are the "four old codgers."
54. Drives + Drave (river in Hungary).
55. I.e., the Poolbeg Lighthouse beyond (this lighthouse is in Dublin Bay). "Pharphar": far far + Pharphar (river in Damascus) + *pharos* (lighthouse; Greek).
56. Near + Nyar (river in India).
57. City in ancient Mesopotamia, traditionally the ruling city after the Flood + Krishna (Hindu god of joy) + Kistna (river in India) + the Kish lightship (in Dublin Bay).
58. Loon (boy; Scottish) + *luna* (moon; Latin). "Honeying of the lune": honeymoon, etc.
59. From a children's game in which a swing is

wonder in your eye. We'll meet again, we'll part once more. The spot I'll seek if the hour you'll find. My chart shines high where the blue milk's upset. Forgivemequick. I'm going! Bubye! And you, pluck your watch, forgetmenot. Your evenlode.[60] So save to jurna's[61] end! My sights are swimming thicker on me by the shadows to this place. I sow[62] home slowly now by own way, moy-valley way. Towy I too, rathmine.[63]

Ah, but she was the queer old skeowsha[64] anyhow, Anna Livia, trinkettoes! And sure he was the quare old buntz too, Dear Dirty Dumpling,[65] foosther-father of fingalls[66] and dotthergills. Gammer and gaffer we're all their gang-sters. Hadn't he seven dams to wive him? And every dam had her seven crutches. And every crutch had its seven hues.[67] And each hue had a differing cry. Sudds[68] for me and supper for you and the doctor's bill for Joe John. Befor! Bifur![69] He married his markets, cheap by foul, I know, like any Etrurian Catholic Heathen, in their pinky limony creamy birnies[70] and their turkiss indienne mauves. But at milkidmass[71] who was the spouse? Then all that was was fair. Tys Elvenland![72] Teems of times and happy returns. The seim anew.[73] Ordovico or viricordo. Anna was, Livia is, Plurabelle's to be.[74] Northmen's thing made southfolk's place but howmulty plurators made each one in person?[75] Latin me that, my trinity scholar, out of eure sanscreed into oure eryan![76] *Hircus Civis Eblanensis![77]* He had buckgoat paps on him, soft ones for orphans. Ho,[78] Lord! Twins of his bosom. Lord save us! And ho! Hey? What all men. Hot? His tittering daughters of. Whawk?

Can't hear with the waters of. The chittering waters of. Flittering bats, fieldmice bawk talk. Ho! Are you not gone ahome? What Thom Malone? Can't hear with bawk of bats, all thim liffeying waters of. Ho, talk save us! My foos won't moos.[79] I feel as old as yonder elm. A tale told of Shaun or Shem? All

---

allowed to slow down to the refrain "She's dead, little Eva, little Eva, she's dead."

60. Evening load + Evenlode (river in England).
61. Journey + Jurna (river in Brazil).
62. Sow (river in England).
63. Moy is the name of an Irish river; Towy, a Welsh river. Moyvalley and Rathmine are names of Dublin suburbs.
64. Old timer, in Dublin.
65. "Dumpling" suggests Humpty Dumpty, whose fall is one of the many involved in the vastly symbolic fall of Finnegan. The phrase "Dear Dirty Dublin" occurs in *Ulysses.*
66. Blond and dark Scandinavian invaders of Ireland.
67. Colors of the rainbow (suggested a few lines later by "pinky limony creamy" and "turkiss indienne mauves"). In these sentences Joyce is parodying the nursery rhyme "As I was going to St. Ives / I met a man with seven wives."
68. Suds (slang for beer) + soap suds + sudd (the floating vegetable matter that often obstructs navigation on the White Nile).
69. Bifurcated creature! This image of human as a forked being suggests HCE (cf. "Etrurian Catholic Heathen," next sentence). HCE's marital history, in his role as the Great Parent or generator, is one theme in this passage.
70. Coats of mail.
71. Milking time + Michaelmas (September 29).
72. 'Tis the land of Elves + Tys Elv (Norway).
73. The same again + Seim (river in Ireland).
74. The Ordovices were an ancient British tribe in northern Wales, and *Ordovician* is a term for a geo-

logical period. "Ordovico" is also a pun on Vico and his order of historical phases. Joyce is suggesting the cyclical nature of things: the marital history of HCE is the history of ever-renewing life ("the seim anew"), and HCE's bride is Everywoman, past, present, and future ("Anna was, Livia is, Plurabelle's to be"). "Viricordo" is another verbal twist to Vico and his cycles, suggesting his *ricorso* ("recurrence," i.e., the fourth stage of the cycle that brings back the first), as well as overtones from the Latin *vir* (man) and *cor* (heart): the heart of the individual beats on, through all phases of civilization.
75. This sentence may be paraphrased: "The Northmen's assembly (thing) is now in Suffolk Place, but how many ancestors went into the making of each one of us?"
76. I.e., out of your Sanskrit into your Aryan. "Sanscreed" has further punning meanings: *sans* screed (without script) + *sans* creed (without faith). Thus the phrase can read: "out of your illiteracy or faithlessness into Irish" (Eire-an). I.e., the greatest skeptic must pause in reverence before the endless flow of life, represented by Irish history. "Trinity": Trinity College, Dublin.
77. The Goat-Citizen of Dublin! (Latin). The goat is the symbol of lust and so of fecundity; "*Eblanensis*" is the adjective form of Eblana, the name given by the 3rd-century Alexandrian geographer Ptolemy to what may have been the site of the modern Dublin.
78. River (Chinese).
79. Move + *Moos* (moss; German). Her foot ("foos") won't move; it is also turning to moss.

Livia's daughter-sons. Dark hawks hear us. Night! Night! My ho head halls. I feel as heavy as yonder stone. Tell me of John or Shaun? Who were Shem and Shaun the living sons or daughters of? Night now! Tell me, tell me, tell me, elm! Night night! Telmetale of stem or stone.[80] Beside the rivering waters of, hitherandthithering waters of. Night!

1923–38   1939

80. Stone and elm tree are important symbols in *Finnegans Wake*. Signifying permanence and change, time and space, mercy and justice, they undergo many changes of symbolic meaning throughout the book.

D. H. LAWRENCE
1885–1930

David Herbert Lawrence was born in the midland mining village of Eastwood, Nottinghamshire. His father was a miner; his mother, better educated than her husband and self-consciously genteel, fought all her married life to lift her children out of the working class. Lawrence was aware from a young age of the struggle between his parents, and allied himself with his mother's delicacy and refinement, resenting his father's coarse and sometimes drunken behavior. In his early novel *Sons and Lovers* (1913), against a background of paternal coarseness conflicting with maternal refinement, Lawrence sets the theme of the demanding mother who has given up the prospect of achieving a true emotional life with her husband and turns to her sons with a stultifying and possessive love. Many years later Lawrence came to feel that he had failed to appreciate his father's vitality and wholeness, even if they were distorted by the culture in which he lived.

Spurred on by his mother, Lawrence escaped from the mining world through education. He won a scholarship to Nottingham high school and later, after working first as a clerk and then as an elementary-school teacher, studied for two years at University College, Nottingham, where he obtained his teacher's certificate. Meanwhile he was reading on his own a great deal of literature and some philosophy and was working on his first novel. Publishing a group of poems in 1909, his first short story and his first novel, *The White Peacock*, in 1910, he was regarded in London literary circles as a promising young writer. He taught school from 1908 to 1912 in Croydon, a southern suburb of London, but he gave this up after falling in love with Frieda von Richthofen Weekley, the German wife of a professor at Nottingham. They went to Germany together and married in 1914, after Frieda's divorce.

Abroad with Frieda, Lawrence finished *Sons and Lovers*, at which he had been working off and on for years. The war brought them back to England, where Frieda's German origins and Lawrence's pacifist objection to the war gave him trouble with the authorities. More and more—especially after the almost immediate banning for indecency of his next novel, *The Rainbow*, in 1915—Lawrence came to feel that the forces of modern civilization were arrayed against him. As soon as he could leave England after the war, he sought refuge in Italy, Australia, Mexico, then again in Italy, and finally in the south of France, often desperately ill, restlessly searching for an ideal, or at least a tolerable, community in which to live. He died of tuberculosis in the south of France at the age of forty-four.

In his poetry and his fiction, Lawrence seeks to express the deep-rooted, the elemental, the instinctual in people and nature. He is at constant war with the mechanical and artificial, with the constraints and hypocrisies that civilization imposes. Because he had new things to say and a new way of saying them, he was not easily or quickly appreciated. Although his early novels are more conventional in style and treatment, from the publication of *The Rainbow* the critics turned away in bewilderment and condemnation. The rest of his life, during which he produced about a dozen more novels and many poems, short stories, sketches, and miscellaneous articles, was, in his own words, "a savage enough pilgrimage," marked by incessant struggle and by periods of frustration and despair. Phrases such as "supreme impulse" and "quickening spontaneous emotion" were characteristic of Lawrence's belief in intuition, in the dark forces of the inner self, that must not be allowed to be swamped by the rational faculties but must be brought into a harmonious relation with them.

The genteel culture of Lawrence's mother came more and more to represent death for Lawrence. In much of his later work, and especially in some of his short stories, he sets the deadening restrictiveness of middle-class conventional living against the forces of liberation that are often represented by an outsider—a peasant, a gypsy, a worker, a primitive of some kind, someone free by circumstance or personal effort. The recurring theme of his short stories—which contain some of his best work—is the distortion of love by possessiveness or gentility or a false romanticism or a false conception of the life of the artist and the achievement of a living relation between a man and a woman against the pressure of class-feeling or tradition or habit or prejudice.

In his two masterpieces, *The Rainbow* and *Women in Love* (both of which developed out of what was originally conceived as a single novel to be called *The Sisters*), Lawrence probes with both subtlety and power into various aspects of relationship— the relationship between humans and their environment, the relationship between the generations, the relationship between man and woman, the relationship between instinct and intellect, and above all the proper basis for the marriage relationship as he conceived it. Lawrence's view of marriage as a struggle, bound up with the deepest rhythms and most profound instincts, derived from his own relationship with his strong-minded wife. He explores this and other kinds of human relationships with a combination of uncanny psychological precision and intense poetic feeling. His novels have an acute surface realism, a sharp sense of time and place, and brilliant topographical detail; at the same time their high symbolism, both of the total pattern of action and of incidents and objects within it, establishes a formal and emotional rhythm.

In poetry as in fiction Lawrence sought out new modes of expression. He began writing in traditional verse forms but, especially after 1912, came to feel that poetry had to be unshackled from habit and fixed form, if it is to make contact with what he called the "insurgent naked throb of the instant moment." Harkening back to the experiments of the American poet Walt Whitman and anticipating the more "open" and "organic" forms of the later twentieth century, Lawrence claimed poetry must be spontaneous, flexible, alive, "direct utterance from the instant, whole man," and should express the "pulsating, carnal self" ("The Poetry of the Present," 1919). To convey the dynamism of animals and people, the emotional intensity of human relationships, his poems repeat and develop symbols or layer clauses in ritualistic cadences or unfold parallels with ancient myths. Vehemently autobiographical, the vital and even ecstatic encounters with nature, sex, and raw feeling in his poems assert the primacy of the unconscious and instinctual self, from which he felt the cerebral-intellectual self had alienated the English middle classes.

In the late 1950s the critic A. Alvarez judged: "The only native English poet of any importance to survive the First World War was D. H. Lawrence." Although there are complex reasons for the posthumous critical triumph of this writer who was so much reviled in his lifetime, there is also a simple and striking reason that must not be forgotten. Lawrence had vision; he responded intensely to life; he had a keen ear and a piercing eye for vitality and color and sound, for landscape—be it of England or Italy or New Mexico—for the individuality and concreteness of things in nature, and for the individuality and concreteness of people. His travel sketches are as impressive in their way as his novels and poems; he seizes both on the symbolic incident and on the concrete reality, and each is interpreted in terms of the other. He looked at the world freshly, with his own eyes, avoiding formulas and clichés; and he forged for himself a kind of utterance that, at his best, was able to convey powerfully and vividly what his original vision showed him. A restless pilgrim, he had uncanny perceptions into the depths of physical things and an uncompromising honesty in his view of human beings and the world.

Odour of Chrysanthemums

I

The small locomotive engine, Number 4, came clanking, stumbling down from Selston with seven full wagons. It appeared round the corner with loud threats of speed, but the colt that it startled from among the gorse,[1] which still flickered indistinctly in the raw afternoon, out-distanced it at a canter. A woman, walking up the railway line to Underwood, drew back into the hedge, held her basket aside, and watched the footplate of the engine advancing. The trucks[2] thumped heavily past, one by one, with slow inevitable movement, as she stood insignificantly trapped between the jolting black wagons and the hedge; then they curved away towards the coppice[3] where the withered oak leaves dropped noiselessly, while the birds, pulling at the scarlet hips beside the track, made off into the dusk that had already crept into the spinney.[4] In the open, the smoke from the engine sank and cleaved to the rough grass. The fields were dreary and forsaken, and in the marshy strip that led to the whim-sey,[5] a reedy pit-pond, the fowls had already abandoned their run among the alders, to roost in the tarred fowl-house. The pit-bank loomed up beyond the pond, flames like red sores licking its ashy sides, in the afternoon's stagnant light. Just beyond rose the tapering chimneys and the clumsy black headstocks of Brinsley Colliery.[6] The two wheels were spinning fast up against the sky, and the winding engine rapped out its little spasms. The miners were being turned up.

The engine whistled as it came into the wide bay of railway lines beside the colliery, where rows of trucks stood in harbour.

Miners, single, trailing and in groups, passed like shadows diverging home. At the edge of the ribbed level of sidings squat a low cottage, three steps down from the cinder track. A large bony vine clutched at the house, as if to claw down the tiled roof. Round the bricked yard grew a few wintry primroses. Beyond, the long garden sloped down to a bush-covered brook course. There were some twiggy apple trees, winter-crack trees, and ragged cabbages. Beside the path hung disheveled pink chrysanthemums, like pink cloths hung on bushes. A woman came stooping out of the felt-covered fowl-house, half-way down the garden. She closed and padlocked the door, then drew herself erect, having brushed some bits from her white apron.

She was a tall woman of imperious mien, handsome, with definite black eyebrows. Her smooth black hair was parted exactly. For a few moments she stood steadily watching the miners as they passed along the railway: then she

1. Common prickly bush with yellow flowers.
2. Open freight cars.
3. A wood of small trees or shrubs.
4. Thicket.

5. Machine for raising ore or water from a mine.
6. Coal mine. "Headstocks" support revolving parts of a machine.

2246 / D. H. Lawrence

turned towards the brook course. Her face was calm and set, her mouth was closed with disillusionment. After a moment she called:

"John!" There was no answer. She waited, and then said distinctly: "Where are you?"

"Here!" replied a child's sulky voice from among the bushes. The woman looked piercingly through the dusk.

"Are you at that brook?" she asked sternly.

For answer the child showed himself before the raspberry-canes that rose like whips. He was a small, sturdy boy of five. He stood quite still, defiantly.

"Oh!" said the mother, conciliated. "I thought you were down at that wet brook—and you remember what I told you——"

The boy did not move or answer.

"Come, come on in," she said more gently, "it's getting dark. There's your grandfather's engine coming down the line!"

The lad advanced slowly, with resentful, taciturn movement. He was dressed in trousers and waistcoat of cloth that was too thick and hard for the size of the garments. They were evidently cut down from a man's clothes.

As they went slowly towards the house he tore at the ragged wisps of chrysanthemums and dropped the petals in handfuls along the path.

"Don't do that—it does look nasty," said his mother. He refrained, and she, suddenly pitiful, broke off a twig with three or four wan flowers and held them against her face. When mother and son reached the yard her hand hesitated, and instead of laying the flower aside, she pushed it in her apron-band. The mother and son stood at the foot of the three steps looking across the bay of lines at the passing home of the miners. The trundle of the small train was imminent. Suddenly the engine loomed past the house and came to a stop opposite the gate.

The engine-driver, a short man with round grey beard, leaned out of the cab high above the woman.

"Have you got a cup of tea?" he said in a cheery, hearty fashion.

It was her father. She went in, saying she would mash.[7] Directly, she returned.

"I didn't come to see you on Sunday," began the little grey-bearded man.

"I didn't expect you," said his daughter.

The engine-driver winced; then, reassuming his cheery, airy manner, he said:

"Oh, have you heard then? Well, and what do you think——?"

"I think it is soon enough," she replied.

At her brief censure the little man made an impatient gesture, and said coaxingly, yet with dangerous coldness:

"Well, what's a man to do? It's no sort of life for a man of my years, to sit at my own hearth like a stranger. And if I'm going to marry again it may as well be soon as late—what does it matter to anybody?"

The woman did not reply, but turned and went into the house. The man in the engine-cab stood assertive, till she returned with a cup of tea and a piece of bread and butter on a plate. She went up the steps and stood near the footplate of the hissing engine.

"You needn't 'a' brought me bread an' butter," said her father. "But a cup of tea"—he sipped appreciatively—"it's very nice." He sipped for a moment or

7. Steep the tea.

two, then: "I hear as Walter's got another bout[8] on," he said.

"When hasn't he?" said the woman bitterly.

"I heerd tell of him in the 'Lord Nelson' braggin' as he was going to spend that b—— afore he went: half a sovereign[9] that was."

"When?" asked the woman.

"A' Sat'day night—I know that's true."

"Very likely," she laughed bitterly. "He gives me twenty-three shillings."

"Aye, it's a nice thing, when a man can do nothing with his money but make a beast of himself!" said the grey-whiskered man. The woman turned her head away. Her father swallowed the last of his tea and handed her the cup.

"Aye," he sighed, wiping his mouth. "It's a settler,[1] it is——"

He put his hand on the lever. The little engine strained and groaned, and the train rumbled towards the crossing. The woman again looked across the metals. Darkness was settling over the spaces of the railway and trucks: the miners, in grey somber groups, were still passing home. The winding engine pulsed hurriedly, with brief pauses. Elizabeth Bates looked at the dreary flow of men, then she went indoors. Her husband did not come.

The kitchen was small and full of firelight; red coals piled glowing up the chimney mouth. All the life of the room seemed in the white, warm hearth and the steel fender reflecting the red fire. The cloth was laid for tea; cups glinted in the shadows. At the back, where the lowest stairs protruded into the room, the boy sat struggling with a knife and a piece of white wood. He was almost hidden in the shadow. It was half-past four. They had but to await the father's coming to begin tea. As the mother watched her son's sullen little struggle with the wood, she saw herself in his silence and pertinacity; she saw the father in her child's indifference to all but himself. She seemed to be occupied by her husband. He had probably gone past his home, slunk past his own door, to drink before he came in, while his dinner spoiled and wasted in waiting. She glanced at the clock, then took the potatoes to strain them in the yard. The garden and fields beyond the brook were closed in uncertain darkness. When she rose with the saucepan, leaving the drain steaming into the night behind her, she saw the yellow lamps were lit along the high road that went up the hill away beyond the space of the railway lines and the field.

Then again she watched the men trooping home, fewer now and fewer.

Indoors the fire was sinking and the room was dark red. The woman put her saucepan on the hob,[2] and set a batter-pudding near the mouth of the oven. Then she stood unmoving. Directly, gratefully, came quick young steps to the door. Someone hung on the latch a moment, then a little girl entered and began pulling off her outdoor things, dragging a mass of curls, just ripening from gold to brown, over her eyes with her hat.

Her mother chid her for coming late from school, and said she would have to keep her at home the dark winter days.

"Why, mother, it's hardly a bit dark yet. The lamp's not lighted, and my father's not home."

"No, he isn't. But it's a quarter to five! Did you see anything of him?"

The child became serious. She looked at her mother with large, wistful blue eyes.

8. Session; i.e., bout of drinking.
9. Gold coin worth twenty shillings. Half a sovereign is worth ten. Lord Nelson is the name of a

public house (pub).
1. Crushing (or final) blow.
2. Part of the fireplace.

"No, mother, I've never seen him. Why? Has he come up an' gone past, to Old Brinsley? He hasn't, mother, 'cos I never saw him."

"He'd watch that," said the mother bitterly, "he'd take care as you didn't see him. But you may depend upon it, he's seated in the 'Prince o' Wales.'[3] He wouldn't be this late."

The girl looked at her mother piteously.

"Let's have our teas, mother, should we?" said she.

The mother called John to table. She opened the door once more and looked out across the darkness of the lines. All was deserted: she could not hear the winding-engines.

"Perhaps," she said to herself, "he's stopped to get some ripping[4] done."

They sat down to tea. John, at the end of the table near the door, was almost lost in the darkness. Their faces were hidden from each other. The girl crouched against the fender[5] slowly moving a thick piece of bread before the fire. The lad, his face a dusky mark on the shadow, sat watching her who was transfigured in the red glow.

"I do think it's beautiful to look in the fire," said the child.

"Do you?" said her mother. "Why?"

"It's so red, and full of little caves—and it feels so nice, and you can fair smell it."

"It'll want mending directly," replied her mother, "and then if your father comes he'll carry on and say there never is a fire when a man comes home sweating from the pit. A public-house is always warm enough."

There was silence till the boy said complainingly: "Make haste, our Annie."

"Well, I am doing! I can't make the fire do it no faster, can I?"

"She keeps wafflin' it about so's to make 'er slow," grumbled the boy.

"Don't have such an evil imagination, child," replied the mother.

Soon the room was busy in the darkness with the crisp sound of crunching. The mother ate very little. She drank her tea determinedly, and sat thinking. When she rose her anger was evident in the stern unbending of her head. She looked at the pudding in the fender, and broke out:

"It is a scandalous thing as a man can't even come home to his dinner! If it's crozzled[6] up to a cinder I don't see why I should care. Past his very door he goes to get to a public-house, and here I sit with his dinner waiting for him——"

She went out. As she dropped piece after piece of coal on the red fire, the shadows fell on the walls, till the room was almost in total darkness.

"I canna see," grumbled the invisible John. In spite of herself, the mother laughed.

"You know the way to your mouth," she said. She set the dust pan outside the door. When she came again like a shadow on the hearth, the lad repeated, complaining sulkily:

"I canna see."

"Good gracious!" cried the mother irritably, "you're as bad as your father if it's a bit dusk!"

Nevertheless, she took a paper spill from a sheaf on the mantelpiece and proceeded to light the lamp that hung from the ceiling in the middle of the

3. Name of a pub.
4. Taking out or cutting away coal or stone (a mining and quarrying term).
5. Frame that keeps coals in the fireplace.
6. Curled.

room. As she reached up, her figure displayed itself just rounding with maternity.

"Oh, mother——!" exclaimed the girl.

"What?" said the woman, suspended in the act of putting the lamp-glass over the flame. The copper reflector shone handsomely on her, as she stood with uplifted arm, turning to face her daughter.

"You've got a flower in your apron!" said the child, in a little rapture at this unusual event.

"Goodness me!" exclaimed the woman, relieved. "One would think the house was afire." She replaced the glass and waited a moment before turning up the wick. A pale shadow was seen floating vaguely on the floor.

"Let me smell!" said the child, still rapturously, coming forward and putting her face to her mother's waist.

"Go along, silly!" said the mother, turning up the lamp. The light revealed their suspense so that the woman felt it almost unbearable. Annie was still bending at her waist. Irritably, the mother took the flowers out from her apron-band.

"Oh, mother—don't take them out!" Annie cried, catching her hand and trying to replace the sprig.

"Such nonsense!" said the mother, turning away. The child put the pale chrysanthemums to her lips, murmuring:

"Don't they smell beautiful!"

Her mother gave a short laugh.

"No," she said, "not to me. It was chrysanthemums when I married him, and chrysanthemums when you were born, and the first time they ever brought him home drunk, he'd got brown chrysanthemums in his buttonhole."

She looked at the children. Their eyes and their parted lips were wondering. The mother sat rocking in silence for some time. Then she looked at the clock.

"Twenty minutes to six!" In a tone of fine bitter carelessness she continued: "Eh, he'll not come now till they bring him. There he'll stick! But he needn't come rolling in here in his pit-dirt, for *I* won't wash him. He can lie on the floor——Eh, what a fool I've been, what a fool! And this is what I came here for, to this dirty hole, rats and all, for him to slink past his very door. Twice last week—he's begun now——"

She silenced herself and rose to clear the table.

While for an hour or more the children played, subduedly intent, fertile of imagination, united in fear of the mother's wrath, and in dread of their father's home-coming, Mrs Bates sat in her rocking chair making a "singlet" of thick cream-coloured flannel, which gave a dull wounded sound as she tore off the grey edge. She worked at her sewing with energy, listening to the children, and her anger wearied itself, lay down to rest, opening its eyes from time to time and steadily watching, its ears raised to listen. Sometimes even her anger quailed and shrank, and the mother suspended her sewing, tracing the foot-steps that thudded along the sleepers[7] outside; she would lift her head sharply to bid the children "hush," but she recovered herself in time, and the footsteps went past the gate, and the children were not flung out of their play-world.

But at last Annie sighed, and gave in. She glanced at her wagon of slippers, and loathed the game. She turned plaintively to her mother.

"Mother!"—but she was inarticulate.

7. Railroad ties.

John crept out like a frog from under the sofa. His mother glanced up. "Yes," she said, "just look at those shirt-sleeves!"

The boy held them out to survey them, saying nothing. Then somebody called in a hoarse voice away down the line, and suspense bristled in the room, till two people had gone by outside, talking.

"It is time for bed," said the mother.

"My father hasn't come," wailed Annie plaintively. But her mother was primed with courage.

"Never mind. They'll bring him when he does come—like a log." She meant there would be no scene. "And he may sleep on the floor till he wakes himself. I know he'll not go to work to-morrow after this!"

The children had their hands and faces wiped with a flannel. They were very quiet. When they had put on their night-dresses, they said their prayers, the boy mumbling. The mother looked down at them, at the brown silken bush of intertwining curls in the nape of the girl's neck, at the little black head of the lad, and her heart burst with anger at their father, who caused all three such distress. The children hid their faces in her skirts for comfort.

When Mrs Bates came down, the room was strangely empty, with a tension of expectancy. She took up her sewing and stitched for some time without raising her head. Meantime her anger was tinged with fear.

II

The clock struck eight and she rose suddenly, dropping her sewing on her chair. She went to the stair-foot door, opened it, listening. Then she went out, locking the door behind her.

Something scuffled in the yard, and she started, though she knew it was only the rats with which the place was over-run. The night was very dark. In the great bay of railway lines, bulked with trucks, there was no trace of light, only away back she could see a few yellow lamps at the pit-top, and the red smear of the burning pit-bank on the night. She hurried along the edge of the track, then, crossing the converging lines, came to the stile by the white gates, whence she emerged on the road. Then the fear which had led her shrank. People were walking up to New Brinsley; she saw the lights in the houses; twenty yards farther on were the broad windows of the "Prince of Wales," very warm and bright, and the loud voices of men could be heard distinctly. What a fool she had been to imagine that anything had happened to him! He was merely drinking over there at the "Prince of Wales." She faltered. She had never yet been to fetch him, and she never would go. So she continued her walk towards the long straggling line of houses, standing back on the highway. She entered a passage between the dwellings.

"Mr Rigley?—Yes! Did you want him? No, he's not in at this minute."

The raw-boned woman leaned forward from her dark scullery[8] and peered at the other, upon whom fell a dim light through the blind of the kitchen window.

"Is it Mrs Bates?" she asked in a tone tinged with respect.

"Yes. I wondered if your Master was at home. Mine hasn't come yet."

" 'Asn't 'e! Oh, Jack's been 'ome an' 'ad 'is dinner an' gone out. 'E's just gone for 'alf an hour afore bed-time. Did you call at the 'Prince of Wales'?"

8. Back kitchen.

"No——"

"No, you didn't like——! It's not very nice." The other woman was indulgent. There was an awkward pause. "Jack never said nothink about—about your Master," she said.

"No!—I expect he's stuck in there!"

Elizabeth Bates said this bitterly, and with recklessness. She knew that the woman across the yard was standing at her door listening, but she did not care. As she turned:

"Stop a minute! I'll just go an' ask Jack if 'e knows anythink," said Mrs Rigley.

"Oh no—I wouldn't like to put——!"

"Yes, I will, if you'll just step inside an' see as th' childer doesn't come downstairs and set theirselves afire."

Elizabeth Bates, murmuring a remonstrance, stepped inside. The other woman apologised for the state of the room.

The kitchen needed apology. There were little frocks and trousers and childish undergarments on the squab[9] and on the floor, and a litter of playthings everywhere. On the black American cloth[1] of the table were pieces of bread and cake, crusts, slops, and a teapot with cold tea.

"Eh, ours is just as bad," said Elizabeth Bates, looking at the woman, not at the house. Mrs Rigley put a shawl over her head and hurried out, saying:

"I shanna be a minute."

The other sat, noting with faint disapproval the general untidiness of the room. Then she fell to counting the shoes of various sizes scattered over the floor. There were twelve. She sighed and said to herself: "No wonder!"—glancing at the litter. There came the scratching of two pairs of feet on the yard, and the Rigleys entered. Elizabeth Bates rose. Rigley was a big man, with very large bones. His head looked particularly bony. Across his temple was a blue scar, caused by a wound got in the pit, a wound in which the coal dust remained blue like tattooing.

" 'Asna 'e come whoam yit?" asked the man, without any form of greeting, but with deference and sympathy. "I couldna say wheer he is—'e's non ower theer!"—he jerked his head to signify the "Prince of Wales."

" 'E's 'appen gone up to th' Yew,"[2] said Mrs Rigley.

There was another pause. Rigley had evidently something to get off his mind:

"Ah left 'im finishin' a stint," he began. "Loose-all[3] 'ad bin gone about ten minutes when we com'n away, an' I shouted: 'Are ter comin', Walt?' an' 'e said: 'Go on, Ah shanna be but a'ef a minnit,' so we com'n ter th' bottom, me an' Bowers, thinkin' as 'e wor just behint, an' 'ud come up i' th' next bantle[4]——"

He stood perplexed, as if answering a charge of deserting his mate. Elizabeth Bates, now again certain of disaster, hastened to reassure him:

"I expect 'e's gone up to th' 'Yew Tree,' as you say. It's not the first time. I've fretted myself into a fever before now. He'll come home when they carry him."

"Ay, isn't it too bad!" deplored the other woman.

"I'll just step up to Dick's an' see if 'e is theer," offered the man, afraid of appearing alarmed, afraid of taking liberties.

---

9. Couch.
1. Oilcloth.
2. I.e., the Yew Tree (a pub).

3. Signal for end of work.
4. Group.

"Oh, I wouldn't think of bothering you that far," said Elizabeth Bates, with emphasis, but he knew she was glad of his offer.

As they stumbled up the entry, Elizabeth Bates heard Rigley's wife run across the yard and open her neighbour's door. At this, suddenly all the blood in her body seemed to switch away from her heart.

"Mind!" warned Rigley. "Ah've said many a time as Ah'd fill up them ruts in this entry, sumb'dy 'll be breakin' their legs yit."

She recovered herself and walked quickly along with the miner.

"I don't like leaving the children in bed, and nobody in the house," she said.

"No, you dunna!" he replied courteously. They were soon at the gate of the cottage.

"Well, I shanna be many minnits. Dunna you be frettin' now, 'e'll be all right," said the butty.[5]

"Thank you very much, Mr Rigley," she replied.

"You're welcome!" he stammered, moving away. "I shanna be many minnits."

The house was quiet. Elizabeth Bates took off her hat and shawl, and rolled back the rug. When she had finished, she sat down. It was a few minutes past nine. She was startled by the rapid chuff of the winding-engine at the pit, and the sharp whirr of the brakes on the rope as it descended. Again she felt the painful sweep of her blood, and she put her hand to her side, saying aloud: "Good gracious!—it's only the nine o'clock deputy[6] going down," rebuking herself.

She sat still, listening. Half an hour of this, and she was wearied out.

"What am I working myself up like this for?" she said pitiably to herself, "I s'll only be doing myself some damage."

She took out her sewing again.

At a quarter to ten there were footsteps. One person! She watched for the door to open. It was an elderly woman, in a black bonnet and a black woollen shawl—his mother. She was about sixty years old, pale, with blue eyes, and her face all wrinkled and lamentable. She shut the door and turned to her daughter-in-law peevishly.

"Eh, Lizzie, whatever shall we do, whatever shall we do!" she cried.

Elizabeth drew back a little, sharply.

"What is it, mother?" she said.

The elder woman seated herself on the sofa.

"I don't know, child, I can't tell you!"—she shook her head slowly. Elizabeth sat watching her, anxious and vexed.

"I don't know," replied the grandmother, sighing very deeply. "There's no end to my troubles, there isn't. The things I've gone through, I'm sure it's enough——!" She wept without wiping her eyes, the tears running.

"But, mother," interrupted Elizabeth, "what do you mean? What is it?"

The grandmother slowly wiped her eyes. The fountains of her tears were stopped by Elizabeth's directness. She wiped her eyes slowly.

"Poor child! Eh, you poor thing!" she moaned. "I don't know what we're going to do, I don't—and you as you are—it's a thing, it is indeed!"

Elizabeth waited.

"Is he dead?" she asked, and at the words her heart swung violently, though she felt a slight flush of shame at the ultimate extravagance of the question. Her words sufficiently frightened the old lady, almost brought her to herself. "Don't say so, Elizabeth! We'll hope it's not as bad as that; no, may the Lord spare us that, Elizabeth. Jack Rigley came just as I was sittin' down to a glass afore going to bed, an' 'e said: ' 'Appen you'll go down th' line, Mrs. Bates. Walt's had an accident. 'Appen you'll go an' sit wi' 'er till we can get him home.' I hadn't time to ask him a word afore he was gone. An' I put my bonnet on an' come straight down, Lizzie. I thought to myself: 'Eh, that poor blessed child, if anybody should come an' tell her of a sudden, there's no knowin' what'll 'appen to 'er.' You mustn't let it upset you, Lizzie—or you know what to expect. How long is it, six months—or is it five, Lizzie? Ay!"—the old woman shook her head—"time slips on, it slips on! Ay!"

Elizabeth's thoughts were busy elsewhere. If he was killed—would she be able to manage on the little pension and what she could earn?—she counted up rapidly. If he was hurt—they wouldn't take him to the hospital—how tiresome he would be to nurse!—but perhaps she'd be able to get him away from the drink and his hateful ways. She would—while he was ill. The tears offered to come to her eyes at the picture. But what sentimental luxury was this she was beginning? She turned to consider the children. At any rate she was absolutely necessary for them. They were her business.

"Ay!" repeated the old woman, "it seems but a week or two since he brought me his first wages. Ay—he was a good lad, Elizabeth, he was, in his way. I don't know why he got to be such a trouble, I don't. He was a happy lad at home, only full of spirits. But there's no mistake he's been a handful of trouble, he has! I hope the Lord'll spare him to mend his ways. I hope so, I hope so. You've had a sight o' trouble with him, Elizabeth, you have indeed. But he was a jolly enough lad wi' me, he was, I can assure you. I don't know how it is. . . ."

The old woman continued to muse aloud, a monotonous irritating sound, while Elizabeth thought concentratedly, startled once, when she heard the winding-engine chuff quickly, and the brakes skirr with a shriek. Then she heard the engine more slowly, and the brakes made no sound. The old woman did not notice. Elizabeth waited in suspense. The mother-in-law talked, with lapses into silence.

"But he wasn't your son, Lizzie, an' it makes a difference. Whatever he was, I remember him when he was little, an' I learned to understand him and to make allowances. You've got to make allowances for them——"

It was half-past ten, and the old woman was saying: "But it's trouble from beginning to end; you're never too old for trouble, never too old for that—— " when the gate banged back, and there were heavy feet on the steps.

"I'll go, Lizzie, let me go," cried the old woman, rising. But Elizabeth was at the door. It was a man in pit-clothes.

"They're bringin' 'im, Missis," he said. Elizabeth's heart halted a moment. Then it surged on again, almost suffocating her.

"Is he—is it bad?" she asked.

The man turned away, looking at the darkness:

"The doctor says 'e'd been dead hours. 'E saw 'im i' th' lamp-cabin."

The old woman, who stood just behind Elizabeth, dropped into a chair, and folded her hands, crying: "Oh, my boy, my boy!"

"Hush!" said Elizabeth, with a sharp twitch of a frown. "Be still, mother, don't waken th' children: I wouldn't have them down for anything!"

The old woman moaned softly, rocking herself. The man was drawing away. Elizabeth took a step forward.

"How was it?" she asked.

"Well, I couldn't say for sure," the man replied, very ill at ease. " 'E wor finishin' a stint an' th' butties 'ad gone, an' a lot o' stuff come down atop 'n 'im."

"And crushed him?" cried the widow, with a shudder.

"No," said the man, "it fell at th' back of 'im. 'E wor under th' face an' it niver touched 'im. It shut 'im in. It seems 'e wor smothered."

Elizabeth shrank back. She heard the old woman behind her cry:

"What?—what did 'e say it was?"

The man replied, more loudly: " 'E wor smothered!"

Then the old woman wailed aloud, and this relieved Elizabeth.

"Oh, mother," she said, putting her hand on the old woman, "don't waken th' children, don't waken th' children."

She wept a little, unknowing, while the old mother rocked herself and moaned. Elizabeth remembered that they were bringing him home, and she must be ready. "They'll lay him in the parlour," she said to herself, standing a moment pale and perplexed.

Then she lighted a candle and went into the tiny room. The air was cold and damp, but she could not make a fire, there was no fireplace. She set down the candle and looked round. The candlelight glittered on the lustre-glasses, on the two vases that held some of the pink chrysanthemums, and on the dark mahogany. There was a cold, deathly smell of chrysanthemums in the room. Elizabeth stood looking at the flowers. She turned away, and calculated whether there would be room to lay him on the floor, between the couch and the chiffonier. She pushed the chairs aside. There would be room to lay him down and to step round him. Then she fetched the old red tablecloth, and another old cloth, spreading them down to save her bit of carpet. She shivered on leaving the parlour; so, from the dresser drawer she took a clean shirt and put it at the fire to air. All the time her mother-in-law was rocking herself in the chair and moaning.

"You'll have to move from there, mother," said Elizabeth. "They'll be bringing him in. Come in the rocker."

The old mother rose mechanically, and seated herself by the fire, continuing to lament. Elizabeth went into the pantry for another candle, and there, in the little pent-house under the naked tiles, she heard them coming. She stood still in the pantry doorway, listening. She heard them pass the end of the house, and come awkwardly down the three steps, a jumble of shuffling footsteps and muttering voices. The old woman was silent. The men were in the yard.

Then Elizabeth heard Matthews, the manager of the pit, say: "You go in first, Jim. Mind!"

The door came open, and the two women saw a collier backing into the room, holding one end of a stretcher, on which they could see the nailed pit-boots of the dead man. The two carriers halted, the man at the head stooping to the lintel of the door.

"Wheer will you have him?" asked the manager, a short, white-bearded man.

Elizabeth roused herself and came from the pantry carrying the unlighted candle.

"In the parlour," she said.

"In there, Jim!" pointed the manager, and the carriers backed round into the tiny room. The coat with which they had covered the body fell off as they awkwardly turned through the two doorways, and the women saw their man, naked to the waist, lying stripped for work. The old woman began to moan in a low voice of horror.

"Lay th' stretcher at th' side," snapped the manager, "an' put 'im on th' cloths. Mind now, mind! Look you now——!"

One of the men had knocked off a vase of chrysanthemums. He stared awkwardly, then they set down the stretcher. Elizabeth did not look at her husband. As soon as she could get in the room, she went and picked up the broken vase and the flowers.

"Wait a minute!" she said.

The three men waited in silence while she mopped up the water with a duster.

"Eh, what a job, what a job, to be sure!" the manager was saying, rubbing his brow with trouble and perplexity. "Never knew such a thing in my life, never! He'd no business to ha' been left. I never knew such a thing in my life! Fell over him clean as a whistle, an' shut him in. Not four foot of space, there wasn't—yet it scarce bruised him."

He looked down at the dead man, lying prone, half naked, all grimed with coal-dust.

" ' 'Sphyxiated,' the doctor said. It *is* the most terrible job I've ever known. Seems as if it was done o' purpose. Clean over him, an' shut 'im in, like a mouse-trap"—he made a sharp, descending gesture with his hand.

The colliers standing by jerked aside their heads in hopeless comment.

The horror of the thing bristled upon them all.

Then they heard the girl's voice upstairs calling shrilly: "Mother, mother—who is it? Mother, who is it?"

Elizabeth hurried to the foot of the stairs and opened the door:

"Go to sleep!" she commanded sharply. "What are you shouting about? Go to sleep at once—there's nothing——"

Then she began to mount the stairs. They could hear her on the boards, and on the plaster floor of the little bedroom. They could hear her distinctly:

"What's the matter now?—what's the matter with you, silly thing?"—her voice was much agitated, with an unreal gentleness.

"I thought it was some men come," said the plaintive voice of the child. "Has he come?"

"Yes, they've brought him. There's nothing to make a fuss about. Go to sleep now, like a good child."

They could hear her voice in the bedroom, they waited whilst she covered the children under the bedclothes.

"Is he drunk?" asked the girl, timidly, faintly.

"No! No—he's not! He—he's asleep."

"Is he asleep downstairs?"

"Yes—and don't make a noise."

There was silence for a moment, then the men heard the frightened child again:

"What's that noise?"

"It's nothing, I tell you, what are you bothering for?"

The noise was the grandmother moaning. She was oblivious of everything, sitting on her chair rocking and moaning. The manager put his hand on her arm and bade her "Sh—sh! !"

The old woman opened her eyes and looked at him. She was shocked by this interruption, and seemed to wonder.

"What time is it?" the plaintive thin voice of the child, sinking back unhappily into sleep, asked this last question.

"Ten o'clock," answered the mother more softly. Then she must have bent down and kissed the children.

Matthews beckoned to the men to come away. They put on their caps and took up the stretcher. Stepping over the body, they tiptoed out of the house. None of them spoke till they were far from the wakeful children.

When Elizabeth came down she found her mother alone on the parlour floor, leaning over the dead man, the tears dropping on him.

"We must lay him out," the wife said. She put on the kettle, then returning knelt at the feet, and began to unfasten the knotted leather laces. The room was clammy and dim with only one candle, so that she had to bend her face almost to the floor. At last she got off the heavy boots and put them away.

"You must help me now," she whispered to the old woman. Together they stripped the man.

When they arose, saw him lying in the naïve dignity of death, the women stood arrested in fear and respect. For a few moments they remained still, looking down, the old mother whimpering. Elizabeth felt countermanded.[7] She saw him, how utterly inviolable he lay in himself. She had nothing to do with him. She could not accept it. Stooping, she laid her hand on him, in claim. He was still warm, for the mine was hot where he had died. His mother had his face between her hands, and was murmuring incoherently. The old tears fell in succession as drops from wet leaves; the mother was not weeping, merely her tears flowed. Elizabeth embraced the body of her husband, with cheek and lips. She seemed to be listening, inquiring, trying to get some connection. But she could not. She was driven away. He was impregnable.

She rose, went into the kitchen where she poured warm water into a bowl, brought soap and flannel and a soft towel. "I must wash him," she said.

Then the old mother rose stiffly, and watched Elizabeth as she carefully washed his face, carefully brushing his big blond moustache from his mouth with the flannel. She was afraid with a bottomless fear, so she ministered to him. The old woman, jealous, said:

"Let me wipe him!"—and she kneeled on the other side drying slowly as Elizabeth washed, her big black bonnet sometimes brushing the dark head of her daughter-in-law. They worked thus in silence for a long time. They never forgot it was death, and the touch of the man's dead body gave them strange emotions, different in each of the women; a great dread possessed them both, the mother felt the lie was given to her womb, she was denied; the wife felt the utter isolation of the human soul, the child within her was a weight apart from her.

At last it was finished. He was a man of handsome body, and his face showed no traces of drink. He was blond, full-fleshed, with fine limbs. But he was dead.

"Bless him," whispered his mother, looking always at his face, and speaking out of sheer terror. "Dear lad—bless him!" She spoke in a faint, sibilant ecstasy of fear and mother love.

Elizabeth sank down again to the floor, and put her face against his neck, and trembled and shuddered. But she had to draw away again. He was dead, and her living flesh had no place against his. A great dread and weariness held her: she was so unavailing. Her life was gone like this.

7. Contradicted.

"White as milk he is, clear as a twelve-month baby, bless him, the darling!" the old mother murmured to herself. "Not a mark on him, clear and clean and white, beautiful as ever a child was made," she murmured with pride. Elizabeth kept her face hidden.

"He went peaceful, Lizzie—peaceful as sleep. Isn't he beautiful, the lamb? Ay—he must ha' made his peace, Lizzie. 'Appen he made it all right, Lizzie, shut in there. He'd have time. He wouldn't look like this if he hadn't made his peace. The lamb, the dear lamb. Eh, but he had a hearty laugh. I loved to hear it. He had the heartiest laugh, Lizzie, as a lad——"

Elizabeth looked up. The man's mouth was fallen back, slightly open under the cover of the moustache. The eyes, half shut, did not show glazed in the obscurity. Life with its smoky burning gone from him, had left him apart and utterly alien to her. And she knew what a stranger he was to her. In her womb was ice of fear, because of this separate stranger with whom she had been living as one flesh. Was this what it all meant—utter, intact separateness, obscured by heat of living? In dread she turned her face away. The fact was too deadly. There had been nothing between them, and yet they had come together, exchanging their nakedness repeatedly. Each time he had taken her, they had been two isolated beings, far apart as now. He was no more responsible than she. The child was like ice in her womb. For as she looked at the dead man, her mind, cold and detached, said clearly: "Who am I? What have I been doing? I have been fighting a husband who did not exist. *He* existed all the time. What wrong have I done? What was that I have been living with? There lies the reality, this man." And her soul died in her for fear: she knew she had never seen him, he had never seen her, they had met in the dark and had fought in the dark, not knowing whom they met or whom they fought. And now she saw, and turned silent in seeing. For she had been wrong. She had said he was something he was not; she had felt familiar with him. Whereas he was apart all the while, living as she never lived, feeling as she never felt.

In fear and shame she looked at his naked body, that she had known falsely. And he was the father of her children. Her soul was torn from her body and stood apart. She looked at his naked body and was ashamed, as if she had denied it. After all, it was itself. It seemed awful to her. She looked at his face, and she turned her own face to the wall. For his look was other than hers, his way was not her way. She had denied him what he was—she saw it now. She had refused him as himself. And this had been her life, and his life. She was grateful to death, which restored the truth. And she knew she was not dead.

And all the while her heart was bursting with grief and pity for him. What had he suffered? What stretch of horror for this helpless man! She was rigid with agony. She had not been able to help him. He had been cruelly injured, this naked man, this other being, and she could make no reparation. There were the children—but the children belonged to life. This dead man had nothing to do with them. He and she were only channels through which life had flowed to issue in the children. She was a mother—but how awful she knew it now to have been a wife. And he, dead now, how awful he must have felt it to be a husband. She felt that in the next world he would be a stranger to her. If they met there, in the beyond, they would only be ashamed of what had been before. The children had come, for some mysterious reason, out of both of them. But the children did not unite them. Now he was dead, she knew how eternally he was apart from her, how eternally he had nothing more to do with her. She saw this episode of her life closed. They had denied each other in life. Now he had withdrawn. An anguish came over her. It was finished then: it had become hopeless between them long before he died. Yet he had been her husband. But how little!

"Have you got his shirt, 'Lizabeth?"

Elizabeth turned without answering, though she strove to weep and behave as her mother-in-law expected. But she could not, she was silenced. She went into the kitchen and returned with the garment.

"It is aired," she said, grasping the cotton shirt here and there to try. She was almost ashamed to handle him; what right had she or anyone to lay hands on him; but her touch was humble on his body. It was hard work to clothe him. He was so heavy and inert. A terrible dread gripped her all the while: that he could be so heavy and utterly inert, unresponsive, apart. The horror of the distance between them was almost too much for her—it was so infinite a gap she must look across.

At last it was finished. They covered him with a sheet and left him lying, with his face bound. And she fastened the door of the little parlour, lest the children should see what was lying there. Then, with peace sunk heavy on her heart, she went about making tidy the kitchen. She knew she submitted to life, which was her immediate master. But from death, her ultimate master, she winced with fear and shame.

1911, 1914

The Horse Dealer's Daughter

"Well, Mabel, and what are you going to do with yourself?" asked Joe, with foolish flippancy. He felt quite safe himself. Without listening for an answer, he turned aside, worked a grain of tobacco to the tip of his tongue, and spat it out. He did not care about anything, since he felt safe himself.

The three brothers and the sister sat round the desolate breakfast-table, attempting some sort of desultory consultation. The morning's post had given the final tap to the family fortunes, and all was over. The dreary dining-room itself, with its heavy mahogany furniture, looked as if it were waiting to be done away with.

But the consultation amounted to nothing. There was a strange air of ineffectuality about the three men, as they sprawled at table, smoking and reflecting vaguely on their own condition. The girl was alone, a rather short, sullen-looking young woman of twenty-seven. She did not share the same life as her brothers. She would have been good-looking, save for the impressive fixity of her face, "bull-dog," as her brothers called it.

There was a confused tramping of horses' feet outside. The three men all sprawled round in their chairs to watch. Beyond the dark holly bushes that separated the strip of lawn from the high-road, they could see a cavalcade of shire horses swinging out of their own yard, being taken for exercise. This was the last time. These were the last horses that would go through their hands. The young men watched with critical, callous look. They were all frightened at the collapse of their lives, and the sense of disaster in which they were involved left them no inner freedom.

Yet they were three fine, well-set fellows enough. Joe, the eldest, was a man of thirty-three, broad and handsome in a hot, flushed way. His face was red, he twisted his black moustache over a thick finger, his eyes were shallow and restless. He had a sensual way of uncovering his teeth when he laughed, and his bearing was stupid. Now he watched the horses with a glazed look of helplessness in his eyes, a certain stupor of downfall.

The great draught horses swung past. They were tied head to tail, four of them, and they heaved along to where a lane branched off from the high-road, planting their great hoofs floutingly in the fine black mud, swinging their great rounded haunches sumptuously, and trotting a few sudden steps as they were led into the lane, round the corner. Every movement showed a massive, slumbrous strength, and a stupidity which held them in subjection. The groom at the head looked back, jerking the leading rope. And the cavalcade moved out of sight up the lane, the tail of the last horse, bobbed up tight and stiff, held out taut from the swinging great haunches as they rocked behind the hedges in a motion-like sleep.

Joe watched with glazed hopeless eyes. The horses were almost like his own body to him. He felt he was done for now. Luckily he was engaged to a woman as old as himself, and therefore her father, who was steward of a neighbouring estate, would provide him with a job. He would marry and go into harness. His life was over, he would be a subject animal now.

He turned uneasily aside, the retreating steps of the horses echoing in his ears. Then, with foolish restlessness, he reached for the scraps of bacon-rind from the plates, and making a faint whistling sound, flung them to the terrier that lay against the fender. He watched the dog swallow them, and waited till the creature looked into his eyes. Then a faint grin came on his face, and in a high, foolish voice he said:

"You won't get much more bacon, shall you, you little b——?"

The dog faintly and dismally wagged its tail, then lowered its haunches, circled round, and lay down again.

There was another helpless silence at the table. Joe sprawled uneasily in his seat, not willing to go till the family conclave was dissolved. Fred Henry, the second brother, was erect, clean-limbed, alert. He had watched the passing of the horses with more *sang-froid*.[1] If he was an animal, like Joe, he was an animal which controls, not one which is controlled. He was master of any horse, and he carried himself with a well-tempered air of mastery. But he was not master of the situations of life. He pushed his coarse brown moustache upwards, off his lip, and glanced irritably at his sister, who sat impassive and inscrutable.

"You'll go and stop with Lucy for a bit, shan't you?" he asked. The girl did not answer.

"I don't see what else you can do," persisted Fred Henry.

"Go as a skivvy,"[2] Joe interpolated laconically.

The girl did not move a muscle.

"If I was her, I should go in for training for a nurse," said Malcolm, the youngest of them all. He was the baby of the family, a young man of twenty-two, with a fresh, jaunty *museau*.[3]

But Mabel did not take any notice of him. They had talked at her and round her for so many years, that she hardly heard them at all.

---

1. Cold blood (French, literal trans.); here calm detachment.
2. Servant girl.
3. Muzzle (French); here face.

The marble clock on the mantelpiece softly chimed the half-hour, the dog rose uneasily from the hearth-rug and looked at the party at the breakfast-table. But still they sat in an ineffectual conclave.

"Oh, all right," said Joe suddenly, apropos of nothing. "I'll get a move on."

He pushed back his chair, straddled his knees with a downward jerk, to get them free, in horsey fashion, and went to the fire. Still he did not go out of the room; he was curious to know what the others would do or say. He began to charge his pipe, looking down at the dog and saying in a high, affected voice:

"Going wi' me? Going wi' me are ter? Tha'rt goin' further than tha counts on just now, dost hear?"

The dog faintly wagged his tail, the man stuck out his jaw and covered his pipe with his hands, and puffed intently, losing himself in the tobacco, looking down all the while at the dog with an absent brown eye. The dog looked up at him in mournful distrust. Joe stood with his knees stuck out, in real horsey fashion.

"Have you had a letter from Lucy?" Fred Henry asked of his sister.

"Last week," came the neutral reply.

"And what does she say?"

There was no answer.

"Does she *ask* you to go and stop there?" persisted Fred Henry.

"She says I can if I like."

"Well, then, you'd better. Tell her you'll come on Monday."

This was received in silence.

"That's what you'll do then, is it?" said Fred Henry, in some exasperation.

But she made no answer. There was a silence of futility and irritation in the room. Malcolm grinned fatuously.

"You'll have to make up your mind between now and next Wednesday," said Joe loudly, "or else find yourself lodgings on the kerbstone."

The face of the young woman darkened, but she sat on immutable.

"Here's Jack Ferguson!" exclaimed Malcolm, who was looking aimlessly out of the window.

"Where?" exclaimed Joe loudly.

"Just gone past."

"Coming in?"

Malcolm craned his neck to see the gate.

"Yes," he said.

There was a silence. Mabel sat on like one condemned, at the head of the table. Then a whistle was heard from the kitchen. The dog got up and barked sharply. Joe opened the door and shouted:

"Come on."

After a moment a young man entered. He was muffled up in overcoat and a purple woollen scarf, and his tweed cap, which he did not remove, was pulled down on his head. He was of medium height, his face was rather long and pale, his eyes looked tired.

"Hello, Jack! Well, Jack!" exclaimed Malcolm and Joe. Fred Henry merely said: "Jack."

"What's doing?" asked the newcomer, evidently addressing Fred Henry.

"Same. We've got to be out by Wednesday. Got a cold?"

"I have—got it bad, too."

"Why don't you stop in?"

"*Me* stop in? When I can't stand on my legs, perhaps I shall have a chance." The young man spoke huskily. He had a slight Scotch accent.

"It's a knock-out, isn't it," said Joe, boisterously, "if a doctor goes round croaking with a cold. Looks bad for the patients, doesn't it?"

The young doctor looked at him slowly.

"Anything the matter with *you*, then?" he asked sarcastically.

"Not as I know of. Damn your eyes, I hope not. Why?"

"I thought you were very concerned about the patients, wondered if you might be one yourself."

"Damn it, no, I've never been patient to no flaming doctor, and hope I never shall be," returned Joe.

At this point Mabel rose from the table, and they all seemed to become aware of her existence. She began putting the dishes together. The young doctor looked at her, but did not address her. He had not greeted her. She went out of the room with the tray, her face impassive and unchanged.

"When are you off then, all of you?" asked the doctor.

"I'm catching the eleven-forty," replied Malcolm. "Are you goin' down wi' th' trap, Joe?"

"Yes, I've told you I'm going down wi' th' trap, haven't I?"

"We'd better be getting her in then. So long Jack, if I don't see you before I go," said Malcolm, shaking hands.

He went out, followed by Joe, who seemed to have his tail between his legs.

"Well, this is the devil's own," exclaimed the doctor, when he was left alone with Fred Henry. "Going before Wednesday, are you?"

"That's the orders," replied the other.

"Where, to Northampton?"

"That's it."

"The devil!" exclaimed Ferguson, with quiet chagrin.

And there was silence between the two.

"All settled up, are you?" asked Ferguson.

"About."

There was another pause.

"Well, I shall miss yer, Freddy, boy," said the young doctor.

"And I shall miss thee, Jack," returned the other.

"Miss you like hell," mused the doctor.

Fred Henry turned aside. There was nothing to say. Mabel came in again, to finish clearing the table.

"What are *you* going to do, then, Miss Pervin?" asked Ferguson. "Going to your sister's, are you?"

Mabel looked at him with her steady, dangerous eyes, that always made him uncomfortable, unsettling his superficial ease.

"No," she said.

"Well, what in the name of fortune *are* you going to do? Say what you mean to do," cried Fred Henry, with futile intensity.

But she only averted her head, and continued her work. She folded the white table-cloth, and put on the chenille cloth.

"The sulkiest bitch that ever trod!" muttered her brother.

But she finished her task with perfectly impassive face, the young doctor watching her interestedly all the while. Then she went out.

Fred Henry stared after her, clenching his lips, his blue eyes fixing in sharp antagonism, as he made a grimace of sour exasperation.

"You could bray[4] her into bits, and that's all you'd get out of her," he said, in a small, narrowed tone.

The doctor smiled faintly.

"What's she *going* to do, then?" he asked.

"Strike me if *I* know!" returned the other.

There was a pause. Then the doctor stirred.

"I'll be seeing you tonight, shall I?" he said to his friend.

"Ay—where's it to be? Are we going over to Jessdale?"

"I don't know. I've got such a cold on me. I'll come round to the 'Moon and Stars,'[5] anyway."

"Let Lizzie and May miss their night for once, eh?"

"That's it—if I feel as I do now."

"All's one——"

The two young men went through the passage and down to the back door together. The house was large, but it was servantless now, and desolate. At the back was a small bricked house-yard and beyond that a big square, gravelled fine and red, and having stables on two sides. Sloping, dank, winter-dark fields stretched away on the open sides.

But the stables were empty. Joseph Pervin, the father of the family, had been a man of no education, who had become a fairly large horse dealer. The stables had been full of horses, there was a great turmoil and come-and-go of horses and of dealers and grooms. Then the kitchen was full of servants. But of late things had declined. The old man had married a second time, to retrieve his fortunes. Now he was dead and everything was gone to the dogs,[6] there was nothing but debt and threatening.

For months, Mabel had been servantless in the big house, keeping the home together in penury for her ineffectual brothers. She had kept house for ten years. But previously it was with unstinted means. Then, however brutal and coarse everything was, the sense of money had kept her proud, confident. The men might be foul-mouthed, the women in the kitchen might have had reputations, her brothers might have illegitimate children. But so long as there was money, the girl felt herself established, and brutally proud, reserved.

No company came to the house, save dealers and coarse men. Mabel had no associates of her own sex, after her sister went away. But she did not mind. She went regularly to church, she attended to her father. And she lived in the memory of her mother, who had died when she was fourteen, and whom she had loved. She had loved her father, too, in a different way, depending upon him, and feeling secure in him, until at the age of fifty-four, he married again. And then she had set hard against him. Now he had died and left them all hopelessly in debt.

She had suffered badly during the period of poverty. Nothing, however, could shake the curious, sullen, animal pride that dominated each member of the family. Now, for Mabel, the end had come. Still she would not cast about her. She would follow her own way just the same. She would always hold the keys of her own situation. Mindless and persistent, she endured from day to day. Why should she think? Why should she answer anybody? It was enough that this was the end, and there was no way out. She need not pass any more darkly along the main street of the small town, avoiding every eye. She need

---

4. Grind.
5. Name of a public house (pub).

6. Gone wrong (slang).

not demean herself any more, going into the shops and buying the cheapest food. This was at an end. She thought of nobody, not even of herself. Mindless and persistent, she seemed in a sort of ecstasy to be coming nearer to her fulfilment, her own glorification, approaching her dead mother, who was glorified.

In the afternoon, she took a little bag, with shears and sponge and a small scrubbing-brush, and went out. It was a grey, wintry day, with saddened, dark green fields and an atmosphere blackened by the smoke of foundries not far off. She went quickly, darkly along the causeway, heeding nobody, through the town to the churchyard.

There she always felt secure, as if no one could see her, although as a matter of fact she was exposed to the stare of everyone who passed along under the churchyard wall. Nevertheless, once under the shadow of the great looming church, among the graves, she felt immune from the world, reserved within the thick churchyard wall as in another country.

Carefully she clipped the grass from the grave, and arranged the pinky-white, small chrysanthemums in the tin cross. When this was done, she took an empty jar from a neighbouring grave, brought water, and carefully, most scrupulously sponged the marble headstone and the coping-stone.

It gave her sincere satisfaction to do this. She felt in immediate contact with the world of her mother. She took minute pains, went through the park in a state bordering on pure happiness, as if in performing this task she came into a subtle, intimate connection with her mother. For the life she followed here in the world was far less real than the world of death she inherited from her mother.

The doctor's house was just by the church. Ferguson, being a mere hired assistant, was slave to the country-side. As he hurried now to attend to the out-patients in the surgery, glancing across the graveyard with his quick eye, he saw the girl at her task at the grave. She seemed so intent and remote, it was like looking into another world. Some mystical element was touched in him. He slowed down as he walked, watching her as if spellbound.

She lifted her eyes, feeling him looking. Their eyes met. And each looked away again at once, each feeling, in some way, found out by the other. He lifted his cap and passed on down the road. There remained distinct in his consciousness, like a vision, the memory of her face, lifted from the tombstone in the churchyard, and looking at him with slow, large, portentous eyes. It *was* portentous, her face. It seemed to mesmerise him. There was a heavy power in her eyes which laid hold of his whole being, as if he had drunk some powerful drug. He had been feeling weak and done before. Now the life came back into him, he felt delivered from his own fretted, daily self.

He finished his duties at the surgery as quickly as might be, hastily filling up the bottles of the waiting people with cheap drugs. Then, in perpetual haste, he set off again to visit several cases in another part of his round, before tea-time. At all times he preferred to walk if he could, but particularly when he was not well. He fancied the motion restored him.

The afternoon was falling. It was grey, deadened, and wintry, with a slow, moist, heavy coldness sinking in and deadening all the faculties. But why should he think or notice? He hastily climbed the hill and turned across the dark green fields, following the black cinder-track. In the distance, across a shallow dip in the country, the small town was clustered like smouldering ash, a tower, a spire, a heap of low, raw, extinct houses. And on the nearest fringe of the town, sloping into the dip, was Oldmeadow, the Pervins' house. He could see the stables and the outbuildings distinctly, as they lay towards him on the slope. Well, he would not go there many more times! Another resource would be lost to him, another place gone: the only company he cared for in the alien, ugly little town he was losing. Nothing but work, drudgery, constant hastening from dwelling to dwelling among the colliers and the iron-workers. It wore him out, but at the same time he had a craving for it. It was a stimulant to him to be in the homes of the working people, moving, as it were, through the innermost body of their life. His nerves were excited and gratified. He could come so near, into the very lives of the rough, inarticulate, powerfully emotional men and women. He grumbled, he said he hated the hellish hole. But as a matter of fact it excited him, the contact with the rough, strongly-feeling people was a stimulant applied direct to his nerves.

Below Oldmeadow, in the green, shallow, soddened hollow of fields, lay a square, deep pond. Roving across the landscape, the doctor's quick eye detected a figure in black passing through the gate of the field, down towards the pond. He looked again. It would be Mabel Pervin. His mind suddenly became alive and attentive.

Why was she going down there? He pulled up on the path on the slope above, and stood staring. He could just make sure of the small black figure moving in the hollow of the failing day. He seemed to see her in the midst of such obscurity, that he was like a clairvoyant, seeing rather with the mind's eye than with ordinary sight. Yet he could see her positively enough, whilst he kept his eye attentive. He felt, if he looked away from her, in the thick, ugly falling dusk, he would lose her altogether.

He followed her minutely as she moved, direct and intent, like something transmitted rather than stirring in voluntary activity, straight down the field towards the pond. There she stood on the bank for a moment. She never raised her head. Then she waded slowly into the water.

He stood motionless as the small black figure walked slowly and deliberately towards the centre of the pond, very slowly, gradually moving deeper into the motionless water, and still moving forward as the water got up to her breast. Then he could see her no more in the dusk of the dead afternoon.

"There!" he exclaimed. "Would you believe it?"

And he hastened straight down, running over the wet, soddened fields, pushing through the hedges, down into the depression of callous wintry obscurity. It took him several minutes to come to the pond. He stood on the bank, breathing heavily. He could see nothing. His eyes seemed to penetrate the dead water. Yes, perhaps that was the dark shadow of her black clothing beneath the surface of the water.

He slowly ventured into the pond. The bottom was deep, soft clay, he sank in, and the water clasped dead cold round his legs. As he stirred he could smell the cold, rotten clay that fouled up into the water. It was objectionable in his lungs. Still, repelled and yet not heeding, he moved deeper into the pond. The cold water rose over his thighs, over his loins, upon his abdomen. The lower part of his body was all sunk in the hideous cold element. And the bottom was so deeply soft and uncertain, he was afraid of pitching with his mouth underneath. He could not swim, and was afraid.

He crouched a little, spreading his hands under the water and moving them round, trying to feel for her. The dead cold pond swayed upon his chest. He moved again, a little deeper, and again, with his hands underneath, he felt all around under the water. And he touched her clothing. But it evaded his fingers. He made a desperate effort to grasp it.

And so doing he lost his balance and went under, horribly, suffocating in the foul earthy water, struggling madly for a few moments. At last, after what seemed an eternity, he got his footing, rose again into the air and looked around. He gasped, and knew he was in the world. Then he looked at the water. She had risen near him. He grasped her clothing, and drawing her nearer, turned to take his way to land again.

He went very slowly, carefully, absorbed in the slow progress. He rose higher, climbing out of the pond. The water was now only about his legs; he was thankful, full of relief to be out of the clutches of the pond. He lifted her and staggered on to the bank, out of the horror of wet, grey clay.

He laid her down on the bank. She was quite unconscious and running with water. He made the water come from her mouth, he worked to restore her. He did not have to work very long before he could feel the breathing begin again in her; she was breathing naturally. He worked a little longer. He could feel her live beneath his hands; she was coming back. He wiped her face, wrapped her in his overcoat, looked round into the dim, dark grey world, then lifted her and staggered down the bank and across the fields.

It seemed an unthinkably long way, and his burden so heavy he felt he would never get to the house. But at last he was in the stable-yard, and then in the house-yard. He opened the door and went into the house. In the kitchen he laid her down on the hearth-rug and called. The house was empty. But the fire was burning in the grate.

Then again he kneeled to attend to her. She was breathing regularly, her eyes were wide open and as if conscious, but there seemed something missing in her look. She was conscious in herself, but unconscious of her surroundings.

He ran upstairs, took blankets from a bed, and put them before the fire to warm. Then he removed her saturated, earthy-smelling clothing, rubbed her dry with a towel, and wrapped her naked in the blankets. Then he went into the dining room, to look for spirits. There was a little whisky. He drank a gulp himself, and put some into her mouth.

The effect was instantaneous. She looked full into his face, as if she had been seeing him for some time, and yet had only just become conscious of him.

"Dr. Ferguson?" she said.

"What?" he answered.

He was divesting himself of his coat, intending to find some dry clothing upstairs. He could not bear the smell of the dead, clayey water, and he was mortally afraid for his own health.

"What did I do?" she asked.

"Walked into the pond," he replied. He had begun to shudder like one sick, and could hardly attend to her. Her eyes remained full on him, he seemed to be going dark in his mind, looking back at her helplessly. The shuddering became quieter in him, his life came back to him, dark and unknowing, but strong again.

"Was I out of my mind?" she asked, while her eyes were fixed on him all the time.

"Maybe, for the moment," he replied. He felt quiet, because his strength had come back. The strange fretful strain had left him.

"Am I out of my mind now?" she asked.

"Are you?" he reflected a moment. "No," he answered truthfully. "I don't see that you are." He turned his face aside. He was afraid now, because he felt dazed, and felt dimly that her power was stronger than his, in this issue. And she continued to look at him fixedly all the time. "Can you tell me where I shall find some dry things to put on?" he asked.

"Did you dive into the pond for me?" she asked.

"No," he answered. "I walked in. But I went in overhead as well."

There was silence for a moment. He hesitated. He very much wanted to go upstairs to get into dry clothing. But there was another desire in him. And she seemed to hold him. His will seemed to have gone to sleep, and left him, standing there slack before her. But he felt warm inside himself. He did not shudder at all, though his clothes were sodden on him.

"Why did you?" she asked.

"Because I didn't want you to do such a foolish thing," he said.

"It wasn't foolish," she said, still gazing at him as she lay on the floor, with a sofa cushion under her head. "It was the right thing to do. *I* knew best, then."

"I'll go and shift these wet things," he said. But still he had not the power to move out of her presence, until she sent him. It was as if she had the life of his body in her hands, and he could not extricate himself. Or perhaps he did not want to.

Suddenly she sat up. Then she became aware of her own immediate condition. She felt the blankets about her, she knew her own limbs. For a moment it seemed as if her reason were going. She looked round, with wild eye, as if seeking something. He stood still with fear. She saw her clothing lying scattered.

"Who undressed me?" she asked, her eyes resting full and inevitable on his face.

"I did," he replied, "to bring you round."

For some moments she sat and gazed at him awfully, her lips parted.

"Do you love me, then?" she asked.

He only stood and stared at her, fascinated. His soul seemed to melt.

She shuffled forward on her knees, and put her arms round him, round his legs, as he stood there, pressing her breasts against his knees and thighs, clutching him with strange, convulsive certainty, pressing his thighs against her, drawing him to her face, her throat, as she looked up at him with flaring, humble eyes of transfiguration, triumphant in first possession.

"You love me," she murmured, in strange transport, yearning and triumphant and confident. "You love me. I know you love me, I know."

And she was passionately kissing his knees, through the wet clothing, passionately and indiscriminately kissing his knees, his legs, as if unaware of everything.

He looked down at the tangled wet hair, the wild, bare, animal shoulders. He was amazed, bewildered, and afraid. He had never thought of loving her. He had never wanted to love her. When he rescued her and restored her, he was a doctor, and she was a patient. He had had no single personal thought of her. Nay, this introduction of the personal element was very distasteful to him, a violation of his professional honour. It was horrible to have her there embracing his knees. It was horrible. He revolted from it, violently. And yet—and yet—he had not the power to break away.

She looked at him again, with the same supplication of powerful love, and that same transcendent, frightening light of triumph. In view of the delicate flame which seemed to come from her face like a light, he was powerless. And yet he had never intended to love her. He had never intended. And something stubborn in him could not give way.

"You love me," she repeated, in a murmur of deep, rhapsodic assurance. "You love me."

Her hands were drawing him, drawing him down to her. He was afraid, even a little horrified. For he had, really, no intention of loving her. Yet her hands were drawing him towards her. He put out his hand quickly to steady himself, and grasped her bare shoulder. A flame seemed to burn the hand that grasped her soft shoulder. He had no intention of loving her: his whole will was against his yielding. It was horrible. And yet wonderful was the touch of her shoulders, beautiful the shining of her face. Was she perhaps mad? He had a horror of yielding to her. Yet something in him ached also.

He had been staring away at the door, away from her. But his hand remained on her shoulder. She had gone suddenly very still. He looked down at her. Her eyes were now wide with fear, with doubt, the light was dying from her face, a shadow of terrible greyness was returning. He could not bear the touch of her eyes' question upon him, and the look of death behind the question.

With an inward groan he gave way, and let his heart yield towards her. A sudden gentle smile came on his face. And her eyes, which never left his face, slowly, slowly filled with tears. He watched the strange water rise in her eyes, like some slow fountain coming up. And his heart seemed to burn and melt away in his breast.

He could not bear to look at her any more. He dropped on his knees and caught her head with his arms and pressed her face against his throat. She was very still. His heart, which seemed to have broken, was burning with a kind of agony in his breast. And he felt her slow, hot tears wetting his throat. But he could not move.

He felt the hot tears wet his neck and the hollows of his neck, and he remained motionless, suspended through one of man's eternities. Only now it had become indispensable to him to have her face pressed close to him; he could never let her go again. He could never let her head go away from the close clutch of his arm. He wanted to remain like that for ever, with his heart hurting him in a pain that was also life to him. Without knowing, he was looking down on her damp, soft brown hair.

Then, as it were suddenly, he smelt the horrid stagnant smell of that water. And at the same moment she drew away from him and looked at him. Her eyes were wistful and unfathomable. He was afraid of them, and he fell to kissing her, not knowing what he was doing. He wanted her eyes not to have that terrible, wistful, unfathomable look.

When she turned her face to him again, a faint delicate flush was glowing, and there was again dawning that terrible shining of joy in her eyes, which really terrified him, and yet which he now wanted to see, because he feared the look of doubt still more.

"You love me?" she said, rather faltering.

"Yes." The word cost him a painful effort. Not because it wasn't true. But because it was too newly true, the *saying* seemed to tear open again his newly-torn heart. And he hardly wanted it to be true, even now.

She lifted her face to him, and he bent forward and kissed her on the mouth, gently, with the one kiss that is an eternal pledge. And as he kissed her his heart strained again in his breast. He never intended to love her. But now it was over. He had crossed over the gulf to her, and all that he had left behind had shrivelled and become void.

After the kiss, her eyes again slowly filled with tears. She sat still, away from him, with her face drooped aside, and her hands folded in her lap. The tears fell very slowly. There was complete silence. He too sat there motionless and silent on the hearth-rug. The strange pain of his heart that was broken seemed to consume him. That he should love her? That this was love! That he should be ripped open in this way! Him, a doctor! How they would all jeer if they knew! It was agony to him to think they might know.

In the curious naked pain of the thought he looked again to her. She was sitting there drooped into a muse. He saw a tear fall, and his heart flared hot. He saw for the first time that one of her shoulders was quite uncovered, one arm bare, he could see one of her small breasts; dimly, because it had become almost dark in the room.

"Why are you crying?" he asked, in an altered voice.

She looked up at him, and behind her tears the consciousness of her situation for the first time brought a dark look of shame to her eyes.

"I'm not crying, really," she said, watching him, half frightened.

He reached his hand, and softly closed it on her bare arm.

"I love you! I love you!" he said in a soft, low vibrating voice, unlike himself.

She shrank, and dropped her head. The soft, penetrating grip of his hand on her arm distressed her. She looked up at him.

"I want to go," she said. "I want to go and get you some dry things."

"Why?" he said. "I'm all right."

"But I want to go," she said. "And I want you to change your things."

He released her arm, and she wrapped herself in the blanket, looking at him, rather frightened. And still she did not rise.

"Kiss me," she said wistfully.

He kissed her, but briefly, half in anger.

Then, after a second, she rose nervously, all mixed up in the blanket. He watched her in her confusion as she tried to extricate herself and wrap herself up so that she could walk. He watched her relentlessly, as she knew. And as she went, the blanket trailing, and as he saw a glimpse of her feet and her white leg, he tried to remember her as she was when he had wrapped her in the blanket. But then he didn't want to remember, because she had been nothing to him then, and his nature revolted from remembering her as she was when she was nothing to him.

A tumbling muffled noise from within the dark house startled him. Then he heard her voice: "There are clothes." He rose and went to the foot of the stairs, and gathered up the garments she had thrown down. Then he came back to the fire, to rub himself down and dress. He grinned at his own appearance when he had finished.

The fire was sinking, so he put on coal. The house was now quite dark, save for the light of a street-lamp that shone in faintly from beyond the holly trees. He lit the gas with matches he found on the mantelpiece. Then he emptied the pockets of his own clothes, and threw all his wet things in a heap into the scullery. After which he gathered up her sodden clothes, gently, and put them in a separate heap on the copper-top in the scullery.

It was six o'clock on the clock. His own watch had stopped. He ought to go back to the surgery. He waited, and still she did not come down. So he went to the foot of the stairs and called:

"I shall have to go."

Almost immediately he heard her coming down. She had on her best dress of black voile, and her hair was tidy, but still damp. She looked at him—and in spite of herself, smiled.

"I don't like you in those clothes," she said.

"Do I look a sight?" he answered.

They were shy of one another.

"I'll make you some tea," she said.

"No, I must go."

"Must you?" And she looked at him again with the wide, strained, doubtful eyes. And again, from the pain of his breast, he knew how he loved her. He went and bent to kiss her, gently, passionately, with his heart's painful kiss.

"And my hair smells so horrible," she murmured in distraction. "And I'm so awful, I'm so awful! Oh no, I'm too awful." And she broke into bitter, heart-broken sobbing. "You can't want to love me, I'm horrible."

"Don't be silly, don't be silly," he said, trying to comfort her, kissing her, holding her in his arms. "I want you, I want to marry you, we're going to be married, quickly, quickly—to-morrow if I can."

But she only sobbed terribly, and cried:

"I feel awful. I feel awful. I feel I'm horrible to you."

"No, I want you, I want you," was all he answered, blindly, with that terrible intonation which frightened her almost more than her horror lest he should *not* want her.

1922

Why the Novel Matters

We have curious ideas of ourselves. We think of ourselves as a body with a spirit in it, or a body with a soul in it, or a body with a mind in it. *Mens sana in corpore sano.*[1] The years drink up the wine, and at last throw the bottle away, the body, of course, being the bottle.

It is a funny sort of superstition. Why should I look at my hand, as it so cleverly writes these words, and decide that it is a mere nothing compared to the mind that directs it? Is there really any huge difference between my hand and my brain? Or my mind? My hand is alive, it flickers with a life of its own. It meets all the strange universe in touch, and learns a vast number of things, and knows a vast number of things. My hand, as it writes these words, slips gaily along, jumps like a grasshopper to dot an *i*, feels the table rather cold, gets a little bored if I write too long, has its own rudiments of thought, and is just as much *me* as is my brain, my mind, or my soul. Why should I imagine that there is a *me* which is more *me* than my hand is? Since my hand is absolutely alive, me alive.

Whereas, of course, as far as I am concerned, my pen isn't alive at all. My pen *isn't me* alive. Me alive ends at my finger tips.

Whatever is me alive is me. Every tiny bit of my hands is alive, every little

---

1. A healthy mind in a healthy body (Latin).

freckle and hair and fold of skin. And whatever is me alive is me. Only my finger-nails, those ten little weapons between me and an inanimate universe, they cross the mysterious Rubicon[2] between me alive and things like my pen, which are not alive, in my own sense.

So, seeing my hand is all alive, and me alive, wherein is it just a bottle, or a jug, or a tin can, or a vessel of clay, or any of the rest of that nonsense? True, if I cut it it will bleed, like a can of cherries. But then the skin that is cut, and the veins that bleed, and the bones that should never be seen, they are all just as alive as the blood that flows. So the tin can business, or vessel of clay, is just bunk.

And that's what you learn, when you're a novelist. And that's what you are very liable *not* to know, if you're a parson, or a philosopher, or a scientist, or a stupid person. If you're a parson, you talk about souls in heaven. If you're a novelist, you know that paradise is in the palm of your hand, and on the end of your nose, because both are alive; and alive, and man alive, which is more than you can say, for certain, of paradise. Paradise is after life, and I for one am not keen on anything that is *after* life. If you are a philosopher, you talk about infinity, and the pure spirit which knows all things. But if you pick up a novel, you realise immediately that infinity is just a handle to this self-same jug of a body of mine; while as for knowing, if I find my finger in the fire, I know that fire burns, with a knowledge so emphatic and vital, it leaves Nirvana[3] merely a conjecture. Oh, yes, my body, me alive, *knows*, and knows intensely. And as for the sum of all knowledge, it can't be anything more than an accumulation of all the things I know in the body, and you, dear reader, know in the body.

These damned philosophers, they talk as if they suddenly went off in steam, and were then much more important than they are when they're in their shirts. It is nonsense. Every man, philosopher included, ends in his own finger-tips. That's the end of his man alive. As for the words and thoughts and sighs and aspirations that fly from him, they are so many tremulations in the ether, and not alive at all. But if the tremulations reach another man alive, he may receive them into his life, and his life may take on a new colour, like a chameleon creeping from a brown rock on to a green leaf. All very well and good. It still doesn't alter the fact that the so-called spirit, the message or teaching of the philosopher or the saint, isn't alive at all, but just a tremulation upon the ether, like a radio message. All this spirit stuff is just tremulations upon the ether. If you, as man alive, quiver from the tremulation of the ether into new life, that is because you are man alive, and you take sustenance and stimulation into your alive man in a myriad ways. But to say that the message, or the spirit which is communicated to you, is more important than your living body, is nonsense. You might as well say that the potato at dinner was more important.

Nothing is important but life. And for myself, I can absolutely see life nowhere but in the living. Life with a capital L is only man alive. Even a cabbage in the rain is cabbage alive. All things that are alive are amazing. And all things that are dead are subsidiary to the living. Better a live dog than a dead lion. But better a live lion than a live dog. *C'est la vie!*

---

2. When Julius Caesar crossed the river Rubicon (near Rimini, Italy) in 49 B.C.E., in defiance of the Senate, he indicated his intention of advancing against Pompey and thus involving the country in civil war. Hence to "cross the Rubicon" means to take an important and irrevocable decision.
3. In Buddhist theology the extinction of the self and its desires and the attainment of perfect beatitude.

It seems impossible to get a saint, or a philosopher, or a scientist, to stick to this simple truth. They are all, in a sense, renegades. The saint wishes to offer himself up as spiritual food for the multitude. Even Francis of Assisi[4] turns himself into a sort of angel-cake, of which anyone may take a slice. But an angel-cake is rather less than man alive. And poor St Francis might well apologise to his body, when he is dying: "Oh, pardon me, my body, the wrong I did you through the years!" It was no wafer,[5] for others to eat.

The philosopher, on the other hand, because he can think, decides that nothing but thoughts matter. It is as if a rabbit, because he can make little pills, should decide that nothing but little pills matter. As for the scientist, he has absolutely no use for me so long as I am man alive. To the scientist, I am dead. He puts under the microscope a bit of dead me, and calls it me. He takes me to pieces, and says first one piece, and then another piece, is me. My heart, my liver, my stomach have all been scientifically me, according to the scientist; and nowadays I am either a brain, or nerves, or glands, or something more up-to-date in the tissue line.

Now I absolutely flatly deny that I am a soul, or a body, or a mind, or an intelligence, or a brain, or a nervous system, or a bunch of glands, or any of the rest of these bits of me. The whole is greater than the part. And therefore, I, who am man alive, am greater than my soul, or spirit, or body, or mind, or consciousness, or anything else that is merely a part of me. I am a man, and alive. I am man alive, and as long as I can, I intend to go on being man alive.

For this reason I am a novelist. And being a novelist, I consider myself superior to the saint, the scientist, the philosopher, and the poet, who are all great masters of different bits of man alive, but never get the whole hog.

The novel is the one bright book of life. Books are not life. They are only tremulations on the ether. But the novel as a tremulation can make the whole man alive tremble. Which is more than poetry, philosophy, science, or any other book-tremulation can do.

The novel is the book of life. In this sense, the Bible is a great confused novel. You may say, it is about God. But it is really about man alive. Adam, Eve, Sarai, Abraham, Isaac, Jacob, Samuel, David, Bath-Sheba, Ruth, Esther, Solomon, Job, Isaiah, Jesus, Mark, Judas, Paul, Peter: what is it but man alive, from start to finish? Man alive, not mere bits. Even the Lord is another man alive, in a burning bush, throwing the tablets of stone at Moses's head.

I do hope you begin to get my idea, why the novel is supremely important, as a tremulation on the ether. Plato makes the perfect ideal being tremble in me. But that's only a bit of me. Perfection is only a bit, in the strange make-up of man alive. The Sermon on the Mount[6] makes the selfless spirit of me quiver. But that, too, is only a bit of me. The Ten Commandments set the old Adam shivering in me, warning me that I am a thief and a murderer, unless I watch it. But even the old Adam is only a bit of me.

I very much like all these bits of me to be set trembling with life and the wisdom of life. But I do ask that the whole of me shall tremble in its wholeness, some time or other.

And this, of course, must happen in me, living.

But as far as it can happen from a communication, it can only happen when

4. Roman Catholic saint (1181 or 1182–1226).   Communion.
5. Consumed as Christ's body in Roman Catholic   6. See Matthew 5.7.

a whole novel communicates itself to me. The Bible—but *all* the Bible—and Homer, and Shakespeare: these are the supreme old novels. These are all things to all men. Which means that in their wholeness they affect the whole man alive, which is the man himself, beyond any part of him. They set the whole tree trembling with a new access of life, they do not just stimulate growth in one direction.

I don't want to grow in any one direction any more. And, if I can help it, I don't want to stimulate anybody else into some particular direction. A particular direction ends in a *cul-de-sac*. We're in a *cul-de-sac* at present.

I don't believe in any dazzling revelation, or in any supreme Word. "The grass withereth, the flower fadeth, but the Word of the Lord shall stand for ever."[7] That's the kind of stuff we've drugged ourselves with. As a matter of fact, the grass withereth, but comes up all the greener for that reason, after the rains. The flower fadeth, and therefore the bud opens. But the Word of the Lord, being man-uttered and a mere vibration on the ether, becomes staler and staler, more and more boring, till at last we turn a deaf ear and it ceases to exist, far more finally than any withered grass. It is grass that renews its youth like the eagle, not any Word.

We should ask for no absolutes, or absolute. Once and for all and for ever, let us have done with the ugly imperialism of any absolute. There is no absolute good, there is nothing absolutely right. All things flow and change, and even change is not absolute. The whole is a strange assembly of apparently incongruous parts, slipping past one another.

Me, man alive, I am a very curious assembly of incongruous parts. My yea! of today is oddly different from my yea! of yesterday. My tears of to-morrow will have nothing to do with my tears of a year ago. If the one I love remains unchanged and unchanging, I shall cease to love her. It is only because she changes and startles me into change and defies my inertia, and is herself staggered in her inertia by my changing, that I can continue to love her. If she stayed put, I might as well love the pepper pot.

In all this change, I maintain a certain integrity. But woe betide me if I try to put my finger on it. If I say of myself, I am this, I am that!—then, if I stick to it, I turn into a stupid fixed thing like a lamp-post. I shall never know wherein lies my integrity, my individuality, my me. I *can* never know it. It is useless to talk about my ego. That only means that I have made up an *idea* of myself, and that I am trying to cut myself out to pattern. Which is no good. You can cut your cloth to fit your coat, but you can't clip bits off your living body, to trim it down to your idea. True, you can put yourself into ideal corsets. But even in ideal corsets, fashions change.

Let us learn from the novel. In the novel, the characters can do nothing but *live*. If they keep on being good, according to pattern, or bad, according to pattern, or even volatile, according to pattern, they cease to live, and the novel falls dead. A character in a novel has got to live, or it is nothing.

We, likewise, in life have got to live, or we are nothing.

What we mean by living is, of course, just as indescribable as what we mean by *being*. Men get ideas into their heads, of what they mean by Life, and they proceed to cut life out to pattern. Sometimes they go into the desert to seek God, sometimes they go into the desert to seek cash, sometimes it is wine, woman, and song, and again it is water, political reform, and votes. You never

---

7. Isaiah 40.8.

know what it will be next: from killing your neighbour with hideous bombs and gas that tears the lungs, to supporting a Foundlings' Home[8] and preaching infinite Love, and being co-respondent in a divorce.

In all this wild welter, we need some sort of guide. It's no good inventing Thou Shalt Nots!

What then? Turn truly, honourably to the novel, and see wherein you are man alive, and wherein you are dead man in life. You may love a woman as man alive, and you may be making love to a woman as sheer dead man in life. You may eat your dinner as man alive, or as a mere masticating corpse. As man alive you may have shot at your enemy. But as a ghastly simulacrum of life you may be firing bombs into men who are neither your enemies nor your friends, but just things you are dead to. Which is criminal, when the things happen to be alive.

To be alive, to be man alive, to be whole man alive: that is the point. And at its best, the novel, and the novel supremely, can help you. It can help you not to be dead man in life. So much of a man walks about dead and a carcass in the street and house, to-day: so much of women is merely dead. Like a pianoforte with half the notes mute.

But the novel you can see, plainly, when the man goes dead, the woman goes inert. You can develop an instinct for life, if you will, instead of a theory of right and wrong, good and bad.

In life, there is right and wrong, good and bad, all the time. But what is right in one case is wrong in another. And in the novel you see one man becoming a corpse, because of his so-called goodness, another going dead because of his so-called wickedness. Right and wrong is an instinct: but an instinct of the whole consciousness in a man, bodily, mental, spiritual at once. And only in the novel are *all* things given full play, or at least, they may be given full play, when we realize that life itself, and not inert safety, is the reason for living. For out of the full play of all things emerges the only thing that is anything, the wholeness of a man, the wholeness of a woman, man live, and live woman.

1936

Love on the Farm[1]

What large, dark hands are those at the window
Grasping in the golden light
Which weaves its way through the evening wind
    At my heart's delight?

5   Ah, only the leaves! But in the west
I see a redness suddenly come
Into the evening's anxious breast—
    'Tis the wound of love goes home!

8. Orphanage.
1. Called "Cruelty and Love" when first published

in 1913 and "Love on the Farm" when it appeared in *Collected Poems* (1928).

The woodbine° creeps abroad   *honeysuckle*
10   Calling low to her lover:
     The sunlit flirt who all the day
     Has poised above her lips in play
     And stolen kisses, shallow and gay
     Of pollen, now has gone away—
15   She woos the moth with her sweet, low word;
     And when above her his moth-wings hover
     Then her bright breast she will uncover
     And yield her honey-drop to her lover.

     Into the yellow, evening glow
20   Saunters a man from the farm below;
     Leans, and looks in at the low-built shed
     Where the swallow has hung her marriage bed.
     The bird lies warm against the wall.
     She glances quick her startled eyes
25   Towards him, then she turns away
     Her small head, making warm display
     Of red upon the throat. Her terrors sway
     Her out of the nest's warm, busy ball,
     Whose plaintive cry is heard as she flies
30   In one blue stoop from out the sties°   *pens for animals*
     Into the twilight's empty hall.
     Oh, water-hen, beside the rushes
     Hide your quaintly scarlet blushes,
     Still your quick tail, lie still as dead,
35   Till the distance folds over his ominous tread!

     The rabbit presses back her ears,
     Turns back her liquid, anguished eyes
     And crouches low; then with wild spring
     Spurts from the terror of *his* oncoming;
40   To be choked back, the wire ring
     Her frantic effort throttling:
        Piteous brown ball of quivering fears!
     Ah, soon in his large, hard hands she dies,
     And swings all loose from the swing of his walk!
45   Yet calm and kindly are his eyes
     And ready to open in brown surprise
     Should I not answer to his talk
     Or should he my tears surmise.

     I hear his hand on the latch, and rise from my chair
50   Watching the door open; he flashes bare
     His strong teeth in a smile, and flashes his eyes
     In a smile like triumph upon me; then careless-wise
     He flings the rabbit soft on the table board
     And comes towards me: ah! the uplifted sword
55   Of his hand against my bosom! and oh, the broad
     Blade of his glance that asks me to applaud
     His coming! With his hand he turns my face to him
     And caresses me with his fingers that still smell grim

Of the rabbit's fur! God, I am caught in a snare!
60 I know not what fine wire is round my throat;
I only know I let him finger there
My pulse of life, and let him nose like a stoat°   weasel
Who sniffs with joy before he drinks the blood.

And down his mouth comes to my mouth! and down
65 His bright dark eyes come over me, like a hood
Upon my mind! his lips meet mine, and a flood
Of sweet fire sweeps across me, so I drown
Against him, die, and find death good.

                                                            1913, 1928

Piano[1]

Softly, in the dusk, a woman is singing to me;
Taking me back down the vista of years, till I see
A child sitting under the piano, in the boom of the tingling strings
And pressing the small, poised feet of a mother who smiles as she sings.

5   In spite of myself, the insidious mastery of song
Betrays me back, till the heart of me weeps to belong
To the old Sunday evenings at home, with winter outside
And hymns in the cozy parlour, the tinkling piano our guide.

So now it is vain for the singer to burst into clamour
10 With the great black piano appassionato.° The glamour   played with passion
Of childish days is upon me, my manhood is cast
Down in the flood of remembrance, I weep like a child for the past.

                                                            1918

Tortoise Shout

I thought he was dumb,
I said he was dumb,
Yet I've heard him cry.

First faint scream,
5 Out of life's unfathomable dawn,
Far off, so far, like a madness, under the horizon's dawning rim,
Far, far off, far scream.

Tortoise *in extremis.*[1]

---

1. For an earlier version of this poem, see "Poems   1. At the point of death (Latin).
in Process," in the appendices to this volume.

Why were we crucified into sex?
10 Why were we not left rounded off, and finished in ourselves.
As we began,
As he certainly began, so perfectly alone?

A far, was-it-audible scream,
Or did it sound on the plasm direct?

15 Worse than the cry of the new-born,
A scream,
A yell,
A shout,
A pæan,
20 A death-agony,
A birth-cry,
A submission,
All, tiny, far away, reptile under the first dawn.

War-cry, triumph, acute-delight, death-scream reptilian,
25 Why was the veil torn?[2]
The silken shriek of the soul's torn membrane?
The male soul's membrane
Torn with a shriek half music, half horror.

Crucifixion.
30 Male tortoise, cleaving behind the hovel-wall of that dense female,
Mounted and tense, spread-eagle, outreaching out of the shell
In tortoise-nakedness,
Long neck, and long vulnerable limbs extruded, spread-eagle over her
      house-roof,
And the deep, secret, all-penetrating tail curved beneath her walls,
35 Reaching and gripping tense, more reaching anguish in uttermost tension
Till suddenly, in the spasm of coition, tupping[3] like a jerking leap, and oh!
Opening its clenched face from his outstretched neck
And giving that fragile yell, that scream,
Super-audible,
40 From his pink, cleft, old-man's mouth,
Giving up the ghost,
Or screaming in Pentecost,[4] receiving the ghost.

His scream, and his moment's subsidence,
The moment of eternal silence,
45 Yet unreleased, and after the moment, the sudden, startling jerk of coition,
      and at once
The inexpressible faint yell—
And so on, till the last plasm of my body was melted back
To the primeval rudiments of life, and the secret.

2. Cf. Matthew 27.50–51, describing Jesus' death: "Jesus, when he had cried again with a loud voice, yielded up the ghost. And, behold, the veil [curtain] of the temple was rent in twain, from the top to the bottom; and the earth did quake, and the rocks rent."
3. Copulating.
4. The religious holiday celebrating the descent of the Holy Ghost on Jesus' apostles.

So he tups, and screams
50   Time after time that frail, torn scream
After each jerk, the longish interval,
The tortoise eternity,
Age-long, reptilian persistence,
Heart-throb, slow heart-throb, persistent for the next spasm.

55   I remember, when I was a boy,
I heard the scream of a frog, which was caught with his foot in the mouth
        of an up-starting snake;
I remember when I first heard bull-frogs break into sound in the spring;
I remember hearing a wild goose out of the throat of night
Cry loudly, beyond the lake of waters;
60   I remember the first time, out of a bush in the darkness, a nightingale's
        piercing cries and gurgles startled the depths of my soul;
I remember the scream of a rabbit as I went through a wood at midnight;
I remember the heifer in her heat, blorting and blorting through the hours,
        persistent and irrepressible;
I remember my first terror hearing the howl of weird, amorous cats;
I remember the scream of a terrified, injured horse, the sheet lightning,
65   And running away from the sound of a woman in labour, something like an
        owl whooing,
And listening inwardly to the first bleat of a lamb,
The first wail of an infant,
And my mother singing to herself,
And the first tenor singing of the passionate throat of a young
        collier,° who has long since drunk himself to death,   coal miner
70   The first elements of foreign speech
On wild dark lips.

And more than all these,
And less than all these,
This last,
75   Strange, faint coition yell
Of the male tortoise at extremity,
Tiny from under the very edge of the farthest far-off horizon of life.

The cross,
The wheel on which our silence first is broken,
80   Sex, which breaks up our integrity, our single inviolability, our deep silence,
Tearing a cry from us.

Sex, which breaks us into voice, sets us calling across the deeps, calling,
        calling for the complement,
Singing, and calling, and singing again, being answered, having found.
Torn, to become whole again, after long seeking for what is lost,
85   The cry from the tortoise as from Christ, the Osiris⁵-cry of abandonment,
That which is whole, torn asunder,
That which is in part, finding its whole again throughout the universe.

1921

5. The Egyptian vegetation god, murdered by his
brother Set, who cut the corpse into fourteen
pieces and scattered them throughout Egypt. Osiris, like Christ, was resurrected, and became an
important ruler in the other world.

Bavarian Gentians

Not every man has gentians in his house
in soft September, at slow, sad Michaelmas.[1]

Bavarian gentians, big and dark, only dark
darkening the daytime torchlike with the smoking blueness of Pluto's[2]
    gloom,
5 ribbed and torchlike, with their blaze of darkness spread blue
down flattening into points, flattened under the sweep of white day
torch-flower of the blue-smoking darkness, Pluto's dark-blue daze,
black lamps from the halls of Dis, burning dark blue,
giving off darkness, blue darkness, as Demeter's pale lamps give off light,
10 lead me then, lead me the way.

Reach me a gentian, give me a torch
let me guide myself with the blue, forked torch of this flower
down the darker and darker stairs, where blue is darkened on blueness
even where Persephone goes, just now, from the frosted September
15 to the sightless realm where darkness was awake upon the dark
and Persephone herself is but a voice
or a darkness invisible enfolded in the deeper dark
of the arms Plutonic, and pierced with the passion of dense gloom,
among the splendour of torches of darkness, shedding darkness on the lost
    bride and her groom.

1923

Snake

A snake came to my water-trough
On a hot, hot day, and I in pyjamas for the heat,
To drink there.

In the deep, strange-scented shade of the great dark
    carob-tree°   *Mediterranean evergreen*
5 I came down the steps with my pitcher
And must wait, must stand and wait, for there he was at the trough before
    me.

He reached down from a fissure in the earth-wall in the gloom
And trailed his yellow-brown slackness soft-bellied down, over the edge of
    the stone trough
And rested his throat upon the stone bottom,
10 And where the water had dripped from the tap, in a small clearness,

---

1. September 29, the feast celebrating the Archangel Michael.
2. God of the underworld in classical mythology.
Also called Dis, he abducted Persephone, daughter
of the goddess of agriculture, Demeter. Persephone was allowed to return to the earth every spring,
but had to descend again to Hades in the autumn,
"the frosted September" (line 14). Demeter and
Persephone were central figures in ancient fertility
myths, where Persephone's annual descent and
return were linked with the death and rebirth of
vegetation.

He sipped with his straight mouth,
Softly drank through his straight gums, into his slack long body,
Silently.

Someone was before me at my water-trough,
15   And I, like a second comer, waiting.

He lifted his head from his drinking, as cattle do,
And looked at me vaguely, as drinking cattle do,
And flickered his two-forked tongue from his lips, and mused a moment,
And stooped and drank a little more,
20   Being earth-brown, earth-golden from the burning bowels of
        the earth
On the day of Sicilian July, with Etna° smoking.   *the volcano*

The voice of my education said to me
He must be killed,
For in Sicily the black, black snakes are innocent, the gold are venomous.

25   And voices in me said, If you were a man
You would take a stick and break him now, and finish him off.

But must I confess how I liked him,
How glad I was he had come like a guest in quiet, to drink at my water-
        trough
And depart peaceful, pacified, and thankless
30   Into the burning bowels of this earth?

Was it cowardice, that I dared not kill him?
Was it perversity, that I longed to talk to him?
Was it humility, to feel so honoured?
I felt so honoured.

35   And yet those voices:
If you were not afraid, you would kill him!

And truly I was afraid, I was most afraid,
But even so, honoured still more
That he should seek my hospitality
40   From out the dark door of the secret earth.

He drank enough
And lifted his head, dreamily, as one who has drunken,
And flickered his tongue like a forked night on the air, so black;
Seeming to lick his lips,
45   And looked around like a god, unseeing, into the air,
And slowly turned his head,
And slowly, very slowly, as if thrice adream
Proceeded to draw his slow length curving round
And climb the broken bank of my wall-face.

50   And as he put his head into that dreadful hole,
And as he slowly drew up, snake-easing his shoulders, and entered farther,

A sort of horror, a sort of protest against his withdrawing into that horrid
    black hole,
Deliberately going into the blackness, and slowly drawing himself after,
Overcame me now his back was turned.

55 I looked round, I put down my pitcher,
I picked up a clumsy log
And threw it at the water-trough with a clatter.

I think it did not hit him;
But suddenly that part of him that was left behind convulsed in undignified
    haste,
60 Writhed like lightning, and was gone
Into the black hole, the earth-lipped fissure in the wall-front
At which, in the intense still noon, I stared with fascination.

And immediately I regretted it.
I thought how paltry, how vulgar, what a mean act!
65 I despised myself and the voices of my accursed human education.

And I thought of the albatross,[1]
And I wished he would come back, my snake.

For he seemed to me again like a king,
Like a king in exile, uncrowned in the underworld,
70 Now due to be crowned again.

And so, I missed my chance with one of the lords
Of life.
And I have something to expiate;
A pettiness.

                                                                1923

Cypresses[1]

Tuscan cypresses,
What is it?

Folded in like a dark thought,
For which the language is lost,
5 Tuscan cypresses,
Is there a great secret?
Are our words no good?

The undeliverable secret,
Dead with a dead race and a dead speech, and yet
10 Darkly monumental in you,
Etruscan cypresses.

---

1. In Coleridge's *Rime of the Ancient Mariner.*   1. Tall dark coniferous evergreen trees, associated

Ah, how I admire your fidelity,
Dark cypresses!

Is it the secret of the long-nosed Etruscans?[2]
15   The long-nosed, sensitive-footed, subtly-smiling Etruscans,
Who made so little noise outside the cypress groves?

Among the sinuous, flame-tall cypresses
That swayed their length of darkness all around
Etruscan-dusky, wavering men of old Etruria:
20   Naked except for fanciful long shoes,
Going with insidious, half-smiling quietness
And some of Africa's imperturbable sang-froid[3]
About a forgotten business.

What business, then?
25   Nay, tongues are dead, and words are hollow as hollow seed-pods,
Having shed their sound and finished all their echoing
Etruscan syllables,
That had the telling.

Yet more I see you darkly concentrate,
30   Tuscan cypresses,
On one old thought:
On one old slim imperishable thought, while you remain
Etruscan cypresses;
Dusky, slim marrow-thought of slender, flickering men of Etruria,
35   Whom Rome called vicious.

Vicious, dark cypresses:
Vicious, you supple, brooding, softly-swaying pillars of dark flame.
Monumental to a dead, dead race
Embowered in you!

40   Were they then vicious, the slender, tender-footed
Long-nosed men of Etruria?
Or was their way only evasive and different, dark, like cypress-trees in a
    wind?

They are dead, with all their vices,
And all that is left
45   Is the shadowy monomania of some cypresses
And tombs.

The smile, the subtle Etruscan smile still lurking
Within the tombs,
Etruscan cypresses.

50   He laughs longest who laughs last;°   (proverbial)
Nay, Leonardo[4] only bungled the pure Etruscan smile.

2. The most important of the pre-Roman inhabi-   4. Leonardo da Vinci (1452–1519), Italian painter
tants of Italy.   whose portrait known as the *Mona Lisa* or *La Gio-*
3. Cold blood (French, literal trans.); here calm   *conda* has a famous mysterious smile.
detachment.

2282 / D. H. LAWRENCE

What would I not give
To bring back the rare and orchid-like
Evil-yclept° Etruscan?   °called (archaic)
55   For as to the evil
We have only Roman word for it,
Which I, being a little weary of Roman virtue,
Don't hang much weight on.

For oh, I know, in the dust where we have buried
60   The silenced races and all their abominations,
We have buried so much of the delicate magic of life.

There in the deeps
That churn the frankincense and ooze the myrrh,
Cypress shadowy,
65   Such an aroma of lost human life!

They say the fit survive,
But I invoke the spirits of the lost.
Those that have not survived, the darkly lost,
To bring their meaning back into life again,
70   Which they have taken away
And wrap inviolable in soft cypress-trees,
Etruscan cypresses.

Evil, what is evil?
There is only one evil, to deny life
75   As Rome denied Etruria
And mechanical America Montezuma⁵ still.

Fiesole.   1923

How Beastly the Bourgeois Is

How beastly the bourgeois is
especially the male of the species—

Presentable, eminently presentable—
shall I make you a present of him?

5   Isn't he handsome? Isn't he healthy? Isn't he a fine specimen?
Doesn't he look the fresh clean englishman, outside?
Isn't it god's own image? tramping his thirty miles a day
after partridges, or a little rubber ball?
wouldn't you like to be like that, well off, and quite the thing?

10   Oh, but wait!
Let him meet a new emotion, let him be faced with another man's need,
let him come home to a bit of moral difficulty, let life face him with a new
     demand on his understanding

5. Aztec war chief or emperor of ancient Mexico at the time of the Spanish conquest early 16th century.

and then watch him go soggy, like a wet meringue.
Watch him turn into a mess, either a fool or a bully.
15   Just watch the display of him, confronted with a new demand on his
        intelligence,
a new life-demand.

How beastly the bourgeois is
especially the male of the species—
Nicely groomed, like a mushroom
20   standing there so sleek and erect and eyeable—
and like a fungus, living on the remains of bygone life
sucking his life out of the dead leaves of greater life than his own.

And even so, he's stale, he's been there too long.
Touch him, and you'll find he's all gone inside
25   just like an old mushroom, all wormy inside, and hollow
under a smooth skin and an upright appearance.

Full of seething, wormy, hollow feelings
rather nasty—
How beastly the bourgeois is!

30   Standing in their thousands, these appearances, in damp England
what a pity they can't all be kicked over
like sickening toadstools, and left to melt back, swiftly
into the soil of England.

1929

The Ship of Death[1]

I

Now it is autumn and the falling fruit
and the long journey towards oblivion.

The apples falling like great drops of dew
to bruise themselves an exit from themselves.

5   And it is time to go, to bid farewell
to one's own self, and find an exit
from the fallen self.

II

Have you built your ship of death, O have you?
O build your ship of death, for you will need it.

10   The grim frost is at hand, when the apples will fall
thick, almost thundrous, on the hardened earth.

---

1. Lawrence is remembering "the sacred treasures of the dead, the little bronze ship of death that should bear him over to the other world," found in Etruscan tombs and described in his book *Etruscan Places* (1932).

And death is on the air like a smell of ashes!
Ah! can't you smell it?

And in the bruised body, the frightened soul
15   finds itself shrinking, wincing from the cold
that blows upon it through the orifices.

III

And can a man his own quietus make
with a bare bodkin?[2]

With daggers, bodkins, bullets, man can make
20   a bruise or break of exit for his life;
but is that a quietus, O tell me, is it quietus?

Surely not so! for how could murder, even self-murder
ever a quietus make?

IV

O let us talk of quiet that we know,
25   that we can know, the deep and lovely quiet
of a strong heart at peace!

How can we this, our own quietus, make?

V

Build then the ship of death, for you must take
the longest journey, to oblivion.

30   And die the death, the long and painful death
that lies between the old self and the new.

Already our bodies are fallen, bruised, badly bruised,
already our souls are oozing through the exit
of the cruel bruise.

35   Already the dark and endless ocean of the end
is washing in through the breaches of our wounds,
already the flood is upon us.

Oh build your ship of death, your little ark
and furnish it with food, with little cakes, and wine
40   for the dark flight down oblivion.

VI

Piecemeal the body dies, and the timid soul
has her footing washed away, as the dark flood rises.

---

2. Cf. Shakespeare's *Hamlet* 3.1.70–76: "For who would bear the whips and scorns of time, / . . . When
he himself might his quietus make / With a bare bodkin?" "Bodkin": dagger.

We are dying, we are dying, we are all of us dying
and nothing will stay the death-flood rising within us
45   and soon it will rise on the world, on the outside world.

We are dying, we are dying, piecemeal our bodies are dying
and our strength leaves us,
and our soul cowers naked in the dark rain over the flood,
cowering in the last branches of the tree of our life.

VII

50   We are dying, we are dying, so all we can do
is now to be willing to die, and to build the ship
of death to carry the soul on the longest journey.

A little ship, with oars and food
and little dishes, and all accoutrements
55   fitting and ready for the departing soul.

Now launch the small ship, now as the body dies
and life departs, launch out, the fragile soul
in the fragile ship of courage, the ark of faith
with its store of food and little cooking pans
60   and change of clothes,
upon the flood's black waste
upon the waters of the end
upon the sea of death, where still we sail
darkly, for we cannot steer, and have no port.

65   There is no port, there is nowhere to go
only the deepening blackness darkening still
blacker upon the soundless, ungurgling flood
darkness at one with darkness, up and down
and sideways utterly dark, so there is no direction any more
70   and the little ship is there; yet she is gone.
She is not seen, for there is nothing to see her by.
She is gone! gone! and yet
somewhere she is there.
Nowhere!

VIII

75   And everything is gone, the body is gone
completely under, gone, entirely gone.
The upper darkness is heavy as the lower,
between them the little ship
is gone
80   she is gone.

It is the end, it is oblivion.

IX

And yet out of eternity a thread
separates itself on the blackness,

a horizontal thread
85   that fumes a little with pallor upon the dark.

Is it illusion? or does the pallor fume
A little higher?
Ah wait, wait, for there's the dawn,
the cruel dawn of coming back to life
90   out of oblivion.

Wait, wait, the little ship
drifting, beneath the deathly ashy grey
of a flood-dawn.

Wait, wait! even so, a flush of yellow
95   and strangely, O chilled wan soul, a flush of rose.

A flush of rose, and the whole thing starts again.

X

The flood subsides, and the body, like a worn sea-shell
emerges strange and lovely.
And the little ship wings home, faltering and lapsing
100   on the pink flood,
and the frail soul steps out, into her house again
filling the heart with peace.

Swings the heart renewed with peace
even of oblivion.

105   Oh build your ship of death, oh build it!
for you will need it.
For the voyage of oblivion awaits you.

1929–30   1933

T. S. ELIOT
1888–1965

Thomas Stearns Eliot was born in St. Louis, Missouri, of New England stock. He entered Harvard in 1906 and was influenced there by the anti-Romanticism of Irving Babbitt and the philosophical and critical interests of George Santayana, as well as by the enthusiastic study of Renaissance literature and of South Asian religions. He wrote his Harvard dissertation on the English idealist philosopher F. H. Bradley, whose emphasis on the private nature of individual experience, "a circle enclosed on the outside," influenced Eliot's poetry considerably. He also studied literature and philosophy in France and Germany, before going to England shortly after the outbreak of World War I in 1914. He studied Greek philosophy at Oxford, taught school in London, and then obtained a position with Lloyd's Bank. In 1915 he married an English writer, Vivienne Haigh-Wood, but the marriage was not a success. She suffered from poor emotional and physical health. The strain told on Eliot, too. By November 1921 distress and worry had brought him to the verge of a nervous break-down, and on medical advice he went to recuperate in a Swiss sanitorium. Two months later he returned, pausing in Paris long enough to give his early supporter and adviser Ezra Pound the manuscript of *The Waste Land*. Eliot left his wife in 1933, and she was eventually committed to a mental home, where she died in 1947. Ten years later he was happily remarried to his secretary, Valerie Fletcher.

Eliot started writing literary and philosophical reviews soon after settling in London and was assistant editor of *The Egoist* magazine from 1917 to 1919. In 1922 he founded the influential quarterly *The Criterion*, which he edited until it ceased pub-lication in 1939. His poetry first appeared in 1915, when, at Pound's urging, "The Love Song of J. Alfred Prufrock" was printed in *Poetry* magazine (Chicago) and a few other short poems were published in the short-lived periodical *Blast*. His first pub-lished collection of poems was *Prufrock and Other Observations*, 1917; two other small collections followed in 1919 and 1920; in 1922 *The Waste Land* appeared, first in *The Criterion* in October, then in *The Dial* (in America) in November, and finally in book form. Meanwhile he was also publishing collections of his critical essays. In 1925 he joined the London publishing firm Faber & Gwyer, and he was made a director when the firm was renamed Faber & Faber. He became a British subject and joined the Church of England in 1927.

"Our civilization comprehends great variety and complexity, and this variety and com-plexity, playing upon a refined sensibility, must produce various and complex results. The poet must become more and more comprehensive, more allusive, more indirect, in order to force, to dislocate if necessary, language into his meaning." This remark, from Eliot's essay "The Metaphysical Poets" (1921), gives one clue to his poetic method from "Prufrock" through *The Waste Land*. When he settled in London he saw poetry in English as exhausted, with no verbal excitement or original craftsman-ship. He sought to make poetry more subtle, more suggestive, and at the same time more precise. Like the imagists, he emphasized the necessity of clear and precise images. From the philosopher poet T. E. Hulme and from Pound, he learned to fear what was seen as Romantic self-indulgence and vagueness, and to regard the poetic medium rather than the poet's personality as the important factor. At the same time the "hard, dry" images advocated by Hulme were not enough for him; he wanted wit, allusiveness, irony. He saw in the Metaphysical poets how wit and passion could be combined, and he saw in the French symbolists, such as Charles Baudelaire, Sté-phane Mallarmé, Paul Verlaine, and Arthur Rimbaud, how an image could be both absolutely precise in what it referred to physically and endlessly suggestive in its meanings because of its relationship to other images. The combination of precision, symbolic suggestion, and ironic mockery in the poetry of the late-nineteenth-century French poet Jules Laforgue attracted and influenced him, as did Laforgue's verse technique that Eliot described in an interview as "rhyming lines of irregular length, with the rhymes coming in irregular places." He also found in the Jacobean drama-tists, such as Thomas Middleton, Cyril Tourneur, and John Webster, a flexible blank verse with overtones of colloquial movement, a way of counterpointing the accent of conversation and the note of terror. Eliot's fluency in French and German, his study of Western and non-Western literary and religious texts in their original languages, his rigorous knowledge of philosophy, his exacting critical intellect, his keen sensitiv-ity to colloquial rhythm and idiom, his ability to fuse anguished emotional states with sharply etched intellectual satire—all of these contributed to his crafting one of the twentieth century's most distinctive and influential bodies of poetry.

Hulme's protests against the Romantic concept of poetry reinforced what Eliot had learned from Babbitt at Harvard; yet for all his severity with poets such as Percy Shelley and Walt Whitman, for all his cultivation of a classical viewpoint and his insistence on order and discipline rather than on mere self-expression in art, one side of Eliot's poetic genius is Romantic. The symbolist influence on his imagery, his elegiac lamentation over loss and fragmentation, his interest in the evocative and the suggestive, lines such as "And fiddled whisper music on those strings / And bats with baby faces in the violet light / Whistled, and beat their wings," and recurring images such as the hyacinth girl and the rose garden show what could be called a Romantic element in his poetry. But it is combined with a dry ironic allusiveness, a play of wit and satire, and a colloquial element, which are not normally found in poets of the Romantic tradition.

Eliot's real novelty—and the cause of much bewilderment when his poems first appeared—was his deliberate elimination of all merely connective and transitional passages, his building up of the total pattern of meaning through the immediate juxtaposition of images without overt explanation of what they are doing, together with his use of oblique references to other works of literature (some of them quite obscure to most readers of his time). "Prufrock" presents a symbolic landscape where the meaning emerges from the mutual interaction of the images, and that meaning is enlarged by echoes, often ironic, of Hesiod and Dante and Shakespeare. *The Waste Land* is a series of scenes and images with no author's voice intervening to tell us where we are but with the implications developed through multiple contrasts and through analogies with older literary works often referred to in a distorted quotation or half-concealed allusion. Furthermore, the works referred to are not necessarily central in the Western literary tradition: besides Dante and Shakespeare there are pre-Socratic philosophers; major and minor seventeenth-century poets and dramatists; works of anthropology, history, and philosophy; texts of Buddhism and Hinduism; even popular songs and vaudeville. Ancient and modern voices, high and low art, Western and non-Western languages clash, coincide, jostle alongside one another. In a culture where the poet's public might lack a common cultural heritage, a shared knowledge of works of the past, Eliot felt it necessary to accumulate his own body of references. In this his use of earlier literature differs from, say, John Milton's. Both poets are difficult for the modern reader, who needs editorial assistance in recognizing and understanding many of the allusions—but Milton was drawing on a body of knowledge common to educated people in his day. Nevertheless, this aspect of Eliot can be exaggerated; his imagery and the movement of his verse set the tone he requires, establish the area of meaning to be developed, so that even a reader ignorant of most of the literary allusions can often get the feel of the poem and achieve some understanding of what it says.

Eliot's early poetry, until at least the middle 1920s, is mostly concerned in one way or another with the Waste Land, with aspects of cultural decay in the modern Western world. After his formal acceptance of Anglican Christianity, a penitential note appears in much of his verse, a note of quiet searching for spiritual peace, with considerable allusion to biblical, liturgical, and mystical religious literature and to Dante. *Ash Wednesday* (1930), a poem in six parts, much less fiercely concentrated in style than the earlier poetry, explores with gentle insistence a mood both penitential and questioning. The Ariel poems (so called because published in Faber's Ariel pamphlet series) present or explore aspects of religious doubt or discovery or revelation, sometimes, as in "Journey of the Magi," drawing on biblical incident. In *Four Quartets* (of which the first, "Burnt Norton," appeared in the *Collected Poems* of 1936, though all four were not completed until 1943, when they were published together), Eliot further explored essentially religious moods, dealing with the relation between time and eternity and the cultivation of that selfless passivity that can yield the moment of timeless revelation in the midst of time. The mocking irony, the savage humor, the collage of quotations, the deliberately startling juxtaposition of the sordid and the romantic give way in these later poems to a quieter poetic idiom that is less jagged and more abstract, less fragmentary and more formally patterned.

As a critic Eliot worked out in his reading of older literature what he needed as a poet to hold and to admire. He lent the growing weight of his authority to a shift in literary taste that replaced Milton by John Donne as the great seventeenth-century English poet and replaced Alfred, Lord Tennyson in the nineteenth century by Gerard Manley Hopkins. Rewriting English literary history, he saw the late-seventeenth-century "dissociation of sensibility"—the segregation of intellect and emotion—as determining the course of English poetry throughout the eighteenth and nineteenth centuries. This theory also explained what he was aiming at in his own poetry: the reestablishment of that *unified* sensibility he found in Donne and other early-seventeenth-century poets and dramatists, who were able, he suggests in "The Metaphysical Poets," to "feel their thought as immediately as the odour of a rose." His view of tradition, his dislike of the poetic exploitation of the author's personality, his advocacy of what he called "orthodoxy," made him suspicious of what he considered eccentric geniuses such as William Blake and D. H. Lawrence. On the other side, his dislike of the grandiloquent and his insistence on complexity and on the mingling of the formal with the conversational made him distrust Milton's influence on English poetry. He considered himself a "classicist in literature, royalist in politics, and Anglo-Catholic in religion" (*For Lancelot Andrewes*, 1928), in favor of order against chaos, tradition against eccentricity, authority against rampant individualism; yet his own poetry is in many respects untraditional and certainly highly individual in tone. His conservative and even authoritarian habit of mind, his anti-Semitic remarks and missionary zeal, alienated some who admire—and some whose own poetry has been much influenced by—his poetry.

Eliot's plays address, directly or indirectly, religious themes. *Murder in the Cathedral* (1935) deals in an appropriately ritual manner with the killing of Archbishop Thomas à Becket, using a chorus and presenting its central speech as a sermon by the archbishop. *The Family Reunion* (1939) deals with the problem of guilt and redemption in a modern upper-class English family; combining choric devices from Greek tragedy with a poetic idiom subdued to the accents of drawing-room conversation. In his three later plays, all written in the 1950s, *The Cocktail Party*, *The Confidential Clerk*, and *The Elder Statesman*, he achieved popular success by casting a serious religious theme in the form of a sophisticated modern social comedy, using a verse that is so conversational in movement that when spoken in the theater it does not sound like verse at all.

Critics differ on the degree to which Eliot succeeded in his last plays in combining box-office success with dramatic effectiveness. But there is no disagreement on his importance as one of the great renovators of poetry in English, whose influence on a whole generation of poets, critics, and intellectuals was enormous. His range as a poet is limited, and his interest in the great middle ground of human experience (as distinct from the extremes of saint and sinner) deficient; but when in 1948 he was awarded the rare honor of the Order of Merit by King George VI and also gained the Nobel Prize in literature, his positive qualities were widely and fully recognized—his poetic cunning, his fine craftsmanship, his original accent, his historical importance as *the* poet of the modern symbolist-Metaphysical tradition.

The Love Song of J. Alfred Prufrock[1]

S'io credesse che mia risposta fosse
a persona che mai tornasse al mondo,
questa fiamma staria senza più scosse.
Ma per cio cche giammai di questo fondo
non torno vivo alcun, s'i'odo il vero,
senza tema d'infamia ti rispondo.[2]

1. The title implies an ironic contrast between the romantic suggestions of "love song" and the dully prosaic name "J. Alfred Prufrock."

2. "If I thought that my reply would be to one who would ever return to the world, this flame would stay without further movement; but since none has

Let us go then, you and I,
When the evening is spread out against the sky
Like a patient etherised upon a table;
Let us go, through certain half-deserted streets,
5   The muttering retreats
Of restless nights in one-night cheap hotels
And sawdust restaurants with oyster shells:
Streets that follow like a tedious argument
Of insidious intent
10   To lead you to an overwhelming question . . .
Oh, do not ask, 'What is it?'
Let us go and make our visit.

In the room the women come and go
Talking of Michelangelo.

15   The yellow fog that rubs its back upon the window-panes,
The yellow smoke that rubs its muzzle on the window-panes
Licked its tongue into the corners of the evening,
Lingered upon the pools that stand in drains,
Let fall upon its back the soot that falls from chimneys,
20   Slipped by the terrace, made a sudden leap,
And seeing that it was a soft October night,
Curled once about the house, and fell asleep.

And indeed there will be time[3]
For the yellow smoke that slides along the street,
25   Rubbing its back upon the window-panes;
There will be time, there will be time
To prepare a face to meet the faces that you meet;
There will be time to murder and create,
And time for all the works and days of hands[4]
30   That lift and drop a question on your plate;
Time for you and time for me,
And time yet for a hundred indecisions,
And for a hundred visions and revisions,
Before the taking of a toast and tea.

35   In the room the women come and go
Talking of Michelangelo.

And indeed there will be time
To wonder, 'Do I dare?' and, 'Do I dare?'
Time to turn back and descend the stair,
40   With a bald spot in the middle of my hair—
(They will say: 'How his hair is growing thin!')
My morning coat, my collar mounting firmly to the chin,

---

ever returned alive from this depth, if what I hear
is true, I answer you without fear of infamy"
(Dante, *Inferno* 27.61–66). Guido da Montefeltro,
shut up in his flame (the punishment given to false
counselors), tells the shame of his evil life to Dante
because he believes Dante will never return to
earth to report it.

3. Cf. Andrew Marvell, "To His Coy Mistress,"
line 1: "Had we but world enough, and time."
4. *Works and Days* is a poem about the farming
year by the Greek poet Hesiod (8th century B.C.E.).
Eliot contrasts useful agricultural labor with the
futile "works and days of hands" engaged in meaningless social gesturing.

My necktie rich and modest, but asserted by a simple pin—
(They will say: 'But how his arms and legs are thin!')
45 Do I dare
Disturb the universe?
In a minute there is time
For decisions and revisions which a minute will reverse.

For I have known them all already, known them all—
50 Have known the evenings, mornings, afternoons,
I have measured out my life with coffee spoons;
I know the voices dying with a dying fall[5]
Beneath the music from a farther room.
       So how should I presume?

55 And I have known the eyes already, known them all—
The eyes that fix you in a formulated phrase,
And when I am formulated, sprawling on a pin,
When I am pinned and wriggling on the wall,
Then how should I begin
60 To spit out all the butt-ends of my days and ways?
       And how should I presume?

And I have known the arms already, known them all—
Arms that are braceleted and white and bare
(But in the lamplight, downed with light brown hair!)
65 Is it perfume from a dress
That makes me so digress?
Arms that lie along a table, or wrap about a shawl.
       And should I then presume?
       And how should I begin?

· · · · ·

70 Shall I say, I have gone at dusk through narrow streets
And watched the smoke that rises from the pipes
Of lonely men in shirt-sleeves, leaning out of windows? . . .
I should have been a pair of ragged claws
Scuttling across the floors of silent seas.[6]

· · · · ·

75 And the afternoon, the evening, sleeps so peacefully!
Smoothed by long fingers,
Asleep . . . tired . . . or it malingers,
Stretched on the floor, here beside you and me.
Should I, after tea and cakes and ices,
80 Have the strength to force the moment to its crisis?
But though I have wept and fasted, wept and prayed,
Though I have seen my head (grown slightly bald) brought in upon a
       platter,[7]

5. Cf. Shakespeare's *Twelfth Night* 1.1.4: "That
strain again, it had a dying fall."
6. I.e., he would have been better as a crab on the
ocean bed. Perhaps, too, the motion of a crab suggests futility and growing old. Cf. Shakespeare's

Hamlet 2.2.201–02: "for you yourself, sir, should
be old as I am—if, like a crab, you could go backward."
7. Like that of John the Baptist. See Mark 6.17–
28 and Matthew 14.3–11.

I am no prophet—and here's no great matter;
I have seen the moment of my greatness flicker,
85 And I have seen the eternal Footman hold my coat, and snicker,
And in short, I was afraid.

And would it have been worth it, after all,
After the cups, the marmalade, the tea,
Among the porcelain, among some talk of you and me,
90 Would it have been worth while,
To have bitten off the matter with a smile,
To have squeezed the universe into a ball[8]
To roll it toward some overwhelming question,
To say: 'I am Lazarus,[9] come from the dead,
95 Come back to tell you all, I shall tell you all'—
If one, settling a pillow by her head,
      Should say: 'That is not what I meant at all.
      That is not it, at all.'

And would it have been worth it, after all,
100 Would it have been worth while,
After the sunsets and the dooryards and the sprinkled streets,
After the novels, after the teacups, after the skirts that trail along the floor—
And this, and so much more?—
It is impossible to say just what I mean!
105 But as if a magic lantern threw the nerves in patterns on a screen:
Would it have been worth while
If one, settling a pillow or throwing off a shawl,
And turning toward the window, should say:
      'That is not it at all,
110   That is not what I meant, at all.'

                    . . . . .

No! I am not Prince Hamlet, nor was meant to be;
Am an attendant lord, one that will do
To swell a progress,[1] start a scene or two,
Advise the prince; no doubt, an easy tool,
115 Deferential, glad to be of use,
Politic, cautious, and meticulous;
Full of high sentence,[2] but a bit obtuse;
At times, indeed, almost ridiculous—
Almost, at times, the Fool.

120 I grow old . . . I grow old . . .
I shall wear the bottoms of my trousers rolled.

Shall I part my hair behind? Do I dare to eat a peach?
I shall wear white flannel trousers, and walk upon the beach.
I have heard the mermaids singing, each to each.

8. Cf. "To His Coy Mistress," lines 41–44: "Let us roll all our strength and all / Our sweetness up into one ball, / And tear our pleasures with rough strife / Thorough the iron gates of life."
9. Raised by Jesus from the dead (Luke 16.19–31 and John 11.1–44).
1. In the Elizabethan sense of a state journey made by a royal or noble person. Elizabethan plays sometimes showed such "progresses" crossing the stage. Cf. Chaucer's General Prologue to The Canterbury Tales, line 308.
2. In its older meanings: "opinions," "sententiousness."

125 I do not think that they will sing to me.

[handwritten: Dramatic monologue]

I have seen them riding seaward on the waves
Combing the white hair of the waves blown back
When the wind blows the water white and black.

[handwritten: love song → that would have been first H lines best that he can do. that are sonnet like.]

We have lingered in the chambers of the sea
130 By sea-girls wreathed with seaweed red and brown
Till human voices wake us, and we drown.

1910–11 *[handwritten: Intentionally difficult, allusions to many older sources, no neat, consistent patterns of imagry. Irony. Form → line length, vary. Rhym but no pattern.]* 1915, 1917

Sweeney among the Nightingales

[handwritten: versification: nothing in particular meter, Rhym pattern none. Not Blank or free verse.]

ὤμοι, πέπληγμαι καιρίαν πληγὴν ἔσω.[1]

Apeneck Sweeney spreads his knees
Letting his arms hang down to laugh,
The zebra stripes along his jaw
Swelling to maculate° giraffe.   spotted, stained

5   The circles of the stormy moon
Slide westward toward the River Plate,[2]
Death and the Raven[3] drift above
And Sweeney guards the hornèd gate.[4]

Gloomy Orion and the Dog
10   Are veiled;[5] and hushed the shrunken seas;
The person in the Spanish cape
Tries to sit on Sweeney's knees

Slips and pulls the table cloth
Overturns a coffee-cup,
15   Reorganized upon the floor
She yawns and draws a stocking up;

The silent man in mocha brown
Sprawls at the window-sill and gapes;
The waiter brings in oranges
20   Bananas figs and hothouse grapes;

The silent vertebrate in brown
Contracts and concentrates, withdraws;
Rachel *née* Rabinovitch
Tears at the grapes with murderous paws;

1. "Alas, I am struck with a mortal blow within"
(Aeschylus, *Agamemnon*, line 1343); the voice of
Agamemnon heard crying out from the palace as
he is murdered by his wife, Clytemnestra.
2. Or Rio de la Plata, an estuary on the South
American coast between Argentina and Uruguay,
formed by the Uruguay and Paraná rivers.

3. The constellation Corvus.
4. The gates of horn, in Hades, through which
true dreams come to the upper world.
5. For Sweeney and his female friend, the gate of
vision is blocked and the great myth-making constellations—"Orion and the Dog"—are "veiled."

25 She and the lady in the cape
Are suspect, thought to be in league;
Therefore the man with heavy eyes
Declines the gambit, shows fatigue,

Leaves the room and reappears
30 Outside the window, leaning in,
Branches of wistaria
Circumscribe a golden grin;

The host with someone indistinct
Converses at the door apart,
35 The nightingales are singing near
The Convent of the Sacred Heart,

And sang within the bloody wood
When Agamemnon cried aloud[6]
And let their liquid siftings fall
40 To stain the stiff dishonoured shroud.

1918, 1919

The Waste Land   In the essay "*Ulysses*, Order, and Myth" (1923), Eliot hinted
at the ambitions of *The Waste Land* when he declared that others would follow James
Joyce "in manipulating a continuous parallel between contemporaneity and antiquity.
. . . It is simply a way of controlling, of ordering, of giving a shape and a significance
to the immense panorama of futility and anarchy which is contemporary history. . . .
It is, I seriously believe, a step toward making the modern world possible in art." Eliot
labeled this new technique "the mythical method."

He gave another clue to the theme and structure of *The Waste Land* in a general
note, in which he stated that "not only the title, but the plan and a good deal of the
symbolism of the poem were suggested by Miss Jessie L. Weston's book on the Grail
legend: *From Ritual to Romance* [1920]." He further acknowledged a general indebt-
edness to Sir James Frazer's *Golden Bough* (thirteen volumes, 1890–1915), "especially the . . . volumes *Adonis, Attis, Osiris*," in which Frazer deals with ancient
vegetation myths and fertility ceremonies. Drawing on material from Frazer and other
anthropologists, Weston traces the relationship of these myths and rituals to Christianity and especially to the legend of the Holy Grail. She finds an archetypal fertility
myth in the story of the Fisher King, whose death, infirmity, or impotence (there are
many forms of the myth) brought drought and desolation to the land and failure of
the power to reproduce themselves among both humans and beasts. This symbolic
Waste Land can be revived only if a "questing knight" goes to the Chapel Perilous,
situated in the heart of it, and there asks certain ritual questions about the Grail (or
Cup) and the Lance—originally fertility symbols, female and male, respectively. The
proper asking of these questions revives the king and restores fertility to the land.
The relation of this original Grail myth to fertility cults and rituals found in many
different civilizations, and represented by stories of a god who dies and is later resurrected (e.g., Tammuz, Adonis, Attis), shows their common origin in a response to

---

6. Agamemnon is murdered not in a "bloody
wood" but in his bath. Eliot here telescopes Agamemnon's murder with the wood where, in Greek
myth, Philomela was raped by her sister's husband,
Tereus (she was subsequently turned into a nightingale), and also with the ancient "bloody wood" of
Nemi, where the old priest was slain by his successor (as described in the first chapter of Sir
James Frazer's *Golden Bough*).

the cyclical movement of the seasons, with vegetation dying in winter to be resurrected again in the spring. Christianity, according to Weston, gave its own spiritual meaning to the myth; it "did not hesitate to utilize the already existing medium of instruction, but boldly identified the Deity of Vegetation, regarded as Life Principle, with the God of the Christian Faith." The Fisher King is related to the use of the fish symbol in early Christianity. Weston states "with certainty that the Fish is a Life symbol of immemorial antiquity, and that the title of Fisher has, from the earliest ages, been associated with the Deities who were held to be specially connected with the origin and preservation of Life." Eliot, following Weston, thus uses a great variety of mythological and religious material, both Western and Eastern, to paint a symbolic picture of the modern Waste Land and the need for regeneration. He vividly presents the terror of that desiccated life—its loneliness, emptiness, and irrational apprehensions—as well as its misuse of sexuality, but he paradoxically ends the poem with a benediction. The mass death and social collapse of World War I inform the poem's vision of a Waste Land strewn with corpses, wreckage, and ruin. Another significant general source for the poem is the German composer Richard Wagner's operas *Götterdämmerung* (*Twilight of the Gods*), *Parsifal*, *Das Rheingold*, and *Tristan und Isolde*.

The poem as published owes a great deal to the severe pruning of Ezra Pound; the original manuscript, with Pound's excisions and comments, provides fascinating information about the genesis and development of the poem, and was reproduced in facsimile in 1971, edited by Eliot's widow, Valerie Eliot. Reprinted below is the text as first published in book form in December 1922, including Eliot's notes, which are supplemented by the present editors' notes.

The Waste Land

"NAM Sibyllam quidem Cumis ego ipse oculis meis vidi in ampulla pendere, et cum illi pueri dicerent: Σίβυλλα τί θέλεις; respondebat illa: ἀποθανεῖν θέλω."[1]

FOR EZRA POUND
il miglior fabbro[2]

I. *The Burial of the Dead*[3]

April is the cruellest month, breeding
Lilacs out of the dead land, mixing
Memory and desire, stirring
Dull roots with spring rain.
5 Winter kept us warm, covering
Earth in forgetful snow, feeding
A little life with dried tubers.
Summer surprised us, coming over the Starnbergersee[4]

---

1. From the *Satyricon* of Petronius (1st century C.E.): "For once I myself saw with my own eyes the Sibyl at Cumae hanging in a cage, and when the boys said to her 'Sibyl, what do you want?' she replied, 'I want to die.' " (The Greek may be transliterated, "Sibylla tí théleis?" and "apothanéin thélo.") The Cumaean Sibyl was the most famous of the Sibyls, the prophetic old women of Greek mythology; she guided Aeneas through Hades in Virgil's *Aeneid*. She had been granted immortality by Apollo, but because she forgot to ask for perpetual youth, she shrank into withered old age and her authority declined.
2. The better craftsman (Italian); a tribute origi-

nally paid to the Provençal poet Arnaut Daniel in Dante's *Purgatorio* 26.117. Ezra Pound (1885–1972), American expatriate poet who was a key figure in the modern movement in poetry, helped Eliot massively revise the manuscript.
3. The title comes from the Anglican burial service.
4. Lake a few miles south of Munich, where the "mad" King Ludwig II of Bavaria drowned in 1886 in mysterious circumstances. This romantic, melancholy king passionately admired Richard Wagner and especially Wagner's opera *Tristan und Isolde*, which plays a significant part in *The Waste Land*. Ludwig's suffering of "death by water" in the

With a shower of rain; we stopped in the colonnade,
10   And went on in sunlight, into the Hofgarten,[5]
And drank coffee, and talked for an hour.
Bin gar keine Russin, stamm' aus Litauen, echt deutsch.[6]
And when we were children, staying at the archduke's,
My cousin's, he took me out on a sled,
15   And I was frightened. He said, Marie,
Marie, hold on tight. And down we went.
In the mountains, there you feel free.
I read, much of the night, and go south in the winter.

What are the roots that clutch, what branches grow
20   Out of this stony rubbish? Son of man,[7]
You cannot say, or guess, for you know only
A heap of broken images, where the sun beats,
And the dead tree gives no shelter, the cricket no relief,[8]
And the dry stone no sound of water. Only
25   There is shadow under this red rock,[9]
(Come in under the shadow of this red rock),
And I will show you something different from either
Your shadow at morning striding behind you
Or your shadow at evening rising to meet you;
30   I will show you fear in a handful of dust.

    Frisch weht der Wind
    Der Heimat zu,
    Mein Irisch Kind,
    Wo weilest du?[1]

35   "You gave me hyacinths first a year ago;
"They called me the hyacinth girl."
—Yet when we came back, late, from the Hyacinth[2] garden,
Yours arms full, and your hair wet, I could not
Speak, and my eyes failed, I was neither
40   Living nor dead, and I knew nothing,
Looking into the heart of light, the silence.
Oed' und leer das Meer.[3]

Starnbergersee thus evokes a cluster of themes central to the poem. Eliot had met King Ludwig's second cousin Countess Marie Larisch and talked with her. Although he had probably not read the countess's book *My Past*, which discusses King Ludwig at length, he got information about her life and times from her in person, and the remarks made in lines 8–18 are hers.
5. A small public park in Munich.
6. I am not Russian at all; I come from Lithuania, a true German (German).
7. Cf. Ezekiel II, i [Eliot's note]. God, addressing Ezekiel, continues: "stand upon thy feet, and I will speak unto thee."
8. Cf. Ecclesiastes XII, v [Eliot's note]. The verse Eliot cites is part of the preacher's picture of the desolation of old age, "when they shall be afraid of that which is high, and fears shall be in the way and the almond tree shall flourish, and the grass-

hopper shall be a burden, and desire shall fail."
9. Cf. Isaiah 32.2: the "righteous king" "shall be . . . as rivers of water in a dry place, as the shadow of a great rock in a weary land."
1. V. [see] *Tristan und Isolde,* I, verses 5–8 [Eliot's note]. In Wagner's opera a sailor recalls the girl he has left behind: "Fresh blows the wind to the homeland; my Irish child, where are you waiting?"
2. Name of a young man loved and accidentally killed by Apollo in Greek mythology; from his blood sprang the flower named for him, inscribed with "AI," a cry of grief.
3. Id. [Ibid] III, verse 24 [Eliot's note]. In act 3 of *Tristan und Isolde,* Tristan lies dying. He is waiting for Isolde to come to him from Cornwall, but a shepherd, appointed to watch for her sail, can report only, "Waste and empty is the sea." *Oed'* (or *Öd'*) was originally misspelled *Od'*.

Madame Sosostris,[4] famous clairvoyante,
Had a bad cold, nevertheless
45   Is known to be the wisest woman in Europe,
With a wicked pack of cards.[5] Here, said she,
Is your card, the drowned Phoenician Sailor,[6]
(Those are pearls that were his eyes. Look!)
Here is Belladonna,[7] the Lady of the Rocks,
50   The lady of situations.
Here is the man with three staves, and here the Wheel,[8]
And here is the one-eyed merchant,[9] and this card,
Which is blank, is something he carries on his back,
Which I am forbidden to see. I do not find
55   The Hanged Man.[1] Fear death by water.
I see crowds of people, walking round in a ring.
Thank you. If you see dear Mrs. Equitone,
Tell her I bring the horoscope myself:
One must be so careful these days.

60   Unreal City,[2]
Under the brown fog of a winter dawn,
A crowd flowed over London Bridge, so many,[3]
I had not thought death had undone so many.
Sighs, short and infrequent, were exhaled,[4]

4. A mock Egyptian name (suggested to Eliot by "Sesostris, the Sorceress of Ecbatana," the name assumed by a character in Aldous Huxley's novel *Crome Yellow* [1921] who dresses up as a gypsy to tell fortunes at a fair).
5. I.e., the deck of Tarot cards. The four suits of the Tarot pack, discussed by Jessie Weston in *From Ritual to Romance*, are the cup, lance, sword, and dish—the life symbols found in the Grail story. Weston noted that "today the Tarot has fallen somewhat into disrepute, being principally used for purposes of divination." Some of the cards mentioned in lines 46–56 are discussed by Eliot in his note to this passage: "I am not familiar with the exact constitution of the Tarot pack of cards, from which I have obviously departed to suit my own convenience. The Hanged Man, a member of the traditional pack, fits my purpose in two ways: because he is associated in my mind with the Hanged God of Frazer, and because I associate him with the hooded figure in the passage of the disciples to Emmaus in part V. The Phoenician Sailor and the Merchant appear later; also the 'crowds of people,' and Death by Water is executed in part IV. The Man with Three Staves (an authentic member of the Tarot pack) I associate, quite arbitrarily, with the Fisher King himself."
6. See part 4. Phlebas the Phoenician and Mr. Eugenides, the Smyrna merchant—both of whom appear later in the poem—are different phases of the same symbolic character, here identified as the "Phoenician Sailor." Mr. Eugenides exports "currants" (line 210); the drowned Phlebas floats in the "current" (line 315). Line 48 draws from Ariel's song in Shakespeare's *The Tempest* (1.2.400–08) to the shipwrecked Ferdinand, who was "sitting on a bank / Weeping again the King my father's wrack," when "this music crept by me on the waters." The song is about the supposed drowning of Ferdinand's father, Alonso. *The Waste Land* contains many references to *The Tempest*. Ferdi-

nand is associated with Phlebas and Mr. Eugenides and, therefore, with the "drowned Phoenician Sailor."
7. Beautiful lady (Italian). The word also suggests Madonna (the Virgin Mary) and, therefore, the Madonna of the Rocks (as in Leonardo da Vinci's painting); the rocks symbolize the Church. Belladonna is also an eye cosmetic and a poison—the deadly nightshade.
8. I.e., the wheel of fortune, whose turning represents the reversals of human life.
9. I.e., Mr. Eugenides, "one-eyed" because the figure is in profile on the card. Unlike the man with three staves and the wheel, which are Tarot cards, he is Eliot's creation.
1. On his card in the Tarot pack he is shown hanging by one foot from a T-shaped cross. He symbolizes the self-sacrifice of the fertility god who is killed so that his resurrection may restore fertility to land and people.
2. Cf. Baudelaire: "Fourmillante cité, cité pleine de rêves, / Où le spectre en plein jour raccroche le passant" [Eliot's note]. The lines are quoted from "Les Sept Vieillards" ("The Seven Old Men") of *Les Fleurs du Mal* (*The Flowers of Evil*), by the French poet Charles Baudelaire (1821–1867): "Swarming city, city full of dreams, / Where the specter in broad daylight accosts the passerby." The word *rêve* was originally misspelled *rève*.
3. Cf. Inferno III, 55–57 [Eliot's note]. The note goes on to quote Dante's lines, which may be translated: "So long a train of people, / that I should never have believed / That death had undone so many." Dante, just outside the gate of hell, has seen "the wretched souls of those who lived without disgrace and without praise."
4. Cf. Inferno IV, 25–27 [Eliot's note]. In Limbo, the first circle of hell, Dante has found the virtuous heathens, who lived before Christianity and are, therefore, eternally unable to achieve their desire

65 And each man fixed his eyes before his feet.
Flowed up the hill and down King William Street,
To where Saint Mary Woolnoth kept the hours
With a dead sound on the final stroke of nine.[5]
There I saw one I knew, and stopped him, crying: "Stetson![6]
70 "You who were with me in the ships at Mylae![7]
"That corpse you planted last year in your garden,
"Has it begun to sprout?[8] Will it bloom this year?
"Or has the sudden frost disturbed its bed?
"Oh keep the Dog far hence, that's friend to men,
75 "Or with his nails he'll dig it up again![9]
"You! hypocrite lecteur!—mon semblable—mon frère!"[1]

II. A Game of Chess[2]

The Chair she sat in, like a burnished throne,[3]
Glowed on the marble, where the glass
Held up by standards wrought with fruited vines
80 From which a golden Cupidon peeped out
(Another hid his eyes behind his wing)
Doubled the flames of sevenbranched candelabra
Reflecting light upon the table as
The glitter of her jewels rose to meet it,
85 From satin cases poured in rich profusion;
In vials of ivory and coloured glass
Unstoppered, lurked her strange synthetic perfumes,
Unguent, powdered, or liquid—troubled, confused
And drowned the sense in odours; stirred by the air
90 That freshened from the window, these ascended
In fattening the prolonged candle-flames,
Flung their smoke into the laquearia,[4]
Stirring the pattern on the coffered ceiling.

---

of seeing God. Dante's lines, cited by Eliot, mean "Here, so far as I could tell by listening, / there was no lamentation except sighs, / which caused the eternal air to tremble."
5. A phenomenon which I have often noticed [Eliot's note]. St. Mary Woolnoth is a church in the City of London (the financial district); the crowd is flowing across London Bridge to work in the City. According to the Bible, Jesus died at the ninth hour.
6. Presumably representing the "average business-man."
7. The battle of Mylae (260 B.C.E.) in the First Punic War, which, in some measure like World War I, was fought for economic reasons.
8. A distortion of the fertility god's ritual death, which heralded rebirth.
9. Cf. the Dirge in Webster's White Devil [Eliot's note]. In the play by John Webster (d. 1625), the dirge, sung by Cornelia, has the lines "But keep the wolf far thence, that's foe to men, / For with his nails he'll dig them up again." Eliot makes the "wolf" into a "dog," which is not a foe but a friend to humans.
1. V. Baudelaire, Preface to Fleurs du Mal [Eliot's note]. The passage is the last line of the introductory poem "Au Lecteur" ("To the Reader"), in Baudelaire's Fleurs du Mal; it may be translated:

"Hypocrite reader!—my likeness—my brother!" "Au Lecteur" describes humans as sunk in stupidity, sin, and evil, but the worst in "each man's foul menagerie of sin" is boredom, the "monstre délicat"—"You know him, reader."
2. The title suggests two plays by Thomas Middleton (1580–1627): A Game at Chess and, more significant, Women Beware Women, which has a scene in which a mother-in-law is distracted by a game of chess while her daughter-in-law is seduced: every move in the chess game represents a move in the seduction.
3. Cf. Antony and Cleopatra, II, ii, l. 190 [Eliot's note]. In Shakespeare's play, Enobarbus's famous description of the first meeting of Antony and Cleopatra begins, "The barge she sat in, like a burnish'd throne, / Burn'd on the water." Eliot's language in the opening lines of part 2 echoes ironically Enobarbus's speech.
4. Laquearia. V. Aeneid, I, 726 [Eliot's note]. Laquearia means "a paneled ceiling," and Eliot's note quotes the passage in the Aeneid that was his source for the word. The passage may be translated: "Blazing torches hang from the gold-paneled ceiling [laquearibus aureis], and torches conquer the night with flames." Virgil is describing the banquet given by Dido, queen of Carthage, for Aeneas, with whom she fell in love.

Huge sea-wood fed with copper
95 Burned green and orange, framed by the coloured stone,
In which sad light a carvèd dolphin swam.
Above the antique mantel was displayed
As though a window gave upon the sylvan scene[5]
The change of Philomel,[6] by the barbarous king
00 So rudely forced; yet there the nightingale
Filled all the desert with inviolable voice
And still she cried, and still the world pursues,
"Jug Jug"[7] to dirty ears.
And other withered stumps of time
05 Were told upon the walls; staring forms
Leaned out, leaning, hushing the room enclosed.
Footsteps shuffled on the stair.
Under the firelight, under the brush, her hair
Spread out in fiery points
10 Glowed into words, then would be savagely still.

"My nerves are bad tonight. Yes, bad. Stay with me.
"Speak to me. Why do you never speak. Speak.
"What are you thinking of? What thinking? What?
"I never know what you are thinking. Think."

15 I think we are in rats' alley[8]
Where the dead men lost their bones.

"What is that noise?"
                    The wind under the door.[9]
"What is that noise now? What is the wind doing?"
20   Nothing again nothing.
                                        "Do
"You know nothing? Do you see nothing? Do you remember
"Nothing?"

          I remember
25 Those are pearls that were his eyes.[1]
"Are you alive, or not? Is there nothing in your head?"
                                        But
O O O O that Shakespeherian Rag[2]—
It's so elegant
30 So intelligent

"What shall I do now? What shall I do?"
"I shall rush out as I am, and walk the street

5. Sylvan scene. V. Milton, *Paradise Lost*, IV, 140 [Eliot's note]. The phrase is part of the first description of Eden, seen through Satan's eyes.
6. V. Ovid, *Metamorphoses*, VI, Philomela [Eliot's note]. Philomela was raped by "the barbarous king" Tereus, husband of her sister, Procne. Philomela was then transformed into a nightingale. Eliot's note for line 100 refers ahead to his elaboration of the nightingale's song.
7. Conventional representation of nightingale's song in Elizabethan poetry.

8. Cf. Part III, l. 195 [Eliot's note].
9. Cf. Webster: "Is the wind in that door still?" [Eliot's note]. In John Webster's *The Devil's Law Case* (3.2.162), a physician asks this question on finding that the victim of a murderous attack is still breathing, meaning "Is he still alive?"
1. Cf. Part I, l. 37, 48 [Eliot's note].
2. American ragtime song, which was a hit of Ziegfeld's Follies in 1912. The chorus is "That Shakespherean Rag, most intelligent, very elegant."

2300 / T. S. ELIOT

"With my hair down, so. What shall we do tomorrow?
"What shall we ever do?"
135   The hot water at ten.
And if it rains, a closed car at four.
And we shall play a game of chess,[3]
Pressing lidless eyes and waiting for a knock upon the door.

When Lil's husband got demobbed,[4] I said—
140   I didn't mince my words, I said to her myself,
HURRY UP PLEASE ITS TIME[5]
Now Albert's coming back, make yourself a bit smart.
He'll want to know what you done with that money he gave you
To get yourself some teeth. He did, I was there.
145   You have them all out, Lil, and get a nice set,
He said, I swear, I can't bear to look at you.
And no more can't I, I said, and think of poor Albert,
He's been in the army four years, he wants a good time,
And if you dont give it him, there's others will, I said.
150   Oh is there, she said. Something o' that, I said.
Then I'll know who to thank, she said, and give me a straight look.
HURRY UP PLEASE ITS TIME
If you dont like it you can get on with it, I said,
Others can pick and choose if you can't.
155   But if Albert makes off, it wont be for lack of telling.
You ought to be ashamed, I said, to look so antique.
(And her only thirty-one.)
I can't help it, she said, pulling a long face,
It's them pills I took, to bring it off, she said.
160   (She's had five already, and nearly died of young George.)
The chemist[6] said it would be alright, but I've never been the same.
You *are* a proper fool, I said.
Well, if Albert wont leave you alone, there it is, I said,
What you get married for if you dont want children?
165   HURRY UP PLEASE ITS TIME
Well, that Sunday Albert was home, they had a hot gammon,°   *ham, bacon*
And they asked me in to dinner, to get the beauty of it hot—
HURRY UP PLEASE ITS TIME
HURRY UP PLEASE ITS TIME
170   Goonight Bill. Goonight Lou. Goonight May. Goonight.
Ta ta. Goonight. Goonight.
Good night, ladies, good night, sweet ladies, good night, good night.[7]

III. The Fire Sermon[8]

The river's tent is broken: the last fingers of leaf
Clutch and sink into the wet bank. The wind

---

3. Cf. the game of chess in Middleton's *Women Beware Women* [Eliot's note]. The significance of this chess game is discussed in the first note to part 2.
4. British slang for "demobilized" (discharged from the army after World War I).
5. The traditional call of the British bartender at closing time.
6. Pharmacist. "To bring it off": to cause an abor-

tion.
7. Cf. the mad Ophelia's departing words (Shakespeare, *Hamlet* 4.5.69–70). Ophelia, too, met "death by water." Cf. also the popular song lyric "Good night ladies, we're going to leave you now."
8. The Buddha preached the Fire Sermon, against the fires of lust and other passions that destroy people and prevent their regeneration.

175 Crosses the brown land, unheard. The nymphs are departed.
Sweet Thames, run softly, till I end my song.[9]
The river bears no empty bottles, sandwich papers,
Silk handkerchiefs, cardboard boxes, cigarette ends
Or other testimony of summer nights. The nymphs are departed.
180 And their friends, the loitering heirs of city directors;
Departed, have left no addresses.
By the waters of Leman I sat down and wept[1] . . .
Sweet Thames, run softly till I end my song,
Sweet Thames, run softly, for I speak not loud or long.
185 But at my back in a cold blast I hear[2]
The rattle of the bones, and chuckle spread from ear to ear.

A rat crept softly through the vegetation
Dragging its slimy belly on the bank
While I was fishing in the dull canal
190 On a winter evening round behind the gashouse
Musing upon the king my brother's wreck
And on the king my father's death before him.[3]
White bodies naked on the low damp ground
And bones cast in a little low dry garret,
195 Rattled by the rat's foot only, year to year.
But at my back from time to time I hear
The sound of horns and motors,[4] which shall bring
Sweeney to Mrs. Porter in the spring.[5]
O the moon shone bright on Mrs. Porter
200 And on her daughter
They wash their feet in soda water[6]
Et O ces voix d'enfants, chantant dans la coupole![7]

Twit twit twit
Jug jug jug jug jug jug
205 So rudely forc'd.
Tereu[8]

9. V. Spenser, *Prothalamion* [Eliot's note]. Eliot's line is the refrain from Edmund Spenser's marriage song, which is also set by the river Thames in London.
1. Cf. Psalms 137.1, in which the exiled Hebrews mourn for their homeland: "By the rivers of Babylon, there we sat down, yea, we wept, when we remembered Zion." Lake Leman is another name for Lake Geneva, in Switzerland; Eliot wrote *The Waste Land* in Lausanne, by that lake. The noun *leman* is an archaic word meaning lover.
2. An ironic distortion of Andrew Marvell's "To His Coy Mistress," lines 21–22: "But at my back I always hear / Time's wingèd chariot hurrying near." Cf. lines 196–97.
3. Cf. *The Tempest*, I, ii [Eliot's note]. See line 48.
4. Cf. Marvell, *To His Coy Mistress* [Eliot's note].
5. Cf. Day, *Parliament of Bees*: "When of the sudden, listening, you shall hear, / A noise of horns and hunting, which shall bring / Actaeon to Diana in the spring, / Where all shall see her naked skin" [Eliot's note]. Actaeon was changed to a stag and hunted to death after he saw Diana, the goddess of chastity, bathing with her nymphs. John Day

(1574–ca. 1640), English poet.
6. I do not know the origin of the ballad from which these lines are taken; it was reported to me from Sydney, Australia [Eliot's note]. One of the less bawdy versions of the song, which was popular among Australian troops in World War I, went as follows: "O the moon shines bright on Mrs. Porter / And on the daughter / Of Mrs. Porter. / They wash their feet in soda water / And so they oughter / To keep them clean."
7. V. Verlaine, *Parsifal* [Eliot's note]: "And O those children's voices singing in the dome!" The sonnet by the French poet Paul Verlaine (1844–1896) describes Parsifal, the questing knight, resisting all sensual temptations to keep himself pure for the Grail and heal the Fisher King; Wagner's *Parsifal* had his feet washed before entering the castle of the Grail.
8. A reference to Tereus, who "rudely forc'd" Philomela; it was also one of the conventional words for a nightingale's song in Elizabethan poetry. Cf. the song from John Lyly's *Alexander and Campaspe* (1564): "Oh, 'tis the ravished nightingale. / Jug, jug, jug, jug, tereu! she cries." Cf. also lines 100ff.

Unreal City
Under the brown fog of a winter noon
Mr. Eugenides, the Smyrna[9] merchant
210 Unshaven, with a pocket full of currants
C.i.f.[1] London: documents at sight,
Asked me in demotic° French   *colloquial*
To luncheon at the Cannon Street Hotel
Followed by a weekend at the Metropole.[2]

215 At the violet hour, when the eyes and back
Turn upward from the desk, when the human engine waits
Like a taxi throbbing waiting,
I Tiresias,[3] though blind, throbbing between two lives,
Old man with wrinkled female breasts, can see
220 At the violet hour, the evening hour that strives
Homeward, and brings the sailor home from sea,[4]
The typist home at teatime, clears her breakfast, lights
Her stove, and lays out food in tins.
Out of the window perilously spread
225 Her drying combinations° touched by the sun's last rays,   *undergarments*
On the divan are piled (at night her bed)
Stockings, slippers, camisoles, and stays.°   *corset*
I Tiresias, old man with wrinkled dugs
Perceived the scene, and foretold the rest—
230 I too awaited the expected guest.
He, the young man carbuncular,° arrives,   *pimply*
A small house agent's clerk, with one bold stare,
One of the low on whom assurance sits
As a silk hat on a Bradford[5] millionaire.

9. Now Izmir, a seaport in western Turkey; here associated with Carthage and the ancient Phoenician and Syrian merchants, who spread the old mystery cults.
1. The currants were quoted at a price "carriage and insurance free to London"; and the Bill of Lading etc. were to be handed to the buyer upon payment of the sight draft [Eliot's note]. Another gloss of *C.i.f.* is "cost, insurance and freight."
2. Luxury hotel in the seaside resort of Brighton. Cannon Street Hotel, near the station that was then chief terminus for travelers to the Continent, was a favorite meeting place for businesspeople going or coming from abroad; it was also a locale for homosexual liaisons.
3. Tiresias, although a mere spectator and not indeed a "character," is yet the most important personage in the poem, uniting all the rest. Just as the one-eyed merchant, seller of currants, melts into the Phoenician Sailor, and the latter is not wholly distinct from Ferdinand Prince of Naples, so all the women are one woman, and the two sexes meet in Tiresias. What Tiresias *sees*, in fact, is the substance of the poem. The whole passage from Ovid is of great anthropological interest [Eliot's note]. The note then quotes, from the Latin text of Ovid's *Metamorphoses*, the story of Tiresias's change of sex: "[The story goes that once Jove, having drunk a great deal,] jested with Juno. He said, 'Your pleasure in love is really greater than that enjoyed by men.' She denied it; so they decided to seek the opinion of the wise Tiresias, for he knew both

aspects of love. For once, with a blow of his staff, he had committed violence on two huge snakes as they copulated in the green forest; and—wonderful to tell—was turned from a man into a woman and thus spent seven years. In the eighth year he saw the same snakes again and said: 'If a blow struck at you is so powerful that it changes the sex of the giver, I will now strike at you again.' With these words she struck the snakes, and again became a man. So he was appointed arbitrator in the playful quarrel, and supported Jove's statement. It is said that Saturnia [i.e., Juno] was quite disproportionately upset, and condemned the arbitrator to perpetual blindness. But the almighty father (for no god may undo what has been done by another god), in return for the sight that was taken away, gave him the power to know the future and so lightened the penalty paid by the honor."
4. This may not appear as exact as Sappho's lines, but I had in mind the "longshore" or "dory" fisherman, who returns at nightfall [Eliot's note]. Sappho's poem addressed Hesperus, the evening star, as the star that brings everyone home from work to evening rest; her poem is here distorted by Eliot. There is also an echo of the 19th-century Scottish writer Robert Louis Stevenson's "Requiem," line 221: "Home is the sailor, home from sea."
5. Either the Yorkshire woolen manufacturing town, where many fortunes were made in World War I, or the pioneer oil town of Bradford, Pennsylvania, the home of one of Eliot's wealthy Harvard contemporaries, T. E. Hanley.

235 The time is now propitious, as he guesses,
The meal is ended, she is bored and tired,
Endeavours to engage her in caresses
Which still are unreproved, if undesired.
Flushed and decided, he assaults at once;
240 Exploring hands encounter no defence;
His vanity requires no response,
And makes a welcome of indifference.
(And I Tiresias have foresuffered all
Enacted on this same divan or bed;
245 I who have sat by Thebes[6] below the wall
And walked among the lowest of the dead.)
Bestows one final patronising kiss,
And gropes his way, finding the stairs unlit . . .

She turns and looks a moment in the glass,
250 Hardly aware of her departed lover;
Her brain allows one half-formed thought to pass:
"Well now that's done: and I'm glad it's over."
When lovely woman stoops to folly and
Paces about her room again, alone,
255 She smoothes her hair with automatic hand,
And puts a record on the gramophone.[7]

"This music crept by me upon the waters"[8]
And along the Strand, up Queen Victoria Street.
O City, City, I can sometimes hear
260 Beside a public bar in Lower Thames Street,
The pleasant whining of a mandoline
And a clatter and a chatter from within
Where fishmen lounge at noon: where the walls
Of Magnus Martyr hold
265 Inexplicable splendour of Ionian white and gold.[9]

The river sweats[1]
Oil and tar
The barges drift
With the turning tide

6. For many generations, Tiresias lived in Thebes, where he witnessed the tragic fates of Oedipus and Creon; he prophesied in the marketplace by the wall of Thebes.
7. V. Goldsmith, the song in *The Vicar of Wakefield* [Eliot's note]. Olivia, a character in Oliver Goldsmith's 1766 novel, sings the following song when she returns to the place where she was seduced: "When lovely woman stoops to folly / And finds too late that men betray / What charm can soothe her melancholy, / What art can wash her guilt away? / The only art her guilt to cover, / To hide her shame from every eye, / To give repentance to her lover / And wring his bosom—is to die."
8. V. *The Tempest*, as above [Eliot's note]. Cf. line 48. The line is from Ferdinand's speech, continuing after "weeping again the King my father's wrack."

9. The interior of St. Magnus Martyr is to my mind one of the finest among [Sir Christopher] Wren's interiors. See *The Proposed Demolition of Nineteen City Churches*: (P. S. King & Son, Ltd.) [Eliot's note]. In these lines the "pleasant" music, the "fishmen" resting after labor, and the splendor of the church interior suggest a world of true values, where work and relaxation are both real and take place in a context of religious meaning.
1. The Song of the (three) Thames-daughters begins here. From line 292 to 306 inclusive they speak in turn. V. *Götterdämmerung*, III, i: the Rhinedaughters [Eliot's note]. Eliot parallels the Thames-daughters with the Rhinemaidens in Wagner's opera *Götterdämmerung* (*The Twilight of the Gods*), who lament that, with the gold of the Rhine stolen, the beauty of the river is gone. The refrain in lines 277–78 is borrowed from Wagner.

270   Red sails
       Wide
       To leeward, swing on the heavy spar.
       The barges wash
       Drifting logs
275   Down Greenwich reach
       Past the Isle of Dogs.[2]
                Weialala leia
                Wallala leialala

       Elizabeth and Leicester[3]
280   Beating oars
       The stern was formed
       A gilded shell
       Red and gold
       The brisk swell
285   Rippled both shores
       Southwest wind
       Carried down stream
       The peal of bells
       White towers
290   Weialala leia
                Wallala leialala

       "Trams and dusty trees.
       Highbury bore me. Richmond and Kew
       Undid me.[4] By Richmond I raised my knees
295   Supine on the floor of a narrow canoe."

       "My feet are at Moorgate,[5] and my heart
       Under my feet. After the event
       He wept. He promised 'a new start.'
       I made no comment. What should I resent?"

300   "On Margate[6] Sands.
       I can connect
       Nothing with nothing.
       The broken fingernails of dirty hands.
       My people humble people who expect
305   Nothing."
                la la

       To Carthage then I came[7]

---

2. Greenwich is a borough in London on the south side of the Thames; opposite is the Isle of Dogs (a peninsula).
3. The fruitless love of Queen Elizabeth and the earl of Leicester (Robert Dudley) is recalled in Eliot's note: "V. [J. A.] Froude, *Elizabeth*, Vol. I, ch. iv, letter of De Quadra to Philip of Spain: 'In the afternoon we were in a barge, watching the games on the river. (The queen) was alone with Lord Robert and myself on the poop, when they began to talk nonsense, and went so far that Lord Robert at last said, as I was on the spot there was no reason why they should not be married if the queen pleased.'" Queen Elizabeth I was born in the old Greenwich House, by the river, where

Greenwich Hospital now stands.
4. Cf. *Purgatorio*, V, 133 [Eliot's note]. The *Purgatorio* lines, which Eliot here parodies, may be translated: "Remember me, who am La Pia. / Siena made me, Maremma undid me." "Highbury": a residential London suburb. "Richmond": a pleasant part of London westward up the Thames, with boating and riverside hotels. "Kew": adjoining Richmond, has the famous Kew Gardens.
5. Underground (i.e., subway) station Eliot used daily while working at Lloyds Bank.
6. Popular seaside resort on the Thames estuary.
7. V. St. Augustine's *Confessions*: "to Carthage then I came, where a caldron of unholy loves sang all about mine ears" [Eliot's note]. The passage

Burning burning burning burning[8]
O Lord Thou pluckest me out[9]
10   O Lord Thou pluckest

burning

IV. Death by Water[1]

Phlebas the Phoenician, a fortnight dead,
Forgot the cry of gulls, and the deep sea swell
And the profit and loss.
15   A current under sea
Picked his bones in whispers. As he rose and fell
He passed the stages of his age and youth
Entering the whirlpool.
                        Gentile or Jew
20   O you who turn the wheel and look to windward,
Consider Phlebas, who was once handsome and tall as you.

V. What the Thunder Said[2]

After the torchlight red on sweaty faces
After the frosty silence in the gardens
After the agony in stony places
25   The shouting and the crying
Prison and palace and reverberation
Of thunder of spring over distant mountains
He who was living is now dead[3]
We who were living are now dying
30   With a little patience

Here is no water but only rock
Rock and no water and the sandy road
The road winding above among the mountains
Which are mountains of rock without water
35   If there were water we should stop and drink
Amongst the rock one cannot stop or think
Sweat is dry and feet are in the sand
If there were only water amongst the rock

---

from the *Confessions* quoted here occurs in St.
Augustine's account of his youthful life of lust. Cf.
line 92 and its note.
8. The complete text of the Buddha's Fire Sermon
(which corresponds in importance to the Sermon
on the Mount) from which these words are taken,
will be found translated in the late Henry Clarke
Warren's *Buddhism in Translation* (Harvard Oriental Series). Mr. Warren was one of the great pioneers of Buddhist studies in the occident [Eliot's
note]. In the sermon, the Buddha instructs his
priests that all things "are on fire. . . . The eye . . .
is on fire; forms are on fire; eye-consciousness is
on fire; impressions received by the eye are on fire;
and whatever sensation, pleasant, unpleasant, or
indifferent, originates in dependence on impressions received by the eye, that also is on fire. And
with what are these on fire? With the fire of passion, say I, with the fire of hatred, with the fire of

infatuation." For Jesus' Sermon on the Mount, see
Matthew 5–7.
9. From St. Augustine's *Confessions* again. The
collocation of these two representatives of eastern
and western asceticism, as the culmination of this
part of the poem, is not an accident [Eliot's note].
1. This section has been interpreted as signifying
death by water without resurrection or as symbolizing the sacrificial death that precedes rebirth.
2. In the first part of Part V three themes are
employed: the journey to Emmaus, the approach
to the Chapel Perilous (see Miss Weston's book),
and the present decay of eastern Europe [Eliot's
note]. On the journey to Emmaus, the resurrected
Jesus walks alongside and converses with two disciples, who think he is a stranger until he reveals
his identity (Luke 24.13–14).
3. These lines allude to Jesus' agony in the Garden
of Gethsemane, his trial, and his crucifixion.

Dead mountain mouth of carious° teeth that cannot spit   *decayed*
340 Here one can neither stand nor lie nor sit
There is not even silence in the mountains
But dry sterile thunder without rain
There is not even solitude in the mountains
But red sullen faces sneer and snarl
345 From doors of mudcracked houses
              If there were water
  And no rock
  If there were rock
  And also water
350   And water
  A spring
  A pool among the rock
  If there were the sound of water only
  Not the cicada[4]
355   And dry grass singing
  But sound of water over a rock
  Where the hermit-thrush[5] sings in the pine trees
  Drip drop drip drop drop drop drop
  But there is no water

360 Who is the third who walks always beside you?[6]
When I count, there are only you and I together
But when I look ahead up the white road
There is always another one walking beside you
Gliding wrapt in a brown mantle, hooded
365 I do not know whether a man or a woman
—But who is that on the other side of you?

What is that sound high in the air[7]
Murmur of maternal lamentation
Who are those hooded hordes swarming
370 Over endless plains, stumbling in cracked earth
Ringed by the flat horizon only
What is the city over the mountains
Cracks and reforms and bursts in the violet air
Falling towers
375 Jerusalem Athens Alexandria
Vienna London
Unreal

---

4. Cf. Ecclesiastes' prophecy "the grasshopper shall be a burden, and desire shall fail." Cf. also line 23 and its note.
5. This is *Turdus aonalaschkae pallasii*, the hermit-thrush which I have heard in Quebec County. Chapman says (*Handbook of Birds of Eastern North America*) "it is most at home in secluded woodland and thickety retreats. . . . Its notes are not remarkable for variety or volume, but in purity and sweetness of tone and exquisite modulation they are unequaled." Its "water-dripping song" is justly celebrated [Eliot's note].
6. The following lines were stimulated by the account of one of the Antarctic expeditions (I forget which, but I think one of Shackleton's): it was related that the party of explorers, at the extremity of their strength, had the constant delusion that there was *one more member* than could actually be counted [Eliot's note]. This reminiscence is associated with Jesus' unrecognized presence on the way to Emmaus.
7. Eliot's note for lines 367–77 is: "Cf. Herman Hesse, *Blick ins Chaos* ["A Glimpse into Chaos"]." The note then quotes a passage from the German text, which is translated: "Already half of Europe, already at least half of Eastern Europe, on the way to Chaos, drives drunk in sacred infatuation along the edge of the precipice, sings drunkenly, as though hymn singing, as Dmitri Karamazov [in Dostoyevsky's *Brothers Karamazov*] sang. The offended bourgeois laughs at the songs; the saint and the seer hear them with tears."

A woman drew her long black hair out tight
And fiddled whisper music on those strings
380 And bats with baby faces in the violet light
Whistled, and beat their wings
And crawled head downward down a blackened wall
And upside down in air were towers
Tolling reminiscent bells, that kept the hours
385 And voices singing out of empty cisterns and exhausted wells.

In this decayed hole among the mountains
In the faint moonlight, the grass is singing
Over the tumbled graves, about the chapel
There is the empty chapel, only the wind's home.[8]
390 It has no windows, and the door swings,
Dry bones can harm no one.
Only a cock stood on the rooftree
Co co   rico   co co   rico[9]
In a flash of lightning. Then a damp gust
395 Bringing rain

Ganga[1] was sunken, and the limp leaves
Waited for rain, while the black clouds
Gathered far distant, over Himavant.[2]
The jungle crouched, humped in silence.
400 Then spoke the thunder
DA[3]
Datta: what have we given?
My friend, blood shaking my heart
The awful daring of a moment's surrender
405 Which an age of prudence can never retract
By this, and this only, we have existed
Which is not to be found in our obituaries
Or in memories draped by the beneficent spider[4]
Or under seals broken by the lean solicitor°   *lawyer*
410 In our empty rooms
DA
Dayadhvam: I have heard the key[5]

8. Suggesting the moment of near despair before the Chapel Perilous, when the questing knight sees nothing there but decay. This illusion of nothingness is the knight's final test.
9. The crowing of the cock signals the departure of ghosts and evil spirits. Cf. *Hamlet* 1.1.157ff. In Matthew 26.34 and 74 the cock crows after Peter betrays Jesus three times.
1. Sanskrit name for the major sacred river in India.
2. I.e., snowy mountain (Sanskrit); usually applied to the Himalayas.
3. Datta, dayadhvam, damyata (Give, sympathize, control). The fable of the meaning of the Thunder is found in the *Brihadaranyaka—Upanishad*, 5, 1. A translation is found in Deussen's *Sechzig Upanishads des Veda*, p. 489 [Eliot's note]. In the Old Indian fable The Three Great Disciplines, the Creator God Prajapati utters the enigmatic syllable *DA* to three groups. Lesser gods, naturally unruly, interpret it as "Control yourselves" (*Damyata*); humans, naturally greedy, as "Give" (*Datta*);

demons, naturally cruel, as "Be compassionate" (*Dayadhvam*); "That very thing is repeated even today by the heavenly voice, in the form of thunder as '*DA' 'DA' 'DA,*' which means 'Control yourselves,' 'Give,' and 'Have compassion.' Therefore one should practice these three things: self-control, giving, and mercy." The Upanishads are ancient philosophical dialogues in Sanskrit. They are primary texts for an early form of Hinduism sometimes called Brahminism.
4. Cf. Webster, *The White Devil*, V, vi: ". . . they'll remarry / Ere the worm pierce your winding-sheet, ere the spider / Make a thin curtain for your epitaphs" [Eliot's note].
5. Cf. *Inferno*, XXXIII, 46 [Eliot's note]. In this passage from the *Inferno* Ugolino recalls his imprisonment in the tower with his children, where they starved to death: "And I heard below the door of the horrible tower being nailed shut." Eliot's note for this line goes on to quote F. H. Bradley, *Appearance and Reality*, p. 346: " 'My external sensations are no less private to myself

Turn in the door once and turn once only
We think of the key, each in his prison
415 Thinking of the key, each confirms a prison
Only at nightfall, æthereal rumours
Revive for a moment a broken Coriolanus[6]
DA
Damyata: The boat responded
420 Gaily, to the hand expert with sail and oar
The sea was calm, your heart would have responded
Gaily, when invited, beating obedient
To controlling hands

                    I sat upon the shore
425 Fishing,[7] with the arid plain behind me
Shall I at least set my lands in order?[8]

London Bridge is falling down falling down falling down[9]
Poi s'ascose nel foco che gli affina[1]
Quando fiam uti chelidon[2]—O swallow swallow[3]
430 *Le Prince d'Aquitaine à la tour abolie*[4]
These fragments I have shored against my ruins
Why then Ile fit you. Hieronymo's mad againe.[5]
Datta. Dayadhvam. Damyata.

            Shantih   shantih   shantih[6]

1921   1922

---

than are my thoughts or my feelings. In either case
my experience falls within my own circle, a circle
closed on the outside; and, with all its elements
alike, every sphere is opaque to the others which
surround it. . . . In brief, regarded as an existence
which appears in a soul, the whole world for each
is peculiar and private to that soul.' " Eliot wrote
his doctoral thesis on Bradley's philosophy.
6. Coriolanus, who acted out of pride rather than
duty, exemplifies a man locked in the prison of
himself. He led the enemy against his native city
out of injured pride (cf. Shakespeare's *Coriolanus*).
7. V. Weston: *From Ritual to Romance;* chapter
on the Fisher King [Eliot's note].
8. Cf. Isaiah 38.1: "Thus saith the Lord, Set thine
house in order, for thou shalt die, and not live."
9. One of the later lines of this nursery rhyme is
"Take the key and lock her up, my fair lady."
1. V. *Purgatorio,* XXVI, 148 [Eliot's note]. The
note goes on to quote lines 145–148 of the *Purgatorio,* in which the Provençal poet Arnaut Daniel
addresses Dante: " 'Now I pray you, by that virtue
which guides you to the summit of the stairway, be
mindful in due time of my pain.' " Then (in the line
Eliot quotes here) "he hid himself in the fire which
refines them."
2. V. *Pervigilium Veneris.* Cf. Philomela in parts
II and III [Eliot's note]. The Latin phrase in the
text, originally misquoting *uti* as *ceu,* means,
"When shall I be as the swallow?" It comes from

the late Latin poem "*Pervigilium Veneris*" ("Vigil of
Venus"), "When will my spring come? When shall
I be as the swallow that I may cease to be silent? I
have lost the Muse in silence, and Apollo regards
me not."
3. Cf. A. C. Swinburne's "Itylus," which begins,
"Swallow, my sister, O sister swallow, / How can
thine heart be full of spring?" and Tennyson's lyric
in *The Princess:* "O Swallow, Swallow, flying, flying
south."
4. V. Gerard de Nerval, Sonnet *El Desdichado*
[Eliot's note]. The French line may be translated:
"The Prince of Aquitaine in the ruined tower." One
of the cards in the Tarot pack is "the tower struck
by lightning."
5. V. Kyd's *Spanish Tragedy* [Eliot's note]. Subtitled *Hieronymo's Mad Againe,* Kyd's play (1594) is
an early example of the Elizabethan tragedy of
revenge. Hieronymo, driven mad by the murder of
his son, has his revenge when he is asked to write
a court entertainment. He replies, "Why then Ile
fit you!" (i.e., accommodate you), and assigns the
parts in the entertainment so that, in the course of
the action, his son's murderers are killed.
6. Shantih. Repeated as here, a formal ending to
an Upanishad. "The Peace which passeth understanding" is a feeble translation of the content of
this word [Eliot's note]. On the Upanishads see the
note to line 401 above.

The Hollow Men

Mistah Kurtz—he dead.[1]
A penny for the Old Guy[2]

I

We are the hollow men
We are the stuffed men
Leaning together
Headpiece filled with straw. Alas!
5   Our dried voices, when
We whisper together
Are quiet and meaningless
As wind in dry glass
Or rats' feet over broken glass
10   In our dry cellar[3]

Shape without form, shade without colour,
Paralysed force, gesture without motion;

Those who have crossed
With direct eyes, to death's other Kingdom
15   Remember us—if at all—not as lost
Violent souls, but only
As the hollow men
The stuffed men.

II

Eyes I dare not meet in dreams
20   In death's dream kingdom[4]
These do not appear:
There, the eyes are
Sunlight on a broken column
There, is a tree swinging
25   And voices are
In the wind's singing
More distant and more solemn
Than a fading star.

Let me be no nearer
30   In death's dream kingdom
Let me also wear
Such deliberate disguises
Rat's coat, crowskin, crossed staves

1. From Joseph Conrad's *Heart of Darkness* (see p. 1941).
2. Every year on Nov. 5, British children build bonfires, on which they burn a scarecrow effigy of the traitor Guido [Guy] Fawkes, who in 1605 attempted to blow up the Parliament buildings. For some days before this, they ask people in the streets for pennies with which to buy fireworks.
3. Cf. *The Waste Land*, lines 115 and 195.
4. At the end of Dante's *Purgatorio* and in *Paradiso* 4, he cannot meet the gaze of Beatrice (see Eliot's 1929 essay "Dante").

In a field[5]
35 Behaving as the wind behaves
No nearer—

Not that final meeting
In the twilight kingdom[6]

III

This is the dead land
40 This is cactus land
Here the stone images[7]
Are raised, here they receive
The supplication of a dead man's hand
Under the twinkle of a fading star.

45 Is it like this
In death's other kingdom
Waking alone
At the hour when we are
Trembling with tenderness
50 Lips that would kiss
Form prayers to broken stone.

IV

The eyes are not here
There are no eyes here
In this valley of dying stars
55 In this hollow valley
This broken jaw of our lost kingdoms

In this last of meeting places
We grope together
And avoid speech
60 Gathered on this beach of the tumid river[8]

Sightless, unless
The eyes reappear
As the perpetual star
Multifoliate rose[9]
65 Of death's twilight kingdom
The hope only
Of empty men.

5. The traditional British scarecrow is made from two sticks tied in the form of a cross (the vertical one stuck in the ground), dressed in cast-off clothes, and sometimes draped with dead vermin.
6. Perhaps a reference to Dante's meeting with Beatrice after he has crossed the river Lethe. There reminded of his sins, he is allowed to proceed to Paradise (*Purgatorio* 30).
7. Cf. *The Waste Land*, line 22.
8. Dante's Acheron, which encircles hell, and the Congo of Conrad's *Heart of Darkness*.
9. The image of heaven in Dante's *Paradiso* 32.

V

Here we go round the prickly pear
Prickly pear prickly pear
70 *Here we go round the prickly pear*
At five o'clock in the morning.[1]

Between the idea
And the reality
Between the motion
75 And the act[2]
Falls the Shadow[3]
                    For Thine is the Kingdom[4]

Between the conception
And the creation
80 Between the emotion
And the response
Falls the Shadow
                    Life is very long

Between the desire
85 And the spasm
Between the potency
And the existence
Between the essence
And the descent
90 Falls the Shadow
                    For Thine is the Kingdom

For Thine is
Life is
For Thine is the

95 *This is the way the world ends*
This is the way the world ends
This is the way the world ends
Not with a bang but a whimper.

1924–25   1925

---

1. Parodic version of the children's rhyme ending
"Here we go round the mulberry bush / On a cold
and frosty morning."
2. Cf. Shakespeare's *Julius Caesar* 2.1.63–5:
"Between the acting of a dreadful thing / And the
first motion, all the interim is / Like a phantasma

or a hideous dream."
3. Cf. Ernest Dowson's "*Non sum qualis eram
bonae sub regno Cynarae*," lines 1–2: "Last night,
ah, yesternight, betwixt her lips and mine / There
fell thy shadow, Cynara!"
4. Cf. The Lord's Prayer.

Journey of the Magi[1]

'A cold coming we had of it,
Just the worst time of the year
For a journey, and such a long journey:
The ways deep and the weather sharp,
5   The very dead of winter.'[2]
And the camels galled, sore-footed, refractory,
Lying down in the melting snow.
There were times we regretted
The summer palaces on slopes, the terraces,
10   And the silken girls bringing sherbet.
Then the camel men cursing and grumbling
And running away, and wanting their liquor and women,
And the night-fires going out, and the lack of shelters,
And the cities hostile and the towns unfriendly
15   And the villages dirty and charging high prices:
A hard time we had of it.
At the end we preferred to travel all night,
Sleeping in snatches,
With the voices singing in our ears, saying
20   That this was all folly.

Then at dawn we came down to a temperate valley,
Wet, below the snow line, smelling of vegetation;
With a running stream and a water mill beating the darkness,
And three trees on the low sky.[3]
25   And an old white horse galloped away in the meadow.
Then we came to a tavern with vine-leaves over the lintel,
Six hands at an open door dicing for pieces of silver,
And feet kicking the empty wine-skins.
But there was no information, and so we continued
30   And arrived at evening, not a moment too soon
Finding the place; it was (you may say) satisfactory.

All this was a long time ago, I remember,
And I would do it again, but set down
This set down
35   This: were we led all that way for
Birth or Death? There was a Birth, certainly,
We had evidence and no doubt. I had seen birth and death,
But had thought they were different; this Birth was
Hard and bitter agony for us, like Death, our death.
40   We returned to our places, these Kingdoms,
But no longer at ease here, in the old dispensation,

---

1. One of the wise men who came from the east to Jerusalem to do homage to the infant Jesus (Matthew 2.1–12) is recalling in old age the meaning of the experience.
2. Adapted from a passage in a 1622 Christmas sermon by Bishop Lancelot Andrewes: "A cold coming they had of it at this time of the year, just the worst time of the year to take a journey, and specially a long journey in. The ways deep, the weather sharp, the days short, the sun farthest off, *in solstitio brumali*, 'the very dead of winter.' "
3. The "three trees" suggest the three crosses, with Jesus crucified on the center one; the men "dicing for pieces of silver" (line 27) suggest the soldiers dicing for Jesus' garments and Judas's betrayal of him for thirty pieces of silver; the empty wineskins recall one of Jesus' parables of old and new (Mark 2.22).

With an alien people clutching their gods.
I should be glad of another death.

1927

FROM FOUR QUARTETS

Little Gidding[1]

I

Midwinter spring is its own season
Sempiternal° though sodden towards sundown,   *eternal, everlasting*
Suspended in time, between pole and tropic,
When the short day is brightest, with frost and fire,
5   The brief sun flames the ice, on pond and ditches,
In windless cold that is the heart's heat,
Reflecting in a watery mirror
A glare that is blindness in the early afternoon.
And glow more intense than blaze of branch, or brazier,
10   Stirs the dumb spirit: no wind, but pentecostal fire[2]
In the dark time of the year. Between melting and freezing
The soul's sap quivers. There is no earth smell
Or smell of living thing. This is the springtime
But not in time's covenant. Now the hedgerow
15   Is blanched for an hour with transitory blossom
Of snow, a bloom more sudden
Than that of summer, neither budding nor fading,
Not in the scheme of generation.
Where is the summer, the unimaginable
Zero summer?

20   If you came this way,
Taking the route you would be likely to take
From the place you would be likely to come from,
If you came this way in may time, you would find the hedges
White again, in May, with voluptuary sweetness.
25   It would be the same at the end of the journey,
If you came at night like a broken king,[3]

---

1. This is the last of Eliot's *Four Quartets,* four related poems each divided into five "movements" in a manner reminiscent of the structure of a quartet or a sonata and each dealing with some aspect of the relation of time and eternity, the meaning of history, the achievement of the moment of timeless insight. Although the *Four Quartets* constitute a unified sequence, they were each written separately and can be read as individual poems. "*Little Gidding* can be understood by itself, without reference to the preceding poems, which it yet so beautifully completes" (Helen Gardner, *The Composition of Four Quartets*). Each of the four is named after a place. Little Gidding is a village in Huntingdonshire where in 1625 Nicholas Ferrar established an Anglican religious community; the community was broken up in 1647, toward the end of the English Civil War, by the victorious Puritans; the chapel, however, was rebuilt in the 19th century and still exists. Eliot wrote the poem in 1942, when he was taking his turn as a nighttime fire-watcher during the incendiary bombings of London in World War II.
2. On the Pentecost day after the death and resurrection of Jesus, there appeared to his apostles "cloven tongues like as of fire . . . And they were all filled with the Holy Ghost" (Acts 2).
3. King Charles I visited Ferrar's community more than once and is said to have paid his last visit in secret after his final defeat at the battle of Naseby in the civil war.

If you came by day not knowing what you came for,
It would be the same, when you leave the rough road
And turn behind the pig-sty to the dull façade
30 And the tombstone. And what you thought you came for
Is only a shell, a husk of meaning
From which the purpose breaks only when it is fulfilled
If at all. Either you had no purpose
Or the purpose is beyond the end you figured
35 And is altered in fulfilment. There are other places
Which also are the world's end, some at the sea jaws,
Or over a dark lake, in a desert or a city[4]—
But this is the nearest, in place and time,
Now and in England.

                              If you came this way,
40 Taking any route, starting from anywhere,
At any time or at any season,
It would always be the same: you would have to put off
Sense and notion. You are not here to verify,
Instruct yourself, or inform curiosity
45 Or carry report. You are here to kneel
Where prayer has been valid. And prayer is more
Than an order of words, the conscious occupation
Of the praying mind, or the sound of the voice praying.
And what the dead had no speech for, when living,
50 They can tell you, being dead: the communication
Of the dead is tongued with fire beyond the language of the living.
Here, the intersection of the timeless moment
Is England and nowhere. Never and always.

II

Ash on an old man's sleeve
55 Is all the ash the burnt roses leave.
Dust in the air suspended
Marks the place where a story ended.[5]
Dust inbreathed was a house—
The wall, the wainscot, and the mouse.
60 The death of hope and despair,
    This is the death of air.[6]

There are flood and drouth
Over the eyes and in the mouth,
Dead water and dead sand

4. "The 'sea jaws' [Eliot] associated with Iona and St. Columba and with Lindisfarne and St. Cuthbert: the 'dark lake' with the lake of Glendalough and St. Kevin's hermitage in County Wicklow: the desert with the hermits of the Thebaid and St. Antony: the city with Padua and the other St. Antony" (Gardner).
5. Eliot wrote to a friend: "During the Blitz [bombing] the accumulated debris was suspended in the London air for hours after a bombing. Then it would slowly descend and cover one's sleeves and coat with a fine white ash."
6. "The death of air," like that of "earth" and of "water and fire" in the succeeding stanzas, recalls the theory of the creative strife of the four elements propounded by Heraclitus (Greek philosopher of 4th and 5th centuries B.C.E.): "Fire lives in the death of air; water lives in the death of earth; and earth lives in the death of water."

65 Contending for the upper hand.
The parched eviscerate soil
Gapes at the vanity of toil,
Laughs without mirth.
    This is the death of earth.

70 Water and fire succeed
The town, the pasture, and the weed.
Water and fire deride
The sacrifice that we denied.
Water and fire shall rot
75 The marred foundations we forgot,
Of sanctuary and choir.
    This is the death of water and fire.

In the uncertain hour before the morning[7]
    Near the ending of interminable night
80   At the recurrent end of the unending
After the dark dove with the flickering tongue[8]
Had passed below the horizon of his homing
While the dead leaves still rattled on like tin
Over the asphalt where no other sound was
85 Between three districts whence the smoke arose
I met one walking, loitering and hurried
As if blown towards me like the metal leaves
Before the urban dawn wind unresisting.
And as I fixed upon the down-turned face
90 That pointed scrutiny with which we challenge
The first-met stranger in the waning dusk
I caught the sudden look of some dead master
Whom I had known, forgotten, half recalled
Both one and many; in the brown baked features
95 The eyes of a familiar compound ghost[9]
Both intimate and unidentifiable.
So I assumed a double part, and cried
And heard another's voice cry: 'What! are *you* here?'
Although we were not. I was still the same,
100 Knowing myself yet being someone other—
And he a face still forming; yet the words sufficed
To compel the recognition they preceded.
And so, compliant to the common wind,
Too strange to each other for misunderstanding,
105 In concord at this intersection time
Of meeting nowhere, no before and after,
We trod the pavement in a dead patrol.
I said: 'The wonder that I feel is easy,
Yet ease is cause of wonder. Therefore speak:

7. The pattern of indentation in the left margin of lines 78–149, their movement and elevated diction, are meant to suggest the terza rima of Dante's *Divine Comedy*.
8. The German dive bomber.
9. This encounter with a ghost "compounded" of W. B. Yeats and his fellow Irishman Jonathan Swift is modeled on Dante's meeting with Brunetto Latini (*Inferno* 15), including a direct translation (line 98) of Dante's cry of horrified recognition: "*Siete voi qui, ser Brunetto?*" Cf. also Shakespeare's sonnet 86, line 9: "that affable familiar ghost."

110   I may not comprehend, may not remember.'
And he: 'I am not eager to rehearse
My thought and theory which you have forgotten.
These things have served their purpose: let them be.
So with your own, and pray they be forgiven
115   By others, as I pray you to forgive
Both bad and good. Last season's fruit is eaten
And the fullfed beast shall kick the empty pail.
For last year's words belong to last year's language
And next year's words await another voice.
120   But, as the passage now presents no hindrance
To the spirit unappeased and peregrine°   *foreign, wandering*
Between two worlds become much like each other,
So I find words I never thought to speak
In streets I never thought I should revisit
125   When I left my body on a distant shore.[1]
Since our concern was speech, and speech impelled us
To purify the dialect of the tribe[2]
And urge the mind to aftersight and foresight,
Let me disclose the gifts reserved for age
130   To set a crown upon your lifetime's effort.
First, the cold friction of expiring sense
Without enchantment, offering no promise
But bitter tastelessness of shadow fruit
As body and soul begin to fall asunder.
135   Second, the conscious impotence of rage[3]
At human folly, and the laceration
Of laughter at what ceases to amuse.[4]
And last, the rending pain of re-enactment
Of all that you have done, and been;[5] the shame
140   Of motives late revealed, and the awareness
Of things ill done and done to others' harm
Which once you took for exercise of virtue.
Then fools' approval stings, and honour stains.
From wrong to wrong the exasperated spirit
145   Proceeds, unless restored by that refining fire[6]
Where you must move in measure, like a dancer.'[7]
The day was breaking. In the disfigured street
He left me, with a kind of valediction,
And faded on the blowing of the horn.[8]

---

1. Yeats died on Jan. 28, 1939, at Roquebrune in the south of France.
2. A rendering of the line *"Donner un sens plus pur aux mots de la tribu"* in Stéphane Mallarmé's 1877 sonnet "Le Tombeau d'Edgar Poe" ("The Tomb of Edgar Poe").
3. Cf. Yeats's "The Spur": "You think it horrible that lust and rage / Should dance attention upon my old age."
4. Cf. Yeats's "Swift's Epitaph" (translated from Swift's own Latin): "Savage indignation there / Cannot lacerate his breast."
5. Cf. Yeats's "Man and the Echo": "All that I have said and done, / Now that I am old and ill, / Turns into a question till / I lie awake night after night / And never get the answer right. / Did that play of mine send out / Certain men the English shot?"

6. Cf. *The Waste Land*, line 428 and its note; also the refining fire in Yeats's "Byzantium," lines 25–32.
7. Cf. Yeats's "Among School Children," line 64: "How can we know the dancer from the dance?"
8. Cf. *Hamlet* 1.2.157: "It faded on the crowing of the cock." The horn is the all-clear signal after an air raid (the dialogue has taken place between the dropping of the last bomb and the sounding of the all clear). Eliot called the section that ends with this line "the nearest equivalent to a canto of the *Inferno* or *Purgatorio*" that he could achieve and spoke of his intention to present "a parallel, by means of contrast, between the *Inferno* and the *Purgatorio* . . . and a hallucinated scene after an air raid."

III

150 There are three conditions which often look alike
Yet differ completely, flourish in the same hedgerow:
Attachment to self and to things and to persons, detachment
From self and from things and from persons; and, growing between
them, indifference
Which resembles the others as death resembles life,
155 Being between two lives—unflowering, between
The live and the dead nettle.⁹ This is the use of memory:
For liberation—not less of love but expanding
Of love beyond desire, and so liberation
From the future as well as the past. Thus, love of a country
160 Begins as attachment to our own field of action
And comes to find that action of little importance
Though never indifferent. History may be servitude,
History may be freedom. See, now they vanish,
The faces and places, with the self which, as it could, loved them,
165 To become renewed, transfigured, in another pattern.

Sin is Behovely, but
All shall be well, and
All manner of thing shall be well.¹
If I think, again, of this place,
170 And of people, not wholly commendable,
Of no immediate kin or kindness,
But some of peculiar genius,
All touched by a common genius,
United in the strife which divided them;
175 If I think of a king at nightfall,²
Of three men, and more, on the scaffold
And a few who died forgotten
In other places, here and abroad,
And of one who died blind and quiet³
180 Why should we celebrate
These dead men more than the dying?
It is not to ring the bell backward
Nor is it an incantation
To summon the spectre of a Rose.
185 We cannot revive old factions
We cannot restore old policies
Or follow an antique drum.
These men, and those who opposed them
And those whom they opposed
190 Accept the constitution of silence
And are folded in a single party.

---

9. Eliot wrote to a friend: "The dead nettle is the family of flowering plants of which the White Archangel is one of the commonest and closely resembles the stinging nettle and is found in its company."
1. A quotation from the 14th-century English mystic Dame Julian of Norwich: "Sin is behovabil [inevitable and fitting], but all shall be well and all shall be well and all manner of thing shall be well."
2. I.e., Charles I. He died "on the scaffold" in 1649, while his principal advisers, Archbishop Laud and Thomas Wentworth, earl of Strafford, were both executed earlier by the victorious parliamentary forces.
3. I.e., Milton, who sided with Cromwell against the king.

Whatever we inherit from the fortunate
We have taken from the defeated
What they had to leave us—a symbol:
195 A symbol perfected in death.
And all shall be well and
All manner of thing shall be well
By the purification of the motive
In the ground of our beseeching.[4]

IV

200 The dove[5] descending breaks the air
With flame of incandescent terror
Of which the tongues declare
The one discharge from sin and error.
The only hope, or else despair
205 Lies in the choice of pyre or pyre—
To be redeemed from fire by fire.

Who then devised the torment? Love.
Love is the unfamiliar Name
Behind the hands that wove
210 The intolerable shirt of flame[6]
Which human power cannot remove.
We only live, only suspire°   breathe, sigh
Consumed by either fire or fire.

V

What we call the beginning is often the end
215 And to make an end is to make a beginning.
The end is where we start from. And every phrase
And sentence that is right (where every word is at home,
Taking its place to support the others,
The word neither diffident nor ostentatious,
220 And easy commerce of the old and the new,
The common word exact without vulgarity,
The formal word precise but not pedantic,
The complete consort[7] dancing together)
Every phrase and every sentence is an end and a beginning,
225 Every poem an epitaph. And any action
Is a step to the block, to the fire, down the sea's throat
Or to an illegible stone: and that is where we start.
We die with the dying:
See, they depart, and we go with them.
230 We are born with the dead:
See, they return, and bring us with them.
The moment of the rose and the moment of the yew-tree[8]

4. Dame Julian of Norwich was instructed in a vision that "the ground of our beseeching" is love.
5. Both a dive bomber and the Holy Spirit with its Pentecostal tongues of fire.
6. Out of love for her husband, Hercules, Deianira gave him the poisoned shirt of Nessus. She had been told that it would increase his love for her, but instead it so corroded his flesh that in his agony he mounted a funeral pyre and burned himself to death.
7. Company; also harmony of sounds.
8. Traditional symbol of death and grief.

Are of equal duration. A people without history
Is not redeemed from time, for history is a pattern
235 Of timeless moments. So, while the light fails
On a winter's afternoon, in a secluded chapel
History is now and England.

With the drawing of this Love and the voice of this Calling[9]

We shall not cease from exploration
240 And the end of all our exploring
Will be to arrive where we started
And know the place for the first time.
Through the unknown, remembered gate
When the last of earth left to discover
245 Is that which was the beginning;
At the source of the longest river
The voice of the hidden waterfall
And the children in the apple tree
Not known, because not looked for
250 But heard, half-heard, in the stillness
Between two waves of the sea.[1]
Quick now, here, now, always—
A condition of complete simplicity
(Costing not less than everything)
255 And all shall be well and
All manner of thing shall be well
When the tongues of flame are in-folded
Into the crowned knot of fire
And the fire and the rose are one.

1942   1942, 1943

Tradition and the Individual Talent[1]

I

In English writing we seldom speak of tradition, though we occasionally apply its name in deploring its absence. We cannot refer to 'the tradition' or to 'a tradition'; at most, we employ the adjective in saying that the poetry of So-and-so is 'traditional' or even 'too traditional.' Seldom, perhaps, does the word appear except in a phrase of censure. If otherwise, it is vaguely approbative, with the implication, as to the work approved, of some pleasing archæological reconstruction. You can hardly make the word agreeable to English ears without this comfortable reference to the reassuring science of archæology.

Certainly the word is not likely to appear in our appreciations of living or dead writers. Every nation, every race, has not only its own creative, but its

---

9. This line is from the *Cloud of Unknowing*, an anonymous 14th-century mystical work.
1. The voices of the children in the apple tree symbolize the sudden moment of insight. Cf. the conclusion to "Burnt Norton" (the first of the *Four Quartets*), where the laughter of the children in the

garden has a like meaning: "Sudden in a shaft of sunlight / Even while the dust moves / There rises the hidden laughter / Of children in the foliage / Quick now, here, now, always."
1. First published in *The Egoist* magazine (1919) and later collected in *The Sacred Wood* (1920).

own critical turn of mind; and is even more oblivious of the shortcomings and limitations of its critical habits than of those of its creative genius. We know, or think we know, from the enormous mass of critical writing that has appeared in the French language the critical method or habit of the French; we only conclude (we are such unconscious people) that the French are 'more critical' than we, and sometimes even plume ourselves a little with the fact, as if the French were the less spontaneous. Perhaps they are; but we might remind ourselves that criticism is as inevitable as breathing, and that we should be none the worse for articulating what passes in our minds when we read a book and feel an emotion about it, for criticizing our own minds in their work of criticism. One of the facts that might come to light in this process is our tendency to insist, when we praise a poet, upon those aspects of his work in which he least resembles anyone else. In these aspects or parts of his work we pretend to find what is individual, what is the peculiar essence of the man. We dwell with satisfaction upon the poet's difference from his predecessors, especially his immediate predecessors; we endeavour to find something that can be isolated in order to be enjoyed. Whereas if we approach a poet without this prejudice we shall often find that not only the best, but the most individual parts of his work may be those in which the dead poets, his ancestors, assert their immortality most vigorously. And I do not mean the impressionable period of adolescence, but the period of full maturity.

Yet if the only form of tradition, of handing down, consisted in following the ways of the immediate generation before us in a blind or timid adherence to its successes, 'tradition' should positively be discouraged. We have seen many such simple currents soon lost in the sand; and novelty is better than repetition. Tradition is a matter of much wider significance. It cannot be inherited, and if you want it you must obtain it by great labour. It involves, in the first place, the historical sense, which we may call nearly indispensable to any one who would continue to be a poet beyond his twenty-fifth year; and the historical sense involves a perception, not only of the pastness of the past, but of its presence; the historical sense compels a man to write not merely with his own generation in his bones, but with a feeling that the whole of the literature of Europe from Homer and within it the whole of the literature of his own country has a simultaneous existence and composes a simultaneous order. This historical sense, which is a sense of the timeless as well as of the temporal and of the timeless and of the temporal together, is what makes a writer traditional. And it is at the same time what makes a writer most acutely conscious of his place in time, of his own contemporaneity.

No poet, no artist of any art, has his complete meaning alone. His significance, his appreciation is the appreciation of his relation to the dead poets and artists. You cannot value him alone; you must set him, for contrast and comparison, among the dead. I mean this as a principle of æsthetic, not merely historical, criticism. The necessity that he shall conform, that he shall cohere, is not one-sided; what happens when a new work of art is created is something that happens simultaneously to all the works of art which preceded it. The existing monuments form an ideal order among themselves, which is modified by the introduction of the new (the really new) work of art among them. The existing order is complete before the new work arrives; for order to persist after the supervention of novelty, the *whole* existing order must be, if ever so slightly, altered; and so the relations, proportions, values of each work of art toward the whole are readjusted; and this is conformity between the old and the new.

Whoever has approved this idea of order, of the form of European, of English literature will not find it preposterous that the past should be altered by the present as much as the present is directed by the past. And the poet who is aware of this will be aware of great difficulties and responsibilities.

In a peculiar sense he will be aware also that he must inevitably be judged by the standards of the past. I say judged, not amputated, by them; not judged to be as good as, or worse or better than, the dead; and certainly not judged by the canons of dead critics. It is a judgment, a comparison, in which two things are measured by each other. To conform merely would be for the new work not really to conform at all; it would not be new, and would therefore not be a work of art. And we do not quite say that the new is more valuable because it fits in; but its fitting in is a test of its value—a test, it is true, which can only be slowly and cautiously applied, for we are none of us infallible judges of conformity. We say: it appears to conform, and is perhaps individual, or it appears individual, and may conform; but we are hardly likely to find that it is one and not the other.

To proceed to a more intelligible exposition of the relation of the poet to the past: he can neither take the past as a lump, an indiscriminate bolus,[2] nor can he form himself wholly on one or two private admirations, nor can he form himself wholly upon one preferred period. The first course is inadmissible, the second is an important experience of youth, and the third is a pleasant and highly desirable supplement. The poet must be very conscious of the main current, which does not at all flow invariably through the most distinguished reputations. He must be quite aware of the obvious fact that art never improves, but that the material of art is never quite the same. He must be aware that the mind of Europe—the mind of his own country—a mind which he learns in time to be much more important than his own private mind—is a mind which changes, and that this change is a development which abandons nothing *en route,* which does not superannuate either Shakespeare, or Homer, or the rock drawing of the Magdalenian[3] draftsmen. That this development, refinement perhaps, complication certainly, is not, from the point of view of the artist, any improvement. Perhaps not even an improvement from the point of view of the psychologist or not to the extent which we imagine; perhaps only in the end based upon a complication in economics and machinery. But the difference between the present and the past is that the conscious present is an awareness of the past in a way and to an extent which the past's awareness of itself cannot show.

Someone said: 'The dead writers are remote from us because we *know* so much more than they did.' Precisely, and they are that which we know.

I am alive to a usual objection to what is clearly part of my programme for the *métier*[4] of poetry. The objection is that the doctrine requires a ridiculous amount of erudition (pedantry), a claim which can be rejected by appeal to the lives of poets in any pantheon. It will even be affirmed that much learning deadens or perverts poetic sensibility. While, however, we persist in believing that a poet ought to know as much as will not encroach upon his necessary receptivity and necessary laziness, it is not desirable to confine knowledge to whatever can be put into a useful shape for examinations, drawing-rooms, or the still more pretentious modes of publicity. Some can absorb knowledge,

2. A round mass of anything: a large pill.
3. The most advanced culture of the European Paleolithic period (from discoveries at La Made-

leine, France).
4. Vocation (French).

the more tardy must sweat for it. Shakespeare acquired more essential history from Plutarch[5] than most men could from the whole British Museum. What is to be insisted upon is that the poet must develop or procure the consciousness of the past and that he should continue to develop this consciousness throughout his career.

What happens is a continual surrender of himself as he is at the moment to something which is more valuable. The progress of an artist is a continual self-sacrifice, a continual extinction of personality.

There remains to define this process of depersonalisation and its relation to the sense of tradition. It is in this depersonalization that art may be said to approach the condition of science. I, therefore, invite you to consider, as a suggestive analogy, the action which takes place when a bit of finely filiated[6] platinum is introduced into a chamber containing oxygen and sulphur dioxide.

II

Honest criticism and sensitive appreciation are directed not upon the poet but upon the poetry. If we attend to the confused cries of the newspaper critics and the susurrus[7] of popular repetition that follows, we shall hear the names of poets in great numbers; if we seek not Blue-book[8] knowledge but the enjoyment of poetry, and ask for a poem, we shall seldom find it. I have tried to point out the importance of the relation of the poem to other poems by other authors, and suggested the conception of poetry as a living whole of all the poetry that has ever been written. The other aspect of this Impersonal theory of poetry is the relation of the poem to its author. And I hinted, by an analogy, that the mind of the mature poet differs from that of the immature one not precisely in any valuation of 'personality,' not being necessarily more interesting, or having 'more to say,' but rather by being a more finely perfected medium in which special, or very varied, feelings are at liberty to enter into new combinations.

The analogy was that of the catalyst.[9] When the two gases previously mentioned are mixed in the presence of a filament of platinum, they form sulphurous acid. This combination takes place only if the platinum is present; nevertheless the newly formed acid contains no trace of platinum, and the platinum itself is apparently unaffected; has remained inert, neutral, and unchanged. The mind of the poet is the shred of platinum. It may partly or exclusively operate upon the experience of the man himself; but, the more perfect the artist, the more completely separate in him will be the man who suffers and the mind which creates; the more perfectly will the mind digest and transmute the passions which are its material.

The experience, you will notice, the elements which enter the presence of the transforming catalyst, are of two kinds: emotions and feelings. The effect of a work of art upon the person who enjoys it is an experience different in kind from any experience not of art. It may be formed out of one emotion, or may be a combination of several; and various feelings, inhering for the writer

---

5. Greek biographer (1st century C.E.) of famous Greeks and Romans; from his work Shakespeare drew the plots of his Roman plays.
6. Drawn out like a thread.
7. Murmuring, buzzing (Latin).
8. British government publication.
9. Substance that triggers a chemical change without being affected by the reaction.

in particular words or phrases or images, may be added to compose the final result. Or great poetry may be made without the direct use of any emotion whatever: composed out of feelings solely. Canto XV of the *Inferno* (Brunetto Latini)[1] is a working up of the emotion evident in the situation; but the effect, though single as that of any work of art, is obtained by considerable complexity of detail. The last quatrain gives an image, a feeling attaching to an image, which 'came,' which did not develop simply out of what precedes, but which was probably in suspension in the poet's mind until the proper combination arrived for it to add itself to.[2] The poet's mind is in fact a receptacle for seizing and storing up numberless feelings, phrases, images, which remain there until all the particles which can unite to form a new compound are present together.

If you compare several representative passages of the greatest poetry you see how great is the variety of types of combination, and also how completely any semi-ethical criterion of 'sublimity' misses the mark. For it is not the 'greatness,' the intensity, of the emotions, the components, but the intensity of the artistic process, the pressure, so to speak, under which the fusion takes place, that counts. The episode of Paolo and Francesca[3] employs a definite emotion, but the intensity of the poetry is something quite different from whatever intensity in the supposed experience it may give the impression of. It is no more intense, furthermore, than Canto XXVI,[4] the voyage of Ulysses, which has not the direct dependence upon an emotion. Great variety is possible in the process of transmutation of emotion: the murder of Agamemnon, or the agony of Othello,[5] gives an artistic effect apparently closer to a possible original than the scenes from Dante. In the *Agamemnon*, the artistic emotion approximates to the emotion of an actual spectator; in *Othello* to the emotion of the protagonist himself. But the difference between art and the event is always absolute; the combination which is the murder of Agamemnon is probably as complex as that which is the voyage of Ulysses. In either case there has been a fusion of elements. The ode of Keats contains a number of feelings which have nothing particular to do with the nightingale, but which the nightingale, partly, perhaps, because of its attractive name, and partly because of its reputation, served to bring together.

The point of view which I am struggling to attack is perhaps related to the metaphysical theory of the substantial unity of the soul: for my meaning is, that the poet has, not a 'personality' to express, but a particular medium, which is only a medium and not a personality, in which impressions and experiences combine in peculiar and unexpected ways. Impressions and experiences which are important for the man may take no place in the poetry, and those which become important in the poetry may play quite a negligible part in the man, the personality.

I will quote a passage which is unfamiliar enough to be regarded with fresh attention in the light—or darkness—of these observations:

1. Dante meets in hell his old master, Brunetto Latini, suffering eternal punishment for unnatural lust yet still loved and admired by Dante, who addresses him with affectionate courtesy.
2. Dante's strange interview with Brunetto is over, and Brunetto moves off to continue his punishment: "Then he turned round, and seemed like one of those / Who run for the green cloth [in the footrace] at Verona / In the field; and he seemed among them / Not the loser but the winner."

3. Illicit lovers whom Dante meets in the second circle of hell (*Inferno* 5) and at whose punishment and sorrows he swoons with pity.
4. Of the *Inferno*. Ulysses, suffering in hell for "false counseling," tells Dante of his final voyage.
5. Shakespeare's character kills himself after being duped into jealously murdering his wife. In Aeschylus's play *Agamemnon* the title character is murdered by his wife, Clytemnestra.

And now methinks I could e'en chide myself
For doating on her beauty, though her death
Shall be revenged after no common action.
Does the silkworm expend her yellow labours
For thee? For thee does she undo herself?
Are lordships sold to maintain ladyships
For the poor benefit of a bewildering minute?
Why does yon fellow falsify highways,
And put his life between the judge's lips,
To refine such a thing—keeps horse and men
To beat their valours for her? . . . [6]

In this passage (as is evident if it is taken in its context) there is a combination of positive and negative emotions: an intensely strong attraction toward beauty and an equally intense fascination by the ugliness which is contrasted with it and which destroys it. This balance of contrasted emotion is in the dramatic situation to which the speech is pertinent, but that situation alone is inadequate to it. This is, so to speak, the structural emotion, provided by the drama. But the whole effect, the dominant tone, is due to the fact that a number of floating feelings, having an affinity to this emotion by no means superficially evident, have combined with it to give us a new art emotion.

It is not in his personal emotions, the emotions provoked by particular events in his life, that the poet is in any way remarkable or interesting. His particular emotions may be simple, or crude, or flat. The emotion in his poetry will be a very complex thing, but not with the complexity of the emotions of people who have very complex or unusual emotions in life. One error, in fact, of eccentricity in poetry is to seek for new human emotions to express; and in this search for novelty in the wrong place it discovers the perverse. The business of the poet is not to find new emotions, but to use the ordinary ones and, in working them up into poetry, to express feelings which are not in actual emotions at all. And emotions which he has never experienced will serve his turn as well as those familiar to him. Consequently, we must believe that 'emotion recollected in tranquillity'[7] is an inexact formula. For it is neither emotion, nor recollection, nor, without distortion of meaning, tranquility. It is a concentration, and a new thing resulting from the concentration, of a very great number of experiences which to the practical and active person would not seem to be experiences at all; it is a concentration which does not happen consciously or of deliberation. These experiences are not 'recollected,' and they finally unite in an atmosphere which is 'tranquil' only in that it is a passive attending upon the event. Of course this is not quite the whole story. There is a great deal, in the writing of poetry, which must be conscious and deliberate. In fact, the bad poet is usually unconscious where he ought to be conscious, and conscious where he ought to be unconscious. Both errors tend to make him 'personal.' Poetry is not a turning loose of emotion, but an escape from emotion; it is not the expression of personality, but an escape from personality. But, of course, only those who have personality and emotions know what it means to want to escape from these things.

6. From Cyril Tourneur's *Revenger's Tragedy* 3.4 (1607).
7. In his preface to *Lyrical Ballads* (2nd ed.,

1800), Wordsworth writes that poetry "takes its origin from emotion recollected in tranquility."

III

ὁ δὲ νοῦζ ἴσωζ θειό τερόν τι καὶ ἀπαθέζ ἐστιν.[8]

This essay proposes to halt at the frontier of metaphysics or mysticism, and confine itself to such practical conclusions as can be applied by the responsible person interested in poetry. To divert interest from the poet to the poetry is a laudable aim: for it would conduce to a juster estimation of actual poetry, good and bad. There are many people who appreciate the expression of sincere emotion in verse, and there is a smaller number of people who can appreciate technical excellence. But very few know when there is an expression of *significant* emotion, emotion which has its life in the poem and not in the history of the poet. The emotion of art is impersonal. And the poet cannot reach this impersonality without surrendering himself wholly to the work to be done. And he is not likely to know what is to be done unless he lives in what is not merely the present, but the present moment of the past, unless he is conscious, not of what is dead, but of what is already living.

1919, 1920

The Metaphysical Poets

By collecting these poems[1] from the work of a generation more often named than read, and more often read than profitably studied, Professor Grierson has rendered a service of some importance. Certainly the reader will meet with many poems already preserved in other anthologies, at the same time that he discovers poems such as those of Aurelian Townshend or Lord Herbert of Cherbury here included. But the function of such an anthology as this is neither that of Professor Saintsbury's admirable edition of Caroline poets nor that of the *Oxford Book of English Verse.* Mr. Grierson's book is in itself a piece of criticism and a provocation of criticism; and we think that he was right in including so many poems of Donne, elsewhere (though not in many editions) accessible, as documents in the case of 'metaphysical poetry.' The phrase has long done duty as a term of abuse or as the label of a quaint and pleasant taste. The question is to what extent the so-called metaphysicals formed a school (in our own time we should say a 'movement'), and how far this so-called school or movement is a digression from the main current.

Not only is it extremely difficult to define metaphysical poetry, but difficult to decide what poets practise it and in which of their verses. The poetry of Donne (to whom Marvell and Bishop King are sometimes nearer than any of the other authors) is late Elizabethan, its feeling often very close to that of Chapman. The 'courtly' poetry is derivative from Jonson, who borrowed liberally from the Latin; it expires in the next century with the sentiment and witticism of Prior. There is finally the devotional verse of Herbert, Vaughan, and Crashaw (echoed long after by Christina Rossetti and Francis Thompson); Crashaw, sometimes more profound and less sectarian than the others, has a

---

8. Aristotle's "De Anima" ("On the Soul") 1.4: "The mind is doubtless something more divine and unimpressionable."
1. *Metaphysical Lyrics and Poems of the Seven-*

teenth Century: Donne to Butler (1921), selected and edited, with an essay, by Herbert J. C. Grierson. Eliot's essay was originally a review of this book in the London *Times Literary Supplement.*

quality which returns through the Elizabethan period to the early Italians. It is difficult to find any precise use of metaphor, simile, or other conceit, which is common to all the poets and at the same time important enough as an element of style to isolate these poets as a group. Donne, and often Cowley, employ a device which is sometimes considered characteristically 'metaphysical'; the elaboration (contrasted with the condensation) of a figure of speech to the furthest stage to which ingenuity can carry it. Thus Cowley develops the commonplace comparison of the world to a chess-board through long stanzas (*To Destiny*), and Donne, with more grace, in *A Valediction*,[2] the comparison of two lovers to a pair of compasses. But elsewhere we find, instead of the mere explication of the content of a comparison, a development by rapid association of thought which requires considerable agility on the part of the reader.

> *On a round ball*
> *A workeman that hath copies by, can lay*
> *An Europe, Afrique, and an Asia,*
> *And quickly make that, which was nothing, All,*
> > *So doth each teare,*
> > *Which thee doth weare,*
> *A globe, yea world by that impression grow,*
> *Till thy tears mixt with mine doe overflow*
> *This world, by waters sent from thee, my heaven dissolved so.*[3]

Here we find at least two connexions which are not implicit in the first figure, but are forced upon it by the poet: from the geographer's globe to the tear, and the tear to the deluge. On the other hand, some of Donne's most successful and characteristic effects are secured by brief words and sudden contrasts:

> *A bracelet of bright hair about the bone,*[4]

where the most powerful effect is produced by the sudden contrast of associations of 'bright hair' and of 'bone'. This telescoping of images and multiplied associations is characteristic of the phrase of some of the dramatists of the period which Donne knew: not to mention Shakespeare, it is frequent in Middleton, Webster, and Tourneur, and is one of the sources of the vitality of their language.

Johnson, who employed the term 'metaphysical poets', apparently having Donne, Cleveland, and Cowley chiefly in mind, remarks of them that 'the most heterogeneous ideas are yoked by violence together'.[5] The force of this impeachment lies in the failure of the conjunction, the fact that often the ideas are yoked but not united; and if we are to judge of styles of poetry by their abuse, enough examples may be found in Cleveland to justify Johnson's condemnation. But a degree of heterogeneity of material compelled into unity by the operation of the poet's mind is omnipresent in poetry. We need not select for illustration such a line as:

> *Notre âme est un trois-mâts cherchant son Icarie;*[6]

2. I.e., "A Valediction: Forbidding Mourning."
3. Donne's "A Valediction: Of Weeping," lines 10–18.
4. "The Relic," line 6.
5. See Samuel Johnson's *Cowley*.

6. From Charles Baudelaire's "Le Voyage": "Our soul is a three-masted ship searching for her Icarie"; Icarie is an imaginary utopia in *Voyage en Icarie* (1840), a novel by the French socialist Etienne Cabet.

we may find it in some of the best lines of Johnson himself (*The Vanity of Human Wishes*):

> *His fate was destined to a barren strand,*
> *A petty fortress, and a dubious hand;*
> *He left a name at which the world grew pale,*
> *To point a moral, or adorn a tale.*

where the effect is due to a contrast of ideas, different in degree but the same in principle, as that which Johnson mildly reprehended. And in one of the finest poems of the age (a poem which could not have been written in any other age), the *Exequy* of Bishop King, the extended comparison is used with perfect success: the idea and the simile become one, in the passage in which the Bishop illustrates his impatience to see his dead wife, under the figure of a journey:

> *Stay for me there; I will not faile*
> *To meet thee in that hollow Vale.*
> *And think not much of my delay;*
> *I am already on the way,*
> *And follow thee with all the speed*
> *Desire can make, or sorrows breed.*
> *Each minute is a short degree,*
> *And ev'ry hour a step towards thee,*
> *At night when I betake to rest,*
> *Next morn I rise nearer my West*
> *Of life, almost by eight houres sail,*
> *Than when sleep breath'd his drowsy gale. . . .*
> *But heark! My Pulse, like a soft Drum*
> *Beats my approach, tells Thee I come;*
> *And slow howere my marches be,*
> *I shall at last sit down by Thee.*

(In the last few lines there is that effect of terror which is several times attained by one of Bishop King's admirers, Edgar Poe.) Again, we may justly take these quatrains from Lord Herbert's Ode,[7] stanzas which would, we think, be immediately pronounced to be of the metaphysical school:

> *So when from hence we shall be gone,*
> *And be no more, nor you, nor I,*
> *As one another's mystery,*
> *Each shall be both, yet both but one.*

> *This said, in her up-lifted face,*
> *Her eyes, which did that beauty crown,*
> *Were like two stars, that having faln down,*
> *Look up again to find their place:*

> *While such a moveless silent peace*
> *Did seize on their becalmed sense,*
> *One would have thought some influence*
> *Their ravished spirits did possess.*

---

7. Edward, Lord Herbert of Cherbury (1583–1648), brother of George Herbert. The "Ode" is his "Ode upon a Question moved, whether Love should continue forever?"

There is nothing in these lines (with the possible exception of the stars, a simile not at once grasped, but lovely and justified) which fits Johnson's general observations on the metaphysical poets in his essay on Cowley. A good deal resides in the richness of association which is at the same time borrowed from and given to the word 'becalmed'; but the meaning is clear, the language simple and elegant. It is to be observed that the language of these poets is as a rule simple and pure; in the verse of George Herbert this simplicity is carried as far as it can go—a simplicity emulated without success by numerous modern poets. The *structure* of the sentences, on the other hand, is sometimes far from simple, but this is not a vice; it is a fidelity to thought and feeling. The effect, at its best, is far less artificial than that of an ode by Gray. And as this fidelity induces variety of thought and feeling, so it induces variety of music. We doubt whether, in the eighteenth century, could be found two poems in nominally the same metre, so dissimilar as Marvell's *Coy Mistress* and Crashaw's *Saint Teresa*; the one producing an effect of great speed by the use of short syllables, and the other an ecclesiastical solemnity by the use of long ones:

> *Love, thou art absolute sole lord*
> *Of life and death.*

If so shrewd and sensitive (though so limited) a critic as Johnson failed to define metaphysical poetry by its faults, it is worth while to inquire whether we may not have more success by adopting the opposite method: by assuming that the poets of the seventeenth century (up to the Revolution)[8] were the direct and normal development of the precedent age; and, without prejudicing their case by the adjective 'metaphysical', consider whether their virtue was not something permanently valuable, which subsequently disappeared, but ought not to have disappeared. Johnson has hit, perhaps by accident, on one of their peculiarities, when he observes that 'their attempts were always analytic'; he would not agree that, after the dissociation, they put the material together again in a new unity.

It is certain that the dramatic verse of the later Elizabethan and early Jacobean poets expresses a degree of development of sensibility which is not found in any of the prose, good as it often is. If we except Marlowe, a man of prodigious intelligence, these dramatists were directly or indirectly (it is at least a tenable theory) affected by Montaigne.[9] Even if we except also Jonson and Chapman, these two were probably erudite, and were notably men who incorporated their erudition into their sensibility: their mode of feeling was directly and freshly altered by their reading and thought. In Chapman especially there is a direct sensuous apprehension of thought, or a recreation of thought into feeling, which is exactly what we find in Donne:

> *in this one thing, all the discipline*
> *Of manners and of manhood is contained;*
> *A man to join himself with th' Universe*
> *In his main sway, and make in all things fit*
> *One with that All, and go on, round as it;*
> *Not plucking from the whole his wretched part,*
> *And into straits, or into nought revert,*

---

8. Of 1688; when James II was replaced by William and Mary.

9. Michel de Montaigne (1533–1592), French essayist.

> Wishing the complete Universe might be
> Subject to such a rag of it as he;
> But to consider great Necessity.[1]

We compare this with some modern passage:

> No, when the fight begins within himself,
> A man's worth something. God stoops o'er his head,
> Satan looks up between his feet—both tug—
> He's left, himself, i' the middle; the soul wakes
> And grows. Prolong that battle through his life![2]

It is perhaps somewhat less fair, though very tempting (as both poets are concerned with the perpetuation of love by offspring), to compare with the stanzas already quoted from Lord Herbert's Ode the following from Tennyson:

> One walked between his wife and child,
> With measured footfall firm and mild,
> And now and then he gravely smiled.
>
> The prudent partner of his blood
> Leaned on him, faithful, gentle, good,
> Wearing the rose of womanhood.
>
> And in their double love secure,
> The little maiden walked demure,
> Pacing with downward eyelids pure.
>
> These three made unity so sweet,
> My frozen heart began to beat,
> Remembering its ancient heat.[3]

The difference is not a simple difference of degree between poets. It is something which had happened to the mind of England between the time of Donne or Lord Herbert of Cherbury and the time of Tennyson and Browning; it is the difference between the intellectual poet and the reflective poet. Tennyson and Browning are poets, and they think; but they do not feel their thought as immediately as the odour of a rose. A thought to Donne was an experience; it modified his sensibility. When a poet's mind is perfectly equipped for its work, it is constantly amalgamating disparate experience; the ordinary man's experience is chaotic, irregular, fragmentary. The latter falls in love, or reads Spinoza,[4] and these two experiences have nothing to do with each other, or with the noise of the typewriter or the smell of cooking; in the mind of the poet these experiences are always forming new wholes.

We may express the difference by the following theory: The poets of the seventeenth century, the successors of the dramatists of the sixteenth, possessed a mechanism of sensibility which could devour any kind of experience. They are simple, artificial, difficult, or fantastic, as their predecessors were; no less nor more than Dante, Guido Cavalcanti, Guinicelli, or Cino.[5] In the seventeenth century a dissociation of sensibility set in, from which we have never recovered; and this dissociation, as is natural, was aggravated by the influence of the two most powerful poets of the century, Milton and Dryden.

1. From *The Revenge of Bussy d'Ambois* (4.1.137–46).
2. Robert Browning, "Bishop Blougram's Apology," lines 693–97.
3. "The Two Voices," lines 412–23.
4. 17th-century Dutch philosopher.

5. These last three poets, all of whom lived in the 13th century, were members of the Tuscan school of lyric love poets. Guido Guinicelli was hailed by Dante in the *Purgatorio* as "father of Italian poets." Cino da Pistoia was a friend of Dante and Petrarch.

Each of these men performed certain poetic functions so magnificently well that the magnitude of the effect concealed the absence of others. The language went on and in some respects improved; the best verse of Collins, Gray, Johnson, and even Goldsmith satisfies some of our fastidious demands better than that of Donne or Marvell or King. But while the language became more refined, the feeling became more crude. The feeling, the sensibility, expressed in the *Country Churchyard*[6] (to say nothing of Tennyson and Browning) is cruder than that in the *Coy Mistress*.

The second effect of the influence of Milton and Dryden followed from the first, and was therefore slow in manifestation. The sentimental age began early in the eighteenth century, and continued. The poets revolted against the ratiocinative, the descriptive; they thought and felt by fits, unbalanced; they reflected. In one or two passages of Shelley's *Triumph of Life*, in the second *Hyperion*, there are traces of a struggle toward unification of sensibility. But Keats and Shelley died, and Tennyson and Browning ruminated.

After this brief exposition of a theory—too brief, perhaps, to carry conviction—we may ask, what would have been the fate of the 'metaphysical' had the current of poetry descended in a direct line from them, as it descended in a direct line to them? They would not, certainly, be classified as metaphysical. The possible interests of a poet are unlimited; the more intelligent he is the better; the more intelligent he is the more likely that he will have interests: our only condition is that he turn them into poetry, and not merely meditate on them poetically. A philosophical theory which has entered into poetry is established, for its truth or falsity in one sense ceases to matter, and its truth in another sense is proved. The poets in question have, like other poets, various faults. But they were, at best, engaged in the task of trying to find the verbal equivalent for states of mind and feeling. And this means both that they are more mature, and that they wear better, than later poets of certainly not less literary ability.

It is not a permanent necessity that poets should be interested in philosophy, or in any other subject. We can only say that it appears likely that poets in our civilization, as it exists at present, must be *difficult*. Our civilization comprehends great variety and complexity, and this variety and complexity, playing upon a refined sensibility, must produce various and complex results. The poet must become more and more comprehensive, more allusive, more indirect, in order to force, to dislocate if necessary, language into his meaning. (A brilliant and extreme statement of this view, with which it is not requisite to associate oneself, is that of M Jean Epstein, *La Poésie d'aujourd'hui*.[7]) Hence we get something which looks very much like the conceit—we get, in fact, a method curiously similar to that of the 'metaphysical poets', similar also in its use of obscure words and of simple phrasing.

> O géraniums diaphanes, guerroyeurs sortilèges,
> Sacrilèges monomanes!
> Emballages, dévergondages, douches! O pressoirs
> Des vendanges des grands soirs!
> Layettes aux abois,
> Thyrses au fond des bois!
> Transfusions, représailles,

Relevailles, compresses et l'éternal potion,
Angélus! n'en pouvoir plus
De débâcles nuptiales! de débâcles nuptiales![8]

The same poet could write also simply:

Elle est bien loin, elle pleure,
Le grand vent se lamente aussi . . .[9]

Jules Laforgue, and Tristan Corbière[1] in many of his poems, are nearer to the 'school of Donne' than any modern English poet. But poets more classical than they have the same essential quality of transmuting ideas into sensations, of transforming an observation into a state of mind.

Pour l'enfant, amoureux de cartes et d'estampes,
L'univers est égal à son vaste appétit.
Ah, que le monde est grand à la clarté des lampes!
Aux yeux du souvenir que le monde est petit![2]

In French literature the great master of the seventeenth century—Racine— and the great master of the nineteenth—Baudelaire—are in some ways more like each other than they are like anyone else. The greatest two masters of diction are also the greatest two psychologists, the most curious explorers of the soul. It is interesting to speculate whether it is not a misfortune that two of the greatest masters of diction in our language, Milton and Dryden, triumph with a dazzling disregard of the soul. If we continued to produce Miltons and Drydens it might not so much matter, but as things are it is a pity that English poetry has remained so incomplete. Those who object to the 'artificiality' of Milton or Dryden sometimes tell us to 'look into our hearts and write.'[3] But that is not looking deep enough; Racine or Donne looked into a good deal more than the heart. One must look into the cerebral cortex, the nervous system, and the digestive tracts.

May we not conclude, then, that Donne, Crashaw, Vaughan, Herbert and Lord Herbert, Marvell, King, Cowley at his best, are in the direct current of English poetry, and that their faults should be reprimanded by this standard rather than coddled by antiquarian affection? They have been enough praised in terms which are implicit limitations because they are 'metaphysical' or 'witty,' 'quaint' or 'obscure,' though at their best they have not these attributes more than other serious poets. On the other hand, we must not reject the criticism of Johnson (a dangerous person to disagree with) without having mastered it, without having assimilated the Johnsonian canons of taste. In reading the celebrated passage in his essay on Cowley we must remember that by wit he clearly means something more serious than we usually mean to-day; in his criticism of their versification we must remember in what a narrow discipline he was trained, but also how well trained; we must remember that

8. From *Derniers Vers* (*Last Poems*, 1890) 10, by Jules Laforgue (1860–1887): "O transparent geraniums, warrior incantations, / Monomaniac sacrileges! / Packing materials, shamelessnesses, shower baths! O wine presses / Of great evening vintages! / Hard-pressed baby linen, / Thyrsis in the depths of the woods! / Transfusions, reprisals, / Churchings, compresses, and the eternal potion, / Angelus! no longer to be borne [are] / Catastrophic marriages! catastrophic marriages!"
9. From *Derniers Vers* 11, "Sur une Défunte" ("On

a Dead Woman"): "She is far away, she weeps / The great wind mourns also."
1. French symbolist poet (1845–1875).
2. From Charles Baudelaire's "Le Voyage": "For the child, in love with maps and prints, / The universe matches his vast appetite. / Ah, how big the world is by lamplight! How small the world is to the eyes of memory!"
3. An adaptation of the last line of the first sonnet of *Astrophil and Stella*, by Sir Philip Sidney (1554–1586).

Johnson tortures chiefly the chief offenders, Cowley and Cleveland. It would be a fruitful work, and one requiring a substantial book, to break up the classification of Johnson (for there has been none since) and exhibit these poets in all their difference of kind and of degree, from the massive music of Donne to the faint, pleasing tinkle of Aurelian Townshend—whose *Dialogue between a Pilgrim and Time* is one of the few regrettable omissions from the excellent anthology of Professor Grierson.

1921

KATHERINE MANSFIELD
1888–1923

Kathleen Mansfield Beauchamp was born in Wellington, New Zealand, daughter of a respected businessman who was later knighted. In 1903 the family moved to London, where Kathleen and her sisters entered Queen's College, the first institution in England founded expressly for the higher education of women. The family returned to New Zealand, leaving the girls in London, but the Beauchamps brought their daughters home in 1906. By this time Kathleen had written a number of poems, sketches, and stories; and after experimenting with different pen names, she adopted that of Katherine Mansfield. She was restless and ambitious and chafed against the narrowness of middle-class life in New Zealand, at that time still very much a new country in the shadow of the British Empire.

In July 1908 Mansfield left again for London; she never returned to New Zealand. In 1909 she suddenly married G. C. Bowden, a teacher of singing and elocution, but left him the same evening. Shortly afterward she became pregnant by another man and went to Germany to await the birth, but she had a miscarriage there. Her experiences in Germany are told in carefully observed sketches full of ironic detail in her first published book, *In a German Pension* (1911).

In 1910 she briefly resumed life with Bowden, who put her in touch with A. R. Orage, editor of the avant-garde periodical *The New Age*. There she published a number of her stories and sketches. At the end of 1911 she met the critic John Middleton Murry, editor of the modernist magazine *Rhythm*, and eventually married him. She developed intense but conflicted friendships with D. H. Lawrence, Virginia Woolf, and other writers of the day. During all this time Mansfield experimented in technique and refined her art, attempting within the short story to illuminate the ambivalences and complexities of friendship and family, gender and class. The death in World War I in October 1915 of her much-loved younger brother sent her imagination back to their childhood days in New Zealand and in doing so gave a fresh charge and significance to her writing. Using her newly developed style with an ever greater subtlety and sensitivity, she now produced her best stories, including "Prelude," "Daughters of the Late Colonel," "At the Bay," and "The Garden Party." With the publication of *The Garden Party and Other Stories* in February 1922, Mansfield's place as a master of the modern short story was ensured. But she was gravely ill with tuberculosis and died suddenly at the age of thirty-four in Fontainebleau, France, where she had gone to try to find a cure by adopting the methods of the controversial mystic George Ivanovich Gurdjieff.

Mansfield produced her best and most characteristic work in her last years, when she combined incident, image, symbol, and structure in a way comparable with, yet interestingly different from, James Joyce's method in *Dubliners*, both writers sharing an influence in the precise and understated art of the Russian writer Anton Chekhov. "Daughters of the Late Colonel," a story of two middle-aged sisters and their devotion to a tyrannical father, shows her working characteristically through suggestion rather than explicit development to illuminate a late-Victorian world, with the subdued elegiac sense of female lives wasted in the service of an outmoded patriarchal order, although the story's ironic surface is restrained comedy. The meaning is achieved most of all through the atmosphere, built up by the accumulation of small strokes, none of which seems more than a shrewdly observed realistic detail. Mansfield also manipulates time masterfully: she makes particularly effective use of the unobtrusive flashback, where we find ourselves in an earlier phase of the action without quite knowing how we got there but fully aware of its relevance to the total action and atmosphere.

The Daughters of the Late Colonel

I

The week after was one of the busiest weeks of their lives. Even when they went to bed it was only their bodies that lay down and rested; their minds went on, thinking things out, talking things over, wondering, deciding, trying to remember where . . .

Constantia lay like a statue, her hands by her sides, her feet just overlapping each other, the sheet up to her chin. She stared at the ceiling.

'Do you think father would mind if we gave his top-hat to the porter?'

'The porter?' snapped Josephine. 'Why ever the porter? What a very extraordinary idea!'

'Because,' said Constantia slowly, 'he must often have to go to funerals. And I noticed at—at the cemetery that he only had a bowler.' She paused. 'I thought then how very much he'd appreciate a top-hat. We ought to give him a present, too. He was always very nice to father.'

'But,' cried Josephine, flouncing on her pillow and staring across the dark at Constantia, 'father's head!' And suddenly, for one awful moment, she nearly giggled. Not, of course, that she felt in the least like giggling. It must have been habit. Years ago, when they had stayed awake at night talking, their beds had simply heaved. And now the porter's head, disappearing, popped out, like a candle, under father's hat. . . . The giggle mounted, mounted; she clenched her hands; she fought it down; she frowned fiercely at the dark and said 'Remember' terribly sternly.

'We can decide tomorrow,' she sighed.

Constantia had noticed nothing; she sighed.

'Do you think we ought to have our dressing-gowns dyed as well?'

'Black?' almost shrieked Josephine.

'Well, what else?' said Constantia. 'I was thinking—it doesn't seem quite sincere, in a way, to wear black out of doors and when we're fully dressed, and then when we're at home—'

'But nobody sees us,' said Josephine. She gave the bedclothes such a twitch that both her feet became uncovered and she had to creep up the pillows to get them well under again.

'Kate does,' said Constantia. 'And the postman very well might.'

Josephine thought of her dark-red slippers, which matched her dressing-gown, and of Constantia's favourite indefinite green ones which went with hers. Black! Two black dressing-gowns and two pairs of black woolly slippers, creeping off to the bathroom like black cats.

'I don't think it's absolutely necessary,' said she.

Silence. Then Constantia said, 'We shall have to post the papers with the notice in them tomorrow to catch the Ceylon mail. . . . How many letters have we had up till now?'

'Twenty-three.'

Josephine had replied to them all, and twenty-three times when she came to 'We miss our dear father so much' she had broken down and had to use her handkerchief, and on some of them even to soak up a very light-blue tear with an edge of blotting-paper. Strange! She couldn't have put it on—but twenty-three times. Even now, though, when she said over to herself sadly 'We miss our dear father so much,' she could have cried if she'd wanted to.

'Have you got enough stamps?' came from Constantia.

'Oh, how can I tell?' said Josephine crossly. 'What's the good of asking me that now?'

'I was just wondering,' said Constantia mildly.

Silence again. There came a little rustle, a scurry, a hop.

'A mouse,' said Constantia.

'It can't be a mouse because there aren't any crumbs,' said Josephine.

'But it doesn't know there aren't,' said Constantia.

A spasm of pity squeezed her heart. Poor little thing! She wished she'd left a tiny piece of biscuit on the dressing-table. It was awful to think of it not finding anything. What would it do?

'I can't think how they manage to live at all,' she said slowly.

'Who?' demanded Josephine.

And Constantia said more loudly than she meant to, 'Mice.'

Josephine was furious. 'Oh, what nonsense, Con!' she said. 'What have mice got to do with it? You're asleep.'

'I don't think I am,' said Constantia. She shut her eyes to make sure. She was.

Josephine arched her spine, pulled up her knees, folded her arms so that her fists came under her ears, and pressed her cheek hard against the pillow.

II

Another thing which complicated matters was they had Nurse Andrews staying on with them that week. It was their own fault; they had asked her. It was Josephine's idea. On the morning—well, on the last morning, when the doctor had gone, Josephine had said to Constantia, 'Don't you think it would be rather nice if we asked Nurse Andrews to stay on for a week as our guest?'

'Very nice,' said Constantia.

'I thought,' went on Josephine quickly, 'I should just say this afternoon, after I've paid her, "My sister and I would be very pleased, after all you've done for us, Nurse Andrews, if you would stay on for a week as our guest." I'd have to put that in about being our guest in case—'

'Oh, but she could hardly expect to be paid!' cried Constantia.

'One never knows,' said Josephine sagely.

Nurse Andrews had, of course, jumped at the idea. But it was a bother. It meant they had to have regular sit-down meals at the proper times, whereas if they'd been alone they could just have asked Kate if she wouldn't have minded bringing them a tray wherever they were. And meal-times now that the strain was over were rather a trial.

Nurse Andrews was simply fearful about butter. Really they couldn't help feeling that about butter, at least, she took advantage of their kindness. And she had that maddening habit of asking for just an inch more bread to finish what she had on her plate, and then, at the last mouthful, absent-mindedly—of course it wasn't absent-mindedly—taking another helping. Josephine got very red when this happened, and she fastened her small, bead-like eyes on the tablecloth as if she saw a minute strange insect creeping through the web of it. But Constantia's long, pale face lengthened and set, and she gazed away—away—far over the desert, to where that line of camels unwound like a thread of wool. . . .

'When I was with Lady Tukes,' said Nurse Andrews, 'she had such a dainty little contrayvance for the buttah. It was a silvah cupid balanced on the—on the bordah of a glass dish, holding a tayny fork. And when you wanted some buttah you simply pressed his foot and he bent down and speared you a piece. It was quite a gayme.'

Josephine could hardly bear that. But 'I think those things are very extravagant' was all she said.

'But whey?' asked Nurse Andrews, beaming through her eyeglasses. 'No one, surely, would take more buttah than one wanted—would one?'

'Ring, Con,' cried Josephine. She couldn't trust herself to reply.

And proud young Kate, the enchanted princess, came in to see what the old tabbies wanted now. She snatched away their plates of mock something or other and slapped down a white terrified blancmange.[1]

'Jam, please, Kate,' said Josephine kindly.

Kate knelt and burst open the sideboard, lifted the lid of the jam-pot, saw it was empty, put it on the table, and stalked off.

'I'm afraid,' said Nurse Andrews a moment later, 'there isn't any.'

'Oh, what a bother!' said Josephine. She bit her lip. 'What had we better do?'

Constantia looked dubious. 'We can't disturb Kate again,' she said softly.

Nurse Andrews waited, smiling at them both. Her eyes wandered, spying at everything behind her eyeglasses. Constantia in despair went back to her camels. Josephine frowned heavily—concentrated. If it hadn't been for this idiotic woman she and Con would, of course, have eaten their blancmange without. Suddenly the idea came.

'I know,' she said. 'Marmalade. There's some marmalade in the sideboard. Get it, Con.'

'I hope,' laughed Nurse Andrews—and her laugh was like a spoon tinkling against a medicine glass—'I hope it's not very bittah marmalayde.'

III

But, after all, it was not long now, and then she'd be gone for good. And there was no getting over the fact that she had been very kind to father. She had nursed him day and night at the end. Indeed, both Constantia and Josephine felt privately she had rather overdone the not leaving him at the very last. For when they had gone in to say goodbye Nurse Andrews had sat beside

---

1. A gelatinous dessert.

his bed the whole time, holding his wrist and pretending to look at her watch. It couldn't have been necessary. It was so tactless, too. Supposing father had wanted to say something—something private to them. Not that he had. Oh, far from it! He lay there, purple, a dark, angry purple in the face, and never even looked at them when they came in. Then, as they were standing there, wondering what to do, he had suddenly opened one eye. Oh, what a difference it would have made, what a difference to their memory of him, how much easier to tell people about it, if he had only opened both! But no—one eye only. It glared at them a moment and then . . . went out.

IV

It had made it very awkward for them when Mr Farolles, of St John's, called the same afternoon.

'The end was quite peaceful, I trust?' were the first words he said as he glided towards them through the dark drawing-room.

'Quite,' said Josephine faintly. They both hung their heads. Both of them felt certain that eye wasn't at all a peaceful eye.

'Won't you sit down?' said Josephine.

'Thank you, Miss Pinner,' said Mr Farolles gratefully. He folded his coattails and began to lower himself into father's armchair, but just as he touched it he almost sprang up and slid into the next chair instead.

He coughed. Josephine clasped her hands; Constantia looked vague.

'I want you to feel, Miss Pinner,' said Mr Farolles, 'and you, Miss Constantia, that I'm trying to be helpful. I want to be helpful to you both, if you will let me. These are the times,' said Mr Farolles, very simply and earnestly, 'when God means us to be helpful to one another.'

'Thank you very much, Mr Farolles,' said Josephine and Constantia.

'Not at all,' said Mr Farolles gently. He drew his kid gloves through his fingers and leaned forward. 'And if either of you would like a little Communion, either or both of you, here and now, you have only to tell me. A little Communion is often very help—a great comfort,' he added tenderly.

But the idea of a little Communion terrified them. What! In the drawing room by themselves—with no—no altar or anything! The piano would be much too high, thought Constantia, and Mr Farolles could not possibly lean over it with the chalice. And Kate would be sure to come bursting in and interrupt them, thought Josephine. And supposing the bell rang in the middle? It might be somebody important—about their mourning. Would they get up reverently and go out, or would they have to wait . . . in torture?

'Perhaps you will send round a note by your good Kate if you would care for it later,' said Mr Farolles.

'Oh yes, thank you very much!' they both said.

Mr Farolles got up and took his black straw hat from the round table.

'And about the funeral,' he said softly. 'I may arrange that—as your dear father's old friend and yours, Miss Pinner—and Miss Constantia?'

Josephine and Constantia got up too.

'I should like it to be quite simple,' said Josephine firmly, 'and not too expensive. At the same time, I should like—'

'A good one that will last,' thought dreamy Constantia, as if Josephine were buying a nightgown. But of course Josephine didn't say that. 'One suitable to our father's position.' She was very nervous.

'I'll run round to our good friend Mr Knight,' said Mr Farolles soothingly. 'I will ask him to come and see you. I am sure you will find him very helpful indeed.'

V

Well, at any rate, all that part of it was over, though neither of them could possibly believe that father was never coming back. Josephine had had a moment of absolute terror at the cemetery, while the coffin was lowered, to think that she and Constantia had done this thing without asking his permission. What would father say when he found out? For he was bound to find out sooner or later. He always did. 'Buried. You two girls had me buried?' She heard his stick thumping. Oh, what would they say? What possible excuse could they make? It sounded such an appallingly heartless thing to do. Such a wicked advantage to take of a person because he happened to be helpless at the moment. The other people seemed to treat it all as a matter of course. They were strangers; they couldn't be expected to understand that father was the very last person for such a thing to happen to. No, the entire blame for it all would fall on her and Constantia. And the expense, she thought, stepping into the tight-buttoned cab. When she had to show him the bills. What would he say then?

She heard him absolutely roaring, 'And do you expect me to pay for this gimcrack excursion of yours?'

'Oh,' groaned poor Josephine aloud, 'we shouldn't have done it, Con!'

And Constantia, pale as a lemon in all that blackness, said in a frightened whisper, 'Done what, Jug?'

'Let them bu-bury father like that,' said Josephine, breaking down and crying into her new, queer-smelling mourning handkerchief.

'But what else could we have done?' asked Constantia wonderingly. 'We couldn't have kept him unburied. At any rate, not in a flat that size.'

Josephine blew her nose; the cab was dreadfully stuffy.

'I don't know,' she said forlornly. 'It is all so dreadful. I feel we ought to have tried to, just for a time at least. To make perfectly sure. One thing's certain'—and her tears sprang out again—'father will never forgive us for this—never!'

VI

Father would never forgive them. That was what they felt more than ever when, two mornings later, they went into his room to go through his things. They had discussed it quite calmly. It was even down on Josephine's list of things to be done. Go through father's things and settle about them. But that was a very different matter from saying after breakfast:

'Well, are you ready, Con?'

'Yes, Jug—when you are.'

'Then I think we'd better get it over.'

It was dark in the hall. It had been a rule for years never to disturb father in the morning, whatever happened. And now they were going to open the door without knocking even . . . . Constantia's eyes were enormous at the idea; Josephine felt weak in the knees.

'You—you go first,' she gasped, pushing Constantia.

But Constantia said, as she always had said on those occasions, 'No, Jug, that's not fair. You're the eldest.'

Josephine was just going to say—what at other times she wouldn't have owned to for the world—what she kept for her very last weapon, 'But you're the tallest,' when they noticed that the kitchen door was open, and there stood Kate. . . .

'Very stiff,' said Josephine, grasping the door-handle and doing her best to turn it. As if anything ever deceived Kate!

It couldn't be helped. That girl was . . . Then the door was shut behind them, but—but they weren't in father's room at all. They might have suddenly walked through the wall by mistake into a different flat altogether. Was the door just behind them? They were too frightened to look. Josephine knew that if it was it was holding itself tight shut; Constantia felt that, like the doors in dreams, it hadn't any handle at all. It was the coldness which made it so awful. Or the whiteness—which? Everything was covered. The blinds were down, a cloth hung over the mirror, a sheet hid the bed, a huge fan of white paper filled the fireplace. Constantia timidly put out her hand; she almost expected a snowflake to fall. Josephine felt a queer tingling in her nose, as if her nose was freezing. Then a cab klop-klopped over the cobbles below, and the quiet seemed to shake into little pieces.

'I had better pull up a blind,' said Josephine bravely.

'Yes, it might be a good idea,' whispered Constantia.

They only gave the blind a touch, but it flew up and the cord flew after, rolling round the blind-stick, and the little tassel tapped as if trying to get free. That was too much for Constantia.

'Don't you think—don't you think we might put it off for another day?' she whispered.

'Why?' snapped Josephine, feeling, as usual, much better now that she knew for certain that Constantia was terrified. 'It's got to be done. But I do wish you wouldn't whisper, Con.'

'I didn't know I was whispering,' whispered Constantia.

'And why do you keep on staring at the bed?' said Josephine, raising her voice almost defiantly. 'There's nothing on the bed.'

'Oh, Jug, don't say so!' said poor Connie. 'At any rate, not so loudly.'

Josephine felt herself that she had gone too far. She took a wide swerve over to the chest of drawers, put out her hand, but quickly drew it back again.

'Connie!' she gasped, and she wheeled round and leaned with her back against the chest of drawers.

'Oh, Jug—what?'

Josephine could only glare. She had the most extraordinary feeling that she had just escaped something simply awful. But how could she explain to Constantia that father was in the chest of drawers? He was in the top drawer with his handkerchiefs and neckties, or in the next with his shirts and pyjamas, or in the lowest of all with his suits. He was watching there, hidden away—just behind the door-handle—ready to spring.

She pulled a funny old-fashioned face at Constantia, just as she used to in the old days when she was going to cry.

'I can't open,' she nearly wailed.

'No, don't, Jug,' whispered Constantia earnestly. 'It's much better not to. Don't let's open anything. At any rate, not for a long time.'

'But—but it seems so weak,' said Josephine, breaking down.

'But why not be weak for once, Jug?' argued Constantia, whispering quite fiercely. 'If it is weak.' And her pale stare flew from the locked writing-table—so safe—to the huge glittering wardrobe, and she began to breathe in a queer, panting way. 'Why shouldn't we be weak for once in our lives, Jug? It's quite excusable. Let's be weak—be weak, Jug. It's much nicer to be weak than to be strong.'

And then she did one of those amazingly bold things that she'd done about twice before in their lives: she marched over to the wardrobe, turned the key, and took it out of the lock. Took it out of the lock and held it up to Josephine, showing Josephine by her extraordinary smile that she knew what she'd done—she'd risked deliberately father being in there among his overcoats.

If the huge wardrobe had lurched forward, had crashed down on Constantia, Josephine wouldn't have been surprised. On the contrary, she would have thought it the only suitable thing to happen. But nothing happened. Only the room seemed quieter than ever, and bigger flakes of cold air fell on Josephine's shoulders and knees. She began to shiver.

'Come, Jug,' said Constantia, still with that awful callous smile; and Josephine followed just as she had that last time, when Constantia had pushed Benny into the round pond.

VII

But the strain told on them when they were back in the dining-room. They sat down, very shaky, and looked at each other.

'I don't feel I can settle to anything,' said Josephine, 'until I've had something. Do you think we could ask Kate for two cups of hot water?'

'I really don't see why we shouldn't,' said Constantia carefully. She was quite normal again. 'I won't ring. I'll go to the kitchen door and ask her.'

'Yes, do,' said Josephine, sinking down into a chair. 'Tell her, just two cups, Con, nothing else—on a tray.'

'She needn't even put the jug on, need she?' said Constantia, as though Kate might very well complain if the jug had been there.

'Oh, no, certainly not! The jug's not at all necessary. She can pour it direct out of the kettle,' cried Josephine, feeling that would be a labour-saving indeed.

Their cold lips quivered at the greenish brims. Josephine curved her small red hands round the cup; Constantia sat up and blew on the wavy stream, making it flutter from one side to the other.

'Speaking of Benny,' said Josephine.

And though Benny hadn't been mentioned Constantia immediately looked as though he had.

'He'll expect us to send him something of father's, of course. But it's so difficult to know what to send to Ceylon.'

'You mean things get unstuck so on the voyage,' murmured Constantia.

'No, lost,' said Josephine sharply. 'You know there's no post. Only runners.'

Both paused to watch a black man in white linen drawers running through the pale fields for dear life, with a large brown-paper parcel in his hands. Josephine's black man was tiny; he scurried along glistening like an ant. But there was something blind and tireless about Constantia's tall, thin fellow, which made him, she decided, a very unpleasant person indeed . . . . On the veranda, dressed all in white and wearing a cork helmet, stood Benny. His right hand shook up and down, as father's did when he was impatient. And behind him, not in the least interested, sat Hilda, the unknown sister-in-law. She swung in a cane rocker and flicked over the leaves of the *Tatler*.

'I think his watch would be the most suitable present,' said Josephine. Constantia looked up; she seemed surprised.

'Oh, would you trust a gold watch to a native?'

'But of course I'd disguise it,' said Josephine. 'No one would know it was a watch.' She liked the idea of having to make a parcel such a curious shape that no one could possibly guess what it was. She even thought for a moment of hiding the watch in a narrow cardboard corset-box that she'd kept by her for a long time, waiting for it to come in for something. It was such beautiful firm cardboard. But, no, it wouldn't be appropriate for this occasion. It had lettering on it: *Medium Women's 28. Extra Firm Busks*. It would be almost too much of a surprise for Benny to open that and find father's watch inside.

'And of course it isn't as though it would be going—ticking, I mean,' said Constantia, who was still thinking of the native love of jewelery. 'At least,' she added, 'it would be very strange if after all that time it was.'

VIII

Josephine made no reply. She had flown off on one of her tangents. She had suddenly thought of Cyril. Wasn't it more usual for the only grandson to have the watch? And then dear Cyril was so appreciative and a gold watch meant so much to a young man. Benny, in all probability, had quite got out of the habit of watches; men so seldom wore waistcoats in those hot climates. Whereas Cyril in London wore them from year's end to year's end. And it would be so nice for her and Constantia, when he came to tea, to know it was there. 'I see you've got on grandfather's watch, Cyril.' It would be somehow so satisfactory.

Dear boy! What a blow his sweet, sympathetic little note had been! Of course they quite understood; but it was most unfortunate.

'It would have been such a point, having him,' said Josephine.

'And he would have enjoyed it so,' said Constantia, not thinking what she was saying.

However, as soon as he got back he was coming to tea with his aunties. Cyril to tea was one of their rare treats.

'Now, Cyril, you mustn't be frightened of our cakes. Your Auntie Con and I bought them at Buszard's this morning. We know what a man's appetite is. So don't be ashamed of making a good tea.'

Josephine cut recklessly into the rich dark cake that stood for her winter gloves or the soling and heeling of Constantia's only respectable shoes. But Cyril was most unmanlike in appetite.

'I say, Aunt Josephine, I simply can't. I've only just had lunch, you know.'

'Oh, Cyril, that can't be true! It's after four,' cried Josephine. Constantia sat with her knife poised over the chocolate-roll.

'It is, all the same,' said Cyril. 'I had to meet a man at Victoria,[2] and he kept me hanging about till . . . there was only time to get lunch and to come on here. And he gave me—phew'—Cyril put his hand to his forehead—'a terrific blow-out,'[3] he said.

---

2. London railroad station, connecting with the Channel ports. 3. Feast.

It was disappointing—today of all days. But still he couldn't be expected to know.

'But you'll have a meringue, won't you, Cyril?' said Aunt Josephine. 'These meringues were bought specially for you. Your dear father was so fond of them. We were sure you are, too.'

'I *am*, Aunt Josephine,' cried Cyril ardently. 'Do you mind if I take half to begin with?'

'Not at all, dear boy; but we mustn't let you off with that.'

'Is your dear father still so fond of meringues?' asked Auntie Con gently. She winced faintly as she broke through the shell of hers.

'Well, I don't quite know, Auntie Con,' said Cyril breezily.

At that they both looked up.

'Don't know?' almost snapped Josephine. 'Don't know a thing like that about your own father, Cyril?'

'Surely,' said Auntie Con softly.

Cyril tried to laugh it off. 'Oh, well,' he said, 'it's such a long time since—' He faltered. He stopped. Their faces were too much for him.

'Even *so*,' said Josephine.

And Auntie Con looked.

Cyril put down his teacup. 'Wait a bit,' he cried. 'Wait a bit, Aunt Josephine. What am I thinking of?'

He looked up. They were beginning to brighten. Cyril slapped his knee.

'Of course,' he said, 'it was meringues. How could I have forgotten? Yes, Aunt Josephine, you're perfectly right. Father's most frightfully keen on meringues.'

They didn't only beam. Aunt Josephine went scarlet with pleasure; Auntie Con gave a deep, deep sigh.

'And now, Cyril, you must come and see father,' said Josephine. 'He knows you were coming today.'

'Right,' said Cyril, very firmly and heartily. He got up from his chair; suddenly he glanced at the clock.

'I say, Auntie Con, isn't your clock a bit slow? I've got to meet a man at—at Paddington[4] just after five. I'm afraid I shan't be able to stay very long with grandfather.'

'Oh, he won't expect you to stay *very* long!' said Aunt Josephine.

Constantia was still gazing at the clock. She couldn't make up her mind if it was fast or slow. It was one or the other, she felt almost certain of that. At any rate, it had been.

Cyril still lingered. 'Aren't you coming along, Auntie Con?'

'Of course,' said Josephine, 'we shall all go. Come on, Con.'

IX

They knocked at the door, and Cyril followed his aunts into grandfather's hot, sweetish room.

'Come on,' said Grandfather Pinner. 'Don't hang about. What is it? What've you been up to?'

He was sitting in front of a roaring fire, clasping his stick. He had a thick

4. London railroad station, serving the west of England and Wales.

2342 / <small>KATHERINE MANSFIELD</small>

rug over his knees. On his lap there lay a beautiful pale yellow silk handkerchief.

'It's Cyril, father,' said Josephine shyly. And she took Cyril's hand and led him forward.

'Good afternoon, grandfather,' said Cyril, trying to take his hand out of Aunt Josephine's. Grandfather Pinner shot his eyes at Cyril in the way he was famous for. Where was Auntie Con? She stood on the other side of Aunt Josephine; her long arms hung down in front of her; her hands were clasped. She never took her eyes off grandfather.

'Well,' said Grandfather Pinner, beginning to thump, 'what have you got to tell me?'

What had he, what had he got to tell him? Cyril felt himself smiling like a perfect imbecile. The room was stifling, too.

But Aunt Josephine came to his rescue. She cried brightly, 'Cyril says his father is still very fond of meringues, father dear.'

'Eh?' said Grandfather Pinner, curving his hand like a purple meringue-shell over one ear.

Josephine repeated, 'Cyril says his father is still very fond of meringues.'

'Can't hear,' said old Colonel Pinner. And he waved Josephine away with his stick, then pointed with his stick to Cyril. 'Tell me what she's trying to say,' he said.

(My God!) 'Must I?' said Cyril, blushing and staring at Aunt Josephine.

'Do, dear,' she smiled. 'It will please him so much.'

'Come on, out with it!' cried Colonel Pinner testily, beginning to thump again.

And Cyril leaned forward and yelled, 'Father's still very fond of meringues.'

At that Grandfather Pinner jumped as though he had been shot.

'Don't shout!' he cried. 'What's the matter with the boy? Meringues! What about 'em?'

'Oh, Aunt Josephine, must we go on?' groaned Cyril desperately.

'It's quite all right, dear boy,' said Aunt Josephine, as though he and she were at the dentist's together. 'He'll understand in a minute.' And she whispered to Cyril, 'He's getting a bit deaf, you know.' Then she leaned forward and really bawled at Grandfather Pinner, 'Cyril only wanted to tell you, father dear, that his father is still very fond of meringues.'

Colonel Pinner heard that time, heard and brooded, looking Cyril up and down.

'What an esstrordinary thing!' said old Grandfather Pinner. 'What an esstrordinary thing to come all this way here to tell me!'

And Cyril felt it *was*.

'Yes, I shall send Cyril the watch,' said Josephine.

'That would be very nice,' said Constantia. 'I seem to remember last time he came there was some little trouble about the time.'

<h1 style="text-align:center">X</h1>

They were interrupted by Kate bursting through the door in her usual fashion, as though she had discovered some secret panel in the wall.

'Fried or boiled?' asked the bold voice.

Fried or boiled? Josephine and Constantia were quite bewildered for the moment. They could hardly take it in.

'Fried or boiled what, Kate?' asked Josephine, trying to begin to concentrate. Kate gave a loud sniff. 'Fish.'

'Well, why didn't you say so immediately?' Josephine reproached her gently. 'How could you expect us to understand, Kate? There are a great many things in this world, you know, which are fried or boiled.' And after such a display of courage she said quite brightly to Constantia, 'Which do you prefer, Con?'

'I think it might be nice to have it fried,' said Constantia. 'On the other hand, of course boiled fish is very nice. I think I prefer both equally well . . . Unless you . . . In that case—'

'I shall fry it,' said Kate, and she bounced back, leaving their door open and slamming the door of her kitchen.

Josephine gazed at Constantia; she raised her pale eyebrows until they rippled away into her pale hair. She got up. She said in a very lofty, imposing way, 'Do you mind following me into the drawing-room, Constantia? I've something of great importance to discuss with you.'

For it was always to the drawing-room they retired when they wanted to talk over Kate.

Josephine closed the door meaningly. 'Sit down, Constantia,' she said, still very grand. She might have been receiving Constantia for the first time. And Con looked round vaguely for a chair, as though she felt indeed quite a stranger.

'Now the question is,' said Josephine, bending forward, 'whether we shall keep her or not.'

'That is the question,' agreed Constantia.

'And this time,' said Josephine firmly, 'we must come to a definite decision.'

Constantia looked for a moment as though she might begin going over all the other times, but she pulled herself together and said, 'Yes, Jug.'

'You see, Con,' explained Josephine, 'everything is so changed now.' Constantia looked up quickly. 'I mean,' went on Josephine, 'we're not dependent on Kate as we were.' And she blushed faintly. 'There's not father to cook for.'

'That is perfectly true,' agreed Constantia. 'Father certainly doesn't want any cooking now, whatever else—'

Josephine broke in sharply, 'You're not sleepy, are you, Con?'

'Sleepy, Jug?' Constantia was wide-eyed.

'Well, concentrate more,' said Josephine sharply, and she returned to the subject. 'What it comes to is, if we did'—and this she barely breathed, glancing at the door—'give Kate notice'—she raised her voice again—'we could manage our own food.'

'Why not?' cried Constantia. She couldn't help smiling. The idea was so exciting. She clasped her hands. 'What should we live on, Jug?'

'Oh, eggs in various forms!' said Jug, lofty again. 'And, besides, there are all the cooked foods.'

'But I've always heard,' said Constantia, 'they are considered so very expensive.'

'Not if one buys them in moderation,' said Josephine. But she tore herself away from this fascinating bypath and dragged Constantia after her.

'What we've got to decide now, however, is whether we really do trust Kate or not.'

Constantia leaned back. Her flat little laugh flew from her lips.

'Isn't it curious, Jug,' said she, 'that just on this one subject I've never been able to quite make up my mind?'

XI

She never had. The whole difficulty was to prove anything. How did one prove things, how could one? Suppose Kate had stood in front of her and deliberately made a face. Mightn't she very well have been in pain? Wasn't it impossible, at any rate, to ask Kate if she was making a face at her? If Kate answered 'No'—and of course she would say 'No'—what a position! How undignified! Then again Constantia suspected, she was almost certain that Kate went to her chest of drawers when she and Josephine were out, not to take things but to spy. Many times she had come back to find her amethyst cross in the most unlikely places, under her lace ties or on top of her evening Bertha.[5] More than once she had laid a trap for Kate. She had arranged things in a special order and then called Josephine to witness.

'You see, Jug?'

'Quite, Con.'

'Now we shall be able to tell.'

But, oh dear, when she did go to look, she was as far off from a proof as ever! If anything was displaced, it might so very well have happened as she closed the drawer; a jolt might have done it so easily.

'You come, Jug, and decide. I really can't. It's too difficult.'

But after a pause and a long glare Josephine would sigh. 'Now you've put the doubt into my mind, Con, I'm sure I can't tell myself.'

'Well, we can't postpone it again,' said Josephine. 'If we postpone it this time—'

XII

But at that moment in the street below a barrel-organ struck up. Josephine and Constantia sprang to their feet together.

'Run, Con,' said Josephine. 'Run quickly. There's sixpence on the—'

Then they remembered. It didn't matter. They would never have to stop the organ-grinder again. Never again would she and Constantia be told to make that monkey take his noise somewhere else. Never would sound that loud, strange bellow when father thought they were not hurrying enough. The organ-grinder might play there all day and the stick would not thump.

It never will thump again,
It never will thump again,

played the barrel-organ.

What was Constantia thinking? She had such a strange smile; she looked different. She couldn't be going to cry.

'Jug, Jug,' said Constantia softly, pressing her hands together. 'Do you know what day it is? It's Saturday. It's a week today, a whole week.'

A week since father died,
A week since father died,

5. Detachable lace collar for low-necked dresses.

cried the barrel-organ. And Josephine, too, forgot to be practical and sensible; she smiled faintly, strangely. On the Indian carpet there fell a square of sunlight, pale red; it came and went and came—and stayed, deepened—until it shone almost golden.

'The sun's out,' said Josephine, as though it really mattered.

A perfect fountain of bubbling notes shook from the barrel-organ, round, bright notes, carelessly scattered.

Constantia lifted her big, cold hands as if to catch them, and then her hands fell again. She walked over to the mantelpiece to her favourite Buddha. And the stone and gilt image, whose smile always gave her such a queer feeling, almost a pain and yet a pleasant pain, seemed today to be more than smiling. He knew something; he had a secret. 'I know something that you don't know,' said her Buddha. Oh, what was it, what could it be? And yet she had always felt there was . . . something.

The sunlight pressed through the windows, thieved its way in, flashed its light over the furniture and the photographs. Josephine watched it. When it came to mother's photograph, the enlargement over the piano, it lingered as though puzzled to find so little remained of mother, except the ear-rings shaped like tiny pagodas and a black feather boa. Why did the photographs of dead people always fade so? wondered Josephine. As soon as a person was dead their photograph died too. But, of course, this one of mother was very old. It was thirty-five years old. Josephine remembered standing on a chair and pointing out that feather boa to Constantia and telling her that it was a snake that had killed their mother in Ceylon . . . . Would everything have been different if mother hadn't died? She didn't see why. Aunt Florence had lived with them until they had left school, and they had moved three times and had their yearly holiday and . . . and there'd been changes of servants, of course.

Some little sparrows, young sparrows they sounded, chirped on the window-ledge. *Yeep—eyeep—yeep.* But Josephine felt they were not sparrows, not on the window-ledge. It was inside her, that queer little crying noise. *Yeep—eyeep—yeep.* Ah, what was it crying, so weak and forlorn?

If mother had lived, might they have married? But there had been nobody for them to marry. There had been father's Anglo-Indian friends before he quarreled with them. But after that she and Constantia never met a single man except clergymen. How did one meet men? Or even if they'd met them, how could they have got to know men well enough to be more than strangers? One read of people having adventures, being followed, and so on. But nobody had ever followed Constantia and her. Oh yes, there had been one year at Eastbourne[6] a mysterious man at their boarding-house who had put a note on the jug of hot water outside their bedroom door! But by the time Connie had found it the steam had made the writing too faint to read; they couldn't even make out to which of them it was addressed. And he had left next day. And that was all. The rest had been looking after father and at the same time keeping out of father's way. But now? But now? The thieving sun touched Josephine gently. She lifted her face. She was drawn over to the window by gentle beams . . . .

Until the barrel-organ stopped playing Constantia stayed before the Buddha, wondering, but not as usual, not vaguely. This time her wonder was like longing. She remembered the times she had come in here, crept out of bed in

6. Seaside resort on Sussex coast.

her nightgown when the moon was full, and lain on the floor with her arms outstretched, as though she was crucified. Why? The big, pale moon had made her do it. The horrible dancing figures on the carved screen had leered at her and she hadn't minded. She remembered too how, whenever they were at the seaside, she had gone off by herself and got as close to the sea as she could, and sung something, something she had made up, while she gazed all over that restless water. There had been this other life, running out, bringing things home in bags, getting things on approval, discussing them with Jug, and taking them back to get more things on approval, and arranging father's trays and trying not to annoy father. But it all seemed to have happened in a kind of tunnel. It wasn't real. It was only when she came out of the tunnel into the moonlight or by the sea or into a thunderstorm that she really felt herself. What did it mean? What was it she was always wanting? What did it all lead to? Now? Now?

She turned away from the Buddha with one of her vague gestures. She went over to where Josephine was standing. She wanted to say something to Josephine, something frightfully important, about—about the future and what . . .

'Don't you think perhaps—' she began.

But Josephine interrupted her. 'I was wondering if now—' she murmured. They stopped; they waited for each either.

'Go on, Con,' said Josephine.

'No, no, Jug; after you,' said Constantia.

'No, say what you were going to say. You began,' said Josephine.

'I . . . I'd rather hear what you were going to say first,' said Constantia.

'Don't be absurd, Con.'

'Really, Jug.'

'Connie!'

'Oh, Jug!'

A pause. Then Constantia said faintly, 'I can't say what I was going to say, Jug, because I've forgotten what it was . . . that I was going to say.'

Josephine was silent for a moment. She stared at a big cloud where the sun had been. Then she replied shortly, 'I've forgotten too.'

1920   1922

The Garden Party[1]

And after all the weather was ideal. They could not have had a more perfect day for a garden party if they had ordered it. Windless, warm, the sky without a cloud. Only the blue was veiled with a haze of light gold, as it is sometimes in early summer. The gardener had been up since dawn, mowing the lawns and sweeping them, until the grass and the dark flat rosettes where the daisy plants had been seemed to shine. As for the roses, you could not help feeling they understood that roses are the only flowers that impress people at garden parties; the only flowers that everybody is certain of knowing. Hundreds, yes, literally hundreds, had come out in a single night; the green bushes bowed down as though they had been visited by archangels.

---

1. This story draws on an incident from Mansfield's life. In March 1907 her mother gave a garden party in their Wellington house, but a street accident befell a neighbor living in a poor quarter nearby.

Breakfast was not yet over before the men came to put up the marquee.
'Where do you want the marquee put, mother?'

'My dear child, it's no use asking me. I'm determined to leave everything to you children this year. Forget I am your mother. Treat me as an honoured guest.'

But Meg could not possibly go and supervise the men. She had washed her hair before breakfast, and she sat drinking her coffee in a green turban, with a dark wet curl stamped on each cheek. Jose, the butterfly, always came down in a silk petticoat and a kimono jacket.

'You'll have to go, Laura; you're the artistic one.'

Away Laura flew, still holding her piece of bread-and-butter. It's so delicious to have an excuse for eating out of doors, and besides, she loved having to arrange things; she always felt she could do it so much better than anybody else.

Four men in their shirt-sleeves stood grouped together on the garden path. They carried staves covered with rolls of canvas, and they had big tool-bags slung on their backs. They looked impressive. Laura wished now that she had not got the bread-and-butter, but there was nowhere to put it, and she couldn't possibly throw it away. She blushed and tried to look severe and even a little bit short-sighted as she came up to them.

'Good morning,' she said, copying her mother's voice. But that sounded so fearfully affected that she was ashamed, and stammered like a little girl, 'Oh—er—have you come—is it about the marquee?'

'That's right, miss,' said the tallest of the men, a lanky, freckled fellow, and he shifted his tool-bag, knocked back his straw hat and smiled down at her. 'That's about it.'

His smile was so easy, so friendly that Laura recovered. What nice eyes he had, small, but such a dark blue! And now she looked at the others, they were smiling too. 'Cheer up, we won't bite,' their smile seemed to say. How very nice workmen were! And what a beautiful morning! She mustn't mention the morning; she must be business-like. The marquee.

'Well, what about the lily-lawn? Would that do?'

And she pointed to the lily-lawn with the hand that didn't hold the bread-and-butter. They turned, they stared in the direction. A little fat chap thrust out his under-lip, and the tall fellow frowned.

'I don't fancy it,' said he. 'Not conspicuous enough. You see, with a thing like a marquee,' and he turned to Laura in his easy way, 'you want to put it somewhere where it'll give you a bang slap in the eye, if you follow me.'

Laura's upbringing made her wonder for a moment whether it was quite respectful of a workman to talk to her of bangs slap in the eye. But she did quite follow him.

'A corner of the tennis-court,' she suggested. 'But the band's going to be in one corner.'

'H'm, going to have a band, are you?' said another of the workmen. He was pale. He had a haggard look as his dark eyes scanned the tennis-court. What was he thinking?

'Only a very small band,' said Laura gently. Perhaps he wouldn't mind so much if the band was quite small. But the tall fellow interrupted.

'Look here, miss, that's the place. Against those trees. Over there. That'll do fine.'

Against the karakas. Then the karaka-trees would be hidden. And they were so lovely, with their broad, gleaming leaves, and their clusters of yellow fruit. They were like trees you imagined growing on a desert island, proud, solitary, lifting their leaves and fruits to the sun in a kind of silent splendour. Must they be hidden by a marquee?

They must. Already the men had shouldered their staves and were making for the place. Only the tall fellow was left. He bent down, pinched a sprig of lavender, put his thumb and forefinger to his nose and snuffed up the smell. When Laura saw that gesture she forgot all about the karakas in her wonder at him caring for things like that—caring for the smell of lavender. How many men that she knew would have done such a thing? Oh, how extraordinarily nice workmen were, she thought. Why couldn't she have workmen for friends rather than the silly boys she danced with and who came to Sunday night supper? She would get on much better with men like these.

It's all the fault, she decided, as the tall fellow drew something on the back of an envelope, something that was to be looped up or left to hang, of these absurd class distinctions. Well, for her part, she didn't feel them. Not a bit, not an atom . . . And now there came the chock-chock of wooden hammers. Some one whistled, some one sang out, 'Are you right there, matey?' 'Matey!' The friendliness of it, the—the—Just to prove how happy she was, just to show the tall fellow how at home she felt, and how she despised stupid conventions, Laura took a big bite of her bread-and-butter as she stared at the little drawing. She felt just like a work-girl.

'Laura, Laura, where are you? Telephone, Laura!' a voice cried from the house.

'Coming!' Away she skimmed, over the lawn, up the path, up the steps, across the veranda, and into the porch. In the hall her father and Laurie were brushing their hats ready to go to the office.

'I say, Laura,' said Laurie very fast, 'you might just give a squiz[2] at my coat before this afternoon. See if it wants pressing.'

'I will,' said she. Suddenly she couldn't stop herself. She ran at Laurie and gave him a small, quick squeeze. 'Oh, I do love parties, don't you?' gasped Laura.

'Ra-ther,' said Laurie's warm, boyish voice, and he squeezed his sister too, and gave her a gentle push. 'Dash off to the telephone, old girl.'

The telephone. 'Yes, yes; oh yes. Kitty? Good morning, dear. Come to lunch? Do, dear. Delighted of course. It will only be a very scratch meal—just the sandwich crusts and broken meringue-shells and what's left over. Yes, isn't it a perfect morning? Your white? Oh, I certainly should. One moment—hold the line. Mother's calling.' And Laura sat back. 'What, mother? Can't hear.'

Mrs Sheridan's voice floated down the stairs. 'Tell her to wear that sweet hat she had on last Sunday.'

'Mother says you're to wear that sweet hat you had on last Sunday. Good. One o'clock. Bye-bye.'

Laura put back the receiver, flung her arms over her head, took a deep breath, stretched and let them fall. 'Huh,' she sighed, and the moment after the sigh she sat up quickly. She was still, listening. All the doors in the house seemed to be open. The house was alive with soft, quick steps and running voices. The green baize[3] door that led to the kitchen regions swung open and

2. Glance.　　　　　　　　　　3. Coarse woolen.

shut with a muffled thud. And now there came a long, chuckling absurd sound. It was the heavy piano being moved on its stiff castors. But the air! If you stopped to notice, was the air always like this? Little faint winds were playing chase in at the tops of the windows, out at the doors. And there were two tiny spots of sun, one on the inkpot, one on a silver photograph frame, playing too. Darling little spots. Especially the one on the inkpot lid. It was quite warm. A warm little silver star. She could have kissed it.

The front door bell pealed, and there sounded the rustle of Sadie's print skirt on the stairs. A man's voice murmured; Sadie answered, careless, 'I'm sure I don't know. Wait. I'll ask Mrs Sheridan.'

'What is it, Sadie?' Laura came into the hall.

'It's the florist, Miss Laura.'

It was, indeed. There, just inside the door, stood a wide, shallow tray full of pots of pink lilies. No other kind. Nothing but lilies—canna lilies, big pink flowers, wide open, radiant, almost frighteningly alive on bright crimson stems.

'O-oh, Sadie!' said Laura, and the sound was like a little moan. She crouched down as if to warm herself at that blaze of lilies; she felt they were in her fingers, on her lips, growing in her breast.

'It's some mistake,' she said faintly. 'Nobody ever ordered so many. Sadie, go and find mother.'

But at that moment Mrs Sheridan joined them.

'It's quite right,' she said calmly. 'Yes, I ordered them. Aren't they lovely?' She pressed Laura's arm. 'I was passing the shop yesterday, and I saw them in the window. And I suddenly thought for once in my life I shall have enough canna lilies. The garden party will be a good excuse.'

'But I thought you said you didn't mean to interfere,' said Laura. Sadie had gone. The florist's man was still outside at his van. She put her arm round her mother's neck and gently, very gently, she bit her mother's ear.

'My darling child, you wouldn't like a logical mother, would you? Don't do that. Here's the man.'

He carried more lilies still, another whole tray.

'Bank them up, just inside the door, on both sides of the porch, please,' said Mrs Sheridan. 'Don't you agree, Laura?'

'Oh, I *do* mother.'

In the drawing-room Meg, Jose and good little Hans had at last succeeded in moving the piano.

'Now, if we put this chesterfield against the wall and move everything out of the room except the chairs, don't you think?'

'Quite.'

'Hans, move these tables into the smoking-room, and bring a sweeper to take these marks off the carpet and—one moment, Hans—' Jose loved giving orders to the servants, and they loved obeying her. She always made them feel they were taking part in some drama. 'Tell mother and Miss Laura to come here at once.'

'Very good, Miss Jose.'

She turned to Meg. 'I want to hear what the piano sounds like, just in case I'm asked to sing this afternoon. Let's try over "This life is Weary."'

Pom! Ta-ta-ta *Tee*-ta! The piano burst out so passionately that Jose's face changed. She clasped her hands. She looked mournfully and enigmatically at her mother and Laura as they came in.

> This Life is Wee-ary,
> A Tear—a Sigh.
> A Love that Chan-ges,
> This Life is Wee-ary,
> A Tear—a Sigh.
> A Love that Chan-ges,
> And then . . . Good-bye!

But at the word 'Good-bye,' and although the piano sounded more desperate than ever, her face broke into a brilliant, dreadfully unsympathetic smile.

'Aren't I in good voice, mummy?' she beamed.

> This Life is Wee-ary,
> Hope comes to Die.
> A Dream—a Wa-kening.

But now Sadie interrupted them. 'What is it, Sadie?'

'If you please, m'm, cook says have you got the flags[4] for the sandwiches?'

'The flags for the sandwiches, Sadie?' echoed Mrs Sheridan dreamily. And the children knew by her face that she hadn't got them. 'Let me see.' And she said to Sadie firmly, 'Tell cook I'll let her have them in ten minutes.'

Sadie went.

'Now, Laura,' said her mother quickly. 'Come with me into the smoking-room. I've got the names[5] somewhere on the back of an envelope. You'll have to write them out for me. Meg, go upstairs this minute and take that wet thing off your head. Jose, run and finish dressing this instant. Do you hear me, children, or shall I have to tell your father when he comes home to-night? And—and, Jose, pacify cook if you do go into the kitchen, will you? I'm terrified of her this morning.'

The envelope was found at last behind the dining-room clock, though how it had got there Mrs Sheridan could not imagine.

'One of you children must have stolen it out of my bag, because I remember vividly—cream cheese and lemon-curd. Have you done that?'

'Yes.'

'Egg and—' Mrs Sheridan held the envelope away from her. 'It looks like mice. It can't be mice, can it?'

'Olive, pet,' said Laura, looking over her shoulder.

'Yes, of course, olive. What a horrible combination it sounds. Egg and olive.'

They were finished at last, and Laura took them off to the kitchen. She found Jose there pacifying the cook, who did not look at all terrifying.

'I have never seen such exquisite sandwiches,' said Jose's rapturous voice. 'How many kinds did you say there were, cook? Fifteen?'

'Fifteen, Miss Jose.'

'Well, cook, I congratulate you.'

Cook swept up crusts with the long sandwich knife and smiled broadly.

'Godber's has come,' announced Sadie, issuing out of the pantry. She had seen the man pass the window.

That meant the cream puffs had come. Godber's were famous for their cream puffs. Nobody ever thought of making them at home.

---

4. Little paper flags stuck in a plate of small tri-angular sandwiches indicating what is inside the sandwiches on each plate—an English custom adopted by the New Zealand middle class as a sign of gentility.

5. I.e., the names of the sandwich fillings to be written on each flag.

'Bring them in and put them on the table, my girl,' ordered cook.

Sadie brought them in and went back to the door. Of course Laura and Jose were far too grown-up to really care about such things. All the same, they couldn't help agreeing that the puffs looked very attractive. Very. Cook began arranging them, shaking off the extra icing sugar.

'Don't they carry one back to all one's parties?' said Laura.

'I suppose they do,' said practical Jose, who never liked to be carried back. 'They look beautifully light and feathery, I must say.'

'Have one each, my dears,' said cook in her comfortable voice. 'Yer ma won't know.'

Oh, impossible. Fancy cream puffs so soon after breakfast. The very idea made one shudder. All the same, two minutes later Jose and Laura were licking their fingers with that absorbed inward look that only comes from whipped cream.

'Let's go into the garden, out by the back way,' suggested Laura. 'I want to see how the men are getting on with the marquee. They're such awfully nice men.'

But the back door was blocked by cook, Sadie, Godber's man and Hans. Something had happened.

'Tuk-tuk-tuk,' clucked cook like an agitated hen. Sadie had her hand clapped to her cheek as though she had toothache. Hans's face was screwed up in the effort to understand. Only Godber's man seemed to be enjoying himself; it was his story.

'What's the matter? What's happened?'

'There's been a horrible accident,' said cook. 'A man killed.'

'A man killed! Where? How? When?'

But Godber's man wasn't going to have his story snatched from under his very nose.

'Know those little cottages just below here, miss?' Know them? Of course, she knew them. 'Well, there's a young chap living there, name of Scott, a carter. His horse shied at a traction-engine, corner of Hawke Street this morning, and he was thrown out on the back of his head. Killed.'

'Dead!' Laura stared at Godber's man.

'Dead when they picked him up,' said Godber's man with relish. 'They were taking the body home as I come up here.' And he said to the cook, 'He's left a wife and five little ones.'

'Jose, come here.' Laura caught hold of her sister's sleeve and dragged her through the kitchen to the other side of the green baize door. There she paused and leaned against it. 'Jose!' she said, horrified, 'however are we going to stop everything?'

'Stop everything, Laura!' cried Jose in astonishment. 'What do you mean?'

'Stop the garden party, of course.' Why did Jose pretend?

But Jose was still more amazed. 'Stop the garden party? My dear Laura, don't be so absurd. Of course we can't do anything of the kind. Nobody expects us to. Don't be so extravagant.'

'But we can't possibly have a garden party with a man dead just outside the front gate.'

That really was extravagant, for the little cottages were in a lane to themselves at the very bottom of a steep rise that led up to the house. A broad road ran between. True, they were far too near. They were the greatest possible eyesore, and they had no right to be in that neighbourhood at all. They were

2352 / Katherine Mansfield

little mean dwellings painted a chocolate brown. In the garden patches there was nothing but cabbage stalks, sick hens and tomato cans. The very smoke coming out of their chimneys was poverty-stricken. Little rags and shreds of smoke, so unlike the great silvery plumes that uncurled from the Sheridans' chimneys. Washerwomen lived in the lane and sweeps and a cobbler, and a man whose house-front was studded all over with minute bird-cages. Children swarmed. When the Sheridans were little they were forbidden to set foot there because of the revolting language and of what they might catch. But since they were grown up, Laura and Laurie on their prowls sometimes walked through. It was disgusting and sordid. They came out with a shudder. But still one must go everywhere; one must see everything. So through they went.

'And just think of what the band would sound like to that poor woman,' said Laura.

'Oh, Laura!' Jose began to be seriously annoyed. 'If you're going to stop a band playing every time some one has an accident, you'll lead a very strenuous life. I'm every bit as sorry about it as you. I feel just as sympathetic.' Her eyes hardened. She looked at her sister just as she used to when they were little and fighting together. 'You won't bring a drunken workman back to life by being sentimental,' she said softly.

'Drunk! Who said he was drunk?' Laura turned furiously on Jose. She said, just as they had used to say on those occasions, 'I'm going straight up to tell mother.'

'Do, dear,' cooed Jose.

'Mother, can I come into your room?' Laura turned the big glass door-knob.

'Of course, child. Why, what's the matter? What's given you such a colour?' And Mrs Sheridan turned round from her dressing-table. She was trying on a new hat.

'Mother, a man's been killed,' began Laura.

'Not in the garden?' interrupted her mother.

'No, no!'

'Oh, what a fright you gave me!' Mrs Sheridan sighed with relief, and took off the big hat and held it on her knees.

'But listen, mother,' said Laura. Breathless, half-choking, she told the dreadful story. 'Of course, we can't have our party, can we?' she pleaded. 'The band and everybody arriving. They'd hear us, mother; they're nearly neighbours!'

To Laura's astonishment her mother behaved just like Jose; it was harder to bear because she seemed amused. She refused to take Laura seriously.

'But, my dear child, use your common sense. It's only by accident we've heard of it. If some one had died there normally—and I can't understand how they keep alive in those poky little holes—we should still be having our party, shouldn't we?'

Laura had to say 'yes' to that, but she felt it was all wrong. She sat down on her mother's sofa and pinched the cushion frill.

'Mother, isn't it really terribly heartless of us?' she asked.

'Darling!' Mrs Sheridan got up and came over to her, carrying the hat. Before Laura could stop her she had popped it on. 'My child!' said her mother, 'the hat is yours. It's made for you. It's much too young for me. I have never seen you look such a picture. Look at yourself!' And she held up her hand-mirror.

'But, mother,' Laura began again. She couldn't look at herself; she turned aside.

This time Mrs Sheridan lost patience just as Jose had done.

'You are being very absurd, Laura,' she said coldly. 'People like that don't expect sacrifices from us. And it's not very sympathetic to spoil everybody's enjoyment as you're doing now.'

'I don't understand,' said Laura, and she walked quickly out of the room into her own bedroom. There, quite by chance, the first thing she saw was this charming girl in the mirror, in her black hat trimmed with gold daisies, and a long black velvet ribbon. Never had she imagined she could look like that. Is mother right? she thought. And now she hoped her mother was right. Am I being extravagant? Perhaps it was extravagant. Just for a moment she had another glimpse of that poor woman and those little children, and the body being carried into the house. But it all seemed blurred, unreal, like a picture in the newspaper. I'll remember it again after the party's over, she decided. And somehow that seemed quite the best plan . . .

Lunch was over by half past one. By half past two they were all ready for the fray. The green-coated band had arrived and was established in a corner of the tennis-court.

'My dear!' trilled Kitty Maitland, 'aren't they too like frogs for words? You ought to have arranged them round the pond with the conductor in the middle on a leaf.'

Laurie arrived and hailed them on his way to dress. At the sight of him Laura remembered the accident again. She wanted to tell him. If Laurie agreed with the others, then it was bound to be all right. And she followed him into the hall.

'Laurie!'

'Hallo!' He was half-way upstairs, but when he turned round and saw Laura he suddenly puffed out his cheeks and goggled his eyes at her. 'My word, Laura! You do look stunning,' said Laurie. 'What an absolutely topping hat!'

Laura said faintly 'Is it?' and smiled up at Laurie, and didn't tell him after all.

Soon after that people began coming in streams. The band struck up; the hired waiters ran from the house to the marquee. Wherever you looked there were couples strolling, bending to the flowers, greeting, moving on over the lawn. They were like bright birds that had alighted in the Sheridans' garden for this one afternoon, on their way to—where? Ah, what happiness it is to be with people who all are happy, to press hands, press cheeks, smile into eyes.

'Darling Laura, how well you look!'

'What a becoming hat, child!'

'Laura, you look quite Spanish. I've never seen you look so striking.'

And Laura, glowing, answered softly, 'Have you had tea? Won't you have an ice? The passion-fruit ices really are rather special.' She ran to her father and begged him. 'Daddy darling, can't the band have something to drink?'

And the perfect afternoon slowly ripened, slowly faded, slowly its petals closed.

'Never a more delightful garden party . . . ' 'The greatest success . . . ' 'Quite the most . . . '

Laura helped her mother with the goodbyes. They stood side by side in the porch till it was all over.

'All over, all over, thank heaven,' said Mrs Sheridan. 'Round up the others, Laura. Let's go and have some fresh coffee. I'm exhausted. Yes, it's been very successful. But oh, these parties, these parties! Why will you children insist on giving parties!' And they all of them sat down in the deserted marquee.

'Have a sandwich, daddy dear. I wrote the flag.'

'Thanks.' Mr Sheridan took a bite and the sandwich was gone. He took another. 'I suppose you didn't hear of a beastly accident that happened to-day?' he said.

'My dear,' said Mrs Sheridan, holding up her hand, 'we did. It nearly ruined the party. Laura insisted we should put it off.'

'Oh, mother!' Laura didn't want to be teased about it.

'It was a horrible affair all the same,' said Mr Sheridan. 'The chap was married too. Lived just below in the lane, and leaves a wife and half a dozen kiddies, so they say.'

An awkward little silence fell. Mrs Sheridan fidgeted with her cup. Really, it was very tactless of father . . .

Suddenly she looked up. There on the table were all those sandwiches, cakes, puffs, all un-eaten, all going to be wasted. She had one of her brilliant ideas.

'I know,' she said. 'Let's make up a basket. Let's send that poor creature some of this perfectly good food. At any rate, it will be the greatest treat for the children. Don't you agree? And she's sure to have neighbours calling in and so on. What a point to have it all ready prepared. Laura!' She jumped up. 'Get me the big basket out of the stairs cupboard.'

'But, mother, do you really think it's a good idea?' said Laura.

Again, how curious, she seemed to be different from them all. To take scraps from their party. Would the poor woman really like that?

'Of course! What's the matter with you today? An hour or two ago you were insisting on us being sympathetic, and now—'

Oh well! Laura ran for the basket. It was filled, it was heaped by her mother.

'Take it yourself, darling,' said she. 'Run down just as you are. No, wait, take the arum lilies too. People of that class are so impressed by arum lilies.'

'The stems will ruin her lace frock,' said practical Jose.

So they would. Just in time. 'Only the basket, then. And, Laura!'—her mother followed her out of the marquee—'don't on any account—'

'What mother?'

No, better not put such ideas into the child's head! 'Nothing! Run along.'

It was just growing dusky as Laura shut their garden gates. A big dog ran by like a shadow. The road gleamed white, and down below in the hollow the little cottages were in deep shade. How quiet it seemed after the afternoon. Here she was going down the hill to somewhere where a man lay dead, and she couldn't realize it. Why couldn't she? She stopped a minute. And it seemed to her that kisses, voices, tinkling spoons, laughter, the smell of crushed grass were somehow inside her. She had no room for anything else. How strange! She looked up at the pale sky, and all she thought was, 'Yes, it was the most successful.'

Now the broad road was crossed. The lane began, smoky and dark. Women in shawls and men's tweed caps hurried by. Men hung over the palings; the children played in the doorways. A low hum came from the mean little cottages. In some of them there was a flicker of light, and a shadow, crab-like, moved across the window. Laura bent her head and hurried on. She wished now she had put on a coat. How her frock shone! And the big hat with the velvet streamer—if only it was another hat! Were the people looking at her? They must be. It was a mistake to have come; she knew all along it was a mistake. Should she go back even now?

No, too late. This was the house. It must be. A dark knot of people stood outside. Beside the gate an old, old woman with a crutch sat in a chair, watching. She had her feet on a newspaper. The voices stopped as Laura drew near. The group parted. It was as though she was expected, as though they had known she was coming here.

Laura was terribly nervous. Tossing the velvet ribbon over her shoulder, she said to a woman standing by, 'Is this Mrs Scott's house?' and the woman, smiling queerly, said, 'It is, my lass.'

Oh, to be away from this! She actually said, 'Help me, God,' as she walked up the tiny path and knocked. To be away from those staring eyes, or to be covered up in anything, one of those women's shawls even. I'll just leave the basket and go, she decided. I shan't even wait for it to be emptied.

Then the door opened. A little woman in black showed in the gloom.

Laura said, 'Are you Mrs Scott?' But to her horror the woman answered, 'Walk in please, miss,' and she was shut in the passage.

'No,' said Laura, 'I don't want to come in. I only want to leave this basket. Mother sent—'

The little woman in the gloomy passage seemed not to have heard her. 'Step this way, please, miss,' she said in an oily voice, and Laura followed her.

She found herself in a wretched little low kitchen, lighted by a smoky lamp. There was a woman sitting before the fire.

'Em,' said the little creature who had let her in. 'Em! It's a young lady.' She turned to Laura. She said meaningly, 'I'm her sister, Miss. You'll excuse 'er, won't you?'

'Oh, but of course!' said Laura. 'Please, please don't disturb her. I—I only want to leave—'

But at that moment the woman at the fire turned round. Her face, puffed up, red, with swollen eyes and swollen lips, looked terrible. She seemed as though she couldn't understand why Laura was there. What did it mean? Why was this stranger standing in the kitchen with a basket? What was it all about? And the poor face puckered up again.

'All right, my dear,' said the other. 'I'll thenk the young lady.'

And again she began, 'You'll excuse her, miss, I'm sure,' and her face, swollen too, tried an oily smile.

Laura only wanted to get out, to get away. She was back in the passage. The door opened. She walked straight through into the bedroom where the dead man was lying.

'You'd like a look at 'im, wouldn't you?' said Em's sister, and she brushed past Laura over to the bed. 'Don't be afraid, my lass,'—and now her voice sounded fond and sly, and fondly she drew down the sheet—' 'e looks a picture. There's nothing to show. Come along, my dear.'

Laura came.

There lay a young man, fast asleep—sleeping so soundly, so deeply, that he was far, far away from them both. Oh, so remote, so peaceful. He was dreaming. Never wake him up again. His head was sunk in the pillow, his eyes were closed; they were blind under the closed eyelids. He was given up to his dream. What did garden parties and baskets and lace frocks matter to him? He was far from all those things. He was wonderful, beautiful. While they were laughing and while the band was playing, this marvel had come to the lane. Happy . . . happy . . . All is well, said that sleeping face. This is just as it should be. I am content.

But all the same you had to cry, and she couldn't go out of the room without saying something to him. Laura gave a loud childish sob.

'Forgive my hat,' she said.

And this time she didn't wait for Em's sister. She found her way out of the door, down the path, past all those dark people. At the corner of the lane she met Laurie.

He stepped out of the shadow. 'Is that you, Laura?'

'Yes.'

'Mother was getting anxious. Was it all right?'

'Yes, quite. Oh, Laurie!' She took his arm, she pressed up against him.

'I say, you're not crying, are you?' asked her brother.

Laura shook her head. She was.

Laurie put his arm round her shoulder. 'Don't cry,' he said in his warm, loving voice. 'Was it awful?'

'No,' sobbed Laura. 'It was simply marvellous. But, Laurie—' She stopped, she looked at her brother. 'Isn't life,' she stammered, 'isn't life—' But what life was she couldn't explain. No matter. He quite understood.

'*Isn't* it, darling?' said Laurie.

1921   1922

JEAN RHYS
1890–1979

Jean Rhys was born Ella Gwendolen Rees Williams on the small island of Dominica in the West Indies. Her father was a Welsh doctor; her mother, a Creole (that is, a white West Indian) descended from wealthy, slave-holding plantation owners. Rhys was educated at a convent school in Roseau, Dominica, before, at the age of seventeen, leaving Dominica to attend the Perse School in Cambridge, England; she returned to her birthplace only once, in 1936. Her feelings toward her Caribbean background and childhood were mixed: she deeply appreciated the rich sensations and cross-racial engagements of her tropical experience, yet she was haunted by the knowledge of her violent heritage and carried a heavy burden of historical guilt. As a West Indian she felt estranged from mainstream European culture and identified with the suffering of Afro-Caribbeans, yet as a white Creole she grew up feeling out of place amid the predominantly black population of Dominica.

After studying briefly at the Academy of Dramatic Art in London, Rhys worked as a traveling chorus girl, mannequin, film extra, and—during World War I—volunteer cook. In 1919 she left England to marry the first of three husbands, and for many years she lived abroad, mainly in Paris, where she began to write the stories of her first book, *The Left Bank: Sketches and Studies of Present-Day Bohemian Paris* (1927). It was published with an introduction by the established novelist and poet Ford Madox Ford, who was for a time her lover. Ford grasped the link between her vulnerability as a person and her strength as a writer; he perceived her "terrifying insight . . . and passion for stating the case of the underdog." Rhys declared, "I have only ever written about myself," and indeed much of her writing is semiautobiographical. Her fiction frequently depicts single, economically challenged women, rootless outsiders living in bohemian London or Paris. Her early "sketches" were followed by her first novel, *Postures* (1928, reprinted as *Quartet* in 1969), in part an account of her affair with Ford; *After Leaving Mr. Mackenzie* (1930), about sexual betrayal; *Voyage in the Dark*

(1934), an account of a nineteen-year-old chorus girl in London who has come from Dominica; and *Good Morning, Midnight* (1939), another first-person narrative of a lonely drifter, this time in Paris.

She published nothing more for many years, dropping out of sight and often living in poverty, until, following the enthusiastic reception of a radio adaptation of *Good Morning, Midnight* in 1957, she began to work in earnest on her masterpiece, *Wide Sargasso Sea* (1966). In this novel, set in Jamaica and Dominica in the 1830s and 1840s, Rhys returns to her Caribbean childhood and, in a brilliant act of imaginative sympathy, creates a West Indian prehistory for the first Mrs. Rochester, the madwoman in the attic of Charlotte Brontë's *Jane Eyre*. Altogether Rhys worked on the novel for twenty-one years, amid bouts of depression, loneliness, and alcoholism, but its immediate acclaim gave her the recognition she had so long been denied. She continued to publish works of fiction and autobiography and in the year before her death received the Commander of the Order of the British Empire.

During the long period when she was writing *Wide Sargasso Sea*, Rhys produced only two published stories, both of which draw like the novel on her Caribbean youth. In "The Day They Burned the Books," set in the West Indies, a white girl who only partly understands the painful entanglements of class, race, and cultural prejudice tells how a lower-class Englishman has accumulated a trove of books he values for their cultural prestige, while his mulatto wife, embittered by her husband's racism, comes to despise them as emblems of British imperial oppression. "Let Them Call It Jazz" also has a first-person female narrator, but this time she is a West Indian mulatto, who speaks in West Indian English of her struggle against racial and class barriers after immigrating to London, an outsider in the metropolitan heart of the empire, ultimately jailed—as was Rhys for a few days after assaulting a neighbor—in Royal Holloway Prison. The shattering of a stained-glass window in this story—like the book burning in the first story and the house burning in *Wide Sargasso Sea*—represents an eruption of Afro-Caribbean rage in response to the circumscriptions and deceptions of white racism.

Whether working in Standard or West Indian English, Rhys is one of the great prose stylists of the twentieth century, her language spare yet lyrical, her sentences exactly written and rewritten to suggest the most in the fewest possible words. Her writing is almost painfully alert to sensory detail, sensitive to the terrible fears and frustrated longings of marginalized people, and fierce in its unmasking of the social and psychic consequences of racial and gender oppression.

The Day They Burned the Books

My friend Eddie was a small, thin boy. You could see the blue veins in his wrists and temples. People said that he had consumption[1] and wasn't long for this world. I loved, but sometimes despised him.

His father, Mr Sawyer, was a strange man. Nobody could make out what he was doing in our part of the world at all. He was not a planter or a doctor or a lawyer or a banker. He didn't keep a store. He wasn't a schoolmaster or a government official. He wasn't—that was the point—a gentleman. We had several resident romantics who had fallen in love with the moon on the Caribbees[2]—they were all gentlemen and quite unlike Mr Sawyer who hadn't an 'h' in his composition.[3] Besides, he detested the moon and everything else about the Caribbean and he didn't mind telling you so.

1. Wasting of the body associated with tuberculosis.
2. Or Caribbees: old term for the group of islands

in the southeastern West Indies, now called the Lesser Antilles.
3. His pronunciation marks him as lower-class.

He was agent for a small steamship line which in those days linked up Venezuela and Trinidad[4] with the smaller islands, but he couldn't make much out of that. He must have a private income, people decided, but they never decided why he had chosen to settle in a place he didn't like and to marry a coloured woman. Though a decent, respectable, nicely educated coloured woman, mind you.

Mrs Sawyer must have been very pretty once but, what with one thing and another, that was in days gone by.

When Mr Sawyer was drunk—this often happened—he used to be very rude to her. She never answered him.

'Look at the nigger showing off,' he would say; and she would smile as if she knew she ought to see the joke but couldn't. 'You damned, long-eyed, gloomy half-caste,[5] you don't smell right,' he would say; and she never answered, not even to whisper, 'You don't smell right to me, either.'

The story went that once they had ventured to give a dinner party and that when the servant, Mildred, was bringing in coffee, he had pulled Mrs Sawyer's hair. 'Not a wig, you see,' he bawled. Even then, if you can believe it, Mrs Sawyer had laughed and tried to pretend that it was all part of the joke, this mysterious, obscure, sacred English joke.

But Mildred told the other servants in the town that her eyes had gone wicked, like a soucriant's[6] eyes, and that afterwards she had picked up some of the hair he pulled out and put it in an envelope, and that Mr Sawyer ought to look out (hair is obeah[7] as well as hands).

Of course, Mrs Sawyer had her compensations. They lived in a very pleasant house in Hill Street. The garden was large and they had a fine mango tree, which bore prolifically. The fruit was small, round, very sweet and juicy—a lovely, red-and-yellow colour when it was ripe. Perhaps it was one of the compensations, I used to think.

Mr Sawyer built a room on to the back of this house. It was unpainted inside and the wood smelt very sweet. Bookshelves lined the walls. Every time the Royal Mail steamer[8] came in it brought a package for him, and gradually the empty shelves filled.

Once I went there with Eddie to borrow *The Arabian Nights*.[9] That was on a Saturday afternoon, one of those hot, still afternoons when you felt that everything had gone to sleep, even the water in the gutters. But Mrs Sawyer was not asleep. She put her head in at the door and looked at us, and I knew that she hated the room and hated the books.

It was Eddie with the pale blue eyes and straw-coloured hair—the living image of his father, though often as silent as his mother—who first infected me with doubts about 'home', meaning England. He would be so quiet when others who had never seen it—none of us had ever seen it—were talking about its delights, gesticulating freely as we talked—London, the beautiful, rosy-cheeked ladies, the theatres, the shops, the fog, the blazing coal fires in winter, the exotic food (whitebait[1] eaten to the sound of violins), strawberries and

4. Formerly British, Caribbean island off northeast Venezuela.
5. Offensive term for a person of mixed racial descent.
6. Female vampire, in Caribbean legend.
7. A charm or fetish used in Afro-Caribbean witchcraft or sorcery.
8. Ship, owned by the Royal Mail Steam Packet Company, that ferried mail from London to the West Indies beginning in 1841.
9. Also called *The Thousand and One Nights*, a collection of old stories, largely Persian, Arabian, and Indian in origin.
1. Young of a small fish, such as herring, considered a delicacy when cooked whole.

cream—the word 'strawberries' always spoken with a guttural and throaty sound which we imagined to be the proper English pronunciation.

'I don't like strawberries,' Eddie said on one occasion.

'You *don't like* strawberries?'

'No, and I don't like daffodils either. Dad's always going on about them. He says they lick the flowers here into a cocked hat[2] and I bet that's a lie.'

We were all too shocked to say, 'You don't know a thing about it.' We were so shocked that nobody spoke to him for the rest of the day. But I for one admired him. I also was tired of learning and reciting poems in praise of daffodils, and my relations with the few 'real' English boys and girls I had met were awkward. I had discovered that if I called myself English they would snub me haughtily: 'You're not English; you're a horrid colonial.' 'Well, I don't much want to be English,' I would say. 'It's much more fun to be French or Spanish or something like that—and, as a matter of fact, I am a bit.' Then I was too killingly funny, quite ridiculous. Not only a horrid colonial, but also ridiculous. Heads I win, tails you lose—that was the English. I had thought about all this, and thought hard, but I had never dared to tell anybody what I thought and I realized that Eddie had been very bold.

But he was bold, and stronger than you would think. For one thing, he never felt the heat; some coldness in his fair skin resisted it. He didn't burn red or brown, he didn't freckle much.

Hot days seemed to make him feel especially energetic. 'Now we'll run twice round the lawn and then you can pretend you're dying of thirst in the desert and that I'm an Arab chieftain bringing you water.'

'You must drink slowly,' he would say, 'for if you're very thirsty and you drink quickly you die.'

So I learnt the voluptuousness of drinking slowly when you are very thirsty—small mouthful by small mouthful, until the glass of pink, iced Coca-Cola was empty.

Just after my twelfth birthday Mr Sawyer died suddenly, and as Eddie's special friend I went to the funeral, wearing a new white dress. My straight hair was damped with sugar and water the night before and plaited into tight little plaits, so that it should be fluffy for the occasion.

When it was all over everybody said how nice Mrs Sawyer had looked, walking like a queen behind the coffin and crying her eyeballs out at the right moment, and wasn't Eddie a funny boy? He hadn't cried at all.

After this Eddie and I took possession of the room with the books. No one else ever entered it, except Mildred to sweep and dust in the mornings, and gradually the ghost of Mr Sawyer pulling Mrs Sawyer's hair faded, though this took a little time. The blinds were always halfway down and going in out of the sun was like stepping into a pool of brown-green water. It was empty except for the bookshelves, a desk with a green baize[3] top and a wicker rocking-chair.

'My room,' Eddie called it. 'My books,' he would say, 'my books.'

I don't know how long this lasted. I don't know whether it was weeks after Mr Sawyer's death or months after, that I see myself and Eddie in the room. But there we are and there, unexpectedly, are Mrs Sawyer and Mildred. Mrs Sawyer's mouth tight, her eyes pleased. She is pulling all the books out of the

---

2. From *knocked into a cocked hat*: make them look terrible by comparison. Daffodils are common in English poetry, but do not grow in the West Indies.

3. Feltlike fabric.

shelves and piling them into two heaps. The big, fat glossy ones—the good-looking ones, Mildred explains in a whisper—lie in one heap. The *Encyclopaedia Britannica, British Flowers, Birds and Beasts,* various histories, books with maps, Froude's *English in the West Indies*[4] and so on—they are going to be sold. The unimportant books, with paper covers or damaged covers or torn pages, lie in another heap. They are going to be burnt—yes, burnt.

Mildred's expression was extraordinary as she said that—half hugely delighted, half shocked, even frightened. And as for Mrs Sawyer—well, I knew bad temper (I had often seen it), I knew rage, but this was hate. I recognized the difference at once and stared at her curiously. I edged closer to her so that I could see the titles of the books she was handling.

It was the poetry shelf. *Poems,* Lord Byron, *Poetical Works,* Milton, and so on. Vlung, vlung, vlung—all thrown into the heap that were to be sold. But a book by Christina Rossetti, though also bound in leather, went into the heap that was to be burnt, and by a flicker in Mrs Sawyer's eyes I knew that worse than men who wrote books were women who wrote books—infinitely worse. Men could be mercifully shot; women must be tortured.

Mrs Sawyer did not seem to notice that we were there, but she was breathing free and easy and her hands had got the rhythm of tearing and pitching. She looked beautiful, too—beautiful as the sky outside which was a very dark blue, or the mango tree, long sprays of brown and gold.

When Eddie said 'no', she did not even glance at him.

'No,' he said again in a high voice. 'Not that one. I was reading that one.'

She laughed and he rushed at her, his eyes starting out of his head, shrieking, 'Now I've got to hate you too. Now I hate you too.'

He snatched the book out of her hand and gave her a violent push. She fell into the rocking-chair.

Well, I wasn't going to be left out of all this, so I grabbed a book from the condemned pile and dived under Mildred's outstretched arm.

Then we were both in the garden. We ran along the path, bordered with crotons.[5] We pelted down the path though they did not follow us and we could hear Mildred laughing—kyah, kyah, kyah, kyah. As I ran I put the book I had taken into the loose front of my brown holland dress. It felt warm and alive.

When we got into the street we walked sedately, for we feared the black children's ridicule. I felt very happy, because I had saved this book and it was my book and I would read it from the beginning to the triumphant words 'The End'. But I was uneasy when I thought of Mrs Sawyer.

'What will she do?' I said.

'Nothing,' Eddie said. 'Not to me.'

He was white as a ghost in his sailor suit, a blue-white even in the setting sun, and his father's sneer was clamped on his face.

'But she'll tell your mother all sorts of lies about you,' he said. 'She's an awful liar. She can't make up a story to save her life, but she makes up lies about people all right.'

'My mother won't take any notice of her,' I said. Though I was not at all sure.

'Why not? Because she's . . . because she isn't white?'

Well, I knew the answer to that one. Whenever the subject was brought

4. Published in 1888 by the English historian James Anthony Froude (1818–1894).   5. Tropical plants.

up—people's relations and whether they had a drop of coloured blood or whether they hadn't—my father would grow impatient and interrupt. 'Who's white?' he would say. 'Damned few.'

So I said, 'Who's white? Damned few.'

'You can go to the devil,' Eddie said. 'She's prettier than your mother. When she's asleep her mouth smiles and she has your curling eyelashes and quantities and quantities and *quantities* of hair.'

'Yes,' I said truthfully. 'She's prettier than my mother.'

It was a red sunset that evening, a huge, sad, frightening sunset.

'Look, let's go back,' I said. 'If you're sure she won't be vexed with you, let's go back. It'll be dark soon.'

At his gate he asked me not to go. 'Don't go yet, don't go yet.'

We sat under the mango tree and I was holding his hand when he began to cry. Drops fell on my hand like the water from the dripstone in the filter[6] in our yard. Then I began to cry too and when I felt my own tears on my hand I thought, 'Now perhaps we're married.'

'Yes, certainly, now we're married,' I thought. But I didn't say anything. I didn't say a thing until I was sure he had stopped. Then I asked, 'What's your book?'

'It's *Kim*,'[7] he said. 'But it got torn. It starts at page twenty now. What's the one you took?'

'I don't know, it's too dark to see,' I said.

When I got home I rushed into my bedroom and locked the door because I knew that this book was the most important thing that had ever happened to me and I did not want anybody to be there when I looked at it.

But I was very disappointed, because it was in French and seemed dull. *Fort Comme La Mort*,[8] it was called. . . .

1960

Let Them Call It Jazz

One bright Sunday morning in July I have trouble with my Notting Hill[1] landlord because he ask for a month's rent in advance. He tell me this after I live there since winter, settling up every week without fail. I have no job at the time, and if I give the money he want there's not much left. So I refuse. The man drunk already at that early hour, and he abuse me—all talk, he can't frighten me. But his wife is a bad one—now she walk in my room and say she must have cash. When I tell her no, she give my suitcase one kick and it burst open. My best dress fall out, then she laugh and give another kick. She say month in advance is usual, and if I can't pay find somewhere else.

Don't talk to me about London. Plenty people there have heart like stone. Any complaint—the answer is 'prove it'. But if nobody see and bear witness for me, how to prove anything? So I pack up and leave. I think better not have dealings with that woman. She too cunning, and Satan don't lie worse.

---

6. Dripstone is a sandstone used as a filter to clean water for household use.
7. Novel (1901) by the English writer Rudyard Kipling (1865–1936), about an Irish orphan boy growing up in India.

8. *Strong as Death*, 1889 novel by the French writer Guy de Maupassant (1850–1893).
1. Area of London, then slums with Afro-Caribbean immigrants.

I walk about till a place nearby is open where I can have coffee and a sandwich. There I start talking to a man at my table. He talk to me already, I know him, but I don't know his name. After a while he ask, 'What's the matter? Anything wrong?' and when I tell him my trouble he say I can use an empty flat he own till I have time to look around.

This man is not at all like most English people. He see very quick, and he decide very quick. English people take long time to decide—you three-quarter dead before they make up their mind about you. Too besides, he speak very matter of fact, as if it's nothing. He speak as if he realize well what it is to live like I do—that's why I accept and go.

He tell me somebody occupy the flat till last week, so I find everything all right, and he tell me how to get there—three-quarters of an hour from Victoria Station,[2] up a steep hill, turn left, and I can't mistake the house. He give me the keys and an envelope with a telephone number on the back. Underneath is written 'After 6 P.M. ask for Mr Sims'.

In the train that evening I think myself lucky, for to walk about London on a Sunday with nowhere to go—that take the heart out of you.

I find the place and the bedroom of the downstairs flat is nicely furnished—two looking glass, wardrobe, chest of drawers, sheets, everything. It smell of jasmine scent, but it smell strong of damp too.

I open the door opposite and there's a table, a couple chairs, a gas stove and a cupboard, but this room so big it look empty. When I pull the blind up I notice the paper peeling off and mushrooms growing on the walls—you never see such a thing.

The bathroom the same, all the taps rusty. I leave the two other rooms and make up the bed. Then I listen, but I can't hear one sound. Nobody come in, nobody go out of that house. I lie awake for a long time, then I decide not to stay and in the morning I start to get ready quickly before I change my mind. I want to wear my best dress, but it's a funny thing—when I take up that dress and remember how my landlady kick it I cry. I cry and I can't stop. When I stop I feel tired to my bones, tired like old woman. I don't want to move again—I have to force myself. But in the end I get out in the passage and there's a postcard for me. 'Stay as long as you like. I'll be seeing you soon—Friday probably. Not to worry.' It isn't signed, but I don't feel so sad and I think, 'All right, I wait here till he come. Perhaps he know of a job for me.'

Nobody else live in the house but a couple on the top floor—quiet people and they don't trouble me. I have no word to say against them.

First time I meet the lady she's opening the front door and she give me a very inquisitive look. But next time she smile a bit and I smile back—once she talk to me. She tell me the house very old, hundred and fifty year old, and she had her husband live there since long time. 'Valuable property,' she says, 'it could have been saved, but nothing done of course.' Then she tells me that as to the present owner—if he is the owner—well he have to deal with local authorities and she believe they make difficulties. 'These people are determined to pull down all the lovely old houses—it's shameful.'

So I agree that many things shameful. But what to do? What to do? I say it have an elegant shape, it make the other houses in the street look cheap trash, and she seem pleased. That's true too. The house sad and out of place, especially at night. But it have style. The second floor shut up, and as for my flat, I go in the two empty rooms once, but never again.

2. Train station in London.

Underneath was the cellar, full of old boards and broken-up furniture—I see a big rat there one day. It was no place to be alone in I tell you, and I get the habit of buying a bottle of wine most evenings, for I don't like whisky and the rum here no good. It don't even *taste* like rum. You wonder what they do to it.

After I drink a glass or two I can sing and when I sing all the misery goes from my heart. Sometimes I make up songs but next morning I forget them, so other times I sing the old ones like 'Tantalizin' ' or 'Don't Trouble Me Now.'

I think I go but I don't go. Instead I wait for the evening and the wine and that's all. Everywhere else I live—well, it doesn't matter to me, but this house is different—empty and no noise and full of shadows, so that sometimes you ask yourself what make all those shadows in an empty room.

I eat in the kitchen, then I clean up everything and have a bath for coolness. Afterwards I lean my elbows on the windowsill and look at the garden. Red and blue flowers mix up with the weeds and there are five-six apple trees. But the fruit drop and lie in the grass, so sour nobody want it. At the back, near the wall, is a bigger tree—this garden certainly take up a lot of room, perhaps that's why they want to pull the place down.

Not much rain all the summer, but not much sunshine either. More of a glare. The grass get brown and dry, the weeds grow tall, the leaves on the trees hang down. Only the red flowers—the poppies—stand up to that light, everything else look weary.

I don't trouble about money, but what with wine and shillings for the slot-meters,[3] it go quickly; so I don't waste much on food. In the evening I walk outside—not by the apple trees but near the street—it's not so lonely.

There's no wall here and I can see the woman next door looking at me over the hedge. At first I say good evening, but she turn away her head, so afterwards I don't speak. A man is often with her, he wear a straw hat with a black ribbon and goldrim spectacles. His suit hang on him like it's too big. He's the husband it seems and he stare at me worse than his wife—he stare as if I'm wild animal let loose. Once I laugh in his face because why these people have to be like that? I don't bother them. In the end I get that I don't even give them one single glance. I have plenty other things to worry about.

To show you how I felt. I don't remember exactly. But I believe it's the second Saturday after I come that when I'm at the window just before, I go for my wine I feel somebody's hand on my shoulder and it's Mr Sims. He must walk very quiet because I don't know a thing till he touch me.

He says hullo, then he tells me I've got terrible thin, do I ever eat. I say of course I eat but he goes on that it doesn't suit me at all to be so thin and he'll buy some food in the village. (That's the way he talk. There's no village here. You don't get away from London so quick.)

It don't seem to me he look very well himself, but I just say bring a drink instead, as I am not hungry.

He come back with three bottles—vermouth, gin and red wine. Then he ask if the little devil who was here last smash all the glasses and I tell him she smash some, I find the pieces. But not all. 'You fight with her, eh?'

He laugh, and he don't answer. He pour out the drinks then he says, 'Now, you eat up those sandwiches.'

Some men when they are there you don't worry so much. These sort of men you do all they tell you blindfold because they can take the trouble from your

3. Coin-fed meters for gas and electricity.

heart and make you think you're safe. It's nothing they say or do. It's a feeling they can give you. So I don't talk with him seriously—I don't want to spoil that evening. But I ask about the house and why it's so empty and he says:

'Has the old trout upstairs been gossiping?'

I tell him, 'She suppose they make difficulties for you.'

'It was a damn bad buy,' he says and talks about selling the lease or something. I don't listen much.

We were standing by the window then and the sun low. No more glare. He puts his hand over my eyes. 'Too big—much too big for your face,' he says and kisses me like you kiss a baby. When he takes his hand away I see he's looking out at the garden and he says this—'It gets you. My God it does.'

I know very well it's not me he means, so I ask him, 'Why sell it then? If you like it, keep it.'

'Sell what?' he says. 'I'm not talking about this damned house.'

I ask what he's talking about. 'Money,' he says. 'Money. That's what I'm talking about. Ways of making it.'

'I don't think so much of money. It don't like me and what do I care?' I was joking, but he turns around, his face quite pale and he tells me I'm a fool. He tells me I'll get pushed around all my life and die like a dog, only worse because they'd finish off a dog, but they'll let me live till I'm a caricature of myself. That's what he say, 'Caricature of yourself.' He say I'll curse the day I was born and everything and everybody in this bloody world before I'm done.

I tell him, 'No I'll never feel like that,' and he smiles, if you can call it a smile, and says he's glad I'm content with my lot. 'I'm disappointed in you, Selina. I thought you had more spirit.'

'If I contented that's all right,' I answer him. 'I don't see very many looking contented over here.' We're standing staring at each other when the doorbell rings. 'That's a friend of mine,' he says. 'I'll let him in.'

As to the friend, he's all dressed up in stripe pants and a black jacket and he's carrying a brief-case. Very ordinary looking but with a soft kind of voice.

'Maurice, this is Selina Davis,' says Mr Sims, and Maurice smiles very kind but it don't mean much, then he looks at his watch and says they ought to be getting along.

At the door Mr Sims tells me he'll see me next week and I answer straight out, 'I won't be here next week because I want a job and I won't get one in this place.'

'Just what I'm going to talk about. Give it a week longer, Selina.'

I say, 'Perhaps I stay a few more days. Then I go. Perhaps I go before.'

'Oh no you won't go,' he says.

They walk to the gates quickly and drive off in a yellow car. Then I feel eyes on me and it's the woman and her husband in the next door garden watching. The man make some remark and she look at me so hateful, so hating I shut the front door quick.

I don't want more wine. I want to go to bed early because I must think. I must think about money. It's true I don't care for it. Even when somebody steal my savings—this happen soon after I get to the Notting Hill house—I forget it soon. About thirty pounds they steal. I keep it roll up in a pair of stockings, but I go to the drawer one day, and no money. In the end I have to tell the police. They ask me exact sum and I say I don't count it lately, about thirty pounds. 'You don't know how much?' they say. 'When did you count it last? Do you remember? Was it before you move or after?'

I get confuse, and I keep saying, 'I don't remember,' though I remember well I see it two days before. They don't believe me and when a policeman come to the house I hear the landlady tell him, 'She certainly had no money when she came here. She wasn't able to pay a month's rent in advance for her room though it's a rule in this house.' 'These people terrible liars,' she say and I think 'it's you a terrible liar, because when I come you tell me weekly or monthly as you like.' It's from that time she don't speak to me and perhaps it's she take it. All I know is I never see one penny of my savings again, all I know is they pretend I never have any, but as it's gone, no use to cry about it. Then my mind goes to my father, for my father is a white man and I think a lot about him. If I could see him only once, for I too small to remember when he was there. My mother is fair coloured woman, fairer than I am they say, and she don't stay long with me either. She have a chance to go to Venezuela when I three-four year old and she never come back. She send money instead. It's my grandmother take care of me. She's quite dark and what we call 'country-cookie' but she's the best I know.

She save up all the money my mother send, she don't keep one penny for herself—that's how I get to England. I was a bit late in going to school regular, getting on for twelve years, but I can sew very beautiful, excellent—so I think I get a good job—in London perhaps.

However, here they tell me all this fine handsewing take too long. Waste of time—too slow. They want somebody to work quick and to hell with the small stitches. Altogether it don't look so good for me, I must say, and I wish I could see my father. I have his name—Davis. But my grandmother tell me, 'Every word that comes out of that man's mouth a damn lie. He is certainly first class liar, though no class otherwise.' So perhaps I have not even his real name.

Last thing I see before I put the light out is the postcard on the dressing table. 'Not to worry.'

Not to worry! Next day is Sunday, and it's on the Monday the people next door complain about me to the police. That evening the woman is by the hedge, and when I pass her she says in very sweet quiet voice, '*Must* you stay? *Can't* you go?' I don't answer. I walk out in the street to get rid of her. But she run inside her house to the window, she can still see me. Then I start to sing, so she can understand I'm not afraid of her. The husband call out: 'If you don't stop that noise I'll send for the police.' I answer them quite short. I say, 'You go to hell and take your wife with you.' And I sing louder.

The police come pretty quick—two of them. Maybe they just round the corner. All I can say about police, and how they behave is I think it all depends who they dealing with. Of my own free will I don't want to mix up with police. No.

One man says, you can't cause this disturbance here. But the other asks a lot of questions. What is my name? Am I tenant of a flat in No. 17? How long have I lived there? Last address and so on. I get vexed the way he speak and I tell him, 'I come here because somebody steal my savings. Why you don't look for my money instead of bawling at me? I work hard for my money. All-you don't do one single thing to find it.'

'What's she talking about?' the first one says, and the other one tells me, 'You can't make that noise here. Get along home. You've been drinking.'

I see that woman looking at me and smiling, and other people at their windows, and I'm so angry I bawl at them too. I say, 'I have absolute and perfect right to be in the street same as anybody else, and I have absolute and perfect

2366 / JEAN RHYS

right to ask the police why they don't even look for my money when it disappear. It's because a dam' English thief take it you don't look,' I say. The end
of all this is that I have to go before a magistrate, and he fine me five pounds
for drunk and disorderly, and he give me two weeks to pay.

When I get back from the court I walk up and down the kitchen, up and
down, waiting for six o'clock because I have no five pounds left, and I don't
know what to do. I telephone at six and a woman answers me very short and
sharp, then Mr Sims comes along and he don't sound too pleased either when
I tell him what happen. 'Oh Lord!' he says, and I say I'm sorry. 'Well don't
panic,' he says, 'I'll pay the fine. But look, I don't think. . . .' Then he breaks
off and talk to some other person in the room. He goes on, 'Perhaps better
not stay at No. 17. I think I can arrange something else. I'll call for you
Wednesday—Saturday latest. Now behave till then.' And he hang up before I
can answer that I don't want to wait till Wednesday, much less Saturday.
I want to get out of that house double quick and with no delay. First I think
I ring back, then I think better now as he sound so vex.

I get ready, but Wednesday he don't come, and Saturday he don't come. All
the week I stay in the flat. Only once I go out and arrange for bread, milk and
eggs to be left at the door, and seems to me I meet up with a lot of policemen.
They don't look at me, but they see me all right. I don't want to drink—I'm all
the time listening, listening and thinking, how can I leave before I know if my
fine is paid? I tell myself the police let me know, that's certain. But I don't
trust them. What they care? The answer is Nothing. Nobody care. One afternoon I knock at the old lady's flat upstairs, because I get the idea she give me
good advice. I can hear her moving about and talking, but she don't answer
and I never try again.

Nearly two weeks pass like that, then I telephone. It's the woman speaking
and she say, 'Mr Sims is not in London at present.' I ask, 'When will he be
back—it's urgent,' and she hang up. I'm not surprised. Not at all. I knew that
would happen. All the same I feel heavy like lead. Near the phone box is a
chemist's shop, so I ask him for something to make me sleep, the day is bad
enough, but to lie awake all night—Ah no! He gives me a little bottle marked
'*One or two tablets only*' and I take three when I go to bed because more and
more I think that sleeping is better than no matter what else. However, I lie
there, eyes wide open as usual, so I take three more. Next thing I know the
room is full of sunlight, so it must be late afternoon, but the lamp is still on.
My head turn around and I can't think well at all. At first I ask myself how I
get to the place. Then it comes to me, but in pictures—like the landlady kicking my dress, and when I take my ticket at Victoria Station, and Mr Sims
telling me to eat the sandwiches, but I can't remember everything clear, and
I feel very giddy and sick. I take in the milk and eggs at the door, go in the
kitchen, and try to eat but the food hard to swallow.

It's when I'm putting the things away that I see the bottles—pushed back
on the lowest shelf in the cupboard.

There's a lot of drink left, and I'm glad I tell you. Because I can't bear the
way I feel. Not any more. I mix a gin and vermouth and I drink it quick, then
I mix another and drink it slow by the window. The garden looks different,
like I never see it before. I know quite well what I must do, but it's late now—
tomorrow I have one more drink, of wine this time, and then a song comes in
my head, I sing it and I dance it, and more I sing, more I am sure this is the
best tune that has ever come to me in all my life.

The sunset light from the window is gold colour. My shoes sound loud on the boards. So I take them off, my stockings too and go on dancing but the room feel shut in, I can't breathe, and I go outside still singing. Maybe I dance a bit too. I forget all about that woman till I hear her saying, 'Henry, look at this.' I turn around and I see her at the window. 'Oh yes, I wanted to speak with you,' I say, 'Why bring the police and get me in bad trouble? Tell me that.'

'And you tell me what you're doing here at all,' she says. 'This is a respectable neighbourhood.'

Then the man come along. 'Now young woman, take yourself off. You ought to be ashamed of this behaviour.'

'It's disgraceful,' he says, talking to his wife, but loud so I can hear, and she speaks loud too—for once. 'At least the other tarts that crook installed here were *white* girls,' she says.

'You a dam' fouti⁴ liar,' I say. 'Plenty of those girls in your country already. Numberless as the sands on the shore. You don't need me for that.'

'You're not a howling success at it certainly.' Her voice sweet sugar again. 'And you won't be seeing much more of your friend Mr Sims. He's in trouble too. Try somewhere else. Find somebody else. If you can, of course.' When she say that my arm moves of itself. I pick up a stone and bam! through the window. Not the one they are standing at but the next, which is of coloured glass, green and purple and yellow.

I never see a woman look so surprise. Her mouth fall open she so full of surprise. I start to laugh, louder and louder—I laugh like my grandmother, with my hands on my hips and my head back. (When she laugh like that you can hear her to the end of our street.) At last I say, 'Well, I'm sorry. An accident. I get it fixed tomorrow early.' 'That glass is irreplaceable,' the man says. 'Irreplaceable.' 'Good thing,' I say, 'those colours look like they sea-sick to me. I buy you a better windowglass.'

He shake his fist at me. 'You won't be let off with a fine this time,' he says. Then they draw the curtains, I call out at them. 'You run away. Always you run away. Ever since I come here you hunt me down because I don't answer back. It's you shameless.' I try to sing 'Don't Trouble Me Now'.

> Don't trouble me now
> You without honour
> Don't walk in my footstep
> You without shame.

But my voice don't sound right, so I get back indoors and drink one more glass of wine—still wanting to laugh, and still thinking of my grandmother for that is one of her songs.

It's about a man whose doudou give him the go-by⁵ when she find somebody rich and he sail away to Panama. Plenty people die there of fever when they make that Panama canal so long ago. But he don't die. He come back with dollars and the girl meet him on the jetty, all dressed up and smiling. Then he sing to her, 'You without honour, you without shame'. It sound good in Martinique patois too: '*Sans honte*'.⁶

Afterwards I ask myself, 'Why I do that? It's not like me. But if they treat

4. West Indian expletive.
5. Intentionally snub by leaving behind. "Dou-

dou": darling (French Creole).
6. Without shame (French Creole).

you wrong over and over again the hour strike when you burst out that's what.'

Too besides, Mr Sims can't tell me now I have no spirit I don't care, I sleep quickly and I'm glad I break the woman's ugly window. But as to my own song it go *right* away and it never come back. A pity.

Next morning the doorbell ringing wake me up. The people upstairs don't come down, and the bell keeps on like fury self. So I go to look, and there is a policeman and a policewoman outside. As soon as I open the door the woman put her foot in it. She wear sandals and thick stockings and I never see a foot so big or so bad. It look like it want to mash up the whole world. Then she come in after the foot, and her face not so pretty either. The policeman tell me my fine is not paid and people make serious complaints about me, so they're taking me back to the magistrate. He show me a paper and I look at it, but I don't read it. The woman push me in the bedroom, and tell me to get dress quickly, but I just stare at her, because I think perhaps I wake up soon. Then I ask her what I must wear. She say she suppose I had some clothes on yesterday. Or not? 'What's it matter, wear anything,' she says. But I find clean underclothes and stockings and my shoes with high heels and I comb my hair. I start to file my nails, because I think they too long for magistrate's court but she get angry. 'Are you coming quietly or aren't you?' she says. So I go with them and we get in a car outside.

I wait for a long time in a room full of policemen. They come in, they go out, they telephone, they talk in low voices. Then it's my turn, and first thing I notice in the court room is a man with frowning black eyebrows. He sit below the magistrate, he dressed in black and he so handsome I can't take my eyes off him. When he see that he frowns worse than before.

First comes a policeman to testify I cause disturbance, and then comes the old gentleman from next door. He repeat that bit about nothing but the truth so help me God. Then he says I make dreadful noise at night and use abominable language, and dance in obscene fashion. He says when they try to shut the curtains because his wife so terrify of me, I throw stones and break a valuable stain-glass window. He say his wife get serious injury if she'd been hit, and as it is she in terrible nervous condition and the doctor is with her. I think, 'Believe me, if I aim at your wife I hit your wife—that's certain.' 'There was no provocation,' he says. 'None at all.' Then another lady from across the street says this is true. She heard no provocation whatsoever, and she swear that they shut the curtains but I go on insulting them and using filthy language and she saw all this and heard it.

The magistrate is a little gentleman with a quiet voice, but I'm very suspicious of these quiet voices now. He ask me why I don't pay any fine, and I say because I haven't the money. I get the idea they want to find out all about Mr Sims—they listen so very attentive. But they'll find out nothing from me. He ask how long I have the flat and I say I don't remember. I know they want to trip me up like they trip me up about my savings so I won't answer. At last he ask if I have anything to say as I can't be allowed to go on being a nuisance. I think, 'I'm nuisance to you because I have no money that's all.' I want to speak up and tell him how they steal all my savings, so when my landlord asks for month's rent I haven't got it to give. I want to tell him the woman next door provoke me since long time and call me bad names but she have a soft sugar voice and nobody hear—that's why I broke her window, but I'm ready to buy another after all. I want to say all I do is sing in that old garden, and I want to say this in decent quiet voice. But I hear myself talking loud and I see my hands wave in the air. Too besides it's no use, they won't believe me, so I don't finish. I stop, and I feel the tears on my face. 'Prove it.' That's all they will say. They whisper, they whisper. They nod, they nod.

Next thing I'm in a car again with a different policewoman, dressed very smart. Not in uniform. I ask her where she's taking me and she says 'Holloway' just that 'Holloway'.[7]

I catch hold of her hand because I'm afraid. But she takes it away. Cold and smooth her hand slide away and her face is china face—smooth like a doll and I think, 'This is the last time I ask anything from anybody. So help me God.'

The car come up to a black castle and little mean streets are all round it. A lorry was blocking up the castle gates. When it get by we pass through and I am in jail. First I stand in a line with others who are waiting to give up hand-bags and all belongings to a woman behind bars like in a post office. The girl in front bring out a nice compact, look like gold to me, lipstick to match and a wallet full of notes. The woman keep the money, but she give back the powder and lipstick and she half-smile. I have two pounds seven shillings and sixpence in pennies. She take my purse, then she throw me my compact (which is cheap) my comb and my handkerchief like everything in my bag is dirty. So I think, 'Here too, here too.' But I tell myself, 'Girl, what you expect, eh? They all like that. All.'

Some of what happen afterwards I forget, or perhaps better not remember. Seems to me they start by trying to frighten you. But they don't succeed with me for I don't care for nothing now, it's as if my heart hard like a rock and I can't feel.

Then I'm standing at the top of a staircase with a lot of women and girls. As we are going down I notice the railing very low on one side, very easy to jump, and a long way below there's the grey stone passage like it's waiting for you.

As I'm thinking this a uniform woman step up alongside quick and grab my arm. She say, 'Oh no you don't.'

I was just noticing the railing very low that's all—but what's the use of saying so.

Another long line waits for the doctor. It move forward slowly and my legs terrible tired. The girl in front is very young and she cry and cry. 'I'm scared,' she keeps saying. She's lucky in a way—as for me I never will cry again. It all dry up and hard in me now. That, and a lot besides. In the end I tell her to stop, because she doing just what these people want her to do.

She stop crying and start a long story, but while she is speaking her voice get very far away, and I find I can't see her face clear at all.

Then I'm in a chair, and one of those uniform women is pushing my head down between my knees, but let her push—everything go away from me just the same.

They put me in the hospital because the doctor say I'm sick. I have cell by myself and it's all right except I don't sleep. The things they say you mind I don't mind.

When they clang the door on me I think, 'You shut me in, but you shut all those other dam' devils *out*. They can't reach me now.'

At first it bothers me when they keep on looking at me all through the night.

7. Prison in London.

They open a little window in the doorway to do this. But I get used to it and get used to the night chemise[8] they give me. It very thick, and to my mind it not very clean either—but what's that matter to me? Only the food I can't swallow—especially the porridge. The woman ask me sarcastic, 'Hunger striking?' But afterwards I can leave most of it, and she don't say nothing.

One day a nice girl comes around with books and she give me two, but I don't want to read so much. Beside one is about a murder, and the other is about a ghost and I don't think it's at all like those books tell you.

There is nothing I want now. It's no use. If they leave me in peace and quiet that's all I ask. The window is barred but not small, so I can see a little thin tree through the bars, and I like watching it.

After a week they tell me I'm better and I can go out with the others for exercise. We walk round and round one of the yards in that castle—it is fine weather and the sky is a kind of pale blue, but the yard is a terrible sad place. The sunlight fall down and die there. I get tired walking in high heels and I'm glad when that's over.

We can talk, and one day an old woman come up and ask me for dog-ends. I don't understand, and she start muttering at me like she very vexed. Another woman tell me she mean cigarette ends, so I say I don't smoke. But the old woman still look angry, and when we're going in she give me one push and I nearly fall down. I'm glad to get away from these people, and hear the door clang and take my shoes off.

Sometimes I think, 'I'm here because I wanted to sing' and I have to laugh. But there's a small looking glass in my cell and I see myself and I'm like somebody else. Like some strange new person. Mr Sims tells me I too thin, but what he say now to this person in the looking glass? So I don't laugh again.

Usually I don't think at all. Everything and everybody seem small and far away, that is the only trouble.

Twice the doctor come to see me. He don't say much and I don't say anything, because a uniform woman is always there. She looks like she thinking, 'Now the lies start.' So I prefer not to speak. Then I'm sure they can't trip me up. Perhaps I there still, or in a worse place. But one day this happen.

We were walking round and round in the yard and I hear a woman singing— the voice come from high up, from one of the small barred windows. At first I don't believe it. Why should anybody sing here? Nobody want to sing in jail, nobody want to do anything. There's no reason, and you have no hope. I think I must be asleep, dreaming, but I'm awake all right and I see all the others are listening too. A nurse is with us that afternoon, not a policewoman. She stop and look up at the window.

It's a smoky kind of voice, and a bit rough sometimes, as if those old dark walls theyselves are complaining, because they see too much misery—too much. But it don't fall down and die in the courtyard; seems to me it could jump the gates of the jail easy and travel far, and nobody could stop it. I don't hear the words—only the music. She sing one verse and she begin another, then she break off sudden. Everybody starts walking again, and nobody says one word. But as we go in I ask the woman in front who was singing. 'That's the Holloway song,' she says. 'Don't you know it yet? She was singing from the punishment cells, and she tell the girls cheerio and never say die.' Then I have to go one way to the hospital block and she goes another so we don't speak again.

---

8. Loosely fitting nightgown.

When I'm back in my cell I can't just wait for bed. I walk up and down and I think. 'One day I hear that song on trumpets and these walls will fall and rest.'[9] I want to get out so bad I could hammer on the door, for I know now that anything can happen, and I don't want to stay lock up here and miss it.

Then I'm hungry. I eat everything they bring and in the morning I'm still so hungry I eat the porridge. Next time the doctor come he tells me I seem much better. Then I say a little of what really happen in that house. Not much. Very careful.

He look at me hard and kind of surprised. At the door he shake his finger and says, 'Now don't let me see you here again.'

That evening the woman tells me I'm going, but she's so upset about it I don't ask questions. Very early, before it's light she bangs the door open and shouts at me to hurry up. As we're going along the passages I see the girl who gave me the books. She's in a row with others doing exercises. Up Down, Up Down, Up. We pass quite close and I notice she's looking very pale and tired. It's crazy, it's all crazy. This up down business and everything else too. When they give me my money I remember I leave my compact in the cell, so I ask if I can go back for it. You should see that policewoman's face as she shoo me on.

There's no car, there's a van and you can't see through the windows. The third time it stop I get out with one other, a young girl, and it's the same magistrates' court as before.

The two of us wait in a small room, nobody else there, and after a while the girl say, 'What the hell are they doing? I don't want to spend all day here.' She go to the bell and she keep her finger press on it. When I look at her she say, 'Well, what are they *for*?' That girl's face is hard like a board— she could change faces with many and you wouldn't know the difference. But she get results certainly. A policeman comes in, all smiling, and we go in the court. The same magistrate, the same frowning man sits below, and when I hear my fine is paid I want to ask who paid it, but he yells at me, 'Silence.'

I think I will never understand the half of what happen, but they tell me I can go, and I understand that. The magistrate ask if I'm leaving the neighbourhood and I say yes, then I'm out in the streets again, and it's the same fine weather, same feeling I'm dreaming.

When I get to the house I see two men talking in the garden. The front door and the door of the flat are both open. I go in, and the bedroom is empty, nothing but the glare streaming inside because they take the Venetian blinds away. As I'm wondering where my suitcase is, and the clothes I leave in the wardrobe, there's a knock and it's the old lady from upstairs carrying my case packed, and my coat is over her arm. She says she sees me come in. 'I kept your things for you.' I start to thank her but she turn her back and walk away. They like that here, and better not expect too much. Too besides, I bet they tell her I'm terrible person.

I go in the kitchen, but when I see they are cutting down the big tree at the back I don't stay to watch.

At the station I'm waiting for the train and a woman asks if I feel well. 'You look so tired,' she says. 'Have you come a long way?' I want to answer, 'I come so far I lose myself on that journey.' But I tell her, 'Yes, I am quite well. But I can't stand the heat.' She says she can't stand it either, and we talk about the weather till the train come in.

9. The walls of Jericho fall when trumpets sound (Joshua 6).

I'm not frightened of them any more—after all what else can they do? I know what to say and everything go like a clock works.

I get a room near Victoria where the landlady accept one pound in advance, and next day I find a job in the kitchen of a private hotel close by. But I don't stay there long. I hear of another job going in a big store—altering ladies' dresses and I get that. I lie and tell them I work in very expensive New York shop. I speak bold and smooth faced, and they never check up on me. I make a friend there—Clarice—very light coloured, very smart, she have a lot to do with the customers and she laugh at some of them behind their backs. But I say it's not their fault if the dress don't fit. Special dress for one person only—that's very expensive in London. So it's take in, or let out all the time. Clarice have two rooms not far from the store. She furnish herself gradual and she gives parties sometimes Saturday nights. It's there I start whistling the Holloway Song. A man comes up to me and says, 'Let's hear that again.' So I whistle it again (I never sing now) and he tells me 'Not bad'. Clarice have an old piano somebody give her to store and he plays the tune, jazzing it up. I say, 'No, not like that,' but everybody else say the way he do it is first class. Well I think no more of this till I get a letter from him telling me he has sold the song and as I was quite a help he encloses five pounds with thanks.

I read the letter and I could cry. For after all, that song was all I had. I don't belong nowhere really, and I haven't money to buy my way to belonging. I don't want to either.

But when that girl sing, she sing to me and she sing for me. I was there because I was *meant* to be there. It was *meant* I should hear it—this I *know*.

Now I've let them play it wrong, and it will go from me like all the other songs—like everything. Nothing left for me at all.

But then I tell myself all this is foolishness. Even if they played it on trumpets, even if they played it just right, like I wanted—no walls would fall so soon. 'So let them call it jazz,' I think, and let them play it wrong. That won't make no difference to the song I heard.

I buy myself a dusty pink dress with the money.

1961   1962

STEVIE SMITH
1902–1971

Stevie Smith's real name was Florence Margaret Smith, but she was nicknamed "Stevie" after a famous jockey because of her small stature. She was born in Hull, Yorkshire, but at the age of three went with her mother and sister to live with an aunt in Palmer's Green, a suburb north of London. She worked as a secretary at the magazine-publishing firm of Newnes, Pearson, while continuing to live with her aunt, to whom she was devoted. When her aunt grew old and infirm, Smith gave up her job to look after her, although she herself was often in ill health. At the same time she managed to lead a lively social life in London and was known for the vividness and range of her conversation.

Smith brought out her first novel, *Novel on Yellow Paper* (1936), at the suggestion of a publisher who rejected a collection of poems. This was followed by her first volume of poetry, *A Good Time Was Had by All* (1937), and in due course by eight further poetry collections and two further novels.

Smith's work is utterly original, fitting into no category and showing none of the characteristic influences of the age. Her poetry sometimes seems to be light verse, and it draws on nursery rhyme and often employs simple language, but its humor can shade into dread, its whimsy into metaphysical pondering. She illustrated many of her poems with line drawings (she called them "doodles") that reinforce the effect of mock-naïveté. This stance is akin to the cunning innocence of the fool or the trickster, and can be seen, in part, as a gendered deflection and subversion of masculine cultural norms. Her diction ranges from the matter-of-fact to the archaic, from colloquialism ("Poor chap"), slang ("you ass"), and nonsense ("Our Bog Is Dood") to didacticism ("My point which upon this has been obscured") and foreign phrases ("Sunt Leones"). Her verse moves from free conversational rhythms to traditional verse patterns, on occasion becoming—to ironic effect—almost doggerel. Her tone can be satiric, solemn, or both at once. A poem such as "Not Waving but Drowning" belies the apparent guilelessness of Smith's art. Like the dying man's ambiguous gesture here, her poetry waves to us, with its songlike lyricism and comedy, and yet also reveals much about "drowning"—about death, suicide, and other painful human issues. A religious skeptic, Smith said she was always in danger of falling into belief, and her poetry shows her to be fascinated by theological speculation, the language of the Bible, and religious experience.

Sunt Leones[1]

The lions who ate the Christians on the sands of the arena
By indulging native appetites played what has now been seen a
Not entirely negligible part
In consolidating at the very start
5   The position of the Early Christian Church.
Initiatory rites are always bloody
And the lions, it appears
From contemporary art, made a study
Of dyeing Coliseum sands a ruddy
10   Liturgically sacrificial hue
And if the Christians felt a little blue—
Well people being eaten often do.
Theirs was the death, and theirs the crown undying,[2]
A state of things which must be satisfying.
15   My point which up to this has been obscured
Is that it was the lions who procured
By chewing up blood gristle flesh and bone
The martyrdoms on which the Church has grown.
I only write this poem because I thought it rather looked
20   As if the part the lions played was being overlooked.
By lions' jaws great benefits and blessings were begotten
And so our debt to Lionhood must never be forgotten.

1937

---

1. There be lions (Latin). Christians were attacked and eaten by lions in the public games held in the Colosseum during the Roman Empire.

2. I.e., of martyrdom, in heaven. The Christian liturgy, or system of worship, prescribes certain colors for certain festivals (line 10).

Our Bog Is Dood

Our Bog is dood, our Bog is dood,
They lisped in accents mild,
But when I asked them to explain
They grew a little wild.
How do you know your Bog is dood   5
My darling little child?

We know because we wish it so
That is enough, they cried,
And straight within each infant eye
Stood up the flame of pride,   10
And if you do not think it so
You shall be crucified.

Then tell me, darling little ones,
What's dood, suppose Bog is?
Just what we think, the answer came,   15
Just what we think it is.
They bowed their heads. Our Bog is ours
And we are wholly his.

But when they raised them up again
They had forgotten me   20
Each one upon each other glared
In pride and misery
For what was dood, and what their Bog
They never could agree.

Oh sweet it was to leave them then,   25
And sweeter not to see,
And sweetest of all to walk alone
Beside the encroaching sea,
The sea that soon should drown them all,
That never yet drowned me.   30

1950

Not Waving but Drowning

Nobody heard him, the dead man,
But still he lay moaning:
I was much further out than you thought
And not waving but drowning.

Poor chap, he always loved larking   5
And now he's dead
It must have been too cold for him his heart gave way,
They said.

Oh, no no no, it was too cold always
10 (Still the dead one lay moaning)
I was much too far out all my life
And not waving but drowning.

1957

Thoughts About the Person from Porlock[1]

Coleridge received the Person from Porlock
And ever after called him a curse,
Then why did he hurry to let him in?
He could have hid in the house.

5   It was not right of Coleridge in fact it was wrong
(But often we all do wrong)
As the truth is I think he was already stuck
With Kubla Khan.

He was weeping and wailing: I am finished, finished,
10 I shall never write another word of it,

1. See Coleridge, "Kubla Khan," (p. 446).

When along comes the Person from Porlock
And takes the blame for it.

It was not right, it was wrong,
But often we all do wrong.

          . . .

15   May we inquire the name of the Person from Porlock?
Why, Porson, didn't you know?
He lived at the bottom of Porlock Hill
So had a long way to go,

He wasn't much in the social sense
20   Though his grandmother was a Warlock,
One of the Ruthlandshire ones I fancy
And nothing to do with Porlock.

And he lived at the bottom of the hill as I said
And had a cat named Flo,
25   And had a cat named Flo.

I long for the Person from Porlock
To bring my thoughts to an end,
I am becoming impatient to see him
I think of him as a friend,

30   Often I look out of the window
Often I run to the gate
I think, He will come this evening,
I think it is rather late.

I am hungry to be interrupted
35   Forever and ever amen
O Person from Porlock come quickly
And bring my thoughts to an end.

          . . .

I felicitate the people who have a Person from Porlock
To break up everything and throw it away
40   Because then there will be nothing to keep them
And they need not stay.

          . . .

Why do they grumble so much?
He comes like a benison
They should be glad he has not forgotten them
45   They might have had to go on.

          . . .

These thoughts are depressing I know. They are depressing,
I wish I was more cheerful, it is more pleasant,
Also it is a duty, we should smile as well as submitting
To the purpose of One Above who is experimenting

50 With various mixtures of human character which goes best,
    All is interesting for him it is exciting, but not for us.
    There I go again, Smile, smile, and get some work to do
    Then you will be practically unconscious without positively having to go.

                                                                    1962

                                    Pretty

            Why is the word pretty so underrated?
            In November the leaf is pretty when it falls
            The stream grows deep in the woods after rain
            And in the pretty pool the pike stalks

        5   He stalks his prey, and this is pretty too,
            The prey escapes with an underwater flash
            But not for long, the great fish has him now
            The pike is a fish who always has his prey

            And this is pretty. The water rat is pretty
        10 His paws are not webbed, he cannot shut his nostrils
            As the otter can and the beaver, he is torn between
            The land and water, Not "torn," he does not mind.

            The owl hunts in the evening and it is pretty
            The lake water below him rustles with ice
        15 There is frost coming from the ground, in the air mist
            All this is pretty, it could not be prettier.

            Yes, it could always be prettier, the eye abashes
            It is becoming an eye that cannot see enough,
            Out of the wood the eye climbs. This is prettier
        20 A field in the evening, tilting up.

            The field tilts to the sky. Though it is late
            The sky is lighter than the hill field
            All this looks easy but really it is extraordinary
            Well, it is extraordinary to be so pretty.

        25 And it is careless, and that is always pretty
            This field, this owl, this pike, this pool are careless,
            As Nature is always careless and indifferent
            Who sees, who steps, means nothing, and this is pretty.

            So a person can come along like a thief—pretty!—
        30 Stealing a look, pinching the sound and feel,
            Lick the icicle broken from the bank
            And still say nothing at all, only cry pretty.

            Cry pretty, pretty, pretty and you'll be able
            Very soon not even to cry pretty

35   And so be delivered entirely from humanity
      This is prettiest of all, it is very pretty.

1966

GEORGE ORWELL
1903–1950

"George Orwell" was the pseudonym of Eric Blair, who was born in the village of Motihari in Bengal, India, where his father was a British civil servant. He was sent to private school in England and won a scholarship to Eton, the foremost "public school" (i.e., private boarding school) in the country. At these schools he became conscious of the difference between his own background and the wealthy backgrounds of many of his schoolmates. On leaving school he joined the Imperial Police in Burma (both Burma—now called Myanmar—and India were then still part of the British Empire). His service in Burma from 1922 to 1927 produced a sense of guilt about British colonialism and a feeling that he had to make some personal expiation for it. This he would later do with an anticolonial novel, *Burmese Days* (1934), and essays such as "Shooting an Elephant" (1936), which subordinates lingering colonial attitudes to fiercely anti-imperial insights. He returned to England determined to be a writer and adopted his pseudonym as one way of escaping from the class position in which his elite education placed him. He went to Paris to try to earn a living by teaching while he made his first attempts at writing. His extremely difficult time in Paris was followed by a spell as a tramp in England, and he vividly recorded both experiences in his first book, *Down and Out in Paris and London* (1933). Orwell did not have to suffer the dire poverty that he seems to have courted (he had influential friends who would have been glad to help him); he wanted, however, to learn firsthand about the life of the poor, both out of humane curiosity and because, as he wrote, if he did so "part of my guilt would drop from me."

The Road to Wigan Pier (1937) discusses the experiences Orwell shared with unemployed miners in the north of England. The book pleased neither the left nor the right, for by now Orwell was showing what was to become his characteristic independence of mind on political and social questions: he wrote of what he knew firsthand to be true and was contemptuous of ideologies. He never joined a political party but regarded himself as a man of the uncommitted and independent left.

When the Spanish Civil War broke out in 1936 after General Franco raised his military rebellion against the elected government, Orwell went there as a reporter and stayed to fight on the Republican side, rising to the rank of second lieutenant and suffering a throat wound. His *Homage to Catalonia* (1938) strongly criticized the Communist part in the civil war and showed from his own experience how the Communist Party in Spain was out to destroy anarchists, Trotskyists, and any others on the Republican side who were suspected of not toeing the Stalinist line; it aroused great indignation on the left in Britain and elsewhere, for many leftists believed that they should solidly support the Soviet Union and the Communist Party as the natural leaders in the struggle against international fascism. Orwell never wavered in his belief that while profound social change was necessary and desirable in capitalist countries of the West, the so-called socialism established in Soviet Russia was a perversion of socialism and a wicked tyranny. In *Animal Farm* (1945) he wrote a fable showing how such a perversion of socialism could develop, while in *Nineteen-Eighty-Four* (1949), when he was an embittered man dying of tuberculosis, he wrote a savagely powerful novel depicting a totalitarian future, where the government uses the language of socialism to cover a tyranny that systematically destroys the human spirit. In that vision of hell on Earth, language has become one of the principal instruments of oppression. The Ministry of Truth is there concerned with the transmission of untruth, and the white face of its pyramidal structure proclaims in "Newspeak" the three slogans of the party: "WAR IS PEACE / FREEDOM IS SLAVERY / IGNO-RANCE IS STRENGTH." Three years before Orwell formulated "Newspeak," "doublespeak," and "Big Brother is watching you," he had explored in one of his most influential essays, "Politics and the English Language," the decay of language and the ways in which that decay might be resisted. The fifty years that have passed since he wrote the piece have only confirmed the accuracy of its diagnosis and the value of its prescription.

Orwell was an outstanding journalist, and the essays he wrote regularly for the left-wing British journal *Tribune* and other periodicals include some of his best work. His independent eye made him both a permanent misfit politically and a brilliantly original writer.

Shooting an Elephant

In Moulmein, in Lower Burma, I was hated by large numbers of people—the only time in my life that I have been important enough for this to happen to me. I was sub-divisional police officer of the town, and in an aimless, petty kind of way anti-European feeling was very bitter. No one had the guts to raise a riot, but if a European woman went through the bazaars alone somebody would probably spit betel[1] juice over her dress. As a police officer I was an obvious target and was baited whenever it seemed safe to do so. When a nimble Burman tripped me up on the football field and the referee (another Burman) looked the other way, the crowd yelled with hideous laughter. This happened more than once. In the end the sneering yellow faces of young men that met me everywhere, the insults hooted after me when I was at a safe distance, got badly on my nerves. The young Buddhist priests were the worst of all. There were several thousands of them in the town and none of them seemed to have anything to do except stand on street corners and jeer at Europeans.

All this was perplexing and upsetting. For at that time I had already made up my mind that imperialism was an evil thing and the sooner I chucked up my job and got out of it the better. Theoretically—and secretly, of course—I was all for the Burmese and all against their oppressors, the British. As for the job I was doing, I hated it more bitterly than I can perhaps make clear. In a job like that you see the dirty work of Empire at close quarters. The wretched prisoners huddling in the stinking cages of the lock-ups, the grey, cowed faces of the long-term convicts, the scarred buttocks of the men who had been flogged with bamboos—all these oppressed me with an intolerable sense of guilt. But I could get nothing into perspective. I was young and ill-educated and I had had to think out my problems in the utter silence that is imposed on every Englishman in the East. I did not even know that the British Empire is dying, still less did I know that it is a great deal better than the younger empires that are going to supplant it. All I knew was that I was stuck between my hatred of the empire I served and my rage against the evil-spirited little beasts who tried to make my job impossible. With one part of my mind I

---

1. Leaf of a plant chewed as a delicacy in Burma and other Eastern countries.

thought of the British Raj as an unbreakable tyranny, as something clamped down, *in saecula saeculorum*,[2] upon the will of prostrate peoples; with another part I thought that the greatest joy in the world would be to drive a bayonet into a Buddhist priest's guts. Feelings like these are the normal by-products of imperialism; ask any Anglo-Indian official, if you can catch him off duty.

One day something happened which in a roundabout way was enlightening. It was a tiny incident in itself, but it gave me a better glimpse than I had had before of the real nature of imperialism—the real motives for which despotic governments act. Early one morning the sub-inspector at a police station the other end of the town rang me up on the phone and said that an elephant was ravaging the bazaar. Would I please come and do something about it? I did not know what I could do, but I wanted to see what was happening and I got on to a pony and started out. I took my rifle, an old .44 Winchester and much too small to kill an elephant, but I thought the noise might be useful *in terrorem*.[3] Various Burmans stopped me on the way and told me about the elephant's doings. It was not, of course, a wild elephant, but a tame one which had gone "must."[4] It had been chained up as tame elephants always are when their attack of "must" is due, but on the previous night it had broken its chain and escaped. Its mahout,[5] the only person who could manage it when it was in that state, had set out in pursuit, but he had taken the wrong direction and was now twelve hours' journey away, and in the morning the elephant had suddenly reappeared in the town. The Burmese population had no weapons and were quite helpless against it. It had already destroyed somebody's bamboo hut, killed a cow and raided some fruit-stalls and devoured the stock; also it had met the municipal rubbish van, and, when the driver jumped out and took to his heels, had turned the van over and inflicted violence upon it.

The Burmese sub-inspector and some Indian constables were waiting for me in the quarter where the elephant had been seen. It was a very poor quarter, a labyrinth of squalid bamboo huts, thatched with palm-leaf, winding all over a steep hillside. I remember that it was a cloudy stuffy morning at the beginning of the rains. We began questioning the people as to where the elephant had gone, and, as usual, failed to get any definite information. That is invariably the case in the East; a story always sounds clear enough at a distance, but the nearer you get to the scene of events the vaguer it becomes. Some of the people said that the elephant had gone in one direction, some said that he had gone in another, some professed not even to have heard of any elephant. I had almost made up my mind that the whole story was a pack of lies, when we heard yells a little distance away. There was a loud, scandalised cry of "Go away, child! Go away this instant!" and an old woman with a switch in her hand came round the corner of a hut, violently shooing away a crowd of naked children. Some more women followed, clicking their tongues and exclaiming; evidently there was something there that the children ought not to have seen. I rounded the hut and saw a man's dead body sprawling in the mud. He was an Indian, a black Dravidian coolie,[6] almost naked, and he could not have been dead many minutes. The people said that the elephant had come suddenly upon him round the corner of the hut, caught him with its trunk, put its foot on his back and ground him into the earth. This was the

2. For ever and ever (Latin). "Raj": rule (Hindi).
3. To frighten it (Latin).
4. A state of sexual frenzy to which certain animals are subject at irregular intervals.
5. Elephant driver (Hindi).
6. Hired laborer (disputed origin). "Dravidian": a South Asian people.

rainy season and the ground was soft, and his face had scored a trench a foot deep and a couple of yards long. He was lying on his belly with arms crucified and head sharply twisted to one side. His face was coated with mud, the eyes wide open, the teeth bared and grinning with an expression of unendurable agony. (Never tell me, by the way, that the dead look peaceful. Most of the corpses I have seen looked devilish.) The friction of the great beast's foot had stripped the skin from his back as neatly as one skins a rabbit. As soon as I saw the dead man I sent an orderly to a friend's house nearby to borrow an elephant rifle. I had already sent back the pony, not wanting it to go mad with fright and throw me if it smelled the elephant.

The orderly came back in a few minutes with a rifle and five cartridges, and meanwhile some Burmans had arrived and told us that the elephant was in the paddy fields below, only a few hundred yards away. As I started forward practically the whole population of the quarter flocked out of their houses and followed me. They had seen the rifle and were all shouting excitedly that I was going to shoot the elephant. They had not shown much interest in the elephant when he was merely ravaging their homes, but it was different now that he was going to be shot. It was a bit of fun to them, as it would be to an English crowd; besides, they wanted the meat. It made me vaguely uneasy. I had no intention of shooting the elephant—I had merely sent for the rifle to defend myself if necessary—and it is always unnerving to have a crowd following you. I marched down the hill, looking and feeling a fool, with the rifle over my shoulder and an ever-growing army of people jostling at my heels. At the bottom, when you got away from the huts, there was a metalled road and beyond that a miry waste of paddy fields a thousand yards across, not yet ploughed but soggy from the first rains and dotted with coarse grass. The elephant was standing eighty yards from the road, his left side towards us. He took not the slightest notice of the crowd's approach. He was tearing up bunches of grass, beating them against his knees to clean them and stuffing them into his mouth.

I had halted on the road. As soon as I saw the elephant I knew with perfect certainty that I ought not to shoot him. It is a serious matter to shoot a working elephant—it is comparable to destroying a huge and costly piece of machinery—and obviously one ought not to do it if it can possibly be avoided. And at that distance, peacefully eating, the elephant looked no more dangerous than a cow. I thought then and I think now that his attack of "must" was already passing off; in which case he would merely wander harmlessly about until the mahout came back and caught him. Moreover, I did not in the least want to shoot him. I decided that I would watch him for a little while to make sure that he did not turn savage again, and then go home.

But at that moment I glanced round at the crowd that had followed me. It was an immense crowd, two thousand at the least and growing every minute. It blocked the road for a long distance on either side. I looked at the sea of yellow faces above the garish clothes—faces all happy and excited over this bit of fun, all certain that the elephant was going to be shot. They were watching me as they would watch a conjuror about to perform a trick. They did not like me, but with the magical rifle in my hands I was momentarily worth watching. And suddenly I realised that I should have to shoot the elephant after all. The people expected it of me and I had got to do it; I could feel their two thousand wills pressing me forward, irresistibly. And it was at this moment, as I stood there with the rifle in my hands, that I first grasped the hollowness, the futility of the white man's dominion in the East. Here was I,

the white man with his gun, standing in front of the unarmed native crowd—
seemingly the leading actor of the piece; but in reality I was only an absurd
puppet pushed to and fro by the will of those yellow faces behind. I perceived
in this moment that when the white man turns tyrant it is his own freedom
that he destroys. He becomes a sort of hollow, posing dummy, the conven-
tionalised figure of a sahib.[7] For it is the condition of his rule that he shall
spend his life in trying to impress the "natives" and so in every crisis he has
got to do what the "natives" expect of him. He wears a mask, and his face
grows to fit it. I had got to shoot the elephant. I had committed myself to doing
it when I sent for the rifle. A sahib has got to act like a sahib; he has got to
appear resolute, to know his own mind and do definite things. To come all
that way, rifle in hand, with two thousand people marching at my heels, and
then to trail feebly away, having done nothing—no, that was impossible. The
crowd would laugh at me. And my whole life, every white man's life in the
East, was one long struggle not to be laughed at.

But I did not want to shoot the elephant. I watched him beating his bunch
of grass against his knees, with that preoccupied grandmotherly air that elephants have. It seemed to me that it would be murder to shoot him. At that
age I was not squeamish about killing animals, but I had never shot an elephant and never wanted to. (Somehow it always seems worse to kill a *large*
animal.) Besides, there was the beast's owner to be considered. Alive, the
elephant was worth at least a hundred pounds; dead, he would only be worth
the value of his tusks—five pounds, possibly. But I had got to act quickly. I
turned to some experienced-looking Burmans who had been there when we
arrived, and asked them how the elephant had been behaving. They all said
the same thing: he took no notice of you if you left him alone, but he might
charge if you went too close to him.

It was perfectly clear to me what I ought to do. I ought to walk up to within,
say, twenty-five yards of the elephant and test his behaviour. If he charged I
could shoot, if he took no notice of me it would be safe to leave him until the
mahout came back. But also I knew that I was going to do no such thing. I
was a poor shot with a rifle and the ground was soft mud into which one would
sink at every step. If the elephant charged and I missed him, I should have
about as much chance as a toad under a steam-roller. But even then I was not
thinking particularly of my own skin, only the watchful yellow faces behind.
For at that moment, with the crowd watching me, I was not afraid in the
ordinary sense, as I would have been if I had been alone. A white man mustn't
be frightened in front of "natives"; and so, in general, he isn't frightened. The
sole thought in my mind was that if anything went wrong those two thousand
Burmans would see me pursued, caught, trampled on and reduced to a grinning corpse like that Indian up the hill. And if that happened it was quite
probable that some of them would laugh. That would never do. There was
only one alternative. I shoved the cartridges into the magazine and lay down
on the road to get a better aim.

The crowd grew very still, and a deep, low, happy sigh, as of people who see
the theatre curtain go up at last, breathed from innumerable throats. They
were going to have their bit of fun after all. The rifle was a beautiful German
thing with cross-hair sights. I did not then know that in shooting an elephant
one should shoot to cut an imaginary bar running from ear-hole to ear-hole.
I ought therefore, as the elephant was sideways on, to have aimed straight at

7. White gentleman (Urdu).

his ear-hole; actually I aimed several inches in front of this, thinking the brain would be further forward.

When I pulled the trigger I did not hear the bang or feel the kick—one never does when a shot goes home—but I heard the devilish roar of glee that went up from the crowd. In that instant, in too short a time, one would have thought, even for the bullet to get there, a mysterious, terrible change had come over the elephant. He neither stirred nor fell, but every line of his body had altered. He looked suddenly stricken, shrunken, immensely old, as though the frightful impact of the bullet had paralysed him without knocking him down. At last, after what seemed a long time—it might have been five seconds, I dare say—he sagged flabbily to his knees. His mouth slobbered. An enormous senility seemed to have settled upon him. One could have imagined him thousands of years old. I fired again into the same spot. At the second shot he did not collapse but climbed with desperate slowness to his feet and stood weakly upright, with legs sagging and head drooping. I fired a third time. That was the shot that did for him. You could see the agony of it jolt his whole body and knock the last remnant of strength from his legs. But in falling he seemed for a moment to rise, for as his hind legs collapsed beneath him he seemed to tower upwards like a huge rock toppling, his trunk reaching skyward like a tree. He trumpeted, for the first and only time. And then down he came, his belly towards me, with a crash that seemed to shake the ground even where I lay.

I got up. The Burmans were already racing past me across the mud. It was obvious that the elephant would never rise again, but he was not dead. He was breathing very rhythmically with long rattling gasps, his great mound of a side painfully rising and falling. His mouth was wide open—I could see far down into caverns of pale pink throat. I waited a long time for him to die, but his breathing did not weaken. Finally I fired my two remaining shots into the spot where I thought his heart must be. The thick blood welled out of him like red velvet, but still he did not die. His body did not even jerk when the shots hit him, the tortured breathing continued without a pause. He was dying, very slowly and in great agony, but in some world remote from me where not even a bullet could damage him further. I felt that I had got to put an end to that dreadful noise. It seemed dreadful to see the great beast lying there, powerless to move and yet powerless to die, and not even to be able to finish him. I sent back for my small rifle and poured shot after shot into his heart and down his throat. They seemed to make no impression. The tortured gasps continued as steadily as the ticking of a clock.

In the end I could not stand it any longer and went away. I heard later that it took him half an hour to die. Burmans were arriving with dahs[8] and baskets even before I left, and I was told they had stripped his body almost to the bones by the afternoon.

Afterwards, of course, there were endless discussions about the shooting of the elephant. The owner was furious, but he was only an Indian and could do nothing. Besides, legally I had done the right thing, for a mad elephant has to be killed, like a mad dog, if its owner fails to control it. Among the Europeans opinion was divided. The older men said I was right, the younger men said it was a damn shame to shoot an elephant for killing a coolie, because an elephant was worth more than any damn Coringhee[9] coolie. And afterwards I

8. Short heavy swords (Burmese).
9. From the seaport Coringa, on the east coast of Madras in British India.

was very glad that the coolie had been killed; it put me legally in the right and it gave me a sufficient pretext for shooting the elephant. I often wondered whether any of the others grasped that I had done it solely to avoid looking a fool.

1936

Politics and the English Language

Most people who bother with the matter at all would admit that the English language is in a bad way, but it is generally assumed that we cannot by conscious action do anything about it. Our civilisation is decadent, and our language—so the argument runs—must inevitably share in the general collapse. It follows that any struggle against the abuse of language is a sentimental archaism, like preferring candles to electric light or hansom cabs to aeroplanes. Underneath this lies the half-conscious belief that language is a natural growth and not an instrument which we shape for our own purposes.

Now, it is clear that the decline of a language must ultimately have political and economic causes: it is not due simply to the bad influence of this or that individual writer. But an effect can become a cause, reinforcing the original cause and producing the same effect in an intensified form, and so on indefinitely. A man may take to drink because he feels himself to be a failure, and then fail all the more completely because he drinks. It is rather the same thing that is happening to the English language. It becomes ugly and inaccurate because our thoughts are foolish, but the slovenliness of our language makes it easier for us to have foolish thoughts. The point is that the process is reversible. Modern English, especially written English, is full of bad habits which spread by imitation and which can be avoided if one is willing to take the necessary trouble. If one gets rid of these habits one can think more clearly, and to think clearly is a necessary first step towards political regeneration: so that the fight against bad English is not frivolous and is not the exclusive concern of professional writers. I will come back to this presently, and I hope that by that time the meaning of what I have said here will have become clearer. Meanwhile, here are five specimens of the English language as it is now habitually written.

These five passages have not been picked out because they are especially bad—I could have quoted far worse if I had chosen—but because they illustrate various of the mental vices from which we now suffer. They are a little below the average, but are fairly representative samples. I number them so that I can refer back to them when necessary:

> 1. I am not, indeed, sure whether it is not true to say that the Milton who once seemed not unlike a seventeenth-century Shelley had not become, out of an experience ever more bitter in each year, more alien (sic)[1] to the founder of that Jesuit sect which nothing could induce him to tolerate.
>
> Professor Harold Laski (Essay in *Freedom of Expression*).

---

1. Thus, i.e., that's the way it was written.

2. Above all, we cannot play ducks and drakes with a native battery of idioms which prescribes such egregious collocations of vocables as the Basic *put up with* for *tolerate* or *put at a loss* for *bewilder*.

> Professor Lancelot Hogben (*Interglossa*).

3. On the one side we have the free personality: by definition it is not neurotic, for it has neither conflict nor dream. Its desires, such as they are, are transparent, for they are just what institutional approval keeps in the forefront of consciousness; another institutional pattern would alter their number and intensity; there is little in them that is natural, irreducible, or culturally dangerous. But *on the other side,* the social bond itself is nothing but the mutual reflection of these self-secure integrities. Recall the definition of love. Is not this the very picture of a small academic? Where is there a place in this hall of mirrors for either personality or fraternity?

> Essay on psychology in *Politics* (New York).

4. All the "best people" from the gentlemen's clubs, and all the frantic Fascist captains, united in common hatred of Socialism and bestial horror of the rising tide of the mass revolutionary movement, have turned to acts of provocation, to foul incendiarism, to medieval legends of poisoned wells, to legalise their own destruction to proletarian organisations, and rouse the agitated petty-bourgeoisie to chauvinistic fervour on behalf of the fight against the revolutionary way out of the crisis.

> Communist pamphlet.

5. If a new spirit *is* to be infused into this old country, there is one thorny and contentious reform which must be tackled, and that is the humanisation and galvanisation of the BBC.[2] Timidity here will bespeak canker and atrophy of the soul. The heart of Britain may be sound and of strong beat, for instance, but the British lion's roar at present is like that of Bottom in Shakespeare's *Midsummer Night's Dream*—as gentle as any sucking dove. A virile new Britain cannot continue indefinitely to be traduced in the eyes, or rather ears, of the world by the effete languors of Langham Place, brazenly masquerading as "standard English." When the Voice of Britain is heard at nine o'clock, better far and infinitely less ludicrous to hear aitches[3] honestly dropped than the present priggish, inflated, inhibited, school-ma'amish arch braying of blameless bashful mewing maidens!

> Letter in *Tribune*.

Each of these passages has faults of its own, but, quite apart from avoidable ugliness, two qualities are common to all of them. The first is staleness of imagery: the other is lack of precision. The writer either has a meaning and cannot express it, or he inadvertently says something else, or he is almost indifferent as to whether his words mean anything or not. This mixture of vagueness and sheer incompetence is the most marked characteristic of mod-

2. British Broadcasting Corporation.
3. I.e., *h* sounds, which are not aspirated in colloquial speech. During—and for some time after—World War II, few programs had a larger audience than the evening nine o'clock news. Langham Place is the location of the BBC's main offices in London.

ern English prose, and especially of any kind of political writing. As soon as certain topics are raised, the concrete melts into the abstract and no one seems able to think of turns of speech that are not hackneyed: prose consists less and less of *words* chosen for the sake of their meaning, and more of *phrases* tacked together like the sections of a prefabricated hen-house. I list below, with notes and examples, various of the tricks by means of which the work of prose construction is habitually dodged:

Dying metaphors. A newly invented metaphor assists thought by evoking a visual image, while on the other hand a metaphor which is technically "dead" (e.g., *iron resolution*) has in effect reverted to being an ordinary word and can generally be used without loss of vividness. But in between these two classes there is a huge dump of worn-out metaphors which have lost all evocative power and are merely used because they save people the trouble of inventing phrases for themselves. Examples are: *Ring the changes on, take up the cudgels for, toe the line, ride roughshod over, stand shoulder to shoulder with, play into the hands of, no axe to grind, grist to the mill, fishing in troubled waters, rift within the lute, on the order of the day, Achilles' heel, swan song, hotbed.* Many of these are used without knowledge of their meaning (What is a "rift," for instance?), and incompatible metaphors are frequently mixed, a sure sign that the writer is not interested in what he is saying. Some metaphors now current have been twisted out of their original meaning without those who use them even being aware of the fact. For example, *toe the line* is sometimes written *tow the line.* Another example is *the hammer and the anvil,* now always used with the implication that the anvil gets the worst of it. In real life it is always the anvil that breaks the hammer, never the other way about: a writer who stopped to think what he was saying would be aware of this, and would avoid perverting the original phrase.

Operators, or *verbal false limbs.* These save the trouble of picking out appropriate verbs and nouns, and at the same time pad each sentence with extra syllables which give it an appearance of symmetry. Characteristic phrases are: *render inoperative, militate against, prove unacceptable, make contact with, be subjected to, give rise to, give grounds for, have the effect of, play a leading part* (*rôle*) *in, make itself felt, take effect, exhibit a tendency to, serve the purpose of,* etc etc. The keynote is the elimination of simple verbs. Instead of being a single word, such as *break, stop, spoil, mend, kill,* a verb becomes a *phrase,* made up of a noun or adjective tacked on to some general-purposes verb such as *prove, serve, form, play, render.* In addition, the passive voice is wherever possible used in preference to the active, and noun constructions are used instead of gerunds (*by examination of* instead of *by examining*). The range of verbs is further cut down by means of the *-ise* and *de-* formations, and banal statements are given an appearance of profundity by means of the *not un-* formation. Simple conjunctions and prepositions are replaced by such phrases as *with respect to, having regard to, the fact that, by dint of, in view of, in the interests of, on the hypothesis that;* and the ends of sentences are saved from anticlimax by such resounding commonplaces as *greatly to be desired, cannot be left out of account, a development to be expected in the near future, deserving of serious consideration, brought to a satisfactory conclusion,* and so on and so forth.

Pretentious diction. Words like *phenomenon, element, individual* (as noun), *objective, categorical, effective, virtual, basic, primary, promote, constitute, exhibit, exploit, utilise, eliminate, liquidate,* are used to dress up simple statements and give an air of scientific impartiality to biassed judgements. Adjectives like *epoch-making, epic, historic, unforgettable, triumphant, age-old, inevitable, inexorable, veritable,* are used to dignify the sordid processes of international politics, while writing that aims at glorifying war usually takes on an archaic colour, its characteristic words being: *realm, throne, chariot, mailed fist, trident, sword, shield, buckler, banner, jackboot, clarion.* Foreign words and expressions such as *cul de sac, ancien régime, deus ex machina, mutatis mutandis, status quo, Gleichschaltung, Weltanschauung,*[4] are used to give an air of culture and elegance. Except for the useful abbreviations *i.e., e.g.,* and *etc.,* there is no real need for any of the hundreds of foreign phrases now current in English. Bad writers, and especially scientific, political and sociological writers, are nearly always haunted by the notion that Latin or Greek words are grander than Saxon ones, and unnecessary words like *expedite, ameliorate, predict, extraneous, deracinated, clandestine, sub-aqueous* and hundreds of others constantly gain ground from their Anglo-Saxon opposite numbers.[5] The jargon peculiar to Marxist writing (*hyena, hangman, cannibal, petty bourgeois, these gentry, lacquey, flunkey, mad dog, White Guard,* etc.) consists largely of words and phrases translated from Russian, German or French; but the normal way of coining a new word is to use a Latin or Greek root with the appropriate affix and, where necessary, the *-ise* formation. It is often easier to make up words of this kind (*deregionalise, impermissible, extra-marital, non-fragmentatory* and so forth) than to think up the English words that will cover one's meaning. The result, in general, is an increase in slovenliness and vagueness.

Meaningless words. In certain kinds of writing, particularly in art criticism and literary criticism, it is normal to come across long passages which are almost completely lacking in meaning.[6] Words like *romantic, plastic, values, human, dead, sentimental, natural, vitality,* as used in art criticism, are strictly meaningless, in the sense that they not only do not point to any discoverable object, but are hardly even expected to do so by the reader. When one critic writes, "The outstanding features of Mr X's work is its living quality," while another writes, "The immediately striking thing about Mr X's work is its peculiar deadness," the reader accepts this as a simple difference of opinion. If words like *black* and *white* were involved, instead of the jargon words *dead* and *living,* he would see at once that language was being used in an improper way. Many political words are similarly abused. The word *Fascism* has now no meaning

4. Respectively: dead end (French), former system of government (French), the god from the machine (Latin), with the necessary changes (Latin), the existing state of things (Latin), standardization of political institutions among authoritarian states (German), and philosophy of life (German).
5. An interesting illustration of this is the way in which the English flower names which were in use till very recently are being ousted by Greek ones, *snapdragon* becoming *antirrhinum, forget-me-not* becoming *myosotis,* etc. It is hard to see any practical reason for this change of fashion: it is probably due to an instinctive turning-away from the more homely word and a vague feeling that the Greek word is scientific [Orwell's note].
6. Example: "Comfort's catholicity of perception and image, strangely Whitmanesque in range, almost the exact opposite in aesthetic compulsion, continues to evoke that trembling atmospheric accumulative hinting at a cruel, an inexorably serene timelessness . . . Wrey Gardiner scores by aiming at simple bullseyes with precision. Only they are not so simple, and through this contented sadness runs more than the surface bitter-sweet of resignation." (*Poetry Quarterly.*) [Orwell's note].

except in so far as it signifies "something not desirable." The words *democracy, socialism, freedom, patriotic, realistic, justice,* have each of them several different meanings which cannot be reconciled with one another. In the case of a word like *democracy,* not only is there no agreed definition, but the attempt to make one is resisted from all sides. It is almost universally felt that when we call a country democratic we are praising it: consequently the defenders of every kind of régime claim that it is a democracy, and fear that they might have to stop using the word if it were tied down to any one meaning. Words of this kind are often used in a consciously dishonest way. That is, the person who uses them has his own private definition, but allows his hearer to think he means something quite different. Statements like *Marshal Pétain[7] was a true patriot, The Soviet press is the freest in the world, The Catholic Church is opposed to persecution,* are almost always made with intent to deceive. Other words used in variable meanings, in most cases more or less dishonestly, are: *class, totalitarian, science, progressive, reactionary, bourgeois, equality.*

Now that I have made this catalogue of swindles and perversions, let me give another example of the kind of writing that they lead to. This time it must of its nature be an imaginary one. I am going to translate a passage of good English into modern English of the worst sort. Here is a well-known verse from *Ecclesiastes:*

> I returned, and saw under the sun, that the race is not to the swift, nor the battle to the strong, neither yet bread to the wise, nor yet riches to men of understanding, nor yet favour to men of skill; but time and chance happeneth to them all.

Here it is in modern English:

> Objective consideration of contemporary phenomena compels the conclusion that success or failure in competitive activities exhibits no tendency to be commensurate with innate capacity, but that a considerable element of the unpredictable must invariably be taken into account.

This is a parody, but not a very gross one. Exhibit 3, above, for instance, contains several patches of the same kind of English. It will be seen that I have not made a full translation. The beginning and ending of the sentence follow the original meaning fairly closely, but in the middle the concrete illustrations—race, battle, bread—dissolve into the vague phrase "success or failure in competitive activities". This had to be so, because no modern writer of the kind I am discussing—no one capable of using phrases like "objective consideration of contemporary phenomena"—would ever tabulate his thoughts in that precise and detailed way. The whole tendency of modern prose is away from concreteness. Now analyse these two sentences a little more closely. The first contains 49 words but only 60 syllables, and all its words are those of everyday life. The second contains 38 words of 90 syllables: 18 of its words are from Latin roots, and one from Greek. The first sentence contains six vivid images, and only one phrase ("time and chance") that could be called vague. The second contains not a single fresh, arresting phrase, and in spite of its 90 syllables it gives only a shortened version of the meaning contained in the first. Yet without a doubt it is the second kind of sentence

---

7. French army officer (1856–1951), head of the Vichy government that collaborated with Germany in World War II.

that is gaining ground in modern English. I do not want to exaggerate. This kind of writing is not yet universal, and outcrops of simplicity will occur here and there in the worst-written page. Still, if you or I were told to write a few lines on the uncertainty of human fortunes, we should probably come much nearer to my imaginary sentence than to the one from *Ecclesiastes*.

As I have tried to show, modern writing at its worst does not consist in picking out words for the sake of their meaning and inventing images in order to make the meaning clearer. It consists in gumming together long strips of words which have already been set in order by someone else, and making the results presentable by sheer humbug. The attraction of this way of writing is that it is easy. It is easier—even quicker, once you have the habit—to say *In my opinion it is a not unjustifiable assumption that* than to say *I think*. If you use ready-made phrases, you not only don't have to hunt about for words; you also don't have to bother with the rhythms of your sentences, since these phrases are generally so arranged as to be more or less euphonious. When you are composing in a hurry—when you are dictating to a stenographer, for instance, or making a public speech—it is natural to fall into a pretentious, latinised style. Tags like *a consideration which we should do well to bear in mind* or *a conclusion to which all of us would readily assent* will save many a sentence from coming down with a bump. By using stale metaphors, similes and idioms, you save much mental effort, at the cost of leaving your meaning vague, not only for your reader but for yourself. This is the significance of mixed metaphors. The sole aim of a metaphor is to call up a visual image. When these images clash—as in *The Fascist octopus has sung its swan song, the jackboot is thrown into the melting-pot*—it can be taken as certain that the writer is not seeing a mental image of the objects he is naming; in other words he is not really thinking. Look again at the examples I gave at the beginning of this essay. Professor Laski (1) uses five negatives in 53 words. One of these is superfluous, making nonsense of the whole passage, and in addition there is the slip *alien* for akin, making further nonsense, and several avoidable pieces of clumsiness which increase the general vagueness. Professor Hogben (2) plays ducks and drakes with a battery which is able to write prescriptions, and, while disapproving of the everyday phrase *put up with,* is unwilling to look *egregious* up in the dictionary and see what it means. (3), if one takes an uncharitable attitude towards it, is simply meaningless: probably one could work out its intended meaning by reading the whole of the article in which it occurs. In (4) the writer knows more or less what he wants to say, but an accumulation of stale phrases chokes him like tea-leaves blocking a sink. In (5) words and meaning have almost parted company. People who write in this manner usually have a general emotional meaning—they dislike one thing and want to express solidarity with another—but they are not interested in the detail of what they are saying. A scrupulous writer, in every sentence that he writes, will ask himself at least four questions, thus: What am I trying to say? What words will express it? What image or idiom will make it clearer? Is this image fresh enough to have an effect? And he will probably ask himself two more: Could I put it more shortly? Have I said anything that is avoidably ugly? But you are not obliged to go to all this trouble. You can shirk it by simply throwing your mind open and letting the ready-made phrases come crowding in. They will construct your sentences for you—even think your thoughts for you, to a certain extent—and at need they will perform the important service of partially concealing your meaning even from yourself. It is at this point that the special connection between politics and the debasement of language becomes clear.

In our time it is broadly true that political writing is bad writing. Where it is not true, it will generally be found that the writer is some kind of rebel, expressing his private opinions, and not a "party line." Orthodoxy, of whatever colour, seems to demand a lifeless, imitative style. The political dialects to be found in pamphlets, leading articles, manifestos, White Papers and the speeches of Under-Secretaries[8] do, of course, vary from party to party, but they are all alike in that one almost never finds in them a fresh, vivid, home-made turn of speech. When one watches some tired hack on the platform mechanically repeating the familiar phrases—*bestial atrocities, iron heel, blood-stained tyranny, free peoples of the world, stand shoulder to shoulder*—one often has a curious feeling that one is not watching a live human being but some kind of dummy: a feeling which suddenly becomes stronger at moments when the light catches the speaker's spectacles and turns them into blank discs which seem to have no eyes behind them. And this is not altogether fanciful. A speaker who uses that kind of phraseology has gone some distance towards turning himself into a machine. The appropriate noises are coming out of his larynx, but his brain is not involved as it would be if he were choosing his words for himself. If the speech he is making is one that he is accustomed to make over and over again, he may be almost unconscious of what he is saying, as one is when one utters the responses in church. And this reduced state of consciousness, if not indispensable, is at any rate favourable to political conformity.

In our time, political speech and writing are largely the defence of the indefensible. Things like the continuance of British rule in India,[9] the Russian purges and deportations, the dropping of the atom bombs on Japan, can indeed be defended, but only by arguments which are too brutal for most people to face, and which do not square with the professed aims of political parties. Thus political language has to consist largely of euphemism, question-begging and sheer cloudy vagueness. Defenceless villages are bombarded from the air, the inhabitants driven out into the countryside, the cattle machine-gunned, the huts set on fire with incendiary bullets: this is called *pacification*. Millions of peasants are robbed of their farms and sent trudging along the roads with no more than they can carry: this is called *transfer of population* or *rectification of frontiers*. People are imprisoned for years without trial, or shot in the back of the neck or sent to die of scurvy in Arctic lumber camps: this is called *elimination of unreliable elements*. Such phraseology is needed if one wants to name things without calling up mental pictures of them. Consider for instance some comfortable English professor defending Russian totalitarianism. He cannot say outright, "I believe in killing off your opponents when you can get good results by doing so." Probably, therefore, he will say something like this:

> While freely conceding that the Soviet régime exhibits certain features which the humanitarian may be inclined to deplore, we must, I think, agree that a certain curtailment of the right to political opposition is an unavoidable concomitant of transitional periods, and that the rigours which the Russian people have been called upon to undergo have been amply justified in the sphere of concrete achievement.

The inflated style is itself a kind of euphemism. A mass of Latin words falls upon the facts like soft snow, blurring the outlines and covering up all the details. The great enemy of clear language is insincerity. When there is a gap between one's real and one's declared aims, one turns as it were instinctively to long words and exhausted idioms, like a cuttlefish squirting out ink. In our age there is no such thing as "keeping out of politics." All issues are political issues, and politics itself is a mass of lies, evasions, folly, hatred and schizophrenia. When the general atmosphere is bad, language must suffer. I should expect to find—this is a guess which I have not sufficient knowledge to verify—that the German, Russian and Italian languages have all deteriorated in the last ten or fifteen years, as a result of dictatorship.

But if thought corrupts language, language can also corrupt thought. A bad usage can spread by tradition and imitation, even among people who should and do know better. The debased language that I have been discussing is in some ways very convenient. Phrases like a *not unjustifiable assumption, leaves much to be desired, would serve no good purpose, a consideration which we should do well to bear in mind,* are a continuous temptation, a packet of aspirins always at one's elbow. Look back through this essay, and for certain you will find that I have again and again committed the very faults I am protesting against. By this morning's post I have received a pamphlet dealing with conditions in Germany. The author tells me that he "felt impelled" to write it. I open it at random, and here is almost the first sentence that I see: "(The Allies) have an opportunity not only of achieving a radical transformation of Germany's social and political structure in such a way as to avoid a nationalistic reaction in Germany itself, but at the same time of laying the foundations of a co-operative and unified Europe." You see, he "feels impelled" to write—feels, presumably, that he has something new to say—and yet his words, like cavalry horses answering the bugle, group themselves automatically into the familiar dreary pattern. This invasion of one's mind by ready-made phrases (*lay the foundations, achieve a radical transformation*) can only be prevented if one is constantly on guard against them, and every such phrase anaesthetises a portion of one's brain.

I said earlier that the decadence of our language is probably curable. Those who deny this would argue, if they produced an argument at all, that language merely reflects existing social conditions, and that we cannot influence its development by any direct tinkering with words and constructions. So far as the general tone or spirit of a language goes, this may be true, but it is not true in detail. Silly words and expressions have often disappeared, not through any evolutionary process but owing to the conscious action of a minority. Two recent examples were *explore every avenue* and *leave no stone unturned,* which were killed by the jeers of a few journalists. There is a long list of fly-blown metaphors which could similarly be got rid of if enough people would interest themselves in the job; and it should also be possible to laugh the *not un-* formation out of existence,[1] to reduce the amount of Latin and Greek in the average sentence, to drive out foreign phrases and strayed scientific words, and, in general, to make pretentiousness unfashionable. But all these are minor points. The defence of the English language implies more than this, and perhaps it is best to start by saying what it does *not* imply.

To begin with, it has nothing to do with archaism, with the salvaging of

---

1. One can cure oneself of the *not un-* formation by memorising this sentence: A *not unblack dog was chasing a not unsmall rabbit across a not ungreen field* [Orwell's note].

obsolete words and turns of speech, or with the setting-up of a "standard English" which must never be departed from. On the contrary, it is especially concerned with the scrapping of every word or idiom which has outworn its usefulness. It has nothing to do with correct grammar and syntax, which are of no importance so long as one makes one's meaning clear, or with the avoidance of Americanisms, or with having what is called a "good prose style." On the other hand it is not concerned with fake simplicity and the attempt to make written English colloquial. Nor does it even imply in every case preferring the Saxon word to the Latin one, though it does imply using the fewest and shortest words that will cover one's meaning. What is above all needed is to let the meaning choose the word, and not the other way about. In prose, the worst thing one can do with words is to surrender to them. When you think of a concrete object, you think wordlessly, and then, if you want to describe the thing you have been visualising, you probably hunt about till you find the exact words that seem to fit it. When you think of something abstract you are more inclined to use words from the start, and unless you make a conscious effort to prevent it, the existing dialect will come rushing in and do the job for you, at the expense of blurring or even changing your meaning. Probably it is better to put off using words as long as possible and get one's meaning as clear as one can through pictures or sensations. Afterwards one can choose—not simply *accept*—the phrases that will best cover the meaning, and then switch round and decide what impression one's words are likely to make on another person. This last effort of the mind cuts out all stale or mixed images, all prefabricated phrases, needless repetitions, and humbug and vagueness generally. But one can often be in doubt about the effect of a word or a phrase, and one needs rules that one can rely on when instinct fails. I think the following rules will cover most cases:

    i. Never use a metaphor, simile or other figure of speech which you are used to seeing in print.

    ii. Never use a long word where a short one will do.

    iii. If it is possible to cut a word out, always cut it out.

    iv. Never use the passive where you can use the active.

    v. Never use a foreign phrase, a scientific word or a jargon word if you can think of an everyday English equivalent.

    vi. Break any of these rules sooner than say anything outright barbarous.

These rules sound elementary, and so they are, but they demand a deep change of attitude in anyone who has grown used to writing in the style now fashionable. One could keep all of them and still write bad English, but one could not write the kind of stuff that I quoted in those five specimens at the beginning of this article.

I have not here been considering the literary use of language, but merely language as an instrument for expressing and not for concealing or preventing thought. Stuart Chase and others have come near to claiming that all abstract words are meaningless, and have used this as a pretext for advocating a kind of political quietism. Since you don't know what Fascism is, how can you struggle against Fascism? One need not swallow such absurdities as this, but one ought to recognise that the present political chaos is connected with the decay of language, and that one can probably bring about some improvement by starting at the verbal end. If you simplify your English, you are freed from the worst follies of orthodoxy. You cannot speak any of the necessary dialects, and when you make a stupid remark its stupidity will be obvious, even to yourself. Political language—and with variations this is true of all political parties, from Conservatives to Anarchists—is designed to make lies sound truthful and murder respectable, and to give an appearance of solidity to pure wind. One cannot change this all in a moment, but one can at least change one's own habits, and from time to time one can even, if one jeers loudly enough, send some worn-out and useless phrase—some *jackboot, Achilles' heel, hotbed, melting pot, acid test, veritable inferno* or other lump of verbal refuse—into the dustbin where it belongs.

1946, 1947

SAMUEL BECKETT
1906–1989

Samuel Beckett was born near Dublin. Like W. B. Yeats, Bernard Shaw, and Oscar Wilde, he came from an Anglo-Irish Protestant family. He received a B.A. from Trinity College, Dublin, and after teaching English at the École Normale Supérieure in Paris for two years, returned to Trinity College to take his M.A. in 1931. He gave up teaching in 1932 to write, and having produced an insightful essay on the early stages of James Joyce's *Finnegans Wake* in 1929, he also worked as Joyce's amanuensis (secretary) and translator. In 1937 he settled permanently in Paris, where during World War II he joined an underground group in the anti-Nazi resistance and, after his group was betrayed, barely escaped into unoccupied France. From the mid-1940s he generally wrote in French and subsequently translated some of his work into an eloquent Irish-inflected English. His early novels—*Murphy* (1938; Eng. trans., 1957), *Watt* (1953), and the trilogy, *Molloy* (1951; 1955), *Malone Dies* (1951; 1956), and *The Unnameable* (1953; 1958)—have been hailed as masterpieces and precursors of postmodern fiction; but he is best-known for his plays, especially *Waiting for Godot* (1952; 1954) and *Endgame* (1957; 1958). He received the Nobel Prize in Literature in 1969.

Not much happens in a Beckett play; there is little plot, little incident, and little characterization. Characters engage in dialogue or dialectical monologues that go nowhere. There is no progression, no development, no resolution. Rambling exchanges and repetitive actions enact the lack of a fixed center, of meaning, of purpose, in the lives depicted. Yet the characters persist in their habitual, almost ritualistic, activities; they go on talking, even if only to themselves. In spite of a reiterated theme of nonexistence, the characters go on existing—if minimally: a stream of discourse, of thought and will, a consciousness questioning its own meaning and purpose. In *Waiting for Godot* the main characters wait for an arrival that is constantly deferred. They inhabit a bleak landscape seemingly confined to one road, one tree; they talk of moving on, yet never leave. Subsequent plays restrict the acting space to a room, to urns, to a mound in which the actor is buried; characters are physically confined or disabled, until *Not I* (1973) presents the most minimal embodiment of human consciousness available to theatrical representation: a disembodied mouth.

Beckett focuses his work on fundamental questions of existence and nonexistence, the mind and the body, the self as known from within and as seen from the outside or in retrospect. Joyce's artistic integrity and stream-of-consciousness technique influenced him, but the minimalism of Beckett's plays and fiction contrast with the maximalism of Joyce's *Ulysses* and *Finnegans Wake*. "I realised that Joyce had gone as far as one could in the direction of knowing more, in control of one's material," he told the biographer James Knowlson. "I realised my own way was in impoverishment, in lack of knowledge and in taking away, in subtracting rather than adding."

At the heart of *Endgame* is the vexed relationship between Hamm, the master, and Clov, his servant and nurse. These irritable, resentful, spiteful characters talk of leaving, dying, or otherwise ending, but they continue repetitively in their peevish ways. They live inside a room with two high windows that afford ambiguous views of an exterior world, where everything may or may not be dead. The play's only other characters are Hamm's parents, Nell and Nagg, but they live in two garbage cans and appear from the shoulders up; their relationship is hardly robust. Like other Beckett plays, this one juxtaposes vaudeville, slapstick, and other comic traditions with the intellectual and the grotesque. While denying the audience the comfortable security of a recognizable world, *Endgame* provides laughs, sometimes at the audience's expense. It shares its tragicomic quality with absurdist drama, which disrupts the conventions of realist drama, draws attention to its own fictionality, and refuses to provide hierarchies of significance. Reduced to bare essentials, the maimed, struggling, incomplete characters of *Endgame*—though often behaving as if they were the bumbling protagonists of a farce—raise unsettling questions about meaning and absurdity, power and dependency, time and repetition, language and the void.

Endgame[1]

For Roger Blin[2]

THE CHARACTERS

NAGG
NELL
HAMM
CLOV

Bare interior.
Grey light.
Left and right back, high up, two small windows, curtains drawn.
Front right, a door. Hanging near door, its face to wall, a picture.
Front left, touching each other, covered with an old sheet, two ashbins.
Centre, in an armchair on castors, covered with an old sheet, HAMM.
Motionless by the door, his eyes fixed on HAMM, CLOV. *Very red face.*
Brief tableau.

[CLOV *goes and stands under window left. Stiff, staggering walk. He looks up at window left. He turns and looks at window right. He goes and stands under window right. He looks up at window right. He turns and looks at window left. He goes out, comes back immediately with a small step-ladder, carries it over and sets it down under window left, gets up on it, draws back curtain. He gets down, takes six steps (for example) towards window right, goes back for ladder, carries it over and sets it down under window right, gets up on it, draws back curtain. He gets down, takes three steps towards window left, goes back for ladder,*

---

1. Translated by the author.
2. Frenchman (1907–1984), who directed the

premieres of *Waiting for Godot, Endgame,* and other Beckett plays.

carries it over and sets it down under window left, gets up on it, looks out of window. Brief laugh. He gets down, takes one step towards window right, goes back for ladder, carries it over and sets it down under window right, gets up on it, looks out of window. Brief laugh. He gets down, goes with ladder towards ashbins, halts, turns, carries back ladder and sets it down under window right, goes to ashbins, removes sheet covering them, folds it over his arm. He raises one lid, stoops and looks into bin. Brief laugh. He closes lid. Same with other bin. He goes to HAMM, *removes sheet covering him, folds it over his arm. In a dressing-gown, a stiff toque[3] on his head, a large blood-stained handkerchief over his face, a whistle hanging from his neck, a rug over his knees, thick socks on his feet,* HAMM *seems to be asleep.* CLOV *looks him over. Brief laugh. He goes to door, halts, turns towards auditorium.*]

CLOV   [*Fixed gaze, tonelessly.*] Finished, it's finished, nearly finished, it must be nearly finished. [*Pause.*] Grain upon grain, one by one, and one day, suddenly, there's a heap, a little heap, the impossible heap. [*Pause.*] I can't be punished any more. [*Pause.*] I'll go now to my kitchen, ten feet by ten feet by ten feet, and wait for him to whistle me. [*Pause.*] Nice dimensions, nice proportions, I'll lean on the table, and look at the wall, and wait for him to whistle me. [*He remains a moment motionless, then goes out. He comes back immediately, goes to window right, takes up the ladder and carries it out. Pause.* HAMM *stirs. He yawns under the handkerchief. He removes the handkerchief from his face. Very red face. Black glasses.*]

HAMM   Me—[*He yawns.*]—to play.[4] [*He holds the handkerchief spread out before him.*] Old Stancher![5] [*He takes off his glasses, wipes his eyes, his face, the glasses, puts them on again, folds the handkerchief and puts it back neatly in the breast-pocket of his dressing-gown. He clears his throat, joins the tips of his fingers.*] Can there be misery—[*He yawns.*]—loftier than mine? No doubt. Formerly. But now? [*Pause.*] My father? [*Pause.*] My mother? [*Pause.*] My . . . dog? [*Pause.*] Oh I am willing to believe they suffer as much as such creatures can suffer. But does that mean their sufferings equal mine? No doubt. [*Pause.*] No, all is a—[*He yawns.*]—bsolute, [*Proudly.*] the bigger a man is the fuller he is. [*Pause. Gloomily.*] And the emptier. [*He sniffs.*] Clov! [*Pause.*] No, alone. [*Pause.*] What dreams! Those forests! [*Pause.*] Enough, it's time it ended, in the shelter too. [*Pause.*] And yet I hesitate, I hesitate to . . . to end. Yes, there it is, it's time it ended and yet I hesitate to—[*He yawns.*]—to end. [*Yawns.*] God, I'm tired, I'd be better off in bed. [*He whistles. Enter* CLOV *immediately. He halts beside the chair.*] You pollute the air! [*Pause.*] Get me ready, I'm going to bed.

CLOV   I've just got you up.

HAMM   And what of it?

CLOV   I can't be getting you up and putting you to bed every five minutes, I have things to do. [*Pause.*]

HAMM   Did you ever see my eyes?

CLOV   No.

HAMM   Did you never have the curiosity, while I was sleeping, to take off my glasses and look at my eyes?

---

3. Small cap with no brim.
4. Hamm announces that it is his move, as it were in a game of chess, of which the final stage is called

the "endgame."
5. Handkerchief that stanches (checks the flow of) blood.

CLOV   Pulling back the lids? [*Pause.*] No.

HAMM   One of these days I'll show them to you. [*Pause.*] It seems they've gone all white. [*Pause.*] What time is it?

CLOV   The same as usual.

HAMM   [*Gesture towards window right.*] Have you looked?

CLOV   Yes.

HAMM   Well?

CLOV   Zero.

HAMM   It'd need to rain.

CLOV   It won't rain. [*Pause.*]

HAMM   Apart from that, how do you feel?

CLOV   I don't complain.

HAMM   You feel normal?

CLOV   [*Irritably.*] I tell you I don't complain.

HAMM   I feel a little queer. [*Pause.*] Clov!

CLOV   Yes.

HAMM   Have you not had enough?

CLOV   Yes! [*Pause.*] Of what?

HAMM   Of this . . . this . . . thing.

CLOV   I always had. [*Pause.*] Not you?

HAMM   [*Gloomily.*] Then there's no reason for it to change.

CLOV   It may end. [*Pause.*] All life long the same questions, the same answers.

HAMM   Get me ready. [CLOV *does not move.*] Go and get the sheet. [CLOV *does not move.*] Clov!

CLOV   Yes.

HAMM   I'll give you nothing more to eat.

CLOV   Then we'll die.

HAMM   I'll give you just enough to keep you from dying. You'll be hungry all the time.

CLOV   Then we won't die. [*Pause.*] I'll go and get the sheet. [*He goes towards the door.*]

HAMM   No! [CLOV *halts.*] I'll give you one biscuit per day. [*Pause.*] One and a half. [*Pause.*] Why do you stay with me?

CLOV   Why do you keep me?

HAMM   There's no one else.

CLOV   There's nowhere else. [*Pause.*]

HAMM   You're leaving me all the same.

CLOV   I'm trying.

HAMM   You don't love me.

CLOV   No.

HAMM   You loved me once.

CLOV   Once!

HAMM   I've made you suffer too much. [*Pause.*] Haven't I?

CLOV   It's not that.

HAMM   [*Shocked.*] I haven't made you suffer too much?

CLOV   Yes!

HAMM   [*Relieved.*] Ah you gave me a fright! [*Pause. Coldly.*] Forgive me. [*Pause. Louder.*] I said, Forgive me.

CLOV   I heard you. [*Pause.*] Have you bled?

HAMM   Less. [*Pause.*] Is it not time for my pain-killer?

CLOV   No. [*Pause.*]

HAMM   How are your eyes?

CLOV   Bad.

HAMM   How are your legs?

CLOV   Bad.

HAMM   But you can move.

CLOV   Yes.

HAMM   [*Violently.*] Then move! [CLOV *goes to back wall, leans against it with his forehead and hands.*] Where are you?

CLOV   Here.

HAMM   Come back! [CLOV *returns to his place beside the chair.*] Where are you?

CLOV   Here.

HAMM   Why don't you kill me?

CLOV   I don't know the combination of the cupboard. [*Pause.*]

HAMM   Go and get two bicycle-wheels.

CLOV   There are no more bicycle-wheels.

HAMM   What have you done with your bicycle?

CLOV   I never had a bicycle.

HAMM   The thing is impossible.

CLOV   When there were still bicycles I wept to have one. I crawled at your feet. You told me to go to hell. Now there are none.

HAMM   And your rounds? When you inspected my paupers. Always on foot?

CLOV   Sometimes on horse. [*The lid of one of the bins lifts and the hands of* NAGG *appear, gripping the rim. Then his head emerges. Nightcap. Very white face.* NAGG *yawns, then listens.*] I'll leave you, I have things to do.

HAMM   In your kitchen?

CLOV   Yes.

HAMM   Outside of here it's death. [*Pause.*] All right, be off. [*Exit* CLOV. *Pause.*] We're getting on.

NAGG   Me Pap![6]

HAMM   Accursed progenitor![7]

NAGG   Me pap!

HAMM   The old folks at home! No decency left! Guzzle, guzzle, that's all they think of. [*He whistles. Enter* CLOV. *He halts beside the chair.*] Well! I thought you were leaving me.

CLOV   Oh not just yet, not just yet.

NAGG   Me pap!

HAMM   Give him his pap.

CLOV   There's no more pap.

HAMM   [*To* NAGG.] Do you hear that? There's no more pap. You'll never get any more pap.

NAGG   I want me pap!

HAMM   Give him a biscuit. [*Exit* CLOV.] Accursed fornicator! How are your stumps?

NAGG   Never mind me stumps. [*Enter* CLOV *with biscuit.*]

CLOV   I'm back again, with the biscuit. [*He gives biscuit to* NAGG *who fingers it, sniffs it.*]

NAGG   [*Plaintively.*] What is it?

CLOV   Spratt's medium.[8]

NAGG   [*As before.*] It's hard! I can't!

---

6. Mushy food.
7. Parent.

8. Brand name of a biscuit (cookie).

HAMM   Bottle him! [CLOV *pushes* NAGG *back into the bin, closes the lid.*]
CLOV   [*Returning to his place beside the chair.*] If age but knew!
HAMM   Sit on him!
CLOV   I can't sit.
HAMM   True. And I can't stand.
CLOV   So it is.
HAMM   Every man his speciality. [*Pause.*] No phone calls? [*Pause.*] Don't we laugh?
CLOV   [*After reflection.*] I don't feel like it.
HAMM   [*After reflection.*] Not I. [*Pause.*] Clov!
CLOV   Yes.
HAMM   Nature has forgotten us.
CLOV   There's no more nature.
HAMM   No more nature! You exaggerate.
CLOV   In the vicinity.
HAMM   But we breathe, we change! We lose our hair, our teeth! Our bloom! Our ideals!
CLOV   Then she hasn't forgotten us.
HAMM   But you say there is none.
CLOV   [*Sadly.*] No one that ever lived ever thought so crooked as we.
HAMM   We do what we can.
CLOV   We shouldn't. [*Pause.*]
HAMM   You're a bit of all right,[9] aren't you?
CLOV   A smithereen. [*Pause.*]
HAMM   This is slow work. [*Pause.*] Is it not time for my pain-killer?
CLOV   No. [*Pause.*] I'll leave you, I have things to do.
HAMM   In your kitchen?
CLOV   Yes.
HAMM   What, I'd like to know.
CLOV   I look at the wall.
HAMM   The wall! And what do you see on your wall? Mene, mene?[1] Naked bodies?
CLOV   I see my light dying.
HAMM   Your light dying! Listen to that! Well, it can die just as well here, *your* light. Take a look at me and then come back and tell me what you think of *your* light. [*Pause.*]
CLOV   You shouldn't speak to me like that. [*Pause.*]
HAMM   [*Coldly.*] Forgive me. [*Pause. Louder.*] I said, Forgive me.
CLOV   I heard you. [*The lid of* NAGG's *bin lifts. His hands appear, gripping the rim. Then his head emerges. In his mouth the biscuit. He listens.*]
HAMM   Did your seeds come up?
CLOV   No.
HAMM   Did you scratch round them to see if they had sprouted?
CLOV   They haven't sprouted.
HAMM   Perhaps it's still too early.
CLOV   If they were going to sprout they would have sprouted. [*Violently.*] They'll never sprout! [*Pause.* NAGG *takes biscuit in his hand.*]

---

9. You're pretty good (British slang).
1. "Mene mene, tekel, upharsin": words written by a heavenly hand on the wall during the feast of

Balshazzar, king of Babylon. Translated as "Thou art weighed in the balance and found wanting," it foretells his ruin (Daniel 5.25–28).

HAMM   This is not much fun. [*Pause.*] But that's always the way at the end of the day, isn't it, Clov?

CLOV   Always.

HAMM   It's the end of the day like any other day, isn't it, Clov?

CLOV   Looks like it. [*Pause.*]

HAMM   [*Anguished.*] What's happening, what's happening?

CLOV   Something is taking its course. [*Pause.*]

HAMM   All right, be off. [*He leans back in his chair, remains motionless.* CLOV *does not move, heaves a great groaning sigh.* HAMM *sits up.*] I thought I told you to be off.

CLOV   I'm trying. [*He goes to door, halts.*] Ever since I was whelped.[2] [*Exit* CLOV.]

HAMM   We're getting on. [*He leans back in his chair, remains motionless.* NAGG *knocks on the lid of the other bin. Pause. He knocks harder. The lid lifts and the hands of* NELL *appear, gripping the rim. Then her head emerges. Lace cap. Very white face.*]

NELL   What is it, my pet? [*Pause.*] Time for love?

NAGG   Were you asleep?

NELL   Oh no!

NAGG   Kiss me.

NELL   We can't.

NAGG   Try. [*Their heads strain towards each other, fail to meet, fall apart again.*]

NELL   Why this farce, day after day? [*Pause.*]

NAGG   I've lost me tooth.

NELL   When?

NAGG   I had it yesterday.

NELL   [*Elegiac.*[3]] Ah yesterday! [*They turn painfully towards each other.*]

NAGG   Can you see me?

NELL   Hardly. And you?

NAGG   What?

NELL   Can you see me?

NAGG   Hardly.

NELL   So much the better, so much the better.

NAGG   Don't say that. [*Pause.*] Our sight has failed.

NELL   Yes. [*Pause. They turn away from each other.*]

NAGG   Can you hear me?

NELL   Yes. And you?

NAGG   Yes. [*Pause.*] Our hearing hasn't failed.

NELL   Our what?

NAGG   Our hearing.

NELL   No. [*Pause.*] Have you anything else to say to me?

NAGG   Do you remember—

NELL   No.

NAGG   When we crashed on our tandem[4] and lost our shanks. [*They laugh heartily.*]

NELL   It was in the Ardennes. [*They laugh less heartily.*]

NAGG   On the road to Sedan.[5] [*They laugh still less heartily.*] Are you cold?

---

2. Born (usually applied to puppies: whelps).
3. As though lamenting something lost.
4. A bicycle made for two.
5. Town in northern France where the French Army was defeated in 1870 during the Franco-Prussian War. Ardennes is a forest in northern France, which was the scene of fierce fighting in both World Wars.

NELL   Yes, perished. And you?

NAGG   [*Pause.*] I'm freezing. [*Pause.*] Do you want to go in?

NELL   Yes.

NAGG   Then go in. [NELL *does not move.*] Why don't you go in?

NELL   I don't know. [*Pause.*]

NAGG   Has he changed your sawdust?

NELL   It isn't sawdust. [*Pause. Wearily.*] Can you not be a little accurate, Nagg?

NAGG   Your sand then. It's not important.

NELL   It is important. [*Pause.*]

NAGG   It was sawdust once.

NELL   Once!

NAGG   And now it's sand. [*Pause.*] From the shore. [*Pause. Impatiently.*] Now it's sand he fetches from the shore.

NELL   Now it's sand.

NAGG   Has he changed yours?

NELL   No.

NAGG   Nor mine. [*Pause.*] I won't have it! [*Pause. Holding up the biscuit.*] Do you want a bit?

NELL   No. [*Pause.*] Of what?

NAGG   Biscuit. I've kept you half. [*He looks at the biscuit. Proudly.*] Three quarters. For you. Here. [*He proffers the biscuit.*] No? [*Pause.*] Do you not feel well?

HAMM   [*Wearily.*] Quiet, quiet, you're keeping me awake. [*Pause.*] Talk softer. [*Pause.*] If I could sleep I might make love. I'd go into the woods. My eyes would see . . . the sky, the earth. I'd run, run, they wouldn't catch me. [*Pause.*] Nature! [*Pause.*] There's something dripping in my head. [*Pause.*] A heart, a heart in my head. [*Pause.*]

NAGG   [*Soft.*] Do you hear him? A heart in his head! [*He chuckles cautiously.*]

NELL   One mustn't laugh at those things, Nagg. Why must you always laugh at them?

NAGG   Not so loud!

NELL   [*Without lowering her voice.*] Nothing is funnier than unhappiness, I grant you that. But—

NAGG   [*Shocked.*] Oh!

NELL   Yes, yes, it's the most comical thing in the world. And we laugh, we laugh, with a will, in the beginning. But it's always the same thing. Yes, it's like the funny story we have heard too often, we still find it funny, but we don't laugh any more. [*Pause.*] Have you anything else to say to me?

NAGG   No.

NELL   Are you quite sure? [*Pause.*] Then I'll leave you.

NAGG   Do you not want your biscuit? [*Pause.*] I'll keep it for you. [*Pause.*] I thought you were going to leave me.

NELL   I am going to leave you.

NAGG   Could you give me a scratch before you go?

NELL   No. [*Pause.*] Where?

NAGG   In the back.

NELL   No. [*Pause.*] Rub yourself against the rim.

NAGG   It's lower down. In the hollow.

NELL   What hollow?

NAGG   The hollow! [*Pause.*] Could you not? [*Pause.*] Yesterday you scratched me there.

NELL   [*Elegiac.*] Ah yesterday!

NAGG   Could you not? [*Pause.*] Would you like me to scratch you? [*Pause.*] Are you crying again?

NELL   I was trying. [*Pause.*]

HAMM   Perhaps it's a little vein. [*Pause.*]

NAGG   What was that he said?

NELL   Perhaps it's a little vein.

NAGG   What does that mean? [*Pause.*] That means nothing. [*Pause.*] Will I tell you the story of the tailor?

NELL   No. [*Pause.*] What for?

NAGG   To cheer you up.

NELL   It's not funny.

NAGG   It always made you laugh. [*Pause.*] The first time I thought you'd die.

NELL   It was on Lake Como.⁶ [*Pause.*] One April afternoon. [*Pause.*] Can you believe it?

NAGG   What?

NELL   That we once went out rowing on Lake Como. [*Pause.*] One April afternoon.

NAGG   We had got engaged the day before.

NELL   Engaged!

NAGG   You were in such fits that we capsized. By rights we should have been drowned.

NELL   It was because I felt happy.

NAGG   [*Indignant.*] It was not, it was not, it was my story and nothing else. Happy! Don't you laugh at it still? Every time I tell it. Happy!

NELL   It was deep, deep. And you could see down to the bottom. So white. So clean.

NAGG   Let me tell it again. [*Raconteur's voice.*] An Englishman, needing a pair of striped trousers in a hurry for the New Year festivities, goes to his tailor who takes his measurements. [*Tailor's voice.*] "That's the lot, come back in four days, I'll have it ready." Good. Four days later. [*Tailor's voice.*] "So sorry, come back in a week, I've made a mess of the seat." Good, that's all right, a neat seat can be very ticklish. A week later. [*Tailor's voice.*] "Frightfully sorry, come back in ten days. I've made a hash of the crotch." Good, can't be helped, a snug crotch is always a teaser. Ten days later. [*Tailor's voice.*] "Dreadfully sorry, come back in a fortnight, I've made a balls of the fly." Good, at a pinch, a smart fly is a stiff proposition. [*Pause. Normal voice.*] I never told it worse. [*Pause. Gloomy.*] I tell this story worse and worse. [*Pause. Raconteur's voice.*] Well, to make it short, the bluebells are blowing and he ballockses⁷ the buttonholes. [*Customer's voice.*] "God damn you to hell, Sir, no, it's indecent, there are limits! In six days, do you hear me, six days, God made the world. Yes Sir, no less Sir, the WORLD! And you are not bloody well capable of making me a pair of trousers in three months!" [*Tailor's voice, scandalised.*] "But my dear Sir, my dear Sir, look—[*Disdainful gesture, disgustedly.*]—at the world—[*Pause.*] and look—[*Loving gesture, proudly.*]—at my TROUSERS!" [*Pause. He looks at* NELL *who has remained impassive, her eyes unseeing, breaks into a high forced laugh, cuts it short, pokes his head towards* NELL, *launches his laugh again.*]

HAMM   Silence!
        [NAGG *starts, cuts short his laugh.*]

---

6. Large lake in northern Italy.   7. Botches.

NELL   You could see down to the bottom.

HAMM   [*Exasperated.*] Have you not finished? Will you never finish? [*With sudden fury.*] Will this never finish? [NAGG *disappears into his bin, closes the lid behind him.* NELL *does not move. Frenziedly.*] My kingdom for a night-man![8] [*He whistles. Enter* CLOV.] Clear away this muck! Chuck it in the sea! [CLOV *goes to bins, halts.*]

NELL   So white.

HAMM   What? What's she blathering about? [CLOV *stoops, takes* NELL's *hand, feels her pulse.*]

NELL   [*To* CLOV.] Desert! [CLOV *lets go her hand, pushes her back in the bin, closes the lid.*]

CLOV   [*Returning to his place beside the chair.*] She has no pulse.

HAMM   What was she drivelling about?

CLOV   She told me to go away, into the desert.

HAMM   Damn busybody! Is that all?

CLOV   No.

HAMM   What else?

CLOV   I didn't understand.

HAMM   Have you bottled her?

CLOV   Yes.

HAMM   Are they both bottled?

CLOV   Yes.

HAMM   Screw down the lids. [CLOV *goes towards door.*] Time enough. [CLOV *halts.*] My anger subsides, I'd like to pee.

CLOV   [*With alacrity.*] I'll go and get the catheter. [*He goes towards door.*]

HAMM   Time enough. [CLOV *halts.*] Give me my pain-killer.

CLOV   It's too soon. [*Pause.*] It's too soon on top of your tonic, it wouldn't act.

HAMM   In the morning they brace you up and in the evening they calm you down. Unless it's the other way round. [*Pause.*] That old doctor, he's dead naturally?

CLOV   He wasn't old.

HAMM   But he's dead?

CLOV   Naturally. [*Pause.*] *You* ask *me* that? [*Pause.*]

HAMM   Take me for a little turn. [CLOV *goes behind the chair and pushes it forward.*] Not too fast! [CLOV *pushes chair.*] Right round the world! [CLOV *pushes chair.*] Hug the walls, then back to the centre again. [CLOV *pushes chair.*] I was right in the centre, wasn't I?

CLOV   [*Pushing.*] Yes.

HAMM   We'd need a proper wheel-chair. With big wheels. Bicycle wheels! [*Pause.*] Are you hugging?

CLOV   [*Pushing.*] Yes.

HAMM   [*Groping for wall.*] It's a lie! Why do you lie to me?

CLOV   [*Bearing closer to wall.*] There! There!

HAMM   Stop! [CLOV *stops chair close to back wall.* HAMM *lays his hand against wall.*] Old wall! [*Pause.*] Beyond is the . . . other hell. [*Pause. Violently.*] Closer! Closer! Up against!

CLOV   Take away your hand. [HAMM *withdraws his hand.* CLOV *rams chair against wall.*] There! [HAMM *leans towards wall, applies his ear to it.*]

---

8. A collector of nightsoil (excrement). Cf. Shakespeare's *Richard III* 5.7.7: "A horse! A horse! My kingdom for a horse!"

HAMM   Do you hear? [*He strikes the wall with his knuckles.*] Do you hear? Hollow bricks! [*He strikes again.*] All that's hollow! [*Pause. He straightens up. Violently.*] That's enough. Back!

CLOV   We haven't done the round.

HAMM   Back to my place! [CLOV *pushes chair back to centre.*] Is that my place?

CLOV   Yes, that's your place.

HAMM   Am I right in the centre?

CLOV   I'll measure it.

HAMM   More or less! More or less!

CLOV   [*Moving chair slightly.*] There!

HAMM   I'm more or less in the centre?

CLOV   I'd say so.

HAMM   You'd say so! Put me right in the centre!

CLOV   I'll go and get the tape.

HAMM   Roughly! Roughly! [CLOV *moves chair slightly.*] Bang in the centre!

CLOV   There! [*Pause.*]

HAMM   I feel a little too far to the left. [CLOV *moves chair slightly.*] Now I feel a little too far to the right. [CLOV *moves chair slightly.*] I feel a little too far forward. [CLOV *moves chair slightly.*] Now I feel a little too far back. [CLOV *moves chair slightly.*] Don't stay there, [*I.e., behind the chair.*] you give me the shivers. [CLOV *returns to his place beside the chair.*]

CLOV   If I could kill him I'd die happy. [*Pause.*]

HAMM   What's the weather like?

CLOV   As usual.

HAMM   Look at the earth.

CLOV   I've looked.

HAMM   With the glass?

CLOV   No need of the glass.

HAMM   Look at it with the glass.

CLOV   I'll go and get the glass. [*Exit* CLOV.]

HAMM   No need of the glass! [*Enter* CLOV *with telescope.*]

CLOV   I'm back again, with the glass. [*He goes to window right, looks up at it.*] I need the steps.

HAMM   Why? Have you shrunk? [*Exit* CLOV *with telescope.*] I don't like that, I don't like that. [*Enter* CLOV *with ladder, but without telescope.*]

CLOV   I'm back again, with the steps. [*He sets down ladder under window right, gets up on it, realises he has not the telescope, gets down.*] I need the glass. [*He goes towards door.*]

HAMM   [*Violently.*] But you have the glass!

CLOV   [*Halting, violently.*] No, I haven't the glass! [*Exit* CLOV.]

HAMM   This is deadly. [*Enter* CLOV *with telescope. He goes towards ladder.*]

CLOV   Things are livening up. [*He gets up on ladder, raises the telescope, lets it fall.*] I did it on purpose. [*He gets down, picks up the telescope, turns it on auditorium.*] I see . . . a multitude . . . in transports . . . of joy.[9] [*Pause.*] That's what I call a magnifier. [*He lowers the telescope, turns towards* HAMM.] Well? Don't we laugh?

HAMM   [*After reflection.*] I don't.

CLOV   [*After reflection.*] Nor I. [*He gets up on ladder, turns the telescope on*

9. Cf. Revelation 7.9–10: "After this I beheld, and lo, a great multitude, which . . . cried with a loud voice . . . Salvation."

the without.] Let's see. [*He looks, moving the telescope.*] Zero . . . [*He looks.*] . . . zero . . . [*He looks.*] . . . and zero.

HAMM   Nothing stirs. All is—

CLOV   Zer—

HAMM   [*Violently.*] Wait till you're spoke to! [*Normal voice.*] All is . . . all is . . . all is what? [*Violently.*] All is what?

CLOV   What all is? In a word? Is that what you want to know? Just a moment. [*He turns the telescope on the without, looks, lowers the telescope, turns towards* HAMM.] Corpsed. [*Pause.*] Well? Content?

HAMM   Look at the sea.

CLOV   It's the same.

HAMM   Look at the ocean! [CLOV *gets down, takes a few steps towards window left, goes back for ladder, carries it over and sets it down under window left, gets up on it, turns the telescope on the without, looks at length. He starts, lowers the telescope, examines it, turns it again on the without.*]

CLOV   Never seen anything like that!

HAMM   [*Anxious.*] What? A sail? A fin? Smoke?

CLOV   [*Looking.*] The light is sunk.

HAMM   [*Relieved.*] Pah! We all knew that.

CLOV   [*Looking.*] There was a bit left.

HAMM   The base.

CLOV   [*Looking.*] Yes.

HAMM   And now?

CLOV   [*Looking.*] All gone.

HAMM   No gulls?

CLOV   [*Looking.*] Gulls!

HAMM   And the horizon? Nothing on the horizon?

CLOV   [*Lowering the telescope, turning towards* HAMM, *exasperated.*] What in God's name could there be on the horizon? [*Pause.*]

HAMM   The waves, how are the waves?

CLOV   The waves? [*He turns the telescope on the waves.*] Lead.

HAMM   And the sun?

CLOV   [*Looking.*] Zero.

HAMM   But it should be sinking. Look again.

CLOV   [*Looking.*] Damn the sun.

HAMM   Is it night already then?

CLOV   [*Looking.*] No.

HAMM   Then what is it?

CLOV   [*Looking.*] Grey. [*Lowering the telescope, turning towards* HAMM, *louder.*] Grey! [*Pause. Still louder.*] GRREY! [*Pause. He gets down, approaches* HAMM *from behind, whispers in his ear.*]

HAMM   [*Starting.*] Grey! Did I hear you say grey?

CLOV   Light black. From pole to pole.

HAMM   You exaggerate. [*Pause.*] Don't stay there, you give me the shivers. [CLOV *returns to his place beside the chair.*]

CLOV   Why this farce, day after day?

HAMM   Routine. One never knows. [*Pause.*] Last night I saw inside my breast. There was a big sore.

CLOV   Pah! You saw your heart.

HAMM   No, it was living. [*Pause. Anguished.*] Clov!

CLOV   Yes.

HAMM   What's happening?

CLOV   Something is taking its course. [*Pause.*]

HAMM   Clov!

CLOV   [*Impatiently.*] What is it?

HAMM   We're not beginning to . . . to . . . mean something?

CLOV   Mean something! You and I, mean something! [*Brief laugh.*] Ah that's a good one!

HAMM   I wonder. [*Pause.*] Imagine if a rational being came back to earth, wouldn't he be liable to get ideas into his head if he observed us long enough. [*Voice of rational being.*] Ah, good, now I see what it is, yes, now I understand what they're at! [CLOV *starts, drops the telescope and begins to scratch his belly with both hands. Normal voice.*] And without going so far as that, we ourselves . . . [*With emotion.*] . . . we ourselves . . . at certain moments . . . [*Vehemently.*] To think perhaps it won't all have been for nothing!

CLOV   [*Anguished, scratching himself.*] I have a flea!

HAMM   A flea! Are there still fleas?

CLOV   On me there's one. [*Scratching.*] Unless it's a crablouse.

HAMM   [*Very perturbed.*] But humanity might start from there all over again! Catch him, for the love of God!

CLOV   I'll go and get the powder. [*Exit* CLOV.]

HAMM   A flea! This is awful! What a day! [*Enter* CLOV *with a sprinkling-tin.*]

CLOV   I'm back again, with the insecticide.

HAMM   Let him have it! [CLOV *loosens the top of his trousers, pulls it forward and shakes powder into the aperture. He stoops, looks, waits, starts, frenziedly shakes more powder, stoops, looks, waits.*]

CLOV   The bastard!

HAMM   Did you get him?

CLOV   Looks like it. [*He drops the tin and adjusts his trousers.*] Unless he's laying doggo.

HAMM   Laying! Lying you mean. Unless he's *lying* doggo.

CLOV   Ah? One says lying? One doesn't say laying?

HAMM   Use your head, can't you. If he was laying we'd be bitched.

CLOV   Ah. [*Pause.*] What about that pee?

HAMM   I'm having it.

CLOV   Ah that's the spirit, that's the spirit! [*Pause.*]

HAMM   [*With ardour.*] Let's go from here, the two of us! South! You can make a raft and the currents will carry us away, far away, to other . . . mammals!

CLOV   God forbid!

HAMM   Alone, I'll embark alone! Get working on that raft immediately. Tomorrow I'll be gone for ever.

CLOV   [*Hastening towards door.*] I'll start straight away.

HAMM   Wait! [CLOV *halts.*] Will there be sharks, do you think?

CLOV   Sharks? I don't know. If there are there will be. [*He goes towards door.*]

HAMM   Wait! [CLOV *halts.*] Is it not yet time for my pain-killer?

CLOV   [*Violently.*] No! [*He goes towards door.*]

HAMM   Wait! [CLOV *halts.*] How are your eyes?

CLOV   Bad.

HAMM   But you can see.

CLOV   All I want.

HAMM   How are your legs?

CLOV   Bad.

HAMM   But you can walk.

CLOV   I come . . . and go.

HAMM   In my house. [*Pause. With prophetic relish.*] One day you'll be blind, like me. You'll be sitting there, a speck in the void, in the dark, for ever, like me. [*Pause.*] One day you'll say to yourself, I'm tired, I'll sit down, and you'll go and sit down. Then you'll say, I'm hungry, I'll get up and get something to eat. But you won't get up. You'll say, I shouldn't have sat down, but since I have I'll sit on a little longer, then I'll get up and get something to eat. But you won't go up and you won't get anything to eat. [*Pause.*] You'll look at the wall a while, then you'll say, I'll close my eyes, perhaps have a little sleep, after that I'll feel better, and you'll close them. And when you open them again there'll be no wall any more. [*Pause.*] Infinite emptiness will be all around you, all the resurrected dead of all the ages wouldn't fill it, and there you'll be like a little bit of grit in the middle of the steppe.[1] [*Pause.*] Yes, one day you'll know what it is, you'll be like me, except that you won't have anyone with you, because you won't have had pity on anyone and because there won't be anyone left to have pity on. [*Pause.*]

CLOV   It's not certain. [*Pause.*] And there's one thing you forget.

HAMM   Ah?

CLOV   I can't sit down.

HAMM   [*Impatiently.*] Well you'll lie down then, what the hell! Or you'll come to a standstill, simply stop and stand still, the way you are now. One day you'll say, I'm tired, I'll stop. What does the attitude matter? [*Pause.*]

CLOV   So you all want me to leave you.

HAMM   Naturally.

CLOV   Then I'll leave you.

HAMM   You can't leave us.

CLOV   Then I won't leave you. [*Pause.*]

HAMM   Why don't you finish us? [*Pause.*] I'll tell you the combination of the cupboard if you promise to finish me.

CLOV   I couldn't finish you.

HAMM   Then you won't finish me. [*Pause.*]

CLOV   I'll leave you, I have things to do.

HAMM   Do you remember when you came here?

CLOV   No. Too small, you told me.

HAMM   Do you remember your father?

CLOV   [*Wearily.*] Same answer. [*Pause.*] You've asked me these questions millions of times.

HAMM   I love the old questions. [*With fervour.*] Ah the old questions, the old answers, there's nothing like them! [*Pause.*] It was I was a father to you.

CLOV   Yes. [*He looks at* HAMM *fixedly.*] You were that to me.

HAMM   My house a home for you.

CLOV   Yes. [*He looks about him.*] This was that for me.

HAMM   [*Proudly.*] But for me, [*Gesture towards himself.*] no father. But for Hamm, [*Gesture towards surroundings.*] no home. [*Pause.*]

CLOV   I'll leave you.

HAMM   Did you ever think of one thing?

CLOV   Never.

HAMM   That here we're down in a hole. [*Pause.*] But beyond the hills? Eh?

1. Level grassy plain devoid of forest, especially in southeast Europe and Siberia.

Perhaps it's still green. Eh? [*Pause.*] Flora! Pomona! [*Ecstatically.*] Ceres![2]
[*Pause.*] Perhaps you won't need to go very far.

CLOV I can't go very far. [*Pause.*] I'll leave you.

HAMM Is my dog ready?

CLOV He lacks a leg.

HAMM Is he silky?

CLOV He's a kind of Pomeranian.

HAMM Go and get him.

CLOV He lacks a leg.

HAMM Go and get him! [*Exit* CLOV.] We're getting on. [*Enter* CLOV *holding by one of its three legs a black toy dog.*]

CLOV Your dogs are here. [*He hands the dog to* HAMM *who feels it, fondles it.*]

HAMM He's white, isn't he?

CLOV Nearly.

HAMM What do you mean, nearly? Is he white or isn't he?

CLOV He isn't. [*Pause.*]

HAMM You've forgotten the sex.

CLOV [*Vexed.*] But he isn't finished. The sex goes on at the end. [*Pause.*]

HAMM You haven't put on his ribbon.

CLOV [*Angrily.*] But he isn't finished, I tell you! First you finish your dog and then you put on his ribbon! [*Pause.*]

HAMM Can he stand?

CLOV I don't know.

HAMM Try. [*He hands the dog to* CLOV *who places it on the ground.*] Well?

CLOV Wait! [*He squats down and tries to get the dog to stand on its three legs, fails, lets it go. The dog falls on its side.*]

HAMM [*Impatiently.*] Well?

CLOV He's standing.

HAMM [*Groping for the dog.*] Where? Where is he? [CLOV *holds up the dog in a standing position.*]

CLOV There. [*He takes* HAMM's *hand and guides it towards the dog's head.*]

HAMM [*His hand on the dog's head.*] Is he gazing at me?

CLOV Yes.

HAMM [*Proudly.*] As if he were asking me to take him for a walk?

CLOV If you like.

HAMM [*As before.*] Or as if he were begging me for a bone. [*He withdraws his hand.*] Leave him like that, standing there imploring me. [CLOV *straightens up. The dog falls on its side.*]

CLOV I'll leave you.

HAMM Have you had your visions?

CLOV Less.

HAMM Is Mother Pegg's light on?

CLOV Light! How could anyone's light be on?

HAMM Extinguished!

CLOV Naturally it's extinguished. If it's not on it's extinguished.

HAMM No, I mean Mother Pegg.

CLOV But naturally she's extinguished! [*Pause.*] What's the matter with you today?

HAMM I'm taking my course. [*Pause.*] Is she buried?

2. In Roman mythology, respectively, the goddesses of flowers, fruit, and crops.

CLOV Buried! Who would have buried her?
HAMM You.
CLOV Me! Haven't I enough to do without burying people?
HAMM But you'll bury me.
CLOV No I won't bury you. [*Pause.*]
HAMM She was bonny once, like a flower of the field. [*With reminiscent leer.*] And a great one for the men!
CLOV We too were bonny—once. It's a rare thing not to have been bonny—once. [*Pause.*]
HAMM Go and get the gaff.[3] [CLOV *goes to door, halts.*]
CLOV Do this, do that, and I do it. I never refuse. Why?
HAMM You're not able to.
CLOV Soon I won't do it any more.
HAMM You won't be able to any more. [*Exit* CLOV.] Ah the creatures, the creatures, everything has to be explained to them. [*Enter* CLOV *with gaff.*]
CLOV Here's your gaff. Stick it up. [*He gives the gaff to* HAMM *who, wielding it like a puntpole,[4] tries to move his chair.*]
HAMM Did I move?
CLOV No. [HAMM *throws down the gaff.*]
HAMM Go and get the oilcan.
CLOV What for?
HAMM To oil the castors.
CLOV I oiled them yesterday.
HAMM Yesterday! What does that mean? Yesterday!
CLOV [*Violently.*] That means that bloody awful day, long ago, before this bloody awful day. I use the words you taught me. If they don't mean anything any more, teach me others. Or let me be silent. [*Pause.*]
HAMM I once knew a madman who thought the end of the world had come. He was a painter—and engraver. I had a great fondness for him. I used to go and see him, in the asylum. I'd take him by the hand and drag him to the window. Look! There! All that rising corn! And there! Look! The sails of the herring fleet! All that loveliness! [*Pause.*] He'd snatch away his hand and go back into his corner. Appalled. All he had seen was ashes. [*Pause.*] He alone had been spared. [*Pause.*] Forgotten. [*Pause.*] It appears the case is . . . was not so . . . so unusual.
CLOV A madman! When was that?
HAMM Oh way back, way back, you weren't in the land of the living.
CLOV God be with the days! [*Pause.* HAMM *raises his toque.*]
HAMM I had a great fondness for him. [*Pause. He puts on his toque again.*] He was a painter—and engraver.
CLOV There are so many terrible things.
HAMM No, no, there are not so many now. [*Pause.*] Clov!
CLOV Yes.
HAMM Do you not think this has gone on long enough?
CLOV Yes! [*Pause.*] What?
HAMM This . . . this . . . thing.
CLOV I've always thought so. [*Pause.*] You not?
HAMM [*Gloomily.*] Then it's a day like any other day.

---

3. Barbed fishing spear.
4. Long pole, pushed against the bottom of a river to propel a punt (a shallow flat-bottomed boat).

CLOV   As long as it lasts. [*Pause.*] All life long the same inanities.
HAMM   I can't leave you.
CLOV   I know. And you can't follow me. [*Pause.*]
HAMM   If you leave me how shall I know?
CLOV   [*Briskly.*] Well you simply whistle me and if I don't come running it means I've left you. [*Pause.*]
HAMM   You won't come and kiss me goodbye?
CLOV   Oh I shouldn't think so. [*Pause.*]
HAMM   But you might be merely dead in your kitchen.
CLOV   The result would be the same.
HAMM   Yes, but how would I know, if you were merely dead in your kitchen?
CLOV   Well . . . sooner or later I'd start to stink.
HAMM   You stink already. The whole place stinks of corpses.
CLOV   The whole universe.
HAMM   [*Angrily.*] To hell with the universe. [*Pause.*] Think of something.
CLOV   What?
HAMM   An idea, have an idea. [*Angrily.*] A bright idea!
CLOV   Ah good. [*He starts pacing to and fro, his eyes fixed on the ground, his hands behind his back. He halts.*] The pains in my legs! It's unbelievable! Soon I won't be able to think any more.
HAMM   You won't be able to leave me. [CLOV *resumes his pacing.*] What are you doing?
CLOV   Having an idea. [*He paces.*] Ah! [*He halts.*]
HAMM   What a brain! [*Pause.*] Well?
CLOV   Wait! [*He meditates. Not very convinced.*] Yes . . . [*Pause. More convinced.*] Yes! [*He raises his head.*] I have it! I set the alarm. [*Pause.*]
HAMM   This is perhaps not one of my bright days, but frankly—
CLOV   You whistle me. I don't come. The alarm rings. I'm gone. It doesn't ring. I'm dead. [*Pause.*]
HAMM   Is it working? [*Pause. Impatiently.*] The alarm, is it working?
CLOV   Why wouldn't it be working?
HAMM   Because it's worked too much.
CLOV   But it's hardly worked at all.
HAMM   [*Angrily.*] Then because it's worked too little!
CLOV   I'll go and see. [*Exit* CLOV. *Brief ring of alarm off. Enter* CLOV *with alarm-clock. He holds it against* HAMM's *ear and releases alarm. They listen to it ringing to the end. Pause.*] Fit to wake the dead! Did you hear it?
HAMM   Vaguely.
CLOV   The end is terrific!
HAMM   I prefer the middle. [*Pause.*] Is it not time for my pain-killer?
CLOV   No! [*He goes to door, turns.*] I'll leave you.
HAMM   It's time for my story. Do you want to listen to my story.
CLOV   No.
HAMM   Ask my father if he wants to listen to my story. [CLOV *goes to bins, raises the lid of* NAGG's, *stoops, looks into it. Pause. He straightens up.*]
CLOV   He's asleep.
HAMM   Wake him. [CLOV *stoops, wakes* NAGG *with the alarm. Unintelligible words.* CLOV *straightens up.*]
CLOV   He doesn't want to listen to your story.
HAMM   I'll give him a bon-bon. [CLOV *stoops. As before.*]
CLOV   He wants a sugar-plum.

HAMM   He'll get a sugar-plum. [CLOV *stoops. As before.*]
CLOV   It's a deal. [*He goes towards door.* NAGG's *hands appear, gripping the rim. Then the head emerges.* CLOV *reaches door, turns.*] Do you believe in the life to come?
HAMM   Mine was always that. [*Exit* CLOV.] Got him that time!
NAGG   I'm listening.
HAMM   Scoundrel! Why did you engender me?
NAGG   I didn't know.
HAMM   What? What didn't you know?
NAGG   That it'd be you. [*Pause.*] You'll give me a sugar-plum?
HAMM   After the audition.
NAGG   You swear?
HAMM   Yes.
NAGG   On what?
HAMM   My honour. [*Pause. They laugh heartily.*]
NAGG   Two.
HAMM   One.
NAGG   One for me and one for—
HAMM   One! Silence! [*Pause.*] Where was I? [*Pause. Gloomily.*] It's finished, we're finished. [*Pause.*] Nearly finished. [*Pause.*] There'll be no more speech. [*Pause.*] Something dripping in my head, ever since the fontanelles.[5] [*Stifled hilarity of* NAGG.] Splash, splash, always on the same spot. [*Pause.*] Perhaps it's a little vein. [*Pause.*] A little artery. [*Pause. More animated.*] Enough of that, it's story time, where was I? [*Pause. Narrative tone.*] The man came crawling towards me, on his belly. Pale, wonderfully pale and thin, he seemed on the point of—[*Pause. Normal tone.*] No, I've done that bit. [*Pause. Narrative tone.*] I calmly filled my pipe—the meerschaum, lit it with . . . let us say a vesta,[6] drew a few puffs. Aah! [*Pause.*] Well, what is it you want? [*Pause.*] It was an extra-ordinarily bitter day, I remember, zero by the thermometer. But considering it was Christmas Eve there was nothing . . . extra-ordinary about that. Seasonable weather, for once in a way. [*Pause.*] Well, what ill wind blows you my way? He raised his face to me, black with mingled dirt and tears. [*Pause. Normal tone.*] That should do it. [*Narrative tone.*] No, no, don't look at me, don't look at me. He dropped his eyes and mumbled something, apologies I presume. [*Pause.*] I'm a busy man, you know, the final touches, before the festivities, you know what it is. [*Pause. Forcibly.*] Come on now, what is the object of this invasion? [*Pause.*] It was a glorious bright day, I remember, fifty by the heliometer,[7] but already the sun was sinking down into the . . . down among the dead. [*Normal tone.*] Nicely put, that. [*Narrative tone.*] Come on now, come on, present your petition and let me resume my labours. [*Pause. Normal tone.*] There's English for you. Ah well . . . [*Narrative tone.*] It was then he took the plunge. It's my little one, he said. Tsstss, a little one, that's bad. My little boy, he said, as if the sex mattered. Where did he come from? He named the hole. A good half-day, on horse. What are you insinuating? That the place is still inhabited? No no, not a soul, except himself and the child—assuming he existed. Good. I enquired about the situation at Kov,[8] beyond the gulf. Not

5. Membranous space in infant's skull at the angles of the parietal bones.
6. Vesta is the brand name of a type of match (from Vesta, Roman goddess of the hearth).
7. Literally, a sun meter.
8. Conceivably the town of Kova in southern Siberia (except that it has no gulf); more probably Hamm's invention.

a sinner. Good. And you expect me to believe you have left your little one back there, all alone, and alive into the bargain? Come now! [*Pause.*] It was a howling wild day, I remember, a hundred by the anemometer.[9] The wind was tearing up the dead pines and sweeping them . . . away. [*Pause. Normal tone.*] A bit feeble, that. [*Narrative tone.*] Come on, man, speak up, what is it you want from me, I have to put up my holly. [*Pause.*] Well to make it short it finally transpired that what he wanted from me was . . . bread for his brat? Bread? But I have no bread, it doesn't agree with me. Good. Then perhaps a little corn? [*Pause. Normal tone.*] That should do it. [*Narrative tone.*] Corn, yes, I have corn, it's true, in my granaries. But use your head. I give you some corn, a pound, a pound and a half, you bring it back to your child and you make him—if he's still alive—a nice pot of porridge, [NAGG reacts.] a nice pot and a half of porridge, full of nourishment. Good. The colours come back into his little cheeks—perhaps. And then? [*Pause.*] I lost patience. [*Violently.*] Use your head, can't you, use your head, you're on earth, there's no cure for that! [*Pause.*] It was an exceedingly dry day, I remember, zero by the hygrometer. Ideal weather, for my lumbago.[1] [*Pause. Violently.*] But what in God's name do you imagine? That the earth will awake in spring? That the rivers and seas will run with fish again? That there's manna in heaven still for imbeciles like you? [*Pause.*] Gradually I cooled down, sufficiently at least to ask him how long he had taken on the way. Three whole days. Good. In what condition he had left the child. Deep in sleep. [*Forcibly.*] But deep in what sleep, deep in what sleep already? [*Pause.*] Well to make it short I finally offered to take him into my service. He had touched a chord. And then I imagined already that I wasn't much longer for this world. [*He laughs. Pause.*] Well? [*Pause.*] Well? Here if you were careful you might die a nice natural death, in peace and comfort. [*Pause.*] Well? [*Pause.*] In the end he asked me would I consent to take in the child as well—if he were still alive. [*Pause.*] It was the moment I was waiting for. [*Pause.*] Would I consent to take in the child . . . [*Pause.*] I can see him still, down on his knees, his hands flat on the ground, glaring at me with his mad eyes, in defiance of my wishes. [*Pause. Normal tone.*] I'll soon have finished with this story. [*Pause.*] Unless I bring in other characters. [*Pause.*] But where would I find them? [*Pause.*] Where would I look for them? [*Pause. He whistles. Enter* CLOV.] Let us pray to God.

NAGG Me sugar-plum!
CLOV There's a rat in the kitchen!
HAMM A rat! Are there still rats?
CLOV In the kitchen there's one.
HAMM And you haven't exterminated him?
CLOV Half. You disturbed us.
HAMM He can't get away?
CLOV No.
HAMM You'll finish him later. Let us pray to God.
CLOV Again!
NAGG Me sugar-plum!
HAMM God first! [*Pause.*] Are you right?
CLOV [*Resigned.*] Off we go.

9. A wind meter.
1. Rheumatic pain in the lumbar region of the lower back. "Hygrometer": a moisture meter.

HAMM [*To* NAGG.] And you?

NAGG [*Clasping his hands, closing his eyes, in a gabble.*] Our Father which art—

HAMM Silence! In silence! Where are your manners? [*Pause.*] Off we go. [*Attitudes of prayer. Silence. Abandoning his attitude, discouraged.*] Well?

CLOV [*Abandoning his attitude.*] What a hope! And you?

HAMM Sweet damn all! [*To* NAGG.] And you?

NAGG Wait! [*Pause. Abandoning his attitude.*] Nothing doing!

HAMM The bastard! He doesn't exist!

CLOV Not yet.

NAGG Me sugar-plum!

HAMM There are no more sugar-plums! [*Pause.*]

NAGG It's natural. After all I'm your father. It's true if it hadn't been me it would have been someone else. But that's no excuse. [*Pause.*] Turkish Delight,[2] for example, which no longer exists, we all know that, there is nothing in the world I love more. And one day I'll ask you for some, in return for a kindness, and you'll promise it to me. One must live with the times. [*Pause.*] Whom did you call when you were a tiny boy, and were frightened, in the dark? Your mother? No. Me. We let you cry. Then we moved you out of earshot, so that we might sleep in peace. [*Pause.*] I was asleep, as happy as a king, and you woke me up to have me listen to you. It wasn't indispensable, you didn't really need to have me listen to you. [*Pause.*] I hope the day will come when you'll really need to have me listen to you, and need to hear my voice, any voice. [*Pause.*] Yes, I hope I'll live till then, to hear you calling me like when you were a tiny boy, and were frightened, in the dark, and I was your only hope. [*Pause.* NAGG *knocks on lid of* NELL's *bin. Pause.*] Nell! [*Pause. He knocks louder. Pause. Louder.*] Nell! [*Pause.* NAGG *sinks back into his bin, closes the lid behind him. Pause.*]

HAMM Our revels now are ended.[3] [*He gropes for the dog*] The dog's gone.

CLOV He's not a real dog, he can't go.

HAMM [*Groping.*] He's not there.

CLOV He's lain down.

HAMM Give him up to me. [CLOV *picks up the dog and gives it to* HAMM. HAMM *holds it in his arms. Pause.* HAMM *throws away the dog.*] Dirty brute! [CLOV *begins to pick up the objects lying on the ground.*] What are you doing?

CLOV Putting things in order. [*He straightens up. Fervently.*] I'm going to clear everything away! [*He starts picking up again.*]

HAMM Order!

CLOV [*Straightening up.*] I love order. It's my dream. A world where all would be silent and still and each thing in its last place, under the last dust. [*He starts picking up again.*]

HAMM [*Exasperated.*] What in God's name do you think you are doing?

CLOV [*Straightening up.*] I'm doing my best to create a little order.

HAMM Drop it! [CLOV *drops the objects he has picked up.*]

CLOV After all, there or elsewhere. [*He goes towards door.*]

HAMM [*Irritably.*] What's wrong with your feet?

CLOV My feet?

HAMM Tramp! Tramp!

2. A sticky sweet candy (originally from Turkey).
3. Words spoken by Prospero in Shakespeare's *The Tempest* 4.1.148.

CLOV   I must have put on my boots.
HAMM   Your slippers were hurting you? [*Pause.*]
CLOV   I'll leave you.
HAMM   No!
CLOV   What is there to keep me here?
HAMM   The dialogue. [*Pause.*] I've got on with my story. [*Pause.*] I've got on with it well. [*Pause. Irritably.*] Ask me where I've got to.
CLOV   Oh, by the way, your story?
HAMM   [*Surprised.*] What story?
CLOV   The one you've been telling yourself all your days.
HAMM   Ah you mean my chronicle?
CLOV   That's the one. [*Pause.*]
HAMM   [*Angrily.*] Keep going, can't you, keep going!
CLOV   You've got on with it, I hope.
HAMM   [*Modestly.*] Oh not very far, not very far. [*He sighs.*] There are days like that, one isn't inspired. [*Pause.*] Nothing you can do about it, just wait for it to come. [*Pause.*] No forcing, no forcing, it's fatal. [*Pause.*] I've got on with it a little all the same. [*Pause.*] Technique, you know. [*Pause. Irritably.*] I say I've got on with it a little all the same.
CLOV   [*Admiringly.*] Well I never! In spite of everything you were able to get on with it!
HAMM   [*Modestly.*] Oh not very far, you know, not very far, but nevertheless, better than nothing.
CLOV   Better than nothing! Is it possible?
HAMM   I'll tell you how it goes. He comes crawling on his belly—
CLOV   Who?
HAMM   What?
CLOV   Who do you mean, he?
HAMM   Who do I mean! Yet another.
CLOV   Ah him! I wasn't sure.
HAMM   Crawling on his belly, whining for bread for his brat. He's offered a job as gardener. Before— [CLOV *bursts out laughing.*] What is there so funny about that?
CLOV   A job as gardener!
HAMM   Is that what tickles you?
CLOV   It must be that.
HAMM   It wouldn't be the bread?
CLOV   Or the brat. [*Pause.*]
HAMM   The whole thing is comical, I grant you that. What about having a good guffaw the two of us together?
CLOV   [*After reflection.*] I couldn't guffaw again today.
HAMM   [*After reflection.*] Nor I. [*Pause.*] I continue then. Before accepting with gratitude he asks if he may have his little boy with him.
CLOV   What age?
HAMM   Oh tiny.
CLOV   He would have climbed the trees.
HAMM   All the little odd jobs.
CLOV   And then he would have grown up.
HAMM   Very likely. [*Pause.*]
CLOV   Keep going, can't you, keep going!
HAMM   That's all. I stopped there. [*Pause.*]

CLOV   Do you see how it goes on.
HAMM   More or less.
CLOV   Will it not soon be the end?
HAMM   I'm afraid it will.
CLOV   Pah! You'll make up another.
HAMM   I don't know. [*Pause.*] I feel rather drained. [*Pause.*] The prolonged creative effort. [*Pause.*] If I could drag myself down to the sea! I'd make a pillow of sand for my head and the tide would come.
CLOV   There's no more tide. [*Pause.*]
HAMM   Go and see is she dead. [CLOV *goes to bins, raises the lid of* NELL'*s, stoops, looks into it. Pause.*]
CLOV   Looks like it. [*He closes the lid, straightens up.* HAMM *raises his toque. Pause. He puts it on again.*]
HAMM   [*With his hand to his toque.*] And Nagg? [CLOV *raises lid of* NAGG'*s bin, stoops, looks into it. Pause.*]
CLOV   Doesn't look like it. [*He closes the lid, straightens up.*]
HAMM   [*Letting go his toque.*] What's he doing? [CLOV *raises lid of* NAGG'*s bin, stoops, looks into it. Pause.*]
CLOV   He's crying. [*He closes lid, straightens up.*]
HAMM   Then he's living. [*Pause.*] Did you ever have an instant of happiness?
CLOV   Not to my knowledge. [*Pause.*]
HAMM   Bring me under the window. [CLOV *goes towards chair.*] I want to feel the light on my face. [CLOV *pushes chair.*] Do you remember, in the beginning, when you took me for a turn? You used to hold the chair too high. At every step you nearly tipped me out. [*With senile quaver.*] Ah great fun, we had, the two of us, great fun. [*Gloomily.*] And then we got into the way of it. [CLOV *stops the chair under window right.*] There already? [*Pause. He tilts back his head.*] Is it light?
CLOV   It isn't dark.
HAMM   [*Angrily*] I'm asking you is it light.
CLOV   Yes. [*Pause.*]
HAMM   The curtain isn't closed?
CLOV   No.
HAMM   What window is it?
CLOV   The earth.
HAMM   I knew it! [*Angrily.*] But there's no light there! The other! [CLOV *stops the chair under window left.* HAMM *tilts back his head.*] That's what I call light! [*Pause.*] Feels like a ray of sunshine. [*Pause.*] No?
CLOV   No.
HAMM   It isn't a ray of sunshine I feel on my face?
CLOV   No. [*Pause.*]
HAMM   Am I very white? [*Pause. Angrily.*] I'm asking you am I very white!
CLOV   Not more so than usual. [*Pause.*]
HAMM   Open the window.
CLOV   What for?
HAMM   I want to hear the sea.
CLOV   You wouldn't hear it.
HAMM   Even if you opened the window?
CLOV   No.
HAMM   Then it's not worth while opening it?
CLOV   No.

HAMM [*Violently*] Then open it! [CLOV *gets up on the ladder, opens the window. Pause.*] Have you opened it?
CLOV Yes. [*Pause.*]
HAMM You swear you've opened it?
CLOV Yes. [*Pause.*]
HAMM Well . . . ! [*Pause.*] It must be very calm. [*Pause. Violently.*] I'm asking you is it very calm!
CLOV Yes.
HAMM It's because there are no more navigators. [*Pause.*] You haven't much conversation all of a sudden. Do you not feel well?
CLOV I'm cold.
HAMM What month are we? [*Pause.*] Close the window, we're going back. [CLOV *closes the window, gets down, pushes the chair back to its place, remains standing behind it, head bowed.*] Don't stay there, you give me the shivers! [CLOV *returns to his place beside the chair.*] Father! [*Pause. Louder.*] Father! [*Pause.*] Go and see did he hear me. [CLOV *goes to* NAGG's *bin, raises the lid, stoops. Unintelligible words.* CLOV *straightens up.*]
CLOV Yes.
HAMM Both times? [CLOV *stoops. As before.*]
CLOV Once only.
HAMM The first time or the second? [CLOV *stoops. As before.*]
CLOV He doesn't know.
HAMM It must have been the second.
CLOV We'll never know. [*He closes lid.*]
HAMM Is he still crying?
CLOV No.
HAMM The dead go fast. [*Pause.*] What's he doing?
CLOV Sucking his biscuit.
HAMM Life goes on. [CLOV *returns to his place beside the chair.*] Give me a rug. I'm freezing.
CLOV There are no more rugs. [*Pause.*]
HAMM Kiss me. [*Pause.*] Will you not kiss me?
CLOV No.
HAMM On the forehead.
CLOV I won't kiss you anywhere. [*Pause.*]
HAMM [*Holding out his hand.*] Give me your hand at least. [*Pause.*] Will you not give me your hand?
CLOV I won't touch you. [*Pause.*]
HAMM Give me the dog. [CLOV *looks round for the dog.*] No!
CLOV Do you not want your dog?
HAMM No.
CLOV Then I'll leave you.
HAMM [*Head bowed, absently.*] That's right. [CLOV *goes to door, turns.*]
CLOV If I don't kill that rat he'll die.
HAMM [*As before.*] That's right. [*Exit* CLOV. *Pause.*] Me to play. [*He takes out his handkerchief, unfolds it, holds it spread out before him.*] We're getting on. [*Pause.*] You weep, and weep, for nothing, so as not to laugh, and little by little . . . you begin to grieve. [*He folds the handkerchief, puts it back in his pocket, raises his head.*] All those I might have helped. [*Pause.*] Helped! [*Pause.*] Saved. [*Pause.*] Saved! [*Pause.*] The place was crawling with them! [*Pause. Violently.*] Use your head, can't you, use your head, you're on earth,

there's no cure for that! [*Pause.*] Get out of here and love one another! Lick your neighbour as yourself![4] [*Pause. Calmer.*] When it wasn't bread they wanted it was crumpets. [*Pause. Violently.*] Out of my sight and back to your petting parties! [*Pause.*] All that, all that! [*Pause.*] Not even a real dog! [*Calmer.*] The end is in the beginning and yet you go on. [*Pause.*] Perhaps I could go on with my story, end it and begin another. [*Pause.*] Perhaps I could throw myself out on the floor. [*He pushes himself painfully off his seat, falls back again.*] Dig my nails into the cracks and drag myself forward with my fingers. [*Pause.*] It will be the end and there I'll be, wondering what can have brought it on and wondering what can have . . . [*He hesitates.*] . . . why it was so long coming. [*Pause.*] There I'll be, in the old shelter, alone against the silence and . . . [*He hesitates.*] . . . the stillness. If I can hold my peace, and sit quiet, it will be all over with sound, and motion, all over and done with. [*Pause.*] I'll have called my father and I'll have called my . . . [*He hesitates.*] . . . my son. And even twice, or three times, in case they shouldn't have heard me, the first time, or the second. [*Pause.*] I'll say to myself, He'll come back. [*Pause.*] And then? [*Pause.*] And then? [*Pause.*] He couldn't, he has gone too far. [*Pause.*] And then? [*Pause. Very agitated.*] All kinds of fantasies! That I'm being watched! A rat! Steps! Breath held and then . . . [*He breathes out.*] Then babble, babble, words, like the solitary child who turns himself into children, two, three, so as to be together, and whisper together, in the dark. [*Pause.*] Moment upon moment, pattering down, like the millet grains of . . . [*He hesitates.*] . . . that old Greek,[5] and all life long you wait for that to mount up to a life. [*Pause. He opens his mouth to continue, renounces.*] Ah let's get it over! [*He whistles. Enter* CLOV *with alarm-clock. He halts beside the chair.*] What? Neither gone nor dead?

CLOV   In spirit only.

HAMM   Which?

CLOV   Both.

HAMM   Gone from me you'd be dead.

CLOV   And vice versa.

HAMM   Outside of here it's death! [*Pause.*] And the rat?

CLOV   He's got away.

HAMM   He can't go far. [*Pause. Anxious.*] Eh?

CLOV   He doesn't need to go far. [*Pause.*]

HAMM   Is it not time for my pain-killer?

CLOV   Yes.

HAMM   Ah! At last! Give it to me! Quick! [*Pause.*]

CLOV   There's no more pain-killer. [*Pause.*]

HAMM   [*Appalled.*] Good . . . ! [*Pause.*] No more pain-killer!

CLOV   No more pain-killer. You'll never get any more pain-killer. [*Pause.*]

HAMM   But the little round box. It was full!

CLOV   Yes. But now it's empty. [*Pause.* CLOV *starts to move about the room. He is looking for a place to put down the alarm-clock.*]

HAMM   [*Soft.*] What'll I do? [*Pause. In a scream.*] What'll I do? [CLOV *sees the picture, takes it down, stands it on the floor with its face to the wall, hangs up the alarm-clock in its place.*] What are you doing?

---

4. Parody of Jesus' instruction: "Thou shalt love thy neighbor as thyself" (Matthew 19.19).
5. Zeno of Elea (ca. 450 B.C.E.), a Greek philosopher famous for his paradoxes; e.g., "If a grain of millet falling makes no sound, how can a bushel of grains make any sound?" (reported by Aristotle in his *Physics* 5:250 a.19).

CLOV Winding up.

HAMM Look at the earth.

CLOV Again!

HAMM Since it's calling to you.

CLOV Is your throat sore? [*Pause.*] Would you like a lozenge? [*Pause.*] No. [*Pause.*] Pity. [CLOV *goes, humming, towards window right, halts before it, looks up at it.*]

HAMM Don't sing.

CLOV [*Turning towards* HAMM.] One hasn't the right to sing any more?

HAMM No.

CLOV Then how can it end?

HAMM You want it to end?

CLOV I want to sing.

HAMM I can't prevent you. [*Pause.* CLOV *turns towards window right.*]

CLOV What did I do with that steps? [*He looks around for ladder.*] You didn't see that steps? [*He sees it.*] Ah, about time. [*He goes towards window left.*] Sometimes I wonder if I'm in my right mind. Then it passes over and I'm as lucid as before. [*He gets up on ladder, looks out of window.*] Christ, she's under water! [*He looks.*] How can that be? [*He pokes forward his head, his hand above his eyes.*] It hasn't rained. [*He wipes the pane, looks. Pause.*] Ah what a fool I am! I'm on the wrong side! [*He gets down, takes a few steps towards window right.*] Under water! [*He goes back for ladder.*] What a fool I am! [*He carries ladder towards window right.*] Sometimes I wonder if I'm in my right senses. Then it passes off and I'm as intelligent as ever. [*He sets down ladder under window right, gets up on it, looks out of window. He turns towards* HAMM.] Any particular sector you fancy? Or merely the whole thing?

HAMM Whole thing.

CLOV The general effect? Just a moment. [*He looks out of window. Pause.*]

HAMM Clov.

CLOV [*Absorbed.*] Mmm.

HAMM Do you know what it is?

CLOV [*As before.*] Mmm.

HAMM I was never there. [*Pause.*] Clov!

CLOV [*Turning towards* HAMM, *exasperated.*] What is it?

HAMM I was never there.

CLOV Lucky for you. [*He looks out of window.*]

HAMM Absent, always. It all happened without me. I don't know what's happened. [*Pause.*] Do you know what's happened? [*Pause.*] Clov!

CLOV [*Turning towards* HAMM, *exasperated.*] Do you want me to look at this muckheap, yes or no?

HAMM Answer me first.

CLOV What?

HAMM Do you know what's happened?

CLOV When? Where?

HAMM [*Violently.*] When! What's happened? Use your head, can't you! What has happened?

CLOV What for Christ's sake does it matter? [*He looks out of window.*]

HAMM I don't know. [*Pause.* CLOV *turns towards* HAMM.]

CLOV [*Harshly.*] When old Mother Pegg asked you for oil for her lamp and you told her to get out to hell, you knew what was happening then, no? [*Pause.*] You know what she died of, Mother Pegg? Of darkness.

HAMM   [*Feebly.*] I hadn't any.

CLOV   [*As before.*] Yes, you had. [*Pause.*]

HAMM   Have you the glass?

CLOV   No, it's clear enough as it is.

HAMM   Go and get it. [*Pause.* CLOV *casts up his eyes, brandishes his fists. He loses balance, clutches on to the ladder. He starts to get down, halts.*]

CLOV   There's one thing I'll never understand. [*He gets down.*] Why I always obey you. Can you explain that to me?

HAMM   No. . . . Perhaps it's compassion. [*Pause.*] A kind of great compassion. [*Pause.*] Oh you won't find it easy, you won't find it easy. [*Pause.* CLOV *begins to move about the room in search of the telescope.*]

CLOV   I'm tired of our goings on, very tired. [*He searches.*] You're not sitting on it? [*He moves the chair, looks at the place where it stood, resumes his search.*]

HAMM   [*Anguished.*] Don't leave me there! [*Angrily* CLOV *restores the chair to its place.*] Am I right in the centre?

CLOV   You'd need a microscope to find this— [*He sees the telescope.*] Ah, about time. [*He picks up the telescope, gets up on the ladder, turns the telescope on the without.*]

HAMM   Give me the dog.

CLOV   [*Looking.*] Quiet!

HAMM   [*Angrily.*] Give me the dog! [CLOV *drops the telescope, clasps his hands to his head. Pause. He gets down precipitately, looks for the dog, sees it, picks it up, hastens towards* HAMM *and strikes him violently on the head with the dog.*]

CLOV   There's your dog for you! [*The dog falls to the ground. Pause.*]

HAMM   He hit me!

CLOV   You drive me mad, I'm mad!

HAMM   If you must hit me, hit me with the axe. [*Pause.*] Or with the gaff, hit me with the gaff. Not with the dog. With the gaff. Or with the axe. [CLOV *picks up the dog and gives it to* HAMM *who takes it in his arms.*]

CLOV   [*Imploringly.*] Let's stop playing!

HAMM   Never! [*Pause.*] Put me in my coffin.

CLOV   There are no more coffins.

HAMM   Then let it end! [CLOV *goes towards ladder.*] With a bang! [CLOV *gets up on ladder, gets down again, looks for telescope, sees it, picks it up, gets up ladder, raises telescope.*] Of darkness! And me? Did anyone ever have pity on me?

CLOV   [*Lowering the telescope, turning towards* HAMM.] What? [*Pause.*] Is it me you're referring to?

HAMM   [*Angrily.*] An aside, ape! Did you never hear an aside before? [*Pause.*] I'm warming up for my last soliloquy.

CLOV   I warn you. I'm going to look at this filth since it's an order. But it's the last time. [*He turns the telescope on the without.*] Let's see. [*He moves the telescope.*] Nothing . . . nothing . . . good . . . good . . . nothing . . . goo— [*He starts, lowers the telescope, examines it, turns it again on the without. Pause.*] Bad luck to it!

HAMM   More complications! [CLOV *gets down.*] Not an underplot, I trust. [CLOV *moves ladder nearer window, gets up on it, turns telescope on the without.*]

CLOV   [*Dismayed.*] Looks like a small boy!

HAMM   [*Sarcastic.*] A small . . . boy!

CLOV I'll go and see. [*He gets down, drops the telescope, goes towards door, turns.*] I'll take the gaff. [*He looks for the gaff, sees it, picks it up, hastens towards door.*]

HAMM No! [CLOV *halts.*]

CLOV No? A potential procreator?

HAMM If he exists he'll die there or he'll come here. And if he doesn't . . . [*Pause.*]

CLOV You don't believe me? You think I'm inventing? [*Pause.*]

HAMM It's the end, Clov, we've come to the end. I don't need you any more. [*Pause.*]

CLOV Lucky for you. [*He goes towards door.*]

HAMM Leave me the gaff. [CLOV *gives him the gaff, goes towards door, halts, looks at alarm-clock, takes it down, looks round for a better place to put it, goes to bins, puts it on lid of* NAGG's *bin. Pause.*]

CLOV I'll leave you. [*He goes towards door.*]

HAMM Before you go . . . [CLOV *halts near door.*] . . . say something.

CLOV There is nothing to say.

HAMM A few words . . . to ponder . . . in my heart.

CLOV Your heart!

HAMM Yes. [*Pause. Forcibly.*] Yes! [*Pause.*] With the rest, in the end, the shadows, the murmurs, all the trouble, to end up with. [*Pause.*] Clov. . . . He never spoke to me. Then, in the end, before he went, without my having asked him, he spoke to me. He said . . .

CLOV [*Despairingly.*] Ah . . . !

HAMM Something . . . from your heart.

CLOV My heart!

HAMM A few words . . . from your heart. [*Pause.*]

CLOV [*Fixed gaze, tonelessly, towards auditorium.*] They said to me, That's love, yes, yes, not a doubt, now you see how—

HAMM Articulate!

CLOV [*As before.*] How easy it is. They said to me, That's friendship, yes, yes, no question, you've found it. They said to me, Here's the place, stop, raise your head and look at all that beauty. That order! They said to me. Come now, you're not a brute beast, think upon these things and you'll see how all becomes clear. And simple! They said to me, What skilled attention they get, all these dying of their wounds.

HAMM Enough!

CLOV [*As before.*] I say to myself—sometimes, Clov, you must learn to suffer better than that if you want them to weary of punishing you—one day. I say to myself—sometimes, Clov, you must be there better than that if you want them to let you go—one day. But I feel too old, and too far, to form new habits. Good, it'll never end, I'll never go. [*Pause.*] Then one day, suddenly, it ends, it changes, I don't understand, it dies, or it's me, I don't understand, that either. I ask the words that remain—sleeping, waking, morning, evening. They have nothing to say. [*Pause.*] I open the door of the cell and go. I am so bowed I only see my feet, if I open my eyes, and between my legs a little trail of black dust. I say to myself that the earth is extinguished, though I never saw it lit. [*Pause.*] It's easy going. [*Pause.*] When I fall I'll weep for happiness. [*Pause. He goes towards door.*]

HAMM Clov! [CLOV *halts, without turning.*] Nothing. [CLOV *moves on.*] Clov! [CLOV *halts, without turning.*]

CLOV This is what we call making an exit.

HAMM   I'm obliged to you, Clov. For your services.

CLOV   [*Turning, sharply.*] Ah pardon, it's I am obliged to you.

HAMM   It's we are obliged to each other. [*Pause.* CLOV *goes towards door.*] One thing more. [CLOV *halts.*] A last favour. [*Exit* CLOV.] Cover me with the sheet. [*Long pause.*] No? Good. [*Pause.*] Me to play. [*Pause. Wearily.*] Old endgame lost of old, play and lose and have done with losing. [*Pause. More animated.*] Let me see. [*Pause.*] Ah yes! [*He tries to move the chair, using the gaff as before. Enter* CLOV, *dressed for the road. Panama hat, tweed coat, raincoat over his arm, umbrella, bag. He halts by the door and stands there, impassive and motionless, his eyes fixed on* HAMM, *till the end.* HAMM *gives up.*] Good. [*Pause.*] Discard. [*He throws away the gaff, makes to throw away the dog, thinks better of it.*] Take it easy. [*Pause.*] And now? [*Pause.*] Raise hat. [*He raises his toque.*] Peace to our . . . arses. [*Pause.*] And put on again. [*He puts on his toque.*] Deuce. [*Pause. He takes off his glasses.*] Wipe. [*He takes out his handkerchief and, without unfolding it, wipes his glasses.*] And put on again. [*He puts on his glasses, puts back the handkerchief in his pocket.*] We're coming. A few more squirms like that and I'll call. [*Pause.*] A little poetry. [*Pause.*] You prayed— [*Pause. He corrects himself.*] You CRIED for night; it comes— [*Pause. He corrects himself.*] It FALLS: now cry in darkness. [*He repeats, chanting.*] You cried for night; it falls: now cry in darkness.⁶ [*Pause.*] Nicely put, that. [*Pause.*] And now? [*Pause.*] Moments for nothing, now as always, time was never and time is over, reckoning closed and story ended. [*Pause. Narrative tone.*] If he could have his child with him. . . . [*Pause.*] It was the moment I was waiting for. [*Pause.*] You don't want to abandon him? You want him to bloom while you are withering? Be there to solace your last million last moments? [*Pause.*] He doesn't realize, all he knows is hunger, and cold, and death to crown it all. But you! You ought to know what the earth is like, nowadays. Oh I put him before his responsibilities! [*Pause. Normal tone.*] Well, there we are, there I am, that's enough. [*He raises the whistle to his lips, hesitates, drops it. Pause.*] Yes, truly! [*He whistles. Pause. Louder. Pause.*] Good. [*Pause.*] Father! [*Pause. Louder.*] Father! [*Pause.*] Good. [*Pause.*] We're coming. [*Pause.*] And to end up with? [*Pause.*] Discard. [*He throws away the dog. He tears the whistle from his neck.*] With my compliments. [*He throws whistle towards auditorium. Pause. He sniffs. Soft.*] Clov! [*Long pause.*] No? Good. [*He takes out the handkerchief.*] Since that's the way we're playing it . . . [*He unfolds handkerchief.*] . . . let's play it that way . . . [*He unfolds.*] . . . and speak no more about it . . . [*He finishes unfolding.*] . . . speak no more. [*He holds handkerchief spread out before him.*] Old stancher! [*Pause.*] You . . . remain. [*Pause. He covers his face with handkerchief, lowers his arms to armrests, remains motionless.*] [*Brief tableau.*]

CURTAIN

1958

6. Parody of a line from Charles Baudelaire's poem "Meditation" that can be translated as: "You were calling for evening; it falls; it is here."

W. H. AUDEN
1907–1973

Wystan Hugh Auden was born in York, England, the son of a doctor and of a former nurse. He was educated at private schools and Christ Church, Oxford. After graduation from Oxford he traveled abroad, taught school in England from 1930 to 1935, and later worked for a government film unit. His sympathies in the 1930s were with the left, like those of most intellectuals of his age, and he went to Spain during its Civil War, intending to serve as an ambulance driver on the left-wing Republican side. To his surprise he felt so disturbed by the sight of the many Roman Catholic churches gutted and looted by the Republicans that he returned to England without fulfilling his ambition. He traveled in Iceland and China before moving to the United States in 1939; in 1946 he became an American citizen. He taught at a number of American colleges and was professor of poetry at Oxford from 1956 to 1960. Most of his later life was shared between residences in New York City and in Europe—first in southern Italy, then in Austria.

Auden was the most prominent of the young English poets who, in the late 1920s and early 1930s, saw themselves bringing new techniques and attitudes to English poetry. Stephen Spender, C. Day Lewis, and Louis MacNeice were other liberal and leftist poets in this loosely affiliated group. Auden learned metrical and verbal techniques from Gerard Manley Hopkins and Wilfred Owen, and from T. S. Eliot he took a conversational and ironic tone, an acute inspection of cultural decay. Thomas Hardy's metrical variety, formal irregularity, and fusion of panoramic and intimate perspectives also proved a useful example, and Auden admired W. B. Yeats's "serious reflective" poems of "personal and public interest," though he later came to disavow Yeats's grand aspirations and rhetoric. Auden's English studies at Oxford familiarized him with the rhythms and long alliterative line of Anglo-Saxon poetry. He learned, too, from popular and folk culture, particularly the songs of the English music hall and, later, American blues singers.

The Depression that hit America in 1929 hit England soon afterward, and Auden and his contemporaries looked out at an England of industrial stagnation and mass unemployment, seeing not Eliot's metaphorical Waste Land but a more literal Waste Land of poverty and "depressed areas." Auden's early poetry diagnoses the ills of his country. This diagnosis, conducted in a verse that combines irreverence with craftsmanship, draws on both Freud and Marx to show England now as a nation of neurotic invalids, now as the victim of an antiquated economic system. The intellectual liveliness and nervous force of this work made a great impression, even though the compressed, elliptical, impersonal style created difficulties of interpretation.

Gradually Auden sought to clarify his imagery and syntax, and in the late 1930s he produced "Lullaby," "Musée des Beaux Arts," "In Memory of W. B. Yeats," and other poems of finely disciplined movement, pellucid clarity, and deep yet unsentimental feeling. Some of the poems he wrote at this time, such as "Spain" and "September 1, 1939," aspire to a visionary perspective on political and social change; but as Auden became increasingly skeptical of poetry in the grand manner, of poetry as revelation or as a tool for political change, he removed these poems from his canon. (He came to see as false his claim in "September 1, 1939" that "We must love one another or die.") "Poetry is not magic," he said in the essay "Writing," but a form of truth telling that should "disenchant and disintoxicate." As he continued to remake his style during World War II, he created a voice that, in contrast not only to Romanticism but also to the authoritarianism devastating Europe, was increasingly flat, ironic, and conversational. He never lost his ear for popular speech or his ability to combine elements from popular art with technical formality. He daringly mixed the grave and the flippant, vivid detail and allegorical abstraction. He always experimented, particularly in ways of bringing together high artifice and a colloquial tone.

The poems of Auden's last phase are increasingly personal in tone and combine an air of offhand informality with remarkable technical skill in versification. He turned out, as if effortlessly, poems in numerous verse forms, including sestinas, sonnets, ballads, canzones, syllabics, haiku, the blues, even limericks. As he became ever more mistrustful of a prophetic role for the poet, he embraced the ordinary—the hours of the day, the rooms of a house, a changeable landscape. He took refuge in love and friendship, particularly the love and friendship he shared with the American writer Chester Kallmann. Like Eliot, Auden became a member of the Church of England, and the emotions of his late poetry—sometimes comic, sometimes solemn—were grounded in an ever deepening but rarely obtrusive religious feeling. In the last year of his life he returned to England to live in Oxford, feeling the need to be part of a university community as a protection against loneliness. Auden is now generally recognized as one of the masters of twentieth-century English poetry, a thoughtful, seriously playful poet, combining extraordinary intelligence and immense craftsmanship.

A note on the texts: Auden heavily revised his poems, sometimes omitting stanzas (as in "Spain" and "In Memory of W. B. Yeats") or even entire poems ("Spain" and "September 1, 1939"). The texts below are reprinted as they first appeared in book form and again in his *Selected Poems: A New Edition*, ed. Edward Mendelson (1989).

Petition[1]

Sir, no man's enemy, forgiving all
But will his negative inversion, be prodigal:
Send to us power and light, a sovereign touch[2]
Curing the intolerable neural itch,
5   The exhaustion of weaning, the liar's quinsy,°   *tonsillitis*
And the distortions of ingrown virginity.
Prohibit sharply the rehearsed response
And gradually correct the coward's stance;
Cover in time with beams those in retreat
10   That, spotted, they turn though the reverse were great;
Publish each healer that in city lives
Or country houses at the end of drives;
Harrow the house of the dead; look shining at
New styles of architecture, a change of heart.

Oct. 1929   1930

On This Island[1]

Look, stranger, at this island now
The leaping light for your delight discovers,
Stand stable here
And silent be,

---

1. This title, by which the poem is widely known, is from Auden's later collections. Many of his early poems first appeared without titles.
2. The king's touch was often regarded as mirac-

ulous cure for disease (cf. "sovereign" as an adjective, meaning "supreme, all-dominating").
1. The title is from Auden's later collections.

5   That through the channels of the ear
    May wander like a river
    The swaying sound of the sea.

    Here at the small field's ending pause
    Where the chalk wall falls to the foam, and its tall ledges
10 Oppose the pluck
    And knock of the tide,
    And the shingle scrambles after the suck-
    ing surf, and the gull lodges
    A moment on its sheer side.

15 Far off like floating seeds the ships
    Diverge on urgent voluntary errands;
    And the full view
    Indeed may enter
    And move in memory as now these clouds do,
20 That pass the harbour mirror
    And all the summer through the water saunter.

Nov. 1935

1936

Lullaby[1]

    Lay your sleeping head, my love,
    Human on my faithless arm;
    Time and fevers burn away
    Individual beauty from
5 Thoughtful children, and the grave
    Proves the child ephemeral:
    But in my arms till break of day
    Let the living creature lie,
    Mortal, guilty, but to me
10 The entirely beautiful.

    Soul and body have no bounds:
    To lovers as they lie upon
    Her tolerant enchanted slope
    In their ordinary swoon,
15 Grave the vision Venus° sends   *Roman goddess of love*
    Of supernatural sympathy,
    Universal love and hope;
    While an abstract insight wakes
    Among the glaciers and the rocks
20 The hermit's sensual ecstasy.

    Certainty, fidelity
    On the stroke of midnight pass

1. Title from Auden's later collections.

Like vibrations of a bell,
And fashionable madmen raise
25 Their pedantic boring cry:
Every farthing[2] of the cost,
All the dreaded cards foretell,
Shall be paid, but from this night
Not a whisper, not a thought,
30 Not a kiss nor look be lost.

Beauty, midnight, vision dies:
Let the winds of dawn that blow
Softly round your dreaming head
Such a day of sweetness show
35 Eye and knocking heart may bless,
Find the mortal world enough;
Noons of dryness see you fed
By the involuntary powers,
Nights of insult let you pass
40 Watched by every human love.

Jan. 1937   1937, 1940

Spain[1]

Yesterday all the past. The language of size
Spreading to China along the trade-routes; the diffusion
        Of the counting-frame and the cromlech;[2]
Yesterday the shadow-reckoning in the sunny climates.

5 Yesterday the assessment of insurance by cards,
The divination of water; yesterday the invention
        Of cartwheels and clocks, the taming of
Horses. Yesterday the bustling world of the navigators.

Yesterday the abolition of fairies and giants,
10 The fortress like a motionless eagle eyeing the valley,
        The chapel built in the forest;
Yesterday the carving of angels and alarming gargoyles;

The trial of heretics among the columns of stone;
Yesterday the theological feuds in the taverns
15   And the miraculous cure at the fountain;
Yesterday the Sabbath of witches; but to-day the struggle.

---

2. At one time the smallest and least valuable British coin.
1. The Spanish Civil War, which began in 1936 as a rebellion by General Franco's right-wing army against the left-wing, elected Spanish government, was viewed by British liberal intellectuals as a testing struggle between fascism and democracy. Written while the war was raging this poem appeared separately in 1937, the proceeds of its sale going to Medical Aid for Spain. In 1940 Auden retitled the poem "Spain 1937," deleted lines 69–76, and made other changes; later he removed the poem from his canon.
2. Ancient stone circle.

Yesterday the installation of dynamos and turbines,
The construction of railways in the colonial desert;
       Yesterday the classic lecture
20 On the origin of Mankind. But to-day the struggle.

Yesterday the belief in the absolute value of Greek,
The fall of the curtain upon the death of a hero;
       Yesterday the prayer to the sunset
And the adoration of madmen. But to-day the struggle.

25 As the poet whispers, startled among the pines,
Or where the loose waterfall sings compact, or upright
       On the crag by the leaning tower:
"O my vision. O send me the luck of the sailor."

And the investigator peers through his instruments
30 At the inhuman provinces, the virile bacillus
       Or enormous Jupiter finished:
"But the lives of my friends. I inquire. I inquire."

And the poor in their fireless lodgings, dropping the sheets
Of the evening paper: "Our day is our loss, O show us
35   History the operator, the
Organiser, Time the refreshing river."

And the nations combine each cry, invoking the life
That shapes the individual belly and orders
       The private nocturnal terror:
40 "Did you not found the city state of the sponge,

"Raise the vast military empires of the shark
And the tiger, establish the robin's plucky canton?°   *district*
       Intervene. O descend as a dove or
A furious papa or a mild engineer,[3] but descend."

45 And the life, if it answers at all, replies from the heart
And the eyes and the lungs, from the shops and squares of the city
       "O no, I am not the mover;
Not to-day; not to you. To you, I'm the

"Yes-man, the bar-companion, the easily-duped;
50 I am whatever you do. I am your vow to be
       Good, your humorous story.
I am your business voice. I am your marriage.

"What's your proposal? To build the just city? I will.
I agree. Or is it the suicide pact, the romantic
55   Death? Very well, I accept, for
I am your choice, your decision. Yes, I am Spain."

---

3. Auden plays on the idea of a *deus ex machina,*
literally a god from a machine, who appears suddenly in a play to resolve an impasse. "Dove": in
the Bible the form taken by the Holy Spirit when
descending to Earth.

Many have heard it on remote peninsulas,
On sleepy plains, in the aberrant fishermen's islands
      Or the corrupt heart of the city,
60 Have heard and migrated like gulls or the seeds of a flower.

They clung like burrs to the long expresses that lurch
Through the unjust lands, through the night, through the alpine tunnel;
      They floated over the oceans;
They walked the passes. All presented their lives.

65 On that arid square, that fragment nipped off from hot
Africa, soldered so crudely to inventive Europe;
      On that tableland scored by rivers,
Our thoughts have bodies; the menacing shapes of our fever

Are precise and alive. For the fears which made us respond
70 To the medicine ad. and the brochure of winter cruises
      Have become invading battalions;
And our faces, the institute-face, the chain-store, the ruin

Are projecting their greed as the firing squad and the bomb.
Madrid is the heart. Our moments of tenderness blossom
75   As the ambulance and the sandbag;
Our hours of friendship into a people's army.

To-morrow, perhaps the future. The research on fatigue
And the movements of packers; the gradual exploring of all the
      Octaves of radiation;
80 To-morrow the enlarging of consciousness by diet and breathing.

To-morrow the rediscovery of romantic love,
The photographing of ravens; all the fun under
      Liberty's masterful shadow;
To-morrow the hour of the pageant-master and the musician,

85 The beautiful roar of the chorus under the dome;
To-morrow the exchanging of tips on the breeding of terriers,
      The eager election of chairmen
By the sudden forest of hands. But to-day the struggle.

To-morrow for the young the poets exploding like bombs,
90 The walks by the lake, the weeks of perfect communion;
      To-morrow the bicycle races
Through the suburbs on summer evenings. But to-day the struggle.

To-day the deliberate increase in the chances of death,
The conscious acceptance of guilt in the necessary murder;[4]
95   To-day the expending of powers
On the flat ephemeral pamphlet and the boring meeting.

---

4. After these two lines were criticized by George Orwell, Auden revised them to read "the inevitable increase" and "the fact of murder."

To-day the makeshift consolations: the shared cigarette,
The cards in the candlelit barn, and the scraping concert,
The masculine jokes; to-day the
100　Fumbled and unsatisfactory embrace before hurting.

The stars are dead. The animals will not look.
We are left alone with our day, and the time is short, and
History to the defeated
May say Alas but cannot help nor pardon.

Mar. 1937   1937

As I Walked Out One Evening[1]

As I walked out one evening,
　　Walking down Bristol Street,
The crowds upon the pavement
　　Were fields of harvest wheat.

5　And down by the brimming river
　　I heard a lover sing
Under an arch of the railway:
　　"Love has no ending.

"I'll love you, dear, I'll love you
10　　Till China and Africa meet
And the river jumps over the mountain
　　And the salmon sing in the street.

"I'll love you till the ocean
　　Is folded and hung up to dry
15　And the seven stars[2] go squawking
　　Like geese about the sky.

"The years shall run like rabbits
　　For in my arms I hold
The Flower of the Ages
20　　And the first love of the world."

But all the clocks in the city
　　Began to whirr and chime:
"O let not Time deceive you,
　　You cannot conquer Time.

25　"In the burrows of the Nightmare
　　Where Justice naked is,
Time watches from the shadow
　　And coughs when you would kiss.

1. Title from Auden's later collections.
2. The constellation of the Pleiades, supposed by the ancients to be seven sisters.

"In headaches and in worry
30   Vaguely life leaks away,
And Time will have his fancy
To-morrow or to-day.

"Into many a green valley
Drifts the appalling³ snow;
35 Time breaks the threaded dances
And the diver's brilliant bow.

"O plunge your hands in water,
Plunge them in up to the wrist;
Stare, stare in the basin
40   And wonder what you've missed.

"The glacier knocks in the cupboard,
The desert sighs in the bed,
And the crack in the tea-cup opens
A lane to the land of the dead.

45 "Where the beggars raffle the banknotes
And the Giant is enchanting to Jack,
And the Lily-white Boy is a Roarer
And Jill goes down on her back.⁴

"O look, look in the mirror,
50   O look in your distress;
Life remains a blessing
Although you cannot bless.

"O stand, stand at the window
As the tears scald and start;
55 You shall love your crooked neighbour
With your crooked heart."

It was late, late in the evening,
The lovers they were gone;
The clocks had ceased their chiming
60   And the deep river ran on.

Nov. 1937   1938, 1940

Musée des Beaux Arts¹

About suffering they were never wrong,
The Old Masters: how well they understood
Its human position; how it takes place

3. Literally, making white.
4. The giant of "Jack and the Bean Stalk" is trying
to seduce Jack; the "lily-white Boy" (presumably

pure) becomes a boisterous reveler; Jill, of "Jack
and Jill," is seduced.
1. Museum of Fine Arts (French).

While someone else is eating or opening a window or just walking dully
    along;
5 How, when the aged are reverently, passionately waiting
For the miraculous birth, there always must be
Children who did not specially want it to happen, skating
On a pond at the edge of the wood:
They never forgot
10 That even the dreadful martyrdom must run its course
Anyhow in a corner, some untidy spot
Where the dogs go on with their doggy life and the torturer's horse
Scratches its innocent behind on a tree.

In Brueghel's *Icarus*,[2] for instance: how everything turns away
15 Quite leisurely from the disaster; the ploughman may
Have heard the splash, the forsaken cry,
But for him it was not an important failure; the sun shone
As it had to on the white legs disappearing into the green
Water; and the expensive delicate ship that must have seen
20 Something amazing, a boy falling out of the sky,
Had somewhere to get to and sailed calmly on.

Dec. 1938   1940

In Memory of W. B. Yeats[1]

(d. January 1939)

I

He disappeared in the dead of winter:
The brooks were frozen, the air-ports almost deserted,
And snow disfigured the public statues;
The mercury sank in the mouth of the dying day.
5 O all the instruments agree
The day of his death was a dark cold day.

Far from his illness
The wolves ran on through the evergreen forests,
The peasant river was untempted by the fashionable quays;
10 By mourning tongues
The death of the poet was kept from his poems.

But for him it was his last afternoon as himself,
An afternoon of nurses and rumours;

2. *The Fall of Icarus*, by the Flemish painter Pieter Brueghel (ca. 1525–1569), in the Musées Royaux des Beaux Arts in Brussels. In one corner of Brueghel's painting, Icarus's legs are seen disappearing into the sea, his wings having melted when he flew too close to the sun. Auden also alludes to other paintings by Brueghel: the nativity scene in *The Numbering at Bethlehem*, skaters in *Winter Landscape with Skaters and a Bird Trap*, a horse scratching its behind in *The Massacre of the Innocents*.
1. The Irish poet William Butler Yeats, born in 1865, died on January 29, 1939, in Roquebrune (southern France).

The provinces of his body revolted,
15   The squares of his mind were empty,
Silence invaded the suburbs,
The current of his feeling failed: he became his admirers.

Now he is scattered among a hundred cities
And wholly given over to unfamiliar affections;
20   To find his happiness in another kind of wood[2]
And be punished under a foreign code of conscience.
The words of a dead man
Are modified in the guts of the living.

But in the importance and noise of to-morrow
25   When the brokers are roaring like beasts on the floor of the Bourse,[3]
And the poor have the sufferings to which they are fairly accustomed,
And each in the cell of himself is almost convinced of his freedom;
A few thousand will think of this day
As one thinks of a day when one did something slightly unusual.

30   O all the instruments agree
The day of his death was a dark cold day.

II

You were silly like us: your gift survived it all;
The parish of rich women,[4] physical decay,
Yourself; mad Ireland hurt you into poetry.
35   Now Ireland has her madness and her weather still,
For poetry makes nothing happen: it survives
In the valley of its saying where executives
Would never want to tamper; it flows south
From ranches of isolation and the busy griefs,
40   Raw towns that we believe and die in; it survives,
A way of happening, a mouth.

III[5]

Earth, receive an honoured guest;
William Yeats is laid to rest:
Let the Irish vessel lie
45   Emptied of its poetry.

Time that is intolerant
Of the brave and innocent,
And indifferent in a week
To a beautiful physique,

2. Cf. the beginning of Dante's *Inferno*: "In the middle of the journey of our life I came to myself in a dark wood where the straight way was lost" (1.1–3).
3. The French stock exchange.
4. Several wealthy women, including Lady Augusta Gregory (1852–1932), provided financial help to Yeats.
5. The stanza pattern of this section echoes that of Yeats's late poem "Under Ben Bulben." Auden later omitted the section's second, third, and fourth stanzas.

50 Worships language and forgives
     Everyone by whom it lives;
     Pardons cowardice, conceit,
     Lays its honours at their feet.

     Time that with this strange excuse
55   Pardoned Kipling[6] and his views,
     And will pardon Paul Claudel,[7]
     Pardons him for writing well.

     In the nightmare of the dark
     All the dogs of Europe bark,[8]
60   And the living nations wait,
     Each sequestered in its hate;

     Intellectual disgrace
     Stares from every human face,
     And the seas of pity lie
65   Locked and frozen in each eye.

     Follow, poet, follow right
     To the bottom of the night,
     With your unconstraining voice
     Still persuade us to rejoice;

70   With the farming of a verse
     Make a vineyard of the curse,
     Sing of human unsuccess
     In a rapture of distress;

     In the deserts of the heart
75   Let the healing fountain start,
     In the prison of his days
     Teach the free man how to praise.

Feb. 1939   1939, 1940

The Unknown Citizen

To JS/07/M/378
This Marble Monument is Erected by the State

He was found by the Bureau of Statistics to be
One against whom there was no official complaint,
And all the reports on his conduct agree
That, in the modern sense of an old-fashioned word, he was a saint,
5   For in everything he did he served the Greater Community.

---

6. The British writer Rudyard Kipling (1865–
1936) championed imperialism.
7. French author (1868–1955) with extremely

conservative politics. Yeats was at times antidemocratic and appeared to favor dictatorship.
8. World War II began in September 1939.

Except for the War till the day he retired
He worked in a factory and never got fired,
But satisfied his employers, Fudge Motors Inc.
Yet he wasn't a scab or odd in his views,
10 For his Union reports that he paid his dues,
(Our report on his Union shows it was sound)
And our Social Psychology workers found
That he was popular with his mates and liked a drink.
The Press are convinced that he bought a paper every day
15 And that his reactions to advertisements were normal in every way.
Policies taken out in his name prove that he was fully insured,
And his Health-card shows he was once in hospital but left it cured.
Both Producers Research and High-Grade Living declare
He was fully sensible to the advantages of the Installment Plan
20 And had everything necessary to the Modern Man,
A gramophone, a radio, a car and a frigidaire.
Our researchers into Public Opinion are content
That he held the proper opinions for the time of year;
When there was peace, he was for peace; when there was war, he
    went.
25 He was married and added five children to the population,
Which our Eugenist[1] says was the right number for a parent of his
    generation,
And our teachers report that he never interfered with their education.
Was he free? Was he happy? The question is absurd:
Had anything been wrong, we should certainly have heard.

Mar. 1939   1939, 1940

September 1, 1939[1]

I sit in one of the dives
On Fifty-Second Street[2]
Uncertain and afraid
As the clever hopes expire
5   Of a low dishonest decade:
Waves of anger and fear
Circulate over the bright
And darkened lands of the earth,
Obsessing our private lives;
10 The unmentionable odour of death
Offends the September night.

Accurate scholarship can
Unearth the whole offence
From Luther[3] until now
15 That has driven a culture mad,
Find what occurred at Linz,[4]

1. An expert in eugenics, a pseudoscience for the genetic "improvement" of humans.
1. The date of Germany's invasion of Poland and the outbreak of World War II.
2. In New York City, where Auden was living.
3. Martin Luther (1483–1546), founder of the Protestant Reformation.
4. Austrian city where Hitler spent his childhood.

What huge imago[5] made
A psychopathic god:
I and the public know
20   What all schoolchildren learn,
Those to whom evil is done
Do evil in return.

Exiled Thucydides[6] knew
All that a speech can say
25   About Democracy,
And what dictators do,
The elderly rubbish they talk
To an apathetic grave;
Analysed all in his book,
30   The enlightenment driven away,
The habit-forming pain,
Mismanagement and grief:
We must suffer them all again.

Into this neutral air
35   Where blind skyscrapers use
Their full height to proclaim
The strength of Collective Man,
Each language pours its vain
Competitive excuse:
40   But who can live for long
In an euphoric dream;
Out of the mirror they stare,
Imperialism's face
And the international wrong.

45   Faces along the bar
Cling to their average day:
The lights must never go out,
The music must always play,
All the conventions conspire
50   To make this fort assume
The furniture of home;
Lest we should see where we are,
Lost in a haunted wood,
Children afraid of the night
55   Who have never been happy or good.

The windiest militant trash
Important Persons shout
Is not so crude as our wish:
What mad Nijinsky wrote
60   About Diaghilev[7]
Is true of the normal heart;

---

5. Psychoanalytic term for the unconscious representation of a parental figure.
6. Greek general (d. ca. 401 B.C.E.) and historian of the Peloponnesian War, exiled from Athens

because he failed to prevent the Spartans from seizing a colony.
7. The Russian dancer and choreographer Vaslav Nijinsky (1890–1950) wrote that his former lover

For the error bred in the bone
Of each woman and each man
Craves what it cannot have,
65 Not universal love
But to be loved alone.

From the conservative dark
Into the ethical life
The dense commuters come,
70 Repeating their morning vow,
"I *will* be true to the wife,
I'll concentrate more on my work,"
And helpless governors wake
To resume their compulsory game:
75 Who can release them now,
Who can reach the deaf,
Who can speak for the dumb?[8]

All I have is a voice
To undo the folded lie,
80 The romantic lie in the brain
Of the sensual man-in-the-street
And the lie of Authority
Whose buildings grope the sky:
There is no such thing as the State
85 And no one exists alone;
Hunger allows no choice
To the citizen or the police;
We must love one another or die.[9]

Defenceless under the night
90 Our world in stupor lies;
Yet, dotted everywhere,
Ironic points of light
Flash out wherever the Just
Exchange their messages:
95 May I, composed like them
Of Eros° and of dust,   *Greek god of desire*
Beleaguered by the same
Negation and despair,
Show an affirming flame.

Sept. 1939   1939, 1940

the ballet impresario Sergey Diaghilev (1872–
1929) "does not want universal love, but to be
loved alone."
8. Proverbs 31.8.

9. Auden later revised this line, which struck him
as "dishonest." In one version of the poem the line
reads "We must love one another and die." Another
version leaves out the entire stanza.

In Praise of Limestone[1]

If it form the one landscape that we the inconstant ones
  Are consistently homesick for, this is chiefly
Because it dissolves in water. Mark these rounded slopes
  With their surface fragrance of thyme and beneath
5 A secret system of caves and conduits; hear these springs
  That spurt out everywhere with a chuckle
Each filling a private pool for its fish and carving
  Its own little ravine whose cliffs entertain
The butterfly and the lizard; examine this region
10   Of short distances and definite places:
What could be more like Mother or a fitter background
  For her son, for the nude young male who lounges
Against a rock displaying his dildo,° never doubting   *penis*
  That for all his faults he is loved, whose works are but
15 Extensions of his power to charm? From weathered outcrop
    To hill-top temple, from appearing waters to
Conspicuous fountains, from a wild to a formal vineyard,
  Are ingenious but short steps that a child's wish
To receive more attention than his brothers, whether
20   By pleasing or teasing, can easily take.

Watch, then, the band of rivals as they climb up and down
  Their steep stone gennels[2] in twos and threes, sometimes
Arm in arm, but never, thank God, in step; or engaged
  On the shady side of a square at midday in
25 Voluble discourse, knowing each other too well to think
  There are any important secrets, unable
To conceive a god whose temper-tantrums are moral
  And not to be pacified by a clever line
Or a good lay: for, accustomed to a stone that responds,
30   They have never had to veil their faces in awe
Of a crater whose blazing fury could not be fixed;
  Adjusted to the local needs of valleys
Where everything can be touched or reached by walking,
  Their eyes have never looked into infinite space
35 Through the lattice-work of a nomad's comb; born lucky,
  Their legs have never encountered the fungi
And insects of the jungle, the monstrous forms and lives
  With which we have nothing, we like to hope, in common.
So, when one of them goes to the bad, the way his mind works
40   Remains comprehensible: to become a pimp
Or deal in fake jewelry or ruin a fine tenor voice
  For effects that bring down the house could happen to all
But the best and the worst of us . . .
                        That is why, I suppose,
  The best and worst never stayed here long but sought

1. Inspired by the limestone landscape outside Florence, Italy, where Auden and his longtime companion Chester Kallman (1921–1975) were staying; the poem also recalls the poet's native Yorkshire. In a letter to Elizabeth Mayer, Auden wrote: "I hadn't realised till I came how like Italy is to my 'Mutterland', the Pennines [hills in the north of England]. Am in fact starting on a poem, 'In Praise of Limestone', the theme of which is that rock creates the only truly human landscape."
2. Narrow passages between houses (Yorkshire dialect) or, as here, rocks.

45   Immoderate soils where the beauty was not so external,
        The light less public and the meaning of life
     Something more than a mad camp. "Come!" cried the granite wastes,
     "How evasive is your humor, how accidental
     Your kindest kiss, how permanent is death." (Saints-to-be
50   Slipped away sighing.) "Come!" purred the clays and gravels
     "On our plains there is room for armies to drill; rivers
        Wait to be tamed and slaves to construct you a tomb
     In the grand manner: soft as the earth is mankind and both
        Need to be altered." (Intendant Caesars rose and
55   Left, slamming the door.) But the really reckless were fetched
        By an older colder voice, the oceanic whisper:
     "I am the solitude that asks and promises nothing;
        That is how I shall set you free. There is no love;
     There are only the various envies, all of them sad."

60   They were right, my dear, all those voices were right
     And still are; this land is not the sweet home that it looks,
        Nor its peace the historical calm of a site
     Where something was settled once and for all: A backward
        And dilapidated province, connected
65   To the big busy world by a tunnel, with a certain
        Seedy appeal, is that all it is now? Not quite:
     It has a worldly duty which in spite of itself
        It does not neglect, but calls into question
     All the Great Powers assume; it disturbs our rights. The poet,
70   Admired for his earnest habit of calling
     The sun the sun, his mind Puzzle, is made uneasy
        By these solid statues which so obviously doubt
     His antimythological myth; and these gamins,°   urchins
        Pursuing the scientist down the tiled colonnade
75   With such lively offers, rebuke his concern for Nature's
        Remotest aspects: I, too, am reproached, for what
     And how much you know. Not to lose time, not to get caught,
        Not to be left behind, not, please! to resemble
     The beasts who repeat themselves, or a thing like water
80   Or stone whose conduct can be predicted, these
     Are our Common Prayer,[3] whose greatest comfort is music
        Which can be made anywhere, is invisible,
     And does not smell. In so far as we have to look forward
        To death as a fact, no doubt we are right: But if
85   Sins can be forgiven, if bodies rise from the dead,
        These modifications of matter into
     Innocent athletes and gesticulating fountains,
        Made solely for pleasure, make a further point:
     The blessed will not care what angle they are regarded from,
90   Having nothing to hide. Dear, I know nothing of
     Either, but when I try to imagine a faultless love
        Or the life to come, what I hear is the murmur
     Of underground streams, what I see is a limestone landscape.

May 1948   1948, 1951

3. The Book of Common Prayer is the liturgical book of the Anglican Church.

The Shield of Achilles[1]

She looked over his shoulder
    For vines and olive trees,
    Marble well-governed cities,
    And ships upon untamed seas,
5   But there on the shining metal
    His hands had put instead
    An artificial wilderness
    And a sky like lead.

A plain without a feature, bare and brown,
10   No blade of grass, no sign of neighborhood,
    Nothing to eat and nowhere to sit down,
    Yet, congregated on its blankness, stood
    An unintelligible multitude,
    A million eyes, a million boots in line,
15   Without expression, waiting for a sign.

Out of the air a voice without a face
    Proved by statistics that some cause was just
In tones as dry and level as the place:
    No one was cheered and nothing was discussed;
20   Column by column in a cloud of dust
    They marched away enduring a belief
    Whose logic brought them, somewhere else, to grief.

She looked over his shoulder
    For ritual pieties,
25   White flower-garlanded heifers,
    Libation and sacrifice,[2]
    But there on the shining metal
    Where the altar should have been,
    She saw by his flickering forge-light
30   Quite another scene.

Barbed wire enclosed an arbitrary spot
    Where bored officials lounged (one cracked a joke)
And sentries sweated, for the day was hot:
    A crowd of ordinary decent folk
35   Watched from without and neither moved nor spoke
    As three pale figures were led forth and bound
    To three posts driven upright in the ground.

---

1. In Homer's *Iliad* Achilles, the chief Greek hero in the war with Troy, lends his armor to his great friend Patroclus and loses it when Patroclus is killed by Hector. While Achilles is mourning the death of his friend, his mother, the goddess Thetis, goes to Mt. Olympus to beg Hephaestos, the god of fire, to forge new armor for Achilles. The splendid shield of Achilles that Hephaestos then makes is described in book 18 (lines 478–608). On it he depicts the earth, the heavens, the sea, and the planets; a city in peace (with a wedding and a trial) and a city at war; scenes from country life, animal life, and the joyful life of young men and women. The ocean, as the outer border, flows around all these scenes.

2. Cf. John Keats's "Ode on a Grecian Urn" (1820): "Who are these coming to the sacrifice? / To what green altar, O mysterious priest, / Lead'st thou that heifer lowing at the skies, / And all her silken flanks with garlands dressed?" "Libation": sacrifice of wine or other liquid.

The mass and majesty of this world, all
That carries weight and always weighs the same,
40 Lay in the hands of others; they were small
And could not hope for help and no help came:
What their foes liked to do was done, their shame
Was all the worst could wish; they lost their pride
And died as men before their bodies died.

45   She looked over his shoulder
      For athletes at their games,
    Men and women in a dance
      Moving their sweet limbs
    Quick, quick, to music,
50   But there on the shining shield
    His hands had set no dancing-floor
      But a weed-choked field.

A ragged urchin, aimless and alone,
Loitered about that vacancy; a bird
55 Flew up to safety from his well-aimed stone:
That girls are raped, that two boys knife a third,
Were axioms to him, who'd never heard
Of any world where promises were kept
Or one could weep because another wept.

60   The thin-lipped armorer,
      Hephaestos, hobbled away;
    Thetis of the shining breasts
      Cried out in dismay
    At what the god had wrought
65   To please her son, the strong
    Iron-hearted man-slaying Achilles
      Who would not live long.

1952   1952, 1955

[Poetry as Memorable Speech][1]

Of the many definitions of poetry, the simplest is still the best: 'memorable speech.' That is to say, it must move our emotions, or excite our intellect, for only that which is moving or exciting is memorable, and the stimulus is the audible spoken word and cadence, to which in all its power of suggestion and incantation we must surrender, as we do when talking to an intimate friend. We must, in fact, make exactly the opposite kind of mental effort to that we make in grasping other verbal uses, for in the case of the latter the aura of suggestion round every word through which, like the atom radiating lines of force through the whole of space and time, it becomes ultimately a sign for the sum of all possible meanings, must be rigorously suppressed and its meaning confined to a single dictionary one. For this reason the exposition of a

1. Excerpted from Auden and John Garrett's introduction to their anthology of verse, *The Poet's Tongue*.

scientific theory is easier to read than to hear. No poetry, on the other hand, which when mastered is not better heard than read is good poetry.

All speech has rhythm, which is the result of the combination of the alternating periods of effort and rest necessary to all living things, and the laying of emphasis on what we consider important; and in all poetry there is a tension between the rhythm due to the poet's personal values, and those due to the experiences of generations crystallised into habits of language such as the English tendency to alternate weak and accented syllables, and conventional verse forms like the hexameter, the heroic pentameter, or the French Alexandrine. Similes, metaphors of image or idea, and auditory metaphors such as rhyme, assonance, and alliteration help further to clarify and strengthen the pattern and internal relations of the experience described.

Poetry, in fact, bears the same kind of relation to Prose, using prose simply in the sense of all those uses of words that are not poetry, that algebra bears to arithmetic. The poet writes of personal or fictitious experiences, but these are not important in themselves until the reader has realised them in his own consciousness.

> Soldier from the war returning,
> Spoiler of the taken town.[2]

It is quite unimportant, though it is the kind of question not infrequently asked, who the soldier is, what regiment he belongs to, what war he had been fighting in, etc. The soldier is you or me, or the man next door. Only when it throws light on our own experience, when these lines occur to us as we see, say, the unhappy face of a stockbroker in the suburban train, does poetry convince us of its significance. The test of a poet is the frequency and diversity of the occasions on which we remember his poetry.

Memorable speech then. About what? Birth, death, the Beatific Vision,[3] the abysses of hatred and fear, the awards and miseries of desire, the unjust walking the earth and the just scratching miserably for food like hens, triumphs, earthquakes, deserts of boredom and featureless anxiety, the Golden Age promised or irrevocably past, the gratifications and terrors of childhood, the impact of nature on the adolescent, the despairs and wisdoms of the mature, the sacrificial victim, the descent into Hell, the devouring and the benign mother? Yes, all of these, but not these only. Everything that we remember no matter how trivial: the mark on the wall, the joke at luncheon, word games, these, like the dance of a stoat[4] or the raven's gamble, are equally the subject of poetry.

We shall do poetry a great disservice if we confine it only to the major experiences of life:

> The soldier's pole is fallen,
> Boys and girls are level now with men,
> And there is nothing left remarkable
> Beneath the visiting moon.

> They had a royal wedding.
> All his courtiers wished him well.

2. Beginning lines of a poem (in which "war" is plural) by the English poet A. E. Housman (1859–1936).

3. A sight of the glories of heaven.
4. Weasel.

The horses pranced and the dancers danced.
O Mister it was swell.

And masculine is found to be
Hadria the Adriatic Sea,[5]

have all their rightful place, and full appreciation of one depends on full appreciation of the others.

A great many people dislike the idea of poetry as they dislike over-earnest people, because they imagine it is always worrying about the eternal verities. Those, in Mr Spender's[6] words, who try to put poetry on a pedestal only succeed in putting it on the shelf. Poetry is no better and no worse than human nature; it is profound and shallow, sophisticated and naïve, dull and witty, bawdy and chaste in turn.

In spite of the spread of education and the accessibility of printed matter, there is a gap between what is commonly called 'highbrow' and 'lowbrow' taste, wider perhaps than it has ever been.

The industrial revolution broke up the agricultural communities, with their local conservative cultures, and divided the growing population into two classes: those whether employers or employees who worked and had little leisure, and a small class of shareholders who did no work, had leisure but no responsibilities or roots, and were therefore preoccupied with themselves. Literature has tended therefore to divide into two streams, one providing the first with a compensation and escape, the other the second with a religion and a drug. The Art for Art's sake[7] of the London drawing-rooms of the '90's, and towns like Burnley and Rochdale,[8] are complementary.

Nor has the situation been much improved by the increased leisure and educational opportunities which the population to-day as a whole possess. Were leisure all, the unemployed would have created a second Athens.

Artistic creations may be produced by individuals, and because their work is only appreciated by a few it does not necessarily follow that it is not good; but a universal art can only be the product of a community united in sympathy, sense of worth, and aspiration; and it is improbable that the artist can do his best except in such a society.

✻   ✻   ✻

The 'average' man says: 'When I get home I want to spend my time with my wife or in the nursery; I want to get out on to the links[9] or go for a spin in the car, not to read poetry. Why should I? I'm quite happy without it.' We must be able to point out to him that whenever, for example, he makes a good joke he is creating poetry, that one of the motives behind poetry is curiosity, the wish to know what we feel and think, and how, as E. M. Forster[1] says, can I know what I think till I see what I say, and that curiosity is the only human passion that can be indulged in for twenty-four hours a day without satiety.

The psychologist maintains that poetry is a neurotic symptom, an attempt

5. A mnemonic to help remember that Hadria, Latin for the Adriatic Sea, is masculine, despite its typically feminine ending. The first quotation is a remembered version of Cleopatra's speech after Antony dies in Shakespeare's *Antony and Cleopatra* (4.16.67–70). The source of the middle quotation has not been identified.

6. Stephen Spender (1909–1995), English poet.
7. Phrase associated with aestheticism.
8. Once industrial mill towns in Lancashire, England.
9. Ground on which golf is played.
1. English novelist (1879–1970).

to compensate by phantasy for a failure to meet reality. We must tell him that phantasy is only the beginning of writing; that, on the contrary, like psychology, poetry is a struggle to reconcile the unwilling subject and object; in fact, that since psychological truth depends so largely on context, poetry, the parabolic[2] approach, is the only adequate medium for psychology.

The propagandist, whether moral or political, complains that the writer should use his powers over words to persuade people to a particular course of action, instead of fiddling while Rome burns.[3] But Poetry is not concerned with telling people what to do, but with extending our knowledge of good and evil, perhaps making the necessity for action more urgent and its nature more clear, but only leading us to the point where it is possible for us to make a rational and moral choice.

※　※　※

1935

2. I.e., akin to parable.
3. The Roman emperor Nero (37–68) reputedly fiddled while Rome burned.

LOUIS MacNEICE
1907–1963

Born in Belfast, the son of a strong-willed Anglican rector (later to become a courageously independent bishop), Louis MacNeice illustrates the English critic Cyril Connolly's dictum that "the one golden recipe for Art is the ferment of an unhappy childhood working through a noble imagination." MacNeice's mother fell ill and died. "When I was five the black dreams came; / Nothing after was quite the same." Sent to English schools, where he lost his Irish accent, he was educated at Marlborough College and Merton College, Oxford. He became a lecturer in classics at Birmingham University and, later, at Bedford College, London. Following the breakup of his first marriage, he traveled to Iceland with his friend the poet W. H. Auden, then to Spain on the eve of—and again during—the Spanish Civil War, and to the United States at the beginning of World War II. After returning to England in 1940, he joined the British Broadcasting Corporation as a feature writer and producer and, except for a year and a half spent in Athens as director of the British Institute, worked for the BBC for the rest of his life.

He was a pioneer of radio drama, a playwright, a translator (of Aeschylus' *Agamemnon* and Goethe's *Faust*), and a literary critic. Best-known as a poet, however, he was early identified with the other liberal and leftist Oxford poets, Auden, Stephen Spender, and C. Day Lewis. Openness, honesty, and a consistently high level of craft characterize his poems. In a responsive, flexible voice, they ruminate tentatively and ponder without resolution. MacNeice delights in the surface of the world his senses apprehend and celebrates "the drunkenness of things being various," often (as in "Bagpipe Music") with wit and a wild gaiety. In love with life's irreducible multiplicity, he strives to embrace life's flux, despite an underlying sense of sadness and, sometimes, tragedy: "All our games are funeral games."

Sunday Morning

Down the road someone is practising scales,
The notes like little fishes vanish with a wink of tails,
Man's heart expands to tinker with his car
For this is Sunday morning, Fate's great bazaar,
5 Regard these means as ends, concentrate on this Now,
And you may grow to music or drive beyond Hindhead[1] anyhow,
Take corners on two wheels until you go so fast
That you can clutch a fringe or two of the windy past,
That you can abstract this day and make it to the week of time
10 A small eternity, a sonnet self-contained in rhyme.

But listen, up the road, something gulps, the church spire
Opens its eight bells out, skulls' mouths which will not tire
To tell how there is no music or movement which secures
Escape from the weekday time. Which deadens and endures.

1933   1935

The Sunlight on the Garden

The sunlight on the garden
Hardens and grows cold,
We cannot cage the minute
Within its nets of gold,
5 When all is told
We cannot beg for pardon.

Our freedom as free lances
Advances towards its end;
The earth compels, upon it
10 Sonnets and birds descend;
And soon, my friend,
We shall have no time for dances.

The sky was good for flying
Defying the church bells
15 And every evil iron
Siren and what it tells:
The earth compels,
We are dying, Egypt, dying[1]

And not expecting pardon,
20 Hardened in heart anew,
But glad to have sat under
Thunder and rain with you,

1. An upland district in Surrey popular for outings.

1. Cf. Antony's speech in Shakespeare's *Antony and Cleopatra* 4.16.19: "I am dying, Egypt, dying."

And grateful too
For sunlight on the garden.

1937, 1938

Bagpipe Music

It's no go the merrygoround, it's no go the rickshaw,
All we want is a limousine and a ticket for the peepshow.
Their knickers° are made of crêpe-de-chine,° their   *panties / silky material*
    shoes are made of python,
Their halls are lined with tiger rugs and their walls with heads of bison.

5   John MacDonald found a corpse, put it under the sofa,
Waited till it came to life and hit it with a poker,
Sold its eyes for souvenirs, sold its blood for whisky,
Kept its bones for dumb-bells to use when he was fifty.

It's no go the Yogi-Man, it's no go Blavatsky,[1]
10 All we want is a bank balance and a bit of skirt in a taxi.
Annie MacDougall went to milk, caught her foot in the heather,
Woke to hear a dance record playing of Old Vienna.
It's no go your maidenheads, it's no go your culture,
All we want is a Dunlop tyre and the devil mend the puncture.

15 The Laird o' Phelps spent Hogmanay[2] declaring he was sober,
Counted his feet to prove the fact and found he had one foot over.
Mrs Carmichael had her fifth, looked at the job with repulsion,
Said to the midwife "Take it away; I'm through with overproduction."

It's no go the gossip column, it's no go the Ceilidh,[3]
20 All we want is a mother's help and a sugar-stick for the baby.

Willie Murray cut his thumb, couldn't count the damage,
Took the hide of an Ayrshire cow and used it for a bandage.
His brother caught three hundred cran[4] when the seas were lavish,
Threw the bleeders back in the sea and went upon the parish.[5]

25 It's no go the Herring Board, it's no go the Bible,
All we want is a packet of fags° when our hands are idle.   *cigarettes*

It's no go the picture palace, it's no go the stadium,
It's no go the country cot° with a pot of pink geraniums.   *cottage*
It's no go the Government grants, it's no go the elections,
30 Sit on your arse for fifty years and hang your hat on a pension.

1. Madame Blavatsky (1831–1891), famous theosophist whose ideas were popular in some quarters in 1930s Britain. The poem is set in Depression-era Scotland, before World War II.
2. New Year's Eve (Scots).
3. A Scottish Gaelic word pronounced *kaley* for a social evening spent singing and storytelling.
4. A measure of fresh herrings, about 750 fish. The Scottish herring industry failed in the 1930s; the Herring Board (line 25) was a government attempt to provide direction.
5. I.e., "went on the county" (on relief).

It's no go my honey love, it's no go my poppet;
Work your hands from day to day, the winds will blow the profit.
The glass is falling hour by hour, the glass will fall forever,
But if you break the bloody glass you won't hold up the weather.

1937

Star-Gazer

Forty-two years ago (to me if to no one else
The number is of some interest) it was a brilliant starry night
And the westward train was empty and had no corridors
So darting from side to side I could catch the unwonted sight
5   Of those almost intolerably bright
Holes, punched in the sky, which excited me partly because
Of their Latin names and partly because I had read in the textbooks
How very far off they were, it seemed their light
Had left them (some at least) long years before I was.

10   And this remembering now I mark that what
Light was leaving some of them at least then,
Forty-two years ago, will never arrive
In time for me to catch it, which light when
It does get here may find that there is not
15   Anyone left alive
To run from side to side in a late night train
Admiring it and adding noughts in vain.

Jan. 1963   1963

DYLAN THOMAS
1914–1953

Dylan Thomas was born in Swansea, Wales, and educated at Swansea Grammar School. After working for a time as a newspaper reporter, he was "discovered" as a poet in 1933 through a poetry contest in a popular newspaper. The following year his *Eighteen Poems* caused considerable excitement because of their powerfully suggestive obscurity and the strange violence of their imagery. It looked as though a new kind of visionary Romanticism had been restored to English poetry after the deliberately muted ironic tones of T. S. Eliot and his followers. Over time it became clear that Thomas was also a master of poetic craft, not merely a shouting rhapsodist. His verbal panache played against strict verse forms, such as the villanelle ("Do Not Go Gentle into That Good Night"). "I am a painstaking, conscientious, involved and devious craftsman in words," he wrote in his "Poetic Manifesto." His images were carefully ordered in a patterned sequence, and his major theme was the unity of all life, the continuing *process* of life and death and new life that linked the generations. Thomas saw the workings of biology as a magical transformation producing unity out of diversity, and again and again in his poetry he sought a poetic ritual to celebrate this unity ("The force that through the green fuse drives the flower / Drives my green age"). He saw men and women locked in cycles of growth, love, procreation, new growth, death, and new life again. Hence each image engenders its opposite in what he called "my dialectical method": "Each image holds within it the seed of its own destruction." Thomas derives his closely woven, sometimes self-contradictory images from the Bible, Welsh folklore and preaching, and Freud. In his poems of reminiscence and autobiographical emotion, such as "Poem in October," he communicates more immediately through compelling use of lyrical feeling and simple natural images. His autobiographical work *Portrait of the Artist as a Young Dog* (1940) and his radio play *Under Milk Wood* (1954) reveal a vividness of observation and a combination of violence and tenderness in expression that show he could handle prose as excitingly as verse.

Thomas was a brilliant talker, an alcoholic, a reckless and impulsive man whose short life was packed with emotional ups and downs. His poetry readings in the United States between 1950 and 1953 were enormous successes, in spite of his sometimes reckless antics. He died suddenly in New York of what was diagnosed as "an insult to the brain," precipitated by alcohol. He played the part of the wild bohemian poet, and while some thought this behavior wonderful, others deplored it. He was a stirring reader of his own and others' poems, and many people who do not normally read poetry were drawn to Thomas's by the magic of his own reading. After his premature death a reaction set in: some critics declared that he had been overrated as a poet because of his sensational life. The "Movement" poets, such as Philip Larkin, repudiated his rhetorical extravagance. Even so, Thomas is still considered an original poet of great power and beauty.

The Force That Through the Green Fuse Drives the Flower

The force that through the green fuse drives the flower
Drives my green age; that blasts the roots of trees
Is my destroyer.
And I am dumb to tell the crooked rose
5   My youth is bent by the same wintry fever.

The force that drives the water through the rocks
Drives my red blood; that dries the mouthing streams
Turns mine to wax.
And I am dumb to mouth unto my veins
10   How at the mountain spring the same mouth sucks.

The hand that whirls the water in the pool[1]
Stirs the quicksand; that ropes the blowing wind
Hauls my shroud sail.
And I am dumb to tell the hanging man
15   How of my clay is made the hangman's lime.[2]

The lips of time leech to the fountain head;
Love drips and gathers, but the fallen blood
Shall calm her sores.

1. The hand of the angel who troubles the water of the pool Bethesda, thus rendering it curative, in John 5.1–4.

2. Quicklime was sometimes poured into the graves of public hangmen's victims to accelerate decomposition.

2446 / D<small>YLAN</small> T<small>HOMAS</small>

And I am dumb to tell a weather's wind
20 How time has ticked a heaven round the stars.

And I am dumb to tell the lover's tomb
How at my sheet goes the same crooked worm.

                                                                        1933

The Hunchback in the Park

The hunchback in the park
A solitary mister
Propped between trees and water
From the opening of the garden lock
5   That lets the trees and water enter
Until the Sunday sombre bell at dark[1]

Eating bread from a newspaper
Drinking water from the chained cup
That the children filled with gravel
10 In the fountain basin where I sailed my ship
Slept at night in a dog kennel
But nobody chained him up.

Like the park birds he came early
Like the water he sat down
15 And Mister they called Hey mister
The truant boys from the town
Running when he had heard them clearly
On out of sound

Past lake and rockery°   rock garden
20 Laughing when he shook his paper
Hunchbacked in mockery
Through the loud zoo of the willow groves
Dodging the park keeper
With his stick that picked up leaves.

25 And the old dog sleeper
Alone between nurses and swans
While the boys among willows
Made the tigers jump out of their eyes
To roar on the rockery stones
30 And the groves were blue with sailors

Made all day until bell time
A woman figure without fault
Straight as a young elm
Straight and tall from his crooked bones

---

1. The bell indicates the park's closing for the night.

35 That she might stand in the night
    After the locks and chains

    All night in the unmade park
    After the railings and shrubberies
    The birds the grass the trees the lake
40 And the wild boys innocent as strawberries
    Had followed the hunchback
    To his kennel in the dark.

1941   1946

Poem in October

    It was my thirtieth year to heaven
    Woke to my hearing from harbour and neighbour wood
    And the mussel pooled and the heron
            Priested shore
5   The morning beckon
    With water praying and call of seagull and rook°   *crow*
    And the knock of sailing boats on the net webbed wall
            Myself to set foot
            That second
10 In the still sleeping town and set forth.

    My birthday began with the water-
    Birds and the birds of the winged trees flying my name
    Above the farms and the white horses
            And I rose
15   In rainy autumn
    And walked abroad in a shower of all my days.
    High tide and the heron dived when I took the road
            Over the border
            And the gates
20 Of the town closed as the town awoke.

    A springful of larks in a rolling
    Cloud and the roadside bushes brimming with whistling
    Blackbirds and the sun of October
            Summery
25   On the hill's shoulder,
    Here were fond climates and sweet singers suddenly
    Come in the morning where I wandered and listened
            To the rain wringing
            Wind blow cold
30 In the wood faraway under me.

    Pale rain over the dwindling harbour
    And over the sea wet church the size of a snail
    With its horns through mist and the castle
            Brown as owls

35   But all the gardens
Of spring and summer were blooming in the tall tales
Beyond the border and under the lark full cloud.
        There could I marvel
            My birthday
40 Away but the weather turned around.

It turned away from the blithe country
And down the other air and the blue altered sky
Streamed again a wonder of summer
            With apples
45   Pears and red currants
And I saw in the turning so clearly a child's
Forgotten mornings when he walked with his mother
        Through the parables
            Of sun light
50 And the legends of the green chapels

And the twice told fields of infancy
That his tears burned my cheeks and his heart moved in mine.
These were the woods the river and sea
            Where a boy
55   In the listening
Summertime of the dead whispered the truth of his joy
To the trees and the stones and the fish in the tide.
        And the mystery
            Sang alive
60 Still in the water and singingbirds.

And there could I marvel my birthday
Away but the weather turned around. And the true
Joy of the long dead child sang burning
            In the sun.
65   It was my thirtieth
Year to heaven stood there then in the summer noon
Though the town below lay leaved with October blood.
        O may my heart's truth
            Still be sung
70 On this high hill in a year's turning.

1944   1946

Fern Hill[1]

Now as I was young and easy under the apple boughs
About the lilting house and happy as the grass was green,
        The night above the dingle[2] starry,
            Time let me hail and climb

1. Name of the Welsh farmhouse, home of his
aunt Ann Jones, where Thomas spent summer holidays as a boy.
2. Deep dell or hollow, usually wooded.

5   Golden in the heydays of his eyes,
And honoured among wagons I was prince of the apple towns
And once below a time I lordly had the trees and leaves
            Trail with daisies and barley
        Down the rivers of the windfall light.

10   And as I was green and carefree, famous among the barns
About the happy yard and singing as the farm was home,
            In the sun that is young once only,
                Time let me play and be
        Golden in the mercy of his means,
15   And green and golden I was huntsman and herdsman, the calves
Sang to my horn, the foxes on the hills barked clear and cold,
            And the sabbath rang slowly
        In the pebbles of the holy streams.

     All the sun long it was running, it was lovely, the hay
20   Fields high as the house, the tunes from the chimneys, it was air
            And playing, lovely and watery
                And fire green as grass.
            And nightly under the simple stars
        As I rode to sleep the owls were bearing the farm away,
25   All the moon long I heard, blessed among stables, the night-jars³
            Flying with the ricks,° and the horses   *haystacks*
        Flashing into the dark.

     And then to awake, and the farm, like a wanderer white
With the dew, come back, the cock on his shoulder: it was all
30   Shining, it was Adam and maiden,⁴
            The sky gathered again
        And the sun grew round that very day.
So it must have been after the birth of the simple light
In the first, spinning place, the spellbound horses walking warm
35   Out of the whinnying green stable
            On to the fields of praise.

     And honoured among foxes and pheasants by the gay house
Under the new made clouds and happy as the heart was long,
            In the sun born over and over,
40   I ran my heedless ways,
            My wishes raced through the house high hay
And nothing I cared, at my sky blue trades, that time allows
In all his tuneful turning so few and such morning songs
            Before the children green and golden
45   Follow him out of grace,

     Nothing I cared, in the lamb white days, that time would take me
Up to the swallow thronged loft by the shadow of my hand,
            In the moon that is always rising,
                Nor that riding to sleep

---

3. Species of bird.   4. Cf. Genesis 1.

50   I should hear him fly with the high fields
And wake to the farm forever fled from the childless land.
Oh as I was young and easy in the mercy of his means,
     Time held me green and dying
Though I sang in my chains like the sea.

1945   1946

Do Not Go Gentle into That Good Night

Do not go gentle into that good night,
Old age should burn and rave at close of day;
Rage, rage against the dying of the light.

Though wise men at their end know dark is right,
5   Because their words had forked no lightning they
Do not go gentle into that good night.

Good men, the last wave by, crying how bright
Their frail deeds might have danced in a green bay,
Rage, rage against the dying of the light.

10   Wild men who caught and sang the sun in flight,
And learn, too late, they grieved it on its way,
Do not go gentle into that good night.

Grave men, near death, who see with blinding sight
Blind eyes could blaze like meteors and be gay,
15   Rage, rage against the dying of the light.

And you, my father, there on the sad height,
Curse, bless, me now with your fierce tears, I pray.
Do not go gentle into that good night.
Rage, rage against the dying of the light.

1951   1952

Voices from World War II

In December 1939, a few months after the start of World War II, a leading article in *The Times Literary Supplement* urged poets to do their duty: "it is for the poets to sound the trumpet call. . . . The monstrous threat to belief and freedom which we are fighting should urge new psalmists to fresh songs of deliverance." The biblical diction reveals the underlying expectation that the poets of 1940 would come forward, like those of 1914, to sanctify the cause with images of sacrifice derived from Jesus Christ's precedent and precept: "greater love hath no man than this, that a man lay down his life for his friends." Far from taking up trumpets, the poets responded bitterly—C. Day Lewis with the poem "Where Are the War Poets?":

> They who in folly or mere greed
> Enslaved religion, markets, laws,
> Borrow our language now and bid
> Us to speak up in freedom's cause.
>
> It is the logic of our times,
> No subject for immortal verse—
> That we who lived by honest dreams
> Defend the bad against the worse.

Stephen Spender responded with an essay, in which he wrote: "At the beginning of the last war Rupert Brooke and others were 'trumpets singing to battle.' Why did not Rupert Brooke step forward 'young and goldenhaired' this time? No doubt, in part, precisely because one had done so last time. There is another reason: the poetry of the war of democracy versus fascism had already been written by English, French, Spanish, German and Italian émigré poets during the Spanish war."

With few exceptions the British poets of the 1930s had been born shortly before the outbreak of World War I, and those who were to be the poets of World War II were born during that earlier conflict. They grew up not, as Rupert Brooke, in the sunlit peace of Georgian England but amid wars and rumors of wars. They lived through the Great Depression and the rise of fascism. Introduced to the horrors of the last war—increased to mythic proportions by their fathers, uncles, and elder brothers—they were continually reminded of it by a flood of best-selling battle memoirs: Edmund Blunden's *Undertones of War* (1928), Robert Graves's *Goodbye to All That* (1929), Siegfried Sassoon's *Memoirs of an Infantry Officer* (1930) and *Sherston's Progress* (1936), and David Jones's *In Parenthesis* (1937). By then another myth, that of the Next War, was taking even more terrifying shape. Western intellectuals' last hope for the 1930s rested with the ragged troops of the left-wing Spanish Republic in their civil war against the right-wing Spanish Army that had mutinied in 1936 against the country's elected government. Democracy and fascism were at last in the open, fighting a war that many thought would determine not simply the future of Spain but the future of Europe. The conscience of the West was aroused as never since the Greek War of Independence against the Turks in 1821–29, in which Byron had lost his life. With the final defeat of the Spanish Republicans in 1938, the Next War ceased to be a myth so much as an all-but-inescapable certainty. At the start of W. B. Yeats's poem "Lapis Lazuli" (1938), "hysterical women say":

> everybody knows or else should know
> That if nothing drastic is done

2451

> Aeroplane and Zeppelin will come out,
> Pitch like King Billy bomb-balls in
> Until the town lie beaten flat.

World War I had been fought, for the most part, on the land, and its emblem in popular mythology was the trench. After the indiscriminate killing of civilians in a bombing raid—by German aircraft—on the Spanish town of Guernica in 1937, everyone knew or else should have known that the emblem of the Next War would be the bomb, the fire from heaven.

So it proved. On September 1, 1939, Germany, in pursuit of imperial ambitions and without warning, launched a savage attack on Poland by land and air. Two days later Britain and France declared war on Germany. By the end of the month, Germany and its ally Russia had between them defeated and partitioned Poland. Russia then attacked Finland, and in April 1940 Germany invaded Denmark and Norway. For Britain and France the period of inactivity that came to be known as "The Phoney War" ended in May, when the German Army overran Luxembourg and invaded The Netherlands and Belgium; their armored columns raced for the English Channel. Cut off, the British forces were evacuated by sea, with heavy losses, from Dunkirk, and in June France signed an armistice with Germany. In August, as prelude to an invasion, the German *Luftwaffe* (Air Force) attacked England. Over the months that followed, the fighter pilots of the Royal Air Force (RAF) challenged the enemy bombers' nightly blitz of London and other major cities. The Battle of Britain, as it came to be called, cost the *Luftwaffe* twenty-three hundred planes and the RAF, nine hundred and caused the Germans to abandon their plans for invasion.

In 1941, Virginia Woolf imagined the coming fury, which would be a factor in her suicide. At the end of Woolf's novel *Between the Acts,* the village pageant of English history is over, and Mr. Streatfield's speech of thanks is interrupted: "A zoom severed it. Twelve aeroplanes in perfect formation like a flight of wild duck came overhead." The following year Edith Sitwell depicted the blitz in "Still Falls the Rain," as did T. S. Eliot in part 2 of "Little Gidding." The Battle of Britain, however, was not the only battle, and British poets were already responding to war on land and at sea as well as in the air. Some of their work shows the influence of their predecessors: Alun Lewis acknowledges a debt to Edward Thomas, whereas the diction and pararhyming of Keith Douglas's poems clearly owe something to Wilfred Owen's. Their voices, however, are their own, and the dominant mood of their poetry is strikingly unlike that from and about the trenches of the Western Front. Just as the heroics of 1914 were impossible in 1940 (although there was no lack of heroism), so too was the antipropagandist indignation of a Siegfried Sassoon. Now that everybody knew about the Battle of the Somme, the bombing of Guernica, London, Dresden, who could be surprised by evidence of "Man's inhumanity to man"? In the draft preface to his poems, one of the more influential poetic manifestos of the twentieth century, Owen had written: "All a poet can do today is warn. That is why the true poets must be truthful." His warnings and those of his contemporaries had been uttered in vain, but the poets of World War II knew they must be truthful, true to their wartime experience of boredom and brutality, true to their humanity, and above all resistant to the murderous inhumanity of the machines.

EDITH SITWELL
1887–1964

Edith Sitwell's father was an extremely eccentric English baronet; her mother, the daughter of an earl. Sitwell, an eccentrically gifted poet, objected to the subdued rural descriptions and reflections of the Georgian poets (of whom Rupert Brooke was the most popular) and reacted in favor of a highly abstract verbal experimentation that exploited the sounds and rhythms and suggestions of words and phrases, often with remarkable pyrotechnic display. She edited and was a substantial contributor to the six "cycles" of *Wheels* (1916–21), an annual anthology of modern poems, in which she displayed her verbal and rhythmic virtuosity and encouraged others to follow her example. Her poem sequence *Façade* (1922), with its cunning exploration of rhymes and rhythms, was set to music by the composer Sir William Walton, whose intensely sympathetic treatment of the words enhanced their impact. The 1923 performance in London's Aeolian Hall was a sensation: Sitwell intoned the poems from behind a screen, and Walton conducted the orchestra.

But Sitwell was more than a flashy manipulator of surfaces. Throughout her poetry she hints at profounder meanings, sometimes with mocking laughter, sometimes with anguish, and in her later work she attacks the pettiness and philistinism of the high society of her time. In still later poems, influenced by William Blake, W. B. Yeats, and her friend Dylan Thomas, Sitwell wished to achieve, she said in her autobiography, "a greater expressiveness, a greater formality, and a return to rhetoric," rejecting "the outcry for understatement, for quietness, for neutral tints in poetry." These poems, such as "Still Falls the Rain," are much concerned with the horrors of war, the varieties of human suffering produced by modern civilization, and the healing powers of a faith in God, combined with a sense of the richness and variety of nature.

Still Falls the Rain

The Raids, 1940.[1] *Night and Dawn*

Still falls the Rain—
Dark as the world of man, black as our loss—
Blind as the nineteen hundred and forty nails
Upon the Cross.

5 Still falls the Rain
With a sound like the pulse of the heart that is changed to the hammer-
    beat
In the Potter's Field,[2] and the sound of the impious feet
On the Tomb:
        Still falls the Rain
In the Field of Blood where the small hopes breed and the human brain
10 Nurtures its greed, that worm with the brow of Cain.[3]

Still falls the Rain
At the feet of the Starved Man hung upon the Cross.
Christ that each day, each night, nails there, have mercy on us—
On Dives and on Lazarus:[4]
15 Under the Rain the sore and the gold are as one.

1. During the Battle of Britain the German air force carried out many raids on London, often with incendiary bombs (see lines 27 and 30).
2. Cf. Matthew 27.3–8: "Then Judas, which betrayed [Jesus], when he saw that he was condemned, repented himself, and brought back the 30 pieces of silver to the chief priests and elders, saying, I have sinned in that I betrayed innocent blood. But they said, What is that to us? see thou to it. And he cast down the pieces of silver into the sanctuary, and departed; and he went away and hanged himself. And the chief priests took the pieces of silver . . . and bought with them the potter's field, to bury strangers in. Wherefore that field was called, The field of blood, unto this day."
3. The first murderer (Genesis 4).
4. In Jesus' parable the rich man Dives was sent to hell, while the leprous beggar Lazarus went to heaven (Luke 16.19–31). This is not the same Lazarus who was raised from the dead.

Still falls the Rain—
Still falls the Blood from the Starved Man's wounded Side:
He bears in His Heart all wounds,—those of the light that died,
The last faint spark
20 In the self-murdered heart, the wounds of the sad uncomprehending dark,
The wounds of the baited bear,[5]—
The blind and weeping bear whom the keepers beat
On his helpless flesh . . . the tears of the hunted hare.

Still falls the Rain—
25 Then—O Ile leape up to my God: who pulles me doune—
See, see where Christ's blood streames in the firmament:[6]
It flows from the Brow we nailed upon the tree
Deep to the dying, to the thirsting heart
That holds the fires of the world,—dark-smirched with pain
30 As Caesar's laurel crown.[7]

Then sounds the voice of One who like the heart of man
Was once a child who among beasts has lain—
"Still do I love, still shed my innocent light, my Blood, for thee."

1942

5. A medieval and Elizabethan sport in which dogs fought a bear chained to a post.
6. Faustus's despairing cry at the end of Christopher Marlowe's play *Doctor Faustus* (1604), when he realizes that he has been damned for his pact with Mephistopheles.
7. Traditionally worn by victorious generals, and perhaps here associated with Jesus' crown of thorns (Matthew 27.29).

HENRY REED
1914–1986

Henry Reed was born and educated in Birmingham, at the King Edward VI School and at Birmingham University, where he gained a first-class degree in classics (having taught himself Greek) and began an M.A. thesis on Thomas Hardy. After leaving the university in 1934, he tried teaching, like many other British writers of the 1930s, but, again like most of them, hated it and left to make his way as a freelance writer and critic. During World War II he served—"or rather *studied*," as he put it—in the Royal Army Ordnance Corps for a year. A notable mimic, he would entertain his friends with a comic imitation of a sergeant instructing new recruits. After a few performances he noticed that the words of the weapon-training instructor, couched in the style of the military manual, fell into certain rhythmic patterns. His fascination with these patterns eventually informed his *Lessons of the War,* the first of which, "Naming of Parts," is probably the most anthologized poem prompted by World War II.

From 1942 to 1945 Reed worked as a cryptographer and translator at the Government Code and Cypher School at Bletchley. In the evenings he wrote much of his first radio play—an adaptation of Melville's *Moby-Dick*—and many of the poems to be published in *A Map of Verona* (1946). After the war, he produced a number of other successful—and often funny—radio plays, verse translations of the Italian poet Giacomo Leopardi (1798–1837), and more fine poems. Many of the best of these were found in manuscript at his death, and with the posthumous publication of his *Collected Poems* (1991), he emerged as a poet whose lifelong quest for lasting homosexual love—which he never found—led him through Edenic landscapes of desire, like the setting of "Naming of Parts."

From Lessons of the War

To Alan Michell

Vixi duellis nuper idoneus
Et militavi non sine gloria[1]

1. Naming of Parts

Today we have naming of parts. Yesterday,
We had daily cleaning. And tomorrow morning,
We shall have what to do after firing. But today,
Today we have naming of parts. Japonica[2]
5 Glistens like coral in all of the neighbouring gardens,
    And today we have naming of parts.

This is the lower sling swivel. And this
Is the upper sling swivel, whose use you will see,
When you are given your slings. And this is the piling swivel,
10 Which in your case you have not got. The branches
Hold in the gardens their silent, eloquent gestures,
    Which in our case we have not got.

This is the safety-catch, which is always released
With an easy flick of the thumb. And please do not let me
15 See anyone using his finger. You can do it quite easy
If you have any strength in your thumb. The blossoms
Are fragile and motionless, never letting anyone see
    Any of them using their finger.

And this you can see is the bolt. The purpose of this
20 Is to open the breech, as you see. We can slide it
Rapidly backwards and forwards: we call this
Easing the spring.[3] And rapidly backwards and forwards
The early bees are assaulting and fumbling the flowers:
    They call it easing the Spring.

25 They call it easing the Spring: it is perfectly easy
If you have any strength in your thumb; like the bolt,
And the breech, and the cocking-piece, and the point of balance,
Which in our case we have not got; and the almond-blossom

1. "Lately I have lived in the midst of battles, creditably enough, / and have soldiered, not without glory" (Horace's *Odes* 3.26.1–2, with the letter *p* of *puellis*—girls—turned upside down to produce *duellis*—battles; an emendation, an exchange, that encapsulates the theme of the *Lessons*).
2. A shrub with brilliant scarlet flowers.
3. An operation that, by ejecting the bullets from the magazine of a rifle, takes the pressure off the magazine spring.

Silent in all of the gardens and the bees going backwards and forwards,
30   For today we have naming of parts.

1945

KEITH DOUGLAS
1920–1944

Keith Douglas was born in Tunbridge Wells, the son of a regular army officer, who had won the Military Cross in World War I and who, in 1927, deserted his wife and son. Like Byron, whose army officer father died in the poet's youth, Douglas developed an almost obsessive interest in warfare. At the age of ten he wrote a poem about the Battle of Waterloo, and later, at Christ's Hospital School in London, he divided his leisure time between developing his precocious talents as poet and artist, riding, playing rugby football, and participating enthusiastically in the Officer Cadet Corps. At Merton College, Oxford, he was tutored by Edmund Blunden, a distinguished soldier poet of World War I. In 1940 Douglas enlisted in a cavalry regiment that was soon obliged to exchange its horses for tanks and in August 1942 he went into battle against German field marshal Rommel's Africa Corps in the Egyptian desert. Forced to remain in reserve behind the lines, Douglas commandeered a truck and, directly disobeying orders, drove off to join his regiment.

His subsequent achievement as a poet and as the author of a brilliant memoir of the desert campaign, *Alamein to Zem Zem* (1966), was to celebrate the last stand of the chivalric hero. His poem "Aristocrats" ends perhaps with a distant echo of Roland's horn, sounded in the Pass of Roncevalles at the end of the twelfth-century French chivalric epic *La Chanson de Roland (The Song of Roland)*. Douglas's poem succeeds where most of the would-be heroic poems of 1914 and 1915 fail. Sharply focused, it acknowledges both the stupidity and the chivalry, the folly and the glamour of cavalrymen on mechanical mounts, dueling in the desert. Douglas's language, spare and understated, finely responsive to his theme, fuses ancient and modern: his heroes are "gentle"—like Chaucer's "verray parfit gentil knight" in *The Canterbury Tales*— and at the same time "obsolescent."

Douglas survived the desert campaign, but was killed in the assault on the Normandy beaches, on June 6, 1944.

Gallantry

The Colonel[1] in a casual voice
spoke into the microphone a joke
Which through a hundred earphones broke
into the ears of a doomed race.[2]

---

1. Lt. Col. J. D. Player, killed in Tunisia, Enfidaville, February 1943, left £3,000 to the Beaufort Hunt, and directed that the incumbent of the living in his gift [i.e., the church whose vicar he was entitled to appoint] should be a 'man who approves of hunting, shooting, and all manly sports, which are the backbone of the nation.' [Douglas's note on one of the manuscripts of "Aristocrats." Player was in fact killed in April.]
2. Cf. Wilfred Owen's "Anthem for Doomed Youth" (p. 1971).

5   Into the ears of the doomed boy, the fool
whose perfectly mannered flesh fell
in opening the door for a shell
as he had learnt to do at school.

Conrad luckily survived the winter:
10   he wrote a letter to welcome
the auspicious spring: only his silken
intentions severed with a single splinter.

Was George fond of little boys?
We always suspected it,
15   but who will say: since George was hit
we never mention our surmise.

It was a brave thing the Colonel said,
but the whole sky turned too hot
and the three heroes never heard what
20   it was, gone deaf with steel and lead.

But the bullets cried with laughter,
the shells were overcome with mirth,
plunging their heads in steel and earth—
(the air commented in a whisper).

El Ballah, General Hospital, Apr. 1943   1949

Vergissmeinnicht[1]

Three weeks gone and the combatants gone
returning over the nightmare ground
we found the place again, and found
the soldier sprawling in the sun.

5   The frowning barrel of his gun
overshadowing. As we came on
that day, he hit my tank with one
like the entry of a demon.

Look. Here in the gunpit spoil
10   the dishonoured picture of his girl
who has put: Steffi. Vergissmeinnicht
in a copybook gothic script.

We see him almost with content,
abased, and seeming to have paid
15   and mocked at by his own equipment
that's hard and good when he's decayed.

1. Forget me not (German).

But she would weep to see today
how on his skin the swart° flies move;   *black*
the dust upon the paper eye
20   and the burst stomach like a cave.

For here the lover and killer are mingled
who had one body and one heart.
And death who had the soldier singled
has done the lover mortal hurt.

Tunisia, 1943   1944

Aristocrats[1]

"I think I am becoming a God"[2]

The noble horse with courage in his eye
clean in the bone, looks up at a shellburst:
away fly the images of the shires[3]
but he puts the pipe back in his mouth.

5   Peter was unfortunately killed by an 88:[4]
it took his leg away, he died in the ambulance.
I saw him crawling on the sand; he said
It's most unfair, they've shot my foot off.

How can I live among this gentle
10   obsolescent breed of heroes, and not weep?
Unicorns, almost,
for they are falling into two legends
in which their stupidity and chivalry
are celebrated. Each, fool and hero, will be an immortal.

15   The plains were their cricket pitch[5]
and in the mountains the tremendous drop fences[6]
brought down some of the runners. Here then
under the stones and earth they dispose themselves,
I think with their famous unconcern.
20   It is not gunfire I hear but a hunting horn.[7]

Enfidaville, Tunisia, 1943   1946

1. Another version of this poem is entitled "Sportsmen."
2. The dying words of Roman Emperor Vespasian were supposedly "Alas! I suppose I am turning into a god."
3. Counties. Cf. Owen's "Anthem for Doomed Youth," line 8 (p. 1971).
4. A German tank fitted with an eighty-eight-millimeter gun.
5. Field on which the game of cricket is played.
6. Fences in the course of a steeplechase horse race.
7. See n. 1, p. 2456.

CHARLES CAUSLEY
1917–2003

Born and educated in Launceston, Cornwall, Charles Causley followed the tradition of his seafaring people and served in the Royal Navy from 1940 to 1946. His experiences on a destroyer and an aircraft carrier had a catalytic effect on him as a poet. "It was Hitler who pushed a subject under my nose," he wrote. "I think the event that affected me more than anything else in those years was the fact that the companion who had left my home-town with me for the navy in 1940 was later lost in a convoy to Russia. From the moment I heard this news, I found myself haunted by the words in the twenty-fourth chapter of St Matthew: 'Then shall two be in the field; the one shall be taken, and the other left.' If my poetry is 'about' anything, it is this."

Causley's Cornishness shows in his skillful use of verse forms and narrative strategies drawn from an oral folk tradition. A formally conservative poet, he was a master of the ballad told in a voice that is at once impersonal—the voice of the anonymous early balladeers—and unmistakably his own. Causley's seeming simplicity, like that of the early balladeers, can be misleading; his jaunty cadences, his spry interweaving of ancient and modern diction, heighten the poignancy of elegies such as the ones printed here.

From 1947 to 1976 he taught at a school in Cornwall. He wrote many volumes of poems and several plays—some of each, with great success, for children.

At the British War Cemetery, Bayeux[1]

I walked where in their talking graves
And shirts of earth five thousand lay,
When history with ten feasts of fire
Had eaten the red air away.

5   I am Christ's boy, I cried, I bear
In iron hands the bread, the fishes.[2]
I hang with honey and with rose
This tidy wreck of all your wishes.

On your geometry of sleep
10   The chestnut and the fir-tree fly,
And lavender and marguerite
Forge with their flowers an English sky.

Turn now towards the belling town
Your jigsaws of impossible bone,
15   And rising read your rank of snow
Accurate as death upon the stone.

About your easy heads my prayers
I said with syllables of clay.
What gift, I asked, shall I bring now
20   Before I weep and walk away?

1. Near the coast of northwest France, the scene of heavy fighting following the Normandy landings in June 1944. 2. Cf. Matthew 14.19–20.

Take, they replied, the oak and laurel.[3]
Take our fortune of tears and live
Like a spendthrift lover. All we ask
Is the one gift you cannot give.

1957

Armistice Day

I stood with three comrades in Parliament Square[1]
November her freights of grey fire unloading,
No sound from the city upon the pale air
Above us the sea-bell eleven exploding.

5   Down by the bands and the burning memorial
Beats all the brass in a royal array,
But at our end we are not so sartorial:
Out of (as usual) the rig of the day.

Starry is wearing a split pusser's flannel[2]
10   Rubbed, as he is, by the regular tide;
Oxo the ducks[3] that he ditched in the Channel
In June, 1940 (when he was inside).

Kitty recalls his abandon-ship station,
Running below at the Old Man's salute[4]
15   And (with a deck-watch) going down for duration[5]
Wearing his oppo's pneumonia-suit.[6]

Comrades, for you the black captain of carracks[7]
Writes in Whitehall[8] his appalling decisions,
But as was often the case in the Barracks
20   Several ratings are not at Divisions.[9]

Into my eyes the stiff sea-horses stare,
Over my head sweeps the sun like a swan.
As I stand alone in Parliament Square
A cold bugle calls, and the city moves on.

1957

---

3. Trees whose leaves are traditionally taken as emblems of courage and victory, respectively.
1. An annual "Remembrance Sunday" service is held at the Cenotaph, a stone memorial to the dead of the two World Wars, in London's Parliament Square. It includes a two-minute silence after the last stroke of eleven o'clock.
2. A torn navy-issue shirt.
3. Sailor's white tunic and trousers.
4. A British naval tradition calls for the Captain
(Old Man) of a sinking ship to go down saluting.
5. I.e., for the duration of the war; a phrase common during World War II.
6. Canvas suit—belonging to his friend ("opposite number")—worn while painting the ship.
7. Large merchant ships equipped for warfare.
8. London street in which stands the Admiralty (navy headquarters).
9. I.e., noncommissioned sailors are absent from church parade, the religious service on board ship.

Nation and Language

Armies and navies, cannons and guns helped spread and consolidate British rule across vast areas of the earth's surface, but so too did the English language. Over many years, in many different parts of the world, the language of the British Empire displaced or commingled with indigenous languages. Then the twentieth century witnessed the decolonization and devolution of the British Empire, from early-century Ireland to midcentury India and Africa and the Caribbean to late-century Hong Kong. Imaginative writers from these and other regions have thus had to wrestle with questions of nation and language. Should they write stories, plays, and poems in the language and traditions of the colonizer, or should they repudiate English and employ their indigenous languages? Is English an enabling tool by which peoples of different nationalities can express their identities, or is it contaminated by a colonial history and mentality that it insidiously perpetuates? If English is chosen for imaginative writing, should it be a standardized English of the imperial center or an English inflected by contact with indigenous languages—a creole, patois, pidgin, even a synthetic composite of a local vernacular and Standard English? Since American power has sustained the global reach of English long after the withdrawal of British colonial administrators and armies, debates over such questions have persisted in many parts of the world where English still thrives in the aftermath of a dead empire.

Having tried to subdue the Irish people for centuries, the British outlawed the use of the Irish language (or Gaelic) in Ireland, and Brian Friel explores the painful effects of the forcible displacement of Irish in his important historical play, *Translations*. Because of Ireland's long and bloody colonial history and the flowering there of cultural nationalism, early-twentieth-century Irish writers were already expressing a powerful ambivalence toward English as both a vital literary inheritance and the language of colonial subjugation. Recalling the sixteenth- and seventeenth-century English "wars of extermination" against the Irish, W. B. Yeats acknowledges a historical hatred of the English but then reminds himself that, as an English-language writer, "I owe my soul to Shakespeare, to Spenser and to Blake, perhaps to William Morris, and to the English language in which I think, speak and write, that everything I love has come to me through English; my hatred tortures me with love, my love with hate" (see his "Introduction," excerpted in this volume). In the novel *A Portrait of the Artist as a Young Man*, James Joyce's autobiographical persona, Stephen Dedalus, reflects on his conversation with an academic dean, an Englishman: "The language in which we are speaking is his before it is mine. . . . I cannot speak or write these [English] words without unrest of spirit. His language, so familiar and so foreign, will always be for me an acquired speech. I have not made or accepted its words. My voice holds them at bay. My soul frets in the shadow of his language." Yet Yeats and Joyce, despite this vexed relation to the language, wrote some of the most innovative English-language poetry and fiction of the twentieth century. Indeed, their conflicted relation to the English language and its literary inheritance—that "unrest of spirit" in its shadow—may paradoxically have impelled their massive literary achievements.

Transplanted in different parts of the world, English has sometimes seemed strange and estranging. When African and Caribbean schoolchildren with British colonial educations tried to write poems, as Kamau Brathwaite and other writers have attested, they would follow the conventions of English poetry, composing iambic pentameter verse about snowfall or daffodils, which they had never seen. English language and

English literature thus risked alienating colonized peoples from their local environments and distinctive cultural histories.

The feeling that the English language is alienating, inextricably bound to colonialism, has led some nativist writers, such as the Kenyan novelist Ngũgĩ wa Thiong'o, to reject it outright. If language is a "collective memory bank," then a people cannot recover its colonially suppressed identity and history without returning to an indigenous language. But the novelist Salman Rushdie, who often writes in an Indianized, or "chutnified," English, takes the opposite stance: "The English language ceased to be the sole possession of the English some time ago," he asserts. English has become a local language even in parts of the world, such as India, where it was once imposed. Rushdie and other cosmopolitan writers reject the assumption that the English language has an inherent relationship to only one kind of national or ethnic experience. "The English language is nobody's special property," asserts the Caribbean poet Derek Walcott.

For the colonial or postcolonial writer who embraces English, the question remains, Which English? The imported standard or a local vernacular? Or if both, should they be intermingled or kept apart? At one end of the spectrum are writers, such as V. S. Naipaul and Wole Soyinka, who think Standard English, perhaps slightly altered, can bespeak a postcolonial experience of race, identity, and history. At the other end are vernacular writers who feel the language of the center cannot do justice to their experience at the margins of empire. The poet Louise Bennett, for example, gives voice to everyday Jamaican experience in her witty and wily use of Jamaican Creole or Patois; she mocks its denigration as a "corruption of the English language," pointing out that Standard English is but an amalgam of dialects and foreign languages. "It was in language that the slave was perhaps most successfully imprisoned by his master," Brathwaite has written, "and it was in his (mis-)use of it that he perhaps most effectively rebelled."

Between the Standard English writer and the vernacular writer range a host of other possibilities. Some poets and novelists, such as the Jamaican-born Claude McKay and the Scottish nationalist Hugh MacDiarmid, spend a substantial part of their careers writing in one version of English and then shift dramatically to another. Others employ either Standard English or a local vernacular depending on the perspective they are presenting. Two of Caribbean-born writer Jean Rhys's stories written during the same period offer two distinct points of view, one in the normative English of a white West Indian child, the other in the creolized (or hybridized) English of a mulatto immigrant in London. Finally, many writers, such as Walcott, Brathwaite, and the Yorkshire poet Tony Harrison, switch between standard and "dialect" within or across individual works, creating juxtapositions, tensions, and new relationships between languages that have traditionally been kept hierarchically discrete. They linguistically embody their interstitial experience of living in between metropolis and margin, canon and creole, schoolbooks and the street.

Whether using slightly or heavily creolized English, or a medley of both, writers from across the world—Barbadians and Bombayites and "Black Britons"—have employed a diverse array of distinctive idioms, dialects, creoles to defy imperial norms, express emerging cultural identities, and inaugurate rich new possibilities for literature in English.

CLAUDE McKAY
1890–1948

Claude McKay was born into a poor farmworking family in Sunny Ville, Clarendon Parish, Jamaica, and spent the first half of his life on the British Caribbean island. He was apprenticed to a cabinetmaker and then a wheelwright and served for less than a year as a police constable in Kingston. An English linguist and folklorist, Walter Jekyll, encouraged him to write in Jamaican dialect, or Creole. Drawing on the example of the Scottish-dialect poet Robert Burns, McKay harnessed Jamaican idiom in poems collected in two books published in 1912, *Constab Ballads* and *Songs of Jamaica*, including "Old England," a seemingly reverent imaginative journey, in a new literary language, to the imperial "homeland." The first major poet to make effective literary use of Jamaican English, he influenced many later Afro-Caribbean poets who went further, such as Louise Bennett.

For his poetry McKay won a prize that enabled him to travel to the United States and study at Alabama's Tuskegee Institute and at Kansas State College, before moving to Harlem in 1914. Switching in his poetry from Jamaican to Standard English, he helped precipitate the Harlem Renaissance with his *Harlem Shadows* (1922), which included sonnets addressing the vexed racial experience of an Afro-Caribbean immigrant. For most of the 1920s into the mid-1930s, McKay, identifying with the radical left, lived and wrote novels and short stories mainly in England, France, and Morocco. He died in poverty in Chicago, where he taught in his last years for a Catholic youth organization. His sonnet "If We Must Die," written in response to the American antiblack riots of the summer of 1919, became a World War II rallying cry after Winston Churchill read it, without attribution, to the British people.

Old England

I've a longin' in me dept's of heart dat I can conquer not,
'Tis a wish dat I've been havin' from since I could form a t'o't,°   *thought*
'Tis to sail athwart the ocean an' to hear de billows roar,
When dem ride aroun' de steamer,° when dem beat on England's   *steamship*
    shore.

5   Just to view de homeland England, in de streets of London walk,
An' to see de famous sights dem 'bouten which dere's so much talk,
An' to watch de fact'ry chimneys pourin' smoke up to de sky,
An' to see de matches-children, dat I hear 'bout, passin' by.[1]

I would see Saint Paul's Cathedral,[2] an' would hear some of de great
10 Learnin' comin' from de bishops, preachin' relics of old fait';
I would ope me mout' wid wonder at de massive organ soun',
An' would 'train me eyes to see de beauty lyin' all aroun'.

I'd go to de City Temple,[3] where de old fait' is a wreck,
An' de parson is a-preachin' views dat most folks will not tek;
15 I'd go where de men of science meet togeder in deir hall,
To give light unto de real truths, to obey king Reason's call.

---

1. Cf. the short story "The Little-Match Seller," by the Danish writer Hans Christian Andersen (1805–1875), and the poem "The Little Match Girl," by the Scottish writer William McGonagall (1830?–1902), both about a poor match-selling girl who freezes to death on New Year's Eve.
2. In London, cathedral of the Anglican bishop.
3. Victorian church in central London.

I would view Westminster Abbey,[4] where de great of England sleep,
An' de solemn marble statues o'er deir ashes vigil keep;
I would see immortal Milton an' de wul'-famous Shakespeare,
20 Past'ral Wordswort', gentle Gray,[5] an' all de great souls buried dere.

I would see de ancient chair where England's kings deir crowns put on,
Soon to lay dem by again when all de vanity is done;
An' I'd go to view de lone spot where in peaceful solitude
Rests de body of our Missis Queen,[6] Victoria de Good.

25 An' dese places dat I sing of now shall afterwards impart
All deir solemn sacred beauty to a weary searchin' heart;
So I'll rest glad an' contented in me min'° for evermore,   mind
When I sail across de ocean back to my own native shore.

1912

If We Must Die

If we must die, let it not be like hogs
Hunted and penned in an inglorious spot,
While round us bark the mad and hungry dogs,
Making their mock at our accursed lot.
5   If we must die, O let us nobly die,
So that our precious blood may not be shed
In vain; then even the monsters we defy
Shall be constrained to honor us though dead!
O kinsmen! we must meet the common foe!
10 Though far outnumbered let us show us brave,
And for their thousand blows deal one deathblow!
What though before us lies the open grave?
Like men we'll face the murderous, cowardly pack,
Pressed to the wall, dying, but fighting back!

1919, 1922

4. London church, where monarchs are crowned and the famous, including poets, are buried.
5. Thomas Gray (1716–1771), English poet and author of "Elegy Written in a Country Church-yard."
6. So-called in Jamaica, Victoria reigned during the emancipation of slaves in 1837.

HUGH MacDIARMID
1892–1978

Hugh MacDiarmid, often said to be the greatest Scottish poet since Robert Burns, was born Christopher Murray Grieve in the Scottish border town of Langholm. After a short period of training as a teacher, he turned to journalism. His political convictions made for a turbulent life. He was a founding member of the National Party of Scotland, but it expelled him in 1933 because of his communism. He then joined the

Communist Party of Great Britain, but it expelled him as well, because of his Scottish nationalism.

From the 1920s MacDiarmid was the central figure of the Scottish Renaissance movement. He published short lyrics in a revived Scots, or "Lallans" (i.e., Lowland Scots), a language that fused the rich vocabulary of medieval Scottish poets, modern dialect Scots, and Standard English. In *A Drunk Man Looks at the Thistle* (1926), he built up an epic statement about Scotland out of a series of related lyrics and passages of descriptive and reflective poetry. In such early poems MacDiarmid proved the vigor and robust physicality of Scots as a medium for modern poetry, after the Burns tradition had declined into sentimentality and imitation. In essays such as "English Ascendancy in British Literature" (excerpted below), he argued vehemently against confining "British literature" to the Standard English literature of England, championing instead the varieties of Scottish, Irish, and Welsh literatures written in locally distinctive forms of English and other languages of the British Isles.

MacDiarmid wrote little poetry in Scots after the mid-1930s, when he turned to an ambitious "poetry of fact and first-hand experience and scientific knowledge," including the long poem *In Memoriam James Joyce* (1955), written in colloquial English but formally patterned by carefully controlled shifts in tempo. In it he affirms the essential kinship of everything in the world that is fully realized and properly possessed of its identity—a theme that clearly bears on his lifelong preoccupation with Scottish nationality, language, and culture.

[The Splendid Variety of Languages and Dialects][1]

* * * Burns[2] knew what he was doing when he reverted from 18th century English to a species of synthetic Scots and was abundantly justified in the result. He was not contributing to English literature but to a clearly defined and quite independent tradition of Scottish poetry hailing from the days of Dunbar and the other great 15th century 'makars'[3]—the golden age of Scottish poetry when the English impulse seemed to have gone sterile and Scotland, not England, was apparently destined to produce the great poetry of the United Kingdom. To ask why this promise was not redeemed and why English, a far less concentrated and expressive language, became the medium of such an incomparably greater succession of poets, involves deep questions of the relationship of literature to economic, political and other considerations and both the causal and the casual in history: but at the moment it is more germane to ask if the potentialities of the Scottish literary tradition can yet be realized? There are signs that they may be. The problem of the British Isles is the problem of English Ascendancy. Ireland after a protracted struggle has won a considerable measure of autonomy;[4] Scotland and Wales may succeed in doing the same; but what is of importance to my point in the meantime is that, in breaking free (or fairly free) politically, Ireland not only experienced the Literary Revival associated with the names of Yeats, 'A. E.', Synge[5] and the others, but has during the past half century recovered almost entirely her ancient Gaelic literature. * * *

1. Excerpted from "English Ascendancy in British Literature," first published in T. S. Eliot's journal *The Criterion*. "Ascendancy": dominance.
2. Robert Burns (1759–1796), Scottish poet.
3. Poets (Scots); term used for the courtly poets known as the Scottish Chaucerians. William Dunbar (1460?–1530?) was the dominant poet among them.
4. The Irish Free State was established in 1922, though Northern Ireland remained part of the U.K.
5. John Millington Synge (1871–1909), Irish playwright. William Butler Yeats (1865–1939), Irish poet. "A. E." was the pseudonym of the Irish poet and mystic George Russell (1867–1935).

* * *

* * * Literature, so far from manifesting any trend towards uniformity or standardization, is evolving in the most disparate ways; and there are few literatures in which dialect elements, and even such extreme employments of—and plays upon—them as render them permanently untranslatable and unintelligible to all but a handful of readers in their own countries, are not peculiarly and significantly active. On this account (as isolating it from general contemporary tendency which must have some deep-seated relation to the needs of modern, and prospective, consciousness) it is a pity that English literature is maintaining a narrow ascendancy tradition instead of broad-basing itself on all the diverse cultural elements and the splendid variety of languages and dialects, in the British Isles. (I do not refer here to the Empire, and the United States of America, though the evolution of genuine independent literatures in all of these is a matter of no little consequence and, already clearly appreciated in America, is being increasingly so realized in most of the Dominions,[6] which is perhaps the cultural significance of the anti-English and other tendencies in most of them which are making for those changes in the Imperial organization which will deprive England of the hegemony it has maintained too long.) To recognize and utilize these, instead of excluding them, could only make for its enrichment. It is absurd that intelligent readers of English, who would be ashamed not to know something (if only the leading names, and roughly, what they stand for) of most Continental literatures, are content to ignore Scottish, Irish, and Welsh Gaelic literatures, and Scots Vernacular literature. Surely the latter are nearer to them than the former, and the language difficulty no greater. These Gaelic, and Scots dialect poets were products of substantially the same environment and concerned for the most part with the same political, psychological, and practical issues, the same traditions and tendencies, the same landscapes, as poets in English to whom, properly regarded, they are not only valuably complementary, but (in view of their linguistic, technical, and other divergencies) corrective. Confinement to the English central stream is like refusing to hear all but one side of a complicated case—and in view of the extent to which the English language is definitely adscripted[7] in certain important moral and psychological directions, and incapable of dealing with certain types of experience which form no inconsiderable part of certain other European literatures and may well be of far greater consequence to the future of humanity as a whole than the more 'normal matters' with which it is qualified to deal, becomes a sort of self-infliction of an extensive spiritual and psychological blindness. * * *

1931

From A Drunk Man Looks at the Thistle

1. Farewell to Dosioevski[1]

The wan leafs shak, atour° us like the snaw. *around*
Here is the cavaburd[2] in which Earth's tint.° *lost*

---

6. Self-governing nations in the British Commonwealth.
7. Attached (to the soil).

1. Fyodor Dostoyevsky (1821–1881), Russian novelist.
2. Dense snowstorm.

There's naebody but Oblivion and us,
Puir gangrel° buddies, waunderin' hameless in't.   *wanderer*

5   The stars are larochs° o' auld cottages,   *foundations*
And a' Time's glen is fu' o' blinnin'° stew.°   *blinding / storm*
Nae freen'ly lozen° skimmers:° and the wund°   *window / gleams / wind*
Rises and separates even me and you.

I ken nae Russian and you ken nae Scots.
10 We canna tell oor voices frae the wund.
The snaw is seekin' everywhere: oor herts
At last like roofless ingles° it has f'und.   *hearths*

And gethers there in drift on endless drift,
Oor broken herts that it can never fill;
15 And still—its leafs like snaw, its growth like wund—
The thistle[3] rises and forever will!

                                1926

2. Yet Ha'e I Silence Left

Yet ha'e I Silence left, the croon° o' a'.   *crown*

No' her, wha on the hills langsyne° I saw   *long ago*
Liftin' a foreheid o' perpetual snaw.

No' her, wha in the how-dumb-deid o' nicht[4]
5 Kyths,[5] like Eternity in Time's despite.

No' her, withooten° shape, wha's name is Daith,°   *without / death*
No' Him, unkennable° abies° to faith   *unknowable / except*

—God whom, gin° e'er He saw a Man,'ud be   *if*
E'en mair dumfooner'd[6] at the sicht° than he.   *sight*

10 —But Him, whom nocht° in man or Deity,   *nothing*
Or Daith or Dreid or Laneliness can touch,
Wha's deed owre often and has seen owre much.[7]

O I ha'e Silence left.

                                1926

From In Memoriam James Joyce

We Must Look at the Harebell[1]

We must look at the harebell as if
We had never seen it before.

---

3. The emblem of Scotland.
4. The still center of night.
5. Makes herself known, appears.
6. More dumbfounded.

7. Who has died too often and seen too much.
1. The Scottish bluebell, a blue flower with a bell-shaped blossom.

Remembrance gives an accumulation of satisfaction
Yet the desire for change is very strong in us
5   And change is in itself a recreation.
To those who take any pleasure
In flowers, plants, birds, and the rest
An ecological change is recreative.
(Come. Climb with me. Even the sheep are different
10   And of new importance.
The coarse-fleeced, hardy Herdwick,
The Hampshire Down, artificially fed almost from birth,
And butcher-fat from the day it is weaned,
The Lincoln-Longwool, the biggest breed in England,
15   With the longest fleece, and the Southdown
Almost the smallest—and between them thirty other breeds,
Some whitefaced, some black,
Some with horns and some without,
Some long-wooled, some short-wooled,
20   In England where the men, and women too,
Are almost as interesting as the sheep.)
Everything is different, everything changes,
Except for the white bedstraw which climbs all the way
Up from the valleys to the tops of the high passes
25   The flowers are all different and more precious
Demanding more search and particularity of vision.
Look! Here and there a pinguicula² eloquent of the Alps
Still keeps a purple-blue flower
On the top of its straight and slender stem.
30   Bog-asphodel, deep-gold, and comely in form,
The queer, almost diabolical, sundew,
And when you leave the bog for the stag moors and the rocks
The parsley fern—a lovelier plant
Than even the proud Osmunda Regalis³—
35   Flourishes in abundance
Showing off oddly contrasted fronds
From the cracks of the lichened stones.
It is pleasant to find the books
Describing it as "very local."
40   Here is a change indeed!
The universal *is* the particular.

1955

Another Epitaph on an Army of Mercenaries¹

It is a God-damned lie to say that these
Saved, or knew, anything worth any man's pride.
They were professional murderers and they took
Their blood money and impious risks and died.

---

2. The butterwort, a genus of small herbs whose leaves secrete a sticky substance in which small insects are caught.
3. The flowering, or royal, fern; a plant with large fronds.

1. Cf. A. E. Housman's "Epitaph on an Army of Mercenaries" (p. 1953), to which this is a response.

5   In spite of all their kind some elements of worth
     With difficulty persist here and there on earth.

                                                    1935

LOUISE BENNETT
b. 1919

Louise Bennett, the preeminent West Indian poet of Creole verse, was born and grew up in Kingston, Jamaica, in the British West Indies, her mother a dressmaker, her father a baker. After she had published her first book of poetry, *Dialect Verses* (1942), she attended London's Royal Academy of Dramatic Art. As "Miss Lou" she won a mass following in the Caribbean through her vibrant stage performances of her poetry and of folk song; her weekly "dialect" poems published from 1943 in Jamaica's national newspaper, the *Gleaner;* her radio show, "Miss Lou's Views" (1966–82); and her children's-television program, "Ring Ding" (1970–82).

Bennett helped dismantle the view that Jamaican English is a corruption of Standard English, a prejudice she lambastes in radio monologues such as "Jamaica Language" and in poems such as "Dry-Foot Bwoy," which humorously juxtaposes a metaphor-rich Creole with a hollowly imitative British English. From a young age she felt the humor, wit, and vigor of Creole were largely untapped possibilities for writing and performing poetry, even though this commitment to Jamaican English prevented her from being recognized as a poet until after the black cultural revolution of the late 1960s and 1970s. In her poetry she often assumes the perspective of a West Indian trickster, such as the woman who cunningly subverts gender and geographic hierarchies in "Jamaica Oman [Woman]." Bennett makes wily and ebullient use of received forms, employing the ironic possibilities of dramatic monologue, the contrasts and inversions afforded by the ballad stanza, and the time-tested wisdom and pith of Jamaican proverbs. Both on the page and in her recorded performances, Bennett's vital characters and robust imagination help win over readers unfamiliar with Jamaican English, who can join in the laughing seriousness of poems such as "Colonization in Reverse," which ironically inverts Britain's xenophobic apprehension at the postwar influx of Jamaican immigrants, while also casting a suspicious eye on some Jamaicans' reverse exploitation of their exploiters. No one is safe from the multiple ironies and carnivalesque irreverence of Bennett's verse.

Jamaica Language[1]

Listen, na!
My Aunty Roachy seh dat it bwile[2] Her temper an really bex[3] Her fi true anytime she hear anybody a style we Jamaican dialec as "corruption of the English language." For if dat be de case, den dem shoulda call English Language corruption of Norman French an Latin an all dem tarra[4] language what dem seh dat English is derived from.

Oonoo[5] hear de wud? "Derived." English is a derivation but Jamaica Dialec is corruption! What a unfairity!

---

1. Originally broadcast sometime between 1979   3. Vexes.
and 1981, this radio monologue has been reprinted   4. Other.
from *Aunty Roachy Seh* (1993), ed. Mervyn Morris.   5. You (plural).
2. Boils.

Aunty Roachy seh dat if Jamaican Dialec is corruption of de English Language, den it is also a corruption of de African Twi Language to, a oh!
For Jamaican Dialec did start when we English forefahders did start mus-an-boun[6] we African ancestors fi stop talk fi-dem African Language altogedder an learn fi talk so-so[7] English, because we English forefahders couldn understan what we African ancestors-dem wasa seh to dem one anodder when dem wasa talk eena dem African Language to dem one annodder!
But we African ancestors-dem pop[8] we English forefahders-dem. Yes! Pop dem an disguise up de English Language fi projec fi-dem African Language in such a way dat we English forefahders-dem still couldn understan what we African ancestors-dem wasa talk bout when dem wasa talk to dem one annodder!
Yes, bwoy!
So till now, aldoah plenty a we Jamaica Dialec wuds-dem come from English wuds, yet, still an for all, de talkin is so-so Jamaican, an when we ready we can meck it soun like it no got no English at all eena it! An no so-so English-talkin smaddy cyaan[9] understan weh we a seh if we doan want dem to understan weh we a seh, a oh!
An we fix up we dialec wud fi soun like whatsoever we a talk bout, look like! For instance, when we seh sinting "kooroo-kooroo"[1] up, yuh know seh dat it mark-up mark-up. An if we seh one house "rookoo-rookoo"[2] up, it is plain to see dat it ole an shaky-shaky. An when we seh smaddy "boogoo-yagga", everybody know seh dat him outa-order; an if we seh dem "boonoonoonoos",[3] yuh know seh dat dem nice an we like dem. Mmmm.
Aunty Roachy seh dat Jamaica Dialec is more direc an to de point dan English. For all like how English smaddy would seh "Go away", Jamaican jus seh "Gweh!" An de only time we use more wuds dan English is when we want fi meck someting soun strong: like when dem seh sinting "batter-batter" up, it soun more expressive dan if yuh seh "it is battered." But most of all we fling weh all de bangarang an trimmins[4]-dem an only lef what wantin, an dat's why when English smaddy seh "I got stuck by a prickle" Jamaican jus seh "Macca[5] jook me"!
So fi-we Jamaica Language is not no English Language corruption at all, a oh! An we no haffi shame a it, like one gal who did go a Englan go represent we Jamaican folk-song "One shif me got" as "De sole underwear garment I possess", and go sing "Mumma, Mumma, dem ketch Puppa" as "Mother, Mother, they apprehended Father"!
Ay ya yie!

1979–81   1993

Dry-Foot Bwoy[1]

Wha wrong wid Mary dry-foot bwoy?
Dem gal got him fi mock,°   *The girls are mocking him*

---

6. Compel.
7. Only.
8. Outwitted.
9. Can't. "Smaddy": people.
1. Rough; rocky. "Sinting": something.
2. Unsteady.

3. Beautiful; wonderful (term of endearment). "Boogoo-yagga": ill-mannered.
4. Miscellaneous trash and trimmings.
5. A prickly plant.
1. Thin-legged (inexperienced) boy.

An when me meet him tarra night
De bwoy gi me a shock!

5   Me tell him seh him auntie an
Him cousin dem sen howdy[2]
An ask him how him getting awn.
Him seh, 'Oh, jolley, jolley!'

Me start fi feel so sorry fi
10   De po bad-lucky soul,
Me tink him come a foreign lan
Come ketch bad foreign cole!

Me tink him got a bad sore-troat,
But as him chat-chat gwan
15   Me fine out seh is foreign twang
De bwoy wasa put awn![3]

For me notice dat him answer
To nearly all me seh
Was 'Actually', 'What', 'Oh deah!'
20   An all dem sinting deh.°   *All of them things there*

Me gi a joke, de gal dem laugh;
But hear de bwoy, 'Haw-haw!
I'm sure you got that bally-dash°   *nonsense, balderdash*
Out of the cinema!'

25   Same time me laas me temper, an
Me holler, 'Bwoy, kirout!°   *clear out*
No chat to me wid no hot pittata
Eena yuh mout!'

Him tan° up like him stunted, den   *stand*
30   Hear him no, 'How silley!
I don't think that I really
Understand you, actually.'

Me seh, 'Yuh understan me, yaw!
No yuh name Cudjoe Scoop?
35   Always visit Nana kitchen an
Gi laugh fi gungoo soup![4]

'An now all yuh can seh is "actually"?
Bwoy, but tap!
Wha happen to dem sweet Jamaica
40   Joke yuh use fi pop?'

---

2. I told him that his auntie and his cousins sent [or send] greetings.
3. But as he kept talking I realized his foreign accent was put on.

4. Chastising the boy for his pretensions, the speaker reminds him that he is Afro-Jamaican. Cudjoe and Nana are African names used in Jamaica. "Gungoo": congo pea.

Him get bex° and walk tru de door,   *vexed*
Him head eena de air;
De gal-dem bawl out affa him,⁵
'Not going? What! Oh deah!'

45   An from dat night till tedeh, mah,
Dem all got him fi mock.
Miss Mary dry-foot bwoy!
Cyaan get over de shock!

                                                      1957

Colonization in Reverse

What a joyful news, Miss Mattie;
Ah feel like me heart gwine burs—
Jamaica people colonizin
Englan in reverse.¹

5   By de hundred, by de tousan,
From country an from town,
By de ship-load, by de plane-load,
Jamaica is Englan boun.

Dem a pour out a Jamaica;
10   Everybody future plan
Is fi get a big-time job
An settle in de motherlan.

What a islan! What a people!
Man an woman, ole an young
15   Jussa pack dem bag an baggage
An tun history upside dung!°   *down*

Some people doan like travel,
But fi show dem loyalty
Dem all a open up cheap-fare-
20   To-Englan agency;

An week by week dem shippin off
Dem countryman like fire
Fi immigrate an populate
De seat a de Empire.

25   Oonoo° se how life is funny,   *you (plural)*
Oonoo see de tunabout?
Jamaica live fi box bread
Out a English people mout.

5. The girls went crying after him.
1. Encouraged by the postwar labor shortage in
England and the scarcity of work at home, three
hundred thousand Jamaicans migrated to Britain
from 1948 to 1962.

For when dem catch a Englan
30 An start play dem different role
Some will settle down to work
An some will settle fi de dole.°   *for unemployment benefits*

Jane seh de dole is not too bad
Because dey payin she
35 Two pounds a week fi seek a job
Dat suit her dignity.

Me seh Jane will never fine work
At de rate how she dah look
For all day she stay pon Aunt Fan couch
40 An read love-story book.

What a devilment a Englan!
Dem face war an brave de worse;
But ah wonderin how dem gwine stan
Colonizin in reverse.

1957

Jamaica Oman[1]

Jamaica oman cunny, sah!°   *cunning, sir*
Is how dem jinnal so?°   *how are they so tricky?*
Look how long dem liberated
An de man dem never know!

5 Look how long Jamaica oman
—Modder, sister, wife, sweetheart—
Outa road an eena yard° deh pon   *home*
A dominate her part!

From Maroon Nanny[2] teck her body
10 Bounce bullet back pon man,
To when nowadays gal-pickney° tun   *girl-child*
Spellin-Bee champion.

From de grass root to de hill-top,
In profession, skill an trade,
15 Jamaica oman teck her time
Dah mount an meck de grade.

Some backa man a push, some side-a
Man a hole him han,
Some a lick sense eena man head,
20 Some a guide him pon him plan!

1. Woman.
2. Jamaican national hero who led the Maroons, fugitive slaves, in battle during the eighteenth century. Bullets reputedly ricocheted off her and killed her enemies.

Neck an neck an foot an foot wid man
She buckle hole° her own;   *she take hold*
While man a call her 'so-so rib'
Oman a tun backbone!³

25   An long before Oman Lib⁴ bruck out
Over foreign lan
Jamaica female wasa work
Her liberated plan!

Jamaica oman know she strong,
30   She know she tallawah,°   *sturdy*
But she no want her pickney° dem   *children*
Fi start call her 'Puppa'.°   *Papa*

So de cunny Jamma° oman   *Jamaican*
Gwan like pants-suit is a style,
35   An Jamaica man no know she wear
De trousiz all de while!

So Jamaica oman coaxin
Fambly budget from explode
A so Jamaica man a sing
40   'Oman a heaby load!'⁵

But de cunny Jamma oman
Ban her belly,⁶ bite her tongue,
Ketch water, put pot pon fire
An jus dig her toe a grung.⁷

45   For 'Oman luck deh a dungle',⁸
Some rooted more dan some,
But as long as fowl a scratch dungle heap
Oman luck mus come!

Lickle by lickle man start praise her,
50   Day by day de praise a grow;
So him praise her, so it sweet her,
For she wonder if him know.

1975

BRIAN FRIEL
b. 1929

For the renowned playwright Brian Friel, as for his Irish predecessors W. B. Yeats and James Joyce, the vexed issue of language and national identity has been a central preoccupation. His play *Translations* (1980), which reimagines the transitional moment when the language of the colonizer is supplanting the language of the colonized, is one of the richest late-twentieth century meditations on the role of the English language in British colonialism.

Set in 1833 in the rural village of Baile Beag, County Donegal, on the northwest corner of Ireland, the play dramatizes two key processes in the linguistic transformation of a colonized nation: remapping and education. Captain Lancey and Lieutenant Yolland, English officers in the Royal Engineers, have been sent to Ireland to help remap it with anglicized and standardized place-names. An intermediary figure, Owen, originally from Baile Beag but employed by the English as an interpreter, is helping the imperial military, as he puts it, "to translate the quaint, archaic tongue" of the Irish "into the King's good English." To produce Britain's first Ordnance Survey of Ireland, ordered by Parliament in 1824, each Gaelic name is replaced either by a translated English equivalent (Cnoc na Ri becomes Kings Head) or a similar English sound (Druim Dubh becomes Dromduff). Language is crucial in claiming the land for the British crown—ridding it of ambiguity and opacity, making it readable, knowable, taxable, militarily penetrable, evacuating its linguistically embodied history and memory. After Lieutenant Yolland and the Irishwoman Maire fall in love—a crosslinguistic and cross-ethnic romance with tragic consequences—the psychic violence of this colonial renaming becomes a matter of brutal physical force. The play widens the scope of its profound reflection on naming and identity through suggestive parallels with other acts of nomination—the nearly mute Sarah's vocalizing her name, the ritual naming of a baby, Owen's accidental renaming as Roland by the English officers, even an allusion to Adam's naming of the animals.

At the very time when the Ordnance Survey is remaking Irish topography, a new English-language system of National Education is being put into place, and it will supplant the local Irish-speaking schools, or hedge schools, greatly accelerating the anglicization of the still-Gaelic-speaking regions of Ireland. Hugh O'Donnell presides over the hedge school, and while his classroom is a barn where the English language and its literary canon (e.g., William Wordsworth) are unknown, the ancient Greek and Roman gods and goddesses, such as flashing-eyed Athena, are vital and immediate presences in classical languages. The conflicted schoolmaster, who initially dismisses English as useful "for the purposes of commerce" and then seeks employment in the new English schools, foresees the loss of an educational system and, to a significant degree, of a culture; he muses elegiacally but realistically that a community's language cannot remain frozen in the face of massive historical change: "We must learn where we live. We must learn to make [the new English names] our own. We must make them our new home." The English language, the play evocatively suggests, has both dispossessed and rehoused, unified and fragmented, advanced and oppressed the Irish, like the many other peoples remapped and reeducated by the empire.

Friel was born in Omagh, County Tyrone, Northern Ireland, and spent much of his youth in Derry (or Londonderry), Northern Ireland, with vacations across the border in County Donegal, in the Irish Republic, with his maternal relatives. He attended St. Patrick's College, Ireland's national seminary, in Maynooth, but instead of becoming a Roman Catholic priest, taught school in Derry for ten years, before turning full-time to writing in 1960. Having published short stories, essays, and radio plays, he increasingly devoted himself to writing stage dramas, such as *Philadelphia, Here I Come!* (first produced in 1964), *Faith Healer* (1979), and *Dancing at Lughnasa*

(1990), which have been performed and garnered prizes in Derry, Dublin, New York, London, and elsewhere. In 1969 Friel moved across the border from Northern Ireland into Derry's hinterland in County Donegal, and in 1980 he cofounded the Field Day Theatre Company, which has brought professional drama to many parts of Ireland and Northern Ireland, while seeking to break down calcified polarities of Northern Irish politics (Catholic vs. Protestant, Unionist vs. Republican, etc.). *Translations* was Field Day's first production, with the company's cofounder, the actor Stephen Rea, playing the role of Owen, and Liam Neeson playing Doalty.

PRONOUNCING GLOSSARY

As an aid for performance and reading, the following phonetic spellings provide a rough guide to the pronunciation of Irish names and words. Standard Irish diacritical marks are given in the glossary, though omitted by Friel in the playscript.

Anna na mBréag: ANN-na nuh MRAYG

Baile Beag: BOLL-ya bYUG (BOLL rhymes with *doll*)

Baile na gGall: BOLL-ya nuh NOWL (NOWL rhymes with *owl*; *nuh* has the *u* sound as in English *up*)

Beann na Gaoithe: bYOWN na GWEE-ha (YOWN rhymes with *town*)

Buncrana: bunn KRAAH-na (where *AA* is an elongated version of the *a* sound in *apple*)

Bun na hAbhann: BUNN nuh HOW-un

Caitlín Dubh Nic Reactainn: katt-LEEN DUV neek ROK-tin

Carraig na Rí: KORR-ig nuh REE (KORR: the *o* sound as in English *on* and *off*)

Carraig an Phoill: KORR-ig on f-WEEL

Catach: KOTT-ukh

Ceann Balor: kYOWN BA-lor (YOWN as above; "Balor" rhymes with *valor*)

Cnoc na Móna: k-NUKH nuh MOW-na (MOW as in English)

Cnoc na nGabhar: k-NUKH nuh NOW-er (NOW as in English)

Cnoc na Rí: k-NUCK nuh REE

Cúchulainn: KOO-kuhl-lin

Diarmuid: DEER-med

Donegal: dunny-GAWL

Druim Dubh: drimm DUV (the *u* sound of the English *un*-)

Druim Luachra: Drim LOO-krah

Éamon: AIM-en

Grania: GRAW-nya

Inis Meadhon: IN-ish MAAN (where *AA* is an elongated version of the *a* sound in *apple*)

Lag: log (exactly like the English word *log*)

Lis Maol: liss MAY-ull (*liss* rhymes with English *kiss*)

Lis na Muc: LISS nuh MUK

Lis na nGall: Liss nuh nALL

Lis na nGradh: LISS nuh nRAW (a gentle little *n* sound before the *RAW*)

Loch an Iubhair: LUKH un OO-er

Loch na nÉan: LUKH nuh NAY-un

Luachra: LOO-akh-ra

Machaire bán: MOKH-ur-uh BAWN

Machaire Buidhe: MOKH-i-reh bWEE (the middle *i* is short like the English *in*)

Machaire Mór: MOKH-i-reh MOOR

Máire Chatach: MAW-reh KHOTT-ukh

Manus: MAAH-nuss

Mullach Dearg: MULL-ukh JA-rug (hard *J* as in *John*)

Poll na gCaorach: POWL nuh GAY-rukh (POWL rhymes with *cowl*)

Port: purt (rhymes with *hurt*)

Poteen: puh-TCHEEN

Ruadh: ROO-uh

Séamus: SHAY-muss

Seán: shawn

Tobair Bhriain: TUB-er vr-EE-un

Tobair Vree: TUB-er vrEE (the letter V is an anglicization)

Tor: tur (as in the first syllable of the English word *turret*)

Trá Bhán: traW VAWN

Tulach Álainn: TULL-ukh AW-linn

Translations

MANUS	BRIDGET
SARAH	HUGH
JIMMY JACK	OWEN
MAIRE	CAPTAIN LANCEY
DOALTY	LIEUTENANT YOLLAND

The action takes place in a hedge-school[1] *in the townland of Baile Beag/Ballybeg, an Irish-speaking community in County Donegal.*[2]

ACT ONE   *An afternoon in late August 1833.*
ACT TWO   *A few days later.*
ACT THREE *The evening of the following day.*

Act One

The hedge-school is held in a disused barn or hay-shed or byre. Along the back wall are the remains of five or six stalls—wooden posts and chains—where cows were once milked and bedded. A double door left, large enough to allow a cart to enter. A window right. A wooden stairway without a banister leads to the upstairs living-quarters (off) of the schoolmaster and his son. Around the room are broken and forgotten implements: a cart-wheel, some lobster-pots, farming tools, a battle[3] *of hay, a churn, etc. There are also the stools and bench-seats which the pupils use and a table and chair for the master. At the door a pail of water and a soiled towel. The room is comfortless and dusty and functional—there is no trace of a woman's hand.*

When the play opens, MANUS *is teaching* SARAH *to speak. He kneels beside her. She is sitting on a low stool, her head down, very tense, clutching a slate on her knees. He is coaxing her gently and firmly and—as with everything he does—with a kind of zeal.*

MANUS *is in his late twenties/early thirties; the master's older son. He is pale-faced, lightly built, intense, and works as an unpaid assistant—a monitor—to his father. His clothes are shabby; and when he moves we see that he is lame.*

SARAH'S *speech defect is so bad that all her life she has been considered locally to be dumb and she has accepted this: when she wishes to communicate, she grunts and makes unintelligible nasal sounds. She has a waiflike*[4] *appearance and could be any age from seventeen to thirty-five.*

JIMMY JACK CASSIE—*known as the Infant Prodigy—sits by himself, contentedly reading Homer in Greek and smiling to himself. He is a bachelor in his sixties,*

1. Peasant school in which the Irish language was the primary medium of instruction; the hedge school was so called because it was beside a hedge (or in the open air or in a barn). Such schools were formed because education of Roman Catholics in Ireland had been officially proscribed by the Penal Laws passed in the 17th and 18th centuries.

2. In the northwest corner of Ireland, now in the Republic of Ireland. Baile Beag/Ballybeg is the imaginary community in which many of Friel's plays are set.
3. Compact bundle.
4. Like a homeless child.

lives alone, and comes to these evening classes partly for the company and partly for the intellectual stimulation. He is fluent in Latin and Greek but is in no way pedantic—to him it is perfectly normal to speak these tongues.[5] He never washes. His clothes—heavy top coat, hat, mittens, which he wears now—are filthy and he lives in them summer and winter, day and night. He now reads in a quiet voice and smiles in profound satisfaction. For JIMMY the world of the gods and the ancient myths is as real and as immediate as everyday life in the townland of Baile Beag.

MANUS holds SARAH's hands in his and he articulates slowly and distinctly into her face.

MANUS   We're doing very well. And we're going to try it once more—just once more. Now—relax and breathe in . . . deep . . . and out . . . in . . . and out . . .

[SARAH shakes her head vigorously and stubbornly.]

MANUS   Come on, Sarah. This is our secret.

[Again vigorous and stubborn shaking of SARAH's head.]

MANUS   Nobody's listening. Nobody hears you.

JIMMY   'Ton d'emeibet epeita thea glaukopis Athene . . .'[6]

MANUS   Get your tongue and your lips working. 'My name—' Come on. One more try. 'My name is—' Good girl.

SARAH   My . . .

MANUS   Great. 'My name—'

SARAH   My . . . my . . .

MANUS   Raise your head. Shout it out. Nobody's listening.

JIMMY   '. . . alla hekelos estai en Atreidao domois . . .'[7]

MANUS   Jimmy, please! Once more—just once more—'My name—' Good girl. Come on now. Head up. Mouth open.

SARAH   My . . .

MANUS   Good.

SARAH   My . . .

MANUS   Great.

SARAH   My name . . .

MANUS   Yes?

[SARAH pauses. Then in a rush.]

SARAH   My name is Sarah.

MANUS   Marvellous! Bloody marvellous!

[MANUS hugs SARAH. She smiles in shy, embarrassed pleasure.]

Did you hear that, Jimmy?—'My name is Sarah'—clear as a bell. [To SARAH.] The Infant Prodigy doesn't know what we're at.

[SARAH laughs at this. MANUS hugs her again and stands up.]

Now we're really started! Nothing'll stop us now! Nothing in the wide world!

[JIMMY, chuckling at his text, comes over to them.]

JIMMY   Listen to this, Manus.

MANUS   Soon you'll be telling me all the secrets that have been in that head of yours all these years.

5. Latin and Greek were taught and used in the hedge schools.
6. But the grey-eyed goddess Athene then replied to him (Odyssey, XIII, 420) [Friel's note]. Athena, ancient Greek goddess of war, wisdom, and the city, was a tutelary god to the hero Odysseus, also known by the Roman name Ulysses. In this scene

of Homer's epic, she plots Odysseus' return home, after his ten-year absence. A disguise, as a dirty and shriveled old man, will enable him to trick and kill the suitors to his wife, Penelope.
7. But he sits at ease in the halls of the Sons of Athens (Odyssey, XIII, 423–4) [Friel's note].

Certainly, James—what is it?
[*To* SARAH.] Maybe you'd set out the stools?
   [MANUS *runs up the stairs.*]
JIMMY Wait till you hear this, Manus.
MANUS Go ahead. I'll be straight down.
JIMMY '*Hos ara min phamene rabdo epemassat Athene*—' 'After Athene had said this, she touched Ulysses with her wand. She withered the fair skin of his supple limbs and destroyed the flaxen[8] hair from off his head and about his limbs she put the skin of an old man . . . '! The divil! The divil!
   [MANUS *has emerged again with a bowl of milk and a piece of bread.*]
JIMMY And wait till you hear! She's not finished with him yet!
   [As MANUS *descends the stairs he toasts* SARAH *with his bowl.*]
JIMMY '*Knuzosen de oi osse*—' 'She dimmed his two eyes that were so beautiful and clothed him in a vile ragged cloak begrimed with filthy smoke . . .'! D'you see! Smoke! Smoke! D'you see! Sure look at what the same turf-smoke has done to myself! [*He rapidly removes his hat to display his bald head.*] Would you call that flaxen hair?
MANUS Of course I would.
JIMMY 'And about him she cast the great skin of a filthy hind,[9] stripped of the hair, and into his hand she thrust a staff and a wallet'! Ha-ha-ha! Athene did that to Ulysses! Made him into a tramp! Isn't she the tight one?
MANUS You couldn't watch her, Jimmy.
JIMMY You know what they call her?
MANUS '*Glaukopis Athene.*'
JIMMY That's it! The flashing-eyed Athene! By God, Manus, sir, if you had a woman like that about the house, it's not stripping a turf[1]-bank you'd be thinking about—eh?
MANUS She was a goddess, Jimmy.
JIMMY Better still. Sure isn't our own Grania a class of a goddess and—
MANUS Who?
JIMMY Grania—Grania—Diarmuid's Grania.[2]
MANUS Ah.
JIMMY And sure she can't get her fill of men.
MANUS Jimmy, you're impossible.
JIMMY I was just thinking to myself last night: if you had the choosing between Athene and Artemis and Helen of Troy—all three of them Zeus's girls[3]—imagine three powerful-looking daughters like that all in the one parish of Athens!—now, if you had the picking between them, which would you take?
MANUS [*To* SARAH.] Which should I take, Sarah?
JIMMY No harm to Helen; and no harm to Artemis; and indeed no harm to our own Grania, Manus. But I think I've no choice but to go bull-straight for Athene. By God, sir, them flashing eyes would fair keep a man jigged[4] up constant!

---

8. A pale strawlike color. Jimmy is continuing with the same scene of the *Odyssey*.
9. Female red deer.
1. Peat; dried and used for fuel.
2. Young and beautiful Irish princess betrothed to the aged but powerful Fionn mac Cumhaill; many medieval stories recount the flight of Grania and her lover, Dairmud, over the Irish countryside in their attempt to escape capture by Fionn.
3. I.e., daughters of the most powerful Greek god. As goddess of wild animals, vegetation, and the hunt, Artemis was contrasted with Athena, goddess of the city. Helen's abduction was the legendary cause of the Trojan War.
4. Jerked, caught.

[*Suddenly and momentarily, as if in spasm,* JIMMY *stands to attention and salutes, his face raised in pained ecstasy.*
MANUS *laughs. So does* SARAH. JIMMY *goes back to his seat, and his reading.*]

MANUS You're a dangerous bloody man, Jimmy Jack.

JIMMY 'Flashing-eyed'! Hah! Sure Homer knows it all, boy. Homer knows it all.

[MANUS *goes to the window and looks out.*]

MANUS Where the hell has he got to?

[SARAH *goes to* MANUS *and touches his elbow. She mimes rocking a baby.*]

MANUS Yes, I know he's at the christening; but it doesn't take them all day to put a name on a baby, does it?

[SARAH *mimes pouring drinks and tossing them back quickly.*]

MANUS You may be sure. Which pub?

[SARAH *indicates.*]

MANUS Gracie's?

[*No. Further away.*]

MANUS Con Connie Tim's?

[*No. To the right of there.*]

MANUS Anna na mBreag's?

[*Yes. That's it.*]

MANUS Great. She'll fill him up. I suppose I may take the class then.

[MANUS *begins to distribute some books, slates and chalk, texts etc. beside the seats.*

SARAH *goes over to the straw and produces a bunch of flowers she has hidden there.*

During this.]

JIMMY '*Autar o ek limenos prosebe—*' 'But Ulysses went forth from the harbour and through the woodland to the place where Athene had shown him he could find the good swineherd who—*o oi biotoio malista kedeto*'—what's that, Manus?

MANUS 'Who cared most for his substance'.

JIMMY That's it! 'The good swineherd who cared most for his substance above all the slaves that Ulysses possessed . . .'[5]

[SARAH *presents the flowers to* MANUS.]

MANUS Those are lovely, Sarah.

[*But* SARAH *has fled in embarrassment to her seat and has her head buried in a book.* MANUS *goes to her.*]

MANUS Flow—ers.

[*Pause.* SARAH *does not look up.*]

MANUS Say the word: flow—ers. Come on—flow—ers.

SARAH Flowers.

MANUS You see?—you're off!

[MANUS *leans down and kisses the top of* SARAH's *head.*]

MANUS And they're beautiful flowers. Thank you.

[MAIRE *enters, a strong-minded, strong-bodied woman in her twenties with a head of curly hair. She is carrying a small can of milk.*]

---

5. At the beginning of book 14 of the *Odyssey*, Odysseus seeks, at Athena's instruction, the field hand who has been most attentive to the hero's estate in his absence.

MAIRE   Is this all's here? Is there no school this evening?
MANUS   If my father's not back, I'll take it.
         [MANUS *stands awkwardly, having been caught kissing* SARAH *and with the flowers almost formally at his chest.*]
MAIRE   Well now, isn't that a pretty sight. There's your milk. How's Sarah? [SARAH *grunts a reply.*]
MANUS   I saw you out at the hay.
         [MAIRE *ignores this and goes to* JIMMY.]
MAIRE   And how's Jimmy Jack Cassie?
JIMMY   Sit down beside me, Maire.
MAIRE   Would I be safe?
JIMMY   No safer man in Donegal.
         [MAIRE *flops on a stool beside* JIMMY.]
MAIRE   Ooooh. The best harvest in living memory, they say; but I don't want to see another like it. [*Showing* JIMMY *her hands.*] Look at the blisters.
JIMMY   *Esne fatigata?*
MAIRE   *Sum fatigatissima.*
JIMMY   *Bene! Optime!*⁶
MAIRE   That's the height of my Latin. Fit me better if I had even that much English.
JIMMY   English? I thought you had some English?
MAIRE   Three words. Wait—there was a spake⁷ I used to have off by heart. What's this it was?
         [*Her accent is strange because she is speaking a foreign language and because she does not understand what she is saying.*]
         'In Norfolk⁸ we besport ourselves around the maypoll.' What about that!
MANUS   Maypole.⁹
         [*Again* MAIRE *ignores* MANUS.]
MAIRE   God have mercy on my Aunt Mary—she taught me that when I was about four, whatever it means. Do you know what it means, Jimmy?
JIMMY   Sure you know I have only Irish like yourself.
MAIRE   And Latin. And Greek.
JIMMY   I'm telling you a lie: I know one English word.
MAIRE   What?
JIMMY   Bo–som.
MAIRE   What's a bo–som?
JIMMY   You know—[*He illustrates with his hands.*]—bo–som—bo–som—you know—Diana, the huntress,¹ she has two powerful bosom.
MAIRE   You may be sure that's the one English word you would know. [*Rises.*] Is there a drop of water about?
         [MANUS *gives* MAIRE *his bowl of milk.*]
MANUS   I'm sorry I couldn't get up last night.
MAIRE   Doesn't matter.
MANUS   Biddy Hanna sent for me to write a letter to her sister in Nova Scotia. All the gossip of the parish. 'I brought the cow to the bull three times last week but no good. There's nothing for it now but Big Ned Frank.'
MAIRE   [*Drinking.*]   That's better.

---

6. Are you tired? / I am very tired. / Good! Excellent! [Friel's note].
7. Speech.
8. County of eastern England.

9. Tall decorated pole around which traditional English dances were conducted in springtime.
1. Roman goddess, comparable to the Greek Artemis.

MANUS   And she got so engrossed in it that she forgot who she was dictating to: 'The aul drunken schoolmaster and that lame son of his are still footering about in the hedge-school, wasting people's good time and money.'
    [MAIRE *has to laugh at this.*]
MAIRE   She did not!
MANUS   And me taking it all down. 'Thank God one of them new national schools[2] is being built above at Poll na gCaorach.' It was after midnight by the time I got back.
MAIRE   Great to be a busy man.
    [MAIRE *moves away.* MANUS *follows.*]
MANUS   I could hear music on my way past but I thought it was too late to call.
MAIRE   [*To* SARAH.]   Wasn't your father in great voice last night?
    [SARAH *nods and smiles.*]
MAIRE   It must have been near three o'clock by the time you got home?
    [SARAH *holds up four fingers.*]
MAIRE   Was it four? No wonder we're in pieces.
MANUS   I can give you a hand at the hay tomorrow.
MAIRE   That's the name of a hornpipe,[3] isn't it?—'The Scholar In The Hay-field'—or is it a reel?[4]
MANUS   If the day's good.
MAIRE   Suit yourself. The English soldiers below in the tents, them sapper[5] fellas, they're coming up to give us a hand. I don't know a word they're saying, nor they me; but sure that doesn't matter, does it?
MANUS   What the hell are you so crabbed[6] about?!
    [DOALTY *and* BRIDGET *enter noisily. Both are in their twenties.*
      DOALTY *is brandishing a surveyor's pole. He is an open-minded, open-hearted, generous and slightly thick young man.*
      BRIDGET *is a plump, fresh young girl, ready to laugh, vain, and with a countrywoman's instinctive cunning.*
      DOALTY *enters doing his imitation of the master.*]
DOALTY   Vesperal[7] salutations to you all.
BRIDGET   He's coming down past Carraig na Ri and he's as full as a pig!
DOALTY   *Ignari, stulti, rustici*[8]—pot-boys and peasant whelps[9]—semi-literates and illegitimates.
BRIDGET   He's been on the batter[1] since this morning; he sent the wee ones home at eleven o'clock.
DOALTY   Three questions. Question A—Am I drunk? Question B—Am I sober? [*Into* MAIRE's *face.*] *Responde—responde!*[2]
BRIDGET   Question C, Master—When were you last sober?
MAIRE   What's the weapon, Doalty?
BRIDGET   I warned him. He'll be arrested one of these days.
DOALTY   Up in the bog with Bridget and her aul fella, and the Red Coats were

---

2. In 1831, two years earlier, a new system of English-speaking schools had been introduced; these would eventually supplant the hedge schools.
3. Vigorous dance performed by a sole person to a wind instrument.
4. Lively dance performed by couples facing each other.
5. Soldier who works in saps, i.e., fortifications, or does field work.

6. Annoyed.
7. Evening.
8. Ignoramuses, fools, peasants [Latin; Friel's note].
9. Young wild animals. "Pot-boys": assistants who serve beer in a pub.
1. On the bottle.
2. Answer—answer! [Latin; Friel's note].

just across at the foot of Cnoc na Mona, dragging them aul chains and peeping through that big machine they lug about everywhere with them— you know the name of it, Manus?

MAIRE   Theodolite.[3]

BRIDGET   How do you know?

MAIRE   They leave it in our byre[4] at night sometimes if it's raining.

JIMMY   Theodolite—what's the etymology of that word, Manus?

MANUS   No idea.

BRIDGET   Get on with the story.

JIMMY   *Theo—theos*[5]—something to do with a god. Maybe *thea*—a goddess! What shape's the yoke?

DOALTY   'Shape!' Will you shut up, you aul eejit[6] you! Anyway, every time they'd stick one of these poles into the ground and move across the bog, I'd creep up and shift it twenty or thirty paces to the side.

BRIDGET   God!

DOALTY   Then they'd come back and stare at it and look at their calculations and stare at it again and scratch their heads. And Cripes[7], d'you know what they ended up doing?

BRIDGET   Wait till you hear!

DOALTY   They took the bloody machine apart! [*And immediately he speaks in gibberish—an imitation of two very agitated and confused sappers in rapid conversation.*]

BRIDGET   That's the image of them!

MAIRE   You must be proud of yourself, Doalty.

DOALTY   What d'you mean?

MAIRE   That was a very clever piece of work.

MANUS   It was a gesture.

MAIRE   What sort of a gesture?

MANUS   Just to indicate . . . a presence.

MAIRE   Hah!

BRIDGET   I'm telling you—you'll be arrested.

[*When* DOALTY *is embarrassed—or pleased—he reacts physically. He now grabs* BRIDGET *around the waist.*]

DOALTY   What d'you make of that for an implement, Bridget? Wouldn't that make a great aul shaft for your churn?

BRIDGET   Let go of me, you dirty brute! I've a headline to do before Big Hughie comes.

MANUS   I don't think we'll wait for him. Let's get started.

[*Slowly, reluctantly they begin to move to their seats and specific tasks.* DOALTY *goes to the bucket of water at the door and washes his hands.* BRIDGET *sets up a hand-mirror and combs her hair.*]

BRIDGET   Nellie Ruadh's baby was to be christened this morning. Did any of yous hear what she called it? Did you, Sarah?

[SARAH *grunts: No.*]

BRIDGET   Did you, Maire?

MAIRE   No.

BRIDGET   Our Seamus says she was threatening she was going to call it after its father.

---

3. A portable instrument for surveying.
4. Barn.
5. God (Greek).

6. Idiot.
7. Christ (mild oath).

DOALTY Who's the father?

BRIDGET That's the point, you donkey you!

DOALTY Ah.

BRIDGET So there's a lot of uneasy bucks about Baile Beag this day.

DOALTY She told me last Sunday she was going to call it Jimmy.

BRIDGET You're a liar, Doalty.

DOALTY Would I tell you a lie? Hi, Jimmy, Nellie Ruadh's aul fella's looking for you.

JIMMY For me?

MAIRE Come on, Doalty.

DOALTY Someone told him . . .

MAIRE Doalty!

DOALTY He heard you know the first book of the Satires of Horace[8] off by heart . . .

JIMMY That's true.

DOALTY . . . and he wants you to recite it for him.

JIMMY I'll do that for him certainly, certainly.

DOALTY He's busting to hear it.

[JIMMY *fumbles in his pockets.*]

JIMMY I came across this last night—this'll interest you—in Book Two of Virgil's *Georgics.*[9]

DOALTY Be God, that's my territory alright.

BRIDGET You clown you! [*To* SARAH.] Hold this for me, would you? [*Her mirror.*]

JIMMY Listen to this, Manus. '*Nigra fere et presso pinguis sub vomere terra . . .*'

DOALTY Steady on now—easy, boys, easy—don't rush me, boys—[*He mimes great concentration.*]

JIMMY Manus?

MANUS 'Land that is black and rich beneath the pressure of the plough . . .'

DOALTY Give *me* a chance!

JIMMY 'And with *cui putre*—with crumbly soil—is in the main best for corn.' There you are!

DOALTY There you are.

JIMMY 'From no other land will you see more wagons wending homeward behind slow bullocks.'[1] Virgil! There!

DOALTY 'Slow bullocks'!

JIMMY Isn't that what I'm always telling you? Black soil for corn. *That's* what you should have in that upper field of yours—corn, not spuds.

DOALTY Would you listen to that fella! Too lazy be Jasus to wash himself and he's lecturing me on agriculture! Would you go and take a running race at yourself, Jimmy Jack Cassie! [*Grabs* SARAH.] Come away out of this with me, Sarah, and we'll plant some corn together.

MANUS Alright—alright. Let's settle down and get some work done. I know Sean Beag isn't coming—he's at the[2] salmon. What about the Donnelly twins? [*To* DOALTY.] Are the Donnelly twins not coming any more?

---

8. Latin lyric poet (65–8 B.C.E.).
9. Four books of poems on farming and rural life by the Roman poet (70–19 B.C.E.).

1. Bulls or, loosely, cattle.
2. Fishing for.

[DOALTY *shrugs and turns away.*]
Did you ask them?
DOALTY   Haven't seen them. Not about these days.
[DOALTY *begins whistling through his teeth.*
   Suddenly the atmosphere is silent and alert.]
MANUS   Aren't they at home?
DOALTY   No.
MANUS   Where are they then?
DOALTY   How would I know?
BRIDGET   Our Seamus says two of the soldiers' horses were found last night
at the foot of the cliffs at Machaire Buide and . . .
[*She stops suddenly and begins writing with chalk on her slate.*]
D'you hear the whistles of this aul slate? Sure nobody could write on an aul
slippery thing like that.
MANUS   What headline did my father set you?
BRIDGET   'It's easier to stamp out learning than to recall it.'
JIMMY   Book Three, the *Agricola* of Tacitus.[3]
BRIDGET   God but you're a dose.[4]
MANUS   Can you do it?
BRIDGET   There. Is it bad? Will he ate me?
MANUS   It's very good. Keep your elbow in closer to your side. Doalty?
DOALTY   I'm at the seven-times table. I'm perfect, skipper.
[MANUS *moves to* SARAH.]
MANUS   Do you understand those sums?
[SARAH *nods: Yes.* MANUS *leans down to her ear.*]
MANUS   My name is Sarah.
[MANUS *goes to* MAIRE. *While he is talking to her the others swop books,*
   talk quietly, etc.]
MANUS   Can I help you? What are you at?
MAIRE   Map of America. [*Pause.*] The passage money came last Friday.
MANUS   You never told me that.
MAIRE   Because I haven't seen you since, have I?
MANUS   You don't want to go. You said that yourself.
MAIRE   There's ten below me to be raised and no man in the house. What do
you suggest?
MANUS   Do you want to go?
MAIRE   Did you apply for that job in the new national school?
MANUS   No.
MAIRE   You said you would.
MANUS   I said I might.
MAIRE   When it opens, this is finished: nobody's going to pay to go to a hedge-
school.
MANUS   I know that and I . . . [*He breaks off because he sees* SARAH, *obviously*
listening, at his shoulder. She moves away again.] I was thinking that maybe
I could . . .
MAIRE   It's £56 a year you're throwing away.
MANUS   I can't apply for it.

---

3. Roman historian (ca. 56–ca. 120 C.E.), author
of *De Vita Julii Agricolae* (*The Life of Julius Agric-*
ola), or the *Agricola*, a biography of his father-in-

law, including an account of his career in Britain.
4. I.e., a dose of medicine, or an unpleasant experience.

MAIRE You *promised* me you would.
MANUS My father has applied for it.
MAIRE He has not!
MANUS Day before yesterday.
MAIRE For God's sake, sure you know he'd never—
MANUS I couldn't—I can't go in against him.
   [MAIRE *looks at him for a second. Then.*]
MAIRE Suit yourself. [*To* BRIDGET.] I saw your Seamus heading off to the Port fair early this morning.
BRIDGET And wait till you hear this—I forgot to tell you this. He said that as soon as he crossed over the gap at Cnoc na Mona—just beyond where the soldiers are making the maps—the sweet smell was everywhere.
DOALTY You never told me that.
BRIDGET It went out of my head.
DOALTY He saw the crops in Port?
BRIDGET Some.
MANUS How did the tops look?
BRIDGET Fine—I think.
DOALTY In flower?
BRIDGET I don't know. I think so. He didn't say.
MANUS Just the sweet smell—that's all?
BRIDGET They say that's the way it snakes in, don't they? First the smell; and then one morning the stalks are all black and limp.
DOALTY Are you stupid? It's the rotting stalks makes the sweet smell for God's sake. That's what the smell is—rotting stalks.
MAIRE Sweet smell! Sweet smell! Every year at this time somebody comes back with stories of the sweet smell. Sweet God, did the potatoes ever fail in Baile Beag? Well, did they ever—ever? Never! There was never blight here. Never. Never. But we're always sniffing about for it, aren't we?—looking for disaster. The rents are going to go up again—the harvest's going to be lost—the herring have gone away for ever—there's going to be evictions. Honest to God, some of you people aren't happy unless you're miserable and you'll not be right content until you're dead!
DOALTY Bloody right, Maire. And sure St. Colmcille prophesied there'd never be blight here. He said:

> The spuds will bloom in Baile Beag
> Till rabbits grow an extra lug.[5]

And sure that'll never be. So we're alright.
   Seven threes are twenty-one; seven fours are twenty-eight; seven fives are forty-nine— Hi, Jimmy, do you fancy my chances as boss of the new national school?
JIMMY What's that?—what's that?
DOALTY Agh, g'way back home to Greece, son.
MAIRE You ought to apply, Doalty.
DOALTY D'you think so? Cripes, maybe I will. Hah!
BRIDGET Did you know that you start at the age of six and you have to stick

---

5. Ear. St. Comcille (521–597), also known as St. Columba, was born in Donegal and established monasteries and churches throughout Ireland and Scotland. Cf. Friel's play about his life, *The Enemy Within* (1962).

at it until you're twelve at least—no matter how smart you are or how much you know.

DOALTY   Who told you that yarn?

BRIDGET   And every child from every house has to go all day, every day, summer or winter. That's the law.

DOALTY   I'll tell you something—nobody's going to go near them—they're not going to take on—law or no law.

BRIDGET   And everything's free in them. You pay for nothing except the books you use; that's what our Seamus says.

DOALTY   'Our Seamus'. Sure your Seamus wouldn't pay anyway. She's making this all up.

BRIDGET   Isn't that right, Manus?

MANUS   I think so.

BRIDGET   And from the very first day you go, you'll not hear one word of Irish spoken. You'll be taught to speak English and every subject will be taught through English and everyone'll end up as cute as the Buncrana[6] people.

[SARAH *suddenly grunts and mimes a warning that the master is coming. The atmosphere changes. Sudden business. Heads down.*]

DOALTY   He's here, boys. Cripes, he'll make yella meal out of me for those bloody tables.

BRIDGET   Have you any extra chalk, Manus?

MAIRE   And the atlas for me.

[DOALTY *goes to* MAIRE *who is sitting on a stool at the back.*]

DOALTY   Swop you seats.

MAIRE   Why?

DOALTY   There's an empty one beside the Infant Prodigy.

MAIRE   I'm fine here.

DOALTY   Please, Maire. I want to jouk[7] in the back here.

[MAIRE *rises.*]

God love you. [*Aloud.*] Anyone got a bloody table-book? Cripes, I'm wrecked.

[SARAH *gives him one.*]

God, I'm dying about you.

[*In his haste to get to the back seat* DOALTY *bumps into* BRIDGET *who is kneeling on the floor and writing laboriously on a slate resting on top of a bench-seat.*]

BRIDGET   Watch where you're going, Doalty!

[DOALTY *gooses*[8] BRIDGET. *She squeals.*

Now the quiet hum of work: JIMMY *reading Homer in a low voice;* BRIDGET *copying her headline;* MAIRE *studying the atlas;* DOALTY, *his eyes shut tight, mouthing his tables;* SARAH *doing sums.*

After a few seconds.]—

BRIDGET   Is this 'g' right, Manus? How do you put a tail on it?

DOALTY   Will you shut up! I can't concentrate!

[*A few more seconds of work. Then* DOALTY *opens his eyes and looks around.*]

False alarm, boys. The bugger's[9] not coming at all. Sure the bugger's hardly fit to walk.

---

6. Small coastal town northwest of Derry.
7. Perch.

8. Pokes or tickles in an erogenous place.
9. Vulgar term of abuse.

[*And immediately* HUGH *enters. A large man, with residual dignity, shabbily dressed, carrying a stick. He has, as always, a large quantity of drink taken, but he is by no means drunk. He is in his early sixties.*]

HUGH Adsum, Doalty, *adsum.*[1] Perhaps not in *sobrietate perfecta*[2] but adequately *sobrius*[3] to overhear your quip. Vesperal salutations to you all.

[*Various responses.*]

JIMMY Ave,[4] Hugh.

HUGH James.

[*He removes his hat and coat and hands them and his stick to* MANUS, *as if to a footman.*]

Apologies for my late arrival: we were celebrating the baptism of Nellie Ruadh's baby.

BRIDGET [*Innocently.*] What name did she put on it, Master?

HUGH Was it Eamon? Yes, it was Eamon.

BRIDGET Eamon Donal from Tor! Cripes!

HUGH And after the *caerimonia nominationis*[5]—Maire?

MAIRE The ritual of naming.

HUGH Indeed—we then had a few libations to mark the occasion. Altogether very pleasant. The derivation of the word 'baptise'?—where are my Greek scholars? Doalty?

DOALTY Would it be—ah—ah—

HUGH Too slow. James?

JIMMY 'Baptizein'—to dip or immerse.

HUGH Indeed—our friend Pliny Minor[6] speaks of the 'baptisterium'—the cold bath.

DOALTY Master.

HUGH Doalty?

DOALTY I suppose you could talk then about baptising a sheep at sheep-dipping, could you?

[*Laughter. Comments.*]

HUGH Indeed—the precedent is there—the day you were appropriately named Doalty—seven nines?

DOALTY What's that, Master?

HUGH Seven times nine?

DOALTY Seven nines—seven nines—seven times nine—seven times nine are—Cripes, it's on the tip of my tongue, Master—I knew it for sure this morning—funny that's the only one that foxes[7] me—

BRIDGET [*Prompt.*] Sixty-three.

DOALTY What's wrong with me: sure seven nines are fifty-three, Master.

HUGH Sophocles from Colonus would agree with Doalty Dan Doalty from Tulach Alainn: 'To know nothing is the sweetest life.'[8] Where's Sean Beag?

MANUS He's at the salmon.

HUGH And Nora Dan?

MAIRE She says she's not coming back any more.

---

1. I am present [Latin; Friel's note].
2. With complete sobriety [Latin; Friel's note].
3. Sober [Latin; Friel's note].
4. Hail [Latin; Friel's note].
5. Ceremony of naming [Latin; Friel's note].
6. Or Pliny the Younger (61 or 62–ca. 113 C.E.),

Roman administrator who wrote an important collection of letters.
7. Befuddles.
8. From *Ajax*, by the ancient Greek playwright Sophocles (ca. 496–406 B.C.E.), born in the village of Colonus, near Athens.

HUGH   Ah. Nora Dan can now write her name—Nora Dan's education is complete. And the Donnelly twins?
        [*Brief pause. Then.*]
BRIDGET   They're probably at the turf.[9] [*She goes to* HUGH.] There's the one-and-eight I owe you for last quarter's arithmetic and there's my one-and-six[1] for this quarter's writing.
HUGH   *Gratias tibi ago.*[2] [*He sits at his table.*] Before we commence our *studia*[3] I have three items of information to impart to you—[*To* MANUS.] a bowl of tea, strong tea, black—
        [MANUS *leaves.*]
        Item A: on my perambulations today—Bridget? Too slow. Maire?
MAIRE   *Perambulare*—to walk about.
HUGH   Indeed—I encountered Captain Lancey of the Royal Engineers who is engaged in the ordnance survey of this area. He tells me that in the past few days two of his horses have strayed and some of his equipment seems to be mislaid. I expressed my regret and suggested he address you himself on these matters. He then explained that he does not speak Irish. Latin? I asked. None. Greek? Not a syllable. He speaks—on his own admission—only English; and to his credit he seemed suitably verecund—James?
JIMMY   *Verecundus*—humble.
HUGH   Indeed—he voiced some surprise that we did not speak his language. I explained that a few of us did, on occasion—outside the parish of course—and then usually for the purposes of commerce, a use to which his tongue seemed particularly suited—[*Shouts.*] and a slice of soda bread—and I went on to propose that our own culture and the classical tongues made a happier conjugation—Doalty?
DOALTY   *Conjugo*—I join together.
        [DOALTY *is so pleased with himself that he prods and winks at* BRIDGET.]
HUGH   Indeed—English, I suggested, couldn't really express us. And again to his credit he acquiesced to my logic. Acquiesced—Maire?
        [MAIRE *turns away impatiently.* HUGH *is unaware of the gesture.*]
        Too slow. Bridget?
BRIDGET   *Acquiesco.*[4]
HUGH   *Procede.*
BRIDGET   *Acquiesco, acquiescere, acquievi, acquietum.*
HUGH   Indeed—and Item B . . .
MAIRE   Master.
HUGH   Yes?
        [MAIRE *gets to her feet uneasily but determinedly. Pause.*]
        Well, girl?
MAIRE   We should all be learning to speak English. That's what my mother says. That's what I say. That's what Dan O'Connell[5] said last month in Ennis. He said the sooner we all learn to speak English the better.
        [*Suddenly several speak together.*]

---

9. I.e., cutting turf.
1. One and a half shillings—eighteen pennies—in the old British currency. "One-and-eight": one shilling and eight pence, or twenty pennies.
2. I thank you [Latin; Friel's note].
3. Studies [Latin; Friel's note].
4. Acquiescere: to rest, to find comfort in [Latin; Friel's note].

5. Irish lawyer and nationalist leader (1775–1847), born in Kerry and known as the Liberator, who argued for Ireland's adoption of the English language. The first Roman Catholic member of Parliament, he regained civil rights for Irish Catholics and urged the reestablishment of the Irish Parliament in Dublin.

JIMMY What's she saying? What? What?

DOALTY It's Irish he uses when he's travelling around scrounging votes.

BRIDGET And sleeping with married women. Sure no woman's safe from that fella.

JIMMY Who-who-who? Who's this? Who's this?

HUGH *Silentium!* [*Pause.*] Who is she talking about?

MAIRE I'm talking about Daniel O'Connell.

HUGH Does she mean that little Kerry politician?

MAIRE I'm talking about the Liberator, Master, as you well know. And what he said was this: 'The old language is a barrier to modern progress.' He said that last month. And he's right. I don't want Greek. I don't want Latin. I want English.

[MANUS *reappears on the platform above.*]

I want to be able to speak English because I'm going to America as soon as the harvest's all saved.

[MAIRE *remains standing.* HUGH *puts his hand into his pocket and produces a flask of whisky. He removes the cap, pours a drink into it, tosses it back, replaces the cap, puts the flask back into his pocket. Then.*]

HUGH We have been diverted—*diverto—divertere*—Where were we?

DOALTY Three items of information, Master. You're at Item B.

HUGH Indeed—Item B—Item B—yes—On my way to the christening this morning I chanced to meet Mr George Alexander, Justice of the Peace. We discussed the new national school. Mr Alexander invited me to take charge of it when it opens. I thanked him and explained that I could do that only if I were free to run it as I have run this hedge-school for the past thirty-five years—filling what our friend Euripides[6] calls the '*aplestos pithos*'—James?

JIMMY 'The cask that cannot be filled'.

HUGH Indeed—and Mr Alexander retorted courteously and emphatically that he hopes that is how it will be run.

[MAIRE *now sits.*]

Indeed. I have had a strenuous day and I am weary of you all. [*He rises.*] Manus will take care of you.

[HUGH *goes towards the steps.*

OWEN *enters.* OWEN *is the younger son, a handsome, attractive young man in his twenties. He is dressed smartly—a city man. His manner is easy and charming: everything he does is invested with consideration and enthusiasm. He now stands framed in the doorway, a travelling bag across his shoulder.*]

OWEN Could anybody tell me is this where Hugh Mor O'Donnell holds his hedge-school?

DOALTY It's Owen—Owen Hugh! Look, boys—it's Owen Hugh!

[OWEN *enters. As he crosses the room he touches and has a word for each person.*]

OWEN Doalty! [*Playful punch.*] How are you, boy? *Jacobe, quid agis?*[7] Are you well?

JIMMY Fine. Fine.

OWEN And Bridget! Give us a kiss. Aaaaaah!

BRIDGET You're welcome, Owen.

---

6. Greek playwright (ca. 484–406 B.C.E.).

7. James, how are you? [Latin; Friel's note].

OWEN   It's not—? Yes, it *is* Maire Chatach! God! A young woman!

MAIRE   How are you, Owen?

[OWEN *is now in front of* HUGH. *He puts his two hands on his father's shoulders.*]

OWEN   And how's the old man himself?

HUGH   Fair—fair.

OWEN   Fair? For God's sake you never looked better! Come here to me. [*He embraces* HUGH *warmly and genuinely.*] Great to see you, Father. Great to be back.

[HUGH's *eyes are moist—partly joy, partly the drink.*]

HUGH   I—I'm—I'm—pay no attention to—

OWEN   Come on—come on—come on—[*He gives* HUGH *his handkerchief.*] Do you know what you and I are going to do tonight? We are going to go up to Anna na mBreag's . . .

DOALTY   Not there, Owen.

OWEN   Why not?

DOALTY   Her poteen's[8] worse than ever.

BRIDGET   They say she puts frogs in it!

OWEN   All the better. [*To* HUGH.] And you and I are going to get footless drunk. That's arranged.

[OWEN *sees* MANUS *coming down the steps with tea and soda bread. They meet at the bottom.*]

And Manus!

MANUS   You're welcome, Owen.

OWEN   I know I am. And it's great to be here. [*He turns round, arms outstretched.*] I can't believe it. I come back after six years and everything's just as it was! Nothing's changed! Not a thing! [*Sniffs.*] Even that smell—that's the same smell this place always had. What is it anyway? Is it the straw?

DOALTY   Jimmy Jack's feet.

[*General laughter. It opens little pockets of conversation round the room.*]

OWEN   And Doalty Dan Doalty hasn't changed either!

DOALTY   Bloody right, Owen.

OWEN   Jimmy, are you well?

JIMMY   Dodging about.

OWEN   Any word of the big day?

[*This is greeted with 'ohs' and 'ahs'.*]

Time enough, Jimmy. Homer's easier to live with, isn't he?

MAIRE   We heard stories that you own ten big shops in Dublin[9]—is it true?

OWEN   Only nine.

BRIDGET   And you've twelve horses and six servants.

OWEN   Yes—that's true. God Almighty, would you listen to them—taking a hand at me!

MANUS   When did you arrive?

OWEN   We left Dublin yesterday morning, spent last night in Omagh and got here half an hour ago.

MANUS   You're hungry then.

HUGH   Indeed—get him food—get him a drink.

---

8. Local whiskey illegally distilled to evade British taxation.

9. Ireland's capital was the site of English military and political power.

OWEN   Not now, thanks; later. Listen—am I interrupting you all?

HUGH   By no means. We're finished for the day.

OWEN   Wonderful. I'll tell you why. Two friends of mine are waiting outside the door. They'd like to meet you and I'd like you to meet them. May I bring them in?

HUGH   Certainly. You'll all eat and have . . .

OWEN   Not just yet, Father. You've seen the sappers working in this area for the past fortnight, haven't you? Well, the older man is Captain Lancey . . .

HUGH   I've met Captain Lancey.

OWEN   Great. He's the cartographer in charge of this whole area. Cartographer—James?

[OWEN *begins to play this game—his father's game—partly to involve his classroom audience, partly to show he has not forgotten it, and indeed partly because he enjoys it.*]

JIMMY   A maker of maps.

OWEN   Indeed—and the younger man that I travelled with from Dublin, his name is Lieutenant Yolland and he is attached to the toponymic department—Father?—*responde—responde!*

HUGH   He gives names to places.

OWEN   Indeed—although he is in fact an orthographer—Doalty?—too slow—Manus?

MANUS   The correct spelling of those names.

OWEN   Indeed—indeed!

[OWEN *laughs and claps his hands. Some of the others join in.*]

Beautiful! Beautiful! Honest to God, it's such a delight to be back here with you all again—'*civilised*' people. Anyhow—may I bring them in?

HUGH   Your friends are our friends.

OWEN   I'll be straight back.

[*There is general talk as* OWEN *goes towards the door. He stops beside* SARAH.]

OWEN   That's a new face. Who are you?

[*A very brief hesitation. Then.*]

SARAH   My name is Sarah.

OWEN   Sarah who?

SARAH   Sarah Johnny Sally.

OWEN   Of course! From Bun na hAbhann! I'm Owen—Owen Hugh Mor. From Baile Beag. Good to see you.

[*During this* OWEN–SARAH *exchange.*]

HUGH   Come on now. Let's tidy this place up. [*He rubs the top of his table with his sleeve.*] Move, Doalty—lift those books off the floor.

DOALTY   Right, Master; certainly, Master; I'm doing my best, Master.

[OWEN *stops at the door.*]

OWEN   One small thing, Father.

HUGH   *Silentium!*

OWEN   I'm on their pay-roll.

[SARAH, *very elated at her success, is beside* MANUS.]

SARAH   I said it, Manus!

[MANUS *ignores* SARAH. *He is much more interested in* OWEN *now.*]

MANUS   You haven't enlisted, have you?!

[SARAH *moves away.*]

OWEN   Me a soldier? I'm employed as a part-time, underpaid, civilian interpreter. My job is to translate the quaint, archaic tongue you people persist in speaking into the King's good English. [*He goes out.*]

HUGH   Move—move—move! Put some order on things! Come on, Sarah— hide that bucket. Whose are these slates? Somebody take these dishes away. *Festinate! Festinate!*[1]

[HUGH *pours another drink.*

MANUS *goes to* MAIRE *who is busy tidying.*]

MANUS   You didn't tell me you were definitely leaving.

MAIRE   Not now.

HUGH   Good girl, Bridget. That's the style.

MANUS   You might at least have told me.

HUGH   Are these your books, James?

JIMMY   Thank you.

MANUS   Fine! Fine! Go ahead! Go ahead!

MAIRE   You talk to me about getting married—with neither a roof over your head nor a sod of ground under your foot. I suggest you go for the new school; but no—'My father's in for that.' Well now he's got it and now this is finished and now you've nothing.

MANUS   I can always . . .

MAIRE   What? Teach classics to the cows? Agh—

[MAIRE *moves away from* MANUS.

OWEN *enters with* LANCEY *and* YOLLAND. CAPTAIN LANCEY *is middle-aged; a small, crisp officer, expert in his field as cartographer but uneasy with people—especially civilians, especially these foreign civilians. His skill is with deeds, not words.*

LIEUTENANT YOLLAND *is in his late twenties/early thirties. He is tall and thin and gangling, blond hair, a shy, awkward manner. A soldier by accident.*]

OWEN   Here we are. Captain Lancey—my father.

LANCEY   Good evening.

[HUGH *becomes expansive, almost courtly with his visitors.*]

HUGH   You and I have already met, sir.

LANCEY   Yes.

OWEN   And Lieutenant Yolland—both Royal Engineers—my father.

HUGH   You're very welcome, gentlemen.

YOLLAND   How do you do.

HUGH   *Gaudeo vos hic adesse.*[2]

OWEN   And I'll make no other introductions except that these are some of the people of Baile Beag and—what?—well you're among the best people in Ireland now. [*He pauses to allow* LANCEY *to speak.* LANCEY *does not.*] Would you like to say a few words, Captain?

HUGH   What about a drop, sir?

LANCEY   A what?

HUGH   Perhaps a modest refreshment? A little sampling of our aqua vitae?[3]

LANCEY   No, no.

HUGH   Later perhaps when . . .

LANCEY   I'll say what I have to say, if I may, and as briefly as possible. Do they speak *any* English, Roland?

---

1. Hurry! [Latin; Friel's note].
2. Welcome! [Latin; Friel's note].

3. "Aqua vitae": spirits; literally, in Latin, water of life.

OWEN   Don't worry. I'll translate.

LANCEY   I see. [*He clears his throat. He speaks as if he were addressing chil-dren—a shade too loudly and enunciating excessively.*] You may have seen me—seen me—working in this section—section?—working. We are here—here—in this place—you understand?—to make a map—a map—a map and—

JIMMY   *Nonne Latine loquitur?*[4]

[HUGH *holds up a restraining hand.*]

HUGH   James.

LANCEY   [*To* JIMMY.]   I do not speak Gaelic, sir. [*He looks at* OWEN.]

OWEN   Carry on.

LANCEY   A map is a representation on paper—a picture—you understand pic-ture?—a paper picture—showing, representing this country—yes?—show-ing your country in miniature—a scaled drawing on paper of—of—of—

[*Suddenly* DOALTY *sniggers. Then* BRIDGET. *Then* SARAH. OWEN *leaps in quickly.*]

OWEN   It might be better if you *assume* they understand you—

LANCEY   Yes?

OWEN   And I'll translate as you go along.

LANCEY   I see. Yes. Very well. Perhaps you're right. Well. What we are doing is this. [*He looks at* OWEN. OWEN *nods reassuringly.*] His Majesty's govern-ment has ordered the first ever comprehensive survey of this entire coun-try—a general triangulation which will embrace detailed hydrographic and topographic information and which will be executed to a scale of six inches to the English mile.

HUGH [*Pouring a drink.*]   Excellent—excellent.

[LANCEY *looks at* OWEN.]

OWEN   A new map is being made of the whole country.

[LANCEY *looks to* OWEN: *Is that all?* OWEN *smiles reassuringly and indi-cates to proceed.*]

LANCEY   This enormous task has been embarked on so that the military authorities will be equipped with up-to-date and accurate information on every corner of this part of the Empire.

OWEN   The job is being done by soldiers because they are skilled in this work.

LANCEY   And also so that the entire basis of land valuation can be reassessed for purposes of more equitable taxation.

OWEN   This new map will take the place of the estate-agent's map so that from now on you will know exactly what is yours in law.

LANCEY   In conclusion I wish to quote two brief extracts from the white paper which is our governing charter: [*Reads.*] 'All former surveys of Ireland orig-inated in forfeiture and violent transfer of property; the present survey has for its object the relief which can be afforded to the proprietors and occu-piers of land from unequal taxation.'

OWEN   The captain hopes that the public will cooperate with the sappers and that the new map will mean that taxes are reduced.

HUGH   A worthy enterprise—*opus honestum!* And Extract B?

LANCEY   'Ireland is privileged. No such survey is being undertaken in England. So this survey cannot but be received as proof of the disposition of this government to advance the interests of Ireland.' My sentiments, too.

---

4. Does he not speak Latin? [Friel's note].

OWEN   This survey demonstrates the government's interest in Ireland and the captain thanks you for listening so attentively to him.

HUGH   Our pleasure, Captain.

LANCEY   Lieutenant Yolland?

YOLLAND   I—I—I've nothing to say—really—

OWEN   The captain is the man who actually makes the new map. George's task is to see that the place-names on this map are . . . correct. [*To* YOLLAND.] Just a few words—they'd like to hear you. [*To class.*] Don't you want to hear George, too?

MAIRE   Has he anything to say?

YOLLAND [*To* MAIRE.]   Sorry—sorry?

OWEN   She says she's dying to hear you.

YOLLAND [*To* MAIRE.]   Very kind of you—thank you . . . [*To class.*] I can only say that I feel—I feel very foolish to—to be working here and not to speak your language. But I intend to rectify that—with Roland's help—indeed I do.

OWEN   He wants me to teach him Irish!

HUGH   You are doubly welcome, sir.

YOLLAND   I think your countryside is—is—is—is very beautiful. I've fallen in love with it already. I hope we're not too—too crude an intrusion on your lives. And I know that I'm going to be happy, very happy, here.

OWEN   He is already a committed Hibernophile⁵—

JIMMY   He loves—

OWEN   Alright, Jimmy—we know—he loves Baile Beag; and he loves you all.

HUGH   Please . . . May I . . . ?

[HUGH *is now drunk. He holds on to the edge of the table.*]

OWEN   Go ahead, Father. [*Hands up for quiet.*] Please—please.

HUGH   And we, gentlemen, we in turn are happy to offer you our friendship, our hospitality, and every assistance that you may require. Gentlemen—welcome!

[*A few desultory⁶ claps. The formalities are over. General conversation. The soldiers meet the locals.*
MANUS *and* OWEN *meet down stage.*]

OWEN   Lancey's a bloody ramrod but George's alright. How are you anyway?

MANUS   What sort of a translation was that, Owen?

OWEN   Did I make a mess of it?

MANUS   You weren't saying what Lancey was saying!

OWEN   'Uncertainty in meaning is incipient poetry'—who said that?

MANUS   There was nothing uncertain about what Lancey said: it's a bloody military operation, Owen! And what's Yolland's function? What's 'incorrect' about the place-names we have here?

OWEN   Nothing at all. They're just going to be standardised.

MANUS   You mean changed into English?

OWEN   Where there's ambiguity, they'll be Anglicised.

MANUS   And they call you Roland! They both call you Roland!

OWEN   Shhhhh. Isn't it ridiculous? They seemed to get it wrong from the very beginning—or else they can't pronounce Owen. I was afraid some of you bastards would laugh.

MANUS   Aren't you going to tell them?

5. Lover of Ireland (in Latin, Hibernia).   6. Scattered.

OWEN   Yes—yes—soon—soon.

MANUS   But they . . .

OWEN   Easy, man, easy. Owen—Roland—what the hell. It's only a name. It's the same me, isn't it? Well, isn't it?

MANUS   Indeed it is. It's the same Owen.

OWEN   And the same Manus. And in a way we complement each other.

[*He punches* MANUS *lightly, playfully and turns to join the others. As he goes.*]

Alright—who has met whom? Isn't this a job for the go-between?

[MANUS *watches* OWEN *move confidently across the floor, taking* MAIRE *by the hand and introducing her to* YOLLAND.

HUGH *is trying to negotiate the steps.*

JIMMY *is lost in a text.*

DOALTY *and* BRIDGET *are reliving their giggling.*

SARAH *is staring at* MANUS.]

Act Two

SCENE ONE

The sappers have already mapped most of the area. YOLLAND'*s official task, which* OWEN *is now doing, is to take each of the Gaelic names—every hill, stream, rock, even every patch of ground which possessed its own distinctive Irish name— and Anglicise it, either by changing it into its approximate English sound or by translating it into English words. For example, a Gaelic name like Cnoc Ban could become Knockban or—directly translated—Fair Hill. These new standardised names were entered into the Name-Book, and when the new maps appeared they contained all these new Anglicised names.* OWEN'*s official function as translator is to pronounce each name in Irish and then provide the English translation.*

The hot weather continues. It is late afternoon some days later.

Stage right: an improvised clothes-line strung between the shafts of the cart and a nail in the wall; on it are some shirts and socks.

A large map—one of the new blank maps—is spread out on the floor. OWEN *is on his hands and knees, consulting it. He is totally engrossed in his task, which he pursues with great energy and efficiency.*

YOLLAND'*s hesitancy has vanished—he is at home here now. He is sitting on the floor, his long legs stretched out before him, his back resting against a creel,[7] his eyes closed. His mind is elsewhere. One of the reference books—a church registry—lies open on his lap.*

Around them are various reference books, the Name-Book, a bottle of poteen, some cups etc.

OWEN *completes an entry in the Name-Book and returns to the map on the floor.*

OWEN   Now. Where have we got to? Yes—the point where that stream enters the sea—that tiny little beach there. George!

YOLLAND   Yes. I'm listening. What do you call it? Say the Irish name again?

OWEN   Bun na hAbhann.

YOLLAND   Again.

OWEN   Bun na hAbhann.

---

7. Large wicker basket.

YOLLAND Bun na hAbhann.
OWEN That's terrible, George.
YOLLAND I know. I'm sorry. Say it again.
OWEN Bun na hAbhann.
YOLLAND Bun na hAbhann.
OWEN That's better. Bun is the Irish word for bottom. And Abha means river.
So it's literally the mouth of the river.
YOLLAND Let's leave it alone. There's no English equivalent for a sound like
that.
OWEN What is it called in the church registry?
[*Only now does* YOLLAND *open his eyes.*]
YOLLAND Let's see . . . Banowen.
OWEN That's wrong. [*Consults text.*] The list of freeholders calls it Owen-
more—that's completely wrong: Owenmore's the big river at the west end
of the parish. [*Another text.*] And in the grand jury lists it's called—God!—
Binhone!—wherever they got that. I suppose we could Anglicize it to Bun-
owen; but somehow that's neither fish nor flesh.
[YOLLAND *closes his eyes again.*]
YOLLAND I give up.
OWEN [*At map.*] Back to first principles. What are we trying to do?
YOLLAND Good question.
OWEN We are trying to denominate and at the same time describe that tiny
area of soggy, rocky, sandy ground where that little stream enters the sea,
an area known locally as Bun na hAbhann . . . Burnfoot![8] What about
Burnfoot?
YOLLAND [*Indifferently.*] Good, Roland. Burnfoot's good.
OWEN George, my name isn't . . .
YOLLAND B-u-r-n-f-o-o-t?
OWEN I suppose so. What do you think?
YOLLAND Yes.
OWEN Are you happy with that?
YOLLAND Yes.
OWEN Burnfoot it is then. [*He makes the entry into the Name-Book.*] Bun na
nAbhann—B-u-r-n-
YOLLAND You're becoming very skilled at this.
OWEN We're not moving fast enough.
YOLLAND [*Opens eyes again.*] Lancey lectured me again last night.
OWEN When does he finish here?
YOLLAND The sappers are pulling out at the end of the week. The trouble is,
the maps they've completed can't be printed without these names. So Lon-
don screams at Lancey and Lancey screams at me. But I wasn't intimidated.
[MANUS *emerges from upstairs and descends.*]
'I'm sorry, sir,' I said, 'But certain tasks demand their own tempo. You cannot
rename a whole country overnight.' Your Irish air has made me bold. [*To*
MANUS.] Do you want us to leave?
MANUS Time enough. Class won't begin for another half-hour.
YOLLAND Sorry—sorry?
OWEN Can't you speak English?
[MANUS *gathers the things off the clothes-line.* OWEN *returns to the map.*]

8. "Burn" is an Ulster-Scots word for river.

OWEN We now come across that beach . . .

YOLLAND Tra—that's the Irish for beach. [*To* MANUS.] I'm picking up the odd word, Manus.

MANUS So.

OWEN . . . on past Burnfoot; and there's nothing around here that has any name that I know of until we come down here to the south end, just about here . . . and there should be a ridge of rocks there . . . Have the sappers marked it? They have. Look, George.

YOLLAND Where are we?

OWEN There.

YOLLAND I'm lost.

OWEN Here. And the name of that ridge is Druim Dubh. Put English on that, Lieutenant.

YOLLAND Say it again.

OWEN Druim Dubh.

YOLLAND Dubh means black.

OWEN Yes.

YOLLAND And Druim means . . . what? a fort?

OWEN We met it yesterday in Druim Luachra.

YOLLAND A ridge! The Black Ridge! [*To* MANUS.] You see, Manus?

OWEN We'll have you fluent at the Irish before the summer's over.

YOLLAND Oh I wish I were. [*To* MANUS *as he crosses to go back upstairs.*] We got a crate of orange from Dublin today. I'll send some up to you.

MANUS Thanks. [*To* OWEN.] Better hide that bottle. Father's just up and he'd be better without it.

OWEN Can't you speak English before your man?

MANUS Why?

OWEN Out of courtesy.

MANUS Doesn't he want to learn Irish? [*To* YOLLAND.] Don't you want to learn Irish?

YOLLAND Sorry—sorry? I—I—

MANUS I understand the Lanceys perfectly but people like you puzzle me.

OWEN Manus, for God's sake!

MANUS [*Still to* YOLLAND.] How's the work going?

YOLLAND The work?—the work? Oh, it's—it's staggering along—I think—[*To* OWEN.]—isn't it? But we'd be lost without Roland.

MANUS [*Leaving.*] I'm sure. But there are always the Rolands, aren't there? [*He goes upstairs and exits.*]

YOLLAND What was that he said?—something about Lancey, was it?

OWEN He said we should hide that bottle before Father gets his hands on it.

YOLLAND Ah.

OWEN He's always trying to protect him.

YOLLAND Was he lame from birth?

OWEN An accident when he was a baby: Father fell across his cradle. That's why Manus feels so responsible for him.

YOLLAND Why doesn't he marry?

OWEN Can't afford to, I suppose.

YOLLAND Hasn't he a salary?

OWEN What salary? All he gets is the odd shilling Father throws him—and that's seldom enough. I got out in time, didn't I?

[YOLLAND *is pouring a drink.*]

Easy with that stuff—it'll hit you suddenly.

YOLLAND I like it.

OWEN Let's get back to the job. Druim Dubh—what's it called in the jury lists? [*Consults texts.*]

YOLLAND Some people here resent us.

OWEN Dramduff—wrong as usual.

YOLLAND I was passing a little girl yesterday and she spat at me.

OWEN And it's Drimdoo here. What's it called in the registry?

YOLLAND Do you know the Donnelly twins?

OWEN Who?

YOLLAND The Donnelly twins.

OWEN Yes. Best fishermen about here. What about them?

YOLLAND Lancey's looking for them.

OWEN What for?

YOLLAND He wants them for questioning.

OWEN Probably stolen somebody's nets. Dramduffy! Nobody ever called it Dramduffy. Take your pick of those three.

YOLLAND My head's addled. Let's take a rest. Do you want a drink?

OWEN Thanks. Now, every Dubh we've come across we've changed to Duff. So if we're to be consistent, I suppose Druim Dubh has to become Dromduff.

[YOLLAND *is now looking out the window.*]

You can see the end of the ridge from where you're standing. But D-r-u-m or D-r-o-m? [*Name-Book.*] Do you remember—which did we agree on for Druim Luachra?

YOLLAND That house immediately above where we're camped—

OWEN Mm?

YOLLAND The house where Maire lives.

OWEN Maire? Oh, Maire Chatach.

YOLLAND What does that mean?

OWEN Curly-haired; the whole family are called the Catachs. What about it?

YOLLAND I hear music coming from that house almost every night.

OWEN Why don't you drop in?

YOLLAND Could I?

OWEN Why not? We used D-r-o-m then. So we've got to call it D-r-o-m-d-u-f-f—alright?

YOLLAND Go back up to where the new school is being built and just say the names again for me, would you?

OWEN That's a good idea. Poolkerry, Ballybeg—

YOLLAND No, no; as they still are—in your own language.

OWEN Poll na gCaorach,

[YOLLAND *repeats the names silently after him.*]

Baile Beag, Ceann Balor, Lis Maol, Machaire Buidhe, Baile na gGall, Carraig na Ri, Mullach Dearg—

YOLLAND Do you think I could live here?

OWEN What are you talking about?

YOLLAND Settle down here—live here.

OWEN Come on, George.

YOLLAND I mean it.

OWEN Live on what? Potatoes? Buttermilk?

YOLLAND It's really heavenly.

OWEN   For God's sake! The first hot summer in fifty years and you think it's Eden. Don't be such a bloody romantic. You wouldn't survive a mild winter here.

YOLLAND   Do you think not? Maybe you're right.

[DOALTY *enters in a rush.*]

DOALTY   Hi, boys, is Manus about?

OWEN   He's upstairs. Give him a shout.

DOALTY   Manus!

The cattle's going mad in that heat—Cripes, running wild all over the place.

[*To* YOLLAND.] How are you doing, skipper?

[MANUS *appears.*]

YOLLAND   Thank you for—I—I'm very grateful to you for—

DOALTY   Wasting your time. I don't know a word you're saying. Hi, Manus, there's two bucks down the road there asking for you.

MANUS [*Descending.*]   Who are they?

DOALTY   Never clapped eyes on them. They want to talk to you.

MANUS   What about?

DOALTY   They wouldn't say. Come on. The bloody beasts'll end up in Loch an Iubhair if they're not capped.[9] Good luck, boys!

[DOALTY *rushes off.* MANUS *follows him.*]

OWEN   Good luck! What were you thanking Doalty for?

YOLLAND   I was washing outside my tent this morning and he was passing with a scythe across his shoulder and he came up to me and pointed to the long grass and then cut a pathway round my tent and from the tent down to the road—so that my feet won't get wet with the dew. Wasn't that kind of him? And I have no words to thank him . . .

I suppose you're right: I suppose I couldn't live here . . .

Just before Doalty came up to me this morning, I was thinking that at that moment I might have been in Bombay instead of Ballybeg. You see, my father was at his wits end with me and finally he got me a job with the East India Company[1]—some kind of a clerkship. This was ten, eleven months ago. So I set off for London. Unfortunately I—I—I missed the boat. Literally. And since I couldn't face Father and hadn't enough money to hang about until the next sailing, I joined the Army. And they stuck me into the Engineers and posted me to Dublin. And Dublin sent me here. And while I was washing this morning and looking across the Tra Bhan, I was thinking how very, very lucky I am to be here and not in Bombay.

OWEN   Do you believe in fate?

YOLLAND   Lancey's so like my father. I was watching him last night. He met every group of sappers as they reported in. He checked the field kitchens. He examined the horses. He inspected every single report—even examining the texture of the paper and commenting on the neatness of the handwriting. The perfect colonial servant: not only must the job be done—it must be done with excellence. Father has that drive, too; that dedication; that indefatigable energy. He builds roads—hopping from one end of the Empire to the other. Can't sit still for five minutes. He says himself the longest time

9. Surpassed.
1. English trade company in India, South Asia, and Southeast Asia, chartered in 1600 and central   to 18th- and 19th-century British imperialism in the region.

he ever sat still was the night before Waterloo when they were waiting for
Wellington to make up his mind to attack.[2]

OWEN   What age is he?

YOLLAND   Born in 1789—the very day the Bastille fell.[3] I've often thought
maybe that gave his whole life its character. Do you think it could? He
inherited a new world the day he was born—the Year One. Ancient time
was at an end. The world had cast off its old skin. There were no longer any
frontiers to man's potential. Possibilities were endless and exciting. He still
believes that. The Apocalypse is just about to happen . . . I'm afraid I'm a
great disappointment to him. I've neither his energy, nor his coherence, nor
his belief. Do I believe in fate? The day I arrived in Ballybeg,—no, Baile
Beag—the moment you brought me in here, I had a curious sensation. It's
difficult to describe. It was a momentary sense of discovery; no—not quite
a sense of discovery—a sense of recognition, of confirmation of something
I half knew instinctively as if I had stepped . . .

OWEN   Back into ancient time?

YOLLAND   No, no. It wasn't an awareness of *direction* being changed but of
experience being of a totally different order. I had moved into a consciousness that wasn't striving nor agitated, but at its ease and with its own conviction and assurance. And when I heard Jimmy Jack and your father
swopping stories about Apollo and Cuchulain and Paris and Ferdia[4]—as if
they lived down the road—it was then that I thought—I knew—perhaps I
could live here . . . [*Now embarrassed.*] Where's the pot-een?

OWEN   Poteen.

YOLLAND   Poteen—poteen—poteen. Even if I did speak Irish I'd always be an
outsider here, wouldn't I? I may learn the password but the language of the
tribe will always elude me, won't it? The private will always be . . . hermetic,[5]
won't it?

OWEN   You can learn to decode us.

[HUGH *emerges from upstairs and descends. He is dressed for the road.
Today he is physically and mentally jaunty and alert—almost self-
consciously jaunty and alert. Indeed, as the scene progresses, one has
the sense that he is deliberately parodying himself.*

The moment HUGH *gets to the bottom of the steps* YOLLAND *leaps
respectfully to his feet.*]

HUGH   [*As he descends.*]

   *Quantumvis cursum longum fessumque moratur
   Sol, sacro tandem carmine vesper adest.*

I dabble in verse, Lieutenant, after the style of Ovid.[6]
[*To* OWEN.] A drop of that to fortify me.

YOLLAND   You'll have to translate it for me.

HUGH   Let's see—

   No matter how long the sun may linger on his long and weary journey
   At length evening comes with its sacred song.

---

2. Dublin-born Arthur Wellesley (1769–1852),
duke of Wellington, vanquished the French
emperor Napoleon's army on June 18, 1815, in
Waterloo, Belgium.
3. The French Revolution began on July 14, 1789,
with the storming of the Bastille (a jail in Paris).
The French monarchy was later overthrown and
replaced by the First Republic.
4. Mythical Irish warrior, slain by his foster

brother, Cuchulainn, the greatest hero of the
medieval Ulster Cycle, an extensive series of stories
focused on the warriors of King Conchobar's court
in Northern Ireland. "Apollo": Greek god of arts,
music, and prophecy, who helped the Trojan
prince Paris kill the greatest Greek hero, Achilles,
in the Trojan War.
5. Secret, hidden.
6. Roman poet (43 B.C.E.–17? C.E.).

YOLLAND   Very nice, sir.
HUGH   English succeeds in making it sound . . . plebeian.[7]
OWEN   Where are you off to, Father?
HUGH   An *expeditio*[8] with three purposes. Purpose A: to acquire a testimonial from our parish priest—[*To* YOLLAND.] a worthy man but barely literate; and since he'll ask me to write it myself, how in all modesty can I do myself justice?
      [*To* OWEN.] Where did this [*Drink.*] come from?
OWEN   Anna na mBreag's.
HUGH [*To* YOLLAND.]   In that case address yourself to it with circumspection.
      [*And* HUGH *instantly tosses the drink back in one gulp and grimaces.*]
Aaaaaaagh!
      [*Holds out his glass for a refill.*]
Anna na mBreag means Anna of the Lies. And Purpose B: to talk to the builders of the new school about the kind of living accommodation I will require there. I have lived too long like a journeyman[9] tailor.
YOLLAND   Some years ago we lived fairly close to a poet—well, about three miles away.
HUGH   His name?
YOLLAND   Wordsworth—William Wordsworth.[1]
HUGH   Did he speak of me to you?
YOLLAND   Actually I never talked to him. I just saw him out walking—in the distance.
HUGH   Wordsworth? . . . no. I'm afraid we're not familiar with your literature, Lieutenant. We feel closer to the warm Mediterranean.[2] We tend to over-look your island.
YOLLAND   I'm learning to speak Irish, sir.
HUGH   Good.
YOLLAND   Roland's teaching me.
HUGH   Splendid.
YOLLAND   I mean—I feel so cut off from the people here. And I was trying to explain a few minutes ago how remarkable a community this is. To meet people like yourself and Jimmy Jack who actually converse in Greek and Latin. And your place-names—what was the one we came across this morn-ing?—Termon, from Terminus, the god of boundaries.[3] It—it—it's really astonishing.
HUGH   We like to think we endure around truths immemorially posited.
YOLLAND   And your Gaelic literature—you're a poet yourself—
HUGH   Only in Latin, I'm afraid.
YOLLAND   I understand it's enormously rich and ornate.
HUGH   Indeed, Lieutenant. A rich language. A rich literature. You'll find, sir, that certain cultures expend on their vocabularies and syntax acquisitive energies and ostentations entirely lacking in their material lives. I suppose you could call us a spiritual people.
OWEN [*Not unkindly; more out of embarrassment before* YOLLAND.]   Will you stop that nonsense, Father.
HUGH   Nonsense? What nonsense?

---

7. Of the common people.
8. Expedition [Latin; Friel's note].
9. Hireling, subservient.
1. Romantic poet (1770–1850), who composed

poetry while walking through England's Lake Dis-trict.
2. I.e., Greek and Latin literature.
3. In Roman mythology.

OWEN   Do you know where the priest lives?

HUGH   At Lis na Muc, over near . . .

OWEN   No, he doesn't. Lis na Muc, the Fort of the Pigs, has become Swine-fort. [*Now turning the pages of the Name-Book—a page per name.*] And to get to Swinefort you pass through Greencastle and Fair Head and Strandhill and Gort and Whiteplains. And the new school isn't at Poll na gCaorach—it's at Sheepsrock. Will you be able to find your way?

[HUGH *pours himself another drink. Then.*]

HUGH   Yes, it is a rich language, Lieutenant, full of the mythologies of fantasy and hope and self-deception—a syntax opulent with tomorrows. It is our response to mud cabins and a diet of potatoes; our only method of replying to . . . inevitabilities.

[*To* OWEN.] Can you give me the loan of half-a-crown? I'll repay you out of the subscriptions I'm collecting for the publication of my new book. [*To* YOLLAND.] It is entitled: 'The Pentaglot Preceptor[4] or Elementary Institute of the English, Greek, Hebrew, Latin and Irish Languages; Particularly Cal-culated for the Instruction of Such Ladies and Gentlemen as may Wish to Learn without the Help of a Master'.

YOLLAND [*Laughs.*]   That's a wonderful title!

HUGH   Between ourselves—the best part of the enterprise. Nor do I, in fact, speak Hebrew. And that last phrase—'without the Help of a Master'—that was written before the new national school was thrust upon me—do you think I ought to drop it now? After all you don't dispose of the cow just because it has produced a magnificent calf, do you?

YOLLAND   You certainly do not.

HUGH   The phrase goes. And I'm interrupting work of moment. [*He goes to the door and stops there.*]

To return briefly to that other matter, Lieutenant. I understand your sense of exclusion, of being cut off from a life here; and I trust you will find access to us with my son's help. But remember that words are signals, counters. They are not immortal. And it can happen—to use an image you'll under-stand—it can happen that a civilisation can be imprisoned in a linguistic contour which no longer matches the landscape of . . . fact.

Gentlemen. [*He leaves.*]

OWEN   'An *expeditio* with three purposes': the children laugh at him: he always promises three points and he never gets beyond A and B.

YOLLAND   He's an astute man.

OWEN   He's bloody pompous.

YOLLAND   But so astute.

OWEN   And he drinks too much. Is it astute not to be able to adjust for sur-vival? Enduring around truths immemorially posited—hah!

YOLLAND   He knows what's happening.

OWEN   What is happening?

YOLLAND   I'm not sure. But I'm concerned about my part in it. It's an eviction of sorts.

OWEN   We're making a six-inch map of the country. Is there something sin-ister in that?

YOLLAND   Not in . . .

OWEN   And we're taking place-names that are riddled with confusion and . . .

4. I.e., the five-tongued head teacher.

YOLLAND   Who's confused? Are the people confused?

OWEN   . . . and we're standardising those names as accurately and as sensitively as we can.

YOLLAND   Something is being eroded.

OWEN   Back to the romance again. Alright! Fine! Fine! Look where we've got to. [*He drops on his hands and knees and stabs a finger at the map.*] We've come to this crossroads. Come here and look at it, man! Look at it! And we call that crossroads Tobair Vree. And why do we call it Tobair Vree? I'll tell you why. Tobair means a well. But what does Vree mean? It's a corruption of Brian—[*Gaelic pronunciation.*] Brian—an erosion of Tobair Bhriain. Because a hundred-and-fifty years ago there used to be a well there, not at the crossroads, mind you—that would be too simple—but in a field close to the crossroads. And an old man called Brian, whose face was disfigured by an enormous growth, got it into his head that the water in that well was blessed; and every day for seven months he went there and bathed his face in it. But the growth didn't go away; and one morning Brian was found drowned in that well. And ever since that crossroads is known as Tobair Vree—even though that well has long since dried up. I know the story because my grandfather told it to me. But ask Doalty—or Maire—or Bridget—even my father—even Manus—why it's called Tobair Vree; and do you think they'll know? I know they don't know. So the question I put to you, Lieutenant, is this: What do we do with a name like that? Do we scrap Tobair Vree altogether and call it—what?—The Cross? Crossroads? Or do we keep piety with a man long dead, long forgotten, his name 'eroded' beyond recognition, whose trivial little story nobody in the parish remembers?

YOLLAND   Except you.

OWEN   I've left here.

YOLLAND   You remember it.

OWEN   I'm asking you: what do we write in the Name-Book?

YOLLAND   Tobair Vree.

OWEN   Even though the well is a hundred yards from the actual crossroads—and there's no well anyway—and what the hell does Vree mean?

YOLLAND   Tobair Vree.

OWEN   That's what you want?

YOLLAND   Yes.

OWEN   You're certain?

YOLLAND   Yes.

OWEN   Fine. Fine. That's what you'll get.

YOLLAND   That's what you want, too, Roland.
        [*Pause.*]

OWEN [*Explodes.*]   George! For God's sake! *My name is not Roland!*

YOLLAND   What?

OWEN [*Softly.*]   My name is Owen.
        [*Pause.*]

YOLLAND   Not Roland?

OWEN   Owen.

YOLLAND   You mean to say—?

OWEN   Owen.

YOLLAND   But I've been—

OWEN   O-w-e-n.

YOLLAND Where did Roland come from?
OWEN I don't know.
YOLLAND It was never Roland?
OWEN Never.
YOLLAND O my God!
[*Pause. They stare at one another. Then the absurdity of the situation strikes them suddenly. They explode with laughter.* OWEN *pours drinks. As they roll about their lines overlap.*]
YOLLAND Why didn't you tell me?
OWEN Do I look like a Roland?
YOLLAND Spell Owen again.
OWEN I was getting fond of Roland.
YOLLAND O my God!
OWEN O-w-e-n.
YOLLAND What'll we write—
OWEN —in the Name-Book?!
YOLLAND R-o-w-e-n!
OWEN Or what about Ol-
YOLLAND Ol- what?
OWEN Oland!
[*And again they explode.*
MANUS *enters. He is very elated.*]
MANUS What's the celebration?
OWEN A christening!
YOLLAND A baptism!
OWEN A hundred christenings!
YOLLAND A thousand baptisms! Welcome to Eden!
OWEN Eden's right! We name a thing and—bang!—it leaps into existence![5]
YOLLAND Each name a perfect equation with its roots.
OWEN A perfect congruence with its reality.
[*To* MANUS.] Take a drink.
YOLLAND Poteen—beautiful.
OWEN Lying Anna's poteen.
YOLLAND Anna na mBreag's poteen.
OWEN Excellent, George.
YOLLAND I'll decode you yet.
OWEN [*Offers drink.*] Manus?
MANUS Not if that's what it does to you.
OWEN You're right. Steady—steady—sober up—sober up.
YOLLAND Sober as a judge, Owen.
[MANUS *moves beside* OWEN.]
MANUS I've got good news! Where's Father?
OWEN He's gone out. What's the good news?
MANUS I've been offered a job.
OWEN Where? [*Now aware of* YOLLAND.] Come on, man—speak in English.
MANUS For the benefit of the colonist?
OWEN He's a decent man.
MANUS Aren't they all at some level?
OWEN Please.

5. Cf. Adam's naming of every creature (Genesis 2.19–20).

[MANUS *shrugs.*]
He's been offered a job.
YOLLAND   Where?
OWEN   Well—tell us!
MANUS   I've just had a meeting with two men from Inis Meadhon.[6] They want me to go there and start a hedge-school. They're giving me a free house, free turf, and free milk; a rood[7] of standing corn; twelve drills[8] of potatoes; and— [*He stops.*]
OWEN   And what?
MANUS   A salary of £42 a year!
OWEN   Manus, that's wonderful!
MANUS   You're talking to a man of substance.
OWEN   I'm delighted.
YOLLAND   Where's Inis Meadhon?
OWEN   An island south of here. And they came looking for you?
MANUS   Well, I mean to say . . .
    [OWEN *punches* MANUS.]
OWEN   Aaaaagh! This calls for a real celebration.
YOLLAND   Congratulations.
MANUS   Thank you.
OWEN   Where are you, Anna?
YOLLAND   When do you start?
MANUS   Next Monday.
OWEN   We'll stay with you when we're there.
    [*To* YOLLAND.] How long will it be before we reach Inis Meadhon?
YOLLAND   How far south is it?
MANUS   About fifty miles.
YOLLAND   Could we make it by December?
OWEN   We'll have Christmas together. [*Sings.*] 'Christmas Day on Inis Meadhon . . .'
YOLLAND [*Toast.*]   I hope you're very content there, Manus.
MANUS   Thank you.
    [YOLLAND *holds out his hand.* MANUS *takes it. They shake warmly.*]
OWEN [*Toast.*]   Manus.
MANUS [*Toast.*]   To Inis Meadhon. [*He drinks quickly and turns to leave.*]
OWEN   Hold on—hold on—refills coming up.
MANUS   I've got to go.
OWEN   Come on, man; this is an occasion. Where are you rushing to?
MANUS   I've got to tell Maire.
    [MAIRE *enters with her can of milk.*]
MAIRE   You've got to tell Maire what?
OWEN   He's got a job!
MAIRE   Manus?
OWEN   He's been invited to start a hedge-school in Inis Meadhon.
MAIRE   Where?
MANUS   Inis Meadhon—the island! They're giving me £42 a year and . . .
OWEN   A house, fuel, milk, potatoes, corn, pupils, what-not!

---

6. Middle Island; one of the three Aran Islands, off the west coast of Ireland, south of Donegal.
7. A cubic measure.
8. Rows.

MANUS I start on Monday.

OWEN You'll take a drink. Isn't it great?

MANUS I want to talk to you for . . .

MAIRE There's your milk. I need the can back.

[MANUS *takes the can and runs up the steps.*]

MANUS [*As he goes.*] How will you like living on an island?

OWEN You know George, don't you?

MAIRE We wave to each other across the fields.

YOLLAND Sorry-sorry?

OWEN She says you wave to each other across the fields.

YOLLAND Yes, we do; oh yes, indeed we do.

MAIRE What's he saying?

OWEN He says you wave to each other across the fields.

MAIRE That's right. So we do.

YOLLAND What's she saying?

OWEN Nothing—nothing—nothing.

[*To* MAIRE.] What's the news?

[MAIRE *moves away, touching the text books with her toe.*]

MAIRE Not a thing. You're busy, the two of you.

OWEN We think we are.

MAIRE I hear the Fiddler O'Shea's about. There's some talk of a dance tomorrow night.

OWEN Where will it be?

MAIRE Maybe over the road. Maybe at Tobair Vree.

YOLLAND Tobair Vree!

MAIRE Yes.

YOLLAND Tobair Vree! Tobair Vree!

MAIRE Does he know what I'm saying?

OWEN Not a word.

MAIRE Tell him then.

OWEN Tell him what?

MAIRE About the dance.

OWEN Maire says there may be a dance tomorrow night.

YOLLAND [*To* OWEN.] Yes? May I come?

[*To* MAIRE.] Would anybody object if I came?

MAIRE [*To* OWEN.] What's he saying?

OWEN [*To* YOLLAND.] Who would object?

MAIRE [*To* OWEN.] Did you tell him?

YOLLAND [*To* MAIRE.] Sorry-sorry?

OWEN [*To* MAIRE.] He says may he come?

MAIRE [*To* YOLLAND.] That's up to you.

YOLLAND [*To* OWEN.] What does she say?

OWEN [*To* YOLLAND.] She says—

YOLLAND [*To* MAIRE.] What-what?

MAIRE [*To* OWEN.] Well?

YOLLAND [*To* OWEN.] Sorry-sorry?

OWEN [*To* YOLLAND.] Will you go?

YOLLAND [*To* MAIRE.] Yes, yes, if I may.

MAIRE [*To* OWEN.] What does he say?

YOLLAND [*To* OWEN.] What is she saying?

OWEN   O for God's sake!
    [*To* MANUS *who is descending with the empty can.*] You take on this job, Manus.
MANUS   I'll walk you up to the house. Is your mother at home? I want to talk to her.
MAIRE   What's the rush? [*To* OWEN.] Didn't you offer me a drink?
OWEN   Will you risk Anna na mBreag?
MAIRE   Why not.
    [YOLLAND *is suddenly intoxicated. He leaps up on a stool, raises his glass and shouts.*]
YOLLAND   Anna na mBreag! Baile Beag! Inis Meadhon! Bombay! Tobair Vree! Eden! And poteen—correct, Owen?
OWEN   Perfect.
YOLLAND   And bloody marvellous stuff it is, too. I love it! Bloody, bloody, bloody marvellous!
    [*Simultaneously with his final 'bloody marvellous' bring up very loud the introductory music of the reel. Then immediately go to black. Retain the music throughout the very brief interval.*]

SCENE TWO

The following night.
This scene may be played in the schoolroom, but it would be preferable to lose—by lighting—as much of the schoolroom as possible, and to play the scene down front in a vaguely 'outside' area.
The music rises to a crescendo. Then in the distance we hear MAIRE *and* YOLLAND *approach—laughing and running. They run on, hand-in-hand. They have just left the dance.*
Fade the music to distant background. Then after a time it is lost and replaced by guitar music.
    MAIRE *and* YOLLAND *are now down front, still holding hands and excited by their sudden and impetuous escape from the dance.*

MAIRE   O my God, that leap across the ditch nearly killed me.
YOLLAND   I could scarcely keep up with you.
MAIRE   Wait till I get my breath back.
YOLLAND   We must have looked as if we were being chased.
    [*They now realise they are alone and holding hands—the beginnings of embarrassment. The hands disengage. They begin to drift apart. Pause.*]
MAIRE   Manus'll wonder where I've got to.
YOLLAND   I wonder did anyone notice us leave.
    [*Pause. Slightly further apart.*]
MAIRE   The grass must be wet. My feet are soaking.
YOLLAND   Your feet must be wet. The grass is soaking.
    [*Another pause. Another few paces apart. They are now a long distance from one another.*]
YOLLAND   [*Indicating himself.*]   George.
    [MAIRE *nods:* Yes—yes. *Then.*]
MAIRE   Lieutenant George.
YOLLAND   Don't call me that. I never think of myself as Lieutenant.
MAIRE   What-what?
YOLLAND   Sorry-sorry? [*He points to himself again.*] George.

[MAIRE *nods: Yes-yes. Then points to herself.*]
MAIRE Maire.
YOLLAND Yes, I know you're Maire. Of course I know you're Maire. I mean
I've been watching you night and day for the past . . .
MAIRE [*Eagerly.*] What-what?
YOLLAND [*Points.*] Maire. [*Points.*] George. [*Points both.*] Maire and George.
[MAIRE *nods: Yes-yes-yes.*]
I—I—I—
MAIRE Say anything at all. I love the sound of your speech.
YOLLAND [*Eagerly.*] Sorry-sorry?
[*In acute frustration he looks around, hoping for some inspiration that
will provide him with communicative means. Now he has a thought: he
tries raising his voice and articulating in a staccato style and with equal
and absurd emphasis on each word.*]
Every-morning-I-see-you-feeding-brown-hens-and-giving-meal-to-black-
calf—[*The futility of it.*]—O my God.
[MAIRE *smiles. She moves towards him. She will try to communicate in
Latin.*]
MAIRE *Tu es centurio in—in—in exercitu Britannico—*[9]
YOLLAND Yes-yes? Go on—go on—say anything at all—I love the sound of
your speech.
MAIRE *—et es in castris quae—quae—quae sunt in agro*[1]—[*The futility of
it.*]—O my God.
[YOLLAND *smiles. He moves towards her.*
Now for her English words.] George—water.
YOLLAND 'Water'? Water! Oh yes—water—water—very good—water—good—
good.
MAIRE Fire.
YOLLAND Fire—indeed—wonderful—fire, fire, fire—splendid—splendid!
MAIRE Ah . . . ah . . .
YOLLAND Yes? Go on.
MAIRE Earth.
YOLLAND 'Earth'?
MAIRE Earth. Earth.
[YOLLAND *still does not understand.*
MAIRE *stoops down and picks up a handful of clay. Holding it out.*]
Earth.
YOLLAND Earth! Of course—earth! Earth. Earth. Good Lord, Maire, your
English is perfect!
MAIRE [*Eagerly.*] What-what?
YOLLAND Perfect English. English perfect.
MAIRE George—
YOLLAND That's beautiful—oh that's really beautiful.
MAIRE George—
YOLLAND Say it again—say it again—
MAIRE Shhh. [*She holds her hand up for silence—she is trying to remember
her one line of English. Now she remembers it and she delivers the line as if*

9. You are a centurion in the British Army [Latin;
Friel's note]. "Centurion": an officer in command
of a hundred soldiers.

1. And you are in the camp in the field [Latin;
Friel's note].

English were her language—easily, fluidly, conversationally.] George, in Norfolk we besport ourselves around the maypoll.

YOLLAND   Good God, do you? That's where my mother comes from—Norfolk. Norwich actually. Not exactly Norwich town but a small village called Little Walsingham close beside it. But in our own village of Winfarthing we have a maypole too and every year on the first of May— [*He stops abruptly, only now realising. He stares at her. She in turn misunderstands his excitement.*]

MAIRE   [*To herself.*]   Mother of God, my Aunt Mary wouldn't have taught me something dirty, would she?

[*Pause.*

YOLLAND *extends his hand to* MAIRE. *She turns away from him and moves slowly across the stage.*]

YOLLAND   Maire.

[*She still moves away.*]

YOLLAND   Maire Chatach.

[*She still moves away.*]

YOLLAND   Bun na hAbhann?[2] [*He says the name softly, almost privately, very tentatively, as if he were searching for a sound she might respond to. He tries again.*] Druim Dubh?[3]

[MAIRE *stops. She is listening.* YOLLAND *is encouraged.*]

Poll na gCaorach. Lis Maol.[4]

[MAIRE *turns towards him.*]

Lis na nGall.[5]

MAIRE   Lis na nGradh.[6]

[*They are now facing each other and begin moving—almost imperceptibly—towards one another.*]

MAIRE   Carraig an Phoill.[7]

YOLLAND   Carraig na Ri. Loch na nEan.[8]

MAIRE   Loch an Iubhair. Machaire Buidhe.[9]

YOLLAND   Machaire Mor. Cnoc na Mona.[1]

MAIRE   Cnoc na nGabhar.[2]

YOLLAND   Mullach.[3]

MAIRE   Port.[4]

YOLLAND   Tor.[5]

MAIRE   Lag.[6] [*She holds out her hands to* YOLLAND. *He takes them. Each now speaks almost to himself/herself.*]

YOLLAND   I wish to God you could understand me.

MAIRE   Soft hands; a gentleman's hands.

YOLLAND   Because if you could understand me I could tell you how I spend my days either thinking of you or gazing up at your house in the hope that you'll appear even for a second.

MAIRE   Every evening you walk by yourself along the Tra Bhan and every morning you wash yourself in front of your tent.

YOLLAND   I would tell you how beautiful you are, curly-headed Maire. I would so like to tell you how beautiful you are.

2. Mouth of the River?
3. Black Ridge?
4. Pit of the Sheep. Bald Fairy Fort.
5. Fairy Fort of the Foreigner.
6. Fairy Fort of Love.
7. Rock of the Hole.
8. Rock of the King. Lake of the Bird.

9. Lake of the Yew Tree. The Great Plain.
1. The Big Plain. Hill of the Nobles.
2. Hill of the Goat.
3. Summit.
4. Port (i.e., same meaning in Gaelic and English).
5. Bush or heavy.
6. Weak.

MAIRE Your arms are long and thin and the skin on your shoulders is very white.

YOLLAND I would tell you . . .

MAIRE Don't stop—I know what you're saying.

YOLLAND I would tell you how I want to be here—to live here—always—with you—always, always.

MAIRE 'Always'? What is that word—'always'?

YOLLAND Yes-yes; always.

MAIRE You're trembling.

YOLLAND Yes, I'm trembling because of you.

MAIRE I'm trembling, too. [*She holds his face in her hand.*]

YOLLAND I've made up my mind . . .

MAIRE Shhhh.

YOLLAND I'm not going to leave here . . .

MAIRE Shhh—listen to me. I want you, too, soldier.

YOLLAND Don't stop—I know what you're saying.

MAIRE I want to live with you—anywhere—anywhere at all—always—always.

YOLLAND 'Always'? What is that word—'always'?

MAIRE Take me away with you, George.
[*Pause.*
Suddenly they kiss.
SARAH *enters. She sees them. She stands shocked, staring at them. Her mouth works. Then almost to herself.*]

SARAH Manus . . . Manus!
[SARAH *runs off.*
Music to crescendo.]

Act Three

The following evening. It is raining.
SARAH *and* OWEN *alone in the schoolroom.* SARAH, *more waiflike than ever, is sitting very still on a stool, an open book across her knee. She is pretending to read but her eyes keep going up to the room upstairs.* OWEN *is working on the floor as before, surrounded by his reference books, map, Name-Book etc. But he has neither concentration nor interest; and like* SARAH *he glances up at the upstairs room.*
After a few seconds MANUS *emerges and descends, carrying a large paper bag which already contains his clothes. His movements are determined and urgent. He moves around the classroom, picking up books, examining each title carefully, and choosing about six of them which he puts into his bag. As he selects these books.*

OWEN You know that old limekiln[7] beyond Con Connie Tim's pub, the place we call The Murren?—do you know why it's called The Murren?
[MANUS *does not answer.*]
I've only just discovered: it's a corruption of Saint Muranus. It seems Saint Muranus had a monastery somewhere about there at the beginning of the seventh century. And over the years the name became shortened to The Murren. Very unattractive name, isn't it? I think we should go back to the

---

7. Furnace for making lime out of shells or limestone.

original—Saint Muranus. What do you think? The original's Saint Muranus. Don't you think we should go back to that?

[*No response.* OWEN *begins writing the name into the Name-Book.* MANUS *is now rooting about among the forgotten implements for a piece of rope. He finds a piece. He begins to tie the mouth of the flimsy, overloaded bag—and it bursts, the contents spilling out on the floor.*]

MANUS   Bloody, bloody, bloody hell!

[*His voice breaks in exasperation: he is about to cry.*
OWEN *leaps to his feet.*]

OWEN   Hold on. I've a bag upstairs.

[*He runs upstairs.* SARAH *waits until* OWEN *is off. Then.*]

SARAH   Manus . . . Manus, I . . .

[MANUS *hears* SARAH *but makes no acknowledgement. He gathers up his belongings.*
OWEN *reappears with the bag he had on his arrival.*]

OWEN   Take this one—I'm finished with it anyway. And it's supposed to keep out the rain.

[MANUS *transfers his few belongings.* OWEN *drifts back to his task. The packing is now complete.*]

MANUS   You'll be here for a while? For a week or two anyhow?

OWEN   Yes.

MANUS   You're not leaving with the army?

OWEN   I haven't made up my mind. Why?

MANUS   Those Inis Meadhon men will be back to see why I haven't turned up. Tell them—tell them I'll write to them as soon as I can. Tell them I still want the job but that it might be three or four months before I'm free to go.

OWEN   You're being damned stupid, Manus.

MANUS   Will you do that for me?

OWEN   Clear out now and Lancey'll think you're involved somehow.

MANUS   Will you do that for me?

OWEN   Wait a couple of days even. You know George—he's a bloody romantic—maybe he's gone out to one of the islands and he'll suddenly reappear tomorrow morning. Or maybe the search party'll find him this evening lying drunk somewhere in the sandhills. You've seen him drinking that poteen—doesn't know how to handle it. Had he drink on him last night at the dance?

MANUS   I had a stone in my hand when I went out looking for him—I was going to fell him. The lame scholar turned violent.

OWEN   Did anybody see you?

MANUS   [*Again close to tears.*]   But when I saw him standing there at the side of the road—smiling—and her face buried in his shoulder—I couldn't even go close to them. I just shouted something stupid—something like, 'You're a bastard, Yolland.' If I'd even said it in English . . . 'cos he kept saying 'Sorry-sorry?' The wrong gesture in the wrong language.

OWEN   And you didn't see him again?

MANUS   'Sorry?'

OWEN   Before you leave tell Lancey that—just to clear yourself.

MANUS   What have I to say to Lancey? You'll give that message to the island-men?

OWEN   I'm warning you: run away now and you're bound to be . . .

MANUS   [*To* SARAH.]   Will you give that message to the Inis Meadhon men?

SARAH   I will.

[MANUS *picks up an old sack and throws it across his shoulders.*]
OWEN   Have you any idea where you're going?
MANUS   Mayo, maybe. I remember Mother saying she had cousins somewhere
away out in the Erris Peninsula.[8] [*He picks up his bag.*] Tell father I took
only the Virgil and the Caesar and the Aeschylus[9] because they're mine
anyway—I bought them with the money I get for that pet lamb I reared—
do you remember that pet lamb? And tell him that Nora Dan never returned
the dictionary and that she still owes him two-and-six[1] for last quarter's
reading—he always forgets those things.
OWEN   Yes.
MANUS   And his good shirt's ironed and hanging up in the press and his clean
socks are in the butter-box under the bed.
OWEN   Alright.
MANUS   And tell him I'll write.
OWEN   If Maire asks where you've gone . . . ?
MANUS   He'll need only half the amount of milk now, won't he? Even less
than half—he usually takes his tea black. [*Pause.*] And when he comes in
at night—you'll hear him; he makes a lot of noise—I usually come down
and give him a hand up. Those stairs are dangerous without a banister.
Maybe before you leave you'd get Big Ned Frank to put up some sort of a
handrail. [*Pause.*] And if you can bake, he's very fond of soda bread.
OWEN   I can give you money. I'm wealthy. Do you know what they pay me?
Two shillings a day for this—this—this—
         [MANUS *rejects the offer by holding out his hand.*]
Goodbye, Manus.
         [MANUS *and* OWEN *shake hands.*]
         Then MANUS *picks up his bag briskly and goes towards the door. He*
         stops a few paces beyond SARAH, *turns, comes back to her. He addresses*
         her as he did in Act One but now without warmth or concern for her.]
MANUS   What is your name? [*Pause.*] Come on. What is your name?
SARAH   My name is Sarah.
MANUS   Just Sarah? Sarah what? [*Pause.*] Well?
SARAH   Sarah Johnny Sally.
MANUS   And where do you live? Come on.
SARAH   I live in Bun na hAbhann. [*She is now crying quietly.*]
MANUS   Very good, Sarah Johnny Sally. There's nothing to stop you now—
nothing in the wide world. [*Pause. He looks down at her.*] It's alright—it's
alright—you did no harm—you did no harm at all. [*He stoops over her and*
kisses the top of her head—as if in absolution. Then briskly to the door and
off.]
OWEN   Good luck, Manus!
SARAH [*Quietly.*]   I'm sorry . . . I'm sorry . . . I'm so sorry, Manus . . .
         [OWEN *tries to work but cannot concentrate. He begins folding up the*
         map. As he does.]
OWEN   Is there class this evening?
         [SARAH *nods: yes.*]
I suppose Father knows. Where is he anyhow?

---

8. Northwest corner of County Mayo, south of
Donegal.
9. Ancient Greek playwright (525–456 B.C.E.).
The surviving works of the Roman general and
statesman Julius Caesar (100–44 B.C.E) are his
military commentaries.
1. Two shillings and sixpence—thirty pennies—in
the old British currency.

[SARAH *points.*]
Where?
[SARAH *mimes rocking a baby.*]
I don't understand—where?
[SARAH *repeats the mime and wipes away tears.* OWEN *is still puzzled.*]
It doesn't matter. He'll probably turn up.
    [BRIDGET *and* DOALTY *enter, sacks over their heads against the rain. They are self-consciously noisier, more ebullient, more garrulous than ever—brimming over with excitement and gossip and brio.*]
DOALTY You're missing the crack,[2] boys! Cripes, you're missing the crack! Fifty more soldiers arrived an hour ago!
BRIDGET And they're spread out in a big line from Sean Neal's over to Lag and they're moving straight across the fields towards Cnoc na nGabhar!
DOALTY Prodding every inch of the ground in front of them with their bayonets and scattering animals and hens in all directions!
BRIDGET And tumbling everything before them—fences, ditches, hay-stacks, turf-stacks!
DOALTY They came to Barney Petey's field of corn—straight through it be God as if it was heather![3]
BRIDGET Not a blade of it left standing!
DOALTY And Barney Petey just out of his bed and running after them in his drawers: 'You hoors[4] you! Get out of my corn, you hoors you!'
BRIDGET First time he ever ran in his life.
DOALTY Too lazy, the wee get,[5] to cut it when the weather was good.
    [SARAH *begins putting out the seats.*]
BRIDGET Tell them about Big Hughie.
DOALTY Cripes, if you'd seen your aul fella, Owen.
BRIDGET They were all inside in Anna na mBreag's pub—all the crowd from the wake—
DOALTY And they hear the commotion and they all come out to the street—
BRIDGET Your father in front; the Infant Prodigy footless[6] behind him!
DOALTY And your aul fella, he sees the army stretched across the countryside—
BRIDGET O my God!
DOALTY And Cripes he starts roaring at them!
BRIDGET 'Visigoths! Huns! Vandals!'[7]
DOALTY '*Ignari! Stulti! Rustici!*'[8]
BRIDGET And wee Jimmy Jack jumping up and down and shouting, 'Thermopylae! Thermopylae!'[9]
DOALTY You never saw crack like it in your life, boys. Come away on out with me, Sarah, and you'll see it all.
BRIDGET Big Hughie's fit to take no class. Is Manus about?
OWEN Manus is gone.
BRIDGET Gone where?
OWEN He's left—gone away.

---

2. Excitement.
3. Plant with small leaves and flowers.
4. Whores.
5. Little bastard or little fool.
6. Barefoot.
7. Nomadic tribes that militarily challenged the (Western) Roman Empire in the fourth and fifth

centuries.
8. Ignoramuses! Fools! Peasants! [Latin; Friel's note].
9. A narrow valley on the Aegean Sea, where in 480 B.C.E. a small number of Greek soldiers attempted to stave off a much larger Persian force.

DOALTY Where to?

OWEN He doesn't know. Mayo, maybe.

DOALTY What's on in Mayo?

OWEN [*To* BRIDGET.] Did you see George and Maire Chatach leave the dance last night?

BRIDGET We did. Didn't we, Doalty?

OWEN Did you see Manus following them out?

BRIDGET I didn't see him going out but I saw him coming in by himself later.

OWEN Did George and Maire come back to the dance?

BRIDGET No.

OWEN Did you see them again?

BRIDGET He left her home. We passed them going up the back road—didn't we, Doalty?

OWEN And Manus stayed till the end of the dance?

DOALTY We know nothing. What are you asking us for?

OWEN Because Lancey'll question me when he hears Manus's gone. [*Back to* BRIDGET.] That's the way George went home? By the back road? That's where you saw him?

BRIDGET Leave me alone, Owen. I know nothing about Yolland. If you want to know about Yolland, ask the Donnelly twins.

    [*Silence.* DOALTY *moves over to the window.*]

    [*To* SARAH.] He's a powerful fiddler, O'Shea, isn't he? He told our Seamus he'll come back for a night at Hallowe'en.

    [OWEN *goes to* DOALTY *who looks resolutely out the window.*]

OWEN What's this about the Donnellys? [*Pause.*] Were they about last night?

DOALTY Didn't see them if they were. [*Begins whistling through his teeth.*]

OWEN George is a friend of mine.

DOALTY So.

OWEN I want to know what's happened to him.

DOALTY Couldn't tell you.

OWEN What have the Donnelly twins to do with it? [*Pause.*] Doalty!

DOALTY I know nothing, Owen—nothing at all—I swear to God. All I know is this: on my way to the dance I saw their boat beached at Port. It wasn't there on my way home, after I left Bridget. And that's all I know. As God's my judge.

    The half-dozen times I met him I didn't know a word he said to me; but he seemed a right enough sort . . . [*With sudden excessive interest in the scene outside.*] Cripes, they're crawling all over the place! Cripes, there's millions of them! Cripes, they're levelling the whole land!

    [OWEN *moves away.*

        MAIRE *enters. She is bareheaded and wet from the rain; her hair in disarray. She attempts to appear normal but she is in acute distress, on the verge of being distraught. She is carrying the milk-can.*]

MAIRE Honest to God, I must be going off my head. I'm half-way here and I think to myself, 'Isn't this can very light?' and I look into it and isn't it empty.

OWEN It doesn't matter.

MAIRE How will you manage for tonight?

OWEN We have enough.

MAIRE Are you sure?

OWEN Plenty, thanks.

MAIRE It'll take me no time at all to go back up for some.

OWEN   Honestly, Maire.

MAIRE   Sure it's better you have it than that black calf that's . . . that . . . [*She looks around.*] Have you heard anything?

OWEN   Nothing.

MAIRE   What does Lancey say?

OWEN   I haven't seen him since this morning.

MAIRE   What does he *think*?

OWEN   We really didn't talk. He was here for only a few seconds.

MAIRE   He left me home, Owen. And the last thing he said to me—he tried to speak in Irish—he said, 'I'll see you yesterday'—he meant to say 'I'll see you tomorrow.' And I laughed that much he pretended to get cross and he said 'Maypoll! Maypoll!' because I said that word wrong. And off he went, laughing—laughing, Owen! Do you think he's alright? What do *you* think?

OWEN   I'm sure he'll turn up, Maire.

MAIRE   He comes from a tiny wee place called Winfarthing. [*She suddenly drops on her hands and knees on the floor—where* OWEN *had his map a few minutes ago—and with her finger traces out an outline map.*]
Come here till you see. Look. There's Winfarthing. And there's two other wee villages right beside it; one of them's called Barton Bendish—it's there; and the other's called Saxingham Nethergate—it's about there. And there's Little Walsingham—that's his mother's townland. Aren't they odd names? Sure they make no sense to me at all. And Winfarthing's near a big town called Norwich. And Norwich is in a county called Norfolk. And Norfolk is in the east of England. He drew a map for me on the wet strand and wrote the names on it. I have it all in my head now: Winfarthing—Barton Bendish—Saxingham Nethergate—Little Walsingham—Norwich—Norfolk. Strange sounds, aren't they? But nice sounds; like Jimmy Jack reciting his Homer.
[*She gets to her feet and looks around; she is almost serene now. To* SARAH.]
You were looking lovely last night, Sarah. Is that the dress you got from Boston? Green suits you.
[*To* OWEN.] Something very bad's happened to him, Owen. I know. He wouldn't go away without telling me. Where is he, Owen? You're his friend—where is he? [*Again she looks around the room; then sits on a stool.*]
I didn't get a chance to do my geography last night. The master'll be angry with me. [*She rises again.*]
I think I'll go home now. The wee ones have to be washed and put to bed and that black calf has to be fed . . .
My hands are that rough; they're still blistered from the hay. I'm ashamed of them. I hope to God there's no hay to be saved in Brooklyn.
[*She stops at the door.*] Did you hear? Nellie Ruadh's baby died in the middle of the night. I must go up to the wake. It didn't last long, did it?
[MAIRE *leaves. Silence. Then.*]

OWEN   I don't think there'll be any class. Maybe you should . . .
[OWEN *begins picking up his texts.* DOALTY *goes to him.*]

DOALTY   Is he long gone?—Manus.

OWEN   Half an hour.

DOALTY   Stupid bloody fool.

OWEN   I told him that.

DOALTY   Do they know he's gone?

OWEN   Who?

DOALTY   The army.

OWEN   Not yet.

DOALTY   They'll be after him like bloody beagles. Bloody, bloody fool, limping along the coast. They'll overtake him before night for Christ's sake.

[DOALTY *returns to the window.* LANCEY *enters—now the commanding officer.*]

OWEN   Any news? Any word?

[LANCEY *moves into the centre of the room, looking around as he does.*]

LANCEY   I understood there was a class. Where are the others?

OWEN   There was to be a class but my father . . .

LANCEY   This will suffice. I will address them and it will be their responsibility to pass on what I have to say to every family in this section.

[LANCEY *indicates to* OWEN *to translate.* OWEN *hesitates, trying to assess the change in* LANCEY's *manner and attiude.*]

I'm in a hurry, O'Donnell.

OWEN   The captain has an announcement to make.

LANCEY   Lieutenant Yolland is missing. We are searching for him. If we don't find him, or if we receive no information as to where he is to be found, I will pursue the following course of action. [*He indicates to* OWEN *to translate.*]

OWEN   They are searching for George. If they don't find him—

LANCEY   Commencing twenty-four hours from now we will shoot all livestock in Ballybeg.

[OWEN *stares at* LANCEY.]

At once.

OWEN   Beginning this time tomorrow they'll kill every animal in Baile Beag—unless they're told where George is.

LANCEY   If that doesn't bear results, commencing forty-eight hours from now we will embark on a series of evictions and levelling of every abode in the following selected areas—

OWEN   You're not—!

LANCEY   Do your job. Translate.

OWEN   If they still haven't found him in two days' time they'll begin evicting and levelling every house starting with these townlands.

[LANCEY *reads from his list.*]

LANCEY   Swinefort.

OWEN   Lis na Muc.

LANCEY   Burnfoot.

OWEN   Bun na hAbhann.

LANCEY   Dromduff.

OWEN   Druim Dubh.

LANCEY   Whiteplains.

OWEN   Machaire Ban.

LANCEY   Kings Head.

OWEN   Cnoc na Ri.

LANCEY   If by then the lieutenant hasn't been found, we will proceed until a complete clearance is made of this entire section.

OWEN   If Yolland hasn't been got by then, they will ravish the whole parish.

LANCEY   I trust they know exactly what they've got to do.

[*Pointing to* BRIDGET.] I know you. I know where you live.

[*Pointing to* SARAH.] Who are you? Name!

[SARAH'S *mouth opens and shuts, opens and shuts. Her face becomes contorted.*]

What's your name?

[*Again* SARAH *tries frantically.*]

OWEN Go on, Sarah. You can tell him.

[*But* SARAH *cannot. And she knows she cannot. She closes her mouth. Her head goes down.*]

OWEN Her name is Sarah Johnny Sally.

LANCEY Where does she live?

OWEN Bun na hAbhann.

LANCEY Where?

OWEN Burnfoot.

LANCEY I want to talk to your brother—is he here?

OWEN Not at the moment.

LANCEY Where is he?

OWEN He's at a wake.

LANCEY What wake?

[DOALTY, *who has been looking out the window all through* LANCEY's *announcements, now speaks—calmly, almost casually.*]

DOALTY Tell him his whole camp's on fire.

LANCEY What's your name? [*To* OWEN.] Who's that lout?

OWEN Doalty Dan Doalty.

LANCEY Where does he live?

OWEN Tulach Alainn.

LANCEY What do we call it?

OWEN Fair Hill. He says your whole camp is on fire.

[LANCEY *rushes to the window and looks out. Then he wheels on* DOALTY.]

LANCEY I'll remember you, Mr Doalty. [*To* OWEN.] You carry a big responsibility in all this. [*He goes off.*]

BRIDGET Mother of God, does he mean it, Owen?

OWEN Yes, he does.

BRIDGET We'll have to hide the beasts somewhere—our Seamus'll know where. Maybe at the back of Lis na nGradh—or in the caves at the far end of the Tra Bhan. Come on, Doalty! Come on! Don't be standing about there!

[DOALTY *does not move.* BRIDGET *runs to the door and stops suddenly. She sniffs the air. Panic.*]

The sweet smell! Smell it! It's the sweet smell! Jesus, it's the potato blight!

DOALTY It's the army tents burning, Bridget.

BRIDGET Is it? Are you sure? Is that what it is? God, I thought we were destroyed altogether. Come on! Come on!

[*She runs off* OWEN *goes to* SARAH *who is preparing to leave.*]

OWEN How are you? Are you alright?

[SARAH *nods: Yes.*]

OWEN Don't worry. It will come back to you again.

[SARAH *shakes her head.*]

OWEN It will. You're upset now. He frightened you. That's all's wrong.

[*Again* SARAH *shakes her head, slowly, emphatically, and smiles at* OWEN. *Then she leaves.*

OWEN *busies himself gathering his belongings.* DOALTY *leaves the window and goes to him.*]

DOALTY He'll do it, too.

OWEN Unless Yolland's found.

DOALTY Hah!

OWEN Then he'll certainly do it.

DOALTY When my grandfather was a boy they did the same thing. [*Simply, altogether without irony.*] And after all the trouble you went to, mapping the place and thinking up new names for it.

> [OWEN *busies himself. Pause.*
>
> DOALTY *almost dreamily.*]

I've damned little to defend but he'll not put me out without a fight. And there'll be others who think the same as me.

OWEN That's a matter for you.

DOALTY If we'd all stick together. If we knew how to defend ourselves.

OWEN Against a trained army.

DOALTY The Donnelly twins know how.

HUGH If they could be found.

DOALTY If they could be found. [*He goes to the door.*] Give me a shout after you've finished with Lancey. I might know something then. [*He leaves.*]

> [OWEN *picks up the Name-Book. He looks at it momentarily, then puts it on top of the pile he is carrying. It falls to the floor. He stoops to pick it up—hesitates—leaves it. He goes upstairs.*
>
> As OWEN *ascends,* HUGH *and* JIMMY JACK *enter. Both wet and drunk.* JIMMY *is very unsteady. He is trotting behind* HUGH, *trying to break in on* HUGH's *declamation.*
>
> HUGH *is equally drunk but more experienced in drunkenness: there is a portion of his mind which retains its clarity.*]

HUGH There I was, appropriately dispositioned to proffer my condolences to the bereaved mother . . .

JIMMY Hugh—

HUGH . . . and about to enter the *domus lugubris*[1]—Maire Chatach?

JIMMY The wake house.

HUGH Indeed—when I experience a plucking at my elbow: Mister George Alexander, Justice of the Peace. 'My tidings are infelicitous,' said he—Bridget? Too slow. Doalty?

JIMMY *Infelix*—unhappy.

HUGH Unhappy indeed. 'Master Bartley Timlin has been appointed to the new national school.'

'Timlin? Who is Timlin?'

'A schoolmaster from Cork.[2] And he will be a major asset to the community: he is also a very skilled bacon-curer'!

JIMMY Hugh—

HUGH Ha-ha-ha-ha-ha! The Cork bacon-curer! *Barbarus hic ego sum quia non intelligor ulli*—James?

JIMMY Ovid.

HUGH *Procede.*

JIMMY 'I am a barbarian in this place because I am not understood by anyone.'[3]

---

1. House of mourning [Latin; Friel's note].
2. Influential city on Ireland's south coast.
3. From Ovid's *Tristia*, written after the Roman

poet was exiled to live by the Black Sea in what is Romania today.

HUGH   Indeed—[*Shouts.*] Manus! Tea!
  I will compose a satire on Master Bartley Timlin, schoolmaster and bacon-
  curer. But it will be too easy, won't it?
  [*Shouts.*] Strong tea! Black!
  [*The only way* JIMMY *can get* HUGH's *attention is by standing in front of
  him and holding his arms.*]
JIMMY   Will you listen to me, Hugh!
HUGH   James.
  [*Shouts.*] And a slice of soda bread.
JIMMY   I'm going to get married.
HUGH   Well!
JIMMY   At Christmas.
HUGH   Splendid.
JIMMY   To Athene.
HUGH   Who?
JIMMY   Pallas Athene.
HUGH   *Glaukopis Athene?*
JIMMY   Flashing-eyed, Hugh, flashing-eyed! [*He attempts the gesture he has
  made before: standing to attention, the momentary spasm, the salute, the face
  raised in pained ecstasy—but the body does not respond efficiently this time.
  The gesture is grotesque.*]
HUGH   The lady has assented?
JIMMY   She asked *me—I* assented.
HUGH   Ah. When was this?
JIMMY   Last night.
HUGH   What does her mother say?
JIMMY   Metis from Hellespont?[4] Decent people—good stock.
HUGH   And her father?
JIMMY   I'm meeting Zeus tomorrow. Hugh, will you be my best man?
HUGH   Honoured, James; profoundly honoured.
JIMMY   You know what I'm looking for, Hugh, don't you? I mean to say—you
  know—I—I—I joke like the rest of them—you know?—[*Again he attempts
  the pathetic routine but abandons it instantly.*] You know yourself, Hugh—
  don't you?—You know all that. But what I'm really looking for, Hugh—what
  I really want—companionship, Hugh—at my time of life, companionship,
  company, someone to talk to. Away up in Beann na Gaoithe—you've no idea
  how lonely it is. Companionship—correct, Hugh? Correct?
HUGH   Correct.
JIMMY   And I always liked her, Hugh. Correct?
HUGH   Correct, James.
JIMMY   Someone to talk to.
HUGH   Indeed.
JIMMY   That's all, Hugh. The whole story. You know it all now, Hugh. You
  know it all.
  [*As* JIMMY *says those last lines he is crying, shaking his head, trying to
  keep his balance, and holding a finger up to his lips in absurd gestures
  of secrecy and intimacy. Now he staggers away, tries to sit on a stool,*

---

4. Renowned for her wisdom, Metis was impregnated by and then swallowed by Zeus, whose head began
to ache until Athena sprang from his head.

misses it, slides to the floor, his feet in front of him, his back against the broken cart. Almost at once he is asleep.

HUGH *watches all of this. Then he produces his flask and is about to pour a drink when he sees the Name-Book on the floor. He picks it up and leafs through it, pronouncing the strange names as he does. Just as he begins,* OWEN *emerges and descends with two bowls of tea.*]

HUGH   Ballybeg. Burnfoot. Kings Head. Whiteplains. Fair Hill. Dunboy. Green Bank.

[OWEN *snatches the book from* HUGH.]

OWEN   I'll take that. [*In apology.*] It's only a catalogue of names.

HUGH   I know what it is.

OWEN   A mistake—my mistake—nothing to do with us. I hope that's strong enough. [*Tea.*]

[*He throws the book on the table and crosses over to* JIMMY.]
Jimmy. Wake up, Jimmy. Wake up, man.

JIMMY   What—what-what?

OWEN   Here. Drink this. Then go on away home. There may be trouble. Do you hear me, Jimmy? There may be trouble.

HUGH [*Indicating Name-Book.*]   We must learn those new names.

OWEN [*Searching around.*]   Did you see a sack lying about?

HUGH   We must learn where we live. We must learn to make them our own. We must make them our new home.

[OWEN *finds a sack and throws it across his shoulders.*]

OWEN   I know where I live.

HUGH   James thinks he knows, too. I look at James and three thoughts occur to me: A—that it is not the literal past, the 'facts' of history, that shape us, but images of the past embodied in language. James has ceased to make that discrimination.

OWEN   Don't lecture me, Father.

HUGH   B—we must never cease renewing those images; because once we do, we fossilise. Is there no soda bread?

OWEN   And C, Father—one single, unalterable 'fact': if Yolland is not found, we are all going to be evicted. Lancey has issued the order.

HUGH   Ah. *Edictum imperatoris.*[5]

OWEN   You should change out of those wet clothes. I've got to go. I've got to see Doalty Dan Doalty.

HUGH   What about?

OWEN   I'll be back soon.

[*As* OWEN *exits.*]

HUGH   Take care, Owen. To remember everything is a form of madness. [*He looks around the room, carefully, as if he were about to leave it forever. Then he looks at* JIMMY, *asleep again.*]

The road to Sligo.[6] A spring morning. 1798.[7] Going into battle. Do you remember, James? Two young gallants with pikes across their shoulders and the *Aeneid*[8] in their pockets. Everything seemed to find definition that

5. The decree of the commander [Latin; Friel's note].
6. Port town south of County Donegal.
7. That year a force of Catholics and Protestants known as the United Irishmen launched a rebellion throughout Ireland. After the British quashed the uprising, the Irish Parliament was abolished, and two years later the Act of Union incorporated Ireland into the United Kingdom.
8. Virgil's epic, about the Trojan hero Aeneas, who escapes the destruction of Troy and founds Rome.

spring—a congruence, a miraculous matching of hope and past and present and possibility. Striding across the fresh, green land. The rhythms of perception heightened. The whole enterprise of consciousness accelerated. We were gods that morning, James; and I had recently married *my* goddess, Caitlin Dubh Nic Reactainn, may she rest in peace. And to leave her and my infant son in his cradle—that was heroic, too. By God, sir, we were magnificent. We marched as far as—where was it?—Glenties![9] All of twenty-three miles in one day. And it was there, in Phelan's pub, that we got homesick for Athens, just like Ulysses. The *desiderium nostrorum*—the need for our own. Our *pietas,*[1] James, was for older, quieter things. And that was the longest twenty-three miles back I ever made. [*Toasts* JIMMY.] My friend, confusion is not an ignoble condition.

[MAIRE *enters.*]

MAIRE I'm back again. I set out for somewhere but I couldn't remember where. So I came back here.

HUGH Yes, I will teach you English, Maire Chatach.

MAIRE Will you, Master? I must learn it. I need to learn it.

HUGH Indeed you may well be my only pupil. [*He goes towards the steps and begins to ascend.*]

MAIRE When can we start?

HUGH Not today. Tomorrow, perhaps. After the funeral. We'll begin tomorrow. [*Ascending.*] But don't expect too much. I will provide you with the available words and the available grammar. But will that help you to interpret between privacies? I have no idea. But it's all we have. I have no idea at all. [*He is now at the top.*]

MAIRE Master, what does the English word 'always' mean?

HUGH *Semper—per omnia saecula.*[2] The Greeks called it *'aei'.* It's not a word I'd start with. It's a silly word, girl. [*He sits.*]

[JIMMY *is awake. He gets to his feet.*

MAIRE *sees the Name-Book, picks it up, and sits with it on her knee.*]

MAIRE When he comes back, this is where he'll come to. He told me this is where he was happiest.

[JIMMY *sits beside* MAIRE.]

JIMMY Do you know the Greek word *endogamein?* It means to marry within the tribe. And the word *exogamein* means to marry outside the tribe. And you don't cross those borders casually—both sides get very angry. Now, the problem is this: Is Athene sufficiently mortal or am I sufficiently godlike for the marriage to be acceptable to her people and to my people? You think about that.

HUGH *Urbs antiqua fuit*—there was an ancient city which,'tis said, Juno[3] loved above all the lands. And it was the goddess's aim and cherished hope that here should be the capital of all nations—should the fates perchance allow that. Yet in truth she discovered that a race was springing from Trojan

9. A region of intersecting glens on the coast of central Donegal.
1. Piety [Friel's note]. The Latin term for the trait associated especially with Virgil's dutiful hero Aeneas. The story of Ulysses', or Odysseus', ten-year wandering on the way home is told in Homer's *Odyssey.*
2. Always—for all time. *Aei,* always [Friel's note].
3. In Roman mythology queen of the gods, who loved ancient Carthage (now in Tunisia) above all. Hugh's recitation is from the beginning of the nar-

rative of Virgil's *Aeneid.* Here Juno angrily foresees the destruction of Carthage by Aeneas's Roman descendants ("a race was springing from Trojan blood") and the extension of Roman rule over this North African colony (Rome and Carthage fought the Punic Wars in the 3rd and 2nd centuries B.C.E.). While vaunting Rome's imperial mission to civilize the world, Virgil's epic also includes a tragic love story: Aeneas and the Carthaginian queen Dido fall in love, but she commits suicide after he abandons her for his imperial duty.

blood to overthrow some day these Tyrian[4] towers—a people *late regem belloque superbum*—kings of broad realms and proud in war who would come forth for Lybia's[5] downfall—such was—such was the course—such was the course ordained—ordained by fate . . . What the hell's wrong with me? Sure I know it backways. I'll begin again. *Urbs antiqua fuit*—there was an ancient city which,'tis said, Juno loved above all the lands.
    [*Begin to bring down the lights.*]
    And it was the goddess's aim and cherished hope that here should be the capital of all nations—should the fates perchance allow that. Yet in truth she discovered that a race was springing from Trojan blood to overthrow some day these Tyrian towers—a people kings of broad realms and proud in war who would come forth for Lybia's downfall . . .
    [*Black.*]

4. I.e., Carthaginian. Carthage had been founded by Phoenicians from the city of Tyre (now in Leb- anon).
5. Carthage's.

KAMAU BRATHWAITE
b. 1930

As a poet and historian Kamau Brathwaite has been the most prominent West Indian spokesman for "the literature of reconnection": he has sought to recover and revalue the African inheritance in the Caribbean—a religious, linguistic, and cultural inheritance seen as embarrassing or taboo through most of the twentieth century. In *History of the Voice*, a lecture first delivered in 1979, Brathwaite argues that Afro-Caribbeans, their ancestors uprooted by slavery, were further cut off from their specific history and their local environment by Standard English models of language and literature. He proposes "nation language," a creolized English saturated with African words, rhythms, even grammar, as a crucial tool for writers to recuperate Afro-Caribbean history and experience. His own poetry draws on West Indian syncopations, orality, and musical traditions, but also adapts imported models, such as the modernist dislocations of persona, rhythm, and tone in T. S. Eliot's verse.

He was born Lawson Edward Brathwaite in Bridgetown, Barbados, at the eastern edge of the West Indies. His undergraduate studies in history were at Cambridge University; his graduate studies, at the University of Sussex. He worked as an education officer for the Ministry of Education in Ghana (1955–62) and taught history at the University of the West Indies, before taking a position in comparative literature at New York University in 1991. His many books of poetry include a work of epic scope and scale, *The Arrivants: A New World Trilogy* (1973), which gathers *Rights of Passage* (1967), *Masks* (1968), and *Islands* (1969).

[Nation Language][1]

What I am going to talk about this morning is language from the Caribbean, the process of using English in a different way from the "norm". English in a new sense as I prefer to call it. English in an ancient sense. English

1. First printed separately in 1984, Brathwaite's lecture *History of the Voice* was slightly modified and incorporated in his essay collection *Roots* (1986, 1993), from which this selection is excerpted.

2524 / Nation and Language

in a very traditional sense. And sometimes not English at all, but *language*.
I start my thoughts, taking up from the discussion that developed after Dennis Brutus's[2] very excellent presentation. Without logic, and through instinct, the people who spoke with Dennis from the floor yesterday brought up the question of language.* * * In his case, it was English, and English as spoken by Africans, and the native languages as spoken by Africans.

We in the Caribbean have a similar kind of plurality: we have English, which is the imposed language on much of the archipelago. English is an imperial language, as are French, Dutch, and Spanish. We have what we call creole English, which is a mixture of English and an adaptation that English took in the new environment of the Caribbean when it became mixed with the other imported languages. We have also what is called *nation language*, which is the kind of English spoken by the people who were brought to the Caribbean, not the official English now, but the language of slaves and labourers, the servants who were brought in by the conquistadors. Finally, we have the remnants of ancestral languages still persisting in the Caribbean. There is Amerindian, which is active in certain parts of Central America but not in the Caribbean because the Amerindians are a destroyed people, and their languages were practically destroyed. We have Hindi, spoken by some of the more traditional East Indians who live in the Caribbean, and there are also varieties of Chinese. And, miraculously, there are survivals of African languages still persisting in the Caribbean. So we have that spectrum—that prism—of languages similar to the kind of structure that Dennis described for South Africa. Now, I have to give you some kind of background to the development of these languages, the historical development of this plurality, because I can't take it for granted that you know and understand the history of the Caribbean.

The Caribbean is a set of islands stretching out from Florida in a mighty curve. You must know of the Caribbean at least from television, at least now with hurricane David (—) coming right into it. The islands stretch out on an arc of some two thousand miles from Florida through the Atlantic to the South American coast, and they were originally inhabited by Amerindian people, Taino, Siboney, Carib, Arawak. In 1492, Columbus "discovered" (as it is said) the Caribbean, and with that discovery came the intrusion of European culture and peoples and a fragmentation of the original Amerindian culture. We had Europe "nationalizing" itself into Spanish, French, English and Dutch so that people had to start speaking (and *thinking*) in four metropolitan languages rather than possibly a single native language. Then, with the destruction of the Amerindians, which took place within 30 years of Columbus' discovery (one million dead a year), it was necessary for the Europeans to import new labour bodies into the Caribbean. And the most convenient form of labour was the labour on the very edge of the trade winds—the labour on the edge of the *slave* trade winds, the labour on the edge of the hurricane, the labour on the edge of West Africa—. And so the peoples of Ashanti,[3] Congo, Nigeria, from all that mighty coast of western Africa were imported into the Caribbean. And we had the arrival in that area of a new language structure. It consisted of many languages, but basically they had a common semantic and stylistic form. What these languages had to do, however, was to submerge themselves, because officially the conquering peoples—the Spaniards, the English, the French, and the Dutch—did not wish to hear people speaking Ashanti or any

2. South African poet (b. 1924).   3. Region in present-day central Ghana.

of the Congolese languages. So there was a submergence of this imported language. Its status became one of inferiority. Similarly, its speakers were slaves. They were conceived of as inferiors—nonhuman, in fact—. But this very submergence served an interesting intercultural purpose, because although people continued to speak English as it was spoken in Elizabethan times and on through the Romantic and Victorian ages, that English was, nonetheless, still being influenced by the underground language, the sub-merged language that the slaves had brought. And that underground language was itself constantly transforming itself into new forms. It was moving from a purely African form to a form that was African, but which was adapting to the new environment and to the cultural imperatives of the European languages. And it was influencing the way in which the French, Dutch, and Spanish spoke their own languages. So there was a very complex process taking place which is now beginning to surface in our literature.

In the Caribbean, as in South Africa (and in any area of cultural imperialism for that matter), the educational system did not recognize the presence of these various languages. What our educational system did was to recognize and maintain the language of the conquistador—the language of the planter, the language of the official, the language of the Anglican preacher—. It insisted that not only would English be spoken in the anglophone Caribbean, but that the educational system would carry the contours of an English heritage. Hence, as Dennis said, Shakespeare, George Eliot, Jane Austen—British lit-erature and literary forms, the models that were intimate to Great Britain, that had very little to do, really, with the environment and the reality of the Carib-bean—were dominant in the Caribbean educational system. People were forced to learn things that had no relevance to themselves. Paradoxically, in the Caribbean (as in many other "cultural disaster" areas), the people educated in this system came to know more, even today, about English kings and queens than they do about our own national heroes, our own slave rebels—the people who helped to build and to destroy our society—. We are more excited by English literary models, by the concept of, say, Sherwood Forest and Robin Hood, than we are by Nanny of the Maroons,[4] a name some of us didn't even know until a few years ago. And in terms of what we write, our perceptual models, we are more conscious (in terms of sensibility) of the falling of snow for instance—the models are all there for the falling of the snow—than of the force of the hurricanes that take place every year. In other words, we haven't got the syllables, the syllabic intelligence, to describe the hurricane, which is our own experience; whereas we can describe the imported alien experience of the snowfall. It is that kind of situation that we are in.

Now the creole adaptation to all this is the child who, instead of writing in an essay "The snow was falling on the fields of Shropshire"[5] (which is what our children literally were writing until a few years ago, below drawings they made of white snow fields and the corn-haired people who inhabited such a landscape), wrote "The snow was falling on the cane fields." The child had not yet reached the obvious statement that it wasn't snow at all, but rain that

4. The Maroons were Africans and escaped slaves who, after running away or participating in suc-cessful rebellions, set up autonomous societies throughout plantation America in marginal and certainly inaccessible areas outside European influence. . . . Nanny of the Maroons, an ex-

Ashanti (?) Queen Mother, is regarded as one of the greatest of the Jamaican freedom fighters [Brathwaite's note].
5. Region of western England on the Welsh bor-der, written about by the English poet A. E. Hous-man (1859–1936).

2526 / NATION AND LANGUAGE

was probably falling on the cane fields. She was trying to have both cultures at the same time. But that is creolization.

What is even more important, as we develop this business of emergent language in the Caribbean, is the actual rhythm and the syllables, the very body work, in a way, of the language. What English has given us as a model for poetry, and to a lesser extent, prose (but poetry is the basic tool here), is the pentameter: "The curfew tolls the knell of parting day."[6] There have, of course, been attempts to break it. And there were other dominant forms like, for example, *Beowulf* (c. 750), *The Seafarer*,[7] and what Langland (1322?–1400) had produced:

> *For trewthe telleth that love. is triacle of hevene;*
> *May no synne be on him sene. that useth that spise,*
> *And alle his werkes he wrougte. with love as him liste.*

Or, from *Piers the Plowman* (which does not make it into *Palgrave's Golden Treasury*,[8] but which we all had to "do" at school) the haunting prologue:

> *In a somer seson. whan soft was the sonne*
> *I shope me into shroudes. as I a shepe were*

Which has recently inspired our own Derek Walcott to his first major nation language effort:

> *In idle August, while the sea soft,*
> *and leaves of brown islands stick to the rim*
> *of this Caribbean, I blow out the light*
> *by the dreamless face of Maria Concepcion*
> *to ship as a seaman on the schooner Flight.*[9]

But by the time we reach Chaucer (1345–1400), the pentameter prevails. Over in the New World, the Americans—Walt Whitman—tried to bridge or to break the pentameter through a cosmic movement, a large movement of sound. Cummings tried to fragment it. And Marianne Moore attacked it with syllabics.[1] But basically the pentameter remained, and it carries with it a certain kind of experience, which is not the experience of a hurricane. The hurricane does not roar in pentameter. And that's the problem: how do you get a rhythm that approximates the natural experience, the environmental experience. We have been trying to break out of the entire pentametric model in the Caribbean and to move into a system that more closely and intimately approaches our own experience. So that is what we are talking about now.

It is nation language in the Caribbean that, in fact, largely ignores the pentameter. Nation language is the language that is influenced very strongly by the African model, the African aspect of our New World/Caribbean heritage. English it may be in terms of its lexicon, but it is not English in terms of its syntax. And English it certainly is not in terms of its rhythm and timbre, its own sound explosion. In its contours, it is not English, even though the words, as you hear them, would be English to a greater or lesser degree. And this brings us back to the question that some of you raised yesterday: can English be a rev-

---

6. The opening line of "Elegy Written in a Country Churchyard," by the English poet Thomas Gray (1716–1771).
7. Poem in Old English.
8. Collection of songs and lyric poems published in London. *Piers the Plowman*: Middle English poem believed to have been written by William

Langland (ca. 1330–1387).
9. Beginning of "The Schooner *Flight*," by the Saint Lucian poet Derek Walcott (b. 1930).
1. Verses based on the number of syllables, not accents, in a line. E. E. Cummings (1894–1962), American poet. Marianne Moore (1887–1972), American poet.

olutionary language? And the lovely answer that came back was: it is not English that is the agent. It is not language, but people, who make revolutions. I think, however, that language does really have a role to play here, certainly in the Caribbean. But it is an English that is not the standard, imported, educated English, but that of the submerged, surrealist experience and sensibility, which has always been there and which is now increasingly coming to the surface and influencing the perception of contemporary Caribbean people. It is what I call, as I say, *nation language*. I use the term in contrast to *dialect*. The word dialect has been bandied about for a long time, and it carries very pejorative overtones. Dialect is thought of as "bad" English. Dialect is "inferior" English. Dialect is the language when you want to make fun of someone. Caricature speaks in dialect. Dialect has a long history coming from the plantation where people's dignity was distorted through their languages and the descriptions that the dialect gave to them. Nation language, on the other hand, is the submerged area of that dialect that is much more closely allied to the African aspect of experience in the Caribbean. It may be in English, but often it is in an English which is like a howl, or a shout, or a machine-gun, or the wind, or a wave. It is also like the blues. And sometimes it is English and African at the same time.* * *

※   ※   ※

The mainstream poets who were moving from standard English to nation language were influenced basically, I think (again the models are important), by T. S. Eliot. What T. S. Eliot did for Caribbean poetry and Caribbean literature was to introduce the notion of the speaking voice, the conversational tone.[2] That is what really attracted us to Eliot. And you can see how the Caribbean poets introduced here have been influenced by him, although they eventually went on to create their own environmental expression.

※   ※   ※

1979–81   1984, 1986

Calypso[1]

1

The stone had skidded arc'd and bloomed into islands:
Cuba and San Domingo
Jamaica and Puerto Rico
Grenada Guadeloupe Bonaire[2]

5   curved stone hissed into reef
       wave teeth fanged into clay

---

2. For those of us who really made the breakthrough, it was Eliot's actual voice—or rather his recorded voice, property of the British Council (Barbados)—reading "Preludes", "The Love Song of J. Alfred Prufrock", *The Waste Land,* and later the *Four Quartets*—not the texts—which turned us on. In that dry deadpan delivery, the "riddims" of St. Louis (though we did not know the source then) were stark and clear for those of us who at the same time were listening to the dislocations of Bird, Dizzy, and Klook. And it is interesting that, on the whole, the establishment could not stand Eliot's voice—and far less jazz [Brathwaite's note].

Bird: American jazz musician Charlie "Bird" Parker (1920–1955). Dizzy: American jazz trumpeter Dizzy Gillespie (1917–1993). Klook: American jazz drummer Kenny Clarke (1914–1985).
1. Type of folk song originating in Trinidad, often involving commentary on current events and improvised wordplay with syncopated rhythms. This poem is from *Rights of Passage,* the first of three books collected as *The Arrivants.*
2. Caribbean Islands. The first two stanzas suggest a creation myth in which the islands are formed in a rock-skipping game called ducks and drakes.

white splash flashed into spray
Bathsheba Montego Bay[3]

bloom of the arcing summers . . .

2

10   The islands roared into green plantations
ruled by silver sugar cane
sweat and profit
cutlass profit
islands ruled by sugar cane

15   And of course it was a wonderful time
a profitable hospitable well-worth-your-time
when captains carried receipts for rices
letters spices wigs
opera glasses swaggering asses
20   debtors vices pigs

O it was a wonderful time
an elegant benevolent redolent time—
and young Mrs. P.'s quick irrelevant crime
at four o'clock in the morning . . .

3

25   But what of black Sam
with the big splayed toes
and the shoe black shiny skin?

He carries bucketfulls of water
'cause his Ma's just had another daughter.

30   And what of John with the European name
who went to school and dreamt of fame
his boss one day called him a fool
and the boss hadn't even been to school . . .

4

Steel drum steel drum
35   hit the hot calypso dancing
hot rum hot rum
who goin' stop this bacchanalling?[4]

For we glance the banjo
dance the limbo
40   grow our crops by maljo[5]

3. Jamaican city and tourist resort. "Bathsheba":
seaside resort in Barbados.
4. From *Bacchanalia*: festival of Bacchus, the
Roman god of wine, celebrated with song, dancing,
and revelry.
5. Evil eye (Trinidadian dialect; from the French
mal yeux).

have loose morals
gather corals
father our neighbour's quarrels

perhaps when they come
45   with their cameras and straw
hats: sacred pink tourists from the frozen Nawth

we should get down to those
white beaches
where if we don't wear breeches

50   it becomes an island dance
Some people doin' well
while others are catchin' hell

o the boss gave our Johnny the sack
though we beg him please
55   please to take 'im back

so the boy now nigratin' overseas . . .

1967

WOLE SOYINKA
b. 1934

Wole Soyinka was born in Abeokuta, near Ibadan, in western Nigeria, and educated at Government College and University College, in Ibadan. In 1954 he began his studies at the University of Leeds. After six years in England he returned to Nigeria, where he founded a national theater in 1960 and, at the cost of repeated imprisonment, intervened in tumultuous political struggles. He has taught at universities in Ibadan, Lagos, and Ife, as well as at North American universities. In 1986 he became the first black African writer to receive the Nobel Prize in Literature, recognized for plays, such as *Death and the King's Horseman* (1975), that inventively hybridize Yoruba oral traditions with European literary paradigms, fuse African rhetoric, myth, and ritual with the verbal extravagance of Elizabethan and Jacobean theater. He has also written poems, including "Telephone Conversation," a mini verse drama of sorts in which two characters, a racist English landlady and an African trying to rent an apartment, are wittily pitted against one another.

Telephone Conversation

The price seemed reasonable, location
Indifferent. The landlady swore she lived
Off premises. Nothing remained
But self-confession. 'Madam', I warned,
5   'I hate a wasted journey—I am African.'

Silence. Silenced transmission of
Pressurised good-breeding. Voice, when it came,
Lip-stick coated, long gold-rolled
Cigarette-holder pipped. Caught I was, foully.

10 'HOW DARK?' . . . I had not misheard . . . 'ARE YOU LIGHT
'OR VERY DARK?' Button B. Button A.[1] Stench
Of rancid breath of public hide-and-speak.
Red booth. Red pillar-box.° Red double-tiered   *mailbox*
Omnibus° squelching tar. It *was* real! Shamed   *double-decker bus*
15 By ill-mannered silence, surrender
Pushed dumbfoundment to beg simplification.
Considerate she was, varying the emphasis—

'ARE YOU DARK? OR VERY LIGHT?' Revelation came.
'You mean—like plain or milk chocolate?'
20 Her assent was clinical, crushing in its light
Impersonality. Rapidly, wave-length adjusted,
I chose. 'West African sepia'°—and as afterthought,   *reddish brown*
'Down in my passport.' Silence for spectroscopic[2]
Flight of fancy, till truthfulness clanged her accent
25 Hard on the mouthpiece. 'WHAT'S THAT?' conceding
'DON'T KNOW WHAT THAT IS.' 'Like brunette.'

'THAT'S DARK, ISN'T IT?' 'Not altogether.
'Facially, I am brunette, but madam, you should see
'The rest of me. Palm of my hand, soles of my feet
30 'Are a peroxide blonde. Friction, caused—
'Foolishly madam—by sitting down, has turned
'My bottom raven black—One moment madam'—sensing
Her receiver rearing on the thunderclap
About my ears—'Madam', I pleaded, 'Wouldn't you rather
35 'See for yourself?'

1960, 1962

1. Buttons on old British telephones.   2. Related to study of the spectrum.

TONY HARRISON
b. 1937

Tony Harrison was born in Leeds, where his father was a baker, and where he learned
a regional Yorkshire dialect from his mother. At the age of eleven, a scholarship to
the prestigious Leeds Grammar School dislocated him from his working-class background: he was told he would have to learn to speak "properly" and forbidden, because
of his accent, to read his poetry aloud in the classroom. He later studied classics at
Leeds University. While a lecturer in English at Ahmadu Bello University in northern
Nigeria, he translated (with fellow poet James Simmons) Aristophanes' *Lysistrata* into
the pidgin English of the Hausa people; at the same time he wrote poems in the
voices of working-class British expatriates. He has been resident dramatist at the

National Theatre in London, has undertaken commissions for the Metropolitan Opera in New York, and has published verse translations of classical Greek and French plays.

As a poet Harrison has been faithful to his modest origins. His poems give speech to the speechless, to the exploited and oppressed—the two uncles of "Heredity," for example, or a bereaved father unable to articulate his grief, or a terrified convict—exposing their predicaments with passion and indignation. Attributing to working-class speech of the north of England a "richer engagement, a more sensual engagement, with language," he brings that sensual vigor, wit, and immediacy of working-class Yorkshire speech into an exciting amalgam with literary English. Like Caribbean poets, Irish poets, Scottish poets, and others, he combines Standard English with nonstandard oral sounds, with the diction, syntax, and grammar of regional speech, in an unstable, sometimes explosive compound. His sixteen-line near-sonnets from the long work called *The School of Eloquence*, like his important long poem *v.*, richly interweave the literary and the oral, learned allusion and raw directness, Standard English and working-class Yorkshire speech.

Heredity

How you became a poet's a mystery!
Wherever did you get your talent from?

I say: I had two uncles, Joe and Harry—
one was a stammerer, the other dumb.

1978

National Trust[1]

Bottomless pits. There's one in Castleton,[2]
and stout upholders of our law and order
one day thought its depth worth wagering on
and borrowed a convict hush-hush from his warder
5 and winched him down; and back, flayed, grey, mad, dumb.

Not even a good flogging made him holler!

O gentlemen, a better way to plumb
the depths of Britain's dangling a scholar,
say, here at the booming shaft at Towanroath,[3]
10 now National Trust, a place where they got tin,
those gentlemen who silenced the men's oath
and killed the language that they swore it in.

The dumb go down in history and disappear
and not one gentleman's been brought to book:

---

1. A British association to preserve places of natural beauty or buildings of architectural or historical importance.

2. In the Derby coalfields.
3. A tin mine in Cornwall.

15 *Mes den hep tavas a-gollas y dyr*

(Cornish)—
"the tongueless man gets his land took."

1978

Book Ends

I

Baked the day she suddenly dropped dead
we chew it slowly that last apple pie.

Shocked into sleeplessness you're scared of bed.
We never could talk much, and now don't try.

5 *You're like book ends, the pair of you,* she'd say,
Hog that grate, say nothing, sit, sleep, stare . . .

The "scholar" me, you, worn out on poor pay,
only our silence made us seem a pair.

Not as good for staring in, blue gas,
10 too regular each bud, each yellow spike.[1]

A night you need my company to pass
and she not here to tell us we're alike!

Your life's all shattered into smithereens.

Back in our silences and sullen looks,
15 for all the Scotch we drink, what's still between's
not the thirty or so years, but books, books, books.

1978

II

The stone's too full. The wording must be terse.
There's scarcely room to carve the FLORENCE on it—

Come on, it's not as if we're wanting verse.
It's not as if we're wanting a whole sonnet!

5 After tumblers of neat *Johnny Walker*
(I think that both of us were on our third)

you said you'd always been a clumsy talker
and couldn't find another, shorter word
for "beloved" or for "wife" in the inscription,
10 but not too clumsy that you can't still cut:

---

1. Flames from the gas fire common in lower-class English homes.

You're supposed to be the bright boy at description
and you can't tell them what the fuck to put!

I've got to find the right words on my own.

I've got the envelope that he'd been scrawling,
15 mis-spelt, mawkish, stylistically appalling
but I can't squeeze more love into their stone.

                                  1981

Long Distance

I

Your bed's got two wrong sides. Your life's all grouse.°   *grumble*
I let your phone-call take its dismal course:

Ah can't stand it no more, this empty house!

Carrots choke us wi'out your mam's white sauce!

5 *Them sweets you brought me, you can have 'em back.*
Ah'm diabetic now. Got all the facts.
(The diabetes comes hard on the track
of two coronaries and cataracts.)

Ah've allus liked things sweet! But now ah push
10 *food down mi throat! Ah'd sooner do wi'out.*
And t'only reason now for beer 's to flush
(so t'dietician said) mi kidneys out.

When I come round, they'll be laid out, the sweets,
Lifesavers, my father's New World treats,
15 still in the big brown bag, and only bought
rushing through JFK[1] as a last thought.

II

Though my mother was already two years dead
Dad kept her slippers warming by the gas,
put hot water bottles her side of the bed
and still went to renew her transport pass.

5 You couldn't just drop in. You had to phone.
He'd put you off an hour to give him time
to clear away her things and look alone
as though his still raw love were such a crime.

He couldn't risk my blight of disbelief
10 though sure that very soon he'd hear her key

---

1. A New York airport.

scrape in the rusted lock and end his grief.
He *knew* she'd just popped out to get the tea.

I believe life ends with death, and that is all.
You haven't both gone shopping; just the same,
15 in my new black leather phone book there's your name
and the disconnected number I still call.

                                                        1981

Turns

I thought it made me look more "working class"
(as if a bit of chequered cloth could bridge that gap!)
I did a turn in it before the glass.
My mother said: *It suits you, your dad's cap.*
5 (She preferred me to wear suits and part my hair:
You're every bit as good as that lot are!)

All the pension queue[1] came out to stare.
Dad was sprawled beside the postbox (still VR),[2]
his cap turned inside up beside his head,
10 smudged H A H in purple Indian ink
and Brylcreem slicks[3] displayed so folk might think
he wanted charity for dropping dead.

He never begged. For nowt![4] Death's reticence
crowns his life's, and *me,* I'm opening my trap
15 to busk[5] the class that broke him for the pence
that splash like brackish tears into our cap.

                                                        1981

Marked with D.[1]

When the chilled dough of his flesh went in an oven
not unlike those he fuelled all his life,
I thought of his cataracts ablaze with Heaven
and radiant with the sight of his dead wife,
5 light streaming from his mouth to shape her name,
"not Florence and not Flo but always Florrie."
I thought how his cold tongue burst into flame
but only literally, which makes me sorry,

---

1. Line of retired people waiting for their pension (social security) payments.
2. Sidewalk mailbox dating from the reign of Queen Victoria and carrying the initials of her name and Latin title: Victoria Regina.
3. Play on Brylcreem Sticks, a hairstyling wax.
4. Nothing (northern dialect).

5. Take around the hat; i.e., solicit money for street entertainment (from members of the middle class, in this case).
1. Cf. the anonymous nursery rhyme "Pat-a-cake, pat-a-cake, baker's man / Bake me a cake as fast as you can / Pat it and prick it, and mark it with B, / Put it in the oven for baby and me."

sorry for his sake there's no Heaven to reach.
10 I get it all from Earth my daily bread
but he hungered for release from mortal speech
that kept him down, the tongue that weighed like lead.

The baker's man that no-one will see rise
and England made to feel like some dull oaf
15 is smoke, enough to sting one person's eyes
and ash (not unlike flour) for one small loaf.

1981

NGŨGĨ WA THIONG'O
b. 1938

Ngũgĩ wa Thiong'o was born in Limuru, Kenya, where his father was a peasant farmer. He was educated at the Alliance High School in Kikuyu, Kenya; Makerere University in Kampala, Uganda; and Leeds University in England. In the late 1960s, while teaching at University College, Nairobi, Kenya, he was one of the prime movers behind the abolition of the college's English department, arguing for its replacement by a Department of African Literature and Languages (two departments were formed, one of literature, the other of language). His novels include *Weep Not, Child* (1964), about the 1950s Mau Mau rebellion against British rule in Kenya, *A Grain of Wheat* (1967), about the war's aftermath, and *Petals of Blood* (1977), about the failure of the East African state, and he has written plays and novels in his native Gĩkũyũ, also sharply critical of post-independence Kenya, such as the novel *Matigarima Njiruungi* (1986). In 1982, after his imprisonment in Kenya and the banning of his books there, Ngũgĩ left to teach abroad, most recently at New York University.

At the beginning of *Decolonising the Mind* (1986), Ngũgĩ declares the book "my farewell to English as a vehicle for any of my writings. From now on it is Gĩkũyũ and Kiswahili all the way." Although Ngũgĩ has subsequently modified this position, he lays out starkly the case against English language and literature as tools of colonialism, which continue to have insidious effects long after formal decolonization. As the student of a British colonial education, Ngũgĩ came to feel that, because of the close relation between language and cultural memory, the imposition of English language and literature severs colonized peoples from their cultural experience—an experience best recovered and explored in indigenous languages.

From Decolonising the Mind
From *The Language of African Literature*

III

I was born into a large peasant family: father, four wives and about twenty-eight children. I also belonged, as we all did in those days, to a wider extended family and to the community as a whole.

We spoke Gĩkũyũ[1] as we worked in the fields. We spoke Gĩkũyũ in and

---

1. Bantu language spoken in western Kenya by approximately five million people.

outside the home. I can vividly recall those evenings of story-telling around the fireside. It was mostly the grown-ups telling the children but everybody was interested and involved. We children would re-tell the stories the following day to other children who worked in the fields picking the pyrethrum flowers,[2] tea-leaves or coffee beans of our European and African landlords.

The stories, with mostly animals as the main characters, were all told in Gĩkũyũ. Hare, being small, weak but full of innovative wit and cunning, was our hero. We identified with him as he struggled against the brutes of prey like lion, leopard, hyena. His victories were our victories and we learnt that the apparently weak can outwit the strong. We followed the animals in their struggle against hostile nature—drought, rain, sun, wind—a confrontation often forcing them to search for forms of co-operation. But we were also interested in their struggles amongst themselves, and particularly between the beasts and the victims of prey. These twin struggles, against nature and other animals, reflected real-life struggles in the human world.

Not that we neglected stories with human beings as the main characters. There were two types of characters in such human-centred narratives: the species of truly human beings with qualities of courage, kindness, mercy, hatred of evil, concern for others; and a man-eat-man two-mouthed species with qualities of greed, selfishness, individualism and hatred of what was good for the larger co-operative community. Co-operation as the ultimate good in a community was a constant theme. It could unite human beings with animals against ogres and beasts of prey, as in the story of how dove, after being fed with castor-oil seeds, was sent to fetch a smith working far away from home and whose pregnant wife was being threatened by these man-eating two-mouthed ogres.

There were good and bad story-tellers. A good one could tell the same story over and over again, and it would always be fresh to us, the listeners. He or she could tell a story told by someone else and make it more alive and dramatic. The differences really were in the use of words and images and the inflexion of voices to effect different tones.

We therefore learnt to value words for their meaning and nuances. Language was not a mere string of words. It had a suggestive power well beyond the immediate and lexical meaning. Our appreciation of the suggestive magical power of language was reinforced by the games we played with words through riddles, proverbs, transpositions of syllables, or through nonsensical but musically arranged words. So we learnt the music of our language on top of the content. The language, through images and symbols, gave us a view of the world, but it had a beauty of its own. The home and the field were then our pre-primary school but what is important, for this discussion, is that the language of our evening teach-ins, and the language of our immediate and wider community, and the language of our work in the fields were one.

And then I went to school, a colonial school, and this harmony was broken. The language of my education was no longer the language of my culture. I first went to Kamaandura, missionary run, and then to another called Maanguuũ run by nationalists grouped around the Gĩkũyũ Independent and Karinga Schools Association. Our language of education was still Gĩkũyũ. The very first time I was ever given an ovation for my writing was over a composition in Gĩkũyũ. So for my first four years there was still harmony between the language of my formal education and that of the Limuru peasant community.

2. Flower used to produce a natural insecticide.

It was after the declaration of a state of emergency over Kenya in 1952[3] that all the schools run by patriotic nationalists were taken over by the colonial regime and were placed under District Education Boards chaired by Englishmen. English became the language of my formal education. In Kenya, English became more than a language: it was *the* language, and all the others had to bow before it in deference.

Thus one of the most humiliating experiences was to be caught speaking Gĩkũyũ in the vicinity of the school. The culprit was given corporal punishment—three to five strokes of the cane on bare buttocks—or was made to carry a metal plate around the neck with inscriptions such as I AM STUPID or I AM A DONKEY. Sometimes the culprits were fined money they could hardly afford. And how did the teachers catch the culprits? A button was initially given to one pupil who was supposed to hand it over to whoever was caught speaking his mother tongue. Whoever had the button at the end of the day would sing who had given it to him and the ensuing process would bring out all the culprits of the day. Thus children were turned into witch-hunters and in the process were being taught the lucrative value of being a traitor to one's immediate community.

The attitude to English was the exact opposite: any achievement in spoken or written English was highly rewarded; prizes, prestige, applause; the ticket to higher realms. English became the measure of intelligence and ability in the arts, the sciences, and all the other branches of learning. English became *the* main determinant of a child's progress up the ladder of formal education.

As you may know, the colonial system of education in addition to its apartheid racial demarcation had the structure of a pyramid: a broad primary base, a narrowing secondary middle, and an even narrower university apex. Selections from primary into secondary were through an examination, in my time called Kenya African Preliminary Examination, in which one had to pass six subjects ranging from Maths to Nature Study and Kiswahili.[4] All the papers were written in English. Nobody could pass the exam who failed the English language paper no matter how brilliantly he had done in the other subjects. I remember one boy in my class of 1954 who had distinctions in all subjects except English, which he had failed. He was made to fail the entire exam. He went on to become a turn boy[5] in a bus company. I who had only passes but a credit in English got a place at the Alliance High School, one of the most elitist institutions for Africans in colonial Kenya. The requirements for a place at the University, Makerere University College,[6] were broadly the same: nobody could go on to wear the undergraduate red gown, no matter how brilliantly they had performed in all the other subjects unless they had a credit—not even a simple pass!—in English. Thus the most coveted place in the pyramid and in the system was only available to the holder of an English language credit card. English was the official vehicle and the magic formula to colonial elitedom.

Literary education was now determined by the dominant language while also reinforcing that dominance. Orature (oral literature) in Kenyan languages stopped. In primary school I now read simplified Dickens and Stevenson alongside Rider Haggard. Jim Hawkins, Oliver Twist, Tom Brown—not Hare,

---

3. The Mau Mau, militant African nationalists, led a revolt in 1952 that resulted in four years of British military operations and the deaths of more than eleven thousand insurgents.
4. Swahili, a Bantu language that is the most widely understood language in Africa.
5. I.e., the person who operates a turnstile.
6. University in Kampala, Uganda, that was connected with the University of London in the 1950s and 1960s.

Leopard and Lion—were now my daily companions in the world of imagination.[7] In secondary school, Scott and G. B. Shaw vied with more Rider Haggard, John Buchan, Alan Paton, Captain W. E. Johns.[8] At Makerere I read
English: from Chaucer to T. S. Eliot with a touch of Graham Greene.[9]

Thus language and literature were taking us further and further from ourselves to other selves, from our world to other worlds.

*   *   *

IV

*   *   *

* * * Language carries culture, and culture carries, particularly through orature and literature, the entire body of values by which we come to perceive
ourselves and our place in the world. How people perceive themselves affects
how they look at their culture, at their politics and at the social production of
wealth, at their entire relationship to nature and to other beings. Language is
thus inseparable from ourselves as a community of human beings with a specific form and character, a specific history, a specific relationship to the world.

V

So what was the colonialist imposition of a foreign language doing to us
children?

The real aim of colonialism was to control the people's wealth: what they
produced, how they produced it, and how it was distributed; to control, in
other words, the entire realm of the language of real life. Colonialism imposed
its control of the social production of wealth through military conquest and
subsequent political dictatorship. But its most important area of domination
was the mental universe of the colonised, the control, through culture, of how
people perceived themselves and their relationship to the world. Economic
and political control can never be complete or effective without mental control. To control a people's culture is to control their tools of self-definition in
relationship to others.

For colonialism this involved two aspects of the same process: the destruction or the deliberate undervaluing of a people's culture, their art, dances,
religions, history, geography, education, orature and literature, and the conscious elevation of the language of the coloniser. The domination of a people's
language by the languages of the colonising nations was crucial to the domination of the mental universe of the colonised.

*   *   *

7. The English novelist Charles Dickens (1812–
1870) wrote *Oliver Twist*. Jim Hawkins is the hero
of *Treasure Island*, by the Scottish fiction writer
and essayist Robert Louis Stevenson (1850–1894).
The English novelist Rider Haggard (1856–1925)
wrote African adventure stories. *Tom Brown's
Schooldays* is by the English novelist Thomas
Hughes (1822–1896).
8. Sir Walter Scott (1771–1832), Scottish novelist. George Bernard Shaw (1856–1950), Anglo-

Irish dramatist. John Buchan (1875–1940),
Scottish author of adventure stories. Alan Paton
(1903–1988), South African novelist. William Earl
Johns (1893–1968), English author of children's
fiction.
9. Geoffrey Chaucer (ca. 1343–1400), English
poet. T. S. Eliot (1888–1965), Anglo-American
poet. Graham Greene (1904–1991), English novelist. "Read": here "majored in."

IX

I started writing in Gĩkũyũ language in 1977 after seventeen years of involvement in Afro-European literature, in my case Afro-English literature.* * * Wherever I have gone, particularly in Europe, I have been confronted with the question: why are you now writing in Gĩkũyũ? Why do you now write in an African language? In some academic quarters I have been confronted with the rebuke, 'Why have you abandoned us?' It was almost as if, in choosing to write in Gĩkũyũ, I was doing something abnormal. But Gĩkũyũ is my mother tongue! The very fact that what common sense dictates in the literary practice of other cultures is being questioned in an African writer is a measure of how far imperialism has distorted the view of African realities. It has turned reality upside down: the abnormal is viewed as normal and the normal is viewed as abnormal. Africa actually enriches Europe: but Africa is made to believe that it needs Europe to rescue it from poverty. Africa's natural and human resources continue to develop Europe and America: but Africa is made to feel grateful for aid from the same quarters that still sit on the back of the continent. Africa even produces intellectuals who now rationalise this upside-down way of looking at Africa.

I believe that my writing in Gĩkũyũ language, a Kenyan language, an African language, is part and parcel of the anti-imperialist struggles of Kenyan and African peoples. In schools and universities our Kenyan languages—that is the languages of the many nationalities which make up Kenya—were associated with negative qualities of backwardness, underdevelopment, humiliation and punishment. We who went through that school system were meant to graduate with a hatred of the people and the culture and the values of the language of our daily humiliation and punishment. I do not want to see Kenyan children growing up in that imperialist-imposed tradition of contempt for the tools of communication developed by their communities and their history. I want them to transcend colonial alienation.

❉   ❉   ❉

We African writers are bound by our calling to do for our languages what Spenser, Milton and Shakespeare did for English; what Pushkin and Tolstoy[1] did for Russian; indeed what all writers in world history have done for their languages by meeting the challenge of creating a literature in them, which process later opens the languages for philosophy, science, technology and all the other areas of human creative endeavours.

1986

1. Aleksandr Pushkin (1799–1837), Russian poet, and Leo Tolstoy (1828–1910), Russian novelist.

SALMAN RUSHDIE

In these excerpts from his essay " 'Commonwealth Literature' Does Not Exist,' " fiction writer Salman Rushdie (b. 1947; see the headnote to him and see his story "The Prophet's Hair," later in this volume) counters the nativist view of English as an imperial yoke that must be thrown off. Recounting the spread of English as a world language and describing its indigenization by the non-English, Rushdie claims it as a vital and expressive South Asian literary language, with its own history and tradition.

[English Is an Indian Literary Language]

I'll begin from an obvious starting place. English is by now the world language. It achieved this status partly as a result of the physical colonization of a quarter of the globe by the British, and it remains ambiguous but central to the affairs of just about all the countries to whom it was given, along with mission schools, trunk roads[1] and the rules of cricket, as a gift of the British colonizers.

But its present-day pre-eminence is not solely—perhaps not even primarily—the result of the British legacy. It is also the effect of the primacy of the United States of America in the affairs of the world. This second impetus towards English could be termed a kind of linguistic neo-colonialism, or just plain pragmatism on the part of many of the world's governments and educationists, according to your point of view.

As for myself, I don't think it is always necessary to take up the anti-colonial—or is it post-colonial?—cudgels against English. What seems to me to be happening is that those peoples who were once colonized by the language are now rapidly remaking it, domesticating it, becoming more and more relaxed about the way they use it—assisted by the English language's enormous flexibility and size, they are carving out large territories for themselves within its frontiers.

To take the case of India, only because it's the one with which I'm most familiar. The debate about the appropriateness of English in post-British India has been raging ever since 1947;[2] but today, I find, it is a debate which has meaning only for the older generation. The children of independent India seem not to think of English as being irredeemably tainted by its colonial provenance. They use it as an Indian language, as one of the tools they have to hand.

(I am simplifying, of course, but the point is broadly true.)

There is also an interesting North–South divide in Indian attitudes to English. In the North, in the so-called 'Hindi belt', where the capital, Delhi, is located, it is possible to think of Hindi as a future national language; but in South India, which is at present suffering from the attempts of central government to *impose* this national language on it, the resentment of Hindi is far greater than of English. After spending quite some time in South India, I've become convinced that English is an essential language in India, not only because of its technical vocabularies and the international communication which it makes possible, but also simply to permit two Indians to talk to each other in a tongue which neither party hates.

Incidentally, in West Bengal, where there is a State-led move against English, the following graffito, a sharp dig at the State's Marxist chief minister, Jyoti Basu, appeared on a wall, in English: it said, 'My son won't learn English; your son won't learn English; but Jyoti Basu will send his son abroad to learn English.'

---

1. Main roads, such as the Grand Trunk Road, the immense highway between Calcutta and Amritsar constructed during the British Raj.
2. When the British relinquished control of India.

One of the points I want to make is that what I've said indicates, I hope, that Indian society and Indian literature have a complex and developing relationship with the English language. * * *

English literature has its Indian branch. By this I mean the literature of the English language. This literature is also Indian literature. There is no incompatibility here. If history creates complexities, let us not try to simplify them.

So: English is an Indian literary language, and by now, thanks to writers like Tagore, Desani, Chaudhuri, Mulk Raj Anand, Raja Rao, Anita Desai[3] and others, it has quite a pedigree. * * *

* * *

In my own case, I have constantly been asked whether I am British, or Indian. The formulation 'Indian-born British writer' has been invented to explain me. But, as I said last night, my new book deals with Pakistan. So what now? 'British-resident Indo-Pakistani writer'? You see the folly of trying to contain writers inside passports.

One of the most absurd aspects of this quest for national authenticity is that—as far as India is concerned, anyway—it is completely fallacious to suppose that there is such a thing as a pure, unalloyed tradition from which to draw. The only people who seriously believe this are religious extremists. The rest of us understand that the very essence of Indian culture is that we possess a mixed tradition, a *mélange* of elements as disparate as ancient Mughal[4] and contemporary Coca-Cola American. To say nothing of Muslim, Buddhist, Jain,[5] Christian, Jewish, British, French, Portuguese, Marxist, Maoist, Trotskyist, Vietnamese, capitalist, and of course Hindu elements. Eclecticism, the ability to take from the world what seems fitting and to leave the rest, has always been a hallmark of the Indian tradition, and today it is at the centre of the best work being done both in the visual arts and in literature. * * *

* * *

* * * As far as Eng. Lit. itself is concerned, I think that if *all* English literatures could be studied together, a shape would emerge which would truly reflect the new shape of the language in the world, and we could see that Eng. Lit. has never been in better shape, because the world language now also possesses a world literature, which is proliferating in every conceivable direction.

The English language ceased to be the sole possession of the English some time ago. * * *

1983

3. Rabindranath Tagore (1861–1941), Bengali poet; G. V. Desani (1909–2000), Nirad C. Chaudhuri (1897–1999), Mulk Raj Anand (1905–2004), Raja Rao (b. 1909), Anita Desai (b. 1937): Indian fiction and nonfiction writers.
4. Dynasty of Muslim emperors who reigned in India, 1526–1858.
5. Jainism is one of India's oldest religions.

JOHN AGARD
b. 1949

John Agard was born and raised in British Guiana (now Guyana) and attended a Roman Catholic high school there, before immigrating to England in 1977. Along with his own collections of poetry, steeped in Caribbean wordplay, rhythms, and idioms that are vivified especially in oral performance, he has also published verse collections, plays, and stories for children. In "Listen Mr Oxford don" he represents his use of West Indian Creole as political and poetic rebellion, while playfully acknowledging, for all his defiance, the complexity of his relation to the Queen's English.

[handwritten: decolonising the English language!]

Listen Mr Oxford don

[handwritten: non standard English, addressing Oxford]

Me not no Oxford don°   *tutor*
me a simple immigrant
from Clapham Common[1]
I didn't graduate
5   I immigrate

But listen Mr Oxford don
I'm a man on de run
and a man on de run
is a dangerous one

10   I ent° have no gun *[handwritten: playing on]*   *don't*
I ent have no knife *[handwritten: an Oxford's racism]*
but mugging de Queen's English[2]
is the story of my life

I dont need no axe
15   to split/   up yu syntax
I dont need no hammer
to mash/   up yu grammar

I warning you Mr Oxford don
I'm a wanted man
20   and a wanted man
is a dangerous one

[handwritten: I'm not a dangerous one, but I have breath.]   Dem accuse me of assault
on de Oxford dictionary/
imagine a concise peaceful man like me/
25   dem want me serve time
for inciting rhyme to riot
but I tekking it quiet
down here in Clapham Common

---

1. In Brixton, a part of London settled by Afro-Caribbean immigrants.

2. English regarded as under the queen's guardianship; hence correct.

I'm not a violent man Mr Oxford don
30 I only armed wit mih human breath
but human breath
is a dangerous weapon

So mek dem send one big word after me
I ent° serving no jail sentence   *am not*
35 I slashing suffix in self-defence
I bashing future wit present tense
and if necessary

I making de Queen's English accessory/to my offence

*Standard English is   1985
subject and target
of the poem.*

DORIS LESSING
b. 1919

Born in Persia (now Iran) to British parents, Doris Lessing (née Tayler) lived in southern Rhodesia (now Zimbabwe) from 1924 to 1949, before settling in England. Her five-novel sequence with the general title *Children of Violence* (beginning with *Martha Quest*, 1952) combines psychological autobiography with powerful explorations of the relationship between blacks and whites in southern Africa. Her combination of psychological introspection, political analysis, social documentary, and feminism gives a characteristic tone to her novels and short stories. These elements are effectively combined in her novel *The Golden Notebook* (1962), which explores with unexhibitionist frankness the sexual problems of an independent woman while at the same time probing the political conscience of an ex-communist and the needs and dilemmas of a creative writer. In the early 1970s, influenced by the writings of the renegade psychologist R. D. Laing and by the principles of Sufism (the mystical, ecstatic aspects of Islam), Lessing's realistic investigations of social issues took a different turn. In *Briefing for a Descent into Hell* (1971) and *The Memoirs of a Survivor* (1974), she explores myth and fantasy, restrained within a broadly realist context. In a series of novels with the general title *Canopus in Argos: Archives* (written between 1979 and 1983), she draws on her reading of the Old and New Testaments, the Apocrypha, and the Koran and borrows conventions from science fiction to describe the efforts of a superhuman, extraterrestrial race to guide human history. The novels convey the scope of human suffering in the twentieth century with a rare imaginative power. On completion of this novel sequence, Lessing took the unusual step of publishing two pseudonymous novels (now known jointly as *The Diaries of Jane Somers*, 1983–84), in which she reverted to the realist mode with which she is most widely associated. *The Good Terrorist* (1985) is also written in the style of documentary realism, but *The Fifth Child* (1988) combines elements of realism and fantasy, exploring the effect on a happy family of the birth of a genetically abnormal, nonhuman child. Her work since the early 1990s has included two candid volumes of autobiography, *Under My Skin* (1994) and *Walking in the Shade* (1997), the four short novels that comprise *The Grandmothers* (2004), several other novels, and a series of short stories. Some of these stories—which deal with racial and social dilemmas as well as with loneliness, the claims of politics, the problems of aging (especially for women), the conflict between the generations, and a whole spectrum of problems of alienation and isolation—have a special pungency and force. Lessing is very much a writer of her time, deeply involved with the changing patterns of thought, feeling, and culture during the last fifty years. She has consistently explored and tested the boundaries of realist technique, without resort to formal experimentalism. Published just on the cusp of second-wave feminism, the story reprinted here, "To Room Nineteen," is a psychologically penetrating study of a woman who finds ultimate fulfillment in neither her marriage nor her children and, feeling trapped by traditional gender roles, seeks solitude in—to echo the title of Virginia Woolf's feminist classic about gender, space, and identity—a room of her own.

To Room Nineteen

This is a story, I suppose, about a failure in intelligence: the Rawlings' marriage was grounded in intelligence.

They were older when they married than most of their married friends: in their well-seasoned late twenties. Both had had a number of affairs, sweet rather than bitter; and when they fell in love—for they did fall in love—had known each other for some time. They joked that they had saved each other "for the real thing." That they had waited so long (but not too long) for this real thing was to them a proof of their sensible discrimination. A good many of their friends had married young, and now (they felt) probably regretted lost opportunities; while others, still unmarried, seemed to them arid, self-doubting, and likely to make desperate or romantic marriages.

Not only they, but others, felt they were well matched: their friends' delight was an additional proof of their happiness. They had played the same roles, male and female, in this group or set, if such a wide, loosely connected, constantly changing constellation of people could be called a set. They had both become, by virtue of their moderation, their humour, and their abstinence from painful experience people to whom others came for advice. They could be, and were, relied on. It was one of those cases of a man and a woman linking themselves whom no one else had ever thought of linking, probably because of their similarities. But then everyone exclaimed: Of course! How right! How was it we never thought of it before!

And so they married amid general rejoicing, and because of their foresight and their sense for what was probable, nothing was a surprise to them.

Both had well-paid jobs. Matthew was a subeditor on a large London newspaper, and Susan worked in an advertising firm. He was not the stuff of which editors or publicised journalists are made, but he was much more than "a subeditor," being one of the essential background people who in fact steady, inspire and make possible the people in the limelight. He was content with this position. Susan had a talent for commercial drawing. She was humorous about the advertisements she was responsible for, but she did not feel strongly about them one way or the other.

Both, before they married, had had pleasant flats, but they felt it unwise to base a marriage on either flat, because it might seem like a submission of personality on the part of the one whose flat it was not. They moved into a new flat in South Kensington on the clear understanding that when their marriage had settled down (a process they knew would not take long, and was in fact more a humorous concession to popular wisdom than what was due to themselves) they would buy a house and start a family.

And this is what happened. They lived in their charming flat for two years, giving parties and going to them, being a popular young married couple, and then Susan became pregnant, she gave up her job, and they bought a house in Richmond. It was typical of this couple that they had a son first, then a daughter, then twins, son and daughter. Everything right, appropriate, and what everyone would wish for, if they could choose. But people did feel these two had chosen; this balanced and sensible family was no more than what was due to them because of their infallible sense for *choosing* right.

And so they lived with their four children in their gardened house in Richmond and were happy. They had everything they had wanted and had planned for.

And yet . . .

Well, even this was expected, that there must be a certain flatness. . . .

Yes, yes, of course, it was natural they sometimes felt like this. Like what?

Their life seemed to be like a snake biting its tail. Matthew's job for the sake of Susan, children, house, and garden—which caravanserai[1] needed a well-paid job to maintain it. And Susan's practical intelligence for the sake of Matthew, the children, the house and the garden—which unit would have collapsed in a week without her.

But there was no point about which either could say: "For the sake of *this* is all the rest." Children? But children can't be a centre of life and a reason for being. They can be a thousand things that are delightful, interesting, satisfying, but they can't be a wellspring to live from. Or they shouldn't be. Susan and Matthew knew that well enough.

Matthew's job? Ridiculous. It was an interesting job, but scarcely a reason for living. Matthew took pride in doing it well; but he could hardly be expected to be proud of the newspaper: the newspaper he read, *his* newspaper, was not the one he worked for.

Their love for each other? Well, that was nearest it. If this wasn't a centre, what was? Yes, it was around this point, their love, that the whole extraordinary structure revolved. For extraordinary it certainly was. Both Susan and Matthew had moments of thinking so, of looking in secret disbelief at this thing they had created: marriage, four children, big house, garden, charwomen,[2] friends, cars . . . and this *thing,* this entity, all of it had come into existence, been blown into being out of nowhere, because Susan loved Matthew and Matthew loved Susan. Extraordinary. So that was the central point, the wellspring.

And if one felt that it simply was not strong enough, important enough, to support it all, well whose fault was that? Certainly neither Susan's nor Matthew's. It was in the nature of things. And they sensibly blamed neither themselves nor each other.

On the contrary, they used their intelligence to preserve what they had created from a painful and explosive world: they looked around them, and took lessons. All around them, marriages collapsing, or breaking, or rubbing along (even worse, they felt). They must not make the same mistakes, they must not.

They had avoided the pitfall so many of their friends had fallen into—of buying a house in the country *for the sake of the children*; so that the husband became a weekend husband, a weekend father, and the wife always careful not to ask what went on in the town flat which they called (in joke) a bachelor flat. No, Matthew was a full-time husband, a full-time father, and at nights,

---

1. Inn with large courtyard, in West Asia.　　2. Household workers.

in the big married bed in the big married bedroom (which had an attractive view of the river) they lay beside each other talking and he told her about his day, and what he had done, and whom he had met; and she told him about her day (not as interesting, but that was not her fault) for both knew of the hidden resentments and deprivations of the woman who has lived her own life—and above all, has earned her own living—and is now dependent on a husband for outside interests and money.

Nor did Susan make the mistake of taking a job for the sake of her independence, which she might very well have done, since her old firm, missing her qualities of humour, balance, and sense, invited her often to go back. Children needed their mother to a certain age, that both parents knew and agreed on; and when these four healthy wisely brought-up children were of the right age, Susan would work again, because she knew, and so did he, what happened to women of fifty at the height of their energy and ability, with grown-up children who no longer needed their full devotion.

So here was this couple, testing their marriage, looking after it, treating it like a small boat full of helpless people in a very stormy sea. Well, of course, so it was. . . . The storms of the world were bad, but not too close—which is not to say they were selfishly felt: Susan and Matthew were both well-informed and responsible people. And the inner storms and quicksands were understood and charted. So everything was all right. Everything was in order. Yes, things were under control.

So what did it matter if they felt dry, flat? People like themselves, fed on a hundred books (psychological, anthropological, sociological) could scarcely be unprepared for the dry, controlled wistfulness which is the distinguishing mark of the intelligent marriage. Two people, endowed with education, with discrimination, with judgement, linked together voluntarily from their will to be happy together and to be of use to others—one sees them everywhere, one knows them, one even is that thing oneself: sadness because so much is after all so little. These two, unsurprised, turned towards each other with even more courtesy and gentle love: this was life, that two people, no matter how carefully chosen, could not be everything to each other. In fact, even to say so, to think in such a way, was banal, they were ashamed to do it.

It was banal, too, when one night Matthew came home late and confessed he had been to a party, taken a girl home and slept with her. Susan forgave him, of course. Except that forgiveness is hardly the word. Understanding, yes. But if you understand something, you don't forgive it, you are the thing itself: forgiveness is for what you *don't* understand. Nor had he *confessed*—what sort of word is that?

The whole thing was not important. After all, years ago they had joked: Of course I'm not going to be faithful to you, no one can be faithful to one other person for a whole lifetime. (And there was the word *faithful*—stupid, all these words, stupid, belonging to a savage old world.) But the incident left both of them irritable. Strange, but they were both bad-tempered, annoyed. There was something unassimilable about it.

Making love splendidly after he had come home that night, both had felt that the idea that Myra Jenkins, a pretty girl met at a party, could be even relevant was ridiculous. They had loved each other for over a decade, would love each other for years more. Who, then, was Myra Jenkins?

Except, thought Susan, unaccountably bad-tempered, she was (is?) the first. In ten years. So either the ten years' fidelity was not important, or she isn't.

TO ROOM NINETEEN / 2547

(No, no, there is something wrong with this way of thinking, there must be.) But if she isn't important, presumably it wasn't important either when Matthew and I first went to bed with each other that afternoon whose delight even now (like a very long shadow at sundown) lays a long, wand-like finger over us. (Why did I say sundown?) Well, if what we felt that afternoon was not important, nothing is important, because if it hadn't been for what we felt, we wouldn't be Mr and Mrs Rawlings with four children, etc., etc. The whole thing is *absurd*—for him to have come home and told me was absurd. For him not to have told me was absurd. For me to care, or for that matter not to care, is absurd . . . and who is Myra Jenkins? Why, no one at all.

There was only one thing to do, and of course these sensible people did it: they put the thing behind them, and consciously, knowing what they were doing, moved forward into a different phase of their marriage, giving thanks for past good fortune as they did so.

For it was inevitable that the handsome, blond, attractive, manly man, Matthew Rawlings, should be at times tempted (oh, what a word!) by the attractive girls at parties she could not attend because of the four children; and that sometimes he would succumb (a word even more repulsive, if possible) and that she, a good-looking woman in the big well-tended garden at Richmond, would sometimes be pierced as by an arrow from the sky with bitterness. Except that bitterness was not in order, it was out of court. Did the casual girls touch the marriage? They did not. Rather it was they who knew defeat because of the handsome Matthew Rawlings' marriage body and soul to Susan Rawlings.

In that case why did Susan feel (though luckily not for longer than a few seconds at a time) as if life had become a desert, and that nothing mattered, and that her children were not her own?

Meanwhile her intelligence continued to assert that all was well. What if her Matthew did have an occasional sweet afternoon, the odd affair? For she knew quite well, except in her moments of aridity, that they were very happy, that the affairs were not important.

Perhaps that was the trouble? It was in the nature of things that the adventures and delights could no longer be hers, because of the four children and the big house that needed so much attention. But perhaps she was secretly wishing, and even knowing that she did, that the wildness and the beauty could be his. But he was married to her. She was married to him. They were married inextricably. And therefore the gods could not strike him with the real magic, not really. Well, was it Susan's fault that after he came home from an adventure he looked harassed rather than fulfilled? (In fact, that was how she knew he had been *unfaithful*, because of his sullen air, and his glances at her, similar to hers at him: What is it that I share with this person that shields all delight from me?) But none of it by anybody's fault. (But what did they feel ought to be somebody's fault?) Nobody's fault, nothing to be at fault, no one to blame, no one to offer or to take it . . . and nothing wrong, either, except that Matthew never was really struck, as he wanted to be, by joy; and that Susan was more and more often threatened by emptiness. (It was usually in the garden that she was invaded by this feeling: she was coming to avoid the garden, unless the children or Matthew were with her.) There was no need to use the dramatic words, unfaithful, forgive, and the rest: intelligence forbade them. Intelligence barred, too, quarrelling, sulking, anger, silences of withdrawal, accusations and tears. Above all, intelligence forbids tears.

A high price has to be paid for the happy marriage with the four healthy children in the large white gardened house.

And they were paying it, willingly, knowing what they were doing. When they lay side by side or breast to breast in the big civilised bedroom overlooking the wild sullied river, they laughed, often, for no particular reason; but they knew it was really because of these two small people, Susan and Matthew, supporting such an edifice on their intelligent love. The laugh comforted them; it saved them both, though from what, they did not know.

They were now both fortyish. The older children, boy and girl were ten and eight, at school. The twins, six, were still at home. Susan did not have nurses or girls to help her: childhood is short; and she did not regret the hard work. Often enough she was bored, since small children can be boring; she was often very tired; but she regretted nothing. In another decade, she would turn herself back into being a woman with a life of her own.

Soon the twins would go to school, and they would be away from home from nine until four. These hours, so Susan saw it, would be the preparation for her own slow emancipation away from the role of hub-of-the-family into woman-with-her-own-life. She was already planning for the hours of freedom when all the children would be "off her hands." That was the phrase used by Matthew and by Susan and by their friends, for the moment when the youngest child went off to school. "They'll be off your hands, darling Susan, and you'll have time to yourself." So said Matthew, the intelligent husband, who had often enough commended and consoled Susan, standing by her in spirit during the years when her soul was not her own, as she said, but her children's.

What it amounted to was that Susan saw herself as she had been at twenty-eight, unmarried; and then again somewhere about fifty, blossoming from the root of what she had been twenty years before. As if the essential Susan were in abeyance, as if she were in cold storage. Matthew said something like this to Susan one night: and she agreed that it was true—she did feel something like that. What, then, was this essential Susan? She did not know. Put like that it sounded ridiculous, and she did not really feel it. Anyway, they had a long discussion about the whole thing before going off to sleep in each other's arms.

So the twins went off to their school, two bright affectionate children who had no problems about it, since their older brother and sister had trodden this path so successfully before them. And now Susan was going to be alone in the big house, every day of the school term, except for the daily woman who came in to clean.

It was now, for the first time in this marriage, that something happened which neither of them had foreseen.

This is what happened. She returned, at nine-thirty, from taking the twins to the school by car, looking forward to seven blissful hours of freedom. On the first morning she was simply restless, worrying about the twins "naturally enough" since this was their first day away at school. She was hardly able to contain herself until they came back. Which they did happily, excited by the world of school, looking forward to the next day. And the next day Susan took them, dropped them, came back, and found herself reluctant to enter her big and beautiful home because it was as if something was waiting for her there that she did not wish to confront. Sensibly, however, she parked the car in the garage, entered the house, spoke to Mrs Parkes the daily woman about her duties, and went up to her bedroom. She was possessed by a fever which

drove her out again, downstairs, into the kitchen, where Mrs Parkes was making cake and did not need her, and into the garden. There she sat on a bench
and tried to calm herself, looking at trees, at a brown glimpse of the river. But
she was filled with tension, like a panic: as if an enemy was in the garden with
her. She spoke to herself severely, thus: All this is quite natural. First, I spent
twelve years of my adult life working, *living my own life*. Then I married, and
from the moment I became pregnant for the first time I signed myself over,
so to speak, to other people. To the children. Not for one moment in twelve
years have I been alone, had time to myself. So now I have to learn to be
myself again. That's all.

And she went indoors to help Mrs Parkes cook and clean, and found some
sewing to do for the children. She kept herself occupied every day. At the end
of the first term she understood she felt two contrary emotions. First: secret
astonishment and dismay that during those weeks when the house was empty
of children she had in fact been more occupied (had been careful to keep
herself occupied) than ever she had been when the children were around her
needing her continual attention. Second: that now she knew the house would
be full of them, and for five weeks, she resented the fact she would never be
alone. She was already looking back at those hours of sewing, cooking (but by
herself), as at a lost freedom which would not be hers for five long weeks. And
the two months of term which would succeed the five weeks stretched allur-
ingly open to her—freedom. But what freedom—when in fact she had been
so careful *not* to be free of small duties during the last weeks? She looked at
herself, Susan Rawlings, sitting in a big chair by the window in the bedroom,
sewing shirts or dresses, which she might just as well have bought. She saw
herself making cakes for hours at a time in the big family kitchen: yet usually
she bought cakes. What she saw was a woman alone, that was true, but she
had not felt alone. For instance, Mrs Parkes was always somewhere in the
house. And she did not like being in the garden at all, because of the closeness
there of the enemy—irritation, restlessness, emptiness, whatever it was, which
keeping her hands occupied made less dangerous for some reason.

Susan did not tell Matthew of these thoughts. They were not sensible. She
did not recognize herself in them. What should she say to her dear friend and
husband Matthew? "When I go into the garden, that is, if the children are not
there, I feel as if there is an enemy there waiting to invade me." "What enemy,
Susan darling?" "Well I don't know, really. . . ." "Perhaps you should see a
doctor?"

No, clearly this conversation should not take place. The holidays began and
Susan welcomed them. Four children, lively, energetic, intelligent, demanding: she was never, not for a moment of her day, alone. If she was in a room,
they would be in the next room, or waiting for her to do something for them;
or it would soon be time for lunch or tea, or to take one of them to the dentist.
Something to do: five weeks of it, thank goodness.

On the fourth day of these so welcome holidays, she found she was storming
with anger at the twins, two shrinking beautiful children who (and this is what
checked her) stood hand in hand looking at her with sheer dismayed disbelief.
This was their calm mother, shouting at them. And for what? They had come
to her with some game, some bit of nonsense. They looked at each other,
moved closer for support, and went off hand in hand, leaving Susan holding
on to the windowsill of the living room, breathing deep, feeling sick. She went
to lie down, telling the older children she had a headache. She heard the boy

Harry telling the little ones: "It's all right, Mother's got a headache." She heard that *It's all right* with pain.

That night she said to her husband: "Today I shouted at the twins, quite unfairly." She sounded miserable, and he said gently: "Well, what of it?"

"It's more of an adjustment than I thought, their going to school."

"But Susie, Susie darling. . . ." For she was crouched weeping on the bed. He comforted her: "Susan, what is all this about? You shouted at them? What of it? If you shouted at them fifty times a day it wouldn't be more than the little devils deserve." But she wouldn't laugh. She wept. Soon he comforted her with his body. She became calm. Calm, she wondered what was wrong with her, and why she should mind so much that she might, just once, have behaved unjustly with the children. What did it matter? They had forgotten it all long ago: Mother had a headache and everything was all right.

It was a long time later that Susan understood that that night, when she had wept and Matthew had driven the misery out of her with his big solid body, was the last time, ever in their married life, that they had been—to use their mutual language—with each other. And even that was a lie, because she had not told him of her real fears at all.

The five weeks passed, and Susan was in control of herself, and good and kind, and she looked forward to the end of the holidays with a mixture of fear and longing. She did not know what to expect. She took the twins off to school (the elder children took themselves to school) and she returned to the house determined to face the enemy wherever he was, in the house, or the garden or—where?

She was again restless, she was possessed by restlessness. She cooked and sewed and worked as before, day after day, while Mrs Parkes remonstrated: "Mrs Rawlings, what's the need for it? I can do that, it's what you pay me for."

And it was so irrational that she checked herself. She would put the car into the garage, go up to her bedroom, and sit, hands in her lap, forcing herself to be quiet. She listened to Mrs Parkes moving around the house. She looked out into the garden and saw the branches shake the trees. She sat defeating the enemy, restlessness. Emptiness. She ought to be thinking about her life, about herself. But she did not. Or perhaps she could not. As soon as she forced her mind to think about Susan (for what else did she want to be alone for?) it skipped off to thoughts of butter or school clothes. Or it thought of Mrs Parkes. She realised that she sat listening for the movements of the cleaning woman, following her every turn, bend, thought. She followed her in her mind from kitchen to bathroom, from table to oven, and it was as if the duster, the cleaning cloth, the saucepan, were in her own hand. She would hear herself saying: No, not like that, don't put that there. . . . Yet she did not give a damn what Mrs Parkes did, or if she did it at all. Yet she could not prevent herself from being conscious of her, every minute. Yes, this was what was wrong with her: she needed, when she was alone, to be really alone, with no one near. She could not endure the knowledge that in ten minutes or in half an hour Mrs Parkes would call up the stairs: "Mrs Rawlings, there's no silver polish. Madam, we're out of flour."

So she left the house and went to sit in the garden where she was screened from the house by trees. She waited for the demon to appear and claim her, but he did not.

She was keeping him off, because she had not, after all, come to an end of arranging herself.

She was planning how to be somewhere where Mrs Parkes would not come after her with a cup of tea, or a demand to be allowed to telephone (always irritating since Susan did not care who she telephoned or how often), or just a nice talk about something. Yes, she needed a place, or a state of affairs, where it would not be necessary to keep reminding herself: In ten minutes I must telephone Matthew about . . . and at half past three I must leave early for the children because the car needs cleaning. And at ten o'clock tomorrow I must remember. . . . She was possessed with resentment that the seven hours of freedom in every day (during weekdays in the school term) were not free, that never, not for one second, ever, was she free from the pressure of time, from having to remember this or that. She could never forget herself; never really let herself go into forgetfulness.

Resentment. It was poisoning her. (She looked at this emotion and thought it was absurd. Yet she felt it.) She was a prisoner. (She looked at this thought too, and it was no good telling herself it was a ridiculous one.) She must tell Matthew—but what? She was filled with emotions that were utterly ridiculous, that she despised, yet that nevertheless she was feeling so strongly she could not shake them off.

The school holidays came round, and this time they were for nearly two months, and she behaved with a conscious controlled decency that nearly drove her crazy. She would lock herself in the bathroom, and sit on the edge of the bath, breathing deep, trying to let go into some kind of calm. Or she went up into the spare room, usually empty, where no one would expect her to be. She heard the children calling "Mother, Mother," and kept silent, feeling guilty. Or she went to the very end of the garden, by herself, and looked at the slow-moving brown river; she looked at the river and closed her eyes and breathed slow and deep, taking it into her being, into her veins.

Then she returned to the family, wife and mother, smiling and responsible, feeling as if the pressure of these people—four lively children and her husband—were a painful pressure on the surface of her skin, a hand pressing on her brain. She did not once break down into irritation during these holidays, but it was like living out a prison sentence, and when the children went back to school, she sat on a white stone seat near the flowing river, and she thought: It is not even a year since the twins went to school, since *they were off my hands* (What on earth did I think I meant when I used that stupid phrase?) and yet I'm a different person. I'm simply not myself. I don't understand it.

Yet she had to understand it. For she knew that this structure—big white house, on which the mortgage still cost four hundred a year, a husband, so good and kind and insightful, four children, all doing so nicely, and the garden where she sat, and Mrs Parkes the cleaning woman—all this depended on her, and yet she could not understand why, or even what it was she contributed to it.

She said to Matthew in their bedroom: "I think there must be something wrong with me."

And he said: "Surely not, Susan? You look marvelous—you're as lovely as ever."

She looked at the handsome blond man, with his clear, intelligent, blue-eyed face, and thought: Why is it I can't tell him? Why not? And she said: "I need to be alone more than I am."

At which he swung his slow blue gaze at her, and she saw what she had been dreading: Incredulity. Disbelief. And fear. An incredulous blue stare from a stranger who was her husband, as close to her as her own breath.

He said: "But the children are at school and off your hands."

She said to herself: I've got to force myself to say: Yes, but do you realise that I never feel free? There's never a moment I can say to myself: There's nothing I have to remind myself about, nothing I have to do in half an hour, or an hour, or two hours. . . .

But she said: "I don't feel well."

He said: "Perhaps you need a holiday."

She said, appalled: "But not without you, surely?" For she could not imagine herself going off without him. Yet that was what he meant. Seeing her face, he laughed, and opened his arms, and she went into them, thinking: Yes, yes, but why can't I say it? And what is it I have to say?

She tried to tell him, about never being free. And he listened and said: "But Susan, what sort of freedom can you possibly want—short of being dead! Am I ever free? I go to the office, and I have to be there at ten—all right, half past ten, sometimes. And I have to do this or that, don't I? Then I've got to come home at a certain time—I don't mean it, you know I don't—but if I'm not going to be back home at six I telephone you. When can I ever say to myself: I have nothing to be responsible for in the next six hours?"

Susan, hearing this, was remorseful. Because it was true. The good marriage, the house, the children, depended just as much on his voluntary bondage as it did on hers. But why did he not feel bound? Why didn't he chafe and become restless? No, there was something really wrong with her and this proved it.

And that word *bondage*—why had she used it? She had never felt marriage, or the children, as bondage. Neither had he, or surely they wouldn't be together lying in each other's arms content after twelve years of marriage.

No, her state (whatever it was) was irrelevant, nothing to do with her real good life with her family. She had to accept the fact that after all, she was an irrational person and to live with it. Some people had to live with crippled arms, or stammers, or being deaf. She would have to live knowing she was subject to a state of mind she could not own.

Nevertheless, as a result of this conversation with her husband, there was a new regime next holidays.

The spare room at the top of the house now had a cardboard sign saying: PRIVATE! DO NOT DISTURB! on it. (This sign had been drawn in coloured chalks by the children, after a discussion between the parents in which it was decided this was psychologically the right thing.) The family and Mrs Parkes knew this was "Mother's Room" and that she was entitled to her privacy. Many serious conversations took place between Matthew and the children about not taking Mother for granted. Susan overheard the first, between father and Harry, the older boy, and was surprised at her irritation over it. Surely she could have a room somewhere in that big house and retire into it without such a fuss being made? Without it being so solemnly discussed? Why couldn't she simply have announced: "I'm going to fit out the little top room for myself, and when I'm in it I'm not to be disturbed for anything short of fire"? Just that, and finished; instead of long earnest discussions. When she heard Harry and Matthew explaining it to the twins with Mrs Parkes coming in—"Yes, well, a family sometimes gets on top of a woman"—she had to go right away to the bottom of the garden until the devils of exasperation had finished their dance in her blood.

But now there was a room, and she could go there when she liked, she used it seldom: she felt even more caged there than in her bedroom. One day she had gone up there after a lunch for ten children she had cooked and served because Mrs Parkes was not there, and had sat alone for a while looking into the garden. She saw the children stream out from the kitchen and stand looking up at the window where she sat behind the curtains. They were all—her children and their friends—discussing Mother's Room. A few minutes later, the chase of children in some game came pounding up the stairs, but ended as abruptly as if they had fallen over a ravine, so sudden was the silence. They had remembered she was there, and had gone silent in a great gale of "Hush! Shhhhh! Quiet, you'll disturb her. . . ." And they went tiptoeing downstairs like criminal conspirators. When she came down to make tea for them, they all apologised. The twins put their arms around her, from front and back, making a human cage of loving limbs, and promised it would never occur again. "We forgot, Mummy, we forgot all about it!"

What it amounted to was that Mother's Room, and her need for privacy, had become a valuable lesson in respect for other people's rights. Quite soon Susan was going up to the room only because it was a lesson it was a pity to drop. Then she took sewing up there, and the children and Mrs Parkes came in and out: it had become another family room.

She sighed, and smiled, and resigned herself—she made jokes at her own expense with Matthew over the room. That is, she did from the self she liked, she respected. But at the same time, something inside her howled with impatience, with rage. . . . And she was frightened. One day she found herself kneeling by her bed and praying: "Dear God, keep it away from me, keep him away from me." She meant the devil, for she now thought of it, not caring if she were irrational, as some sort of demon. She imagined him, or it, as a youngish man, or perhaps a middle-aged man pretending to be young. Or a man young-looking from immaturity? At any rate, she saw the young-looking face which, when she drew closer, had dry lines about mouth and eyes. He was thinnish, meagre in build. And he had a reddish complexion, and ginger hair. That was he—a gingery, energetic man, and he wore a reddish hairy jacket, unpleasant to the touch.

Well, one day she saw him. She was standing at the bottom of the garden, watching the river ebb past, when she raised her eyes and saw this person, or being, sitting on the white stone bench. He was looking at her, and grinning. In his hand was a long crooked stick, which he had picked off the ground, or broken off the tree above him. He was absent-mindedly, out of an absent-minded or freakish impulse of spite, using the stick to stir around in the coils of a blindworm or a grass snake (or some kind of snakelike creature: it was whitish and unhealthy to look at, unpleasant). The snake was twisting about, flinging its coils from side to side in a kind of dance of protest against the teasing prodding stick.

Susan looked at him thinking: Who is the stranger? What is he doing in our garden? Then she recognised the man around whom her terrors had crystallised. As she did so, he vanished. She made herself walk over to the bench. A shadow from a branch lay across thin emerald grass, moving jerkily over its roughness, and she could see why she had taken it for a snake, lashing and twisting. She went back to the house thinking: Right, then, so I've seen him with my own eyes, so I'm not crazy after all—there *is* a danger because I've seen him. He is lurking in the garden and sometimes even in the house, and he wants *to get into me and to take me over.*

She dreamed of having a room or a place, anywhere, where she could go and sit, by herself, no one knowing where she was.

Once, near Victoria, she found herself outside a news agent that had Rooms to Let advertised. She decided to rent a room, telling no one. Sometimes she could take the train in to Richmond and sit alone in it for an hour or two. Yet how could she? A room would cost three or four pounds a week, and she earned no money, and how could she explain to Matthew that she needed such a sum? What for? It did not occur to her that she was taking it for granted she wasn't going to tell him about the room.

Well, it was out of the question, having a room; yet she knew she must.

One day, when a school term was well established, and none of the children had measles or other ailments, and everything seemed in order, she did the shopping early, explained to Mrs Parkes she was meeting an old school friend, took the train to Victoria, searched until she found a small quiet hotel, and asked for a room for the day. They did not let rooms by the day, the manageress said, looking doubtful, since Susan so obviously was not the kind of woman who needed a room for unrespectable reasons. Susan made a long explanation about not being well, being unable to shop without frequent rests for lying down. At last she was allowed to rent the room provided she paid a full night's price for it. She was taken up by the manageress and a maid, both concerned over the state of her health . . . which must be pretty bad if, living at Richmond (she had signed her name and address in the register), she needed a shelter at Victoria.

The room was ordinary and anonymous, and was just what Susan needed. She put a shilling in the gas fire, and sat, eyes shut, in a dingy armchair with her back to a dingy window. She was alone. She was alone. She was alone. She could feel pressures lifting off her. First the sounds of traffic came very loud; then they seemed to vanish; she might even have slept a little. A knock on the door: it was Miss Townsend the manageress, bringing her a cup of tea with her own hands, so concerned was she over Susan's long silence and possible illness.

Miss Townsend was a lonely woman of fifty, running this hotel with all the rectitude expected of her, and she sensed in Susan the possibility of understanding companionship. She stayed to talk. Susan found herself in the middle of a fantastic story about her illness, which got more and more improbable as she tried to make it tally with the large house at Richmond, well-off husband, and four children. Suppose she said instead: Miss Townsend, I'm here in your hotel because I need to be alone for a few hours, above all *alone and with no one knowing where I am.* She said it mentally, and saw, mentally, the look that would inevitably come on Miss Townsend's elderly maiden's face. "Miss Townsend, my four children and my husband are driving me insane, do you understand that? Yes, I can see from the gleam of hysteria in your eyes that comes from loneliness controlled but only just contained that I've got everything in the world you've ever longed for. Well, Miss Townsend, I don't want any of it. You can have it, Miss Townsend. I wish I was absolutely alone in the world, like you. Miss Townsend, I'm besieged by seven devils, Miss Townsend, Miss Townsend, let me stay here in your hotel where the devils can't get me. . . ." Instead of saying all this, she described her anaemia, agreed to try Miss Townsend's remedy for it, which was raw liver, minced, between whole-meal bread, and said yes, perhaps it would be better if she stayed at home and let a friend do shopping for her. She paid her bill and left the hotel, defeated.

At home Mrs Parkes said she didn't really like it, no, not really, when Mrs Rawlings was away from nine in the morning until five. The teacher had telephoned from school to say Joan's teeth were paining her, and she hadn't known what to say; and what was she to make for the children's tea, Mrs Rawlings hadn't said.

All this was nonsense, of course. Mrs Parkes's complaint was that Susan had withdrawn herself spiritually, leaving the burden of the big house on her.

Susan looked back at her day of "freedom" which had resulted in her becoming a friend to the lonely Miss Townsend, and in Mrs Parkes's remonstrances. Yet she remembered the short blissful hour of being alone, really alone. She was determined to arrange her life, no matter what it cost, so that she could have that solitude more often. An absolute solitude, where no one knew her or cared about her.

But how? She thought of saying to her old employer: I want you to back me up in a story with Matthew that I am doing part-time work for you. The truth is that . . . but she would have to tell him a lie too, and which lie? She could not say: I want to sit by myself three or four times a week in a rented room. And besides, he knew Matthew, and she could not really ask him to tell lies on her behalf, apart from his being bound to think it meant a lover.

Suppose she really took a part-time job, which she could get through fast and efficiently, leaving time for herself. What job? Addressing envelopes? Canvassing?

And there was Mrs Parkes, working widow, who knew exactly what she was prepared to give to the house, who knew by instinct when her mistress withdrew in spirit from her responsibilities. Mrs Parkes was one of the servers of this world, but she needed someone to serve. She had to have Mrs Rawlings, her madam, at the top of the house or in the garden, so that she could come and get support from her: "Yes, the bread's not what it was when I was a girl. . . . Yes, Harry's got a wonderful appetite, I wonder where he puts it all. . . . Yes, it's lucky the twins are so much of a size, they can wear each other's shoes, that's a saving in these hard times. . . . Yes, the cherry jam from Switzerland is not a patch on the jam from Poland, and three times the price. . . ." And so on. That sort of talk Mrs Parkes must have, every day, or she would leave, not knowing herself why she left.

Susan Rawlings, thinking these thoughts, found that she was prowling through the great thicketed garden like a wild cat: she was walking up the stairs, down the stairs, through the rooms, into the garden, along the brown running river, back, up through the house, down again. . . . It was a wonder Mrs Parkes did not think it strange. But on the contrary, Mrs Rawlings could do what she liked, she could stand on her head if she wanted, provided she was *there*. Susan Rawlings prowled and muttered through her house, hating Mrs Parkes, hating poor Miss Townsend, dreaming of her hour of solitude in the dingy respectability of Miss Townsend's hotel bedroom, and she knew quite well she was mad. Yes, she was mad.

She said to Matthew that she must have a holiday. Matthew agreed with her. This was not as things had been once—how they had talked in each other's arms in the marriage bed. He had, she knew, diagnosed her finally as *unreasonable*. She had become someone outside himself that he had to manage. They were living side by side in this house like two tolerably friendly strangers.

Having told Mrs Parkes, or rather, asked for her permission, she went off

2556 / DORIS LESSING

on a walking holiday in Wales. She chose the remotest place she knew of. Every morning the children telephoned her before they went off to school, to encourage and support her, just as they had over Mother's Room. Every evening she telephoned them, spoke to each child in turn, and then to Matthew. Mrs Parkes, given permission to telephone for instructions or advice, did so every day at lunchtime. When, as happened three times, Mrs Rawlings was out on the mountainside, Mrs Parkes asked that she should ring back at such and such a time, for she would not be happy in what she was doing without Mrs Rawlings' blessing.

Susan prowled over wild country with the telephone wire holding her to her duty like a leash. The next time she must telephone, or wait to be telephoned, nailed her to her cross. The mountains themselves seemed trammelled by her unfreedom. Everywhere on the mountains, where she met no one at all, from breakfast time to dusk, excepting sheep, or a shepherd, she came face to face with her own craziness which might attack her in the broadest valleys, so that they seemed too small; or on a mountaintop from which she could see a hundred other mountains and valleys, so that they seemed too low, too small, with the sky pressing down too close. She would stand gazing at a hillside brilliant with ferns and bracken, jewelled with running water, and see nothing but her devil, who lifted inhuman eyes at her from where he leaned negligently on a rock, switching at his ugly yellow boots with a leafy twig.

She returned to her home and family, with the Welsh emptiness at the back of her mind like a promise of freedom.

She told her husband she wanted to have an *au pair* girl.[3]

They were in their bedroom, it was late at night, the children slept. He sat, shirted and slippered, in a chair by the window, looking out. She sat brushing her hair and watching him in the mirror. A time-hallowed scene in the connubial bedroom. He said nothing, while she heard the arguments coming into his mind, only to be rejected because every one was *reasonable.*

"It seems strange to get one now, after all, the children are in school most of the day. Surely the time for you to have help was when you were stuck with them day and night. Why don't you ask Mrs Parkes to cook for you? She's even offered to—I can understand if you are tired of cooking for six people. But you know that an *au pair* girl means all kinds of problems, it's not like having an ordinary char[4] in during the day. . . ."

Finally he said carefully: "Are you thinking of going back to work?"

"No," she said, "no, not really," She made herself sound vague, rather stupid. She went on brushing her black hair and peering at herself so as to be oblivious of the short uneasy glances her Matthew kept giving her. "Do you think we can't afford it?" she went on vaguely, not at all the old efficient Susan who knew exactly what they could afford.

"It's not that," he said, looking out of the window at dark trees, so as not to look at her. Meanwhile she examined a round, candid, pleasant face with clear dark brows and clear grey eyes. A sensible face. She brushed thick healthy black hair and thought: Yet that's the reflection of a madwoman. How very strange! Much more to the point if what looked back at me was the gingery green-eyed demon with his dry meagre smile. . . . Why wasn't Matthew agreeing? After all, what else could he do? She was breaking her part of the bargain

3. Live-in foreigner who serves a family in exchange for learning its language.   4. Charwoman.

and there was no way of forcing her to keep it: that her spirit, her soul, should live in this house, so that the people in it could grow like plants in water, and Mrs Parkes remain content in their service. In return for this, he would be a good loving husband, and responsible towards the children. Well, nothing like this had been true of either of them for a long time. He did his duty, perfunctorily; she did not even pretend to do hers. And he had become like other husbands, with his real life in his work and the people he met there, and very likely a serious affair. All this was her fault.

At last he drew heavy curtains, blotting out the trees, and turned to force her attention: "Susan, are you really sure we need a girl?" But she would not meet his appeal at all: She was running the brush over her hair again and again, lifting fine black clouds in a small hiss of electricity. She was peering in and smiling as if she were amused at the clinging hissing hair that followed the brush.

"Yes, I think it would be a good idea on the whole," she said, with the cunning of a madwoman evading the real point.

In the mirror she could see her Matthew lying on his back, his hands behind his head, staring upwards, his face sad and hard. She felt her heart (the old heart of Susan Rawlings) soften and call out to him. But she set it to be indifferent.

He said: "Susan, the children?" It was an appeal that *almost* reached her. He opened his arms, lifting them from where they had lain by his sides, palms up, empty. She had only to run across and fling herself into them, onto his hard, warm chest, and melt into herself, into Susan. But she could not. She would not see his lifted arms. She said vaguely: "Well, surely it'll be even better for them? We'll get a French or a German girl and they'll learn the language."

In the dark she lay beside him, feeling frozen, a stranger. She felt as if Susan had been spirited away. She disliked very much this woman who lay here, cold and indifferent beside a suffering man, but she could not change her.

Next morning she set about getting a girl, and very soon came Sophie Traub from Hamburg, a girl of twenty, laughing, healthy, blue-eyed, intending to learn English. Indeed, she already spoke a good deal. In return for a room— "Mother's Room"—and her food, she undertook to do some light cooking, and to be with the children when Mrs Rawlings asked. She was an intelligent girl and understood perfectly what was needed. Susan said: "I go off sometimes, for the morning or for the day—well, sometimes the children run home from school, or they ring up, or a teacher rings up. I should be here, really. And there's the daily woman. . . ." And Sophie laughed her deep fruity *Fräulein's* laugh, showed her fine white teeth and her dimples, and said: "You want some person to play mistress of the house sometimes, not so?"

"Yes, that is just so," said Susan, a bit dry, despite herself, thinking in secret fear how easy it was, how much nearer to the end she was than she thought. Healthy Fräulein Traub's instant understanding of their position proved this to be true.

The *au pair* girl, because of her own common sense, or (as Susan said to herself with her new inward shudder) because she had been *chosen* so well by Susan, was a success with everyone, the children liking her, Mrs Parkes forgetting almost at once that she was German, and Matthew finding her "nice to have around the house." For he was now taking things as they came, from the surface of life, withdrawn both as a husband and a father from the household.

One day Susan saw how Sophie and Mrs Parkes were talking and laughing in the kitchen, and she announced that she would be away until teatime. She knew exactly where to go and what she must look for. She took the District Line to South Kensington, changed to the Circle, got off at Paddington, and walked around looking at the smaller hotels until she was satisfied with one which had FRED'S HOTEL painted on windowpanes that needed cleaning. The façade was a faded shiny yellow, like unhealthy skin. A door at the end of a passage said she must knock; she did, and Fred appeared. He was not at all attractive, not in any way, being fattish, and run-down, and wearing a tasteless striped suit. He had small sharp eyes in a white creased face, and was quite prepared to let Mrs Jones (she chose the farcical name deliberately, staring him out) have a room three days a week from ten until six. Provided of course that she paid in advance each time she came? Susan produced fifteen shillings (no price had been set by him) and held it out, still fixing him with a bold unblinking challenge she had not known until then she could use at will. Looking at her still, he took up a ten-shilling note from her palm between thumb and forefinger, fingered it; then shuffled up two half crowns, held out his own palm with these bits of money displayed thereon, and let his gaze lower broodingly at them. They were standing in the passage, a red-shaded light above, bare boards beneath, and a strong smell of floor polish rising about them. He shot his gaze up at her over the still-extended palm, and smiled as if to say: What do you take me for? "I shan't," said Susan, "be using this room for the purposes of making money." He still waited. She added another five shillings, at which he nodded and said: "You pay, and I ask no questions." "Good," said Susan. He now went past her to the stairs, and there waited a moment: the light from the street door being in her eyes, she lost sight of him momentarily. Then she saw a sober-suited, white-faced, white-balding little man trotting up the stairs like a waiter, and she went after him. They proceeded in utter silence up the stairs of this house where no questions were asked— Fred's Hotel, which could afford the freedom for its visitors that poor Miss Townsend's hotel could not. The room was hideous. It had a single window, with thin green brocade curtains, a three-quarter bed that had a cheap green satin bedspread on it, a fireplace with a gas fire and a shilling meter by it, a chest of drawers, and a green wicker armchair.

"Thank you," said Susan, knowing that Fred (if this was Fred, and not George, or Herbert or Charlie) was looking at her not so much with curiosity, an emotion he would not own to, for professional reasons, but with a philosophical sense of what was appropriate. Having taken her money and shown her up and agreed to everything, he was clearly disapproving of her for coming here. She did not belong here at all, so his look said. (But she knew, already, how very much she did belong: the room had been waiting for her to join it.) "Would you have me called at five o'clock, please?" and he nodded and went downstairs.

It was twelve in the morning. She was free. She sat in the armchair, she simply sat, she closed her eyes and sat and let herself be alone. She was alone and no one knew where she was. When a knock came on the door she was annoyed, and prepared to show it: but it was Fred himself, it was five o'clock and he was calling her as ordered. He flicked his sharp little eyes over the room—bed, first. It was undisturbed. She might never have been in the room at all. She thanked him, said she would be returning the day after tomorrow, and left. She was back home in time to cook supper, to put the children to

bed, to cook a second supper for her husband and herself later. And to welcome Sophie back from the pictures where she had gone with a friend. All
these things she did cheerfully, willingly. But she was thinking all the time of
the hotel room, she was longing for it with her whole being.

Three times a week. She arrived promptly at ten, looked Fred in the eyes,
gave him twenty shillings, followed him up the stairs, went into the room, and
shut the door on him with gentle firmness. For Fred, disapproving of her being
here at all, was quite ready to let friendship, or at least acquaintanceship,
follow his disapproval, if only she would let him. But he was content to go off
on her dismissing nod, with the twenty shillings in his hand.

She sat in the armchair and shut her eyes.

What did she *do* in the room? Why, nothing at all. From the chair, when it
had rested her, she went to the window, stretching her arms, smiling, treas-
uring her anonymity, to look out. She was no longer Susan Rawlings, mother
of four, wife of Matthew, employer of Mrs Parkes and of Sophie Traub, with
these and those relations with friends, schoolteachers, tradesmen. She no
longer was mistress of the big white house and garden, owning clothes suitable
for this and that activity or occasion. She was Mrs Jones, and she was alone,
and she had no past and no future. Here I am, she thought, after all these
years of being married and having children and playing those roles of responsibility—and I'm just the same. Yet there have been times I thought that nothing existed of me except the roles that went with being Mrs Matthew Rawlings.
Yes, here I am, and if I never saw any of my family again, here I would still be
. . . how very strange that is! And she leaned on the sill, and looked into the
street, loving the men and women who passed, because she did not know them.
She looked at the downtrodden buildings over the street, and at the sky, wet
and dingy, or sometimes blue, and she felt she had never seen buildings or
sky before. And then she went back to the chair, empty, her mind a blank.
Sometimes she talked aloud, saying nothing—an exclamation, meaningless,
followed by a comment about the floral pattern on the thin rug, or a stain on
the green satin coverlet. For the most part, she wool-gathered—what word is
there for it?—brooded, wandered, simply went dark, feeling emptiness run
deliciously through her veins like the movement of her blood.

This room had become more her own than the house she lived in. One
morning she found Fred taking her a flight higher than usual. She stopped,
refusing to go up, and demanded her usual room, Number 19. "Well, you'll
have to wait half an hour then," he said. Willingly she descended to the dark
disinfectant-smelling hall, and sat waiting until the two, man and woman,
came down the stairs, giving her swift indifferent glances before they hurried
out into the street, separating at the door. She went up to the room, *her* room,
which they had just vacated. It was no less hers, though the windows were set
wide open, and a maid was straightening the bed as she came in.

After these days of solitude, it was both easy to play her part as mother and
wife, and difficult—because it was so easy: she felt an impostor. She felt as if
her shell moved here, with her family, answering to Mummy, Mother, Susan,
Mrs Rawlings. She was surprised no one saw through her, that she wasn't
turned out of doors, as a fake. On the contrary, it seemed the children loved
her more; Matthew and she "got on" pleasantly, and Mrs Parkes was happy in
her work under (for the most part, it must be confessed) Sophie Traub. At
night she lay beside her husband, and they made love again, apparently just
as they used to, when they were really married. But she, Susan, or the being

2560 / DORIS LESSING

who answered so readily and improbably to the name of Susan, was not there: she was in Fred's Hotel, in Paddington, waiting for the easing hours of solitude to begin.

Soon she made a new arrangement with Fred and with Sophie. It was for five days a week. As for the money, five pounds, she simply asked Matthew for it. She saw that she was not even frightened he might ask what for: he would give it to her, she knew that, and yet it was terrifying it could be so, for this close couple, these partners, had once known the destination of every shilling they must spend. He agreed to give her five pounds a week. She asked for just so much, not a penny more. He sounded indifferent about it. It was as if he were paying her, she thought: *paying her off*—yes, that was it. Terror came back for a moment, when she understood this, but she stilled it: things had gone too far for that. Now, every week, on Sunday nights, he gave her five pounds, turning away from her before their eyes could meet on the transaction. As for Sophie Traub, she was to be somewhere in or near the house until six at night, after which she was free. She was not to cook, or to clean, she was simply to be there. So she gardened or sewed, and asked friends in, being a person who was bound to have a lot of friends. If the children were sick, she nursed them. If teachers telephoned, she answered them sensibly. For the five daytimes in the school week, she was altogether the mistress of the house.

One night in the bedroom, Matthew asked: "Susan, I don't want to interfere—don't think that, please—but are you sure you are well?"

She was brushing her hair at the mirror. She made two more strokes on either side of her head, before she replied: "Yes, dear, I am sure I am well."

He was again lying on his back, his big blond head on his hands, his elbows angled up and part-concealing his face. He said: "Then Susan, I have to ask you this question, though you must understand, I'm not putting any sort of pressure on you." (Susan heard the word pressure with dismay, because this was inevitable, of course she could not go on like this.) "Are things going to go on like this?"

"Well," she said, going vague and bright and idiotic again, so as to escape: "Well, I don't see why not."

He was jerking his elbows up and down, in annoyance or in pain, and, looking at him, she saw he had got thin, even gaunt; and restless angry movements were not what she remembered of him. He said: "Do you want a divorce, is that it?"

At this, Susan only with the greatest difficulty stopped herself from laughing: she could hear the bright bubbling laughter she *would* have emitted, had she let herself. He could only mean one thing: she had a lover, and that was why she spent her days in London, as lost to him as if she had vanished to another continent.

Then the small panic set in again: she understood that he hoped she did have a lover, he was begging her to say so, because otherwise it would be too terrifying.

She thought this out, as she brushed her hair, watching the fine black stuff fly up to make its little clouds of electricity, hiss, hiss, hiss. Behind her head, across the room, was a blue wall. She realised she was absorbed in watching the black hair making shapes against the blue. She should be answering him. "Do *you* want a divorce, Matthew?"

He said: "That surely isn't the point, is it?"

"You brought it up, I didn't," she said, brightly, suppressing meaningless tinkling laughter.

Next day she asked Fred: "Have enquiries been made for me?"

He hesitated, and she said: "I've been coming here a year now. I've made no trouble, and you've been paid every day. I have a right to be told."

"As a matter of fact, Mrs Jones, a man did come asking."

"A man from a detective agency?"

"Well, he could have been, couldn't he?"

"I was asking you . . . well, what did you tell him?"

"I told him a Mrs Jones came every weekday from ten until five or six and stayed in Number Nineteen by herself."

"Describing me?"

"Well Mrs Jones, I had no alternative. Put yourself in my place."

"By rights I should deduct what that man gave you for the information."

He raised shocked eyes: she was not the sort of person to make jokes like this! Then he chose to laugh: a pinkish wet slit appeared across his white crinkled face: his eyes positively begged her to laugh, otherwise he might lose some money. She remained grave, looking at him.

He stopped laughing and said: "You want to go up now?"—returning to the familiarity, the comradeship, of the country where no questions are asked, on which (and he knew it) she depended completely.

She went up to sit in her wicker chair. But it was not the same. Her husband had searched her out. (The world had searched her out.) The pressures were on her. She was here with his connivance. He might walk in at any moment, here, into Room 19. She imagined the report from the detective agency: "A woman calling herself Mrs Jones, fitting the description of your wife (etc., etc., etc.), stays alone all day in room No. 19. She insists on this room, waits for it if it is engaged. As far as the proprietor knows she receives no visitors there, male or female." A report something on these lines, Matthew must have received.

Well of course he was right: things couldn't go on like this. He had put an end to it all simply by sending the detective after her.

She tried to shrink herself back into the shelter of the room, a snail pecked out of its shell and trying to squirm back. But the peace of the room had gone. She was trying consciously to revive it, trying to let go into the dark creative trance (or whatever it was) that she had found there. It was no use, yet she craved for it, she was as ill as a suddenly deprived addict.

Several times she returned to the room, to look for herself there, but instead she found the unnamed spirit of restlessness, a prickling fevered hunger for movement, an irritable self-consciousness that made her brain feel as if it had coloured lights going on and off inside it. Instead of the soft dark that had been the room's air, were now waiting for her demons that made her dash blindly about, muttering words of hate; she was impelling herself from point to point like a moth dashing itself against a windowpane, sliding to the bottom, fluttering off on broken wings, then crashing into the invisible barrier again. And again and again. Soon she was exhausted, and she told Fred that for a while she would not be needing the room, she was going on holiday. Home she went, to the big white house by the river. The middle of a weekday, and she felt guilty at returning to her own home when not expected. She stood unseen, looking in at the kitchen window. Mrs Parkes, wearing a discarded floral overall of Susan's, was stooping to slide something into the oven. Sophie, arms folded, was leaning her back against a cupboard and laughing at some joke made by a girl not seen before by Susan—a dark foreign girl, Sophie's visitor. In an armchair Molly, one of the twins, lay curled, sucking her thumb and watching the grownups. She must have some sickness, to be kept from school. The child's listless face, the dark circles under her eyes, hurt Susan: Molly was looking at the three grownups working and talking in exactly the same way Susan looked at the four through the kitchen window: she was remote, shut off from them.

But then, just as Susan imagined herself going in, picking up the little girl, and sitting in an armchair with her, stroking her probably heated forehead, Sophie did just that: she had been standing on one leg, the other knee flexed, its foot set against the wall. Now she let her foot in its ribbon-tied red shoe slide down the wall, and stood solid on two feet, clapping her hands before and behind her, and sang a couple of lines in German, so that the child lifted her heavy eyes at her and began to smile. Then she walked, or rather skipped, over to the child, swung her up, and let her fall into her lap at the same moment she sat herself. She said "Hopla! Hopla! Molly . . ." and began stroking the dark untidy young head that Molly laid on her shoulder for comfort.

Well. . . . Susan blinked the tears of farewell out of her eyes, and went quietly up the house to her bedroom. There she sat looking at the river through the trees. She felt at peace, but in a way that was new to her. She had no desire to move, to talk, to do anything at all. The devils that had haunted the house, the garden, were not there; but she knew it was because her soul was in Room 19 in Fred's Hotel; she was not really here at all. It was a sensation that should have been frightening: to sit at her own bedroom window, listening to Sophie's rich young voice sing German nursery songs to her child, listening to Mrs Parkes clatter and move below, and to know that all this had nothing to do with her: she was already out of it.

Later, she made herself go down and say she was home: it was unfair to be here unannounced. She took lunch with Mrs Parkes, Sophie, Sophie's Italian friend Maria, and her daughter Molly, and felt like a visitor.

A few days later, at bedtime, Matthew said: "Here's your five pounds," and pushed them over at her. Yet he must have known she had not been leaving the house at all.

She shook her head, gave it back to him, and said, in explanation, not in accusation: "As soon as you knew where I was, there was no point."

He nodded, not looking at her. He was turned away from her: thinking, she knew, how best to handle this wife who terrified him.

He said: "I wasn't trying to . . . it's just that I was worried."

"Yes, I know."

"I must confess that I was beginning to wonder . . ."

"You thought that I had a lover?"

"Yes, I am afraid I did."

She knew that he wished she had. She sat wondering how to say: "For a year now I've been spending all my days in a very sordid hotel room. It's the place where I'm happy. In fact, without it I don't exist." She heard herself saying this, and understood how terrified he was that she might. So instead she said: "Well, perhaps you're not far wrong."

Probably Matthew would think the hotel proprietor lied: he would want to think so.

"Well," he said, and she could hear his voice spring up, so to speak, with relief: "in that case I must confess I've got a bit of an affair on myself."

She said, detached and interested: "Really? Who is she?" and saw Matthew's startled look because of this reaction.

"It's Phil. Phil Hunt."

She had known Phil Hunt well in the old unmarried days. She was thinking: No, she won't do, she's too neurotic and difficult. She's never been happy yet. Sophie's much better: Well Matthew will see that himself, as sensible as he is.

This line of thought went on in silence, while she said aloud: "It's no point in telling you about mine, because you don't know him."

Quick, quick, invent, she thought. Remember how you invented all that nonsense for Miss Townsend.

She began slowly, careful not to contradict herself: "His name is Michael"— (*Michael What?*)—"Michael Plant." (What a silly name!) "He's rather like you—in looks, I mean." And indeed, she could imagine herself being touched by no one but Matthew himself. "He's a publisher." (Really? Why?) "He's got a wife already and two children."

She brought out this fantasy, proud of herself.

Matthew said: "Are you two thinking of marrying?"

She said, before she could stop herself: "Good God, *no!*"

She realised, if Matthew wanted to marry Phil Hunt, that this was too emphatic, but apparently it was all right, for his voice sounded relieved as he said: "It is a bit impossible to imagine oneself married to anyone else, isn't it?" With which he pulled her to him, so that her head lay on his shoulder. She turned her face into the dark of his flesh, and listened to the blood pounding through her ears saying: I am alone, I am alone, I am alone.

In the morning Susan lay in bed while he dressed.

He had been thinking things out in the night, because now he said: "Susan, why don't we make a foursome?"

Of course, she said to herself, of course he would be bound to say that. If one is sensible, if one is reasonable, if one never allows oneself a base thought or an envious emotion, naturally one says: Let's make a foursome!

"Why not?" she said.

"We could all meet for lunch. I mean, it's ridiculous, you sneaking off to filthy hotels, and me staying late at the office, and all the lies everyone has to tell."

What on earth did I say his name was?—she panicked, then said: "I think it's a good idea, but Michael is away at the moment. When he comes back though—and I'm sure you two would like each other."

"He's away, is he? So that's why you've been . . ." Her husband put his hand to the knot of his tie in a gesture of male coquetry she would not before have associated with him; and he bent to kiss her cheek with the expression that goes with the words: Oh you naughty little puss! And she felt its answering look, naughty and coy, come onto her face.

Inside she was dissolving in horror at them both, at how far they had both sunk from honesty of emotion.

So now she was saddled with a lover, and he had a mistress! How ordinary, how reassuring, how jolly! And now they would make a foursome of it, and go about to theatres and restaurants. After all, the Rawlings could well afford that sort of thing, and presumably the publisher Michael Plant could afford to do himself and his mistress quite well. No, there was nothing to stop the four of them developing the most intricate relationship of civilised tolerance, all enveloped in a charming afterglow of autumnal passion. Perhaps they would all go off on holidays together? She had known people who did. Or perhaps Matthew would draw the line there? Why should he, though, if he was capable of talking about "foursomes" at all?

She lay in the empty bedroom, listening to the car drive off with Matthew in it, off to work. Then she heard the children clattering off to school to the accompaniment of Sophie's cheerfully ringing voice. She slid down into the hollow of the bed, for shelter against her own irrelevance. And she stretched out her hand to the hollow where her husband's body had lain, but found no comfort there: he was not her husband. She curled herself up in a small tight ball under the clothes: she could stay here all day, all week, indeed, all her life.

But in a few days she must produce Michael Plant, and—but how? She must presumably find some agreeable man prepared to impersonate a publisher called Michael Plant. And in return for which she would—what? Well, for one thing they would make love. The idea made her want to cry with sheer exhaustion. Oh no, she had finished with all that—the proof of it was that the words "make love," or even imagining it, trying hard to revive no more than the pleasures of sensuality, let alone affection, or love, made her want to run away and hide from the sheer effort of the thing. . . . Good Lord, why make love at all? Why make love with anyone? Or if you are going to make love, what does it matter who with? Why shouldn't she simply walk into the street, pick up a man and have a roaring sexual affair with him? Why not? Or even with Fred? What difference did it make?

But she had let herself in for it—an interminable stretch of time with a lover, called Michael, as part of a gallant civilised foursome. Well, she could not, and she would not.

She got up, dressed, went down to find Mrs Parkes, and asked her for the loan of a pound, since Matthew, she said, had forgotten to leave her money. She exchanged with Mrs Parkes variations on the theme that husbands are all the same, they don't think, and without saying a word to Sophie, whose voice could be heard upstairs from the telephone, walked to the underground, travelled to South Kensington, changed to the Inner Circle, got out at Paddington, and walked to Fred's Hotel. There she told Fred that she wasn't going on holiday after all, she needed the room. She would have to wait an hour, Fred said. She went to a busy tearoom-cum-restaurant around the corner, and sat watching the people flow in and out the door that kept swinging open and shut, watched them mingle and merge and separate, felt her being flow into them, into their movement. When the hour was up she left a half crown for her pot of tea, and left the place without looking back at it, just as she had left her house, the big, beautiful white house, without another look, but silently dedicating it to Sophie. She returned to Fred, received the key of No. 19, now free, and ascended the grimy stairs slowly, letting floor after floor fall away below her, keeping her eyes lifted, so that floor after floor descended jerkily to her level of vision, and fell away out of sight.

No. 19 was the same. She saw everything with an acute, narrow, checking glance: the cheap shine of the satin spread, which had been replaced carelessly after the two bodies had finished their convulsions under it; a trace of powder on the glass that topped the chest of drawers; an intense green shade in a fold of the curtain. She stood at the window, looking down, watching people pass and pass and pass until her mind went dark from the constant movement. Then she sat in the wicker chair, letting herself go slack. But she had to be careful, because she did not want, today, to be surprised by Fred's knock at five o'clock.

The demons were not here. They had gone forever, because she was buying her freedom from them. She was slipping already into the dark fructifying dream that seemed to caress her inwardly, like the movement of her blood . . . but she had to think about Matthew first. Should she write a letter for the coroner? But what should she say? She would like to leave him with the look on his face she had seen this morning—banal, admittedly, but at least confidently healthy. Well, that was impossible, one did not look like that with a wife dead from suicide. But how to leave him believing she was dying because of a man—because of the fascinating publisher Michael Plant? Oh, how ridiculous! How absurd! How humiliating! But she decided not to trouble about it, simply not to think about the living. If he wanted to believe she had a lover, he would believe it. And he *did* want to believe it. Even when he had found out that there was no publisher in London called Michael Plant, he would think: Oh poor Susan, she was afraid to give me his real name.

And what did it matter whether he married Phil Hunt or Sophie? Though it ought to be Sophie, who was already the mother of those children . . . and what hypocrisy to sit here worrying about the children, when she was going to leave them because she had not got the energy to stay.

She had about four hours. She spent them delightfully, darkly, sweetly, letting herself slide gently, gently, to the edge of the river. Then, with hardly a break in her consciousness, she got up, pushed the thin rug against the door, made sure the windows were tight shut, put two shillings in the meter, and turned on the gas. For the first time since she had been in the room she lay on the hard bed that smelled stale, that smelled of sweat and sex.

She lay on her back on the green satin cover, but her legs were chilly. She got up, found a blanket folded in the bottom of the chest of drawers, and carefully covered her legs with it. She was quite content lying there, listening to the faint soft hiss of the gas that poured into the room, into her lungs, into her brain, as she drifted off into the dark river.

1963

PHILIP LARKIN
1922–1985

Philip Larkin was born in Coventry; was educated at its King Henry VIII School and at St. John's College, Oxford; and was for many years librarian of the Hull University Library. He wrote the poems of his first book, *The North Ship* (1945), under W. B. Yeats's strong enchantment. Although this influence persisted in the English poet's formal skill and subdued visionary longings, Larkin began to read Thomas Hardy seriously after World War II, and Hardy's rugged language, local settings, and ironic tone helped counter Yeats's influence. "After that," Larkin said, "Yeats came to seem so artificial—all that crap about masks and Crazy Jane and all the rest. It all rang so completely unreal." Also rejecting the international modernism of Eliot and Pound because of its mythical allusions, polyglot discourse, and fragmentary syntax, Larkin reclaimed a more direct, personal, formally regular model of poetry, supposedly rooted in a native English tradition of Wordsworth, Hardy, A. E. Housman, Wilfred Owen, and W. H. Auden. Even so, his poetry is not so thoroughly antimodernist as are his declarations: witness his imagist precision and alienated personae, his blending of revulsion and attraction toward modernity.

Larkin was the dominant figure in what came to be known as "the Movement," a group of university poets that included Kingsley Amis, Donald Davie, and Thom Gunn, gathered together in Robert Conquest's landmark anthology of 1956, *New Lines*. Their work was seen as counteracting not only the extravagances of modernism but also the influence of Dylan Thomas's high-flown, apocalyptic rhetoric: like Larkin, these poets preferred a civil grammar and rational syntax over prophecy, suburban realities over mythmaking.

No other poet presents the welfare-state world of postimperial Britain so vividly, so unsparingly, and so tenderly. "Poetry is an affair of sanity, of seeing things as they are," Larkin said; "I don't want to transcend the commonplace, I love the commonplace life. Everyday things are lovely to me." Eschewing the grandiose, he writes poetry that, in its everyday diction and melancholy wryness, worldly subjects and regular meters, affirms rather than contravenes the restrictions of ordinary life. Love's failure, the erosion of religious and national abutments, the loneliness of age and death—Larkin does not avert his poetic gaze from these bleak realities. As indicated by the title of his 1955 collection *The Less Deceived*, disillusionment, drabness, and resignation color these poems. Yet Larkin's drearily mundane world often gives way to muted promise, his speakers' alienation to possible communion, his skepticism to encounters even with the sublime. At the end of "High Windows," the characteristically ironic and self-deprecating speaker glimpses both radiant presence and total absence in the sunlit glass: "And beyond it, the deep blue air, that shows / Nothing, and is nowhere, and is endless."

Like Hardy, Larkin wrote novels—*Jill* (1946) and *A Girl in Winter* (1947)—and his poems have a novelist's sense of place and skill in the handling of direct speech. He also edited a controversial anthology, *The Oxford Book of Twentieth-Century English Verse* (1973), which attempted to construct a modern native tradition in England. But his most significant legacy was his poetry, although his output was limited to four volumes. Out of "the commonplace life" he fashioned uncommon poems—some of the most emotionally complex, rhythmically polished, and intricately rhymed poems of the second half of the twentieth century.

Church Going

Once I am sure there's nothing going on
I step inside, letting the door thud shut.
Another church: matting, seats, and stone,
And little books; sprawlings of flowers, cut
5 For Sunday, brownish now; some brass and stuff
Up at the holy end; the small neat organ;
And a tense, musty, unignorable silence,
Brewed God knows how long. Hatless, I take off
My cycle-clips in awkward reverence,

10 Move forward, run my hand around the font.
From where I stand, the roof looks almost new—
Cleaned, or restored? Someone would know: I don't.
Mounting the lectern, I peruse a few

Hectoring large-scale verses,[1] and pronounce
15 "Here endeth" much more loudly than I'd meant.
The echoes snigger briefly. Back at the door
I sign the book, donate an Irish sixpence,[2]
Reflect the place was not worth stopping for.

Yet stop I did: in fact I often do,
20 And always end much at a loss like this,
Wondering what to look for; wondering, too,
When churches fall completely out of use
What we shall turn them into, if we shall keep
A few cathedrals chronically on show,
25 Their parchment, plate and pyx[3] in locked cases,
And let the rest rent-free to rain and sheep.
Shall we avoid them as unlucky places?

Or, after dark, will dubious women come
To make their children touch a particular stone;
30 Pick simples° for a cancer; or on some   *medicinal herbs*
Advised night see walking a dead one?
Power of some sort or other will go on
In games, in riddles, seemingly at random;
But superstition, like belief, must die,
35 And what remains when disbelief has gone?
Grass, weedy pavement, brambles, buttress, sky,

A shape less recognisable each week,
A purpose more obscure. I wonder who
Will be the last, the very last, to seek
40 This place for what it was; one of the crew
That tap and jot and know what rood-lofts[4] were?
Some ruin-bibber, randy for antique,
Or Christmas-addict, counting on a whiff
Of gown-and-bands and organ-pipes and myrrh?[5]
45 Or will he be my representative,

Bored, uninformed, knowing the ghostly silt
Dispersed, yet tending to this cross of ground[6]
Through suburb scrub because it held unspilt
So long and equably what since is found
50 Only in separation—marriage, and birth,
And death, and thoughts of these—for which was built
This special shell? For, though I've no idea
What this accoutred frowsty barn is worth,
It pleases me to stand in silence here;

---

1. I.e., Bible verses printed in large type for reading aloud.
2. An Irish sixpence has no value in England.
3. Box in which communion wafers are kept.
4. Galleries on top of carved screens separating the nave of a church from the choir.

5. Gum resin used in the making of incense; one of three presents given by the Three Wise Men to the infant Jesus. "Gown-and-bands": gown and decorative collar worn by clergypeople.
6. Most churches were built in the shape of a cross.

55 A serious house on serious earth it is,
In whose blent air all our compulsions meet,
Are recognised, and robed as destinies.
And that much never can be obsolete,
Since someone will forever be surprising
60 A hunger in himself to be more serious,
And gravitating with it to this ground,
Which, he once heard, was proper to grow wise in,
If only that so many dead lie round.

1954   1955

MCMXIV[1]

Those long uneven lines
Standing as patiently
As if they were stretched outside
The Oval or Villa Park,[2]
5 The crowns of hats, the sun
On moustached archaic faces
Grinning as if it were all
An August bank Holiday lark;

And the shut shops, the bleached,
10 Established names on the sunblinds,
The farthings and sovereigns,[3]
And dark-clothed children at play
Called after kings and queens,
The tin advertisements
15 For cocoa and twist,° and the pubs   *tobacco*
Wide open all day;

And the countryside not caring:
The place-names all hazed over
With flowering grasses, and fields
20 Shadowing Domesday lines[4]
Under wheat's restless silence;
The differently-dressed servants
With tiny rooms in huge houses,
The dust behind limousines;

25 Never such innocence,
Never before or since,
As changed itself to past
Without a word—the men
Leaving the gardens tidy,

1. 1914, in Roman numerals, as incised on stone memorials to the dead of World War I.
2. London cricket ground and Birmingham football ground.
3. At that time the least valuable and the most

valuable British coins, respectively.
4. The still-visible boundaries of medieval farmers' long and narrow plots, ownership of which is recorded in William the Conqueror's *Domesday Book* (1085–86).

30   The thousands of marriages
Lasting a little while longer:
Never such innocence again.

1960   1964

Talking in Bed

Talking in bed ought to be easiest,
Lying together there goes back so far,
An emblem of two people being honest.

Yet more and more time passes silently.
5   Outside, the wind's incomplete unrest
Builds and disperses clouds about the sky,

And dark towns heap up on the horizon.
None of this cares for us. Nothing shows why
At this unique distance from isolation

10   It becomes still more difficult to find
Words at once true and kind,
Or not untrue and not unkind.

1960   1964

Ambulances

Closed like confessionals,[1] they thread
Loud noons of cities, giving back
None of the glances they absorb.
Light glossy grey, arms on a plaque,
5   They come to rest at any kerb:
All streets in time are visited.

Then children strewn on steps or road,
Or women coming from the shops
Past smells of different dinners, see
10   A wild white face that overtops
Red stretcher-blankets momently
As it is carried in and stowed,

And sense the solving emptiness
That lies just under all we do,
15   And for a second get it whole,
So permanent and blank and true.
The fastened doors recede. *Poor soul,*
They whisper at their own distress;

---

1. Enclosed stalls in Roman Catholic churches in which priests hear confession.

For borne away in deadened air
20　May go the sudden shut of loss
Round something nearly at an end,
And what cohered in it across
The years, the unique random blend
Of families and fashions, there

25　At last begin to loosen. Far
From the exchange of love to lie
Unreachable inside a room
The traffic parts to let go by
Brings closer what is left to come,
30　And dulls to distance all we are.

1961   1964

High Windows

When I see a couple of kids
And guess he's fucking her and she's
Taking pills or wearing a diaphragm,
I know this is paradise

5　Everyone old has dreamed of all their lives—
Bonds and gestures pushed to one side
Like an outdated combine harvester,[1]
And everyone young going down the long slide

To happiness, endlessly. I wonder if
10　Anyone looked at me, forty years back,
And thought, *That'll be the life;*
No God any more, or sweating in the dark

About hell and that, or having to hide
What you think of the priest. He
15　*And his lot will all go down the long slide*
Like free bloody birds. And immediately

Rather than words comes the thought of high windows:
The sun-comprehending glass,
And beyond it, the deep blue air, that shows
20　Nothing, and is nowhere, and is endless.

1967   1974

1. Farm machine for harvesting grain.

Sad Steps[1]

Groping back to bed after a piss
I part thick curtains, and am startled by
The rapid clouds, the moon's cleanliness.

Four o'clock: wedge-shadowed gardens lie
5   Under a cavernous, a wind-picked sky.
There's something laughable about this,

The way the moon dashes through clouds that blow
Loosely as cannon-smoke to stand apart
(Stone-coloured light sharpening the roofs below)

10 High and preposterous and separate—
Lozenge° of love! Medallion of art!   *diamondlike shape*
O wolves of memory! Immensements! No,

One shivers slightly, looking up there.
The hardness and the brightness and the plain
15 Far-reaching singleness of that wide stare

Is a reminder of the strength and pain
Of being young; that it can't come again,
But is for others undiminished somewhere.

1968   1974

Homage to a Government

Next year we are to bring the soldiers home
For lack of money, and it is all right.
Places they guarded, or kept orderly,
Must guard themselves, and keep themselves orderly.
5   We want the money for ourselves at home
Instead of working. And this is all right.

It's hard to say who wanted it to happen,
But now it's been decided nobody minds.
The places are a long way off, not here,
10 Which is all right, and from what we hear
The soldiers there only made trouble happen.
Next year we shall be easier in our minds.

Next year we shall be living in a country
That brought its soldiers home for lack of money.
15 The statues will be standing in the same
Tree-muffled squares, and look nearly the same.

1. Cf. Sir Philip Sidney's *Astrophil and Stella* 31: "With how sad steps, O Moon, thou climb'st the skies."

Our children will not know it's a different country.
All we can hope to leave them now is money.

Jan. 10, 1969   1974

The Explosion

On the day of the explosion
Shadows pointed towards the pithead:°   *mine entrance*
In the sun the slagheap° slept.   *pile of scrap, refuse*

Down the lane came men in pitboots
5   Coughing oath-edged talk and pipe-smoke,
Shouldering off the freshened silence.

One chased after rabbits; lost them;
Came back with a nest of lark's eggs;
Showed them; lodged them in the grasses.

10   So they passed in beards and moleskins,[1]
Fathers, brothers, nicknames, laughter,
Through the tall gates standing open.

At noon, there came a tremor; cows
Stopped chewing for a second; sun,
15   Scarfed as in a heat-haze, dimmed.

The dead go on before us, they
Are sitting in God's house in comfort,
We shall see them face to face—

Plain as lettering in the chapels
20   It was said, and for a second
Wives saw men of the explosion

Larger than in life they managed—
Gold as on a coin, or walking
Somehow from the sun towards them,

25   One showing the eggs unbroken.

1970   1974

This Be The Verse[1]

They fuck you up, your mum and dad.
They may not mean to, but they do.

1. Clothes of heavy fabric.
1. Cf. the elegy "Requiem," by Robert Louis Stevenson (1850–1894), of which the final verse reads, "This be the verse you grave for me: / Here

he lies where he longed to be, / Home is the sailor, home from sea, / And the hunter home from the hill."

They fill you with the faults they had
And add some extra, just for you.

5   But they were fucked up in their turn
By fools in old-style hats and coats,
Who half the time were soppy-stern
And half at one another's throats.

Man hands on misery to man.
10   It deepens like a coastal shelf.[2]
Get out as early as you can,
And don't have any kids yourself.

Apr. ? 1971   1974

Aubade[1]

I work all day, and get half-drunk at night.
Waking at four to soundless dark, I stare.
In time the curtain-edges will grow light.
Till then I see what's really always there:
5   Unresting death, a whole day nearer now,
Making all thought impossible but how
And where and when I shall myself die.
Arid interrogation: yet the dread
Of dying, and being dead,
10   Flashes afresh to hold and horrify.

The mind blanks at the glare. Not in remorse
—The good not done, the love not given, time
Torn off unused—nor wretchedly because
An only life can take so long to climb
15   Clear of its wrong beginnings, and may never;
But at the total emptiness for ever,
The sure extinction that we travel to
And shall be lost in always. Not to be here,
Not to be anywhere,
20   And soon; nothing more terrible, nothing more true.

This is a special way of being afraid
No trick dispels. Religion used to try,
That vast moth-eaten musical brocade
Created to pretend we never die,
25   And specious stuff that says *No rational being
Can fear a thing it will not feel*, not seeing
That this is what we fear—no sight, no sound,
No touch or taste or smell, nothing to think with,
Nothing to love or link with,
30   The anaesthetic from which none come round.

2. Underwater land off a coast   1. Music or poem announcing dawn.

And so it stays just on the edge of vision,
A small unfocused blur, a standing chill
That slows each impulse down to indecision.
Most things may never happen: this one will,
35   And realisation of it rages out
In furnace-fear when we are caught without
People or drink. Courage is no good:
It means not scaring others. Being brave
Lets no one off the grave.
40   Death is no different whined at than withstood.

Slowly light strengthens, and the room takes shape.
It stands plain as a wardrobe, what we know,
Have always known, know that we can't escape,
Yet can't accept. One side will have to go.
45   Meanwhile telephones crouch, getting ready to ring
In locked-up offices, and all the uncaring
Intricate rented world begins to rouse.
The sky is white as clay, with no sun.
Work has to be done.
50   Postmen like doctors go from house to house.

1977   1977

NADINE GORDIMER
b. 1923

Nadine Gordimer's fiction has given imaginative and moral shape to the recent history of South Africa. Since the publication of her first book, *The Lying Days* (1953), she has charted the changing patterns of response and resistance to apartheid by exploring the place of the European in Africa, selecting representative themes and governing motifs for novels and short stories, and shifting her ideological focus from a liberal to a more radical position. In recognition of this achievement, of having borne untiring and lucid narrative witness, Gordimer was awarded the 1991 Nobel Prize in Literature.

Born to Jewish immigrant parents in the South African mining town of Springs, Gordimer began writing early, from the beginning taking as her subject the pathologies and everyday realities of a racially divided society. Her decision to remain in Johannesburg through the years of political repression reflected her commitment to her subject and to her vision of a postapartheid future. In the years since apartheid was dismantled in 1994, Gordimer has continued to live and write in South Africa, and her recent novels, such as *The House Gun* (1998) and *The Pickup* (2001), retain an uncompromising focus on the inhabitants of a racially fractured culture.

In her nonfiction Gordimer self-consciously places her writing within a tradition of European realism, most notably that defined by the Hungarian philosopher and critic Georg Lukács (1885–1971). Her aim—as shown in her incisive and highly acclaimed novels of the 1970s, *The Conservationist* (1974) and *Burger's Daughter* (1979)—is to evoke by way of the personal and of the precisely observed particular a broader political and historical totality. This method gives her characters, and the stories in which they reside, their representativeness. As Gordimer has famously said, "politics is character in South Africa." Yet throughout the long years of political polarization in that country and the banning of three of her own books, Gordimer has distanced herself from polemics and retained a firm humanist belief in what she variously describes as the objectivity and the inwardness of the writer. Although she has referred to an engagement with political reality as imperative and explores permutations of the question of engagement in novels such as *Burger's Daughter* and *July's People* (1981), she nevertheless asserts the autonomy of the writer's perspective, "the last true judgment." Narrative for Gordimer helps define and clarify historical experience. Her keen sense of history as formation, and as demanding a continual rewriting, has ensured that her novels can be read as at once contemporary in their reference and symbolic of broader social and historical patterns, as in the paranoia surrounding the case of the buried black body on a white farm in *The Conservationist*, or in the psychosocial portrait of Rosa Burger in *Burger's Daughter*.

Gordimer has drawn criticism both for her apparent lack of attention to feminism in favor of race issues and for the wholeness and unfashionable completeness of her novels—their plottedness, meticulous scene paintings, fully realized characters. However, the searching symbolism and complexity of her narratives generally work against such judgments. As the following short story shows, a prominent feature of her writing is to give a number of different perspectives on a situation, in some cases most poignantly those of apartheid's supporters, and in this way to represent the broader anatomy of a diseased politics and, more generally, of the human being in history.

The Moment before the Gun Went Off

Marais Van der Vyver shot one of his farm labourers, dead. An accident, there are accidents with guns every day of the week—children playing a fatal game with a father's revolver in the cities where guns are domestic objects, nowadays, hunting mishaps like this one, in the country—but these won't be reported all over the world. Van der Vyver knows his will be. He knows that the story of the Afrikaner farmer—regional Party leader and Commandant of the local security commando—shooting a black man who worked for him will fit exactly *their* version of South Africa, it's made for them. They'll be able to use it in their boycott and divestment campaigns, it'll be another piece of evidence in their truth about the country. The papers at home will quote the story as it has appeared in the overseas press, and in the back-and-forth he and the black man will become those crudely-drawn figures on anti-apartheid banners, units in statistics of white brutality against the blacks quoted at the United Nations—he, whom they will gleefully be able to call "a leading member" of the ruling Party.

People in the farming community understand how he must feel. Bad enough to have killed a man, without helping the Party's, the government's, the country's enemies, as well. They see the truth of that. They know, reading the Sunday papers, that when Van der Vyver is quoted saying he is "terribly shocked," he will "look after the wife and children," none of those Americans and English, and none of those people at home who want to destroy the white man's power will believe him. And how they will sneer when he even says of the farm boy (according to one paper, if you can trust any of those reporters), "He was my friend, I always took him hunting with me." Those city and overseas people don't know it's true: farmers usually have one particular black boy they like to take along with them in the lands; you could call it a kind of friend, yes, friends are not only your own white people, like yourself, you take into your house, pray with in church and work with on the Party committee. But how can those others know that? They don't want to know it. They think all blacks are like the big-mouth agitators in town. And Van der Vyver's face, in the photographs, strangely opened by distress—everyone in the district remembers Marais Van der Vyver as a little boy who would go away and hide himself if he caught you smiling at him, and everyone knows him now as a man who hides any change of expression round his mouth behind a thick, soft moustache, and in his eyes by always looking at some object in hand, leaf of a crop fingered, pen or stone picked up, while concentrating on what he is saying, or while listening to you. It just goes to show what shock can do; when you look at the newspaper photographs you feel like apologising, as if you had stared in on some room where you should not be.

There will be an inquiry; there had better be, to stop the assumption of yet another case of brutality against farm workers, although there's nothing in doubt—an accident, and all the facts fully admitted by Van der Vyver. He made a statement when he arrived at the police station with the dead man in his bakkie.[1] Captain Beetge knows him well, of course; he gave him brandy. He was shaking, this big, calm, clever son of Willem Van der Vyver, who inherited the old man's best farm. The black was stone dead, nothing to be done for him. Beetge will not tell anyone that after the brandy Van der Vyver wept. He sobbed, snot running onto his hands, like a dirty kid. The Captain was ashamed, for him, and walked out to give him a chance to recover himself.

Marais Van der Vyver left his house at three in the afternoon to cull a buck from the family of kudu[2] he protects in the bush areas of his farm. He is interested in wildlife and sees it as the farmers' sacred duty to raise game as well as cattle. As usual, he called at his shed workshop to pick up Lucas, a twenty-year-old farmhand who had shown mechanical aptitude and whom Van der Vyver himself had taught to maintain tractors and other farm machinery. He hooted, and Lucas followed the familiar routine, jumping onto the back of the truck. He liked to travel standing up there, spotting game before his employer did. He would lean forward, braced against the cab below him.

Van der Vyver had a rifle and .300 ammunition beside him in the cab. The rifle was one of his father's, because his own was at the gunsmith's in town. Since his father died (Beetge's sergeant wrote "passed on") no one had used the rifle and so when he took it from a cupboard he was sure it was not loaded. His father had never allowed a loaded gun in the house; he himself had been taught since childhood never to ride with a loaded weapon in a vehicle. But this gun was loaded. On a dirt track, Lucas thumped his fist on the cab roof three times to signal: look left. Having seen the white-ripple-marked flank of a kudu, and its fine horns raking through disguising bush, Van der Vyver drove rather fast over a pot-hole. The jolt fired the rifle. Upright, it was pointing straight through the cab roof at the head of Lucas. The bullet pierced the roof and entered Lucas's brain by way of his throat.

That is the statement of what happened. Although a man of such standing in the district, Van der Vyver had to go through the ritual of swearing that it was the truth. It has gone on record, and will be there in the archive of the local police station as long as Van der Vyver lives, and beyond that, through

1. Pickup truck.
2. Large African antelope. The males have long, spirally twisted horns.

the lives of his children, Magnus, Helena and Karel—unless things in the country get worse, the example of black mobs in the towns spreads to the rural areas and the place is burned down as many urban police stations have been. Because nothing the government can do will appease the agitators and the whites who encourage them. Nothing satisfies them, in the cities: blacks can sit and drink in white hotels, now, the Immorality Act[3] has gone, blacks can sleep with whites. . . . It's not even a crime any more.

Van der Vyver has a high barbed security fence round his farmhouse and garden which his wife, Alida, thinks spoils completely the effect of her artificial stream with its tree-ferns beneath the jacarandas.[4] There is an aerial soaring like a flag-pole in the back yard. All his vehicles, including the truck in which the black man died, have aerials that swing their whips when the driver hits a pot-hole: they are part of the security system the farmers in the district maintain, each farm in touch with every other by radio, twenty-four hours out of twenty-four. It has already happened that infiltrators from over the border have mined remote farm roads, killing white farmers and their families out on their own property for a Sunday picnic. The pot-hole could have set off a land-mine, and Van der Vyver might have died with his farm boy. When neighbours use the communications system to call up and say they are sorry about "that business" with one of Van der Vyver's boys, there goes unsaid: it could have been worse.

It is obvious from the quality and fittings of the coffin that the farmer has provided money for the funeral. And an elaborate funeral means a great deal to blacks; look how they will deprive themselves of the little they have, in their lifetime, keeping up payments to a burial society so they won't go in boxwood to an unmarked grave. The young wife is pregnant (of course) and another little one, wearing red shoes several sizes too large, leans under her jutting belly. He is too young to understand what has happened, what he is witnessing that day, but neither whines nor plays about; he is solemn without knowing why. Blacks expose small children to everything, they don't protect them from the sight of fear and pain the way whites do theirs. It is the young wife who rolls her head and cries like a child, sobbing on the breast of this relative and that.

All present work for Van der Vyver or are the families of those who work; and in the weeding and harvest seasons, the women and children work for him, too, carried—wrapped in their blankets, on a truck, singing—at sunrise to the fields. The dead man's mother is a woman who can't be more than in her late thirties (they start bearing children at puberty) but she is heavily mature in a black dress between her own parents, who were already working for old Van der Vyver when Marais, like their daughter, was a child. The parents hold her as if she were a prisoner or a crazy woman to be restrained. But she says nothing, does nothing. She does not look up; she does not look at Van der Vyver, whose gun went off in the truck, she stares at the grave. Nothing will make her look up; there need be no fear that she will look up; at him. His wife, Alida, is beside him. To show the proper respect, as for any white funeral, she is wearing the navy-blue-and-cream hat she wears to church this summer. She is always supportive, although he doesn't seem to notice it; this coldness and reserve—his mother says he didn't mix well as a child—she

<hr>

3. South African government act prohibiting sexual relations between whites and other races.

4. Tropical trees with blue flowers.

accepts for herself but regrets that it has prevented him from being nominated, as he should be, to stand as the Party's parliamentary candidate for the district. He does not let her clothing, or that of anyone else gathered closely, make contact with him. He, too, stares at the grave. The dead man's mother and he stare at the grave in communication like that between the black man outside and the white man inside the cab the moment before the gun went off.

The moment before the gun went off was a moment of high excitement shared through the roof of the cab, as the bullet was to pass, between the young black man outside and the white farmer inside the vehicle. There were such moments, without explanation, between them, although often around the farm the farmer would pass the young man without returning a greeting, as if he did not recognize him. When the bullet went off what Van der Vyver saw was the kudu stumble in fright at the report and gallop away. Then he heard the thud behind him, and past the window saw the young man fall out of the vehicle. He was sure he had leapt up and toppled—in fright, like the buck. The farmer was almost laughing with relief, ready to tease, as he opened his door, it did not seem possible that a bullet passing through the roof could have done harm.

The young man did not laugh with him at his own fright. The farmer carried him in his arms, to the truck. He was sure, sure he could not be dead. But the young black man's blood was all over the farmer's clothes, soaking against his flesh as he drove.

How will they ever know, when they file newspaper clippings, evidence, proof, when they look at the photographs and see his face—guilty! guilty! they are right!—how will they know, when the police stations burn with all the evidence of what has happened now, and what the law made a crime in the past. How could they know that *they do not know.* Anything. The young black callously shot through the negligence of the white man was not the farmer's boy; he was his son.

1991

A. K. RAMANUJAN
1929–1993

Born in Mysore, India, Attipat Krishnaswami Ramanujan grew up amid the different languages that later informed his life's work as poet, translator, and linguist: he spoke Kannada in the streets, Tamil with his mother, and English with his father, a mathematics professor at Mysore University. Educated there and at Deccan College, he traveled for graduate studies to Indiana University, staying on in the U.S. to teach at the University of Chicago from 1961. He was the recipient of a MacArthur Fellowship, and in 1976 the Indian government honored him with the Padma Shri for distinguished service to the nation.

Ramanujan affirmed that "cultural traditions in India are indissolubly plural and often conflicting," and his poetry—in its texture and subject matter—embodies this complex intercultural mingling within India and across much of the contemporary world. His poems reflect the influence of modern English-language poets, such as W. B. Yeats, Ezra Pound, William Carlos Williams, and Wallace Stevens, while also drawing on the vivid and structural use of metaphor, the flowing imagery and syntax, the spare diction and paradoxes of ancient and medieval poetry of south India. A poem such as the wittily entitled "Elements of Composition" recalls a traditional Indian vision of identity as embedded in endlessly fluid, concentrically arranged contexts at the same time that it suggests a postmodern vision of the self as decentered, composite, and provisional. "India does not have one past," Ramanujan emphasized, "but many pasts," and the same is true of the self whose multiple pasts he composes and decomposes in his poetry.

Self-Portrait

I resemble everyone
but myself, and sometimes see
in shop-windows,
   despite the well-known laws
5   of optics,
the portrait of a stranger,
date unknown,
often signed in a corner
by my father.

1966

Elements of Composition

Composed as I am, like others,
  of elements on certain well-known lists,
father's seed and mother's egg

gathering earth, air, fire, mostly
5   water, into a mulberry mass,
moulding calcium,

carbon, even gold, magnesium and such,
  into a chattering self tangled
in love and work,

10   scary dreams, capable of eyes that can see,
  only by moving constantly,
the constancy of things

like Stonehenge or cherry trees;

add uncle's eleven fingers
15   making shadow-plays of rajas°   *Indian kings or princes*
and cats, hissing,

becoming fingers again, the look
  of panic on sister's face
an hour before

20 her wedding, a dated newspaper map
of a place one has never seen, maybe
no longer there

after the riots, downtown Nairobi,°   *capital of Kenya*
that a friend carried in his passport
25 as others would

a woman's picture in their wallets;

add the lepers of Madurai,°   *city in south India*
male, female, married,
with children,

30 lion faces, crabs for claws,
clotted on their shadows
under the stone-eyed

goddesses of dance, mere pillars,
moving as nothing on earth
35 can move—

I pass through them
as they pass through me
taking and leaving

affections, seeds, skeletons,

40 millennia of fossil records
of insects that do not last
a day,

body-prints of mayflies,
a legend half-heard
45 in a train

of the half-man searching
for an ever-fleeing
other half[1]

through Muharram tigers,[2]
50 hyacinths in crocodile waters,
and the sweet

twisted lives of epileptic saints,

1. In an essay Ramanujan compares the Hindu myth of the god that "splits himself into male and female" to "the androgynous figure in Plato's *Symposium*, halved into male and female segments which forever seek each other and crave union."

2. During the first month of the Islamic calendar, Muharram processions, often including dancers in tiger masks, commemorate the martyrdom of Muhammad's grandson, Husein.

and even as I add,
I lose, decompose
55   into my elements,

into other names and forms,
    past, and passing, tenses
without time,

caterpillar on a leaf, eating,
60   being eaten.[3]

1986

Foundlings in the Yukon

In the Yukon[1] the other day
miners found the skeleton
of a lemming
curled around some seeds
5   in a burrow:
sealed off by a landslide
in Pleistocene times.°   *the Great Ice Age*

Six grains were whole,
unbroken: picked and planted
10   ten thousand
years after their time,
they took root
within forty-eight hours
and sprouted
15   a candelabra of eight small leaves.

A modern Alaskan lupine,°   *a wildflower*
I'm told, waits three years to come
to flower, but these
upstarts drank up sun
20   and unfurled early
with the crocuses of March
as if long deep
burial had made them hasty

for birth and season, for names,
25   genes, for passing on:
like the kick
and shift of an intra-uterine
memory, like

---

3. According to a poem in the ancient Sanskrit *Taittiriya Upanishad*, "What eats is eaten, / and what's eaten, eats / in turn" (Ramanujan's translation, in his essay "Some Thoughts on 'Non-Western' Classics").
1. Mountainous territory in northwestern Canada.

this morning's dream of being
30   born in an eagle's
nest with speckled eggs and the screech

of nestlings, like a pent-up
centenarian's sudden burst
of lust, or maybe
35   just elegies in Duino[2] unbound
from the dark,
these new aborigines biding
their time
for the miner's night-light

40   to bring them their dawn,
these infants compact with age,
older than the oldest
things alive, having skipped
a million falls
45   and the registry of tree-rings,
suddenly younger
by an accident of flowering

than all their timely descendants.

1995

2. The Austro-German poet Rainer Maria Rilke (1875–1926) overcame thirteen years of writer's block in
Duino Castle (near Trieste), where he wrote a famous series of elegies.

THOM GUNN
1929–2004

The son of a London journalist, Thomson Gunn was educated at University College
School, London, then Trinity College, Cambridge, and Stanford University, where
he studied under the antimodernist, classically inclined poet Yvor Winters. In a poem
addressed to Winters, he wrote: "You keep both Rule and Energy in view, / Much
power in each, most in the balanced two." The poems of Gunn's *Fighting Terms*
(1954) and *The Sense of Movement* (1957) aimed for the same balance. They were
influenced by the seventeenth-century English poet John Donne and the twentieth-
century French philosopher Jean-Paul Sartre and introduced a modern Metaphysical
poet able to give powerfully concrete expression to abstract ideas. Along with Philip
Larkin, he was seen as a member of "the Movement"—English poets who preferred
inherited verse forms to either modernist avant-gardism or high-flown Romanticism.
In the second half of *My Sad Captains* (1961), he began to move away from the will-
driven heroes and the tight-fitting stanzas of his early work into more tentative explorations of experience and more supple syllabic or open verse forms. "Most of my
poems are ambivalent," he said. Moving from England to San Francisco, he experimented with LSD and moved also from poems presumably addressed to women to
poems frankly homosexual. *The Man with Night Sweats* (1992) ends with a sequence
of poems remarkable for their unflinching directness, compassion, and grace about

the deaths of friends from AIDS. Gunn was a poet of rare intelligence and power in all his protean changes.

Black Jackets

In the silence that prolongs the span
Rawly of music when the record ends,
The red-haired boy who drove a van
In weekday overalls but, like his friends,

5   Wore cycle boots and jacket here
To suit the Sunday hangout he was in,
Heard, as he stretched back from his beer,
Leather creak softly round his neck and chin.

Before him, on a coal-black sleeve
10   Remote exertion had lined, scratched, and burned
Insignia that could not revive
The heroic fall or climb where they were earned.

On the other drinkers bent together,
Concocting selves for their impervious kit,
15   He saw it as no more than leather
Which, taut across the shoulders grown to it,

Sent through the dimness of a bar
As sudden and anonymous hints of light
As those that shipping give, that are
20   Now flickers in the Bay, now lost in night.

He stretched out like a cat, and rolled
The bitterish taste of beer upon his tongue,
And listened to a joke being told:
The present was the things he stayed among.

25   If it was only loss he wore,
He wore it to assert, with fierce devotion,
Complicity and nothing more.
He recollected his initiation,

And one especially of the rites.
30   For on his shoulders they had put tattoos:
The group's name on the left, The Knights,
And on the right the slogan Born To Lose.

1961

My Sad Captains

One by one they appear in
the darkness: a few friends, and

a few with historical
names. How late they start to shine!
5   but before they fade they stand
perfectly embodied, all

the past lapping them like a
cloak of chaos. They were men
who, I thought, lived only to
10   renew the wasteful force they
spent with each hot convulsion.
They remind me, distant now.

True, they are not at rest yet,
but now that they are indeed
15   apart, winnowed from failures,
they withdraw to an orbit
and turn with disinterested
hard energy, like the stars.

1961

From the Wave

It mounts at sea, a concave wall
   Down-ribbed with shine,
And pushes forward, building tall
   Its steep incline.

5 Then from their hiding rise to sight
   Black shapes on boards
Bearing before the fringe of white
   It mottles towards.

Their pale feet curl, they poise their weight
10   With a learn'd skill.
It is the wave they imitate
   Keeps them so still.

The marbling bodies have become
   Half wave, half men,
15 Grafted it seems by feet of foam
   Some seconds, then,

Late as they can, they slice the face
   In timed procession:
Balance is triumph in this place,
20   Triumph possession.

The mindless heave of which they rode
   A fluid shelf
Breaks as they leave it, falls and, slowed,
   Loses itself.

25 Clear, the sheathed bodies slick as seals
        Loosen and tingle;
    And by the board the bare foot feels
        The suck of shingle.

    They paddle in the shallows still;
30   Two splash each other;
    Then all swim out to wait until
        The right waves gather.

                                                    1971

Still Life

    I shall not soon forget
    The greyish-yellow skin
    To which the face had set:
    Lids tight: nothing of his,
5   No tremor from within,
    Played on the surfaces.

    He still found breath, and yet
    It was an obscure knack.
    I shall not soon forget
10 The angle of his head,
    Arrested and reared back
    On the crisp field of bed,

    Back from what he could neither
    Accept, as one opposed,
15 Nor, as a life-long breather,
    Consentingly let go,
    The tube his mouth enclosed
    In an astonished O.

                                                    1992

The Missing

    Now as I watch the progress of the plague,°   AIDS
    The friends surrounding me fall sick, grow thin,
    And drop away. Bared, is my shape less vague
    —Sharply exposed and with a sculpted skin?

5   I do not like the statue's chill contour,
    Not nowadays. The warmth investing me
    Led outward through mind, limb, feeling, and more
    In an involved increasing family.

    Contact of friend led to another friend,
10 Supple entwinement through the living mass

Which for all that I knew might have no end,
Image of an unlimited embrace.

I did not just feel ease, though comfortable:
Aggressive as in some ideal of sport,
15 With ceaseless movement thrilling through the whole,
Their push kept me as firm as their support.

But death—Their deaths have left me less defined:
It was their pulsing presence made me clear.
I borrowed from it, I was unconfined,
20 Who tonight balance unsupported here,

Eyes glaring from raw marble, in a pose
Languorously part-buried in the block,
Shins perfect and no calves, as if I froze
Between potential and a finished work.

25 —Abandoned incomplete, shape of a shape,
In which exact detail shows the more strange,
Trapped in unwholeness, I find no escape
Back to the play of constant give and change.

Aug. 1987   1992

DEREK WALCOTT
b. 1930

Derek Walcott was born on the island of Saint Lucia in the British West Indies, where
he had a Methodist upbringing in a largely Roman Catholic society. He was educated
at St. Mary's College in Saint Lucia and the University of the West Indies in Jamaica.
He then moved to Trinidad, where he worked as a book reviewer, art critic, playwright,
and artistic director of a theater workshop. Since the early 1980s he has also taught
at a number of American colleges and universities, especially Boston University; in
1992 he received the Nobel Prize in Literature.

As a black poet writing from within both the English literary tradition and the
history of a colonized people, Walcott has self-mockingly referred to his split alle-
giances to his Afro-Caribbean and his European inheritances as those of a "schizophrenic," a "mongrel," a "mulatto of style." His background is indeed racially and
culturally mixed: his grandmothers were of African descent; his grandfathers were
white, a Dutchman and an Englishman. Schooled in the Standard English that is the
official language of Saint Lucia, Walcott also grew up speaking the predominantly
French Creole (or patois) that is the primary language of everyday life (the island had
traded hands fourteen times in colonial wars between the British and the French).
In his poetry this cross-cultural inheritance is sometimes the source of pain and
ambivalence, as when in "A Far Cry from Africa" he refers to himself as being "poisoned with the blood of both." At other times it fuels a celebratory integration of
multiple forms, visions, and energies, as in parts of his long poem *Omeros,* which
transposes elements of Homeric epic from the Aegean to the Caribbean.

Even as a schoolboy Walcott knew he was not alone in his effort to sort through his vexed postcolonial affiliations. From a young age he felt a special affinity with Irish writers such as W. B. Yeats, James Joyce, and J. M. Synge, whom he saw as fellow colonials—"They were the niggers of Britain"—with the same paradoxical hatred for the British Empire and worship of the English language. He has repeatedly asked how the postcolonial poet can both grieve the agonizing harm of British colonialism and appreciate the empire's literary gift. Walcott has also acknowledged other English and American writers—T. S. Eliot, Ezra Pound, Hart Crane, W. H. Auden, and Robert Lowell—as enabling influences.

Over the course of his prolific career, Walcott has adapted various European literary archetypes (e.g., the Greek character Philoctetes) and forms (epic, quatrains, terza rima, English meters). He has ascribed his rigorous concern with craft to his youthful Protestantism. At once disciplined and flamboyant as a poet, he insists on the specifically Caribbean opulence of his art: "I come from a place that likes grandeur; it likes large gestures; it is not inhibited by flourish; it is a rhetorical society; it is a society of physical performance; it is a society of style." Although much of his poetry is in a rhetorically elevated Standard English, Walcott adapts the calypso rhythms of a lightly creolized English in "The Schooner *Flight*," and he braids together West Indian English, Standard English, and French patois in *Omeros*. He has a great passion for metaphor, by which he deftly weaves imaginative connections across cultural and racial boundaries. His plays, written in an accurate and energetic language, are similarly infused with the spirit of syncretism, vividly conjoining Caribbean and European motifs, images, and idioms.

A Far Cry from Africa

Standard English

A wind is ruffling the tawny pelt
Of Africa. Kikuyu,[1] quick as flies,
Batten upon the bloodstreams of the veldt.[2]
Corpses are scattered through a paradise.
5 Only the worm, colonel of carrion, cries:
"Waste no compassion on these separate dead!"
Statistics justify and scholars seize
The salients of colonial policy.
What is that to the white child hacked in bed?
10 To savages, expendable as Jews?

Threshed out by beaters,[3] the long rushes break
In a white dust of ibises whose cries
Have wheeled since civilization's dawn
From the parched river or beast-teeming plain.
15 The violence of beast on beast is read
As natural law, but upright man
Seeks his divinity by inflicting pain.
Delirious as these worried beasts, his wars
Dance to the tightened carcass of a drum,
20 While he calls courage still that native dread
Of the white peace contracted by the dead.

1. An east African ethnic group whose members, as Mau Mau fighters, conducted an eight-year campaign of violent resistance against British colonial settlers in Kenya in the 1950s.
2. Open country, neither cultivated nor forest

(Afrikaans).
3. In big-game hunting, natives are hired to beat the brush, driving birds—such as ibises—and other animals into the open.

Again brutish necessity wipes its hands
Upon the napkin of a dirty cause, again
A waste of our compassion, as with Spain,[4]
25 The gorilla wrestles with the superman.
I who am poisoned with the blood of both,
Where shall I turn, divided to the vein?
I who have cursed
The drunken officer of British rule, how choose
30 Between this Africa and the English tongue I love?
Betray them both, or give back what they give?
How can I face such slaughter and be cool?
How can I turn from Africa and live?

Poisoned, not enriched

1956, 1962

From The Schooner *Flight*

1 Adios, Carenage[1]

In idle August, while the sea soft,
and leaves of brown islands stick to the rim
of this Caribbean, I blow out the light
by the dreamless face of Maria Concepcion
5 to ship as a seaman on the schooner *Flight*.
Out in the yard turning grey in the dawn,
I stood like a stone and nothing else move
but the cold sea rippling like galvanize
and the nail holes of stars in the sky roof,
10 till a wind start to interfere with the trees.
I pass me dry neighbour sweeping she yard
as I went downhill, and I nearly said:
"Sweep soft, you witch, 'cause she don't sleep hard,"
but the bitch look through me like I was dead.
15 A route taxi pull up, park-lights still on.
The driver size up my bags with a grin:
"This time, Shabine, like you really gone!"
I ain't answer the ass, I simply pile in
the back seat and watch the sky burn
20 above Laventille[2] pink as the gown
in which the woman I left was sleeping,
and I look in the rearview and see a man
exactly like me, and the man was weeping
for the houses, the streets, the whole fucking island.

25 Christ have mercy on all sleeping things!
From that dog rotting down Wrightson Road
to when I was a dog on these streets;
if loving these islands must be my load,

---

4. The Spanish Civil War (1936–39).
1. Waterfront where schooners are cleaned and

repaired. "Adios": goodbye (Spanish).
2. Hillside slum outside Port of Spain, Trinidad.

out of corruption my soul takes wings,
30   But they had started to poison my soul
with their big house, big car, big-time bohbohl,[3]
coolie, nigger, Syrian, and French Creole,
so I leave it for them and their carnival—
I taking a sea-bath, I gone down the road.
35   I know these islands from Monos to Nassau,[4]
a rusty head sailor with sea-green eyes
that they nickname Shabine, the patois° for   *spoken dialect*
any red nigger, and I, Shabine, saw
when these slums of empire was paradise.
40   I'm just a red nigger who love the sea,
I had a sound colonial education,
I have Dutch, nigger, and English in me,
and either I'm nobody, or I'm a nation.

But Maria Concepcion was all my thought
45   watching the sea heaving up and down
as the port side of dories, schooners, and yachts
was painted afresh by the strokes of the sun
signing her name with every reflection;
I knew when dark-haired evening put on
50   her bright silk at sunset, and, folding the sea,
sidled under the sheet with her starry laugh,
that there'd be no rest, there'd be no forgetting.
Is like telling mourners round the graveside
about resurrection, they want the dead back,
55   so I smile to myself as the bow rope untied
and the *Flight* swing seaward: "Is no use repeating
that the sea have more fish. I ain't want her
dressed in the sexless light of a seraph,°   *angel*
I want those round brown eyes like a marmoset,[5] and
60   till the day when I can lean back and laugh,
those claws that tickled my back on sweating
Sunday afternoons, like a crab on wet sand."
As I worked, watching the rotting waves come
past the bow that scissor the sea like silk,
65   I swear to you all, by my mother's milk,
by the stars that shall fly from tonight's furnace,
that I loved them, my children, my wife, my home;
I loved them as poets love the poetry
that kills them, as drowned sailors the sea.

70   You ever look up from some lonely beach
and see a far schooner? Well, when I write
this poem, each phrase go be soaked in salt;
I go draw and knot every line as tight
as ropes in this rigging; in simple speech

---

3. Or *bobol*: corrupt practices or fraud, organized
by people in positions of power (Eastern Caribbean
English).

4. Capital of the Bahamas. "Monos": island off the
northwest coast of Trinidad.

5. South American monkey.

75   my common language go be the wind,
     my pages the sails of the schooner *Flight*.

                                                              1979

The Season of Phantasmal Peace

Then all the nations of birds lifted together
the huge net of the shadows of this earth
in multitudinous dialects, twittering tongues,
stitching and crossing it. They lifted up
5   the shadows of long pines down trackless slopes,
the shadows of glass-faced towers down evening streets,
the shadow of a frail plant on a city sill—
the net rising soundless as night, the birds' cries soundless, until
there was no longer dusk, or season, decline, or weather,
10   only this passage of phantasmal light
that not the narrowest shadow dared to sever.

And men could not see, looking up, what the wild geese drew,
what the ospreys trailed behind them in silvery ropes
that flashed in the icy sunlight; they could not hear
15   battalions of starlings waging peaceful cries,
bearing the net higher, covering this world
like the vines of an orchard, or a mother drawing
the trembling gauze over the trembling eyes
of a child fluttering to sleep;
                                        it was the light
20   that you will see at evening on the side of a hill
in yellow October, and no one hearing knew
what change had brought into the raven's cawing,
the killdeer's screech, the ember-circling chough°   *bird in crow family*
such an immense, soundless, and high concern
25   for the fields and cities where the birds belong,
except it was their seasonal passing, Love,
made seasonless, or, from the high privilege of their birth,
something brighter than pity for the wingless ones
below them who shared dark holes in windows and in houses,
30   and higher they lifted the net with soundless voices
above all change, betrayals of falling suns,
and this season lasted one moment, like the pause
between dusk and darkness, between fury and peace,
but, for such as our earth is now, it lasted long.

                                                              1981

FROM OMEROS[1]

Book One

Chapter III

III

"*Mais qui ça qui rivait-'ous, Philoctete?*"[2]
　　　　　　　　　　"*Moin blessé.*"[3]
"But what is wrong wif you, Philoctete?"
　　　　　　　　　"I am blest
wif this wound, Ma Kilman,[4] *qui pas ka guérir pièce.*

Which will never heal."
　　　　　　　"Well, you must take it easy.
5　Go home and lie down, give the foot a lickle°　　　*little (West Indian English)*
　rest."
Philoctete, his trouser-legs rolled, stares out to sea

from the worn rumshop window. The itch in the sore
tingles like the tendrils of the anemone,
and the puffed blister of Portuguese man-o'-war.°　　　*jellyfish*

10　He believed the swelling came from the chained ankles
　of his grandfathers. Or else why was there no cure?
　That the cross he carried was not only the anchor's

but that of his race, for a village black and poor
as the pigs that rooted in its burning garbage,
15　then were hooked on the anchors of the abattoir.°　　　*slaughterhouse*

Ma Kilman was sewing. She looked up and saw his face
squinting from the white of the street. He was waiting
to pass out on the table. This went on for days.

The ice turned to warm water near the self-hating
20　gesture of clenching his head tight in both hands. She
heard the boys in blue uniforms, going to school,

screaming at his elbow: "Pheeloh! Pheelosophee!"
A mummy embalmed in Vaseline and alcohol.
In the Egyptian silence she muttered softly:

1. Modern Greek version of the name Homer. Homer's *Iliad* and *Odyssey* are, along with Dante's *Divine Comedy*, from which Walcott adapts the terza rima stanza, and James Joyce's *Ulysses* (1922), major influences on this Caribbean epic, which moves across centuries and geographies, from Saint Lucia to Africa to Ireland.
2. Pronounced *fee-lock-TET*; a name shared with Philoctetes, who, in the *Iliad* and Sophocles' eponymous play, is abandoned on an island on the way to the Trojan War after receiving a snakebite. The wound never heals and continually torments Philoctetes, who moans uncontrollably. Later the gods decide that the war cannot be won without him, and the Greek soldiers have to go back to the island and beg him to return with them to battle.
3. French patois, punningly mistranslated below, since *blessé* actually means "wounded."
4. The owner of the No Pain Café, Ma Kilman serves in the poem as a sibyl (female prophet) and an obeah woman (one practicing a kind of West Indian sorcery).

25   "It have a flower somewhere, a medicine, and ways
my grandmother would boil it. I used to watch ants
climbing her white flower-pot. But, God, in which place?"

Where was this root? What senna,° what tepid   *medicinal herb*
    tisanes,°   *medicinal beverages*
could clean the branched river of his corrupted blood,
30   whose sap was a wounded cedar's? What did it mean,

this name that felt like a fever? Well, one good heft
of his garden-cutlass would slice the damned name clean
from its rotting yam. He said, *"Merci."*° Then he left.   *Thank you (French)*

Book Six

Chapter XLIX

I

She bathed him in the brew of the root.[1] The basin
was one of those cauldrons from the old sugar-mill,
with its charred pillars, rock pasture, and one grazing

horse, looking like helmets that have tumbled downhill
5   from an infantry charge. Children rang them with stones.
Wildflowers sprung in them when the dirt found a seam.

She had one in her back yard, close to the crotons,°   *tree or shrub*
agape in its crusted, agonized O: the scream
of centuries. She scraped its rusted scabs, she scoured

10   the mouth of the cauldron, then fed a crackling pyre
with palms and banana-trash. In the scream she poured
tin after kerosene tin, its base black from fire,

of seawater and sulphur. Into this she then fed
the bubbling root and leaves. She led Philoctete
15   to the gurgling lava. Trembling, he entered

his bath like a boy. The lime leaves leeched to his wet
knuckled spine like islands that cling to the basin
of the rusted Caribbean. An icy sweat

glazed his scalp, but he could feel the putrescent shin
20   drain in the seethe like sucked marrow, he felt it drag
the slime from his shame. She rammed him back to his place

as he tried climbing out with: *"Not yet!"* With a rag
sogged in a basin of ice she rubbed his squeezed face
the way boys enjoy their mother's ritual rage,

---

1. Ma Kilman is bathing Philoctete to heal his wound.

25 and as he surrendered to her, the foul flower
on his shin whitened and puckered, the corolla
closed its thorns like the sea-egg. What else did it cure?

II

The bow leapt back to the palm of the warrior.
The yoke of the wrong name lifted from his shoulders.
30 His muscles loosened like those of a brown river

that was dammed with silt, and then silkens its boulders
with refreshing strength. His ribs thudded like a horse
cantering on a beach that bursts into full gallop

while a boy yanks at its rein with terrified "Whoas!"
35 The white foam unlocked his coffles, his ribbed shallop
broke from its anchor, and the water, which he swirled

like a child, steered his brow into the right current,
as calm as *In God We Troust*[2] to that other world,
and his flexed palm enclosed an oar with the identi-

40 ical closure of a mouth around its own name,
the way a sea-anemone closes slyly
into a secrecy many mistake for shame.

Centuries weigh down the head of the swamp-lily,
its tribal burden arches the sea-almond's° spine,   *a tree*
45 in barracoon[3] back yards the soul-smoke still passes,

but the wound has found her own cure. The soft days spin
the spittle of the spider in webbed glasses,
as she drenches the burning trash to its last flame,

and the embers steam and hiss to the schoolboys' cries
50 when he'd weep in the window for their tribal shame.
A shame for the loss of words, and a language tired

of accepting that loss, and then all accepted.
That was why the sea stank from the frothing urine
of surf, and fish-guts reeked from the government shed,

55 and why God pissed on the village for months of rain.
But now, quite clearly the tears trickled down his face
like rainwater down a cracked carafe from Choiseul,[4]

as he stood like a boy in his bath with the first clay's
innocent prick! So she threw Adam a towel.
60 And the yard was Eden. And its light the first day's.

1990

2. Near the poem's beginning, the character   and mine" (1.1.2).
Achille chisels this misspelled phrase into his   3. Barracks for housing convicts or slaves.
canoe and then decides, "Leave it! Is God' spelling   4. A village in Saint Lucia.

TED HUGHES
1930–1998

Ted Hughes was born in Yorkshire, the son of one of seventeen men from a regiment of several hundred to return from Gallipoli in World War I, a tragedy that imprinted the imagination of the poet. He was educated at Mexborough Grammar School and Pembroke College, Cambridge, where in his last year he changed his course of study from English to archaeology and anthropology, pursuing his interest in the mythic structures that were later to inform his poetry. In 1956 he married the American-born poet Sylvia Plath, who committed suicide in 1963. As poets they explored the world of raw feeling and sensation, a world that Hughes's poems tended to view through the eye of the predator, Plath's through the eye of the victim.

In contrast to the rational lucidity and buttoned-up forms of Philip Larkin and other English poets of "the Movement," Hughes fashions a mythical consciousness in his poems, embodied in violent metaphors, blunt syntax, harsh alliterative clusters, bunched stresses, incantatory repetitions, insistent assonances, and a dark brooding tone. His early books, *The Hawk in the Rain* (1957) and *Lupercal* (1960), show the influence of D. H. Lawrence's *Birds, Beasts and Flowers* (1923), and Hughes's electrifying descriptions of jaguars, thrushes, and pike similarly generate metaphors that relate such creatures to forces underlying all animal and human experience. With *Crow* (1970) and *Gaudete* (1977) he abandoned at once the semblance of realism and the traditional metrical patterning of his early work, in the belief that "the very sound of metre calls up the ghosts of the past and it is difficult to sing one's own tune against that choir. It is easier to speak a language that raises no ghosts." Returning from the wilder shores of myth, Hughes showed in *Moortown* (1979), *Remains of Elmet* (1979), *River* (1983), and *Flowers and Insects* (1989) that he could render the natural world with a delicacy and tenderness as arresting as his earlier ferocity. In *Tales from Ovid* (1997) he brilliantly re-created—rather than translated—twenty-four passages from the Roman poet Ovid's *Metamorphoses*. In the poems of his last volume, *Birthday Letters* (1998), all but two of which are addressed to Plath, Hughes broke a silence of thirty-five years to lift the curtain on the tragic drama of their marriage. That same year he was appointed a member of the Order of Merit, having served as poet laureate of the United Kingdom since 1984. His *Collected Poems* was published in 2003.

Wind

This house has been far out at sea all night,
The woods crashing through darkness, the booming hills,
Winds stampeding the fields under the window
Floundering black astride and blinding wet

5 Till day rose; then under an orange sky
The hills had new places, and wind wielded
Blade-light, luminous and emerald,
Flexing like the lens of a mad eye.

At noon I scaled along the house-side as far as
10 The coal-house door. I dared once to look up—
Through the brunt wind that dented the balls of my eyes
The tent of the hills drummed and strained its guyrope,

The fields quivering, the skyline a grimace,
At any second to bang and vanish with a flap:
15   The wind flung a magpie away and a black-
Back gull bent like an iron bar slowly. The house

Rang like some fine green goblet in the note
That any second would shatter it. Now deep
In chairs, in front of the great fire, we grip
20   Our hearts and cannot entertain book, thought,

Or each other. We watch the fire blazing,
And feel the roots of the house move, but sit on,
Seeing the window tremble to come in,
Hearing the stones cry out under the horizons.

1957

Relic

I found this jawbone at the sea's edge:
There, crabs, dogfish, broken by the breakers or tossed
To flap for half an hour and turn to a crust
Continue the beginning. The deeps are cold:
5   In that darkness camaraderie does not hold:

Nothing touches but, clutching, devours. And the jaws,
Before they are satisfied or their stretched purpose
Slacken, go down jaws; go gnawn bare. Jaws
Eat and are finished and the jawbone comes to the beach:
10   This is the sea's achievement; with shells,
Vertebrae, claws, carapaces, skulls.

Time in the sea eats its tail, thrives, casts these
Indigestibles, the spars of purposes
That failed far from the surface. None grow rich
15   In the sea. This curved jawbone did not laugh
But gripped, gripped and is now a cenotaph.[1]

1960

Pike

Pike, three inches long, perfect
Pike in all parts, green tigering the gold.
Killers from the egg: the malevolent aged grin.
They dance on the surface among the flies.

---

1. Monument to the dead.

5 Or move, stunned by their own grandeur,
   Over a bed of emerald, silhouette
   Of submarine delicacy and horror.
   A hundred feet long in their world.

   In ponds, under the heat-struck lily pads—
10 Gloom of their stillness:
   Logged on last year's black leaves, watching upwards.
   Or hung in an amber cavern of weeds

   The jaws' hooked clamp and fangs
   Not to be changed at this date;
15 A life subdued to its instrument;
   The gills kneading quietly, and the pectorals.

   Three we kept behind glass,
   Jungled in weed: three inches, four,
   And four and a half: fed fry° to them—   young fish
20 Suddenly there were two. Finally one

   With a sag belly and the grin it was born with.
   And indeed they spare nobody.
   Two, six pounds each, over two feet long,
   High and dry and dead in the willow-herb—

25 One jammed past its gills down the other's gullet:
   The outside eye stared: as a vice locks—
   The same iron in this eye
   Though its film shrank in death.

   A pond I fished, fifty yards across,
30 Whose lilies and muscular tench¹
   Had outlasted every visible stone
   Of the monastery that planted them—

   Stilled legendary depth:
   It was as deep as England. It held
35 Pike too immense to stir, so immense and old
   That past nightfall I dared not cast

   But silently cast and fished
   With the hair frozen on my head
   For what might move, for what eye might move.
40 The still splashes on the dark pond,

   Owls hushing the floating woods
   Frail on my ear against the dream
   Darkness beneath night's darkness had freed,
   That rose slowly towards me, watching.

                                          1959, 1960

1. Variety of freshwater fish.

Out

1 The Dream Time

My father sat in his chair recovering
From the four-year mastication° by gunfire and mud,   *grinding; chewing*
Body buffeted wordless, estranged by long soaking
In the colors of mutilation.
                   His outer perforations
5 Were valiantly healed, but he and the hearth-fire, its blood-flicker
On biscuit-bowl and piano and table leg,
Moved into strong and stronger possession
Of minute after minute, as the clock's tiny cog
Labored and on the thread of his listening
10 Dragged him bodily from under
The mortised° four-year strata of dead Englishmen   *firmly fixed*
He belonged with. He felt his limbs clearing
With every slight, gingerish movement. While I, small and four,
Lay on the carpet as his luckless double,
15 His memory's buried, immovable anchor,
Among jawbones and blown-off boots, tree-stumps, shell-cases and craters,
Under rain that goes on drumming its rods and thickening
Its kingdom, which the sun has abandoned, and where nobody
Can ever again move from shelter.

2

20 The dead man in his cave beginning to sweat;
The melting bronze visor of flesh
Of the mother in the baby-furnace—

Nobody believes, it
Could be nothing, all
25 Undergo smiling at
The lulling of blood in
Their ears, their ears, their ears, their eyes
Are only drops of water and even the dead man suddenly
Sits up and sneezes—Atishoo!
30 Then the nurse wraps him up, smiling,
And, though faintly, the mother is smiling,
And it's just another baby.

As after being blasted to bits
The reassembled infantryman
35 Tentatively totters out, gazing around with the eyes
Of an exhausted clerk.

3 *Remembrance Day*[1]

The poppy is a wound, the poppy is the mouth
Of the grave, maybe of the womb searching—

A canvas-beauty puppet on a wire
40 Today whoring everywhere. It is years since I wore one.

It is more years
The shrapnel that shattered my father's paybook

Gripped me, and all his dead
Gripped him to a time

45 He no more than they could outgrow, but, cast into one, like iron,
Hung deeper than refreshing of ploughs

In the woe-dark under my mother's eye—
One anchor

Holding my juvenile neck bowed to the dunkings of the Atlantic.
50 So goodbye to that bloody-minded flower.

You dead bury your dead.
Goodbye to the cenotaphs° on my mother's breasts.   *empty tombs*

Goodbye to all the remaindered charms of my father's survival.
Let England close. Let the green sea-anemone close.

                                                              1967

Theology

No, the serpent did not
Seduce Eve to the apple.
All that's simply
Corruption of the facts.

5 Adam ate the apple.
Eve ate Adam.
The serpent ate Eve.
This is the dark intestine.

The serpent, meanwhile,
10 Sleeps his meal off in Paradise—
Smiling to hear
God's querulous calling.

                                                              1967

---

1. Holiday (November 11) commemorating soldiers who lost their lives in battle. The practice of
wearing red poppies in honor of lost soldiers recalls
John McCrae's poem "In Flanders Fields" (1915),
which depicts the flowers growing between the
graves on a battlefield.

Crow's Last Stand

Burning
    burning
        burning[1]
            there was finally something
5 The sun could not burn, that it had rendered
Everything down to—a final obstacle
Against which it raged and charred

And rages and chars

Limpid° among the glaring furnace clinkers°   *clear / coal remains*
10 The pulsing blue tongues and the red and the yellow
The green lickings of the conflagration

Limpid and black—

Crow's eye-pupil, in the tower of its scorched fort.

1970

Daffodils

Remember how we[1] picked the daffodils?
Nobody else remembers, but I remember.
Your daughter came with her armfuls, eager and happy,
Helping the harvest. She has forgotten.
5 She cannot even remember you. And we sold them.
It sounds like sacrilege, but we sold them.
Were we so poor? Old Stoneman, the grocer,
Boss-eyed, his blood-pressure purpling to beetroot
(It was his last chance,
10 He would die in the same great freeze as you),
He persuaded us. Every Spring
He always bought them, sevenpence a dozen,
'A custom of the house'.

Besides, we still weren't sure we wanted to own
15 Anything. Mainly we were hungry
To convert everything to profit.
Still nomads—still strangers
To our whole possession. The daffodils
Were incidental gilding of the deeds,[2]
20 Treasure trove. They simply came,
And they kept on coming.
As if not from the sod but falling from heaven.

---

1. Cf. "Burning burning burning burning," line 308 of T. S. Eliot's *Waste Land,* where it is quoted from the Buddha's Fire Sermon.
1. Hughes is addressing his first wife, the Ameri-

can poet Sylvia Plath (1932–1963).
2. Document establishing legal possession of a house.

Our lives were still a raid on our own good luck.
We knew we'd live for ever. We had not learned
25   What a fleeting glance of the everlasting
Daffodils are. Never identified
The nuptial flight of the rarest ephemera[3]—
Our own days!
           We thought they were a windfall.
Never guessed they were a last blessing.
30   So we sold them. We worked at selling them
As if employed on somebody else's
Flower-farm. You bent at it
In the rain of that April—your last April.
We bent there together, among the soft shrieks
35   Of their jostled stems, the wet shocks shaken
Of their girlish dance-frocks—
Fresh-opened dragonflies, wet and flimsy,
Opened too early.

We piled their frailty lights on a carpenter's bench,
40   Distributed leaves among the dozens—
Buckling blade-leaves, limber, groping for air, zinc-silvered—
Propped their raw butts in bucket water,
Their oval, meaty butts,
And sold them, sevenpence a bunch—

45   Wind-wounds, spasms from the dark earth,
With their odourless metals,
A flamy purification of the deep grave's stony cold
As if ice had a breath—

We sold them, to wither.
50   The crop thickened faster than we could thin it.
Finally, we were overwhelmed
And we lost our wedding-present scissors.

Every March since they have lifted again
Out of the same bulbs, the same
55   Baby-cries from the thaw,
Ballerinas too early for music, shiverers
In the draughty wings of the year.
On that same groundswell of memory, fluttering
They return to forget you stooping there
60   Behind the rainy curtains of a dark April,
Snipping their stems.

But somewhere your scissors remember. Wherever they are.
Here somewhere, blades wide open,
April by April
65   Sinking deeper
Through the sod—an anchor, a cross of rust.

                                                1998

3. Insect that lives only a few days.

HAROLD PINTER
b. 1930

Harold Pinter is one of the most original and challenging of the many important playwrights who have emerged in Britain in the last half-century. He was born and educated in East London, studied briefly at the Academy of Dramatic Art, and from the age of nineteen to the age of twenty-seven acted in a repertory company. His first play (in one act), *The Room*, was written and produced in 1957 and was followed immediately by *The Dumb Waiter* and *The Birthday Party*, his first real success. In addition to his prize-winning work for theater and television, he has written a number of screenplays based on novels such as Marcel Proust's *A la Recherche du Temps Perdu* (*In Search of Lost Time*), John Fowles's *The French Lieutenant's Woman*, and Margaret Atwood's *The Handmaid's Tale*; his screenplays were collected and published in three volumes in 2000.

Pinter's early work shows the influence of Samuel Beckett and of absurdist drama, notably that of the French playwright Eugène Ionesco, but his vision rapidly established itself as more naturalistic (though no less alarming) than theirs. His territory is typically a room (refuge, prison cell, trap) symbolic of its occupants' world. Into this, and into their ritualized relationship with its rules and taboos, comes a stranger on to whom—as on to a screen—the occupants project their deepest desires, guilts, neuroses. The breakdown that follows is mirrored in the breakdown of language. Pinter, who has a poet's ear for the rhythms of spoken English, is a master of the pauses, double entendres, and silences that communicate a secondary level of meaning often opposed to the first. He has said of language:

> The speech we hear is an indication of that which we don't hear. It is a necessary avoidance, a violent, sly, and anguished or mocking smoke screen which keeps the other in its true place. When true silence falls we are left with echo but are nearer nakedness. One way of looking at speech is to say that it is a constant stratagem to cover nakedness.

The critic Lois Gordon has well said that "one way of looking at Pinter's plays is to say that they are dramatic stratagems that uncover nakedness."

The Dumb Waiter

SCENE: *A basement room. Two beds, flat against the back wall. A serving hatch, closed, between the beds. A door to the kitchen and lavatory, left. A door to a passage, right.*

BEN *is lying on a bed, left, reading a paper.* GUS *is sitting on a bed, right, tying his shoelaces, with difficulty. Both are dressed in shirts, trousers and braces.*
Silence.
GUS *ties his laces, rises, yawns and begins to walk slowly to the door, left. He stops, looks down, and shakes his foot.*
BEN *lowers his paper and watches him.* GUS *kneels and unties his shoelace and slowly takes off the shoe. He looks inside it and brings out a flattened matchbox. He shakes it and examines it. Their eyes meet.* BEN *rattles his paper and reads.* GUS *puts the matchbox in his pocket and bends down to put on his shoe. He ties his lace, with difficulty.* BEN *lowers his paper and watches him.* GUS *walks to the door, left, stops, and shakes the other foot. He kneels, unties his shoelace, and slowly takes off the shoe. He looks inside it and brings out a flattened cigarette*

packet. He shakes it and examines it. Their eyes meet. BEN *rattles his paper and reads.* GUS *puts the packet in his pocket, bends down, puts on his shoe and ties the lace.*

He wanders off, left.

BEN *slams the paper down on the bed and glares after him. He picks up the paper and lies on his back, reading.*

Silence.

A lavatory chain is pulled twice off left, but the lavatory does not flush.

Silence.

GUS *re-enters, left, and halts at the door, scratching his head.*

BEN *slams down the paper.*

BEN   Kaw!

      [*He picks up the paper.*]

  What about this? Listen to this!

      [*He refers to the paper.*]

  A man of eighty-seven wanted to cross the road. But there was a lot of traffic, see? He couldn't see how he was going to squeeze through. So he crawled under a lorry.[1]

GUS   He what?

BEN   He crawled under a lorry. A stationary lorry.

GUS   No?

BEN   The lorry started and ran over him.

GUS   Go on!

BEN   That's what it says here.

GUS   Get away.

BEN   It's enough to make you want to puke, isn't it?

GUS   Who advised him to do a thing like that?

BEN   A man of eighty-seven crawling under a lorry!

GUS   It's unbelievable.

BEN   It's down here in black and white.

GUS   Incredible.

      [*Silence.*

        GUS *shakes his head and exits.* BEN *lies back and reads.*

        The lavatory chain is pulled once off left, but the lavatory does not flush.

        BEN *whistles at an item in the paper.*

        GUS *re-enters.*]

  I want to ask you something.

BEN   What are you doing out there?

GUS   Well, I was just—

BEN   What about the tea?

GUS   I'm just going to make it.

BEN   Well, go on, make it.

GUS   Yes, I will. [*He sits in a chair. Ruminatively.*] He's laid on some very nice crockery this time, I'll say that. It's sort of striped. There's a white stripe.

      [BEN *reads.*]

  It's very nice. I'll say that.

      [BEN *turns the page.*]

---

1. Truck.

You know, sort of round the cup. Round the rim. All the rest of it's black, you see. Then the saucer's black, except for right in the middle, where the cup goes, where it's white.

[BEN *reads.*]

Then the plates are the same, you see. Only they've got a black stripe—the plates—right across the middle. Yes, I'm quite taken with the crockery.

BEN [*Still reading.*] What do you want plates for? You're not going to eat.

GUS I've brought a few biscuits.

BEN Well, you'd better eat them quick.

GUS I always bring a few biscuits. Or a pie. You know I can't drink tea without anything to eat.

BEN Well, make the tea then, will you? Time's getting on.

[GUS *brings out the flattened cigarette packet and examines it.*]

GUS You got any cigarettes? I think I've run out.

[*He throws the packet high up and leans forward to catch it.*]

I hope it won't be a long job, this one.

[*Aiming carefully, he flips the packet under his bed.*]

Oh, I wanted to ask you something.

BEN [*Slamming his paper down.*] Kaw!

GUS What's that?

BEN A child of eight killed a cat!

GUS Get away.

BEN It's a fact. What about that, eh? A child of eight killing a cat!

GUS How did he do it?

BEN It was a girl.

GUS How did she do it?

BEN She—

[*He picks up the paper and studies it.*]

It doesn't say.

GUS Why not?

BEN Wait a minute. It just says—Her brother, aged eleven, viewed the incident from the toolshed.

GUS Go on!

BEN That's bloody ridiculous.

[*Pause.*]

GUS I bet he did it.

BEN Who?

GUS The brother.

BEN I think you're right.

[*Pause.*]

[*Slamming down the paper.*] What about that, eh? A kid of eleven killing a cat and blaming it on his little sister of eight! It's enough to—

[*He breaks off in disgust and seizes the paper.* GUS *rises.*]

GUS What time is he getting in touch?

[BEN *reads.*]

What time is he getting in touch?

BEN What's the matter with you? It could be any time. Any time.

GUS [*Moves to the foot of* BEN's *bed.*] Well, I was going to ask you something.

BEN What?

GUS Have you noticed the time that tank takes to fill?

BEN What tank?

GUS   In the lavatory.
BEN   No. Does it?
GUS   Terrible.
BEN   Well, what about it?
GUS   What do you think's the matter with it?
BEN   Nothing.
GUS   Nothing?
BEN   It's got a deficient ballcock, that's all.
GUS   A deficient what?
BEN   Ballcock.
GUS   No? Really?
BEN   That's what I should say.
GUS   Go on! That didn't occur to me.
       [GUS *wanders to his bed and presses the mattress.*]
       I didn't have a very restful sleep today, did you? It's not much of a bed. I
       could have done with another blanket too. [*He catches sight of a picture on
       the wall.*] Hello, what's this? [*Peering at it.*] "The First Eleven."² Cricketers.
       You seen this, Ben?
BEN   [*Reading.*] What?
GUS   The first eleven.
BEN   What?
GUS   There's a photo here of the first eleven.
BEN   What first eleven?
GUS   [*Studying the photo.*] It doesn't say.
BEN   What about that tea?
GUS   They all look a bit old to me.
       [GUS *wanders downstage, looks out front, then all about the room.*]
       I wouldn't like to live in this dump. I wouldn't mind if you had a window,
       you could see what it looked like outside.
BEN   What do you want a window for?
GUS   Well, I like to have a bit of a view, Ben. It whiles away the time.
       [*He walks about the room.*]
       I mean, you come into a place when it's still dark, you come into a room
       you've never seen before, you sleep all day, you do your job, and then you
       go away in the night again.
       [*Pause.*]
       I like to get a look at the scenery. You never get the chance in this job.
BEN   You get your holidays, don't you?
GUS   Only a fortnight.
BEN   [*Lowering the paper.*] You kill me. Anyone would think you're working
       every day. How often do we do a job? Once a week? What are you com-
       plaining about?
GUS   Yes, but we've got to be on tap though, haven't we? You can't move out
       of the house in case a call comes.
BEN   You know what your trouble is?
GUS   What?
BEN   You haven't got any interests.
GUS   I've got interests.
BEN   What? Tell me one of your interests.

2. A school's top team of cricketers.

[*Pause.*]

GUS   I've got interests.

BEN   Look at me. What have I got?

GUS   I don't know. What?

BEN   I've got my woodwork. I've got my model boats. Have you ever seen me idle? I'm never idle. I know how to occupy my time, to its best advantage. Then when a call comes, I'm ready.

GUS   Don't you ever get a bit fed up?

BEN   Fed up? What with?

> [*Silence.*
>
> > BEN *reads.* GUS *feels in the pocket of his jacket, which hangs on the bed.*]

GUS   You got any cigarettes? I've run out.

> [*The lavatory flushes off left.*]

There she goes.

> [GUS *sits on his bed.*]

No, I mean, I say the crockery's good. It is. It's very nice. But that's about all I can say for this place. It's worse than the last one. Remember that last place we were in? Last time, where was it? At least there was a wireless there. No, honest. He doesn't seem to bother much about our comfort these days.

BEN   When are you going to stop jabbering?

GUS   You'd get rheumatism in a place like this, if you stay long.

BEN   We're not staying long. Make the tea, will you? We'll be on the job in a minute.

> [GUS *picks up a small bag by his bed and brings out a packet of tea. He examines it and looks up.*]

GUS   Eh, I've been meaning to ask you.

BEN   What the hell is it now?

GUS   Why did you stop the car this morning, in the middle of that road?

BEN   [*Lowering the paper.*] I thought you were asleep.

GUS   I was, but I woke up when you stopped. You did stop, didn't you?

> [*Pause.*]

In the middle of that road. It was still dark, don't you remember? I looked out. It was all misty. I thought perhaps you wanted to kip,³ but you were sitting up dead straight, like you were waiting for something.

BEN   I wasn't waiting for anything.

GUS   I must have fallen asleep again. What was all that about then? Why did you stop?

BEN   [*Picking up the paper.*] We were too early.

GUS   Early? [*He rises.*] What do you mean? We got the call, didn't we, saying we were to start right away. We did. We shoved out on the dot. So how could we be too early?

BEN   [*Quietly.*] Who took the call, me or you?

GUS   You.

BEN   We were too early.

GUS   Too early for what?

> [*Pause.*]

You mean someone had to get out before we got in?

3. Nap.

2606 / Harold Pinter

[*He examines the bedclothes.*]
I thought these sheets didn't look too bright. I thought they ponged[4] a bit.
I was too tired to notice when I got in this morning. Eh, that's taking a bit
of a liberty, isn't it? I don't want to share my bed-sheets. I told you things
were going down the drain. I mean, we've always had clean sheets laid on
up till now. I've noticed it.

BEN   How do you know those sheets weren't clean?

GUS   What do you mean?

BEN   How do you know they weren't clean? You've spent the whole day in
them, haven't you?

GUS   What, you mean it might be my pong? [*He sniffs sheets.*] Yes. [*He sits
slowly on bed.*] It could be my pong, I suppose. It's difficult to tell. I don't
really know what I pong like, that's the trouble.

BEN   [*Referring to the paper.*] Kaw!

GUS   Eh, Ben.

BEN   Kaw!

GUS   Ben.

BEN   What?

GUS   What town are we in? I've forgotten.

BEN   I've told you. Birmingham.

GUS   Go on!
      [*He looks with interest about the room.*]
That's in the Midlands. The second biggest city in Great Britain. I'd never
have guessed.
      [*He snaps his fingers.*]
Eh, it's Friday today, isn't it? It'll be Saturday tomorrow.

BEN   What about it?

GUS   [*Excited.*] We could go and watch the Villa.[5]

BEN   They're playing away.

GUS   No, are they? Caarr! What a pity.

BEN   Anyway, there's no time. We've got to get straight back.

GUS   Well, we have done in the past, haven't we? Stayed over and watched a
game, haven't we? For a bit of relaxation.

BEN   Things have tightened up, mate. They're tightened up.
      [GUS *chuckles to himself.*]

GUS   I saw the Villa get beat in a cup tie once. Who was it against now? White
shirts. It was one-all at half time. I'll never forget it. Their opponents won
by a penalty. Talk about drama. Yes, it was a disputed penalty. Disputed.
They got beat two–one, anyway, because of it. You were there yourself.

BEN   Not me.

GUS   Yes, you were there. Don't you remember that disputed penalty?

BEN   No.

GUS   He went down just inside the area. Then they said he was just acting. I
didn't think the other bloke touched him myself. But the referee had the
ball on the spot.

BEN   Didn't touch him! What are you talking about? He laid him out flat!

GUS   Not the Villa. The Villa don't play that sort of game.

BEN   Get out of it.

---

4. Smelled.
5. Aston Villa, popularly known as "the Villa," Birmingham's soccer team.

[*Pause.*]

GUS Eh, that must have been here, in Birmingham.

BEN What must?

GUS The Villa. That must have been here.

BEN They were playing away.

GUS Because you know who the other team was? It was the Spurs. It was Tottenham Hotspur.[6]

BEN Well, what about it?

GUS We've never done a job in Tottenham.

BEN How do you know?

GUS I'd remember Tottenham.

> [BEN *turns on his bed to look at him.*]

BEN Don't make me laugh, will you?

> [BEN *turns back and reads.* GUS *yawns and speaks through his yawn.*]

GUS When's he going to get in touch?

> [*Pause.*]

Yes, I'd like to see another football match. I've always been an ardent football fan. Here, what about coming to see the Spurs tomorrow?

BEN [*Tonelessly.*] They're playing away.

GUS Who are?

BEN The Spurs.

GUS Then they might be playing here.

BEN Don't be silly.

GUS If they're playing away they might be playing here. They might be playing the Villa.

BEN [*Tonelessly.*] But the Villa are playing away.

> [*Pause. An envelope slides under the door, right.* GUS *sees it. He stands, looking at it.*]

GUS Ben.

BEN Away. They're all playing away.

GUS Ben, look here.

BEN What?

GUS Look.

> [BEN *turns his head and sees the envelope. He stands.*]

BEN What's that?

GUS I don't know.

BEN Where did it come from?

GUS Under the door.

BEN Well, what is it?

GUS I don't know.

> [*They stare at it.*]

BEN Pick it up.

GUS What do you mean?

BEN Pick it up!

> [GUS *slowly moves towards it, bends and picks it up.*]

What is it?

GUS An envelope.

BEN Is there anything on it?

GUS No.

---

6. A soccer team; Tottenham is in north London.

BEN   Is it sealed?
GUS   Yes.
BEN   Open it.
GUS   What?
BEN   Open it!
  [GUS *opens it and looks inside.*]
 What's in it?
  [GUS *empties twelve matches into his hand.*]
GUS   Matches.
BEN   Matches?
GUS   Yes.
BEN   Show it to me.
  [GUS *passes the envelope.* BEN *examines it.*]
 Nothing on it. Not a word.
GUS   That's funny, isn't it?
BEN   It came under the door?
GUS   Must have done.
BEN   Well, go on.
GUS   Go on where?
BEN   Open the door and see if you catch anyone outside.
GUS   Who, me?
BEN   Go on!
  [GUS *stares at him, puts the matches in his pocket, goes to his bed and brings a revolver from under the pillow. He goes to the door, opens it, looks out and shuts it.*]
GUS   No one.
  [*He replaces the revolver.*]
BEN   What did you see?
GUS   Nothing.
BEN   They must have been pretty quick.
  [GUS *takes the matches from pocket and looks at them.*]
GUS   Well, they'll come in handy.
BEN   Yes.
GUS   Won't they?
BEN   Yes, you're always running out, aren't you?
GUS   All the time.
BEN   Well, they'll come in handy then.
GUS   Yes.
BEN   Won't they?
GUS   Yes, I could do with them. I could do with them too.
BEN   You could, eh?
GUS   Yes.
BEN   Why?
GUS   We haven't any.
BEN   Well, you've got some now, haven't you?
GUS   I can light the kettle now.
BEN   Yes, you're always cadging matches. How many have you got there?
GUS   About a dozen.
BEN   Well, don't lose them. Red too. You don't even need a box.
  [GUS *probes his ear with a match.*]
 [*Slapping his hand.*] Don't waste them! Go on, go and light it.

GUS Eh?
BEN Go and light it.
GUS Light what?
BEN The kettle.
GUS You mean the gas.
BEN Who does?
GUS You do.
BEN [*His eyes narrowing.*] What do you mean, I mean the gas?
GUS Well, that's what you mean, don't you? The gas.
BEN [*Powerfully.*] If I say go and light the kettle I mean go and light the kettle.
GUS How can you light a kettle?
BEN It's a figure of speech! Light the kettle. It's a figure of speech!
GUS I've never heard it.
BEN Light the kettle! It's common usage!
GUS I think you've got it wrong.
BEN [*Menacing.*] What do you mean?
GUS They say put on the kettle.
BEN [*Taut.*] Who says?

[*They stare at each other, breathing hard.*]

[*Deliberately.*] I have never in all my life heard anyone say put on the kettle.
GUS I bet my mother used to say it.
BEN Your mother? When did you last see your mother?
GUS I don't know, about—
BEN Well, what are you talking about your mother for?

[*They stare.*]

Gus, I'm not trying to be unreasonable. I'm just trying to point out something to you.
GUS Yes, but—
BEN Who's the senior partner here, me or you?
GUS You.
BEN I'm only looking after your interests, Gus. You've got to learn, mate.
GUS Yes, but I've never heard—
BEN [*Vehemently.*] Nobody says light the gas! What does the gas light?
GUS What does the gas—?
BEN [*Grabbing him with two hands by the throat, at arm's length.*] THE KETTLE, YOU FOOL!

[GUS *takes the hands from his throat.*]

GUS All right, all right.

[*Pause.*]

BEN Well, what are you waiting for?
GUS I want to see if they light.
BEN What?
GUS The matches.

[*He takes out the flattened box and tries to strike.*]

No.

[*He throws the box under the bed.*
BEN *stares at him.*
GUS *raises his foot.*]

Shall I try it on here?

[BEN *stares.* GUS *strikes a match on his shoe. It lights.*]

Here we are.

BEN [*Wearily.*] Put on the bloody kettle, for Christ's sake.

[BEN *goes to his bed, but, realizing what he has said, stops and half turns. They look at each other.* GUS *slowly exits, left.* BEN *slams his paper down on the bed and sits on it, head in hands.*]

GUS [*Entering.*] It's going.

BEN What?

GUS The stove.

[GUS *goes to his bed and sits.*]

I wonder who it'll be tonight.

[*Silence.*]

Eh, I've been wanting to ask you something.

BEN [*Putting his legs on the bed.*] Oh, for Christ's sake.

GUS No. I was going to ask you something.

[*He rises and sits on* BEN's *bed.*]

BEN What are you sitting on my bed for?

[GUS *sits.*]

What's the matter with you? You're always asking me questions. What's the matter with you?

GUS Nothing.

BEN You never used to ask me so many damn questions. What's come over you?

GUS No, I was just wondering.

BEN Stop wondering. You've got a job to do. Why don't you just do it and shut up?

GUS That's what I was wondering about.

BEN What?

GUS The job.

BEN What job?

GUS [*Tentatively.*] I thought perhaps you might know something.

[BEN *looks at him.*]

I thought perhaps you—I mean—have you got any idea—who it's going to be tonight?

BEN Who what's going to be?

[*They look at each other.*]

GUS [*At length.*] Who it's going to be.

[*Silence.*]

BEN Are you feeling all right?

GUS Sure.

BEN Go and make the tea.

GUS Yes, sure.

[GUS *exits, left,* BEN *looks after him. He then takes his revolver from under the pillow and checks it for ammunition.* GUS *re-enters.*]

The gas has gone out.

BEN Well, what about it?

GUS There's a meter.[7]

BEN I haven't got any money.

GUS Nor have I.

BEN You'll have to wait.

---

7. One that controls the supply of gas and must be fed with shilling coins.

GUS   What for?

BEN   For Wilson.

GUS   He might not come. He might just send a message. He doesn't always come.

BEN   Well, you'll have to do without it, won't you?

GUS   Blimey.

BEN   You'll have a cup of tea afterwards. What's the matter with you?

GUS   I like to have one before.

[BEN *holds the revolver up to the light and polishes it.*]

BEN   You'd better get ready anyway.

GUS   Well, I don't know, that's a bit much, you know, for my money.

[*He picks up a packet of tea from the bed and throws it into the bag.*] I hope he's got a shilling, anyway, if he comes. He's entitled to have. After all, it's his place, he could have seen there was enough gas for a cup of tea.

BEN   What do you mean, it's his place?

GUS   Well, isn't it?

BEN   He's probably only rented it. It doesn't have to be his place.

GUS   I know it's his place. I bet the whole house is. He's not even laying on any gas now either.

[GUS *sits on his bed.*]

It's his place all right. Look at all the other places. You go to this address, there's a key there, there's a teapot, there's never a soul in sight—[*He pauses.*] Eh, nobody ever hears a thing, have you ever thought of that? We never get any complaints, do we, too much noise or anything like that? You never see a soul, do you?—except the bloke who comes. You ever noticed that? I wonder if the walls are soundproof. [*He touches the wall above his bed.*] Can't tell. All you do is wait, eh? Half the time he doesn't even bother to put in an appearance, Wilson.

BEN   Why should he? He's a busy man.

GUS   [*Thoughtfully.*] I find him hard to talk to, Wilson. Do you know that, Ben?

BEN   Scrub round it, will you?

[*Pause.*]

GUS   There are a number of things I want to ask him. But I can never get round to it, when I see him.

[*Pause.*]

I've been thinking about the last one.

BEN   What last one?

GUS   That girl.

[BEN *grabs the paper, which he reads.*]

[*Rising, looking down at* BEN.] How many times have you read that paper?

[BEN *slams the paper down and rises.*]

BEN   [*Angrily.*] What do you mean?

GUS   I was just wondering how many times you'd—

BEN   What are you doing, criticizing me?

GUS   No, I was just—

BEN   You'll get a swipe round your earhole if you don't watch your step.

GUS   Now look here, Ben—

BEN   I'm not looking anywhere! [*He addresses the room.*] How many times have I—! A bloody liberty!

GUS   I didn't mean that.

BEN   You just get on with it, mate. Get on with it, that's all.
[BEN *gets back on the bed.*]
GUS   I was just thinking about that girl, that's all.
[GUS *sits on his bed.*]
She wasn't much to look at, I know, but still. It was a mess though, wasn't it? What a mess. Honest, I can't remember a mess like that one. They don't seem to hold together like men, women. A looser texture, like. Didn't she spread, eh? She didn't half spread. Kaw! But I've been meaning to ask you.
[BEN *sits up and clenches his eyes.*]
Who clears up after we've gone? I'm curious about that. Who does the clearing up? Maybe they don't clear up. Maybe they just leave them there, eh? What do you think? How many jobs have we done? Blimey, I can't count them. What if they never clear anything up after we've gone.
BEN   [*Pityingly.*] You mutt. Do you think we're the only branch of this organization? Have a bit of common. They got departments for everything.
GUS   What, cleaners and all?
BEN   You birk!
GUS   No, it was that girl made me start to think—
[*There is a loud clatter and racket in the bulge of wall between the beds, of something descending. They grab their revolvers, jump up and face the wall. The noise comes to a stop. Silence. They look at each other. BEN gestures sharply towards the wall. GUS approaches the wall slowly. He bangs it with his revolver. It is hollow. BEN moves to the head of his bed, his revolver cocked. GUS puts his revolver on his bed and pats along the bottom of the centre panel. He finds a rim. He lifts the panel. Disclosed is a serving-hatch, a "dumb waiter." A wide box is held by pulleys. GUS peers into the box. He brings out a piece of paper.*]
BEN   What is it?
GUS   You have a look at it.
BEN   Read it.
GUS   [*Reading.*] Two braised steak and chips. Two sago puddings. Two teas without sugar.
BEN   Let me see that. [*He takes the paper.*]
GUS   [*To himself.*] Two teas without sugar.
BEN   Mmnn.
GUS   What do you think of that?
BEN   Well—
[*The box goes up,* BEN *levels his revolver.*]
GUS   Give us a chance! They're in a hurry, aren't they?
[BEN *rereads the note.* GUS *looks over his shoulder.*]
That's a bit—that's a bit funny, isn't it?
BEN   [*Quickly.*] No, it's not funny. It probably used to be a café here, that's all. Upstairs. These places change hands very quickly.
GUS   A café?
BEN   Yes.
GUS   What, do you mean this was the kitchen, down here?
BEN   Yes, they change hands overnight, these places. Go into liquidation. The people who run it, you know, they don't find it a going concern, they move out.
GUS   You mean the people who ran this place didn't find it a going concern and moved out?

BEN   Sure.

GUS   WELL, WHO'S GOT IT NOW?

      [Silence.]

BEN   What do you mean, who's got it now?

GUS   Who's got it now? If they moved out, who moved in?

BEN   Well, that all depends—

      [The box descends with a clatter and bang. BEN *levels his revolver.* GUS *goes to the box and brings out a piece of paper.]*

GUS   *[Reading.]* Soup of the day. Liver and onions. Jam tart.

      [A pause. GUS *looks at* BEN. BEN *takes the note and reads it. He walks slowly to the hatch.* GUS *follows.* BEN *looks into the hatch but not up it.* GUS *puts his hand on* BEN's *shoulder.* BEN *throws it off.* GUS *puts his finger to his mouth. He leans on the hatch and swiftly looks up it.* BEN *flings him away in alarm.* BEN *looks at the note. He throws his revolver on the bed and speaks with decision.]*

BEN   We'd better send something up.

GUS   Eh?

BEN   We'd better send something up.

GUS   Oh! Yes. Yes. Maybe you're right.

      [They are both relieved at the decision.]

BEN   *[Purposefully.]* Quick! What have you got in that bag?

GUS   Not much.

      [GUS goes to the hatch and shouts up it.]

  Wait a minute!

BEN   Don't do that!

      [GUS examines the contents of the bag and brings them out, one by one.]

GUS   Biscuits. A bar of chocolate. Half a pint of milk.

BEN   That all?

GUS   Packet of tea.

BEN   Good.

GUS   We can't send the tea. That's all the tea we've got.

BEN   Well, there's no gas. You can't do anything with it, can you?

GUS   Maybe they can send us down a bob.[8]

BEN   What else is there?

GUS   *[Reaching into bag.]* One Eccles cake.[9]

BEN   One Eccles cake?

GUS   Yes.

BEN   You never told me you had an Eccles cake.

GUS   Didn't I?

BEN   Why only one? Didn't you bring one for me?

GUS   I didn't think you'd be keen.

BEN   Well, you can't send up one Eccles cake, anyway.

GUS   Why not?

BEN   Fetch one of those plates.

GUS   All right.

      [GUS goes towards the door, left, and stops.]

  Do you mean I can keep the Eccles cake then?

BEN   Keep it?

---

8. A shilling (i.e., to insert in the gas meter).
9. A small cake originally made in the Lancashire town of Eccles.

GUS   Well, they don't know we've got it, do they?

BEN   That's not the point.

GUS   Can't I keep it?

BEN   No, you can't. Get the plate.

>   [GUS *exits, left.* BEN *looks in the bag. He brings out a packet of crisps.*[1] *Enter* GUS *with a plate.*]

>   [*Accusingly, holding up the crisps.*] Where did these come from?

GUS   What?

BEN   Where did these crisps come from?

GUS   Where did you find them?

BEN   [*Hitting him on the shoulder.*] You're playing a dirty game, my lad!

GUS   I only eat those with beer!

BEN   Well, where were you going to get the beer?

GUS   I was saving them till I did.

BEN   I'll remember this. Put everything on the plate.

>   [*They pile everything on to the plate. The box goes up without the plate.*]

Wait a minute!

>   [*They stand.*]

GUS   It's gone up.

BEN   It's all your stupid fault, playing about!

GUS   What do we do now?

BEN   We'll have to wait till it comes down.

>   [BEN *puts the plate on the bed, puts on his shoulder holster, and starts to put on his tie.*]

You'd better get ready.

>   [GUS *goes to his bed, puts on his tie, and starts to fix his holster.*]

GUS   Hey, Ben.

BEN   What?

GUS   What's going on here?

>   [*Pause.*]

BEN   What do you mean?

GUS   How can this be a café?

BEN   It used to be a café.

GUS   Have you seen the gas stove?

BEN   What about it?

GUS   It's only got three rings.

BEN   So what?

GUS   Well, you couldn't cook much on three rings, not for a busy place like this.

BEN   [*Irritably.*] That's why the service is slow!

>   [BEN *puts on his waistcoat.*]

GUS   Yes, but what happens when we're not here? What do they do then? All these menus coming down and nothing going up. It might have been going on like this for years.

>   [BEN *brushes his jacket.*]

What happens when we go?

>   [BEN *puts on his jacket.*]

They can't do much business.

>   [*The box descends. They turn about.* GUS *goes to the hatch and brings out a note.*]

---

1. Potato chips.

GUS   [*Reading.*] Macaroni Pastitsio. Ormitha Macarounada.
BEN   What was that?
GUS   Macaroni Pastitsio. Ormitha Macarounada.
BEN   Greek dishes.
GUS   No.
BEN   That's right.
GUS   That's pretty high class.
BEN   Quick before it goes up.
        [GUS *puts the plate in the box.*]
GUS   [*Calling up the hatch.*] Three McVitie and Price! One Lyons Red Label!
    One Smith's Crisps!² One Eccles cake! One Fruit and Nut!
BEN   Cadbury's.³
GUS   [*Up the hatch.*] Cadbury's!
BEN   [*Handing the milk.*] One bottle of milk.
GUS   [*Up the hatch.*] One bottle of milk! Half a pint! [*He looks at the label.*]
    Express Dairy! [*He puts the bottle in the box.*]
        [*The box goes up.*]
    Just did it.
BEN   You shouldn't shout like that.
GUS   Why not?
BEN   It isn't done.
        [BEN *goes to his bed.*]
    Well, that should be all right, anyway, for the time being.
GUS   You think so, eh?
BEN   Get dressed, will you? It'll be any minute now.
        [GUS *puts on his waistcoat.* BEN *lies down and looks up at the ceiling.*]
GUS   This is some place. No tea and no biscuits.
BEN   Eating makes you lazy, mate. You're getting lazy, you know that? You
    don't want to get slack on your job.
GUS   Who me?
BEN   Slack, mate, slack.
GUS   Who me? Slack?
BEN   Have you checked your gun? You haven't even checked your gun. It
    looks disgraceful, anyway. Why don't you ever polish it?
        [GUS *rubs his revolver on the sheet.* BEN *takes out a pocket mirror and
        straightens his tie.*]
GUS   I wonder where the cook is. They must have had a few, to cope with
    that. Maybe they had a few more gas stoves. Eh! Maybe there's another
    kitchen along the passage.
BEN   Of course there is! Do you know what it takes to make an Ormitha
    Macarounada?
GUS   No, what?
BEN   An Ormitha—! Buck your ideas up, will you?
GUS   Takes a few cooks, eh?
        [GUS *puts his revolver in its holster.*]
    The sooner we're out of this place the better.
        [*He puts on his jacket.*]
    Why doesn't he get in touch? I feel like I've been here years. [*He takes his
    revolver out of its holster to check the ammunition.*] We've never let him

2. Brands, respectively, of cookies, tea, and potato   3. A brand of chocolate bar.
chips.

down though, have we? We've never let him down. I was thinking only the other day, Ben. We're reliable, aren't we?
[*He puts his revolver back in its holster.*]
Still, I'll be glad when it's over tonight.
[*He brushes his jacket.*]
I hope the bloke's not going to get excited tonight, or anything. I'm feeling a bit off. I've got a splitting headache.
[*Silence.*
The box descends. BEN *jumps up.*
GUS *collects the note.*]
[*Reading.*] One Bamboo Shoots, Water Chestnuts, and Chicken. One Char Siu and Beansprouts.
BEN   Beansprouts?
GUS   Yes.
BEN   Blimey.
GUS   I wouldn't know where to begin.
[*He looks back at the box. The packet of tea is inside it. He picks it up.*]
They've sent back the tea.
BEN   [*Anxious.*] What'd they do that for?
GUS   Maybe it isn't teatime.
[*The box goes up. Silence.*]
BEN   [*Throwing the tea on the bed, and speaking urgently.*] Look here. We'd better tell them.
GUS   Tell them what?
BEN   That we can't do it, we haven't got it.
GUS   All right then.
BEN   Lend us your pencil. We'll write a note.
[GUS, *turning for a pencil, suddenly discovers the speaking tube, which hangs on the right wall of the hatch facing his bed.*]
GUS   What's this?
BEN   What?
GUS   This.
BEN   [*Examining it.*] This? It's a speaking tube.
GUS   How long has that been there?
BEN   Just the job. We should have used it before, instead of shouting up there.
GUS   Funny I never noticed it before.
BEN   Well, come on.
GUS   What do you do?
BEN   See that? That's a whistle.
GUS   What, this?
BEN   Yes, take it out. Pull it out.
[GUS *does so.*]
That's it.
GUS   What do we do now?
BEN   Blow into it.
GUS   Blow?
BEN   It whistles up there if you blow. Then they know you want to speak. Blow.
[GUS *blows. Silence.*]
GUS   [*Tube at mouth.*] I can't hear a thing.
BEN   Now you speak! Speak into it!

[GUS *looks at* BEN, *then speaks into the tube.*]
GUS   The larder's bare!
BEN   Give me that!
    [*He grabs the tube and puts it to his mouth.*]
    [*Speaking with great deference.*] Good evening. I'm sorry to—bother you, but we just thought we'd better let you know that we haven't got anything left. We sent up all we had. There's no more food down here.
    [*He brings the tube slowly to his ear.*]
    What?
    [*To mouth.*]
    What?
    [*To ear. He listens. To mouth.*]
    No, all we had we sent up.
    [*To ear. He listens. To mouth.*]
    Oh, I'm very sorry to hear that.
    [*To ear. He listens. To* GUS.]
    The Eccles cake was stale.
    [*He listens. To* GUS.]
    The chocolate was melted.
    [*He listens. To* GUS.]
    The milk was sour.
GUS   What about the crisps?
BEN   [*Listening.*] The biscuits were mouldy.
    [*He glares at* GUS. *Tube to mouth.*]
    Well, we're sorry about that.
    [*Tube to ear.*]
    What?
    [*To mouth.*]
    What?
    [*To ear.*]
    Yes. Yes.
    [*To mouth.*]
    Yes certainly. Right away.
    [*To ear. The voice has ceased. He hangs up the tube.*]
    [*Excitedly.*] Did you hear that?
GUS   What?
BEN   You know what he said? Light the kettle! Not put on the kettle! Not light the gas! But light the kettle!
GUS   How can we light the kettle?
BEN   What do you mean?
GUS   There's no gas.
BEN   [*Clapping hand to head.*] Now what do we do?
GUS   What did he want us to light the kettle for?
BEN   For tea. He wanted a cup of tea.
GUS   *He* wanted a cup of tea! What about me? I've been wanting a cup of tea all night!
BEN   [*Despairingly.*] What do we do now?
GUS   What are we supposed to drink?
    [BEN *sits on his bed, staring.*]
    What about us?
    [BEN *sits.*]

I'm thirsty too. I'm starving. And he wants a cup of tea. That beats the band, that does.

[BEN *lets his head sink on his chest.*]

I could do with a bit of sustenance myself. What about you? You look as if you could do with something too.

[GUS *sits on his bed.*]

We send him up all we've got and he's not satisfied. No, honest, it's enough to make the cat laugh. Why did you send him up all that stuff? [*Thoughtfully.*] Why did I send it up?

[*Pause.*]

Who knows what he's got upstairs? He's probably got a salad bowl. They must have something up there. They won't get much from down here. You notice they didn't ask for any salads? They've probably got a salad bowl up there. Cold meat, radishes, cucumbers. Watercress. Roll mops.

[*Pause.*]

Hardboiled eggs.

[*Pause.*]

The lot. They've probably got a crate of beer too. Probably eating my crisps with a pint of beer now. Didn't have anything to say about those crisps, did he? They do all right, don't worry about that. You don't think they're just going to sit there and wait for stuff to come up from down here, do you? That'll get them nowhere.

[*Pause.*]

They do all right.

[*Pause.*]

And he wants a cup of tea.

[*Pause.*]

That's past a joke, in my opinion.

[*He looks over at* BEN, *rises, and goes to him.*]

What's the matter with you? You don't look too bright. I feel like an Alka-Seltzer myself.

[BEN *sits up.*]

BEN   [*In a low voice.*] Time's getting on.

GUS   I know. I don't like doing a job on an empty stomach.

BEN   [*Wearily.*] Be quiet a minute. Let me give you your instructions.

GUS   What for? We always do it the same way, don't we?

BEN   Let me give you your instructions.

[GUS *sighs and sits next to* BEN *on the bed. The instructions are stated and repeated automatically.*]

When we get the call, you go over and stand behind the door.

GUS   Stand behind the door.

BEN   If there's a knock on the door you don't answer it.

GUS   If there's a knock on the door I don't answer it.

BEN   But there won't be a knock on the door.

GUS   So I won't answer it.

BEN   When the bloke comes in—

GUS   When the bloke comes in—

BEN   Shut the door behind him.

GUS   Shut the door behind him.

BEN   Without divulging your presence.

GUS   Without divulging my presence.

BEN   He'll see me and come towards me.
GUS   He'll see you and come towards you.
BEN   He won't see you.
GUS   [*Absently.*] Eh?
BEN   He won't see you.
GUS   He won't see me.
BEN   But he'll see me.
GUS   He'll see you.
BEN   He won't know you're there.
GUS   He won't know you're there.
BEN   He won't know *you're* there.
GUS   He won't know I'm there.
BEN   I take out my gun.
GUS   You take out your gun.
BEN   He stops in his tracks.
GUS   He stops in his tracks.
BEN   If he turns round—
GUS   If he turns round—
BEN   You're there.
GUS   I'm here.
        [BEN *frowns and presses his forehead.*]
    You've missed something out.
BEN   I know. What?
GUS   I haven't taken my gun out, according to you.
BEN   You take your gun out—
GUS   After I've closed the door.
BEN   After you've closed the door.
GUS   You've never missed that out before, you know that?
BEN   When he sees you behind him—
GUS   Me behind him—
BEN   And me in front of him—
GUS   And you in front of him—
BEN   He'll feel uncertain—
GUS   Uneasy.
BEN   He won't know what to do.
GUS   So what will he do?
BEN   He'll look at me and he'll look at you.
GUS   We won't say a word.
BEN   We'll look at him.
GUS   He won't say a word.
BEN   He'll look at us.
GUS   And we'll look at him.
BEN   Exactly.
        [*Pause.*]
GUS   What do we do if it's a girl?
BEN   We do the same.
GUS   Exactly the same?
BEN   Exactly.
        [*Pause.*]
GUS   We don't do anything different?
BEN   We do exactly the same.

GUS Oh.
> [GUS *rises, and shivers.*]

Excuse me.
> [*He exits through the door on the left.* BEN *remains sitting on the bed, still.*
> *The lavatory chain is pulled once off left, but the lavatory does not flush.*
> *Silence.*
> GUS *re-enters and stops inside the door, deep in thought. He looks at* BEN, *then walks slowly across to his own bed. He is troubled. He stands, thinking. He turns and looks at* BEN. *He moves a few paces towards him.*]

[*Slowly in a low, tense voice.*] Why did he send us matches if he knew there was no gas?
> [*Silence.*
> BEN *stares in front of him.* GUS *crosses to the left side of* BEN, *to the foot of his bed, to get to his other ear.*]

Ben. Why did he send us matches if he knew there was no gas?
> [BEN *looks up.*]

Why did he do that?
BEN Who?
GUS Who sent us those matches?
BEN What are you talking about?
> [GUS *stares down at him.*]
GUS [*Thickly.*] Who is it upstairs?
BEN [*Nervously.*] What's one thing to do with another?
GUS Who is it, though?
BEN What's one thing to do with another?
> [BEN *fumbles for his paper on the bed.*]
GUS I asked you a question.
BEN Enough!
GUS [*With growing agitation.*] I asked you before. Who moved in? I asked you. You said the people who had it before moved out. Well, who moved in?
BEN [*Hunched.*] Shut up.
GUS I told you, didn't I?
BEN [*Standing.*] Shut up!
GUS [*Feverishly.*] I told you before who owned this place, didn't I? I told you.
> [BEN *hits him viciously on the shoulder.*]
I told you who ran this place, didn't I?
> [BEN *hits him viciously on the shoulder.*]
[*Violently.*] Well, what's he playing all these games for? That's what I want to know. What's he doing it for?
BEN What games?
GUS [*Passionately, advancing.*] What's he doing it for? We've been through our tests, haven't we? We got right through our tests, years ago, didn't we? We took them together, don't you remember, didn't we? We've proved ourselves before now, haven't we? We've always done our job. What's he doing all this for? What's the idea? What's he playing these games for?
> [*The box in the shaft comes down behind them. The noise is this time accompanied by a shrill whistle, as it falls.* GUS *rushes to the hatch and seizes the note.*]

[*Reading.*] Scampi!

    [*He crumples the note, picks up the tube, takes out the whistle, blows and speaks.*]

WE'VE GOT NOTHING LEFT! NOTHING! DO YOU UNDERSTAND?

    [BEN *seizes the tube and flings* GUS *away. He follows* GUS *and slaps him hard, back-handed, across the chest.*]

BEN   Stop it! You maniac!

GUS   But you heard!

BEN   [*Savagely.*] That's enough! I'm warning you!

    [*Silence.*

        BEN *hangs the tube. He goes to his bed and lies down. He picks up his paper and reads.*

        Silence.

        The box goes up.

        They turn quickly, their eyes meet. BEN *turns to his paper.*

        Slowly GUS *goes back to his bed, and sits.*

        Silence.

        The hatch falls back into place.

        They turn quickly, their eyes meet. BEN *turns back to his paper.*

        Silence.

        BEN *throws his paper down.*]

BEN   Kaw!

    [*He picks up the paper and looks at it.*]

Listen to this!

    [*Pause.*]

What about that, eh?

    [*Pause.*]

Kaw!

    [*Pause.*]

Have you ever heard such a thing?

GUS   [*Dully.*] Go on!

BEN   It's true.

GUS   Get away.

BEN   It's down here in black and white.

GUS   [*Very low.*] Is that a fact?

BEN   Can you imagine it.

GUS   It's unbelievable.

BEN   It's enough to make you want to puke, isn't it?

GUS   [*Almost inaudible.*] Incredible.

    [BEN *shakes his head. He puts the paper down and rises. He fixes the revolver in his holster.*

        GUS *stands up. He goes towards the door on the left.*]

BEN   Where are you going?

GUS   I'm going to have a glass of water.

    [*He exits.* BEN *brushes dust off his clothes and shoes. The whistle in the speaking tube blows. He goes to it, takes the whistle out and puts the tube to his ear. He listens. He puts it to his mouth.*]

BEN   Yes.

    [*To ear. He listens. To mouth.*]

Straight away. Right.

    [*To ear. He listens. To mouth.*]

Sure we're ready.

[*To ear. He listens. To mouth.*]
Understood. Repeat. He has arrived and will be coming in straight away.
The normal method to be employed. Understood.
[*To ear. He listens. To mouth.*]
Sure we're ready.
[*To ear. He listens. To mouth.*]
Right.
[*He hangs the tube up.*]
Gus!
[*He takes out a comb and combs his hair, adjusts his jacket to diminish
the bulge of the revolver. The lavatory flushes off left.* BEN *goes quickly
to the door, left.*]
Gus!
[*The door right opens sharply.* BEN *turns, his revolver leveled at the door.*
GUS *stumbles in.*
He is stripped of his jacket, waistcoat, tie, holster, and revolver.
He stops, body stooping, his arms at his sides.
He raises his head and looks at BEN.
A long silence.
They stare at each other.]

CURTAIN

1960

CHINUA ACHEBE
b. 1930

The most celebrated African novelist is Chinua Achebe, whose *Things Fall Apart*
(1958) permanently transformed the landscape of African fiction, both in his own
continent and in the Western imagination. His novels, while steadfastly refusing to
sentimentalize their Nigerian subjects, effectively challenged many of the West's
entrenched impressions of African life and culture, replacing simplistic stereotypes
with portrayals of a complex society still suffering from a legacy of Western colonial
oppression.

Achebe was born in Ogidi, an Igbo-speaking town in eastern Nigeria, and educated—in English—at church schools and University College, Ibadan, where he subsequently taught (briefly) before joining the Nigerian Broadcasting Corporation in
Lagos. He was director of external broadcasting from 1961 to 1966, and then
launched a publishing company with Christopher Okigbo, a poet soon to die in the
Nigerian civil war (1967–70). After the war Achebe taught in the United States,
before returning for a time to the University of Nigeria at Nsukka. Since 1990 Achebe
has been Charles P. Stevenson Jr. Professor of Languages and Literature at Bard
College.

A volume of Achebe's poems was joint winner of the Commonwealth Poetry Prize
in 1972. He also has written short stories and essays, including an attack on corruption in Nigerian politics, *The Trouble with Nigeria* (1983). A more famous attack of
another kind, his essay "An Image of Africa: Racism in Conrad's *Heart of Darkness*,"
is a vigorous polemic that accuses Conrad of racism, while perhaps deflecting attention from Achebe's debt to his Polish-born precursor. Achebe is best-known for his

novels, however: *Things Fall Apart* (1958), *No Longer at Ease* (1960), *Arrow of God* (1964), *A Man of the People* (1966), and *Anthills of the Savannah* (1987). The first of these is a response to Joyce Cary's *Mr. Johnson* (1939), a novel famous in its day for its depiction of Nigerian tribal society. Cary had been a British district officer in Nigeria, and his account of the life and tragic death of a young African clerk, although well meaning, was written from an outsider's patronizing perspective. By contrast, Achebe's *Things Fall Apart*, written with an insider's understanding of the African world and its history, depicts the destruction of an individual, a family, and a culture at the moment of colonial incursion. This novel's hero, Okonkwo, is dignified and courageous, a noble figure, whereas Cary's Mr. Johnson is charming but undignified. Like other tragic heroes, however, Okonkwo is flawed and falls through lack of the balance everywhere celebrated in Achebe's writings.

Taking his title from W. B. Yeats's poem "The Second Coming," Achebe shows how "the blood-dimmed tide is loosed" in a Nigerian village by European colonizers, drowning the ceremonies of the indigenous society. The novel is set in the fictional village of Umuofia during the late nineteenth century, before the arrival of Europeans, and in the ensuing period of British imperial "pacification" of southeast Nigeria from 1900 to 1920, including the Ahiara massacre of 1905 (fictionalized in chapter 15 as the Abame incident) and the destruction of Igbo opposition groups by the Bende-Onitsha Hinterland Expedition. The British asserted colonial authority over the Igbo through a combination of economic trade, missionary religion, and political control, and Achebe represents this process of colonization from the vantage point of villagers who are puzzled, intrigued, co-opted, enraged, divided against themselves, or killed. The imperial incursion seems all the more bewildering and violent because the novel has immersed the reader in this village society's finely calibrated cultural practices in religion and government, athletics and storytelling, agriculture and the family. Helping to rebut Western preconceptions about African primitivism, this rich portrait of a culture also advances Achebe's ambition to help his "society regain belief in itself and put away the complexes of the years of denigration and self-abasement" produced by the distortions of colonialism. He has said he wants his novels to teach his African "readers that their past—with all its imperfections—was not one long night of savagery from which the first Europeans acting on God's behalf delivered them." But while *Things Fall Apart* lays considerable blame for the destruction of Igbo village society at the door of the whites, Achebe carefully avoids rosily idealizing the precolonial Igbo world, and he has frankly acknowledged that "internal problems" also made this African society vulnerable. *Things Fall Apart* is at once Okonkwo's tragedy and that of a complex tribal society, whose members speak a resonantly proverbial language that operates in the book as an image of all the beautiful and traditional structures transformed irrevocably by colonialism.

PRONOUNCING GLOSSARY

The following list uses common English syllables and stress accents to provide rough equivalents of selected words. Most of the names in *Things Fall Apart* are pronounced basically as they would be in English (for example, Okonkwo as *oh-kon'-kwo*), except that Igbo (like other African languages and Chinese) is a tonal language and therefore uses high or low tones for individual syllables.

Chielo: *chee'-ay-loh*

egwugwu: *eg-woog'-woo*

Erulu: *air-oo'-loo*

Ezeani: *ez-ah'-nee*

Ezeugo: *e'-zoo-goh*

Idemili: *ee-day-mee'-lee*

Igbo: *ee'-boh*

Ikemefuna: *ee-kay-may'-foo-na*

mbari: *mbah'-ree*

Ndulue: *in'-doo-loo'-eh*

Nwakibie: *nwa'-kee-ee'-bee-yay*

Nwayieke: *nwah'-ee-eh'-kay*

Umuofia: *oo'-moo-off'-yah*

Things Fall Apart

Turning and turning in the widening gyre
The falcon cannot hear the falconer;
Things fall apart; the centre cannot hold;
Mere anarchy is loosed upon the world.
W. B. Yeats: 'The Second Coming'

Part One

CHAPTER ONE

Okonkwo[1] was well known throughout the nine villages and even beyond. His fame rested on solid personal achievements. As a young man of eighteen he had brought honour to his village by throwing Amalinze the Cat. Amalinze was the great wrestler who for seven years was unbeaten, from Umuofia to Mbaino.[2] He was called the Cat because his back would never touch the earth. It was this man that Okonkwo threw in a fight which the old men agreed was one of the fiercest since the founder of their town engaged a spirit of the wild for seven days and seven nights.

The drums beat and the flutes sang and the spectators held their breath. Amalinze was a wily craftsman, but Okonkwo was as slippery as a fish in water. Every nerve and every muscle stood out on their arms, on their backs and their thighs, and one almost heard them stretching to breaking point. In the end Okonkwo threw the Cat.

That was many years ago, twenty years or more, and during this time Okonkwo's fame had grown like a bush-fire in the harmattan.[3] He was tall and huge, and his bushy eyebrows and wide nose gave him a very severe look. He breathed heavily, and it was said that, when he slept, his wives and children in their out-houses could hear him breathe. When he walked, his heels hardly touched the ground and he seemed to walk on springs, as if he was going to pounce on somebody. And he did pounce on people quite often. He had a slight stammer and whenever he was angry and could not get his words out quickly enough, he would use his fists. He had no patience with unsuccessful men. He had had no patience with his father.

Unoka,[4] for that was his father's name, had died ten years ago. In his day he was lazy and improvident and was quite incapable of thinking about tomorrow. If any money came his way, and it seldom did, he immediately bought gourds of palm-wine, called round his neighbours and made merry. He always said that whenever he saw a dead man's mouth he saw the folly of not eating what one had in one's lifetime. Unoka was, of course, a debtor, and he owed every neighbour some money, from a few cowries[5] to quite substantial amounts.

He was tall but very thin and had a slight stoop. He wore a haggard and mournful look except when he was drinking or playing on his flute. He was

---

1. Man [oko] born on Nkwo Day; the name also suggests stubborn male pride.
2. Four settlements. Umuofia means "children of the forest" (literal trans.); but ofia ("forest") also means "bush," or land untouched by European influence.
3. A dusty wind from the Sahara.

4. Home is supreme.
5. Glossy half-inch-long tan-and-white shells, collected in strings and used as money. A bag of twenty-four thousand cowries weighed about sixty pounds and, at the time of the story, was worth approximately £1 British.

very good on his flute, and his happiest moments were the two or three moons after the harvest when the village musicians brought down their instruments, hung above the fireplace. Unoka would play with them, his face beaming with blessedness and peace. Sometimes another village would ask Unoka's band and their dancing *egwugwu*[6] to come and stay with them and teach them their tunes. They would go to such hosts for as long as three or four markets,[7] making music and feasting. Unoka loved the good fare and the good fellowship, and he loved this season of the year, when the rains had stopped and the sun rose every morning with dazzling beauty. And it was not too hot either, because the cold and dry harmattan wind was blowing down from the north. Some years the harmattan was very severe and a dense haze hung on the atmosphere. Old men and children would then sit round log fires, warming their bodies. Unoka loved it all, and he loved the first kites[8] that returned with the dry season, and the children who sang songs of welcome to them. He would remember his own childhood, how he had often wandered around looking for a kite sailing leisurely against the blue sky. As soon as he found one he would sing with his whole being, welcoming it back from its long, long journey, and asking it if it had brought home any lengths of cloth.

That was years ago, when he was young. Unoka, the grown-up, was a failure. He was poor and his wife and children had barely enough to eat. People laughed at him because he was a loafer, and they swore never to lend him any more money because he never paid back. But Unoka was such a man that he always succeeded in borrowing more, and piling up his debts.

One day a neighbour called Okoye[9] came in to see him. He was reclining on a mud bed in his hut playing on the flute. He immediately rose and shook hands with Okoye, who then unrolled the goatskin which he carried under his arm, and sat down. Unoka went into an inner room and soon returned with a small wooden disc containing a kola nut, some alligator pepper and a lump of white chalk.[1]

"I have kola," he announced when he sat down, and passed the disc over to his guest.

"Thank you. He who brings kola brings life. But I think you ought to break it," replied Okoye passing back the disc.

"No, it is for you, I think," and they argued like this for a few moments before Unoka accepted the honour of breaking the kola. Okoye, meanwhile, took the lump of chalk, drew some lines on the floor, and then painted his big toe.[2]

As he broke the kola, Unoka prayed to their ancestors for life and health, and for protection against their enemies. When they had eaten they talked about many things: about the heavy rains which were drowning the yams, about the next ancestral feast and about the impending war with the village of Mbaino. Unoka was never happy when it came to wars. He was in fact a coward and could not bear the sight of blood. And so he changed the subject

---

6. Here masked performers as part of musical entertainment.
7. Counting one important market day a week, roughly two English weeks. The Igbo week has four days: Eke, Oye, Afo, and Nkwo. Eke is a rest day and the main market day; Afo, a half day on the farm; Oye and Nkwo, full workdays.
8. A kind of hawk.
9. Man born on Oye Day; a generic "Everyman" name.

1. Signifies coolness and peace and is offered in rituals of hospitality so that the guest may draw his personal emblem on the floor. "Kola nut": a bitter, caffeine-rich nut that is broken and eaten ceremonially; it indicates life or vitality. "Alligator pepper": black pepper, known as the "pepper for kola" to distinguish it from cooking pepper, or chilies.
2. If the guest has taken the first title, he marks his big toe. Higher titles require different facial markings.

2626 / CHINUA ACHEBE

and talked about music, and his face beamed. He could hear in his mind's ear the blood-stirring and intricate rhythms of the *ekwe* and the *udu* and the *ogene*,[3] and he could hear his own flute weaving in and out of them, decorating them with a colourful and plaintive tune. The total effect was gay and brisk, but if one picked out the flute as it went up and down and then broke up into short snatches, one saw that there was sorrow and grief there.

Okoye was also a musician. He played on the *ogene*. But he was not a failure like Unoka. He had a large barn full of yams and he had three wives. And now he was going to take the Idemili title,[4] the third highest in the land. It was a very expensive ceremony and he was gathering all his resources together. That was in fact the reason why he had come to see Unoka. He cleared his throat and began:

"Thank you for the kola. You may have heard of the title I intend to take shortly."

Having spoken plainly so far, Okoye said the next half a dozen sentences in proverbs. Among the Ibo the art of conversation is regarded very highly, and proverbs are the palm-oil with which words are eaten. Okoye was a great talker and he spoke for a long time, skirting round the subject and then hitting it finally. In short, he was asking Unoka to return the two hundred cowries he had borrowed from him more than two years before. As soon as Unoka understood what his friend was driving at, he burst out laughing. He laughed loud and long and his voice rang out clear as the *ogene*, and tears stood in his eyes. His visitor was amazed, and sat speechless. At the end, Unoka was able to give an answer between fresh outbursts of mirth.

"Look at that wall," he said, pointing at the far wall of his hut, which was rubbed with red earth so that it shone. "Look at those lines of chalk;" and Okoye saw groups of short perpendicular lines drawn in chalk. There were five groups, and the smallest group had ten lines. Unoka had a sense of the dramatic and so he allowed a pause, in which he took a pinch of snuff and sneezed noisily, and then he continued: "Each group there represents a debt to someone, and each stroke is one hundred cowries. You see, I owe that man a thousand cowries. But he has not come to wake me up in the morning for it. I shall pay you, but not today. Our elders say that the sun will shine on those who stand before it shines on those who kneel under them. I shall pay my big debts first." And he took another pinch of snuff, as if that was paying the big debts first. Okoye rolled his goatskin and departed.

When Unoka died he had taken no title at all and he was heavily in debt. Any wonder then that his son Okonkwo was ashamed of him? Fortunately, among these people a man was judged according to his worth and not according to the worth of his father. Okonkwo was clearly cut out for great things. He was still young but he had won fame as the greatest wrestler in the nine villages. He was a wealthy farmer and had two barns full of yams, and had just married his third wife. To crown it all he had taken two titles and had shown incredible prowess in two inter-tribal wars. And so although Okonkwo was still young, he was already one of the greatest men of his time. Age was respected

---

3. A bell-shaped gong made from two pieces of sheet iron. "Ekwe": a wooden drum, about three feet long, that produces high and low tones (as does the Igbo language). "Udu": a clay pot with a hole to one side of the neck opening; various resonant tones are produced when the hole is struck with one hand while the other hand covers or uncovers the top.

4. A title of honor named after the river god Idemili, to whom the python is sacred. "Barn": not a building but a walled enclosure for the yam stacks (frames on which individual yams are tied, shaded with palm leaves, and exposed to circulating air).

among his people, but achievement was revered. As the elders said, if a child washed his hands he could eat with kings. Okonkwo had clearly washed his hands and so he ate with kings and elders. And that was how he came to look after the doomed lad who was sacrificed to the village of Umuofia by their neighbours to avoid war and bloodshed. The ill-fated lad was called Ikemefuna.[5]

CHAPTER TWO

Okonkwo had just blown out the palm-oil lamp and stretched himself on his bamboo bed when he heard the *ogene* of the town-crier piercing the still night air. *Gome, gome, gome, gome,* boomed the hollow metal. Then the crier gave his message, and at the end of it beat his instrument again. And this was the message. Every man of Umuofia was asked to gather at the market-place tomorrow morning. Okonkwo wondered what was amiss, for he knew certainly that something was amiss. He had discerned a clear overtone of tragedy in the crier's voice, and even now he could still hear it as it grew dimmer and dimmer in the distance.

The night was very quiet. It was always quiet except on moonlight nights. Darkness held a vague terror for these people, even the bravest among them. Children were warned not to whistle at night for fear of evil spirits. Dangerous animals became even more sinister and uncanny in the dark. A snake was never called by its name at night, because it would hear. It was called a string. And so on this particular night as the crier's voice was gradually swallowed up in the distance, silence returned to the world, a vibrant silence made more intense by the universal trill of a million million forest insects.

On a moonlight night it would be different. The happy voices of children playing in open fields would then be heard. And perhaps those not so young would be playing in pairs in less open places, and old men and women would remember their youth. As the Ibo say: "When the moon is shining the cripple becomes hungry for a walk."

But this particular night was dark and silent. And in all the nine villages of Umuofia a town-crier with his *ogene* asked every man to be present tomorrow morning. Okonkwo on his bamboo bed tried to figure out the nature of the emergency—war with a neighbouring clan? That seemed the most likely reason, and he was not afraid of war. He was a man of action, a man of war. Unlike his father he could stand the look of blood. In Umuofia's latest war he was the first to bring home a human head. That was his fifth head; and he was not an old man yet. On great occasions such as the funeral of a village celebrity he drank his palm-wine from his first human head.

In the morning the market-place was full. There must have been about ten thousand men there, all talking in low voices. At last Ogbuefi Ezeugo stood up in the midst of them and bellowed four times, "*Umuofia kwenu,*"[6] and on each occasion he faced a different direction and seemed to push the air with a clenched fist. And ten thousand men answered "*Yaa!*" each time. Then there was perfect silence. Ogbuefi Ezeugo was a powerful orator and was always chosen to speak on such occasions. He moved his hand over his white head

---

5. My strength should not be dissipated.
6. United Umuofia! An orator's call on the audience to respond as a group. "Ogbuefi": cow killer (literal trans.); indicates someone who has taken a

high title (e.g., the Idemili title) for which the celebration ceremony requires the slaughter of a cow. "Ezeugo": a name denoting a priest or high initiate, someone who wears the eagle feather.

and stroked his white beard. He then adjusted his cloth, which was passed under his right arm-pit and tied above his left shoulder.

"*Umuofia kwenu,*" he bellowed a fifth time, and the crowd yelled in answer. And then suddenly like one possessed he shot out his left hand and pointed in the direction of Mbaino, and said through gleaming white teeth firmly clenched: "Those sons of wild animals have dared to murder a daughter of Umuofia." He threw his head down and gnashed his teeth, and allowed a murmur of suppressed anger to sweep the crowd. When he began again, the anger on his face was gone and in its place a sort of smile hovered, more terrible and more sinister than the anger. And in a clear unemotional voice he told Umuofia how their daughter had gone to market at Mbaino and had been killed. That woman, said Ezeugo, was the wife of Ogbuefi Udo,[7] and he pointed to a man who sat near him with a bowed head. The crowd then shouted with anger and thirst for blood.

Many others spoke, and at the end it was decided to follow the normal course of action. An ultimatum was immediately dispatched to Mbaino asking them to choose between war on the one hand, and on the other the offer of a young man and a virgin as compensation.

Umuofia was feared by all its neighbours. It was powerful in war and in magic, and its priests and medicine-men were feared in all the surrounding country. Its most potent war-medicine was as old as the clan itself. Nobody knew how old. But on one point there was general agreement—the active principle in that medicine had been an old woman with one leg. In fact, the medicine itself was called *agadi-nwayi,* or old woman. It had its shrine in the centre of Umuofia, in a cleared spot. And if anybody was so foolhardy as to pass by the shrine after dusk he was sure to see the old woman hopping about.

And so the neighbouring clans who naturally knew of these things feared Umuofia, and would not go to war against it without first trying a peaceful settlement. And in fairness to Umuofia it should be recorded that it never went to war unless its case was clear and just and was accepted as such by its Oracle—the Oracle of the Hills and the Caves. And there were indeed occasions when the Oracle had forbidden Umuofia to wage a war. If the clan had disobeyed the Oracle they would surely have been beaten, because their dreaded *agadi-nwayi* would never fight what the Ibo call *a fight of blame.*

But the war that now threatened was a just war. Even the enemy clan knew that. And so when Okonkwo of Umuofia arrived at Mbaino as the proud and imperious emissary of war, he was treated with great honour and respect, and two days later he returned home with a lad of fifteen and a young virgin. The lad's name was Ikemefuna, whose sad story is still told in Umuofia unto this day.

The elders, or *ndichie,* met to hear a report of Okonkwo's mission. At the end they decided, as everybody knew they would, that the girl should go to Ogbuefi Udo to replace his murdered wife. As for the boy, he belonged to the clan as a whole, and there was no hurry to decide his fate. Okonkwo was, therefore, asked on behalf of the clan to look after him in the interim. And so for three years Ikemefuna lived in Okonkwo's household.

Okonkwo ruled his household with a heavy hand. His wives, especially the youngest, lived in perpetual fear of his fiery temper, and so did his little chil-

7. Peace.

dren. Perhaps down in his heart Okonkwo was not a cruel man. But his whole life was dominated by fear, the fear of failure and of weakness. It was deeper and more intimate than the fear of evil and capricious gods and of magic, the fear of the forest, and of the forces of nature, malevolent, red in tooth and claw. Okonkwo's fear was greater than these. It was not external but lay deep within himself. It was the fear of himself, lest he should be found to resemble his father. Even as a little boy he had resented his father's failure and weakness, and even now he still remembered how he had suffered when a playmate had told him that his father was *agbala*. That was how Okonkwo first came to know that *agbala* was not only another name for a woman, it could also mean a man who had taken no title. And so Okonkwo was ruled by one passion— to hate everything that his father Unoka had loved. One of those things was gentleness and another was idleness.

During the planting season Okonkwo worked daily on his farms from cockcrow until the chickens went to roost. He was a very strong man and rarely felt fatigue. But his wives and young children were not as strong, and so they suffered. But they dared not complain openly. Okonkwo's first son, Nwoye,[8] was then twelve years old but was already causing his father great anxiety for his incipient laziness. At any rate, that was how it looked to his father, and he sought to correct him by constant nagging and beating. And so Nwoye was developing into a sad-faced youth.

Okonkwo's prosperity was visible in his household. He had a large compound enclosed by a thick wall of red earth. His own hut, or *obi*, stood immediately behind the only gate in the red walls. Each of his three wives had her own hut, which together formed a half moon behind the *obi*. The barn was built against one end of the red walls, and long stacks of yam stood out prosperously in it. At the opposite end of the compound was a shed for the goats, and each wife built a small attachment to her hut for the hens. Near the barn was a small house, the 'medicine house' or shrine where Okonkwo kept the wooden symbols of his personal god and of his ancestral spirits. He worshipped them with sacrifices of kola nut, food and palm-wine, and offered prayers to them on behalf of himself, his three wives and eight children.

So when the daughter of Umuofia was killed in Mbaino, Ikemefuna came into Okonkwo's household. When Okonkwo brought him home that day he called his most senior wife and handed him over to her.

"He belongs to the clan," he told her. "So look after him."

"Is he staying long with us?" she asked.

"Do what you are told, woman," Okonkwo thundered, and stammered. "When did you become one of the *ndichie* of Umuofia?"

And so Nwoye's mother took Ikemefuna to her hut and asked no more questions.

As for the boy himself, he was terribly afraid. He could not understand what was happening to him or what he had done. How could he know that his father had taken a hand in killing a daughter of Umuofia? All he knew was that a few men had arrived at their house, conversing with his father in low tones, and at the end he had been taken out and handed over to a stranger. His mother had wept bitterly, but he had been too surprised to weep. And so the stranger had brought him, and a girl, a long, long way from home, through

8. Child born on Oye Day.

lonely forest paths. He did not know who the girl was, and he never saw her again.

CHAPTER THREE

Okonkwo did not have the start in life which many young men usually had. He did not inherit a barn from his father. There was no barn to inherit. The story was told in Umuofia of how his father, Unoka, had gone to consult the Oracle of the Hills and the Caves to find out why he always had a miserable harvest.

The Oracle was called Agbala,[9] and people came from far and near to consult it. They came when misfortune dogged their steps or when they had a dispute with their neighbours. They came to discover what the future held for them or to consult the spirits of their departed fathers.

The way into the shrine was a round hole at the side of a hill, just a little bigger than the round opening into a hen-house. Worshippers and those who came to seek knowledge from the god crawled on their belly through the hole and found themselves in a dark, endless space in the presence of Agbala. No one had ever beheld Agbala, except his priestess. But no one who had ever crawled into his awful shrine had come out without the fear of his power. His priestess stood by the sacred fire which she built in the heart of the cave and proclaimed the will of the god. The fire did not burn with a flame. The glowing logs only served to light up vaguely the dark figure of the priestess.

Sometimes a man came to consult the spirit of his dead father or relative. It was said that when such a spirit appeared, the man saw it vaguely in the darkness, but never heard its voice. Some people even said that they had heard the spirits flying and flapping their wings against the roof of the cave.

Many years ago when Okonkwo was still a boy his father, Unoka, had gone to consult Agbala. The priestess in those days was a woman called Chika.[1] She was full of the power of her god, and she was greatly feared. Unoka stood before her and began his story.

"Every year," he said sadly, "before I put any crop in the earth, I sacrifice a cock to Ani, the owner of all land. It is the law of our fathers. I also kill a cock at the shrine of Ifejioku, the god of yams. I clear the bush and set fire to it when it is dry. I sow the yams when the first rain has fallen, and stake them when the young tendrils appear. I weed——"

"Hold your peace!" screamed the priestess, her voice terrible as it echoed through the dark void. "You have offended neither the gods nor your fathers. And when a man is at peace with his gods and his ancestors, his harvest will be good or bad according to the strength of his arm. You, Unoka, are known in all the clan for the weakness of your matchet[2] and your hoe. When your neighbours go out with their axe to cut down virgin forests, you sow your yams on exhausted farms that take no labour to clear. They cross seven rivers to make their farms; you stay at home and offer sacrifices to a reluctant soil. Go home and work like a man."

Unoka was an ill-fated man. He had a bad *chi* or personal god, and evil fortune followed him to the grave, or rather to his death, for he had no grave. He died of the swelling which was an abomination to the earth goddess. When a man was afflicted with swelling in the stomach and the limbs he was not

---

9. The Oracle is masculine, but his priestess, or Voice, is feminine.
1. Sky is supreme.
2. Machete.

allowed to die in the house. He was carried to the Evil Forest and left there to die. There was the story of a very stubborn man who staggered back to his house and had to be carried again to the forest and tied to a tree. The sickness was an abomination to the earth, and so the victim could not be buried in her bowels. He died and rotted away above the earth, and was not given the first or the second burial. Such was Unoka's fate. When they carried him away, he took with him his flute.

With a father like Unoka, Okonkwo did not have the start in life which many young men had. He neither inherited a barn nor a title, nor even a young wife. But in spite of these disadvantages, he had begun even in his father's lifetime to lay the foundations of a prosperous future. It was slow and painful. But he threw himself into it like one possessed. And indeed he was possessed by the fear of his father's contemptible life and shameful death.

There was a wealthy man in Okonkwo's village who had three huge barns, nine wives and thirty children. His name was Nwakibie[3] and he had taken the highest but one title which a man could take in the clan. It was for this man that Okonkwo worked to earn his first seed yams.

He took a pot of palm-wine and a cock to Nwakibie. Two elderly neighbours were sent for, and Nwakibie's two grown-up sons were also present in his *obi*. He presented a kola nut and an alligator pepper, which was passed round for all to see and then returned to him. He broke it, saying: "We shall all live. We pray for life, children, a good harvest and happiness. You will have what is good for you and I will have what is good for me. Let the kite perch and let the egret perch too. If one says no to the other, let his wing break."

After the kola nut had been eaten Okonkwo brought his palm-wine from the corner of the hut where it had been placed and stood it in the centre of the group. He addressed Nwakibie, calling him 'Our father'.

"*Nna ayi*," he said. "I have brought you this little kola. As our people say, a man who pays respect to the great paves the way for his own greatness. I have come to pay you my respects and also to ask a favour. But let us drink the wine first."

Everybody thanked Okonkwo and the neighbours brought out their drinking horns from the goatskin bags they carried. Nwakibie brought down his own horn, which was fastened to the rafters. The younger of his sons, who was also the youngest man in the group, moved to the centre, raised the pot on his left knee and began to pour out the wine. The first cup went to Okonkwo, who must taste his wine before anyone else.[4] Then the group drank, beginning with the eldest man. When everyone had drunk two or three horns, Nwakibie sent for his wives. Some of them were not at home and only four came in.

"Is Anasi not in?" he asked them. They said she was coming. Anasi was the first[5] wife and the others could not drink before her, and so they stood waiting.

Anasi was a middle-aged woman, tall and strongly built. There was authority in her bearing and she looked every inch the ruler of the womenfolk in a large and prosperous family. She wore the anklet of her husband's titles, which the first wife alone could wear.

She walked up to her husband and accepted the horn from him. She then went down on one knee, drank a little and handed back the horn. She rose,

<hr />

3. The child surpasses his neighbors.
4. A ceremonial gesture; one who gives wine tastes

it first to show that it is not poisoned.
5. First or favorite wife—not always the same.

called him by his name and went back to her hut. The other wives drank in the same way, in their proper order, and went away.

The men then continued their drinking and talking. Ogbuefi Idigo was talking about the palm-wine tapper, Obiako, who suddenly gave up his trade.

"There must be something behind it," he said, wiping the foam of wine from his moustache with the back of his left hand. "There must be a reason for it. A toad does not run in the daytime for nothing."

"Some people say the Oracle warned him that he would fall off a palm tree and kill himself," said Akukalia.

"Obiako has always been a strange one," said Nwakibie. "I have heard that many years ago, when his father had not been dead very long, he had gone to consult the Oracle. The Oracle said to him, 'Your dead father wants you to sacrifice a goat to him.' Do you know what he told the Oracle? He said, 'Ask my dead father if he ever had a fowl when he was alive.'" Everybody laughed heartily except Okonkwo, who laughed uneasily because, as the saying goes, an old woman is always uneasy when dry bones are mentioned in a proverb. Okonkwo remembered his own father.

At last the young man who was pouring out the wine held up half a horn of the thick, white dregs and said, "What we are eating is finished." "We have seen it," the others replied. "Who will drink the dregs?" he asked. "Whoever has a job in hand," said Idigo, looking at Nwakibie's elder son Igwelo with a malicious twinkle in his eye.

Everybody agreed that Igwelo should drink the dregs. He accepted the half-full horn from his brother and drank it. As Idigo had said, Igwelo had a job in hand because he had married his first wife a month or two before. The thick dregs of palm-wine were supposed to be good for men who were going in to their wives.

After the wine had been drunk Okonkwo laid his difficulties before Nwakibie.

"I have come to you for help," he said. "Perhaps you can already guess what it is. I have cleared a farm but have no yams to sow. I know what it is to ask a man to trust another with his yams, especially these days when young men are afraid of hard work. I am not afraid of work. The lizard that jumped from the high iroko tree to the ground said he would praise himself if no one else did. I began to fend for myself at an age when most people still suck at their mothers' breasts. If you give me some yam seeds I shall not fail you."

Nwakibie cleared his throat. "It pleases me to see a young man like you these days when our youth have gone so soft. Many young men have come to me to ask for yams but I have refused because I knew they would just dump them in the earth and leave them to be choked by weeds. When I say no to them they think I am hard-hearted. But it is not so. Eneke the bird[6] says that since men have learnt to shoot without missing, he has learnt to fly without perching. I have learnt to be stingy with my yams. But I can trust you. I know it as I look at you. As our fathers said, you can tell a ripe corn by its look. I shall give you twice four hundred yams. Go ahead and prepare your farm."

Okonkwo thanked him again and again and went home feeling happy. He knew that Nwakibie would not refuse him, but he had not expected he would be so generous. He had not hoped to get more than four hundred seeds. He would now have to make a bigger farm. He hoped to get another four hundred yams from one of his father's friends at Isiuzo.[7]

---

6. Proverbial.

7. Head of the road; a small town.

Share-cropping was a very slow way of building up a barn of one's own. After all the toil one only got a third of the harvest. But for a young man whose father had no yams, there was no other way. And what made it worse in Okonkwo's case was that he had to support his mother and two sisters from his meagre harvest. And supporting his mother also meant supporting his father. She could not be expected to cook and eat while her husband starved. And so at a very early age when he was striving desperately to build a barn through share-cropping Okonkwo was also fending for his father's house. It was like pouring grains of corn into a bag full of holes. His mother and sisters worked hard enough, but they grew women's crops, like coco-yams, beans and cassava. Yam, the king of crops, was a man's crop.[8]

The year that Okonkwo took eight hundred seed-yams from Nwakibie was the worst year in living memory. Nothing happened at its proper time; it was either too early or too late. It seemed as if the world had gone mad. The first rains were late, and, when they came, lasted only a brief moment. The blazing sun returned, more fierce than it had ever been known, and scorched all the green that had appeared with the rains. The earth burned like hot coals and roasted all the yams that had been sown. Like all good farmers, Okonkwo had begun to sow with the first rains. He had sown four hundred seeds when the rains dried up and the heat returned. He watched the sky all day for signs of rain-clouds and lay awake all night. In the morning he went back to his farm and saw the withering tendrils. He had tried to protect them from the smouldering earth by making rings of thick sisal leaves around them. But by the end of the day the sisal rings were burnt dry and grey. He changed them every day, and prayed that the rain might fall in the night. But the drought continued for eight market weeks and the yams were killed.

Some farmers had not planted their yams yet. They were the lazy easy-going ones who always put off clearing their farms as long as they could. This year they were the wise ones. They sympathised with their neighbours with much shaking of the head, but inwardly they were happy for what they took to be their own foresight.

Okonkwo planted what was left of his seed-yams when the rains finally returned. He had one consolation. The yams he had sown before the drought were his own, the harvest of the previous year. He still had the eight hundred from Nwakibie and the four hundred from his father's friend. So he would make a fresh start.

But the year had gone mad. Rain fell as it had never fallen before. For days and nights together it poured down in violent torrents, and washed away the yam heaps. Trees were uprooted and deep gorges appeared everywhere. Then the rain became less violent. But it went on from day to day without a pause. The spell of sunshine which always came in the middle of the wet season did not appear. The yams put on luxuriant green leaves, but every farmer knew that without sunshine the tubers would not grow.

That year the harvest was sad, like a funeral, and many farmers wept as they dug up the miserable and rotting yams. One man tied his cloth to a tree branch and hanged himself.

Okonkwo remembered that tragic year with a cold shiver throughout the

8. Yams, a staple food in Western Africa, were a sacred crop generally cultivated only by men and eaten either roasted or boiled. "Coco-yams" (a brown root also called taro) and "cassava" (or man- ioc, which is refined in various ways to remove natural cyanide) were low-status root vegetables, prepared for eating by boiling and pounding.

rest of his life. It always surprised him when he thought of it later that he did not sink under the load of despair. He knew he was a fierce fighter, but that year had been enough to break the heart of a lion.

"Since I survived that year," he always said, "I shall survive anything." He put it down to his inflexible will.

His father, Unoka, who was then an ailing man, had said to him during that terrible harvest month: "Do not despair. I know you will not despair. You have a manly and a proud heart. A proud heart can survive a general failure because such a failure does not prick its pride. It is more difficult and more bitter when a man fails *alone*."

Unoka was like that in his last days. His love of talk had grown with age and sickness. It tried Okonkwo's patience beyond words.

CHAPTER FOUR

"Looking at a king's mouth," said an old man, "one would think he never sucked at his mother's breast." He was talking about Okonkwo, who had risen so suddenly from great poverty and misfortune to be one of the lords of the clan. The old man bore no ill-will towards Okonkwo. Indeed he respected him for his industry and success. But he was struck, as most people were, by Okonkwo's brusqueness in dealing with less successful men. Only a week ago a man had contradicted him at a kindred meeting which they held to discuss the next ancestral feast. Without looking at the man Okonkwo had said: "This meeting is for men." The man who had contradicted him had no titles. That was why he had called him a woman. Okonkwo knew how to kill a man's spirit.

Everybody at the kindred meeting took sides with Osugo[9] when Okonkwo called him a woman. The oldest man present said sternly that those whose palm-kernels were cracked for them by a benevolent spirit should not forget to be humble. Okonkwo said he was sorry for what he had said, and the meeting continued.

But it was really not true that Okonkwo's palm-kernels had been cracked for him by a benevolent spirit. He had cracked them himself. Anyone who knew his grim struggle against poverty and misfortune could not say he had been lucky. If ever a man deserved his success, that man was Okonkwo. At an early age he had achieved fame as the greatest wrestler in all the land. That was not luck. At the most one could say that his *chi* or personal god was good. But the Ibo people have a proverb that when a man says yes his *chi* says yes also. Okonkwo said yes very strongly; so his *chi* agreed. And not only his *chi* but his clan too, because it judged a man by the work of his hands. That was why Okonkwo had been chosen by the nine villages to carry a message of war to their enemies unless they agreed to give up a young man and a virgin to atone for the murder of Udo's wife. And such was the deep fear that their enemies had for Umuofia that they treated Okonkwo like a king and brought him a virgin who was given to Udo as wife, and the lad Ikemefuna.

The elders of the clan had decided that Ikemefuna should be in Okonkwo's care for a while. But no one thought it would be as long as three years. They seemed to forget all about him as soon as they had taken the decision.

At first Ikemefuna was very much afraid. Once or twice he tried to run away,

9. Low-status (*osu*) person.

but he did not know where to begin. He thought of his mother and his three-year-old sister and wept bitterly. Nwoye's mother was very kind to him and treated him as one of her own children. But all he said was: "When shall I go home?" When Okonkwo heard that he would not eat any food he came into the hut with a big stick in his hand and stood over him while he swallowed his yams, trembling. A few moments later he went behind the hut and began to vomit painfully. Nwoye's mother went to him and placed her hands on his chest and on his back. He was ill for three market weeks, and when he recovered he seemed to have overcome his great fear and sadness.

He was by nature a very lively boy and he gradually became popular in Okonkwo's household, especially with the children. Okonkwo's son, Nwoye, who was two years younger, became quite inseparable from him because he seemed to know everything. He could fashion out flutes from bamboo stems and even from the elephant grass. He knew the names of all the birds and could set clever traps for the little bush rodents. And he knew which trees made the strongest bows.

Even Okonkwo himself became very fond of the boy—inwardly of course. Okonkwo never showed any emotion openly, unless it be the emotion of anger. To show affection was a sign of weakness; the only thing worth demonstrating was strength. He therefore treated Ikemefuna as he treated everybody else— with a heavy hand. But there was no doubt that he liked the boy. Sometimes when he went to big village meetings or communal ancestral feasts he allowed Ikemefuna to accompany him, like a son, carrying his stool and his goatskin bag. And, indeed, Ikemefuna called him father.

Ikemefuna came to Umuofia at the end of the carefree season between harvest and planting. In fact he recovered from his illness only a few days before the Week of Peace began. And that was also the year Okonkwo broke the peace, and was punished, as was the custom, by Ezeani, the priest of the earth goddess.

Okonkwo was provoked to justifiable anger by his youngest wife, who went to plait her hair at her friend's house and did not return early enough to cook the afternoon meal. Okonkwo did not know at first that she was not at home. After waiting in vain for her dish he went to her hut to see what she was doing. There was nobody in the hut and the fireplace was cold.

"Where is Ojiugo?" he asked his second wife, who came out of her hut to draw water from a gigantic pot in the shade of a small tree in the middle of the compound.

"She has gone to plait her hair."

Okonkwo bit his lips as anger welled up within him.

"Where are her children? Did she take them?" he asked with unusual coolness and restraint.

"They are here," answered his first wife, Nwoye's mother. Okonkwo bent down and looked into her hut. Ojiugo's children were eating with the children of his first wife.

"Did she ask you to feed them before she went?"

"Yes," lied Nwoye's mother, trying to minimise Ojiugo's thoughtlessness.

Okonkwo knew she was not speaking the truth. He walked back to his *obi* to await Ojiugo's return. And when she returned he beat her very heavily. In his anger he had forgotten that it was the Week of Peace. His first two wives ran out in great alarm pleading with him that it was the sacred week. But

2636 / CHINUA ACHEBE

Okonkwo was not the man to stop beating somebody half-way through, not even for fear of a goddess.

Okonkwo's neighbours heard his wife crying and sent their voices over the compound walls to ask what was the matter. Some of them came over to see for themselves. It was unheard-of to beat somebody during the sacred week.

Before it was dusk Ezeani, who was the priest of the earth goddess, Ani, called on Okonkwo in his *obi*. Okonkwo brought out kola nut and placed it before the priest.

"Take away your kola nut. I shall not eat in the house of a man who has no respect for our gods and ancestors."

Okonkwo tried to explain to him what his wife had done, but Ezeani seemed to pay no attention. He held a short staff in his hand which he brought down on the floor to emphasise his points.

"Listen to me," he said when Okonkwo had spoken. "You are not a stranger in Umuofia. You know as well as I do that our forefathers ordained that before we plant any crops in the earth we should observe a week in which a man does not say a harsh word to his neighbour. We live in peace with our fellows to honour our great goddess of the earth without whose blessing our crops will not grow. You have committed a great evil." He brought down his staff heavily on the floor. "Your wife was at fault, but even if you came into your *obi* and found her lover on top of her, you would still have committed a great evil to beat her." His staff came down again. "The evil you have done can ruin the whole clan. The earth goddess whom you have insulted may refuse to give us her increase, and we shall all perish." His tone now changed from anger to command. "You will bring to the shrine of Ani tomorrow one she-goat, one hen, a length of cloth and a hundred cowries." He rose and left the hut.

Okonkwo did as the priest said. He also took with him a pot of palm-wine. Inwardly, he was repentant. But he was not the man to go about telling his neighbours that he was in error. And so people said he had no respect for the gods of the clan. His enemies said his good fortune had gone to his head. They called him the little bird *nza*[1] who so far forgot himself after a heavy meal that he challenged his *chi*.

No work was done during the Week of Peace. People called on their neighbours and drank palm-wine. This year they talked of nothing else but the *nso-ani*[2] which Okonkwo had committed. It was the first time for many years that a man had broken the sacred peace. Even the oldest men could only remember one or two other occasions somewhere in the dim past.

Ogbuefi Ezeudu, who was the oldest man in the village, was telling two other men who came to visit him that the punishment for breaking the Peace of Ani had become very mild in their clan.

"It has not always been so," he said. "My father told me that he had been told that in the past a man who broke the peace was dragged on the ground through the village until he died. But after a while this custom was stopped because it spoilt the peace which it was meant to preserve."

"Somebody told me yesterday," said one of the younger men, "that in some clans it is an abomination for a man to die during the Week of Peace."

---

1. The one that talks back (literal trans.); a small aggressive bird. In the traditional story, it is easily defeated (alternatively, caught by a hawk) when it becomes bold enough to challenge its personal god.

2. Sin, abomination against the Earth goddess Ani.

"It is indeed true," said Ogbuefi Ezeudu. "They have that custom in Obo-doani.[3] If a man dies at this time he is not buried but cast into the Evil Forest. It is a bad custom which these people observe because they lack understanding. They throw away large numbers of men and women without burial. And what is the result? Their clan is full of the evil spirits of these unburied dead, hungry to do harm to the living."

After the Week of Peace every man and his family began to clear the bush to make new farms. The cut bush was left to dry and fire was then set to it. As the smoke rose into the sky kites appeared from different directions and hovered over the burning field in silent valediction. The rainy season was approaching when they would go away until the dry season returned.

Okonkwo spent the next few days preparing his seed-yams. He looked at each yam carefully to see whether it was good for sowing. Sometimes he decided that a yam was too big to be sown as one seed and he split it deftly along its length with his sharp knife. His eldest son, Nwoye, and Ikemefuna helped him by fetching the yams in long baskets from the barn and in counting the prepared seeds in groups of four hundred. Sometimes Okonkwo gave them a few yams each to prepare. But he always found fault with their effort, and he said so with much threatening.

"Do you think you are cutting up yams for cooking?" he asked Nwoye. "If you split another yam of this size, I shall break your jaw. You think you are still a child. I began to own a farm at your age. And you," he said to Ikemefuna, "do you not grow yams where you come from?"

Inwardly Okonkwo knew that the boys were still too young to understand fully the difficult art of preparing seed-yams. But he thought that one could not begin too early. Yam stood for manliness, and he who could feed his family on yams from one harvest to another was a very great man indeed. Okonkwo wanted his son to be a great farmer and a great man. He would stamp out the disquieting signs of laziness which he thought he already saw in him.

"I will not have a son who cannot hold up his head in the gathering of the clan. I would sooner strangle him with my own hands. And if you stand staring at me like that," he swore, "Amadiora[4] will break your head for you!"

Some days later, when the land had been moistened by two or three heavy rains, Okonkwo and his family went to the farm with baskets of seed-yams, their hoes and matchets, and the planting began. They made single mounds of earth in straight lines all over the field and sowed the yams in them.

Yam, the king of crops, was a very exacting king. For three or four moons it demanded hard work and constant attention from cock-crow till the chickens went back to roost. The young tendrils were protected from earth-heat with rings of sisal leaves. As the rains became heavier the women planted maize, melons and beans between the yam mounds. The yams were then staked, first with little sticks and later with tall and big tree branches. The women weeded the farm three times at definite periods in the life of the yams, neither early nor late.

And now the rains had really come, so heavy and persistent that even the village rain-maker no longer claimed to be able to intervene. He could not

---

3. The town of the land (literal trans.); i.e., Any-town, Nigeria.   4. God of thunder and lightning.

stop the rain now, just as he would not attempt to start it in the heart of the dry season, without serious danger to his own health. The personal dynamism required to counter the forces of these extremes of weather would be far too great for the human frame.

And so nature was not interfered with in the middle of the rainy season. Sometimes it poured down in such thick sheets of water that earth and sky seemed merged in one grey wetness. It was then uncertain whether the low rumbling of Amadiora's thunder came from above or below. At such times, in each of the countless thatched huts of Umuofia, children sat around their mother's cooking fire telling stories, or with their father in his *obi* warming themselves from a log fire, roasting and eating maize. It was a brief resting period between the exacting and arduous planting season and the equally exacting but light-hearted month of harvests.

Ikemefuna had begun to feel like a member of Okonkwo's family. He still thought about his mother and his three-year-old sister, and he had moments of sadness and depression. But he and Nwoye had become so deeply attached to each other that such moments became less frequent and less poignant. Ikemefuna had an endless stock of folk tales. Even those which Nwoye knew already were told with a new freshness and the local flavour of a different clan. Nwoye remembered this period very vividly till the end of his life. He even remembered how he had laughed when Ikemefuna told him that the proper name for a corn-cob with only a few scattered grains was *eze-agadi-nwayi*, or the teeth of an old woman. Nwoye's mind had gone immediately to Nwayieke, who lived near the udala tree.[5] She had about three teeth and was always smoking her pipe.

Gradually the rains became lighter and less frequent, and earth and sky once again became separate. The rain fell in thin, slanting showers through sunshine and quiet breeze. Children no longer stayed indoors but ran about singing:

> *"The rain is falling, the sun is shining,*
> *Alone Nnadi[6] is cooking and eating."*

Nwoye always wondered who Nnadi was and why he should live all by himself, cooking and eating. In the end he decided that Nnadi must live in that land of Ikemefuna's favourite story where the ant holds his court in splendour and the sands dance forever.

CHAPTER FIVE

The Feast of the New Yam was approaching and Umuofia was in a festival mood. It was an occasion for giving thanks to Ani, the earth goddess and the source of all fertility. Ani played a greater part in the life of the people than any other deity. She was the ultimate judge of morality and conduct. And what was more, she was in close communion with the departed fathers of the clan whose bodies had been committed to earth.

The Feast of the New Yam was held every year before the harvest began, to honour the earth goddess and the ancestral spirits of the clan. New yams could not be eaten until some had first been offered to these powers. Men and

---

5. African star apple tree. "Nwayieke": Woman born on Eke Day. 6. Father is there or Father exists.

women, young and old, looked forward to the New Yam Festival because it began the season of plenty—the new year. On the last night before the festival, yams of the old year were all disposed of by those who still had them. The new year must begin with tasty, fresh yams and not the shrivelled and fibrous crop of the previous year. All cooking-pots, calabashes and wooden bowls were thoroughly washed, especially the wooden mortar in which yam was pounded. Yam foo-foo[7] and vegetable soup was the chief food in the celebration. So much of it was cooked that, no matter how heavily the family ate or how many friends and relations they invited from neighbouring villages, there was always a huge quantity of food left over at the end of the day. The story was always told of a wealthy man who set before his guests a mound of foo-foo so high that those who sat on one side could not see what was happening on the other, and it was not until late in the evening that one of them saw for the first time his in-law who had arrived during the course of the meal and had fallen to on the opposite side. It was only then that they exchanged greetings and shook hands over what was left of the food.

The New Yam Festival was thus an occasion for joy throughout Umuofia. And every man whose arm was strong, as the Ibo people say, was expected to invite large numbers of guests from far and wide. Okonkwo always asked his wives' relations, and since he now had three wives his guests would make a fairly big crowd.

But somehow Okonkwo could never become as enthusiastic over feasts as most people. He was a good eater and he could drink one or two fairly big gourds of palm-wine. But he was always uncomfortable sitting around for days waiting for a feast or getting over it. He would be very much happier working on his farm.

The festival was now only three days away. Okonkwo's wives had scrubbed the walls and the huts with red earth until they reflected light. They had then drawn patterns on them in white, yellow and dark green. They then set about painting themselves with cam wood and drawing beautiful black patterns on their stomachs and on their backs. The children were also decorated, especially their hair, which was shaved in beautiful patterns. The three women talked excitedly about the relations who had been invited, and the children revelled in the thought of being spoilt by these visitors from mother-land. Ikemefuna was equally excited. The New Yam Festival seemed to him to be a much bigger event here than in his own village, a place which was already becoming remote and vague in his imagination.

And then the storm burst. Okonkwo, who had been walking about aimlessly in his compound in suppressed anger, suddenly found an outlet.

"Who killed this banana tree?" he asked.

A hush fell on the compound immediately.

"Who killed this tree? Or are you all deaf and dumb?"

As a matter of fact the tree was very much alive. Okonkwo's second wife had merely cut a few leaves off it to wrap some food, and she said so. Without further argument Okonkwo gave her a sound beating and left her and her only daughter weeping. Neither of the other wives dared to interfere beyond an occasional and tentative, "It is enough, Okonkwo," pleaded from a reasonable distance.

---

7. A mashed edible base that is shaped into balls with the fingers and then indented for cupping and eating soup.

His anger thus satisfied, Okonkwo decided to go out hunting. He had an old rusty gun made by a clever blacksmith who had come to live in Umuofia long ago. But although Okonkwo was a great man whose prowess was universally acknowledged, he was not a hunter. In fact he had not killed a rat with his gun. And so when he called Ikemefuna to fetch his gun, the wife who had just been beaten murmured something about guns that never shot. Unfortunately for her, Okonkwo heard it and ran madly into his room for the loaded gun, ran out again and aimed at her as she clambered over the dwarf wall of the barn. He pressed the trigger and there was a loud report accompanied by the wail of his wives and children. He threw down the gun and jumped into the barn, and there lay the woman, very much shaken and frightened but quite unhurt. He heaved a heavy sigh and went away with the gun.

In spite of this incident the New Yam Festival was celebrated with great joy in Okonkwo's household. Early that morning as he offered a sacrifice of new yam and palm-oil to his ancestors he asked them to protect him, his children and their mothers in the new year.

As the day wore on his in-laws arrived from three surrounding villages, and each party brought with them a huge pot of palm-wine. And there was eating and drinking till night, when Okonkwo's in-laws began to leave for their homes.

The second day of the new year was the day of the great wrestling match between Okonkwo's village and their neighbours. It was difficult to say which the people enjoyed more—the feasting and fellowship of the first day or the wrestling contest of the second. But there was one woman who had no doubt whatever in her mind. She was Okonkwo's second wife, Ekwefi, whom he nearly shot. There was no festival in all the seasons of the year which gave her as much pleasure as the wrestling match. Many years ago when she was the village beauty Okonkwo had won her heart by throwing the Cat in the greatest contest within living memory. She did not marry him then because he was too poor to pay her bride-price. But a few years later she ran away from her husband and came to live with Okonkwo. All this happened many years ago. Now Ekwefi[8] was a woman of forty-five who had suffered a great deal in her time. But her love of wrestling contests was still as strong as it was thirty years ago.

It was not yet noon on the second day of the New Yam Festival. Ekwefi and her only daughter, Ezinma,[9] sat near the fireplace waiting for the water in the pot to boil. The fowl Ekwefi had just killed was in the wooden mortar. The water began to boil, and in one deft movement she lifted the pot from the fire and poured the boiling water on to the fowl. She put back the empty pot on the circular pad in the corner, and looked at her palms, which were black with soot. Ezinma was always surprised that her mother could lift a pot from the fire with her bare hands.

"Ekwefi," she said, "is it true that when people are grown up, fire does not burn them?" Ezinma, unlike most children, called her mother by her name.

"Yes," replied Ekwefi, too busy to argue. Her daughter was only ten years old but she was wiser than her years.

---

8. An abbreviation of "Do you have a cow?"; the cow being a symbol of wealth. Okonkwo would presumably have repaid Ekwefi's bride-price to her first husband.

9. True beauty (literal trans.), or goodness.

"But Nwoye's mother dropped her pot of hot soup the other day and it broke on the floor."

Ekwefi turned the hen over in the mortar and began to pluck the feathers.

"Ekwefi," said Ezinma, who had joined in plucking the feathers, "my eyelid is twitching."

"It means you are going to cry," said her mother.

"No," Ezinma said, "it is this eyelid, the top one."

"That means you will see something."

"What will I see?" she asked.

"How can I know?" Ekwefi wanted her to work it out herself.

"Oho," said Ezinma at last. "I know what it is—the wrestling match."

At last the hen was plucked clean. Ekwefi tried to pull out the horny beak but it was too hard. She turned round on her low stool and put the beak in the fire for a few moments. She pulled again and it came off.

"Ekwefi!" a voice called from one of the other huts. It was Nwoye's mother, Okonkwo's first wife.

"Is that me?" Ekwefi called back. That was the way people answered calls from outside. They never answered yes for fear it might be an evil spirit calling.

"Will you give Ezinma some fire to bring to me?" Her own children and Ikemefuna had gone to the stream.

Ekwefi put a few live coals into a piece of broken pot and Ezinma carried it across the clean-swept compound to Nwoye's mother.

"Thank you, Nma," she said. She was peeling new yams, and in a basket beside her were green vegetables and beans.

"Let me make the fire for you," Ezinma offered.

"Thank you, Ezigbo," she said. She often called her Ezigbo, which means "the good one."

Ezinma went outside and brought some sticks from a huge bundle of firewood. She broke them into little pieces across the sole of her foot and began to build a fire, blowing it with her breath.

"You will blow your eyes out," said Nwoye's mother, looking up from the yams she was peeling. "Use the fan." She stood up and pulled out the fan which was fastened into one of the rafters. As soon as she got up, the troublesome nanny-goat, which had been dutifully eating yam peelings, dug her teeth into the real thing, scooped out two mouthfuls and fled from the hut to chew the cud in the goats' shed. Nwoye's mother swore at her and settled down again to her peeling. Ezinma's fire was now sending up thick clouds of smoke. She went on fanning it until it burst into flames. Nwoye's mother thanked her and she went back to her mother's hut.

Just then the distant beating of drums began to reach them. It came from the direction of the *ilo*, the village playground. Every village had its own *ilo* which was as old as the village itself and where all the great ceremonies and dances took place. The drums beat the unmistakable wrestling dance—quick, light and gay, and it came floating on the wind.

Okonkwo cleared his throat and moved his feet to the beat of the drums. It filled him with fire as it had always done from his youth. He trembled with the desire to conquer and subdue. It was like the desire for woman.

"We shall be late for the wrestling," said Ezinma to her mother.

"They will not begin until the sun goes down."

"But they are beating the drums."

"Yes. The drums begin at noon but the wrestling waits until the sun begins to sink. Go and see if your father has brought out yams for the afternoon."

"He has. Nwoye's mother is already cooking."

"Go and bring our own, then. We must cook quickly or we shall be late for the wrestling."

Ezinma ran in the direction of the barn and brought back two yams from the dwarf wall.

Ekwefi peeled the yams quickly. The troublesome nanny-goat sniffed about, eating the peelings. She cut the yams into small pieces and began to prepare a pottage, using some of the chicken.

At that moment they heard someone crying just outside their compound. It was very much like Obiageli,[1] Nwoye's sister.

"Is that not Obiageli weeping?" Ekwefi called across the yard to Nwoye's mother.

"Yes," she replied. "She must have broken her water-pot."

The weeping was now quite close and soon the children filed in, carrying on their heads various sizes of pots suitable to their years. Ikemefuna came first with the biggest pot, closely followed by Nwoye and his two younger brothers. Obiageli brought up the rear, her face streaming with tears. In her hand was the cloth pad on which the pot should have rested on her head.

"What happened?" her mother asked, and Obiageli told her mournful story. Her mother consoled her and promised to buy her another pot.

Nwoye's younger brothers were about to tell their mother the true story of the accident when Ikemefuna looked at them sternly and they held their peace. The fact was that Obiageli had been making *inyanga*[2] with her pot. She had balanced it on her head, folded her arms in front of her and began to sway her waist like a grown-up young lady. When the pot fell down and broke she burst out laughing. She only began to weep when they got near the iroko tree outside their compound.

The drums were still beating, persistent and unchanging. Their sound was no longer a separate thing from the living village. It was like the pulsation of its heart. It throbbed in the air, in the sunshine, and even in the trees, and filled the village with excitement.

Ekwefi ladled her husband's share of the pottage into a bowl and covered it. Ezinma took it to him in his *obi*.

Okonkwo was sitting on a goatskin already eating his first wife's meal. Obiageli, who had brought it from her mother's hut, sat on the floor waiting for him to finish. Ezinma placed her mother's dish before him and sat with Obiageli.

"Sit like a woman!" Okonkwo shouted at her. Ezinma brought her two legs together and stretched them in front of her.

"Father, will you go to see the wrestling?" Ezinma asked after a suitable interval.

"Yes," he answered. "Will you go?"

"Yes." And after a pause she said: "Can I bring your chair for you?"

"No, that is a boy's job." Okonkwo was specially fond of Ezinma. She looked very much like her mother, who was once the village beauty. But his fondness only showed on very rare occasions.

"Obiageli broke her pot today," Ezinma said.

"Yes, she has told me about it," Okonkwo said between mouthfuls.

---

1. Born to eat (born into prosperity). 2. Had been showing off.

"Father," said Obiageli, "people should not talk when they are eating or pepper may go down the wrong way."
"That is very true. Do you hear that, Ezinma? You are older than Obiageli but she has more sense."
He uncovered his second wife's dish and began to eat from it. Obiageli took the first dish and returned to her mother's hut. And then Nkechi came in, bringing the third dish. Nkechi was the daughter of Okonkwo's third wife.
In the distance the drums continued to beat.

CHAPTER SIX

The whole village turned out on the *ilo*, men, women and children. They stood round in a huge circle leaving the centre of the playground free. The elders and grandees of the village sat on their own stools brought there by their young sons or slaves. Okonkwo was among them. All others stood except those who came early enough to secure places on the few stands which had been built by placing smooth logs on forked pillars.

The wrestlers were not there yet and the drummers held the field. They too sat just in front of the huge circle of spectators, facing the elders. Behind them was the big and ancient silk-cotton tree which was sacred. Spirits of good children lived in that tree waiting to be born. On ordinary days young women who desired children came to sit under its shade.

There were seven drums and they were arranged according to their sizes in a long wooden basket. Three men beat them with sticks, working feverishly from one drum to another. They were possessed by the spirit of the drums.

The young men who kept order on these occasions dashed about, consulting among themselves and with the leaders of the two wrestling teams, who were still outside the circle, behind the crowd. Once in a while two young men carrying palm fronds ran round the circle and kept the crowd back by beating the ground in front of them or, if they were stubborn, their legs and feet.

At last the two teams danced into the circle and the crowd roared and clapped. The drums rose to a frenzy. The people surged forward. The young men who kept order flew around, waving their palm fronds. Old men nodded to the beat of the drums and remembered the days when they wrestled to its intoxicating rhythm.

The contest began with boys of fifteen or sixteen. There were only three such boys in each team. They were not the real wrestlers; they merely set the scene. Within a short time the first two bouts were over. But the third created a big sensation even among the elders who did not usually show their excitement so openly. It was as quick as the other two, perhaps even quicker. But very few people had ever seen that kind of wrestling before. As soon as the two boys closed in, one of them did something which no one could describe because it had been as quick as a flash. And the other boy was flat on his back. The crowd roared and clapped and for a while drowned the frenzied drums. Okonkwo sprang to his feet and quickly sat down again. Three young men from the victorious boy's team ran forward, carried him shoulder-high and danced through the cheering crowd. Everybody soon knew who the boy was. His name was Maduka, the son of Obierika.[3]

The drummers stopped for a brief rest before the real matches. Their bodies

3. The heart eats [enjoys] more.

shone with sweat, and they took up fans and began to fan themselves. They also drank water from small pots and ate kola nuts. They became ordinary human beings again, talking and laughing among themselves and with others who stood near them. The air, which had been stretched taut with excitement, relaxed again. It was as if water had been poured on the tightened skin of a drum. Many people looked around, perhaps for the first time, and saw those who stood or sat next to them.

"I did not know it was you," Ekwefi said to the woman who had stood shoulder to shoulder with her since the beginning of the matches.

"I do not blame you," said the woman. "I have never seen such a large crowd of people. Is it true that Okonkwo nearly killed you with his gun?"

"It is true indeed, my dear friend. I cannot yet find a mouth with which to tell the story."

"Your *chi* is very much awake, my friend. And how is my daughter, Ezinma?"

"She has been very well for some time now. Perhaps she has come to stay."

"I think she has. How old is she now?"

"She is about ten years old."

"I think she will stay. They usually stay if they do not die before the age of six."

"I pray she stays," said Ekwefi with a heavy sigh.

The woman with whom she talked was called Chielo.[4] She was the priestess of Agbala, the Oracle of the Hills and the Caves. In ordinary life Chielo was a widow with two children. She was very friendly with Ekwefi and they shared a common shed in the market. She was particularly fond of Ekwefi's only daughter, Ezinma, whom she called "my daughter". Quite often she bought bean-cakes and gave Ekwefi some to take home to Ezinma. Anyone seeing Chielo in ordinary life would hardly believe she was the same person who prophesied when the spirit of Agbala was upon her.

The drummers took up their sticks again and the air shivered and grew tense like a tightened bow.

The two teams were ranged facing each other across the clear space. A young man from one team danced across the centre to the other side and pointed at whomever he wanted to fight. They danced back to the centre together and then closed in.

There were twelve men on each side and the challenge went from one side to the other. Two judges walked around the wrestlers and when they thought they were equally matched, stopped them. Five matches ended in this way. But the really exciting moments were when a man was thrown. The huge voice of the crowd then rose to the sky and in every direction. It was even heard in the surrounding villages.

The last match was between the leaders of the teams. They were among the best wrestlers in all the nine villages. The crowd wondered who would throw the other this year. Some said Okafo was the better man; others said he was not the equal of Ikezue.[5] Last year neither of them had thrown the other even though the judges had allowed the contest to go on longer than was the custom. They had the same style and one saw the other's plans beforehand. It might happen again this year.

Dusk was already approaching when their contest began. The drums went

4. *Chi* who plants.   5. Strength is complete (a boastful name).

mad and the crowds also. They surged forward as the two young men danced into the circle. The palm fronds were helpless in keeping them back.

Ikezue held out his right hand. Okafo seized it, and they closed in. It was a fierce contest. Ikezue strove to dig in his right heel behind Okafo so as to pitch him backwards in the clever *ege* style. But the one knew what the other was thinking. The crowd had surrounded and swallowed up the drummers, whose frantic rhythm was no longer a mere disembodied sound but the very heart-beat of the people.

The wrestlers were now almost still in each other's grip. The muscles on their arms and their thighs and on their backs stood out and twitched. It looked like an equal match. The two judges were already moving forward to separate them when Ikezue, now desperate, went down quickly on one knee in an attempt to fling his man backwards over his head. It was a sad miscalculation. Quick as the lightning of Amadiora, Okafo raised his right leg and swung it over his rival's head. The crowd burst into a thunderous roar. Okafo was swept off his feet by his supporters and carried home shoulder-high. They sang his praise and the young women clapped their hands:

> "Who will wrestle for our village?
> Okafo will wrestle for our village.
> Has he thrown a hundred men?
> He has thrown four hundred men.
> Has he thrown a hundred Cats?
> He has thrown four hundred Cats.
> Then send him word to fight for us."

CHAPTER SEVEN

For three years Ikemefuna lived in Okonkwo's household and the elders of Umuofia seemed to have forgotten about him. He grew rapidly like a yam tendril in the rainy season, and was full of the sap of life. He had become wholly absorbed into his new family. He was like an elder brother to Nwoye, and from the very first seemed to have kindled a new fire in the younger boy. He made him feel grown-up; and they no longer spent the evenings in mother's hut while she cooked, but now sat with Okonkwo in his *obi*, or watched him as he tapped his palm tree for the evening wine. Nothing pleased Nwoye now more than to be sent for by his mother or another of his father's wives to do one of those difficult and masculine tasks in the home, like splitting wood, or pounding food. On receiving such a message through a younger brother or sister, Nwoye would feign annoyance and grumble aloud about women and their troubles.

Okonkwo was inwardly pleased at his son's development, and he knew it was due to Ikemefuna. He wanted Nwoye to grow into a tough young man capable of ruling his father's household when he was dead and gone to join the ancestors. He wanted him to be a prosperous man, having enough in his barn to feed the ancestors with regular sacrifices. And so he was always happy when he heard him grumbling about women. That showed that in time he would be able to control his women-folk. No matter how prosperous a man was, if he was unable to rule his women and his children (and especially his women) he was not really a man. He was like the man in the song who had ten and one wives and not enough soup for his foo-foo.

So Okonkwo encouraged the boys to sit with him in his *obi*, and he told them stories of the land—masculine stories of violence and bloodshed. Nwoye knew that it was right to be masculine and to be violent, but somehow he still preferred the stories that his mother used to tell, and which she no doubt still told to her younger children—stories of the tortoise and his wily ways, and of the bird eneke-nti-oba[6] who challenged the whole world to a wrestling contest and was finally thrown by the cat. He remembered the story she often told of the quarrel between Earth and Sky long ago, and how Sky withheld rain for seven years, until crops withered and the dead could not be buried because the hoes broke on the stony Earth. At last Vulture was sent to plead with Sky, and to soften his heart with a song of the suffering of the sons of men. Whenever Nwoye's mother sang this song he felt carried away to the distant scene in the sky where Vulture, Earth's emissary, sang for mercy. At last Sky was moved to pity, and he gave to Vulture rain wrapped in leaves of coco-yam. But as he flew home his long talon pierced the leaves and the rain fell as it had never fallen before. And so heavily did it rain on Vulture that he did not return to deliver his message but flew to a distant land, from where he had espied a fire. And when he got there he found it was a man making a sacrifice. He warmed himself in the fire and ate the entrails.

That was the kind of story that Nwoye loved. But he now knew that they were for foolish women and children, and he knew that his father wanted him to be a man. And so he feigned that he no longer cared for women's stories. And when he did this he saw that his father was pleased, and no longer rebuked him or beat him. So Nwoye and Ikemefuna would listen to Okonkwo's stories about tribal wars, or how, years ago, he had stalked his victim, overpowered him and obtained his first human head. And as he told them of the past they sat in darkness or the dim glow of logs, waiting for the women to finish their cooking. When they finished, each brought her bowl of foo-foo and bowl of soup to her husband. An oil lamp was lit and Okonkwo tasted from each bowl, and then passed two shares to Nwoye and Ikemefuna.

In this way the moons and the seasons passed. And then the locusts came. It had not happened for many a long year. The elders said locusts came once in a generation, reappeared every year for seven years and then disappeared for another lifetime. They went back to their caves in a distant land, where they were guarded by a race of stunted men. And then after another lifetime these men opened the caves again and the locusts came to Umuofia.

They came in the cold harmattan season after the harvests had been gathered, and ate up all the wild grass in the fields.

Okonkwo and the two boys were working on the red outer walls of the compound. This was one of the lighter tasks of the after-harvest season. A new cover of thick palm branches and palm leaves was set on the walls to protect them from the next rainy season. Okonkwo worked on the outside of the wall and the boys worked from within. There were little holes from one side to the other in the upper levels of the wall, and through these Okonkwo passed the rope, or tie-tie,[7] to the boys and they passed it round the wooden stays and then back to him; and in this way the cover was strengthened on the wall.

The women had gone to the bush to collect firewood, and the little children

6. The swallow with the ear of a crocodile [who is deaf] (literal trans.); a bird who proverbially flies without perching.

7. A creeper used as a rope to lash sections in building (pidgin English from "to tie").

to visit their playmates in the neighbouring compounds. The harmattan was in the air and seemed to distil a hazy feeling of sleep on the world. Okonkwo and the boys worked in complete silence, which was only broken when a new palm frond was lifted on to the wall or when a busy hen moved dry leaves about in her ceaseless search for food.

And then quite suddenly a shadow fell on the world, and the sun seemed hidden behind a thick cloud. Okonkwo looked up from his work and wondered if it was going to rain at such an unlikely time of the year. But almost immediately a shout of joy broke out in all directions, and Umuofia, which had dozed in the noon-day haze, broke into life and activity.

"Locusts are descending," was joyfully chanted everywhere, and men, women and children left their work or their play and ran into the open to see the unfamiliar sight. The locusts had not come for many, many years, and only the old people had seen them before.

At first, a fairly small swarm came. They were the harbingers sent to survey the land. And then appeared on the horizon a slowly-moving mass like a boundless sheet of black cloud drifting towards Umuofia. Soon it covered half the sky, and the solid mass was now broken by tiny eyes of light like shining star-dust. It was a tremendous sight, full of power and beauty.

Everyone was now about, talking excitedly and praying that the locusts should camp in Umuofia for the night. For although locusts had not visited Umuofia for many years, everybody knew by instinct that they were very good to eat. And at last the locusts did descend. They settled on every tree and on every blade of grass; they settled on the roofs and covered the bare ground. Mighty tree branches broke away under them, and the whole country became the brown-earth colour of the vast, hungry swarm.

Many people went out with baskets trying to catch them, but the elders counselled patience till nightfall. And they were right. The locusts settled in the bushes for the night and their wings became wet with dew. Then all Umuofia turned out in spite of the cold harmattan, and everyone filled his bags and pots with locusts. The next morning they were roasted in clay pots and then spread in the sun until they became dry and brittle. And for many days this rare food was eaten with solid palm-oil.

Okonkwo sat in his *obi* crunching happily with Ikemefuna and Nwoye, and drinking palm-wine copiously, when Ogbuefi Ezeudu came in. Ezeudu was the oldest man in this quarter of Umuofia. He had been a great and fearless warrior in his time, and was now accorded great respect in all the clan. He refused to join in the meal, and asked Okonkwo to have a word with him outside. And so they walked out together, the old man supporting himself with his stick. When they were out of ear-shot, he said to Okonkwo:

"That boy calls you father. Do not bear a hand in his death." Okonkwo was surprised, and was about to say something when the old man continued:

"Yes, Umuofia has decided to kill him. The Oracle of the Hills and the Caves has pronounced it. They will take him outside Umuofia as is the custom, and kill him there. But I want you to have nothing to do with it. He calls you his father."

The next day a group of elders from all the nine villages of Umuofia came to Okonkwo's house early in the morning, and before they began to speak in low tones Nwoye and Ikemefuna were sent out. They did not stay very long, but when they went away Okonkwo sat still for a very long time supporting his chin in his palms. Later in the day he called Ikemefuna and told him that he was to be taken home the next day. Nwoye overheard it and burst into tears, whereupon his father beat him heavily. As for Ikemefuna, he was at a loss. His own home had gradually become very faint and distant. He still missed his mother and his sister and would be very glad to see them. But somehow he knew he was not going to see them. He remembered once when men had talked in low tones with his father; and it seemed now as if it was happening all over again.

Later, Nwoye went to his mother's hut and told her that Ikemefuna was going home. She immediately dropped the pestle with which she was grinding pepper, folded her arms across her breast and sighed, "Poor child".

The next day, the men returned with a pot of wine. They were all fully dressed as if they were going to a big clan meeting or to pay a visit to a neighbouring village. They passed their cloths under the right arm-pit, and hung their goatskin bags and sheathed matchets over their left shoulders. Okonkwo got ready quickly and the party set out with Ikemefuna carrying the pot of wine. A deathly silence descended on Okonkwo's compound. Even the very little children seemed to know. Throughout that day Nwoye sat in his mother's hut and tears stood in his eyes.

At the beginning of their journey the men of Umuofia talked and laughed about the locusts, about their women, and about some effeminate men who had refused to come with them. But as they drew near to the outskirts of Umuofia silence fell upon them too.

The sun rose slowly to the centre of the sky, and the dry, sandy footway began to throw up the heat that lay buried in it. Some birds chirruped in the forests around. The men trod dry leaves on the sand. All else was silent. Then from the distance came the faint beating of the *ekwe*. It rose and faded with the wind—a peaceful dance from a distant clan.

"It is an *ozo* dance,"[8] the men said among themselves. But no one was sure where it was coming from. Some said Ezimili, others Abame or Aninta. They argued for a short while and fell into silence again, and the elusive dance rose and fell with the wind. Somewhere a man was taking one of the titles of his clan, with music and dancing and a great feast.

The footway had now become a narrow line in the heart of the forest. The short trees and sparse undergrowth which surrounded the men's village began to give way to giant trees and climbers which perhaps had stood from the beginning of things, untouched by the axe and the bush-fire. The sun breaking through their leaves and branches threw a pattern of light and shade on the sandy footway.

Ikemefuna heard a whisper close behind him and turned round sharply. The man who had whispered now called out aloud, urging the others to hurry up.

"We still have a long way to go," he said. Then he and another man went before Ikemefuna and set a faster pace.

Thus the men of Umuofia pursued their way, armed with sheathed matchets, and Ikemefuna, carrying a pot of palm-wine on his head, walked in their midst. Although he had felt uneasy at first, he was not afraid now. Okonkwo walked behind him. He could hardly imagine that Okonkwo was not his real father. He had never been fond of his real father, and at the end of three years he had become very distant indeed. But his mother and his three-year-old sister . . . of course she would not be three now, but six. Would he recognise

---

8. Part of the *ozo* rituals, the spiritual ceremonies that accompanied the taking of titles.

her now? She must have grown quite big. How his mother would weep for joy, and thank Okonkwo for having looked after him so well and for bringing him back. She would want to hear everything that had happened to him in all these years. Could he remember them all? He would tell her about Nwoye and his mother, and about the locusts. . . . Then quite suddenly a thought came upon him. His mother might be dead. He tried in vain to force the thought out of his mind. Then he tried to settle the matter the way he used to settle such matters when he was a little boy. He still remembered the song:

> *Eze elina, elina!*
> *Sala*
> *Eze ilikwa ya*
> *Ikwaba akwa oligholi*
> *Ebe Danda nechi eze*
> *Ebe Uzuzu nete egwu*
> *Sala*[9]

He sang it in his mind, and walked to its beat. If the song ended on his right foot, his mother was alive. If it ended on his left, she was dead. No, not dead, but ill. It ended on the right. She was alive and well. He sang the song again, and it ended on the left. But the second time did not count. The first voice gets to Chukwu, or God's house. That was a favourite saying of children. Ikemefuna felt like a child once more. It must be the thought of going home to his mother.

One of the men behind him cleared his throat. Ikemefuna looked back, and the man growled at him to go on and not stand looking back. The way he said it sent cold fear down Ikemefuna's back. His hands trembled vaguely on the black pot he carried. Why had Okonkwo withdrawn to the rear? Ikemefuna felt his legs melting under him. And he was afraid to look back.

As the man who had cleared his throat drew up and raised his matchet, Okonkwo looked away. He heard the blow. The pot fell and broke in the sand. He heard Ikemefuna cry, "My father, they have killed me!" as he ran towards him. Dazed with fear, Okonkwo drew his matchet and cut him down. He was afraid of being thought weak.

As soon as his father walked in, that night, Nwoye knew that Ikemefuna had been killed, and something seemed to give way inside him, like the snapping of a tightened bow. He did not cry. He just hung limp. He had had the same kind of feeling not long ago, during the last harvest season. Every child loved the harvest season. Those who were big enough to carry even a few yams in a tiny basket went with grown-ups to the farm. And if they could not help in digging up the yams, they could gather firewood together for roasting the ones that would be eaten there on the farm. This roasted yam soaked in red palm-oil and eaten in the open farm was sweeter than any meal at home. It was after such a day at the farm during the last harvest that Nwoye had felt for the first time a snapping inside him like the one he now felt. They were returning home with baskets of yams from a distant farm across the stream when they had heard the voice of an infant crying in the thick forest. A sudden

---

9. King don't eat, don't eat / Sala / King if you eat it / You will weep for the abomination / Where Danda installs a king / Where Uzuzu dances / Sala. "Sala": meaningless refrain. "Danda": the ant.

"Uzuzu": sand. Ikemefuna reassures himself by singing his favorite song about the country where the "sands dance forever" (see p. 2632).

hush had fallen on the women, who had been talking, and they had quickened their steps. Nwoye had heard that twins were put in earthenware pots and thrown away in the forest, but he had never yet come across them. A vague chill had descended on him and his head had seemed to swell, like a solitary walker at night who passes an evil spirit on the way. Then something had given way inside him. It descended on him again, this feeling, when his father walked in, that night after killing Ikemefuna.

CHAPTER EIGHT

Okonkwo did not taste any food for two days after the death of Ikemefuna. He drank palm-wine from morning till night, and his eyes were red and fierce like the eyes of a rat when it was caught by the tail and dashed against the floor. He called his son, Nwoye, to sit with him in his *obi*. But the boy was afraid of him and slipped out of the hut as soon as he noticed him dozing.

He did not sleep at night. He tried not to think about Ikemefuna, but the more he tried the more he thought about him. Once he got up from bed and walked about his compound. But he was so weak that his legs could hardly carry him. He felt like a drunken giant walking with the limbs of a mosquito. Now and then a cold shiver descended on his head and spread down his body.

On the third day he asked his second wife, Ekwefi, to roast plantains for him. She prepared it the way he liked—with slices of oil-bean and fish.

"You have not eaten for two days," said his daughter Ezinma when she brought the food to him. "So you must finish this." She sat down and stretched her legs in front of her. Okonkwo ate the food absent-mindedly. 'She should have been a boy,' he thought as he looked at his ten-year-old daughter. He passed her a piece of fish.

"Go and bring me some cold water," he said. Ezinma rushed out of the hut, chewing the fish, and soon returned with a bowl of cool water from the earthen pot in her mother's hut.

Okonkwo took the bowl from her and gulped the water down. He ate a few more pieces of plantain and pushed the dish aside.

"Bring me my bag," he asked, and Ezinma brought his goatskin bag from the far end of the hut. He searched in it for his snuff-bottle. It was a deep bag and took almost the whole length of his arm. It contained other things apart from his snuff-bottle. There was a drinking horn in it, and also a drinking gourd, and they knocked against each other as he searched. When he brought out the snuff-bottle he tapped it a few times against his knee-cap before taking out some snuff on the palm of his left hand. Then he remembered that he had not taken out his snuff-spoon. He searched his bag again and brought out a small, flat, ivory spoon, with which he carried the brown snuff to his nostrils.

Ezinma took the dish in one hand and the empty water bowl in the other and went back to her mother's hut. 'She should have been a boy,' Okonkwo said to himself again. His mind went back to Ikemefuna and he shivered. If only he could find some work to do he would be able to forget. But it was the season of rest between the harvest and the next planting season. The only work that men did at this time was covering the walls of their compound with new palm fronds. And Okonkwo had already done that. He had finished it on the very day the locusts came, when he had worked on one side of the wall and Ikemefuna and Nwoye on the other.

'When did you become a shivering old woman,' Okonkwo asked himself, 'you, who are known in all the nine villages for your valour in war? How can a man who has killed five men in battle fall to pieces because he has added a boy to their number? Okonkwo, you have become a woman indeed.'

He sprang to his feet, hung his goatskin bag on his shoulder and went to visit his friend, Obierika.

Obierika was sitting outside under the shade of an orange tree making thatches from leaves of the raffia-palm. He exchanged greetings with Okonkwo and led the way into his *obi*.

"I was coming over to see you as soon as I finished that thatch," he said, rubbing off the grains of sand that clung to his thighs.

"Is it well?" Okonkwo asked.

"Yes," replied Obierika. "My daughter's suitor is coming today and I hope we will clinch the matter of the bride-price. I want you to be there."

Just then Obierika's son, Maduka, came into the *obi* from outside, greeted Okonkwo and turned towards the compound.

"Come and shake hands with me," Okonkwo said to the lad. "Your wrestling the other day gave me much happiness." The boy smiled, shook hands with Okonkwo and went into the compound.

"He will do great things," Okonkwo said. "If I had a son like him I should be happy. I am worried about Nwoye. A bowl of pounded yams can throw him in a wrestling match. His two younger brothers are more promising. But I can tell you, Obierika, that my children do not resemble me. Where are the young suckers that will grow when the old banana tree dies? If Ezinma had been a boy I would have been happier. She has the right spirit."

"You worry yourself for nothing," said Obierika. "The children are still very young."

"Nwoye is old enough to impregnate a woman. At his age I was already fending for myself. No, my friend, he is not too young. A chick that will grow into a cock can be spotted the very day it hatches. I have done my best to make Nwoye grow into a man, but there is too much of his mother in him."

'Too much of his grandfather,' Obierika thought, but he did not say it. The same thought also came to Okonkwo's mind. But he had long learnt how to lay that ghost. Whenever the thought of his father's weakness and failure troubled him he expelled it by thinking about his own strength and success. And so he did now. His mind went to his latest show of manliness.

"I cannot understand why you refused to come with us to kill that boy," he asked Obierika.

"Because I did not want to," Obierika replied sharply. "I had something better to do."

"You sound as if you question the authority and the decision of the Oracle, who said he should die."

"I do not. Why should I? But the Oracle did not ask me to carry out its decision."

"But someone had to do it. If we were all afraid of blood, it would not be done. And what do you think the Oracle would do then?"

"You know very well, Okonkwo, that I am not afraid of blood; and if anyone tells you that I am, he is telling a lie. And let me tell you one thing, my friend. If I were you I would have stayed at home. What you have done will not please the Earth. It is the kind of action for which the goddess wipes out whole families."

"The Earth cannot punish me for obeying her messenger," Okonkwo said.

"A child's fingers are not scalded by a piece of hot yam which its mother puts into its palm."

"That is true," Obierika agreed. "But if the Oracle said that my son should be killed I would neither dispute it nor be the one to do it."

They would have gone on arguing had Ofoedu[1] not come in just then. It was clear from his twinkling eyes that he had important news. But it would be impolite to rush him. Obierika offered him a lobe of the kola nut he had broken with Okonkwo. Ofoedu ate slowly and talked about the locusts. When he finished his kola nut he said:

"The things that happen these days are very strange."

"What has happened?" asked Okonkwo.

"Do you know Ogbuefi Ndulue?"[2] Ofoedu asked.

"Ogbuefi Ndulue of Ire village," Okonkwo and Obierika said together.

"He died this morning," said Ofoedu.

"That is not strange. He was the oldest man in Ire," said Obierika.

"You are right," Ofoedu agreed. "But you ought to ask why the drum has not been beaten to tell Umuofia of his death."

"Why?" asked Obierika and Okonkwo together.

"That is the strange part of it. You know his first wife who walks with a stick?"

"Yes. She is called Ozoemena."[3]

"That is so," said Ofoedu. "Ozoemena was, as you know, too old to attend Ndulue during his illness. His younger wives did that. When he died this morning, one of these women went to Ozoemena's hut and told her. She rose from her mat, took her stick and walked over to the *obi*. She knelt on her knees and hands at the threshold and called her husband, who was laid on a mat. 'Ogbuefi Ndulue,' she called, three times, and went back to her hut. When the youngest wife went to call her again to be present at the washing of the body, she found her lying on the mat, dead."

"That is very strange indeed," said Okonkwo. "They will put off Ndulue's funeral until his wife has been buried."[4]

"That is why the drum has not been beaten to tell Umuofia."

"It was always said that Ndulue and Ozoemena had one mind," said Obierika. "I remember when I was a young boy there was a song about them. He could not do anything without telling her."

"I did not know that," said Okonkwo. "I thought he was a strong man in his youth."

"He was indeed," said Ofoedu.

Okonkwo shook his head doubtfully.

"He led Umuofia to war in those days," said Obierika.

Okonkwo was beginning to feel like his old self again. All that he required was something to occupy his mind. If he had killed Ikemefuna during the busy planting season or harvesting it would not have been so bad; his mind would have been centred on his work. Okonkwo was not a man of thought but of action. But in the absence of work, talking was the next best.

Soon after Ofoedu left, Okonkwo took up his goatskin bag to go.

"I must go home to tap my palm trees for the afternoon," he said.

---

1. The ancestors are our guide.
2. Life has arrived.
3. Another bad thing will not happen.
4. A wife dying shortly after her husband was

sometimes considered guilty of his death, so the village preserves appearances by burying Ozoemena before announcing Ogbuefi Ndulue's death.

"Who taps your tall trees for you?" asked Obierika.

"Umezulike," replied Okonkwo.

"Sometimes I wish I had not taken the *ozo* title," said Obierika. "It wounds my heart to see these young men killing palm trees in the name of tapping."

"It is so indeed," Okonkwo agreed. "But the law of the land must be obeyed."

"I don't know how we got that law," said Obierika. "In many other clans a man of title is not forbidden to climb the palm tree. Here we say he cannot climb the tall tree but he can tap the short ones standing on the ground. It is like Dimaragana, who would not lend his knife for cutting up dog-meat because the dog was taboo to him, but offered to use his teeth."

"I think it is good that our clan holds the *ozo* title in high esteem," said Okonkwo. "In those other clans you speak of, *ozo* is so low that every beggar takes it."

"I was only speaking in jest," said Obierika. "In Abame and Aninta the title is worth less than two cowries. Every man wears the thread of title on his ankle, and does not lose it even if he steals."

"They have indeed soiled the name of *ozo*," said Okonkwo as he rose to go.

"It will not be very long now before my in-laws come," said Obierika.

"I shall return very soon," said Okonkwo, looking at the position of the sun.

There were seven men in Obierika's hut when Okonkwo returned. The suitor was a young man of about twenty-five, and with him were his father and uncle. On Obierika's side were his two elder brothers and Maduka, his sixteen-year-old son.

"Ask Akueke's mother to send us some kola nuts," said Obierika to his son. Maduka vanished into the compound like lightning. The conversation at once centred on him, and everybody agreed that he was as sharp as a razor.

"I sometimes think he is too sharp," said Obierika, somewhat indulgently. "He hardly ever walks. He is always in a hurry. If you are sending him on an errand he flies away before he has heard half of the message."

"You were very much like that yourself," said his eldest brother. "As our people say, 'When mother-cow is chewing grass its young ones watch its mouth.' Maduka has been watching your mouth."

As he was speaking the boy returned, followed by Akueke,[5] his half-sister, carrying a wooden dish with three kola nuts and alligator pepper. She gave the dish to her father's eldest brother and then shook hands, very shyly, with her suitor and his relatives. She was about sixteen and just ripe for marriage. Her suitor and his relatives surveyed her young body with expert eyes as if to assure themselves that she was beautiful and ripe.

She wore a coiffure which was done up into a crest in the middle of the head. Cam wood was rubbed lightly into her skin, and all over her body were black patterns drawn with *uli*.[6] She wore a black necklace which hung down in three coils just above her full, succulent breasts. On her arms were red and yellow bangles, and on her waist four or five rows of *jigida*, or waist-beads.

When she had shaken hands, or rather held out her hand to be shaken, she returned to her mother's hut to help with the cooking.

"Remove your *jigida* first," her mother warned as she moved near the fire-

---

5. Wealth of Eke (a divinity). Similar names built on *ako* ("wealth") connote riches and are associated with the idea of women as a form of exchangeable material wealth.

6. A liquid made from crushed seeds, which caused the skin to pucker temporarily. It was used to create black tattoolike decorations. "Cam wood": a shrub. The powdered red heartwood of the shrub was used as a cosmetic dye.

place to bring the pestle resting against the wall. "Every day I tell you that *jigida* and fire are not friends. But you will never hear. You grew your ears for decoration, not for hearing. One of these days your *jigida* will catch fire on your waist, and then you will know."

Akueke moved to the other end of the hut and began to remove the waist-beads. It had to be done slowly and carefully, taking each string separately, else it would break and the thousand tiny rings would have to be strung together again. She rubbed each string downwards with her palms until it passed the buttocks and slipped down to the floor around her feet.

The men in the *obi* had already begun to drink the palm-wine which Akueke's suitor had brought. It was a very good wine and powerful, for in spite of the palm fruit hung across the mouth of the pot to restrain the lively liquor, white foam rose and spilled over.

"That wine is the work of a good tapper," said Okonkwo.

The young suitor, whose name was Ibe, smiled broadly and said to his father: "Do you hear that?" He then said to the others: "He will never admit that I am a good tapper."

"He tapped three of my best palm trees to death," said his father, Ukegbu.

"That was about five years ago," said Ibe, who had begun to pour out the wine, "before I learnt how to tap." He filled the first horn and gave to his father. Then he poured out for the others. Okonkwo brought out his big horn from the goatskin bag, blew into it to remove any dust that might be there, and gave it to Ibe to fill.

As the men drank, they talked about everything except the thing for which they had gathered. It was only after the pot had been emptied that the suitor's father cleared his voice and announced the object of their visit.

Obierika then presented to him a small bundle of short broomsticks. Ukegbu counted them.

"They are thirty?" he asked.

Obierika nodded in agreement.

"We are at last getting somewhere," Ukegbu said, and then turning to his brother and his son he said: "Let us go out and whisper together." The three rose and went outside. When they returned Ukegbu handed the bundle of sticks back to Obierika. He counted them; instead of thirty there were now only fifteen. He passed them over to his eldest brother, Machi, who also counted them and said:

"We had not thought to go below thirty. But as the dog said, 'If I fall down for you and you fall down for me, it is play'. Marriage should be a play and not a fight; so we are falling down again." He then added ten sticks to the fifteen and gave the bundle to Ukegbu.

In this way Akueke's bride-price was finally settled at twenty bags of cowries. It was already dusk when the two parties came to this agreement.

"Go and tell Akueke's mother that we have finished," Obierika said to his son, Maduka. Almost immediately the woman came in with a big bowl of foo-foo. Obierika's second wife followed with a pot of soup, and Maduka brought in a pot of palm-wine.

As the men ate and drank palm-wine they talked about the customs of their neighbours.

"It was only this morning," said Obierika, "that Okonkwo and I were talking about Abame and Aninta, where titled men climb trees and pound foo-foo for their wives."

"All their customs are upside-down. They do not decide bride-price as we do, with sticks. They haggle and bargain as if they were buying a goat or a cow in the market."

"That is very bad," said Obierika's eldest brother. "But what is good in one place is bad in another place. In Umunso they do not bargain at all, not even with broomsticks. The suitor just goes on bringing bags of cowries until his in-laws tell him to stop. It is a bad custom because it always leads to a quarrel."

"The world is large," said Okonkwo. "I have even heard that in some tribes a man's children belong to his wife and her family."

"That cannot be," said Machi. "You might as well say that the woman lies on top of the man when they are making the children."

"It is like the story of white men who, they say, are white like this piece of chalk," said Obierika. He held up a piece of chalk, which every man kept in his *obi* and with which his guests drew lines on the floor before they ate kola nuts. "And these white men, they say, have no toes."[7]

"And have you never seen them?" asked Machi.

"Have you?" asked Obierika.

"One of them passes here frequently," said Machi. "His name is Amadi."

Those who knew Amadi laughed. He was a leper, and the polite name for leprosy was 'the white skin'.

CHAPTER NINE

For the first time in three nights, Okonkwo slept. He woke up once in the middle of the night and his mind went back to the past three days without making him feel uneasy. He began to wonder why he had felt uneasy at all. It was like a man wondering in broad daylight why a dream had appeared so terrible to him at night. He stretched himself and scratched his thigh where a mosquito had bitten him as he slept. Another one was wailing near his right ear. He slapped the ear and hoped he had killed it. Why do they always go for one's ears? When he was a child his mother had told him a story about it. But it was as silly as all women's stories. Mosquito, she had said, had asked Ear to marry him, whereupon Ear fell on the floor in uncontrollable laughter. "How much longer do you think you will live?" she asked. "You are already a skeleton." Mosquito went away humiliated, and any time he passed her way he told Ear that he was still alive.

Okonkwo turned on his side and went back to sleep. He was roused in the morning by someone banging on his door.

"Who is that?" he growled. He knew it must be Ekwefi. Of his three wives Ekwefi was the only one who would have the audacity to bang on his door.

"Ezinma is dying," came her voice, and all the tragedy and sorrow of her life were packed in those words.

Okonkwo sprang from his bed, pushed back the bolt on his door and ran into Ekwefi's hut.

Ezinma lay shivering on a mat beside a huge fire that her mother had kept burning all night.

"It is *iba*,"[8] said Okonkwo as he took his matchet and went into the bush to collect the leaves and grasses and barks of trees that went into making the medicine for *iba*.

7. They wear shoes.
8. A fever accompanied by jaundice, probably caused by malaria.

Ekwefi knelt beside the sick child, occasionally feeling with her palm the wet, burning forehead.

Ezinma was an only child and the centre of her mother's world. Very often it was Ezinma who decided what food her mother should prepare. Ekwefi even gave her such delicacies as eggs, which children were rarely allowed to eat because such food tempted them to steal. One day as Ezinma was eating an egg Okonkwo had come in unexpectedly from his hut. He was greatly shocked and swore to beat Ekwefi if she dared to give the child eggs again. But it was impossible to refuse Ezinma anything. After her father's rebuke she developed an even keener appetite for eggs. And she enjoyed above all the secrecy in which she now ate them. Her mother always took her into their bedroom and shut the door.

Ezinma did not call her mother Nne like all children. She called her by her name, Ekwefi, as her father and other grown-up people did. The relationship between them was not only that of mother and child. There was something in it like the companionship of equals, which was strengthened by such little conspiracies as eating eggs in the bedroom.

Ekwefi had suffered a good deal in her life. She had borne ten children and nine of them had died in infancy, usually before the age of three. As she buried one child after another her sorrow gave way to despair and then to grim resignation. The birth of her children, which should be a woman's crowning glory, became for Ekwefi mere physical agony devoid of promise. The naming ceremony after seven market weeks became an empty ritual. Her deepening despair found expression in the names she gave her children. One of them was a pathetic cry, Onwumbiko—'Death, I implore you.' But Death took no notice; Onwumbiko died in his fifteenth month. The next child was a girl, Ozoemena—'May it not happen again.' She died in her eleventh month, and two others after her. Ekwefi then became defiant and called her next child Onwuma—'Death may please himself.' And he did.

After the death of Ekwefi's second child, Okonkwo had gone to a medicine-man, who was also a diviner of the Afa Oracle,[9] to inquire what was amiss. This man told him that the child was an *ogbanje,* one of those wicked children who, when they died, entered their mothers' wombs to be born again.

"When your wife becomes pregnant again," he said, "let her not sleep in her hut. Let her go and stay with her people. In that way she will elude her wicked tormentor and break its evil cycle of birth and death."

Ekwefi did as she was asked. As soon as she became pregnant she went to live with her old mother in another village. It was there that her third child was born and circumcised on the eighth day. She did not return to Okonkwo's compound until three days before the naming ceremony. The child was called Onwumbiko.

Onwumbiko was not given proper burial when he died. Okonkwo had called in another medicine-man who was famous in the clan for his great knowledge about *ogbanje* children. His name was Okagbue Uyanwa. Okagbue was a very striking figure, tall, with a full beard and a bald head. He was light in complexion and his eyes were red and fiery. He always gnashed his teeth as he listened to those who came to consult him. He asked Okonkwo a few questions about the dead child. All the neighbours and relations who had come to mourn gathered round them.

---

9. One who communicates with the clients' ancestors by reading patterns made by objects (e.g., seeds, teeth, shells) thrown on a flat surface.

"On what market-day was it born?" he asked.

"*Oye*," replied Okonkwo.

"And it died this morning?"

Okonkwo said yes, and only then realised for the first time that the child had died on the same market-day as it had been born. The neighbours and relations also saw the coincidence and said among themselves that it was very significant.

"Where do you sleep with your wife, in your *obi* or in her own hut?" asked the medicine-man.

"In her hut."

"In future call her into your *obi*."

The medicine-man then ordered that there should be no mourning for the dead child. He brought out a sharp razor from the goatskin bag slung from his left shoulder and began to mutilate the child. Then he took it away to bury in the Evil Forest, holding it by the ankle and dragging it on the ground behind him. After such treatment it would think twice before coming again, unless it was one of the stubborn ones who returned, carrying the stamp of their mutilation—a missing finger or perhaps a dark line where the medicine-man's razor had cut them.

By the time Onwumbiko died Ekwefi had become a very bitter woman. Her husband's first wife had already had three sons, all strong and healthy. When she had borne her third son in succession, Okonkwo had slaughtered a goat for her, as was the custom. Ekwefi had nothing but good wishes for her. But she had grown so bitter about her own *chi* that she could not rejoice with others over their good fortune. And so, on the day that Nwoye's mother celebrated the birth of her three sons with feasting and music, Ekwefi was the only person in the happy company who went about with a cloud on her brow. Her husband's wife took this for malevolence, as husband's wives were wont to. How could she know that Ekwefi's bitterness did not flow outwards to others but inwards into her own soul; that she did not blame others for their good fortune but her own evil *chi* who denied her any?

At last Ezinma was born, and although ailing she seemed determined to live. At first Ekwefi accepted her, as she had accepted others—with listless resignation. But when she lived on to her fourth, fifth and sixth years, love returned once more to her mother, and, with love, anxiety. She determined to nurse her child to health, and she put all her being into it. She was rewarded by occasional spells of health during which Ezinma bubbled with energy like fresh palm-wine. At such times she seemed beyond danger. But all of a sudden she would go down again. Everybody knew she was an *ogbanje*. These sudden bouts of sickness and health were typical of her kind. But she had lived so long that perhaps she had decided to stay. Some of them did become tired of their evil rounds of birth and death, or took pity on their mothers, and stayed. Ekwefi believed deep inside her that Ezinma had come to stay. She believed because it was that faith alone that gave her own life any kind of meaning. And this faith had been strengthened when a year or so ago a medicine-man had dug up Ezinma's *iyi-uwa*.[1] Everyone knew then that she would live because her bond with the world of *ogbanje* had been broken. Ekwefi was reassured. But such was her anxiety for her daughter that she could not rid herself completely of her fear. And although she believed that the *iyi-uwa* which had been

---

1. Stone that forms the link between an *ogbanje* child and the spirit world. If the *iyi-uwa* is found and destroyed, the cycle is broken and the child will not die.

dug up was genuine, she could not ignore the fact that some really evil children sometimes misled people into digging up a specious one.

But Ezinma's *iyi-uwa* had looked real enough. It was a smooth pebble wrapped in a dirty rag. The man who dug it up was the same Okagbue who was famous in all the clan for his knowledge in these matters. Ezinma had not wanted to co-operate with him at first. But that was only to be expected. No *ogbanje* would yield her secrets easily, and most of them never did because they died too young—before they could be asked questions.

"Where did you bury your *iyi-uwa*?" Okagbue had asked Ezinma. She was nine then and was just recovering from a serious illness.

"What is *iyi-uwa*?" she asked in return.

"You know what it is. You buried it in the ground somewhere so that you can die and return again to torment your mother."

Ezinma looked at her mother, whose eyes, sad and pleading, were fixed on her.

"Answer the question at once," roared Okonkwo, who stood beside her. All the family were there and some of the neighbours too.

"Leave her to me," the medicine-man told Okonkwo in a cool, confident voice. He turned again to Ezinma. "Where did you bury your *iyi-uwa*?"

"Where they bury children," she replied, and the quiet spectators murmured to themselves.

"Come along then and show me the spot," said the medicine-man.

The crowd set out with Ezinma leading the way and Okagbue following closely behind her. Okonkwo came next and Ekwefi followed him. When she came to the main road, Ezinma turned left as if she was going to the stream.

"But you said it was where they bury children?" asked the medicine-man.

"No," said Ezinma, whose feeling of importance was manifest in her sprightly walk. She sometimes broke into a run and stopped again suddenly. The crowd followed her silently. Women and children returning from the stream with pots of water on their heads wondered what was happening until they saw Okagbue and guessed that it must be something to do with *ogbanje*. And they all knew Ekwefi and her daughter very well.

When she got to the big udala tree Ezinma turned left into the bush, and the crowd followed her. Because of her size she made her way through trees and creepers more quickly than her followers. The bush was alive with the tread of feet on dry leaves and sticks and the moving aside of tree branches. Ezinma went deeper and deeper and the crowd went with her. Then she suddenly turned round and began to walk back to the road. Everybody stood to let her pass and then filed after her.

"If you bring us all this way for nothing I shall beat sense into you," Okonkwo threatened.

"I have told you to let her alone. I know how to deal with them," said Okagbue.

Ezinma led the way back to the road, looked left and right and turned right. And so they arrived home again.

"Where did you bury your *iyi-uwa*?" asked Okagbue when Ezinma finally stopped outside her father's *obi*. Okagbue's voice was unchanged. It was quiet and confident.

"It is near that orange tree," Ezinma said.

"And why did you not say so, you wicked daughter of Akalogoli?" Okonkwo swore furiously. The medicine-man ignored him.

"Come and show me the exact spot," he said quietly to Ezinma.

"It is here," she said when they got to the tree.

"Point at the spot with your finger," said Okagbue.

"It is here," said Ezinma touching the ground with her finger. Okonkwo stood by, rumbling like thunder in the rainy season.

"Bring me a hoe," said Okagbue.

When Ekwefi brought the hoe, he had already put aside his goatskin bag and his big cloth and was in his underwear, a long and thin strip of cloth wound round the waist like a belt and then passed between the legs to be fastened to the belt behind. He immediately set to work digging a pit where Ezinma had indicated. The neighbours sat around watching the pit becoming deeper and deeper. The dark top-soil soon gave way to the bright-red earth with which women scrubbed the floor and walls of huts. Okagbue worked tirelessly and in silence, his back shining with perspiration. Okonkwo stood by the pit. He asked Okagbue to come up and rest while he took a hand. But Okagbue said he was not tired yet.

Ekwefi went into her hut to cook yams. Her husband had brought out more yams than usual because the medicine-man had to be fed. Ezinma went with her and helped in preparing the vegetables.

"There is too much green vegetable," she said.

"Don't you see the pot is full of yams?" Ekwefi asked.

"And you know how leaves become smaller after cooking."

"Yes," said Ezinma, "that was why the snake-lizard killed his mother."

"Very true," said Ekwefi.

"He gave his mother seven baskets of vegetables to cook and in the end there were only three. And so he killed her," said Ezinma.

"That is not the end of the story."

"Oho," said Ezinma. "I remember now. He brought another seven baskets and cooked them himself. And there were again only three. So he killed himself too."

Outside the *obi* Okagbue and Okonkwo were digging the pit to find where Ezinma had buried her *iyi-uwa*. Neighbours sat around, watching. The pit was now so deep that they no longer saw the digger. They only saw the red earth he threw up mounting higher and higher. Okonkwo's son, Nwoye, stood near the edge of the pit because he wanted to take in all that happened.

Okagbue had again taken over the digging from Okonkwo. He worked, as usual, in silence. The neighbours and Okonkwo's wives were now talking. The children had lost interest and were playing.

Suddenly Okagbue sprang to the surface with the agility of a leopard.

"It is very near now," he said. "I have felt it."

There was immediate excitement and those who were sitting jumped to their feet.

"Call your wife and child," he said to Okonkwo. But Ekwefi and Ezinma had heard the noise and run out to see what it was.

Okagbue went back into the pit, which was now surrounded by spectators. After a few more hoe-fuls of earth he struck the *iyi-uwa*. He raised it carefully with the hoe and threw it to the surface. Some women ran away in fear when it was thrown. But they soon returned and everyone was gazing at the rag from a reasonable distance. Okagbue emerged and without saying a word or even looking at the spectators he went to his goatskin bag, took out two leaves and began to chew them. When he had swallowed them, he took up the rag with his left hand and began to untie it. And then the smooth, shiny pebble fell out. He picked it up.

"Is this yours?" he asked Ezinma.

"Yes," she replied. All the women shouted with joy because Ekwefi's troubles were at last ended.

All this had happened more than a year ago and Ezinma had not been ill since. And then suddenly she had begun to shiver in the night. Ekwefi brought her to the fireplace, spread her mat on the floor and built a fire. But she had got worse and worse. As she knelt by her, feeling with her palm the wet, burning forehead, she prayed a thousand times. Although her husband's wives were saying that it was nothing more than *iba*, she did not hear them.

Okonkwo returned from the bush carrying on his left shoulder a large bundle of grasses and leaves, roots and barks of medicinal trees and shrubs. He went into Ekwefi's hut, put down his load and sat down.

"Get me a pot," he said, "and leave the child alone."

Ekwefi went to bring the pot and Okonkwo selected the best from his bundle, in their due proportions, and cut them up. He put them in the pot and Ekwefi poured in some water.

"Is that enough?" she asked when she had poured in about half of the water in the bowl.

"A little more . . . I said a *little*. Are you deaf?" Okonkwo roared at her.

She set the pot on the fire and Okonkwo took up his matchet to return to his *obi*.

"You must watch the pot carefully," he said as he went, "and don't allow it to boil over. If it does its power will be gone." He went away to his hut and Ekwefi began to tend the medicine pot almost as if it was itself a sick child. Her eyes went constantly from Ezinma to the boiling pot and back to Ezinma.

Okonkwo returned when he felt the medicine had cooked long enough. He looked it over and said it was done.

"Bring a low stool for Ezinma," he said, "and a thick mat."

He took down the pot from the fire and placed it in front of the stool. He then roused Ezinma and placed her on the stool, astride the steaming pot. The thick mat was thrown over both. Ezinma struggled to escape from the choking and overpowering steam, but she was held down. She started to cry.

When the mat was at last removed she was drenched in perspiration. Ekwefi mopped her with a piece of cloth and she lay down on a dry mat and was soon asleep.

CHAPTER TEN

Large crowds began to gather on the village *ilo* as soon as the edge had worn off the sun's heat and it was no longer painful on the body. Most communal ceremonies took place at that time of the day, so that even when it was said that a ceremony would begin "after the midday meal" everyone understood that it would begin a long time later, when the sun's heat had softened.

It was clear from the way the crowd stood or sat that the ceremony was for men. There were many women, but they looked on from the fringe like outsiders. The titled men and elders sat on their stools waiting for the trials to begin. In front of them was a row of stools on which nobody sat. There were nine of them. Two little groups of people stood at a respectable distance beyond the stools. They faced the elders. There were three men in one group and three men and one woman in the other. The woman was Mgbafo and the three men with her were her brothers. In the other group were her husband, Uzowulu, and his relatives. Mgbafo and her brothers were as still as statues into whose faces the artist has moulded defiance. Uzowulu and his relative, on the other hand, were whispering together. It looked like whispering, but they were really talking at the top of their voices. Everybody in the crowd was talking. It was like the market. From a distance the noise was a deep rumble carried by the wind.

An iron gong sounded, setting up a wave of expectation in the crowd. Everyone looked in the direction of the *egwugwu*[2] house. *Gome, gome, gome, gome* went the gong, and a powerful flute blew a high-pitched blast. Then came the voices of the *egwugwu*, guttural and awesome. The wave struck the women and children and there was a backward stampede. But it was momentary. They were already far enough where they stood and there was room for running away if any of the *egwugwu* should go towards them.

The drum sounded again and the flute blew. The *egwugwu* house was now a pandemonium of quavering voices: *Aru oyim de de de dei!*[3] filled the air as the spirits of the ancestors, just emerged from the earth, greeted themselves in their esoteric language. The *egwugwu* house into which they emerged faced the forest, away from the crowd, who saw only its back with the many-coloured patterns and drawings done by specially chosen women at regular intervals. These women never saw the inside of the hut. No woman ever did. They scrubbed and painted the outside walls under the supervision of men. If they imagined what was inside, they kept their imagination to themselves. No woman ever asked questions about the most powerful and the most secret cult in the clan.

Aru oyim de de de dei! flew around the dark, closed hut like tongues of fire. The ancestral spirits of the clan were abroad. The metal gong beat continuously now and the flute, shrill and powerful, floated on the chaos.

And then the *egwugwu* appeared. The women and children sent up a great shout and took to their heels. It was instinctive. A woman fled as soon as an *egwugwu* came in sight. And when, as on that day, nine of the greatest masked spirits in the clan came out together it was a terrifying spectacle. Even Mgbafo took to her heels and had to be restrained by her brothers.

Each of the nine *egwugwu* represented a village of the clan. Their leader was called Evil Forest. Smoke poured out of his head.

The nine villages of Umuofia had grown out of the nine sons of the first father of the clan. Evil Forest represented the village of Umueru, or the children of Eru, who was the eldest of the nine sons.

"*Umuofia kwenu!*" shouted the leading *egwugwu*, pushing the air with his raffia arms. The elders of the clan replied, "*Yaa!*"

"*Umuofia kwenu!*"

"*Yaa!*"

"*Umuofia kwenu!*"

"*Yaa!*"

Evil Forest then thrust the pointed end of his rattling staff into the earth.

2. Here the term refers to the village's highest spiritual and judicial authority, prominent men who, after putting on elaborate ceremonial costumes, embody the village's ancestral spirits.
3. Body of my friend, greetings!

And it began to shake and rattle, like something agitating with a metallic life. He took the first of the empty stools and the eight other *egwugwu* began to sit in order of seniority after him.

Okonkwo's wives, and perhaps other women as well, might have noticed that the second *egwugwu* had the springy walk of Okonkwo. And they might also have noticed that Okonkwo was not among the titled men and elders who sat behind the row of *egwugwu*. But if they thought these things they kept them within themselves. The *egwugwu* with the springy walk was one of the dead fathers of the clan. He looked terrible with the smoked raffia body, a huge wooden face painted white except for the round hollow eyes and the charred teeth that were as big as a man's fingers. On his head were two powerful horns.

When all the *egwugwu* had sat down and the sound of the many tiny bells and rattles on their bodies had subsided, Evil Forest addressed the two groups of people facing them.

"Uzowulu's body, I salute you," he said. Spirits always addressed humans as 'bodies'. Uzowulu bent down and touched the earth with his right hand as a sign of submission.

"Our father, my hand has touched the ground," he said.

"Uzowulu's body, do you know me?" asked the spirit.

"How can I know you, father? You are beyond our knowledge."

Evil Forest then turned to the other group and addressed the eldest of the three brothers.

"The body of Odukwe, I greet you," he said, and Odukwe bent down and touched the earth. The hearing then began.

Uzowulu stepped forward and presented his case.

"That woman standing there is my wife, Mgbafo. I married her with my money and my yams. I do not owe my in-laws anything. I owe them no yams. I owe them no coco-yams. One morning three of them came to my house, beat me up and took my wife and children away. This happened in the rainy season. I have waited in vain for my wife to return. At last I went to my in-laws and said to them, 'You have taken back your sister. I did not send her away. You yourselves took her. The law of the clan is that you should return her bride-price.' But my wife's brothers said they had nothing to tell me. So I have brought the matter to the fathers of the clan. My case is finished. I salute you."

"Your words are good," said the leader of the *egwugwu*. "Let us hear Odukwe. His words may also be good."

Odukwe was short and thick-set. He stepped forward, saluted the spirits and began his story.

"My in-law has told you that we went to his house, beat him up and took our sister and her children away. All that is true. He told you that he came to take back her bride-price and we refused to give it him. That also is true. My in-law, Uzowulu, is a beast. My sister lived with him for nine years. During those years no single day passed in the sky without his beating the woman. We have tried to settle their quarrels time without number and on each occasion Uzowulu was guilty——"

"It is a lie!" Uzowulu shouted.

"Two years ago," continued Odukwe, "when she was pregnant, he beat her until she miscarried."

"It is a lie. She miscarried after she had gone to sleep with her lover."

"Uzowulu's body, I salute you," said Evil Forest, silencing him. "What kind of lover sleeps with a pregnant woman?" There was a loud murmur of approbation from the crowd. Odukwe continued:

"Last year when my sister was recovering from an illness, he beat her again so that if the neighbours had not gone in to save her she would have been killed. We heard of it, and did as you have been told. The law of Umuofia is that if a woman runs away from her husband her bride-price is returned. But in this case she ran away to save her life. Her two children belong to Uzowulu. We do not dispute it, but they are too young to leave their mother. If, on the other hand, Uzowulu should recover from his madness and come in the proper way to beg his wife to return she will do so on the understanding that if he ever beats her again we shall cut off his genitals for him."

The crowd roared with laughter. Evil Forest rose to his feet and order was immediately restored. A steady cloud of smoke rose from his head. He sat down again and called two witnesses. They were both Uzowulu's neighbours, and they agreed about the beating. Evil Forest then stood up, pulled out his staff and thrust it into the earth again. He ran a few steps in the direction of the women; they all fled in terror, only to return to their places almost immediately. The nine *egwugwu* then went away to consult together in their house. They were silent for a long time. Then the metal gong sounded and the flute was blown. The *egwugwu* had emerged once again from their underground home. They saluted one another and then reappeared on the *ilo*.

"*Umuofia kwenu!*" roared Evil Forest, facing the elders and grandees of the clan.

"*Yaa!*" replied the thunderous crowd; then silence descended from the sky and swallowed the noise.

Evil Forest began to speak and all the while he spoke everyone was silent. The eight other *egwugwu* were as still as statues.

"We have heard both sides of the case," said Evil Forest. "Our duty is not to blame this man or to praise that, but to settle the dispute." He turned to Uzowulu's group and allowed a short pause.

"Uzowulu's body, I salute you," he said.

"Our father, my hand has touched the ground," replied Uzowulu, touching the earth.

"Uzowulu's body, do you know me?"

"How can I know you, father? You are beyond our knowledge," Uzowulu replied.

"I am Evil Forest. I kill a man on the day that his life is sweetest to him."

"That is true," replied Uzowulu.

"Go to your in-laws with a pot of wine and beg your wife to return to you. It is not bravery when a man fights with a woman." He turned to Odukwe, and allowed a brief pause.

"Odukwe's body, I greet you," he said.

"My hand is on the ground," replied Odukwe.

"Do you know me?"

"No man can know you," replied Odukwe.

"I am Evil Forest, I am Dry-meat-that-fills-the-mouth, I am Fire-that-burns-without-faggots. If your in-law brings wine to you, let your sister go with him. I salute you." He pulled his staff from the hard earth and thrust it back.

"*Umuofia kwenu!*" he roared, and the crowd answered.

"I don't know why such a trifle should come before the *egwugwu*," said one elder to another.

"Don't you know what kind of man Uzowulu is? He will not listen to any other decision," replied the other.

As they spoke two other groups of people had replaced the first before the *egwugwu*, and a great land case began.

CHAPTER ELEVEN

The night was impenetrably dark. The moon had been rising later and later every night until now it was seen only at dawn. And whenever the moon forsook evening and rose at cock-crow the nights were as black as charcoal.

Ezinma and her mother sat on a mat on the floor after their supper of yam foo-foo and bitter-leaf soup. A palm-oil lamp gave out yellowish light. Without it, it would have been impossible to eat; one could not have known where one's mouth was in the darkness of that night. There was an oil lamp in all the four huts on Okonkwo's compound, and each hut seen from the others looked like a soft eye of yellow half-light set in the solid massiveness of night.

The world was silent except for the shrill cry of insects, which was part of the night, and the sound of wooden mortar and pestle as Nwayieke pounded her foo-foo. Nwayieke lived four compounds away, and she was notorious for her late cooking. Every woman in the neighbourhood knew the sound of Nwayieke's mortar and pestle. It was also part of the night.

Okonkwo had eaten from his wives' dishes and was now reclining with his back against the wall. He searched his bag and brought out his snuff-bottle. He turned it on to his left palm, but nothing came out. He hit the bottle against his knee to shake up the tobacco. That was always the trouble with Okeke's snuff. It very quickly went damp, and there was too much saltpetre in it. Okonkwo had not bought snuff from him for a long time. Idigo was the man who knew how to grind good snuff. But he had recently fallen ill.

Low voices, broken now and again by singing, reached Okonkwo from his wives' huts as each woman and her children told folk stories. Ekwefi and her daughter, Ezinma, sat on a mat on the floor. It was Ekwefi's turn to tell a story.

"Once upon a time," she began, "all the birds were invited to a feast in the sky. They were very happy and began to prepare themselves for the great day. They painted their bodies with red cam wood and drew beautiful patterns on them with *uli*.

"Tortoise saw all these preparations and soon discovered what it all meant. Nothing that happened in the world of the animals ever escaped his notice; he was full of cunning. As soon as he heard of the great feast in the sky his throat began to itch at the very thought. There was a famine in those days and Tortoise had not eaten a good meal for two moons. His body rattled like a piece of dry stick in his empty shell. So he began to plan how he would go to the sky."

"But he had no wings," said Ezinma.

"Be patient," replied her mother. "That is the story. Tortoise had no wings, but he went to the birds and asked to be allowed to go with them.

" 'We know you too well,' said the birds when they had heard him. 'You are full of cunning and you are ungrateful. If we allow you to come with us you will soon begin your mischief.'

" 'You do not know me,' said Tortoise. 'I am a changed man. I have learnt that a man who makes trouble for others is also making it for himself.'

"Tortoise had a sweet tongue, and within a short time all the birds agreed that he was a changed man, and they each gave him a feather, with which he made two wings.

"At last the great day came and Tortoise was the first to arrive at the meeting-place. When all the birds had gathered together, they set off in a body. Tortoise was very happy and voluble as he flew among the birds, and he was soon chosen as the man to speak for the party because he was a great orator.

" 'There is one important thing which we must not forget,' he said as they flew on their way. 'When people are invited to a great feast like this, they take new names for the occasion. Our hosts in the sky will expect us to honour this age-old custom.'

"None of the birds had heard of this custom but they knew that Tortoise, in spite of his failings in other directions, was a widely-travelled man who knew the customs of different peoples. And so they each took a new name. When they had all taken, Tortoise also took one. He was to be called *All of you*.

"At last the party arrived in the sky and their hosts were very happy to see them. Tortoise stood up in his many-coloured plumage and thanked them for their invitation. His speech was so eloquent that all the birds were glad they had brought him, and nodded their heads in approval of all he said. Their hosts took him as the king of the birds, especially as he looked somewhat different from the others.

"After kola nuts had been presented and eaten, the people of the sky set before their guests the most delectable dishes Tortoise had ever seen or dreamt of. The soup was brought out hot from the fire and in the very pot in which it had been cooked. It was full of meat and fish. Tortoise began to sniff aloud. There was pounded yam and also yam pottage cooked with palm-oil and fresh fish. There were also pots of palm-wine. When everything had been set before the guests, one of the people of the sky came forward and tasted a little from each pot. He then invited the birds to eat. But Tortoise jumped to his feet and asked: 'For whom have you prepared this feast?'

" 'For all of you,' replied the man.

"Tortoise turned to the birds and said: 'You remember that my name is *All of you*. The custom here is to serve the spokesman first and the others later. They will serve you when I have eaten.'

"He began to eat and the birds grumbled angrily. The people of the sky thought it must be their custom to leave all the food for their king. And so Tortoise ate the best part of the food and then drank two pots of palm-wine, so that he was full of food and drink and his body filled out in his shell.

"The birds gathered round to eat what was left and to peck at the bones he had thrown all about the floor. Some of them were too angry to eat. They chose to fly home on an empty stomach. But before they left each took back the feather he had lent to Tortoise. And there he stood in his hard shell full of food and wine but without any wings to fly home. He asked the birds to take a message for his wife, but they all refused. In the end Parrot, who had felt more angry than the others, suddenly changed his mind and agreed to take the message.

" 'Tell my wife,' said Tortoise, 'to bring out all the soft things in my house and cover the compound with them so that I can jump down from the sky without very great danger.'

"Parrot promised to deliver the message, and then flew away. But when he reached Tortoise's house he told his wife to bring out all the hard things in the house. And so she brought out her husband's hoes, matchets, spears, guns and even his cannon. Tortoise looked down from the sky and saw his wife bringing things out, but it was too far to see what they were. When all seemed ready he let himself go. He fell and fell and fell until he began to fear that he would never stop falling. And then like the sound of his cannon he crashed on the compound."

"Did he die?" asked Ezinma.

"No," replied Ekwefi. "His shell broke into pieces. But there was a great medicine-man in the neighbourhood. Tortoise's wife sent for him and he gathered all the bits of shell and stuck them together. That is why Tortoise's shell is not smooth."

"There is no song in the story," Ezinma pointed out.

"No," said Ekwefi. "I shall think of another one with a song. But it is your turn now."

"Once upon a time," Ezinma began, "Tortoise and Cat went to wrestle against Yams—no, that is not the beginning. Once upon a time there was a great famine in the land of animals. Everybody was lean except Cat, who was fat and whose body shone as if oil was rubbed on it . . ."

She broke off because at that very moment a loud and high-pitched voice broke the outer silence of the night. It was Chielo, the priestess of Agbala, prophesying. There was nothing new in that. Once in a while Chielo was possessed by the spirit of her god and she began to prophesy. But tonight she was addressing her prophecy and greetings to Okonkwo, and so everyone in his family listened. The folk stories stopped.

"Agbala do-o-o-o! Agbala ekeneo-o-o-o-o,"[4] came the voice like a sharp knife cutting through the night. "Okonkwo! Agbala ekene gio-o-o-o! Agbala cholu ifu ada ya Ezinmao-o-o-o!"[5]

At the mention of Ezinma's name Ekwefi jerked her head sharply like an animal that had sniffed death in the air. Her heart jumped painfully within her.

The priestess had now reached Okonkwo's compound and was talking with him outside his hut. She was saying again and again that Agbala wanted to see his daughter, Ezinma. Okonkwo pleaded with her to come back in the morning because Ezinma was now asleep. But Chielo ignored what he was trying to say and went on shouting that Agbala wanted to see his daughter. Her voice was as clear as metal, and Okonkwo's women and children heard from their huts all that she said. Okonkwo was still pleading that the girl had been ill of late and was asleep. Ekwefi quickly took her to their bedroom and placed her on their high bamboo bed.

The priestess suddenly screamed. "Beware, Okonkwo!" she warned. "Beware of exchanging words with Agbala. Does a man speak when a god speaks? Beware!"

She walked through Okonkwo's hut into the circular compound and went straight towards Ekwefi's hut. Okonkwo came after her.

4. Agbala wants something! Agbala greets.
5. Agbala greets you! Agbala wants to see his daughter Ezinma!

"Ekwefi," she called, "Agbala greets you. Where is my daughter, Ezinma? Agbala wants to see her."

Ekwefi came out from her hut carrying her oil lamp in her left hand. There was a light wind blowing, so she cupped her right hand to shelter the flame. Nwoye's mother, also carrying an oil lamp, emerged from her hut. Her children stood in the darkness outside their hut watching the strange event. Okonkwo's youngest wife also came out and joined the others.

"Where does Agbala want to see her?" Ekwefi asked.

"Where else but in his house in the hills and the caves?" replied the priestess.

"I will come with you, too," Ekwefi said firmly.

"*Tufia-a!*"[6] the priestess cursed, her voice cracking like the angry bark of thunder in the dry season. "How dare you, woman, to go before the mighty Agbala of your own accord? Beware, woman, lest he strike you in his anger. Bring me my daughter."

Ekwefi went into her hut and came out again with Ezinma.

"Come, my daughter," said the priestess. "I shall carry you on my back. A baby on its mother's back does not know that the way is long."

Ezinma began to cry. She was used to Chielo calling her 'my daughter'. But it was a different Chielo she now saw in the yellow half-light.

"Don't cry, my daughter," said the priestess, "lest Agbala be angry with you."

"Don't cry," said Ekwefi, "she will bring you back very soon. I shall give you some fish to eat." She went into the hut again and brought down the smoke-black basket in which she kept her dried fish and other ingredients for cooking soup. She broke a piece in two and gave it to Ezinma, who clung to her.

"Don't be afraid," said Ekwefi, stroking her head, which was shaved in places, leaving a regular pattern of hair. They went outside again. The priestess bent down on one knee and Ezinma climbed on her back, her left palm closed on her fish and her eyes gleaming with tears.

"*Agbala do-o-o-o! Agbala ekeneo-o-o-o,*" Chielo began once again to chant greetings to her god. She turned round sharply and walked through Okonkwo's hut, bending very low at the eaves. Ezinma was crying loudly now, calling on her mother. The two voices disappeared into the thick darkness.

A strange and sudden weakness descended on Ekwefi as she stood gazing in the direction of the voices like a hen whose only chick has been carried away by a kite. Ezinma's voice soon faded away and only Chielo was heard moving farther and farther into the distance.

"Why do you stand there as though she had been kidnapped?" asked Okonkwo as he went back to his hut.

"She will bring her back soon," Nwoye's mother said.

But Ekwefi did not hear these consolations. She stood for a while, and then, all of a sudden, made up her mind. She hurried through Okonkwo's hut and went outside.

"Where are you going?" he asked.

"I am following Chielo," she replied and disappeared in the darkness. Okonkwo cleared his throat, and brought out his snuff-bottle from the goatskin bag by his side.

---

6. A curse in words meaning "spitting" or "clearing out," often accompanied by spitting.

The priestess's voice was already growing faint in the distance. Ekwefi hurried to the main footpath and turned left in the direction of the voice. Her eyes were useless to her in the darkness. But she picked her way easily on the sandy footpath hedged on either side by branches and damp leaves. She began to run, holding her breasts with her hands to stop them flapping noisily against her body. She hit her left foot against an outcropped root, and terror seized her. It was an ill omen. She ran faster. But Chielo's voice was still a long way away. Had she been running too? How could she go so fast with Ezinma on her back? Although the night was cool, Ekwefi was beginning to feel hot from her running. She continually ran into the luxuriant weeds and creepers that walled in the path. Once she tripped up and fell. Only then did she realise, with a start, that Chielo had stopped her chanting. Her heart beat violently and she stood still. Then Chielo's renewed outburst came from only a few paces ahead. But Ekwefi could not see her. She shut her eyes for a while and opened them again in an effort to see. But it was useless. She could not see beyond her nose.

There were no stars in the sky because there was a rain-cloud. Fireflies went about with their tiny green lamps, which only made the darkness more profound. Between Chielo's outbursts the night was alive with the shrill tremor of forest insects woven into the darkness.

"*Agbala do-o-o-o!* . . . *Agbala ekeneo-o-o-o!* . . ." Ekwefi trudged behind, neither getting too near nor keeping too far back. She thought they must be going towards the sacred cave. Now that she walked slowly she had time to think. What would she do when they got to the cave? She would not dare to enter. She would wait at the mouth, all alone in that fearful place. She thought of all the terrors of the night. She remembered the night, long ago, when she had seen *Ogbu-agali-odu*, one of those evil essences loosed upon the world by the potent 'medicines' which the tribe had made in the distant past against its enemies but had now forgotten how to control. Ekwefi had been returning from the stream with her mother on a dark night like this when they saw its glow as it flew in their direction. They had thrown down their water-pots and lain by the roadside expecting the sinister light to descend on them and kill them. That was the only time Ekwefi ever saw *Ogbu-agali-odu*. But although it had happened so long ago, her blood still ran cold whenever she remembered that night.

The priestess's voice came at longer intervals now, but its vigour was undiminished. The air was cool and damp with dew. Ezinma sneezed. Ekwefi muttered, "Life to you." At the same time the priestess also said, "Life to you, my daughter." Ezinma's voice from the darkness warmed her mother's heart. She trudged slowly along.

And then the priestess screamed. "Somebody is walking behind me!" she said. "Whether you are spirit or man, may Agbala shave your head with a blunt razor! May he twist your neck until you see your heels!"

Ekwefi stood rooted to the spot. One mind said to her: 'Woman, go home before Agbala does you harm.' But she could not. She stood until Chielo had increased the distance between them and she began to follow again. She had already walked so long that she began to feel a slight numbness in the limbs and in the head. Then it occurred to her that they could not have been heading for the cave. They must have by-passed it long ago; they must be going towards Umuachi, the farthest village in the clan. Chielo's voice now came after long intervals.

It seemed to Ekwefi that the night had become a little lighter. The cloud had lifted and a few stars were out. The moon must be preparing to rise, its sullenness over. When the moon rose late in the night, people said it was refusing food, as a sullen husband refuses his wife's food when they have quarrelled.

"*Agbala do-o-o-o! Umuachi! Agbala ekene unuo-o-o!*" It was just as Ekwefi had thought. The priestess was now saluting the village of Umuachi. It was unbelievable, the distance they had covered. As they emerged into the open village from the narrow forest track the darkness was softened and it became possible to see the vague shape of trees. Ekwefi screwed her eyes up in an effort to see her daughter and the priestess, but whenever she thought she saw their shape it immediately dissolved like a melting lump of darkness. She walked numbly along.

Chielo's voice was now rising continuously, as when she first set out. Ekwefi had a feeling of spacious openness, and she guessed they must be on the village *ilo*, or playground. And she realised too with something like a jerk that Chielo was no longer moving forward. She was, in fact, returning. Ekwefi quickly moved away from her line of retreat. Chielo passed by, and they began to go back the way they had come.

It was a long and weary journey and Ekwefi felt like a sleep-walker most of the way. The moon was definitely rising, and although it had not yet appeared on the sky its light had already melted down the darkness. Ekwefi could now discern the figure of the priestess and her burden. She slowed down her pace so as to increase the distance between them. She was afraid of what might happen if Chielo suddenly turned round and saw her.

She had prayed for the moon to rise. But now she found the half-light of the incipient moon more terrifying than darkness. The world was now peopled with vague, fantastic figures that dissolved under her steady gaze and then formed again in new shapes. At one stage Ekwefi was so afraid that she nearly called out to Chielo for companionship and human sympathy. What she had seen was the shape of a man climbing a palm tree, his head pointing to the earth and his legs skywards. But at that very moment Chielo's voice rose again in her possessed chanting, and Ekwefi recoiled, because there was no humanity there. It was not the same Chielo who sat with her in the market and sometimes bought bean-cakes for Ezinma, whom she called her daughter. It was a different woman—the priestess of Agbala, the Oracle of the Hills and Caves. Ekwefi trudged along between two fears. The sound of her benumbed steps seemed to come from some other person walking behind her. Her arms were folded across her bare breasts. Dew fell heavily and the air was cold. She could no longer think, not even about the terrors of night. She just jogged along in a half-sleep, only waking to full life when Chielo sang.

At last they took a turning and began to head for the caves. From then on, Chielo never ceased in her chanting. She greeted her god in a multitude of names—the owner of the future, the messenger of earth, the god who cut a man down when his life was sweetest to him. Ekwefi was also awakened and her benumbed fears revived.

The moon was now up and she could see Chielo and Ezinma clearly. How a woman could carry a child of that size so easily and for so long was a miracle. But Ekwefi was not thinking about that. Chielo was not a woman that night.

"Agbala do-o-o-o! Agbala ekeno-o-o-o! Chi negbu madu ubosi ndu ya nato ya uto daluo-o-o! . . ."[7]

Ekwefi could already see the hills looming in the moonlight. They formed a circular ring with a break at one point through which the foot-track led to the centre of the circle.

As soon as the priestess stepped into this ring of hills her voice was not only doubled in strength but was thrown back on all sides. It was indeed the shrine of a great god. Ekwefi picked her way carefully and quietly. She was already beginning to doubt the wisdom of her coming. Nothing would happen to Ezinma, she thought. And if anything happened to her could she stop it? She would not dare to enter the underground caves. Her coming was quite useless, she thought.

As these things went through her mind she did not realise how close they were to the cave mouth. And so when the priestess with Ezinma on her back disappeared through a hole hardly big enough to pass a hen, Ekwefi broke into a run as though to stop them. As she stood gazing at the circular darkness which had swallowed them, tears gushed from her eyes, and she swore within her that if she heard Ezinma cry she would rush into the cave to defend her against all the gods in the world. She would die with her.

Having sworn that oath, she sat down on a stony ledge and waited. Her fear had vanished. She could hear the priestess's voice, all its metal taken out of it by the vast emptiness of the cave. She buried her face in her lap and waited.

She did not know how long she waited. It must have been a very long time. Her back was turned on the footpath that led out of the hills. She must have heard a noise behind her and turned round sharply. A man stood there with a matchet in his hand. Ekwefi uttered a scream and sprang to her feet.

"Don't be foolish," said Okonkwo's voice. "I thought you were going into the shrine with Chielo," he mocked.

Ekwefi did not answer. Tears of gratitude filled her eyes. She knew her daughter was safe.

"Go home and sleep," said Okonkwo. "I shall wait here."

"I shall wait too. It is almost dawn. The first cock has crowed."

As they stood there together, Ekwefi's mind went back to the days when they were young. She had married Anene because Okonkwo was too poor then to marry. Two years after her marriage to Anene she could bear it no longer and she ran away to Okonkwo. It had been early in the morning. The moon was shining. She was going to the stream to fetch water. Okonkwo's house was on the way to the stream. She went in and knocked at his door and he came out. Even in those days he was not a man of many words. He just carried her into his bed and in the darkness began to feel around her waist for the loose end of her cloth.

CHAPTER TWELVE

On the following morning the entire neighbourhood wore a festive air because Okonkwo's friend, Obierika, was celebrating his daughter's *uri*. It was the day on which her suitor (having already paid the greater part of her bride-price) would bring palm-wine not only to her parents and immediate relatives but to the wide and extensive group of kinsmen called *umunna*. Everybody had been invited—men, women and children. But it was really a

---

7. Agbala wants something! Agbala greets! God who kills a man on the day his life is so pleasant he give thanks! . . .

woman's ceremony and the central figures were the bride and her mother.

As soon as day broke, breakfast was hastily eaten and women and children began to gather at Obierika's compound to help the bride's mother in her difficult but happy task of cooking for a whole village.

Okonkwo's family was astir like any other family in the neighbourhood. Nwoye's mother and Okonkwo's youngest wife were ready to set out for Obierika's compound with all their children. Nwoye's mother carried a basket of coco-yams, a cake of salt and smoked fish which she would present to Obierika's wife. Okonkwo's youngest wife, Ojiugo, also had a basket of plantains and coco-yams and a small pot of palm-oil. Their children carried pots of water.

Ekwefi was tired and sleepy from the exhausting experiences of the previous night. It was not very long since they had returned. The priestess, with Ezinma sleeping on her back, had crawled out of the shrine on her belly like a snake. She had not as much as looked at Okonkwo and Ekwefi or shown any surprise at finding them at the mouth of the cave. She looked straight ahead of her and walked back to the village. Okonkwo and his wife followed at a respectful distance. They thought the priestess might be going to her house, but she went to Okonkwo's compound, passed through his *obi* and into Ekwefi's hut and walked into her bedroom. She placed Ezinma carefully on the bed and went away without saying a word to anybody.

Ezinma was still sleeping when everyone else was astir, and Ekwefi asked Nwoye's mother and Ojiugo to explain to Obierika's wife that she would be late. She had got ready her basket of coco-yams and fish, but she must wait for Ezinma to wake.

"You need some sleep yourself," said Nwoye's mother. "You look very tired."

As they spoke Ezinma emerged from the hut, rubbing her eyes and stretching her spare frame. She saw the other children with their water-pots and remembered that they were going to fetch water for Obierika's wife. She went back to the hut and brought her pot.

"Have you slept enough?" asked her mother.

"Yes," she replied. "Let us go."

"Not before you have had your breakfast," said Ekwefi. And she went into her hut to warm the vegetable soup she had cooked last night.

"We shall be going," said Nwoye's mother. "I will tell Obierika's wife that you are coming later." And so they all went to help Obierika's wife—Nwoye's mother with her four children and Ojiugo with her two.

As they trooped through Okonkwo's *obi* he asked: "Who will prepare my afternoon meal?"

"I shall return to do it," said Ojiugo.

Okonkwo was also feeling tired and sleepy, for although nobody else knew it, he had not slept at all last night. He had felt very anxious but did not show it. When Ekwefi had followed the priestess, he had allowed what he regarded as a reasonable and manly interval to pass and then gone with his matchet to the shrine, where he thought they must be. It was only when he had got there that it had occurred to him that the priestess might have chosen to go round the villages first. Okonkwo had returned home and sat waiting. When he thought he had waited long enough he again returned to the shrine. But the Hills and the Caves were as silent as death. It was only on his fourth trip that he had found Ekwefi, and by then he had become gravely worried.

Obierika's compound was as busy as an ant-hill. Temporary cooking tripods were erected on every available space by bringing together three blocks of sun-dried earth and making a fire in their midst. Cooking pots went up and down the tripods, and foo-foo was pounded in a hundred wooden mortars. Some of the women cooked the yams and the cassava, and others prepared vegetable soup. Young men pounded the foo-foo or split firewood. The children made endless trips to the stream.

Three young men helped Obierika to slaughter the two goats with which the soup was made. They were very fat goats, but the fattest of all was tethered to a peg near the wall of the compound. It was as big as a small cow. Obierika had sent one of his relatives all the way to Umuike to buy that goat. It was the one he would present alive to his in-laws.

"The market of Umuike is a wonderful place," said the young man who had been sent by Obierika to buy the giant goat. "There are so many people on it that if you threw up a grain of sand it would not find a way to fall to earth again."

"It is the result of a great medicine," said Obierika. "The people of Umuike wanted their market to grow and swallow up the markets of their neighbours. So they made a powerful medicine. Every market-day, before the first cock-crow, this medicine stands on the market-ground in the shape of an old woman with a fan. With this magic fan she beckons to the market all the neighbouring clans. She beckons in front of her and behind her, to her right and to her left."

"And so everybody comes," said another man, "honest men and thieves. They can steal your cloth from off your waist in that market."

"Yes," said Obierika. "I warned Nwankwo to keep a sharp eye and a sharp ear. There was once a man who went to sell a goat. He led it on a thick rope which he tied round his wrist. But as he walked through the market he realised that people were pointing at him as they do to a madman. He could not understand it until he looked back and saw that what he led at the end of the tether was not a goat but a heavy log of wood."

"Do you think a thief can do that kind of thing singlehanded?" asked Nwankwo.

"No," said Obierika. "They use medicine."

When they had cut the goats' throats and collected the blood in a bowl, they held them over an open fire to burn off the hair, and the smell of burning hair blended with the smell of cooking. Then they washed them and cut them up for the women who prepared the soup.

All this ant-hill activity was going smoothly when a sudden interruption came. It was a cry in the distance: *Oji odu achu ijiji-o-o!* (*The one that uses its tail to drive flies away!*) Every woman immediately abandoned whatever she was doing and rushed out in the direction of the cry.

"We cannot all rush out like that, leaving what we are cooking to burn in the fire," shouted Chielo, the priestess. "Three or four of us should stay behind."

"It is true," said another woman. "We will allow three or four women to stay behind."

Five women stayed behind to look after the cooking-pots, and all the rest rushed away to see the cow that had been let loose. When they saw it they drove it back to its owner, who at once paid the heavy fine which the village imposed on anyone whose cow was let loose on his neighbours' crops. When the women had exacted the penalty they checked among themselves to see if any woman had failed to come out when the cry had been raised.

"Where is Mgbogo?" asked one of them.

"She is ill in bed," said Mgbogo's next-door neighbour. "She has *iba*."

"The only other person is Udenkwo," said another woman, "and her child is not twenty-eight days yet."

Those women whom Obierika's wife had not asked to help her with the cooking returned to their homes, and the rest went back, in a body, to Obierika's compound.

"Whose cow was it?" asked the women who had been allowed to stay behind.

"It was my husband's," said Ezelagbo. "One of the young children had opened the gate of the cow-shed."

Early in the afternoon the first two pots of palm-wine arrived from Obierika's in-laws. They were duly presented to the women, who drank a cup or two each, to help them in their cooking. Some of it also went to the bride and her attendant maidens, who were putting the last delicate touches of razor to her coiffure and cam wood on her smooth skin.

When the heat of the sun began to soften, Obierika's son, Maduka, took a long broom and swept the ground in front of his father's *obi*. And as if they had been waiting for that, Obierika's relatives and friends began to arrive, every man with his goatskin bag hung on one shoulder and a rolled goatskin mat under his arm. Some of them were accompanied by their sons bearing carved wooden stools. Okonkwo was one of them. They sat in a half circle and began to talk of many things. It would not be long before the suitors came.

Okonkwo brought out his snuff-bottle and offered it to Ogbuefi Ezenwa, who sat next to him. Ezenwa[8] took it, tapped it on his knee-cap, rubbed his left palm on his body to dry it before tipping a little snuff into it. His actions were deliberate, and he spoke as he performed them:

"I hope our in-laws will bring many pots of wine. Although they come from a village that is known for being close-fisted, they ought to know that Akueke is the bride for a king."

"They dare not bring fewer than thirty pots," said Okonkwo. "I shall tell them my mind if they do."

At that moment Obierika's son, Maduka, led out the giant goat from the inner compound, for his father's relatives to see. They all admired it and said that that was the way things should be done. The goat was then led back to the inner compound.

Very soon after, the in-laws began to arrive. Young men and boys in single file, each carrying a pot of wine, came first. Obierika's relatives counted the pots as they came in. Twenty, twenty-five. There was a long break, and the hosts looked at each other as if to say, 'I told you.' Then more pots came. Thirty, thirty-five, forty, forty-five. The hosts nodded in approval and seemed to say, 'Now they are behaving like men.' Altogether there were fifty pots of wine. After the pot-bearers came Ibe, the suitor, and the elders of his family. They sat in a half-moon, thus completing a circle with their hosts. The pots of wine stood in their midst. Then the bride, her mother and half a dozen other women and girls emerged from the inner compound, and went round the circle shaking hands with all. The bride's mother led the way, followed by the bride and the other women. The married women wore their best cloths and the girls wore red and black waist-beads and anklets of brass.

When the women retired, Obierika presented kola nuts to his in-laws. His

8. King from childhood (strong praise).

2674 / CHINUA ACHEBE

eldest brother broke the first one. "Life to all of us," he said as he broke it. "And let there be friendship between your family and ours."

The crowd answered: *"Ee-e-e!"*

"We are giving you our daughter today. She will be a good wife to you. She will bear you nine sons like the mother of our town."

"Ee-e-e!"

The oldest man in the camp of the visitors replied: "It will be good for you and it will be good for us."

"Ee-e-e!"

"This is not the first time my people have come to marry your daughter. My mother was one of you."

"Ee-e-e!"

"And this will not be the last, because you understand us and we understand you. You are a great family."

"Ee-e-e!"

"Prosperous men and great warriors." He looked in the direction of Okonkwo. "Your daughter will bear us sons like you."

"Ee-e-e!"

The kola was eaten and the drinking of palm-wine began. Groups of four or five men sat round with a pot in their midst. As the evening wore on, food was presented to the guests. There were huge bowls of foo-foo and steaming pots of soup. There were also pots of yam pottage. It was a great feast.

As night fell, burning torches were set on wooden tripods and the young men raised a song. The elders sat in a big circle and the singers went round singing each man's praise as they came before him. They had something to say for every man. Some were great farmers, some were orators who spoke for the clan; Okonkwo was the greatest wrestler and warrior alive. When they had gone round the circle they settled down in the centre, and girls came from the inner compound to dance. At first the bride was not among them. But when she finally appeared holding a cock in her right hand, a loud cheer rose from the crowd. All the other dancers made way for her. She presented the cock to the musicians and began to dance. Her brass anklets rattled as she danced and her body gleamed with cam wood in the soft yellow light. The musicians with their wood, clay and metal instruments went from song to song. And they were all gay. They sang the latest song in the village:

> *"If I hold her hand*
> *She says, 'Don't touch!'*
> *If I hold her foot*
> *She says, 'Don't touch!'*
> *But when I hold her waist-beads*
> *She pretends not to know."*

The night was already far spent when the guests rose to go, taking their bride home to spend seven market weeks with her suitor's family. They sang songs as they went, and on their way they paid short courtesy visits to prominent men like Okonkwo, before they finally left for their village. Okonkwo made a present of two cocks to them.

CHAPTER THIRTEEN

Go-di-di-go-go-di-go. Di-go-go-di-go. It was the *ekwe* talking to the clan. One of the things every man learned was the language of the hollowed-out wooden instrument. Diim! Diim! Diim! boomed the cannon at intervals. The first cock had not crowed, and Umuofia was still swallowed up in sleep and silence when the *ekwe* began to talk, and the cannon shattered the silence. Men stirred on their bamboo beds and listened anxiously. Somebody was dead. The cannon seemed to rend the sky. Di-go-go-di-go-di-di-go-go floated in the message-laden night air. The faint and distant wailing of women settled like a sediment of sorrow on the earth. Now and again a full-chested lamentation rose above the wailing whenever a man came into the place of death. He raised his voice once or twice in manly sorrow and then sat down with the other men listening to the endless wailing of the women and the esoteric language of the *ekwe*. Now and again the cannon boomed. The wailing of the women would not be heard beyond the village, but the *ekwe* carried the news to all the nine villages and even beyond. It began by naming the clan: *Umuofia obodo dike*, 'the land of the brave.' *Umuofia obodo dike! Umuofia obodo dike!* It said this over and over again, and as it dwelt on it, anxiety mounted in every heart that heaved on a bamboo bed that night. Then it went nearer and named the village: *Iguedo*⁹ *of the yellow grinding-stone!* It was Okonkwo's village. Again and again Iguedo was called and men waited breathlessly in all the nine villages. At last the man was named and people sighed "E-u-u, Ezeudu is dead." A cold shiver ran down Okonkwo's back as he remembered the last time the old man had visited him. "That boy calls you father," he had said. "Bear no hand in his death."

Ezeudu was a great man, and so all the clan was at his funeral. The ancient drums of death beat, guns and cannon were fired, and men dashed about in frenzy, cutting down every tree or animal they saw, jumping over walls and dancing on the roof. It was a warrior's funeral, and from morning till night warriors came and went in their age-groups. They all wore smoked raffia skirts and their bodies were painted with chalk and charcoal. Now and again an ancestral spirit or *egwugwu* appeared from the underworld, speaking in a tremulous, unearthly voice and completely covered in raffia. Some of them were very violent, and there had been a mad rush for shelter earlier in the day when one appeared with a sharp matchet and was only prevented from doing serious harm by two men who restrained him with the help of a strong rope tied round his waist. Sometimes he turned round and chased those men, and they ran for their lives. But they always returned to the long rope he trailed behind. He sang, in a terrifying voice, that Ekwensu, or Evil Spirit, had entered his eye.

But the most dreaded of all was yet to come. He was always alone and was shaped like a coffin. A sickly odour hung in the air wherever he went, and flies went with him. Even the greatest medicine-men took shelter when he was near. Many years ago another *egwugwu* had dared to stand his ground before him and had been transfixed to the spot for two days. This one had only one hand and with it carried a basket full of water.

But some of the *egwugwu* were quite harmless. One of them was so old and infirm that he leaned heavily on a stick. He walked unsteadily to the place where the corpse was laid, gazed at it a while and went away again—to the underworld.

The land of the living was not far removed from the domain of the ancestors. There was coming and going between them, especially at festivals and also when an old man died, because an old man was very close to the ancestors. A

---

9. The yellow grindstone.

man's life from birth to death was a series of transition rites which brought him nearer and nearer to his ancestors.

Ezeudu had been the oldest man in his village, and at his death there were only three men in the whole clan who were older, and four or five others in his own age-group. Whenever one of these ancient men appeared in the crowd to dance unsteadily the funeral steps of the tribe, younger men gave way and the tumult subsided.

It was a great funeral, such as befitted a noble warrior. As the evening drew near, the shouting and the firing of guns, the beating of drums and the brandishing and clanging of matchets increased.

Ezeudu had taken three titles in his life. It was a rare achievement. There were only four titles in the clan, and only one or two men in any generation ever achieved the fourth and highest. When they did, they became the lords of the land. Because he had taken titles, Ezeudu was to be buried after dark with only a glowing brand to light the sacred ceremony.

But before this quiet and final rite, the tumult increased tenfold. Drums beat violently and men leaped up and down in frenzy. Guns were fired on all sides and sparks flew out as matchets clanged together in warriors' salutes. The air was full of dust and the smell of gunpowder. It was then that the one-handed spirit came, carrying a basket full of water. People made way for him on all sides and the noise subsided. Even the smell of gunpowder was swallowed in the sickly smell that now filled the air. He danced a few steps to the funeral drums and then went to see the corpse.

"Ezeudu!" he called in his guttural voice. "If you had been poor in your last life I would have asked you to be rich when you come again. But you were rich. If you had been a coward, I would have asked you to bring courage. But you were a fearless warrior. If you had died young, I would have asked you to get life. But you lived long. So I shall ask you to come again the way you came before. If your death was the death of nature, go in peace. But if a man caused it, do not allow him a moment's rest." He danced a few more steps and went away.

The drums and the dancing began again and reached fever-heat. Darkness was around the corner, and the burial was near. Guns fired the last salute and the cannon rent the sky. And then from the centre of the delirious fury came a cry of agony and shouts of horror. It was as if a spell had been cast. All was silent. In the centre of the crowd a boy lay in a pool of blood. It was the dead man's sixteen-year-old son, who with his brothers and half-brothers had been dancing the traditional farewell to their father. Okonkwo's gun had exploded and a piece of iron had pierced the boy's heart.

The confusion that followed was without parallel in the tradition of Umuofia. Violent deaths were frequent, but nothing like this had ever happened.

The only course open to Okonkwo was to flee from the clan. It was a crime against the earth goddess to kill a clansman, and a man who committed it must flee from the land. The crime was of two kinds, male and female. Okonkwo had committed the female, because it had been inadvertent. He could return to the clan after seven years.

That night he collected his most valuable belongings into head-loads. His wives wept bitterly and their children wept with them without knowing why. Obierika and half a dozen other friends came to help and to console him. They each made nine or ten trips carrying Okonkwo's yams to store in Obierika's barn. And before the cock crowed Okonkwo and his family were fleeing to his motherland. It was a little village called Mbanta,[1] just beyond the borders of Mbaino.

As soon as the day broke, a large crowd of men from Ezeudu's quarter stormed Okonkwo's compound, dressed in garbs of war. They set fire to his houses, demolished his red walls, killed his animals and destroyed his barn. It was the justice of the earth goddess, and they were merely her messengers. They had no hatred in their hearts against Okonkwo. His greatest friend, Obierika, was among them. They were merely cleansing the land which Okonkwo had polluted with the blood of a clansman.

Obierika was a man who thought about things. When the will of the goddess had been done, he sat down in his *obi* and mourned his friend's calamity. Why should a man suffer so grievously for an offence he had committed inadvertently? But although he thought for a long time he found no answer. He was merely led into greater complexities. He remembered his wife's twin children, whom he had thrown away. What crime had they committed? The Earth had decreed that they were an offence on the land and must be destroyed. And *if* the clan did not exact punishment for an offence against the great goddess, her wrath was loosed on all the land and not just on the offender. As the elders said, if one finger brought oil it soiled the others.

Part Two

CHAPTER FOURTEEN

Okonkwo was well received by his mother's kinsmen in Mbanta. The old man who received him was his mother's younger brother, who was now the eldest surviving member of that family. His name was Uchendu,[2] and it was he who had received Okonkwo's mother twenty and ten years before when she had been brought home from Umuofia to be buried with her people. Okonkwo was only a boy then and Uchendu still remembered him crying the traditional farewell: "Mother, mother, mother is going."

That was many years ago. Today Okonkwo was not bringing his mother home to be buried with her people. He was taking his family of three wives and eleven children to seek refuge in his motherland. As soon as Uchendu saw him with his sad and weary company he guessed what had happened, and asked no questions. It was not until the following day that Okonkwo told him the full story. The old man listened silently to the end and then said with some relief: "It is a female *ochu*."[3] And he arranged the requisite rites and sacrifices.

Okonkwo was given a plot of ground on which to build his compound, and two or three pieces of land on which to farm during the coming planting season. With the help of his mother's kinsmen he built himself an *obi* and three huts for his wives. He then installed his personal god and the symbols of his departed fathers. Each of Uchendu's five sons contributed three hundred seed-yams to enable their cousin to plant a farm, for as soon as the first rain came farming would begin.

At last the rain came. It was sudden and tremendous. For two or three moons the sun had been gathering strength till it seemed to breathe a breath of fire on the earth. All the grass had long been scorched brown, and the sands

1. Small town.
2. The thought created by life.

3. Murder, manslaughter.

felt like live coals to the feet. Evergreen trees wore a dusty coat of brown. The birds were silenced in the forests, and the world lay panting under the live, vibrating heat. And then came the clap of thunder. It was an angry, metallic and thirsty clap, unlike the deep and liquid rumbling of the rainy season. A mighty wind arose and filled the air with dust. Palm trees swayed as the wind combed their leaves into flying crests like strange and fantastic coiffure.

When the rain finally came, it was in large, solid drops of frozen water which the people called 'the nuts of the water of heaven'. They were hard and painful on the body as they fell, yet young people ran about happily picking up the cold nuts and throwing them into their mouths to melt.

The earth quickly came to life and the birds in the forests fluttered around and chirped merrily. A vague scent of life and green vegetation was diffused in the air. As the rain began to fall more soberly and in smaller liquid drops, children sought for shelter, and all were happy, refreshed and thankful.

Okonkwo and his family worked very hard to plant a new farm. But it was like beginning life anew without the vigour and enthusiasm of youth, like learning to become left-handed in old age. Work no longer had for him the pleasure it used to have, and when there was no work to do he sat in a silent half-sleep.

His life had been ruled by a great passion—to become one of the lords of the clan. That had been his life-spring. And he had all but achieved it. Then everything had been broken. He had been cast out of his clan like a fish on to a dry, sandy beach, panting. Clearly his personal god or *chi* was not made for great things. A man could not rise beyond the destiny of his *chi*. The saying of the elders was not true—that if a man said yea his *chi* also affirmed. Here was a man whose *chi* said nay despite his own affirmation.

The old man, Uchendu, saw clearly that Okonkwo had yielded to despair and he was greatly troubled. He would speak to him after the *isa-ifi* ceremony.[4]

The youngest of Uchendu's five sons, Amikwu, was marrying a new wife. The bride-price had been paid and all but the last ceremony had been performed. Amikwu and his people had taken palm-wine to the bride's kinsmen about two moons before Okonkwo's arrival in Mbanta. And so it was time for the final ceremony of confession.

The daughters of the family were all there, some of them having come a long way from their homes in distant villages. Uchendu's eldest daughter had come from Obodo, nearly half a day's journey away. The daughters of Uchendu's brothers were also there. It was a full gathering of *umuada*,[5] in the same way as they would meet if a death occurred in the family. There were twenty-two of them.

They sat in a big circle on the ground and the bride sat in the centre with a hen in her right hand. Uchendu sat by her, holding the ancestral staff of the family. All the other men stood outside the circle, watching. Their wives watched also. It was evening and the sun was setting.

Uchendu's eldest daughter, Njide, asked the questions.

"Remember that if you do not answer truthfully you will suffer or even die

4. A ceremony to ascertain that a wife (here a promised bride) had been faithful to her husband during a separation.
5. The daughters, who, according to Igbo custom, married outside the clan, perform a special initiation upon returning home for important gatherings.

at child-birth," she began. "How many men have lain with you since my brother first expressed the desire to marry you?"

"None," she replied simply.

"Answer truthfully," urged the other women.

"None?" asked Njide.

"None," she answered.

"Swear on this staff of my fathers," said Uchendu.

"I swear," said the bride.

Uchendu took the hen from her, slit its throat with a sharp knife and allowed some of the blood to fall on his ancestral staff.

From that day Amikwu took the young bride to his hut and she became his wife. The daughters of the family did not return to their homes immediately but spent two or three days with their kinsmen.

On the second day Uchendu called together his sons and daughters and his nephew, Okonkwo. The men brought their goatskin mats, with which they sat on the floor, and the women sat on a sisal mat spread on a raised bank of earth. Uchendu pulled gently at his grey beard and gnashed his teeth. Then he began to speak, quietly and deliberately, picking his words with great care:

"It is Okonkwo that I primarily wish to speak to," he began. "But I want all of you to note what I am going to say. I am an old man and you are all children. I know more about the world than any of you. If there is any one among you who thinks he knows more let him speak up." He paused, but no one spoke.

"Why is Okonkwo with us today? This is not his clan. We are only his mother's kinsmen. He does not belong here. He is an exile, condemned for seven years to live in a strange land. And so he is bowed with grief. But there is just one question I would like to ask him. Can you tell me, Okonkwo, why it is that one of the commonest names we give our children is Nneka, or 'Mother is Supreme'? We all know that a man is the head of the family and his wives do his bidding. A child belongs to its father and his family and not to its mother and her family. A man belongs to his fatherland and not to his motherland. And yet we say Nneka—'Mother is Supreme.' Why is that?"

There was silence. "I want Okonkwo to answer me," said Uchendu.

"I do not know the answer," Okonkwo replied.

"You do not know the answer? So you see that you are a child. You have many wives and many children—more children than I have. You are a great man in your clan. But you are still a child, *my* child. Listen to me and I shall tell you. But there is one more question I shall ask you. Why is it that when a woman dies she is taken home to be buried with her own kinsmen? She is not buried with her husband's kinsmen. Why is that? Your mother was brought home to me and buried with my people. Why was that?"

Okonkwo shook his head.

"He does not know that either," said Uchendu, "and yet he is full of sorrow because he has come to live in his motherland for a few years." He laughed a mirthless laughter, and turned to his sons and daughters. "What about you? Can you answer my question?"

They all shook their heads.

"Then listen to me," he said and cleared his throat. "It's true that a child belongs to its father. But when a father beats his child, it seeks sympathy in its mother's hut. A man belongs to his fatherland when things are good and life is sweet. But when there is sorrow and bitterness he finds refuge in his motherland. Your mother is there to protect you. She is buried there. And that is why we say that mother is supreme. Is it right that you, Okonkwo, should bring to your mother a heavy face and refuse to be comforted? Be careful or you may displease the dead. Your duty is to comfort your wives and children and take them back to your fatherland after seven years. But if you allow sorrow to weigh you down and kill you, they will all die in exile." He paused for a long while. "These are now your kinsmen." He waved at his sons and daughters. "You think you are the greatest sufferer in the world. Do you know that men are sometimes banished for life? Do you know that men sometimes lose all their yams and even their children? I had six wives once. I have none now except that young girl who knows not her right from her left. Do you know how many children I have buried—children I begot in my youth and strength? Twenty-two. I did not hang myself, and I am still alive. If you think you are the greatest sufferer in the world ask my daughter, Akueni, how many twins she has borne and thrown away. Have you not heard the song they sing when a woman dies?

" 'For whom is it well, for whom is it well?
" 'There is no one for whom it is well.'

"I have no more to say to you."

CHAPTER FIFTEEN

It was in the second year of Okonkwo's exile that his friend, Obierika, came to visit him. He brought with him two young men, each of them carrying a heavy bag on his head. Okonkwo helped them put down their loads. It was clear that the bags were full of cowries.

Okonkwo was very happy to receive his friend. His wives and children were very happy too, and so were his cousins and their wives when he sent for them and told them who his guest was.

"You must take him to salute our father," said one of the cousins.

"Yes," replied Okonkwo. "We are going directly." But before they went he whispered something to his first wife. She nodded, and soon the children were chasing one of their cocks.

Uchendu had been told by one of his grandchildren that three strangers had come to Okonkwo's house. He was therefore waiting to receive them. He held out his hands to them when they came into his *obi*, and after they had shaken hands he asked Okonkwo who they were.

"This is Obierika, my great friend. I have already spoken to you about him."

"Yes," said the old man, turning to Obierika. "My son has told me about you, and I am happy you have come to see us. I knew your father, Iweka. He was a great man. He had many friends here and came to see them quite often. Those were good days when a man had friends in distant clans. Your generation does not know that. You stay at home, afraid of your next-door neighbour. Even a man's motherland is strange to him nowadays." He looked at Okonkwo. "I am an old man and I like to talk. That is all I am good for now." He got up painfully, went into an inner room and came back with a kola nut.

"Who are the young men with you?" he asked as he sat down again on his goatskin. Okonkwo told him.

"Ah," he said. "Welcome, my sons." He presented the kola nut to them, and when they had seen it and thanked him, he broke it and they ate.

"Go into that room," he said to Okonkwo, pointing with his finger. "You will find a pot of wine there."

Okonkwo brought the wine and they began to drink. It was a day old, and very strong.

"Yes," said Uchendu after a long silence. "People travelled more in those days. There is not a single clan in these parts that I do not know very well. Aninta, Umuazu, Ikeocha, Elumelu, Abame—I know them all."

"Have you heard," asked Obierika, "that Abame is no more?"

"How is that?" asked Uchendu and Okonkwo together.

"Abame has been wiped out," said Obierika. "It is a strange and terrible story. If I had not seen the few survivors with my own eyes and heard their story with my own ears, I would not have believed. Was it not on an Eke day that they fled into Umuofia?" he asked his two companions, and they nodded their heads.

"Three moons ago," said Obierika, "on an Eke market-day a little band of fugitives came into our town. Most of them were sons of our land whose mothers had been buried with us. But there were some too who came because they had friends in our town, and others who could think of nowhere else open to escape. And so they fled into Umuofia with a woeful story." He drank his palm-wine, and Okonkwo filled his horn again. He continued:

"During the last planting season a white man had appeared in their clan."

"An albino," suggested Okonkwo.

"He was not an albino. He was quite different." He sipped his wine. "And he was riding an iron horse.[6] The first people who saw him ran away, but he stood beckoning to them. In the end the fearless ones went near and even touched him. The elders consulted their Oracle and it told them that the strange man would break their clan and spread destruction among them." Obierika again drank a little of his wine. "And so they killed the white man and tied his iron horse to their sacred tree because it looked as if it would run away to call the man's friends. I forgot to tell you another thing which the Oracle said. It said that other white men were on their way. They were locusts, it said, and that first man was their harbinger sent to explore the terrain. And so they killed him."

"What did the white man say before they killed him?" asked Uchendu.

"He said nothing," answered one of Obierika's companions.

"He said something, only they did not understand him," said Obierika. "He seemed to speak through his nose."

"One of the men told me," said Obierika's other companion, "that he repeated over and over again a word that resembled Mbaino. Perhaps he had been going to Mbaino and had lost his way."

"Anyway," resumed Obierika, "they killed him and tied up his iron horse. This was before the planting season began. For a long time nothing happened. The rains had come and yams had been sown. The iron horse was still tied to the sacred silk-cotton tree. And then one morning three white men led by a band of ordinary men like us came to the clan. They saw the iron horse and went away again. Most of the men and women of Abame had gone to their farms. Only a few of them saw these white men and their followers. For many market weeks nothing else happened. They have a big market in Abame on every other Afo day and, as you know, the whole clan gathers there. That was

6. Bicycle.

the day it happened. The three white men and a very large number of other men surrounded the market. They must have used a powerful medicine to make themselves invisible until the market was full. And they began to shoot. Everybody was killed, except the old and the sick who were at home and a handful of men and women whose *chi* were wide awake and brought them out of that market."[7] He paused.

"Their clan is now completely empty. Even the sacred fish in their mysterious lake have fled and the lake has turned the colour of blood. A great evil has come upon their land as the Oracle had warned."

There was a long silence. Uchendu ground his teeth together audibly. Then he burst out:

"Never kill a man who says nothing. Those men of Abame were fools. What did they know about the man?" He ground his teeth again and told a story to illustrate his point. "Mother Kite once sent her daughter to bring food. She went, and brought back a duckling. 'You have done very well,' said Mother Kite to her daughter, 'but tell me, what did the mother of this duckling say when you swooped and carried its child away?' 'It said nothing,' replied the young kite. 'It just walked away.' 'You must return the duckling,' said Mother Kite. 'There is something ominous behind the silence.' And so Daughter Kite returned the duckling and took a chick instead. 'What did the mother of this chick do?' asked the old kite. 'It cried and raved and cursed me,' said the young kite. 'Then we can eat the chick,' said her mother. 'There is nothing to fear from someone who shouts.' Those men of Abame were fools."

"They were fools," said Okonkwo after a pause. "They had been warned that danger was ahead. They should have armed themselves with their guns and their matchets even when they went to market."

"They have paid for their foolishness," said Obierika. "But I am greatly afraid. We have heard stories about white men who made the powerful guns and the strong drinks and took slaves away across the seas, but no one thought the stories were true."

"There is no story that is not true," said Uchendu. "The world has no end, and what is good among one people is an abomination with others. We have albinos among us. Do you not think that they came to our clan by mistake, that they have strayed from their way to a land where everybody is like them?"

Okonkwo's first wife soon finished her cooking and set before their guests a big meal of pounded yams and bitter-leaf soup. Okonkwo's son, Nwoye, brought in a pot of sweet wine tapped from the raffia palm.

"You are a big man now," Obierika said to Nwoye. "Your friend Anene asked me to greet you."

"Is he well?" asked Nwoye.

"We are all well," said Obierika.

Ezinma brought them a bowl of water with which to wash their hands. After that they began to eat and to drink the wine.

"When did you set out from home?" asked Okonkwo.

"We had meant to set out from my house before cock-crow," said Obierika. "But Nweke did not appear until it was quite light. Never make an early morning appointment with a man who has just married a new wife." They all laughed.

---

7. Achebe bases his account on a similar incident in 1905 when British troops massacred the town of Ahiara in reprisal for the death of a missionary.

"Has Nweke married a wife?" asked Okonkwo.

"He has married Okadigbo's second daughter," said Obierika.

"That is very good," said Okonkwo. "I do not blame you for not hearing the cock crow."

When they had eaten, Obierika pointed at the two heavy bags.

"That is the money from your yams," he said. "I sold the big ones as soon as you left. Later on I sold some of the seed-yams and gave out others to share-croppers. I shall do that every year until you return. But I thought you would need the money now and so I brought it. Who knows what may happen tomorrow? Perhaps green men will come to our clan and shoot us."

"God will not permit it," said Okonkwo. "I do not know how to thank you."

"I can tell you," said Obierika. "Kill one of your sons for me."

"That will not be enough," said Okonkwo.

"Then kill yourself," said Obierika.

"Forgive me," said Okonkwo, smiling. "I shall not talk about thanking you any more."

CHAPTER SIXTEEN

When nearly two years later Obierika paid another visit to his friend in exile the circumstances were less happy. The missionaries had come to Umuofia. They had built their church there, won a handful of converts and were already sending evangelists to the surrounding towns and villages. That was a source of great sorrow to the leaders of the clan; but many of them believed that the strange faith and the white man's god would not last. None of his converts was a man whose word was heeded in the assembly of the people. None of them was a man of title. They were mostly the kind of people that were called efulefu, worthless, empty men. The imagery of an efulefu in the language of the clan was a man who sold his matchet and wore the sheath to battle. Chielo, the priestess of Agbala, called the converts the excrement of the clan, and the new faith was a mad dog that had come to eat it up.

What moved Obierika to visit Okonkwo was the sudden appearance of the latter's son, Nwoye, among the missionaries in Umuofia.

"What are you doing here?" Obierika had asked when after many difficulties the missionaries had allowed him to speak to the boy.

"I am one of them," replied Nwoye.

"How is your father?" Obierika asked, not knowing what else to say.

"I don't know. He is not my father," said Nwoye, unhappily.

And so Obierika went to Mbanta to see his friend. And he found that Okonkwo did not wish to speak about Nwoye. It was only from Nwoye's mother that he heard scraps of the story.

The arrival of the missionaries had caused a considerable stir in the village of Mbanta. There were six of them and one was a white man. Every man and woman came out to see the white man. Stories about these strange men had grown since one of them had been killed in Abame and his iron horse tied to the sacred silk-cotton tree. And so everybody came to see the white man. It was the time of the year when everybody was at home. The harvest was over.

When they had all gathered, the white man began to speak to them. He spoke through an interpreter who was an Ibo man, though his dialect was different and harsh to the ears of Mbanta. Many people laughed at his dialect and the way he used words strangely. Instead of saying 'myself' he always said 'my buttocks.'[8] But he was a man of commanding presence and the clansmen listened to him. He said he was one of them, as they could see from his colour and his language. The other four black men were also their brothers, although one of them did not speak Ibo. The white man was also their brother because they were all sons of God. And he told them about this new God, the Creator of all the world and all the men and women. He told them that they worshipped false gods, gods of wood and stone. A deep murmur went through the crowd when he said this. He told them that the true God lived on high and that all men when they died went before Him for judgment. Evil men and all the heathen who in their blindness bowed to wood and stone were thrown into a fire that burned like palm-oil. But good men who worshipped the true God lived for ever in His happy kingdom. "We have been sent by this great God to ask you to leave your wicked ways and false gods and turn to Him so that you may be saved when you die," he said.

"Your buttocks understand our language," said someone light-heartedly and the crowd laughed.

"What did he say?" the white man asked his interpreter. But before he could answer, another man asked a question: "Where is the white man's horse?" he asked. The Ibo evangelists consulted among themselves and decided that the man probably meant bicycle. They told the white man and he smiled benevolently.

"Tell them," he said, "that I shall bring many iron horses when we have settled down among them. Some of them will even ride the iron horse themselves." This was interpreted to them but very few of them heard. They were talking excitedly among themselves because the white man had said he was going to live among them. They had not thought about that.

At this point an old man said he had a question. "Which is this god of yours," he asked, "the goddess of the earth, the god of the sky, Amadiora of the thunderbolt, or what?"

The interpreter spoke to the white man and he immediately gave his answer. "All the gods you have named are not gods at all. They are gods of deceit who tell you to kill your fellows and destroy innocent children. There is only one true God and He has the earth, the sky, you and me and all of us."

"If we leave our gods and follow your god," asked another man, "who will protect us from the anger of our neglected gods and ancestors?"

"Your gods are not alive and cannot do you any harm," replied the white man. "They are pieces of wood and stone."

When this was interpreted to the men of Mbanta they broke into derisive laughter. These men must be mad, they said to themselves. How else could they say that Ani and Amadiora were harmless? And Idemili and Ogwugwu too? And some of them began to go away.

Then the missionaries burst into song. It was one of those gay and rollicking tunes of evangelism which had the power of plucking at silent and dusty chords in the heart of an Ibo man. The interpreter explained each verse to the audience, some of whom now stood enthralled. It was a story of brothers who lived in darkness and in fear, ignorant of the love of God. It told of one sheep out on the hills, away from the gates of God and from the tender shepherd's care.

---

8. The Igbo language has high and low tones, so that the same word may have different meanings according to its pronunciation. Here Achebe is probably referring to a famous pair of near-homonyms: *íké* (strength) and *íkè* (buttocks).

After the singing the interpreter spoke about the Son of God whose name was Jesu Kristi. Okonkwo, who only stayed in the hope that it might come to chasing the men out of the village or whipping them, now said:

"You told us with your own mouth that there was only one god. Now you talk about his son. He must have a wife, then." The crowd agreed.

"I did not say He had a wife," said the interpreter, somewhat lamely.

"Your buttocks said he had a son," said the joker. "So he must have a wife and all of them must have buttocks."

The missionary ignored him and went on to talk about the Holy Trinity. At the end of it Okonkwo was fully convinced that the man was mad. He shrugged his shoulders and went away to tap his afternoon palm-wine.

But there was a young lad who had been captivated. His name was Nwoye, Okonkwo's first son. It was not the mad logic of the Trinity that captivated him. He did not understand it. It was the poetry of the new religion, something felt in the marrow. The hymn about brothers who sat in darkness and in fear seemed to answer a vague and persistent question that haunted his young soul—the question of the twins crying in the bush and the question of Ikemefuna who was killed. He felt a relief within as the hymn poured into his parched soul. The words of the hymn were like the drops of frozen rain melting on the dry palate of the panting earth. Nwoye's callow mind was greatly puzzled.

CHAPTER SEVENTEEN

The missionaries spent their first four or five nights in the market-place, and went into the village in the morning to preach the gospel. They asked who the king of the village was, but the villagers told them that there was no king. "We have men of high title and the chief priests and the elders," they said.

It was not very easy getting the men of high title and the elders together after the excitement of the first day. But the missionaries persevered, and in the end they were received by the rulers of Mbanta. They asked for a plot of land to build their church.

Every clan and village had its 'evil forest'. In it were buried all those who died of the really evil diseases, like leprosy and smallpox. It was also the dumping ground for the potent fetishes of great medicine-men when they died. An 'evil forest' was, therefore, alive with sinister forces and powers of darkness. It was such a forest that the rulers of Mbanta gave to the missionaries. They did not really want them in their clan, and so they made them that offer which nobody in his right senses would accept.

"They want a piece of land to build their shrine," said Uchendu to his peers when they consulted among themselves. "We shall give them a piece of land." He paused, and there was a murmur of surprise and disagreement. "Let us give them a portion of the Evil Forest. They boast about victory over death. Let us give them a real battlefield in which to show their victory." They laughed and agreed, and sent for the missionaries, whom they had asked to leave them for a while so that they might 'whisper together'. They offered them as much of the Evil Forest as they cared to take. And to their greatest amazement the missionaries thanked them and burst into song.

"They do not understand," said some of the elders. "But they will understand when they go to their plot of land tomorrow morning." And they dispersed.

The next morning the crazy men actually began to clear a part of the forest and to build their house. The inhabitants of Mbanta expected them all to be dead within four days. The first day passed and the second and third and fourth, and none of them died. Everyone was puzzled. And then it became known that the white man's fetish had unbelievable power. It was said that he wore glasses on his eyes so that he could see and talk to evil spirits. Not long after, he won his first three converts.

Although Nwoye had been attracted to the new faith from the very first day, he kept it secret. He dared not go too near the missionaries for fear of his father. But whenever they came, to preach in the open market-place or the village playground, Nwoye was there. And he was already beginning to know some of the simple stories they told.

"We have now built a church," said Mr Kiaga, the interpreter, who was now in charge of the infant congregation. The white man had gone back to Umuofia, where he built his headquarters and from where he paid regular visits to Mr Kiaga's congregation at Mbanta.

"We have now built a church," said Mr Kiaga, "and we want you all to come in every seventh day to worship the true God."

On the following Sunday, Nwoye passed and re-passed the little red-earth and thatch building without summoning enough courage to enter. He heard the voice of singing and although it came from a handful of men it was loud and confident. Their church stood on a circular clearing that looked like the open mouth of the Evil Forest. Was it waiting to snap its teeth together? After passing and re-passing by the church, Nwoye returned home.

It was well known among the people of Mbanta that their gods and ancestors were sometimes long-suffering and would deliberately allow a man to go on defying them. But even in such cases they set their limit at seven market weeks or twenty-eight days. Beyond that limit no man was suffered to go. And so excitement mounted in the village as the seventh week approached since the impudent missionaries built their church in the Evil Forest. The villagers were so certain about the doom that awaited these men that one or two converts thought it wise to suspend their allegiance to the new faith.

At last the day came by which all the missionaries should have died. But they were still alive, building a new red-earth and thatch house for their teacher, Mr Kiaga. That week they won a handful more converts. And for the first time they had a woman. Her name was Nneka, the wife of Amadi, who was a prosperous farmer. She was very heavy with child.

Nneka had had four previous pregnancies and childbirths. But each time she had borne twins, and they had been immediately thrown away. Her husband and his family were already becoming highly critical of such a woman and were not unduly perturbed when they found she had fled to join the Christians. It was a good riddance.

One morning Okonkwo's cousin, Amikwu, was passing by the church on his way from the neighbouring village, when he saw Nwoye among the Christians. He was greatly surprised, and when he got home he went straight to Okonkwo's hut and told him what he had seen. The women began to talk excitedly, but Okonkwo sat unmoved.

It was late afternoon before Nwoye returned. He went into the *obi* and saluted his father, but he did not answer. Nwoye turned round to walk into the inner compound when his father, suddenly overcome with fury, sprang to his feet and gripped him by the neck.

"Where have you been?" he stammered.

Nwoye struggled to free himself from the choking grip.

"Answer me," roared Okonkwo, "before I kill you!" He seized a heavy stick that lay on the dwarf wall and hit him two or three savage blows. "Answer me!" he roared again. Nwoye stood looking at him and did not say a word. The women were screaming outside, afraid to go in.

"Leave that boy at once!" said a voice in the outer compound. It was Okonkwo's uncle, Uchendu. "Are you mad?"

Okonkwo did not answer. But he left hold of Nwoye, who walked away and never returned.

He went back to the church and told Mr Kiaga that he had decided to go to Umuofia, where the white missionary had set up a school to teach young Christians to read and write.

Mr Kiaga's joy was very great. "Blessed is he who forsakes his father and his mother for my sake," he intoned. "Those that hear my words are my father and my mother."

Nwoye did not fully understand. But he was happy to leave his father. He would return later to his mother and his brothers and sisters and convert them to the new faith.

As Okonkwo sat in his hut that night, gazing into a log fire, he thought over the matter. A sudden fury rose within him and he felt a strong desire to take up his matchet, go to the church and wipe out the entire vile and miscreant gang. But on further thought he told himself that Nwoye was not worth fighting for. Why, he cried in his heart, should he, Okonkwo, of all people, be cursed with such a son? He saw clearly in it the finger of his personal god or *chi*. For how else could he explain his great misfortune and exile and now his despicable son's behaviour? Now that he had time to think of it, his son's crime stood out in its stark enormity. To abandon the gods of one's father and go about with a lot of effeminate men clucking like old hens was the very depth of abomination. Suppose when he died all his male children decided to follow Nwoye's steps and abandon their ancestors? Okonkwo felt a cold shudder run through him at the terrible prospect, like the prospect of annihilation. He saw himself and his fathers crowding round their ancestral shrine waiting in vain for worship and sacrifice and finding nothing but ashes of bygone days, and his children the while praying to the white man's god. If such a thing were ever to happen, he, Okonkwo, would wipe them off the face of the earth.

Okonkwo was popularly called the "Roaring Flame." As he looked into the log fire he recalled the name. He was a flaming fire. How then could he have begotten a son like Nwoye, degenerate and effeminate? Perhaps he was not his son. No! he could not be. His wife had played him false. He would teach her! But Nwoye resembled his grandfather, Unoka, who was Okonkwo's father. He pushed the thought out of his mind. He, Okonkwo, was called a flaming fire. How could he have begotten a woman for a son? At Nwoye's age Okonkwo had already become famous throughout Umuofia for his wrestling and his fearlessness.

He sighed heavily, and as if in sympathy the smouldering log also sighed. And immediately Okonkwo's eyes were opened and he saw the whole matter clearly. Living fire begets cold, impotent ash. He sighed again, deeply.

CHAPTER EIGHTEEN

The young church in Mbanta had a few crises early in its life. At first the clan had assumed that it would not survive. But it had gone on living and gradually becoming stronger. The clan was worried, but not overmuch. If a gang of *efulefu* decided to live in the Evil Forest it was their own affair. When one came to think of it, the Evil Forest was a fit home for such undesirable people. It was true they were rescuing twins from the bush, but they never brought them into the village. As far as the villagers were concerned, the twins still remained where they had been thrown away. Surely the earth goddess would not visit the sins of the missionaries on the innocent villagers?

But on one occasion the missionaries had tried to overstep the bounds. Three converts had gone into the village and boasted openly that all the gods were dead and impotent and that they were prepared to defy them by burning all their shrines.

"Go and burn your mothers' genitals," said one of the priests. The men were seized and beaten until they streamed with blood. After that nothing happened for a long time between the church and the clan.

But stories were already gaining ground that the white man had not only brought a religion but also a government. It was said that they had built a place of judgment in Umuofia to protect the followers of their religion. It was even said that they had hanged one man who killed a missionary.

Although such stories were now often told they looked like fairy-tales in Mbanta and did not as yet affect the relationship between the new church and the clan. There was no question of killing a missionary here, for Mr Kiaga, despite his madness, was quite harmless. As for his converts, no one could kill them without having to flee from the clan, for in spite of their worthlessness they still belonged to the clan. And so nobody gave serious thought to the stories about the white man's government or the consequences of killing the Christians. If they became more troublesome than they already were they would simply be driven out of the clan.

And the little church was at that moment too deeply absorbed in its own troubles to annoy the clan. It all began over the question of admitting outcasts.

These outcasts, or *osu*, seeing that the new religion welcomed twins and such abominations, thought that it was possible that they would also be received. And so one Sunday two of them went into the church. There was an immediate stir; but so great was the work the new religion had done among the converts that they did not immediately leave the church when the outcasts came in. Those who found themselves nearest to them merely moved to another seat. It was a miracle. But it only lasted till the end of the service. The whole church raised a protest and were about to drive these people out, when Mr Kiaga stopped them and began to explain.

"Before God," he said, "there is no slave or free. We are all children of God and we must receive these our brothers."

"You do not understand," said one of the converts. "What will the heathen say of us when they hear that we receive *osu* into our midst? They will laugh."

"Let them laugh," said Mr Kiaga. "God will laugh at them on the judgment day. Why do the nations rage and the peoples imagine a vain thing? He that sitteth in the heavens shall laugh. The Lord shall have them in derision."

"You do not understand," the convert maintained. "You are our teacher, and you can teach us the things of the new faith. But this is a matter which we know." And he told him what an *osu* was.

He was a person dedicated to a god, a thing set apart—a taboo for ever, and his children after him. He could neither marry nor be married by the free-born. He was in fact an outcast, living in a special area of the village, close to the Great Shrine. Wherever he went he carried with him the mark of his forbidden caste—long, tangled and dirty hair. A razor was taboo to him. An *osu* could not attend an assembly of the free-born, and they, in turn, could not shelter under his roof. He could not take any of the four titles of the clan, and when he died he was buried by his kind in the Evil Forest. How could such a man be a follower of Christ?

"He needs Christ more than you and I," said Mr Kiaga.

"Then I shall go back to the clan," said the convert. And he went. Mr Kiaga stood firm, and it was his firmness that saved the young church. The wavering converts drew inspiration and confidence from his unshakable faith. He ordered the outcasts to shave off their long, tangled hair. At first they were afraid they might die.

"Unless you shave off the mark of your heathen belief I will not admit you into the church," said Mr Kiaga. "You fear that you will die. Why should that be? How are you different from other men who shave their hair? The same God created you and them. But they have cast you out like lepers. It is against the will of God, who has promised everlasting life to all who believe in His holy name. The heathen say you will die if you do this or that, and you are afraid. They also said I would die if I built my church on this ground. Am I dead? They said I would die if I took care of twins. I am still alive. The heathen speak nothing but falsehood. Only the word of our God is true."

The two outcasts shaved off their hair, and soon they were among the strong-est adherents of the new faith. And what was more, nearly all the *osu* in Mbanta followed their example. It was in fact one of them who in his zeal brought the church into serious conflict with the clan a year later by killing the sacred python, the emanation of the god of water.

The royal python was the most revered animal in Mbanta and all the sur-rounding clans. It was addressed as 'Our Father', and was allowed to go wherever it chose, even into people's beds. It ate rats in the house and some-times swallowed hens' eggs. If a clansman killed a royal python accidentally, he made sacrifices of atonement and performed an expensive burial ceremony such as was done for a great man. No punishment was prescribed for a man who killed the python knowingly. Nobody thought that such a thing could ever happen.

Perhaps it never did happen. That was the way the clan at first looked at it. No one had actually seen the man do it. The story had arisen among the Christians themselves.

But, all the same, the rulers and elders of Mbanta assembled to decide on their action. Many of them spoke at great length and in fury. The spirit of war was upon them. Okonkwo, who had begun to play a part in the affairs of his motherland, said that until the abominable gang was chased out of the village with whips there would be no peace.

But there were many others who saw the situation differently, and it was their counsel that prevailed in the end.

"It is not our custom to fight for our gods," said one of them. "Let us not presume to do so now. If a man kills the sacred python in the secrecy of his hut, the matter lies between him and the god. We did not see it. If we put ourselves between the god and his victim we may receive blows intended for the offender. When a man blasphemes, what do we do? Do we go and stop his mouth? No. We put our fingers into our ears to stop us hearing. That is a wise action."

"Let us not reason like cowards," said Okonkwo. "If a man comes into my hut and defæcates on the floor, what do I do? Do I shut my eyes? No! I take a stick and break his head. That is what a man does. These people are daily pouring filth over us, and Okeke says we should pretend not to see." Okonkwo made a sound full of disgust. This was a womanly clan, he thought. Such a thing could never happen in his fatherland, Umuofia.

"Okonkwo has spoken the truth," said another man. "We should do something. But let us ostracise these men. We would then not be held accountable for their abominations."

Everybody in the assembly spoke, and in the end it was decided to ostracise the Christians. Okonkwo ground his teeth in disgust.

That night a bell-man went through the length and breadth of Mbanta proclaiming that the adherents of the new faith were thenceforth excluded from the life and privileges of the clan.

The Christians had grown in number and were now a small community of men, women and children, self-assured and confident. Mr Brown, the white missionary, paid regular visits to them. "When I think that it is only eighteen months since the Seed was first sown among you," he said, "I marvel at what the Lord hath wrought."

It was Wednesday in Holy Week and Mr Kiaga had asked the women to bring red earth and white chalk and water to scrub the church for Easter; and the women had formed themselves into three groups for this purpose. They set out early that morning, some of them with their water-pots to the stream, another group with hoes and baskets to the village red-earth pit, and the others to the chalk quarry.

Mr Kiaga was praying in the church when he heard the women talking excitedly. He rounded off his prayer and went to see what it was all about. The women had come to the church with empty water-pots. They said that some young men had chased them away from the stream with whips. Soon after, the women who had gone for red earth returned with empty baskets. Some of them had been heavily whipped. The chalk women also returned to tell a similar story.

"What does it all mean?" asked Mr Kiaga, who was greatly perplexed.

"The village has outlawed us," said one of the women. "The bell-man announced it last night. But it is not our custom to debar anyone from the stream or the quarry."

Another woman said, "They want to ruin us. They will not allow us into the markets. They have said so."

Mr Kiaga was going to send into the village for his men-converts when he saw them coming on their own. Of course they had all heard the bell-man, but they had never in all their lives heard of women being debarred from the stream.

"Come along," they said to the women. "We will go with you to meet those cowards." Some of them had big sticks and some even matchets.

But Mr Kiaga restrained them. He wanted first to know why they had been outlawed.

"They say that Okoli killed the sacred python," said one man.

"It is false," said another. "Okoli told me himself that it was false."

Okoli was not there to answer. He had fallen ill on the previous night. Before the day was over he was dead. His death showed that the gods were still able to fight their own battles. The clan saw no reason then for molesting the Christians.

CHAPTER NINETEEN

The last big rains of the year were falling. It was the time for treading red earth with which to build walls. It was not done earlier because the rains were too heavy and would have washed away the heap of trodden earth; and it could not be done later because harvesting would soon set in, and after that the dry season.

It was going to be Okonkwo's last harvest in Mbanta. The seven wasted and weary years were at last dragging to a close. Although he had prospered in his motherland Okonkwo knew that he would have prospered even more in Umuofia, in the land of his fathers where men were bold and warlike. In these seven years he would have climbed to the utmost heights. And so he regretted every day of his exile. His mother's kinsmen had been very kind to him, and he was grateful. But that did not alter the facts. He had called the first child born to him in exile Nneka—'Mother is Supreme'—out of politeness to his mother's kinsmen. But two years later when a son was born he called him Nwofia—'Begotten in the Wilderness'.

As soon as he entered his last year in exile Okonkwo sent money to Obierika to build him two huts in his old compound where he and his family would live until he built more huts and the outside wall of his compound. He could not ask another man to build his own *obi* for him, nor the walls of his compound. Those things a man built for himself or inherited from his father.

As the last heavy rains of the year began to fall, Obierika sent word that the two huts had been built and Okonkwo began to prepare for his return, after the rains. He would have liked to return earlier and build his compound that year before the rains stopped, but in doing so he would have taken something from the full penalty of seven years. And that could not be. So he waited impatiently for the dry season to come.

It came slowly. The rain became lighter and lighter until it fell in slanting showers. Sometimes the sun shone through the rain and a light breeze blew. It was a gay and airy kind of rain. The rainbow began to appear, and sometimes two rainbows, like a mother and her daughter, the one young and beautiful, and the other an old and faint shadow. The rainbow was called the python of the sky.

Okonkwo called his three wives and told them to get things together for a great feast. "I must thank my mother's kinsmen before I go," he said.

Ekwefi still had some cassava left on her farm from the previous year. Neither of the other wives had. It was not that they had been lazy, but that they had many children to feed. It was therefore understood that Ekwefi would provide cassava for the feast. Nwoye's mother and Ojiugo would provide the other things like smoked fish, palm-oil and pepper for the soup. Okonkwo would take care of meat and yams.

Ekwefi rose early on the following morning and went to her farm with her daughter, Ezinma, and Ojiugo's daughter, Obiageli, to harvest cassava tubers. Each of them carried a long cane basket, a matchet for cutting down the soft cassava stem, and a little hoe for digging out the tuber. Fortunately, a light rain had fallen during the night and the soil would not be very hard.

"It will not take us long to harvest as much as we like," said Ekwefi.

"But the leaves will be wet," said Ezinma. Her basket was balanced on her head, and her arms folded across her breasts. She felt cold. "I dislike cold water dropping on my back. We should have waited for the sun to rise and dry the leaves."

Obiageli called her "Salt" because she said that she disliked water. "Are you afraid you may dissolve?"

The harvesting was easy, as Ekwefi had said. Ezinma shook every tree violently with a long stick before she bent down to cut the stem and dig out the tuber. Sometimes it was not necessary to dig. They just pulled the stump, and earth rose, roots snapped below, and the tuber was pulled out.

When they had harvested a sizeable heap they carried it down in two trips to the stream, where every woman had a shallow well for fermenting her cassava.

"It should be ready in four days or even three," said Obiageli. "They are young tubers."

"They are not all that young," said Ekwefi. "I planted the farm nearly two years ago. It is a poor soil and that is why the tubers are so small."

Okonkwo never did things by halves. When his wife Ekwefi protested that two goats were sufficient for the feast he told her that it was not her affair.

"I am calling a feast because I have the wherewithal. I cannot live on the bank of a river and wash my hands with spittle. My mother's people have been good to me and I must show my gratitude."

And so three goats were slaughtered and a number of fowls. It was like a wedding feast. There was foo-foo and yam pottage, egusi[9] soup and bitter-leaf soup and pots and pots of palm-wine.

All the *umunna*[1] were invited to the feast, all the descendants of Okolo, who had lived about two hundred years before. The oldest member of this extensive family was Okonkwo's uncle, Uchendu. The kola nut was given to him to break, and he prayed to the ancestors. He asked them for health and children. "We do not ask for wealth because he that has health and children will also have wealth. We do not pray to have more money but to have more kinsmen. We are better than animals because we have kinsmen. An animal rubs its itching flank against a tree, a man asks his kinsman to scratch him." He prayed especially for Okonkwo and his family. He then broke the kola nut and threw one of the lobes on the ground for the ancestors.

As the broken kola nuts were passed round, Okonkwo's wives and children and those who came to help them with the cooking began to bring out the food. His sons brought out the pots of palm-wine. There was so much food and drink that many kinsmen whistled in surprise. When all was laid out, Okonkwo rose to speak.

"I beg you to accept this little kola," he said. "It is not to pay you back for all you did for me in these seven years. A child cannot pay for its mother's

9. Melon seed, which is roasted, ground, and cooked in soup.

1. Children of the father (literal trans.); the clan (male).

milk. I have only called you together because it is good for kinsmen to meet."

Yam pottage was served first because it was lighter than foo-foo and because yam always came first. Then the foo-foo was served. Some kinsmen ate it with egusi soup and others with bitter-leaf soup. The meat was then shared so that every member of the *umunna* had a portion. Every man rose in order of years and took a share. Even the few kinsmen who had not been able to come had their shares taken out for them in due turn.

As the palm-wine was drunk one of the oldest members of the *umunna* rose to thank Okonkwo:

"If I say that we did not expect such a big feast I will be suggesting that we did not know how open-handed our son, Okonkwo, is. We all know him, and we expected a big feast. But it turned out to be even bigger than we expected. Thank you. May all you took out return again tenfold. It is good in these days when the younger generation consider themselves wiser than their sires to see a man doing things in the grand, old way. A man who calls his kinsmen to a feast does not do so to save them from starving. They all have food in their own homes. When we gather together in the moonlit village ground it is not because of the moon. Every man can see it in his own compound. We come together because it is good for kinsmen to do so. You may ask why I am saying all this. I say it because I fear for the younger generation, for you people." He waved his arm where most of the young men sat. "As for me, I have only a short while to live, and so have Uchendu and Unachukwu and Emefo. But I fear for you young people because you do not understand how strong is the bond of kinship. You do not know what it is to speak with one voice. And what is the result? An abominable religion has settled among you. A man can now leave his father and his brothers. He can curse the gods of his fathers and his ancestors, like a hunter's dog that suddenly goes mad and turns on his master. I fear for you; I fear for the clan." He turned again to Okonkwo and said, "Thank you for calling us together."

Part Three

CHAPTER TWENTY

Seven years was a long time to be away from one's clan. A man's place was not always there, waiting for him. As soon as he left, someone else rose and filled it. The clan was like a lizard; if it lost its tail it soon grew another.

Okonkwo knew these things. He knew that he had lost his place among the nine masked spirits who administered justice in the clan. He had lost the chance to lead his warlike clan against the new religion, which he was told, had gained ground. He had lost the years in which he might have taken the highest titles in the clan. But some of these losses were not irreparable. He was determined that his return should be marked by his people. He would return with a flourish, and regain the seven wasted years.

Even in his first year in exile he had begun to plan for his return. The first thing he would do would be to rebuild his compound on a more magnificent scale. He would build a bigger barn than he had had before and he would build huts for two new wives. Then he would show his wealth by initiating his sons into the *ozo* society. Only the really great men in the clan were able to do this. Okonkwo saw clearly the high esteem in which he would be held, and he saw himself taking the highest title in the land.

As the years of exile passed one by one it seemed to him that his *chi* might now be making amends for the past disaster. His yams grew abundantly, not only in his motherland but also in Umuofia, where his friend gave them out year by year to share-croppers.

Then the tragedy of his first son had occurred. At first it appeared as if it might prove too great for his spirit. But it was a resilient spirit, and in the end Okonkwo overcame his sorrow. He had five other sons and he would bring them up in the way of the clan.

He sent for the five sons and they came and sat in his *obi*. The youngest of them was four years old.

"You have all seen the great abomination of your brother. Now he is no longer my son or your brother. I will only have a son who is a man, who will hold his head up among my people. If any one of you prefers to be a woman, let him follow Nwoye now while I am alive so that I can curse him. If you turn against me when I am dead I will visit you and break your neck."

Okonkwo was very lucky in his daughters. He never stopped regretting that Ezinma was a girl. Of all his children she alone understood his every mood. A bond of sympathy had grown between them as the years had passed.

Ezinma grew up in her father's exile and became one of the most beautiful girls in Mbanta. She was called Crystal of Beauty, as her mother had been called in her youth. The young ailing girl who had caused her mother so much heartache had been transformed, almost overnight, into a healthy buoyant maiden. She had, it was true, her moments of depression when she would snap at everybody like an angry dog. These moods descended on her suddenly and for no apparent reason. But they were very rare and short-lived. As long as they lasted, she could bear no other person but her father.

Many young men and prosperous middle-aged men of Mbanta came to marry her. But she refused them all, because her father had called her one evening and said to her: "There are many good and prosperous people here, but I shall be happy if you marry in Umuofia when we return home."

That was all he had said. But Ezinma had seen clearly all the thought and hidden meaning behind the few words. And she had agreed.

"Your half-sister, Obiageli, will not understand me," Okonkwo said. "But you can explain to her."

Although they were almost the same age, Ezinma wielded a strong influence over her half-sister. She explained to her why they should not marry yet, and she agreed also. And so the two of them refused every offer of marriage in Mbanta.

"I wish she were a boy," Okonkwo thought within himself. She understood things so perfectly. Who else among his children could have read his thought so well? With two beautiful grown-up daughters his return to Umuofia would attract considerable attention. His future sons-in-law would be men of authority in the clan. The poor and unknown would not dare to come forth.

Umuofia had indeed changed during the seven years Okonkwo had been in exile. The church had come and led many astray. Not only the low-born and the outcast but sometimes a worthy man had joined it. Such a man was Ogbuefi Ugonna,[2] who had taken two titles, and who like a madman had cut the anklet of his titles and cast it away to join the Christians. The white missionary was very proud of him and he was one of the first men in Umuofia to

2. Father's honor (with the eagle feather).

receive the sacrament of Holy Communion, or Holy Feast as it was called in Ibo. Ogbuefi Ugonna had thought of the Feast in terms of eating and drinking, only more holy than the village variety. He had therefore put his drinking-horn into his goatskin bag for the occasion.

But apart from the church, the white men had also brought a government. They had built a court where the District Commissioner judged cases in ignorance. He had court messengers who brought men to him for trial. Many of these messengers came from Umuru on the bank of the Great River, where the white men first came many years before and where they had built the centre of their religion and trade and government. These court messengers were greatly hated in Umuofia because they were foreigners and also arrogant and high-handed. They were called *kotma*,[3] and because of their ash-coloured shorts they earned the additional name of Ashy-Buttocks. They guarded the prison, which was full of men who had offended against the white man's law. Some of these prisoners had thrown away their twins and some had molested the Christians. They were beaten in the prison by the *kotma* and made to work every morning clearing the government compound and fetching wood for the white Commissioner and the court messengers. Some of these prisoners were men of title who should be above such mean occupation. They were grieved by the indignity and mourned for their neglected farms. As they cut grass in the morning the younger men sang in time with the strokes of their matchets:

> "Kotma *of the ash buttocks,*
> *He is fit to be a slave.*
> *The white man has no sense,*
> *He is fit to be a slave."*

The court messengers did not like to be called Ashy-Buttocks, and they beat the men. But the song spread in Umuofia.

Okonkwo's head was bowed in sadness as Obierika told him these things. "Perhaps I have been away too long," Okonkwo said, almost to himself. "But I cannot understand these things you tell me. What is it that has happened to our people? Why have they lost the power to fight?"

"Have you not heard how the white man wiped out Abame?" asked Obierika.

"I have heard," said Okonkwo. "But I have also heard that Abame people were weak and foolish. Why did they not fight back? Had they no guns and matchets? We would be cowards to compare ourselves with the men of Abame. Their fathers had never dared to stand before our ancestors. We must fight these men and drive them from the land."

"It is already too late," said Obierika sadly. "Our own men and our sons have joined the ranks of the stranger. They have joined his religion and they help to uphold his government. If we should try to drive out the white men in Umuofia we should find it easy. There are only two of them. But what of our own people who are following their way and have been given power? They would go to Umuru and bring the soldiers, and we would be like Abame." He paused for a long time and then said: "I told you on my last visit to Mbanta how they hanged Aneto."

"What has happened to that piece of land in dispute?" asked Okonkwo.

"The white man's court has decided that it should belong to Nnama's family, who had given much money to the white man's messengers and interpreter."

---

3. Court messenger (pidgin English).

"Does the white man understand our custom about land?"

"How can he when he does not even speak our tongue? But he says that our customs are bad; and our own brothers who have taken up his religion also say that our customs are bad. How do you think we can fight when our own brothers have turned against us? The white man is very clever. He came quietly and peaceably with his religion. We were amused at his foolishness and allowed him to stay. Now he has won our brothers, and our clan can no longer act like one. He has put a knife on the things that held us together and we have fallen apart."

"How did they get hold of Aneto to hang him?" asked Okonkwo.

"When he killed Oduche in the fight over the land, he fled to Aninta to escape the wrath of the earth. This was about eight days after the fight, because Oduche had not died immediately from his wounds. It was on the seventh day that he died. But everybody knew that he was going to die and Aneto got his belongings together in readiness to flee. But the Christians had told the white man about the accident, and he sent his *kotma* to catch Aneto. He was imprisoned with all the leaders of his family. In the end Oduche died and Aneto was taken to Umuru and hanged. The other people were released, but even now they have not found the mouth with which to tell of their suffering."

The two men sat in silence for a long while afterwards.

CHAPTER TWENTY-ONE

There were many men and women in Umuofia who did not feel as strongly as Okonkwo about the new dispensation. The white man had indeed brought a lunatic religion, but he had also built a trading store and for the first time palm-oil and kernel[4] became things of great price, and much money flowed into Umuofia.

And even in the matter of religion there was a growing feeling that there might be something in it after all, something vaguely akin to method in the overwhelming madness.

This growing feeling was due to Mr Brown, the white missionary, who was very firm in restraining his flock from provoking the wrath of the clan. One member in particular was very difficult to restrain. His name was Enoch and his father was the priest of the snake cult. The story went around that Enoch had killed and eaten the sacred python, and that his father had cursed him.

Mr Brown preached against such excess of zeal. Everything was possible, he told his energetic flock, but everything was not expedient. And so Mr Brown came to be respected even by the clan, because he trod softly on its faith. He made friends with some of the great men of the clan and on one of his frequent visits to the neighbouring villages he had been presented with a carved elephant tusk, which was a sign of dignity and rank. One of the great men in that village was called Akunna[5] and he had given one of his sons to be taught the white man's knowledge in Mr Brown's school.

Whenever Mr Brown went to that village he spent long hours with Akunna in his *obi* talking through an interpreter about religion. Neither of them succeeded in converting the other but they learnt more about their different beliefs.

---

4. The red fleshy husk of the palm nut is crushed manually to produce cooking oil, leaving a fibrous residue along with hard kernels. The Europeans bought both the red oil and the kernels, from which they could extract a very fine oil by using machines.
5. Father's wealth.

"You say that there is one supreme God who made heaven and earth," said Akunna on one of Mr Brown's visits. "We also believe in Him and call Him Chukwu. He made all the world and the other gods."

"There are no other gods," said Mr Brown. "Chukwu is the only God and all others are false. You carve a piece of wood—like that one" (he pointed at the rafters from which Akunna's carved *Ikenga*[6] hung), "and you call it a god. But it is still a piece of wood."

"Yes," said Akunna. "It is indeed a piece of wood. The tree from which it came was made by Chukwu, as indeed all minor gods were. But He made them for His messengers so that we could approach Him through them. It is like yourself. You are the head of your church."

"No," protested Mr Brown. "The head of my church is God Himself."

"I know," said Akunna, "but there must be a head in this world among men. Somebody like yourself must be the head here."

"The head of my church in that sense is in England."

"That is exactly what I am saying. The head of your church is in your country. He has sent you here as his messenger. And you have also appointed your own messengers and servants. Or let me take another example, the District Commissioner. He is sent by your king."

"They have a queen," said the interpreter on his own account.

"Your queen sends her messenger, the District Commissioner. He finds that he cannot do the work alone and so he appoints *kotma* to help him. It is the same with God, or Chukwu. He appoints the smaller gods to help Him because His work is too great for one person."

"You should not think of him as a person," said Mr Brown. "It is because you do so that you imagine He must need helpers. And the worst thing about it is that you give all the worship to the false gods you have created."

"That is not so. We make sacrifices to the little gods, but when they fail and there is no one else to turn to we go to Chukwu. It is right to do so. We approach a great man through his servants. But when his servants fail to help us, then we go to the last source of hope. We appear to pay greater attention to the little gods but that is not so. We worry them more because we are afraid to worry their Master. Our fathers knew that Chukwu was the Overlord and that is why many of them gave their children the name Chukwuka—'Chukwu is Supreme'."

"You said one interesting thing," said Mr Brown. "You are afraid of Chukwu. In my religion Chukwu is a loving Father and need not be feared by those who do His will."

"But we must fear Him when we are not doing His will," said Akunna. "And who is to tell His will? It is too great to be known."

In this way Mr Brown learnt a good deal about the religion of the clan and he came to the conclusion that a frontal attack on it would not succeed. And so he built a school and a little hospital in Umuofia. He went from family to family begging people to send their children to his school. But at first they only sent their slaves or sometimes their lazy children. Mr Brown begged and argued and prophesied. He said that the leaders of the land in the future would be men and women who had learnt to read and write. If Umuofia failed to send her children to the school, strangers would come from other places to rule them. They could already see that happening in the Native Court, where

---

6. A carved wooden figure with the horns of a ram that symbolized the strength of a man's right hand. Every adult male kept an *Ikenga* in his personal shrine.

the D.C. was surrounded by strangers who spoke his tongue. Most of these strangers came from the distant town of Umuru on the bank of the Great River where the white man first went.

In the end Mr Brown's arguments began to have an effect. More people came to learn in his school, and he encouraged them with gifts of singlets[7] and towels. They were not all young, these people who came to learn. Some of them were thirty years old or more. They worked on their farms in the morning and went to school in the afternoon. And it was not long before the people began to say that the white man's medicine was quick in working. Mr Brown's school produced quick results. A few months in it were enough to make one a court messenger or even a court clerk. Those who stayed longer became teachers; and from Umuofia labourers went forth into the Lord's vineyard. New churches were established in the surrounding villages and a few schools with them. From the very beginning religion and education went hand in hand.

Mr Brown's mission grew from strength to strength, and because of its link with the new administration it earned a new social prestige. But Mr Brown himself was breaking down in health. At first he ignored the warning signs. But in the end he had to leave his flock, sad and broken.

It was in the first rainy season after Okonkwo's return to Umuofia that Mr Brown left for home. As soon as he had learnt of Okonkwo's return five months earlier, the missionary had immediately paid him a visit. He had just sent Okonkwo's son, Nwoye, who was now called Isaac,[8] to the new training college for teachers in Umuru. And he had hoped that Okonkwo would be happy to hear of it. But Okonkwo had driven him away with the threat that if he came into his compound again, he would be carried out of it.

Okonkwo's return to his native land was not as memorable as he had wished. It was true his two beautiful daughters aroused great interest among suitors and marriage negotiations were soon in progress, but, beyond that, Umuofia did not appear to have taken any special notice of the warrior's return. The clan had undergone such profound change during his exile that it was barely recognisable. The new religion and government and the trading stores were very much in the people's eyes and minds. There were still many who saw these new institutions as evil, but even they talked and thought about little else, and certainly not about Okonkwo's return.

And it was the wrong year too. If Okonkwo had immediately initiated his two sons into the *ozo* society as he had planned he would have caused a stir. But the initiation rite was performed once in three years in Umuofia, and he had to wait for nearly two years for the next round of ceremonies.

Okonkwo was deeply grieved. And it was not just a personal grief. He mourned for the clan, which he saw breaking up and falling apart, and he mourned for the warlike men of Umuofia, who had so unaccountably become soft like women.

CHAPTER TWENTY-TWO

Mr Brown's successor was the Reverend James Smith, and he was a different kind of man. He condemned openly Mr Brown's policy of compromise and

7. Undershirts, T-shirts.
8. Son of Abraham, offered to God as a sacrifice (Genesis 22).

accommodation. He saw things as black and white. And black was evil. He saw the world as a battlefield in which the children of light were locked in mortal conflict with the sons of darkness. He spoke in his sermons about sheep and goats and about wheat and tares. He believed in slaying the prophets of Baal.

Mr Smith was greatly distressed by the ignorance which many of his flock showed even in such things as the Trinity and the Sacraments. It only showed that they were seeds sown on a rocky soil. Mr Brown had thought of nothing but numbers. He should have known that the kingdom of God did not depend on large crowds. Our Lord Himself stressed the importance of fewness. Narrow is the way and few the number. To fill the Lord's holy temple with an idolatrous crowd clamouring for signs was a folly of everlasting consequence. Our Lord used the whip only once in His life—to drive the crowd away from His church.

Within a few weeks of his arrival in Umuofia Mr Smith suspended a young woman from the church for pouring new wine into old bottles. This woman had allowed her heathen husband to mutilate her dead child. The child had been declared an *ogbanje*, plaguing its mother by dying and entering her womb to be born again. Four times this child had run its evil round. And so it was mutilated to discourage it from returning.

Mr Smith was filled with wrath when he heard of this. He disbelieved the story which even some of the most faithful confirmed, the story of really evil children who were not deterred by mutilation, but came back with all the scars. He replied that such stories were spread in the world by the Devil to lead men astray. Those who believed such stories were unworthy of the Lord's table.

There was a saying in Umuofia that as a man danced so the drums were beaten for him. Mr Smith danced a furious step and so the drums went mad. The over-zealous converts who had smarted under Mr Brown's restraining hand now flourished in full favour. One of them was Enoch, the son of the snake-priest who was believed to have killed and eaten the sacred python. Enoch's devotion to the new faith had seemed so much greater than Mr Brown's that the villagers called him The outsider who wept louder than the bereaved.

Enoch was short and slight of build, and always seemed in great haste. His feet were short and broad, and when he stood or walked his heels came together and his feet opened outwards as if they had quarrelled and meant to go in different directions. Such was the excessive energy bottled up in Enoch's small body that it was always erupting in quarrels and fights. On Sundays he always imagined that the sermon was preached for the benefit of his enemies. And if he happened to sit near one of them he would occasionally turn to give him a meaningful look, as if to say, 'I told you so'. It was Enoch who touched off the great conflict between church and clan in Umuofia which had been gathering since Mr Brown left.

It happened during the annual ceremony which was held in honour of the earth deity. At such times the ancestors of the clan who had been committed to Mother Earth at their death emerged again as *egwugwu* through tiny ant-holes.

One of the greatest crimes a man could commit was to unmask an *egwugwu* in public, or to say or do anything which might reduce its immortal prestige in the eyes of the uninitiated. And this was what Enoch did.

The annual worship of the earth goddess fell on a Sunday, and the masked spirits were abroad. The Christian women who had been to church could not therefore go home. Some of their men had gone out to beg the egwugwu to retire for a short while for the women to pass. They agreed and were already retiring, when Enoch boasted aloud that they would not dare to touch a Christian. Whereupon they all came back and one of them gave Enoch a good stroke of the cane, which was always carried. Enoch fell on him and tore off his mask. The other egwugwu immediately surrounded their desecrated companion, to shield him from the profane gaze of women and children, and led him away. Enoch had killed an ancestral spirit, and Umuofia was thrown into confusion.

That night the Mother of the Spirits walked the length and breadth of the clan, weeping for her murdered son. It was a terrible night. Not even the oldest man in Umuofia had ever heard such a strange and fearful sound, and it was never to be heard again. It seemed as if the very soul of the tribe wept for a great evil that was coming—its own death.

On the next day all the masked egwugwu of Umuofia assembled in the market-place. They came from all the quarters of the clan and even from the neighbouring villages. The dreaded Otakagu came from Imo, and Ekwensu, dangling a white cock, arrived from Uli. It was a terrible gathering. The eerie voices of countless spirits, the bells that clattered behind some of them, and the clash of matchets as they ran forwards and backwards and saluted one another, sent tremors of fear into every heart. For the first time in living memory the sacred bull-roarer was heard in broad daylight.

From the market-place the furious band made for Enoch's compound. Some of the elders of the clan went with them, wearing heavy protections of charms and amulets. These were men whose arms were strong in ogwu, or medicine. As for the ordinary men and women, they listened from the safety of their huts.

The leaders of the Christians had met together at Mr Smith's parsonage on the previous night. As they deliberated they could hear the Mother of Spirits wailing for her son. The chilling sound affected Mr Smith, and for the first time he seemed to be afraid.

"What are they planning to do?" he asked. No one knew, because such a thing had never happened before. Mr Smith would have sent for the District Commissioner and his court messengers, but they had gone on tour on the previous day.

"One thing is clear," said Mr Smith. "We cannot offer physical resistance to them. Our strength lies in the Lord." They knelt down together and prayed to God for delivery.

"O Lord save Thy people," cried Mr Smith.

"And bless Thine inheritance," replied the men.

They decided that Enoch should be hidden in the parsonage for a day or two. Enoch himself was greatly disappointed when he heard this, for he had hoped that a holy war was imminent; and there were a few other Christians who thought like him. But wisdom prevailed in the camp of the faithful and many lives were thus saved.

The band of egwugwu moved like a furious whirlwind to Enoch's compound and with matchet and fire reduced it to a desolate heap. And from there they made for the church, intoxicated with destruction.

Mr Smith was in his church when he heard the masked spirits coming. He walked quietly to the door which commanded the approach to the church compound, and stood there. But when the first three or four *egwugwu* appeared on the church compound he nearly bolted. He overcame this impulse and instead of running away he went down the two steps that led up to the church and walked towards the approaching spirits.

They surged forward, and a long stretch of the bamboo fence with which the church compound was surrounded gave way before them. Discordant bells clanged, matchets clashed and the air was full of dust and weird sounds. Mr Smith heard a sound of footsteps behind him. He turned round and saw Okeke, his interpreter. Okeke had not been on the best of terms with his master since he had strongly condemned Enoch's behaviour at the meeting of the leaders of the church during the night. Okeke had gone as far as to say that Enoch should not be hidden in the parsonage, because he would only draw the wrath of the clan on the pastor. Mr Smith had rebuked him in very strong language, and had not sought his advice that morning. But now, as he came up and stood by him confronting the angry spirits, Mr Smith looked at him and smiled. It was a wan smile, but there was deep gratitude there.

For a brief moment the onrush of the *egwugwu* was checked by the unexpected composure of the two men. But it was only a momentary check, like the tense silence between blasts of thunder. The second onrush was greater than the first. It swallowed up the two men. Then an unmistakable voice rose above the tumult and there was immediate silence. Space was made around the two men, and Ajofia began to speak.

Ajofia was the leading *egwugwu* of Umuofia. He was the head and spokesman of the nine ancestors who administered justice in the clan. His voice was unmistakable and so he was able to bring immediate peace to the agitated spirits. He then addressed Mr Smith, and as he spoke clouds of smoke rose from his head.

"The body of the white man, I salute you," he said, using the language in which immortals spoke to men.

"The body of the white man, do you know me?" he asked.

Mr Smith looked at his interpreter, but Okeke, who was a native of distant Umuru, was also at a loss.

Ajofia laughed in his guttural voice. It was like the laugh of rusty metal. "They are strangers," he said, "and they are ignorant. But let that pass." He turned round to his comrades and saluted them, calling them the fathers of Umuofia. He dug his rattling spear into the ground and it shook with metallic life. Then he turned once more to the missionary and his interpreter.

"Tell the white man that we will not do him any harm," he said to the interpreter. "Tell him to go back to his house and leave us alone. We liked his brother who was with us before. He was foolish, but we liked him, and for his sake we shall not harm his brother. But this shrine which he built must be destroyed. We shall no longer allow it in our midst. It has bred untold abominations and we have come to put an end to it." He turned to his comrades. "Fathers of Umuofia, I salute you;" and they replied with one guttural voice. He turned again to the missionary. "You can stay with us if you like our ways. You can worship your own god. It is good that a man should worship the gods and the spirits of his fathers. Go back to your house so that you may not be hurt. Our anger is great but we have held it down so that we can talk to you."

Mr Smith said to his interpreter: "Tell them to go away from here. This is the house of God and I will not live to see it desecrated."

Okeke interpreted wisely to the spirits and leaders of Umuofia: "The white man says he is happy you have come to him with your grievances, like friends. He will be happy if you leave the matter in his hands."

"We cannot leave the matter in his hands because he does not understand our customs, just as we do not understand his. We say he is foolish because he does not know our ways, and perhaps he says we are foolish because we do not know his. Let him go away."

Mr Smith stood his ground. But he could not save his church. When the *egwugwu* went away the red-earth church which Mr Brown had built was a pile of earth and ashes. And for the moment the spirit of the clan was pacified.

CHAPTER TWENTY-THREE

For the first time in many years Okonkwo had a feeling that was akin to happiness. The times which had altered so unaccountably during his exile seemed to be coming round again. The clan which had turned false on him appeared to be making amends.

He had spoken violently to his clansmen when they had met in the market-place to decide on their action. And they had listened to him with respect. It was like the good old days again, when a warrior was a warrior. Although they had not agreed to kill the missionary or drive away the Christians, they had agreed to do something substantial. And they had done it. Okonkwo was almost happy again.

For two days after the destruction of the church, nothing happened. Every man in Umuofia went about armed with a gun or a matchet. They would not be caught unawares, like the men of Abame.

Then the District Commissioner returned from his tour. Mr Smith went immediately to him and they had a long discussion. The men of Umuofia did not take any notice of this, and if they did, they thought it was not important. The missionary often went to see his brother white man. There was nothing strange in that.

Three days later the District Commissioner sent his sweet-tongued messenger to the leaders of Umuofia asking them to meet him in his headquarters. That also was not strange. He often asked them to hold such palavers, as he called them. Okonkwo was among the six leaders he invited.

Okonkwo warned the others to be fully armed. "An Umuofia man does not refuse a call," he said. "He may refuse to do what he is asked; he does not refuse to be asked. But the times have changed, and we must be fully prepared."

And so the six men went to see the District Commissioner, armed with their matchets. They did not carry guns, for that would be unseemly. They were led into the court-house where the District Commissioner sat. He received them politely. They unslung their goatskin bags and their sheathed matchets, put them on the floor, and sat down.

"I have asked you to come," began the Commissioner, "because of what happened during my absence. I have been told a few things but I cannot believe them until I have heard your own side. Let us talk about it like friends and find a way of ensuring that it does not happen again."

Ogbuefi Ekwueme[9] rose to his feet and began to tell the story.

9. A person who does what he says (a praise name).

"Wait a minute," said the Commissioner. "I want to bring in my men so that they too can hear your grievances and take warning. Many of them come from distant places and although they speak your tongue they are ignorant of your customs. James! Go and bring in the men." His interpreter left the court-room and soon returned with twelve men. They sat together with the men of Umuofia, and Ogbuefi Ekwueme began again to tell the story of how Enoch murdered an *egwugwu*.

It happened so quickly that the six men did not see it coming. There was only a brief scuffle, too brief even to allow the drawing of a sheathed matchet. The six men were handcuffed and led into the guardroom.

"We shall not do you any harm," said the District Commissioner to them later, "if only you agree to co-operate with us. We have brought a peaceful administration to you and your people so that you may be happy. If any man ill-treats you we shall come to your rescue. But we will not allow you to ill-treat others. We have a court of law where we judge cases and administer justice just as it is done in my own country under a great queen. I have brought you here because you joined together to molest others, to burn people's houses and their place of worship. That must not happen in the dominion of our queen, the most powerful ruler in the world. I have decided that you will pay a fine of two hundred bags of cowries. You will be released as soon as you agree to this and undertake to collect that fine from your people. What do you say to that?"

The six men remained sullen and silent and the Commissioner left them for a while. He told the court messengers, when he left the guardroom, to treat the men with respect because they were the leaders of Umuofia. They said, "Yes, sir," and saluted.

As soon as the District Commissioner left, the head messenger, who was also the prisoners' barber, took down his razor and shaved off all the hair on the men's heads. They were still handcuffed, and they just sat and moped.

"Who is the chief among you?" the court messengers asked in jest. "We see that every pauper wears the anklet of title in Umuofia. Does it cost as much as ten cowries?"

The six men ate nothing throughout that day and the next. They were not even given any water to drink, and they could not go out to urinate or go into the bush when they were pressed. At night the messengers came in to taunt them and to knock their shaven heads together.

Even when the men were left alone they found no words to speak to one another. It was only on the third day, when they could no longer bear the hunger and the insults, that they began to talk about giving in.

"We should have killed the white man if you had listened to me," Okonkwo snarled.

"We could have been in Umuru now waiting to be hanged," someone said to him.

"Who wants to kill the white man?" asked a messenger who had just rushed in. Nobody spoke.

"You are not satisfied with your crime, but you must kill the white man on top of it." He carried a strong stick, and he hit each man a few blows on the head and back. Okonkwo was choked with hate.

As soon as the six men were locked up, court messengers went into Umuofia to tell the people that their leaders would not be released unless they paid a fine of two hundred and fifty bags of cowries.

"Unless you pay the fine immediately," said their headman, "we will take your leaders to Umuru before the big white man, and hang them."

This story spread quickly through the villages, and was added to as it went. Some said that the men had already been taken to Umuru and would be hanged on the following day. Some said that their families would also be hanged. Others said that soldiers were already on their way to shoot the people of Umuofia as they had done in Abame.

It was the time of the full moon. But that night the voice of children was not heard. The village *ilo* where they always gathered for a moon-play was empty. The women of Iguedo did not meet in their secret enclosure to learn a new dance to be displayed later to the village. Young men who were always abroad in the moonlight kept their huts that night. Their manly voices were not heard on the village paths as they went to visit their friends and lovers. Umuofia was like a startled animal with ears erect, sniffing the silent, ominous air and not knowing which way to run.

The silence was broken by the village crier beating his sonorous *ogene*. He called every man in Umuofia, from the Akakanma age-group upwards, to a meeting in the market-place after the morning meal. He went from one end of the village to the other and walked all its breadth. He did not leave out any of the main footpaths.

Okonkwo's compound was like a deserted homestead. It was as if cold water had been poured on it. His family was all there, but everyone spoke in whispers. His daughter Ezinma had broken her twenty-eight-day visit to the family of her future husband, and returned home when she heard that her father had been imprisoned, and was going to be hanged. As soon as she got home she went to Obierika to ask what the men of Umuofia were going to do about it. But Obierika had not been home since morning. His wives thought he had gone to a secret meeting. Ezinma was satisfied that something was being done.

On the morning after the village crier's appeal the men of Umuofia met in the market-place and decided to collect without delay two hundred and fifty bags of cowries to appease the white man. They did not know that fifty bags would go to the court messengers, who had increased the fine for that purpose.

CHAPTER TWENTY-FOUR

Okonkwo and his fellow prisoners were set free as soon as the fine was paid. The District Commissioner spoke to them again about the great queen, and about peace and good government. But the men did not listen. They just sat and looked at him and at his interpreter. In the end they were given back their bags and sheathed matchets and told to go home. They rose and left the court-house. They neither spoke to anyone nor among themselves.

The court-house, like the church, was built a little way outside the village. The footpath that linked them was a very busy one because it also led to the stream, beyond the court. It was open and sandy. Footpaths were open and sandy in the dry season. But when the rains came the bush grew thick on either side and closed in on the path. It was now dry season.

As they made their way to the village the six men met women and children going to the stream with their waterpots. But the men wore such heavy and fearsome looks that the women and children did not say '*nno*' or 'welcome' to them, but edged out of the way to let them pass. In the village little groups of men joined them until they became a sizeable company. They walked silently.

As each of the six men got to his compound, he turned in, taking some of the crowd with him. The village was astir in a silent, suppressed way.

Ezinma had prepared some food for her father as soon as news spread that the six men would be released. She took it to him in his *obi*. He ate absent-mindedly. He had no appetite; he only ate to please her. His male relations and friends had gathered in his *obi*, and Obierika was urging him to eat. Nobody else spoke, but they noticed the long stripes on Okonkwo's back where the warder's whip had cut into his flesh.

The village crier was abroad again in the night. He beat his iron gong and announced that another meeting would be held in the morning. Everyone knew that Umuofia was at last going to speak its mind about the things that were happening.

Okonkwo slept very little that night. The bitterness in his heart was now mixed with a kind of child-like excitement. Before he had gone to bed he had brought down his war dress, which he had not touched since his return from exile. He had shaken out his smoked raffia skirt and examined his tall feather head-gear and his shield. They were all satisfactory, he had thought.

As he lay on his bamboo bed he thought about the treatment he had received in the white man's court, and he swore vengeance. If Umuofia decided on war, all would be well. But if they chose to be cowards he would go out and avenge himself. He thought about wars in the past. The noblest, he thought, was the war against Isike. In those days Okudo[1] was still alive. Okudo sang a war song in a way that no other man could. He was not a fighter, but his voice turned every man into a lion.

'Worthy men are no more,' Okonkwo sighed as he remembered those days. 'Isike will never forget how we slaughtered them in that war. We killed twelve of their men and they killed only two of ours. Before the end of the fourth market week they were suing for peace. Those were days when men were men.'

As he thought of these things he heard the sound of the iron gong in the distance. He listened carefully, and could just hear the crier's voice. But it was very faint. He turned on his bed and his back hurt him. He ground his teeth. The crier was drawing nearer and nearer until he passed by Okonkwo's compound.

'The greatest obstacle in Umuofia,' Okonkwo thought bitterly, 'is that coward, Egonwanne.[2] His sweet tongue can change fire into cold ash. When he speaks he moves our men to impotence. If they had ignored his womanish wisdom five years ago, we would not have come to this.' He ground his teeth. 'Tomorrow he will tell them that our fathers never fought a "war of blame". If they listen to him I shall leave them and plan my own revenge.'

The crier's voice had once more become faint, and the distance had taken the harsh edge off his iron gong. Okonkwo turned from one side to the other and derived a kind of pleasure from the pain his back gave him. 'Let Egonwanne talk about a "war of blame" tomorrow and I shall show him my back and head.' He ground his teeth.

The market-place began to fill as soon as the sun rose. Obierika was waiting in his *obi* when Okonkwo came along and called him. He hung his goatskin bag and his sheathed matchet on his shoulder and went out to join him. Obi-

---

1. Great eagle feather (a praise name).   2. Wealth of a sibling.

erika's hut was close to the road and he saw every man who passed to the market-place. He had exchanged greetings with many who had already passed that morning.

When Okonkwo and Obierika got to the meeting-place there were already so many people that if one threw up a grain of sand it would not find its way to the earth again. And many more people were coming from every quarter of the nine villages. It warmed Okonkwo's heart to see such strength of numbers. But he was looking for one man in particular, the man whose tongue he dreaded and despised so much.

"Can you see him?" he asked Obierika.

"Who?"

"Egonwanne," he said, his eyes roving from one corner of the huge market-place to the other. Most of the men were seated on goatskins on the ground. A few of them sat on wooden stools they had brought with them.

"No," said Obierika, casting his eyes over the crowd. "Yes, there he is, under the silk-cotton tree. Are you afraid he would convince us not to fight?"

"Afraid? I do not care what he does to *you*. I despise him and those who listen to him. I shall fight alone if I choose."

They spoke at the top of their voices because everybody was talking, and it was like the sound of a great market.

'I shall wait till he has spoken,' Okonkwo thought. 'Then I shall speak.'

"But how do you know he will speak against war?" Obierika asked after a while.

"Because I know he is a coward," said Okonkwo. Obierika did not hear the rest of what he said because at that moment somebody touched his shoulder from behind and he turned round to shake hands and exchange greetings with five or six friends. Okonkwo did not turn round even though he knew the voices. He was in no mood to exchange greetings. But one of the men touched him and asked about the people of his compound.

"They are well," he replied without interest.

The first man to speak to Umuofia that morning was Okika, one of the six who had been imprisoned. Okika was a great man and an orator. But he did not have the booming voice which a first speaker must use to establish silence in the assembly of the clan. Onyeka[3] had such a voice; and so he was asked to salute Umuofia before Okika began to speak.

"*Umuofia kwenu!*" he bellowed, raising his left arm and pushing the air with his open hand.

"*Yaa!*" roared Umuofia.

"*Umuofia kwenu!*" he bellowed again, and again and again, facing a new direction each time. And the crowd answered, "*Yaa!*"

There was immediate silence as though cold water had been poured on a roaring flame.

Okika sprang to his feet and also saluted his clansmen four times. Then he began to speak:

"You all know why we are here, when we ought to be building our barns or mending our huts, when we should be putting our compounds in order. My father used to say to me: 'Whenever you see a toad jumping in broad daylight, then know that something is after its life.' When I saw you all pouring into this meeting from all the quarters of our clan so early in the morning, I knew

3. "Who surpasses [God]?" (a rhetorical question).

that something was after our life." He paused for a brief moment and then
began again:

"All our gods are weeping. Idemili is weeping, Ogwugwu is weeping, Agbala
is weeping, and all the others. Our dead fathers are weeping because of the
shameful sacrilege they are suffering and the abomination we have all seen
with our eyes." He stopped again to steady his trembling voice.

"This is a great gathering. No clan can boast of greater numbers or greater
valour. But are we all here? I ask you: Are all the sons of Umuofia with us
here?" A deep murmur swept through the crowd.

"They are not," he said. "They have broken the clan and gone their several
ways. We who are here this morning have remained true to our fathers, but
our brothers have deserted us and joined a stranger to soil their fatherland. If
we fight the stranger we shall hit our brothers and perhaps shed the blood of
a clansman. But we must do it. Our fathers never dreamt of such a thing, they
never killed their brothers. But a white man never came to them. So we must
do what our fathers would never have done. Eneke the bird was asked why he
was always on the wing and he replied: 'Men have learnt to shoot without
missing their mark and I have learnt to fly without perching on a twig.' We
must root out this evil. And if our brothers take the side of evil we must root
them out too. And we must do it *now*. We must bale this water now that it is
only ankle-deep. . . ."

At this point there was a sudden stir in the crowd and every eye was turned
in one direction. There was a sharp bend in the road that led from the market
place to the white man's court, and to the stream beyond it. And so no one
had seen the approach of the five court messengers until they had come round
the bend, a few paces from the edge of the crowd. Okonkwo was sitting at the
edge.

He sprang to his feet as soon as he saw who it was. He confronted the head
messenger, trembling with hate, unable to utter a word. The man was fearless
and stood his ground, his four men lined up behind him.

In that brief moment the world seemed to stand still, waiting. There was
utter silence. The men of Umuofia were merged into the mute backcloth of
trees and giant creepers, waiting.

The spell was broken by the head messenger. "Let me pass!" he ordered.

"What do you want here?"

"The white man whose power you know too well has ordered this meeting
to stop."

In a flash Okonkwo drew his matchet. The messenger crouched to avoid
the blow. It was useless. Okonkwo's matchet descended twice and the man's
head lay beside his uniformed body.

The waiting backcloth jumped into tumultuous life and the meeting was
stopped. Okonkwo stood looking at the dead man. He knew that Umuofia
would not go to war. He knew because they had let the other messengers
escape. They had broken into tumult instead of action. He discerned fright in
that tumult. He heard voices asking: "Why did he do it?"

He wiped his matchet on the sand and went away.

CHAPTER TWENTY-FIVE

When the District Commissioner arrived at Okonkwo's compound at the
head of an armed band of soldiers and court messengers he found a small

crowd of men sitting wearily in the *obi*. He commanded them to come outside, and they obeyed without a murmur.

"Which among you is called Okonkwo?" he asked through his interpreter.

"He is not here," replied Obierika.

"Where is he?"

"He is not here!"

The Commissioner became angry and red in the face. He warned the men that unless they produced Okonkwo forthwith he would lock them all up. The men murmured among themselves, and Obierika spoke again.

"We can take you where he is, and perhaps your men will help us."

The Commissioner did not understand what Obierika meant when he said, "Perhaps your men will help us." One of the most infuriating habits of these people was their love of superfluous words, he thought.

Obierika with five or six others led the way. The Commissioner and his men followed, their firearms held at the ready. He had warned Obierika that if he and his men played any monkey tricks they would be shot. And so they went.

There was a small bush behind Okonkwo's compound. The only opening into this bush from the compound was a little round hole in the red-earth wall through which fowls went in and out in their endless search for food. The hole would not let a man through. It was to this bush that Obierika led the Commissioner and his men. They skirted round the compound, keeping close to the wall. The only sound they made was with their feet as they crushed dry leaves.

Then they came to the tree from which Okonkwo's body was dangling, and they stopped dead.

"Perhaps your men can help us bring him down and bury him," said Obierika. "We have sent for strangers from another village to do it for us, but they may be a long time coming."

The District Commissioner changed instantaneously. The resolute administrator in him gave way to the student of primitive customs.

"Why can't you take him down yourselves?" he asked.

"It is against our custom," said one of the men. "It is an abomination for a man to take his own life. It is an offence against the Earth, and a man who commits it will not be buried by his clansmen. His body is evil, and only strangers may touch it. That is why we ask your people to bring him down, because you are strangers."

"Will you bury him like any other man?" asked the Commissioner.

"We cannot bury him. Only strangers can. We shall pay your men to do it. When he has been buried we will then do our duty by him. We shall make sacrifices to cleanse the desecrated land."

Obierika, who had been gazing steadily at his friend's dangling body, turned suddenly to the District Commissioner and said ferociously: "That man was one of the greatest men in Umuofia. You drove him to kill himself; and now he will be buried like a dog. . . ." He could not say any more. His voice trembled and choked his words.

"Shut up!" shouted one of the messengers, quite unnecessarily.

"Take down the body," the Commissioner ordered his chief messenger, "and bring it and all these people to the court."

"Yes, sah," the messenger said, saluting.

The Commissioner went away, taking three or four of the soldiers with him. In the many years in which he had toiled to bring civilisation to different parts of Africa he had learnt a number of things. One of them was that a District Commissioner must never attend to such undignified details as cutting down a hanged man from the tree. Such attention would give the natives a poor opinion of him. In the book which he planned to write he would stress that point. As he walked back to the court he thought about that book. Every day brought him some new material. The story of this man who had killed a messenger and hanged himself would make interesting reading. One could almost write a whole chapter on him. Perhaps not a whole chapter but a reasonable paragraph, at any rate. There was so much else to include, and one must be firm in cutting out details. He had already chosen the title of the book, after much thought: *The Pacification of the Primitive Tribes of the Lower Niger*.

1958

From An Image of Africa: Racism in Conrad's *Heart of Darkness*

Heart of Darkness projects the image of Africa as 'the other world', the antithesis of Europe and therefore of civilization, a place where man's vaunted intelligence and refinement are finally mocked by triumphant bestiality. The book opens on the River Thames, tranquil, resting peacefully 'at the decline of day after ages of good service done to the race that peopled its banks' (1892).[1] But the actual story will take place on the River Congo, the very antithesis of the Thames. The River Congo is quite decidedly not a River Emeritus.[2] It has rendered no service and enjoys no old-age pension. We are told that 'going up that river was like travelling back to the earliest beginning of the world'.

Is Conrad saying then that these two rivers are very different, one good, the other bad? Yes, but that is not the real point. It is not the differentness that worries Conrad but the lurking hint of kinship, of common ancestry. For the Thames too 'has been one of the dark places of the earth'. It conquered its darkness, of course, and is now in daylight and at peace. But if it were to visit its primordial relative, the Congo, it would run the terrible risk of hearing grotesque echoes of its own forgotten darkness, and falling victim to an avenging recrudescence of the mindless frenzy of the first beginnings.

These suggestive echoes comprise Conrad's famed evocation of the African atmosphere in *Heart of Darkness*. In the final consideration his method amounts to no more than a steady, ponderous, fake-ritualistic repetition of two antithetical sentences, one about silence and the other about frenzy. We can inspect samples of this on pages 1914 and 1916: (a) 'It was the stillness of an implacable force brooding over an inscrutable intention' and (b) 'The steamer toiled along slowly on the edge of a black and incomprehensible frenzy.' Of course there is a judicious change of adjective from time to time, so that instead of inscrutable', for example, you might have 'unspeakable', even plain 'mysterious', etc., etc.

The eagle-eyed English critic F. R. Leavis[3] drew attention long ago to

---

1. Page numbers refer to this volume of *The Norton Anthology of English Literature*.
2. Honorably discharged from service.

3. Frank Raymond Leavis (1895–1978), famous English literary critic and Cambridge University academic.

Conrad's 'adjectival insistence upon inexpressible and incomprehensible mystery'. That insistence must not be dismissed lightly, as many Conrad critics have tended to do, as a mere stylistic flaw; for it raises serious questions of artistic good faith. When a writer while pretending to record scenes, incidents and their impact is in reality engaged in inducing hypnotic stupor in his readers through a bombardment of emotive words and other forms of trickery, much more has to be at stake than stylistic felicity. Generally normal readers are well armed to detect and resist such underhand activity. But Conrad chose his subject well—one which was guaranteed not to put him in conflict with the psychological predisposition of his readers or raise the need for him to contend with their resistance. He chose the role of purveyor of comforting myths.

The most interesting and revealing passages in *Heart of Darkness* are, however, about people. I must crave the indulgence of my reader to quote almost a whole page from about the middle of the story when representatives of Europe in a steamer going down the Congo encounter the denizens of Africa:

> We were wanderers on a prehistoric earth, on an earth that wore the aspect of an unknown planet. We could have fancied ourselves the first of men taking possession of an accursed inheritance, to be subdued at the cost of profound anguish and of excessive toil. But suddenly, as we struggled round a bend, there would be a glimpse of rush walls, of peaked grass-roofs, a burst of yells, a whirl of black limbs, a mass of hands clapping, of feet stamping, of bodies swaying, of eyes rolling, under the droop of heavy and motionless foliage. The steamer toiled along slowly on the edge of the black and incomprehensible frenzy. The prehistoric man was cursing us, praying to us, welcoming us—who could tell? We were cut off from the comprehension of our surroundings; we glided past like phantoms, wondering and secretly appalled, as sane men would be before an enthusiastic outbreak in a madhouse. We could not understand because we were too far and could not remember because we were travelling in the night of first ages, of those ages that are gone, leaving hardly a sign—and no memories.
>
> The earth seemed unearthly. We are accustomed to look upon the shackled form of a conquered monster, but there—there you could look at a thing monstrous and free. It was unearthly, and the men were—No, they were not inhuman. Well, you know, that was the worst of it—this suspicion of their not being inhuman. It would come slowly to one. They howled and leaped, and spun, and made horrid faces; but what thrilled you was just the thought of their humanity—like yours—the thought of your remote kinship with this wild and passionate uproar. Ugly. Yes, it was ugly enough; but if you were man enough you would admit to yourself that there was in you just the faintest trace of a response to the terrible frankness of that noise, a dim suspicion of there being a meaning in it which you—you so remote from the night of first ages—could comprehend. (1916)

Herein lies the meaning of *Heart of Darkness* and the fascination it holds over the Western mind: 'What thrilled you was just the thought of their humanity—like yours . . . Ugly.'

Having shown us Africa in the mass, Conrad then zeros in, half a page later, on a specific example, giving us one of his rare descriptions of an African who is not just limbs or rolling eyes:

And between whiles I had to look after the savage who was fireman. He was an improved specimen; he could fire up a vertical boiler. He was there below me, and, upon my word, to look at him was as edifying as seeing a dog in a parody of breeches and a feather hat, walking on his hind legs. A few months of training had done for that really fine chap. He squinted at the steam gauge and at the water gauge with an evident effort of intrepidity—and he had filed his teeth, too, the poor devil, and the wool of his pate shaved into queer patterns, and three ornamental scars on each of his cheeks. He ought to have been clapping his hands and stamping his feet on the bank, instead of which he was hard at work, a thrall to strange witchcraft, full of improving knowledge. (1916–17)

As everybody knows, Conrad is a romantic on the side. He might not exactly admire savages clapping their hands and stamping their feet but they have at least the merit of being in their place, unlike this dog in a parody of breeches. For Conrad things being in their place is of the utmost importance.

'Fine fellows—cannibals—in their place,' he tells us pointedly. Tragedy begins when things leave their accustomed place, like Europe leaving its safe stronghold between the policeman and the baker to take a peep into the heart of darkness.

Before the story takes us into the Congo basin proper we are given this nice little vignette as an example of things in their place:

Now and then a boat from the shore gave one a momentary contact with reality. It was paddled by black fellows. You could see from afar the white of their eyeballs glistening. They shouted, sang; their bodies streamed with perspiration; they had faces like grotesque masks—these chaps; but they had bone, muscle, a wild vitality, an intense energy of movement, that was as natural and true as the surf along their coast. They wanted no excuse for being there. They were a great comfort to look at. (1899)

Towards the end of the story Conrad lavishes a whole page quite unexpectedly on an African woman who has obviously been some kind of mistress to Mr Kurtz and now presides (if I may be permitted a little liberty) like a formidable mystery over the inexorable imminence of his departure:

She was savage and superb, wild-eyed and magnificent . . . She stood looking at us without a stir and like the wilderness itself, with an air of brooding over an inscrutable purpose. (1935)

This Amazon is drawn in considerable detail, albeit of a predictable nature, for two reasons. First, she is in her place and so can win Conrad's special brand of approval; and second, she fulfils a structural requirement of the story: a savage counterpart to the refined, European woman who will step forth to end the story:

She came forward, all in black with a pale head, floating toward me in the dusk. She was in mourning . . . She took both my hands in hers and murmured, 'I had heard you were coming' . . . She had a mature capacity for fidelity, for belief, for suffering. (1945)

The difference in the attitude of the novelist to these two women is conveyed in too many direct and subtle ways to need elaboration. But perhaps the most significant difference is the one implied in the author's bestowal of human expression to the one and the withholding of it from the other. It is clearly not part of Conrad's purpose to confer language on the 'rudimentary souls' of Africa. In place of speech they made 'a violent babble of uncouth sounds'. They 'exchanged short grunting phrases' even among themselves. But most of the time they were too busy with their frenzy. There are two occasions in the book, however, when Conrad departs somewhat from his practice and confers speech, even English speech, on the savages. The first occurs when cannibalism gets the better of them:

'Catch 'im,' he snapped, with a bloodshot widening of his eyes and a flash of sharp white teeth—'catch 'im. Give 'im to us.' 'To you, eh?' I asked; 'what would you do with them?' 'Eat 'im!' he said curtly. (1919)

The other occasion was the famous announcement: 'Mistah Kurtz—he dead' (1941).

At first sight these instances might be mistaken for unexpected acts of generosity from Conrad. In reality they constitute some of his best assaults. In the case of the cannibals the incomprehensible grunts that had thus far served them for speech suddenly proved inadequate for Conrad's purpose of letting the European glimpse the unspeakable craving in their hearts. Weighing the necessity for consistency in the portrayal of the dumb brutes against the sensational advantages of securing their conviction by clear, unambiguous evidence issuing out of their own mouth Conrad chose the latter. As for the announcement of Mr Kurtz's death by the 'insolent black head in the doorway', what better or more appropriate *finis* could be written to the horror story of that wayward child of civilization who wilfully had given his soul to the powers of darkness and 'taken a high seat amongst the devils of the land' than the proclamation of his physical death by the forces he had joined?

It might be contended, of course, that the attitude to the African in *Heart of Darkness* is not Conrad's but that of his fictional narrator, Marlow, and that far from endorsing it Conrad might indeed be holding it up to irony and criticism. Certainly Conrad appears to go to considerable pains to set up layers of insulation between himself and the moral universe of his story. He has, for example, a narrator behind a narrator. The primary narrator is Marlow but his account is given to us through the filter of a second, shadowy person. But if Conrad's intention is to draw a cordon sanitaire[4] between himself and the moral and psychological *malaise* of his narrator his care seems to me totally wasted because he neglects to hint, clearly and adequately, at an alternative frame of reference by which we may judge the actions and opinions of his characters. It would not have been beyond Conrad's power to make that provision if he had thought it necessary. Conrad seems to me to approve of Marlow, with only minor reservations—a fact reinforced by the similarities between their two careers.

Marlow comes through to us not only as a witness of truth, but one holding those advanced and humane views appropriate to the English liberal tradition which required all Englishmen of decency to be deeply shocked by atrocities in Bulgaria or the Congo of King Leopold of the Belgians[5] or wherever.

Thus Marlow is able to toss out such bleeding-heart sentiments as these:

---

4. A guarded line between infected and uninfected areas.
5. Leopold II (1835–1909) satisfied a lust for personal wealth by the brutal exploitation of the people of the Belgian Congo.

They were all dying slowly—it was very clear. They were not enemies, they were not criminals, they were nothing earthly now—nothing but black shadows of disease and starvation, lying confusedly in the greenish gloom. Brought from all the recesses of the coast in all the legality of time contracts, lost in uncongenial surroundings, fed on unfamiliar food, they sickened, became inefficient, and were then allowed to crawl away and rest. (1901)

The kind of liberalism espoused here by Marlow/Conrad touched all the best minds of the age in England, Europe and America. It took different forms in the minds of different people but almost always managed to sidestep the ultimate question of equality between white people and black people. That extraordinary missionary, Albert Schweitzer,[6] who sacrificed brilliant careers in music and theology in Europe for a life of service to Africans in much the same area as Conrad writes about, epitomizes the ambivalence. In a comment which has often been quoted Schweitzer says: 'The African is indeed my brother but my junior brother.' And so he proceeded to build a hospital appropriate to the needs of junior brothers with standards of hygiene reminiscent of medical practice in the days before the germ theory of disease came into being. Naturally he became a sensation in Europe and America. Pilgrims flocked, and I believe still flock even after he has passed on, to witness the prodigious miracle in Lamberene, on the edge of the primeval forest.

Conrad's liberalism would not take him quite as far as Schweitzer's, though. He would not use the word 'brother' however qualified; the farthest he would go was 'kinship'. When Marlow's African helmsman falls down with a spear in his heart he gives his white master one final disquieting look:

And the intimate profundity of that look he gave me when he received his hurt remains to this day in my memory—like a claim of distant kinship affirmed in a supreme moment.

It is important to note that Conrad, careful as ever with his words, is concerned not so much about 'distant kinship' as about someone *laying a claim* on it. The black man lays a claim on the white man which is well-nigh intolerable. It is the laying of this claim which frightens and at the same time fascinates Conrad, 'the thought of their humanity—like yours . . . Ugly.'

The point of my observations should be quite clear by now, namely that Joseph Conrad was a thoroughgoing racist. That this simple truth is glossed over in criticisms of his work is due to the fact that white racism against Africa is such a normal way of thinking that its manifestations go completely unremarked. Students of *Heart of Darkness* will often tell you that Conrad is concerned not so much with Africa as with the deterioration of one European mind caused by solitude and sickness. They will point out to you that Conrad is, if anything, less charitable to the Europeans in the story than he is to the natives, that the point of the story is to ridicule Europe's civilizing mission in Africa. A Conrad student informed me in Scotland that Africa is merely a setting for the disintegration of the mind of Mr Kurtz.

Which is partly the point. Africa as setting and backdrop which eliminates the African as human factor. Africa as a metaphysical battlefield devoid of all recognizable humanity, into which the wandering European enters at his peril.

6. Medical missionary (1875–1965), who established a hospital at Lambaréné, Gabon (then in French Equatorial Africa), famous for its treatment of lepers.

Can nobody see the preposterous and perverse arrogance in thus reducing Africa to the role of props for the break-up of one petty European mind? But that is not even the point. The real question is the dehumanization of Africa and Africans which this age-long attitude has fostered and continues to foster in the world. And the question is whether a novel which celebrates this dehumanization, which depersonalizes a portion of the human race, can be called a great work of art. My answer is: No, it cannot.

1975   1977

ALICE MUNRO
b. 1931

Alice Munro has become one of the leading short-story writers of her generation. Her fiction combines spareness and realism—an uncompromising look at a panorama of faltering lives—with magisterial vision and expansiveness. Munro's signature approach to the short story, in which she uses a deceptively simple style to produce complex, layered, and emotionally potent effects, has influenced many of her English-language contemporaries, both within and outside Canada. In addition to one novel, *Lives of Girls and Women* (1972), she has published numerous collections of short stories, including *Dance of the Happy Shades* (1968), *Something I've Been Meaning to Tell You* (1974), *The Moons of Jupiter* (1982), *Friend of My Youth* (1990), *The Love of a Good Woman* (1998), *Hateship, Friendship, Courtship, Loveship, Marriage* (2001), and *Runaway* (2004).

Many of Munro's stories are written in the first person, often from the perspective of women whose voices and experiences suggest the author's history. She was born Alice Anne Laidlaw to a poor family in Wingham, Ontario, and her parents' struggles within a variety of rural occupations continued throughout her childhood. She began writing in her teens and in 1949 enrolled in the University of Western Ontario; she left the university two years later, to marry and raise three daughters. She typically sets her stories in small towns where poverty stamps itself on all facets of life, and where women confront—often in a spirit that combines resignation with stubborn resistance—the triple binds of economic, gender, and cultural confinement. Through a precise and particular emphasis on setting and character, she evokes rural Canadian life in the decades following midcentury, when modernity and the promise of the future are often crowded out by a hardening sense of the past.

In an early writing Munro describes an approach to the outside world that effectively captures her sense of the mystery within the ordinary—the hallmark of her realist style: "It seems as if there are feelings that have to be translated into a next-door language, which might blow them up and burst them altogether; or else they have to be let alone. The truth about them is always suspected, never verified, the light catches but doesn't define them. . . . Yet there is the feeling—I have the feeling—that at some level these things open; fragments, moments, suggestions, open, full of power." This aura of openness and suggestion, conveyed through "next-door language," gives Munro's stories their haunting aspect, their quality of movement, rippling and widening from the small-scale to the magnificent. The story included here, "Walker Brothers Cowboy," exemplifies her ability to imbue "fragments, moments, suggestions" with fullness and power, as we view through a young girl's eyes both the pathos and the degradation of men and women whose lives have fallen into a potentially deadening cycle of promise and decay.

Walker Brothers Cowboy[1]

After supper my father says, "Want to go down and see if the Lake's still there?" We leave my mother sewing under the dining-room light, making clothes for me against[2] the opening of school. She has ripped up for this purpose an old suit and an old plaid wool dress of hers, and she has to cut and match very cleverly and also make me stand and turn for endless fittings, sweaty, itching from the hot wool, ungrateful. We leave my brother in bed in the little screened porch at the end of the front veranda, and sometimes he kneels on his bed and presses his face against the screen and calls mournfully, "Bring me an ice-cream cone!" but I call back, "You will be asleep," and do not even turn my head.

Then my father and I walk gradually down a long, shabby sort of street, with Silverwoods Ice Cream signs standing on the sidewalk, outside tiny, lighted stores. This is in Tuppertown, an old town on Lake Huron,[3] an old grain port. The street is shaded, in some places, by maple trees whose roots have cracked and heaved the sidewalk and spread out like crocodiles into the bare yards. People are sitting out, men in shirtsleeves and undershirts and women in aprons—not people we know but if anybody looks ready to nod and say, "Warm night," my father will nod too and say something the same. Children are still playing. I don't know them either because my mother keeps my brother and me in our own yard, saying he is too young to leave it and I have to mind him. I am not so sad to watch their evening games because the games themselves are ragged, dissolving. Children, of their own will, draw apart, separate into islands of two or one under the heavy trees, occupying themselves in such solitary ways as I do all day, planting pebbles in the dirt or writing in it with a stick.

Presently we leave these yards and houses behind; we pass a factory with boarded-up windows, a lumberyard whose high wooden gates are locked for the night. Then the town falls away in a defeated jumble of sheds and small junkyards, the sidewalk gives up and we are walking on a sandy path with burdocks, plantains, humble nameless weeds all around. We enter a vacant lot, a kind of park really, for it is kept clear of junk and there is one bench with a slat missing on the back, a place to sit and look at the water. Which is generally gray in the evening, under a lightly overcast sky, no sunsets, the horizon dim. A very quiet, washing noise on the stones of the beach. Further along, towards the main part of town, there is a stretch of sand, a water slide, floats bobbing around the safe swimming area, a lifeguard's rickety throne. Also a long dark-green building, like a roofed veranda, called the Pavilion, full of farmers and their wives, in stiff good clothes, on Sundays. That is the part of the town we used to know when we lived at Dungannon and came here three or four times a summer, to the Lake. That, and the docks where we would go and look at the grain boats, ancient, rusty, wallowing, making us wonder how they got past the breakwater let alone to Fort William.

Tramps hang around the docks and occasionally on these evenings wander up the dwindling beach and climb the shifting, precarious path boys have

---

1. Refers to a traveling salesman for a Canadian company, which is probably modeled on the American direct marketer Watkins Products.
2. In time for.

3. One of the Great Lakes, bordering on Ontario and eastern Michigan. Place-names are both real and invented.

made, hanging on to dry bushes, and say something to my father which, being
frightened of tramps, I am too alarmed to catch. My father says he is a bit
hard up himself. "I'll roll you a cigarette if it's any use to you," he says, and
he shakes tobacco out carefully on one of the thin butterfly papers, flicks it
with his tongue, seals it and hands it to the tramp, who takes it and walks
away. My father also rolls and lights and smokes one cigarette of his own.

He tells me how the Great Lakes came to be. All where Lake Huron is now,
he says, used to be flat land, a wide flat plain. Then came the ice, creeping
down from the North, pushing deep into the low places. Like *that*—and he
shows me his hand with his spread fingers pressing the rock-hard ground
where we are sitting. His fingers make hardly any impression at all and he
says, "Well, the old ice cap had a lot more power behind it than this hand
has." And then the ice went back, shrank back towards the North Pole where
it came from, and left its fingers of ice in the deep places it had gouged, and
ice turned to lakes and there they were today. They were *new*, as time went.
I try to see that plain before me, dinosaurs walking on it, but I am not able
even to imagine the shore of the Lake when the Indians were there, before
Tuppertown. The tiny share we have of time appalls me, though my father
seems to regard it with tranquillity. Even my father, who sometimes seems to
me to have been at home in the world as long as it has lasted, has really lived
on this earth only a little longer than I have, in terms of all the time there has
been to live in. He has not known a time, any more than I, when automobiles
and electric lights did not at least exist. He was not alive when this century
started. I will be barely alive—old, old—when it ends. I do not like to think of
it. I wish the Lake to be always just a lake, with the safe-swimming floats
marking it, and the breakwater and the lights of Tuppertown.

My father has a job, selling for Walker Brothers. This is a firm that sells
almost entirely in the country, the back country. Sunshine, Boylesbridge,
Turnaround—that is all his territory. Not Dungannon where we used to live,
Dungannon is too near town and my mother is grateful for that. He sells cough
medicine, iron tonic, corn plasters, laxatives, pills for female disorders, mouth-
wash, shampoo, liniment, salves, lemon and orange and raspberry concentrate
for making refreshing drinks, vanilla, food coloring, black and green tea, ginger, cloves, and other spices, rat poison. He has a song about it, with these
two lines:

> And have all liniments and oils,
> For everything from corns to boils. . . .

Not a very funny song, in my mother's opinion. A peddler's song, and that
is what he is, a peddler knocking at backwoods kitchens. Up until last winter
we had our own business, a fox farm. My father raised silver foxes and sold
their pelts to the people who make them into capes and coats and muffs. Prices
fell, my father hung on hoping they would get better next year, and they fell
again, and he hung on one more year and one more and finally it was not
possible to hang on anymore, we owed everything to the feed company. I have
heard my mother explain this, several times, to Mrs. Oliphant, who is the only
neighbor she talks to. (Mrs. Oliphant also has come down in the world, being
a schoolteacher who married the janitor.) We poured all we had into it, my
mother says, and we came out with nothing. Many people could say the same
thing, these days, but my mother has no time for the national calamity, only

ours. Fate has flung us onto a street of poor people (it does not matter that we were poor before; that was a different sort of poverty), and the only way to take this, as she sees it, is with dignity, with bitterness, with no reconciliation. No bathroom with a claw-footed tub and a flush toilet is going to comfort her, nor water on tap and sidewalks past the house and milk in bottles, not even the two movie theatres and the Venus Restaurant and Woolworths so marvellous it has live birds singing in its fan-cooled corners and fish as tiny as fingernails, as bright as moons, swimming in its green tanks. My mother does not care.

In the afternoons she often walks to Simon's Grocery and takes me with her to help carry things. She wears a good dress, navy blue with little flowers, sheer, worn over a navy-blue slip. Also a summer hat of white straw, pushed down on the side of the head, and white shoes I have just whitened on a newspaper on the back steps. I have my hair freshly done in long damp curls which the dry air will fortunately soon loosen, a stiff large hair ribbon on top of my head. This is entirely different from going out after supper with my father. We have not walked past two houses before I feel we have become objects of universal ridicule. Even the dirty words chalked on the sidewalk are laughing at us. My mother does not seem to notice. She walks serenely like a lady shopping, like a *lady* shopping, past the housewives in loose beltless dresses torn under the arms. With me her creation, wretched curls and flaunting hair bow, scrubbed knees and white socks—all I do not want to be. I loathe even my name when she says it in public, in a voice so high, proud, and ringing, deliberately different from the voice of any other mother on the street.

My mother will sometimes carry home, for a treat, a brick of ice cream—pale Neapolitan; and because we have no refrigerator in our house we wake my brother and eat it at once in the dining room, always darkened by the wall of the house next door. I spoon it up tenderly, leaving the chocolate till last, hoping to have some still to eat when my brother's dish is empty. My mother tries then to imitate the conversations we used to have at Dungannon, going back to our earliest, most leisurely days before my brother was born, when she would give me a little tea and a lot of milk in a cup like hers and we would sit out on the step facing the pump, the lilac tree, the fox pens beyond. She is not able to keep from mentioning those days. "Do you remember when we put you in your sled and Major pulled you?" (Major our dog, that we had to leave with neighbors when we moved.) "Do you remember your sandbox outside the kitchen window?" I pretend to remember far less than I do, wary of being trapped into sympathy or any unwanted emotion.

My mother has headaches. She often has to lie down. She lies on my brother's narrow bed in the little screened porch, shaded by heavy branches. "I look up at that tree and I think I am at home," she says.

"What you need," my father tells her, "is some fresh air and a drive in the country." He means for her to go with him, on his Walker Brothers route.

That is not my mother's idea of a drive in the country.

"Can I come?"

"Your mother might want you for trying on clothes."

"I'm beyond sewing this afternoon," my mother says.

"I'll take her then. Take both of them, give you a rest."

What is there about us that people need to be given a rest from? Never mind. I am glad enough to find my brother and make him go to the toilet and get us both into the car, our knees unscrubbed, my hair unringleted. My father brings from the house his two heavy brown suitcases, full of bottles, and sets them on the back seat. He wears a white shirt, brilliant in the sunlight, a tie, light trousers belonging to his summer suit (his other suit is black, for funerals, and belonged to my uncle before he died), and a creamy straw hat. His sales-man's outfit, with pencils clipped in the shirt pocket. He goes back once again, probably to say goodbye to my mother, to ask her if she is sure she doesn't want to come, and hear her say, "No. No thanks, I'm better just to lie here with my eyes closed." Then we are backing out of the driveway with the rising hope of adventure, just the little hope that takes you over the bump into the street, the hot air starting to move, turning into a breeze, the houses growing less and less familiar as we follow the shortcut my father knows, the quick way out of town. Yet what is there waiting for us all afternoon but hot hours in stricken farmyards, perhaps a stop at a country store and three ice-cream cones or bottles of pop, and my father singing? The one he made up about himself has a title—"The Walker Brothers Cowboy"—and it starts out like this:

> Old Ned Fields, he now is dead,
> So I am ridin' the route instead. . . .

Who is Ned Fields? The man he has replaced, surely, and if so he really is dead; yet my father's voice is mournful-jolly, making his death some kind of nonsense, a comic calamity. "Wisht I was back on the Rio Grande,[4] plungin' through the dusky sand." My father sings most of the time while driving the car. Even now, heading out of town, crossing the bridge and taking the sharp turn onto the highway, he is humming something, mumbling a bit of a song to himself, just tuning up, really, getting ready to improvise, for out along the highway we pass the Baptist Camp, the Vacation Bible Camp, and he lets loose:

> Where are the Baptists, where are the Bapists,
>   where are all the Baptists today?
> They're down in the water, in Lake Huron water,
>   with their sins all a-gittin' washed away.

My brother takes this for straight truth and gets up on his knees trying to see down to the Lake. "I don't see any Baptists," he says accusingly. "Neither do I, son," says my father. "I told you, they're down in the Lake."

No roads paved when we left the highway. We have to roll up the windows because of dust. The land is flat, scorched, empty. Bush lots at the back of the farms hold shade, black pine-shade like pools nobody can ever get to. We bump up a long lane and at the end of it what could look more unwelcoming, more deserted than the tall unpainted farmhouse with grass growing uncut right up to the front door, green blinds down, and a door upstairs opening on nothing but air? Many houses have this door, and I have never yet been able to find out why. I ask my father and he says they are for walking in your sleep. *What?* Well, if you happen to be walking in your sleep and you want to step outside. I am offended, seeing too late that he is joking, as usual, but my brother says sturdily, "If they did that they would break their necks."

The 1930s. How much this kind of farmhouse, this kind of afternoon seem

---

4. A large river that begins in Colorado and flows south, becoming the border between Mexico and the United States.

to me to belong to that one decade in time, just as my father's hat does, his bright flared tie, our car with its wide running board (an Essex, and long past its prime). Cars somewhat like it, many older, none dustier, sit in the farm-yards. Some are past running and have their doors pulled off, their seats removed for use on porches. No living things to be seen, chickens or cattle. Except dogs. There are dogs lying in any kind of shade they can find, dreaming, their lean sides rising and sinking rapidly. They get up when my father opens the car door, he has to speak to them. "Nice boy, there's a boy, nice old boy." They quiet down, go back to their shade. He should know how to quiet ani-mals, he has held desperate foxes with tongs around their necks. One gentling voice for the dogs and another, rousing, cheerful, for calling at doors. "Hello there, missus, it's the Walker Brothers man and what are you out of today?" A door opens, he disappears. Forbidden to follow, forbidden even to leave the car, we can just wait and wonder what he says. Sometimes trying to make my mother laugh, he pretends to be himself in a farm kitchen, spreading out his sample case. "Now then, missus, are you troubled with parasitic life? Your children's scalps, I mean. All those crawly little things we're too polite to men-tion that show up on the heads of the best of families? Soap alone is useless, kerosene is not too nice a perfume, but I have here—" Or else, "Believe me, sitting and driving all day the way I do I *know* the value of these fine pills. Natural relief. A problem common to old folks too, once their days of activity are over—How about you, Grandma?" He would wave the imaginary box of pills under my mother's nose and she would laugh finally, unwillingly. "He doesn't say that really, does he?" I said, and she said no of course not, he was too much of a gentleman.

One yard after another, then, the old cars, the pumps, dogs, views of gray barns and falling-down sheds and unturning windmills. The men, if they are working in the fields, are not in any fields that we can see. The children are far away, following dry creek beds or looking for blackberries, or else they are hidden in the house, spying at us through cracks in the blinds. The car seat has grown slick with our sweat. I dare my brother to sound the horn, wanting to do it myself but not wanting to get the blame. He knows better. We play I Spy, but it is hard to find many colors. Gray for the barns and sheds and toilets and houses, brown for the yard and fields, black or brown for the dogs. The rusting cars show rainbow patches, in which I strain to pick out purple or green; likewise I peer at doors for shreds of old peeling paint, maroon or yellow. We can't play with letters, which would be better, because my brother is too young to spell. The game disintegrates anyway. He claims my colors are not fair, and wants extra turns.

In one house no door opens, though the car is in the yard. My father knocks and whistles, calls, "Hullo there ! Walker Brothers man!" but there is not a stir of reply anywhere. This house has no porch, just a bare, slanting slab of cement on which my father stands. He turns around, searching the barnyard, the barn whose mow must be empty because you can see the sky through it, and finally he bends to pick up his suitcases. Just then a window is opened upstairs, a white pot appears on the sill, is tilted over and its contents splash down the outside wall. The window is not directly above my father's head, so only a stray splash would catch him. He picks up his suitcases with no partic-ular hurry and walks, no longer whistling, to the car. "Do you know what that was?" I say to my brother. "*Pee.*" He laughs and laughs.

My father rolls and lights a cigarette before he starts the car. The window has been slammed down, the blind drawn, we never did see a hand or face. "Pee, pee," sings my brother ecstatically. "Somebody dumped down pee!" "Just don't tell your mother that," my father says. "She isn't liable to see the joke." "Is it in your song?" my brother wants to know. My father says no but he will see what he can do to work it in.

I notice in a little while that we are not turning in any more lanes, though it does not seem to me that we are headed home. "Is this the way to Sunshine?" I ask my father, and he answers, "No, ma'am, it's not." "Are we still in your territory?" He shakes his head. "We're going *fast*," my brother says approvingly, and in fact we are bouncing along through dry puddle-holes so that all the bottles in the suitcases clink together and gurgle promisingly.

Another lane, a house, also unpainted, dried to silver in the sun.

"I thought we were out of your territory."

"We are."

"Then what are we going in here for?"

"You'll see."

In front of the house a short, sturdy woman is picking up washing, which had been spread on the grass to bleach and dry. When the car stops she stares at it hard for a moment, bends to pick up a couple more towels to add to the bundle under her arm, comes across to us and says in a flat voice, neither welcoming nor unfriendly, "Have you lost your way?"

My father takes his time getting out of the car. "I don't think so," he says. "I'm the Walker Brothers man."

"George Golley is our Walker Brothers man," the woman says, "and he was out here no more than a week ago. Oh, my Lord God," she says harshly, "it's you."

"It was, the last time I looked in the mirror," my father says.

The woman gathers all the towels in front of her and holds on to them tightly, pushing them against her stomach as if it hurt. "Of all the people I never thought to see. And telling me you were the Walker Brothers man."

"I'm sorry if you were looking forward to George Golley," my father says humbly.

"And look at me, I was prepared to clean the henhouse. You'll think that's just an excuse but it's true. I don't go round looking like this every day." She is wearing a farmer's straw hat, through which pricks of sunlight penetrate and float on her face, a loose, dirty print smock, and canvas shoes. "Who are those in the car, Ben? They're not yours?"

"Well, I hope and believe they are," my father says, and tells our names and ages. "Come on, you can get out. This is Nora, Miss Cronin. Nora, you better tell me, is it still Miss, or have you got a husband hiding in the woodshed?"

"If I had a husband that's not where I'd keep him, Ben," she says, and they both laugh, her laugh abrupt and somewhat angry. "You'll think I got no manners, as well as being dressed like a tramp," she says. "Come on in out of the sun. It's cool in the house."

We go across the yard ("Excuse me taking you in this way but I don't think the front door has been opened since Papa's funeral, I'm afraid the hinges might drop off"), up the porch steps, into the kitchen, which really is cool, high-ceilinged, the blinds of course down, a simple, clean, threadbare room with waxed worn linoleum, potted geraniums, drinking-pail and dipper, a round table with scrubbed oilcloth. In spite of the cleanness, the wiped and swept surfaces, there is a faint sour smell—maybe of the dishrag or the tin dipper or the oilcloth, or the old lady, because there is one, sitting in an easy chair under the clock shelf. She turns her head slightly in our direction and says, "Nora? Is that company?"

"Blind," says Nora in a quick explaining voice to my father. Then, "You won't guess who it is, Momma. Hear his voice."

My father goes to the front of her chair and bends and says hopefully, "Afternoon, Mrs. Cronin."

"Ben Jordan," says the old lady with no surprise. "You haven't been to see us in the longest time. Have you been out of the country?"

My father and Nora look at each other.

"He's married, Momma," says Nora cheerfully and aggressively. "Married and got two children and here they are." She pulls us forward, makes each of us touch the old lady's dry, cool hand while she says our names in turn. Blind! This is the first blind person I have ever seen close up. Her eyes are closed, the eyelids sunk away down, showing no shape of the eyeball, just hollows. From one hollow comes a drop of silver liquid, a medicine, or a miraculous tear.

"Let me get into a decent dress," Nora says. "Talk to Momma. It's a treat for her. We hardly ever see company, do we, Momma?"

"Not many makes it out this road," says the old lady placidly. "And the ones that used to be around here, our old neighbors, some of them have pulled out."

"True everywhere," my father says.

"Where's your wife then?"

"Home. She's not too fond of the hot weather, makes her feel poorly."

"Well." This is a habit of country people, old people, to say "well," meaning, "Is that so?" with a little extra politeness and concern.

Nora's dress, when she appears again—stepping heavily on Cuban heels down the stairs in the hall—is flowered more lavishly than anything my mother owns, green and yellow on brown, some sort of floating sheer crêpe, leaving her arms bare. Her arms are heavy, and every bit of her skin you can see is covered with little dark freckles like measles. Her hair is short, black, coarse and curly, her teeth very white and strong. "It's the first time I knew there was such a thing as green poppies," my father says, looking at her dress.

"You would be surprised all the things you never knew," says Nora, sending a smell of cologne far and wide when she moves and displaying a change of voice to go with the dress, something more sociable and youthful. "They're not poppies anyway, they're just flowers. You go and pump me some good cold water and I'll make these children a drink." She gets down from the cupboard a bottle of Walker Brothers Orange syrup.

"You telling me you were the Walker Brothers man!"

"It's the truth, Nora. You go and look at my sample cases in the car if you don't believe me. I got the territory directly south of here."

"Walker Brothers? Is that a fact? You selling for Walker Brothers?"

"Yes, ma'am."

"We always heard you were raising foxes over Dungannon way."

"That's what I was doing, but I kind of run out of luck in that business."

"So where're you living? How long've you been out selling?"

"We moved into Tuppertown. I been at it, oh, two, three months. It keeps the wolf from the door. Keeps him as far away as the back fence."

Nora laughs. "Well, I guess you count yourself lucky to have the work.

Isabel's husband in Brantford, he was out of work the longest time. I thought if he didn't find something soon I was going to have them all land in here to feed, and I tell you I was hardly looking forward to it. It's all I can manage with me and Momma."

"Isabel married," my father says. "Muriel married too?"

"No, she's teaching school out West. She hasn't been home for five years. I guess she finds something better to do with her holidays. I would if I was her." She gets some snapshots out of the table drawer and starts showing him. "That's Isabel's oldest boy, starting school. That's the baby sitting in her carriage. Isabel and her husband. Muriel. That's her roommate with her. That's a fellow she used to go around with, and his car. He was working in a bank out there. That's her school, it has eight rooms. She teaches Grade Five." My father shakes his head. "I can't think of her any way but when she was going to school, so shy I used to pick her up on the road—I'd be on my way to see you—and she would not say one word, not even to agree it was a nice day."

"She's got over that."

"Who are you talking about?" says the old lady.

"Muriel. I said she's got over being shy."

"She was here last summer."

"No, Momma, that was Isabel. Isabel and her family were here last summer. Muriel's out West."

"I meant Isabel."

Shortly after this the old lady falls asleep, her head on the side, her mouth open. "Excuse her manners," Nora says. "It's old age." She fixes an afghan over her mother and says we can all go into the front room where our talking won't disturb her.

"You two," my father says. "Do you want to go outside and amuse yourselves?"

Amuse ourselves how? Anyway, I want to stay. The front room is more interesting than the kitchen, though barer. There is a gramophone and a pump organ and a picture on the wall of Mary, Jesus' mother—I know that much—in shades of bright blue and pink with a spiked band of light around her head. I know that such pictures are found only in the homes of Roman Catholics and so Nora must be one. We have never known any Roman Catholics at all well, never well enough to visit in their houses. I think of what my grandmother and my Aunt Tena, over in Dungannon, used to always say to indicate that somebody was a Catholic. *So-and-so digs with the wrong foot*, they would say. *She digs with the wrong foot.* That was what they would say about Nora.[5]

Nora takes a bottle, half full, out of the top of the organ and pours some of what is in it into the two glasses that she and my father have emptied of the orange drink.

"Keep it in case of sickness?" my father says.

"Not on your life," says Nora. "I'm never sick. I just keep it because I keep it. One bottle does me a fair time, though, because I don't care for drinking alone. Here's luck!" She and my father drink and I know what it is. Whisky. One of the things my mother has told me in our talks together is that my father never drinks whisky. But I see he does. He drinks whisky and he talks of people whose names I have never heard before. But after a while he turns to a familiar

---

5. Relations between Protestants and Catholics within the Irish population in southern Ontario were often strained.

incident. He tells about the chamberpot that was emptied out the window. "Picture me there," he says, "hollering my heartiest. *Oh, lady, it's your Walker Brothers man, anybody home?*" He does himself hollering, grinning absurdly, waiting, looking up in pleased expectation, and then—oh, ducking, covering his head with his arms, looking as if he begged for mercy (when he never did anything like that, I was watching), and Nora laughs, almost as hard as my brother did at the time.

"That isn't true! That's not a word true!"

"Oh, indeed it is, ma'am. We have our heroes in the ranks of Walker Brothers. I'm glad you think it's funny," he says sombrely.

I ask him shyly, "Sing the song."

"What song? Have you turned into a singer on top of everything else?"

Embarrassed, my father says, "Oh, just this song I made up while I was driving around, it gives me something to do, making up rhymes."

But after some urging he does sing it, looking at Nora with a droll, apologetic expression, and she laughs so much that in places he has to stop and wait for her to get over laughing so he can go on, because she makes him laugh too. Then he does various parts of his salesman's spiel. Nora when she laughs squeezes her large bosom under her folded arms. "You're crazy," she says. "That's all you are." She sees my brother peering into the gramophone and she jumps up and goes over to him. "Here's us sitting enjoying ourselves and not giving you a thought, isn't it terrible?" she says. "You want me to put a record on, don't you? You want to hear a nice record? Can you dance? I bet your sister can, can't she?"

I say no. "A big girl like you and so good-looking and can't dance!" says Nora. "It's high time you learned. I bet you'd make a lovely dancer. Here, I'm going to put on a piece I used to dance to and even your daddy did, in his dancing days. You didn't know your daddy was a dancer, did you? Well, he is a talented man, your daddy!"

She puts down the lid and takes hold of me unexpectedly around the waist, picks up my other hand, and starts making me go backwards. "This is the way, now, this is how they dance. Follow me. This foot, see. One and one-two. One and one-two. That's fine, that's lovely, don't look at your feet! Follow me, that's right, see how easy? You're going to be a lovely dancer! One and one-two. One and one-two. Ben, see your daughter dancing!" *Whispering while you cuddle near me, Whispering so no one can hear me . . .*[6]

Round and round the linoleum, me proud, intent, Nora laughing and moving with great buoyancy, wrapping me in her strange gaiety, her smell of whisky, cologne, and sweat. Under the arms her dress is damp, and little drops form along her upper lip, hang in the soft black hairs at the corners of her mouth. She whirls me around in front of my father—causing me to stumble, for I am by no means so swift a pupil as she pretends—and lets me go, breathless.

"Dance with me, Ben."

"I'm the world's worst dancer, Nora, and you know it."

"I certainly never thought so."

"You would now."

She stands in front of him, arms hanging loose and hopeful, her breasts,

---

6. From the popular song "Whispering," whose original 1920 recording was one of the first records to sell a million copies.

which a moment ago embarrassed me with their warmth and bulk, rising and falling under her loose flowered dress, her face shining with the exercise, and delight.

"Ben."

My father drops his head and says quietly, "Not me, Nora."

So she can only go and take the record off. "I can drink alone but I can't dance alone," she says. "Unless I am a whole lot crazier than I think I am."

"Nora," says my father, smiling. "You're not crazy."

"Stay for supper."

"Oh, no. We couldn't put you to the trouble."

"It's no trouble. I'd be glad of it."

"And their mother would worry. She'd think I'd turned us over in a ditch."

"Oh, well. Yes."

"We've taken a lot of your time now."

"Time," says Nora bitterly. "Will you come by ever again?"

"I will if I can," says my father.

"Bring the children. Bring your wife."

"Yes, I will," says my father. "I will if I can."

When she follows us to the car he says, "You come to see us too, Nora. We're right on Grove Street, left-hand side going in, that's north, and two doors this side—east—of Baker Street."

Nora does not repeat these directions. She stands close to the car in her soft, brilliant dress. She touches the fender, making an unintelligible mark in the dust there.

On the way home my father does not buy any ice cream or pop, but he does go into a country store and get a package of licorice, which he shares with us. She digs with the wrong foot, I think, and the words seem sad to me as never before, dark, perverse. My father does not say anything to me about not mentioning things at home, but I know, just from the thoughtfulness, the pause when he passes the licorice, that there are things not to be mentioned. The whisky, maybe the dancing. No worry about my brother, he does not notice enough. At most he might remember the blind lady, the picture of Mary.

"Sing," my brother commands my father, but my father says gravely, "I don't know, I seem to be fresh out of songs. You watch the road and let me know if you see any rabbits."

So my father drives and my brother watches the road for rabbits and I feel my father's life flowing back from our car in the last of the afternoon, darkening and turning strange, like a landscape that has an enchantment on it, making it kindly, ordinary and familiar while you are looking at it, but changing it, once your back is turned, into something you will never know, with all kinds of weathers, and distances you cannot imagine.

When we get closer to Tuppertown the sky becomes gently overcast, as always, nearly always, on summer evenings by the Lake.

1968

GEOFFREY HILL
b. 1932

Geoffrey Hill, born in the Worcestershire village of Bromsgrove, educated at its high school and at Keble College, Oxford, has been a professor of English at Leeds University and a lecturer at Cambridge, and is a professor at Boston University. As a boy he was drawn to the Metaphysical poets' "fusion of intellectual strength with simple, sensuous, and passionate immediacy," and his own poems offer something of the same fusion. What he has said of "Annunciations: 2" might have been said of many of his poems: "But I want the poem to have this dubious end; because I feel dubious; and the whole business is dubious." He is a religious poet but a poet of religious doubt—a skeptic confronting the extremes of human experience, "man's inhumanity to man," on the cross and in the concentration camps—or delight in the abundance of the natural world: pain and pleasure alike rendered with a Keatsian richness and specificity, a modernist allusiveness and syntactic contortion. Distinctively resonant as is the voice of Hill's poems, they are consistently impersonal. Even when the poet's earlier self is conflated with that of Offa, eighth-century king of a large part of Britain, in *Mercian Hymns* (1971), subjectivity is dissolved in the objective projection of a historical imagination of great range and power. That book had been concerned at one level with what medieval historians called "the matter of Britain," but a later collection, *Canaan* (1996), bleakly attempts to diagnose the matter *with* Britain (identifying the U.K. with "Canaan, the land of the Philistines," excoriated in the Bible). Hill is at once one of the most ambitious, most difficult, and most rewarding poets now writing in English.

In Memory of Jane Fraser

When snow like sheep lay in the fold°   *shelter for sheep*
And winds went begging at each door,
And the far hills were blue with cold,
And a cold shroud lay on the moor,

5   She kept the siege. And every day
We watched her brooding over death
Like a strong bird above its prey.
The room filled with the kettle's breath.

Damp curtains glued against the pane
10   Sealed time away. Her body froze
As if to freeze us all, and chain
Creation to a stunned repose.

She died before the world could stir.
In March the ice unloosed the brook
15   And water ruffled the sun's hair.
Dead cones upon the alder shook.

1959

Requiem for the Plantagenet Kings[1]

For whom the possessed sea littered, on both shores,
Ruinous arms; being fired, and for good,
To sound the constitution of just wars,
Men, in their eloquent fashion, understood.

5 Relieved of soul, the dropping-back of dust,
Their usage, pride, admitted within doors;
At home, under caved chantries,[2] set in trust,
With well-dressed alabaster and proved spurs
They lie; they lie; secure in the decay
10 Of blood, blood-marks, crowns hacked and coveted,
Before the scouring fires of trial-day
Alight on men; before sleeked groin, gored head,
Budge through the clay and gravel, and the sea
Across daubed rock evacuates its dead.

1959

September Song[1]

born 19.6.32—deported 24.9.42

Undesirable you may have been, untouchable
you were not. Not forgotten
or passed over at the proper time.

As estimated, you died. Things marched,
5 sufficient, to that end.
Just so much Zyklon and leather, patented
terror, so many routine cries.

(I have made
an elegy for myself it
10 is true)[2]

---

1. Dynastic succession of 12th- to 15th-century English kings, beginning with Henry II, who was followed in turn by Richard I, John, Henry III, Edward I, Edward II, Edward III, and Richard II. They ruled not only over England but also over much of France ("on both shores"). The last Plantagenet king was Richard III, who was killed at the Battle of Bosworth on Aug. 22, 1485.
2. Chapels endowed for priests to sing Masses for the souls of those who founded them. Many chantries have cavelike ceilings of vaulted stone and contain effigies—sometimes in alabaster—of their founders.
1. The poem is about the gassing of Jews in German extermination camps; Zyklon-B was the gas used. Hill's fellow poet Jon Silkin has drawn attention to the kind of wit involved in the subtitle, "where the natural event of birth is placed, simply, beside the human and murderous 'deported' as if the latter were of the same order and inevitability for the victim"; he discusses, too, "the irony of conjuncted meanings between 'undesirable' (touching on both sexual desire and racism) and 'untouchable,' which exploits a similar ambiguity but reverses the emphases" and is "unusually dense *and* simple."
2. As the critic Christopher Ricks pointed out, Hill was born on 18.6.32 (June 18, 1932).

September fattens on vines. Roses
flake from the wall. The smoke
of harmless fires drifts to my eyes.

This is plenty. This is more than enough.

1968

From Mercian Hymns[1]

6

The princes of Mercia were badger and raven. Thrall
to their freedom, I dug and hoarded. Orchards
fruited above clefts. I drank from honeycombs of
chill sandstone.

5   "A boy at odds in the house, lonely among brothers."
But I, who had none, fostered a strangeness; gave
myself to unattainable toys.

Candles of gnarled resin, apple-branches, the tacky
mistletoe. "Look" they said and again "look." But
10   I ran slowly; the landscape flowed away, back to
its source.

In the schoolyard, in the cloakrooms, the children
boasted their scars of dried snot; wrists and
knees garnished with impetigo.

7

Gasholders,[2] russet among fields. Milldams, marlpools[3]
that lay unstirring. Eel-swarms. Coagulations of
frogs: once, with branches and half-bricks, he
battered a ditchful; then sidled away from the
5   stillness and silence.

Ceolred[4] was his friend and remained so, even after
the day of the lost fighter: a biplane, already
obsolete and irreplaceable, two inches of heavy
snub silver. Ceolred let it spin through a hole
10   in the classroom-floorboards, softly, into the rat-
droppings and coins.

---

1. The historical Offa reigned over Mercia (and the greater part of England south of the Humber) in the years 757–96 C.E. During early medieval times he was already becoming a creature of legend. The Offa who figures in this sequence might perhaps most usefully be regarded as the presiding genius of the West Midlands, his dominion enduring from the middle of the 8th century until the middle of the 20th (and possibly beyond). The indi-cation of such a timespan will, I trust, explain and to some extent justify a number of anachronisms [Hill's note].
2. Or gasometers, large metal receptacles for gas.
3. Pools in deposits of crumbling clay and chalk.
4. A 9th-century bishop of Leicester, but the name is here used as a characteristic Anglo-Saxon Mercian name.

After school he lured Ceolred, who was sniggering
  with fright, down to the old quarries, and flayed
  him. Then, leaving Ceolred, he journeyed for hours,
15 calm and alone, in his private derelict sandlorry
  named *Albion*.[5]

28

Processes of generation; deeds of settlement. The
  urge to marry well; wit to invest in the proper
  ties of healing-springs. Our children and our
  children's children, o my masters.

5 Tracks of ancient occupation. Frail ironworks rusting in the thorn-thicket. Hearthstones; charred
  lullabies. A solitary axe-blow that is the echo
  of a lost sound.

Tumult recedes as though into the long rain. Groves
10 of legendary holly; silverdark the ridged gleam.

30

And it seemed, while we waited, he began to walk towards us   he vanished

he left behind coins, for his lodging, and traces of
  red mud.

                                                        1971

From An Apology for the Revival of Christian Architecture in England

the spiritual, Platonic old England . . .
                              —STC,[1] *Anima Poetae*

"Your situation," said Coningsby, looking up
the green and silent valley, "is absolutely
poetic."

"I try sometimes to fancy," said Mr Millbank,
with a rather fierce smile, "that I am in the
New World."
                              —BENJAMIN DISRAELI,[2] *Coningsby*

9. The Laurel Axe

Autumn resumes the land, ruffles the woods
with smoky wings, entangles them. Trees shine

5. An old Celtic name for England; also the name of a famous make of British truck. "Sandlorry": sand truck.
1. Samuel Taylor Coleridge (1772–1834), English poet and philosopher. The "old England" here is an idealized orderly rural one.
2. British novelist and statesman (1804–1881). The "New World" referred to is that of an idealized rural America.

out from their leaves, rocks mildew to moss-green;
the avenues are spread with brittle floods.

5   Platonic England, house of solitudes,
rests in its laurels and its injured stone,
replete with complex fortunes that are gone,
beset by dynasties of moods and clouds.

It stands, as though at ease with its own world,
10   the mannerly extortions, languid praise,
all that devotion long since bought and sold,

the rooms of cedar and soft-thudding baize,[3]
tremulous boudoirs where the crystals kissed
in cabinets of amethyst and frost.

1978

3. Billiard rooms in British "stately homes." The "soft-thudding baize" may refer either to the soft green cloth covering billiard tables or to the door traditionally covered with green baize dividing the family side of the home from the servants' quarters.

V. S. NAIPAUL
b. 1932

Widely regarded as the most accomplished novelist from the English-speaking Caribbean, Vidiadhar Surajprasad Naipaul was born to a family of Indian descent in Trinidad and educated at Queen's Royal College, Port of Spain, and at University College, Oxford. After settling in England, he became editor of the *Caribbean Voices* program for the British Broadcasting Corporation (1954–56) and fiction reviewer for the *New Statesman* (1957–61). The recipient of many prestigious prizes and awards, he won the Booker Prize in 1971 for *In a Free State*, was knighted in 1990, and received the Nobel Prize in Literature in 2001. He continues to live and write in England.

Naipaul's first three books, *The Mystic Masseur* (1957), *The Suffrage of Elvira* (1958), and *Miguel Street* (short stories, 1959), are comedies of manners, set in a Trinidad viewed with an exile's acute and ironic eye. These early works present a starkly satiric vision, but a more modulated tone appears in Naipaul's first major novel, partly based on his father's experience, *A House for Mr. Biswas* (1961). Following the declining fortunes of its gentle hero from cradle to grave, this tragicomic novel traces the disintegration of a traditional way of life, on something approaching an epic scale. Subsequent novels, including *The Mimic Men* (1967), *Guerrillas* (1973), *The Enigma of Arrival* (1987), and *Half a Life* (2001), have continued to explore the desperate and destructive conditions facing individuals as they struggle with cultures in complicated states of transition and development. Because of his often bitter, even withering critiques of so-called Third World states and societies, he is controversial among readers of postcolonial fiction.

Naipaul has also produced essays on a variety of themes, including a travel narrative about the southern United States, *A Turn in the South* (1988), and two studies—what he calls "cultural explorations"—of Islam: *Among the Believers: An Islamic Journey* (1981) and *Beyond Belief: Islamic Excursions among the Converted Peoples* (1998). Like his novels, these writings range widely, carrying readers to Africa, England, the Indian subcontinent, the Middle East, South and North America. With the years Naipaul's vision of the human condition has grown darker and more pessimistic, as he brilliantly lays bare the insensitivities and disconnections that bedevil relations among individuals, races, and nations.

Such tremendous disjunctions and dire consequences are revealed in "One Out of Many," the second of three stories that, with two linking diary entries, make up *In a Free State*, a bleakly ironic yet emotionally engaging study of what it means to be enslaved and what it means to be free. The story—its title playing on the American motto "*E pluribus unum*" ("from many, one")—follows the fortunes of Santosh, an Indian immigrant to the U.S., whose sense of self changes dramatically in relation to various liberating and imprisoning spaces, various ethnic, cultural, and sexual others. In contrast to narratives of immigration as empowerment, the story represents the promise of more freedom, more status, more economic opportunity in America as coming at the price of an intensified isolation and alienation. As in the literary journeys of other innocents abroad, Santosh's immersion in America satirically reveals as much about the culture he assumes as about the culture he leaves behind.

One Out of Many

I am now an American citizen and I live in Washington, capital of the world. Many people, both here and in India, will feel that I have done well. But.

I was so happy in Bombay. I was respected, I had a certain position. I worked for an important man. The highest in the land came to our bachelor chambers and enjoyed my food and showered compliments on me. I also had my friends. We met in the evenings on the pavement below the gallery of our chambers. Some of us, like the tailor's bearer[1] and myself, were domestics who lived in the street. The others were people who came to that bit of pavement to sleep. Respectable people; we didn't encourage riff-raff.

In the evenings it was cool. There were few passers-by and, apart from an occasional double-decker bus or taxi, little traffic. The pavement was swept and sprinkled, bedding brought out from daytime hiding-places, little oil-lamps lit. While the folk upstairs chattered and laughed, on the pavement we read newspapers, played cards, told stories and smoked. The clay pipe passed from friend to friend; we became drowsy. Except of course during the monsoon,[2] I preferred to sleep on the pavement with my friends, although in our chambers a whole cupboard below the staircase was reserved for my personal use.

It was good after a healthy night in the open to rise before the sun and before the sweepers came. Sometimes I saw the street lights go off. Bedding was rolled up; no one spoke much; and soon my friends were hurrying in silent competition to secluded lanes and alleys and open lots to relieve themselves. I was spared this competition; in our chambers I had facilities.[3]

Afterwards for half an hour or so I was free simply to stroll. I liked walking beside the Arabian Sea, waiting for the sun to come up. Then the city and the ocean gleamed like gold. Alas for those morning walks, that sudden ocean dazzle, the moist salt breeze on my face, the flap of my shirt, that first cup of hot sweet tea from a stall, the taste of the first leaf-cigarette.

Observe the workings of fate. The respect and security I enjoyed were due to the importance of my employer. It was this very importance which now all at once destroyed the pattern of my life.

My employer was seconded[4] by his firm to Government service and was

---

1. Servant.
2. Rainy season.
3. I.e., a toilet.
4. Temporarily transferred.

posted to Washington. I was happy for his sake but frightened for mine. He was to be away for some years and there was nobody in Bombay he could second me to. Soon, therefore, I was to be out of a job and out of the chambers. For many years I had considered my life as settled. I had served my apprenticeship, known my hard times. I didn't feel I could start again. I despaired. Was there a job for me in Bombay? I saw myself having to return to my village in the hills, to my wife and children there, not just for a holiday but for good. I saw myself again becoming a porter during the tourist season, racing after the buses as they arrived at the station and shouting with forty or fifty others for luggage. Indian luggage, not this lightweight American stuff! Heavy metal trunks!

I could have cried. It was no longer the sort of life for which I was fitted. I had grown soft in Bombay and I was no longer young. I had acquired possessions, I was used to the privacy of my cupboard. I had become a city man, used to certain comforts.

My employer said, "Washington is not Bombay, Santosh. Washington is expensive. Even if I was able to raise your fare, you wouldn't be able to live over there in anything like your present style."

But to be barefoot in the hills, after Bombay! The shock, the disgrace! I couldn't face my friends. I stopped sleeping on the pavement and spent as much of my free time as possible in my cupboard among my possessions, as among things which were soon to be taken from me.

My employer said, "Santosh, my heart bleeds for you."

I said, "Sahib,[5] if I look a little concerned it is only because I worry about you. You have always been fussy, and I don't see how you will manage in Washington."

"It won't be easy. But it's the principle. Does the representative of a poor country like ours travel about with his cook? Will that create a good impression?"

"You will always do what is right, sahib."

He went silent.

After some days he said, "There's not only the expense, Santosh. There's the question of foreign exchange. Our rupee[6] isn't what it was."

"I understand, sahib. Duty is duty."

A fortnight later, when I had almost given up hope, he said, "Santosh, I have consulted Government. You will accompany me. Government has sanctioned, will arrange accommodation. But no expenses. You will get your passport and your P form. But I want you to think, Santosh. Washington is not Bombay."

I went down to the pavement that night with my bedding.

I said, blowing down my shirt, "Bombay gets hotter and hotter."

"Do you know what you are doing?" the tailor's bearer said. "Will the Americans smoke with you? Will they sit and talk with you in the evenings? Will they hold you by the hand and walk with you beside the ocean?"

It pleased me that he was jealous. My last days in Bombay were very happy.

I packed my employer's two suitcases and bundled up my own belongings in lengths of old cotton. At the airport they made a fuss about my bundles. They said they couldn't accept them as luggage for the hold because they didn't like the responsibility. So when the time came I had to climb up to the aircraft with all my bundles. The girl at the top, who was smiling at everybody else, stopped smiling when she saw me. She made me go right to the back of the plane, far from my employer. Most of the seats there were empty, though, and I was able to spread my bundles around and, well, it was comfortable.

It was bright and hot outside, cool inside. The plane started, rose up in the air, and Bombay and the ocean tilted this way and that. It was very nice. When we settled down I looked around for people like myself, but I could see no one among the Indians or the foreigners who looked like a domestic. Worse, they were all dressed as though they were going to a wedding and, brother, I soon saw it wasn't they who were conspicuous. I was in my ordinary Bombay clothes, the loose long-tailed shirt, the wide-waisted pants held up with a piece of string. Perfectly respectable domestic's wear, neither dirty nor clean, and in Bombay no one would have looked. But now on the plane I felt heads turning whenever I stood up.

I was anxious. I slipped off my shoes, tight even without the laces, and drew my feet up. That made me feel better. I made myself a little betel-nut[7] mixture and that made me feel better still. Half the pleasure of betel, though, is the spitting; and it was only when I had worked up a good mouthful that I saw I had a problem. The airline girl saw too. That girl didn't like me at all. She spoke roughly to me. My mouth was full, my cheeks were bursting, and I couldn't say anything. I could only look at her. She went and called a man in uniform and he came and stood over me. I put my shoes back on and swallowed the betel juice. It made me feel quite ill.

The girl and the man, the two of them, pushed a little trolley of drinks down the aisle. The girl didn't look at me but the man said, "You want a drink, chum?" He wasn't a bad fellow. I pointed at random to a bottle. It was a kind of soda drink, nice and sharp at first but then not so nice. I was worrying about it when the girl said, "Five shillings sterling or sixty cents U.S." That took me by surprise. I had no money, only a few rupees. The girl stamped, and I thought she was going to hit me with her pad when I stood up to show her who my employer was.

Presently my employer came down the aisle. He didn't look very well. He said, without stopping, "Champagne, Santosh? Already we are overdoing?" He went on to the lavatory. When he passed back he said, "Foreign exchange, Santosh! Foreign exchange!" That was all. Poor fellow, he was suffering too.

The journey became miserable for me. Soon, with the wine I had drunk, the betel juice, the movement and the noise of the aeroplane, I was vomiting all over my bundles, and I didn't care what the girl said or did. Later there were more urgent and terrible needs. I felt I would choke in the tiny, hissing room at the back. I had a shock when I saw my face in the mirror. In the fluorescent light it was the colour of a corpse. My eyes were strained, the sharp air hurt my nose and seemed to get into my brain. I climbed up on the lavatory seat and squatted. I lost control of myself. As quickly as I could I ran back out into the comparative openness of the cabin and hoped no one had noticed. The lights were dim now; some people had taken off their jackets and were sleeping. I hoped the plane would crash.

The girl woke me up. She was almost screaming. "It's you, isn't it? Isn't it?" I thought she was going to tear the shirt off me. I pulled back and leaned

---

7. Evergreen plant, the leaves of which are chewed in the East with areca-nut parings.

hard on the window. She burst into tears and nearly tripped on her sari as she ran up the aisle to get the man in uniform.

Nightmare. And all I knew was that somewhere at the end, after the airports and the crowded lounges where everybody was dressed up, after all those take-offs and touchdowns, was the city of Washington. I wanted the journey to end but I couldn't say I wanted to arrive at Washington. I was already a little scared of that city, to tell the truth. I wanted only to be off the plane and to be in the open again, to stand on the ground and breathe and to try to understand what time of day it was.

At last we arrived. I was in a daze. The burden of those bundles! There were more closed rooms and electric lights. There were questions from officials.

"Is he diplomatic?"[8]

"He's only a domestic," my employer said.

"Is that his luggage? What's in that pocket?"

I was ashamed.

"Santosh," my employer said.

I pulled out the little packets of pepper and salt, the sweets, the envelopes with scented napkins, the toy tubes of mustard. Airline trinkets. I had been collecting them throughout the journey, seizing a handful, whatever my condition, every time I passed the galley.

"He's a cook," my employer said.

"Does he always travel with his condiments?"

"Santosh, Santosh," my employer said in the car afterwards, "in Bombay it didn't matter what you did. Over here you represent your country. I must say I cannot understand why your behaviour has already gone so much out of character."

"I am sorry, sahib."

"Look at it like this, Santosh. Over here you don't only represent your country, you represent me."

For the people of Washington it was late afternoon or early evening, I couldn't say which. The time and the light didn't match, as they did in Bombay. Of that drive I remember green fields, wide roads, many motor cars travelling fast, making a steady hiss, hiss, which wasn't at all like our Bombay traffic noise. I remember big buildings and wide parks; many bazaar areas; then smaller houses without fences and with gardens like bush, with the *hubshi*[9] standing about or sitting down, more usually sitting down, everywhere. Especially I remember the *hubshi*. I had heard about them in stories and had seen one or two in Bombay. But I had never dreamt that this wild race existed in such numbers in Washington and were permitted to roam the streets so freely. O father, what was this place I had come to?

I wanted, I say, to be in the open, to breathe, to come to myself, to reflect. But there was to be no openness for me that evening. From the aeroplane to the airport building to the motor car to the apartment block to the elevator to the corridor to the apartment itself, I was forever enclosed, forever in the hissing, hissing sound of air-conditioners.

I was too dazed to take stock of the apartment. I saw it as only another halting place. My employer went to bed at once, completely exhausted, poor fellow. I looked around for my room. I couldn't find it and gave up. Aching for

8. In the Diplomatic Corps.
9. Derogatory Indian term for African blacks (Hindustani).

the Bombay ways, I spread my bedding in the carpeted corridor just outside our apartment door. The corridor was long: doors, doors. The illuminated ceiling was decorated with stars of different sizes; the colours were grey and blue and gold. Below that imitation sky I felt like a prisoner.

Waking, looking up at the ceiling, I thought just for a second that I had fallen asleep on the pavement below the gallery of our Bombay chambers. Then I realized my loss. I couldn't tell how much time had passed or whether it was night or day. The only clue was that newspapers now lay outside some doors. It disturbed me to think that while I had been sleeping, alone and defenceless, I had been observed by a stranger and perhaps by more than one stranger.

I tried the apartment door and found I had locked myself out. I didn't want to disturb my employer. I thought I would get out into the open, go for a walk. I remembered where the elevator was. I got in and pressed the button. The elevator dropped fast and silently and it was like being in the aeroplane again. When the elevator stopped and the blue metal door slid open I saw plain concrete corridors and blank walls. The noise of machinery was very loud. I knew I was in the basement and the main floor was not far above me. But I no longer wanted to try; I gave up ideas of the open air. I thought I would just go back up to the apartment. But I hadn't noted the number and didn't even know what floor we were on. My courage flowed out of me. I sat on the floor of the elevator and felt the tears come to my eyes. Almost without noise the elevator door closed, and I found I was being taken up silently at great speed. The elevator stopped and the door opened. It was my employer, his hair uncombed, yesterday's dirty shirt partly unbuttoned. He looked frightened.

"Santosh, where have you been at this hour of morning? Without your shoes."

I could have embraced him. He hurried me back past the newspapers to our apartment and I took the bedding inside. The wide window showed the early morning sky, the big city; we were high up, way above the trees.

I said, "I couldn't find my room."

"Government sanctioned," my employer said. "Are you sure you've looked?"

We looked together. One little corridor led past the bathroom to his bedroom; another, shorter corridor led to the big room and the kitchen. There was nothing else.

"Government sanctioned," my employer said, moving about the kitchen and opening cupboard doors. "Separate entrance, shelving. I have the correspondence." He opened another door and looked inside. "Santosh, do you think it is possible that this is what Government meant?"

The cupboard he had opened was as high as the rest of the apartment and as wide as the kitchen, about six feet. It was about three feet deep. It had two doors. One door opened into the kitchen; another door, directly opposite, opened into the corridor.

"Separate entrance," my employer said. "Shelving, electric light, power point, fitted carpet."

"This must be my room, sahib."

"Santosh, some enemy in Government has done this to me."

"Oh no, sahib. You mustn't say that. Besides, it is very big. I will be able to make myself very comfortable. It is much bigger than my little cubby-hole in the chambers. And it has a nice flat ceiling. I wouldn't hit my head."

"You don't understand, Santosh. Bombay is Bombay. Here if we start living in cupboards we give the wrong impression. They will think we all live in cupboards in Bombay."

"O sahib, but they can just look at me and see I am dirt."

"You are very good, Santosh. But these people are malicious. Still, if you are happy, then I am happy."

"I am very happy, sahib."

And after all the upset, I was. It was nice to crawl in that evening, spread my bedding and feel protected and hidden. I slept very well.

In the morning my employer said, "We must talk about money, Santosh. Your salary is one hundred rupees a month. But Washington isn't Bombay. Everything is a little bit more expensive here, and I am going to give you a Dearness Allowance. As from today you are getting one hundred and fifty rupees."

"Sahib."

"And I'm giving you a fortnight's pay in advance. In foreign exchange. Seventy-five rupees. Ten cents to the rupee, seven hundred and fifty cents. Seven fifty U.S. Here, Santosh. This afternoon you go out and have a little walk and enjoy. But be careful. We are not among friends, remember."

So at last, rested, with money in my pocket, I went out in the open. And of course the city wasn't a quarter as frightening as I had thought. The buildings weren't particularly big, not all the streets were busy, and there were many lovely trees. A lot of the *hubshi* were about, very wild-looking some of them, with dark glasses and their hair frizzed out, but it seemed that if you didn't trouble them they didn't attack you.

I was looking for a café or a tea-stall where perhaps domestics congregated. But I saw no domestics, and I was chased away from the place I did eventually go into. The girl said, after I had been waiting some time, "Can't you read? We don't serve hippies or bare feet here."

O father! I had come out without my shoes. But what a country, I thought, walking briskly away, where people are never allowed to dress normally but must forever wear their very best! Why must they wear out shoes and fine clothes for no purpose? What occasion are they honouring? What waste, what presumption! Who do they think is noticing them all the time?

And even while these thoughts were in my head I found I had come to a roundabout with trees and a fountain where—and it was like a fulfilment in a dream, not easy to believe—there were many people who looked like my own people. I tightened the string around my loose pants, held down my flapping shirt and ran through the traffic to the green circle.

Some of the *hubshi* were there, playing musical instruments and looking quite happy in their way. There were some Americans sitting about on the grass and the fountain and the kerb. Many of them were in rough, friendly-looking clothes; some were without shoes; and I felt I had been over hasty in condemning the entire race. But it wasn't these people who had attracted me to the circle. It was the dancers. The men were bearded, barefooted and in saffron robes, and the girls were in saris and canvas shoes that looked like our own Bata shoes.[1] They were shaking little cymbals and chanting and lifting their heads up and down and going round in a circle, making a lot of dust. It

---

1. I.e., from the Bata Shoe Company.

2736 / V. S. NAIPAUL

was a little bit like a Red Indian dance in a cowboy movie, but they were chanting Sanskrit words in praise of Lord Krishna.[2]

I was very pleased. But then a disturbing thought came to me. It might have been because of the half-caste[3] appearance of the dancers; it might have been their bad Sanskrit pronunciation and their accent. I thought that these people were now strangers, but that perhaps once upon a time they had been like me. Perhaps, as in some story, they had been brought here among the *hubshi* as captives a long time ago and had become a lost people, like our own wandering gipsy folk, and had forgotten who they were. When I thought that, I lost my pleasure in the dancing; and I felt for the dancers the sort of distaste we feel when we are faced with something that should be kin but turns out not to be, turns out to be degraded, like a deformed man, or like a leper, who from a distance looks whole.

I didn't stay. Not far from the circle I saw a café which appeared to be serving bare feet. I went in, had a coffee and a nice piece of cake and bought a pack of cigarettes; matches they gave me free with the cigarettes. It was all right, but then the bare feet began looking at me, and one bearded fellow came and sniffed loudly at me and smiled and spoke some sort of gibberish, and then some others of the bare feet came and sniffed at me. They weren't unfriendly, but I didn't appreciate the behaviour; and it was a little frightening to find, when I left the place, that two or three of them appeared to be following me. They weren't unfriendly, but I didn't want to take any chances. I passed a cinema; I went in. It was something I wanted to do anyway. In Bombay I used to go once a week.

And that was all right. The movie had already started. It was in English, not too easy for me to follow, and it gave me time to think. It was only there, in the darkness, that I thought about the money I had been spending. The prices had seemed to me very reasonable, like Bombay prices. Three for the movie ticket, one fifty in the café, with tip. But I had been thinking in rupees and paying in dollars. In less than an hour I had spent nine days' pay.

I couldn't watch the movie after that. I went out and began to make my way back to the apartment block. Many more of the *hubshi* were about now and I saw that where they congregated the pavement was wet, and dangerous with broken glass and bottles. I couldn't think of cooking when I got back to the apartment. I couldn't bear to look at the view. I spread my bedding in the cupboard, lay down in the darkness and waited for my employer to return.

When he did I said, "Sahib, I want to go home."

"Santosh, I've paid five thousand rupees to bring you here. If I send you back now, you will have to work for six or seven years without salary to pay me back."

I burst into tears.

"My poor Santosh, something has happened. Tell me what has happened."

"Sahib, I've spent more than half the advance you gave me this morning. I went out and had a coffee and cake and then I went to a movie."

His eyes went small and twinkly behind his glasses. He bit the inside of his top lip, scraped at his moustache with his lower teeth, and he said, "You see, you see. I told you it was expensive."

2. Great Hindu deity.
3. Mixed-race, usually in India, descended from or born to an Indian mother and a European father.

I understood I was a prisoner. I accepted this and adjusted. I learned to live within the apartment, and I was even calm.

My employer was a man of taste and he soon had the apartment looking like something in a magazine, with books and Indian paintings and Indian fabrics and pieces of sculpture and bronze statues of our gods. I was careful to take no delight in it. It was of course very pretty, especially with the view. But the view remained foreign and I never felt that the apartment was real, like the shabby old Bombay chambers with the cane chairs, or that it had anything to do with me.

When people came to dinner I did my duty. At the appropriate time I would bid the company goodnight, close off the kitchen behind its folding screen and pretend I was leaving the apartment. Then I would lie down quietly in my cupboard and smoke. I was free to go out; I had my separate entrance. But I didn't like being out of the apartment. I didn't even like going down to the laundry room in the basement.

Once or twice a week I went to the supermarket on our street. I always had to walk past groups of *hubshi* men and children. I tried not to look, but it was hard. They sat on the pavement, on steps and in the bush around their redbrick houses, some of which had boarded-up windows. They appeared to be very much a people of the open air, with little to do; even in the mornings some of the men were drunk.

Scattered among the *hubshi* houses were others just as old but with gas-lamps that burned night and day in the entrance. These were the houses of the Americans. I seldom saw these people; they didn't spend much time on the street. The lighted gas-lamp was the American way of saying that though a house looked old outside it was nice and new inside. I also felt that it was like a warning to the *hubshi* to keep off.

Outside the supermarket there was always a policeman with a gun. Inside, there were always a couple of *hubshi* guards with truncheons, and, behind the cashiers, some old *hubshi* beggar men in rags. There were also many young *hubshi* boys, small but muscular, waiting to carry parcels, as once in the hills I had waited to carry Indian tourists' luggage.

These trips to the supermarket were my only outings, and I was always glad to get back to the apartment. The work there was light. I watched a lot of television and my English improved. I grew to like certain commercials very much. It was in these commercials I saw the Americans whom in real life I so seldom saw and knew only by their gas-lamps. Up there in the apartment, with a view of the white domes and towers and greenery of the famous city, I entered the homes of the Americans and saw them cleaning those homes. I saw them cleaning floors and dishes. I saw them buying clothes and cleaning clothes, buying motor cars and cleaning motor cars. I saw them cleaning, cleaning.

The effect of all this television on me was curious. If by some chance I saw an American on the street I tried to fit him or her into the commercials; and I felt I had caught the person in an interval between his television duties. So to some extent Americans have remained to me, as people not quite real, as people temporarily absent from television.

Sometimes a *hubshi* came on the screen, not to talk of *hubshi* things, but to do a little cleaning of his own. That wasn't the same. He was too different from the *hubshi* I saw on the street and I knew he was an actor. I knew that his television duties were only make-believe and that he would soon have to return to the street.

One day at the supermarket, when the *hubshi* girl took my money, she sniffed and said, "You always smell sweet, baby."

She was friendly, and I was at last able to clear up that mystery, of my smell. It was the poor country weed I smoked. It was a peasant taste of which I was slightly ashamed, to tell the truth; but the cashier was encouraging. As it happened, I had brought a quantity of the weed with me from Bombay in one of my bundles, together with a hundred razor blades, believing both weed and blades to be purely Indian things. I made an offering to the girl. In return she taught me a few words of English. "Me black and beautiful"[4] was the first thing she taught me. Then she pointed to the policeman with the gun outside and taught me: "He pig."

My English lessons were taken a stage further by the *hubshi* maid who worked for someone on our floor in the apartment block. She too was attracted by my smell, but I soon began to feel that she was also attracted by my small-ness and strangeness. She herself was a big woman, broad in the face, with high cheeks and bold eyes and lips that were full but not pendulous. Her largeness disturbed me; I found it better to concentrate on her face. She mis-understood; there were times when she frolicked with me in a violent way. I didn't like it, because I couldn't fight her off as well as I would have liked and because in spite of myself I was fascinated by her appearance. Her smell mixed with the perfumes she used could have made me forget myself.

She was always coming into the apartment. She disturbed me while I was watching the Americans on television. I feared the smell she left behind. Sweat, perfume, my own weed: the smells lay thick in the room, and I prayed to the bronze gods my employer had installed as living-room ornaments that I would not be dishonoured. Dishonoured, I say; and I know that this might seem strange to people over here, who have permitted the *hubshi* to settle among them in such large numbers and must therefore esteem them in certain ways. But in our country we frankly do not care for the *hubshi*. It is written in our books, both holy and not so holy, that it is indecent and wrong for a man of our blood to embrace the *hubshi* woman. To be dishonoured in this life, to be born a cat or a monkey or a *hubshi* in the next!

But I was falling. Was it idleness and solitude? I was found attractive: I wanted to know why. I began to go to the bathroom of the apartment simply to study my face in the mirror. I cannot easily believe it myself now, but in Bombay a week or a month could pass without my looking in the mirror; then it wasn't to consider my looks but to check whether the barber had cut off too much hair or whether a pimple was about to burst. Slowly I made a discovery. My face was handsome. I had never thought of myself in this way. I had thought of myself as unnoticeable, with features that served as identification alone.

The discovery of my good looks brought its strains. I became obsessed with my appearance, with a wish to see myself. It was like an illness. I would be watching television, for instance, and I would be surprised by the thought: are you as handsome as that man? I would have to get up and go to the bathroom and look in the mirror.

I thought back to the time when these matters hadn't interested me, and I saw how ragged I must have looked, on the aeroplane, in the airport, in that café for bare feet, with the rough and dirty clothes I wore, without doubt or question, as clothes befitting a servant. I was choked with shame. I saw, too, how good people in Washington had been, to have seen me in rags and yet to have taken me for a man.

I was glad I had a place to hide. I had thought of myself as a prisoner. Now I was glad I had so little of Washington to cope with: the apartment, my cupboard, the television set, my employer, the walk to the supermarket, the *hubshi* woman. And one day I found I no longer knew whether I wanted to go back to Bombay. Up there, in the apartment, I no longer knew what I wanted to do.

I became more careful of my appearance. There wasn't much I could do. I bought laces for my old black shoes, socks, a belt. Then some money came my way. I had understood that the weed I smoked was of value to the *hubshi* and the bare feet; I disposed of what I had, disadvantageously as I now know, through the *hubshi* girl at the supermarket. I got just under two hundred dollars. Then, as anxiously as I had got rid of my weed, I went out and bought some clothes.

I still have the things I bought that morning. A green hat, a green suit. The suit was always too big for me. Ignorance, inexperience; but I also remember the feeling of presumption. The salesman wanted to talk, to do his job. I didn't want to listen. I took the first suit he showed me and went into the cubicle and changed. I couldn't think about size and fit. When I considered all that cloth and all that tailoring I was proposing to adorn my simple body with, that body that needed so little, I felt I was asking to be destroyed. I changed back quickly, went out of the cubicle and said I would take the green suit. The salesman began to talk; I cut him short; I asked for a hat. When I got back to the apartment I felt quite weak and had to lie down for a while in my cupboard.

I never hung the suit up. Even in the shop, even while counting out the precious dollars, I had known it was a mistake. I kept the suit folded in the box with all its pieces of tissue paper. Three or four times I put it on and walked about the apartment and sat down on chairs and lit cigarettes and crossed my legs, practising. But I couldn't bring myself to wear the suit out of doors. Later I wore the pants, but never the jacket. I never bought another suit; I soon began wearing the sort of clothes I wear today, pants with some sort of zippered jacket.

Once I had had no secrets from my employer; it was so much simpler not to have secrets. But some instinct told me now it would be better not to let him know about the green suit or the few dollars I had, just as instinct had already told me I should keep my growing knowledge of English to myself.

Once my employer had been to me only a presence. I used to tell him then that beside him I was as dirt. It was only a way of talking, one of the courtesies of our language, but it had something of truth. I meant that he was the man who adventured in the world for me, that I experienced the world through him, that I was content to be a small part of his presence. I was content, sleeping on the Bombay pavement with my friends, to hear the talk of my employer and his guests upstairs. I was more than content, late at night, to be identified among the sleepers and greeted by some of those guests before they drove away.

Now I found that, without wishing it, I was ceasing to see myself as part of my employer's presence, and beginning at the same time to see him as an outsider might see him, as perhaps the people who came to dinner in the apartment saw him. I saw that he was a man of my own age, around thirty-five; it astonished me that I hadn't noticed this before. I saw that he was plump, in need of exercise, that he moved with short, fussy steps; a man with glasses, thinning hair, and that habit, during conversation, of scraping at his moustache with his teeth and nibbling at the inside of his top lip; a man who was frequently anxious, took pains over his work, was subjected at his own table to unkind remarks by his office colleagues; a man who looked as uneasy in Washington as I felt, who acted as cautiously as I had learned to act.

I remember an American who came to dinner. He looked at the pieces of sculpture in the apartment and said he had himself brought back a whole head from one of our ancient temples; he had got the guide to hack it off.

I could see that my employer was offended. He said, "But that's illegal."

"That's why I had to give the guide two dollars. If I had a bottle of whisky he would have pulled down the whole temple for me."

My employer's face went blank. He continued to do his duties as host but he was unhappy throughout the dinner. I grieved for him.

Afterwards he knocked on my cupboard. I knew he wanted to talk. I was in my underclothes but I didn't feel underdressed, with the American gone. I stood in the door of my cupboard; my employer paced up and down the small kitchen; the apartment felt sad.

"Did you hear that person, Santosh?"

I pretended I hadn't understood, and when he explained I tried to console him. I said, "Sahib, but we know these people are Franks[5] and barbarians."

"They are malicious people, Santosh. They think that because we are a poor country we are all the same. They think an official in Government is just the same as some poor guide scraping together a few rupees to keep body and soul together, poor fellow."

I saw that he had taken the insult only in a personal way, and I was disappointed. I thought he had been thinking of the temple.

A few days later I had my adventure. The *hubshi* woman came in, moving among my employer's ornaments like a bull. I was greatly provoked. The smell was too much; so was the sight of her armpits. I fell. She dragged me down on the couch, on the saffron spread which was one of my employer's nicest pieces of Punjabi folk-weaving. I saw the moment, helplessly, as one of dishonour. I saw her as Kali,[6] goddess of death and destruction, coal-black, with a red tongue and white eyeballs and many powerful arms. I expected her to be wild and fierce; but she added insult to injury by being very playful, as though, because I was small and strange, the act was not real. She laughed all the time. I would have liked to withdraw, but the act took over and completed itself. And then I felt dreadful.

I wanted to be forgiven, I wanted to be cleansed, I wanted her to go. Nothing frightened me more than the way she had ceased to be a visitor in the apartment and behaved as though she possessed it. I looked at the sculpture and the fabrics and thought of my poor employer, suffering in his office somewhere.

I bathed and bathed afterwards. The smell would not leave me. I fancied that the woman's oil was still on that poor part of my poor body. It occurred to me to rub it down with half a lemon. Penance and cleansing; but it didn't

---

5. Here foreigners of Western origin. 6. Great Hindu deity.

hurt as much as I expected, and I extended the penance by rolling about naked on the floor of the bathroom and the sitting-room and howling. At last the tears came, real tears, and I was comforted.

It was cool in the apartment; the air-conditioning always hummed; but I could see that it was hot outside, like one of our own summer days in the hills. The urge came upon me to dress as I might have done in my village on a religious occasion. In one of my bundles I had a dhoti[7]-length of new cotton, a gift from the tailor's bearer that I had never used. I draped this around my waist and between my legs, lit incense sticks, sat down cross-legged on the floor and tried to meditate and become still. Soon I began to feel hungry. That made me happy; I decided to fast.

Unexpectedly my employer came in. I didn't mind being caught in the attitude and garb of prayer; it could have been so much worse. But I wasn't expecting him till late afternoon.

"Santosh, what has happened?"

Pride got the better of me. I said, "Sahib, it is what I do from time to time."

But I didn't find merit in his eyes. He was far too agitated to notice me properly. He took off his lightweight fawn jacket, dropped it on the saffron spread, went to the refrigerator and drank two tumblers of orange juice, one after the other. Then he looked out at the view, scraping at his moustache.

"Oh, my poor Santosh, what are we doing in this place? Why do we have to come here?"

I looked with him. I saw nothing unusual. The wide window showed the colours of the hot day: the pale-blue sky, the white, almost colourless, domes of famous buildings rising out of dead-green foliage; the untidy roofs of apartment blocks where on Saturday and Sunday mornings people sunbathed; and, below, the fronts and backs of houses on the tree-lined street down which I walked to the supermarket.

My employer turned off the air-conditioning and all noise was absent from the room. An instant later I began to hear the noises outside: sirens far and near. When my employer slid the window open the roar of the disturbed city rushed into the room. He closed the window and there was near-silence again. Not far from the supermarket I saw black smoke, uncurling, rising, swiftly turning colourless. This was not the smoke which some of the apartment blocks gave off all day. This was the smoke of a real fire.

"The *hubshi* have gone wild, Santosh. They are burning down Washington."

I didn't mind at all. Indeed, in my mood of prayer and repentance, the news was even welcome. And it was with a feeling of release that I watched and heard the city burn that afternoon and watched it burn that night. I watched it burn again and again on television; and I watched it burn in the morning. It burned like a famous city and I didn't want it to stop burning. I wanted the fire to spread and spread and I wanted everything in the city, even the apartment block, even the apartment, even myself, to be destroyed and consumed. I wanted escape to be impossible; I wanted the very idea of escape to become absurd. At every sign that the burning was going to stop I felt disappointed and let down.

For four days my employer and I stayed in the apartment and watched the city burn. The television continued to show us what we could see and what, whenever we slid the window back, we could hear. Then it was over. The view

7. Loincloth (Hindi).

from our window hadn't changed. The famous buildings stood; the trees remained. But for the first time since I had understood that I was a prisoner I found that I wanted to be out of the apartment and in the streets.

The destruction lay beyond the supermarket. I had never gone into this part of the city before, and it was strange to walk in those long wide streets for the first time, to see trees and houses and shops and advertisements, everything like a real city, and then to see that every signboard on every shop was burnt or stained with smoke, that the shops themselves were black and broken, that flames had burst through some of the upper windows and scorched the red bricks. For mile after mile it was like that. There were *hubshi* groups about, and at first when I passed them I pretended to be busy, minding my own business, not at all interested in the ruins. But they smiled at me and I found I was smiling back. Happiness was on the faces of the *hubshi*. They were like people amazed they could do so much, that so much lay in their power. They were like people on holiday. I shared their exhilaration.

The idea of escape was a simple one, but it hadn't occurred to me before. When I adjusted to my imprisonment I had wanted only to get away from Washington and to return to Bombay. But then I had become confused. I had looked in the mirror and seen myself, and I knew it wasn't possible for me to return to Bombay to the sort of job I had had and the life I had lived. I couldn't easily become part of someone else's presence again. Those evening chats on the pavement, those morning walks: happy times, but they were like the happy times of childhood: I didn't want them to return.

I had taken, after the fire, to going for long walks in the city. And one day, when I wasn't even thinking of escape, when I was just enjoying the sights and my new freedom of movement, I found myself in one of those leafy streets where private houses had been turned into business premises. I saw a fellow countryman superintending the raising of a signboard on his gallery. The signboard told me that the building was a restaurant, and I assumed that the man in charge was the owner. He looked worried and slightly ashamed, and he smiled at me. This was unusual, because the Indians I had seen on the streets of Washington pretended they hadn't seen me; they made me feel that they didn't like the competition of my presence or didn't want me to start asking them difficult questions.

I complimented the worried man on his signboard and wished him good luck in his business. He was a small man of about fifty and he was wearing a double-breasted suit with old-fashioned wide lapels. He had dark hollows below his eyes and he looked as though he had recently lost a little weight. I could see that in our country he had been a man of some standing, not quite the sort of person who would go into the restaurant business. I felt at one with him. He invited me in to look around, asked my name and gave his. It was Priya.

Just past the gallery was the loveliest and richest room I had ever seen. The wallpaper was like velvet; I wanted to pass my hand over it. The brass lamps that hung from the ceiling were in a lovely cut-out pattern and the bulbs were of many colours. Priya looked with me, and the hollows under his eyes grew darker, as though my admiration was increasing his worry at his extravagance. The restaurant hadn't yet opened for customers and on a shelf in one corner I saw Priya's collection of good-luck objects: a brass plate with a heap of uncooked rice, for prosperity; a little copybook and a little diary pencil, for good luck with the accounts; a little clay lamp, for general good luck.

"What do you think, Santosh? You think it will be all right?"

"It is bound to be all right, Priya."

"But I have enemies, you know, Santosh. The Indian restaurant people are not going to appreciate me. All mine, you know, Santosh. Cash paid. No mortgage or anything like that. I don't believe in mortgages. Cash or nothing."

I understood him to mean that he had tried to get a mortgage and failed, and was anxious about money.

"But what are you doing here, Santosh? You used to be in Government or something?"

"You could say that, Priya."

"Like me. They have a saying here. If you can't beat them, join them. I joined them. They are still beating me." He sighed and spread his arms on the top of the red wall-seat. "Ah, Santosh, why do we do it? Why don't we renounce and go and meditate on the riverbank?" He waved about the room. "The yemblems[8] of the world, Santosh. Just yemblems."

I didn't know the English word he used, but I understood its meaning; and for a moment it was like being back in Bombay, exchanging stories and philosophies with the tailor's bearer and others in the evening.

"But I am forgetting, Santosh. You will have some tea or coffee or something?"

I shook my head from side to side to indicate that I was agreeable, and he called out in a strange harsh language to someone behind the kitchen door.

"Yes, Santosh. Yem-*blems*!" And he sighed and slapped the red seat hard.

A man came out from the kitchen with a tray. At first he looked like a fellow countryman, but in a second I could tell he was a stranger.

"You are right," Priya said, when the stranger went back to the kitchen. "He is not of Bharat. He is a Mexican. But what can I do? You get fellow countrymen, you fix up their papers and everything. And then? Then they run away. Run-run-runaway. Crooks this side, crooks that side, I can't tell you. Listen, Santosh. I was in cloth business before. Buy for fifty rupees that side, sell for fifty dollars this side. Easy. But then. Caftan, everybody wants caftan. Caftan-aftan, I say, I will settle your caftan. I buy one thousand, Santosh. Delays India-side,[9] of course. They come one year later. Nobody wants caftan then. We're not organized, Santosh. We don't do enough consumer research. That's what the fellows at the embassy tell me. But if I do consumer research, when will I do my business? The trouble, you know, Santosh, is that this shopkeeping is not in my blood. The damn thing goes *against* my blood. When I was in cloth business I used to hide sometimes for shame when a customer came in. Sometimes I used to pretend I was a shopper myself. Consumer research! These people make us dance, Santosh. You and I, we will renounce. We will go together and walk beside Potomac and meditate."

I loved his talk. I hadn't heard anything so sweet and philosophical since the Bombay days. I said, "Priya, I will cook for you, if you want a cook."

"I feel I've known you a long time, Santosh. I feel you are like a member of my own family. I will give you a place to sleep, a little food to eat and a little pocket money, as much as I can afford."

I said, "Show me the place to sleep."

He led me out of the pretty room and up a carpeted staircase. I was expecting

8. Emblems.
9. In India. "Caftan": long loose tunic or shirt (Turkish).

the carpet and the new paint to stop somewhere, but it was nice and new all the way. We entered a room that was like a smaller version of my employer's apartment.

"Built-in cupboards and everything, you see, Santosh."

I went to the cupboard. It had a folding door that opened outward. I said, "Priya, it is too small. There is room on the shelf for my belongings. But I don't see how I can spread my bedding inside here. It is far too narrow."

He giggled nervously. "Santosh, you are a joker. I feel that we are of the same family already."

Then it came to me that I was being offered the whole room. I was stunned.

Priya looked stunned too. He sat down on the edge of the soft bed. The dark hollows under his eyes were almost black and he looked very small in his double-breasted jacket. "This is how they make us dance over here, Santosh. You say staff quarters and they say staff quarters. This is what they mean."

For some seconds we sat silently, I fearful, he gloomy, meditating on the ways of this new world.

Someone called from downstairs, "Priya!"

His gloom gone, smiling in advance, winking at me, Priya called back in an accent of the country, "Hi, Bab!"

I followed him down.

"Priya," the American said, "I've brought over the menus."

He was a tall man in a leather jacket, with jeans that rode up above thick white socks and big rubber-soled shoes. He looked like someone about to run in a race. The menus were enormous; on the cover there was a drawing of a fat man with a moustache and a plumed turban, something like the man in the airline advertisements.

"They look great, Bab."

"I like them myself. But what's that, Priya? What's that shelf doing there?"

Moving like the front part of a horse, Bab walked to the shelf with the rice and the brass plate and the little clay lamp. It was only then that I saw that the shelf was very roughly made.

Priya looked penitent and it was clear he had put the shelf up himself. It was also clear he didn't intend to take it down.

"Well, it's yours," Bab said. "I suppose we had to have a touch of the East somewhere. Now, Priya—"

"Money-money-money, is it?" Priya said, racing the words together as though he was making a joke to amuse a child. "But, Bab, how can *you ask me* for money? Anybody hearing you would believe that this restaurant is mine. But this restaurant isn't mine, Bab. This restaurant is yours."

It was only one of our courtesies, but it puzzled Bab and he allowed himself to be led to other matters.

I saw that, for all his talk of renunciation and business failure, and for all his jumpiness, Priya was able to cope with Washington. I admired this strength in him as much as I admired the richness of his talk. I didn't know how much to believe of his stories, but I liked having to guess about him. I liked having to play with his words in my mind. I liked the mystery of the man. The mystery came from his solidity. I knew where I was with him. After the apartment and the green suit and the *hubshi* woman and the city burning for four days, to be with Priya was to feel safe. For the first time since I had come to Washington I felt safe.

I can't say that I moved in. I simply stayed. I didn't want to go back to the apartment even to collect my belongings. I was afraid that something might

ONE OUT OF MANY / 2745

happen to keep me a prisoner there. My employer might turn up and demand his five thousand rupees. The *hubshi* woman might claim me for her own; I might be condemned to a life among the *hubshi*. And it wasn't as if I was leaving behind anything of value in the apartment. The green suit I was even happy to forget. But.

Priya paid me forty dollars a week. After what I was getting, three dollars and seventy-five cents, it seemed a lot; and it was more than enough for my needs. I didn't have much temptation to spend, to tell the truth. I knew that my old employer and the *hubshi* woman would be wondering about me in their respective ways and I thought I should keep off the streets for a while. That was no hardship; it was what I was used to in Washington. Besides, my days at the restaurant were pretty full; for the first time in my life I had little leisure.

The restaurant was a success from the start, and Priya was fussy. He was always bursting into the kitchen with one of those big menus in his hand, saying in English, "Prestige job, Santosh, prestige." I didn't mind. I liked to feel I had to do things perfectly; I felt I was earning my freedom. Though I was in hiding, and though I worked every day until midnight, I felt I was much more in charge of myself than I had ever been.

Many of our waiters were Mexicans, but when we put turbans on them they could pass. They came and went, like the Indian staff. I didn't get on with these people. They were frightened and jealous of one another and very treacherous. Their talk amid the biryanis and the pillaus[1] was all of papers and green cards. They were always about to get green cards or they had been cheated out of green cards or they had just got green cards. At first I didn't know what they were talking about. When I understood I was more than depressed.

I understood that because I had escaped from my employer I had made myself illegal in America. At any moment I could be denounced, seized, jailed, deported, disgraced. It was a complication. I had no green card; I didn't know how to set about getting one; and there was no one I could talk to.

I felt burdened by my secrets. Once I had none; now I had so many. I couldn't tell Priya I had no green card. I couldn't tell him I had broken faith with my old employer and dishonoured myself with a *hubshi* woman and lived in fear of retribution. I couldn't tell him that I was afraid to leave the restaurant and that nowadays when I saw an Indian I hid from him as anxiously as the Indian hid from me. I would have felt foolish to confess. With Priya, right from the start, I had pretended to be strong; and I wanted it to remain like that. Instead, when we talked now, and he grew philosophical, I tried to find bigger causes for being sad. My mind fastened on to these causes, and the effect of this was that my sadness became like a sickness of the soul.

It was worse than being in the apartment, because now the responsibility was mine and mine alone. I had decided to be free, to act for myself. It pained me to think of the exhilaration I had felt during the days of the fire; and I felt mocked when I remembered that in the early days of my escape I had thought I was in charge of myself.

The year turned. The snow came and melted. I was more afraid than ever of going out. The sickness was bigger than all the causes. I saw the future as a hole into which I was dropping. Sometimes at night when I awakened my body would burn and I would feel the hot perspiration break all over.

I leaned on Priya. He was my only hope, my only link with what was real.

---

1. "Biryanis" and "pillaus": Indian dishes.

He went out; he brought back stories. He went out especially to eat in the restaurants of our competitors.

He said, "Santosh, I never believed that running a restaurant was a way to God. But it is true. I eat like a scientist. Every day I eat like a scientist. I feel I have already renounced."

This was Priya. This was how his talk ensnared me and gave me the bigger causes that steadily weakened me. I became more and more detached from the men in the kitchen. When they spoke of their green cards and the jobs they were about to get I felt like asking them: Why? Why?

And every day the mirror told its own tale. Without exercise, with the sickening of my heart and my mind, I was losing my looks. My face had become pudgy and sallow and full of spots; it was becoming ugly. I could have cried for that, discovering my good looks only to lose them. It was like a punishment for my presumption, the punishment I had feared when I bought the green suit.

Priya said, "Santosh, you must get some exercise. You are not looking well. Your eyes are getting like mine. What are you pining for? Are you pining for Bombay or your family in the hills?"

But now, even in my mind, I was a stranger in those places.

Priya said one Sunday morning, "Santosh, I am going to take you to see a Hindi movie today. All the Indians of Washington will be there, domestics and everybody else."

I was very frightened. I didn't want to go and I couldn't tell him why. He insisted. My heart began to beat fast as soon as I got into the car. Soon there were no more houses with gas-lamps in the entrance, just those long wide burnt-out *hubshi* streets, now with fresh leaves on the trees, heaps of rubble on bulldozed, fenced-in lots, boarded-up shop windows, and old smoke-stained signboards announcing what was no longer true. Cars raced along the wide roads; there was life only on the roads. I thought I would vomit with fear.

I said, "Take me back, *sahib*."

I had used the wrong word. Once I had used the word a hundred times a day. But then I had considered myself a small part of my employer's presence, and the word was not servile; it was more like a name, like a reassuring sound, part of my employer's dignity and therefore part of mine. But Priya's dignity could never be mine; that was not our relationship. Priya I had always called Priya; it was his wish, the American way, man to man. With Priya the word was servile. And he responded to the word. He did as I asked; he drove me back to the restaurant. I never called him by his name again.

I was good-looking; I had lost my looks. I was a free man; I had lost my freedom.

One of the Mexican waiters came into the kitchen late one evening and said, "There is a man outside who wants to see the chef."

No one had made this request before, and Priya was at once agitated. "Is he an American? Some enemy has sent him here. Sanitary-anitary, health-ealth, they can inspect my kitchens at any time."

"He is an Indian," the Mexican said.

I was alarmed. I thought it was my old employer; that quiet approach was like him. Priya thought it was a rival. Though Priya regularly ate in the restaurants of his rivals he thought it unfair when they came to eat in his. We both went to the door and peeked through the glass window into the dimly lit dining-room.

"Do you know that person, Santosh?"

"Yes, sahib."

It wasn't my old employer. It was one of his Bombay friends, a big man in Government, whom I had often served in the chambers. He was by himself and seemed to have just arrived in Washington. He had a new Bombay haircut, very close, and a stiff dark suit, Bombay tailoring. His shirt looked blue, but in the dim multi-coloured light of the dining-room everything white looked blue. He didn't look unhappy with what he had eaten. Both his elbows were on the curry-spotted tablecloth and he was picking his teeth, half closing his eyes and hiding his mouth with his cupped left hand.

"I don't like him," Priya said. "Still, big man in Government and so on. You must go to him, Santosh."

But I couldn't go.

"Put on your apron, Santosh. And that chef's cap. Prestige. You must go, Santosh."

Priya went out to the dining-room and I heard him say in English that I was coming.

I ran up to my room, put some oil on my hair, combed my hair, put on my best pants and shirt and my shining shoes. It was so, as a man about town rather than as a cook, I went to the dining-room.

The man from Bombay was as astonished as Priya. We exchanged the old courtesies, and I waited. But, to my relief, there seemed little more to say. No difficult questions were put to me; I was grateful to the man from Bombay for his tact. I avoided talk as much as possible. I smiled. The man from Bombay smiled back. Priya smiled uneasily at both of us. So for a while we were, smiling in the dim blue-red light and waiting.

The man from Bombay said to Priya, "Brother, I just have a few words to say to my old friend Santosh."

Priya didn't like it, but he left us.

I waited for those words. But they were not the words I feared. The man from Bombay didn't speak of my old employer. We continued to exchange courtesies. Yes, I was well and he was well and everybody else we knew was well; and I was doing well and he was doing well. That was all. Then, secretively, the man from Bombay gave me a dollar. A dollar, ten rupees, an enormous tip for Bombay. But, from him, much more than a tip: an act of graciousness, part of the sweetness of the old days. Once it would have meant so much to me. Now it meant so little. I was saddened and embarrassed. And I had been anticipating hostility!

Priya was waiting behind the kitchen door. His little face was tight and serious, and I knew he had seen the money pass. Now, quickly, he read my own face, and without saying anything to me he hurried out into the dining-room.

I heard him say in English to the man from Bombay, "Santosh is a good fellow. He's got his own room with bath and everything. I am giving him a hundred dollars a week from next week. A thousand rupees a week. This is a first-class establishment."

A thousand chips a week! I was staggered. It was much more than any man in Government got, and I was sure the man from Bombay was also staggered, and perhaps regretting his good gesture and that precious dollar of foreign exchange.

"Santosh," Priya said, when the restaurant closed that evening, "that man

was an enemy. I knew it from the moment I saw him. And because he was an
enemy I did something very bad, Santosh."

"Sahib."

"I lied, Santosh. To protect you. I told him, Santosh, that I was going to
give you seventy-five dollars a week after Christmas."

"Sahib."

"And now I have to make that lie true. But, Santosh, you know that is money
we can't afford. I don't have to tell you about overheads and things like that.
Santosh, I will give you sixty."

I said, "Sahib, I couldn't stay on for less than a hundred and twenty-five."

Priya's eyes went shiny and the hollows below his eyes darkened. He giggled
and pressed out his lips. At the end of that week I got a hundred dollars. And
Priya, good man that he was, bore me no grudge.

Now here was a victory. It was only after it happened that I realized how
badly I had needed such a victory, how far, gaining my freedom, I had begun
to accept death not as the end but as the goal. I revived. Or rather, my senses
revived. But in this city what was there to feed my senses? There were no walks
to be taken, no idle conversations with understanding friends. I could buy new
clothes. But then? Would I just look at myself in the mirror? Would I go
walking, inviting passers-by to look at me and my clothes? No, the whole
business of clothes and dressing up only threw me back into myself.

There was a Swiss or German woman in the cake-shop some doors away,
and there was a Filipino woman in the kitchen. They were neither of them
attractive, to tell the truth. The Swiss or German could have broken my back
with a slap, and the Filipino, though young, was remarkably like one of our
older hill women. Still, I felt I owed something to the senses, and I thought I
might frolic with these women. But then I was frightened of the responsibility.
Goodness, I had learned that a woman is not just a roll and a frolic but a big
creature weighing a hundred-and-so-many pounds who is going to be around
afterwards.

So the moment of victory passed, without celebration. And it was strange,
I thought, that sorrow lasts and can make a man look forward to death, but
the mood of victory fills a moment and then is over. When my moment of
victory was over I discovered below it, as if waiting for me, all my old sickness
and fears: fear of my illegality, my former employer, my presumption, the
hubshi woman. I saw then that the victory I had had was not something I had
worked for, but luck; and that luck was only fate's cheating, giving an illusion
of power.

But that illusion lingered, and I became restless. I decided to act, to challenge fate. I decided I would no longer stay in my room and hide. I began to
go out walking in the afternoons. I gained courage; every afternoon I walked
a little farther. It became my ambition to walk to that green circle with the
fountain where, on my first day out in Washington, I had come upon those
people in Hindu costumes, like domestics abandoned a long time ago, singing
their Sanskrit gibberish and doing their strange Red Indian dance. And one
day I got there.

One day I crossed the road to the circle and sat down on a bench. The
hubshi were there, and the bare feet, and the dancers in saris and the saffron
robes. It was mid-afternoon, very hot, and no one was active. I remembered
how magical and inexplicable that circle had seemed to me the first time I saw

it. Now it seemed so ordinary and tired: the roads, the motor cars, the shops, the trees, the careful policemen: so much part of the waste and futility that was our world. There was no longer a mystery. I felt I knew where everybody had come from and where those cars were going. But I also felt that everybody there felt like me, and that was soothing. I took to going to the circle every day after the lunch rush and sitting until it was time to go back to Priya's for the dinners.

Late one afternoon, among the dancers and the musicians, the *hubshi* and the bare feet, the singers and the police, I saw her. The *hubshi* woman. And again I wondered at her size; my memory had not exaggerated. I decided to stay where I was. She saw me and smiled. Then, as if remembering anger, she gave me a look of great hatred; and again I saw her as Kali, many-armed, goddess of death and destruction. She looked hard at my face; she considered my clothes. I thought: is it for this I bought these clothes? She got up. She was very big and her tight pants made her much more appalling. She moved towards me. I got up and ran. I ran across the road and then, not looking back, hurried by devious ways to the restaurant.

Priya was doing his accounts. He always looked older when he was doing his accounts, not worried, just older, like a man to whom life could bring no further surprises. I envied him.

"Santosh, some friend brought a parcel for you."

It was a big parcel wrapped in brown paper. He handed it to me, and I thought how calm he was, with his bills and pieces of paper, and the pen with which he made his neat figures, and the book in which he would write every day until that book was exhausted and he would begin a new one.

I took the parcel up to my room and opened it. Inside there was a cardboard box; and inside that, still in its tissue paper, was the green suit.

I felt a hole in my stomach. I couldn't think. I was glad I had to go down almost immediately to the kitchen, glad to be busy until midnight. But then I had to go up to my room again, and I was alone. I hadn't escaped; I had never been free. I had been abandoned. I was like nothing; I had made myself nothing. And I couldn't turn back.

In the morning Priya said, "You don't look very well, Santosh."

His concern weakened me further. He was the only man I could talk to and I didn't know what I could say to him. I felt tears coming to my eyes. At that moment I would have liked the whole world to be reduced to tears. I said, "Sahib, I cannot stay with you any longer."

They were just words, part of my mood, part of my wish for tears and relief. But Priya didn't soften. He didn't even look surprised. "Where will you go, Santosh?"

How could I answer his serious question?

"Will it be different where you go?"

He had freed himself of me. I could no longer think of tears. I said, "Sahib, I have enemies."

He giggled. "You are a joker, Santosh. How can a man like yourself have enemies? There would be no profit in it. *I* have enemies. It is part of your happiness and part of the equity of the world that you cannot have enemies. That's why you can run-run-runaway." He smiled and made the running gesture with his extended palm.

So, at last, I told him my story. I told him about my old employer and my escape and the green suit. He made me feel I was telling him nothing he hadn't already known. I told him about the *hubshi* woman. I was hoping for some rebuke. A rebuke would have meant that he was concerned for my honour, that I could lean on him, that rescue was possible.

But he said, "Santosh, you have no problems. Marry the *hubshi*. That will automatically make you a citizen. Then you will be a free man."

It wasn't what I was expecting. He was asking me to be alone forever. I said, "Sahib, I have a wife and children in the hills at home."

"But this is your home, Santosh. Wife and children in the hills, that is very nice and that is always there. But that is over. You have to do what is best for you here. You are alone here. *Hubshi-ubshi*, nobody worries about that here, if that is your choice. This isn't Bombay. Nobody looks at you when you walk down the street. Nobody cares what you do."

He was right. I was a free man; I could do anything I wanted. I could, if it were possible for me to turn back, go to the apartment and beg my old employer for forgiveness. I could, if it were possible for me to become again what I once was, go to the police and say, "I am an illegal immigrant here. Please deport me to Bombay." I could run away, hang myself, surrender, confess, hide. It didn't matter what I did, because I was alone. And I didn't know what I wanted to do. It was like the time when I felt my senses revive and I wanted to go out and enjoy and I found there was nothing to enjoy.

To be empty is not to be sad. To be empty is to be calm. It is to renounce. Priya said no more to me; he was always busy in the mornings. I left him and went up to my room. It was still a bare room, still like a room that in half an hour could be someone else's. I had never thought of it as mine. I was frightened of its spotless painted walls and had been careful to keep them spotless. For just such a moment.

I tried to think of the particular moment in my life, the particular action, that had brought me to that room. Was it the moment with the *hubshi* woman, or was it when the American came to dinner and insulted my employer? Was it the moment of my escape, my sight of Priya in the gallery, or was it when I looked in the mirror and bought the green suit? Or was it much earlier, in that other life, in Bombay, in the hills? I could find no one moment; every moment seemed important. An endless chain of action had brought me to that room. It was frightening; it was burdensome. It was not a time for new decisions. It was time to call a halt.

I lay on the bed watching the ceiling, watching the sky. The door was pushed open. It was Priya.

"My goodness, Santosh! How long have you been here? You have been so quiet I forgot about you."

He looked about the room. He went into the bathroom and came out again. "Are you all right, Santosh?"

He sat on the edge of the bed and the longer he stayed the more I realized how glad I was to see him. There was this: when I tried to think of him rushing into the room I couldn't place it in time; it seemed to have occurred only in my mind. He sat with me. Time became real again. I felt a great love for him. Soon I could have laughed at his agitation. And later, indeed, we laughed together.

I said, "Sahib, you must excuse me this morning. I want to go for a walk. I will come back about tea time."

He looked hard at me, and we both knew I had spoken truly.

"Yes, yes, Santosh. You go for a good long walk. Make yourself hungry with walking. You will feel much better."

Walking, through streets that were now so simple to me, I thought how nice it would be if the people in Hindu costumes in the circle were real. Then I might have joined them. We would have taken to the road; at midday we would have halted in the shade of big trees; in the late afternoon the sinking sun would have turned the dust clouds to gold; and every evening at some village there would have been welcome, water, food, a fire in the night. But that was a dream of another life. I had watched the people in the circle long enough to know that they were of their city; that their television life awaited them; that their renunciation was not like mine. No television life awaited me. It didn't matter. In this city I was alone and it didn't matter what I did.

As magical as the circle with the fountain the apartment block had once been to me. Now I saw that it was plain, not very tall, and faced with small white tiles. A glass door; four tiled steps down; the desk to the right, letters and keys in the pigeonholes; a carpet to the left, upholstered chairs, a low table with paper flowers in the vase; the blue door of the swift, silent elevator. I saw the simplicity of all these things. I knew the floor I wanted. In the corridor, with its illuminated star-decorated ceiling, an imitation sky, the colours were blue, grey and gold. I knew the door I wanted. I knocked.

The *hubshi* woman opened. I saw the apartment where she worked. I had never seen it before and was expecting something like my old employer's apartment, which was on the same floor. Instead, for the first time, I saw something arranged for a television life.

I thought she might have been angry. She looked only puzzled. I was grateful for that.

I said to her in English, "Will you marry me?"

And there, it was done.

"It is for the best, Santosh," Priya said, giving me tea when I got back to the restaurant. "You will be a free man. A citizen. You will have the whole world before you."

I was pleased that he was pleased.

So I am now a citizen, my presence is legal, and I live in Washington. I am still with Priya. We do not talk together as much as we did. The restaurant is one world, the parks and green streets of Washington are another, and every evening some of these streets take me to a third. Burnt-out brick houses, broken fences, overgrown gardens; in a levelled lot between the high brick walls of two houses, a sort of artistic children's playground which the *hubshi* children never use; and then the dark house in which I now live.

Its smells are strange, everything in it is strange. But my strength in this house is that I am a stranger. I have closed my mind and heart to the English language, to newspapers and radio and television, to the pictures of *hubshi* runners and boxers and musicians on the wall. I do not want to understand or learn any more.

I am a simple man who decided to act and see for himself, and it is as though I have had several lives. I do not wish to add to these. Some afternoons I walk to the circle with the fountain. I see the dancers but they are separated from me as by glass. Once, when there were rumours of new burnings, someone scrawled in white paint on the pavement outside my house: *Soul Brother.* I understand the words; but I feel, brother to what or to whom?

I was once part of the flow, never thinking of myself as a presence. Then I looked in the mirror and decided to be free. All that my freedom has brought me is the knowledge that I have a face and have a body, that I must feed this body and clothe this body for a certain number of years. Then it will be over.

1971

TOM STOPPARD
b. 1937

Tom Stoppard was born Tomas Straussler in the former Czechoslovakia. His family emigrated to Singapore in 1939 to escape the Nazis and moved to India in 1941 to escape the Japanese. His father stayed behind and was killed in the invasion of Singapore. Tom and his mother went to England in 1946; on her remarriage he took his stepfather's name of Stoppard. After leaving Pocklington School in Yorkshire at seventeen, he became a journalist, wrote a novel, and in 1962 had two short plays broadcast on the radio. The British theater had been dominated for a decade by realistic "kitchen sink" dramas when Stoppard's *Rosencrantz and Guildenstern Are Dead* (1966) appeared and was hailed as a major theatrical event. Critics recognized a debt to *Waiting for Godot,* but where Samuel Beckett had focused on the hopelessness of his two abandoned characters, Stoppard celebrates the gaiety and perverse vitality that can be generated from despair.

He frequently uses plays by other playwrights as launching pads for his own: Rosencrantz and Guildenstern step out of the shadows of Shakespeare's *Hamlet; The Real Inspector Hound* (1968) parodies Agatha Christie's classic country-house murder-mystery play, *The Mousetrap*; and the plot of *Travesties* (1974) is entwined with that of Oscar Wilde's *The Importance of Being Earnest.* Past and present are again entwined, though not intertextually, in his masterpiece, *Arcadia* (1993), which explores the nature of Nature, classical and Romantic theories of landscape gardening, literary history and historians, truth and time. As is appropriate for a play with a double time frame (early nineteenth century spliced with late twentieth century), *Arcadia* has the intricate movement of a grandfather clock, its characters and their concerns interacting with finely geared precision. Appropriately again, the classical mechanism is driven by a Romantic power source: sex—"the attraction which Newton left out."

Newton's classical mechanics posited an order underlying a seemingly disordered world. He saw its "laws" operating via cause-and-effect mechanisms, leading to determinism: given adequate information, one could predict future events. His near-contemporary, however, the wittily named heroine of Stoppard's play, Thomasina [*Tom 'as seen a*] Coverly, has seen another future, one ordered by disorder, what is now known as "chaos theory." (Stoppard found the seed of his play in James Gleick's *Chaos: The Making of a New Science.*) The opposition of order and disorder, past and future (our present), provides the structuring principle of *Arcadia.*

Its action takes place in a large room in a large English country house. Here in 1809 Thomasina, a mathematically and scientifically precocious thirteen-year-old, is being tutored by Septimus, whose friend the poet Lord Byron visits long enough to shoot a hare and, perhaps, another visiting poet, Ezra Chater, in a duel. The opposition of science and poetry is repeated, more than a century and a half later, in the second scene and the same room, when a twentieth-century member of the Coverly family, Valentine, a graduate student "chaotician," tells a visiting literary biographer and theoretician, Hannah Jarvis, about his researches in the new science. The analytically inclined Hannah and a rival, romantically inclined literary critic, Bernard Nightingale, are each embarked on a quest for the truth of Byron's role (if any) in the death of Ezra Chater.

The five principal characters of *Arcadia* are, thus, each engaged in the quest for knowledge. While truth, the whole truth scientific and humanistic, eludes the questers, the interwoven themes of the play reach their resolution in a final scene of astonishing technical virtuosity. After three scenes set in the past and three in the present, the seventh and longest brings past and present—the Romantic age and the postmodern—together. Characters from both periods are on stage simultaneously, all wearing Regency costume (the modern ones for a fancy-dress ball). The scene is at once "chaotic" and supremely ordered, ending—like so many Renaissance and later comedies—with a dance. Here, on the verge of tragedy, humanist and mathematician/scientist from each period join hands and start to waltz. As the Russian Yevgeny Yevtushenko put it in a war poem called "Weddings," even on the verge of tragedy, "you can't not dance."

Stoppard's most recent plays are *Indian Ink* (1993); *The Invention of Love* (1997), which brings together in one galaxy A. E. Housman, Oscar Wilde, and a sparkling constellation of Victorian worthies; and *The Coast of Utopia* (2002), an epic trilogy that follows the trajectory of romantics and revolutionaries in the twilight of Czarist Russia. He shared an Oscar for the screenplay of *Shakespeare in Love* (1998) and has also written for radio and television, alternating—sometimes in the same work—between a serious handling of political themes and arabesques of exuberant fantasy. As he says: "I never quite know whether I want to be a serious artist or a siren." He has succeeded in being both, often—as in *Arcadia*—at the same time.

Stoppard was knighted in 1997 and three years later was appointed a member of the Order of Merit.

Arcadia[1]

CHARACTERS (IN ORDER OF APPEARANCE)

THOMASINA COVERLY, *aged thirteen, later sixteen*
SEPTIMUS HODGE, *her tutor, aged twenty-two, later twenty-five*
JELLABY, *a butler, middle-aged*
EZRA CHATER, *a poet, aged thirty-one*
RICHARD NOAKES, *a landscape architect, middle-aged*
LADY CROOM, *middle thirties*
CAPT. BRICE, RN,[2] *middle thirties*

HANNAH JARVIS, *an author, late thirties*
CHLOË COVERLY, *aged eighteen*
BERNARD NIGHTINGALE, *a don,[3] late thirties*
VALENTINE COVERLY, *aged twenty-five to thirty*
GUS COVERLY, *aged fifteen*
AUGUSTUS COVERLY, *aged fifteen*

Act One

SCENE ONE

A room on the garden front of a very large country house in Derbyshire in April 1809. Nowadays, the house would be called a stately home. The upstage wall is mainly tall, shapely, uncurtained windows, one or more of which work as doors. Nothing much need be said or seen of the exterior beyond. We come to learn that

1. A mountainous region of central Peloponnese, Greece; scene of idealized and idyllic country life in the pastoral poetry of ancient Greece, notably that of Theocritus, and Italy, notably that of Virgil; its shepherds are called "Arcades."
2. Royal Navy.
3. University teacher of English literature.

*the house stands in the typical English park of the time. Perhaps we see an indi-
cation of this, perhaps only light and air and sky.
The room looks bare despite the large table which occupies the centre of it.
The table, the straight-backed chairs and, the only other item of furniture, the
architect's stand or reading stand, would all be collectable pieces now but here,
on an uncarpeted wood floor, they have no more pretension than a schoolroom,
which is indeed the main use of this room at this time. What elegance there is,
is architectural, and nothing is impressive but the scale. There is a door in each
of the side walls. These are closed, but one of the french windows[4] is open to a
bright but sunless morning.
There are two people, each busy with books and paper and pen and ink, separately occupied. The pupil is* THOMASINA COVERLY, *aged 13. The tutor is* SEPTI-
MUS HODGE, *aged 22. Each has an open book. Hers is a slim mathematics primer.[5]
His is a handsome thick quarto,[6] brand new, a vanity production,[7] with little
tapes to tie when the book is closed. His loose papers, etc, are kept in a stiff-
backed portfolio which also ties up with tapes.
Septimus has a tortoise which is sleepy enough to serve as a paperweight.
Elsewhere on the table there is an old-fashioned theodolite[8] and also some other
books stacked up.*

THOMASINA   Septimus, what is carnal embrace?[9]
SEPTIMUS   Carnal embrace is the practice of throwing one's arms around a
side of beef.
THOMASINA   Is that all?
SEPTIMUS   No . . . a shoulder of mutton, a haunch of venison well hugged,[1]
an embrace of grouse . . . *caro, carnis;*[2] feminine; flesh.
THOMASINA   Is it a sin?
SEPTIMUS   Not necessarily, my lady, but when carnal embrace is sinful it is a
sin of the flesh, QED.[3] We had *caro* in our Gallic Wars[4]—'The Britons live
on milk and meat'—'*lacte et carne vivunt*'. I am sorry that the seed fell on
stony ground.[5]
THOMASINA   That was the sin of Onan,[6] wasn't it, Septimus?
SEPTIMUS   Yes. He was giving his brother's wife a Latin lesson and she was
hardly the wiser after it than before. I thought you were finding a proof for
Fermat's last theorem.[7]
THOMASINA   It is very difficult, Septimus. You will have to show me how.
SEPTIMUS   If I knew how, there would be no need to ask *you*. Fermat's last
theorem has kept people busy for a hundred and fifty years, and I hoped it
would keep *you* busy long enough for me to read Mr Chater's poem in praise
of love with only the distraction of its own absurdities.

4. Glass-panelled door in the outside wall of a
house, serving as a window and a door.
5. Textbook.
6. Book, a quarter of the size of a traditional printing sheet, approximately the size of a modern
novel.
7. Published at author's expense.
8. Surveyor's measuring instrument, a telescope
mounted on a tripod.
9. Sexual intercourse.
1. Wordplay on *well-hung*.
2. Latin.
3. Initials indicating a problem has been solved:
quod erat demonstrandum ("as has been demonstrated," Latin).

4. Julius Caesar's history of his wars in Gaul
(France), *De Bello Gallico*.
5. Cf. Matthew 13.3–8: Christ's parable of the
sower who "went forth to sow."
6. Cf. Genesis 38.9. Thomasina mischievously
confuses the sower's seed with the semen Onan
"spilled . . . on the ground" rather than impregnate
his brother's wife.
7. Famous problem proposed by the French mathematician Pierre de Fermat (1601–1665) and
described by Septimus on p. 2755. See also
p. 2757. Often held to be unprovable, Fermat's last
theorem was proved by Professor Andrew Wiles a
few months after *Arcadia* was first performed.

THOMASINA Our Mr Chater has written a poem?
SEPTIMUS He believes he has written a poem, yes. I can see that there might be more carnality in your algebra than in Mr Chater's 'Couch of Eros'.[8]
THOMASINA Oh, it was not my algebra. I heard Jellaby telling cook that Mrs Chater was discovered in carnal embrace in the gazebo.
SEPTIMUS [*Pause*] Really? With whom, did Jellaby happen to say?
  [THOMASINA *considers this with a puzzled frown.*]
THOMASINA What do you mean, with whom?
SEPTIMUS With what? Exactly so. The idea is absurd. Where did this story come from?
THOMASINA Mr Noakes.
SEPTIMUS Mr Noakes!
THOMASINA Papa's landskip[9] architect. He was taking bearings in the garden when he saw—through his spyglass—Mrs Chater in the gazebo in carnal embrace.
SEPTIMUS And do you mean to tell me that Mr Noakes told the butler?
THOMASINA No. Mr Noakes told Mr Chater. *Jellaby* was told by the groom, who overheard Mr Noakes telling Mr Chater, in the stable yard.
SEPTIMUS Mr Chater being engaged in closing the stable door.[1]
THOMASINA What do you mean, Septimus?
SEPTIMUS So, thus far, the only people who know about this are Mr Noakes the landskip architect, the groom, the butler, the cook and, of course, Mrs Chater's husband, the poet.
THOMASINA And Arthur who was cleaning the silver, and the bootboy. And now you.
SEPTIMUS Of course. What else did he say?
THOMASINA Mr Noakes?
SEPTIMUS No, not Mr Noakes. Jellaby. You heard Jellaby telling the cook.
THOMASINA Cook hushed him almost as soon as he started. Jellaby did not see that I was being allowed to finish yesterday's upstairs[2] rabbit pie before I came to my lesson. I think you have not been candid with me, Septimus. A gazebo is not, after all, a meat larder.
SEPTIMUS I never said my definition was complete.
THOMASINA Is carnal embrace kissing?
SEPTIMUS Yes.
THOMASINA And throwing one's arms around Mrs Chater?
SEPTIMUS Yes. Now, Fermat's last theorem—
THOMASINA I thought as much. I hope you are ashamed.
SEPTIMUS I, my lady?
THOMASINA If *you* do not teach me the true meaning of things, who will?
SEPTIMUS Ah. Yes, I am ashamed. Carnal embrace is sexual congress, which is the insertion of the male genital organ into the female genital organ for purposes of procreation and pleasure. Fermat's last theorem, by contrast, asserts that when x, y and z are whole numbers each raised to power of n, the sum of the first two can never equal the third when n is greater than 2.
  [*Pause.*]
THOMASINA Eurghhh!

8. Greek god of love.
9. Landscape.
1. Proverbial saying that continues "after the horse has bolted."

2. As prepared for Lord and Lady Croom and their guests ("upstairs," as distinct from the servants "below stairs").

SEPTIMUS   Nevertheless, that is the theorem.

THOMASINA   It is disgusting and incomprehensible. Now when I am grown to practise it myself I shall never do so without thinking of you.

SEPTIMUS   Thank you very much, my lady. Was Mrs Chater down this morning?

THOMASINA   No. Tell me more about sexual congress.

SEPTIMUS   There is nothing more to be said about sexual congress.

THOMASINA   Is it the same as love?

SEPTIMUS   Oh no, it is much nicer than that.

[*One of the side doors leads to the music room. It is the other side door which now opens to admit* JELLABY, *the butler.*]

I am teaching, Jellaby.

JELLABY   Beg your pardon, Mr Hodge, Mr Chater said it was urgent you receive his letter.

SEPTIMUS   Oh, very well. [SEPTIMUS *takes the letter.*] Thank you. [*And to dismiss* JELLABY.] Thank you.

JELLABY [*Holding his ground.*]   Mr Chater asked me to bring him your answer.

SEPTIMUS   My answer?

[*He opens the letter. There is no envelope as such, but there is a 'cover' which, folded and sealed, does the same service.*

SEPTIMUS *tosses the cover negligently aside and reads.*]

Well, my answer is that as is my custom and my duty to his lordship I am engaged until a quarter to twelve in the education of his daughter. When I am done, and if Mr Chater is still there, I will be happy to wait upon him in—[*He checks the letter.*]—in the gunroom.

JELLABY   I will tell him so, thank you, sir.

[SEPTIMUS *folds the letter and places it between the pages of 'The Couch of Eros'.*]

THOMASINA   What is for dinner, Jellaby?

JELLABY   Boiled ham and cabbages, my lady, and a rice pudding.

THOMASINA   Oh, goody.

[JELLABY *leaves.*]

SEPTIMUS   Well, so much for Mr Noakes. He puts himself forward as a gentleman, a philosopher of the picturesque,[3] a visionary who can move mountains and cause lakes, but in the scheme of the garden he is as the serpent.[4]

THOMASINA   When you stir your rice pudding, Septimus, the spoonful of jam spreads itself round making red trails like the picture of a meteor in my astronomical atlas. But if you stir backward, the jam will not come together again. Indeed, the pudding does not notice and continues to turn pink just as before. Do you think this is odd?

SEPTIMUS   No.

THOMASINA   Well, I do. You cannot stir things apart.

SEPTIMUS   No more you can, time must needs run backward, and since it will not, we must stir our way onward mixing as we go, disorder out of disorder into disorder until pink is complete, unchanging and unchangeable, and we are done with it for ever.[5] This is known as free will or self-determination.

---

3. Italianate landscape associated with the writers and landscape gardeners of the early-nineteenth-century Romantic movement.
4. Noakes spies on and spoils the happiness of the lovers in the gazebo, as the serpent in the Garden of Eden poisoned the bliss of Adam and Eve (Genesis 3).
5. Evidence offered, with no awareness of its significance, of the then-undiscovered second law of thermodynamics.

[*He picks up the tortoise and moves it a few inches as though it had strayed, on top of some loose papers, and admonishes it.*]
Sit!

THOMASINA Septimus, do you think God is a Newtonian?[6]

SEPTIMUS An Etonian?[7] Almost certainly, I'm afraid. We must ask your brother to make it his first enquiry.

THOMASINA No, Septimus, a Newtonian. Septimus! Am I the first person to have thought of this?

SEPTIMUS No.

THOMASINA I have not said yet.

SEPTIMUS 'If everything from the furthest planet to the smallest atom of our brain acts according to Newton's law of motion, what becomes of free will?'

THOMASINA No.

SEPTIMUS God's will.

THOMASINA No.

SEPTIMUS Sin.

THOMASINA [*Derisively.*] No!

SEPTIMUS Very well.

THOMASINA If you could stop every atom in its position and direction, and if your mind could comprehend all the actions thus suspended, then if you were really, *really* good at algebra you could write the formula for all the future; and although nobody can be so clever to do it, the formula must exist just as if one could.

SEPTIMUS [*Pause.*] Yes. [*Pause.*] Yes, as far as I know, you are the first person to have thought of this. [*Pause. With an effort.*] In the margin of his copy of *Arithmetica*, Fermat wrote that he had discovered a wonderful proof of his theorem but, the margin being too narrow for his purpose, did not have room to write it down. The note was found after his death, and from that day to this—

THOMASINA Oh! I see now! The answer is perfectly obvious.

SEPTIMUS This time you may have overreached yourself.

[*The door is opened, somewhat violently.* CHATER *enters.*] Mr Chater! Perhaps my message miscarried. I will be at liberty at a quarter to twelve, if that is convenient.

CHATER It is not convenient, sir. My business will not wait.

SEPTIMUS Then I suppose you have Lord Croom's opinion that your business is more important than his daughter's lesson.

CHATER I do not, but, if you like, I will ask his lordship to settle the point.

SEPTIMUS [*Pause.*] My lady, take Fermat into the music room. There will be an extra spoonful of jam if you find his proof.

THOMASINA There is no proof, Septimus. The thing that is perfectly obvious is that the note in the margin was a joke to make you all mad.

[THOMASINA *leaves.*]

SEPTIMUS Now, sir, what is this business that cannot wait?

CHATER I think you know it, sir. You have insulted my wife.

SEPTIMUS Insulted her? That would deny my nature, my conduct, and the admiration in which I hold Mrs Chater.

---

6. Believer in the scientific theories of Isaac Newton (1642–1727).
7. Alumnus of the famous English public (i.e., in the U.S., private) school, Eton, which Thomasina's brother Augustus will later attend.

CHATER   I have heard of your admiration, sir! You insulted my wife in the gazebo yesterday evening!

SEPTIMUS   You are mistaken. I made love to your wife in the gazebo. She asked me to meet her there, I have her note somewhere, I dare say I could find it for you, and if someone is putting it about that I did not turn up, by God, sir, it is a slander.

CHATER   You damned lecher! You would drag down a lady's reputation to make a refuge for your cowardice. It will not do! I am calling you out![8]

SEPTIMUS   Chater! Chater, Chater, Chater! My dear friend!

CHATER   You dare to call me that. I demand satisfaction!

SEPTIMUS   Mrs Chater demanded satisfaction and now you are demanding satisfaction. I cannot spend my time day and night satisfying the demands of the Chater family. As for your wife's reputation, it stands where it ever stood.

CHATER   You blackguard!

SEPTIMUS   I assure you. Mrs Chater is charming and spirited, with a pleasing voice and a dainty step, she is the epitome of all the qualities society applauds in her sex—and yet her chief renown is for a readiness that keeps her in a state of tropical humidity as would grow orchids in her drawers in January.

CHATER   Damn you, Hodge, I will not listen to this! Will you fight or not?

SEPTIMUS   [Definitively.]   Not! There are no more than two or three poets of the first rank now living, and I will not shoot one of them dead over a perpendicular poke in a gazebo with a woman whose reputation could not be adequately defended with a platoon of musketry deployed by rota.

CHATER   Ha! You say so! Who are the others? In your opinion?—no—no—!—this goes very ill, Hodge. I will not be flattered out of my course. You say so, do you?

SEPTIMUS   I do. And I would say the same to Milton[9] were he not already dead. Not the part about his wife, of course—

CHATER   But among the living? Mr Southey?[1]

SEPTIMUS   Southey I would have shot on sight.

CHATER   [Shaking his head sadly.]   Yes, he has fallen off. I admired 'Thalaba' quite, but 'Madoc', [He chuckles.] oh dear me!—but we are straying from the business here—you took advantage of Mrs Chater, and if that were not bad enough, it appears every stableboy and scullery maid on the strength—

SEPTIMUS   Damn me! Have you not listened to a word I said?

CHATER   I have heard you, sir, and I will not deny I welcome your regard, God knows one is little appreciated if one stands outside the coterie of hacks and placemen[2] who surround Jeffrey and the Edinburgh—[3]

SEPTIMUS   My dear Chater, they judge a poet by the seating plan of Lord Holland's table![4]

CHATER   By heaven, you are right! And I would very much like to know the name of the scoundrel who slandered my verse drama 'Maid of Turkey' in the Piccadilly Recreation, too!

---

8. Challenging you to a duel.
9. John Milton (1608–1674), English poet.
1. Robert Southey (1774–1843), English poet, author of the long poems Thalaba and Madoc.
2. Clique of those who write only for money or social advantage.
3. Frances Lord Jeffrey (1773–1850), cofounder

and editor of The Edinburgh Review (1802–29), was a stern but generally perceptive literary critic.
4. Henry Richard Vassall Fox, Lord Holland (1773–1840), British politician, exerted considerable influence on literature and politics through the hospitality that Holland House offered the brilliant and distinguished people of his day.

SEPTIMUS   'The Maid of Turkey'! I have it by my bedside! When I cannot sleep
I take up 'The Maid of Turkey' like an old friend!
CHATER [*Gratified.*]   There you are! And the scoundrel wrote he would not
give it to his dog for dinner were it covered in bread sauce and stuffed with
chestnuts. When Mrs Chater read that, she wept, sir, and would not give
herself to me for a fortnight—which recalls me to my purpose—
SEPTIMUS   The new poem, however, will make your name perpetual—
CHATER   Whether it do or not—
SEPTIMUS   It is not a question, sir. No coterie can oppose the acclamation of
the reading public. 'The Couch of Eros' will take the town.
CHATER   Is that your estimation?
SEPTIMUS   It is my intent.
CHATER   Is it, is it? Well, well! I do not understand you.
SEPTIMUS   You see I have an early copy—sent to me for review. I say review,
but I speak of an extensive appreciation of your gifts and your rightful place
in English literature.
CHATER   Well, I must say. That is certainly . . . You have written it?
SEPTIMUS [*Crisply.*]   Not yet.
CHATER   Ah. And how long does . . . ?
SEPTIMUS   To be done right, it first requires a careful re-reading of your book,
of both your books, several readings, together with outlying works[5] for an
exhibition of deference or disdain as the case merits. I make notes, of course,
I order my thoughts, and finally, when all is ready and I am *calm in my
mind* . . .
CHATER [*Shrewdly.*]   Did Mrs Chater know of this before she—before you—
SEPTIMUS   I think she very likely did.
CHATER [*Triumphantly.*]   There is nothing that woman would not do for me!
Now you have an insight to her character. Yes, by God, she is a wife to me,
sir!
SEPTIMUS   For that alone, I would not make her a widow.
CHATER   Captain Brice once made the same observation!
SEPTIMUS   Captain Brice did?
CHATER   Mr Hodge, allow me to inscribe your copy in happy anticipation.
Lady Thomasina's pen will serve us.
SEPTIMUS   Your connection with Lord and Lady Croom you owe to your fight-
ing her ladyship's brother?
CHATER   No! It was all nonsense, sir—a canard![6] But a fortunate mistake, sir.
It brought me the patronage of a captain of His Majesty's Navy and the
brother of a countess. I do not think Mr Walter Scott[7] can say as much, and
here I am, a respected guest at Sidley Park.
SEPTIMUS   Well, sir, you can say you have received satisfaction.
[CHATER *is already inscribing the book, using the pen and ink-pot on
the table.* NOAKES *enters through the door used by* CHATER. *He carries
rolled-up plans.* CHATER, *inscribing, ignores* NOAKES. NOAKES *on seeing
the occupants, panics.*]
NOAKES   Oh!
SEPTIMUS   Ah, Mr Noakes—my muddy-mettled[8] rascal! Where's your
spyglass?

---

5. Other writers' books.   (1771–1832).
6. Malicious gossip.   8. Dirty-minded.
7. Best-selling Scottish poet and, later, novelist

NOAKES   I beg your leave—I thought her ladyship—excuse me—
[*He is beating an embarrassed retreat when he becomes rooted by* CHA-
TER's *voice.* CHATER *reads his inscription in ringing tones.*]
CHATER   'To my friend Septimus Hodge, who stood up[9] and gave his best on
behalf of the Author—Ezra Chater, at Sidley Park, Derbyshire, April 10th,
1809.' [*Giving the book to* SEPTIMUS.] There, sir—something to show your
grandchildren!
SEPTIMUS   This is more than I deserve, this is handsome, what do you say,
Noakes?
    [*They are interrupted by the appearance, outside the windows, of* LADY
    CROOM *and* CAPTAIN EDWARD BRICE, RN.[1] *Her first words arrive through
    the open door.*]
LADY CROOM   Oh, no! Not the gazebo!
    [*She enters, followed by* BRICE *who carries a leatherbound sketch book.*]
Mr Noakes! What is this I hear?
BRICE   Not only the gazebo, but the boat-house, the Chinese bridge, the
shrubbery—
CHATER   By God, sir! Not possible!
BRICE   Mr Noakes will have it so.
SEPTIMUS   Mr Noakes, this is monstrous!
LADY CROOM   I am glad to hear it from *you*, Mr Hodge.
THOMASINA [*Opening the door from the music room.*]   May I return now?
SEPTIMUS [*Attempting to close the door.*]   Not just yet—
LADY CROOM   Yes, let her stay. A lesson in folly is worth two in wisdom.
    [BRICE *takes the sketch book to the reading stand, where he lays it open.
    The sketch book is the work of* MR NOAKES, *who is obviously an admirer
    of Humphry Repton's 'Red Books'.*[2] *The pages, drawn in watercolours,
    show 'before' and 'after' views of the landscape, and the pages are cun-
    ningly cut to allow the latter to be superimposed over portions of the
    former, though Repton did it the other way round.*]
BRICE   Is Sidley Park to be an Englishman's garden or the haunt of Corsican
brigands?
SEPTIMUS   Let us not hyperbolize, sir.
BRICE   It is rape, sir!
NOAKES [*Defending himself.*]   It is the modern style.
CHATER [*Under the same misapprehension as* SEPTIMUS.]   Regrettable, of
course, but so it is.
    [THOMASINA *has gone to examine the sketch book.*]
LADY CROOM   Mr Chater, you show too much submission. Mr Hodge. I appeal
to you.
SEPTIMUS   Madam, I regret the gazebo, I sincerely regret the gazebo—and the
boat-house up to a point—but the Chinese bridge, fantasy!—and the shrub-
bery I reject with contempt! Mr Chater!—would you take the word of a
jumped-up jobbing gardener[3] who sees carnal embrace in every nook and
cranny of the landskip!
THOMASINA   Septimus, they are not speaking of carnal embrace, are you,
Mama?

9. Cf. Septimus's "perpendicular poke in a
gazebo" (p. 2758).
1. See p. 2753, n. 2.
2. Repton (1752–1818), a landscape architect,
presented his designs in so-called Red Books showing "before" and "after" views of his clients'
grounds. Noakes is proposing to Gothicize the classical English landscape of Sidley Park.
3. Presumptuously conceited odd-job gardener.

LADY CROOM   Certainly not. What do you know of carnal embrace?
THOMASINA   Everything, thanks to Septimus. In my opinion, Mr Noakes's
scheme for the garden is perfect. It is a Salvator!⁴
LADY CROOM   What does she mean?
NOAKES [*Answering the wrong question.*]   Salvator Rosa, your ladyship, the
painter. He is indeed the very exemplar of the picturesque style.
BRICE   Hodge, what is this?
SEPTIMUS   She speaks from innocence not from experience.
BRICE   You call it innocence? Has he ruined you, child?
    [*Pause.*]
SEPTIMUS   Answer your uncle!
THOMASINA [*To* SEPTIMUS.]   How is a ruined child different from a ruined
castle?
SEPTIMUS   On such questions I defer to Mr Noakes.
NOAKES [*Out of his depth.*]   A ruined castle is picturesque, certainly.
SEPTIMUS   That is the main difference. [*To* BRICE.] I teach the classical
authors. If I do not elucidate their meaning, who will?
BRICE   As her tutor you have a duty to keep her in ignorance.
LADY CROOM   Do not dabble in paradox, Edward, it puts you in danger of
fortuitous wit. Thomasina, wait in your bedroom.
THOMASINA [*Retiring.*]   Yes, mama. I did not intend to get you into trouble,
Septimus. I am very sorry for it. It is plain that there are some things a girl
is allowed to understand, and these include the whole of algebra, but there
are others, such as embracing a side of beef, that must be kept from her
until she is old enough to have a carcass of her own.
LADY CROOM   One moment.
BRICE   What is she talking about?
LADY CROOM   Meat.
BRICE   Meat?
LADY CROOM   Thomasina, you had better remain. Your knowledge of the picturesque obviously exceeds anything the rest of us can offer. Mr Hodge,
ignorance should be like an empty vessel waiting to be filled at the well of
truth—not a cabinet of vulgar curios.⁵ Mr Noakes—now at last it is your
turn—
NOAKES   Thank you, your ladyship—
LADY CROOM   Your drawing is a very wonderful transformation. I would not
have recognized my own garden but for your ingenious book—is it not?—
look! Here is the Park as it appears to us now, and here as it might be when
Mr Noakes has done with it. Where there is the familiar pastoral refinement
of an Englishman's garden, here is an eruption of gloomy forest and towering crag, of ruins where there was never a house, of water dashing against
rocks where there was neither spring nor a stone I could not throw the
length of a cricket pitch.⁶ My hyacinth dell is become a haunt for hobgoblins, my Chinese bridge, which I am assured is superior to the one at Kew,⁷
and for all I know at Peking, is usurped by a fallen obelisk overgrown with
briars—
NOAKES [*Bleating.*]   Lord Little has one very similar—

LADY CROOM   I cannot relieve Lord Little's misfortunes by adding to my own. Pray, what is this rustic hovel that presumes to superpose itself on my gazebo?

NOAKES   That is the hermitage,[8] madam.

LADY CROOM   I am bewildered.

BRICE   It is all irregular, Mr Noakes.

NOAKES   It is, sir. Irregularity is one of the chiefest principles of the picturesque style—

LADY CROOM   But Sidley Park is already a picture, and a most amiable picture too. The slopes are green and gentle. The trees are companionably grouped at intervals that show them to advantage. The rill[9] is a serpentine ribbon unwound from the lake peaceably contained by meadows on which the right amount of sheep are tastefully arranged—in short, it is nature as God intended, and I can say with the painter, '*Et in Arcadia ego!*'[1] 'Here I am in Arcadia,' Thomasina.

THOMASINA   Yes, mama, if you would have it so.

LADY CROOM   Is she correcting my taste or my translation?

THOMASINA   Neither are beyond correction, mama, but it was your geography caused the doubt.

LADY CROOM   Something has occurred with the girl since I saw her last, and surely that was yesterday. How old are you this morning?

THOMASINA   Thirteen years and ten months, mama.

LADY CROOM   Thirteen years and ten months. She is not due to be pert for six months at the earliest, or to have notions of taste for much longer. Mr Hodge, I hold you accountable. Mr Noakes, back to you—

NOAKES   Thank you, my—

LADY CROOM   You have been reading too many novels by Mrs Radcliffe, that is my opinion. This is a garden for *The Castle of Otranto* or *The Mysteries of Udolpho*—[2]

CHATER   *The Castle of Otranto*, my lady, is by Horace Walpole.

NOAKES   [*Thrilled.*]   Mr Walpole the gardener?!

LADY CROOM   Mr Chater, you are a welcome guest at Sidley Park but while you are one, *The Castle of Otranto* was written by whomsoever I say it was, otherwise what is the point of being a guest or having one?

[*The distant popping of guns heard.*]

Well, the guns have reached the brow[3]—I will speak to his lordship on the subject, and we will see by and by—[*She stands looking out.*] Ah!—your friend has got down a pigeon, Mr Hodge. [*Calls out.*] Bravo, sir!

SEPTIMUS   The pigeon, I am sure, fell to your husband or to your son, your ladyship—my schoolfriend was never a sportsman.

BRICE [*Looking out.*]   Yes, to Augustus!—bravo, lad!

LADY CROOM [*Outside.*]   Well, come along! Where are my troops?

[BRICE, NOAKES *and* CHATER *obediently follow her,* CHATER *making a detour to shake* SEPTIMUS's *hand fervently.*]

CHATER   My dear Mr Hodge!

[CHATER *leaves also. The guns are heard again, a little closer.*]

---

8. Hermit's residence.
9. Stream.
1. Latin phrase, inscribed on a tomb in a painting by the French artist Nicolas Poussin (1594–1665). Lady Groom translates it literally, but the speaker is often taken—as Septimus does below—to be Death.

2. Ann Radcliffe (1764–1823) wrote Gothic novels, the most famous of which is *The Mysteries of Udolpho* (1794). Horace Walpole (1717–1797), author of *The Castle of Otranto* (1764), also pioneered the Gothic style of picturesque landscaping.
3. Top of the hill.

THOMASINA   Pop, pop, pop . . . I have grown up in the sound of guns like the child of a siege. Pigeons and rooks in the close season,[4] grouse on the heights from August, and the pheasants to follow—partridge, snipe, woodcock, and teal—pop—pop—pop, and the culling of the herd. Papa has no need of the recording angel, his life is written in the game book.[5]

SEPTIMUS   A calendar of slaughter. 'Even in Arcadia, there am I!'

THOMASINA   Oh, phooey to Death!
    [*She dips a pen and takes it to the reading stand.*]
    I will put in a hermit, for what is a hermitage without a hermit? Are you in love with my mother, Septimus?

SEPTIMUS   You must not be cleverer than your elders. It is not polite.

THOMASINA   Am I cleverer?

SEPTIMUS   Yes. Much.

THOMASINA   Well, I am sorry, Septimus. [*She pauses in her drawing and produces a small envelope from her pocket.*] Mrs Chater came to the music room with a note for you. She said it was of scant importance, and that therefore I should carry it to you with the utmost safety, urgency and discretion. Does carnal embrace addle the brain?

SEPTIMUS   [*Taking the letter.*]   Invariably. Thank you. That is enough education for today.

THOMASINA   There. I have made him like the Baptist in the wilderness.[6]

SEPTIMUS   How picturesque.

    [LADY CROOM *is heard calling distantly for* THOMASINA *who runs off into the garden, cheerfully, an uncomplicated girl.*

    SEPTIMUS *opens Mrs Chater's note. He crumples the envelope and throws it away. He reads the note, folds it and inserts it into the pages of 'The Couch of Eros'.*]

SCENE TWO

The lights come up on the same room, on the same sort of morning, in the present day, as is instantly clear from the appearance of HANNAH JARVIS; *and from nothing else.*

Something needs to be said about this. The action of the play shuttles back and forth between the early nineteenth century and the present day, always in this same room. Both periods must share the state of the room, without the additions and subtractions which would normally be expected. The general appearance of the room should offend neither period. In the case of props—books, paper, flowers, etc., there is no absolute need to remove the evidence of one period to make way for another. However, books, etc., used in both periods should exist in both old and new versions. The landscape outside, we are told, has undergone changes. Again, what we see should neither change nor contradict.

On the above principle, the ink and pens etc., of the first scene can remain. Books and papers associated with Hannah's research, in Scene Two, can have been on the table from the beginning of the play. And so on. During the course of the play the table collects this and that, and where an object from one scene would be an anachronism in another (say a coffee mug) it is simply deemed to have become invisible. By the end of the play the table has collected an inventory of objects.

HANNAH *is leafing through the pages of Mr Noakes's sketch book. Also to hand,*

---

4. Closed to hunters.
5. For recording a sportsman's or sportswoman's kill.

6. Thomasina's hermit looks like John the Baptist (cf. Luke 1.4), who lived many years in the desert.

opened and closed, are a number of small volumes like diaries (these turn out to be Lady Croom's 'garden books'). After a few moments, HANNAH *takes the sketch book to the windows, comparing the view with what has been drawn, and then she replaces the sketch book on the reading stand.*

She wears nothing frivolous. Her shoes are suitable for the garden, which is where she goes now after picking up the theodolite from the table. The room is empty for a few moments.

One of the other doors opens to admit CHLOË *and* BERNARD. *She is the daughter of the house and is dressed casually.* BERNARD, *the visitor, wears a suit and a tie. His tendency is to dress flamboyantly, but he has damped it down for the occasion, slightly. A peacock-coloured display handkerchief boils over in his breast pocket. He carries a capacious leather bag which serves as a briefcase.*

CHLOË   Oh! Well, she *was* here . . .
BERNARD   Ah . . . the french window . . .
CHLOË   Yes. Hang on.
    [CHLOË *steps out through the garden door and disappears from view.* BERNARD *hangs on. The second door opens and* VALENTINE *looks in.*]
VALENTINE   Sod.[7]
    [VALENTINE *goes out again, closing the door.* CHLOË *returns, carrying a pair of rubber boots. She comes in and sits down and starts exchanging her shoes for the boots, while she talks.*]
CHLOË   The best thing is, you wait here, save you tramping around. She spends a good deal of time in the garden, as you may imagine.
BERNARD   Yes. Why?
CHLOË   Well, she's writing a history of the garden, didn't you know?
BERNARD   No, I knew she was working on the Croom papers but . . .
CHLOË   Well, it's not exactly a history of the garden either. I'll let Hannah explain it. The trench you nearly drove into is all to do with it. I was going to say make yourself comfortable but that's hardly possible, everything's been cleared out, it's en route[8] to the nearest lavatory.
BERNARD   Everything is?
CHLOË   No, this room is. They drew the line at chemical 'Ladies' '.[9]
BERNARD   Yes, I see. Did you say Hannah?
CHLOË   Hannah, yes. Will you be all right?
    [*She stands up wearing the boots.*]
    I won't be . . . [*But she has lost him.*] Mr Nightingale?
BERNARD   [*Waking up.*]   Yes. Thank you. Miss Jarvis is Hannah Jarvis the author?
CHLOË   Yes. Have you read her book?
BERNARD   Oh, yes. Yes.
CHLOË   I bet she's in the hermitage, can't see from here with the marquee . . .[1]
BERNARD   Are you having a garden party?
CHLOË   A dance for the district, our annual dressing up and general drunkenness. The wrinklies won't have it in the house, there was a teapot we once had to bag back from Christie's[2] in the nick of time, so anything that can be destroyed, stolen or vomited on has been tactfully removed; tactlessly, I should say—

---

7. Angry expletive.
8. On the way to.
9. They would not allow portable toilets for women in the garden.

1. Large tent.
2. Rescue from Christie's, famous London firm of auctioneers.

[*She is about to leave.*]

BERNARD   Um—look—would you tell her—would you mind not mentioning my name just yet?

CHLOË   Oh. All right.

BERNARD [*Smiling.*]   More fun to surprise her. Would you mind?

CHLOË   No. But she's bound to ask . . . Should I give you another name, just for the moment?

BERNARD   Yes, why not?

CHLOË   Perhaps another bird, you're not really a Nightingale.

[*She leaves again.* BERNARD *glances over the books on the table. He puts his briefcase down. There is the distant pop-pop of a shotgun. It takes* BERNARD *vaguely to the window. He looks out. The door he entered by now opens and* GUS *looks into the room.* BERNARD *turns and sees him.*]

BERNARD   Hello.

[GUS *doesn't speak. He never speaks. Perhaps he cannot speak. He has no composure, and faced with a stranger, he caves in and leaves again. A moment later the other door opens again and* VALENTINE *crosses the room, not exactly ignoring* BERNARD *and yet ignoring him.*]

VALENTINE   Sod, sod, sod, sod, sod, sod . . . [*As many times as it takes him to leave by the opposite door, which he closes behind him. Beyond it, he can be heard shouting.* Chlo! Chlo! BERNARD's *discomfort increases. The same door opens and* VALENTINE *returns. He looks at* BERNARD.]

BERNARD   She's in the garden looking for Miss Jarvis.

VALENTINE   Where is everything?

BERNARD   It's been removed for the, er . . .

VALENTINE   The dance is all in the tent, isn't it?

BERNARD   Yes, but this is the way to the nearest toilet.

VALENTINE   I need the commode.[3]

BERNARD   Oh. Can't you use the toilet?

VALENTINE   It's got all the game books in it.

BERNARD   Ah. The toilet has or the commode has?

VALENTINE   Is anyone looking after you?

BERNARD   Yes. Thank you. I'm Bernard Nigh—I've come to see Miss Jarvis. I wrote to Lord Croom but unfortunately I never received a reply, so I—

VALENTINE   Did you type it?

BERNARD   Type it?

VALENTINE   Was your letter typewritten?

BERNARD   Yes.

VALENTINE   My father never replies to typewritten letters.

[*He spots a tortoise which has been half-hidden on the table.*]

Oh! Where have you been hiding, Lightning? [*He picks up the tortoise.*]

BERNARD   So I telephoned yesterday and I think I spoke to you—

VALENTINE   To me? Ah! Yes! Sorry! You're doing a talk about—someone—and you wanted to ask Hannah—something—

BERNARD   Yes. As it turns out. I'm hoping Miss Jarvis will look kindly on me.

VALENTINE   I doubt it.

BERNARD   Ah, you know about research?

VALENTINE   I know Hannah.

BERNARD   Has she been here long?

---

3. Lavatory bowl enclosed in a chair or box with a cover.

VALENTINE Well in possession,[4] I'm afraid. My mother had read her book, you see. Have you?

BERNARD No. Yes. Her book. Indeed.

VALENTINE She's terrifically pleased with herself.

BERNARD Well, I dare say if I wrote a bestseller—

VALENTINE No, for reading it. My mother basically reads gardening books.

BERNARD She must be delighted to have Hannah Jarvis writing a book about her garden.

VALENTINE Actually it's about hermits.

[GUS *returns through the same door, and turns to leave again.*]

It's all right, Gus—what do you want?—

[*But* GUS *has gone again.*]

Well . . . I'll take Lightning for his run.

BERNARD Actually, we've met before. At Sussex,[5] a couple of years ago, a seminar . . .

VALENTINE Oh. Was I there?

BERNARD Yes. One of my colleagues believed he had found an unattributed short story by D. H. Lawrence,[6] and he analysed it on his home computer, most interesting, perhaps you remember the paper?

VALENTINE Not really. But I often sit with my eyes closed and it doesn't necessarily mean I'm awake.

BERNARD Well, by comparing sentence structures and so forth, this chap showed that there was a ninety per cent chance that the story had indeed been written by the same person as *Women in Love.* To my inexpressible joy, one of your maths mob was able to show that on the same statistical basis there was a ninety per cent chance that Lawrence also wrote the *Just William* books and much of the previous day's *Brighton and Hove Argus.*[7]

VALENTINE [*Pause.*] Oh, Brighton. Yes. I was there. [*And looking out.*] Oh— here she comes, I'll leave you to talk. By the way, is yours the red Mazda?

BERNARD Yes.

VALENTINE If you want a tip I'd put it out of sight through the stable arch before my father comes in. He won't have anyone in the house with a Japanese car. Are you queer?

BERNARD No, actually.

VALENTINE Well, even so.

[VALENTINE *leaves, closing the door.* BERNARD *keeps staring at the closed door. Behind him,* HANNAH *comes to the garden door.*]

HANNAH Mr Peacock?

[BERNARD *looks round vaguely then checks over his shoulder for the missing Peacock, then recovers himself and turns on the Nightingale bonhomie.*]

BERNARD Oh . . . hello! Hello. Miss Jarvis, of course. Such a pleasure. I was thrown for a moment—the photograph doesn't do you justice.

HANNAH Photograph?

[*Her shoes have got muddy and she is taking them off.*]

BERNARD On the book. I'm sorry to have brought you indoors, but Lady Chloë kindly insisted she—

---

4. In a position of power.
5. Sussex University at Brighton.
6. English novelist and short-story writer (1885–1930), author of *Women in Love* (1920).

7. A local newspaper. "*Just William* books": series of "schoolboy" novels by the best-selling children's author Richmal Crompton (1890–1969).

HANNAH   No matter—you would have muddied your shoes.
BERNARD   How thoughtful. And how kind of you to spare me a little of your time.
    [*He is overdoing it. She shoots him a glance.*]
HANNAH   Are you a journalist?
BERNARD   [*Shocked.*]   No!
HANNAH   [*Resuming.*]   I've been in the ha-ha,[8] very squelchy.
BERNARD   [*Unexpectedly.*]   Ha-*hah!*
HANNAH   What?
BERNARD   A theory of mine. Ha-hah, not ha-ha. If you were strolling down the garden and all of a sudden the ground gave way at your feet, you're not going to go 'ha-ha', you're going to jump back and go 'ha-hah!', or more probably, 'Bloody 'ell!' . . . though personally I think old Murray was up the pole[9] on that one—in France, you know, 'ha-ha' is used to denote a strikingly ugly woman, a much more likely bet for something that keeps the cows off the lawn.
    [*This is not going well for* BERNARD *but he seems blithely unaware.*
    HANNAH *stares at him for a moment.*]
HANNAH   Mr Peacock, what can I do for you?
BERNARD   Well, to begin with, you can call me Bernard, which is my name.
HANNAH   Thank you.
    [*She goes to the garden door to bang her shoes together and scrape off the worst of the mud.*]
BERNARD   The book!—the book is a revelation! To see Caroline Lamb[1] through your eyes is really like seeing her for the first time. I'm ashamed to say I never read her fiction, and how right you are, it's extraordinary stuff— Early Nineteenth is my period as much as anything is.
HANNAH   You teach?
BERNARD   Yes. And write, like you, like we all, though I've never done anything which has sold like *Caro.*[2]
HANNAH   I don't teach.
BERNARD   No. All the more credit to you. To rehabilitate a forgotten writer, I suppose you could say that's the main reason for an English don.[3]
HANNAH   Not to teach?
BERNARD   Good God, no, let the brats sort it out for themselves. Anyway, many congratulations. I expect someone will be bringing out Caroline Lamb's oeuvre[4] now?
HANNAH   Yes, I expect so.
BERNARD   How wonderful! Bravo! Simply as a document shedding reflected light on the character of Lord Byron, it's bound to be—
HANNAH   Bernard. You did say Bernard, didn't you?
BERNARD   I did.
HANNAH   I'm putting my shoes on again.
BERNARD   Oh. You're not going to go out?
HANNAH   No, I'm going to kick you in the balls.

---

8. Ditch with a wall on its inner side below ground level, forming a boundary to a lawn without interrupting the view from the house.
9. James Murray (1837–1915), editor of the original *Oxford English Dictionary*. Bernard thinks him misguided—"up the [greasy] pole" (slang)—in the pronunciation of "ha-ha" recommended in his

OED.
1. Novelist (1785–1828), best-known as the mistress of Lord Byron (1788–1824).
2. Title of Hannah's biography. Cf. p. 2754, n. 2.
3. See p. 2753, n. 3.
4. A writer's body of work.

2846 / TOM STOPPARD

Right. Point taken. Ezra Chater.

BERNARD   Right. Point taken. Ezra Chater.
HANNAH   Ezra Chater.
BERNARD   Born Twickenham, Middlesex, 1778, author of two verse narra-
tives, 'The Maid of Turkey', 1808, and 'The Couch of Eros', 1809. Nothing
known after 1809, disappears from view.
HANNAH   I see. And?
BERNARD   [Reaching for his bag.]   There is a Sidley Park connection.
    [He produces 'The Couch of Eros' from the bag. He reads the inscrip-
    tion.]
    'To my friend Septimus Hodge, who stood up and gave his best on behalf
    of the Author—Ezra Chater, at Sidley Park, Derbyshire, April 10th 1809.'
    [He gives her the book.]
    I am in your hands.
HANNAH   'The Couch of Eros'. Is it any good?
BERNARD   Quite surprising.
HANNAH   You think there's a book in him?
BERNARD   No, no—a monograph perhaps for the Journal of English Studies.
    There's almost nothing on Chater, not a word in the DNB,[5] of course—by
    that time he'd been completely forgotten.
HANNAH   Family?
BERNARD   Zilch. There's only one other Chater in the British Library
    database.
HANNAH   Same period?
BERNARD   Yes, but he wasn't poet like our Ezra, he was a botanist who
    described a dwarf dahlia in Martinique[6] and died there after being bitten
    by a monkey.
HANNAH   And Ezra Chater?
BERNARD   He gets two references in the periodical index, one for each book,
    in both cases a substantial review in the Piccadilly Recreation, a thrice
    weekly folio sheet, but giving no personal details.
HANNAH   And where was this [the book]?
BERNARD   Private collection. I've got a talk to give next week, in London, and
    I think Chater is interesting, so anything on him, or this Septimus Hodge,
    Sidley Park, any leads at all . . . I'd be most grateful.
    [Pause.]
HANNAH   Well! This is a new experience for me. A grovelling academic.
BERNARD   Oh, I say.
HANNAH   Oh, but it is. All the academics who reviewed my book patronized
    it.
BERNARD   Surely not.
HANNAH   Surely yes. The Byron gang unzipped their flies and patronized all
    over it. Where is it you don't bother to teach, by the way?
BERNARD   Oh, well, Sussex, actually.
HANNAH   Sussex. [She thinks a moment.] Nightingale. Yes; a thousand words
    in the Observer[7] to see me off the premises with a pat on the bottom. You
    must know him.
BERNARD   As I say, I'm in your hands.
HANNAH   Quite. Say please, then.

5. British Dictionary of National Biography.   7. British Sunday newspaper.
6. One of the Windward Islands of the Caribbean.

BERNARD Please.

HANNAH Sit down, do.

BERNARD Thank you.

[*He takes a chair. She remains standing. Possibly she smokes; if so, perhaps now. A short cigarette-holder sounds right, too. Or brown-paper cigarillos.*]

HANNAH How did you know I was here?

BERNARD Oh, I didn't. I spoke to the son on the phone but he didn't mention you by name . . . and then he forgot to mention me.

HANNAH Valentine. He's at Oxford,[8] technically.

BERNARD Yes, I met him. Brideshead Regurgitated.[9]

HANNAH My fiancé.

[*She holds his look.*]

BERNARD [*Pause.*] I'll take a chance. You're lying.

HANNAH [*Pause*] Well done, Bernard.

BERNARD Christ.

HANNAH He calls me his fiancée.

BERNARD Why?

HANNAH It's a joke.

BERNARD You turned him down?

HANNAH Don't be silly, do I look like the next Countess of—

BERNARD No, no—a freebie. The joke that consoles. My tortoise Lightning, my fiancée Hannah.

HANNAH Oh. Yes. You have a way with you, Bernard. I'm not sure I like it.

BERNARD What's he doing, Valentine?

HANNAH He's a postgrad. Biology.

BERNARD No, he's a mathematician.

HANNAH Well, he's doing grouse.[1]

BERNARD Grouse?

HANNAH Not actual grouse. Computer grouse.

BERNARD Who's the one who doesn't speak?

HANNAH Gus.

BERNARD What's the matter with him?

HANNAH I didn't ask.

BERNARD And the father sounds like a lot of fun.

HANNAH Ah yes.

BERNARD And the mother is the gardener. What's going on here?

HANNAH What do you mean?

BERNARD I nearly took her head off—she was standing in a trench at the time.

HANNAH Archaeology. The house had a formal Italian garden until about 1740. Lady Croom is interested in garden history. I sent her my book—it contains, as you know if you've read it—which I'm not assuming, by the way—a rather good description of Caroline's garden at Brocket Hall. I'm here now helping Hermione.

BERNARD [*Impressed*] Hermione.

HANNAH The records are unusually complete and they have never been worked on.

---

8. University, attended by Sebastian Flyte, anti-hero of Evelyn Waugh's satirical novel of British upper-class life, *Brideshead Revisited* (1945).

9. Vomited up.
1. Valentine is researching into changes in the Sidley Park population of the grouse, a game bird.

BERNARD   I'm beginning to admire you.

HANNAH   Before was bullshit?

BERNARD   Completely. Your photograph does you justice, I'm not sure the book does.

[*She considers him. He waits, confident.*]

HANNAH   Septimus Hodge was the tutor.

BERNARD [*Quietly.*]   Attagirl.

HANNAH   His pupil was the Croom daughter. There was a son at Eton. Septimus lived in the house: the pay book specifies allowances for wine and candles. So, not quite a guest but rather more than a steward.[2] His letter of self-recommendation is preserved among the papers. I'll dig it out for you. As far as I remember he studied mathematics and natural philosophy at Cambridge. A scientist, therefore, as much as anything.

BERNARD   I'm impressed. Thank you. And Chater?

HANNAH   Nothing.

BERNARD   Oh. Nothing at all?

HANNAH   I'm afraid not.

BERNARD   How about the library?

HANNAH   The catalogue was done in the 1880s. I've been through the lot.

BERNARD   Books or catalogue?

HANNAH   Catalogue.

BERNARD   Ah. Pity.

HANNAH   I'm sorry.

BERNARD   What about the letters? No mention?

HANNAH   I'm afraid not. I've been very thorough in your period because, of course, it's my period too.

BERNARD   Is it? Actually, I don't quite know what it is you're . . .

HANNAH   The Sidley hermit.

BERNARD   Ah. Who's he?

HANNAH   He's my peg[3] for the nervous breakdown of the Romantic Imagination. I'm doing landscape and literature 1750 to 1834.

BERNARD   What happened in 1834?

HANNAH   My hermit died.

BERNARD   Of course.

HANNAH   What do you mean, of course?

BERNARD   Nothing.

HANNAH   Yes, you do.

BERNARD   No, no . . . However, Coleridge[4] also died in 1834.

HANNAH   So he did. What a stroke of luck. [*Softening.*] Thank you, Bernard.

[*She goes to the reading stand and opens Noakes's sketch book.*]
Look—there he is.

[BERNARD *goes to look.*]

BERNARD   Mmm.

HANNAH   The only known likeness of the Sidley hermit.

BERNARD   Very biblical.[5]

HANNAH   Drawn in by a later hand, of course. The hermitage didn't yet exist when Noakes did the drawings.

---

2. Chief servant.
3. On which to hang the argument of a book about the Romantic Imagination.

4. Samuel Taylor Coleridge (1722–1834), English Romantic poet.
5. See p. 2763, n. 6.

BERNARD Noakes . . . the painter?

HANNAH Landscape gardener. He'd do these books for his clients, as a sort of prospectus. [*She demonstrates.*] Before and after, you see. This is how it all looked until, say, 1810–smooth, undulating, serpentine—open water, clumps of trees, classical boat-house—

BERNARD Lovely. The real England.

HANNAH You can stop being silly now, Bernard. English landscape was invented by gardeners imitating foreign painters who were evoking classical authors. The whole thing was brought home in the luggage from the grand tour. Here, look—Capability Brown doing Claude, who was doing Virgil.[6] Arcadia! And here, superimposed by Richard Noakes, untamed nature in the style of Salvator Rosa. It's the Gothic novel expressed in landscape. Everything but vampires. There's an account of my hermit in a letter by your illustrious namesake.

BERNARD Florence?[7]

HANNAH What?

BERNARD No. You go on.

HANNAH Thomas Love Peacock.[8]

BERNARD Ah yes.

HANNAH I found it in an essay on hermits and anchorites[9] published in the *Cornhill Magazine* in the 1860s . . . [*She fishes for the magazine itself among the books on the table, and finds it.*] . . . 1862 . . . Peacock calls him [*She quotes from memory.*] 'Not one of your village simpletons to frighten the ladies, but a savant[1] among idiots, a sage of lunacy.'

BERNARD An oxy-moron,[2] so to speak.

HANNAH [*Busy*] Yes. What?

BERNARD Nothing.

HANNAH [*Having found the place.*] Here we are. 'A letter we have seen, written by the author of *Heading Hall* nearly thirty years ago, tells of a visit to the Earl of Croom's estate, Sidley Park—'

BERNARD Was the letter to Thackeray?[3]

HANNAH [*Brought up short.*] I don't know. Does it matter?

BERNARD No. Sorry.

[*But the gaps he leaves for her are false promises—and she is not quick enough. That's how it goes.*]

Only, Thackeray edited the *Cornhill* until '63 when, as you know, he died. His father had been with the East India Company where Peacock, of course, had held the position of Examiner, so it's quite possible that if the essay were by Thackeray, the *letter* . . . Sorry. Go on.

Of course, the East India Library in Blackfriars has most of Peacock's letters, so it would be quite easy to . . . Sorry. Can I look?

[*Silently she hands him the* Cornhill.]

---

6. Hannah sees Lancelot "Capability" Brown (1715–1783), England's most celebrated landscape designer, imitating ("doing") Claude Lorrain (1600–1682), French landscape painter, who was imitating Virgil's *Georgics*, poems celebrating the country/pastoral life of an idealized Arcadia.
7. Florence Nightingale (1820–1910), English nurse considered the founder of modern nursing (Bernard has temporarily forgotten his alias).
8. English novelist and poet (1785–1866), author of *Headlong* [not *Heading*] *Hall* (1816), and one-

time "Examiner" (investigator) with the British East India Company in India.
9. People who have withdrawn from the world, usually for religious reasons.
1. Learned man.
2. Phrase that seems to contradict itself ("sage of lunacy"), here prompting Bernard's pun on "moron" (meaning "idiot").
3. William Makepeace Thackeray (1811–1863), English novelist and poet.

Yes, it's been topped and tailed, of course. It might be worth . . . Go on. I'm listening . . .

[*Leafing through the essay, he suddenly chuckles.*] Oh yes, it's Thackeray all right . . .

[*He slaps the book shut.*] Unbearable . . .

[*He hands it back to her.*] What were you saying?

HANNAH   Are you always like this?

BERNARD   Like what?

HANNAH   The point is, the Crooms, of course, had the hermit under their noses for twenty years so hardly thought him worth remarking. As I'm finding out. The Peacock letter is still the main source, unfortunately. When I read this [*the magazine in her hand*], well, it was one of those moments that tell you what your next book is going to be. The hermit of Sidley Park was my . . .

BERNARD   Peg.

HANNAH   Epiphany.

BERNARD   Epiphany, that's it.

HANNAH   The hermit was *placed* in the landscape exactly as one might place a pottery gnome. And there he lived out his life as a garden ornament.

BERNARD   Did he do anything?

HANNAH   Oh, he was very busy. When he died, the cottage was stacked solid with paper. Hundreds of pages. Thousands. Peacock says he was suspected of genius. It turned out, of course, he was off his head. He'd covered every sheet with cabalistic[4] proofs that the world was coming to an end. It's perfect, isn't it? A perfect symbol, I mean.

BERNARD   Oh, yes. Of what?

HANNAH   The whole Romantic sham, Bernard! It's what happened to the Enlightenment, isn't it? A century of intellectual rigour turned in on itself. A mind in chaos suspected of genius. In a setting of cheap thrills and false emotion. The history of the garden says it all, beautifully. There's an engraving of Sidley Park in 1730 that makes you want to weep. Paradise in the age of reason. By 1760 everything had gone—the topiary, pools and terraces, fountains, an avenue of limes—the whole sublime geometry was ploughed under by Capability Brown. The grass went from the doorstep to the horizon and the best box hedge in Derbyshire was dug up for the ha-ha so that the fools could pretend they were living in God's countryside. And then Richard Noakes came in to bring God up to date. By the time he'd finished it looked like this [*the sketch book*]. The decline from thinking to feeling, you see.

BERNARD   [*A judgement.*]   That's awfully good.

[HANNAH *looks at him in case of irony but he is professional.*]
No, that'll stand up.

HANNAH   Thank you.

BERNARD   Personally I like the ha-ha. Do you like hedges?

HANNAH   I don't like sentimentality.

BERNARD   Yes, I see. Are you sure? You seem quite sentimental over geometry. But the hermit is very very good. The genius[5] of the place.

HANNAH   [*Pleased.*]   That's my title!

BERNARD   Of course.

---

4. Coded.
5. With a pun on the meaning "attendant spirit of a person or a place."

HANNAH [*Less pleased.*] Of course?

BERNARD Of course. Who was he when he wasn't being a symbol?

HANNAH I don't know.

BERNARD Ah.

HANNAH I mean, yet.

BERNARD Absolutely. What did they do with all the paper? Does Peacock say?

HANNAH Made a bonfire.

BERNARD Ah, well.

HANNAH I've still got Lady Croom's garden books to go through.

BERNARD Account books or journals?

HANNAH A bit of both. They're gappy but they span the period.

BERNARD Really? Have you come across Byron at all? As a matter of interest.

HANNAH A first edition of 'Childe Harold' in the library, and *English Bards*, I think.[6]

BERNARD Inscribed?

HANNAH No.

BERNARD And he doesn't pop up in the letters at all?

HANNAH Why should he? The Crooms don't pop up in his.

BERNARD [*Casually.*] That's true, of course. But Newstead[7] isn't so far away. Would you mind terribly if I poked about a bit? Only in the papers you've done with, of course.

[HANNAH twigs[8] *something.*]

HANNAH Are you looking into Byron or Chater?

[CHLOË *enters in stockinged feet through one of the side doors, laden with an armful of generally similar leather-covered ledgers. She detours to collect her shoes.*]

CHLOË Sorry—just cutting through—there's tea in the pantry if you don't mind mugs—

BERNARD How kind.

CHLOË Hannah will show you.

BERNARD Let me help you.

CHLOË No, it's all right—

[BERNARD *opens the opposite door for her.*]

Thank you—I've been saving Val's game books. Thanks.

[BERNARD *closes the door.*]

BERNARD Sweet girl.

HANNAH Mmm.

BERNARD Oh, really?

HANNAH Oh really what?

[CHLOË'*s door opens again and she puts her head round it.*]

CHLOË Meant to say, don't worry if father makes remarks about your car, Mr Nightingale, he's got a thing about—[*and the Nightingale now being out of the bag*] ooh—ah, how was the surprise?—not yet, eh? Oh, well—sorry—tea, anyway—so sorry if I—[*Embarrassed, she leaves again, closing the door. Pause.*]

HANNAH You absolute shit.

[*She heads off to leave.*]

---

6. Two of Byron's long poems: *English Bards and Scotch Reviewers* (1809) and *Childe Harold's Pilgrimage* (1812).

7. Newstead Abbey, Byron's family home.
8. Perceives.

BERNARD   The thing is, there's a Byron connection too.
[HANNAH *stops and faces him.*]
HANNAH   I don't care.
BERNARD   You should. The Byron gang are going to get their dicks caught in their zip.
HANNAH [*Pause.*]   Oh really?
BERNARD   If we collaborate.
HANNAH   On what?
BERNARD   Sit down, I'll tell you.
HANNAH   I'll stand for the moment.
BERNARD   This copy of 'The Couch of Eros' belonged to Lord Byron.
HANNAH   It belonged to Septimus Hodge.
BERNARD   Originally, yes. But it was in Byron's library which was sold to pay his debts when he left England for good in 1816. The sales catalogue is in the British Library. 'Eros' was lot 74A and was bought by the bookseller and publisher John Nightingale of Opera Court, Pall Mall . . . whose name survives in the firm of Nightingale and Matlock, the present Nightingale being my cousin.
[*He pauses.* HANNAH *hesitates and then sits down at the table.*]
I'll just give you the headlines. 1939, stock removed to Nightingale country house in Kent. 1945, stock returned to bookshop. Meanwhile, overlooked box of early nineteenth-century books languish in country house cellar until house sold to make way for the Channel Tunnel rail-link.[9] 'Eros' discovered with sales slip from 1816 attached—photocopy available for inspection.
[*He brings this from his bag and gives it to* HANNAH *who inspects it.*]
HANNAH   All right. It was in Byron's library.
BERNARD   A number of passages have been underlined.
[HANNAH *picks up the book and leafs through it.*]
All of them, and only them—no, no, look at me, not at the book—all the underlined passages, word for word, were used as quotations in the review of 'The Couch of Eros' in the *Piccadilly Recreation* of April 30th 1809. The reviewer begins by drawing attention to his previous notice in the same periodical of 'The Maid of Turkey'.
HANNAH   The reviewer is obviously Hodge. 'My friend Septimus Hodge who stood up and gave his best on behalf of the Author.'
BERNARD   That's the point. The *Piccadilly* ridiculed both books.
HANNAH [*Pause.*]   Do the reviews read like Byron?
BERNARD [*Producing two photocopies from his case.*]   They read a damn sight more like Byron than Byron's review of Wordsworth the previous year.
[HANNAH *glances over the photocopies.*]
HANNAH   I see. Well, congratulations. Possibly. Two previously unknown book reviews by the young Byron. Is that it?
BERNARD   No. Because of the tapes, three documents survived undisturbed in the book.
[*He has been carefully opening a package produced from his bag. He has the originals. He holds them carefully one by one.*]
'Sir—we have a matter to settle. I wait on you in the gun room. E. Chater, Esq.'

---

9. High-speed railway line linking London with the tunnel that crosses the English Channel.

'My husband has sent to town for pistols. Deny what cannot be proven—
for Charity's sake—I keep my room this day.' Unsigned.

'Sidley Park, April 11th 1809. Sir—I call you a liar, a lecher, a slanderer in
the press and a thief of my honour. I wait upon your arrangements for giving
me satisfaction as a man and a poet. E. Chater, Esq.'

[*Pause.*]

HANNAH   Superb. But inconclusive. The book had seven years to find its way
into Byron's possession. It doesn't connect Byron with Chater, or with Sidley
Park. Or with Hodge for that matter. Furthermore, there isn't a hint in
Byron's letters and this kind of scrape is the last thing he would have kept
quiet about.

BERNARD   *Scrape?*

HANNAH   He would have made a comic turn out of it.

BERNARD   Comic turn, fiddlesticks! [*He pauses for effect.*] He killed Chater!

HANNAH   [*A raspberry.*]   Oh, really!

BERNARD   Chater was thirty-one years old. The author of two books. Nothing
more is heard from him after 'Eros'. He disappears completely after April
1809. And Byron—Byron had just published his satire, *English Bards
and Scotch Reviewers*, in March. He was just getting a name. Yet he sailed
for Lisbon[1] as soon as he could find a ship, and stayed abroad for two
years. Hannah, *this is fame*. Somewhere in the Croom papers there will be
something—

HANNAH   There isn't, I've looked.

BERNARD   But you were looking for something else! It's not going to jump out
at you like 'Lord Byron remarked wittily at breakfast!'

HANNAH   Nevertheless his presence would be unlikely to have gone unremarked. But there is nothing to suggest that Byron was here, and I don't
believe he ever was.

BERNARD   All right, but let me have a look.

HANNAH   You'll queer my pitch.[2]

BERNARD   Dear girl, I know how to handle myself—

HANNAH   And don't call me dear girl. If I find anything on Byron, or Chater,
or Hodge, I'll pass it on. Nightingale, Sussex.

[*Pause. She stands up.*]

BERNARD   Thank you. I'm sorry about that business with my name.

HANNAH   Don't mention it . . .

BERNARD   What was Hodge's college,[3] by the way?

HANNAH   Trinity.

BERNARD   Trinity?

HANNAH   Yes. [*She hesitates.*] Yes. Byron's old college.

BERNARD   How old was Hodge?

HANNAH   I'd have to look it up but a year or two older than Byron. Twenty-
two . . .

BERNARD   Contemporaries at Trinity?

HANNAH   [*Wearily.*]   Yes, Bernard, and no doubt they were both in the cricket
eleven when Harrow played Eton at Lords!⁴

1. Capital of Portugal.
2. Spoil my chances.
3. At Cambridge University.
4. Contemporaries also at Harrow School, Byron

and Hodge could have been in the same team (of
eleven players) that played against Eton at Lords
cricket ground in London.

[BERNARD *approaches her and stands close to her.*]

BERNARD [*Evenly.*] Do you mean that Septimus Hodge was at school with Byron?

HANNAH [*Falters slightly.*] Yes . . . he must have been . . . as a matter of fact.

BERNARD Well, you silly cow.

[*With a large gesture of pure happiness,* BERNARD *throws his arms around* HANNAH *and gives her a great smacking kiss on the cheek.* CHLOË *enters to witness the end of this.*]

CHLOË Oh—erm . . . I thought I'd bring it to you.

[*She is carrying a small tray with two mugs on it.*]

BERNARD I have to go and see about my car.

HANNAH Going to hide it?

BERNARD Hide it? I'm going to sell it! Is there a pub I can put up at in the village?

[*He turns back to them as he is about to leave through the garden.*] Aren't you glad I'm here?

[*He leaves.*]

CHLOË He said he knew you.

HANNAH He couldn't have.

CHLOË No, perhaps not. He said he wanted to be a surprise, but I suppose that's different. I thought there was a lot of sexual energy there, didn't you?

HANNAH What?

CHLOË Bouncy on his feet, you see, a sure sign. Should I invite him for you?

HANNAH To what? No.

CHLOË You can invite him—that's better. He can come as your partner.

HANNAH Stop it. Thank you for the tea.

CHLOË If you don't want him, I'll have him. Is he married?

HANNAH I haven't the slightest idea. Aren't you supposed to have a pony?

CHLOË I'm just trying to fix you up, Hannah.

HANNAH Believe me, it gets less important.

CHLOË I mean for the dancing. He can come as Beau Brummel[5]

HANNAH I don't want to dress up and I don't want a dancing partner, least of all Mr Nightingale. I don't dance.

CHLOË Don't be such a prune. You were kissing him, anyway.

HANNAH He was kissing me, and only out of general enthusiasm.

CHLOË Well, don't say I didn't give you first chance. My genius brother will be much relieved. He's in love with you, I suppose you know.

HANNAH [*Angry.*] That's a joke!

CHLOË It's not a joke to him.

HANNAH Of course it is—not even a joke—how can you be so ridiculous?

[GUS *enters from the garden, in his customary silent awkwardness.*]

CHLOË Hello, Gus, what have you got?

[GUS *has an apple, just picked, with a leaf or two still attached. He offers the apple to* HANNAH.][6]

HANNAH [*Surprised.*] Oh! . . . Thank you!

CHLOË [*Leaving.*] Told you.

---

5. George Bryan Brummel (1778–1840), known as "Beau" because of his elegant clothes.
6. Cf. Genesis 3.1–6, specifically Eve's gift of an apple to Adam in the Garden of Eden; cf. also the golden apple of discord given by Paris to the goddess Aphrodite in Greek legend.

[CHLOË *close the door on herself.*]
HANNAH   Thank you. Oh dear.

SCENE THREE

The schoolroom. The next morning. Present are: THOMASINA, SEPTIMUS, JEL-
LABY. *We have seen this composition before:* THOMASINA *at her place at the table;*
SEPTIMUS *reading a letter which has just arrived;* JELLABY *waiting, having just
delivered the letter.*
'*The Couch of Eros' is in front of* SEPTIMUS, *open, together with sheets of paper
on which he has been writing. His portfolio is on the table. Plautus (the tortoise)
is the paperweight. There is also an apple on the table now, the same apple from
all appearances.*

SEPTIMUS [*With his eyes on the letter.*]   Why have you stopped?
   [THOMASINA *is studying a sheet of paper, a 'Latin unseen' lesson.*⁷ *She is
   having some difficulty.*]
THOMASINA   Solio insessa . . . *in igne* . . . seated on a throne . . . in the fire . . .
   and also on a ship . . . *sedebat regina* . . . sat the queen . . .
SEPTIMUS   There is no reply, Jellaby. Thank you.
   [*He folds the letter up and places it between the leaves of 'The Couch
   of Eros'.*]
JELLABY   I will say so, sir.
THOMASINA   . . . the wind smelling sweetly . . . *purpureis velis* . . . by, with or
   from purple sails—
SEPTIMUS [*To* JELLABY]   I will have something for the post, if you would be so
   kind.
JELLABY [*Leaving.*]   Yes sir.
THOMASINA   . . . was like as to—something—by, with or from lovers—oh,
   Septimus!—*musica tibiarum imperabat* . . . music of pipes commanded . . .
SEPTIMUS   'Ruled' is better.
THOMASINA   . . . the silver oars—exciting the ocean—as if—as if—amorous—
SEPTIMUS   That is very good.
   [*He picks up the apple. He picks off the twig and leaves, placing these
   on the table. With a pocket knife he cuts a slice of apple, and while he
   eats it, cuts another slice which he offers to Plautus.*]
THOMASINA   Regina reclinabat . . . the queen—was reclining—*praeter des-
   criptionem*—indescribably—in a golden tent . . . like Venus and yet more—
SEPTIMUS   Try to put some poetry into it.
THOMASINA   How can I if there is none in the Latin?
SEPTIMUS   Oh, a critic!
THOMASINA   Is it Queen Dido?⁸
SEPTIMUS   No.
THOMASINA   Who is the poet?
SEPTIMUS   Known to you.
THOMASINA   Known to me?
SEPTIMUS   Not a Roman.

7. Latin passage that a student is required to
translate: here the Roman historian Plutarch's
description of Cleopatra in her barge, on which
Shakespeare based a famous speech by Enobarbus
(*Antony and Cleopatra* 2.2.196ff.) Below Septimus
pretends Shakespeare's lines are his own translation.
8. Legendary queen of Carthage who, abandoned
by her lover Aeneas, in Virgil's *Aeneid*, commits
suicide.

THOMASINA   Mr Chater?
SEPTIMUS   Your translation is quite like Chater.
    [SEPTIMUS *picks up his pen and continues with his own writing.*]
THOMASINA   I know who it is, it is your friend Byron.
SEPTIMUS   Lord Byron, if you please.
THOMASINA   Mama is in love with Lord Byron.
SEPTIMUS [*Absorbed.*]   Yes. Nonsense.
THOMASINA   It is not nonsense. I saw them together in the gazebo.
    [SEPTIMUS'*s pen stops moving, he raises his eyes to her at last.*]
    Lord Byron was reading to her from his satire, and mama was laughing, with
    her head in her best position.
SEPTIMUS   She did not understand the satire, and was showing politeness to
    a guest.
THOMASINA   She is vexed with papa for his determination to alter the park,
    but that alone cannot account for her politeness to a guest. She came down-
    stairs hours before her custom. Lord Byron was amusing at breakfast. He
    paid you a tribute, Septimus.
SEPTIMUS   Did he?
THOMASINA   He said you were a witty fellow, and he had almost by heart an
    article you wrote about—well, I forget what, but it concerned a book called
    'The Maid of Turkey' and how you would not give it to your dog for dinner.
SEPTIMUS   Ah. Mr Chater was at breakfast, of course.
THOMASINA   He was, not like certain lazybones.
SEPTIMUS   He does not have Latin to set and mathematics to correct.
    [*He takes Thomasina's lesson book from underneath Plautus and tosses
    it down the table to her.*]
THOMASINA   Correct? What was incorrect in it? [*She looks into the book.*]
    Alpha minus?[9] Pooh! What is the minus for?
SEPTIMUS   For doing more than was asked.
THOMASINA   You did not like my discovery?
SEPTIMUS   A fancy is not a discovery.
THOMASINA   A gibe is not a rebuttal.
    [SEPTIMUS *finishes what he is writing. He folds the pages into a letter.
    He has sealing wax and the means to melt it. He seals the letter and
    writes on the cover. Meanwhile—*]
    You are churlish with me because mama is paying attention to your friend.
    Well, let them elope, they cannot turn back the advancement of knowledge.
    I think it is an excellent discovery. Each week I plot your equations dot
    for dot, *x*s against *y*s in all manner of algebraical relation, and every week
    they draw themselves as commonplace geometry, as if the world of forms
    were nothing but arcs and angles. God's truth, Septimus, if there is an
    equation for a curve like a bell, there must be an equation for one like a
    bluebell, and if a bluebell, why not a rose? Do we believe nature is written
    in numbers?
SEPTIMUS   We do.
THOMASINA   Then why do your equations only describe the shapes of manu-
    facture?
SEPTIMUS   I do not know.
THOMASINA   Armed thus, God could only make a cabinet.

9. A grade of A minus.

SEPTIMUS   He has mastery of equations which lead into infinities where we cannot follow.

THOMASINA   What a faint-heart! We must work outward from the middle of the maze. We will start with something simple. [*She picks up the apple leaf.*] I will plot this leaf and deduce its equation. You will be famous for being my tutor when Lord Byron is dead and forgotten.

[SEPTIMUS *completes the business with his letter. He puts the letter in his pocket.*]

SEPTIMUS [*Firmly.*]   Back to Cleopatra.[1]

THOMASINA   Is it Cleopatra?—I hate Cleopatra!

SEPTIMUS   You hate her? Why?

THOMASINA   Everything is turned to love with her. New love, absent love, lost love—I never knew a heroine that makes such noodles of our sex. It only needs a Roman general to drop anchor outside the window and away goes the empire like a christening mug into a pawn shop. If Queen Elizabeth had been a Ptolemy history would have been quite different—we would be admiring the pyramids of Rome and the great Sphinx of Verona.[2]

SEPTIMUS   God save us.

THOMASINA   But instead, the Egyptian noodle made carnal embrace with the enemy who burned the great library of Alexandria without so much as a fine for all that is overdue. Oh, Septimus!—can you bear it? All the lost plays of the Athenians! Two hundred at least by Aeschylus, Sophocles, Euripides— thousands of poems—Aristotle's own library brought to Egypt by the noodle's ancestors![3] How can we sleep for grief?

SEPTIMUS   By counting our stock. Seven plays from Aeschylus, seven from Sophocles, *nineteen* from Euripides, my lady! You should no more grieve for the rest than for a buckle lost from your first shoe, or for your lesson book which will be lost when you are old. We shed as we pick up, like travellers who must carry everything in their arms, and what we let fall will be picked up by those behind. The procession is very long and life is very short. We die on the march. But there is nothing outside the march so nothing can be lost to it. The missing plays of Sophocles will turn up piece by piece, or be written again in another language. Ancient cures for diseases will reveal themselves once more. Mathematical discoveries glimpsed and lost to view will have their time again. You do not suppose, my lady, that if all of Archimedes[4] had been hiding in the great library of Alexandria, we would be at a loss for a corkscrew? I have no doubt that the improved steam-driven heat-engine which puts Mr Noakes into an ecstasy that he and it and the modern age should all coincide, was described on papyrus. Steam and brass were not invented in Glasgow. Now, where are we? Let me see if I can attempt a free translation for you. At Harrow I was better at this than Lord Byron.

[*He takes the piece of paper from her and scrutinizes it, testing one or two Latin phrases speculatively before committing himself.*]

Yes—'The barge she sat in, like a burnished throne . . . burned on the water

1. Queen of Egypt (69–30 B.C.E.), mistress of the Roman Marc Antony.
2. In Italy. I.e., if Queen Elizabeth I of England (1533–1603) had been Cleopatra (a member of the Ptolemy family), says Thomasina, Egypt would have overthrown the Roman Empire.
3. The plays of Aeschylus (525–456 B.C.E.), Soph-ocles (ca. 496–406 B.C.E.), and Euripides (ca. 484–406 B.C.E.) and the library of the philosopher Aristotle (384–322 B.C.E.) had been brought to Egypt from Greece by Cleopatra's forebears.
4. All the writings of the Greek scientist Archi-medes (ca. 287–212 B.C.E.), who invented the Archimedean screw to raise water.

...the—something—the poop was beaten gold, purple the sails, and—what's this?—oh yes,—so perfumed that—

THOMASINA [*Catching on and furious.*] Cheat!

SEPTIMUS [*Imperturbably.*] '—the winds were lovesick with them . . .'

THOMASINA Cheat!

SEPTIMUS '. . . the oars were silver which to the tune of flutes kept stroke . . .'

THOMASINA [*Jumping to her feet.*] Cheat! Cheat! Cheat!

SEPTIMUS [*As though it were too easy to make the effort worthwhile.*] '. . . and made the water which they beat to follow faster, as *amorous* of their strokes. For her own person, it beggared all description—she did lie in her pavilion—'

[THOMASINA, *in tears of rage, is hurrying out through the garden.*]

THOMASINA I hope you die!

[*She nearly bumps into* BRICE *who is entering. She runs out of sight.* BRICE *enters.*]

BRICE Good God, man, what have you told her?

SEPTIMUS Told her? Told her what?

BRICE Hodge!

[SEPTIMUS *looks outside the door, slightly contrite about* THOMASINA, *and sees that* CHATER *is skulking out of view.*]

SEPTIMUS Chater! My dear fellow! Don't hang back—come in, sir!

[CHATER *allows himself to be drawn sheepishly into the room, where* BRICE *stands on his dignity.*]

CHATER Captain Brice does me the honour—I mean to say, sir, whatever you have to say to me, sir, address yourself to Captain Brice.[5]

SEPTIMUS How unusual. [*To* BRICE.] Your wife did not appear yesterday, sir. I trust she is not sick?

BRICE My wife? I have no wife. What the devil do you mean, sir?

[SEPTIMUS *makes to reply, but hesitates, puzzled. He turns back to* CHATER.]

SEPTIMUS I do not understand the scheme, Chater. Whom do I address when I want to speak to Captain Brice?

BRICE Oh, slippery, Hodge—slippery!

SEPTIMUS [*To* CHATER] By the way, Chater—[*He interrupts himself and turns back to* BRICE, *and continues as before.*] by the way, Chater, I have amazing news to tell you. Someone has taken to writing wild and whirling letters in your name. I received one not half an hour ago.

BRICE [*Angrily.*] Mr Hodge! Look to your honour, sir! If you cannot attend to me without this foolery, nominate your second who might settle the business as between gentlemen. No doubt your friend Byron would do you the service.

[SEPTIMUS *gives up the game.*]

SEPTIMUS Oh yes, he would do me the service. [*His mood changes, he turns to* CHATER.] Sir—I repent your injury. You are an honest fellow with no more malice in you than poetry.

CHATER [*Happily.*] Ah well!—that is more like the thing! [*Overtaken by doubt.*] Is he apologizing?

BRICE There is still the injury to his conjugal[6] property, Mrs Chater's—

CHATER Tush,[7] sir!

---

5. Brice has done Chater "the honour" of agreeing to act as his "second" (supporter) in the duel to which Chater has challenged Septimus. Dueling etiquette required the two seconds to arrange the time, place, and choice of weapons.
6. Marital.
7. Expression of mild irritation, which Brice turns into a vulgar joke.

BRICE   As you will—her tush. Nevertheless—
         [*But they are interrupted by* LADY CROOM, *also entering from the garden.*]
LADY CROOM   Oh—excellently found! Mr Chater, this will please you very much. Lord Byron begs a copy of your new book. He dies to read it and intends to include your name in the second edition of his *English Bards and Scotch Reviewers.*
CHATER   *English Bards and Scotch Reviewers,* your ladyship, is a doggerel aimed at Lord Byron's seniors and betters. If he intends to include me, he intends to insult me.
LADY CROOM   Well, of course he does, Mr Chater. Would you rather be thought not worth insulting? You should be proud to be in the company of Rogers and Moore and Wordsworth—[8] ah! 'The Couch of Eros.' [*For she has spotted Septimus's copy of the book on the table.*]
SEPTIMUS   That is my copy, madam.
LADY CROOM   So much the better—what are a friend's books for if not to be borrowed?
         [*Note: 'The Couch of Eros' now contains the three letters, and it must do so without advertising the fact. This is why the volume has been described as a substantial quarto.*]
         Mr Hodge, you must speak to your friend[9] and put him out of his affectation of pretending to quit us. I will not have it. He says he is determined on the Malta packet sailing out of Falmouth! His head is full of Lisbon and Lesbos, and his portmanteau[1] of pistols, and I have told him it is not to be thought of. The whole of Europe is in a Napoleonic fit,[2] all the best ruins will be closed, the roads entirely occupied with the movement of armies, the lodgings turned to billets[3] and the fashion for godless republicanism not yet arrived at its natural reversion. He says his aim is poetry. One does not aim at poetry with pistols. At poets, perhaps. I charge you to take command of his pistols, Mr Hodge! He is not safe with them. His lameness, he confessed to me, is entirely the result of his habit from boyhood of shooting himself in the foot.[4] What is that *noise?*
         [*The noise is a badly played piano in the next room. It has been going on for some time since* THOMASINA *left.*]
SEPTIMUS   The new Broadwood pianoforte,[5] madam. Our music lessons are at an early stage.
LADY CROOM   Well, restrict your lessons to the *piano* side of the instrument and let her loose on the *forte* when she has learned something.
         [LADY CROOM, *holding the book, sails out back into the garden.*]
BRICE   Now! If that was not God speaking through Lady Croom, he never spoke through anyone!
CHATER [*Awed.*]   Take command of Lord Byron's pistols!
BRICE   You hear Mr Chater, sir—how will you answer him?
         [SEPTIMUS *has been watching* LADY CROOM's *progress up the garden. He turns back.*]

8. Samuel Rogers (1763–1855), English poet; Thomas Moore (1779–1852), Irish poet, friend and biographer of Byron; William Wordsworth (1770–1850), English poet.
9. Lord Byron.
1. Suitcase. "Packet": mail boat, which also carried passengers. "Lesbos": Greek island.
2. France, under Napoleon, was fighting the Pen-insula War (1804–14) against Great Britain, Portugal, and Spanish guerrillas in the Iberian Peninsula.
3. Accommodation for troops.
4. Byron was born with a clubfoot.
5. An early form of the piano, its name combining the Italian words for soft and loud, respectively.

SEPTIMUS By killing him. I am tired of him.

CHATER [*Startled.*] Eh?

BRICE [*Pleased.*] Ah!

SEPTIMUS Oh, damn your soul, Chater! Ovid[6] would have stayed a lawyer and Virgil a farmer if they had known the bathos[7] to which love would descend in your sportive satyrs and noodle nymphs![8] I am at your service with a half-ounce ball[9] in your brain. May it satisfy you—behind the boat-house at daybreak—shall we say five o'clock? My compliments to Mrs Chater—have no fear for her, she will not want for protection while Captain Brice has a guinea[1] in his pocket, he told her so himself.

BRICE You lie, sir!

SEPTIMUS No, sir. Mrs Chater, perhaps.

BRICE You lie, or you will answer to me!

SEPTIMUS [*Wearily.*] Oh, very well—I can fit you in at five minutes after five. And then it's off to the Malta packet out of Falmouth. You two will be dead, my penurious[2] schoolfriend will remain to tutor Lady Thomasina, and I trust everybody including Lady Croom will be satisfied!

[SEPTIMUS *slams the door behind him.*]

BRICE He is all bluster and bladder. Rest assured, Chater, I will let the air out of him.

[BRICE *leaves by the other door.* CHATER's *assurance lasts only a moment. When he spots the flaw . . .*[3]]

CHATER Oh! But . . .

[*He hurries out after* BRICE.]

SCENE FOUR

HANNAH *and* VALENTINE. *She is reading aloud. He is listening. Lightning, the tortoise, is on the table and is not readily distinguishable from Plautus. In front of* VALENTINE *is Septimus's portfolio, recognizably so but naturally somewhat faded. It is open. Principally associated with the portfolio (although it may contain sheets of blank paper also) are three items: a slim maths primer; a sheet of drawing paper on which there is a scrawled diagram and some mathematical notations, arrow marks, etc.; and Thomasina's mathematics lesson book, i.e. the one she writes in, which* VALENTINE *is leafing through as he listens to* HANNAH *reading from the primer.*

HANNAH 'I, Thomasina Coverly, have found a truly wonderful method whereby all the forms of nature must give up their numerical secrets and draw themselves through number alone. This margin being too mean for my purpose, the reader must look elsewhere for the New Geometry of Irregular Forms discovered by Thomasina Coverly.'

[*Pause. She hands* VALENTINE *the text book.* VALENTINE *looks at what she has been reading.*

From the next room, a piano is heard, beginning to play quietly, unintrusively, improvisationally.]

Does it mean anything?

---

6. Roman poet (43 B.C.E.–17? C.E.)
7. Rhetorical descent from the exalted to the commonplace.
8. Your lustful men and foolish young women.
9. Bullet.

1. British gold coin with a value (in the nineteenth century) of twenty-one shillings.
2. Penniless.
3. Brice, as Chater's "second," could duel with Septimus only if Chater were dead or wounded.

VALENTINE   I don't know. I don't know what it means, except mathematically.
HANNAH   I meant mathematically.
VALENTINE [*Now with the lesson book again.*]   It's an iterated algorithm.[4]
HANNAH   What's that?
VALENTINE   Well, it's . . . Jesus . . . it's an algorithm that's been . . . iterated. How'm I supposed to . . . ? [*He makes an effort.*] The left-hand pages are graphs of what the numbers are doing on the right-hand pages. But all on different scales. Each graph is a small section of the previous one, blown up. Like you'd blow up a detail of a photograph, and then a detail of the detail, and so on, forever. Or in her case, till she ran out of pages.
HANNAH   Is it difficult?
VALENTINE   The maths isn't difficult. It's what you did at school. You have some x-and-y equation. Any value for x gives you a value for y. So you put a dot where it's right for both x and y. Then you take the next value for x which gives you another value for y, and when you've done that a few times you join up the dots and that's your graph of whatever the equation is.
HANNAH   And is that what she's doing?
VALENTINE   No. Not exactly. Not at all. What she's doing is, every time she works out a value for y, she's using *that* as her next value for x. And so on. Like a feedback. She's feeding the solution back into the equation, and then solving it again. Iteration, you see.
HANNAH   And that's surprising, is it?
VALENTINE   Well, it is a bit. It's the technique I'm using on my grouse numbers, and it hasn't been around for much longer than, well, call it twenty years.
   [*Pause.*]
HANNAH   Why would she be doing it?
VALENTINE   I have no idea.
   [*Pause.*]
   I thought you were doing the hermit.
HANNAH   I am. I still am. But Bernard, damn him . . . Thomasina's tutor turns out to have interesting connections. Bernard is going through the library like a bloodhound. The portfolio was in a cupboard.
VALENTINE   There's a lot of stuff around. Gus loves going through it. No old masters or anything . . .
HANNAH   The maths primer she was using belonged to him—the tutor; he wrote his name in it.
VALENTINE [*Reading.*]   'Septimus Hodge.'
HANNAH   Why were these things saved, do you think?
VALENTINE   Why should there be a reason?
HANNAH   And the diagram, what's it of?
VALENTINE   How would I know?
HANNAH   Why are you cross?
VALENTINE   I'm not cross. [*Pause.*] When your Thomasina was doing maths it had been the same maths for a couple of thousand years. Classical. And for a century after Thomasina. Then maths left the real world behind, just like modern art really. Nature was classical, maths was suddenly Picassos. But now nature is having the last laugh. The freaky stuff is turning out to be the mathematics of the natural world.

---

4. Mathematical procedure for computing results through a series of repeated operations.

HANNAH This feedback thing?

VALENTINE For example.

HANNAH Well, could Thomasina have—

VALENTINE [*Snaps.*] No, of course she bloody couldn't!

HANNAH All right, you're not cross. What did you mean you were doing the same thing she was doing? [*Pause.*] What *are* you doing?

VALENTINE Actually I'm doing it from the other end. She started with an equation and turned it into a graph. I've got a graph—real data—and I'm trying to find the equation which would give you the graph if you used it the way she's used hers. Iterated it.

HANNAH What for?

VALENTINE It's how you look at population changes in biology. Goldfish in a pond, say. This year there are x goldfish. Next year there'll be y goldfish. Some get born, some get eaten by herons, whatever. Nature manipulates the x and turns it into y. Then y goldfish is your starting population for the following year. Just like Thomasina. Your value for y becomes your next value for x. The question is: what is being done to x? What is the manipulation? Whatever it is, it can be written down as mathematics. It's called an algorithm.

HANNAH It can't be the same every year.

VALENTINE The details change, you can't keep tabs on everything, it's not nature in a box. But it isn't necessary to know the details. When they are all put together, it turns out the population is obeying a mathematical rule.

HANNAH The goldfish are?

VALENTINE Yes. No. The numbers. It's not about the behaviour of fish. It's about the behaviour of numbers. This thing works for any phenomenon which eats its own numbers—measles epidemics, rainfall averages, cotton prices, it's a natural phenomenon in itself. Spooky.

HANNAH Does it work for grouse?

VALENTINE I don't know yet. I mean, it does undoubtedly, but it's hard to show. There's more noise with grouse.

HANNAH Noise?

VALENTINE Distortions. Interference. Real data is messy. There's a thousand acres of moorland that had grouse on it, always did till about 1930. But nobody counted the grouse. They shot them. So you count the grouse they shot. But burning the heather interferes, it improves the food supply. A good year for foxes interferes the other way, they eat the chicks. And then there's the weather. It's all very, very noisy out there. Very hard to spot the tune. Like a piano in the next room, it's playing your song, but unfortunately it's out of whack, some of the strings are missing, and the pianist is tone deaf and drunk—I mean, the *noise*! Impossible!

HANNAH What do you do?

VALENTINE You start guessing what the tune might be. You try to pick it out of the noise. You try this, you try that, you start to get something—it's half-baked but you start putting in notes which are missing or not quite the right notes . . . and bit by bit . . . [*He starts to dumdi-da to the tune of 'Happy Birthday'.*] Dumdi-dum-dum, dear Val-en-tine, dumdi-dum-dum to you—the lost algorithm!

HANNAH [*Soberly.*] Yes, I see. And then what?

VALENTINE I publish.

HANNAH Of course. Sorry. Jolly good.

VALENTINE   That's the theory. Grouse are bastards compared to goldfish.
HANNAH   Why did you choose them?
VALENTINE   The game books. My true inheritance. Two hundred years of real data on a plate.
HANNAH   Somebody wrote down everything that's shot?
VALENTINE   Well, that's what a game book is. I'm only using from 1870, when butts and beaters[5] came in.
HANNAH   You mean the game books go back to Thomasina's time?
VALENTINE   Oh yes. Further. [*And then getting ahead of her thought.*] No—really. I promise you. I *promise* you. Not a schoolgirl living in a country house in Derbyshire in eighteen-something!
HANNAH   Well, what was she doing?
VALENTINE   She was just playing with the numbers. The truth is, she wasn't doing anything.
HANNAH   She must have been doing something.
VALENTINE   Doodling. Nothing she understood.
HANNAH   A monkey at a typewriter?[6]
VALENTINE   Yes. Well, a piano.
    [HANNAH *picks up the algebra book and reads from it.*]
HANNAH   ' . . . a method whereby all the forms of nature must give up their numerical secrets and draw themselves through number alone.' This feedback, is it a way of making pictures of forms in nature? Just tell me if it is or it isn't.
VALENTINE [*Irritated.*]   To *me* it is. Pictures of turbulence—growth—change—creation—it's not a way of drawing an elephant, for God's sake!
HANNAH   I'm sorry.
    [*She picks up an apple leaf from the table. She is timid about pushing the point.*]
    So you couldn't make a picture of this leaf by iterating a whatsit?
VALENTINE [*Off-hand.*]   Oh yes, you could do that.
HANNAH [*Furiously.*]   Well, tell me! Honestly, I could kill you!
VALENTINE   If you knew the algorithm and fed it back say ten thousand times, each time there'd be a dot somewhere on the screen. You'd never know where to expect the next dot. But gradually you'd start to see this shape, because every dot will be inside the shape of this leaf. It wouldn't *be* a leaf, it would be a mathematical object. But yes. The unpredictable and the pre-determined unfold together to make everything the way it is. It's how nature creates itself, on every scale, the snowflake and the snowstorm. It makes me so happy. To be at the beginning again, knowing almost nothing. People were talking about the end of physics. Relativity and quantum[7] looked as if they were going to clean out the whole problem between them. A theory of everything. But they only explained the very big and the very small. The universe, the elementary particles. The ordinary-sized stuff which is our lives, the things people write poetry about—clouds—daffodils—waterfalls—and what happens in a cup of coffee when the cream goes in—these things

5. "Butts": concealed stands (blinds) for shooting birds. "Beaters": people employed to drive the birds toward the guns.
6. Refers to a once-popular belief that, given sufficient time, a monkey jabbing typewriter keys at random would eventually produce the complete plays of Shakespeare.
7. Twentieth-century advances in physics made by Albert Einstein (1879–1955) and others. Valentine continues with a simplified description of chaos theory.

are full of mystery, as mysterious to us as the heavens were to the Greeks. We're better at predicting events at the edge of the galaxy or inside the nucleus of an atom than whether it'll rain on auntie's garden party three Sundays from now. Because the problem turns out to be different. We can't even predict the next drip from a dripping tap when it gets irregular. Each drip sets up the conditions for the next, the smallest variation blows prediction apart, and the weather is unpredictable the same way, will always be unpredictable. When you push the numbers through the computer you can see it on the screen. The future is disorder. A door like this has cracked open five or six times since we got up on our hind legs. It's the best possible time to be alive, when almost everything you thought you knew is wrong.

[*Pause.*]

HANNAH   The weather is fairly predictable in the Sahara.

VALENTINE   The scale is different but the graph goes up and down the same way. Six thousand years in the Sahara looks like six months in Manchester, I bet you.

HANNAH   How much?

VALENTINE   Everything you have to lose.

HANNAH [*Pause.*]   No.

VALENTINE   Quite right. That's why there was corn in Egypt.[8]

[*Hiatus. The piano is heard again.*]

HANNAH   What is he playing?

VALENTINE   I don't know. He makes it up.

HANNAH   Chloë called him 'genius'.

VALENTINE   It's what my mother calls him—only *she* means it. Last year some expert had her digging in the wrong place for months to find something or other—the foundations of Capability Brown's boat-house—and Gus put her right first go.

HANNAH   Did he ever speak?

VALENTINE   Oh yes. Until he was five. You've never asked about him. You get high marks here for good breeding.

HANNAH   Yes, I know. I've always been given credit for my unconcern.

[BERNARD *enters in high excitement and triumph.*]

BERNARD   *English Bards and Scotch Reviewers.* A pencilled superscription.[9] Listen and kiss my cycle-clips!

[*He is carrying the book. He reads from it.*]

'O harbinger of Sleep, who missed the press[1]
And hoped his drone might thus escape redress!
The wretched Chater, bard of Eros' Couch,
For his narcotic[2] let my pencil vouch!'

You see, *you have to turn over every page.*

HANNAH   Is it his[3] handwriting?

BERNARD   Oh, come *on.*

HANNAH   Obviously not.

BERNARD   Christ, what do you want?

HANNAH   Proof.

VALENTINE   Quite right. Who are you talking about?

8. Cf. Exodus 42.1.
9. Note.
1. O herald . . . who published his poem too late

to be included in the first edition of Byron's work.
2. Sleep-inducing drug.
3. Byron's.

BERNARD   Proof? *Proof?* You'd have to be there, you silly bitch!

VALENTINE [*Mildly.*]   I say, you're speaking of my fiancée.

HANNAH   Especially when I have a present for you. Guess what I found. [*Producing the present for* BERNARD.] Lady Croom writing from London to her husband. Her brother, Captain Brice, married a Mrs Chater. In other words, one might assume, a widow.

[BERNARD *looks at the letter.*]

BERNARD   I *said* he was dead. What year? 1810! Oh my God, 1810! Well *done,* Hannah! Are you going to tell me it's a different Mrs Chater?

HANNAH   Oh no. It's her all right. Note her Christian name.

BERNARD   Charity. Charity . . . 'Deny what cannot be proven for Charity's sake!'

HANNAH   Don't kiss me!

VALENTINE   She won't let anyone kiss her.

BERNARD   You see! They wrote—they scribbled—they put it on paper. It was their employment. Their diversion. Paper is what they had. And there'll be more. There is always more. We can find it!

HANNAH   Such passion. First Valentine, now you. It's moving.

BERNARD   The aristocratic friend of the tutor—under the same roof as the poor sod whose book he savaged—the first thing he does is seduce Chater's wife. All is discovered. There is a duel. Chater dead, Byron fled! P.S. guess what?, the widow married her ladyship's brother! Do you honestly think no one wrote a word? How could they not! It dropped from sight but we will write it again!

HANNAH   You can, Bernard. I'm not going to take any credit, I haven't done anything.

[*The same thought has clearly occurred to* BERNARD. *He becomes instantly po-faced.*][4]

BERNARD   Well, that's—very fair—generous—

HANNAH   Prudent. Chater could have died of anything, anywhere.

[*The po-face is forgotten.*]

BERNARD   But he fought a duel with Byron!

HANNAH   You haven't established it was fought. You haven't established it was Byron. For God's sake, Bernard, you haven't established Byron was even here!

BERNARD   I'll tell you your problem. No guts.

HANNAH   Really?

BERNARD   By which I mean a visceral belief in yourself. Gut instinct. The part of you which doesn't reason. The certainty for which there is no back-reference. Because time is reversed. Tock, tick goes the universe and then recovers itself, but it was enough, you were in there and you bloody *know.*

VALENTINE   Are you talking about Lord Byron, the poet?

BERNARD   No, you fucking idiot, we're talking about Lord Byron the chartered[5] accountant.

VALENTINE [*Unoffended.*]   Oh well, *he* was here all right, the poet.

[*Silence.*]

HANNAH   How do you know?

VALENTINE   He's in the game book. I think he shot a hare. I read through the whole lot once when I had mumps—some quite interesting people—

4. Pompously serious.   5. Certified.

HANNAH Where's the book?

VALENTINE It's not one I'm using—too early, of course—

HANNAH 1809.

VALENTINE They've always been in the commode. Ask Chloë.

[HANNAH *looks to* BERNARD. BERNARD *has been silent because he has been incapable of speech. He seems to have gone into a trance, in which only his mouth tries to work.* HANNAH *steps over to him and gives him a demure kiss on the cheek. It works.* BERNARD *lurches out into the garden and can be heard croaking for 'Chloë . . . Chloë!'*]

VALENTINE My mother's lent him her bicycle. Lending one's bicycle is a form of safe sex, possibly the safest there is. My mother is in a flutter about Bernard, and he's no fool. He gave her a first edition of Horace Walpole, and now she's lent him her bicycle.

[*He gathers up the three items [the primer, the lesson book and the diagram] and puts them into the portfolio.*]

Can I keep these for a while?

HANNAH Yes, of course.

[*The piano stops.* GUS *enters hesitantly from the music room.*]

VALENTINE [*To* GUS.] Yes, finished . . . coming now. [*To* HANNAH.] I'm trying to work out the diagram.

[GUS *nods and smiles, at* HANNAH *too, but she is preoccupied.*]

HANNAH What I don't understand is . . . why nobody did this feedback thing before—it's not like relativity, you don't have to be Einstein.

VALENTINE You couldn't see to look before. The electronic calculator was what the telescope was for Galileo.[6]

HANNAH Calculator?

VALENTINE There wasn't enough time before. There weren't enough *pencils*! [*He flourishes Thomasina's lesson book.*] This took her I don't know how many days and she hasn't scratched the paintwork. Now she'd only have to press a button, the same button over and over. Iteration. A few minutes. And what I've done in a couple of months, with only a *pencil* the calculations would take me the rest of my life to do again—thousands of pages—tens of thousands! And so boring!

HANNAH Do you mean—?

[*She stops because* GUS *is plucking* VALENTINE's *sleeve.*]

Do you mean—?

VALENTINE All right, Gus, I'm coming.

HANNAH Do you mean that was the only problem? Enough time? And paper? And the boredom?

VALENTINE We're going to get out the dressing-up box.

HANNAH [*Driven to raising her voice.*] Val! Is that what you're saying?

VALENTINE [*Surprised by her. Mildly.*] No, I'm saying you'd have to have a reason for doing it.

[GUS *runs out of the room, upset.*]

[*Apologetically.*] He hates people shouting.

HANNAH I'm sorry.

[VALENTINE *starts to follow* GUS.]

But anything else?

VALENTINE Well, the other thing is, you'd have to be insane.

---

6. Galileo Galilei (1564–1642), Italian astronomer.

[VALENTINE *leaves.*
HANNAH *stays, thoughtful. After a moment, she turns to the table and picks up the* Cornhill Magazine. *She looks into it briefly, then closes it, and leaves the room, taking the magazine with her.*
The empty room.
The light changes to early morning. From a long way off, there is a pistol shot. A moment later there is the cry of dozens of crows disturbed from the unseen trees.]

Act Two

SCENE FIVE

BERNARD *is pacing around, reading aloud from a handful of typed sheets.* VALENTINE *and* CHLOË *are his audience.* VALENTINE *has his tortoise and is eating a sandwich from which he extracts shreds of lettuce to offer the tortoise.*

BERNARD   'Did it happen? Could it happen?
Undoubtedly it could. Only three years earlier the Irish poet Tom Moore appeared on the field of combat to avenge a review by Jeffrey of the *Edinburgh.* These affairs were seldom fatal and sometimes farcical but, potentially, the duellist stood in respect to the law no differently from a murderer. As for the murderee, a minor poet like Ezra Chater could go to his death in a Derbyshire glade as unmissed and unremembered as his contemporary and namesake, the minor botanist who died in the forests of the West Indies, lost to history like the monkey that bit him. On April 16th 1809, a few days after he left Sidley Park, Byron wrote to his solicitor John Hanson: 'If the consequences of my leaving England were ten times as ruinous as you describe, I have no alternative; there are circumstances which render it absolutely indispensable, and quit the country I must immediately.' To which, the editor's note in the Collected Letters reads as follows: 'What Byron's urgent reasons for leaving England were at this time has never been revealed.' The letter was written from the family seat, Newstead Abbey, Nottinghamshire. A long day's ride to the north-west lay Sidley Park, the estate of the Coverlys—a far grander family, raised by Charles II to the Earldom of Croom . . . '
[HANNAH *enters briskly, a piece of paper in her hand.*]
HANNAH   Bernard . . . ! Val . . .
BERNARD   Do you mind?
[HANNAH *puts her piece of paper down in front of* VALENTINE.]
CHLOË [*Angrily.*]   Hannah!
HANNAH   What?
CHLOË   She's so *rude!*
HANNAH [*Taken aback.*]   What? Am I?
VALENTINE   Bernard's reading us his lecture.
HANNAH   Yes, I know. [*Then recollecting herself.*] Yes—yes—that *was* rude. I'm sorry, Bernard.
VALENTINE [*With the piece of paper.*]   What is this?
HANNAH [*To* BERNARD.]   Spot on—the India Office Library. [*To* VALENTINE.] Peacock's letter in holograph,[7] I got a copy sent—

---

7. Handwriting.

CHLOË   *Hannah!* Shut up!
HANNAH [*Sitting down.*] Yes, sorry.
BERNARD It's all right, I'll read it to myself.
CHLOË   *No.*
[HANNAH *reaches for the Peacock letter and takes it back.*]
HANNAH Go on, Bernard. Have I missed anything? Sorry.
[BERNARD *stares at her balefully but then continues to read.*]
BERNARD 'The Byrons of Newstead in 1809 comprised an eccentric widow
and her undistinguished son, the "lame brat", who until the age of ten when
he came into the title, had been carted about the country from lodging to
lodging by his vulgar hectoring monster of a mother—' [HANNAH's *hand has
gone up.*]—overruled—'and who four months past his twenty-first birthday
was master of nothing but his debts and his genius. Between the Byrons
and the Coverlys there was no social equality and none to be expected. The
connection, undisclosed to posterity until now, was with Septimus Hodge,
Byron's friend at Harrow and Trinity College—' [HANNAH's *hand goes up
again.*]—sustained—[*He makes an instant correction with a silver pencil.*]
'Byron's contemporary at Harrow and Trinity College, and now tutor in
residence to the Croom daughter, Thomasina Coverly. Byron's letters tell
us where he was on April 8th and on April 12th. He was at Newstead. But
on the 10th he was at Sidley Park, as attested by the game book preserved
there: "April 10th 1809—forenoon. High cloud, dry, and sun between times,
wind southeasterly. Self—Augustus—Lord Byron. Fourteen pigeon, one
hare (Lord B.)." But, as we know now, the drama of life and death at Sidley
Park was not about pigeons but about sex and literature.'
VALENTINE Unless you were the pigeon.
BERNARD I don't have to do this. I'm paying you a compliment.
CHLOË   Ignore him, Bernard—go on, get to the duel.
BERNARD Hannah's not even paying attention.
HANNAH Yes I am, it's all going in. I often work with the radio on.
BERNARD Oh thanks!
HANNAH Is there much more?
CHLOË   *Hannah!*
HANNAH No, it's fascinating. I just wondered how much more there was. I
need to ask Valentine about this [*letter.*]—sorry, Bernard, go on, this will
keep.
VALENTINE Yes—sorry, Bernard.
CHLOË   Please, Bernard!
BERNARD Where was I?
VALENTINE Pigeons.
CHLOË   Sex.
HANNAH Literature.
BERNARD Life and death. Right. 'Nothing could be more eloquent of that
than the three documents I have quoted: the terse demand to settle a matter
in private; the desperate scribble of "my husband has sent for pistols"; and
on April 11th, the gauntlet thrown down by the aggrieved and cuckolded
author Ezra Chater. The covers[8] have not survived. What is certain is that
all three letters were in Byron's possession when his books were sold in

8. Envelopelike wrappers of letters. "Cuckolded": whose wife is adulterous.

1816—preserved in the pages of "The Couch of Eros" which seven years earlier at Sidley Park Byron had borrowed from Septimus Hodge.'

HANNAH   Borrowed?

BERNARD   I will be taking questions at the end. Constructive comments will be welcome. Which is indeed my reason for trying out in the provinces before my London opening[9] under the auspices of the Byron Society prior to publication. By the way, Valentine, do you want a credit?—'the game book recently discovered by'?

VALENTINE   It was never lost, Bernard.

BERNARD   'As recently pointed out by.' I don't normally like giving credit where it's due, but with scholarly articles as with divorce, there is a certain cachet[1] in citing a member of the aristocracy. I'll pop it in ad lib[2] for the lecture, and give you a mention in the press release. How's that?

VALENTINE   Very kind.

HANNAH   Press release? What happened to the *Journal of English Studies*?

BERNARD   That comes later with the apparatus,[3] and in the recognized tone— very dry, very modest, absolutely gloat-free, and yet unmistakably 'Eat your heart out, you dozy bastards'. But first, it's 'Media Don,[4] book early to avoid disappointment'. Where was I?

VALENTINE   Game book.

CHLOË   Eros.

HANNAH   Borrowed.

BERNARD   Right. '—borrowed from Septimus Hodge. Is it conceivable that the letters were already in the book when Byron borrowed it?'

VALENTINE   Yes.

CHLOË   Shut up, Val.

VALENTINE   Well, it's conceivable.

BERNARD   'Is it *likely* that Hodge would have lent Byron the book without first removing the three private letters?'

VALENTINE   Look, sorry—I only meant, Byron could have borrowed the book without asking.

HANNAH   That's true.

BERNARD   Then why wouldn't Hodge get them back?

HANNAH   I don't know, I wasn't there.

BERNARD   That's right, you bloody weren't.

CHLOË   Go on, Bernard.

BERNARD   'It is the third document, the challenge itself, that convinces. Chater "as a man and a poet", points the finger at his "slanderer in the press". Neither as a man nor a poet did Ezra Chater cut such a figure as to be habitually slandered or even mentioned in the press. It is surely indisputable that the slander was the review of "The Maid of Turkey" in the *Piccadilly Recreation*. Did Septimus Hodge have any connection with the London periodicals? No. Did Byron? Yes! He had reviewed Wordsworth two years earlier, he was to review Spencer[5] two years later. And do we have any clue as to Byron's opinion of Chater the poet? Yes! Who but Byron could have written

9. New plays in Britain are frequently first performed outside London in preparation for more-sophisticated audiences in the capital.
1. Distinction.
2. Short for *ad libitum* (Latin): as an extemporaneous aside.
3. In the later version with footnotes.
4. Professor in the media spotlight.
5. William Robert Spencer (1769–1834), poet and wit.

the four lines pencilled into Lady Croom's copy of *English Bards and Scotch Reviewers'*—

HANNAH   Almost anybody.

BERNARD   Darling—

HANNAH   Don't call me darling.

BERNARD   Dickhead, then, is it likely that the man Chater calls his friend Septimus Hodge is the same man who screwed his wife and kicked the shit out of his last book?

HANNAH   Put it like that, almost certain.

CHLOË   [*Earnestly.*]   You've been deeply wounded in the past, haven't you, Hannah?

HANNAH   Nothing compared to listening to this. Why is there nothing in Byron's letters about the *Piccadilly* reviews?

BERNARD   Exactly. Because he killed the author.

HANNAH   But the first one, 'The Maid of Turkey', was the year before. Was he clairvoyant?

CHLOË   Letters get lost.

BERNARD   Thank you! Exactly! There is a platonic[6] letter which confirms everything—lost but ineradicable, like radio voices rippling through the universe for all eternity. "My dear Hodge—here I am in Albania and you're the only person in the whole world who knows why. Poor C! I never wished him any harm—except in the *Piccadilly*, of course—it was the woman who bade me eat,[7] dear Hodge!—what a tragic business, but thank God it ended well for poetry. Yours ever, B.—PS. Burn this.'

VALENTINE   How did Chater find out the reviewer was Byron?

BERNARD   [*Irritated.*]   I don't know, I wasn't there, was I? [*Pause. To* HANNAH.] You wish to say something?

HANNAH   Moi?[8]

CHLOË   I know. Byron told Mrs Chater in bed. Next day he dumped her so she grassed on him, and pleaded date rape.

BERNARD   [*Fastidiously.*]   Date rape? What do you mean, date rape?

HANNAH   April the tenth.

[BERNARD *cracks. Everything becomes loud and overlapped as* BERNARD *threatens to walk out and is cajoled into continuing.*]

BERNARD   Right!—forget it!

HANNAH   Sorry—

BERNARD   No—I've had nothing but sarcasm and childish interruptions—

VALENTINE   What did I do?

BERNARD   No credit for probably the most sensational literary discovery of the century—

CHLOË   I think you're jolly unfair—they're jealous, Bernard—

HANNAH   I won't say another word—

VALENTINE   Yes, go on, Bernard—we promise.

BERNARD   [*Finally.*]   Well, only if you stop *feeding tortoises!*

VALENTINE   Well, it's his lunch time.

BERNARD   And on condition that I am afforded the common courtesy of a scholar among scholars—

HANNAH   Absolutely mum till you're finished—

---

6. Nonexistent ideal.   8. Me? (French).
7. Cf. Genesis 3.12.

BERNARD   After which, any comments are to be couched in terms of accepted academic—

HANNAH   Dignity—you're right, Bernard.

BERNARD   —respect.

HANNAH   Respect. Absolutely. The language of scholars. Count on it.

[*Having made a great show of putting his pages away,* BERNARD *reassembles them and finds his place, glancing suspiciously at the other three for signs of levity.*]

BERNARD   Last paragraph. 'Without question, Ezra Chater issued a challenge to *somebody*. If a duel was fought in the dawn mist of Sidley Park in April 1809, his opponent, on the evidence, was a critic with a gift for ridicule and a taste for seduction. Do we need to look far? Without question, Mrs Chater was a widow by 1810. If we seek the occasion of Ezra Chater's early and unrecorded death, do we need to look far? Without question, Lord Byron, in the very season of his emergence as a literary figure, quit the country in a cloud of panic and mystery, and stayed abroad for two years at a time when Continental travel was unusual and dangerous. If we seek his reason—*do we need to look far?*'

[*No mean performer, he is pleased with the effect of his peroration. There is a significant silence.*]

HANNAH   Bollocks.[9]

CHLOË   Well, I think it's true.

HANNAH   You've left out everything which doesn't fit. Byron had been banging on[1] for months about leaving England—there's a letter in *February*—

BERNARD   But he didn't go, did he?

HANNAH   And then he didn't sail until the beginning of July!

BERNARD   Everything moved more slowly then. Time was different. He was two weeks in Falmouth waiting for wind or something—

HANNAH   Bernard, I don't know why I'm bothering—you're arrogant, greedy and reckless. You've gone from a glint in your eye to a sure thing in a hop, skip and a jump. You deserve what you get and I think you're mad. But I can't help myself, you're like some exasperating child pedalling its tricycle towards the edge of a cliff, and I have to do something. So listen to me. If Byron killed Chater in a duel I'm Marie of Romania.[2] You'll end up with so much *fame* you won't leave the house without a paper bag over your head.

VALENTINE   Actually, Bernard, as a scientist, your theory is incomplete.

BERNARD   But I'm not a scientist.

VALENTINE   [*Patiently.*]   No, *as a scientist*—

BERNARD   [*Beginning to shout.*]   I have yet to hear a proper argument.

HANNAH   Nobody would kill a man and then pan his book. I mean, not in that order. So he must have borrowed the book, written the review, *posted it*, seduced Mrs Chater, fought a duel and departed, all in the space of two or three days. Who would do that?

BERNARD   Byron.

HANNAH   It's hopeless.

BERNARD   You've never understood him, as you've shown in your novelette.[3]

HANNAH   In my what?

9. Nonsense (slang).
1. Talking (slang).
2. Cf. Dorothy Parker's poem "Comment," lines

3–4: "And love is a thing that can never go wrong; / And I am Marie of Roumania."
3. Sentimental short novel.

BERNARD   Oh, sorry—did you think it was a work of historical revisionism?
Byron the spoilt child promoted beyond his gifts by the spirit of the age!
And Caroline the closet intellectual shafted by a male society!
VALENTINE   I read that somewhere—
HANNAH   It's his review.
BERNARD   And bloody well said, too!
       [*Things are turning a little ugly and* BERNARD *seems in a mood to push
       them that way.*]
You got them backwards, darling. Caroline was Romantic waffle on wheels
with no talent, and Byron was an eighteenth-century Rationalist[4] touched
by genius. And he killed Chater.
HANNAH   [*Pause.*]   If it's not too late to change my mind, I'd like you to go
ahead.
BERNARD   I intend to. Look to the mote in your own eye![5]—you even had the
wrong bloke on the dust-jacket!
HANNAH   Dust-jacket?
VALENTINE   What about my computer model? Aren't you going to mention it?
BERNARD   It's inconclusive.
VALENTINE   [*To* HANNAH.]   The *Piccadilly* reviews aren't a very good fit with
Byron's other reviews, you see.
HANNAH   [*To* BERNARD.]   What do you mean, the wrong bloke?
BERNARD   [*Ignoring her.*]   The other reviews aren't a very good fit for each
other, are they?
VALENTINE   No, but differently. The parameters—[6]
BERNARD   [*Jeering.*]   Parameters! You can't stick Byron's head in your laptop!
Genius isn't like your average grouse.
VALENTINE   [*Casually.*]   Well, it's all trivial anyway.
BERNARD   What is?
VALENTINE   Who wrote what when . . .
BERNARD   Trivial?
VALENTINE   Personalities.
BERNARD   I'm sorry—did you say trivial?
VALENTINE   It's a technical term.[7]
BERNARD   Not where I come from, it isn't.
VALENTINE   The questions you're asking don't matter, you see. It's like arguing
who got there first with the calculus. The English say Newton, the Germans
say Leibnitz.[8] But it doesn't *matter*. Personalities. What matters is the cal-
culus. Scientific progress. Knowledge.
BERNARD   Really? Why?
VALENTINE   Why what?
BERNARD   Why does scientific progress matter more than personalities?
VALENTINE   Is he serious?
HANNAH   No, he's trivial. Bernard—
VALENTINE   [*Interrupting, to* BERNARD.]   Do yourself a favour, you're on a loser.
BERNARD   Oh, you're going to zap me with penicillin and pesticides. Spare
me that and I'll spare you the bomb and aerosols. But don't confuse progress
with perfectibility. A great poet is always timely. A great philosopher is an

---

4. Person whose opinions are based on pure reasoning. "Waffle": gossip.
5. Cf. Matthew 7.3.
6. Distinguishing or defining characteristics.

7. From mathematics.
8. Gottfried Wilhelm, Baron von Leibnitz (1646–
1716), German philosopher and mathematician.

urgent need. There's no rush for Isaac Newton. We were quite happy with Aristotle's cosmos. Personally, I preferred it. Fifty-five crystal spheres geared to God's crankshaft is my idea of a satisfying universe. I can't think of anything more trivial than the speed of light. Quarks, quasars—big bangs, black holes—who gives a shit? How did you people[9] con us out of all that status? All that money? And why are you so pleased with yourselves?

CHLOË   Are you against penicillin, Bernard?

BERNARD   Don't feed the animals.[1] [*Back to* VALENTINE.] I'd push the lot of you over a cliff myself. Except the one in the wheelchair,[2] I think I'd lose the sympathy vote before people had time to think it through.

HANNAH [*Loudly.*]   What the hell do you mean, the dust-jacket?

BERNARD [*Ignoring her.*]   If knowledge isn't self-knowledge it isn't doing much, mate. Is the universe expanding? Is it contracting? Is it standing on one leg and singing 'When Father Painted the Parlour'? Leave me out. I can expand my universe without you. 'She walks in beauty, like the night of cloudless climes and starry skies, and all that's best of dark and bright meet in her aspect and her eyes.'[3] There you are, he wrote it after coming home from a party. [*With offensive politeness.*] What is it that you're doing with grouse, Valentine, I'd love to know?

[VALENTINE *stands up and it is suddenly apparent that he is shaking and close to tears.*]

VALENTINE [*To* CHLOË.]   He's not against penicillin, and he knows I'm not against poetry. [*To* BERNARD.] I've given up on the grouse.

HANNAH   You haven't, Valentine!

VALENTINE [*Leaving.*]   I can't do it.

HANNAH   Why?

VALENTINE   Too much noise. There's just too much *bloody noise*!

[*On which,* VALENTINE *leaves the room.* CHLOË, *upset and in tears, jumps up and briefly pummels* BERNARD *ineffectually with her fists.*]

CHLOË   You bastard, Bernard!

[*She follows* VALENTINE *out. Pause.*]

HANNAH   Well, I think that's everybody. You can leave now, give Gus a kick on your way out.

BERNARD   Yes, I'm sorry about that. It's no fun when it's not among pros, is it?

HANNAH   No.

BERNARD   Oh, well . . . [*He begins to put his lecture sheets away in his briefcase, and is thus reminded . . .*] do you want to know about your book jacket? 'Lord Byron and Caroline Lamb at the Royal Academy'? Ink study by Henry Fuseli?[4]

HANNAH   What about it?

BERNARD   It's not them.

HANNAH [*She explodes.*]   Who says!?

[BERNARD *brings the* Byron Society Journal *from his briefcase.*]

BERNARD   This Fuseli expert in the *Byron Society Journal*. They sent me the latest . . . as a distinguished guest speaker.

HANNAH   But of course it's them! Everyone knows—

---

9. Scientists.
1. Don't encourage them; i.e., don't keep the discussion going.
2. Stephen Hawking (b. 1942), physicist.

3. Lord Byron, "She walks in beauty," lines 1–4.
4. Swiss-born artist (1741–1825) who lived and worked in England.

BERNARD   Popular tradition only. [*He is finding the place in the journal.*] Here we are. 'No earlier than 1820'. He's analysed it. [*Offers it to her.*] Read at your leisure.

HANNAH [*She sounds like* BERNARD *jeering.*] Analysed it?

BERNARD   Charming sketch, of course, but Byron was in Italy . . .

HANNAH   But, Bernard—I *know* it's them.

BERNARD   How?

HANNAH   How? It just *is.* 'Analysed it', my big toe!

BERNARD   Language!

HANNAH   He's wrong.

BERNARD   Oh, gut instinct, you mean?

HANNAH [*Flatly.*]   He's wrong.

  [BERNARD *snaps shut his briefcase.*]

BERNARD   Well, it's all trivial, isn't it? Why don't you come?

HANNAH   Where?

BERNARD   With me.

HANNAH   To London? What for?

BERNARD   What for.

HANNAH   Oh, your lecture.

BERNARD   No, no, bugger that. Sex.

HANNAH   Oh . . . No. Thanks . . . [*Then, protesting.*] *Bernard!*

BERNARD   You should try it. It's very underrated.

HANNAH   Nothing against it.

BERNARD   Yes, you have. You should let yourself go a bit. You might have written a better book. Or at any rate the right book.

HANNAH   Sex and literature. Literature and sex. Your conversation, left to itself, doesn't have many places to go. Like two marbles rolling around a pudding basin. One of them is always sex.

BERNARD   Ah well, yes. Men all over.

HANNAH   No doubt. Einstein—relativity and sex. Chippendale—[5] sex and furniture. Galileo—'Did the earth move?' What the hell is it with you people? Chaps sometimes wanted to marry me, and I don't know a worse bargain. Available sex against not being allowed to fart in bed. What do you mean the right book?

BERNARD   It takes a romantic to make a heroine of Caroline Lamb. You were cut out for Byron.

  [*Pause.*]

HANNAH   So, cheerio.

BERNARD   Oh, I'm coming back for the dance, you know. Chloë asked me.

HANNAH   She meant well, but I don't dance.

BERNARD   No, no—I'm going with her.

HANNAH   Oh, I see. I don't, actually.

BERNARD   I'm her date. Sub rosa.[6] Don't tell Mother.

HANNAH   She doesn't want her mother to know?

BERNARD   No—*I* don't want her mother to know. This is my first experience of the landed aristocracy. I tell you, I'm boggle-eyed.

HANNAH   Bernard!—you haven't seduced that girl?

BERNARD   Seduced her? Every time I turned round she was up a library ladder.

---

5. Thomas Chippendale (1718–1779), famous English cabinetmaker.   6. Secretly (Latin).

In the end I gave in. That reminds me—I spotted something between her legs that made me think of you.
[*He instantly receives a sharp stinging slap on the face but manages to remain completely unperturbed by it. He is already producing from his pocket a small book. His voice has hardly hesitated.*]
The Peaks Traveller and Gazetteer—James Godolphin 1832—unillustrated, I'm afraid. [*He has opened the book to a marked place.*] Sidley Park in Derbyshire, property of the Earl of Croom . . . '
HANNAH [*Numbly.*]   The world is going to hell in a handcart.
BERNARD   'Five hundred acres including forty of lake—the Park by Brown and Noakes has pleasing features in the horrid style—viaduct, grotto,[7] etc—a hermitage occupied by a lunatic since twenty years without discourse or companion save for a pet tortoise, Plautus by name, which he suffers children to touch on request.' [*He holds out the book for her.*] A tortoise. They must be a feature.
   [*After a moment* HANNAH *takes the book.*]
HANNAH   Thank you.
   [VALENTINE *comes to the door.*]
VALENTINE   The station taxi is at the front . . .
BERNARD   Yes . . . thanks . . . Oh—did Peacock come up trumps?[8]
HANNAH   For some.
BERNARD   Hermit's name and CV?
   [*He picks up and glances at the Peacock letter.*]
'My dear Thackeray . . . ' God, I'm good.
   [*He puts the letter down.*]
Well, wish me luck— [*Vaguely to* VALENTINE] Sorry about . . . you know . . .
[*and to* HANNAH] and about your . . .
VALENTINE   Piss off, Bernard.
BERNARD   Right.
   [BERNARD *goes.*]
HANNAH   Don't let Bernard get to you. It's only performance art, you know. Rhetoric, they used to teach it in ancient times, like PT.[9] It's not about being right, they had philosophy for that. Rhetoric was their chat show. Bernard's indignation is a sort of aerobics for when he gets on television.
VALENTINE   I don't care to be rubbished by the dustbin man.[1]
   [*He has been looking at the letter.*] The what of the lunatic?
   [HANNAH *reclaims the letter and reads it for him.*]
HANNAH   'The testament of the lunatic serves as a caution against French fashion . . . for it was Frenchified mathematick that brought him to the melancholy certitude of a world without light or life . . . as a wooden stove that must consume itself until ash and stove are as one, and heat is gone from the earth.'
VALENTINE [*Amused, surprised.*]   Huh!
HANNAH   'He died aged two score years and seven, hoary as Job[2] and meagre as a cabbage-stalk, the proof of his prediction even yet unyielding to his labours for the restitution of hope through good English algebra.'

---

7. Artificial cave or cavern. "Horrid": Gothic. "Viaduct": bridgelike structure designed to carry a road over a valley, river, etc.
8. Give you what you wanted.
9. Physical training. "Performance art": nontraditional art form that involves presentation to an audience and sometimes involves acting.
1. Garbage collector.
2. As old as Job, who, according to the Bible, lived to be 140. "Two score years and seven": forty-seven.

VALENTINE That's it?
HANNAH [*Nods.*] Is there anything in it?
VALENTINE In what? We are all doomed? [*Casually.*] Oh yes, sure—it's called the second law of thermodynamics.
HANNAH Was it known about?
VALENTINE By poets and lunatics from time immemorial.
HANNAH Seriously.
VALENTINE No.
HANNAH Is it anything to do with . . . you know, Thomasina's discovery?
VALENTINE She didn't discover anything.
HANNAH Her lesson book.
VALENTINE No.
HANNAH A coincidence, then?
VALENTINE What is?
HANNAH [*Reading.*] 'He died aged two score years and seven.' That was in 1834. So he was born in 1787. So was the tutor. He says so in his letter to Lord Croom when he recommended himself for the job: 'Date of birth— 1787.' The hermit was born in the same year as Septimus Hodge.
VALENTINE [*Pause.*] Did Bernard bite you in the leg?[3]
HANNAH Don't you see? I thought my hermit was a perfect symbol. An idiot in the landscape. But this is better. The Age of Enlightenment banished into the Romantic wilderness! The genius of Sidley Park living on in a hermit's hut!
VALENTINE You don't *know* that.
HANNAH Oh, but I do. I do. Somewhere there will be *something* . . . if only I can find it.

SCENE SIX

The room is empty.
A reprise: early morning—a distant pistol shot—the sound of the crows.
JELLABY *enters the dawn-dark room with a lamp. He goes to the windows and looks out. He sees something. He returns to put the lamp on the table, and then opens one of the french windows and steps outside.*

JELLABY [*Outside.*] Mr Hodge!
    [SEPTIMUS *comes in, followed by* JELLABY, *who closes the garden door.* SEPTIMUS *is wearing a greatcoat.*]
SEPTIMUS Thank you, Jellaby. I was expecting to be locked out. What time is it?
JELLABY Half past five.
SEPTIMUS That is what I have. Well!—what a bracing experience!
    [*He produces two pistols from inside his coat and places them on the table.*]
The dawn, you know. Unexpectedly lively. Fishes, birds, frogs . . . rabbits . . . [*he produces a dead rabbit from inside his coat.*] and very beautiful. If only it did not occur so early in the day. I have brought Lady Thomasina a rabbit. Will you take it?
JELLABY It's dead.

---

3. Like a mad dog, whose bite transmits madness (rabies).

SEPTIMUS   Yes. Lady Thomasina loves a rabbit pie.

[JELLABY *takes the rabbit without enthusiasm. There is a little blood on it.*]

JELLABY   You were missed, Mr Hodge.

SEPTIMUS   I decided to sleep last night in the boat-house. Did I see a carriage leaving the Park?

JELLABY   Captain Brice's carriage, with Mr and Mrs Chater also.

SEPTIMUS   Gone?!

JELLABY   Yes, sir. And Lord Byron's horse was brought round at four o'clock.

SEPTIMUS   Lord Byron too!

JELLABY   Yes, sir. The house has been up and hopping.

SEPTIMUS   But I have his rabbit pistols! What am I to do with his rabbit pistols?

JELLABY   You were looked for in your room.

SEPTIMUS   By whom?

JELLABY   By her ladyship.

SEPTIMUS   In my room?

JELLABY   I will tell her ladyship you are returned.

[*He starts to leave.*]

SEPTIMUS   Jellaby! Did Lord Byron leave a book for me?

JELLABY   A book?

SEPTIMUS   He had the loan of a book from me.

JELLABY   His lordship left nothing in his room, sir, not a coin.[4]

SEPTIMUS   Oh. Well, I'm sure he would have left a coin if he'd had one. Jellaby—here is a half-guinea for you.

JELLABY   Thank you very much, sir.

SEPTIMUS   What has occurred?

JELLABY   The servants are told nothing, sir.

SEPTIMUS   Come, come, does a half-guinea buy nothing any more?

JELLABY [*Sighs.*]   Her ladyship encountered Mrs Chater during the night.

SEPTIMUS   Where?

JELLABY   On the threshold of Lord Byron's room.

SEPTIMUS   Ah. Which one was leaving and which entering?

JELLABY   Mrs Chater was leaving Lord Byron's room.

SEPTIMUS   And where was Mr Chater?

JELLABY   Mr Chater and Captain Brice were drinking cherry brandy. They had the footman to keep the fire up until three o'clock. There was a loud altercation upstairs, and—

[LADY CROOM *enters the room.*]

LADY CROOM   Well, Mr Hodge.

SEPTIMUS   My lady.

LADY CROOM   All this to shoot a hare?

SEPTIMUS   A rabbit. [*She gives him one of her looks.*] No, indeed, a hare, though very rabbit-like—

[JELLABY *is about to leave.*]

LADY CROOM   My infusion.[5]

JELLABY   Yes, my lady.

---

4. Guests staying in country houses were expected   5. Tea.
to leave tips for the servants.

[*He leaves.* LADY CROOM *is carrying two letters. We have not seen them before. Each has an envelope which has been opened. She flings them on the table.*]

LADY CROOM How dare you!

SEPTIMUS I cannot be called to account for what was written in private and read without regard to propriety.

LADY CROOM Addressed to me!

SEPTIMUS Left in my room, in the event of my death—

LADY CROOM Pah!—what earthly use is a love letter from beyond the grave?

SEPTIMUS As much, surely, as from this side of it. The second letter, however, was not addressed to your ladyship.

LADY CROOM I have a mother's right to open a letter addressed by you to my daughter, whether in the event of your life, your death, or your imbecility. What do you mean by writing to her of rice pudding when she has just suffered the shock of violent death in our midst?

SEPTIMUS Whose death?

LADY CROOM Yours, you wretch!

SEPTIMUS Yes, I see.

LADY CROOM I do not know which is the madder of your ravings. One envelope full of rice pudding, the other of the most insolent familiarities regarding several parts of my body, but have no doubt which is the more intolerable to me.

SEPTIMUS Which?

LADY CROOM Oh, aren't we saucy when our bags are packed! Your friend has gone before you, and I have despatched the harlot Chater and her husband—and also my brother for bringing them here. Such is the sentence, you see, for choosing unwisely in your acquaintance. Banishment. Lord Byron is a rake and a hypocrite, and the sooner he sails for the Levant[6] the sooner he will find society congenial to his character.

SEPTIMUS It has been a night of reckoning.

LADY CROOM Indeed, I wish it had passed uneventfully with you and Mr Chater shooting each other with the decorum due to a civilized house. You have no secrets left, Mr Hodge. They spilled out between shrieks and oaths and tears. It is fortunate that a lifetime's devotion to the sporting gun has halved my husband's hearing to the ear he sleeps on.

SEPTIMUS I'm afraid I have no knowledge of what has occurred.

LADY CROOM Your trollop[7] was discovered in Lord Byron's room.

SEPTIMUS Ah. Discovered by Mr Chater?

LADY CROOM Who else?

SEPTIMUS I am very sorry, madam, for having used your kindness to bring my unworthy friend to your notice. He will have to give an account of himself to me, you may be sure.

[*Before* LADY CROOM *can respond to this threat,* JELLABY *enters the room with her 'infusion'. This is quite an elaborate affair: a pewter tray on small feet on which there is a kettle suspended over a spirit lamp. There is a cup and saucer and the silver 'basket' containing the dry leaves for the tea.* JELLABY *places the tray on the table and is about to offer further assistance with it.*]

6. Eastern part of the Mediterranean. "Rake": sexually promiscuous man.   7. Loose woman (Mrs. Chater).

LADY CROOM   I will do it.

JELLABY   Yes, my lady. [To SEPTIMUS.] Lord Byron left a letter for you with the valet,[8] sir.

SEPTIMUS   Thank you.

[SEPTIMUS *takes the letter off the tray.* JELLABY *prepares to leave.* LADY CROOM *eyes the letter.*]

LADY CROOM   When did he do so?

JELLABY   As he was leaving, your ladyship.

[JELLABY *leaves.* SEPTIMUS *puts the letter into his pocket.*]

SEPTIMUS   Allow me.

[*Since she does not object, he pours a cup of tea for her. She accepts it.*]

LADY CROOM   I do not know if it is proper for you to receive a letter written in my house from someone not welcome in it.

SEPTIMUS   Very improper, I agree. Lord Byron's want of delicacy is a grief to his friends, among whom I no longer count myself. I will not read his letter until I have followed him through the gates.

[*She considers that for a moment.*]

LADY CROOM   That may excuse the reading but not the writing.

SEPTIMUS   Your ladyship should have lived in the Athens of Pericles![9] The philosophers would have fought the sculptors for your idle hour!

LADY CROOM [*Protesting.*]   Oh, really! . . . [*Protesting less.*] Oh really . . .

[SEPTIMUS *has taken Byron's letter from his pocket and is now setting fire to a corner of it using the little flame from the spirit lamp.*]

Oh . . . really . . .

[*The paper blazes in* SEPTIMUS*'s hand and he drops it and lets it burn out on the metal tray.*]

SEPTIMUS   Now there's a thing—a letter from Lord Byron never to be read by a living soul. I will take my leave, madam, at the time of your desiring it.

LADY CROOM   To the Indies?[1]

SEPTIMUS   The Indies! Why?

LADY CROOM   To follow the Chater, of course. She did not tell you?

SEPTIMUS   She did not exchange half-a-dozen words with me.

LADY CROOM   I expect she did not like to waste the time. The Chater sails with Captain Brice.

SEPTIMUS   Ah. As a member of the crew?

LADY CROOM   No, as wife to Mr Chater, plant-gatherer to my brother's expedition.

SEPTIMUS   I knew he was no poet. I did not know it was botany under the false colours.

LADY CROOM   He is no more a botanist. My brother paid fifty pounds to have him published, and he will pay a hundred and fifty to have Mr Chater picking flowers in the Indies for a year while the wife plays mistress of the Captain's quarters. Captain Brice has fixed his passion on Mrs Chater, and to take her on voyage he has not scrupled to deceive the Admiralty, the Linnean Society and Sir Joseph Banks, botanist to His Majesty at Kew.[2]

SEPTIMUS   Her passion is not as fixed as his.

---

8. Manservant.
9. Athenian military commander, statesman, and patron of the arts (ca. 495–429 B.C.E.).
1. West Indies.

2. See p. 2761, n. 7. "Admiralty": headquarters of the British navy. "Linnean Society": Britain's leading botanical association. Sir Joseph Banks (1743–1820), naturalist and patron of the sciences.

LADY CROOM   It is a defect of God's humour that he directs our hearts everywhere but to those who have a right to them.
SEPTIMUS   Indeed, madam. [*Pause.*] But is Mr Chater deceived?
LADY CROOM   He insists on it, and finds the proof of his wife's virtue in his
eagerness to defend it. Captain Brice is *not* deceived but cannot help himself. He would die for her.
SEPTIMUS   I think, my lady, he would have Mr Chater die for her.
LADY CROOM   Indeed, I never knew a woman worth the duel, or the other way
about. Your letter to me goes very ill with your conduct to Mrs Chater, Mr
Hodge. I have had experience of being betrayed before the ink is dry, but
to be betrayed before the pen is even dipped, and with the village notice-
board, what am I to think of such a performance?
SEPTIMUS   My lady, I was alone with my thoughts in the gazebo, when Mrs
Chater ran me to ground, and I being in such a passion, in an agony of
unrelieved desire—
LADY CROOM   Oh . . . !
SEPTIMUS   —I thought in my madness that the Chater with her skirts over
her head would give me the momentary illusion of the happiness to which
I dared not put a face.
   [*Pause.*]
LADY CROOM   I do not know when I have received a more unusual compli-
ment, Mr Hodge. I hope I am more than a match for Mrs Chater with her
head in a bucket. Does she wear drawers?
SEPTIMUS   She does.
LADY CROOM   Yes, I have heard that drawers are being worn now. It is unnat-
ural for women to be got up like jockeys. I cannot approve.
   [*She turns with a whirl of skirts and moves to leave.*]
I know nothing of Pericles or the Athenian philosophers. I can spare them
an hour, in my sitting room when I have bathed. Seven o'clock. Bring a
book.
   [*She goes out.* SEPTIMUS *picks up the two letters, the ones he wrote, and
   starts to burn them in the flame of the spirit lamp.*]

SCENE SEVEN

VALENTINE *and* CHLOË *are at the table.* GUS *is in the room.*
CHLOË *is reading from two Saturday newspapers. She is wearing workaday
period clothes, a Regency dress,[3] no hat.*
VALENTINE *is pecking at a portable computer. He is wearing unkempt Regency
clothes, too.*
*The clothes have evidently come from a large wicker laundry hamper, from
which* GUS *is producing more clothes to try on himself. He finds a Regency coat
and starts putting it on.*
*The objects on the table now include two geometrical solids, pyramid and cone,
about twenty inches high, of the type used in a drawing lesson; and a pot of dwarf
dahlias (which do not look like modern dahlias).*

CHLOË   'Even in Arcadia—Sex, Literature and Death at Sidley Park'. Picture
of Byron.

---

3. Fashionable in the "Regency" period, 1811–20, when George, Prince of Wales, was regent, ruling
England after his father, George III, had been judged insane.

VALENTINE   Not of Bernard?

CHLOË   'Byron Fought Fatal Duel, Says Don' . . . Valentine, do you think I'm the first person to think of this?

VALENTINE   No.

CHLOË   I haven't said yet. The future is all programmed like a computer—that's a proper theory, isn't it?

VALENTINE   The deterministic[4] universe, yes.

CHLOË   Right. Because everything including us is just a lot of atoms bouncing off each other like billiard balls.

VALENTINE   Yes. There was someone, forget his name, 1820s, who pointed out that from Newton's laws you could predict everything to come—I mean, you'd need a computer as big as the universe but the formula would exist.

CHLOË   But it doesn't work, does it?

VALENTINE   No. It turns out the maths is different.

CHLOË   No, it's all because of sex.

VALENTINE   Really?

CHLOË   That's what I think. The universe is deterministic all right, just like Newton said, I mean it's trying to be, but the only thing going wrong is people fancying people who aren't supposed to be in that part of the plan.

VALENTINE   Ah. The attraction that Newton left out. All the way back to the apple in the garden.[5] Yes. [Pause.] Yes, I think you're the first person to think of this.

[HANNAH enters, carrying a tabloid paper, and a mug of tea.]

HANNAH   Have you seen this? 'Bonking[6] Byron Shot Poet'.

CHLOË [Pleased.]   Let's see.

[HANNAH gives her the paper, smiles at GUS.]

VALENTINE   He's done awfully well, hasn't he? How did they all know?

HANNAH   Don't be ridiculous. [To CHLOË] Your father wants it back.

CHLOË   All right.

HANNAH   What a fool.

CHLOË   Jealous. I think it's brilliant. [She gets up to go. To GUS.] Yes, that's perfect, but not with trainers. Come on, I'll lend you a pair of flatties,[7] they'll look period on you—

HANNAH   Hello, Gus. You all look so romantic.

[GUS following CHLOË out, hesitates, smiles at her.]

CHLOË [Pointedly.]   Are you coming?

[She holds the door for GUS and follows him out, leaving a sense of her disapproval behind her.]

HANNAH   The important thing is not to give two monkeys for what young people think about you.

[She goes to look at the other newspapers.]

VALENTINE [Anxiously.]   You don't think she's getting a thing about[8] Bernard, do you?

HANNAH   I wouldn't worry about Chloë, she's old enough to vote on her back. 'Byron Fought Fatal Duel, Says Don'. Or rather—[Sceptically.] 'Says Don!'

VALENTINE   It may all prove to be true.

HANNAH   It can't prove to be true, it can only not prove to be false yet.

4. Predetermined (see Valentine and Chloë's discussion below).
5. Of Eden; cf. Genesis 3. Also the apple whose fall from the tree alerted Isaac Newton to the law of gravity.
6. Fucking (slang).
7. Flat-soled shoes. "Trainers": sneakers.
8. A crush on.

VALENTINE [*Pleased.*] Just like science.

HANNAH If Bernard can stay ahead of getting the rug pulled till he's dead, he'll be a success.

VALENTINE Just like science . . . The ultimate fear is of posterity . . .

HANNAH Personally I don't think it'll take that long.

VALENTINE . . . and then there's the afterlife. An afterlife would be a mixed blessing. 'Ah—Bernard Nightingale, I don't believe you know Lord Byron.' It must be heaven up there.

HANNAH You can't believe in an afterlife, Valentine.

VALENTINE Oh, you're going to disappoint me at last.

HANNAH Am I? Why?

VALENTINE Science and religion.

HANNAH No, no, been there, done that, boring.

VALENTINE Oh, Hannah. Fiancée. Have pity. Can't we have a trial marriage and I'll call it off in the morning?

HANNAH [*Amused.*] I don't know when I've received a more unusual proposal.

VALENTINE [*Interested.*] Have you had many?

HANNAH That would be telling.

VALENTINE Well, why not? Your classical reserve is only a mannerism; and neurotic.

HANNAH Do you want the room?

VALENTINE You get nothing if you give nothing.

HANNAH I ask nothing.

VALENTINE No, stay.

[VALENTINE *resumes work at his computer.* HANNAH *establishes herself among her references at 'her' end of the table. She has a stack of pocket-sized volumes,* Lady Croom's 'garden books'.]

HANNAH What are you doing? Valentine?

VALENTINE The set of points on a complex plane[9] made by—

HANNAH Is it the grouse?

VALENTINE Oh, the grouse. The damned grouse.

HANNAH You mustn't give up.

VALENTINE Why? Didn't you agree with Bernard?

HANNAH Oh, that. It's *all* trivial—your grouse, my hermit, Bernard's Byron. Comparing what we're looking for misses the point. It's wanting to know that makes us matter. Otherwise we're going out the way we came in. That's why you can't believe in the afterlife, Valentine. Believe in the after, by all means, but not the life. Believe in God, the soul, the spirit, the infinite, believe in angels if you like, but not in the great celestial get-together for an exchange of views. If the answers are in the back of the book I can wait, but what a drag. Better to struggle on knowing that failure is final. [*She looks over* VALENTINE's *shoulder at the computer screen. Reacting.*] Oh!, but . . . how beautiful!

VALENTINE The Coverly set.[1]

HANNAH The Coverly set! My goodness, Valentine!

VALENTINE Lend me a finger.

[*He takes her finger and presses one of the computer keys several times.*]

---

9. The "complex numbers" of mathematics laid out in a two-dimensional plane.

1. Graphic patterns of changes in Sidley Park's grouse population.

See? In an ocean of ashes, islands of order. Patterns making themselves out of nothing.

I can't show you how deep it goes. Each picture is a detail of the previous one, blown up. And so on. For ever. Pretty nice, eh?

HANNAH Is it important?

VALENTINE Interesting. Publishable.

HANNAH Well done!

VALENTINE Not me. It's Thomasina's. I just pushed her equations through the computer a few million times further than she managed to do with her pencil.

[*From the old portfolio he takes Thomasina's lesson book and gives it to* HANNAH. *The piano starts to be heard.*]

You can have it back now.

HANNAH What does it mean?

VALENTINE Not what you'd like it to.

HANNAH Why not?

VALENTINE Well, for one thing, she'd be famous.

HANNAH No, she wouldn't. She was dead before she had time to be famous . . .

VALENTINE She died?

HANNAH . . . burned to death.

VALENTINE [*Realizing.*] Oh . . . the girl who died in the fire!

HANNAH The night before her seventeenth birthday. You can see where the dormer[2] doesn't match. That was her bedroom under the roof. There's a memorial in the Park.

VALENTINE [*Irritated.*] I know—it's my house.

[VALENTINE *turns his attention back to his computer.* HANNAH *goes back to her chair. She looks through the lesson book.*]

HANNAH Val, Septimus was her tutor—he and Thomasina would have—

VALENTINE You do yours.

[*Pause. Two researchers.*

LORD AUGUSTUS, *fifteen years old, wearing clothes of 1812, bursts in through the non–music room door. He is laughing. He dives under the table. He is chased into the room by* THOMASINA, *aged sixteen and furious. She spots* AUGUSTUS *immediately.*]

THOMASINA You swore! You crossed your heart!

[AUGUSTUS *scampers out from under the table and* THOMASINA *chases him around it.*]

AUGUSTUS I'll tell mama! I'll tell mama!

THOMASINA You beast!

[*She catches* AUGUSTUS *as* SEPTIMUS *enters from the other door, carrying a book, a decanter[3] and a glass, and his portfolio.*]

SEPTIMUS Hush! What is this? My lord! Order, order!

[THOMASINA *and* AUGUSTUS *separate.*]

I am obliged.[4]

---

2. Vertical window that projects from a sloping roof.
3. Glass bottle (with a stopper) from which wine is served.
4. Thank you.

[SEPTIMUS *goes to his place at the table. He pours himself a glass of wine.*]

AUGUSTUS   Well, good day to you, Mr Hodge!

[*He is smirking about something.*

THOMASINA *dutifully picks up a drawing book and settles down to draw the geometrical solids.*

SEPTIMUS *opens his portfolio.*]

SEPTIMUS   Will you join us this morning, Lord Augustus? We have our drawing lesson.

AUGUSTUS   I am a master of it at Eton, Mr Hodge, but we only draw naked women.

SEPTIMUS   You may work from memory.

THOMASINA   Disgusting!

SEPTIMUS   We will have silence now, if you please.

[*From the portfolio* SEPTIMUS *takes Thomasina's lesson book and tosses it to her; returning homework. She snatches it and opens it.*]

THOMASINA   No marks?! Did you not like my rabbit equation?

SEPTIMUS   I saw no resemblance to a rabbit.

THOMASINA   It eats its own progeny.[5]

SEPTIMUS   [*Pause.*]   I did not see that.

[*He extends his hand for the lesson book. She returns it to him.*]

THOMASINA   I have not room to extend it.

[SEPTIMUS *and* HANNAH *turn the pages doubled by time.* AUGUSTUS *indolently starts to draw the models.*]

HANNAH   Do you mean the world is saved after all?

VALENTINE   No, it's still doomed. But if this is how it started, perhaps it's how the next one will come.

HANNAH   From good English algebra?

SEPTIMUS   It will go to infinity or zero, or nonsense.

THOMASINA   No, if you set apart the minus roots they square back to sense.

[SEPTIMUS *turns the pages.*

THOMASINA *starts drawing the models.*

HANNAH *closes the lesson book and turns her attention to her stack of 'garden books'.*]

VALENTINE   Listen—you know your tea's getting cold.

HANNAH   I like it cold.

VALENTINE   [*Ignoring that.*]   I'm telling you something. Your tea gets cold by itself, it doesn't get hot by itself. Do you think that's odd?

HANNAH   No.

VALENTINE   Well, it is odd. Heat goes to cold. It's a one-way street. Your tea will end up at room temperature. What's happening to your tea is happening to everything everywhere. The sun and the stars. It'll take a while but we're all going to end up at room temperature. When your hermit set up shop nobody understood this. But let's say you're right, in 18-whatever nobody knew more about heat than this scribbling nutter[6] living in a hovel in Derbyshire.

5. See p. 2783. VALENTINE: "She's feeding the solution back into the equation."

6. Madman.

HANNAH   He was at Cambridge—a scientist.

VALENTINE   Say he was. I'm not arguing. And the girl was his pupil, she had a genius for her tutor.

HANNAH   Or the other way round.

VALENTINE   Anything you like. But not *this!* Whatever he thought he was doing to save the world with good English algebra it wasn't this!

HANNAH   Why? Because they didn't have calculators?

VALENTINE   No. Yes. Because there's an order things can't happen in. You can't open a door till there's a house.

HANNAH   I thought that's what genius was.

VALENTINE   Only for lunatics and poets.

[*Pause.*]

HANNAH   'I had a dream which was not all a dream.
The bright sun was extinguished, and the stars
Did wander darkling in the eternal space,
Rayless, and pathless, and the icy earth
Swung blind and blackening in the moonless air . . . '[7]

VALENTINE   Your own?

HANNAH   Byron.

[*Pause. Two researchers again.*]

THOMASINA   Septimus, do you think that I will marry Lord Byron?

AUGUSTUS   Who is he?

THOMASINA   He is the author of 'Childe Harold's Pilgrimage', the most poetical and pathetic and bravest hero of any book I ever read before, and the most modern and the handsomest, for Harold is Lord Byron himself to those who know him, like myself and Septimus. Well, Septimus?

SEPTIMUS   [*Absorbed.*]   No.

[*Then he puts her lesson book away into the portfolio and picks up his own book to read.*]

THOMASINA   Why not?

SEPTIMUS   For one thing, he is not aware of your existence.

THOMASINA   We exchanged many significant glances when he was at Sidley Park. I do wonder that he has been home almost a year from his adventures and has not written to me once.

SEPTIMUS   It is indeed improbable, my lady.

AUGUSTUS   Lord Byron?!—he claimed my hare, although my shot was the earlier! He said I missed by a hare's breadth. His conversation was very facetious. But I think Lord Byron will not marry you, Thom, for he was only lame and not blind.

SEPTIMUS   Peace! Peace until a quarter to twelve. It is intolerable for a tutor to have his thoughts interrupted by his pupils.

AUGUSTUS   You are not *my* tutor, sir. I am visiting your lesson by my free will.

SEPTIMUS   If you are so determined, my lord.

[THOMASINA *laughs at that, the joke is for her.* AUGUSTUS, *not included, becomes angry.*]

AUGUSTUS   Your peace is nothing to me, sir. You do not rule over me.

THOMASINA   [*Admonishing.*]   Augustus!

SEPTIMUS   I do not rule here, my lord. I inspire by reverence for learning and the exaltation of knowledge whereby man may approach God. There will be a shilling[8] for the best cone and pyramid drawn in silence by a quarter to twelve *at the earliest.*

AUGUSTUS   You will not buy my silence for a shilling, sir. What I know to tell is worth much more than that.

[*And throwing down his drawing book and pencil, he leaves the room on his dignity, closing the door sharply. Pause.* SEPTIMUS *looks enquiringly at* THOMASINA.]

THOMASINA   I told him you kissed me. But he will not tell.

SEPTIMUS   When did I kiss you?

THOMASINA   What! Yesterday!

SEPTIMUS   Where?

THOMASINA   On the lips!

SEPTIMUS   In which country?

THOMASINA   In the hermitage, Septimus!

SEPTIMUS   On the lips in the hermitage! That? That was not a shilling kiss! I would not give sixpence to have it back. I had almost forgot it already.

THOMASINA   Oh, cruel! Have you forgotten our compact?

SEPTIMUS   God save me! Our compact?

THOMASINA   To teach me to waltz! Sealed with a kiss, and a second kiss due when I can dance like mama!

SEPTIMUS   Ah yes. Indeed. We were all waltzing like mice in London.

THOMASINA   I must waltz, Septimus! I will be despised if I do not waltz! It is the most fashionable and gayest and boldest invention conceivable—started in Germany!

SEPTIMUS   Let them have the waltz, they cannot have the calculus.

THOMASINA   Mama has brought from town a whole book of waltzes for the Broadwood,[9] to play with Count Zelinsky.

SEPTIMUS   I need not be told what I cannot but suffer. Count Zelinsky banging on the Broadwood without relief has me reading in waltz time.

THOMASINA   Oh, stuff! What is your book?

SEPTIMUS   A prize essay of the Scientific Academy in Paris. The author deserves your indulgence, my lady, for you are his prophet.

THOMASINA   I? What does he write about? The waltz?

SEPTIMUS   Yes. He demonstrates the equation of the propagation of heat in a solid body.[1] But in doing so he has discovered heresy—a natural contradiction of Sir Isaac Newton.

THOMASINA   Oh!—he contradicts determinism?

SEPTIMUS   No! . . . Well, perhaps. He shows that the atoms do not go according to Newton.

[*Her interest has switched in the mercurial way characteristic of her— she has crossed to take the book.*]

THOMASINA   Let me see—oh! In French?

SEPTIMUS   Yes. Paris is the capital of France.

THOMASINA   Show me where to read.

[*He takes the book back from her and finds the page for her. Meanwhile,*

8. British coin (before decimalization) equal to twelve old pennies/pence, or one-twentieth of a pound.
9. Brand of piano.
1. "Paris was the center of such studies: in 1807 Jean-Baptiste Fourier had written about heat flow.

The French scientist most relevant is Sadi Carnot, founder of thermodynamics; but he was only sixteen in 1812. The essay is about the passing of heat from one body to another, which is why Septimus can humourously agree that it is 'about' the 'waltz'" (Jim Hunter, *Tom Stoppard*, 2000).

the piano music from the next room has doubled its notes and its emotion.]

THOMASINA   Four-handed now! Mama is in love with the Count.

SEPTIMUS   He is a Count in Poland. In Derbyshire he is a piano tuner.

[*She has taken the book and is already immersed in it. The piano music becomes rapidly more passionate, and then breaks off suddenly in mid-phrase. There is an expressive silence next door which makes* SEPTIMUS *raise his eyes. It does not register with* THOMASINA. *The silence allows us to hear the distant regular thump of the steam engine which is to be a topic. A few moments later* LADY CROOM *enters from the music room, seeming surprised and slightly flustered to find the schoolroom occupied. She collects herself, closing the door behind her. And remains watching, aimless and discreet, as though not wanting to interrupt the lesson.* SEP-TIMUS *has stood, and she nods him back into his chair.*

CHLOË, *in Regency dress, enters from the door opposite the music room. She takes in* VALENTINE *and* HANNAH *but crosses without pausing to the music room door.*]

CHLOË   Oh!—where's Gus?

VALENTINE   Dunno.

[CHLOË *goes into the music room.*]

LADY CROOM [*Annoyed*]   Oh!—Mr Noakes's engine!

[*She goes to the garden door and steps outside.*

CHLOË *re-enters.*]

CHLOË   Damn.

LADY CROOM [*Calls out.*]   Mr Noakes!

VALENTINE   He was there not long ago . . .

LADY CROOM   Halloo!

CHLOË   Well, he has to be in the photograph—is he dressed?

HANNAH   Is Bernard back?

CHLOË   No—he's late!

[*The piano is heard again, under the noise of the steam engine.* LADY CROOM *steps back into the room.*

CHLOË *steps outside the garden door. Shouts.*] Gus!

LADY CROOM   I wonder you can teach against such a disturbance and I am sorry for it, Mr Hodge.

[CHLOË *comes back inside.*]

VALENTINE [*Getting up.*]   Stop ordering everybody about.

LADY CROOM   It is an unendurable noise.

VALENTINE   The photographer will wait.

[*But, grumbling, he follows* CHLOË *out of the door she came in by, and closes the door behind them.* HANNAH *remains absorbed. In the silence, the rhythmic thump can be heard again.*]

LADY CROOM   The ceaseless dull overbearing monotony of it! It will drive me distracted. I may have to return to town to escape it.

SEPTIMUS   Your ladyship could remain in the country and let Count Zelinsky return to town where you would not hear him.

LADY CROOM   I mean Mr Noakes's engine! [*Semi-aside to* SEPTIMUS.] *Would you sulk? I will not have my daughter study sulking.*

THOMASINA [*Not listening.*] What, mama?

[THOMASINA *remains lost in her book.* LADY CROOM *returns to close the garden door and the noise of the steam engine subsides.*

HANNAH *closes one of the 'garden books', and opens the next. She is making occasional notes.*

The piano ceases.]

LADY CROOM [*To* THOMASINA.] What are we learning today? [*Pause.*] Well, not manners.

SEPTIMUS We are drawing today.

[LADY CROOM *negligently examines what* THOMASINA *had started to draw.*]

LADY CROOM Geometry. I approve of geometry.

SEPTIMUS Your ladyship's approval is my constant object.

LADY CROOM Well, do not despair of it. [*Returning to the window impatiently.*] Where is 'Culpability' Noakes?[2] [*She looks out and is annoyed.*] Oh!—he has gone for his hat so that he may remove it.

[*She returns to the table and touches the bowl of dahlias.*

HANNAH *sits back in her chair, caught by what she is reading.*]

For the widow's dowry of dahlias I can almost forgive my brother's marriage. We must be thankful the monkey bit the husband. If it had bit the wife the monkey would be dead and we would not be first in the kingdom to show a dahlia. [HANNAH, *still reading the garden book, stands up.*] I sent one potted to Chatsworth.[3] The Duchess was most satisfactorily put out[4] by it when I called at Devonshire House. Your friend was there lording it as a poet.

[HANNAH *leaves through the door, following* VALENTINE *and* CHLOË.

Meanwhile, THOMASINA *thumps the book down on the table.*]

THOMASINA Well! Just as I said! Newton's machine which would knock our atoms from cradle to grave by the laws of motion is incomplete! Determinism leaves the road at every corner, as I knew all along, and the cause is very likely hidden in this gentleman's observation.

LADY CROOM Of what?

THOMASINA The action of bodies in heat.

LADY CROOM Is this geometry?

THOMASINA This? No, I despise geometry!

[*Touching the dahlias she adds, almost to herself.*] The Chater would overthrow the Newtonian system in a weekend.

SEPTIMUS Geometry, Hobbes assures us in the *Leviathan*,[5] is the only science God has been pleased to bestow on mankind.

LADY CROOM And what does he mean by it?

SEPTIMUS Mr Hobbes or God?

LADY CROOM I am sure I do not know what either means by it.

2. Noakes is called "culpable" (deserving of blame) for ruining the landscape designed by the "capable" Brown (so called because of his habit of saying a landscape had "capabilities," or potential). See p. 2771, n. 6.
3. Derbyshire "stately home" of the duke and duchess of Devonshire, whose London residence is Devonshire House.
4. Jealously annoyed.
5. Philosophic treatise, published in 1651, by Thomas Hobbes (1588–1679).

THOMASINA   Oh, pooh to Hobbes! Mountains are not pyramids and trees are not cones. God must love gunnery and architecture if Euclid[6] is his only geometry. There is another geometry which I am engaged in discovering by trial and error, am I not, Septimus?

SEPTIMUS   Trial and error perfectly describes your enthusiasm, my lady.

LADY CROOM   How old are you today?

THOMASINA   Sixteen years and eleven months, mama, and three weeks.

LADY CROOM   Sixteen years and eleven months. We must have you married before you are educated beyond eligibility.[7]

THOMASINA   I am going to marry Lord Byron.

LADY CROOM   Are you? He did not have the manners to mention it.

THOMASINA   You have spoken to him?!

LADY CROOM   Certainly not.

THOMASINA   Where did you see him?

LADY CROOM   [With some bitterness.]   Everywhere.

THOMASINA   Did you, Septimus?

SEPTIMUS   At the Royal Academy where I had the honour to accompany your mother and Count Zelinsky.

THOMASINA   What was Lord Byron doing?

LADY CROOM   Posing.

SEPTIMUS   [Tactfully.]   He was being sketched during his visit . . . by the Professor of Painting . . . Mr Fuseli.[8]

LADY CROOM   There was more posing at the pictures than in them. His companion likewise reversed the custom of the Academy that the ladies viewing wear more than the ladies viewed—well, enough! Let him be hanged there for a Lamb.[9] I have enough with Mr Noakes, who is to a garden what a bull is to a china shop.

[This as NOAKES enters.]

THOMASINA   The Emperor of Irregularity!

[She settles down to drawing the diagram which is to be the third item in the surviving portfolio.]

LADY CROOM   Mr Noakes!

NOAKES   Your ladyship—

LADY CROOM   What have you done to me!

NOAKES   Everything is satisfactory, I assure you. A little behind, to be sure, but my dam will be repaired within the month—

LADY CROOM   [Banging the table.]   Hush!

[In the silence, the steam engine thumps in the distance.]

Can you hear, Mr Noakes?

NOAKES   [Pleased and proud.]   The Improved Newcomen steam pump[1]—the only one in England!

LADY CROOM   That is what I object to. If everybody had his own I would bear my portion of the agony without complaint. But to have been singled out by the only Improved Newcomen steam pump in England, this is hard, sir, this is not to be borne.

NOAKES   Your lady—

6. Greek mathematician (flourished ca. 300 B.C.E.), famous for his *Elements*, a presentation of the geometry and other mathematics known in his day.
7. Suitability (as a partner in marriage).

8. See p. 2795, n. 4.
9. Cf. the old proverb "One might as well be hung for a sheep as a lamb."
1. Thomas Newcomen had produced his first, very inefficient, steam pump in 1712.

LADY CROOM   And for what? My lake is drained to a ditch for no purpose I can understand, unless it be that snipe and curlew² have deserted three counties so that they may be shot in our swamp. What you painted as forest is a mean plantation, your greenery is mud, your waterfall is wet mud, and your mount is an opencast mine for the mud that was lacking in the dell.³ [*Pointing through the window.*] What is that cowshed?

NOAKES   The hermitage, my lady?

LADY CROOM   It is a cowshed.

NOAKES   Madam, it is, I assure you, a very habitable cottage, properly founded and drained, two rooms and a closet under a slate roof and a stone chimney—

LADY CROOM   And who is to live in it?

NOAKES   Why, the hermit.

LADY CROOM   Where is he?

NOAKES   Madam?

LADY CROOM   You surely do not supply a hermitage without a hermit?

NOAKES   Indeed, madam—

LADY CROOM   Come, come, Mr Noakes. If I am promised a fountain I expect it to come with water. What hermits do you have?

NOAKES   I have no hermits, my lady.

LADY CROOM   Not one? I am speechless.

NOAKES   I am sure a hermit can be found. One could advertise.

LADY CROOM   Advertise?

NOAKES   In the newspapers.

LADY CROOM   But surely a hermit who takes a newspaper is not a hermit in whom one can have complete confidence.

NOAKES   I do not know what to suggest, my lady.

SEPTIMUS   Is there room for a piano?

NOAKES   [*Baffled.*]   A piano?

LADY CROOM   We are intruding here—this will not do, Mr Hodge. Evidently, nothing is being learned. [*To* NOAKES.] Come along, sir!

THOMASINA   Mr Noakes—bad news from Paris!

NOAKES   Is it the Emperor Napoleon?

THOMASINA   No. [*She tears the page off her drawing block, with her 'diagram' on it.*] It concerns your heat engine. Improve it as you will, you can never get out of it what you put in. It repays eleven pence in the shilling at most. The penny is for this author's thoughts.

[*She gives the diagram to* SEPTIMUS *who looks at it.*]

NOAKES   [*Baffled again.*]   Thank you, my lady.

[NOAKES *goes out into the garden.*]

LADY CROOM   [To SEPTIMUS.]   Do you understand her?

SEPTIMUS   No.

LADY CROOM   Then this business is over. I was married at seventeen. *Ce soir il faut qu'on parle français, je te demande,*⁴ Thomasina, as a courtesy to the Count. Wear your green velvet, please, I will send Briggs to do your hair. Sixteen and eleven months . . . !

[*She follows* NOAKES *out of view.*]

THOMASINA   Lord Byron was with a lady?

2. Two species of game bird.
3. Small valley.

4. This evening I must ask you to speak French (French).

SEPTIMUS   Yes.

THOMASINA   Huh!

> [*Now* SEPTIMUS *retrieves his book from* THOMASINA. *He turns the pages, and also continues to study Thomasina's diagram. He strokes the tortoise absently as he reads.* THOMASINA *takes up pencil and paper and starts to draw* SEPTIMUS *with Plautus.*]

SEPTIMUS   Why does it mean Mr Noakes's engine pays eleven pence in the shilling? Where does he say it?

THOMASINA   Nowhere. I noticed it by the way. I cannot remember now.

SEPTIMUS   Nor is he interested by determinism—

THOMASINA   Oh . . . yes. Newton's equations go forwards and backwards, they do not care which way. But the heat equation cares very much, it goes only one way. That is the reason Mr Noakes's engine cannot give the power to drive Mr Noakes's engine.

SEPTIMUS   Everybody knows that.

THOMASINA   Yes, Septimus, they know it about engines!

SEPTIMUS   [*Pause. He looks at his watch.*]   A quarter to twelve. For your essay this week, explicate[5] your diagram.

THOMASINA   I cannot, I do not know the mathematics.

SEPTIMUS   Without mathematics, then.

> [THOMASINA *has continued to draw. She tears the top page from her drawing pad and gives it to* SEPTIMUS.]

THOMASINA   There. I have made a drawing of you and Plautus.

SEPTIMUS   [*Looking at it.*]   Excellent likeness. Not so good of me.

> [THOMASINA *laughs, and leaves the room.*
>
> AUGUSTUS *appears at the garden door. His manner cautious and diffident.*[6] SEPTIMUS *does not notice him for a moment.*
>
> SEPTIMUS *gathers his papers together.*]

AUGUSTUS   Sir . . .

SEPTIMUS   My lord . . . ?

AUGUSTUS   I gave you offence, sir, and I am sorry for it.

SEPTIMUS   I took none, my lord, but you are kind to mention it.

AUGUSTUS   I would like to ask you a question, Mr Hodge. [*Pause.*] You have an elder brother, I dare say, being a Septimus?[7]

SEPTIMUS   Yes, my lord. He lives in London. He is the editor of a newspaper, the *Piccadilly Recreation.* [*Pause.*] Was that your question?

> [AUGUSTUS, *evidently embarrassed about something, picks up the drawing of Septimus.*]

AUGUSTUS   No. Oh . . . it is you? . . . I would like to keep it. [SEPTIMUS *inclines his head in assent.*] There are things a fellow cannot ask his friends. Carnal things. My sister has told me . . . my sister believes such things as I cannot, I assure you, bring myself to repeat.

SEPTIMUS   You must not repeat them, then. The walk between here and dinner will suffice to put us straight, if we stroll by the garden. It is an easy business. And then I must rely on you to correct your sister's state of ignorance.

> [*A commotion is heard outside*—BERNARD'S *loud voice in a sort of agony.*]

5. Explain.
6. Shy.

7. Latin for "seventh."

BERNARD [*outside the door.*]   Oh no—no—no—oh, bloody hell!—
AUGUSTUS   Thank you, Mr Hodge, I will.
  [*Taking the drawing with him,* AUGUSTUS *allows himself to be shown out through the garden door, and* SEPTIMUS *follows him.*

  BERNARD *enters the room, through the door* HANNAH *left by.* VALENTINE *comes in with him, leaving the door open and they are followed by* HANNAH *who is holding the 'garden book'.*]
BERNARD   Oh, no—no—
HANNAH   I'm sorry, Bernard.
BERNARD   Fucked by a dahlia! Do you think? Is it open and shut? Am I fucked? What does it really amount to? When all's said and done? Am I fucked? What do *you* think, Valentine? Tell me the truth.
VALENTINE   You're fucked.
BERNARD   Oh God! Does it mean that?
HANNAH   Yes, Bernard, it does.
BERNARD   I'm not sure. Show me where it says. I want to see it. No—read it—no, wait . . .
  [BERNARD *sits at the table. He prepares to listen as though listening were an oriental art.*]
Right.
HANNAH [*Reading.*]   'October 1st, 1810. Today under the direction of Mr Noakes, a parterre[8] was dug on the south lawn and will be a handsome show next year, a consolation for the picturesque catastrophe of the second and third distances. The dahlia having propagated under glass with no ill effect from the sea voyage, is named by Captain Brice 'Charity' for his bride, though the honour properly belongs to the husband who exchanged beds with my dahlia, and an English summer for everlasting night in the Indies.'
  [*Pause.*]
BERNARD   Well, it's so round the houses, isn't it? Who's to say what it means?
HANNAH [*Patiently.*]   It means that Ezra Chater of the Sidley Park connection is the same Chater who described a dwarf dahlia in Martinique in 1810 and died there, of a monkey bite.
BERNARD [*Wildly.*]   Ezra wasn't a botanist! He was a poet!
HANNAH   He was not much of either, but he was both.
VALENTINE   It's not a disaster.
BERNARD   Of course it's a disaster! I was on 'The Breakfast Hour'![9]
VALENTINE   It doesn't mean Byron didn't fight a duel, it only means Chater wasn't killed in it.
BERNARD   Oh, pull yourself together!—do you think I'd have been on 'The Breakfast Hour' if Byron had *missed*!
HANNAH   Calm down, Bernard. Valentine's right.
BERNARD [*Grasping at straws.*]   Do you think so? You mean the *Piccadilly* reviews? Yes, two completely unknown Byron essays—*and* my discovery of the lines he added to 'English Bards'. That counts for something.
HANNAH [*Tactfully.*]   Very possible—persuasive, indeed.
BERNARD   Oh, bugger persuasive! I've proved Byron was here and as far as I'm concerned he wrote those lines as sure as he shot that hare. If only I

---

8. Level space in a garden occupied by an orna-   9. Popular British TV program.
mental arrangement of flower beds.

hadn't somehow . . . made it all about *killing Chater*. Why didn't you stop me?! It's bound to get out, you know—I mean this—this *gloss*[1] on my discovery—I mean how long do you think it'll be before some botanical pedant[2] blows the whistle on me?

HANNAH   The day after tomorrow. A letter in *The Times*.

BERNARD   You wouldn't.

HANNAH   It's a dirty job but somebody—

BERNARD   Darling. Sorry. Hannah—

HANNAH   —and, after all, it is my discovery.

BERNARD   Hannah.

HANNAH   Bernard.

BERNARD   Hannah.

HANNAH   Oh, shut up. It'll be very short, very dry, absolutely gloat-free. Would you rather it were one of your friends?

BERNARD   [*Fervently.*]   Oh God, no!

HANNAH   And then in *your* letter to *The Times*—

BERNARD   Mine?

HANNAH   Well, of course. Dignified congratulations to a colleague, in the language of scholars, I trust.

BERNARD   Oh, eat shit, you mean?

HANNAH   Think of it as a breakthrough in dahlia studies.

[CHLOË *hurries in from the garden.*]

CHLOË   Why aren't you coming?!—Bernard! And you're not dressed! How long have you been back?

[BERNARD *looks at her and then at* VALENTINE *and realizes for the first time that* VALENTINE *is unusually dressed.*]

BERNARD   Why are you wearing those clothes?

CHLOË   Do be quick!

[*She is already digging into the basket and producing odd garments for* BERNARD.]

Just put anything on. We're all being photographed. Except Hannah.

HANNAH   I'll come and watch.

[VALENTINE *and* CHLOË *help* BERNARD *into a decorative coat and fix a lace collar round his neck.*]

CHLOË [*To* HANNAH.]   Mummy says have you got the theodolite?

VALENTINE   What are you supposed to be, Chlo? Bo-Peep?

CHLOË   Jane Austen![3]

VALENTINE   Of course.

HANNAH [*To* CHLOË.]   Oh—it's in the hermitage! Sorry.

BERNARD   I thought it wasn't till this evening. What photograph?

CHLOË   The local paper, of course—they always come before we start. We want a good crowd of us—Gus looks gorgeous—

BERNARD [*Aghast.*]   The newspaper!

[*He grabs something like a bishop's mitre*[4] *from the basket and pulls it down completely over his face.*]

[*Muffled.*] I'm ready!

[*And he staggers out with* VALELNTINE *and* CHLOË, *followed by* HANNAH.

1. Explanatory comment.
2. Person excessively concerned with minor details.
3. English novelist (1775–1817). "Bo-Peep": Little Bo-Peep, subject of an eighteenth-century nursery rhyme.
4. Bishop's ceremonial headdress.

A light change to evening. The paper lanterns outside begin to glow. Piano music from the next room.

SEPTIMUS *enters with an oil lamp. He carries Thomasina's algebra primer, and also her essay on loose sheets. He settles down to read at the table. It is nearly dark outside, despite the lanterns.*

THOMASINA *enters, in a nightgown and barefoot, holding a candlestick. Her manner is secretive and excited.*]

SEPTIMUS   My lady! What is it?

THOMASINA   Septimus! Shush!

[*She closes the door quietly.*]

Now is our chance!

SEPTIMUS   For what, dear God?

[*She blows out the candle and puts the candlestick on the table.*]

THOMASINA   Do not act the innocent! Tomorrow I will be seventeen!

[*She kisses* SEPTIMUS *full on the mouth.*]

There!

SEPTIMUS   Dear Christ!

THOMASINA   Now you must show me, you are paid in advance.

SEPTIMUS [*Understanding.*]   Oh!

THOMASINA   The Count plays for us, it is God-given! I cannot be seventeen and not waltz.

SEPTIMUS   But your mother—

THOMASINA   While she swoons, we can dance. The house is all abed. I heard the Broadwood. Oh, Septimus, teach me now!

SEPTIMUS   Hush! I cannot now!

THOMASINA   Indeed you can, and I am come barefoot so mind my toes.

SEPTIMUS   I cannot because it is not a waltz.

THOMASINA   It is not?

SEPTIMUS   No, it is too quick for waltzing.

THOMASINA   Oh! Then we will wait for him to play slow.

SEPTIMUS   My lady—

THOMASINA   Mr Hodge!

[*She takes a chair next to him and looks at his work.*]

Are you reading my essay? Why do you work here so late?

SEPTIMUS   To save my candles.

THOMASINA   You have my old primer.

SEPTIMUS   It is mine again. You should not have written in it.

[*She takes it, looks at the open page.*]

THOMASINA   It was a joke.

SEPTIMUS   It will make me mad as you promised. Sit over there. You will have us in disgrace.

[THOMASINA *gets up and goes to the furthest chair.*]

THOMASINA   If mama comes I will tell her we only met to kiss, not to waltz.

SEPTIMUS   Silence or bed.

THOMASINA   Silence!

[SEPTIMUS *pours himself some more wine. He continues to read her essay.*

The music changes to party music from the marquee. And there are fireworks—small against the sky, distant flares of light like exploding meteors.

HANNAH *enters. She has dressed for the party. The difference is not, however, dramatic. She closes the door and crosses to leave by the garden door. But as she gets there,* VALENTINE *is entering. He has a glass of wine in his hand.*]

HANNAH   Oh . . .

[*But* VALENTINE *merely brushes past her, intent on something, and half-drunk.*]

VALENTINE [*To her.*]   Got it!

[*He goes straight to the table and roots about in what is now a considerable mess of papers, books and objects.* HANNAH *turns back, puzzled by his manner. He finds what he has been looking for—the 'diagram'.*

Meanwhile, SEPTIMUS, *reading Thomasina's essay, also studies the diagram.*

SEPTIMUS *and* VALENTINE *study the diagram doubled by time.*]

VALENTINE   It's heat.

HANNAH   Are you tight,[5] Val?

VALENTINE   It's a diagram of heat exchange.

SEPTIMUS   So, we are all doomed!

THOMASINA [*Cheerfully.*]   Yes.

VALENTINE   Like a steam engine, you see—

[HANNAH *fills Septimus's glass from the same decanter, and sips from it.*] She didn't have the maths, not remotely. She saw what things meant, way ahead, like seeing a picture.

SEPTIMUS   This is not science. This is story-telling.

THOMASINA   Is it a waltz now?

SEPTIMUS   No.

[*The music is still modern.*]

VALENTINE   Like a film.

HANNAH   What did she see?

VALENTINE   That you can't run the film backwards. Heat was the first thing which didn't work that way. Not like Newton. A film of a pendulum, or a ball falling through the air—backwards, it looks the same.

HANNAH   The ball would be going the wrong way.

VALENTINE   You'd have to know that. But with heat—friction—a ball breaking a window—

HANNAH   Yes.

VALENTINE   It won't work backwards.

HANNAH   Who thought it did?

VALENTINE   She saw why. You can put back the bits of glass but you can't collect up the heat of the smash. It's gone.

SEPTIMUS   So the Improved Newtonian Universe must cease and grow cold. Dear me.

VALENTINE   The heat goes into the mix.

[*He gestures to indicate the air in the room, in the universe.*]

THOMASINA   Yes, we must hurry if we are going to dance.

VALENTINE   And everything is mixing the same way, all the time, irreversibly . . .

SEPTIMUS   Oh, we have time, I think.

5. Drunk.

VALENTINE . . . till there's no time left. That's what time means.

SEPTIMUS When we have found all the mysteries and lost all the meaning, we will be alone, on an empty shore.

THOMASINA Then we will dance. Is this a waltz?

SEPTIMUS It will serve.

[*He stands up.*]

THOMASINA [*Jumping up.*] Goody!

[SEPTIMUS *takes her in his arms carefully and the waltz lesson, to the music from the marquee, begins.*

BERNARD *in unconvincing Regency dress, enters carrying a bottle.*]

BERNARD Don't mind me, I left my jacket . . .

[*He heads for the area of the wicker basket.*]

VALENTINE Are you leaving?

[BERNARD *is stripping off his period coat. He is wearing his own trousers, tucked into knee socks and his own shirt.*]

BERNARD Yes, I'm afraid so.

HANNAH What's up, Bernard?

BERNARD Nothing I can go into—

VALENTINE Should I go?

BERNARD No, *I'm* going!

[VALENTINE *and* HANNAH *watch* BERNARD *struggling into his jacket and adjusting his clothes.*

SEPTIMUS, *holding* THOMASINA, *kisses her on the mouth. The waltz lesson pauses. She looks at him. He kisses her again, in earnest. She puts her arms round him.*]

THOMASINA Septimus . . .

[SEPTIMUS *hushes her. They start to dance again, with the slight awkwardness of a lesson.*

CHLOË *bursts in from the garden.*]

CHLOË I'll kill her! I'll *kill* her!

BERNARD Oh dear.

VALENTINE What the hell is it, Chlo?

CHLOË [*Venomously.*] Mummy!

BERNARD [*To* VALENTINE.] Your mother caught us in that cottage.

CHLOË She snooped!

BERNARD I don't think so. She was rescuing a theodolite.

CHLOË I'll come with you, Bernard.

BERNARD No, you bloody won't.

CHLOË Don't you want me to?

BERNARD Of course not. What for? [*To* VALENTINE.] I'm sorry.

CHLOË [*In furious tears.*] What are you saying sorry to *him* for?

BERNARD Sorry to you too. Sorry one and all. Sorry, Hannah—sorry, Hermione—sorry, Byron—sorry, sorry, sorry, now can I go?

[CHLOË *stands stiffly, tearfully.*]

CHLOË Well . . .

[THOMASINA *and* SEPTIMUS *dance.*]

HANNAH What a bastard you are, Bernard.

[CHLOË *rounds on her.*]

CHLOË   And you mind your own business! What do you know about anything?
HANNAH   Nothing.
CHLOË [*To* BERNARD.]   It *was* worth it, though, wasn't it?
BERNARD   It was wonderful.
[CHLOË *goes out, through the garden door, towards the party.*]
HANNAH [*An echo.*]   Nothing.
VALENTINE   Well, you shit. I'd drive you but I'm a bit sloshed.
[VALENTINE *follows* CHLOË *out and can be heard outside calling* 'Chlo! Chlo!']
BERNARD   A scrape.
HANNAH   Oh . . . [*She gives up.*] Bernard!
BERNARD   I look forward to *The Genius of the Place.* I hope you find your hermit. I think out front is the safest.
[*He opens the door cautiously and looks out.*]
HANNAH   Actually, I've got a good idea who he was, but I can't prove it.
BERNARD [*With a carefree expansive gesture.*]   Publish!
[*He goes out closing the door.*]

SEPTIMUS *and* THOMASINA *are now waltzing freely. She is delighted with herself.*]
THOMASINA   Am I waltzing?
SEPTIMUS   Yes, my lady.
[*He gives her a final twirl, bringing them to the table where he bows to her. He lights her candlestick.*

HANNAH *goes to sit at the table, playing truant from the party. She pours herself more wine. The table contains the geometrical solids, the computer, decanter, glasses, tea mug, Hannah's research books, Septimus's books, the two portfolios, Thomasina's candlestick, the oil lamp, the dahlia, the Sunday papers . . .*
GUS *appears in the doorway. It takes a moment to realize that he is not Lord Augustus; perhaps not until* HANNAH *sees him.*]
SEPTIMUS   Take your essay, I have given it an alpha[6] in blind faith. Be careful with the flame.
THOMASINA   I will wait for you to come.
SEPTIMUS   I cannot.
THOMASINA   You may.
SEPTIMUS   I may not.
THOMASINA   You must.
SEPTIMUS   I will not.
[*She puts the candlestick and the essay on the table.*]
THOMASINA   Then I will not go. Once more, for my birthday.
[SEPTIMUS *and* THOMASINA *start to waltz together.*

GUS *comes forward, startling* HANNAH.]
HANNAH   Oh!—you made me jump.
[GUS *looks resplendent. He is carrying an old and somewhat tattered stiff-backed folio fastened with a tape tied in a bow. He comes to* HANNAH *and thrusts this present at her.*]

---

6. An A grade.

Oh . . .

[*She lays the folio down on the table and starts to open it. It consists only of two boards hinged, containing Thomasina's drawing.*]

'Septimus with Plautus'. [*To* GUS.] I was looking for that. Thank you.

[GUS *nods several times. Then, rather awkwardly, he bows to her. A Regency bow, an invitation to dance.*]

Oh, dear, I don't really . . .

[*After a moment's hesitation, she gets up and they hold each other, keeping a decorous distance between them, and start to dance, rather awkwardly.*

SEPTIMUS *and* THOMASINA *continue to dance, fluently, to the piano.*]

END

1993

LES MURRAY
b. 1938

Leslie Allan Murray was born at Nabiac on the north coast of New South Wales, Australia, and grew up on a dairy farm at nearby Bunyah. He was educated at Taree High School and the University of Sydney, where he studied modern languages. After military service with the Royal Australian Naval Reserve, he worked as a translator in the Australian National University, Canberra, and as an officer in the prime minister's department. Since 1971 he has been a full-time writer.

Remaining true to his roots in the Australian "outback" (despite the global shuttling expected of a major poet in the late twentieth century), Murray has emerged as a powerful celebrant of the natural world and agricultural work. His substantial *Collected Poems* (1998), dedicated "to the glory of God," bears witness to a staunch and highly individual Roman Catholicism. His celebration of nature includes human nature and reveals a sensibility generously attuned to the hopes and fears, hurts and happinesses of ordinary lives.

Murray seems intent on proving that the provincial farmer living at the margins of the former British Empire can write poetry as learned, authoritative, and technically virtuosic as any from the metropolitan center. The language of his poetry startles and amuses, reveling in the fecundity and elasticity of English. In poems of metaphorical lushness and sonic opulence, he plays on the eddying reflections of homonyms and rhymes, alliterations and consonances, to suggest a profound interconnectedness among things. As Derek Walcott has said of Murray's work: "There is no poetry in the English language so rooted in its sacredness, so broad-leafed in its pleasures, and yet so intimate and conversational."

Morse

Tuckett. Bill Tuckett. Telegraph operator, Hall's Creek,
which is way out back of the Outback, but he stuck it,
quite likely liked it, despite heat, glare, dust and the lack
of diversion or doctors. Come disaster you trusted to luck,
5 ingenuity and pluck. This was back when nice people said pluck,
the sleevelink and green eyeshade epoch.[1]
                                    Faced, though, like Bill Tuckett
with a man needing surgery right on the spot, a lot
would have done their dashes. It looked hopeless (dot dot dot)
Lift him up on the table, said Tuckett, running the key hot
10 till Head Office turned up a doctor who coolly instructed
up a thousand miles of wire, as Tuckett advanced slit by slit
with a safety razor blade, pioneering on into the wet,
copper-wiring the rivers off, in the first operation conducted
along dotted lines, with rum drinkers gripping the patient:
d-d-dash it, take care, Tuck!
15   And the vital spark stayed unshorted.
Yallah![2] breathed the camelmen. Tuckett, you did it, you did it!
cried the spattered la-de-dah jodhpur[3]-wearing Inspector of Stock.
We imagine, some weeks later, a properly laconic
convalescent averring Without you, I'd have kicked the bucket . . .

20 From Chungking to Burrenjuck,[4] morse keys have mostly gone silent
and only old men meet now to chit-chat in their electric
bygone dialect. The last letter many will forget
is dit-dit-dit-dah, V for Victory. The coders' hero had speed,
resource and a touch. So ditditdit daah for Bill Tuckett.

1983

On Removing Spiderweb

Like summer silk its denier
but stickily, oh, ickilier,
miffed bunny-blinder, silver tar,
gesticuli-gesticular,
5 crepe when cobbed, crap when rubbed,
stretchily adhere-and-there
and everyway, nap-snarled or sleek,
glibly hubbed with grots to tweak:
ehh weakly bobbined tae yer neb,
10 spit it Phuoc Tuy! filthy web!

1990

1. I.e., the nineteenth century. "Sleevelink": cuff
link.
2. God be praised! (Arabic).
3. Long breeches for riding, close-fitting from
knee to ankle.
4. I.e., from southwest China to southeast Australia.

2822 / SEAMUS HEANEY

Corniche[1]

I work all day and hardly drink at all.[2]
I can reach down and feel if I'm depressed.
I adore the Creator because I made myself
and a few times a week a wire jags in my chest.

5 The first time, I'd been coming apart all year,
weeping, incoherent; cigars had given me up:
any road round a cliff edge I'd whimper along in low gear
then: cardiac horror. Masking my pulse's calm lub-dub.

It was the victim-sickness. Adrenaline howling in my head,
10 the black dog was my brain. Come to drown me in my breath
was energy's black hole, depression, compere° of   *master of ceremonies*
    the predawn show
when, returned from a pee, you stew and welter in your death.

The rogue space rock is on course to snuff your world,
sure. But go acute, and its oncoming fills your day.
15 The brave die but once? I could go a hundred times a week,
clinging to my pulse with the world's edge inches away.

Laugh, who never shrank around wizened genitals there
or killed themselves to stop dying. The blow that never falls
batters you stupid. Only gradually do
20 you notice a slight scorn in you for what appals.

A self inside self, cool as conscience, one to be erased
in your final night, or faxed, still knows beneath
all the mute grand opera and uncaused effect—
that death which can be imagined is not true death.

1996

1. Coastal road.
2. Cf. the opening of "Aubade," by the English
poet Philip Larkin (1922–1985): "I work all day,
and get half drunk at night."

SEAMUS HEANEY
b. 1939

Seamus Heaney was born into a Roman Catholic family in predominantly Protestant
North Ireland (or Ulster), and he grew up on a farm in County Derry bordered on
one side by a stream that marked the frontier with the largely Catholic Irish Republic
(or Eire) to the south. He won scholarships first to St. Columb's College, a Catholic
boarding school, and then to Queen's University in Belfast. There he became one of
an extraordinary group of Northern Irish poets from both Protestant and Catholic
backgrounds, including Michael Longley and Derek Mahon, who read, discussed,
and spurred on one another's work. He taught at Queen's University, before moving
in 1972 to the Irish Republic, where he became a citizen and full-time writer. He has

been Boylston Professor of Rhetoric and Oratory at Harvard and Professor of Poetry at Oxford, and in 1995 won the Nobel Prize in Literature.

With "Digging," placed appropriately as the first poem of his first book, Heaney defined his territory. He dug into his memory, uncovering first his father and then, going deeper, his grandfather. This idea of poetry as an archaeological process of recovery took on a darker cast after the eruption of internecine violence in Northern Ireland in 1969, culminating in the 1972 Bloody Sunday killing of thirteen Catholic civilians by British paratroopers during a civil rights march in Derry. Across several volumes, especially *North* (1975), Heaney wrote a series of grim "bog poems," about well-preserved Iron Age corpses discovered in the peat of Northern Europe and Ireland. In these poems he sees the bog as a "memory bank," or unconscious, that preserves everything thrown into it, including the victims of ritual killings. He views contemporary violence through the lens of ancient myths, sacrifices, and feuds, an oblique approach that gives his poetry about the Troubles an unusual depth and resonance. He had discovered emblems for the violence in Northern Ireland in *The Bog People*, a book by the Danish archaeologist P. V. Glob, published in translation in 1969, "the year the killing started." Heaney wrote of it:

> It was chiefly concerned with preserved bodies of men and women found in the bogs of Jutland, naked, strangled or with their throats cut, disposed under the peat since early Iron Age times. The author . . . argues convincingly that a number of these, and in particular, the Tollund Man, whose head is now preserved near Aarhus in the museum of Silkeburg, were ritual sacrifices to the Mother Goddess, the goddess of the ground who needed new bridegrooms each winter to bed with her in her sacred place, in the spring. Taken in relation to the tradition of Irish political martyrdom for the cause whose icon is Kathleen Ni Houlihan [mythic figure emblematic of Mother Ireland], this is more than an archaic barbarous rite: it is an archetypal pattern. And the unforgettable photographs of these victims blended in my mind with photographs of atrocities, past and present, in the long rites of Irish political and religious struggles. ("Feeling into Words")

In the bog poems Heaney reflects on the poet's responsibilities to write about the dead, yet to do so without prettifying or exploiting them. He probes the vexed relations between lyric song and historical suffering, "beauty and atrocity": the need to be true to his calling as artist, but also to represent the irredeemable carnage of modern political violence—"the actual weight / of each hooded victim / slashed and dumped" ("The Grauballe Man"). The result is a tough-minded witnessing, an ethically scrupulous and self-aware mourning of collective loss and sectarian murder. (For more on the Troubles, see "Imagining Ireland" at Norton Literature Online.)

Since the late 1970s Heaney has continued to elegize victims of the Troubles, such as his acquaintance Louis O'Neill, in "Casualty," as well as more personal losses, such as the natural death of his mother, in "Clearances." He has also written poems about domestic love, such as "The Skunk" and "The Sharping Stone." Heaney is thus both a private poet—skillfully kneading grief, love, and wonder into poems about his family and his humble origins—and a public poet, affirming his affinities with the Catholic civil rights movement, which has struggled against British and Protestant domination. Even in his public poetry he refuses slogans, journalistic reportage, and political pieties, scrutinizing instead the wellsprings of collective identity, the ambivalences of individual response to history.

An Irishman writing in the language of the British Empire, he has translated Gaelic poetry and renewed specifically Irish traditions, such as the *aisling*, or vision poem, but he is also steeped in the English literary canon, drawing on British poetry from *Beowulf* (his prize-winning translation appears in volume 1 of this anthology) to the works of William Wordsworth, Gerard Manley Hopkins, and Ted Hughes. Straddling in his verse a multiplicity of divisions, transubstantiating crisscross feelings into unexpected images and intricate sonorities, Heaney has been embraced by popular audiences for his accessible style and yet also admired by poets and academic critics for his lyric subtlety and rigorous technique.

Formally, his poetry ranges from strenuous free verse—the clipped lines and unrhymed quatrains of the bog poems—to more traditional forms, such as the modified terza rima of "Station Island" and the sonnet sequence "Clearances." His poems are earthy and matter-of-fact, saturated with the physical textures, sights, smells, and sounds of farm life, and they are also visionary, lit up by hope and spirit, enacting penitential pilgrimages and unbridled imaginings. That Heaney's poetry is both earthbound and airborne, free and formed, public and private helps explain why he is seen by many as the most gifted English-language poet of his generation.

Digging

Between my finger and my thumb
The squat pen rests; snug as a gun.

Under my window, a clean rasping sound
When the spade sinks into gravelly ground:
5 My father, digging. I look down

Till his straining rump among the flowerbeds
Bends low, comes up twenty years away
Stooping in rhythm through potato drills[1]
Where he was digging.

10 The coarse boot nestled on the lug, the shaft
Against the inside knee was levered firmly.
He rooted out tall tops, buried the bright edge deep
To scatter new potatoes that we picked
Loving their cool hardness in our hands.

15 By God, the old man could handle a spade.
Just like his old man.

My grandfather cut more turf[2] in a day
Than any other man on Toner's bog.
Once I carried him milk in a bottle
20 Corked sloppily with paper. He straightened up
To drink it, then fell to right away
Nicking and slicing neatly, heaving sods
Over his shoulder, going down and down
For the good turf. Digging.

25 The cold smell of potato mould, the squelch and slap
Of soggy peat, the curt cuts of an edge
Through living roots awaken in my head.
But I've no spade to follow men like them.

1. Small furrows in which seeds are sown.
2. Slabs of peat that, when dried, are a common domestic fuel in Ireland.

Between my finger and my thumb
30   The squat pen rests.
I'll dig with it.

1966

The Forge

All I know is a door into the dark.
Outside, old axles and iron hoops rusting;
Inside, the hammered anvil's short-pitched ring,
The unpredictable fantail of sparks
5   Or hiss when a new shoe toughens in water.
The anvil must be somewhere in the centre,
Horned as a unicorn, at one end square,
Set there immoveable: an altar
Where he expends himself in shape and music.
10   Sometimes, leather-aproned, hairs in his nose,
He leans out on the jamb, recalls a clatter
Of hoofs where traffic is flashing in rows;
Then grunts and goes in, with a slam and flick
To beat real iron out, to work the bellows.

1969

The Grauballe Man[1]

As if he had been poured
in tar, he lies
on a pillow of turf
and seems to weep

5   the black river of himself.
The grain of his wrists
is like bog oak,
the ball of his heel

like a basalt egg.
10   His instep has shrunk
cold as a swan's foot
or a wet swamp root.

His hips are the ridge
and purse of a mussel,
15   his spine an eel arrested
under a glisten of mud.

---

1. A body exhumed from a Danish bog and photographed in P.V. Glob's book *The Bog People*.

The head lifts,
the chin is a visor
raised above the vent
20   of his slashed throat

that has tanned and toughened.
The cured wound
opens inwards to a dark
elderberry place.

25   Who will say 'corpse'
to his vivid cast?
Who will say 'body'
to his opaque repose?

And his rusted hair,
30   a mat unlikely
as a foetus's.
I first saw his twisted face

in a photograph,
a head and shoulder
35   out of the peat,
bruised like a forceps baby,

but now he lies
perfected in my memory,
down to the red horn
40   of his nails,

hung in the scales
with beauty and atrocity:
with the Dying Gaul[2]
too strictly compassed

45   on his shield,
with the actual weight
of each hooded victim,
slashed and dumped.

1969

Punishment[1]

I can feel the tug
of the halter at the nape

2. Roman marble reproduction of a Greek bronze sculpture depicting a wounded soldier of Gaul, whose matted hair identifies him as a Celt, in Rome's Capitoline Museum.
1. In 1951 the peat-stained body of a young girl, who lived in the late 1st century c.e., was recovered from a bog in Windeby, Germany. As P. V. Glob describes her in *The Bog People*, she "lay naked in the hole in the peat, a bandage over the eyes and a collar round the neck. The band across the eyes was drawn tight and had cut into the neck and the base of the nose. We may feel sure that it had been used to close her eyes to this world. There was no mark of strangulation on the neck, so that it had not been used for that purpose." Her hair "had been shaved off with a razor on the left side

of her neck, the wind
on her naked front.

5   It blows her nipples
to amber beads,
it shakes the frail rigging
of her ribs.

I can see her drowned
10   body in the bog,
the weighing stone,
the floating rods and boughs.

Under which at first
she was a barked sapling
15   that is dug up
oak-bone, brain-firkin:°   *small cask*

her shaved head
like a stubble of black corn,
her blindfold a soiled bandage,
20   her noose a ring

to store
the memories of love.
Little adultress,
before they punished you

25   you were flaxen-haired,
undernourished, and your
tar-black face was beautiful.
My poor scapegoat,

I almost love you
30   but would have cast, I know,
the stones of silence.
I am the artful voyeur

of your brain's exposed
and darkened combs,°   *valleys*
35   your muscles' webbing
and all your numbered bones:

I who have stood dumb
when your betraying sisters,
cauled° in tar,   *wrapped, enclosed*
40   wept by the railings,

---

of the head. . . . When the brain was removed the
convolutions and folds of the surface could be
clearly seen [Glob reproduces a photograph of her
brain]. . . . This girl of only fourteen had had an
inadequate winter diet. . . . To keep the young
body under, some birch branches and a big stone
were laid upon her." According to the Roman historian Tacitus, the Germanic peoples punished
adulterous women by shaving off their hair and
then scourging them out of the village or killing
them. More recently, her "betraying sisters" were
sometimes shaved, stripped, tarred, and handcuffed by the Irish Republican Army (IRA) to the
railings of Belfast in punishment for keeping company with British soldiers.

who would connive
in civilized outrage
yet understand the exact
and tribal, intimate revenge.

1975

Casualty

1

He would drink by himself
And raise a weathered thumb
Towards the high shelf,
Calling another rum
5   And blackcurrant, without
Having to raise his voice,
Or order a quick stout°   strong dark beer
By a lifting of the eyes
And a discreet dumb-show
10 Of pulling off the top;
At closing time would go
In waders and peaked cap
Into the showery dark,
A dole-kept[1] breadwinner
15 But a natural for work.
I loved his whole manner,
Sure-footed but too sly,
His deadpan sidling tact,
His fisherman's quick eye
20 And turned observant back.
Incomprehensible
To him, my other life.
Sometimes, on his high stool,
Too busy with his knife
25 At a tobacco plug
And not meeting my eye
In the pause after a slug°   gulp of liquor
He mentioned poetry.
We would be on our own
30 And, always politic
And shy of condescension,
I would manage by some trick
To switch the talk to eels
Or lore of the horse and cart
35 Or the Provisionals.[2]

But my tentative art
His turned back watches too:
He was blown to bits
Out drinking in a curfew

---

1. I.e., receiving unemployment benefits.   2. The Provisional branch of the IRA.

40　Others obeyed, three nights
　　After they shot dead
　　The thirteen men in Derry.
　　PARAS THIRTEEN, the walls said,
　　BOGSIDE NIL.[3] That Wednesday
45　Everybody held
　　His breath and trembled.

2

　　It was a day of cold
　　Raw silence, wind-blown
　　Surplice and soutane:[4]
50　Rained-on, flower-laden
　　Coffin after coffin
　　Seemed to float from the door
　　Of the packed cathedral
　　Like blossoms on slow water.
55　The common funeral
　　Unrolled its swaddling band,[5]
　　Lapping, tightening
　　Till we were braced and bound
　　Like brothers in a ring.

60　But he would not be held
　　At home by his own crowd
　　Whatever threats were phoned,
　　Whatever black flags waved.
　　I see him as he turned
65　In that bombed offending place,
　　Remorse fused with terror
　　In his still knowable face,
　　His cornered outfaced stare
　　Blinding in the flash.

70　He had gone miles away
　　For he drank like a fish
　　Nightly, naturally
　　Swimming towards the lure
　　Of warm lit-up places,
75　The blurred mesh and murmur
　　Drifting among glasses
　　In the gregarious smoke.
　　How culpable was he
　　That last night when he broke
80　Our tribe's complicity?[6]
　　'Now you're supposed to be
　　An educated man,'

3. This graffito records—in the form of a soccer match score—that the British Army's Parachute Regiment had killed thirteen people; the Roman Catholic inhabitants of Derry's Bogside district, none. The IRA bombing occurred after the killing of Catholic demonstrators on Bloody Sunday, January 30, 1972.
4. Vestments worn by Roman Catholic priests.
5. Long cloth in which babies were once wrapped to restrain and warm them.
6. The Roman Catholic community's agreement to obey the curfew (of lines 39–40).

I hear him say. 'Puzzle me
The right answer to that one.'

3

85   I missed his funeral,
Those quiet walkers
And sideways talkers
Shoaling out of his lane
To the respectable
90   Purring of the hearse . . .
They move in equal pace
With the habitual
Slow consolation
Of a dawdling engine,
95   The line lifted, hand
Over fist, cold sunshine
On the water, the land
Banked under fog: that morning
I was taken in his boat,
100   The screw° purling, turning   *propellor*
Indolent fathoms white,
I tasted freedom with him.
To get out early, haul
Steadily off the bottom,
105   Dispraise the catch, and smile
As you find a rhythm
Working you, slow mile by mile,
Into your proper haunt
Somewhere, well out, beyond . . .

110   Dawn-sniffing revenant,[7]
Plodder through midnight rain,
Question me again.

1979

The Skunk

Up, black, striped and damasked like the chasuble[1]
At a funeral mass, the skunk's tail
Paraded the skunk. Night after night
I expected her like a visitor.

5   The refrigerator whinnied into silence.
My desk light softened beyond the verandah.
Small oranges loomed in the orange tree.
I began to be tense as a voyeur.

7. One returned from the dead.
1. Sleeveless vestment worn by the priest celebrating Mass, its color regulated by the feast of the
day. "Damasked": woven with elaborate designs.

After eleven years I was composing
10 Love-letters again, broaching the word 'wife'
Like a stored cask, as if its slender vowel
Had mutated into the night earth and air

Of California. The beautiful, useless
Tang of eucalyptus spelt your absence.
15 The aftermath of a mouthful of wine
Was like inhaling you off a cold pillow.

And there she was, the intent and glamorous,
Ordinary, mysterious skunk,
Mythologized, demythologized,
20 Snuffing the boards five feet beyond me.

It all came back to me last night, stirred
By the sootfall of your things at bedtime,
Your head-down, tail-up hunt in a bottom drawer
For the black plunge-line nightdress.

1979

From Station Island[1]

12

Like a convalescent, I took the hand
stretched down from the jetty, sensed again
an alien comfort as I stepped on ground

to find the helping hand still gripping mine,
5 fish-cold and bony, but whether to guide
or to be guided I could not be certain

for the tall man in step at my side
seemed blind, though he walked straight as a rush
upon his ash plant,[2] his eyes fixed straight ahead.

10 Then I knew him in the flesh
out there on the tarmac° among the cars,   blacktop surface
wintered hard and sharp as a blackthorn bush.

1. *Station Island* is a sequence of dream encounters with familiar ghosts, set on Station Island on
Lough Derg in Co. Donegal. The island is also
known as St. Patrick's Purgatory because of a tradition that Patrick was the first to establish the
penitential vigil of fasting and praying which still
constitutes the basis of the three-day pilgrimage.
Each unit of the contemporary pilgrim's exercises
is called a 'station,' and a large part of each station
involves walking barefoot and praying round the
'beds,' stone circles which are said to be the
remains of early medieval monastic cells [Heaney's
note]. In this last section of the poem, the familiar
ghost is that of Heaney's countryman James Joyce.
Cf. the stanza form and encounter with a ghost in
T. S. Eliot's "Little Gidding."
2. Walking stick made of ash, like the one carried
by Stephen Dedalus in Joyce's *Ulysses*. (See the
opening paragraphs of "Proteus," p. 2200). Joyce
was almost blind.

His voice eddying with the vowels of all rivers[3]
came back to me, though he did not speak yet,
15   a voice like a prosecutor's or a singer's,

cunning,[4] narcotic, mimic, definite
as a steel nib's downstroke, quick and clean,
and suddenly he hit a litter basket

with his stick, saying, "Your obligation
20   is not discharged by any common rite.
What you must do must be done on your own

so get back in harness. The main thing is to write
for the joy of it. Cultivate a work-lust
that imagines its haven like your hands at night

25   dreaming the sun in the sunspot of a breast.
You are fasted now, light-headed, dangerous.
Take off from here. And don't be so earnest,

let others wear the sackcloth and the ashes.[5]
Let go, let fly, forget.
30   You've listened long enough. Now strike your note."

It was as if I had stepped free into space
alone with nothing that I had not known
already. Raindrops blew in my face

as I came to. "Old father, mother's son,
35   there is a moment in Stephen's diary
for April the thirteenth, a revelation

set among my stars—that one entry
has been a sort of password in my ears,
the collect of a new epiphany,[6]

40   the Feast of the Holy Tundish."[7] "Who cares,"
he jeered, "any more? The English language
belongs to us. You are raking at dead fires,

a waste of time for somebody your age.
That subject° people stuff is a cod's° game,   *colonized / fool's*
45   infantile, like your peasant pilgrimage.

---

3. The Anna Livia Plurabelle episode of *Finnegans Wake* (p. 2239) resounds with the names of many rivers.
4. "The only arms I allow myself to use—silence, exile, and cunning" (Joyce, *A Portrait of the Artist as a Young Man*).
5. As worn by penitents in biblical times and later.
6. Manifestation of a superhuman being, as of the infant Jesus to the Magi (Matthew 2). In the Christian calendar, the Feast of the Epiphany is January 6. "Epiphany" was also Joyce's term for the

"sudden revelation of the whatness of a thing." "Collect": short prayer assigned to a particular day.
7. See the end of James Joyce's *Portrait of the Artist as a Young Man* [Heaney's note]: "13 April: That tundish [funnel] has been on my mind for a long time. I looked it up and find it English and good old blunt English too. Damn the dean of studies and his funnel! What did he come here for to teach us his own language or to learn it from us? Damn him one way or the other!"

You lose more of yourself than you redeem
doing the decent thing. Keep at a tangent.
When they make the circle wide, it's time to swim

out on your own and fill the element
50   with signatures on your own frequency,
echo soundings, searches, probes, allurements,

elver-gleams[8] in the dark of the whole sea."
The shower broke in a cloudburst, the tarmac
fumed and sizzled. As he moved off quickly

55   the downpour loosed its screens round his straight walk.

1984

Clearances

in memoriam M.K.H.,[1] 1911–1984

She taught me what her uncle once taught her:
How easily the biggest coal block split
If you got the grain and hammer angled right.

The sound of that relaxed alluring blow,
5   *Its co-opted and obliterated echo,*
Taught me to hit, taught me to loosen,

Taught me between the hammer and the block
To face the music. Teach me now to listen,
To strike it rich behind the linear black.

1

10   A cobble thrown a hundred years ago
Keeps coming at me, the first stone
Aimed at a great-grandmother's turncoat brow.[2]
The pony jerks and the riot's on.
She's crouched low in the trap
15   Running the gauntlet that first Sunday
Down the brae° to Mass at a panicked gallop.   *steep slope*
He whips on through the town to cries of 'Lundy!'[3]

Call her 'The Convert'. 'The Exogamous[4] Bride'.
Anyhow, it is a genre piece
20   Inherited on my mother's side

8. Gleams as of young eels.
1. Margaret Kathleen Heaney, the poet's mother.
2. Heaney's Protestant great-grandmother married a Catholic.
3. I.e., traitor. In 1688 the Irish colonel Robert

Lundy knew that Derry (or Londonderry) would be invaded by the English, but failed to prepare adequate defenses.
4. Married outside the group.

And mine to dispose with now she's gone.
Instead of silver and Victorian lace,
The exonerating, exonerated stone.

2

Polished linoleum shone there. Brass taps shone.
25 The china cups were very white and big—
An unchipped set with sugar bowl and jug.
The kettle whistled. Sandwich and teascone
Were present and correct. In case it run,
The butter must be kept out of the sun.
30 And don't be dropping crumbs. Don't tilt your chair.
Don't reach. Don't point. Don't make noise when you stir.

It is Number 5, New Row, Land of the Dead,
Where grandfather is rising from his place
With spectacles pushed back on a clean bald head
35 To welcome a bewildered homing daughter
Before she even knocks. 'What's this? What's this?'
And they sit down in the shining room together.

3

When all the others were away at Mass
I was all hers as we peeled potatoes.
40 They broke the silence, let fall one by one
Like solder weeping off the soldering iron:
Cold comforts set between us, things to share
Gleaming in a bucket of clean water.
And again let fall. Little pleasant splashes
45 From each other's work would bring us to our senses.

So while the parish priest at her bedside
Went hammer and tongs at the prayers for the dying
And some were responding and some crying
I remembered her head bent towards my head,
50 Her breath in mine, our fluent dipping knives—
Never closer the whole rest of our lives.

4

Fear of affectation made her affect
Inadequacy whenever it came to
Pronouncing words 'beyond her'. *Bertold Brek.*[5]
55 She'd manage something hampered and askew
Every time, as if she might betray
The hampered and inadequate by too
Well-adjusted a vocabulary.
With more challenge than pride, she'd tell me, 'You

---

5. Bertolt Brecht (1898–1956), German playwright.

60　Know all them things.' So I governed my tongue
　　In front of her, a genuinely well-
　　adjusted adequate betrayal
　　Of what I knew better. I'd *naw* and *aye*
　　And decently relapse into the wrong
65　Grammar which kept us allied and at bay.

5

　　The cool that came off sheets just off the line
　　Made me think the damp must still be in them
　　But when I took my corners of the linen
　　And pulled against her, first straight down the hem
70　And then diagonally, then flapped and shook
　　The fabric like a sail in a cross-wind,
　　They made a dried-out undulating thwack.
　　So we'd stretch and fold and end up hand to hand
　　For a split second as if nothing had happened
75　For nothing had that had not always happened
　　Beforehand, day by day, just touch and go,
　　Coming close again by holding back
　　In moves where I was x and she was o
　　Inscribed in sheets she'd sewn from ripped-out flour sacks.

6

80　In the first flush of the Easter holidays
　　The ceremonies during Holy Week
　　Were highpoints of our *Sons and Lovers*[6] phase.
　　The midnight fire. The paschal candlestick.[7]
　　Elbow to elbow, glad to be kneeling next
85　To each other up there near the front
　　Of the packed church, we would follow the text
　　And rubrics° for the blessing of the font.[8]　　　　　　　*rules*
　　As the hind longs for the streams, so my soul . . .[9]
　　Dippings. Towellings. The water breathed on.
90　The water mixed with chrism[1] and with oil.
　　Cruet[2] tinkle. Formal incensation
　　And the psalmist's outcry taken up with pride:
　　Day and night my tears have been my bread.[3]

7

　　In the last minutes he said more to her
95　Almost than in all their life together.
　　'You'll be in New Row on Monday night
　　And I'll come up for you and you'll be glad
　　When I walk in the door . . . Isn't that right?'

6. Novel (1913) by the English writer D. H.
Lawrence (1885–1930) that largely centers on the
oedipal relationship between a mother and son.
7. Large candle lit during a ceremony on Holy Saturday, which precedes Easter.

8. Receptacle for holy water.
9. Psalms 42.1.
1. Mixture of olive oil and balsam.
2. Small vessel for wine or water.
3. Psalms 42.3.

His head was bent down to her propped-up head.
100 She could not hear but we were overjoyed.
He called her good and girl. Then she was dead,
The searching for a pulsebeat was abandoned
And we all knew one thing by being there.
The space we stood around had been emptied
105 Into us to keep, it penetrated
Clearances that suddenly stood open.
High cries were felled and a pure change happened.

8

I thought of walking round and round a space
Utterly empty, utterly a source
110 Where the decked chestnut tree had lost its place
In our front hedge above the wallflowers.
The white chips jumped and jumped and skited[4] high.
I heard the hatchet's differentiated
Accurate cut, the crack, the sigh
115 And collapse of what luxuriated
Through the shocked tips and wreckage of it all.
Deep planted and long gone, my coeval[5]
Chestnut from a jam jar in a hole,
Its heft and hush become a bright nowhere,
120 A soul ramifying and forever
Silent, beyond silence listened for.

1987

The Sharping Stone[1]

In an apothecary's° chest of drawers,   *pharmacist's*
Sweet cedar that we'd purchased second hand,
In one of its weighty deep-sliding recesses
I found the sharping stone that was to be
5 Our gift to him. Still in its wrapping paper.
Like a baton of black light I'd failed to pass.

•

Airless cinder-depths. But all the same,
The way it lay there, it wakened something too . . .
I thought of us that evening on the logs,
10 Flat on our backs, the pair of us, parallel,
Supported head to heel, arms straight, eyes front,
Listening to the rain drip off the trees
And saying nothing, braced to the damp bark.
What possessed us? The bare, lopped loveliness
15 Of those two winter trunks, the way they seemed

4. Shot off obliquely.
5. Of the same age.

1. Whetstone for sharpening metal blades.

Prepared for launching, at right angles across
A causeway of short fence-posts set like rollers.
Neither of us spoke. The puddles waited.
The workers had gone home, saws fallen silent.
20 And next thing down we lay, babes in the wood,
Gazing up at the flood-face of the sky
Until it seemed a flood was carrying us
Out of the forest park, feet first, eyes front,
Out of November, out of middle age,
25 Together, out, across the Sea of Moyle.[2]

•

Sarcophage des époux.[3] In terra cotta.
Etruscan couple shown side by side,
Recumbent on left elbows, husband pointing
With his right arm and watching where he points,
30 Wife in front, her earrings in, her braids
Down to her waist, taking her sexual ease.
He is all eyes, she is all brow and dream,
Her right forearm and hand held out as if
Some bird she sees in her deep inward gaze
35 Might be about to roost there. Domestic
Love, the artist thought, warm tones and property,
The frangibility of terra cotta . . .
Which is how they figured on the colour postcard
(*Louvre, Département des Antiquités*)[4]
40 That we'd sent him once, then found among his things.

•

He loved inspired mistakes: his Spanish grandson's
English transliteration, thanking him
For a boat trip: 'That was a marvellous
Walk on the water, granddad.' And indeed
45 He walked on air himself, never more so
Than when he had been widowed and the youth
In him, the athlete who had wooed her—
Breasting tapes and clearing the high bars—
Grew lightsome once again. Going at eighty
50 On the bendiest roads, going for broke
At every point-to-point[5] and poker-school,
'He commenced his wild career' a second time
And not a bother on him. Smoked like a train
And took the power mower in his stride.
55 Flirted and vaunted. Set fire to his bed.
Fell from a ladder. Learned to microwave.

•

So set the drawer on freshets° of thaw water   *surges*
And place the unused sharping stone inside it:

---

2. Channel between the northwestern coast of
County Antrim in Ireland and the southwestern
coast of Scotland.
3. Coffin for a married couple.

4. Department of Antiquities, Louvre Museum,
Paris, in which this Etruscan funerary statue,
known as *The Cerveteri Couple*, is to be found.
5. Horse race over jumps.

To be found next summer on a riverbank
60   Where scythes once hung all night in alder trees
And mowers played dawn scherzos[6] on the blades,
Their arms like harpists' arms, one drawing towards,
One sweeping the bright rim of the extreme.

1996

6. Vigorous light and playful musical compositions.

J. M. COETZEE
b. 1940

John Michael Coetzee was born in Cape Town, South Africa. His mother was a schoolteacher; his father, a lawyer who became a sheepherder after losing his job. When Coetzee was eight, his family left the provinces, and he chronicles this and other parts of his childhood in third-person memoirs, *Boyhood: Scenes from a Provincial Life* (1997) and *Youth: Scenes from a Provincial Life II* (2002). Coetzee was educated in Cape Town and then lived in London for a few years, working as a computer programmer, before earning his Ph.D. from the University of Texas at Austin, where he wrote a dissertation on the fiction of Samuel Beckett—a major influence along with Kafka and Dostoyevsky, on Coetzee's fiction. He was appointed, first, assistant professor and, subsequently, Butler Professor of English at the State University of New York at Buffalo. In 1984 he returned to South Africa as professor of general literature at the University of Cape Town, and since 2002 he has lived in Australia. Coetzee is the first novelist to win the prestigious Booker Prize twice, and in 2003 he was awarded the Nobel Prize in Literature.

The central concern of Coetzee's fiction—the oppressive nature of colonialism—made its appearance with his first book, *Dusklands* (1974). This consists of two novellas, one set in the U.S. State Department during the Vietnam War, the other in southern Africa two hundred years earlier. The protagonists of these seemingly different stories—Eugene Dawn, an expert in psychological warfare, and Jacobus Coetzee, an explorer and pioneer—are engaged in similar projects, each leading to oppression and murder. Coetzee's subsequent novels include *In the Heart of the Country* (1977), a feminist anticolonial fable in the voice of a mad South African farmwoman; *Life and Times of Michael K* (1983), about a homeless man trying to survive in war-torn Africa; *Foe* (1986), a retelling of Daniel Defoe's *Robinson Crusoe* from the perspective of a female castaway; *The Master of Petersburg* (1994), a fictionalized account of Dostoyevsky's life; *Disgrace* (1999), about sexual harassment, rape, and race relations; and *Elizabeth Costello: Eight Lessons* (2003), which blends essay and fiction. His many essays and works of criticism have concerned censorship, the rights of animals, South African history, and other themes.

Coetzee is at once a passionate political novelist and an intensely literary one, both qualities emerging in his most compelling indictment of colonialism, *Waiting for the Barbarians* (1980). This novel takes its title and theme from a well-known poem by the Greek poet Constantine Cavafy (1863–1933), which ends (in Rae Dalven's translation):

> . . . night is here but the barbarians have not come.
> Some people arrived from the frontiers,
> And they said that there are no longer any barbarians.

And now what shall become of us without any barbarians?
Those people were a kind of solution.

In Coetzee's novel the rulers of the unnamed empire claim it is threatened by barbarians, but the barbarian threat is, at least in part, a fantasy concocted by the empire
to hold itself together. The narrator is a magistrate in charge of a frontier post, poised
uneasily between the harmless inhabitants of the region and the empire's ruthless
officials, and unable to protect either the natives or himself from his brutal colleague,
Colonel Joll. Imprisoned and stripped of his duties, the magistrate becomes increasingly skeptical of the empire's motives. When the imperial army arrives to subdue
supposed insurgents, its vicious treatment of prisoners calls into question the relation
of "civilization" to "barbarism" and demonstrates, in harrowing scenes of abuse and
torture, the ethical dangers of one people's dominance over another. In this medley
of realist particularism and allegorical parable, Coetzee leaves the landscape and time
of the novel hauntingly unspecified, suggesting that colonialism's degradation and
coercion, violence and moral corruption can occur anywhere, at any time.

From Waiting for the Barbarians

First there is the sound of muskets far away, as diminutive as popguns.[1]
Then from nearer by, from the ramparts themselves, come volleys of answering
shots. There is a stampede of footsteps across the barracks yard. "The barbarians!" someone shouts; but I think he is wrong. Above all the clamour the great
bell begins to peal.
    Kneeling with an ear to the crack of the door I try to make out what is going
on.
    The noise from the square mounts from a hubbub to a steady roar in which
no single voice can be distinguished. The whole town must be pouring out in
welcome, thousands of ecstatic souls. Volleys of musket-shots keep cracking.
Then the tenor of the roar changes, rises in pitch and excitement. Faintly above
it come the brassy tones of bugles.
    The temptation is too great. What have I to lose? I unlock the door. In glare
so blinding that I must squint and shade my eyes, I cross the yard, pass through
the gate, and join the rear of the crowd. The volleys and the roar of applause
continue. The old woman in black beside me takes my arm to steady herself
and stands on her toes. "Can you see?" she says. "Yes, I can see men on
horseback," I reply; but she is not listening.
    I can see a long file of horsemen who, amid flying banners, pass through
the gateway and make their way to the centre of the square where they dis-
mount. There is a cloud of dust over the whole square, but I see that they are
smiling and laughing: one of them rides with his hands raised high in triumph,
another waves a garland of flowers. They progress slowly, for the crowd presses
around them, trying to touch them, throwing flowers, clapping their hands
above their heads in joy, spinning round and round in private ecstasies. Children dive past me, scrambling through the legs of the grownups to be nearer
to their heroes. Fusillade after fusillade comes from the ramparts, which are
lined with cheering people.
    One part of the cavalcade does not dismount. Headed by a stern-faced young
corporal bearing the green and gold banner of the battalion, it passes through

---

1. The magistrate, narrator of the novel, listens from the prison in which the empire has incarcerated him.

the press of bodies to the far end of the square and then begins a circuit of the perimeter, the crowd surging slowly in its wake. The word runs like fire from neighbour to neighbour: *"Barbarians!"*

The standard-bearer's horse is led by a man who brandishes a heavy stick to clear his way. Behind him comes another trooper trailing a rope; and at the end of the rope, tied neck to neck, comes a file of men, barbarians, stark naked, holding their hands up to their faces in an odd way as though one and all are suffering from toothache. For a moment I am puzzled by the posture, by the tiptoeing eagerness with which they follow their leader, till I catch a glint of metal and at once comprehend. A simple loop of wire runs through the flesh of each man's hands and through holes pierced in his cheeks. "It makes them meek as lambs," I remember being told by a soldier who had once seen the trick: "they think of nothing but how to keep very still." My heart grows sick. I know now that I should not have left my cell.

I have to turn my back smartly to avoid being seen by the two who, with their mounted escort, bring up the rear of the procession: the bareheaded young captain whose first triumph this is, and at his shoulder, leaner and darker after his months of campaigning, Colonel of Police Joll.

The circuit is made, everyone has a chance to see the twelve miserable captives, to prove to his children that the barbarians are real. Now the crowd, myself reluctantly in its wake, flows towards the great gate, where a half-moon of soldiers blocks its way until, compressed at front and rear, it cannot budge.

"What is going on?" I ask my neighbour.

"I don't know," he says, "but help me to lift him." I help him to lift the child he carries on his arm on to his shoulders. "Can you see?" he asks the child.

"Yes."

"What are they doing?"

"They are making those barbarians kneel. What are they going to do to them?"

"I don't know. Let's wait and see."

Slowly, titanically, with all my might, I turn and begin to squeeze my body out, "Excuse me . . . excuse me . . ." I say: "the heat—I'm going to be sick." For the first time I see heads turn, fingers point.

I ought to go back to my cell. As a gesture it will have no effect, it will not even be noticed. Nevertheless, for my own sake, as a gesture to myself alone, I ought to return to the cool dark and lock the door and bend the key and stop my ears to the noise of patriotic bloodlust and close my lips and never speak again. Who knows, perhaps I do my fellow-townsmen an injustice, perhaps at this very minute the shoemaker is at home tapping on his last, humming to himself to drown the shouting, perhaps there are housewives shelling peas in their kitchens, telling stories to occupy their restless children, perhaps there are farmers still going calmly about the repair of the ditches. If comrades like these exist, what a pity I do not know them! For me, at this moment, striding away from the crowd, what has become important above all is that I should neither be contaminated by the atrocity that is about to be committed nor poison myself with impotent hatred of its perpetrators. I cannot save the prisoners, therefore let me save myself. Let it at the very least be said, if it ever comes to be said, if there is ever anyone in some remote future interested to know the way we lived, that in this farthest outpost of the Empire of light there existed one man who in his heart was not a barbarian.

I pass through the barracks gate into my prison yard. At the trough in the middle of the yard I pick up an empty bucket and fill it. With the bucket held up before me, slopping water over its sides, I approach the rear of the crowd again. "Excuse me," I say, and push. People curse me, give way, the bucket tilts and splashes, I forge forward till in a minute I am suddenly clear in the frontmost rank of the crowd behind the backs of the soldiers who, holding staves between them, keep an arena clear for the exemplary spectacle.

Four of the prisoners kneel on the ground. The other eight, still roped together, squat in the shade of the wall watching, their hands to their cheeks.

The kneeling prisoners bend side by side over a long heavy pole. A cord runs from the loop of wire through the first man's mouth, under the pole, up to the second man's loop, back under the pole, up to the third loop, under the pole, through the fourth loop. As I watch a soldier slowly pulls the cord tighter and the prisoners bend further till finally they are kneeling with their faces touching the pole. One of them writhes his shoulders in pain and moans. The others are silent, their thoughts wholly concentrated on moving smoothly with the cord, not giving the wire a chance to tear their flesh.

Directing the soldier with little gestures of the hand is Colonel Joll. Though I am only one in a crowd of thousands, though his eyes are shaded as ever, I stare at him so hard with a face so luminous with query that I know at once he sees me.

Behind me I distinctly hear the word *magistrate*. Do I imagine it or are my neighbours inching away from me?

The Colonel steps forward. Stooping over each prisoner in turn he rubs a handful of dust into his naked back and writes a word with a stick of charcoal. I read the words upside down: ENEMY . . . ENEMY . . . ENEMY . . . ENEMY. He steps back and folds his hands. At a distance of no more than twenty paces he and I contemplate each other.

Then the beating begins. The soldiers use the stout green cane staves, bringing them down with the heavy slapping sounds of washing-paddles, raising red welts on the prisoners' backs and buttocks. With slow care the prisoners extend their legs until they lie flat on their bellies, all except the one who had been moaning and who now gasps with each blow.

The black charcoal and ochre dust begin to run with sweat and blood. The game, I see, is to beat them till their backs are washed clean.

I watch the face of a little girl who stands in the front rank of the crowd gripping her mother's clothes. Her eyes are round, her thumb is in her mouth: silent, terrified, curious, she drinks in the sight of these big naked men being beaten. On every face around me, even those that are smiling, I see the same expression: not hatred, not bloodlust, but a curiosity so intense that their bodies are drained by it and only their eyes live, organs of a new and ravening appetite.

The soldiers doing the beating grow tired. One stands with his hands on his hips panting, smiling, gesturing to the crowd. There is a word from the Colonel: all four of them cease their labour and come forward offering their canes to the spectators.

A girl, giggling and hiding her face, is pushed forward by her friends. "Go on, don't be afraid!" they urge her. A soldier puts a cane in her hand and leads her to the place. She stands confused, embarrassed, one hand still over her face. Shouts, jokes, obscene advice are hurled at her. She lifts the cane, brings it down smartly on the prisoner's buttocks, drops it, and scuttles to safety to a roar of applause.

2842 / J. M. COETZEE

There is a scramble for the canes, the soldiers can barely keep order, I lose sight of the prisoners on the ground as people press forward to take a turn or simply watch the beating from nearer. I stand forgotten with my bucket between my feet.

Then the flogging is over, the soldiers reassert themselves, the crowd scrambles back, the arena is reconstituted, though narrower than before.

Over his head, exhibiting it to the crowd, Colonel Joll holds a hammer, an ordinary four-pound hammer used for knocking in tent-pegs. Again his gaze meets mine. The babble subsides.

"No!" I hear the first word from my throat, rusty, not loud enough. Then again: "No!" This time the word rings like a bell from my chest. The soldier who blocks my way stumbles aside. I am in the arena holding up my hands to still the crowd: "No! No! No!"

When I turn to Colonel Joll he is standing not five paces from me, his arms folded. I point a finger at him. "You!" I shout. Let it all be said. Let him be the one on whom the anger breaks. "You are depraving these people!"

He does not flinch, he does not reply.

"You!" My arm points at him like a gun. My voice fills the square. There is utter silence; or perhaps I am too intoxicated to hear.

Something crashes into me from behind. I sprawl in the dust, gasp, feel the sear of old pain in my back. A stick thuds down on me. Reaching out to ward it off, I take a withering blow on my hand.

It becomes important to stand up, however difficult the pain makes it. I come to my feet and see who it is that is hitting me. It is the stocky man with the sergeant's stripes who helped with the beatings. Crouched at the knees, his nostrils flaring, he stands with his stick raised for the next blow. "Wait!" I gasp, holding out my limp hand. "I think you have broken it!" He strikes, and I take the blow on the forearm. I hide my arm, lower my head, and try to grope towards him and grapple. Blows fall on my head and shoulders. Never mind: all I want is a few moments to finish what I am saying now that I have begun. I grip his tunic and hug him to me. Though he wrestles, he cannot use his stick; over his shoulder I shout again.

"Not with that!" I shout. The hammer lies cradled in the Colonel's folded arms. "You would not use a hammer on a beast, not on a beast!" In a terrible surge of rage I turn on the sergeant and hurl him from me. Godlike strength is mine. In a minute it will pass: let me use it well while it lasts! "Look!" I shout. I point to the four prisoners who lie docilely on the earth, their lips to the pole, their hands clasped to their faces like monkeys' paws, oblivious of the hammer, ignorant of what is going on behind them, relieved that the offending mark has been beaten from their backs, hoping that the punishment is at an end. I raise my broken hand to the sky. "Look!" I shout. "We are the great miracle of creation! But from some blows this miraculous body cannot repair itself! How—!" Words fail me. "Look at these men!" I recommence. "Men!" Those in the crowd who can crane to look at the prisoners, even at the flies that begin to settle on their bleeding welts.

I hear the blow coming and turn to meet it. It catches me full across the face. "I am blind!" I think, staggering back into the blackness that instantly falls. I swallow blood; something blooms across my face, starting as a rosy warmth, turning to fiery agony. I hide my face in my hands and stamp around in a circle trying not to shout, trying not to fall.

What I wanted to say next I cannot remember. A miracle of creation—I pursue the thought but it eludes me like a wisp of smoke. It occurs to me that we crush insects beneath our feet, miracles of creation too, beetles, worms, cockroaches, ants, in their various ways.

I take my fingers from my eyes and a grey world re-emerges swimming in tears. I am so profoundly grateful that I cease to feel pain. As I am hustled, a man at each elbow, back through the murmuring crowd to my cell, I even find myself smiling.

That smile, that flush of joy, leave behind a disturbing residue. I know that they commit an error in treating me so summarily. For I am no orator. What would I have said if they had let me go on? That it is worse to beat a man's feet to pulp than to kill him in combat? That it brings shame on everyone when a girl is permitted to flog a man? That spectacles of cruelty corrupt the hearts of the innocent? The words they stopped me from uttering may have been very paltry indeed, hardly words to rouse the rabble. What, after all, do I stand for besides an archaic code of gentlemanly behaviour towards captured foes, and what do I stand against except the new science of degradation that kills people on their knees, confused and disgraced in their own eyes? Would I have dared to face the crowd to demand justice for these ridiculous barbarian prisoners with their backsides in the air? *Justice:* once that word is uttered, where will it all end? Easier to shout *No!* Easier to be beaten and made a martyr. Easier to lay my head on a block than to defend the cause of justice for the barbarians: for where can that argument lead but to laying down our arms and opening the gates of the town to the people whose land we have raped? The old magistrate, defender of the rule of law, enemy in his own way of the State, assaulted and imprisoned, impregnably virtuous, is not without his own twinges of doubt.

My nose is broken, I know, and perhaps also the cheekbone where the flesh was laid open by the blow of the stick. My left eye is swelling shut.

As the numbness wears off the pain begins to come in spasms a minute or two apart so intense that I can no longer lie still. At the height of the spasm I trot around the room holding my face, whining like a dog; in the blessed valleys between the peaks I breathe deeply, trying to keep control of myself, trying not to make too disgraceful an outcry. I seem to hear surges and lulls in the noise from the mob on the square but cannot be sure that the roar is not simply in my eardrums.

They bring me my evening meal as usual but I cannot eat. I cannot keep still, I have to walk back and forth or rock on my haunches to keep myself from screaming, tearing my clothes, clawing my flesh, doing whatever people do when the limit of their endurance is reached. I weep, and feel the tears stinging the open flesh. I hum the old song about the rider and the juniper bush over and over again, clinging to the remembered words even after they have ceased to make any sense. One, two, three, four . . . I count. It will be a famous victory, I tell myself, if you can last the night.

In the early hours of the morning, when I am so giddy with exhaustion that I reel on my feet, I finally give way and sob from the heart like a child: I sit in a corner against the wall and weep, the tears running from my eyes without stop. I weep and weep while the throbbing comes and goes according to its own cycles. In this position sleep bursts upon me like a thunderbolt. I am amazed to come to myself in the thin grey light of day, slumped in a corner, with not the faintest sense that time has passed. Though the throbbing is still there I find I can endure it if I remain still. Indeed, it has lost its strangeness. Soon, perhaps, it will be as much part of me as breathing.

So I lie quietly against the wall, folding my sore hand under my armpit for

2844 / J. M. COETZEE

comfort, and fall into a second sleep, into a confusion of images among which I search out one in particular, brushing aside the others that fly at me like leaves. It is of the girl. She is kneeling with her back to me before the snow-castle or sandcastle she has built. She wears a dark blue robe. As I approach I see that she is digging away in the bowels of the castle.

She becomes aware of me and turns. I am mistaken, it is not a castle she has built but a clay oven. Smoke curls up from the vent at the back. She holds out her hands to me offering me something, a shapeless lump which I peer at unwillingly through a mist. Though I shake my head my vision will not clear.

She is wearing a round cap embroidered in gold. Her hair is braided in a heavy plait which lies over her shoulder: there is gold thread worked into the braid. "Why are you dressed in your best?" I want to say: "I have never seen you looking so lovely." She smiles at me: what beautiful teeth she has, what clear jet-black eyes! Also now I can see that what she is holding out to me is a loaf of bread, still hot, with a coarse steaming broken crust. A surge of gratitude sweeps through me. "Where did a child like you learn to bake so well in the desert?" I want to say. I open my arms to embrace her, and come to myself with tears stinging the wound on my cheek. Though I scrabble back at once into the burrow of sleep I cannot re-enter the dream or taste the bread that has made my saliva run.

• •

Colonel Joll sits behind the desk in my office. There are no books or files; the room is starkly empty save for a vase of fresh flowers.

The handsome warrant officer whose name I do not know lifts the cedar-wood chest on to the desk and steps back.

Looking down to refer to his papers, the Colonel speaks. "Among the items found in your apartment was this wooden chest. I would like you to consider it. Its contents are unusual. It contains approximately three hundred slips of white poplar-wood, each about eight inches by two inches, many of them wound about with lengths of string.[2] The wood is dry and brittle. Some of the string is new, some so old that it has perished.

"If one loosens the string one finds that the slip splits open revealing two flat inner surfaces. These surfaces are written on in an unfamiliar script.

"I think you will concur with this description."

I stare into the black lenses. He goes on.

"A reasonable inference is that the wooden slips contain messages passed between yourself and other parties, we do not know when. It remains for you to explain what the messages say and who the other parties were."

He takes a slip from the chest and flicks it across the polished surface of the desk towards me.

I look at the lines of characters written by a stranger long since dead. I do not even know whether to read from right to left or from left to right. In the long evenings I spent poring over my collection I isolated over four hundred different characters in the script, perhaps as many as four hundred and fifty. I have no idea what they stand for. Does each stand for a single thing, a circle for the sun, a triangle for a woman, a wave for a lake; or does a circle merely stand for "circle", a triangle for "triangle", a wave for "wave"? Does each sign

---

2. Over the years the magistrate has conducted archaeological digs outside the city, unearthing these poplar slips and other artifacts.

represent a different state of the tongue, the lips, the throat, the lungs, as they combine in the uttering of some multifarious unimaginable extinct barbarian language? Or are my four hundred characters nothing but scribal embellishments of an underlying repertory of twenty or thirty whose primitive forms I am too stupid to see?

"He sends greetings to his daughter," I say. I hear with surprise the thick nasal voice that is now mine. My finger runs along the line of characters from right to left. "Whom he says he has not seen for a long time. He hopes she is happy and thriving. He hopes the lambing season has been good. He has a gift for her, he says, which he will keep till he sees her again. He sends his love. It is not easy to read his signature. It could be simply 'Your father' or it could be something else, a name."

I reach over into the chest and pick out a second slip. The warrant officer, who sits behind Joll with a little notebook open on his knee, stares hard at me, his pencil poised above the paper.

"This one reads as follows," I say: " 'I am sorry I must send bad news. The soldiers came and took your brother away. I have been to the fort every day to plead for his return. I sit in the dust with my head bare. Yesterday for the first time they sent a man to speak to me. He says your brother is no longer here. He says he has been sent away. "Where?" I asked, but he would not say. Do not tell your mother, but join me in praying for his safety.'

"And now let us see what this next one says." The pencil is still poised, he has not written anything, he has not stirred. " 'We went to fetch your brother yesterday. They showed us into a room where he lay on a table sewn up in a sheet.' " Slowly Joll leans back in his chair. The warrant officer closes his notebook and half-rises; but with a gesture Joll restrains him. " 'They wanted me to take him away like that, but I insisted on looking first. "What if it is the wrong body you are giving me?" I said—"You have so many bodies here, bodies of brave young men." So I opened the sheet and saw that it was indeed he. Through each eyelid, I saw that there was a stitch, "Why have you done that?" I said. "It is our custom," he said. I tore the sheet wide open and saw bruises all over his body, and saw that his feet were swollen and broken. "What happened to him?" I said. "I do not know," said the man, "it is not on the paper; if you have questions you must go to the sergeant, but he is very busy." We have had to bury your brother here, outside their fort, because he was beginning to stink. Please tell your mother and try to console her.'

"Now let us see what the next one says. See, there is only a single character. It is the barbarian character war, but it has other senses too. It can stand for vengeance, and, if you turn it upside down like this, it can be made to read justice. There is no knowing which sense is intended. That is part of barbarian cunning.

"It is the same with the rest of these slips." I plunge my good hand into the chest and stir. "They form an allegory. They can be read in many orders. Further, each single slip can be read in many ways. Together they can be read as a domestic journal, or they can be read as a plan of war, or they can be turned on their sides and read as a history of the last years of the Empire— the old Empire, I mean. There is no agreement among scholars about how to interpret these relics of the ancient barbarians. Allegorical sets like this one can be found buried all over the desert. I found this one not three miles from here in the ruins of a public building. Graveyards are another good place to look in, though it is not always easy to tell where barbarian burial sites lie. It

2846 / J. M. Coetzee

is recommended that you simply dig at random: perhaps at the very spot where you stand you will come upon scraps, shards, reminders of the dead. Also the air: the air is full of sighs and cries. These are never lost: if you listen carefully, with a sympathetic ear, you can hear them echoing forever within the second sphere. The night is best: sometimes when you have difficulty in falling asleep it is because your ears have been reached by the cries of the dead which, like their writings, are open to many interpretations.

"Thank you. I have finished translating."

I have not failed to keep an eye on Joll through all this. He has not stirred again, save to lay a hand on his subordinate's sleeve at the moment when I referred to the Empire and he rose, ready to strike me.

If he comes near me I will hit him with all the strength in my body. I will not disappear into the earth without leaving my mark on them.

The Colonel speaks. "You have no idea how tiresome your behaviour is. You are the one and only official we have had to work with on the frontier who has not given us his fullest co-operation. Candidly, I must tell you I am not interested in these sticks." He waves a hand at the slips scattered on the desk. "They are very likely gambling-sticks. I know that other tribes on the border gamble with sticks.

"I ask you to consider soberly: what kind of future do you have here? You cannot be allowed to remain in your post. You have utterly disgraced yourself. Even if you are not eventually prosecuted—"

"I am waiting for you to prosecute me!" I shout. "When are you going to do it? When are you going to bring me to trial? When am I going to have a chance to defend myself?" I am in a fury. None of the speechlessness I felt in front of the crowd afflicts me. If I were to confront these men now, in public, in a fair trial, I would find the words to shame them. It is a matter of health and strength: I feel my hot words swell in my breast. But they will never bring a man to trial while he is healthy and strong enough to confound them. They will shut me away in the dark till I am a muttering idiot, a ghost of myself; then they will haul me before a closed court and in five minutes dispose of the legalities they find so tiresome.

"For the duration of the emergency, as you know," says the Colonel, "the administration of justice is out of the hands of civilians and in the hands of the Bureau." He sighs. "Magistrate, you seem to believe that we do not dare to bring you to trial because we fear you are too popular a figure in this town. I do not think you are aware of how much you forfeited by neglecting your duties, shunning your friends, keeping company with low people. There is no one I have spoken to who has not at some time felt insulted by your behaviour."

"My private life is none of their business!"

"Nevertheless, I may tell you that our decision to relieve you of your duties has been welcomed in most quarters. Personally I have nothing against you. When I arrived back a few days ago, I had decided that all I wanted from you was a clear answer to a simple question, after which you could have returned to your concubines a free man."

It strikes me suddenly that the insult may not be gratuitous, that perhaps for different reasons these two men might welcome it if I lost my temper. Burning with outrage, tense in every muscle, I guard my silence.

"However, you seem to have a new ambition," he goes on. "You seem to want to make a name for yourself as the One Just Man, the man who is prepared to sacrifice his freedom to his principles.

"But let me ask you: do you believe that that is how your fellow-citizens see you after the ridiculous spectacle you created on the square the other day? Believe me, to people in this town you are not the One Just Man, you are simply a clown, a madman. You are dirty, you stink, they can smell you a mile away. You look like an old beggar-man, a refuse-scavenger. They do not want you back in any capacity. You have no future here.

"You want to go down in history as a martyr, I suspect. But who is going to put you in the history books? These border troubles are of no significance. In a while they will pass and the frontier will go to sleep for another twenty years. People are not interested in the history of the back of beyond."

"There were no border troubles before you came," I say.

"That is nonsense," he says. "You are simply ignorant of the facts. You are living in a world of the past. You think we are dealing with small groups of peaceful nomads. In fact we are dealing with a well organized enemy. If you had travelled with the expeditionary force you would have seen that for yourself."

"Those pitiable prisoners you brought in—are *they* the enemy I must fear? Is that what you say? *You* are the enemy, Colonel!" I can restrain myself no longer. I pound the desk with my fist. "*You* are the enemy, *you* have made the war, and *you* have given them all the martyrs they need—starting not now but a year ago when you committed your first filthy barbarities here! History will bear me out!"

"Nonsense. There will be no history, the affair is too trivial." He seems impassive, but I am sure I have shaken him.

"You are an obscene torturer! You deserve to hang!"

"Thus speaks the judge, the One Just Man," he murmurs.

We stare into each other's eyes.

"Now," he says, squaring the papers before him: "I would like a statement on everything that passed between you and the barbarians on your recent and unauthorized visit to them."

"I refuse."

"Very well. Our interview is over." He turns to his subordinate. "He is your responsibility." He stands up, walks out. I face the warrant officer.

•   •

The wound on my cheek, never washed or dressed, is swollen and inflamed. A crust like a fat caterpillar has formed on it. My left eye is a mere slit, my nose a shapeless throbbing lump. I must breathe through my mouth.

I lie in the reek of old vomit obsessed with the thought of water. I have had nothing to drink for two days.

In my suffering there is nothing ennobling. Little of what I call suffering is even pain. What I am made to undergo is subjection to the most rudimentary needs of my body: to drink, to relieve itself, to find the posture in which it is least sore. When Warrant Officer Mandel and his man first brought me back here and lit the lamp and closed the door, I wondered how much pain a plump comfortable old man would be able to endure in the name of his eccentric notions of how the Empire should conduct itself. But my torturers were not interested in degrees of pain. They were interested only in demonstrating to me what it meant to live in a body, as a body, a body which can entertain notions of justice only as long as it is whole and well, which very soon forgets them when its head is gripped and a pipe is pushed down its gullet and pints of salt water are poured into it till it coughs and retches and flails and voids itself. They did not come to force the story out of me of what I had said to the barbarians and what the barbarians had said to me. So I had no chance to throw the high-sounding words I had ready in their faces. They came to my cell to show me the meaning of humanity, and in the space of an hour they showed me a great deal.

1980

EAVAN BOLAND
b. 1944

Eavan Boland was born in Dublin, the youngest daughter of an Irish diplomat and a painter, but as recalled in "Fond Memory" and other poems, she was displaced as a six-year-old from Ireland to London, where her father was Irish ambassador, and then to New York, where he was his country's representative at the United Nations, before finally returning to Ireland in adolescence. She attended convent schools in these various locations. In Ireland she studied—and then taught—English at Trinity College, Dublin, and since then she has taught at University College, the University of Iowa, and Stanford University.

Boland said in a 1994 lecture, "I am an Irish poet. A woman poet. In the first category I enter the tradition of the English language at an angle. In the second, I enter my own tradition at an even more steep angle." The great puzzle of Boland's career has been how to embrace Irish identity while rejecting certain male-centered assumptions that have long dominated Irish literary culture. For Boland as a young woman writer, the frozen, mythical images of the Irish nation as an idealized woman—Mother Ireland, Dark Rosaleen, Cathleen Ni Houlihan—were inhibiting and insufficient. To bring into Irish verse a national narrative, a "herstory" that interweaves private life and public life, Boland seized on an alternative tradition to that of Irish male poets—namely, the example of American women poets such as Sylvia Plath and Adrienne Rich. Her eye for symbolic detail, her ear for musical structure, her use of form to mirror content have served her well in her effort to recover and vivify Irish women's historical experiences, including domestic labor, motherhood, famine, prostitution, and emigration.

Fond Memory

It was a school where all the children wore darned worsted;°   *woolen fabric*
where they cried—or almost all—when the Reverend Mother
announced at lunch-time that the King[1] had died

peacefully in his sleep. I dressed in wool as well,
5   ate rationed food, played English games and learned
how wise the Magna Carta was, how hard the Hanoverians[2]

---

1. King George VI of the United Kingdom died in 1952. Boland's father was a diplomat, and she spent much of her childhood in London.

2. Family of English monarchs who reigned from 1714 to 1901. "Magna Carta": charter of English liberties granted by King John in 1215.

had tried, the measure and complexity of verse,
the hum and score of the whole orchestra.
At three-o-clock I caught two buses home

10 where sometimes in the late afternoon
    at a piano pushed into a corner of the playroom
    my father would sit down and play the slow

    lilts of Tom Moore[3] while I stood there trying
    not to weep at the cigarette smoke stinging up
15 from between his fingers and—as much as I could think—

    I thought this is my country, was, will be again,
    this upward-straining song made to be
    our safe inventory of pain. And I was wrong.

                                                    1987

That the Science of Cartography[1] Is Limited

    —and not simply by the fact that this shading of
    forest cannot show the fragrance of balsam,
    the gloom of cypresses
    is what I wish to prove.

5   When you and I were first in love we drove
    to the borders of Connacht[2]
    and entered a wood there.

    Look down you said: this was once a famine road.

    I looked down at ivy and the scutch grass
10 rough-cast stone had
    disappeared into as you told me
    in the second winter of their ordeal, in

    1847, when the crop[3] had failed twice,
    Relief Committees gave
15 the starving Irish such roads to build.

    Where they died, there the road ended

    and ends still and when I take down
    the map of this island, it is never so
    I can say here is
20 the masterful, the apt rendering of

    the spherical as flat, nor
    an ingenious design which persuades a curve

3. Irish poet and singer (1779–1852).
1. Mapmaking.
2. Western province of Ireland.

3. Of potatoes, staple diet of Irish peasants in the
19th century. Over a million people died in the
Irish Famine of 1845–49.

into a plane,
but to tell myself again that

25   the line which says woodland and cries hunger
and gives out among sweet pine and cypress,
and finds no horizon

will not be there.

1994

The Dolls Museum in Dublin

The wounds are terrible. The paint is old.
The cracks along the lips and on the cheeks
cannot be fixed. The cotton lawn[1] is soiled.
The arms are ivory dissolved to wax.

5   Recall the Quadrille.[2] Hum the waltz.
Promenade on the yacht-club terraces.
Put back the lamps in their copper holders,
the carriage wheels on the cobbled quays.

And recreate Easter in Dublin.[3]
10   Booted officers. Their mistresses.
Sunlight criss-crossing College Green.
Steam hissing from the flanks of horses.

Here they are. Cradled and cleaned,
held close in the arms of their owners.
15   Their cold hands clasped by warm hands,
their faces memorized like perfect manners.

The altars are mannerly with linen.
The lilies are whiter than surplices.[4]
The candles are burning and warning:
20   Rejoice, they whisper. After sacrifice.

Horse-chestnuts hold up their candles.
The Green is vivid with parasols.
Sunlight is pastel and windless.
The bar of the Shelbourne[5] is full.

25   Laughter and gossip on the terraces.
Rumour and alarm at the barracks.
The Empire is summoning its officers.
The carriages are turning: they are turning back.

---

1. Usually fine linen, but also, as here, fine cotton.
2. A square dance and the music for it.
3. What became known as the "Easter Rising" began on Easter Monday, 1916, when over sixteen hundred Irish Nationalists seized key points in Dublin and an Irish Republic was proclaimed from the General Post Office. See W. B. Yeats's "Easter, 1916" (p. 2031).
4. White linen vestments worn over cassocks.
5. Large Dublin hotel.

Past children walking with governesses,
30 Looking down, cossetting their dolls,
then looking up as the carriage passes,
the shadow chilling them. Twilight falls.

It is twilight in the dolls' museum. Shadows
remain on the parchment-coloured waists,
35 are bruises on the stitched cotton clothes,
are hidden in the dimples on the wrists.

The eyes are wide. They cannot address
the helplessness which has lingered in
the airless peace of each glass case:
40 to have survived. To have been stronger than

a moment. To be the hostages ignorance
takes from time and ornament from destiny. Both.
To be the present of the past. To infer the difference
with a terrible stare. But not feel it. And not know it.

1994

The Lost Land

I have two daughters.

They are all I ever wanted from the earth.

Or almost all.

I also wanted one piece of ground:

5   One city trapped by hills. One urban river.
An island in its element.

So I could say *mine. My own.*
And mean it.

Now they are grown up and far away

10   and memory itself
has become an emigrant,
wandering in a place
where love dissembles itself as landscape:

Where the hills
15   are the colours of a child's eyes,
where my children are distances, horizons:

At night,
on the edge of sleep,

I can see the shore of Dublin Bay.
20   Its rocky sweep and its granite pier.

Is this, I say
how they must have seen it,
backing out on the mailboat at twilight,

shadows falling
25   on everything they had to leave?
And would love forever?
And then

I imagine myself
at the landward rail of that boat
30   searching for the last sight of a hand.

I see myself
on the underworld side of that water,
the darkness coming in fast, saying
all the names I know for a lost land:

35   *Ireland. Absence. Daughter.*

1998

SALMAN RUSHDIE
b. 1947

The most influential novelist to have come from South Asia in the last fifty years is Ahmed Salman Rushdie, whose dynamic narratives—stories of magic, suffering, and the vitality of human beings in the grip of history—have helped generate the literary renaissance flowering in India today. "I come from Bombay," Rushdie has said, "and from a Muslim family, too. 'My' India has always been based on ideas of multiplicity, pluralism, hybridity: ideas to which the ideologies of the communalists are diametrically opposed. To my mind, the defining image of India is the crowd, and a crowd is by its very nature superabundant, heterogeneous, many things at once." Rushdie was educated at Cathedral School, Bombay (now Mumbai), and from the age of thirteen, at Rugby School, Warwickshire, and King's College, Cambridge. After living briefly in Pakistan, where his prosperous family had moved, Rushdie eventually settled in England, working as an actor and as a freelance advertising copywriter (1970–80).

His first novel, *Grimus* (1979), passed unnoticed, but his second, *Midnight's Children* (1981), announced the arrival of a major writer. Taking its title from those who were born—two months later than its author—around midnight on August 15, 1947, when the independent state of India was born, *Midnight's Children* is a work of prodigious prodigality, a cornucopia as richly fertile in character, incident, and language as the subcontinent that is its setting. The book's triumphant progress across the world culminated in its being judged "the Booker of Bookers," the best novel to have won Britain's premier fiction prize in its first twenty-five years. Rushdie has said that "we're all radio-active with history," and the books that have followed *Midnight's Children* have again shown a form of "magical realism"—learned from Latin American writers such as Jorge Luis Borges and Gabriel García Márquez—deployed in the service of a powerful political-historical imagination.

In 1988 Rushdie found himself at the perilous center of a real, rather than a magical realist, political-historical storm. His novel *The Satanic Verses* provoked riots in India, Pakistan, and South Africa, and was judged by senior religious figures in Iran to have blasphemed the Prophet Muhammad (called by the offensive name "Mahound" in the novel), founder of the Muslim faith, and a fatwa, or legal decree, calling for his death was pronounced. He was obliged to go into hiding, and for almost a decade lived under round-the-clock protection from British Secret Service agents, while governments argued for and against the lifting of the fatwa, and the author himself became symbolic of the vulnerability of the intellectual in the face of fundamentalism. The lifting of the fatwa in 1998 allowed Rushdie to reappear in public, but it is seen as irrevocable by some religious groups, and so his life remains under constant threat. He has defended his book in the essay "In Good Faith" (1990), while defining the irreverently pluralistic vision behind his "mongrel" aesthetic—a vision that has repeatedly resulted in the burning or banning of his books by political nationalists and religious purists in South Asia and other parts of the world:

> If *The Satanic Verses* is anything, it is a migrant's-eye view of the world. It is written from the very experience of uprooting, disjuncture and metamorphosis (slow or rapid, painful or pleasurable) that is the migrant condition, and from which, I believe, can be derived a metaphor for all humanity.
>
> Standing at the centre of the novel is a group of characters most of whom are British Muslims, or not particularly religious persons of Muslim background, struggling with just the sort of great problems of hybridization and ghettoization, of reconciling the old and the new. Those who oppose the novel most vociferously today are of the opinion that intermingling with a different culture will inevitably weaken and ruin their own. I am of the opposite opinion. *The Satanic Verses* celebrates hybridity, impurity, intermingling, the transformation that comes of new and unexpected combinations of human beings, cultures, ideas, politics, movies, songs. It rejoices in mongrelization and fears the absolutism of the Pure. *Mélange*, hotchpotch, a bit of this and a bit of that is *how newness enters the world*. It is the great possibility that mass migration gives the world, and I have tried to embrace it. *The Satanic Verses* is for change-by-fusion, change-by-conjoining. It is a love-song to our mongrel selves.

An earlier story, published the same year as his groundbreaking *Midnight's Children*, had invoked the Prophet uncontroversially. Like *Midnight's Children*, the story "The Prophet's Hair" buoyantly fuses Standard English with an exuberantly Indianized English, peppered with words of Hindi, Persian, Sanskrit, and Arabic origin—among the many languages that have been used in the extraordinarily polyglot Indian subcontinent. Like *The Satanic Verses*, "The Prophet's Hair" risks playfulness, satire, caricature, and whimsy in its treatment of the religion of his youth (though Rushdie has indicated he was brought up not as a believer but within a relaxed Muslim climate, almost secularized by the variety of other religions surrounding it). The story is at once a moral fable in the tradition of *The Thousand and One Nights* and a magical realist extravaganza, packed with incident, poetic detail ("water to which the cold of the night had given the cloudy consistency of wild honey"), and humor, all brilliantly interwoven at breakneck speed.

RL = hair stolen
From a shrine, riots,
order to find the hair,
found, Priest authenticated.

The Prophet's[1] Hair

Early in the year 19—, when Srinagar[2] was under the spell of a winter so fierce it could crack men's bones as if they were glass, a young man upon whose cold-pinked skin there lay, like a frost, the unmistakable sheen of wealth was to be seen entering the most wretched and disreputable part of the city, where the houses of wood and corrugated iron seemed perpetually on the verge of losing their balance, and asking in low, grave tones where he might go to engage the services of a dependably professional burglar. The young man's name was Atta, and the rogues in that part of town directed him gleefully into ever darker and less public alleys, until in a yard wet with the blood of a slaughtered chicken he was set upon by two men whose faces he never saw, robbed of the substantial bank-roll which he had insanely brought on his solitary excursion, and beaten within an inch of his life.

Night fell. His body was carried by anonymous hands to the edge of the lake, whence it was transported by shikara[3] across the water and deposited, torn and bleeding, on the deserted embankment of the canal which led to the gardens of Shalimar. At dawn the next morning a flower-vendor was rowing his boat through water to which the cold of the night had given the cloudy consistency of wild honey when he saw the prone form of young Atta, who was just beginning to stir and moan, and on whose now deathly pale skin the sheen of wealth could still be made out dimly beneath an actual layer of frost.

The flower-vendor moored his craft and by stooping over the mouth of the injured man was able to learn the poor fellow's address, which was mumbled through lips that could scarcely move; whereupon, hoping for a large tip, the hawker rowed Atta home to a large house on the shores of the lake, where a beautiful but inexplicably bruised young woman and her distraught, but equally handsome mother, neither of whom, it was clear from their eyes, had slept a wink from worrying, screamed at the sight of their Atta—who was the elder brother of the beautiful young woman—lying motionless amidst the funereally stunted winter blooms of the hopeful florist.

The flower-vendor was indeed paid off handsomely, not least to ensure his silence, and plays no further part in our story. Atta himself, suffering terribly from exposure as well as a broken skull, entered a coma which caused the city's finest doctors to shrug helplessly. It was therefore all the more remarkable that on the very next evening the most wretched and disreputable part of the city received a second unexpected visitor. This was Huma, the sister of the unfortunate young man, and her question was the same as her brother's, and asked in the same low, grave tones:

'Where may I hire a thief?'

The story of the rich idiot who had come looking for a burglar was already common knowledge in those insalubrious[4] gullies, but this time the young woman added: 'I should say that I am carrying no money, nor am I wearing any jewellery items. My father has disowned me and will pay no ransom if I am kidnapped; and a letter has been lodged with the Deputy Commissioner

---

1. The Prophet Muhammad, founder of the Muslim religion, was born in Mecca about 570 and died in 632.
2. Capital of the state of Kashmir.
3. Long swift Kashmiri boat.
4. Unhealthy.

of Police, my uncle, to be opened in the event of my not being safe at home by morning. In that letter he will find full details of my journey here, and he will move Heaven and Earth to punish my assailants.'

Her exceptional beauty, which was visible even through the enormous welts and bruises disfiguring her arms and forehead, coupled with the oddity of her inquiries, had attracted a sizable group of curious onlookers, and because her little speech seemed to them to cover just about everything, no one attempted to injure her in any way, although there were some raucous comments to the effect that it was pretty peculiar for someone who was trying to hire a crook to invoke the protection of a high-up policeman uncle.

She was directed into ever darker and less public alleys until finally in a gully as dark as ink an old woman with eyes which stared so piercingly that Huma instantly understood she was blind motioned her through a doorway from which darkness seemed to be pouring like smoke. Clenching her fists, angrily ordering her heart to behave normally, Huma followed the old woman into the gloom-wrapped house.

The faintest conceivable rivulet of candlelight trickled through the darkness; following this unreliable yellow thread (because she could no longer see the old lady), Huma received a sudden sharp blow to the shins and cried out involuntarily, after which she at once bit her lip, angry at having revealed her mounting terror to whoever or whatever waited before her, shrouded in blackness.

She had, in fact, collided with a low table on which a single candle burned and beyond which a mountainous figure could be made out, sitting cross-legged on the floor. 'Sit, sit,' said a man's calm, deep voice, and her legs, needing no more flowery invitation, buckled beneath her at the terse command. Clutching her left hand in her right, she forced her voice to respond evenly:

'And you, sir, will be the thief I have been requesting?'

Shifting its weight very slightly, the shadow-mountain informed Huma that all criminal activity originating in this zone was well organised and also centrally controlled, so that all requests for what might be termed freelance work had to be channelled through this room.

He demanded comprehensive details of the crime to be committed, including a precise inventory of items to be acquired, also a clear statement of all financial inducements being offered with no gratuities excluded, plus, for filing purposes only, a summary of the motives for the application.

At this, Huma, as though remembering something, stiffened both in body and resolve and replied loudly that her motives were entirely a matter for herself; that she would discuss details with no one but the thief himself; but that the rewards she proposed could only be described as 'lavish'.

'All I am willing to disclose to you, sir, since it appears that I am on the premises of some sort of employment agency, is that in return for such lavish rewards I must have the most desperate criminal at your disposal, a man for whom life holds no terrors, not even the fear of God.

'The worst of fellows, I tell you—nothing less will do!'

At this a paraffin storm-lantern was lighted, and Huma saw facing her a grey-haired giant down whose left cheek ran the most sinister of scars, a cicatrice

2856 / SALMAN RUSHDIE

in the shape of the letter *sín* in the Nastaliq[5] script. She was gripped by the insupportably nostalgic notion that the bogeyman of her childhood nursery had risen up to confront her, because her ayah[6] had always forestalled any incipient acts of disobedience by threatening Huma and Atta: 'You don't watch out and I'll send that one to steal you away—that Sheikh[7] Sín, the Thief of Thieves!'

Here, grey-haired but unquestionably scarred, was the notorious criminal himself—and was she out of her mind, were her ears playing tricks, or had he truly just announced that, given the stated circumstances, he himself was the only man for the job?

Struggling hard against the newborn goblins of nostalgia, Huma warned the fearsome volunteer that only a matter of extreme urgency and peril would have brought her unescorted into these ferocious streets.

'Because we can afford no last-minute backings-out,' she continued, 'I am determined to tell you everything, keeping back no secrets whatsoever. If, after hearing me out, you are still prepared to proceed, then we shall do everything in our power to assist you, and to make you rich.'

The old thief shrugged, nodded, spat. Huma began her story.

Six days ago, everything in the household of her father, the wealthy money-lender Hashim, had been as it always was. At breakfast her mother had spooned khichri[8] lovingly on to the moneylender's plate; the conversation had been filled with those expressions of courtesy and solicitude on which the family prided itself.

Hashim was fond of pointing out that while he was not a godly man he set great store by 'living honourably in the world'. In that spacious lakeside residence, all outsiders were greeted with the same formality and respect, even those unfortunates who came to negotiate for small fragments of Hashim's large fortune, and of whom he naturally asked an interest rate of over seventy per cent, partly, as he told his khichri-spooning wife, 'to teach these people the value of money; let them only learn that, and they will be cured of this fever of borrowing borrowing all the time—so you see that if my plans succeed, I shall put myself out of business!'

In their children, Atta and Huma, the moneylender and his wife had successfully sought to inculcate the virtues of thrift, plain dealing and a healthy independence of spirit. On this, too, Hashim was fond of congratulating himself.

Breakfast ended; the family members wished one another a fulfilling day. Within a few hours, however, the glassy contentment of that household, of that life of porcelain delicacy and alabaster sensibilities, was to be shattered beyond all hope of repair.

The moneylender summoned his personal shikara and was on the point of stepping into it when, attracted by a glint of silver, he noticed a small vial floating between the boat and his private quay. On an impulse, he scooped it out of the glutinous water.

5. A Persian cursive script, characterized by rounded forms and elongated horizontal strokes. "Cicatrice": scar of a healed wound.
6. Child's nurse (Anglo-Indian, from Portuguese).
7. Chief (Arabic).
8. Rice and lentils cooked together (Hindi).

It was a cylinder of tinted glass cased in exquisitely wrought silver, and Hashim saw within its walls a silver pendant bearing a single strand of human hair.

Closing his fist around this unique discovery, he muttered to the boatman that he'd changed his plans, and hurried to his sanctum,[9] where, behind closed doors, he feasted his eyes on his find.

There can be no doubt that Hashim the moneylender knew from the first that he was in possession of the famous relic of the Prophet Muhammad, that revered hair whose theft from its shrine at Hazratbal mosque the previous morning had created an unprecedented hue and cry in the valley.

The thieves—no doubt alarmed by the pandemonium, by the procession through the streets of endless ululating[1] crocodiles of lamentation, by the riots, the political ramifications and by the massive police search which was commanded and carried out by men whose entire careers now hung upon the finding of this lost hair—had evidently panicked and hurled the vial into the gelatine bosom of the lake.

Having found it by a stroke of great good fortune, Hashim's duty as a citizen was clear: the hair must be restored to its shrine, and the state to equanimity and peace.

But the moneylender had a different notion.

All around him in his study was the evidence of his collector's mania. There were enormous glass cases full of impaled butterflies from Gulmarg, three dozen scale models in various metals of the legendary cannon Zamzama, innumerable swords, a Naga spear, ninety-four terracotta camels of the sort sold on railway station platforms, many samovars,[2] and a whole zoology of tiny sandalwood animals, which had originally been carved to serve as children's bathtime toys.

'And after all,' Hashim told himself, 'the Prophet would have disapproved mightily of this relic-worship. He abhorred the idea of being deified! So, by keeping this hair from its distracted devotees, I perform—do I not?—a finer service than I would by returning it! Naturally, I don't want it for its religious value . . . I'm a man of the world, of this world. I see it purely as a secular object of great rarity and blinding beauty. In short, it's the silver vial I desire, more than the hair.

'They say there are American millionaires who purchase stolen art masterpieces and hide them away—they would know how I feel. I must, must have it!'

Every collector must share his treasures with one other human being, and Hashim summoned—and told—his only son Atta, who was deeply perturbed but, having been sworn to secrecy, only spilled the beans when the troubles became too terrible to bear.

The youth excused himself and left his father alone in the crowded solitude of his collections. Hashim was sitting erect in a hard, straight-backed chair, gazing intently at the beautiful vial.

9. Private room.
1. Howling.

2. Apparatuses for making tea (Russian for self-boilers).

It was well known that the moneylender never ate lunch, so it was not until evening that a servant entered the sanctum to summon his master to the dining-table. He found Hashim as Atta had left him. The same, and not the same—for now the moneylender looked swollen, distended. His eyes bulged even more than they always had, they were red-rimmed, and his knuckles were white.

He seemed to be on the point of bursting! As though, under the influence of the misappropriated relic, he had filled up with some spectral fluid which might at any moment ooze uncontrollably from his every bodily opening.

He had to be helped to the table, and then the explosion did indeed take place.

Seemingly careless of the effect of his words on the carefully constructed and fragile constitution of the family's life, Hashim began to gush, to spume long streams of awful truths. In horrified silence, his children heard their father turn upon his wife, and reveal to her that for many years their marriage had been the worst of his afflictions. 'An end to politeness!' he thundered. 'An end to hypocrisy!'

Next, and in the same spirit, he revealed to his family the existence of a mistress; he informed them also of his regular visits to paid women. He told his wife that, far from being the principal beneficiary of his will, she would receive no more than the eighth portion which was her due under Islamic law. Then he turned upon his children, screaming at Atta for his lack of academic ability—'A dope! I have been cursed with a dope!'—and accusing his daughter of lasciviousness, because she went around the city barefaced, which was unseemly for any good Muslim girl to do. She should, he commanded, enter purdah[3] forthwith.

Hashim left the table without having eaten and fell into the deep sleep of a man who has got many things off his chest, leaving his children stunned, in tears, and the dinner going cold on the sideboard under the gaze of an anticipatory bearer.[4]

At five o'clock the next morning the moneylender forced his family to rise, wash and say their prayers. From then on, he began to pray five times daily for the first time in his life, and his wife and children were obliged to do likewise.

Before breakfast, Huma saw the servants, under her father's direction, constructing a great heap of books in the garden and setting fire to it. The only volume left untouched was the Qur'an,[5] which Hashim wrapped in a silken cloth and placed on a table in the hall. He ordered each member of his family to read passages from this book for at least two hours per day. Visits to the cinema were forbidden. And if Atta invited male friends to the house, Huma was to retire to her room.

By now, the family had entered a state of shock and dismay; but there was worse to come.

That afternoon, a trembling debtor arrived at the house to confess his inability to pay the latest instalment of interest owed, and made the mistake of

---

3. Area of certain traditional Indian houses in which Hindu or Muslim women live secluded from the sight of men outside their family circle.

4. Servant.
5. Muslims' sacred book: collection of the Prophet Muhammad's oral revelations.

reminding Hashim, in somewhat blustering fashion, of the Qur'an's strictures against usury. The moneylender flew into a rage and attacked the fellow with one of his large collection of bullwhips.

By mischance, later the same day a second defaulter came to plead for time, and was seen fleeing Hashim's study with a great gash in his arm, because Huma's father had called him a thief of other men's money and had tried to cut off the wretch's right hand with one of the thirty-eight kukri knives[6] hanging on the study walls.

These breaches of the family's unwritten laws of decorum alarmed Atta and Huma, and when, that evening, their mother attempted to calm Hashim down, he struck her on the face with an open hand. Atta leapt to his mother's defence and he, too, was sent flying.

'From now on,' Hashim bellowed, 'there's going to be some discipline around here!'

The moneylender's wife began a fit of hysterics which continued throughout that night and the following day, and which so provoked her husband that he threatened her with divorce, at which she fled to her room, locked the door and subsided into a raga[7] of sniffling. Huma now lost her composure, challenged her father openly, and announced (with that same independence of spirit which he had encouraged in her) that she would wear no cloth over her face; apart from anything else, it was bad for the eyes.

On hearing this, her father disowned her on the spot and gave her one week in which to pack her bags and go.

By the fourth day, the fear in the air of the house had become so thick that it was difficult to walk around. Atta told his shock-numbed sister: 'We are descending to gutter-level—but I know what must be done.'

That afternoon, Hashim left home accompanied by two hired thugs to extract the unpaid dues from his two insolvent clients. Atta went immediately to his father's study. Being the son and heir, he possessed his own key to the moneylender's safe. This he now used, and removing the little vial from its hiding-place, he slipped it into his trouser pocket and re-locked the safe door.

Now he told Huma the secret of what his father had fished out of Lake Dal, and exclaimed: 'Maybe I'm crazy—maybe the awful things that are happening have made me cracked—but I am convinced there will be no peace in our house until this hair is out of it.'

His sister at once agreed that the hair must be returned, and Atta set off in a hired shikara to Hazratbal mosque. Only when the boat had delivered him into the throng of the distraught faithful which was swirling around the desecrated shrine did Atta discover that the relic was no longer in his pocket. There was only a hole, which his mother, usually so attentive to household matters, must have overlooked under the stress of recent events.

Atta's initial surge of chagrin was quickly replaced by a feeling of profound relief.

'Suppose', he imagined, 'that I had already announced to the mullahs[8] that

---

6. Curved knives broadening toward the point (Hindi).
7. Musical improvisation (Sanskrit).

8. Muslims learned in Islamic theology and sacred law.

the hair was on my person! They would never have believed me now—and this mob would have lynched me! At any rate, it has gone, and that's a load off my mind.' Feeling more contented than he had for days, the young man returned home.

Here he found his sister bruised and weeping in the hall; upstairs, in her bedroom, his mother wailed like a brand-new widow. He begged Huma to tell him what had happened, and when she replied that their father, returning from his brutal business trip, had once again noticed a glint of silver between boat and quay, had once again scooped up the errant relic, and was consequently in a rage to end all rages, having beaten the truth out of her—then Atta buried his face in his hands and sobbed out his opinion, which was that the hair was persecuting them, and had come back to finish the job.

It was Huma's turn to think of a way out of their troubles.

While her arms turned black and blue and great stains spread across her forehead, she hugged her brother and whispered to him that she was determined to get rid of the hair *at all costs*—she repeated this last phrase several times.

'The hair', she then declared, 'was stolen from the mosque; so it can be stolen from this house. But it must be a genuine robbery, carried out by a bona-fide thief, not by one of us who are under the hair's thrall—by a thief so desperate that he fears neither capture nor curses.'

Unfortunately, she added, the theft would be ten times harder to pull off now that their father, knowing that there had already been one attempt on the relic, was certainly on his guard.

'Can you do it?'

Huma, in a room lit by candle and storm-lantern, ended her account with one further question: 'What assurances can you give that the job holds no terrors for you still?'

The criminal, spitting, stated that he was not in the habit of providing references, as a cook might, or a gardener, but he was not alarmed so easily, certainly not by any children's djinni[9] of a curse. Huma had to be content with this boast, and proceeded to describe the details of the proposed burglary.

'Since my brother's failure to return the hair to the mosque, my father has taken to sleeping with his precious treasure under his pillow. However, he sleeps alone, and very energetically; only enter his room without waking him, and he will certainly have tossed and turned quite enough to make the theft a simple matter. When you have the vial, come to my room,' and here she handed Sheikh Sín a plan of her home, 'and I will hand over all the jewellery owned by my mother and myself. You will find . . . it is worth . . . that is, you will be able to get a fortune for it . . . '

It was evident that her self-control was weakening and that she was on the point of physical collapse.

'Tonight,' she burst out finally. 'You must come tonight!'

No sooner had she left the room than the old criminal's body was convulsed by a fit of coughing: he spat blood into an old vanaspati[1] can. The great Sheikh,

---

9. In Muslim demonology a spirit (genie) with supernatural powers.

1. Vegetable fat used as butter in India.

the 'Thief of Thieves', had become a sick man, and every day the time drew nearer when some young pretender to his power would stick a dagger in his stomach. A lifelong addiction to gambling had left him almost as poor as he had been when, decades ago, he had started out in this line of work as a mere pickpocket's apprentice; so in the extraordinary commission he had accepted from the moneylender's daughter he saw his opportunity of amassing enough wealth at a stroke to leave the valley for ever, and acquire the luxury of a respectable death which would leave his stomach intact.

As for the Prophet's hair, well, neither he nor his blind wife had ever had much to say for prophets—that was one thing they had in common with the moneylender's thunderstruck clan.

It would not do, however, to reveal the nature of this, his last crime, to his four sons. To his consternation, they had all grown up to be hopelessly devout men, who even spoke of making the pilgrimage to Mecca some day. 'Absurd!' their father would laugh at them. 'Just tell me how you will go?' For, with a parent's absolutist love, he had made sure they were all provided with a lifelong source of high income by crippling them at birth, so that, as they dragged themselves around the city, they earned excellent money in the begging business.

The children, then, could look after themselves.

He and his wife would be off soon with the jewel-boxes of the moneylender's women. It was a timely chance indeed that had brought the beautiful bruised girl into his corner of the town.

That night, the large house on the shore of the lake lay blindly waiting, with silence lapping at its walls. A burglar's night: clouds in the sky and mists on the winter water. Hashim the moneylender was asleep, the only member of his family to whom sleep had come that night. In another room, his son Atta lay deep in the coils of his coma with a blood-clot forming on his brain, watched over by a mother who had let down her long greying hair to show her grief, a mother who placed warm compresses on his head with gestures redolent of impotence. In a third bedroom Huma waited, fully dressed, amidst the jewel-heavy caskets of her desperation.

At last a bulbul[2] sang softly from the garden below her window and, creeping downstairs, she opened a door to the bird, on whose face there was a scar in the shape of the Nastaliq letter *sín*.

Noiselessly, the bird flew up the stairs behind her. At the head of the staircase they parted, moving in opposite directions along the corridor of their conspiracy without a glance at one another.

Entering the moneylender's room with professional ease, the burglar, Sín, discovered that Huma's predictions had been wholly accurate. Hashim lay sprawled diagonally across his bed, the pillow untenanted by his head, the prize easily accessible. Step by padded step, Sín moved towards the goal.

It was at this point that, in the bedroom next door, young Atta sat bolt upright in his bed, giving his mother a great fright, and without any warning—prompted by goodness knows what pressure of the blood-clot upon his brain—began screaming at the top of his voice:

'Thief! Thief! Thief!'

2. Asian song thrush.

It seems probable that his poor mind had been dwelling, in these last moments, upon his own father; but it is impossible to be certain, because having uttered these three emphatic words the young man fell back upon his pillow and died.

At once his mother set up a screeching and a wailing and a keening and a howling so earsplittingly intense that they completed the work which Atta's cry had begun—that is, her laments penetrated the walls of her husband's bedroom and brought Hashim wide awake.

Sheikh Sín was just deciding whether to dive beneath the bed or brain the moneylender good and proper when Hashim grabbed the tiger-striped swords-tick which always stood propped up in a corner beside his bed, and rushed from the room without so much as noticing the burglar who stood on the opposite side of the bed in the darkness. Sín stooped quickly and removed the vial containing the Prophet's hair from its hiding-place.

Meanwhile Hashim had erupted into the corridor, having unsheathed the sword inside his cane. In his right hand he held the weapon and was waving it about dementedly. His left hand was shaking the stick. A shadow came rushing towards him through the midnight darkness of the passageway and, in his somnolent anger, the moneylender thrust his sword fatally through its heart. Turning up the light, he found that he had murdered his daughter, and under the dire influence of this accident he was so overwhelmed by remorse that he turned the sword upon himself, fell upon it and so extinguished his life. His wife, the sole surviving member of the family, was driven mad by the general carnage and had to be committed to an asylum for the insane by her brother, the city's Deputy Commissioner of Police.

Sheikh Sín had quickly understood that the plan had gone awry.

Abandoning the dream of the jewel-boxes when he was but a few yards from its fulfilment, he climbed out of Hashim's window and made his escape during the appalling events described above. Reaching home before dawn, he woke his wife and confessed his failure. It would be necessary, he whispered, for him to vanish for a while. Her blind eyes never opened until he had gone.

The noise in the Hashim household had roused their servants and even man-aged to awaken the night-watchman, who had been fast asleep as usual on his charpoy[3] by the street-gate. They alerted the police, and the Deputy Commis-sioner himself was informed. When he heard of Huma's death, the mournful officer opened and read the sealed letter which his niece had given him, and instantly led a large detachment of armed men into the light-repellent gullies of the most wretched and disreputable part of the city.

The tongue of a malicious cat-burglar named Huma's fellow-conspirator; the finger of an ambitious bank-robber pointed at the house in which he lay concealed; and although Sín managed to crawl through a hatch in the attic and attempt a roof-top escape, a bullet from the Deputy Commissioner's own rifle penetrated his stomach and brought him crashing messily to the ground at the feet of Huma's enraged uncle.

From the dead thief's pocket rolled a vial of tinted glass, cased in filigree silver.

---

3. Light Indian bedstead.

The recovery of the Prophet's hair was announced at once on All-India Radio. One month later, the valley's holiest men assembled at the Hazratbal mosque and formally authenticated the relic. It sits to this day in a closely guarded vault by the shores of the loveliest of lakes in the heart of the valley which was once closer than any other place on earth to Paradise.

But before our story can properly be concluded, it is necessary to record that when the four sons of the dead Sheikh awoke on the morning of his death, having unwittingly spent a few minutes under the same roof as the famous hair, they found that a miracle had occurred, that they were all sound of limb and strong of wind, as whole as they might have been if their father had not thought to smash their legs in the first hours of their lives. They were, all four of them, very properly furious, because the miracle had reduced their earning powers by 75 per cent, at the most conservative estimate; so they were ruined men.

Only the Sheikh's widow had some reason for feeling grateful, because although her husband was dead she had regained her sight, so that it was possible for her to spend her last days gazing once more upon the beauties of the valley of Kashmir.

, Don't steAL
, DAngers of Religious Extremeism

1981

ANNE CARSON
b. 1950

Anne Carson was born in Toronto, Canada, and grew up in Ontario, and she received both her B.A. and her Ph.D. in classics from the University of Toronto. The recipient of a MacArthur Fellowship, she has taught classics at McGill University and the University of Michigan, among other schools. Along with poetry, she has published books of criticism on classical literature; translations from Greek; and a novel-in-verse, *Autobiography of Red* (1998).

In her poetry Carson braids together the ruminative texture of the essay, the narrative propulsion of the novel, the self-analysis of autobiography, and the lapidary compression of lyric. In "The Glass Essay," a long poem that reflects on the dislocations of identity through time, love, and madness, she vividly narrates the end of a love affair, a visit with a difficult mother, and the degeneration of a father with Alzheimer's in a nursing home. Into this semiautobiographical tale she weaves commentary on the writings of Charlotte and Emily Brontë, whose works function—like the classical texts she often incorporates into her poetry—as oblique and remote points of comparison for the poet's experience. Both personal and impersonal, Carson's poetry bridges the gap between private narrative and philosophical speculation, between self-excavation and literary-critical analysis. Tightly wound with crisp diction, studded with striking metaphors, etched with epigrams and ironies, her poems are lucid in feeling and intense in thought. They are as intellectually crystalline as they are emotionally volcanic.

From The Glass Essay

Hero

I can tell by the way my mother chews her toast
whether she had a good night
and is about to say a happy thing
or not.

5 Not.
She puts her toast down on the side of her plate.
You know you can pull the drapes in that room, she begins.

This is a coded reference to one of our oldest arguments,
from what I call The Rules Of Life series.
10 My mother always closes her bedroom drapes tight before going to bed at
    night.

I open mine as wide as possible.
I like to see everything, I say.
What's there to see?

Moon. Air. Sunrise.
15 All that light on your face in the morning. Wakes you up.
I like to wake up.

At this point the drapes argument has reached a delta
and may advance along one of three channels.
There is the What You Need Is A Good Night's Sleep channel,

20 the Stubborn As Your Father channel
and random channel.
More toast? I interpose strongly, pushing back my chair.

Those women! says my mother with an exasperated rasp.
Mother has chosen random channel.
25 Women?

Complaining about rape all the time—
I see she is tapping one furious finger on yesterday's newspaper
lying beside the grape jam.

The front page has a small feature
30 about a rally for International Women's Day—
have you had a look at the Sears Summer Catalogue?

Nope.
Why, it's a disgrace! Those bathing suits—
cut way up to here! (she points) No wonder!

35 You're saying women deserve to get raped
because Sears bathing suit ads
have high-cut legs? Ma, are you serious?

Well someone has to be responsible.
Why should women be responsible for male desire? My voice is high.
Oh I see you're one of Them.

One of Whom? My voice is very high. Mother vaults it.
And whatever did you do with that little tank suit you had last year the
    green one?
It looked so smart on you.

The frail fact drops on me from a great height
that my mother is afraid.
She will be eighty years old this summer.

Her tiny sharp shoulders hunched in the blue bathrobe
make me think of Emily Brontë's little merlin hawk Hero
that she fed bits of bacon at the kitchen table when Charlotte[1] wasn't
    around.

So Ma, we'll go—I pop up the toaster
and toss a hot slice of pumpernickel lightly across onto her plate—
visit Dad today? She eyes the kitchen clock with hostility.

Leave at eleven, home again by four? I continue.
She is buttering her toast with jagged strokes.
Silence is assent in our code. I go into the next room to phone the taxi.

My father lives in a hospital for patients who need chronic care
about 50 miles from here.
He suffers from a kind of dementia

characterized by two sorts of pathological change
first recorded in 1907 by Alois Alzheimer.[2]
First, the presence in cerebral tissue

of a spherical formation known as neuritic plaque,
consisting mainly of degenerating brain cells.
Second, neurofibrillary snarlings

in the cerebral cortex and in the hippocampus.[3]
There is no known cause or cure.
Mother visits him by taxi once a week

for the last five years.
Marriage is for better or for worse, she says,
this is the worse.

So about an hour later we are in the taxi
shooting along empty country roads towards town.
The April light is clear as an alarm.

1. Charlotte Brontë (1816–1855), English novelist, author of *Jane Eyre*, and sister of Emily (1818–
1848), author of *Wuthering Heights*. Throughout
"The Glass Essay," the poet compares her own life
with Emily Brontë's.
2. German neurologist (1864–1915).
3. Parts of the brain. Neurofibrils are nerve fibers.

As we pass them it gives a sudden sense of every object
75 existing in space on its own shadow.
I wish I could carry this clarity with me

into the hospital where distinctions tend to flatten and coalesce.
I wish I had been nicer to him before he got crazy.
These are my two wishes.

80 It is hard to find the beginning of dementia.
I remember a night about ten years ago
when I was talking to him on the telephone.

It was a Sunday night in winter.
I heard his sentences filling up with fear.
85 He would start a sentence—about weather, lose his way, start another.
It made me furious to hear him floundering—

my tall proud father, former World War II navigator!
It made me merciless.
I stood on the edge of the conversation,

90 watching him thrash about for cues,
offering none,
and it came to me like a slow avalanche

that he had no idea who he was talking to.
Much colder today I guess. . . .
95 his voice pressed into the silence and broke off,

snow falling on it.
There was a long pause while snow covered us both.
Well I won't keep you,

he said with sudden desperate cheer as if sighting land.
100 I'll say goodnight now,
I won't run up your bill. Goodbye.

Goodbye.
Goodbye. Who are you?
I said into the dial tone.

105 At the hospital we pass down long pink halls
through a door with a big window
and a combination lock (5–25–3)

to the west wing, for chronic care patients.
Each wing has a name.
110 The chronic wing is Our Golden Mile

although mother prefers to call it The Last Lap.
Father sits strapped in a chair which is tied to the wall
in a room of other tied people tilting at various angles.

My father tilts least, I am proud of him.
115   Hi Dad how y'doing?
His face cracks open it could be a grin or rage

and looking past me he issues a stream of vehemence at the air.
My mother lays her hand on his.
Hello love, she says. He jerks his hand away. We sit.

120   Sunlight flocks through the room.
Mother begins to unpack from her handbag the things she has brought for
        him,
grapes, arrowroot biscuits, humbugs.°   *hard candies*

He is addressing strenuous remarks to someone in the air between us.
He uses a language known only to himself,
125   made of snarls and syllables and sudden wild appeals.

Once in a while some old formula floats up through the wash—
You don't say! or Happy birthday to you!—
but no real sentence

for more than three years now.
130   I notice his front teeth are getting black.
I wonder how you clean the teeth of mad people.

He always took good care of his teeth. My mother looks up.
She and I often think two halves of one thought.
Do you remember that gold-plated toothpick

135   you sent him from Harrod's⁴ the summer you were in London? she asks.
Yes I wonder what happened to it.
Must be in the bathroom somewhere.

She is giving him grapes one by one.
They keep rolling out of his huge stiff fingers.
140   He used to be a big man, over six feet tall and strong,

but since he came to hospital his body has shrunk to the merest bone
        house—
except the hands. The hands keep growing.
Each one now as big as a boot in Van Gogh,⁵

they go lumbering after the grapes in his lap.
145   But now he turns to me with a rush of urgent syllables
that break off on a high note—he waits,

staring into my face. That quizzical look.
One eyebrow at an angle.
I have a photograph taped to my fridge at home.

4. Department store.
5. Vincent van Gogh (1853–1890), Dutch postimpressionist, painted *A Pair of Boots* (1887).

150 It shows his World War II air crew posing in front of the plane.
Hands firmly behind backs, legs wide apart,
chins forward.

Dressed in the puffed flying suits
with a wide leather strap pulled tight through the crotch.
155 They squint into the brilliant winter sun of 1942.

It is dawn.
They are leaving Dover[6] for France.
My father on the far left is the tallest airman,

with his collar up,
160 one eyebrow at an angle.
The shadowless light makes him look immortal,

for all the world like someone who will not weep again.
He is still staring into my face.
Flaps down! I cry.
165 His black grin flares once and goes out like a match.

1995

Epitaph: Zion[1]

Murderous little world once our objects had gazes. Our lives
    Were fragile, the wind
Could dash them away. Here lies the refugee breather
    Who drank a bowl of elsewhere.

2000

6. Port on the English Channel.
1. In the Hebrew Bible the eastern hill of Jerusalem. In Judaism it came to symbolize a promised

homeland; in Christianity, a heavenly or ideal city
of faith.

PAUL MULDOON
b. 1951

Paul Muldoon was born in Portadown, County Armagh, Northern Ireland. His
mother was a schoolteacher; his father, a farm laborer and mushroom grower. He
grew up in, as he put it, "a little enclave of Roman Catholics living within the predominantly Protestant parish of Loughgall, the village where the Orange Order was
founded in 1795." Despite inheriting strong Republican sympathies, he depicts the
Catholic Church unsympathetically, even going so far as to state that there is "a very
fine line between organized religion and organized crime." He was educated at the
primary school in Collegelands (where his mother taught); St. Patrick's College,
Armagh; and Queen's University, Belfast, where he was tutored by Seamus Heaney
and came to know other poets of the "Belfast Group," such as Derek Mahon and

Michael Longley. He worked as a radio and television producer for the British Broadcasting Corporation in Belfast until, in the mid-1980s, he became a freelance writer and moved to the United States, where he teaches at Princeton University.

Muldoon's first published poems were written in Irish, and although he soon switched to English, Irish words and phrases continued to appear in his work. As with many other Irish poets, America soon loomed large in his imagination. Excited by American films, he adapted cinematic techniques in hectic, hallucinatory long poems. Other poems, such as "Meeting the British," parallel the plight of American Indians with that of Northern Irish Catholics. Still others, such as "The Grand Conversation," turn his marriage to the American Jewish writer Jean Korelitz into a densely specific yet allegorical poem about identity and intercultural experience. His earliest literary influence was, he said, Robert Frost's "strong, classic, lyric line. But the most important thing . . . was his mischievous, shy, multi-layered quality under the surface." It would be hard to improve on that last sentence as a description of Muldoon's own mature style, the expression of an omnivorous imagination that—in "Milkweed and Monarch," for example—mixes his parents' Collegelands grave with other geographically scattered memories into a kaleidoscopic pattern that is at once moving, musically satisfying, and a brilliant postmodern variation on the ancient poetic form of villanelle (with the repetition of its first and third lines).

Meeting the British

We met the British in the dead of winter.
The sky was lavender

and the snow lavender-blue.
I could hear, far below,

5   the sound of two streams coming together
(both were frozen over)

and, no less strange,
myself calling out in French

across that forest-
10   clearing. Neither General Jeffrey Amherst[1]

nor Colonel Henry Bouquet
could stomach our willow-tobacco.

As for the unusual
scent when the Colonel shook out his hand-

1. Commander-in-chief of British forces in the French and Indian War (1754–63); fought against France and its Native American allies. During Pontiac's Rebellion (1763–64), led by Ottawa chief Pontiac in the Great Lakes region, Amherst wrote to the British officer Colonel Bouquet, "Could it not be contrived to Send the *Small Pox* among those Disaffected Tribes of Indians?" Bouquet replied, "I will try to inoculate the Indians by means of Blankets that may fall in their hands, tak- ing care however not to get the disease myself," to which Amherst responded, "You will Do well to try to Innoculate the Indians by means of Blanketts, as well as to try Every other method that can serve to Extirpate this Execreble Race." Apparently as a result of this and similar plans of other British officers, many Native Americans in the area, never having been exposed to smallpox, were killed by the disease in 1763–64. Pontiac concluded a peace treaty with the British in July 1766.

15   kerchief: *C'est la lavande,*
une fleur mauve comme le ciel.[2]

They gave us six fishhooks
and two blankets embroidered with smallpox.

1987

Gathering Mushrooms

The rain comes flapping through the yard
like a tablecloth that she hand-embroidered.
My mother has left it on the line.
It is sodden with rain.
5   The mushroom shed is windowless, wide,
its high-stacked wooden trays
hosed down with formaldehyde.[1]
And my father has opened the Gates of Troy[2]
to that first load of horse manure.
10   Barley straw. Gypsum.[3] Dried blood. Ammonia.
Wagon after wagon
blusters in, a self-renewing gold-black dragon
we push to the back of the mind.
We have taken our pitchforks to the wind.

15   All brought back to me that September evening
fifteen years on. The pair of us
tripping through Barnett's fair demesne°   *domain*
like girls in long dresses
after a hail-storm.
20   We might have been thinking of the fire-bomb
that sent Malone House[4] sky-high
and its priceless collection of linen
sky-high.
We might have wept with Elizabeth McCrum.
25   We were thinking only of psilocybin.[5]
You sang of the maid you met on the dewy grass—
And she stooped so low gave me to know
it was mushrooms she was gathering O.

He'll be wearing that same old donkey-jacket[6]
30   and the sawn-off waders.
He carries a knife, two punnets,[7] a bucket.
He reaches far into his own shadow.
We'll have taken him unawares
and stand behind him, slightly to one side.

2. It is lavender, a flower purple as the sky (French).
1. Formic-acid disinfectant.
2. City besieged by the Greeks in Homer's *Iliad*. Its walls could not be destroyed from without, and it was finally captured only by a trick.
3. Hydrated calcium sulfate, used for making plas-

ter of Paris.
4. A mansion in Barnett Demesne, Belfast, bombed in 1976.
5. Hallucinogenic drug made from mushrooms.
6. Strong jacket with leather shoulder patches.
7. Small shallow baskets for fruit or vegetables.

35　He is one of those ancient warriors
　　before the rising tide.
　　He'll glance back from under his peaked cap
　　without breaking rhythm:
　　his coaxing a mushroom—a flat or a cup—
40　the nick against his right thumb;
　　the bucket then, the punnet to left or right,
　　and so on and so forth till kingdom come.

　　We followed the overgrown tow-path by the Lagan.[8]
　　The sunset would deepen through cinnamon
45　to aubergine,
　　the wood-pigeon's concerto for oboe and strings,
　　allegro, blowing your mind.
　　And you were suddenly out of my ken, hurtling
　　towards the ever-receding ground,
50　into the maw
　　of a shimmering green-gold dragon.
　　You discovered yourself in some outbuilding
　　with your long-lost companion, me,
　　though my head had grown into the head of a horse
55　that shook its dirty-fair mane
　　and spoke this verse:

　　Come back to us. However cold and raw, your feet
　　were always meant
　　to negotiate terms with bare cement.
60　*Beyond this concrete wall is a wall of concrete*
　　and barbed wire. Your only hope
　　is to come back. If sing you must, let your song
　　tell of treading your own dung,
　　let straw and dung give a spring to your step.
65　*If we never live to see the day we leap*
　　into our true domain,
　　lie down with us now and wrap
　　yourself in the soiled grey blanket of Irish rain
　　that will, one day, bleach itself white.
70　*Lie down with us and wait.*

　　　　　　　　　　　　　　　　　　　　　　　　　　1983

Milkweed and Monarch

　　As he knelt by the grave of his mother and father
　　the taste of dill, or tarragon—
　　he could barely tell one from the other—

　　filled his mouth. It seemed as if he might smother.
5　Why should he be stricken
　　with grief, not for his mother and father,

but a woman slinking from the fur of a sea-otter
in Portland, Maine, or, yes, Portland, Oregon—
he could barely tell one from the other—

10   and why should he now savour
the tang of her, her little pickled gherkin,
as he knelt by the grave of his mother and father?

                            •

He looked about. He remembered her palaver
on how both earth and sky would darken—
15   "You could barely tell one from the other"—

while the Monarch butterflies passed over
in their milkweed-hunger: "A wing-beat, some reckon,
may trigger off the mother and father

of all storms, striking your Irish Cliffs of Moher
20   with the force of a hurricane."
Then: "Milkweed and Monarch 'invented' each other."

                            •

He looked about. Cow's-parsley in a samovar.[1]
He'd mistaken his mother's name, "Regan", for "Anger":
as he knelt by the grave of his mother and father
25   he could barely tell one from the other.

                                             1994

The Grand Conversation

She. My people came from Korelitz[1]
where they grew yellow cucumbers
and studied the Talmud.[2]
He. Mine pored over the mud
5   of mangold-° and potato-pits   *a beet*
or flicked through kale plants from Comber[3]
as bibliomancers of old
went a-flicking through deckle-mold.[4]

She. Mine would lie low in the shtetl[5]
10   when they heard the distant thunder
stolen by the Cossacks.[6]
He. It was potato sacks
lumped together on a settle°   *long wooden bed or bench*

---

1. Russian tea urn.
1. Town, now in Belarus, once famous for its cucumbers. During World War II the Nazis largely massacred its population.
2. Collection of writings that constitutes the Jewish civil and religious law.
3. Village in Northern Ireland.
4. Rough edges of pages before they are trimmed.

"Bibliomancers": people who predicted the future from the text in a book opened at random.
5. Former Jewish village-communities of Eastern Europe.
6. A Polish people known for their horsemanship, they massacred perhaps a hundred thousand Polish Jews in 1648–49.

mine found themselves lying under,
15   the Peep O'Day Boys from Loughgall
making Defenders[7] of us all.

She. Mine once controlled the sugar trade
from the islets of Langerhans[8]
and were granted the deed
20   to Charlottesville.° *He.* Indeed?   city in Virginia
My people called a spade a spade
and were admitted to the hanse°   merchant guild
of pike- and pickax-men, shovels
leaning to their lean-to hovels.

25   *She.* Mine were trained to make a suture
after the bomb and the bombast
have done their very worst.
He. Between *fearsad* and *verst*[9]
we may yet construct our future
30   as we've reconstructed our past
and cry out, my love, each to each
from his or her own quicken-queach.[1]

She. Each from his stand of mountain ash
will cry out over valley farms
35   spotlit with pear blossom.
He. There some young Absalom[2]
picks his way through cache after cache
of ammunition and small arms
hidden in grain wells, while his nag
40   tugs at a rein caught on a snag.

2002

7. Eighteenth-century Catholic group in Ireland that fought Protestants who called themselves the Peep O'Day Boys. "Loughgall": village where Protestants formed a larger coalition, the Orange Order, at the beginning of the nineteenth century.
8. The groups of cells in the pancreas that produce the hormone insulin, which regulates the sugar level in the bloodstream.
9. Russian land measure, roughly two-thirds of a mile. "Fearsad": sandbank (Irish).
1. "Queach": dense growth of bushes. Cf. T. S. Eliot's "Love Song of J. Alfred Prufrock": "Do I dare to eat a peach? / . . . I have heard the mermaids singing, each to each."
2. King David's son, killed leading a rebellion against his father (2 Samuel). Riding his mule, he was accidentally hung up on a low branch and was thus made vulnerable to enemy spears.

CAROL ANN DUFFY
b. 1955

Carol Ann Duffy was born in Glasgow, Scotland, to an Irish mother and a Scottish father in a working-class Catholic family. After moving as a child to Stafford, England, she was educated there at St. Joseph's Convent and at Stafford Girls' High School, before studying philosophy at the University of Liverpool. She worked in television, edited a poetry magazine, and taught creative writing in London's schools, and since 1996 she has lectured at Manchester Metropolitan University.

A playwright as well as poet, Duffy is especially skillful in her use of dramatic monologue, fashioning and assuming the voices of mythological, historical, and fictive characters, such as Medusa or Lazarus's imaginary wife. Such poetic ventriloquism is well suited to her feminist revisions of myth and history: it enables her to dramatize a silenced or marginalized female perspective, wittily playing on the ironic contrast between the traditional version of a narrative and her own. The biblical story of Lazarus's resurrection, for example, looks different from the perspective of his wife, who upon his miraculous return from the dead scoffs: "I breathed / his stench."

The author of love poetry and political satire as well as dramatic monologues, Duffy has a sharp eye for detail and uses it deftly in poems characterized by their sensuality, economy, and exuberance. Working in well-constructed stanzas, carefully pacing her rhythms, playing on half-rhymes, effectively conjuring the senses of touch, smell, and sight, she mobilizes the resources of traditional lyric and turns them to contemporary ends—the remaking of master narratives, the celebration of lesbian desire.

Warming Her Pearls

for Judith Radstone[1]

Next to my own skin, her pearls. My mistress
bids me wear them, warm then, until evening
when I'll brush her hair. At six, I place them
round her cool, white throat. All day I think of her,

5   resting in the Yellow Room, contemplating silk
or taffeta, which gown tonight? She fans herself
whilst I work willingly, my slow heat entering
each pearl. Slack on my neck, her rope.

She's beautiful. I dream about her
10   in my attic bed; picture her dancing
with tall men, puzzled by my faint, persistent scent
beneath her French perfume, her milky stones.

I dust her shoulders with a rabbit's foot,
watch the soft blush seep through her skin
15   like an indolent sigh. In her looking-glass
my red lips part as though I want to speak.

Full moon. Her carriage brings her home. I see
her every movement in my head . . . Undressing,
taking off her jewels, her slim hand reaching
20   for the case, slipping naked into bed, the way

she always does . . . And I lie here awake,
knowing the pearls are cooling even now
in the room where my mistress sleeps. All night
I feel their absence and I burn.

1987

1. British political activist and bookseller (1925–
2001). According to Radstone's obituary in *The
Guardian*, the poem was inspired by a conversation
with Radstone about the practice of ladies' maids
increasing the luster of their mistresses' pearls by
wearing them beneath their clothes.

Medusa[1]

A suspicion, a doubt, a jealousy
grew in my mind,
which turned the hairs on my head to filthy snakes,
as though my thoughts
5   hissed and spat on my scalp.

My bride's breath soured, stank
in the grey bags of my lungs.
I'm foul mouthed now, foul tongued,
yellow fanged.
10   There are bullet tears in my eyes.
Are you terrified?

Be terrified.
It's you I love,
perfect man, Greek God, my own;
15   but I know you'll go, betray me, stray
from home.
So better by far for me if you were stone.

I glanced at a buzzing bee,
a dull grey pebble fell
20   to the ground.
I glanced at a singing bird,
a handful of dusty gravel
spattered down.

I looked at a ginger cat,
25   a housebrick
shattered a bowl of milk.
I looked at a snuffling pig,
a boulder rolled
in a heap of shit.

30   I stared in the mirror.
Love gone bad
showed me a Gorgon.
I stared at a dragon.
Fire spewed
35   from the mouth of a mountain.

And here you come
with a shield for a heart
and a sword for a tongue
and your girls, your girls.

1. In Greek mythology the mortal, snake-haired gorgon with the power to turn anyone who gazed upon her into stone. Looking at her reflection in a shield given him by Athena, Perseus cut off Medusa's head as she slept.

40   Wasn't I beautiful?
      Wasn't I fragrant and young?

      Look at me now.

1999

Mrs Lazarus[1]

I had grieved. I had wept for a night and a day
over my loss, ripped the cloth I was married in
from my breasts, howled, shrieked, clawed
at the burial stones till my hands bled, retched
5   his name over and over again, dead, dead.

Gone home. Gutted the place. Slept in a single cot,
widow, one empty glove, white femur
in the dust, half. Stuffed dark suits
into black bags, shuffled in a dead man's shoes,
10   noosed the double knot of a tie round my bare neck,

gaunt nun in the mirror, touching herself. I learnt
the Stations of Bereavement,[2] the icon of my face
in each bleak frame; but all those months
he was going away from me, dwindling
15   to the shrunk size of a snapshot, going,

going. Till his name was no longer a certain spell
for his face. The last hair on his head
floated out from a book. His scent went from the house.
The will was read. See, he was vanishing
20   to the small zero held by the gold of my ring.

Then he was gone. Then he was legend, language;
my arm on the arm of the schoolteacher—the shock
of a man's strength under the sleeve of his coat—
along the hedgerows. But I was faithful
25   for as long as it took. Until he was memory.

So I could stand that evening in the field
in a shawl of fine air, healed, able
to watch the edge of the moon occur to the sky
and a hare thump from a hedge; then notice
30   the village men running towards me, shouting,

1. Lazarus was the man raised from the dead by
Jesus (John 11).
2. Allusion to the Stations of the Cross, a series of

fourteen icons (pictures or carvings) corresponding to the stages of Jesus' crucifixion and over each
of which a prayer is said.

behind them the women and children, barking dogs,
and I knew. I knew by the sly light
on the blacksmith's face, the shrill eyes
of the barmaid, the sudden hands bearing me
35   into the hot tang of the crowd parting before me.

He lived. I saw the horror on his face.
I heard his mother's crazy song. I breathed
his stench; my bridegroom in his rotting shroud,
moist and dishevelled from the grave's slack chew,
40   croaking his cuckold name, disinherited, out of his time.

1999

Poems in Process

Poets have often claimed that their poems were not willed but were inspired, whether by a muse or by divine visitation, or that they emerged full-blown from the poet's unconscious mind. But poets' often untidy manuscripts tell another story, suggesting that, however involuntary the origin of a poem, vision has usually been followed by revision.

Writers have described the second thoughts recorded in their working manuscripts in a number of ways. Revision may be viewed as a work of refinement and clarification, a process revealing or bringing out more vividly a meaning the author always had in mind. In this account, revision involves the perfection of an original, singular intention. But this understanding of revision has not satisfied authors who reject a notion of identity as something given and unchanging and who might be inclined to see revision as a process that makes something new. As W. B. Yeats, a compulsive reviser, wrote in 1908: "The friends that have it I do wrong / Whenever I remake a song, / Should know what issue is at stake: / It is myself that I remake." And people besides the poet can have a hand in the process of revision. As the "Publishing History, Censorship" section of our literary terms appendix outlines, many individuals participate in the labor that takes texts from the forms in which authors produce them to the forms in which they are presented to readers; in a similar if more limited way, revision, too, involves a range of collaborators, both institutional and personal, witting and unwitting. A revised text might, for instance, incorporate changes introduced by the amanuensis who recopies the draft so as to prepare a fair copy for the printer (a role women such as Dorothy Wordsworth and Mary Shelley often played in the nineteenth century—on occasion, Mary Shelley seems to have had primary responsibility for Lord Byron's punctuation). The second thoughts at stake in a revision might reflect the input of trusted advisors and editors, the poet's attempt to anticipate the response of hostile critics or readers, or (as was often the case with the revisions in which William Wordsworth and Yeats engaged) the poet's efforts to bring the political and aesthetic values of the poem into line with the changing times.

Although some earlier manuscripts have survived, it was not until the nineteenth century, when a relatively new conception of authorship as a career gained widespread acceptance, that poets' working drafts began to be preserved with any regularity. The examples from major poets that are transcribed here represent various stages in the composition of a poem, and a variety of procedures by individual poets. The selections from William Blake, Byron, Percy Shelley, John Keats, and Elizabeth Barrett Browning are drafts that were written, emended, crossed out, and rewritten in the heat of first invention; while poems by William Wordsworth, Gerard Manley Hopkins, and Yeats are shown in successive stages of revision over an extended period of time. Shelley's "O World, O Life, O Time" originated in a few key nouns, together with an abstract rhythmic pattern that was only later fleshed out with words. Still other poems—Alfred, Lord Tennyson's "The Lady of Shalott"; Yeats's "The Sorrow of Love"—were subjected to radical revision long after the initial versions had been committed to print. In these examples we look on as poets (no matter how rapidly they achieve a result they are willing to let stand) carry on their inevitably tentative efforts to meet the multiple requirements of meaning, syntax, meter, sound pattern, and the constraints imposed by a chosen stanza.

Our transcriptions from the poets' drafts attempt to reproduce, as accurately as the change from script to print will allow, the appearance of the original manuscript page.

A1

A poet's first attempt at a line or phrase is reproduced in larger type, the emendations in smaller type. The line numbers in the headings that identify an excerpt are those of the final form of the complete poem, as reprinted in this anthology, above.

SELECTED BIBLIOGRAPHY

Autograph Poetry in the English Language, 2 vols., 1973, compiled by P. J. Croft, reproduces and transcribes one or more pages of manuscript in the poet's own hand, from the fourteenth century to the late twentieth century. Volume 1 includes William Blake and Robert Burns; volume 2 includes many of the other poets represented in this volume of *The Norton Anthology of English Literature*, from William Wordsworth to Dylan Thomas. Books that discuss the process of composition and revision, with examples from the manuscripts and printed versions of poems, are Charles D. Abbott, ed., *Poets at Work*, 1948; Phyllis Bartlett, *Poems in Process*, 1951; A. F. Scott, *The Poet's Craft*, 1957; George Bornstein, *Poetic Remaking: The Art of Browning, Yeats, and Pound*, 1988; and Robert Brinkley and Keith Hanley, eds., *Romantic Revisions*, 1992. In *Word for Word: A Study of Authors' Alterations*, 1965, Wallace Hildick analyzes the composition of prose fiction as well as poems. *Byron's "Don Juan,"* ed. T. G. Steffan and W. W. Pratt, 4 vols., 1957, transcribes the manuscript drafts; the Cornell Wordsworth, in process, reproduces, transcribes, and discusses various versions of Wordsworth's poems from the first manuscript drafts to the final publication in his lifetime, and the Cornell Yeats, also in process, does the same for Yeats. The *Bodleian Shelley Manuscripts*, under the general editorship of Donald Reiman, reproduces facsimiles of Percy Shelley's manuscripts. For facsimiles and transcripts of Keats's poems, see *John Keats: Poetry Manuscripts at Harvard*, ed. Jack Stillinger, 1990. Jon Stallworthy, *Between the Lines: Yeats's Poetry in the Making*, 1963, reproduces and analyzes the sequential drafts of a number of Yeats's major poems. Valerie Eliot has edited T. S. Eliot's *The Waste Land: A Facsimile and Transcript of the Original Drafts Including the Annotations of Ezra Pound*, 1971, while Dame Helen Gardner has transcribed and analyzed the manuscript drafts of Eliot's *Four Quartets* in *The Composition of Four Quartets*, 1978.

WILLIAM BLAKE
The Tyger[1]
[First Draft]

The Tyger

1   Tyger Tyger burning bright
In the forests of the night
What immortal hand or eye
~~Dare~~ ~~Could~~ frame thy fearful symmetry

         Burnt in
2   ~~In what distan~~t deeps or skies
~~The cruel Burnt the~~ fire of thine eyes
On what wings dare he aspire
What the hand dare sieze the fire

3   And what shoulder & what art
Could twist the sinews of thy heart
And when thy heart began to beat
What dread hand & what dread feet

1. These drafts have been taken from a notebook used by William Blake, called the Rossetti MS because it was once owned by Dante Gabriel Rossetti, the Victorian poet and painter; David V. Erd-man's edition of *The Notebook of William Blake* (1973) contains a photographic facsimile. The stanza and line numbers were written by Blake in the manuscript.

~~Could fetch it from the furnace deep~~
~~And in thy horrid ribs dare steep~~
~~In the well of sanguine woe~~
~~In what clay & what mould~~
~~Were thy eyes of fury rolld~~

4   ~~Where~~
     ~~What~~ the hammer ~~what~~ the chain
     In what furnace was thy brain
                          dread grasp
     What the anvil what ~~the arm~~ ~~arm~~ ~~grasp~~ ~~clasp~~
     Dare ~~Could~~ its deadly terrors ~~clasp~~ ~~grasp~~ clasp

6   Tyger Tyger burning bright
     In the forests of the night
     What immortal hand & eye
           frame
     Dare ~~form~~ thy fearful symmetry

                [*Trial Stanzas*]

     Burnt in distant deeps or skies
     The cruel fire of thine eye,
     Could heart descend or wings aspire
     What the hand dare sieze the fire

                dare he ~~smile laugh~~
5 3 And ~~did he laugh~~ his work to see
                ankle
     ~~What the shoulder what the knee~~
     Dare
4   ~~Did~~ he who made the lamb make thee
1   When the stars threw down their spears
2   And waterd heaven with their tears

                [*Second Full Draft*]

     Tyger Tyger burning bright
     In the forests of the night
     What Immortal hand & eye
     Dare frame thy fearful symmetry

     And what shoulder & what art
     Could twist the sinews of thy heart
     And when thy heart began to beat
     What dread hand & what dread feet

     When the stars threw down their spears
     And waterd heaven with their tears
     Did he smile his work to see
     Did he who made the lamb make thee

Tyger Tyger burning bright
In the forests of the night
What immortal hand & eye
Dare frame thy fearful symmetry

[*Final Version, 1794*][2]

The Tyger

Tyger Tyger, burning bright,
In the forests of the night;
What immortal hand or eye,
Could frame thy fearful symmetry?

In what distant deeps or skies
Burnt the fire of thine eyes!
On what wings dare he aspire?
What the hand, dare sieze the fire?

And what shoulder, & what art,
Could twist the sinews of thy heart?
And when thy heart began to beat,
What dread hand? & what dread feet?

What the hammer? what the chain,
In what furnace was thy brain?
What the anvil? what dread grasp,
Dare its deadly terrors clasp?

When the stars threw down their spears
And water'd heaven with their tears:
Did he smile his work to see?
Did he who made the Lamb make thee?

Tyger, Tyger burning bright,
In the forests of the night:
What immortal hand or eye,
Dare frame thy fearful symmetry?

WILLIAM WORDSWORTH
She dwelt among the untrodden ways

[*Version in a Letter to Coleridge,*
December 1798 or January 1799][1]

My hope was one, from cities far
Nursed on a lonesome heath:
Her lips were red as roses are,
Her hair a woodbine wreath.

2. As published in *Songs of Experience*.
1. Printed in Ernest de Selincourt's *Early Letters of William and Dorothy Wordsworth* (1935). By deleting two stanzas, and making a few verbal changes, Wordsworth achieved the terse published form of his great dirge.

She lived among the untrodden ways
  Beside the springs of Dove,
A maid whom there were none to praise,
  And very few to love;

A violet by a mossy stone
  Half-hidden from the eye!
Fair as a star when only one
  Is shining in the sky!

And she was graceful as the broom
  That flowers by Carron's side;[2]
But slow distemper checked her bloom,
  And on the Heath she died.

Long time before her head lay low
  Dead to the world was she:
But now she's in her grave, and Oh!
  The difference to me!

[*Final Version, 1800*][3]

Song

She dwelt among th' untrodden ways
  Beside the springs of Dove,
A Maid whom there were none to praise
  And very few to love.

A Violet by a mossy stone
  Half-hidden from the Eye!
—Fair, as a star when only one
  Is shining in the sky!

She *liv'd* unknown, and few could know
  When Lucy ceas'd to be;
But she is in her Grave, and Oh!
  The difference to me.

LORD BYRON
From Don Juan[1]

[*First Draft: Canto 3, Stanza 9*]

~~Life is a play and men~~
All tragedies are finished by a death,
All Comedies are ended by a marriage,

2. The Carron is a river in northwestern Scotland. "Broom" (preceding line) is a shrub with long slender branches and yellow flowers.
3. As published in the second edition of *Lyrical Ballads.*

1. Reproduced from transcripts made of Byron's manuscripts in T. G. Steffan and W. W. Pratt, *Byron's "Don Juan"* (1957). The stanzas were published by Byron in their emended form.

~~For Life can go no further~~
~~These two form the last gasp of Passion's breath~~
~~All further is a blank—I won't disparage~~
~~That holy state—but certainly beneath~~
~~The Sun—of human things—~~
~~These two are levellers, and human breath.~~
~~So~~ ~~These point the epigram of human breath,~~
~~Or any~~ The future states of both are left to faith,
~~Though Life and love I like not to disparage~~
~~The~~ For authors ~~think~~ description might disparage
  fear
~~Tis strange that poets never try to wreathe~~ [sic?]
~~With eith~~ ~~Tis strange that poets of the Catholic faith~~
~~Neer go beyond—and~~ ~~but seem to dread miscarriage~~
~~So dramas close with death or settlement for life~~
~~Veiling~~ ~~Leaving the future states of Love and Life~~
~~The paradise beyond like that of life~~
~~And neer describing either—~~
~~To more conjecture of a devil~~ ~~and~~ ~~or wife~~
~~And don't say much of paradise or wife.~~
The worlds to come of both—~~or~~ or fall beneath,
And ~~all~~ ~~both the worlds would blame them for miscarriage~~
And then both worlds would punish their miscarriage—
~~So leaving both with priest & prayerbook ready~~
So leaving ~~Clerg both a~~ each their Priest and prayerbook ready,
They say no more of death or of the Lady.

[*First Draft: Canto 14, Stanza 95*]

   quote   seldom
Alas! ~~I speak by~~ Experience—~~never~~ yet
~~I had a paramour—and I've had many—~~
     ~~some small~~
~~To whom I did not cause a deep~~ regret—
~~Whom I had not some reason to~~ regret
~~For Whom—I did not feel myself~~ a Zany—
Alas! by all experience, seldom yet
(I merely quote what I have heard from many)
Had lovers not some reason to regret
The passion which made Solomon a Zany.
~~I also had a wife—~~not to forget—
I've also seen some wives—not to forget—
The marriage state—the best or worst of any—
  were   paragons
Who ~~was~~ the very ~~paragon~~ of wives,
Yet made the misery of ~~both our~~ lives.
     ~~many~~
     ~~several~~
    ~~of~~ at least two

PERCY BYSSHE SHELLEY

The three stages of this poem labeled "First Draft" are scattered through one of Shelley's notebooks, now in the Huntington Library, San Marino, California; these drafts have been transcribed and analyzed by Bennett Weaver, "Shelley Works Out the Rhythm of A *Lament*," *PMLA* 47 (1932): 570–76. They show Shelley working with fragmentary words and phrases, and simultaneously with a wordless pattern of pulses that marked out the meter of the single lines and the shape of the lyric stanzas. Shelley left this draft unfinished.

Apparently at some later time, Shelley returned to the poem and wrote what is here called the "Second Draft"; from this he then made, on a second page, a revised fair copy that provided the text that Mary Shelley published in 1824, after the poet's death. These two manuscript pages are now in the Bodleian Library, Oxford; the first page is photographically reproduced and discussed by John Carter and John Sparrow, "Shelley, Swinburne, and Housman," *Times Literary Supplement*, November 21, 1968, pp. 1318–19.

O World, O Life, O Time

[*First Draft, Stage 1*]

Ah time, oh night, oh day
~~Ni na! ni na, na ni~~
~~Ni na ni na, ni na~~
Oh life O death, O time
   Time a di
~~Never Time~~
Ah time, a time O-time
  ~~Time!~~

[*First Draft, Stage 2*]

Oh time, oh night oh day
~~O day oh night, alas~~
  ~~O~~ Death time night ~~oh~~
Oh, Time
Oh time o night oh day

[*First Draft, Stage 3*]

Na na, na na ná na
Nǎ nǎ na na na—nǎ nǎ
  Nǎ nǎ nǎ nǎ nā nā
Na na nǎ nǎ nâ ǎ na

Na na na—nǎ nǎ—na na
  Na na na na—na na na na na
Na na na na na.
  Na na
Na na na na na

Na na
Na na na na na ˇ na!

Oh time, oh night, o day
        alas
O day ~~serenest~~, o day
O day alas the day
That thou shouldst sleep when we awake to say

O time time—o death—o day
      for
O day, o death life is far from thee
O thou wert never free
For death is now with thee
~~And life is far from~~
O death, o day for life is far from thee

[*Second Draft*][1]

I am despair

Out of the day & night
A joy has taken flight
Fresh spring & summer   & winter hoar
Fill my faint heart with grief, but with
                      delight
    No more—o never more!

~~Wo~~
   O World, o life, o time
  ~~Will ye~~ On whose last steps I climb
Trembling at those which I have trod[2] before
When will return the glory of yr prime
    No more   Oh never more

Out of the day & night
A joy has taken flight—
        autumn
~~From~~ Green spring, & ~~summer gra~~[3] & winter hoar

[FAIR COPY]

O World o Life o Time
On whose last steps I climb
Trembling at that where I had stood before
When will return the glory of yr prime?
    No more, o never more

1. Shelley apparently wrote the first stanza of this draft low down on the page, and ran out of space after crowding in the third line of the second stanza; he then, in a lighter ink, wrote a revised form of the whole of the second stanza at the top of the page. In this revision he left a space after "summer" in line 3, indicating that he planned an insertion that would fill out the four-foot meter of this line, and so make it match the five feet in the corresponding line of the first stanza.

In the upper right-hand corner of this manuscript page, Shelley wrote "I am despair"—seemingly to express his bleak mood at the time he wrote the poem.

For this draft and information, and for the transcript of the fair copy that follows, the editors are indebted to Donald H. Reiman.

2. Shelley at first wrote "trod," then overwrote that with "stood." In the following line, Shelley at first wrote "yr," then overwrote "thy."

3. Not clearly legible; it is either "gra" or "gre." A difference in the ink from the rest of the line indicates that Shelley, having left a blank space, later started to fill it in, but thought better of it and crossed out the fragmentary insertion.

2
Out of the day & night
A joy has taken flight
Fresh spring & summer   ⁴ & winter hoar
Move my faint heart with grief but with delight
No more, o, never more

JOHN KEATS
From The Eve of St. Agnes¹

[*Stanza 26*]

~~But soon his heart revives—her prayers said~~
~~She lays aside her veil~~ pearled
strips her hair of all its ^ wreaths pearl
~~Unclasps her bosom jewels~~
~~And twist it in one knot upon her head~~

soon
~~But soon his heart revives—her praying done,~~
~~Of all its wreathed pearl she strips her hair~~
~~Unclasps her warmed jewels one by one~~
her warming
~~Loosens the boddice from her~~
~~her Boddice lace string~~
~~her Boddice and her bosom bare~~
her

[HERE KEATS BEGINS A NEW SHEET]

Loosens ~~her fragrant~~ boddice and doth bare
~~Her.~~

26

Anon
~~But soon~~ his heart revives—her praying done,
frees:
Of all its wreathe'd pearl her hair she ~~strips~~
Unclasps her warmed jewels one by one
by degrees

4. This fair copy of the second draft retains, and even enlarges, the blank space, indicating that Shelley still hasn't made up his mind what to insert after the word "summer." We may speculate, by reference to the fragmentary version of this stanza in the second draft, that he had in mind as possibilities either an adjective, "gray" or "green," or else the noun "autumn." Mary Shelley closed up this space when she published the poem in 1824, with the result that editors, following her version, have until very recently printed this line as though Shelley had intended it to be one metric foot shorter than the corresponding line of stanza 1.

1. Transcribed from Keats's first draft of all but the first seven stanzas of *The Eve of St. Agnes*; the manuscript is now in the Houghton Library, Harvard University. Keats's published version of the poem contains additional changes in wording. That published version also incorporates revisions introduced by other hands. Because Keats's friend Richard Woodhouse and his publisher, John Taylor, took alarm at the suggestion, made more explicit in one of the stanzas Keats added to his original draft, that the pleasure of which Madeline would dream would include sexual pleasure particularly, they worked over Woodhouse's transcripts of the poem and produced a less risqué text that combined Keats's draft and his revised fair copy along with, as Jack Stillinger has conjectured, their own suggestions.

For a photographic reproduction of the page of the holograph manuscript of *The Eve of St. Agnes* containing the poem's stanza 30, see the color insert.

~~to her knees~~
Loosens her fragrant boddice: ~~and down slips~~
Her sweet attire ~~falls light creeps down by~~
 creeps rusteling to her knees
 Mermaid in sea weed
Half hidden like ~~a Syren of the Sea~~
~~And more melodious~~
 dreaming
She stands awhile in ∧ thought; and sees
 on
In fancy fair Saint Agnes ~~in~~ her bed
But dares not look behind or all the charm is ~~a~~ dead

[*Stanza 30*]

 But
~~And still she slept~~:
And still she slept an azure-lidded sleep
In blanched linen, smooth and lavender'd
While he from frorth the closet brough a heap
 ~~fruits~~
Of candied ~~sweets sweets, with~~
 apple Quince and plumb and gourd
 creamed
With jellies soother than the ~~dairy~~ curd
 tinct
And lucent syrups ~~smooth~~ with ciannamon
~~And sugar'd dates from that oer Euphrates ford~~
 ~~in Brigantine transferred~~
Manna and daites in ~~Bragtine transferred~~
 ~~and manna wild transferred~~
~~And Manna wild and Bragantine~~
 sugar'd dates transferred
~~In Brigantine from Fez~~
From fez—and spiced danties every one
 ~~glutted~~
From ~~wealthy~~ Samarchand to cedard lebanon
 silken

argosy]

To Autumn[2]

Season of Mists and mellow fruitfulness
 Close bosom friend of the naturring sun;
Conspiring with him how to load and bless
 The Vines with fruit that round the thatch eves run
  To bend with apples the moss'd Cottage trees
And fill all furuits with sweeness to the core
 To swell the gourd, and plump the hazle shells
  With a white kernel; to set budding more
And still more later flowers for the bees
 Until they think wam days with never cease
  For Summer has o'erbrimm'd their clammy cells—

2. From an untitled manuscript—apparently Keats's first draft of the poem—in the Houghton Library, Harvard University. The many pen-slips and errors in spelling indicate that Keats wrote rap- idly, in a state of creative excitement. Keats made a few further changes before publishing the poem in the form included in the selections above.

oft amid thy stores?
Who hath not seen thee? ~~for thy haunts are many~~
abroad
Sometimes whoeever seeks ~~for thee~~ may find
Thee sitting careless on a granary floorr
Thy hair soft lifted by the winnowing wind

~~While bright the Sun slants through the~~ ^ barn;—
~~on a half reap'd furrow sound asleep~~
~~Or sound asleep in a half reaped field~~
~~Dos'd with~~ read poppies; while thy reaping hook
~~Spares form some slumbrous~~
~~minutes while warm slumpers creep~~
Or on a half reap'd furrow sound asleep
Dos'd with the fume of poppies, while thy hook
Spares the next swath and all its twined flowers
~~Spares for some slumbrous minutes the next swath;~~
And sometimes like a gleans thost dost keep
Steady thy laden head across the brook;
Or by a Cyder-press with patent look
Thou watchest the last oozing hours by hours

Where are the songs of Sping? Aye where are they?
Think not of them thou hast thy music too—
barred   bloom
While ~~a gold~~ clouds ~~gilds~~ the soft-dying day
And   with
~~And~~ Touching ~~the~~ the stibble plains ^ rosy hue—
Then in a waiful quire the small gnats mourn
Among the river sallows, ~~on the~~ borne afots
Or sinking as the light wind lives and dies;
And full grown Lambs loud bleat from hilly bourn,
Hedge crickets sing, and now again full soft
The Redbreast whistles from a garden croft:
~~And now flock still~~
And Gather'd Swallows twiter in the Skies—

ALFRED, LORD TENNYSON
From The Lady of Shalott[1]

[*Version of 1832*]

PART THE FIRST.

On either side the river lie
Long fields of barley and of rye,
That clothe the wold, and meet the sky.
And thro' the field the road runs by

1. First published in Tennyson's *Poems* of 1832 (dated 1833 on the title page). The volume was severely criticized by some reviewers; partly in response to this criticism, Tennyson radically revised a number of the poems, including "The Lady of Shalott," before reprinting them in his *Poems* (1842).

   Parts 1 and 4 are reproduced here in the version of 1832. The final form of the poem reprinted in the selections from Tennyson, above, differs from the revised version that Tennyson published in 1842 only in line 157, which in 1842 read "A corse between the houses high"; Tennyson changed the line to "Dead-pale between the houses high" in 1855.

         To manytowered Camelot.
The yellowleavèd waterlily,
The greensheathèd daffodilly,
Tremble in the water chilly,
        Round about Shallot.

Willows whiten, aspens shiver,
The sunbeam-showers break and quiver
In the stream that runneth ever
By the island in the river,
         Flowing down to Camelot.
Four gray walls and four gray towers
Overlook a space of flowers,
And the silent isle imbowers
        The Lady of Shallot.

Underneath the bearded barley,
The reaper, reaping late and early,
Hears her ever chanting cheerly,
Like an angel, singing clearly,
        O'er the stream of Camelot.
Piling the sheaves in furrows airy,
Beneath the moon, the reaper weary
Listening whispers, " 'tis the fairy
        Lady of Shalott."

The little isle is all inrailed
With a rose-fence, and overtrailed
With roses: by the marge unhailed
The shallop flitteth silkensailed,
        Skimming down to Camelot.
A pearlgarland winds her head:
She leaneth on a velvet bed,
Full royally apparellèd,
        The Lady of Shalott.

        *   *   *

PART THE FOURTH.

In the stormy eastwind straining
The pale-yellow woods were waning,
The broad stream in his banks complaining,
Heavily the low sky raining
        Over towered Camelot:
Outside the isle a shallow boat
Beneath a willow lay afloat,
Below the carven stern she wrote,
        THE LADY OF SHALOTT.

A cloudwhite crown of pearl she dight.
All raimented in snowy white
That loosely flew, (her zone in sight,
Clasped with one blinding diamond bright,)

Her wide eyes fixed on Camelot,
Though the squally eastwind keenly
Blew, with folded arms serenely
By the water stood the queenly
      Lady of Shalott.

With a steady, stony glance—
Like some bold seer in a trance,
Beholding all his own mischance,
Mute, with a glassy countenance—
      She looked down to Camelot.
It was the closing of the day,
She loosed the chain, and down she lay,
The broad stream bore her far away,
      The Lady of Shalott.

As when to sailors while they roam,
By creeks and outfalls far from home,
Rising and dropping with the foam,
From dying swans wild warblings come,
      Blown shoreward; so to Camelot
Still as the boathead wound along
The willowy hills and fields among,
They heard her chanting her deathsong,
      The Lady of Shalott.

A longdrawn carol, mournful, holy,
She chanted loudly, chanted lowly,
Till her eyes were darkened wholly,
And her smooth face sharpened slowly
      Turned to towered Camelot:
For ere she reached upon the tide
The first house by the waterside,
Singing in her song she died,
      The Lady of Shalott.

Under tower and balcony,
By gardenwall and gallery,
A pale, pale corpse she floated by,
Deadcold, between the houses high.
      Dead into towered Camelot.
Knight and burgher, lord and dame,
To the plankèd wharfage came:
Below the stern they read her name,
      "The Lady of Shalott."

They crossed themselves, their stars they blest,
Knight, ministrel, abbot, squire and guest.
There lay a parchment on her breast,
That puzzled more than all the rest,
      The wellfed wits at Camelot.
"The web was woven curiously

The charm is broken utterly,
Draw near and fear not—this is I,
The Lady of Shalott."

From Tithonus²

[Lines 1–10]

[TRINITY COLLEGE MANUSCRIPT]

Ay me! Ay me! the woods decay & fall

~~The stars blaze out & never rise again.~~

the
The vapours weep their substance to ground
Man͜ comes & tills the earth & lies beneath
And after many summers dies the ~~rose~~ swan
Me only fatal immortality
Consumes: I wither slowly in thine arms:
Here at the quiet limit of the world
                      e   yet
A white-haired shad~~ow~~roaming like a dream
The ever-silent spaces‸of the East
Far-folded mists & gleaming halls of morn.

[HEATH MANUSCRIPT]

Tithon

Ay me! ay me! the woods decay and fall,
The vapours weep their substance to the ground,
Man comes and tills the earth and lies beneath,
And after many summers dies the rose.
Me only fatal immortality
Consumes: I wither slowly in thine arms,
Here at the quiet limit of the world,
A white-haired shadow roaming like a dream
The ever-silent spaces of the East,
Far-folded mists, and gleaming halls of morn.

[AS PRINTED IN 1864]

Tithonus

The woods decay, the woods decay and fall,
The vapours weep their burthen to the ground,
Man comes and tills the field and lies beneath,
And after many a summer dies the swan.

2. Three manuscript drafts of "Tithonus" are extant. Two are in Tennyson's Notebooks Nos. 20 and 21, at Trinity College, Cambridge; a third one, written 1833, is in the Commonplace Book compiled by Tennyson's friend J. M. Heath, which is in the Fitzwilliam Museum at Cambridge University. According to Tennyson's editor, Christopher Ricks, the Heath version is later than those in the Trinity Manuscripts. The transcriptions here of Tennyson's opening lines are from the first draft (Trinity College manuscript, Notebook 20), and from the Heath manuscript, where the poem is titled "Tithon." These are followed by the final version of "Tithonus" Tennyson published in 1864. As late as in the edition of 1860, the opening words had remained "Ay me! ay me!" and "field" (line 3) had remained "earth."

Me only cruel immortality
Consumes: I wither slowly in thine arms,
Here at the quiet limit of the world,
A white-haired shadow roaming like a dream
The ever-silent spaces of the East,
Far-folded mists, and gleaming halls of morn.

ELIZABETH BARRETT BROWNING
From The Runaway Slave at Pilgrim's Point[1]

[*From the British Library manuscript, 1846*]

Why
~~And~~ in that single glance I had
Of my child's face . . I tell you all . .
I saw a look that made me mad—!
The master's look, that used to fall
On my soul like his lash . . or worse:
And so, to save it from my curse
I twisted it round in my shawl.   Does this <u>sound</u> like a slave's article of clothing?[2]

               trembled
And he moaned and ~~struggled~~ from foot to head—
  shivered
He ~~trembled~~ from head to foot—
Till after a time he lay instead
Too suddenly still and mute . .
And I felt, beside, a creeping cold—
I dared to lift up just a fold,
As in lifting a leaf of the mango-fruit.

But <u>my</u> fruit . . . ha, ha—there, had been . .
(I laugh to think on't at this hour . .)
Your fine white angels, (who have seen
God's secrets nearest to His power)
And plucked my fruit to make them wine,
And sucked the soul of that child of mine,
              the soul of
As the hummingbird sucks **∧** the flower.

Ha, ha, for the trick of the angels white!
They freed the white child's spirit so,
I said not a word, but day and night

1. One part of Barrett Browning's manuscript draft of her abolitionist poem is in the British Library in London; another, fittingly, given the poem's initial publication by a Boston abolitionist society, is on the other side of the Atlantic, in Baylor University's Armstrong Library; a third is in the hands of a private collector. We give six stanzas from the British Library manuscript, along with, first, their counterparts in the initial printed version of the poem in *The Liberty Bell for 1848* (published in December 1847 for the National Anti-Slavery Bazaar), and, then, their counterparts in Barrett Browning's *Poems* of 1850. Barrett Browning added a stanza to the poem after 1847 (the seventh stanza of the 1850 version); stanza 20 in the *Liberty Bell* version corresponds accordingly to stanza 21 in *Poems* and so forth. For discussion of Barrett Browning's revision of the *Liberty Bell* version, see Andrew M. Stauffer, "Elizabeth Barrett Browning's (Re)Vision of Slavery," in *English Language Notes* 34 (1997): 29–48.
2. Written sideways in the right-hand margin of the manuscript, in Robert Browning's handwriting.

I carried the body to and fro—
And it lay on my heart like a stone . . as chill.
The sun may shine out as much as he will.

month
I am cold, though it happened a ~~year~~ ago.

From the white man's house, and the black man's hut
I carried the little body on—

's arms
The forest ~~trees~~ did around us shut

trees
And silence through the leaves did run—
They asked no questions as I went:

They stood
~~The trees were~~ too high, for astonishment;
They could see God rise on His throne.

My little body, kerchiefed fast,
I bore it on through the forest . . on:
And, when I felt it was tired at last,
I scooped a hole beneath the moon—
Through the forest-tops the angels far
With a white fine finger from every star,

and mock
Did point ∧ at what was done.

[*First printed version, from* The Liberty Bell for 1848]

XX.

Even in that single glance I had
  Of my child's face,—I tell you all,—
I saw a look that made me mad,—
  The master's look, that used to fall
On my soul like this lash, or worse,—
Therefore, to save it from my curse,
  I twisted it round in my shawl.

XXI.

And he moaned and trembled from foot to head,—
  He shivered from head to foot,—
Till, after a time, he lay, instead,
  Too suddenly still and mute;
And I felt, beside, a creeping cold,—
I dared to lift up just a fold,
  As in lifting a leaf of the mango fruit.

XXII.

But MY fruit! ha, ha!—there had been
  (I laugh to think on 't at this hour!)
Your fine white angels,—who have seen
  God's secret nearest to His power,—
And gathered my fruit to make them wine,

And sucked the soul of that child of mine,
  As the humming-bird sucks the soul of the flower.

XXIII.

Ha, ha! for the trick of the angels white!
  They freed the white child's spirit so;
I said not a word, but day and night
  I carried the body to and fro;
And it lay on my heart like a stone—as chill;
The sun may shine out as much as he will,—
  I am cold, though it happened a month ago.

XXIV.

From the white man's house and the black man's hut
  I carried the little body on;
The forest's arms did around us shut,
  And silence through the trees did run!
They asked no questions as I went,—
They stood too high for astonishment,—
  They could see God rise on his throne.

XXV.

My little body, kerchiefed fast,
  I bore it on through the forest—on—
And when I felt it was tired at last,
  I scooped a hole beneath the moon.
Through the forest-tops the angels far,
With a white fine finger in every star
  Did point and mock at what was done.

[*From* Poems, *1850*]

XXI.

Why, in that single glance I had
  Of my child's face, . . . I tell you all,
I saw a look that made me mad!
  The *master's* look, that used to fall
On my soul like his lash . . . or worse!
And so, to save it from my curse,
  I twisted it round in my shawl.

XXII.

And he moaned and trembled from foot to head,
  He shivered from head to foot;
Till after a time, he lay instead
  Too suddenly still and mute.
I felt, beside, a stiffening cold:
I dared to lift up just a fold,
  As in lifting a leaf of the mango-fruit.

XXIII.

But *my* fruit . . . ha, ha!—there, had been
(I laugh to think on't at this hour!)
Your fine white angels (who have seen
Nearest the secret of God's power)
And plucked my fruit to make them wine,
And sucked the soul of that child of mine
As the humming-bird sucks the soul of the flower.

XXIV.

Ha, ha, the trick of the angels white!
They freed the white child's spirit so.
I said not a word, but day and night
I carried the body to and fro,
And it lay on my heart like a stone, as chill.
—The sun may shine out as much as he will:
I am cold, though it happened a month ago.

XXV.

From the white man's house, and the black man's hut,
I carried the little body on;
The forest's arms did round us shut,
And silence through the trees did run:
They asked no question as I went,
They stood too high for astonishment,
They could see God sit on His throne.

XXVI.

My little body, kerchiefed fast,
I bore it on through the forest, on;
And when I felt it was tired at last,
I scooped a hole beneath the moon:
Through the forest-tops the angels far,
With a white sharp finger from every star,
Did point and mock at what was done.

GERARD MANLEY HOPKINS
Thou art indeed just, Lord[1]

*Justus quidem tu es, Domine, si disputem tecum; verumtamen
justa loquar ad te: quare via impiorum prosperatur?* etc.
—Jer. xii 1.

1. From a manuscript in the Bodleian Library, Oxford University; it is a clean copy, made after earlier drafts, which Hopkins goes on to revise further. Differences in the ink show that the emendation "lacèd they are" (line 10) was made during the first writing, but that the other verbal changes were made later. The interlinear markings are Hopkins's metrical indicators; he explains their sig- nificance in the "Author's Preface," included in *Poems of Gerard Manley Hopkins* (1970), ed. W. H. Gardner and N. H. MacKenzie.

The epigraph is from the Vulgate translation of Jeremiah 12.1; a literal translation of the Latin is "Thou art indeed just, Lord, [even] if I plead with Thee; nevertheless I will speak what is just to Thee: Why does the way of the wicked prosper? etc."

March 17 1889

Lord, if I
Thou art indeed just, ~~were I to~~ contend
     sir,   plead
With thee; but, ~~Lord~~, so what I ~~speak~~ is just.

Why do sinners' ways prosper? and why must

Disappointment all I endeavour end?
Wert thou my enemy, O thou my friend,
How wouldst thou worse, I wonder, than thou dost
                O the sots and   of
Defeat, thwart me? ~~Ah! sots, revellers~~, thralls to lust
Do in   that
Do spare hours do more thrive than I ~~who~~ spend,
    great   See,
Sir, ~~my~~ life on thy cause. ~~Look~~, banks and brakes
Now, leavèd   lacèd they are
~~Leavèd~~ how thick! ~~broidered all~~ again
           look
With fretty chervil, ~~now~~, and fresh wind shakes
Them; birds build—but not I build; no, but strain,
Time's eunuch, and not breed one work that wakes.
   Mine, O   send my
~~Then send~~, thou lord of life, ~~these~~ roots ~~their~~ rain.

WILLIAM BUTLER YEATS

Yeats usually composed very slowly and with painful effort. He tells us in his autobiography that "five or six lines in two or three laborious hours were a day's work, and I longed for somebody to interrupt me." His manuscripts show the slow evolution of his best poems, which sometimes began with a prose sketch, were then versified, and underwent numerous revisions. In many instances, even after the poems had been published, Yeats continued to revise them, sometimes drastically, in later printings.

The Sorrow of Love[1]

[Manuscript, 1891][2]

The quarrel of the sparrows in the eaves,
The full round moon and the star-laden sky,
The song of the ever-singing leaves,
Had hushed away earth's old and weary cry.

1. Originally composed in Yeats's Pre-Raphaelite mode of the early 1890s, "The Sorrow of Love" was one of his most popular poems. Nonetheless, some thirty years after publication, Yeats rewrote the lyric in accordance with modernism's emphasis on precision and colloquial vigor.
2. Manuscript version composed in October 1891, as transcribed by Jon Stallworthy, *Between the Lines: Yeats's Poetry in the Making* (Oxford University Press, 1963), pp. 47–48.

And then you came with those red mournful lips,
And with you came the whole of the world's tears,
And all the sorrows of her labouring ships,
And all the burden of her million years.

And now the angry sparrows in the eaves,
The withered moon, the white stars in the sky,
The wearisome loud chanting of the leaves,
Are shaken with earth's old and weary cry.

[First Printed Version, 1892][3]

The quarrel of the sparrows in the eaves,
The full round moon and the star-laden sky,
And the loud song of the ever-singing leaves
Had hid away earth's old and weary cry.

And then you came with those red mournful lips,
And with you came the whole of the world's tears,
And all the sorrows of her labouring ships,
And all burden of her myriad years.

And now the sparrows warring in the eaves,
The crumbling moon, the white stars in the sky,
And the loud chanting of the unquiet leaves,
Are shaken with earth's old and weary cry.

[Final Printed Version, 1925][4]

The brawling of a sparrow in the eaves,
The brilliant moon and all the milky sky,
And all that famous harmony of leaves,
Had blotted out man's image and his cry.

A girl arose that had red mournful lips
And seemed the greatness of the world in tears,
Doomed like Odysseus and the labouring ships
And proud as Priam murdered with his peers;

---

3. From Yeats's *The Countess Kathleen and Various Legends and Lyrics* (1892). In a corrected page proof for this printing, now in the Garvan Collection of the Yale University Library, lines 7–8 originally read "And all the sorrows of his labouring ships, / And all the burden of his married years." Also, in lines 4 and 12, the adjective was "bitter" instead of "weary." In his *Poems* (1895), Yeats inserted the missing "the" in line 8 and changed "sorrows" (line 7) to "trouble"; "burden" (line 8) to "trouble"; and "crumbling moon" (line 10) to "curd-pale moon."
4. From *Early Poems and Stories* (1925). Yeats wrote in his *Autobiographies* (New York, 1999),

p. 321, that "in later years" he had "learnt that occasional prosaic words gave the impression of an active man speaking," so that "certain words must be dull and numb. Here and there in correcting my early poems I have introduced such numbness and dullness, turned, for instance, 'the curd-pale moon' into the 'brilliant moon', that all might seem, as it were, remembered with indifference, except some one vivid image." Yeats, however, did not recall his emendations accurately. He had in 1925 altered "the full round moon" (line 2) to "the brilliant moon," and "the curd-pale moon" (line 10, version of 1895) to "a climbing moon."

Arose, and on the instant clamorous eaves,
A climbing moon upon an empty sky,
And all that lamentation of the leaves,
Could but compose man's image and his cry.

Leda and the Swan[5]

[First Version]

Annunciation

Now can the swooping Godhead have his will
Yet hovers, though her helpless thighs are pressed
By the webbed toes; and that all powerful bill
Has suddenly bowed her face upon his breast.
How can those terrified vague fingers push
The feathered glory from her loosening thighs?
All the stretched body's laid on that white rush
      strange
And feels the ~~strong~~ heart beating where it lies
A shudder in the loins engenders there
The broken wall, the burning roof and tower
And Agamemnon dead. . . .
                Being so caught up
Did nothing pass before her in the air?
Did she put on his knowledge with his power
Before the indifferent beak could let her drop
            Sept 18 1923

      swooping
The ~~trembl~~ godhead is half hovering still,
     climbs
Yet ~~climbs~~ upon her trembling body pressed
   webbed
By the toes; & ~~through~~ that all powerful bill
        ~~through~~ bowed
Has suddenly ~~bowed~~ her face upon his breast.
How can those terrified vague fingers push
The feathered glory from her loosening thighs
             laid
All the stretched body leans on ~~that~~ white rush
       or
Her ~~falling body thrown on the white white rush~~

5. From Yeats's manuscript *Journal*, Sections 248 and 250. This *Journal*, including facsimiles and transcriptions of the drafts of "Leda and the Swan," has been published in W. B. Yeats, *Memoirs*, ed. Denis Donoghue (London, 1972).

The first version, entitled "Annunciation," seems to be a clean copy of earlier drafts; Yeats went on to revise it further, especially the opening octave. Neither of the other two complete drafts, each of which Yeats labeled "Final Version," was in fact final. Yeats crossed out the first draft. The second, although Yeats published it in 1924, was subjected to further revision before he published the poem in *The Tower* (1928), in the final form reprinted in the selections from Yeats, above.

Yeats's handwriting is hasty and very difficult to decipher. The readings of some words in the manuscript are uncertain.

   Can feel etc
or Her body can but lean on the white rush

   But mounts until her trembling thighs are pressed[6]
   B
   By the webbed toes; & that all powerful bill
   Has suddenly bowed her head on his breast

Can hold

       Final Version

       Annunciation

   The swooping godhead is half hovering still
   But mounts, until her trembling thighs are pressed
   By the webbed toes, & that all powerful bill
    Has hung her helpless body
   Has suddenly bowed her head upon his breast.
   How can those terrified vague fingers push
   The feathered glory from her loosening thighs?
    How now its body leans on
   With her body laid on the white rush
    all the stretched body laid on the white rush
  and Can feel the strange heart beating where it lies?
   A shudder in the loins engenders there
   The broken wall, the burning roof & tower
   And Agamemnon dead . . .
        Being mastered so
      Being so caught up
    So
   And mastered by the brute blood of the air
       Being mastered so
   Did nothing pass before her in the air
   Did she put on his knowledge with his power
   Before the indifferent beak could let her drop.
       WBY Sept 18 1923
    swoop
   A rush upon great wings & hovering still
   He sinks until
   He has sunk on her down, & her hair
   The great bird sinks, till
   The bird descends, & her frail thigh thighs are pressed
   By the webbed toes, & that all

    that
   Now all her body's laid on that white rush[7]
   All the stretched body laid on that white rush
   Now that whole

6. This passage is written across the blank page opposite the first version; Yeats drew a line indicating that it was to replace the revised lines 2–4, which he had written below the first version.

7. Written on the blank page across from the complete version, with an arrow indicating that it was a revision of the seventh line.

N~~ow t~~... rush

~~Can~~ ~~ee~~

Final Version

Leda & the Swan

A rush, a sudden wheel and

~~A swoop upon great wings &~~ hovering still

sinks down ~~bare frail~~

stet The bird descends & her ~~frail~~ thighs are pressed

By the toes ⸱webbed toes, & that all powerful bill

laid

Has ~~driven~~ her helpless face upon his breast.

How can those terrified vague fingers push

The feathered glory from her loosening thighs?

s laid

All the stretched body ~~laid~~ on that white rush

And ~~feel~~ feels the strange heart beating where it lies.

A shudder in the loins engenders there

The broken wall, the burning roof & tower

And Agamemnon dead.

Being so caught up

So mastered by the ~~br~~ brute blood of the air

Did she put on his knowledge with his power

Before the indifferent beak could let her drop.

D. H. LAWRENCE

The Piano[1]

Somewhere beneath that piano's superb sleek ~~black~~

Must hide my mother's piano, little and ~~brown~~, with
the back

stood close to

That ~~was against~~ the wall, and the front's faded silk, both torn

And the keys with little hollows, that my mother's fingers
had worn.

Softly, in the shadows, a woman is singing to me

Quietly, through the years I have crept back to see

A child sitting under the piano, in the boom of the
shaking ~~tingling~~ strings.

---

1. Transcribed from a notebook in which Lawrence at first entered various academic assignments while he was a student at the University College of Nottingham, 1906–8, but then used to write drafts of some of his early poems. These were probably composed in the period from 1906 to 1910. The text reproduced here was revised and published with the title "Piano" in Lawrence's *New Poems*, 1918. A comparison of this draft with "Piano," reprinted above, will show that Lawrence eliminated the first and fourth stanzas (as well as the last two lines of the third stanza); revised the remaining three stanzas, sometimes radically; and most surprisingly, reversed his original conclusion. As Lawrence explained, some of his early poems "had to be altered, where sometimes the hand of commonplace youth had been laid on the mouth of the demon. It is not for technique that these poems are altered: it is to say the real say."

For transcriptions and discussions of this and other poems in Lawrence's early notebook, see Vivian de Sola Pinto, "D. H. Lawrence: Letter-Writer and Craftsman in Verse," in *Renaissance and Modern Studies* 1 (1957): 5–34.

Pressing the little ~~poised~~ feet of the mother who smiles
as she sings

The full throated woman has chosen a winning, living[2]
song
And surely the heart that is in me must belong
To the old Sunday evenings, when darkness wandered
outside
And hymns gleamed on our warm lips, as we watched
mother's fingers glide
                  is
Or ~~is~~ this my sister at home in the old front room
Singing love's first surprised gladness, alone in
the gloom.
She will start when she sees me, and blushing,
spread out her hands
To cover my mouth's raillery, til I'm bound in
            heart-spun
her shame's ~~pleading~~ hands.

A woman is singing me a wild Hungarian
air
And her arms, and her bosom and the whole
of her soul is bare
And the great black piano is clamouring as my
mother's never could clamour
        my mother's [   ][3] tunes are
And ~~the tunes of the past is~~ devoured of this music's
ravaging glamour.

2. A conjectural reading; the word is not clearly   3. An undecipherable word is crossed out here.
legible.

Selected Bibliographies

The Selected Bibliographies consist of a list of Suggested General Readings on English literature, followed by bibliographies for each of the literary periods in this volume. For ease of reference, the authors within each period are arranged in alphabetical order. Entries for certain classes of writings (e.g., "Light Verse") are included, in alphabetical order, within the listings for individual authors.

SUGGESTED GENERAL READINGS

Histories of England and of English Literature

New research and new perspectives have made even the most distinguished of the comprehensive general histories written in past generations seem outmoded. Innovative research in social, cultural, and political history has made it difficult to write a single coherent account of England from the Middle Ages to the present, let alone to accommodate in a unified narrative the complex histories of Scotland, Ireland, Wales, and the other nations where writing in English has flourished. Readers who wish to explore the historical matrix out of which the works of literature collected in this anthology emerged are advised to consult the studies of particular periods listed in the appropriate sections of this bibliography. The multivolume *Oxford History of England* and *New Oxford History of England* are useful, as are the three-volume *Peoples of the British Isles: A New History*, ed. Stanford Lehmberg, 1992, the nine-volume *Cambridge Cultural History of Britain*, ed. Boris Ford, 1992, and the multivolume *Penguin History of Britain*, gen. ed. David Cannadine, 1996–. Given the cultural centrality of London, readers may find *The London Encyclopaedia*, ed. Ben Weinreb and Christopher Hibbert, 1986, and Roy Porter's *London: A Social History*, 1994, valuable.

Similar observations may be made about literary history. In the light of such initiatives as women's studies, new historicism, and postcolonialism, the range of authors deemed most significant has expanded in recent years, along with the geographical and conceptual boundaries of literature in English. Attempts to capture in a unified account the great sweep of literature from *Beowulf* to late last night have largely given way to studies of individual genres, carefully delimited time periods, and specific authors. For these more focused accounts, see the listings by

period. Among the large-scale literary surveys, *The Cambridge Guide to Literature in English*, 1993, is useful, as is the seven-volume *Penguin History of Literature*, 1993–94. The *Feminist Companion to Literature in English*, ed. Virginia Blain, Isobel Grundy, and Patricia Clements, 1990, is an important resource, and the editorial materials in *The Norton Anthology of Literature by Women*, 2nd ed., 1996, ed. Sandra M. Gilbert and Susan Gubar, constitute a concise history and set of biographies of women authors since the Middle Ages. *Annals of English Literature, 1475–1950*, rev. 1961, lists important publications year by year, together with the significant literary events for each year. Four volumes have been published in the *Oxford English Literary History*, gen. ed. Jonathan Bate, 2002–: James Simpson, *Reform and Cultural Revolution, 1350–1547*; Philip Davis, *The Victorians, 1830–1880*; Randall Stevenson, *The Last of England? 1960–2000*; and Bruce King, *The Internationalization of English Literature, 1948–2000*. See also *The Cambridge History of Medieval English Literature*, ed. David Wallace, 1999, and *The Cambridge History of Early Modern English Literature*, ed. David Loewenstein and Janel Mueller, 2002.

Helpful treatments and surveys of English meter, rhyme, and stanza forms are Paul Fussell Jr., *Poetic Meter and Poetic Form*, rev. 1979; Donald Wesling, *The Chances of Rhyme: Device and Modernity*, 1980; Derek Attridge, *The Rhythms of English Poetry*, 1982; Charles O. Hartman, *Free Verse: An Essay in Prosody*, 1983; John Hollander, *Vision and Resonance: Two Senses of Poetic Form*, rev. 1985; and Robert Pinsky, *The Sounds of Poetry: A Brief Guide*, 1998.

On the development of the novel as a form, see Ian Watt, *The Rise of the Novel*, 1957; *The Columbia History of the British Novel*, ed. John Richetti, 1994; Margaret Doody, *The True Story* of the Novel, 1996; Theory of the Novel: A Historical Approach, ed. Michael McKeon, 2000; and McKeon, The Origins of the English Novel, 1600–1740, 15th anniversary ed., 2002. On women novelists and readers, see Nancy Armstrong, Desire and Domestic Fiction: A Political History of the Novel, 1987; and Catherine Gallagher, Nobody's Story: The Vanishing Acts of Women Writers in the Marketplace, 1670–1820, 1994.

On the history of playhouse design, see Richard Leacroft, The Development of the English Playhouse: An Illustrated Survey of Theatre Building in England from Medieval to Modern Times, 1988. For a survey of the plays that have appeared on these and other stages, see Allardyce Nicoll, British Drama, rev. 1962, the eight-volume Revels History of Drama in English, gen. eds. Clifford Leech and T. W. Craik, 1975–83; and Alfred Harbage, Annals of English Drama, 975–1700, 3rd ed., 1989, rev. S. Schoenbaum and Sylvia Wagonheim.

On some of the key intellectual currents that are at once reflected in and shaped by literature, Arthur O. Lovejoy's classic studies The Great Chain of Being, 1936, and Essays in the History of Ideas, 1948, remain valuable, along with such works as Lovejoy and George Boas, Primitivism and Related Ideas in Antiquity, 1935; Ernst Kantorowicz, The King's Two Bodies: A Study in Medieval Political Theology, 1957, new ed. 1997; Richard Popkin, The History of Skepticism from Erasmus to Descartes, 1960; M. H. Abrams, Natural Supernaturalism: Tradition and Revolution in Romantic Literature, 1971; Michel Foucault, Madness and Civilization: A History of Insanity in the Age of Reason, Eng. trans. 1965, The Order of Things: An Archaeology of the Human Sciences, Eng. trans. 1970; Mikhail Bakhtin, Rabelais and his World, Eng. trans. 1968, and The Dialogic Imagination, Eng. trans. 1981; Roland Barthes, The Pleasure of the Text, Eng. trans. 1975; Jacques Derrida, Of Grammatology, Eng. trans. 1976, and Dissemination, Eng. trans. 1981; Raymond Williams, Keywords: A Vocabulary of Culture and Society, rev. 1983; Pierre Bourdieu, Distinction: A Social Critique of the Judgment of Taste, Eng. trans. 1984; Michel de Certeau, The Practice of Everyday Life, Eng. trans. 1984; and Sigmund Freud, Writings on Art and Literature, ed. Neil Hertz, 1997.

Reference Works

The single most important tool for the study of literature in English is the Oxford English Dictionary, 2nd ed., 1989, also available on CD-ROM, and online to subscribers. The OED is written on historical principles: that is, it attempts not only to describe current word use but also to record the history and development of the language from its origins before the Norman conquest to the present. It thus provides,

for familiar as well as archaic and obscure words, the widest possible range of meanings and uses, organized chronologically and illustrated with quotations. Beyond the OED there are many other valuable dictionaries, such as The American Heritage Dictionary, The Oxford Dictionary of Etymology, and an array of reference works from The Cambridge Encyclopedia of the English Language, ed. David Crystal, 1995, to guides to specialized vocabularies, slang, regional dialects, and the like.

There is a steady flow of new editions of most major and many minor writers in English, along with a ceaseless outpouring of critical appraisals and scholarship. The MLA International Bibliography (also online) is the best way to keep abreast of the most recent work and to conduct bibliographic searches. The New Cambridge Bibliography of English Literature, ed. George Watson, 1969–77, updated shorter ed. 1981, is a valuable guide to the huge body of earlier literary criticism and scholarship. A Guide to English and American Literature, ed. F. W. Bateson and Harrison Meserole, rev. 1976, is a selected list of editions, as well as scholarly and critical treatments. Further bibliographical aids are described in Arthur G. Kennedy, A Concise Bibliography for Students of English, rev. 1972; Richard D. Altick and Andrew Wright, Selective Bibliography for the Study of English and American Literature, rev. 1979, and James L. Harner, Literary Research Guide, rev. 1998.

For compact biographies of English authors, see the multivolume Oxford Dictionary of National Biography, ed. H. C. G. Matthew and Brian Harrison, 2004; condensed biographies will be found in the Concise Dictionary of National Biography, 2 parts (1920, 1988). Handy reference books of authors, works, and various literary terms and allusions are The Oxford Companion to the Theatre, Phyllis Hartnoll, rev. 1990; Princeton Encyclopedia of Poetry and Poetics, ed. Alex Preminger and others, rev. 1993; and The Oxford Companion to English Literature, ed. Margaret Drabble, rev. 1998. Handbooks that define and illustrate literary concepts and terms are The Penguin Dictionary of Literary Terms and Literary Theory, ed. J. A. Cuddon, 1991; W. F. Thrall and Addison Hibbard, A Handbook to Literature, ed. C. Hugh Holman, rev. 1992; Critical Terms for Literary Study, ed. Frank Lentricchia and Thomas McLaughlin, rev. 1995; and M. H. Abrams, A Glossary of Literary Terms, rev. 1992. Also useful are Richard Lanham, A Handlist of Rhetorical Terms, 2nd ed., 1991; Arthur Quinn, Figures of Speech: 60 Ways to Turn a Phrase, 1993; and the Barnhart Concise Dictionary of Etymology, ed. Robert K. Barnhart, 1995. On the Greek and Roman background, see G. M. Kirkwood, A Short Guide to Classical Mythology, 1959; The Oxford Classical Dictionary, rev. 1996; and The Oxford Companion to Classical Literature, ed.

M. C. Howatson and Ian Chilvers, rev. 1993. Useful online resources include Early English Books Online; University of Pennsylvania's SCETI Furness Shakespeare Library; Michael Best's Internet Shakespeare Editions; and the University of Toronto Early Modern English Dictionaries Database, ed. Ian Lancashire.

Literary Criticism and Theory
Seven volumes of the *Cambridge History of Literary Criticism* have been published, 1989– : *Classical Criticism*, ed. George A. Kennedy; *The Renaissance*, ed. Glyn P. Norton; *The Eighteenth Century*, ed. H. B. Nisbet and Claude Rawson; *Romanticism*, ed. Marshall Brown; *Modernism and the New Criticism*, ed. A. Walton Litz, Louis Menand, and Lawrence Rainey; *From Formalism to Poststructuralism*, ed. Raman Selden; and *Twentieth-Century Historical, Philosophical, and Psychological Perspectives*, ed. Christa Knellwolf and Christopher Norris. See also M. H. Abrams, *The Mirror and the Lamp: Romantic Theory and the Critical Tradition*, 1953; William K. Wimsatt and Cleanth Brooks, *Literary Criticism: A Short History*, 1957; René Wellek, *A History of Modern Criticism: 1750–1950*, 9 vols., 1955–93; Frank Lentricchia, *After the New Criticism*, 1980; *Redrawing the Boundaries: The Transformation of English and American Literary Studies*, ed. Stephen Greenblatt and Giles Gunn, 1992; and J. Hillis Miller, *On Literature*, 2002. Raman Selden, Peter Widdowson, and Peter Brooker have written *A Reader's Guide to Contemporary Literary Theory*, 1997. Other useful resources include *The Johns Hopkins Guide to Literary Theory and Criticism*, ed. Michael Groden and Martin Kreiswirth, 1994 (also online); *Literary Theory, an Anthology*, ed. Julie Rivkin and Michael Ryan, 1998; and *The Norton Anthology of Theory and Criticism*, gen. ed. Vincent Leitch, 2001.

The following is a selection of books in literary criticism that have been notably influential in shaping modern approaches to English literature and literary forms: Lionel Trilling, *The Liberal Imagination*, 1950; T. S. Eliot, *Selected Essays*, 3rd ed. 1951, and *On Poetry and Poets*, 1957; Erich Auerbach, *Mimesis: The Representation of Reality in Western Literature*, 1953; William Empson, *Some Versions of Pastoral*, 1935, rpt. 1986, and *Seven Types of Ambiguity*, 3rd ed. 1953; William K. Wimsatt, *The Verbal Icon*, 1954; Northrop Frye, *Anatomy of Criticism*, 1957; Wayne C. Booth, *The Rhetoric of Fiction*, 1961, rev. ed. 1983; W. J. Bate, *The Burden of the Past and the English Poet*, 1970; Harold Bloom, *The Anxiety of Influence*, 1973; Paul de Man, *Allegories of Reading*, 1979; and Stanley Fish, *Is There a Text in This Class?: The Authority of Interpretive Communities*, 1980.

René Wellek and Austin Warren, *Theory of Literature*, rev. 1970, is a useful introduction to the variety of scholarly and critical approaches to literature up to the time of its publication. Jonathan Culler's *Literary Theory: A Very Short Introduction*, 1997, discusses recurrent issues and debates. See also Terry Eagleton, *After Theory*, 2003. Modern feminist literary criticism was fashioned by such works as Patricia Meyer Spacks, *The Female Imagination*, 1975; Ellen Moers, *Literary Women*, 1976; Elaine Showalter, *A Literature of Their Own*, 1977; and Sandra Gilbert and Susan Gubar, *The Madwoman in the Attic*, 1979. More recent studies include Jane Gallop, *The Daughter's Seduction: Feminism and Psychoanalysis*, 1982; Gayatri Chakravorty Spivak, *In Other Worlds: Essays in Cultural Politics*, 1987; Sandra Gilbert and Susan Gubar, *No Man's Land: The Place of the Woman Writer in the Twentieth Century*, 2 vols., 1988–89; Barbara Johnson, *A World of Difference*, 1989; Judith Butler, *Gender Trouble*, 1990; and the critical views sampled in Elaine Showalter, *The New Feminist Criticism*, 1985; *Feminist Literary Theory: A Reader*, ed. Mary Eagleton, 2nd ed., 1995; and *Feminisms: An Anthology of Literary Theory and Criticism*, ed. Robyn R. Warhol and Diane Price Herndl, 2nd ed. 1997. Gay and lesbian studies and criticism are represented in *The Lesbian and Gay Studies Reader*, ed. Henry Abelove, Michele Barale, and David Halperin, 1993, and by such books as Eve Sedgwick, *Between Men: English Literature and Male Homosocial Desire*, 1985, and *Epistemology of the Closet*, 1990; Diana Fuss, *Essentially Speaking: Feminism, Nature, and Difference*, 1989; Gregory Woods, *A History of Gay Literature: The Male Tradition*, 1998; and David Halperin, *How to Do the History of Homosexuality*, 2002.

Convenient introductions to structuralist literary criticism include Robert Scholes, *Structuralism in Literature: An Introduction*, 1974, and Jonathan Culler, *Structuralist Poetics*, 1975. The poststructuralist challenges to this approach are discussed in Jonathan Culler, *On Deconstruction*, 1982; Fredric Jameson, *Poststructuralism; or the Cultural Logic of Late Capitalism*, 1991; John McGowan, *Postmodernism and Its Critics*, 1991; and *Beyond Structuralism*, ed. Wendell Harris, 1996. For Marxism, see *Selections from the Prison Notebooks of Antonio Gramsci*, ed. and trans. Quintin Hoare and Geoffrey Smith, 1971; Raymond Williams, *Marxism and Literature*, 1977; Fredric Jameson, *The Political Unconscious: Narrative as a Socially Symbolic Act*, 1981; and Terry Eagleton, *Literary Theory: An Introduction*, 1983. New historicism is represented in Stephen Greenblatt, *Learning to Curse*, 1990; in the essays collected in *The New Historicism*, ed. Harold Veeser, 1989; and *New Historical Literary Study: Essays on Reproducing Texts, Representing History*, ed. Jeffrey N. Cox and Larry J. Reynolds, 1993; and in Catherine Gallagher and Stephen Greenblatt, *Practicing New Histori-*

cism, 2000. The related social and historical dimension of texts is discussed in Jerome McGann, *Critique of Modern Textual Criticism*, 1983; D. F. McKenzie, *Bibliography and Sociology of Texts*, 1986; Roger Chartier, *The Order of Books*, 1994; and *Scholarly Editing: A Guide to Research*, ed. D. C. Greetham, 1995. Characteristic of new historicism is an expansion of the field of literary interpretation extended still further in cultural studies; for a broad sampling of the range of interests, see *The Cultural Studies Reader*, ed. Simon During, 1993, and *A Cultural Studies Reader: History, Theory, Practice*, ed. Jessica Munns and Gita Rajan, 1997. This expansion of the field is similarly reflected in postcolonial studies: see *The Post-Colonial*

Studies Reader, ed. Bill Ashcroft, Gareth Griffiths, and Helen Tiffin, 1995, and such influential books as Ranajit Guha and Gayatri Chakravorty Spivak, *Selected Subaltern Studies*, 1988; Edward Said, *Culture and Imperialism*, 1993; Homi Bhabha, *The Location of Culture*, 1994; Anne McClintock, *Imperial Leather: Race, Gender, and Sexuality in the Colonial Contest*, 1995; and Jonathan Goldberg, *Tempest in the Caribbean*, 2004.

Anthologies representing a range of recent approaches include *Modern Criticism and Theory*, ed. David Lodge, 1988, and *Contemporary Literary Criticism*, ed. Robert Con Davis and Ronald Schlieffer, rev. 1998.

THE ROMANTIC PERIOD

Bibliographies and Reference Works
The most convenient starting points are the surveys by Frank Jordan and others in *The English Romantic Poets: A Review of Research and Criticism*, rev. ed. 1985, on Blake, Wordsworth, Coleridge, Byron, Shelley, and Keats; and Carolyn W. Houtchens and Lawrence H. Houtchens, *The English Romantic Poets and Essayists*, rev. ed. 1966, on Blake, the less studied poets, and the essayists. Annual bibliographies of publications about these writers are to be found in *The Romantic Movement: A Selective and Critical Bibliography*, ed. David V. Erdman, 1980–.

See also the topical bibliographies in *The Cambridge Companion to British Romanticism*, ed. Stuart Curran, 1993; *A Companion to Romanticism*, ed. Duncan Wu, 1997; *An Oxford Companion to the Romantic Age*, ed. Iain McCalman, 1999; *The Cambridge Companion to British Literature, 1740–1830*, ed. Thomas Keymer and Jon Mee, 2004; and the Scholarly Resources section of the *Romantic Circles* Web page (www.rc.umd.edu/reference).

Political and Social, and Intellectual Backgrounds
Histories of the political and social events in this period are Asa Briggs, *The Making of Modern England: 1783–1867*, 1959; E. P. Thompson, *The Making of the English Working Class*, 1963, and *Customs in Common*, 1991; James Walvin, *Slavery and British Society, 1776–1834*, 1982; and Linda Colley, *Britons: Forging the Nation, 1707–1837*, 1992. See also Carl Woodring, *Politics in English Romantic Poetry*, 1970; Marilyn Butler, *Romantics, Rebels, and Reactionaries: English Literature and Its Background, 1760–1830*, 1982; Gillian Russell, *The Theatres of War: Performance, Politics, and Society, 1793–1815*, 1995; and James Chandler, *England in 1819: The Politics of Literary Culture and the*

Case of Romantic Historicism, 1998.

For English literary relations to the French Revolution, see *The Debate on the French Revolution, 1789–1800*, ed. Alfred Cobban, 2nd ed. 1960; Ronald Paulson, *Representations of Revolution (1789–1820)*, 1983; *Burke, Paine, Godwin, and the Revolution Controversy*, ed. Marilyn Butler, 1984; Olivia Smith, *The Politics of Language, 1791–1819*, 1984; H. T. Dickinson, *British Radicalism and the French Revolution, 1789–1815*, 1985; *The French Revolution and British Popular Politics*, ed. Mark Philp, 1991; Simon Bainbridge, *Napoleon and English Romanticism*, 1995; Kevin Gilmartin, *Print Politics: The Press and Radical Opposition in Early Nineteenth-Century England*, 1996; and John Barrell, *Imagining the King's Death*, 2000.

Illuminating analysis of important intellectual movements will be found in A. O. Lovejoy, *The Great Chain of Being*, 1936, chaps. 9–10. Other useful works on intellectual history are Basil Willey, *Nineteenth Century Studies: Coleridge to Matthew Arnold*, 1949; James Engell, *The Creative Imagination: Enlightenment to Romanticism*, 1981; Marilyn Gaull, *English Romanticism: The Human Context*, 1988; and Robert M. Ryan, *The Romantic Reformation: Religious Politics in English Literature, 1789–1824*, 1997. On Romantic literature in its social matrix, see Raymond Williams, *Culture and Society, 1780–1950*, 1960; Jon Klancher, *The Making of English Reading Audiences, 1790–1832*, 1987; Alan Richardson, *Literature, Education, and Romanticism: Reading as Social Practice, 1780–1832*, 1994; Lee Erickson, *The Economy of Literary Form: English Literature and the Industrialization of Publishing, 1800–1850*, 1996; and Clifford Siskin, *The Work of Writing: Literature and Social Change in Britain, 1700–1830*, 1997.

For literary responses to the expansion in this era of the Second British Empire, see *Romanticism, Race, and Imperial Culture, 1780–1834*, ed. Alan Richardson and Sonia Hofkosh, 1996, and *Romanticism and Colonialism: Writing and Empire, 1780–1830*, ed. Timothy Fulford and Peter J. Kitson, 1998. Nigel Leask discusses writers' relationship to the Orientalism of the period in *British Romantic Writers and the East*, 1994, as does Saree Makdisi in *Romantic Imperialism: Universal Empire and the Culture of Modernity*, 1997. For discussion of the Romantics and the beginnings of environmentalism, see Jonathan Bate, *Romantic Ecology*, 1991, and James McKusick, *Green Writing: Romanticism and Ecology*, 2000.

Literary History and Criticism
Among the histories of Romantic literature are Ian Jack, *English Literature, 1815–1832*, 1963, and J. R. de J. Jackson, *Poetry of the Romantic Period*, 1980. Douglas Bush, *Mythology and the Romantic Tradition in English Poetry*, 1937, is so broad in its range that it constitutes an excellent survey of Romantic poetry in general. Harold Bloom, *The Visionary Company*, rev. ed. 1971, which relates the poets to the prophetic tradition of Spenser and Milton, includes brief and stimulating commentaries on many important poems; Bloom, *The Ringers in the Tower*, 1971, consists of essays on nineteenth- and twentieth-century "Romantic" writers. David Perkins treats Wordsworth, Shelley, and Keats in *The Quest for Permanence*, 1959. In *Natural Supernaturalism: Tradition and Revolution in Romantic Literature*, 1971, and in *The Correspondent Breeze: Essays on English Romanticism*, 1984, M. H. Abrams deals with persistent themes, concepts, and designs in English and German Romantic literature, and stresses their relation both to the biblical tradition and to the intellectual ambiance of a revolutionary age. Peter L. Thorslev Jr., *The Byronic Hero: Types and Prototypes*, 1962, discusses the alienated hero in other writers as well as Byron; see also Frank Kermode, *Romantic Image*, 1957, on the concept of the poet at odds with society, from the Romantic period to Yeats. Other useful books are Thomas Weiskel, *The Romantic Sublime: Studies in the Structure and Psychology of Transcendence*, 1976; Anne K. Mellor, *English Romantic Irony*, 1980; Thomas McFarland, *Romanticism and the Forms of Ruin: Wordsworth, Coleridge, and Modalities of Fragmentation*, 1981; Jerome J. McGann, *The Romantic Ideology*, 1983; Charles J. Rzepka, *The Self as Mind: Vision and Identity in Wordsworth, Coleridge, and Keats*, 1986; Clifford Siskin, *The Historicity of Romantic Discourse*, 1988; Peter J. Manning, *Reading Romantics: Texts and Contexts*, 1990; William H. Galperin, *The Return of the Visible in British Romanticism*, 1993; McGann, *The Poetics of Sensibility: A Revolution in Literary Style*, 1996; and Lucy Newlyn, *Reading, Writing, and Romanticism: The Anxiety of Reception*, 2000. See also the essays in

Romantic Poetry: Recent Revisionary Criticism, ed. Karl Kroeber and Gene W. Ruoff, 1993. For critical opinions of the poets during their lifetime, see Donald H. Reiman, *The Romantics Reviewed: Contemporary Reviews of British Romantic Writers*, 9 vols., 1972.

Following are studies of various forms of Romantic literature. On literary criticism: M. H. Abrams, *The Mirror and the Lamp: Romantic Theory and the Critical Tradition*, 1953; and *The Cambridge History of Literary Criticism*, vol. 5, *The Romantic Period*, ed. Marshall Brown, 2000. On poetic genres: Stuart Curran, *Poetic Form and British Romanticism*, 1986, and Susan J. Wolfson, *Formal Charges: The Shaping of Poetry in British Romanticism*, 1997. On the fragment: Marjorie Levinson, *The Romantic Fragment Poem*, 1986. On the novel: Robert Kiely, *The Romantic Novel in England*, 1972; Gary Kelly, *English Fiction of the Romantic Period, 1789–1830*, 1989; Ian Duncan, *Modern Romance and Transformations of the Novel*, 1992; Nicola J. Watson, *Revolution and the Form of the British Novel, 1790–1825*, 1994; Katie Trumpener, *Bardic Nationalism: The Romantic Novel and the British Empire*, 1997. On the gothic: Montague Summers, *The Gothic Quest: A History of the Gothic Novel*, 1938; Mario Praz, *The Romantic Agony*, 2nd ed. 1951; E. J. Clery, *The Rise of Supernatural Fiction, 1762–1800*, 1995; and Michael Gamer, *Romanticism and the Gothic: Genre, Reception, and Canon Formation, 1790–1820*, 2000. On drama: Allardyce Nicoll, *History of Early Nineteenth-Century Drama*, 1800–50, 2 vols., rev. ed. 1955; Jeffrey N. Cox, *In the Shadows of Romance: Romantic Tragic Drama in Germany, England, and France*, 1987; Alan Richardson, *A Mental Theatre: Poetic Drama and Consciousness in the Romantic Age*, 1988; and William Jewett, *Fatal Autonomy: Romantic Drama and the Rhetoric of Agency*, 1997. On Romantic prose: Annette Wheeler Cafarelli, *Prose in the Age of Poets: Romanticism and Biographical Narrative from Johnson to De Quincey*, 1990; Mark Parker, *Literary Magazines and British Romanticism*, 2000; and *Romantic Periodicals and Print Culture*, ed. Kim Wheatley, 2003.

On women writers of the period, see Sandra M. Gilbert and Susan Gubar, *The Madwoman in the Attic: The Woman Writer and the Nineteenth-Century Literary Imagination*, 1979; Mary Poovey, *The Proper Lady and the Woman Writer: Ideology as Style in the Works of Mary Wollstonecraft, Mary Shelley, and Jane Austen*, 1984; Margaret Homans, *Bearing the Word: Language and Female Experience in Nineteenth-Century Women's Writing*, 1986; Marlon B. Ross, *The Contours of Masculine Desire: Romanticism and the Rise of Women's Poetry*, 1989; Gary Kelly, *Women, Writing, and Revolution, 1790–1827*, 1993; Anne K. Mellor, *Romanti-*

cism and Gender, 1993; Judith Pascoe, *Romantic Theatricality: Gender, Poetry, and Spectatorship*, 1997; Mellor, *Mothers of the Nation: Women's Political Writing in England, 1780–1830*, 2002; *Romanticism and Feminism*, ed. Mellor, 1988; *Re-Visioning Romanticism: British Women Writers, 1776–1837*, ed. Carol Shiner Wilson and Joel Haefner, 1994; *Romantic Women Writers: Voices and Countervoices*, ed. Paula R. Feldman and Theresa M. Kelley, 1995; and *Romanticism and Women Poets: Opening the Doors of Perception*, ed. Stephen Behrendt and Harriet Kramer Linkin, 1999. A good starting guide specifically to the poets is J. R. de J. Jackson, *Romantic Poetry by Women: A Bibliography, 1770–1835*, 1993.

Jane Austen

The standard edition remains the one prepared by R. W. Chapman (1923–54), later updated by Mary Lascelles (1965–67); however, the novels are currently being reedited on new principles under the general editorship of Janet Todd. Margaret Anne Doody and Douglas Murray have produced a both delightful and scholarly edition of Austen's juvenilia, *Catharine and Other Writings*, 1993; see also Brian Southam, *Jane Austen's Literary Manuscripts*, 1964. Austen's letters have been newly edited by Deirdre Le Faye, 1995. The first biography of Austen was written by her nephew J. E. Austen-Leigh in 1870; his *Memoir of Jane Austen* has been reissued with illuminating commentary in an edition by Kathryn Sutherland, 2002. Of the many modern biographies, see in particular Park Honan, *Jane Austen: Her Life*, 1987, and Clare Tomalin, *Jane Austen: A Life*, 1997. Modern critical discussion of Jane Austen as a participant in the history of her time got underway in Alistair Duckworth, *The Improvement of the Estate*, 1971, and Marilyn Butler, *Jane Austen and the War of Ideas*, 1975, and was continued in Mary Poovey's *The Proper Lady and the Woman Writer*, 1984, and Claudia L. Johnson's *Jane Austen: Women, Politics, and the Novel*, 1988. For additional discussions of Austen in relationship to the Romantic period, see Warren Roberts, *Jane Austen and the French Revolution*, 1979; Susan Morgan, *In the Meantime: Character and Perception in Jane Austen's Fiction*, 1980; Mary A. Favret, *Romantic Correspondence: Women, Politics, and the Fiction of Letters*, 1993; Clara Tuite, *Romantic Austen: Sexual Politics and the Literary Canon*, 2002; and William H. Galperin, *The Historical Austen*, 2003. See also *The Cambridge Companion to Jane Austen*, ed. Edward Copeland and Juliet McMaster, 1997.

Joanna Baillie

A modern selection is Keith Hanley and Amanda Gilroy, *Joanna Baillie: A Selection of Plays and Poems*, 1997; the most recent full-scale biogra-phy is Margaret S. Carhart's dissertation, *The Life and Work of Joanna Baillie*, 1923. For recent commentary see Anne K. Mellor, "Joanna Baillie and the Counter-Public Sphere," *Studies in Romanticism*, 1994; Catherine B. Burroughs, *Closet Stages: Joanna Baillie and the Theater Theory of British Romantic Women Writers*, 1997; Andrea Henderson, "Passion and Fashion in Joanna Baillie's 'Introductory Discourse,' " *PMLA*, 1997; and the pieces collected in *Joanna Baillie, Romantic Dramatist: Critical Essays*, ed. Thomas Crochunis, 2004.

Anna Letitia Barbauld

The Poems of Anna Letitia Barbauld, ed. William McCarthy and Elizabeth Kraft, 1994, is now the standard edition. For a biography see Betsy Rodgers, *Georgian Chronicle: Mrs. Barbauld and Her Family*, 1958. Among recent critical essays see Julie Ellison, "The Politics of Fancy in the Age of Sensibility," in *Re-Visioning Romanticism*, ed. Wilson and Haefner, 1994; William Keach, "A Regency Prophecy and the End of Anna Barbauld's Career," *Studies in Romanticism*, 1994; Isobel Armstrong, "The Gush of the Feminine," in *Romantic Women Writers*, ed. Feldman and Kelley, 1995; William McCarthy, "Repression, Desire, and Gender in Anna Letitia Barbauld's Early Poems," also in Feldman and Kelley; and Daniel White, "The 'Joineriana': Anna Barbauld, the Aikin Family Circle, and the Dissenting Public Sphere," *Eighteenth-Century Studies*, 1994.

William Blake

The standard scholarly edition is *The Poetry and Prose of William Blake*, ed. David Erdman and Harold Bloom, rev. ed. 1982, which includes painstaking textual notes and brief commentaries on many of the poems. Erdman also prepared a modernized text of all Blake's verse, with copious explanatory notes by W. H. Stevenson, *The Poems of William Blake* (Longman-Norton Annotated English Poets), 1971. A useful annotated selection of *Blake's Poetry and Designs* has been edited by Mary Lynn Johnson and John E. Grant, 1979. The first full account of Blake's life, Alexander Gilchrist's *The Life of William Blake*, 1863, has been a source for all later biographers and remains widely available. The most recent biographies are James King, *William Blake: His Life*, 1991, and Peter Ackroyd, *Blake*, 1996.

The modern era of the scholarly explication of Blake symbolism was begun by S. Foster Damon, *William Blake: His Philosophy and Symbols*, 1924; Damon also published *Blake Dictionary: The Ideas and Symbols of William Blake*, 1965. Some of the most useful later books are Northrop Frye's classic analysis of Blake's moral allegory, *Fearful Symmetry*, 1947; David V. Erdman's investigation of the relation of Blake's poetry to the historical events of his time, *Blake: Prophet against Empire*, rev. ed. 1969; J. A. Wittreich, *Angel of Apocalypse: Blake's Idea of Milton*, 1975; W. J. T. Mitchell, *Blake's Composite Art: A Study of the Illuminated Poetry*, 1978; Leopold Damrosch Jr., *Symbol and Truth in Blake's Myth*, 1980; Robert N. Essick, *William Blake and the Language of Albion*, 1989; Morris Eaves, *The Counter-Arts Conspiracy: Art and Identity in the Age of Blake*, 1992; Jon Mee, *Dangerous Enthusiasm: William Blake and the Culture of Radicalism in the 1790s*, 1994; Nicholas Williams, *Ideology and Utopia in the Poetry of William Blake*, 1998; and Saree Makdisi, *William Blake and the Impossible History of the 1790s*, 2003.

The Cambridge Companion to William Blake, ed. Morris Eaves, 2003, is a useful general introduction to the man and his work. Studies emphasizing the shorter poems are Robert F. Gleckner, *The Piper and the Bard*, 1959, and E. D. Hirsch Jr., *Innocence and Experience: An Introduction to Blake*, 1964. *Blake's Sublime Allegory*, ed. Stuart Curran and Joseph Anthony Wittreich Jr., 1973, includes essays by various scholars on the major prophecies. On Blake's graphic work see Robert N. Essick, *William Blake, Printmaker*, 1980; Eaves, *William Blake's Theory of Art*, 1982; and Joseph Viscomi, *Blake and the Idea of the Book*, 1993. There is a large and growing list of books that reproduce (some of them in color) Blake's etched poems, drawings, and engravings; especially useful are *The Illuminated Blake*, ed. David V. Erdman, 1974, and Erdman's reproduction, with transcripts and commentary, of *The Notebooks of William Blake*, rev. ed. 1977. See also the excellent website *The Blake Archive* (www.blakearchive.org).

Robert Burns
The standard references for Burns's poems are the Centenary Edition, ed. W. E. Henley and T. F. Henderson, 4 vols., 1896–97, and *The Poems and Songs of Robert Burns*, ed. James Kinsley, 3 vols., 1968. Kinsley also prepared a good one-volume edition, Oxford Standard Authors, 1969. J. De Lancey Ferguson has given us a reliable edition of *The Letters of Robert Burns*, 2 vols., 1931 (2nd ed., ed. G. Ross Roy, 1985), and a brilliant portrait of Burns, *Pride and Passion*, 1939. The most recent among many biographies are James Mackay, *A Biography of Robert Burns*, 1992; Ian McIntyre, *Dirt and Deity: A Life of Robert Burns*, 1995; and Hugh Douglas, *Robert Burns: The Tinder Heart*, 1996. David Daiches, *Robert Burns*, 1950, provides a critical analysis of the major poems, and Thomas Crawford, *Burns: A Study of the Poems and Songs*, 1960, is a detailed and comprehensive commentary. See also Mary Ellen Brown, *Burns and Tradition*, 1984; Raymond Bentman, *Robert Burns*, 1987; *Robert Burns and Cultural Authority*, ed. Robert Crawford, 1997; and Liam Mc-Ilvanney, *Burns the Radical*, 2002.

George Gordon, Lord Byron
For the poetry the standard edition is *Lord Byron: The Complete Poetical Works*, ed. Jerome J. McGann, 7 vols., 1980–93; for the letters, *Byron's Letters and Journals*, ed. Leslie A. Marchand, 12 vols., 1973–82 (with a supplementary volume in 1994); Marchand also edited the one-volume *Selected Letters and Journals*, 1982. Ernest J. Lovell Jr., *His Very Self and Voice*, 1954, is a compilation of Byron's conversations. The standard biography is Marchand, *Byron: A Biography*, 3 vols., 1957. Fiona MacCarthy, *Byron: Life and Legend*, 2002, met with much acclaim. See also Louis Crompton, *Byron and Greek Love: Homophobia in 19th-Century England*, 1985.

Among the many useful books on Byron as poet are McGann, *Fiery Dust: Byron's Poetic Development*, 1968; Peter J. Manning, *Byron and His Fictions*, 1978; Jerome Christensen, *Lord Byron's Strength: Romantic Writing and Commercial Society*, 1993; Jane Stabler, *Byron, Politics and History*, 2002. See also *Critical Essays on Lord Byron*, ed. Robert F. Gleckner, 1991, and *Rereading Byron*, ed. Alice Levine and Robert N. Keane, 1993. On Byron's nineteenth-century reception see Andrew Elfenbein, *Byron and the Victorians*, 1995. On Byron and gender see Sonia Hofkosh, "Women and the Romantic Author: The Example of Byron," in *Romanticism and Feminism*, ed. Anne K. Mellor, 1988; Caroline Franklin, *Byron's Heroines*, 1992; and Susan Wolfson, " 'Their She Condition': Cross-Dressing and the Politics of Gender in *Don Juan*," *ELH*, 1987. Other discussions of *Don Juan* include McGann, "*Don Juan*" in Context, 1976; Peter W. Graham, "*Don Juan*" and Regency England, 1990; and Moyra Haslett, *Byron's "Don Juan" and the Don Juan Legend*, 1997.

John Clare
The most recent scholarly presentation of Clare's poems is the series of Oxford English Texts volumes under the general editorship of Eric Robinson: *Later Poems*, 2 vols., 1984; *Early Poems*, 1989; and *Poems of the Middle Period*, 5 vols., 1996–2003. Robinson and his associate David Powell have also produced an Oxford Standard Authors *John Clare*, 1984. An accessible modern-spelling selection has been edited by Jonathan Bate, "*I Am*": *The Selected Poetry of John Clare*, 2003. J. W. Tibble and Anne Tibble edited Clare's *Prose* and his *Letters*, both 1951. Clare's autobiographical writings have been collected by Eric Robinson in *John Clare by Himself*, 1996. An acclaimed recent biography is Jonathan Bate, *John Clare*, 2003. The essays on Clare by J. Middleton Murry, collected in his *John Clare and Other Studies*, 1959, indicate the sudden leap forward of Clare's reputation when he was "rediscovered" in the 1920s. For more-recent commentary see John Barrell, *The Idea*

of Landscape and the Sense of Place, 1730–1840: An Approach to the Poetry of John Clare, 1972; Mark Storey, The Poetry of John Clare: A Critical Introduction, 1974; Elizabeth Helsinger, "Clare and the Place of the Peasant Poet," Critical Inquiry, 1987; John Clare in Context, ed. Hugh Haughton, Adam Phillips, and Geoffrey Summerfield, 1994; and John Clare: New Approaches, ed. John Goodridge and Simon Kövesi, 2000.

Samuel Taylor Coleridge
The Collected Works under the general editorship of Kathleen Coburn is now complete, 16 vols., 1969–2003. E. H. Coleridge, Complete Poetical Works, 2 vols., 1912 (with a one-volume edition of Poetical Works by the same editor in the Oxford Standard Authors series), has been replaced as the standard by J. C. C. Mays's edition of the poems and plays in volume 16 of the Collected Works. The most fully annotated edition of Biographia Literaria is that by James Engell and W. Jackson Bate, 2 vols., 1983 (vol. 7 of the Collected Works).

Richard Holmes, Coleridge: Early Visions, 1989, and Coleridge: Darker Reflections, 1998, together constitute the most recent biography, following close upon Rosemary Ashton, The Life of Samuel Taylor Coleridge: A Critical Biography, 1987. Walter Jackson Bate, Coleridge, 1968, remains valuable. The definitive edition of Coleridge's Collected Letters is by E. L. Griggs, 6 vols., 1956–71; see also Selected Letters, ed. H. J. Jackson, 1987. Five volumes of Coleridge's Notebooks are available, meticulously edited by Kathleen Coburn and associates, 1957–2002. A fascinating one-volume selection from the notebooks has been edited by Seamus Perry, Coleridge's Notebooks, 2002.

H. M. Margoliouth has described the most fruitful literary association on record in his Wordsworth and Coleridge, 1795–1834, 1953. More sophisticated studies are Paul Magnuson, Coleridge and Wordsworth: A Lyrical Dialogue, 1988; Gene W. Ruoff, Wordsworth and Coleridge: The Making of the Major Lyrics, 1802–1804, 1989; and Susan Eilenberg, Strange Power of Speech: Wordsworth, Coleridge, and Literary Possession, 1992. Studies of Coleridge as a poet include Magnuson, Coleridge's Nightmare Poetry, 1974; Reeve Parker, Coleridge's Meditative Art, 1975; Kelvin Everest, Coleridge's Secret Ministry, 1979; M. H. Abrams, The Correspondent Breeze, 1984; and Morton D. Paley, Coleridge's Later Poetry, 1996. J. L. Lowes, The Road to Xanadu, 1927, rev. ed. 1930, which investigates the sources and composition of The Ancient Mariner and "Kubla Khan," is a critical classic. Discussion of Coleridge as critic will be found in M. H. Abrams, The Mirror and the Lamp, 1953; for a more recent discussion see Seamus Perry, Coleridge and the Uses of Divi-

sion, 1999. Among the excellent studies of Coleridge's philosophical, theological, and moral interests and achievements are Thomas McFarland's wide-ranging study, Coleridge and the Pantheist Tradition, 1969; Owen Barfield, What Coleridge Thought, 1971; and Lawrence S. Lockridge, Coleridge the Moralist, 1977. Studies of his political views include Nicholas Roe, Wordsworth and Coleridge: The Radical Years, 1988; John Morrow, Coleridge's Political Thought, 1990; and Patrick J. Keane, Coleridge's Submerged Politics, 1994. On his sexual politics, see Karen Swann, "Literary Gentlemen and Lovely Ladies: The Debate on the Character of Christabel," ELH, 1985, and Julie A. Carlson, In the Theatre of Romanticism: Coleridge, Nationalism, Women, 1994. On opium, dreaming, and Coleridge's poetry, see Alethea Hayter, Opium and the Romantic Imagination, 1968; M. H. Abrams, The Milk of Paradise, rev. ed. 1970; and Jennifer Ford, Coleridge on Dreaming: Romanticism, Dreams and the Medical Imagination, 1998. On his developing reputation see Coleridge: The Critical Heritage, ed. J. R. de J. Jackson, 2 vols., 1970, 1991. Modern essays in criticism have been collected by, among others, John Beer, Coleridge's Variety, 1974; Frederick Burwick, Coleridge's "Biographia Literaria": Text and Meaning, 1989; Leonard Orr, Critical Essays, 1994; and Lucy Newlyn, ed., The Cambridge Companion to Coleridge, 2002.

Thomas De Quincey
The now-complete Pickering Masters series edition of The Works of Thomas De Quincey, gen. ed. Grevel Lindop, 21 vols. (2000–2003), has superseded David Masson's edition of The Collected Writings, 14 vols., 1889–90. There are numerous books of selections from De Quincey, and The Confessions of an English Opium-Eater has been frequently reprinted. The most recent full-scale biography is Lindop, The Opium-Eater: A Life of Thomas De Quincey, 1981. For the effect of opium addiction on De Quincey's writings, see Alethea Hayter, Opium and the Romantic Imagination, 1968, and M. H. Abrams, The Milk of Paradise, rev. ed. 1970. Recent critical studies include John Barrell, The Infection of Thomas De Quincey: A Psychopathology of Imperialism, 1991; Alina Clej, A Genealogy of the Modern Self: Thomas De Quincey and the Intoxication of Writing, 1995; Charles J. Rzepka, Sacramental Commodities: Gift, Text, and the Sublime in De Quincey, 1995; and Margaret Russett, De Quincey's Romanticism: Canonical Minority and the Forms of Transmission, 1997.

Maria Edgeworth
For scholarly texts and critical apparatus, we now have The Works of Maria Edgeworth, 12 vols., 1999–2003, under the general editorship of Marilyn Butler. Butler is also the author of a

modern biography, *Maria Edgeworth: A Literary Biography*, 1972. A modern edition of Edgeworth's correspondence has been produced by Christina Colvin, *Letters from England, 1813– 1844*, 1971. For critical commentary see, most recently, Elizabeth Kowaleski-Wallace, *Their Fathers' Daughters: Hannah More, Maria Edgeworth, and Patriarchal Complicity*, 1991; Catherine Gallagher, *Nobody's Story: The Vanishing Acts of Women Writers in the Marketplace*, 1994; Mitzi Myers, "Goring John Bull: Maria Edgeworth's Hibernian High Jinks," in *Cutting Edges: Postmodern Essays on Eighteenth-Century Satire*, ed. James Gill, 1995; and Mary Jean Corbett, *Allegories of Union in Irish and English Writing, 1790–1870*, 2000.

William Hazlitt

The Complete Works of William Hazlitt, 21 vols., 1930–34, is well edited by P. P. Howe; the final volume includes an overall index, as well as an index of Hazlitt's quotations. Useful selections of Hazlitt's writings are *Selected Writings*, ed. John Cook, 1998, and *The Plain Speaker: Key Essays*, ed. Duncan Wu, 1999. The most detailed biographies are Ralph M. Wardle, *Hazlitt*, 1971, and Stanley Jones, *Hazlitt: A Life, from Winterslow to Frith Street*, 1989. For the correspondence see *The Letters of William Hazlitt*, ed. Herschel M. Sikes, 1978. For introductions to the life and works, see Catherine M. Maclean, *Born under Saturn*, 1944; Herschel Baker's comprehensive study, *William Hazlitt*, 1962; and Tom Paulin, *The Day-Star of Liberty: William Hazlitt's Radical Style*, 1998. On Hazlitt as a critic, see John Kinnaird, *William Hazlitt: Critic of Power*, 1978; David Bromwich, *Hazlitt: The Mind of a Critic*, 1983; John Whale, *Imagination under Pressure, 1789–1832*, 2000; and Julie A. Carlson, "Hazlitt and the Sociability of Theatre," in *Romantic Sociability: Social Networks and Literary Culture in Britain, 1770– 1840*, ed. Gillian Russell and Clara Tuite, 2002.

Felicia Dorothea Hemans

Excellent modern selections are *Felicia Hemans: Selected Poems, Letters, Reception Materials*, ed. Susan J. Wolfson, 2000, and *Felicia Hemans: Selected Poems, Prose, and Letters*, ed. Gary Kelly, 2002. For criticism see Angela Leighton, *Victorian Women Poets: Writing against the Heart*, 1992; Isobel Armstrong, *Victorian Poetry*, 1993; *Felicia Hemans: Reimagining Poetry in the Nineteenth Century*, ed. Nanora Sweet and Julie Melnyk, 2001; Tricia Lootens, "Hemans and Home," *PMLA*, 1994; Sweet, "Hemans and the Post-Napoleonic Moment," in *At the Limits of Romanticism*, ed. Mary A. Favret and Nicola J. Watson, 1994; Susan J. Wolfson, "Felicia Hemans and the Dilemma of Gender," in *Re-Visioning Romanticism*, ed. Carol Shiner Wilson and Joel Haefner, 1994; and Paula R. Feldman,

"Felicia Hemans and the Literary Marketplace," *Keats-Shelley Journal*, 1997.

John Keats

The standard edition of the poetry is by Jack Stillinger, *The Poems of John Keats*, 1978. Miriam Allott, *The Poems of John Keats*, 1970, is generously annotated. Hyder E. Rollins, *The Letters of John Keats*, 2 vols., 1958, provides exact texts based on the manuscripts, and a copious *Selected Letters* has been edited by Grant F. Scott, 2002. The most frequently cited biographies are Walter Jackson Bate, *John Keats*, 1963; Robert Gittings, *John Keats*, 1968; and Aileen Ward, *John Keats: The Making of a Poet*, rev. ed. 1986. Andrew Motion, *Keats*, 1997, is the most recent.

Among the many critical studies, the following are especially useful: Earl Wasserman, *The Finer Tone*, 1953 (a close analysis of the major poems); David Perkins, *The Quest for Permanence*, 1959; Jack Stillinger, *The Hoodwinking of Madeline and Other Essays on Keats's Poems*, 1971; Stuart Sperry, *Keats the Poet*, 1973; Christopher Ricks's lively and wide-ranging study, *Keats and Embarrassment*, 1974; Robert M. Ryan's analysis of Keats's personal creed, *Keats: The Religious Sense*, 1976; Helen Vendler, *The Odes of John Keats*, 1983; Leon Waldoff, *Keats and the Silent Work of Imagination*, 1985; Susan J. Wolfson, *The Questioning Presence: Wordsworth, Keats, and the Interrogative Mode in Romantic Poetry*, 1986; John Barnard, *John Keats*, 1987; Marjorie Levinson, *Keats's Life of Allegory*, 1988; Daniel P. Watkins, *Keats's Poetry and the Poetics of Imagination*, 1989; Nicholas Roe, *John Keats and the Culture of Dissent*, 1997; Stillinger, *Reading "The Eve of St. Agnes,"* 1999; *The Persistence of Poetry: Bicentennial Essays on Keats*, ed. Robert M. Ryan and Ronald A. Sharp, 1998. On Keats in his social milieu, see Jeffrey N. Cox, *Poetry and Politics in the Cockney School*, 1998. For the poet's nineteenth-century reputation, see *Keats: The Critical Heritage*, ed. G. M. Matthews, 1971. Recent collections of essays include *Critical Essays on John Keats*, ed. Hermione de Almeida, 1990; *Keats and History*, ed. Roe, 1995; and *The Cambridge Companion to Keats*, ed. Susan J. Wolfson, 2001.

Charles Lamb

We are indebted to E. V. Lucas for the standard *Works of Charles and Mary Lamb*, 7 vols., 1903– 05; for the standard edition of their *Letters*, 3 vols., 1935; and for the standard *Life of Charles Lamb*, 2 vols., rev. ed. 1921. *The Letters of Charles and Mary Anne Lamb*, ed. Edwin W. Marrs Jr., appeared in 3 vols., 1975–78. Winifred F. Courtney, *Young Charles Lamb, 1775– 1802*, 1982, is a biography. For commentary see Fred V. Randall, *The World of Elia: Charles Lamb's Essayistic Romanticism*, 1975; Jane

Aaron, A Double Singleness: Gender and the Writing of Charles and Mary Lamb, 1991; Alison Hickey, "Double Bonds: Charles Lamb's Romantic Collaborations," ELH, 1996; Mark Parker, Literary Magazines and British Romanticism, 2000; and Peter J. Manning, "Detaching Lamb's Thoughts," in Romantic Periodicals and Print Culture, ed. Kim Wheatley, 2003.

Letitia Elizabeth Landon
For scholarly texts consult Letitia Elizabeth Landon: Selected Writings, ed. Jerome McGann and Daniel Riess, 1997. Laman Blanchard, Life and Literary Remains of L.E.L., 1841, is still a valuable biographical source. For criticism see Angela Leighton, Victorian Women Poets: Writing against the Heart, 1992; Isobel Armstrong, Victorian Poetry, 1993; Glennis Stephenson, Letitia Landon: The Woman behind L.E.L., 1995; Judith Pascoe, Romantic Theatricality, 1997; and Adriana Craciun, Fatal Women of Romanticism, 2003.

Mary Robinson
For scholarly texts and critical apparatus, we now have Mary Robinson: Selected Poems, ed. Judith Pascoe, 1999. The fullest biography is Paula Byrne, Perdita: The Life of Mary Robinson, 2004. For commentary consult Stuart Curran, "Mary Robinson's Lyrical Tales in Context," in Re-Visioning Romanticism, ed. Carol Shiner Wilson and Joel Haefner, 1994; Linda H. Peterson, "Mary Robinson's Memoirs and the Origins of the Woman Artist's Autobiography," also in Wilson and Haefner; McGann, "Mary Robinson and the Myth of Sappho," Modern Language Quarterly, 1995; and Judith Pascoe, Romantic Theatricality, 1997.

Sir Walter Scott
Scott's novels have been often reprinted, collectively and individually, and most of the best ones are available in cheap editions. A new scholarly edition of the complete Waverley Novels is in progress, gen. ed. David Hewitt. A useful collection of the Poetical Works is that in the Oxford Standard Authors, ed. J. L. Robertson, 1904. The letters have been edited by H. J. C. Grierson in 12 vols., 1932–37, and the Journal has been edited by W. E. K. Anderson, 1972. The official Memoirs of the Life of Sir Walter Scott by Scott's son-in-law, J. G. Lockhart, 7 vols., 1837–38, is a classic; its facts and evaluations are supplemented by Edgar Johnson, Sir Walter Scott: The Great Unknown, 2 vols., 1970. A more recent biography is John Sutherland's The Life of Walter Scott, 1995. For commentary see David Daiches, Sir Walter Scott and His World, 1971; Jane Millgate, Walter Scott: The Making of the Novelist, 1984; Nancy Moore Goslee, Scott the Rhymer, 1988; Ina Ferris, The Achievement of Literary Authority: Gender, History, and the Waverley Novels, 1991; Ian Duncan, Modern Romance and Transformations of the Novel,

1992; Alexander Welsh, The Hero of the Waverley Novels, rev. ed. 1992; and Katie Trumpener, Bardic Nationalism: The Romantic Novel and the British Empire, 1997. On The Lay of the Last Minstrel, see the essays by Celeste Langan and Peter J. Manning in Studies in Romanticism, 2001.

Mary Wollstonecraft Shelley
At last we have a collected edition, The Novels and Selected Works of Mary Shelley, ed. Nora Crook, 8 vols., 1996, supplemented in 2002 by an additional 4 vols., also edited by Crook, of Mary Shelley's Literary Lives and Other Writings. The recent explosion of interest in Shelley means that there are inexpensive scholarly editions of almost all her novels. For separate versions of Frankenstein, see especially the editions by James Rieger, 1974, and J. Paul Hunter, 1996, both of which have reliable texts, a record of changes from the first to the third editions of 1818 and 1831, and much useful supplementary material. Charles E. Robinson has meticulously edited The "Frankenstein" Notebooks, 2 vols., 1996. The short fictional writings have been edited by Charles E. Robinson, Mary Shelley: Collected Tales and Stories, 1976. Her prefaces and notes to her husband's poems are accessible in Oxford Standard Authors, The Complete Poetical Works of Percy Bysshe Shelley, ed. Thomas Hutchinson, and rev. G. M. Matthews, 1970. Betty T. Bennett edited The Letters of Mary Wollstonecraft Shelley, 3 vols., 1980–88. Paula R. Feldman and Diana Scott-Kilvert edited her Journals, 2 vols., 1987. A good place to begin a survey of her wide range of achievements is The Cambridge Companion to Mary Shelley, ed. Esther Schor, 2003. See also the biography by Miranda Seymour, 2001. Also among the more recent biographical and critical studies are Paul A. Cantor, Creature and Creator: Myth-Making and English Romanticism, 1984; Mary Poovey, The Proper Lady and the Woman Writer, 1984; William R. Veeder, Mary Shelley and Frankenstein: The Fate of Androgyny, 1986; Anne K. Mellor, Mary Shelley: Her Life, Her Fiction, Her Monsters, 1988; William St. Clair, The Shelleys and the Godwins: The Biography of a Family, 1989; and Emily W. Sunstein, Mary Shelley: Romance and Reality, 1989. See also the essays collected in The Endurance of Frankenstein, ed. George Levine and U. C. Knoepflmacher, 1979; The Other Mary Shelley: Beyond "Frankenstein," ed. Audrey A. Fisch, Mellor, and Esther H. Schor, 1993; Critical Essays on Mary Wollstonecraft Shelley, ed. Mary Lowe-Evans, 1998; and Mary Shelley in Her Times, ed. Betty T. Bennett and Stuart Curran, 2000.

Percy Bysshe Shelley
The nearest to a complete collection of Shelley's writings is The Complete Works, ed. Roger Ingpen and Walter E. Peck, 10 vols., 1926–30. The

most widely used single-volume edition of the poems has been that in the Oxford Standard Authors, ed. Thomas Hutchinson and rev. G. M. Matthews, 1970. *Shelley's Prose* was collected by David Lee Clark in 1954, and *The Letters* was edited by Frederick L. Jones, 2 vols., 1964. Because of the erratic way in which Shelley's poems and essays were published, all the collected editions are faulty; Shelley's writings are now in the process of being revised and reprinted by a number of editors. The best texts are those in *The Lyrics of Shelley*, edited and sensitively interpreted by Judith Chernaik, 1972; and in the large selection, *Shelley's Poetry and Prose*, A Norton Critical Edition, rev. Donald H. Reiman and Neil Fraistat, 2002, which also includes a collection of critical essays. Reiman and Fraistat are currently editing *The Complete Poetry of Percy Bysshe Shelley*; vol. 1 appeared in 2000.

The classic life is Newman Ivey White, *Shelley*, 2 vols., 1940, which is also available in a condensed single volume, *Portrait of Shelley*, 1945. Richard Holmes, *Shelley: The Pursuit*, 1974, is not so detailed as White's biography, but provides a vivid sense of Shelley as a person. Kenneth Neill Cameron, in *The Young Shelley*, 1950, and in the sequel, *Shelley: The Golden Years*, 1974, emphasizes the development of Shelley's radical social and political thinking. As early as 1900 W. B. Yeats, in "The Philosophy of Shelley's Poetry" (reprinted in *Essays*, 1924), dealt with Shelley as one of the great symbolist poets. Harold Bloom's *Shelley's Mythmaking*, 1959, puts Shelley in the line of visionary poets whose imaginative processes were instinctively mythopoetic. Earl Wasserman, *Shelley: A Critical Reading*, 1971, is a series of close readings of Shelley's most important poems and essays. Other useful critical works are R. G. Woodman, *The Apocalyptic Tradition in the Poetry of Shelley*, 1964; Stuart Curran's study, *Shelley's Annus Mirabilis: The Maturing of an Epic Vision*, 1975; Timothy Webb, *Shelley: A Voice Not Understood*, 1977; Michael Scrivener, *Radical Shelley*, 1982; William Keach, *Shelley's Style*, 1984; Stuart M. Sperry, *Shelley's Major Verse: The Narrative and Dramatic Poetry*, 1988; Stephen C. Behrendt, *Shelley and His Audiences*, 1989; Donald Reiman, *Percy Bysshe Shelley*, rev. ed. 1990; and Susan Wolfson, *Formal Charges*, 1997. Charles Robinson discusses personal and poetic relations in *Byron and Shelley: The Snake and the Eagle Wreathed in Fight*, 1975.

Charlotte Smith

The Poems of Charlotte Smith, ed. Stuart Curran, 1993, is the standard edition. The recent explosion of interest in Smith has led to the republication of a number of her novels in inexpensive scholarly editions. A *Collected Works*, under the general editorship of Curran, is in progress. Judith Phillips Stanton has recently edited *The Collected Letters of Charlotte Smith*, 2002. For a biography see Lorraine Fletcher, *Charlotte Smith: A Critical Biography*, 1998. For commentary see Judith Phillips Stanton, "Charlotte Smith's 'Literary Business,' " *The Age of Johnson*, 1987; Judith Pascoe, "Female Botanists and the Poetry of Charlotte Smith," in *Re-Visioning Romanticism*, ed. Carol Shiner Wilson and Joel Haefner, 1994; Adela Pinch, *Strange Fits of Passion: Epistemologies of Emotion, Hume to Austen*, 1996; Sarah Zimmerman, *Romanticism, Lyricism, and History*, 1999; Anne D. Wallace, "Picturesque Fossils, Sublime Geology? The Crisis of Authority in Charlotte Smith's *Beachy Head*," *European Romantic Review*, 2002.

Mary Wollstonecraft

There is a collected edition, *The Works of Mary Wollstonecraft*, ed. Janet Todd and Marilyn Butler, 7 vols., 1989. Todd has also edited *A Wollstonecraft Anthology*, 1989; *Mary Wollstonecraft: Political Writings*, 1993; and a new edition of the *Collected Letters of Mary Wollstonecraft*, 2004. The most important reprints of single works are *A Vindication of the Rights of Men*, facsimile edition by Eleanor Louise Nicholes, 1960; *A Vindication of the Rights of Woman*, Norton Critical Edition by Carol H. Poston, 1988; *Letters Written during a Short Residence in Sweden, Norway, and Denmark*, ed. Poston, 1976; and a reprint in a single volume (ed. Gary Kelly, 1976) of her two novels, the early *Mary, A Fiction*, and *The Wrongs of Woman; or Maria*, which she left unfinished at her death.

Biographers rely for many facts on William Godwin's candid *Memoirs of the Author of "A Vindication of the Rights of Woman,"* 1798, now in a modern edition by Pamela Clemit and Gina Luria Walker, 2001. The first modern critical biography is Ralph Wardle, *Mary Wollstonecraft*, 1951; see also Claire Tomalin, *The Life and Death of Mary Wollstonecraft*, 1974; Emily Sunstein, *A Different Face: The Life of Mary Wollstonecraft*, 1975; and Janet Todd, *Mary Wollstonecraft: A Revolutionary Life*, 2000. An excellent place to begin a review of Wollstonecraft's ideas and writings is *The Cambridge Companion to Mary Wollstonecraft*, ed. Claudia L. Johnson, 2002. Other recent studies include Mary Poovey, *The Proper Lady and the Woman Writer*, 1984; Gary Kelly, *Revolutionary Feminism: The Mind and Career of Mary Wollstonecraft*, 1992; Virginia Sapiro, *A Vindication of Political Virtue: The Political Theory of Mary Wollstonecraft*, 1992; Johnson, *Equivocal Beings: Politics, Gender, and Sentimentality in the 1790s*, 1995; and Barbara Taylor, *Mary Wollstonecraft and the Feminist Imagination*, 2003.

Dorothy Wordsworth

For the journals the best editions are *Journals of Dorothy Wordsworth*, ed. Mary Moorman, 1971, and *The Grasmere Journals,* ed. Pamela Woof, 1991. For the poems consult the appendix of Susan M. Levin's critical study, *Dorothy Wordsworth and Romanticism,* 1987. Dorothy Wordsworth's letters are collected with those of her brother in *The Letters of William and Dorothy Wordsworth,* rev. Chester L. Shaver and others, 7 vols., 1967–92; there is a one-volume selection of her letters, ed. Alan G. Hill, 1985. The standard biography is Robert Gittings and Jo Manton, *Dorothy Wordsworth,* 1985. See also Margaret Homans, *Women Writers and Poetic Identity: Dorothy Wordsworth, Emily Brontë, and Emily Dickinson,* 1980, and the essays by Susan Wolfson and Kurt Heinzelman in *Romanticism and Feminism,* ed. Anne K. Mellor, 1988.

William Wordsworth
Ernest de Selincourt edited *The Poetical Works* (with Helen Darbishire), 5 vols., 1940–49, and the variorum edition of *The Prelude,* with the texts of 1805 and 1850 on facing pages (rev. Helen Darbishire, 1959). *The Letters of William and Dorothy Wordsworth,* ed. de Selincourt, have been revised by C. L. Shaver, Mary Moorman, and Alan G. Hill, 7 vols., 1967–92. The 1805 and 1850 *Preludes* on facing pages, together with the "Two-Part *Prelude*" of 1799, various manuscript fragments of *The Prelude,* and a selection of recent critical essays on the poem, are available in *The Prelude: 1799, 1805, 1850,* A Norton Critical Edition, ed. Jonathan Wordsworth, M. H. Abrams, and Stephen Gill, 1979. Wordsworth's poems in one volume were edited for the Oxford Authors by Gill, 1984. A comprehensive series, the Cornell Wordsworth, gen. ed. Stephen Parrish, begun in 1975 and now close to completion, prints texts of the poems, together with variant readings from the manuscripts (which are reproduced and transcribed) through the final printings in Wordsworth's lifetime. W. J. B. Owen and Jane Worthington Smyser have edited *The Prose Works,* 3 vols., 1974, and there is a *Selected Prose,* ed. John O. Hayden, 1988. Owen has also printed from his edition a convenient collection of *Wordsworth's Literary Criticism,* 1974. For biography see Gill's reliable *William Wordsworth: A Life,* 1984, and Kenneth R. Johnston's lively and well-researched, if at times speculative, *The Hidden Wordsworth,* 1998, whose emphases are indicated by its subtitle: *Poet, Lover, Rebel, Spy.* Mark L. Reed's dating of

Wordsworth's poems, manuscripts, and the events of his daily life has reached two volumes, *Wordsworth: The Chronology of the Early Years,* 1967, and *The Chronology of the Middle Years,* 1975.

For modern discussion of *Lyrical Ballads,* see Stephen M. Parrish, *The Art of the "Lyrical Ballads,"* 1973; Mary Jacobus, *Tradition and Experiment in Wordsworth's "Lyrical Ballads," 1798,* 1976; John E. Jordan, *Why the "Lyrical Ballads"?* 1976; Don H. Bialostosky, *Making Tales,* 1984; and *1798: The Year of "Lyrical Ballads,"* ed. Richard Cronin, 1998. Herbert Lindenberger, *On Wordsworth's "Prelude,"* 1963, explores Wordsworth's major achievement; and Mary Jacobus deals with it from a feminist standpoint in *Romanticism, Writing, and Sexual Difference: Essays on "The Prelude,"* 1989. Aspects of Wordsworth's thought are explored by James A. W. Heffernan, *Wordsworth's Theory of Poetry,* 1969; James K. Chandler, *Wordsworth's Second Nature: A Study of the Poetry and the Politics,* 1984; and Alan Bewell, *Wordsworth and the Enlightenment,* 1989. Prominent critical studies of Wordsworth's poetry are David Perkins, *Wordsworth and the Poetry of Sincerity,* 1964; Geoffrey Hartman's impressive study of *Wordsworth's Poetry, 1787–1814,* 1964, and his *The Unremarkable Wordsworth,* 1987; James H. Averill, *Wordsworth and the Poetry of Human Suffering,* 1980; Kenneth R. Johnston, *Wordsworth and "The Recluse,"* 1984; Marjorie Levinson, *Wordsworth's Great Period Poems,* 1986; Susan J. Wolfson, *The Questioning Presence: Wordsworth, Keats, and the Interrogative Mode in Romantic Poetry,* 1986; David Simpson, *Wordsworth's Historical Imagination,* 1987; Nicholas Roe, *Wordsworth and Coleridge: The Radical Years,* 1988; Theresa M. Kelley, *Wordsworth's Revisionary Aesthetics,* 1988; William H. Galperin, *Revision and Authority in Wordsworth,* 1989; Alan Liu, *Wordsworth, the Sense of History,* 1989; Peter J. Manning, *Reading Romantics,* 1990; and Judith W. Page, *Wordsworth and the Cultivation of Women,* 1994. The range and diversity of critical studies are represented in *The Age of William Wordsworth: Critical Essays on the Romantic Tradition,* ed. Johnston and Gene W. Ruoff, 1987; *Critical Essays on William Wordsworth,* ed. George Gilpin, 1990; and *The Cambridge Companion to Wordsworth,* ed. Gill, 2003.

THE VICTORIAN AGE

General studies and histories of the Victorian age and its frame of mind include Walter E. Houghton, *The Victorian Frame of Mind, 1830–1870,* 1957; Asa Briggs, *The Age of Improvement,* 1962; Richard D. Altick, *Victorian People*

and Ideas: A Companion for the Modern Reader of Victorian Literature, 1973; *Victorian Britain: An Encyclopedia,* ed. Sally Mitchell, 1988; Richard L. Stein, *Victoria's Year: English Literature and Culture, 1837–38,* 1988; F. M. L. Thompson, *The Rise of Respectable Society: A Social History of Victorian Britain, 1830–1900*, 1988; Robin Gilmour, *The Victorian Period: The Intellectual and Cultural Context of Victorian Literature, 1830–1890*, 1993; David Newsome, *The Victorian World Picture: Perceptions and Introspections in a World of Change*, 1997; Philip Davis, *The Victorians*, 2002; and A. N. Wilson, *The Victorians*, 2002. G. M. Young, *Victorian England: Portrait of an Age*, 1936 (republished in 1977 with 215 pages of explanatory notes by George Kitson Clark), is a brilliant synthesis, but it can be incomprehensible to readers who are not yet adequately familiar with the history of the age. Such readers should consult David Thomson, *England in the Nineteenth Century*, 1950, or Derek Beales, *From Castlereagh to Gladstone: 1815–1885*, 1970. The historical spread of Raymond Williams, *Culture and Society, 1780–1950*, 1960, exceeds the Victorian period, but the work continues to be important for those interested in this era.

Some interesting studies of special aspects of the age include Richard Altick, *The English Common Reader*, 1957; E. P. Thompson, *The Making of the English Working Class*, 1963; Steven Marcus, *The Other Victorians: A Study of Sexuality and Pornography in Mid-Nineteenth-Century England*, 1964; *The Victorian City*, ed. H. J. Dyos and Michael Wolff, 2 vols., 1973; Frank M. Turner, *The Greek Heritage in Victorian Britain*, 1981; Jeffrey Weeks, *Sex, Politics and Society: The Regulation of Sexuality since 1800*, 1981; Peter Gay, *The Bourgeois Experience: From Victoria to Freud*, 2 vols., 1984–86; Briggs, *Victorian Things*, 1989; David Cannadine, *The Decline and Fall of the British Aristocracy*, 1990; Christopher Herbert, *Culture and Anomie: Ethnographic Imagination and the Nineteenth Century*, 1991, and *Victorian Relativity: Radical Thought and Scientific Discovery*, 2001; Michael Wheeler, *Death and the Future Life in Victorian Literature and Theology*, 1991; Michael Mason, *The Making of Victorian Sexuality*, 1994; Margaret Homans, *Royal Representations: Queen Victoria and British Culture, 1837–1876*, 1998; and Rick Rylance, *Victorian Psychology and British Culture, 1850–1888*, 2000. Leonore Davidoff and Catherine Hall, *Family Fortunes: Men and Women of the English Middle Class, 1780–1850*, 1987, provides a useful prehistory of this topic for the high Victorian period. For pictures and paintings of the Victorian scene, see Jeremy Maas, *Victorian Painters*, 1969; Christopher Wood, *The Pre-Raphaelites*, 1981; and Julian Treuherz, *Victorian Painting*, 1993. Also revealing are the illustrations for Henry Mayhew, *London Labour and London Poor*, originally published 1851 and reprinted 1967, and Gustav Doré, *London: A Pilgrimage*, originally published 1872 and reprinted 1970. *Nature and the Victorian Imagination*, ed. U. C. Knoepflmacher and G. B.

Tennyson, 1977; George Landow, *Victorian Types, Victorian Shadows: Biblical Typology in Victorian Literature, Art, and Thought*, 1980; and *Victorian Literature and the Victorian Visual Imagination*, ed. Carol T. Christ and John O. Jordan, 1995, feature valuable treatments of literature and the visual arts; see also the individual entries for **Dante Gabriel Rossetti** and **William Morris**.

Books and collections of writings on Victorian poetry include Robert Langbaum, *The Poetry of Experience*, 1957; Carol T. Christ, *The Finer Optic: The Aesthetic of Particularity in Victorian Poetry*, 1975, and *Victorian and Modern Poetics*, 1984; Angela Leighton, *Victorian Women Poets: Writing against the Heart*, 1992; Isobel Armstrong, *Victorian Poetry: Poetry, Poetics, and Politics*, 1993; Antony Harrison, *Victorian Poets and the Politics of Culture*, 1998; *Women's Poetry, Late Romantic to Late Victorian: Gender and Genre 1730–1930*, ed. Armstrong and Virginia Blain, 1999; Yopie Prins, *Victorian Sappho*, 1999; *The Cambridge Companion to Victorian Poetry*, ed. Joseph Bristow, 2000; Matthew Reynolds, *Realms of Verse: English Poetry in a Time of Nation Building*, 2001; and *A Companion to Victorian Poetry*, ed. Richard Cronin, Alison Chapman, and Harrison, 2002. Studies with a particular interest in the novel include J. Hillis Miller, *The Form of Victorian Fiction*, 1968; Peter Garrett, *The Victorian Multiplot Novel*, 1980; Donald Stone, *The Romantic Impulse in Victorian Fiction*, 1980; George Levine, *The Realistic Imagination*, 1981; Gillian Beer, *Darwin's Plots: Evolutionary Narrative in Darwin, George Eliot and Nineteenth-Century Fiction*, 1983; Peter Brooks, *Reading for the Plot: Design and Intention in Narrative*, 1984; Garrett Stewart, *Death Sentences: Styles of Dying in British Fiction*, 1984; Catherine Gallagher, *The Industrial Reformation of English Fiction: Social Discourse and Narrative Form, 1832–1867*, 1985; D. A. Miller, *The Novel and the Police*, 1988; Joseph W. Childers, *Novel Possibilities: Fiction and the Formation of Early Victorian Culture*, 1995; William A. Cohen, *Sex Scandal: The Private Parts of Victorian Fiction*, 1996; and Nicholas Dames, *Nostalgia, Forgetting and British Fiction, 1810–1870*, 2001. John Sutherland, *The Stanford Companion to Victorian Fiction*, 1989, and *The Cambridge Companion to the Victorian Novel*, ed. Deirdre David, 2000, are useful volumes.

Works that address other prose genres include John Holloway, *The Victorian Sage: Studies in Argument*, 1953; Peter Allan Dale, *The Victorian Critic and the Idea of History*, 1977; Avrom Fleischman, *Figures of Autobiography: The Language of Self in Victorian and Modern England*, 1983; Linda H. Peterson, *Victorian Autobiography: The Tradition of Self-Interpretation*, 1986; Hilary Fraser with David Brown, *English Prose of the Nineteenth Century*,

1997; and *Traditions of Victorian Women's Auto-
biography: The Poetics and Politics of Life-
Writing*, 1999. For drama consult George
Rowell, *The Victorian Theatre, 1792–1914: A
Survey*, 1956; Michael R. Booth, *Theatre in the
Victorian Age*, 1991; Kerry Powell, *Women and
the Victorian Theatre*, 1997; and *The Cambridge
Companion to Victorian and Edwardian Theatre*,
ed. Powell, 2004.

Studies that cut across generic lines include
J. Hillis Miller, *The Disappearance of God: Five
Nineteenth-Century Writers*, 1963; John R.
Reed, *Victorian Conventions*, 1975; John P.
McGowan, *Representation and Revelation: Vic-
torian Realism from Carlyle to Yeats*, 1986; and
Amanda Anderson, *The Powers of Distance: Cos-
mopolitanism and the Cultivation of Detach-
ment*, 2001. Interesting works focusing on
gender and sexuality in Victorian life and liter-
ature include *Suffer and Be Still*, 1972, and
A Widening Sphere, 1977, both ed. Martha
Vicinus; Ellen Moers, *Literary Women*, 1976;
Elaine Showalter, *A Literature of Their Own*,
1977; Sandra Gilbert and Susan Gubar, *The
Madwoman in the Attic*, 1979; Elizabeth Helsinger, Robin Lauterbach Sheets, and William
Veeder, *The Woman Question*, 3 vols., 1980;
Nina Auerbach, *Woman and the Demon*, 1982,
and *Romantic Imprisonment*, 1985; Eve Kosof-
sky Sedgwick, *Between Men: English Litera-
ture and Male Homosexual Desire*, 1985; Mar-
garet Homans, *Bearing the Word: Language
and Female Experience in Nineteenth-Century
Women's Writing*, 1986; Mary Poovey, *Uneven
Developments: The Ideological Work of Gender
in Mid-Victorian England*, 1988; Kate Flint, *The
Woman Reader: 1837–1914*, 1993; James Eli
Adams, *Dandies and Desert Saints: Styles of Victorian Masculinity*, 1995; Elizabeth Langland,
*Nobody's Angels: Middle Class Women and
Domestic Ideology in Victorian Culture*, 1995;
Victorian Sexual Dissidence, ed. Richard Della-
mora, 1999; and *Women and Literature in Brit-
ain, 1800–1900*, ed. Joanne Shattock, 2001. For
studies that join a concern with gender or iden-
tity with an interest in issues of empire and
nation, see Jenny Sharpe, *Allegories of Empire:
The Figure of Woman in the Colonial Text*,
1993; Graham Dawson, *Soldier Heroes: British
Adventure, Empire and the Imagining of Mas-
culinities*, 1994; Deirdre David, *Rule Britannia:
Women, Empire, and Victorian Writing*, 1996;
Susan Meyer, *Imperialism at Home: Race and
Victorian Women's Fiction*, 1996; and Ian
Baucom, *Out of Place: Englishness, Empire, and
the Locations of Identity*, 1999. Patrick Brantlin-
ger, *Rule of Darkness: British Literature and
Imperialism, 1830–1914*, 1988, provides a
good introduction to the topic. *A Companion to
Victorian Literature and Culture*, ed. Herbert
Tucker, 1999, contains a wide range of inter-
esting and helpful essays. Articles on aspects
of Victorian literature and culture appear

in many general journals in the field; specialized
periodicals include *ELT: English Literature in
Transition, 1880–1920*; *Journal of Victorian Culture*; *Nineteenth-Century Contexts*;
Nineteenth-Century Literature; *Nineteenth Century Studies*; *Novel*, *Victorian Literature and
Culture*; *Victorian Poetry*; and *Victorian
Studies*. Once a year *Victorian Studies* issues a bibliography for the previous year, covering books,
articles, and reviews; since 2001 it has been
available in a searchable electronic form online.
Other useful research tools are the *Victoria
Research Web* (www.victorianresearch.org) and
specialized bibliographies, which include Rich-
ard C. Tobias, *Bibliographies of Studies in Victorian Literature*, 1991; Sharon W. Propas,
Victorian Studies: A Research Guide, 1992; and
Laurence W. Mazzeno, *Victorian Poetry: An
Annotated Bibliography*, 1995.

Matthew Arnold
The standard edition of Arnold's poetry is the
elaborately annotated *Poems of Arnold*, ed. Miriam Allott, 1979. Cecil Lang has edited *The Letters of Matthew Arnold*, 6 vols., 1996–2001.
R. H. Super has produced an authoritative edition of *The Complete Prose Works*, 11 vols.,
1960–77. For a study of those prose works, see
Joseph Carroll, *The Cultural Theory of Matthew
Arnold*, 1982.

The most satisfactory biography is Park
Honan's *Matthew Arnold: A Life*, 1981, but see
also Nicholas Murray, *A Life of Matthew Arnold*,
1996, and Ian Hamilton, *A Gift Imprisoned: The
Poetic Life of Matthew Arnold*, 1998. Lionel Tril-
ling's excellent *Matthew Arnold*, 1949, remains
a standard critical and biographical study, but
see also G. Robert Stange's *The Poet as Human-
ist*, 1967, and Dwight Culler's *Imaginative Rea-
son*, 1966. Other assessments include Stefan
Collini, *Arnold*, 1988; David G. Riede, *Matthew
Arnold and the Betrayal of Language*, 1988; and
Alan Grob, *A Longing Like Despair: Arnold's
Poetry of Pessimism*, 2002. Two investigations of
Arnold's literary and intellectual background are
Ruth apRoberts, *Arnold and God*, 1983, and
Leon Gottfried, *Matthew Arnold and the
Romantics*, 1983. See also the selection of
essays edited by Harold Bloom, *Matthew Arnold*,
1987.

Emily Brontë
The Complete Poems were first edited by C. W.
Hatfield in 1941. A more-recent edition is *The
Poems of Emily Brontë*, ed. Derek Roper and
Edward Chitham, 1995. Information about the
Gondal narrative is supplied by Fannie R.
Ratchford, *The Brontës' Web of Childhood*,
1941, and *Gondal's Queen, A Novel in Verse*,
1955. The most satisfactory biography is
Edward Chitham, *A Life of Emily Brontë*, 1988.
Essays on the poetry are contained in *The Art of
Emily Brontë*, ed. Anne Smith, 1977; *Critical
Essays on Emily Brontë*, ed. Thomas John Win-

nifrith, 1997; and *The Cambridge Companion to the Brontës*, ed. Heather Glen, 2002. See also Margaret Homans, *Women Writers and Poetic Identity*, 1980, and Irene Taylor, *Holy Ghosts: The Male Muses of Emily and Charlotte Brontë*, 1990. William M. Sale, Jr., and Richard J. Dunn have edited the Norton Critical Edition of *Wuthering Heights*, 4th ed. 2003.

Elizabeth Barrett Browning
There is no complete modern standard edition, so readers still rely on the *Complete Works*, ed. Charlotte Porter and Helen Clarke, 6 vols., 1900. Julia Markus edited *Casa Guidi Windows*, 1977, and Margaret Reynolds edited a Norton Critical Edition of *Aurora Leigh*, 1996. Of a projected forty-volume collection, *The Brownings' Correspondence*, ed. Philip Kelley and Ronald Hudson, 1984–, fourteen volumes have been published. The best critical biography is Dorothy Mermin, *Elizabeth Barrett Browning: The Origins of a New Poetry*, 1989. See also Angela Leighton, *Elizabeth Barrett Browning*, 1986, and Rebecca Stott and Simon Avery, *Elizabeth Barrett Browning*, 2003. Interesting discussions of Barrett Browning can be found in Ellen Moers, *Literary Women*, 1976; Sandra Gilbert and Susan Gubar, *The Madwoman in the Attic*, 1979; Deirdre David, *Intellectual Women and Victorian Patriarchy*, 1987; Helen Cooper, *Elizabeth Barrett Browning, Woman and Artist*, 1988; and Marjorie Stone, *Elizabeth Barrett Browning*, 1995. See also the collections of essays edited by Sandra Donaldson, *Critical Essays on Elizabeth Barrett Browning*, 1999, and Harold Bloom, *Elizabeth Barrett Browning*, 2002.

Robert Browning
There are several competing modern editions, some of which are still in progress: *The Complete Works of Robert Browning, with Variant Readings and Annotations*, ed. Roma A. King Jr., 16 vols., 1969–99; *The Poetical Works of Robert Browning*, ed. Ian Jack, 9 vols., 1983–2004; and *The Poems of Browning*, ed. John Woolford and Daniel Karlin, 2 vols., 1991. A convenient two-volume collection is *Robert Browning: The Poems*, ed. John Pettigrew and Thomas J. Collins, 1981. For the Brownings' correspondence see entry under **Elizabeth Barrett Browning.** The standard biography is William Irvine and Park Honan, *The Book, the Ring, and the Poet*, 1974; see also Clyde de L. Ryals, *The Life of Robert Browning: A Critical Biography*, 1993. Gertrude Reese Hudson provides a study of his critical reception in *Robert Browning's Literary Life*, 1993. W. C. DeVane, *A Browning Handbook*, rev. ed. 1955, is a compilation of factual data concerning each of Browning's poems: sources, composition, and reputation. Further information is supplied by Norman B. Crowell, *A Reader's Guide to Robert Browning*, 1972, which also offers simplified summaries of criti-

cal discussions for twenty-three monologues. The critical assessments in G. K. Chesterton, *Robert Browning*, 1903, are colorfully expressed and often shrewd. Robert Langbaum, *The Poetry of Experience*, 1957, begins the modern critical discussion of Browning. See also W. O. Raymond, *The Infinite Moment*, 1965; Donald Hair, *Browning's Experiments with Genre*, 1972; Ian Jack, *Browning's Major Poetry*, 1973; Herbert Tucker, *Browning's Beginnings*, 1980; Loy Martin, *Browning's Dramatic Monologues and the Post-Romantic Subject*, 1985; Joseph Bristow, *Robert Browning*, 1991; Daniel Karlin, *Browning's Hatreds*, 1993; Donald Hair, *Robert Browning's Language*, 1999; and Stefan Hawlin, *The Complete Critical Guide to Robert Browning*, 2002. Useful collections of essays include *The Browning Critics*, ed. Boyd Litzinger and K. L. Knickerbocker, 1965; *Robert Browning: A Collection of Critical Essays*, ed. Philip Drew, 1966; *Browning: The Critical Heritage*, ed. Litzinger and Donald Smalley, 1970; *Robert Browning*, ed. Isobel Armstrong, 1974; *Robert Browning: A Collection of Critical Essays*, ed. Harold Bloom and Adrienne Munich, 1979; *Critical Essays on Robert Browning*, ed. Mary Ellis Gibson, 1992; and *Robert Browning*, ed. Bloom, 2002.

Thomas Carlyle
H. D Traill edited the *Works*, 30 vols., 1898–1901. Twenty-one volumes of the *Collected Letters*, projected to extend to thirty volumes, have been published since 1971 (ed. C. R. Sanders et al.). There is a modern edition of *Sartor Resartus*, ed. Kerry McSweeney and Peter Sabot, 1987. J. A. Froude, *Thomas Carlyle*, 1882–84, for years the standard biography, has been replaced by Fred Kaplan, *Thomas Carlyle*, 1983. Recommended studies are Albert J. LaValley, *Carlyle and the Idea of the Modern*, 1968; Philip Rosenberg, *The Seventh Hero: Thomas Carlyle and the Theory of Radical Activism*, 1974; J. D. Rosenberg, *Carlyle and the Burden of History*, 1985; Ruth apRoberts, *The Ancient Dialect: Thomas Carlyle and Comparative Religion*, 1988; and Chris Vanden Bossche, *Carlyle and the Search for Authority*, 1991. John Holloway, *The Victorian Sage*, 1953, includes a chapter analyzing Carlyle's rhetoric. George B. Tennyson, *Sartor Called Resartus*, 1965, is an important critical study. See also George Levine, *The Boundaries of Fiction*, 1968; the collection of essays edited by K. J. Fielding and Rodger L. Tarr, *Carlyle Past and Present*, 1976; and B. V. Qualls, *The Secular Pilgrims of Victorian Fiction*, 1982. Tarr has also compiled *Thomas Carlyle: A Descriptive Bibliography*, 1990.

Lewis Carroll
The standard edition is *The Complete Writings of Lewis Carroll*, 1939. Martin Gardner has edited *The Annotated Alice: The Definitive Edition*, 2000; there is a Norton Critical Edition, *Alice in Wonderland*, ed. Donald J. Gray, 2nd

ed. 1992. For his life see Morton N. Cohen, *Lewis Carroll: A Biography*, 1995. See also William Empson, *Some Versions of Pastoral*, 1935. For a variety of recent critical views, see *Soaring with the Dodo: Essays on Lewis Carroll's Life and Art*, ed. Edward Giuliano and James R. Kincaid, 1982, and *Lewis Carroll*, ed. Harold Bloom, 1987. Francis Huxley, *The Raven and the Writing Desk*, 1976, is a brilliant and idiosyncratic discussion of Carroll's work.

Mary Elizabeth Coleridge
The only edition of Coleridge's poetry is *Collected Poems*, ed. Theresa Whistler, 1954. A posthumous collection of selections from her stories and journals is contained in *Gathered Leaves from the Prose of Mary E. Coleridge*, with a memoir by Edith Sichel, 1910. Sandra M. Gilbert and Susan Gubar, *The Madwoman in the Attic*, 1979, contains a discussion of "The Other Side of a Mirror."

Charles Dickens
The standard modern edition of Dickens's works is the Clarendon Edition, 1966–. Norton Critical Editions exist for *Bleak House*, ed. George Ford and Sylvere Monod, 1977; *David Copperfield*, ed. Jerome H. Buckley, 1990; *Oliver Twist*, ed. Fred Kaplan, 1993; *Great Expectations*, ed. Edgar Rosenberg, 1999; and *Hard Times*, ed. George Ford and Sylvere Monod, 2001. A modern edition of *The Letters of Charles Dickens*, ed. Madeline House et al., 1965–, is in progress.

Two classic biographies are John Forster, *The Life of Charles Dickens*, 2 vols., 1876, and Edward Johnson, *Charles Dickens*, 2 vols., 1952. For modern biographies see Fred Kaplan, *Dickens: A Biography*, 1988; Peter Ackroyd, *Dickens*, 1990; and Grahame Smith, *Charles Dickens: A Literary Life*, 1996. *Dickens: Interviews and Recollections*, ed. Philip Collins, 2 vols., 1981, is another biographical source.

Classic early studies include George Gissing, *Charles Dickens: A Critical Study*, 1903; G. K. Chesterton, *Charles Dickens*, 1906; Humphry House, *The Dickens World*, 1941; Edmund Wilson, "Dickens: The Two Scrooges," in his *The Wound and the Bow*, 1952; and George Orwell, "Charles Dickens," in his *A Collection of Essays*, 1954. Other valuable critical studies are George H. Ford, *Dickens and His Readers*, 1955; J. Hillis Miller, *Charles Dickens: The World of His Novels*, 1958; Philip Collins, *Dickens and Crime*, 1962; Robert Garis, *The Dickens Theatre*, 1965; Steven Marcus, *Dickens: From Pickwick to Dombey*, 1965; Angus Wilson, *The World of Charles Dickens*, 1970; Alexander Welsh, *The City of Dickens*, 1971; and John Carey, *Here Comes Dickens*, 1974. More-recent books include D. A. Miller, *The Novel and the Police*, 1988; Andrew Sanders, *Dickens and the Spirit of the Age*, 1999; and Robert Newsom, *Dickens Revisited*, 2000. Critical responses to Dickens are collected in *Dickens: The Critical Heritage*, ed. Philip Collins, 1971, and *Charles Dickens*,

ed. Stephen Wall, 1970. *The Cambridge Companion to Charles Dickens*, ed. John Jordan, 2001, contains valuable essays, as does *Charles Dickens*, ed. Harold Bloom, 2003.

Ernest Dowson
The standard modern edition of Dowson's poems is *The Poetry of Ernest Dowson*, ed. Desmond Flower, 1st American ed. 1970. The best biography is Jad Adams, *Madder Music, Stronger Wine*, 2002. Much lively and illuminating comment on Dowson will be found in W. B. Yeats, *Autobiography*, 1955; a short chapter on Dowson in Geoffrey Tillotson, *Essays in Criticism and Research*, 1967, assesses his relationship with other poets. See also *Letters of Ernest Dowson*, ed. Desmond Flower and Henry Maas, 1967. See also entries under **Late Victorians**.

George Eliot
There is no twentieth-century standard edition of Eliot's complete works. The collected edition of the works, corrected by Eliot, is the Cabinet Edition, 20 vols., 1878–80. Thomas Pinney edited the *Essays*, 1963, and Gordon S. Haight edited *The George Eliot Letters*, 9 vols., 1954–78. Margaret Harris and Judith Johnston edited *The Journals of George Eliot*, 1999. Clarendon has published annotated editions of the novels. Norton Critical Editions exist for *Middlemarch*, ed. Bert Hornback, 2000, and *The Mill on the Floss*, ed. Carol Christ, 1994. The best critical biography is Ruby V. Redinger, *George Eliot: The Emergent Self*, 1975; Gordon Haight, *George Eliot: A Biography*, 1968, remains the most exhaustive account of her life. See also Rosemary Ashton, *George Eliot: A Life*, 1997; Rosemarie Bodenheimer, *The Real Life of Mary Ann Evans: George Eliot, Her Letters and Fiction*, 1994; and Frederick R. Karl, *George Eliot, Voice of a Century: A Biography*, 1995.

F. R. Leavis's influential discussion of Eliot in *The Great Tradition*, 1948, revived critical interest in Eliot's work in the twentieth century. See also Barbara Hardy, *Novels of George Eliot: A Study in Form*, 1959; W. J. Harvey, *The Art of George Eliot*, 1962; U. C. Knoepflmacher, *George Eliot's Early Novels: The Limits of Realism*, 1968; Alexander Welsh, *George Eliot and Blackmail*, 1985; Gillian Beer, *George Eliot*, 1986; Deirdre David, *Intellectual Women and Victorian Patriarchy: Harriet Martineau, Elizabeth Barrett Browning, George Eliot*, 1987; Dorothea Barrett, *Vocation and Desire: George Eliot's Heroines*, 1989; David Carroll, *George Eliot and the Conflict of Interpretations: A Reading of the Novels*, 1992; and Pauline Nestor, *George Eliot: Critical Issues*, 2002. Useful collections of essays include *George Eliot: The Critical Heritage*, ed. David Carroll, 1971; *The Cambridge Companion to George Eliot*, ed. George Levine, 2001; and *George Eliot*, ed. Harold Bloom, 2003. A useful reference work is Levine, *An Annotated Critical Bibliography of George Eliot*, 1988.

THE VICTORIAN AGE / A41

Michael Field

Michael Field's poetry has not been collected. Individual volumes are *Long Ago*, 1889; *Sight and Song*, 1892; *Underneath the Bough, A Book of Verses*, 1893; *Wild Honey from Various Thyme*, 1908; *Mystic Trees*, 1913; *Dedicated: An Early Work of Michael Field*, 1914; *Whym Chow: Flame of Love*, 1914; and *The Wattlefold: Unpublished Poems*, 1930.

Works and Days: From the Journal of Michael Field, ed. T. and D. C. Sturge Moore, 1933, contains selections from the diaries. For a critical biography see Emma Donoghue, *We Are Michael Field*, 1998; for critical commentary see Angela Leighton, *Victorian Women Poets*, 1992, and see *Women Poets 1830–1894*, a special issue of *Victorian Poetry*.

Edward FitzGerald

George Bentham edited *The Variorum Edition of the . . . Writings of Edward FitzGerald*, 7 vols., 1902; a critical edition of the *Rubáiyát* has been edited by Christopher Decker, 1997. See also the *Letters*, ed. A. McKinley Terhune, 4 vols., 1980. The biography is Robert Bernard Martin, *With Friends Possessed: A Life of Edward Fitz-Gerald*, 1985. For a collection of critical essays, see *Edward Fitzgerald's The Rubáiyát of Omar Khayyám*, 2004, ed. Harold Bloom.

Elizabeth Gaskell

The standard edition of Gaskell's fiction is the Knutsford Edition, ed. A. W. Ward, 8 vols., 1906–20; the best modern editions are by Penguin. A modern edition exists of *The Letters of Mrs. Gaskell*, ed. J. A. V. Chapple and Arthur Pollard, rev. ed. 1997, augmented by *Further Letters*, ed. Chapple and A. Shelston, 2000. Biographies include Chapple, *Elizabeth Gaskell: The Early Years*, 1997; Winifred Gerin, *Elizabeth Gaskell*, 1980; and Jenny Uglow, *Elizabeth Gaskell: A Habit of Stories*, 1993. For critical studies see W. A. Craik, *Elizabeth Gaskell and the English Provincial Novel*, 1975; Angus Easson, *Elizabeth Gaskell*, 1979; Patsy Stoneman, *Elizabeth Gaskell*, 1987; *Elizabeth Gaskell: The Critical Heritage*, ed. Angus Easson, 1991; Hilary M. Schor, *Scheherezade in the Marketplace: Elizabeth Gaskell and the Victorian Novel*, 1992; and Deirdre D'Albertis, *Elizabeth Gaskell and the Victorian Social Text*, 1997.

W. S. Gilbert

Gilbert's librettos for Sullivan in their finally revised form comprise *The Complete Plays of Gilbert and Sullivan*, 1976. The earliest published versions, often substantially different from those performed today, are reprinted in Reginald Allen, *The First Night Gilbert and Sullivan*, 1958. Earlier works by Gilbert include *Gilbert before Sullivan: Six Comic Plays*, ed. Jane W. Stedman, 1967, and *The Bab Ballads*, ed. James Ellis, 1970. Stedman, *W. S. Gilbert: A Classic Victorian and His Theatre*, 1996, is a useful modern biography. A sampling of Gilbert

criticism is offered in John B. Hones, *W. S. Gilbert: A Century of Scholarship and Commentary*, 1970. See also Alan Fischler, *Modified Rapture: Comedy in W. S. Gilbert's Savoy Operas*, 1991.

William Ernest Henley

The standard edition, which includes essays and plays as well as poetry, is *The Works of William Ernest Henley*, 7 vols., 1970 (reprint of 1908 edition). See B. Ifor Evans, *English Poetry in the Later Nineteenth Century*, 1933, chap. 12, and Jerome H. Buckley, *William Ernest Henley: A Study of the "Counter-Decadence" of the Nineties*, 1945. Also useful on Henley as a figure of the nineties is a study by André Guillaume, *William Ernest Henley et Son Groupe*, 1973.

See also entries under **Late Victorians.**

Gerard Manley Hopkins

In 1918 Robert Bridges edited the first (posthumous) edition of Hopkins's poems, which has been the nucleus of all subsequent editions. The most recent is *The Poetical Works of Gerard Manley Hopkins*, ed. Norman H. MacKenzie, 1990. In addition to the poems, Hopkins's letters and parts of his notebooks have been published: *The Letters of Gerard Manley Hopkins to Robert Bridges* and *The Correspondence of G. M. Hopkins and Richard Watson Dixon*, ed. C. C. Abbot, 2 vols., 1935; *Further Letters of Gerard Manley Hopkins*, ed. Abbott, 1938, rev. ed. 1956; *The Journals and Papers of Gerard Manley Hopkins*, ed. Humphry House and Graham Storey, 1969; and *The Sermons and Devotional Writings of Gerard Manley Hopkins*, ed. Christopher Devlin, 1959. A helpful introduction to these works is Norman H. MacKenzie, *A Reader's Guide to Gerard Manley Hopkins*, 1981.

The two best biographies are Robert Bernard Martin, *Gerard Manley Hopkins: A Very Private Life*, 1991, and Norman White, *Hopkins: A Literary Biography*, 1992. Some useful critical studies are W. H. Gardner, *G. M. Hopkins: A Study of Poetic Idiosyncrasy in Relation to Poetic Tradition*, 2 vols., 1944, 1949; Paul L. Mariani, *A Commentary on the Complete Poems of Gerard Manley Hopkins*, 1970; Alison Sulloway, *Gerard Manley Hopkins and the Victorian Temper*, 1972; Daniel Harris, *Inspirations Unbidden: The "Terrible Sonnets" of Gerard Manley Hopkins*, 1982; Walter J. Ong, *Hopkins, the Self, and God*, 1986; Virginia Ridley Ellis, *Gerard Manley Hopkins and the Language of Mystery*, 1991; Julia Saville, *A Queer Chivalry: The Homoerotic Asceticism of Gerard Manley Hopkins*, 2000; and Bernadette Waterman, *Word as World: Philosophical Theology in Gerard Manley Hopkins*, 2002. Two good collections of critical essays are *Hopkins*, ed. Geoffrey Hartmann, 1966, and *Hopkins among the Poets: Studies in Modern Responses to Gerard Manley Hopkins*, ed. Richard F. Giles, 1985.

Thomas Henry Huxley

Alan Barr has edited *The Major Prose of Thomas Henry Huxley*, 1997. Huxley's son, Leonard

Huxley, compiled *The Life and Letters of Thomas Henry Huxley*, 2 vols., 1900. William Irvine, *Apes, Angels, and Victorians*, 1955, is lively and informative. Adrian Desmond offers the standard biography in *The Devil's Disciple*, 1994, and *Huxley: Evolution's High Priest*, 1997. See also Harold Cyril Bibby, *Scientist Extraordinary: The Life and Scientific Work of Thomas Henry Huxley*, 1972, and Sherrie L. Lyons, *Thomas Henry Huxley: The Evolution of a Scientist*, 1999.

Rudyard Kipling
The standard complete works is the Sussex Edition, 35 vols., 1937–39. *Rudyard Kipling's Verse: Definitive Edition*, 1940, is supplemented by *Early Verse by Rudyard Kipling, 1879–1889: Unpublished, Uncollated and Rarely Collected Poems*, ed. Andrew Rutherford, 1986. T. S. Eliot edited, with an appreciative and discerning introduction, *A Choice of Kipling's Verse*, 1941. Thomas Pinney edited *The Letters of Rudyard Kipling* (1872–99), 3 vols., 1988–96. Charles E. Carrington, *Rudyard Kipling*, 1955, is the official biography; two recent and worthy ones are Harry Ricketts, *Rudyard Kipling: A Life*, 2001, and David Gilmour, *The Long Recessional*, 2002. Philip Mason, *Kipling: The Glass, the Shadow, and the Fire*, 1975, offers an informative account of Kipling's complex relationship with India. Three important midcentury critics have written interesting essays on Kipling: Edmund Wilson in *The Wound and the Bow*, 1941; George Orwell in *Critical Essays*, 1946; and Lionel Trilling in *The Liberal Imagination*, 1950. Studies of his fiction include Elliot L. Gilbert, *The Good Kipling: Studies in the Short Story*, 1971; Sandra Kemp, *Kipling's Hidden Narratives*, 1987; Mark Paffard, *Kipling's Indian Fiction*, 1989; Zohreh T. Sullivan, *Narratives of Empire: Fictions of Rudyard Kipling*, 1992; and Helen Pike Bauer, *Rudyard Kipling: A Study of the Short Fiction*, 1994. Peter Keating has written a study of his poetry, *Kipling the Poet*, 1994. There are a number of useful collections of critical essays: *Kipling's Mind and Art*, ed. Andrew Rutherford, 1964; *Kipling and the Critics*, ed. E. L. Gilbert, 1965; Roger Lancelyn Green, *Kipling: The Critical Heritage*, 1971; *Rudyard Kipling*, ed. John Gross, 1972; *Critical Essays on Rudyard Kipling*, ed. Harold Orel, 1989; and *Rudyard Kipling*, ed. Harold Bloom, 2004. See also entries under **Late Victorians.**

Late Victorians
On the special qualities of the literature of the end of the period, see *Edwardians and Late Victorians*, ed. Richard Ellmann, 1960. See also Holbrook Jackson, *The Eighteen Nineties*, 1913, rev. ed. 1976; Graham Hough, *The Last Romantics*, 1947; R. K. R. Thornton, *The Decadent Dilemma*, 1983; John R. Reed, *Decadent Style*, 1985; Linda C. Dowling, *Language and Decadence in the Victorian Fin de Siècle*, 1986; Rich-

ard Dellamora, *Masculine Desire: The Sexual Politics of Victorian Aestheticism*, 1990; Elaine Showalter, *Sexual Anarchy: Gender and Culture at the Fin de Siècle*, 1990; Karl Beckson, *London in the 1890's: A Cultural History*, 1992; *The 1890's: An Encyclopedia of British Literature, Art, and Culture*, ed. G. A. Cevasco, 1993; Rhonda K. Garelick, *Rising Star: Dandyism, Gender, and Performance in the Fin de Siècle*, 1998; *Women and British Aestheticism*, ed. Talia Schaffer and Kathy Alexis Psomiades, 1999; Schaffer, *The Forgotten Female Aesthetes: Literary Culture in Late-Victorian Britain*, 2000; *The New Woman in Fiction and Fact: Fin-de-Siècle Feminisms*, ed. Angelique Richardson and Chris Willis, 2001. Three useful anthologies are *An Anthology of "Nineties" Verse*, ed. A. J. A. Symons, 1928; *Aesthetes and Decadents of the 1890's: An Anthology of British Poetry and Prose*, ed. K. Beckson, 1966; and *Poetry of the Nineties*, ed. R. K. R. Thornton, 1971.

See also entries under **Ernest Dowson, William Ernest Henley, Rudyard Kipling, Walter Pater,** and **Oscar Wilde.**

Edward Lear
See *The Complete Nonsense*, ed. Holbrook Jackson, 1947; Elizabeth Sewell, *The Field of Nonsense*, 1952; and Ina Rae Hark, *Edward Lear*, 1982. See also Thomas Byrom, *Nonsense and Wonder: The Poems and Cartoons of Edward Lear*, 1978. Edward Gorey, *Gorey x 3*, 1976, provides delightful illustrations for Lear's verse narratives. Vivien Noakes has edited the *Selected Letters*, 1988, and Peter Levi has written *Edward Lear: A Biography*, 1995.

Light Verse
Interesting collections of light verse include *The Oxford Book of Light Verse*, ed. W. H. Auden, 1938; *Parodies: An Anthology from Chaucer to Beerbohm*, ed. Dwight Macdonald, 1969; and *The New Oxford Book of Light Verse*, ed. Kingsley Amis, 1978.

See also entries under **Lewis Carroll, W. S. Gilbert,** and **Edward Lear.**

George Meredith
Phyllis Bartlett's edition of the *Poems*, 1978, supersedes G. M. Trevelyan's edition of 1928. *The Letters*, ed. C. L. Cline, 3 vols., were published in 1970. See C. Day Lewis, *Introduction to Modern Love*, 1948; Lionel Stevenson, *The Ordeal of George Meredith*, 1953; and Norman Kelvin, *A Troubled Eden*, 1961. A Norton Critical Edition of Meredith's novel, *The Egoist*, was edited by Robert M. Adams in 1979.

John Stuart Mill
Collected Works, ed. John Robson et al., 27 vols., was published from 1963 to 1990. A Norton Critical Edition of *Mill: The Spirit of the Age, On Liberty, The Subjection of Women* was edited by Alan Ryan in 1998. Ann P. Robson and John M. Robson edited *Sexual Equality: Writ-*

ings by John Stuart Mill, Harriet Taylor Mill, and Helen Taylor, 1994. M. St. J. Packe, The Life of J. S. Mill, 1954, is the standard biography; an excellent recent biography is Nicholas Capaldi, John Stuart Mill, 2004. Studies include Maurice Cowling, Mill and Liberalism, 1963; John Robson, The Improvement of Mankind, 1968; Alan Ryan, John Stuart Mill, 1970; Fred Berger, Happiness, Justice, and Freedom, 1984; Janice Carlisle, John Stuart Mill and the Writing of Character, 1991; and Elizabeth Raeder, John Stuart Mill and the Religion of Humanity, 2002. Collections of essays include Mill: A Collection of Critical Essays, ed. J. B. Schneewind, 1968; J. S. Mill: On Liberty in Focus, ed. John Gray and G. W. Smith, 1991; and A Cultivated Mind: Essays on J. S. Mill Presented to John M. Robson, ed. Michael Laine, 1991.

William Morris
May Morris edited the Collected Works, 24 vols., 1910–15; Norman Kelvin edited The Collected Letters of William Morris, 4 vols., 1984–96. Biographies include J. W. Mackail, The Life of William Morris, 2 vols., 1899; Philip Henderson, William Morris, His Life, Work and Friends, 1967; E. P. Thompson, William Morris: Romantic to Revolutionary, 1977; Peter Stansky, William Morris, 1983; and Fiona MacCarthy, William Morris: A Life for Our Time, 1995. See also George Bernard Shaw, William Morris, As I Knew Him, 1936; William Morris: The Critical Heritage, ed. Peter Faulkner, 1973; Peter Faulkner, Against the Age: An Introduction to William Morris, 1980; Carole Silver, The Romance of William Morris, 1982; Jerome McGann, Black Riders: The Visible Language of Modernism, 1993; and Ruth Kinna, William Morris and the Art of Socialism, 2000.

John Henry Cardinal Newman
The only complete edition of Newman's works is the Longman edition, 41 vols., 1908–18. His Letters and Diaries have been collected and edited by C. S. Dessain et al., 31 vols., 1961–84. There is a Norton Critical Edition of Apologia Pro Vita Sua, ed. David J. DeLaura, 1968, and a Clarendon edition of The Idea of a University, ed. I. T. Ker, 1976. Ker, John Henry Newman, 1988, is the standard biography. See also Sheridan Gilley, Newman and His Age, 1990; Dwight Culler, The Imperial Intellect, 1955; and Francis McGrath, John Henry Newman: Universal Revelation, 1997. His literary skill is analyzed in John Holloway, The Victorian Sage, 1953.

Walter Pater
The standard edition is Works, 10 vols., 1910; Donald Hill has done an annotated edition of The Renaissance, 1980. Thomas Wright, The Life of Walter Pater, 2 vols., 1907, is a standard but unreliable source. Better is Denis Donoghue, Walter Pater: Lover of Strange Souls,

1995. For critical studies see Wolfgang Iser, Walter Pater: The Aesthetic Moment, 1987; Carolyn Williams, Transfigured World: Walter Pater's Aesthetic Historicism, 1989; and Kenneth Daley, The Rescue of Romanticism: Walter Pater and John Ruskin, 2001. T. S. Eliot's essay "Arnold and Pater," in Selected Essays 1917–32, 1932, has been influential. For collections of essays see Walter Pater: Modern Critical Views, ed. Harold Bloom, 1985, and Elinor Shaffer, Walter Pater and the Culture of the Fin-de-Siècle, 1995.
See also entries under **Late Victorians.**

Christina Rossetti
The standard variorum edition is The Complete Poems of Christina Rossetti, ed. R. W. Crump, 3 vols., 1979–90. Antony Harrison has edited The Letters of Christina Rossetti, 3 vols., 1997–2000. See also Selected Prose of Christina Rossetti, ed. David A. Kent and P. G. Stanwood, 1998. Two recent biographies are Kathleen Jones, Learning Not to Be First: The Life of Christina Rossetti, 1991, and Jan Marsh, Christina Rossetti: A Writer's Life, 1995. Virginia Woolf, Second Common Reader, 1932, contains an essay on the poet. Dolores Rosenblum, Christina Rossetti: The Poetry of Endurance, 1986, and Harrison, Christina Rossetti in Context, 1988, are good book-length studies of the poetry. Collections of critical essays are The Culture of Christina Rossetti: Female Politics and Victorian Contexts, ed. Mary Arseneau, Harrison, and Lorraine Janzen Kooistra, 1999, and David Kent, The Achievement of Christina Rossetti, 1987.

Dante Gabriel Rossetti
Rossetti's collected works were edited by W. M. Rossetti, 1911; Collected Writings, ed. Jan Marsh, 2000, and Collected Poetry and Prose, ed. Jerome McGann, 2003, are excellent modern editions. Readers had relied on The Letters, an incomplete collection, ed. Oswald Doughty and J. R. Wahl, 4 vols., 1965–67, but The Correspondence of Dante Gabriel Rossetti, ed. William Fredeman, 5 vols., 2002–05, will supplant this edition once it is complete. For critical biographies see Robert M. Cooper, Lost on Both Sides, 1970, and Marsh, Dante Gabriel Rossetti: Painter and Poet, 1999. For critical studies see Joan Rees, The Poetry of Dante Gabriel Rossetti, 1981; David Riede, Dante Gabriel Rossetti and the Limits of Victorian Vision, 1983, and Dante Gabriel Rossetti Revisited, 1992; and McGann, Dante Gabriel Rossetti and the Game That Must Be Lost, 2000. An online resource, edited by McGann, is The Rossetti Archive (www.iath .virginia.edu/rossetti/fullarch.html).

John Ruskin
Ruskin's collected works were edited by E. T. Cook and Alexander Wedderburn, 39 vols., 1903–12. See also Deborah Nord's edition of Sesame and Lilies, 2002. Cook's early biography

of Ruskin, 1911, has been superseded by John Batchelor's *John Ruskin: No Wealth but Life*, 2000, and Tim Hilton's two volumes, *John Ruskin: The Early Years*, 1985, and *The Later Years*, 2000. For critical studies see John D. Rosenberg, *The Darkening Glass*, 1961; George P. Landow, *The Aesthetic and Critical Theories of John Ruskin*, 1971; Robert Hewison, *John Ruskin and the Argument of the Eye*, 1976; Elizabeth Helsinger, *Ruskin and the Art of the Beholder*, 1982; Paul L. Sawyer, *Ruskin's Poetic Argument: The Design of the Major Works*, 1985; Linda M. Austin, *The Practical Ruskin: Economics and Audience in the Late Work*, 1991; Sharon Weltman, *Ruskin's Mythic Queen: Gender Subversion in Victorian Culture*, 1999; Michael Wheeler, *Ruskin's God*, 1999; and Kenneth Daley, *The Rescue of Romanticism: Walter Pater and John Ruskin*, 2001. For collections of essays see *New Approaches to Ruskin*, ed. Robert Hewison, 1981; *Ruskin and the Dawn of the Modern*, ed. Dinah Birch, 1999; and *Ruskin and Gender*, ed. Birch and Francis O'Gorman, 2002.

Bernard Shaw
The first volume of *The Collected Works of Bernard Shaw*, in the Ayot St. Lawrence Edition, 30 vols., appeared in 1930. *Collected Plays with Their Prefaces*, 7 vols., 1975, contains the fully revised texts of all the published plays, together with historical data and miscellaneous Shavian pronouncements on each play. There is a Norton Critical Edition, *Bernard Shaw's Plays*, ed. Sandie Byrne, 2002. Selections of prose include *Bernard Shaw, Selected Prose*, ed. Diarmuid Russell, 1952; *Plays and Players*, ed. A. C. Ward, 1952; *Bernard Shaw on Language*, ed. Abraham Tauber, 1963; *The Nondramatic Literary Criticism of Bernard Shaw*, ed. Stanley Weintraub, 1972; and *Shaw on Music*, ed. Eric Bentley, 1972. The *Collected Letters of Bernard Shaw*, ed. Dan H. Laurence, 1965–, collects his voluminous correspondence.
  The standard biography is Michael Holroyd, *Bernard Shaw*, 4 vols., 1988–93, also abridged in a single volume, 1998. Also of interest is Hesketh Pearson, *George Bernard Shaw: His Life and Personality*, 1963. Other biographical sources are *Shaw: An Autobiography, Selected from His Writings*, ed. Stanley Weintraub, 2 vols., 1969–70, and *Shaw: Interviews and Recollections*, ed. A. M. Gibbs, 1990.
  Critical studies include Eric Bentley, *Bernard Shaw: A Reconsideration*, 1947; Charles A. Carpenter, *Bernard Shaw and the Art of Destroying Ideals*, 1969; Louis Crompton, *Shaw the Dramatist*, 1969; *Shaw and Politics*, ed. T. F. Evans, 1991; J. Ellen Gainor, *Shaw's Daughters: Dramatic and Narrative Constructions of Gender*, 1991; Gareth Griffith, *Socialism and Superior Brains: The Political Thought of Bernard Shaw*, 1992; and Sally Peters, *Bernard Shaw: The Ascent of the Superman*, 1996. Useful col-

lections of essays are *Critical Essays on George Bernard Shaw*, ed. Elsie B. Adams, 1991; *The Cambridge Companion to George Bernard Shaw*, ed. Christopher Innes, 1998; and *George Bernard Shaw*, ed. Harold Bloom, 2000.

Robert Louis Stevenson
The standard edition of *The Works of Robert Louis Stevenson* was published by Scribner's, 32 vols., 1911–12; Ian Bell edited *The Complete Short Stories*, 1993, and Roger Lewis edited *The Collected Poems*, 2003. There is a Norton Critical Edition of *The Strange Case of Dr. Jekyll and Mr. Hyde*, ed. Katherine Lineham, 2003. Bradford Booth and Ernest Mehew edited *The Letters of Robert Louis Stevenson*, 8 vols., 1994–95. Graham Balfour, *Life of Robert Louis Stevenson*, 1901, has been an important source for subsequent biographers; modern biographies include Jenni Calder, *Robert Louis Stevenson: A Life Study*, 1980, and Bell, *Robert Louis Stevenson: Dreams of Exile*, 1992. For critical studies see David Daiches, *Robert Louis Stevenson*, 1947; Robert Kiely, *Robert Louis Stevenson and the Fiction of Adventure*, 1964; E. Eigner, *Robert Louis Stevenson and the Romantic Tradition*, 1966; Alan Sandison, *Robert Louis Stevenson and the Appearance of Modernism*, 1995; Peter Garrett, *Gothic Reflections*, 2003; and Ann Coley, *Robert Louis Stevenson and the Colonial Imagination*, 2004. For collections of essays see *Dr. Jekyll and Mr. Hyde after One Hundred Years*, ed. William Veeder and Gordon Hirsch, 1988; *Stevenson and Victorian Scotland*, ed. Jenni Calder, 2001; and *Robert Louis Stevenson Reconsidered*, ed. William Jones Jr., 2003.

Algernon Charles Swinburne
Complete Works was edited by E. W. Gosse and T. J. Wise, 20 vols., 1925–27, and *The Swinburne Letters* was edited by Cecil Y. Lang, 6 vols., 1959–62. They have been supplemented by *Uncollected Letters*, ed. Terry Meyers, 2004. Rikky Rooksby, *A. C. Swinburne: A Poet's Life*, 1997, is the best biography. For an attack on Swinburne's shortcomings as a poet, see A. E. Housman's essay of 1910, first published in *American Scholar*, Winter 1969–70. For more sympathetic readings see the special Swinburne issue of *Victorian Poetry*, Spring–Summer 1971, and see also Jerome J. McGann, *Swinburne: An Experiment in Criticism*, 1972; David Riede, *Swinburne: A Study of Romantic Mythmaking*, 1978; Margot K. Louis, *Swinburne and His Gods: The Roots and Growth of an Agnostic Poetry*, 1990; the chapter on Swinburne in Camille Paglia, *Sexual Personae*, 1990; *The Whole Music of Passion: New Essays on Swinburne*, ed. Rikky Rooksby and Nicholas Shrimpton, 1993; and Yopie Prins, *Victorian Sappho*, 1999.

Alfred, Lord Tennyson
Works was edited by his son Hallam, Lord Tennyson, 9 vols., 1907–08. The poems were edited

by Christopher Ricks in one volume, 1969, and extensively revised in three volumes, 1988. Norton Critical Editions of Tennyson's work are *Tennyson's Poetry*, ed. Robert W. Hill, Jr., 1999, and *In Memoriam*, ed. Erik Gray, 2003. *In Memoriam* has been edited by Susan Shatto and Marion Shaw, 1982. *The Letters of Alfred, Lord Tennyson*, to 1870, are edited by Cecil Y. Lang and Edgar F. Shannon, 4 vols., 1981–91. Hallam Tennyson's *Alfred, Lord Tennyson: A Memoir*, 2 vols., 1897, is a mine of anecdotes and valuable information. *The Tennyson Archive*, ed. Christopher Ricks and Aidan Day, 23 vols., 1987–89, is a monumental production concerning the manuscripts. The standard biography is Robert Martin, *Tennyson*, 1980. Critical studies include Jerome H. Buckley, *Tennyson: The Growth of a Poet*, 1961; Christopher Ricks, *Tennyson*, 1972; F. E. L. Priestley, *Language and Structure in Tennyson's Poetry*, 1973; James R. Kincaid, *Tennyson's Major Poems: The Comic and Ironic Patterns*, 1975; W. David Shaw, *Tennyson's Style*, 1976; and A. Dwight Culler, *The Poetry of Tennyson*, 1977. See also Daniel Albright, *Tennyson: The Muses' Tug-of-War*, 1986; Alan Sinfield, *Alfred Tennyson*, 1986; Herbert F. Tucker, *Tennyson and the Doom of Romanticism*, 1988; Donald S. Hair, *Tennyson's Language*, 1991; and Gerhard Joseph, *Tennyson and the Text: The Weaver's Shuttle*, 1992.

Some of the most interesting discussions are in introductory essays to Tennyson's poems by T. S. Eliot, 1936; W. H. Auden, 1944; and H. Marshall McLuhan, 1956. Also useful are A. C. Bradley, *A Commentary on Tennyson's "In Memoriam,"* 1901; E. D. H. Johnson, *The Alien Vision of Victorian Poetry*, 1952; *Critical Essays on the Poetry of Tennyson*, ed. John Kilham, 1960; *Critical Essays on Alfred Lord Tennyson*, ed. Herbert F. Tucker, 1993; and *Alfred Lord Tennyson*, ed. Harold Bloom, 1999. Book-length studies of the *Idylls* have been published by Clyde de L. Ryals, 1967; John R. Reed, 1969; and John D. Rosenberg, 1973. A collection of critical essays on *In Memoriam* was edited by John Dixon Hunt, 1970, and Timothy Peltason has published a study of the poem, *Reading In Memoriam*, 1985.

Oscar Wilde

There is no standard complete edition, but a convenient one-volume collection is *The Complete Works of Oscar Wilde*, 1989. Merlin Holland and Rupert Hart-Davis edited *Complete Letters*, 2000. The standard biography is Richard Ellmann, *Oscar Wilde*, 1988. See also the psychoanalytic biography by Melissa Knox, *Oscar Wilde: A Long and Lovely Suicide*, 1994, and Barbara Belford, *Oscar Wilde: A Certain Genius*, 2000. Earlier biographies include Hesketh Pearson, *The Life of Oscar Wilde: His Life and Wit*, 1946, and H. Montgomery Hyde, *Oscar Wilde: A Biography*, 1975. *Oscar Wilde, a Pictorial Biography*, by Wilde's son, Vyvyan Holland, 1960, has splendid photographs of Wilde and his contemporaries and also provides a concise factual account of his life. The essays by Ian Fletcher and John Stokes in *Anglo-Irish Literature: A Review of Research*, 1976, and *Recent Research on Anglo-Irish Writers*, 1983, both ed. Richard J. Finneran, provide a full-scale guide to editions of Wilde and studies of his life and work.

Oscar Wilde: A Collection of Critical Essays, ed. Richard Ellmann, 1969, is valuable for its coverage of responses to Wilde by writers such as Yeats and Shaw. *Oscar Wilde: The Critical Heritage*, ed. Karl Beckson, 1970, is especially helpful with regard to the plays; it covers the period 1881–1927. For an account of the contemporary reception of Wilde, see Regenia Gagnier, *Idylls of the Marketplace: Oscar Wilde and the Victorian Public*, 1986. See also Camille Paglia, *Sexual Personae*, 1990; Ed Cohen, *Talk on the Wilde Side: Toward a Genealogy of Discourse on Male Sexualities*, 1993; Gary Schmidgall, *The Stranger Wilde: Interpreting Oscar*, 1994; Lawrence Damson, *Wilde's Intentions: The Artist in His Criticism*, 1997; and Knox, *Oscar Wilde in the 1990s: The Critic as Creator*, 2001. Useful collections of essays are *Critical Essays on Oscar Wilde*, ed. Gagnier, 1991; *The Cambridge Companion to Oscar Wilde*, ed. Peter Raby, 1997; and *Oscar Wilde*, ed. Harold Bloom, 2002. Karl Beckson, *The Oscar Wilde Encyclopedia*, 1998, and Ian Small, *Oscar Wilde: Recent Research*, 2000, are also valuable resources.

See also entries under **Late Victorians.**

THE TWENTIETH CENTURY AND AFTER

The Twentieth Century and After

Martin Gilbert, *A History of the Twentieth Century*, 3 vols., 1997–99, offers a richly informative account of the first half-century, while Peter Conrad, *Modern Times, Modern Places*, 1999, skillfully interweaves the history of the period with its artistic and intellectual movements.

The social and political background is well covered in Robert Graves and Alan Hodge's *The* *Long Week End: A Social History of Great Britain, 1918–1939*, 1940; *The Baldwin Age*, ed. John Raymond, 1960; Julian Symons's *The Thirties: A Dream Revolved*, 1960, rev. ed. 1975; Hugh Thomas's *The Spanish Civil War*, 1961, 3rd ed. 1986; Malcolm Bradbury's *The Social Context of Modern English Literature*, 1971; *The Twentieth-Century Mind: History, Ideas, and Literature in Britain*, 3 vols., ed. C. B. Cox and

A. E. Dyson, 1972; Paul Fussell's *The Great War and Modern Memory*, 1975, and *Wartime: Understanding and Behavior in the Second World War*, 1989; Samuel Hynes's *The Auden Generation: Literature and Politics in England in the 1930s*, 1976, and *A War Imagined: The First World War and English Culture*, 1991; Valentine Cunningham's *British Writers of the Thirties*, 1988; Alan Sinfield's *Literature, Politics, and Culture in Postwar Britain*, 1989; all of which include useful bibliographies.

The following critical works deal with general aspects of modern English literature: Stephen Spender's *The Struggle of the Modern*, 1963; C. K. Stead's *The New Poetic: Yeats to Eliot*, 1964, rev. ed. 1987, and *Pound, Yeats, Eliot, and the Modernist Movement*, 1986; *The Modern Tradition: Backgrounds of Modern Literature*, ed. Richard Ellmann and Charles Feidelson, 1965; Irving Howe's *The Idea of the Modern in Literature and the Arts*, 1967; Hugh Kenner's *The Pound Era*, 1971; *Modernism 1890–1930*, ed. Malcolm Bradbury and James McFarlane, 1976; David Perkins's *A History of Modern Poetry*, 2 vols., 1976–87; Robert Hughes's *The Shock of the New*, 1981, rev. ed. 1991; Michael Levenson's *A Genealogy of Modernism*, 1984; Carol T. Christ's *Victorian and Modern Poetics*, 1984; Sanford Schwartz's *The Matrix of Modernism: Pound, Eliot and Early Twentieth-Century Thought*, 1985; Maud Ellmann's *The Poetics of Impersonality: T. S. Eliot and Ezra Pound*, 1987; Perry Meisel's *The Myth of the Modern: A Study in British Literature and Criticism after 1850*, 1987; James Longenbach's *Stone Cottage: Pound, Yeats, and Modernism*, 1988; John Bayley's *The Short Story: Henry James to Elizabeth Bowen*, 1988; Sandra M. Gilbert and Susan Gubar's *No Man's Land: The Place of the Woman Writer in the Twentieth Century*, 3 vols., 1988–94; George Watson's *British Literature since 1945*, 1991; Daniel Albright's *Quantum Poetics: Yeats, Pound, Eliot, and the Science of Modernism*, 1997; Lawrence Rainey's *Institutions of Modernism*, 1998; *The Cambridge Companion to Modernism*, ed. Michael Levenson, 1999; Jed Esty's *A Shrinking Island: Modernism and National Culture in England*, 2004; and vols. 11, 12, and 13 of the *Oxford English Literary History*: Chris Baldick's *The Modern Movement*, 2004, which covers 1910–40, Randall Stevenson's *The Last of England?*, 2004, which covers 1960–2000, and Bruce King's *The Internationalization of English Literature*, 2004, which surveys black and Asian British literature from 1948 to 2000.

Useful reference books include John L. Somer and Barbara Eck Cooper's *American and British Literature 1945–1975: An Annotated Bibliography of Contemporary Scholarship*, 1980; Alistair Davies's *An Annotated Critical Bibliography of Modernism*, 1982; *Contemporary Novelists*, ed. D. L. Kirkpatrick and James Vin-

son, 4th ed. 1986; *Contemporary Dramatists*, ed. K. A. Berney, 5th ed. 1993; *The Oxford Companion to Twentieth-Century Poetry*, ed. Ian Hamilton, 1994; *The Oxford Companion to Irish Literature*, ed. Robert Welch and Bruce Stewart, 1996; *Contemporary Poets*, ed. Thomas Riggs, 7th ed. 2001; Neil Roberts's *A Companion to Twentieth-Century Poetry*, 2001; and entries in the many volumes of the *Dictionary of Literary Biography* (also available online). The British Council/Book Trust Web site (www .contemporarywriters.com) is a useful source of information about contemporary British authors.

See also entries for **Voices from World War I**, **Modernist Manifestos**, **Voices from World War II**, and **Nation and Language**.

Chinua Achebe

Achebe's first novel, *Things Fall Apart*, 1958, was the first of three known collectively as *The African Trilogy*; the other two novels, *No Longer at Ease* and *Arrow of God*, were published in 1960 and 1964, respectively. *A Man of the People* was published in 1966; *Anthills of the Savannah*, in 1987. Collections of Achebe's short stories include *The Sacrificial Egg and Other Stories*, 1962, and *Girls at War and Other Stories*, 1972, and he has written other books for children. A collection of poems, *Beware, Soul-Brother, and Other Poems*, was published in 1971 and revised and enlarged the following year. Achebe's nonfiction includes *Morning Yet on Creation Day: Essays*, 1975; *The Trouble with Nigeria*, 1983; *Hopes and Impediments: Selected Essays 1965–1987*, 1988; *The University and the Leadership Factor in Nigerian Politics*, 1988; *Beyond Hunger in Africa: Conventional Wisdom and a Vision of Africa in 2057*, 1990; *Home and Exile*, 2000; and *The Short Century: Independence and Liberation in Africa, 1945–1994*, cowritten with Okwui Enwezor, 2001. He is editor of *The Heinemann Book of Contemporary African Short Stories*, 1992, and coeditor of *The Insider: Stories of War and Peace from Nigeria*, 1971, and *African Short Stories*, 1985. For his life, see *Chinua Achebe: A Biography*, ed. Ezenwa Ohaeto, 1997; Tijan M. Sallah and Ngozi Okonjo-Iweala, *Chinua Achebe, Teacher of Light: A Biography*, 2003. Bibliographies include B. M. Okpu, *Chinua Achebe: A Bio-Bibliography*, 1984, and *Chinua Achebe: A Bio-Bibliography*, compiled by the staff of Nnamdi Azikiwe Library, University of Nigeria, Nsukka, 1990.

Studies of Achebe's work include Arthur Ravenscroft's *Chinua Achebe*, 1977; C. L. Innes's *Chinua Achebe*, 1990; David Carroll's *Chinua Achebe: Novelist, Poet, Critic*, 2nd ed. 1990; Simon Gikandi's *Reading Chinua Achebe: Language and Ideology in Fiction*, 1991; Chinwe Okechukwu's *Achebe the Orator: The Art of Persuasion in Chinua Achebe's Novels*, 2001; and

Ode Ogede's *Achebe and the Politics of Representation: Form against Itself, From Colonial Conquest and Occupation to Post-Independence Disillusionment*, 2001. Useful contextual information is provided by Robert M. Wren's *Achebe's World: The Historical and Cultural Context of the Novels of Chinua Achebe*, 1980; Emmanuel Meziemadu Okoye's *The Traditional Religion and Its Encounter with Christianity in Achebe's Novels*, 1987; Olawale Awosika's *Form and Technique in the African Novel*, 1997; Bernth Lindfors's *Conversations with Chinua Achebe*, Literary Conversations Series, 1997; and M. Keith Booker's *The Chinua Achebe Encyclopedia*, 2003. A collection of essays celebrating Achebe's achievement, *Chinua Achebe: A Celebration*, ed. Kirsten Holst Petersen and Anna Rutherford, was published in 1991.

Studies of *Things Fall Apart* include Kate Turkington's *Chinua Achebe, Things Fall Apart*, 1977; Christopher Heywood's *Chinua Achebe, Things Fall Apart: A Critical View*, ed. Yolande Cantú, 1985; Solomon Ogbede Iyasere's *Understanding Things Fall Apart: Selected Essays and Criticism*, 1998; Emmanuel Edame Egar's *The Rhetorical Implications of Chinua Achebe's Things Fall Apart*, 2000; *Chinua Achebe's Things Fall Apart*, ed. Harold Bloom, 2002; and Isidore Okpweho's *Chinua Achebe's Things Fall Apart: A Casebook*, 2003.

John Agard

Agard's poetry includes the volumes *Shoot Me with Flowers*, 1974; *Man to Pan: A Cycle of Poems to Be Performed with Drums and Steelpans*, 1982; *Mangoes & Bullets: Selected and New Poems, 1972–1984*, 1985; *Lovelines for a Goat-Born Lady*, 1990; *Laughter Is an Egg*, 1990; *Get Back, Pimple!*, 1996; *From the Devil's Pulpit*, 1997; and *Weblines*, 2000. He has written prolifically for children, both fiction and poetry. With Grace Nichols he has edited *A Caribbean Dozen: Poems from Caribbean Poets*, 1994; *No Hickory No Dickory No Dock: Caribbean Nursery Rhymes*, 1995; and *Under the Moon & Over the Sea: A Collection of Caribbean Poems*, 2002. He has also compiled a collection of poetry for teenagers, *Life Doesn't Frighten Me at All*, 1989.

W. H. Auden

Auden's *Selected Poems*, ed. Edward Mendelson, 1979, rev. ed. 1989, reprints many of Auden's poems as they first appeared in his volumes of poetry. *The English Auden: Poems, Essays and Dramatic Writings, 1927–1939*, ed. Mendelson, 1977, also reprints Auden's poems in their original versions—all those published in book form in the 1930s—as well as many previously unpublished and uncollected poems and early prose writings. *W. H. Auden: Collected Poems*, ed. Mendelson, 1976, rev. ed. 1991, contains the poems Auden wished to preserve in their final revised form.

The definitive collected editions of Auden's works proceed under Mendelson's editorship: *Plays and Other Dramatic Writings by W. H. Auden, 1928–1938*, 1989; *W. H. Auden and Chester Kallman: Libretti and Other Dramatic Writings by W. H. Auden, 1939–1973*, 1993; *Prose and Travel Books in Prose and Verse, Volume I, 1926–1938*, 1996; and *Prose: Volume II, 1939–1948*, 2002. *Juvenilia 1922–1928*, ed. Katherine Bucknell, 1994, contains Auden's earliest work and appeared in an expanded edition in 2003. *"The Dyer's Hand" and Other Essays*, 1968, is an essential collection of Auden's lectures and essays. Other such collections include *Forewords and Afterwards*, 1973, and two posthumous editions, *"In Solitude, for Company": W. H. Auden after 1940*, ed. Bucknell and Nicholas Jenkins, 1995, and *Lectures on Shakespeare*, ed. Arthur C. Kirsch, 2000. Auden edited a number of anthologies, including *The Poet's Tongue*, with John Garrett, 1935; *The Oxford Book of Light Verse*, 1938; *Poets of the English Language*, with Norman Holmes Pearson, 1950; *An Elizabethan Songbook*, with Noah Greenberg and Chester Kallman, 1955; and *The Elder Edda: A Selection*, 1969. For Auden's life see Humphrey Carpenter's *W. H. Auden: A Biography*, 1981; *The Map of All My Youth: Early Works, Friends, and Influences*, ed. Bucknell and Jenkins, 1990; R. P. T. Davenport-Hines's *Auden*, 1995; Thekla Clark's *Wystan and Chester: A Personal Memoir of W. H. Auden and Chester Kallman*, 1995, rev. ed 1996; and David Garrett Izzo's *W. H. Auden Encyclopedia*, 2002, rev. ed. 2004. The standard bibliography is B. C. Bloomfield and Mendelson's *W. H. Auden: A Bibliography 1924–1969*, 1972, and is updated in *Auden Studies*, ed. Bucknell and Jenkins, 1990–95.

W. H. Auden: The Critical Heritage, ed. John Haffenden, 1983, traces Auden's critical reception and provides contemporary criticism. For helpful glosses on individual poems, see John Fuller's *W. H. Auden: A Commentary*, 1998. Useful studies include Monroe K. Spears's *The Poetry of W. H. Auden*, 1963; Justin Replogle's *Auden's Poetry*, 1969; Samuel Hynes's *The Auden Generation*, 1976, rev. ed. 1992; Edward Mendelson's *Early Auden*, 1981; Edward Callan's *Auden: A Carnival of Intellect*, 1983; Stan Smith's *W. H. Auden*, 1985; Lucy McDiarmid's *Auden's Apologies for Poetry*, 1990; John R. Boly's *Reading Auden: The Returns of Caliban*, 1991; Anthony Hecht's *The Hidden Law*, 1993; Marsha Bryant's *Auden and Documentary in the 1930s*, 1997; Mendelson's *Later Auden*, 1999; Rainer Emig's *W. H. Auden: Towards a Postmodern Poetics*, 2000; Richard R. Bozorth's *Auden's Games of Knowledge: Poetry and the Meanings of Homosexuality*, 2001; Peter Edgerly Firchow's *W. H. Auden: Contexts for Poetry*, 2002; and Susannah Young-ah Gottlieb's *Regions of Sorrow: Anxiety and Messianism in*

Hannah Arendt and W. H. Auden, 2003. Useful essays are collected in *Auden: A Collection of Critical Essays*, ed. Monroe K. Spears, 1964, and *Critical Essays on W. H. Auden*, ed. George W. Bahlke, 1991.

Samuel Beckett
Beckett's dramatic works include *Waiting for Godot: Tragicomedy in 2 Acts*, 1954, ed. Dougald McMillan and James Knowlson in the revised edition published in 1994; *Endgame*, 1958, ed. S. E. Gontarski, rev. ed. 1992; *Krapp's Last Tape and Other Dramatic Pieces*, 1960, ed. Knowlson, rev. ed. 1992; *Happy Days: A Play in Two Acts*, 1961; and *The Shorter Plays: With Revised Texts for Footfalls, Come and Go, and What Where*, ed. Gontarski, 2000. Beckett's novels include *Murphy*, 1938; *Molloy*, 1951; *Watt*, 1953; *Malone Dies*, 1956; *The Unnamable*, 1958; *Four Novellas*, 1977; and *Nohow On: Three Novels*, 1980. Short prose fiction can be found in *More Pricks than Kicks*, 1930, rev. ed. 1970; *As the Story Was Told: Uncollected and Late Prose*, 1990; *The Complete Short Prose, 1929–1989*, ed. Gontarski, 1995; and *I Can't Go On, I'll Go On: A Selection from Samuel Beckett's Work*, ed. Richard W. Seaver, 1976. Beckett's poetry can be found in *Poems in English*, 1961, and *Collected Poems in English and French*, 1977. Beckett also edited *Our Exagmination Round His Factification for Incamination of Work in Progress*, a symposium on James Joyce's *Finnegans Wake*, 1929, 2nd ed. 1962. The standard biography is Knowlson's *Damned to Fame: The Life of Samuel Beckett*, 1996. Anthony Cronin's *Samuel Beckett: The Last Modernist*, 1996; *Conversations with and about Beckett*, ed. Mel Gussow, 1996; and Anne Atik's *How It Was: A Memoir of Samuel Beckett*, 2001, are also useful. For biographical background for Beckett's early work, see John Pilling's *Beckett before Godot*, 1997. Bibliographic reference sources include Raymond Federman and John Fletcher's *Samuel Beckett: His Works and His Critics: An Essay in Bibliography*, 1970; P. J. Murphy's *Critique of Beckett Criticism: A Guide to Research in English, French, and German*, 1994; and Ruby Cohn's *A Beckett Canon*, 2001.
Alvarez's *Samuel Beckett*, 1973; Hugh Kenner's *A Reader's Guide to Samuel Beckett*, 1973; and C. J. Ackerly's *The Grove Companion to Samuel Beckett: A Reader's Guide to His Work, Life, and Thought*, 2004, are good introductions to Beckett's work. Criticism of the plays includes Cohn's *Just Play: Beckett's Theatre*, 1980; Beryl Fletcher and John Fletcher's *A Student's Guide to the Plays of Samuel Beckett*, 1985; Gontarksi's *The Intent of Undoing in Samuel Beckett's Dramatic Texts*, 1985; and, specifically on the later drama, Rosemary Pountney's *Theatre of Shadows: Samuel Beckett's Drama 1956–76: From All*

That Fall to Footfalls with Commentaries on the Late Plays, 1988.
On *Endgame* see *Twentieth Century Interpretations of* Endgame, ed. B. G. Chevigny, 1969, and Arthur N. Athanason's Endgame: *The Ashbin Play*, 1993. On the later work in general, see Steven Connor's *Samuel Beckett: Repetition Theory and Text*, 1986, and Enoch Brater's *Beyond Minimalism: Beckett's Late Style in the Theatre*, 1987, and *The Drama in the Text: Beckett's Late Fiction*, 1994.
Among many good general studies are Vivian Mercier's *Beckett/Beckett*, 1977; *Samuel Beckett–Humanistic Perspectives*, ed. Morris Beja, 1983; Christopher Ricks's *Beckett's Dying Words*, 1993; and *The Cambridge Companion to Beckett*, ed. John Pilling, 1994. Also very useful is *Samuel Beckett: The Critical Heritage*, ed. Lawrence Graver and Ray Federman, 1979, and David Pattie's *The Complete Critical Guide to Samuel Beckett*, 2000. The Beckett Archive is housed at the University of Reading, and the twice-yearly *Journal of Beckett Studies* began publication in 1976; Gontarski is editor of *The Beckett Studies Reader*, published in 1993.

Louise Bennett
Bennett's *Selected Poems*, 1982, corr. ed. 1983, was edited by Mervyn Morris and contains his excellent introduction and notes; an earlier selection, also important, is *Jamaica Labrish*, ed. by Rex Nettleford, 1966. Other volumes of poetry, folktales, and stories include *Jamaica Dialect Verses*, comp. George R. Bowen, 1942; *Anancy Stories and Poems in Dialect*, 1944; *Jamaican Dialect Poems*, 1949; *Anancy Stories and Dialect Verse*, with others, 1950, 1957; *Laugh with Louise: A Pot-Pourri of Jamaican Folklore, Stories, Songs, Verses*, with Lois Kelle-Barrow, 1961; and *Anancy and Miss Lou*, 1979. *Aunty Roachy Seh*, ed. Mervyn Morris, 1993, is a collection of monologues from Bennett's popular radio broadcasts; her funny and vivid performances of her poetry can be heard on recordings such as *Yes M'Dear: Miss Lou Live!*, 1983.
Discussions of Bennett's works can be found in Rex Nettleford's introduction to Bennett's *Jamaica Labrish*, 1966; Lloyd W. Brown's *West Indian Poetry*, 1978; Edward Kamau Brathwaite's *History of the Voice: The Development of Nation Language in Anglophone Caribbean Poetry*, 1984; Carolyn Cooper's *Noises in the Blood: Orality, Gender and the "Vulgar" Body of Jamaican Popular Culture*, 1993; Mervyn Morris's *"Is English We Speaking" and Other Essays*, 1999; and Jahan Ramazani's *The Hybrid Muse*, 2001.

Eavan Boland
An Origin Like Water: Collected Poems, 1967–1987 appeared in 1996; it includes selections from *New Territory*, 1967; *The War Horse*, 1975;

In Her Own Image, 1980; *Night Feed*, 1982; and *The Journey*, 1987. Subsequent volumes include *Outside History: Selected Poems 1980–1990*, 1990; *In a Time of Violence*, 1994; *The Lost Land*, 1998; *Against Love Poetry*, 2001; and *Code*, 2001. Boland's nonfiction includes *A Kind of Scar: The Woman Poet in a National Tradition*, 1989, and *Object Lessons: The Life of the Woman and the Poet in Our Time*, 1995, both of which provide essential insight into her work. She is coeditor, with Mark Strand, of *The Making of a Poem: A Norton Anthology of Poetic Forms*, 2000, and edited *Three Irish Poets: An Anthology*, 2003.

For her life see Patricia L. Hagen and Thomas W. Zelman's biography *Eavan Boland and the History of the Ordinary*, 2004. Critical studies of Boland's poetry may be found in Patricia Boyle Haberstroh's *Women Creating Women: Contemporary Irish Women Poets*, 1996; Susan Shaw Sailer's *Representing Ireland: Gender, Class, Nationality*, 1997; and William H. Gass and Lorin Cuoco's *The Writer and Religion*, 2000. *Irish University Review*, Spring/Summer 1993, and *Colby Quarterly* 35.4, 1999 are special issues dedicated to Boland.

Kamau Brathwaite

Brathwaite's volumes of poetry are *The Arrivants: A New World Trilogy*, 1973, which includes *Rights of Passage*, 1967, *Masks*, 1968, and *Islands*, 1969; *Days and Nights*, 1975; *Other Exiles*, 1975; *Black + Blues*, 1976; *Mother Poem*, 1977; *Soweto*, 1979; *Word Making Man: A Poem for Nicólas Guillén*, 1979; *Sun Poem*, 1982; *Third World Poems*, 1983; *Jah Music*, 1986; *X/Self*, 1987; *Sappho Sakyi's Meditations*, 1989; *Middle Passages*, 1992; *Shar/Hurricane Poem*, 1992; *Trench Town Rock*, 1994; *Words Need Love Too*, 2000; and *Ancestors: A Reinvention of Mother Poem, Sun Poem, and X/Self*, 2001. Brathwaite has also written plays, including *Four Plays for Primary Schools*, 1964, and *Odale's Voice*, 1967. A revised edition of his *Roots: Essays in Caribbean Literature*, 1986, appeared in 1993, incorporating his influential lecture, first published separately, *History of the Voice: The Development of Nation Language in Anglophone Caribbean Poetry*, 1984. His historical studies of Caribbean culture include *The Development of Creole Society in Jamaica, 1770–1820*, 1971. Brathwaite has also edited collections of literature, including *Iouanaloa: Recent Writing from St. Lucia*, 1963, and *New Poets from Jamaica*, 1979, and he contributed an interview to *Talk Yuh Talk: Interviews with Anglophone Caribbean Poets*, ed. Kwame Dawes, 2001. Doris Monica Brathwaite's *A Descriptive and Chronological Bibliography (1950–1982) of the Work of Edward Kamau Brathwaite* was published in 1988.

Studies of Brathwaite's work include Gordon Rohlehr's *Pathfinder: Black Awakening in The Arrivants of Edward Kamau Brathwaite*, 1981; June D. Bobb's *Beating a Restless Drum: The Poetics of Kamau Brathwaite and Derek Walcott*, 1998; and Paul Naylor's *Poetic Investigations: Singing the Holes in History*, 1999. Collections of essays concerned with Brathwaite's work include *The Art of Kamau Brathwaite*, ed. Stewart Brown, 1995; *For the Geography of a Soul: Emerging Perspectives on Kamau Brathwaite*, ed. Timothy J. Reiss, 2001; and *Questioning Creole: Creolisation Discourses in Caribbean Literature*, ed. Verene A. Shepherd and Glen L. Richards, 2002. *World Literature Today* 68.4, 1994, is a special issue dedicated to Brathwaite.

Rupert Brooke

The Poetical Works, 2nd ed. 1970, and *The Letters*, 1968, are both edited by Geoffrey Keynes. *The Prose*, 1956, is edited by Christopher Hassall, who wrote the standard biography, *Rupert Brooke: A Biography*, 1964; Nigel Jones's *Rupert Brooke: Life, Death and Myth* was published in 1999. Volumes of Brooke's correspondence include *Song of Love: The Letters of Rupert Brooke and Noel Olivier, 1909–1915*, ed. Pippa Harris, 1991, and *Friends and Apostles: The Correspondence of Rupert Brooke and James Strachey, 1905–1914*, ed. Keith Hale, 1998. Paul Delany's *The Neo-Pagans: Rupert Brooke and the Ordeal of Youth*, 1987, provides a group portrait, and useful context and criticism appear in Kenneth Millard's *Edwardian Poetry*, 1991.

Studies of Brooke's work include Walter de la Mare's "Rupert Brooke and the Intellectual Imagination," in his *Pleasures and Speculations*, 1940; John H. Johnston's *English Poetry of the First World War*, 1964; Bernard Bergonzi's *Heroes' Twilight: A Study of the Literature of the Great War*, 1966, 2nd ed. 1980; *Rupert Brooke: A Reappraisal and Selection from His Writings, Some Hitherto Unpublished*, ed. Timothy Rogers, 1971; Jon Silkin's *Out of Battle: The Poetry of the Great War*, 1972, 2nd ed. 1998; John Lehmann's *The Strange Destiny of Rupert Brooke*, 1980; Adrian Caesar's *Taking It like a Man: Suffering, Sexuality, and the War Poets: Brooke, Sassoon, Owen, Graves*, 1993; Jonathan Rutherford's *Forever England: Reflections on Race, Masculinity, and Empire*, 1997; and *Poets of World War I: Rupert Brooke & Siegfried Sassoon*, ed. Harold Bloom, 2003.

May Wedderburn Cannan

Cannan's collections of poems include *In War Time*, 1917; *The Splendid Days*, 1919; and *The House of Hope*, 1923. She is also author of the novel *The Lonely Generation*, 1934. Her unfinished autobiography, *Grey Ghosts and Voices*, appeared posthumously in 1976. *The Tears of War: The Love Story of a Young Poet and a War Hero*, ed. Charlotte Fyfe, 2000, combines her poetry with personal narratives.

Anne Carson

Poetry and prose are often combined in Carson's books, which include *Short Talks*, 1992; *Plainwater: Essays and Poetry*, 1995; *Glass, Irony, and God*, 1995; *Autobiography of Red: A Novel in Verse*, 1998; *Men in the Off Hours*, 2000; *The Beauty of the Husband: A Fictional Essay in 29 Tangos*, 2001; and *If Not, Winter: Fragments of Sappho*, 2002. Other works include her classical study *Eros the Bittersweet: An Essay*, 1986, and *Economy of the Unlost: Reading Simonides of Keos with Paul Celan*, 1999. Criticism of her work can be found in *American and Canadian Women Poets, 1930–Present*, ed. Harold Bloom, 2002.

Charles Causley

Causley's many publications include his *Collected Poems, 1951–2000*, rev. ed. 2000, as well as plays, short stories, and anthologies. Critical discussions of his poetry can be found in Elizabeth Jennings, *Poetry Today 1957–60*, 1961; Vernon Scannell, *Not Without Glory: Poets of the Second World War*, 1976; Edward Levy, "The Poetry of Charles Causley," in *PN Review* 5.2, 1978; Michael Schmidt, *An Introduction to 50 Modern British Poets*, 1979; *Causley at Seventy*, ed. Harry Chambers, 1987; Anthony Thwaite, *Poetry Today: A Critical Guide to British Poetry, 1960–95*, 1996; and Dana Gioia, *Barrier of a Common Language*, 2003.

See also entries for **Voices from World War II.**

J. M. Coetzee

Dusklands, 1974, consists of two linked novellas. It was followed by the novels *In the Heart of the Country*, 1977; *Waiting for the Barbarians*, 1980; *Life & Times of Michael K.*, 1983; *Foe*, 1986; *Age of Iron*, 1990; *The Master of Petersburg*, 1994; *Disgrace*, 1999; and *Elizabeth Costello*, 2003. Coetzee's nonfiction includes *White Writing: On the Culture of Letters in South Africa*, 1988; *Doubling the Point: Essays and Interviews*, 1992; *Giving Offense: Essays on Censorship*, 1996; the fictionalized lecture *The Lives of Animals*, 1999; and *Stranger Shores: Literary Essays, 1986–1999*, 2001. He coedited, with André Philippus Brink, *A Land Apart: A Contemporary South African Reader*, 1986. He edited and translated *Landscape with Rowers: Poetry from the Netherlands*, 2004, a facing-page collection of six twentieth-century Dutch poets. Kevin Goddard, John Read, and Teresa Dovey's *J. M. Coetzee: A Bibliography*, 1990, is comprehensive of his work to 1990. For Coetzee's life see his fictionalized memoirs *Boyhood: Scenes from Provincial Life*, 1997, and *Youth: Scenes from Provincial Life II*, 2002.

An inclusive overview of Coetzee's fiction is Dominic Head's *J. M. Coetzee*, 1997. Allen Penner's *Countries of the Mind: The Fiction of J. M. Coetzee*, 1989, illuminates work up to and including *Foe*. For a range of criticism see Graham Huggan and Stephen Watson's *Critical Perspectives on J. M. Coetzee*, 1996. Coetzee is examined as a specifically South African post-colonial writer in Susan Gallagher's *A Story of South Africa: J. M. Coetzee's Fiction in Context*, 1991; David Attwell's *J. M. Coetzee: South Africa and the Politics of Writing*, 1993; Sue Kossew's *Critical Essays on J. M. Coetzee*, 1998; and Derek Attridge's *J. M. Coetzee & the Ethics of Reading*, 2004. A special issue of *South Atlantic Quarterly*, 93.1, ed. Michael Valdez Moses, 1994, is devoted to Coetzee's work.

Joseph Conrad

The standard edition of Conrad's works is *The Uniform Edition of the Works of Joseph Conrad*, 22 vols., 1923–38, reprinted 1946–55 as the *Collected Edition of the Works of Joseph Conrad*. Useful essays and notes to the novels are provided by the Norton Critical Editions of *Lord Jim*, ed. Thomas C. Moser, 2nd ed. 1996; *The Nigger of the "Narcissus,"* ed. Robert Kimbrough, 1979; and *Heart of Darkness*, ed. Robert Kimbrough, 3rd ed. 1988. The Modern Library edition of *Nostromo*, 1951, also contains an illuminating introductory essay by Robert Penn Warren. Conrad's letters have been published as *The Collected Letters of Joseph Conrad*, 6 vols., ed. Frederick R. Karl and Laurence Davies, 1983–2002, and the selection *Letters from Joseph Conrad, 1895–1924*, 1 vol., ed. Edward Garnett, 1928; these are supplemented by material in *Joseph Conrad's Letters to R. B. Cunninghame Graham*, ed. C. T. Watts, 1969; the collection *A Portrait in Letters: Correspondence to and about Conrad*, ed. J. H. Stape and Owen Knowles, 1996, is also helpful. Biographies include Zdzislaw Najder's *Joseph Conrad: A Chronicle*, 1983; Cedric Watts's *Joseph Conrad: A Literary Life*, 1989; Jeffrey Meyers's *Joseph Conrad: A Biography*, 1991; and John Batchelor's *The Life of Joseph Conrad: A Critical Biography*, 1994. Memoirs of Conrad include Jessie Conrad's *Joseph Conrad as I Knew Him*, 1926, and *Joseph Conrad and His Circle*, 1935; and Ford Madox Ford's *Joseph Conrad: A Personal Remembrance*, 1965. See also material collected in *Joseph Conrad: Interviews and Recollections*, ed. Martin Ray, 1990. The standard bibliography is *Joseph Conrad: An Annotated Bibliography*, ed. Bruce Teets, 1990.

Ian Watt's *Conrad in the Nineteenth Century*, 1979; Fredric Jameson's *The Political Unconscious: Narrative as a Socially Symbolic Act*, 1981; Jakob Lothe's *Conrad's Narrative Method*, 1989; Vincent P. Pecora's *Self and Form in Modern Narrative*, 1989, and Michael Greaney's *Conrad, Language, and Narrative*, 2002, examine Conrad's narrative strategies. Heliéna Krenn's *Conrad's Lingard Trilogy: Empire, Race and Women in the Malay Novels*, 1990, and Ruth Nadelhaft's *Joseph Conrad*, 1991, offer feminist perspectives, and gender-theoretical

THE TWENTIETH CENTURY AND AFTER / A51

criticism includes Andrew Michael Roberts's
Conrad and Gender, 1993, and *Conrad and Mas-
culinity*, 2000. Christopher GoGwilt's *The
Invention of the West: Joseph Conrad and the
Double-Mapping of Europe and Empire*, 1995,
presents a postcolonial perspective. Peter J.
Glassman's *Language and Being: Joseph Conrad
and the Literature of Personality*, 1976, offers a
psychological analysis. *Conrad on Film*, ed.
Gene M. Moore, 1997, is also helpful.
A guide to Conrad's work is *The Cambridge
Companion to Joseph Conrad*, ed. J. H. Stape,
1996. In addition to the essays in the Norton
Critical Editions, criticism on both *Heart of
Darkness* and *The Nigger of the "Narcissus"* can
be found in *Conrad: The Critical Heritage*, ed.
Norman Sherry, 1973; *Joseph Conrad*, ed. Har-
old Bloom, 1986; *Joseph Conrad: Critical Assess-
ments*, 4 vols., ed. Keith Carabine, 1992; *A
Joseph Conrad Companion*, ed. Leonard Orr and
Theodore Billy, 1999; and *Essays on Conrad*, ed.
Ian Watt, 2000.
For further reading on *The Nigger of the "Nar-
cissus,"* see *Conrad's Manifesto: Preface to a
Career: The History of the Preface to* The Nigger
of the "Narcissus," *with Facsimiles of the Man-
uscripts*, ed. David R. Smith and Leonard Bas-
kin, 1966; James W. Parins and Todd K.
Bender's *A Concordance to Conrad's* The Nigger
of the "Narcissus," 1981; and chapters in
Michael Levenson's *A Genealogy of Modernism*,
1984, and in Michael North's *The Dialect of
Modernism*, 1994.
For works concerning *Heart of Darkness*, see
Gary Adelman's *Heart of Darkness: Search for
the Unconscious*, 1987; *Joseph Conrad's* Heart of
Darkness, ed. Harold Bloom, 1987; *Heart of
Darkness: A Case Study in Contemporary Criti-
cism*, ed. Ross C. Murfin, 1989; *Marlow*, ed.
Harold Bloom, 1992; Nicolas Tredell's *Joseph
Conrad: Heart of Darkness*, 1999; Peter Edger-
ley Firchow's *Envisioning Africa: Racism and
Imperialism in Conrad's Heart of Darkness*,
2000; an essay in J. Hillis Miller's *Others*, 2001,
and another by Richard J. Ruppel in *Imperial
Desire: Dissident Sexualities and Colonial Literature*, ed. Philip Holden and Richard J. Ruppel,
2003.

Keith Douglas
Alamein to Zem Zem, ed. John Waller, 1966, a
memoir of Douglas's World War II experience
in North Africa; *A Prose Miscellany*, 1985; *The
Complete Poems*, 3rd ed. 1998; and *The Letters*,
2000, are all edited by Desmond Graham,
author of *Keith Douglas, 1920–1944: A Biography*, 1974. Further critical discussion of Douglas's poems can be found in Vernon Scannell's
*Not without Glory: Poets of the Second World
War*, 1976; Penny Pittman Merliss's *In Another
Country: Three Poets of the Second World War*,
1987; and William Scammell's *Keith Douglas: A
Study*, 1988.

Carol Ann Duffy
Duffy's volumes of poetry include *"Fleshweath-
ercock" and Other Poems*, 1973; *Fifth Last Song*,
1982; *Standing Female Nude*, 1985; *Thrown
Voices*, 1986; *Selling Manhattan*, 1987; *The
Other Country*, 1990; *Mean Time*, 1993;
Selected Poems, 1994; *The Pamphlet*, 1998; *The
World's Wife: Poems*, 1999; *The Salmon Carol
Ann Duffy: Poems Selected and New 1985–
1999*, 2000; and *Feminine Gospels: Poems*,
2003. Along with many books for younger read-
ers, she has also written plays, including *Take
My Husband*, 1982; *Cavern of Dreams*, 1984;
Little Women, Big Boys, 1986; and the radio play
Loss, 1986. Collections edited by Duffy include
*I Wouldn't Thank You for a Valentine: Poems for
Young Feminists*, 1992, and *Stopping for Death:
Poems of Death and Loss*, 1996, both illustrated
by Trisha Rafferty. In 1999, when she appeared
to be a leading candidate for British poet lau-
reate, a number of profiles and interviews
appeared in *The Guardian*, *The Independent*,
and other British newspapers.
A book-length study of Duffy's work is Deryn
Rees-Jones's *Carol Ann Duffy*, 1999. Other dis-
cussions include *Four Women Poets*, ed. Judith
Baxter, 1995, and *The Poetry of Carol Ann
Duffy: "Choosing Tough Words,"* ed. Angelica
Michelis and Antony Rowland, 2003.

T. S. Eliot
The *Complete Poems and Plays of T. S. Eliot* was
published in 1969. *Inventions of the March
Hare: Poems, 1909–1917*, ed. Christopher
Ricks, brought early unpublished work to light
in 1996. The fascinating manuscripts of *The
Waste Land* are available as *The Waste Land: A
Facsimile and Transcript of the Original Drafts
Including the Annotations of Ezra Pound*, ed.
Valerie Eliot, 1971. Also immensely useful is the
Norton Critical Edition of *The Waste Land*, ed.
Michael North, 2001, which contains contextual documents and criticism in addition to the
poem. Eliot's most important critical essays are
to be found in *The Sacred Wood: Essays on Poetry
and Criticism*, 1920; *The Use of Poetry and the
Use of Criticism: Studies in the Relation of Criticism to Poetry in England*, 1933; *The Idea of a
Christian Society*, 1939; *Notes towards the Definition of Culture*, 1948; *On Poetry and Poets*,
1957; *To Criticize the Critic and Other Writings*,
1965; and *The Varieties of Metaphysical Poetry*,
ed. Ronald Schuchard, 1994. Important biographies include Peter Ackroyd's *T. S. Eliot: A
Life*, 1984, and Lyndall Gordon's *T. S. Eliot: An
Imperfect Life*, 1999. Also helpful is *The Letters
of T. S. Eliot, Vol. I: 1898–1922*, ed. Valerie
Eliot, 1988.
Studies of Eliot's work include F. O. Mat-
thiessen's *The Achievement of T. S. Eliot*, 3rd
ed. 1958; Northrop Frye's *T. S. Eliot*, 1963; Bernard Bergonzi's *T. S. Eliot*, 1972; Stephen
Spender's *T. S. Eliot*, 1976; Ronald Bush's *T. S.*

Eliot: A Study in Character and Style, 1983; Robert Crawford's *The Savage and the City in the Work of T. S. Eliot*, 1987; Louis Menand's *Discovering Modernism*, 1987; Richard Shusterman's *T. S. Eliot and the Philosophy of Criticism*, 1988; Christopher Ricks's *T. S. Eliot and Prejudice*, 1988; Eric Sigg's *The American T. S. Eliot: A Study of the Early Writings*, 1989; Michael North's *The Political Aesthetic of Yeats, Eliot, and Pound*, 1991; Jewel Spears Brooker's *Mastery and Escape: T. S. Eliot and the Dialectic of Modernism*, 1994; Anthony Julius's *T. S. Eliot, Anti-Semitism and Literary Form*, 1995; *T. S. Eliot*, ed. Harriet Davidson, 1999; Ronald Schuchard's *Eliot's Dark Angel: Intersections of Life and Art*, 1999; and Donald J. Childs's *From Philosophy to Poetry: T. S. Eliot's Study of Knowledge and Experience*, 2001.

Valuable collections of essays include *T. S. Eliot: A Collection of Critical Essays*, ed. Hugh Kenner, 1962; *T. S. Eliot: A Collection of Criticism*, ed. Linda Wagner-Martin, 1974; *T. S. Eliot: The Critical Heritage*, ed. Michael Grant, 1982; *T. S. Eliot: Modern Critical Views*, ed. Harold Bloom, 1985; *T. S. Eliot, A Voice Descanting: Centenary Essays*, ed. Shyamal Bagchee, 1990; *T. S. Eliot: The Modernist in History*, ed. Ronald Bush, 1991; *T. S. Eliot*, ed. Harold Bloom, 1999; and *T. S. Eliot and Our Turning World*, ed. Jewel Spears Brooker, 2001. Donald C. Gallup's *T. S. Eliot: A Bibliography*, rev. ed. 1969, is also useful.

Helpful guides to the poetry and plays are Grover Smith's *T. S. Eliot's Poetry and Plays: A Study in Sources and Meanings*, 1956; Carol H. Smith's *T. S. Eliot's Dramatic Theory and Practice, from Sweeney Agonistes to The Elder Statesman*, 1963; *The Cambridge Companion to T. S. Eliot*, ed. A. David Moody, 1994; and *A Concordance to the Complete Poems and Plays of T. S. Eliot*, ed. J. L. Dawson et al., 1995.

For further reading on Eliot's poetry, see Elizabeth Drew's *T. S. Eliot, The Design of His Poetry*, 1949; Helen Gardner's *The Art of T. S. Eliot*, 1950; Hugh Kenner's *The Invisible Poet*, 1959; David Moody's *Thomas Stearns Eliot, Poet*, 1979; Maud Ellmann's *The Poetics of Impersonality: T. S. Eliot and Ezra Pound*, 1987; Lee Oser's *T. S. Eliot and American Poetry*, 1998; and Denis Donoghue's *Words Alone: The Poet, T. S. Eliot*, 2000. On *Four Quartets* see Helen Gardner's *The Composition of Four Quartets*, 1978.

For further reading on *The Waste Land*, see *Eliot in His Time: Essays on the Occasion of the Fiftieth Anniversary of The Waste Land*, ed. A. Walton Litz, 1973; Harriet Davidson's *T. S. Eliot and Hermeneutics: Absence and Interpretation in The Waste Land*, 1985; Calvin Bedient's *He Do the Police in Different Voices: The Waste Land and Its Protagonists*, 1986; *T. S. Eliot's The Waste Land*, ed. Harold Bloom, 1986; Nancy K. Gish's *The Waste Land: A Poem of Memory and Desire*, 1988; and Jewel Spears Brooker and Joseph Bentley's *Reading The Waste Land: Modernism and the Limits of Interpretation*, 1990.

E. M. Forster

Forster's major novels are *Where Angels Fear to Tread*, 1905; *The Longest Journey*, 1907; *A Room with a View*, 1908; *Howards End*, 1910; and *A Passage to India*, 1924. A sixth novel, *Maurice*, was finished in 1914 but published posthumously in 1971. *The Collected Tales of E. M. Forster* appeared in 1947, and *The Life to Come and Other Stories* was published posthumously in 1972. Philip Gardner edited Forster's *Commonplace Book* in 1985. *Abinger Harvest*, a collection of some eighty essays, was published in 1936, and *Two Cheers for Democracy*, a second collection, was published in 1951. Forster's provocative study of fictional technique, *Aspects of the Novel*, appeared in 1927. His biography of his aunt, *Marianne Thornton: A Domestic Biography, 1797–1887*, 1956, is a contribution to Victorian social history. For his life see *E. M. Forster: A Life*, 1978, by P. N. Furbank, who, with Mary Lago, edited Forster's *Selected Letters*, 2 vols., 1983, 1985; Nicola Beauman's *E. M. Forster: A Biography*, 1994, is also useful. See also P. J. Kirkpatrick's *A Bibliography of E. M. Forster*, 2nd ed. 1985.

Studies of Forster's work include Frederick Crews's *E. M. Forster: The Perils of Humanism*, 1962; Lionel Trilling's *E. M. Forster*, 2nd ed. 1965; Wilfred Stone's *The Cave and the Mountain: A Study of E. M. Forster*, 1966; G. K. Das's *E. M. Forster's India*, 1977; Robin Jared Lewis's *E. M. Forster's Passages to India*, 1979; Barbara Rosecrance's *Forster's Narrative Vision*, 1982; Claude J. Summers's *E. M. Forster*, 1983; David Medalie's *E. M. Forster's Modernism*, 2002; *Narrative Dynamics: Essays on Time, Plot, Closure, and Frames*, ed. Brian Richardson, 2002; James J. Miracky's *Regenerating the Novel: Gender and Genre in Woolf, Forster, Sinclair, and Lawrence*, 2003; and Muhammad Shahin's *E. M. Forster and the Politics of Imperialism*, 2004. Valuable collections of essays are *E. M. Forster: The Critical Heritage*, ed. Philip Gardner, 1973; *Critical Essays on E. M. Forster*, ed. Alan Wilde, 1985; and *E. M. Forster*, ed. Harold Bloom, 1987.

Brian Friel

Plays One, 1984, 1996, and *Plays Two*, 1999, draw from Friel's dramatic works, including *The Saucer of Larks*, 1962; *Philadelphia, Here I Come!*, 1965; *The Gold in the Sea*, 1966; *The Loves of Cass McGuire*, 1967; *Lovers*, 1968; *Crystal and Fox*, 1970; *The Mundy Scheme*, 1970; *The Gentle Island*, 1973; *The Freedom of the City*, 1974; *The Enemy Within*, 1975; *Living Quarters*, 1978; *Volunteers*, 1979; *Aristocrats*, 1980; *Faith Healer*, 1980; *Anton Chekhov's Three Sisters: A Translation*, 1981; *Translations*, 1981; *The Communication Cord*, 1983; *Fathers* and Sons: After the Novel by Ivan Turgenev, 1987; Making History, 1989; Dancing at Lughnasa, 1990; The London Vertigo, Based on a Play The True Born Irishman, or, The Irish Fine Lady, by Charles Macklin, 1990; A Month in the Country: After Turgenev, 1992; Wonderful Tennessee, 1993; Molly Sweeney, 1994; Give Me Your Answer, Do!, 1997; Uncle Vanya: A Version of the Play by Anton Chekhov, 1998; The Yalta Game: After Chekhov, 2001; Three Plays After, 2002. Friel's fiction can be found in Selected Stories, 1979, and The Diviner: The Best Stories of Brian Friel, 1982. Friel is also editor of Charles McGlinchey's The Last of the Name, 1986, 1999.

For biographical information and criticism see Brian Friel: Essays, Diaries, Interviews, 1964–1999, ed. Christopher Murray, 1999, and Brian Friel in Conversation, ed. Paul Delaney, 2000. Ten Modern Irish Playwrights: A Comprehensive Annotated Bibliography, ed. Kimball King, 1979, is a helpful resource.

Brian Friel: A Reference Guide, 1962–1992, ed. George O'Brien, 1995, provides a useful guide to most of Friel's work. For criticism of Friel's work see D. E. S. Maxwell's Brian Friel, 1973; Seamus Deane's Essays in Modern Irish Literature: 1880–1980, 1985; Ulf Dantanus's Brian Friel: The Growth of an Irish Dramatist, 1985, and Brian Friel: A Study, 1988; Critical Approaches to Anglo-Irish Literature, ed. Michael Allen and Angela Wilcox, 1989; George O'Brien's Brian Friel, 1990; Elmer Kennedy-Andrews's The Art of Brian Friel: Neither Reality nor Dreams, 1995; Brian Friel: A Casebook, ed. William Kerwin, 1997; Nicholas Grene's The Politics of Irish Drama: Plays in Context from Boucicault to Friel, 1999; Richard Pine's The Diviner: The Art of Brian Friel, 2nd ed. 1999; F. C. McGrath's Brian Friel's (Post)Colonial Drama: Language, Illusion, and Politics, 1999; and Tony Corbett's Brian Friel: Decoding the Language of the Tribe, 2002. The Norton Critical Edition Modern Irish Drama, ed. John P. Harrington, 1991, includes backgrounds and criticism for Translations. For criticism of Friel's drama and short stories, see A Companion to Brian Friel, ed. Richard Harp and Robert C. Evans, 2002.

Nadine Gordimer

Gordimer's novels include The Lying Days, 1953; A World of Strangers, 1958; Occasion for Loving, 1963; The Late Bourgeois World, 1966; A Guest of Honour, 1970; The Conservationist, 1974; Burger's Daughter, 1979; July's People, 1981; A Sport of Nature, 1987; My Son's Story, 1990; None to Accompany Me, 1994; The House Gun, 1998; and The Pickup, 2001. Gordimer's short-story collections include Face to Face, 1949; The Soft Voice of the Serpent, 1952; Six Feet of the Country, 1956; Friday's Footprints, 1960; Not for Publication, 1965; Livingstone's

Companions, 1971; Some Monday for Sure, 1976; A Soldier's Embrace, 1980; Something Out There, 1984; Jump, 1991; and Loot, and Other Stories, 2003. Collected editions of her stories include Why Haven't You Written?: Selected Stories, 1950–1972, 1992, and Selected Stories, 2000. Gordimer's essays are collected in The Essential Gesture: Writing, Politics and Places, ed. Stephen Clingman, 1988; Writing and Being, 1995; and Living in Hope and History: Notes from Our Century, 1999.

A celebration of Gordimer's work, A Writing Life: Celebrating Nadine Gordimer, ed. Andries Walter Oliphant, was published in 1998. For her life see Conversations with Nadine Gordimer, ed. Nancy Topping Bazin and Marilyn Dallman Seymour, 1990. For a bibliography see Nadine Gordimer: A Bibliography of Primary and Secondary Sources, 1937–1992, ed. Dorothy Driver, 1994.

The following critical accounts include postcolonial, feminist, and political perspectives on Gordimer's work: Abdul R. JanMohamed's Manichean Aesthetics: The Politics of Literature in Colonial Africa, 1983; Stephen Clingman's The Novels of Nadine Gordimer: History from the Inside, 1986; Judie Newman's Nadine Gordimer, 1988; Critical Essays on Nadine Gordimer, ed. Rowland Smith, 1990; The Later Fiction of Nadine Gordimer, ed. Bruce King, 1993; Andrew V. Ettin's Betrayals of the Body Politic: The Literary Commitments of Nadine Gordimer, 1993; Dominic Head's Nadine Gordimer, 1994; Kathrin M. Wagner's Rereading Nadine Gordimer, 1994; Barbara Temple-Thurston's Nadine Gordimer Revisited, 1999; Martine Watson Brownley's Deferrals of Domain: Contemporary Women Novelists and the State, 2000; Joya F. Uraizee's This Is No Place for a Woman: Nadine Gordimer, Buchi Emecheta, and Nayantara Saghal and the Politics of Gender, 2000; and Brighton J. Uledi Kamanga's Cracks in the Wall: Nadine Gordimer's Fiction and the Irony of Apartheid, 2002.

Robert Graves

Graves's Complete Poems, ed. Beryl Graves and Dunstan Ward, was published in three volumes in 1995, 1997, and 1999. His Complete Short Stories, ed. Lucia Graves, was published in 1996. A selection of Graves's criticism is Collected Writings on Poetry, ed. Paul O'Prey, 1995. Other important prose works include On English Poetry, 1922; The Meaning of Dreams, 1924; A Survey of Modernist Poetry, with Laura Riding, 1927; The Long Week End: A Social History of England 1919–1939, with Alan Hodge, 1940; The White Goddess, 1948, enl. ed., 1966; The Common Asphodel: Collected Essays on Poetry, 1922–1949, 1949; and On Poetry: Collected Talks and Essays, 1969. Graves also published many historical novels, including I, Claudius, 1934; Claudius the God, 1935; Count

Belisarius, 1938; *Sergeant Lamb's America*, 1940; *Wife to Mr. Milton*, 1943; and *Homer's Daughter*, 1955. Interviews are collected in *Conversations with Robert Graves*, ed. Frank L. Kersnowski, 1989. Selected letters appear in *In Broken Images: Selected Letters of Robert Graves, 1914–1946*, ed. O'Prey, 1982; *Between Moon and Moon: Selected Letters of Robert Graves, 1946–1972*, ed. O'Prey, 1984; and *Dear Robert, Dear Spike: The Graves–Milligan Correspondence*, ed. Pauline Scudamore, 1991. Graves's autobiography, *Good-Bye to All That*, was first published in 1929 and then in several revised editions. Biographies include Martin Seymour-Smith's *Robert Graves: His Life and Work*, 1983; Miranda Seymour's *Robert Graves: Life on the Edge*, 1995; and Richard Perceval Graves's *Robert Graves*, 3 vols., 1987–95. An updated version of Fred H. Higginson and William Proctor Williams's *A Bibliography of the Writings of Robert Graves* was published in 1987.

Studies of Graves's work include Seymour-Smith's *Robert Graves*, 1956; J. M. Cohen's *Robert Graves*, 1960; Douglas Day's *Swifter than Reason: The Poetry and Criticism of Robert Graves*, 1963; George Stade's *Robert Graves*, 1967; Michael Kirkham's *The Poetry of Robert Graves*, 1969; John B. Vickery's *Robert Graves and the White Goddess*, 1972; Paul Fussell's *The Great War and Modern Memory*, 1975; James S. Mehoke's *Robert Graves: Peace-Weaver*, 1975; Katherine Snipes's *Robert Graves*, 1979; Patrick J. Keane's *A Wild Civility: Interactions in the Poetry and Thought of Robert Graves*, 1980; D. N. G. Carter's *Robert Graves: The Lasting Poetic Achievement*, 1989; Patrick J. Quinn's *The Great War and the Missing Muse: The Early Writings of Robert Graves and Siegfried Sassoon*, 1994; and Kersnowski's *The Early Poetry of Robert Graves: The Goddess Beckons*, 2002. Collections of essays include *Robert Graves*, ed. Harold Bloom, 1987, and *New Perspectives on Robert Graves*, ed. Quinn, 1999.

Thom Gunn
Thom Gunn's *Collected Poems* appeared in 1994; *Boss Cupid*, in 2000. *The Occasions of Poetry: Essays in Criticism and Autobiography*, ed. Clive Wilmer, 1982, and *Shelf Life: Essays, Memoirs, and an Interview*, 1993, are collections of essays and autobiographical writings. For his life see the interview Gunn contributed to *Viewpoints: Poets in Conversation with John Haffenden*, 1981, and *Thom Gunn in Conversation with James Campbell*, 2000. Jack W. C. Hagstrom and George Bixby's *Thom Gunn: A Bibliography 1940–1978*, 1979, lists interviews as well as poems and articles.

Studies of Gunn's work include Alan Norman Bold's *Thom Gunn and Ted Hughes*, 1976; *Three Contemporary Poets: Thom Gunn, Ted Hughes, and R. S. Thomas: A Casebook*, ed. A. E. Dyson, 1990. Discussions of Gunn's work can be found in John Press's *Rule and Energy: Trends in British Poetry since the Second World War*, 1963; *British Poetry since 1960: A Critical Survey*, ed. Michael Schmidt and Grevel Lindop, 1972; and *Contemporary British Poetry: Essays in Theory and Criticism*, ed. James Acheson and Romana Huk, 1996. *PN Review 70*, 1989, is devoted chiefly to Gunn and contains useful discussions of his work. For further reading on Gunn and "The Movement," see Jerry Bradley's *The Movement: British Poets of the 1950s*, 1993.

Ivor Gurney
During his lifetime Gurney published two volumes: *Severn and Somme*, 1917, and *War's Embers*, 1919, but at his death some seven hundred poems remained unpublished. *Collected Poems of Ivor Gurney*, ed. P. J. Kavanagh, 1982, includes many of the works Gurney left unpublished at his death. Gurney was also a musical composer; of special note are his song accompaniments to *Severn and Somme*. Gurney's letters have been published as *War Letters: A Selection*, 1983, and *Collected Letters*, 1991, both edited by R. K. R. Thornton. For his life see Michael Hurd's *The Ordeal of Ivor Gurney*, 1978, and John Lucas's *Ivor Gurney*, 2001. Thornton and George Walter's *Ivor Gurney: Towards a Bibliography* was published in 1996.

Discussions of Gurney's work can be found in Jon Silkin's *Out of Battle: The Poetry of the Great War*, 1972, 2nd ed. 1998; Paul Fussell's *The Great War and Modern Memory*, 1975; Piers Gray's *Marginal Men: Edward Thomas, Ivor Gurney, J. R. Ackerley*, 1991; Jon Stallworthy's *Great Poets of World War I: Poetry from the Great War*, 2002. The Ivor Gurney Society publishes its journal annually.

Thomas Hardy
Hardy published over a dozen volumes of poetry in his lifetime. His complete poems can be found in *Thomas Hardy: The Complete Poems*, ed. James Gibson, 1978, or *The Complete Poetical Works of Thomas Hardy*, 3 vols., ed. Samuel Lynn Hynes, 1982–95. There are several collected editions of Hardy's complete works, notably the Wessex Edition, 21 vols., 1912–14, and the Mellstock Edition, 37 vols., 1919–20. Useful essays and notes to Hardy's novels are provided by the Norton Critical Editions of *The Return of the Native*, ed. James Gindin, 1969; *Far from the Madding Crowd*, ed. Robert C. Schweik, 1986; *Tess of the D'Urbervilles*, ed. Scott Elledge, 3rd ed. 1991; *Jude the Obscure*, ed. Norman Page, 2nd ed. 1999; and *The Mayor of Casterbridge*, 2nd ed., ed. Phillip Mallett, 2001. Michael Millgate and Richard Little Purdy have edited *The Collected Letters of Thomas Hardy*, 7 vols., 1978–88. Millgate has also edited *Selected Letters*, 1990, and *Thomas Hardy's Public Voice: The Essays, Speeches, and*

Miscellaneous Prose, 2001. Harold Orel has edited *Thomas Hardy's Personal Writings: Prefaces, Literary Opinions, Reminiscences*, 1990. For Hardy's life see Robert Gittings's *Young Thomas Hardy*, 1975, and *Thomas Hardy's Later Years*, 1978; Millgate's *Thomas Hardy: A Biography*, 1982; F. B. Pinion's *Thomas Hardy: His Life and Friends*, 1992; Gibson's *Thomas Hardy: A Literary Life*, 1996; and Paul Turner's *The Life of Thomas Hardy: A Critical Biography*, 1998. *Thomas Hardy: Interviews and Recollections*, ed. Gibson, 1999, is also worth consulting.

The Cambridge Companion to Thomas Hardy, ed. Dale Kramer, 1999, and *The Oxford Reader's Companion to Hardy*, ed. Page, 2000, are good guides to Hardy's work. Pinion's *A Hardy Companion: A Guide to the Works of Thomas Hardy and Their Background*, 1968, continues to be useful. Helpful reference works include Sarah Bird Wright's *Thomas Hardy A to Z: The Essential Reference to His Life and Work*, 2002, and Geoffrey Harvey's *The Complete Critical Guide to Thomas Hardy*, 2003.

For criticism on Hardy's prose and poetry, see *Hardy: A Collection of Critical Essays*, ed. Albert Guérard, 1963; J. Hillis Miller's *Thomas Hardy: Distance and Desire*, 1970; Jean R. Brooks's *Thomas Hardy: The Poetic Structure*, 1971; John Bayley's *An Essay on Hardy*, 1978; *Thomas Hardy: The Writer and His Background*, ed. Page, 1980; *Thomas Hardy*, ed. Harold Bloom, 1982, 2003; and *Thomas Hardy*, ed. Patricia Ingham, 1990, 2003.

For criticism concerning Hardy's poetry, see Hynes's *The Pattern of Hardy's Poetry*, 1956; Donald Davie's *Thomas Hardy and British Poetry*, 1972; Tom Paulin's *Thomas Hardy: The Poetry of Perception*, 1975; *The Poetry of Thomas Hardy*, ed. Patricia Clements and Juliet Grindle, 1980; William Earl Buckler's *The Poetry of Thomas Hardy: A Study in Art and Ideas*, 1983; and James Persoon's *Hardy's Early Poetry: Romanticism through a "Dark Bilberry Eye,"* 2000. For criticism of individual poems J. O. Bailey's *The Poetry of Thomas Hardy: A Handbook and Commentary*, 1970, and Pinion's *A Commentary on the Poems of Thomas Hardy*, 1976, are useful.

For criticism concerning Hardy's fiction see Shirley A. Stave's *The Decline of the Goddess: Nature, Culture, and Women in Thomas Hardy's Fiction*, 1995; Shanta Dutta's *Ambivalence in Hardy: A Study of His Attitude to Women*, 2000; Rosemary Sumner's *A Route to Modernism: Hardy, Lawrence, Woolf*, 2000; and Joanna Devereux's *Patriarchy and Its Discontents: Sexual Politics in Selected Novels and Stories of Thomas Hardy*, 2003.

The Hardy Centennial Number of *The Southern Review*, 1940, was influential in shaping Hardy's critical reputation; the special Hardy issues of *Agenda*, 1970, and *Victorian Poetry*, 1979, are also notable.

Tony Harrison

Harrison's volumes of poetry include *Earthworks*, 1964; *Newcastle Is Peru*, 1969; *The Loiners*, 1970; *From "The School of Eloquence" and Other Poems*, 1978; *Continuous: Fifty Sonnets from "The School of Eloquence,"* 1981; *A Kumquat for John Keats*, 1981; *U. S. Martial*, 1981; *Selected Poems*, 1984, 1987; *"V." and Other Poems*, 1990; *A Cold Coming*, 1991; *The Gaze of the Gorgon*, 1992; and *Permanently Bard: Selected Poetry*, 1995. Among his collections of dramatic verse are *Theatre Works: 1973–1985*, 1986; *Plays Three*, 1996; *Plays One*, 2001; *Plays Two*, 2002; and *Plays Four*, 2002. Harrison's television and screen credits include *Black Daisies for the Bride*, 1993; *Prometheus*, 1998; and *"The Shadow of Hiroshima" and Other Film/Poems*, 1995. For his life see Joe Kelleher's *Tony Harrison*, 1996. John R. Kaiser's *Tony Harrison: A Bibliography, 1957–1987* was published in 1989.

Collections of essays focusing on Harrison's work include *Tony Harrison*, ed. Neil Astley, 1991, and *Tony Harrison: Loiner*, ed. Sandie Byrne, 1997. Other criticism of his work includes Luke Spencer's *The Poetry of Tony Harrison*, 1994; Byrne's *H, v. & O: The Poetry of Tony Harrison*, 1998; and Antony Rowland's *Tony Harrison and the Holocaust*, 2001.

Seamus Heaney

Heaney's volumes of poetry include *Death of a Naturalist*, 1966; *Door into the Dark*, 1969; *Wintering Out*, 1972; *North*, 1975; *Field Work*, 1979; *Sweeney Astray: A Version from the Irish*, 1983; *Station Island*, 1984; *The Haw Lantern*, 1987; *Seeing Things*, 1991; *Sweeney's Flight*, 1992; *The Spirit Level*, 1996; *Opened Ground: Selected Poems, 1966–1996*, 1998; and *Electric Light*, 2001. He is translator of *The Cure at Troy: A Version of Sophocles's Philoctetes*, 1990, and of *The Midnight Verdict*, based on Ovid's *Metamorphoses* and Brian Merriman's *Cúirt an Mheán Oíche*, 1993; he is cotranslator, with Stanislaw Baranczak, of Jan Kochanowski's *Laments*, 1995. His translation of Ozef Kalda's poems set into a song cycle by Leoš Janáček, *Diary of One Who Vanished: A Song Cycle*, was published in 2000; his translation of *Beowulf* was published in 1999 and released in a Norton Critical Edition edited by Daniel Donoghue in 2002. Heaney is also editor of *The Essential Wordsworth*, 1988. Heaney's essays are collected in *Preoccupations: Selected Prose, 1968–1978*, 1980; *The Government of the Tongue: Selected Prose, 1978–1987*, 1988; *The Redress of Poetry: Oxford Lectures*, 1995; and *Finders Keepers: Selected Prose, 1971–2001*, 2002. For his life see Blake Morrison's *Seamus Heaney*, 1982, and Michael Parker's *Seamus Heaney: The Making of the Poet*, 1993. Bibliographical information can be found in Michael J. Durkan and Rand Brandes's *Seamus Heaney: A Reference Guide*, 1996.

For guides to Heaney's poetry see Neil Corcoran's *Seamus Heaney*, 1986, and *Seamus Heaney: Comprehensive Research and Study Guide*, ed. Harold Bloom, 2003. Studies of Heaney's work include Elmer Andrews's *The Poetry of Seamus Heaney: All the Realms of Whisper*, 1988; Thomas C. Foster's *Seamus Heaney*, 1989; Henry Hart's *Seamus Heaney: Poet of Contrary Progressions*, 1992; Bernard O'Donoghue's *Seamus Heaney and the Language of Poetry*, 1994; John Wilson Foster's *The Achievement of Seamus Heaney*, 1995; Helen Vendler's *Seamus Heaney*, 1998; Eugene O'Brien's *Seamus Heaney and the Place of Writing* and *Seamus Heaney: Creating Irelands of the Mind*, 2002; and Floyd Collins's *Seamus Heaney: The Crisis of Identity*, 2003. Collections of essays focusing on Heaney's work include *Seamus Heaney*, ed. Harold Bloom, 1986; *Seamus Heaney: A Collection of Critical Essays*, ed. Andrews, 1992; *The Art of Seamus Heaney*, ed. Tony Curtis, 3rd ed. 1993; and *Critical Essays on Seamus Heaney*, ed. Robert F. Garratt, 1995.

Geoffrey Hill

Hill's *New and Collected Poems, 1952–1992* was published in 1994. Subsequent works include *Canaan*, 1996; *The Triumph of Love*, 1998; *Speech! Speech!*, 2000; and *The Orchards of Syon*, 2002. His prose works include *The Lords of Limit: Essays on Literature and Ideas*, 1984; *Illuminating Shadows: The Mythic Power of Film*, 1992; and *Style and Faith*, 2003. An interview appears in *Viewpoints: Poets in Conversation with John Haffenden*, 1981.

For an overview of Hill's work, see W. S. Milne's *An Introduction to Geoffrey Hill*, 1998. Collections of criticism include *Geoffrey Hill: Essays on His Work*, ed. Peter Robinson, 1985; and *Geoffrey Hill*, ed. Harold Bloom, 1986. Studies of Hill's work include Henry Hart's *The Poetry of Geoffrey Hill*, 1986; Vincent Sherry's *The Uncommon Tongue: The Poetry and Criticism of Geoffrey Hill*, 1987; E. M. Knottenbelt's *Passionate Intelligence: The Poetry of Geoffrey Hill*, 1990; Eleanor J. McNees's *Eucharistic Poetry: The Search for Presence in the Writings of John Donne, Gerard Manley Hopkins, Dylan Thomas, and Geoffrey Hill*, 1992; and Andrew Michael Roberts's *Geoffrey Hill*, 2003. Critical discussions can also be found in John Silkin's chapter in *British Poetry since 1960*, ed. Michael Schmidt and Grevel Lindop, 1972; Christopher Ricks's *The Force of Poetry*, 1984; John Hollander's *The Work of Poetry*, 1997; William Logan's *Reputations of the Tongue: On Poets and Poetry*, 1999; and Peter McDonald's *Serious Poetry: Form and Authority from Yeats to Hill*, 2002. *Agenda* 17.1, 1979, and *Agenda* 23, 1985–86, are special issues dedicated to Hill.

A. E. Housman

The Poems of A. E. Housman, ed. Archie Burnett, was published in 1997. *Collected Poems and Selected Prose*, ed. Christopher Ricks, 1988, is also valuable. Much of Housman's work as a classicist is available in *The Classical Papers of A. E. Housman*, 3 vols., ed. J. Diggle and F. R. D. Goodyear, 1972. Other essays are published in *Selected Prose*, ed. John Carter, 1961. Henry Maas edited *The Letters of A. E. Housman*, 1971. For Housman's life see Laurence Housman's *My Brother, A. E. Housman*, 1938, and Norman Page's *A. E. Housman: A Critical Biography*, 1983. Important reference materials include John Carter, John Sparrow, and William White's *A. E. Housman: A Bibliography*, 2nd ed. 1982, and Clyde Kenneth Hyder's *A Concordance to the Poems of A. E. Housman*, 1966.

Book-length studies of Housman's work include B. J. Leggett's *The Poetic Art of A. E. Housman: Theory and Practice*, 1978; Richard Perceval Graves's *A. E. Housman: The Scholar-Poet*, 1979; John Bayley's *Housman's Poems*, 1992; Keith Jebb's *A. E. Housman*, 1992; Terence Allan Hoagwood's *A. E. Housman Revisited*, 1995; and Carol Efrati's *The Road of Danger, Guilt, and Shame: The Lonely Way of A. E. Housman*, 2002. Collections of essays about Housman's work include *A. E. Housman: A Collection of Critical Essays*, ed. Ricks, 1968; *A. E. Housman: The Critical Heritage*, ed. Philip Gardner, 1992; and *A. E. Housman: A Reassessment*, ed. Alan W. Holden and J. Roy Birch, 2000. The Housman Society also publishes a journal.

Ted Hughes

Ted Hughes: Collected Poems, ed. Paul Keegan, was published in 2003 and includes poetry from *The Hawk in the Rain*, 1957; *Lupercal*, 1960; *Wodwo*, 1967; *Crow*, 1970; *Season Songs*, 1975; *Gaudete*, 1977; *Cave Birds: An Alchemical Cave Drama*, 1978; *Moortown*, 1979; *Remains of Elmet*, 1979; *River*, 1983; *Flowers and Insects: Some Birds and a Pair of Spiders*, 1986; *Wolfwatching*, 1989; *Capriccio*, 1990; *"Rain-Charm for the Duchy" and Other Laureate Poems*, 1992; *New Selected Poems, 1957–1994*, 1995; *Difficulties of a Bridegroom*, 1995; *Tales from Ovid*, 1997; and *Birthday Letters*, 1998. Hughes's prose works include *Poetry in the Making*, 1967; *Shakespeare and the Goddess of Complete Being*, 1992; and *Winter Pollen: Occasional Prose*, 1994. His translations include Seneca's *Oedipus*, 1969, and Jean Racine's *Phèdre*, 1998. He has also published much literature for children and has edited collections of Shakespeare, Coleridge, Dickinson, Keith Douglas, and Sylvia Plath. For his life see Elaine Feinstein's *Ted Hughes: The Life of a Poet*, 2001, and Diane Middlebrook's *Her Husband: Hughes and Plath— A Marriage*, 2003. Keith Sagar's *The Art of Ted*

Hughes, 2nd ed. 1978, offers a detailed critical account of his work as well as a comprehensive bibliography of writings by and about him; Sagar and Stephen Tabor's Ted Hughes: A Bibliography, 1946–1995, 1998, is also useful.

Book-length studies of Hughes's work include Sagar's The Art of Ted Hughes, 1978; Terry Gifford and Neil Roberts's Ted Hughes: A Critical Study, 1981; Thomas West's Ted Hughes, 1985; Dennis Walder's Ted Hughes, 1987; Craig Robinson's Ted Hughes as Shepherd of Being, 1989; Nick Bishop's Re-Making Poetry: Ted Hughes and a New Critical Psychology, 1991; Ann Skea's Ted Hughes: The Poetic Quest, 1994; Paul Bentley's The Poetry of Ted Hughes: Language, Illusion, and Beyond, 1998; and Sagar's The Laughter of Foxes: A Study of Ted Hughes, 2000. Collections of essays include The Achievement of Ted Hughes, ed. Sagar, 1983; Critical Essays on Ted Hughes, ed. Leonard M. Scigaj, 1992; and The Epic Poise: A Celebration of Ted Hughes, ed. Nick Gammage, 1999.

David Jones

Jones's major works are the two long poems, In Parenthesis, 1937, and The Anathémata, 1952. Posthumous volumes of poetry were published as "The Sleeping Lord" and Other Fragments, 1974, and The Roman Quarry and Other Sequences, ed. Harman Grisewood and René Hague, 1981. A useful selection of Jones's work appears in Introducing David Jones, ed. John Matthias, 1980, with a preface by Stephen Spender. Important prose works can be found in Epoch and Artist: Selected Writings, 1959, and "The Dying Gaul" and Other Writings, 1978, both edited by Grisewood. Jones was also a gifted artist; books he illustrated include Harold Monro's The Winter Solstice, 1928, and Roy Fisher's The Ship's Orchestra, 1966, as well as his own In Parenthesis. Letters are available in David Jones: Letters to Vernon Watkins, ed. Ruth Pryor, 1976; Dai Greatcoat: A Self-Portrait of David Jones in His Letters, ed. Hague, 1980; Letters to a Friend, ed. Aneirin Talfan Davies, 1980; and Inner Necessities: The Letters of David Jones to Desmond Chute, ed. Thomas Dilworth, 1984. Samuel Rees's David Jones: An Annotated Bibliography and Guide to Research was published in 1977.

For an introduction to Jones see Jon Stallworthy's Great Poets of World War I: Poetry from the Great War, 2002. Studies of Jones's poetry include David Blamires's David Jones: Artist and Writer, 1972; Jeremy Hooker's David Jones: An Exploratory Study of the Writings, 1975; Elizabeth Ward's David Jones: Mythmaker, 1983; Dilworth's The Shape of Meaning in the Poetry of David Jones, 1988; Kathleen Henderson Staudt's At the Turn of a Civilization: David Jones and Modern Poetics, 1994; and Jonathan Miles and Derek Shiel's David Jones: The Maker

Unmade, 1995. Numerous helpful essays are collected in David Jones: Artist and Poet, ed. Paul Hills, 1997. For further reading on In Parenthesis, see discussions in John H. Johnston's English Poetry of the First World War, 1964; Bernard Bergonzi's Heroes' Twilight: A Study of the Literature of the Great War, 1966, 2nd ed. 1980; Jon Silkin's Out of Battle: The Poetry of the Great War, 1972, 2nd ed. 1998; and Paul Fussell's The Great War and Modern Memory, 1975.

James Joyce

The most reliable edition of Ulysses, 1922, is Ulysses: A Critical and Synoptic Edition, 3 vols., ed. Hans Walter Gabler with Wolfhard Steppe and Claus Melchoir, 1984, rev. ed. 1986. Annotated editions of Dubliners, 1914, and A Portrait of the Artist as a Young Man, 1916, are available from Viking, Penguin, and Oxford World's Classics; the Oxford World's Classics edition of Ulysses, ed. Jeri Johnson, 1993, uses the 1922 text and has extensive notes and supportive critical material. Stephen Hero, ed. John J. Slocum and Herbert Cahoon, 1963, is the novel that provided the basis for Portrait. Faber, Minerva, Palladin, and Penguin have all produced good editions of Finnegans Wake, which was originally published in 1939. The Portable James Joyce, ed. Harry Levin, rev. ed. 1966, conveniently contains selections from Ulysses and Finnegans Wake, the entire Portrait, selections from Dubliners, and Joyce's poetry. For Joyce's critical writing see Critical Writings of James Joyce, ed. Richard Ellmann and Ellsworth Mason, 1989, and for his poems and shorter pieces see James Joyce: Poems and Shorter Writings, ed. Richard Ellmann, A. Walton Litz, and John Whittier-Ferguson, 1991. The Letters of James Joyce, 3 vols., was edited by Stuart Gilbert with Ellmann and James F. Spoerri, 1957–66; Selected Letters of James Joyce, ed. Ellmann, 1975, is also available. The standard biography of Joyce is Ellmann's James Joyce, 3rd ed. 1982. Also useful are Sylvia Beach's Shakespeare and Company, 1959; Stanislaus Joyce's My Brother's Keeper: James Joyce's Early Years, ed. Ellmann, 1958, and The Complete Dublin Diary of Stanislaus Joyce, 1971; Arthur Power's Conversations with James Joyce, 1975; Portraits of the Artist in Exile: Recollections of James Joyce by Europeans, ed. Willard Potts, 1979; Brenda Maddox's Nora: A Biography of Nora Joyce, 1988; and E. H. Mikhail's James Joyce: Interviews and Recollections, 1990. The standard bibliography of Joyce's work is A Bibliography of James Joyce, ed. Slocum and Cahoon, 2nd ed. 1971. Thomas Jackson Rice's James Joyce: A Guide to Research, 1982, and Thomas F. Staley's An Annotated Critical Bibliography of James Joyce, 1989, are helpful bibliographies of the secondary literature.

Good general accounts of Joyce's work can be found in Hugh Kenner's *Dublin's Joyce*, 1956, and *Joyce's Voices*, 1978; *James Joyce: The Critical Heritage*, 2 vols., ed. Robert H. Deming, 1970; C. H. Peake's *James Joyce: The Citizen and the Artist*, 1976; Ellmann's *The Consciousness of Joyce*, 1977; Colin MacCabe's *James Joyce and the Revolution of the Word*, 1979; *James Joyce: New Perspectives*, ed. MacCabe, 1982; *A Companion to Joyce Studies*, ed. Zack Bowen and James F. Carens, 1984; Patrick Parrinder's *James Joyce*, 1984; Vicki Mahaffey's *Reauthorizing Joyce*, 1988; *The Cambridge Companion to James Joyce*, ed. Derek Attridge, 1990, 2nd ed. 2004, and Jean-Michel Rabaté's *James Joyce: Authorized Reader*, 1991.

More-specialized studies include Dominic Manganiello's *Joyce's Politics*, 1980; *Women in Joyce*, ed. Suzette A. Henke and Elaine Unkeless, 1982; Fritz Senn's *Joyce's Dislocations: Essays on Reading as Translation*, 1984; *Post-Structuralist Joyce: Essays from the French*, ed. Attridge and Daniel Ferrer, 1984; Richard Brown's *James Joyce and Sexuality*, 1985; Patrick McGee's *Paperspace: Style as Ideology in Joyce's Ulysses*, 1988; Henke's *James Joyce and the Politics of Desire*, 1990; Margot Norris's *Joyce's Web: The Social Unraveling of Modernism*, 1992; Robert Spoo's *James Joyce and the Language of History: Dedalus's Nightmare*, 1994; Kevin J. H. Dettmar's *The Illicit Joyce of Postmodernism: Reading against the Grain*, 1996; *Semicolonial Joyce*, ed. Attridge and Marjorie Howes, 2000; *Joyce and the City: The Significance of Place*, ed. Michael Begnal, 2002; David Spurr's *Joyce and the Scene of Modernity*, 2002; *Joyce and the Joyceans*, ed. Morton Levitt, 2002; and *James Joyce and the Difference of Language*, ed. Laurent Milesi, 2003.

Don Gifford's *Joyce Annotated: Notes for Dubliners and A Portrait of the Artist as a Young Man*, 2nd ed. 1982, is a useful guide for both works. Studies of *Dubliners* include *Twentieth-Century Interpretations of Dubliners: A Collection of Critical Essays*, ed. Peter K. Garrett, 1968; *James Joyce's Dubliners: Critical Essays*, ed. Clive Hart, 1969. *Concordance to James Joyce's Dubliners: With a Reverse Index, a Frequency List, and a Conversion Tab*, ed. Wilhelm Füger, 1980, provides a unique reference source. Critical studies of *A Portrait of the Artist as a Young Man* include Maud Ellmann's essay in *Untying the Text: A Post-Structuralist Reader*, ed. Robert Young, 1981; *James Joyce's A Portrait of the Artist as a Young Man*, ed. Harold Bloom, 1999; *Readings on A Portrait of the Artist as a Young Man*, ed. Clarice Swisher, 2000; *James Joyce's A Portrait of the Artist as Young Man: A Casebook*, ed. Mark A. Wollaeger, 2003. *A Portrait of the Artist as a Young Man: Complete, Authoritative Text with Biographical and Historical Contexts, Critical History, and Essays from Five Contemporary Critical Perspectives*,

ed. R. B. Kershner, 1993, is a helpful compendium.

Critical studies of *Ulysses* include Frank Budgen's *James Joyce and the Making of Ulysses*, 1934, rpt. 1960; Stuart Gilbert's *James Joyce's Ulysses: A Study*, 2nd. ed. 1952; William Schutte's *Joyce and Shakespeare: A Study in the Meaning of Ulysses*, 1957; Richard Ellmann's *Ulysses on the Liffey*, 1972; Weldon Thornton's *Allusions in Ulysses: An Annotated List*, 1973; *Ulysses: Fifty Years*, ed. Staley, 1974; *James Joyce's Ulysses: Critical Essays*, ed. Hart and David Hayman, 1974; Michael Seidel's *Epic Geography: James Joyce's Ulysses*, 1976; Marilyn French's *The Book as World: James Joyce's Ulysses*, 1976; Michael Groden's *Ulysses in Progress*, 1977; James H. Maddox's *Joyce's Ulysses and the Assault upon Character*, 1978; Karen Lawrence's *The Odyssey of Style in Ulysses*, 1981; Hayman's *Ulysses: The Mechanics of Meaning*, rev. ed. 1982; Hugh Kenner's *Ulysses*, rev. ed. 1987; Gifford and Robert J. Seidman's *Ulysses Annotated: Notes for Joyce's Ulysses*, 2nd. ed. 1988; Enda Duffy's *The Subaltern Ulysses*, 1994; *A Companion to James Joyce's Ulysses: Biographical and Historical Contexts, Critical History, and Essays from Five Contemporary Critical Perspectives*, ed. Norris, 1998; *Joycean Cultures, Culturing Joyces*, ed. Vincent J. Cheng, Kimberly J. Devlin, and Norris, 1998; Marilyn Reizbaum's *James Joyce's Judaic Other*, 1999; Paul Schwaber's *The Cast of Characters: A Reading of Ulysses*, 1999; and Andrew Gibson's *Joyce's Revenge: History, Politics, and Aesthetics in Ulysses*, 2002. Collections of essays include *James Joyce's Ulysses: A Casebook*, ed. Attridge, 2004; *Leopold Bloom*, ed. Harold Bloom, 2004; and *James Joyce's Ulysses*, ed. Bloom, 2004. David Pierce's *James Joyce's Ireland*, 1992, provides other useful background material. Phillip F. Herring has edited notes and drafts for the novel and compiled them in *Joyce's Ulysses Notesheets in the British Museum*, 1972, and *Joyce's Notes and Early Drafts for Ulysses: Selections from the Buffalo Collection*, 1977.

Studies of *Finnegans Wake* include Samuel Beckett et al., *Our Examination Round His Factification for Incamination of Work in Progress*, 2nd ed. 1962; Hart's *Structure and Motif in Finnegans Wake*, 1962; James S. Atherton's *The Books at the Wake: A Study of Literary Allusions in James Joyce's Finnegans Wake*, 2nd ed. 1974; Hart's *A Concordance to Finnegans Wake*, rev. ed. 1974; Adaline Glasheen's *A Third Census of Finnegans Wake: An Index of the Characters and Their Roles*, 1977; Roland McHugh's *Annotations to Finnegans Wake*, 1980; John Bishop's *Joyce's Book of the Dark: Finnegans Wake*, 1986; Kimberly J. Devlin's *Wandering and Return in Finnegans Wake: An Integrative Approach to Joyce's Fictions*, 1991; Thomas C. Hofheinz's *Joyce and the Invention of Irish History: Finnegans Wake in Context*, 1995.

Philip Larkin

Larkin's *Collected Poems*, ed. Anthony Thwaite, 2nd ed. 2004, contains a number of hitherto unpublished poems in addition to the contents of his four collections: *The North Ship*, 1945; *The Less Deceived*, 1955; *The Whitsun Weddings*, 1964; and *High Windows*, 1974. *Philip Larkin: The Whitsun Weddings and Selected Poems*, ed. David Punter, was published in 2003. Thwaite edited *Selected Letters of Philip Larkin, 1940–1985*, 1993, and *Further Requirements: Interviews, Broadcasts, Statements, and Book Reviews, 1952–1985*, 2001. Larkin's other works include his novels, *Jill*, 1946, and *A Girl in Winter*, 1947; a collection of music reviews, *All What Jazz: A Record Diary, 1961–1971*, 1985; and *The Oxford Book of Twentieth-Century English Verse*, 1973, which Larkin edited. Previously unpublished material has recently been published in two posthumous collections: *Larkin's Jazz: Essays and Reviews, 1940–84*, ed. Richard Palmer and John White, 2001, and *"Trouble at Willow Gables" and Other Fictions*, ed. James Booth, 2002. *Required Writing: Miscellaneous Pieces, 1955–1982*, 1983, contains much of Larkin's important prose, including recollections, interviews, and essays on literature and jazz. (For further reading on Larkin and jazz, see B. J. Leggett's *Larkin's Blues: Jazz, Popular Music, and Poetry*, 1999.) The standard biography is Andrew Motion's *Philip Larkin: A Writer's Life*, 1993. B. C. Bloomfield's *Philip Larkin: A Bibliography, 1933–1994*, was first published in 1979 and revised and enlarged in 2002.

Studies of Larkin's work include David Timms's *Philip Larkin*, 1973; Bruce K. Martin's *Philip Larkin*, 1978; Motion's *Philip Larkin*, 1982; Terrence Whalen's *Philip Larkin and English Poetry*, 1986; Salem K. Hassan's *Philip Larkin and His Contemporaries: An Air of Authenticity*, 1988; Janice Rossen's *Philip Larkin: His Life's Work*, 1989; Stephen Regan's *Philip Larkin*, 1992; Booth's *Philip Larkin: Writer*, 1992; Andrew Swarbrick's *Out of Reach: The Poetry of Philip Larkin*, 1995; and A. T. Tolley's *Larkin at Work: A Study of Larkin's Mode of Composition as Seen in His Workbooks*, 1997. Collections of essays include *Larkin at Sixty*, ed. Thwaite, 1982; *Critical Essays on Philip Larkin: The Poems*, ed. Linda Cookson and Bryan Loughrey, 1989; *Philip Larkin: The Man and His Work*, ed. Dale Salwak, 1989; *Philip Larkin*, ed. Regan, 1997; and *New Larkins for Old: Critical Essays*, ed. Booth, 2000.

D. H. Lawrence

The Cambridge Edition of Lawrence's works is nearing completion and will prove definitive. Penguin's paperback editions of Lawrence's novels and short fiction are based on the Cambridge Edition; Oxford World's Classics also offers paperbacks of *The White Peacock*, *Sons and Lovers*, *The Rainbow*, and *Women in Love*, among others. *The Portable D. H. Lawrence*, ed. Diana Trilling, 1947, offers selections from *The Rainbow* and *Women in Love* as well as from Lawrence's poems, short stories, criticism, and letters. The eight volumes of Lawrence's *Letters*, ed. James T. Boulton et al., were issued by Cambridge between 1979 and 2000. The best edition of Lawrence's poetry remains the third edition of *The Complete Poems*, ed. Vivian de Sola Pinto and Warren Roberts, 1977. For Lawrence's life see the Cambridge triptych: John Worthen's *D. H. Lawrence: The Early Years, 1885–1912*, 1991; Mark Kinkead-Weekes's *D. H. Lawrence: Triumph to Exile, 1912–1922*, 1996; and David Ellis's *D. H. Lawrence: Dying Game, 1922–1930*, 1998.

Recent bibliographies of secondary sources include Paul Poplawski and Worthen's *D. H. Lawrence: A Reference Companion*, 1996, and Warren Roberts and Poplawski's *A Bibliography of D. H. Lawrence*, 3rd ed. 2001. Pioneering studies include F. R. Leavis's *D. H. Lawrence: Novelist*, 1956; Graham Hough's *The Dark Sun*, 1957; H. M. Daleski's *The Forked Flame*, 1965; George Ford's *Double Measure: A Study of the Novels and Stories of D. H. Lawrence*, 1965; and Colin Clarke's *River of Dissolution: D. H. Lawrence and English Romanticism*, 1969. More recent studies include *D. H. Lawrence: The Critical Heritage*, ed. Ronald P. Draper, 1970; Emile Delavenay's *D. H. Lawrence: The Man and His Work: The Formative Years, 1885–1919*, trans. Katherine M. Delavenay, 1972; Frank Kermode's *D. H. Lawrence*, 1973; *D. H. Lawrence: Novelist, Poet, Prophet*, ed. Stephen Spender, 1973; Paul Delaney's *D. H. Lawrence's Nightmare: The Writer and His Circle in the Years of the Great War*, 1978; *D. H. Lawrence*, ed. Harold Bloom, 1986; Christopher Heywood's *D. H. Lawrence: New Studies*, 1987; *The Challenge of D. H. Lawrence*, ed. Michael Squires and Keith Cushman, 1990; Tony Pinkney's *D. H. Lawrence and Modernism*, 1990; *Rethinking Lawrence*, ed. Keith Brown, 1990; *D. H. Lawrence*, ed. Peter Widdowson, 1992; *The Cambridge Companion to D. H. Lawrence*, ed. Anne Fernihough, 2001; *The Complete Critical Guide to D. H. Lawrence*, ed. Fiona Becket, 2002; *D. H. Lawrence: New Worlds*, ed. Cushman and Earl G. Ingersoll, 2003.

For studies of Lawrence and gender, see *Lawrence and Women*, ed. Anne Smith, 1978; Hilary Simpson's *D. H. Lawrence and Feminism*, 1982; Sheila Macleod's *Lawrence's Men and Women*, 1985; Cornelia Nixon's *Lawrence's Leadership Politics and the Turn Against Women*, 1986; James C. Cowan's *D. H. Lawrence: Self and Sexuality*, 2002; and James J. Miracky's *Regenerating the Novel: Gender and Genre in Woolf, Forster, Sinclair, and Lawrence*, 2003. For studies of Lawrence's poetry, see

M. J. Lockwood's *A Study of the Poems of D. H. Lawrence: Thinking in Poetry*, 1987; Holly A. Laird's *Self and Sequence: The Poetry of D. H. Lawrence*, 1988; Sandra Gilbert's *Acts of Attention: The Poems of D. H. Lawrence*, 2nd ed. 1990; and Amit Chaudhuri, *D. H. Lawrence and 'Difference': Postcoloniality and the Poetry of the Present*, 2003.

For further reading on Lawrence and philosophy, see Aidan Burns's *Nature and Culture in D. H. Lawrence*, 1980; Colin Milton's *Lawrence and Nietzsche: A Study in Influence*, 1987; Michael H. Black's *D. H. Lawrence: The Early Philosophical Works: A Commentary*, 1992; Michael Bell's *D. H. Lawrence: Language and Being*, 1992; and Robert E. Montgomery's *The Visionary D. H. Lawrence: Beyond Philosophy and Art*, 1994. For Lawrence's aesthetics and politics, see Graham Holderness's *D. H. Lawrence: History, Ideology and Fiction*, 1982, and Fernihough's *D. H. Lawrence: Aesthetics and Ideology*, 1993. For Lawrence's theories of the novel, see Scott R. Sanders's *D. H. Lawrence: The World of the Five Major Novels*, 1974; Alastair Niven's *D. H. Lawrence: The Novels*, 1978; Worthen's *D. H. Lawrence and the Idea of the Novel*, 1979; Charles L. Ross's *Women in Love: A Novel of Mythic Realism*, 1991; and *D. H. Lawrence*, ed. Bloom, 2002.

Doris Lessing

Lessing's first novel, *The Grass Is Singing*, 1950, was followed two years later by the first of the quintet *Children of Violence*, the remaining volumes of which appeared between 1954 and 1969. Lessing published one of her best-known works, *The Golden Notebook*, in 1962. Her other fiction includes *Briefing for a Descent into Hell*, 1971; *The Summer before the Dark*, 1973; *Memoirs of a Survivor*, 1974; the monumental sequence *Canopus in Argus: Archives*, 1979–83; *Diaries of Jane Somers*, 1983; *The Good Terrorist*, 1985; *The Fifth Child*, 1988; *Love, Again*, 1995; *Mara and Dann*, 1999; and *The Grandmothers*, 2004. Lessing's *Collected Stories*, 2 vols., was published in 1978. In 1967 she published a biography of female English novelists and cat owners, *Particularly Cats*; the latest revision appeared in 2000. For Lessing's life see *Under My Skin: The First Volume of My Autobiography, to 1949*, 1994, and *Walking in the Shade: Volume Two of My Autobiography, 1949 to 1962*, 1997. Carole Klein's *Doris Lessing: A Biography*, 2000, and *Doris Lessing: Conversations*, ed. Earl G. Ingersoll, 1994, supplement Lessing's autobiography with helpful second-person and third-person perspectives. *The Doris Lessing Reader*, 1988, contains selections from Lessing's fiction and memoirs; *A Small Personal Voice: Essays, Reviews, Interviews*, ed. Paul Schlueter, 1974, contains a selection of her essays. Useful reference works include Selma R. Burkom's *Doris Lessing: A Checklist of Primary*

and Secondary Sources, 1973, and Dee Seligman's *Doris Lessing: An Annotated Bibliography of Criticism*, 1981.

Studies of Lessing's work include Schlueter's *The Novels of Doris Lessing*, 1973; *Doris Lessing: Critical Studies*, ed. Annis Pratt and L. S. Dembo, 1974; Mary Ann Singleton's *The City and the Veld: The Fiction of Doris Lessing*, 1977; Roberta Rubenstein's *The Novelistic Vision of Doris Lessing: Breaking the Forms of Consciousness*, 1979; *Notebooks, Memoirs, Archives: Reading and Rereading Doris Lessing*, ed. Jenny Taylor, 1982; Lorna Sage's *Doris Lessing*, 1983; Betsy Draine's *Substance under Pressure: Artistic Coherence and Evolving Form*, 1983; Mona Knapp's *Doris Lessing*, 1984; Katherine Fishburn's *The Unexpected Universe of Doris Lessing: A Study in Narrative Technique*, 1985; *Doris Lessing*, ed. Harold Bloom, 1986, 2003; *Critical Essays on Doris Lessing*, ed. Claire Sprague and Virginia Tiger, 1986; *Doris Lessing: The Alchemy of Survival*, ed. Carey Kaplan and Ellen Cronan Rose, 1988; Jean Pickering's *Understanding Doris Lessing*, 1990; Gayle Greene's *Doris Lessing: The Poetics of Change*, 1994; Louise Yelin's *From the Margins of Empire: Christina Stead, Doris Lessing, Nadine Gordimer*, 1998; Yuan-Jung Cheng's *Heralds of the Postmodern: Madness and Fiction in Conrad, Woolf, and Lessing*, 1999; and Deborah Martinson's *In the Presence of Audience: The Self in Diaries and Fiction*, 2003. For theoretical criticisms of Lessing's work, see Jeannette King's *Doris Lessing*, 1989, and Sprague's *Rereading Doris Lessing: Narrative Patterns of Doubling and Repetition*, 1987. Michael Thorpe's *Doris Lessing's Africa*, 1978, examines Lessing's work through the lens of her home continent.

Hugh MacDiarmid

Hugh MacDiarmid: The Complete Poems, 1920–1976, 2 vols., 1978, rev. ed. 1994, was edited by Michael Grieve and W. R. Aitken. *Selected Poetry*, ed. Grieve and Alan Riach, and *Selected Prose*, ed. Riach, were both published in 1992 and are part of Carcanet Press's projected sixteen-volume *Collected Works of Hugh MacDiarmid*. MacDiarmid is editor of *The Golden Treasury of Scottish Poetry*, 1940. His correspondence is available in *The Letters of Hugh MacDiarmid*, ed. Alan Bold, 1984; *The Hugh MacDiarmid–George Ogilvie Letters*, ed. Catherine Kerrigan, 1988; and *New Selected Letters*, ed. Dorian Grieve, Owen Dudley Edwards, and Riach, 2001. An autobiography, *Lucky Poet*, was published in 1943, and Gordon Wright's *MacDiarmid: An Illustrated Biography*, 1977, covers eighty-five years of the poet's life in photographs, caricatures, poems, press cuttings, and other documents. Bold's *MacDiarmid: Christopher Murray Grieve, A Critical Biography*, 1988, is also very informative. *Hugh MacDiarmid: A Critical Survey*, ed. Duncan Glen, 1972, contains critical essays as well as a comprehensive bibliography.

For a helpful study of MacDiarmid's themes and perspective, see Bold's *MacDiarmid: The Terrible Crystal*, 1983. Kerrigan's *Whaur Extremes Meet: The Poetry of Hugh MacDiarmid 1920–1934*, 1983, and Harvey Oxenhorn's *Elemental Things: The Poetry of Hugh MacDiarmid*, 1984, also provide perceptive critical discussions of his early and middle poetry. A valuable general account of MacDiarmid and his poetry is Kenneth Buthlay's *Hugh MacDiarmid*, 1981. On the Scottish cultural background and MacDiarmid's part in Scottish literary movements, see Glen's *Hugh MacDiarmid and the Scottish Renaissance*, 1964. *Hugh MacDiarmid, A Festschrift*, ed. Kugan Dalby Duval and Sydney Goodsir Smith, 1982, is the most important single critical book on MacDiarmid. Other useful studies include Edwin Morgan's *Hugh MacDiarmid*, 1976; John Baglow's *Hugh MacDiarmid: The Poetry of Self*, 1987; Peter McCarey's *Hugh MacDiarmid and the Russians*, 1987; Riach's *Hugh MacDiarmid's Epic Poetry*, 1991; Ruth McQuillan's *Hugh MacDiarmid: The Patrimony*, 1992; and W. N. Herbert's *To Circumjack MacDiarmid*, 1992. Collections of critical essays include *The Age of MacDiarmid*, ed. P. H. Scott and A. C. Davis, 1980, and *Hugh MacDiarmid: Man and Poet*, ed. Nancy Gish, 1992. The chapter "A Torchlight Procession of One: On Hugh MacDiarmid," in Seamus Heaney's *The Redress of Poetry*, 1995, is also helpful. *Akros* 23, August 1977, and *Scottish Literary Journal* 5, December 1978, are special MacDiarmid issues.

Louis MacNeice

The Collected Poems, 1966, and MacNeice's posthumously published unfinished autobiography, *The Strings Are False*, 1965, were both edited by E. R. Dodds. MacNeice made verse translations of Aeschylus's *Agamemnon*, 1936, and, with E. L. Stahl, of Goethe's *Faust* (an abridged version of parts one and two), 1951. MacNeice and Stephen Spender edited the anthology *Oxford Poetry 1929*, 1929. His Clark Lectures at Cambridge were published as *Varieties of Parable*, 1965. Alan Heuser has edited *Selected Literary Criticism of Louis MacNeice*, 1987; *Selected Prose of Louis MacNeice*, 1990; and, with Peter McDonald, *Selected Plays of Louis MacNeice*, 1993. A collection of MacNeice's BBC radio plays is *"The Dark Tower" and Other Radio Scripts*, 1947; Barbara Coulton's *Louis MacNeice in the BBC*, 1980, is a biographical and critical study of his work for radio. *A Bibliography of the Works of Louis MacNeice*, ed. C. M. Armitage and Neil Clark, 1973, lists most of his many other publications. A fine biography is Jon Stallworthy's *Louis MacNeice*, 1995.

Studies of MacNeice's work include Elton

Edward Smith's *Louis MacNeice*, 1970; William T. McKinnon's *Apollo's Blended Dream: A Study of the Poetry of Louis MacNeice*, 1971; D. B. Moore's *The Poetry of Louis MacNeice*, 1972; Terence Brown's *Louis MacNeice: Sceptical Vision*, 1975; Robyn Marsack, *The Cave of Making: The Poetry of Louis MacNeice*, 1982; Edna Longley's *Louis MacNeice: A Study*, 1988; and Peter McDonald's *Louis MacNeice: The Poet in His Contexts*, 1991. Numerous useful essays are collected in *Time Was Away: The World of Louis MacNeice*, ed. Brown and Alec Reid, 1974, and *Louis MacNeice and His Influence*, ed. Kathleen Devine and Alan J. Peacock, 1998.

MacNeice is also often discussed in connection with the group of poets identified with Auden in the 1930s; for more information on this group of poets, see Derek Stanford's *Stephen Spender, Louis MacNeice, Cecil Day Lewis: A Critical Survey*, 1969; Smith, *The Angry Young Men of the Thirties*, 1975; Samuel Hynes's *The Auden Generation: Literature and Politics in the 1930s*, 1976; Michael O'Neill's and Gareth Reeves's *Auden, MacNeice, Spender: The Thirties Poetry*, 1992; and John Whitehead's *A Commentary on the Poetry of W. H. Auden, C. Day Lewis, Louis MacNeice, and Stephen Spender*, 1992.

Katherine Mansfield

The Short Stories of Katherine Mansfield, 1937, contains all of Mansfield's stories, and her poetry is contained in *Poems of Katherine Mansfield*, ed. Vincent O'Sullivan, 1988. *The Critical Writings of Katherine Mansfield*, ed. Clare Hanson, was published in 1987. *Journal of Katherine Mansfield*, ed. John Middleton Murry, 1927; *The Collected Letters of Katherine Mansfield*, 4 vols., ed. O'Sullivan and Margaret Scott, 1984–96; and *The Katherine Mansfield Notebooks*, ed. Scott, 1997, 2002, provide autobiographical resources useful in studying Mansfield's work in depth, and Alexandra Johnson's *The Hidden Writer: Diaries and the Creative Life*, 1997, is a supplement to the volumes of Mansfield's life-writing. For biographical accounts of her life, see Antony Alpers's *The Life of Katherine Mansfield*, 1980; Claire Tomalin's *Katherine Mansfield: A Secret Life*, 1988; and Angela Smith's *Katherine Mansfield: A Literary Life*, 2000.

Critical studies of Mansfield's work include Marvin Magalener's *The Fiction of Katherine Mansfield*, 1971; Ian A. Gordon's *Undiscovered Country: The New Zealand Stories of Katherine Mansfield*, 1974; Clare Hanson and Andrew Gurr's *Katherine Mansfield*, 1981; C. A. Hankin's *Katherine Mansfield and Her Confessional Stories*, 1983; Kate Fullbrook's *Katherine Mansfield*, 1986; *Critical Essays on Katherine Mansfield*, ed. Rhoda B. Nathan, 1993; *The Critical Response to Katherine Mansfield*, ed. Jan Pilditch, 1996; Patricia Moran's *Word of Mouth: Body Language in Katherine Mansfield and Vir-*

ginia Woolf, 1996; Pamela Dunbar's *Radical Mansfield: Double Discourse in Katherine Mansfield's Short Stories*, 1997; Smith's *Katherine Mansfield and Virginia Woolf: A Public of Two*, 1999; and Deborah Martinson's *In the Presence of Audience: The Self in Diaries and Fiction*, 2003.

Claude McKay

Complete Poems, ed. William J. Maxwell, was published in 2004. McKay's volumes of poetry include *Constab Ballads*, 1912; *Songs of Jamaica*, 1912; "*Spring in New Hampshire*" *and Other Poems*, 1920; and *Harlem Shadows*, 1922. Collections published posthumously include *Selected Poems*, 1953; *The Dialect Poetry*, 1972; and *The Passion of Claude McKay: Selected Poetry and Prose, 1912–1948*, ed. Wayne F. Cooper, 1973. McKay also published the collection of short stories *Gingertown*, 1932, and three novels: *Home to Harlem*, 1928; *Banjo*, 1929; and *Banana Bottom*, 1933. Posthumously published collections of stories are *Trial by Lynching: Stories about Negro Life in America*, ed. A. L. MacLeod, 1977, and *My Green Hills of Jamaica*, ed. Mervyn Morris, 1979. Essay collections include *Harlem: Negro Metropolis*, 1940, and *The Negroes in America*, 1979. McKay's autobiography, *A Long Way from Home*, was published in 1937. Biographies include James R. Giles's *Claude McKay*, 1976; Cooper's *Claude McKay: Rebel Sojourner in the Harlem Renaissance*, 1987; and Tyrone Tillery's *Claude McKay: A Black Poet's Struggle for Identity*, 1992.

Studies of McKay's work include Harold Cruse's *The Crisis of the Negro Intellectual*, 1967; Addison Gayle's *Claude McKay: The Black Poet at War*, 1972; Houston A. Baker's *Modernism and the Harlem Renaissance*, 1987; Michael North's *The Dialect of Modernism*, 1994; George Hutchinson's *The Harlem Renaissance in Black and White*, 1995; Laurence A. Breiner's *An Introduction to West Indian Poetry*, 1998; Heather Hathaway's *Caribbean Waves: Relocating Claude McKay and Paule Marshall*, 1999; Maxwell's *New Negro, Old Left*, 1999; and Winston James's *A Fierce Hatred of Injustice: Claude McKay's Jamaica and his Poetry of Rebellion*, 2001. Numerous useful essays are collected in *Claude McKay: Centennial Studies*, ed. McLeod, 1992, and useful essays appear in A. B. Christa Schwartz's *Gay Voices of the Harlem Renaissance*, 2003, and (by Maxwell) in *Left of the Color Line: Race, Radicalism, and Twentieth Century Literature of the United States*, ed. Bill V. Mullen and James Smethurst, 2003.

Modernist Manifestos

Janet Lyon's *Manifestoes: Provocations of the Modern*, 1999, provides a study of the manifesto as a genre uniquely suited to modernist politics. Helpful literary-historical introductions include Hugh Kenner's *The Pound Era*, 1971, and

Michael H. Levenson's *A Genealogy of Modernism: A Study of English Literary Doctrine, 1908–1922*, 1984. Marjorie Perloff's *The Futurist Moment: Avant-garde, Avant Guerre, and the Language of Rupture*, 1986, and Peter Nicholls's *Modernisms: A Literary Guide*, 1995, offer needed context by examining imagism and vorticism alongside surrealism, Dada, and futurism. *On Modern Poetry: Essays Presented to Donald Davie*, ed. Vereen M. Bell and Laurence Lerner, 1988, includes discussions of Loy, H. D., and Pound.

Helpful studies of imagism include Glenn Hughes's *Imagism and the Imagists: A Study in Modern Poetry*, 1931; Stanley K. Coffman's *Imagism: A Chapter for the History of Modern Poetry*, 1951; *The Imagist Poem: Modern Poetry in Miniature*, ed. William Pratt, 1963, rev. ed. 2001; *Imagist Poetry*, ed. Peter Jones, 1972; J. B. Harmer's *Victory in Limbo: Imagism, 1908–1917*, 1975; John T. Gage's *In the Arresting Eye: The Rhetoric of Imagism*, 1981; and *Homage to Imagism*, ed. Pratt and Robert Richardson, 1992.

For more on vorticism, see William Wees's *Vorticism and the English Avant-Garde*, 1972; Richard Cork's *Vorticism and Abstract Art in the First Machine Age*, 1976; Timothy Materer's *Vortex: Pound, Eliot, and Lewis*, 1979; *Blast: Vorticism 1914–1918*, ed. Paul Edwards, 2000; Paul Peppis's *Literature, Politics, and the English Avant-Garde: Nation and Empire, 1901–1918*, 2000; and Jonathan Black's *Blasting the Future!: Vorticism in Britain 1910–1920*, 2004.

Paul Muldoon

Muldoon's collected *Poems, 1968–1998* appeared in 2001; he published *Moy Sand and Gravel* in 2002. He has also published translations, including one of Nuala Ní Dhomhnaill's *The Astrakhan Cloak*, 1993, and one of Aristophanes's *The Birds*, with Richard Martin, 1999. Muldoon is editor of *The Scrake of Dawn: Poems by Young People from Northern Ireland*, 1979; *The Faber Book of Contemporary Irish Poetry*, 1986; *The Essential Byron*, 1989; and *The Faber Book of Beasts*, 1997. His lectures on Irish literature were published as *To Ireland, I*, 2000. He has also written the libretti for Daron Hagen's operas *Shining Brow*, 1993, and *Bandanna*, 1999; his play, *Six Honest Serving Men*, was published in 1995.

For an introduction to Muldoon's poetry, see Tim Kendall's *Paul Muldoon*, 1996. Studies of Muldoon's work include Clair Wills's *Improprieties: Politics and Sexuality in Northern Irish Poetry*, 1993, and *Reading Paul Muldoon*, 1998. Wills's essay in *The Chosen Ground: Essays on the Contemporary Poetry of Northern Ireland*, ed. Neil Corcoran, 1992, and a chapter in Ian Gregson's *The Male Image: Representations of Masculinity in Postwar Poetry*, 1999, are also useful.

Alice Munro

Munro's works include *"Dance of the Happy Shades" and Other Stories*, 1968; *Lives of Girls and Women: A Novel*, 1971; *Something I've Been Meaning to Tell You: Thirteen Stories*, 1974; *Who Do You Think You Are?: Stories*, 1978; *The Beggar Maid: Stories of Flo and Rose*, 1979; *The Moons of Jupiter*, 1983; *The Progress of Love*, 1986; *Friend of My Youth: Stories*, 1990; *Open Secrets: Stories*, 1994; *The Love of a Good Woman: Stories*, 1998; and *Hateship, Friendship, Courtship, Loveship, Marriage: Stories*, 2001. For Munro's life see Catherine Sheldrick Ross's *Alice Munro: A Double Life*, 1992.

Studies of Munro's work include *Probable Fictions: Alice Munro's Narrative Acts*, ed. Louis K. MacKendrick, 1983; W. R. Martin's *Alice Munro: Paradox and Parallel*, 1987; E. D. Blodgett's *Alice Munro*, 1988; Beverly Jean Rasporich's *Dance of the Sexes: Art and Gender in the Fiction of Alice Munro*, 1990; Magdalene Redekop's *Mothers and Other Clowns: The Stories of Alice Munro*, 1992; Karen E. Smythe's *Figuring Grief: Gallant, Munro, and the Poetics of Elegy*, 1992; James Carscallen's *The Other Country: Patterns in the Writing of Alice Munro*, 1993; Ajay Heble's *The Tumble of Reason: Alice Munro's Discourse of Absence*, 1994; Coral Ann Howells's *Alice Munro*, 1998; and *The Rest of the Story: Critical Essays on Alice Munro*, ed. Robert Thacker, 1999. For archival material accompanying criticism see JoAnn McCaig's *Reading In: Alice Munro's Archives*, 2002.

Les Murray

Murray's volumes of poetry include *The Ilex Tree*, with Geoffrey Lehmann, 1965; *The Weatherboard Cathedral*, 1969; *Poems against Economics*, 1972; *Lunch & Counter Lunch*, 1974; *Selected Poems: The Vernacular Republic*, 1976, rev. ed. 1982; *Ethnic Radio*, 1977; *The People's Otherworld*, 1983; *The Daylight Moon*, 1987; *Dog Fox Field*, 1990; *The Rabbiter's Bounty: Collected Poems*, 1991; *Translations from the Natural World*, 1992; *Subhuman Redneck Poems*, 1996; *Collected Poems*, 1998, rev. ed. 2002; *Conscious and Verbal*, 1999; *Learning Human: Selected Poems*, 2000; and *Poems the Size of Photographs*, 2002. Murray has also composed two verse novels, *The Boys who Stole the Funeral: a Novel Sequence*, 1980, and *Fredy Neptune: A Novel in Verse*, 1999. Murray's essays and reviews are collected in *The Peasant Mandarin: Prose Pieces*, 1978; *Persistence in Folly: Selected Prose Writings*, 1984; *Blocks and Tackles: Articles and Essays 1982–1990*, 1990; and *The Paperbark Tree: Selected Prose*, 1992. Murray is editor of *The New Oxford Book of Australian Verse*, 1986, exp. ed. 1991; *The Anthology of Australian Religious Poetry*, 1986; and *Fivefathers: Five Australian Poets of the Pre-academic Era*, 1994. Peter F. Alexander's

biography, *Les Murray: A Life in Progress*, appeared in 2000.

For an introduction to Murray's work, see Lawrence Bourke's *A Vivid Steady State: Les Murray and Australian Poetry*, 1992. Collections of essays on Murray's work include *Counterbalancing Light: Essays on Les Murray*, ed. Carmel Gaffney, 1997; *The Poetry of Les Murray: Critical Essays*, ed. Laurie Hergenhan and Bruce Clunies Ross, 2001; Steven Matthews's *Les Murray*, 2001; and *Les Murray and Australian Poetry*, ed. Angela Smith, 2002. The chapter "Crocodile Dandy: Les Murray," in Derek Walcott's *What the Twilight Says: Essays*, 1998, is also helpful. *Australian Literary Studies* 20.2, 2001, is a special issue dedicated to Murray and contains Carol Hetherington's bibliographical "Les Murray: A Selective Checklist."

V. S. Naipaul

Naipaul's novels include *The Mystic Masseur*, 1957; *The Suffrage of Elvira*, 1958; *Miguel Street*, 1959; *A House for Mr. Biswas*, 1961; *Mr. Stone and the Knights Companion*, 1963; *The Mimic Men*, 1967; *A Flag on the Island*, 1967; *In a Free State*, 1971; *Guerrillas*, 1975; *A Bend in the River*, 1979; *The Enigma of Arrival*, 1987; *A Way in the World*, 1994; and *Half a Life*, 2001. His literary essays include *Reading and Writing: A Personal Account*, 2000; *The Writer and the World: Essays*, 2002; and *Literary Occasions: Essays*, ed. Pankaj Mishra, 2003. Naipaul's journalism and travel writings include *The Middle Passage: Impressions of Five Societies, British, French and Dutch, in the West Indies and South America*, 1962; *An Area of Darkness*, 1964; *"The Return of Eva Perón," with "The Killings in Trinidad,"* 1966; *The Loss of El Dorado: A Colonial History*, 1969; *The Overcrowded Barracoon and Other Articles*, 1972; *India: A Wounded Civilization*, 1977; *Among the Believers: An Islamic Journey*, 1981; *A Turn in the South*, 1989; *India: A Million Mutinies Now*, 1990; and *Beyond Belief: Islamic Excursions among the Converted Peoples*, 1998. For his life see *Finding the Center: Two Narratives*, 1984, and *Between Father and Son: Family Letters*, ed. Gillon Aitken, 1999; Richard Michael Kelly's biography, *V. S. Naipaul*, 1989, is also useful. For a guide to secondary sources, see Kelvin Jarvis's *V. S. Naipaul: A Selective Bibliography with Annotations, 1957–1987*, 1989.

Introductions to Naipaul can be found in Paul Theroux's *V. S. Naipaul: An Introduction to His Work*, 1972, and Landeg White's *V. S. Naipaul: A Critical Introduction*, 1975. Studies of Naipaul's work include Robert D. Hamner's *V. S. Naipaul*, 1973; Peggy Nightingale's *Journey through Darkness: The Writing of V. S. Naipaul*, 1987; Peter Hughes's *V. S. Naipaul*, 1988; Rob Nixon's *London Calling: V. S. Naipaul, Postcolonial Mandarin*, 1992; Timothy Weiss's *On the Margins: The Art of Exile in V. S. Naipaul*,

1992; Bruce King's *V. S. Naipaul*, 1993; Judith Levy's *V. S. Naipaul: Displacement and Autobiography*, 1995; Helen Hayward's *The Enigma of V. S. Naipaul: Sources and Contexts*, 2002; and John Ball's *Satire and the Postcolonial Novel: V. S. Naipaul, Chinua Achebe, and Salman Rushdie*, 2003. Useful book chapters include Derek Walcott's "The Garden Path: V. S. Naipaul," in *What the Twilight Says: Essays*, 1998; Edward Said's "Among the Believers: On V. S. Naipaul," in *Reflections on Exile and Other Essays*, 2000; and "V. S. Naipaul, Modernity, and Postcolonial Excrement," in Subramanian Shankar's *Textual Traffic: Colonialism, Modernity, and the Economy of the Text*, 2001.

Nation and Language
Useful introductory collections of essays on world English include *English Literature: Opening up the Canon*, ed. Leslie A. Fiedler and Houston A. Baker, 1981, and *The Language, Ethnicity and Race Reader*, ed. Roxy Harris and Ben Rampton, 2003. I. A. Richard's *So Much Nearer: Essays toward a World English*, 1968; Richard W. Bailey's *Images of English: A Cultural History of the Language*, 1991; David Crystal's *English as a Global Language*, 1997; *The Oxford Guide to World English*, ed. Tom McArthur, 2002; and Janina Brutt-Griffler, *World English: A Study of Its Development*, 2003, provide linguistic contexts.

A book exploring the varieties of English worldwide is Braj B. Kachru's *The Other Tongue: English across Cultures*, 1982, 2nd ed. 1992, along with his *The Indianization of English: The English Language in India*, 1983. Bill Ashcroft, Gareth Griffiths, and Helen Tiffin's *The Empire Writes Back*, 2nd ed. 2002, examines the role of language in postcolonial literatures. Kwame Anthony Appiah probes the connections between language and nation in "Topologies of Nativism," reprinted in his *In My Father's House: Africa in the Philosophy of Culture*, 1992. Charles Bernstein's essay "Poetics of the Americas," reprinted in his book *My Way: Speeches and Poems*, 1999, offers an account of literary resistances to Standard English. Jed Esty's *A Shrinking Island: Modernism and National Culture in England*, 2004, explores the effects of the explosion of world literature on postimperial England.

See also **Chinua Achebe, John Agard, Louise Bennett, Kamau Brathwaite, Brian Friel, Tony Harrison, Hugh MacDiarmid, Claude McKay, Salman Rushdie,** and **Wole Soyinka.**

Ngũgĩ Wa Thiong'o
Ngũgĩ's novels in English include *Weep Not, Child*, 1964; *The River Between*, 1965; *A Grain of Wheat*, 1967; and *Petals of Blood*, 1977. *Devil on the Cross*, 1982, and *Matigari*, 1989, were written first in Gĩkũyũ. *Secret Lives*, a collection of short fiction, was published in 1975. Ngũgĩ's published plays include *The Black Hermit*,

1968; *This Time Tomorrow*, 1970; *The Trial of Dedan Kimathi*, with Micere Mugo, 1976; and *I Will Marry When I Want*, with Ngũgĩ wa Mĩrĩĩ, 1982. Ngũgĩ is a prolific essayist whose collections include *Homecoming: Essays on African and Caribbean Literature, Culture and Politics*, 1972; *Writers in Politics*, 1981, rev. ed. 1997; *Barrel of a Pen: Resistance to Oppression in Neo-Colonial Kenya*, 1983; *Decolonising the Mind: The Politics of Language in African Literature*, 1986; *Mother, Sing for Me: People's Theatre in Kenya*, with Ingrid Björkman, 1989; *Moving the Centre: The Struggle for Cultural Freedoms*, 1992; and *Penpoints, Gunpoints, and Dreams: Toward a Critical Theory of the Arts and the State in Africa*, 1998. Ngũgĩ's autobiographical writings include *Detained: A Writer's Prison Diary*, 1981, and a chapter in Wendy Lesser's *The Genius of Language: Fifteen Writers Reflect on their Mother Tongues*, 2004. *The World of Ngũgĩ wa Thiong'o*, ed. Charles Cantalupo, 1995, contains interviews with the author. See also Carol Sicherman's *Ngugi wa Thiong'o: A Bibliography of Primary and Secondary Sources, 1957–1987*, 1989.

For guides to Ngũgĩ, see *An Introduction to the Writings of Ngugi*, 1980, by G. D. Killam, who also edited *Critical Perspectives on Ngugi's wa Thiong'o*, 1984. Other studies of Ngũgĩ's works include Clifford B. Robson, *Ngugi wa Thiong'o*, 1979; David Cook, *Ngũgĩ wa Thiong'o: An Exploration of his Writings*, 1983, 2nd. ed. 1997; *Ngũgĩ wa Thiong'o: Texts and Contexts*, ed. Cantalupo, 1995; Patrick Williams, *Ngugi wa Thiong'o*, 1998; Simon Gikandi, *Ngugi wa Thiong'o*, 2000; Oliver Lovesey, *Ngũgĩ wa Thiong'o*, 2000; and *Critical Essays on Ngũgĩ wa Thiong'o*, ed. Peter Nazareth, 2000.

George Orwell
The standard edition of Orwell's work is *The Complete Works of George Orwell*, 20 vols., ed. Peter Davison with Ian Angus and Sheila Davison, 1998. Orwell is best-known for two works of fiction: *Animal Farm*, 1945, and *Nineteen Eighty-four*, 1949. Orwell's other fiction includes the autobiographical novels *Down and Out in Paris and London: A Novel*, 1933, and *Burmese Days: A Novel*, 1934, as well as *A Clergyman's Daughter*, 1935; *Keep the Aspidistra Flying*, 1936; and *Coming Up for Air*, 1939. Other nonfiction works also based on his experiences include *The Road to Wigan Pier*, 1937, and *Homage to Catalonia*, 1938. Orwell's collections of essays include *Inside the Whale and Other Essays*, 1940; *The Lion and the Unicorn: Socialism and the English Genius*, 1941; *Shooting an Elephant*, 1950; *England Your England*, 1953; and *Such, Such Were the Joys*, 1953. *Collected Essays, Journalism and Letters*, 4 vols., ed. Angus and Sonia Orwell, was first published in 1968. For his life see Bernard Crick's *George Orwell: A Life*, 1980; Michael Shelden's *Orwell: The*

Authorised Biography, 1991; Peter Davison's *Orwell: A Literary Life*, 1996; and Gordon Bowker's *Inside George Orwell*, 2003. Gillian Fenwick's *George Orwell: A Bibliography*, 1998, is also quite useful for secondary sources.

Studies of Orwell's work include George Woodcock's *The Crystal Spirit: A Study of George Orwell*, 1966; *The World of George Orwell*, ed. Miriam Gross, 1971; *George Orwell: A Collection of Critical Essays*, ed. Raymond Williams, 1974; *George Orwell: The Critical Heritage*, ed. Jeffrey Meyers, 1975; *Critical Essays on George Orwell*, ed. Bernard Oldsey and Joseph Browne, 1986; Patrick Reilly's *George Orwell: The Age's Adversary*, 1986; *George Orwell*, ed. Harold Bloom, 1987; Alok Rai's *Orwell and the Politics of Despair: A Critical Study of the Writings of George Orwell*, 1988; *George Orwell*, ed. Graham Holderness, Bryan Loughrey, and Nahem Yousaf, 1998; John Newsinger's *Orwell's Politics*, 1999; Christopher Hitchens's *Why Orwell Matters*, 2002; Anthony Stewart's *George Orwell, Doubleness, and the Value of Decency*, 2003; and James M. Decker's *Ideology*, 2004. Edward Said's chapter "Tourism among the Dogs: On George Orwell," in *Reflections on Exile and Other Essays*, 2000, is also useful.

Many of the aforementioned works contain material on *Animal Farm*, but for further reading on this piece, see Richard I. Smyer's *Animal Farm: Pastoralism and Politics*, 1988; *George Orwell's* Animal Farm, ed. Harold Bloom, 1998; and *Readings on* Animal Farm, ed. Terry O'Neill, 1998. For further reading on *Nineteen Eighty-four* see *Twentieth Century Interpretations of 1984: A Collection of Critical Essays*, ed. Samuel Hynes, 1971; William Steinhoff's *The Origins of 1984*, 1975; *1984 Revisited: Totalitarianism in Our Century*, ed. Irving Howe, 1983; *George Orwell's 1984*, ed. Harold Bloom, 1987; Peter Buitenhuis and Ira B. Nadel's *George Orwell: A Reassessment*, 1988; *The Orwellian Moment: Hindsight and Foresight in a Post-1984 World*, ed. Robert L. Savage, James Combs, and Dan Nimmo, 1989; and Reilly's *Nineteen Eighty-Four: Past, Present, and Future*, 1989.

Wilfred Owen
The Complete Poems and Fragments of Wilfred Owen, 2 vols., 1984, and *The Poems of Wilfred Owen*, 1985, both edited by Jon Stallworthy, are the standard scholarly edition and the standard reader's edition, respectively. The *Collected Letters*, ed. Harold Owen and John Bell, was published in 1967; Bell also edited *Selected Letters*, 1985. For his life see Stallworthy's *Wilfred Owen*, 1974; Harold Owen's *Journey from Obscurity: Memoirs of the Owen Family*, 3 vols., 1963–65; and Dominic Hibberd's *Wilfred Owen: A New Biography*, 2002. William White's *Wilfred Owen (1893–1918): A Bibliography* was published in 1967.

For an introduction to Owen see Stallworthy's *Great Poets of World War I: Poetry from the Great War*, 2002. Studies of Owen's work include Gertrude M. White's *Wilfred Owen*, 1969; Arthur E. Lane's *An Adequate Response: The War Poetry of Wilfred Owen and Siegfried Sassoon*, 1972; Dennis Welland's *Wilfred Owen: A Critical Study*, rev. ed. 1978; Sven Bäckman's *Tradition Transformed: Studies in the Poetry of Wilfred Owen*, 1979; Desmond Graham's *The Truth of War: Owen, Blunden and Rosenberg*, 1984; Hibberd's *Owen the Poet*, 1986; Adrian Caesar's *Taking It like a Man: Suffering, Sexuality, and the War Poets: Brooke, Sassoon, Owen, Graves*, 1993; Douglas Kerr's *Wilfred Owen's Voices: Language and Community*, 1993; John Purkis's *A Preface to Wilfred Owen*, 1999; and *Poets of WWI: Wilfred Owen and Isaac Rosenberg*, ed. Harold Bloom, 2002. Discussions of Owen's work can also be found in Jon Silkin's *Out of Battle: The Poetry of the Great War*, 1972, 2nd ed. 1998; Jahan Ramazani's *Poetry of Mourning: The Modern Elegy from Hardy to Heaney*, 1994; Patrick J. Quinn's *Recharting the Thirties*, 1996; and *The Literature of the Great War Reconsidered: Beyond Modern Memory*, ed. Quinn and Steven Trout, 2001.

Harold Pinter
Pinter's plays, poetry, and selected prose have been published in paperback as *Complete Works*, 4 vols., 1976–81; and in *Collected Poems and Prose*, 1986. *Collected Screenplays*, 2000, includes *The Proust Screenplay: À la recherche du temps perdu*, written with Joseph Losey and Barbara Bray, 1977, and *The French Lieutenant's Woman and Other Screenplays*, 1982. Pinter's dramatic works include *The Caretaker* and *The Dumb Waiter: Two Plays*, 1960; *The Birthday Party* and *The Room: Two Plays*, 1961; *Three Plays: A Slight Ache, The Collection, The Dwarfs*, 1962; *The Homecoming*, 1966; *The Lover, Tea Party, The Basement: Two Plays and a Film Script*, 1967; *A Night Out: Night School, Revue Sketches: Early Plays*, 1967; *Landscape and Silence*, 1970; *Old Times*, 1971; *Five Screenplays*, 1973; *No Man's Land*, 1975; *Betrayal*, 1978; *The Hothouse: A Play*, 1980; *Other Places: Three Plays*, 1983; *Mountain Language*, 1988; *The Heat of the Day*, 1989; *The Dwarfs: A Novel*, 1990; *Party Time*, 1991; *Moonlight*, 1993; *Ashes to Ashes*, 1996. His nonfiction includes *Various Voices: Prose, Poetry, and Politics*, 1998. For Pinter's life see *Conversations with Pinter*, ed. Mel Gussow, 1994, or Michael Billington's *The Life and Work of Harold Pinter*, 1996. Steven H. Gale published *Harold Pinter: An Annotated Bibliography* in 1978.

The Cambridge Companion to Harold Pinter, ed. Peter Raby, 2001, is a good introduction to Pinter's work. Critical studies include Walter Kerr's *Harold Pinter*, 1967; Lois G. Gordon's *Stratagems to Uncover Nakedness: The Dramas* of Harold Pinter, 1969; Martin Esslin's The Peopled Wound: The Work of Harold Pinter, 1970; James R. Hollis's Harold Pinter: The Poetics of Silence, 1970; Pinter: A Collection of Critical Essays, ed. Arthur Ganz, 1972; Ronald Hayman's Harold Pinter, 1973; Simon Trussler's The Plays of Harold Pinter: An Assessment, 1973; William Baker and Stephen Ely Tabachnick's Harold Pinter, 1973; Austin E. Quigley's The Pinter Problem, 1975; Esslin's Pinter: A Study of His Plays, exp. 2nd ed. 1976; Bernard F. Dukore's Where Laughter Stops: Pinter's Tragicomedy, 1976; Gale's Butter's Going Up: A Critical Analysis of Harold Pinter's Work, 1977; Guido Almansi and Simon Henderson's Harold Pinter, 1983; Harold Pinter: Critical Approaches, 1986, and Critical Essays on Harold Pinter, 1990, both edited by Gale; Harold Pinter: A Casebook, ed. Gordon, 1990; Victor L. Cahn's Gender and Power in the Plays of Harold Pinter, 1993; Marc Silverstein's Harold Pinter and the Language of Cultural Power, 1993; Pinter at Sixty, ed. Katherine H. Burkman and John L. Kundert-Gibbs, 1993; Penelope Prentice's The Pinter Ethic: The Erotic Aesthetic, 1994; Stephen Watt's Postmodern/drama: Reading the Contemporary Stage, 1998; Raymond Armstrong's Kafka and Pinter: Shadow-Boxing: The Struggle between Father and Son, 1999; Pinter at 70: A Casebook, ed. Gordon, 2001; and Gale's Sharp Cut: Harold Pinter's Screenplays and the Artistic Process, 2002.

A. K. Ramanujan

The Collected Poems of A. K. Ramanujan was published in 1995; The Collected Essays of A. K. Ramanujan, ed. Vinay Dharwadker and Stuart H. Blackburn, in 1999. Uncollected Poems and Prose, ed. Molly Daniels-Ramanujan and Keith Harrison, was published in 2001. A Flowering Tree and Other Oral Tales from India, ed. Blackburn and Alan Dundes, was published in 1997. Ramanujan published many important translations from Tamil and Kannada, including The Interior Landscape: Love Poems from a Classical Tamil Anthology, 1967; Speaking of Siva, 1973; Hymns for the Drowning: Poems for Visnu, 1981; and Poems of Love and War: From the Eight Anthologies and the Ten Long Poems of Classical Tamil, 1985. He is coeditor, with Blackburn, of Another Harmony: New Essays on the Folklore of India, 1986; editor of Folktales from India: A Selection of Oral Tales from Twenty-Two Languages, 1991; coeditor and cotranslator, with Velcheru Narayana Rao and David Dean Shulman, of When God Is a Customer: Telugu Courtesan Songs, 1994; and coeditor, with Dharwadker, of The Oxford Anthology of Modern Indian Poetry, 1994.

A. N. Dwivedi has published two studies of Ramanujan's work: A. K. Ramanujan and His Poetry, 1983, and The Poetic Art of A. K. Ramanujan, 1995. Other studies of Ramanujan's

poetry include Emmanuel Narendra Lall's The Poetry of Encounter: Three Indo-Anglian Poets: Dom Moraes, A. K. Ramanujan, and Nissim Ezekiel, 1983; Bruce King's Modern Poetry in English, 1987, rev. ed. 2001, and his Three Indian Poets: Nissim Ezekiel, A. K. Ramanujan, Dom Moraes, 1991; Dharwadker's introduction to Collected Poems; Shirish Chindhade's Five Indian Poets: Nissim Ezekiel, A. K. Ramanujan, Arun Kolatkar, Dilip Chitre, R. Parthasarathy, 1996; and Jahan Ramazani's The Hybrid Muse: Postcolonial Poetry in English, 2001.

Henry Reed

Reed's Collected Poems, edited with a biographical and critical introduction by Jon Stallworthy 1991, contains not only the contents of his one published volume of poetry, A Map of Verona, 1946, but also many uncollected and unpublished poems. The best of his radio plays are to be found in The Streets of Pompeii and Other Plays for Radio, 1971, and Hilda Tablet and Others: Four Pieces for Radio, 1971. Studies of Reed's poetry include James S. Beggs's The Poetic Character of Henry Reed, 1999, and the chapter "Henry Reed and Others," in Vernon Scannell's Not without Glory: Poets of the Second World War, 1976.

Jean Rhys

Rhys's first collection of short stories is The Left Bank and Other Stories, with an introduction by Ford Madox Ford, 1927. Her second collection, Postures, 1928, is best-known as the novel Quartet, under which title it was republished in 1957. Rhys's other works include After Leaving Mr. Mackenzie, 1931; Voyage in the Dark, 1934; Good Morning, Midnight, 1938; and Wide Sargasso Sea, 1966, which appeared with notes, essays, and contextual documents in Judith Raiskin's Norton Critical Edition in 1999. The Collected Short Stories was published in 1987 and includes stories from Tigers Are Better-Looking, 1968; My Day: Three Pieces, 1974; and Sleep It Off, Lady, 1976. Smile Please: An Unfinished Autobiography was published posthumously in 1979. A selection of her letters, The Letters of Jean Rhys, ed. Francis Wyndham and Diana Melly, was published in 1984. For her life see Carole Angier's Jean Rhys: Life and Work, 1990, and Elaine Savory's Jean Rhys, 1998. Elgin W. Mellown's Jean Rhys: A Descriptive and Annotated Bibliography, 1984, is a useful reference source.

Studies of Rhys's work include Thomas F. Staley's Jean Rhys: A Critical Study, 1979; Peter Wolfe's Jean Rhys, 1980; Judith Kegan Gardiner's Rhys, Stead, Lessing and the Politics of Empathy, 1989; Coral Ann Howells's Jean Rhys, 1991; George B. Handley's Postslavery Literatures in the Americas: Family Portraits in Black and White, 2000; and Delia Caparoso Konzett's Ethnic Modernisms: Anzia Yezierska, Zora Neale Hurston, Jean Rhys, and the Aesthetics of Dislo-

cation, 2002. For readings of Rhys as a specifically Caribbean writer, see Louis James's *Jean Rhys*, 1978; Margaret Paul Joseph's *Caliban in Exile: The Outsider in Caribbean Fiction*, 1992; and Mervyn Morris's *"Is English We Speaking" and Other Essays*, 1999. Helen Nebeker's *Jean Rhys, Woman in Passage: A Critical Study of the Novels of Jean Rhys*, 1981; Nancy R. Harrison's *Jean Rhys and the Novel as Women's Text*, 1988; and Deborah Kelly Kloepfer's *The Unspeakable Mother: Forbidden Discourse in Jean Rhys and H. D*, 1989, offer feminist perspectives on Rhys's work. For analysis of the shorter fiction, see Cheryl Alexander Malcolm and David Malcolm's *Jean Rhys: A Study of the Short Fiction*, 1996. For further reading concerning *Wide Sargasso Sea*, see Selma James's *The Ladies and the Mammies: Jane Austen and Jean Rhys*, 1983, and Veronica Marie Gregg's *Jean Rhys's Historical Imagination: Reading and Writing the Creole*, 1995.

Isaac Rosenberg

The Collected Works of Isaac Rosenberg: Poetry, Prose, Letters, Paintings and Drawings, ed. Ian Parsons, 1979, with a foreword by Siegfried Sassoon, is the standard edition of Rosenberg's work. *Isaac Rosenberg: Selected Poems and Letters*, ed. Jean Liddiard, was published in 2003. Rosenberg's play, *Moses*, was published in 1916. Biographies include Liddiard's *Isaac Rosenberg: The Half Used Life*, 1975; Jean Moorcroft Wilson's *Isaac Rosenberg, Poet and Painter: A Biography*, 1975; Joseph Cohen's *Journey to the Trenches: The Life of Isaac Rosenberg, 1890–1918*, 1975; and Deborah Maccoby's *God Made Blind: Isaac Rosenberg, His Life and Poetry*, 1999.

For studies of Rosenberg's work see D. W. Harding's *Experience into Words: Essays on Poetry*, 1963; John H. Johnston's *English Poetry of the First World War: A Study in the Evolution of Lyric and Narrative Form*, 1964; Jon Silkin's *Out of Battle: The Poetry of the Great War*, 1972, 2nd ed. 1998; Desmond Graham's *The Truth of War: Owen, Rosenberg and Blunden*, 1984; Frank Field's *British and French Writers of the First World War: Comparative Studies in Cultural History*, 1991; *British Poets of the Great War: Brooke, Rosenberg, Thomas: A Documentary Volume*, ed. Patrick Quinn, 2000; Jon Stallworthy's *Great Poets of World War I: Poetry from the Great War*, 2002; and *Poets of WWI: Wilfred Owen & Isaac Rosenberg*, ed. Harold Bloom, 2002. Diana Collecott's essay "Isaac Rosenberg (1890–1913): A Cross-Cultural Study," in *The Jewish East End, 1840–1939*, ed. Aubrey Newman, 1981, is also useful.

Salman Rushdie

Rushdie's first full-length work of fiction, *Grimus*, 1975, was followed by *Midnight's Children*, 1980; *Shame*, 1983; *The Satanic Verses*, 1988; *The Moor's Last Sigh*, 1995; *The Ground beneath Her Feet*, 1999; and *Fury*, 2001. He also has written the children's novel *Haroun and the Sea of Stories*, 1990, and the volume of short fiction *East, West: Stories*, 1994. Rushdie's nonfiction includes *The Jaguar Smile: A Nicaraguan Journey*, 1987; *In Good Faith*, 1990; *The Wizard of Oz*, 1992; and the collections *Imaginary Homelands: Essays and Criticism, 1981–1991*, 1991, and *Step across This Line: Collected Nonfiction 1992–2002*, 2002. With Elizabeth West, Rushdie is coeditor of *Mirrorwork: Fifty Years of Indian Writing, 1947–1997*, 1997. For biographical material and the author's perspective on his work, see *Conversations with Salman Rushdie*, ed. Michael Reder, 2000, and *Salman Rushdie Interviews: A Sourcebook of His Ideas*, ed. Pradyumna S. Chauhan, 2001. Joel Kuortti's *The Salman Rushdie Bibliography: A Bibliography of Salman Rushdie's Work and Rushdie Criticism*, 1997, is a helpful guide to primary and secondary sources.

Studies of Rushdie's works include Timothy Brennan's *Salman Rushdie and the Third World*, 1989; *The Rushdie File*, ed. Lisa Appignanesi and Sara Maitland, 1989; Malise Ruthven's *A Satanic Affair: Salman Rushdie and the Rage of Islam*, 1990; James Harrison's *Salman Rushdie*, 1992; Catherine Cundy's *Salman Rushdie*, 1996; D. C. R. A. Goonetilleke's *Salman Rushdie*, 1998; *Critical Essays on Salman Rushdie*, ed. M. Keith Booker, 1999; and Sabrina Hassumani's *Salman Rushdie: A Postmodern Reading of His Major Works*, 2002. Criticism of Rushdie's work from a postcolonial perspective includes Fawzia Afzal-Khan's *Cultural Imperialism and the Indo-English Novel: Genre and Ideology in R. K. Narayan, Anita Desai, Kamala Markandaya, and Salman Rushdie*, 1993; Michael Gorra's *After Empire: Scott, Naipaul, Rushdie*, 1997; Anuradha Dingwaney Needham's *Using the Master's Tools: Resistance and the Literature of the African and South-Asian Diasporas*, 2000; Jaina C. Sanga's *Salman Rushdie's Postcolonial Metaphors: Migration, Translation, Hybridity, Blasphemy, and Globalization*, 2001; Deepika Bahri's *Native Intelligence: Aesthetics, Politics, and Postcolonial Literature*, 2003; John Clement Ball's *Satire and the Postcolonial Novel: V. S. Naipaul, Chinua Achebe, Salman Rushdie*, 2003; and Alexandra W. Schultheis's *Regenerative Fictions: Postcolonialism, Psychoanalysis, and the Nation as Family*, 2004.

Siegfried Sassoon

Sassoon's *Collected Poems, 1908–1956* was published in 1961 and reprinted in 1984; the selection *The War Poems of Siegfried Sassoon*, ed. Rupert Hart-Davis, was published in 1983. Sassoon is also author of six volumes of autobiographical prose; the first three semifictional volumes, *Memoirs of a Fox-Hunting Man*, 1928; *Memoirs of an Infantry Officer*, 1930; and *Sher-*

ston's *Progress*, 1936, were collectively published in 1937 as *The Memoirs of George Sherston*; Sassoon followed these with *The Old Century and Seven More Years*, 1938; *In the Weald of Youth*, 1942; and *Siegfried's Journey*, 1945. Hart-Davis edited Sassoon's *Diaries, 1920–1922*, 1981; *Diaries, 1915–1918*, 1983; and *Diaries, 1923–1925*, 1985, as well as Sassoon's letters in *Siegfried Sassoon: Letters to Max Beerbohm: With a Few Answers*, 1986. Michael Thorpe edited *Letters to a Critic*, 1976. The first volume of Jean Moorcroft Wilson's biography, *Siegfried Sassoon: The Making of a War Poet: A Biography (1886–1918)*, was published in 1998, and her *Siegfried Sassoon: The Journey from the Trenches: A Biography (1918–1967)*, appeared in 2003. Geoffrey Keynes's *A Bibliography of Siegfried Sassoon* was published in 1962.

For studies of Sassoon's poetry see Bernard Bergonzi's *Heroes' Twilight: A Study of the Literature of the Great War*, 1966; John H. Johnston's *English Poetry of the First World War: A Study in the Evolution of Lyric and Narrative Form*, 1964; Arthur E. Lane's *An Adequate Response: The War Poetry of Wilfred Owen and Siegfried Sassoon*, 1972; Jon Silkin's *Out of Battle: The Poetry of the Great War*, 1972, 2nd ed. 1998; John Lehmann's *The English Poets of the First World War*, 1981; Adrian Caesar's *Taking It like a Man: Suffering, Sexuality, and the War Poets: Brooke, Sassoon, Owen, Graves*, 1993; Patrick J. Quinn's *The Great War and the Missing Muse: The Early Writings of Robert Graves and Siegfried Sassoon*, 1994; Paul Moeyes's *Siegfried Sassoon, Scorched Glory: A Critical Study*, 1997; Patrick Campbell's *Siegfried Sassoon: A Study of the War Poetry*, 1999; Jon Stallworthy's *Great Poets of World War I: Poetry from the Great War*, 2002; and *Poets of World War I: Rupert Brooke & Siegfried Sassoon*, ed. Harold Bloom, 2003. For further discussions of Sassoon's diaries and prose works, see Thorpe's *Siegfried Sassoon: A Critical Study*, 1966, and Paul Fussell's *The Great War and Modern Memory*, 1975.

Edith Sitwell

Sitwell's more than thirty volumes of poetry were assembled as *Collected Poems* first in 1954 and then again in 1967; *The Early Unpublished Poems*, ed. Gerald W. Morton and Karen P. Helgeson, was published in 1994. A volume of *Selected Poems*, with an introduction by John Lehmann, was published in 1965. Important works of criticism include *Alexander Pope*, 1930; *The English Eccentrics*, 1933, rev. ed. 1957; *Aspects of Modern Poetry*, 1934; and *A Poet's Notebook*, 1943. Richard Greene edited *Selected Letters of Edith Sitwell*, 1997. For her life see Sitwell's *Taken Care Of: An Autobiography*, 1965; biographies include Geoffrey Elborn's *Edith Sitwell: A Biography*, 1981, and Victoria Glendinning's *Edith Sitwell: A Unicorn*

among Lions, 1981. Portraits of the Sitwell family can be found in Elizabeth Salter's *The Last Years of a Rebel: A Memoir of Edith Sitwell*, 1967; other biographies of the Sitwell family include Lehmann's *A Nest of Tigers: The Sitwells in Their Times*, 1968; John Pearson's *Façades: Edith, Osbert, and Sacheverell Sitwell*, 1978; and G. A. Cevasco's *The Sitwells: Edith, Osbert, and Sacheverell*, 1987. Bibliographic information is available in Richard Fifoot's *A Bibliography of Edith, Osbert, and Sacheverell Sitwell*, 1971.

Studies of Sitwell's work includes Lehmann's *Edith Sitwell*, 1952; Geoffrey Singleton's *Edith Sitwell: The Hymn to Life*, 1960; Ralph J. Mills's *Edith Sitwell: A Critical Essay*, 1966; J. D. Brophy's *Edith Sitwell: The Symbolist Order*, 1968; and John Press's *A Map of Modern English Verse*, 1969. Useful essays include Kenneth Rexroth's "Poets Old and New: Edith Sitwell," in *Assays*, 1961, and two chapters dedicated to Sitwell in Susan Kavaler-Adler's *The Compulsion to Create: A Psychoanalytic Study of Women Artists*, 1993.

Stevie Smith

The Collected Poems of Stevie Smith, ed. James MacGibbon, was published in 1975 and contains many of Smith's drawings. Other works are available in *Me Again: Uncollected Writings*, ed. Jack Barbera and William McBrien, 1981. Smith also published three novels: *Novel on Yellow Paper*, 1936; *Over the Frontier*, 1938; and *The Holiday*, 1949. Short prose is collected in *A Very Pleasant Evening with Stevie Smith: Selected Short Prose*, 1995, and drawings in *Some Are More Human than Others: A Sketchbook*, 1958. For her life see Barbera and McBrien's *Stevie: A Biography of Stevie Smith*, 1985, and Frances Spalding's *Stevie Smith*, 1989. Interviews appear in *The Poet Speaks: Interviews with Contemporary Poets Conducted by Hilary Morrish, Peter Orr, John Press and Ian Scott-Kilvert*, ed. Peter Orr, 1966, and Kay Dick's *Ivy and Stevie: Ivy Compton-Burnett and Stevie Smith: Conversations and Reflections*, 1971. Barbera, McBrien, and Helen Bajan compiled *Stevie Smith: A Bibliography* in 1987.

Studies of Smith's work include Arthur C. Rankin's *The Poetry of Stevie Smith, "Little Girl Lost,"* 1985; Sanford Sternlicht's *Stevie Smith*, 1990, and *In Search of Stevie Smith*, 1991; Catherine A. Civello's *Patterns of Ambivalence: The Fiction and Poetry of Stevie Smith*, 1997; and Laura Severin's *Stevie Smith's Resistant Antics*, 1997. Other discussions of her work can be found in chapters of Calvin Bedient's *Eight Contemporary Poets: Charles Tomlinson, Donald Davie, R. S. Thomas, Philip Larkin, Ted Hughes, Thomas Kinsella, Stevie Smith, W. S. Graham*, 1974; Seamus Heaney's *Preoccupations: Selected Prose, 1968–1978*, 1980; Philip Larkin's *Required Writing: Miscellaneous Pieces*,

1955–1982, 1983; Christopher Ricks's *The Force of Poetry*, 1984; Gill Plain's *Women's Fiction of the Second World War: Gender, Power, and Resistance*, 1996; Jacqueline Rose's essay on Smith and Virginia Woolf in *Between "Race" and Culture: Representations of "the Jew" in English and American Literature*, ed. Bryan Cheyette, 1996; and Laura Severin's *Poetry Off the Page: Twentieth-Century British Women Poets in Performance*, 2004.

Wole Soyinka

Soyinka's volumes of poetry include *"Idanre" and Other Poems*, 1967; *Poems from Prison*, 1969, expanded as *A Shuttle in the Crypt*, 1972; *Ogun Abibiman*, 1976; and *"Mandela's Earth" and Other Poems*, 1988. Oxford published a selection of Soyinka's plays, *Collected Plays*, 2 vols., 1973–74, which includes *The Lion and the Jewel*, 1959; *The Swamp Dwellers*, 1959; *A Dance of the Forests*, 1960; *The Strong Breed*, 1963; *The Trials of Brother Jero*, 1963; *The Road*, 1965; *Kongi's Harvest*, 1966; *Madmen and Specialists*, 1970; *The Bacchae of Euripides: A Communion Rite*, 1973; and *Jero's Metamorphosis*, 1973. Other major plays include *Camwood on the Leaves*, 1960; *Death and the King's Horseman*, 1975, also available in a Norton Critical Edition, ed. Simon Gikandi, 2003; *Opera Wonyosi*, 1981; *A Play of Giants*, 1984; *From Zia, with Love*, 1992; and *The Beatification of Area Boy: A Lagosian Kaleidoscope*, 1995. Soyinka is also the author of two novels—*The Interpreters*, 1965, and *Season of Anomy*, 1973— and he has written scripts for radio, television, and film. Works dealing with the politics of Nigeria include his prison diary, *The Man Died: Prison Notes*, 1972, and his lectures in *The Open Sore of a Continent: A Personal Narrative of the Nigerian Crisis*, 1996. Other prose works include *Myth, Literature, and the African World*, 1976; the autobiographical *Aké: The Years of Childhood*, 1981; *The Critic and Society: Barthes, Leftocracy and Other Mythologies*, 1982; *Art, Dialogue and Outrage: Essays on Literature and Culture*, 1988; his 1986 Nobel lecture, *This Past Must Address Its Present*, 1988; *Isara, A Voyage Around Essay*, 1989; *Ibadan: The Penkelemes Years: A Memoir: 1946–1965*, 1994; and *The Burden of Memory, The Muse of Forgiveness*, 1999. Soyinka has also edited the anthology *Poems of Black Africa*, 1975. Biodun Jeyifo edited a book of interviews, *Conversations with Wole Soyinka*, in 2001. B. M. Okpu's *Wole Soyinka: A Bibliography* was published in 1984; James Gibbs, Ketu H. Katrak, and Henry Louis Gates Jr.'s *Wole Soyinka: A Bibliography of Primary and Secondary Sources* appeared in 1986.

For guides to Soyinka see K. L. Goodwin's *Understanding African Poetry: A Study of Ten Poets*, 1982; Obi Maduakor's *Wole Soyinka: An Introduction to His Writing*, 1986; and Aderemi Bamikunle's *Introduction to Soyinka's Poetry:*

Analysis of A Shuttle in the Crypt, 1991. Studies of Soyinka's work include Gerald Moore's *Wole Soyinka* 1971, 2nd ed. 1978; Gibbs's *Wole Soyinka*, 1986; Eldred D. Jones's *The Writing of Wole Soyinka*, 3rd ed. 1988; Akomaye Oko's *The Tragic Paradox: A Study of Wole Soyinka and His Works*, 1992; Derek Wright's *Wole Soyinka Revisited*, 1993; Tanure Ojaide's *The Poetry of Wole Soyinka*, 1994; and Tunde Adeniran's *The Politics of Wole Soyinka*, 1994. Collections of essays dedicated to Soyinka include *Critical Perspectives on Wole Soyinka*, ed. Gibbs, 1980; *Before Our Very Eyes: Tribute to Wole Soyinka*, ed. Dapo Adelugba, 1987; *Research on Wole Soyinka*, ed. Bernth Lindfors and Gibbs, 1993; *Soyinka: A Collection of Critical Essays*, ed. Oyin Ogunba, 1994; and Jeyifo's *Perspectives on Wole Soyinka: Freedom and Complexity*, 2001. Other useful discussions of Soyinka's work include Nyong J. Udoeyop's *Three Nigerian Poets: A Critical Study of the Poetry of Soyinka, Clark, and Okigbo*, 1973; Kole Omotoso's *Achebe or Soyinka?: A Study in Contrasts*, 1996; Chii P. Akporji's *Figures in a Dance: The Theater of Yeats and Soyinka*, 2003; and Olakunle George's *Relocating Agency: Modernity and African Letters*, 2003.

Tom Stoppard

Stoppard's published plays include *Rosencrantz and Guildenstern Are Dead*, 1967; *The Real Inspector Hound*, 1968; *Enter a Free Man*, 1968; *Albert's Bridge*, 1969; *If You're Glad I'll Be Frank*, 1969; *A Separate Peace*, 1969; *After Magritte*, 1971; *Jumpers*, 1972; *Artist Descending a Staircase*, 1973; *Where Are They Now?*, 1973; *Travesties*, 1974; *Dirty Linen*, 1976; *New-Found-Land*, 1976; *The Fifteen Minute Hamlet*, 1976; *Every Good Boy Deserves Favour*, 1978; *Professional Foul*, 1978; *Night and Day*, 1978; *On the Razzle*, 1981; *The Real Thing*, 1982; *Rough Crossing*, 1985; *Dalliance*, 1986; *Hapgood*, 1988; *Arcadia*, 1993; *Indian Ink*, 1995; *The Seagull*, 1997; *The Invention of Love*, 1997; and *The Coast of Utopia*, 2002. He has also published screenplays, radio and television plays, opera libretti, a novel, and short stories. Ira Nadel's *Tom Stoppard: A Life*, 2002, is the standard biography. Interviews can be found in Paul Delaney, *Tom Stoppard in Conversation*, 1994, and Mel Gussow, *Conversations with Stoppard*, 1995.

Critical studies of his works include C. W. E. Bigsby, *Tom Stoppard*, 1976; Ronald Hayman, *Tom Stoppard*, 1977; Victor L. Cahn, *Beyond Absurdity: The Plays of Tom Stoppard*, 1979; Felicia Hardison Londré, *Tom Stoppard*, 1981; David Bratt, *Tom Stoppard: A Reference Guide*, 1982; Susan Rusinko, *Tom Stoppard*, 1986; Anthony Jenkins, *The Theatre of Tom Stoppard*, 1987, 2nd ed. 1989; Jim Hunter, *Tom Stoppard*, 2000; and *Tom Stoppard*, ed. Harold Bloom, 2003. For Studies of *Arcadia*, see Jeffrey and

Prapassaree Kramer's article "Stoppard's *Arcadia*: Research, Time, Loss" in *Modern Drama* 40.1, 1997; Paul Edwards's chapter "Science in *Hapgood* and *Arcadia*" in *The Cambridge Companion to Tom Stoppard*, ed. Katherine E. Kelly, 2001; and Shaun McCarthy's *Arcadia*, 2001.

Dylan Thomas
Collected Poems, ed. Walford Davies and Ralph Maud, 1988, is the standard edition of Thomas's poetry. *Dylan Thomas Selected Poems, 1934–1952* was published in 2003. Thomas also wrote the autobiographical prose work *Portrait of the Artist as a Young Dog*, 1940; a radio play, *Under Milk Wood: A Play for Voices*, 1954; *Quite Early One Morning*, 1954, a collection of stories, essays, and minor pieces broadcast over BBC; and the short-fiction collection *Adventures in the Skin Trade and Other Stories*, 1955. Maud edited *The Notebooks of Dylan Thomas*, 1967; Paul Ferris edited *The Collected Letters of Dylan Thomas*, 1985; and Peter Lynch edited *The Love-Letters of Dylan Thomas*, 2001. For his life see Constantine FitzGibbon's *The Life of Dylan Thomas*, 1965; Ferris's *Dylan Thomas: The Biography*, 1977, 2nd ed. 1999; and Andrew Sinclair's *Dylan the Bard: A Life of Dylan Thomas*, 1999. Bill Read's *The Days of Dylan Thomas*, 1964, supplements a straightforward narrative with many photographs.

For introductions to Thomas see William York Tindall's *A Reader's Guide to Dylan Thomas*, 1962, 3rd ed. 1996; Maud's *Entrances to Dylan Thomas' Poetry*, 1963, and *Where Have All the Old Words Got Me?: Explications of Dylan Thomas's Collected Poems*, 2003; William T. Moynahan's *The Craft and Art of Dylan Thomas*, 1966; and John Ackerman's *A Dylan Thomas Companion*, 1991. For criticism of Thomas's work see C. B. Cox's *Dylan Thomas: A Collection of Critical Essays*, 1966; R. B. Kershner's *Dylan Thomas*, 1976; *Critical Essays on Dylan Thomas*, ed. Georg Gaston, 1989; Barbara Hardy's *Dylan Thomas: An Original Language*, 2000; and *Dylan Thomas*, ed. John Goodby and Chris Wigginton, 2001.

Edward Thomas
The Collected Poems of Edward Thomas, ed. R. George Thomas, was published in 1978. Thomas's prose can be found in *A Language Not to Be Betrayed: Selected Prose of Edward Thomas*, ed. Edna Longley, 1981. R. George Thomas edited *Selected Letters*, 1995, and *Letters from Edward Thomas to Gordon Bottomley*, 1968. The *Diary of Edward Thomas: 1 January–8 April 1917*, with an introduction by Roland Gant, was published in 1977. Thomas's accounts of his travels around England include *Oxford*, illustrated by John Fulleylove, 1903; *The South Country*, 1909; and *A Literary Pilgrim in England*, 1917. For his life see *As It Was*, 1927, and *World without End*, 1956, both by his wife, Helen Thomas. The first book of Eleanor Farjeon's *Memoirs*, *Edward Thomas: The Last Four Years*, 1958; R. George Thomas's *Edward Thomas: A Portrait*, 1985; and William Cooke's *Edward Thomas: A Critical Biography 1878–1917*, 1970, are all quite helpful. An autobiographical fragment, *The Childhood of Edward Thomas*, was published in 1983 with a preface by Roland Gant. Bibliographic information is available in Robert P. Eckert's *Edward Thomas: A Biography and Bibliography*, 1937.

For introductions to Thomas see *British Poets of the Great War*, ed. Patrick Quinn, 2000, and Jon Stallworthy's *Great Poets of World War I: Poetry from the Great War*, 2002. For discussions of Thomas's life and work, see H. Coombes's *Edward Thomas*, 1956; Jon Silkin's *Out of Battle: The Poetry of the Great War*, 1972, 2nd ed. 1998; Jan Marsh's *Edward Thomas: A Poet for His Country*, 1978; Andrew Motion's *The Poetry of Edward Thomas*, 1980; Stan Smith's *Edward Thomas*, 1986; Edna Longley's *Poetry in the Wars*, 1987; Piers Gray's *Marginal Men: Edward Thomas, Ivor Gurney, J. R. Ackerley*, 1991; Jeremy Hooker's *Writers in a Landscape*, 1996; and Rennie Parker's *The Georgian Poets*, 1999. Numerous helpful essays are collected in *The Imagination of Edward Thomas*, ed. Michael Kirkham, 1986, and *The Art of Edward Thomas*, ed. Jonathan Barker, 1987.

Voices from World War I
The best anthologies are *Up the Line to Death: The War Poets, 1914–1918*, ed. Brian Gardner, 1964; *Men Who March Away: Poems of the First World War*, ed. I. M. Parsons, 1965; *The Penguin Book of First World War Poetry*, ed. Jon Silkin, 2nd ed. 1981, rev. ed. 1996; and *The Penguin Book of First World War Prose*, ed. Jon Glover and Jon Silkin, 1989. Jon Stallworthy's *Great Poets of World War I: Poetry from the Great War*, 2002, complements an anthology of twelve war poets with critical and biographical introductions for each. The literature is set in much-needed new perspectives by Samuel Hynes's *A War Imagined: The First World War and English Culture*, 1991, and *The Cambridge Companion to the Literature of the First World War*, ed. Vincent Sherry, 2005. Bernard Bergonzi's *Heroes' Twilight: A Study of the Literature of the Great War*, 1966, 2nd ed. 1980, is a balanced introduction to both the poetry and the literary prose of the period, while one of the many strengths of Paul Fussell's *The Great War and Modern Memory*, 1975, is a range of references that includes nonliterary as well as literary writing. Other noteworthy critical studies include John H. Johnston's *English Poetry of the First World War: A Study in the Evolution of Lyric and Narrative Form*, 1964; Desmond Graham's *The Truth of War: Owen, Rosenberg and Blunden*, 1984; Hugh Cecil's *The Flower of Battle: British Fiction Writers of the First World War*, 1995; Allyson Booth's *Postcards from the*

Trenches: Negotiating the Space between Modernism and the First World War, 1996; Jon Silkin's Out of Battle: The Poetry of the Great War, 1972, 2nd ed. 1998; and Vincent Sherry's The Great War and the Language of Modernism, 2003. The British experience is usefully set in an international context by Patrick Bridgwater's The German Poets of the First World War, 1985; The Lost Voices of World War I: An International Anthology of Writers, Poets & Playwrights, ed. Tim Cross, 1989; and Frank Field's British and French Writers of the First World War, 1991. Modernism/Modernity 9.1, 2002, is a special issue devoted to "Men, Women, and World War I."

See also entries under **Rupert Brooke, May Wedderburn Cannan, Robert Graves, Ivor Gurney, David Jones, Wilfred Owen, Isaac Rosenberg, Siegfried Sassoon,** and **Edward Thomas.**

Voices from World War II
The best anthologies are The Poetry of War, 1939–45, ed. Ian Hamilton, 1965, and The Terrible Rain: The War Poets, 1939–45, ed. Brian Gardner, 1966; and the fullest critical accounts of this poetry are Vernon Scannell's Not without Glory: Poets of the Second World War, 1976, and Linda M. Shires's British Poetry of the Second World War, 1985. The Second World War in Fiction, ed. Holger Michael Klein, J. E. Flower, and Eric Homberger, 1984; Paul Fussell's Wartime: Understanding and Behavior in the Second World War, 1989; Sebastian D. G. Knowles's A Purgatorial Flame: Seven British Writers in the Second World War, 1990; Bernard Bergonzi's Wartime and Aftermath: English Literature and Its Background, 1939–60, 1993; and Mark Rawlinson's British Writing of the Second World War, 2000, are useful contextual studies. For studies of the home front in England during the war, see Robert Hewison's Under Siege: Literary Life in London, 1939–1945, 1977, and Jed Esty's A Shrinking Island: Modernism and National Culture in England, 2004.

See also entries under **Charles Causley, Keith Douglas, Henry Reed,** and **Edith Sitwell.**

Derek Walcott
Walcott's Collected Poems, 1948–1984, 1986, included selections from In a Green Night: Poems 1948–60, 1960; The Castaway and Other Poems, 1965; The Gulf and Other Poems, 1969; Another Life, 1973; Sea Grapes, 1976; The Fortunate Traveler, 1981; and Midsummer, 1984. Subsequent volumes include The Arkansas Testament, 1987; Omeros, 1990; The Bounty, 1997; Tiepolo's Hound, 2000; and The Prodigal, 2004. His many plays include Ti-Jean and His Brothers, 1958; Dream on Monkey Mountain, 1967; The Joker of Seville, 1978; O Babylon!, 1978; Three Plays: The Last Carnival; Beef, No Chicken; A Branch of the Blue Nile, 1986; and

The Odyssey, 1993. What the Twilight Says: Essays, 1998, offers a selection of Walcott's essays, and Conversations with Derek Walcott, ed. William Baer, 1996, is a collection of interviews. Walcott's autobiography, Another Life: Fully Annotated, ed. Edward Baugh and Colbert I. Nepaulsingh, was published in 2004. A fine biography is Bruce King's Derek Walcott: A Caribbean Life, 2000. The standard bibliography is Irma E. Goldstraw's Derek Walcott: An Annotated Bibliography of His Works, 1984. Studies of Walcott's work include Edward Baugh's Derek Walcott: Memory as Vision, 1978; Ned Thomas's Derek Walcott: Poet of the Islands, 1980; The Art of Derek Walcott, ed. Stewart Brown, 1991; Rei Terada's Walcott's Poetry: American Mimicry, 1992; Robert D. Hamner's Derek Walcott, 1981, 2nd ed. 1993; Postcolonial Literatures: Achebe, Ngugi, Desai, Walcott, ed. Michael Parker and Roger Starkey, 1995; June D. Bobb's Beating a Restless Drum: The Poetics of Kamau Brathwaite and Derek Walcott, 1998; John Thieme's Derek Walcott, 1999; Paula Burnett's Derek Walcott: Politics and Poetics, 2000; Paul Breslin's Nobody's Nation: Reading Derek Walcott, 2001; Approaches to the Poetics of Derek Walcott, ed. José Luis Martínez-Dueñas Espejo and José María Pérez Fernández, 2001; Patricia Ismond's Abandoning Dead Metaphors: The Caribbean Phase of Derek Walcott's Poetry, 2001; and Derek Walcott, ed. Harold Bloom, 2003. An essential collection of primary and secondary materials is Critical Perspectives on Derek Walcott, ed. Hamner, 1993. Verse 11.2, 1994, South Atlantic Quarterly 96.2, 1997, and Callaloo 28.1, 2005, are special issues dedicated to Walcott.

For further discussion of Omeros see Hamner's Epic of the Dispossessed: Derek Walcott's Omeros, 1997; Jahan Ramazani's The Hybrid Muse, 2001; and Lance Callahan's In the Shadows of Divine Perfection: Derek Walcott's Omeros, 2003.

Virginia Woolf
Woolf's ten novels are The Voyage Out, 1915; Night and Day, 1919; Jacob's Room, 1922; Mrs. Dalloway, 1925; To the Lighthouse, 1927; Orlando: A Biography, 1928; The Waves, 1931; Flush: A Biography, 1933; The Years, 1937; and the posthumously published Between the Acts, 1941. Roger Fry: A Biography, 1940, is an actual biography. Mrs. Dalloway's Party: A Short Story Sequence, 1973, and Freshwater: A Comedy, 1976, were both published posthumously; Woolf's short stories have been compiled in The Complete Shorter Fiction, ed. Susan Dick, 1985.

Woolf was a prolific essayist, and A Room of One's Own, 1929, and Three Guineas, 1938, are major works of sociopolitical and literary criticism; The Common Reader, 1925, and The Second Common Reader, 1932, provide selections of her literary criticism; and The Essays of Virginia Woolf, 3 vols., ed. Andrew McNeillie, 1986–88, contains much of her prose. Woolf's complete diaries are available in *The Diary of Virginia Woolf*, 5 vols., ed. Anne Olivier Bell and McNeillie, 1977–84; the selection *A Writer's Diary: Being Extracts from the Diary of Virginia Woolf*, ed. Leonard Woolf, 1954, describes the composition of *The Years* and *Three Guineas*. Woolf's prolific correspondence is collected in *The Letters of Virginia Woolf*, 6 vols., ed. Nigel Nicolson and Joanne Trautmann Banks, 1975–80. For Woolf's early development see *A Passionate Apprentice: The Early Journals, 1897–1909*, ed. Mitchell A. Leaska, 1990. *Moments of Being: Unpublished Autobiographical Writings*, ed. Jeanne Schulkind, 1976, 2nd ed. 1985, contains her autobiographical writings. Quentin Bell's *Virginia Woolf*, 1972, is the standard biography, but Lyndall Gordon's *Virginia Woolf: A Writer's Life*, 1984, and Hermione Lee's *Virginia Woolf*, 1997, are both useful. Phyllis Rose, *Woman of Letters: A Life of Virginia Woolf*, 1978, focuses on her feminism, and Louise A. DeSalvo's *Virginia Woolf: The Impact of Childhood Sexual Abuse on Her Life and Work*, 1989, offers a revised picture of Woolf's childhood and its effect on her writing. For a guide to secondary sources, see B. J. Kirkpatrick and Stuart N. Clarke's *A Bibliography of Virginia Woolf*, 4th ed. 1997.

Perceptive critical studies of Woolf's work include David Daiches's *Virginia Woolf*, 1942, rev. ed. 1963; Joan Bennett, *Virginia Woolf: Her Art as a Novelist*, 2nd ed. 1964; Avrom Fleishman's *Virginia Woolf: A Critical Reading*, 1975; Lee's *The Novels of Virginia Woolf*, 1977; *New Feminist Essays on Virginia Woolf*, ed. Jane Marcus, 1981; *Virginia Woolf: New Critical Essays*, ed. Patricia Clements and Isobel Grundy, 1983; Alex Zwerdling's *Virginia Woolf and the Real World*, 1986; Elizabeth Abel's *Virginia Woolf and the Fictions of Psychoanalysis*, 1989; *Virginia Woolf and War: Fiction, Reality, and Myth*, ed. Mark Hussey, 1991; Michael Tratner's *Modernism and Mass Politics: Joyce, Woolf, Eliot, Yeats*, 1995; Gillian Beer's *Virginia Woolf: The Common Ground*, 1996; *Ambiguous Discourse: Feminist Narratology and British Women Writers*, ed. Kathy Mezei, 1996; Juliet Dusinberre's *Virginia Woolf's Renaissance: Woman Reader or Common Reader?*, 1997; and James J. Miracky's *Regenerating the Novel: Gender and Genre in Woolf, Forster, Sinclair, and Lawrence*, 2003. Since she was a central member of the "Bloomsbury Group," studies of Woolf may also be aided by *Bloomsbury Group: A Collection of Memoirs, Commentary, and Criticism*, ed. S. P. Rosenbaum, 1975, and Mary Ann Caws and Sarah Bird Wright's *Bloomsbury and France: Art and Friends*, 2000.

For further reading on Woolf and feminism, especially regarding *A Room of One's Own*, see Elaine Showalter's *A Literature of Their Own: British Women Novelists from Brontë to Lessing*,

1977, 2nd ed. 1999; Ellen Bayuk Rosenman's *A Room of One's Own: Women Writers and the Politics of Creativity*, 1995; and Rachel Bowlby's *Virginia Woolf: Feminist Destinations*, 1988, rev. ed. 1997.

William Butler Yeats
In addition to poems and plays, Yeats was author to a number of memoirs, works of short fiction, and essays; with Edwin Ellis he was editor of the first complete works of William Blake, 1893, and in 1936 he selected and introduced poems for *The Oxford Book of Modern Verse*. An authoritative edition of Yeats's poetry is available in the revised edition of *The Poems*, ed. Richard J. Finneran, the first volume of *The Collected Works of W. B. Yeats*, gen. ed. Finneran and George Mills Harper, 1989. Other published texts in this series include, in order by volume number, *The Plays*, ed. David R. Clark and Rosalind E. Clark, 2001; *Autobiographies*, ed. William H. O'Donnell and Douglas N. Archibald, 1999; *Later Essays*, ed. O'Donnell with Elizabeth Bergmann Loizeaux, 1994; *Prefaces and Introductions*, ed. O'Donnell, 1989; *Letters to the New Island*, ed. George Bornstein and Hugh Witemeyer, 1989; *The Irish Dramatic Movement*, ed. Mary FitzGerald and Finneran, 2003; *Early Articles and Reviews*, ed. John P. Frayne and Madeleine Marchaterre, 2004; *Later Articles and Reviews*, ed. Colton Johnson, 2000; and the two short pseudonymous novels, *John Sherman* and *Dhoya*, ed. Finneran, 1991. Important scholarly editions include *The Variorum Edition of the Poems*, ed. Peter Allt and Russell K. Alspach, 1957; and *The Variorum Edition of the Plays*, ed. Alspach and Catherine C. Alspach, 1966. An excellent paperback selection is the Norton Critical Edition of Yeats's *Poetry, Drama, and Prose*, ed. James Pethica, 2000, which contains secondary criticism in addition to Yeats's work and reprints the poems in their earlier published versions. Also of note are *Mythologies*, 1959, which contains much of Yeats's prose fiction; *Essays and Introductions*, 1961; and the miscellaneous prose in *Explorations*, 1962; and *Memoirs*, ed. Denis Donoghue, 1973, which contains journals and the first published version of the *Autobiographies*. Yeats's mythological system is available in *A Vision*, first published in 1925, substantially revised and reissued in 1937. John Kelly, Eric Domville, and Ronald Schuchard have to date published three volumes of *The Collected Letters of W. B. Yeats*, 1986, 1994, 1997.

R. F. Foster has published the standard biography, *W. B. Yeats: A Life*, 2 vols., 1997, 2003. Also useful is A. N. Jeffares's *W. B. Yeats: A New Biography*, 1989. Bibliographic information is available in Wade's *A Bibliography of the Writings of W. B. Yeats*, 1958, revised by Alspach 1968.

W. B. Yeats: The Critical Heritage, ed. Jeffares, 1977, provides a reception history and contemporary reviews. Jeffares's *A New Commentary on the Poems of W. B. Yeats*, rev. ed. 1984, and *A Commentary on the Plays of W. B. Yeats*, 1975, are indispensable references. Also valuable are Sam McCready's *A William Butler Yeats Encyclopedia*, 1997, and Lester I. Conner's *A Yeats Dictionary*, 1998.

In the vast body of Yeats criticism, some important studies are Richard Ellmann's *Yeats: The Man and the Masks*, 1948, and *The Identity of Yeats*, 2nd ed. 1964; Thomas Parkinson's *W. B. Yeats, Self-Critic: A Study of his Early Verse*, 1951, rpt. 1971 with *The Later Poetry* and a new foreword; Frank Kermode's *Romantic Image*, 1957; Jon Stallworthy's *Between the Lines: W. B. Yeats's Poetry in the Making*, 1963; Helen Vendler's *Yeats's Vision and Later Plays*, 1963; Thomas R. Whitaker's *Swan and Shadow: Yeats's Dialogue with History*, 1964; Harold Bloom's *Yeats*, 1970; Bornstein's *Yeats and Shelley*, 1970; Donoghue's *William Butler Yeats*, 1971; Mary Helen Thuente's *W. B. Yeats and Irish Folklore*, 1981; Elizabeth Butler Cullingford's *Yeats, Ireland and Fascism*, 1981; Loizeaux's *Yeats and the Visual Arts*, 1986; Paul Scott Stanfield's *Yeats and Politics in the 1930s*, 1988; Finneran's *Editing Yeats's Poems*, 1990; Stan Smith's *W. B. Yeats: A Critical Introduction*, 1990; Jahan Ramazani's *Yeats and the Poetry of Death: Elegy, Self-Elegy, and the Sublime*, 1990; Hazard Adams's *The Book of Yeats's Poems*, 1991; Michael North's *The Political Aesthetic of Yeats, Eliot, and Pound*, 1991; Cullingford's *Gender and History in Yeats's Love Poetry*, 1993; M. L. Rosenthal's *Running to Paradise: Yeats's Poetic Art*, 1994; Marjorie Howes's *Yeats's Nations: Gender, Class, and Irishness*, 1996; Michael J. Sidnell's *Yeats's Poetry and Poetics*, 1996; Vicki Mahaffey's *States of Desire: Wilde, Yeats, Joyce, and the Irish Experiment*, 1998; Bornstein's *Material Modernism: The Politics of the Page*, 2001; Gregory Castle's *Modernism and the Celtic Revival*, 2001; Richard Greaves's *Transition, Reception, and Modernism in W. B. Yeats*, 2002. Collections of essays include *William Butler Yeats*, ed. Bloom, 1986; *Yeats's Political Identities*, ed. Jonathan Allison, 1996; and *W. B. Yeats: Critical Assessments*, ed. David Pierce, 2000. Many essays have appeared annually in the journals *Yeats* and *Yeats Annual*.

Literary Terminology*

Using simple technical terms can sharpen our understanding and streamline our discussion of literary works. Some terms, such as the ones in Sections A, B, and C of this appendix, help us address the internal style, form, and structure of works. Other terms, such as those in Section D, provide insight into the material forms in which literary works have been produced.

In analyzing what they called "rhetoric," ancient Greek and Roman writers determined the elements of what we call "style" and "structure." Our literary terms are derived, via medieval and Renaissance intermediaries, from the Greek and Latin sources. In the definitions that follow, the etymology, or root, of the word is given when it helps illuminate the word's current usage.

Most of the examples are drawn from texts in this anthology.

Words **boldfaced** within definitions are themselves defined in this appendix. Some terms are defined within definitions; such words are *italicized*.

A. Style

In literary works the manner in which something is expressed contributes substantially to its meaning. The manner of a literary work is its "style," the effect of which is its "tone." We often can intuit the tone of a text; the following terms offer a set of concepts by which we can analyze the stylistic features that produce the tone. The groups within this section move from the micro to the macro level internal to works.

(i) Diction

"Diction," or "lexis" (from, respectively, Latin "dictio" and Greek "lexis," each meaning "word"), designates the actual words used in any utterance—speech, writing, and, for our purposes here, literary works. The choice of words contributes significantly to the style of a given work.

Connotation: To understand connotation, we need to understand **denotation**. While many words can denote the same concept—that is, have the same basic meaning—those words can evoke different associations, or connotations. Contrast, for example, the clinical-sounding term "depression" and the more colorful, musical, even poetic phrase "the blues."

Denotation: A word has a basic, "prosaic" (factual) meaning prior to the associations it connotes (see **connotation**). The word "steed," for example, might call to mind a horse fitted with battle gear, to be ridden by a warrior, but its denotation is simply "horse."

---

* This appendix was devised and compiled by James Simpson with the collaboration of all the editors.

Register: The register of a word is its stylistic level, which can be distinguished by degree of technicality but also by degree of formality. We choose our words from different registers according to context, that is, audience and/ or environment. Thus a chemist in a laboratory will say "sodium chloride," a cook in a kitchen "salt." A formal register designates the kind of language used in polite society (e.g., "Mr. President"), while an informal or colloquial register is used in less formal or more relaxed social situations (e.g., "the boss"). In **classical** and medieval rhetoric, these registers of formality were called *high style* and *low style*. A *middle style* was defined as the style fit for narrative, not drawing attention to itself.

Lexical set: Words that habitually recur together (e.g., January, February, March, etc.; or red, white, and blue) form a lexical set.

(ii) Rhetorical Figures: Figures of Speech

Literary language often employs patterns perceptible to the eye and/or to the ear. Such patterns are called "figures of speech"; in **classical** *rhetoric they were called* **"schemes"** *(from Greek "schema," meaning "form, figure").*

Alliteration (from Latin "litera," alphabetic letter): the repetition of an initial consonant sound or consonant cluster in consecutive or closely positioned words. This pattern is often an inseparable part of the meter in Germanic languages, where the tonic, or accented **syllable,** is usually the first syllable. Thus all Old English poetry and some varieties of Middle English poetry use alliteration as part of their basic metrical practice. *Sir Gawain and the Green Knight,* line 1: "Sithen the sege and the assaut was sesed at Troye" (see vol. 1, p. 161). Otherwise used for local effects; Stevie Smith, "Pretty," lines 4–5: "And in the pretty pool the pike stalks / He stalks his prey . . ." (see vol. 2, p. 2377).

Anaphora (Greek "carrying back"): the repetition of words or groups of words at the beginning of consecutive sentences, clauses, or phrases. Blake, "London," lines 5–8: "In every cry of every Man, / In every Infant's cry of fear, / In every voice, in every ban . . ." (see vol. 2, p. 94); Louise Bennett, "Jamaica Oman," lines 17–20: "Some backa man a push, some side-a / Man a hole him han, / Some a lick sense eena him head, / Some a guide him pon him plan!" (see vol. 2, p. 2473).

Assonance (Latin "sounding to"): the repetition of identical or near identical stressed vowel sounds in words whose final consonants differ, producing half-rhyme. Tennyson, "The Lady of Shalott," line 100: "His broad clear brow in sunlight glowed" (see vol. 2, p. 1116).

Chiasmus (Greek "crosswise"): the inversion of an already established sequence. This can involve verbal echoes: Pope, "Eloisa to Abelard," line 104, "The crime was common, common be the pain" (see vol. 1, p. 2535); or it can be purely a matter of syntactic inversion: Pope, *Epistle to Dr. Arbuthnot,* line 8: "They pierce my thickets, through my grot they glide" (see vol. 1, p. 2549).

Consonance (Latin "sounding with"): the repetition of final consonants in words or stressed syllables whose vowel sounds are different. Herbert, "Easter," line 13: "Consort, both heart and lute . . ." (see vol. 1, p. 1608).

Homophone (Greek "same sound"): a word that sounds identical to another word but has a different meaning ("bear" / "bare").

Onomatopoeia (Greek "name making"): verbal sounds that imitate and evoke the sounds they denotate. Hopkins, "Binsey Poplars," lines 10–12 (about some felled trees): "O if we but knew what we do / When we delve [dig] or hew— / Hack and rack the growing green!" (see vol. 2, p. 1519).

Rhyme: the repetition of identical vowel sounds in stressed syllables whose initial consonants differ ("dead" / "head"). In poetry, rhyme often links the end of one line with another. *Masculine rhyme*: full rhyme on the final syllable of the line ("decays" / "days"). *Feminine rhyme*: full rhyme on syllables that are followed by unaccented syllables ("fountains"/"mountains"). *Internal rhyme*: full rhyme within a single line; Coleridge, *The Rime of the Ancient Mariner*, line 7: "The guests are met, the feast is set" (see vol. 2, p. 430). *Rhyme riche*: rhyming on **homophones**; Chaucer, *General Prologue*, lines 17/18: "seeke" / "seke." *Off rhyme* (also known as *half rhyme, near rhyme,* or *slant rhyme*): differs from perfect rhyme in changing the vowel sound and/or the concluding consonants expected of perfect rhyme; Byron, "They say that Hope is Happiness," lines 5–7: "most" / "lost" (see vol. 2, p. 613). *Pararhyme*: stressed vowel sounds differ but are flanked by identical or similar consonants; Owen, "Miners," lines 9–11: "simmer" / "summer" (see vol. 2, p. 1973).

(iii) Rhetorical Figures: Figures of Thought

Language can also be patterned conceptually, even outside the rules that normally govern it. Literary language in particular exploits this licensed linguistic irregularity. Synonyms for figures of thought are "trope" (Greek "twisting," referring to the irregularity of use) and "conceit" (Latin "concept," referring to the fact that these figures are perceptible only to the mind). Be careful not to confuse "trope" with "topos" (a common error).

Allegory (Greek "saying otherwise"): saying one thing (the "vehicle" of the allegory) and meaning another (the allegory's "tenor"). Allegories may be momentary aspects of a work, as in **metaphor** ("John is a lion"), or, through extended metaphor, may constitute the basis of narrative, as in Bunyan's *Pilgrim's Progress*; this second meaning is the dominant one. See also **symbol** and **type**.

Antithesis (Greek "placing against"): juxtaposition of opposed terms in clauses or sentences that are next to or near each other; Milton, *Paradise Lost* 1.777–80: "They but now who seemed / In bigness to surpass Earth's giant sons / Now less than smallest dwarfs, in narrow room / Throng numberless" (see vol. 1, p. 1849).

Bathos (Greek "depth"): a sudden and sometimes ridiculous descent of tone; Pope, *The Rape of the Lock* 3.157–58: "Not louder shrieks to pitying heaven are cast, / When husbands, or when lapdogs breathe their last" (see vol. 1, p. 2524).

Emblem (Greek "an insertion"): a picture allegorically expressing a moral, or a verbal picture open to such interpretation. Donne, "A Hymn to Christ," lines 1–2: "In what torn ship soever I embark, / That ship shall be my emblem of thy ark" (see vol. 1, p. 1300).

Euphemism (Greek "sweet saying"): the figure by which something distasteful is described in alternative, less repugnant terms (e.g., "he passed away").

Hyperbole (Greek "throwing over"): overstatement, exaggeration; Marvell, "To His Coy Mistress," lines 11–12: "My vegetable love would grow / Vaster than empires, and more slow" (see vol. 1, p. 1703); Auden, "As I Walked Out One Evening," lines 9–12: " 'I'll love you, dear, I'll love you / Till China and Africa meet / And the river jumps over the mountain / And the salmon sing in the street" (see vol. 2, p. 2427).

Irony (Greek "dissimulation"): strictly, a subset of allegory: whereas allegory says one thing and means another, irony says one thing and means its opposite; Byron, *Don Juan* 1.1–2: "I want a hero: an uncommon want, / When every year and month sends forth a new one" (see vol. 2, p. 670). For an extended example of irony, see Swift's "Modest Proposal."

Litotes (from Greek "smooth"): strictly, understatement by denying the contrary; More, *Utopia:* "differences of no slight import" (see vol. 1, p. 524). More loosely, understatement; Swift, "A Tale of a Tub": "Last week I saw a woman flayed, and you will hardly believe how much it altered her person for the worse" (see vol. 1, p. 2320). Stevie Smith, "Sunt Leones," lines 11–12: "And if the Christians felt a little blue— / Well people being eaten often do" (see vol. 2, p. 2373).

Metaphor (Greek "carrying across," etymologically parallel to Latin "translation"): the identification or implicit identification of one thing with another with which it is not literally identifiable. Blake, "London," lines 11–12: "And the hapless Soldier's sigh / Runs in blood down Palace walls" (see vol. 2, p. 94).

Metonymy (Greek "change of name"): using a word to **denote** another concept or other concepts, by virtue of habitual association. Thus "The Press," designating printed news media. Fictional names often work by associations of this kind. A figure closely related to **synecdoche.**

Occupatio (Latin "taking possession"): denying that one will discuss a subject while actually discussing it; also known as "praeteritio" (Latin "passing by"). See Chaucer, *Nun's Priest's Tale,* lines 414–32 (see vol. 1, p. 308).

Oxymoron (Greek "sharp blunt"): conjunction of normally incompatible terms; Milton, *Paradise Lost* 1.63: "darkness visible" (see vol. 1, p. 1833). Ramanujan, "Foundlings in the Yukon," line 41: "these infants compact with age" (see vol. 2, p. 2582).

Paradox (Greek "contrary to received opinion"): an apparent contradiction that requires thought to reveal an inner consistency. Chaucer, "Troilus's Song," line 12: "O sweete harm so quainte" (see vol. 1, p. 316).

Periphrasis (Greek "declaring around"): circumlocution; the use of many words to express what could be expressed in few or one; Sidney, *Astrophil and Stella* 39.1–4 (vol. 1, p. 982).

Personification, or prosopopoeia (Greek "person making"): the attribution of human qualities to nonhuman forces or objects; Shakespeare, *King Lear* 3.2.1: "Blow winds and crack your cheeks, rage! Blow!" (see vol. 1, p. 1182).

Pun: a sometimes irresolvable doubleness of meaning in a single word or expression; Shakespeare, Sonnet 135, line 1: "Whoever hath her wish, thou hast thy Will" (see vol. 1, p. 1075).

Sarcasm (Greek "flesh tearing"): a wounding remark, often expressed ironically; Boswell, *Life of Johnson:* Johnson [asked if any man of the modern age could have written the **epic** poem *Fingal*] replied, "Yes, Sir, many men, many women, and many children" (see vol. 1, p. 2792).

Simile (Latin "like"): comparison, usually using the word "like" or "as," of one thing with another so as to produce sometimes surprising analogies. Donne, "The Storm," lines 29–30: "Sooner than you read this line did the gale, / Like shot, not feared till felt, our sails assail." Frequently used, in extended form, in **epic** poetry; Milton, *Paradise Lost* 1.338–46 (see vol. 1, p. 1839).

Symbol (Greek "token"): something that stands for something else, and yet seems necessarily to evoke that other thing. Blake, "The Sick Rose," lines 1–8: "O Rose, thou art sick. / The invisible worm / That flies in the night / In the howling storm / Has found out thy bed / Of crimson joy, And his dark secret love / Does thy life destroy" (see vol. 2, p. 91). In Neoplatonic, and therefore Romantic, theory, to be distinguished from **allegory** thus: whereas allegory involves connections between vehicle and tenor agreed by convention or made explicit, the meanings of a symbol are supposedly inherent to it. For discussion, see Coleridge, "On Symbol and Allegory" (vol. 2, p. 488).

Synecdoche (Greek "to take with something else"): using a part to express the whole, or vice versa; "Donne, "A Hymn to Christ," lines 1–2: "In what torn ship soever I embark / That ship shall be my emblem of thy ark" (see vol. 1, p. 1300).

Type (Greek "impression, figure"): In Christian allegorical interpretation of the Old Testament, pre-Christian figures were regarded as "types," or foreshadowings, of Christ or the Christian dispensation. *Typology* has been the source of much visual and literary art in which the parallelisms between old and new are extended to nonbiblical figures; thus the virtuous plowman in *Piers Plowman* becomes a type of Christ.

Zeugma (Greek "a yoking"): a syntactic pun whereby the one word is revealed to have more than one sense in the sentence as a whole; Pope, *Rape of the Lock* 3.7–8, in which the word "take" is used in two senses: "Here thou, great Anna! whom three realms obey, / Dost sometimes counsel take—and sometimes tea" (see vol. 1, p. 2521).

(iv) Meter, Rhythm

Verse (from Latin "versus," turned) is distinguished from prose (from Latin "prorsus," straightforward) as a more compressed form of expression, shaped by metrical norms. **Meter** *(Greek "measure") refers to the regularly recurring sound pattern of verse lines. The means of producing sound patterns across lines differ in different poetic traditions. Verse may be* **quantitative,** *or determined by the quantities of syllables (set patterns of long and short syllables), as in Latin and Greek poetry. It may be* **syllabic,** *determined by fixed numbers of syllables in the line, as in the verse of Romance languages (e.g., French and Italian). It may be* **accentual,** *determined by the number of accents, or stresses in the line, with variable numbers of syllables, as in Old English and some varieties of Middle English alliterative verse. Or it may be* **accentual-syllabic,** *determined by the numbers of accents, but possessing a regular pattern of stressed and unstressed syllables, so as to produce regular numbers of syllables per line. Since Chaucer, English verse has worked primarily within the many possibilities of accentual-syllabic meter. The unit of meter is the* **foot.** *In English verse the number of feet per line corresponds to the number of accents in a line. For the types and examples of different meters, see* **monometer, dimeter, trimeter, tetrameter, pentameter,** *and* **hexameter.** *In the definitions below, "u" designates one unstressed syllable, and "/" one stressed syllable.*

Rhythm is not absolutely distinguishable from meter. One way of making a clear distinction between these terms is to say that rhythm (from the Greek "to flow") denotes the patterns of sound within the feet of verse lines and the combination of those feet. Very often a particular meter will raise expectations that a given rhythm will be used regularly through a whole line or a whole poem. Thus in English verse the pentameter regularly uses an iambic rhythm. Rhythm, however, is much more fluid than meter, and many lines within the same poem using a single meter will frequently exploit different rhythmic possibilities. For examples of different rhythms, see **iamb, trochee, anapest, spondee,** *and* **dactyl.**

Accent (synonym "stress"): the special force devoted to the voicing of one syllable in a word over others. In the noun "accent," for example, the stress is on the first syllable.

Alexandrine: in French verse a line of twelve syllables, and, by analogy, in English verse a line of six stresses. See **hexameter.**

Anapest: a three-syllable foot following the rhythmic pattern, in English verse, of two unstressed (uu) syllables followed by one stressed (/). Thus, for example, "Illinois."

Caesura (Latin "cut"): a pause or breathing space within a line of verse, generally occurring between syntactic units; Louise Bennett, "Colonization in Reverse," lines 5–8: "By de hundred, by de tousan, / From country an from town, / By de ship-load, by de plane-load, / Jamaica is Englan boun" (see vol. 2, p. 2472).

Dactyl (Greek "finger," because of the finger's three joints): a three-syllable foot following the rhythmic pattern, in English verse, of one stressed (/) followed by two unstressed (uu) syllables. Thus, for example, "Oregon."

Dimeter (Greek "two measure"): a two-stress line, rarely used as the meter of whole poems, though used with great frequency in single poems by Skelton, e.g., "The Tunning of Elinour Rumming" (see vol. 1, p. 516). Otherwise used for single lines, as in Herbert, "Discipline," line 3: "O my God" (see vol. 1, p. 1623).

End-stopping: the placement of a complete syntactic unit within a complete metrical pattern; Auden, "In Memory of W. B. Yeats," line 42: "Earth, receive an honoured guest" (see vol. 2, p. 2430). Compare **enjambment.**

Enjambment (French "striding," encroaching): The opposite of **end-stopping,** enjambment occurs when the syntactic unit does not end with the metrical pattern, i.e., when the sense of the line overflows its meter and, therefore, the line break; Auden, "In Memory of W. B. Yeats," lines 44–45: "Let the Irish vessel lie / Emptied of its poetry" (see vol. 2, p. 2430).

Hexameter (Greek "six measure"): The hexameter line (a six-stress line) is the meter of **classical** Latin **epic;** while not imitated in that form for epic verse in English, some instances of the hexameter exist. See, for example, the last line of a Spenserian stanza, *Faerie Queene* 1.1.2: "O help thou my weake wit, and sharpen my dull tong" (vol. 1, p. 720), or Yeats, "The Lake Isle of Innisfree," line 1: "I will arise and go now, and go to Innisfree" (vol. 2, p. 2025).

Hypermetrical (adj.; Greek "over measured"): describes a breaking of the expected metrical pattern by at least one extra syllable.

Iamb: the basic foot of English verse; two syllables following the rhythmic pattern of unstressed (u) followed by stressed (/) and producing a rising effect. Thus, for example, "Vermont."

Monometer (Greek "one measure"): an entire line with just one stress; *Sir*

Gawain and the Green Knight, line 15, "wyth (u) wynne (/)" (see vol. 1, p. 162).

Pentameter (Greek "five measure"): in English verse, a five-stress line. Between the late fourteenth and the nineteenth centuries, this meter, frequently employing an iambic rhythm, was the basic line of English verse. Chaucer, Shakespeare, Milton, and Wordsworth each, for example, deployed this very flexible line as their primary resource; Milton, *Paradise Lost* 1.128: "O Prince, O Chief of many thronèd Powers" (see vol. 1, p. 1835).

Spondee: a two-syllable foot following the rhythmic pattern, in English verse, of two stressed (//) syllables. Thus, for example, "Utah."

Syllable: the smallest unit of sound in a pronounced word. The syllable that receives the greatest stress is called the *tonic* syllable.

Tetrameter (Greek "four measure"): a line with four stresses. Coleridge, *Christabel*, line 31: "She stole along, she nothing spoke" (see vol. 2, p. 450).

Trimeter (Greek "three measure"): a line with three stresses. Herbert, "Discipline," line 1: "Throw away thy rod" (see vol. 1, p. 1623).

Trochee: a two-syllable foot following the pattern, in English verse, of stressed (/) followed by unstressed (u) syllable, producing a falling effect. Thus, for example, "Texas."

(vi) Verse Forms

The terms related to meter and rhythm describe the shape of individual lines. Lines of verse are combined to produce larger groupings, called verse forms. These larger groupings are in the first instance **stanzas** *(Italian "rooms"): groupings of two or more lines, though "stanza" is usually reserved for groupings of at least four lines. Stanzas are often joined by rhyme, often in sequence, where each group shares the same metrical pattern and, when rhymed, rhyme scheme. Stanzas can themselves be arranged into larger groupings. Poets often invent new verse forms, or they may work within established forms, a list of which follows.*

Ballad stanza: usually a **quatrain** in alternating **iambic tetrameter** and **iambic trimeter** lines, rhyming abcb. See "Sir Patrick Spens" (vol. 1, p. 2902); Louise Bennett's poems (vol. 2, pp. 2469–74); Eliot, "Sweeney among the Nightingales" (vol. 2, p. 2293); Larkin, "This Be The Verse" (vol. 2, p. 2572).

Ballade: a form consisting usually of three stanzas followed by a four-line envoi (French, "send off"). The last line of the first stanza establishes a **refrain**, which is repeated, or subtly varied, as the last line of each stanza. The form was derived from French medieval poetry; English poets, from the fourteenth to the sixteenth centuries especially, used it with varying stanza forms. Chaucer, "Complaint to His Purse" (see vol. 1, p. 318).

Blank verse: unrhymed **iambic pentameter** lines. Blank verse has no stanzas, but is broken up into uneven units (verse paragraphs) determined by sense rather than form. First devised in English by Henry Howard, Earl of Surrey, in his translation of two books of Virgil's *Aeneid* (see vol. 1, p. 614), this very flexible verse type became the standard form for dramatic poetry in the seventeenth century, as in most of Shakespeare's plays. Milton and Wordsworth, among many others, also used it to create an English equivalent to **classical epic**.

Couplet: in English verse two consecutive, rhyming lines usually containing the same number of stresses. Chaucer first introduced the **iambic pentameter** couplet into English (*Canterbury Tales*); the form was later used in many types of writing, including drama; imitations and translations of **classical epic** (thus *heroic couplet*); essays; and **satire** (see Dryden and Pope). The *distich* (Greek "two lines") is a couplet usually making complete sense; Aemilia Lanyer, *Salve Deus Rex Judaeorum*, lines 5–6: "Read it fair queen, though it defective be, / Your excellence can grace both it and me" (see vol. 1, p. 1315).

Ottava rima: an eight-line stanza form, rhyming abababcc, using **iambic pentameter;** Yeats, "Sailing to Byzantium" (see vol. 2, p. 2040). Derived from the Italian poet Boccaccio, an eight-line stanza was used by fifteenth-century English poets for inset passages (e.g., Christ's speech from the Cross in Lydgate's *Testament*, lines 754–897). The form in this rhyme scheme was used in English poetry for long narrative by, for example, Byron (*Don Juan*; see vol. 2, p. 669).

Quatrain: a stanza of four lines, usually rhyming abcb, abab, or abba. Of many possible examples, see Crashaw, "On the Wounds of Our Crucified Lord" (see vol. 1, p. 1644).

Refrain: usually a single line repeated as the last line of consecutive stanzas, sometimes with subtly different wording and ideally with subtly different meaning as the poem progresses. See, for example, Wyatt, "Blame not my lute" (vol. 1, p. 602).

Rhyme royal: a stanza form of seven **iambic pentameter** lines, rhyming ababbcc; first introduced by Chaucer and called "royal" because the form was used by James I of Scotland for his *Kingis Quair* in the early fifteenth century. Chaucer, "Troilus's Song" (see vol. 1, p. 316).

Sonnet: a form combining a variable number of units of rhymed lines to produce a fourteen-line poem, usually in rhyming **iambic pentameter** lines. In English there are two principal varieties: the Petrarchan sonnet, formed by an octave (an eight-line stanza, often broken into two **quatrains** having the same rhyme scheme, typically abba abba) and a sestet (a six-line stanza, typically cdecde or cdcdcd); and the Shakespearean sonnet, formed by three quatrains (abab cdcd efef) and a **couplet** (gg). The declaration of a sonnet can take a sharp turn, or "volta," often at the decisive formal shift from octave to sestet in the Petrarchan sonnet, or in the final couplet of a Shakespearean sonnet, introducing a trenchant counterstatement. Derived from Italian poetry, and especially from the poetry of Petrarch, the sonnet was first introduced to English poetry by Wyatt, and initially used principally for the expression of unrequited erotic love, though later poets used the form for many other purposes. See Wyatt, "Whoso list to hunt" (vol. 1, p. 595); Sidney, *Astrophil and Stella* (vol. 1, p. 975); Shakespeare, *Sonnets* (vol. 1, p. 1060); Wordsworth, "London, 1802" (vol. 2, p. 319); McKay, "If We Must Die" (vol. 2, p. 2464); Heaney, "Clearances" (vol. 2, p. 2833).

Spenserian stanza: the stanza developed by Spenser for *The Faerie Queene*; nine **iambic** lines, the first eight of which are **pentameters,** followed by one **hexameter,** rhyming ababbcbcc. See also, for example, Shelley, *Adonais* (vol. 2, p. 822), and Keats, *The Eve of St. Agnes* (vol. 2, p. 888).

Tercet: a stanza or group of three lines, used in larger forms such as **terza rima,** the **Petrarchan sonnet,** and the **villanelle.**

Terza rima: a sequence of rhymed **tercets** linked by rhyme thus: aba bcb cdc, etc. First used extensively by Dante in *The Divine Comedy*, the form was adapted in English **iambic pentameters** by Wyatt and revived in the nineteenth century. See Wyatt, "Mine own John Poins" (vol. 1, pp. 604); Shelley, "Ode to the West Wind" (vol. 2, pp. 772); and Morris, "The Death of Guinevere" (vol. 2, pp. 1483). For modern adaptations see Eliot, lines 78–149 (though unrhymed) of "Little Gidding" (vol. 2, pp. 2315–16); Heaney, "Station Island" (vol. 2, p. 2831); Walcott, *Omeros* (vol. 2, p. 2591).

Triplet: a **tercet** rhyming on the same sound. Pope inserts triplets among heroic **couplets** to emphasize a particular thought; see *Essay on Criticism*, 315–17 (vol. 1, p. 2504).

Villanelle: a fixed form of usually five **tercets** and a **quatrain** employing only two rhyme sounds altogether, rhyming aba for the tercets and abaa for the quatrain, with a complex pattern of two **refrains**. Derived from a French fixed form. Thomas, "Do Not Go Gentle into That Good Night" (see vol. 2, p. 2450).

(v) Syntax

Syntax (Greek "ordering with") designates the rules by which sentences are constructed in a given language. Discussion of meter is impossible without some reference to syntax, since the overall effect of a poem is, in part, always the product of a subtle balance of meter and sentence construction. Syntax is also essential to the understanding of prose style, since prose writers, deprived of the full shaping possibilities of meter, rely all the more heavily on syntactic resources. A working command of syntactical practice requires an understanding of the parts of speech (nouns, verbs, adjectives, adverbs, conjunctions, pronouns, prepositions, and interjections), since writers exploit syntactic possibilities by using particular combinations and concentrations of the parts of speech. The list below offers some useful terms for the description of syntactic features of a work.

Apposition: the repetition of elements serving an identical grammatical function in one sentence. The effect of this repetition is to arrest the flow of the sentence, but in doing so to add extra semantic nuance to repeated elements. This is an especially important feature of Old English poetic style. See, for example, Caedmon's Hymn (vol. 1, p. 24), where the phrases "heaven kingdom's guardian," "the Measurer's might," "his mind-plans," and "the work of the Glory-Father" each serve an identical syntactic function as the direct objects of "praise."

Hypotaxis, or subordination (respectively Greek and Latin "ordering under"): the subordination, by the use of subordinate clauses, of different elements of a sentence to a single main verb. Milton, *Paradise Lost* 9.513–15: "As when a ship by skillful steersman wrought / Nigh river's mouth or foreland, where the wind / Veers oft, as oft so steers, and shifts her sail; So varied he" (vol. 1, p. 1984). The contrary principle to **parataxis.**

Hyperbaton (Greek "overstepping"): the rearrangement, or inversion, of the expected word order in a sentence or clause. Gray, "Elegy Written in a Country Churchyard," line 38: "If Memory o'er their tomb no trophies raise" (vol. 1, p. 2867). Poets can suspend the expected syntax over many lines, as in the first sentences of the *Canterbury Tales* (vol. 1, p. 218) and of *Paradise Lost* (vol. 1, p. 1832).

Parataxis, or coordination (respectively Greek and Latin "ordering beside"):

the coordination, by the use of coordinating conjunctions, of different main clauses in a single sentence. Malory, "Morte Darthur": "So Sir Lancelot departed and took his sword under his arm, and so he walked in his mantel, that noble knight, and put himself in great jeopardy" (see vol. 1, p. 442). The opposite principle to **hypotaxis.**

(vii) Point of View

*All of the many kinds of writing (see "B. Genre and Mode," below) involve a point of view from which a text is, or seems to be, generated. The presence of such a point of view may be powerful and explicit, as in many novels, or deliberately invisible, as in much drama. In some genres, such as the **novel**, the narrator does not necessarily tell the story from a position we can predict; that is, the needs of a particular story, not the **conventions** of the genre, determine the narrator's position. In other genres, the narrator's position is fixed by convention; in certain kinds of love poetry, for example, the narrating voice is always that of a suffering lover. Not only does the point of view significantly inform the style of a work, but it also informs the structure of that work. Most of the terms below are especially relevant to narrative in either verse or prose, but many also apply to other modes of writing.*

Deixis (Greek "pointing"): Every work has, implicitly or explicitly, a "here" and a "now" from which it is narrated. Words that refer to or imply this point from which the voice of the work is projected (such as "here," "there," "this," "that," "now," "then") are examples of deixis, or "deictics." This technique is especially important in drama, where it is used to create a sense of the events happening as the spectator witnesses them.

First-person narration: a narrative in which the voice narrating refers to itself with forms of the first-person pronoun ("I," "me," "my," etc., or possibly "we," "us," "our"), and in which the narrative is determined by the limitations of that voice. Thus Mary Wollstonecraft Shelley, *Frankenstein.*

Frame narrative: Some narratives, particularly collections of narratives, involve a frame narrative that explains the genesis of, and/or gives a perspective on, the main narrative or narratives to follow. Thus Chaucer, *Canterbury Tales;* Mary Wollstonecraft Shelley, *Frankenstein;* or Conrad, *Heart of Darkness.*

Free indirect style: a narratorial voice that manages, without explicit reference, to imply, and often implicitly to comment on, the voice of a **character** in the narrative itself. Virginia Woolf, "A Sketch of the Past," where the voice, although strictly that of the adult narrator, manages to convey the child's manner of perception: "—I begin: the first memory. This was of red and purple flowers on a black background—my mother's dress" (see vol. 2, p. 2155).

Omniscient narrator (Latin "all-knowing narrator"): a narrator who, in the fiction of the narrative, has complete access to both the deeds and the thoughts of all **characters** in the narrative. Thus Thomas Hardy, "On the Western Circuit" (see vol. 2, p. 1852).

Order: A story may be told in different orders. A narrator might use the sequence of events as they happened, and thereby follow what **classical** rhetoricians called the *natural order;* alternatively, the narrator might reorder the sequence of events, beginning the narration either in the middle or

at the end of the sequence of events, thereby following an *artificial order.*
If a narrator begins in the middle of events, he or she is said to begin *in
medias res* (Latin "in the middle of the matter"). For a brief discussion of
these concepts, see Spenser, *Faerie Queene,* "A Letter of the Authors" (vol.
1, p. 716). Modern narratology makes a related distinction, between *histoire*
(French "story") for the natural order that readers mentally reconstruct,
and *discours* (French, here "narration") for the narrative as presented.

Plot: the sequence of events in a story as narrated.

Stream of consciousness: usually a **first-person** narrative that seems to give
the reader access to the narrator's mind as it perceives or reflects on events,
prior to organizing those perceptions into a coherent narrative. Thus
(though generated from a **third-person** narrative) Joyce, *Ulysses,* "Lestrygonians" (see vol. 2, p. 2213).

Third-person narration: a narration in which the narrator recounts a narrative of **characters** referred to explicitly or implicitly by third-person pronouns ("he," she," etc.), without the limitation of a **first-person narration.**
Thus Johnson, *The History of Rasselas.*

Unities: According to a theory supposedly derived from Aristotle's *Poetics,* the
events represented in a play should have unity of time, place, and action:
that the play take up no more time than the time of the play, or at most a
day; that the space of action should be within a single city; and that there
should be no subplot. See Johnson, *The Preface to Shakespeare* (vol. 1.,
p. 2756).

B. Genre and Mode

*The style, structure, and, often, length of a work, when coupled with a certain
subject matter, raise expectations that a literary work conforms to a certain **genre**
(French "kind"). Good writers might upset these expectations, but they remain
aware of the expectations and thwart them purposefully. Works in different genres may nevertheless participate in the same **mode,** a broader category designating the fundamental perspectives governing various genres of writing. For mode,
see **tragic, comic, satiric,** and **didactic modes.** All the other terms in this list
refer to more or less specific literary genres. Genres are fluid, sometimes very fluid
(e.g., the **novel**); the word "usually" should be added to almost every statement!*

Animal fable: a short narrative of speaking animals, followed by moralizing
comment, written in a low style and gathered into a collection. Robert
Henryson, "The Cock and the Fox" (see vol. 1, p. 457).

Aubade (originally from Spanish "alba," dawn): a lover's dawn song or lyric
bewailing the arrival of the day and the necessary separation of the lovers;
Donne, "The Sun Rising" (see vol. 1, p. 1266). Larkin recasts the genre in
"Aubade" (see vol. 2, p. 2573).

Autobiography (Greek "self-life writing"): a narrative of a life written by the
subject; Wordsworth, *The Prelude* (see vol. 2, p. 322). There are subgenres,
such as the spiritual autobiography, narrating the author's path to conversion and subsequent spiritual trials, as in Bunyan's *Grace Abounding.*

Beast epic: a continuous, unmoralized narrative, in prose or verse, relating
the victories of the wholly unscrupulous but brilliant strategist Reynard the

Fox over all adversaries. Chaucer arouses, only to deflate, expectations of the genre in *The Nun's Priest's Tale* (see vol. 1, p. 298).

Biography (Greek "life-writing"): a life as the subject of an extended narrative. Thus Izaak Walton, *The Life of Dr. Donne* (see vol. 1, p. 1309).

Comedy: a term primarily applied to drama, and derived from ancient drama, in opposition to **tragedy**. Comedy deals with humorously confusing, sometimes ridiculous situations in which the ending is, nevertheless, happy. Shakespeare, *Twelfth Night* (see vol. 1, p. 1079).

Comic mode: many genres (e.g., **romance, fabliau, comedy**) involve a happy ending in which justice is done, the ravages of time are arrested, and that which is lost is found. Such genres participate in a comic mode.

Dialogue (Greek "conversation"): Dialogue is a feature of many genres, especially in both the **novel** and drama. As a genre itself, dialogue is used in philosophical traditions especially (most famously in Plato's *Dialogues*), as the representation of a conversation in which a philosophical question is pursued among various speakers.

Didactic mode (Greek "teaching mode"): genres in a didactic mode are designed to instruct or teach, sometimes explicitly (e.g., sermons, philosophical **discourses, georgic**), and sometimes through the medium of fiction (e.g., **animal fable, parable**).

Discourse (Latin "running to and fro"): broadly, any nonfictional speech or writing; as a more specific genre, a philosophical meditation on a set theme. Thus Newman, *The Idea of a University* (see vol. 2, p. 1035).

Dramatic monologue (Greek "single speaking"): a poem in which the voice of a historical or fictional **character** speaks, unmediated by any narrator, to an implied though silent audience. See Tennyson, "Ulysses" (vol. 2, p. 1123); Browning, "The Bishop Orders His Tomb" (vol. 2, p. 1259); Eliot, "The Love Song of J. Alfred Prufrock" (vol. 2, p. 2289); Carol Ann Duffy, "Medusa" and "Mrs Lazarus" (vol. 2, pp. 2875–76).

Elegy: In **classical** literature elegy was a form written in elegiac **couplets** (a **hexameter** followed by a **pentameter**) devoted to many possible topics. In Ovidian elegy a lover meditates on the trials of erotic desire (e.g., Ovid's *Amores*). The **sonnet** sequences of both Sidney and Shakespeare exploit this genre, and, while it was still practiced in classical tradition by Donne ("On His Mistress" [see vol. 1, p. 1281]), by the later seventeenth century the term came to denote the poetry of loss, especially through the death of a loved person. See Tennyson, *In Memoriam* (vol. 2, p. 1138); Yeats, "In Memory of Major Robert Gregory" (vol. 2, p. 2034); Auden, "In Memory of W. B. Yeats" (see vol. 2, p. 2429); Heaney, "Clearances" (vol. 2, p. 2833).

Epic (synonym, *heroic poetry*): an extended narrative poem celebrating martial heroes, invoking divine inspiration, beginning in medias res (see **order**), written in a high style (including the deployment of **epic similes**; on high style, see **register**), and divided into long narrative sequences. Homer's *Iliad* and Virgil's *Aeneid* were the prime models for English writers of epic verse. Thus Milton, *Paradise Lost* (see vol. 1, p. 1829); Wordsworth, *The Prelude* (see vol. 2, p. 322); and Walcott, *Omeros* (see vol. 2, p. 2591). With its precise repertoire of stylistic resources, epic lent itself easily to **parodic** and **burlesque** forms, known as **mock epic;** thus Pope, *The Rape of the Lock* (see vol. 1, p. 2513).

Epigram: a short, pithy poem wittily expressed, often with wounding intent. See Jonson, *Epigrams* (see vol. 1, p. 1427).

Epigraph (Greek "inscription"): any formal statement inscribed on stone; also the brief formulation on a book's title page, or a quotation at the beginning of a poem, introducing the work's themes in the most compressed form possible.

Epistle (Latin "letter"): the letter can be shaped as a literary form, involving an intimate address often between equals. The *Epistles* of Horace provided a model for English writers from the sixteenth century. Thus Wyatt, "Mine own John Poins" (see vol. 1, p. 604), or Pope, "Epistle to a Lady" (vol. 1, p. 2598). Letters can be shaped to form the matter of an extended fiction, as the eighteenth-century epistolary **novel** (e.g., Samuel Richardson's *Pamela*).

Epitaph: a pithy formulation to be inscribed on a funeral monument. Thus Ralegh, "The Author's Epitaph, Made by Himself" (see vol. 1, p. 923).

Epithalamion (Greek "concerning the bridal chamber"): a wedding poem, celebrating the marriage and wishing the couple good fortune. Thus Spenser, *Epithalamion* (see vol. 1, p. 907).

Essay (French "trial, attempt"): an informal philosophical meditation, usually in prose and sometimes in verse. The journalistic periodical essay was developed in the early eighteenth century. Thus Addison and Steele, periodical essays (see vol. 1, p. 2470); Pope, *An Essay on Criticism* (see vol. 1, p. 2496).

Fabliau (French "little story," plural *fabliaux*): a short, funny, often bawdy narrative in low style (see **register**) imitated and developed from French models most subtly by Chaucer; see *The Miller's Prologue and Tale* (vol. 1, p. 239).

Farce: a play designed to provoke laughter through the often humiliating antics of stock **characters.** Congreve's *The Way of the World* (see vol. 1, p. 2228) draws on this tradition.

Georgic (Greek "farming"): Virgil's *Georgics* treat agricultural and occasionally scientific subjects, giving instructions on the proper management of farms. Unlike **pastoral,** which treats the countryside as a place of recreational idleness among shepherds, the georgic treats it as a place of productive labor. For an English poem that critiques both genres, see Crabbe, "The Village" (vol. 1, p. 2887).

Heroic poetry: see **epic.**

Homily (Greek "discourse"): a sermon, to be preached in church; *Book of Homilies* (see vol. 1, p. 635). Writers of literary fiction sometimes exploit the homily, or sermon, as in Chaucer, *The Pardoner's Tale* (see vol. 1, p. 284).

Journal (French "daily"): a diary, or daily record of ephemeral experience, whose perspectives are concentrated on, and limited by, the experiences of single days. Thus Pepys, *Diary* (see vol. 1, p. 2134).

Lai: a short narrative, often characterized by images of great intensity; a French term, and a form practiced by Marie de France (see vol. 1, p. 141).

Legend (Latin "requiring to be read"): a narrative of a celebrated, possibly historical, but mortal **protagonist.** To be distinguished from **myth.** Thus the "Arthurian legend" but the "myth of Proserpine."

Lyric (from Greek "lyre"): Initially meaning a song, "lyric" refers to a short poetic form, without restriction of meter, in which the expression of personal emotion, often by a voice in the first person, is given primacy over narrative sequence. Thus "The Wife's Lament" (see vol. 1, p. 113); Yeats, "The Wild Swans at Coole" (see vol. 2, p. 2033).

Lullaby: a bedtime, sleep-inducing song for children, in simple and regular meter. Adapted by Auden, "Lullaby" (see vol. 2, p. 2423).

Masque: costly entertainments of the Stuart court, involving dance, song, speech, and elaborate stage effects, in which courtiers themselves participated. See Jonson, *The Masque of Blackness* (see vol. 1, p. 1327).

Myth: the narrative of **protagonists** with, or subject to, superhuman powers. A myth expresses some profound foundational truth, often by accounting for the origin of natural phenomena. To be distinguished from **legend.** Thus the "Arthurian legend" but the "myth of Proserpine."

Novel: an extremely flexible genre in both form and subject matter. Usually in prose, giving high priority to narration of events, with a certain expectation of length, novels are preponderantly rooted in a specific, and often complex, social world; sensitive to the realities of material life; and often focused on one **character** or a small circle of central characters. By contrast with chivalric **romance** (the main European narrative genre prior to the novel), novels tend to eschew the marvelous in favor of a recognizable social world and credible action. The novel's openness allows it to participate in all modes, and to be co-opted for a huge variety of subgenres. In English literature the novel dates from the late seventeenth century and has been astonishingly successful in appealing to a huge readership, particularly in the nineteenth and twentieth centuries. The English and Irish tradition of the novel includes, for example, Fielding, Austen, the Brontë sisters, Dickens, George Eliot, Conrad, Woolf, Lawrence, Joyce, to name but a few very great exponents of the genre.

Novella: a short **novel,** often characterized by imagistic intensity. Conrad, *Heart of Darkness* (see vol. 2, p. 1890).

Ode (Greek "song"): a **lyric** poem in elevated, or high style (see **register),** often addressed to a natural force, a person, or an abstract quality. The Pindaric ode in English is made up of **stanzas** of unequal length, while the Horatian ode has stanzas of equal length. For examples of both types, see, respectively, Wordsworth, "Ode: Intimations of Immortality" (vol. 2, p. 306); and Marvell, "An Horatian Ode" (vol. 1, p. 1712), or Keats, "Ode on Melancholy" (vol. 2, p. 906). For a fuller discussion, see the headnote to Jonson's "Ode on Cary and Morison" (vol. 1, p. 1439).

Panegyric: Demonstrative, or epideictic (Greek "showing"), rhetoric was a branch of **classical** rhetoric. Its own two main branches were the rhetoric of praise on the one hand and of vituperation on the other. Panegyric, or eulogy (Greek "sweet speaking"), or encomium (plural *encomia),* is the term used to describe the speeches or writings of praise.

Parable: a simple story designed to provoke, and often accompanied by, **allegorical** interpretation, most famously by Christ as reported in the Gospels.

Pastoral (from Latin "pastor," shepherd): Pastoral is set among shepherds, making often refined **allusion** to other apparently unconnected subjects (sometimes politics) from the potentially idyllic world of highly literary if illiterate shepherds. Pastoral is distinguished from **georgic** by representing recreational rural idleness, whereas the georgic offers instruction on how to manage rural labor. English writers had classical models in the *Idylls* of Theocritus in Greek and Virgil's *Eclogues* in Latin. Pastoral is also called bucolic (from the Greek word for "herdsman"). Thus Spenser, *Shepheardes Calender* (see vol. 1, p. 708).

Romance: From the twelfth to the sixteenth century, the main form of European narrative, in either verse or prose, was that of chivalric romance.

Romance, like the later **novel,** is a very fluid genre, but romances are often characterized by (i) a tripartite structure of social integration, followed by disintegration, involving moral tests and often marvelous events, itself the prelude to reintegration in a happy ending, frequently of marriage; (ii) **high-style** diction; (iii) aristocratic social mileux. Thus *Sir Gawain and the Green Knight* (see vol. 1, p. 160); Spenser's (unfinished) *Faerie Queene* (vol. 1, p. 713). The immensely popular, fertile genre was absorbed, in both domesticated and undomesticated form, by the novel. For an adaptation of romance, see Chaucer, *Wife of Bath's Tale* (vol. 1, p. 256).

Satire: In Roman literature (e.g., Juvenal), the communication, in the form of a letter between equals, complaining of the ills of contemporary society. The genre in this form is characterized by a first-person narrator exasperated by social ills; the letter form; a high frequency of contemporary reference; and the use of invective in **low-style** language. Pope practices the genre thus in the *Epistle to Dr. Arbuthnot* (see vol. 1, p. 2548). Wyatt's "Mine own John Poins" (see vol. 1, p. 604) draws ultimately on a gentler, Horatian model of the genre.

Satiric mode: Works in a very large variety of genres are devoted to the more or less savage attack on social ills. Thus Swift's travel narrative *Gulliver's Travels* (see vol. 1, p. 2323), his **essay** "A Modest Proposal" (vol. 1, p. 2462), Pope's mock-**epic** *The Dunciad* (vol. 1, p. 2559), and Gay's *Beggar's Opera* (vol. 1, p. 2613), to look no further than the eighteenth century, are all within a satiric mode.

Short story: generically similar to, though shorter and more concentrated than, the **novel;** often published as part of a collection. Thus Mansfield, "The Daughters of the Late Colonel" (see vol. 2, p. 2333).

Topographical poem (Greek "place writing"): a poem devoted to the meditative description of particular places. Thus Gray, "Ode on a Distant Prospect of Eton College" (see vol. 1, p. 2863).

Tragedy: a dramatic representation of the fall of kings or nobles, beginning in happiness and ending in catastrophe. Later transferred to other social mileux. The opposite of **comedy.** Shakespeare, *King Lear* (see vol. 1, p. 1139).

Tragic mode: Many genres (**epic** poetry, **legend**ary chronicles, **tragedy,** the **novel**) either do or can participate in a tragic mode, by representing the fall of noble **protagonists** and the irreparable ravages of human society and history.

Tragicomedy: a play in which potentially tragic events turn out to have a happy, or **comic,** ending. Thus Shakespeare, *Measure for Measure.*

C. Miscellaneous

Act: the major subdivision of a play, usually divided into **scenes.**

Aesthetics (from Greek, "to feel, apprehend by the senses"): the philosophy of artistic meaning as a distinct mode of apprehending untranslatable truth, defined as an alternative to rational enquiry, which is purely abstract. Developed in the late eighteenth century by the German philosopher Immanuel Kant especially.

Allusion: Literary allusion is a passing but illuminating reference within a literary text to another, well-known text (often biblical or **classical**). Topical allusions are also, of course, common in certain modes, especially **satire.**

Anagnorisis (Greek "recognition"): the moment of **protagonists'** recognition in a narrative, which is also often the moment of moral understanding.

Apostrophe (from Greek "turning away"): an address, often to an absent person, a force, or a quality. For example, a poet makes an apostrophe to a Muse when invoking her for inspiration.

Blazon: strictly, a heraldic shield; in rhetorical usage, a **topos** whereby the individual elements of a beloved's face and body are singled out for **hyperbolic** admiration. Spenser, *Epithalamion*, lines 167–84 (see vol. 1, p. 907). For an inversion of the **topos**, see Shakespeare, Sonnet 130 (vol. 1, p. 1074).

Burlesque (French and Italian "mocking"): a work that adopts the **conventions** of a genre with the aim less of comically mocking the genre than of satirically mocking the society so represented (see **satire**). Thus Pope's *Rape of the Lock* (see vol. 1, p. 2513) does not mock **classical epic** so much as contemporary mores.

Canon (Greek "rule"): the group of texts regarded as worthy of special respect or attention by a given institution. Also, the group of texts regarded as definitely having been written by a certain author.

Catastrophe (Greek "overturning"): the decisive turn in **tragedy** by which the plot is resolved and, usually, the **protagonist** dies.

Catharsis (Greek "cleansing"): According to Aristotle, the effect of **tragedy** on its audience, through their experience of pity and terror, was a kind of spiritual cleansing, or catharsis.

Character (Greek "stamp, impression"): a person, personified animal, or other figure represented in a literary work, especially in narrative and drama. The more a character seems to generate the action of a narrative, and the less he or she seems merely to serve a preordained narrative pattern, the "fuller," or more "rounded," a character is said to be. A "stock" character, common particularly in many comic genres, will perform a predictable function in different works of a given genre.

Classical, Classicism, Classic: Each term can be widely applied, but in English literary discourse, "classical" primarily describes the works of either Greek or Roman antiquity. "Classicism" denotes the practice of art forms inspired by classical antiquity, in particular the observance of rhetorical norms of **decorum** and balance, as opposed to following the dictates of untutored inspiration, as in Romanticism. "Classic" denotes an especially famous work within a given **canon.**

Climax (Greek "ladder"): a moment of great intensity and structural change, especially in drama. Also a figure of speech whereby a sequence of verbally linked clauses is made, in which each successive clause is of greater consequence than its predecessor. Bacon, *Of Studies:* "Studies serve for pastimes, for ornaments, and for abilities. Their chief use for pastimes is in privateness and retiring; for ornament, is in discourse; and for ability, is in judgement" (see vol. 1, p. 1561).

Convention: a repeatedly recurring feature (in either form or content) of works, occurring in combination with other recurring formal features, constitutes a convention of a particular genre.

Decorum (Latin "that which is fitting"): a rhetorical principle whereby each formal aspect of a work should be in keeping with its subject matter and/ or audience.

Denouement (French "unknotting"): the point at which a narrative can be resolved and so ended.

Dramatic irony: a feature of narrative and drama, whereby the audience knows that the outcome of an action will be the opposite of that intended by a **character.**

Ecphrasis (Greek "speaking out"): a **topos** whereby a work of visual art is represented in a literary work. Auden, "Musée des Beaux Arts" (see vol. 2, p. 2428).

Exegesis (Greek "leading out"): interpretation, traditionally of the biblical text, but, by transference, of any text.

Exemplum (Latin "example"): an example inserted into a usually nonfictional writing (e.g., sermon or **essay**) to give extra force to an abstract thesis. Thus Johnson's example of "Sober" in his essay "On Idleness" (see vol. 1, p. 2678).

Hermeneutics (from the Greek god Hermes, messenger between the gods and humankind): the science of interpretation, first formulated as such by the German philosophical theologian Friedrich Schleiermacher in the early nineteenth century.

Imitation: the practice whereby writers strive ideally to reproduce and yet renew the **conventions** of an older form, often derived from **classical** civilization. Such a practice will be praised in periods of classicism (e.g., the eighteenth century) and repudiated in periods dominated by a model of inspiration (e.g., Romanticism).

Parody: a work that uses the **conventions** of a particular genre with the aim of comically mocking a **topos**, a genre, or a particular exponent of a genre. Shakespeare parodies the topos of **blazon** in Sonnet 130 (see vol. 1, p. 1074).

Pathetic fallacy: the attribution of sentiment to natural phenomena, as if they were in sympathy with human feelings. Thus Milton, *Lycidas*, lines 146–47: "With cowslips wan that hang the pensive head, / And every flower that sad embroidery wears" (see vol. 1, p. 1810). For critique of the practice, see Ruskin (who coined the term), "Of the Pathetic Fallacy" (vol. 2, p. 1322).

Peripeteia (Greek "turning about"): the sudden reversal of fortune (in both directions) in a dramatic work.

Persona (Latin "sound through"): originally the mask worn in the Roman theater to magnify an actor's voice; in literary discourse persona (plural *personae*) refers to the narrator or speaker of a text, by whose voice the author may mask him- or herself. Eliot, "The Love Song of J. Alfred Prufrock" (see vol. 2, p. 2289).

Protagonist (Greek "first actor"): the hero or heroine of a drama or narrative.

Rhetoric: the art of verbal persuasion. **Classical** rhetoricians distinguished three areas of rhetoric: the forensic, to be used in law courts; the deliberative, to be used in political or philosophical deliberations; and the demonstrative, or epideictic, to be used for the purposes of public praise or blame. Rhetorical manuals covered all the skills required of a speaker, from the management of style and structure to delivery. These manuals powerfully influenced the theory of poetics as a separate branch of verbal practice, particularly in the matter of style.

Scene: a subdivision of an **act,** itself a subdivision of a dramatic performance and/or text. The action of a scene usually occurs in one place.

Sensibility (from Latin, "capable of being perceived by the senses"): as a literary term, an eighteenth-century concept derived from moral philosophy that stressed the social importance of fellow feeling and particularly of sympathy in social relations. The concept generated a literature of "sensibility," such as the sentimental **novel** (the most famous of which was Goethe's *Sorrows of the Young Werther* [1774]), or sentimental poetry, such as Cowper's passage on the stricken deer in *The Task* (see vol. 1, p. 2893).

Soliloquy (Latin "single speaking"): a **topos** of drama, in which a **character,** alone or thinking to be alone on stage, speaks so as to give the audience access to his or her private thoughts. Thus Viola's soliloquy in Shakespeare, *Twelfth Night* 2.2.17–41 (vol. 1, p. 1095).

Sublime: As a concept generating a literary movement, the sublime refers to the realm of experience beyond the measurable, and so beyond the rational, produced especially by the terrors and grandeur of natural phenomena. Derived especially from the first-century Greek treatise *On the Sublime,* sometimes attributed to Longinus, the notion of the sublime was in the later eighteenth century a spur to Romanticism.

Taste (from Italian "touch"): Although medieval monastic traditions used eating and tasting as a metaphor for reading, the concept of taste as a personal ideal to be cultivated by, and applied to, the appreciation and judgment of works of art in general was developed in the eighteenth century.

Topos (Greek "place," plural *topoi*): a commonplace in the content of a given kind of literature. Originally, in **classical** rhetoric, the topoi were tried-and-tested stimuli to literary invention: lists of standard headings under which a subject might be investigated. In medieval narrative poems, for example, it was commonplace to begin with a description of spring. Writers did, of course, render the commonplace uncommon, as in Chaucer's spring scene at the opening of *The Canterbury Tales* (see vol. 1, p. 218).

Tradition (from Latin "passing on"): A literary tradition is whatever is passed on or revived from the past in a single literary culture, or drawn from others to enrich a writer's culture. "Tradition" is fluid in reference, ranging from small to large referents: thus it may refer to a relatively small aspect of texts (e.g., the tradition of **iambic pentameter**), or it may, at the other extreme, refer to the body of texts that constitute a **canon.**

Translation (Latin "carrying across"): the rendering of a text written in one language into another.

Vernacular (from Latin "verna," servant): the language of the people, as distinguished from learned and arcane languages. From the later Middle Ages especially, the "vernacular" languages and literatures of Europe distinguished themselves from the learned languages and literatures of Latin, Greek, and Hebrew.

Wit: Originally a synonym for "reason" in Old and Middle English, "wit" became a literary ideal in the Renaissance as brilliant play of the full range of mental resources. For eighteenth-century writers, the notion necessarily involved pleasing expression, as in Pope's definition of true wit as "Nature to advantage dressed, / What oft was thought, but ne'er so well expressed" (*Essay on Criticism,* lines 297–98; (see vol. 1, p. 2503). See also Johnson, *Lives of the Poets,* "Cowley," on "metaphysical wit" (see vol. 1, p. 2766). Romantic theory of the imagination deprived wit of its full range of apprehension, whence the word came to be restricted to its modern sense, as the clever play of mind that produces laughter.

D. Publishing History, Censorship

By the time we read texts in published books, they have already been treated— that is, changed by authors, editors, and printers—in many ways. Although there are differences across history, in each period literary works are subject to pressures of many kinds, which apply before, while, and after an author writes. The pressures might be financial, as in the relations of author and patron; commercial, as in the marketing of books; and legal, as in, during some periods, the negotiation through official and unofficial censorship. In addition, texts in all periods undergo technological processes, as they move from the material forms in which an author produced them to the forms in which they are presented to readers. Some of the terms below designate important material forms in which books were produced, disseminated, and surveyed across the historical span of this anthology. Others designate the skills developed to understand these processes. The anthology's introductions to individual periods discuss the particular forms these phenomena took in different eras.

Bookseller: In England, and particularly in London, commercial bookmaking and -selling enterprises came into being in the early fourteenth century. These were loose organizations of artisans who usually lived in the same neighborhoods (around St. Paul's Cathedral in London). A bookseller or dealer would coordinate the production of hand-copied books for wealthy patrons (see **patronage**), who would order books to be custom-made. After the introduction of **printing** in the late fifteenth century, authors generally sold the rights to their work to booksellers, without any further **royalties.** Booksellers, who often had their own shops, belonged to the **Stationers' Company.** This system lasted into the eighteenth century. In 1710, however, authors were for the first time granted **copyright,** which tipped the commercial balance in their favor, against booksellers.

Censorship: The term applies to any mechanism for restricting what can be published. Historically, the reasons for imposing censorship are heresy, sedition, blasphemy, libel, or obscenity. External censorship is imposed by institutions having legislative sanctions at their disposal. Thus the pre-Reformation Church imposed the Constitutions of Archbishop Arundel of 1409, aimed at repressing the Lollard "heresy." After the Reformation, some key events in the history of censorship are as follows: 1547, when anti-Lollard legislation and legislation made by Henry VIII concerning treason by writing (1534) were abolished; the Licensing Order of 1643, which legislated that works be licensed, through the Stationers' Company, prior to publication; and 1695, when the last such Act stipulating prepublication licensing lapsed. Postpublication censorship continued in different periods for different reasons. Thus, for example, British publication of D. H. Lawrence's *Lady Chatterley's Lover* (1928) was obstructed (though unsuccessfully) in 1960, under the Obscene Publications Act of 1959. Censorship can also be international: although not published in Iran, Salman Rushdie's *Satanic Verses* (1988) was censored in that country, where the leader, Ayatollah Ruhollah Khomeini, proclaimed a fatwa (religious decree) promising the author's execution. Very often censorship is not imposed externally, however: authors or publishers can censor work in anticipation of what will incur the wrath of readers or the penalties of the law. Victorian and Edwardian publishers of **novels,** for example, urged authors to remove potentially offensive material, especially for serial publication in popular magazines.

Codex (Latin "book"): having the format of a book (usually applied to manuscript books), as distinguished originally from the scroll, which was the standard form of written document in ancient Rome.

Copyright: the legal protection afforded to authors for control of their work's publication, in an attempt to ensure due financial reward. Some key dates in the history of copyright in the United Kingdom are as follows: 1710, when a statute gave authors the exclusive right to publish their work for fourteen years, and fourteen years more if the author were still alive when the first term had expired; 1842, when the period of authorial control was extended to forty-two years; and 1911, when the term was extended yet further, to fifty years after the author's death. In 1995 the period of protection was harmonized with the laws in other European countries to be the life of the author plus seventy years. In the United States no works first published before 1923 are in copyright. Works published since 1978 are, as in the United Kingdom, protected for the life of the author plus seventy years.

Copy text: the particular text of a work used by a textual editor as the basis of an edition of that work.

Folio: Books come in different shapes, depending originally on the number of times a standard sheet of paper is folded. One fold produces a large volume, a *folio* book; two folds produce a *quarto,* four an *octavo,* and six a very small *duodecimo.* Generally speaking, the larger the book, the grander and more expensive. Shakespeare's plays were, for example, first printed in quartos, but were gathered into a folio edition in 1623.

Foul papers: versions of a work before an author has produced, if she or he has, a final copy (a "fair copy") with all corrections removed.

Manuscript (Latin, "written by hand"): Any text written physically by hand is a manuscript. Before the introduction of **printing** with moveable type in 1476, all texts in England were produced and reproduced by hand, in manuscript. This is an extremely labor-intensive task, using expensive materials (e.g., animal skins); the cost of books produced thereby was, accordingly, very high. Even after the introduction of printing, many texts continued to be produced in manuscript. This is obviously true of letters, for example, but until the eighteenth century, poetry written within aristocratic circles was often transmitted in manuscript copies.

Paleography (Greek "ancient writing"): the art of deciphering, describing, and dating forms of handwriting.

Patronage (Latin "protector"): Many technological, legal, and commercial supports were necessary before professional authorship became possible. Although some playwrights (e.g., Shakespeare) made a living by writing for the theater, other authors needed, principally, the large-scale reproductive capacities of **printing** and the security of **copyright** to make a living from writing. Before these conditions obtained, many authors had another main occupation, and most authors had to rely on patronage. In different periods, institutions or individuals offered material support, or patronage, to authors. Thus in Anglo-Saxon England, monasteries afforded the conditions of writing to monastic authors. Between the twelfth and the seventeenth centuries, the main source of patronage was the royal court. Authors offered patrons prestige and ideological support in return for financial support. Even as the conditions of professional authorship came into being at the beginning of the eighteenth century, older forms of direct patronage were not altogether displaced until the middle of the century.

Periodical: Whereas journalism, strictly, applies to daily writing (from French "jour," day), periodical writing appears at larger, but still frequent, intervals, characteristically in the form of the **essay.** Periodicals were developed especially in the eighteenth century.

Printing: Printing, or the mechanical reproduction of books using moveable type, was invented in Germany in the mid-fifteenth century by Johannes Gutenberg; it quickly spread throughout Europe. William Caxton brought printing into England from the Low Countries in 1476. Much greater powers of reproduction at much lower prices transformed every aspect of literary culture.

Publisher: the person or company responsible for the commissioning and publicizing of printed matter. In the early period of **printing,** publisher, printer, and bookseller were often the same person. This trend continued in the ascendancy of the **Stationers' Company,** between the middle of the sixteenth and the end of the seventeenth centuries. Toward the end of the seventeenth century, these three functions began to separate, leading to their modern distinctions.

Royalties: an agreed-upon proportion of the price of each copy of a work sold, paid by the publisher to the author, or an agreed-upon fee paid to the playwright for each performance of a play.

Scribe: in **manuscript** culture, the scribe is the copyist who reproduces a text by hand.

Stationers' Company: The Stationers' Company was an English guild incorporating various tradesmen, including printers, publishers, and booksellers, skilled in the production and selling of books. It was formed in 1403, received its royal charter in 1557, and served as a means both of producing and of regulating books. Authors would sell the manuscripts of their books to individual stationers, who incurred the risks and took the profits of producing and selling the books. The stationers entered their rights over given books in the Stationers' Register. They also regulated the book trade and held their monopoly by licensing books and by being empowered to seize unauthorized books and imprison resisters. This system of licensing broke down in the social unrest of the Civil War and Interregnum (1640–60), and it ended in 1695. Even after the end of licensing, the Stationers' Company continued to be an intrinsic part of the **copyright** process, since the 1710 copyright statute directed that copyright had to be registered at Stationers' Hall.

Subscription: An eighteenth-century system of bookselling somewhere between direct **patronage** and impersonal sales. A subscriber paid half the cost of a book before publication and half on delivery. The author received these payments directly. The subscriber's name appeared in the prefatory pages.

Textual criticism: works in all periods often exist in many subtly or not so subtly different forms. This is especially true with regard to manuscript textual reproduction, but it also applies to printed texts. Textual criticism is the art, developed from the fifteenth century in Italy but raised to new levels of sophistication from the eighteenth century, of deciphering different historical states of texts. This art involves the analysis of textual variants, often with the aim of distinguishing authorial from scribal forms.

Geographic Nomenclature

The British Isles refers to the prominent group of islands off the northwest coast of Europe, especially to the two largest, **Great Britain** and **Ireland**. At present these comprise two sovereign states: **the Republic of Ireland**, or **Éire**, and **the United Kingdom of Great Britain and Northern Ireland**—known for short as the **United Kingdom** or the **U.K.** Most of the smaller islands are part of the **U.K.** but a few, like the **Isle of Man** and the tiny **Channel Islands**, are largely independent. The **U.K.** is often loosely referred to as "**Britain**" or "**Great Britain**" and is sometimes called simply, if inaccurately, "**England**." For obvious reasons, the latter usage is rarely heard among the inhabitants of the other countries of the **U.K.**—Scotland, Wales, and **Northern Ireland** (sometimes called **Ulster**). England is by far the most populous part of the kingdom, as well as the seat of its capital, London.

From the first to the fifth century C.E. most of what is now **England** and **Wales** was a province of the Roman Empire called **Britain** (in Latin, **Britannia**). After the fall of Rome, much of the island was invaded and settled by peoples from northern Germany and Denmark speaking what we now call Old English. These peoples are collectively known as the Anglo-Saxons, and the word **England** is related to the first element of their name. By the time of the Norman Conquest (1066) most of the kingdoms founded by the Anglo-Saxons and subsequent Viking invaders had coalesced into the kingdom of **England**, which, in the latter Middle Ages, conquered and largely absorbed the neighboring Celtic kingdom of **Wales**. In 1603 James VI of **Scotland** inherited the island's other throne as James I of **England**, and for the next hundred years—except for the brief period of Puritan rule—**Scotland** (both its English-speaking **Lowlands** and its Gaelic-speaking **Highlands**) and **England** (with **Wales**) were two kingdoms under a single king. In 1707 the Act of Union welded them together as **the United Kingdom of Great Britain. Ireland,** where English rule had begun in the twelfth century and been tightened in the sixteenth, was incorporated by the 1800–1801 Act of Union into **the United Kingdom of Great Britain and Ireland**. With the division of Ireland and the establishment of **the Irish Free State** after World War I, this name was modified to its present form, and in 1949 **the Irish Free State** became **the Republic of Ireland**. In 1999 **Scotland** elected a separate parliament it had relinquished in 1707, and **Wales** elected an assembly it lost in 1409; neither Scotland nor Wales ceased to be part of the **United Kingdom**.

The **British Isles** are further divided into counties, which in **Great Britain** are also known as shires. This word, with its vowel shortened in pronunciation, forms the suffix in the names of many counties, such as **Yorkshire, Wiltshire, Somersetshire**.

The Latin names **Britannia (Britain), Caledonia (Scotland)**, and **Hibernia (Ireland)** are sometimes used in poetic diction; so too is **Britain**'s ancient Celtic name, **Albion**. Because of its accidental resemblance to *albus* (Latin for "white"), **Albion** is especially associated with the chalk cliffs that seem to gird much of the English coast like defensive walls.

The British Empire took its name from **the British Isles** because it was created not only by the **English** but also by the **Irish, Scots,** and **Welsh**, as well as by civilians and servicemen from other constituent countries of the empire. Some of the empire's **overseas colonies**, or **crown colonies**, were populated largely by settlers of European origin and their descendants. These predominantly white **settler colonies**, such as **Canada, Australia**, and **New Zealand**, were allowed significant self-government in the nineteenth century and recognized as **dominions** in the early twentieth century.

The **white dominions** became members of **the Commonwealth of Nations**, also called **the Commonwealth, the British Commonwealth,** and "**the Old Commonwealth**" at different times, an association of sovereign states under the symbolic leadership of the British monarch.

Other **overseas colonies** of the empire had mostly indigenous populations (or, in the Caribbean, the descendants of imported slaves, indentured servants, and others). These **colonies** were granted political independence after World War II, later than the **dominions**, and have often been referred to since as **postcolonial** nations. In South and Southeast Asia, **India** and **Pakistan** gained independence in 1947, followed by other countries including **Sri Lanka** (formerly **Ceylon**), **Burma** (now **Myanmar**), **Malaya** (now **Malaysia**), and **Singapore**. In West and East Africa, the **Gold Coast** was decolonized as **Ghana** in 1957, **Nigeria** in 1960, **Sierra Leone** in 1961, **Uganda** in 1962, **Kenya** in 1963, and so forth, while in southern Africa, the white minority government of **South Africa** was already independent in 1931, though majority rule did not come until 1994. In the Caribbean, **Jamaica** and **Trinidad and Tobago** won independence in 1962, followed by **Barbados** in 1966, and other islands of the British West Indies in the 1970s and '80s. Other regions with nations emerging out of British colonial rule included Central America (**British Honduras**, now **Belize**), South America (**British Guiana**, now **Guyana**), the Pacific islands (**Fiji**), and Europe (**Cyprus, Malta**). After decolonization, many of these nations chose to remain within a newly conceived **Commonwealth** and are sometimes referred to as "**New Commonwealth**" countries. Some nations, such as **Ireland, Pakistan,** and **South Africa,** withdrew from the **Commonwealth,** though **South Africa** and **Pakistan** eventually rejoined, and others, such as **Burma** (**Myanmar**), gained independence outside the **Commonwealth**. Britain's last major overseas colony, **Hong Kong,** was returned to Chinese sovereignty in 1997, but while Britain retains only a handful of dependent territories, such as **Bermuda** and **Montserrat,** the scope of the **Commonwealth** remains vast, with 30 percent of the world's population.

British Money

One of the most dramatic changes to the system of British money came in 1971. In the system previously in place, the pound consisted of 20 shillings, each containing 12 pence, making 240 pence to the pound. Since 1971, British money has been calculated on the decimal system, with 100 pence to the pound. Britons' experience of paper money did not change very drastically: as before, 5- and 10-pound notes constitute the majority of bills passing through their hands (in addition, 20- and 50-pound notes have been added). But the shift necessitated a whole new way of thinking about and exchanging coins and marked the demise of the shilling, one of the fundamental units of British monetary history. Many other coins, still frequently encountered in literature, had already passed. These include the groat, worth 4 pence (the word "groat" is often used to signify a trifling sum); the angel (which depicted the archangel Michael triumphing over a dragon), valued at 10 shillings; the mark, worth in its day two-thirds of a pound or 13 shillings 4 pence; and the sovereign, a gold coin initially worth 22 shillings 6 pence, later valued at 1 pound, last circulated in 1932. One prominent older coin, the guinea, was worth a pound and a shilling; though it has not been minted since 1813, a very few quality items or prestige awards (like the purse in a horse race) may still be quoted in guineas. (The table below includes some other well-known, obsolete coins.) Colloquially, a pound was (and is) called a quid; a shilling a bob; sixpence, a tanner; a copper could refer to a penny, a half-penny, or a farthing ($\frac{1}{4}$ penny).

Old Currency	New Currency
1 pound note	1 pound coin (or note in Scotland)
10 shilling (half-pound note)	50 pence
5 shilling (crown)	
2½ shilling (half crown)	20 pence
2 shilling (florin)	10 pence
1 shilling	5 pence
6 pence	
2½ pence	1 penny
2 pence	
1 penny	
½ penny	
¼ penny (farthing)	

In recent years, the British government and people have been contemplating and debating a change even greater than the shift to the decimal system. Britain, a member of the European Union, may adopt the EU's common currency, the Euro, and eventually see the pound itself become obsolete. More than many other EU-member countries, Britain has resisted this change: many people strongly identify their country with its rich commercial history and tend to view their currency patriotically as a national symbol.

Even more challenging than sorting out the values of obsolete coins is calculating for any given period the purchasing power of money, which fluctuates over time by its very nature. At the beginning of the twentieth century, 1 pound was worth about 5 American dollars, though those bought three to four times what they now do. Now, the pound buys anywhere from $1.50 to $1.90. As difficult as it is to generalize, it is clear that money used to be worth much more than it is currently. In Anglo-Saxon times, the most valuable circulating coin was the silver penny: four would buy a sheep. Beyond long-term inflationary trends, prices varied from times of plenty to those marked by poor harvests; from peacetime to wartime; from the country to the metropolis (life in London has always been very expensive); and wages varied according to the availability of labor (wages rose sharply, for instance, during the devastating Black Death in the fourteenth century). The chart below provides a glimpse of some actual prices of given periods and their changes across time, though all the variables mentioned above prevent them from being definitive. Even from one year to the next, an added tax on gin or tea could drastically raise prices, and a lottery ticket could cost much more the night before the drawing than just a month earlier. Still, the prices quoted below do indicate important trends, such as the disparity of incomes in British society and the costs of basic commodities. In the chart below, the symbol £ is used for pound, s. for shilling, d. for a penny (from Latin *denarius*); a sum would normally be written £2.19.3, i.e., 2 pounds, 19 shillings, 3 pence. (This is Leopold Bloom's budget for the day depicted in Joyce's novel *Ulysses* [1922]; in the new currency, it would be about £2.96.)

circa	1390	1590	1650	1750	1815	1875	1950
food and drink	gallon (8 pints) of ale, 1.5d.	tankard of beer, .5d.	coffee, 1d. a dish	"drunk for a penny, dead drunk for twopence" (gin shop sign in Hogarth print)	ounce of laudanum, 3d.	pint of beer, 3d.	pint of Guinness stout, 11d.
	gallon (8 pints) of wine, 3 to 4d.	pound of beef, 2s. 5d.	chicken, 1s. 4d.	dinner at a steakhouse, 1s.	ham and potato dinner for two, 7s.	dinner in a good hotel, 5s.	pound of beef, 2s. 2d.
	pound of cinnamon, 1 to 3s.	pound of cinnamon, 10s. 6d.	pound of tea, £3 10s.	pound of tea, 16s.	Prince Regent's dinner party for 2000, £12.000	pound of tea, 2s.	dinner on railway car, 7s. 6d.
entertainment	no cost to watch a cycle play	admission to public theater, 1 to 3d.	falcon, £11 5s.	theater tickets, 1 to 5s.	admission to Covent Garden theater, 1 to 7s.	theater tickets, 6d. to 7s.	admission to Old Vic theater, 1s. 6d. to 10s. 6d.
	contributory admission to professional troupe theater	cheap seat in private theater, 6d.	billiard table, £25	admission to Vauxhall Gardens, 1s.	annual subscription to Almack's (exclusive club), 10 guineas	admission to Madam Tussaud's waxworks, 1s.	admission to Odeon cinema, Manchester, 1s. 3d.
	maintenance for royal hounds at Windsor, .75d. a day	"to see a dead Indian" (qtd. in *The Tempest*), 1.25d. (ten "doits")	three-quarter-length portrait painting, £31	lottery ticket, £20 (shares were sold)	Jane Austen's piano, 30 guineas	annual fees at a gentleman's club, 7–10 guineas	tropical fish tank, £4 4s.
reading	cheap romance, 1s.	play quarto, 6d.	pamphlet, 1 to 6d.	issue of *The Gentleman's Magazine*, 6d.	issue of *Edinburgh Review*, 6s.	copy of *The Times*, 3d.	copy of *The Times*, 3d.

circa	1390	1590	1650	1750	1815	1875	1950
	a Latin Bible, 2 to £4	Shakespeare's *First Folio* (1623), £1	student Bible, 6s.	cheap edition of Milton, 2s.	membership in circulating library (3rd class), £1 4s. a year	illustrated edition of *Through the Looking-glass*, 6s.	issue of *Eagle* comics, 4.5d.
	payment for illuminating a liturgical book, £22 9s.	Foxe's *Acts and Monuments*, 24s.	Hobbes's *Leviathan*, 8s.	Johnson's *Dictionary*, folio, 2 vols., £4 10s.	1st edition of Austen's *Pride and Prejudice*, 18s.	1st edition of Trollope's *The Way We Live Now*, 2 vols., £1 1s.	Orwell's *Nineteen Eighty Four*, paperback, 3s. 6d.
transportation	night's supply of hay for horse, 2d.	wherry (whole boat) across Thames, 1d.	day's journey, coach, 10s.	boat across Thames, 4d.	coach ride, outside, 2 to 3d. a mile; inside, 4 to 5d. a mile	15-minute journey in a London cab, 1s. 6d.	London tube fare, about 2d. a mile
	coach, £8	hiring a horse for a day, 12d.	coach horse, £30	coach fare, London to Edinburgh, £4 10s.	palanquin transport in Madras, 5s. a day	railway, 3rd class, London to Plymouth, 18s. 8d. (about 1d. a mile)	petrol, 3s. a gallon
	quality horse, £10	hiring a coach for a day, 10s.	fancy carriage, £170	transport to America, £5	passage, Liverpool to New York, £10	passage to India, 1st class, £50	midsize Austin sedan, £449 plus £188 4s. 2d. tax
clothes	clothing allowance for peasant, 3s. a year	shoes with buckles, 8d.	footman's frieze coat, 15s.	working woman's gown, 6s. 6d.	checked muslin, 7s. per yard	flannel for a cheap petticoat, 1s. 3d. a yard	woman's sun frock, £3 13s. 10d.

circa			labor/incomes			
1390	shoes for gentry wearer, 4d.	hat for gentry wearer, 10d.	hiring a skilled building worker, 4d. a day	wage for professional scribe, £2 3s. 4d. a year + cloak	minimum income to be called gentleman, £10 a year; for knighthood, 40 to £400	income from land of richest magnates, £3,500 a year
1590	woman's gloves, £1 5s.	fine cloak, £16	actor's daily wage during playing season, 1s.	household servant 2 to £5 a year + food, clothing	minimum income for eligibility for knighthood, £30 a year	income from land of average earl, £4000 a year
1650	falconer's hat, 10s.	black cloth for mourning household of an earl, £100	agricultural laborer, 6s. 5d. a week	tutor to nobleman's children, £30 a year	Milton's salary as Secretary of Foreign Tongues, £288 a year	Earl of Bedford's income, £8,000 a year
1750	gentleman's suit, £8	very fine wig, £30	price of boy slave, £32	housemaid's wage, £6 to £8 a year	Boswell's allowance, £200 a year	Duke of Newcastle's income, £40,000 a year
1815	hiring a dressmaker for a pelisse, 8s.	ladies silk stockings, 12s.	lowest-paid sailor on Royal Navy ship, 10s. 9d. a month	contributor to *Quarterly Review*, 10 guineas per sheet	minimum income for a "genteel" family, £100 a year	Mr. Darcy's income, *Pride and Prejudice*, £10,000
1875	overcoat for an Eton schoolboy, £1 1s.	set of false teeth, £2 10s.	seasonal agricultural laborer, 14s. a week	housemaid's wage, £10 to £25 a year	income of the "comfortable" classes, £800 and up a year	Trollope's income, £4,000 a year
1950	tweed sports jacket, £3 16s. 6d.	"Teddy boy" drape suit, £20	minimum wage, agricultural laborer, £4 14s. per 47-hour week	shorthand typist, £367 a year	middle manager's salary, £1,480 a year	barrister's salary, £2,032 a year

The British Baronage

The English monarchy is in principle hereditary, though at times during the Middle Ages the rules were subject to dispute. In general, authority passes from father to eldest surviving son, from daughters in order of seniority if there is no son, to a brother if there are no children, and in default of direct descendants to collateral lines (cousins, nephews, nieces) in order of closeness. There have been breaks in the order of succession (1066, 1399, 1688), but so far as possible the usurpers have always sought to paper over the break with a legitimate, i.e., hereditary, claim. When a queen succeeds to the throne and takes a husband, he does not become king unless he is in the line of blood succession; rather, he is named prince consort, as Albert was to Victoria. He may father kings, but is not one himself.

The original Saxon nobles were the king's thanes, ealdormen, or earls, who provided the king with military service and counsel in return for booty, gifts, or landed estates. William the Conqueror, arriving from France, where feudalism was fully developed, considerably expanded this group. In addition, as the king distributed the lands of his new kingdom, he also distributed dignities to men who became known collectively as "the baronage." "Baron" in its root meaning signifies simply "man," and barons were the king's men. As the title was common, a distinction was early made between greater and lesser barons, the former gradually assuming loftier and more impressive titles. The first English "duke" was created in 1337; the title of "marquess," or "marquis" (pronounced "markwis"), followed in 1385, and "viscount" ("vyekount") in 1440. Though "earl" is the oldest title of all, an earl now comes between a marquess and a viscount in order of dignity and precedence, and the old term "baron" now designates a rank just below viscount."Baronets" were created in 1611 as a means of raising revenue for the crown (the title could be purchased for about £1000); they are marginal nobility and have never sat in the House of Lords.

Kings and queens are addressed as "Your Majesty," princes and princesses as "Your Highness," the other hereditary nobility as "My Lord" or "Your Lordship." Peers receive their titles either by inheritance (like Lord Byron, the sixth baron of that line) or from the monarch (like Alfred Lord Tennyson, created first Baron Tennyson by Victoria). The children, even of a duke, are commoners unless they are specifically granted some other title or inherit their father's title from him. A peerage can be forfeited by act of attainder, as for example when a lord is convicted of treason; and, when forfeited, or lapsed for lack of a successor, can be bestowed on another family. Thus in 1605 Robert Cecil was made first earl of Salisbury in the third creation, the first creation dating from 1149, the second from 1337, the title having been in abeyance since 1539. Titles descend by right of succession and do not depend on tenure of land; thus, a title does not always indicate where a lord dwells or holds power. Indeed, noble titles do not always refer to a real place at all. At Prince Edward's marriage in 1999, the queen created him earl of Wessex, although the old kingdom of Wessex has had no political existence since the Anglo-Saxon period, and the name was all but forgotten until it was resurrected by Thomas Hardy as the setting of his novels. (This is perhaps but one of many ways in which the world of the aristocracy increasingly resembles the realm of literature.)

The king and queen	(These are all of the royal line.)
Prince and princess	
Duke and duchess	(These may or may not be of the royal line, but are
Marquess and marchioness	ordinarily remote from the succession.)
Earl and countess	
Viscount and viscountess	
Baron and baroness	
Baronet and lady	

Scottish peers sat in the parliament of Scotland, as English peers did in the parliament of England, till at the Act of Union (1707) Scottish peers were granted sixteen seats in the English House of Lords, to be filled by election. (In 1963, all Scottish lords were allowed to sit.) Similarly, Irish peers, when the Irish parliament was abolished in 1801, were granted the right to elect twenty-eight of their number to the House of Lords in Westminster. (Now that the Republic of Ireland is a separate nation, this no longer applies.) Women members (peeresses) were first allowed to sit in the House as nonhereditary Life Peers in 1958 (when that status was created for members of both genders); women first sat by their own hereditary right in 1963. Today the House of Lords still retains some power to influence or delay legislation, but its future is uncertain. In 1999, the hereditary peers (then amounting to 750) were reduced to 92 temporary members elected by their fellow peers. Holders of Life Peerages remain, as do senior bishops of the Church of England and high-court judges (the "Law Lords").

Below the peerage the chief title of honor is "knight." Knighthood, which is not hereditary, is generally a reward for services rendered. A knight (Sir John Black) is addressed, using his first name, as "Sir John"; his wife, using the last name, is "Lady Black"—unless she is the daughter of an earl or nobleman of higher rank, in which case she will be "Lady Arabella." The female equivalent of a knight bears the title of "Dame." Though the word itself comes from the Anglo-Saxon cniht, there is some doubt as to whether knighthood amounted to much before the arrival of the Normans. The feudal system required military service as a condition of land tenure, and a man who came to serve his king at the head of an army of tenants required a title of authority and badges of identity—hence the title of knighthood and the coat of arms. During the Crusades, when men were far removed from their land (or even sold it in order to go on crusade), more elaborate forms of fealty sprang up that soon expanded into orders of knighthood. The Templars, Hospitallers, Knights of the Teutonic Order, Knights of Malta, and Knights of the Golden Fleece were but a few of these companionships; not all of them were available at all times in England.

Gradually, with the rise of centralized government and the decline of feudal tenures, military knighthood became obsolete, and the rank largely honorific; sometimes, as under James I, it degenerated into a scheme of the royal government for making money. For hundreds of years after its establishment in the fourteenth century, the Order of the Garter was the only English order of knighthood, an exclusive courtly companionship. Then, during the late seventeenth, the eighteenth, and the nineteenth centuries, a number of additional orders were created, with names such as the Thistle, Saint Patrick, the Bath, Saint Michael and Saint George, plus a number of special Victorian and Indian orders. They retain the terminology, ceremony, and dignity of knighthood, but the military implications are vestigial.

Although the British Empire now belongs to history, appointments to the Order of the British Empire continue to be conferred for services to that empire at home or abroad. Such honors (commonly referred to as "gongs") are granted by the monarch in her New Year's and Birthday lists, but the decisions are now made by the government in power. In recent years there have been efforts to popularize and democratize the dispensation of honors, with recipients including rock stars and actors. But this does not prevent large sectors of British society from regarding both knighthood and the peerage as largely irrelevant to modern life.

The Royal Lines of England and Great Britain

England

SAXONS AND DANES

Egbert, king of Wessex	802–839
Ethelwulf, son of Egbert	839–858
Ethelbald, second son of Ethelwulf	858–860
Ethelbert, third son of Ethelwulf	860–866
Ethelred I, fourth son of Ethelwulf	866–871
Alfred the Great, fifth son of Ethelwulf	871–899
Edward the Elder, son of Alfred	899–924
Athelstan the Glorious, son of Edward	924–940
Edmund I, third son of Edward	940–946
Edred, fourth son of Edward	946–955
Edwy the Fair, son of Edmund	955–959
Edgar the Peaceful, second son of Edmund	959–975
Edward the Martyr, son of Edgar	975–978 (murdered)
Ethelred II, the Unready, second son of Edgar	978–1016
Edmund II, Ironside, son of Ethelred II	1016–1016
Canute the Dane	1016–1035
Harold I, Harefoot, natural son of Canute	1035–1040
Hardecanute, son of Canute	1040–1042
Edward the Confessor, son of Ethelred II	1042–1066
Harold II, brother-in-law of Edward	1066–1066 (died in battle)

HOUSE OF NORMANDY

William I the Conqueror	1066–1087
William II, Rufus, third son of William I	1087–1100 (shot from ambush)
Henry I, Beauclerc, youngest son of William I	1100–1135

HOUSE OF BLOIS

Stephen, son of Adela, daughter of William I	1135–1154

HOUSE OF PLANTAGENET

Henry II, son of Geoffrey Plantagenet by Matilda, daughter of Henry I	1154–1189
Richard I, Coeur de Lion, son of Henry II	1189–1199
John Lackland, son of Henry II	1199–1216
Henry III, son of John	1216–1272
Edward I, Longshanks, son of Henry III	1272–1307
Edward II, son of Edward I	1307–1327 (deposed)
Edward III of Windsor, son of Edward II	1327–1377
Richard II, grandson of Edward III	1377–1399 (deposed)

HOUSE OF LANCASTER

Henry IV, son of John of Gaunt, son of Edward III	1399–1413
Henry V, Prince Hal, son of Henry IV	1413–1422
Henry VI, son of Henry V	1422–1461 (deposed), 1470–1471 (deposed)

HOUSE OF YORK

Edward IV, great-great-grandson of Edward III	1461–1470 (deposed), 1471–1483
Edward V, son of Edward IV	1483–1483 (murdered)
Richard III, Crookback	1483–1485 (died in battle)

HOUSE OF TUDOR

Henry VII, married daughter of Edward IV	1485–1509
Henry VIII, son of Henry VII	1509–1547
Edward VI, son of Henry VIII	1547–1553
Mary I, "Bloody," daughter of Henry VIII	1553–1558
Elizabeth I, daughter of Henry VIII	1558–1603

HOUSE OF STUART

James I (James VI of Scotland)	1603–1625
Charles I, son of James I	1625–1649 (executed)

COMMONWEALTH & PROTECTORATE

Council of State	1649–1653
Oliver Cromwell, Lord Protector	1653–1658
Richard Cromwell, son of Oliver	1658–1660 (resigned)

HOUSE OF STUART (RESTORED)

Charles II, son of Charles I	1660–1685
James II, second son of Charles I	1685–1688

(INTERREGNUM, 11 DECEMBER 1688 TO 13 FEBRUARY 1689)

William III of Orange, by Mary, daughter of Charles I	1689–1701
and Mary II, daughter of James II	–1694
Anne, second daughter of James II	1702–1714

Great Britain

HOUSE OF HANOVER

George I, son of Elector of Hanover and Sophia, granddaughter of James I	1714–1727
George II, son of George I	1727–1760
George III, grandson of George II	1760–1820
George IV, son of George III	1820–1830
William IV, third son of George III	1830–1837
Victoria, daughter of Edward, fourth son of George III	1837–1901

HOUSE OF SAXE-COBURG AND GOTHA

Edward VII, son of Victoria	1901–1910

HOUSE OF WINDSOR (NAME ADOPTED 17 JULY 1917)

George V, second son of Edward VII	1910–1936
Edward VIII, eldest son of George V	1936–1936 (abdicated)
George VI, second son of George V	1936–1952
Elizabeth II, daughter of George VI	1952–

Religions in England

In the sixth century C.E., missionaries from Ireland and the Continent introduced Christianity to the Anglo-Saxons—actually, reintroduced it, since it had briefly flourished in the southern parts of the British Isles during the Roman occupation, and even after the Roman withdrawal had persisted in the Celtic regions of Scotland and Wales. By the time the earliest poems included in the *Norton Anthology* were composed, therefore, the English people had been Christians for hundreds of years; such Anglo-Saxon poems as "The Dream of the Rood" bear witness to their faith. Our knowledge of the religion of pre-Christian Britain is sketchy, but it is likely that vestiges of paganism assimilated into, or coexisted with, the practice of Christianity: fertility rites were incorporated into the celebration of Easter resurrection, rituals commemorating the dead into All-Hallows Eve and All Saints Day, and elements of winter solstice festivals into the celebration of Christmas. In English literature such "folkloric" elements often elicit romantic nostalgia. Geoffrey Chaucer's Wife of Bath looks back to a magical time before the arrival of Christianity in which the land was "fulfilled of fairye." Hundreds of years later, the seventeenth-century writer Robert Herrick honors the amalgamation of Christian and pagan elements in agrarian British culture in such poems as "Corinna's Gone A-Maying" and "The Hock Cart."

Medieval Christianity was fairly uniform across Western Europe—hence called "catholic," or universally shared—and its rituals and expectations, common to the whole community, permeated everyday life. The Catholic Church was also an international power structure. In its hierarchy of pope, cardinals, archbishops, and bishops, it resembled the feudal state, but the church power structure coexisted alongside a separate hierarchy of lay authorities with a theoretically different sphere of social responsibilities. The sharing out of lay and ecclesiastical authority in medieval England was sometimes a source of conflict. Chaucer's pilgrims are on their way to visit the memorial shrine to one victim of such struggle: Thomas a Becket, Archbishop of Canterbury, who opposed the policies of King Henry III, was assassinated on the king's orders in 1120 and later made a saint. As an international organization, the church conducted its business in the universal language of Latin, and thus although statistically in the period the largest segment of literate persons were monks and priests, the clerical contribution to great writing in English was relatively modest. Yet the lay writers of the period reflect the importance of the church as an institution and the pervasiveness of religion in everyday life.

Beginning in 1517 the German monk Martin Luther, in Wittenberg, Germany, openly challenged many aspects of Catholic practice and by 1520 had completely repudiated the authority of the Pope, setting in train the Protestant Reformation. Luther argued that the Roman Catholic Church had strayed far from the pattern of Christianity laid out in scripture. He rejected Catholic doctrines for which no biblical authority was to be found, such as the belief in Purgatory, and translated the Bible into German, on the grounds that the importance of scripture for all Christians made its translation into the vernacular tongue essential. Luther was not the first to advance such views—followers of the Englishman John Wycliffe had translated the Bible in the fourteenth century. But Luther, protected by powerful German rulers, was able to speak out with impunity and convert others to his views, rather than suffer the persecution usually meted out to heretics. Soon other reformers were following in Luther's footsteps: of these, the Swiss Ulrich Zwingli and the French Jean Calvin would be especially influential for English religious thought.

At first England remained staunchly Catholic. Its king, Henry VIII, was so severe to heretics that the Pope awarded him the title "Defender of the Faith," which British monarchs have retained to this day. In 1534, however, Henry rejected the authority of the Pope to prevent his divorce from his queen, Catherine of Aragon, and his marriage to his mistress, Ann Boleyn. In doing so, Henry appropriated to himself ecclesiastical as well as secular authority. Thomas More, author of *Utopia*, was executed for refusing to endorse Henry's right to govern the English church. Over the following six years, Henry consolidated his grip on the ecclesiastical establishment by dissolving the powerful, populous Catholic monasteries and redistributing their massive landholdings to his own lay followers. Yet Henry's church largely retained Catholic doctrine and liturgy. When Henry died and his young son, Edward, came to the throne in 1547, the English church embarked on a more Protestant path, a direction abruptly reversed when Edward died and his older sister Mary, the daughter of Catherine of Aragon, took the throne in 1553 and attempted to reintroduce Roman Catholicism. Mary's reign was also short, however, and her successor, Elizabeth I, the daughter of Ann Boleyn, was a Protestant. Elizabeth attempted to establish a "middle way" Christianity, compromising between Roman Catholic practices and beliefs and reformed ones.

The Church of England, though it laid claim to a national rather than pan-European authority, aspired like its predecessor to be the universal church of all English subjects. It retained the Catholic structure of parishes and dioceses and the Catholic hierarchy of bishops, though the ecclesiastical authority was now the Archbishop of Canterbury and the Church's "Supreme Governor" was the monarch. Yet disagreement and controversy persisted. Some members of the Church of England wanted to retain many of the ritual and liturgical elements of Catholicism. Others, the Puritans, advocated a more thoroughgoing reformation. Most Puritans remained within the Church of England, but a minority, the "Separatists" or "Congregationalists," split from the established church altogether. These dissenters no longer thought of the ideal church as an organization to which everybody belonged; instead, they conceived it as a more exclusive group of likeminded people, one not necessarily attached to a larger body of believers.

In the seventeenth century, the succession of the Scottish king James to the English throne produced another problem. England and Scotland were separate nations, and in the sixteenth century Scotland had developed its own national Presbyterian church, or "kirk," under the leadership of the reformer John Knox. The kirk retained fewer Catholic liturgical elements than did the Church of England, and its authorities, or "presbyters," were elected by assemblies of their fellow clerics, rather than appointed by the king. James I and his son Charles I, especially the latter, wanted to bring the Scottish kirk into conformity with Church of England practices. The Scots violently resisted these efforts, with the collaboration of many English Puritans, in a conflict that eventually developed into the English Civil War in the mid-seventeenth century. The effect of these disputes is visible in the poetry of such writers as John Milton, Robert Herrick, Henry Vaughan, and Thomas Traherne, and in the prose of Thomas Browne, Lucy Hutchinson, and Dorothy Waugh. Just as in the mid-sixteenth century, when a succession of monarchs with different religious commitments destabilized the church, so the seventeenth century endured spiritual whiplash. King Charles I's highly ritualistic Church of England was violently overturned by the Puritan victors in the Civil War—until 1660, after the death of the Puritan leader, Oliver Cromwell, when the Church of England was restored along with the monarchy.

The religious and political upheavals of the seventeenth century produced Christian sects that de-emphasized the ceremony of the established church and rejected as well its top-down authority structure. Some of these groups were ephemeral, but the Baptists (founded in 1608 in Amsterdam by the English expatriate John Smyth) and Quakers, or Society of Friends (founded by George Fox in the 1640s), flourished outside the established church, sometimes despite cruel persecution. John Bunyan, a Baptist, wrote the Christian allegory *Pilgrim's Progress* while in prison. Some dissenters, like the Baptists, shared the reformed reverence for the absolute authority of scripture but interpreted the scriptural texts differently from their fellow Protestants. Others, like the Quakers, favored, even over the authority of the Bible, the "inner light" or voice of individual conscience, which they took to be the working of the Holy Spirit in the lives of individuals.

The Protestant dissenters were not England's only religious minorities. Despite crushing fines and the threat of imprisonment, a minority of Catholics under Elizabeth and James openly refused to give their allegiance to the new church, and others remained secret adherents to the old ways. John Donne was brought up in an ardently Catholic family, and several other writers converted to Catholicism as adults—Ben Jonson for a considerable part of his career, Elizabeth Carey and Richard Crashaw permanently, and at profound personal cost. In the eighteenth century, Catholics remained objects of suspicion as possible agents of sedition, especially after the "Glorious Revolution" in 1688 deposed the Catholic James II in favor of the Protestant William and Mary. Anti-Catholic prejudice affected John Dryden, a Catholic convert, as well as the lifelong Catholic Alexander Pope. By contrast, the English colony of Ireland remained overwhelmingly Roman Catholic, the fervor of its religious commitment at least partly inspired by resistance to English occupation. Starting in the reign of Elizabeth, England shored up its own authority in Ireland by encouraging Protestant immigrants from Scotland to settle in northern Ireland, producing a virulent religious divide the effects of which are still playing out today.

A small community of Jews had moved from France to London after 1066, when the Norman William the Conqueror came to the English throne. Although despised and persecuted by many Christians, they were allowed to remain as moneylenders to the Crown, until the thirteenth century, when the king developed alternative sources of credit. At this point, in 1290, the Jews were expelled from England. In 1655 Oliver Cromwell permitted a few to return, and in the late seventeenth and early eighteenth centuries the Jewish population slowly increased, mainly by immigration from Germany. In the mid-eighteenth century some prominent Jews had their children brought up as Christians so as to facilitate their full integration into English society: thus the nineteenth-century writer and politician Benjamin Disraeli, although he and his father were members of the Church of England, was widely considered a Jew insofar as his ancestry was Jewish.

In the late seventeenth century, as the Church of England reasserted itself, Catholics, Jews, and dissenting Protestants found themselves subject to significant legal restrictions. The Corporation Act, passed in 1661, and the Test Act, passed in 1673, excluded all who refused to take communion in the Church of England from voting, attending university, or working in government or in the professions. Members of religious minorities, as well as Church of England communicants, paid mandatory taxes in support of Church of England ministers and buildings. In 1689 the dissenters gained the right to worship in public, but Jews and Catholics were not permitted to do so.

During the eighteenth century, political, intellectual, and religious history remained closely intertwined. The Church of England came to accommodate a good deal of variety. "Low church" services resembled those of the dissenting Protestant churches, minimizing ritual and emphasizing the sermon; the "high church" retained more elaborate ritual elements, yet its prestige was under attack on several fronts. Many Enlightenment thinkers subjected the Bible to rational critique and found it wanting: the philosopher David Hume, for instance, argued that the "miracles" described therein were more probably lies or errors than real breaches of the laws of nature. Within the Church of England, the "broad church" Latitudinarians welcomed this rationalism, advocating theological openness and an emphasis on ethics rather than dogma. More radically, the Unitarian movement rejected the divinity of Christ while professing to accept his ethical teachings. Taking a different tack, the preacher John Wesley, founder of Methodism, responded to the rationalists' challenge with a newly fervent call to evangelism and personal discipline; his movement was particularly successful in Wales. Revolutions in America and France at the end of the century generated considerable millenarian excitement and fostered more new religious ideas, often in conjunction with a radical social agenda. Many important writers of the Romantic period were indebted to traditions of protestant dissent: Unitarian and rationalist protestant ideas influenced William Hazlitt, Anna Barbauld, Mary Wollstonecraft, and the young Samuel Taylor Coleridge. William Blake created a highly idiosyncratic poetic mythology loosely indebted to radical strains of Christian mysticism. Others were even more heterodox: Lord Byron and Robert Burns, brought up as Scots Presbyterians, rebelled fiercely, and Percy Shelley's writing of an atheistic pamphlet resulted in his expulsion from Oxford.

Great Britain never erected an American-style "wall of separation" between church and state, but in practice religion and secular affairs grew more and more distinct during the nineteenth century. In consequence, members of religious minorities no longer seemed to pose a threat to the commonweal. A movement to repeal the Test Act failed in the 1790s, but a renewed effort resulted in the extension of the franchise to dissenting Protestants in 1828 and to Catholics in 1829. The numbers of Roman Catholics in England were swelled by immigration from Ireland, but there were also some prominent English adherents. Among writers, the converts John Newman and Gerard Manley Hopkins are especially important. The political participation and social integration of Jews presented a thornier challenge. Lionel de Rothschild, repeatedly elected to represent London in Parliament during the 1840s and 1850s, was not permitted to take his seat there because he refused to take his oath of office "on the true faith of a Christian"; finally, in 1858, the Jewish Disabilities Act allowed him to omit these words. Only in 1871, however, were Oxford and Cambridge opened to non-Anglicans.

Meanwhile geological discoveries and Charles Darwin's evolutionary theories increasingly cast doubt on the literal truth of the Creation story, and close philological analysis of the biblical text suggested that its origins were human rather than divine. By the end of the nineteenth century, many writers were bearing witness to a world in which Christianity no longer seemed fundamentally plausible. In his poetry and prose, Thomas Hardy depicts a world devoid of benevolent providence. Matthew Arnold's poem "Dover Beach" is in part an elegy to lost spiritual assurance, as the "Sea of Faith" goes out like the tide: "But now I only hear / Its melancholy, long, withdrawing roar / Retreating." For Arnold, literature must replace religion as a source of spiritual truth, and intimacy between individuals substitute for the lost communal solidarity of the universal church.

The work of many twentieth-century writers shows the influence of a religious upbringing or a religious conversion in adulthood. T. S. Eliot and W. S. Auden embrace Anglicanism, William Butler Yeats spiritualism. James Joyce repudiates Irish Catholicism but remains obsessed with it. Yet religion, or lack of it, is a matter of individual choice and conscience, not social or legal mandate. In the past fifty years, church attendance has plummeted in Great Britain. Although 71 percent of the population still identified itself as "Christian" on the 2000 census, only about 7 percent of these regularly attend religious services of any denomination. Meanwhile, immigration from former British colonies has swelled the ranks of religions once alien to the British Isles—Muslim, Sikh, Hindu, Buddhist—though the numbers of adherents remain small relative to the total population.

PERMISSIONS ACKNOWLEDGMENTS

Chinua Achebe: THINGS FALL APART. Copyright © 1958 by Chinua Achebe. First published by William Heinemann Ltd., 1958. Reprinted by permission of Harcourt Education Limited. Excerpt from "An Image of Africa: Racism in Conrad's HEART OF DARKNESS" from HOPES AND IMPEDIMENTS: SELECTED ESSAYS. Copyright © by Chinua Achebe. Reprinted by permission of the author.

John Agard: "Listen Mr Oxford Don" from MANGOES & BULLETS: SELECTED AND NEW POEMS. Serpent's Tail: London, 1990. Reprinted with permission

W. H. Auden: Introduction to THE POET'S TONGUE [Poetry as a Memorable Speech] by W. H. Auden. Copyright © 1935 by W. H. Auden. Reprinted by permission of Curtis Brown Ltd. "Petition" ("Sir, no man's enemy") and "Spain 1937" from THE ENGLISH AUDEN by W. H. Auden, edited by Edward Mendelson. Copyright © 1934, 1940 and renewed 1962, 1968 by W. H. Auden. Reprinted by permission of Random House, Inc., and Faber & Faber Ltd. "On This Island," "Musée des Beaux Arts," "Lullaby," "In Memory of W. B. Yeats," "In Praise of Limestone," "The Shield of Achilles," "The Unknown Citizen," and "September 1, 1939" all from W. H. AUDEN: COLLECTED POEMS by W. H. Auden, edited by Edward Mendelson. Copyright © 1937, 1940, 1951, 1952 and renewed 1965, 1968 by W. H. Auden. Reprinted by permission of Random House, Inc. and Faber & Faber Ltd. "As I Walked Out One Evening" copyright © 1940 & renewed 1968 by W. H. Auden, from COLLECTED POEMS by W. H. Auden. Used by permission of Random House, Inc.

Jane Austen: *Love and Friendship* from OXFORD ILLUSTRATED AUSTEN, VOLUME THE SECOND, edited by R. W. Chapman. "Plan of a Novel" from OXFORD ILLUSTRATED AUSTEN—VOLUME VI: THE MINOR WORKS, edited by R. W. Chapman, copyright © 1963. Reprinted with the permission of Oxford University Press.

Samuel Beckett: *Endgame*. Copyright © 1958 by Samuel Beckett; copyright renewed © 1986 by Samuel Beckett. Used by permission of Grove/Atlantic, Inc., and Faber & Faber Ltd.

Louise Bennett: "Jamaica Language" from AUNTY ROACHY SEH. "Dry-Foot Bwoy," "Jamaica Oman," "Colonization in Reverse" from SELECTED POEMS OF LOUISE BENNETT. Reprinted by permission of Sangster Books.

Annie Besant: "The White Slavery of London Match Workers" from STRONG-MINDED WOMEN by Janet H. Murray. Copyright © 1982 by Janet H. Murray. Reprinted by permission of Pantheon Books, a division of Random House, Inc., and the author.

William Blake: Poems from THE COMPLETE POETRY AND PROSE OF WILLIAM BLAKE, edited by David V. Erdman, copyright © 1965, 1981, Doubleday & Company. Blake engravings: reproduced from the Lessing J. Rosenwald Collection, Library of Congress.

Eavan Boland: "Fond Memory" and "The Lost Land" from THE LOST LAND. "That the Science of Cartography Is Limited" and "The Dolls Museum in Dublin" from IN A TIME OF VIOLENCE by Eavan Boland. Copyright © 1994 by Eavan Boland. Reprinted by permission of W. W. Norton & Company, Inc., and Carcanet Press Ltd.

Kamau Brathwaite: Extract from HISTORY OF THE VOICE by Kamau Brathwaite, published by New Beacon Books in 1994. Reprinted with the permission of the publisher. "Calypso" from THE ARRIVANTS, copyright © 1981. Reprinted by permission of Oxford University Press.

Emily Brontë: All poems from THE COMPLETE POEMS OF EMILY JANE BRONTË by C. W. Hatfield, copyright © 1941 by Columbia University Press. Reprinted with the permission of the publisher.

Robert Burns: Selections from THE POEMS AND SONGS OF ROBERT BURNS, edited by James Kinsley (1968). Reprinted by permission of Oxford University Press.

Lord Byron: Selections as indicated from LORD BYRON: THE COMPLETE POETICAL WORKS, edited by Jerome J. McGann (Vol I., 1980). Reprinted by permission of Oxford University Press. Letters are reprinted by permission of the publisher from BYRON'S LETTERS AND JOURNALS, Volumes I–VII, edited by Leslie A. Marchand, Cambridge, Mass.: The Belknap Press of Harvard University Press: Copyright © Editorial 1973, 1975, 1976, 1977 by Leslie A. Marchand. Reproduced by permission of John Murray Publishers.

May Cannan: Excerpt from GRAY GHOSTS AND VOICES and "Rouen" from IN WAR TIME, POEMS. Reprinted by permission of James Cannan Slater.

Anne Carson: "Hero" by Anne Carson, from GLASS IRONY AND GOD, copyright © 1995 by Anne Carson. Reprinted by permission of New Directions Publishing Corp. "Epitaph: Zion" from MEN IN THE OFF HOURS by Anne Carson, copyright © 2000 by Anne Carson. Used by permission of Alfred A. Knopf, a division of Random House, Inc.

Charles Causley: "At the British Cemetery, Bayeux" and "Armistice Day" from UNION STREET. Reprinted by permission of David Higham Associates.

Ada Nield Chew: Extract from THE LIFE AND WRITINGS OF A WORKING WOMAN by Ada Nield Chew. Published by Virago Press, London. Reprinted by permission.

John Clare: "Mouse's Nest" and "Pastoral Poetry" from THE POEMS OF JOHN CLARE, edited by J. W. Tibble (J. M. Dent). Reprinted by permission Everyman's Library, London. "The Nightingale's Nest" from SELECTED POEMS AND PROSE OF JOHN CLARE, edited by Eric Robinson and Geoffrey Summerfield. Reproduced with permission of Curtis Brown Ltd., London, on behalf of Eric Robinson. Copyright © Eric Robinson 1984, 1967. All other poems from THE LATER POEMS OF JOHN CLARE 1837–1864, edited by Eric Robinson and David Powell. Reproduced with permission of Curtis Brown Ltd., London, on behalf of Eric Robinson. Copyright © Eric Robinson 1984, 1967.

permission of Scribner, an imprint of Simon & Schuster Adult Publishing Group, from THE COLLECTED WORKS OF W. B. YEATS, VOLUME I: THE POEMS, revised, edited by Richard J. Finneran. Copyright © 1940 by Georgie Yeats; copyright renewed © 1968 by Bertha Georgie Yeats, Michael Butler Yeats, and Anne Yeats.

Every effort has been made to contact the copyright holders of each of the selections. Rights holders of any selections not credited should contact W. W. Norton & Company, Inc., 500 Fifth Avenue, New York, NY 10110 for a correction to be made in the next reprinting of our work.

Index

The British Isles

in the

19th and 20th Centuries

North Sea

North Channel

ATLANTIC OCEAN

ORKNEY ISLANDS

CAITHNESS
SUTHERLAND
ROSS & CROMARTY
NORTH MINCH
LITTLE MINCH
ROSS
OUTER HEBRIDES
ISLE OF SKYE
INNER HEBRIDES

Highlands

INVERNESS
Spey
MORAY FIRTH
NAIRN
MORAY
BANFF
KINCARDINE
Aberdeen

GRAMPIAN MOUNTAINS
ARGYLE
Loch Lomond
DUMBARTON
ANGUS
PERTH
Dundee
St. Andrews
FIFE
KINROSS
Dunfermline
FIRTH OF FORTH
STIRLING
CLACKMANNAN
Glasgow
R. Clyde
LANARK
Ayr
BUTE
ARRAN I.

WEST LOTHIAN
Edinburgh
EAST LOTHIAN
MIDLOTHIAN
Pentland Hills
Lammermuir Hills
PEEBLES
SELKIRK
R. Tweed
Abbotsford
Berwick-upon-Tweed
HOLY I.

Cheviot Hills
CRAIGENPUTTOCK
DUMFRIES
KIRKCUDBRIGHT
Galloway
WIGTOWN
Solway Firth
Carlisle
HADRIAN'S WALL
Hadrian's Wall
Newcastle
R. Tyne
CO. DURHAM
R. Tees
NORTHUMBERLAND
RYDAL MT.
CUMBERLAND
Lake District
Grasmere

ISLE OF MAN

PARTITION OF IRELAND IN 1921

Northern Ireland
ULSTER
Derry
DONEGAL EAST
Donegal
ANTRIM
Belfast
DOWN
TYRONE
Armagh
FERMANAGH
MONAGHAN
CAVAN
BEN BULBEN
Sligo
LEITRIM
LONGFORD
Edgeworthstown
ROSCOMMON
MAYO
CONNAUGHT
Galway
ARAN ISLANDS
CLARE
WESTMEATH
MEATH
R. Boyne
OFFALY
R. Shannon
LOUTH